D0881929

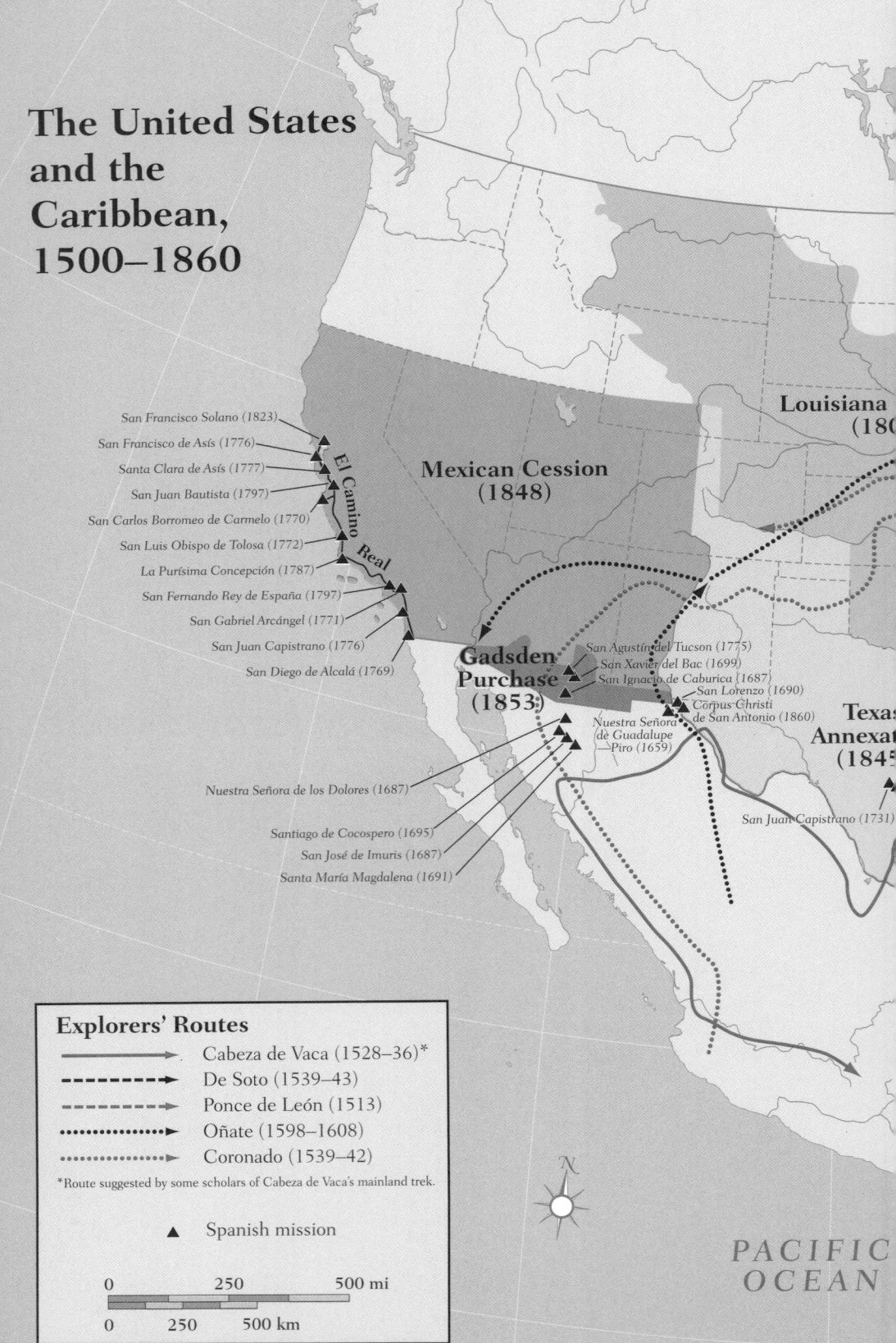

# The United States and the Caribbean, 1500–1860

San Francisco Solano (1823)
San Francisco de Asís (1776)
Santa Clara de Asís (1777)
San Juan Bautista (1797)
San Carlos Borromeo de Carmelo (1770)
San Luis Obispo de Tolosa (1772)
La Purísima Concepción (1787)
San Fernando Rey de España (1797)
San Gabriel Arcángel (1771)
San Juan Capistrano (1776)
San Diego de Alcalá (1769)

El Camino Real

**Mexican Cession (1848)**

**Louisiana (180**

**Gadsden Purchase (1853)**

San Agustín del Tucson (1775)
San Xavier del Bac (1699)
San Ignacio de Caburica (1687)
San Lorenzo (1690)
Corpus Christi de San Antonio (1860)

**Texas Annexa (1845**

Nuestra Señora de Guadalupe
—Piro (1659)

Nuestra Señora de los Dolores (1687)

Santiago de Cocospero (1695)
San José de Imuris (1687)
Santa María Magdalena (1691)

San Juan Capistrano (1731)

## Explorers' Routes

| | |
|---|---|
| → | Cabeza de Vaca (1528–36)* |
| ▪▪▪▶ | De Soto (1539–43) |
| - - -▶ | Ponce de León (1513) |
| ●●●▶ | Oñate (1598–1608) |
| ••••▶ | Coronado (1539–42) |

*Route suggested by some scholars of Cabeza de Vaca's mainland trek.

▲ Spanish mission

N

0     250     500 mi

0   250   500 km

**PACIFIC OCEAN**

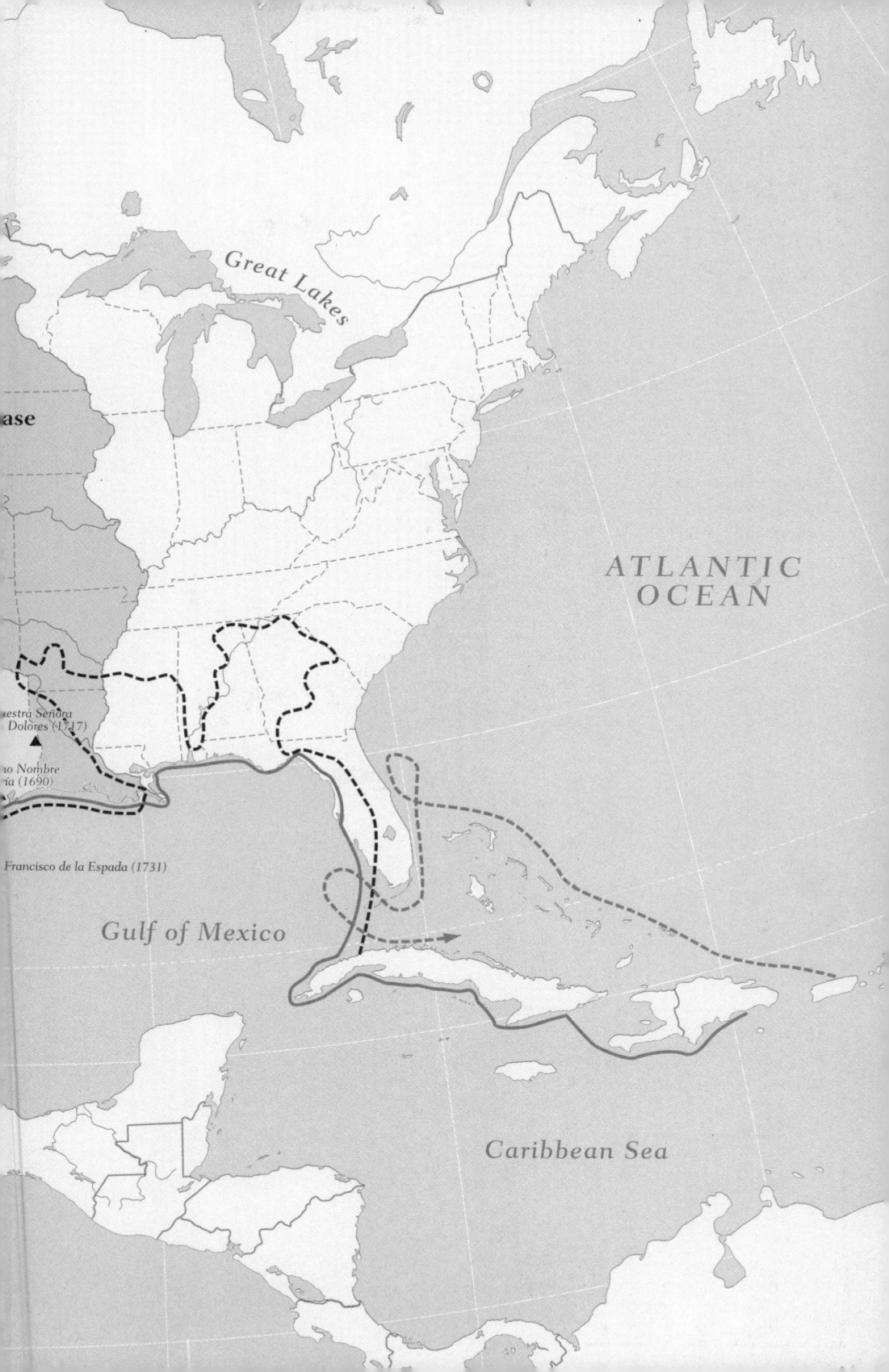

Great Lakes

ase

ATLANTIC OCEAN

uestra Señora
Dolores (1717)

o Nombre
ía (1690)

Francisco de la Espada (1731)

Gulf of Mexico

Caribbean Sea

# The Norton Anthology
## of Latino Literature

# The Norton Anthology of Latino Literature

Ilan Stavans, *General Editor*

Lewis-Sebring Professor in Latin American and
Latino Culture
AMHERST COLLEGE

W · W · NORTON & COMPANY · *New York* · *London*

Editor: Julia Reidhead
Developmental, Manuscript, and Project Editor: Kurt Wildermuth
Associate Editor: Carly Fraser
Editorial Assistants: Rivka Genesen, Erin Granville
Marketer: Scott Berzon
Emedia Editor: Eileen Connell
Managing Editor, College: Marian Johnson
Production Managers: Christine D'Antonio, Eric Pier-Hocking,
    Devon Zahn
Permissions Manager: Nancy Rodwan
Permissions Associate: Katrina Washington
Art Director: Hope Miller Goodell
Text Designer: Antonina Krass
Cover Art Director: Albert Tang

Manufacturing by RR Donnelley, Crawfordsville

    Library of Congress has cataloged the trade edition as follows:

The Norton anthology of Latino literature / Ilan Stavans, general editor ;
[editors], Edna Acosta-Belén ... [et al.]. —1st ed.
        p. cm.
    Includes bibliographical references and index.

    ISBN 978-0-393-08007-0 (hardcover)

    1. American literature—Hispanic American authors. 2. Hispanic
Americans—Literary collections. I. Stavans, Ilan. II. Acosta-Belén,
Edna.
    PS508.H57N65 2010
    810.8'0868073—dc22

                                                    2010015108

This edition: ISBN 978-0-393-97532-1

W. W. Norton & Company, Inc., 500 Fifth Avenue, New York, N.Y. 10110
www.wwnorton.com

W. W. Norton & Company Ltd., Castle House, 75/76 Wells Street, London
W1T 3QT

1 2 3 4 5 6 7 8 9 0

# Contents

## ACCULTURATION: 1899–1945                                        359

# POPULAR DIMENSIONS

# Alternate Table of Contents

### POPULAR DIMENSIONS

## DOMINICAN REPUBLIC

# GUATEMALA

# MEXICO

### POPULAR DIMENSIONS

## PERU

# PUERTO RICO

## SPAIN

# Preface

*The Norton Anthology of Latino Literature* celebrates five centuries of diverse writing by Latinos in what is now the United States. Thirteen years in the making, the book seeks to represent, classify, and explore the ways that the Latino literary tradition has grown organically as an essential, though insufficiently studied and perhaps underappreciated, component of the nation's literature.

Anthologies are different things to different audiences. They are resources for reading pleasure; they are critical tools for students and instructors; and, for the culture at large, they are the portable libraries in which memory is deposited. They enable past, present, and future readers to appreciate the literary past through a particular lens. Three central ideas define the "library" that this volume seeks to be.

First: At its core, Latino literature is about the tension between double attachments to place, to language, and to identity. Many Latinos did not come as immigrants to the United States; the United States came to them in the form of colonial enterprises. Those Latinos that came as immigrants are unlike any other immigrant group in the United States, because for centuries they have maintained strong ties to the places once called home and with the languages of those homelands. This double attachment results in a double loyalty. Thus, to understand Latino literature, it is important to keep in mind both the ambivalence at the core of the tradition and the literary works' connection to two different intellectual mores, the Anglo and the Hispanic.

Second: This volume also suggests that the multinational quality of Latinos as a group—Mexicans, Puerto Ricans, Cubans, Colombians, Dominicans, and others—and the ongoing influx of immigrants across the Rio Grande and the Caribbean allow Latinos to exist in a state of constant mutation. This mutability, deftly conveyed by Julia Alvarez in her novel *How the García Girls Lost Their Accent* in the motif of the accent, is a defining characteristic of the collective Latino identity. Stressing the polyphonic language and polymorphic forms of the Latino tradition, this volume features writers working in many genres: poetry, short fiction, drama, novels, manifestos, memoirs, journals, letters, graphic novels, songs, tales, sayings, and more.

Third: For a long time, because of their different national backgrounds, the individual groups of people within this minority perceived themselves as independent from one another. From the 1980s onward—especially after the finding by the Census Bureau, at the dawn of this century, that Latinos have become the country's largest and fastest-growing ethnic group—a feeling of unity has begun to emerge. This change is particularly evident on college and university campuses. Since the civil rights era, Chicano Studies and Puerto Rican Studies have matured in the American academy. In the 1990s, scholars across the United States made a collective effort to consider

Latino culture generally. Academic institutions offered new courses and established interdisciplinary departments devoted to understanding the Hispanic experience in the United States from diverse academic disciplines: sociology, history, anthropology, literature, linguistics, and political science. Thus the intellectual scene was ripe for the harvest of the most important and widely acknowledged works by Latinos in a single volume that would provide students with a simultaneously in-depth and panoramic view of the Latino literary tradition.

How have the editors defined and presented this 2,600-page panorama? Early in the planning stages, we identified—and argued over—four thematic emphases that now play out across the volume.

First there is the question of appellation. Why is the word *Latino* used in the anthology's title? In popular parlance, this rubric describes the people living in the United States who come from Spanish-speaking countries (Mexico, Central and South America, as well as the Caribbean Basin. Brazil, Portugal, and the Philippines are not included). Other names are used interchangeably with it or have been fashionable in the past, including *Hispanic*, *Hispano*, *iberoamericano*, *Latin*, and *Spanish-speaking*. Nationality-inclusive terms have also been in vogue, such as *Mexican*, *Cuban*, *Puerto Rican*, and *Dominican*, as have more geographically or generationally defined rubrics, such as *Boricua*, *Pachuco*, and *Marielito*. The plethora of names illustrates that the minority is looking for a definition, trying to answer the questions *Who are we?*, *Where do we come from?*, and *What should we call ourselves?* In contrast with these appellations, *Latino*—a derivation of *Latin American*, the name coined at the end of the nineteenth century to refer to the people of the newly independent community of republics that the South American liberator Simón Bolívar struggled to merge into a federation—has been endorsed by the minority itself and does not derive from outside forces. Not only has *Latino* proven to be the most neutral and the least exclusive term; it is also favored by Latinos. Still, as in this preface, the anthology does not shy away from juxtaposing the preferred term with other valuable ones.

Second comes the issue of provenance, which carries with it questions of class. As noted above, a large number of Latinos in the United States are immigrants, typically having traveled from distant places in search of better opportunities for themselves and their children. Like many such newcomers, they have undergone the odyssey from being described as trespassers and interlopers to being embraced for their contributions to society. Yet, as noted in the introduction to the anthology, scores of other Latinos, especially those in certain parts of the Southwest, Florida, and Puerto Rico, have never moved from the terrain where their families have lived for centuries. Their presence in the country dates back to 1819, when the Adams-Onis Treaty transferred ownership of Florida from Spain to the United States; to 1848, when the Treaty of Guadalupe Hidalgo forced Mexico to give up the territories that today constitute large parts of the Southwest; and to 1917, when the Jones Act granted U.S. citizenship to all citizens of Puerto Rico. A few Latinos trace their roots to an even earlier era, the colonial period, during which the Spanish and indigenous populations interacted for the first time. Hence the multifaceted disposition of Latinos allows for various narratives within the literary tradition, all invariably framed around the topic of belonging. Some of these narratives are about immigration: The writer describes a journey—of arrival, accommodation, and ultimate redemption—across a minefield that is typical of immigrant writing. Other narratives treat usurpation, territorial and psychological. These variant narratives might be completely independent from one another or they might intersect. In a particular historical period, one type might recur while another lies dormant.

Third is the issue of race. Unlike blacks and Asians, Latinos are not composed of a single racial background. Some trace their roots to indigenous civilizations in the pre-Columbian past. Others define themselves as *mestizos*. A considerable portion is of African descent, some of their ancestors having arrived as slaves to the shores of Mexico, the northeastern part of South America, and the Caribbean Basin. A few others have a Caucasian lineage or else have a genealogical tree linking them to Creole cultures. And still others are the offspring of immigrants to the Spanish-speaking Americas from Italy, Russia, Japan, and other countries. Somewhat related issues are social status and religion. While most Latinos remain in the lower-income strata, a growing number are middle class. There are, of course, wealthy Latinos, just as there are Catholic, Protestant, Muslim, Jewish, Buddhist, agnostic, and atheist Latinos. In other words, *e pluribus unum*.

Fourth is the concept of nation. Any serious analysis of the Latino literary tradition needs to pay equal attention to two parallel, at times colliding, narratives: the United States and Latin America, the latter of which is broken into 21 national parts. Latinos exist at the crossroads of all these narratives. To understand the circumstances of individual Latinos, it is thus essential to view people against their multiple backdrops. For instance, the Mexican American civil rights activist César Chávez was influenced as much by the American civil rights leader Martin Luther King Jr. as by the Mexican revolutionary Emiliano Zapata. Likewise, the works of the Cuban poet José Martí owe as much to the Spanish-language aesthetic movement *Modernismo* as to the writing of Walt Whitman and other English-language precursors.

*The Norton Anthology of Latino Literature* is organized chronologically, from the age of exploration and colonization to the present. Each of the six sections begins with an introduction about the major historical, political, intellectual, and aesthetic motifs that shaped the chronological period. "Colonization" includes chronicles written by Spaniards about life in what are now Florida, Arizona, New Mexico, Texas, California, and the Pacific Northwest, starting in 1552, when Fray Bartolomé de Las Casas published his accusatory account, *The Devastation of the Indies*. While the section introduction traces the journeys of the various conquistadors, explorers, and missionaries, the section is organized not geographically but by significance, beginning with the authors of the most significant descriptions of the natural and human landscape of the colonial era. This first section concludes in 1810, when Mexico engaged in a war of independence.

The second section, "Annexations," starts in 1811, when the struggle for emancipation from the Iberian Peninsula spread throughout Latin America, and concludes in 1898, with the Spanish-American War, after which the United States became the hegemonic power in the Caribbean Basin and the

Philippines. The influences of the Monroe Doctrine and the widespread conception of Manifest Destiny are the driving ideas in this section, galvanizing fierce support and equally fierce resistance.

"Acculturation" begins in the aftermath of the Spanish-American War, when Cuba and Puerto Rico struggled to define themselves as nations, and continues through World War I and to the end of World War II. During this period, Latinos enlisted in the U.S. military and fought in the two global wars, thus displaying their loyalty for the country; also during this period, xenophobic acts increased against Mexican Americans and Puerto Ricans, especially in California, Texas, and New York City.

Section four, "Upheaval," includes writing from the civil rights era and focuses on the contemporaneous Chicano Movement, in which César Chávez and his United Farm Workers fought for justice, dignity, and equality for Mexican Americans, Puerto Ricans, and Filipinos. A concurrent Puerto Rican movement was carried out by different grassroots organizations (e.g., the Young Lords, PRDELF, ASPIRA), especially in New York and Chicago.

"Into the Mainstream" is the anthology's largest section. During this period, Latino identity takes shape as an umbrella encompassing people in the United States whose backgrounds are from all over the Spanish-speaking world. Discussions of Latino identity focus on concepts such as Latinidad, *mestizaje*, and brownness. Language also becomes a focus of attention, as Spanglish—the hybrid of Spanish and English used in everyday life, from homes to streets to classrooms—becomes a useful if controversial tool of expression among writers in the literary tradition.

The last section, "Popular Dimensions," focuses on forms directed toward popular audiences. These forms—the folklore traditions of anonymous *chistes* and *cuentos*, the popular theater, the comic strip, the editorial cartoon, the graphic novel, the lyrics of popular songs, from corrido to salsa to Chicano rock and Latin pop—reflect the concerns that prevail in other sections of the anthology: the concept of nationhood; race, class, and provenance; the varieties of linguistic expression.

The anthology concludes with three appendixes. Appendix 1 is a comprehensive chronology that highlights not only major Latino events, political and cultural, but also decisive events in Latin America. Appendix 2 presents historic documents that have defined the body politic for Latinos since the middle of the nineteenth century, namely the Treaty of Guadalupe Hidalgo, the Treaty of Paris, the Jones Act, the Bracero Agreement, and Proposition 187. Appendix 3 consists of selections from four defining essays by south-of-the-border intellectuals about U.S.–Latin American relations, *mestizaje*, Mexicanness in Los Angeles, imperialism, and colonialism. These essays have affected Latinos' perceptions of themselves as citizens of two empires, first Spain and then the United States.

Readers who wish to explore the traditions of different national subgroups within the Latino literary tradition can refer to the alternate table of contents at the front of the anthology.

*The Norton Anthology of Latino Literature* includes works by 201 writers. Not every "Latino" author in the anthology has an equally rounded Latino identity. Is Fray Bartolomé de Las Casas, whose activism against Spanish abuses of the indigenous population in the Americas made him a hero in some quarters and infamous in others, a proto-Latino, since he did not set foot in any part of what constitutes the United States today? Is Isabel Allende, who writes her novels in Spanish, a Latina? Or is she a Chilean émigré living permanently in San Francisco, and thus a Latin American novelist in the United States? Engaged in these questions, the editors have defined Latino literature in elastic terms, as the artistic, written manifestation, in Spanish, English, Spanglish, or any combination of these three, by an author of Hispanic ancestry who has either lived most of his or her existence in the United States or, while having only some tangential connection to the Latino community, has helped define that community through his or her work.

This flexible definition leaves a number of gray areas. Rudolfo A. Anaya is an English-language Mexican American author, but he occasionally writes about countries other than the United States, as in his book *A Chicano in China*. William Carlos Williams, whose mother was Puerto Rican, belongs to the tradition even though his Spanish was minimal. Heberto Padilla—a Cuban exile who arrived in the United States in middle age, then shifted his focus from life in Cuba under Fidel Castro's regime to life in Princeton, New Jersey, where Padilla lived for years—never perceived himself as a Latino. Among the "gray area" authors who did not make the cut is María Luisa Bombal. A Chilean who lived at various times in England, France, Argentina, the United States, and her native country, Bombal translated her Spanish-language novella *La amortajada* (1938) into Shakespeare's tongue as *The Shrouded Woman*, but her oeuvre has no connection to Latino identity, and thus she is not included in the anthology. Neither is the work of Carlos Fuentes, who was born in Washington, D.C., is the son of a career diplomat, and for decades was at ease in American intellectual circles, but who has positioned himself as a central player in Mexican literature.

Each of the anthology's period editors defined, chose the selections within, and wrote the introduction for the period corresponding to his or her field of expertise, as well as collaborated on the "Popular Dimensions" section and the appendixes. María Herrera-Sobek was responsible for the works in "Colonization"; Edna Acosta-Belén for the works by Puerto Ricans on the mainland and, when appropriate, on the island; Rolando Hinojosa for the works by Mexican Americans of the twentieth century; Gustavo Pérez Firmat for the works by Cuban Americans; and Harold Augenbraum for the works by Mexican Americans of the nineteenth century as well as those by authors from national groups other than Puerto Ricans on the mainland, Mexican Americans of the twentieth century, and Cuban Americans.

Unfortunately, as a result of permissions limitations, *The Norton Anthology of Latino Literature* has left out works deemed canonical. Prominent among these are Aristeo Brito's novel *The Devil in Texas* and Sandra Cisneros's novel *The House on Mango Street*. Fortunately, the anthology includes a significant number of texts in their entirety: Tomás Rivera's *This Migrant Earth*, Rodolfo "Corky" Gonzales's *I Am Joaquín*, Rolando Hinojosa's *Becky and Her Friends*, Luis Valdez's *Zoot Suit*, María Irene Fornés's *Fefu and Her Friends*, Dolores Prida's *Coser y Cantar*, Carlos Morton's *The Many Deaths of Danny Rosales*, José Rivera's *The House of Ramón Iglesia*, and Cherríe Moraga's *Giving Up the Ghost*. The documents in Appendix 2 are also complete.

A word about translation: Unlike some other ethnic literatures in the United States, the Latino tradition has led a double life, one part in the ancestral language and one part in English. At times during the past five centuries, Spanish and English have existed side by side; at other times, they have intermingled, resulting in the hybrid known as Spanglish. The editors of this anthology have selected texts for an English-language readership in the United States, approaching the content as an essential part of American literature. Still, at least a fourth of the material was originally in Spanish and is hereby presented in translation. Whenever a fluid rendition was available and had been available to at least a generation of readers, it was chosen for inclusion. However, a number of selections from the colonial period were translated anew, or for the first time, into English, as was much of the Mexican American, Cuban American, and Puerto Rican poetry from the second half of the nineteenth century. The translator's name is given in the introductory footnote for the selection.

We generally follow the editorial procedures of the Norton Anthology series. After each work, we cite the date of first publication on the right; for some works, this date is accompanied by that of a revised edition. A date of composition, when it is known and when it differs from the publication date, is given on the left. We use square brackets to indicate the titles and other information supplied by the editors. Whenever we have omitted a portion of a text, we have indicated that omission with three asterisks. In addition, we have used accents and other diacritics consistently with Spanish usage except when an author employs them differently. The name César Chávez, for example, has been properly accented in Spanish except when an author's original omits the accents. In our editorial material, we have paid particular attention to anthologized authors' wishes regarding the treatment of their names. Richard Rodriguez, for example, does not accent the *i* in his surname.

And, finally, a note on footnoting: An anthology of this scope about Latinos in the United States, for whom bilingualism has been a way of life for centuries, necessarily involves a considerable amount of code switching and other linguistic devices. In general, our footnoting method is based on the least possible intrusion but also on the widest possible inclusion of English-only readers. We have annotated Spanish and Spanglish terms unless those terms lack precise cultural referents or are, as in Luis Valdez's play *Zoot Suit*, clearly part of an aesthetic strategy to erase the border between linguistic codes. We have also footnoted geographical, historical, political, and cultural items unfamiliar to the average college undergraduate in the United States at the beginning of the twenty-first century. For some texts, we have retained the footnotes of the outside editors and translators. Where we have adapted those footnotes to follow the Norton style, an acknowledgment is made in the first footnote to the text.

The editors want to express their special gratitude to a number of advisors, colleagues, institutions, friends, and family members whose aid facilitated the work on this edition. The late Luis Leal, at the University of California, Santa Barbara, advised on the colonial period. Francisco Lomelí, at the University of California, Santa Barbara, suggested entries for "Popular Dimensions." Jaime Mejía, at Texas State University–San Marcos, advised on Mexican American literature since World War II. Jennifer Acker read the editorial apparatus with fine-combed attention. Her judicious comments were invaluable.

The editors offer a heartfelt *gracias* to the staff at Norton, whose dedication to the project allowed it to flourish. Without the indefatigable support of the acquiring editor, Julia Reidhead, this 13-year-long endeavor would not have come to fruition. Kurt Wildermuth, senior developmental editor, did a titanic job streamlining the manuscript and is as close to the "best reader" as the anthology will ever have. Rivka Genesen and Erin Granville ably assisted bringing the manuscript to final form, as did Carly Fraser, who also oversaw the creation of the endpaper maps. Christine D'Antonio and Eric Pier-Hocking managed the production process flawlessly. Nancy Rodwan and Katrina Washington patiently handled more than their share of obstacles while securing the permissions. David Hawkins proofread the galleys with enviable acuity.

Richard Rodriguez, in his memoir *Hunger of Memory*, ponders his quest for self-definition as he looks at the page he has just written, and states: "Now it exists—a weight in my hand." The same might be said of *The Norton Anthology of Latino Literature*.

Ilan Stavans
Amherst, Massachusetts
April 7, 2010

# Acknowledgments

This mammoth endeavor required the support, encouragement, and expertise of countless people. Naming them all is impossible. Thanks to the dozens of readers who offered comments at various stages of the manuscript. Thanks also to the myriad teachers who used parts of the material in their classrooms, thus enabling the editors to judge the value of different selections.

The counsel of the following people—listed in alphabetical order—proved indispensable: Marjorie Agosín (Wellesley College), Verónica Albin (Rice University), Lalo López Alcaraz, Cèsar Alegre, René Alegría (Harper-Collins), Terry Allen, Patricia Alvarado (PBS-WGBH), Julia Alvarez (Middlebury College), Isabel Alvarez-Borland (College of the Holy Cross), José F. Aranda Jr. (Rice University), Ruth Behar (University of Michigan), the late Antonio Benítez-Rojo (Amherst College), Sue Betz (Chicago Review Press), P. Scott Brown, Lee and Bobby Byrd (Cinco Puntos Press), Gregory S. Call (Amherst College), Cass Canfield Jr. (HarperCollins), Mari Castaneda (University of Massachusetts Amherst), Linda Chavez, Susana Chávez-Silverman (Pomona College), Daisy Cocco de Filippis (Hostos Community College), Jerry Cohen, Jonathan Cohen, Martin A. Cohen (Hebrew Union College), Constantine Contogenis, Javier Corrales (Amherst College), Juan Debesis, Richard Delgado (University of Pittsburgh), Ariel Dorfman (Duke University), Elizabeth Eddy, Laszlo Erdelyi (*El País*), Martín Espada (University of Massachusetts Amherst), Margarite Fernández Olmos (Brooklyn College), Pat Fraker, Jonathan Galassi (Farrar, Straus and Giroux), Regina Galasso (Johns Hopkins University), Héctor García (Loyola University), Marcela García (*El Planeta*), Mario T. García (University of California, Santa Barbara), Henry Louis Gates Jr. (Harvard University), Anne Gendler (Northwestern University), Dagoberto Gilb (Texas State University), Isaac Goldemberg (Hostos Community College), Erica González (*El Diario/La Prensa*), Mariá C. Gonzáles (University of Houston), Rigoberto González (Rutgers University), Jorge J. E. Gracia (State University of New York at Buffalo), Franklin Gutiérrez (York College), Roberta Helinski (Amherst College), Juan Felipe Herrera (University of California, Riverside), Andrew Hurley (Universidad de Puerto Rico), Iván Jaksic (Stanford University), Nicolás Kanellos (Arte Público Press), Steven G. Kellman (University of Texas at San Antonio), Bridget Kevane (Montana State University), Jacqueline Kiefer, Casey Kittrel (University of Texas Press), Jeffrey T. Lawrence (Princeton University), Mark Linn-Baker, Rick A. López (Amherst College), Elena Machado (Florida Atlantic University), Reed Malcolm (University of California, Berkeley), Jaime Manrique, James E. Maraniss (Amherst College), Roberto Márquez (Mount Holyoke College), Ellen McCracken (University of California, Santa Barbara), Joe McCullough (University of Nevada, Las Vegas), A. Gabriel Meléndez (University of New Mexico), Juan Fernando

Merino (*El Diario/La Prensa*), Doris Meyer (Connecticut College), Tom Miller, Michael Millman (Penguin Books), Carlos Morton (University of California, Santa Barbara), Antonio Muñoz Molina (Cervantes Institute, New York), Frances Negrón-Muntaner (Columbia University), Susana Nuccetelli (St. Cloud State University), Achy Obejas (DePaul University), Tess O'Dwyer (Americas Society, New York), Ricardo Ortiz (Georgetown University), Judith Ortiz Cofer (University of Georgia), Jay Parini (Middlebury College), Paul S. Park (César E. Chávez Foundation), Marian Perales (ABC-Clio), Mary Anne Pérez, Lisa Pierce (Greenwood Publishing), José Prado (University of Southern California), Jennifer Prather, Josef Raab (Universität Duisburg-Essen), Jorge Ramos (Univisión), Richard Rodriguez, Elda Rotor (Penguin Books), Stephen A. Sadow (Northeastern University), Sonia Saldívar-Hull (University of Texas at San Antonio), Esmeralda Santiago, Donna Sanzone (HarperCollins), Margaret Sayers Peden, Moacyr Scliar, Daniel Shapiro (Americas Society, New York), Kirsten Silva Gruesz (University of California, Santa Cruz), Neal Sokol, Werner Sollors (Harvard University), Doris Sommer (Harvard University), Alison Sparks, Silvia Spitta (Dartmouth College), Jean Stefancic (University of Pittsburgh), Lucía Suárez (Amherst College), Ray Suárez (PBS), Virgil Suárez (Florida State University), Yvette Sánchez (Universität St. Gallen), the late Sandy Taylor (Curbstone Press), Hector Torres (University of New Mexico), Silvio Torres-Saillant (Syracuse University), Joseph Tovares (PBS-WGBH), Sergio Troncoso, Tom Viator (Rowan University), Gerardo Villacrés, Oscar Villalón (*San Francisco Chronicle*), Teresa Villegas, Kristi Ward (ABC-Clio), Roberto Weil, Cheryl Wilson, Karen Winkler (*Chronicle of Higher Education*), Pablo Yglesias, and Julián Zugazagoitia (El Museo del Barrio, New York).

The staffs of the following libraries were helpful: Bancroft Library, University of California, Berkeley; Benson Latin American Collection, University of Texas; Denver Public Library; Institute of Dominican Studies, City College, CUNY; Microfilm Library, Sterling Library, Yale University; Museum of New Mexico; Newberry Library; New Mexico State Library; New York Public Library; State Historical Society of Colorado; and University of New Mexico Library.

# Introduction:
# The Search for Wholeness

The urgent duty of our America is to show herself as she is, one in soul and intent, rapidly overcoming the crushing weight of her past and stained only by the fertile bloodshed by hands that do battle against ruins and by veins that were punctured by our former masters. The disdain of the formidable neighbor who does not know her is our America's greatest danger, and it is urgent—for the day of the visit is near—that her neighbor come to know her, and quickly, so that he will not disdain her. Out of ignorance, he may perhaps begin to covet her. But when he knows her, he will remove his hands from her in respect. One must have faith in the best in man and distrust the worst. One must give the best every opportunity, so that the worst will be laid bare and overcome. If not, the worst will prevail.

Thus wrote José Martí, the Cuban poet and freedom fighter, in "Nuestra América (Our America)," his seminal essay published in 1894. The quest to look at the Spanish-speaking Americas whole, in a hemispheric context, was a recurrent theme before this time, but Martí helped turn it into an ideology.

The purpose of that quest was to form the Americas with roots in the Iberian Peninsula into a cohesive, harmonious entity, defined by its shared ancestry and common goals. Martí sees the 21 countries of Latin America as unified by language, political views, social structures, and religious persuasion. He sees them as having a coalescing body: "one in soul and intent." Believing there are fundamental differences between *nuestra América* and *la América sajona, la América ajena*, he discards the English-speaking Americas as alien, invasive, disconnected from the other planets in the galaxy he is looking to assemble. He is sympathetic only to those Americas recognized by ruins and "veins that were punctured by our former masters." His essay is a manifesto for a Latin America victimized by "the disdain of the formidable neighbor who does not know her."

Martí lived most of his adult life in the United States, during a time when the country defined itself as Anglo-Saxon and suppressed its other cultural roots, including the Hispanic ones. He ultimately developed a deep understanding of the Anglo nation, its great achievements, and its flaws, especially its expansionist goals and determination to become the hegemonic power in the hemisphere. He died a martyr three years before the Spanish-American War, in which Spain lost control of Cuba, Puerto Rico, and the Philippines and the United States became the centripetal empire in the Caribbean Basin. But for Martí the Spanish-speaking Americas were always in great danger, at the mercy of a nation eager to lay hands on them.

Despite the imbalance of power created by U.S. imperialism, however, Martí hoped to avert confrontation. He suggests in his essay that the weak Latin American nations should seek not enmity but pride. Since they are not capable of fighting the United States with force, their upset has to be achieved through creativity. "One must give the best every opportunity, so that the worst will be laid bare and overcome."

Clearly, in his mental map, Martí does not envision a translinguistic utopia from Alaska and Greenland to the Pampas and the Caribbean Basin. That overarching concept—encompassing English-, French-, Portuguese-, Spanish-, and Creole-speaking areas—is of more recent origin. Yet Martí is its source of inspiration.

Latinos are a byproduct of the age of empire: transplanted, uprooted, in a process of constant reinvention. The first representatives of this uprootedness are the indigenous tribes who went head-to-head with the conquistadors, explorers, missionaries, and other imperial envoys, such as Pánfilo de Narváez, Alvar Núñez Cabeza de Vaca, and Hernando de Soto, in the territories that now are part of the southwestern United States. From the early sixteenth century on, the encounter between these two civilizations, Spanish and aboriginal, established the foundation on which Latino life would eventually be built. These beginnings preceded, by a substantial amount of time, the arrival of the Puritans on the *Mayflower*, in 1620. Indeed, despite the frequent misconception, Latinos are not invariably immigrants or the children of immigrants. In Florida and the Southwest, it was not that the Latinos came to the United States. As is shown in the work of Southwestern writers such as Eulalia Pérez, Andrew García, and Eusebio Chacón, it was the other way around.

Approximately three centuries after the arrival of the Spaniards, the people of Latin America became feverish for independence. In a domino effect that started in 1810 and continued unabated for many decades, these people severed their ties with the Iberian Peninsula and established autonomous republics. But at the end of the nineteenth century, the United States sought to compete with Europe for world domination and became the reigning force on the western side of the Atlantic. In this effort, the nation was guided by the Monroe Doctrine (President James Monroe's proclamation, in 1823, that European nations were not to interfere in the activities of the Americas and the United States would reciprocate by not interfering in the affairs of Europe) and the concept of Manifest Destiny (the belief, articulated during the presidency of Andrew Jackson, between 1829 and 1837, that the United States was destined to expand from the Atlantic coast to the Pacific coast). Under President Theodore Roosevelt's Big Stick policy, his corollary to the Monroe Doctrine—"Speak softly and carry a big stick," Roosevelt explained in 1901—the U.S. invaded Mexico, Cuba, and the Dominican Republic, and it annexed Puerto Rico, which remains an unincorporated territory under commonwealth status.

Throughout the nineteenth and twentieth centuries, a series of stunning political and economic shifts—following from conquests, annexations, and migrations—relocated millions of people from these Iberian-colonized places to the United States. Over time, this unrest has resulted in the formation of a minority that, more than a hundred years after Martí, is the nation's largest. The writer who surfaces from this sea of changes exists at the borders of Hispanic and Anglo worlds, a hybrid vessel navigating within the English and Spanish languages, literarily between the American poet Walt Whitman (Martí's contemporary), whose *Leaves of Grass* sang to the American multitudes, and the Colombian novelist Gabriel García Márquez, our contemporary, whose *Cien años de soledad* (One Hundred Years of Solitude) presents a fictional Caribbean family at the mercy of major natural, historical, and magical forces. The Latino writer inhabits a liminal zone, a Latin America *inside* the United States.

Martí understood the agony of exile and felt the meaning of *diaspora*, or the dispersion of a group of people from their homeland. Yet what Martí did not and perhaps could not have conceived of is the ultimate richness and complexity of Latino literature, birthed from the confrontation of the two worlds he believed should be kept apart, separate but respectful of each other. During his time in the United States, in the late 1800s, the country had more than 61 million people, of which around 250,000 were Latino. Could Martí have imagined that within a century, roughly one out of every seven U.S. citizens would be of Hispanic descent? Could he have foretold that in parts of Texas the Latino population would outnumber that of any other ethnic group? That Mexican cuisine, Caribbean music, and South American folklore would become essential cultural ingredients north of the Rio Grande? To visualize these scenarios, Martí would have needed to accept that the English-speaking United States could become part of a more inclusive, less either/or *nuestra América*. More than a century after Martí wrote his piece, the Americas are inhabited by 900 million people, roughly 14 percent of the world population. These people belong to diverse groups. One out of every five Mexicans in the world, one out of every two Puerto Ricans, and one out of every ten Cubans now lives north of the Rio Grande.

The Latino writer now resides at a unique junction of traditions: Latin American literature, Anglo American literature, and minority literature. The writer no longer develops in a monolithic culture, but absorbs many cultures during the course of a life. For instance, Jaime Manrique was born in Barranquilla, Colombia; immigrated to the United States in his adolescence; switched from Spanish to English; and is at once a Colombian writer, a U.S. writer, and a Latino writer, reacting to creative impulses from several places. Like Manrique, the Mexican-born critic Luis Leal, the Cuban-born poet Lourdes Casal, the Dominican-born writer Franklin Gutiérrez, and many other Latino writers moved to the United States to look for a more open intellectual atmosphere or even to escape political persecution. Surely Martí would have perceived the irony in this reversal of fortunes: The same "formidable neighbor" supporting the tyrannical regimes that propel some writers out of their homelands also opens its doors as a safe haven.

Some exiles return home when the political situation in their home country stabilizes, but many never do. The latter is the case for hundreds of thousands of Cubans who left the island soon after Fidel Castro's takeover in 1958–59. While waiting (hoping) for Castro's downfall, they became full-fledged residents, even naturalized citizens, of the United States. Cuban-exile writers in the U.S. include Heberto Padilla, Dolores Prida, Reinaldo Arenas, and Carlos M. N. Eire. And, of course, Martí himself. What would Martí have made of the effort to see him as a cornerstone of the foundation of a Latino community he could not visualize? Is Martí a U.S. Latino in spite of himself?

Each intellectual who moves to the United States as a political exile faces a unique set of circumstances in creating a self-identity. Mariano Azuela, a Mexican doctor and author of novels such as *Los de abajo* (The Underdogs, 1915), lived on the north side of the Rio Grande during the Mexican Revolution (1910–21). This temporary stay did not significantly affect his worldview. José Vasconcelos, who in 1914 (during the presidency of Eulalio Gutiérrez) was briefly Mexico's Minister of Education and went on to become chancellor of the National Autonomous University of Mexico and the founder of the Ministry of Public Education, also spent time in exile north of the Rio Grande. Yet he always saw himself as *mexicano*. Likewise, the Argentine writers Manuel Puig and Luisa Valenzuela and the Chilean writers Gabriela Mistral and José Donoso always identified primarily with their home countries, despite years of living as exiles in other places. Among the countless intellectuals and artists from the Hispanic world who passed time in the U.S. as students, teachers, lecturers, diplomats, and tourists are Domingo Faustino Sarmiento, Luis Muñoz Marín, Pedro Henríquez Ureña, Jorge Mañach, Diego Rivera, Frida Kahlo, Mario Vargas Llosa, Octavio Paz, and Elena Poniatowska. None considered himself or herself Latino. Among those who do, Latino identity has not always been a matter of choice. The writers Rosario Ferré, Isabel Allende, and Ariel Dorfman might have embraced a Latino identity as a survival strategy, to make themselves comfortable in their new habitats, or as a sign of empathy or solidarity with a downtrodden population with which they share cultural and linguistic commonalities. But José María Heredia, Eugenio María de Hostos, Felipe Alfau, and Reinaldo Arenas never contemplated such a decision, and they might even have been opposed to the idea since it suggested a rejection of their roots. These writers' inclusion in the Latino tradition is less a matter of self-identification than of the way literary culture has considered each author's work.

Unlike the exiles, however, most of the Latino writers in the United States today have little relationship with the south-of-the-border educated elite. Whatever strings connect them to the elite are often tenuous. These Latinos are part of the immigration route, legal and otherwise, through which people look for *un futuro más estable*, a better life elsewhere. Because the Latin American economies have often been unstable over long periods, people move north seeking *el sueño americano*, the (often elusive) American dream.

Just before the census was taken in 2010, the Latino minority in the United States was estimated to be around 48 million. Almost seven out of every ten of its members are of Mexican descent, but the rest are from or trace their roots to all over the Americas. This minority "group" is therefore extremely diverse in terms of national background, class, ethnicity, race, religion, and political affiliation. It is more unified in terms of age: Compared to other Americans, the Latino community is young, a majority being between 17 and 25 years of age. In addition, far more than other immigrant groups, Latinos have through generations retained their connections with their homelands through language, in this case through *el español*, which was present in the lands that now make up the United States even before the arrival of the *Mayflower*. In fact, as a result of demographic growth, Spanish has become the unofficial second language of the United States.

Parts of Miami, Los Angeles, and New York seem Latin American because of the amount of Spanish spoken there: After Havana, Miami has the greatest concentration of Cubans in the world; after Mexico City, Los Angeles has the largest Mexican population; and there are almost as many Puerto Ricans in New York as there are in San Juan's metropolitan area.

Latinos differ from earlier immigrant groups in four crucial ways. In shaping people's lives, these differences have helped create a uniquely Latino literature. The first difference is the closeness of home. An Italian immigrant in the 1880s, for example, needed substantial amounts of money and time to travel to Italy. An Ashkenazi Jew in the 1880s would not have been able to visit the homeland, in Russia's Pale of Settlement, because of anti-Semitic violence there. For Latinos, particularly those on the U.S.-Mexico border, returning home can be dangerous, but generally it is quick and relatively inexpensive. Air travel has contributed to back-and-forth migration and thus to stronger transnational connections between most U.S. Latino groups and their countries of origin. The second difference is that the waves of immigration from Spanish-speaking countries have not been limited to a particular period. No sooner have Guatemalans ceased moving north, for example, than they are followed by Salvadorans, Nicaraguans, Colombians, and Venezuelans. Key countries such as Mexico continuously generate immigrants. The third difference lies in the immense influence of the media on Latinos and, in turn, their growing influence on the media. The global movement of information and capital reinforces confused notions of "home" as, more than ever before, technology enables immigrants to live, virtually, both in their home countries and in their adopted one.

The fourth difference is arguably the most significant. Large portions of the Southwest (parts of present-day Colorado, Arizona, New Mexico, and Wyoming; all of California, Nevada, and Utah) were sold under pressure by the Mexican government under General Antonio López de Santa Anna to the United States in 1848, as part of the settlement of the Mexican-American War. Some descendants of the Spanish-speaking population in the region see the subsequent "occupation" of lands previously owned by Mexico as a form of colonialism. A similar notion exists in Puerto Rico. After the U.S. annexation of the island as a result of the Spanish-American War, through the Jones Act (1917), Puerto Ricans became U.S. citizens—a prelude to the island's becoming a commonwealth (known in Spanish as the *Estado Libre Asociado*), in 1952. As U.S. citizens, Puerto Ricans have many of the same rights and privileges as stateside citizens. Yet because the United States exercises territorial jurisdiction over this still-unincorporated territory, many island Puerto Ricans perceive their status as second-class. Despite their U.S. citizenship, they are not allowed to vote in presidential or congressional elections, and thus they do not choose the ultimate authorities in any decisions affecting their future. Mainland Puerto Ricans, too, are subject to discrimination and remain part of an underprivileged minority. Like the American Indians, the Puerto Ricans ask why they are not treated equally when they are citizens by birthright.

Therefore it is not surprising that the Latino literary tradition is characterized by a deep sense of rupture. That same sense, for African Americans, was defined by the scholar W. E. B. Du Bois as one of "double consciousness." As an exile, Martí knew of such displacement. In 1869, the "apostle of Cuban independence" was arrested for sedition against Cuba's Spanish rule; he was, as the government at the time put it, "repatriated" to Spain, and he then traveled to France and Guatemala before arriving in New York City in 1880. But the displacement of many Latino writers is less related to globe-trotting. It comes from racism, anti-Hispanism, and the feeling of being an alien in one's own homeland, the feeling of constantly being pushed and shoved because of one's skin, one's background, and the language one speaks. René Marqués, in his controversial essay "The Docile Puerto Rican" (1962), meditates on the psychological impact of U.S. colonialism on the Puerto Rican people. Some Latinos in the United States see themselves as an extremity of Hispanic civilization living under occupation. For others, the Latino minority is an integral part of the American mosaic, yet one that suffers from ingrained racism and xenophobia.

But not every writer sees darkness instead of light. Latinos' double consciousness and the plurality of views exhibited in their worldview is the result of the historical journey they have traveled, individually and collectively. Many Latinos value their divided selves, which allow them to exist in multiple states of being at the same time. They are Latin Americans. They are U.S. citizens. They identify by their individual national backgrounds. More than anything else, they are their own creations, whether they struggle with or celebrate their complex identities.

This self-creation surfaces in the search for wholeness. In "Our America," Martí described that wholeness rhetorically, but since the 1980s it has been seen as representing the community-building that Latinos must do. Before then, the various groups within the Latino minority, differentiated by national backgrounds, most often perceived themselves as traversing their own paths. For example, Chicano letters—whose moment of political determination came during *El Movimiento*, as the Chicano Movement was known during the civil rights era—were defined as works by writers of Mexican ancestry living and writing in the United States, such as Ernesto Galarza, Fray Angélico Chávez, Daniel Venegas, Mario Suárez, and Sabine Ulibarrí, some of whom wrote their work in the preceding decades. While authors such as the Mexican poet Sor Juana Inés de la Cruz were included in anthologies of Chicano literature, and while literary critics such as Luis Leal invited readers to think of the colonial period in Latin America as part of Mexican American history, historical figures of the colonial period, such as Alvar Núñez Cabeza de Vaca, were often left out. Nor did the movement embrace *vendidos*, "sell-outs" such as the nineteenth-century California and Texas politicos Antonio María Osio y Higuera and Juan Nepomuceno Seguín. The links between Chicano literature and that of Puerto Ricans on the mainland, from Bernardo Vega to Nuyorican "street" poets such as Miguel Piñero and Miguel Algarín, were contemplated in journals such as the *Revista Chicano-Riqueña*, but the impact of those links was limited. And vice versa: Mainland Puerto Rican writers did not necessarily see themselves as connected with Chicanos or, for that matter, with their Cuban counterparts in the United States.

In other words, before there was an entity called the Latino literary tradition there were parallel national literatures by writers from the Spanish-language Americas living in the United States. The Latino minority did not yet see itself as a unit. With the Chicano Movement opening things up, the decisive change took place in the 1970s, as multiculturalism came to the fore. Economic, political, and cultural forces consolidated Latinos from all nations and ethnicities, urging them to become a whole just like African Americans, Asian Americans, Native Americans, and other ethnic groups. The media played an important role, especially Spanish-language TV and radio, which stressed a feeling of commonality across class, geographic, and cultural divides within this continuously growing demographic. The Latin music market enlarged exponentially. The first anthologies presenting cross-national Latino literature belong to that time. And politics was crucial in that local, state, and federal leaders embraced the idea of "a Hispanic electorate." The term *Hispanic* was adopted by the U.S. government on September 12, 1969, when President Richard M. Nixon signed into law the celebration of a Hispanic Heritage Week. The term was then consistently used in government documents as an umbrella category for Spanish-speakers, regardless of their ethnic and national backgrounds. In 2000, the U.S. Census began using the term *Latino* as well.

The search for wholeness manifests itself differently in each writer, but Latin America serves as a rich well of possibilities. When regional differences are downplayed to the point of being inconsequential, camaraderie increases among Latino artists. Thus, breaching geographical borders within the Spanish-speaking world, the Puerto Rican poet Martín Espada embraces the Chilean poet Pablo Neruda as a model, while the Cuban poet Pablo Medina selects the Spanish poet Federico García Lorca as his precursor. The Chicana writer Ana Castillo sees the Argentine novelist Julio Cortázar as an inspiration, while the Cuban novelist Cristina García draws upon the Colombian novelist Gabriel García Márquez. Publishers confirm, even "prove," this unity by marketing a book such as Junot Díaz's *The Brief Wondrous Life of Oscar Wao* (2007) to a wide, non–ethnically delineated readership. In advertising terms, *Latino* has become a buzzword. The 48 million members of the minority are not necessarily viewed as Mexican, Cuban, Puerto Rican, and the like. They are Latinos one and all.

Arguably the most significant concept defining a pluralistic Latino identity, one stressed by writers such as Gloria Anzaldúa and Richard Rodriguez from the eighties on, is *mestizaje*, understood as the physical, social, religious, political, and cultural miscegenation of foreign and indigenous elements. The notion of *mestizaje* goes back to the colonial period, when the crossbreeding between Spaniards and native people in the New World resulted in the formation of a third ethnicity: *el mestizo*. The non–English-speaking Americas were born of this encounter.

However, at the time of the European arrival in 1492, the lands were unevenly populated, so *mestizaje* was more evident in certain regions than in others. Around the River Plate, for instance, in what is today Argentina and Uruguay, there were few Indian tribes. And into the countries that touched the Caribbean (Cuba, Puerto Rico, the Dominican Republic, Colombia, Venezuela, and Brazil), as well as in Mexican states such as Veracruz, Guerrero, and Morelos, the Spanish and Portuguese Crowns brought black slaves from Africa. From the transformed racial mix predominantly on the western side of the Atlantic emerged mulatos, zambos, and other hybrid ethnicities.

In the first half of the twentieth century, the Mexican politician, educator, and philosopher José Vasconcelos infused the notion of *mestizaje* with a political drive. In his book *La raza cósmica* (The Cosmic Race, 1925), Vasconcelos suggested that *la raza de bronce*, the Bronze Race, which is how he described *mestizos*, would dominate the globe in the near future, not only demographically but culturally. Anzaldúa, in her seminal book *Borderlands/La Frontera: The New Mestiza* (1987), explores the idea:

> José Vasconcelos, Mexican philosopher, envisaged *una raza mestiza, una mezcla de razas afines, una raza de color*—la primera raza síntesis del globo. He called it a cosmic race, *la raza cósmica*, a fifth race embracing the four major races of the world. Opposite to the theory of the pure Aryan, and to the policy of racial purity that white America practices, his theory is one of inclusivity. At the confluence of two or more generic streams, with chromosomes constantly "crossing over," this mixture of races, rather than resulting in an inferior being, provides hybrid progeny, a mutable, more malleable species with a rich gene pool. From this racial, ideological, cultural and biological cross-pollinization, an "alien" consciousness is presently in the making.

Mobility + mutability + renewal = inclusivity. Latinos: people of many colors, unified by a single language: Spanish. Latinos: part *gringos*, part *indios*, part black, and fully hybrid. *La unión hace la fuerza*: For Anzaldúa, the act of mixing races is also an art. To engage in miscegenation is to embrace a vision of unity.

Rodriguez takes a similar approach to *mestizaje*. He is fascinated by Vasconcelos's idea of the Bronze Race, but adapts it to the U.S. racial context. Between the social constructs of whiteness and blackness, through which the nation has defined itself since its inception, brownness is a third option. Brown, not bronze. The concept comes from the Chicano Movement, in the 1960s, when as part of the struggle for civil rights, César Chávez, Dolores Huerta, and other leaders of the United Farm Workers, as well as intellectuals such as the *Los Angeles Times* reporter Rubén Salazar and the lawyer Oscar "Zeta" Acosta, meditated on brownness as a metaphor for collective identity.

In his book *Brown: The Last Discovery of America* (2002), Rodriguez emphasizes brownness as an alternative to the black/white dichotomy:

> I write of a color that is not a singular color, not a strict recipe, not an expected result, but a color produced by careless desire, even by accident; by two or several. I write of blood that is blended. I write of brown as complete freedom of substance and narrative. I extol impurity.
>
> I eulogize a literature that is suffused with brown, with allusion, irony, paradox—ha!—pleasure.
>
> I write about race in America in hopes of understanding the notion of race in America.
>
> Brown bleeds through the straight line, unstaunchable—the line separating black from white, for example. Brown confuses. Brown forms at the border of contradiction (the ability of language to express two or several things at once, the ability of bodies to experience two or several things at once).
>
> It is that brown faculty I uphold by attempting to write brownly.

Impurity + contradiction + renewal = freedom. For Rodriguez, miscegenation has given place to a new self that reaches beyond the old U.S. paradigm of race, a self that, in its uncleanness, is emancipated in a way impossible to find anywhere else.

Just as the concept *mestizaje* refers mostly to particular regions in the Spanish-speaking world, so brownness is limited to Latinos whose ancestors are from Mexico and Central American countries, where *mestizos* play a fundamental role in the shaping of culture. The *mestizo* category is somewhat foreign to Cubans and Puerto Ricans. For them, blackness—African heritage—is more familiar. But Anzaldúa and Rodriguez do not want to be too specific about color. They want to discuss hybridity broadly and theoretically. For *them*, the image of an *América completa*, a whole America, is about finding a common ground for people of diverse backgrounds and upbringings.

José Martí advocated the idea of equal dignity and harmony among the races, but he viewed life as either/or, defined by separation and by keeping one culture at bay from another. The Latino writer today, living in a more complex, challenging time and realizing that polarity is no longer suitable, prefers both/and. In the in-between, wholeness is not about choosing between the north and the south. From this perspective, a new Latino nation has been born in the United States, a country within a country, *gringa* and *latina*, broad and limitless—black and white and brown and multicolored.

# The Norton Anthology
## of Latino Literature

# Colonization: 1537–1810

More than a century before the appearance of John Smith's *A Description of New England* (1616), William Bradford's *Of Plymouth Plantation* (1608–47), and Anne Bradstreet's poems of the 1660s—that is, long before the foundational works of present-day American literature were created—accounts of the Iberian conquest, exploration, and colonization of the Americas were published in Spain. These narratives are the origins of the Latino literary tradition, announcing the environmental, racial, class, religious, political, and economic structures on which the future would be built. They include Álvar Núñez Cabeza de Vaca's *Chronicle of the Narváez Expedition* (1542, 1555), Fray Bartolomé de Las Casas's *The Devastation of the Indies* (1552), and Juan de Castellanos's *Elegías de varones ilustres de Indias* (Elegies of Illustrious Men of the Indies, 1589). Via these reports, the Spanish colonial period in the Americas, which historians consider to have lasted more than three centuries, can be understood. In literary terms, the period starts in 1537, when Cabeza de Vaca first set foot in Florida (after the collapse of Pánfilo de Narváez's sea expedition); continues through the American Revolution (1775–83), by which the 13 original colonies gained their independence from Britain and became the United States; and concludes in 1810, when Mexico's war of independence erupted with the Catholic priest Father Miguel Hidalgo y Costilla's ringing the bells of freedom in Dolores, Mexico.

The conquest was, first and foremost, a military quest for territory. Yet it can also be seen from religious, ethnic, cultural, and linguistic perspectives. By 1492, the Catholic monarchy of Spain, King Ferdinand II of Aragón and Queen Isabella I of Castile, in a process known as *La Reconquista*, had succeeded in campaigning against "outside" forces (e.g., Arab civilization) to create a unified Catholic, Spanish-speaking nation. Through the Holy Office of the Inquisition, which was charged with persecuting non-Catholics and practitioners of deviant behavior, Catholicism became a centralized ideology. *El castellano*, or Castilian—the dialect of the region of Castile, Spain—metamorphosed into *el español*, or Spanish, the language of the empire; previously, many conflicting languages had been spoken in the nascent country. The efforts by the lexicographer, humanist, and grammarian Antonio de Nebrija (1444–1522), whose academic career evolved first at the University of Salamanca and then at the University of Alcalá de Henares, were critical. The author of influential philological studies, Nebrija wrote bilingual lexicons such as *Introductiones latinae* (1486), *Diccionario latino-español* (1492), *Vocabulario español-latino* (circa 1495), and *Tabla de la diversidad de los días* (1499). His *Gramática de la lengua castellana*, released in 1492, just as Christopher Columbus, a Spanish admiral from Genoa, was organizing his first trip across the Atlantic Ocean and as the monarchs Isabella and Ferdinand were preparing to expel the Jews from the kingdom, established Spanish as a tool in the effort to homogenize the country's population.

In the prologue to his *Gramática de la lengua castellana*, which he dedicated to Queen Isabella, Nebrija states (the italics are added):

> Whenever I think to myself, much enlightened Queen, and I place before the eyes the antiquity of all things that were written for our remembrance and memory, I come to one single and truthful conclusion: that *language was always a companion of empire*; and to such a degree it accompanied it, that together they were born, grew up and flourished, and their demise came together later on as well.

Hence the arrival and dissemination of Spanish in the New World was a colonial enterprise. As the language was forced upon and embraced by the peoples in successive territories, it became the signature aspect of the emerging nations of the Americas.

The first indigenous tribes encountered by Columbus were the Taíno peoples, in what are now Puerto Rico (where they called the island Boriquén and themselves Boricuas), Haiti and the Dominican Republic, both on the island of Hispaniola (where they called the island Quisqueya and themselves Quisqueyanos), and Cuba (which was also inhabited by the Ciboneys). Florida was inhabited by the Ais, Apalachee, Calusa, Timucua, and Tocobaga peoples. Estimates of the population of the Americas before the Iberians arrived vary enormously from one source to another. Some historians believe the number to be between 13 million and 18 million; others push for as much as 180 million. The latter number is likely too high, but it reflects the scale of the decimation of the "Indians" through warfare, malnutrition, and epidemics. Whatever the population count, it is still bewildering (no adjective does more justice) that the Spanish conquistador Hernán Cortés was able to vanquish the Aztec Empire in a single battle (1521) in which he had somewhere between 200 and 670 soldiers. In the key fight of the conquest of Peru (1533), the conquistador Francisco Pizarro had an equally small battalion: 200 soldiers dominated the Inca emperor Atahualpa's army of 80,000.

How did such small forces bring down the powerful empires of the pre-Columbian world? According to one theory, the Aztecs believed that one of their gods, Quetzalcóatl, would soon return from his cosmic journey in the guise of a bearded man in an iron suit, so the arrival of the bearded, armored Cortés was heralded as a religious watershed. Other theories emphasize the Iberians' technological superiority in warfare, such as in their use of gunpowder (imported from China). Still other theories argue that the indigenous populations were already so weakened and traumatized by disease that they were not able to rally sufficient defensive forces. In his encounter with the Spanish invaders, including Pizarro and Hernando de Soto, Atahualpa acted complacently. As a leading historian of the conquest of Peru once put it, while Atahualpa was planning to have Pizarro for lunch, Pizarro had him for breakfast.

At the time of the Iberian invasion, the Aztecs and Incas were heterogeneous populations. The Aztec Empire, which reached its height 100 years before the arrival of Cortés, was a coalition of three powerful Meso-american peoples: the Mexicans and their allies, the Texcocans, and the Tlacopans. They subjugated the Huastec people (to the north) and the Mixtec and Zapotec peoples (to the south). With a tributary system of government centralized in Tenochtitlán (now Mexico City), this religious, economic, and political partnership is known as *la triple alianza*, the triple alliance. To-gether the three entities are often described as Nahuas because the language they spoke was classical Nahuatl, labeled "classical" to distinguish it from the Nahuatl spoken now in enclaves of the Mexican population. As the com-mon tongue of Mesoamerica, Nahuatl took two forms: *pipiltin*, used by the nobles, and *mācehualtin*, spoken by the lower classes.

The Inca Empire was larger than that of the Aztecs, covering more than 772,000 square miles on the Pacific coast of South America and passing through present-day Ecuador, Peru, Bolivia, Colombia, Chile, and Argen-tina. Its capital was the city of Cuzco. Unlike the warring Aztecs, the Incas expanded their empire through coercive assimilation, and their empire should be seen as a federation divided into four parts, called *suyus*. The complex societal structure that resulted from the Incas' invasions allowed for mul-tiple forms of religious worship, but the primary deity of the population of Cuzco was the sun god Inti. The primary tongue was Quechua (one of the official languages in Bolivia and Peru, spoken by roughly 10 million people today), followed by Aymara, Puquina, and scores of others.

To nineteenth- and early-twentieth-century English-language historians such as William Hickling Prescott, the hero of the conquest and coloniza-tion of the Americas was unquestionable. In Prescott's *History of the Con-quest of Mexico* (1843), praise goes not to Moctezuma, the Aztec emperor and defender of Aztec civilization, but Cortés, the brave, white knight who "civilized" a barbarous, idolatrous empire. The same is true in *Hernán Cortés: Conqueror of Mexico* (1941), by Salvador de Madariaga, an Oxford scholar of Iberian descent. Although this biography describes the conquista-dor's self-righteous acts against the native population and is sensitive to the anti-imperialism that was sweeping Europe in the early twentieth century, it gives the Aztecs minor roles and puts the Iberians at center stage. In *The Rise of the Spanish Empire* (1947), Madariaga paints the conquistadors as coura-geous, flamboyant, sexually permissive adventurers eager to find wealth, fame, and glory:

> The men who explored and conquered America did so with the scantiest material means. Their spirit did it all. Colón [Christopher Columbus] had set the example discovering the New World with the three caravels [sailing ships], the biggest of which was 140 tons. Cabeza de Vaca walked through thousands of miles of unexplored country in both the northern and the southern parts of the continent. Cortés conquered Mexico with four hundred men and sixteen horses. Official help was seldom given, in fact seldom asked for, by these men who preferred to go ahead without shackles. They nearly always applied for some official sanction before starting on their expeditions of exploration and conquest, but what they sought at Court was less money, weapons, ships and horses, than the moral force to legitimate authority. No man will ever understand the Conquest who does not give its due value to this feature of it: spirited,

undisciplined, anarchical, the conquerors are nevertheless obsessed by the majesty of the law and not only do they never . . . stand up against the King of Spain, who, distant and enigmatic, follows their fabulous adventures with an eye worried and distracted by [the Protestant Reformation in] Europe, but they actually seek the sanction of the royal word for their deeds and status.

Why? Because these Spaniards were all imbued with the sense of common fellowship fostered in Spain as in all the Latin world by the twofold tradition of Rome—the Imperial and the Christian. They were, in one world, deeply *civilized*. Many of them behaved damnably. The extermination of the natives of the islands was in part at least due to the outburst of violence which followed the first discoveries and conquests. But this very outburst of disorder and anarchy which took place in the first years was but the explosion of energies restrained by civilized standards, on finding themselves suddenly liberated on the edge of the world of authority.

By the last decades of the twentieth century, historians had begun to ponder these events more even-handedly. They recognized that representing pre-Columbian civilizations as primitive elided understanding the political, economic, religious, and intellectual systems developed by groups such as the Aztecs and Incas. History, of course, is written by the conquerors. Yet these conquered peoples had developed sophisticated worldviews, whose echoes are fundamental to understanding Hispanic life today, not only in Mexico, Peru, and other modern republics, but among Latinos in the United States.

## *Relaciones, Derroteros,* and *Diarios*

By 1600, the submission of the native peoples in the Caribbean and in Florida was complete. For the most part, the southwestern regions of the United States were seen by the Spanish Crown as a buffer against British and French settlement efforts, and the monarchy encouraged its settlers to explore these territories. In 1598, Juan de Oñate imposed Spanish rule over the Pueblo Indians in New Mexico, followed shortly by ones in Arizona. Within half a century, other tribes (such as the Anasazi, who lived in the Colorado Plateau) and other groups of Pueblo Indians (such as the Hopi, in Arizona), would also be subdued, first through military means and then through religious education delivered in Spanish. *Misiones* (missions), established by priests of the Franciscan, Dominican, and Augustinian orders, were the principal tool for spreading Catholicism throughout the colonies. Self-sufficient establishments that included irrigation systems, schools, jails, ranches, and carpentries, missions complemented other institutions, such as *presidios* (military garrisons) and *pueblos* (towns).

The Spanish aimed to convert the aboriginal population to Catholicism and turn it into a solid labor force capable of making pottery, ranching and husbanding various animals, and harvesting and processing wheat. The native peoples sometimes resisted these forms of "acculturation," and the Spanish punished transgressions such as theft, idolatry, adultery, and sodomy to various degrees with prison, flagellation, and torture. Fray Junípero Serra, a famous and controversial missionary of the period, is considered successful for having converted to Catholicism close to 5,000 people. Pope John Paul II beatified him in 1988, and he represents a learned aspect of the missions because he taught himself many indigenous languages, but he was also known to treat his pupils and laborers harshly. Indians confined to missions often ran away. Organized, large-scale rebellions include the Pueblo Revolt, of 1680, and the Chumash Revolt, of 1824. During the seventeenth century, the Seminoles rebelled in Florida. In the nineteenth century, after Mexico became independent, a wave of anticlericalism swept the northern territories, the mission system fell into disarray, and secularization overtook the population.

Most of the literature produced by the Spaniards in the New World during this era consists of *relaciones* (chronicles) and *derroteros* (itineraries). These generally were written not by the conquistadors (e.g. Cortés, Pizarro, de Soto, and Narváez), although several left behind invaluable correspondence, but by the soldiers and attachés in their regiments. Many missionaries, educators, and scholars living in the colonies wrote personal letters, diaries, guidebooks, memoirs, prayer books, manuals of religious instruction, epic poetry, religious and secular theater scripts, and full-fledged histories. The missionaries were extraordinarily successful as explorers, ethnographers, and chroniclers, being able to travel mostly unhindered across vast expanses (because the Indians did not view them with the same hostility as the Indians viewed the soldiers) and having the erudition with which to write scientifically about and evaluate their observations. However, most of the colonial observers' accounts were not written journalistically, at the time of the events. Instead, years later, these people sat down to recount their experiences of the invasion and occupation of the American landscape, trusting memory as their primary tool in the retrieval of information. Thus the writer's objectivity is always at question in reading these narratives. Whether a particular author had a vested interest in glorifying the Spanish enterprise or vilifying it, truth and myth were often interchangeable.

The sole narrative about an unintentional transcontinental trek during this period is *La relación*, known in the standard English-language version as *Chronicle of the Narváez Expedition*, by Álvar Núñez Cabeza de Vaca. Cabeza de Vaca was a member of the disastrous sea voyage to Florida headed by Pánfilo de Narváez. Five ships sailed from San Lúcar de Barrameda, Spain, in mid-1527. On April 16, 1528, after a series of heavy storms, the expedition foundered off the coast of Florida. Few of the 600 men survived the shipwreck. The would-be conquistadors were left naked and hungry on the shore, where they were rescued by a group of Native Americans who took pity on them. With the eyes of a proto-biologist and -anthropologist, Cabeza de Vaca describes in detail his odyssey, which probably took him from Florida to the Southwest, through present-day Georgia, Alabama, Mississippi, Louisiana, Texas, New Mexico, and Arizona.

A close reading of works by the most significant explorers and missionaries after Cabeza de Vaca offers a transhistorical map of the Spanish expansionist drive, from Florida to Arizona, Texas to the Pacific Northwest. The oldest accounts are from Florida, the first area settled by the Spanish colonists. The region was explored by Hernando de Soto, whose journey is described by authors including the Caballero de Elvas, "El Inca" Garcilaso de la Vega, and de Soto's personal secretary, Rodrigo Ranjel. Their combined reports describe a trek that lasted from 1539 to 1543. Fray Bartolomé de Las Casas also provided early descriptions of these explorations. Between 1588 and 1609, the missionary priest Fray Alonso Gregorio de Escobedo penned an epic poem, *La Florida*, published in English in 1966 as *Pirates, Indians, and Spaniards: Father Escobedo's "La Florida."* The poem provides an ethnographic and historical study of the region and includes descriptions of local customs.

Another geographical area widely chronicled is New Mexico. In 1538, Fray Marcos de Niza became one of the first Spaniards to lead an expedition into New Mexican territory. His goal was to find the Seven Cities of Cíbola and Quivira, fabled places that were said to be paved with gold and precious stones and that fueled the imaginations of several explorers. De Niza kept a diary of the expedition, which he headed with the Moroccan slave Estevanico (1500?–1539). Their exploratory effort began in Mexico City and ended in complete chaos and tragedy; most of the 300 men accompanying them were massacred by Indian tribes in Zuñi territory in northern New Mexico.

De Niza's journey inspired wild exaggerations that egged on other glory-seeking explorers. The Francisco Vázquez de Coronado expedition left northern Mexico on February 23, 1540, and followed de Niza's route in an exhausting effort to locate the elusive and phantasmagoric Seven Cities. The chronicler accompanying Coronado, Pedro Castañeda de Nájera, detailed the journey taken between 1540 and 1542 through New Mexican lands, the Texas Plains, and Kansas territory. Juan de Oñate led an ill-fated expedition to New Mexico in 1595–1601. In 1610, a member of the expedition, Gaspar Pérez de Villagrá, published his account as *Historia de la Nueva México*, an epic poem written in hendecasyllabic meter.

In 1573, to protect the Indians from the abuses of the conquistadors, the Spanish Crown passed the Colonization Laws. These laws stipulated that, for example, anyone wanting to initiate an expedition to the so-called New Spain's northern frontier was required to obtain written permission from the king. (What was then the Viceroyalty of New Spain is now Mexico and the American Southwest. The Viceroyalty of New Granada is now Colombia, Panama, Venezuela, and Ecuador.) However, several unauthorized expeditions occurred in the 1580s and early 1590s. In 1581, Fray Agustín Rodríguez, Francisco Sánchez Chamuscado, and 30 others "rediscovered" New Mexico, following first the Conchos River and then the Rio Grande and arriving at settlements of Pueblo Indians before returning south. Nine years later, Gaspar Castaño de Sosa made illegal entries into New Mexican territories. In 1593, Captain Francisco Leyva de Bonilla made unauthorized incursions into northern lands. Members of these various expeditions left valuable written records of their journeys.

Important accounts of early journeys into Texas include diaries by Alonso de León, written in 1655, and by Fernando del Bosque, translated as *Diary of Fernando del Bosque 1675*. In *Historia del Nuevo Reino de León: 1630–1690*, translated as *Texas and Northeastern Mexico 1630–1690*, Juan Bautista Chapa describes in great detail the exploration of eastern and southeastern Texas. In *Memorias para la historia de Texas* (Memoirs for the History of Texas, 1778) and the highly regarded *Historia de Texas 1673–1779* (translated as *History of Texas 1673–1779*), Fray Juan Agustín Morfi narrates the often harrowing explorations of the areas around the Rio Grande in south Texas as well as of the San Antonio area.

In 1587, Fray Eusebio Francisco Kino, of Italian descent, arrived in southern Arizona, where he founded the first mission in that area, Nuestra Señora de los Dolores (Our Lady of the Sorrows). The well-educated missionary extensively explored the Colorado River and wrote about his experiences in his autobiographical *Favores Celestiales*, translated in 1919 as *Kino's Historical Memoir of Pimería Alta: A Contemporary Account of the Beginnings of California, Sonora, and Arizona by Father Eusebio Kino, S.J. Pioneer Missionary Explorer, Cartographer, and Ranchman—1683–1711.*

The Spanish exploration of California, by land and sea, was fueled in part by the conquerors' imaginations. The conquests of Mexico and Peru had not satisfied the Spaniards' overwhelming urge to "discover" more kingdoms. *Plus ultra* (Latin for "further beyond," "further yet," "more beyond," or "yet beyond," and Spain's national motto) became the rallying cry and motivating force compelling these hardened and ferocious men into the vast unknown. The conquistadors were driven by seemingly inexhaustible energy and by visions of fabulous kingdoms filled with comely Amazons. (Indeed, the name California is derived from that of the Amazons' supposed queen, Califia, and originally referred to the mythical island on which the Amazons lived, off the coast of the Indies.) Expeditions were continually organized, some by seasoned soldiers from the Aztec and Inca conquests, others by new and raw recruits, who wanted to test their luck and build fortunes. Most of the explorers died during these quixotic adventures.

In addition to the personal incentives motivating many Spaniards to explore California and the Pacific coast were the directives of the Spanish Crown, which constantly feared losing its newly acquired lands to other European nations, particularly from the second half of the sixteenth century through the eighteenth century. France and England were major competitors, continually making incursions into Spanish holdings in New Spain, Central America, and South America, and causing extensive damage through their surrogates, greatly feared pirates such as Francis Drake and Henry Morgan. After Spain acquired the Philippine Islands, commerce developed between these islands and Mexico. Spanish galleons sailing to and from Manila required safe ports on the California coastline, to moor and replenish their provisions after the long ocean voyage, and the Crown sent expeditions to indentify and colonize suitable harbors on the Pacific coast.

Captain Juan Bautista de Anza's expedition into Arizona and California included two excellent chroniclers: Frays Hermenegildo Garcés and Pedro Font. Their diaries, translated as *Diary of Garcés* and *Diary of Pedro Font*, describe the de Anza expedition up to 1774, providing detailed accounts of journeys from the royal presidio of San Ignacio de Tubac, near present-day Sonora, Mexico, into California. Font's writings afford splendid insights into the lives, customs, foods, and clothing of the Native Americans encountered in Arizona; they stand as an excellent ethnographic study as well as a literary gem. Diaries by the intrepid de Anza have also been translated.

Rodríguez Cabrillo was one of the earliest explorers to sail along California and the Pacific coast. His expedition is recorded in the diary kept by either Bartolomé Ferrel or Juan Páez (authorship is unconfirmed) and translated in 1908 as *Relation of the Voyage Made by Juan Rodríguez Cabrillo*. Equally interesting are the writings of Miguel de Constansó, an ensign and engineer accompanying the Gaspar de Portolá expedition. He left a detailed narrative of the expedition, known as *The Narrative*, and a diary. In his diary, the explorer Sebastián Vizcaíno recorded the exploits and travails of the expedition on which he and his men discovered Monterey Bay.

During the second half of the eighteenth century, Franciscan friars were sent to aid the establishment of a strong foothold by founding missions in the vast territory of Alta California (Upper California; now the U.S. state of California) and Baja California (Lower California; now the Mexican states of Baja California Sur and Baja California). Noted for their dedication, their letters, and their diaries are Fray Junípero Serra, Fray Juan Crespi, and Fray Francisco Palóu. Particularly zealous, Serra is famous for having established the 21 missions in the state of California whose buildings are still standing.

While images of the fabled Amazons and their Queen Califia permeated many a conquistador's imagination, the equally mythical Strait of Anián, supposedly a watery thoroughfare connecting the Pacific and Atlantic Oceans through the upper parts of what is now Canada, motivated the Spanish Crown to finance expeditions farther north. Among the several groups sent from Acapulco to find the strait were the Juan Pérez expedition, of 1774, and the Alejandro Malaspina expedition, of 1789–94; each left behind a member's detailed diary.

## The Memory of Antiquity

Antonio de Herrera y Tordesillas was the royal chronicler of Spain's Philip II. In his *Historia general de los hechos de los castellanos en las islas y tierra firme del mar océano* (1601–15, translated in 1725–26 as *General History of the Spaniards*), a multivolume account of the conquest of the New World, he writes:

> The nations of New Spain preserved the memory of their antiquities. In Yucatán and Honduras there were certain books in which the Indians recorded the events of their times, together with their knowledge of plants, animals and other natural things.
>
> In the Province of Mexico, they had libraries of histories and calendars, which they painted with pictures. Whatever had a concrete form was painted in its own image, while if it lacked a form, they represented it by other characters. Thus they set down what they wished.

A library is a suitable image for the pre-Columbian peoples' wealth of knowledge and spirituality. For what is a library—whether it consists of symbols, codices, alphabetical transcriptions of oral tales, multivolume histories, or what have you—but a depository of memory? The past had been essential for the Aztecs, the Incas, and other pre-Columbian civilizations, just as it was for the Spaniards. In dismantling the material culture they found in the New World, the Spaniards over time sought to destroy memories of it. Some missionaries might have attempted to rescue oral traditions, even codices, but the rescuing was performed in such a way as to divorce that material from the society that had nurtured it. In essence, colonization became a program of devastation meant to undermine not only the future of the indigenous population but its past as well.

Still available to readers are Mayan texts—such as the *Popol Vuh* and *Chilam Balam of Chumayet*—in which religious doctrines are among the information presented in detail. A substantial number of love and epic poems remain. Often they were written anonymously, in part because many pre-Columbian civilizations did not emphasize individualism, but the recognized aboriginal poets included Axayacatl, Nezahualpilli, and Cacamatzin. The most talented of them, capable of depicting extreme varieties of feeling and thought, is Nezahualcóyotl, a fifteenth-century king of Tezcoco. A product of Chichimeca and Toltec cultures, he is at once a proto-existentialist, a lover of *pulque* (a traditional beverage made from the fermented juice of maguey), a battle-hardened warrior, and a tortured political leader. Brutality infused the poet-king's life. At a young age, he witnessed the assassination of his father. As an adult, Nezahualcóyotl arranged the death of his loyal follower Cuacuauhtzin to marry his friend's wife. But the king was also a promoter of the arts, devoted to building a gathering place for artists and intellectuals. Nezahualcóyotl's poetry is ingrained with a philosophical inquisitiveness that makes it surprisingly modern. Consider his poem "I Shall Never Disappear":

> I shall never disappear.
> I am intoxicated.
> I weep, I grieve,
> I think, I speak,
> within myself I discover this:
> I shall never die,
> never disappear.
> Let me go to the place
> where there is no death,
> where death is overcome:
> I shall never disappear.

Or "Song of the Flight":

> Live peacefully,
> pass life calmly!
> I am bent over,
> I live with my head bowed
> beside the people.
> For this I am weeping,
> I am wretched!
> I have remained alone
> beside the people on earth.
> How has Your heart decided,
> Giver of Life?
> Dismiss Your displeasure!
> Extend Your compassion,
> I am at Your side, You are God.
> Perhaps You would bring death to me?
> Is it true that we are happy,
> that we live on the earth?
> It is certain that we live.

Is it possible to unravel the ways in which the pre-Columbian mind approached the universe? What were its ethos and pathos? Which obsessions overwhelmed it? How did these ancient civilizations use language to explore their social and spiritual conditions? By the seventeenth century, Spanish-language writers such as Sor Juana Inés de La Cruz and Carlos de Sigüenza y Góngora were embracing the Indian legacy in their work. The fragmented texts available today have passed through various editorial filters, as the quest to understand pre-Columbian societies has inspired experts and aficionados from the nineteenth-century German scientist Alexander von Humboldt to the twentieth-century U.S. anthropologist Franz Boas and beyond. In the Americas, during the twentieth century, influential work opening up the pre-Hispanic mind was done by scholars such as Manuel Gamio, Pablo González Casanova, Angel María Garibay, Fernando Horcasitas Pimentel, and Miguel León Portilla. Inspired in part by work such as theirs have been Spanish-language writers such as Miguel Angel Asturias and José María Arguedas.

For centuries, however, the Indian worldview lay dormant in the Latino literary traditions. It was not until the arrival of *Modernismo*, an aesthetic movement that swept through Latin America, from Nicaragua to Colombia, between 1885 and 1915, that a renewed appreciation for aboriginal civilizations took shape south of the Rio Grande. *Modernismo* was followed by a determination—known as *Indigenismo*—not only to recover indigenous traditions but to place them decisively at the center of Latin American identity. The echoes of *Indigenismo* reverberated during the Chicano Movement in the United States, from the late 1960s to the 1970s. The poet Alurista (Alberto Baltazar Heredia Urista; see p. 1657) introduced the concept of Aztlán, a mythological Chicano homeland, at the first National Chicano Youth Liberation Conference, sponsored by Rodolfo "Corky" Gonzales's Crusade for Justice organization (p. 787). Attendees of this conference drafted the *Plan Espiritual de Aztlán*, a political manifesto that underscored the Indian and mestizo (mixed European and Indian) heritage of the Chicano people. Other early Chicano Movement writers, such as Rudolfo A. Anaya (p. 1160), Luis Valdez (p. 1244), Ana Castillo (p. 1978), and Lorna Dee Cervantes (p. 2011), emphasized their indigenous roots. Carlos Castaneda— a subversive, UCLA-trained anthropologist of Peruvian descent—explored Yaqui culture in early works such as his doctoral dissertation, *The Teachings of Don Juan* (1968). Such uses of the indigenous ancestry, grounding political and cultural searches in the pre-Columbian past, make clear how essential the colonial period is to the Latino literary tradition.

## An Effort at Replenishment

Many works featured in this anthology were translated by or influenced by Herbert Eugene Bolton, the superb historian of the Spanish heritage in the United States, at times described as "a historian of the borderlands." Born in Wisconsin in 1870 and a professor at the University of California, Berkeley, for over four decades, Bolton was an avid, erudite interpreter of the colonial past in the Southwest, responsible for almost a hundred books. His overall view was that American history needed to be approached holistically. In an address he delivered in 1932 at the American Historical Association, in Toronto, he stated: "European history cannot be learned from books dealing alone with England or France, or Germany, or Italy, or Russia; nor can American history be adequately presented if confined to Brazil, or Chile, or Mexico, or Canada, or the United States. In my own country the study of thirteen English colonies and the United States in isolation has obscured many of the larger factors in their development and helped to raise up a nation of chauvinists." What Bolton, who died in 1953, promoted was an understanding that north and south in these hemispheres are conventions, not actual divisions. To know American history is to appreciate it beyond linguistic, cultural, and national parameters.

Bolton's books on the Spanish explorers from Florida to California are essential reading. He not only translated Fray Eusebio Francisco Kino, Fray Juan Crespi, Juan Bautista de Anza, Fray Francisco Palóu, and many others; he established a context in which to appreciate them collectively, as actors in a Spanish Golden Age play. Bolton was instrumental in making the Bancroft Library, at Berkeley, a crucial research center for colonial history, including, of course, the foundation of the Latino literary tradition.

# FRAY BARTOLOMÉ DE LAS CASAS
## 1484–1566

Fray Bartolomé de Las Casas has acquired mythical stature. Since the mid-twentieth century, when his works were widely disseminated in accessible editions in the Spanish-language world, he has been associated with movements such as *Indigenismo*, which sought to vindicate the rights of the aboriginal population in Latin America. Political figures such as Rigoberta Menchú, the Guatemalan human rights activist and winner of the Nobel Peace Prize in 1992, and Subcomandante Marcos, leader of the Zapatista uprising in Chiapas, Mexico, in 1994, have taken inspiration from him.

Known even in his time as the "Father of the Indians" and "Defender of the Indians," Las Casas was one of the first missionaries in the New World to denounce the atrocities of the Spanish conquest and to document the decimation of the indigenous population. He was born in Seville, Spain, to a family of *conversos*, that is, Jewish converts. The experiences of his father, a merchant who accompanied Columbus on his second voyage, in 1493, inspired Las Casas to visit the New World colonies. After being trained in Latin and humanistic studies, he traveled to the West Indies in 1502, and there he joined the Diego de Velásquez expedition to Cuba. He then traveled to Hispaniola (Haiti and the Dominican Republic), where he spent a few years as an *encomendero*, a titleholder granted control of land and of native workers. He gradually came to abhor this system and its allocation of forced Indian labor among the Spanish colonists.

Las Casas's political awakening came in 1511, when he heard a sermon preached by the Dominican friar Antonio de Montesinos indicting the Spanish settlers for their mistreatment of the Indians. A year later, he became the first priest ordained in the colonies, and from then on he spoke out against Indian slavery and in favor of the evangelization of the islands' native populations. Recognition of their humanity, he hoped, would lead to their humane treatment. In 1515, he returned to Spain and—to anyone who would listen—presented his grievances related to the unjust manner of Spanish colonization.

In 1527, Las Casas began writing his *Historia de las Indias* (History of the Indies), which he worked on for over three decades but died before completing. Published in three volumes in 1875, it combines valuable ethnographic information with the polemical discourse and rhetorical strategies that characterized most of Las Casas's narratives about the disastrous encounter between Spaniards and Indians. In addition to providing detailed information from Columbus's travel journal, describing the character and customs of the Indians, and detailing the flora and fauna he encountered in the Caribbean Basin, the friar decries the brutal methods employed by the Spaniards in their conquest and settlement of the Americas.

Las Casas's most enduring work is *Brevísima relación de la destrucción de las Indias* (1552), an exposé and a passionate indictment of rapacious plundering. It was translated almost immediately into French and Dutch, and in 1599 it was translated into English as *The Destruction of the Indies: A Brief Account*. In Europe, Las Casas's treatise generated controversy regarding the humanity of the Indians, galvanized perceptions of the Spaniards as a cruel and violent people, and gave origin to the *leyenda negra*, that is, the Black Legend, constructed to demean the Spanish people. Ultimately, the work and the legend derived from it served as an ideological and political tool against the power of the Spanish Empire.

*The Destruction of the Indies*, here translated as *The Devastation of the Indies*, provides an overall view of the Native American peoples, focusing on those in the Caribbean islands where the Spaniards first set foot after their long voyage across the Atlantic. Las Casas discusses the natives' mild dispositions, humility, lack of avarice, obedience, innocence, and so forth. He then proceeds to detail the ways in which the settlers are destroying these peoples. According to Las Casas's eyewitness account, Hispaniola had a population of over three million; he estimates that on the mainland over 15 million died. Some of Las Casas's critics point out his tendency to exaggerate not only the virtues of the indigenous populations but also the cruelty of the Spaniards and the number of deaths. Nevertheless, by the end of the first century of colonization most of the indigenous populations of the New World islands had vanished as a result of war, mistreatment, illnesses to which they had no immunity, or suicide.

Las Casas takes two approaches to criticizing the abuses against the natives. The less successful approach consists of inconclusive scientific experiments designed to demonstrate more-intelligent methods of carrying out the colonization. More persuasive is Las Casas's theoretical approach, based on juridical and philosophical issues. He argues that although Pope Alexander VI—in his Papal Bull *Inter Caetera*, published May 4, 1493—gave the Spanish Crown the rights to American territories, (1) the Spaniards had no right to enslave the Indians; (2) the Spaniards had no right to claim the Indians' land and property; and (3) the Spanish Crown, seeking the conversion of the Indians to Catholicism, continually promulgated laws to protect the Indians and did not approve of the violence against them.

Las Casas begins with a preface about his impetus for writing the book. He follows that with a prologue advising Spain's King Philip of the horrors being perpetrated against the Indians in the colonies and imploring the king to stop the decimation. In the 21 sections of the main text, Las Casas reviews the colonization process throughout Latin America. Focusing on one geographic area at a time, he describes the systematic destruction of the Indians. Colonists wantonly kill Indians for sport; punish minor infractions by cutting off hands, feet, heads; work men to death in the mines and women to death in the agricultural fields; starve people; let dogs loose on them; steal women from their parents and husbands and violate them; spear pregnant women with swords; kill babies by throwing them "against the crags" or "into the rivers."

In this anthology, the first selection from the work is Las Casas's overview of the Caribbean islands and of the Spaniards' depopulation of the islands. The second selection, "Hispaniola," enumerates the cruelest ways in which the colonists are murdering the Indians. "That Part of the Mainland Called Florida" focuses on the four major expeditions undertaken to Florida, most likely those of Juan Ponce de León (1513); Lucas Vázquez de Ayllón (1526); Pánfilo de Narváez, in which Álvar Núñez Cabeza de Vaca participated (1527); and Hernando de Soto (1539–40). Las Casas underscores these expeditions' tyrannical treatment of the Indians in the Florida territories.

In his introduction to *The Devastation of the Indies*, the historian Bill M. Donovan ponders the essential questions posed by Las Casas, such as *How should one react to horrific injustice? How is one's reaction affected by cultural and geographic distance? Do the colonized (representing "barbarism") have the same rights as the colonizers (representing "civilization"), such as to their own land and their own culture? If the colonizers do not recognize the rights of the colonized—if in fact the "civilized" eradicate the "barbarous"—are the colonizers truly "civilized"?*

Las Casas is often viewed as the moral conscience of the Spanish Conquest. One of the major contradictions of the friar's life, however, was that while he argued for the humane treatment of the islands' native populations, he condoned the importation of African slaves to replace the declining Indian laborers, an approach he later regretted. Among his additional writings are tracts, letters, memorials, legal arguments, and the historical works *Apologética historia sumaria de las Indias* (Apologetic Summary History of the Indies, 1561) and *Historia general de las Indias* (General History of the Indies, 1561).

## From THE DEVASTATION OF THE INDIES: A BRIEF ACCOUNT[1]

The Indies[2] were discovered in the year one thousand four hundred and ninety-two. In the following year a great many Spaniards went there with the intention of settling the land. Thus, forty-nine years have passed since the first settlers penetrated the land, the first so-claimed being the large and most happy isle called Hispaniola,[3] which is six hundred leagues in circumference.[4] Around it in all directions are many other islands, some very big, others very small, and all of them were, as we saw with our own eyes, densely populated with native peoples called Indians. This large island was perhaps the most densely populated place in the world. There must be close to two hundred leagues of land on this island, and the seacoast has been explored for more than ten thousand leagues, and each day more of it is being explored. And all the land so far discovered is a beehive of people; it is as though God had crowded into these lands the great majority of mankind.

And of all the infinite universe of humanity, these people are the most guileless, the most devoid of wickedness and duplicity, the most obedient and faithful to their native masters and to the Spanish Christians whom they serve. They are by nature the most humble, patient, and peaceable, holding no grudges, free from embroilments, neither excitable nor quarrelsome. These people are the most devoid of rancors, hatreds, or desire for vengeance of any people in the world. And because they are so weak and complaisant, they are less able to endure heavy labor and soon die of no matter what malady. The sons of nobles among us, brought up in the enjoyments of life's refinements, are no more delicate than are these Indians, even those among them who are of the lowest rank of laborers. They are also poor people, for they not only possess little but have no desire to possess worldly goods. For this reason they are not arrogant, embittered, or greedy. Their repasts are such that the food of the holy fathers in the desert can scarcely be more parsimonious, scanty, and poor. As to their dress, they are generally naked, with only their pudenda covered somewhat. And when they cover their shoulders it is with a square cloth no more than two varas in size.[5] They have no beds, but sleep on a kind of matting or else in a kind of suspended net called *hamacas*. They are very clean in their persons, with alert, intelligent minds, docile and open to doctrine, very apt to receive our holy Catholic faith, to be endowed with virtuous customs, and to behave in a godly fashion. And once they begin to hear the tidings of the Faith, they are so insistent on knowing more and on taking the sacraments of the Church and on observing the divine cult that, truly, the missionaries who are here need to be endowed by God with great patience in order to cope with such eagerness. Some of the secular Spaniards who have been here for many years say that the goodness of the Indians is undeniable and that if this

1. Translated by Herma Briffault. Except as indicated, all footnotes are Briffault's. The anthology editors have transposed one note, omitted one, and made minor, stylistic changes to others.
2. India—*Las Indias*—was what the Spanish discoverers called the islands in the Caribbean and the coasts of Central and South America, being as we know under the misapprehension of having found the sea route to India.
3. Hispaniola—Small Spain—° ° ° is the Caribbean island that comprises the Dominican Republic and the Republic of Haiti.
4. A Spanish *legua* comprises roughly 3½ miles.
5. A *vara* is a unit of length about 2.4 ft.

gifted people could be brought to know the one true God they would be the most fortunate people in the world.

Yet into this sheepfold, into this land of meek outcasts there came some Spaniards who immediately behaved like ravening wild beasts, wolves, tigers, or lions that had been starved for many days. And Spaniards have behaved in no other way during the past forty years, down to the present time, for they are still acting like ravening beasts, killing, terrorizing, afflicting, torturing, and destroying the native peoples, doing all this with the strangest and most varied new methods of cruelty, never seen or heard of before, and to such a degree that this Island of Hispaniola, once so populous (having a population that I estimated to be more than three millions), has now a population of barely two hundred persons.

The island of Cuba is nearly as long as the distance between Valladolid and Rome; it is now almost completely depopulated. San Juan[6] and Jamaica are two of the largest, most productive and attractive islands; both are now deserted and devastated. On the northern side of Cuba and Hispaniola lie the neighboring Lucayos[7] comprising more than sixty islands including those called *Gigantes*, beside numerous other islands, some small some large. The least felicitous of them were more fertile and beautiful than the gardens of the King of Seville. They have the healthiest lands in the world, where lived more than five hundred thousand souls; they are now deserted, inhabited by not a single living creature. All the people were slain or died after being taken into captivity and brought to the Island of Hispaniola to be sold as slaves. When the Spaniards saw that some of these had escaped, they sent a ship to find them, and it voyaged for three years among the islands searching for those who had escaped being slaughtered, for a good Christian[8] had helped them escape, taking pity on them and had won them over to Christ; of these there were eleven persons and these I saw.

More than thirty other islands in the vicinity of San Juan are for the most part and for the same reason depopulated, and the land laid waste. On these islands I estimate there are 2,100 leagues of land that have been ruined and depopulated, empty of people.

As for the vast mainland, which is ten times larger than all Spain, even including Aragón and Portugal, containing more land than the distance between Seville and Jerusalem, or more than two thousand leagues, we are sure that our Spaniards, with their cruel and abominable acts, have devastated the land and exterminated the rational people who fully inhabited it. We can estimate very surely and truthfully that in the forty years that have passed, with the infernal actions of the Christians, there have been unjustly slain more than twelve million men, women, and children. In truth, I believe without trying to deceive myself that the number of the slain is more like fifteen million.

The common way mainly employed by the Spaniards who call themselves Christian and who have gone there to extirpate those pitiful nations and wipe them off the earth is by unjustly waging cruel and bloody wars. Then, when they have slain all those who fought for their lives or to escape the

6. San Juan is the old name of the island of Puerto Rico.
7. The Lucayos and Gigantes comprise today's Bahamas.
8. Briffault identifies him as Pedro de Ysla, a trader. [Anthology editors' note]

tortures they would have to endure, that is to say, when they have slain all the native rulers and young men (since the Spaniards usually spare only the women and children, who are subjected to the hardest and bitterest servitude ever suffered by man or beast), they enslave any survivors. With these infernal methods of tyranny they debase and weaken countless numbers of those pitiful Indian nations.

Their reason for killing and destroying such an infinite number of souls is that the Christians have an ultimate aim, which is to acquire gold, and to swell themselves with riches in a very brief time and thus rise to a high estate disproportionate to their merits. It should be kept in mind that their insatiable greed and ambition, the greatest ever seen in the world, is the cause of their villainies. And also, those lands are so rich and felicitous, the native peoples so meek and patient, so easy to subject, that our Spaniards have no more consideration for them than beasts. And I say this from my own knowledge of the acts I witnessed. But I should not say "than beasts" for, thanks be to God, they have treated beasts with some respect; I should say instead like excrement on the public squares. And thus they have deprived the Indians of their lives and souls, for the millions I mentioned have died without the Faith and without the benefit of the sacraments. This is a well-known and proven fact which even the tyrant Governors, themselves killers, know and admit. And never have the Indians in all the Indies committed any act against the Spanish Christians, until those Christians have first and many times committed countless cruel aggressions against them or against neighboring nations. For in the beginning the Indians regarded the Spaniards as angels from Heaven.[9] Only after the Spaniards had used violence against them, killing, robbing, torturing, did the Indians ever rise up against them.

## Hispaniola

On the Island Hispaniola was where the Spaniards first landed, as I have said. Here those Christians perpetrated their first ravages and oppressions against the native peoples. This was the first land in the New World to be destroyed and depopulated by the Christians, and here they began their subjection of the women and children, taking them away from the Indians to use them and ill use them, eating the food they provided with their sweat and toil. The Spaniards did not content themselves with what the Indians gave them of their own free will, according to their ability, which was always too little to satisfy enormous appetites, for a Christian eats and consumes in one day an amount of food that would suffice to feed three houses inhabited by ten Indians for one month. And they committed other acts of force and violence and oppression which made the Indians realize that these men had not come from Heaven. And some of the Indians concealed their foods while others concealed their wives and children

9. "Come and behold the men who have stepped down from heaven, and bring them food and drink." According to Columbus' ship's diary, these were the words uttered by the inhabitants of the Antilles upon first greeting the Spaniards. The Mayas and Aztecs, too, regarded the Europeans as of supernatural descent—because of their height, their skin color, and their beards.

and still others fled to the mountains to avoid the terrible transactions of the Christians.

And the Christians attacked them with buffets[1] and beatings, until finally they laid hands on the nobles of the villages. Then they behaved with such temerity and shamelessness that the most powerful ruler of the islands had to see his own wife raped by a Christian officer.

From that time onward the Indians began to seek ways to throw the Christians out of their lands. They took up arms, but their weapons were very weak and of little service in offense and still less in defense. (Because of this, the wars of the Indians against each other are little more than games played by children.) And the Christians, with their horses and swords and pikes began to carry out massacres and strange cruelties against them. They attacked the towns and spared neither the children nor the aged nor pregnant women nor women in childbed, not only stabbing them and dismembering them but cutting them to pieces as if dealing with sheep in the slaughter house. They laid bets as to who, with one stroke of the sword, could split a man in two or could cut off his head or spill out his entrails with a single stroke of the pike. They took infants from their mothers' breasts, snatching them by the legs and pitching them headfirst against the crags or snatched them by the arms and threw them into the rivers, roaring with laughter and saying as the babies fell into the water, "Boil there, you offspring of the devil!" Other infants they put to the sword along with their mothers and anyone else who happened to be nearby. They made some low wide gallows on which the hanged victim's feet almost touched the ground, stringing up their victims in lots of thirteen, in memory of Our Redeemer and His twelve Apostles, then set burning wood at their feet and thus burned them alive. To others they attached straw or wrapped their whole bodies in straw and set them afire. With still others, all those they wanted to capture alive, they cut off their hands and hung them round the victim's neck, saying, "Go now, carry the message," meaning, Take the news to the Indians who have fled to the mountains. They usually dealt with the chieftains and nobles in the following way: they made a grid of rods which they placed on forked sticks, then lashed the victims to the grid and lighted a smoldering fire underneath, so that little by little, as those captives screamed in despair and torment, their souls would leave them.

I once saw this, when there were four or five nobles lashed on grids and burning; I seem even to recall that there were two or three pairs of grids where others were burning, and because they uttered such loud screams that they disturbed the captain's sleep, he ordered them to be strangled. And the constable, who was worse than an executioner, did not want to obey that order (and I know the name of that constable and know his relatives in Seville), but instead put a stick over the victims' tongues, so they could not make a sound, and he stirred up the fire, but not too much, so that they roasted slowly, as he liked. I saw all these things I have described, and countless others.

And because all the people who could do so fled to the mountains to escape these inhuman, ruthless, and ferocious acts, the Spanish captains, enemies of the human race, pursued them with the fierce dogs they kept which attacked the Indians, tearing them to pieces and devouring them. And because on few and far between occasions, the Indians justifiably killed

---

1. Blows. [Anthology editors' note]

some Christians, the Spaniards made a rule among themselves that for every Christian slain by the Indians, they would slay a hundred Indians.

*　　*　　*

## That Part of the Mainland Called Florida

Into these mainland provinces have gone three tyrants at different times from the year one thousand five hundred and ten or eleven, to commit the nefarious acts that have been committed by other tyrants, especially two of them, in other parts of the Indies, so as to rise in rank beyond their merits.[2] And all three tyrants have come to a bad end, losing their lives and possessions, the houses they built in other times with the blood and sweat of the Indians, and their memory is erased from the earth as if they had never lived. They left the entire world scandalized and their names have become a byword of horror and infamy. God ended their lives before they could do more harm. And God has punished them for the evil deeds they committed, deeds I know about, having seen them with my own eyes.

The fourth and the latest tyrant-Governor[3] was appointed with a great to-do in this year one thousand five hundred and thirty-eight. Nothing has been heard of him for three years but we are sure that if he is still alive, wherever he has gone he will have inflicted many cruelties, will have destroyed many nations, for he is of the same breed as those who have ravaged and destroyed most provinces and perpetrated most vile deeds, along with his comrades, but we believe still more strongly that God may have given him the same ending to his life that He gave the other tyrants.

Three or four years after writing the above, I learn that those tyrants who conquered Florida have departed that land, leaving behind them their dead leader. He had committed unheard-of cruelties, which his inhuman comrades repeated against those innocent and harmless peoples. Thus my surmise has been proven not to have been false. His vile deeds were too many and too terrible to recount. I will only reaffirm what I said at the beginning, to wit: The more the conquerors discover new lands, the more lands and peoples do they destroy and with ever greater iniquities against God and man. It is wearisome to dwell on their bloody deeds, the deeds not of men but of wild beasts. I will not tell of their cruelties in detail, but will only relate as an example the following.

On these lands lived a population that was wise, well disposed, politically well organized. As usual, the tyrants perpetrated massacres with the aim of instilling and spreading terror. They afflicted, they killed the people, they took captives and compelled them to carry intolerable loads, like beasts of burden. And when one of the burden-bearers sank under the load, they cut off his head at the neck-chain, so as not to interrupt the march of the others, since they were all chained together, and as I have related above, the head fell to one side of the road, while the body fell to the other.

---

2. Briffault identifies them as Pánfilo de Narváez, Juan Ponce de León, and Álvar Núñez Cabeza de Vaca. [Anthology editors' note]
3. * * * Hernando de Soto.

When the conquerors entered a town, they were greeted cheerfully and were given all the food they required and were assigned six hundred Indians to carry their loads and attend to their horses for their journeys into the interior.

A relative of the leading tyrant returned unexpectedly from one of these journeys to rob and slay all these people who had thought themselves secure, and he killed with his pike the ruler of the land and committed many other atrocities.

In another village where the people appeared to be more reserved and grudging and were so, because of what they had heard about the horrible acts of the Spaniards, they put all the people to the sword, men, women, and children, young and old, chieftains and subjects, for they spared no one.

Then there was the time when they summoned a great number of Indians, more than two hundred, from another village, or perhaps they came of their own accord. The Spaniards cut their faces from the nose and lips down to the chin and sent them in this lamentable condition, streaming with blood, to carry the news of the miraculous things being done by the Spaniards, advocates of the holy Faith of baptized Catholics. And judge, then, how those people felt, how much love they could have for the Christians, and how they could believe in a God who considered such things good and just, or in the religion the Spaniards professed or in the immaculate Faith of which they boasted. Very great and strange were the evil deeds committed there by those wretched men, children of perdition. And thus, the worst of those wretches, the captain-general, died as if by accident, without confession, and thus no doubt he is now deep in the infernal regions suffering eternal torment, unless perhaps God in His infinite mercy intervenes to ease his punishment, an undeserved relief, considering his execrable misdeeds.

1550–52

---

# ÁLVAR NÚÑEZ CABEZA DE VACA
## ca. 1490–ca. 1560

The first voyager ácross the American continent to have survived the journey and written about it, Álvar Núñez Cabeza de Vaca has become an emblem of the trekker misconstrued as an explorer. From 1528 to 1536, having survived the disastrous expedition to Florida of Pánfilo de Narváez, he traversed a large portion of land from present-day Florida through present-day Georgia, Alabama, Mississippi, Louisiana, Texas, New Mexico, and Arizona. Like a modern-day biologist and anthropologist, he observed the flora and fauna in these lands, as well as the social behavior of the natives he encountered (almost a dozen recognizable tribes, from the Apalachees to the Coahuiltecans).

Cabeza de Vaca was born between 1485 and 1492. Roughly between 1502 and 1527, he worked for a series of dukes of Medina Sidonia, one of the oldest Spanish ducal houses to be formed by the king. (Other members of the Cabeza de Vaca family also lived at the duke's court.) He was one of the duke's stewards—a *camarero*, or personal attendant.

His military career included participation in the company that traveled to Italy to take Naples. He appears to have taken part in the Spanish attack on Bologna and in the decisive battle of Ravenna (1512), in which the French all but destroyed the Spanish forces in Italy. He participated in the 1520 effort by the duke of Medina Sidonia to put down a *Comunero* revolt in Seville, a popular uprising against converted Jews known as *conversos*, and was supported by the ducal house of Arcos, in Andalusia. Probably around the same time, he married María Marmolejo, who, some scholars believe, came from a *converso* family. Between then and his decision to join the Narváez expedition, little is known of his whereabouts or activities.

The Narváez expedition embarked from Spain with five ships and a crew of some 600 men. They sailed out of San Lúcar de Barrameda, a Mediterranean port at the mouth of the Guadalquivir River, stopped briefly in the Canary Islands, in mid-August arrived in Hispaniola, and then went onward to Cuba. In Cuba, they encountered a hurricane and lost two ships and scores of men. After crossing to the mainland, they found the inhabitants hostile and the food scarce. At some point, they abandoned their ships, and three-quarters of the expeditionary force marched inland. About 300 men died on this trek and, later, in small boats. The four survivors—the Moroccan slave Estevanico, Andrés Dorantes, Alonso del Castillo Maldonado, and Cabeza de Vaca—began an inland journey that, in today's geography, started near Austin and San Antonio, went northward toward the Colorado River and then on to the region of Midland, Pecos, and Carlsbad; the region of El Paso; and finally south to Culiacán, Guadalajara, and Mexico City. Soon after Cabeza de Vaca and his three companions reached Mexico City, he cowrote with Dorantes and Maldonado an account of the expedition, known as the "Joint Report," which has been lost.

In the spring of 1537, Cabeza de Vaca returned to Spain, where he spent the next three years seeking a royal commission and preparing his *La relación* (1542), known in English as *Chronicle of the Narváez Expedition*. His dream was to become *Adelantado* (governor of a border province) of Florida, and he asked the king to name him to that post. When the king instead gave it to Hernando de Soto, Cabeza de Vaca sought a similar position in the Río de la Plata, in the region known today as Argentina and Paraguay, after news of the death by starvation of the person who had held the job, Pedro de Mendoza. In 1540, by royal contract, Cabeza de Vaca became governor of the province of La Plata and also *Adelantado* of any new lands that might be discovered.

The age of Spanish exploration in the New World was quickly coming to an end, replaced by a move to institutionalize the viceroyship of the various lands conquered in these efforts. "Just as he and his fellows returning to New Spain from the wilderness of Florida in 1537 had to come to grips with the end of the period of freewheeling entrepreneurship on the American mainland," argue Rolena Adorno and Charles Pautz in their scholarly edition of the *Chronicle*, "so too his appointment in 1540 to the exalted titles of *Adelantado* and governor came at a time when the power and privilege therein promised were harder than ever to achieve." He held these positions between 1541 and 1545, but his power, if any, quickly eroded. The title of *Adelantado* usually generated animosity, and those under Cabeza de Vaca's tutelage rebelled against him. He was eventually arrested and brought back to Spain in chains. In his only other book, *Comentarios*, Cabeza de Vaca chronicles his period in South America, his return home, and subsequent events.

On the Iberian Peninsula, in 1546, four lawsuits were brought against him concerning abuse of power and violence against the Native American populations. He first was imprisoned and subsequently was put under house arrest. He suffered intensely during this time, mainly from public embarrassment. In 1551, a court stripped him of his titles, banned him from returning to the New World, and sentenced him to time in an Algerian penal colony. He appealed, the case was reopened, and his sentence was reduced the following year to the stripping of his titles and banishment from only the Río de la Plata; he did not have to go to the penal colony. After negotiations with the authorities, Cabeza de Vaca received some compensation for lost assets. Still, he had endured an eight-year affront.

When the 1555 edition of *Relación y comentarios* was released, Cabeza de Vaca apparently was stationed in Seville. Sometime between then and his death, he returned to Jerez de la Frontera, a municipality in Andalusia. In his biography *The Odyssey of Cabeza de Vaca* (1933), Morris Bishop claimed that Cabeza de Vaca had died "penniless, old, and broken-hearted" from his trial, but recent scholarship indicates that Cabeza de Vaca paid a ransom for a relative held captive in Algiers; he was alive and well in the late winter and early spring of 1559; and he was buried in the Real Convento de Santo Domingo, where one of his grandfathers, a military man, had been laid to rest.

The portrait of Cabeza de Vaca and his three close companions that emerges from *La relación* is colored by its author's stupefaction. Cabeza de Vaca's account is a veritable descent to chaos and should be read as a Dantean pilgrimage through the chambers of hell and purgatory. In it, order (a well-planned expedition) becomes disorder (physical and linguistic disorientation), which, through lessons learned and a tale told, returns to order (a document useful for future expeditions). Cabeza de Vaca offers an excruciating account of his journey, emphasizing that his faith in Jesus Christ kept him alive. After the expedition's internal struggle for power, the men encountered obstacles such as terrible weather, swamps, snakes, and treacherous paths through brutal vegetation. He and Narváez parted ways, and Cabeza de Vaca's group went on to suffer illness and starvation.

In this anthology, the first excerpts from *La relación* are chapters 1–4, about the Narváez expedition's collapse. In the subsequent selections, chapters 19–26, Cabeza de Vaca assesses his adventures with the Indians, whom he claims to have healed with his Christ-like powers. (He was actually distributing bogus remedies that he thought were medicines.) Often he feels at odds with what he sees, but more often he is humble and nonjudgmental. He perceives the natives as friends, but he is constantly on guard and criticizes their behavior, describing acts of back-stabbing, ambush, and revenge. In one of the most controversial sections of the book, chapter 19, he presents the Indian population as uncivilized: "All over the land there are vast and handsome pastures, with good grass for cattle, and it strikes me that the soil would be very fertile were the country inhabited and improved by reasoning people."

William T. Pilkington, an American scholar of southwestern literature, has called Cabeza de Vaca "not only a physical trailblazer; he was also a literary pioneer, and he deserves the distinction of being called the Southwest's first writer." He adds: "The *Relación*, while not fiction, possesses most of the attributes of a good novel." In fact, it might be better described as a fictional account, or perhaps a factual novel, for Cabeza de Vaca has a most unorthodox approach to facts. Even when it was first published, the narrative's accuracy was in question. Speaking for many, Trinidad Barrera, a scholar of Spanish culture in the Americas, has called Cabeza de Vaca's account "*el máximo ejemplo de la insensatez e improvisación*" (the supreme example of insensibility and improvisation).

What was Cabeza de Vaca's objective in *La relación*, written about half a decade after the events took place? "No service is left to me," he explains in the prologue, which is dedicated to the king,

> but to bring an account to Your Majesty of the nine years I wandered. . . . In this way you will know and understand the manner of the lands and the provinces in them, what foods and animals grow there, the customs of the many barbarous nations with which I had contact and lived, and many other details that I was able to experience and know so that in some way I will have been of service to Your Majesty.

To judge Cabeza de Vaca's truthfulness and objectivity, one can read his book against another account of the Narváez expedition, by Gonzalo Fernández de Oviedo y Valdés (1478–1557), included in *Historia general y natural de las Indias* (General and Natural History of the Indies; book 35, chapters 1–7).

## FROM CHRONICLE OF THE NARVÁEZ EXPEDITION[1]

## Chapter One. When the Fleet Left Spain and the Men Who Went with It

On the twenty-seventh day of the month of June 1527,[2] Governor Pánfilo de Narváez departed from the port of San Lúcar de Barrameda,[3] with power and mandate from Your Majesty[4] to conquer and govern the provinces that extend from the River of the Palms[5] to the Cape of Florida,[6] which lie on the mainland. Five vessels went with him, and about six hundred men. His officers, who need to be mentioned here, were the following: Cabeza de Vaca, treasurer and chief legal officer;[7] Alonso Enríquez, comptroller; and Alonso de Solís, Your Majesty's tax agent and inspector.[8] A friar of the order of Saint Francis named Fray Juan Xuárez went as commissary,[9] along with four other monks of the order.

We arrived at the Island of Santo Domingo,[1] where we remained for nearly forty-five days, supplying ourselves with what was needed, horses in particular. Here more than 140 men of our army left us, wishing to remain as a result of the proposals and promises they had received from the people of the country.

Leaving there, we arrived at Santiago, a port on the island of Cuba[2] where, in the few days we were there, the governor resupplied himself with men, arms, and horses. A gentleman there named Vasco Porcallo,[3] a resident of Trinidad,[4] which is on the same island, offered to give the governor certain supplies he had at a distance of one hundred leagues[5] from the aforementioned harbor of Santiago.

The governor sailed in that direction with the whole fleet, but halfway there, at a port named Cape Santa Cruz,[6] he thought it best to stop and send

1. Translated by Fanny Bandelier, revised and annotated by Harold Augenbraum. Except as indicated, all footnotes are Harold Augenbraum's. The anthology editors have moved one of the notes.
2. Dates are reckoned in the Julian calendar. For dates according to the Gregorian calendar, add ten days. [Introduced by the Roman emperor Julius Caesar in 46 BC, the "Julian" calendar was used in the Western world until 1582, when Pope Gregory XIII replaced it with the "Gregorian" calendar. (In England, the latter was not adopted until 1751.)]
3. San Lúcar de Barrameda is located near the mouth of the Guadalquivir River in southern Spain. In the sixteenth century, it was the point of departure for many expeditions to the Indies.
4. The Emperor Charles V.
5. The modern-day Río de Soto la Marina in the State of Tamaulipas (Mexico).
6. The present-day Florida peninsula.
7. As the expedition's treasurer, Cabeza de Vaca was expected to give an accounting of all income and collect taxes for the crown. His claim to having been appointed to the position of chief legal officer (*alguacil mayor*) may be specious. According to [Rolena] Adorno and [Patrick Charles] Pautz [in *Álvar Núñez Cabeza de Vaca: His Account, His Life, and the Expedition of Pánfilo de Narváez*, 1997], not only is there no documentary

evidence to support this appointment, but contrary evidence exists that this post was occupied by the expedition's leader, Narváez.
8. Like the treasurer, the comptroller, tax agent, and inspector are officials of the royal treasury.
9. In the opening to the 1542 edition, Cabeza de Vaca identifies the commissary as "Gutiérrez." Later in the text, he will be called Xuárez (Suárez, in modern Spanish). In the 1555 edition, he is identified only as "Xuárez," which is consistent with administrative documents of the expedition.
1. The island of Hispañola, or Hispaniola, in the Caribbean Sea. The island is currently divided between the Spanish-speaking Dominican Republic on the east and the French-speaking Haiti on the west.
2. Santiago lies on the southeastern coast of the island of Cuba, in the northeastern Caribbean.
3. Vasco Porcallo de Figueroa was a major figure in the early Spanish development of Cuba. He also accompanied Hernando de Soto on his 1539 expedition on the North American mainland. For more information on Porcallo, see the chronicle of the de Soto expedition by the Gentleman of Elvas.
4. Trinidad lies on the south-central coast of Cuba.
5. A Spanish league varied between 2.7 and 3.1 miles, depending on the region of the country in which it was measured.
6. A spur of land on the southern coast of Cuba. The original Spanish reads "Cabo Cruz."

a single ship to bring back these supplies. He ordered a certain Captain Pantoja to go with his craft and, for increased security, directed me to accompany him, while he stayed with four ships, having purchased one on the Island of Santo Domingo. When we arrived at the port of Trinidad with these two ships, Captain Pantoja went with Vasco Porcallo to the town, which is one league away, in order to take possession of the supplies. I stayed on board with the pilots, who told us that we should leave as soon as possible, since the harbor was very poor and many ships had been lost in it. Now, since what happened to us there was very remarkable, it appears to me not unsuitable for the aims and ends of my narrative to recount it here.[7]

The following morning the weather looked ominous. It began to rain, and the sea became so rough that, although I gave permission for the men to land, when they saw the weather and that the town was a league away, in order to avoid being out in the wet and cold, many came back to the ship. At the same time, a canoe came from the town bringing a letter from a person living there, begging me to come, and saying that I would be given the supplies and whatever else might be necessary.[8] I excused myself, saying that I could not leave the ships.

At noon the canoe came again with another letter, repeating the request, but with a great deal of insistence. They also brought a horse for me to ride. I gave the same reply as the first time, saying that I could not leave the ships. But the pilots and men begged me to leave in order to hasten the transfer of the supplies to the ships so that we would be able to sail soon from a place where they were very much afraid that the ships would be lost if they had to remain for much time. I decided to go, but before I went I left the pilots with instructions and orders that if the south wind should rise, which in those parts often causes ships to be lost, and they found themselves in great danger, they should beach the ships in order to save the men and horses. Then I left, wanting some of the men to accompany me. They refused, however, saying that it was too cold and rainy, and the town too far away. They promised to come, God willing, to hear mass on the following day, which was Sunday.

An hour after my departure, the sea became very rough and the north wind blew so fiercely that the small boats did not dare land, nor could the men beach the ships, since the wind was blowing from the shore. They spent that day and Sunday in great difficulty because of two contrary storms and considerable rain, until nightfall. Then the rain and storm increased in violence at the village as well as on the sea, and all the houses and the churches came crashing down. We had to lock arms and walk seven or eight men together to prevent the wind from carrying us off. It was no less dangerous under the trees than among the houses, since they were also being blown down and we were in danger of being killed underneath them. We wandered about all night in this storm and in danger, without finding anywhere we might feel safe for even half an hour.

In this plight we heard, all night long but especially after midnight, a great uproar, the sound of many voices, and a great noise of small bells, flutes,

7. This is often thought to be the first European account of a hurricane.
8. It is unclear why it was requested that Cabeza de Vaca receive the supplies or who made the request. If it had been Porcallo or Pantoja, one would assume that Cabeza de Vaca would have identified him.

tambourines, and other instruments. Most of this noise lasted until morning, when the storm ended. Such a terrifying thing has never been experienced in these parts.[9] I took depositions about it, and sent them, certified, to Your Majesty.

On Monday morning we went down to the harbor, but did not find the ships. We saw their buoys in the water, and from this knew that the ships were lost, so we followed the shore, looking for wreckage. Not finding any, we turned into the forest. Walking through it we saw, on top of the trees a quarter of a league from the water, a small boat from one of the ships, and ten leagues further, on the coast, were two men of my crew and the tops of several crates. The men's bodies were so disfigured by having been dashed against the rocks that we could not identify them. We also found a cape and a tattered quilt, but nothing else. Sixty people and twenty horses perished on the ships. Those who went on land the day we arrived, some thirty men, were all who survived from the crews of both ships.

We remained in this state for several days, in considerable need and hardship, since the food and supplies at the village had also been destroyed, as well as some cattle. The country was pitiful to see. Trees had fallen and the woods were blighted, with neither leaves nor grass.

The situation continued until the fifth day of the month of November, when the governor arrived with his four ships. They had also weathered a great storm and had escaped by moving to a safe place in time. The people on board the ships and those he found with us were so terrified by what had happened that they were afraid to set to sea again in winter and begged the governor to remain there for the season. In view of their wishes and those of the inhabitants, he decided to winter there. He put me in charge of the ships and their crews, and I was to go with them to the port of Xagua,[1] twelve leagues away, where I remained until the twentieth day of February.

## Chapter Two. How the Governor Came to Xagua and Brought a Pilot with Him

At that point the governor came with a brig he had bought at Trinidad, and with him was a pilot named Miruelo. The governor had brought the man because they said he knew the way and had been on the river of the Palms and was a very good pilot for the whole northern coast. The governor left another ship, which he had bought on the coast of Havana,[2] on which Álvaro de la Cerda remained as captain with forty men and twelve cavalry. Two days after the governor arrived he embarked again. He took along four hundred men and eighty horses, on four ships and one brigantine. The pilot we had taken with us ran the ships aground on what is known as the Canarreo shoals,[3] so that the next day we were stranded and remained stranded for

9. A reference to Spain, to which Cabeza de Vaca had already returned when he wrote this account.
1. The present-day port of Cienfuegos, on the south-central coast of Cuba.
2. Though the original reads "on the coast of

Lixarte," in the 1555 edition, Cabeza de Vaca changed it to "the coast of Havana," and Bandelier follows suit.
3. The Canarroe shoals are an archipelago off the southern coast of Cuba.

fifteen days, the keels often lying on the bottom. Then a southerly storm drove so much water onto the shoals that we were able to get off, though not without considerable danger.

After leaving there, we went to Guaniguanico,[4] where another storm came up and we nearly perished. At Cape Corrientes[5] we had another, which lasted three days. Afterward we rounded the Cape of San Anton[6] and sailed against contrary winds until we were twelve leagues off Havana. On the following day, when we attempted to enter the bay, a southerly storm drove us away, so that we crossed to the coast of Florida, reaching land on Tuesday, the twelfth day of the month of April. We sailed along the coast of Florida, and on Holy Thursday, entered the mouth of a bay on that coast, at the head of which we saw several Indian lodges and dwellings.

## Chapter Three. How We Arrived in Florida

On that day the comptroller, Alonso Enríquez, left his ship and went to an island in the bay and called to the Indians, who came over and spent a good while with him. By way of trade they gave him fish and some venison. The following day, which was Good Friday, the governor left the ship with as many men as his small boats would hold. When we arrived at the Indian huts and lodges we had seen, we found them abandoned and deserted, the people having left that night in their canoes. One of the lodges was so large it could hold more than three hundred people. The others were smaller, and we found a golden rattle among the fishnets. The next day the governor raised standards in behalf of Your Majesty and took possession of the country in Your Royal name. He showed his credentials and was acknowledged as governor according to Your Majesty's commands. We likewise presented our titles to him and he complied, as was required. He then ordered the remainder of the men to disembark, along with the remaining forty-two horses, the others having perished from the great storms and the long time they had been at sea. The few that remained were so thin and weak that they would be of little use for the time being. The following day the Indians of that village arrived and, although they spoke to us, we had no interpreters and did not understand them; but they made many gestures and threats, and it seemed as if they were telling us to leave the country. With that, they left us alone, making no attempt to impede us in any way, and departed.

## Chapter Four. How We Went to the Interior

After another day the governor resolved to go inland to explore the country and see what was there. The commissary, the inspector, and I went with him, along with forty men, among whom were six men with horses, which would be of little use. We took a northerly direction and at the hour of

---

4. A town in western Cuba (Pilar del Río Province).

5. A spur of land on the western edge of Cuba.

6. Again, a section on the western edge of Cuba.

vespers[7] reached a very large bay, which appeared to sweep far inland. After remaining there that night and the next day, we returned to where the ships and men were. The governor ordered the brigantine to ply the coast toward Florida in search of the port that Miruelo, the pilot, had said he knew, but he had missed it and did not know where we were or where the port was. So word was sent to the brigantine that if the port were not found, to cross over to Havana to find Álvaro de la Cerda's ship and, after taking on supplies, to come to look for us.

After the brigantine left the same men as before went inland again, with the addition of a few more. We followed the bay's shoreline and, after a march of four leagues, captured four Indians, to whom we showed corn[8] in order to find out if they knew it, for until then we had seen no trace of it. They told us that they would take us to where there was corn and they led us to their village, at the end of the bay nearby. There they showed us some that was not yet fit to be picked. We also found many cargo boxes from Castile.[9] In each was a corpse, each corpse covered with painted deerskins. The commissary believed this to be some idolatrous practice, so he burned the crates with the corpses inside. We also found pieces of canvas and cloth, and feather headdresses that seemed to be from New Spain.[1] We also found traces of gold.

Using signs, we asked the Indians where they had obtained these things and they indicated to us that very far away there was a province called Apalache[2] in which there was a great deal of gold. They also indicated that in that province we would find everything we held to be of value.

Once they told us about the bounty in Apalache, taking them as guides, we set out for there. After walking ten or twelve leagues, we came to another village of fifteen houses, where there was a large cultivated patch of corn almost ready for harvest, and some that was already ripe. After staying there two days, we returned to where we had left the comptroller and those from the ships and told the comptroller and the pilots what we had seen and the information the Indians had given us.

The next day, which was the first of May, the governor took aside the commissary, the comptroller, the inspector, myself, a sailor named Bartolomé Fernández, and a notary by the name of Jerónimo de Albaniz, and told us that he had in mind to move inland, while the ships should follow the coast as far as the harbor. The pilots believed and had stated that if they went in the direction of the river of the Palms they would reach it soon. He asked us to give our opinions on this.

I replied that it seemed to me in no way advisable to leave the ships until they were in a safe, occupied port. I told him to consider that the pilots were at a loss, disagreeing among themselves and undecided as to what course to

---

7. In Catholicism, an hour of the day canonically appointed for vespers, one of the ritual observances of devotion; typically at sunset. [Anthology editors' note]
8. Bandelier translates the Spanish *maíz* as "maize," except when the text refers to the meal made from *maíz*, which she translates as "cornmeal." Though the English word *maize* often brings with it connotations of Mesoamerica, and Adorno and Pautz make a case for the specific type of maize that probably migrated thousands

of years ago from Mexico, I prefer the more commonly used English word.
9. The central province of Spain, where the capital city of Madrid lies. From there, Ferdinand and Isabella conquered the remaining Moorish states and created the modern Spanish state.
1. The Spanish settlements of Central Mexico, in which the capital city lay.
2. The section of contemporary Florida that runs approximately from Tampa Bay to the Apalachicola River.

pursue. Moreover, the horses would not be with us in case we needed them, and, furthermore, we had no interpreter to make ourselves understood by the natives, and would not be able to converse with them. Neither did we know what to expect from the land we were entering, having no knowledge of what it was, what it might contain, and by what kind of people it was inhabited, nor in what part of it we were, and, finally, that we did not have the supplies required for penetrating into an unknown country, since of the supplies left in the ships not more than one pound of biscuit and one of bacon could be given as rations to each man for the journey. In my opinion, we should go back on ship and sail in search of a land and harbor better adapted to settlement, since the country we had seen was the poorest and most desolate ever found in those parts.

The commissary was of the opposite opinion and said that we should not go by ship, but should follow the coast in search of a harbor, since the pilots asserted that Pánuco[3] was not more than ten or fifteen leagues away and that by following the coast it was impossible to miss it, since the coast bent inland for twelve leagues. The first to arrive should wait for the others. As for going by ship, he said it would be to tempt God, after all the vicissitudes of storms, losses of men and ships, and hardships we had suffered from the time we left Castile until we arrived there. His advice would be to follow the coast as far as the harbor, while the ships with the other men would follow along to the same port.

To all the others this seemed to be the best idea, except to the notary, who said that before leaving the ships they should be put into a well-known harbor, safe and in a settled country, after which we might go inland and do as we liked. But the governor clung to his own view and to the advice of the others.

Seeing his determination, I required him in Your Majesty's name not to leave the ships until they were in port and safe, and I asked the notary to testify to what I said. The governor replied that he agreed with the opinion of the other officers and of the commissary and that I had no authority to make such demands, and he asked the notary to give him a certified statement that because that country lacked the means for supporting a settlement and a harbor for the ships, he was breaking the current encampment he had established there to go in search of the port and of better land.

He then ordered the people who were to accompany him to get ready and to provide themselves with what was needed for the journey. After this he turned to me and told me in the presence of all who were there that, since I so strongly opposed the expedition into the interior and was afraid of it, I should take charge of the ships and men remaining, and in case I reached the port before him, establish a settlement there. This I declined.

After leaving there, that same day he sent me a message and begged me again to take charge of that task, saying that it seemed to him that he could trust no one else. Seeing that despite his insistence, I still declined, he asked the reasons for my refusal. I then told him that I refused to accept because I felt sure that he would never see the ships again, nor the ships him, and that seeing how utterly unprepared he was for moving inland, I preferred to share

---

3. The Spanish settlements in the vicinity of the Pánuco River (Río Pánuco), on the northeastern coast of contemporary Mexico.

the risk with him and his people and suffer what they would have to suffer rather than take charge of the ships and thus give occasion for saying that I opposed the journey and remained with the ships out of fear, which would place my honor in jeopardy. Under these circumstances, I would much rather risk my life than my good name.

Seeing that he was getting nowhere, he asked others to speak with me to ask me to do it, but I gave them the same answer. Finally he appointed as his lieutenant to remain with the ships a magistrate[4] named Caravallo.

## Chapter Nineteen. How the Indians Separated Us

When I had been with the Christians for six months, waiting to execute our plans, the Indians went for prickly pears, at a distance of thirty leagues from there, and when we were about to run away, the Indians began fighting among themselves over a woman, cuffing and striking and hurting each other, so that each one took his lodge and went his own way in a great rage. So we Christians had to part, and there was no way we could get together again until the following year. During that time I fared very badly, as much from lack of food as from the abuse the Indians gave me. I was treated so badly that I had to flee from my masters three times, and they all went in pursuit, ready to kill me. But God, our Lord, in his infinite goodness, protected me and saved my life.

When the prickly pear time arrived we met each other again at the same spot. We had already agreed to escape and appointed a day for it, when on that very day the Indians separated us, sending each one to a different place, and I told my companions that I would wait for them at the prickly pears until full moon. It was the first of September and the first day of the new moon, and I told them that if at the set time they did not appear I would go on alone without them. We parted, each one going off with his Indians.

I remained with mine until the thirteenth of the moon, determined to escape to other Indians as soon as the moon was full, and on that day Andrés Dorantes and Estevanico arrived. They said they had left Castillo with other people nearby called Anagados and told me how they had suffered many hardships and been lost. On the following day our Indians moved toward where Castillo was. They were going to join those who were holding him and make friends with them, since until then they had been at war. In this way we got Castillo as well.

During the entire time we ate prickly pears we were thirsty. To allay our thirst we drank the fruit's juice, first pouring it into a pit, which we dug in the soil, and when that was full drinking to satisfaction. The Indians do it in that way, because they lack drinking glasses. The juice is sweet and has the color of must. There are many kinds of prickly pears, some very good ones, although to me they all tasted alike. Hunger never left me time to select or even stop to think about which ones were better. Most of the people drink rainwater that collects here and there, for, even though there

4. The original text reads "alcalde" [mayor].

are rivers, they never have a fixed dwelling place and have no knowledge of springs or established water holes.

All over the land there are vast and handsome pastures, with good grass for cattle, and it strikes me that the soil would be very fertile were the country inhabited and improved by reasoning people. We saw no mountains the entire time we were in this country. These Indians told us that further on there were others called Camones, who live nearer the coast, and that it was they who had killed everyone who had come in Peñalosa and Téllez's boat. They had been so emaciated and feeble that when they were being killed they offered no resistance, so the Indians finished them off. They showed us some of their clothes and weapons and said the boat was still beached there. This is the fifth of the missing boats. That of the governor we have already said had been swept out to sea. That of the comptroller and the monks was seen stranded on the beach and Esquivel told us of their end. Of the two in which Castillo, Dorantes, and I had been, I have recounted how they sank close to the Isle of Misfortune.

## Chapter Twenty. How We Fled

Two days after we moved we commended ourselves to God, our Lord, and fled, hoping that, although it was late in the season and the fruit of the prickly pears was giving out, by remaining in the field we might still get over a good portion of the land. As we proceeded that day, in great fear lest the Indians follow us, we spied smoke, and, going toward it, reached a place after sundown, where we found an Indian who, when he saw us coming, did not want to come toward us and ran away. We sent the Negro after him, and since the Indian saw him approaching alone he waited. The Negro told him that we were going in search of the people who had made the smoke. He answered that their dwellings were nearby and that he would guide us, and we followed. He hurried ahead to let them know of our coming. At sunset we came in sight of the lodges, and two crossbow shots before reaching them we met four Indians waiting for us, who received us well. We told them in the language of the Marianes[5] that we had come to see them. They appeared to be pleased with our company and took us to their homes. They lodged Dorantes and the Negro at the house of a medicine man, and me and Castillo at that of some other people. These Indians speak another language and are called Avavares. They were the ones who used to bring bows to our Indians and barter with them, and, although they are of another nation and language, they understood the language of those with whom we had been and had arrived there on that very day with their lodges. They soon offered us many prickly pears, because they had heard of us and of how we cured people and of the marvels our Lord worked through us. And surely, even if there had been no other tokens, it was wonderful how he prepared the way for us through a barely inhabited country, causing us to meet people where for a long time there had been none, saving us from so many dangers, not

5. In chapter 26, Cabeza de Vaca identifies them as one of the Native American peoples on the Isle of Misfortune (present-day East Island, Louisiana); but see note 7, p. 36. [Anthology editors' note]

permitting us to be killed, maintaining us through starvation and misfortune, and moving the hearts of the people to treat us well, as we shall relate further on.

## Chapter Twenty-One. How We Cured Several Sick People

On the night we arrived there, some Indians came to Castillo complaining that their heads ached and begging him for relief. At the very moment he had made the sign of the cross over them and commended them to God, the Indians said that all the pain was gone. They went back to their homes and brought us a number of prickly pears and a piece of venison, which we did not recognize. As the news spread that same night there came many other sick people for him to cure, and each brought a piece of venison, and there were so many that we did not know where to store the meat. We thanked God for his mercy and kindness, which increased daily, and after they were all well they began to dance and celebrate and feast until sunrise of the following day.

They celebrated our coming for three days, at the end of which we asked them about the land further on, the people we might meet there, and the food we might find. They replied that there were plenty of prickly pears all through that country, but that the season was over and nobody was there because they had all gone home after gathering prickly pears and that the country was very cold and had very few hides in it. Hearing this, and since winter and its cold weather were setting in, we decided to spend it with those Indians. Five days after our arrival they left to get more prickly pears where there were people of other nations and languages. We traveled for five days, during which we suffered greatly from hunger since on the way there were neither prickly pears nor any kind of fruit, until we came to a river, where we pitched our lodges.

As soon as we were settled we went out to hunt for the fruit of a certain type of tree, which is like spring bitter vetch. Since throughout that land there are no paths, I took too much time hunting for them and the people went back without me. That night, as I started to rejoin them, I went astray and got lost. It pleased God to let me find a burning tree, by the fire of which I spent that very cold night, and in the morning I loaded myself with wood, taking two burning sticks, and continued my journey. Thus I went on for five days, always with my firebrands and load of wood, so that in case the fire went out where there was no timber, since in many parts there is none, I would always have the means to make other torches and not be without firewood. It was my only protection against the cold, for I was as naked as the day I was born. For the night I used the following artifice.

I went to the brush in the timber near the rivers and stopped in it every evening before sunset. Then I scratched a hole in the ground and threw a great deal of firewood from the numerous trees in it. I also picked up fallen dry wood and built four fires crosswise around the hole, being very careful to stir them from time to time. I made bundles from the long grass that grows there, with which I covered myself in the hole and so was protected from the night cold. One night fire fell on the straw covering me, and while I was asleep in the hole, it began to burn so rapidly that, although I hurried out as quickly as possible, I still have marks on my hair from this dangerous accident. During all that time I did not eat a mouthful, nor could I find anything to eat, and my feet, because they were bare, bled a great deal. God had mercy upon me, that in all this time there was no norther or I could not have survived.

At the end of five days I reached the bank of a river and met my Indians. They, as well as the Christians, had given me up for dead, thinking that perhaps some snake had bitten me. They all were greatly pleased to see me, the Christians especially, and told me that thus far they had wandered about famished and therefore had not hunted for me, and that night they gave me some of their prickly pears. On the next day we left and went where we found a great number of that fruit with which everyone satisfied their hunger, and we gave many thanks to our Lord, whose help to us never failed.

## Chapter Twenty-Two. How the Following Day They Brought Other Sick People

Early the next day many Indians came and brought five people who were paralyzed and very ill and who had come for Castillo to cure them. Each patient offered him his bow and arrows, which Castillo accepted, and by sunset he had made the sign of the cross over each of the sick people, commending them to God, our Lord. We all prayed to him as well as we could to restore them to health and he, seeing there was no other way of getting those people to help us so that we might be saved from our miserable existence, had mercy on us. In the morning they all woke up well and hearty and went away in such good health that it was as if they never had had any ailment at all. This created great admiration among them and moved us to thank our Lord and to greater faith in his goodness and the hope that he would save us, guiding us to where we could serve him. For myself I may say that I always had full faith in his mercy and that he would liberate me from captivity, and I always told my companions so.

When the Indians had gone with their now healthy Indians, we moved on to others called Cultalchulches and Maliacones, who speak a different language and who were eating prickly pears as well. With them were still others, called Coayos and Susolas, and in another area were the Atayos, who were at war with the Susolas and exchanged arrow shots with them every day.

In this whole country, nothing was spoken of but the wonderful mysteries that God, our Lord, performed through us. They came from far and wide to be cured, and after having been with us two days, some of the Susolas begged Castillo to go and attend to a man who had been wounded, as well as to others that were sick and among whom, they said, was one who was on the verge of death. Castillo was very fearful, especially in frightening and dangerous cases, always afraid that his sins might interfere and prevent the cures from being effective. Therefore the Indians told me to go and perform the cure. They liked me. They remembered that I had cured them while they were out gathering walnuts, for which they had given us walnuts and hides, which had taken place at the time I was on my way to join the Christians. So I had to go, and Dorantes and Estevanico went with me.

When I got close to their huts I saw that the sick man we had been called to cure was dead, for there were many people around him weeping and his lodge was torn down, which is a sign that the owner has died. I found the Indian with his eyes rolled back, without pulse and with all the marks of death, at least it seemed so to me, and Dorantes said the same thing. I removed the mat with which he was covered, and as best I could I prayed to our Lord to restore him to health as well as any others in need. After I had made the sign of the cross and breathed on him many times, they brought his bow and presented it to me, as well as a basket of ground prickly pears, and then they took me to many others who were suffering from sleeping sickness. They gave me two more baskets of prickly pears, which I left for the Indians that had come with us. Then we returned to our living quarters.

Our Indians, to whom I had given the prickly pears, remained. At night they returned, saying that the dead man whom I attended to in their presence had resuscitated, risen from his bed, walked about, eaten, and talked to them, and that everyone I had treated was well and in very good spirits. This caused great surprise and awe, and all over the land nothing else was spoken of. Everyone who heard about it came to us so that we might cure them and bless their children. When the Cultalchulches, who were in the company of our Indians, had to return to their country, before parting they offered us all the prickly pears they had for their journey, not keeping a single one. They gave us flint stones as long as one and a half palms, which are greatly prized among them and with which they cut. They begged us to remember them and pray to God to keep them healthy always, which we promised to do. Then they left, the happiest people on earth, having given us the very best of what they owned.

We remained with the Avavares for eight months, according to our reckoning of the moons. During that time people came to us from far and wide and said that we were truly the children of the sun. Until then Dorantes and the Negro had not cured anyone, but we found ourselves so pressed by the Indians coming from all sides that all of us had to become medicine men. I was the most daring and reckless of all in undertaking cures. We never treated anyone that did not afterward say he was well, and they had such confidence in our skill that they believed that none of them would die as long as we were among them.

These Indians and the ones we left behind told us a very strange tale. From their account it may have occurred fifteen or sixteen years ago. They said that at that time there wandered about the country a man whom they called "Bad Thing," who was short and bearded. Although they could never see his features clearly, whenever he would approach their dwellings their hair would stand on end and they would begin to tremble. In the doorway of the lodge a firebrand would then appear. The man would come in and take hold of anyone he chose. With a sharp knife made of flint, as broad as a hand and two palms in length, he would then make a cut in that person's flank, thrust his hand through the gash, and take out the person's entrails. Then he would cut off a piece one palm long, which he would throw into the fire. Afterward he would make three cuts in one of the person's arms, the second one at a place where people are usually bled, and twist the arm, but would reset it soon afterward. Then he would place his hands on the wounds, which, they told us, would close up at once. Many times he appeared among them while they were dancing, sometimes in the dress of a woman and other times as a man, and whenever he took a notion to do it he would seize a hut or lodge, take it up into the air, and come down with it again with a great crash. They also told us how, many a time, they set food before him, but he would never partake of it. When they asked him where he came from and where he had his home, he pointed to a rent in the earth and said his house was down below.

We laughed a great deal at those stories and made fun of them. Seeing our disbelief they brought us many of those he had taken, they said, and we saw the scars from his slashes in the places they had said. We told them he was a demon and explained as best we could that if they would believe in God, our Lord, and be Christians like ourselves, they would not have to fear that man, nor would he come and do these things to them, and they might be sure that as long as we were in this country he would not dare to appear again. This pleased them greatly and they lost much of their apprehension.

The same Indians told us they had seen the Asturian and Figueroa[6] with other Indians from further along the coast whom we had named the People of the Figs. None of them know how to reckon the seasons by either sun or moon, nor do they count by months and years; they judge the seasons by the ripening of fruit, by the time that fish die, and by the appearance of the stars, and in all of this they are very clever and expert. While with them we were always well treated, although our food was never too plentiful, and we had to carry our own water and wood. Their dwellings and their food are like those of the others we had known, but they are much more prone to hunger, having neither corn nor acorns or walnuts. We always went naked like them and at night covered ourselves with deerskins.

During six of the eight months we were with them we suffered greatly from hunger, because they do not have fish either. At the end of that time the prickly pears began to ripen. Without their noticing it the Negro and I left and went to other Indians further ahead, called Maliacones, at a distance of one day's travel. Three days after we arrived I sent him back to get Castillo and Dorantes, and after they rejoined me we all departed in company of the Indians, who went to eat a small fruit of a certain type of tree, on which they subsist for ten or twelve days, until the prickly pears are fully ripe. There they joined other Indians called Arbadaos, whom we found to be so sick, emaciated, and bloated that we were greatly astonished. The Indians with whom we had come went back on the same trail, and we told them that we wished to remain with the others, which made them sad. So we remained with the others in a field near their dwellings.

When the Indians saw us, they gathered together and, after having talked among themselves, each one took the one of us he had claimed by the hand and led us to their homes. While we were with them we suffered more from hunger than we had with any of the others. In the course of a whole day we did not eat more than two handfuls of the fruit, which was green and contained so much milky juice that it burned our mouths. Since water was very scarce, whoever ate them became very thirsty. Finally we grew so hungry that

6. Members of the expedition. *The Asturian*: a priest from Asturias, an autonomous community in Spain. [Anthology editors' note]

we purchased two dogs in exchange for nets and other things and a hide that I used to cover myself.

I have said already that we went naked in that land, and not being accustomed to it, we shed our skin twice a year, like snakes. Exposure to the sun and air covered our chests and backs with great sores that made it very painful to carry big and heavy loads, the ropes of which cut into the flesh on our arms.

The country is so rough and overgrown that often after we had gathered firewood in the forest and dragged it out, we would bleed freely from the thorns and spines that cut and slashed us wherever they touched us. Sometimes it happened that I was unable to carry or drag out the firewood after I had gathered it with great loss of blood. In all that trouble my only relief or consolation was to remember the passion of our Savior, Jesus Christ, and the blood he shed for me, and to consider how much greater his sufferings had been from those thorns than I from the ones I was then enduring.

I made a contract with the Indians to make combs, arrows, bows, and nets for them. We also made the matting from which their lodges are constructed and which they greatly need, for, although they know how to make it, they do not like to do any work, in order to be able to go in search of food. Whenever they work they suffer greatly from hunger.

At other times, they would make me scrape skins and tan them, and the greatest luxury I enjoyed was on the day they would give me a skin to scrape, because I scraped it very deeply in order to eat the parings, which would last me two or three days. It also happened that, while we were with these Indians and those mentioned before, we would eat a piece of meat they gave us raw, because if we broiled it the first Indian who came along would snatch it away and eat it. It seemed useless to take any pains, in view of what we might expect, nor did we care to go to any trouble in order to have it broiled and might just as well eat it raw. Such was the life we led there, and we had to earn even that scant sustenance by bartering the objects we made with our own hands.

## Chapter Twenty-Five. How Ready the Indians Are with Weapons

These Indians are the readiest people with their weapons of any I have seen in the world. When they fear an enemy's approach they lie awake all night with their bows and a dozen arrows within reach. Before one goes to sleep he tries his bow and, should the string not be to his liking, he arranges it to suit him. Often they crawl out of their dwellings so as not to be seen and look around in every direction. If they detect anything, in less than no time they are all out in the field with their bows and arrows. Thus they remain until daybreak, running hither and thither whenever they see danger or suspect their enemies might approach. At daybreak, they unstring their bows until the time comes for them to go out to hunt.

Their bowstrings are made of deer sinews. They fight in a crouch, and while shooting at each other they talk and dart from side to side to dodge their foe's arrows. Because of this our crossbows and harquebuses will do them little damage. On the contrary, the Indians laugh at those weapons, because they present no danger to them on the plains over which they roam. They are only good in narrow areas and in swamps. Horses are what the Indians dread most, and the means by which they will be overcome.

Whoever has to fight Indians must take great care not to let them think he is disheartened or that he covets what they own. In war they must be treated very harshly, for should they notice either fear or greed, as a people they know how to bide their time waiting for revenge and take courage from their enemies' fears. After using up all their arrows, they part, each going his own way, without attempting pursuit, although one side might have more men than the other. Such is their custom.

Many times they are shot all over their bodies with arrows, but they do not die from the wounds as long as their bowels or heart is not affected. On the contrary, they recover quickly. Their eyesight, hearing, and senses in general are better, I believe, than those of any other men on earth. They can stand, and they have to stand, severe hunger, thirst, and cold, and are more accustomed and used to it than others. I wished to state this here, since, apart from the curiosity all men have about the habits and devices of others, those who might come in contact with those people should be informed of their customs and deeds, which will be of no small profit to them.

## Chapter Twenty-Six. On Nations and Languages

I also do wish to tell of the nations and languages encountered from the Island of Misfortune to the most recent ones, the Cuchendados. On the Isle of Misfortune two languages are spoken, one they call Cavoques, the other Han. On the mainland, facing the island, there are others, called Charruco Indians, who take their name from the woods in which they live. Further on, along the seashore, there are others who call themselves Deguenes, and across from them still others named the Mendicans. Further on, on the coast, are the Quevenes, and further inland the Marianes. Following the coast we come to the Guaycones, and in front of them inland the Yguaces. After those come the Atayos, and behind them others, called Decubadaos, of whom there are a great many further on in this direction. On the coast live the Quitoles, and in front of them, inland, the Chavavares. These are joined by the Maliacones and the Cultalchulches and others called Susolas and Comos. Ahead on the coast are the Camolas, and further on those whom we call the People of the Figs.[7]

All of them have houses and villages and speak different languages. Among them is a language in which when they call men to look at something they say "arraca" and for dogs they say "xó."

---

7. This list of Indian nations evidences Cabeza de Vaca's temporal and spatial viewpoint. His characterization of Indians as "recent" reflects the point in time he has reached in his travel narrative. Instead of the directions of north, south, east, and west, he situates tribes in relation to each other and local landmarks. Bandelier is highly skeptical of the reliability of the names of these tribes and does not believe that Cabeza de Vaca had much understanding of the tribal names or locations.

Throughout the country, they get inebriated by using a certain smoke, and will give everything they have in order to get it. They also drink something that they extract from leaves of a tree similar to a water-oak, toasting them on the fire in a container like a low-necked bottle. When the leaves are toasted they fill the container with water and hold it over the fire for long enough for the water to boil twice. Then they pour the liquid into a bowl made of a gourd cut in half. When there is a lot of foam on it they drink it as hot as they can stand, and from the time they take it out of the first vessel until they drink they shout, "Who wants to drink?" When women hear this they stand still, and although they may be carrying a very heavy load they do not dare to move. Should one of them stir, she is dishonored and beaten. In a great rage they spill the liquid they have prepared and spit up what they drank, easily and without pain. The reason for this custom, they say, is that when they want to drink that water and the women stir from the spot where they first hear the shouts, an evil substance gets into the liquid that penetrates their bodies, causing them to die before long. All the time the water boils the vessel must be kept covered. Should it be uncovered while a woman comes along they pour it out and do not drink it. It is yellow and they drink it for three days without partaking of any food, each consuming an *arroba*[8] and a half every day.

When the women have their cycle they seek food only for themselves, because nobody else will eat what they bring.

During the time I was among them I saw something very repulsive, namely, a man married to another. These are impotent and womanish beings who dress like and do the work of women. They carry heavy loads but do not use a bow. Among these Indians we saw many of them. They are more robust than other men, taller, and can bear heavy loads.

1537–41                                                              1542, 1555

---

8. A liquid measure that is reckoned by weight, generally about twenty-five pounds, more or less between two and four gallons.

# FRAY MARCOS DE NIZA
## ca. 1495–1558

The first Spanish explorers of New Mexican lands were Álvar Núñez Cabeza de Vaca and the other survivors of the Pánfilo de Narvaéz expedition of 1527. But the first major expedition of the area took place under the leadership of Fray Marcos de Niza.

Biographical information on de Niza is scarce. He was born in Nice (hence the surname under which he is known), which at the time was part of the Duchy of Savoy. He joined the Franciscan order in 1531 and soon thereafter was sent to the New World. In Nicaragua and Peru, he witnessed the atrocities committed against the Incas by the conquistadors, and he later reported on these to the bishop of

Mexico, Fray Juan Zumárraga. In 1536, he was in what is now Guatemala with the expedition of Pedro de Alvarado.

The viceroy of New Spain, Antonio de Mendoza, was intensely interested in having an explorer find the fabled Seven Cities of Cíbola and Quivira. Fray Marcos de Niza was not his first choice to head an expedition to find the Seven Cities, however. Since the Spaniards Cabeza de Vaca and Andrés Dorantes were not available, and the Moroccan explorer Estevanico was not eligible because he was a slave, de Niza was deemed acceptable. According to early legends, the Seven Cities were founded by a Portuguese bishop in some mid-Atlantic continent. Later they were thought to be in the Caribbean. By the time of de Niza's expedition, the site had been moved to the northwestern frontier.

In the fall of 1539, de Niza initiated his journey, traveling from Mexico City to San Miguel de Culiacán, now in the state of Sinaloa, Mexico. In the nineteenth century, the anthropologist and historian Adolph F. Bandelier (husband of Fanny Bandelier, Cabeza de Vaca's English translator) proposed that de Niza's route from Culiacán to the northern frontier was most likely north to Banámichi and Ojo de Agua, both in Sonora, Mexico; on to Arizona; following the route in Arizona from Charleston to Fort Grant to Fort Apache; and on to Zuñi territory in New Mexico. Among nineteenth-century scholars, opinions differed as to exactly what places de Niza had happened upon when he thought he had arrived in the regions of Cíbola and Quivira. Lewis H. Morgan, for example, thought de Niza's Cíbola was a group of villages, including Pueblo Bonita, in what is today Chaco Canyon National Monument. James H. Simpson claimed Cíbola was the village of Toyoalana, in Old Zuñi. In 1895, Frederick W. Hodge proposed that Cíbola was the Zuñi pueblo Hawikuh, and his theory was accepted in the twentieth century by Herbert E. Bolton, among others.

Fray Marcos de Niza has defenders and detractors. Some of the latter accuse him of fabricating the whole journey, in fact of being a liar. Pedro Castañeda de Nájera, a member and chronicler of the Francisco Vásquez Coronado expedition (1540)—of which de Niza was also a member—blames the tragic ending of that expedition on de Niza's having created false expectations of the wonders to be found in the New World. However, in his extensive writing on de Niza's life and works, Adolph Bandelier insists that the explorer presented at least kernels of truth and that the exaggerations merely reflect the Spaniards' Eurocentric perspective on the Indians. According to Bandalier, simply by inspiring future expeditions—such as those of Coronado, Chamuscado, Espejo, Castaño de Sosa, Oñate, and Diego de Vargas—de Niza achieved something by opening up the Southwest for later development.

The following excerpt from de Niza's after-the-fact testimony describes in broad strokes his journey from San Miguel de Culiacán to Cíbola, where events proved first tragic and then, he claims, triumphant. His expedition included several hundred Indians and was led by Estevanico, whom he calls Estevan de Dorantes (at the time, he was owned by the explorer Andrés Dorantes; he was also known as Black Stephen and Stephen the Moor). Before proceeding into Cíbola, de Niza sent an exploratory party of about 300 Indians, led by Estevanico; all were killed, as intruders, by the inhabitants upon arrival there. De Niza claims to have continued toward the Seven Cities and, in the name of the king of Spain, taken possession of them from a distance. His description of the Seven Cities as being bigger than "the city of Mexico" (Tenochtitlán) is one of de Niza's clearly false notes. Still, his writing style creates suspense and excitement as well as empathy for all the people killed in the massacre at "Cíbola."

## FROM NARRATIVE OF FRAY MARCOS DE NIZA[1]

With the aid and protection of the Most Holy Virgin Mary, Our Lady, and of the Seráfico,[2] our father Saint Francis, I, Fray Marcos de Niza, a professed friar of the order of Saint Francis, in compliance with the instructions above contained,[3] from the Illustrious Lord Don Antonio de Mendoza, viceroy and governor for His Majesty of New Spain, departed from the *villa* of San Miguel,[4] in the province of Culiacán, Friday, the seventh day of March,[5] year of one thousand five hundred and thirty nine, taking with me as companion the Father Friar Honoratus, and also taking with me Estevan de Dorantes, a black,[6] and certain Indians of those which the said Lord Viceroy liberated and purchased for this purpose, the which were brought to me by Francisco Vázquez de Coronado, governor of New Galicia,[7] and with many other Indians from Petatlán and from the town that is called Cuchillo,[8] that would be fifty leagues[9] from the said *villa* [of San Miguel]. These came to the valley of Culiacán showing great joy, because it had been proclaimed that the Indians are free men, the said governor having previously sent word to them to inform them of their liberty, and to assure them that they would not be made slaves nor warred upon nor mistreated, telling them that this was the will and command of His Majesty.[1] And with the company that I have said, I took my way toward the town of Petatlán, receiving on the way many hospitalities and presents of food, roses and other things of this sort, and huts that they built for me of mats and brush in those districts where were no people.[2] In this town of Petatlán I rested three days, because my companion, Fray Honoratus, was seized with illness, and I found it advisable to leave him there. So, conforming to the said instructions, I pursued my journey, wherein I was guided by the Holy Spirit, though I was unworthy. And with me went the said Estevan de Dorantes, the black, and some of the freed Indians and many people of the region, arranging for me, in all places that I reached, much hospitality and celebrations and triumphal arches. They gave me of the food they had, though it was little because they said they had three years without rain, and because the Indians of that region think more of hiding themselves

1. Translated by Cleve Hallenbeck. Within the text, parenthetical and bracketed insertions are Hallenbeck's; the anthology editors have made a few minor, stylistic changes to the text. Within the footnotes, bracketed insertions are the anthology editors'. Except as indicated, all footnotes are Hallenbeck's. The editors have omitted some notes and made minor changes to others.

2. *Seráfico*, usually rendered as "seraphic," is here used as a noun to designate Saint Francis, the founder of the Franciscan order, which also is known as the "Seraphic Order." * * *

3. De Niza attached to his narrative a copy of the viceroy's instructions.

4. The *villa* of San Miguel later became known as Culiacán * * *.

5. March 7 on the Julian calendar would be March 17 on our calendar, the Gregorian. (The "Julian" calendar was introduced by the Roman emperor Julius Caesar in 46 BC and used in the Western world until 1582, when Pope Gregory XIII replaced it with the "Gregorian" calendar. [In England, the latter was not adopted until 1751.]) [Anthology editors' note]

6. Most writers refer to Estevan as a Negro because de Niza speaks of him as a *negro*, which is Spanish for "a black." The Spanish called all the Hamitic races, as well as the Negroes, "blacks." Cabeza de Vaca, who was associated with Estevan for nine years, says he was an Arab from Azamor, Africa. * * * Nájera, who also knew him, says he was a *moreno*—a brown man.

7. I.e., Nueva Galicia, a region of New Spain, in what is now western Mexico. [Anthology editors' note]

8. Cuchillo and Petatlán were Indian villages, the latter about 65 miles and the former 150 miles above Culiacán.

9. The official Spanish linear league at that time was equal to 3.1 miles * * *.

1. Charles V had ordered that Indians be treated in all respects as subjects of the Crown of Spain. Pope Paul III shortly before this time issued a decree that any person found guilty of enslaving Indians would be excommunicated.

2. That is, in districts having no fixed populations. The "huts" de Niza speaks of were brush shelters.

than of planting crops, through fear of the Christians of the *villa* of San Miguel, who until then had been accustomed to go there to make war and slaves. On all this road, which would be for twenty-five or thirty leagues [after leaving Petatlán[3]] I saw nothing worthy of being placed herein, except that to me came Indians from the island that had been visited by the Marqués del Valle;[4] these informed me that it was an island and not, as some would say, the mainland; and I saw that they passed to the mainland, and from the mainland back to the island, on rafts. The distance from the island to the mainland may be half a sea league, a little more or less.

Also, there came to see me Indians of another island, larger than the first one, and farther away; from these Indians I received information of thirty other, small, islands occupied by people having little food, except two which they said had maize. These Indians wore, hanging from their necks, many shells of the kind that contain pearls. I showed them a pearl that I carried as a specimen, and they told me that such were found in the islands, but I saw none of them.

I pursued my way through a *despoblado*[5] for four days, Indians from the islands I mentioned as well as from the towns that I have passed, going with me, and at the end of the *despoblado*[6] I reached other Indians who marveled at seeing me, as they had no knowledge of Christians,[7] because they have no dealings with those below the *despoblado*. These Indians gave me many receptions and much food, and they tried to touch my robe, calling me *Sayota*, which would be to say, in their language, "man from Heaven." Through my interpreters, I made them understand, the best I could, the tenor of my instructions, which is [to impart to them] the knowledge of Our Lord in Heaven and of His Majesty on the earth. And always, by every means I had, I sought information of a country of numerous settlements and of people more enlightened than those which I had encountered; but I learned nothing more than that, as they told me, the country beyond [inland], four or five *jornadas*[8] from where the ranges of mountains ended, contained an extensive and level valley[9] wherein they said were many and very large settlements, wherein were people possessing cotton garments. Showing them some metals that I carried in order to learn of the metals of the country, they took the piece of gold and told me that they had vessels of that metal among the people of the valley, and that there they wore, hanging from their ears and noses, certain round ornaments of gold, and that they had some small golden plates (*paletillas*) with which they scrape themselves to remove their sweat. But as this tract is away from the coast [i.e., inland] and my instructions are not to depart farther from it, I decided to leave it [the valley] until my return, because then I would be able to see it better (or, "see more of it"). And so I went on three days through country inhabited by the same tribe,[1] by whom I was received

3. The district between Petatlán and the Compostela River. * * *

4. The Marques del Valle (Marquis of the Valley) was Cortés, the title having been conferred upon him in 1529. The island referred to was Guayaval.

5. A region with no fixed population. [Anthology editors' note]

6. The end of this *despoblado* probably was at the Petatlán-Sinaloa River.

7. I.e., Europeans.

8. A *jornada* was a day's journey, but it is to be kept in mind that the Indians along the way stated distances in terms of day's journeys *for them*.

9. *Una abra llana y de mucha tierra.* [The translator Percy M.] Baldwin renders this as "an extensive and level open tract." "*Abra*" connotes narrowness, as a gorge or canyon, so I have compromised with "extensive and level valley." De Niza here really gives us an extensive plain in a mountain gorge! See also note 2, p. 47.

1. The Cahitas.

the same as by those before. I then came to a fair-sized settlement that they called Vacapa, where they made me a great reception and gave me much food, of which they had an abundance because their land is irrigated. From this settlement to the sea [the coast of the Gulf of California] is forty leagues, and as I found myself so far removed from the sea, and as it was two days before Passion Sunday,[2] I decided to stay there until Easter, in order to learn more about the islands of which I said, above, I had been told. So I sent Indian messengers by three routes to the sea, charging them to bring me people from the coast and from some of those islands, that I might inform myself of them. On another route I sent Estevan de Dorantes, the black, whom I instructed to follow to the north for fifty or sixty leagues, to see if by that route he would be able to learn of any great thing such as we sought; and I agreed with him that if he received any information of a rich, peopled land, that was something great, he should not go farther, but that he return in person or send me Indians with this signal, which we arranged: that if the thing was of moderate importance, he send me a white cross the size of a hand; if it was something great he send me one of two hands; and if it was something bigger and better than New Spain, he send me a large cross.[3]

And so the said Estevan, the black, departed from me on Passion Sunday after dinner (or, "after eating"), while I stayed on in this settlement which, as I say, is called Vacapa. And after four days there came messengers from Estevan with a very large cross, of the height of a man, and they told me on the part of Estevan that I should at once ("on the hour") depart and follow him, because he had reached people who gave him information of the greatest thing in the world; and that he had found Indians who had been there, of whom he was sending me one. This Indian told me so many wonderful things of the land that I forebore to credit him until I should have seen them or have more information of the place. He told me that it was thirty *jornadas* from the place where he had left Estevan to the first city of that country, which city he said was called Cíbola.[4] And as it appears to me worth placing in this paper that which this Indian, whom Estevan sent me, said of the country, I will do so. He affirmed and said that in that province were seven very great cities, all under one lord; that the houses, of stone and lime, were large, the smallest being of one story with a terrace above, and others of two and three stories, and that of the lord had four, all joined under his rule, and in the porches (*portadas*) of the main houses were worked many designs of turquoises, of which, he said, there was a great abundance, and that the people of those cities went very well clothed. Many other particulars he told me of these seven cities, as well as of other provinces farther away, each of which, he said, was much greater than the seven cities; and in order to comprehend it as he knew it, I asked him many questions, and I found him to be of very good intelligence.

I gave thanks to Our Lord, but deferred my departure in pursuit of Estevan de Dorantes, believing he would await me as I had arranged with him, and also because I had promised the messengers whom I had sent to the sea that

2. In branches of Christianity such as Roman Catholicism, the fifth Sunday in the period known as Lent. Lent consists of the 40 days from Ash Wednesday until Easter. [Anthology editors' note]
3. Estevan could not read or write; hence this arrangement for transmitting information.
4. This is the first time this name, Cíbola, later to become known throughout the civilized world, appears in historical literature.

I would await them; for I proposed always to treat truthfully the people with whom I dealt. The messengers arrived on Easter Sunday, and with them were people from the coast and from the islands which, as I said before, are poor in food, though populated. These wore shells on their foreheads and said that such contain pearls. They informed me that there were thirty-four islands, near to each other, whose names I place in another paper,[5] wherein I give the names of the islands and settlements. The people of the coast say they have as little food as those of the islands, and that they trade among themselves by means of rafts. They say that the coast goes almost directly to the north. These Indians of the coast brought me shields of cowhide, very well made, so large that they cover them from feet to head, with some holes above the handle in order to be able to see from behind them: they are so thick (or "strong") that I believe a crossbow arrow would not pass through them.

This day there came to me three Indians, of those that are called *Pintados*,[6] their faces, chests and arms all decorated; these are in a district to the east and they border on a people who are next to the seven cities. They told me that having heard of me, they had come to see me, and, among other things, they gave me much information concerning the seven cities and the provinces that Estevan's Indian had told me of, in the same manner that Estevan's told me. And so I sent back the people of the coast; and two Indians of the islands said they wished to go with me seven or eight days. And with them and with the three *Pintados* that I mentioned, I left Vacapa the second day of Easter[7] by way of the road that Estevan had followed, from whom I had received other messengers, with another cross the size of the first one he sent, urging me to hurry, and declaring that the land we sought was the best and greatest thing of which he ever had heard. Those same messengers told me in detail, without differing on any point, that which the first one had told me, except that they told me much more and gave me a clearer description.

And so I traveled that day, the second day of Easter, and two other days, traveling the same *jornadas* as had Estevan, at the end of which I reached the people who had given him information of the seven cities and of the country farther away, the which told me that from there it was thirty *jornadas* to the city of Cíbola, which is the first of the seven, and I had the account not only from one, but from many: and very particularly they told me of the grandeur of the houses and the style of them, just as the first one had. They told me that beyond these seven cities are other kingdoms that they call Marata and Acus and Totonteac. I wished to know for what they went so far from their homes, and they told me that they went for turquoises and for cowhides and other things; and of both they had a quantity in that town. I also wished to know what they exchanged for what they obtained, and they told me, with sweat and with the service of their bodies; that they went to the first city, which is called Cíbola, and there served by digging in the ground and in other labor, and that [in payment] they were given cowhides, which they had there, and turquoises. All the people of this town wear fine and beautiful turquoises hanging from their ears and from their noses, and they say that these [turquoises] are worked into the principal doorways (*portales*) of Cíbola.

---

5. This other document has never been found * * *.
6. *Pintado* means "a painted man." These Indians were probably tattooed, as no southwestern Indians wore paint except in war and in religious ceremonials.
7. I.e., the Monday after Easter Sunday.

They told me that the form of clothing of the people of Cíbola is a cotton shirt reaching to the instep of the foot, with a button at the throat and a large tassel that hangs from it; the sleeves of the shirt being of the same width above as below: to me it appeared like the Bohemian [gipsy] dress. They say that they go girt with belts of turquoises, and that over these they wear the shirts: some wear very good blankets (*mantas*) and others cowhides,[8] very well processed, which they hold to be the better clothing and of which that country, they say, has a very great quantity. The women, likewise, go clothed and covered to the feet in the same manner. These Indians received me very well, and took great care to learn the day I left Vacapa,[9] so as to take food and shelter for me on the road. They brought me their sick, that I might cure them,[1] and tried to touch my robe. I recited the Gospel over them. They gave me some cowhides so well tanned and dressed that they appeared to be the work of men of much culture, and they said that all these had come from Cíbola.[2]

Next day I continued my journey, taking with me the *Pintados*, who did not want to remain behind. I reached another settlement where I was very well received by its people, who tried to touch my robe, and they informed me of the land which was my destination, as particularly as I had been told before, and they told me how people from that village had gone four or five *jornadas* with Estevan Dorantes. Here I came upon a large cross erected by Estevan to indicate that the news of the good country always increases, and he left word for me to hurry on and that he would await me at the end of the next *despoblado* Here I erected two crosses and took possession, in compliance with instructions, because it appeared to me that this was a better land than that which I had passed,[3] and so it was proper to perform there the acts of possession. And after this manner I continued for five days, always finding well-populated settlements where I was received with great hospitality and receptions and where I found many turquoises and cowhides, and the same report of the country. They all spoke to me of Cíbola and that province as people who knew that I was going in search of it and they told me how Estevan had preceded me; and from him I there received messengers who were natives of that town, and who had gone some distance with him; and always he overloaded my hand (*cargándome la mano*)[4] in speaking of the grandeur of the land and urged me to make haste.

---

8. All other writers have taken it for granted that these "cowhides" were buffalo hides. But they were deerskins. Buffalo skins are so thick and stiff that no tribe ever used them for clothing if deer or antelope skins were to be had. Cabeza de Vaca remarked the great number of deerskins possessed by these same people, and each of the chroniclers of Coronado's expedition—Nájera, Jaramillo, and the unidentified author of *Relación del Suceso*—says they were deerskins. Marcos' later praise of the way these skins were processed is merited, for as prepared by Indians they were as soft and flexible as cotton flannel, and thrice as durable.

9. De Niza's recollections are tangled here. He had left Vacapa three days before.

1. When Cabeza de Vaca and his companions passed this way, their reputation as healers ran far ahead of them, and Indians flocked to them to be cured, believing that beneficial results would accrue from merely touching them. Here the Indians were assuming that de Niza was one of the same breed of white magicians.

2. De Niza is mistaken here. The traffic in these skins was in the opposite direction. There were plenty of deer in the mountains of Sonora and Sinaloa—witness the more than six hundred dried deer-hearts given to Cabeza de Vaca at one village—while the Zuñi district had no deer. But the blankets may have come from Cíbola.

3. De Niza is traveling along the little Cedros and Chico valleys, between the Río Mayo and Río Yaqui, and in the valley of the Yaqui, among the Nebomes (Southern Pimas).

4. *Cargándome la mano* is a Spanish idiom meaning, here, that Estevan taxed the friar's credulity to the limit.

Estevan evidently understood something of Indian character, for he used as messengers Indians he had picked up at their villages and had taken long distances with him. These, sent back with messages for de Niza, would be heading toward home and so would lose no time on the road. In this town, messengers had reached home before reaching de Niza, and, of course, stopped there.

Here I learned that after two more *jornadas* I would reach a *despoblado* of four *jornadas* extent, in which there was no food more than was provided by making me shelters and carrying food: I went on, expecting to meet Estevan, because he had sent to tell me that he would await me. Before reaching the *despoblado*, I came to a fresh, cool town,[5] irrigated, where came to meet me a considerable number of people, men and women, clothed in cotton [garments] and some covered with cowhides which in general they hold to be better garments than those of cotton. All in this town wear *encaconados*[6] of turquoises which they hang from their noses and ears, and which they call *cacona*. Among them came the lord of that town and his two brothers (or "two of his brothers") very well clothed in cotton and *encaconados*, and each with necklaces of turquoises on his neck, and they brought me much meat of deer, coneys[7] and quails, and maize and meal, all in great abundance. They offered me many turquoises and cowhides and very handsome bowls and other things, of which I took nothing, for such has been my custom ever since I entered country wherein they have no knowledge of us. Here I had the same account as before of the seven cities and the kingdoms and provinces. I was dressed in a habit of dark woolen cloth of the kind known as Saragossa, which was given to me by Francisco Vázquez de Coronado, governor of New Galicia, and the lord of this town and other Indians touched the habit with their hands and told me that there was a great deal of that material in Totonteac, and that the natives in that place were clothed with it. At this I laughed and declared that it could not be so; that the blankets that those people wore were made of cotton; and they replied, "Think you that we know not that what you wear and what we wear is different? Know that in Cíbola all the houses are full of this cloth that we wear, but in Totonteac they have some small animals from which they take the fiber with which they make cloth like yours." I was surprised, because I had not heard of any such thing before arriving here. I desired to inform myself very particularly of it, and they told me that the animals are of the size of the two Castilian greyhounds that Estevan had with him: they said they had many of them in Totonteac, but I could not learn what genus of animals they were.[8]

*       *       *

Upon resuming our journey, one *jornada* from Cíbola, we met two other Indians of those who had gone with Estevan; they arrived covered with blood and with many wounds, and at their arrival they and those that were with me began such a weeping that from compassion and fear they made me cry also, and there was so much outcry ("so many voices") that I was not able to inquire of them about Estevan, or of what they had suffered. I entreated them to be silent that we might learn what had happened, and they replied, "How can we be silent, since we know that of our fathers, sons and brothers, of those who were with Estevan, more than three hundred are dead? And we dare no more to go to Cíbola, as [we were] accus-

---

5. Probably Matape; but it may have been Tepupa, on the Moctezuma River, at or near its juncture with the Yaqui.

6. This word was coined by de Niza from the Indian word *cacona*. It meant some sort of turquoise ornament.

7. *Conejos*, ordinary rabbits.

8. No wool was used by any southwestern tribe prior to the introduction of sheep into New Mexico in 1598.

tomed." Nevertheless, I tried to pacify them the best I could, and rid them of fear, although I was not without need of some one to rid me of it. I asked the Indians who were wounded about Estevan and what had happened. They remained a while without speaking a word to me, weeping with those of their towns. Finally, they told me that when Estevan arrived at one *jornada* from the city of Cíbola, he sent his messengers with his calabash[9] to Cíbola, to the lord, to make it known to them that he was coming to make peace [i.e., in peace] and to cure them. When they gave him the calabash and he saw the cascabels,[1] he angrily threw the calabash to the ground and said: "I know these people, for these cascabels are not of the fashion of ours; tell them to turn back at once; if not, no man of them will remain [alive]," and thus he remained much enraged. And the messengers returned, but feared to tell Estevan of what had happened; however, they [finally] told him, and he told them that they should have no fear; that he wished to go there, because, although they had answered him badly, they would receive him well. So he went on and arrived at the city of Cíbola just before the setting of the sun, with all the people who went with him, which would be more than three hundred men, not counting the many women; and they [the Cíbolans] would not consent for him to enter the city, but [put them] into a large house with good apartments that was outside the city, and they presently took from Estevan all that he carried, telling him that the lord so ordered, and "in all that night they gave us nothing to eat or to drink. The next day, when the sun was a lance-length high,[2] Estevan went from the house and some of the chiefs with him, and at once there came many people from the city and, when he saw them, he began to flee and we with him. Immediately they gave us these arrow-strokes and gashes and we fell, and upon us fell some dead men. And so we remained until night, without daring to move. We heard loud voices in the city, and on the terraces we saw many men and women watching. We saw no more of Estevan, but we believe that they shot him with arrows as they did the rest who were with him, of whom there escaped none but us."

In view of what the Indians told, and the bad prospects for continuing my journey as I wished, I could not but sense their loss and mine, and God is witness of how much I wished to have some one of whom to beg counsel and assistance, for I confess that it seemed to me I was at fault. I told them that Our Lord would punish Cíbola and that when the Emperor learned what had happened he would send many Christians to chastise them; but they did not believe me, because they say that none can withstand the might of Cíbola. I begged that they be comforted and not weep, and I consoled them with the best words I could, the which would be too long to place here. And after telling them this, I then withdrew a stone's throw or two, to commend myself to God, therein tarrying an hour and a half; and when I returned to

9. A symbol of religious authority, made from the hard shell of a gourd known as a calabash. [Anthology editors' note]
1. Spherical bells enclosing pellets, used like rattles; these appear to have been made by another tribe. [Anthology editors' note]
2. The Spanish copy of the *Relación* carries this explanatory note, probably added by the copyist:

"That is to say, the sun was on the horizon at the altitude of one lance, a little after having risen." That well-meant explanation leaves us exactly where we were before. The height of the sun would depend upon the length of the lance and its distance from the observer. We can conclude only that it was early in the morning.

them, I found, crying, one of my Indians[3] who was called Mark, and whom I had brought from Mexico, and he told me, "Father, these people have plotted to kill you, because they say that through you and through Estevan their kinsfolk are dead, and that there will not remain, of them all, a man or woman who will not die" [i.e., if they continue on to Cíbola]. I proceeded to distribute among them what I still had of garments and trade-articles, to pacify them, and I told them to observe that if they killed me, they would do no evil to me, because I would die a Christian and would go to heaven, and that those who killed me would suffer for it, because the Christians would come in search for me and, against my will, kill all of them. With these and many other words that I spoke I appeased them somewhat, although they still felt great resentment because of the people that were killed. I asked that some of them should go with me to Cíbola, for to see if any other Indian had escaped and to learn anything new of Estevan, but I could do nothing with them. In the end, seeing me determined, two chiefs said that they would go with me. With these and my own Indians and interpreters, I pursued my journey until within sight of Cíbola, which is situated on a plain at the skirt of a round hill. It has the appearance of a very beautiful town,[4] the best that I have seen in these parts. The houses are of the fashion that the Indians had described to me, all of stone, with their stories and terraces, as it appeared to me from a hill where I was able to view it. The city is bigger than the city of Mexico. At times I was tempted to go to it, because I knew that I ventured only life, which I had offered to God the day I commenced the journey. At the end I feared [to do so], considering my danger and that, if I died, I would not be able to make a report of this country, which to me appears the greatest and best of the discoveries.[5] Saying to the chiefs who had come with me how beautiful Cíbola appeared to me, they told me that it was the least of the seven cities, and that Totonteac is much bigger and better than all the seven, and that it has so many houses and people that it has no end. Viewing the situation of the city, it appeared appropriate to me to call that country the new kingdom of Saint Francis; and there, with the aid of the Indians, I made a great heap of stones, and on top of it I placed a cross, small and light because I had not the equipment for making it larger, and I announced that I erected that cross and monument in the name of Don Antonio de Mendoza, viceroy of New Spain, for the Emperor, our lord, in token of possession, conforming to the instructions, which possession I proclaimed that I took of all the seven cities and of the kingdoms of Totonteac and of Acus and of Marata, and that I went not to them in order to return to give account of what I did and saw.

And so I returned, more satiated with fear than with food, and with the greatest haste I could went to overtake the people I had left behind. I over-

3. I.e., one of his permanent attendants who had accompanied him from Culiacán. These are not to be confused with the local Indians who traveled with the party from time to time.

4. The friar's words, *tiene muy hermoso parescer de pueblo*, have been translated in half a dozen different ways. Often they are incorrectly rendered as "it is a very beautiful city." Baldwin does better with "it appears to be a very beautiful city," but [The translator George Parker] Winship gives us "it has a fine appearance for a village" (note the introduced derogatory implication). "It has the appearance of a very beautiful town" is as nearly exact as is possible in English. Here is the only instance where de Niza calls Cíbola a town, and he next refers to it as a *población*. Thereafter he always speaks of it as a city.

5. By "the discoveries" de Niza refers to all that had till then been discovered in the New World. He therefore rates the country of Cíbola above that of the Incas and the Aztecs, both of which he had seen.

took them after two days of travel and went with them until past the *despoblado*, where[6] they did not make me so good a reception as the first time,[7] because the men, as well as the women, made great lament for the people who were killed at Cíbola. And with fear I hurried immediately from the people of that valley,[8] and went ten leagues the first day, and then eight, and then ten leagues, without stopping until past the second *despoblado*.[9]

Returning, and still not rid of fear, I determined to approach the gorge where the mountain ranges ended, of which I said before I had information,[1] and there I had information that the valley was peopled many *jornadas* to the eastward, but I dared not enter it, because it appeared to me that we have to go to occupy and dominate that other country of the seven cities and the kingdoms that I spoke of; that then (or, "at that time") we could see it better, without placing my person in jeopardy, and leaving it in order to give an account of what I had seen. I saw only, from the mouth of the gorge, seven settlements of fair size, at some distance a valley farther below, very green and of very good land,[2] from which arose many smokes: I was informed that in it is much gold, and that the natives of it trade in vessels and jewels for the ears, and little plates with which they scrape themselves and remove the sweat, and that these people do not consent that those of the other part of the valley trade with them: they were unable to tell the reason for that. Here I placed two crosses and took possession of all the gorge and valley after the manner and ritual of the possessions above, conforming to the instructions.

From there I turned back to my journey, with all the haste I could, until I arrived at the *villa* of San Miguel, of the province of Culiacán, expecting to find there Francisco Vázquez de Coronado, governor of New Galicia, and as I did not find him, I continued my journey to the City of Compostela, where I found him. And from there I presently wrote of my arrival to the most illustrious lord, the viceroy of New Spain, and to our Father Friar Antonio de Ciudad-Rodrigo, Provincial, asking him to send me orders what to do.

I do not place here many details, because they have nothing to do with the case: I only tell what I saw and was told me of the countries where I went and of those of which I was given information, for to give it to our Father Provincial, so that he might show it to the Father of our Order, who may advise him, or to the Assembly[3] at whose command I went, that they give it to the Most Illustrious Lord, the Viceroy of New Spain, at whose request they sent me on this journey.

ca. 1540

---

6. "Where" has reference to the northernmost village of the Sonora Valley, whence these disgruntled Ópatas [a collective name for three indigenous peoples of Sonora] came.
7. That is, on the occasion of his three days' stay at that village when he was en route toward Cíbola.
8. The Sonora Valley.
9. Past the second *despoblado*, he would have been in the Yaqui Valley and out of reach of the Ópatas.

1. This refers to the well-populated valley of which de Niza says the Indians told him, on his outbound trip.
2. This suggests that the "mountain gorge of much land" was a broad valley, pinched into a gorge at its lower end by the convergence of flanking mountain ranges. See note 9, p. 40.
3. The Assembly (*Capítulo*) was formed of the prelates of the Franciscan order in New Spain.

# HERNANDO DE SOTO
## ca. 1496–1542

As discussed in the period introduction, the Spanish conquistadors and colonizers documented the exploration and conquest of America through various forms of writing: memoirs, letters, itineraries, diaries, memorials, ethnographies, epic poems, log books, historical accounts, official reports, manuals, legal documents such as treaties, and *relaciones*. In part, they were preserving their experiences for posterity. In part, they were responding to the requirements of the Crown or the exigencies of local government officials.

Four written narratives detail the adventures and exploits of the Spanish explorer Hernando de Soto during his expedition of 1539–43, into Florida and the American South. One was written by a mysterious Portuguese known as Caballero de Elvas, or Gentleman of Elvas; the second by "El Inca" Garcilaso de la Vega; the third, the official diary of the expedition, by de Soto's personal secretary, Rodrigo Ranjel; and the fourth, an official report to the king of Spain, by the broker of the expedition, Luys Hernández de Biedma. However, historians favor Elvas's eyewitness account, which was written in 1557, not too long after the events. Published in Portugal in 1904 as *Relação verdadeira dos trabalhos que o governador d. Fernando de Souto e certos fidalgos portugueses passaram no descobrimento da província da Flórida agora novamente feita por um fidalgo de Elvas* (True Relation of the Vicissitudes That Attended the Governor Don Hernando de Soto and Some Nobles of Portugal in the Discovery of the Province of Florida Now Just Given by a Fidalgo of Elvas), it was first translated into English in 1607 with the quite descriptive title *Virginia Richly Valued by the Description of the Main Land of Florida, Her Next Neighbor; Out of Four Years Continued Travel and Discovery for Above One Thousand Miles East and West, of Don Fernando de Soto, and Six Hundred Able Men in His Company. Wherein Are Truly Observed the Riches and Fertility of Those Parts Abounding with Things Necessary, Pleasant, and Profitable for the Life of Man; with the Nature and Dispositions of the Inhabitants. Written by a Portugal Gentleman of Elvas, Employed in All the Action, and Translated Out of Portuguese by Richard Hakluyt.*

*True Relation*, a fairly straightforward account of the expedition in 44 chapters, begins by describing the early life of its protagonist. Hernado de Soto was born between 1496 and 1500, in Xerez de Badajoz, Spain. As a member of the Francisco Hernández de Córdova expedition, he arrived in Balboa, Panama, in 1514. Soon thereafter, he began to distinguish himself by participating in some of the first expeditions to the Pacific Ocean. The conquistador Pedrárias Dávila (also spelled Pedro Arias de Ávila), governor of what is now Panamá, appointed him captain of a horse troop and also directed him to join Francisco Pizarro in the conquest of Peru. In Peru, he distinguished himself in all the battles including the capture of the Inca emperor Atahualpa, and he is considered second in importance in the conquest of Peru only to Francisco and Hernando Pizarro. De Soto's success in the battlefield yielded him rich rewards, and he soon returned to Spain a wealthy man, with 180,000 *cruzados* (approximately $75,000). While in Spain, he married Doña Ysabel de Bobadilla, daughter of Pedrárias Dávila. He presented himself in court, and the king of Spain named him governor of Cuba and *Adelantado* (governor of a border province) of Florida. He was also granted the title of marquis as his reward for the future conquest and colonization of the Florida territory.

When de Soto began to organize his expedition, many Spaniards who had been with him in the conquest of Peru, and had acquired wealth as a result, joined him. For four years, these explorers, between 600 and 800 men, journeyed through what is today Florida, Georgia, North and South Carolina, Tennessee, Alabama, Mississippi, Arkansas, Texas, Missouri, and Louisiana. This vast territory was occupied by numerous Indian nations: Timuguas, Cherokees, Creek, Choctaws, Chickasaws, Quapaws or Arkansas, and the Pani nation. After tracing de Soto's footsteps from his days at the court of Spain to Seville, where the men assembled to depart for the Americas, Elvas describes perilous journeys: first to the Canary Islands and later from San Lúcar de Barrameda, Santiago de Cuba (present-day Havana), to the coast of Florida. The Spaniards experience both friendly and bellicose encounters with the local Native Americans, and Elvas frequently cites the bravery of de Soto and his men. When de Soto dies during the expedition, Luis Moscoso assumes command.

The following selection is a letter de Soto wrote in July 1539, in Tampa Bay, Florida. Addressing the justice and board of magistrates in Santiago de Cuba, de Soto details his quest for domination; his unquenchable desire for gold, silver, and pearls; his deep faith in God; the righteousness of his endeavor; his loyalty to the king of Spain; and his desire to bring glory and financial gain to the Crown. He explicitly presents the harsh nature of the Spaniards' encounters with the Native Americans: Whole towns flee as the conquistadors approach; if the Indians lie to de Soto, "it will cost them their lives." Evident also is the Spaniards' belief in their right to take the Native Americans' food, their clothing, or whatever else the soldiers desire. Written in elegant, albeit bureaucratic Spanish, this letter provides an excellent glimpse into de Soto's personality, motives, and plans.

## Letter of Hernando de Soto at Tampa Bay to the Justice and Board of Magistrates in Santiago de Cuba[1]

VERY NOBLE GENTLEMEN:

The being in a new country, not very distant indeed from that where you are, still with some sea between, a thousand years appear to me to have gone by since any thing has been heard from you; and although I left some letters written at Havana, to go off in three ways, it is indeed long since I have received one. However, since opportunity offers by which I may send an account of what it is always my duty to give, I will relate what passes, and I believe will be welcome to persons I know favourably, and are earnest for my success.

I took my departure from Havana with all my armament on Sunday, the XVIIIth of May, although I wrote that I should leave on the XXVth of the month. I anticipated the day, not to lose a favourable wind, which changed, nevertheless, for calms, upon our getting into the Gulf; still these were not so continuous as to prevent our casting anchor on this coast, as we did at the end of eight days, which was on Sunday, the festival of Espíritu Santo.[2]

Having fallen four or five leagues[3] below the port, without any one of my pilots being able to tell where we were, it became necessary that I should go in the brigantines and look for it.[4] In doing so, and in entering the mouth of the port, we were detained three days; and likewise because we had no knowledge of the passage—a bay that runs up a dozen leagues or more from

1. Translated in 1866 by Buckingham Smith from the unpublished, handwritten original (housed at the Archivo de Indias, Seville, Spain). *Santiago de Cuba*: capital city of the Santiago de Cuba Province, in the southeastern area of Cuba.
2. Holy Spirit; along with God and the Son, the third person in the Christian Trinity (Godhead). The descent of the Holy Spirit on Jesus' disciples is celebrated on the feast day called Pentecost, the seventh Sunday after Easter.
3. Between roughly 140 and 175 miles.
4. I.e., sail the ships to find the port.

the sea—we were so long delayed that I was obliged to send my Lieutenant-General, Vasco Porcallo de Figueroa,[5] in the brigantines, to take possession of a town at the end of the bay. I ordered all the men and horses to be landed on a beach, whence, with great difficulty, we went on Trinity Sunday[6] to join Vasco Porcallo. The Indians of the coast, because of some fears of us, have abandoned all the country, so that for thirty leagues not a man of them has halted.

At my arrival here I received news of there being a Christian in the possession of a Cacique, and I sent Baltazar de Gallegos,[7] with XL. men of the horse, and as many of the foot, to endeavour to get him. He found the man a day's journey from this place, with eight or ten Indians, whom he brought into my power. We rejoiced no little over him, for he speaks the language; and although he had forgotten his own, it directly returned to him. His name is Juan Ortiz, an hidalgo, native of Sevilla.

In consequence of this occurrence, I went myself for the Cacique, and came back with him in peace. I then sent Baltazar de Gallegos, with eighty lancers, and a hundred foot-soldiers, to enter the country. He has found fields of maize, beans, and pumpkins, with other fruits, and provision in such quantity as would suffice to subsist a very large army without its knowing a want. Having been allowed, without interruption, to reach the town of a Cacique named Urripacoxit, master of the one we are in, also of many other towns, some Indians were sent to him to treat for peace. This, he writes, having been accomplished, the Cacique failed to keep certain promises, whereupon he seized about XVII. persons, among whom are some of the principal men; for in this way, it appears to him, he can best secure a performance. Among those he detains are some old men of authority, as great as can be among such people, who have information of the country farther on. They say that three days' journey from where they are, going by some towns and huts, all well inhabited, and having many maize-fields, is a large town called Acuera, where with much convenience we might winter; and that afterwards, farther on, at the distance of two days' journey, there is another town, called Ocale. It is so large, and they so extol it, that I dare not repeat all that is said. There is to be found in it a great plenty of all the things mentioned; and fowls, a multitude of turkeys, kept in pens, and herds of tame deer that are tended. What this means I do not understand, unless it be the cattle, of which we brought the knowledge with us. They say there are many trades among that people, and much intercourse,[8] an abundance of gold and silver, and many pearls. May it please God that this may be so; for of what these Indians say I believe nothing but what I see, and must well see; although they know, and have it for a saying, that if they lie to me it will cost them their lives. This interpreter puts a new life into us, in affording the means of our understanding these people, for without him I know not what would become of us. Glory be to God, who by His goodness has directed all, so that it appears as if He had taken this enterprise in His especial keeping, that it may be for His service, as I have supplicated, and do dedicate it to Him.

---

5. Spanish nobleman who, among other accomplishments, founded the Cuban city of Remedios between 1513 and 1524.
6. In the Christian liturgical calendar, the first Sunday after Pentecost.
7. Spanish officer in the de Soto expedition. *Cacique*: a chief or leader of a tribe.
8. Dealings, exchanges.

I sent eighty soldiers by sea in boats, and my General by land with XL. horsemen, to fall upon a throng of some thousand Indians, or more, whom Juan de Añasco[9] had discovered. The General got back last night, and states that they fled from him; and although he pursued them, they could not be overtaken, for the many obstructions in the way. On our coming together we will march to join Baltazar de Gallegos, that we may go thence to pass the winter at the Ocale,[1] where, if what is said be true, we shall have nothing to desire. Heaven be pleased that something may come of this that shall be for the service of our Divine Master, and whereby I may be enabled to serve Your Worships, and each of you, as I desire, and is your due.

Notwithstanding my continual occupation here, I am not forgetful of the love I owe to objects at a distance; and since I may not be there in person, I believe that where you, Gentlemen, are, there is little in which my presence can be necessary. This duty weighs upon me more than every other, and for the attentions you will bestow, as befits your goodness, I shall be under great obligations. I enjoin it upon you, to make the utmost exertions to maintain the repose and well-being of the public, with the proper administration of justice, always reposing in the Licentiate,[2] that every thing may be so done in accordance with law, that God and the King may be served, myself gratified, and every one be content and pleased with the performance of his trust, in such a manner as you, Gentlemen, have ever considered for my honour, not less than your own, although I still feel that I have the weight thereof, and bear the responsibility.

As respects the bastion which I left begun, if labouring on it have been neglected, or perhaps discontinued, with the idea that the fabric is not now needed, you, Gentlemen, will favour me by having it finished, since every day brings change; and although no occasion should arise for its employment, the erection is provident for the well-being and safety of the town: an act that will yield me increased satisfaction, through your very noble personages.

That our Lord may guard and increase your prosperity is my wish and your deserving.

In this town and Port of Espiritu Santo, in the Province of Florida, July the IX., in the year 1539.

The servant of you, Gentlemen.

EL ADELANTADO DON HERNANDO DE SOTO.

July 9, 1539                                                                 1866

---

9. The Spanish king's comptroller. According to the account of "El Inca" Garcilaso de la Vega, Añasco was dispatched from Cuba to explore Florida's coast during the year before de Soto sailed from Havana.
1. A Timucua Indian village in which de Soto and his army stayed several weeks before continuing their northward journey. In the sixteenth and seventeenth centuries, the accepted spellings were Ocali, Ocale, Ocaly, Cale, and Elo-cale.
2. I.e., drawing on legal experts.

# PEDRO CASTAÑEDA DE NÁJERA
## ca. 1512–death unknown

Not much is known about Pedro Castañeda de Nájera, and most of the information about him comes directly from his writings. He was a native of the Biscayan town of Nájera (hence the surname under which he is known), in northern Spain. By 1540, he was living in the northern Mexican outpost of Culiacán (now a city in the state of Sinaloa). In 1540–42, he served as a soldier in and chronicler of the Francisco Vásquez de Coronado expedition. We know he was married with eight children because his wife presented a claim against the Mexican treasury for the time he served and the travails he experienced in the Coronado adventure.

Coronado—"the general," as Castañeda de Nájera calls him—was born in Salamanca, Spain, in 1510, to an aristocratic family. Through his wife, Beatriz Estrada, he inherited a sizeable estate. At the age of 25, he traveled to New Spain, where he worked closely with the viceroy, Don Antonio de Mendoza. Possibly as a reward for this work, he was made governor of Nueva Galicia, in western Mexico. Mendoza subsidized Coronado's expedition, which was intended to find the Seven Cities of Cíbola and Quivira, supposedly located somewhere in what is now the southwestern United States.

The journey began on February 23, 1540, in Compostela, on the Pacific coast. Coronado had assembled 250 horsemen, 70 Spanish foot soldiers armed with crossbows and harquebuses, 300 Indian allies, a thousand Afro-Hispanic and Indian servants and followers, horses, pack mules, oxen, cows, sheep, and swine. Among the members of the expedition was Fray Marcos de Niza, the Spanish explorer whose account of the Seven Cities had whetted Coronado's appetite for exploring the Southwest. De Niza had claimed that the Seven Cities were in present-day New Mexico, and Coronado followed de Niza's path. Even the very small chance of finding gold or a fabulous empire inspired these explorers, as it inspired many other conquistadors, and de Niza wanted to be at the head of the expedition even if it proved as fruitless as his own actually had.

After reaching Culiacán on March 23, 1540, Coronado reorganized the expedition, sending 200 men ahead to explore the terrain as the rest of the members followed at a more leisurely pace. Three months later, Coronado reached what is now Arizona. On July 7, he arrived at the place in New Mexico that de Niza had identified as Cíbola. Instead of the legendary gold-paved city, Coronado found, to his disappointment, the pueblo of Hawikuh, which consisted of adobe dwellings where Zuñi Indians still live today. The Zuñi were unhappy that the expedition had interrupted their summer ceremonies, and they were particularly annoyed at Coronado's taking possession of their lands for the pope and for the king and queen of Spain. After an hour-long battle, the Spaniards took the pueblo.

By August 7, the expedition had found seven villages, which were inhabited by the Moqui tribes of Tusayan. In the spring of 1541, still searching for Quivira, Coronado continued eastward, crossing the Rio Grande and the Great Plains of Texas. The only settlements he and his men found in the east were those of the Plains Indians in Kansas. In 1542, exhausted and defeated, Coronado returned to central Mexico to quell a rebellion. (De Niza had returned to Mexico after the expedition failed to substantiate his claims about New Mexico.) In Mexico City, he served as governor of Nueva Galicia until Viceroy Mendoza relieved him of this post, and he died on September 22, 1545.

Like de Niza's exploratory journey, Coronado's expedition was instrumental in opening up the Southwest and the Midwest for the expeditions that came during the second half of the sixteenth century. Coronado was not celebrated during his lifetime, but he was honored in 1952 with the naming of the Coronado National Memorial, in Bisbee, Arizona.

The following selections are two chapters from the journal in which Castañeda de Nájera details Coronado's journey from Culiacán to the Midwestern plains. The first chapter matter-of-factly yet paternalistically presents the relentless quest for Cíbola, the Spaniards' approaches to the environment, and the native peoples' customs and ceremonies. The second chapter narrates the rape of an Indian woman by a Spaniard and the aftermath of that attack.

---

*FROM* NARRATIVE OF THE EXPEDITION OF CORONADO[1]

## Chapter 9. Of How the Army Started from Culiacán and the Arrival of the General at Cíbola, and of the Army at Señora and of Other Things That Happened

The general, as has been said, started to continue his journey from the valley of Culiacán somewhat lightly equipped, taking with him the friars, since none of them wished to stay behind with the army. After they had gone three days, a regular friar who could say mass, named Friar Antonio Victoria, broke his leg, and they brought him back from the camp to have it treated. He stayed with the army after this, which was no slight consolation for all. The general and his force crossed the country without trouble, as they found everything peaceful, because the Indians knew Friar Marcos and some of the others who had been with Melchor Díaz when he went with Juan de Saldíbar to investigate. After the general had crossed the inhabited region and came to Chichilticalli, where the wilderness begins, and saw nothing favorable, he could not help feeling somewhat downhearted, for, although the reports were very fine about what was ahead, there was nobody who had seen it except the Indians who went with the negro,[2] and these had already been caught in some lies. Besides all this, he was much affected by seeing that the fame of Chichilticalli was summed up in one tumbledown house without any roof, although it appeared to have been a strong place at some former time when it was inhabited, and it was very plain that it had been built by a civilized and warlike race of strangers who had come from a distance. This building was made of red earth.[3] From here they went on through the wilderness, and in fifteen days came to a river about eight leagues from Cíbola which they called Red River,[4] because its waters were muddy and reddish. In this river they found mullets like those of Spain. The first Indians from that country were seen here—two of them, who ran away to give the news. During the night following the next day, about two leagues from the village, some

1. Translated by George Parker Winship. Except as indicated, all footnotes are by Frederick Webb Hodge and Theodore H. Lewis, as editors of *Spanish Explorers in the Southwestern United States, 1528–1543* (1907). The anthology editors have omitted two notes and made minor, stylistic changes to the text and notes.
2. Estevanico (1500?–1539), also known as Estevan, Black Stephen, and Stephen the Moor, a Moroccan explorer and slave (at one time, owned by the explorer Andrés Dorantes). [Anthology editors' note]
3. Chichilticalli, or the "Red House," was so named by the Aztec Indians on account of its color. It was situated on or near the Río Gila, east of the mouth of the San Pedro, probably not far from present Solomonsville in southern Arizona.
4. The Zuñi River, within the present Arizona. Its waters are muddy in springtime, the only time it flows into the Little Colorado.

Indians in a safe place yelled so that, although the men were ready for any-thing, some were so excited that they put their saddles on hind-side before; but these were the new fellows. When the veterans had mounted and ridden round the camp, the Indians fled. None of them could be caught because they knew the country.

The next day they entered the settled country in good order, and when they saw the first village, which was Cíbola, such were the curses that some hurled at Friar Marcos that I pray God may protect him from them.

It is a little, crowded village,[5] looking as if it had been crumpled all up together. There are haciendas in New Spain which make a better appear-ance at a distance. It is a village of about two hundred warriors, is three and four stories high, with the houses small and having only a few rooms, and without a courtyard. One yard serves for each section.[6] The people of the whole district had collected here, for there are seven villages in the province, and some of the others are even larger and stronger than Cíbola. These folks waited for the army, drawn up by divisions in front of the village. When they refused to have peace on the terms the interpreters extended to them, but appeared defiant, the Santiago[7] was given, and they were at once put to flight. The Spaniards then attacked the village, which was taken with not a little difficulty, since they held the narrow and crooked entrance. During the attack they knocked the general down with a large stone, and would have killed him but for Don García López de Cárdenas and Hernando de Alvarado, who threw themselves above him and drew him away, receiving the blows of the stones, which were not few. But the first fury of the Span-iards could not be resisted, and in less than an hour they entered the village and captured it. They discovered food there, which was the thing they were most in need of. After this the whole province was at peace.

The army which had stayed with Don Tristán de Arellano started to follow their general, all loaded with provisions, with lances on their shoulders, and all on foot, so as to have the horses loaded. With no slight labor from day to day, they reached a province which Cabeza de Vaca had named Hearts (Cora-zones), because the people here offered him many hearts of animals.[8] He founded a town here and named it San Hieronimo de los Corazones (Saint Jerome of the Hearts). After it had been started, it was seen that it could not be kept up here, and so it was afterward transferred to a valley which had been called Señora. The Spaniards call it Señora,[9] and so it will be known by this name.

5. The Zuñi Indian pueblo of Hawikuh, one of their seven villages, from which Coronado wrote to the Viceroy Mendoza, dating his letter "from the province of Cevola, and this city of Granada, the 3d of August, 1540." (See Winship's transla-tion in Fourteenth Report of the Bureau of Ethnol-ogy, pp. 552–563.) Hawikuh, or "Granada," was situated about fifteen miles southwest of the pres-ent Zuñi, near the Zuñi River, in New Mexico, and its ruins are still to be seen. This was the pueblo in which Estevan lost his life the year be-fore, and which was viewed from an adjacent height by Fray Marcos. Hawikuh was the seat of a mission established by the Franciscans in 1629; it was abandoned in 1670 after having been raided by the Apaches and its priest killed. The name

"Cíbola," now and later applied to Hawikuh, is believed to be a Spanish form of Shiwina, the Zuñi name for their tribal range. Cíbolo later be-came the term by which the Spaniards of Mexico designated the bison.
6. The houses were built in terrace fashion, one above the other, the roof of one tier forming a sort of front yard for the tier of houses next above it.
7. The war cry or "loud invocation addressed to Saint James before engaging in battle with the Infidels." —Captain John Stevens's Dictionary [an English/Spanish dictionary of 1705].
8. ° ° ° The place was at or near the present Ures, on the Río Sonora in Sonora, Mexico.
9. Whence the name of the present state of Sonora.

From here a force went down the river to the seacoast to find the harbor and to find out about the ships. Don Rodrigo Maldonado, who was captain of those who went in search of the ships, did not find them, but he brought back with him an Indian so large and tall that the best man in the army reached only to his chest.[1] It was said that other Indians were even taller on that coast. After the rains ceased the army went on to where the town of Señora was afterward located,[2] because there were provisions in that region, so that they were able to wait there for orders from the general.

About the middle of the month of October,[3] Captains Melchor Díaz and Juan Gallego came from Cíbola, Juan Gallego on his way to New Spain and Melchor Díaz to stay in the new town of Hearts, in command of the men who remained there. He was to go along the coast in search of the ships.

## Chapter 15. Of Why Tiguex Revolted, and How They Were Punished, without Being to Blame for It

It has been related how the general reached Tiguex,[4] where he found Don García López de Cárdenas and Hernando de Alvarado, and how he sent the latter back to Cicuye, where he took the captain Whiskers and the governor of the village, who was an old man, prisoners. The people of Tiguex did not feel well about this seizure. In addition to this, the general wished to obtain some clothing to divide among his soldiers, and for this purpose he summoned one of the chief Indians of Tiguex, with whom he had already had much intercourse[5] and with whom he was on good terms, who was called Juan Alemán by our men, after a Juan Alemán who lived in Mexico, whom he was said to resemble. The general told him that he must furnish about three hundred or more pieces of cloth, which he needed to give his people. He said that he was not able to do this, but that it pertained to the governors; and that besides this, they would have to consult together and divide it among the villages, and that it was necessary to make the demand of each town separately. The general did this, and ordered certain of the gentlemen who were with him to go and make the demand; and as there were twelve villages, some of them went on one side of the river and some on the other. As they were in very great need, they did not give the natives a chance to consult about it, but when they came to a village they demanded what they had to give, so that they could proceed at once. Thus these people could do nothing except take off their own cloaks and give them to make up the number demanded of them. And some of the soldiers who were in these parties, when the collectors

---

1. A Seri Indian. The Seri are a tribe speaking an independent language and occupying the island of Tiburón and the adjacent Sonora coast of the Gulf of California. * * * For an account of this people, see [W. J.] McGee in *Seventeenth Report of the Bureau of American Ethnology*, pt. 1 (1898).
2. In the present Sonora valley, where it opens out into a broader plain a number of miles above Ures.
3. This should be September.
4. Tiguex (pronounced Tee-guaysh') is the name of a group of Pueblo tribes, now consisting of Isleta, Sandía, Taos, and Picuris, speaking the Tigua language, as it is now designated. Their principal village in Coronado's time was also called Tiguex by the Spaniards; this was the Puaray of forty years later (1583), the first time the native name was recorded. It was situated at the site of Bernalillo, on the Rio Grande, and was inhabited up to the time of the Pueblo rebellion of 1680, when it contained two hundred Tiguas and Spaniards.
5. Dealings, exchanges. [Anthology editors' note]

gave them some blankets or cloaks which were not such as they wanted, if they saw any Indian with a better one on, they exchanged with him without more ado, not stopping to find out the rank of the man they were stripping, which caused not a little hard feeling.

Besides what I have just said, one whom I will not name, out of regard for him, left the village where the camp was and went to another village about a league distant, and seeing a pretty woman there he called her husband down to hold his horse by the bridle while he went up; and as the village was entered by the upper story, the Indian supposed he was going to some other part of it. While he was there the Indian heard some slight noise, and then the Spaniard came down, took his horse, and went away. The Indian went up and learned that he had violated, or tried to violate, his wife, and so he came with the important men of the town to complain that a man had violated his wife, and he told how it happened. When the general made all the soldiers and the persons who were with him come together, the Indian did not recognize the man, either because he had changed his clothes or for whatever other reason there may have been, but he said that he could tell the horse, because he had held his bridle, and so he was taken to the stables, and found the horse, and said that the master of the horse must be the man. He denied doing it, seeing that he had not been recognized, and it may be that the Indian was mistaken in the horse; anyway, he went off without getting any satisfaction. The next day one of the Indians, who was guarding the horses of the army, came running in, saying that a companion of his had been killed, and that the Indians of the country were driving off the horses toward their villages. The Spaniards tried to collect the horses again, but many were lost, besides seven of the general's mules.

The next day Don García López de Cárdenas went to see the villages and talk with the natives. He found the villages closed by palisades and a great noise inside, the horses being chased as in a bull fight and shot with arrows. They were all ready for fighting. Nothing could be done, because they would not come down on to the plain and the villages are so strong that the Spaniards could not dislodge them. The general then ordered Don García López de Cárdenas to go and surround one village with all the rest of the force. This village was the one where the greatest injury had been done and where the affair with the Indian woman occurred. Several captains who had gone on in advance with the general, Juan de Saldívar and Barrionuevo and Diego López and Melgosa, took the Indians so much by surprise that they gained the upper story, with great danger, for they wounded many of our men from within the houses. Our men were on top of the houses in great danger for a day and a night and part of the next day, and they made some good shots with their crossbows and muskets. The horsemen on the plain with many of the Indian allies from New Spain smoked them out from the cellars[6] into which they had broken, so that they begged for peace. Pablo de Melgosa and Diego López, the alderman from Seville, were left on the roof and answered the Indians with the same signs they were making for peace, which was to make a cross. They then put down their arms and received pardon. They were taken to the tent of Don García, who, according to what he said, did not know about the peace and thought that they had given themselves up

---

6. *Kivas*, underground ceremonial chambers. [Anthology editors' note]

of their own accord because they had been conquered. As he had been ordered by the general not to take them alive, but to make an example of them so that the other natives would fear the Spaniards, he ordered two hundred stakes to be prepared at once to burn them alive. Nobody told him about the peace that had been granted them, for the soldiers knew as little as he, and those who should have told him about it remained silent, not thinking that it was any of their business. Then when the enemies saw that the Spaniards were binding them and beginning to roast them, about a hundred men who were in the tent began to struggle and defend themselves with what there was there and with the stakes they could seize. Our men who were on foot attacked the tent on all sides, so that there was great confusion around it, and then the horsemen chased those who escaped. As the country was level, not a man of them remained alive, unless it was some who remained hidden in the village and escaped that night to spread throughout the country the news that the strangers did not respect the peace they had made, which afterward proved a great misfortune. After this was over, it began to snow, and they abandoned the village and returned to the camp just as the army came from Cíbola.

1540–42                                                                    1896

# JUAN DE CASTELLANOS
## 1522–1607

As an adolescent, in the late 1530s, Juan de Castellanos traveled from Spain to the Spanish colony of New Granada. He was an altar boy, a pearl fisherman, a soldier, and an adventurer before becoming a priest and writing about his New World experiences. In 1589, de Castellanos published his *Elegías de varones ilustres de Indias* (Elegies of Illustrious Men of the Indies). At about 150,000 lines, this work remains the longest epic poem written in Spanish. Starting with an account of Columbus's first trip to the New World, it glorifies many of the Spanish conquistadors, describing their heroic adventures, their physical and spiritual qualities, and their bravery in battling Indians to secure Spanish domination of the new territories.

De Castellanos wrote the *Elegías* from memory. The abundant details in it demonstrate his extensive knowledge of the recounted events, of the localities where they took place, and of the people at the center of the action. Critics generally consider the work a valuable historical document of the conquest of the West Indies, but are not equally impressed with the author's often tedious and unadorned artistic style. The poem certainly lacks the literary merit of similar efforts, such as Alonso de Ercilla's *La araucana* (1569), the masterpiece of Latin American epic poetry.

The selection in this anthology, "Revolt of the Borinqueños," is part of the poem's sixth elegy. It focuses on the violent encounter between the Spaniards and the Taínos in the island the native inhabitants called Boriquén and Columbus had named Isla de San Juan Bautista upon his arrival in 1493, during his second voyage. In the colonial period, the island's Spanish name was interchanged with the name of its main port, Puerto Rico (literally, Rich Port), while its indigenous name was adapted into the Spanish language as Borinquen and its inhabitants were called *borinqueños*. In the original Spanish text, Castellanos refers to them as *boriquenes*. The historical characters in this selection are Juan Ponce de León, the Spaniard sent to the Island of San Juan Bautista in 1508 to begin colonization and who was later appointed governor of the island; Diego de Salcedo, a conquistador killed by the Indians to test the presumed immortality of the Spaniards and dispel the myth that they were gods; and Agüeybana II, the Taíno chieftain who led the last major indigenous rebellion against the Spanish invaders, in 1511.

# Revolt of the Borinqueños[1]

Juan Ponce[2] having readied men and store,
Under the powers given to his hand,
Made the journey without delaying more,
With interpreters from Haiti in his command
And since on St. John's Day[3] he went ashore,     5
San Juan de Puerto Rico he called the land.
The men that he brought with him on that day
Stepped forth on sandy beaches of a bay.

## Salcedo

As the Chief[4] was pondering how best to play
His game ensuring the success he planned,     10
Diego de Salcedo[5] passed that way,
Unaccompanied by any of his band;
Whereat Urayoan,[6] hospitable and gay,
Giving no hint of what he had in hand,
Every attention to Salcedo showed,     15
And sent men to companion him on the road.
He set out with those Indians and their scheme,
He who wotted not what might betide.
And most courteously when they neared a stream,
They offered to bear him to the other side     20
Upon their shoulders; best way it would seem,
To keep his clothes dry from the river's tide.
He should have known such promises not to keep.
They flung him in where the water runs most deep.

Watching him flounder as the waters rose     25
Above where two or three had let him lour,

---

1. Translated into English in 1957 by Muna Lee, the first wife of Luis Muñoz Marín (see p. 482).
2. Juan Ponce de León (1460–1521), Spanish conquistador; after taking part in Columbus's second voyage, he was appointed governor of Puerto Rico by the Spanish Crown and later was the first European to explore Florida.
3. Christian feast in honor of St. John the Baptist. It takes place on June 24.
4. I.e., one of the principal *caciques*, or leaders, of the Taínos in Puerto Rico: Agüeybaná II (d. 1511).
5. Spanish soldier (d. 1510). According to legend, the Taínos drowned him to test the presumed divinity and immortality of the Spaniards. Their discovery that the Spaniards were not gods reportedly led the Indians—two months later, in January 1511—to begin the last major indigenous rebellion against the invaders.
6. The Taíno cacique said to have ordered the killing of Diego de Salcedo.

All the Indians beset him now with blows,
And kept him under water a full hour,
Till seeing him still dead, at last each knows
He had been mortal, with but a mortal's power.      30
Yet even then remained with them a dread
Lest 'spite all seeming, he be not wholly dead.
And so they waited there till the third day,
Fearful of what that drowned corpse yet might do.
Begging its pardon, they would softly say      35
How their ill action toward him they must rue,
Until the corpse was putrefying in such way
That by its look and smell at last they knew
Truth could no longer be doubted nor denied:
Here was no feigning: this man indeed had died . . .      40
I am not shocked by this, their show of might,
Nor by the evil deeds they had in mind;
For they had seen their pleasures vanish quite,
Nor security nor any hope could find.
Their wives and children, each unhappy wight      45
Knew a life-long servitude would bind.
They had all seen those precious freedoms fly
Which no amount of money can ever buy.

### Agüeybana

When in one place they were at last aligned,
In a town-meeting there, as you might say,      50
Agüeybana, who has the master mind
And planned in everything to have his way,
Addressed that gathering in a speech designed
To give his eloquent argument full sway.
His words not many, but he chose them well,      55
This, more or less, is what he had to tell:

"If extremes of frenzy cease at long last,
If thinking man feels thought begin to fail,
If you can still remember the good past:
Then no man here can check an anguished wail      60
For object wretchedness that holds us fast
In this fell present where all woes assail.
How much we suffer, how bitter is our bread,
How many of us are failing, fleeing—dead!

"While suffering such evils night and day,      65
We serve these foreigners in our land of birth;
And this our only freedom is: we may
Work their mines and till for them the earth.
Our fields, our plains, our coastlands—and it is they
Who possess all, and leave us to our dearth      70
Here in the land that always was our own,
Where we were born and wherein we have grown.

"Each of us to a master now belongs,
And must render him complete obedience;
Useless it is to tell you of your wrongs,                    75
Who make no effort in your own defense.
So meekly now do you endure your thongs[7]
It seems that suffering has benumbed your sense.
You let your master as he will enjoy
Your wife, your child, as past-time or as toy.              80

"Before the shame and evil that they do,
We like vile cowards have only given way,
I have no knowledge any one of you
Is planning aught such injuries to withstay.
Men who no more than cowed endurance show               85
When suffering or disgraced, what breed are they
If not ourselves, for whom shame has no sting,
We who it seems put up with anything!

"Speak up, forgetful dwellers in this land,
Snoring at ease, who not e'en in sleep complain.            90
Were you not born with weapons in your hand?
Rather than headlong flight across the plain
Were it not better in the hills to stand?
Speaking of war, must I speak to you in vain?
How is it we have not in all our host                       95
One voice to tell the good of the good we lost?

"The Caribs[8] in their fierce and wild estate
—The man that daunts them never casts a shade—[9]
Whose cruelties are so many and so great
That even recounting them makes men afraid,               100
At a high value do your friendship rate,
And tremble when Borinquen's name is said.
And we, shall we in our turn tremble then
Before two hundred worn-out, crippled, starving men?

"My grandmother, that old bestial crone,                   105
And my uncle, dull and slow of wit,
Gave us to believe a fiction all their own,
Which I held monstrous, always doubting it.
By now at last the simple truth is shown
By our own river, the Gurabo. This is it:                  110
Christians are not immortal. Understand
At last that they can meet death by your hand!"

1589

7. Whips.
8. A seafaring, warring native people who raided Puerto Rico's coast from the Virgin Islands.
9. The man would not cast a shade because he does not exist; i.e., the Caribs cannot be daunted.

# "EL INCA" GARCILASO DE LA VEGA
## ca. 1539–1616

The figure known as "El Inca" was a mestizo, a person of mixed European and American Indian ancestry. He was born Gómez Suárez de Figueroa, in Cuzco, Peru. While in Spain in 1563, he changed his name to "El Inca" Garcilaso de la Vega.

His father was Sebastian Garcí Lasso de la Vega Vargas, a Spanish soldier who had participated in the conquest of Peru with Francisco Pizarro and other major conquistadors. His mother was the Peruvian Inca princess Chimpu Ocllo, who was baptized as a Catholic with the name Isabel Suárez. Her father, Huallpa Tupac, was the fourth son of the Inca emperor Tupac Yupanqui and first cousin of the emperor Huáscar, deposed brother of the fallen emperor Atahualpa. "El Inca" Garcilaso lived his early years in Cuzco, under the tutelage of his mother. From her and his Inca relatives, he heard grief-stricken narratives about the fall of the Inca Empire and of their royal ancestors. Until about the age of six or seven, "El Inca" Garcilaso spoke only his mother's language, Quechua. After that, he was tutored in Spanish.

In 1560, "El Inca" Garcilaso traveled to Spain, to further his formal education. For a time, he lived with a favorite uncle, the military leader Don Alonso de Vargas y Figueroa, in the small town of Montilla, in the Andalucía area. He then moved to the city of Córdoba, again to facilitate his studies. Around 1563–66, he happened to meet Gonzalo Silvestre, an old soldier who had accompanied Hernando de Soto on de Soto's expedition of 1539, through present-day Florida and surrounding areas. "El Inca" Garcilaso became interested in writing about the expedition, but exactly when he began composing his account is unknown. By 1592, he had finished the first complete manuscript, *La Florida del Inca: Historia del adelantado Hernando de Soto, Gobernador y capitán general del reino de la Florida, y de otros Heroicos caballeros españoles e indios, escrita por el Inca Garcilaso de la Vega, Capitan de su majestad, natural de la gran ciudad de Coszco, Cabeza de los reinos y provincias del Perú* (The Florida of the Inca: A History of Adelantado Hernando de Soto, Governor and Captain General of the Kingdom of Florida, and of Other Heroic Spanish and Indian Cavaliers, Written by the Inca Garcilaso de la Vega, an Officer of His Majesty, and a Native of the Great City of Cuzco, Capital of the Realms and Provinces of Peru).

"El Inca" Garcilaso's primary source was Gonzalo Silvestre, who was then living in Las Posadas, near Córdoba. In addition to recounting the adventures and misadventures of the expedition, Silvestre was closely involved with the editing of various drafts of "El Inca" Garcilaso's narrative. "El Inca" Garcilaso continued rewriting and polishing the manuscript until 1605, when 750 copies of his work were printed in Portugal. In the published version, "El Inca" Garcilaso acknowledges the influence of two manuscripts about the expedition—Alonso de Carmona's *Peregrinaciones* and Juan Colés's *Relación*—both of which he found in a printing house in Córdoba where a chronicler, a priest belonging to the Franciscan order, had deposited them.

"El Inca" Garcilaso's account of the de Soto expedition is controversial. Some critics believe that in preserving Silvestre's memories it offers important historical information about the expedition; others consider it a fact-based novel with little historical value. Indeed, as noted by the scholar Sylvia L. Hilton, "El Inca" Garcilaso's account draws on the conventions of the Byzantine novel (e.g., felicitous chance encounters, misadventures in vast territories, shipwrecks), the Italian Renaissance novel ("fiestas and celebrations, the medieval and Renaissance courtesy exhibited, the description of placid and tranquil waters, the sweet and refreshing breezes"), and the knight errant novel (adventures through exotic lands, physically invincible heroes' battles against extraordinary enemies, the "rites of combat, the promises rendered between the lady and her suitor, the love messages sent by the lady to the beloved knight, the gallantry and bravery of the young men"). These three literary genres were popular during the fifteenth and sixteenth centuries, and they greatly influenced the writings of both Spanish conquistadors and chroniclers of the conquest of the Americas. In addition, like chroniclers such as Bernal Díaz del Castillo, "El Inca" Garcilaso seeks to make the American experience accessible to Europeans by providing analogies between the exploits of the Spanish conquistadors and those of ancient Greek and Roman mythological and/or historical heroes.

The selections in this anthology provide a view of the battles between the Spanish and the Native Americans. They describe the Indians' extraordinary efforts to expel the Spaniards from their lands or fight the intruders to the death. They also show the Spaniards' unquenchable thirst to dominate, together with their superior weaponry and war strategies. Both sides of this tragic encounter appear brave and dignified. "El Inca" Garcilaso's other works include the highly regarded first part of *Los comentarios reales* (The Royal Commentaries, 1609) and *Historia general del Perú* (General History of Peru; the second part of *Los comentarios reales*, published in 1617). These writings chronicle Inca life before and after the Spanish conquest, addressing the economic, political, and cultural aspects of the Inca Empire. While based in a centuries-old oral tradition, they reflect their author's perspective as a member of the royal family from Cuzco.

---

## *FROM* THE FLORIDA OF THE INCA[1]

### From *Book Two, Part One*

### Chapter XXIV. How They Seized Vitachuco.[2] The Outbreak of the Battle Which Occurred between the Spaniards and the Indians

The people having been ordered out from both sides, as has been stated, the Spaniards sallied forth magnificently decorated and armed, their squadrons arranged in battle formation with the horsemen divided from the footsoldiers. The Governor,[3] in order further to conceal his knowledge of the treason of the Indians, had resolved to accompany the Curaca[4] on foot.

Near the village there was a great plain, on one side of which was a tall, dense and extensive forest, and on the other, two lagoons. The first lagoon was small, measuring only a league in circumference, but it was clear of underbrush and mud, and so deep that at three or four steps from its bank, one could not find footing. The second, which was farther from the town, was very large, for it was more than half a league in width and so long that it looked like a great river, and they had no idea as to where it ended. Between the forest and the two lagoons, the Indians placed their battalion in such a way that water lay to their right and trees to their left. There must

---

1. Translated by John Grier Varner and Jeannette Johnson Varner.
2. A *cacique*—chief or leader of a tribe—in Caliquin, present-day Alachua County, Florida.
3. Hernando de Soto (see p. 48); later in the selection, "El Inca" calls him "their Captain General."
4. The indigenous elected authority in the Quechua communities in Peru.

have been almost ten thousand of these warriors, all of whom were chosen people, valiant and well disposed. On their heads were their finest adornments, some large feather ornaments, prepared and worn in such a way as to rise a half-fathom high and thus make the wearers appear taller than they actually were. Their bows and arrows they had laid on the ground and covered with grass so as to leave the impression that as friends they were unarmed; their squadron they had arranged in the utmost military perfection, not squared but elongated, with the rows straight and somewhat open, and with two flanks on each side of the commanding officers. Indeed their battalion was so excellently organized that it was a beautiful sight to behold. In this manner, they waited for their lord Vitachuco and Hernando de Soto to come out to review them. And eventually these two men did approach on foot, each accompanied by twelve of his own soldiers and each harboring the same motive and desire against the other. To the right of the Governor marched the Spanish battalions, the infantry remaining close to the forest and the cavalry holding to the middle of the plain.

When they came to the place where Vitachuco had promised to give a signal for his Indians to seize the Governor, the latter, who was playing the same game, gave his signal first lest his opponent win over him by a hand; for it was with this signal that the stakes between them were to be won. So it was that the Governor now had a crossbow fired, this being the indication that his men were to act. (Alonso de Carmona says that the signal was the blowing of a trumpet, and it could have been either the one or the other.) With that, the twelve Spaniards who were near Vitachuco seized the Cacique in spite of the fact that the Indians accompanying him made an effort in his defense.

Being secretly armed, Hernando de Soto now mounted one of the two horses standing nearby. This was a dappled gray called Aceytuno, after Mateo de Aceytuno[5] who had presented it to the Governor. (We have told before how this man had gone to rebuild Havana. Remaining there, he became warden of a fortress which he himself founded, and which is the one that at present protects the city and port, although in his time it was not so large and majestic as it is today.) It was a very brave and beautiful animal and was indeed worthy of having had such masters. Once mounted, the Governor attacked and penetrated the squadron of Indians before any other Castilian had an opportunity to do so, for this valiant captain was nearest the foe, and furthermore he prided himself on being first always in each of the battles and encounters that were offered him by day or by night in both the conquest of Florida and that of Peru. And indeed he was one of the four best lancers that could have come or did come to the West Indies. Many times his captains complained about his subjecting himself to such risk and danger, since in the preservation of the life and health of the head of the army lay the safety of the army itself; and although it is possible that he realized that they were right, still he could not curb his bellicose spirit, and he disliked victories unless he were the first in gaining them. Leaders should not be so audacious.

The Indians who at this point already had their arms in their hands, received the Governor with the same spirit and gallantry that he himself

---

5. Also spelled Aceituno; according to "El Inca" Garcilaso in book 1, chapter 12, he was "a cavalier captain born in Talavera de la Reyna," and he was among those ordered by Hernando de Soto to go by sea and rebuild Havana, which had been sacked and burned by French corsairs.

displayed; and they did not permit him to break many lines of their battalion, for, of the numerous arrows which they discharged when he reached the first line, eight struck his horse. As we shall see in the process of this history, the Indians always tried to kill the horses first because of the advantage these animals gave the cavaliers. Thus they nailed the General's horse with four arrows through the chest and four in the knees, two on each side; and they did so with such skill and ferocity that, just as if hit in the forehead with a piece of artillery, the animal fell dead without so much as moving a foot.

Meanwhile the Spaniards, having heard the shot from the crossbow, followed the lead of their Captain General and rushed at the squadron of Indians. Their horses passed so near the Governor that they were able to assist him before the enemy could do further harm. At this time one of the Governor's pages, an hidalgo called something-or-other Viota, who was a native of Zamora,[6] dismounted and, offering the Governor his horse, helped him upon it. Then both the Governor and his men fell upon the Indians once more, and the latter being without pikes were unable to resist the combined impact of the three hundred cavalrymen. Consequently they turned their backs without making further proof of their strength and valor, which was quite contrary to what they and their Cacique had thought it to be a short while before, when it had appeared to them impossible for so few Spaniards to conquer so many and such valiant Indians as they prided themselves on being.

Their squadron broken, the Indians fled to the nearest shelters they could find. A great band of them saved their lives by entering the forest; whereas many others escaped by plunging into the large lagoon. But some of the rearguard not near shelter fled forward across the plain, where a few of them were captured, while more than three hundred were lanced and killed. Those of the advance guard who were the best soldiers and as such are accustomed always to pay in battle for everyone else, were less fortunate because they received the first encounter and the greatest impact of the cavalry. Not being able to take refuge in the woods or in the large lagoon, which were the best shelters, more than nine hundred of them threw themselves into the small lagoon. This first demonstration of Vitachuco's bravery took place at nine or ten o'clock in the morning.

The Spaniards pursued the Indians in every direction, even entering the woods and the large lagoon; but when they saw that all of their perseverance was not resulting in their taking a single Indian, they rushed back to the small lagoon, within which, as we have said, more than nine hundred men had sought shelter. With these men, they fought the entire day, more with threats and terror, however, than with arms since they merely wished to make them surrender. Hence in firing their crossbows and arquebuses, it was not their intention to kill but to frighten, for they were loath to harm men who were exhausted and unable to flee.

The Indians for their part continued to discharge arrows throughout the day, not ceasing until their supply was gone. Because of the depth of the water they were unable to stand, and in order to fire one man would mount three or four of his companions as they swam and, suspended thus in the air, shoot until he had used up the ammunition of his team. In this manner,

6. The capital of the province of Zamora, Spain.

they occupied themselves for the entire day without any one of them surrendering. Then when night came groups of Spaniards stationed themselves at short intervals so that no one could escape in the darkness—the cavalry being arranged in pairs and the infantry in groups of six. And now they continued to torment the Indians, never once letting them set foot on the shore, for when they heard them near, they shot at them and drove them away, hoping that they would become exhausted by the swimming and as a result give up the more quickly. Thus they threatened with death those who would not surrender, at the same time offering pardon, peace and fellowship to those who were willing to receive them.

## Chapter XXV. The Gradual Surrender of the Conquered Indians, and the Constancy of Seven of Them

Regardless of how much the Castilians afflicted the Indians in the lake, they could not do enough to keep them from showing their spirit and strength; for even though these men realized that they were without hope of help in the hardships and danger they were experiencing, they chose death as a lesser evil to that of showing weakness in adversity. This obstinacy they maintained until twelve o'clock that night, for there was not one of them who would yield in spite of the fact that all had spent fourteen hours in the water. From that time on, however, because of the many persuasions of Juan Ortiz[7] and the four Indian interpreters with him who promised and assured them of their lives, the weakest began to come out and surrender one at a time and in pairs, but with such reluctance that by dawn not more than fifty had done so. Then, persuaded by their comrades who had yielded and seeing that they had not been killed or harmed but on the contrary well treated, those remaining in the water now surrendered in greater numbers, although with so much hesitation and so much urging that many, after they were near the bank, returned to the depth of the lagoon. But eventually the will to live brought them once again to the shore. In this manner they continued, fearing to come out and submit, until ten o'clock in the day when those who remained, about two hundred in all, yielded in a body. They had been swimming twenty-four hours, and it was a great pity to see them emerge from the lagoon, half drowned and swollen by the large amount of water they had swallowed, and transfixed by the toil, hunger, fatigue and lack of sleep they had suffered.

Only seven Indians now remained in the water. They were so obstinate that the pleas of the interpreters, the promises of the Governor, and even the example of those who had yielded, were insufficient to persuade them to do the same. On the contrary they appeared to have absorbed the spirit that the others had lost and to prefer death to being conquered. Thus, forcing themselves to answer what was said to them as best they could, they responded that they neither wanted the promises of the Spaniards nor feared their threats or even death itself. With this constancy and strength, they remained

---

7. A native of Seville and an interpreter in the de Soto expedition. According to "El Inca" Garcilaso in book 1, chapters 2–4, he was tortured by a *cacique* and became a captive go-between.

in the lagoon until three o'clock in the afternoon and would have ended their lives there but for the fact that at that hour the Governor decided it was inhuman to permit men of so much magnanimity and virtue (which even in enemies inspires our admiration) to perish. He therefore ordered twelve Spaniards who were great swimmers to go with their swords in their mouths (in imitation of Julius Caesar at Alexandria, Egypt,[8] and of the few Spaniards who did likewise on another occasion in the river Albis, when they conquered the Duke of Saxony[9] and all of his league) and take those seven valiant Indians from the lagoon. At that the swimmers plunged into the water and seizing the men by the leg, arm or hair, dragged them out and threw them on the ground, more drowned than alive, for they were almost unconscious. Thus they remained stretched on the sand in a condition one may well imagine of men who had struggled in water for almost thirty hours without having put foot on dry land (as it appeared) or received any other relief. Their performance was indeed incredible, and I would not dare tell of it were it not verified by the testimony of so many cavaliers and illustrious men who spoke of it in the Indies and in Spain, as well as of others who saw it in this conquest, and in addition by the authority and truthfulness of the individual who related this history to me, a person who is worthy of faith in all respects.

\* \* \*

Moved to pity and compassion by the hardship the seven Indians had suffered in the water, and admiring the strength and constancy of spirit they manifested, the Spaniards now carried them to their camp and did everything possible to recall them to life. Because of these attentions as well as of their own good spirits the miserable ones were revived during the night, but it required the whole of the night to free them from danger. Then when morning came, the Governor commanded that all seven of them be brought before him; and feigning anger, he ordered them to be questioned as to the cause of their persistence and rebellion, and as to why, seeing themselves in such a circumstance and without hope of help, they would not surrender as the rest of their companions had done. Four of these Indians, who were approximately thirty-five years of age, responded. They talked in turns, first one and then the other, this one taking up the account where that one, because of being nervous or not happening to relate it well, had left off. At other times one who had been silent would supply a word that the speaker happened to omit, it being their custom to assist each other in discourse with serious persons before whom they feared they would be ill at ease. Thus maintaining this style of communication, they answered the Governor in many long discourses, the sum of which was understood to be as follows. They had realized that they were in danger of losing their lives and had had no hope of assistance, but in spite of this fact, had felt and confidently believed that in surrendering themselves, they would not be complying in any manner with the obligations of the military offices and charges which

8. Caesar (100 BC–44 BC), a Roman military and political leader, eventually emperor, lived for a time in Alexandria with the Egyptian queen Cleopatra (69 BC–30 BC).

9. The medieval Duchy of Saxony was in northern Germany. Garcisalo might be referring to Augustus I (1526–1586), elector of Saxony. *River Albis*: river in central Europe.

they exercised. Their lord and prince had selected them in time of prosperity and had honored them with the titles and insignia of captain because he had looked upon them as men of strength, spirit and constancy; therefore, they said, it was only just that in times of adversity they should fulfill the obligations of their offices and thus show themselves worthy of those charges lest their Curaca and lord feel that he had erred in choosing them. But in addition to satisfying the military obligations which they owed their lord, they added, they wished likewise to set an example for their sons and successors and for all soldiers and fighting men as to how they should act in similar circumstances, especially in the position of captain and superior; for as such their deeds of spirit and strength or of weakness and cowardice were more conspicuous to those who would honor or censure them than they would be were they base plebeians with no responsibility or charge to fulfill. For this reason, they said, even though they had experienced and survived what his lordship had witnessed, they were not satisfied that they had done their duty or fulfilled their obligations as chiefs and leaders, and it would have been a greater favor and honor for the Governor to have permitted them to perish in the lagoon than to have given them their lives. Hence they refused to recognize any beneficence in his act, and they begged his lordship to command that they be killed, since, not having died for their lord Vitachuco, who had honored and esteemed them so very much, they would not dare appear before him again and would live in the world in great infamy and shame.

## From *Book Three*

## Chapter X. The Mistress of Cofachiqui[1] Comes to Talk with the Governor, Offering Him Both Provisions and Passage for his Army

A little after the news had been carried to the village, there issued from that place six principal Indians who, from what was understood, must have been town magistrates. All were of goodly appearance and of about the same age, being between forty and fifty years old. They entered a large canoe which was managed by servants. Afterward, when the six of them stood before the Governor, they at one and the same time made three different and sweeping bows: the first to the Sun, as all turned their faces toward the east; the second to the Moon, as all turned toward the west; and the third to the Governor, as all addressed themselves to him. The Governor was seated on a chair known as a rest seat, which it was the custom to carry for his use wherever he went so that he might receive the curacas and emissaries with a gravity and embellishment befitting the grandeur of his station. Their salutations completed, the six Indians said to the Governor: "My Lord, do you seek peace or war?" Now you must know that it was a general rule for the Indians to make this their initial question, and that always when the

---

1. *La Señora de Cofachiqui*—literally, the lady of Cofachiqui. Other translators have referred to her as the *Cacica*, but Garcilaso tells us that the Spaniards simply called her "la Señora." We have used the word mistress to indicate that she is a woman with authority. [Translators' note]

Governor entered a new province these were the first words that he heard from its inhabitants.

The General replied that he wished peace and not war, and that he asked no more of them than passage and supplies to enable him to continue on his way to certain provinces for which he was searching. He said that since they knew that food was something that could not be done without, he hoped they would pardon him the bother occasioned in granting it; and promising that he would try to trouble them as little as possible, he begged that they provide him rafts and canoes to cross that river and moreover that they grant him their friendship while his army was passing through their lands.

The Indians responded that they accepted the peace but that they had little food because a great pestilence with many consequent deaths had ravaged their province during the past year, a pestilence from which their town alone had been free. For this reason the inhabitants of the other villages of that province had fled to the forests without sowing their fields. And now, although the disease had passed, these people had not yet been gathered to their homes and towns. They added, however, that they themselves were the vassals of a lady, a young maiden who had recently inherited and was ready for marriage; that they would return to this lady to acquaint her with what his lordship had requested and then apprise him at once concerning her response; and that he meanwhile should await with confidence because it was their belief that their lady, since she was a woman of discretion and of queenly heart, would do everything that she could in the service of the Christians.

Having spoken these words and then obtained the Governor's permission to withdraw, the Indians returned to their village to inform their mistress of what the Captain of the Christians had requested for their journey. They could scarcely have delivered their message when the Castilians observed them making ready two large canoes. Afterward, the mistress of the town[2] and eight of her ladies embarked in one of these canoes, which had been covered with a great canopy and adorned with ornaments. No one else traveled in this canoe, and it was towed by the second one which bore the six principal Indians and many oarsmen. In this manner all crossed the river and came to the place where the Governor was awaiting them.

Although less spectacular in grandeur and majesty, this scene indeed resembles that one in which Cleopatra went forth to receive Marc Anthony on the river Cydnus in Cilicia.[3] There the fates altered in such a fashion that she who had been accused of the crime of *lèse majesté* eventually became the judge of the man who had come to condemn her; and an emperor and lord became the slave of his serf, rendered thus by force of love and by the excellencies, beauty and discretion of that most famous Egyptian. This scene is copiously and ornately described by the teacher of the great Spaniard, Trajan,[4] a disciple worthy of such a master; and because of the simi-

2. [Luys Hernández de] Biedma [broker of the de Soto expedition] says that this woman was only a niece of the ruling dowager. He speaks of her as "brown but well proportioned." [Translators' note]
3. This ancient region of southeast Asia Minor was at one time part of the Roman Empire. After the assassination of Emperor Julius Caesar, the

Roman political and military leader Marc Anthony (ca. 82 BC–30 BC) formed an official political alliance, the Second Triumvirate, under which he controlled Egypt. In Egypt, he met Cleopatra and became her lover.
4. Roman emperor (AD 53–117), reigned 98–117.

larity of events, I could pilfer useful material from that same master, as others have done, since he has sufficient for everyone. But I would fear that his rich brocade, if so openly exposed, would be detected against the background of my base sackcloth.

The mistress of the province of Cofachiqui came before the Governor and after paying her respects seated herself upon a chair which her subjects had brought for her. She alone spoke with the Governor, no other man or woman of her people saying a word. She referred once more to the message delivered by her vassals and declared that the scourge of the previous year had robbed her of the supplies she would like to have had in order to minister to his lordship more adequately, but that she would do all possible in his service. And that he might judge of her sincerity by her actions, she offered him immediately one of two deposits in that town, in each of which there were six hundred bushels of corn that had been gathered for the relief of those of her vassals who had escaped the pestilence. She begged him, however, to agree to leave her the other deposit for her own great need, assuring him that should his lordship require corn further on, he could take what he wanted from a deposit of two thousand bushels which had been gathered in a nearby town for the same purpose. As for accommodations, she declared that she would vacate her own house for his lordship, command half the town to be emptied for his captains and most illustrious soldiers, and have constructed very pleasant bowers of branches in which the remainder of his people could be at ease, but that if the Governor desired she would clear the entire town of Indians and send them to another one nearby. And then she assured him that rafts and wooden canoes would be provided quickly for the army to cross the river, and that on the morrow there would be a complete supply of them so that his lordship might perceive with what promptitude and willingness she served him.

The Governor responded to the lady's fine words and promises with profound gratitude, for he was much impressed by the fact that at a time when her own land suffered from want, she should offer him more than he had requested. So in deference to her beneficence, he said that both he and his people would try to be satisfied with as little food as possible in order not to afford her so much inconvenience, and that her plans for lodging and other provisions were well ordained. He added, moreover, that in the name of his lord, the Emperor of the Christians and the King of Spain, he received her kindness in service so that his sovereign might show gratitude in his own time and occasion; and he assured her that he on his own part as well as that of the army, was accepting her generosity as a particular favor never to be forgotten.

Besides these things, they talked of additional matters which concerned that and other provinces in the district; and all that the Governor asked, the lady answered to the great satisfaction of those present and in such a manner that the Spaniards were amazed to hear of such fine and well coordinated words, disclosing the wisdom of a barbarian, born and reared far from all good teaching and refinement. But those who possess natural excellence, wherever they may be, grow in wisdom and gentility of themselves and without training; whereas the foolish reveal their stupidity all the more with an increase of instruction.

Our Spaniards noted especially that the Indians of this province and of the two previous provinces were of a more gentle and affable disposition and less

ferocious than all the others they found in their expedition. For even though
the inhabitants of the other provinces offered and maintained peace, it was
always suspected that in their gestures and harsh words, one might detect a
friendship more feigned than real. But there was nothing false about the
people of Cofachiqui or those of Cofaqui and Cofa;[5] rather they seemed to
have passed their entire lives among Spaniards. Not only were they subservient, but in all their actions and words they made an effort to disclose and
demonstrate their sincere affection. And the fact that people who had never
seen them before should be so cordial was indeed gratifying to our men.

ca. 1592                                                                         1605

5. *Cofaqui and Cofa*: designations for two aboriginal tribes related to the Cofachiqui but of unknown origins and locations.

# SEBASTIÁN VIZCAÍNO
## 1548–1624

Little is known about Sebastián Vizcaíno's early life. As an adult, he was a successful merchant, trading with China and captaining a galleon along the route from
Manila to Mexico City.

In 1602–03, he led a naval expedition along the California coast, searching for
harbors and scouting out the topography to prepare for future colonization. For this
effort, Vizcaíno had been commissioned by Luis de Velasco, Antonio de Mendoza's
replacement as viceroy of New Spain. Some 60 years earlier, Mendoza had commissioned Juan Rodríguez Cabrillo to explore the California coast. However, the Cabrillo
expedition (1542–43) was devastated by harrowing storms, starvation, and disease.

On May 5, 1602, Vizcaíno and his crew set sail from Acapulco on the *San Diego*
and *Santo Tomás* ships and the *Tres Reyes* frigate. The three vessels basically retraced
Cabrillo's steps, stopping at what are now San Diego Bay (November 10, 1602), Santa
Catalina Island, Santa Barbara, and so forth. One of Vizcaíno's great achievements
was discovering Monterey Bay (December 16, 1602), which Cabrillo had missed. Owing to both nature's wrath on the open seas and an extreme lack of provisions, the
Vizcaíno expedition suffered even more hardships than the Cabrillo expedition had.
After most of the crew members, including the pilot of the *Tres Reyes*, had died, the
remaining explorers returned to Acapulco, reaching it on March 23, 1603.

Published in Francisco Carrasco y Gisacola's *Documentos referentes al recono-
cimiento de las costas de las Californias desde el cabo de San Lucas al de Mendocino
recopilados en el Archivo de Indias* (Documents Referring to the Recognizance of
the California Coasts from San Lucas to Mendocino, Collected in the Archivo de
Indias, 1882), the diary from the Vizcaíno expedition has no title and does not specify
its author. In addition to valuable descriptions of the California coast, it provides a
lively and engrossing account of the encounters between the Spanish seamen, missionaries, and officers and the Indians along the coast. From the shore, the Native
Americans generally shouted and made menacing gestures; but after disembarking,
the Spaniards often won them over with gifts. In the first of the two chapters presented here, the Spaniards disembark to find the Indians ready for a battle that
proves brief but deadly.

*FROM* DIARY OF SEBASTIÁN VIZCAÍNO[1]

## Chapter 11. Departure from the Bay of the Eleven Thousand Virgins and Arrival at the Port of San Diego

We sailed, as we have said, on Sunday, the 20th of the said month, from the Bay of the Eleven Thousand Virgins,[2] and at dawn of the following day the general ordered a sailor to the topmast-head, from there to look for the admiral's ship, which was causing much anxiety, lest some misfortune should have happened to her since she had separated from us.[3] The sailor saw a ship about six leagues[4] out at sea, and immediately Ensign Sebastián Melendez was ordered to go in the frigate to inspect her, carrying orders that if she were the admiral's ship she should be told that we were there, and that if she were some other ship she should wait, in order to carry a package of letters to the viceroy. We also approached her, and at two o'clock in the afternoon we were all together. We recognized her to be the admiral's ship, which gave the greatest pleasure.

After we had saluted the general asked the admiral, Father Fray Antonio, and Captain Peguero where they had taken shelter during the past storm, and whether they were in need of anything. They said that they carried eight quarters of water, and that the late tempest obliged them to put into the Bay of Pescado Blanco, but, not being very safe there, they went to Serros Island, where they remained during the storm; and that on the 25th of the past month Ensign Juan de Azevedo Tejeda had died. This news gave great pain to the general, for he was a good soldier. After sailing forty leagues from the mainland they had discovered a large island, but the weather did not permit them to go to it.

Seeing that the weather was so favorable the general ordered us to continue our voyage, and, following along the coast, the next day we discovered an island some two leagues from the mainland; we did not cast anchor at it, in order not to lose time. It was given the name of San Marcos.[5] We proceeded, tacking back and forth, and on the eve of the feast of San Simón and San Judas, the 27th of the month, we being in latitude 32° scant, a strong northwest wind came up, with a heavy sea, so that the admiral's ship and the frigate could not weather it unaided. Thereupon the general, with the admiral and the members of the council, determined to put in at a bay which was nine leagues to leeward, to take shelter from the storm, and to provide the admiral's ship with water. This was done, and at sunset of the same day we cast anchor in the said bay.

The next day Captain Peguero and Ensign Juan Francisco, with some soldiers, went on shore with orders to search diligently for water and to treat

---

1. Translated by Herbert Eugene Bolton. All footnotes are by the anthology editors, but most are based on Bolton's research. The editors have omitted Bolton's original, more technical footnotes.
2. Present-day San Quintin Bay (Baja California, Mexico). Vizcaíno named it the Bay of the Eleven Thousand Virgins in allusion to the legend of the Virgins of Cologne (11,000 virgins said to have

been martyred in Cologne, Germany, around AD 383).
3. The historian Iván de Torquemada gives the sailing date as the 24th; the admiral's ship, one of the three on the expedition, had not been seen for 28 days. *The general*: Vizcaíno.
4. Approximately 16 miles (a Spanish league then equaling about 2.6 miles).
5. Today, San Martín Island.

well the Indians who were on the beach. When they arrived on the land they made wells near the sea and found plenty of good water. More than a hundred Indian warriors came to the place with their bows and arrows and with clubs for throwing. These Indians were very insolent, to the extent of drawing their bows and picking up stones to throw at us. Without taking notice of them except to make signs of peace, the captain and ensign embarked, and having come on board reported to the general what had happened.

The next day Captain Peguero, Ensign Pascual de Alarcón, and the chief pilot, Francisco Bolaños, went ashore to take water. To them the general gave orders to treat the Indians well and to deal with them with great care and prudence, especially in embarking and disembarking. Arriving on land we found a multitude of Indians arrayed for battle, and although, on our part, we gave them to understand that we intended to do them no harm, but to get water, and although we gave them biscuits and other things, the Indians took no notice of what was given them; on the contrary, they tried to prevent the taking of water and to take from us the bottles and barrels. This made it necessary to fire three arquebus shots at them; whereupon, with the noise of the powder and someone's crying at the death of some of the others, they fled with great outcries; but at the end of two hours a multitude of Indians returned, assembling from different rancherías, holding councils among themselves, apparently, as to what they should do, and then, with arms in hand, they came toward us, who to them seemed few, with their women and children, bows and arrows. Ensign Pascual de Alarcón went out to meet them, telling them by signs that they must be quiet, and that they should be friends. Thereupon the Indians said they would do so upon condition that we would not fire any more arquebuses at them, which appeared to them many. They gave a female dog as a hostage, and with this they went away to their rancherías very well satisfied, and we took on water. At midnight, the 30th of the month, the general ordered us to set sail. This bay was named San Simón y San Judas.[6]

Skirting alone the coast with much difficulty because the wind was at the prow, on November 5 we discovered two small islands at the mouth of a large bay.[7] As we were entering it night came on and the wind went down, and the chief pilot told the general that he did not think it best to enter the bay that night, and so he stood out to sea, leaving it for the next day. At dawn we found ourselves at the mouth of the bay. As we were entering it a light breeze came up from the east and prevented our going in. The general consulted the admiral, captains, ensign, counsellors, and pilots as to what should be done and all were of the opinion that he should go on and not lose this wind, which was in our favor; we therefore continued our voyage. This bay was given the name of Islas de Todos los Santos.

On the 9th of the said month we discovered two other islands and three farallones,[8] in latitude 33° full, a little more than two leagues from the mainland, and a very large bay. The general ordered Ensign Meléndes to go ahead in the frigate, the captain's and admiral's ships following him. Then, while the frigate sailed along the coast of the mainland, the captain's ship went up to the islands. There was so much kelp around them in the bottom

---

6. Colnett Bay, east of Cape Colnett.
7. Todos Santos Islands, off Grajero Point.

8. High, vertical rock formations that emerge from the sea.

of the sea, that, although the water was fourteen fathoms deep, the kelp extended more than six fathoms above the water. The captain's ship passed over it as if it were a green meadow. Some of the kelp looked as large as gourds and was very highly colored, with fruit resembling very large capers and with tubes like sackbuts. These islands were given the name San Martín.[9] The Indians made so many columns of smoke on the mainland that at night it looked like a procession and in the daytime the sky was overcast. We did not land here because the coast was wild.

The next day, Sunday, the 10th of the month, we arrived at a port, which must be the best to be found in all the South Sea, for, besides being protected on all sides and having good anchorage, it is in latitude 33½°.[1] It has very good wood and water, many fish of all kinds, many of which we caught with seine and hooks. On land there is much game, such as rabbits, hares, deer, very large quail, royal ducks, thrushes, and many other birds.

On the 12th of the said month, which was the day of the glorious San Diego, the general, admiral, religious, captains, ensigns, and almost all the men went on shore. A hut was built and mass was said in celebration of the feast of Señor San Diego.[2] When it was over the general called a council to consider what was to be done in this port, in order to get through quickly. It was decided that the admiral, with the chief pilot, the pilots, the masters, calkers, and seamen should scour the ships, giving them a good cleaning, which they greatly needed, and that Captain Peguero, Ensign Alarcon, and Ensign Martín de Aguilar should each attend to getting water for his ship, while Ensign Juan Francisco, and Sergeant Miguel de Lagar, with the carpenters, should provide wood.

When this had all been agreed upon, a hundred Indians appeared on a hill with bows and arrows and with many feathers on their heads, yelling noisily at us. The general ordered Ensign Juan Francisco to go to them with four arquebusiers, Father Fray Antonio following him in order to win their friendship. The ensign was instructed that if the Indians fled he should let them go, but that if they waited he should regale them. The Indians waited, albeit with some fear. The ensign and soldiers returned, and the general, his son, and the admiral went toward the Indians. The Indians seeing this, two men and two women came down from a hill. They having reached the general, and the Indian women weeping, he cajoled and embraced them, giving them some things. Reassuring the others by signs, they descended peacefully, whereupon they were given presents. The net was cast and fish were given them. Whereupon the Indians became more confident and went to their rancherías and we to our ships to attend to our affairs.

Friday, the 15th of the month, the general went aboard the frigate, taking with him his son, Father Fray Antonio, the chief pilot, and fifteen arquebusiers, to go and take the soundings of a large bay which entered the land. He did not take the cosmographer with him, as he was ill and occupied with the papers of the voyage. That night, rowing with the flood tide, he got under way and at dawn he was six leagues within the bay, which he found to be the best, large enough for all kinds of vessels, more secure than at the

9. Los Coronados Islands.
1. San Diego Bay.
2. The date of the feast of San Diego, or the Roman Catholic saint Didacus, has changed over time; in 1602, it took place on November 13. Bolton believes the diary's "12th" should be "11th."

anchorage, and better for careening the ships, for they could be placed high and dry during the flood tide and taken down at the ebb tide, even if they were of a thousand tons.

I do not place in this report the sailing directions, descriptions of the land, or soundings, because the cosmographer and pilots are keeping an itinerary in conformity with the art of navigation.

In this bay the general, with his men, went ashore. After they had gone more than three leagues along it a number of Indians appeared with their bows and arrows, and although signs of peace were made to them, they did not dare to approach, excepting a very old Indian woman who appeared to be more than one hundred and fifty years old and who approached weeping. The general cajoled her and gave her some beads and something to eat. This Indian woman, from extreme age, had wrinkles on her belly which looked like a blacksmith's bellows, and the navel protruded bigger than a gourd. Seeing this kind treatment the Indians came peaceably and took us to their rancherías, where they were gathering their crops and where they had made their *paresos*[3] of seeds like flax. They had pots in which they cooked their food, and the women were dressed in skins of animals. The general would not allow any soldier to enter their rancherías; and, it being already late, he returned to the frigate, many Indians accompanying him to the beach. Saturday night he reached the captain's ship, which was ready; wood, water, and fish were brought on board, and on Wednesday, the 20th of the said month, we set sail. I do not state, lest I should be tiresome, how many times the Indians came to our camps with skins of martens and other things. Until the next day, when we set sail, they remained on the beach shouting. This port was given the name of San Diego.

## Chapter 12. Departure from the Port of San Diego and Arrival at the Island of Santa Catalina

We left the port of San Diego, as has been said, on a Wednesday, the 20th of the said month, and the same day the general ordered Ensign Sebastian Meléndes to go ahead with the frigate to examine a bay which was to windward some four leagues,[4] and directed that the pilot should sound it, map it, and find out what was there. He did so, and the next day ordered the return to the captain's ship. He reported to the general that he had entered the said bay, that it was a good port, although it had at its entrance a bar of little more than two fathoms depth, and that there was a very large grove at an estuary which extended into the land, and many Indians: and that he had not gone ashore. Thereupon we continued our voyage, skirting along the coast until the 24th of the month, which was the eve of the feast of the glorious Samta Catalina, when we discovered three large islands.[5] We approached them with difficulty because of a head-wind, and arrived at the middle one, which is more than twenty-five leagues around.

3. Unidentified; perhaps an invented word for this food, in that the Spanish sometimes called the Indians *paresos* or *paresis*.
4. False Bay, just north of San Diego Bay.

5. Santa Catalina, Santa Barbara, and San Nicolas. *Samta Catalina*: Saint Catherine (early fourth century), Christian saint and martyr.

On the 27th of the month, and before casting anchor in a very good cove[6] which was found, a multitude of Indians came out in canoes of cedar and pine, made of planks very well joined and calked, each one with eight oars and with fourteen or fifteen Indians, who looked like galley-slaves. They came alongside without the least fear and came on board our ships, mooring their own. They showed great pleasure at seeing us, telling us by signs that we must land, and guiding us like pilots to the anchorage. The general received them kindly and gave them some presents, especially to the boys. We anchored, and the admiral, Ensign Alarcón, Father Fray Antonio, and Captain Peguero, with some soldiers, went ashore. Many Indians were on the beach, and the women treated us to roasted sardines and a small fruit like sweet potatoes. Fresh water was found, although a long distance from the beach.

The next day the general and the Father Commissary went ashore, a hut was built, and mass was said. More than one hundred and fifty Indian men and women were present, and they marvelled not a little at seeing the altar and the image of our Lord Jesus crucified, and listened attentively to the saying of mass, asking by signs what it was about. They were told that it was about heaven, whereat they marvelled more. When the divine service was ended the general went to their houses, where the women took him by the hand and led him inside, giving him some of the food which they had given before. He brought to the ship six Indian girls from eight to ten years old, whom their mothers willingly gave him, and he clothed them with chemises, petticoats, and necklaces, and sent them ashore. The rest of the women, seeing this, came with their daughters in canoes, asking for gifts. The result was that no one returned empty-handed. The people go dressed in seal skins, the women especially covering their loins, and their faces show them to be modest; but the men are thieves, for anything they saw unguarded they took. They are a people given to trade and traffic and are fond of barter, for in return for old clothes they would give the soldiers skins, shells, nets, thread, and very well twisted ropes, these in great quantities and resembling linen. They have dogs like those in Castile.

※　※　※

On the night of the eve of San Andrés, the 29th of the said month, we set sail, for the Indians had told us by signs that farther along on this same island they had their houses and there was food.[7] On the day of San Andrés, at four o'clock in the afternoon, we arrived at the place which the Indians had designated, they piloting us in their canoes into the port,[8] which is all that could be desired as to convenience and security. On the beach there was a pueblo and more than three hundred Indians, men, women and children. The general and Ensign Alarcón went ashore and inspected it. The next day the general and many of the rest of us went ashore. The Indian men and women embraced him and took him to their houses. These women have good features. The general gave them beads and regaled them, and they gave him prickly pears and a grain like the *gofio*[9] of the Canary Islands, in some willow

6. On Santa Catalina Island.
7. At this time, the weather was good, but the exploration of San Andrés (now San Clemente) was postponed because the men were becoming ill and supplies were running short.

8. Puerto de Santa Catalina, mentioned above.
9. Flour made from roasted grains (typically wheat or certain varieties of maize) or from starchy plants.

baskets very well made, and water in vessels resembling flasks, which were like rattan inside and very thickly varnished outside. They had acorns and some very large skins, apparently of bears, with heavy fur, which they used for blankets.

The general went inland to see the opposite coast. He found on the way a level prairie, very well cleared, where the Indians were assembled to worship an idol which was there. It resembled a demon, having two horns, no head, a dog at its feet, and many children painted all around it. The Indians told the general not to go near it, but he approached it and saw the whole thing, and made a cross, and placed the name of Jesus on the head of the demon, telling the Indians that that was good, and from heaven, but that the idol was the devil. At this the Indians marvelled, and they will readily renounce it and receive our Holy Faith, for apparently they have good intellects and are friendly and desirous of our friendship. The general returned to the pueblo, and an Indian woman brought him two pieces of figured China silk, in fragments, telling him that they had got them from people like ourselves, who had negroes; that they had come on the ship which was driven by a strong wind to the coast and wrecked, and that it was farther on. The general endeavored to take two or three Indians with him, that they might tell him where the ship had been lost, promising to give them clothes. The Indians consented and went with him to the captain's ship, but as we were weighing anchor preparatory to leaving the Indians said they wished to go ahead in their canoe, and that they did not wish to go aboard the ship, fearing that we would abduct them, and the general, in order not to excite them, said: "Very well."

We set sail, and on leaving the port a head-wind struck us, which prevented our going where the Indians indicated; therefore we stood out to sea and the Indians returned to their pueblo. This attempt was given up because we did not have the launch, which had gone to reconnoitre another island,[1] apparently belonging to the mainland, and because the admiral's ship was absent, as it could not make the said port, and because the fog was so very dense that we could not see each other, and also because there seemed to be many islands, keys, and shoals, among which, in such weather, the pilots did not dare take the flagship; and so we continued our voyage.

The next day the admiral's ship and frigate came up with us, for perhaps God willed it that we should be united. On being asked what he had found on the island, Ensign Meléndez said that there were many Indians, who had told him by signs that upon it there were men who were bearded and clothed like ourselves. Thinking them to be Spaniards, he sent them a note, and eight Indians came to him in a canoe, bearded and clothed in skins of animals, but they could learn nothing more. Accordingly the general ordered that we should continue our voyage without further delay, because our men were all becoming ill, leaving for the return any efforts to verify what the Indians of the island of Samta Catalina had told us by signs, for, as we could not understand their language, all was confusion and there was little certainty as to what they said.

after 1603                                                              1882

1. Apparently an island in San Pedro Bay; perhaps El Moro, or Dead Man's Island.

# JUAN DE OÑATE
## 1550–1626

By the late sixteenth century, the Spanish very much wanted to colonize the lands that are now New Mexico. In 1583, inspired by explorers' reports about the Pueblo Indians in the area, the merchant Antonio de Espejo traveled up the Rio Grande, to the Puaray Pueblo (near present-day Albuquerque) and to Hopi settlements. That same year, King Philip II directed Luis de Velasco Hijo—viceroy of New Spain 1590–95, 1607–11—to send an expedition into the New Mexican lands. The king's major goal was to find the legendary Strait of Anián, said to be a waterway from the Pacific to the Atlantic, located in the northern parts of Alaska and Canada.

On September 21, 1595, after much political maneuvering by various candidates, Velasco awarded the coveted assignment to his friend Juan de Oñate. Oñate was wealthy enough to finance the expedition, and he began preparations in the spring of 1596. According to his contract with Velasco, Oñate was initially to be made governor and captain-general, and after he had established his colony he would receive the title of *Adelantado* (governor of a border province). However, before the contract was finalized, Velasco was replaced by a new viceroy, Gaspar de Zúñiga Acevedo y Fonseca, Fifth Count of Monterey. The count never fully supported Oñate and plagued his expedition with delays. Finally, on January 26, 1598, Oñate and his caravan left from San Gerónimo, a northernmost outpost.

In August 1598, Oñate arrived in New Mexico. Early the next month, he founded the town of San Juan de los Caballeros by constructing a church there; that same year, he became *Adelantado*. The town's small colony of settlers, including women and children, established themselves among the local Pueblo Indians, who at first were friendly to the Spaniards but who grew increasingly resentful. The Indians' previous encounters with Spaniards had not been pleasant: Unscrupulous explorers and adventurers had mistreated them and had carried out raids to acquire slaves for the mines and agricultural fields in New Spain. Now, the standard Spanish colonization process required the submission of the Indians and their sworn allegiance and obedience to the king of Spain. The Indians were to be indoctrinated into Catholicism by the friars and priests accompanying the expedition. In addition, the *Requerimiento*, a legal document read to the Indians in Spanish, officially took possession of the Indian lands.

As a result, one group of Pueblo Indians, the Acomas, revolted against the colonizers. They began by killing Oñate's nephew Juan Saldívar, a prominent member of the expedition. Common sentiment among the settlers was that the rebels had to be severely punished, to prove the Spaniards' superior strength and thus prevent other Pueblo Indians from rebelling. Oñate directed his soldiers to attack the town of Acoma and subdue its inhabitants. Because the town was perched on a rock formation 400 feet high, the Spaniards had to strategize: One group of soldiers attacked from the front to distract the Indians while a smaller group of soldiers scaled the rock from behind. After a bloody battle that lasted several days, the Acomas surrendered to avoid being decimated. As punishment for the revolt, Oñate ordered that one hand be cut off every male between the ages of 12 and 25 and that the left foot be cut off every male 25 years old or older. Sixty young girls were sent to convents in Mexico City, never to return to Acoma or to see their relatives. The rest of the females were parceled out as servants to the colonists.

While maintaining his base in New Mexico, Oñate subsequently undertook other expeditions. He traveled west in hope of finding the Strait of Anián and reached the Sea of California, or Gulf of California, which separates the Baja California peninsula and mainland Mexico. He traveled east in search of the fabulous golden city of

Quivira and reached the plains of Kansas. Upon his return from one such excursion, he found his New Mexican colony in shambles. Oñate was already in serious trouble, since many of his followers had deserted and had lodged complaints against him. In fact, on June 17, 1606, King Philip III had directed Luis de Velasco Hijo to recall Oñate and begin investigating the charges against him. On August 24, 1607, disheartened and acknowledging the failure of his enterprise, Oñate sent a letter of resignation to Velasco, who accepted his resignation six months later. The explorer returned to Mexico, where after several years he was tried for 30 crimes he allegedly committed while governor of New Mexico. Some of these crimes were related to the cruelties he inflicted on the Acoma people. Others were tied to the various mutinies that had plagued his colony and the extreme punishments, including death, that he delivered to deserters.

Found guilty on 12 charges, Oñate was stripped of his titles, banished from Mexico City for four years, and exiled from New Mexico for life. He went back to Spain to fight the charges and clear his name, but he regained only some of his prestige, for the king refused to return his titles. Oñate died on June 3, 1626, in a mine in Spain, having been appointed a mine inspector by the Crown. Despite his failure to found a Spanish colony and his subsequent fall from grace, Oñate is considered to have made several lasting contributions to the Spanish Crown. In his book *The Last Conquistador: Juan de Oñate and the Settling of the Far Southwest* (1991), the historian Marc Simmons delineates Oñate's many achievements: He paved the way for future expeditions and colonization projects by establishing, from Zacatecas to Santa Fe, the route known as *el Camino Real* (the Royal Road). His explorations in New Mexico, Arizona, Texas, Oklahoma, and Kansas aided in the mapping of those lands and yielded knowledge of the flora, fauna, minerals, and Indian nations there. He helped establish one of the oldest cities in the United States—Santa Fe—and laid the foundations for the development of New Mexico. To this day, however, many Native Americans and Chicanos in New Mexico consider Oñate a villain guilty of war crimes. In 1998, while some people celebrated the 400th anniversary of this conquistador's *entrada* into New Mexico, others cut off the left foot of the statue of him in Albuquerque.

Among the numerous writings that survive from Oñate are an extensive report in which he detailed the expedition to New Mexico and numerous letters he wrote to the viceroy in Mexico City and to the king in Spain. In addition, his secretary penned *relaciones* chronicling the expeditions Oñate undertook while in New Mexico. The selections that follow are an excerpt from one of Oñate's letters and a *relación* in which his secretary describes the American buffalo and the admiration and awe it elicited from the members of the exploratory party traveling in Kansas.

# Letter Written by Don Juan de Oñate from New Mexico to the Viceroy, the Count of Monterey, on March 2, 1599[1]

From Rio de Nombre de Dios[2] I last wrote to you, Illustrious Sir, giving you an account of my departure, and of the discovery of a wagon road to the Rio del Norte,[3] and of my certain hopes of the successful outcome of my jour-

---

1. Translated by Herbert Eugene Bolton. Except as indicated, all footnotes are Bolton's. The anthology editors have omitted Bolton's more technical notes.
2. Nombre de Diós was reached March 12, 1598,

and was left on the 14th. * * *
3. The reference is to the exploration made by Vicente de Zaldívar [Oñate's nephew, Juan's brother, and an important member of the expedition]. * * *

ney, which hopes God has been pleased to grant, may He be forever praised; for greatly to His advantage and that of his royal Majesty, they have acquired a possession so good that none other of his Majesty in these Indies excels it, judging it solely by what I have seen, by things told of in reliable reports, and by things almost a matter of experience, from having been seen by people in my camp and known by me at present.

This does not include the vastness of the settlements or the riches of the West which the natives praise, or the certainty of pearls promised by the South Sea from the many shells containing them possessed by these Indians, or the many settlements called the seven caves,[4] which the Indians report at the head of this river, which is the Río del Norte; but includes only the provinces which I have seen and traversed, the people of this eastern country, the Apaches, the nation of the Cocóyes,[5] and many others which are daily being discovered in this district and neighborhood, as I shall specify in this letter. I wish to begin by giving your Lordship an account of it, because it is the first since I left New Spain.

I departed, Illustrious Sir, from Río de Nombre de Dios on the sixteenth of March, with the great multitude of wagons, women, and children, which your Lordship very well knows, freed from all my opponents, but with a multitude of evil predictions conforming to their desires and not to the goodness of God. His Majesty was pleased to accede to my desires, and to take pity on my great hardships, afflictions, and expenses, bringing me to these provinces of New Mexico with all his Majesty's army enjoying perfect health.

Although I reached these provinces on the twenty-eighth day of May (going ahead with as many as sixty soldiers to pacify the land and free it from traitors, if in it there should be any, seizing Humaña and his followers,[6] to obtain full information, by seeing with my own eyes, regarding the location and nature of the land, and regarding the nature and customs of the people, so as to order what might be best for the army, which I left about twenty-two leagues[7] from the first pueblos,[8] after having crossed the Río del Norte, at which river I took possession,[9] in the name of his Majesty, of all these kingdoms and pueblos which I discovered before departing from it with scouts), the army did not overtake me at the place where I established it and where I now have it established, in this province of the Teguas,[1] until the nineteenth day of August of the past year. During that time I

---

4. This may be a survival of the older tradition regarding the Seven Caves [Chicomoztoc, or the Seven Caves of Chicomoztoc, the mythical origin place of the Aztec people of central Mexico] existing somewhere to the northward of Mexico. The text is evidently corrupt at this point. It reads, "ni las muchas poblazones que el nacimiento destos indios, que es el del Rio del Norte, llamada las siete quebas" [nor the many towns where these Indians are from, which is the River of the North, known as the Seven Caves].

5. Cicuyé, or Pecos.

6. It was not yet known that Humaña had been slaughtered by the Indians of the plains. [Bolton note]

Around 1594, the Spanish army captains Francisco Leyva de Bonilla and Juan de Humaña were authorized to lead a punitive expedition against some Indian tribes in what is now the Mexican state of Chihuahua. Instead, in search of riches, the captains led an illegal expedition into and beyond New Mexico. As a condition for his appointment as governor and captain-general of New Mexico, Juan de Oñate was ordered to personally find and apprehend the renegades. However, in central Kansas, Humaña killed Leyva de Bonilla after an argument. Indians subsequently killed all but two members of the expedition. [Anthology editors' note]

7. Approximately 572 miles (a Spanish league then equaling about 2.6 miles). [Anthology editors' note]

8. He refers here to reaching the first pueblos above El Paso, having left the caravan at El Sepulcro de Robledo. * * *

9. April 30, 1598. * * *

1. A Pueblo tribe. "The place" is San Juan de Los Caballeros. [Anthology editors' note]

travelled through settlements sixty-one leagues in extent toward the north, and thirty-five in width from east to west. All this district is filled with pueblos, large and small, very continuous and close together.

At the end of August I began to prepare the people of my camp for the severe winter with which both the Indians and the nature of the land threatened me; and the devil, who has ever tried to make good his great loss occasioned by our coming, plotted, as is his wont, exciting a rebellion among more than forty-five soldiers and captains, who under pretext of not finding immediately whole plates of silver lying on the ground, and offended because I would not permit them to maltreat these natives, either in their persons or in their goods, became disgusted with the country, or to be more exact, with me, and endeavored to form a gang in order to flee to that New Spain, as they proclaimed, although judging from what has since come to light their intention was directed more to stealing slaves and clothing and to other acts of effrontery not permitted. I arrested two captains and a soldier, who they said were guilty, in order to garrote them on this charge, but ascertaining that their guilt was not so great, and on account of my situation and of the importunate pleadings of the religious and of the entire army, I was forced to forego the punishment and let bygones be bygones.

Although by the middle of September I succeeded in completely calming and pacifying my camp, from this great conflagration a spark was bound to remain hidden underneath the ashes of the dissembling countenances of four of the soldiers of the said coterie. These fled from me at that time, stealing from me part of the horses, thereby violating not only one but many proclamations which, regarding this matter and others, I had posted for the good of the land in the name of his Majesty.

Since they had violated his royal orders, it appeared to me that they should not go unpunished; therefore I immediately sent post-haste the captain and procurator-general Gaspar Pérez de Villagrá[2] and the captain of artillery Gerónimo Márques, with an express order to follow and overtake them and give them due punishment. They left in the middle of September, as I have said, thinking that they would overtake them at once, but their journey was prolonged more than they or I had anticipated, with the result to two of the offenders[3] which your Lordship already knows from the letter which they tell me they wrote from Santa Bárbara. The other two who fled from them will have received the same at your Lordship's hands, as is just.

I awaited their return and the outcome for some days, during which time I sent my *sargento mayor* to find and utilize the buffalo to the east, where he found an infinite multitude of them, and had the experience which he set forth in a special report.[4] Both he and the others were so long delayed that, in order to lose no time, at the beginning of October, this first church having been founded, wherein the first mass was celebrated on the 8th of September, and the religious having been distributed[5] in various provinces and *doctrinas*, I went in person to the province of Abo and to that of the Xuma-

2. See p. 90. [Anthology editors' note]
3. They were beheaded. * * *
4. The following selection, "Account of the Discovery of the Buffalo," is a report by Oñate's secretary, Juan Gutiérrez Bocanegra, that draws on the account of "the *sargento mayor* Vicente de Saldívar Mendoza." [Anthology editors' note]
5. The pueblos were assigned to the friars on the 9th, and the missionaries went to their new posts within the next few days. * * *

nas and to the large and famous salines[6] of this country, which must be about twenty leagues east of here.

From there I crossed over to the west through the province of Puaray to discover the South Sea, so that I might be able to report to your Lordship. When Captain Villagrá arrived I took him for this purpose.

What more in good time it was possible to accomplish through human efforts is in substance what I shall set forth in the following chapter. For this purpose it shall be day by day, and event by event, especially regarding the death of my nephew and *maese de campo*,[7] who, as my rear-guard, was following me to the South Sea. His process, along with many other papers, I am sending to your Lordship. To despatch them earlier has been impossible. I have, then, discovered and seen up to the present the following provinces:

The province of the Piguis,[8] which is the one encountered in coming from that New Spain; the province of the Xumanas; the province of the Cheguas, which we Spaniards call Puaray; the province of the Cheres; the province of the Trias; the province of the Emmes; the province of the Teguas; the province of the Picuries; the province of the Taos; the province of the Peccos; the province of Abbo and the salines; the province of Juni; and the province of Mohoce.

These last two are somewhat apart from the rest, towards the west, and are the places where we recently discovered the rich mines, as is attested by the papers which your Lordship will see there. I could not work or improve these mines because of the death of my *maese de campo*, Juan de Zaldívar, and of the rectification of the results of it, which I completed at the end of last month.[9] Nor could I complete my journey to the South Sea, which was the purpose with which I went to the said provinces, leaving my camp in this province of the Teguas, whence I am now writing.

There must be in this province and in the others above-mentioned, to make a conservative estimate, seventy thousand[1] Indians, settled after our custom, house adjoining house, with square plazas. They have no streets, and in the pueblos, which contain many plazas or wards, one goes from one plaza to the other through alleys. They are of two and three stories, of an *estado*[2] and a half or an *estado* and a third each, which latter is not so common; and some houses are of four, five, six, and seven stories. Even whole pueblos dress in very highly colored cotton *mantas*, white or black, and some of thread— very good clothes. Others wear buffalo hides, of which there is a great abundance. They have most excellent wool, of whose value I am sending a small example.

It is a land abounding in flesh of buffalo, goats with hideous horns, and turkeys; and in Mohoce there is game of all kinds. There are many wild and ferocious beasts, lions, bears, wolves, tigers, *penicas*,[3] ferrets, porcupines,

6. Salt lakes. *Doctrinas*: frontier missions. *Xumanas*: a Native American tribe, also known as the Humanas and the Jumanos. [Anthology editors' note]

7. Field commander. [Anthology editors' note]

8. [Unidentified tribe.] For each of the other tribes listed in this paragraph, see [Frederick Webb] Hodge, *Handbook of American Indians* [1910], under the following names: Jumano, Tigua, Keres, Sia, Jemez, Tewa, Picuris, Taos, Pecos, Abo, Zuñi, Moqui (or Hopi).

9. He refers to the punishment of the pueblo and the investigation of the uprising. * * *

1. An exaggerated estimate, no doubt. * * *

2. An *estado* is a unit equivalent to the height of a man.

3. Unidentified. [Anthology editors' note]

and other animals, whose hides they tan and use. Towards the west there are bees and very white honey, of which I am sending a sample. Besides, there are vegetables, a great abundance of the best and greatest salines in the world, and a very great many kinds of very rich ores, as I stated above. Some discovered near here do not appear so, although we have hardly begun to see anything of the much there is to be seen. There are very fine grape vines, rivers, forests of many oaks, and some cork trees, fruits, melons, grapes, watermelons, Castilian plums, *capuli*, pine-nuts, acorns, ground-nuts, and *coralejo*,[4] which is a delicious fruit, and other wild fruits. There are many and very good fish in this Río del Norte, and in others. From the ores here are made all the colors which we use, and they are very fine.

The people are in general very comely; their color is like those of that land, and they are much like them in manner and dress, in their grinding, in their food, dancing, singing, and many other things, except in their languages, which are many, and different from those there. Their religion consists in worshipping idols, of which they have many; and in their temples, after their own manner, they worship them with fire, painted reeds, feathers, and universal offering of almost everything they get, such as small animals, birds, vegetables, etc. In their government they are free, for although they have some petty captains, they obey them badly and in very few things.

We have seen other nations such as the Querechos, or herdsmen, who live in tents of tanned hides, among the buffalo. The Apaches, of whom we have also seen some, are innumerable, and although I heard that they lived in rancherías, a few days ago I ascertained that they live like these in pueblos, one of which, eighteen leagues from here, contains fifteen plazas.[5] They are a people whom I have compelled to render obedience to His Majesty, although not by means of legal instruments like the rest of the provinces. This has caused me much labor, diligence, and care, long journeys, with arms on the shoulders, and not a little watching and circumspection; indeed, because my *maese de campo* was not as cautious as he should have been, they killed him with twelve companions in a great pueblo and fortress called Acoma, which must contain about three thousand Indians. As punishment for its crime and its treason against his Majesty, to whom it had already rendered submission by a public instrument, and as a warning to the rest, I razed and burned it completely, in the way in which your Lordship will see by the process of this cause. All these provinces, pueblos, and peoples, I have seen with my own eyes.

There is another nation, that of the Cocóyes, an innumerable people with huts and agriculture. Of this nation and of the large settlements at the source of the Río del Norte and of those to the northwest and west and towards the South Sea, I have numberless reports, and pearls of remarkable size from the said sea, and assurance that there is an infinite number of them on the coast of this country. And as to the east, a person in my camp, an Indian who speaks Spanish and is one of those who came with Humaña, has been in the pueblo of the said herdsmen. It is nine continuous leagues

---

4. Unidentified. *Capuli*: a wild berry, known in Mexico today as capulín, that looks and tastes like a cherry and grows in bunches like a grape. [Anthology editors' note]

5. Unidentified settlement [Anthology editors' note]

in length and two in width, with streets and houses consisting of huts. It is situated in the midst of the multitude of buffalo, which are so numerous that my *sargento mayor*, who hunted them and brought back their hides, meat, tallow, and suet, asserts that in one herd alone he saw more than there are of our cattle in the combined three ranches of Rodrigo del Río, Salvago, and Jerónimo López, which are famed in those regions.

I should never cease were I to recount individually all of the many things which occur to me. I can only say that with God's help I shall see them all, and give new worlds, new, peaceful, and grand, to his Majesty, greater than the good Marquis[6] gave to him, although he did so much, if you, Illustrious Sir, will give to me the aid, the protection, and the help which I expect from such a hand. And although I confess that I am crushed at having been so out of favor when I left that country, and although a soul frightened by disfavor usually loses hope and despairs of success, it is nevertheless true that I never have and never shall lose hope of receiving many and very great favors at the hand of your Lordship, especially in matters of such importance to his Majesty. And in order that you, Illustrious Sir, may be inclined to render them to me, I beg that you take note of the great increase which the royal crown and the rents of his Majesty have and will have in this land, with so many and such a variety of things, each one of which promises very great treasures. I shall only note these four, omitting the rest as being well known and common:

First, the great wealth which the mines have begun to reveal and the great number of them in this land, whence proceed the royal fifths[7] and profits. Second, the certainty of the proximity of the South Sea, whose trade with Pirú, New Spain, and China is not to be depreciated, for it will give birth in time to advantageous and continuous duties, because of its close proximity, particularly to China and to that land. And what I emphasize in this matter as worthy of esteem is the traffic in pearls, reports of which are so certain, as I have stated, and of which we have had ocular experience from the shells. Third, the increase of vassals and tributes, which will increase not only the rents, but his renown and dominion as well, if it be possible that for our king these can increase. Fourth, the wealth of the abundant salines, and of the mountains of brimstone, of which there is a greater quantity than in any other province. Salt is the universal article of traffic of all these barbarians and their regular food, for they even eat or suck it alone as we do sugar. These four things appear as if dedicated solely to his Majesty. I will not mention the founding of so many republics, the many offices, their quittances, vacancies, provisions, etc., the wealth of the wool and hides of buffalo, and many other things, clearly and well known, or, judging from the general nature of the land, the certainty of wines and oils.

In view, then, Illustrious Sir, of things of such honor, profit, and value, and of the great prudence, magnanimity, and nobility of your Lordship, who in all matters is bound to prosper me and overcome the ill fortune of my disgrace, I humbly beg and supplicate, since it is of such importance to the service of God and of his Majesty, that the greatest aid possible be sent to me, both for settling and pacifying, your Lordship giving your favor, mind, zeal, and life for the conservation, progress, and increase of this

6. [Hernán] Cortés, the Marquis of the Valley.
7. *Royal fifths*: taxes related to mining. [Anthology editors' note]

land, through the preaching of the holy gospel and the founding of this republic, giving liberty and favor to all, opening wide the door to them, and, if it should be necessary, even ordering them to come to serve their king in so honorable and profitable a matter, in a land so abundant and of such great beginnings of riches. I call them beginnings, for although we have seen much, we have not yet made a beginning in comparison with what there is to see and enjoy. And if the number should exceed five hundred men, they all would be needed, especially married men, who are the solid rock on which new republics are permanently founded; and noble people, of whom there is such a surplus there. Particularly do I beg your Lordship to give a license to my daughter Mariquita, for whom I am sending, and to those of my relatives who may wish so honorably to end their lives.

For my part, I have sunk my ships and have furnished an example to all as to how they ought to spend their wealth and their lives and those of their children and relatives in the service of their king and lord, on whose account and in whose name I beg your Lordship to order sent to me six small cannon and some powder, all of which will always be at the service of his Majesty, as is this and everything else. Although on such occasions the necessities increase, and although under such circumstances as those in which I now find myself others are wont to exaggerate, I prefer to suffer from lack of necessities rather than to be a burden to his Majesty or to your Lordship, feeling assured that I shall provide them for many poor people who may look to me if your Lordship will grant the favor, which I ask, of sending them to me.

To make this request of you, Illustrious Sir, I am sending the best qualified persons whom I have in my camp, for it is but reasonable that such should go on an errand of such importance to the service of God and his Majesty, in which they risk their health and life, looking lightly upon the great hardships which they must suffer and have suffered. Father Fray Alonso Martínez, apostolic commissary of these provinces of New Mexico, is the most meritorious person with whom I have had any dealings, and of the kind needed by such great kingdoms for their spiritual government. Concerning this I am writing to his Majesty, and I shall be greatly favored if your Lordship will do the same. I believe your Lordship is under a loving obligation to do this, both because the said Father Commissary is your client as well as because of the authority of his person and of the merits of his worthy life, of which I am sending to his Majesty a special report, which your Lordship will see if you desire, and to which I refer. In his company goes my cousin, Father Fray Cristobal de Salazar, concerning whom testimony can be given by his prelate, for in order not to appear an interested witness in my own cause I refrain from saying what I could say with much reason and truth. For all spiritual matters I refer you to the said fathers, whom I beg your Lordship to credit in every respect as you would credit me in person. I say but little to your Lordship as to your crediting them as true priests of my father Saint Francis.[8] With such as these may your Lordship swell these your kingdoms, for there is plenty for them to do.

For temporal matters go such honorable persons as Captain and Procurator-general Gaspar Pérez de Villagrá, captain of the guard Marcos Farfan de los

---

8. Francis of Assisi (1181 or 1182–1226), Italian friar; founder of the Franciscan order. [Anthology editors' note]

Godos, and Captain Juan Pinero, to whom I refer you, as also to the many papers which they carry.[9] In them your Lordship will find authentic information regarding all that you may desire to learn of this country of yours.

I remain as faithful to you, Illustrious Sir, as those who most protest. Your interests will always be mine, for the assurance and confidence which my faithfulness gives me is an evidence that in past undertakings I have found in your Lordship true help and love; for although when I left I did not deserve to receive the cédula[1] from my king dated April 2, I shall deserve to receive it now that I know that I have served him so well.

And in order to satisfy his royal conscience and for the safety of the creatures who were preserved at Acoma, I send them to your Lordship with the holy purpose which the Father Commissary will explain, for I know it is so great a service to God that I consider very well employed the work and expense which I have spent in the matter. And I do not expect a lesser reward for your Lordship on account of the prayers of those few days. Honor it, Illustrious Sir, for it redounds to the service of God. May He prosper and exalt you to greater offices. In His divine service, which is the highest and greatest I can name, I again beg for the aid requested, much, good, and speedy—priests as well as settlers and soldiers.

1599

## Account of the Discovery of the Buffalo
## [Written by Juan Gutiérrez Bocanegra, Oñate's Secretary][1]

The *sargento mayor* Vicente de Saldívar Mendoza, the *proveedor general* Diego de Cubia, Captain Aguilar, and other captains and soldiers, to the number of sixty, set out from camp[2] for the cattle herds on the 15th day of September, well provided with many droves of mares and other supplies. They reached the Pecos River on the 18th and set out from there on the 20th, leaving Father Fray Francisco de San Miguel of the Order of San Francisco as prelate of that province, and Juan de Dios, lay brother and interpreter of that tongue. That province is the one Espejo named Tamas, from which came a certain Indian named Don Pedro Oros, who died in Tlanepantla under control and instruction of the friars of San Francisco.

Having travelled four leagues[3] they reached the place called Las Ciruelas, where there are very great quantities of Castilian plums, Almonacid plums of Cordoba.[4] On the following day they travelled five more leagues, finding water after going three leagues, although they camped for the night without it. Next day they travelled two leagues to a small stream[5] carrying

9. The papers include the following selection, "Account of the Discovery of the Buffalo." [Anthology editors' note]
1. Certificate, authorization. [Anthology editors' note]
1. Translated by Herbert Eugene Bolton. Except as indicated, all footnotes are Bolton's. The anthology editors have omitted Bolton's more technical notes.
2. At San Juan de los Caballeros. * * *
3. Approximately 10 miles (a Spanish league

then equaling about 2.6 miles). [Anthology editors' note]
4. "Ciruela almonaci de la cordoba." Almonacid de Toledo is a village in Spain twelve miles southeast of Toledo. Almonacid de Zorita is a village in Spain nineteen miles southeast of Guadalajara. Both are in Castile. * * *
5. They were now eleven leagues—twenty-five to thirty miles—from Pecos. The stream was probably the Gallinas, near Las Vegas.

but little water but containing a prodigious quantity of excellent fish, pilchard, sardines, prawn, shrimp, and *matalote*.[6] That night five hundred catfish were caught with only a fishhook, and many more on the following day.[7] At that place four Indian herdsmen came to see him; they ordered that the Indians be given food and presents. One of them arose and with a loud voice called many Indians who were hidden and they all came to where the Spaniards were. They are powerful people and expert bowmen. The *sargento mayor* gave presents to all and won them over. He asked them for a guide to the cattle and they furnished one very willingly.

Next day they travelled six leagues and reached some rain water. There three Indians came out from a mountain, and, being asked where their ranchería was, they said that it was a league from there, and that they were very much excited because of our being in that land. In order that they might not become more excited by many people going, the *sargento mayor* went to their ranchería with but one companion, telling the three Indians to go ahead and quiet the people, and that he wished only to go and see them and to be their friend. He told them by means of an interpreter whom he had with him, named Jusepillo, one of the Indians who had been brought by Humayna and Leyba,[8] and who had gone with them to a very great river to the east, in the direction of Florida. We all understand this to be the famous Río de la Magdalena which flows into Florida, and that this was the route followed by Dorantes, Cabeza de Vaca,[9] and the negro who came thence to this land and to the rancherías and mountains of the Patarabueyes.

When he was about three-quarters of a league from his camp a great number of people came out to meet him, by fours and sixes. They asked for the Spaniards' friendship, their method of making the request being to extend the palm of the right hand to the sun and then to bring it down on the person whose friendship they desire. He made them presents also, and they importuned him to go to their ranchería, and although evening was approaching he had to comply so that they would not think he was afraid to go. He reached the ranchería and remained with them in great friendliness, returning to his camp very late at night.

Next day as he travelled many Indians and Indian women came out to meet him, bringing *pinole*.[1] Most of the men go naked, but some are clothed with skins of buffalo and some with blankets. The women wear a sort of trousers made of buckskin, and shoes or leggins, after their own fashion. He gave them some presents and told them by means of the interpreter that Governor Don Juan de Oñate had sent him that they might know that he could protect those who were loyal to his Majesty and punish those who were not. All were friendly and very well pleased. They asked him for aid against the Xumanas,[2] as they call a tribe of Indians who are painted after the manner of the Chichimecos. The *sargento mayor* promised them that he would endeavor to insure peace to them, since he had come to this land for that purpose.

---

6. Matalote opata, a ray-finned fish of Mexico. [Anthology editors' note]

7. [Some names given to the fish here are incorrect.] Villagrá says they caught forty *arrobas*—a thousand pounds—of fish in less than three hours, with hooks only. ° ° °

8. See note 6, p. 79. [Anthology editors' note]

9. See p. 20. [Anthology editors' note]

1. Cornmeal used to make a gruel. [Anthology editors' note]

2. Also known as the Humanas or Jumanos. [Anthology editors' note]

Bidding them goodby, he left that place and travelled ten more leagues in three days, at the end of which time he saw the first buffalo bull,[3] which, being rather old, wandered alone and ran but little. This produced much merriment and was regarded as a great joke, for the least one in the company would not be satisfied with less than ten thousand head of cattle in his own corral.

Shortly afterward more than three hundred buffalo were seen in some pools. During the next day they travelled about seven leagues, when they encountered as many as a thousand head of cattle. In that place there were found very good facilities for the construction of a corral with wings. Orders having been given for its construction, the cattle went inland more than eight leagues. Upon seeing this the *sargento mayor* went on ahead with ten of his soldiers to a river six leagues from there, which flows from the province of the Picuries[4] and the snow-covered range where they are,[5] and where the guide had told him that there were great numbers of cattle. But when he reached the river the cattle had left, because just then many Indian herdsmen crossed it, coming from trading with the Picuries and Taos, populous pueblos of this New Mexico, where they sell meat, hides, tallow, suet, and salt in exchange for cotton blankets, pottery, maize, and some small green stones which they use.

He camped for the night at that river, and on the following day, on his way back to the camp, he found a ranchería in which there were fifty tents made of tanned hides, very bright red and white in color and bell-shaped, with flaps and openings, and built as skilfully as those of Italy and so large that in the most ordinary ones four different mattresses and beds were easily accommodated. The tanning is so fine that although it should rain bucketfuls it will not pass through nor stiffen the hide, but rather upon drying it remains as soft and pliable as before. This being so wonderful, he wanted to experiment, and, cutting off a piece of hide from one of the tents, it was soaked and placed to dry in the sun, but it remained as before, and as pliable as if it had never been wet. The *sargento mayor* bartered for a tent and brought it to this camp, and although it was so very large, as has been stated, it did not weigh over two *arrobas*.[6]

To carry this load, the poles that they use to set it up, and a knapsack of meat and their *pinole*, or maize, the Indians use a medium-sized shaggy dog, which is their substitute for mules. They drive great trains of them. Each, girt round its breast and haunches, and carrying a load of flour of at least one hundred pounds, travels as fast as his master. It is a sight worth seeing and very laughable to see them travelling, the ends of the poles dragging on the ground, nearly all of them snarling in their encounters, travelling one after another on their journey. In order to load them the Indian women seize their heads between their knees and thus load them, or adjust the load, which is seldom required, because they travel along at a steady gait as if they had been trained by means of reins.

---

3. The party had travelled twenty-seven leagues, or perhaps seventy-five miles, from Pecos.
4. An Indian tribe. [Anthology editors' note]
5. They were now forty leagues—a hundred miles or more—from Pecos, and the river must have been the Canadian, near Alamosa. It issues from the Sangre de Cristo Mountains.
6. An *arroba* is twenty-five pounds.

Having returned to camp they had a holiday that day and the next, as it was the feast of Señor San Francisco,[7] and on the 5th of October they continued their march so as to reach the main herd of the cattle. In three days they travelled fourteen leagues, at the end of which they found and killed many cattle. Next day they went three more leagues farther in search of a convenient and suitable site for a corral, and upon finding a place they began to construct it out of large pieces of cottonwood.[8] It took them three days to complete it. It was so large and the wings so long that they thought they could corral ten thousand head of cattle, because they had seen so many, during those days, wandering so near to the tents and houses. In view of this and of the further fact that when they run they act as though fettered, they took their capture for granted. It was declared by those who had seen them that in that place alone there were more buffalo than there are cattle in three of the largest ranches in New Spain.

The corral constructed, they went next day to a plain where on the previous afternoon about a hundred thousand cattle had been seen. Giving them the right of way, the cattle started very nicely towards the corral, but soon they turned back in a stampede towards the men, and, rushing through them in a mass, it was impossible to stop them, because they are cattle terribly obstinate, courageous beyond exaggeration, and so cunning that if pursued they run, and that if their pursuers stop or slacken their speed they stop and roll, just like mules, and with this respite renew their run. For several days they tried a thousand ways of shutting them in or of surrounding them, but in no manner was it possible to do so. This was not due to fear, for they are remarkably savage and ferocious, so much so that they killed three of our horses and badly wounded forty, for their horns are very sharp and fairly long, about a span and a half, and bent upward together. They attack from the side, putting the head far down, so that whatever they seize they tear very badly. Nevertheless, some were killed and over eighty *arrobas*[9] of tallow were secured, which without doubt is greatly superior to that from pork; the meat of the bull is superior to that of our cow, and that of the cow equals our most tender veal or mutton.

Seeing therefore that the full grown cattle could not be brought alive, the *sargento mayor* ordered that calves be captured, but they became so enraged that out of the many which were being brought, some dragged by ropes and others upon the horses, not one got a league toward the camp, for they all died within about an hour. Therefore it is believed that unless taken shortly after birth and put under the care of our cows or goats, they cannot be brought until the cattle become tamer than they now are.

Its shape and form are so marvellous and laughable, or frightful, that the more one sees it the more one desires to see it, and no one could be so melancholy that if he were to see it a hundred times a day he could keep from laughing heartily as many times, or could fail to marvel at the sight of so ferocious an animal. Its horns are black, and a third of a *vara* long,[1] as already stated, and resemble those of the *búfalo*;[2] its eyes are small, its face, snout, feet, and hoofs of the same form as of our cows, with the exception that both the male and female are very much bearded, similar to he-goats.

7. See note 8, p. 84.
8. They were now fifty-one leagues, or perhaps from one hundred and twenty-five to one hundred and forty miles, from Pecos. This took them near to, if not beyond, the borders of New Mexico. * * *

9. More than a ton.
1. The length of the Spanish *vara*, or yard, differed at various times and places, but a third was approximately one foot. [Anthology editors' note]
2. That is, the Asiatic buffalo, or wild ox.

They are so thickly covered with wool that it covers their eyes and face, and the forelock nearly envelops their horns. This wool, which is long and very soft, extends almost to the middle of the body, but from there on the hair is shorter. Over the ribs they have so much wool and the chine is so high that they appear humpbacked, although in reality and in truth they are not greatly so, for the hump easily disappears when the hides are stretched.

In general, they are larger than our cattle. Their tail is like that of a hog, being very short, and having few bristles at the tip, and they twist it upward when they run. At the knee they have natural garters of very long hair. In their haunches, which resemble those of mules, they are hipped and crippled, and they therefore run, as already stated, in leaps, especially down hill. They are all of the same dark color, somewhat tawny, in parts their hair being almost black. Such is their appearance, which at sight is far more ferocious than the pen can depict. As many of these cattle as are desired can be killed and brought to these settlements, which are distant from them thirty or forty leagues, but if they are to be brought alive it will be most difficult unless time and crossing them with those from Spain make them tamer.

In this region and on this road were found some camps and sleeping places made by Leyba and Humaña when they left this land, fleeing from the men who were coming from New Spain to arrest them.[3]

These cattle have their haunts on some very level mesas which extend over many leagues, for, after reaching the top of them by a slight grade, as of low hills, thirty leagues were travelled, continuously covered with an infinite number of cattle, and the end of them was not reached. The mesas have neither mountain, nor tree, nor shrub, and when on them they were guided solely by the sun. To the north in their highest part flows a medium-sized river, which appears to be a marvel, for at that point it is higher than at its source, and seems rather to flow up than down. It contains many fish and crustaceans. At the base of these mesas, in some places where there are glens or valleys, there are many cedars, and an infinite number of springs which issue from these very mesas, and a half league from them there are large cotton groves.

The Indians are numerous in all that land. They live in rancherías in the hide tents hereinbefore mentioned. They always follow the cattle, and in their pursuit they are as well sheltered in their tents as they could be in any house. They eat meat almost raw, and much tallow and suet, which serves them as bread, and with a chunk of meat in one hand and a piece of tallow in the other, they bite first on one and then on the other, and grow up magnificently strong and courageous. Their weapons consist of flint and very large bows, after the manner of the Turks. They saw some arrows with long thick points,[4] although few, for the flint is better than spears to kill cattle. They kill them at the first shot with the greatest skill, while ambushed in brush blinds made at the watering places, as all saw who went there, and who in company with the said *sargento mayor* consumed in the journey fifty-four days and returned to this camp on the 8th of November, 1598, thanks be to God.

✳︎    ✳︎    ✳︎

# 1599

3. See note 6, p. 79.
4. I.e., some spears. [Anthology editors' note]

# GASPAR PÉREZ DE VILLAGRÁ
## ca. 1555–1620

The Spanish soldier-poet Gaspar Pérez de Villagrá played an important role in Juan de Oñate's attempted colonization of New Mexico. As mentioned in the Oñate headnote, Villagrá's epic poem *La historia de la Nueva México* (The History of New Mexico, 1610) chronicles the Oñate expedition from its shaky beginning, in 1595, to the victory over the Acoma rebellion, in 1601. Composed in hendecasyllabic blank verse, the poem is written from the perspective of a loyal officer, full of admiration for his leader, intimately involved in events, and strongly supporting the conquest.

Villagrá was born to Spanish parents in Puebla, Mexico. At one of the oldest and most prestigious universities in Spain, the University of Salamanca, he obtained a degree in humanistic studies and acquired a vast knowledge of classical Greek, classical Roman, and Italian Renaissance literature. He was well acquainted with Spanish Golden Age literature and with the Spanish poets writing in the New World. His work bears the influences of Greek poets such as Homer, Roman poets such as Virgil, Italians such as Ariosto and Tasso, and colonial Spaniards including Alonso de Ercilla y Zúñiga, Pedro de Oña, and Martín del Barco Centenera.

In 1596, Oñate appointed Villagrá a captain and the expedition's legal officer; in 1598, he became ecclesiastical counsel. As a member of Oñate's inner circle, he followed orders unquestioningly, to the point of catching a group of four deserters and executing two of them. For having done so, in 1612 he was charged with a criminal act; in 1614, after a long trial, he was found guilty. His punishment consisted of a six-year banishment from New Mexico, a two-year banishment from Mexico City, a two-year ban on holding any office, and court costs. Perhaps Villagrá wrote his epic to exonerate himself, to explain the Oñate expedition's problems, and to demonstrate the hardships he suffered and the service he had rendered to the Crown. He also wrote several petitions to King Philip II and, in 1614, a memorial in which he tried to justify the harsh treatment of the Acoma nation by Oñate's forces.

*The History of New Mexico* is the first written history of an area that eventually became part of the United States, preceding John Smith's *General History of Virginia* by 14 years. In chronicling history, some critics argue, epic poets such as Villagrá are hampered by the constraints of the topic and tend to recount events in verse that is more like prose. Indeed, with its often flat and cumbersome language, *The History of New Mexico* is often seen as more valuable for its historical information than for its poetic qualities. George Ticknor, a nineteenth-century American critic of Spanish literature, once said that Villagrá's epic belongs less to poetry than to patriotism. Contemporary critics such as Luis Leal (see p. 551), however, champion the literary value of Villagrá's work.

The selections of the poem in this anthology begin with canto 1, which pays homage to the Spaniards' valor and provides a background of the New Mexican Indians. Villagrá brings to the fore the mythical legend of Aztlán and points out that the New Mexican Indians are the ancestors of the Aztecs. The next selection, canto 2, narrates the Aztec migration from New Mexican lands to their new home, Tenochtitlán, and their founding of a new empire. Canto 14 recounts the exploration by the Oñate expedition of the flora and fauna of New Mexico. When they discovered the River of the North, known today as the North Cavedon River—which flows through New Mexico, Texas, and Oklahoma—the Spaniards also found buffalo, which they referred to as "monstrous cows." Included in canto 14 is an excerpt from the *Requerimiento*, the long and complex official document that the Spaniards would read to the Indians in Spanish, announcing that the Indians were now subjects of the Spanish Crown, that they would soon be indoctrinated into Catholicism, and that the invaders would be taking possession of the natives' lands either through their voluntary acquiescence or through warfare.

---

## *FROM* THE HISTORY OF NEW MEXICO[1]

### Canto I

*Which sets forth the outline of the history and the location of New Mexico,[2] and the reports had of it in the traditions of the Indians, and of the true origin and descent of the Mexicans.[3]*

I sing of arms and the heroic man,[4]
The being, courage, care, and high emprise
Of him whose unconquered patience,
Though cast upon a sea of cares,[5]
In spite of envy slanderous,                                              5
Is raising to new heights the feats,
The deeds, of those brave Spaniards who,
In the far India of the West,[6]
Discovering in the world that which was hid,
'Plus ultra'[7] go bravely saying                                        10
By force of valor and strong arms,
In war and suffering as experienced
As celebrated now by pen unskilled.
I beg of thee, most Christian Philip,[8]

1. Translated by Miguel Encinias, Alfred Rodríguez, and Joseph P. Sánchez. Except as indicated, all footnotes are Encinias, Rodríguez, and Sánchez's. The anthology editors have omitted some notes and made minor, stylistic changes to others.
2. This geographic identification, which the area has retained into our own day, does not proceed, as a modern reader might surmise, from what is today known as Mexico, a name that New Spain acquired only after its independence in the nineteenth century. Nueva México, as it was called in the sixteenth century, stems from the Spaniards' hopeful association (after the glowing reports made by Cabeza de Vaca and Father Marcos de Niza of the American southwest) between the unknown lands to the north and the fabulous Aztec Empire found by Cortés. To our knowledge, the term "Nuevo México," used to identify those unknown northern lands, was first employed by Francisco de Ibarra, viceroy of Nueva Vizcaya, after his exploration of the same in 1563 * * *.
3. The reference is to the Aztecs, whose historical-legendary origin in the north, in the general area of the new lands being explored, and settled, intrigued the Spaniards, always hopeful of encoun-

tering similar societies in that area.
4. This is a very direct imitation of the first line of Virgil's *Aeneid*, the primary model of the Renaissance epic. Although less direct, this entire presentation of the hero. Oñate, patiently suffering a multitude of adversities, echoes Virgil's poetic opening.
5. Villagrá's nautical imagery initiates a pattern of usage that, perhaps stemming from the primary Virgilian model but more likely reflecting the novel and extreme experience of New World writers, is an essential characteristic of the New World epic.
6. Villagrá refers to the New World land mass as India of the West.
7. This "further on" became the watchword and motto of those who had broken the geographical limits of the ancient world, forming part of the Castilian coat of arms. [Since the fifteenth century, the region of Castile, Spain, has been the center of Spanish political and administrative power. *Plus ultra* appears on a banner within the Spanish monarchical coat of arms.]
8. The poem is dedicated to Philip III, son of Philip II, still king when Oñate negotiated and started his expedition.

Being the Phoenix[9] of New Mexico                                    15
Now newly brought forth from the flames
Of fire and new produced from ashes
Of the most ardent faith, in whose hot coals
Sublime your sainted Father and our lord
We saw all burned and quite undone,                                  20
Suspend a moment from your back
The great and heavy weight which bears you down
Of this enormous globe which, in all right,
Is by your arm alone upheld,
And, lending, O great King, attentive ear,                           25
Thou here shalt see the load of toil,
Of calumny, affliction, under which
Did plant the evangel holy and the Faith of Christ
That Christian Achilles[1] whom you wished
To be employed in such heroic work.                                  30
And if in fortune good I may succeed
In having you, my Monarch, listener,
Who doubts that, with a wondering fear,
The whole round world shall listen too
To that which holds so high a King intent.                           35
For, being favored thus by you,
It being no less to write of deeds worthy
Of being elevated by the pen
Than to undertake those which are no less
Worthy of being written by this same pen,[2]                         40
'Tis only needed that those same brave men
For whom this task I undertook
Should nourish with their great, heroic valor
The daring flight of this my pen,
Because I think that this time we shall see                          45
The words well equaled by the deeds.
Hear me, great King, for I am witness
Of all that here, my Lord, I say to you.
Beneath the Arctic Pole, in height
Some thirty-three degrees, which the same                            50
Are, we know, of sainted Jerusalem,[3]
Not without mystery and marvel great,
Are spread, extended, sown, and overflow
Some nations barbarous, remote
From the bosom of the Church, where                                  55
The longest day of all the year contains and has
Some fourteen hours and a half when it arrives,

9. The phoenix's rebirth from its own ashes was common to most medieval and Renaissance bestiaries, with their common origin in Pliny's *Historia naturalis* [Natural History (Latin); an encyclopedia by the Roman author Pliny the Elder (AD 23–79)]. Villagrá parallels that rebirth from fire with the renewed faith of Philip II's Counter-Reformation Catholicism.
1. The identification of the epic hero's Christian mission with the Homeric hero, Achilles, is char-

acteristic of the New World epic. * * *
2. Villagrá, like Ercilla (*La araucana*) and several other poets of the conquest of the New World, was an active participant in the events he narrates.
3. This stressed coincidence of latitude between the new land and holy Jerusalem is meant to underscore the then widely held idea that the former, with great significance for Spain's missionary goals, had been especially preserved by God.

The furious sun, at the rising of Cancer,[4]
Through whose zenith he doth usually pass
The image of Andromeda and Perseus,[5]                60
Whose constellation always influences
The quality of Venus and Mercury.
And shows to us its location in longitude,
According as most modern fixed meridian
Doth teach us and we practice,[6]                     65
Two hundred just degrees and seventy
Into the temperate zone and the fourth clime,[7]
Two hundred long leagues[8] from the place
Where the Sea of the North[9] and Gulf of Mexico
Approach the most and nearest to the coast           70
On the southeast; and to the side
Toward the rough Californio[1] and Sea of the Pearls[2]
The distance in that direction is about the same
Toward where the southwest wind strikes the coast[3]
And from the frozen zone its distance is             75
About five hundred full long leagues;
And in a circle round we see it hold,
Beneath the parallel, if we should take
The height of thirty-seven degrees,
Five thousand goodly Spanish leagues,                80
Whose greatness it is a shame it should be held
By so great sum of people ignorant
About the blood of Christ, whose holiness
It causes pain to think so many souls know not.
From these new regions 'tis notorious,               85
Of public voice and fame, that there descended
Those oldest folk of Mexico
Who to the famous city, Mexico,
Did give their name, that it might be
Memorial eternal of their name, and lasting,         90
In imitation of wise Romulus
Who put a measure to the walls of Rome,[4]
Whose truth is drawn from and is proved by
That extremely ancient painting
And hieroglyphic method which they have,[5]          95
By which they deal and speak and are well understood,
Though not with the same excellent perfection

4. The Tropic of Cancer, the northern latitudinal division.
5. Andromeda and Perseus are northern constellations.
6. At that time there was as yet no agreed upon keying meridian (Greenwich), and nations used instead the meridian of their own capital city. The discovery of the New World implied the creation of many new meridians.
7. At that time a "clime" was defined as the geographic area between latitudinal lines. The ancients divided the world into seven climes.
8. The Spanish league, at that time, according to [the ethnologist Miguel] Covarrubias, contained some three miles.
9. The Atlantic Ocean.
1. The Colorado River.
2. The Gulf of California.
3. The use of winds to designate cardinal points was common nautical usage of those times.
4. Romulus and his brother Remus, legendary founders of Rome. Their feat is narrated by Ovid, Metamorphoses XIV.
5. Villagrá may possibly have had some knowledge of Aztec glyph writing. Father Bernardino de Sahagún's Historia antigua de México would have been accessible to him.

Of graceful conversation which is offered
When we converse with absent friends
By means of the excellence and greatness          100
Of the noble writing which we have.[6]
And there reconfirms and corroborates this tradition
That prodigy immense which we did find
When taking road, uncertain and unknown,
For that New Mexico. It happened that             105
In the last towns of what is called New Spain,
And on the border of the Kingdom of Vizcaya,[7]
The whole camp having risen
To make a start upon the route,
Wild, rough, and difficult and hidden yet,        110
One thing we learned for very certain
And talked of through immortal memory
And which had come from hand to hand,
Just as midst us the coming here to Spain
Of those brave hearts who at the first             115
Came here to populate and conquer it.[8]
They told us then, those native folk,
Unanimous, agreed, and with one voice,
That from that land beyond, and pointing out
That section where the North doth hide            120
The hollow cavern, craggy,
Of vigorous and hasty Boreas,[9]
There came two most courageous brethren,[1]
Of high and noble Kings descended,
Sons of a King, and king of highest lineage,      125
Desirous of esteem and elevation
By discovering the marvels of the world,
And all its kings illustrious and all its lords,
With noble triumph and with famous trophies,
By active force of arms, perhaps without them,    130
Like gentle lamblings to the fold,
Reduce, subject, and obedient
To the harsh yoke of their immense empire,
Proud lordship, great estate;
And that, arriving there with a great force        135
Of many soldiers and well armed,
Divided in two camps most large
Of mighty squadrons and well formed,

6. This praise of Castilian, especially as a written language, is a clear indication of Villagrá's humanistic education.
7. Nueva Vizcaya is today the area of Mexico bordering on the Rio Grande.
8. Villagrá refers to the no less legendary prehistory of Iberia.
9. Boreas, the mythological name for the north wind, was held in a cave.
1. The legends that have come down to us regarding the origins of the Aztecs refer to two principal figures, not necessarily brothers, Huitzíton and Tecpátzin. ° ° ° Villagrá may offer here a legend not known to earlier or later historians. But his making the two figures brothers and the manner in which they divide jurisdictions may possibly reflect other influences; on the one hand, Statius's *Thebaid*, much read in its sixteenth-century Spanish translation by Juan de Arjona; on the other, Martín del Barco Centenera's *Argentina y conquista del Río de Plata*, published in Lisbon in 1602, in which the brothers Tupi and Guaraní divide up the lands of that region.

The elder of the two did lead the van[2]
With number great of squadrons,                                    140
And the younger brother reinforced
The rear guard with a number just as great
And led it with great skill,
And in the middle of the force
Great sum of baggage and of apparatus,                            145
Tents and pavilions shining bright
With which their Highnesses did make their camp,
And like to free and tender fawns
Infinity of children and of babes
Here, there, and elsewhere frolicking,                            150
Surrounded by most pretty toys
Of simple, innocent infancy,
And with no sort of plan or concert.
And also in that proud camp
There showed themselves among the deadly arms,                    155
As flowers beautiful are seen mid thorns,
Fair dames and ladies and bright damsels,
As dainty, lovely, and discreet
As noble, beautiful, and well-advised;
And, in the very Hower of youth, young men,                       160
And gentlemen and well dressed, all,
Each one competing with the rest
Such sum of finery and of livery
As in the finest and most lofty courts
Are customed to be worn on festal days                            165
By the most conspicuous courtiers.
And then, also, the mighty squadrons
Showed in the midst of such gallantry
A number terrible, and fearful, too,
Of notable animal disguises:                                      170
One wore the hide of a manéd lion
With which he represented well
The face ferocious and the appearance of the proud animal;
Some the striped hide of fierce Hircanian tiger,
Of speedy ounce, astute monkey, and leopard,                      175
There were the hungry wolf carnivorous,
The fox, the hare and the rabbit shy,
The fishes huge and lordly eagles, too,
With all the rest of the brute beasts
Which occupy the earth and sky and the broad seas.                180
There they appeared all, most natural,
A native, old invention, one that's used
Among all peoples and all nations
Which we have yet discovered in the Indies.
There were of arms, warlike and strong,                           185
A shining, great, and goodly sum:
Bent Turkish bows, well strung,

---

2. Vanguard. [Anthology editors' note]

Broad quivers, broad and of a capacious size,
Well stuffed with arrows light,
Light javelins and maces heavy,                                    190
Strong bucklers and cuirasses strong,
Well made, of knotted, woven work,
Mischievous slings, swung in the air,
Thick clubs with heavy stones
Imbedded in their strong wood,                                     195
And, lined with sharp flints,
Strong, well-wrought, wooden swords;
And lofted in air there fluttered,
With gallantry and grace bizarre,
A quantity of banners and of standards                             200
Of different colors, many hued.
And the well-serried ranks of troops,
Each gripping fast his arms,
Kept marching over the great field
With greatest ease and gallant tread,                              205
And, lashed by tread of many men,
The hard-baked earth sent high into the air
A cloud of dust so thick and dense
It seemed that the whole earth was there dissolved
In blinding dust, whirled on                                       210
By swift and sudden earthquake,
Which through the broad dome of the air
Spreads out in lofty whirlwinds.
Well, going thus and traveling carelessly,
There placed himself before them by intent,                        215
In form of an old and haglike woman,
A valiant and cunning demon
Whose face ferocious dare I not,
If I must with some care depict it,
Set out to paint without new strength.                             220

# Canto II

*How the devil appeared to the whole camp in the shape
of an old woman, and of the scheme he had to separate
the two brothers, and of the great heap of iron that he left so that
everyone might know his true estate.*

When the majesty of God removeth
Some flock from out the Catholic fold,
It is a sign most evident, ignored by none,
That this His justice doth permit
Because this road least evil is                                      5
Of those that their sad souls could take.
And thus, as though to miserable lost souls
Divided from the holy Church,
These poor reprobates marching forward thus,
That accursed one placed himself before them                        10

In form of an old woman well disguised,
Whose great and fearful cleverness
Doth cause both fear and terror to imagine.
He had his gray hair badly dressed,
And like a horrible, fierce skeleton                                    15
His fleshless and emaciated face,
Of an expression wild and fearsome,
Misshapen breasts and dangling teats,
Starved, flaccid, dry, and wrinkled,
Great chest, both wide and spacious,                                    20
With shoulders terrible, well set,
Eyes sunk and colored as of fire,
A mouth malformed, from ear to ear,
Through whose dry and distorted lips
Of fangs just four protruded                                           25
And, curving, showed themselves a good palm's length;
His arms were fearful, feet and legs,
In whose fearsome joints
The bones creaked loud,
Well set, with muscles powerful.                                       30
Just as they picture for us and do show
The ferocious person of brave Atlas,[1]
Upon whose great and robust strength
The great, incomparable weight and thrust
Of highest-lifted heavens doth rest,                                   35
Of which he partook to some degree
In curious and learned Astrology,[2]
Thus of this fierce old woman and astrologer[3]
They say most certainly she bore
Upon her head, so great and strong,                                    40
A huge, enormous weight, almost in form
A tortoise-shell set upright,
Exceeding some eight hundred quintal weight,
Of iron, massive and well molded.
And when he came upon the foreign camp,                                45
Holding it attentive and in suspense,
With a loud voice and unembarrassed,
His head erect, he then addressed them thus:
"I am not pained, O valiant Mexicans,
Because, as raging fire never quenched                                 50
Which rises to its summit high,[4]
You are in no way less moved or beckoned
By the rude haughtiness and gallantry
Of your illustrious, grand, and noble blood,

1. In mythology, Atlas, a Titan, holds the world on his shoulders. Villagrá, given the grotesqueness of the figure described, was perhaps plastically re-calling the often grotesquely topped columns of buildings, which, understandably, also went by that name in Spanish.
2. It would seem that Villagrá would mean "my-thology," which does indicate the Titans' attempt to storm the heavens.
3. The description of the witch-seer appears to echo that of Lucan, *Pharsalia* VI.
4. The comparison with the natural impulse of fire to rise, although applied to the soul's search for God, is found in Dante, *Paradiso* I.

To whose heroic, royal, character                                    55
'Tis natural, inborn, this great desire
With which you go from the paternal nest
Only to seek for lands remote,
New worlds, new stars, as well,
In which the greatness can be shown                                  60
Of these, your strong and warlike arms,
Extending out to either side
As the proud sea extends itself
In powerful waves and stretches them
Out to its far-flung shores and banks,                               65
That thus be spread, extend, and be made known
O'er all created and discovered
The fitting adoration which is due
Unto that prince supreme and powerful
Of that dark shelter which we seek.[5]                               70
And so that you may better take the point,
As a most rapid arrow which flies fast
Into the target waiting it,
Hear ye the will which 'tis best to obey
Of the great lord who sent me here.                                  75
You know already that tired, weary age
Keepeth the royal person of your noble father,
Well-beloved, so painfully oppressed,
Downcast, afflicted, miserable,
That more could not well be within this life,                        80
And that his old age, sick and gray,
Has come to weak decrepitude,
Returning now to childhood once again.
And so that most of his estates,
Like a swift comet which doth set,                                   85
May not remain, by his end and sad death,
Without a natural lord to care for them,
'Tis necessary now that one of you return
And that the other still pursue his noble star,
Its prosperous destiny, and make his place,                          90
Not where the ancient Romans saw the head
Of that huge dead man struck from off his shoulders[6]
Nor where the great hide of the beauteous bull
Took up so much land that it was enough
To close within its mighty strips                                    95
The lofty walls of Carthage,[7]
But where on a hard and solid rock
Girded by waters crystalline

---

5. The reference is to Satan and his dominion. Hell, toward which the evil are headed. The Aztec gods were considered by the Spaniards as manifestations of Satan.
6. The reference may possibly be to the sight the Trojans (ancient Romans) had of the headless body of King Priam when they fled from the burning Troy. It is narrated in Virgil, *Aeneid* II,

749–50.
7. In the legend of the founding of Carthage, Queen Dido was conceded all the land that could be covered by the skin of an ox. By making it into thin strips, she was able to claim an extensive area. Narrated by Virgil, *Aeneid* I, 520–22 and more extensively by Ercilla, *La araucana* III, 33.

A cactus planted you shall see
Upon whose thick and spreading leaves          100
A beautiful red-tailed eagle sits, quite enormous,
And it be eating greedily
On a great snake that in his claws,
As you shall see, is twisting, but well gripped.
Here it is willed that you shall found and raise          105
The lofty, generous, metropolis
Of the strong state indicated,
For which 'tis ordered most express
It Mexico Tenochtitlán be named.
And with that memorable sign          110
You shall make, afterward, new arms
And, for the shields, new blazons.
And because greed, a wicked vice
Of sinful acquiring, is often cause
Of great dissensions and of grudge,          115
To free yourselves from lawsuits and debates
It will be well to mark the limits down,
The borders and the boundaries of the lands
That each for his sole governance
Will accept, nor pretend          120
To any other rule, nor more nor less
Than that which shall be there assigned to him.[8]
And raising from the ground his heels,
Set firm upon his mighty toes,
He raised his powerful, mighty arms          125
And giving to his monstrous load a push,
As though it were a mighty thunderbolt
That 'stonishes with fear and terror great
The many, and does leave them without sense,
There being few it hurts,          130
So with a sudden and horrendous noise
He threw aside the mighty load,
And hardly did it strike the flinty earth
When, trembling and shaking all,
That earth was broken everywhere.          135
And when 'twas done, like Circe skilled,[9]
He vanished thence without their seeing him,
Pointing to one and to the other Pole
The two crowns raised on high.
Just as the Romans and the Greeks          140
When they divided the empire famed,[1]
Which great and wonderful action
The imperial Eagle, double-headed,[2] in symbol
That immense division represents,

8. This summarizes the well-known legend of the founding of Mexico City.
9. Circe is the mythological witch, described by Virgil, *Aeneid* VII, 22–25 and Ovid, *Metamorphoses* XIV.

1. The reference is to the division of the Roman Empire into its eastern and western parts.
2. The two-headed eagle symbolizes the Holy Roman Empire, successor to the Western Roman Empire.

In this same manner, way and sort                               145
They did the powerful earth divide.
And, as the pelota ball, sent forth with strength
Of mighty arm and stick so broad,
Flies back and in an instant,
Quick as we saw it come, returns,[3]                            150
Thus, in a bound, the stricken camp became
From what the woman had proposed to them,
All the rear guard did turn again
Toward that sweet fatherland they'd left
In regions of the hardy North,                                  155
And toward the South there still kept on
The vanguard, marching proudly and content,
First having each embraced the other
Most tenderly and taken leave.
And like that memorable needle                                  160
Which, as a great wonder and marvel,
Still stands upright in place
In the beautiful and holy city, Rome,[4]
Plain to be seen by all who wish to see it,
There still remains, in the same way,                           165
The mighty mass which there was placed,
In height some twenty-seven degrees
And a half more.[5] And there was no man
Of all your camp who did not stop
Astonished, stunned, and almost senseless,                      170
Considering that same story
And seeing with his own two eyes
The greatness of the monstrous mass was there.
And of the horses not one would approach it
Unless one tore their flanks,                                   175
For some stood on their hind legs, rebellious,
With whistlings and snorts,
And others, frightened more, did shy,
Suspicious, to one side or to the other,
From that enormous mass, such as was never seen,               180
Until one day a certain priest
Did celebrate the great, most holy mystery
Of that redemption of the universe,
Taking for altar that same mass of iron,
And ever since we noticed that those beasts                     185
Came, without fear or trembling or suspicion,
Right to its foot
As to a place which has been freed
From some unloosed infernal fury.
And I, as one who is good witness of that sight,               190
Say that it is as pure and smooth a metal,

3. The description is of some form of Basque ball, very popular with the Spanish conquerors in the New World. References to it abound in the New World epic, beginning with Ercilla.
4. The reference is to the Egyptian obelisk in Rome.
5. Despite Villagrá's fairly precise latitudinal reference, no reference has been found to such a metal mountain in the historical accounts of the expedition.

And free of rust, as if it were
Silver refined of Copella.[6]
And what our people wondered most
Is that we saw no sort of vein,                                195
Nor scoria, trace, nor any rock
By means of which we might be shown or see
How the great mass could be created there,
Because there's no more trace of that
Than the swift birds leave traces in the air               200
Through which they make their road,
Or, in the sea, the swimming fish
When they go plying through the waters clean.
And this same story which I here have told
We know, great lord, is oft related                        205
In that same place we call New Mexico,
Where, we ourselves were told,
They all were strangers, and in so narrating
The long journey of those two brethren,
In passing, they do say, their forefathers and ancestors   210
Remained, and they point out
The far off Northland, whence they say
And do affirm themselves to be descended.
And they do say their boundaries do contain
Great sum of nations, different,                           215
In language, laws, rites, and customs,
Each very different from the rest,
Among which they do count the Mexicans,
Tarascans and the folk of Guinea.[7]
Nor stopping here, they do affirm                         220
That they have people white, as in Castile.
All these are grandeurs which do lead us on
To throw to earth the columns
Of that same Non Plus Ultra[8] which they raise,
Folk more for distaff and for parlor fit,                 225
For coifs, for sewing and such labor,
Than for the wielding of the mighty pike,
The generous scepter, and the honored sword.
And having come from these new lands,
The fine Mexicans, is proved to us by                     230
The ruins of that city great
Which we all see in New Galicia,[9]
Of mighty buildings, all laid waste,
Where they, the natives of the land,
Say it was made and founded there                         235
By those New Mexicans who came

6. The reference is to a procedure, using cal-
cined bones, for the melting of precious metals.
7. The Tarascans were an indigenous Indian tribe
located in the northern part of the ancient Aztec
empire. "People of Guinea" refers to blacks. The
whites mentioned below almost certainly refers
to albinos.

8. *Non plus ultra* was the classical signal, on the
columns of Hercules, Straits of Gibraltar, to go
no further.
9. The reference is to the pre-Columbian ruins
of Casas Grandes, in the present state of Chihuahua, then called Nueva Galicia.

Out of the new land that we seek.
From whose foundations and high walls,
With all the area that New Spain contains
Until reaching the very towns                                240
Of what we call New Mexico,
Just like the solicitous scouts,
Who from no more than the wind can detect
The remotest game in hiding,
Thus did the careful soldiery                               245
Constantly find and discover,
In the broad boundaries I said,
Clear traces, signs, and indications
Of this truth we are referring,
Because in all the desert land                              250
Always we found, and without seeking it,
Great store of pottery, both good and bad,
Sometimes heaped up in mounds
And others spread about and broke.
For this they always took for grandeur,                     255
Those rulers Mexican we named,
Because most of the service that they had
Was of baked mud, and just as soon
As it was taken out from its first use
They broke it and destroyed it.                             260
And in those selfsame towns
Most of your people saw
Some edifices, aye, and pictures
Of ancient Mexicans well depicted.
And thus, just as the skillful gambler discovers            265
The much desired card as with compass,
Saving the money he has bet,
E'en so, by these same traces and these signs
Assured, we set up the whole camp
Within this pleasing refuge we'd discovered,                270
Taking such rest as might
Somewhat refresh and comfort us,
Our tired bodies broken down
By weight of heavy arms.
And so, my lord, this was the way we knew                   275
That this is the noble land they trod,
Those brave old ones who came
From New Mexico, great and famous,
Of whom El Peregrino Indiano[1] says
That very few desired to see it won                         280
And very rightly doth it set us right
In truth so evident and well known.
Because in order to extend the lofty walls
Of this our Holy Church, and raise them higher still,
Many are called, but very few                               285

---

1. The reference is to Saavedra Guzmán's epic of the conquest of Mexico, Canto XI.

Are those whom we see chosen
For such high and lofty work.
But let us lay this thing aside,
Which needs a story long to tell it all,
Closing our canto, badly sung,                                    290
By having sung quite all of what
By the most ancient natives here
Could be remembered and discovered
About the ancient descent.
The coming and the settlement of Mexicans,                         295
Who, for myself, I think that they did come
From the great China, all who live
In what we call the Indies.[2] But it matters not,
That here, for now, we leave the matter.
And because your Castilian folk,                                   300
To whom the grandeur of the Universe entire
That we enjoy, to tread and to discover
Seems small,
Did for themselves grasp a great part
Of this new world which we explore,                                305
I shall say later who they were,
Those who the journey undertook
Not seeing it done and ended in a moment.


## Canto XIV

*How the River of the North was discovered and the trials that were borne
in discovering it, and of other things that happened until arriving
at the point of taking possession of the land.*

The value of a thing undertaken
Is esteemed and praised and raised aloft
In such proportion as that is esteemed
With which it is accomplished, gained, and won.
This I do say, great lord, so that I may                            5
Make clearer the great greatness, excellence,
Of warlike exercise practiced
By all those heroes valorous
Who, in exchange for toil and suffering,
Life and blood, have bought and won                               10
Only the famous name of soldiers,
To whose high excellence 'tis proper
To see and to observe in every way
That 'tis useless to bear the trials
Miseries, afflictions, and fatigues                               15
That bloody war always entails
If in the middle of its course unstoppable
Their spirit breaks and becomes cowardly.

---

2. Note Villagrá's insight into the Asian origin of the New World peoples.

And, not to come to such disgrace,
Our tired forces sinking down,                                    20
Seeing no port agreeable, sweet,
When the noble Polca,[1] content,
Her farewell said, had gone to her country,
As goes the huntsman who has lost
A great gyrfalcon, falcon, or saker,                             25
Shouting among the valleys and hills,
Calling it with anxiety,
Showing the lure until he sees him safe
Perched on his hand, where, happily,
Without a memory of his recent fright,                           30
He dandles him and pets him and smooths down
His ruffled plumage, and appeases him,
So went the beautiful barbarian, I think,
She went eagerly after her Milco,[2]
And we, lord, resolute anew,                                     35
Did journey more than fifty days,
Suffering heavy mischances.
And as it had unceasing rained on us
For seven long, hard days' journeyings,
Our clothing sticking to our flesh,                             40
No one of us had any thought
Of coming out with life from that affair.
We went through rough and craggy lands
Of Arabs and of rude barbarians
And other deserts, wild and perilous,                           45
Upon whose wide and spacious soil
No Christian foot had ever trod.
In which long time we did consume
The poor provisions we had brought,
And all with difficulty fed                                      50
Their tired bodies, all worn out,
Only with coarse roots indigestible.
Driving against the hardness of our fate
We ever held unto our course,
Now through thick briars and ravines,                           55
Entangled in whose harsh forests
Even our strong cuisses were torn,
Now over high and rugged peaks,
Over whose summits we did drive
Our tired horses on before,                                      60
Panting and tired and quite worn out,
On foot and hindered by all our arms,
Our swollen feet, now quite naked
And shoeless, without shoes we still did set
On cliffs and ragged looming rocks,                             65
Now over lofty dunes of sand,
So ardent, burning, and fervent

---

1. An Indian first mentioned in canto 13.     2. Polca's husband. [Anthology editors' note]
[Anthology editors' note]

That, wounded by their strong reflection,
Our miserable eyes, burnt up
'Neath our hard helmets, failed us quite.                    70
And as the end of what is hoped
Alone is nourished, thewed, sustained,
By valor and the ring of hope,
Hoping, we did those tasks that were,
But lighter, more endurable, and easier borne.               75
And since a ready diligence
Lent to a careful toil
Is mother of all good outcome,
We had that same, discovering the pass
That the astute barbarian told us of,                        80
Marking the lands all round about
The sites and places that he showed
When we with Milco captured him.
And, like Magellan through his strait,[3]
We all did pass through it,                                   85
Worn down with toil, now quite worn out
By the force of the rigorous fate
Which with a strong and heavy hand
So pressed us down, afflicted us.
Four complete days did pass away                             90
In which we drank no drop of water there,
And now the horses, being blind,
Did give themselves most cruel blows
And bumps against the unseen trees,
And we, as tired as they,                                    95
Exhaling living fire and spitting forth
Saliva more viscous than pitch,
Our hope given up, entirely lost,
Were almost all wishing for death.
But the great Providence, pitying,                          100
Which is always more quick in helping us
As we more firmly trust in it,
The fifth day opened us the door
And we all, happily, did come upon the roaring River
Of the North, for which we all had undergone               105
Such care and such enormous toil.
Unto whose waters the weak horses
Creeping, staggering much, approached
And, all there plunging in their heads,
Two of them drank to such extent                            110
They there, together, burst and died,
And two more, blind, went in so far
That, by the current snatched away,
They also died, with water satisfied.
And as in public taverns there do use                       115

---

3. In 1520, the Portuguese navigator Ferdinand Magellan (ca. 1480–1521), leader of the first expedition to circumnavigate the globe, discovered the strait that now bears his name; it separates Tierra del Fuego from mainland South America. [Anthology editors' note]

To lie upon the floor some wretched ones,
Drunk from the wine they have imbibed,
So our companions remained,
Stretched out upon the watery sand,
As swollen, dropsical, gasping,                                      120
As they had all been toads,
The whole river seeming to them but small
To extinguish and abate their thirst.
And as if in the fresh Elysian Fields[4]
We had arrived, there to refresh ourselves,                          125
Such, lord, there did appear to us
All those beaches and banks,
Among whose goodly pasture the horses
Were gladly grazing and resting
Their tired and exhausted bones                                      130
From the laborious, weary road.
And in the pleasant wood we all
With much pleasure did roam about
'Mid fresh and well-leaved poplar groves
Whose beautiful, agreeable shades                                    135
Gave invitation to our weary limbs,
By their own prostrate trunks nearby
To rest together with them there.
Through their green branches, spreading wide,
As exceeding chaste bees do go,                                      140
With buzzing dull and comforting,
Traveling from one thyme to the next
Tasting the best of many flowers,
Likewise among those lofty trunks,
With dainty, sweet-intoned song,                                     145
There flew a million little birds,
Whose graceful, unembarrassed throats
And lyric tongues did sing the praise
Of that All-powerful Lord who had made them.
And even the waters of the harsh river,                              150
At flood, a furious, roaring stream,
Were all flowing and pouring down
As peaceful, suave, pleasing, and mild
As though they were a quiet pool
Over wide flats and well spread out,                                 155
And, too, with many kinds of fish
Most excellently rich and abounding.
We found, beside this, much hunting,
Of many cranes and ducks and geese,
upon which the astute, prompt hunters there                          160
Made good use of their harquebuses.
And having hunted and fished much,
From out the fire-bearing flints
We struck their hidden fires and made
A great and excellent campfire,                                      165

4. In classical mythology, the abode of the blessed after death. [Anthology editors' note]

And on huge spits and in the coals
We put a huge supply of meat and fish,
Placing with liberal hands all that
Our eager appetites did ask
To conquer in completest sort                                    170
Their great desire for savory food.
And like that memorable dove
Which, after the great storm had passed,
Returned with the green olive branch,[5]
Not otherwise, we all returned,                                  175
Filled wholly with content and joy,
Which is the true reward of work.
And when we came to the army
We were received with much festivity,
And, as 'tis always needed and is pleasant, too,                180
To bring to memory the toils,
The miseries, fatigues, we have endured
When the fierce war was on,
The Sergeant Major, drawn by this pleasure,
Related unto all the camp,                                       185
The General[6] being present, those events,
Journeys, occurrences, endured
until at last we came unto the shores,
The banks and groves of that river,
under whose widely spreading trees                              190
We took our ease after all our fatigues.
And as it always causes great relief
To know one suffers not alone,
When he had done, the skillful General
Took to himself the floor and as a comfort                      195
For our sad trials now gone by,
Told of the trials that his men
Had also borne and undergone,
And how one of them was so hard
That the camp came to the edge of ruin.                         200
And 'twas that, March coming on hot
And settling down with burning suns,
Water began to fail to such extent
That, with their throats all miserably dry,
The tender children, women, and the men,                        205
Afflicted, ruined, quite burnt up,
Did beg for aid from sovereign God,
This being the final remedy
That they could have in such distress.
And the sad, tired animals,                                      210
Feeble as those of Nineveh,[7]
Worn down by unchecked fast,
Thus all did show themselves worn out

---

5. The reference is to Noah's ark [see the Old Testament, Genesis 6–9], an image that Villagrá repeats.
6. Juan de Oñate. *The Sergeant Major*: Vicente de Saldívar Mendoza (see p. 85). [Anthology editors' note]
7. Villagrá recalls the Old Testament, Nahum 1–3.

By the weather that they had borne.[8]
And as He always favors and assists                    215
With His immense sovereign goodness
The ones who truly ask and beg of Him,
The sky, being clear and very calm
In all directions, was disturbed
By huge black clouds, heavy laden,                     220
And without lightning or thunder
They shed and poured down such water
That oxen laden with their yokes
Did satisfy their killing thirst.
And when the afflicted army                            225
Was quite entirely appeased,
The beauty of the sun's bright rays
Was spread so widely over all
That not a single cloud held back
His bright splendor from any place.                    230
And so, for this cause, they did give
The place that holy water fell
The name of "Water of the Miracle" that it
Might have its memory prolonged eternally
And never throughout all time be forgot.               235
O sovereign Good, with what swiftness dost Thou
Assist us in our need if we have but
Such faith as but a grain of mustard-seed
May measure, weigh, and balance with!
Blessed be such a gift and its use                     240
Not only that the lofty clouds
Out of their season might pour water down,
But that the most massive mountains
Might move and change their locations
And the swift-flying sun might halt                    245
His powerful course and hold it back
For no more than the order of a noble Man
At whose feet there do yield and crouch
All things, both great and small,
Finally, as a man upheld                               250
By hands so great and wonderful.
It seems his greatness continued
To carry on this camp as His,
Being sometimes burdened with great woes
And others aided with a thousand joys,                 255
A certain, direct, and true voyage
Of those great laborers who raised
Heroic buildings for his Church.
For, marching thus for many days,
They came unto the waters of this river,               260
And, like the Trojan memorable
Who was favored and protected
By Neptune's water trident

8. This long description of drought echoes that in Statius's *Thebaid* IV.

After the whirlwind and great storm,[9]
The Governor with all his camp                          265
Came to a safe and pleasant port,
And to his sore-tried soldiery
He gave permission free to rest
upon those cooling banks and shores.
And as good government does not consist              270
In industry of no more than the present time,
But in a timely foresight of
What afterward may trouble us,
The Governor ordered that without delay
The Sergeant should set out at once                    275
With five chosen companions,
All skillful in swimming, to seek
Some safe ford through the swift river
So that by it all this your camp
Might pass safely and without fear.                    280
And carrying that order out
There went Caravajal, Antonio Sánchez,
The great Cristóbal Sánchez and Araujo,
And I, too, with them, that I might
Complete the number of the five.                       285
And, traveling all together, studiously,
Careful in search for some good ford,
We suddenly did come upon
Some thatched huts from whence there came out
Great numbers of barbarian warriors.                  290
And as that place was all marshy
And we could not well use our arms,
We went ahead toward the barbarians
Showing ourselves agreeable friends.
And as giving even breaks rocks,                       295
Giving them of the clothes we had
We made them so peaceful, friendly, to us
That four of them did come with us
And showed to us a goodly ford.
For which reason the prudent General                  300
Ordered that all the four be clothed
And treated with much regalement,
Wherefore all four went down the stream
And, as a sign of peace, brought back
A great number of fresh caught fish.                   305
And, ordering us to make proper return,
He then did cause to be made there,
Within a pleasant, leafy wood,
A graceful church, one with a nave
Of such a size that all the camp at once              310
Might be contained in it without crowding.
Within whose shelter, holy and religious,
They sang a very solemn Mass,

9. The reference is to Aeneas, the *Aeneid* 1, 177.

And the learned Commissary, with wisdom,
Did speak a famous sermon, well thought out.          315
And when the services were done
They did present a great drama
The noble Captain Farfán had composed,[1]
Whose argument was but to show to us
The great reception of the Church                    320
That all New Mexico did give,
Congratulating it upon its arrival,
Begging, with thorough reverence,
And kneeling on the ground, it would wash out
Its faults with that holy water                      325
Of precious Baptism which they brought,
With which most salutary sacrament
We saw many barbarians cleansed
When we were traveling through their lands.
There were solemn and pleasing festivals             330
Of splendid men on horseback,
And in honor of that illustrious day
A gallant squadron was released
From that illustrious Captain Cárdenas,
A soldier of courage, modesty                        335
And who, O lord, has served you well.
He, thinking that the expedition
Would be unable to set out,
Remained, so that he never afterward
Could overtake this camp of yours,                   340
Wherefore his standard then was given
To Diego Núñez. And with that we then
Did take possession of that land
In your famous, heroic, lofty name,
Making some record of the case,                      345
Which it is well I give to you,
Nor skip a letter, for it imports much
As being the statement of the General himself.

### *Of how we took and seized upon possession of the new land*

In the name of the most Holy Trinity and of the individual eternal unity, deity, and majesty, Father, Son, and Holy Ghost, three persons and one single being and one single true God, who with his eternal will, omnipotent power, and infinite wisdom rules, governs, and disposes, powerfully and gently, from sea to sea, from end to end, as the beginning and end of all things, and in whose hands are the eternal Pontificate and priesthood, the empires and the kingdoms, principalities and fiefs, republics, greater and lesser, families and persons, as in the eternal Priest, Emperor and king of emperors and kings, Lord of lords, creator of the heavens and earth, elements, birds and fish, animals, plants and of all creatures, spiritual and corporal, rational and irrational, from the most supreme Cherubim to the most despised

---

1. Farfán's play, now lost, would undoubtedly be the first literary work created in what is today the United States.

ant and little butterfly; and to His honor and glory and of His most sacred and blessed Mother, the Virgin, holy Mary, our Lady, gate of heaven, ark of the Testament, in whom the manna of Heaven, the rod of divine justice and arm of God, and his law of grace and love was enclosed, as in the mother of God, sun, moon, north and guide and advocate of the human race; and to the honor of the seraphic father Saint Francis, image of Christ, God, in body and soul, his royal ensign and patriarch of the poor, whom I take for my patrons and advocates, defenders, and intercessors, that they may pray God himself that all my thoughts, sayings, and deeds may go on the road of the service of his infinite Majesty, increase of the faithful and the extension of his holy Church, and to the service of the most Christian King don Felipe, our lord, most strong pillar of the Catholic Faith, may God keep him many years, and the crown of Castile and the increase of its kingdoms and provinces.

I wish that they may know, those who now are here or in time shall be, how I, don Juan de Oñate, Governor and Captain General and Adelantado[2] of New Mexico and of its kingdoms and provinces, and of those neighboring and adjoining, settler and discoverer and pacificator of them and of the aforesaid kingdoms, for the King, our lord, I say that, inasmuch as in virtue of the nomination which of me was made and titles which his Majesty gives me, undoubtedly, as such Governor, Captain General and Adelantado of the aforesaid kingdoms and provinces, beside other greater which he promises me by virtue of his Royal Ordinances and by two Royal Decrees and two other second Royal orders and chapters of the letters of the King, our lord, its date in Valencia the twenty-sixth of January of the year one thousand five hundred and eighty-six, its date in San Lorenzo on the nineteenth of July of the year one thousand five hundred and eighty-nine, its date the sixteenth of January of the year one thousand five hundred and ninety-three, its date the twenty-first of June of the year one thousand five hundred and ninety-five, and by another final Royal Decree, its date the second of April of this past year of one thousand five hundred and ninety-seven, in which, in opposition to certain opinions, his Majesty approves the choice made of my person and estate, exercising and continuing my said office and now come in claim of the aforesaid kingdoms and provinces with my chief officers, captains, ensigns, and people of peace and war, to populate and pacify, and other great number of necessary apparatus, carts, wagons, buggies,[3] horses, oxen, major cattle and other cattle, and many of my aforesaid people married, so that I find myself today with all my camp entire and with more people than I took from the province of Santa Bárbola, beside the river that they call of the North and lodged on the bank, which is a place neighboring and adjoining the first towns of New Mexico, and the aforesaid river passes through them, and I have left a road made open for wagons, wide and flat, so that it is possible without difficulty to go and come by it, after having gone on foot through a hundred leagues of uninhabited land; and because I wish to take possession of the land today, the day of the Ascension of our Lord, which is counted thirty days in the month of April of this present year of one thousand five hundred and ninety-eight,

2. Governor of a border province. [Anthology editors' note]

3. Villagrá has *rasas*, which may be short for *carrozas* [coaches].

through the person of Juan Pérez de Donís, Notary of his Majesty and Secretary of the journey and government of the aforesaid kingdoms and provinces, in the voice and name of the most Christian King, our lord, don Felipe, the Second of this name, and of his successors, may they be many and with the highest felicity, and for the crown of Castile and kings whose glorious stock may reign in it, and by the aforesaid and for the aforesaid my government, basing myself and resting on the unique and absolute power and jurisdiction which the eternal, highest, Pontiff and King, Jesus Christ, son of the living God, universal head of the Church and first and only institutor of its sacraments, base and cornerstone of the Old and New Testaments, foundation and perfection of it, has in heaven and earth, not only as to God and consubstantial with his eternal Father, who as creator of all things is the only absolute, natural, and proprietary lord of them, who as such can make and unmake, order and dispose according to his will and what he may consider good, but also as to man, to whom his eternal Father, as such, and as being the son of man, and for his dolorous and painful death and triumphant and glorious Resurrection and Ascension and the special title of universal Redeemer which he gained thereby, gave omnipotent power, jurisdiction and dominion, civil and criminal, high and low scaffold,[4] and simple mixed empire,[5] in the Kingdom of Heaven and in the kingdoms of the earth, and in whose hands he put the weight and measure, judicature, reward and penalty, of the universal globe, making him not only King and Judge, but also universal shepherd of the sheep, faithful and unfaithful, of those who today believe in and follow his voice and are within his fold and Christian people, and of those who have not heard his voice and Evangelical word, not to the day of today know him, whom he says it suits him to bring to his divine acquaintance, because they are his and he is their legitimate and universal shepherd, for which, having to ascend unto his eternal Father in corporal presence, he had to leave and he left as his Vicar and substitute the prince of the Apostles, Saint Peter and other successors, legitimately chosen, to whom he gave and left the kingdom, power and empire and the keys of Heaven, according to and as the same Christ God received them from his eternal Father, in him, as its head and universal lord, and in the others, as in his successors, servants, ministers, and vicars, and so he left them not only the ecclesiastical jurisdiction and spiritual monarchy, but also he left them habitually temporal jurisdiction and monarchy, and the one arm and the other and the two-edged sword, so that through themselves or through the means of their children, the emperors and kings, when and as might seem suitable to them, for urgent cause, they might reduce the aforesaid jurisdiction and temporal monarchy to fact and put it into execution as soon as the occasion and necessity should be offered they execute it, using the entire temporal power of the secular arm and power as well by itself as by fleets and armies on land and sea, in his own and in different and barbarous nations, with the pennons, banners, and Imperial standard of the Cross, subjecting the barbarous nations, leveling the way for the evangelical preachers, assuring their lives, avenging the injuries which they once received, might receive, restraining and checking the

4. This legal formula indicates the power to impose the death penalty.

5. This refers to the power both to exercise justice and to delegate the same to judges.

impetus and bestial and barbarous wildness of the aforementioned; and in the name of the powerful Christ God who ordered his Evangel preached to all the world, and by his authority and right extending the boundaries of the Christian Republic and amplifying its Empire also by the hand of the aforesaid its sons, emperors, and kings, among whom the King don Felipe, our lord, King of Castile and of Portugal and of the Oriental and Occidental Indies, discovered and to be discovered, found and to be found, under the aforesaid power, jurisdiction and Apostolic and Pontifical Monarchy transferred, conceded, and handed over, entrusted and charged upon the Kings of Castile and Portugal and to their successors since the time of the supreme Pontiff Alexander the Sixth, by divine and singular inspiration, as Christian piety teaches that he infallibly is, since God to his Vicar, who represents his person and supplies his place in such grave things, never fails, and true experience, master, and proof of the truth, has shown for long periods, which testifies with infallible certitude to the consent, permission, and confirmation of the above-mentioned empire and dominion of the Oriental Indies and Occidental in the Kingdoms of Castile and Portugal and their successors, transferred and placed by the hands of the Church militant of all the other Supreme Pontiffs, successors to the aforesaid most holy Pontiff of glorious memory, Alexander the Sixth, up to the present day, upon which solid foundation I strive to take the aforesaid possession of these kingdoms and provinces in the aforesaid name, for which are alleged, as bases and pillars of this edifice, many other grave, urgent, and notorious causes and reasons, which move me to it, and oblige me and give secure entry; and with the aid of God and of his blessed Mother and of the standard of his holy Cross, by means of the evangelical preachers, sons of my seraphic Father Saint Francis, giving much safer, more prosperous, happy success, and the first and of no less consideration for the present case is the innocent death of the preachers of the holy Evangel, true sons of Saint Francis, Fray Juan de Santa María, Fray Francisco López and Fray Agustín Ruiz,[6] first discoverers of this land after that great Father Fray Marcos de Niza,[7] who all gave their lives and blood, as first fruits of the holy Evangel,[8] in it, whose death was innocent and undeserved, for, being once received by these Indians and admitted into their Pueblos and houses and the aforesaid monks remaining alone among them to preach to them the word of God and to better understand their language, trusting the safety of the good appearance and treatment that was shown them, and having come on all occasions to do good to these natives, so in all the time that the few Spaniards who were with them, who were only eight, remained in the land, as they were afterward alone, against the law of nature they gave evil for good and death to the other men as they, innocent and doing them no harm and who gave them what best they could and tried to give them life through the word of the law of grace more advantageously, cause and reason, were there no other, to justify my pretension, beside which the improvement, correction, and punishment of the unnatural sins and the inhumanity which among these bestial nations is found, which it seems proper to my King and Prince, as so powerful a lord, to correct and repress, and to

---

6. Villagrá errs. Fray Agustín Rodríguez. ° ° °
7. See p. 37. [Anthology editors' note]
8. Villagrá forgets the martyrs resulting from the

Coronado expedition: Fray Juan de Padilla, Fray Luis de Escalona, and Fray Juan de la Cruz. ° ° °

me in his Royal name give hand to the present act, and without them the pious course and most Christian opinion of Baptism and salvation of souls of as many children as among these faithless parents at present live and are born, who to their true Father God and chief Father neither obey or recognize, nor can, morally speaking, recognize except through this means, as long experience in these lands has shown, and when they can recognize him, entering through the door of baptism, they cannot preserve the faith nor persevere in their vocation among a people idolatrous and unfaithful, against whose will this work must be done because the will of God is that all be saved and to all shall come the sound and effects of his word and Passion, and God should be obeyed and not men, although they be judges or parents or if they have kingdoms or cities, for but one soul is more precious than all the world nor its commands, riches, and properties; and without these there are other evident causes on which I base myself for this effect, such as the great temporal good, as the spiritual has no price, that these barbarous nations with our commerce and treatment may acquire and gain in their political affairs and government of their cities, living like reasonable folk in modesty and understanding, increasing their professions and arts, mechanic and some the liberal, augmenting their republics with new cattle, livestock, and seeds, vegetables and provisions, clothing and fruits, and ordering discreetly the economic affairs of their families, houses, and persons, the naked being clothed and the now-clothed bettering themselves; and leaving other causes, finally, in being governed in peace and justice, with safety in their homes and on their highways, and defended and sheltered from their enemies by hand and at the expense of so powerful a king, subjection to whom is true advantage and liberty, and to have in him an own father who at his cost and by means of his pay and mercy to such remote lands sends them preachers and ministers, justice and protection, with instructions truly of a father, of peace, concord, suavity, and love, which I shall preserve at cost of my life and I order and shall always order that it be kept under pain of same. And therefore, based on the aforesaid solid foundation, I wish to take the aforesaid possession, and doing so, in the presence of the most reverend Father Fray Alonso Martínez, of the Order of the lord Saint Francis, the Commissary Apostolic, *cum plenitudine potestatis*,[9] of this journey into New Mexico and its provinces, and of the most reverend Fathers, preachers of the holy Evangel, his companions, Fray Francisco de San Miguel, Fray Francisco de Zamora, Fray Juan de Rosas, Fray Alonso de Lugo, Fray Andrés Corchado, Fray Juan Claros and Fray Cristóbal de Salazar, and of my beloved Fathers and brothers, Fray Juan de Buenaventura and Fray Pedro de Vergara, lay friars, monks, who go on this journey and conversion, and of my general Army Master, don Juan de Zaldívar Oñate, and of the chief officers and of the greater part of the Captains and officers of the camp and of the people of peace and war of it, I say that in the voice and in the name of the most Christian King Don Felipe, our lord, only defender and protector of the Holy Mother Church and its true son, and for the crown of Castile and of the kings who

9. With all that he can ever do (Latin). [Anthology editors' note]

of his glorious stock may reign in it, and for the aforesaid my government I take and seize one, two, and three times, one, two, and three times, one, two, and three times, and all those which I can and ought, the Royal tenancy and possession, actual, civil, and criminal, at this aforesaid River of the North, without excepting anything and without any limitation, with the meadows, glens, and their pastures and watering places. And I take this aforesaid possession, and I seize upon it, in the voice and name of the other lands, towns, cities, villas, castles, and strong houses and dwellings, which are now founded in the said kingdoms and provinces of New Mexico, and those neighboring to them, and shall in future time be founded in them, with their mountains, rivers and banks, waters, pastures, meadows, glens, watering places, and all its Indian natives, who in it may be included and comprehended, and with the civil and criminal jurisdiction, high and low, gallows and knife, mere mixed power, from the leaf on the mountain to the rock in the river and sands of it, and from the rock and sands of the river to the leaf on the mountain.[1]

And I, the said Juan Pérez de Donís, notary of his Majesty and above mentioned secretary, certify and give faith that the said Lord Governor, Captain General and Adelantado of the aforesaid kingdoms, in sign of the true and peaceful possession and continuing the acts of it, he set and nailed, with his own hands, on a fixed tree prepared for the purpose, the holy Cross of our Lord Jesus Christ, and returning to it, his knees on the ground, he said: "Holy Cross, who art the divine gate of Heaven, altar of the only and essential sacrifice of the body and blood of the Son of God, road of the saints and possession of their glory, open the gate of Heaven to these infidels, found the church and altars upon which are offered the body and blood of the Son of God, open for us a road of safety and peace for their conversion and our conversion, and give our King, and me in his Royal name, peaceful possession of these kingdoms and provinces, for His holy glory. Amen." And then, immediately, he fixed and set himself, with his own hands, the Royal standard, the Arms of the most Christian King don Felipe, our lord; on the one side the Imperial, and on the other the Royal; and at the time and when he placed it, and did the aforementioned, the trumpet sounded and the musketry fired with most great demonstration of joy, accordingly as notoriously appeared. And his Lordship, the said Governor, Captain General and Adelantado, for perpetual memory, ordained that there be authorized and sealed with the great seal of his office and signed and marked with my name and signet, be kept with his papers of the journey and government, and be taken from this original such transcripts as might be desired, setting it down in the Book of the Government; and he signed it with his name, being witnesses the above-mentioned, most revered Father Commissary Fray Alonso Martínez, the Apostolic Commissary, Fray Francisco de San Miguel, Fray Francisco de Zamora, Fray Juan de Rosas, Fray Alonso de Lugo, Fray Andrés Corchado, Fray Juan Claros, Fray Cristóbal de Salazar, Fray Juan de Buenaventura, Fray Pedro de Vergara and don Juan de Zaldívar Oñate, my Army Master general, and the other major officers, captains, and soldiers of the army aforesaid, the aforesaid day of the Ascension of

---

1. Villagrá's excerpt from the *Requerimiento* ends here. [Anthology editors' note]

the Lord, thirtieth and last of April of the year of one thousand five hundred and ninety-eight.

*This possession taken, the next day the camp began to march, to pass over the River of the North, in the form we shall state.*

1610

---

# FRAY EUSEBIO FRANCISCO KINO
## 1645–1711

The exploration of Arizona is very much linked to the exploration of New Mexico, in particular to the early, feverish expeditions of Fray Marcos de Niza (1538) and Francisco Vázquez Coronado (1540–42). In searching for the mythological Seven Cities of Cíbola and Quivira, these expeditions opened the way into lands never before seen by European eyes. In 1604, Juan de Oñate traversed Arizona in a delirious search for the coast of California and the phantasmagoric Strait of Anián. A more stabilizing force, however, was Fray Eusebio Francisco Kino. By erecting missions in the Sonora area of northern Mexico and of southern Arizona—in places where the landscapes' spectacular beauty continues to draw the faithful— Kino established a firm foundation for the settlement and colonization of the region.

Kino was born in Segno, Tirol, in what is now Italy. After a serious illness in his youth, he dedicated himself to the mission life, and in 1665 he joined the Society of Jesus (Jesuits). Although he wanted to undertake missionary work in China, in 1678 he was commissioned to serve in New Spain, and he arrived there in 1681. His first assignment was in the Lower California desert. Soon he was transferred to Pimería Alta, the northern Sonora area of what is now southern Arizona, where in 1687 he founded his first mission, Nuestra Señora de los Dolores (Our Lady of the Sorrows).

Thereafter, during his 23 years among the Pima Indians in Pimería Alta, Kino established more than 40 missions, including San Ignacio de Caburica, San José de Imuris, Santiago de Cocospero, Santa María Magdalena, and San Xavier del Bac. In addition to bringing Catholicism to the Indians, Kino aided the Pimas in fighting off the continual attacks of the Apache Indians. He also introduced European agricultural products such as wheat and animals such as horses, cattle, and sheep. Thus he established meat farming and dairy production in Arizona, where both industries still flourish.

Kino's missionary work is surpassed only by his explorations of the Arizona desert. He explored the Gila River, the Rio Grande, and the Colorado River, and is credited with being the first European to discover, in 1698, that Baja California is a peninsula and not, as many had conjectured, an island. On his numerous journeys, Kino's training as a mathematician, a cartographer, and a cosmographer enabled him to map the Arizona region, and the map he published in 1705 served as the best reference source for the area until the nineteenth century.

His autobiographical work *Favores celestiales de Jesús y de María Santísima y del Gloriosísimo Apóstol de las Yndias, San Francisco Xavier, experimentados en las nuevas conquistas y nuevas conversiones del nuevo reino de la Nueva Navarra de esta*

*América septentional incógnita, y pasa por la tierra a la California en 35 grados de altura* (Celestial Favors of Jesus and of Mary Most Holy and of the Most Glorious Apostle of the Indies, San Francisco Xavier, Experienced in the New Conquests and New Conversions of This Kingdom of New Navarra of This Unknown North America and Passing by Land onto the California at 35 Degrees High) was translated by Herbert Eugene Bolton in 1919 as *Kino's Historical Memoir of Pimería Alta: A Contemporary Account of the Beginnings of California, Sonora, and Arizona by Father Eusebio Francisco Kino, S.J. Pioneer Missionary Explorer, Cartographer, and Ranchman—1683–1711.* Dedicated to King Philip V, the text narrates Kino's experiences in the Southwest, featuring the letters and reports Kino had written during the mission-building and colonization processes in Sonora and Arizona. As Kino explains, the work's main inspiration was the Royal *Cédulas*, issued by the Spanish kings. These edicts required the missionaries to make reports to the Crown regarding the progress of exploration and colonization efforts, specifically the conversions of and efforts to "civilize" the Indians. The kings' extension of the Spanish Empire throughout the Americas was seen as being justified by the missionaries' imparting of spiritual benefits, in the form of Catholic doctrine, to the Indians. Kino thus presents both the natural wealth of the Pimería Alta and his great success in bringing the Indians into the Catholic faith. For example, the title of the first part of *Favores celestiales* focuses on the conversion of the Indians and the prosperity this conversion can bring to the Spanish Crown in the form of new kingdoms; it can be translated as

> Report and Relation of the New Conversions of This North America Which Comprise More than Two Hundred Leagues of Fertile Country, and Extend to the Recently Discovered Land Route to California, Which Is Not an Island but a Peninsula, and Is Very Populous, and to the Very Large Río Colorado, Which is the True Río del Norte of the Ancients; with New Maps of These Nations and of This North America, Which Hitherto Has Been Regarded as Unknown. Likewise, of the Very Great Advantage to Both Majesties Which Even at Small Cost to the Royal Treasury Can Be Secured by Sending Father Laborers in the Royal Service to These New Conversions, in Which, in the Opinion of Prudent Persons, Can Be Formed a New Kingdom, Which Can Be called Kingdom of New Navarre

The following selections are chapters from the first three books of Kino's work. Included in chapter 2 of book 1 is the Royal *Cédula* signed by Charles II on May 14, 1686. This document states the king's great interest in the conversion of the Indians and his concern for their proper treatment (i.e., they were not to be required to pay tribute, to work in the mines, or to perform other forced labor) because mistreatment interfered with their conversion. Chapters 9–11 of book 3 describe how the Pima, after being falsely accused of murdering Fray Xavier Saeta and four Opata Indian servants on April 2, 1695, revolted and began to burn missions in retaliation for the affront and their unjust punishment.

# [From Memoir of Pimería Alta][1]

## From Book I. First Entry into Pimería, and the Beginnings of Its Spiritual and Temporal Conquest, and of Its Conversion to Our Holy Catholic Faith

### Chapter I. Because of the Suspension of the Conquest and Conversion of California, Two Alms Are Asked for and Obtained from the Royal Treasury for Two Missionary Fathers for This Coast and Mainland Nearest to California

The enterprise of the conquest and conversion of California, in which I took part for more than two years, with two other fathers of the Company, with the offices of superior, or rector, and of cosmographer of his Majesty, may God preserve him, having been suspended,[2] for twelve years and going on thirteen I have been in this extensive Pimería, which has a length from north to south of more than one hundred leagues,[3] reaching from the province and valleys of Sonora almost to the province of Moqui, and a width of as many and even more leagues from east to west, from the land of the Jocomes, Janos, Sumas, Apaches, etc., to the arm of the Sea of California.[4] For, on the occasion of this suspension, I asked of the father provincial, who at the time was Father Luis del Canto,[5] permission to come to the heathen people of these coasts nearest to the above mentioned California, and when his Reverence said to me that there were no alms from his Majesty for this purpose, I told him that if he would give me permission I would ask them of his Excellency. He replied that I should make a report, and with it and one of his own his Reverence asked and obtained two alms for two persons. With one I came at once to this Pimeria, and with the other Father Adán Gil came later to the neighboring Seris. When these alms were conceded, the fiscal of his Majesty, Don Pedro de la Bastilla, may God preserve him, asserted that these coasts would afford the best opportunity possible for continuing afterwards from here with the conquest and conversion of California. Leaving Mexico on November 20, 1686, just after Father Bernabé de Soto had come as provincial, I went to Guadalaxara,[6] whence I set out on December 16, having obtained from the Royal Audiencia the royal provision and the inserted royal cédula which is given in the following chapter.

1. Translated by Herbert Eugene Bolton. Except as indicated, all footnotes are Bolton's. The anthology editors have transposed one of Bolton's notes and omitted his more technical ones. Within the text, bracketed insertions are Bolton's. Within the notes, bracketed insertions are the anthology editors'.
2. The reference is to the attempt of [the Spanish admiral Isidro de] Atondo y Antillón to subdue California, 1683–1685. ° ° °
3. Approximately 260 miles (a Spanish league then equaling about 2.6 miles). [Anthology editors' note]
4. Or the Gulf of California, which separates the Baja California peninsula and mainland Mexico. [Anthology editors' note]

The Janos and Jocomes, now extinct, dwelt between Casas Grandes, Chihuahua, and the Gila. [The anthropologist and historian Adolph F.] Bandelier regarded them as the most southern band of Apaches, and as a composite of broken down tribes. Mission were early established among them at Janos and Carretas. ° ° ° They became absorbed in the main Apache nation. [Bolton's note]
5. Luis del Canto was provincial [i.e., superior of a province of a Catholic religious order] in New Spain, 1683–1686. He was succeeded by Father Bernabé Soto, long a missionary among the Tepehuanes [a native people in northwest Mexico]. ° ° °
6. Old spelling for the Mexican city of Guadalajara. [Anthology editors' note]

## Chapter II. Royal Provision and Royal *Cédula* Which Favor the New Conversions

At the suggestion of the father provincial, Luis del Canto, and of the father provincial elect, Bernabé de Soto, I asked for and obtained from the Royal Audiencia of Guadalaxara, through the very Catholic zeal of the Señor president, Don Alonso Sevallos y Billa Gutierres, and of the Señor judge Don Christobal de la Palma, a royal provision to the effect that during five years no natives whatever should be taken out with seals[7] to work, from the places where I should go for their conversion. I requested this royal provision at a very opportune time, for there had just arrived from Spain the very Catholic royal *cédula* which orders that for twenty years recent converts to our holy faith shall not be taken away with seals. This royal *cédula* is dated at Buen Retiro, May 14, of the said year of 1686. It is so very Catholic and so favorable to the new conquests and new conversions that I will insert here some of its notable paragraphs.

Well, then, our most Catholic monarch, Don Carlos II, may God preserve him many most happy years, writes as follows:

ROYAL CÉDULA. Whereas,[8] in my Royal Council of the Indies information has been received that twenty-four leagues from Mexico the tribes of heathen Indians begin and that they continue without interruption through the provinces of Nueva España Nueva Galicia, Nueva Biscaya, Nueva México, etc., and that care is not given to their conversion; and since this is the first and principal obligation of the ministers, to whose fulfillment they should give very particular care and attention, so that the neglect and omission which even here have been noted and experienced may not continue; since for this conversion no escort of soldiers is needed, as the natives show no resistance, and as some nations and districts assist with others; since this care is the first obligation of the Council, and is kept prominently in mind by it, as in the eighth ordinance I have charged it to do; and wishing to satisfy its conscience, in so far as it may be concerned, as I have satisfied my own by fulfilling so important an obligation, and by applying all means, endeavors, and requests possible, in order to secure the execution of a thing that is so serviceable to God, our Lord, who, in his great providence, always returns a very great and notable increase to my monarchy for what is spent from my royal estate in these new conversions; and wishing to comply with this obligation, which I regard as the principal one of my great desire, I have agreed to issue the present *cédula*, by which I order and command my viceroy of Nueva España and the presidents and judges of my Royal Audiencias of Mexico, Guadalaxara, and Guatemala, and the governors of Nueva Biscaya, that as soon as they shall receive this my *cédula* they shall exercise very especial care and application to the end that all the tribes of heathen Indians which may be found in the district and

---

7. Official permission; i.e., permits. [Anthology editors' note]
8. A comparison of this copy of the *cédula* with the official copy ° ° ° shows that Kino has omitted numerous phrases of the original, as nonessential to his point, and has paraphrased others. ° ° °

jurisdiction comprised in the government of each audiencia and government district, may be reduced and converted to our holy Catholic faith, each one providing, in so far as concerns him, that from now on their reduction and conversion be undertaken with the mildest and most effective means that can be employed and contrived, entrusting it to the ecclesiastics most satisfactory to them and of the virtue and spirit required for so very important a matter, giving to them for the purpose the assistance, favor, and aid that may be necessary, and encouraging them in it in the best manner possible, and promising in my name to all new converts that during the first twenty years of their reduction they will not be required to give tribute or to serve on estates or in mines, since this is one of the reasons why they refuse to be converted. And I charge my ministers to notify me at once of the receipt of this dispatch, of what may be done in virtue thereof, and of the condition which this matter may be assuming, so that upon receipt of this information the orders most important for its continuation may be given, because I desire that all time possible be gained in a matter of such importance and so serviceable to God and to me. Done at Buen Retiro, May 14, 1686.          I, ᴛʜᴇ Kɪɴɢ.

## Chapter III. My Arrival at These Missions of Sonora, and My First Entry into This Pimería, with the Father Visitor, Manuel Gonzales

With this royal provision and royal *cédula*, which by its admirable Catholic zeal might well and should astonish and edify the whole world, I came in February of 1687 to these missions of Sonora, and went to Opossura to see and talk with the father visitor, who then was Father Manuel Gonzales. I found in his Reverence such charity and so holy a zeal for the welfare of souls, that his Reverence in person came at once more than fifty leagues' journey to this pueblo of Nuestra Señora de los Dolores, which is five leagues from the old mission of Cucurpe, of the rectorate of San Francisco Xavier de Sonora. On the way we passed by the mining town of San Juan[9] and saw the Señor alcalde mayor, who, with the great respectfulness that characterizes him, gave obedience to the royal *cédula* and to the royal provision. Coming by the valley of Sonora we saw the father rector of the mission or rectorate, who then was Father Juan Muños de Burgos, and by the valley and pueblo of Opodepe, Tuape, and Cocorpe,[1] divisions or pueblos then administered by Father Josep[h] de Aguilar; and on the thirteenth of March, 1687, we three Fathers together came to Nuestra Señora de los Dolores del Bamotze, or de Cosari, having the day before notified the natives. Their governor was absent, but, nevertheless, they received us with all love, for, months and years before they had asked for fathers and holy baptism.

---

9. Real de San Juan was situated some forty leagues eastward from Dolores, and an equal distance southward of Arizpe. It was at this time the seat of government of the alcaldía [alcalde] mayor of Sonora.

1. Cucurpe was the frontier mission of Sonora at this time. * * * The place, still in existence, is a few miles south of the site of mission Dolores, in the San Miguel River Valley.

The following day the father visitor, leaving us fathers and the children with a very paternal goodbye, returned toward Oposura to the necessary occupations of Holy Week,[2] etc., suggesting to Father Aguilar and me that we should see later if there was opportunity to go somewhat further inland to seek and find a place where a second pueblo might be founded.

## Chapter IV. Expedition to San Ygnacio de Caborica, San Joseph de Los Himiris, and Nuestra Señora de Los Remedios

Upon this advice of the father visitor we at once, the very same day, went inland to the west, and after going ten leagues found the very good post of Caborica, inhabited by affable people, which by order of the father visitor we named San Ygnacio. Then, turning to the north, we found another good post, with plenty of docile and domesticated people. This place we named San Joseph de los Himires. To the east we found another, likewise of industrious Indians, which we named Nuestra Señora de los Remedios. It is distant from Nuestra Señora de los Dolores seven leagues, to the north. In all places they received with love the Word of God for the sake of their eternal salvation. We returned, thanks to the Lord, safe and rejoicing, to Nuestra Señora de los Dolores.[3] Father Aguilar went on to Cucurpe, and I began to catechize the people and to baptize children. The governor of Nuestra Señora de los Dolores came from inland and by him and others I sent to various and even remote parts of this Pimeria divers messages and friendly invitations, requesting that they should endeavor likewise to become Christians, saying that for them would be the good and the advantage, for I had come to aid them in order that they might be eternally saved.

## Chapter V. First Opposition Experienced in This New Conversion

Being always very much aided in everything by the great charity of Father Joseph de Aguilar, by Divine grace everything went, on the part of the natives, with entire prosperity, pleasantness, and satisfaction, and there were welcome additions,[4] but on the part of others there was no lack of hostility, which has endured up to the present day. A false report was despatched to the Señor alcalde mayor of the mining town of San Juan, that these natives, on the coming of the father missionary, had moved far away. These serious but false reports reached the father visitor, Manuel Gonzales, troubling his Reverence greatly, and he wrote to Tuape, where the three fathers, Joseph de Aguilar, Antonio de Roxas, and I were holding Holy Week, with more than one hundred Pimas of this new pueblo of Nuestra Señora de los Dolores. Of

2. Holy Week [in Christianity, a commemoration of the last week of Jesus Christ's life] in 1687 fell between March 23 and March 30.
3. On March 26 (Kino, Letter of May 13, 1687).

4. By May 13, 1687, Kino had baptized at Dolores thirty children and youths, including two sons of the cacique [tribal chief]. Before the end of April he had built a chapel [and a parsonage].

the Pimas there were about forty[5] recently baptized infants and children, whom the Spanish ladies of the mining town of Opodepe dressed richly and adorned with their ornaments and best jewels, like new Christians, for the Procession of the Blessed Sacrament, to the great delight of all; nor was there the least truth in the pretended withdrawal of the natives, which so falsely was reported to the mining town of San Juan. All this we wrote to the father visitor for his consolation, we three fathers signing the letter.

## Chapter VI. Second Opposition and Discord Sown in Pimería

Returning from Holy Week and Easter at Tuape to Nuestra Señora de los Dolores, I went inland to San Ygnacio and San Joseph de los Himires, where in all places things were going very well, in spiritual and temporal matters, in Christian teaching, beginnings of baptisms, buildings, planting of crops, etc., but in Nuestra Señora de los Remedios I found the people so disconsolate that they said to me openly that they neither wished to be Christians nor to have a missionary father. On asking them why, they answered me, first, because they had heard it said that the fathers ordered the people hanged and killed; second, because they required so much labor and sowing for their churches that no opportunity was left the Indians to sow for themselves; third, because they pastured so many cattle that the watering places were drying up; fourth, because they killed the people with the holy oils; fifth, because they deceived the Indians with false promises and words, and because I had falsely said that I had a letter or royal *cédula* of the king our Sovereign, whereas I had no such letter, for if I had I would have shown it to the Señor lieutenant of Bacanuche. These chimeras, discords, and altercations disturbed me very much, but I recognized at once whence they might have come; and although the father visitor and I had shown the royal provision which I carried, with the royal *cédula* inserted, to the Señor alcalde mayor in the mining town of San Juan, which was sufficient there, within two days (on the tenth of May) I went with the justices[6] of Nuestra Señora de los Dolores to the mining town of Bacanuche,[7] which is twenty leagues away. I showed the royal provision and the royal *cédula* to the Señor lieutenant, Captain Francisco Pacheco Zevallos, in whom I found all kindness, and told him of what had happened in Nuestra Señora de los Remedios because of the untruths which had been spread so falsely during the preceding days against the fathers. And gradually things were remedied and the calumnies of the malicious and of the common enemy hushed, and although there was no lack of stories and pretended dangers from persons of little loyalty, the natives of this Pimeria became so inclined to our holy faith that from places further inland, from El Tupo, El Tubutama, and other parts, they asked for fathers and holy baptism.

5. It seems that Kino took his neophytes from Dolores to Tuape to celebrate Holy Week. * * *
6. These were evidently native officials.
7. Bacanuche, a *real*, or mining camp, about

twenty leagues northeast of Dolores and the same distance north of Arizpe and south of Cananea. It is situated on the Bacanuche River, a branch of the Sonora.

From *Book II. Visit and Triennium of the Father Visitor Juan María Salvatierra, 1690, 1691, 1692*

## Chapter VII. Second and Third Expeditions to the Sea of California

FEBRUARY, 1694. In February, 1694, I made another expedition to the same waters of the Sea of California, in company with Father Marcos Antonio Kapus, who was stationed in Cucurpe, and Lieutenant Juan Matheo Manje. We again saw very clearly the same California and its principal and larger hills. We named them San Marcos, San Matheo, San Juan (for the name of San Lucas is already given to the Cape of California), and San Antonio, as may be seen on the map. The natives of the nation of El Soba we found so friendly that, having come thirty, forty, and fifty leagues' journey from the north to see us, they gave us their infants to baptize.

A few months later[1] I made another expedition with Lieut. Juan Matheo Manje, to this nation and to the sea, and we discovered the good port of Santa Sabina on the day of that saint.

During these months and the preceding ones there was built in La Concepción del Caborica a capacious earth-covered hall of adobe and earth, and wheat and maize were sown for the father whom they were asking for and hoping to obtain.

## Chapter VIII. Expedition or Mission to the North and Northwest for More than One Hundred Leagues, as Far as to the Rio Grande and the Casa Grande, and the Discovery of the Two New Nations, the Opa and the Cocomaricopa

In November, 1694, I went inland with my servants and some justices of this Pimería, as far as the *casa grande*, as these Pimas call it, which is on the large River of Hila that flows out of Nuevo México and has its source near Acoma. This river and this large house and the neighboring houses are forty-three leagues beyond and to the northwest of the Sobaipuris of San Francisco Xavier del Bac. The first ranchería, that of El Tusonimo, we named La Encarnación, as we arrived there to say mass on the first Sunday in Advent;[2] and because many other Indians came to see us from the ranchería of El Coatoydag, which was four leagues further on, we named the latter San Andrés, as the following day was the feast of that holy apostle. All were affable and docile people. They told us of two friendly nations living further on, all down the river to the west, and to the northwest on the Río Azul, and still further, on the Río Colorado. These nations are the Opas

---

1. This was evidently the third expedition of 1694. * * *
2. The period that runs through the first four Sundays before Christmas, observed by some Christians as a season of prayer and fasting in celebration of the Incarnation—or unity of divinity and humanity—of Jesus Christ. [Anthology editors' note]

and Cocomaricopas. They speak a language very different [from that of the Pimas], though it is very clear, and as there were some who knew both languages very well, I at once and with ease made a vocabulary of the said tongue, and also a map of those lands, measuring the sun with the astrolabe.

The *casa grande* is a four-story building, as large as a castle and equal to the largest church in these lands of Sonora. It is said that the ancestors of Montezuma deserted and depopulated it, and, beset by the neighboring Apaches, left for the east or Casas Grandes, and that from there they turned towards the south and southwest, finally founding the great city and court of Mexico. Close to this *casa grande* there are thirteen smaller houses, somewhat more dilapidated, and the ruins of many others, which make it evident that in ancient times there had been a city here. On this occasion and on later ones I have learned and heard, and at times have seen, that further to the east, north, and west there are seven or eight more of these large old houses and the ruins of whole cities, with many broken *metates*[3] and jars, charcoal, etc. These certainly must be the Seven Cities mentioned by the holy man, Fray Marcos de Niza,[4] who in his long pilgrimage came clear to the Bacapa ranchería of these coasts, which is about sixty leagues southwest from this *casa grande,* and about twenty leagues from the Sea of California. The guides or interpreters must have given his Reverence the information which he has in his book concerning these Seven Cities, although certainly at that time, and for a long while before, they must have been deserted. The natives and children of the Pimas, Opas, and Cocomaricopas were very well pleased.

## From *Book III. Arrival of the Venerable Father Francisco Xavier Saeta at These New Conversions; His Apostolic Fervor, Work, Zeal, and Holy Letters; His Glorious, Innocent Death; and Various Letters Prophetic of the Great Fruit of These Conversions*

### Chapter VIII. Last Letter of Most Tender Farewell from the Venerable Father

I add the eighth and last letter, which the venerable father wrote me on April 1, a few hours before his glorious death, and which, without his knowing or suspecting it, is a most tender farewell. I received it twenty-seven hours after his holy martyrdom occurred, the news of his death itself having come two hours before. The letter is as follows:

> The great favor of your Reverence reaches me, with the rolls of bread, biscuit, etc., for which I return to your Reverence due and cordial thanks. In regard to the question of our seeing each other one of these days, your Reverence may notify me by an Indian whenever you wish me to go to the post of Santa María; for, although I am badly needed here if I leave for a moment, because I am so very busy, nevertheless, I will

3. Grinding stones. [Anthology editors' note]    4. See p. 37. [Anthology editors' note]

steal that short bit of time and, like fleet Saeta, will fly and place myself at the feet of your Reverence, to receive your commands and discuss many things. I shall be glad if the articles of clothing referred to can be brought at the time of meeting from some of these mining towns for my children, for they are limited to sackcloth, blankets, tunics, and *pisiete*.[1] I will promptly pay what they are worth, either in wheat or in silver, at the latest at wheat harvest, for here work proceeds with vigor—*feruet opus*[2]—and I realize that these attractions are very helpful for the spiritualities as well as for the temporalities. I cannot spend much time on this letter, as the bearer wishes to return. I always remain subject to the orders of your Reverence. *Vale, pater optime, et in tuis sacrificiis, tui yndignisimi famuli ne obliviscaris precor.*[3] Concepción de Nuestra Señora del Caborca, April 1, 1695. Your Reverence's humblest servant in Christ.

XAVIER SAETA.

P.S. I. Through lack of vinegar I have not yet tried my very pretty garden. I appreciate very much the kindness your Reverence does me in writing in my behalf to the superiors, and although I merit nothing except all kinds of confusion (for what I do is nothing in comparison with what I owe to the divine Majesty and to His most beloved souls), nevertheless I do not fail to be grateful for the kindness. *Vale iterum humanissime Pater et felix vive.*[4]

P.S. II. The bearer of your Reverence's letter has grieved me unspeakably by the news he brought me, to the effect that the Hocomes attacked San Pedro del Tubutama the other day and killed poor Martín and the boy Fernando, who were returning from bringing me the cattle.[5] In God's name your Reverence will tell me about what happened, as well as about Father Daniel.[6]

Thus far the venerable father in his last letter, inside; but after it was sealed he wrote me the following on the outside:

I shall be very much pleased if your Reverence receives the bundle of relics and other little things which I sent to you by Father Daniel. I received two sacks of maize by hand of the governor of Bosna. The maize could not be brought from Santa María on account of the enemies, for the news of the deaths of Martín and the boy is confirmed. Let your Reverence not lose sight of me.

Thus far the venerable father. I received this last long and most tender letter at eleven o'clock on Easter day, having received two hours before, at about nine o'clock in the morning, the sad news of his holy death.

APRIL 2, 1695. It occurred at sunrise on the morning of Holy Saturday, or Saturday of the Gloria,[7] April 2, 1695, as I will now tell in chapter nine. The news of it came in twenty-seven hours, a distance of forty-six leagues.

---

1. Tobacco. [Anthology editors' note]
2. "The work glows," i.e., proceeds with vigor (Virgil, *Aeneid*, vol. 1, line 436. *Fervet opus redolentque thymo fragrantia mella*).
3. "Farewell, most excellent Father. In your holy sacrifices do not, I pray, be unmindful of your most unworthy servant" (i.e., in your Masses) [Latin].
4. "Again, farewell, most kindly Father, and be

happy" [Latin].
5. The Hocome (or Jocome), Janos, Suma, Manso, and Apache peoples were stealing livestock from communities in northern Sonora and Nueva Vizcaya. The Pima were often falsely accused of these crimes. [Anthology editors' note]
6. Father Daniel Januske.
7. The Saturday before Easter. [Anthology editors' note]

## Chapter IX. Concerning Three Other Murders Committed in San Pedro del Tubutama

The disturbances and murders which the venerable father mentions in his last letter, and which were attributed to the Jocomes, were not committed by them, but by the Tubutamas themselves, and later, by some others, disgusted, very much stirred up, and irritated at certain bad treatment and new and old severities, and even at some murders in the west and in the north. Those malcontents went to take vengeance on La Concepción, destroying almost all the mission. It is evident that the three murders which took place in El Tubutama on March 29, four days before the death of the venerable father—namely, those of three Opata Indians, Antonio, the herdsman of El Tubutama, Martín and the boy Fernando, who were returning from La Concepción, were committed by the Tubutamas because of the harsh and choleric treatment with which, many times, the said Opata Indian Antonio abused and beat the Pima Indians of El Tubutama. For, on the same day, March 29, Holy Tuesday, he knocked down on the ground and wounded with spur thrusts the overseer of the farm, who cried out to his relatives, "This Opata is killing me;" whereupon the rest of the Pimas shot two arrows at him. Nevertheless, he mounted a horse and fled to the pueblo. They followed and killed him, plundered the other Opata Indians named, burned the house and little church of the venerable father, and killed many cattle, etc., as the father had set out a few hours before for San Ygnacio and Cucurpe with the news of all this.

And it seems that some of these disturbers went to the neighboring ranchería of San Antonio del Vquitoa, eight leagues to the southwest, and the malcontents there, together with others, about forty in all, planned to do the same thing [in Pitquin], which is distant about twelve leagues, the common enemy and others, their following, coöperating to the complete obstruction of our holy faith. On the first day of April these forty-odd sinners came down to San Diego del Pitquin, which is three leagues from La Concepción, and arranged to commit very early on the following morning the sacrilegious iniquities which in fact they so barbarously did commit against the person of the venerable father, his property, and his four servants, Opatas and strangers.

## Chapter X. Happy and Glorious Death of the Venerable Father Francisco Xavier Saeta and of His Four Servants, and the Plundering of His House

At sunrise on Saturday of the Gloria, April 2, 1695, these forty-odd malefactors from San Antonio del Vquitoa entered the house of the venerable father, apparently in peace, but with their bows and arrows. They talked to the venerable father and he with them, and bade them good-bye in a friendly way. They went out, the venerable father accompanying them to the door of the spacious hall, where he at once discovered the evil purpose of the sacrilegists, and although the venerable father called the captain of La Concepción, through fear of the armed people he failed to approach. Then the venerable father knelt down in the very door of his hall (which was the one that still served as a little church) to receive, as he did receive, the two arrow shots, and arising with them he went in to embrace a very pretty crucifix which he had brought with him from Europe, and, seating himself on a box, on account of weakness and pain, and afterwards on the bed, bleeding, he gave his happy spirit to the sovereign Creator.

These cruel barbarians also killed the four servants of the venerable father. One was named Francisco Xavier and was a native of Vris. He served as interpreter and was married to a Pima woman of this Pimeria named Luisa, a native of the great ranchería of Mototicachi, which was so unreasonably destroyed in the year 1688. More than twenty captives were carried off from it to the mining town which they call Los Frayles, and more than fifty natives were beaten, merely because of the malicious suspicion that they were stealing stock and committing the hostilities in this province, although it is thoroughly patent now that they have been committed by the Hocomes, Xanos, Sumas, and Apaches combined, and not by these much persecuted poor Pimas of this extensive Pimería hereabout.

Therefore, his Excellency ordered that these captives should be restored to their liberty and to their nation, whereupon the said Lucía came to this pueblo of Nuestra Señora de los Dolores, where she married the above mentioned Francisco Xavier. The second of the servants was Josep[h], a very good herdsman, a native of Chinapa, who had married in Cocospera. The third was a plainsman,[8] a native of Cumpas, named Francisco. The fourth was another boy, a native of Vres, named Fernando, who had aided in taking the cattle to La Concepción. The barbarians plundered the house of the venerable father, killed and stampeded the cattle, sheep and goats, and the horse-herd, and went away leaving the people of La Concepción grief stricken. Four or five days afterward the governor of El Bosna, whom I had sent to find out in detail about all that had happened, arrived at La Concepción. As he found that the bodies of the dead were decomposing, he burned them, not being able to give them any other burial. Near the body of the venerable father he found the holy crucifix, which he was bringing to me when he met the soldiers from the presidio, who took it away from him.

## Chapter XI. Expedition of the Garrison of This Province of Sonora to Punish the Delinquents and to Remove the Body of the Venerable Father

Upon receiving the news, which I at once despatched to the superiors and to the royal justice, the Señor governor of arms, Don Domingo Jeronsa Petriz de Cruzat, responded and came at once with the soldiers of his presidio and with many friendly Indians, and accompanied by Father Agustin de Campos and Father Fernando Bayerca, for the purpose of redressing the injuries and to remove the body of the venerable father to La Concepción. But from everywhere around there the people fled through fear of the soldiers, whom they

8. *Sabanero* [can also mean cowboy, cattle drover].

had never seen before. Having killed a boy, beaten an Indian woman, and taken captive three little children whom they encountered, they gathered up the bones and ashes of the venerable father, and various papers, books, and other trifles. Returning, the Señor governor observed the day of the Holy Cross in May[9] in this new church of Nuestra Señora de los Dolores, confessing and partaking of the holy Sacrament in the morning, and in the afternoon we all proceeded to the nearby pueblo of Cucurpe. We bore the bones and ashes of the venerable father; and the Señor governor, to the great satisfaction of all, deigned to lead by the bridle the mule which bore the little box containing the bones of the venerable father. The following day the burial occurred, the father rector of this rectorate of Nuestra Señora de los Dolores, Father Marcos Antonio Kappus, singing mass.

## Chapter XII. Second and New Expedition of the Garrison and New and Greater Disturbance than Before

As all the people of El Tubutama and its vicinity, those of La Concepción, and especially the delinquents of San Antonio del Uquitoa, etc., had fled afar through fear of the garrison, the Señor governor of arms was of the opinion that he should wait a little, and that, affecting carelessness, only the chief criminals should be punished, the good Pimas who were not guilty of or accomplices in the crime cooperating. But others urged that return should be made to inflict severe punishment at once. The captain of the presidio returned with more supplies. We summoned the people, with the delinquents of El Tubutama, to make peace. The innocent ones and the justices went inland to seek out and summon the malefactors, and all came with crosses and without arms, but all were killed, both good and bad, to the number of more than fifty, among them being the governor of El Bosna and the governor of El Tupo, who with great friendliness and loyalty had labored so hard and traveled so far in hunting for the criminals, and who had aided in their punishment.

At so many murders of so many innocents, for there were only five or six of the delinquents there, the relatives of the dead were aroused and stirred up to such a degree that after the garrison had retired or gone away, they burned the houses or chapels of San Ignacio, San Joseph de los Hymires, Santa María Magdalena, and La Concepción (which at the time of the murder of the venerable father they had not burned), profaning the holy ornaments and destroying all the supplies, cattle, and horses, etc. But, happily, Father Agustin de Campos with the six soldiers who had remained with him as guard, had left, fleeing to Cucurpe and Opodepe. We were all in great straits, but I sent such quieting messages as I could to all parts, and by Divine grace the trouble went no further.

1683–1711                                                                                       1919

9. Once celebrated by Spaniards with flower-adorned crosses, May 3 has become, in Mexico, the feast day of masons; during the early Spanish colonial period, priests once asked masons to put crosses on churches that were still under construction. [Anthology editors' note]

# FRAY JUNÍPERO SERRA
## 1713–1784

*Siempre adelante, nunca atrás*—"always forward, never backward"—was Fray Junípero Serra's maxim. In the spirit of that maxim, this Franciscan missionary journeyed from the northern frontier of eighteenth-century Mexico into California. His optimism, energy, and deep love for God enabled him to lay the groundwork for California's vast mission system, which today functions as Catholic churches and popular tourist attractions. In 1984—the bicentennial of Serra's death—Leon Panetta, the U.S. Representative from California's Sixteenth District, noted that

> Junípero Serra is to the Pacific Coast what the Pilgrims are to New England, a founding father. . . . He represents the beginning of American history from [a] western perspective [and] a striking contrast to the other explorers of our continent, driven not out of personal adventure or interest but from a spiritual mission. Fray Serra sought not to conquer an unknown region but to cultivate its land and educate its people. [Let us now] recognize his central role in the Spanish settlement of America and the national importance of his efforts.

Serra was born Miguel José Serra y Ferrer in Petra, Majorca (one of the Balearic Islands, in the Mediterranean Sea, near the eastern coast of Spain). His parents, Antonio Nadal Serra y Abram and Margarita Rosa Ferrer y Fornés, were of peasant stock and were highly devoted to the Catholic Church. Their son attended a local Franciscan elementary school, and at a very young age he expressed interest in becoming a friar. Intelligent and studious, he was schooled in subjects such as Aristotelian logic, the works of Saint Augustine and Saint Bonaventure, and the philosophical currents of the day. On September 14, 1730, he received the habit of the Observant Branch of the Mendicant Order of Friars Minor. Upon becoming a priest, he changed his name to Junípero Serra—Junípero, "Jester of God," being associated with humility, "foolish simplicity," and a companion of Saint Francis of Assisi, founder of the Franciscan order.

By 1736, Serra was a deacon of the Church, and by 1740 he was teaching courses in philosophy at the Convent of San Francisco, in Cádiz, Andalusia, Spain. Among his pupils were two Franciscans who would become his lifelong friends and fellow companions in the missions of California: Fray Francisco Palóu and Fray Juan Crespi. In 1742, Serra received his doctorate in sacred theology from the University of Majorca, also known as Llullian University. The next year, he was appointed Catedrático de Prima (highest ranking professor). In spite of this stellar achievement, Serra's desire to become a missionary led him to leave his professorship and seek an appointment in the New World. On April 13, 1749, he sailed from Majorca. He never returned to his native land.

Later that same year, he arrived in Veracruz, and as a first act of humility he decided to walk the 275 miles to Mexico City. In Mexico City, he was appointed to the Franciscan College of San Fernando, where he served until 1767. He first began working with Indians in Jalpán, Querétaro, in the Sierra Gorda region of Mexico. Feeling great compassion toward the indigenous populations, Serra dreamed of ministering to the "gentiles," meaning non-Christians, in the northern frontier. In 1767, he was appointed president of the 15 missions in the Baja California area and was headquartered in Loreto, then the capital of the territory, Las Californias. Two years later—although a wisp of a man, five feet two and weighing no more than 110 pounds, suffering from poor health, with an ulcerating foot and a leg full of sores—he volunteered to accompany the Gaspar de Portolá expedition to Alta California; the expedition left Loreto on March 28, 1769, traveling by land.

On July 16, Serra and Portolá established the first mission in California, the presidio-mission in San Diego de Alcalá. The expedition then traveled by sea from San Diego to Monterey Bay, arriving on May 31, 1770. In what is now Carmel-by-the-Sea, Serra and Portolá established the San Carlos Borromeo presidio-mission. In 1771, having immediately fallen in love with the area and with the native population, Serra made this mission his headquarters. He subsequently built 21 missions along the California coast. However, all was not well with Serra and his fellow early settlers. They often lacked food, clothing, and basic necessities, and the abuses visited by the military upon the Indians led the Indians to rebel and massacre missionaries. At the age of 60, Serra took the three-month journey from Monterey Bay to Mexico City, on a "mission" to convey to the viceroy of New Spain, Antonio María Bucareli y Ursúa, the urgent needs of the mission system in California. He obtained the support he requested. In the *Reglamento para el gobierno de la provincial de California* (Decrees for the government of the province of California, 1784) proposed by Serra, two of his 32 points were most important: He requested continued expansion of the mission system, and he asked that the Indians be placed under the authority of the missions and not of the military. The *Reglamento* became effective in 1774 and, with minor revisions in 1779, lasted until 1821, when Mexico gained its independence from Spain.

After his death, Serra's fame—as a humble spirit with a simple heart, laboring 54 years for the cause of God—grew until he became a candidate for the highest honor granted by the Catholic Church: canonization for sainthood. The long process to canonize him began officially in 1934, but by the 1980s it had become controversial. Native American activists voiced opposition, since from their perspective the mission system had been not idyllic but exploitative and brutal. The controversy persists, and Serra has not been declared a saint by the Church.

The following selections are a letter Serra wrote during the Portolá expedition and one he wrote after it. These documents are a window into the running of the missions as self-sufficient bodies in remote frontier locations. Serra sharply and incisively reports on the missionaries' dire economic situation and health problems, the educational strategies they devised for the Indians, and his enthusiasms, fears, and administrative challenges. Of particular interest are Serra's depictions of the complicated encounters between the Spaniards and the Native Americans, without whose help many more of Serra's compatriots would have died.

For an account of the expedition in its early stages, see the Fray Juan Crespi headnote and selection (a letter to Fray Palóu), below.


# Letter to Fray Juan Andrés[1]

### Hail Jesus, Mary, Joseph!

Very Reverend Father Preacher and Guardian Fray Juan Andrés.

Venerable Father and my dear Sir:

Because of the distance and the lack of all means of communication with the place where I am living, my letters will of necessity be few. Yet I have not passed by, nor will I pass by, any occasion that presents itself for writing.

The last time I wrote was at the beginning of July of last year. The packet boat *San Antonio*, commonly known as *El Príncipe*, was to sail from this

---

1. Translated and edited by Antoine Tibesar. The anthology editors have omitted Tibesar's footnotes. Fray Juan Andrés was guardian of the College of San Fernando, in Mexico City.

Port of San Diego, and so I wrote to Your Reverence of my arrival at this place without any mishap and in good health.

At this time a number of soldiers are leaving here by land, with their Captain. I assure you that I am still blessed with good health because God sees fit to bestow it. On July 14th, as I have told you, Fathers Preachers Fray Juan Crespi, and Fray Francisco Gómez[2] started from here to accompany the expedition by land in quest of the Port of Monterey. And Father Fray Juan Viscaíno, Father Fray Fernando Parrón[3] and I remained here.

The appointments I had in mind were these: ministers here would be Father Murguía,[4] who, I knew by a letter, would come with the boat San José, and Father Fray Fernando Parrón; in Monterey, Father Crespi and I; and in San Buenaventura, Fathers Viscaíno and Gómez.

On July 16th of the same year, the Mission here of San Diego in this port was founded in the usual way; and on the first page of its records we put our names as ministers, the said Father Fray Fernando and I; and we have continued to be such, and still are. Father Fray Juan Viscaíno is staying with us, looking upon this as his home until such time as his own mission shall be erected.

Until today—what with the few of us who were well, while most were sick; the poor condition both of the countryside around, and the houses we live in; and not having an interpreter to communicate in any proper fashion with these poor naked gentiles—little more could be done than to prepare the ground for their eventual conversion and salvation.

When these natives, with whom the soldiers from the very beginning showed much familiarity, noticed how small our numbers were, and that we were continually burying a great number, and that many besides were prostrate in bed, on the Assumption Day of Our Blessed Lady,[5] they imagined they could kill us all very easily. The more so when out of our very limited number they saw four going to the beach to change escort and bring back Father Fernando. He had gone on the preceding Saturday to say Mass for those on the boat.

They broke in all of a sudden; and the only four soldiers present, seeing their ugly mood, immediately snatched up their arms. The fight was on. There were wounded both on our side and theirs. The one worst hurt was a young Spanish lad from the diocese of Guadalaxara. He came to me in Loreto[6] to be my servant on the road, and to be with me wherever I should be established.

At the first shot he darted into my hut, spouting so much blood at the mouth and from his temples, that I had hardly time to absolve him and help him to meet his end. This came in less than a quarter of an hour. He expired on the ground before me bathed in his own blood. And so I was quite a while with him there dead, and my little apartment a pool of blood. Still

2. Fray Francisco Gómez de la Cadena, guardian of the Convent of Santa Fe, in New Mexico.
3. Headmaster of the San Francisco Javier Viggé-Biaundó Mission, in Baja California. Father Fray Juan Viscaíno: unidentified.
4. Fray José Antonio de Murguía, architect and headmaster of Santa Clara Mission, in California.
5. In the Roman Catholic Church, Assumption Day, or the Feast of the Assumption, occurs

on August 15; it celebrates the Virgin Mary's assumption—the passage of her body and soul—into heaven after death.
6. Also known as Concho, and the first Spanish settlement on the Baja California Peninsula. Located on the coast of the Sea of Cortés, about 220 miles north of the state capital, La Paz, it served as the capital of Las Californias from 1697 to 1777. Guadalaxara: old spelling for the Mexican city of Guadalajara.

the exchange of shots—bullets and arrows—went on. There were only four on our side against more than twenty on theirs. And there I was with the dead man, thinking it most probable I would soon have to follow him, but at the same time praying to God that the victory would be for our Catholic Faith without losing a single soul.

And so it turned out, thank God, for seeing many of their companions covered with blood, they all fled. And I believe none of them were killed; therefore they can all yet be baptized. They are all by this time recovered from their wounds, and we are all, since then, living in peace.

Apart from the one man who was killed, Father Viscaíno and a blacksmith, Chacón, from Guadalaxara, were wounded; also a Christian Indian belonging to the San Ignacio Mission.[7]

Father Viscaíno's wound was due to an arrow without flint which first passed through a carpet that had been hung up and was blowing about in the wind. He was hit at the joining of the middle and ring finger of the right hand. The surgeon extracted some small splinters of wood from it. And his fingers are still more or less numb and half paralyzed.

The other two on our side who were wounded made a quick recovery and are now in good health.

One day I began the ceremony of Baptism, and half way through it they snatched the baby from the hands of the godfather. The parents had previously given their free consent to the Baptism; but it was not performed. But with God's blessing some day it will be completed.

On January 24th of this year, the entire Monterey expedition came back, and with them the two Fathers Crespi and Gómez. While they had to face great hardships and endure dire want they met with no hostility in that great stretch of infidel country peopled by gentiles—all the way from here to the Port of Our Father San Francisco.[8] Since these same Fathers, eyewitnesses of it all, are writing at this time to Your Reverence, there is no need for me to linger on what most assuredly should become the subject of a most interesting volume—a book worthy of print—to stir up the world to undertake the spiritual conquest of this New World, and give to God, before very long, thousands of souls.

I am well aware of, my very dear Father Guardian, and I see now with my own eyes, what some time ago I wrote in a letter to Your Reverence: if the hundred religious that the King's Councillors were proposing to give to Father Fray Pablo, should be sought for by Your Reverence and our Venerable Discretorium; and if you were to bring them all over here, win their consent, and ship the whole assemblage of them to California, without one staying at home, I could find a place for them all here. And further I might add that they would be all too few. But if they are anxious not to be put to any annoyance or discomfort, even one of them would be one too many.

Our position here is what you can well imagine. But we are not dead yet, thank God. I ask Your Reverence for two things: your blessing and permission to live here in these parts, relying on Almighty God's Providence when human means and prudence perchance fail, and the the same permission be

---

7. The San Ignacio Kadakaamán Mission, in central Baja California.
8. *Our Father San Francisco*: ecclesiastical reference to Saint Francis of Assisi (1181 or 1182–1226), Italian friar; founder of the Franciscan order.

granted my companion, Father Crespi, who, I feel confident, will not desert me till God disposes otherwise.

Father Viscaíno has told me repeatedly that he would like to return to the College when the next ships come, and that he had written to Your Reverence about the matter. And now that the opportunity comes up of going by land, he would like to go by way of the missions. He felt very much dejected just to see me hesitating about consenting to it. So I gave him permission and he is leaving with my full consent.

The rest of us are looking for the arrival of the boats to see what can be done.

As to the state of religion in California I have not got any news since I left there. The *sínodos*[9] for here might already have been claimed had I been able to send a notice of the foundation here to the Inspector, as I am now doing.

I intend to write to our Father Commissary General; and if I cannot, I ask Your Reverence to make my excuses and to forward to His Very Reverend Paternity the news from here.

I send my heartiest greetings to all the members of our holy Community, likewise to the lowest servant, asking them all to commend us to God and pray for the conversion to our holy Catholic Faith of all these poor gentiles up here. If it is not boldness in a mere nobody such as I am to ask a favor of so distinguished a Community, I ask a Hail Mary to Our Blessed and Spotless Queen in thanksgiving for her protection on the Feast of her Assumption, and at the same time, that she continue to guard over us. I held her picture in one hand, and her Divine Crucified Son in the other when arrows were raining everywhere; and my thoughts were, that with such defense either I would not have to die, or that I would die well, great sinner that I am.

Apart from prayers I know not what to ask of Your Reverence and of our holy College. Should something be sent me, who can tell where I shall be? And so anything Your Reverence might like to send, you had better address to your new mission; yours because founded under obedience to Your Reverence, and while you were Superior. May our Superiors cherish that mission as something costly; and I hope in time it will prove its worth.

And so I end, praying Our Lord God to keep Your Reverence many more years in His holy love and grace.

Mission of San Diego de Alcalá, in this port among the gentiles of Northern California, February 10, 1770.

Kissing the hand of Your Reverence,

Your most affectionate and devoted subject,

Fray Junípero Serra

1770                                                                                  1955–56

---

9. Annual subsidies.

# Letter to Francisco Carlos de Croix[1]

## Hail Jesus, Mary, Joseph!

Most Excellent Sir.

Most Revered and Most Excellent Sir:

Great was the edification and the delight of my heart when, last May 21st, I received two letters from Your Excellency, dated November 12 of last year 1770. I praised God especially at seeing so much zeal and attention paid to every detail that may prove helpful to the happiness and progress of these spiritual conquests. I know that you are weighed down with many important matters and anxieties that unavoidably and ceaselessly call for Your Excellency's attention; such responsibilities are inseparably connected with the high office you occupy with so much distinction. And seeing that the subject discussed—or should I say the purpose of both letters—is the same, I feel confident—and I humbly ask permission—that Your Excellency will permit me to answer both in this single letter.

The ten religious, Most Excellent Sir, who took ship at the Port of San Blás, on the packet boat *San Antonio*, commonly called *El Príncipe*, landed at this Port of Monterey, after a safe voyage, on the said 21st of last month. There arrived also, and undamaged, the cases containing the furnishings and everything else relative to the supplies for said missionaries and missions.

I received the complete vestments—especially chosen and the finest of all that came—by the generosity of Your Excellency as a gift to this your favorite Mission of San Carlos de Monterey.[2] I soon had an opportunity of showing it all off to advantage on the Solemnity of Corpus Christi[3] that was not far off. We made a great event of it this year, with additional splendor, because of the participation of a group of twelve Franciscan priests and the arrival of the boat with all its crew in good health. There were, too, other circumstances which helped, among them particularly the presence of quite a number of convert Christian boys from here who played the part of acolytes and choristers during the procession. For your magnificent gift, I wish to return to Your Excellency all proper thanks—hoping that the Divine Majesty will reward you most abundantly for the help you have rendered to His Divine service.

Mindful of the rules laid down by Your Excellency in the letters you have sent me, and considering the state of affairs as it now is, I have assigned and published the appointments of the ten new religious. The details are contained in the list I am enclosing, which also has been signed by the military Commander of the Royal Presidio here. In doing so I am following the advice given me by the Most Illustrious Inspector General in his letter of instructions.

In reading over the list, Your Excellency may wonder why there is no reference to the Missions of Santa Clara and of Our Seraphic Father San Fran-

---

1. Translated and edited by Antoine Tibesar. The anthology editors have omitted Tibesar's footnotes; the bracketed insertion in the text is his. Francisco Carlos de Croix (1699–1786) was viceroy of New Spain from 1766 to 1771.
2. Also known as Mission of San Carlos Borro-

meo de Carmelo, the Carmel Mission, Mission Carmel.
3. Christian feast honoring the Eucharist (or Communion, a sacrament that is a memorial of Christ's death).

cisco.[4] The reason is that the Officer in command assures me that these missions cannot be founded at least for the time being, for want of an escort, and also in the case of the second mission, because an exploration of the famous port has to be made beforehand in accordance with the commands of Your Excellency.

Concerning this matter the officers in command of the ship and of the presidio held numerous conferences in my presence. I offered to go with them myself if they decided to undertake the said exploration. But, in the end, they came to the conclusion that it was impossible or inadvisable just now, because they were without men to take in hand the expedition by land, and because it would hold up the ship too long if they were to start from here to make the venture by sea. For my own part, I am most anxious to see, as soon as possible, the mission of my dearly beloved Seraphic Father established there; and as far as I am concerned, it will not be delayed an instant, with the help of God.

The reason that two of the said religious are being assigned to the San Buenaventura Mission[5] is that, thus far, it has not been founded for want of an escort; and none of the friars whom I assigned there more than two years ago are at my disposal now. On that account I wrote, last year, to the Most Illustrious Inspector General giving him the assurance that its foundation would not be delayed on our part, because as soon as they could provide an escort, no matter how small, one of the two of us would go there. We were ready to make the sacrifice, for the present, of being all alone in the midst of so vast a pagan country until the arrival of more companions.

As things were last year, Most Excellent Sir, we arrived here to take possession of Monterey with only seven leather-jacket soldiers,[6] two muleteers and twelve volunteers. Among the last mentioned, some were sick, and of no practical use. The same situation continues even until today. For the whole year we have been waiting for an expedition by land which would bring us livestock, or possibly arrive without it. And over and above the fact that it has not arrived, we now know that it is not on its way. And that explains why I had to assign two of these religious as ministers to San Buenaventura. Its foundation, along with that of the others you will find on the same list, we have arranged for in the following manner.

With the eight men from the presidio here, together with eight sailors that Captain Don Juan Pérez[7] is allowing us, this San Carlos Mission is being removed immediately to the banks of the Carmel River, as Your Excellency orders; with ten other men, the San Antonio de Padua Mission is to be founded in the foothills of the Sierra de Santa Lucía, at a place called in the diaries La Cañada de los Robles. It is about twenty-five leagues[8] to the south of this port.

4. Mission Santa Clara de Asís, founded on January 12, 1777, was named for Saint Clare of Assisi, who cofounded the Order of the Poor Clares, also known as the Second Order of Saint Francis, with Saint Francis of Assisi. *Our Seraphic Father San Francisco*: full ecclesiastical reference to Saint Francis.
5. Named for the Franciscan theologian Saint Bonaventure; it was the last mission Serra founded, on Easter Sunday, March 31, 1782.

6. The soldiers at presidios in California were given this name because, for protection against Indians' arrows, they wore *cueras*, long, sleeveless jackets of deerhide, horsehide, or cowhide.
7. Juan José Pérez Hernández (ca. 1725–1775), Spanish explorer.
8. Approximately 65 miles (a Spanish league then equaling about 2.6 miles). *The diaries*: the diaries of pioneering explorers in the region.

The Officer Don Pedro Fages[9] is embarking for San Diego. He intends, with some of the soldiers he expects to find there, and those he may possibly get from San Fernando de Velicatá,[1] to begin at once, if it is at all possible, the San Buenaventura Mission. Now, if over and above what are absolutely necessary there, he can gather ten or twelve more, he will establish with their help the San Gabriel Mission[2] on his way north. It is on the southern bank of the Río de los Temblores where the gentiles have asked to have ministers, and is at a distance of about thirty leagues from the Mission and Port of San Diego.

As for myself—as soon as the boat is actually on its way—I shall start for Carmel. From there immediately, with the Fathers and the escort assigned for the San Antonio Mission, we are to set out for the said place called Los Robles. While establishing the mission there, we expect the arrival of a courier from the said Commander, as agreed between us, to tell me what is possible for him to accomplish there. I am then to resume my journey in order to meet the said Lieutenant at the place where we intend to build San Buenaventura, which is, as I wrote before, at the entrance of the Santa Barbara Channel, at the San Diego end of it, and at a distance of thirty-two leagues from San Gabriel. There I will help as much as I can in that holy enterprise, and I will see with my own eyes how much security the religious can obtain in those parts.

The Fathers appointed as ministers for the two missions, San Gabriel and San Buenaventura, are to set sail with the said officer. They have with them all their belongings and church furnishings. Here there still remain the two Fathers belonging to San Antonio and the two others destined for the San Luis Obispo Mission.[3] The place selected for this mission is what is called in the diaries La Cañada de los Osos [Bear Valley]. Nearby lives the leader of these parts whom our men have nicknamed "El Buchón."[4] This man must already be a familiar figure to Your Excellency from the diaries and stories told by those who have met him, and have had dealings with him, as they passed to and fro in these parts. It is at a distance of twenty-five leagues from the preceding mission of San Antonio, and from the next one—San Buenaventura—about forty leagues or more. Between these two are the Channel settlements[5]—known far and wide for their size and number.

These four missions—that is to say, San Antonio, San Buenaventura, San Gabriel and San Luis Obispo—represent, in my judgment, the utmost that can be founded in the very near future, according to what I am told and what I understand to be the present state of affairs. But alas, may it not be less than what I am now proposing. I am as much afraid I will fall short of my goal as I am anxious to go beyond it.

9. Pedro Fages (1734–1794), governor of Alta California. Earlier, Serra had met him when they took part in an exploration of the east coast of San Francisco Bay. When friction developed at Monterey between Fages and Serra, Fages was recalled, but he returned in 1782 as governor.
1. Mission San Fernando Rey de España—in the San Fernando Valley and named after Saint Ferdinand, king of Castile (1217–52)—was founded by Franciscans under Serra on the Feast of the Birth of Mary, September 8, 1797.
2. Mission San Gabriel Arcángel—in San Ga-

briel, California—was founded by Franciscans under Serra on the Feast of the Birth of Mary, September 8, 1771.
3. On the central coast of California, halfway between Santa Barbara and Monterey; named after Saint Louis of Anjou, the bishop of Toulouse, it was the fifth mission Serra founded, on September 1, 1772.
4. The Double-Chinned.
5. On the California coast off the Santa Barbara Channel.

And, while I am on the subject, I might mention that I have reserved the two religious that remain from the ten newly arrived, to be ministers of the San Diego Mission, because the two Fathers stationed there, until now, are habitually on the sick list, in consequence of the infirmities they contracted during the first trip made by the two boats, during which scurvy took such a distressing toll. Because they took care of the sick, these Fathers themselves became victims of the disease. Furthermore, as regards one of them, his troubles were added to by reason of the exhausting land journey from San Diego to San Francisco, and back again. As regards the second, his sickness was aggravated from constant attendance at the two hospitals that were set up in San Diego during the first expedition to Monterey.

And so it came about, during the course of this year, during which I have been away from Their Reverences, that they both became so weak that on one occasion, one wishing to go to confession to the other, the confessor fell exhausted at the feet of his penitent. The situation has been reported to the Most Illustrious Inspector, who has been in touch with and knows both of them intimately, and understands that, while being religious strong in the spirit, they are very weak physically. Nor will he be surprised that with all that has taken place they are in a more exhausted condition than I can explain.

On the understanding that this is the situation, and since Father Gómez is anxious to be returned to the College, while Father Fray Fernando wants only to be transferred to one of the Californian missions, where, with a robust companion and a little less strain, he might continue his apostolic ministry till he dies, it did not seem fair to me to delay any longer my permission, they having previously applied for and received the consent of the Reverend Father Guardian of our College, especially considering that, by the time the Missions of Santa Clara and of Our Father San Francisco are established, more religious will have arrived both from California and from Mexico. If it turns out otherwise, then we will manage here as best we can; and would that it were tomorrow!

With regard to the individual provision for these ten religious, taken care of by the two hundred and seventy-five pesos of the *sínodo*[6] paid for each of them by order of Your Excellency to the Syndic Don Joseph González Calderón, each missionary takes with him to his own mission what belongs to him for his own use and convenience. Now, since all the missions are entitled to major ratings for such stipends, and all are on an equal footing, no reductions should be made, nor distinctions between them.

The only question that arises is concerning the provision that has come to the two former ministers of San Diego who are sick. If it has been given in advance, for the year yet to come, as for an actual year's residence, they are advised to notify the College concerning their new residence, so that the College may notify Your Excellency. Your Excellency will then decide what should be done about it according to the decrees governing this matter, or as you may see fit. The Father going to California will take with him the provision for the mission assigned to him; and the Father returning to Mexico, being provided with what is necessary for the trip, will leave the rest here; and it will be assigned to that or to some other mission; and Your Excellency will be given a full report of the whole proceedings.

6. Annual subsidy.

All this is being said on the supposition that the provision is to be provided in advance for the year ahead. If it covers the past year, the question does not arise, since they were in San Diego the whole year. I cannot make up my mind definitely because Your Excellency expressly states that for the ten new missionaries the *sínodo* has been paid in advance; whereas in the case of the others no such circumstance was emphasized. And so I am unable to present the matter with all clearness as instructed by Your Excellency.

Concerning the property belonging to the same new missions bought with the thousand pesos allotted to each, Your Excellency tells me that you have given instructions for them to be handed over to the said syndic. In reference to the two Missions of Our Father San Francisco and Santa Clara, since they are not to be established for some while, the share assigned to each remains here on deposit until needed. The packing cases of furnishings for each of the missions—five all told, and the goods marvelous—also arrived. Also an additional supply of tools and permanent furniture which, by order of Your Excellency, the Officer Don Pedro Fages distributed among the missions—as Your Excellency will see from the signed receipt of it all which I have given to the above-mentioned Lieutenant. And so, when I will have apportioned to each, and in good time, the proper amount of corn, flour, groceries, etc., belonging to them, the only thing remaining to be done is to take the road to their various destinations.

I fully agree that there should be no question of transplanting the aborigines from the islands where they were born and are now living; on the other hand, while we are establishing various missions along the Channel, their ministers should aim at winning the good will of those who come regularly from the islands to the mainland; they should also try to understand their language. They should in like manner consider the feasibility of going there, with a good escort, to explore the islands, and see if it be possible and advisable to establish missions there. After that the Government will decide what will be best in view of the information received. Besides, our College will forward, at the proper time, the reports it receives from our religious.

And so, Most Excellent Lord, I think that I have covered, with as much clearness as I could, all the points raised in the two most gracious letters from Your Excellency. It now remains for me to offer to Your Excellency, in my name, and in the name of my religious brethren who arrived on the recent ship, the most profuse thanks for the splendid and lavish provisions for their upkeep during the voyage; for the plentiful supplies which came by boat for the maintenance and convenience of all in our respective missions; for the wonderful outfittings of furnishings and sacred vessels—everything corresponding exactly with the list Your Excellency sent me. In short, I wish to thank Your Excellency for the marvelous way in which you have succeeded in playing the part of our Catholic Monarch, whom God keep, and in displaying your most fervent zeal for the propagation of our Catholic Faith. You have spared no pains or expense to attain the accomplishment of so holy a purpose—a purpose so much in conformity with the wishes of the King of Glory, and the glory of our Lord the King.

I am just now writing to our College giving them a report of everything, and asking for images or paintings of the patron saints of the new missions. The Fathers could not ask for them before, not knowing what names they would be given. I am also asking for whatever else the Fathers need, now that they know where they are being assigned.

What still remains to be desired for the complete achievement of all our hopes is a troop of leather-jacket soldiers, as I said before. Besides that, we are without any bells for the five missions. I had collected some before leaving California, and these would be sufficient now. But seeing that none of them have arrived, it is to be presumed that they were put on board the packet boat *San Joseph*. And being without news of its whereabouts, we are still without information concerning the bells. For an immediate disposition, out of the three bells belonging to this mission, I will keep only one and give one to San Antonio Mission and the other to that of San Luis Obispo. But even to put that plan into execution, as one of the three is cracked and sounds accordingly, I have had to ask for it to be exchanged for the ship's bell, which is undamaged. I promised I would advise Your Excellency of it as I am now doing, and so relieve Captain Pérez of all responsibility. Of the three bells that were here in safe keeping for San Buenaventura, one that is broken I am sending to San Blás in the hope their by an order Your Excellency might be so good as to issue, they may recast it, or send another in exchange. Of the two remaining, one will be for San Gabriel, and the other for the said San Buenaventura. And so it happens that with the exception of San Diego, which keeps the two it had from the very beginning, in each of the other missions we have only one bell. And there are none for the two missions of Santa Clara and Our Father San Francisco.

May I also ask Your Excellency to issue orders that the boat should never sail again, as it did this year, without bringing a supply of meat for our poor men, so that they may work with greater energy and contentment. True it is that there was consigned for each mission a goodly sized package of ham, and all will get the benefit of it as long as it lasts.

For the time being, Most Excellent Sir, it is most necessary that the far-famed generosity of our Sovereign should help us. At present each one of the projected missions has such extensive and fertile lands that, before long, they assuredly will be able to reduce in part that load.

When I see these missions well established, I will apply to Your Excellency for others to be added. Meanwhile, and always, on my part and on the part of the religious with me, rest assured we will do our best to serve the cause of God and that of our Catholic Sovereign.

By God's great mercy, in the short time we have been here, we have already registered twenty Baptisms. Of their number, there are four big boys who not only are able to say their prayers well, but are making much progress in the Castilian tongue;[7] and I, as best I can, am learning from them, as my teachers, the language of this country. At San Diego the number baptized is a little smaller, but the progress of two full-grown boys in the Castilian tongue is greater. These two young Christians serve as interpreters to the gentiles, and as teachers to the Fathers. And so I hope that, by fanning the flame on all sides, by way of these said new missions, in addition to the one here and San Buenaventura, we will see, before long, new and immense territories gathered into the bosom of our Holy Mother the Church, and subjected to the Crown of Spain.

---

7. Spanish (i.e., the dialect of the region of Castile, Spain, adopted as the official national language).

For these most important purposes I pray that Our Lord God may keep and prosper Your Excellency for many years, blessing you with health and daily progress in His holy grace.

From this your Mission of San Carlos de Monterey, June 18, 1771.

Most Excellent Lord Viceroy, My Lord,

Kissing the hand of Your Excellency,

Your most affectionate and devoted servant and chaplain,

Fray Junípero Serra

1771                                                                                                    1955–56

---

# FRAY JUAN CRESPI
## 1721–1782

"On the 24th of March [1769] we set out from Villacatá—the commander, twenty-five leather-jacket soldiers [soldiers from presidios; for protection against Indians' arrows, they wore *cueras*, long, sleeveless jackets of deerhide, horsehide, or cowhide], three muleteers, and about fifty-two Christian Indians from the missions—taking the necessary provisions and a convoy of about one hundred and eighty mules and horses, while I alone accompanied the expedition for its spiritual administration." Thus, as he described it in a letter, began Fray Juan Crespi's multistage journey from Lower California to Alaska. That journey involved three of the period's most spectacular expeditions, by land and sea, providing the friar with some of the most thrilling experiences a person could have had at the time.

Crespi left a record of his adventures through copious letters written to his fellow friars and through diaries that he wrote while en route to the various destinations. "Among the great diarists who recorded explorations in the New World," Herbert Eugene Bolton states in his book *Fray Juan Crespi: Missionary Explorer on the Pacific Coast 1769–1774* (1927; reprinted in 1971), "Juan Fray Crespi occupied a conspicuous place." As Bolton notes, Crespi's writings are deeply carved into the multilayered collective history of the Pacific coast.

Like Fray Francisco Palóu and Fray Junípero Serra (the latter of whom is included in this anthology), Crespi wrote some of the most vivid and stirring narratives of the eighteenth-century explorations of California. All three friars were from the island of Majorca, Spain, where Palóu and Crespi had been students of Serra's and became his close friends and colleagues. All three traveled together to the New World, landing in Mexico in 1749. They all served in the Franciscan College of San Fernando, in Mexico City, and they later journeyed to California and lived for long periods in the Monterey Bay area.

After serving in the Franciscan College of San Fernando, Crespi distinguished himself through his dedication to missionary work in Sierra Gorda, Mexico. In 1767, he was appointed director of the Mission Purísima Concepción, in Villacatá, after Spain's King Charles III expelled the Jesuits from Spain and parts of the New World, including the 15 missions they had established in Baja California. Subsequently, Crespi and Serra joined the Gaspar de Portolá expedition, which traveled by land to what is now San Diego and founded the presidio-mission San Diego de Alcalá (and thus founded the city). The expedition then traveled by sea to Monterey and, at what is now Carmel-by-the-Sea, founded the San Carlos Borromeo presideo-mission.

On March 20, 1772, Crespi joined the Pedro Fages expedition, which reconnoitered the San Francisco area and in the process discovered the San Francisco Bay (and thus led to the founding of that city). On June 11, 1774, Crespi and Fray Tomás de la Peña sailed as chaplains on the ship *Santiago*, as part of the Juan Pérez expedition. This expedition marked the first time Spaniards explored the northern Pacific coast, from California through Canada, and it established a toehold for the Spanish Crown near the 60-degree latitude (near Alaska's southern border).

The following selection is a letter to Fray Palóu in which Crespi relates the Portolá expedition's long journey from Villacatá to San Diego. This valuable historical document describes the expedition's hardships and near starvation, the tough terrain along the way, and various reactions to the encounters with Native Americans. "In his precious diaries," Bolton adds, "the human toils, the adventures, the thrills, the hopes, the fears of [these] historic journeys on the Pacific Coast are embalmed."

## Letter to Fray Francisco Palóu[1]

SAN DIEGO, JUNE 9, 1769.

HAIL JESUS, MARY AND JOSEPH!

TO MY REVEREND FATHER LECTOR, FELLOW-STUDENT AND PRESIDENT, FR. FRANCISCO PALÓU.

My very dear fellow-student and friend: I shall be very glad if this letter finds your Reverence in the perfect health that my deep affection wishes for you. I give thanks to God for this favor to me, and as always I am awaiting orders for your further pleasure.

My dear friend: On the 22d of March, Wednesday of Holy Week,[2] between two and three o'clock in the afternoon, I reached Villacatá well and without any injury to my health. The two boys whom I brought with me and the soldier Islas were likewise sound. Arriving at Villacatá I found the captain well and ready to leave on Holy Thursday, although we did not start on that day. I very much desired to write your Reverence from that place before our departure, but the captain's impatience and the fact of my having just arrived at the place did not permit it. The 24th of March, Good Friday, we left Villacatá in the afternoon, starting our journey in search of the port of San Diego. The 14th of May, the Feast of Espíritu Santo,[3] we arrived with the greatest success at this pleasant port of San Diego, all in good health, thanks to the Lord, having spent fifty-two days on the way, with not a few misadventures on such an unknown road, in danger every instant, since it was all so thickly populated with numerous Indians; but thanks to the Lord we suffered no harm anywhere on the way.

1. Translated by Herbert Eugene Bolton. Unless otherwise indicated, all footnotes are Bolton's; the anthology editors have omitted some of his notes.
2. In Christianity, a commemoration of the last week of Jesus' life, culminating in his crucifixion on Good Friday and his resurrection on Easter Sunday. [Anthology editors' note]

3. Holy Spirit; along with God and the Son, the third person in the Christian Trinity (Godhead). The descent of the Holy Spirit on Jesus' disciples is celebrated on this feast day, Pentecost, the seventh Sunday after Easter. [Anthology editors' note]

When we arrived at this port of San Diego we found in it the two packet-boats, *San Carlos* and *El Príncipe*. The latter arrived here the 11th of April and the former the 29th of the same month. We found the crews of both ships and the soldiers from the *San Carlos* filling a hospital on shore, recovering from the disease of loanda or scurvy. Up to the present twenty-one have died from the crews of both ships, besides one or two of the soldiers on the *San Carlos*. At this time the sailors on *El Príncipe* are very few, since those who are somewhat stronger, and able to walk and do a little work, are only about six or seven, while of the soldiers only three are well, all the rest being sick, many dying, the majority with cramps in the legs or all over the body. With all this trouble your Reverence can easily see how well fitted this sea expedition is to continue its course to Monterey.

At present only those of us who came by land are in good health. We found here Fathers Parrón, Vizcaíno, and Gómez,[4] who, although they have been a little indisposed, are all well once more. Of all our band the one who is frailest and weakest is Father Parrón, who says that he will stay at this port. Of those on the two vessels the strongest are the lieutenant of the volunteers, Sr. Costanzó, the captain of *El Príncipe*, and his pilot. Although some of them have been ill, they have now recovered, and with the few that I brought they are the only ones from the two vessels that are able to do anything. The *San Carlos* spent three months and nineteen days on the voyage, since they went as far as thirty-five degrees in search of this port, and the same thing happened to *El Príncipe*, although, as I have observed, this port is only thirty-two degrees and forty-two minutes north latitude. As a matter of fact, they are disembarking the leather-jacket soldiers from *El Príncipe*, in order to send it to San Blás to inform the visitor-general of what occurred on the sea expedition. Meanwhile, if the *San Joseph*[5] does not come, or the sick do not get relief, I do not know how the commanders will manage to go on to Monterey. God has seen fit to send us the gift of patience and submission to the Most High Providence of the Lord, since He willed that those of us who came by land should arrive at this port in good health. I am much troubled because I do not know when our father lector president and the governor will come.

When we reached this port, since there was no fresh water near, we went back about a league,[6] still in sight of it, where the fathers who arrived the first of the month had already investigated. We found there a good sized river[7] which empties into the sea through an estuary which the ships use as a watering-station. This river has a very large, broad plain on its banks, which seems to be of very good soil, with many willows, some poplars, and some alders, although so far it has not been possible to examine it properly. If the river is permanent it may prove in time to be the best of those discovered in all California. On the banks of this river, which are thickly covered with willows, there are many Castilian rose bushes with very fragrant roses, which I have held in my hand and smelled. All the plain is dotted over with wild grapevines, which look as if they had been planted, and at present their many branches are in bloom. We have been in this port since the second day

---

4. Fray Francisco Gómez de la Cadena, guardian of the Convent of Santa Fe, in New Mexico. *Parrón*: Fray Fernando Parrón, headmaster of the San Francisco Javier Viggé-Biaundó Mission, in Baja California. *Vizcaíno*: Fray Juan Vizcaíno (also spelled Viscaíno). [Anthology editors' note]

5. This supply vessel was lost at sea * * *.

6. A Spanish league then equaled about 2.6 miles. [Anthology editors' note]

7. San Diego River.

of the Feast of Espíritu Santo, but we have not yet been able to begin the mission, and we are much troubled because the river, which flows through the plain and which has very good, clear water, as we have observed every day, is drying up to such a degree that although two weeks ago when we arrived we saw it flowing with an abundant stream, it has now diminished so that it hardly runs at all, and they say now that they can cross it dry shod. If this continues it will be necessary to look for another place to establish the mission and obtain irrigation.

This port is a large, level place in the midst of great meadows and plains, with very good pasturage for all kinds of cattle, and not a stone is found for variety. All the port is well populated with a large number of villages of Indians, too clever, wide awake,[8] and business-like for any Spaniard to get ahead of them. The men are naked and almost all are very much painted. They are well armed with bows and quivers of arrows. We are camped near one of their villages. They received us in peace, thanks to the Lord, and so far there has been no trouble, but strict care is necessary, since they are great thieves. The women, as many as we have seen, are all properly clothed with a thick apron from the waist in front, and skins of deer or seals behind, and some have a garment made of hare or rabbit skins in the shape of a cape with which they cover their breasts and the rest of their bodies, in the manner of a blanket.

We suffered great cold on the way and it still prevails. The northwest and west winds are very cold—too cold. But in spite of it all we have kept our health throughout, except one soldier, who became ill during the week of our departure from Villacatá. I administered all the sacraments to him as he seemed to be in the last extremity, but, thanks to God, he recovered and at present is safe and sound.

Many of the fifty-one Christian Indians who accompanied us were sick. I buried five on the way, and almost all the rest absconded on the road. But this is not to be wondered at, since they did not give them food where there was mescal,[9] which was lacking most of the way. When this failed they had to get along with only a little atole,[1] although the need of water was more urgent than that of atole. Since I could not remedy this at all, it is not strange that they returned to their missions, or that of the whole number only thirteen reached this port, or that some of them were sick.

I do not know how to tell your Reverence what we suffered from hunger on this journey, because the captain brought only sixteen tierces of very old flour and ten packs of jerked beef. This was all the food that was brought; and if he had left eight other tierces of the flour which he did not wish to bring, we surely should have perished from starvation halfway along the road. From what he did bring we had two meals a day of poor tortillas, which were mostly bran, and a bit of roasted jerked beef that was so hard and so salty that only necessity could make one eat it, except some days when they boiled it in water. On those days we considered it a great treat to have a little stew, which was more like brine than anything else, but the beef, which softened with cooking, tasted as if it were the finest chicken.

8. On the alert. [Anthology editors' note]
9. Agave, a genus of plants (such as the aloe) found in deserts of Mexico and the southwestern U.S.; it can be fermented to make a drink, and its base and leaves can be cooked to make a food. [Anthology editors' note]
1. A cornstarch- or chocolate-based Mexican drink. [Anthology editors' note]

This was all the food we had on the journey. The beef gave out eleven days before we reached this port, and the soldiers got along with a single dry tortilla, although mine lasted until we arrived here. This, without any seasoning or sauce, and the morning chocolate, which was more like a poor syrup than anything else, was our only food. Praise God for preserving our health.

Almost all the road was through the mountain, or mountains, some of them very rough, but we found water and good pasturage in them on every day's march. We always traveled on the mountains because the captain had a complete aversion for going down to the seashore, until finally the mountain forced us to descend because of its height, roughness, and steepness, and he was obliged, in spite of himself, to allow us to come down to the beach. In my opinion all our good fortune in not perishing was due to this, because the beach gave us a good and very easy passage by land, was well supplied with pasturage, and had sufficient fresh water for all. We reached this port with only three tierces of flour and part of another, and this only because when the first eight tierces were used up strict orders were given that the two tortillas that were distributed as rations at the two meals should be made very thin, so that we might not perish entirely.

Words fail me in which to tell your Reverence of the danger that this man put us in because of his whim, since, without knowing what road we had to travel over, he left at Villacatá as much flour as he brought with him, considerable corn, four or five boxes of chocolate, and four or five jars of wine and brandy, of which he brought only his case full, although there were a great plenty of mules, for in all one hundred and eighty-nine have come.

Moreover, instead of the fifty-two days that we spent on the way, the journey could have been made in a month or a little over. I do not know why, except that it suited his fancy, we were in some spots two days, and in some even two and a half, as is seen by what I wrote in my diary, a copy of which will not fail to reach your Reverence in time, together with the latitudes and directions on the occasions when they could be observed on the way.

I have reckoned the distance from Santa María to this port as one hundred and twenty-eight leagues, and from Villacatá as one hundred and eight leagues and a half. On all the journey we found about ten good sites, with sufficient land and water for establishing missions, and with soil suitable to raise everything. Many sites have marshes and moist land, as will be seen in the diary in good time. The first place was San Isidoro in thirty-one degrees and five minutes. It has much moist land and some other land for irrigation, with a very good stream of water somewhat larger than that which flows near the Hospice of Tepic, well-wooded with white poplars, many willows, underbrush, and pasturage for the cattle. This stream flows to the northwest by west at the foot of a very high mountain.

Six or seven leagues beyond Río de San Isidoro we came upon a large river very much blocked up and choked with trees. I called it Río de San Dionisio, and although we saw no land good for agriculture where we crossed, we learned from some Indians by signs that it emptied into the sea, and that two or three streams of water joined it; and that beyond the mountain there was a great confluence; hence we did not doubt that near the shore there might be some plains that would be suitable for establishing a mission. Two leagues beyond the river of San Dionisio we came upon a stream which I called the San León. It has a flow of water perhaps as large as the San Joseph Comundú;

and although we did not see any arable land in passing, we were persuaded that some would be found on exploring.

I will mention only one other place, the one which I called San Francisco Solano, since in time you will read about all of them in the diary. This San Francisco Solano is a large valley, which is in 32° and 12', and is entered from the north. In the center of the level ground it has two springs about two hundred feet apart, one larger than the other, and from the two there is a good flow of water. It has also abundant land and pasturage, and I do not doubt that one hundred bushels of wheat could be sown there. Moreover, it is well wooded. The captain and the soldiers told me that there are to the west-northwest of this valley many marshes and much tule land, and that a large amount of moist land could be planted. From the Christian Indians I also learned that by going in the same direction to the beach, which is not very far from this valley, one finds there a large body of water flowing like a river.

Besides this, to the east and northeast, two rivers can be made out in the distance, flowing down from the mountain between green, wooded banks, which we conjectured might also have good water, although we could not explore them. Of all the good places this seems to me the most advantageous. And thus your Reverence has now a good site for establishing the mission of San Francisco Solano, which will be about eighty leagues distant from Villacatá, according to my reckoning. Besides, this is the eighth of the good locations, counting from Villacatá, while from San Francisco Solano to this place there are only two others, namely San Jorge and San Juan Bautista. This last also might be a good mission. It is fifteen leagues distant from this port of San Diego, but I could not take its latitude. It was there that we began to get news of the ships, in some well populated villages of Indians who crowded around us and were very peaceful but wide-awake.

All along the road from Villacatá, as we continually saw from the mountain, there were many footprints, and many well worn paths of the Indians, but, although we came upon many villages, we did not find a very large number of people because the greater part of the mountain is very barren, so that the poor wretches do not have anything to eat. Even the mescal, their daily bread, is not to be found in the greater part of the mountains, and those that we crossed are so very poor that the numerous tribes of Indians on the two slopes are forced to get their living from the sea.

On all the mountain we saw no trees that produce food except some on a peak in the distance that appeared to be pines. Indeed, all the trees that we came upon were on streams, and as far as we have penetrated the mountains continue even barer than those about the old missions. When we descended to the shore because the mountain had closed our road by its height and steepness, our Gracious Lady wished it to be at the great Bay of the Virgins.[2] The map does not show it quite correctly, because it represents it with one island, whereas it has two islands, with all the headlands or farallones[3] that the map shows. The bay is about twenty-eight leagues from this port, and is in 32° and 14' north latitude.

When we reached the coast we began to encounter what we had expected, that is, very well populated Indian villages. From the tops of the nearby hills

2. Crespi's geography is not quite right. They were actually at what is now Todos Santos Bay, a little south of the Bay of Eleven Thousand Virgins (see note 2, p. 71). [Anthology editors' note]
3. High, vertical rock formations that emerge from the sea. [Anthology editors' note]

Indians well armed with their bows and quivers began to shout at us, and although we made signs to them to come to us and that we did not intend to harm them, they never let themselves be seen at close range. For three days one village of twenty-nine Indians followed us along the hill-tops, shouting all the time and too often with gestures of wanting to shoot us with their arrows. Indeed, on the second day they came so near us that they were almost within shooting distance. Fearing an ambush in some pass, the captain ordered the pack animals halted, and that all the soldiers should then show themselves with their shields and their arms in their hands, drawn up in battle array. All the Indians drew up on a small hill in the same valley a little more than a gunshot away. The captain gave orders that none of our men should say a word, but all should be on the lookout. All the Indians were shouting at us and making gestures of intending to shoot us, until finally, although they were not within shooting distance, they shot three arrows into the air, which fell not far from the captain and the soldiers. At this demonstration the captain and another soldier fired twice without hitting the Indians because they were out of range. For this reason they retreated to the top of the Sierra, which was near, and gradually disappeared, giving a loud war whoop.

We were delayed more than two hours in this affray, but when the Indians had disappeared we continued our journey, giving thanks to the Lord. The following day we came upon the river of San Juan Bautista, on which we found a village of very peaceful and friendly Indians, from whom we learned by signs that the port of San Diego was not very far away, and that the two ships were there, and that there were fathers dressed in habits like mine. From this settlement a number of Indians guided us from village to village until we reached this port, which, as I have said, is about fifteen leagues distant from the Río de San Juan Bautista.

Although I should like to enlarge upon this narrative more, I cannot, and although I intend to write to my dear Father Martínez, I shall not be able to do so at such length. Therefore I request you to show him this letter and beg him to consider it as his, and tell all the other father companions that I hope they are enjoying the best of health, begging them all most earnestly to keep me in mind in their sacred devotions, and to pray that we may arrive at the port of Monterey as soon as possible, although I do not know what means will be found, since almost all are sick, including the commander of the ships, Don Vicente Vila, and his pilot.

Please, your Reverence, accept the warmest greetings from the fathers and the captain who are all in perfect health. I remain, your Reverence, as always, entirely yours, begging God that he may guard and keep you many years.

From this port of San Diego, June 9, 1769. As always, your Reverence's most affectionate fellow student, friend, and humble servant, who honors you in all things.

FRAY JUAN CRESPI.

1769                                                                                    1911

# JUAN BAUTISTA DE ANZA
## 1736–1788

The journeys of the Spanish conquistador Juan de Oñate—in New Mexico, then in areas to the west and east—had been of epic proportions (see the Oñate headnote and selection, above). Many smaller-scale but still arduous journeys opened up additional southern and western territories for settlement, and one of the most prominent leaders of these expeditions was Juan Bautista de Anza.

Anza was born on the frontier border between what is now Arizona and Sonora, Mexico. His family was Spanish and had a long history in the colonization of the New World and what the Spaniards euphemistically called "pacification" of the Indians. Anza's exploratory bent was stimulated by Fray Francisco Garcés, who lived nearby and who undertook journeys west and north of Arizona and into California, his missionary work with the local Native American tribes having provided Garcés with rudimentary knowledge about those territories.

By 1772, Anza was captain of the Royal Presidio of San Ignacio, at Tubac, near present-day Tucson. The Spanish Crown, anxious about Russian incursions in the Northwest, was encouraging Spanish settlers to secure a stronghold far north. The northern outposts in California were in dire need of supplies, and the ocean routes were dangerous and unpredictable. The necessity for mapping an inside route from Sonora to Monterey was evident to the Crown and Mexico City government officials. Anza decided to organize an expedition that would have a twofold goal: to open a road from Sonora to Monterey and, once the road was marked and mapped out, to bring colonists who would populate northern California.

In 1774, with the help of New Spain's viceroy, Antonio Bucareli, Anza undertook his first expedition. After establishing an inland route, Anza planned for his next major accomplishment: the establishment of a colony north of Monterey. In 1775, Anza's second incursion into California began in the presidio of San Miguel de Horcasitas (near Culiacán, Sinaloa), where he gathered 300 people (men, women, and children), 340 horses, 165 pack mules, and 305 cattle. From Horcasitas, he and the settlers traveled to Tubac. From there, following the Gila River, they crossed the Colorado River and continued on to San Diego, Monterey, and finally San Francisco, where Anza founded the city. According to the historian Herbert Eugene Bolton, this 1,600-mile journey was unequaled during Europe's colonization of the Americas. Bolton compares Anza to the nineteenth-century Anglo American exploration team of Meriwether Lewis and William Clark, but he points out that not even Lewis and Clark led a large group of colonists through such hostile terrain and for such a long period—and with only one death, that of a woman giving birth at the onset of the trek.

For his brilliant success in the California incursions, Anza was appointed governor of New Mexico and served from 1777 until his death. As governor, he "pacified" the Indians, in particular the Comanches, who tended to attack settlements and war with other Indian tribes. In a famous battle, immortalized in the historical folk play *Los Comanches*, Anza defeated the Comanches, who were led by their chief, Cuerno Verde (Green Horn). The following selection is Anza's diary about this expedition and his encounters with the Comanches. This chronicle is a self-portrait of a sharp, determined, entrepreneurial explorer ready to stop at nothing to accomplish his task. He surveys the landscape as a military leader, using scouts to plan his next move. He brings his enemy to its knees and loots after the battle is over, then states, matter-of-factly: "In this matter we had not the least unpleasantness."

## From Diary of Governor de Anza's Expedition against the Comanche Nation, August 15–September 10, 1779[1]

[Sunday, August 15, 1779] At three o'clock in the afternoon the march was begun, route to the north on which six leagues were covered on the Camino Real.[2] Halt was made to pass the night in the vicinity of the pueblo of Pujuaque.

At half-past six in the morning we continued our march on the road, route north, one-quarter to the northwest. On this six leagues were traveled, in the wood of San Juan de los Caballeros. Camped.

[Monday the 16th] This place I designated for the assembling of the combatants mentioned above. Accordingly, I reviewed all on the afternoon of this day. In this review I found the troops provided with three horses to each soldier with arms, munitions of war, and food supplies more than enough for forty days. This was not the case with the settlers and Indians. Because of their well-known poverty and wretchedness, the best equipped presented themselves with two riding beasts, the most of them almost useless; their guns were the same, very few of them having three charges of powder; in everything else the proportion was similar. In view of this I supplied the most needy, each with a good horse from the two hundred that I have extra in the herd at the presidio and all of them with firearms with ten ball cartridge belts.

I immediately provided for the best arrangement of the people making up the expedition, by forming the whole into three divisions, which can be of advantage to it in any event. I gave each one its respective commander whom I appointed. The divisions understood their position which I also indicated for any affray and for the entire march. The first was the vanguard under my command; the second, the rear-guard under the first lieutenant; and the third, under command of the second lieutenant, the center between the two aforesaid and the reserve corps.

At the end of the afternoon I sent two scouts in advance to reconnoitre the points of entrance and departure of the enemy with orders that if they should find no indication or other development not to return until the 20th.

It will not be out of place to note here that I am directing the present expedition along a route and through regions different from those which have been followed previously.[3] Thus I shall not suffer what has always happened so often, that is, to be discovered long before reaching the country in which the enemy lives, as they inform me this is very common and is the reason for the failure of most of the campaigns, and so that I may be able to

1. Translated and edited by Alfred Barnaby Thomas. Unless otherwise indicated, the anthology editors have omitted Thomas's original, highly technical footnotes and his marginal notes recording how many leagues the expedition traveled. Bracketed insertions within the text are Thomas's; the bracketed dates have been adapted from his marginal dates.
2. Royal Road; originally the route, established by Juan de Oñate, from Mexico to Santa Fe, but subsequently any road under the direct jurisdiction of the Spanish Crown and its viceroys. Six leagues: 15.6 miles (a Spanish league then equaling about 2.6 miles). Before beginning its return

journey on September 1, the expedition traveled 120 leagues, or 312 miles.
3. The usual route northeast of Sante Fe in the pursuit of Comanches was either through Pecos or directly east from Taos over the Taos Mountains thence north to the Arkansas River in present southern Colorado. So far as is known Anza's is the first expedition ever made into eastern Colorado of today over the route he followed. However, Anza's statement on August 23 and 27 that the pass (present Ponca Pass) is rarely crossed is an indication that not all of his route was entirely virgin. ° ° ° [Translator/editor's note]

gain the border or boundary of the country indicated for the best success of the undertaking.

[Tuesday the 17th] At a little after six we proceeded along the same road, the Rio del Norte crossed, route to the north-northwest. On this seven leagues were made as far as the deserted pueblo of Ojo Caliente, where camp was pitched for the night, having reached the end of the Camino Real that we have been following.

The above mentioned pueblo is one of those abandoned on account of the hostilities of the enemy, as well as one proposed for the establishment of a presidio. For this reason I devoted myself today surveying it. I found it lacking all the conditions and advantages required for such an establishment. Those who have left it can only make this [selection] possible. Altogether they are twenty-five or thirty families scattered over more than four leagues, their houses unfortified. For this reason, it is not strange that there were such attacks, as this disorder brought upon them the loss of their poor fields to which in substance the possessions of the inhabitants were reduced.

[Wednesday the 18th] At seven o'clock we set out again on our way with the route to the north through terrain considerably broken. Through this eight leagues were made up to the Río de las Nutrias where the journey ended.

[Thursday the 19th] A little before seven we pushed on toward the north. On this were traveled seven leagues through a country similar to that of the preceding day as far as the Río de San Antonio where we stopped to pass the night.

[Friday the 20th] On this day frost and cold as though it were the months appropriate to this weather. At half-past six we resumed our march toward the north through broken terrain which lasted as far as the Río de los Conejos. To this seven leagues were made with which the day's journey ended.

Today the scouts mentioned on the 16th returned to me. They had found no other sign of the enemy than the trail in this very place of the last ones who encroached on our territory.

At the end of the afternoon two hundred men of the Ute and Apache nation[4] also joined me with one of their principal captains. Of the first were those who ever since my assumption of this government have asked me, and have reiterated incessantly with prayers, that they be admitted into my company in confirmation of our friendship, provided I should go on a campaign against the Comanches. I agreed to grant this to them, as much to take advantage of this increase of people as to try in this way to civilize them so that they may at least be more useful to us against the enemy itself than they have been formerly.

With this intent I indicated that they must be at my orders as to what of spoils belonged to them in case of encounters and defeats of the enemy. This, with the exception of personal captures, they would have to agree to divide equally with all my men. To these proposals they consented, promising to observe them.

4. The Ute nation consisted of groups of ethnically related Indians, originally from the West. The Apache nation consisted of several cultur- ally related groups of Indians, originally from the Southwest.

[Saturday the 21st] At six we again returned to our route to the north-northeast through bad country with many ravines, among which, after two leagues, the Río del Pino was crossed. To these three more leagues were added until Las Jaras was reached where the day's journey ended.

[Sunday the 22nd] It was necessary to make the next march at night so that the enemy might not descry the dust of our troop and horseherd from the sierra, not very distant, which we are keeping on our right. For that reason the march of this day was reserved for the night.

At sunset the journey was taken up with route to the north and after a league was made in that direction, the Río de las Timbres was crossed; beyond that another six leagues were made in the same direction, upon which the Río de San Lorenzo was reached at two in the morning.

[Monday the 23rd] At nightfall we again held our course toward the north in which direction we traveled four leagues through fairly good country. At the end of this march we inclined toward the north-northwest for two more leagues upon which the march ended at the Río del Norte where the ford was named El Paso de San Bartolomé.

This river, as is known, empties into the Mar del Norte and the Bay of Espíritu Santo. It has its own source fifteen leagues more or less from this place in the Sierra de la Grulla, which is that on the skirts of which we have traveled since the 17th, it being the one to the west and closest on this route to the principal Villa[5] of this government under my charge.

The Ute nation which is accompanying me, who reside at the said source, and three civilians who have explored it, tell me that the river above proceeds from a great swamp, this having been formed, in addition to its springs, by the continuous melting of snow from some volcanos which are very close.

The same persons also assure me that after fifteen leagues on the breadth of the sierra, one sees seven rivers in a very short distance. These united form in the same way one of considerable size which flows to the west. For this reason and others which I omit, I judge this river to be that which they call the Río Colorado, which merging with the Gila, empties into the Gulf of California. There from the nations who live on it and with whom I have communicated in my travels along it I have quite detailed information of the Ute nation.[6] From this I infer that the two are not far distant from each other.

The same settlers mentioned, who explored the seven rivers referred to, by order of Governor Don Tomás Velez,[7] affirm that on all of them, which are very fertile, they observed that in ancient times they were well populated with Indians, this being demonstrated by the large size of the formal pueblos of three stories and other remains. Among these was [evidence] that the settlers themselves had practised the art of taking out silver, as their ore dumps and other remains of their use were found. They assured me moreover they delivered these fragments to the aforesaid governor, who, according to other reports, sent them to the city of Mexico.

[Tuesday the 24th] As soon as it was night we picked up our route in the same northern direction, by which, and through good land, eight leagues

---

5. Village.
6. Governor Anza refers to his remarkable expedition which opened a route between Sonora and California via the Gila River region. This aspect of his life has been exhaustively treated in the monumental California studies of Professor Herbert E. Bolton. [Translator/editor's note]
7. Tomás Vélez Cachupín, governor of New Mexico 1749–54.

were made. After this we descended four to the north-northwest, upon which we arrived at the break of day following at a pleasant pond named San Luis.

From the beginning of the march we suffered from bitter cold. When as we ended the journey we promised ourselves relief with fires which we were about to kindle, we discovered many fires to the east of us, and believing them of the enemy, we gave up what we had intended. Later these fires were found to be from a camp of long standing, but the mistake was not learned until eight o'clock in the morning.

At this place, on the 10th of July of the present year, a large number of Comanches attacked a greater force of Utes who were camped there with their families. Although the former succeeded in the darkness of the night in capturing all the Ute horses, the latter recovered them, with the added advantage of killing twelve of the robbers, among them a captain. Their bodies with other evidences proved the fact; besides the very victors themselves pointed it out to us.

[Wednesday the 25th] At nightfall we began our march, route to the north for one league, at the end of which we inclined for another two the north. After three more we made to the northwest, we reached an arroyo which was named Santa Xines.

[Thursday the 26th] At four o'clock in the afternoon we continued our route to the northeast. Along it four leagues were marched at the end of which we halted to pass the night and wait the following day in order to cross the bad land which follows. This place was named El Aguage de los Yutas.

Since the swamp of San Luis was left, up to the above-named water-hole, the sierras that we have had to the right and left of us (between which runs the Río del Norte) have drawn much closer together. Those there conjoined run thus to the northwest, their end being unknown.

[Friday the 27th] At seven we forced our way through a very narrow canyon with almost inaccessible sides, and considerable water, the first that runs generally to the northeast and which is the only one that divides the two sierras mentioned. It, being very rarely crossed, cost us considerable work to conquer. This accomplished after traveling five leagues, we came out at the union of this stream of water with a good sized river, which was named San Agustín. There the day's journey ended.

[Saturday the 28th] Just before seven o'clock we set out on the road toward the northeast, and after a little more than a league we crossed to the Río de Napestle which comes from the northwest. It has its rise in the sierra which as already said runs in this direction. After finishing another league we began to cross another medium-sized sierra, which occupied two more leagues. Upon these four more were made to the east through some ranges of hills, where from two in the afternoon until seven we rested the horses. After this, continuing the march in the last named direction, five more leagues were traveled until we arrived at some hills which were named Las Perdidas,[8] because of the trouble we had from the snow and fog which beset us before nightfall.

[Sunday the 29th] At eight o'clock, the weather still bad, we forged ahead to the east. In this direction and through a good country four leagues were made. These over we paused in a good arroyo, as much to refresh the riding beasts as to give time to all the people of the expedition to prepare and dress

8. The Losses.

the meat of fifty head of buffalo they had succeeded in killing in less than ten minutes from the great number which broke in on our march.

A little before twelve the scouts mentioned on the 26th rejoined us, having found nothing worthy of mention. Twenty others were substituted for them at once with orders to meet me on the 31st if nothing of importance occurred before then.

After these scouts had been sent out at the time spoken of, we again took up our route at six in the afternoon to the east-southeast. Along it six leagues were made through good country, with many small streams. The day's journey terminated, the night being now well advanced, at the foot of a high hill which was called Los Ojos Ciegos.

[Monday the 30th] At a little before seven we began to force our way over Sierra Almagre, which is very rough with its ravines and thick woods, route to the east.[9] After eight leagues traveled in this direction, while we were still within the same sierra, halt was made on a river which rises in it, which I called Santa Rosa, to spend the night and await the reports of the spies who should come in tomorrow.

Since from the heights of this place the regions usually inhabited by the enemies may be descried, I had placed lookouts on three eminences to note what might happen until the following day.

[Tuesday the 31st] At half-past ten one of the aforesaid scouts reported that toward the east of where we were encamped clouds of dust were to be seen three leagues distant, and that in the same direction two [persons] apparently were traveling in search of us. For this reason I ordered that our entire train should be ready to march if necessary.

After eleven o'clock two of the scouts previously mentioned arrived, having been sent by their corporal with the information that a considerable number of enemies were raising the dust. They were encamped about a league and a half from where he was on watch. I proposed to go to this place because the site was still hidden and was nearer those whom he was observing and who he feared might come upon his trail, because he had been at dawn that morning at the very spot where they halted.

With this news I resolved to move to the spot mentioned as a more suitable place. The train of baggage and the horseherd advancing more slowly, I left guarded by two hundred men. To its commander I issued the orders I judged necessary, that is to follow me, watching in case of attack, thus not to be unadvised of my whereabouts.

Arrived at this place, the corporal of the scouts informed me that in his opinion we were discovered by his tracks because a little while after the enemy had halted and set up only six tents, four of the Indians came along the trail that he had made until they were very near the place where he was, and that as soon as those who came went back, he advanced a little to reconnoitre their trail and observed that they had collected their tents and all their horses. Accordingly, he judged the enemy proposed to flee.

Convinced by all that has been said that this would happen and that perhaps they observed everything about us, I resolved to attack without delay. This was made from right, left and center, as because it was daylight, and

9. [In roughly the mid-1700s] the Sierra Almagre was the name given the present Front Range of the Rockies in Colorado. [Translator/editor's note]

because of the nature of the plain in which the savages were, we had no opportunity to put them off from the retreat from our front over the same terrain by which they had come. At twelve o'clock, more than a half a league away from their camp, it was inevitable that they should discover us. They had already caught all their horses, the mounts as well as the spare ones, but withal they did not sally forth as customarily to meet the troop, whom they observed drawn up in a form they had never before seen. Consequently, all being mounted, even to the women and children, they undertook precipitous flight, notwithstanding that the number of families equalled more than one hundred and twenty tents, whose wooden frames only had been set up. Disregarding this, we pursued them in the best order possible. In three leagues we began to overtake the men, who faced us. The fight with them lasted about another league, during which we succeeded in killing eighteen of the most valiant and in wounding many.

It was necessary to take more than thirty women and children, the latter running where their fathers were. Thirty-four of these were captured, besides all the horse herd, more than five hundred head. This was the last thing done, after the horses could run no farther. None escaped except the mounts of the Indians fleeing. They lost all their goods and baggage; even the most necessary articles they abandoned where they had begun to make their camp. There was so much of this material that it could not be loaded on a hundred horses. The spoil our people seized, dividing it equally. In this matter we had not the least unpleasantness.

It is impossible accurately to state the number of the enemy with whom we fought because the men were clothed as their women with whom they fled and veiled in the dust of the horseherd they sought to save. It was impossible to count them, especially when the slaughter began, for the reason that they scattered widely. Accordingly, there is no way to calculate other than by the number of tents they prepared to raise, and which, as already said, were more than one hundred and twenty. It is well known that in each tent six to eight fighting men live.[1]

At half-past four I returned to the watering place and pasture where the defeated enemy had been encamped. To this place the name of Río del Sacramento[2] was given, this expedition having been dedicated to this most Holy Mystery.[3] Notwithstanding that from the time when the first prisoners were taken, I asked questions about the rest of their rancherías to ascertain whether I could strike another blow, I drew nothing certain from them until nine o'clock at night, when the last two informed me that their chief or captain-general, Cuerno Verde, having gone with four of his principal captains and many of his people on a campaign to our country, had ordered them all to gather at this place to receive him and celebrate the triumph that he flattered himself he would secure; that it had been about sixteen days since he had marched away, and that for this purpose for two days a great number of rancherías were marching in the direction whence they had fled and whence those escaped from us had gone.

1. Thomas notes that other estimates, including one by Anza, indicate that in each lodge there were three to four warriors, seven to eight women and children.
2. Present Fountain Creek. ° ° ° The battle was fought apparently near present Wigwam, Colorado. [Translator/editor's note]
3. I.e., to the Christian sacrament of the Eucharist, or Communion.

With this information and without hope of gaining anything from those since they would have news of us very much in advance, I determined, although the time was propitious for my return, to follow the trail of Cuerno Verde, to see if fortune would grant me an encounter with him. I proposed to seek this by whatever means were possible, as much because his punishment would be quick and opportune, as in order to restore the prisoners that he might be bringing from our country in case he had succeeded in striking a blow. The night of this day was passed with the greatest precautions; and nothing happened worthy of mention.

[Wednesday, September 1] In prosecution of my intention at seven o'clock in the morning having set out to discover the trail sought, I came upon it at ten o'clock, and, having ordered that the advance scouts should always travel to the right and left of it, by day as well as by night, I pressed ahead. After seven leagues in the direction of the east-southeast, night forced a stop at the end of the same Sacramento River because many of the settlers' horses were jaded.

[Thursday the 2nd] A little before seven we forged ahead to the south, and after traveling three leagues recrossed the Río de Napestle where we found horses of the enemy whom we were following. Those were caught. After this, without giving any notice, most of the Ute nation left for their country.[4] Along the same route five more leagues were made. At the end of these in a rocky arroyo we rested the horses until four in the afternoon. At this hour we again took up our route, and a league ahead, one of the advance scouts returned with the information that the enemies approaching were unaware of us. So that they should not discover us at a great distance away, I had hid our horseherd and train, and the entire troop, which I placed where it seemed to me most advantageous for surprising the rebels who in a quite large force although considerably scattered were skirting some fairly heavily wooded mountains. Intervening between us was a little narrow valley which I had not time to examine.

At sunset the barbarians reached the valley, and we were forced to attack them with the column under my command, which it seemed they were expecting. However, noting the other two columns about united to surround them, they gave themselves up to a blind and headlong flight. Although eight were killed and a considerable number wounded, not many perished as we had the misfortune to waste considerable time in crossing one by one the bottom of a boggy gully which the valley hid. Our advance was more than a half a league on the other side. During that time they scattered completely. Because night was falling they had been able to escape as much because of this as well as from the previously mentioned loss [of time on our part]. If they had held firm on the side of the gully opposite us, then we might not have been able to cross if they had succeeded in defending it under cover of its woods. From this I infer that they had no knowledge of the gully or that because of the surprise did not think of doing so.

At half-past eight at night I withdrew to this gully which I crossed again with great trouble in the darkness to the place ordered for our horseherd and baggage to pass the rest of the night.

4. The Utes originally occupied eastern Utah, western Colorado, and parts of New Mexico and Wyoming. After the arrival of the Spaniards, the Utes consolidated and are now associated mainly with Utah and Colorado.

Those acquainted with the country and the mode of war usually practised in it advised me to abandon the spot, as they had always done so, warning me that those recently routed could retaliate in the darkness of the night, especially if they should succeed in uniting. Judging this as difficult according to the knowledge that I have of other Indians, as well as this proposal might have something of cowardice in it, I replied that the very thing they feared I desired; that they should understand that even in case the encounter had not been decided so much in our favor, we ought for the honor of our arms to wait on the spot until dawn of the following day, and that, until then, it was proper that we should remain under arms. This was done. We passed the night in great inconvenience because of rain and severe cold which prevailed during the greater part of it, but without any other disturbance whatever.

[Friday the 3rd] Accordingly at daylight I had the immediate neighborhood reconnoitred. Nothing of any consequence having been found, I ordered the whole troop to prepare to march. This was begun at seven o'clock.

At the beginning of our march a few of the enemy showed themselves, apparently wishing to cross the region that we were leaving through the very place which we had opened a road over the gully spoken of above. These few were joined by a great number. Accordingly, lest something untoward should happen I remained with the first and second column on the rear and ordered the third, the reserve corps, as vanguard, and that all should continue the march. For this purpose I required that the first two columns should hold some fair sized woods on our right and left through which we had to pass for a distance of half a league.

At the wood the enemy had already increased to more than forty, and they drew almost within gunshot, firing off their own muskets. In this way was recognized from his insignia and devices the famous chief Cuerno Verde, who, his spirit proud and superior to all his followers, left them and came ahead his horse curvetting spiritedly. Accordingly, I determined to have his life and his pride and arrogance precipitated him to this end.

To accomplish this I ordered the vanguard on coming out of the woods which concealed their formation to join battle with two hundred lightly burdened men, that the cavalry and loaded animals with their guards should aid the vanguard for the purpose of forcing the enemy against this body if I succeeded in enclosing them as I planned with a half circle I was considering forming with the columns of the rear guard, and in order that the rear guard need not remain on watch over the horseherd and train while it was precipitating the enemy into the gully already mentioned. Thus should perish there those most important to us, that is, the party immediately behind the leader of the barbarians, cut off from their right and left flank.

In order to execute both purposes and to fatigue as much as possible the horses of the enemy, in whose swiftness he placed his confidence for attacking and escaping, I withdrew swiftly apart from our Indian auxiliaries as though in retreat, but when my first plan was about to take effect the principal chieftain understood it and ordered all his men to retire. In view of this I proceeded to my second purpose and succeeded at once in cutting off from the larger body Cuerno Verde with his leading followers and they fell into the trap and the said gully. There without other recourse they sprang to the ground and intrenched behind their horses made in this manner a defense as brave as it was glorious. Notwithstanding the aforesaid Cuerno

Verde perished, with his first-born son, the heir to his command, four of his most famous captains, a medicine man who preached that he was immortal, and ten more, who were able to get in the place indicated.

A larger number might have been killed, but I preferred the death of this chief even to more of those who escaped, because of his being constantly in this region the cruel scourge of this kingdom, and because he had exterminated many pueblos, killing hundreds and making as many prisoners whom he afterwards sacrificed in cold blood. His own nation accuse him, ever since he took command, of forcing them to take up arms and volunteer against the Spaniards, a hatred of whom has dominated him because his father who also held the same command and power met death at our hands.

I infer that his death was caused by his own intrepidity and the contempt that he wished to show for our people, being vaunted by the many successes that they have always obtained over us because of the irregularities with which they have always warred. He feared for the main body of his people who were defeated the afternoon before. This defeat had not been unknown to him for a musket lost in the battle by our Indian auxiliaries was in his possession, and withal, he had the temerity with fifty men of his daily and personal guard, to attack six hundred men in good formation. From this should be deduced the arrogance, presumption and pride which characterized this barbarian, and which he manifested until the last moment in various ways, disdaining even to load his own musket, which was done for him three times by another, while in the interval he was in danger.

All of our people and the prisoners say his death will be greatly lamented but I believe that their regret will not exceed the pleasure our people have had in it. Among our force we had no greater disaster than a slight bullet wound received by a light-horse soldier. From some of the dead were taken five muskets, today an article which is plentiful among these heathen.

Although I tarried in this place which was named Los Dolores de María Santíssima until half-past ten to observe if there be any return of the barbarians, nothing was seen but the dust and smoke of their retreat which was made out for a distance of twelve leagues. From this it is inferred that those are the same who were defeated on the previous afternoon.[5]

At the hour mentioned, after much cheering by our people in the name of the king and the superior chief who commands us, I set out toward the south. In this direction through good country, five leagues were made until we reached the first stream and arroyo of La Sangre de Cristo where passed the night.

[Saturday the 4th] A little before seven we continued our route along the same direction, and from the first we began to recross the sierra that we had on our right in going. It was extremely fatiguing from its constant alternations of ascents and descents and to this was added a violent wind and fog. At five in the afternoon we came down to its foot, after eight leagues of travel to the place of the Ciénega.

[Sunday the 5th] At half-past seven we again set out on our march on the said route through good country, during which we progressed ten leagues

5. Anza probably crossed the Arkansas near present Pueblo, Colorado, and continued somewhat east of the San Carlos River towards the foot of the present Greenhorn Peak. It was in this vicinity that the battle occurred. * * * [Translator/editor's note]

in the whole day. At the end of this we arrived at the Río de la Culebra and the day's journey was ended.

Because on reaching this place we found seven horses killed by the enemies whom we had met on the third, and other signs of treatment of wounds, I had it examined with great care. This resulted in the discovery of a grave in which were the same number of bodies [seven] which proved to us that they perished in the attack which we suppose they made on the pueblo of Taos, whence it appears the trail comes.

On this same day, before twelve o'clock, that part of the Ute nation which had remained, left for their country enriched and satisfied, and without farewells, for their barbarity and desire again to see their country did not admit this civility.

[Monday the 6th] At seven o'clock we continued our route with destination for the pueblo of Taos to obtain information of what had happened there. We traveled to the south and after making ten leagues during the entire day, the journey came to an end at the Río del Dátil.

[Tuesday the 7th] A little before seven we proceeded and after concluding three leagues, forded the Río Colorado. Up to this we had had good country. From here we began to skirt the sierra which we had on our left. Along this route and with its many difficulties another five leagues were marched until we arrived at four o'clock in the afternoon at the pueblo of Taos, which is the most northern one of all those of this kingdom.

Before reaching the pueblo, its alcalde,[6] with whom I had communicated in advance my coming in order not to cause him surprise, came out to meet me. He informed me that having been notified by our Apache friends six days before they attacked the pueblo under his command, which occurred on the 31st of last month, that many enemies were coming, he prepared to receive them. He even advised the interior of the kingdom to do the same, in case the attack should turn in another direction. In consequence of this, he placed scouts on the usual roads of the barbarians. In this way it was possible on the night of the 30th for the scouts to signal him with fires that the enemy was marching on the pueblo which he then put under arms. They found it so on the day mentioned.

The first attack of the enemy, made at twilight, he assured me was vigorous, but as soon as they recognized the new state of defense which the place has because it is one of those I had made into a square with triangular fortifications on the corners, their surprise was so great that he was able to fire on them sallying forth from the wall, [tactics] which from [within] they could not attempt, nor attack the enemy. With this foray he succeeded in killing three, wounding many and frightening off all whom he judged to number two hundred and fifty. They then took the prudent part of retiring to much greater distance, to examine the town in this way. There they remained until nine in the morning when their retreat began, preceded by a great havoc which they wrought in the cornfields.

The only loss this pueblo sustained was that of a young man, who, although he was inside at the time of the attack, went out unknown to the alcalde to see if he could save a horse which he saw in a cornfield, judging it to be his own. He found that it belonged to the enemy who killed him.

6. Mayor.

The enemy's loss, from what the alcalde states and from what is related on the 6th, amounts to ten deaths in this attack alone, a disaster which in the many attacks that they have made has never been experienced. This is attributed to the fact that as all its inhabitants were not needed as before to defend the seven corners and as many other salient or exposed parts it had, they employed themselves in attacking the assailants, being able to sally out for the purpose for more than seventy *varas*[7] from the new wall.

[Wednesday the 8th] At half-past seven we continued our march along the Camino Real to Santa Fe, which in general runs towards the south. After ten leagues were made on it we arrived at the pueblo of Embudo.

[Thursday the 9th] At half-past seven we again set out over the above-mentioned route and direction. On this nine leagues were traveled. The march ended at the pueblo of Pujuaque.

[Friday the 10th] At seven o'clock we continued our way by the aforesaid direction and course, and then after six leagues arrived at the Villa of Santa Fe. There I received information communicated by the Ute nation from those who, as recorded, left us on the 2nd at the Río de Napestle, that they had the good fortune to surprise seven Comanches in their houses with their families, the latter being nine, women and children, who perished at their hands with the men, with the exception of one child who surrendered alive to them. At the same time they seized forty saddle horses the barbarians had, with the rest of the articles of their use and service.

With this loss, those which have been referred to, which the Comanches suffered on the 31st, 2nd, and 3rd, with that which is stated at the pueblo of Taos amount to fifty-eight men and sixty-three women and children, making a total of one hundred and thirty-one persons. With this information, and the statement that the sum of leagues amounted to two hundred and five covered on this expedition, ends the diary which it relates.

1779                                                                              1930

---

7. The length of the Spanish *vara*, or yard, differed at various times and places, but 70 *varas* probably equaled about 210 feet.

# Annexations: 1811–1898

From the start of the Spanish Crown's colonization of the New World, the colonies were perceived on the Iberian Peninsula as a bottomless treasure box from which to extract the money needed to keep Spain's economy afloat. However, the Spanish Empire's collapse began as early as 1588, with the defeat of the Spanish Armada—the "invincible" fleet commanded by the legendary Duke of Medina-Sidonia—by the British Navy. This defeat was part of Britain's effort to counterbalance the imperial power gained by the Spanish Crown in the New World. During the next few centuries, the Spanish Empire was weakened by fiscal chaos, diplomatic arrogance and missteps, and poor leadership. The House of Habsburg began ruling Spain in the sixteenth century, but a century later this dynasty was characterized by mismanagement. Beginning in 1635, the Habsburgs fought against the French during the final and bloodiest phase of the Thirty Years War. In 1808, Napoléon Bonaparte, the emperor of France, intervened in a quarrel between Spain's king, Charles IV, and Charles's son Ferdinand. Napoléon invaded Spain, took Charles and Ferdinand prisoner, and placed on the throne his older brother, Joseph Bonaparte, known in Spain as Pepe Botella (Pepe the Bottle) because of his appetite for alcohol. With significant help from England, the Spanish and the Portuguese fought Wars of Liberation against the French, using guerilla tactics. By 1813, the occupiers had been pushed back into France.

All of this unrest caused the Spanish to lose authority in Latin America, where armed uprisings occurred from Argentina to Mexico. The Spanish-speaking Americas (including Mexico, Cuba, and Puerto Rico), still in gestation, were swept by a nationalistic fervor that would define Latino life in the United States for centuries. This period is roughly delineated by the call of the *criollo* (Creole) class in New Spain for Mexican independence, in 1810, and the Spanish-American War, in 1898, when Spain lost control of the Caribbean Basin and the United States initiated a process of geopolitical domination in the region.

By the turn of the nineteenth century, the bourgeoisie in European countries such as Germany, France, England, and Italy had become a driving force for change, embracing freedom and equality and promoting ideals of free enterprise. In Spain, these ideals were consistently crushed by the Counter-Reformation, which kept the Catholic Church as the sole legislator of political, social, and moral affairs. In the colonies, across the Atlantic, the Church tightly regulated the type of literature that was imported. It prohibited the publication and dissemination of fiction (which at the time meant novels), considered dangerously capable of pushing the reader, in the Church's view, "on an evil path."

## The Age of Nationalism

In the New World colonies, the fever for independence began with the Spanish Empire's internal strife and inability to handle its overseas affairs, but it was heightened by the struggles for self-government in the United States and France. In 1776, the British colonies in North America began the American Revolution by seceding from England. Thirteen years later, in Paris, the French Revolution was jump-started by the storming of the Bastille, the fortress-prison where criminals as well as religious and political prisoners were held. Among the educated *criollo* elite from California to the River Plate, widespread skepticism about autonomy turned into a cry for freedom.

In 1810, the Mexican priest Miguel Hidalgo y Costilla rang the church bells in his town of Dolores (now called Dolores Hidalgo, in a state also named after him)—an act called *el grito de Dolores*—to declare the start of an armed struggle against Spain. Simultaneously, in Argentina, the May Revolution established the First Government Junta; in 1816, a congress in the Argentinian capital, Tucumán, declared independence from Spain. Spain would not officially grant Argentina its freedom until 1862, but the declaration itself soon inspired the Argentinian general José de San Martín and his Pan-American army to liberate Chile and Peru. By the 1830s, a vast portion of the southern continent—including countries such as Bolivia, Colombia, Paraguay, and Uruguay—had officially broken ties with Europe.

Father Hildalgo was by no means the first orchestrator of rebellions against Spanish rule; he was predated by revolutionary figures such as the late-eighteenth- and early-nineteenth-century Venezuelan Francisco de Miranda. But the transition to independence was difficult. Internal power struggles made democracy an elusive system of government. Local support was limited, and foreign powers did not offer sustained support. The frequent collapse of civil authority—and a narrow conception of military culture, with *criollo* officers having only limited power—meant the struggle for independence often depended on a particular leader's personality. The famous South American liberator Simón Bolívar embraced *La Gran Colombia*, his contemporary Miranda's idea of uniting territory that encompassed Columbia, Venezuela, Ecuador, Panama, the Caribbean coast of Costa Rica, and small parts of what are today Brazil, Peru, and Guyana. Bolívar attempted to form a centralist government in Bogotá, Columbia, with a lifetime presidency for himself. But a civil society based on universal principles of law and tolerance proved elusive. The historian J. H. Elliott, in his book *Empires of the Atlantic World* (2006), argues that "although the Spanish empire possessed a superficial unity given by its common culture, there was no way in which its territorial integrity could be conserved in the wake of emancipation." The challenge, Elliott adds, stemmed from the vast scale of the territory and its extreme physical and climatic diversity as well as the strength of local and regional traditions that had developed over three centuries of imperial rule. In Mexico, after autonomy was declared in 1821, the Michoacán-born soldier Agustín de Iturbide proclaimed himself the first Mexican emperor. Although his effort was short-lived, it inaugurated a sequence of dictatorial regimes interspersed with periods of democratic rule. In Argentina, opposing ideological groups, the Federales and the Unitarios, were locked in conflict until a constitution was promulgated in 1853.

The prevailing aesthetic movement in Europe at the time was Romanticism, and its central tenets (the celebration of Nature, the exaltation of a supreme being as Nature's sole orchestrator, the belief in individual fate, and the acknowledgment of human emotion as the driving force in life) colored the arts in the Spanish Americas. In literature, a patriotic spirit emerged. Nationalism became the central motif, as reflected in the work of Spanish-speaking writers who lived, at various points in their careers, in the United States. Among these writers is Félix Varela, a Cuban-born religious and philosophical thinker (he was ordained as a priest) who spent his early years in Florida. He also lived in New York City, where he edited a magazine, *El Habanero*, that served as a voice for Cuban exiles. He sought to bring about independence for Cuba, but his feelings toward Spain and the United States are marked by a measured tone. Another expatriate was José María Heredia, a lawyer and one of the most significant Romantic poets in Latin America; for engaging in revolutionary activities, he was exiled from Cuba in 1823. He spent two years living in places along the northeastern coast of the United States—including Boston, New York (where he was a teacher), a town near New Haven, and Philadelphia—after which he moved to Mexico. Heredia's poetry celebrates Nature in a way that became fashionable among the New England Transcendentalists at midcentury. But his nationalistic political engagement makes his literature unique: His work is defined by emotional longing for his abandoned homeland, a nostalgic connection that would become a hallmark of Latino writing in the United States.

Indeed, Varela and Heredia's exiled consciousnesses (their activities served as a matrix for the Cuban-exile community in the 1820s and 1830s), as well as their engagement as Spanish-language writers in U.S. intellectual debates, make them key figures in the creation of the Latino literary tradition. Unlike the Iberian conquistadors, explorers, and missionaries of the colonial period, they are among the foundational figures for Hispanic culture in the United States. It is safe to say that the early writing of Cuban exiles was a particularly crucial element in the construction of the Latino tradition. In 1858, an anthology of poems by Cuban exiles inspired by Varela, *El laúd del desterrado* (The Exile's Lute), was published in New York City. Its contents had originally appeared in small, Spanish-language periodicals in the United States. After Puerto Rico and Cuba declared their independence from Spain—prematurely, in 1868, with the *Grito de Lares* and *Grito de Yara* insurrections—the influx of Antillean expatriates to the United States continued because people feared for their lives. New York was a major center for these exiles, and in the city's Spanish-language press, Puerto Rican patriots such as Ramón Emeterio Betances and Eugenio María de Hostos wrote about the independence struggle and nation-building. Toward the end of the century, José Martí, eventually the most iconic figure in the Cuban-exile community, would redefine the movement's ideological and aesthetic views.

## Mestizaje

The caste system established in the Americas during the colonial period resulted in an ethnic hierarchy that placed *españoles* (Iberians) at the top, followed by the *criollos*, self-described as "Spaniards born in American lands." At the bottom were the *indígenas*, and in between were the black slaves imported from Africa as well as mulattos and other racial combinations resulting from miscegenation between the *españoles*, *criollos*, and *indígenas*. Among these combinations—and unquestionably the largest social class—were the *mestizos*, people born from the intermingling of *españoles* and *indígenas*. (Chronicles from the colonization period consistently refer to the *mestizo* as *el hijo de la conquista*, the child of conquest.) Though this basic hierarchy existed everywhere, racial stratification varied from one country to another. For example, in Mexico and Central America there were relatively few African slaves. In the Caribbean, there were many; their labor was essential to the plantations, around which the colonial economy had been organized.

The concept of miscegenation became the leitmotif of political and cultural matters. In Mexico—which at the time spanned from the territory of Alta California in the north, formed in 1804 with Franciscan and Dominican missions, to Yucatán and Chiapas in the south—the *mestizo* character was omnipresent at all levels of life. For instance, the national symbol, an eagle seated on a cactus emerging from a rock in the middle of a lake, came from the Aztec creation myth of the city of Tenochtitlán, now Mexico City. *La Virgen de Guadalupe*, a *mestiza* version of the Virgin Mary, became the country's matron saint. Brown-skinned and dressed in colorful regalia, she accompanied Father Hidalgo in his quest for independence. The Spanish past, in contrast, was repudiated. In its stead, a pantheon of *mestizo* icons—upheld by leaders beginning with Father Hidalgo and, later, Father José María Morelos y Pavón, as well as President Benito Juárez, the dictator Porfirio Díaz, and, in the early half of the twentieth century, the nationalist leader Lázaro Cárdenas—signaled racial crossbreeding as the nation's makeup of choice. This choice would be decisive in defining Mexico vis-à-vis the United States: *Mestizaje*, defined as racial and cultural mixing, has been Mexico's strategy for distinguishing its population from that of its northern neighbor—during the eighteenth and nineteenth centuries, a mainly white, Anglo-Saxon, and Protestant society with huge numbers of slaves. The countries of South America did not use the term *mestizo*, but had a similar concept.

Defined as a consciousness marked by ambivalence, *mestizaje* serves as a kaleidoscopic lens through which we can understand Latino identity in the United States. José Vasconcelos, in his book *The Cosmic Race* (1925), which includes the influential essay "Mestizaje," offered a rereading of world history from this perspective, stating that in Mexico the miscegenation between Iberians and Indians produced a Bronze Race destined to control the globe. (See Appendix 3: Influential Essays by Latin American Writers, p. A65.) Vasconcelos, who encountered U.S. culture during his childhood and who sought asylum in the United States during crucial moments in his political career, used *mestizaje* as an overarching theme in examining the historical role, from the colonial period onward, of Latinos north of the Rio Grande, along with Mexicans on the other side of the border. He believed that Darwinism was a pseudoscientific theory devised to justify the superiority of Europeans over other people. Vasconcelos offered an alternative social hierarchy of his own, arguing that the "fifth" race, coming from the Americas, would go beyond color to erect a new civilization: *Universópolis.*

The reverberations of the concept of *mestizaje* are manifold among Latinos in the United States. For the Mexican component of the minority, the Virgin of Guadalupe is a central icon. In the late 1960s and the 1970s, César Chávez, Dolores Huerta, and other leaders of the Chicano Movement used her image in marches, meetings, and labor strikes. Furthermore, this *mestizo* worldview is showcased by the mythical Chicano homeland of Aztlán, a Xanadu-like utopia based on the idea that the original Mexicans descended from the northern states. In other words, first were Chicanos and then came Mexico, not the other way around. This idea helps explain why some leaders of the Chicano Movement, in their speeches and writings, rejected any link to Mexico.

The ambivalence of *mestizaje*—that a single race embodying two distinct heritages can be both unified and marginalized—is a ubiquitous ingredient in the Latino literary tradition, starting in the nineteenth century. It appears, tacitly, in Eulalia Pérez's "An Old Woman Remembers," part of a collection of oral histories commissioned by the American historian and ethnologist Hubert Howe Bancroft for his history of California, which details the dispossession felt by people from different classes and eras. In her recollections, Pérez presents herself as proud and self-reliant, seizing her place in the world without loyalties or debts to others, connecting neither with Mexico nor with the United States. In his memoirs, the political leader Juan Nepomuceno Seguín conveys a different kind of ambivalence. Seguín had fought on the Tejano and Anglo side during the Battle of the Alamo and later switched to become a prominent Texan, only to find himself disappointed by the Anglo treatment of *mexicanos.* In covering the years that mark the demise of Mexican rule in Texas and the establishment of the Texas Republic, Seguín describes not knowing how to help his people: On one hand, he was proud of his involvement in bringing down the Mexican domination of the region; on the other hand, he regretted the new state of affairs. In *The Cosmic Race*, Vasconcelos labels this kind of ambivalence "a trait of character among *mestizos.*"

## The Making of the Modern United States

The burning desire of the United States to become a world power, ignited soon after the country became independent, was realized partly at the expense of the Latino population of the Southeast and Southwest. In 1803, the United States bought the territory of Louisiana from France. By the middle of the nineteenth century, the Democratic Party had begun to turn the catchphrase *Manifest Destiny* into an ideology. The belief embodied in the phrase was that the nation was destined to expand from the Atlantic coast to the Pacific coast—"from sea to shining sea." As articulated during the presidency of Andrew Jackson (1829–37), the concept became firmly established as a blueprint for the nation's ambitious future.

The nation's expansion was grounded in the Monroe Doctrine, proclaimed by President James Monroe in 1823, in his seventh annual State of the Union address to Congress. The doctrine established, in part:

> The citizens of the United States cherish sentiments the most friendly, in favor of the liberty and happiness of their fellow men on that side of the Atlantic [i.e., in Europe]. In the wars of the European powers, in matters relating to themselves, we have never taken any part, nor does it comport with our policy to do so. It is only when our rights are invaded, or seriously menaced, that we resent injuries, or make preparation for our defence. With the movements in this hemisphere, we are, of necessity, more immediately connected, and by causes which must be obvious to all enlightened and impartial observers. The political system of the allied powers is essentially different, in this respect, from that of America. This difference proceeds from that which exists in their respective governments. And to the defence of our own, which has been achieved by the loss of so much blood and treasure, and matured by the wisdom of their most enlightened citizens, and under which we have enjoyed unexampled felicity, this whole nation is devoted. We owe it, therefore, to candor, and to the amicable relations existing between the United States and those powers, to declare, that we should consider any attempt on their part to extend their system to any portion of this hemisphere, as dangerous to our peace and safety. With the existing colonies or dependencies of any European power we have not interfered, and shall not interfere. But with the governments who have declared their independence, and maintained it, and whose independence we have, on great consideration, and on just principles, acknowledged, we could not view any interposition for the purpose of oppressing them, or controlling, in any other manner, their destiny, by any European power in any other light than as the manifestation of an unfriendly disposition towards the United States. In the war between those new governments and Spain we declared our neutrality at the time of their recognition, and to this we have adhered, and shall continue to adhere, provided no change shall occur, which, in the judgment of the competent authorities of this government, shall make a corresponding change, on the part of the United States, indispensable to their security.

The Monroe Doctrine came at a time when the countries of the Americas were seeking their national destinies. It suggested that Europeans had no business on the western side of the Atlantic and presented the United States as the protective sibling of the other countries of the Americas. Also stated was that any invasion by foreign powers of American territories was a threat to the national security of the United States. At first, the Monroe Doctrine attracted little attention. But this last idea, of regional stability as national security, created an excuse for the United States to become an invading power. The doctrine was used by later U.S. presidents, from James Polk to Theodore Roosevelt to Ronald Reagan, as a rationale for the military invasion or hegemonic control of other American nations, such as the annexation of Texas (in 1895); the taking control of Cuba and Puerto Rico (during the Spanish-American War, 1898); the support of the Contras, in Honduras, against the Sandinistas, in Nicaragua (in the 1980s); the invasion of Grenada (in 1983); and the invasion of Panama (in 1989).

Manifest Destiny also underlay the U.S. expansion into the Southwest. During Mexico's initial years of self-government, when Agustín de Iturbide proclaimed himself emperor (1822–23), internal chaos extended to the northern frontier, and the Mexican government allowed U.S. settlers to establish themselves there to help stabilize the region. Soon, however, the English-language inhabitants in the region outnumbered the Spanish speakers. In 1836, taking advantage of the nascent country's political disarray and feeling itself geographically and politically disconnected from the trifles taking place in distant Mexico City, the territory of Texas seceded from Mexico. Mexico did not recognize the move and declared Texas a rebel state. A battle occurred in San Jacinto, as Texans, commanded by Sam Houston, fought the Mexican army, led by General Antonio López de Santa Anna. After being captured, the general concluded the fight. The agreement he signed, the Treaty of Velasco, granted Texas its autonomy, but was not recognized by the political elite in Mexico. Soon after adopting a constitution, Texas made efforts to be annexed by the United States. Nine years later, in 1845, this annexation occurred. The following year, after a series of military skirmishes accompanied by diplomatic efforts, a war began, and the United States invaded Mexico.

The war lasted until February 1848, when the Treaty of Guadalupe Hidalgo was signed. (For the text, see Appendix 2: Treaties, Acts, and Propositions, p. A15.) This document established Texas as part of the United States, and under its terms Mexico sold to the United States, for $15 million, more than 500,000 square miles of land. Thus approximately 40 percent of Mexico became parts of the modern-day U.S. states of Colorado, Arizona, New Mexico, and Wyoming, as well as the whole of California, Nevada, and Utah. In the annexed territory, there were about 1,000 Mexican families in Alta California and 7,000 in New Mexico. These people—*españoles*, *criollos*, *mestizos*, and *indios*—had at best a fragile connection to the government in Mexico City. In *Occupied America*, his seminal account of Chicano history (originally published in 1972 but revised several times since), the American historian Rodolfo Acuña notes that approximately 12,000 people lived in the transferred territories that today constitute the Southwest. He writes: "The United States acquired a colony two and a half times the size of France, containing rich farmlands and natural resources such as gold, silver, zinc, copper, oil and uranium, which would make possible its unprecedented industrial boom." In the United States and Mexico, news of the geographical rupture spread rapidly in cities, but failed to penetrate rural areas. The Spanish-speaking population perceived the change with suspicion. The *californios*, residents of Mexican descent living in Alta and Baja Californias, felt betrayed. Meanwhile, the Anglo population concentrated in California and Texas consolidated power.

Article V of the Treaty of Guadalupe Hidalgo stipulated that the border started in the Gulf of Mexico and moved westward to the California Pacific coast. The article stated that the two governments would appoint a commissioner and a surveyor to establish the exact line. Other sections of the treaty dealt with policing and future arbitration should tension arise between the two governments. Articles VIII to X discussed sensitive issues, some of which would be hotly contested by future generations. Article VIII stated:

> Mexicans now established in territories previously belonging to Mexico, and which remain for the future within the limits of the United States, as defined by the present treaty, shall be free to continue where they now reside, or to remove at any time to the Mexican Republic, retaining the property which they possess in the said territories, or disposing thereof, and removing the proceeds wherever they please, without their being subjected, on this account, to any contribution, tax or charge whatever.
>
> Those who shall prefer to remain in the said territories, may either retain the title and rights of Mexican citizens, or acquire those of citizens of the United States. But they shall be under the obligation to make their election within one year from the date of the exchange of ratifications of this treaty: and those who shall remain in the said territories, after the expiration of that year, without having declared their intention to retain the character of Mexicans, shall be considered to have elected to become citizens of the United States.
>
> In the said territories, property of every kind, now belonging to Mexicans, not established there, shall be inviolably respected. The present owners, the heirs of these, and all Mexicans who may hereafter acquire said property by contract, shall enjoy with respect to it, guarantees equally ample as if the same belonged to citizens of the United States.

The statement that within a year Mexicans in the transferred territories were to freely announce if they would remain in the United States or would move to Mexico was ambitious at best and deceitful at worst. First, given the relative isolation of the areas involved, many residents would not receive news for a long time. Second, because many of these people had deep and historical connections to the land, the thought of being uprooted would discomfort them. Article XIX went further:

> The Mexicans who, in the territories aforesaid, shall not preserve the character of citizens of the Mexican Republic, conformably with what is stipulated in the preceding article, shall be incorporated into the Union of the United States, and be admitted at the proper time (to be judged of by the Congress of the United States) to the enjoyment of all the rights of citizens of the United States, according to the principles of the Constitution; and in the mean time, shall be maintained and protected in the free enjoyment of their liberty and property, and secured in the free exercise of their religion without restriction.

Not allowed to voice its own opinion on the matter, the Mexican population in the territories was incorporated into the United States. Immediately, the arrival of Anglos to the region established a new hierarchy of power whereby Mexicans were pushed to the lower strata. Racism, xenophobia, and, more specifically, outright anti-Mexicanism would keep them thus for generations. Before the treaty was signed, the U.S. Senate deleted Article X, which guaranteed the protection of Mexican land grants. Among Chicanos that deletion remains a source of animosity toward the United States.

The effects of the Treaty of Guadalupe Hidalgo on Latino civilization were numerous and enormous. Among the majority of Latinos, the agreement fostered a feeling of usurpation, fragmentation, and resentment. The educated elite found that the coordinates of its world had suddenly changed. The old Spanish way was suddenly replaced by an Anglo approach. The Latina writer María Amparo Ruiz de Burton, in her 1885 novel, *The Squatter and the Don* (along with her 1872 novel, *Who Would Have Thought It?*, which was published anonymously and is the first Latino novel known to have appeared in English), criticized the land appropriations in California by Anglo ranchers and foreigners to the territory, and she sympathized with the frustrated local population. The type of melodrama Ruiz de Burton employed was in vogue in New York literary circles of the age. Her wealthy characters, Anglo and Latino, appear dignified, while the members of the lower classes look brute and immoral. Still, *The Squatter and the Don*, widely read in its day, was essential in publicizing the situation of the Mexican landowners, whose property was supposedly protected by the treaty but who were helpless against the encroachments of squatters and of speculators.

While Ruiz de Burton was among the Latino writers who looked to the northeastern United States for inspiration, other nineteenth-century writers in the Latino literary tradition looked south and embraced Mexican literature. In Santa Fe, which served as a regional capital, newspapers such as *El Crepúsculo de la Libertad* and *El Boletín Popular* regularly featured poetry, stories, anecdotes, and *piezas costumbristas*, impressionistic snapshots of life in the area. Just a handful of the literary pieces, seen today as cornerstones in the shaping of the Latino literary tradition, have survived, among them an early novel by Manuel M. Salazar. Of particular importance are the writings of the Chacóns, a distinguished and well-educated New Mexican family.

In his stories "El hijo de la tempestad" (The Son of the Storm) and "Tras la tormenta la calma" (The Calm after the Storm), first published in serialized form in *El Boletín Popular* in 1892, Eusebio Chacón articulated an aesthetic meant to inspire Mexican Americans in Santa Fe and elsewhere in the territories that had been sold to the United States. He celebrated Mexican outlaws who fought against the Anglo status quo. Believing that the work of Spanish-language authors needed to be as far from the prevalent style of Anglos—whom he described, derogatorily, as *gabachos* (white Americans) and *extranjeros* (foreigners)—as possible, he filled his works with overwrought sentimentality in the narrative mode of melodramas popular in the Spanish-speaking world at the time.

In addition to the frontier memoirs of Juan Nepomuceno Seguín, significant Southwestern memoirs were produced by political figures during this period of annexations. In their personal histories of California, Antonio María Osio y Higuera (included in this anthology), Mariano Guadalupe Vallejo, and Juan Bautista Alvarado reminisced about the transition from life under Mexican rule to the challenges of being of Hispanic descent under U.S. domination. These accounts of power in high society have a counterpoint in the autobiographies of common people such as José Policarpo Rodríguez and Andrew García (both included here), the former a frontier dweller who converted from Catholicism to Protestantism, the latter a trail-rider, cowpoke, and working man in Texas. Rodríguez and García were uneducated. Their reports are plain and straightforward. As such, they allow an understanding of the average person's challenges in the Southwest at a time of dramatic historical upheaval.

## Modernismo

While the American Civil War (1861–65) affected African Americans tremendously, it had less effect on the other nonwhite populations in the United States. It had especially little significance for those in the Confederate states. However, at the beginning of the war an estimated 2,500 Mexican Americans fought on the Confederate side, whereas approximately 950 Hispanics had joined the Union Army. By the end, the total number of Hispanics on both sides grew close to 10,000. (There is no breakdown of how many fought for each side.) There were Spanish-speaking soldiers under Major Salvador Vallejo, who defeated a Confederate invasion of New Mexico. Others were part of the 10th Texas Cavalry, the 55th Alabama Infantry, and the 6th Missouri Infantry. But in the Civil War little was at stake for the Latino minority, which could not have been bigger than 150,000 at the time.

In the Southwest, the war's aftermath was marked by a rapid drive toward modernization. Electricity, the telegraph, railroads, and other modern innovations arrived in southwestern cities, as they did, at a different pace, in Mexico, Cuba, Argentina, and other parts of the Spanish American world. The literary response to this technological transformation was an aesthetic movement called *Modernismo*. In the first half of the nineteenth century, the texts read by the enlightened elite in the Americas were principally imported from Europe. Domestically produced literature had been characterized by realistic depictions of the local customs and fashions, and it had been read mainly by the individual writer's friends and acquaintances. That provincialism changed in the 1880s. For the first time, authors from different provenances (including Rubén Darío, from Nicaragua; José Martí, from Cuba; José Asunción Silva, from Colombia; and Amado Nervo, from Mexico) addressed in their poems, essays, stories, and travel pieces this remarkable, ubiquitous change. (Of these seminal authors, only Martí is included in this anthology, because he lived for a time in the United States.)

The *Modernista* movement was not the same as its English-language counterpart, the Modernism ascribed to writers such as James Joyce, Ezra Pound, T. S. Eliot, and Gertrude Stein. Between 1885 and 1915, roughly a generation earlier than these Europeans and Americans, Darío and his colleagues infused new life into Spanish-language literature and created an aesthetic inspired by French Symbolism, Parnassianism, and Decadentism. In collections of poetry and prose such as *Azul* . . . (Blue . . . ) and *Prosas Profanas* (Profane Prose), Darío wrote about swans, princesses, and obscure Chinese imagery. As he evolved artistically, he became more politically engaged. He denounced corruption, superstition, and ignorance. And he railed against, in his view, the sorrowful deprivation of life in the Americas. In his poem "To Columbus," written in 1892, on the 400th anniversary of Christopher Columbus's first voyage across the Atlantic, Darío pointed to the Spanish abuses during the colonial period in the Americas as well as to U.S. intervention in the Americas. Here (as translated by Greg Simon and Steven White) are the opening three stanzas and the last one:

> Ill-fated admiral! Your poor America,
> your beautiful, hot-blooded Indian virgin,
> the pearl of your dreams, is now some hysterical
> woman who has convulsions, tics, and pallid skin.
>
> A disastrous spirit has occupied your land.
> Where once united tribes lifted their maces high,
> an endless civil war has gotten out of hand:
> those of the same race fight and watch each other die.
>
> Now the pagan idols of stone have been replaced
> by idols of flesh that have taken their throne,
> and every day dawn after white dawn has embraced
> fraternal fields with blood and ashes of our own.
>
>            ✻  ✻  ✻
>
> The horror, the wars, the constant malarias
> are doomed paths from which our luck has not recovered:
> Poor Admiral, yes, you, Christopher Columbus,
> Pray to God for the world you discovered!

Among the quests of *Modernismo* was the recovery, in an idealized form, of the pre-Columbian past. In eulogizing figures such as Tutecotzimi, Caupolicán, and Huitzilopoxtli, Darío began a thread that runs through the Latino literary tradition. In the work of twentieth-century writers such as Rodolfo "Corky" Gonzales, Victor Hernández Cruz, and Pat Mora, pre-Columbian mythology (gods, warriors, poets) is eulogized as a link to a fractured past.

In Cuba, Puerto Rico, and the Dominican Republic, the aesthetics of *Modernismo* combined with aspects of Romanticism. The nationalist writings of intellectuals such as Francisco Gonzalo "Pachín" Marín are infused with a desire to break the old colonial mold and provide the populations of the Americas with a sense of new beginning. The work of figures such as Fabio Fiallo, who openly condemned the U.S. invasion of the Dominican Republic in 1916, is defined less by passionate love for particular individuals than by love as a cosmic condition. Fiallo's sense of religion, like Darío's, is defined by Jesus Christ's sacrifice for humankind—for the *Modernistas*, a symbolic invitation to embrace a just political cause no matter the cost.

Arguably the most celebrated *Modernista* writer is José Martí, whose role in the independence of Cuba has acquired mythical proportions. For a while, Martí lived in Florida and New York, from where he sent journalistic dispatches to major Spanish-language newspapers, such as *La Nación* in Buenos Aires. In those dispatches, he chronicled important events, such as the unveiling of the Statue of Liberty and the building of the Brooklyn Bridge. He also reflected on the lives of minorities, including women and blacks, in Manhattan and, to a lesser extent, of the Caribbean exiles in the United States.

Such is the appeal of Martí as activist and poet that a number of traditions have embraced him as their founding father. Not only were he and Darío the leading *Modernista* writers of their generation, but Fidel Castro's Communist Revolution in Cuba (1958–59) also turned him, posthumously, into a heroic figure. (Others figures made heroic by the same revolution include Karl Marx and Ernesto "Che" Guevara.) Martí's image also recurred in the anti-imperialist war fought in Latin America by revolutionaries such as Emiliano Zapata, Pancho Villa, and Augusto César Sandino. And since the 1980s, he has been ensconced in the Latino literary canon in the line of the Cuban intellectual Félix Varela and the Cuban poet José María Heredia. This reconfiguration stresses Martí's role as a Cuban exile in the United States. He longs for his lost homeland (his poem "Dos Cubas" has become a touchstone for the émigré community in Florida); he opposes the imperialist interpretations of the Monroe Doctrine; and while writing a poetry grounded, like Walt Whitman's, in the individual/society dichotomy, he embraces through essays such as "Our America" a continental Latinidad, in which the one becomes part of the many.

Martí died a martyr, fighting for Cuban independence in 1895. Still to come was the watershed historical moment that defined the *Modernista* generation: the Spanish-American War. Decades before the war, nationalist figures in exile, such as Ramón Emeterio Betances, had embarked on a revolution aimed at independence. Considered "the father of the Puerto Rican nation," Betances, a doctor, was educated in France. As a separatist in Puerto Rico and the founder of an abolitionist society, he had been forced into exile. In 1867, from New York and Saint Thomas, he organized an armed insurrection, but its failure did not curtail his efforts toward independence. He lived alternately in France, Cuba, the Dominican Republic, and the United States, writing—in Spanish and in French—numerous political, scientific, and literary works. In 1867, while in exile in Saint Thomas, Betances wrote the proclamation "Los diez mandamientos de los hombres libres" (The Ten Commandments of Free Men), in which he defended individual rights and called for Puerto Ricans to take up arms against Spain.

In 1898, war broke out between Spain and the United States over political control in the Caribbean. The future U.S. president Theodore Roosevelt and his volunteer cavalry regiment, the Rough Riders, invaded Cuba. The media played a crucial role in disseminating the news through a patriotic prism. A series of battles that started in Matanzas and continued to Cárdenas, Cienfuegos, and Santiago were viewed as benign and even positive by the public in the United States. Cuban *independentistas* were on the U.S. side, doing what they could to bring freedom to their homeland. The hostilities came to an end in December 1898, with the signing of the Treaty of Paris. (For the text, see Appendix 2: Treaties, Acts, and Propositions, p. A15.) As a condition of the treaty, sovereignty over and title to Cuba, Puerto Rico, and the Philippines passed from Spain to the United States. However, the Philippines continued to contest its status, in what came to be known as the Philippine-American War (1899–1901); the Philippines would become an independent commonwealth in 1935 and would achieve complete independence in 1946. In a fascinating counterpoint to the similar issues in the Treaty of Guadalupe Hidalgo, Article IX of the Treaty of Paris states that

> Spanish subjects, natives of the Peninsula, residing in the territory over which Spain by the present treaty relinquishes or cedes her sovereignty, may remain in such territory or may remove therefrom, retaining in either event all their rights of property, including the right to sell or dispose of such property or of its proceeds; and they shall also have the right to carry on their industry, commerce and professions, being subject in respect thereof to such laws as are applicable to other foreigners. In case they remain in the territory they may preserve their allegiance to the Crown of Spain by making, before a court of record, within a year from the date of the exchange of ratifications of this treaty, a declaration of their decision to preserve such allegiance; in default of which declaration they shall be held to have renounced it and to have adopted the nationality of the territory in which they may reside.
>
> The civil rights and political status of the native inhabitants of the territories hereby ceded to the United States shall be determined by the Congress.

From the outset, the annexation of these territories to the United States left more room for the local population to maneuver than had the annexation of Mexican lands. Other entries in the treaty reassured the local populations that their cultures would be respected, as in Article X: "The inhabitants of the territories over which Spain relinquishes or cedes her sovereignty shall be secured in the free exercise of their religion." In other words, just as Spanish power in the Caribbean receded, the United States moved in as the orchestrator in Caribbean—and, by extension, Latin American—affairs.

Latino intellectuals, especially those in Florida and New England, responded to the Spanish-American War by calling for unity against aggression from imperial powers. The quest in the political arena was to fight for autonomy and self-determination. In 1900, the Foraker Act, a U.S. federal law officially known as the Organic Act of 1900, replaced the initial U.S. military government with a civil government. The new government was controlled by the United States, however, and involved only limited representation and participation of Puerto Ricans. The Americanization of Puerto Rico continued. Meanwhile, from New York and other places of exile, revolutionary figures such as Eugenio María de Hostos, Lola Rodríguez de Tió, and Sotero Figueroa continued their efforts to liberate Cuba and Puerto Rico.

# FÉLIX VARELA
## 1787–1853

One of the most important political and literary figures in nineteenth-century Cuba, Félix Varela was also an insightful observer of the United States, where he lived for many years. Born in Havana, Varela spent most of his childhood in St. Augustine, Florida, at the time a Spanish possession. After returning to Cuba in 1802, he was educated at San Carlos Seminary and the University of Havana. He was ordained a priest in 1811, and during the next ten years he taught and published several philosophical treatises, including *Lecciones de filosofía* (Lessons of Philosophy) and *Miscelánea filosófica* (Philosophical Miscellany). His democratic vision led him to political activity in support of independence for Cuba, and in 1821 he was elected a delegate to the Cortes Generales, the Spanish Parliament, where he introduced legislation calling for Cuban independence and the abolition of slavery on the island. Early in 1823, however, King Ferdinand VII of Spain disbanded the Cortes and ended constitutional government, returning Spain to royalist absolute rule and ending the debate on Cuban independence. Varela, having been condemned to death, fled to Gibraltar and then to the United States, where he remained for the rest of his life.

Settled in New York City, Varela continued his work for Cuban independence. He founded the magazine *El Habanero: Papel Político, Científico y Literario*, which provided a forum for the voices of other exiles. Some of the exiles favored annexation of Cuba by the United States; some favored a restoration of constitutional government in Spain, a change they hoped would produce autonomy in Cuba; and others favored an invasion of Cuba, by exiles and their supporters in Latin America and in the United States, to secure its independence. Varela cautioned against political hysteria directed against Spain or the United States, while maintaining his position that Cuba eventually had to become an independent republic, free from foreign control. As the focus of the independence movement, *El Habanero* was banned in Cuba, Puerto Rico, and Spain. In 1825, an attempt on Varela's life, by an assassin sent by the governor of Cuba, failed. Remaining in New York among his mostly Irish Catholic parishioners and his fellow Cuban exiles, Varela prominently opposed anti-Catholic and anti-immigrant movements in the United States. The critic Luis Leal (see p. 551) identified Varela as the most likely author of the novel *Xicoténcatl* (1826), published anonymously in Philadelphia. This work broke ground as one of the first historical novels by a Latin American.

In two series, published in 1835 and 1838, Varela published *Cartas a Elpidio sobre la impiedad, la superstición y el fanatismo en sus relaciones con la sociedad* (translated as *Letters to Elpidio* in 1989), 11 essays combining philosophical commentary, religious commentary, and personal observations on political and cultural matters. He derived the name "Elpidio" from *elpis*, the Greek word for hope, and intended these "letters" as messages to his disciples in Cuba. In them, Varela presented his belief in the noble destiny of the independent human, created in the image of God. He cautioned his readers to resist the threats to democracy and freedom posed by irreligiosity, secularism, superstition, and fanaticism. Convinced that liberal democracy and individual freedom were strengthened by the virtues and moral values that are the basis of religion, he decried both the intellectuals who viewed religion as standing in the way of progress and the zealots who misused religious sentiment to support ignorance and intolerance. In the *Letters*, Varela offers an eloquent synthesis of his philosophical and theological beliefs, his spirituality and faith, and his vision of community and patriotism.

# LETTERS TO ELPIDIO[1]

## Final Observations on the Humor of Irreligious Masks

Let us interrupt these serious thoughts to have some fun remembering the foolishness, the gestures and contests of the *sages of social debates*, whom you have many times observed. Imagine one of these *philosophical frauds* entering a great event, so swollen with pride that it lifts him from the floor, which he barely touches with the tip of his little shiny fitted shoe, in such a way that he could run over fragile crystal without breaking it. The elegance, composition and adornment of attire, curled locks and perfumes indicate the time he has spent dressing; and the well-rehearsed and mysterious looks, symmetrical steps, and stylized gestures and movements complete the signs of spiritual superficiality and an idle life. No sooner does he sit down than he lets it be known that he is a philosopher and a true-blue *liberal*, and without any other proof or guarantee other than his word, he assures us that there cannot be liberty while there are fools that believe in religion and that it has been invented to maintain despotism. He repeats enthusiastically the names of some famous irreligious persons, but does not quote from their works, since he has not even read them. He talks of the contradictions of the Bible (which he has never opened) and speaks against idle clergy (he himself being a prototype of idleness). He ridicules everyone, without noting that he is a model of ridicule. The guests fix their eyes on this *refined fool*, who, taking the soft mockeries as just praises, continues vomiting *sublime foolishness*, and after having wasted time, leaves the gathering, thinking he has discovered the hidden secrets of the deepest philosophy and provided a great service to the cause of liberty.

If these crazy *serious-comedian-philosophers* were treated as such, it would matter little to society that they continue in their delirium; but unfortunately they find many as foolish as they are, although not as vain, who do not perceive their madness and follow their advice using them as models. I consider them as the most efficient agents of despotism, since they do not seem suspicious to their unwary enemies, although they cannot hide from experts who, being so few, scarcely cause concern. These *wise figurines* are like mosquitoes, for, being weak and insignificant, they manage with their first bites and with great presumptuousness to preoccupy the most populous society, and to interrupt the most useful works. We should therefore, scare them off with a puff of indifference and contempt, but never actually hit them in order to prevent their bite. After they play a second political-religious trick without being noticed, they will forego a third, realizing that it is a bad idea. You well know that these *political chameleons* thrive on the air of vanity, and when it does not find support, they leave baffled. How much ground despots would lose if these *erudite jugglers* found another profession!

Only the one who cannot be a slave is truly free, and this prerogative is only fit for the virtuous. Enjoy it, Elpidio, for heaven has granted it to you for the comfort of good people and the glory of the fatherland.

---

1. Translated by Felipe J. Estévez. Estévez's footnote has been omitted.

## Civil Religion in the United States

This country is always looked upon as a model of perfection, and even though I am one of its admirers, at the same time I would not like to see some delude themselves and lose the important lesson that they may learn in this country they so much laud. The faults of great people have always been the best corrective for mending the average; and by the same token, the imperfections of advanced countries should serve as an antidote to the poison that may be introduced into other, less experienced countries. Anyone who is not stupid, or deluded, will perceive that the principle of civil religious tolerance has been degenerating into dogmatic or purely religious tolerance, from which results a new religion, which has no name (and it is difficult to find one for it). When I am among friends, I call it the *religion of the nothings*; and since the pen has already slipped to communicate my jest to you, be patient and allow me to reveal my thoughts.

The people to whom I am referring do not wish to be counted among the irreligious, and in fact many of them are not. Nor are they considered to have an attachment to any religious sect. They have not formed the religious monster propounded by Jerieu, that is, a church formed by all sects; instead they defend each and every one's independence and fight the unity of the Church. If you ask me what these people are, my answer is that they are deluded, or they are irreligious; but if you ask me what they *seem* to be, I think I can say that they are people who, while they think themselves religious, are in fact nothing; and this is why I call it the religion of the nothings. Unfortunately it spreads more and more, serving as a cloak for the irreligious, who do not mind covering themselves with it. They recognize it as the best disguise—the most suitable to gain the esteem of the truly religious without assenting to the dogma or discipline of any religion. That is why they do not cease to praise this system, or better said, this social religious conduct, and they complain bitterly when they encounter someone with enough firmness to refuse to play the fool or the *religious charlatan*, one who acts according to the circumstances, seeking only to please, without realizing or caring much about the degradation they incur to sensible people, even when they are not irreligious.

Besides their religious complaints, the irreligious have the fatal practice of being offended by any minor circumstance that does not satisfy their wishes, and they cause much disquiet to many religious people. These are a new kind of complaint, even though they make use of the religious feelings they find in some persons. We could call them social complaints, or perhaps *philosophical complaints*, since enemies of true philosophy have the boldness to call themselves philosophers and have fashioned themselves as apostles of irreligiosity. If it is your misfortune, Elpidio, to deal with this family, you will observe that they are always complaining and protesting injury. Forget any hope of pleasing them; plan only to fulfill your duty, for they are most ungrateful, always complaining. Consider them maniacs. We should not be perturbed by their complaints nor become vain from their praise, because one will follow the other as soon as they find that they have not gotten all they hoped for or plundered the mine. Ingratitude is their principle, and we should not heed it, for we are not so naive as to expect something different from people who are looking for anything they can get.

The result of this is that they are in constant disagreement among themselves, which proves that it is not precisely for religious considerations but because of frustrated expectations. They proceed like what they say they are, that is, *pure animals* of a kind much more perfect than the others we know. Consequently, their norm is sensitivity, and anything that does not gratify it is bad; and gratefulness, when separated from the vanity that produces a sensitivity to the homage and applause of our neighbors, has no power whatsoever in their hearts, much less in their minds. They complain just as a lion roars for food, or other kinds of animals give other signs.

## On the Quakers

The Quakers are famous in matters of both inspiration and false imputations. Women preach the same as men. At their meetings they remain in silence almost as if asleep, and truly sometimes they are asleep, until the Spirit moves one of them to jump up on the bench and begin preaching.

Several curious Spaniards went to one of these meetings, staying at the door so that it would be evident that they had no other intention than to look in as observers. Once, they were seen by one of those women impostors. Feeling inspired she quickly jumped onto a bench and began to preach against the Spanish Inquisition;[1] she no doubt had recognized them as Spaniards and saw a good opportunity to convert them.

They left outraged but at the same time laughing at the fraud of that truly inspired character, that is to say, inspired by the devil. My friend and companion, Gener, told me with his usual natural jocularity, "this time at least, Varela, the Holy Spirit made a mistake, for there is no inquisition in Spain, nor is it likely that there shall be ever again, and the Spaniards who were at that door, far from being in favor of the inquisition, detested it much more than the preacher lady, so that the inspiration was thus totally useless." My learned and wise friend made many other observations, and we both agreed that fanaticism and superstition did not leave this country with the rise of new institutions, but that they took other forms.

Let us return to the Quakers. They do not swear at all, and thus they disobey the courts and do not give sworn testimony under the pretext that the Gospel, absolutely and without any exception, forbids the taking of any oath. Their rude practice of not doffing their hat for anybody or in any place is the result more of fanaticism and lack of judgment than superstition, even though it has many elements of it, for everything of the kind comes from a false belief.

I remember one time when a Quaker who was decently dressed (in the fashion of a uniform, that is, with dark cloth coat, cut with rounded edges, without lapels, and with a raised collar and wearing a widerimmed white hat) came into my Church. He came in a few minutes before the beginning of Mass on a feast day. The church was full and all the eyes of the congregation

---

1. A notoriously harsh tribunal established in 1478 by the Spanish monarchs to punish the Jews and Muslims who had converted to Catholi- cism but were insincere; formally abolished in 1834. It had powerful branches in the Americas.

turned to that man who walked around the church with his hat firmly in place. The people immediately tried to show him where he could sit, so that he would be less noticeable (even though he would always be noticed because he did not take off his hat). He declined the invitation, for no doubt he came only to walk around the church and attract attention.

I was able to see him from the sacristy and I was immediately going to send someone to tell him that according to our manners men kept their heads uncovered while women kept theirs covered. Once this was established I would be within my rights, by the laws of this country, to call a policeman to remove him from the church. I did not have to do it, however, because he left once he had achieved his purpose.

Once I saw myself free from that Quaker, I meditated that this man's bearing and ease of movement did show some good social upbringing; nevertheless he came uninvited to a gathering in which he had no business. He did not even want to stop but came only to insult those in attendance, or else his rare fanaticism had blinded him to such an extent that he was not aware of his provocation.

One has only to see that he did not respond to the expressions of welcome, for he showed contempt and shocking rudeness. Such is the power of superstition! That wretch walks through the streets of one of the most learned cities glorying in himself for having given public witness that his doctrine is rooted in the Gospel. Yet all he has shown is that he does not understand the Gospel that he sacrilegiously ridicules. He should really blush with shame at his rudeness and lack of prudence, which are always a sign of ignorance.

Those Quakers have studied well the system according to their own convenience. In spite of some of their genuine good qualities, I have always held that it is the most ridiculous and selfish sect. They do not wish to serve in the military, or to take arms to defend the fatherland. nor do they want to contribute to the payment of those who defend it. It seems that we should expect a miracle from heaven each time we are attacked, and that God will send his angels to defend us while we make no effort on our part; or that we should, in conscience, allow the first tyrant who so wishes to take over our fatherland.

What do you think about this morality and about these *virtuous Quakers?* They are opposed to all kinds of entertainment, and here is another virtue that is as serious as it is ridiculous! Their clothing is very simple, but sometimes it is made of good material that is no less expensive than that of other citizens who are less stoic! The ladies usually wear some coatlike blanket of ample dimensions that are no less expensive than the dresses of the ladies of other sects.

What is more interesting, my Elpidio, is that they have an agreement by which the sect money remains within the sect. If there is only one Quaker shoemaker in a city, he is assured that he will make all the shoes of all the Quakers in that city. They would go to another shoemaker only when the Quaker said *he could not, or would not do it.*The same thing happens with all the professions: the Quaker doctor never lacks patients, etc., etc. Besides these economic considerations, this system gives rise to a hypocrisy and religious speculation, which is the greatest of all evils and the most horrible of all sins. How many would stop being Quakers if they stopped turning a profit, and how many are Quakers because they do make a profit!

I had the occasion to observe the spirit of a sect in a particular case. There is in this city a Baptist doctor who is very zealous about the propagation of his sect, and a good friend of his told me that he had been converted by a Quaker lady. Why, I asked him, did she not convert him to her own sect? And the answer was that among the Baptists there is a smaller number of doctors of his specialty and that sect is very generous. What do you think of this! The good lady, no doubt, believes in her sect and the *pious doctor* has a great belief in the one he has adopted.

1835–38

---

# EULALIA PÉREZ
## ca. 1780–death unknown

In the *Historical Society of Southern California Quarterly* (1926), Major Frederick R. Burnham tells the possibly apocryphal story of a 135-year-old woman, Eulalia Periss (sic), who in 1876 was sent from California to the U.S. Centennial Exposition, in Philadelphia. When she returned by rail to her hometown, she disdained the carriage sent to transport her home from the station. Instead, she opted for an oxcart, as Burnham puts it, to "have a real comfortable drive home, after the exhausting Pullmans [passenger cars on the train] and soft spring buggies [horse-drawn carriages] in the East."

In her memoir, dictated to the oral historian Thomas Savage in 1877, Eulalia Pérez never mentions such a trip. It is possible that her memory and some of Savage's assumptions were faulty. Indeed, the text includes a few factual inconsistencies. For example, on the title page Savage notes that Pérez is "of the advanced age of 139," placing her birth in 1738. Yet in her memoir, Pérez notes that she was pregnant during the devastating earthquake of 1812. If she had been born in 1738, she would have been 74 during that earthquake!

Inaccuracies aside, Burnham's characterization of this pioneering woman matches the picture that emerges from her memoir. In her younger years, Pérez was, by turns, the midwife, chief cook, concierge, and supervisor of the Mission San Gabriel Arcángel, in San Gabriel, California. During the early nineteenth century, it was rare for women to hold such responsible positions as concierge and supervisor, and in her memoir Pérez is adamant about her abilities. Into her later years, the remained strong and self-reliant.

The massive collection of oral histories of Mexican Californians was one of the great but controversial efforts of the late nineteenth century in California. Organized in the 1870s by the historian Hubert Howe Bancroft, whose works on California and the American Southwest still resound, modestly trained oral historians fanned out over the state interviewing Spanish-speaking Californians. Pérez was one of about 40 women out of a total of approximately 150 people whose personal testimonies were recorded by Bancroft's oral historians.

Many of these testimonies were nostalgic recollections of the days, before 1848, when the land-owning *californios* ruled Alta California. They depict a world at odds with both the fictional and the historical accounts of the period by Anglo writers, who often depicted the area as lawless or deserted. However, the interviewers' individual abilities in Spanish and the types of questions the interviewers asked may have affected the resulting remembrances.

Most of the female narrators came from prominent families. The few working-class women revealed strong senses of self-pride and desires for economic and social change. Eulalia Pérez's strong personality and the fact that her brief marriages figured insignificantly in her memoirs led the scholar Genaro Padilla to comment that the women seized this unique opportunity for creative self-affirmation, reconstructing and perhaps even reinventing their lives through the Bancroft narratives. A narrative "about the operations of the mission system . . . ," Padilla writes in his book *My History, Not Yours: The Formation of Mexican American Autobiography* (1993), "was for Pérez an opportunity to describe how, alone with five children, she brought the male-dominated world in which she lived into compliance with her own will to be self-sufficient."

## An Old Woman Remembers[1]

I, Eulalia Pérez, was born in the Presidio of Loreto in Baja California.

My father's name was Diego Pérez, and he was employed in the Navy Department of said presidio; my mother's name was Antonia Rosalia Cota. Both were pure white.

I do not remember the date of my birth, but I do know that I was fifteen years old when I married Miguel Antonio Guillén, a soldier of the garrison at Loreto Presidio. During the time of my stay at Loreto I had three children—two boys, who died there in infancy, one girl, Petra, who was eleven years old when we moved to San Diego, and another boy, Isidoro, who came with us to this [Alta] California.

I lived eight years in San Diego with my husband, who continued his service in the garrison of the presidio, and I attended women in childbirth.

I had relatives in the vicinity of Los Angeles, and even farther north, and asked my husband repeatedly to take me to see them. My husband did not want to come along, and the commandant of the presidio did not allow me to go, either, because there was no other woman who knew midwifery.

In San Diego everyone seemed to like me very much, and in the most important homes they treated me affectionately. Although I had my own house, they arranged for me to be with those families almost all the time, even including my children.

In 1812 I was in San Juan Capistrano[2] attending Mass in church when a big earthquake occurred, and the tower fell down. I dashed through the sacristy, and in the doorway the people knocked me down and stepped over me. I was pregnant and could not move. Soon afterwards I returned to San Diego and almost immediately gave birth to my daughter María Antonia, who still lives here in San Gabriel.

After being in San Diego eight years, we came to the Mission of San Gabriel, where my husband had been serving in the guard. In 1814, on the first

1. Translated by Ruth Rodríguez and Vivian C. Fisher under the supervision of Hubert Howe Bancroft. The bracketed insertions are Bancroft's. Rodríguez and Fisher's footnote has been omitted, and its content has been incorporated into the section's headnote.
2. City in southern Orange County, California.

of October, my daughter María del Rosario was born, the one who is the wife of Michael White and in whose home I am now living. . . .

When I first came to San Diego the only house in the presidio was that of the commandant and the barracks where the soldiers lived.

There was no church, and Mass was said in a shelter made out of some old walls covered with branches, by the missionary who came from the Mission of San Diego.

The first sturdy house built in San Diego belonged to a certain Sánchez, the father of Don Vicente Sánchez, alcalde[3] of Los Angeles and deputy of the Territorial Council. The house was very small, and everyone went to look at it as though it were a palace. That house was built about a year after I arrived in San Diego.

My last trip to San Diego would have been in the year 1818, when my daughter María del Rosario was four years old. I seem to remember that I was there when the revolutionaries came to California. I recall that they put a stranger in irons and that afterwards they took them off.

Some three years later I came back to San Gabriel. The reason for my return was that the missionary at San Gabriel, Father José Sánchez, wrote to Father Fernando at San Diego—who was his cousin or uncle—asking him to speak to the commandant of the presidio at San Diego requesting him to give my son Isidoro Guillén a guard to escort me here with all my family. The commandant agreed.

When we arrived here Father José Sánchez lodged me and my family temporarily in a small house until work could be found for me. There I was with my five daughters—my son Isidoro Guillén was taken into service as a soldier in the mission guard.

At that time Father Sánchez was between sixty and seventy years of age—a white Spaniard, heavy set, of medium stature—a very good, kind, charitable man. He, as well as his companion Father José María Zalvidea,[4] treated the Indians very well, and the two were much loved by the Spanish-speaking people and by the neophytes and other Indians.

Father Zalvidea was very tall, a little heavy, white; he was a man of advanced age. I heard it said that they summoned Zalvidea to San Juan Capistrano because there was no missionary priest there. Many years later, when Father Antonio Peyri fled from San Luis Obispo—it was rumored that they were going to kill the priests—I learned that Zalvidea was very sick, and that actually he had been out of his mind ever since they took him away from San Gabriel, for he did not want to abandon the mission. I repeat that the father was afraid, and two Indians came from San Luis Rey to San Juan Capistrano; in a rawhide cart, making him as comfortable as they could, they took him to San Luis, where he died soon after from the grueling hardships he had suffered on the way.

Father Zalvidea was very much attached to his children at the mission, as he called the Indians that he himself had converted to Christianity. He traveled personally, sometimes on horseback and at other times on foot,

3. Spanish for municipal magistrate, whose functions are judicial and administrative.
4. Spanish Franciscan (1780–1846), who in 1805 entered the mission system in California. Over the years, he served at Mission San Fernando Rey de España, Mission San Gabriel Arcángel, Mission San Juan Capistrano, and Mission San Luis Rey de Francia.

and crossed mountains until he came to remote Indian settlements, in order to bring them to our religion.

Father Zalvidea introduced many improvements in the Mission of San Gabriel and made it progress a very great deal in every way. Not content with providing abundantly for the neophytes, he planted [fruit] trees in the mountains, far away from the mission, in order that the untamed Indians might have food when they passed by those spots.

When I came to San Gabriel the last time, there were only two women in this part of California who knew how to cook [well]. One was María Luisa Cota, wife of Claudio López, superintendent of the mission; the other was María Ignacia Amador, wife of Francisco Javier Alvarado. She knew how to cook, sew, read and write and take care of the sick. She was a good healer. She did needlework and took care of the church vestments. She taught a few children to read and write in her home, but did not conduct a formal school.

On special holidays, such as the day of our patron saint, Easter, etc., the two women were called upon to prepare the feast and to make the meat dishes, sweets, etc.

The priests wanted to help me out because I was a widow burdened with a family. They looked for some way to give me work without offending the other women. Fathers Sánchez and Zalvidea conferred and decided that they would have first one woman, then the other and finally me, do the cooking, in order to determine who did it best, with the aim of putting the one who surpassed the others in charge of the Indian cooks so as to teach them how to cook. With that idea in mind, the gentlemen who were to decide on the merits of the three dinners were warned ahead of time. One of these gentlemen was Don Ignacio Tenorio, whom they called the Royal Judge, and who came to live and die in the company of Father Sánchez. He was a very old man, and when he went out, wrapped up in a muffler, he walked very slowly with the aid of a cane. His walk consisted only of going from the missionary's house to the church.

The other judges who also were to give their opinions were Don Ignacio Mancisidor, merchant; Don Pedro Narváez, naval official; Sergeant José Antonio Pico—who later became lieutenant, brother of Governor Pío Pico;[5] Don Domingo Romero, who was my assistant when I was housekeeper at the mission; Claudio López, superintendent at the mission; besides the missionaries. These gentlemen, whenever they were at the mission, were accustomed to eat with the missionaries.

On the days agreed upon for the three dinners, they attended. No one told me anything regarding what it was all about, until one day Father Sánchez called me and said, "Look, Eulalia, tomorrow it is your turn to prepare dinner—because María Ignacia and Luisa have already done so. We shall see what kind of a dinner you will give us tomorrow."

The next day I went to prepare the food. I made several kinds of soup, a variety of meat dishes and whatever else happened to pop into my head that I knew how to prepare: The Indian cook, named Tomás, watched me attentively, as the missionary had told him to do.

At dinner time those mentioned came. When the meal was concluded, Father Sánchez asked for their opinions about it, beginning with the eldest,

5. (1801–1894); last Mexican governor of California (1832, 1845–46).

Don Ignacio Tenorio. This gentleman pondered awhile, saying that for many years he had not eaten the way he had eaten that day—that he doubted that they ate any better at the King's table. The others also praised the dinner highly.

Then the missionary called Tomás and asked him which of the three women he liked best—which one of them knew the most about cooking. He answered that I did.

Because of all this, employment was provided for me at the mission. At first they assigned me two Indians so that I could show them how to cook, the one named Tomás and the other called "The Gentile."[6] I taught them so well that I had the satisfaction of seeing them turn out to be very good cooks, perhaps the best in all this part of the country.

The missionaries were very satisfied; this made them think more highly of me. I spent about a year teaching those two Indians. I did not have to do the work, only direct them, because they already had learned a few of the fundamentals.

After this, the missionaries conferred among themselves and agreed to hand over the mission keys to me. This was in 1821, if I remember correctly. I recall that my daughter María del Rosario was seven years old when she became seriously ill and was attended by Father José Sánchez, who took such excellent care of her that finally we could rejoice at not having lost her. At that time I was already the housekeeper.

The duties of the housekeeper were many. In the first place, every day she handed out the rations for the mess hut. To do this she had to count the un-married women, bachelors, day-laborers, vaqueros—both those with saddles and those who rode bareback. Besides that, she had to hand out daily rations to the heads of households. In short, she was responsible for the distribution of supplies to the Indian population and to the missionaries' kitchen. She was in charge of the key to the clothing storehouse where materials were given out for dresses for the unmarried and married women and children. Then she also had to take care of cutting and making clothes for the men.

Furthermore, she was in charge of cutting and making the vaqueros' out-fits, from head to foot—that is, for the vaqueros who rode in saddles. Those who rode bareback received nothing more than their cotton blanket and loin-cloth, while those who rode in saddles were dressed the same way as the Spanish-speaking inhabitants; that is, they were given shirt, vest, jacket, trousers, hat, cowboy boots, shoes and spurs; and a saddle, bridle and lariat for the horse. Besides, each vaquero was given a big silk or cotton handker-chief, and a sash of Chinese silk or Canton crepe, or whatever there hap-pened to be in the storehouse.

They put under my charge everything having to do with clothing. I cut and fitted, and my five daughters sewed up the pieces. When they could not handle everything, the father was told, and then women from the town of Los Angeles were employed, and the father paid them.

Besides this, I had to attend to the soap-house, which was very large, to the wine-presses, and to the olive-crushers that produced oil, which I worked in myself. Under my direction and responsibility, Domingo Romero took care of changing the liquid.

6. Meaning, at the time, "non-Christian."

Luis the soap-maker had charge of the soap-house, but I directed everything.

I handled the distribution of leather, calf-skin, chamois, sheepskin, Morocco leather, fine scarlet cloth, nails, thread, silk, etc.—everything having to do with the making of saddles, shoes and what was needed for the belt-and shoe-making shops.

Every week I delivered supplies for the troops and Spanish-speaking servants. These consisted of beans, corn, garbanzos, lentils, candles, soap and lard. To carry out this distribution, they placed at my disposal an Indian servant named Lucio, who was trusted completely by the missionaries.

When it was necessary, some of my daughters did what I could not find the time to do. Generally, the one who was always at my side was my daughter María del Rosario.

After all my daughters were married—the last one was Rita, about 1832 or 1833—Father Sánchez undertook to persuade me to marry First Lieutenant Juan Mariné, a Spaniard from Catalonia, a widower with family who had served in the artillery. I did not want to get married, but the father told me that Mariné was a very good man—as, in fact, he turned out to be—besides, he had some money, although he never turned his cash-box over to me. I gave in to the father's wishes because I did not have the heart to deny him anything when he had been father and mother to me and to all my family.

I served as housekeeper of the mission for twelve or fourteen years, until about two years after the death of Father José Sánchez, which occurred in this same mission.

A short while before Father Sánchez died, he seemed robust and in good health, in spite of his advanced age. When Captain Barroso came and excited the Indians in all the missions to rebel, telling them that they were no longer neophytes but free men, Indians arrived from San Luis, San Juan and the rest of the missions. They pushed their way into the college, carrying their arms, because it was raining very hard. Outside the mission, guards and patrols made up of the Indians themselves were stationed. They had been taught to shout "Sentinel—on guard!" and "On guard he is!" but they said "Sentinel—open! Open he is!"

On seeing the Indians demoralized, Father Sánchez was very upset. He had to go to Los Angeles to say Mass, because he was accustomed to do so every week or fortnight, I do not remember which. He said to me, "Eulalia, I am going now. You know what the situation is; keep your eyes open and take care of what you can. Do not leave here, neither you nor your daughters." (My daughter María Antonia's husband, named Leonardo Higuera, was in charge of the Rancho de los Cerritos, which belonged to the mission, and María del Rosario's husband, Michael White, was in San Blas.)

The father left for the pueblo, and in front of the guard some Indians surged forward and cut the traces of his coach. He jumped out of the coach, and then the Indians, pushing him rudely, forced him toward his room. He was sad and filled with sorrow because of what the Indians had done and remained in his room for about a week without leaving it. He became ill and never again was his previous self. Blood flowed from his ears, and his head never stopped paining him until he died. He lived perhaps a little more than a month after the affair with the Indians, dying in the month of

January, I think it was, of 1833. In that month there was a great flood. The river rose very high and for more than two weeks no one could get from one side to the other. Among our grandchildren was one that they could not bring to the mission for burial for something like two weeks, because of the flood. The same month—a few days after the father's death—Claudio López, who had been superintendent of the mission for something like thirty years, also died.

In the Mission of San Gabriel there was a large number of neophytes. The married ones lived on their rancherías with their small children. There were two divisions for the unmarried ones: one for the women, called the nunnery, and another for the men. They brought girls from the ages of seven, eight or nine years to the nunnery, and they were brought up there. They left to get married. They were under the care of a mother in the nunnery, an Indian. During the time I was at the mission this matron was named Polonia—they called her "Mother Superior." The alcalde was in charge of the unmarried men's division. Every night both divisions were locked up, the keys were delivered to me, and I handed them over to the missionaries.

A blind Indian named Andresillo stood at the door of the nunnery and called out each girl's name, telling her to come in. If any girl was missing at admission time, they looked for her the following day and brought her to the nunnery. Her mother, if she had one, was brought in and punished for having detained her, and the girl was locked up for having been careless in not coming in punctually.

In the morning the girls were let out. First they went to Father Zalvidea's Mass, for he spoke the Indian language; afterwards they went to the mess hut to have breakfast, which sometimes consisted of corn gruel with chocolate, and on holidays with sweets and bread. On other days, ordinarily they had boiled barley and beans and meat. After eating breakfast each girl began the task that had been assigned to her beforehand—sometimes it was at the looms, or unloading, or sewing, or whatever there was to be done.

When they worked at unloading, at eleven o'clock they had to come up to one or two of the carts that carried refreshments out to the Indians working in the fields. This refreshment was made of water with vinegar and sugar, or sometimes with lemon and sugar. I was the one who made up that refreshment and sent it out, so the Indians would not get sick. That is what the missionaries ordered.

All work stopped at eleven, and at twelve o'clock the Indians came to the mess hut to eat barley and beans with meat and vegetables. At one o'clock they returned to their work, which ended for the day at sunset. Then all came to the mess hut to eat supper, which consisted of gruel with meat, sometimes just pure gruel. Each Indian carried his own bowl, and the mess attendant filled it up with the allotted portion. . . .

The Indians were taught the various jobs for which they showed an aptitude. Others worked in the fields, or took care of the horses, cattle, etc. Still others were carters, oxherds, etc.

At the mission, coarse cloth, serapes, and blankets were woven, and saddles, bridles, boots, shoes, and similar things were made. There was a soap-house, and a big carpenter shop as well as a small one, where those who were just beginning to learn carpentry worked; when they had mastered enough they were transferred to the big shop.

Wine and oil, bricks and adobe bricks were also made. Chocolate was manufactured from cocoa, brought in from the outside; and sweets were made. Many of these sweets, made by my own hands, were sent to Spain by Father Sánchez.

There was a teacher in every department, an instructed Indian who was Christianized. A white man headed the looms, but when the Indians were finally skilled, he withdrew.

My daughters and I made the chocolate, oil, sweets, lemonade and other things ourselves. I made plenty of lemonade—it was even bottled and sent to Spain.

The Indians also were taught to pray. A few of the more intelligent ones were taught to read and write. Father Zalvidea taught the Indians to pray in their Indian tongue; some Indians learned music and played instruments and sang at Mass. The sextons and pages who helped with Mass were Indians of the mission.

The punishments that were meted out were the stocks and confinement. When the misdemeanor was serious, the delinquent was taken to the guard, where they tied him to a pipe or a post and gave him twenty-five or more lashes, depending on his crime. Sometimes they put them in the headstocks; other times they passed a musket from one leg to the other and fastened it there, and also they tied their hands. That punishment, called "The Law of Bayona," was very painful.

But Fathers Sánchez and Zalvidea were always very considerate with the Indians. I would not want to say what others did because they did not live in the mission. . . .

1877

---

# ANTONIO MARÍA OSIO Y HIGUERA
## 1800–1878

Alta California was the western edge of the Spanish Empire in North America, above the peninsula that was then known as Antigua and is now known as Baja California. It was settled in the late nineteenth century by a combination of soldiers, sea traders, and Franciscan missionaries, led by Fray Junípero Serra (see p. 129). The generations of Spaniards, then Mexicans, who followed these early explorers and adventurers became the *californios*, landed gentry whose massive holdings made up the backbone of Spanish-speaking Californian society. Among the prominent citizens of Mexican California was Antonio María Osio y Higuera

Osio was born in San José del Cabo, in Baja California. In 1832, he and seven of his fellow citizens expelled California's Mexican governor and developed a government based on the theories of the Enlightenment and on the revolutions during the eighteenth century in Europe and North America. By the early 1850s, however, with California under the control of Anglo settlers, the dissipation of the *californio* estates had begun. Pioneers such as Pío de Jesús Pico (the last Mexican governor of Alta California), Mariano Guadalupe Vallejo (at one time, comandante-general of California), and Juan Bandini (a prominent citizen) watched as their lack of political influence and the aggressive business techniques of Anglos whittled away at their land. Osio had pressed a claim for Angel Island and Point Reyes (near San Francisco) without much luck. In 1852, he and his family left Alta California and returned to Mexico, where he continued to take an active role in local politics.

In 1851, a few years after the Mexican-American War, Osio had completed a 220-page manuscript, *La historia de Alta California* (The History of Alta California). The earliest written record of the territory, Osio's work is a representative of the personal accounts, less histories than stories, by prominent Spanish-speaking political figures that chronicled the transition in California from Mexican rule to U.S. rule. Predating more famous historical reminiscences by Vallejo and by Juan Bautista Valentin Alvarado y Vallejo, it offers valuable and colorful details about life in Monterey, Los Angeles, and San Francisco. The book showcases Osio's rhapsodic views on Mexican California. Osio begins the story in 1815, with the death of José Joaquín de Arrillaga and the establishment of the new governor, Colonel Pablo Vicente de Solá, and ends it with the takeover of Alta California by *americanos*. He applauds the *orgullo* (pride) of Mexicans in California and attacks the United States for its imperialist actions in the region. He also explains the background conditions of the 1830s that resulted in Alvarado's becoming governor.

The selection in this anthology consists of the first half of chapter 8. It concerns the personal traits and political work of Mariano Chico, who served in the Mexican Congress and was made governor of Alta California in 1835, the year this selection takes place. Chico was expelled by the *californios* the following year. He went on to be governor of Guanajuato, Mexico, and was involved in the war against the U.S. invasion of Mexico.

---

## *From* The History of Alta California[1]

## *From* Chapter 8

When the news of Señor Figueroa's death reached Mexico, there certainly was no shortage of candidates to replace him. However, men of integrity, reason, and knowledge, who had served the homeland, were not considered, and a congressional delegate from the state of Guanajuato was preferred. Believing that he would improve his fortune with the mission interests, he seized the opportunity and exchanged the rostrum for the political and military command of Alta California. He then set out for his destination with the necessary documents.

The biographical sketches of the representatives to the general congress which appeared in contemporary newspapers provided the *californios* with advance notice of their new governor's character. The following description was accurate to the letter: "Don Mariano Chico, a man who takes up arms, will prove for no reason at all with the tip of his sword that three plus two

---

1. Translated by Rose Marie Beebe and Robert M. Senkewicz. Unless otherwise indicated, all footnotes are Beebe and Senkewicz's. Beebe and Senkewicz's scholarly references and one of their footnotes have been omitted, but can be found in *The History of Alta California: A Memoir of Mexican California* by Antonio María Osio (Madison: University of Wisconsin Press, 1996).

do not equal five. And when he has an attack of excess bile, he does not even respect the Sovereign Power of the universe."[2]

The new *jefe* of the *californios*, a lieutenant colonel, was a contemporary and friend of Don Manuel Victoria. He could have been a distant relative of Don Quixote.[3] He wanted to take revenge on the scoundrels who had caused Victoria so much political and personal harm. With this aim in mind, he began by compiling a list of those involved, a list he intended to use at the appropriate time.

His ship arrived at Santa Bárbara Bay in April 1836, and he disembarked there because he was tired of the sea voyage. When he requested information about recent events, as was customary procedure, they told him about a treacherous murder of a husband in the *pueblo* of Los Angeles. An adulterous wife and her accomplice had been imprisoned and charged with the crime. While the authorities were in the process of drawing up the indictment against them, a large number of people rose up, armed themselves, and took the prisoners out of the jail to shoot them.[4] Chico just stood there in a trance for quite a while. Since he was from Guanajuato, it was not as if crimes of that nature would catch him by surprise. Finally, his body caught fire and exploded in its typical fashion. He wanted to leave for Los Angeles at that very moment to punish those people for their impudence, lawlessness, and the disrespect they had shown for his authority. They had committed the type of crime that would be punished severely during his tenure.

Fortunately both for him and the people of Los Angeles, Don Carlos Carrillo had known Chico for a long time. He had maintained a close friendship with him ever since they both were delegates to the national congress, and he knew how to give Chico sound advice.[5] Carrillo told Chico that he lacked authority because he had not yet assumed the command of the territory, nor had he been formally recognized as the *jefe principal*. Chico agreed and decided to hurry to Monterey to assume the command as governor. Then he could quickly decree whatever measures he pleased about the incident in Los Angeles.

During the few days that he spent in Los Angeles, he constantly tried to find out who had taken part in the conspiracy against Don Manuel Victoria and how they had proceeded. When everything had been arranged for his departure, he left for Monterey. When he arrived, Don Nicolás Gutiérrez

2. Chico came to Alta California with Santa Anna's appointment [Antonio López de Santa Anna (1794–1876), Mexican general and president]. He had a mission to introduce the new centralist administration to that area. That in itself would have turned the *californios* against him. In addition, the recent decision in Mexico to make Los Angeles the capital of the territory would have made the northerners hostile to anyone from Mexico.

3. Title character in the novel (1605, 1615) by the Spanish writer Miguel de Cervantes (1547–1616). *Jefe*: Spanish for chief, leader, superior. *Don Manuel Victoria*: infantry officer appointed to be governor of Baja California. Eventually his jurisdiction included Alta California too. He was engaged in a series of disputes with the *califor-*

*nios*, and a movement was organized to oust him. [Anthology editors' note]

4. In Los Angeles on March 26, 1836, Domingo Félix was killed by Gervasio Alipás. Félix's wife, María del Rosario Villa, had been living with Alipás for two years, and Félix finally had her arrested. After the *alcalde* [municipal magistrate], Manuel Requena, had tried to reconcile the couple, she was released, and as the two were on their way back to their *rancho*, Alipás ambushed them. Assisted by his lover, he then murdered Félix. When the body was discovered, Alipás and Villa were arrested. A group dominated by foreigners soon organized a vigilance committee, which took the prisoners from the jail and shot them.

5. Carrillo had served in the Mexican congress in 1831–32.

surrendered command of the territory to him in the customary fashion.[6] Gutiérrez also circulated orders that Chico be recognized as *jefe principal*. When Gutiérrez had fulfilled that obligation, he was immediately ordered to take some troops to Mission San Gabriel, a short distance from the *pueblo* of Los Angeles, and to establish his barracks there. He was to determine who had instigated and had participated in the shooting of the man and woman who had murdered the husband. He was to imprison whomever he could apprehend and then follow up with criminal proceedings as he saw fit.

At the same time, Chico sent another order to the *alcalde* of Los Angeles, telling him, the moment he received the order, to instruct Don Abel Stearns to present himself to the authorities in the capital without wasting any time. He did not give any reason for summoning Stearns.[7] However, since his reputation for rash action was already well known, Stearns covered the 130 leagues[8] as quickly as possible. Although he arrived after sunset he did not want to delay his appearance, so he barely took enough time to wash up. In the company of various other people, he appeared in the government hall. The *jefe* did not know two of the men, but he received them all in a courteous fashion. He had them sit down and then took his seat.[9]

Assuming a more festive tone than usual, Chico next stated that, even though he did not have the honor of knowing two of the men present, he wished to be of service to them to the extent that his authority permitted, if indeed some issue pertaining to his official position had brought them there. But when he found out that one of those men was Don Abel Stearns, he leaped from his chair as if fifteen scorpions had stung him at once. He turned toward Señor Stearns and began the following interrogation, as he shook his index finger at him: "Are you the rogue, Abel Stearns, whom I summoned to punish because his criminal deeds warrant it? Are you the American scoundrel who rose against Don Manuel Victoria, and whom tomorrow I am going to order hanged on the flagpole in the middle of the *plaza*? Are you the impudent and dishonorable foreigner, who, without introducing himself first, had the arrogance to take a seat in my living room among decent people who honor me with their visit? Get out of my presence immediately. Tomorrow you will suffer the consequences your despicable actions deserve."

Consider the state of confusion that Chico's manner of expressing himself created for Don Abel Stearns. He left that praetorium in such a hurry that he even forgot his hat.[1] Fortunately for him, on the following day there were only a few small particles of ash left over from the huge straw fire, which is an accurate metaphor for Señor Chico's style. It seemed that Chico had been

---

6. When Figueroa became ill in August 1835, he had José Castro, as the senior available member of the *diputación*, assume the political command and Nicolás Gutiérrez, as senior military officer, assume the military command. Castro surrendered the political command to Gutiérrez on January 2, 1836.

7. Stearns held the office of *síndico* [public attorney or advocate/representative of a mission] during the vigilante episode. Since Stearns was the highest-ranking person of U.S. birth in the city government, Chico may well have suspected that he had sympathized with the vigilantes. Also, Chico may have thought that Stearns might prove to be a good scapegoat for the movement against Victoria.

8. About 400 miles. [Anthology editors' note]

9. The vividness of the following description indicates that Osio may have been the second person. Osio's own relationship to Stearns was an interesting example of the complex web in which an official like Osio could be caught as he tried to attain the twin objectives of enforcing the Mexican laws and increasing the overall prosperity of Alta California. Stearns was generally regarded as being involved in smuggling, yet his trade contributed to the economic well-being of the Los Angeles elite. * * *

1. This is a reference to Mark 15.16, where Jesus, having been condemned before Pilate, is led away by soldiers to the praetorium [headquarters of the Roman army].

relieved of the burden of the plans he had made against Don Abel Stearns. He sent Stearns to Los Angeles and promised that he would follow him there very soon to resolve the matter for which he had been summoned.[2]

As soon as Don Nicolás Gutiérrez had quartered his troops as well as he could at Mission San Gabriel, he proceeded to carry out his orders. Don Víctor Prudón was imprisoned based on information which indicated that he was president of the council which had been formed when the *angelinos* gathered, under the command of Don Francisco Araujo, to shoot Gervasio Alipás and Rosario Villa. Don Manuel Arzaga, the council's secretary, was also imprisoned.

In carrying out his instructions, Gutiérrez determined that these three individuals bore the most guilt. He was also very determined to clarify whether Alcalde Don Manuel Requena in his judicial capacity had tried to assert his authority and stop the unlawful execution of the man and woman, or whether he had consented to, or at least not opposed, the action. Fearful that he might not be able to defend himself if charges were brought against him, Señor Requena requested that Don Mariano Romero come down from Monterey. Even though he did not yet have the title of lawyer, Señor Romero possessed a good knowledge of legal matters. He arrived in Los Angeles at the same time as Señor Chico, and he naturally busied himself with anything which could contribute to Requena's defense. However, the *jefe político* had no knowledge whatsoever of criminal proceedings, and so he reduced everything to rhetoric. With his grand eloquence he not only rudely humiliated the prisoners but also insulted other people who were not prisoners and accused them of the same offense.

Furious, he promised the guilty parties that they would shortly receive the severe punishment which he had prepared for them. Believing that he was about to be executed, Araujo almost lost his mind over Señor Chico's terrible threats. But almost instantly Chico's bile decreased, since he had drained his liver more quickly than usual. The moment he ordered the prisoners brought to him turned out to be a favorable one for them. They were in despair as they waited to hear that his threat was to be carried out. But strangely, when he received them Chico spoke to them in a moderate tone. In the end he promised them that if they acknowledged their crime and agreed to make amends, he would pardon them. They immediately provided him with more pledges than they could fulfill, and they were set free.[3] The *jefe* left at the same time on a swift march to Monterey.

The unexpected speed of the pardon and the departure piqued people's curiosity to find out the reason. Since this is something easily accomplished in small towns, it was learned a bit later that a special messenger from Monterey had brought Chico a confidential message. Upon reading it Chico became livid and wanted to leave that very hour. A few more inquiries clarified the matter. It turned out that Señor Chico had brought a "niece" with him to California.[4] She was somewhat elegant and witty, similar to Cervantes' description of Maritornes.[5] He also brought a eunuch, who was to

2. Chico arrived in Los Angeles on June 15 and left on June 28.
3. Apparently, all were released except Prudón and Arzaga, whom Chico had decided to send off to Mexico City for punishment.

4. Her name is given in the sources as Doña Cruz, and little else is known about her. * * *
5. Maritornes is the Asturian servant in Cervantes' *Don Quixote*. [She] is an outgoing person who is fascinated by men. In her relationships

watch over the conduct of this Dulcinea from Guanajuato during Chico's absence.[6] The eunuch performed his duty and notified his loving master that, metaphorically speaking, perhaps the girl was bored during that advent with the constant consumption of slightly rotten salt cod and had sailed out through the bay in search of fresh delights.[7] That thundering machine, propelled by the hurricane created from his own fiery spirit, quickly reached his destination. However, in view of the evidence which surfaced, he was perverted by roguish sorcerers who transformed him into Marrimaquiz. Zapaquilda "the beautiful" had not been seen for three or four days, and when she finally appeared, it seemed that she had recovered, but she had a number of scratches on her face.[8]

The man returned to his primitive behavior. Hearing about this situation from a good-for-nothing man of poor ancestry had highly offended him. Because he had been insulted to the core of his being, he ordered the eunuch jailed even before charging him with a crime. Then he tried to prove that the man had stolen some gold jewelry and a considerable number of stamped ounces of gold. Since no additional facts surfaced other than the premeditated slander of his accuser, whose hostility became more evident as he refused to reveal the real reason for the man's imprisonment, the judge set the prisoner free in due course. This started a fierce legal battle. When the *jefe* found out that two respectable and knowledgeable lawyers were advising the judge, he stopped the proceedings. He decided to take up the matter personally with the judge when the opportunity presented itself.

Chico was outraged by all types of judges because they followed legal procedures which were foreign to him and did not behave according to his whims. He recalled that he had left San Gabriel without resolving some pending matters for Don Nicolás Gutiérrez. He sent Gutiérrez an order to continue the investigation against Alcalde Don Manuel Requena. Chico ordered that Requena be imprisoned in the barracks if the investigation uncovered the slightest evidence indicating that the *alcalde* had been remiss in carrying out his obligation to prevent the shooting of the man and woman. He added that Requena should be handcuffed, and if Requena's lawyer prepared documents citing regulations or demanding compliance

---

with men she demonstrates that she can be both compassionate and cruel to them at the same time. Her physical appearance is rather ordinary and somewhat masculine. * * *

6. Dulcinea is the name that Don Quixote bestows upon the peasant woman from Toboso, Aldonza Lorenzo. In his imagination, Don Quixote elevates Aldonza to the status of the perfect or idealized woman (Dulcinea) whom he can love from afar. The name Dulcinea has become synonymous with the concept of the "beloved one" or "mistress."

7. Advent is the season in the Catholic liturgical year which immediately precedes Christmas. It is a season of waiting for the appearance of the Savior. Osio uses the term ironically here, much as he ironically alluded earlier to the trial of Jesus by Pontius Pilate. Chico's "niece" may have been bored with him and was restless as she awaited her "savior," that is, another man.

8. Marramaquiz and Zapaquilda are two protagonists in Lope de Vega's burlesque poem *La gato-* *maquia*. They did not originate with Lope de Vega, however, for they appear in the fables of Aesop. * * * In Lope de Vega's poem the action centers around the turbulent relationship between Marramaquiz, who is an old, brave, and extremely jealous tabby cat, and Zapaquilda, the beautiful, young cat who is adored by all of the male cats in the vicinity. Eventually, a foreign cat arrives on the scene and seduces Zapaquilda with gifts and exquisite food. Marramaquiz flies into a rage when he witnesses Zapaquilda's interest in the foreigner. She later engages in a fight with another cat and is clawed brutally. Marramaquiz then kidnaps Zapaquilda and locks her away in a tower. Osio is drawing obvious parallels between specific incidents involving these cats and Chico's jealousy and quick temper as demonstrated later by his brutality toward his "niece," when he digs his fingernails into her arm as if his nails were eagle's talons. Osio here seems to imply that it is quite possible that Chico physically abused his "niece." * * *

with the law, Gutiérrez was to handcuff the lawyer as well and place him with his client.

A few days later a husband discovered his wife in a clear act of infidelity.[9] He went and complained to the judge about her guilty accomplice's wickedness, requesting that the judge inflict the punishment which he deserved. The judge began by taking steps to arrest both adulterers, but the complainant stated that he was not pressing charges against his wife. Señor Chico wanted to get involved in this dispute, telling the judge that the woman fell under the same military jurisdiction as her husband. Therefore, the information about her case was of concern to him. Chico ordered her secluded in a respectable house, provided that they put the other adulterer in jail and prepare the case against him.

While this was going on; there was a holiday during which a company of *maromeros* put on a show in the evening.[1] The husband of the woman who was in seclusion pleaded with Señor Chico to allow her to attend the festivities, and without showing any embarrassment, she appeared at the show.[2] When a number of people in the crowd saw her, they decided to have a little fun at the expense of the *jefe político*. They thought it would be very amusing to provoke the *jefe*'s anger and force him to display it in public, since whenever Chico's anger reached its limit, he would act like a clown. So they contrived to get the *alcalde* to come to the performance, even though he had previously declined.[3] With the help of three people who were present, they decided to concoct a dispute between the two officials. As soon as the *alcalde* arrived, they gave him a seat and pointed out the woman by describing where she was seated and how she was dressed. Then they asked the *alcalde* if he knew her. He clearly recognized her and responded that it really surprised him to see her there for no apparent reason. They quickly told him everything and arranged for the prisoner, the woman's accomplice, to take part in the same festivities. While they went to pick up the prisoner, who took his time getting dressed, the *alcalde* enjoyed himself watching the *maromeros* perform some stunts. As one of the stunts ended, the people who had sent for the prisoner saw him arrive and welcomed him with great applause. Without knowing the real reason, others in the crowd joined in as if to applaud some good fortune of his.

They purposely seated the prisoner in front of Señor Chico, where he would be more visible. Chico, however, was enjoying himself conversing with a number of women, including his "niece," and had not noticed the prisoner until the husband informed him of his presence. When Chico saw the prisoner there, the blood raced through his arteries more forcefully than water spewing from a water pump used to extinguish fires. His anger made him virtually rabid. With a voice like the thunder of a violent storm,

9. The husband was José María Herrera, who had returned to Alta California in 1834. His wife was Ildefonsa González, who had become romantically involved with José María Castañares. The case had originally been brought to public attention by Ana González, the wife of Castañares. By the end of May, Herrera had become involved and had secured the imprisonment of Castañares in the jail and the seclusion of González in the house of Francisco Pacheco.

1. The *maromeros* were acrobats who generally performed their stunts while swinging from ropes around a large pole.
2. By the latter part of July, Herrera was softening his position. On July 30 he agreed to withdraw his suit on the condition that Castañares leave Monterey.
3. The *alcalde* was José Ramón Estrada.

he yelled at the *alcalde*, asking him who had granted Don J.M.C. permission to be there when he was supposed to be in jail.[4] The *alcalde* responded with restraint and in a low tone of voice that he had granted the permission because two prisoners accused of the same crime were equally entitled to have a good time, and then be returned to their respective prisons. Señor Chico, already blind with rage, burst forth with a torrent of the highly obscene insults for which the miners of his country are famous. A number of officers of sound judgment and prudence quickly surrounded him. They managed to subdue him by making him understand that this was not the appropriate place for two officials to speak about matters which, if made public, would bring them dishonor, and that they were also interrupting the festivities.

This was perhaps the first time in his wretched life that Chico had heeded prudent and convincing words spoken to him. Like a volcano which spews the last of its lava before subsiding, he threatened the *alcalde* and promised that he would get even with him for everything the following day. Then he went home. After that scene, which was acclaimed by many as the best interlude thanks to the assistance of the clown, the *alcalde* pretended to act very timid. Unknown to them, he hid himself under some women's seats. When the crowd demanded that he come out, he answered as if he were choked by fear. After the crowd had cheered the lead acrobat's finale, the *alcalde* appeared. He claimed that Chico's anger had caused him to fear for his life, because he thought that he had overheard him say that the rope from the swing would be converted into a noose for the harmless little clown's neck. Thanks to the governor's antics, this was the best performance that the *maromeros* ever gave.

Very irritated and unable to sleep, Señor Chico spent the night contemplating how to avenge such a horrible insult. After deciding upon, and then rejecting, one idea after another, he finally settled on one which seemed the best to him. Without considering that every type of scandal is reprehensible, he felt that, since the insult was public, the satisfaction should be public as well. He summoned Captain Don Agustín Zamorano, who served as his secretary and as major of the *plaza*. When Zamorano appeared, Chico ordered him to mobilize the available troops immediately and have them appear before him with arms and munitions. As soon as they were ready, Chico meticulously reviewed them himself, as if an enemy were present and prepared to fight. Satisfied that everything was set, he ordered them to follow him to the *alcalde*'s house. When they arrived, he ordered them to line up in battle formation and to ready themselves to fire at will. He stood by to observe the completion of these maneuvers, which, he was sure, would guarantee his victory in such an important endeavor. Then, without a word, he fearlessly burst into the living room and shouted at the *alcalde*, who stood up from his chair to ask him what he wanted. Chico replied that he had come to the *alcalde*'s house to give orders and the *alcalde* was to grab his staff immediately. The *alcalde* obeyed very quickly, since the staff was at his side. When Chico saw him with the staff in his hand, he became like the black panther of Morocco, which pounces on its prey ferociously and swiftly. He sprang toward the *alcalde* to snatch the staff away from him.

4. The initials J. M. C. refer to José María Castañares.

The *alcalde* released it without resisting. As Chico held it, he told the *alcalde* that that judge's insignia should be in better hands. He then proceeded to leave in the same decorous manner with which he had entered. He wanted to show the judge's staff, which was for him a trophy which he had won in a colossal battle, to the officers and the troops.[5]

Once the insult had been avenged by such a valiant champion, who considered himself superior to the Rolands, Amadises, and other knights of the Round Table,[6] he retired with his men. He ordered them confined to barracks and isolated himself in his house, fearing the inevitable consequences.

When that whole unpleasant event had ended, mounted men could be seen hurrying in every direction to alert the people to the outrageous act committed against their *alcalde*, whom they both loved and respected. As a group they could seek the appropriate satisfaction from the *jefe político*. The members of the *diputación territorial* were at hand, and its president convened an extraordinary session after he received an official communiqué from the *alcalde*. Besides notifying the president of Señor Chico's scandalous behavior, the *alcalde* expressed the general disgust of the local community, which was preparing armed retribution. He could not tell if fatalities might result, but he was warning the president ahead of time so that he would take appropriate steps to prevent a recurrence of the state of anarchy which the country recently experienced.

Since the *diputación* had been informed that groups of fifteen to twenty people, armed with the guns and munitions they were able to obtain, were already gathering, it agreed to ask the *alcalde* to use all his influence and authority to restrain the local community. It also agreed to try to handle the matter in the least disruptive manner possible for the sake of public order. By nightfall there were more armed civilians on the streets than soldiers. The *jefe* could not even count on his own troops, because the cavalry had sided with the *alcalde*, whom they had been very fond of ever since he was a child. He was the son of their former commander, whom they loved and respected as a superior as well as a father.

An enraged and caged lion does not roar as ferociously as the governor was doing in the room where he had isolated himself. Although he was extremely eager to take revenge, he found himself forced to remain behind four walls, since he did not dare stick out his head for fear of being stoned. He believed that he was in his last hours and that a fate similar to that of his friend Don Manuel Victoria would befall him. In addition, there was not a competent doctor available to heal him if one of the *californios* were to shoot him or strike him with a sword as a just punishment for his arbitrary acts.

While Chico was thus confined, he was bombarded with official communiqués from the *diputación*.[7] With due respect and great eloquence, this body informed him of the powers granted it by law. It also stated that the actions which he had taken against the *alcalde* were scandalous and disruptive. Consequently, the *pueblo* had expressed its indignation and was going

5. Chico removed Estrada from office and replaced him with Teodoro González, a member of the *ayuntamiento* [see note 7, below], on July 27, 1836. González proceeded immediately to rouse the people of Monterey against Chico. According to some accounts, Chico also insulted Mariano Estrada, the former commander of Monterey,

who was still extremely popular. That served further to incite the populace against him.
6. In ancient English legend, knights awarded the order of chivalry at King Arthur's court. [Anthology editors' note]
7. In this and the next few paragraphs Osio confuses the two representative bodies in Monterey

to seek satisfaction by force. Since the *diputación* could not restrain the *pueblo,* he alone would be responsible for the consequences. Two well-educated *vocales* in the *diputación* gave counsel to the president.[8] Señor Chico was choking with rage because he did not know how to respond satisfactorily to the official communiqués from the *diputación*. The communiqués actually had been sent to scare him, since he was most arrogant with those who were weak. They achieved their goal perfectly, because Chico ordered, or rather pleaded with, one of those lawyers to advise him about his final decision. He explained that he did not have adequate troops to instill respect. Therefore, to carry out his gubernatorial duties better, he planned to charter the English brigantine *Clementine*, which was anchored in the bay, and take it to Mazatlán to bring back soldiers who were not allied with the *californios* through friendship or family ties. In the interim, he would leave Don Nicolás Gutiérrez in command of the territory.

The lawyer was glad to hear this, since it accorded with his own desires. He then proceeded to overstate the soundness of that admirable idea, to try to persuade Chico not to dismiss it but rather to put it into practice as soon as possible. He promised Chico his assistance, so that he would not encounter any obstacle to his departure. With that aim in mind, he would work to insure that he could leave and that absolutely nothing would be demanded of him because of the incident involving the *alcalde*. The lawyer had considerable influence over the *alcalde* because he was his brother-in-law. When Señor Chico saw that an unexpected port was opening to save him from the storm that was about to overwhelm him, he accepted everything in good faith, expressed his appreciation, and dispatched him to complete his important mission quickly.[9]

The lawyer then went to inform the other delegates of the outcome of his interview with Señor Chico. They in turn informed the *alcalde* and the alarmed *pueblo*. All agreed that, if Chico got out of the territory quickly and left them in peace, he would not have to give satisfaction for the scandal he had committed. Finally, everything was arranged so that he could set sail the next day. Everyone believed that, after the scare he had received, he would not want to return to California once he was in Mazatlán. If he had hesitated before, not knowing how to reply to the official communications sent to him by the *diputación*, he now felt that he had to reply at the last minute before his departure. He could not tolerate remaining silent while the current ruling body was acting arbitrarily right under his whiskers. Therefore, amid his continual attacks of bile, he formulated his response, using the peculiar expressions of his dialect. It consisted of but a few words,

which were involved in the removal of Chico. The body which called for the people to rise against him was the town *ayuntamiento*. The two men who conducted the negotiations with Chico were members of that body. The body to which Chico formally indicated that he was going to leave Alta California was the *diputación*.

8. The two were members of the *ayuntamiento*. They were most likely Teodoro González and Bonifacio Madariaga.

9. The *diputación* demanded that Chico turn over the political command to Alvarado, the most senior member of the *diputación* who happened

to be present in Monterey. It also demanded that the governor turn over the military command to the senior military officer. If he did that, the body promised, it would do its best to protect him until he left the territory. Chico did not split the commands. Instead, he turned them both over to the senior military officer, Nicolás Gutiérrez. The concentration of power stemming from the union of the civil and military commands was one of the most basic complaints the *californio* elite had against Mexico at this time. * * *

and it fit on a fourth of a half sheet of paper. He wrote the message by hand, sealed it in an envelope, and put it in the pocket of his frock coat. He then left to board the ship. When he arrived at the beach, he bid a general farewell to all those present and promised to return promptly. With one foot already on the boat and the other on the rock that served as a pier, he called out to Don David Spence.[1] Because Spence was a delegate, he gave him his written reply and asked him to tell the delegates that, besides what he already had told them in writing, he wanted to add that they were "pricks" and "sons of bitches." Since they did not deserve to be called anything better, this was his gift to them. Consider the elegant terminology that must have been used in drafting the message!

Before Señor Chico set sail, a circular was sent out calling for Don Nicolás Gutiérrez to be recognized as *jefe superior* of the territory. This admirable news was celebrated along all the populated areas through which the circular passed. Because the *californios* were generally disgusted with their governor, they were delighted to hear about the sudden change in command. Gutiérrez was a friend to all, and they held him in high esteem because of his unselfish generosity and the fact that he loved serving everyone. He had acquired that trait under the tutelage of Señor Figueroa, with whom he had served in the military since he had been a young drummer boy in a Spanish regiment. He deserted that regiment in order to follow the insurgents, and from that time on, until the general's death, they were inseparable friends.

While the circular was making its way through the territory, Gutiérrez was hurrying about to carry out the orders which he had recently received from his superior. One morning he left San Gabriel and headed for Los Angeles to attempt to resolve the Don Manuel Requena affair. As usual, he dismounted at the home of one of his friends and then summoned him. The friend appeared immediately because he was extremely afraid that Gutiérrez would be arrested, an illegal act that some people had already vowed to commit.[2] As the friend listened to the substantial charges which were being brought against Gutiérrez, he suggested that his lawyer be summoned so that he could speak on Gutiérrez' behalf and assist him with certain legal points.[3] It so happened that when the lawyer entered the room, the courier who was transporting the circular arrived and was welcomed by Gutiérrez' friend. Letters from Monterey had informed the friend that, on the day after the letters were dated, Señor Chico would set sail, because of the *alcalde* affair.[4] Don Nicolás Gutiérrez would assume both commands in his place.

Gutiérrez was unaware of what was happening around him. He was also angry because of a dispute he had with the lawyer. In a professorial manner, the lawyer was insisting that Gutiérrez judge in accord with explicit laws. Gutiérrez responded with a military directness that his responsibilities did not extend beyond complying with his orders to arrest both of them and take them to his barracks. Gutiérrez' friend was waiting out of sight in another room to see what would happen, and he overheard this conversa-

---

1. Spence was serving on the *diputación*.
2. Osio had succeeded Stearns as *síndico* at the beginning of July.
3. The lawyer was José Mariano Romero.
4. The *Clementine* sailed from Monterey on July

31 with Chico aboard. The letters which Osio received, accordingly, would have been dated July 30. This episode, then, occurred toward the beginning of August. The *Clementine* sailed from San Pedro on August 10.

tion as he peered through a small opening in the room's thin wooden wall. Both the lawyer and Señor Requena turned pale when they heard that prospect. The friend felt sorry for them, but he was also convinced that Gutiérrez would never order such a thing on his own. However, since the order came from a superior, he knew that Gutiérrez would definitely carry it out. The friend wanted to help free them from this predicament, so, acting as if he had neither seen nor heard anything, he knocked and immediately opened the door of the room they were in. He begged their forgiveness if he was interrupting anything important, but he thought that Señor Gutiérrez needed to be informed as soon as possible about the document which had arrived from the political leadership. When he placed the document in his hands, Gutiérrez grabbed it because he was eager to know what it said. He was shocked almost to the point of paralysis when he found out. His imposing seriousness reverted to his customary friendliness. He told Señor Requena and Señor Romero that they should be grateful for their good luck because the circumstances had changed at that critical moment in their lives. The matter at hand would be dealt with on some other occasion. With this, they concluded and went to the living room, where something had been left for them so that they could have a drink.

When Gutiérrez entered the room, he asked his friend, in a tone of disapproval, knowing full well what the document contained, if he had hastened to give it to him to spare him some trouble. He responded affirmatively and then addressed the other two men, who were still deathly pale. He asked them if they would be so kind as to join him in drinking a glass of wine in honor of the *jefe* of the territory, who was there in the fullness of his power. This seemed very puzzling to them, and they both stared at Gutiérrez, as if to ask him to clarify the situation. Gutiérrez pointed his index finger at his friend and said, "This crafty fellow, without being seen by us, was aware of our business when he received the communiqué. He already knew, by letters which probably came from Monterey, that Señor Chico has some very important government business which will take him to Mazatlán. He is leaving me in charge of the command of the territory in the interim. My friend knew that I was following Chico's orders regarding you. He wanted to give me the pleasure of ordering that you be freed from the trouble which was awaiting you. This obviously was why he entered the room we were in, before he was granted permission to do so. It is time to have a drink. We can quench our thirst and enjoy what this crafty operator has already laid out for us." Neither Señor Requena nor Señor Romero was fond of drinking liquor other than at the dinner hour, but this time, because of their happiness and because they knew the proper rules of etiquette, they offered a toast to the new *jefe*.

Unfortunately for Gutiérrez, the brigantine *Clementine* was forced to call at San Pedro Bay. When the ship anchored, Señor Chico ordered that Gutiérrez be summoned. He also ordered that the treasury employee send him a ship's waybill for more than one thousand *arrobas*[5] of tallow which Don J.M.T. of Monterey had put on board to ship to Don J.H. of Mazatlán. The employee wanted to inform Chico in person that he could not ship

---

5. Spanish unit of weight, equal to about 25 pounds. [Anthology editors' note]

cargo on a foreign vessel.[6] So he went down to the beach, where he found his friend Gutiérrez. When they both found out that Señor Chico was on board the *Don Quixote*, they headed for that vessel on the first available boat.[7] When they arrived, the two *jefes* spoke privately, in low voices, for about a quarter of an hour. Then Señor Chico spoke to the employee. He asked him if he had brought the waybill which he had requested. The employee responded calmly that since it was not permissible for a foreign ship to transport cargo from one port of the republic to another, he was sorry, but he would not be able to give him the waybill. Since Chico had paid no attention to the general congress for a number of years, he viewed this refusal as capricious. He became infuriated and threatened to strip the employee of his job. The employee did not take this lightly. He asked Chico if he was willing to comply with regulations or if he himself would be forced to fulfill his duty. Fortunately, Gutiérrez was prepared to speak on the employee's behalf. He finally convinced the man who had spilled his bile that only ships of national registry were permitted to engage in coastal trade and the waybill which he requested would be a detriment, not a protection, if he presented it to the customs authorities in Mazatlán.

A man who has the tendency to become angry for any reason can always find more than enough reasons; for the most part these reasons are baseless. Nevertheless, in this case it is important to acknowledge that Señor Chico did indeed have reason to be angry. The general opinion of those who study such matters is that the most perfect and animated young faces are commonly found among males in the United States of the North. One such individual, a striking seventeen-year-old Adonis,[8] was aboard the *Don Quixote*.[9] Self-infatuation had corrupted him, and his father wanted to keep him occupied on long voyages as a means of correcting his behavior and continuing his studies. But he felt persecuted and assaulted everywhere in different languages which he did not understand. He learned from experience to compensate for this by making himself understood only with his very beautiful and expressive eyes. He had been spending his days aboard ship very depressed until he saw another pair of lively black eyes at Señor Chico's side. The eyes sparkled when they met his, and he was almost in ecstasy. They fell in love the moment their hearts were pierced by the blind boy's arrows. But Señor Chico's vehemence in defending his honor was so apparent that even he became aware of it, to his great humiliation.

---

6. The *Clementine* was an English brigantine.
7. The *Don Quixote* was a U.S. vessel which engaged in trade between Alta California and Hawaii in the 1830s and 1840s. The U.S. trader William Sturgis Hinckley was associated with both it and the *Clementine*, and it would not have been unusual for Chico to have been invited to dine aboard the *Don Quixote* while that vessel and the *Clementine* were both in San Pedro Bay.
8. In Greek mythology Adonis was so handsome that the goddesses Aphrodite and Persephone quarreled over him. Zeus settled the issue by having Adonis spend one-third of the year with each of them, and the remaining third with whomever he chose.
9. Whatever the basis of the following story, the fanciful fashion in which Osio relates it and his

extensive use of mythological characters give it a clearly deliberate air of unreality. He turns the story into a symbol of the self-satisfied United States being able effortlessly to seduce an unsuspecting resident of Alta California with an easy display of luxurious possessions. In another section a bit further along in the manuscript, Osio will try his hand at yet another allegorical story along the same lines and with equally unsatisfactory results, as he himself admits. Both stories indicate that he was trying to make sense of the attraction that the United States obviously had for some *californios*, and he was unable to come up with an explanation or an allegory that accounted for what he thought was such ill-advised behavior.

The captain served wine and brandy to the gathering. Narcissus did not believe that particular liquor was worthy of the beautiful Napea, so he quickly brought out a box filled with exquisite crystal decanters which contained some very high-quality liquors.[1] He offered her four types of liquor in delicately gilded goblets and asked her to take the one she liked best. In one of the secret compartments of the box there were assorted bottles of perfume, and he told her to choose as many as she liked. Bashfully, she took two or three bottles of perfume and paid for them with a sigh and an expressive glance. Then from another of the box's secret compartments he took out a small packet of drawings of the latest fashions. Among the drawings he was able to show her, due to the carelessness of Argos the observer, was a drawing of the latest Parisian fashion of kissing.[2] He showed her others, but no reference can be made to them because, as the time had come to dine in another room, he took the box, put it back in order, and closed it.

The excessive care with which the young man prepared and served meats to the female guest was reason enough for Señor Chico to find the meats rather tasteless, but he finally selected the ones which seemed best to him. When the meal was finished, he took hold of his "niece's" arm and escorted her up to the deck, where he spoke with Gutiérrez and gave him some orders. Gutiérrez was to carry out the orders while Chico was away on a brief trip he was planning. During that time, the brigantine *Clementine* weighed its anchors and approached the stern of the *Don Quixote* to receive its passengers. Señor Chico was notified, and he began to bid farewell. While he was shaking hands with those around him, behind his back the two passionate young people, imitating the latest fashion they had just seen, were also bidding farewell. Unfortunately for her, they were caught by surprise. The offended party took her by the arm and dug his fingernails into her. At that point Chico would have liked to have had fingernails as long as an eagle's talons. As if it were an act of courtesy, he escorted her to the gangway and walked across it behind her toward the boat. As he got halfway up the last few steps, it occurred to him to give Gutiérrez one last assignment. He went back and removed his gold watch, which had a fine gold chain. With his own hands he draped it around Gutiérrez' neck and told him that it ran a bit slow and he wanted Monsieur Praior, a watchmaker in Los Angeles, to fix it while he was away. Chico finally left in October 1836 to request additional troops in order to enable him to return and resolve his problems, but the general government was already aware of the situation and did not heed his request.

*  *  *

1851

---

1. Narcissus was a very handsome youth who one day happened to see his own reflection in a stream and was so taken by its beauty that he remained in that spot gazing upon himself until, due to lack of food and sustenance, he died. Napea is simply a Spanish transliteration of the Latin Napaea, the name for the wood nymphs in Latin bucolic poetry. By using the classical form instead of the generic term *ninfas,* Osio is able to maintain the more fantasy-filled tone that he is seeking here.

2. Argos is a mythological character who has one hundred eyes and is constantly vigilant.

# GASPAR BETANCOURT CISNEROS
## 1803–1866

Known to his contemporaries by the pseudonym *El Lugareño* (The Villager), Gaspar Betancourt Cisneros was a native of the Cuban province of Camagüey. He dedicated most of his life to freeing Cuba from Spanish rule, believing that only by separating itself from Spain would Cuba achieve progress and prosperity. But like many of his contemporaries, Betancourt Cisneros argued that, once Cuba was freed from Spain, the future of the island would lie in its annexation to the United States, which he admired as embodying the spirit of modern civilization. Also a fervent abolitionist, Betancourt freed the slaves working on his properties several years before abolition was decreed in Cuba. Betancourt left Cuba to complete his studies in 1822.

He settled in Philadelphia, where he worked for a commercial house—a combination bank, import/export trader, and clearinghouse for trade—and joined groups promoting Cuban independence. In 1823, he and other exiles traveled to Venezuela, where they and the South American liberator Simón Bolívar planned an insurrection in Cuba. This insurrection never happened, because of opposition from the governments of the United States and England, both of which feared possible slave uprisings in Cuba, such as had occurred in Haiti. (The United States also wanted to keep open the possibility of Cuba's future annexation as a state.) Eleven years later, Betancourt Cisneros returned to Cuba. He dedicated himself to improving economic and social conditions in Camagüey, where he founded schools and introduced railroads. Because of his activity on behalf of Cuban independence, the Spanish authorities ordered him into exile in 1846. For the next 15 years, he lived in Europe and America, finally returning to Cuba five years before his death.

Betancourt Cisneros is best-remembered for his correspondence with José Antonio Saco (1797–1879), another important political figure in the Cuban independence movement. Although Betancourt Cisneros and Saco had deep political differences, their profound love of Cuba was the basis for a warm and long-lasting friendship. In writing to Saco, Betancourt Cisneros used the nickname "Narizotas" (Big Nose). In one letter, Saco responded to Betancourt's request that he take on the editorship of a Cuban exile newspaper in New York. The following selection is Betancourt Cisneros's reply to that letter.

## Letter from Lugareño[1]

New York, February 4, 1849

Saquete mío:

It is with great pleasure that I respond to your most welcome letter of the 10th of last month, and if I let loose with the storm inside my head it's liable to flood all four pages of the letter. Fortunately, you're a good swimmer and you won't drown in the tropical waters I'm sending you.

So you've been down with convulsions, fevers and rheumatism! Poor Saquete! I feel for you, not only because I'm fond of you, but because my luck has been just as bad, and not because I'm going through purifying flames

---

1. Translated by Ilan Stavans.

but because of the northern winds with their glorious retinue of snow, ice, frost, and hail, and the attendant cohort of chilblains, colds, rheumatic pains and the rest of winter's plagues. What can we do, my dear Saquete, to build a little nest for our old age, if only to allow us a *comfortable* one? Poor expatriates, can't we find some place in Lima, Peru, or Puebla, Mexico, which travelers portray as paradises on earth? I can already hear your categorical answer, sung in the style of a *guajiro* from Bayamo:[2]

> Ay! From milk comes cheese,
> from the big cheese comes a little cheese,
> and from the great Spaniards,
> come the little Spaniards!

And, in faith, you're right. We are wisely taught by our learned and virtuous Varela,[3] who has chosen the northern ice and the Florida heat instead of those paradises. For even though Florida came out of Spanish milk, with Confederate salt and Pennsylvania flour one can swallow it without much fear. At least Flores isn't there, nor Paredes, nor Santa Anna[4] or any others who don't allow you to speak or sleep without taking precautions beforehand.

I've received the package of books that rascal Domingo gave me before he went back into the lion's den.[5] In whose paws will his hopes and dreams perish? The Carlista War?[6] Among more moderate forces? Or will he fall under the spell of the progressive ones? Because, as I see it, it isn't the mouse that's making these proposals, but that the mouse is trying to bell such a big cat. And what can you expect from the cat? Or in any case what can mice expect from cats in general? Just scratches and bruises.

Your little essay on annexation has not yet reached the hands of the individuals in this city to whom you said you sent it. I've heard others speak about it, making reference to letters written in La Habana in which they say you are opposed to the annexation project and you recommend suffering and suffering until Cuba enlightens the Iberian sun. I beg you to resend copies of your pamphlet to as many people as you can, so that at least some of them will arrive and they can be distributed to other believers. I'm eager to see how you examine the issue, because your opinion is decisive in regard to what is at stake for Cubans, and appropriately, not only because of your knowledge, but because of the sympathy with which your opinions are received here. Those of us who know you have never doubted you, and even if we don't follow you blindly as one does an oracle, at the very least we see you as a loyal and proven patriot.

2. Town in eastern Cuba. *Guajiro*: Cuban farmer.
3. Félix Varela (1787–1853), Cuban educator and writer who died in St. Augustine, Florida. See p. 173.
4. Antonio López de Santa Anna (1794–1876), Mexican general and president. *Flores*: Juan José Flores (1800–1864), Ecuadorian president. *Paredes*: Mariano Paredes y Arrillaga (1797–1849), Mexican president.
5. In 1844, a slave uprising occurred in Cuba. This rebellion was called *Conspiración de la Escalera* (Year of the Lash) because of the harsh way it was put down by the Spaniards, and Cuban leaders who favored abolition of slavery,

such as the writer and intellectual Domingo del Monte (1804–1853), were expelled from Cuba. During his exile in Madrid, where he died, del Monte traveled in Europe and the United States. Here, Betancourt Cisneros may be referring to del Monte's returning to Spain after a trip to the United States in 1849. At the time, Spain was undergoing a war of political factions (see next note) and the threat of invasion from England and/or France.
6. The Second Carlist War (1846–49), a civil war in Spain between conservative and liberal factions. The First Carlist War occurred in 1833–39, the Third in 1872–76.

I'm ready to explain, to the best of my abilities, the arguments I've heard from the *conscientious annexationists*[7] in support of the project.

They believe that the Island of Cuba is running toward its inevitable ruin under the tutelage of its Metropolis; that Cuba's fate is in the hands of those who have also decided the fate of Santo Domingo, Jamaica, Guadalupe, and all, all of the European colonies in this Archipelago; and that the only way to save Cuba is make it part of the great family of Confederate States of the American Union.

These believers can be divided into two parties: those who see in annexation the way to *keep their slaves*, which no matter how much they pretend otherwise is their *ultimate goal*, not to say the only reason they support annexation; the others believe that achieving annexation should be done slowly, through a series of steps, taking the appropriate measures in order to double the white population in 10 or 20 years, and introduce machinery, instruments, capital, expertise that will replace and improve the present means of labor and wealth. At any rate, my Saco, everyone seeks in annexation the guarantee, the protection of the wise and strong government of the United States against Europe's pretensions no less than against *ourselves*, for although our pride may prevent us from admitting it, we are made of the same stuff as those who have already achieved independence, but have not become free and happy nations. This is the synthesis of what I've heard from those leading the effort of the annexation project.

The fear that the island will lose its way under the guidance of Spain is based on arguments they expound, and which I'll point to as those with the most weight.

Spain, they say, is naturally linked to European politics. Whether it is an absolute, constitutional or republican monarchy, Spain has to follow the trend dictated and delineated by European civilization; and whatever is agreed upon by great nations like England, France, etc., regarding the great political and social issues and measures, that's what Spain will have to accept, of its own free will or by force. What are the guarantees offered to Cuba by the Spanish government today? What kind of guarantee is Narváez[8] and the moderate party? Who answers for their stability? Who will stop the influence of England and France, to which the progressive party may hand over the government tomorrow and give it the power to make decrees, under the support of England and the French Republic, to achieve, suddenly and immediately, the abolition of slavery, which has already been granted in the American colonies?[9] Why did the Cuban government and its people fear Louis-Philippe?[1] Why did everyone tremble while reading the decree of the provisional government granting emancipation to slaves? Why do they tremble every time England renews its claims or reminds Spain of its commitments?

7. Saco opposed annexation, but Betancourt Cisneros favored it. The various groups termed "conscientious annexationists" also favored annexation, but for a different reason than Betancourt Cisneros did: The Congress of Vienna (1815) had allowed Spain just a few years to end the slave trade, but slaves continued to be imported into Cuba. Some proslavery annexationists believed England would enforce the anti-slave trade regulations against Spain forcefully, even through the invasion of Cuba, and so they eagerly sought the protection of the United States.
8. Ramón María Narváez (1800–1868), Spanish prime minister.
9. Slavery had not been abolished in the United States by 1849, the year this letter was written. Betancourt Cisneros is referring to the abolition of the slave trade.
1. King of France from 1830 to 1848.

On the other hand, the annexationists say: What is Spain's conduct toward Cuba? What system has it adopted to govern a people as educated as Castile's, and even more advanced than the peninsula in agriculture, in commerce, in communications, and more in contact, more in touch with the freest nations on earth? Is such a state of affairs feasible between Cuba and Spain? And if it's neither stable nor feasible, what should Cuba do, where should it look for support?

The annexationists believe that Spain's policies are set, and that they will remain as such solely to prolong its domination of Cuba for as long as possible. A permanent army that oppresses and harasses the population; protection for the importing of blacks and the endorsement of the institution of slavery; opposition to the immigration of whites; the restriction of foreign commerce; the systematic division between Spaniards and Cubans; the undermining and negation of political and religious rights; taxes on everything, even breathing; the exclusion of Cubans from all jobs that might influence the education of the young, in the government, in law, and in the political leanings of Cubans. That is Spain's objective, so say the *conscientious annexationists*: to prolong its domination of Cuba. If this is what is good for the island, if this is what will bring peace, property, security, and progress to a civilized people, if this is what Cubans aspire to, then, the annexationist gentlemen say, let them eat Spanish bread and be guided by the Iberian sun. But Cubans are guided by the American sun and therein lays the cause of the conflict between the two lights. Enough with annexation and annexationists and let us move to other matters.

The railway system in Camagüey, under construction, is already thirty miles, and it's presently offering service with all its trains, stores, and businesses. A commissioner has gone to Havana to negotiate *money* with the Junta de Fomento[2] in order to expand and in 1849 build six or seven of the fourteen miles left to reach the banks of the Hatibonico River. What has been built is already bearing the desired fruit. Remember those skeptics in Camagüey who thought the project would ruin them? They were blind, Saquete, incapable of seeing the light of the sun. But now that they can see, they are finally realizing that sometimes one set of eyes is better than two million.

On the 6th of this month, the Conde de Villamar, in the Junta Electoral,[3] denounced me as an enemy of the state, his party and the government, someone unsuitable to be reelected President of the Company. My representatives have asked the Conde to appear in person to prove my crime of infidelity or be subject to the charge of calumny. That's how things are in Cuba today, and it won't be surprising if all those false attacks against me are proven to be right, just as it was proven that that virtuous guardian was even a pervert; he lamented not that he was accused of a crime he didn't commit, but that his opponents proved that it indeed took place.

Tell me how exactly to reach Domingo, because I want to write to him at length. If you write to him, include excerpts of this letter as if I were writing to him.

---

2. Improvement board. The word *money* is in English in the original.
3. Electoral board. *Conde de Villamar*: José

Miguel Hernández y Piñas, nineteenth-century Cuban political figure.

Don't forget to write to me. If I don't lose what I own in Cuba, if I'm left
to idle under the Valencian moon or to fry under the Iberian sun, I might go
to Italy, even if it's in chaos, because I want to see it before I die and retire
where I can have my little nest. If I'm forced into poverty I will work wherever I can find a favorable job. I will eat next to young men, inspiring them
to think. Write to me, my dear Saco, and don't believe anyone who tells you
that they love you more than your friend.

—Narizotas

---

# JOSÉ MARÍA HEREDIA
## 1803–1839

José María Heredia, a lawyer by training, was one of the most important Romantic
poets in Spanish America. As a boy, in his native Cuba, Heredia learned Greek and
Latin and translated Homer, Horace, and other classical authors. He composed
some of his best-known poems when he was still a teenager and achieved wide renown in his lifetime.

In 1823, at age nineteen, he left Cuba clandestinely, as he was sought by the
Spanish authorities for participating in proindependence activities. He spent two
years in New York City, teaching Spanish, publishing poetry, founding a newspaper,
and becoming a key figure in the Cuban-exile community. After moving to Mexico
in 1825, he became active in Mexican cultural and political circles, held various
administrative positions in the Mexican government, wrote for several newspapers,
and published many original works and translations. Heredia returned briefly to
Cuba in 1836, but soon left again for Mexico, where he remained until his death.

Heredia was greatly influenced by the European Romantics, especially English
and French writers such as Byron and Chateaubriand. Like many expatriate writers, Heredia infused his work with melancholy reflections on exile and nostalgic
longings for his homeland. In "Oda al Niágara," written in 1824 and translated here
as "Ode to Niagara" by the legendary U.S. poet, journalist, and political advisor
William Cullen Bryant, Heredia contrasts the fierce power of Niagara Falls with
the softness of his lost tropical home. Asking why he cannot see the palm trees of
his "own native Cuba spring and spread / Their thickly foliaged summits to the
sun," he laments that "I am an exile, and for me / There is no country and there is
no love."

## Ode to Niagara

My lyre! Give me my lyre! My bosom finds
The glow of inspiration. Oh, how long
Have I been left in darkness, since this light
Last visited my brow! Niagara!
Thou with thy rushing waters dost restore          5
The heavenly gift that sorrow took away.
Tremendous torrent! for an instant hush

The terrors of thy voice, and cast aside
Those wide-involving shadows, that my eyes
May see the fearful beauty of thy face!                        10
I am not all unworthy of thy sight,
For from my very boyhood have I loved,
Shunning the meaner track of common minds,
To look on Nature in her loftier moods.
At the fierce rushing of the hurricane,                        15
At the near bursting of the thunderbolt,
I have been touched with joy; and when the sea
Lashed by the wind hath rocked my bark, and showed
Its yawning caves beneath me, I have loved
Its dangers and the wrath of elements.                         20
But never yet the madness of the sea
Hath moved me as thy grandeur moves me now. . . .
The hoarse and rapid whirlpools there! My brain
Grows wild, my senses wander, as I gaze
Upon the hurrying waters, and my sight                         25
Vainly would follow, as toward the verge
Sweeps the wide torrent. Waves innumerable
Meet there and madden—waves innumerable
Urge on and overtake the waves before,
And disappear in thunder and in foam. . . .                    30
What seeks thy restless eye? Why are not here,
About the jaws of this abyss, the palms—
Ah, the delicious palms—that on the plains
Of my own native Cuba spring and spread
Their thickly foliaged summits to the sun . . . ?             35
But no, Niagara—thy forest pines
Are fitter coronal for thee. The palm,
The effeminate myrtle and frail rose may grow
In gardens, and give out their fragrance there,
Unmanning him who breathes it. Thine it is                     40
To do a nobler office. Generous minds
Behold thee, and are moved, and learn to rise
Above earth's frivolous pleasures; they partake
Thy grandeur, at the utterance of thy name
God of all truth! in other lands I've seen                     45
Lying philosophers, blaspheming men,
Questioners of thy mysteries, that draw
Their fellows deep into impiety;
And therefore doth my spirit seek thy face
In earth's majestic solitudes. Even here                       50
My heart doth open all itself to thee. . . .
I see thy never-resting waters run
And I bethink me how the tide of Time
Sweeps by eternity. So pass, of man—
Pass, like a noonday dream—the blossoming days.               55
And he awakes to sorrow. I, alas!—
Feel that my youth is withered, and my brow
Plowed early with the lines of grief and care.
Never have I so deeply felt as now

The hopeless solitude, the abandonment,                                    60
The anguish of a loveless life. Alas!
How can the impassioned, the unfrozen heart
Be happy without love? I would that one
Beautiful, worthy to be loved and joined
In love with me, now shared my lonely walk                                 65
On this tremendous brink. 'Twere sweet to see
Her sweet face touched with paleness, and become
More beautiful from fear, and overspread
With a faint smile, while clinging to my side.
Dreams—dreams! I am an exile, and for me                                   70
There is no country and there is no love.
Hear, dread Niagara, my latest voice!
Yet a few years, and the cold earth shall close
Over the bones of him who sings thee now
Thus feelingly. Would that this, my humble verse,                          75
Might be, like thee, immortal! I, meanwhile,
Cheerfully passing to the appointed rest,
Might raise my radiant forehead in the clouds
To listen to the echoes of my fame.

1824

# Frontier Memoirs

The life and career of Juan Nepomuceno Seguín (aka John N. Seguín) present an object lesson in the difficulties experienced by powerful Mexicans on the American frontier, who at one time worked alongside Anglo settlers but who were later relegated to subordinate positions in a racially charged society. Divided loyalty runs throughout Seguín's memoirs, which are written in several voices and express ambivalence about the situation of Mexican Americans in the mid-nineteenth century.

Seguín was born in San Antonio de Bexar (now known as San Antonio, Texas), in 1806. By the 1830s, he was a prominent politician working to overthrow Mexican rule of Texas. His compatriots in this struggle were Texas Mexican landowners and Anglo newcomers to the region—the latter including Sam Houston and Stephen Austin, who would later become the new republic's first secretary of state. During the Texas Revolution, Seguín served at the San Antonio de Valero Mission, later known as the Alamo. At this now legendary chapel-fort in San Antonio, in the most famous conflict of the revolution, about 180 Texans (or Texians, as these men called themselves) fought against thousands of Mexicans led by the Mexican general Santa Anna. On the eve of the final battle, in which nearly all the Texans were killed, Seguín was ordered to leave in search of reinforcements; thus he survived. His having fought at the Alamo, and his meritorious service at the pivotal Battle of San Jacinto, led to Seguín's being elected a senator of the burgeoning Texas Republic. In 1841, he became mayor of San Antonio.

As discussed in the "Annexations" introduction, Seguín was disheartened by Texas Mexicans' loss of power and prestige in the following years, and he became disillusioned about his role in securing the independence of Texas. In 1858, 13 years after Texas entered the Union, he wrote the book *Personal Memoirs of John N. Seguín, 1834–42*, which is both personal and political. Crossing back and forth between the loyal citizen and the critical outsider, Seguin attempts to convince himself and his readers that the world of the Mexican/Texan Mexican/Mexican American was fluid and situational. Anglo adventurers were flooding into Texas, and as mayor of San Antonio, Seguín believed he needed to defend Mexican Americans from the racist views expounded by the newcomers. "My countrymen ran to me for protection against the assaults or exactions of those adventurers," he writes. As Mexican Americans learn to distrust him, Anglos take advantage of him and accuse him of conspiring with Mexico to take back Texas. On the page, he re-creates his confusion and ambivalence. Writing for history and posterity, he provides the reader—Mexican, Mexican American, or Anglo—with the reasons for his actions in the political sphere.

Seguín published his memoirs ten years after the Treaty of Guadalupe Hidalgo, the chronological point that many scholars view as the beginning of Mexican American literary culture. In the Latino literary tradition, his work is linked to later autobiography and autobiographical fiction through the senses of both divided loyalty and solitariness—that is, through the writer's belief that he or she is alone between cultures, belonging to none but beholden to all. Even the fact that Seguín signs his work *John N.*, rather than using his full, Spanish-language name, reveals his personal divisions. Such discomfort is an important theme in much Latino literature, as in the autobiographical novels *Pocho* (1959), by the Mexican American José Antonio Villarreal, and *Down These Mean Streets* (1967), by the mainland Puerto Rican Piri Thomas.

Seguín's near-contemporary José Policarpio Rodríguez wrote his own life story not as an apology but as a cautionary tale, his wild life on the frontier having led him to a religious conversion. According to its editor, G. B. Winton, Rodríguez's *The Old Guide: Surveyor, Scout, Hunter, Indian Fighter, Ranchman, Preacher: His Life in His Own Words*, the memoir "was dictated to the Reverend D.W. Carter, D.D., at odd times during the years from 1892 to 1897. The unrevised manuscript was by him intrusted to me to be published." It was published around 1897 by the Methodist Episcopal Church in Dallas, Texas, with a picture of a stolid, bearded Rodríguez, dressed in sober black, at the front of the book, as if he were a father introducing the work of his son.

Rodríguez's story begins with his birth, in 1829, in Mexico, near Texas. His father wanted him to enter the Catholic seminary, but Rodríguez received only about a year of formal education. From age 12 to age 15, he was apprenticed to a gunsmith. He then became a surveyor and, at age 20, an army scout. He later married and developed a ranch.

The most significant episode in Rodríguez's memoir is his conversion from Catholicism to Protestantism. One day, to pick up a horse, he travels to his cousin James Tafolla's house, where a prayer session is in progress. Tafolla has recently converted to Methodism and asks Rodríguez to do the same, but Rodríguez refuses. At the prayer session, the visiting preacher, Trinidad Armendáriz, prays for Rodríguez, who then leaves but is unable to get the prayer out of his mind. The following day, while riding in the woods, he gets down off his horse, goes into the bushes, and falls on his face to pray to God for guidance. By the time he gets home, he has undergone a complete conversion. He commands his wife to remove all images of saints and virgins—that is, all Catholic icons—from the house. He soon becomes a traveling preacher, an unusual occupation for a Mexican at the time. The remainder of the memoir tells the story of Rodríguez's life preaching the gospel, and it concludes with "I hope this true record of how I was brought to Christ may lead many to believe in him. Perhaps it will preach the gospel when I can no longer do so."

Though folklore of the nineteenth-century United States includes scouts, mountain men, and cowboys, often as romanticized by the dime novels of the period, the Hispanic presence in the west at that time is rarely represented; when it is, the representatives are often outlaws or *cholos*, low-class squatters and ne'er-do-wells. The publication of Andrew García's *Tough Trip through Paradise 1878–1879*, in 1968, provided the autobiographical account of a late-nineteenth-century Tejano trail rider, cowpoke, and working man, who explored in Montana before settling there. The story of the discovery of the manuscript adds romance to García's tale. In 1948, its editor, Bennett H. Stein, found the manuscript "from which this book was written [i.e., edited]." The original was both handwritten and typed, on several thousand pages of legal-sized paper, and packed solid in dynamite boxes, along with the heavy waxed paper that powder comes in. In these boxes, Stein also found "newspaper clippings showing Andrew García at meetings of the Society of Montana Pioneers" in the 1930s—depicting him as "the most colorful character attending"—as well as letters from "other old-timers."

García was probably born in Texas in 1855. By the mid-1870s, he was in Montana, employed as a herder and, for the U.S. government, a packer (someone who conveys goods by pack animal). In 1878, he went out on his own, living mainly among the Indians for the following two decades. "Little did I know that day that I was giving up all hope to be a white man again—that I was leaving the white man and his ways forever, and that I would become inoculated with the wild life of the old-time Indian and be one of them, to live and run with them, wild and free like a mustang." Though unschooled as a writer or historian, he claims to have resisted all efforts to pare his recollections into publishable form, fearing that any outside assistance would remove the work's personal tone.

# JUAN NEPOMUCENO SEGUÍN
## 1806–1890

## *FROM* PERSONAL MEMOIRS OF JOHN N. SEGUÍN, 1834–42

When we received intelligence from our spies on the Rio Grande, that Santa Anna was preparing to invade Texas, my father, with his, my own, and several other families, removed toward the centre of the country.[1]

My family took with them above three thousand head of sheep. They had reached Gonzales when Santa Anna took possession of San Antonio, and as soon as some other families joined them, they proceeded towards the Colorado, via Columbus. On their arrival at San Felipe de Austin the citizens of that place, terror struck at the sight of the hurried flight of such a number of families, endeavored to take the advance. The confusion and delay caused on the road by that immense straggling column of fugitives were such, that when my family were beginning to cross the Colorado with their cattle, the enemy was at their heels. General Ramirez y Sesma[2] did not fail to take hold of that rich booty; and the shepherds only escaped by swimming over the river. The loss to three of the families was very severe, nay, irretrievable. They did not stop on their flight, until they reached the town of San Augustine, east of Nacogdoches. When the families received the welcome tidings of the victory of San Jacinto, they went to Nacogdoches. There, all the members of my family, without excepting a single person, were attacked by fever. Thus, prostrated on their couches, deprived of all resources, they had to struggle in the midst of their sufferings, to assist one another. Want of money compelled them to part, little by little, with their valuables and articles of clothing. A son, an uncle, and several more remote relatives of mine fell victims to the disease. Seeing that the fever did not abate, the families determined upon moving towards the interior.

The train presented a spectacle which beggars description. Old men and children were lying in the wagons, and for several days, Captain Menchaca,[3]

---

1. As this selection opens, the forces are massing for what would become the Battle of the Alamo (February 23–March 6, 1836). Seguín's family has been living on a ranch in southern Texas. With other families, they travel northeast in Texas: to Gonzales, a city east of San Antonio; toward the city of Columbus, which is on the Colorado River; to the town of San Felipe de Austin, also known as San Felipe; and finally to San Augustine, a town east of the city of Nacogdoches.

2. Joaquín Ramírez y Sesma, captain of the Mexican army during this siege. He arrived on the scene on February 20, and General Santa Anna ordered him to lead a cavalry force to take over the Alamo.

3. A soldier in the Texan forces.

who was the only person able to stand up, had to drive the whole train as well as attend to the sick.

The families reached San Antonio at last. There was not one of them who had not to lament the loss of a relative, and to crown their misfortunes, they found their houses in ruins, their fields laid waste, and their cattle destroyed or dispersed.

I, myself found my ranch despoiled; what little was spared by the retreating enemy, had been wasted by our own army; ruin and misery met me on my return to my unpretending home.

But let me draw a veil over those past and sorrowful days, and resume my narrative.

The tokens of esteem, and evidences of trust and confidence, repeatedly bestowed upon me by the Supreme Magistrate, General Rusk,[4] and other dignitaries of the Republic, could not fail to arouse against me much invidious and malignant feeling. The jealousy evinced against me by several officers of the companies recently arrived at San Antonio, from the United States, soon spread amongst the American straggling adventurers, who were already beginning to work their dark intrigues against the native families, whose only crime was, that they owned large tracts of land and desirable property.

John W. Smith,[5] a bitter enemy of several of the richest families of San Antonio, by whom he had been covered with favors, joined the conspiracy which was organized to ruin me.

I will also point out the origin of another enmity which, on several occasions, endangered my life. In those evil days, San Antonio was swarming with adventurers from every quarter of the globe. Many a noble heart grasped the sword in the defence of the liberty of Texas, cheerfully pouring out their blood for our cause, and to them everlasting public gratitude is due; but there were also many bad men, fugitives from their country, who found in this land on open field for their criminal designs.

San Antonio claimed then, as it claims now, to be the first city of Texas; it was also the receptacle of the scum of society. My political and social situation brought me into continual contact with that class of people. At every hour of the day and night, my countrymen ran to me for protection against the assaults or exactions of those adventurers. Some times, by persuasion, I prevailed on them to desist; some times, also, force had to be resorted to. How could I have done otherwise? Were not the victims my own countrymen, friends and associates? Could I leave them defenceless, exposed to the assaults of foreigners, who, on the pretext that they were Mexicans, treated them worse than brutes? Sound reason and the dictates of humanity would have precluded a different conduct on my part.

1858

---

4. General Thomas Jefferson Rusk (1803–1857), who fought in the Battle of Jacinto, was political and military leader of the Republic of Texas. He became the state's first secretary of war.
5. John William Smith (1792–1845), soldier on the Texas side during the Texas Revolution, last messenger from the Alamo before it fell to the Mexican army, three-term mayor of San Antonio, and member of the Texas Republic Senate from the district of Bexar.

# JOSÉ POLICARPO RODRÍGUEZ
## 1829–1914

## The Old Guide

### Chapter I. Boyhood Days

Many of my friends have asked me to tell the story of my life, and I have consented to do so in the hope that it may prove interesting to them and not entirely valueless for other reasons.

It deals with conditions that have passed away, but which were thrilling and important in the early history of Texas. I have lived in Texas when it was a part of Mexico, when it was an independent republic, while it was one of the Confederate States, and hope to lay my body to rest in its soil in sight of Polly's Peak[1] when my journey is ended.

I was born at Zaragoza, Mexico, thirty-five miles west of Eagle Pass, Tex., January 26, 1829. My father was José Antonio Rodriguez; my mother, Encarnacion Sanchez. My father was a man of means and well educated for his day; he lost much property by the depredations of wild Indians that then infested the country. He was desirous of educating me for the priesthood of the Romish Church;[2] he made three separate attempts to put me in a seminary to educate me for that purpose, but failed, as at each time his plans were broken up by the revolutions which were then so frequent. At the age of six he put me in a school at Nadadores, Coahuila, where I remained about eight months; thence I was taken to Cuatro Ciénegas,[3] where I remained some six months. This was all the schooling I ever received, but my father taught me at home as occasion permitted.

In my twelfth year my father brought me to San Antonio, Tex., and apprenticed me to Jim Goodman to learn the trade of gunsmith. There I remained three years. Goodman killed a man, and was imprisoned; this ended my apprenticeship.

In the meantime my father had moved to Texas, near San Antonio, having bought a place on the Medina River, fifteen miles below town. San Antonio was then a very small place, consisting chiefly of straw-thatched *jacales*.[4] I have played in the high weeds on the river where Commerce Street bridge now crosses. The Indians at that time often came into the town and stole horses, and had been known to kill people in the streets and carry off small boys. I hunted rabbits in the bend of the river between Houston and Commerce Streets. It was difficult at times to bury the dead in the cemetery where Milam Park now is, for fear of the prowling Indians.

1. Or Polley's Peak, a mountain in eastern Bandera County, Texas. The county was formed in 1856, and Rodríguez settled there in 1858. Despite the local legend, the peak was named not after him (i.e., after "Policarpo") but after Joseph B. Polley, who helped survey the area.

2. I.e., Roman Catholic Church.
3. Cuatro Ciénegas and Nadadores are cities in the northern Mexican state of Coahuila.
4. Adobe-style housing structures found throughout Mexico and the U.S. Southwest.

At the end of my apprenticeship, I joined a party of surveyors, a Mr. Tivy, a gunsmith, in charge. A man named Goodman accompanied this party, which operated around where Boerne[5] now stands. The country was then full of game animals and wild cattle; bear, deer, and turkeys especially abounded; the party lived on wild meat. Bee trees were common, and the surveyors had plenty of honey.

On one occasion when out on this survey we were surprised to see a party of Indians coming directly toward us. The only weapon we had with us was one old five-shooter pistol, we having left all our guns in camp. We squatted on the ground and crawled to a neighboring thicket through the tall grass. When the Indians came within half a mile of us they turned to the left and the party divided, some going by the mountain side and others continuing in the direction of San Antonio. Had they found our marks, they would have hunted for us, and we should have perished there. After this we did not go out without horses and arms.

## Chapter II. Surveying

On this trip, at a big cave spring on the Guadalupe[6] below Boerne, we were one day resting, when one of the party, looking into the cave, said, "I believe the devil is here," and gave a yell. Out rushed a big, fat black bear, splashing the water and scattering us from side to side; so scared were we that we forgot our guns and let him get away. We afterwards saw a bear passing with three young cubs, and went out and killed two of the cubs. I never tasted finer meat than young bear. After the survey was finished, we returned to San Antonio. I received the wages of a man—one dollar a day—though but fifteen years old. I could shoot and hunt and work on the survey as well as a man. When we were beginning to carry the chain, one of the men asked Mr. Tivy who was going to carry the chain with him, and he said, "That boy there," meaning me.

The man said: "I won't carry a chain with a boy."

"You won't?"

"No."

"Why?"

"Because he is nothing but a boy, and I won't work with him."

"Then you can go. I'm responsible here, and that boy can carry a chain as well as you can, and can do things that you can't."

So he consented, and was one of my best friends afterwards. From this time I went often with surveyors, as they seemed to pick me for such work. I went with Mr. Zepher and with Mr. Bingham and others.

In San Antonio in 1846 I bought my first horse, and one night with a young fellow who had found a mule lost by the Indians and another boy went hunting turkeys at the head of the San Antonio River. It was drizzling rain, and we built a fire and passed the night mainly in talk. Our horses were tied in the brush near by, and the Indians came and stole them. We

5. City in the Hill Country of central Texas.
6. River that runs from the Hill Country to the Gulf of Mexico.

went to General Harney[7] and asked him for soldiers to go with us to get our horses, but he refused. Another boy and I went and followed them, but did not find them. As we were but two, we thought it dangerous to follow too far, and returned home. So I lost my first horse, to which I was much attached. The boy who went with me after the horse was Jacob Lynn, a German boy raised by a Mexican woman of San Antonio. He was the best shot I ever saw without exception. He could shoot a flying duck with a rifle. And I never saw a braver man than he became.

We went hunting once from San Antonio to Bandera County. We had four horses and six dogs. We killed several deer, a number of turkeys, one bear, and cut several bee trees. We found a bunch of wild cattle, most of them black or brown. We got after one and killed her. We emptied our guns into that cow before we killed her. Lynn had an eight-shooting pistol he had made himself, a rifle, and a pair of holsters; I had a rifle, a six-shooter, and a pair of holsters. Twenty shots went into the body of that black cow before we killed her. Then we camped. The Indians heard our shooting and came toward our camp, which was in a clump of small trees. We had had supper, fed our dogs plenty of beef, and had lain down to rest. Suddenly the dogs jumped up and ran out as if some one were coming, and we heard somebody talking low. We thought sure it was Indians, and we hissed on the dogs in English. The dogs ran out farther and barked as if they had something at bay. We hallooed loud and hissed the dogs. The Indians could not see how many there were of us, and feared to come on us. They thought there was a crowd of us, as we had fired very rapidly at the cow. The Indians stayed around us all night, but feared to charge us. They marched around and around us. They made all kinds of animal calls and cries. They were at one time barking like wolves, then hooting like owls, then fighting like wild cats or quacking like ducks. They thus tried to decoy us out or get us to expose ourselves, but we lay low. The Indians were all afoot, as we found out next morning. There were twenty or thirty of them, as the trail would indicate. Just before daylight we heard them leave. After we found that they were afoot, we decided to follow them, and found where they had killed a deer. They carried away every particle of the deer except the heart. We followed this trail until we saw the smoke rising from the bushes on a little hill, and decided that there were too many of them for us to attack, although we were well mounted and armed. They went on, and we thought it best to go home. We learned later that that party of Indians had killed four men—Germans—on the Medina, who were camped making shingles.[8] They cut open their breasts and took out their hearts. They seemed to have some superstition about the heart. They left the deer's heart, but cut out and carried away the hearts of the men.

ca. 1892–97

---

7. William Selby Harney (1800–1889), cavalry officer in the U.S. Army during the Mexican-American War and the Indian Wars.

8. Materials to cover the roofs or sides of buildings. *The Medina*: river in Bandera County.

# ANDREW GARCÍA
## 1855?–1943

---

## Chapter 34. Murder of John Hays

The miner John Hays had been warned that morning, before leaving Philipsburg,[1] to be careful and to be on the look out for bad Injuns,[2] as the ones who had robbed and murdered the two miners near old Beartown were supposed to be returning Nez Perce[3] warriors, revengeful and bad. They were now thought to be on their way, going up Rock Creek to strike the Salish Indian buffalo trail, after having stolen horses on their way through the Flint Creek country.

John Hays said in Philipsburg that morning, not to fear for him, that he savvied an Injun, and would like to see the color of the Injun's hair who could get near him when he had his old stand-by, his 45-70 Winchester Betsy Jane[4] to fall back on.

No one was ever to know why it was, after quitting his work at the usual time, probably to cook his supper, in the long July daylight and some time yet to sundown, that he left his cabin to go back to the diggins. With his forty-five Colt[5] hanging at his hip, his faithful Winchester on his shoulder, glancing cautiously up and down the gulch, he went on his way to the diggins close by, and saw no danger in this peaceful little valley. And as he goes down the low bank into the diggins, how could he know that a few yards away from him, fierce savage faces, their eyes gleaming with hate, are peering at him? The sluice and pipe head had been shut off for the night to save the water. And only a light head of clear seepage water ran through the ground sluice and sluice boxes.

Leaning his rifle on a rock near him, John Hays starts in cleaning bed rock, shoveling the bedrock dirt into the ground sluice. As the sun sunk lower back in the big hills in the distance, some presentiment must have whispered to him a timely warning that danger lurked here. Twice since coming here John Hays quits his work, as though to go back to his cabin. Taking his rifle, he goes up on the bank of the cut and gazes anxiously up and down the gulch. Seeing no danger each time, he returns to his work.

A few minutes after going up on the bank to look the second time, what his thoughts were only God knows, for sitting on their war ponies like statues between him and the cabin were what appears to be three Injuns with their rifles in their hands. Seeing this, John Hays grabs up his rifle. Quickly stepping behind a pile of boulders, he stands holding his rifle in both hands, ready to shoot if he has to.

---

1. Town in southeastern Montana.
2. Derogatory term for Native Americans.
3. Native American tribe from the Pacific Northwest.

4. I.e., his .45-70 caliber Winchester rifle, which he had nicknamed "Betsy Jane."
5. His .45 caliber Colt revolver.

The Injuns, seeing this, lay their guns across their saddles in front of them, holding up both their arms in the air, to let him know they are friendly to him. The middle Injun, with his arms still held up, steps his horse a step or two closer to the diggins, making signs that they only want to talk.

John Hays waves his rifle at him, making signs at him to go back, not to come nearer to him, and for them to go away, he does not want them there.

Instead of leaving, as Hays told them, the Injuns got off their horses. They laid their rifles down on the ground beside their horses, and one of the Injuns, our friend the Breed,[6] takes off a cartridge belt with two forty-fives in holsters, laying them down on the ground with the rifles. Showing Hays they have no more guns of any kind on them, the three go some ways off to one side of them.

The Breed then, with his hands held up, goes a short way toward the diggins, to where Hays can well hear what he says. He says in good English for the white man not to be afraid of them, that he is a Bitterroot half-breed, and this his two friends are Salish (Flathead) Injuns who live at Stevensville. That they all belong to a large party of Salish who were camped for the night near the mouth of Ross's Fork, on their way back to the Bitterroot Valley from hunting buffalo all last winter across the Big Hills in the land of the Piegans. Yes, for him not to be afraid that they were bad Injuns when they were his friends, who only came here to tell him they had been told by a white man from Philipsburg on their way today, that there were plenty bad Nez Perce warriors robbing and killing white men on their way through here on the Salish trail, for him to look out for them as they would kill him if they found him here alone. Besides he wanted to see how it was the white man washed for gold. He (the Breed) was sure he knew where there was plenty. If he only knew what way the white men did to get it, he would try himself.

John Hays lowered his rifle, knowing well the Salish were always good Injuns and good friends that never yet harmed a white man, many of them camping around here in their fall hunts. After thanking the Breed for warning him, he invited the Breed and two renegades into the diggins.

He told the Breed he would show them all he knowed about washing gold. The Breed and two renegades gladly accepted the invitation, and this trio of hellions lost no time in joining John Hays in his placer diggings.

Still cautious, rifle in hand, the obliging miner shows them the ground sluice and sluice boxes, and tells the highly interested Breed that it was simple as falling off a log to learn, and only required considerable strong-arm labor to loosen up the dirt and gravel.

The Breed asks Hays if he finds plenty gold here. The cautious and wary miner replies, "Alas, no. There is not much to be found here."

Getting more confidential all the time, the Breed brings forth a well-filled buckskin sack, spilling out of it, to the astonished miner's gaze, nuggets and coarse gold, all that the scooped palm of his hand would hold, saying to the white man, as guileless as a child, "Is this gold? If it is, I know where I could find plenty more, where I picked up this sack nearly full among the rocks and gravel with just my hands."

---

6. I.e., half-breed (the offspring of a Native American and a white person).

He sees the nuggets and coarse gold in the Breed's hand at first with envy, then with the inherited greed and avarice of the white man beaming in his face and eyes. Forgetting all caution, he leans his rifle down on a boulder. Eagerly holding out his trembling hand, as the obliging Breed puts the nuggets and coarse gold in his outstretched hand. The gold in his hand sends waves of ecstasy sweeping through him like a prairie fire. He stands entranced, and lovingly as a tenderhearted sweetheart, caresses the nuggets with his other hand. His eyes cannot hide their joy and envy. He tells the Breed in a whisper, "Yes, this is gold. Gold. Gold." Gold, gold, gleaming gold that the white man, since the beginning, has braved death, cold and hunger for, even selling his soul to hell. Wading through rivers of blood to obtain, its cursed lure like the songs of the sirens of old.[7]

As John Hays stands enraptured, the two renegades show no interest in what was going on. The Breed waxes more and more eloquent about what he has already seen in the diggins, but what he would like to see was how the white men washed for gold with a gold pan.

At this the miner John Hays, coming out of his dreams with a sigh of regret, holds out his hand to give the Breed the nuggets and gold dust back. The Breed tells Hays he may keep the largest nugget for himself. Yes, he would give him the big one.

John Hays thanks the Breed for his offered gift, telling him he did not have to give him the nugget for showing him how to use a gold pan, when he would do it for nothing.

The Breed, not to be outdone at this generosity, gently pushes Hays's outstretched hand away, saying that for his friend's heart being so good to him, to show him how to use a gold pan, his good friend must take all the gold in his hand.

The good-hearted miner said that he did not want to do this when the Breed might soon need it himslf.

The Breed said not to fear for that; did not his good friend hear him say that he knew where there were plenty more? He would come back soon and bring his friend with him. There would be plenty gold for both of them.

John Hays objected no more, and took a small buckskin sack out of his pocket. After putting nuggets and gold dust back in it, he returns the sack to his pocket. As he done this, could he only have known that the Breed's gift was a part of the blood-stained gold dust and nuggets of the two murdered miners near old Beartown?

John Hays was now more than willing to reward the Breed's generosity. Leaving his rifle still leaning on the boulder pile nearby, he picked up a gold pan and put a shovel full of rich bedrock dirt in the gold pan. He went to the ground sluice, accompanied by the enthusiastic Breed, the two renegades trailing behind. Their moccasin feet tread the ground as silent as a stalking panther. John Hays kneels down on one knee beside the ground sluice, saying to the Breed, "See, it is just this way." He dips the gold pan in the clear ground sluice water till nearly full and whirls the water and gravel around in the gold pan.

---

7. In ancient Greek mythology, the Sirens were female, partly human creatures who lured sailors to their deaths by singing.

The Breed's beady eyes gleam with interest, his burly form silently crouched down by the white man. The trusting John Hays, unconscious of his peril, with professional pride whirls the water and gravel around in the gold pan. Time and again, dipping the gold pan with a swinging side-motion in the ground sluice water, sending small riffles of water washing the top gravel out of the gold pan. When nearly all of the gravel was washed out, several grains of gold, like little stars, gleam in the black sand in the bottom. All this time the two renegades stand like two statues behind John Hays and the Breed. Not a sign on their faces betrays their hellish thoughts.

The Breed now flashes them a look of understanding. He crouches closer to the white man. The hour and the minute had come. One of the renegades steps in between John Hays and his rifle. The Breed's arm moves with the rapidity of a striking rattler's darting head. His hands grabs the protruding gun butt hanging on John Hays's belt. With a quick twist and a wrench, the forty-five Colt is in his hand. The Breed springs to his feet, flourishing the gun, and gives John Hays a kick in the back that sent him sprawling face downward in the ground sluice. The renegade picks up Hays's rifle as the other renegade hurls a rock striking him between the shoulders. The half-stunned white man had not fully realized what had happened, as seven more red devils came leaping out of the brush and down the bank into the diggins; throwing down their blankets, stripped for action in leggins and breechclout, they picked up rocks as they came.

What John Hays's thoughts were only God knows, as he sprung to his feet, dripping wet, to find himself surrounded by a living wall of savages. He thought they only meant robbery, because they could have shot him dead without going to all this bother to get his rifle and pistol away from him.

With a look of blind fury at the Breed, he tells this limb of Satan just what he thinks of him, saying, since when was it that the Flathead Injuns had become thieves and liars to do a dirty trick like this to a good friend who had always used them well? He told them to take what they wanted and that he would know better next time than to trust a breed or Injun of any kind.

The Breed, with a crafty look, meets this with stoic silence. Then he tells the others in Nez Perce that this was good. The white man still thought they were Flatheads. He had not thought of this before.

The Breed, with Hays's rifle in his hand, stands to one side, encouraging them on. Like a band of hungry wolves, the nine warriors needed no second bidding and hurl themselves at the defenseless white man as though they would tear him to pieces.

John Hays was a large and powerful man and his desperation and fury added strength to his burly form. With a sweep of his powerful arms, he hurls them aside like ninepins. He made a spring toward one renegade and grabbed him by the arm. There was a swift twist and wrench upward, with the cracking of bone. He swung the terrified Injun off his feet, one limp and broken arm hanging at his side. The other warriors in their fury to get at the white man were always in each other's way. Some of them drew their knives, but soon put them back in their sheaths when one of them, making a slash at the white man, cut another warrior instead.

Hays took off his heavy-loaded cartridge belt and met the milling and on-coming renegades, swinging the heavy cartridge belt full of cartridges with telling effect. One crack was enough for the renegade that came within its reach. Charging after them with this improvised weapon, he soon had the astonished redskins on the run, and dodging in and out around him, firing rocks at him whenever they got the chance.

Hays had not much trouble in breaking away from them, and starts off on the run from them down through the diggins, the surprised warriors running after him. Rather than see him escape, the Breed raises the rifle, but could not shoot Hays without hitting some of the renegades.

John Hays's mad dash for his life and liberty was short-lived. Hampered as he was with his heavy hip gum boots, he was no match for his fleet-footed enemies. Running through the loose wash in the diggins, he stumbles in a hole, sprawling on the slippery gravel. Before he could rise, the first of his pursuers came up and, with a whoop of triumph, sprang at him, pulling the cartridge belt out of his hand. Hays ducked a blow in springing to his feet, only to find himself again surrounded by his tormentors, all of them panting and out of breath.

The Breed coming up, gun in hand, is furious at the warriors for letting the white man get away from them. He said they were worse than squaws, who would have killed the white man before this. Since they were only snapping coyotes, afraid to face a white man, only being able to bite him in the back, they should spread out in a circle and he would help them to kill the white dog with rocks. Putting the rifle down, he joined them.

In this circle of death, going up through the diggins amid flying rocks, many of which found their mark, John Hays, now bruised from head to foot, still done his best and fought them back with rocks, but in this unequal struggle there could be but one end. No matter what way he turns and charges them, others would slip around behind him. Smaller and closer to him grew the death circle of determined fiends. Twice whizzing rocks struck him on the head and brought him down on his knees, only for him to spring up on his feet again, but he was getting weaker and weaker, realizing that the end will soon come. John Hays, with superhuman effort born of despair, leaps through a volley of flying rocks, and clutches one of the surprised warriors. In a deadly embrace, as the warrior vainly struggles to release himself, both fell to the ground, the white man on top with a death clutch on the Injun's throat. The Breed and renegades for an instant seem stupefied at the white man's desperate bravery. Hays, with his other hand, reached and grabbed a rock, and smashed in the gurgling warrior's brains. Almost at the same instant one of the renegades leaps at the white man, swinging his rock slingshot, striking Hays with terrible force on the back of his head.

Without a moan or struggle, the powerful arms and clutch on the dead Injun's throat relaxed their grip in death. John Hays's bruised body lay silent in the death embrace of the dead warrior still underneath him.

ca. 1910                                                                                          1967

# Southwestern Newspaper Poetry

The history of journalism in the southwestern United States effectively begins in 1834, when Ramón Abréu brought a printing press from Mexico to what was then the Mexican territory of Santa Fe and began printing the newspaper *El Crepúsculo de la Libertad*. By the following year, the effort had failed, and Father Antonio José Martínez bought the press and began printing texts for schools.

Even after 1848, with the signing of the Treaty of Guadalupe Hidalgo and the ceding of northern Mexican territory to the United States, Mexicans in the Southwest were loyal to their native tongue. Thus Spanish-language newspapers circulated in the region. Indeed, from then until the beginning of World War II, Spanish-language newspapers flourished throughout the United States. Some—such as *El Clamor Público*, in Los Angeles, and *El Boletín Popular*, in Santa Fe, New Mexico—existed for several decades. Others lasted only months.

In addition to reporting the news, these dailies and weeklies carried literary and other cultural pieces, including feature stories on regional cuisine, Spanish American and Mexican American customs, and religion. In this way, they became conservers of local culture and, often, pockets of resistance to English-language-dominated literature and culture. For Mexican Americans, who had lost their patrimony but were intent on maintaining a cultural identity, these newspapers and small-press documents were a way to educate the Spanish-speaking populations about the traditions that were in danger of being lost as Anglo culture swiftly came to dominate the region. They also served to make the English-speaking population aware of the literacy of its Spanish-speaking neighbors.

Editors of these periodicals were often among the best-educated members of the community, and they doubled as poets, essayists, editorialists, and short-story writers. According to the critic Doris Meyer, "Neomexicano newspapers were the de facto literature" for their readership. Written by the editors, staff writers, local freelancers, writers in Mexico, and translators, the newspapers, especially in New Mexico, ran news articles side by side with political literature in the form of poetry and short stories. The types of literature printed, much of it anonymously, were often influenced by a state's particular political circumstances. As Texas, New Mexico, Arizona, and California (for the purposes of this discussion, we consider California part of the Southwest) became states of the Union, their largely Latino populations experienced varied feelings about how they would be treated as U.S. citizens. The expression of this tension and fear often appeared in local newspapers in the form of literature, especially short stories and poetry. In New Mexico, as both Meyer and the critic A. Gabriel Meléndez have noted, newspaper literature in the late nineteenth and early twentieth centuries focused on the development of cultural identity. Eusebio Chacón, one of the region's great orators and scion of the territory's—and, later, the state's—most prominent families, published "A la Patria" (To the Fatherland) in *El Boletín Popular*, next to the gazette of local news. This piece identified the Spanish-language region as worthy of one's loyalty, and its appearance in a newspaper meant it would reach many more readers than if it had been printed in a book.

Newspaper literature ran the gamut from poorly written versions of romantic European- or Mexican-style poetry to reprints of work by the foremost Spanish and Mexican poets of the age; from ardent expressions of U.S. patriotism to calls for local cultural preservation. Poetry that focused on personal issues, such as love of a spouse and/or a family—including a great deal of poetry paying homage to children or friends—also found a place in southwestern newspapers. In many cases, short stories focused less on patriotism and the development of cultural identity than on the changing mores within the culture.

In her seminal study, *Speaking for Themselves: Neomexicano Cultural Identity and the Spanish-Language Press, 1880–1920* (1996), Meyer designates four types of New Mexican newspaper poetry: adversarial political verse, corrido-style narrative verse (employing an epic grandeur), *canción*-style lyric verse (in the manner of folk poetry, folk songs, and folktales), and the work of an unclassifiably wide-ranging poet who identified himself as X.X.X. in public and whom Meyer has identified as Luis Tafoya. Catholic religious images are included in much of this verse, intermingled with cultural and political references. A fifth type of poetry, moral and ethical pedagogy, could be broken out as well.

These categories may not be as useful for newspaper poetry printed beyond New Mexico. In California, after a huge increase in the Anglo American population during the late 1840s, the Spanish-speaking population's search for political and cultural identity took relatively isolated forms of expression, as in oral and written histories. The most published newspaper poet of the time, Dantés, wrote mainly about personal and social issues, as opposed to political and cultural ones. In Texas, newspaper literature took similar forms.

The work of Luis Tafoya demonstrates the late-nineteenth and early-twentieth century literary response to the political situation of New Mexico and many other areas of the Southwest. It focuses on Mexican American culture and includes an attempt to interpret that culture's political concepts. Tafoya was well educated, and in addition to essays, editorials, dialogues, and sermons, he wrote poetry in both folk styles and the sophisticated styles favored in Mexico at the time. Tafoya's poetry is also intriguing because of its broad themes and subject matter. In verse structures that are often simple, Tafoya uses local language to express the unfairness and, often, corruption inherent in New Mexican politics. In fact, the difficult and even dangerous nature of New Mexican political battles is illustrated by the attempt on Tafoya's life made in 1917, about which a story appeared in the newspaper *La Revista de Taos* (as the paper's Santa Fe correspondent, Tafoya himself probably wrote the story). His work was little known until the 1990s, when Meyer, fascinated by the poetry of the anonymous X.X.X. that had appeared in newspapers around the turn of the century, especially in *El Independiente* and *El Nuevo Mexicano* (Santa Fe), began literary detective work to discover his name.

The poems that follow, a representative sample translated by Harold Augenbraum, were all originally published in Spanish-language newspapers: Juan B. Hijar y Jaro's "Heaven Hands Us Our Fate" appeared in San Francisco's *El Nuevo Mundo*, July 19, 1864; J. M. Vigil's "Love and Friendship," in *El Nuevo Mundo*, July 26, 1864; José Rómulo Ribera's "Homeland and Home," in *El Boletín Popular*, December 8, 1892; Luis A. Torres's "Philosophical Truths," anonymously in the same newspaper in 1856; Luis Tafoya's "Same as Usual," in *El Nuevo Mexicano*, February 5, 1898; and Tafoya's "To New Mexico," in *La Revista de Taos*, January 27, 1911. In 1991, "To New Mexico" was made the New Mexico state poem.

# JUAN B. HIJAR Y JARO
## dates unknown

## Heaven Hands Us Our Fate

Beyond the seas they told me:
    In the realm of foreign lands
    I sought a safe harbor
Like the tender birds that left
And sang farewells in tranquil flight.         5
Thus sadly I crossed the seas
And said goodbye to blesséd lares.[1]
    The door of my father's home I closed
And with a cry kissed the lock.
    O! why was I leaving       10
    What I so dearly loved,
    That holy sepulcher?
I passed the place where a holy woman
Lies in eternal sleep;
That holy woman was my mother;      15
    And finding myself alone
Before such a beloved tomb,
I kissed three times the sacred earth,
And in saying my farewell, her soul heard,
    O! I left a piece of my life!      20
A brave figment, the Golden Age,
Rose over the sea like a palace,
And in the calm port awaited me.
In the sea's expanse I set course,
In the sad icuan[2] I crossed the sea,      25
And as I said farewell to my blesséd lares.
    I turned my gaze to Mexican soil,
Where my mother's grave lay,
    And in my deepest sorrow
    O! I let out a sigh:      30
The heart seeking heaven;
Her heart as big as the world . . . !
    The sea welcomed me on its back
    Of boiling mountains.
My ship carved out a luminous trail,      35
Forming transparent skirts
Of crystalline blue from its currents.
    In its depths and its rocks
The giant Pacific slept;
In its dark, sleeping mouth      40
Great eternity is seen

---

1. Personal or household effects; from Lares: in    2. Vessel.
ancient Roman mythology, gods or spirits who
guarded households.

From its breast without end or time,
A wall no longer separated me.
    There I spent my solitary nights,
Swaying in arms of an unstable fate          45
And begging, and wandering in my solitude,
I neither loved life nor summoned death.
    And I crossed the seas
And said farewell to my blesséd lares.
    Then very early one morning:         50
The mist shone from gold to purple,
    And in the mirror of the sea
    The many-faceted light
In every wave rendered a single day.
    Weightless seagulls inhabited         55
The brilliant sky, as souls
    Inhabit memory,
    And in loving flight
Pursue us in the shadows of mist.
    Land! They all shouted, and then         60
The cannon boomed, the harbor welcomed us,
And the resplendent sun, as it rose,
    Lit up the city, the mountains
And the desert, all at once.
The pavilion of stars shivered,         65
In the midst of a hundred pennants,
Adorning with great beauty
The great mist on the waves,
On the fields of silver spray.
There I left the yawning seas         70
And said farewell to my blesséd lares!

    Well, you know the rest, my bosom friends,
Take pity on me. It's a long life,
And without love, life is bitter:
The soul quivers with its mortal pain.         75
Don't ask me to sing, or to laugh,
Since no songs come to mind:
What I loved, I lost, and but
The sad memory of my birthplace remains.

# J. M. VIGIL
## dates unknown

## Love and Friendship

To my good friend E.S.D. Sotero Prieto

Amid the bitterness
Of life's pitiless cast
My heart's holding fast
To a wellspring of tenderness

In whose sacred protection                                     5
My anxious soul will repose
With the love of my spouse
And a good friend's affection.

Illusions one by one
Have quickly expired,                                          10
Passions abjectly desired
Around me undone.

Brows of such innocence
Seen sunk in the mire
While glory lifts higher                                       15
To your grim face such insolence.

It brings to a heart
Such anger and spite, shaking,
Both hands quaking
And stifling a curséd start.                                   20

With utter scorn
It flings looks of despite,
Where eyes shut out light,
Where murder is borne.

Still once I felt fellowship                                   25
Yet offer me flowers
Of inestimable dowers:
Love and friendship,

When on a strange shore
One day I was pained                                          30
That in my homeland remained
Of my love a sweet core.

Where for me eyes would weep,
Where for me hearts would feel,
Lips give breath to appeal                                     35
And my sighs sink in deep.

Where tears that condole
The unfeeling soil lie,
And pleas reach the sky,
As high as the soul.　　　　　　　　　　　　　40

There folks tell my story
In words of great mourning
Misfortune aborning
In my name and my memory.

When I feel these deep glooms　　　　　　　45
To which fates alloy,
Through its whims I'm a toy
Through its strength darkness looms.

I see tenderness allay
My suffering, so inhuman,　　　　　　　　　50
And I'll stretch out my hand,
A hand of amity if I may.

Perhaps one day I'll have grown
Tired of such woe
Abandon my lot and strive to go　　　　　　55
Back to my peaceable home.

Perhaps then I can feel on my cheeks
Those caresses so innocent
Of my children, so impatient
As they bounce on my knees.　　　　　　　60

With my story repeating
Through its deepest pains,
And all my love's gains
Speed the heart's beating.

When a name is impressed　　　　　　　　65
On a childlike soul,
With love on their lips they extol
That name to be blessed.

Then you'll see in the bitterness
Of life's pitiless cast,　　　　　　　　　　70
My heart holding fast
To a wellspring of tenderness.

And that all of humanity
Is not horror and plight,
But that love's full of light　　　　　　　　75
And the voices of amity.

# JOSÉ RÓMULO RIBERA
## birth unknown–1917

### Homeland and Home

In my breast there's a place
And a sanctuary in my memory
Dedicated to the case
That by loving it we embrace
Alone, shamelessly, its glory.                              5

A place, where the glow
Of wild thought always leaps,
And my breast beats to show
Saintly joy fill me, so
That my lyre howls and weeps.                               10

A place whose gleam
Sows a world of illusions in part,
And the most beautiful dreams
In life are these
Inscribed on one's heart.                                   15

A temple, whose great essence
Has a fascinating soul
—And neither time nor absence
Can erase its presence
For it is sculpted in the soul.                             20

A temple of peace and calm,
A shadow of that holy yen.
In his soul, the martyr's balm
When he achieves his longed for palm[1]
And finds himself alone in heaven.                          25

Safe there inside,
Virginal purity can breathe.
There, the warrior is inspired.
Sublime, love sighs
Like a morning breeze.                                      30

That longed-for place
Homeland, as it's known.
And my quivering face
Whispers the beloved phrase
"The Sanctuary of Home."                                    35

1. A palm leaf as a symbol of victory.

# LUIS A. TORRES
dates unknown

## Philosophical Truths

We enter this world innocent,
And grow up thinking,
Foolishly
That our lives expand,
And that the journey to the grave          5
Goes slowly.

But the centuries fly by
Like shadows in the wind,
And we bury
In the very core of a moment          10
What thought conceives
In delirium.

A rushing torrent
We enjoy in life
Briefly,          15
And, intoxicated, we decide
To be eternal, and then it ends
So suddenly.

The centuries roll by
Aged, and tired,          20
They nibble at the edges
Of our selves, tormented
By the masks of pleasure
That crush us.

We pursue each day          25
The happiness that exists only
In the minds of men,
And how sad we do not see it
As just a dream, a tale told,
A jesting.          30

# LUIS TAFOYA aka X.X.X.
## 1851–1922

## Same as Usual

Uncle Samuel answered no,
He won't admit us as a state
And so to faithful New Mexico
Congress has dealt a mighty blow.

It's the silver we are lacking          5
Which worries this land.
Interests have their backing,
Our plans they will derail
And our aspirations fail,
In a feeling not so old,                 10

As we play this sad, sad role
In this state of hope, we're praying,
So this we'll keep on saying
'Though Uncle Samuel has said no.

For half a century, we all know,         15
They have promised us a state
And both earlier and late
These promises they forego;
Not a verbal promise, but more so,
In a treaty they all credited,           20
Fully written and edited,
Approved by two nations,
And still these Solons
Don't admit us as a state.

Like a beggar all in tatters            25
They shoo us from the door,
Decide not in our favor,
And no trial or witness matters;
We lack a faithful friend
Who with his words like honey           30
Could by San Miguel portend
That if the Congress is made of money
It will ease our statehood's entry
For a faithful New Mexico.

Hope's a consolation                    35
To a soul that's so afflicted.
To feel so much constricted
You lift your eyes in search of heaven.
Our desires did not obtain
In the case already past                40
Yet it will be won at last
And its day come back again.

For there really is no reason
For Congress to deal this blow.


## To New Mexico

New Mexico, lift up
    the beat-down brow
that clouds the charms
    of your beaming face,
and clasp with joy the shimmering crown,      5
    symbol of glory and good fortune and peace.

Past now the many years of struggle
    and strife
your luck has turned,
    a victory wrought,      10
the day of success
    finally come about,
the culmination of joy, the font
    of glory.

As empire you have been great,      15
    so crowned with riches
—though great reverses
    you had to suffer,
but now the triumph
    is complete,      20
a reward for constancy
    you should receive.

For three centuries your people
    were isolated and alone,
helped by no one, no one      25
fought for your daring,
    bold existence
and sealed autonomy and mastery
    with their blood.

So past this epic task,      30
    at last you'll get
the good that comes with
    perseverance,
and you are freely brought in
    to the United States      35
with sovereignty that draws
    the souls of free men.

The obstacles and hindrances
    all fade away,
and you have free entry      40
    to that glorious Union,

where citizens prosper
　　and flourish,
with all its guarantees
　　and protection.　　　　　　　　　　　　　　　45

For such remarkable joy
　　we congratulate you,
you, and all your children,
　　for such a signal honor,
and in your new sphere　　　　　　　　　　　　50
　　we truly expect
that as great an empire as you were,
　　so great a state you will be.

# RAMÓN EMETERIO BETANCES
## 1827–1898

Historically regarded as the father of the Puerto Rican nation, Ramón Emeterio Betances is among a select group of nineteenth-century patrician revolutionary leaders who, in support of the abolitionist and separatist causes, struggled against Spanish colonial authority and, as a result, spent a good part of their adult lives in exile. Born in the town of Cabo Rojo, in western Puerto Rico, Betances was sent to France by his father in 1837 to receive a secondary education and university training. He studied at the Royal College (today's Lycée Pierre-de-Fermat) in Toulouse and in 1848 was admitted to the University of Paris, where seven years later he completed a medical degree. In Paris, Betances participated in the 1848 uprising against the monarchy, an event that gave birth to the second French Republic; thus he was undoubtedly influenced by the French people's struggles for freedom, individual rights, and social justice. After completing his studies in 1855, he returned to Puerto Rico to practice medicine and became well known when he played a major role in attending the needy during a cholera epidemic in the western part of the island that same year. Shortly thereafter, he became involved in the island's political struggles against Spain. He was one of the founders of a secret abolitionist society and also became a fervent separatist. As a result, he was exiled in 1856 and went to the Dominican Republic.

During the next decade, Betances was forced out of his homeland three more times, the last time in 1867, never to return. His 1867 exile brought him to New York City. Accompanied by his compatriot Segundo Ruiz Belvis, also a prominent abolitionist and separatist, he joined José Francisco Basora, another well-known Puerto Rican separatist doctor living in New York, who in 1865 had participated in the founding of the Sociedad Republicana de Cuba y Puerto Rico (Republican Society of Cuba and Puerto Rico) and of the separatist newspaper *La Voz de América*. In New York, the three men formed the Comité Revolucionario de Puerto Rico (Puerto Rican Revolutionary Committee) and began to plan the armed insurrection of September 23, 1868, later known as the *Grito de Lares* (Cry of Lares).

This insurrection took place only a few weeks before the *Grito de Yara* (Cry of Yara) insurrection in Cuba, which marked the beginning of the neighboring island's Ten Years' War for independence (1868–78) from Spain. From New York, Betances went to the Caribbean island of Saint Thomas, then a Danish colony, 40 miles east of Puerto Rico. In November 1867, he issued his famous proclamation, "Los diez mandamientos de los hombres libres" (The Ten Commandments of Free Men)—also known as "You Shall Be Free" (as the selection here is titled). This assertion of individual rights was also a call for island independence and for Puerto Ricans to take up arms against Spain, and it served as an inspiration for the *Grito de Lares* insurrection. Betances also put together a shipment of weapons to be taken to Puerto Rico, where separatists were planning the insurrection. But the plan was thwarted by the early interference of Spanish authorities, and the ship and its cargo of weapons were confiscated and never able to leave port, although Betances and his fellow conspirators were able to escape. The insurrection broke out in the town of Lares, but it was crushed within a few days by Spanish troops.

The failure of Puerto Rico's Lares insurrection did not dampen Betances's revolutionary fervor. During the decades that followed, he remained one of most internationally respected crusaders for Antillean independence. Unable to return to his homeland, he spent the rest of his life in France, with occasional returns to the Dominican Republic, Cuba, and New York, to continue his many endeavors on behalf of the separatist movement. In France, he published several scientific studies that were considered important contributions to medicine, including a major study on the prevention and treatment of cholera and research on the causes of tetanus. In 1887, he received the French Legion of Honor for his medical work and for his diplomatic efforts on behalf of Cuba and the Dominican Republic.

Since his younger years as a medical student, Betances had engaged in literary pursuits, writing in French and in Spanish. One of his earlier works is *Les Deux Indiens* (The Two Indians), a romantic novel about the tragic love between a Spanish woman and an Indian man, reflecting an interest in indigenist themes common among Puerto Rican writers of this period. He frequently wrote political essays for newspapers and corresponded with many separatist friends and other intellectual and political leaders. His political writings reflect a firm opposition to the growing support among separatists for the annexation of Cuba and Puerto Rico by the United States. Emulating the Monroe Doctrine, Betances made his celebrated anti-imperialist declaration, "The Antilles for the Antilleans." He was also one of the major proponents of the idea of an Antillean federation, a postindependence political union among the Caribbean islands.

From 1895 to 1898, Betances played an important diplomatic role in Paris, representing Cuba during that island's second war of independence. "Remembrances of a Revolutionary" was written in February 1898, a few months before the explosion of the U.S. battleship *Maine* in Havana Harbor and the United States' subsequent declaration of war against Spain. At this point, the Cuban rebel army had made important gains against the Spaniards and was close to achieving victory. In this text, the Puerto Rican patriot reflects upon his almost half-century involvement in the Antillean separatist struggle and confirms the anticipation shared by most separatists that a victory in the Cuban battlefield was near and that a Spanish defeat in Cuba would also eventually bring liberation to Puerto Rico. Betances died only a few months after the subsequent invasion of Cuba and Puerto Rico by the United States.

"Arriba, Puerto Ricans!", also included here, is one of Betances's major proclamations for Puerto Rico's independence. Like "You Shall Be Free," it denounces Spanish despotism and exhorts the island's population to take up arms against colonial rule.

# Arriba, Puerto Ricans![1]

Puerto Ricans, for more than three centuries, Spanish despotism has oppressed us. Until now, not a single son of this country has occupied a post of

1. Translated and edited by Kal Wagenheim and Olga Jiménez de Wagenheim.

any distinction. On the contrary, any man who has dared to speak for the well-being of his countrymen has been persecuted, banished into exile, or ruined.

For more than three centuries, we have been paying immense taxes, and still we have no roads, railways, telegraph systems, or steamships.

The rabble of Spain—its soldiers and clerks—come to the island without a *peseta*,[2] and, after they have squeezed us dry, return to their homeland with millions that belong to us, who have worked for it.

The *gíbaros*[3] are poor and ignorant because of the Government, which prohibits schools, newspapers, and books, and not long ago refused to found a university, so that the poor, who cannot send their children abroad, shall never see them with the titles of doctor, lawyer, etc.

The Government insists that the *gíbaros* should remain nothing more than lowly day laborers with *libretas*.[4] And, lately, to exploit us even more, it tries to make us hate our brothers, the sons of Santo Domingo,[5] forcing us to take arms and fight against them. . . .

Puerto Ricans, let us not be fools, let us not be deceived by the promises and falsehoods of the Government; we know from experience that Spain never fulfills its promises. Let us not sleep; the occasion is magnificent; there are no soldiers on the Island, and even if there were, the war in Santo Domingo must have convinced us that one *gíbaro* with his machete in hand is worth a hundred Spaniards.

*Arriba* Puerto Ricans! Let us show the rabble, who rob and insult us, that the *gíbaros* of Puerto Rico are neither cowards against their executioners, nor assassins against their brothers.

Let us join together, and rise en masse against the oppressors of our land, of our women and children. Our *grito* of Independence shall be heard, and supported, by all friends of Liberty; and there shall be no lack of arms and money to crush the despots of Cuba, Puerto Rico, and Santo Domingo into the dust.

1864

# You Shall Be Free[1]

### Puerto Ricans![2]

The government of Queen Isabella is making a terrible accusation against us:
    It says that we are bad Spaniards. The government is spreading false-hoods.

2. Official Spanish currency at the time. [Anthology editors' note]

3. Alternative spelling for *jíbaros*, a term used in Puerto Rico to denote peasants. [Anthology editors' note]

4. Each worker had to carry a *libreta*, or notebook, which severely restricted his activities. * * * [Translator-editors' note]

5. Santo Domingo de Guzmán, the capital and largest city in the Dominican Republic. [Anthology editors' note]

1. Translated and edited by Kal Wagenheim and Olga Jiménez de Wagenheim. Wagenheim and Jiménez de Wagenheim's bracketed introduction has been turned into a footnote; their bracketed insertion in the text has been incorporated into the anthology editors' note.

2. After the previous proclamation [i.e., "Arriba, Puerto Ricans!"], General Félix María de Messina, the island's Spanish colonial governor, ordered Betances to appear before him in La Fortaleza, the governor's palace. As Betances told Messina of the need for independence, the governor interrupted and said, "If you continue this, I shall be obliged to hang you from one of the battlements of El Morro [the Spanish main military fort in Old San Juan]." Betances replied, "Well, keep in mind, General Messina, that the night of that day I shall sleep far more peacefully than Your Excellency." Betances was exiled, but he continued to support independence from abroad. The following proclamation, reproduced in leaflet form, was signed by Betances in November, 1867, and distributed on the island. He

We do not want separation; we want peace and union with Spain; but it is only fair that we should also specify the conditions in the contract. They are very simple:

ABOLITION OF SLAVERY
THE RIGHT TO REJECT ALL TAXES
FREEDOM OF RELIGION
FREEDOM OF SPEECH
FREEDOM OF THE PRESS
FREEDOM OF COMMERCE
THE RIGHT TO ASSEMBLE
THE RIGHT TO BEAR ARMS
THE INVIOLABILITY OF THE CITIZEN
THE RIGHT TO ELECT OUR AUTHORITIES

These are the
TEN COMMANDMENTS
of Free Men

If Spain feels capable of giving us these rights and freedoms, and does so, then it may send us a captain general or governor . . . made of straw, and we shall hang him, and have him burned during the days of *carnestolandas*,[3] to commemorate all the Judases who, until today, have sold us out.

THUS, we shall be Spaniards. If not, NO.

If not, Puerto Ricans, PATIENCE! You shall be free.

November 1867

---

# REMEMBRANCES OF A REVOLUTIONARY[1]

## I. [Against Spanish Despotism]

In 1851, a group of Cuban young men, wealthy, happy, and full of promise, came through Paris like a flock of wagtails. They knew that at that moment General Narciso López[2] was embarking with six hundred of his comrades to invade the province of Pinar del Río. Among the Cubans were two Puerto Ricans. One of them was the lawyer Vargas (from Ponce)[3] who later dedicated himself to the defense of liberal ideals. About the other one I

---

was still in exile, this time on nearby Saint Thomas. The proclamation sets forth "Ten Commandments," listing the conditions under which Puerto Rico would retain its association with Spain. It is virtually a declaration of independence. [Translator-editors' note]
3. Three days of carnival before Lent. In the Christian tradition, Lent is a 40-day period during which the faithful are expected to fast, abstain from eating meat and attending festivities, and engage in various penitential practices. [Anthology editors' note]

1. Translated by Susan P. Liberis-Hill and Edna Acosta-Belén.
2. Narciso López (1798–1851) was a Creole born in Venezuela to Spanish parents. He defended Cuba's right to independence and organized four expeditions to liberate the island, in 1848, 1849, 1850, and 1851. He was captured and executed by the Spanish authorities. [Translators' note]
3. A municipality on the south-central coast of Puerto Rico. [Anthology editors' note]

only have one memory: his unquenchable passion for women, that eventually brought him to his grave.

Vargas had met me when I became politically active in 1848. From him, the others learned my name, and they all came many times deep into the Latin Quarter to drag me out when I was starting my medical studies, taking stands on issues and frequently voicing them through newspaper articles coming out in favor of Antillean independence.

On one of these outings, where hopes swell with the clouds of cigar smoke and the fizz of champagne, we entered one of the main restaurants of the Boulevard des Italiens, and settled ourselves in a private room.

Lunch was splendid and the conversation revolved entirely around patriotism.

The same thought kept troubling all of us:

"Who knows"—someone said—"if he has already left?"

"Victory is secure"—said another. "The General carries the support of the North American people with him."

"Do not"—I said—"plant a palm tree in Washington or an apple tree in Havana, because they will both die."

"What else do you want?"—a young comrade responded. "There are no more beautiful women in the world than those from Baltimore. By God, if only I could transplant them to Puerto Rico!"

The conversation continued like that, sometimes happy, other times filled with melancholy, but always reflecting the desires of my fellow comrades to achieve annexation to the United States.

"Ah!"—said the first speaker. "We should not be here. People might think that we are running away from danger. Our duty was to go and wait for the arrival of Narciso López."

"But where?"—added another one. "Nobody knows where he is going to land."

"Then"—a slightly somber voice said—"that indicates that Cuba is not prepared."

Not long ago the King of Piamonte, despairing at not finding the slightest material support against Austrian despotism among European governments, had pronounced the courageous and memorable words: *Italia fará da sé.*[4]

The conversation followed its course, and each of us, when his turn arrived, toasted the great general. When my turn came, I was standing with a glass in my hand, and all of us heard the cries of the newspaper vendors coming from the boulevard:

"Invasion of Cuba by the Yankees!"

"Complete defeat of the filibusters!"

"Mass executions!"

I must say it. As soon as those words reached us, I saw tears misting in the eyes of my comrades, and then running down their cheeks. A strange heat ran through my whole body, my face became inflamed, and with an irresistible impulse I smashed my glass against the table, and it shattered to pieces. With a sob drowning my voice, I screamed: "Cuba will triumph by herself!"

---

4. Italy will do it by herself. [Translator's note]
   An important region in the efforts toward the unification of Italy, Piedmont lost two wars against Austria (1820–21 and 1848–49). [Anthology editors' note]

It was an electric commotion. A single roar rose from our chests: "Long Live Free Cuba!" We fell into each others arms, hands fumbling to find others to shake fervently.

In the middle of our fraternal hugs, tears intermingled; then our stares at the sky became lost into the future, as if under the spell of a mysterious apparition of our splendorous Cuba, liberated by Cubans, and prospering only in the hands of Cubans.

So many hopes!

There was an oath: "To work until death against Spanish despotism, to gain the independence of the two Antilles."

And here I am, doing my part, about to celebrate on February 24, 1898, my diamond wedding anniversary with the Revolution.

## II. Tenth of October

Narciso López's head inclined on the scaffold, his neck bones crushed by the iron tie of the "garrote vil."[5]

"A man dies," Goicouría[6] would say later, "and a nation is born." For seventeen years there was the silence of horror. The peace of the cemeteries. All that time was necessary for the gestation and arrival of the revolutionary Venus,[7]

and the 10th of October,

emerging from the *blue* Antillean Sea, a terrestrial tremor from the deep bottom of the water hurling her onto the beach *red* with blood, over the *white* foam of the waves, and displaying on her forehead *the lone star*[8] of redemption.

It was she who awakened the hero of the Ten Years' War, Carlos Manuel de Céspedes,[9] and who delivered the banner of Narciso López so it could wave in his hands in the mist of battles to salvage Cuban dignity, and she offered him, if not the independence of his beloved motherland, then at least the immortality of his name and an eternal place in the temple of glory.

Céspedes accepted the offering and surrounded himself with a legion of heroes: the venerable Aguilera, and Santa Lucía; Máximo Gómez, our real Liberator; Calixto García, whom the goddess herself anointed with a star

5. A handheld weapon, such as a length of chain, used to strangle someone, especially in an execution or assassination. [Anthology editors' note]

6. I.e., General Domingo de Goicouría (1805–1870), a Cuban separatist involved in the revolutionary activities leading to the Ten Years' War of Independence (1868–78) in Cuba. He was captured during an 1870 expedition and garroted by the Spaniards, and his execution was covered in the American press as an example of Spanish barbarity in Cuba. [Anthology editors' note]

7. In ancient Roman mythology, the goddess of love and beauty, born fully formed out of the sea. Betances is referring to the 17 years that elapsed between the end of the Ten Years' War and the beginning of the second War of Independence (1895–98). The emergence of a revolutionary Venus from the Antillean ocean symbolizes the emergence of the Cuban nation from the blood of its patriots, represented here by the colors of the independence movement's flag (later to become the national flag): red triangle with a lone white star, and sky-blue and white stripes. [Anthology editors' note]

8. In the Cuban flag; see previous note. [Anthology editors' note]

9. Carlos Manuel de Céspedes (1819–1874) was a Cuban separatist and the leader of the *Grito de Yara*'s declaration of independence, which initiated the Ten Years' War. He is often referred to as the *Padre de la Patria* (Father of the Country). The other names listed here are of patriots and soldiers who, in fighting for the independence of Cuba during this period, gave or risked their lives for the revolutionary cause. [Anthology editors' note]

on his forehead; Palma, a man of integrity, taken prisoner defending the archives of the Revolution; Maceo, the invincible, who in the silence of the tropical nights had conversed with Victory; Agramonte, the impetuous and brilliant Agramonte; Rabí, the indomitable Indian; Mármol, who at the capture of Bayamo wrote to his mother the following sublime words: "I had the glory of burning your house"; Quesada, who arrived with all the prestige of the Mexican war fought by the three Indians Juárez, Ramírez y Altamirano; and Collazo and the Sangylys, and the Agueros, and the Arangos, and many others resting in the bosom of the motherland and in the heart of all Cubans.

The desperate struggle lasted ten years to carry on the task considered impossible until then: to convert a timid and enslaved people into a free and fighting people whose efforts, nevertheless, were in vain and who succumbed, once again, waiting for help from abroad, and without relying enough upon themselves.

## III. Realized Dream

Some fell in the battlefield, and those who came from behind picked up their weapons and shouted: "Charge!" Others barefoot, without weapons, sublime *sans-culottes*[1] answered: "Long live death!" and trodded onward.

At the highest point in one of the mountains of the Sierra Maestra,[2] at a spot sculpted into the rock by nature, sat a young man, serious and pensive, holding his forehead with his hands. His lively and penetrating gaze followed with emotion the drama that was unfolding at his feet. From his place his gaze extended to the virgin forest and the boundless oceans, emblems of freedom, and closer, through the thick cloud of smoke, surrounded by flames devouring the sugar cane fields, two armies engaged in combat.

One soldier, more terrified by the fire than by the bullets, looked behind him, afraid of becoming encircled by the flames; the other, heedless of the fire, moved forward with irrepressible momentum and joyfully proclaimed: "Independence or death!"

"What soldiers!" he said to himself. "What a country these revolutions— which should form a united front—will make with these men, now that Cuba wants to fend *for herself*!"

And the mighty dreamer silently came down from those mountains, already pondering the kind of organization that he would give to this great endeavor, which following the labor of seventeen years (1878–1895), was realized today to glorify, in 1898, an independent and free Cuba, and for Cuba and Puerto Rico to glorify the patriotism inspired by the events of February 24th, and by the great citizen, unparalleled organizer, honored departed, defeated in battle, but immortal in his work: JOSÉ MARTÍ.[3]

1898

---

1. Nonuniformed civilian fighters. [Translators' note]
2. Mountain range in southeast Cuba. [Anthology editors' note]
3. See p. 265. [Anthology editors' note]

# MARÍA AMPARO RUIZ DE BURTON
## 1832–1895

According to her marriage certificate, María Amparo Ruiz de Burton was born in Loreto, in Baja California (now Mexico's western peninsula), on July 3, 1832. Her maternal grandfather was José Manuel Ruiz, the governor of Baja California, and her maternal grandmother was related to some of the most prominent Spanish-speaking families of Alta California (now the state of California). Her father's surname was Arango, but his full name and lineage—as well as why she used her mother's surname on her marriage certificate—remain a mystery. In 1848—after the United States and Mexico signed the Treaty of Guadalupe Hidalgo, which forced Mexico to cede nearly half its territory to the United States—Ruiz de Burton and her mother moved from Baja to San Francisco, along with several hundred other refugees. There she met U.S. Army captain Henry S. Burton, a 28-year-old widower. Though she was Catholic and he Protestant, they were married, in civil and religious ceremonies.

At the time, Ruiz de Burton was thought to be one of the most beautiful women in the West and was believed to be the model for the young woman in the ballad "The Maid of Monterey," which for years was sung by Mexican veterans of the war. In the historian Hubert Howe Bancroft's *California Pastoral* (1888) and in various newspaper articles of the 1930s, the marriage of Ruiz and Burton is described in great detail and characterized as one of the great romances of the time. At the outbreak of the Civil War, Burton was posted to the East. During his southern campaign, he contracted malaria, and Ruiz de Burton traveled east to be with him. He died in Rhode Island in 1869, leaving Ruiz de Burton to raise their two children.

Ruiz de Burton's first known work was *Don Quixote de La Mancha: A Comedy in Five Acts Taken from Cervantes' Novel of That Name* (1876), but her novel *Who Would Have Thought It?* (1872) revealed her extraordinary talent. Written in highly assured English prose, it is now believed to be the first novel by a Mexican American (and certainly the first in English). *Who Would Have Thought It?* was published without the author's name on the title page (a common occurrence at the time), but was registered at the Library of Congress under the names H. S. Burton and Mrs. Henry S. Burton. A diligent reporter soon discovered Ruiz de Burton's authorship and made it known to the public. The novel takes place immediately before, during, and after the Civil War. Through the story of Lola, a young Mexican orphan brought to live in the home of a prominent provincial, Anglo family of New England, Ruiz de Burton scrutinizes the national political situation of her time. She begins by focusing on local and personal struggles, but then expands the novel's scope to include views of the racially charged white-versus-black dichotomy that plagues the United States.

The author listed on the title page of Ruiz de Burton's second novel, *The Squatter and the Don* (1885), is "C. Loyal," which stands for *Ciudadano Loyal* (Loyal Citizen). Most critics have interpreted this pseudonym as Ruiz de Burton's declaration of loyalty both to the laudable goals of the United States and to the collective welfare of those Mexican Americans living in the former Mexican territories. By the time of the composition of *The Squatter and the Don*, Ruiz de Burton had returned from the East to California, where governmental corruption had undermined the tenets of the Guadalupe Hidalgo agreement. The treaty, designed to protect the interests of formerly Mexican citizens in former Mexican-controlled territories, undermined the patron/peon-based economy that had existed before the U.S. annexed California.

Though the treaty nominally protected Mexican land grants, in reality corruption of elected representatives made it difficult, if not impossible, for the *californios* to protect their holdings. When, in 1850, California became the twentieth state of the Union, through loose and corrupt interpretations and lax enforcement of the law, representatives and judges could turn a blind eye to the land-grabbing Anglo migrants who appropriated major parts of *californio* land estates, since these white men represented a voting constituency. Gradually, these large areas of private property were, in effect, cut into smaller parcels and the upper-class *californios* relegated to a middle class, in many ways destroying the traditional Mexican class system of the time.

In Ruiz de Burton's book, William Darrell (the squatter) and Mariano Amaro (the don—a courtesy title for a distinguished male), both basically decent men, clash over a large tract of land granted to Amaro by the Mexican government when Alta California was part of Mexico. Darrell has settled on the Amaro rancho, with the understanding that the Don's initial title defense has been rejected, though Darrell's wife insists that he not lay claim to any land whose litigation has not been finalized. Throughout the story, Amaro tries to protect his property by using all the legal means available to him. Though Darrell and Amaro will settle their dispute, less scrupulous, lower-class squatters will pick away at Amaro's territory, until both he and Darrell, weary from these struggles, will die, leaving their families to reconfigure their own lives.

Like species unable to adapt, the "squatter" and the "don" die out as their environment enters a new era, a transition that includes a symbolic act of optimism: marriage between the two families. Yet Ruiz de Burton does not merely portray the lost rights of the *californios*. She vehemently decries the creeping control of outside monied interests over local economies—in essence, the gradual "corporatization" of the entire landscape. For example, when Darrell's son joins with three other San Diegan businessmen to acquire the right-of-way to bring the southern railway to San Diego—a move meant to spur the city's growth into a second major hub for Californian commerce—northern interests in San Francisco, eager to protect their transportation monopoly, quash the attempt through bribery of corrupt officials in California and Washington.

The following selection, the first chapter of *The Squatter and the Don*, provides an idea of Ruiz de Burton's writing style, as well as the conflict at the story's core.

---

## FROM THE SQUATTER AND THE DON

## Chapter 1

### Squatter Darrell Reviews the Past

"To be guided by good advice, is to profit by the wisdom of others; to be guided by experience, is to profit by wisdom of our own," said Mrs. Darrell to her husband, in her own sweet, winning way, as they sat alone in the sitting room of their Alameda farm house, having their last talk that evening, while she darned his stockings and sewed buttons on his shirts. The children (so-called, though the majority were grown up) had all retired for the night. Mr. and Mrs. Darrell sat up later, having much to talk about, as he would leave next day for Southern California, intending to locate—somewhere in a desirable neighborhood—a homestead claim.

"Therefore," continued Mrs. Darrell, seeing that her husband smoked his pipe in silence, adding no observations to her own, "let us this time be guided by our own past history, William—our experience. In other words, let us be wise, my husband."

"By way of variety, you mean," said he smiling. "That is, as far as I am concerned, because I own, frankly, that had I been guided by your advice—your wisdom—we would be much better off today. You have a right to reproach me."

"I do not wish to do anything of the kind. I think reproaches seldom do good."

"No use in crying over spilt milk, eh?"

"That is not my idea, either. On the contrary, if by '*milk*' it is meant all or any earthly good whatever, it is the '*spilt milk*' that we should lament. There is no reason to cry for the milk that has not been wasted, the good that is not lost. So let us cry for the *spilt milk,* by all means, if by doing so we learn how to avoid spilling any more. Let us cry for the *spilt milk,* and remember how, and where, and when, and why, we spilt it. Much wisdom is learnt through tears, but none by forgetting our lessons."

"But how can a man learn when he is born a fool?"

"Only an idiot is, truly speaking, a born fool; a fool to such a degree that he cannot act wisely if he will. It is only when *perversity* is added to foolishness, that a being—not an idiot—is utterly a fool. To persist in acting wrongfully, that is the real folly. To reject good counsel, either of one's own good thoughts or the good thoughts of others. But to act foolishly by deciding hastily, by lack of mature reflection, that I should only call a foolish mistake. So, then, if we have been foolish, let us at least utilize our foolishness by drawing from it lessons of wisdom for the future. We cannot conscientiously plead that we are born fools when we see our errors."

Mr. Darrell smilingly bowed, and with a voice much softer than his usual stentorian tones, said:

"I understand, little wife, but I fear that my streak of perversity is a broad one, and has solely been the bane of my life; it has a fatality accompanying it. I have often seen the right way to act, and yet I have gone with my eyes wide open to do the wrong thing. And this, too, not meaning to do harm to any one, nor wishing to be malicious or mean. I don't know what power impelled me. But if you will forgive my past wickedness, I'll try to do better."

"Don't say that. Don't speak of your wickedness, for real wickedness is perversity. You have acted wrongly at times, when you have misapplied your rights and the rights of others, but you have not intentionally done wrong. You are not perverse; don't say that."

"In a few days it will be twenty-four years since we crossed the plains with our three babies, in our caravan of four wagons, followed by our fine horses and choice Durham cows. I firmly believed then, that with my fine stock and my good bank account, and broad government lands, free to all Americans, I should have given you a nice home before I was five years older; that I would have saved money and would be getting more to make us rich before I was old. But see, at the end of twenty-four years, where and how do I find myself? I am still poor, all I have earned is the name of 'Squatter.' That pretty name (which I hate because you despise it) is what I have earned."

"Don't say that either, William. We will only recommence one of numerous fruitless discussions. We are not poor, because we have enough to live in comfort, and I do not despise the name of Squatter, for it is harmless enough, but I do certainly disapprove of acts done by men because they are squatters, or to become squatters. They have caused much trouble to people who never harmed them."

"They, too, the poor squatters, have suffered as much distress as they have caused, the poor hard-worked toilers."

"That is very true, but I am afraid I shall never be able to see the necessity of any one being a squatter in this blessed country of plentiful broad acres, which a most liberal government gives away for the asking."

"That's exactly it. We aren't squatters. We are 'settlers.' We take up land that belongs to us, American citizens, by paying the government price for it."

"Whenever you take up government land, yes, you are 'settlers,' but not when you locate claims on land belonging to any one else. In that case, you must accept the epithet of 'Squatter.'"

Darrell set his teeth so tightly, that he bit a little chip off his pipe. Mrs. Darrell went on as if she had not observed her husband's flash of irritation.

"But I hope we will never more deserve such name; I trust that before you locate any homestead claim in Southern California, you will first inform yourself, very carefully, whether any one has a previous claim. And more specially, I beg of you, do not go on a Mexican grant unless you buy the land from the owner. This I beg of you specially, and must *insist upon it.*"

"And how am I to know who is the owner of a rancho that has been rejected, for instance?"

"If the rancho is still in litigation, don't buy land in it, or if you do, buy title from the original grantee, on fair conditions and clear understanding."

"I don't know whether that can be done in the Alamar rancho, which I am going to see, and I know it has been rejected. But of one thing you can rest assured, that I shall not forget our sad experience in Napa and Sonoma valleys, where—after years of hard toil—I had to abandon our home and lose the earnings of years and years of hard work."

"That is all I ask, William. To remember our experience in Napa and Sonoma. To remember, also, that we are no longer young. We cannot afford to throw away another twenty years of our life; and really and truly, if you again go into a Mexican grant, William, I shall not follow you there willingly. Do not expect it of me; I shall only go if you compel me."

"Compel you!" he exclaimed, laughing. "Compel you, when you know I have obeyed you all my life."

"Oh! no, William, not all your life, for you were well grown before I ever saw you."

"I mean ever since I went to Washington with my mind made up to jump off the train coming back, if you didn't agree to come North to be my commandant."

"I don't think I have been a very strict disciplinarian," she said, smiling. "I think the subaltern has had pretty much his own way."

"Yes, when he thinks he might. But when the commandant pulls the string, by looking sad or offended, then good-by to the spirit and independence of the subaltern."

"One thing I must not forget to ask you," she said, going back to the point of their digression, "and it is, not to believe what those men have been telling you about the Alamar rancho having been finally rejected. You know John Gasbang could never speak the truth, and years have not made him more reliable. As for Miller, Hughes and Mathews, they are dishonest enough, and though not so brazen as Gasbang, they will misrepresent facts to induce you to go with them, for they want you with them."

"I know they do; I see through all that. But I see, too, that San Diego is sure to have a railroad direct to the Eastern States. Lands will increase in value immediately; so I think, myself, I had better take time by the forelock and get a good lot of land in the Alamar grant, which is quite near town."

"But, are you sure it is finally rejected?"

"I saw the book, where the fact is recorded. Isn't that enough?"

"Yes, if there has been no error."

"Always the same cautious Mary Moreneau, who tortured me with her doubts and would not have me until Father White took compassion on me," said he, smiling, looking at her fondly, for his thoughts reverted back to those days when Miss Mary was *afraid* to marry him; but, after all, he won her and brought her all the way from Washington to his New England home.

William Darrell was already a well-to-do young farmer in those days, a bachelor twenty-eight to thirty years of age, sole heir to a flourishing New England farm, and with a good account in a Boston bank, when Miss Mary Moreneau came to New England from Washington to visit her aunt, Mrs. Newton. As Mrs. Newton's husband was William Darrell's uncle, nothing was more natural than for Mary to meet him at his uncle's house. Nobody expected that William would fall in love with her, as he seemed to be proof against Cupid's darts. The marriageable maidens of William's neighborhood had in vain tried to attract the obdurate young farmer, who seemed to enjoy no other society than that of his uncle Newton and his wife.

But Mary came and William surrendered at once. She, however, gave him no encouragement. Her coldness seemed only to inflame his love the more, until Miss Moreneau thought it was best to shorten her visit and return home about the middle of September.

"Why are you to return home so early?" Darrell asked Mary, after Mrs. Newton had informed him of Mary's intention of going.

"Because I think it is best," she answered.

"Why is it best?"

"For several reasons."

"May I be permitted to ask what are those reasons?"

"Certainly. One reason is, that as I came to see my aunt and at the same time to rest and improve my health, and all those objects have been accomplished, I might as well go home. Then, my other aunt, with whom I reside, is not feeling well. She went to spend the summer in Virginia, but writes that her health has not improved much, and she will soon come back to Washington. Then some of my pupils will want to recommence their lessons soon, and I want to have some little time to myself before I begin to work. You know, Mr. Darrell, I teach to support myself."

"Yes, only because you have a notion to do it."

"A notion! Do you think I am rich?"

"No, but there is no need of your working."

"It is a need to me to feel independent. I don't want to be supported by my aunts, while I know how to earn my own living."

"Miss Mary, please, I beg of you, let me have the happiness of taking care of you. Be my wife, I am not a rich man, but I have enough to provide for you."

"Mr. Darrell, you surprise me. I thank you for the compliment you pay me with your honorable offer, but I have no wish to get married."

"Do you reject me, Miss Mary? Tell me one thing; tell me truly, do you care for any one else?"

"No, I care for nobody. I don't want to marry."

"But you will marry some time. If you knew how very miserable you make me, I think you would not have the heart to refuse me."

"You will get over it. I am going soon. Forget me."

Darrell made no answer. He staggered out of the room and did not return until the following week, when Mary had left for Washington, accompanied by Letitia, her colored servant (called Tisha), who was devotedly attached to her.

Darrell had become rather taciturn and less sociable than ever, Mrs. Newton noticed, and since Mary left he seemed to lose flesh and all his spirits, and passed the winter as if life were a burden to him. But when spring came, he brightened up a little, though he felt far from happy. About that time Mrs. Newton had a letter from Mary, saying that she was going to spend vacation in Maryland with her other aunt, and Tisha for her escort.

"She don't come here, because she fears I shall pester her life with my visits. As she knows I can't keep away from her, she keeps away from you. She hates me. I suppose you, too, will take to hating me, by and by," said Darrell, when he heard that Mary was not coming that summer.

"No danger of that, William," Mrs. Newton replied.

"Yes, there is. You ought to hate me for driving her away. I hate myself worse than I hate the devil."

"William, you mustn't feel so. It isn't right."

"I know it. But when did I ever do anything right, I'd like to know? I wish I could hate her as I hate myself, or as she hates me."

"William, she does not hate you."

"How do you know she don't?"

"Because she would have told me. She is very truthful."

"I know it. She gave me my walking papers in a jiffy. I wish I could hate her."

"William, do you promise not to get angry, if I tell you why Mary declined your offer?"

"Say on. You couldn't well make a burning furnace any hotter. I am too mad already."

"Well, I'll tell you. She likes you, but is afraid of you."

"Afraid? afraid?" said he, aghast—"why! that is awful! I, an object of fear, when I worship the ground she treads on! But, how? What have I done? When did I frighten her?"

"At no particular time; but often you gave her the impression that you have a high temper, and she told me, 'If I loved Mr. Darrell better than my life, I wouldn't marry him, for I could never be happy with a man of a violent temper.' Then she spoke, too, of her being a Roman Catholic and you a Protestant."

"But you are a Catholic and uncle is Protestant."

"Certainly, I think the barrier is not insuperable."

"So, my temper frightened her! It is awful!" He mused in silence for a few minutes and then left the room.

About an hour after, he returned dressed for traveling, carrying a satchel in one hand and a tin box under his arm. He put the box on the table, saying:

"Aunt Newton, I am going away for a few days. Please take care of this box until I return or you hear from me. Good-by!" and he hurried away, for he had only barely time to catch the train going to New York.

Darrell was in New York for a few hours. He bought a finer suit of clothes, a very elegant light overcoat, hat and boots, and gloves to match, and thus equipped so elegantly that he hardly recognized himself, as he surveyed his figure in a large mirror of the furnishing store, where he was so metamorphosed, he took the night train for Washington.

It was early on a Sunday morning that Darrell arrived at Washington. He went to a hotel, entered his name, took a room, a bath and a breakfast, and then called a hack to go in search of Mary. He knew that was not an hour for calling, but he had *business* with Mary. His was no friendly visit; it was a matter of life and death with him.

He rang the bell, and presently he heard Tisha's flapping steps coming. "Lud a massa!"[1] she exclaimed, stepping back. But recovering herself, said with true heartiness—"Come in the parlor, please. It is true glad Miss Mary will be to see ye."

"Do you think so, Tisha?" he asked.

"I know it; no thinking about it, neither. She is going to mass; but she'll see you for a little while, anyway."

Opening the parlor door for Darrell to walk in, Tisha ran up stairs to Mary's room.

"Oh Miss Mary!" said she, "guess who is down stairs."

"I couldn't, Tish, being so early and on Sunday, but I heard a man's voice. Is it a gentleman?"

"You bet; ah! please excuse me, I mean sure as I live it is, and no other than Mr. Darrell, from New England."

"Ah!" said Miss Mary, affecting indifference, but her hands trembled as she tied her bonnet strings.

Darrell knew he must appear self-contained and not in the least impetuous, but when he saw those beautiful dark eyes of Mary's he forgot all his pretended calmness.

"Is my aunt well?" Mary began as she came in.

"Yes, yes, everybody is well; don't be alarmed at my coming, I know it must seem strange to you. Two days ago I had no idea of coming to Washington, but Miss Moreneau, your aunt told me you were not coming North this summer, and this news nearly drove me crazy."

"Oh, Mr. Darrell!"

1. I.e., "Lord have mercy!"

"Wait, don't drive me off yet. Your aunt told me that you refused me because you believed I have a violent temper. Now, I am not going to deny that, but this I am going to say—That I have never violated my word, and never shall, and I make a most solemn oath to you, that if you will marry me you shall never have occasion to be made unhappy or displeased by my quick anger, because you will only have to remind me of this pledge, and I shall curb my temper, if it kills me."

"Mr. Darrell, I believe you are perfectly sincere in what you say, but a strong trait of character is not controlled easily. It is more apt to be uncontrollable."

"For God's sake don't refuse me, I feel I must kill myself if you spurn me. I don't want life without you."

"Don't say that," Mary said, trying to keep calm, but she felt as if being carried away in spite of herself, by the torrent of his impetuosity. She was afraid of him, but she liked him and she liked to be loved in that passionate rebellious way of his; she smiled, adding, "we must postpone this conversation for I must go to church, and it is quite a long walk there."

"The carriage that brought me is at the door, take it, and don't walk, it is quite warm out."

"Will you go with me to church? You see, that is another obstacle; the difference of religions."

"Indeed, that is no obstacle; your religion tells you to pity me."

"We will talk to Father White about that."

"Then Mary, my beloved, will you give me hope?"

"And will you really try to control your anger when you feel it is getting the mastery over you?"

"I will, so help me God," said he, lifting his hand.

"Take care, that is an oath."

"I know it, and mean it," said he, much moved.

They went to church together. After church, Mary had a few moments' conversation with her pastor. She explained everything to him. "Do you love him, my child?" asked the good Father, knowing the human heart only too well. Mary blushed and said—"Yes, Father, I believe I do."

"Very well, send him to see me tomorrow morning."

Darrell had a long talk with Father White, and promised solemnly not to coerce or influence his wife to change her religion, and that should their union be blessed with children, they should be baptized and brought up Catholics.

And his union was blessed. Mary made his New England home a paradise, and eight children, sharing largely their mother's fine qualities, filled to overflowing his cup of happiness.

### The Don's View of the Treaty of Guadalupe Hidalgo

If there had been such a thing as communicating by telephone in the days of '72, and there had been those magic wires spanning the distance between William Darrell's house in Alameda County and that of Don Mariano Alamar in San Diego County, with power to transmit the human voice for five hundred miles, a listener at either end would have heard various discussions upon the same subject, differentiated only by circumstances.

No magic wires crossed San Francisco bay to bring the sound of voices to San Diego, but the law of necessity made the Squatter and the Don, distant as they were—distant in every way, without reckoning the miles between them—talk quite warmly of the same matter. The point of view was of course different, for how could it be otherwise? Darrell thought himself justified, and *authorized,* to "take up lands," as he had done before. He had had more than half of California's population on his side, and though the *"Squatter's Sovereignty"* was now rather on the wane, and the *"squatter vote"* was no longer the power, still, the squatters would not abdicate, having yet much to say about election times.

But Darrell was no longer the active squatter that he had been. He controlled many votes yet, but in his heart he felt the weight which his wife's sad eyes invariably put there when the talk was of litigating against a Mexican land title.

This time, however, Darrell honestly meant to take no land but what belonged to the United States. His promise to his wife was sincere, yet his coming to Southern California had already brought trouble to the Alamar rancho.

Don Mariano Alamar was silently walking up and down the front piazza of his house at the rancho; his hands listlessly clasped behind and his head slightly bent forward in deep thought. He had pushed away to one side the many armchairs and wicker rockers with which the piazza was furnished. He wanted a long space to walk. That his meditations were far from agreeable, could easily be seen by the compressed lips, slight frown, and sad gaze of his mild and beautiful blue eyes. Sounds of laughter, music and dancing came from the parlor; the young people were entertaining friends from town with their usual gay hospitality, and enjoying themselves heartily. Don Mariano, though already in his fiftieth year, was as fond of dancing as his sons and daughters, and not to see him come in and join the quadrille was so singular that his wife thought she must come out and inquire what could detain him. He was so absorbed in his thoughts that he did not hear her voice calling him—"What keeps you away? Lizzie has been looking for you; she wants you for a partner in the lancers," said Doña Josefa, putting her arm under that of her husband, bending her head forward and turning it up to look into his eyes.

"What is the matter?" she asked, stopping short, thus making her husband come to a sudden halt. "I am sure something has happened. Tell me."

"Nothing, dear wife. Nothing has happened. That is to say, nothing new."

"More squatters?" she asked. Señor Alamar bent his head slightly, in affirmative reply.

"More coming, you mean?"

"Yes, wife; more. Those two friends of squatters Mathews and Hagar, who were here last year to locate claims and went away, did not abandon their claims, but only went away to bring proselytes and their families, and a large invoice of them will arrive on tomorrow's steamer. The worst of it all is, that among the new comers is that terrible and most dangerous squatter William Darrell, who some years ago gave so much trouble to the Spanish people in Napa and Sonoma Counties, by locating claims there. John Gasbang wrote to Hogsden that besides Darrell, there will be six or seven other men bringing their families, so that there will be more rifles for my cattle."

"But, didn't we hear that Darrell was no longer a squatter, that he is rich and living quietly in Alameda?"

"Yes, we heard that, and it is true. He is quite well off, but Gasbang and Miller and Mathews went and told him that my rancho had been rejected, and that it is near enough to town to become valuable, as soon as we have a railroad. Darrell believed it, and is coming to locate here."

"Strange that Darrell should believe such men; I suppose he does not know how low they are."

"He ought to know them, for they were his teamsters when he crossed the plains in '48. That is, Miller, Mathews, Hughes and Hager, were his teamsters, and Gasbang was their cook—the cook for the hired men. Mrs. Darrell had a colored woman who cooked for the Darrell family; she despised Gasbang's cooking as we despise his character, I suppose."

Doña Josefa was silent, and holding on to her husband's arm, took a turn with him up and down the piazza.

"Is it possible that there is no law to protect us; to protect our property; what does your lawyer say about obtaining redress or protection; is there no hope?" she asked, with a sigh.

"Protection for our land, or for our cattle, you mean?"

"For both, as we get it for neither," she said.

"In the matter of our land, we have to wait for the attorney general, at Washington, to decide."

"Lizzie was telling Elvira, yesterday, that her uncle Lawrence is a friend of several influential people in Washington, and that George can get him to interest himself in having your title decided."

"But, as George is to marry my daughter, he would be the last man from whom I would ask a favor."

"What is that I hear about not asking a favor from me?" said George Mechlin, coming out on the piazza with Elvira on his arm, having just finished a waltz—"I am interested to know why you would not ask it."

"You know why, my dear boy. It isn't exactly the thing to bother you with my disagreeable business."

"And why not? And who has a better right? And why should it be a bother to me to help you in any way I can? My father spoke to me about a dismissal of an appeal, and I made a note of it. Let me see, I think I have it in my pocket now,"—said George, feeling in his breast pocket for his memorandum book,—"yes, here it is,—'For uncle to write to the attorney general about dismissing the appeal taken by the squatters in the Alamar grant, against Don Mariano's title, which was approved.' Is that the correct idea? I only made this note to ask you for further particulars."

"You have it exactly. When I give you the number of the case, it is all that you need say to your uncle. What I want is to have the appeal dismissed, of course, but if the attorney general does not see fit to do so, he can, at least, remand back the case for a new trial. Anything rather than this killing suspense. Killing literally, for while we are waiting to have my title settled, the *settlers* (I don't mean to make puns), are killing my cattle by the hundred head, and I cannot stop them."

"But are there no laws to protect property in California?" George asked.

"Yes, some sort of laws, which in my case seem more intended to help the law-breakers than to protect the law-abiding," Don Mariano replied.

"How so? Is there no law to punish the thieves who kill your cattle?"

"There are some enactments so obviously intended to favor one class of citizens against another class, that to call them laws is an insult to law, but such as they are, we must submit to them. By those laws any man can come to my land, for instance, plant ten acres of grain, without any fence, and then catch my cattle which, seeing the green grass without a fence, will go to eat it. Then he puts them in a 'corral' and makes me pay damages and so much per head for keeping them, and costs of legal proceedings and many other trumped up expenses, until for such little fields of grain I may be obliged to pay thousands of dollars. Or, if the grain fields are large enough to bring more money by keeping the cattle away, then the settler shoots the cattle at any time without the least hesitation, only taking care that no one sees him in the act of firing upon the cattle. He might stand behind a bush or tree and fire, but then he is not seen. No one can swear that they saw him actually kill the cattle, and no jury can convict him, for although the dead animals may be there, lying on the ground shot, still no one saw the settler kill them. And so it is all the time. I must pay damages and expenses of litigation, or my cattle get killed almost every day."

"But this is infamous. Haven't you—the cattle owners—tried to have some law enacted that will protect your property?" George asked. "It seems to me that could be done."

"It could be done, perhaps, if our positions were reversed, and the Spanish people—'the natives'—were the planters of the grain fields, and the Americans were the owners of the cattle. But as we, the Spaniards, are the owners of the Spanish—or Mexican—land grants and also the owners of the cattle ranchos, our State legislators will not make any law to protect cattle. They make laws 'to protect agriculture' (they say proudly), which means to drive to the wall all owners of cattle ranchos. I am told that at this session of the legislature a law more strict yet will be passed, which will be ostensibly 'to protect agriculture,' but in reality to destroy cattle and ruin the native Californians. The agriculture of this State does not require legislative protection. Such pretext is absurd."

"I thought that the rights of the Spanish people were protected by our treaty with Mexico," George said.

"Mexico did not pay much attention to the future welfare of the children she left to their fate in the hands of a nation which had no sympathies for us," said Doña Josefa, feelingly.

"I remember," calmly said Don Mariano, "that when I first read the text of the treaty of Guadalupe Hidalgo, I felt a bitter resentment against my people; against Mexico, the mother country, who abandoned us—her children—with so slight a provision of obligatory stipulations for protection. But afterwards, upon mature reflection, I saw that Mexico did as much as could have been reasonably expected at the time. In the very preamble of the treaty the spirit of peace and friendship, which animated both nations, was carefully made manifest. That spirit was to be the *foundation* of the relations between the conqueror and conquered. How could Mexico have foreseen then that when scarcely half a dozen years should have elapsed the trusted conquerors would, 'In Congress Assembled,' pass laws which were to be retroactive upon the defenseless, helpless, conquered people, in order to despoil them? The treaty said that our rights would be the same as those enjoyed by all other American citizens. But, you see, Congress takes very good care not to enact retroactive laws for Americans; laws to take away from American citizens the property which they hold now, already, with a recognized legal title. No, indeed. But they do so quickly enough with us—with us, the Spano-Americans, who were to enjoy equal rights, mind you, according to the treaty of peace. This is what seems to me a breach of faith, which Mexico could neither presuppose nor prevent."

"It is nothing else, I am sorry and ashamed to say," George said. "I never knew much about the treaty with Mexico, but I never imagined we had acted so badly."

"I think but few Americans know or believe to what extent we have been wronged by Congressional action. And truly, I believe that Congress itself did not anticipate the effect of its laws upon us, and how we would be despoiled, we, the conquered people," said Don Mariano, sadly.

"It is the duty of law-givers to foresee the effect of the laws they impose upon people," said Doña Josefa.

"That I don't deny, but I fear that the conquered have always but a weak voice, which nobody hears," said Don Mariano.

"We have had no one to speak for us. By the treaty of Guadalupe Hidalgo the American nation pledged its honor to respect our land titles just the same as Mexico would have done. Unfortunately, however, the discovery of gold brought to California the riff-raff of the world, and with it a horde of land sharks, all possessing the privilege of voting, and most of them coveting our lands, for which they very quickly began to clamor. There was, and still is, plenty of good government land, which any one can take. But no. The forbidden fruit is the sweetest. They do not want government land. They want the land of the Spanish people, because we 'have too much,' they say. So, to win their votes, the votes of the squatters, our representatives in Congress helped to pass laws declaring all lands in California open to pre-emption, as in Louisiana, for instance. Then, as a coating of whitewash to the stain on the nation's honor, a 'land commission' was established to examine land titles. Because, having pledged the national word to respect our rights, it would be an act of despoliation, besides an open violation of pledged honor, to take the lands without some pretext of a legal process. So then, we became obliged to present our titles before the said land commission to be examined and approved or rejected. While these legal proceedings are going on, the squatters locate their claims and raise crops on our lands, which they convert into money to fight our titles. But don't let me, with my disagreeable subject spoil your dance. Go back to your lancers, and tell Lizzie to excuse me," said Don Mariano.

Lizzie would not excuse him. With the privilege of a future daughter-in-law, she insisted that Don Mariano should be her partner in the lancers, which would be a far pleasanter occupation than to be walking up and down the porch thinking about squatters.

Don Mariano therefore followed Lizzie to their place in the dance. Mercedes sat at the piano to play for them. The other couples took their respective positions.

The well-balanced mind and kindly spirit of Don Mariano soon yielded to the genial influences surrounding him. He would not bring his trouble to

mar the pleasure of others. He danced with his children as gaily as the gay-
est. He insisted that Mr. Mechlin, too, should dance, and this gentleman
graciously yielded and led Elvira through a quadrille, protesting that he had
not danced for twenty years.

"You have not danced because you were sick, but now you are well. Don't
be lazy," said Mrs. Mechlin.

"You would be paying to San Diego climate a very poor compliment by
refusing to dance now," George added.

"That is so, Papa. Show us how well you feel," Lizzie said.

"I shall have to dance a hornpipe to do that," Mr. Mechlin answered,
laughing.

To understand this remark better, the reader must know that Mr. James
Mechlin had come to San Diego, four years previously, a living skeleton,
not expected to last another winter. He had lost his health by a too close
application to business, and when he sought rest and relaxation his constitution seemed permanently undermined. He tried the climate of Florida.
He spent several years in Italy and in the south of France, but he felt no
better. At last, believing his malady incurable, he returned to his New York
home to die. In New York a friend, who also had been an invalid, but whose
health had been restored in Southern California, advised him to try the
salubrious air of San Diego. With but little hope, and only to please his
family, Mr. Mechlin came to San Diego, and his health improved so rapidly
that he made up his mind to buy a country place and make San Diego his
home. William Mathews heard of this, and offered to sell his place on what
Mr. Mechlin thought very moderate terms. A lawyer was employed to pass
upon the title, and on his recommendation the purchase was made. Mr.
Mechlin had the Mathews house moved back near the barn, and a new and
much larger one built. Mr. Mechlin devoted himself to cultivating trees and
flowers, and his health was bettered every day. This was the compensation
to his wife and two daughters for exiling themselves from New York; for it
was exile to Caroline and Lizzie to give up their fine house in New York City
to come and live on a California rancho.

Soon, however, these two young ladies passed their time more pleasantly,
after making the acquaintance of the Alamar family, and soon their acquaintance ripened into friendship, to be made closer by the intended
marriage of Gabriel—Don Mariano's eldest son—to Lizzie. Shortly after,
George—Mr. Mechlin's only son—came on a visit, and when he returned
to New York he was already engaged to Elvira, third daughter of Señor
Alamar.

Now, George Mechlin was making his second visit to his family. He had
found New York so very dull and stupid on his return from California that
when Christmas was approaching he told his uncle and aunt—with whom
he lived—that he wanted to go and spend Christmas and New Year's Day
with his family in California.

"Very well; I wish I could go with you. Give my love to James, and tell him
I am delighted at his getting so well," Mr. Lawrence Mechlin said, and
George had his leave of absence. Mr. Lawrence Mechlin was president of
the bank of which George was cashier, so it was not difficult for him to get
the assistant cashier to attend to his duties when he was away, particularly
as the assistant cashier himself was George's most devoted friend. George

could have only twelve days in California, but to see Elvira for even so short a time he would have traveled a much longer distance.

Mr. James Mechlin affirmed repeatedly that he owed his improved health to the genial society of the Alamar family as much as to the genial climate of San Diego County. Mr. Mechlin, however, was not the only one who had paid the same tribute to that most delightful family, the most charming of which—the majority vote said—was Don Mariano himself. His nobility of character and great kindness of heart were well known to everybody.

The Alamar family was quite patriarchal in size, if the collateral branches be taken into account, for there were many brothers, nephews and nieces. These, however, lived in the adjoining rancho, and yet another branch in Lower California, in Mexico. Don Mariano's own immediate family was composed of his wife and six children, two sons and four daughters.

All of these, as we have seen, were having a dance. The music was furnished by the young ladies themselves, taking their turn at the piano, assisted by Madam Halier (Mercedes' French governess), who was always ready to play for the girls to dance. Besides the Mechlins, there were three or four young gentlemen from town, but there were so many Alamars (brothers, nieces and nephews, besides) that the room seemed quite well filled. Such family gatherings were frequent, making the Alamar house very gay and pleasant.

George Mechlin would have liked to prolong his visit, but he could not. He consoled himself looking forward to the ninth of June, when he would come again to make a visit of two months' duration. On his return East, before renewing his duties at the bank, he went to Washington to see about the dismissal of the appeal. Unfortunately, the attorney general had to absent himself about that time, and the matter being left with the solicitor general, nothing was done. George explained to Don Mariano how the matter was delayed, and his case remained undecided yet for another year longer.

1885

---

# EUGENIO MARÍA DE HOSTOS
## 1839–1903

Throughout the American hemisphere, no nineteenth-century Puerto Rican intellectual is better known than Eugenio María de Hostos. He has been called "Citizen of the Americas," a designation that indicates his numerous intellectual endeavors and enduring prominence in the many nations of Latin America and the Caribbean. He was an educator, a sociologist, a philosopher, a journalist, a creative writer, and an unwavering supporter of Puerto Rico's and Cuba's independence from Spain.

Born in the western town of Mayagüez, Puerto Rico, Hostos moved to Spain at age 13 to attend high school in Bilbao. He was a law student at the Central University of Madrid, Spain, when he was drawn to Puerto Rico's struggles for political freedom, including the abolition of slavery. During this period he wrote his first novel, *La peregrinación de Bayoán* (Bayoán's Pilgrimage, 1863), a symbolic indictment of Spanish tyrannical rule in the Americas from the perspective of a young liberal reformist. At the time, Hostos was still not fully persuaded that armed struggle was the only course in the pursuit of more representation and civil liberties for Puerto Rico from Spain. This novel, written in the form of an intimate diary, introduces some of the philosophical, sociological, political, and moral concerns that characterized many of Hostos's subsequent writings. However, his more mature writings are deeply influenced by French positivism, a philosophy that emphasized reason, logic, empiricism, and the notion that scientific laws govern human behavior just as they do natural phenomena.

While he was living in Madrid in 1865, Hostos's liberalism was further influenced by Spanish advocates of republican government as they battled conservative supporters of monarchical rule. The failure of Puerto Rico's separatist armed insurrection—the *Grito de Lares* (Cry of Lares) of 1868, a year that also marked the beginning of Cuba's Ten Years' War of independence and the triumph of the first Spanish Republic—inspired Hostos's decision to join the Antillean separatist movement. He left Madrid for New York City in 1869 and became a writer for the newspaper *La Revolución*, the main publication of the Junta Central Republicana de Cuba y Puerto Rico (Republican Central Committee for Cuba and Puerto Rico), an organization promoting Antillean independence. Through his newspaper articles, Hostos became a major proponent of the postindependence ideal of an Antillean federation uniting Cuba, Puerto Rico, and the Dominican Republic. He also strongly opposed annexation of the islands by the United States.

After spending almost a year in New York, Hostos began a long pilgrimage through Venezuela, Colombia, Chile, Peru, Argentina, and Brazil. Through these countries' newspapers, he proved to be one of the most committed defenders of the ongoing Cuban war of independence, enlisting the support of many Latin American intellectuals and political leaders for the Antillean cause. In 1879, Hostos settled in the Dominican Republic, beginning many years of service and intellectual contributions to that nation. During the nine years he spent there, he founded and directed the Escuela Normal (Normal School) and wrote one of his most important collections of ethical essays, *Moral social* (Social Morals, 1888).

In 1888, Hostos returned to Chile, where he was a professor of law, directed a secondary school, and continued his journalistic and literary pursuits. A decade later, he went back to New York, shortly after the U.S. invasion of Cuba and Puerto Rico. In New York, he immediately founded the Liga de Patriotas Puertorriqueños (League of Puerto Rican Patriots) to exert pressure on the United States to establish a civil government on the island and conduct a plebiscite among the Puerto Rican people to determine their future political status. He was also part of a delegation of Puerto Rican leaders who met with U.S. president William McKinley in 1899 to brief him on the island's needs and priorities and persuade him to end military rule and allow Puerto Ricans to participate in their own government. Hostos delivered the speech "Liga de Patriotas Puertorriqueños," included in this anthology, in 1898. He wrote it to enlist island Puerto Ricans into this new organization aimed at educating the population about their civil liberties and improving the social, economic, educational, and political conditions in Puerto Rico after the U.S. takeover.

Hostos's warnings about the dangers of the U.S. occupation of Puerto Rico were thrust aside by the acrimonious partisanship of Puerto Rican political leaders, many of whom had welcomed the U.S. invading forces and favored annexation. In their eagerness to be liberated from Spanish tyrannical rule and their hope to be linked to the nation that was at the time a symbol of democracy and modernity, most island politicians did not foresee the United States' intentions to keep Puerto Rico as an unincorporated colonial possession, a status with a lesser degree of autonomy than the one that had been granted by Spain less than a year before the U.S. invasion, and one that did not provide the island a clear path to independence, annexation, or self-government. Hostos returned to Puerto Rico in 1899, but his disappointment with Puerto Rico's new colonial condition, coupled with the lack of a consensus among island leaders regarding its political future, and the refusal of U.S. authorities to grant a plebiscite to allow Puerto Ricans to express their preferences about their future status, influenced his return to the Dominican Republic, where he remained until his death.

Less than a month before his death, Hostos wrote the final entry in his *diario* (diary), which he started in Madrid in 1866. Many of the entries through the years provide an intimate and self-reflective measure of his principles and moral character, and of his dreams, existential anguish, and passionate dedication to the pursuit of knowledge and freedom. In the fragment presented in this anthology, written in 1870, Hostos expresses his views about the United States and the possible dangers of a future U.S. annexation of any of the Antilles.

## League of Puerto Rican Patriots[1]

Our presence and attendance at this Assembly[2] is compelled by the fulfillment of our duty; it is a response to our belief that we have an obligation as Puerto Ricans, working towards the improvement of the social, economic, and political welfare of our people.

There is nothing that better represents our objectives than the program that is being developed by the League, with its initiation of evening classes and Sunday lectures, as well as setting the foundation for a municipal institute in the town of Juana Díaz. This also will be done in other towns.

The League of Puerto Rican Patriots has as its political objective the quick change of the military government for a civil one; the establishment of a provisional government as soon as Congress meets; the prompt elevation of Puerto Rico to the status of statehood, reserving the right to a plebiscite until the political situation in the United States favors this goal.

The political goal is less important to the League in comparison to the social objectives.

What we are mainly addressing at this moment in the life of the country is for the country to prepare itself so that this generation can contribute its efforts to the improvement of its habits, and the increase of its knowledge in order for subsequent generations to appropriate all the resources that freedom places in the hands of the country.

For that to occur, it is indispensable to establish public education at all levels, and for it to be extended to boys and girls, and also to men and women.

It is indispensable for education to encompass at the same time social, civic, and military concerns.

It is indispensable to foresee and facilitate the functioning of the political, economic, civic, and cultural institutions, so they can give to the whole population the aptitude, ability, and spontaneity that are necessary for an active life, for the improvement of public health, and to exercise the initiative that must be applied to all the necessities of life, individual as well as social.

1. Translated by Edna Acosta-Belén and Susan P. Liberis-Hill.
2. Assembly of all the island's town city halls, held at the San Juan Municipal Theater on October 30, 1898, where Hostos and Dr. Rafael Cestero represented the town of Juana Díaz and also presented this addendum to the conference on public education. * * * [Editor's Note]

The levels of public education are three: the fundamental which Kindergarten and public school must provide; high school, which must offer positive scientific, civic, and technical ideas; professional school, which must offer concrete knowledge of jurisprudence, medicine, engineering, and technology; and university, which must provide all the knowledge of each one of the disciplines of the positivist sciences, not aimed at the practical aspects of life, but at the cultivation of the mind.

For the development and availability of a teaching pool, capable to give classes in these areas and the military ones, there must be:

Public schools for male and female tutors.

Normal schools for teachers.

Public schools for university professors.

Naval schools.

How far teaching goes is not a major concern if it is regarded as the means to make it more effective.

With the ultimate goal of making it so, the League will begin by founding in each of the towns where it works, an evening school, a municipal institute that understands innovative primary and secondary teaching, Sunday lectures, a newspaper about culture in general, and as many rural schools as possible.

In four of the provincial capitals, normal schools for male teachers will be founded, and normal schools for female teachers will be founded in the remaining three county towns.

As long as the League does not have at its disposal the necessary resources to establish special institutions for military and civic training, municipal institutes will satisfy that need, providing the practical aspects of such training.

## II

The League will contribute to facilitating the political culture by cooperating with the establishment of rural town halls which will, as part of their decision-making and administrative tasks, put into practice the talents of the peasant, capabilities that will continue to develop through practice.

The establishment of savings institutions and cooperatives for production and consumption are so urgent for the moral and economic development of the Puerto Rican population, whether it is the one living in urban sectors or the one bursting over the countryside, that the League would be at fault in its goal of elevating the national character if it did not work to establish these truly emancipating institutions.

Not less capable of complying with the objectives of the League are the creation of gymnasiums and target shooting ranges, which are related to the duties of citizenship and are true civic learning.

The League of Patriots is seeing that the countryside worker and those in the cities do not have any resources against the three vices that impair them, not a room to retain at home, nor distraction to keep him away from the tavern, or a gathering scene or prospect that will make him ashamed of gambling. Establishing construction brotherhoods with the goal of building hygienic housing for the workers; inducing men with initiative to pursue popular forms of entertainment; striving to build an association of national choirs to sweeten our customs and solidify the will to be good citizens, these are cultural goals that the League will make a reality.

It is evident that an endeavor of such magnitude will not be completed within a year, nor in one generation since it is a lifetime challenge for the people. That is, precisely, the worthiness of our purpose: until now, men's coalitions have had fleeting motivations and transitory objectives; now with the League of Patriots, those affiliated with it will have their work cut out for their entire lives.

As a result of being corrupted by colonialism, not even the more enlightened men of Puerto Rico (and they are many more than our patriotism would have the right to expect after such a disastrous Spanish domination), not even the more enlightened men of Puerto Rico decide to show their initiative for anything, or rely completely even on themselves, or quit expecting to be handed down to them by the holders of power. What is needed today is the opposite, whether it is to live under the American Federation, or living subjected to the will of the U.S. Congress, it is imperative to acquire the two forces that colonialism has deprived our society of when it inhibited the exercise of rights that invigorate the individual in his particular endeavors and those of the association.

Aware of that malady, the League of Patriots also knows the impossible condition of the country to function as an active part of the Federation, until it has acquired the custom of relying exclusively on itself, and the habit of carrying out its initiatives. That the basis of its ample program.

Puerto Rico, November 1, 1898


# Fragment from Diary[1]

New York, Wednesday, January 12, 1870, morning

Yesterday, for about a quarter hour around midday, I went out for a walk to distract myself from the preoccupations of politics. And, on this bright day, when Broadway is full of enchanting women, I unconsciously found myself doing what matched my state of mind: I was taking great pleasure in following a very attractive young thing who was walking my way, and from whom I parted when our paths separated. I didn't know it then; but this was not why I stopped turning thirty-one: thirty-one years spent imagining and containing my imagination, feeling and drowning feeling, thinking and not thinking, struggling to give reality to my imaginings, my feelings and my thoughts, without obtaining from this struggle other fruit than the creation of a living contradiction which, just as I momentarily felt and, perhaps, for a moment, made that affection felt, I abandoned it when I could have pursued it. In this fashion, swaying perpetually in the realm of conceivable ideals, worshiped by the race, the heart, and the conscience, and unrealizable by a will that wants to move only in a straight path, that only sees this same path as smooth and lacking any obstacles between the goal and the

1. Translated by Bethania Stewart. The bracketed insertion in the text is the anthology editors'.

point of departure, I tell myself that this is not absolutely certain: that I know people too well to not feel with them, to not be amazed at seeing them place their passions where I place my principles, their egoism where I hasten toward self-denial, their calculated coldness where I express my indignation and my enthusiasm; but, if what my inner voice says is true, it is also true that I make my passivity worse, justify my illness less, make more criminal the negligence with which I submit myself to the struggles that I should overcome and lead. The more lucidly I discern the magnitude of the obstacles I confront, the more serenely I can scientifically confront the forces with which I have to deal [I am devastated]. And, on what does this depend? That they put into life a force that I myself economize: willpower. That it is blind, that it is mobile, that it is not reflective, that it is unhealthy, that it can become wicked, all this is true; but they give outwardly into their desires, their passions, while I inwardly ponder and exaggerate my inner thoughts which, being more honorable and more human, can be the more easily interrupted by more insane ambitions and more inhuman struggles. Let's examine, thus, my present situation.

I am in New York to bring about the Puerto Rican revolution and to contribute to the development of the one in Cuba. There is no one else who views the matter with more clarity nor who has for this end the solutions that I would desire to realize. In short, there is no one who is more useful than I. I am organized in my thoughts, and I will not be swayed. The Antilles have the conditions for independence, and I absolutely want to draw their attractiveness away from the Americans. Others believe that it is only a matter of liberating them and freeing them from Spain's oppression and, with that, they violate logic, dignity, and justice, as long as they can achieve their end. I believe annexation will mean absorption, and that absorption is a real, material, evident, tangible, enumerable act, that consists not only of the successive abandonment of the islands by the native people, but also of the immediate economic triumph of the ones who annex, and the resultant impoverishment of those annexed. The others do not make these meticulous observations, they laugh at the notion of absorption, they have money or they dream of having money and position, and they laugh at the goals of a people and at the final objective of the archipelago's predicament. I understand the Americans at this moment. They are strong, they are active, they are industrious, and they love the kind of freedom that safeguards all possessions, those of labor as well as those of thought, those of the earth as well as those of the conscience. Freedom informs them; its culminating moment was attained when independence was achieved, and they, by themselves, could reasonably establish their own institutions and, reasonably, conduct their own lives in general. But since, of all the peoples of the earth, they are the only ones who have not suffered, the only ones for whom the path has been smoothed and with whom all have sympathized, and for whom all obstacle has been triumph, it follows that these people of the easy life, are cold because they are happy, are ambitious because they are cold, and there is coldness because they have struggled little and ambition because they believe, and have been made to believe, that happiness increases to the extent that one believes in happiness. Well, then, I, who am unamazed by the attempts of a government that rules a people such as this; I, who respect it too much to not be hurt by its misconduct; I, who, since 1867 in *El Progreso*, decry its territorial ambition. And here I am, scorning my everyday experience, striving to change reality, insisting on leading a heroic life, I am doing nothing for the Antilles. I am upset with what I see in the past and what I see in the present and in the future; I am more discontented with myself, falling each time into an ever deeper abyss, each time my ideal higher, each time falling still lower, and I have reached the age of thirty-one years without having lived.

Everything is inside; nothing, outside. My response to emotion?: emptiness. María Lozada, when we were both children, felt a passionate affection for me, which I did not know how to appreciate nor correspond. Enriqueta Muriátegui and one of the Chavarry girls, in Ludiema; Lola Ruiz, Cipriana Mangual, in Mayagüez, did well in not reciprocating my hesitant demonstrations of sentiment. Matilde was smart in preferring her husband; having loved her when I encountered obstacles, not loving her when the obstacles were not worthy of my efforts, making that incompleteness of feeling the pretext for the prodigious moral and intellectual activity into which I threw myself. I did not love her like a lover nor would I have loved her as a wife. And in spite of this. . . . Yes, therein is the mystery, in spite of this, I love her, as one loves memories, as one loves the life that one has lived, as one loves the work that one has done. It is, in the history of my emotions, the only reality I stumble over, even when it is a confusing, embryonic, obscure reality, the ideal of an ideal, faded in color, halfway to the end (that's it, that's how I have always done everything, *halfway to the end*), I accept it into my imagination with enthusiasm, I bring it closer to my heart with reverence, I contemplate it in my soul as an ideal. Then, Amparo. There is no letter from A. that says everything? And I left her in the midst of a difficult crisis that I myself may have contributed to bringing about. Then, Asunción. Poor Asunción! Even now in my heart and from my eyes fall the desperate tears shed during our last time together. Then, María, and, perhaps, Candor. One was hesitant, but the other! Never was the feeling more spontaneous, stronger, simpler nor more naïve! And I was able to see it calmly and, even today, when I think about it, I am content to remember and to say: *I was able.* And, now, Memé. I do not know if it is love, but the fire has never so reverently come closer: either when we are alone, and her shining face comes close and kisses me on the lips and then withdraws, or when she watches me silently when others look at us, or when she lets herself be diverted from her feelings and desires, as happened a few days ago, while ignoring those around her and, at my insistence, she transfers the solitary kiss on the lips to my rigid cheeks which barely flush and whose flush no one sees.

Incomplete realities, and I do not want them; the one which has a heart, does not have a face; those with a face do not have a brain; those which have a brain, do not possess the harmony that makes up esthetic beauty; those who have not loved, have not been loved; and those who began to be loved, and remained at onset, remain there in the half-light of unfinished things. Family affection? . . . If anyone in this world has loved his family, it is I. And, nonetheless, I have been the torment of mine. Duration of this relationship? I have never stopped loving those who I have loved even one day, and I have loved all of mankind I have come upon along the way. Nevertheless, I do not have a friend, not one single friend. Intellectual activity? From an imagination that sprouted without needing to be cultivated, and which, before suffering all my moral crises, harmonized so closely with precocious mental powers that were admired by all around me and which were the downfall of my adolescence, to the early acquired good sense that so unswervingly invigorated my hard experience later, all that I have sensed in myself I have eagerly tried to understand and to focus. As proof of my passion, and also as an explanation of my failures, is the fact that I never systematically dedicated myself to study the thinking of others. With less consistent effort, my ignorance would have been shameful, but it is not. Sometimes by intuition, other times by assimilation, the fundamental concepts of the sciences are immediately familiar to me, and it is almost certain that if I were to solely devote myself to the reconstruction of all human thought, its evolutions, its losses, the whole history, I would be able to do it. When I was a boy, nothing clashed more with my passion for reason so much as the ecstasies of others as they realized the fortunate linking of causes and effects. It came so easily to me that, when I started thinking about it, I was astonished that the others found the operation of such a simple mechanism so difficult. They sent me to school, and instead of longing for daily games, I deeply worried about what would be thought of me; an early sense of dignity: in school I was absorbed by the contemplation of the anthill that I can still see under the pine table where I sat; a nascent observation: the first time I heard music, it produced so deep an effect on me that I learned it by heart and spent two straight days remembering it in a very strange way; I lay down on the floor of the living room, spinning around, almost fainting, until the music, the sound of the carnival playing, wounded me in the most intimate place of my soul, and revealed to me the sadness of happiness: this was the moment that emotion was born. When they took me to school, my grammar teacher, Roqué, marveled at my progress, without knowing what it consisted of; it consisted of the powers of deduction which were ever increasing. When I was not going to school, I avoided the company of my brother and sister, and when the sun, at ten in the morning, progressed in intensity, I would be found sitting in one of the corners of the balcony, where my sainted mother would find me contemplating the sun face-on and looking far off at the twinkling of the sea; imagination fueled with notions on the universe. The first time I heard mention of philosophy, I conceived the intention of trying to coordinate the opposing schools of thought. Later, after living more completely, that is to say, through a more consecutive externalization of my senses, the lack of method in my studies, the solitude of my self-education, the continuous trial-and-error way in which I have lived, the examination of conscience to which I have continually devoted myself, have exhausted my energies. Instead of accomplishing this by harmonizing discordant mental faculties, excessive impulses, and a dangerous predominance of faculties, I did it by leaving intact those forces that were too impulsive, and forcibly coordinating them with more moderate faculties.

It was then that random intellectual cultivation coincided with the notion of willpower and its cultivation. I may be, perhaps, the one person who can regard his willpower to be the most uniquely his. I used to have a tremendous will; but when you leave childhood behind, the same way that the shaping of the soul is abandoned by almost all children, that intensity got lost somewhere. What was done by proxy, against my will, by professors and friends, in Bilbao, powerfully contributed to the weakening of it: the self-neglect, the imprudent use I made of my freedom, free time, the absolute denial of any obligations, all destroyed it. It was then that, observing the vices of will, I believed and said that willpower is necessarily and fundamentally perverse. The family obligations that I had with Mamá, Eladia and Carlos, the struggle that I would impose upon myself, the death of my hopes for my own family, the energy that I devoted to making a sacrifice of that semi-love for Matilde, the misfortunes that fell upon me, the ruin that was recompensed in Mayagüez, the martyrdom of Madrid, and the spectacle of indignity, the injustice and tyranny in my poor Puerto Rico, produced a strength of conscience too demanding to permit the freedom of will; and I fell into passivity, half stoic and half stupid, that for some time immobilized me; but then, just as the crisis was coming about, my imagination and my feeling guided by reason and conscience produced my *Peregrinación*.[2] Everyone's silence, the conspiracy of friends and writers against the new man,[3] resulted in one of the gravest struggles I have been through, and from which I have still not recovered. My plans upset for easy glory which would open wide the world of writing, and seeing, for the first time, the difference that exists between conception and reality, astonished me, filled me with wonder and fear of a world of reality that I did not know, and I missed having willpower, and set out to create it, and created it, and in an aphorism, I offered this observation: "Will is half a man. Choose between will and a pistol. If you want to be a whole man, put all the energies of your soul into all the phases of life." Having a total concept of life, as in the last aphorism, and the individual duties that it imposes, it looks like I was well ahead of the crisis; perhaps too much so, because if I had done without willpower before, from this point on I could not exert it except by means of a contest between reason and conscience. And who can make a move among such burdensome companions! The truth is that it revived me, truth is that I owe the idea of organic valor to that moment, and the tranquility with which I have confronted and was able to dominate my fears of danger. But, I do not know how to take action in time. I have a profound timidity of action and never, never carry through with what I think, and always, or almost always, it is others who achieve what I do not dare achieve. The arrival in New York, my resolve to fight with all possible weapons the injustice which paralyzes the Antilles, are transformed here into a constant vacillation, into a perpetual maturing of something I never do. The truth is also that the strength of my will consists of overcoming the forces of inertia; but of what value are these dark triumphs over self, if they do not give the world a reality other than my spirit, which perhaps is in itself a powerful thing, due to the fact that I have never seen myself as having power to do anything? This is probably the man that I am; superimpose on him whatever others make of me and the result is clear: a useless man, unutilized, and discarded.

So, struggling simultaneously with the desires of emotion, with the energy of reason, with the categorical forces of conscience, and with a strong will to do good, but at a standstill with regard to the means, I have arrived

2. Hostos's first novel, *La peregrinación de Bayoán* (Bayoán's Pilgrimage), first published in 1863.
3. Hostos is referring to himself and how his political views changed during the writing and subsequent publication in Madrid of *La peregrinación de Bayoán*. For many years, he had been a liberal reformist. Now, as a convert to the Antillean separatist revolutionary cause, he was denouncing Spanish despotism and advocating the liberation of Cuba and Puerto Rico, positions that displeased Spanish authorities and lost him some friends.

at the age of thirty-one years. To reach this age and not die of shame for the emptiness of a life that I believed to be so full, is perhaps a tribute in itself. I will not rest, not even for one moment, because this constant discontent with myself keeps nibbling at me, the problem of my life always overwhelming me: how to make a reality of such a healthy internal life.

If I persisted in believing, although I do not doubt it, that moral crises resolve themselves through organic crises, I would be happy. Since last night, I have felt a discomfort that gets worse by the moment and I feel a fever coming. My heart continues to ache; indeed, punishing me.

## LOLA RODRÍGUEZ DE TIÓ
### 1843–1924

During the nineteenth century, when women had few opportunities for education or for participation in civic life and were largely relegated to the home, Lola Rodríguez de Tió was a public figure in Puerto Rico's literary and political circles. Her father was a prominent lawyer, and her mother was a descendant of the famous conquistador Juan Ponce de León. Rodríguez was born in San Germán, a town in western Puerto Rico. Educated at home by private tutors, she studied the classics of European literature, but developed an affinity for the Romantics, especially the Spaniards José de Espronceda and Gustavo Adolfo Bécquer, the Frenchman Alfred de Musset, and the German Heinrich Heine. At age 22, Rodríguez married Bonocio Tió, a prominent separatist journalist. From then on, the couple was involved in their respective literary and journalistic pursuits and in promoting the cause of Antillean independence. Rodríguez de Tió's poems and articles appeared often in the pages of the few Puerto Rican newspapers that Spanish authorities allowed. In some of her most provocative articles, she challenged traditional views about women and advocated their education and intellectual development.

Rodríguez de Tió's first encounter with Spanish authorities came in 1868, when she wrote some patriotic verses and adapted them to the music of a popular Cuban *danza* (a *danza* is a song-and-dance form) that had been rearranged and popularized in Puerto Rico by Félix Astol, a Catalan composer and tenor who had been exiled from Spain because of his republican ideals. Rodríguez de Tió used Astol's music to accompany her poetic composition "La Borinqueña" (translated as "The Song of Borinquen"). A call to her people to take up arms against the Spanish colonial regime, Rodríguez de Tió's song had been prompted by a request from the separatist leader Ramón Emeterio Betances. Exiled in New York City, Betances had encouraged his supporters to come up with a revolutionary anthem that during an insurrection would have the inspirational effect of *La Marseillaise*. It was not surprising that a few months after being composed, "La Borinqueña" was adopted as the revolutionary anthem of the Lares insurrection, which began on September 23 of that year and was crushed by the Spanish army less than a week later. (When the Estado Libre Asociado de Puerto Rico [Commonwealth of Puerto Rico] was inaugurated, in 1952, "La Borinqueña" became the official anthem of Puerto Rico, but by then Rodríguez de Tió's lyrics had been replaced with less revolutionary ones.)

Rodríguez de Tió's characteristic audacity and patriotic muse gained her the admiration of other Antillean liberals supporting autonomy or independence for Puerto Rico and Cuba, but put her in disfavor with Spanish colonial authorities. A decade later, the poet and her husband experienced the first of several exiles, spending 1877–80 in Venezuela, where they befriended their compatriot Eugenio

María de Hostos. No matter where exile took them, their home was always a place for *tertulias* (frequent gatherings for conversion and discussion) attended by prominent Latin American intellectuals and other public figures. The couple was back in Puerto Rico in 1887, when a new Spanish governor, Romualdo Palacio, began his tyrannical rule. This period of repressive measures, known as the *Compontes*, led to the incarceration and torture of several prominent Puerto Rican autonomists. Guided by her strong convictions and courageous spirit, Rodríguez de Tió went to Palacio's residence to demand their release and also wrote letters on their behalf to officials in Spain. These efforts led to her second exile, this time to Cuba. But problems with Spanish authorities in Cuba persuaded Rodríguez de Tió and her spouse to move to New York in 1892. There, they joined the Antillean-expatriate separatist movement, and Rodríguez de Tió became a founding member, vice-president, and later honorary president of the first women's club of the Puerto Rico section of the Partido Revolucionario Cubano (Cuban Revolutionary Party). After a few years in New York, the couple, now with a daughter, returned to Cuba. Although Rodríguez de Tió was able to visit Puerto Rico a few more times after the 1898 U.S. takeover of the island, she remained in Cuba until her death.

The anguish and nostalgia produced by her many years of separation from Puerto Rico is a frequent theme in many of Rodríguez de Tió's poems. One of her most memorable verses—"Porque la patria llevo conmigo" (Because I carry the motherland within me), part of her poem "Autógrafo" (Autograph)—expresses the longing, produced by political exile, for the native homeland. Foremost, she was a lyrical poet who used both popular verse forms, such as the *décima* and the *romance*, and more classical forms, such as the sonnet and the *lira*. Her poetry therefore combines Romantic and neoclassical styles. The selections here, "The Song of Borinquen" and "Cuba and Puerto Rico," are two of her most famous patriotic poems. The first one remains a powerful symbol of Puerto Rico's long struggle for independence. The latter—a portion of her longer poem "A Cuba"—captures the spirit of Antillean unity and solidarity among some nineteenth-century separatists, such as Hostos and Betances, and their belief that Cuba and Puerto Rico were part of a common struggle for freedom. As the opening lines put it, "Cuba and Puerto Rico are / the two wings of a bird." For such sentiments, the Nicaraguan *Modernista* poet Rubén Darío called Rodríguez de Tió *"Hija de las Islas"* (Daughter of the Islands). Her best-known collections of poetry include *Mis cantares* (My Songs, 1876), *Claros y nieblas* (Clarities and Mists, 1885), and *Mi libro de Cuba* (My Book of Cuba, 1893).

## The Song of Borinquen[1]

Awake, Borinqueños,
for they've given the signal!

Awake from your sleep
for it's time to fight!

Come! The sound of cannon          5
will be dear to us.

At that patriotic clamor
doesn't your heart burn?

---

1. Translated by José Nieto. *Borinquen:* a name for Puerto Rico; from *Boriquén*, the island's indigenous Taíno name.

Look! The Cuban will soon be free,
the machete will give him freedom.                                    10

The drum of war announces in its beating
that the thicket is the place, the meeting place!

Most beautiful Borinquen, we have to follow Cuba;
you have brave sons who want to fight!

Let us no more seem fearful!                                          15
Let us no more, timid, permit our enslavement!

We want to be free already
and our machete is well sharpened!

Why should we, then, remain so asleep
and deaf, asleep and deaf to that signal?                            20

There's no need to fear, Ricans, the sound of cannon,
for saving the homeland is the duty of the heart!

We want no more despots! Let the tyrant fall!
Women, likewise wild, will know how to fight!

We want freedom and our machete will give it to us!                  25

Let's go, Puerto Ricans, let's go already,
for LIBERTY is waiting, ever so anxious!

1868

## From A Cuba

### Cuba and Puerto Rico[1]

Cuba and Puerto Rico are
the two wings of a bird,
they receive flowers and bullets
on the very same heart.
What a lot if in the illusion                                         5
that glows red in a thousand tones,
Lola's muse dreams
with fervent fantasy
of making one single homeland
of this land and of mine.                                            10

1893

---

1. Translated by José Nieto.

# SOTERO FIGUEROA
## 1851–1923

Sotero Figueroa was born in Ponce, a city in southern Puerto Rico. He was a working-class mulatto with very few options for furthering his education, so he sought training as an artisan typographer and found an opportunity to learn the trade at the famous San Juan print shop owned by the Puerto Rican abolitionist and liberal patrician José Julián Acosta. Like most members of the artisan class in Puerto Rico, Figueroa was largely self-educated; in addition to being a typographer, he became a print journalist, playwright, and poet. His *zarzuela* (Spanish operetta), *Don Mamerto*, performed in Ponce's theater in the early 1880s and published in 1886, poignantly satirizes political opportunists who betray their ideals or are blinded by a materialist yearning for climbing the social ladder.

In 1887, Figueroa participated in the founding of the Partido Autonomista Puerto-rriqueño (Puerto Rican Autonomist Party), whose main goal was to demand from Spain the granting of political and socioeconomic reforms and self-government for the island. The following year, he received a literary prize for his *Ensayo biográfico de los que más han contribuído al progreso de Puerto Rico* (Biographic Essay about Those Who Have Contributed the Most to Puerto Rico's Progress), a collection of laudatory biographies that document the contributions and heroism of several island figures from the past to the development of the Puerto Rican nation. This volume is his best-known publication.

In 1889, Figueroa moved to New York City, where he joined the Antillean separatist movement and became close friends with the exiled Cuban leader José Martí. In 1892, along with compatriots such as Francisco Gonzalo "Pachín" Marín and Arthur A. Schomburg (aka Arturo Alfonso Schomburg), Figueroa collaborated in the founding of the Club Borinquen, the first of several clubs aimed at organizing the participation and representation of Puerto Ricans in the Partido Revolucionario Cubano (Cuban Revolutionary Party), or PRC, which Martí had founded that same year to promote the island's independence from Spain. After a few years, Figueroa became secretary of the PRC Executive Council.

In New York, Figueroa established the print shop Imprenta América (America Press). This press published several Spanish-language newspapers, including *El Americano* and *El Porvenir*. It also printed José Martí's separatist newspaper, *Patria*. Because Martí was traveling frequently to generate support for the Antillean independence struggle, he asked Figueroa to assume most of *Patria*'s editorial and typographical work. Figueroa's journalistic contributions to the paper, along with his strong sense of solidarity and devotion to a unified Antillean separatist cause, gained him the respect and admiration of Cuban and Puerto Rican separatists. Inspired by his working-class background and racial origins, Figueroa urged the Antillean separatist movement to expand its social base and leadership positions to include not only members of the political or intellectual elites, but also *tabaqueros* (cigar makers), typographers, and other artisans who had migrated in large numbers to New York and other parts of the United States during the second half of the nineteenth century. In December 1895, less than a year after José Martí's death, the PRC established the Sección de Puerto Rico (Puerto Rico Section) to reflect its continuing commitment to the Puerto Rican independence struggle, and Figueroa became a prominent member of the Sección's leadership.

The Spanish-American War (1898) ultimately brought independence to Cuba, while Puerto Rico was kept as a colonial possession of the United States. A year after the war, Figueroa left New York for Cuba. After Cuba gained its independence in 1902, he was named director of *La Gaceta Oficial*, the main newspaper of the new Cuban republican government. He also contributed to several other Cuban newspapers, but most of his writings remain scattered in these periodicals and unavailable to readers. Figueroa maintained links with Puerto Rico through his writings for island publications such as *Puerto Rico Ilustrado*, which printed many of his articles and poems in 1911–15. He is buried in Cuba, the island he loved perhaps as much as his native Puerto Rico.

The first of the following selections is a speech Figueroa gave at Hardman Hall, during the founding ceremonies for the PRC. In this text, Figueroa makes an analogy between the struggle for freedom and justice of Antillean separatists and Christ's martyrdom to liberate the Jewish people. The second selection is a speech he gave at a ceremony to honor the memories of those separatists who had given their lives in the first Cuban war for independence (1868–78). In this text, Figueroa foresees the continuation of the revolutionary struggle through united Antillean expatriates. Both speeches were published in *Patria* and reflect his understated but effective militant style.

# Speech Confirming the Proclamation
## of the Cuban Revolutionary Party[1]

My Fellow Antilleans:

Eight days ago, on a memorable date for the Cuban people, all emigrants here with one will united to restore popular sovereignty for a free motherland, and proclaimed the Revolutionary Party unequivocally constituted for the independence of the two sorrowful islands splashed by the Caribbean Sea. The Guáimaro Constitution, statute of a sovereign Cuba, was the emblem around which rallied those who believe that the desired time of reckoning had arrived that day of April 10, 1892. The anniversary of this great date[2] could not have been better revered, this date on which was written this fundamental statute, that restores to the people their natural pride which was taken away by the despotic and incomprehensible right of conquest.

And today, on this glorious day for all humanity when we commemorate the glorification of Christ,[3] who gave us a solid basis for the principles of justice upon which modern law is rooted, we come here, devotedly, to ratify the sworn proclamation, as if we wished to bind our redemptive deed to that of the humble man from Nazareth, who railed against all the injustices of the ancient world, transforming slave into citizen, and planting the seed of hope where there was an inferno of despair.

And what an analogy between that everlasting epic that began in a miserable barn in Bethlehem and the patriotic endeavor that we carry on today, initiated in the small town of Yara, now on its own way to glory, having en-

---

1. Translated by Susan Liberis-Hill and Edna Acosta-Belén.
2. Figueroa delivered this speech on Easter Sunday, April 17, 1892. Here, he is referring to the anniversary of *la Constitución de Guáimaro*, the first Cuban Constitution, which came as a result of the *Grito de Yara* declaration of independence (1868). On April 10, 1869, a Constitutional Assembly ratified the Constitution, which re-

mained in effect until the end of the Ten Years' War (1878).
3. Easter is the chief Christian feast, commemorating Jesus' resurrection after his crucifixion. Beginning with the mention below of Nazareth, Jesus' hometown, this speech includes many references to places and events in Jesus' life. For the four biblical accounts of those places and events, the Gospels, see the New Testament.

dured a path of anguish and splattered with blood the hills of its own Calvary!

Like that other example, this movement of redemption that exists in the conscience and the souls of people does not come from the privileged classes. It rises from below, and that is why it will be rich in satisfying results. It is the meek and the good-hearted, who spread the word with a lofty spirit of justice and without violence or hatred; it is this seed which it carries within that will make it stronger and make it triumph. In the greatest uprisings for human rights, the leaders do not rise from those who live comfortably or who find themselves in perfect agreement with the established order of things, but from the suffering masses, the dispossessed who carry their inspiration in their minds, torture in their hearts, and the truth on their lips. Neither fanatics nor the arrogant have the authority to guide the popular masses; neither are presumptuous scholars able to proclaim themselves the mentors of truth or simplicity that, when surrendered to a rigorous and reflective logic, never reaches overstated prosopopoeia or insulting notoriety. It is virtue, it is purity, it is unpretentious wisdom, it is the rectitude of your intentions which the people embrace with love; and the individual who embodies these beneficent qualities will be the guide and the leader whom the masses will follow in those moments of radical transformations.

In this way, Jesus, the exalted martyr of democratic doctrine, is recorded with noble blood in the annals of honorable countries. He was born, according to the holy Christian tale, of parents who were so deprived they did not have a place where they could find shelter. He grows up, a poor artisan without privilege or favor. He achieves the age of manhood and is already experienced in the school of misfortune, strengthened by redeeming truth, with a faith that moves mountains, with enough of a self-sacrificing soul to be able to forgive offenses, dismiss the attacks of the impertinent, and give his life for the redemption of his people. He forges ahead, poor and unknown, alone and defenseless, throughout Judea, in order to build, in people's hearts, an empire of justice, abolish caste laws, preach the dogma that ignites their conscience and dignifies their humanity, and which is embodied in three sublime words: Liberty, Equality, and Fraternity.[4]

Soon the cedars of Lebanon in Jerico eagerly embraced the consoling words of the Master. The banks of Jordan and the Genazareth slowly resonated with the echoes of that inspiring voice, and Canaan and Bethsaida, Cafarmaum and Naim, Bethage and Bethania, all these confines of ancient Galilee trembled with enthusiasm when they heard the sacred doctrine that elevated the moral level of men, granted them singularity, and recognized their rights.

Along his path, the multitude gathered to insult him first and then follow him. The scribes and pharisees, the ones who prospered with Caesar's[5] benevolence, laughed at that wandering man, that strange madman, who preached absurdities. They would have time to silence him when he became enough of a nuisance. But, in a short time, hundreds of thousands were his

---

4. The national motto of France, derived from one motto of the French Revolution.

5. Augustus Caesar (63 BC–AD 14), Roman emperor at the time of the crucifixion.

followers. Jesus had to instruct the twelve apostles to preach his new doctrine; and these were unknown fishermen, simple and uneducated men, who possessed a great deal of love for humanity in their souls. These were the ones selected for spreading his word. The wave of sacrifice had to crash against the resistant rock of selfishness. The moment that the Master enters high and mighty Jerusalem, surrounded by insults and palms, raging against corruption, regarding the powerful with disdain, casting out, with his whip, the merchants from the temple, is when all the power of the city rulers descends upon him, with the foolish resolution to suppress the proselytizer, without understanding that a seed of salvation had been planted in their hearts, and the death of the Innocent One would only surround, with eternal glory, the triumphant redemption. Great ideas do not prevail without the martyrdom of their most fervent proponents, and Jesus could not have achieved his victorious transfiguration in the Thabor without enduring the horrible torment of Mount Calvary.

The example is both eloquent and consoling for the proponents of freedom for the Antilles. Long live the meek, in this beautiful awakening of the souls; those who are teaching the blind and arrogant supporters of the colony the path to political decency that will ultimately lead to the creation of a free motherland!

The revolutionary ideal triumphantly paraded through the patriotic emigrations of Tampa and Key West.[6] It is the inspired voice with enough internal vigor to not waiver one step of the way, even when everything succumbed to the hesitation of the moment or the trust in the false promises of liberation. The good man who educates the working class to consciously march and demand its rights; the modest man who achieves merit without ostentation and, as the best role model I could have presented to you here tonight, encourages wills, does not hate or curse, and prefers to wait for justice to prevail where palms are more beautiful, the sun brighter and the flowers and fruits more varied, sweeter, and juicier. He has had his own Peter to deny him, but like the man from the biblical legend, he has also cordially and prudently recognized what is just and reasonable. It may pass than an Iscariot could emerge and sell him out, but if that were the case, there is the disarming appeal of the words of the proselytizer.

When, on that holy night, Jesus said to his apostles: "There is one among you who will betray me" and the aggrieved disciples asked for his name in order to punish him, Jesus responded:

"Why do you need to know? His conscience is already punishing him."

Let us then forge ahead, without letting the obstacles that we might find in our path intimidate us, or without letting the pessimism of those who **do not believe** in resurrection overcome us because it is an easy way of being patriotic without collaboration.

Let us forge ahead! And I hope that, very soon, on another anniversary of Christ's redemption, we are able to salute the political redemption of Cuba and Puerto Rico.

April 17, 1832                                                      April 23, 1892

---

6. Focal points for Cuban émigrés in Florida.

# Cubans and Puerto Ricans[1]

My Fellow Cubans and Puerto Ricans:

If the sentiment for a free motherland were not so firmly rooted in our hearts, I would not have, on this solemn and imposingly majestic night, climbed the steps to this podium, built on foreign soil, to glorify our illustrious heroes, legendary combatants of that unforgettable decade;[2] who fell facing the enemy, clutching the flag with its radiant star on a the red triangle, shouting the magic battle cry, ¡Viva Cuba Libre![3]

And, I would not ascend this podium because you, like me, think that the best exaltation that we can give to our revolutionary fathers is a prestigious gravestone in the yet enslaved motherland, waiting to be redeemed by our efforts: that blessed land sanctified by the tears of our women, by the valiant resistance of our men, who do not resign themselves to accept the yoke of incompetent and chaotic Spanish domination, by the abundant outbursts of our proud youth, who will not be bought by selfish rulers, and by the torrent of blood shed by those of the highest nobility, who showed us the way, if it could lead us to Zanjón,[4] it was just a brief rest to allow us, cured now of prejudices and suspicion, and possessing greater energy and shrewder insights, to climb that mountaintop where our rightful Capitol stands.

But, if I dare come to this place, shielded by the benevolence of your uncorrupted patriotism, it is because there is a mysterious voice that arises from the most intimate part of my soul, which tells me that this October 10 is more than a commemoration of the infamous day on which our sovereign flag took to the winds, it is a profession of revolutionary protest by all Antillean expatriates, who stand, with reverence, heads uncovered, to salute, from their exile, the immortals of Demajagua,[5] and to tell their Cuban and Puerto Rican brothers: "Have Faith and Carry On; the glorious days of heroic deeds did not disappear, never to return again. Fervent jubilation arouses our souls; something akin to a vision of glory glimmers in the eyes of the brave who wait impatiently to begin again the magnificent journey to redemption, and today, more than ever, our confidence in the immediate achievement of our cause stirs all hearts. Have Faith and Carry On!"

There are, gentlemen, in the moral world, as in the physical world, certain internal conflicts that are no more than forewarnings of profound clashes that will transform, in some way, the ordinary course of life or nature. The judicious do not ignore these warnings; on the contrary, they take action while they are engulfed by them. The foolish, like the cicada of fable, live obliviously and, in the end, some calamity makes them fall victim to their own lack of foresight.

Those who do not see a just and fortifying revolution filling the air, inciting our conscience, bonding all émigrés with fraternity, and manifesting itself

---

1. Translated by Edna Acosta-Belén and Susan Liberis-Hill. Unless otherwise indicated, all footnotes are Acosta-Belén and Liberis-Hill's. The information from one of their footnotes has been incorporated into the section's headnote.
2. The "unforgettable decade" refers to Cuba's Ten Years' War (1868–78) of independence against Spain.

3. Long Live a Free Cuba!
4. The Treaty of Zanjón put an end to the Ten Years' War.
5. Demajagua was the sugar plantation in Yara, Cuba, where the Ten Years' War of independence began, under the leadership of Carlos Manuel de Céspedes.

through the expressive and threatening discontent of the laboring and productive classes of our enslaved islands. Those who do not see the revolution in the ever-growing respect with which the Cuban Revolutionary Party is treated in Cuba, outside Cuba, in the United States, and all of South America, and are not acquainted with its great deeds, the forces of will it has assembled, the resources it has garnered, the valuable constituents that support it; in a word, the rectitude and purity with which the party has moved forward in fulfilling its vigorous charge; those who do not see the valuable acquiescence of so many fiery eyes shining in this spacious hall, so many virile arms and proud heads moved by patriotism and community of thought; those who do not see revolution despite so many outward signs and others, about which prudence compels me to keep silent; we should forgive those blinded by submission because, like the cicada in the fable, winter will surprise them without their having gathered, during the summer, enough provisions for unity and harmony among fellow revolutionaries, and the frozen blizzard will engulf them ignoring the cries of anger and despair they may send out.

As for us, we are possessed by an indescribable vision. It is as if we see hovering around us, not the frowning countenances of days gone by, but joyously resplendent, the forefathers of our independence, who have not perished and will never perish in the sacred shrine we hold within our hearts: the murmur of palms caresses our ears; a flaming sun quickens the pulse in our veins; a breeze saturated with the intoxicating perfume of our blossoms kisses our foreheads; the Caribbean sea in its undulating transparency reminds us of tranquil childhood days; a splendid sky shows off its even more translucent indigo blue, and light, perfume, harmony, liberty, justice and rights bear before us the image of a happy and independent motherland.

Could it be that we are nearing the end and that an encouraging sign is anticipating our wishes?

We do not know. However, Mohammad, the reformer, tells us, in his sacred book,[6] and in *Patria* it is reiterated: "In the shadows behind you, you will find Paradise." I have finished.

October 14, 1893

6. The Koran, the sacred book accepted by Muslims as revelations made to Muhammad (ca. 570–632), the founder of Islam, by Allah (God). [Anthology editors' note]

---

# JOSÉ MARTÍ
## 1853–1895

Known to Cubans as *"El Apóstol"* (The Apostle), José Martí is revered throughout Latin America. A prolific writer and brilliant orator, Martí was the person most responsible for organizing the insurrection against Spain in 1898 that led to the defeat of the Spanish forces later that year. Born in Havana, Cuba, to Spanish parents, Martí was raised in near poverty. Since his parents could not afford to educate him, his godfather paid for his early studies, at the Municipal School for Boys in Havana. He attended secondary school at the College of San Pablo, which was administered by the radical poet and journalist Rafael María de Mendive.

Through Mendive's tutelage, Martí became active in the Cuban independence movement and began to publish pro-Cuban articles. In 1868, at age 15, Martí founded, with Mendive's help, a political newspaper, *La Patria Libre*, where Martí published "Abdala," a long poem in which a country called "Nuba" fights for its freedom. On October 10 of that year, Carlos Manuel de Céspedes led a revolt to protest exploitative taxes levied on Cubans by the Spaniards. Martí published a sonnet, "El diez de octobre" (The Tenth of October), to express his enthusiastic support for the revolt, but the conflict turned into a ten-year war that ended with the defeat of the Cubans.

In 1869, Martí was arrested by Spanish authorities for a proindependence letter he wrote to a fellow student. Convicted of treason, Martí was imprisoned in El Cárcel Nueva o de Tacón, in central Havana, and sentenced to six years hard labor in the nearby quarries of San Lazaro. After six months, his health was broken, and he was sent to the Isle of Pines to recover. In 1871, he was exiled to Spain. In Spain, Martí studied at the University of Zaragoza and the University of Madrid and earned degrees in philosophy and law. He continued to write and publish political pieces, including "El presidio político de Cuba" (The Political Prison in Cuba), where he described in vivid detail his experience of forced labor.

Martí had hoped that if Spain turned from a monarchy into a republic, Cuba and Spain might exist harmoniously; but in late 1871, he learned that a group of medical students at the University of Havana had been seized by the Spanish authorities and executed. Martí's attitude toward Spain changed completely, and from that point on, he advocated nothing less than complete independence for Cuba. In 1873, at the formation of the First Spanish Republic, he tried but failed to interest the new government in the question of Cuban independence. After the Spanish Parliament confirmed the status of Cuba as a colony, Martí published *La república española ante la revolución cubana* (The Spanish Republic before the Cuban Revolution, 1873), in which he argued that the elected representatives of Spain's democratic government should grant Cubans the same freedoms they were enjoying. Martí began to contemplate a return to Cuba.

In 1875, after a brief stay in France, he traveled to Mexico, where he wrote for the *Revista Universal*, publishing articles on art, drama, and social issues and continuing his quest for Cuban independence. His play *Amor con amor se paga* (Love Is Repaid by Love) was staged successfully in Mexico City. When the Mexican dictator Porfirio Díaz assumed power, in 1876, Martí left Mexico and traveled to Cuba, where he attempted to work under an assumed name, "Julián Pérez." Forced to flee the island again, he settled in Guatemala, where he taught literature and philosophy.

Martí lectured widely in Guatemala, edited the *Revista de la Universidad*, and wrote articles, plays, and poetry, including "La Niña de Guatemala" (The Girl from Guatemala), one of his most famous poems. In 1877, Martí married Carmen Zayas Bazán, the daughter of a wealthy Cuban exile. When the Ten Years' War ended, a general amnesty was declared, and Martí and Zayas Bazán returned to Cuba. In his writings, Martí continued to make clear that in his view the only solution to Cuba's problems was independence from Spain, and once more he was deported to Spain, leaving behind his wife, who did not support his political activities, and their infant son.

Martí exited Spain as soon as possible, and, after brief stays in France and Venezuela, settled in New York City. There he met Charles A. Dana, who gave him a position writing for the newspaper *New York Sun*. In 1880, his illegitimate daughter, María Mantilla, was born of a liaison with Carmen Miyards de Mantilla, his Cuban landlady. The next year, he left New York for Venezuela, where he founded a modernist review, *Revista Venezolana*, which provoked the Venezuelan dictator Antonio Guzmán Blanco by championing independence and individual freedom. Martí soon returned to New York, where he lived for the last 14 years of his life and served as consul for Uruguay and Argentina. He again began contributing to the *Sun*, published short essays in the New York weekly literary magazine *The Hour*, and wrote for many of the major Latin American newspapers: *La Nación*, in Buenos Aires; *La República*, in Honduras; *La Opinión Pública*, in Uruguay; and *El Partido Liberal*, in Mexico. He wrote and lectured on an enormously wide range of subjects, from Walt Whitman and Impressionism to New York landmarks and natural disasters. He spoke at countless meetings for independence, and for the Cuban revolutionary cause he produced many pamphlets, articles, and essays.

His regular columns, especially in *La Nación*, made him famous throughout Latin America. One of his favorite themes was the shared heritage of language and culture that unites the Latin American countries. In some of his best-known essays, such as "Nuestra América" (Our America, 1881), "Emerson" (1882), and "Bolívar" (1893), he points out the similarities and differences between U.S. culture and Latin American culture. The public debate in the United States around the possible purchase of Cuba from Spain included attacks on the Cuban character and Cuban people's values, and in answer to these attacks Martí wrote the essay "A Vindication of Cuba." Since he wrote so much and his thinking was not always consistent, Martí has been claimed as a spiritual mentor for politicians, and social activists, of different ideological persuasions. In Martí's intensely personal prose, admirers as well as critics of U.S. culture can always find support for their conflicting views.

As important as Martí's essays is his poetry, which laid the groundwork for the Latin American literary movement *Modernismo*. Before 1882, Martí's published verses, influenced by Spanish poets, tended to use traditional forms; but in that year he published *Ismaelillo* (Little Ismael), a series of 15 poems addressed to his son, whom he had rarely seen, and in whom he saw the Cuba of the future. Writing of reunion with his son, Martí was also writing of his longing for reunion with his homeland and the end of his exile. Celebrating the laughter and beauty of the boy as a symbol of Cuba, Martí declared his love and explained his absence. The poems in *Versos libres* (Free Verses), written between 1878 and 1882 and published posthumously in Cuba in 1913, represent a departure in form and content. In rough, sometimes abrupt poems, Martí reacts to life in New York and conveys the anguish of exile.

Although he continued to use traditional Spanish hendecasyllables and octosyllables (eleven- and eight-syllable lines), he avoided rhyme, and these poems often give the impression of having been dashed off in a state of agitation. In 1891, Martí published *Versos sencillos* (Simple Verses), written during a summer spent in the Catskill Mountains of New York State. Building on his readings of the Spanish classics, especially of works by the seventeenth-century writers Quevedo and Gracián, and on his familiarity with the new French writers of the Parnassian school—who, reacting against the verbal and emotional excesses of the Romantics, insisted that poetry should be restrained, technically perfect, carefully and precisely shaped—Martí produced poetry that is spare and understated, but often brilliant and subtle in its simplicity. His technical deftness, as well as his use of symbolism, particularly of color, was innovative and influential. His poems initiated a new era in Latin American poetry.

Along with his own writing, Martí produced translations; published a magazine for children, *La Edad de Oro*; and edited *Patria*, the official newspaper of the Partido Revolucionario Cubano (Cuban Revolutionary Party), which he helped found. Under a pseudonym, Adelaida Ral, he wrote a novel, *Amistad Funesta* (1885), as a favor to a friend, Adelaida Baralt, who found herself unable to write the serialized novel she had promised to *El Latino-Americano*, a New York journal. Although Martí composed the work in just seven days to her specifications, it has been recognized as an important step in the movement of the Latin American novel away from the clichés of Romanticism and toward a modern realism.

During his years in the United States, Martí traveled extensively and spent time with many Cuban-exile groups, especially in Tampa and Key West, Florida, in his effort to raise funds and organize support for the independence movement. Despite not always seeing eye to eye with the other leaders of the movement, he was elected *delegado* (he refused to be called president) of the Cuban Revolutionary Party in 1892. Although he was a man of letters and not a soldier, he wished to participate directly in the Cuban resistance movement, and he planned an invasion of Cuba. In late January 1895, he left New York for the Dominican Republic, accompanied by General Máximo Gómez and others. On April 1, this group left to join the uprising that had begun in the village of Baire, on the eastern end of Cuba. Upon arriving on the beach at La Playita on April 11, Martí was declared a general by the Liberating Army. On May 19, he rode into battle against the Spaniards and was shot to death in an ambush at the battle of Dos Ríos. He was buried on May 27, in Santiago de Cuba.

## Coney Island[1]

Nothing in the history of mankind has ever equalled the marvelous prosperity of the United States. Time will tell whether deep roots are lacking here; whether the ties of sacrifice and common sorrow that bind some people together are stronger than those of common interests; whether this colossal nation carries in its entrails ferocious, tremendous elements; whether a lack of that femininity which is the origin of the artistic sense and the complement of nationality hardens and corrupts the heart of this wonderful country.

For the present, the fact is that never has a happier, a jollier, a better equipped, more compact, more jovial, and more frenzied multitude living anywhere on earth, while engaged in useful labors, created and enjoyed greater wealth, nor covered rivers and seas with more gaily dressed ships, nor overflown lovely shores, gigantic wharves, and brilliant, fantastic promenades with more bustling order, more childlike glee.

United States' newspapers are full of hyperbolic descriptions of the unusual beauty and singular attraction of one of these summer resorts, with crowds of people, numerous luxurious hotels, crossed by an elevated railroad, studded with gardens, kiosks, small theatres, saloons, circuses, tents, a multitude of carriages, picturesque assemblies, vending wagons, stands, and fountains.

French newspapers echo its fame. From all over the Union come legions of fearless ladies and country beaux to admire the splendid scenery, lavish wealth, blinding variety, Herculean push, and surprising aspect of famous Coney Island, an island which four years ago was nothing but an abandoned heap of earth and is now an ample place for rest, seclusion, or entertainment for the one hundred thousand New Yorkers who visit its shores daily.

It is composed of four hamlets joined by carriage, tram, and steam railroads. One is *Manhattan Beach*, where, in the dining room of one hotel, four thousand people can comfortably sit at the same time; another, *Rockaway*,

1. Translated by Luis A. Baralt. Except as indicated, all footnotes are Baralt's. Baralt writes: "Published in *La Pluma*, Bogotá, December 3, 1881."

has arisen, as Minerva[2] arose with lance and helmet, armed with steamers, squares, piers, murmuring orchestras, hotels big as cities, nay, as nations; still another, less important, takes its name from its hotel, the vast, heavy *Brighton*. But the most attractive place on the island is neither far off Rockaway, nor monotonous Brighton, nor aristocratic, stuffy Manhattan Beach, but *Cable*, smiling Cable with its elevator, higher than Trinity Church steeple in New York, twice as high as the steeples of our Cathedral, to the top of which people are carried in a tiny, fragile cage to a dizzy height; Cable, with its two iron piers projecting on elegant piles three blocks into the sea, its *Sea Beach Palace*, now only a hotel, but which in the Philadelphia Fair was the famous Agricultural Building, transported to New York and reassembled as if by magic, without a piece missing, on the shores of Coney Island; Cable, with its fifty cent museums where human monsters, freakish fish, bearded ladies, melancholy dwarfs, and rickety elephants, bally-hooed as the biggest elephants in the world, are shown; Cable with its one hundred orchestras, its lively dances, its battalions of baby carriages, its gigantic cow being perpetually milked, its fresh cider at twenty-five cents a glass, its countless couples of loving pilgrims which bring back to our lips García Gutiérrez's tender cries;

> In pairs they go
> Over the hillocks
> The crested larks,
> The turtle-doves; . . .[3]

Cable, where families resort in search of wholesome, invigorating sea breezes instead of New York's foul and nauseating air; where poor mothers, as they open great lunch baskets with provisions for the whole family, press against their breasts their unfortunate babes who seem consumed, emaciated, gnawed by that terrible summer sickness which mows down children as a sickle does wheat, *infantum cholera*.

Steamers come and go, trains whistle and smoke, leave and arrive emptying their serpent belly-full of people on the shore. Women wear rented blue-flannel suits and coarse straw hats which they tie under their chins; men in still simpler suits lead them to the sea, while barefooted children at the water's edge await the roaring breakers and run back when the waves are about to wet them, disguising their fear with laughter. Then, relieved of the smoldering heat of an hour ago, they charge, tirelessly, against the enemy, or, like marine butterflies, they brave the fresh waves, play at filling each other's pails with shovelfuls of burning sand, or, after bathing—imitating in this the behavior of grown-up people of both sexes who do not heed the censure and surprise of those who feel as we do in our countries—they lie on the sand and allow themselves to be buried, patted down, kneaded into the burning sand. This practice, considered a wholesome exercise, lends itself to a certain superficial, vulgar, and boisterous intimacy to which these prosperous people seem so inclined.

---

2. The Roman goddess of wisdom. [Anthology editors' note]
3. Aparejadas / van por las lomas / las cogujadas / y las palomas . . . Antonio García Gutiérrez

(1812–1884), a Spanish Romantic dramatist and lyric poet, was the author of *El trovador*, from which the libretto was taken for Verdi's opera *Il Trovatore*.

But the most surprising thing there is not the way they go bathing, nor the children's cadaverous faces, nor the odd headresses and incomprehensible attire of those girls noted for their extravagance, their eccentricity, and their disordinate inclination to merry-making, nor the spooners, nor the bathing booths, nor the operas that are sung at café tables in the guise of *Edgar* and *Romeo,* and *Lucia* and *Juliet,* nor the grimaces and screams of Negro minstrels, surely not like the Scotch minstrels, alas!, nor the majestic beach, nor the soft, serene sun. The surprising thing there is the size, the quantity, the sudden outburst of human activity, that immense valve of pleasure open to an immense people, those diningrooms which, seen from afar, look like bivouacked armies, those roads which, from two miles away, do not seem like roads but like carpets of heads, that daily out-pouring of a portentous people upon a portentous beach, that mobility, that change of form, that fighting spirit, that push, that feverish rivalry of wealth, that monumental appearance of the whole place which makes a bathing establishment worthy of competing with the majesty of the country that supports it, the sea that caresses it and the sky that crowns it, that swelling tide, that dumbfounding, overwhelming, steady, frenzied expansiveness, and that simplicity in the marvelous; *that* is the surprising thing.

Other peoples—we among them—live devoured by a sublime inner demon who pushes us tirelessly on in search of an ideal of love or glory. When we hold the measure of the ideal we were after, delighted as though we were holding an eagle, a new quest makes us restless, a new ambition spurs us, a new aspiration heads us toward a new vehement desire, and out of the captive eagle emerges a rebel, free butterfly, daring us to follow it, chaining us to her circuitous flight.

Not so these tranquil souls, only disturbed by the craving of owning a fortune. Our eyes scan the reverberating beaches, we go in and out of those halls as vast as pampas,[4] we climb to the peak of those colossal structures as tall as mountains. Promenaders in comfortable chairs by the seaside fill their lungs with that bracing, benign air. But a melancholy sadness, as it were, takes hold of the men of our Latin American countries who live here, for they seek each other in vain and no matter how much first impressions may have lured their senses, charmed their eyes, dazzled and puzzled their reason, they are finally possessed by the anguish of solitude, while the homesickness for a superior spiritual world invades them and grieves them. They feel like stray sheep without their mothers or their shepherd. Tears may or may not flow to their eyes, but their astounded souls break in bitter weeping, because this great land is devoid of spirit.

What a bustle! What flow of money! What facilities for pleasure! What absolute absence of all sadness or visible poverty! Everything is in the open air: the noisy groups, the vast dining halls, that peculiar courtship of North Americans into which enter almost none of the elements which make up the modest, tender, exalted love found in our lands. The theatre, the photographic studio, the bathing booths; everything in the open. Some get weighed, for to North Americans to weigh a pound more or less is a matter of positive joy or real grief; for fifty cents, others receive from a stout German woman an envelope containing their fortune; still others, with incomprehensible

---

4. Pampas, vast prairies of South America.

delight, drink certain unsavory mineral waters out of tall, narrow glasses like mortar shells.

Some ride in roomy carriages from Manhattan to Brighton at the soft twilight time. One fellow shores his boat, in which he had been rowing with his smiling girl friend, who holds on to his shoulder as she jumps, frolicking like a child, onto the bustling beach. A group of people admire an artist who cuts silhouettes out of black paper of whoever wishes to have this kind of portrait of himself and glues them on white cards. Another group watch a woman in a tiny shop less than a yard wide and praise her skill at fashioning strange flowers out of fish skins. Others laugh uproariously when one fellow succeeds in hitting a Negro on the nose with a ball, a poor Negro who, for a miserable wage, sticks his head out of a hole in a cloth and is busied day and night eluding with grotesque movements the balls pitched at him. Bearded, venerable citizens ride gravely on wooden tigers, hippogriffs, sphinxes, and boa constrictors that turn like horses around a central pole where a band of would-be musicians play unharmonious sonatas. The less well-to-do eat crabs and oysters on the beach or pies and meats on tables that some large hotels offer free for such purpose. The wealthier people lavish large sums on fuchsine infusions passed off as wine and on strange, massive dishes which our palates, fond of the artistic and light, would certainly reject. To these people eating is a matter of quantity; to ours, of quality.

And this lavishing, this bustle, these crowds, this astounding ant hill lasts from June to October, from morning till midnight, without respite, without interruption, without change.

What a beautiful spectacle at night! True enough, a thinking man is surprised at seeing so many married women without their husbands and so many mothers strolling by the humid seaside, concerned with their pleasure, and heedless of the piercing wind that might harm the squalid constitution of the babies they hold against their shoulder.

But no city offers a more splendid view than Cable Beach by night. More lights shine at night than heads could be seen by day. When descried from a distance offshore the four towns shine in the darkness as though the stars of heaven had suddenly gathered and fallen to the sea.

The electric lights that bathe with magic brightness the approaches to the hotels, the lawns, the concert pavilions, even the beach whose every grain of sand can be counted, seem from afar like restless sprites, like blithe, diabolic spirits romping about the sickly gas jets, the garlands of red lanterns, the Chinese globes, the Venetian chandeliers. One can read everywhere, as though it were day: newspapers, billboards, announcements, letters. All is heavenly: the orchestras, the dances, the clamor, the rumble of the waves, the noise of men, the ringing of laughter, the air's caresses, the loud calls, the rapid trains, the stately carriages, until the time comes to return home. Then, as a monster emptying its entrails into the hungry gullet of another monster, the colossal, crushed, compact crowds rush to catch the trains, which, bursting under their weight, seem to pant in their ride through solitude, until they deliver their motley load onto gigantic ships. These latter, livened by harps and violins, take the exhausted tourists to the piers of New York and distribute them in the thousand cars and along the thousand tracks that like veins of steel traverse the sleeping city.

December 3, 1881

# Love in the City[1]

Times of gorge and rush are these:
Voices fly like light: lightning,
like a ship hurled upon dread quicksand,
plunges down the high rod, and in delicate craft
man, as if winged, cleaves the air.                                         5
And love, without splendor or mystery,
dies when newly born, of glut.
The city is a cage of dead doves
and avid hunters! If men's bosoms
were to open and their torn flesh                                          10
fall to the earth, inside would be
nothing but a scatter of small, crushed fruit!

Love happens in the street, standing in the dust
of saloons and public squares: the flower
dies the day it's born. The trembling                                      15
virgin who would rather death
have her than some unknown youth;
the joy of trepidation; that feeling of heart
set free from chest; the ineffable
pleasure of deserving; the sweet alarm                                     20
of walking quick and straight
from your love's home and breaking
into tears like a happy child;—
and that gazing of our love at the fire,
as roses slowly blush a deeper color,—                                     25
Bah, it's all a sham! Who has the time
to be noble? Though like a golden
bowl or sumptuous painting
a genteel lady sits in the magnate's home!

But if you're thirsty, reach out your arm,                                 30
and drain some passing cup!
The dirtied cup rolls to the dust, then,
and the expert taster—breast blotted
with invisible blood—goes happily,
crowned with myrtle, on his way!                                           35
Bodies are nothing now but trash,
pits, and tatters! And souls
are not the tree's lush fruit
down whose tender skin runs
sweet juice in time of ripeness,—                                          40
but fruit of the marketplace, ripened
by the hardened laborer's brutal blows!

It is an age of dry lips!
Of undreaming nights! Of life
crushed unripe! What is it that we lack,                                   45

---

1. Translated by Esther Allen.

without which there is no gladness? Like a startled
hare in the wild thicket of our breast,
fleeing, tremulous, from a gleeful hunter,
the spirit takes cover;
and Desire, on Fever's arm,                                    50
beats the thicket, like the rich hunter.

    The city appals me! Full
of cups to be emptied, and empty cups!
I fear—ah me!—that this wine
may be poison, and sink its teeth,                             55
vengeful imp, in my veins!
I thirst—but for a wine that none on earth
knows how to drink! I have not yet
endured enough to break through the wall
that keeps me, ah grief!, from my vineyard!                    60
Take, oh squalid tasters
of humble human wines, these cups
from which, with no fear or pity,
you swill the lily's juice!
Take them! I am honorable, and I am afraid!                    65

April 1882


## The Charleston Earthquake[1]

Charleston has been destroyed by an earthquake. There is nothing but ruins
where once stood a city spreading like a basket of fruit between the sandy
waters of two rivers, merging inland into beautiful villages surrounded by
magnolia trees, orange trees, and gardens.

Since the war, the defeated whites and the now tolerated Negroes have
lived there in languid concord. Trees do not shed their leaves there. There
one can see the ocean from vine-draped balconies. There, in the bay, almost
hidden by the sand, stands Fort Sumter on whose walls the bullet struck
that first called North and South to war. There the unfortunate travelers of
the barge "Puig"[2] were received kindly.

Streets run straight towards both rivers; an avenue of trees borders the
city on the water front. A multitude of ships alongside the wharves load cotton for Europe and India. King Street is the business center; the rich hotels
are on Meeting Street. The garrulous, tightly packed Negroes occupy a
crowded neighborhood. The rest of the city abounds in beautiful residences,
not built shoulder to shoulder like these immodest and slavish houses in
the cold North, but with that noble detachment which contributes so much

1. Translated by Luis A. Baralt. Except as indicated, all footnotes are Baralt's. About this report
from Charleston, South Carolina, Baralt writes:
"Dated New York, September 10, 1886, published
in La Nación, Buenos Aires, October 14 and 15,
1886."
2. In June 1875, a group of political refugees from

Uruguay arrived in Charleston harbor on the vessel Puig. They had sailed from Montevideo, Uruguay, to Havana, Cuba, where Spanish authorities prevented them from landing. They were
permitted to land at Fort Sumter, in Charleston
Bay, and from Charleston the group traveled to
New York. [Anthology editors' note]

to the poetry and decorum of life. The smallest house has its rose bushes and its square patio with a lawn and sunflowers and orange trees at the door.

Brightly colored rugs and ornaments contrasting with the white walls are hung out in the morning on the veranda along the upper floor gallery by smiling Negresses with red or blue bandannas covering their heads. The dust of defeat has dimmed the brick-red color of opulent residences. They live with courage in their soul and light in their minds in this peaceful, black-eyed town.

But today trains have to stop outside of the city on the twisted, broken, sunken, torn-up rails; towers have toppled; the population has been a week on their knees; Negroes and their former masters have slept under the same tent and partaken of the same bread of compassion, in front of the ruined houses, the fallen walls, the grilles wrenched from their stone supports, the broken columns!

Charleston's fifty thousand inhabitants, taken by surprise in the evening by the earthquake which shook their homes like straw nests, are still living in the streets and squares, in wagons, under tents, under huts built with their own clothes. Eight million dollars turned to dust in twenty-five seconds. There have been sixty killed, some by falling walls, others by fright, and in the same tremendous hour many children were born.

Calamities such as this coming from the bowels of the earth must be envisioned from the high heavens! Thus looked upon, earthquakes, with all their fearful accouterments of human suffering, are but an adjustment of the crust of the earth over its shrinking entrails to maintain the equilibrium of creation. Man, with all the majesty of his grief, with all the impact of his judgment, with all the flutter of wings that goes on within his skull, is but one of those shimmering bubbles that dance and stumble blindly on a ray of the sun! Poor warrior of the air, arrayed in gold, always knocked to earth by an invisible enemy, always getting on his feet, stunned by the blow but ready to fight again, his hands never quite enough to wipe from his eyes the streams of his own blood! But he feels himself rising as the bubble on the sunbeam rises! He feels within himself all the joys and lights, all the tempests and sufferings of nature which he tries to uplift! All this majesty lay prone to earth in the hour of horror of the Charleston earthquake.

It was about six in the evening. Our good brothers who make the newspapers were working at their composing stands like golden bees; in the churches the worshipers, who in Charleston, a place of scanty science and abundant imagination, are plentiful, were finishing their prayers; doors were being closed and many sought in love or rest strength with which to fight the following day's battle; Charleston reposed while the suffocating, stilled air could hardly sustain the scent of roses. The misfortune awaiting the town traveled faster than light!

This Charleston earth softly sloping to the sea had never quaked before. The town stretches on alluvial ground along the coast. There never were volcanoes, big or small, vapor spouts, ground disturbances, or *solfataras*; the only vapors rising were aromatic ones, the aroma of orange trees always filled with white blossoms. Nor had the shallow waters of her coast of yellowish sands ever been beaten by those mighty breakers, dark like gorges, which the ocean sends against the shores when its bottom is deranged, broken, or raised, and out of the abyss rises the tremendous force that swells and curves the waves and dashes them like voracious mountains on the beach. In that lordly peace of southern cities night was just taking its leave when a rumble was heard like that of a heavy object being dragged hurriedly along.

To tell the story is to see it. The rumble swelled: lamps and windows shook . . . underground there was a sound like the rolling of heavy artillery. Printers left their type on the composing boxes, clergymen left their cassocks and fled, women ran out onto the streets forgetting their children, men shuttled desperately from one tumbling wall to the next. What was this terrible hand that grasped the city by the waist and shook it in the air, disjointing it?

Floors surged, walls cracked, houses swayed from side to side; half-naked people kissed the earth: Oh, Lord! Oh, dearest Lord! cried suffocated voices. A whole porch collapsed! Courage fled, minds became crazed. Then it subsided, waned, stopped. The dust raised by the crumbling buildings hovered above the trees, above the housetops.

Desperate parents availed themselves of the truce to look for their children. A beautiful young mother removed the rubble from her own door. Brothers and husbands dragged out or carried out fainted women. A poor wretch who threw himself out of a window crawled on his stomach screaming painfully, his arms and legs broken. An old lady started trembling, and died. Another, dying of fright, was left alone to her spasms. The weak gas jets, scarcely perceivable in the thick air, lighted the perplexed crowds which ran to and fro praying, crying out to Jesus, shaking their arms towards heaven. Suddenly, great fires rose out of the shadows, bathing the scene in a red glare and moving heavily their tongues of flame.

The new light shining on every face showed that they had just seen death. About some faces reason seemed to flow stripped to tatters, about others it seemed to wander blindly groping for a foothold. The flames spread like a panoply, the fire rose. Then—how can words describe what then was seen? Again the muffled rumble was heard; people circled around as though seeking the best exit; then fled in all directions; the swell from below grew and expanded; each thought a tiger was upon him.

Some fell on their knees, others face down; old gentlemen were carried by their loyal servants. Great crevices rent the earth; walls waved like wind-blown flags; the cornices of buildings facing each other touched on high; the people's horror was increased by that of beasts: horses, unable to shake themselves away from their wagons, threw them over; another horse bent his fore-legs, another sniffed the ground, still another's eyes shone red in the flames' glare, his body trembling like a reed in a storm. What dreadful tremor in the earth's entrails was calling to battle?

Then, when the second wave was over, when souls could hold no more fear, when the cries of dying people, as though they had hands, pushed their way out of the rubbish, when the trembling horses were tied down as though they were wild elephants, when falling walls had dragged down with them telegraph poles and wires, when the wounded shook off the bricks and lumber that cut off their flight, when the wretched women, with the marvelous sight of love, described in the shadow their tumbled-down houses, when fright sparkled the Negroes' tempestuous imagination, a clamor began to spread over that carpet of prone bodies, which seemed to rise from unfathomed depths rending the air with dart-like wings, a cry that soared over their heads and made it seem as though it were raining tears.

The few brave ones still standing, very few indeed, struggled in vain to quench that growing clamor which pierced their flesh: fifty thousand humans coaxing God at once with the most insane flatteries fear can breed!

The bravest put out fires, raised the fallen, dropped those who had no further reason to be lifted, carried away the horror-stricken aged. No one knew the time: all watches had stopped at the first quake.

Morning revealed the disaster.

Gradually by the day's early light appeared bodies strewn along the streets, mountains of rubbish, walls crumbled to dust, porches cut in slices, iron grilles and posts warped and twisted, houses folded over their foundations, towers upset and the tallest church spire held on only by a thin iron thread.

The sun began to warm all hearts. The dead were taken to the cemetery where Calhoun[3] the great orator, now lies silent, as do Gadsden,[4] Rutledge,[5] Pinckney.[6] Doctors took care of the sick. A priest gave confession to the fearful. Leaves of doors and Venetian blinds served as stretchers.

Rubbish was piled high on the sidewalks. Some entered houses requesting sheets and blankets with which to put up tents. Negroes frantically reached out for the ice that wagons were distributing. Many houses still smoked. A sulphur-smelling sand had oozed from the crannies of the freshly-cracked earth.

Everyone was astir. Some prepared straw beds, others put a baby to sleep on a pillow and shaded it with a parasol. Here a group ran from a collapsing wall; there a fence fell on two old men who did not have time to escape it. Tears streamed down a bearded man's cheeks as he kissed his old father's body he held in his arms. It seems many babies had been born during the night. Under a blue tent one mother had given birth to twins.

The city's best buildings have either collapsed or are out of plumb: St. Michael's, the church of resounding bells; St. Phillip's, the one with the lofty tower; Hibernian Hall, where speeches bristling like bayonets were once delivered; the Guard House . . .

A one-armed man with a thick, black mustache, drawn face, and eyes aflame with joy approached a group of men sitting dejectedly on a broken pediment: ". . . it hasn't fallen, boys; it hasn't fallen!" What had not fallen was the Court House where the spirited McGrath,[7] on hearing the first shot fired by the federalists on Fort Sumter, shed his judge's gown swearing to give the South all his blood, which he did!

3. John Caldwell Calhoun (1782–1850), American statesman and political philosopher; U.S. vice-president 1825–32. [Anthology editors' note]
4. James Gadsden (1788–1858), American soldier, diplomat, and railroad president.
5. John Rutledge (1739–1800), American jurist and statesman, born and died in Charleston, S.C. Delegate to the Continental Congress (1772–1777).

6. The reference may be to any of the Pinckneys: Charles Cotesworth (1746–1825), Charles (1757–1823), Thomas (1750–1828), all born in Charleston, S.C., all soldiers in the War of Independence, diplomats, and statesmen; the first two, signatories of the Constitution.
7. A. G. McGrath, American district-attorney and collector in Charleston, S.C. * * *

Among the homes, what desolation! Not a sound wall remained in the city, nor unrent roof. Many porches, their overhanging roofs unsupported by columns, look like faces without jaws. Some lamps had been nailed into walls or looked like spiders smashed on the floor; statues had descended from their pedestals; water from tanks on the roof-tops had drizzled through wall cracks and flooded the houses; in front even the withered jasmines on the branches and the stooping, faded roses seemed to take their share of the damage.

The first two days the city's anguish was great. No one returned home. No business or trade was transacted. One tremor followed another, though each less violent than the previous. It was like a religious jubilee: the arrogant whites, when fear grew, humbly joined the frantic Negroes in the improvised hymns; many a Negro girl hung to a white woman's skirts as she passed by and weepingly implored her to take her with her—for thus does habit convert crime itself into goodness and invest it with poetry. Thus these creatures, conceived in misery by parents whose spirit had been frozen in slavery, still conceded a supernatural power to the race which wielded that power against their elders! Which gives us the measure of the goodness and humility of this race which only the wicked can disfigure and disdain, because the greater its shame, the greater our obligation to pardon it!

Groups of Negroes went out into the country in search of produce, only to return horrified at what they had seen. Within a radius of twenty miles inland the ground was everywhere parched and cracked; there were bottomless crevices two feet wide; out of many new wells came a fine, white sand mixed with water, or sand alone, spilled over the edges of the well as if from ant holes, or water mixed with blue mud, or little mounds of mud topped with little mounds of sand, as if under the crust of the earth there was mud first and sand deeper down. The new water tasted like sulphur and iron.

A hundred acre reservoir suddenly dried up when the first quake came and was now full of dead fish. A dam had broken, the water sweeping everything before it.

Trains could not reach Charleston because the rails had been lifted or had snapped or wound around raised ties.

At the time of the first quake a locomotive was speeding on proudly when it suddenly jumped, shook the trailing cars like beads of a rosary and plunged with its dead engineer into the crevice that opened across the road. Another, which followed whistling merrily, was lifted in the air and dropped into a nearby reservoir where it lies under forty feet of water.

In all the frightened towns in the area people have taken up their abode in trees. Country folk fill the churches and listen in dread to the words of ire the stupid pastors visit upon their heads. The hymns and prayers in country churches can be heard for miles. The town of Summerville, where it seems this rupture of the earth had its center, was razed to the ground.

In Columbia people held on to the walls as though they were sea-sick. In Abberville the quake caused the bells to ring, now a wild alarm, now a plaintive knell. In Savannah the fright was so great that women were known to jump out of windows with their babes in their arms, and right now a column of smoke can be seen coming up out of the sea a few meters from the coast.

That night the woods were filled with city people who, fleeing from their shaken dwellings, took refuge among the trees, and gathered in the darkness to kneel and sing out their praises to the Lord, imploring His mercy. The earth also shook and was rent in Illinois, Kentucky, Missouri, and Ohio. A man who was being initiated in a Masonic lodge stampeded out to the street with a rope around his waist. A Cherokee Indian who was brutally beating his poor wife, on feeling the ground move under his feet, fell on his knees and swore to the Lord he would never punish her again.

A strange spectacle awaited those who at last, jumping over crevices and wells, succeeded in bringing to Charleston money and tents! They arrived at night. The streets were lined with wagons like western caravans. In the squares, which are small, families slept under tents improvised from blankets, towels, or even woolen clothes. There were purple, red, yellow tents; white and blue tents with red stripes.

The most dangerous walls had already been demolished. Booths, reminiscent of those of fairs, had been set up around the ice wagons, fire engines, ambulances. Wild screams came from afar, from the suburbs. When women met they embraced and wept, and their weeping was the language of gratitude to Heaven. They knelt in silence, prayed, and went their separate ways consoled.

Certain pilgrims come and go with their tents on their backs, sit a while, then march on, then stop and sing. They do not seem to find a sure place for their rags and their fear. They are Negroes, Negroes in whom is reborn, in wailing hymns and terrible dances, the primeval fear with which the phenomena of nature filled their emotional ancestors. It is as though fearful birds, unperceived by other men, had lighted on their heads and plucked at them and furiously lashed at their backs with their wings.

From the moment one had eyes to see in that night's horror, it became apparent that a strange nature began to surge out of the blurred memory of those Negroes and show on their faces: it was the constricted race; it was the Africa of their parents and grandparents; it was that sign of ownership which every nature stamps on its man and which, regardless of accidents and human violations, lives its life and finds its way!

Every race brings with it into the world its mandate and it must be left its right of way, lest the harmony of the universe be disturbed, so that it may employ its strength and fulfill its mission with all the decorum and fruitfulness of its natural independence. Can anyone believe it possible, without incurring a logical punishment, to interrupt the spiritual harmony of the world by closing the way to one of its races, under pretext of a superiority which is but a degree in time?

It seems as though a black sun illumined those men from Africa! Their blood is fire; their passion like biting; their eyes flames, and everything in their nature has the energy of Africa's venoms, the enduring potency of her balms. The Negro has a great native goodness, which neither the martyrdom of slavery has perverted, nor his virile fierceness obscured. But he, more than the men of any other race, lives in such an intimate communion with nature, that he seems more capable than other men of shuddering and rejoicing with her changes.

In his fright and his joy there is something supernatural and marvelous which cannot be found in other primitive races. His movements and his glance bring to mind the majesty of the lion. In his affection there is such a sweet loyalty that we do not think of dogs but of doves; and his passions are so clear, tenacious, and intense that they resemble the sun's rays.

Those deformed creatures whom whip and fear have perhaps spared only in order that they might transmit to their offspring, conceived in the gloomy, tormented nights of slavery, the beastlike emotions of instinct and a vague reflection of their impetuous, free nature, are but a miserable parody of those other superb specimens.

But not even slavery, capable of putting out the sun itself, can completely extinguish the spirit of a race. Thus was it seen rising in these quiet souls when the greatest fright of their lives shook within their veins the inherited sediment of jungle winds, swaying bamboos, rustling reeds! Thus lived again in these Negroes—mostly born in America and educated in American ways—that fear with all its melancholic barbarism, violent and ingenuous like all the fears of their fiery race, the fear of the changes of ravaging nature, which creates among plants the hemlock, among animals, the lion!

Having been taught the Bible, they utter their fright in the Bible's prophetic tongue. The Negroes' horror reached its extremity from the very start of the earthquake.

The greatest love of these disconsolate creatures in all of what they know of Christianity is Jesus, because they see him whipped and meek like themselves. Jesus is theirs, and in their prayers they call him "Jesus, my Master," "my sweet Jesus," "my blessed Christ." They implored Him on their knees, beating their heads and their thighs as spires and columns came crashing down. "This Sodum and Gemorrah" they cried trembling. "Mount Horeb is opening up; it sure is!" And they wept, and opened their arms, and swayed to and fro, and begged not to be left alone until "the judgment was over."

They came and went dragging their children about crazily. When the poor elders of their caste appeared, the elders held sacred by all men but the white men, they prostrated themselves around them in great groups, listened to them on their knees with heads bowed to the ground, repeated together convulsively their mysterious exhortations, which derived from the vigor and candor of their nature and the divine character of old age such sacerdotal strength that even the white folks, the cultured white folks, rapturously joined the music of their distressed souls to that tender and ridiculous dialect.

Some six Negro children, in the night's saddest hour, rolled in a tumble on the ground, possessed with the racial frenzy in the garb of religion. They actually crawled. In their song an unutterable anxiety trembled. Their eyes were bathed in tears. "They're the little angels, the little angels, knocking on the door!"[8] In a low voice they repeated singing the same stanza they had sung out loud. Then came the refrain, heavy with prayer, incisive, desperate: "Oh! Tell Noah to hurry and build his ark, and build his ark, and build his ark!" The elders' prayers are not joined sentences, but the short phrases proper of genuine emotions and simple races.

Their contortions have the monotony, the strength, the weariness of their dances. The surrounding group invented a rhythm after each phrase which

8. This and the following quotations are approximate versions of Negro spirituals most of which can be found in *Jubilee and Plantation Songs* (Boston: Oliver Ditson Company, 1887).

seemed to them musical and appropriate to the mood of the occasion, and, with no previous agreement, all joined in. It is this that imparted a singular power of conviction and a positive charm to these grotesque prayers, at times so purely poetic: "Oh Lord touch not, oh Lord touch not again my city!"

"Birds got their nests. Lord, leave us our nests!" And the whole group, their faces touching the ground, repeated with a heart-breaking anguish: "Leave us our nests!"

In front of a tent we see a Negress whose extreme old age gives her a fantastic appearance. Her lips move, but we do not hear her words. She sways her body incessantly back and forth. Many blacks and whites surround her visibly anxious until the old woman takes up the hymn "Oh let me go, Jacob, let me go!" The crowd joins her singing, swaying like her, raising their hands to heaven, clapping to express their ecstasy. One man falls to the ground imploring mercy. He is the first convert. Several women, bearing a lamp, kneel around him and hold his hand. He shudders, stammers, sings out a prayer. His muscles become taut, he contracts his hands. A veil of blissful death seems to be drawn over his face. He lies fainted in front of the tent. Others follow. There is a similar scene before each tent. When dawn comes the singing and the swaying still continue. In the sinful neighborhoods the beasts which abound in all races indulge, under the pretext of religion, in the most abominable orgies.

Then, after seven and a half days of praying, people began to return to their homes. The women returned first, giving courage to their husbands. Women are easily alarmed, but are first in resignation. The mayor is again living with his family in what remains standing of his sumptuous residence. Trains loaded with bales of cotton ran again on the repaired tracks. Strangers stream into the city once consecrated by bravery in war, now by catastrophy. The town floats a nation-wide ten million dollar loan to reconstruct damaged buildings and replace the ones fallen to earth.

Stock exchanges, theatres, newspapers, banks send their help in money. Many tents, left empty by their occupants, are folded up and removed from gardens and squares where the government had pitched them. The earth continues to quake as though it has not yet settled definitely on its new foundations. What could have been the cause of this shaking of the earth?

Could it be that, as the earth's entrails shrank by the slow loss of heat which they incessantly let out through hot springs and lavas, the outer shell contracted, adjusting itself to a changed and reduced interior that sucked it in? The earth then, when it can no longer resist the tension, shrinks, waves, cracks, one lip of a fissure overlapping the other with a terrific clatter, and the successive tremors caused by the adjacent rocks giving in and pushing the ground up and sideways, until the echo of the clatter subsides.

But there are no volcanos in the vast area where the earthquake was felt, and the sulphuric fumes and vapors that escape through holes and cracks in the surface are those that naturally abound, because of its geologic formation, in this low and sandy Atlantic coastal plain. Could it be that in the sea's far-off bosom, because of a similar gradual cooling of the fiery core, the bottom, too extended to cover the weakened dome, began to undulate and snapped as would a body that contracts violently and then, closing over the broken edge with an enormous impetus, made all the foundations shake, sending the movement surging with a roar to the surface of the waves? But then in that case a monstrous wave would have advanced, wrinkling the face of the sea, and chastised the land with its great jaws, unleashing its wrath on the gallant town that breeds flowers and black-eyed belles on that shore's uncertain sands.

Or perhaps the coast's inclined plain, formed of fragmentary rock, loaded with the rivers' secular residues, broke off violently, yielding at last to the weight of the gneiss that descended from the Alleghanies,[9] then slid along the granitic foundation which three thousand feet below sustains the plain on the seaside, the weight of the highest detached rocks compressing the lower levels, thereby swelling the surface and shaking the cities with each undulatory impact! Such is the general belief: that the Atlantic coastal plain, soft and unsettled, yielding to the weight of sediments deposited upon it by rivers in the course of centuries, slid on its granitic berth toward the sea.

Thus simply did the earth follow its law of formation, swallowing men and snatching from them their homes as winds snatch leaves, with the majesty that becomes Nature's acts of creation and pain!

Wounded man strives to stanch the flow of blood that blinds his eyes, while he feels for the sword hanging from his side to combat the eternal foe; he goes on dancing in the wind, an atom on his way, forever rising, like a scaling warrior, up the sun's beams!

Charleston lives again, though her agony is not yet over, nor has the ground ceased to rumble under her swaying houses. The relatives and friends of the dead find that work reconstructs in the soul the roots that death has pulled out. The humble Negroes, once the fires that burnt in their eyes in the hour of fear have been spent, return to their tame chores and their abundant progeny. The spirited young shake from the mended porches the dust of roses.

And in the public square seem to laugh, one to each side of their mother, the twins born under a blue tent in the very hour of desolation.

September 10, 1886                                          October 14–15, 1886

## Two Homelands[1]

I have two homelands: Cuba and the night.
Or are they one and the same? No sooner
does his majesty, the sun, retire, than Cuba, with long veils,
and a carnation in hand, silently,
like a sad widow, appears before me.                                    5
I know that bleeding carnation
trembling in her hand! It's empty,
my chest is destroyed and empty,
where the heart once was. It's time

---

9. I.e., the Alleghany Mountains, mountains of the Appalachian system, in the southeastern    United States. [Anthology editors' note]
1. Translated by Ilan Stavans.

to begin dying. The night is                                                    10
right to say goodbye. The light is bothersome
and the word is human. The universe
speaks better than man.
                    Like a flag
inviting us to battle, the candle's                                             15
red flame flickers. Too full of myself,
I open the windows.
Silent, plucking
the carnation's leaves, like a cloud
darkening the sky, Cuba, a widow, passes by.                                     20

ca. 1887–88

# Our America[1]

The prideful villager thinks his hometown contains the whole world, and as long as he can stay on as mayor or humiliate the rival who stole his sweetheart or watch his nest egg accumulating in its strongbox he believes the universe to be in good order, unaware of the giants in seven-league boots who can crush him underfoot or the battling comets in the heavens that go through the air devouring the sleeping worlds. Whatever is left of that sleepy hometown in America must awaken. These are not times for going to bed in a sleeping cap, but rather, like Juan de Castellanos's[2] men, with our weapons for a pillow, weapons of the mind, which vanquish all others. Trenches of ideas are worth more than trenches of stone.

A cloud of ideas is a thing no armored prow can smash through. A vital idea set ablaze before the world at the right moment can, like the mystic banner of the last judgment, stop a fleet of battleships. Hometowns that are still strangers to one another must hurry to become acquainted, like men who are about to do battle together. Those who shake their fists at each other like jealous brothers quarreling over a piece of land or the owner of a small house who envies the man with a better one must join hands and interlace them until their two hands are as one. Those who, shielded by a criminal tradition, mutilate, with swords smeared in the same blood that flows through their own veins, the land of a conquered brother whose punishment far exceeds his crimes, must return that land to their brother if they do not wish to be known as a nation of plunderers. The honorable man does not collect his debts of honor in money, at so much per slap. We can no longer be a nation of fluttering leaves, spending our lives in the air, our treetop crowned in flowers, humming or creaking, caressed by the caprices of sunlight or thrashed and felled by tempests. The trees must form ranks to block the seven-league giant! It is the hour of reckoning and of marching

---

1. Translated by Esther Allen. Except as indicated, all footnotes are Allen's.

In this seminal essay, Martí strives to create a pan–Latin American (and, indirectly, a pan-Latino) identity and delineates the relationship between the United States and its Hispanic, Francophone, and Brazilian counterparts in the Americas. Martí's central tenet in the piece has long been a topic of debate among politicians and intellectuals.

2. *Juan de Castellanos* (1522–1607): Spanish poet and chronicler of the conquest of New Granada (now Colombia) in which he took part [see p. 57].

in unison, and we must move in lines as compact as the veins of silver that lie at the roots of the Andes.[3]

Only runts whose growth was stunted will lack the necessary valor, for those who have no faith in their land are like men born prematurely. Having no valor themselves, they deny that other men do. Their puny arms, with bracelets and painted nails, the arms of Madrid or of Paris, cannot manage the lofty tree and so they say the tree cannot be climbed. We must load up the ships with these termites who gnaw away at the core of the patria[4] that has nurtured them; if they are Parisians or Madrileños then let them stroll to the Prado by lamplight or go to Tortoni's[5] for an ice. These sons of carpenters who are ashamed that their father was a carpenter! These men born in America who are ashamed of the mother that raised them because she wears an Indian apron, these delinquents who disown their sick mother and leave her alone in her sickbed! Which one is truly a man, he who stays with his mother to nurse her through her illness, or he who forces her to work somewhere out of sight, and lives off her sustenance in corrupted lands, with a worm for his insignia, cursing the bosom that bore him, sporting a sign that says "traitor" on the back of his paper dress-coat? These sons of our America, which must save herself through her Indians, and which is going from less to more, who desert her and take up arms in the armies of North America, which drowns its own Indians in blood and is going from more to less! These delicate creatures who are men but do not want to do men's work! Did Washington, who made that land for them, go and live with the English during the years when he saw the English marching against his own land? These *incroyables* who drag their honor across foreign soil, like the *incroyables* of the French Revolution,[6] dancing, smacking their lips, and deliberately slurring their words!

And in what patria can a man take greater pride than in our long-suffering republics of America, erected among mute masses of Indians upon the bloodied arms of no more than a hundred apostles, to the sound of the book doing battle against the monk's tall candle? Never before have such advanced and consolidated nations been created from such disparate factors in less historical time. The haughty man thinks that because he wields a quick pen or a vivid phrase the earth was made to be his pedestal, and accuses his native republic of irredeemable incompetence because its virgin jungles do not continually provide him with the means of going about the world a famous plutocrat, driving Persian ponies and spilling champagne. The incapacity lies not in the emerging country, which demands forms that are appropriate to it and a grandeur that is useful, but in the leaders who try to rule unique nations, of a singular and violent composition, with laws inherited from four centuries of free practice in the United States and nineteen centuries of monarchy in France. A gaucho's pony cannot be stopped in midbolt by one of Alexander Hamilton's[7] laws. The sluggish blood

---

3. Mountain system of South America. [Anthology editors' note]
4. Fatherland. [Anthology editors' note]
5. Café in the Latin Quarter of Paris. *The Prado*: major fine-art museum in Madrid. [Anthology editors' note]
6. The *Incroyables* (French for "Incredibles") and

their female counterparts, the *Merveilleuses* ("Marvelouses"), were extravagantly fashionable subcultures in France during the Directory era (1795–99), the second-to-last phase of the French Revolution. [Anthology editors' note]
7. American statesman (1755–1804). [Anthology editors' note]

of the Indian race cannot be quickened by a phrase from Sieyès.[8] To govern well, one must attend closely to the reality of the place that is governed. In America, the good ruler does not need to know how the German or Frenchman is governed, but what elements his own country is composed of and how he can marshal them so as to reach, by means and institutions born from the country itself, the desirable state in which every man knows himself and is active, and all men enjoy the abundance that Nature, for the good of all, has bestowed on the country they make fruitful by their labor and defend with their lives. The government must be born from the country. The spirit of the government must be the spirit of the country. The form of the government must be in harmony with the country's natural constitution. The government is no more than an equilibrium among the country's natural elements.

In America the natural man has triumphed over the imported book. Natural men have triumphed over an artificial intelligentsia. The native mestizo has triumphed over the alien, pure-blooded criollo.[9] The battle is not between civilization and barbarity, but between false erudition and nature. The natural man is good, and esteems and rewards a superior intelligence as long as that intelligence does not use his submission against him or offend him by ignoring him—for that the natural man deems unforgivable, and he is prepared to use force to regain the respect of anyone who wounds his sensibilities or harms his interests. The tyrants of America have come to power by acquiescing to these scorned natural elements and have fallen as soon as they betrayed them. The republics have purged the former tyrannies of their inability to know the true elements of the country, derive the form of government from them, and govern along with them. Governor, in a new country, means Creator.

In countries composed of educated and uneducated sectors, the uneducated will govern by their habit of attacking and resolving their doubts with their fists, unless the educated learn the art of governing. The uneducated masses are lazy and timid about matters of the intellect and want to be well-governed, but if the government injures them they shake it off and govern themselves. How can our governors emerge from the universities when there is not a university in America that teaches the most basic element of the art of governing, which is the analysis of all that is unique to the peoples of America? Our youth go out into the world wearing Yankee- or French-colored glasses and aspire to rule by guesswork a country they do not know. Those unacquainted with the rudiments of politics should not be allowed to embark on a career in politics. The literary prizes must not go to the best ode, but to the best study of the political factors in the student's country. In the newspapers, lecture halls, and academies, the study of the country's real factors must be carried forward. Simply knowing those factors without blindfolds or circumlocutions is enough—for anyone who deliberately or unknowingly sets aside a part of the truth will ultimately fail because of the truth he was lacking, which expands when neglected and

8. *Emmanuel Joseph Sieyès* (1748–1836): Author of the famous tract *The Third Estate* (1789) and leading figure in the French Revolution, who subsequently assisted Napoleon [Napoléon Bonaparte (1769–1821), French emperor 1804–15] in his coup d'état.
9. On the *mestizo* and *criollo* classes, see the "Annexations" introduction. [Anthology editors' note]

brings down whatever is built without it. Solving the problem after knowing its elements is easier than solving it without knowing them. The natural man, strong and indignant, comes and overthrows the authority that is accumulated from books because it is not administered in keeping with the manifest needs of the country. To know is to solve. To know the country and govern it in accordance with that knowledge is the only way of freeing it from tyranny. The European university must yield to the American university. The history of America from the Incas to the present must be taught in its smallest detail, even if the Greek Archons go untaught. Our own Greece is preferable to the Greece that is not ours; we need it more. Statesmen who arise from the nation must replace statesmen who are alien to it. Let the world be grafted onto our republics, but we must be the trunk. And let the vanquished pedant hold his tongue, for there is no patria in which a man can take greater pride than in our long-suffering American republics.

Our feet upon a rosary, our heads white, and our bodies a motley of Indian and criollo we boldly entered the community of nations. Bearing the standard of the Virgin, we went out to conquer our liberty. A priest,[1] a few lieutenants, and a woman built a republic in Mexico upon the shoulders of the Indians. A Spanish cleric, under cover of his priestly cape, taught French liberty to a handful of magnificent students who chose a Spanish general to lead Central America against Spain. Still accustomed to monarchy, and with the sun on their chests, the Venezuelans in the north and the Argentines in the south set out to construct nations. When the two heroes clashed and the continent was about to be rocked, one of them, and not the lesser one, turned back.[2] But heroism is less glorious in peacetime than in war, and thus rarer, and it is easier for a man to die with honor than to think in an orderly way. Exalted and unanimous sentiments are more readily governed than the diverging, arrogant, alien, and ambitious ideas that emerge when the battle is over. The powers that were swept up in the epic struggle, along with the feline wariness of the species and the sheer weight of reality, undermined the edifice that had raised the flags of nations sustained by wise governance in the continual practice of reason and freedom over the crude and singular regions of our mestizo America with its towns of bare legs and Parisian dress-coats. The colonial hierarchy resisted the republic's democracy, and the capital city, wearing its elegant cravat, left the countryside, in its horsehide boots, waiting at the door; the redeemers born from books did not understand that a revolution that had triumphed when the soul of the earth was unleashed by a savior's voice had to govern with the soul of the earth and not against or without it. And for all these reasons, America began enduring and still endures the weary task of reconciling the discordant and hostile elements it inherited from its perverse, despotic colonizer with the imported forms and ideas that have, in their lack of local reality, delayed the advent of a logical form of government. The

---

1. *A priest:* Miguel Hidalgo y Costilla (1753–1811), an elderly priest, initiated Mexico's revolution of independence in the town of Dolores at the head of a band of Indians and with the help of the wife of the mayor of nearby Querétaro, Josefa Ortíz de Domínguez (1768–1829).
2. *Not the lesser one, turned back:* In South America, revolutions of independence emerged in 1810, in Venezuela, under Simón Bolívar (1783–1830), and in 1813, in Argentina, under José de San Martín (1778–1850). Bolívar's forces gradually made their way south, as San Martín's came north, and the two leaders eventually met in July 1822, in Guayaquil. After that meeting, San Martín renounced his title as Protector of Peru and left South America to live in France.

continent, deformed by three centuries of a rule that denied man the right
to exercise his reason, embarked—overlooking or refusing to listen to the
ignorant masses that had helped it redeem itself—upon a government based
on reason, the reason of all directed toward the things that are of concern
to all, and not the university-taught reason of the few imposed upon the
rustic reason of others. The problem of independence was not the change
in form, but the change in spirit.

Common cause had to be made with the oppressed in order to consolidate a system that was opposed to the interests and governmental habits of
the oppressors. The tiger, frightened away by the flash of gunfire, creeps back
in the night to find his prey. He will die with flames shooting from his eyes,
his claws unsheathed, but now his step is inaudible for he comes on velvet
paws. When the prey awakens, the tiger is upon him. The colony lives on in
the republic, but our America is saving itself from its grave blunders—the
arrogance of the capital cities, the blind triumph of the scorned campesinos,
the excessive importation of foreign ideas and formulas, the wicked and
impolitic disdain for the native race—through the superior virtue, confirmed by necessary bloodshed, of the republic that struggles against the
colony. The tiger waits behind every tree, crouches in every corner. He will
die, his claws unsheathed, flames shooting from his eyes.

But "these countries will be saved," in the words of the Argentine Rivadivia,[3] who erred on the side of urbanity during crude times; the machete is
ill-suited to a silken scabbard, nor can the spear be abandoned in a country
won by the spear, for it becomes enraged and stands in the doorway of Iturbide's Congress[4] demanding that "the fair-skinned man be made emperor."
These countries will be saved because, with the genius of moderation that
now seems, by nature's serene harmony, to prevail in the continent of light,
and the influence of the critical reading that has, in Europe, replaced the
fumbling ideas about phalansteries[5] in which the previous generation was
steeped, the real man is being born to America, in these real times.

What a vision we were: the chest of an athlete, the hands of a dandy, and
the forehead of a child. We were a whole fancy dress ball, in English trousers, a Parisian waistcoat, a North American overcoat, and a Spanish bullfighter's hat. The Indian circled about us, mute, and went to the mountaintop
to christen his children. The black, pursued from afar, alone and unknown,
sang his heart's music in the night, between waves and wild beasts. The
campesinos, the men of the land, the creators, rose up in blind indignation
against the disdainful city, their own creation. We wore epaulets and judge's
robes, in countries that came into the world wearing rope sandals and Indian headbands. The wise thing would have been to pair, with charitable

3. *Bernardino Rivadivia* (1780–1845): Argentine
politician who defended his country against English invaders and then fought for its independence. Elected as the first president of the United
Provinces of Río de la Plata in 1826, he was
forced to resign by the caudillo Quiroga [Juan
Facundo Quiroga (1788–1835), Argentine leader]
and went into exile, living out his life in the Spanish city of Cádiz.
4. *Iturbide's Congress:* Agustín de Iturbide (1783–
1824), Mexican general who initially fought
against Mexico's independence movement. He
later joined forces with insurgent general Guerrero to assure Mexico's independence. But instead of the liberal state envisioned by the insurgents, Iturbide ushered in a conservative one.
When his soldiers proclaimed him emperor, the
newly independent Mexican Congress, angry but
cowed, ratified the proclamation (1822). A revolution soon broke out against him, and in 1823 he
was forced to abdicate.
5. Cooperative communities as formulated by the
French sociologist and reformer Charles Fourier
(1772–1837). [Anthology editors' note]

hearts and the audacity of our founders, the Indian headband and the judicial robe, to undam the Indian, make a place for the able black, and tailor
liberty to the bodies of those who rose up and triumphed in its name. What
we had was the judge, the general, the man of letters, and the cleric. Our
angelic youth, as if struggling from the arms of an octopus, cast their heads
into the heavens and fell back with sterile glory, crowned with clouds. The
natural people, driven by instinct, blind with triumph, overwhelmed their
gilded rulers. No Yankee or European book could furnish the key to the
Hispanoamerican enigma. So the people tried hatred instead, and our
countries amounted to less and less each year. Weary of useless hatred, of
the struggle of book against sword, reason against the monk's taper, city
against countryside, the impossible empire of the quarreling urban castes
against the tempestuous or inert natural nation, we are beginning, almost
unknowingly, to try love. The nations arise and salute one another. "What
are we like?" they ask, and begin telling each other what they are like.
When a problem arises in Cojimar they no longer seek the solution in
Dantzig.[6] The frock-coats are still French, but the thinking begins to be
American. The young men of America are rolling up their sleeves and
plunging their hands into the dough, and making it rise with the leavening
of their sweat. They understand that there is too much imitation, and that
salvation lies in creating. Create is this generation's password. Make wine
from plantains; it may be sour, but it is our wine! It is now understood that
a country's form of government must adapt to its natural elements, that
absolute ideas, in order not to collapse over an error of form, must be expressed in relative forms; that liberty, in order to be viable, must be sincere
and full, that if the republic does not open its arms to all and include all in
its progress, it dies. The tiger inside came in through the gap, and so will
the tiger outside. The general holds the cavalry's speed to the pace of the
infantry, for if he leaves the infantry far behind, the enemy will surround
the cavalry. Politics is strategy. Nations must continually criticize themselves, for criticism is health, but with a single heart and a single mind.
Lower yourselves to the unfortunate and raise them up in your arms! Let
the heart's fires unfreeze all that is motionless in America, and let the
country's natural blood surge and throb through its veins! Standing tall, the
workmen's eyes full of joy, the new men of America are saluting each other
from one country to another. Natural statesmen are emerging from the direct study of nature; they read in order to apply what they read, not copy it.
Economists are studying problems at their origins. Orators are becoming
more temperate. Dramatists are putting native characters onstage. Academies are discussing practical subjects. Poetry is snipping off its wild,
Zorilla-esque[7] mane and hanging up its gaudy waistcost on the glorious
tree. Prose, polished and gleaming, is replete with ideas. The rulers of Indian republics are learning Indian languages.

America is saving herself from all her dangers. Over some republics
the octopus sleeps still, but by the law of equilibrium, other republics are

---

6. I.e., Danzig, or Gdańsk, city and port in Poland. *Cojimar*: small fishing village east of Havana,
Cuba. Martí is stressing that the new nations of
the Americas do not turn to Europe for answers to
their problems. Dantzig stands for "European" solutions. [Anthology editors' note]
7. *Zorilla-esque*: A reference to José Zorilla (1817–
93), a Romantic Spanish poet. Martí did not share
in the popular enthusiasm for Zorilla's work.

running into the sea to recover the lost centuries with mad and sublime swiftness. Others, forgetting that Juárez[8] traveled in a coach drawn by mules, hitch their coach to the wind and take a soap bubble for coachman—and poisonous luxury, enemy of liberty, corrupts the frivolous and opens the door to foreigners. The virile character of others is being perfected by the epic spirit of a threatened independence. And others, in rapacious wars against their neighbors, are nurturing an unruly soldier caste that may devour them. But our America may also face another danger, which comes not from within but from the differing origins, methods, and interests of the continent's two factions. The hour is near when she will be approached by an enterprising and forceful nation that will demand intimate relations with her, though it does not know her and disdains her. And virile nations self-made by the rifle and the law love other virile nations, and love only them. The hour of unbridled passion and ambition from which North America may escape by the ascendancy of the purest element in its blood—or into which its vengeful and sordid masses, its tradition of conquest, and the self-interest of a cunning leader could plunge it—is not yet so close, even to the most apprehensive eye, that there is no time for it to be confronted and averted by the manifestation of a discreet and unswerving pride, for its dignity as a republic, in the eyes of the watchful nations of the Universe, places upon North America a brake that our America must not remove by puerile provocation, ostentatious arrogance, or patricidal discord. Therefore the urgent duty of our America is to show herself as she is, one in soul and intent, rapidly overcoming the crushing weight of her past and stained only by the fertile blood shed by hands that do battle against ruins and by veins that were punctured by our former masters. The disdain of the formidable neighbor who does not know her is our America's greatest danger, and it is urgent—for the day of the visit is near—that her neighbor come to know her, and quickly, so that he will not disdain her. Out of ignorance, he may perhaps begin to covet her. But when he knows her, he will remove his hands from her in respect. One must have faith in the best in man and distrust the worst. One must give the best every opportunity, so that the worst will be laid bare and overcome. If not, the worst will prevail. Nations should have one special pillory for those who incite them to futile hatreds, and another for those who do not tell them the truth until it is too late.

There is no racial hatred, because there are no races. Sickly, lamp-lit minds string together and rewarm the library-shelf races that the honest traveler and the cordial observer seek in vain in the justice of nature, where the universal identity of man leaps forth in victorious love and turbulent appetite. The soul, equal and eternal, emanates from bodies that are diverse in form and color. Anyone who promotes and disseminates opposition or hatred among races is committing a sin against humanity. But within that jumble of peoples which lives in close proximity to our peoples, certain peculiar and dynamic characteristics are condensed—ideas and habits of expansion, acquisition, vanity, and greed—that could, in a period of internal

---

8. *Benito Juárez* (1806–72): Widely revered as one of Latin America's greatest nineteenth-century political figures, Juárez was a Zapotec Indian who was president of Mexico from 1857 to 1863, and again from 1867 until his death.

disorder or precipitation of a people's cumulative character, cease to be latent national preoccupations and become a serious threat to the neighboring, isolated and weak lands that the strong country declares to be perishable and inferior. To think is to serve. We must not, out of a villager's antipathy, impute some lethal congenital wickedness to the continent's light-skinned nation simply because it does not speak our language or share our view of what home life should be or resemble us in its political failings, which are different from ours, or because it does not think highly of quick-tempered, swarthy men or look with charity, from its still uncertain eminence, upon those less favored by history who, in heroic stages, are climbing the road that republics travel. But neither should we seek to conceal the obvious facts of the problem, which can, for the peace of the centuries, be resolved by timely study and the urgent, wordless union of the continental soul. For the unanimous hymn is already ringing forth, and the present generation is bearing industrious America along the road sanctioned by our sublime forefathers. From the Rio Bravo to the Straits of Magellan, the Great Cemi,[9] seated on a condor's back, has scattered the seeds of the new America across the romantic nations of the continent and the suffering islands of the sea!

January 20, 1891

9. *Cemi:* A spirit worshiped by the Taino, an indigenous people of the Caribbean. The cemi (or zemi) is often represented in the form of a tricornered clay object.

# MANUEL M. SALAZAR
## 1854–1911 ~

Author of one of the earliest Spanish-language novels written in the United States, Manuel M. Salazar was also a prolific poet whose work is marked by deep sentiment and longing for personal fulfillment. The son of a Civil War veteran, Salazar was born in El Puertecito, New Mexico. He began his working life as a businessman, but in 1874 he became a teacher in Mora. After holding various posts in local government, in 1895 he returned to commerce by opening a retail business.

Written in 1881 on the pages of a business ledger, *La historia de un caminante, o sea Gervacio y Aurora* (The Story of a Wayfarer, or Gervacio and Aurora) has never been published in its entirety, although an excerpt appeared in *The Journal of American Folklore* in 1980. It tells the story of the many loves of Gervacio, a good-natured young man who moves from unhappy affair to unhappy affair.

In *The Story of a Wayfarer*, Salazar portrays New Mexico as idyllic and pastoral, despite the roving groups of outlaws that bedeviled the territory in the 1880s. Like Eusebio Chacón's two stories, which would be published in 1892, *The Story of a Wayfarer* was most likely influenced by French and Spanish pastoral works of the late nineteenth century, evidence that fiction writers of the nascent New Mexican literary tradition may have sought models beyond those of the United States.

## FROM THE STORY OF A WAYFARER, OR GERVACIO AND AURORA[1]

## Chapter 19

After a few days, Don Tadeo and his wife returned, and, finding them in the house when he came back from school, Gervacio was delighted, since he loved Don Tadeo's company. The latter was a man of great wit, an excellent public speaker, a wonderful legal counselor, and a great statesman and politician. They talked for a while and then Don Tadeo said to Gervacio, "I don't know if you'll be very happy with me, but I took it upon myself to get your letters from the post office. Or rather, I should say 'letter', because there was only one, which I've brought with me. If I'm not mistaken, I'm pretty sure it's from Rogerio de la O, since I recognize his hand-writing."

Gervacio replied that, far from being angry, he was actually happy that Don Tadeo had taken the trouble to ask at the post office for his mail. Then he added, "Show me the letter and I assure you that if it's from my dear friend Rogerio, I'll let you read it, whatever is in it, good or bad."

"Well, then," Don Tadeo replied, "here it is."

Gervacio looked at the writing on the envelope and, seeing that it indeed was from Don Rogerio, he gave it back to Don Tadeo to open and read, which he did immediately, aloud.

> Valles de la Luna
> Christmas Eve
> Don Gervacio Morales
>
> Dear Sir:
>
> Please be aware that since you left for Puerto del Navegante, I've been forced to play my instrument by myself, which I found a bit odd, and I think I play so badly that Susana has been grumbling that "I'm not worth the trouble." Maybe that's true because even though we've had dinner parties here, I haven't played at them. Segismundo was here eight days ago, but since Aurora was at the convent, as you know, he quickly went home to the Gulf of Batanes. I spoke to him and it seemed to me that he has taken quite a liking to Aurora, but to be honest I have to say that "he hates you more that he loves her." As for other news, there isn't any, because "if you're talking about the harvest" there's nothing new because when you left we had already harvested the grain and now we're in the first month of the winter, there's nothing if not snow and ice and doors shut tight and people sitting next to their stoves or searching for a bit of warm sun.
>
> In the end, since I can't find anything to tell you because there aren't very many of us around here, I'll ask you to let me in on the uproar your letter to Elmira caused. I can imagine you beaten to a pulp, scolded, thrashed, and I'm even afraid that Luscinda has sent you packing, which would be the worst punishment of all for a trickster like you, since it might cure you of your mania of cheating poor, ignorant folk, which is what happened to me what you read the same letter I was just referring to.

---

1. Translated by Harold Augenbraum.

Let me know, as well, if Don Tadeo Mendoza is alive or dead since I haven't seen him since my wedding and it concerns me that I don't know if he's in good shape. If you see him tell him that the godfather should write to the godson, and tell his wife that a godmother should be sending Christmas presents to her goddaughter and if you see your brother-in-law tell him to say hello to his brother.

Finally, I pray to God for the best for you and your parents and neighbors, those close to you and your brothers. And as for my teacher I send my good wishes, and I hope for more talent than he has to some time hear him play something worthy to be heard.

Don Alfredo and Doña Beatriz are safe and well and surrounded by children, like the moon by the stars. They are only missing Aurora. Goodbye for now and don't forget me.

I remain, Rogerio de la O.

They really enjoyed Don Rogerio's letter since it was so frank. And even more so since it focused on Aurora and Segismundo and the Gulf of Batanes, like Elmira's letter. In the end it gave Gervacio a clear idea of what was happening, and it had taken him two hours to do it.

Soon thereafter Gervacio left for The Enchanted Eye Forest to hunt. As he approached the marshland, he saw something white heading toward him. As it got closer, he realized that this mobile object was none other than a member of the fairer sex. He examined her closely, from head to toe, admiring her beauty. She wore all white, and her clothes reminded him of a wedding dress, and the garland of flowers around her head completed the nuptial dress. There was a shyness in her eyes and a modesty in her lips, humility in her movement and in her cheeks "the fire of love." One of her hands rested on her chest, the other on her mouth, symbolic of internal suffering and, perhaps, a pained silence.

Enchanted, Gervacio screwed up the courage to approach her, to contemplate her beauty, actually. As he did, the young nymph parted her lips, showing off what one could call a line of ivory amid coral lips. Then, fixing her gaze on Gervacio, her tears seemed to tell him about the bitterness of her situation. Perhaps, in the end, by unburdening herself she could convince him of the rectitude of her love while showing him the sad aspect of that love, constricting her chest and bowing her head, as if to expend her final breath.

Gervacio was overcome, and said, "Your very manner conveys such sorrow to me as much as your integrity. I share your pain, and see that your silence proves how great is your affliction. Permit me to know your name and perhaps I can alleviate your suffering."

But the nymph "as serious as thought," in essence proving her heroism by hiding and keeping to herself the reasons for her sufferings, would not reveal who she was.

Finally, removing a piece of paper from among her clothes she placed it on the rock on which Gervacio was leaning. With an ever so slight bow, she withdrew as fast as lightning. Gervacio was so shocked and amazed at what he had seen that he completely forgot about hunting and went back to the house in deep thought. He had taken the piece of paper from the rock, but he was so absorbed in those thoughts that he decided not to read it until he could see Don Tadeo. When the latter arrived, Gervacio told him all about the nymph and Don Tadeo, no less amazed, took the piece of paper Gervacio had brought and read it.

Whoever is reading this, know that I am a poor, unfortunate woman, who, despite my having been born beautiful, rich and innocent, today, owing to my simplicity, I live apart from the world. I find myself destitute, and malice ruins me and causes my destruction. I advise all young women who nature has afforded beauty and innocence, even without wealth, that if the spark of love burns in your heart, that you curry that flame, and that you not try to get everyone to admire your beauty or compliment you, for if you do, you'll fall into the same trap I did, being born beautiful, and having to conform to the gifts nature afforded me, but no, "full of vainglory." With a desire to be admired I loved a young man, but not content with just his affection, I sought to be loved and admired by many men. And when my beloved fiancé found out, it ruined me, for he withdrew his affection since he realized that I did not consider it enough or I would not have sought the love of others. When he abandoned me, I wept, and abandoned the world. I came to these caves to live out my days and share my woes with only these rocks, my only companions. Now I know that no one in the world can care for me, not even the one person who swore he would love me forever. But I don't blame him. I blame my mad fantasies. I'm ready and waiting for death, and I declare that I forgo any legal proceedings through which I could take back my beloved. Now I understand the saying, "If you want everything, you'll lose everything." It's impossible. "If you love everyone, you love no one." It confirms the lesson learned: you love one person and you live happily. Don't try for something that will end badly more than one that can end well. Look at these libertines: they love everyone. But what do they get out of it? Their love is a lie. Afterwards, all those people who have been loved and admired can't even convince themselves that they were loved, much less really possessed any affection from the people they loved. And why does that happen? Because as everyone knows, "what belongs to everyone, belongs to no one."

If you try to find me, you won't. Like an echo, I will raise my voice in lamentation, not in consolation, just like poor Echo who responded to the laments of her beloved Narcissus but with no consolation at all. My home is the world, and my name is

Experience

Having finished reading, Don Tadeo said to Gervacio, "Without any powder or shot, you've hunted down this piece of writing, which is worth a lot more than any plumed duck. This woman who came over to you must have been some poor young girl rejected by her lover, since she herself said so, and I'll tell you that she may be the only creature that has recognized the error of her ways and through them wants to warn others. This idea of loving only one person is a good and smart one, and the idea of loving everyone and coquetting around with everyone is the worst thing that can happen to the reputation of a young man or woman, and they get called all sorts of names, like 'layabout,' 'rascal,' or 'gadabout' or even 'whore,' 'libertine,' or 'nuisance,' if people even notice them. In the end, if young men or women pledge themselves and then their lovers end up seeing that type of behavior, they'll get rid of them quick. That's how they will come to understand (and the community's disdain will remind them) that 'if you want everything, you'll lose everything.'"

"Well," said Gervacio, "I'm glad I went hunting. If I hadn't gone, all of this wouldn't have happened. Meeting the young woman brought out love and compassion, and the fact that she hid her real name under the rubric of 'Experience' made me feel like I actually had had experience itself, and afforded me a good picture of what love is, so if it so happens that I love and lose, it will be on a whim, and not for the lack of good advice. And not just vulgar advice, but that of Experience itself."

After that he want home since night was coming on and shadows falling since there was no moon to provide any light. Days passed, one after the other, and Gervacio couldn't sleep. His heart ached almost to death. He couldn't figure out what was causing it, but his suffering went from bad to worse. Despite a desire to voice his complaints, he couldn't even do that, since he was drying up inside. He grew pale, so much so that his aspect took on the appearance of a skeleton or a dead man.

In the middle of all this suffering, Augusto Estadio of Puerto del Navegante told him his daughter Clara was getting married that very afternoon to Don Alfonso de Vega, the son of Don Andrés de Vega, and that since they were friends he wanted him at the ceremony. Gervacio thanked him for thinking of him and promised to be in Puerto del Navegante that afternoon.

"Well, then," said Don Augusto, "I'm assured that you'll honor my daughter with your presence and I'll say as much to Don Reyes."

"Fine," Gervacio replied, "I'll see you then."

After he said goodbye to Don Augusto, Gervacio went to his classroom. When he got home, he told Don Rómulo of Don Augusto's visit, his news, and the invitation.

"So he invited you?" Don Rómulo asked.

"Yes," Gervacio answered. "I think I'll go right now, and I'll come back tomorrow afternoon, Sunday."

"All best," Don Rómulo replied. "Go, and God be with you."

While Gervacio was getting ready, Don Rómulo saddled his horse, and without much ado Gervacio left for Puerto del Navegante, where he would not arrive until ten at night, and even then it was difficult since the ground was covered with snow, which was still falling heavily. When he got to Don Reyes' house, he called out to Olivero, who immediately set to taking the horse to the stable, while Gervacio ended up between Don Reyes and Marta, warming himself by the fire since the night was very cold. After chatting for a while and warming himself up, he left for the dance hall, accompanied by Don Reyes and Olivero, so he could dance with his beloved Luscinda.

When he arrived, he greeted almost everyone there with great affection, but especially Señor Normando and Amalia. Luscinda greeted him as well but not very heartily. She seemed to be in a bad mood or ill, but he refused to let her sourness affect him. The music filled him with a great desire to dance, so he asked his beloved Luscinda to be his partner. She did but not very willingly. Gervacio had no idea to what to attribute this behavior. At the same time, his heart felt an intense sorrow, since, as the saying goes, "desire creates great emotion."

When the dance was over, a good-looking young man named Alejo took his arm and told him he wanted to speak to him alone. Gervacio agreed, and as they left the room, Alejo said to him, "Gervacio, my friend, would you do me the favor of reading me a letter I just received today, from that young woman Luscinda."

When he heard this, Gervacio started and didn't know how to respond. Finally, recovering from the shock he said to Alejo, "If I'm going to read the letter to you, I think we should go somewhere private, like my uncle Don Reyes's house. I'll read it to you there."

"Agreed, let's go," said Alejo, "I can't think of a better place."

When they arrived, they went into a bedroom, and Alejo gave Gervacio the letter. This is what it said:

Puerto del Navegante
13th of December

Dear Alejo:

I was very sorry to have refused you when your parents very diplomatically and courteously ask for my hand on your behalf. That was because I had already promised myself to Gervacio Morales, whom I believed to be an honest young man, to all appearances.

But now that my cousin has given me clear information about him, I can't in all good conscience marry him. My cousin has sworn to me that what he has told me is true, and if it is, I can in no way marry a young man like that, who embodies the attributes of laziness, thievery, and murder.

Tell me, Alejo, my love, how could I put my trust in someone of such common and evil character? I could not, Alejo mío. My entire happiness is in your hands, and if you love me as much as I love you, I beg of you to ask for my hand and I will marry you as soon as I possibly can. If you're afraid my father will oppose my wishes, we'll elope and "take the Villadiego way."[2] So let me know when to expect you, where, and at what time, since without your letting me know it will not be possible to be sure.

My desire is to take enough money as we need to get far away, since a lot of people will want to come after us. Only my trust in your love leaves me the hope to be yours in any way I can. Rest assured that I am yours, and please forgive all my past mistakes.

Yours forever,

Luscinda Perez

After he had read Luscinda's letter, Gervacio said, "My dear Alejo, I don't want to leave you with the impression that what Luscinda has told you about me has made me unhappy. What I would rather do is congratulate you, since it's great good fortune that this young woman is in love with you.

---

2. I.e., flee; this now obscure expression is related to the history of Villadiego, a municipality in northern Spain.

It's true that I loved her and wanted to marry her, but on seeing that she is more in love with you, I'm happy about your good luck. Believe me, I'm telling the truth. 'Though I do envy your good fortune, I won't stand in the way of your marriage. On the other hand, you yourself have seen Luscinda say in her letter that she promised herself to me, which is true, just like the love she professes for you now. And since I can't deny the facts, I would ask you to let me keep the letter. It would be easy for Señor Normando to accuse me in court of breach of promise if I want to marry someone else and not Luscinda, and if that's the case, this letter will be my best evidence to refute it, and it will show everyone that you are her one true love and the only person for her. So can I keep it?"

"Yes," Alejo replied. "Take it and do what's best and fair for both of us."

That said, they went back to the dance together, arm in arm.

Luscinda, seeing them like that, decided to leave, which she did almost immediately. Both Alejo and Gervacio thought her quick exit rather odd, and they discussed her heavy-handed and crass spitefulness, but, in the end, surrounded by so many other beautiful and more faithful and modest women and in their desire to have a good time, they danced as much as they could and in such an amicable way that anyone seeing them would never have guessed that anything had passed between them. When the dance ended, they went their respective ways.

The following morning Señor Normando came to Don Reyes's house and begged Gervacio to accompany him to his house to see Luscinda, who was depressed and subdued, and he added, "Maybe your presence would cheer her up."

Gervacio went to see Luscinda. When he saw her he greeted her with his usual affection and courtesy. But when he saw her so extraordinarily unresponsive, with such a cruel and angry silence, he left her side and sat down in a chair by the desk, where he took a bit of paper and wrote the following sonnet to Luscinda:

> I would like to sing, with divine accents
> An elegy to your soul, without peer.
> You have dealt my breast a blow so sear,
> That now I perish from its torments.
>
> You alone made this feeling, you ungrateful wretch,
> Your foul lips have sentenced me
> To suffer alone, and now I see mortality
> And that you will cause my final breath.
>
> Heaven will pity me for your cruelty
> And in time my misfortunes leaven,
> 'Though your love will never belong to me.
>
> 'Though this struggle be my burden
> It cannot take from me what I will always see
> As an offering of love in this world and in heaven.

> In praise,

> Gervacio Morales

Luscinda wept copiously when she read Gervacio's sonnet, and he, unable to remain any longer, went to cry in a forest with only God as his witness. Finally, tired of his own tears, he went to Don Reyes's house, where he wished, or at least tried, to hide his feelings. But they weighed so heavily on him that by the time he arrived he was very low and depressed. Not wanting to suppress his emotions, he saddled his horse and said goodbye to his aunt and uncle. As they watched the usually cheerful Gervacio leave bearing such a long face, they too became lost in thought.

From Don Reyes's, Gervacio headed to Señor Normando's house to take leave of him, his wife, and the unfaithful and ungrateful Luscinda. Having said goodbye, he trotted off on his horse, sadder than when Aurora had found him crying in the forest and lower than when Segismundo surprised him with Aurora, and more weighed down by events and lifeless than when Don Augusto had invited him to his daughter's wedding the day before. But he was satisfied that he had uncovered the falsity of women and how little their word meant. He wept and moaned and cried all along his route, and even when he finally got home, he was still cut to the quick.

1881

---

# LUIS MUÑOZ RIVERA
## 1859–1916

More than any other Puerto Rican public figure of his generation, Luis Muñoz Rivera is responsible for plotting the course of the island's political destiny during the crucial years of transition from a Spanish territory to a U.S. territory. He began his working life as a merchant, but after a few years he became a prominent newspaper owner, journalist, poet, and orator. In the 1880s, he joined the ranks of the island's liberal autonomist movement and became a fervent advocate of self-government for Puerto Rico, then still under Spanish rule.

In 1890, Muñoz Rivera founded *La Democracia*, a newspaper that defended liberal autonomist ideals and contributed to his eventual ascent into the leadership of the Partido Autonomista Puertorriqueño (Puerto Rican Autonomist Party). In 1897, when Spain finally granted the *Carta Autonómica* (Charter of Autonomy) to Puerto Rico, Muñoz Rivera was chosen to occupy one of the cabinet's secretary posts in the new provisional government. While most members of this insular parliament were Puerto Ricans elected to their posts, the top government official on the island continued to be a Spanish governor appointed by the colonial metropolis. The opportunity for self-government for Puerto Rico came to an end just a few months later, however, with the advent of the Spanish-American War and the subsequent U.S. invasion of the island. A year after the arrival of the U.S. troops, Muñoz Rivera founded the Partido Federal (Federalist Party) to promote Puerto Rico's incorporation as a state of the American union, but was quickly disillusioned with the U.S. government's Americanization policies, its decision to keep Puerto Rico as an unincorporated territorial possession, and the limited participation of Puerto Ricans in the new colonial administration. The situation was further aggravated by the acrimonious political divisions among Puerto Rican leaders and their conflicting claims for self-government, annexation, or independence. These factors prompted Muñoz Rivera's move from Puerto Rico to New York City in 1901.

During his first year in New York, Muñoz Rivera founded the weekly newspaper *The Puerto Rico Herald*, which he published for the next three years. In the paper's editorials, he kept Puerto Rican communities on the island and in the U.S. aware of Puerto Rico's struggles against unilateral Americanization policies, and he pressed for a resolution to the island's political status. One of Muñoz Rivera's editorials, "Northward Ho!," published in 1903 and included in this anthology, underscores the economic crisis confronted by the now powerless Spanish and Creole commercial and propertied class in Puerto Rico under the new U.S. regime, and the widespread misery that was overwhelming the island's population, even after almost five years of U.S. occupation. Muñoz Rivera presents emigration as the only option left to a population that was being deprived of a role in charting its collective future and encourages the idea of Puerto Ricans going to the United States to seek prosperity. However, he also warns individuals not to emigrate to the United States unless they have some English-language skills and some funds to support themselves while they face the difficult challenges of finding employment.

In 1904, Muñoz Rivera returned to Puerto Rico to cofound the Partido Unión de Puerto Rico (Puerto Rican Unionist Party), which went on to represent the interests of the island's propertied class until 1932. One main objective of the Unionists was to bring together the different political factions and promote a prompt resolution to the issue of the island's colonial status. At the time, there was widespread discontent among Puerto Rico's political leaders with the provisions of the U.S. government's Foraker Act (of 1900), which promoted Americanization policies and provided only limited representation and participation of Puerto Ricans in the U.S.-controlled island government.

With the Unionist Party's triumph in the 1908 local elections, Muñoz Rivera became Puerto Rico's resident commissioner in Washington, D.C. This position, which he occupied until his death, allowed him to speak for the island in the U.S. Congress, but without being able to cast a vote. The second Muñoz Rivera selection in this anthology is a speech he gave at the U.S. House of Representatives in 1916, in response to the hearings on granting U.S. citizenship to Puerto Ricans and on other political-reforms proposals under a new act that would replace the Foraker Act. The speech reflects Muñoz Rivera's frustration with U.S. authorities' disregard for the wishes of the Puerto Rican people and with the island's unresolved political status. He urges Congress to grant the island its independence unless the United States is willing to make Puerto Rico a state of the union or a self-governing entity. The Jones Act, which granted U.S. citizenship to all Puerto Ricans, was approved by Congress in 1917, less than a year after Muñoz Rivera's death.

Muñoz Rivera once stated in a letter to a friend that independence was his desideratum (what he really wanted for Puerto Rico) and autonomy his modus operandi (his method of operation as a politician). In other words, he practiced an ambiguous combination of his true ideals and an opportunistic politics of pragmatism and compromise when negotiating with the colonial authorities. Putting aside the dream of a sovereign Puerto Rico, he instead sought a more easily achievable goal—a larger measure of self-government for Puerto Rico—while maintaining a permanent relationship with the United States that he, and many other leaders of his time, saw as beneficial to the island.

# Northward Ho!

One of the most interesting problems of the moment is that of the emigration of Puerto Ricans to other countries. In the last number of this weekly we devoted an editorial to this topic. We are preoccupied by the condition of our countrymen and we feel that an imperious duty prompts us to offer them our advice, which cannot be suspected of being adulterated by impure and egoistic calculations.

In October, the first five years of American dominion in the island will have gone by. After so short a time, the islanders already feel the need of shaking off this political yoke which oppresses them and the economical servitude which suffocates them. Liberty exists only for the favorites of the Government, while prosperity exists only for its officials.

The youth of the island, notwithstanding their natural endowments, vegetate in a sterile inaction or in a degrading lassitude. All the mountainous regions of the island are in ruins, that is to say, two thirds of the territory. Small cities, formerly enjoying a high degree of prosperity—Coamo, Utuado, Lares, San Sebastián, Aguas Buenas, Hato Grande, Las Marías, Adjuntas, etc., etc., etc—today are homes without life, without hope, without a future.

There is hardly any commerce in those places. We might quote actual cases. In 1898, a merchant of the interior possessed a capital of $100,000 in coffee plantations, in completely new buildings, in merchandise, in fruit, and in sums due to him. In 1903, this same merchant possesses nothing. His buildings were destroyed by the hurricane and his plantations have become worthless on account of the price that he gets for the grain that's produced. His bills are uncollected—they cannot be collected and will never be collected, because the debtors were ruined at the same time as the creditors.

That is the history of hundreds and hundreds of citizens whose credit was worth thousands and thousands of dollars, and whose signature, at this moment, would not be honored. This is the cause of the conflict which is not understood in Washington for a very simple reason—for the reason that it's in the interest of Mr. William H. Hunt, Governor of the colony, to make Puerto Rico appear prosperous, happy and satisfied.

We challenge any one of our adversaries to deny this affirmation or to argue against its truth. We speak of a fact known even to children, a fact which makes every one suffer with the keenness of its actuality and has caused the profound crisis that is daily extending over a wider field, while no one takes the trouble of checking it.

Therefore, as the means for making one's living do not exist, as the poverty of yesterday is converted into the misery of today and will be transformed into the starvation of tomorrow, the Puerto Ricans are looking for individual remedies in a condition for which collective remedies cannot be had.

And while the banner of ostracism, as it might be called, is fluttering in the wind with its colors that will always appear gloomy and sad, the eyes anxiously turn to that ominous flag. The people who never thought of abandoning the land of their affections beg to be led to the Yucatán, to Ecuador, to Oceania, no matter where—to any place that is likely to offer them work and bread.

It is a spectacle that arouses the burning heat of an immense indignation in our veins and makes the blood rise to our cheeks. Yonder garden of the tropics, the refuge of so many immigrants, sees its sons emigrating on the decks of the ships; sees them turning to unknown shores; hears their sobs; and beholds their tears running down from their eyes. While it could prevent the exodus depopulating the island by contracting loans, opening markets, granting bounties, compensating the deficit of some branches of production by the surplus of others, it finds its hands tied by a system lacking the advantages of European paternalism, which at times produces salvation. In Puerto Rico, contrary to the condition prevalent in the United States, the people are deprived of any initiative whatsoever, because the Government has concentrated all the prerogatives and powers onto itself.

Emigration? O certainly! Under so adverse circumstances there is today in the struggle for existence, no other outlet than expatriation. But in an extremity so painful, we ought to meditate quietly, measure our own forces, study the obstacles, reflect on untoward possibilities, and above all, fix on a course and determine to what place the prows of the ships have to turn.

Of the republics of South and Central America—Mexico, the Argentine Republic and Chile seem to have institutions of an admirable stability. It's not easy to reach Chile or Argentina. The voyage is too long. Mexico is quickly reached without much discomfort. But, will the order established by law, will the law itself now in force continue, when, unfortunately, General Diaz[1] should succumb or retire? Will not the rivalry of petty chieftains, which is now destroying Colombia and Venezuela, raise its head also there? Will there not be a return to the barbarism of pronunciamientos and mutinies, which now dishonor Ecuador and Guatemala?

On the other side, will it be feasible to open mountains to cultivation, to found villages in places which are covered by forests that are centuries old, to establish a society where only lagoons and woody regions exist? There, the Creoles will go to test their impulses. There we shall later go to find out whether the attempt produces beneficial results. O, might the colony of Quintana Róo[2] be one day like an iris spreading out over our misfortunes, like a gate opening to our hopes!

But today, we will point out the northern continent to the young men of Puerto Rico. We encourage them in their purpose of finding a road to prosperity far from their native land. We advise them to pursue this course, which, no doubt, is the least difficult and the straightest and safest course.

Here arrive the Italians, humble people from Sicily and Calabria determined and tenacious, in fact, more tenacious and determined than our countrymen generally are, but not more intelligent and industrious. There are not a thousand, not ten thousands, but three hundred thousand of them every year. All of them find their employers and receive their wages. The subterranean railroad, the large bridges, the long tunnels, the enormous buildings of twenty or thirty stories give food to the people of Ferrara and Palermo. An immigration in the same proportion continued for three years would be sufficient to depopulate Puerto Rico entirely.

1. Porfirio Díaz (1830–1915), president of Mexico 1877–80, 1884–1911.
2. An area on the Yucután Peninsula, named after an early patriot of the Mexican Republic, Andrés Quintana Roo. Now a state of Mexico, it was made a territory by decree of President Díaz in November 1902, and until 1911 was used as a penal colony to hold opponents of the Díaz regime.

We, however, are careful in pointing out that no one should emigrate entirely destitute of resources and without the decisive assistance of the language. There is much suffering. Persons arriving must submit to horrible vexations in Ellis Island and in the places of detention. Man descends to the condition of an animal treated with the whip. If a countryman or workman wishes to come to New York, he has to bring some funds, so that he can wait awhile until some favorable opportunity offers itself and the remunerated labor begins.

September 5, 1903

## Speech Given to the House of Representatives

Mr. Speaker, I want to state, in the first place, that I have taken great pleasure in the declaration of the gentleman from Virginia, Mr. Jones, the other day, and also in the declaration of the gentleman from Iowa, Mr. Towner, this morning. Both gentlemen are doing justice to my country. Both have endeavored to make this bill, which I consider a general proposition, a democratic measure, acceptable to all of my countrymen in Porto Rico.

On the 18th day of October 1898, when the flag of this great Republic was unfurled over the fortresses of San Juan, if anyone had said to my countrymen that the United States, the land of liberty, was going to deny their right to form a government of the people, by the people, and for the people of Porto Rico, my countrymen would have refused to believe such a prophecy, considering it sheer madness. The Porto Ricans were living at that time under a regime of ample self-government, discussed and voted by the Spanish Cortes,[1] on the basis of the parliamentary system in use among all the nations of Europe. Spain sent to the islands a Governor, whose power, strictly limited by law, made him the equivalent of those constitutional sovereigns who reign but do not govern. The members of the Cabinet, without whose signature no executive order was valid, were natives of the island; the representatives in the Senate and in the House were natives of the island; and the administration in its entirety was in the hands of natives of the island. The Spanish Cortes, it is true, retained the power to make statutory laws for Porto Rico, but in the Cortes were 16 Porto Rican representatives and 3 Porto Rican senators having voice and vote. And all the insular laws were made by the insular parliament.

Two years later, in 1900, after a long period of military rule, the Congress of the United States approved the Foraker Act. Under this act, all of the 11 members of the executive council were appointed by the President of the United States; 6 of them were the heads of departments; 5 exercised legislative functions only. And this executive council, or, in practice, the bureaucratic majority of the council, was, and is in reality, with the Governor, the supreme arbiter of the island and of its interests. It represents the most absolute contradiction of republican principles.

1. Cortes Generales, the Spanish Parliament.

For 16 years we have endured this system of government, protesting and struggling against it, with energy and without result. We did not lose hope, because if one national party, the Republican, was forcibly enforcing this system upon us, the other national party, the Democratic, was encouraging us by its declarations in the platforms of Kansas City, St. Louis, and Denver. Porto Rico waited, election after election, for the Democratic Party to triumph at the polls and fulfill its promises. At last the Democratic Party did triumph. It is here. It has a controlling majority at this end of the Capitol and at the other end: it is in possession of the White House. On the Democratic Party rests the sole and undivided responsibility for the progress of events at this juncture. It can, by a legislative act, keep alive the hopes for the people of Porto Rico or it can deal these hopes their death blow.

The Republican Party decreed independence for Cuba and thereby covered itself with glory; the Democratic Party is bound by the principles written into its platforms and by the recorded speeches of its leaders to decree liberty for Porto Rico. The legislation you are about to enact will prove whether the platforms of the Democratic Party are more than useless paper, whether the words of its leaders are more than soap bubbles, dissolved by the breath of triumph. Here is the dilemma with its two unescapable horns: You must proceed in accordance with the fundamental principles of your party or you must be untrue to them. The monarchies of the Old World, envious of American success and the republics of the New World, anxious to see clearly the direction in which the American initiative is tending, are watching and studying the Democratic administration. Something more is at stake than the fate of Porto Rico—poor, isolated, and defenseless as she is—the prestige and the good name of the United States are at stake. England learned the hard lessons of Saratoga and Yorktown[2] in the 18th century. And in the 19th century she established self-government, complete, sincere, and honorable in Canada, Australia, and New Zealand. Then in the 20th century, immediately after the Anglo-Boer War, she established self-government, complete, sincere, and honorable, for the Orange Free State and the Transvaal, her enemies of the day before. She turned over the reins of power to insurgents who were still wearing uniforms stained with British blood.[3]

In Porto Rico no blood will be shed. Such a thing is impossible in an island of 3,600 square miles. Its narrow confines never permitted and never will permit armed resistance. For this very reason Porto Rico is a field of experiment unique on the globe. And if Spain, the reactionary monarchy, gave Porto Rico the home rule which she was enjoying in 1898, what should the United States, the progressive Republic, grant her? This is the mute question which Europe and America are writing today in the solitudes of the Atlantic and on the waters of the Panama Canal. The reply is the bill which is now under discussion. This bill cannot meet the earnest aspirations of my country. It is not a measure of self-government ample enough to solve definitely our political problem or to match your national reputation,

2. Sites of British defeats during the American Revolution (1775–83).
3. Economic and territorial disputes led to the war (1899–1902) between the British and two Boer (Dutch) states: the South African Republic (Transvaal) and the Orange Free State. After achieving victory, the British granted amnesty to Boer fighters who had not broken the rules of war.

established by a successful championship for liberty and justice throughout the world since the very beginning of your national life. But, meager and conservative as the bill appears when we look at its provisions from our own point of view, we sincerely recognize its noble purposes and willingly accept it as a step in the right direction and as a reform paving the way for others more acceptable and satisfactory which shall come a little later, provided that my countrymen will be able to demonstrate their capacity, the capacity they possess, to govern themselves. In regard to such capacity, it is my duty, no doubt a pleasant duty, to assure Congress that the Porto Ricans will endeavor to prove their intelligence, their patriotism, and their full preparation to enjoy and to exercise a democratic regime.

Our behavior during the past is a sufficient guarantee for our behavior in the future. Never a revolution there, in spite of our Latin blood; never an attempt to commercialize our political influence; never an attack against the majesty of law. The ever-reigning peace was not at any time disturbed by the illiterate masses, which bear their suffering with such stoic fortitude and only seek comfort in their bitter servitude, confiding in the supreme protection of God.

There is no reason which justifies American statesmen in denying self-government to my country and erasing from their programs the principles of popular sovereignty. Is illiteracy the reason? Because if in Porto Rico 60 percent of the electorate cannot read, in the United States in the early days of the Republic, 80 percent of the population were unable to read; and even today there are 20 Republics and 20 monarchies which acknowledge a higher percentage of illiteracy than Porto Rico. It is not the coexistence of two races on the island, because here in North America more than 10 States show a higher proportion of Negro population than Porto Rico and the District of Columbia has precisely the same proportion, 67 white to 33 percent colored. It is not our small territorial extent, because two States have a smaller area than Porto Rico. It is not a question of population, for by the last census there were 18 States with a smaller population than Porto Rico. Nor is it a matter of real and personal property, for the taxable property in New Mexico is only one-third that of Porto Rico. There is a reason and only one reason—the same sad reason of war and conquest which let loose over the South after the fall of Richmond thousands and thousands of office seekers, hungry for power and authority, and determined to report to their superiors that the rebels of the South were unprepared for self-government. We are the southerners of the 20th century.

The House of Representatives has never been influenced by this class of motive. The House of Representatives has very high motives, and, if they are studied thoroughly, very grave reasons, for redeeming my country from bureaucratic greed and confiding to it at once the responsibility for its own destinies and the power to fix and determine them. They are reasons of an international character which affect the policy of the United States in the rest of America; Porto Rico, the only one of the former colonies of Spain in this hemisphere, which does not fly its own flag or figure in the family of nations, is being closely observed with assiduous vigilance by the Republics of the Caribbean Sea and the Gulf of Mexico. Cuba, Santo Domingo, Venezuela, Colombia, Costa Rica, Honduras, Nicaragua, Salvador, Guatemala maintain with us a constant interchange of ideas and never lose sight of the experiment in the colonial government which is being carried on in Porto Rico. If they see that the Porto Ricans are living happily, that they are not treated with disdain, that their aspirations are being fulfilled, that their character is respected, that they are not being subjected to an imperialistic tutelage, and that the right to govern their own country is not being usurped, these nations will recognize the superiority of American methods and will feel the influence of the American government. This will smooth the way to the moral hegemony which you are called by your greatness, by your wealth, by your traditions, and your institutions to exercise in the New World. On the other hand, if these communities, Latin—like Porto Rico—speaking the same language as Porto Rico, branches of the same ancestral trunk that produced Porto Rico, bound to Porto Rico by so many roots striking deep in a common past, if these communities observe that your insular experiment is a failure and that you have not been able to keep the affections of a people who awaited from you their redemption and their happiness, they will be convinced that they must look, not to Washington but to London, Paris, or Berlin when they seek markets for their products, sympathy in their misfortunes, and guarantees for their liberty.

What do you gain along with the discontent of my countrymen? You as Members of Congress? Nothing. And the Nation loses a part of its prestige, difficulties are created in the path of its policies, its democratic ideals are violated, and it must abdicate its position as leader in every progressive movement on the planet. Therefore if you undertake a reform, do it sincerely. A policy of subterfuge and shadows might be expected in the Italy of the Medicis, in the France of the Valois, in the England of the Stuarts, or the Spain of the Bourbons, but it is hard to explain in the United States of Cleveland, McKinley, Roosevelt, and Wilson.[4]

This bill I am commenting on provides for a full elective legislature. Well, that is a splendid concession you will make to your own principles and to our own rights. But now, after such a magnificent advance, do not permit, gentlemen, do not permit the local powers of the legislature to be diminished in matters so important for us as the education of the children. We are citizens jealous of this dignity; we are fathers anxious to foster our sons toward the future, teaching them how to struggle for life and how to reach the highest standard of honesty, intelligence, and energy. We accept one of your compatriots, a capable American, as head of the department of education, though we have in the island many men capable of filling this high office with distinction. We welcomed his appointment by the President of the United States. In this way the island will have the guarantee to find such a man as Dr. Brumbaugh, the first commissioner of education who went to Porto Rico, or as Dr. Miller, the present commissioner, who deserves all our confidence. But let the legislature regulate the courses of study, cooperating in that manner with the general development of educational work throughout our native country.

---

4. Grover Cleveland (1837–1908), William McKinley (1843–1901), Theodore Roosevelt (1858–1919), and Woodrow Wilson (1856–1924), U.S. presidents. *Medicis:* Italian family that governed Florence from the fifteenth century until 1737. *Valois:* royal house of France from 1328 to 1589. *Stuarts:* royal family of Scotland and England from ca. 1160 until 1714. *Bourbons:* royal family of France, Spain, the two Sicilies, and Parma; ruled Spain from 1700 until 1931 and again after 1975.

I come now to treat of a problem which is really not a problem for Porto Rico, as my constituents look at it, because it has been solved already in the Foraker Act. The Foraker Act recognizes the Porto Rican citizenship of the inhabitants of Porto Rico. We are satisfied with this citizenship and desire to prolong and maintain it—our natural citizenship, founded not on the conventionalism of law but on the fact that we were born on an island and love that island above all else, and would not exchange our country for any other country, though it were one as great and as free as the United States. If Porto Rico were to disappear in a geological catastrophe and there survived a thousand or 10,000 or a hundred thousand Porto Ricans, and they were given their choice of all citizenships of the world, they would choose without a moment's hesitation that of the United States. But so long as Porto Rico exists on the surface of the ocean, poor and small as she is, and even if she were poorer and smaller, Porto Ricans will always choose Porto Rican citizenship. And the Congress of the United States will have performed an indefensible act if it tries to destroy so legitimate a sentiment and to annul through a law of its own making a law of the oldest and wisest legislators of all time—a law of nature.

It is true that my countrymen have asked many times, unanimously, for American citizenship. They asked for it when through the promise of General Miles on his disembarkation in Ponce,[5] and through the promises of the Democratic Party when it adopted the Kansas City platform—they believed it not only possible but probable, not only probable but certain, that American citizenship was the door by which to enter, not after a period of 100 years nor of 10, but immediately into the fellowship of the American people as a State of the Union. Today they no longer believe it. From this floor the most eminent statesmen have made it clear to them that they must not believe it. And my countrymen, who, precisely the same as yours, have their dignity and self-respect to maintain, refuse to accept a citizenship of an inferior order, a citizenship of the second class, which does not permit them to dispose of their own resources nor to live their own lives nor to send to this Capitol their proportional representation. To obtain benefits of such magnitude they were disposed to sacrifice their sentiments of filial love for the motherland. These advantages have vanished, and the people of Porto Rico have decided to continue to be Porto Ricans; to be so each day with increasing enthusiasm, to retain their own name, claiming for it the same consideration, the same respect, which they accord to the names of other countries, above all to the name of the United States. Give us statehood and your glorious citizenship will be welcome to us and to our children. If you deny us statehood, we decline your citizenship, frankly, proudly, as befits a people who can be deprived of their civil liberties but who, although deprived of their civil liberties, will preserve their conception of honor, which none can take from them because they bear it in their souls, a moral heritage from their forefathers.

This bill which I am speaking of grants American citizenship to all my compatriots. It authorizes those who do not accept American citizenship to so declare before a court of justice, and thus retain their Porto Rican citizenship. It provides that—

5. City and port in southern Puerto Rico. *General Miles*: Nelson Appleton Miles (1839–1925), U.S. commanding general, led the invasion of Puerto Rico during the Spanish-American War.

"No person shall be allowed to register as a voter in Porto Rico who is not a citizen of the United States."

My compatriots are generously permitted to be citizens of the only country they possess, but they are eliminated from the body politic; the exercise of political rights is forbidden them and by a single stroke of the pen they are converted into pariahs and there is established in America, on American soil, protected by the Monroe Doctrine, a division into castes like the Brahmans and Sudras of India. The Democratic platform of Kansas City declared 14 years ago, "A nation can not long endure half empire and half republic," and "Imperialism abroad will lead rapidly and irreparably to despotism at home." These are not Porto Rican phrases reflecting our Latin impressionability; they are American phrases, reflecting the Anglo-Saxon spirit, calm in its attitude and jealous—very jealous—of its privileges.

We have a profound consideration for your national ideas; you must treat our local ideas with a similar consideration. As the representative of Porto Rico I propose that you convoke the people of the island to express themselves in full plebiscite on the question of citizenship and that you permit the people of Porto Rico to decide by their votes whether they wish the citizenship of the United States or whether they prefer their own natural citizenship. It would be strange, if, having refused it so long as the majority of people asked for it, you should decide to impose it by force now that the majority of the people decline it.

Someone recently stated that we desire the benefits but shirk the responsibilities and burdens of citizenship. I affirm in reply that we were never consulted as to our status, and that in the Treaty of Paris[6] the people of Porto Rico were disposed of as were the serfs of ancient times, fixtures of the land, who were transferred by force to the service of new masters and subject to new servitudes. The fault is not ours, though ours are the grief and humiliation; the fault lies with our bitter destiny which made us weak and left us an easy prey between the warring interests of mighty powers. If we had our choice, we would be a free and isolated people in the liberty and solitude of the seas, without other advantages than those won by our exertions in industry and in peace, without other responsibilities and burdens than those of our own conduct and our duty toward one another and toward the civilization which surrounds us.

The bill under consideration, liberal and generous in some of its sections—as those creating an elective insular Senate; a Cabinet, the majority of whose members shall be confirmed by the Senate; and a public-service commission, two members of which shall be elected by the people—is exceedingly conservative in other sections, most of all in that which restricts the popular vote, enjoining that the right of registering as electors be limited to those who are able to read and write or who pay taxes to the Porto Rican treasury. By means of this restriction 165,000 citizens who vote at present and who have been voting since the Spanish days would be barred from the polls.

Here are the facts: There exist at present 250,000 registered electors. Seventy percent of the electoral population is illiterate. There will remain,

6. See Appendix 2: Treaties, Acts, and Propositions (p. A15).

then, 75,000 registered electors. Adding 10,000 illiterate taxpayers, there will be a total of 85,000 citizens within the electoral register and 165,000 outside of it. I cannot figure out, hard as I have tried, how those 165,000 Porto Ricans are considered incapable of participating in the elections of their representatives in the legislature and municipalities, while on the other hand they are judged perfectly capable of possessing with dignity American citizenship. This is an inconsistency which I cannot explain, unless the principle is upheld that he who incurs the greatest misfortune—not by his own fault—of living in the shadow of ignorance is not worthy of the honor of being an American citizen. In the case of this being the principle on which the clause is based, it would seem necessary to uphold such principle by depriving 3 million Americans of their citizenship, for this is the number of illiterates in the United States according to the census of 1910. There is no reason that justifies this measure, anyway. Since civil government was established in Porto Rico, superseding military government—that is, 16 years ago—eight general elections have been staged. Eight times the people, with a most ample suffrage law, have elected their legislative bodies, their municipal councils, their municipal courts, and school boards. These various bodies have cooperated to the betterment and progress of the country, which gives evidence that they were prudently chosen.

Perhaps one or a hundred or a thousand electors tried to commercialize their votes, selling them to the bidders.

For the sake of argument I will accept that hypothesis, though it was never proved. But even supposing that we had not to do with a presumption, but with an accomplished fact, I ask: Were there not and are there not in the rest of this Nation those who negotiate their constitutional rights? Did not the courts of a great State—the State of Massachusetts—convict four or five thousand men of that offense? Was there not a case in which the majority of a legislature promised to elect and did elect a high Federal officer for a few dollars? I do not think that these infractions of the law and breaches of honor reflect the least discredit on the clean name of the American people. I do not think that such isolated crimes can lead in any State to the restriction of the vote. They are exceptional cases, which cannot be helped. The courts of justice punish the guilty ones and the social organization continues its march. In Porto Rico, if such cases occur, they should have and do have the same consequences. But it would be a sad and unjust condition of affairs if, through the fault of one, 1,000 men were to be deprived of their privileges; or, to speak in proportion, if, through the fault of 160 electors, 160,000 were to be deprived of their privileges.

The aforesaid motives are fundamental ones that require careful attention from the House. But there are deeper motives yet, those that refer to the history of the United States and of the American Congress. Never was there a single law passed under the dome of the Capitol restrictive of individual rights, of the rights of humanity. Quite the contrary, Congress, even going to the extreme of amending the Constitution, restrained the initiative of the States for the purpose of making them respect the exercise of those rights without marring it with the least drawback. There is the 14th amendment. Congress could not hinder States from making their electoral laws, but it could decree and did decree that in the event of any State decreasing its number of electors it would, ipso facto, decrease its number of

Representatives in this House. The United States always gave to the world examples of a profound respect for the ideal of a sincere democracy.

I feel at ease when I think of the future of my country. I read a solemn declaration of the five American commissioners that signed, in 1898, the Treaty of Paris. When the five Spanish delegates, no less distinguished than the Americans, asked for a guarantee as to the future of Porto Rico, your compatriots answered thus:

"The Congress of a country which never enacted laws to oppress or abridge the rights of residents within its domains, and whose laws permit the largest liberty consistent with the preservation of order and the protection of property, may safely be trusted not to depart from its well-settled practice in dealing with the inhabitants of these islands."

Congress needs not be reminded of its sacred obligations, the obligations which those words impose upon it. Porto Rico had nothing to do with the declaration of war. The Cubans were assured of their national independence. The Porto Ricans were acquired for $20 million, and my country, innocent and blameless, paid with its territory the expenses of the campaign.

The Treaty of Paris says:

"As compensation for the losses and expenses occasioned the United States by the war and for the claims of its citizens by reason of the injuries and damages they may have suffered in their persons and property during the last insurrection of Cuba, Her Catholic Majesty, in the name and representation of Spain, and thereunto constitutionally authorized by the Cortes of the Kingdom, cedes to the United States of America, and the latter accept for themselves, the island of Porto Rico and the other islands now under Spanish sovereignty in the West Indies, as also the island of Guam, in the Marianas or Ladrones Archipelago, which island was selected by the United States of America in virtue of the provisions of article 11 of the protocol signed in Washington on August 12 last."

You, citizens of a free fatherland, with its own laws, its own institutions, and its own flag, can appreciate the unhappiness of the small and solitary people that must await its laws from your authority, that lacks institutions created by their will, and who does not feel the pride of having the colors of a national emblem to cover the homes of its families and the tombs of its ancestors.

Give us now the field of experiment which we ask of you, that we may show that it is easy for us to constitute a stable republican government with all possible guarantees for all possible interests. And afterward, when you acquire the certainty that you can find in Porto Rico a republic like that founded in Cuba and Panama, like the one that you will find at some future day in the Philippines, give us our independence and you will stand before humanity as the greatest of the great; that which neither Greece nor Rome nor England ever were, a great creator of new nationalities and a great liberator of oppressed peoples.

May 15, 1916

# MIGUEL ANTONIO OTERO JR.
## 1859–1944

A premier chronicler of the western frontier, Miguel Antonio Otero Jr. was born in St. Louis, Missouri. His father—one of the most prominent Mexican Americans of the day—had been a professor of Latin and Greek at Pingree College, in Fishkill on the Hudson, New York; three-time delegate to the U.S. Congress from the territory of New Mexico; a prominent banker in Las Vegas, New Mexico; and a railroad baron. The younger Miguel Antonio was educated at a boarding school in Topeka, Kansas, and then at St. Louis University and Notre Dame. After returning from college, Otero joined his father's bank as an accountant. At age 27, he was elected probate clerk of San Miguel County and, in 1891, was selected to represent New Mexico at the Republican National Convention. There, he met the future president William McKinley, who in 1897 named him governor of the territory of New Mexico.

In 1935, at age 76, Otero published the first of his three memoirs, *My Life on the Frontier, 1864–1882*, which he followed with *My Life on the Frontier, 1882–1897* (1939) and *My Nine Years as Governor of the Territory of New Mexico, 1897–1906* (1940). In 1936, he published *The Real Billy the Kid*, a biography of the nineteenth-century outlaw and gunman Henry McCarty, also known as William Bonney. Bonney had been jailed in Las Vegas, New Mexico, in 1880, and Otero and his brother Page had ridden with the prisoner as he was transported by train to Santa Fe, where they remained for a while and visited him in jail many times. In fact, as he recounts in his memoirs, Otero had met many legendary characters, such as the brothel madams Calamity Jane and Lousy Liz, the gunfighter James Butler "Wild Bill" Hickok, and the showman William Frederick "Buffalo Bill" Cody. While telling these stories, he provides exciting accounts of murders, manhunts, and criminal trials, but he also writes about politics and the workings of government. In shaping this chronicle of human interest, Otero drew on both his memory and extensive research in newspaper archives.

---

## FROM MY NINE YEARS AS GOVERNOR OF THE TERRITORY OF NEW MEXICO, 1897–1906

### From Chapter VIII. The Folsom Train Robberies

As I now remember, it was sometime late in the summer of 1897 that I learned that the Black Jack Ketchum gang had established their rendezvous in a thickly wooded canyon in northern New Mexico on the east side of the Taos mountains in Colfax County not far from Elizabethtown and within sight of Old Baldy.[1] Learning this about two months after I became governor, I at once notified the sheriffs of Colfax and Taos counties to keep a close watch on the gang and to notify me promptly should they make any attempt to move. I learned that besides Tom and Sam Ketchum, the gang

---

1. A mountain summit.

consisted of Will Carver, alias G. W. Franks, whose real name I believed to be Harvey Logan; William Walter, alias Broncho Bill; and Ezra Lay, alias William H. McGinnis. All five of these men were at their headquarters. Will Franks was a wonderful shot with either rifle or pistol, and was regarded as the most desperate man in the bunch. He was a plausible sort of fellow, a good mixer and a good talker, so he usually did the scouting for the party, and located the "easy money." Clayton, the county seat of Union County, was a comparatively new town and the headquarters for cattle, horse, and sheep men. In those early days it was overrun with gambling houses, saloons, dance halls, houses of prostitution, and rustlers. Much ready cash was in evidence, and the Colorado and Southern Railroad brought it in to Clayton from Colorado points almost daily. Franks soon learned all the facts and located the best point on the railroad right-of-way for a holdup, which was five miles south of Folsom[2] near Twin Mountain. After acquainting himself with all the details, he mounted his horse and struck the trail for headquarters. He soon made known his plans to the gang and Tom Ketchum said, "We will try it. Let's waste no time, but get ready at once." As soon as arrangements were made, Broncho Bill was left in charge of the "Robbers' Roost" and the others left on good horses in the direction of Folsom.

On the night of September 3, 1897, the south-bound passenger train of the Colorado and Southern Railroad entered New Mexico through Emory Gap without mishap. The engineer was Crowfoot, the fireman Cackley, and the conductor Frank Harrington.

The train stopped for a few minutes in Folsom. As it started south, a man jumped on the front end of the express car to the engine, and quickly climbed over on the tender. At Twin Mountain, where there is a slight grade, the man dropped from the tender into the engine's cab, where he covered the engineer and fireman with his rifle. "Stop the train," he yelled to Crowfoot. Finding himself looking into the barrel of a rifle, the engineer quickly complied with the order. When the train came to a stop, the engineer and fireman were ordered to jump off and line up. The strange visitor was none other than Black Jack and the three men walked back to the door of the express car where Cackley called out to the express messenger to open the door, which he did. At this point, Black Jack was joined by Sam, his brother, and Will Franks. The other member of the gang, McGinnis, was left to guard the four horses. Crowfoot, Cackley, and the two Ketchum boys climbed into the express car, while Franks stood guard at the door. "Open the safe," commanded Black Jack. "I can't," said Drew. "It is a through safe, and I don't have the combination." "You lie," said Sam Ketchum, striking Drew over the head with his rifle. The latter fell to the floor, stunned by the blow. "Hand up those sticks," said Black Jack to Franks. Several sticks of dynamite were passed to him and five of them were placed on the top of the safe. Throwing a quarter of fresh beef on top of the sticks, he lighted the fuse and the men stepped back. The explosion broke open the safe door and damaged the roof of the car. While the Ketchums were in the express car, Conductor Harrington came up from the forward passenger coach toward

2. A village in Union County.

the disconnected express car, swinging his lantern. Franks called out, "Go back where you came from and put out that light before I shoot it out." A sack holding silver dollars had been torn open by the explosion and the contents were scattered over the car floor. Sam Ketchum, however, picked the silver up and made the sack secure. "Now get back to your engine," said Black Jack to the engineer and fireman, "and continue your journey south." On their arrival in Clayton, Harrington reported the robbery. Immediately after the robbery, which took about thirty minutes, the bandits mounted their horses and rode off towards their rendezvous in the Taos mountains.

Dixon, the rear brakeman, jumped off the rear Pullman and hurried back to Folsom to report the robbery. Posses were organized in Trinidad, Clayton, and Folsom. The next morning they visited the scene of the holdup, but the bandits had disappeared. The booty secured on this first holdup was reported to have been $3,500. "I made a careful investigation of the robbery," said W. H. Reno, "and secured information which convinced me the crime was committed by the Black Jack gang, but I was unable to locate their whereabouts."

Shortly after this first holdup of the Colorado and Southern, the Ketchum gang left their Taos Mountain rendezvous and took up their abode in the southwestern part of the territory. For nearly two years, Colfax and Union counties were at peace, so far as the Black Jack gang was concerned; but they made things interesting along the eastern line of Arizona and Grant County, New Mexico, until well-organized posses began a systematic round-up of all bandits. Then the gang found things too warm to remain in that locality. At this time, late in the spring of 1899, the gang had a falling-out with their old leader, Black Jack. Sam Ketchum was delegated to inform his brother of their determination to quit him. Sam had decided to go with the gang, and early one morning Franks and Broncho Bill gathered up their belongings, mounted their horses, and rode north. This time they located their headquarters on Turkey Creek, in a canyon ten miles above the town of Cimarron, where they had several horses and a good supply of grub and ammunition. Franks scouted around for awhile and finally decided it was about time to attempt a second holdup at Twin Mountain. Since the other bandits readily assented to the suggestion, preparations were in order. At this point, Broncho Bill decided to leave the bunch, so he told Sam Ketchum that he was disgusted with camp life and declined to stay in the camp during their absence. They cached their camp outfit, and the remaining three mounted their horses and soon reached their destination between Folsom and Twin Mountain.

On July 11, 1899, the gang again held up the southbound passenger train at the same spot where the first holdup had taken place. Frank Harrington was again the conductor, Engineer Tubbs was in the cab, and Homel Scott was in charge of the express car, which carried considerable money. As the train rounded the curve at Twin Mountain, Tubbs noticed a fire on the prairie ahead of his train. "Some sheepherder's camp," he told his fireman. When the engine reached the fire, an uninvited guest with a pistol in each hand entered the cab from the tender. "Stop her," he ordered. The engineer promptly shut off steam, and the train stopped within three hundred yards of the scene of the first holdup. The stranger, who was Franks, forced the engineer and fireman to walk to the express car where he was joined by

Ketchum and McGinnis. They fired a few shots to frighten the passengers and prevent their interference. The noise of these shots, however, informed the alert express messenger, Scott, that something unusual was happening. Accordingly, he hurriedly seized several valuable packages of currency from one of the safes and threw them among a pile of merchandise and fruit boxes, where the robbers failed to find them. A second safe was blown open with dynamite, and the bandits jumped out of the car with loot, which I was told, amounted to $70,000. The three bandits then crossed the track and made for their horses.

Meanwhile, Conductor Harrington had realized that another holdup was under way. Having secured a gun from a closet in the smoking car, he enlisted the assistance of two deputy sheriffs who happened to be on the train. The three men went through the train to the rear Pullman, and dropped to the ground. Seeing a bunch of horses by the light of the fire, they crawled toward them in the hope of preventing the escape of the robbers. Their share in the adventure being unknown to the engineer, the latter blew his whistle, and started the train without them. However, he soon realized that they had been left behind, and stopped the train and waited for them. As it turned out, the conductor and the two deputy sheriffs were too late. The bandits secured the horses and rode off in the direction of Turkey Canyon.

A posse was soon organized at Trinidad. This consisted of eight men: W. H. Reno; Sheriff Edward Farr, of Huerfano County, Colorado; F. H. Smith, of New York; H. N. Love, a cowboy from Springer, New Mexico; Perfecto Cordova; Miguel Lopez; James H. Morgan; and Captain Thacker. The two last named were employees of the Wells Fargo Express Company. A heavy rain fell in the vicinity of Folsom the night after the holdup and greatly interfered with the work of the posse. However, they were able to locate the camp where the robbers had slept the night before the robbery. Here they found the first real clue to the location of the gang's rendezvous. This was an envelope postmarked "Springer, New Mexico." It bore the address, "G. W. Franks, Cimarron, New Mexico."

Acting on this information, the posse then proceeded to Cimarron, where they were joined by United States Marshall Foraker with several deputies. On July 15, some of the posse drove into Cimarron and reported having seen three men leading several pack horses entering Turkey Canyon that morning. It was, at once, suspected that the trio were Franks, McGinnis, and Sam Ketchum. Quickly mustering their posse, Reno and Farr headed for some smoke which they took to be the Ketchum camp. On the following day, at five o'clock in the afternoon, they came upon the camp. According to one version of the fight which followed, McGinnis, who was on his way to a creek about fifty yards distant, was immediately put out of action by a bullet in his shoulder. Bullets flew so fast for awhile that no two accounts agree as to exactly what did happen. The robbers, unaccustomed to resistance on the part of the law, were cornered but fought desperately. Sam Ketchum was struck in the left arm by a bullet which shattered the bone and left him unable to continue the fight. Franks, the remaining desperado, was able, single-handed, to deal considerable misery to the posse. An expert shot, he fought like a bunch of wildcats against the eight men and got away without a scratch. As for the posse, Sheriff Farr fought with a wounded wrist until he was killed. Smith was wounded in the leg, and Love was killed with a shot through the breast. The battle lasted nearly an hour, Franks keeping up a fusilade of bullets the whole time. Finally he managed to get McGinnis on a horse, and carried him to a hideout in the mountains. Ketchum, painfully wounded, also escaped on horseback, but was captured not long afterwards, about twenty miles from the camp. He was taken to Santa Fe on July 20, 1899, and entered the territorial penitentiary as "No. 129." He refused to have his shattered arm amputated and died four days later of blood poisoning.

On leaving the battlefield, the posse headed for Raton. Realizing that the authorities had located their rendezvous, Franks decided to leave Turkey Canyon at the earliest moment. That same night he washed and dressed the wounds on McGinnis' shoulder. He then saddled two of their best horses and helped his wounded companion to mount. The two then left together for the southern country, keeping close to the mountains. After traveling all night and part of the following day, they succeeded in reaching a ranch belonging to a native family which was very friendly to the bandits, having received many favors from them. Franks gave them considerable money and the man and his wife agreed to care for McGinnis and not allow anyone to enter his room. Franks then went in the direction of Roswell and Carlsbad to a ranch in Eddy County that belonged to a Frenchman named Lusk who was taking care of some horses for the bandits. It was agreed that McGinnis would meet him at the ranch as soon as he was able to travel.

McGinnis remained with this family for about four weeks and received the best attention possible. Either the man or his wife was with him day and night and his wounds were kept clean and dressed every day. So far as McGinnis knew, no one suspected his being there. By the middle of August he had entirely recovered, so he decided to leave for the Lusk ranch. His Mexican friends cried on the day of McGinnis' departure, for they had tended him like one of the family. The robber showed the greatest appreciation and affection for both man and wife and presented each with a goodly sum of money with his thanks and a promise to come back and see them at some future day. His horse was in fine condition, and he left his benefactors at night, well equipped with rifle, pistols, and sufficient food to last until he reached his rendezvous with Franks.

Soon after the arrival of McGinnis at his ranch, Lusk became suspicious and notified M. Cicero Stewart, sheriff of Eddy County, of the two suspicious strangers at his place. Accordingly, on August 22, 1899, Sheriff Stewart, together with two deputies, J. D. Cantrell and Rufus Thomas, went with Lusk to arrest the two men. When they arrived, McGinnis was in the house, eating breakfast, while Franks was outside hunting their horses. A slight noise made by the posse while tying their horses to a wire fence alarmed McGinnis, who dashed out of the door to get his rifle from his saddle. Seeing Thomas approaching the house, he fired at the latter with his 45 Colt revolver, striking him in the shoulder. Observing the ranchman, Lusk, in the group, and being satisfied that he had turned informer, he aimed at him, wounding him in the wrist. By this time Lusk had gotten his rifle into action and fired a shot which struck the outlaw on the side of the head. As McGinnis was stunned, he was quickly disarmed, handcuffed, and tied on a horse. Meanwhile, Franks, who had watched these proceedings from a hill about a mile away, disappeared. He was never captured, but his partner was taken safely back to town. The Colfax County officials having been notified of the arrest, the sheriff and two deputies went to Carlsbad and escorted McGinnis to Raton.

On August 16, 1899, just six days before the arrest of McGinnis in Eddy County, Black Jack Ketchum staged the third holdup of the Colorado and Southern at Twin Mountain. However, the affair turned out rather disastrously for the lone bandit. Having picketed his horse near Twin Mountain, he had walked leisurely to Folsom, where he prepared for his audacious attempt to hold up a passenger train all by himself. No one knows what prompted him to such a foolhardy undertaking. There was only one chance in a thousand that he would succeed. Very likely his pride was pricked because the other members of the gang had discarded him and he wanted to show them that he could accomplish single-handed what it had taken three of them to do. He certainly did not lack nerve, even if his plans were foolhardy. As a matter of fact, he came very near succeeding. He was defeated by one factor which he had not foreseen. He stopped the train on a curve and this made it impossible for the trainmen to uncouple the express car quickly. The resulting loss of time was the direct cause of his downfall.

The same routine was followed as in the two previous holdups. Black Jack boarded the engine's tender at Folsom, and rode to Twin Mountain where he disappeared in the cab and compelled the engineer, Kirchgraber, to stop the train. The engineer and fireman were then marched back to the rear of the express car, and Scotty Drew, the express messenger, was forced to join them. Fred Bartlett, the mail clerk, stuck his head out of the door of the mail car to see what was going on. His curiosity, however, was quickly satisfied. Ketchum promptly sent a bullet through his jaw. The bandit accompanied his shot by yelling, "Get your damn head in there!" and Bartlett complied without delay. On reaching the rear of the express car, the three trainmen were ordered to uncouple it from the rest of the train. In vain they tugged and pulled at the couplings, which would not yield, owing to the train's being on a curve. "Hurry up or I'll kill every damn one of you," roared Black Jack.

Meanwhile, Conductor Harrington was preparing to take a hand in the affair. When the train had come to a stop, he walked to the platform of the car and got off. There was shooting up near the engine and he knew what that meant. His train was being held up again. It was the third time in two years and a second time within five weeks. He was getting tired of this holdup business, fearing the company might think he was in the play, as his train was always selected. Hurriedly, he got back into the car. He knew what the bandits were doing but he did not know how many there were in the party. Securing his double-barreled shotgun, he crawled through a small opening at the bottom of the partition between the smoking room and mail compartment, and pulled his shotgun after him. Harrington made his way to the front door and opened it slightly. The four men were only about ten feet away, all bunched together, so he was afraid to shoot for fear of hitting one of the crew. "Hurry, damn you," said the bandit, while the three men were making poor headway with the couplings. Drew stepped out of the line thus exposing Black Jack who was facing Harrington. "I wanted to hit the robber in the heart," said Harrington, "but in the dim light I misjudged. I had to be quick for I knew that when I opened the door

I would attract the attention of the robber who was facing me, so I aimed as well as I could under the circumstances. I raised my shotgun, opened the door, and fired." Immediately another shot was heard. Eleven buckshot entered Ketchum's right arm just above the elbow, as a bullet from his gun went through the left coat sleeve of Harrington's coat. "His buckshot jiggled my aim," said Black Jack later. "I'd have killed him if he'd waited a fraction of a second; I had a bead on his heart, but he jiggled my aim."

Struck by buckshot from Harrington's gun, Black Jack fell. He got up and crawled under the express car and disappeared in the darkness, trying to reach his horse. His right arm was terribly lacerated and he bled terribly.

Kirchgraber and his fireman returned to the engine, while Drew went to his car. The holdup was over. Sheriff Saturnino Pinard and a posse from Clayton found the outlaw three hundred yards from the track astride his rifle, dazed, his right arm riddled with buckshot, his body drained of blood. He made repeated attempts to mount his horse, but was too weak to do so. As the posse came up, he waved them down with his huge black hat. He was then taken to Trinidad, where his wounded arm was dressed. However, his identity was not known at first. When asked his name he replied, "Stevens." After some correspondence he was taken to Santa Fe and entered at the penitentiary, on August 24, 1899.

As no one could properly identify the prisoner, Sheriff Shields, of San Angelo, Texas, was asked to come to Santa Fe. On his arrival he was taken to Ketchum's cell. "Halloo, Tom," was the sheriff's greeting. "I haven't seen you for some time. Where have you been keeping yourself?" The name of Stevens was no longer used. While Shields was in Santa Fe, Black Jack talked freely with him and told him of many things in which he had been engaged. As soon as it became generally known that Black Jack had been captured, the entire West breathed more freely. The press of the country applauded Conductor Harrington for his courage and two rewards of $1,000 each were paid to Harrington, one by the United States government and one by Wells Fargo Express Company. Several other rewards aggregating $3,000, were never paid. One important matter had been finally settled, and Black Jack's career of crime was ended.

Shortly after Tom Ketchum's arrival at the penitentiary, his wounded arm began to bother him considerably. Dr. Miguel F. Desmarais, of the penitentiary staff, called me on the telephone, saying that gangrene had set in, and requesting that I would speak to Ketchum about the necessity of having it amputated. I drove out and had a talk with Tom, who agreed very readily to do as I advised. The arm was taken off at the shoulder. He recovered rapidly and began putting on flesh. He was an amiable prisoner, usually in a good humor. When Sheriff Stewart visited him in October, 1899, Tom said: "I am getting so fat that when they hang me they can eat me." The warden found in his cell a steel saw and a wooden pistol covered with tin foil. He was evidently preparing to attempt an escape from the penitentiary. The newspapers some times worried him. Thus when he read in the *New Mexican* that the Boers[3] had held up a train and taken two million five hundred thousand dollars in English gold, he wept.

3. The Dutch in South Africa (see note 3, p. 301).

I took my son out to see Ketchum and they became great pals. Tom was very fond of peanuts and Miguel would bring him a sack whenever he visited him, which was quite often. One day Miguel told Tom he was going to beg his father to pardon him and he kept after me every day, saying, "Papa, Tom is an awfully good friend of mine, and I wish you would pardon him, as he promised me that he would be good and settle down."

One day Tom's oldest brother, Berry Ketchum, came to visit him but Tom declined to see him. He said, "Berry is my good brother. He is a Christian and belongs to the church. I will tell you how it all happened. He showed both Sam and me how to hold up a train. The three of us held up a train in Texas and secured about $100,000 in cash. Berry was the oldest, so he took the money and became a real Christian gentleman, and Sam and I had to rustle for a living. Once in a while, he would give us a horse and a few dollars but, believe me, the dollars were very few. He had taught us just how to hold up trains and get the money, so we kept it up. He worried every time we visited him, fearing we might give him away, but we never did. No, I do not wish to see him." Berry came over to see me and seemed to be a quiet and pleasant gentleman. He said Sam and Tom were always wild and would not follow his advice to settle down and go to farming. He said he had promised to give each of them a good farm if they would work it, but they declined. Berry went back to the penitentiary and left some money with the warden to buy Tom what he wanted, such as peanuts, candy, cakes, and pies, as he was very fond of sweets. At the same time, he asked the warden not to tell Tom what he had done. Berry returned to San Angelo without seeing his brother, but he visited Sam's grave and placed some flowers and a wreath on it. I felt sorry for Berry, as he appeared to be quite disappointed.

One day Doctor Sloan called at my office and asked if he might see Tom Ketchum and have a talk with him. Accordingly, I telephoned the necessary permission to Mr. James, the assistant warden. It seems that the doctor had been told of a buried treasure near San Angelo, Texas, where Sam and Tom had cached a considerable sum of money. Tom told the doctor a great story, drawing a map and locating the exact spot. Sloan did not tell any one, not even me, but he took a friend with him and, together, they drove to San Angelo and remained there several days looking for the place, but without success. On his return the doctor told me of his trip and his failure to find a fortune. Tom appeared to be disappointed over the doctor's failure and told him, "If I could go with you, I could show you the place in a minute." The doctor believed Tom and got up a great plan for me to allow him to take a large guard with him, with a promise to return Tom to the penitentiary, but I knocked all his plans into a cocked-hat and told him no, not even if the cache contained millions.

Sheriff Saturnino Pinard brought Black Jack's rifle to Santa Fe and presented it to me. I presented it to Colonel Theodore Roosevelt[4] who was greatly pleased, especially when I told him that Ketchum wanted him to have it.

While the notorious train robber was waiting trial, public opinion all over the Southwest was greatly aroused as to the disposition of him. Arizona wanted to try him for the murder of Rogers and Wingate at Camp Verde,

4. (1858–1919); at this time, leader of the volunteer cavalry regiment the Rough Riders; U.S. president 1901–09.

and made a requisition on New Mexico for him. They said, "Hand him over to us and we will see that he will trouble the frontier no longer." However, I refused to honor the requisition, telling the Arizona officers, "We'll attend to Black Jack ourselves."

He was tried at the regular September term of the district court sitting in Union County, in 1899. The indictment was for holding up a railway train with intent to rob it, which offense, according to territorial law, was punishable with death. Chief Justice Mills presided at the trial, while Jeremiah Leahy, of Raton, was the district attorney in charge of the prosecution. The latter was a splendid lawyer. He was absolutely fearless and was very successful in securing convictions. The court appointed William B. Bunker, a well-known attorney of Las Vegas, to conduct the defense.

Tom Ketchum made a very striking appearance at his trial. He was a tall, handsome man and stood as straight as an Indian warrior. His black hair was brushed back from his forehead and his face was clean-shaven except for a heavy, well-trimmed mustache. His eyes, which resembled black coals of fire, were piercing and radiant. He was neatly dressed, the end of his empty coat sleeve being tucked into a side pocket. His confinement had bleached and softened his usually rough and sunburned features. He stood calmly in the crowded court room, his eyes resting now on the judge, then wandering over the faces of the strange audience gathered to see the leader of the worst gang of outlaws the Southwest had ever known. It was the first time in his life that he had ever been hailed before a high court of justice. Unaccustomed as he was to such surroundings, he showed no signs of nervousness and seemed quite indifferent to what was taking place.

The imperturbable district attorney read the indictment and asked for the death penalty. The defendant's plea of "not guilty" was almost inaudible. Leahy put Kirchgraber, Harrington, and Drew in the witness box, and they testified that the man before them was the one who had held up their train at Twin Mountain on the night of August 16. Drew, the express messenger, was relating what happened when his train came to a stop on the fateful night.

"You say the prisoner pounded on the door of your car and commanded you to open it?" asked Leahy.

"Yes, sir."

"Well, what did he say to you?"

"He said, pointing his gun at me, 'Fall out of there damn quick!'"

"And what did you do?"

"I fell out damn quick. What would you have done, Mr. Leahy?"

"Is that true, Tom?" asked Bunker.

"You bet your goddamn life it's true and he didn't lose any time either."

The court suppressed the ripples of laughter that followed these remarks by Ketchum.

Bunker used his talents well but the testimony of the witnesses was very convincing and the summary by the district attorney was very damaging. The jury deliberated only a few minutes. When their verdict of guilty, which carried a death sentence, was read, the crowded court room was so quiet that a pin dropped on the floor could have been heard. However, Black Jack showed no emotion. He merely crossed his legs and gazed out of the open window. When Judge Mills asked him if he had anything to say, he promptly replied, "I'd like to shave the district attorney." The sentence of the court was that he be hanged in Clayton on October 4, 1900. Closely guarded, he was returned to the penitentiary in Santa Fe for safe keeping. For more than a year the attorneys wrangled on appeal. I ordered a stay of execution and set the day for the execution April 26, 1901.

\* \* \*

1940

# FRANCISCO GONZALO "PACHÍN" MARÍN
## 1863–1897

Francisco Gonzalo Marín—best-known by his nickname, "Pachín Marín"—is considered one of the "pilgrims of freedom." (Introduced by Félix Ojeda Reyes in his 1992 book, *Peregrinos de la libertad*, this term is used widely by scholars to identify nineteenth-century Puerto Rican separatist émigrés who had to endure multiple exiles in different countries because of their involvement in the Puerto Rican and Cuban liberation struggles against Spain. Among the other pilgrims are Rámon Emeterio Betances, Eugenio María de Hostos, Lola Rodríguez de Tío, and Sotero Figueroa.) Marín's brief life cannot be separated from his political ideals. Born in Arecibo, Puerto Rico, he is known mainly for his patriotic poems, revolutionary convictions, and bohemian lifestyle. He was also an eloquent orator, a dedicated journalist-typographer, and an accomplished musician.

In 1887, Marín founded the newspaper *El Postillón* to promote the ideal of political autonomy for the island. He was one of several print journalists forced into exile during the infamous period of *Compontes*, repressive measures implemented by the island's Spanish governor. For Marín, it was the beginning of a long pilgrimage away from his homeland and to the Dominican Republic, Curaçao, Venezuela, Martinique, and Saint Thomas. He returned to Puerto Rico in 1890 and continued to publish *El Postillón*, but in less than a year he was again forced into exile.

For his second exile, Marín chose New York, one of several U.S. cities where nineteenth-century Antillean separatist émigrés had concentrated. In New York, he became friends with the Cuban-independence leader José Martí. Marín joined Martí and other independence supporters in the founding of the Partido Revolucionario Cubano (Cuban Revolutionary Party), or PRC, in 1892, and he was elected secretary of the Club Borinquen, a club started by Puerto Rican separatists affiliated with the PRC, among them Sotero Figueroa and Arthur A. Schomburg (aka Arturo Alfonso Schomburg). He also revived *El Postillón*, turning it into an important voice for the faction of the separatist movement that supported liberation of the islands from Spain but not their annexation by the United States. In 1893, Marín moved to Haiti, where he managed a hotel and continued to support the Antillean revolutionary cause.

He returned to New York in 1895 and several months later was shaken by the news of the death of his brother Wenceslao, who, like Martí, had gone to Cuba to join rebel forces fighting in the second Cuban war of independence (1895–98) and was killed on the battlefield. Like many of the Antillean separatists, both of the Marín brothers had shared the conviction that a victory for Cuban independence would also bring freedom to Puerto Rico. The deaths of his close friend and his brother influenced Marín's decision to join the revolutionary army. In the summer of 1896, he left New York for Cuba and joined the rebel troops fighting in the jungle. There, he contracted malaria, which caused his death less than a year and a half after his arrival.

Influenced by the Spanish Romantic poet Gustavo Adolfo Bécquer, Marín often wrote about love, motherland, and death. His intertwining of lyrical Romanticism with strong revolutionary convictions makes him one of the most radical Puerto Rican voices of the period. The Marín poem that appears in this anthology, "The Rag"—a translation of the sonnet "El trapo," which appeared in his posthumous collection *En la arena* (On the Sand, 1898)—argues that only through the bloodshed of battle against Spanish tyrannical rule will the island find the dignity of freedom.

In addition to his own newspaper, Marín wrote for several other New York Spanish-language newspapers, including *La Gaceta del Pueblo* and *Patria*. Most of his articles await compilation and further study. This anthology's selection "New York from Within: One Aspect of Its Bohemian Life," published in *La Gaceta* in 1892, is considered an important antecedent to the work of subsequent generations of Puerto Rican writers in the city.

## New York from Within: One Aspect of Its Bohemian Life[1]

If you present yourself in this metropolis in the enviable guise of a tourist, and bring, as it is customary, suitcases stuffed with Mexican *soles*[2] or shimmering gold doubloons, things will naturally go very well for you, my amiable reader. But you will not have known New York from within, as it really is, with its grand institutions and prodigious marvels.

To attain an intimate knowledge of this elephant of modern civilization, you will need to set foot to the ground without a quarter to your name, though you may bring a world of hope in your heart.

Indeed! To arrive in New York, check into a comfortable hotel, go out in an elegant carriage pulled by monumental horses every time an occasion presents itself, visit the theaters, museums, *cafés chantants*,[3] cruise the fast-flowing East River, lulled by the ebb and flow and murmur of the waves, visit Brooklyn Bridge—that frenzy of North American initiative—and the Statue of Liberty—that tour de force of French pride—pay twenty dollars or more to hear La Pattissi sing, as she is doing now, at the Metropolitan Opera House, frequent, in short, the places where elegant people of good taste gather, people who can afford to spend three or four hundred dollars in one evening for the sole pleasure of looking at a dancer's legs, oh!, all that is very agreeable, very delicious, and very . . . singular; but it doesn't give you the exact measure of this city which is, at one and the same time, an emporium of sweeping riches and rendezvous-point for all the penniless souls of America.

The convenient—if you prefer, the reasonable—thing to do, is for you to present yourself at one of the vast New York docks without even a semblance of resources; ready and agile as a student and as hungry as a schoolteacher.

1. Translated by Lizabeth Paravasini-Gebert.
2. Coins, although Mexican coins are called *pesos*. *Soles* are Peruvian.

3. Musical cafés (French); intimate cabarets offering musical entertainment.

You have already realized your most cherished dream; you are overjoyed because since childhood your happiness has centered on great voyages . . . What! You don't speak any English? Are you overwhelmed by the incessant howling of the locomotives, the vertiginous agitation of the factories, and the vista of a million people hurrying past, trampling each other, yet going on their way as if nothing had happened? Well, don't you stop. Let's walk, walk! Here in New York time is sacred, since it is the most genuine representation of money. Don't stand there in perplexed contemplation of an eleven- or twelve-story building whose highest windows seem to look down on you as if mocking your smallness. Time is urgent. Walk hurriedly, as if you had most important business at hand. One must find a friend, a friend or countryman, at all cost. Where? How? Don't you know how? Well, by asking everyone. Come on; try it out on that gigantic policeman looking at you so tenaciously. Throw care to the wind and plunge in. Gentleman, would you be so kind as to point out where I can find a friend . . . How stupid of me! Now I get it, this man can't speak any Spanish . . . You're beginning to grow sad. You see no familiar faces. My God! you exclaim. I'm a wretch! Some identical incidents read in novels dart past your imagination with the speed of lightning. Jean Valjean, Jean Valjean[4] . . . If the same thing that happened to Jean Valjean were to happen to you . . .

If there is a civilized country capable of astonishing the most indifferent and stoic, the United States, or better yet, New York, is the place.

Its buildings, its portentous architectural works, its elevated railways fantastically crisscrossing through the air, its streets—broad arteries roamed by inexhaustible hordes from all countries of the world—its parks—austerely and aristocratically designed—its steam engines, its powerful journalistic institutions, its treacherously beautiful women, its wonders, all instill, at first sight, a deep malaise in the foreigner, because it occurs to one that these large cities, deafening in their progress, are like the mouth of a horrible monster constantly busy simultaneously swallowing and vomiting human beings; and it is amidst these great noises and grand centers that our soul finds itself increasingly besieged by that horrendous malady called sadness, and assumes the somber character of isolation and silence . . .

For the poor in money but rich in ambition, arriving here in the circumstances outlined above, however, New York is a great house of asylum where all who believe, more or less vigorously, in the virtue and sanctity of work, ultimately find their niche.

Are you very poor? Have you not succeeded yet in finding something in which to invest your talents and energies? Are you feeling the sting of hunger? Are you cold?

Don't distress yourself. Don't despair in any way. Do you see that establishment on the corner whose door continuously opens and closes? Well, it is commonly known here by the name of Lager Beer Hall. Have you been inside? Such cleanliness and tidiness everywhere! Isn't it true that places like these are better decorated than the presidential palaces of our republics? But

---

4. The protagonist of the novel *Les misérables* (The Miserable Ones, 1862), by the French writer Victor Hugo (1802–1885). Desperately poor and living in a period of economic devastation, Valjean steals bread and is pursued for two decades by a dogged policeman, Javert.

we shouldn't waste time in useless ramblings, not even in here. Take that table nearby; throw five cents on it; it's a tip in advance; don't go believing anything else. Pay attention now. In the first place, they bring you a big mug of beer, fresh, foamy, poured on smooth glass. Drink it. In this country, beer is a necessity; it fortifies and warms limbs numbed by the cold. But . . . don't be a fool! Take care. Let us, before draining the contents of the glass, eat ham, beef, sausage, cheese, etc. That stuff you gobble down for starters. At least that's what gastronomy calls it. Well! Good heavens! But principles be gone! You must eat it all. Here comes the waiter; this time he's bringing you a succulent soup preceded by its wafting aromas. Eat until you've had your fill: I am your host, you honorable Maecenas . . .[5]

Are you pleased? Yes? Let's not waste time, then, take a toothpick, light this cigarette I'm offering you and . . . onto the street.

"But, sir, didn't you offer to pay the check? We can't leave without paying . . . I am an honest man . . ."

"Come now, blockhead. The sum of what you have gobbled down amounts to five cents. You have already paid . . ."

And after leaving the place, satiated and proud of our find, forgetting the novelistic tortures that made Jean Valjean suffer from such acute hunger, then we recall the real New York, the wise and good New York, hospitable and gay; and we laugh our heads off at the admirers of the Brooklyn Bridge and the Statue of Liberty, of the elevated railway and gigantic buildings, of all the great institutions of this surprising republic, since, never fear, I doubt that there is in this country of inventions and colossal enterprises anything as grand, as portentous, as human as those establishments where for five coppers they feed the hungry and give drink to the thirsty.

Ample reason has my philosopher friend, who, every day, upon returning from heaven-knows-where with an enormous toothpick in his hand, says to me:

"Oh! A Lager Beer Hall is indeed an institution."

1892

## The Rag[1]

When a country does not have a flag,
a free flag to raise proudly,
pursuing its sovereign right
and patriotism, the gentle chimera,

if in the achievement of its entire glory it lacks                    5
the strength of combat against the tyrant,
the proud dignity of the citizen,
or the instinctive bravery of the beast;

---

5. An ancient Roman statesman and patron of literature; his name now stands for a patron of the arts, especially of literature.
1. Translated by Barry Luby.

with enormous faith and singular bravery,
let it throw itself into the field of fecund honor,                    10
take a rag, at random, pale or red,

and on staining it with blood the furious soul,
the miserable cloth will be seen transformed
into a rag that astonishes the whole world.

1898

# FABIO FIALLO
## 1866–1942

Fabio Fiallo was one of the great late-Romantic poets of the Dominican Republic. Influenced by European Romantics such as Gustavo Adolfo Bécquer, Heinrich Heine, and Alfred de Musset, he in turn influenced a generation of Dominican poets, many of whom migrated to the United States in the 1960s.

Born in Santo Domingo, the capital of and largest city in the Dominican Republic, Fiallo worked as a teacher and journalist. Several of his articles condemning the U.S. invasion of the Dominican Republic in 1916, as well as several of his patriotic poems (now lost), resulted in a jail term. He served as a diplomat in New York, Hamburg, and Havana, where he died. Though some of Fiallo's work was translated into English in the 1930s and 1940s, he is consistently overlooked in the United States and England.

Fiallo came of age during the *Modernista* period and wrote short stories in the *Modernista* mode—stylistically precise, about exotic and bizarre characters with elitist tastes—some of which were collected in the book *Cuentos frágiles* (Fragile Stories, 1908). However, he resisted the movement's imagism.

His brief, beautiful, subversive lyric poems carry on the Romantic tradition of strong kinship to Nature. The poems' focus on deep feelings of love and spirituality is often marked by a speaker's sweetness and sentimentality, but just as often that speaker's undermining of religious hypocrisy verges on the sacrilegious. In "Golgotha Rose," for example, one of the three Fiallo poems that follow, the speaker indicates a kinship with the artist who created a necklace of Christ and perhaps invested profane feelings in this sacred work. The necklace hangs between the breasts of the speaker's mistress. Unable to focus on the sacred nature of the image, the speaker concentrates on the sexual feelings it invokes and the immanence of sexuality in art. Linking the sacred and the profane, he suggests that Christ's martyrdom was in some ways sexual. In Spanish, the final two stanzas are directed to the golden image of Christ in the familiar form of the pronoun *you* (*tú*).

"Plenilunio," the earliest of the three selections, is in the tradition of Rubén Darío, a leader of the *Modernista* movement. It establishes a connection between love and Nature, as the poet's emotions are a reflection of the movements of the moon and of a nightingale. "Profane Rhyme" echoes Darío's *Prosas profanas* (Profane Prose), suggesting that music is a sublime intonation of the soul.

# Plenilunio[1]

Through the green grove of poplars
    we went, she and I:
the moon rose past the hills,
in the brush sang the nightingale.

And I said . . . I don't know what I said,        5
    in my trembling voice . . .
In the ether the moon paused,
the nightingale broke its song
and this genteel loved one, anxious and mute
    beseeched the sky.        10

Do you know about those mysterious questions
    that form an answer? . . .
Guard, oh moon, the secret of my soul!
    Keep it silent, nightingale!

1898        1902

# Golgotha Rose[1]

A Christ hangs from a loved one's neck,
a gold pendant of the engraver's genius,
and this Christ, in his agony, seems
happy with life as he expires.

In his sweet, dying eyes        5
He conveys such earthly delight,
and I wonder if this genial artist
gave his Christ the spirit of Don Juan.

The equivocal tilt of the forehead,
the curious, knowing look,        10
the lip that intends—if this is anguish,
it's a sensual shudder, too.

Oh, little Christ on your Cross,
let me die in your place
above the temptation of a Calvary        15
formed by the twin peaks of a rose bush.

Give your post to me, lest my hand,
in a fit of sudden passion

---

1. Translated by Harold Augenbraum. *Plenilunio*: under a full moon.
1. Translated by Constantine Contogenis and Harold Augenbraum. *Golgotha*: Like Calvary (below), an English-language, Western Christian name for the site of Jesus' crucifixion.

forces your face to heaven and changes
the oblique direction of your gaze.                    20

1910


### Profane Rhyme[1]

The white girl I adore
carries her prayer to the temple
and, the way pianos intone, the floor
groans beneath the golden bore
of her upturned heel.                                    5

Suggestive and elegant, above
she plays with just one glove
and this time I felt in my soul
jealous of the other's favored role.

Some people lack wine,                                  10
others lack bread.
Woe is me, I lack only
a dinner companion!

1910

1. Translated by Harold Augenbraum.

---

# JOSÉ ESCOBAR
## dates unknown

Of the newspaper writers, editors, and critics in the nineteenth-century Southwest, José Escobar was one of the most peripatetic. His journalistic and literary writing reveals a familiarity with European arts and culture and an impressive understanding of the literary arts of Mexico and Latin America. Thanks to the literary detective work of the critics Doris Meyer and A. Gabriel Meléndez, we now know that Escobar's transformation from a voice reliant on Mexican- and Latin American–tinged literary influences to a vocal supporter of the burgeoning literary climate in New Mexico was crucial in the development of the Latino literary tradition in the Southwest.

In the 1970s, Meyer "rediscovered" Escobar and his writings when she combed through hundreds of newspapers in archives in Texas, New Mexico, and Arizona. Based on information culled from his poetry, Meyer speculates that Escobar was born and educated in Zacatecas, Mexico, and became a political exile from the repressive regime of the Mexican dictator Porfirio Díaz. In the late 1880s, Escobar arrived in the New Mexican territory. He briefly worked at the Albuquerque newspaper *El Defensor del Pueblo*, but left after a few months to found his own newspaper, *El Combate*. As a journalist and editorial writer, he often used pen names such as "Zig-Zag" and "Popé." The evidence of a final poem suggests that after about a decade in the United States, where he rarely edited or wrote for a single newspaper for more than a few months at a time, he returned to Mexico, after which his trail is lost.

Escobar published two types of poems that survive. His lyrical work, written very much according to the custom of the time, focused on beautiful women ("Bird arriving from afar / come and tell me if you saw / that little girl sighing sadly / or if she was happy and lovely as ever"); exile and longing for his homeland ("From the distant and foreign soil / where my pain finds no rest"); and politics ("Keep on shouting; there must be / Pain for genius to shine"). He also produced a series of poems on the history of New Mexico, which seems to have fascinated him more the longer he lived there. In these poems, purportedly by "El Cantor del Popé" (The Bard of Popé), Escobar dons a literary-historical costume to focus on themes similar to those he would explore in his essays, particularly the cultural independence and traditions of New Mexico.

Escobar also revealed this historical interest through essays such as "Progreso literario en Nuevo Mexico," published in *Las Dos Repúblicas* in 1896 and translated here as "Literary Progress in New Mexico." This piece represents one of the first public attempts to construct a New Mexican literary tradition. Bringing together historical precedents and contemporaneous examples, Escobar argues that New Mexico has had a rich, important literary past and has a bright future. His optimism would later be borne out by late-twentieth-century discoveries of much of the poetry and prose that appeared in New Mexican newspapers and from the several related presses in the territory.

## Literary Progress in New Mexico[1]

In our article today we will focus on something truly satisfying: literary progress in the neighboring territory of New Mexico. Our main thought is to breath life into those who fight so zealously in that sacred literary struggle; our wish and hope is that this tiny handful of bright talent persevere in its good work and in the end will be able to overcome the huge obstacles and thorny barriers frequently accompanied by envy—and not rarely by ignorance—and that, like the symbol of the condor, they might rise above the earth's mire to find in the azure mantle of the heavens a worthy place to practice the majesty of their flight.

The efforts of Rev. José A. Martínez, the parish priest of Taos, to initiate the study of letters and public education in New Mexican soil turned out to be entirely sterile. The popular masses were, in those days, beset by distinct circumstances. A complete ignorance enveloped the locals who, removed from great urban centers and lost in the immense sands of a desert that stretched from Missouri to the banks of the Rio Bravo del Norte, could but struggle from day to day to defend their lives and household against the onslaughts of barbarous savages who, with blood and fire, so often devastated the burgeoning colonies of these civilized Creoles. Public education was totally abandoned and the efforts of several illustrious citizens, to which were added from time to time the efforts of the central government

1. Translated by Harold Augenbraum.

and the local territorial government, were, as we said at the beginning, entirely sterile.

A few years passed, when suddenly a complete change took place on that soil. With the arrival of French clergy and under the liberal laws of a U.S. government, academies, institutes and public schools were born, and since that time, in Catholic establishments and lay schools one has seen our youth, thirsty for knowledge, leave their isolated towns for those institutions to drink the blessed and sweet water from those beautiful fountains, with extraordinary desire, and need little time to bring forth the fruits of the bright intelligence of New Mexicans—possessors for the most part of a magnificent, natural aptitude.

Today's travelers, who pass in their comfortable sleeping carriages through the high ranges, fertile valleys, and broad plains of this territory, cannot appreciate in any way the favorable change that the genie of progress has wrought in this soil, but whoever familiarizes himself with the history of this heroic and hospitable country will but admire the energy of both the native and the immigrant, who, by means of consistent hard work, have in the end made from those formerly rude sands such cities of importance as Albuquerque, Las Vegas, and Santa Fe.

Changes in the literary field, despite the short period of time between then and now: In the press, newspapers rise up every day and if at times they disappear soon thereafter, they always leave in their wake something akin to the remnants of light from a setting sun, or the fragrance escaping from a censer that dissipates in white eddies in the high vault of a temple: light and fragrance, which serve to illuminate the community's path and perfume the ideals of its freedoms and rights. If it is true that the field of journalism of the neighboring territory has had several publications of such ephemeral existence, it is also true that there exist accredited organs that number many years of life. Among those that stand out are *La Revista Católica*, *La Voz del Pueblo*, *El Nuevo Mexicano*, *El Boletin Popular* and many others we cannot remember at the moment in which one can always see tendencies of social improvement. The press itself, in recent years, has improved in a notable way, and in its editorials and bulletins one can already see something of the embryonic style of a burgeoning press: logical and just arguments that fight not only for their own, but for something much grander still, the improvement of the masses, without regard to differences of religion or political belief. This is the true mission of an honorable press, and for that reason we feel a justifiable and legitimate pride in sending our affectionate greetings to the faithful defenders of the New Mexican people.

Just as in the press, in the literary circles of that fertile soil a radical change has occurred. Today, both in cities and small towns, literary and debating societies exist in which young people at various times try out the poetic inspiration of the bard, the eminent judgment of the historian, or even the incisive metaphor of the critic or the difficult conception of the novel of manners or a meaningful national romance, all this without plagiarism, without speciousness, without ideas purloined from foreign authors, and one finds in every type of this burgeoning literature a special hue, something truly *sui generis*, that, as in South American poetry, gives it a tinge of the most beautiful originality, filled with delicacy and good taste.

In recent years, such distinguished authors as the Most Reverend Archbishop J.B. Salpointe, the learned archaeologist Adolfo Bandelier, and the priest J. Defouri have taken up the task of writing the history of the Church in New Mexico. And talents as brilliant as the young attorney E. Chacón[2] have dutifully undertaken the writing of the first historical studies in Spanish. The compassionate doctor F.A. Marrón and the astute legal professor Octaviano Larrazolo have, in this respect, written brilliant oratorical pieces, which we have read at length, with real satisfaction.

If in the realm of history several successful attempts have already been made, the divine art of poetry and the difficult genre of the national novel have not yet followed suit. In the former not only have the imaginations of several local poets and those of Cuban bards come together to sing of natural wonders and popular epics, through heartfelt romances full of sentiment and, not infrequently, exalted philosophical ideas, but also the brilliant talents of young native women who write under a pseudonym in order to submit to the press their poetic compositions in which they bring out the purity of their feelings and their souls, as they bring out the immanence of a flower, the splendid rainbow of its colors and the aromatic essences of its perfume.

E. Chacón was the first. Two or three years ago, he gave the public a small book that contained two separate novels, the former in the genre of fantasy, the latter in a realistic style. In the first book, *The Son of the Storm*, one certainly notes the author's relaxed style and astoundingly fertile imagination. As for the second, one can see after reading just a few pages the beauty of a superior talent that from early on observes and reasons. There are events in that volume worthy of the pens of Valera or Father Coloma. As with their works, the young literatus' talent is surprising: at times sarcastic and burlesque, at others elevated, philosophical, or highly moral. In sum, Chacón's little book, though unknown among most locals, is a true jewel in our national literature.

By a happy chance and with thanks to its author, the small book called *Vicente Silva and His Forty Thieves, Their Crimes and Retribution* has dropped into our hands. A better pen than ours will occupy itself with writing a thoughtful critique of that work, so we will do nothing more than make public the impression that we are experiencing in reading such an interesting booklet.

The book just written by the attorney Baca is, in our opinion, the first to bring together all the exigencies and rules of the novel of manners, with the uniqueness of having been written in a particularly national style. The real history of the events themselves have been transferred to these pages with total purity; the plot is so interesting and so expertly woven by the author's expertise that, having read the first few pages, one feels compelled to read, read, and read, until one finishes those pages in which, in addition to good taste and simplicity of style, there is an important moral and educational object for young people.

The author set down the situation with great assurance. With a magisterial hand, he traced the repulsive scenes of crimes that left such a great

2. Eusebio Chacón (see p. 333).

impression on the society of those lowlands, and with a truly masterful pen he copied the differing characters of those personages in a novel full of moving, dramatic incidents, which is why we believe that this work will be received favorably by the entire population of the territory in which Vicente Silva, like the famous Italian bandit Luigi Vampa,[3] ended up making himself so unfortunately famous, by his evil crimes and terrifying audacity.

In conclusion, Baca's book will pass into posterity, with a great deal to offer criminologists and those who pursue the improbable task of physiological dissection of the human heart . . . ! Meanwhile, we wish Baca our warmest and well-deserved congratulations on this literary work of true social usefulness. We hope that his example will stimulate local youth to doings of this sort so we might sweep away the unjust charges and unfair calumny of those turistas who, without knowing us any more than from an express train, charge us with of a lack of culture and an absolute paucity of talent.

Youth of New Mexico, the field is yours! Cultivate your noble ambition to learn! Persevere in your noble struggle, and the laurels of glory and triumph will in the end adorn your high brows. Paladins of ideas, rise up! Apostles of your people, onward!

July 11, 1896

3. Leader of a gang of criminals in the novel *Le comte de Monte-Cristo* (The Count of Monte Cristo, 1844–46), by the French writer Alexandre Dumas (1802–1870). *Vicente Silva*: notorious New Mexican outlaw of the late nineteenth century.

---

# JESSE PÉREZ
## 1870–1927

In 1934, the literary historian J. Frank Dobie discovered memoirs written in the early 1920s, replete with phonetic spelling, by Jesse Pérez. Tapping out his story on an old typewriter, Pérez had chronicled an uncommon life: He was a Mexican American and a Texas Ranger at a time when the Tejano population and *los rinches*, as the Rangers were called, coexisted uneasily.

Pérez notes that he was born in Atascoso County, in south-central Texas. He attended Saint Mary's College, but left to help support his family by hauling coal from Somerset to San Antonio. When the coal mine was exhausted, the sheriff of Bexar County appointed him deputy sheriff, thus initiating his career in law enforcement.

The anecdotes Pérez relates, surrounded by both venial and mortal violence, are often hilarious because of his off-handed manner. However, in his study *My History, Not Yours: The Formation of Mexican-American Autobiography* (1993), the critic Genaro Padilla discusses the anti–Mexican American racism that Pérez displays in his narrative. Living "in a power network from which Mexicanos had been excluded," he explains, Pérez was "largely alienated . . . from his own community."

## FROM MEMOIRS

* * * One day after that wee went to a dance and it was a bunch of boys there by the name of Gusman the was 5 brothers and they was bad out fit the use to go to a dance and at any-time that they wanted to leave the dance they pick up a rowed and get into a fight and brook up the dance. we was there that night at the dance when they gat in a big fight and brook up the dance and whipp a copple of boys puty bad of cause they didnt know us and we was not bodying by them at all after the fight the other boys was telling us that them Gusman boys was awful mean that they do that every time they go to a dance when ever they get ready to leave the dance they pick up a fight and brook up the dance a go one of them came and asked me if I didn't like it I told him I didnt had any-thing to do with it if I would told John and Emet Coy we would had some fun that night but I never told them any thing we came next Saturday and dose fellow had another fight and brook up the dance again that night John come near getting in trouble with one of them on account of a girl that was talking to John true a window but John told this Girl that he was going to make a dance next Sunday so that night those boys brook up the dance that night we went back to the honey ranch and John was talking about that putty girl and what he was going to do with Gusmans out-fit if they intafer with him and his girl. me and Emett knew very well what was going to happing at that dance them Gusmans was going to saddle the rong horse when ever they Jump on John Coy.

so wee went to the dance Old men Bill Butler say to us when we left the house bee care-ful boys dont get into no rows John answere no Mr Butler is no danger. so we left to the dance the house where the dance was was school house only one room they had to bige Lanters one on each Conner of the house it was little after Midnight when them boys commence to start trouble and they had to started with us because we made the dance John came to me and Emett and told us for me to stay close to one of the lamp and Emett neer the other so when dose fellows start any-thing each of you Just blow the lamps and I do the rest. well I went and stand by the lamp and Emitt done the same he was close the other lamp the oldest one of the Gusman drow a quart and the fight comence me and Emett blow the lights out and the shooting commence in the dark after the fight that bige Gusman boy was hanging true a winder he was shot in the arm and true the belley screaming like a callote and his brother was shot true the hip only he rage his but true the brush when every-thing was over and the law came we hide our guns and stay there and swear that them Gusman must a shot each other because the fight commence right in the middle of the hall and we couldn't see any-thing because was dark John says I push and old lady and two Girls true a window and then drag myself out then they asked me what did you see Perez. I didnt see nothing I push every-body that was on my way to get out I didnt care he was going to stay in side. * * *

early 1920s                                                                 ca. 1934

# JULIO G. ARCE aka JORGE ULICA
## 1870–1926

Early Latino prose is rarely funny. By the late nineteenth and early twentieth centuries, however, Latino theater was full of comic interludes. By the second and third decades of the twentieth century, Latino prose writers such as Julio G. Arce, who published under the pen name "Jorge Ulica," had begun to find a comic sensibility. Their humorous takes on everyday life may have been inspired by skits performed before or after theatrical productions, by Mexican and Latin American newspaper *crónicas* (lightly satirical feature chronicles), and by similar columns in Anglo publications such as *The Smart Set* and *Vanity Fair*. Arce's dispatches might be compared to the writings of modern humorists such as Art Buchwald, Fran Lebowitz, and Dave Barry.

Their author was born in Guadalajara, Jalisco, Mexico. His father was a prominent surgeon. At age 14, Arce founded a student newspaper, *El Hijo del Progreso*. Later, as a pharmacology student, he founded *El Amigo del Pueblo*. After he completed his studies, Arce and a friend opened a drugstore in Mazatlán, Sinaloa, Mexico, where Arce edited and contributed articles to various newspapers and founded the literary review *Bohemia Sinaloense*. He later moved to Culiacán, Sinaloa, where he married and worked on the local government's newspaper, *El Occidental*.

In 1909, he became editor of the influential newspaper *El Diario del Pacifico*, which he used to espouse counterrevolutionary ideas. As a result, he was jailed for several months and eventually was forced to flee the area. In October 1915, fearing for his life as a result of his political activities, Arce moved with his second wife and five children to San Francisco, where he began to write for the newspaper *La Crónica*. He soon became its editor and, with the name changed to *Hispano-América*, its proprietor. There, from 1916 until his death, he produced the *Crónicas diabólicas* (Diabolical Tales), brief sketches of life in the United States, set against the backdrop of the Latino community of San Francisco.

The *Crónicas diabólicas* belong to the Mexican tradition of *costumbristas*, or chronicles of daily life. Perhaps because Arce was already middle-aged when he arrived in the United States, his satire conveys affection for the community but with a tone of the outsider. Arce often portrays the fictional Ulica in odd predicaments as a Latino who does not feel himself to be fully a member of the oppressed minority. In one instance, Ulica receives a phone call from someone who asks if he is the "inclito [illustrious] defender of the race," an epithet to which he reluctantly accedes. In another, he attends a Spanish class, only to find a proud group of students butchering the language under the tutelage of a "false Iberian." Because of their light tone and their appearance as newspaper columns surrounded by advertisements, the *Crónicas* have not always been seen as literature. However, because they convey significant aspects of the Latino culture in which they were written, the *Crónicas* are part of the Latino literary tradition.

# The Spanish Plague[1]

You realize, my dear, dear readers, that comes this way influenza of the highest caliber, gigantic, monstrous, capable of finishing us all off if we're not careful, law-abiding and prudent people.

---

1. Translated by Harold Augenbraum.

It is, undoubtedly, the most evil thing imaginable, but it's even more evil than influenza itself. It's bad *influence*, and it's called "Spanish." It's screwing everything up!

On the matter of whether all of us who speak Cervantes's[2] language are Spanish, let's just say we have been cursed, we have been called bores, and we have had "messages" sent to our families and other such shows of affection.

To anyone who has been brought down by this plague, cough by cough, who has been clasped in its sharp talons, who has felt its pains all over and who has had no end of microbes inside and out, it's going to seem normal, this "Spanish" sickness, these "Spanish people," every one of them who claims even a hint of direct, indirect, or circumstantial lineage from our mother country.

Well, all of us were in a way already in quarantine, even before they let some influenza or other in. You can tell because scarcely had someone "de la raza"[3] sneezed, even though he had actually taken snuff, then everyone around would cover their noses and mouths with handkerchiefs soaked in pesticides or disinfectant to impede a blast of bacillus, spiraea, or other micrococcus, or other such great serpent then out you go and the next thing you knew your were stuck in some bed somewhere.

• • •

In the 15-cent restaurant where I usually have "lunch," someone asked me, a few days ago, where I was from. I told them without hesitation. But not happy with the answer, the establishment's owners, administrators and waiters followed me around interrogating me until they dragged the terrible confession out of me that I speak "Spanish" . . .

"Spanish?" said a little Japanese woman who held the joint responsibilities of cashier, accountant, and washerwoman par excellence.

"Yes, pretty 'Musmé,'[4] Spanish."

"It's a very 'fine' language," she exclaimed while, at the same time, keeping a respectable distance from me.

The following day, at meal-time, the jefe[5] and the assistant waiter asked me to come into the private dining room because they had prepared something special for me. Since I'm something of a dreamer, I thought that maybe my friends were throwing a "fiestecita"[6] for me, and I began to imagine a few pretty, sweet-sounding, harmonious, mellifluous words that, gathered together for a toast, would somehow convey my limitless, boundless gratitude for the Champagne, since I thought for sure that any surprise could not be complete without the bubbly or something on the par of that expensive drink, intoxicating to the nth . . .

But, no . . . all I found there was a guy who was attacking the peel of a baked potato.

"They brought you here, too?" he asked me in perfect Spanish.

"Seems that way."

"And you have no idea why?"

"None at all."

2. Miguel de Cervantes (1547–1616), Spanish novelist.
3. Belonging to the *mestizo* race.
4. *La Musmé* (1888) is a portrait of a young woman by the Dutch artist Vincent van Gogh (1853–1890).
5. Spanish for chief, leader, superior.
6. Spanish for little party.

"They say that because we speak 'Spanish' we carry the Spanish Flu."

When I left I noticed that all the plates, knives, napkins, anything we had been served, were getting a dunking in a pot of boiling water to demicrobe them.

The only thing they weren't going to put to this purifying action was my 15 cents, "my nickels," which were going right into the cash box . . .

And the little Japanese woman, with the same sweet and tender voice she used every day, said to me, "Come again," without even moving her lips.

From that moment on, every time I go into a public place, the first thing I do is to flare my nostrils so I don't speak as if I had nasal congestion, and immediately let loose with the sweet tongue God has given me with, "Atalacoyatumichotapolafamugationtinzon . . ."

When they hear me, they think I'm Chinese and they don't figure that a Chinaman, as badly off as he may be, can infect a Christian with The Spanish Flu.

\* \* \*

Unfortunately, not everybody believes I'm a son of China. The other night I went to visit a lady friend of mine who lives in Oakland and is married to a citizen of this country. She greeted me amiably enough, played the guitar for me, sang "Adelita" and a serenade by "Chober"[7]—that's the way she said it—and gave me cookies, port, and eggnog.

When her husband arrived on the scene, he gave me a nasty look after which he called his wife over and then he left. She had invited me to spend the night at her house so the three of us could leave very early the next morning for a nearby ranch. But when she got back from her conjugal discussion, she said to me, "I'm so sorry, paisano,[8] but you're going to have to sleep on the 'porch,' because my husband is really anxious about your being 'Spanish.' He says you're going to bring the plague that's going around."

"But, paisana," I said, "you're 'Spanish,' too and so . . ."

"Ah, but I'm not 'Spanish' anymore, not since I married an American . . ."

"That may be true . . ." I parried, "but the porch, paisana . . . and there are no more boats back to San Francisco . . ."

"Well, paisano, you can sleep with the cook Librada's boy. He has a bit of a cough, but there's no other bed. Anyway, he doesn't wake up during the night."

There was nothing I could do.

\* \* \*

I was just falling asleep when frightening screams awakened me. "The devil! The devil!" shouted the condemned boy, who saw in me the face of Lucifer. Pointing at me, he continued his shouting. "The devil! The devil!"

---

7. I.e., the Austrian composer Franz Schubert (1797–1828). *"Adelita"*: An iconic *soldadera*, female soldier, of the Mexican Revolution (1910), Adelita is the topic and main character of a famous revolutionary corrido.

8. Compatriot. Since there isn't an English word to convey the spoken meaning of *"paisano"* and *"paisana"* in this context, I've kept the original since it is widely understood in the United States. [Translator's note]

La Librada came in and took charge of her kid, but the frightened little snot kept on so much that he gave meaning to the saying that he who sleeps with a boy gets the shelter he deserves.

When the sun came up, my fellow countrywoman had the nerve to ask me how I had slept.

"Terrible, atrocious, paisana."

"Well, Mr. Thompson was afraid you were a carrier."

Ah, paisana, I didn't bring it, but I'm certainly leaving with it! Fool!

And she disappeared like a soul carried off by the devil.

October 5, 1918

# The Chacón Family

Mexican American literature of New Mexico has received more scholarly attention than that of any other southwestern state. Together, the Pasó Por Aquí Series, from the University of New Mexico Press, and studies of literature in New Mexican newspapers, by Doris Meyer and A. Gabriel Meléndez, have presented a broad overview of New Mexican literature from 1598 to the present. This literature is generally divided between folk writing, much of which was collected by the ethnographer Juan Rael and others in the early twentieth century, and that of the educated elite, which was published mainly in New Mexican newspapers.

Among the elite, often educated at universities in Chicago, St. Louis, and Indiana (Notre Dame), there grew up in Santa Fe and other cities of New Mexico during its territorial years and its transition to statehood a coterie of sophisticated editors and writers who worked to develop a dynamic regional literature. Foremost among these were the Oteros (see p. 308) and the Chacón family, especially the two brothers Rafael (1833–1925) and Urbano (1836–1886) and their sons Eusebio (1869–1948) and Felipe Maximiliano (1873–1949); the Chacóns' circle also included the prominent Southwest historian Benjamin M. Read (1853–1927). The Chacón family represented cultured New Mexicans intent on establishing personal and artistic identity in the face of cultured easterners' movement into the region. Even the printing and distribution of the Chacóns' works is of interest, since Spanish-language distribution was limited and overshadowed by the dominant English-language publishers and bookshops.

Rafael Chacón's literary output was limited to *memorias* (memoirs), which he wrote between 1906 and 1912 and which the critic Genaro Padilla has called an important example of the New Mexican autobiographical consciousness, one reflecting the dilemmas of living a Spanish-language life in an Anglo environment. In recounting his long life, Rafael encompasses the vast experience of Mexican Americans in New Mexico before the modern era: the conquest of the state; the transfer of power from the Mexican to the U.S. government; the widespread abrogation of the Treaty of Guadalupe Hidalgo; the arrival of the first printing press in the Southwest (1833); and the Gadsden Purchase (1853), the U.S. procurement from Mexico of a region that finalized the borders of New Mexico and Arizona. He also discusses his youth, education, service in the Union Army during the Civil War, return to the Southwest, and retirement to Colorado. Rafael's *memorias* were not translated and published until 1986, but his social and political prominence was such that he was given an extensive biography, including photographs, in Read's *Illustrated History of New Mexico* (1912). Rafael's brother Urbano was also a prominent citizen, a newspaper publisher and two-term superintendent of schools in Santa Fe. It was the sons of Rafael and Urbano, however, who established the family's literary reputation by producing arguably the most sophisticated and sustained literary work in the Southwest between 1880 and 1925.

Rafael's son Eusebio has only recently become known as the author of the stories "El hijo de la tempestad" (The Son of the Storm) and "Tras la tormenta la calma" (The Calm after the Storm), both first published serially in *El Boletín Popular* in 1892. The same year, they were combined in one volume by El Tipográfia de El

333

*Boletín Popular*, most likely through a private printing on the presses of that newspaper. (In New Mexico during that era, newspapers' presses often printed other materials, to help pay the publishers' bills.) Born in Peñasco, New Mexico, and raised in southern California, Eusebio received his undergraduate degree from the Jesuit institution Las Vegas College, in Las Vegas, New Mexico, in 1887, and a law degree from Notre Dame in 1889. When he returned to New Mexico, he became a teacher of English at Guadalupano College, in Durango, Mexico, where he eventually was appointed vice-director. He returned to New Mexico because of ill health and later became a member of the bar; married Sofía Barela, whose father was a Colorado senator and Mexican consul; and raised a family. From a young age, Eusebio was a powerful orator who spoke at various community events. While at Notre Dame, he was selected to deliver a welcoming address to the Pan-American Congress, which met in St. Paul, Minnesota, in 1889.

Eusebio attempted to develop a style of prose fiction linked more to Mexican and New Mexican traditions than to mainstream, Anglo traditions. He aimed to develop what he called "una literatura nacional" (a national literature). In his introduction to the combined works, Eusebio notes that

> son creación genuina de mi propia fantasía y no robadas ni prestadas de gabachos ni extranjeros. Sobre el suelo Nuevo Mexicano me atrevo á cimentar la semilla de la literatura recreativa para que si después otros autores de más feliz ingenio que el mío siguen el camino que aquí trazo, puedan volver hacia el pasado la vista y señalarme como el primero que emprendió tan áspero camino (they are a genuine creation of my own imagination, neither stolen nor borrowed from *gabachos* [a derogatory term used to describe Anglos] or foreigners. I dare to sow the seeds of recreational literature on New Mexican soil so that other authors of greater imagination than my own may follow the path I have traced, and can turn their eyes to the past and see me as the first to have undertaken such a difficult path).

In reviewing the combined volume, his contemporary José Escobar said that "Chacón's small book, although unknown among many nativos, is a true jewel in our national literature." Yet no reprint or English translation, even partial, of either work appeared until 1997.

The themes of *The Son of the Storm* are derived from local legends and superstitions and mixed with the pervasive fear of the violence of the New Mexican bandoleros of the late nineteenth century. As in other romantic works of the time, the relationship between natural events and emotional development is emphasized, as in the opening of the novel, where pounding thunder joins with the beating of a couple's hearts. (The relationship between Nature and emotion continues to be explored by modern New Mexican novelists such as Rudolfo Anaya and Denise Chavez.) Fortune-telling and spirituality also figure in the work. Unfortunately, the work's spiritual language makes *The Son of the Storm* alien to many contemporary readers, although readers of gothic literature generally feel at home with most of the images.

*Tras la tormenta la calma* is more experimental. Focusing on a love triangle and including the narrator's comments on the action, it examines the concepts of love and honor and their place in then-contemporary society. The critic Francisco Lomelí has situated the work, with its garish sentimentality and melodrama, in the tradition of the *fotonovela*, or dime novel, of the time. Chacón cleverly raises the literary stakes, however, by embedding references to great satirical works of European literature—Cervantes's *Don Quixote* and Byron's *Don Juan*—and to the unwittingly satirical *Campani Treasury of Spanish Eloquence*. Thus flagging "The Calm after the Storm" as a broad melodramatic farce, he then fills it with puffed-up serenades and presents the cuckolded protagonist, gun in hand, chasing an underwear-clad lothario through the streets of Santa Fe.

Urbano's son Felipe Maximiliano was educated first at public schools and then at St. Michael's College, in Santa Fe. From a young age, he had literary inclinations; in fact, by age 14 he had already published verse in local newspapers. He most likely wrote the poems included in his single collection between the ages of 17 and 50. From 1911 to 1918, he edited various New Mexico newspapers, in Las Vegas, Bernalillo, Albuquerque, and Mora. He spent the following four years pursuing business interests, after which he returned to journalism, in Albuqerque, as the editor and general manager of *La Bandera Americana*.

Felipe Maximiliano's writing is marked by expertise in Spanish, a rarity at that time in the Southwest, where English-language education dominated. In his preface to Felipe Maximiliano's book, *Obras de Felipe Maximiliano Chacón, El Cantor Neo-Mexicano: Poesía y Prosa* (1924, most likely printed as a limited edition of several hundred copies on the presses of *La Bandera Americana*), Read notes that "the literary works of Felipe Maximiliano Chacón are destined to mark a distinct era in the literary history of the United States. I say a distinct era because it has produced a clearly American genius, the first to give luster to his homeland in the beautiful language of [the sixteenth- and seventeenth-century Spanish novelist Miguel de] Cervantes."

In his own prologue, Felipe Maximiliano declares that he intends the book as "*una simple contribución a la Lectura Recreativa, para las masas populares de los pueblos*" (a simple contribution to recreational reading, for the popular masses). The desire to create literature to be read by the "popular masses" may seem anomalous in a highly educated *neomexicano*, but of course at the time most newspapers—written by the elite for the masses—included poetry and short stories. Though today Felipe Maximiliano's poetry seems florid, Meyer notes that it was "written in a style extremely popular in the late 19th and 20th centuries, both in Mexico and the United States." However, the contents of Read's preface—which provides details on significant periods of the author's life and sets his poetry into social, political and cultural context—suggest that such a collection, especially in Spanish, was rare and needed explanation for a reading public educated on nineteenth-century poets such as the American Henry Wadsworth Longfellow and the Englishman Lord Byron.

The poetry is divided into "*Cantos patrios y misceláneos*" (Patriotic and Miscellaneous Songs), which include 46 poems of various lengths and dedications, and "*Cantos del hogar y traducciones*" (Songs of the Home and Translations), which consist of nine poems dedicated to his children; one that Felipe Maximiliano claims his maternal uncle has written to Felipe Maximiliano's mother; and seven translations of poems from the English, including works by Byron, John Dryden, and Edward Bulwer-Lytton. This section is followed by "*Saetas políticas y prosa*" (Political Verses and Prose), which consists of a satirical poem on a boastful old soldier and three prose pieces. The prose piece included in this anthology, "Don Julio Berlanga," is delivered in a straightforward reportorial style. It presents a Spanish-speaking New Mexican, an honorable *caballero*, whose life is suddenly altered by a chance encounter with a ticket-taker in Las Vegas. The poem reprinted here is typical of much of the elegiac political verse published in New Mexican newspapers during and after the campaign for statehood (New Mexico became a state in 1912). What makes it exceptional is its dedication to another New Mexican writer of the time, Adelina "Nina" Otero-Warren (see p. 405). The poem is evidence of the political and literary contacts among the New Mexico elite of the time. Despite Otero-Warren's long experience in local Santa Fe politics, she was defeated for the Congressional seat.

In southern Colorado in the 1920s, Felipe's daughter Herminia carried on the family tradition by publishing poetry in local newspapers.

# EUSEBIO CHACÓN
## 1869–1948

### The Calm after the Storm[1]

There are imprudent actions that have serious and grave consequences, but not for that reason should one fail to comment upon them; quite the contrary, they are the source of many others, and people, ever foolish, are not content with heeding the warning of foreign minds but rather appear to go to great pains to transfer to their own personality the inane and indiscreet actions of the latter. In matters of love, so great are the irrational actions that are committed in its name that many books are filled with them; and not because they are novel or original, but because there is something of the old song in all of this, in that the older it is the more beautiful it appears. Helen's love led to the loss of Troy, Caba's dug a sepulchre for the Gothic monarchy in Spain.[2] And, despite the agelessness of love, despite the agelessness of its intrigues and its now adverse, now propitious results, not a soul can resist chasing after it, until they end up like the Count of the drama in which a madman leads a blind man to unheard-of disasters.[3] So embedded in human nature is the influence of the little winged god that even the sublime madman from la Mancha would never have achieved immortality, had he not found in some corner of his mind the memory of one rural Aldonza whose image his fancy summarily converted into a princess, all to the glory of Spanish belles lettres.[4] Slave to this same imperial passion was the young man from my homeland, Luciano, a youth of elegant presence and noble lineage; who, oblivious to the experience of others, dove into an inferno of fortuitous events and misfortunes from which he was rescued thanks to his good luck and a bit of fear. I lament the young man's fortune; but that does not mean that I am not entertained by the teasing he receives from his peers, or by their occasional serenades in which they sing Becquer's famous couplets:

1. Translated by Erlinda González-Berry, with minor changes by Ilan Stavans and Harold Augenbraum.
2. A reference to the eighth-century Visigothic legend of La Cava en Pedroche (in Arabic, *cava* means a "refined prostitute"; Pedroche is a town in the province of Córdoba, Andalusia, Spain). According to the legend, Florinda, the beautiful daughter of the Arab ruler Count Don Julián, was raped by King Don Rodrigo and bore him a child. Seeking revenge, Don Julián fought the king in battle and ultimately took over his kingdom. From then on, Florinda lived in penance, thinking that Gothic Spain had fallen into Arab hands because of her. Before she died, she threw her belongings into a well (known as Fuente de la Cava, the Cava's fountain), where she—and subsequently her spirit—lamented both the death of her child and her fate. This legend might be connected with the myth of La Llorona (for a version, see p. 2452; for a variation on the myth, see p. 2454). *Helen's love . . . Troy:* According to the *Iliad*, an epic poem by the ancient Greek poet Homer, the legendarily beautiful Spartan queen Helen was abducted by her lover, the Trojan prince Paris; this event led to the Trojan War and the resulting fall of Troy.
3. This episode occurs in *El conde Lucanor* (*Tales of Count Lucanor*, 1335), one of the earliest prose works written in Castilian Spanish.
4. In the novel *Don Quixote* (1605, 1615), a foundational text of Spanish literature by Miguel de Cervantes (1547–1616), the title character is "the sublime madman from la Mancha," whose distorted memory of his beloved Aldonza leads him to many misbegotten adventures. *The little winged god:* Eros, also known as Cupid, the incarnation of love.

Are you leaving?

'Tis been a while that I did so
'Tis true also that
My clothes were left to dry
On the sandy beach.[5]

But, let us be honest, the poor devil deserves it. Therefore, for the pleasure and entertainment of those in love, I will recount the story of Luciano's amorous affair, which, due to his indiscretions, trapped him between a rock and a hard place.

It so happened that in one of our barrios in Santa Fe, my dear homeland, there lived one of those dark beauties that bedevil one with glances that turn the most pusillanimous man into a hero, and the most reticent into a magpie. Her name was Lola, and so harsh had been her luck that she had been left without parents or siblings, so her aunt, a jolly and round matron, who during her waking hours stuffed herself with beans and onions and at night snored from both ends like a subchanter,[6] acted in their stead. The auntie's name was Manuela, but her neighbors affectionately called her Aunt Mela.

Aunt Mela was a good soul, there is no doubt about that; and since she had no sons or daughters of her own, she loved her niece Lola, who, as we have already mentioned, was one of those dark beauties that drive men mad, though she was only fifteen years old. At this tender age, what young girl will not be consumed by the divine flames of love? Which of them will not inhabit the paradise of illusions? Which of them has not launched arrows with her blazing eyes nor made to suffer the winged child,[7] holding him prisoner in her net? Lola was not about to be an exception to this venerable tradition; on the contrary, her beauty destined her to be among the most passionate sweethearts in the history of Santa Fe. She was born to love, and she loved a young laborer named Pablo, who so reciprocated her love that there existed no more loving couple.

Pablo was one of those laborers from years gone by. He was not of the indolent, rude, unambitious and lacking in self-respect contemporary type that is content to live without hope or money; who waits like a gypsy in the hope that perhaps some do-gooder will deliver his daily bread and another chew it for him. No, Pablo was not one of these. He was poor, but his poverty incited him to work, to strive to better his lot. He was frugal, attentive, courteous, modest, and industrious: he was above all a Christian, respectful of his bosses, obedient and honorable. He loved Lola with tenderness; he respected her as does the man who hopes to take his loved one to the altar to make her his wife. I dare say that beneath his unpolished exterior there existed a truly noble man. His hands were callused, his face burned

5. A misquotation of the last stanza of "Terecra voz" (Third voice) in "Rima LXXII," by Gustavo Adolfo Domínguez Bastida, better known as Gustavo Adolfo Bécquer (1836–1870), Spanish poet and short-story writer. The correct lines are "¿Te embarcas? gritaban, y yo sonriendo / les dije al pasar: / Yo ya me he embarcado, por señas que aún tengo / la ropa en la playa tendida a secar" ("You're embarking?" they screamed, and laughing / I told them, while passing by: / I've already embarked, leaving behind some signs / like the cloths I left on the beach to dry up").
6. Like the person who sings the second part of a religious chant; i.e., she issued noises from her mouth and her behind.
7. Eros/Cupid.

by the sun, but he was ever pleasant and jovial. The circumstances under which these two children of the land fell in love have a romantic tone, and I would never pardon myself were I to continue with this story without calling attention to this important event.

Pablo and Lola had been neighbors since their childhood; they had grown together, and together they had played as children, chasing butterflies in the gardens, and on moonlit nights contemplating the sky, across which some capricious cloud might cross and inspire them to see in it now a castle, now a battle, or a banquet of the gods. Their imaginations developed simultaneously and, given their likeness of temperament, they loved, desired, wanted, and admired the same thing; and in all matters they were in agreement, including in their sweet and pleasant character. The similarity of their taste, once childhood turned into adolescence, gave birth to a burning passion.

It was a lovely spring night. Gardens were filled with flowers, and aromatic gentle breezes lent a thousand charms to the ambience. On some flower two butterflies met in love, and in the lush apple trees a lovelorn dove sang her tender song. 'Tis clear that conditions were propitious and so Lola and Pablo chose that moment to confess their mutual love. In front of Aunt Mela's house there grew an old apple tree that in its lifetime had seen many things, and was now about to witness an amorous scene played out in front of its tired and withered branches. Lola and Pablo sat on two chairs, close to each other, quietly contemplating the moon and listening to the faraway song of some lover. Inside Aunt Mela made her two adopted children recite their evening prayers, but before the prayers ended she had fallen asleep as had the two neophytes, and from a distance one could hear her rickety, windmill-like, and not at all musical snoring. Meantime the hours flew by; Pablo and Lola felt a deep, immense love, and their hands touched, their gazes met with unsaid tenderness. Not a soul walked by, not a soul saw them, and in the midst of that calm night their lips met and the beats of their hearts became one faint wonder:

> "Oh love, Oh sweet love, in which nestle
> Placid quarrels of illusion."

I would sing out with my countryman and friend Alberto; but enough digression, 'tis better that the heroes of this story speak for themselves and reveal their characters to the readers.

—Lola! said the trembling youth.

—What fear, Pablo! What fear—stuttered the happy girl; and their lips touched once again in a kiss that lasted. . . . How long did it last, oh ye poets? . . . They say here and there that a kiss cannot be measured in time but only in the amount of love that engenders it; and love is immense in two gentle souls when they fall in love for the first time at the tender age of fifteen.

—Know that I love you with all my heart, my dear Lola.

—What happiness, Pablo; I feel tears of pleasure.

—My heart adores you.

—And mine idolizes you.

—Will your love be ever constant? Or will you someday feel shame for having loved a humble dark-skinned laborer?

—Never, Pablo of my heart; nothing on this earth will taint this love.

But is it possible to transfer that scene to the written page? How foolish of me, what a responsibility I have taken on! Tell me, readers, who would dare photograph the sun? Who portray the hurricane, and who those objects that enervate art and human constancy? Am I mad in wanting to capture the words that passed between them? 'Tis true that their eyes and their kisses and their souls with their silent but tender language spoke more than their tongues; and that the language of the soul and of the eyes cannot be captured! In the end I will say that so great was Pablo and Lola's love that time passed without their noticing, and to their astonishment the morning sun would have found them murmuring their words of love had luck not brought their way another young neighbor, given also to romantic inclinations. Her name was Pascuala, and she was as bold as that other Pascuala of fiction.[8]

> Yes, no, maybe so
> Yes, no, maybe so
> Only your grandchildren
> Will ever know.

It so happened that there was a rural girl that was about to marry. The priest asked her name, and she vigorously responded:

—Pascuala, well, what else.

—Where are you from?

—From the ranch, well, where else . . .

—And you wish to marry?

—Yes!!! Be it known that this *yes* was the strongest superlative she could summon.

No less intrepid was this Pascuala who now appeared to interrupt Pablo and Lola's sweet colloquy. For some time now she had been mad about our congenial laborer, but he did not know it. It was that hour at which the lark begins its morning song when Pascuala left her bed and looked out the window. So clear was the night that only a blind person would have missed the activity under the apple tree in front of Aunt Mela's. She did not fail to recognize the actors in that scene, and insane with jealousy she fell upon the two lovers, harassing them in the most horrible manner. The startled Lola ran home, and Pablo remained to fight off the wrath of the offended Pascuala.

Yes, these were her words,—you unfaithful, thankless fool, is that how you dare waste your love, on that conceited flirt, without caring one whit about my sleepless nights. Listen up, you wooden heart, you soulless tyrant, who cares not for me, insults my heart, you petulant oaf.

—But Pascuala . . . reasoned the confused young man: and barely had he put together a response when Pascuala unleashed another vituperation.

8. A character in the comedy *Fuenteovejuna* (1619), by the Spanish poet and playwright Lope de Vega (Félix Lope de Vega y Carpio, 1562–1635).

—You ungrateful dolt, how can I ever be happy, what with that skunk-eyed, prudish wench, enticing you that way: listen, had you chosen to love me, I would have been more faithful than a turtle dove;—and saying this Pascuala sobbed and groaned, and threw herself at Pablo.

Holy smokes, did things get hot for the boy! He wanted to respond, but a knot formed in his throat. So violent was that scene that it must have awakened more than one old busybody, for no sooner had the sun risen than the details of that highly commented, and by now embellished, midnight episode took wing and spread to the four corners of the land.

Such is the true story of this love. The jealous Pascuala was left unheeded, and Pablo and Lola's love, barring that one interruption, flowed smoothly and peacefully for some time without suffering any misfortunes or setbacks.

But it is now time to search out Luciano, who up to this point has remained out of sight. Pablo and Lola had been in love for six months, and word of Lola's beauty had spread like a forest fire, reaching the ears of the students at Saint Michael's College, among them Luciano. Luciano was not a serious student, certainly not a model one. It was preparation time for final exams, and instead of studying he wasted his time reading Byron's *Don Juan, The Student from Salamanca*,[9] and other works along those lines, from whose pages he was absorbing a strong taste for the dishonesties that in them appear. These readings stirred his fantasy in such a way that he could hardly wait for the opportunity to prove himself a daring Don Juan, or a Felix of Montemar. All that he read appeared to him to have in fact taken place as described, and he found those blasphemies, indecent, immoral and totally lacking in honor as they were, ideally suited to the life of a student. He began by falling in love and writing poems such as the following to the gracious dark beauty:

> From the eyes of the moon
> I brought two fine diamonds
> To place them in thine
> O dark beauty of enormous eyes.

And on another occasion pretending to have obtained a date with the beautiful Lola, he put his mind to work on the following composition worthy of being archived for ever and ever, amen; and it went thus:

> That divine look of yours
> Oh my dear dear friend
> Lures me to follow you
> along that road
>
> May your journey not be interrupted
> By the old man with his staff

9. *El estudiante de Salamanca* (published beginning 1837), a long, unfinished combination of poetry and drama, by the Spanish poet José de Espronceda (1808–1842); the central character, Don Félix de Montemar, is based on the legendary Don Juan. The English poet George Gordon, Lord Byron (1788–1824) wrote a narrative poem (1819–24) based on the Don Juan legend.

> For chasing close behind you
> Is this pathetic pilgrim

You must be warned that we have not yet been able to confirm who exactly the old man referred to by the inspired composer might be. But, leaving that concern aside, let us continue with our story. Luciano could hardly wait to be free from school in order to freely pursue Lola's love and after . . . well, afterwards, that's another story. The doling out of awards was one full month away. To his great delight he recalled the words of his model lover:

> To the shepherd's abode I went
> And to palaces I did rise
> Wherever I set foot
> Upon virtue did I trample

The indiscreet boy slipped out through the balcony of his alma mater and with a heart palpitating like the blacksmith's bellows, he headed toward Aunt Mela's. The moon had just appeared and, to the benefit of the hovering student, Lola's love had just turned the corner and disappeared. She remained standing still beneath the old apple tree and did not notice Luciano's arrival until he interrupted her state of contemplation with these words:

—Good evening, lovely Lola!

Startled, Lola took three steps back and, turning, suddenly said:

—Oh! . . . Good evening.

One second later she was inside the house and the bright student of Saint Michael's College was left alone. Alone! In a chaos of lost hope, feeling the abyss of love settle in his heart. Alone! That woman who unnerved his calm had left him alone in the night.

What a disappointment! Luciano was stupefied. He who had dreamed of collecting material for at least a ballad that night was left in the dark. Nonetheless, collecting his scattered thoughts he stepped up to the tree trunk and thought:

—Disillusion, he said to himself, what a severe lesson you have taught me! But in the future I will know how to have my way, and that slippery dark beauty who scorns me today will one day soon sigh upon seeing me draw near this tufted tree. Why was she frightened by my presence? Could it be that she already has a lover? Who was it that turned the corner? I saw a shape there and then I heard the voice of one who sang in this direction. There is not doubt she has a lover. I must proceed cautiously in this matter. Tomorrow I will return at this very hour. I will try my fortune once again and I will bring my guitar. They say I sing well. And for security I shall bring a dagger. Good.

And upon saying this, the boy scratched his head and stretched his eyes toward Aunt Mela's door in the hope of seeing Lola's shape appear. He saw nothing. He went round the back and saw a light in a window; he drew near and looked inside. He saw a lit candle, a folding cot with a mattress, a table with vases and flowers, and, at the head of the cot, he saw an old crucifix before which a young woman knelt; it was Lola. For a moment Luciano contemplated her.

—Pray, he whispered, as he slipped away from the window.

He took a path that led back to the college and half an hour later was sleeping peacefully in his bed.

The following night he repeated his outing, well armed with a dagger and guitar, determined not to be disappointed once again. On this occasion he did not dare speak to Lola so as not to frighten her; instead, he watched her go to her room and proceeded to her window, where he watched her say her prayers and climb into bed; no sooner had she settled in when she heard someone singing softly to the strum of a guitar:

> Awake, dear one,
> Awake from your sleep,
> Come listen to my song
> Come listen to my plea.
>
> If the world is a sweet abode
> Where love does blossom,
> From among its loveliest roses
> I have picked one for you.
>
> Do not fear that it is night time,
> Do not fear; all is quiet,
> Night is the tender bosom
> Where love does lie.
>
> If blue eyes
> Are the color of the sky,
> Your black eyes
> Are the color of love.
>
> Awake, dear one
> Awake from your sleep
> Come listen to my song
> Come listen to my plea.

Such was the student's song. So languid, so soft, so sweetly tender did it sound in the middle of the night that it seemed a dream. Restless, the young lass tossed and turned in her bed, wanting and not wanting to peek out the window in order to hear more clearly. She knew the identity of the troubadour, and she recognized that pleasant voice that merited her attention. Finally she gave in to her female curiosity. Lola arose, raised the window just a bit, and no sooner had she done so than a hand slipped through the window and handed her a note while saying:

—Please read this.

Lola, feeling faint from fear, let the window drop, and the note slipped away. Outside she heard a moan and an emphatic damn! The window caught the lad's hand, smashing his little finger. Afterwards she heard steps, then silence.

The next morning the first thing Lola saw upon arising was the note from the night before. She picked it up carefully, unfolded it and read:

Lovely Lola,
I love you as I have never loved before. For you I would die, and also kill. Please return my love. I know you are poor and I rich. But—what does that matter? Love me anyway. You are far too beautiful to live in obscurity. Please answer.

LAST NIGHT'S VISITOR

—Oh, it's him, murmured Lola as she tore the note into a thousand pieces.
—Last night's visitor, she kept saying over and over, as she trembled. She remembered Pablo; she remembered his love.
Bear with my repeating that the following night Luciano arrived once again, that he took his place at the window, that he sang the same song, and introduced the same letter; or should we say, another note with the same words; and once again he said, damn! when his finger was smashed. And as before, Lola became frightened, ran gingerly to her bed and the next morning found the note from *Last Night's Visitor*. Luciano's serenade was like that of the lover who knew only one verse and sang it all night long at his loved one's door. The verse went like this:

At your door I planted a pine tree
At your window a pear tree
So that on Christmas night
You could eat fresh pears

So many pine and pear trees did the troubadour set forth that one night a cranky old man appeared at his balcony and said to him:
—Son, you've planted a forest at my doors and windows. Tomorrow the carriages won't be able to get through my patio. Beat it already and let people sleep.
If guileless Aunt Mela hadn't slept so soundly, she could well have sent Luciano to plant his groves of love far away from Santa Fe. But the good lady heard nothing. It was sleeping time and nothing could tear her away from her deep sleep. And oh, what misfortune befell her! Oh, cruel destiny, you who cast the fortunes of mortals into a thousand complex paths and even dare to entice in your machinations those of simple and innocent ways. Oh, Aunt Mela, if instead of snoring and dreaming perhaps about turnips and onions and about tomorrow's new porridges you had been alert and kept a vigilant eye on what was going on with your lovely kin a few steps from your window, you might have at least impeded the success of an adventure that was to become so bitter and fatal.
Once upon a time, in my youth, I read in some inconsequential Latin book the proverb that says, *guta cavat lapiden non vi sed saepe cadendo.*[1]

---

1. A steady drip can carve even stone (Latin).

With this in mind and with that other proverb that says, *audaces fortuna juvat*,[2] our bright Luciano continued to besiege the lovely dark maiden; and so hard did he try that in the end the tender beauty surrendered. Humanity loves adulation: most need it for their existence, and Luciano understood this well when he raised his voice in song at Lola's window. From song, he moved to words, from words to friendship, from friendship . . . like Lucifer in the form of the serpent who disclosed gorgeous lies and ephemeral delicacies before the eyes of the first woman, submerging her in a sea of misfortunes,[3] so too did Luciano with golden hypocrisy undo Lola's happiness. Lola trembled, and nonetheless she began to enjoy the danger, and it is written that he who loves danger in it will find his demise. Like the moth that becomes fascinated by the light of a lantern and eventually lights upon its flame, thus was Lola carried away and enchanted by Luciano's doleful flame of love. That youthful heart was undergoing a radical change that caused innumerable tears to flow, yet she was nonetheless deceived. From song Luciano moved to words, but words that caused her to lose her senses and abandon herself to the strangest aberrations of the mind; words that, murmured in the ear of the credulous young maiden, sounded like pure honey when compared to humble Pablo, whose words rang coarse; words which in the end were like those of Luzbel[4] hidden in the branches of the tree of the Garden of Eden. We cannot doubt it: Luciano was winning ground, as he tenaciously tightened the rope, and the prize was to be his. Lola had confided the secret of her amorous adventure with Pablo, and Luciano struggled to destroy it. He reminded her of her lover's humble condition, then praised her beauty, concluding that she was destined to move in a circle of admirers and in conditions of luxury that did not belong to the working man. So obstinate was the astute Luciano in his reasoning that he finally drew from Lola's lips a solemn promise to abandon Pablo and to be his whenever he desired her, on condition that upon finishing school he would marry her.

—I accept, exclaimed Luciano and reached out to shake her hand.

—Seal this contract, replied the maiden as she offered her lips.

A kiss that seemed to burst the very fibers of the soul burst forth in darkness. It was the kiss of betrayal and infidelity.

Dear reader, I would like to represent Lola, dressed anew in the magnificent robes of heroines, lovely and virtuous, adorned in a thousand jewels and cleansed by victory against the fury of passion. I would like to always present her to you as sweet, as pleasant as she was when born in my imagination and as she grew by Pablo's side, in his tender love and happiness. But from this moment on, I can feature her only as a blemished wreath, a faded blossom, an illusion that was a dream that ended. Nonetheless, love her as I love her for her lamentable weakness, pity her as I pity her in her misfortune; and instead of despising her, know that it was not she who worked her calamity but rather that malicious Luciano who had trickery in his soul when he promised to wed her, for in all things he deceived her only to satisfy his diabolical whims. That kiss! That nefarious kiss! How many are the lasses who began like that only to drag themselves in the mire of the most

---

2. Fortune favors the bold (Latin).
3. For the story of Eve's interaction with the serpent in Eden, see the biblical Book of Genesis.
4. A Spanish name for Lucifer.

shameful immorality. Nevertheless, the criminal Lucianos of the world far outnumber the Lolas.

But rather than cut the thread of this narration, I will say that after that kiss the young man, armed with a dagger, nightly entered Lola's window and after a long while left with a diabolical smile on his lips as he murmured a disgusting joke.

Things were just lovely; it would be difficult to conjecture where that adventure was headed, were it not for a coincidence that interrupted its progress and turned it around on its head. Pablo was no fool, and he had begun to suspect his dark beauty's infidelity. He had noticed in her an inexplicable change and he banged his head trying to understand the mystery behind the change, if in fact one existed. Lola on the other hand had been looking for some time for a way to get rid of Pablo without staining her reputation, but she couldn't find a suitable solution. In her dilemma, she approached Luciano, but his mind was as bereft of plans as his soul was of good intentions. In this state of affairs, the laborer Pablo, certain that there was something fishy going on, and bent on figuring things out whatever the loss might be, headed for Aunt Mela's on the night that grades were to be issued at Saint Michael's. A wall that who knows what governor had built to protect his skull from Indian arrows ran along the house, and behind it hid our laborer drawing up all his courage to face whatever might present itself. From that position he could see clearly the objects that surrounded Lola's window, and he could even see a good portion of the interior, since the light was on and he was not too far away. He could see her cot, part of the crucifix and half of the vase with flowers; and in the whitewashed background of the room loomed the shadow of gracious Lola, who without a doubt stood between the candle and the wall. Delighted in his contemplation of that scene, Pablo did not sense the passing of time. Finally the cathedral clock rang out the eleventh hour, a noise nearby broke the silence and Pablo reacted, all eyes and ears. His heart beat wildly. Holding his breath, gritting his teeth, and clenching his fists, he peered into the night. Someone arrived, and in a state of agitation crept toward the window. Then he heard the chords of a guitar followed by a meek song. The window opened and the sound of a kiss landed like ice upon the poor lad's heart, and before he was able to convince himself that what he witnessed was truth and not illusion he saw the recently arrived guest step through the window and into the room like a thief in the night.

Pablo's mind clouded over with anger and, with cocked gun, he took aim calmly and, a moment later, he had nearly fired a bullet in the direction of his rival and his unfaithful love. However, at the very moment that he was about to commit a double murder, a felicitous thought crossed his mind, so he lowered the gun, put it away, and headed hurriedly toward the house. He entered without knocking and found Aunt Mela snoring as one snores when the body is fatigued and the conscience clear. Drawing close to her he shook her abruptly to wake her as he whispered into her ear:

—Aunt Mela, Aunt Mela. Wake up. What deep sleep! Aunt Mela!

The good lady tossed and turned, no doubt dreaming that some evil spirit was about to haul her off. But presently she opened her eyes, red as burning coals, and while rubbing them cut off her snoring and asked in a fright:

—What's the matter? . . . What? . . . What? . . . Pablo! Oh, it's you! What a fright!

—It is I, Aunt Mela, don't be afraid, answered Pablo. But get up and come with me.

The poor matron, with eyes open wide, did not know what to think; but obeying and dressing in a hurry, asked once again.

—Well now, young man, What a fright! What do you want?

—I want you to authorize me to defend her. You cannot defend yourself. I am your friend; and I shall defend her.

—But what's the problem, dear boy? Tell me. Don't keep me in suspense, Aunt Mela stuttered breathlessly.

—There are thieves in your house, Aunt Mela. . . .

—Jesus!!! Don't tell me, dear boy. Help, for my life. Help, help, for I am a helpless woman! And Aunt Mela wrung her hands in sad desperation.

Pablo said no more. He dragged her to Lola's room; and all of this happened so fast that even though Lola and Luciano heard the shouting, they didn't have time to respond, and were still in suspense when Pablo shoved the door open as he and the timorous aunt dashed in. Their arrival was so sudden that Luciano did not even think of hiding under the cot. The candle was lit, the crucifix hanging, the flowers wilted, the room full of scattered shoes, shirts, underwear and stockings, and on the cot lay the unfaithful dark beauty and the fickle student. The Aunt tried to shout out her consternation; she tried to beg for help, moved not by fear but by pain. She imagined that an ogre had Lolita in his plundering claws; that the young maiden was unconscious and that the ogre acted against her will. Oh, what love is capable of! And Pablo was livid. He bore a look of determination on his face and in his right hand his trusty friend. Luciano, whose color was that of wax, kept blinking his eyes, and Lola covered her face. At that moment the two wrongdoers would have wished the earth to part and swallow them.

—Look, Pablo finally said to Aunt Mela, as his mouth turned blue and his eyes flashed in a rage.

—Help, help, cried the poor woman and, overtaken by a most extraordinary pain, she ran madly from one room to another.

—Before you stands the thief, repeated Pablo. Aunt Mela, Aunt Mela. They rob from you your niece's virtue, but that is not all. What is worse is that she allows herself to be robbed, she prostitutes herself.

Upon hearing these words Luciano thought it was all over. Fearing for his life he jumped from the bed to flee, and Pablo, believing he was going to grab for his gun, fired and hit him in the calf. Lola jumped to the other side of the bed; Aunt Mela, shouting that she had been killed, fainted on the floor; Luciano jumped through the window wearing only his underwear; and like a bat out of hell Pablo followed close behind. The noise alerted neighbors, who found the house in major turmoil and the poor woman on the verge of death. They called the priest as she had requested, and before long she lay there pale and stiff. The fright proved to be mortal.

Half an hour later a frightened, half-dressed man ran through the streets, followed closely by what appeared to be a madman. One ran for his life; the other for his honor and vengeance. They had been running for two hours: news spread like the plague that Aunt Mela and her niece had been murdered. How things were exaggerated as they traveled from mouth to mouth!

The townspeople became unruly, dogs barked, bells rang, soldiers fell upon their arms and loaded the artillery, and the evildoer and his foe ran and ran some more. Finally, upon turning a cursed corner, the first one did not see an approaching pedestrian and ran into him head on, knocking him over while he stood there with little stars floating around his head. That encounter was his undoing: for no sooner had it occurred than his determined pursuer took hold of him with an iron hand. Had Pablo not been blind with rage he would have laughed heartily to see the look on his rival's face, which just the day before had been so haughty and now was so ridiculous that, truth be told, he looked like an exact copy of the gentleman from la Mancha doing his penance at the Sierra Morena,[5] the only difference being that the latter was a magnificent madman and the former a flagrant coward. Without bothering to apologize to the roughed-up chap our Pablo, with a few swift kicks and a bit of name-calling that fit the student like a glove, herded Luciano toward Aunt Mela's house. They arrived precisely when the poor woman had swallowed her last breath and handed her guileless soul over to her Creator. Without ceremony and without heeding the solemnity of the occasion, the evildoer and his pursuer made their way through the crowd, and the latter, dragging the former to where she who in life had been Aunt Mela lay, said in a tone that inspired the fear of God in all— Look, coward, at what you have done. For one moment look at this dead woman who moments ago was so full of life; take joy in your deed, you worthless clown, and if you still have a feeling heart, feel the horror of seeing before you the innocent victim of your abominable actions. Oh, Aunt Mela, he sobbed with tenderness before the cadaver; "before the world your untimely death must seem a calamity, but it is your fortune not to have survived to face this dishonor! Woe is me before whom there lies an abyss of shame! Woe is me, for not having died with you and spared myself the occasion of seeing the woman I idolized so dishonored. And all because she desired it! Dishonored! And I deceived at the very moment when I most loved her. Fickle woman, treacherous woman! . . ."

Pablo would have gone on with a long soliloquy worthy of inclusion in the Capmany Treasury of Spanish Eloquence,[6] but pain intervened and sheared the bud that had once been a rose. Luciano, on the other hand, looked like an idiot; his distorted countenance and his dumbfounded look gave him the appearance of one who has just returned from a royal drunken spree. His observers were amazed to see him in such a state; they were shocked to hear Lola's slippery excuses; the old ladies covered their eyes to protect their chaste vision; children were awed by such strange events; some discussed the issue of a quick lynching and others, more given to pity, spoke of a good thrashing; and the honorable priest who had not yet dared to show his face, and not even the tip of his excellent nose, for fear of imminent trouble blessed himself repeatedly as he conjured the evil one, be it demon or spirit, to please depart until some indeterminable future from that god-fearing community. Upon seeing his Reverence's anxiety, Pablo once again raised his voice, causing his audience to tremble:

5. In Part 1, chapters 23–26 of *Don Quixote*, Quixote pauses from his adventures to reflect.
6. Either the *Tesoro de la elocuencia española* (Treasury of Spanish Eloquence, 1774) or the *Fi-* *losofía de la elocuencia* (Philosophy of Eloquence, 1776), by the Spanish scholar and military officer Antonio de Capmany y Montpalau (1742–1813).

—That will not do, Reverend Father! I say that will not do; you have fulfilled your obligations to the dead, now fulfill them to the living.

—Well, what say you, my son? asked his Reverence.

—I say that that woman whom you see lying before you preferred to die from pain rather than see her niece dishonored by this wretched coward, as he pointed at Luciano. Lola was mine, he continued, and this despicable man has dishonored her. I happen to know that he dragged her to ruin with false promises, and I have come here to see that those promises are kept. Yes, he must have promised her a great deal, for Lola was pure and good, and she would never have allowed herself to be deflowered for mere sinful pleasure. Lola was mine, and my soul adored her as the native adores his fetishes. In her I placed my happiness; but now all has ended between us. Nonetheless, I still love her enough to save her from greater harm. Father, there is Lola; here her deceiver. By natural law they belong to each other, and I, from this moment on, renounce all claims that my heart had on Lola's. If you don't want to see that witless girl turn to prostitution tomorrow in order to hide her first insane action, marry them, marry them. I desire it, I command it. I respond in my conscience and before God for the aftermath.

So awful was Pablo's attitude that, without wanting to, all present were left trembling, shocked and stunned. Lola was humbled, Pablo serious and threatening, while Luciano, assisted now by some compassionate souls, altered and agitated, put his boots on the wrong feet, his pants on backwards, as someone had brought him the belongings he had left in Lola's bedroom and the priest had ordered him to get dressed, because it was not decent to stand about in an undershirt before so many women.

Regarding the holy Reverend, speeding through his rosary beads and invoking the assistance of the entire celestial court in his moment of need, and pounding piously on his belly, with a serious tone he approached Luciano and said:

—Let's see, young man. How do you respond to the charges? Are they true?

—Every one of them, my father, replied Luciano, in an imploring tone.

—Do you love Lola and take her for your wife?

—Yes, father.

—And you, child; come, come hither; he said to Lola. Do you love Luciano, and do you take him for your spouse and partner?

A barely perceptible yes escaped the young woman's lips, and she lowered her face, which was red as a tomato.

A muffled sound spread throughout the assembly, and Pablo was white as jasper.

—Do you both promise to right past wrongs and give a good example? And do you repent wholeheartedly for your sins? asked the Reverend as both replied affirmatively in one voice.

They held hands; the priest raised his eyes to heaven, and with his right hand he made the sign of the cross and blessed the young couple. Pablo shed a secret tear, and Lola, falling to his feet and with eyes ablaze from crying, exclaimed:

—Forgive me, Pablo!

Pablo, taking for one last time that beautiful face in his hands, replied:

—May God's forgiveness be yours as my forgiveness is yours, and he immediately disappeared.

In the present, as I walk past the dead aunt's house daily, I seek in vain the joyous countenance of that guileless woman, and I feel like crying. In her stead, absolute heirs to her house, live Luciano and Lola, who repeatedly ask each other's forgiveness for their past iniquities. They have a lovely young son named Pepe, and on moonlit nights when my soul is melancholy I go to the tree at their door, from where I can occasionally hear an evening sermon, of which Luciano has a broad and endless repertoire.

1892

## FELIPE MAXIMILIANO CHACÓN
## 1873–1949

### To Señora Adelina Otero-Warren[1]

*Republican Candidate for Congress, 1922*

A brow weighed down by laurel leaves,[2]
And your name lit up with honors, may
Your star now burst onto the eaves
Of a triumphal arc's new day.

The world moves forth with human thought          5
That life will bear new fruit;
And reflects therein what the morning brought
A new sphere for women's pursuit.

Just like men, from suffrage you come,
But loftier in such spiritual things;          10
Your name in moral purity will thrum
The earth's improvement it brings.

This evolution, a wonderful story,
Marks great steps toward Progress.
And wraps New Mexico in such glory          15
Putting a woman in Congress.

Capable, competent, honest,
A sincere heart, a gentle hero,
This is woman at her best,
Acclaimed by the people, Adelina Otero!          20

1. Translated by Harold Augenbraum and Ilan Stavans.
2. In ancient Greece, laurel leaves symbolized victory.

A noble branch of a Spanish line,
Still, American through and through,
But what do they matter, these external signs,
When such fineness exists in you?

Human grandeur is found                          25
In not just one nation on this earth;
To heaven alone your gifts redound,
Such beauty designed in birth.

I mean not only flattery
With servile words and egoism,                   30
Only such grand thoughts design your mastery
To knit justice into idealism.

A toast! A toast! Be of good cheer!
Joy from a progressive man,
I send you along with this, my air,              35
The best from a sovereign land.

1922                                             1924

## Don Julio Berlanga[1]

It was in August 1918 that I had the honor of meeting Don Julio Berlanga, from ————, in Las Vegas, N. Mex.

Don Julio was an industrious man of 48 years of age, about six feet tall, upright, muscular, with sandy-colored skin and prominent cheekbones, a thick, black mustache and hair, lively eyes, even though they were a bit sunk in their sockets, not ready of wit or humor (though he knew how to appreciate them in others), but always frank and serious in his conversation, even when it was frivolous.

A kind of innocent vanity showed through Don Julio's good qualities; he was sober, hard-working and constant in his occupations, which in a person of such serious character, was very amusing. To give a clearer idea of his particular character, it would be better to tell, in a specific way, the description that he himself gave me of the happiest day of his life.

We were both seated in the waiting room of a railway station, chatting, when he said to me,

"I'll never forget this place, Las Vegas. Do you know why?"

I gave him an inquisitive look and after a brief pause, he went on. "Because it was here, last year, that I spent the happiest day of my life. Well, I arrived here the afternoon of the third of July from Wyoming, where I had been shepherding for a year. I came with the idea of having a few days of rest and recreation, attracted by the reputation of the cowboy gathering that takes place the third, fourth and fifth of the month.

"As soon as I got here I had dinner. Then, I went to the barber's and had a bath, got myself clean, did my hair and beard, and immediately went to a shop to buy clothes. I bought a suit that cost me fifty pesos, a hat that cost

1. Translated by Harold Augenbraum.

ten, shoes that cost twelve, silk socks, a purple silk shirt with a proper collar, and a tie that went with it. My friend, I spent ninety pesos like it was one! But with the three hundred more I had brought with me, and the three hundred I had left in the bank in Rawlings, what did that matter? I went to my room and dressed in my new clothes from head to toe, and since I had brought a watch and fob that had cost me sixty pesos in Rawlings, I was dressed, my friend, to the nines! But I took one last look in that mirror . . .

"In both the barber shop and the street I had heard tell of a dance that was going to be given that same night in a salon named La Favorita. After I got dressed, I poked around Las Vegas's two town squares, and even though I didn't know anyone to speak of, I had a good time. Then I went to the arena to see the roping matches and bronco-busting and bull-riding, all of which I thoroughly enjoyed.

"When I left the park, the idea entered my head to strut my stuff that night at La Favorita, since there are times when one has a desire to strut one's stuff. After supper I went to the shows, and it would be nine o'clock before I arrived at the dance. When I entered the salon, which was full of people, everyone looked me over from head to toe, since to tell you the truth, my friend, not a single local could come near me without being 'eclipsed', to coin a phrase, by the handsomeness of clothes and the elegance of my person.

"I stood looking at all the women there, until I saw the most beautiful woman I had ever seen, chatting with another woman off to the side opposite to where I was. I saw her looking at me and whispering to her friend. Then I went over and invited her to dance and suddenly she took my arm and we walked to the middle of the salon. Everyone was looking at us, and admiring us, my friend, and me showing off with that beautiful woman. Finally, I stopped and said, 'My friends, let's everyone who would like to accompany your humble servant, Julio Berlanga, be my guest and dance a waltz. Be my guest, those who will, it's on me!'"

"All but two or three shouted, 'Long live Julio Berlanga!' like an ocean, my friend, of riotous cheers for Julio Berlanga, and me strutting with that beautiful woman.

"Finally the ticket-taker came over and said to me, 'Twenty-six people have accepted your invitation, are you going to pay for them all?' I replied that I would, giving him a couple of pesos. He gave me back seventy cents, but I said to him, 'Keep the change, son.' Needless to say, my friend, that ticket-taker was all mine. I repeated the same 'aicion'[2] three or four times, and that dance was my throne, my friend, everybody toasting me with their most amiable attention and courtesy, nothing could be better. Of the twenty or so pieces I danced that night, in fifteen my partner was that beautiful woman I told you about. In the end, she let me take her home after the dance. This woman was married, but her husband had left her nine months before and she lived with her sister. In the end I asked her to go with me to Wyoming so we could be together. Three days later I went to St. Louis to see my people, and three days after that I returned and we left.

---

2. Chacón is poking fun at Don Julio's poor diction for *acción*.

"But that woman, in the end, paid me back in spades. I set up house-keeping in Rawlings and gave her plenty of money and necessities until when I returned from working, an absence of about six weeks. Since my work required travel, I almost never expected to get a letter from her, but a week into my absence I got one that said that she was well, that she loved me as much as ever, and that she awaited my return to Rawlings so we could get married. I replied that her pleasure was mine, but after six weeks I returned to find other people living in my house. I later found out that she had sold the furniture and had gone off with an American. I was mad as a hound dog! I never saw her again. But I'll never forget the day I met her, that day I enjoyed the measure of my desires, nor that dance, my friend, because at that dance I was the king, the lion himself! Nothing could be better."

1924

# ISIDORO ARMIJO
## 1871–1949

Isidoro Armijo enjoyed eminent standing as a writer and editor for New Mexican newspapers, but his literary reputation in the non-Hispanic world was based solely on one poorly translated story: "Sesenta minutos en los infiernos," originally published in the newspaper *El Eco del Valle* in 1911, was published in *Laughing Horse* magazine in 1924 as "Sixty Minutes in Hades." The scholar Gabriel Meléndez notes that this translation "represents the lone instance of a Neo-Mexicano writer crossing over to English publication before 1930," though a case can also be made for Vicente J. Bernal's posthumously published *Las primicias* (1916) as having this status (see p. 442).

Armijo graduated from the College of Agriculture and Mechanical Arts, after which he worked as a teacher in Doña Ana County, New Mexico. He later worked as a newspaper writer in Las Cruces, New Mexico, traveled extensively in the United States and Mexico, and in 1899 returned to Las Cruces, where he became active in local and state politics. From 1900 to 1904, Armijo was editor of *El Eco del Valle*, and from 1904 to 1908 he edited *La Flor del Valle*. Beginning in 1914, he served a term in the New Mexico House of Representatives, and he then returned principally to journalism, editing and publishing some of the most prominent newspapers in the state, including *El Eco del Valle*, *La Flor del Valle*, and *La Estrella*.

"Sixty Minutes in Hell," newly translated here, is a brief but vivid story of Florencia True and Eduardo Green, a husband and wife whose prospects of marital happiness have been undermined by the husband's focus on work and worldly success. In this traditional examination of the tension between public achievement and personal intimacy, Armijo's depiction of the relationship between the two main characters may lack moral nuance and the emotional restraint popular in Anglo letters of the time. However, his narrative method, portraying multiple viewpoints through letters in addition to the objective narration, presents mature themes with literary sophistication. Armijo's use of Anglo last names for the main characters and Florencia's paraphrase of *Don Juan* (canto 1, verse 194), by the English poet Lord Byron, may be taken as evidence of Anglo influence in New Mexican letters of the time, a desire to appeal to an Anglo audience, or a veiled criticism of an Anglo way of life that replaces humanistic values with financial striving.

## Sixty Minutes in Hell[1]

For several minutes Eduardo Green remained seated at his writing desk, without moving, in his beautiful home's magnificent, well-lighted library in the suburbs of a western city, contemplating the small sheets of paper he held in his hands. He had read and reread them, each time growing increasingly anxious, until every word was etched on his mind.

It was too awful to be true, too horrible. It had to be a dream, a nightmare, the mind's betrayal. In a moment he would wake up to find everything still in place, including his graceful wife, the bride he had brought to his house and taken to his heart only a year ago.

Florence had run off, had left him. Had she left him for another man? No, that would be impossible, could not be, just must not be! But here was the letter. It was her writing, her signature; the bitter and accusatory words had come from her.

He picked up the letter and read it again, the way an accused man reads his own death sentence. Her words were already familiar. He read them again, with no anger or resentment in his eyes, nothing but silent feeling.

> My dear husband (it would be strange not to call you that, to call you by some other expression, so I address you this way, for the last time),

> I say for the last time, which I mean, because by the time you read these words the sacred terms "husband" and "wife" will no longer hold any meaning for us. By then I will be the wife of another man, perhaps not in the eyes of the law, but surely in my heart and before the only Being who has the right to judge me.

> When I walked down the aisle with you, a year ago, I trusted you, and I abandoned myself to a future happiness in your arms. I didn't dream then that I would be forced to take this step now. I know what the world will say. I know that all the shame will fall on my narrow shoulders, while you will get sympathy and commiseration. But even that does not stem my resolve. In the end, you and I will know the truth, and in the end, after the initial bitterness of your resentment, perhaps you will forget a part of what I am saying to you today.

> During our courtship—when I think back on that time, it seems like a hundred years ago—you always said such sweet words of love, such gallant words poured into such willing ears. But soon after the wedding you tired of me, the way a small child tires of a new toy. My soul starved, and would have been grateful for even empty expressions of love, but even those were not forthcoming . . . nothing but neglect. A few times you spoke blithely of love and you kissed me, but not very

1. Translated by Harold Augenbraum.

often. Even then there was nothing in the brush of your lips against mine, nothing of the old fire, of that electric touch of before. You were merely performing an unwanted task, without even thinking about it. That was all! Even though it may have meant nothing to you, Eduardo, it meant a great deal to me: life, pleasure, honor, everything a woman holds dear!

A hungry rat, in its desperation, will attack even a man. When a woman's soul hungers, when it pines for love, it will risk everything. Love—and a husband's companionship—is the sweetest thing in the world. If a woman doesn't have it, she will go elsewhere for the love and sympathy she so very much desires.

Yet even then I did not go looking for it! It came to me without my having sought it out. Since I no longer had any part of your love, I needed to take what was offered.

It was you who had roused the tender buds of my womanly affection, and then you who, by your studied neglect and indifference, let another man care for them and cultivate them and bring them to bloom.

Yes, Eduardo, you are entirely to blame. Even though your pride has been dealt a blow, in the end having taken you at your word (unspoken, certainly, but no less real), I hope and I believe that you will be better off without me. As for me, whatever my future will be, I can feel no less wretched than I have during the past two months, slighted and forgotten. I feel compelled to say this to the man who had promised to love me and comfort me for the rest of our lives.

I suffered in silence, as much as I could, and now I am free. Yes, Eduardo, free! And the terrible price I will have to pay for this freedom is evidence of how important it is to me and how much I have had to bear in order to reach this point.

I have one more thing to request. If in the first outburst of blind rage—not because of the meaningless loss of an unloved, unappreciated woman but for the indignity dealt you and your abilities as a husband—you believe you can erase the stain from your love by spilling blood, leave him alone and kill me. I alone must bear that guilt. You have hardly spoken a single word of affection since the end of our honeymoon. My heart is starved for love, for your love, Eduardo, if only I could have had it. But no, not once. You were always too busy, taken up with your club, or with politics or with some other affair that kept you out of the house and unable to pay any attention to poor little me. You denied me the love and affection that by rights belonged to me. Maybe you gave them to another woman, but I would know nothing of that. I only know that though my heart asked for love, it got nothing but disdain. Do you remember the last time you even kissed me? Assuredly not. You have so many other important things on your mind!

> For Man love is a thing Apart
> For women it is life itself.

Byron was right. To you, our marriage was just a small thing, a speck. For me it was everything. Our paths came to a crossroads, and they diverged. It was the seventh of August, only two months ago, but to me those two months without your affection have been an eternity. Do you remember, Eduardo, how open and affectionate I was when you arrived home that evening? I was in such a loving mood. I brought my lips to yours and waited for the usual kiss, but instead you tried to shove me aside, saying that the time had come to cease such childishness. Do you remember how I clung to you until I had gotten my kiss, the last one you gave me?

As incoherent as it may be, this letter comes straight from my heart. A soul struggling in its agony does not stop to choose just the right word.

I do not ask for your forgiveness—there is nothing to forgive—the only thing I ask is that you forget me as soon as you can. And when you have accomplished that (which undoubtedly will not take long since I am already half-forgotten), I know you will be much happier than I have ever been able to make you.

If you would like to send me a few words of farewell or communicate with me, you can direct them to me under my maiden name at General Delivery, Chicago, and it will get to me safely. Once more, goodbye, and may God help us both.

Florencia

Flinging the letter onto his desk, Eduardo Green shook violently. He began to pace back and forth with long strides, steadily, the way a tiger paces in his cage. His wife's portrait hung on the wall. Stopping in front of it he raised his hands in supplication.

"My God, my God," he groaned, "she is gone forever. How am I going to face the world without her? What shall I do?"

He stopped speaking and slumped into the chair at his desk. His thoughts were clear. Taking up paper and pencil, with great intensity he began to write the following letter.

My queen, my Cleopatra,[2] my idol,

I have read your farewell letter with the deepest of feelings. Even though I feel weighed down and sickened by the great calamity that has befallen me, I bear no ill will toward you at all. It is all my fault. My heart has been deeply wounded by your accusations, and their truth. God forgive me and take pity on me, they are all too true! I did take you for granted. I did neglect you: pitilessly, cruelly, and, even worse, unintentionally, without even a single thought. You are the only woman I have ever loved, the only one who has ever been important in my life. Until I read your letter I had no idea what a woman's heart needs. I could not have imagined what a delicate flower a woman can be, and how easily that flower can wither. I am a man and I judged a woman's feelings from a man's point of view.

---

2. Legendarily seductive Egyptian queen (69 BC–30 BC).

I was preoccupied by my business affairs during the day and the casino where I went in the evening; in my own unseeing way I was happy. I never thought about your loneliness, or even that a heart might be breaking at home.

I do remember the incident to which you are referring. Business affairs had not gone well in those days, and I was nervous and irritable. I never wanted to treat you as badly as I did, but once it was done, once the words had been uttered, I was too stubborn to take them back. I have wanted to ask your forgiveness a thousand times since then and begin anew. But each time the devil of contrarity who lives deep in the breast of every man said to me: No, let her make the first move. And, stupidly, I listened to his advice instead of following the dictates of my own heart.

Nevertheless, tonight I came home two hours earlier than usual, fully determined to confess my faults to you, but it was too late. I have cast aside the woman with whom I was tied by the greatest of all attachments, the woman who only one year ago placed the happiness of her life and her honor under my protection. I have failed in the great duty I took upon myself, and I have only one manner of redress: to disappear from the world forever and leave you as you should be, legally free to be with the man that you have chosen as a companion and protector.

That is what I must do. By the time you get this note, I will be dead, in these rooms—our rooms—with a bullet in my heart. Then you will be able to come back to your old home and accompany me to my last dwelling. It will be better this way. And then when you have forgotten all about me (which won't be long), you will be able to go back to his side, without anyone being able to cast aspersions on your good name.

I have failed you in everything else, I know, but I will not do so now. Farewell, my beloved wife. When you see that I am dead, I hope that this act of mine and the love you once had for me will make you forget what has happened.

> With great regret,
> Eduardo

P.S. I enclose your letter with my own, so that no one but you will know the cause of my death, and because my body will not be discovered until you return, you will no doubt in some way be able to explain your absence without giving rise to criticism or idle rumors. My final, anxious desire, beloved Florencia, is to help you avoid the censure that may come to pass as a result of the terrible step I am about to take.

Eduardo Green folded the two letters and addressed them to Florence True (writing that name seemed so odd to him), General Delivery, Chicago, Illinois. Then, opening a drawer in his desk, he withdrew a high-caliber, pearl-handled revolver, examining it carefully to make sure it was loaded and ready to use, and put it on top of the letters.

"I think everything is ready. The only thing left to do is to post the letter and then . . . everything will be finished," he said, coldly playing with the weapon.

At that moment he heard the front door open and a familiar sound of steps was heard in the living room. Grabbing the gun, he turned his head and found himself face-to-face with his wife, who was hurrying into the room.

"You here?" she said, and saw her husband's pale face and red-rimmed eyes.

"Yes, me. I thought you had gone with . . . with . . ."

"No. I thought about doing it, but I couldn't. A sudden change of heart came over me when I got to the station where he was waiting for me. I saw the enormity of my mistake, the evil of the act I was about to commit, and I told him so, and I told him we would never see each other again. As soon as I convinced him I was serious and made him understand that our foolish dream was over, I hurried back, thinking that I would get here in time to destroy my letter and continue my life with you, despite its being full of unhappiness. But I see that you've already read it, and I'm sure that you will no longer want me as your wife. You wanted me so little before, and now . . ."

"Florence," he exclaimed, with a tremor in his voice, "whatever you have done is my fault, I made you do it. Me, and only me, I was the cause of your feeling forced to break your sacred marriage vows."

"Please, Eduardo, don't even think such things," she exclaimed, her voice bruised and heavy. "I never broke my marriage vows. I could never bring myself to that point while I lived in the house that bears your name and honor. I would not even let him kiss my hand. There would be time for that, if . . . if . . . I had gone with him.

"But when he spoke of love, Eduardo, I sinned against you in my heart. And perhaps I am only worthy of living with a husband who rejects me. I see you have a gun ready. Take it and kill me if you wish. I am prepared, even willing, to die, if you would be happier without me. Go ahead, Eduardo, I am ready!"

"No, Florencia," he begged, "don't say such things. I cannot bear for you to accuse yourself like this, when my conscience tells me that I am the cause of our unfortunate past. I have made you suffer, cruelly and unjustly. During the past hour, I have suffered the torments of hell, sixty minutes of horrible agony that have made me pay dearly for my neglecting you.

"I read your letter. Most likely you would like to read my reply. I was about to go out to mail it when you arrived. This gun was meant for me, not for you."

He offered her a chair and, tearing open the envelope, handed her the response he had just written.

As she read it, tears filled her eyes and rolled down her cheeks. When she had finished, she flung the letter away and, with a fitful trembling, stretched her arms toward her husband. She tried to get up, but the room began to spin, and she would have fallen had he not gotten up quickly, caught her, and held her tightly to his chest.

For a time, she remained there, more dead than alive, while he stroked her hands and called her name. Bit by bit, the color came back to her lips, and her face regained its expressiveness. Staring into his eyes, which returned her gaze with longing, she whispered, "I'm so sad, so . . ."

"I'm not," her husband replied, with a passionate kiss cutting short the rest of her confession. "This has taught me how little value life would hold without you. Now that my safe haven has been reborn, I'll never make your life unhappy again, nor forget the attention a loving wife deserves."

September 23, 1911

# Acculturation: 1899–1945

The first half of the twentieth century was a period of difficult integration for Latinos. Within recent memory, the western border of the United States had been the Mississippi River. Mexico's transfer of two-thirds of its land to its northern neighbor, under the Treaty of Guadalupe Hidalgo, reshaped the United States, whose new southwestern territories provided attractive real estate for Anglo business expansion. But the former Mexican lands had already developed emphatic local cultures shaped by idiosyncratic *criollo*, *mestizo*, and indigenous populations with an attachment to the soil. For decades, some of those areas, especially in New Mexico, had remained almost totally isolated from the rest of the world. Language, cuisine, and traditions had acquired unique characteristics. It is therefore not surprising that in subsequent decades, Anglos and *mexicanos* in the Southwest engaged in fearful relations.

After the period of the Civil War (1861–65) and Reconstruction (1865–77)—during which the U.S government put down the southern states' secession and attempted to establish order in the South—the country underwent rapid industrialization. Roads, telephone service, postal delivery, radio, and newspapers helped bridge economic internal divisions left by the Civil War, though cultural divides remained deep. President Abraham Lincoln's Emancipation Proclamation (1863) had freed the slaves in the southern states, and the North's victory in the war assured the end of slavery throughout the country, but African Americans continued to be segregated and treated unequally. In 1900, Latinos were a minority of approximately three million out of 76 million, comprising Mexicans in the Southwest plus a small group of Cuban exiles and Puerto Rican migrants in the Northeast. No sense of unity existed among these Latino subgroups, yet alienation defined their status: After the Spanish-American War (1898), the Spanish language was perceived by Anglos as the tongue of a barbaric empire.

As discussed in the "Annexations" introduction, that war had forced the Spanish Crown from the Caribbean Basin, but the power vacuum was filled by the forceful presence of the United States. Using the Monroe Doctrine to justify the control of its neighbors to the south, the United States decisively defined the hemisphere's economic, labor, and diplomatic relations.

Mexico endured the 30-year-plus dictatorship of Porfirio Díaz, who solidified the wealth of a small elite but kept a large portion of the country's population in poverty. The country then underwent a socialist revolution (1910–20). U.S. intellectuals such as the journalist John Reed and the writer

Ambrose Bierce became infatuated with the revolutionary activities. Conversely, Mexican intellectuals and dissidents such as Mariano Azuela, author of the novel *Los de abajo* (The Underdogs, 1915), sought refuge in the United States, predominantly in Texas, where the number of Mexicans exceeded half a million. The demographic map quickly changed, as a million and a half people crossed the border to flee the revolutionary struggle.

This was the first major immigration of *mexicanos* to the United States. More immigrants were drawn during World War I (1914–18; U.S. involvement began in 1917), when the loss of men in the United States for fighting overseas meant that workers were needed north of the Rio Grande for farming, mining, and railroad construction. And as Mexico recovered from the impact of the peasant revolution, it became immersed in *La Cristiada*, an anticlerical crusade and counterrevolutionary uprising that reacted against some provisions of the Mexican Constitution, which had been drafted in 1917 by a liberal government eager to suppress the power of the Catholic Church in the country. Again, especially in southern Mexico, people were pushed to move elsewhere.

## The Great Migration

Immigration by Latinos into the Northeast also intensified during the first two decades of the twentieth century. After the military clash of 1898, the status of Cuba remained in question. Some forces on both sides favored independence, and others favored annexation. U.S. president William McKinley placed the island in a 20-year interregnum. When Theodore Roosevelt, who had fought in the Spanish-American War, succeeded McKinley, Cuba was given its independence (1902), although the U.S. retained the right to intervene in Cuban affairs. This situation was destabilized when an armed revolt took place in 1906. The U.S. then occupied the island and placed Charles Edward Magoon as governor.

Cuba continued to undergo dramatic changes. An elected president was restored in 1908, but racial divisions undercut the efforts by civil governments. In 1912, part of the Afro-Cuban population in Oriente province attempted to create a separate republic. The effort was crushed by Havana's centralized regime. Gerardo Machado, who had fought in the war of independence, became a dictatorial president, and his control of the island lasted from 1925 to 1933. General Fulgencio Batista, a mulatto leader, was involved in a series of coups and debacles. In 1940, backed by the Communist Party and with the initial support of the United States, Batista was elected president. He served a first term (1940–44), retired, and then staged a coup that restored his power (1952–58).

The Cuban literary production in the United States in this period was relatively small. In the tradition of Félix Varela (see p. 173), José María Heredia (p. 203), and José Martí (p. 265), the émigré poet Eugenio Florit lived in New York City, where he taught at Columbia University. Florit wrote most of his mature literary output in the United States, but cases like this were few. In contrast, Puerto Ricans, in successive waves of immigration, solidified their roots in New York and the surrounding areas during this time. Not long after the Spanish-American War, the destinies of Cuba and Puerto Rico split and never again paralleled each other. After the war, Puerto Rico also came under U.S. military rule, and in 1900 the Foraker Act gave the island limited civil governance. Among other liberties, Puerto Ricans were allowed to choose, through a popular vote, their House of Delegates, although the governor and Executive Council were appointed by the U.S. president.

In 1917, the Jones Act made Puerto Ricans—unlike Cubans—U.S. citizens and increased their participation in their own government by adding an elective Senate to the island's legislature. (For the text of the Jones Act, see Appendix 2: Treaties, Acts, and Propositions, p. A15.) The Puerto Rican political leader largely responsible for this early legal transformation of the island was Luis Muñoz Rivera. He had led the political movement that pressured Spain to pass the *Carta Autonómica* (Charter of Autonomy, 1897), which granted self-government and civil liberties to Puerto Rico. He then became secretary of state in the Cabinet of the new autonomist government. A few months later, when the U.S. invasion put an end to Spanish jurisdiction over the island, he was among the supporters of the new American regime.

However, Muñoz Rivera also opposed the initial U.S. military governorship, and after Congress approved the Foraker Act, he pushed for greater participation of Puerto Rican leaders in an island administration run largely by U.S. officials. He voiced the concerns of the island's *criollo* propertied class, which was being hurt by a U.S.-imposed trade blockade, new shipping tariffs, the rapid influx of U.S. corporate capital, and the change from Spanish currency to the American dollar. He also sought free trade between the island and the mainland, to benefit Puerto Rico's landowners and businessmen. Disillusioned with the unilateral policies of the U.S.-controlled government, the increasing power of U.S. corporations, and the acrimonious political divisions among Puerto Ricans leaders, he moved to New York, where in 1901 he founded the bilingual newspaper *The Puerto Rico Herald*. In its editorials, Muñoz Rivera was critical of the Foraker Act's detrimental effects on the island's economy and its propertied class and of Puerto Ricans' lack of self-government.

During the first three decades of U.S. rule, Puerto Rico's intellectual and political elites continued to be absorbed by debate about the effects of unilateral Americanization policies, the unresolved colonial status of the island, and the extreme poverty of most of its population. Muñoz Rivera's son, Luis Muñoz Marín, considered by many the father of modern Puerto Rico, carried on the struggle for self-government by founding, in 1938, the Partido Popular Democrático (Popular Democratic Party). The idea of a self-governing commonwealth, or *Estado Libre Asociado* (Free Associated State), had been supported by political leaders of earlier periods, but change in the island's socioeconomic conditions and internal governance did not begin until the administrations of U.S. presidents Franklin Delano Roosevelt (1933–45) and Harry S. Truman (1945–53). Muñoz Marín and others spearheaded a compromise that culminated in the appointment by Truman in 1946 of the first Puerto Rican–born governor, Jesús T. Piñero. In 1947, the United States granted Puerto Ricans the right to elect their own governor, an important accomplishment in Muñoz Marín's efforts to eventually secure a compact that would allow the island a substantial degree of autonomy while maintaining a permanent union with the United States. Muñoz Marín became the island's first elected governor and served from 1948 to 1964, and the Estado Libre Asociado de Puerto Rico was officially inaugurated in 1952.

Yet Muñoz Marín was not only a career politician. He was also a poet and an essayist fascinated, as a young man, with political philosophers, especially the nineteenth-century German socialist Karl Marx and the nineteenth- and twentieth-century U.S. poet Edwin Markham. Early on, he lived a bohemian life in New York and Washington, D.C. (where he was known as *"El Vate,"* the Bard). During this period, he wrote in English for U.S. liberal and progressive newspapers such as *The Nation, The New Republic,* and *The American Mercury*; he criticized the U.S. colonial government's failure to eradicate poverty in Puerto Rico, denounced the stranglehold of U.S. corporations on the island's economy, advocated for social justice in Puerto Rico and democratic rule for its people, and also supported the island's independence.

Despite Muñoz Marín's political dreams, when his party came to power in Puerto Rico he traded in the ideal of independence for what he considered a more pragmatic political arrangement with the United States—one that would allow self-government, the influx of U.S. capital investment, and the improvement of socioeconomic conditions, but also maintain U.S. military presence and territorial jurisdiction over the island. The lasting contribution of Muñoz Marín to the idea of a Free Associated State was his emphasis, as cultural critic Juan Flores puts it in his book *Divided Borders: Essays on Puerto Rican Identity* (1993), on a "convenient amalgam of cultural nationalism and cultural assimilation." Such an amalgam is clear in reflections by Muñoz Marín such as:

> We know that Puerto Rican culture, like that of the United States, is and has to be part of the great tradition of Western culture. But there is no such thing as a Western man who is not a man from some place in the Western world. If we are not Western with Puerto Rican roots, we will be Western without roots at all. And the vitality of a people has a great need for roots. We are a Western people in the manner of our own roots. We are Americans of the United States and Americans of America and Westerners of the West. And we are still this as Puerto Ricans from Puerto Rico.

Another notable political figure of the period was Pedro Albizu Campos, a leader of the Partido Nacionalista Puertorriqueño (Puerto Rican Nationalist Party). Pushing for complete independence from the United States, he galvanized a movement that defied the U.S. occupation of the island. Nationalist activism eventually moved from the rhetorical to a series of violent confrontations with colonial authorities and the local police. Albizu Campos was imprisoned several times in Puerto Rico and the United States. In 1943, after suffering a heart attack in the Atlanta, Georgia, federal prison, where he had been incarcerated since 1937, Albizu Campos was hospitalized in New York and for several years was not allowed to return to the island. The Nationalists' motto was *la patria es valor y sacrificio* (the motherland requires courage and sacrifice), and many Nationalists gave their lives, went to prison, or were blacklisted by the colonial authorities. During his tenure as governor, Muñoz Marín pardoned Albizu Campos twice in response to local and international pressures.

In the 1930s, economic stagnation in Puerto Rico increased the number of migrants to the United States, especially to New York City, to 1,700 a year. In 1930, there were 52,774 Puerto Ricans in the United States. That number ballooned to 69,967 by 1940 and 301,375 by 1950, after the beginning of *Operación Manos a la Obra* (Operation Put Your Hands to Work; known in English as "Operation Bootstrap"), a U.S.-led mass-industrialization and -modernization program that had a detrimental effect on the island's agricultural economy and displaced a large number of agricultural workers. It was also common during this period for U.S. companies to recruit laborers from Puerto Rico to work in mainland factories. From 1950 to 1960, about half a million Puerto Ricans left the island for the United States. The mobilization of Puerto Ricans, many of whom were *jíbaros*, countryside dwellers in search of better jobs, became known as the Great Migration (echoing the movement of blacks—from the South to the North, Midwest, and West—that started after World War I and continued until 1970). The reasons behind this mass migration were primarily economic. As the island underwent a transition from an agricultural to an industrial society, migration to the United States became an escape valve for surplus labor. Moreover, since the agricultural, manufacturing, construction, and military industries in the United States desperately needed workers—especially because of the labor shortage during World War II (1939–45; U.S. involvement began in 1941) and the economic expansion of later years—recruitment of low-wage workers from the island was encouraged by local and federal authorities.

New York became the unofficial Puerto Rican cultural capital outside the island. It also became an important refuge for many Nationalists who were blacklisted and thus unable to find work in Puerto Rico. But as exemplified in Manhattan neighborhoods such as Spanish Harlem and the Lower East Side, poverty among Puerto Ricans on the mainland was widespread, since the available jobs paid poorly. In addition, the newcomers, many of whom were black or of mixed race, experienced racism and discrimination. The migrants often expressed their experiences, struggles, and sense of alienation through music, dance, and literature. Many were strongly committed to achieving social justice and to building organizations and institutions endowed with the responsibility of advocating for civil rights, improving socioeconomic conditions, and protecting the collective memory.

The foundational figures in the Puerto Rican cultural expansion include scholars and private collectors, poets and memoirists, journalists and political activists. Among the pioneers was Arthur Alfonso Schomburg, the son of a German merchant living in Puerto Rico and a black laundress from Saint Thomas. A scholar attached to the Pan-African and Harlem Renaissance movements, Schomburg was heavily involved in New York's Cuban and Puerto Rican independence movements in the 1890s. In later years, he distanced himself from the Puerto Rican community and established closer ties with African Americans, investing most of his energies in the building of a collection of artifacts from the African diaspora that also included the Caribbean Basin. Schomburg saw the effort as a way "to dig up the past," to show that African Americans in the United States and blacks in other parts of the world had a rich, multifaceted tradition.

William Carlos Williams, a doctor and poet from Paterson, New Jersey, whose mother was Puerto Rican, was among the earliest U.S. writers to look at Latino history as an essential chapter in the nation's history. His influential prose work *In the American Grain* (1925) makes the case for understanding the word *American* in its broadest sense. Williams intertwines provocative profiles of historical figures of diverse extraction—such as the Viking explorer Eric the Red; the Genoese explorer Christopher Columbus; the Aztec emperor Moctezuma; the Spanish conquistadors Hernán Cortés, Juan Ponce de León, and Hernando de Soto; the English courtier and navigator Sir Walter Raleigh; the U.S. Revolutionary War figures George Washington, Benjamin Franklin, and Aaron Burr; and the U.S. pioneer Daniel Boone—to suggest that the United States should be seen together with the rest of the Americas to understand the hemisphere's culturally heterogeneous past. In his essays, memoirs, and poetry, Williams depicted himself and his surroundings as "a nation in transition."

Bernardo Vega was an emblematic community activist. A Puerto Rican *tabaquero* (cigar worker) who had been involved in the socialist labor struggles on the island, he migrated to New York in 1916. There he joined many other migrant *tabaqueros*, who constituted a significant portion of the city's growing Latino community—composed primarily of Puerto Ricans, Cubans, and Spaniards—during the 1910s and '20s. Published in 1977, his memoir of being an artisan in the decades before the Great Migration shows Latinos of Caribbean extraction and Spaniards joining the city's working class and struggling to survive in a racist and unwelcoming metropolis. In 1927, Vega became the owner of *Gráfico* (1926–31), a weekly newspaper started by a group of tobacco workers. Self-described as *defensor de la raza hispana* (defender of the Hispanic race), it was one of several Spanish-language community newspapers that promoted unity among the various Hispanic groups in the city.

Vega's hometown friend Jesús Colón migrated to New York in 1918 and, influenced by the socialist culture of the *tabaqueros*, became a community leader, labor organizer, and prolific newspaper columnist. He wrote for *Gráfico*, among other periodicals, in Spanish and *The Daily Worker* in English. His feelings toward the United States matched the range of Latinos' emotions about the country. An anticolonialist, Colón applauded the democratic spirit in the United States, but denounced the racism and class differences there as well as imperialist interventions in Latin America and the Caribbean. He also embraced the independence movement of his homeland. Colón's forceful narrative dispatches were an attempt to humanize the Puerto Rican people in the eyes of a society that perceived them as stereotypes, typically threatening ones.

## *Braceros* and Zoot Suiters

The demographic face of the Southwest changed in the period after World War I, as a series of natural and economic events prompted waves of refugees, legal laborers, and undocumented Mexican workers to cross the Rio

Grande. Then the Great Depression, triggered by the stock market crash of October 29, 1929, devastated the American economy. When a severe drought turned the Great Plains into the so-called Dust Bowl, in which fierce winds blew away topsoil, displaced families from states such as Oklahoma and Arkansas went to California in search of jobs and a fresh start. From 1935 to 1938, 350,000 to 400,000 destitute people, mostly white and derogatorily referred to as "Okies" and "Arkies," arrived in the West.

During World War II, an estimated 375,000 Latinos, many of them Mexican and Puerto Rican, served in the armed forces. On the home front, as discussed above, a labor shortage was made up for by newly arrived Latinos. In 1942, the U.S. and Mexico, through a diplomatic maneuver, agreed on the Bracero Program, whereby Mexicans were admitted to the United States as field-workers. (In Spanish, *bracero* means "laborer who works with his arms." For the text of the Bracero Agreement, see Appendix 2: Treaties, Acts, and Propositions, p. A15.) The program lasted 23 years and brought north, sometimes temporarily, an estimated one million Mexicans.

While *braceros* were welcome in abstract economic terms, animosity against Mexicans intensified in the social arena. These workers contributed little to local economies, as they remitted substantial amounts of their wages to their families in Mexico. Sometimes, after harvests were finished, government officials would send the workers back to Mexico. These officials, particularly in the 1930s because of the Depression, understood repatriation (return) and deportation (removal) as synonymous—they simply wanted to move the Mexicans. The historian Rodolfo Acuña argues that between 500,000 and 600,000 Mexicans and their U.S.-born children departed the United States from 1929 to 1939: "It is speculated that half of the number came from Texas. . . . Authorities manipulated the process to drive Mexicans out of the country and, in the case of the U.S.-born children, between 60 and 75 percent of the total, they had little choice." Some Latinos supported the Bracero Program; some did not. Some, feeling powerless to change the situation, kept a low profile.

Others, such as Ernesto Galarza, campaigned against repatriation, often testifying before the U.S. Congress to support their views. Galarza had immigrated from the Mexican village of Jalcocotán to Sacramento, California, an ordeal he would later write about in his memoir, *Barrio Boy* (1971). In his eyes and those of other opponents, the Bracero Program and the subsequent repatriation of the laborers were a U.S. government stratagem to provide cheap labor while creating a hostile environment for Mexicans. In the preface to his memoir, Galarza argues that, through cartoons and biased news reports, the media portrayed *braceros* as imbeciles good only for helping companies generate profit. He reacts angrily to the demoralizing psychological attacks:

> The worst thing that has happened to [those like me] is that some psychologist, psychiatrist, social anthropologist and other manner of "shrink" have spread the rumor that these Mexican immigrants and their offspring have lost their "self-image." By this, of course, they mean that a Mexican doesn't know what he is; and if by chance he is something, it isn't any good.

I, for one Mexican, never had any doubts on this score. I can't remember a time I didn't know who I was; and I have heard much testimony from my friends and other more detached persons to the effect that I thought too highly of what I thought I was.

It seemed to me unlikely that out of six or seven million Mexicans in the United States I was the only one who felt this way.

However, as the historian George J. Sánchez has argued in *Becoming Mexican American: Ethnicity, Culture, and Identity in Chicano Los Angeles* (1993), the issue often brought about a dilemma concerning national loyalty. North of the Rio Grande, Mexicans encountered a new culture. To what extent did they benefit from that exposure? Sánchez argues that "returnees often found themselves unable to translate their American experience into tangible economic results in Mexico." Instead, as itinerant workers, they felt neither connected to their Mexican place of origin nor accepted in the United States.

In cities, Mexican American, or Chicano, culture was fluid and changed rapidly. (Reportedly among the earliest uses of the term *Chicano* in print is in the Mexican American writer Mario Suárez's "El Hoyo," a sketch that was part of a cycle Suárez published in *Arizona Quarterly* beginning in 1947. It was preceded by mentions in *décimas* of the 1940s and in Daniel Venegas's novel *The Adventures of Don Chipote*, published in 1928.) During the 1940s, in ghettos in Los Angeles and other cities in California and Texas, a tangible Spanish-speaking underclass emerged that set the stage for pachucos, *mestizo* adolescents who dressed flashily and spoke using their own jargon. Thus pachucos delineated the parameters of their minority culture by stressing their ambivalence—neither Mexican nor American, they belonged to an imagined community that straddled two cultural and linguistic worlds. When Octavio Paz, a middle-class, Caucasian Mexican poet and essayist who would be awarded the Nobel Prize in Literature in 1990, went to Los Angeles in the mid-1940s to write a series of essays in which he would try to unravel the mysteries of the Mexican psyche, his encounter with the pachuco subculture left him in a state of shock. In "The Pachuco and Other Extremes," the first chapter of the book that resulted (published in 1950 as *El Laberinto de la soledad* and translated in 1961 as *The Labyrinth of Solitude*; see Appendix 3: Influential Essays by Latin American Writers, p. A65), Paz describes the Chicanos he encountered as alienated, rowdy, erratic, and violent:

> They have lived in the city for many years, wearing the same clothes and speaking the same language as the other inhabitants, and they feel ashamed of their origin, yet no one would mistake them for authentic North Americans. . . . What distinguishes them, I think, is their furtive, restless air; they act like persons who are wearing disguises, who are afraid of a stranger's look because it could strip them and leave them stark naked.

Paz's reaction was based, in part, on a paternalism he learned from the literature of European travelers to the Americas and, in part, from the psychoanalytical views, of Alfred Adler and others, that prevailed at the time. Paz's portrait of these Mexican Americans as inauthentic generated anger among Latinos and still does. Indeed, it emphasizes the stereotype of Mexican Americans that Galarza adamantly denounced: the ethnic dweller as confused and disoriented. Like the stereotypes of Puerto Ricans in the United States, those of Mexican Americans circulated abundantly in the U.S. media. Stereotypes also emerged from within the minority, either as fleeting verbal exchanges or as full-blown explorations passing for sophisticated literature—for example, Paz's depiction of pachucos; the one-act theater pieces by playwright Josefina Niggli (published in 1938), about *campesinos*, *soldaderas* (female soldiers during the Mexican Revolution), and other "innocent" archetypes; and so on.

Negative stereotypes of Latinos set the stage for a series of violent clashes in California during World War II. The first took place in July 1942, when Chicanos and police fought after the police broke up the Chicanos' streetcorner gambling game. The next month, at a reservoir known as Sleepy Lagoon, some 600 Chicanos were rounded up and 22 indicted for murder after a Mexican American youth, José Díaz, was killed in a brawl. In reporting both incidents, the media depicted young Chicanos as out of control, but failed to depict the historical context of alienation and labor abuse in which they lived.

In Los Angeles in May 1943, the Zoot Suit Riots proved an even larger manifestation of animosity and unrest. In fighting between white sailors and Chicanos, one of the sailors was injured. His friends blamed *zoot suiters*, using a derogatory term based on the fashion style of pachucos, young Filipino Americans, and some young Italian Americans: high-waisted, wide-legged, tight-cuffed pegged trousers (*tramas*); a long coat (*carlango*) with wide lapels and wide, padded shoulders; a felt hat (*tanda*) with a long feather; and pointy shoes (*calcos*). In retaliation for the first injury, the sailors stabbed one pachuco and then targeted other *mexicanos* in East Los Angeles. At the scene, the police arrested only Chicanos.

In the following days, the violence became a full-blown riot. Anglos widened their attacks to include African Americans. Automobiles were burned. Businesses were destroyed. Hundreds of pachucos and nine sailors were arrested. The governor of California, Earl Warren, created an ad hoc committee to investigate the riots. The resulting state report asked that everyone involved be punished, indicated that the press had done much to agitate people, and recommended better training for policemen who interacted with the Mexican American community. Even the Mexican government became involved, asking for damages to be paid to the Mexican American victims.

As the historian Eduardo Pagán notes in his book *Murder at the Sleepy Lagoon: Zoot Suits, Race & Riots in Wartime L.A.* (2003), which analyzes the explosive confluence of ethnicity and alienation, the Zoot Suit Riots were a watershed event in Latino history. The subject of reflection in fiction, nonfiction, poetry, and theater, the riots would prove a decisive factor in shaping Chicano consciousness during the civil rights era. Arguably the most significant artistic representation is Luis Valdez's play *Zoot Suit* (1978), which places the incidents against a large historical canvas that includes the Sleepy Lagoon Incident, the Bracero Program, *mestizaje*, and the Aztec past. The riots have also been represented in mainstream U.S. culture, such as in Thomas Sanchez's novel *Zoot-Suit Murders* (1978) and a scene in Steven Speilberg's movie *1941* (1979).

## Assimilationist Views

While the Latino literary tradition includes many direct responses to historical events, the tradition has been shaped by the tension between standard trends and rebellious visions. Thus the Latino literature of this period expresses much more than the frustration and angst that can arise from questions of ethnic identity. To a large degree, the works of this period take divergent paths, experimenting with genres and styles.

In New Mexico, Latinas such as Adelina "Nina" Otero-Warren, Fabiola Cabeza de Baca Gilbert, and Cleofas Jaramillo produced a "domestic" fiction that has been called "the literature of Spanish fantasy heritage." In response to a more politicized fraction of Latinos, who articulated anxiety and alienation as a dead end, these writers romanticized the colonial past as a time of balance and harmony. Dismissed by generations of readers as escapist, their work recently has been reevaluated as valuable cultural commentary that opens new vistas into Latino life.

Otero-Warren, a native of New Mexico who ran for the U.S. House of Representatives and was a protégée of Eusebio Chacón (see p. 333), celebrated regional Spanish American customs in her book *Old Spain in Our Southwest* (1936). Cleofas Jaramillo's autobiography, *Romance of a Little Village Girl* (not published until 1955), centered on her upper-class "life of etiquette" as the daughter of a prominent New Mexican family. Cabeza de Baca Gilbert's book *We Fed Them Cactus* (1954) chronicles life in New Mexico's Llano Estacado (Staked Plains) region from her idealized perspective as a young girl. Presenting an assimilationist viewpoint that highlights integration as a ticket to happiness, these domestic works ponder questions of biculturalism marginally.

The second experimental path has a dramatically different direction. Felipe Alfau, a Spaniard who immigrated to New York, published in English a novel, *Locos: A Comedy of Gestures* (1936), that automatically opened a new path in the Latino literary tradition. Rejecting realism and politics, Alfau seated his characters in the imaginary Café de los Locos, where they discuss large philosophical questions. The novel's stories about mistaken identity, and its reflections on the purpose of literature, may remind the reader of the metaliterary works of Miguel de Unamuno, Luigi Pirandello, Jorge Luis Borges, and Italo Calvino; however, Alfau, isolated from the world of literature, was unacquainted with any of these writers' works. Although chronologically his work might be considered Modernist in the European/American sense, Alfau was a visionary artist whose writing foreshadowed the aesthetic movement called Postmodernism, which arrived in the 1960s and emphasizes ahistorical plots, baroque identity games, and self-referentiality.

The third experimental path—equally important and far more popular—was set by *The Last Puritan: A Memoir in the Form of a Novel* (1936), the only novel by George Santayana. When it became a best seller, Santayana appeared on the cover of *Time* magazine. Although he was born in Spain and remained a Spanish citizen, Santayana (not included in this anthology) was raised and educated in the United States (at Harvard University, he studied under the psychologist and philosopher William James), he wrote in English, and he is considered a cosmopolitan and a U.S. intellectual. His New

England life did not connect him with Latino life. *The Last Puritan*, a non-realistic narrative of ideas, takes place in the fictional town of Great Falls, Connecticut; in Boston; and in and around Oxford, England. It explores the self-destructive existence of the protagonist, Oliver Alden, a Puritan who rejects his past while seeking self-knowledge.

During the 1940s, academic study began of Latinos, Latino culture, and Latino literature. No courses on these subjects were being taught in colleges and universities, but important scholars did foundational work. Among these scholars is the Mexican-born Luis Leal, who initially studied south-of-the-border literature and then, as historical events such as the Zoot Suit Riots took place, turned to Mexican American experiences. Leal's wide-ranging work looks at Mexican American culture from the colonial period to the present, discussing it as an integral part of Mexican and U.S. literatures.

# ARTHUR A. SCHOMBURG
## 1874–1938

Born in San Juan, Arturo Alfonso Schomburg was a light-skinned mulatto, the son of a black laundress from Saint Thomas, Virgin Islands, and a merchant father from Germany living in Puerto Rico. He spent part of his youth in Puerto Rico and part in the Virgin Islands. As an adult, he said that he became aware of racial prejudice when one of his teachers in Puerto Rico claimed that blacks had no history and no heroes. The teacher's comment set the course for the rest of Schomburg's life, particularly his quest to recover the history of black people around the world. In his adult years, he became an avid bibliophile and devoted most of his time to assembling a remarkable collection of books, manuscripts, drawings, and other materials documenting the African diaspora in the Americas and other parts of the world.

Before he left Puerto Rico for New York City in 1891, Schomburg worked as a typographer in a San Juan print shop and also spent some time among the *tabaqueros*, working-class cigar-manufacturing artisans who were self-educated and politically aware. To New York he brought letters of introduction that placed him in contact with other Puerto Ricans—largely typographers and *tabaqueros*—involved in the Antillean separatist movement. While working as an elevator operator, a bellhop, and a printer, he attended night school to earn his high school diploma.

Schomburg wanted to study law, but racial barriers and a lack of money prevented him from pursuing higher education. He spent most of the 1890s participating in the separatist movement along with many other Puerto Rican and Cuban patriots. With Sotero Figueroa (see p. 260) and Pachín Marín (p. 317), he founded the Club Borinquen, the first of many clubs aimed at organizing Puerto Rican support for Antillean independence. A few years later, he became secretary of the Club Dos Antillas (The Two Antilles Club), another separatist organization. He also was initiated in Freemasonry and joined the El Sol de Cuba (Cuba's Sun) Lodge. This was the beginning of many decades of involvement in the black Masonic movement.

After the Spanish-American War (1898), as many separatists returned to Cuba and Puerto Rico, Schomburg grew estranged from the New York Puerto Rican community. Increasingly connected with his black roots and the African American community, he married an African American woman, anglicized his name, and moved to the black section of Harlem. There he developed long-standing friendships with many prominent black intellectuals and artists from the United States and the Caribbean, and he joined the Pan-African movement, which went on to influence the work of many leading figures of the Harlem Renaissance.

From 1906 to 1929, Schomburg worked at the Bankers Trust Company, first as a messenger and, in later years, as the supervisor of the foreign-mailing section. But the passion that occupied most of his life was collecting items related to the African heritage of the United States and other countries. He accomplished this task primarily by using his modest income to travel and purchase materials for the collection.

Schomburg's embrace of his African heritage and his ever-growing collection led to his cofounding the Negro Society for Historical Research in 1911 and to his election as president of the American Negro Academy in 1922. In 1926, he sold his vast compilation—thousands of books, documents, and so on—to the New York Public Library, which a few years later appointed him curator of the collection. By the end of his life, the Schomburg Center for Research on Black Culture, in New York, had become one of the largest and most-used repositories for recovered materials documenting the African American experience.

Schomburg was not a prolific writer. Most of his available writings consist of newspaper and journal articles. His essay "Juan Latino" (1913) is one of several biographical profiles he wrote of Hispanic black artists. In helping recognize such individuals, Schomburg aimed to keep racism from erasing the historical record. In the essay "The Negro Digs Up His Past" (1925), he stresses the need for blacks to reclaim and document their heritage and to establish a chair of Negro history at a major university, making him a precursor of the African American studies movement of the 1960s and '70s.

# The Negro Digs Up His Past[1]

The American Negro must remake his past in order to make his future. Though it is orthodox to think of America as the one country where it is unnecessary to have a past, what is a luxury for the nation as a whole becomes a prime social necessity for the Negro. For him, a group tradition must supply compensation for persecution, and pride of race the antidote for prejudice. History must restore what slavery took away, for it is the social damage of slavery that the present generations must repair and offset. So among the rising democratic millions we find the Negro thinking more collectively, more retrospectively than the rest, and apt out of the very pressure of the present to become the most enthusiastic antiquarian of them all.

Vindicating evidences of individual achievement have as a matter of fact been gathered and treasured for over a century: Abbé Gregoire's[2] liberal-minded book on Negro notables in 1808 was the pioneer effort; it has been followed at intervals by less known and often less discriminating compendiums of exceptional men and women of African stock. But this sort of thing was on the whole pathetically over-corrective, ridiculously over-laudatory; it was apologetics turned into biography. A true historical sense develops slowly and with difficulty under such circumstances. But today, even if for the ultimate purpose of group justification, history has become less a matter of argument and more a matter of record. There is the definite desire and determination to have a history, well documented, widely known at least within race circles, and administered as a stimulating and inspiring tradition for the coming generations.

Gradually as the study of the Negro's past has come out of the vagaries of rhetoric and propaganda and become systematic and scientific, three outstanding conclusions have been established:

First, that the Negro has been throughout the centuries of controversy an active collaborator, and often a pioneer, in the struggle for his own freedom and advancement. This is true to a degree which makes it the more surprising that it has not been recognized earlier.

Second, that by virtue of their being regarded as something "exceptional," even by friends and well-wishers, Negroes of attainment and genius have been unfairly disassociated from the group, and group credit lost accordingly.

---

1. Except as indicated, all footnotes are by the editors of *The Norton Anthology of African American Literature*, 2nd ed.
2. Henri Grégoire (1750–1831), French author of

*De la littérature des nègres, ou Recherches sur leurs facultés intellectuelles, leurs qualités morales, et leur littérature* (1808).

Third, that the remote racial origins of the Negro, far from being what the race and the world have been given to understand, offer a record of credible group achievement when scientifically viewed, and more important still, that they are of vital general interest because of their bearing upon the beginnings and early development of human culture.

With such crucial truths to document and establish, an ounce of fact is worth a pound of controversy. So the Negro historian today digs under the spot where his predecessor stood and argued. Not long ago, the Public Library of Harlem housed a special exhibition of books, pamphlets, prints and old engravings, that simply said, to skeptic and believer alike, to scholar and schoolchild, to proud black and astonished white, "Here is the evidence." Assembled from the rapidly growing collections of the leading Negro book-collectors and research societies, there were in these cases, materials not only for the first true writing of Negro history, but for the rewriting of many important paragraphs of our common American history. Slow though it be, historical truth is no exception to the proverb.

Here among the rarities of early Negro Americana was Jupiter Hammon's[3] Address to the Negroes of the State of New York, edition of 1787, with the first American Negro poet's famous "If we should ever get to Heaven, we shall find nobody to reproach us for being black, or for being slaves." Here was Phyllis Wheatley's Mss. poem of 1767 addressed to the students of Harvard, her spirited encomiums upon George Washington and the Revolutionary Cause,[4] and John Marrant's[5] St. John's Day eulogy to the "Brothers of African Lodge No. 459" delivered at Boston in 1789. Here too were Lemuel Haynes' Vermont commentaries on the American Revolution and his learned sermons to his white congregation in Rutland, Vermont, and the sermons of the year 1808 by the Rev. Absalom Jones of St. Thomas Church, Philadelphia, and Peter Williams[6] of St. Philip's, New York, pioneer Episcopal rectors who spoke out in daring and influential ways on the Abolition of the Slave Trade. Such things and many others are more than mere items of curiosity: they educate any receptive mind.

Reinforcing these were still rarer items of Africana and foreign Negro interest, the volumes of Juan Latino,[7] the best Latinist of Spain in the reign of Philip V, incumbent of the chair of Poetry at the University of Granada, and author of Poems printed there in 1573 and a book on the Escorial[8] published 1576; the Latin and Dutch treatises of Jacobus Eliza Capitein, a native of West Coast Africa and graduate of the University of Leyden, Gustavus Vassa's celebrated autobiography that supplied so much of the evidence in 1796 for Granville Sharpe's attack on slavery in the British colonies, Julien Raymond's Paris exposé of the disabilities of the free people of color in the then (1791) French colony of Hayti, and Baron de Vastey's *Cry of the Fatherland*, the famous polemic by the secretary of Christophe[9] that

---

3. Poet (c. 1720–c. 1806).
4. Wheatley's poem to Harvard is titled "To the University of Cambridge, in New England" and her poem to Washington, "To His Excellency General Washington" (1776).
5. Born 1755.
6. Williams (c. 1780–1840). Haynes (1753–1833), a New England minister popular with white and black congregations, published his sermon "Uni-

versal Salvation" in 1806. Jones (c. 1746–1818).
7. Latino (c. 1518–1594).
8. A palace and monastery outside Madrid.
9. Henri Christophe (1767–1820), king of Haiti from 1811 to 1820. Capitein (1717–1747), author of *De Vocatione Ethnicorum* (1737) and a thesis defending slavery (1742). Vassa (c. 1745–1797) formerly named Olaudah Equiano, wrote his autobiographical *Interesting Narrative* in 1789. Granville

precipitated the Haytian struggle for independence. The cumulative effect of such evidences of scholarship and moral prowess is too weighty to be dismissed as exceptional.

But weightier surely than any evidence of individual talent and scholarship could ever be, is the evidence of important collaboration and significant pioneer initiative in social service and reform, in the efforts toward race emancipation, colonization and race betterment. From neglected and rust-spotted pages comes testimony to the black men and women who stood shoulder to shoulder in courage and zeal, and often on a parity of intelligence and talent, with their notable white benefactors. There was the already cited work of Vassa that aided so materially the efforts of Granville Sharpe, the record of Paul Cuffee,[1] the Negro colonization pioneer, associated so importantly with the establishment of Sierra Leone as a British colony for the occupancy of free people of color in West Africa; the dramatic and history-making exposé of John Baptist Phillips,[2] African graduate of Edinburgh, who compelled through Lord Bathurst in 1824 the enforcement of the articles of capitulation guaranteeing freedom to the blacks of Trinidad. There is the record of the pioneer colonization project of Rev. Daniel Coker in conducting a voyage of ninety expatriates to West Africa in 1820, of the missionary efforts of Samuel Crowther in Sierra Leone, first Anglican bishop of his diocese, and that of the work of John Russwurm, a leader in the work and foundation of the American Colonization Society.

When we consider the facts, certain chapters of American history will have to be reopened. Just as black men were influential factors in the campaign against the slave trade, so they were among the earliest instigators of the abolition movement. Indeed there was a dangerous calm between the agitation for the suppression of the slave trade and the beginning of the campaign for emancipation. During that interval colored men were very influential in arousing the attention of public men who in turn aroused the conscience of the country. Continuously between 1808 and 1845, men like Prince Saunders, Peter Williams, Absalom Jones, Nathaniel Paul, and Bishops Varick and Richard Allen,[3] the founders of the two wings of African Methodism, spoke out with force and initiative, and men like Denmark Vesey (1822), David Walker (1828) and Nat Turner[4] (1831) advocated and organized schemes for direct action. This culminated in the generally ignored but important conventions of Free People of Color in New York, Philadelphia and other centers, whose platforms and efforts are to the Negro of as great significance as the nationally cherished memories of Faneuil and Independence Halls.[5] Then with Abolition comes the better documented and more recognized collaboration of Samuel R. Ward, William Wells Brown, Henry Highland Garnett, Martin Delany, Harriet Tubman, Sojourner Truth,

Sharp (1735–1813), a leading British abolitionist. Vastey (d. 1820), author of *Le Cri de la Patrie* (1815).
1. Cuffee (c. 1758–1817).
2. Phillips (1799–1851).
3. Allen (c. 1750–1831). Saunders (1775–1839). Paul (1775–1834). James Varick (c. 1750–1827).
4. Turner (1800–1831) and Vesey (1767?–1822)

both led slave conspiracies to revolt in the South. Walker (1785–1830) published his *Appeal to the Colored Citizens of the World* in 1829.
5. Independence Hall (in Philadelphia) hosted both the Second Constitutional Congress and the federal convention of 1787. Faneuil Hall was the meeting place for the participants in the Boston Tea Party incident of 1773.

and Frederick Douglass[6] with their great colleagues, Tappan, Phillips, Sumner, Mott, Stowe and Garrison.[7]

But even this latter group[8] who came within the limelight of national and international notice, and thus into open comparison with the best minds of their generation, the public too often regards as a group of inspired illiterates, eloquent echoes of their Abolitionist sponsors. For a true estimate of their ability and scholarship, however, one must go with the antiquarian to the files of the *Anglo-African Magazine,* where page by page comparisons may be made. Their writings show Douglass, McCune Smith, Wells Brown, Delany, Wilmot Blyden and Alexander Crummell[9] to have been as scholarly and versatile as any of the noted publicists with whom they were associated. All of them labored internationally in the cause of their fellows; to Scotland, England, France, Germany and Africa, they carried their brilliant offensive of debate and propaganda, and with this came instance upon instance of signal foreign recognition, from academic, scientific, public and official sources. Delany's *Principia of Ethnology* won public reception from learned societies, Pennington's[1] discourses an honorary doctorate from Heidelberg, Wells Brown's three year mission the entrée of the salons of London and Paris, and the tours of Frederick Douglass, receptions second only to Henry Ward Beecher's.[2]

After this great era of public interest and discussion, it was Alexander Crummell, who, with the reaction already setting in, first organized Negro brains defensively through the founding of the American Negro Academy in 1897 at Washington. A New York boy whose zeal for education had suffered a rude shock when refused admission to the Episcopal Seminary by Bishop Onderdonk, he had been befriended by John Jay[3] and sent to Cambridge University, England, for his education and ordination. On his return, he was beset with the idea of promoting race scholarship, and the Academy was the final result. It has continued ever since to be one of the bulwarks of our intellectual life, though unfortunately its members have had to spend too much of their energy and effort answering detractors and disproving popular fallacies. Only gradually have the men of this group been able to work toward pure scholarship. Taking a slightly different start, The Negro Society for Historical Research[4] was later organized in New York, and has succeeded in stimulating the collection from all parts of the world of books and documents dealing with the Negro. It has also brought together for the first time cooperatively in a single society African, West Indian and Afro-American scholars. Direct offshoots of this same effort are the extensive private collections[5] of Henry P. Slaughter of Washington, the

6. Brown (1815–1884), Garnet (1815–1882), Tubman (c. 1820–1913), Sojourner Truth (c. 1797–1883), and Douglass (1818–1895) were escaped slaves who joined Delany (1812–1885), a free man of the North, in fighting slavery.
7. Arthur Tappan (1786–1865), Wendell Phillips (1811–1884), Lucretia Mott (1793–1880), and William Lloyd Garrison (1805–1879) were prominent abolitionists. Charles Sumner (1811–1874), an important Radical Republican during the Reconstruction era. Harriet Beecher Stowe (1811–1896), author of *Uncle Tom's Cabin.*
8. I.e., Ward, Brown, etc.

9. Crummell (1819–1898). James McCune Smith (1813–1865). Blyden (1832–1912).
1. James Pennington (1809–1870).
2. A prominent abolitionist (1813–1887).
3. First U.S. Supreme Court chief justice (1745–1829). Benjamin T. Onderdonk (1791–1861).
4. Founded by Schomburg and John E. Bruce (1856–1924).
5. Schomburg's collection had been purchased by the New York Public Library in 1926, but he continued collecting materials and donating them to the library.

Rev. Charles D. Martin of Harlem, of Arthur Schomburg of Brooklyn, and of the late John E. Bruce, who was the enthusiastic and far-seeing pioneer of this movement. Finally and more recently, the Association for the Study of Negro Life and History has extended these efforts into a scientific research project of great achievement and promise. Under the direction of Dr. Carter G. Woodson,[6] it has continuously maintained for nine years the publication of the learned quarterly, *The Journal of Negro History,* and with the assistance and recognition of two large educational foundations has maintained research and published valuable monographs in Negro history. Almost keeping pace with the work of scholarship has been the effort to popularize the results, and to place before Negro youth in the schools the true story of race vicissitude, struggle and accomplishment. So that quite largely now the ambition of Negro youth can be nourished on its own milk.

Such work is a far cry from the puerile controversy and petty braggadocio with which the effort for race history first started. But a general as well as a racial lesson has been learned. We seem lately to have come at last to realize what the truly scientific attitude requires, and to see that the race issue has been a plague on both our historical houses, and that history cannot be properly written with either bias or counterbias. The blatant Caucasian racialist with his theories and assumptions of race superiority and dominance has in turn bred his Ethiopian counterpart—the rash and rabid amateur who has glibly tried to prove half of the world's geniuses to have been Negroes and to trace the pedigree of nineteenth century Americans from the Queen of Sheba.[7] But fortunately to-day there is on both sides of a really common cause less of the sand of controversy and more of the dust of digging.

Of course, a racial motive remains—legitimately compatible with scientific method and aim. The work our race students now regard as important, they undertake very naturally to overcome in part certain handicaps of disparagement and omission too well-known to particularize. But they do so not merely that we may not wrongfully be deprived of the spiritual nourishment of our cultural past, but also that the full story of human collaboration and interdependence may be told and realized. Especially is this likely to be the effect of the latest and most fascinating of all of the attempts to open up the closed Negro past, namely the important study of African cultural origins and sources. The bigotry of civilization which is the taproot of intellectual prejudice begins far back and must be corrected at its source. Fundamentally it has come about from that depreciation of Africa which has sprung up from ignorance of her true rôle and position in human history and the early development of culture. The Negro has been a man without a history because he has been considered a man without a worthy culture. But a new notion of the cultural attainment and potentialities of the African stocks has recently come about, partly through the corrective influence of the more scientific study of African institutions and early cultural history, partly through growing appreciation of the skill and beauty

6. Woodson (1875–1950) began editing the *Journal of Negro History* in 1915. He founded Negro History Week, later Black History Month, in 1926.

7. In antiquity, ruler of the Kingdom of Sheba, which might have included all or parts of what are now Eritrea, Ethiopia, and Yemen.

and in many cases the historical priority of the African native crafts, and finally through the signal recognition which first in France and Germany, but now very generally, the astonishing art of the African sculptures has received. Into these fascinating new vistas, with limited horizons lifting in all directions, the mind of the Negro has leapt forward faster than the slow clearings of scholarship will yet safely permit. But there is no doubt that here is a field full of the most intriguing and inspiring possibilities. Already the Negro sees himself against a reclaimed background, in a perspective that will give pride and self-respect ample scope, and make history yield for him the same values that the treasured past of any people affords.

1925

## Juan Latino

The remark attributed to John C. Calhoun,[1] "that the Negro race was so inferior it could not produce a single individual who could conjugate a Greek verb," was accepted half a century ago in this country as the last word on the subject of the inferiority of the Negro. Thomas Jefferson,[2] one of the fathers of the revolution, and a friend of the Negro race, who was not so dogmatic as Calhoun, said:—"I think one (Negro) could scarcely be found capable of tracing and comprehending the investigations of Euclid:[3] and that in imagination they are dull, tasteless and anomalous. . . . Never yet could I find that a black had uttered a thought above the level of plain narration; never saw even an elementary trait of painting or sculpture. . . . Religion indeed, has produced a Phyllis Wheatley,[4] but it could not produce a poet." So much for the American statesmen. In Europe we have had the historian Hume[5] who said in one of his essays that "there are Negro slaves dispersed all over Europe, of whom none ever discovered any symptoms of ingenuity. . . . In Jamaica, indeed, they talk of one Negro as a man of parts and learning; but it is likely he is admired for slender accomplishments, like a parrot who speaks a few words plainly."

As the world rolls onward, evidence accumulates from day to day to prove that these eminent gentlemen have been unjust in their opinion, not zealous in their research, nor calm in their gifted reasoning, before giving to the public the result of their investigations on this subject.

It has been said time and again from the earliest days that "America has not produced one good poet," and again it has been noted that not one able mathematician" has been produced, because the country is young; when old, like Greece, it may produce a Homer, or, like England, a Shakespeare. Thomas Jefferson said that the "reproach is as unjust it is unkind."

---

1. Politician (1782–1850) from South Carolina; U.S. vice-president 1825–32.
2. Politician (1743–1826) from Virginia; U.S. president 1801–09.
3. Greek geometer (flourished ca. 300 BC).
4. Phillis Wheatley (1753?–1784), American poet born in Africa. Jefferson continued: "The compositions published under her name are below the dignity of criticism." He believed that a black person, even a writer as famous and well-regarded as Wheatley was, might be able to repeat information, but lacked imagination equal to a white person's.
5. David Hume (1711–1776), Scottish philosopher and historian.

There was a Spanish poet known as Juan Latino who was born during the latter part of the sixteenth century in the northern littoral of Africa. Some of his biographers claimed that he was born at Barbery during the year 1515. He was captured by Spanish caravel traders, who made a practice of bringing Negroes to Sevilla, and sold to the family of the famous Gonzalo de Cordova.[6] He was said to have a great aptitude for learning, and he was permitted at the time that his young master was at school to learn grammar and the other studies then in vogue in Spain. His master afterwards granted him his liberty. He lived at Granada and was Professor of Grammar, Latin and Greek in the University of that city. The writer Gallardo,[7] in the first volume of his essays on "Spanish Bibliography," speaks of an anonymous writer who calls Latino the most famous Negro of his day, that he was raised in the city of Granada "in the home of the Duchess of Terranova, widow of the great Captain Gonzalo Fernandez de Cordova; he was servant to their son, the Duke of Sesa and carried daily his books to his study." Latino learned grammar and the Latin language readily because of his very splendid mind. When a young man he fell in love with Anna Carloval, a beautiful woman, and daughter of the custodian of the Duke's estate. Many inducements were made to her to break the engagement, but she refused them all, saying she had given her word to be the Negro's wife. Latino studied the arts, and became a master in them; he wanted to advance further, but was offered the Chair of Grammar at the University of Granada, which he held for more than sixty years, and was highly esteemed by all his fellow professors and students because of his great learning and noble character. He was an excellent declaimer of Terence,[8] and was doubtless a great admirer of that polished writer, and of the quotation from his writing: "Homo sum, nihil humani a me alienum puto,"[9] which so well expresses his feelings on the subject of manhood. He was also a great musician and a good poet, and known for his courageous actions when young. He lived to the ripe age of ninety years, leaving respectable sons and grandsons. The widow of Juan Latino erected a monument in the Church of Saint Ann, where he was buried. Engraved on the marble is the following epitaph, which has been reproduced by Nicholas Antonio in his first tome of the "Bibliotheca Nova" (p. 716): "Juan was an excellent Latin poet. He sang the birth of the Prince Ferdinand II., the deeds of Pius V.'s pontificate, and the times of Don Juan of Austria at Lepanto." The book, a quarto volume, is in Latin, and was printed at Granada in 1573. Mr. Antonio also cites another book in Latin by Latino on the Spanish Royal Cemetery, better known as the Escurial. This book was printed at Granada in 1576.

Those who have waded through the beautiful chapters of Cervantes book, "Don Quixote,"[1] will run across Latino, and will remember that God hath placed him there to refute the statements of Calhoun, Jefferson, and Hume. There is no doubt about Latino's origin and race—his epitaph reads: "Filius Æthiopium, prolesque nigerrima patrum."[2]

6. Gonzalo Fernández de Córdova (1453–1515), Spanish military commander.
7. Bartolomé José Gallardo (1776–1852), Spanish writer, editor, and bibliographer.
8. Publius Terentius Afer (186 or 185–ca. 159 BC), Roman dramatist.

9. I am a man. Nothing human is alien to me (Latin).
1. Novel by the Spanish writer Miguel de Cervantes (1547–1616).
2. The son of Ethiopians, and the blackest offspring (or progeny) by birth (Latin).

Mr. Ticknor,[3] in his work, "The History of Spanish Literature," states that Juan Latino's book," making above a hundred and sixty pages in small quarto, is not only one of the rarest books in the world, but is one of the most remarkable illustrations of the intellectual faculties and possible accomplishments of the African race." It is extremily gratifying to know that at the University of Granada, at such a remote period of the world's history, there was a man learned in the arts and letters who could think, read and write in Latin, and knew men, fellow-professors, who could disentangle the hard problem of Euclid with the same ease and grace that Latino could declaim Terence. In those days, as Raynal[4] charged, "America could not produce one able mathematician, one man of genius in a single art or a single science." Is it too much to ask that the Negro, who has just reached his 50th year of freedom, be given the same opportunity to prove himself as was asked for the Americans against whom a like charge was made, and of which Jefferson said: "We therefore suppose that this reproach is as unjust as it is unkind; and that of the geniuses which adorn the present age America contributes its full share"? The race which Jefferson and Calhoun held up to contempt and scorn did not deserve their reproaches, because it is this race which gave to the Greeks and Romans, who in turn gave it to Europe and America, all their present boasted knowledge of the arts and sciences, religion, and law and government. In geography, Africa, says the learned Blyden,[5] "has been called 'Africa nutrix leonum' (the dry nurse of lions), so in the early political history of the United States the same description is applicable to the gray-haired mother of civilisation. Lions in Church and State were born out of her struggles and sufferings."

1913

3. George Ticknor (1791–1871), American scholar who specialized in the history and criticism of Spanish literature.
4. Guillaume Thomas François Raynal (1711–

1796), French writer.
5. Edward Wilmot Blyden (1832–1912), Liberian educator and statesman.

# LEONOR VILLEGAS DE MAGNÓN
## 1876–1955

Leonor Villegas de Magnón was born into a wealthy and prominent family in Nuevo Laredo, a Mexican city across the Rio Grande from Laredo, Texas. She spent a privileged but lonely childhood in private American schools and endured a dispiriting marriage in Mexico City during the final years of Porfirio Díaz's dictatorship. After the outbreak of the Mexican Revolution in 1910, Villegas de Magnón crossed the border to join the nursing corps of *La cruz blanca* (The White Cross). She became radicalized by her firsthand experiences with injustice to the poor and her involvement with bloody combat. She even met Pancho Villa, a revolutionary general who was notorious for his caprices in politics and with young women. After the revolution ended in 1920, she made her living as a teacher in Texas.

During or shortly before the early 1920s, Villegas de Magnón wrote a 300-page autobiographical Spanish-language narrative, *La rebelde*, intended for a Mexican audience. For decades, she submitted her manuscript to various publishing entities, all of which rejected the work because it could not be called strictly history, memoir, or fiction. Sometime in the 1940s, to improve the work's chances of publication, Villegas de Magnón rewrote *La rebelde*, in English, as the 400-page *The Lady Was a Rebel*. In 1961, *The Laredo Times* published the original *La rebelde*, posthumously, as a serial. Finally, 33 years later—encouraged by the historian Ruth Winegarten, aided by Villegas de Magnón's daughter and then by Villegas de Magnón's granddaughter—the scholar Clara Lomas located the manuscript of *The Lady Was a Rebel*, which she edited and published as *The Rebel*.

Throughout this work, one chapter of which is excerpted here, Villegas de Magnón refers to herself as "the Rebel," making the autobiographer a character in the novel of her own life and of the political world around her. *The Rebel* begins as a bildungsroman, peppered with images that project far into the later parts. At age two, for example, the Rebel is pricked by a rose; later she is burned in the same spot on her arm as one of Mexico's great generals. As the life story becomes a war story, Villegas de Magnón and other women inside and outside *La cruz blanca* play key roles on the border. And as she writes herself into history, the Rebel offers a unique vision of intercultural loyalties.

---

## FROM THE REBEL

## The Rebel Is a Girl

The Río Bravo or Río Grande defines the dividing line between the two nations, Mexico and the United States. As the years pass, the river appears to be in a state of inactivity. Its waters seek a lower level, until it eventually leaves its banks exposed. In some places it becomes a thin stream that can be easily crossed on foot. The least cautious, or perhaps the most daring and hard-pressed, people take advantage of the fertile soil and, at their own risk, build huts, plant vegetables, raise chickens, cows, and a pig or two. The river maintains this happy mood for years, and the poor are hopeful that it will thus continue.

By some whim of nature, or it may be that Neptune, God of the Seas, wishes to amuse himself, the water awakens from its tranquil slumber and transforms itself into a gigantic serpent that crawls slowly, but gains a momentum of such menacing form that it carries with it everything that it contacts. Soon on its surface, floating with the torrent, cows, sheep, chickens, snakes, and huts struggle to keep above the waters until they are finally engulfed by the churning undercurrent. Nothing escapes the furious waters that rush on as if in answer to a challenge presenting a grotesque contrast to the many years of defiant lethargy.

On a night like this, the twelfth of June, 1876, the shrill whistle of the night guards gave the alarm. Civil guards on horses rode from town to town along the river, warning the inhabitants of the approaching peril. Shrill cries and terrifying screams filled the air, and the Laredos, two border towns across the river from each other, rose to the emergency. The darkness of the

night became more terrifying as thunderclap after thunderclap intermingled with the cries of those in danger. The lightning illuminated their
path momentarily only to leave it again and again in intense darkness.

The trees whipped by a gale of wind blew back and forth, beating against
the walls of the big homes, while rampant waters gaining ground curled
around the foundations, menacing homes and huts till they yielded to the
mighty pressure of the water and fell like sugar toys.

The poor who lived on the edge of the river were making powerful efforts
to save the little they possessed. They moved forward like beasts of burden,
carrying as much as their strength allowed them. Women with children
tied to their back in *rebozos* had their hands free to drag their animals. Men
burdened with chattel also dragged their beasts, going ahead to find a safe
foot path to scale the river banks. If they dared to halt, those behind gave a
cry of warning.

"Go up higher! Higher! Higher!"

Again they redoubled their steps in an effort to gain safe ground; the
waters were already flooding Nuevo Laredo on the Mexican side. The town
was in darkness; only the lanterns carried by helpers provided the means to
light the way of the refugees. The *mozos*, caretakers of the rich ones, were
kept busy guarding the homes, and running back and forth with news of
the rising water, its level, its perils. providing an excuse for wild excitement.

Emperor Maximilian had been dethroned, tried, and executed. Benito
Juárez and Porfirio Díaz had dickered for power between themselves. After
overthrowing the government of Lerdo de Tejada, General Porfirio Díaz
had taken the Capital of Mexico, proclaiming his *Plan de Tuxtepec*. Slow
means of communication and the rapid changes in governments left many
guerrilla bands of either side scattered over the country. These groups, unaware of peace, continued to roam about attacking towns.

A band of these scattered rebels, taking advantage of the storm-frightened
people of the little town of Nuevo Laredo, found it opportune to attack and
loot the homes which had been temporarily abandoned or neglected, either
from fear of the rising river or out of curiosity to view the damage. The terror of the night meant nothing to the rebel looters. They rode unchallenged
to the heart of town, determined to break down the gates of a rich Spanish
merchant to whom it was rumored a large consignment of fine wines had
recently arrived by barge from the Gulf of Mexico.

Quickly they made their way through the darkness to the front of a strong
gate, or *portón*, with the master's name, Don Joaquín, on the stone arch
overhead.

"This is the place," they yelled, banging on the gate with the butts of their
guns. "Open the gate! Open!"

Don Joaquín, a prudent man, ordered the gate opened. Pancho, the *mozo*,[1]
was accustomed to obeying orders, but he hesitated.

"Go, Pancho. Open the gate."

Slowly Pancho proceeded to accomplish the task which was always so easy,
but tonight his trembling fingers refused to pull the heavy lock that held the
door tight.

---

1. Servant. This Pancho is not Pancho Villa.

"Señor," he said, "they are bandits."

"You cannot do it, Pancho? I will do it myself." Don Joaquín, carrying a lantern in one hand, approached and opened the door that yielded softly.

Pancho hid behind the door. The Indian guessed the reason for this visit. Holding his lantern high, Don Joaquín got a quick view of the intruders. He saw the group of armed bandits and at once guessed their motive.

"Follow me," he said in a low voice, escorting them down the tile-paved courtyard.

Don Joaquín's establishment covered a long city block on the main plaza, a quarter of a mile from the river. Surrounded by a thick wall well over a man's height were the house, the *bodega* (warehouse), and the store. In the house lived the young master and his family. In rooms built along the side of the warehouse lived the young boys who had come from Spain to learn the merchandising business. Along the back wall was an open space behind the house and the *bodega*, where garlic was stored.

Entering the warehouse, Don Joaquín led the way down into the cellar where the big assortment of Spanish wines has been stowed away. The intruders at once became his guests, sitting around on the benches, but still holding their guns in a prominent position. Wine casks stacked on top of each other lined the sides of the room. The light from Don Joaquín's lantern on the rough wooden table was reflected in the tin wine cups. Where the wine had dripped from the spigots there were stains on the stone floor. The sweet smell of wine was heavy in the air.

Serving the wine Don Joaquín drew, Pancho faltered among the rough men. Grabbing a cup from Pancho, the leader held it up close to his eyes to see if it was full. Then flinging back his head he poured it down his throat. Putting his cup back on the table with a heavy thump he looked meaningfully at Pancho.

"His cup, Pancho. We do not want our friends to leave thirsty." Don Joaquín held out his hand for the empty cup.

"Ah, we are not leaving yet, Señor. Not until we have searched the house." The leader nodded to his men who forgot their wine and jumped up.

Don Joaquín's pushed through the men and started toward the door near the gate, but the men were already attracted by a closed door across the patio, where voices were heard coming from within.

"Open this door, señor," commanded the boldest one, making a sign to his companions to present arms. "Open this door."

Without hesitating, the master raised his lantern to throw a better light in the dimly lit room. At that moment cries of a newborn baby broke the silence.

Outside, the increasing fury of the stormy night threatened at any moment to demolish the house. The waters were slapping against the walls, slipping in through the low windows. Inside the bandit-held mansion, beaten by the wind, threatened by the water, a woman in majestic dignity had given birth to a child.

The rebels were touched by the familiar sacredness of the scene. Putting away their guns, some among them made the sign of the cross on their foreheads and on their hearts. They returned to the patio to resume their drinking.

"Pardon, señor," the leader murmured.

But before the band could descend to the wine cellar, loud knocks and threats of breaking in the gate were heard. A Federal commander in command of his own troops demanded entrance to search for bandits. Frightened by the Federals, the rebels scattered wildly over the courtyard, climbing the wall in back of the warehouse and escaping in the opposite direction.

Gripping his lantern, the master walked to the gate. He again held his light high. Opening the door, he signaled to the Federals to walk in and be quiet.

"Follow me," said Don Joaquín, starting toward the wine cellar.

The Federals in their anxiety to find some victim on whom to discharge their fury, pushed one another into the hall, some bouncing clear across the patio.

"The rebels are here," the commander said, seeing that Don Joaquín was leading them away from the direction of the house.

"Sí, señor," answered Don Joaquín quickly. "I am hiding one rebel." He walked toward the door, hesitated, then flung it open. The crying of the baby silenced the men.

"A man child, señor?" asked the commander.

Pancho shook his head at Don Joaquín.

"No, señor," the master answered. He drew himself up in pride. "My rebel is a girl."

"A girl!" one of the men said, and making excuses for their intrusion, turned away from the door.

"Pardon us, señor. We already knew that you were an honest man. But in these awful times, what about it? Anything may happen. All the people are alarmed with so many rumors of bandits."

Don Joaquín ushered the Federals to the same cellar where the bandits had just been. With their cups filled, the men held them high and offered a toast of welcome to the new arrival, the Rebel. They drank a second toast to the mother of the baby.

"This toast we offer," the commander said, "to the mother of this border town on the banks of the Río Bravo." He wished to appear in a good light before the eyes of the owner of such good wines.

"¡Viva! ¡Viva!" the men called out in high spirits because their bandit hunt had turned into a party.

Finally, Don Joaquín, who was impatiently awaiting their departure, began to show signs of restlessness. Pancho appeared with his lantern to lead the way out. As the Federals filed out of the gate, passersby reported that the river was now at a standstill and the storm had abated.

Pancho, lantern in hand, did not think it time to go to bed, but preferred walking the streets, telling the double good news of the baby and the dying storm. As he started out the gate, Don Joaquín called, "Pancho, go put on dry clothes while Julia makes coffee for us all."

Julia was considered part of the family. She was a young Indian girl whom Doña Valerianna, Don Joaquín's wife, had taken as a child and raised.

Meanwhile, Don Joaquín personally examined all the doors and windows; though the storm had ceased, the strong wind might blow them open. While he was walking about the place, his thoughts were filled with scenes from the year. He remembered that just one year before, his first son had been born in Corpus Christi.[2]

"Strange coincidence," he recalled. On the night Leopoldo was born there had been a tempest and the waves had lashed his home on the bay.

"My son born on American soil. My daughter in Mexican territory, and I, a Spanish subject. Who will be more powerful, he or she?"

In bed, Doña Valerianna held her child in a warm embrace, whispering a benediction.

"A Mexican flag shall be yours. I will wrap it together with your brother's. His shall be an American flag, but they shall be like one to me."

Her eyes searched into the darkness for her husband's flag, murmuring in her semiconsciousness, "His country I shall never see; it is beyond the great ocean."

\* \* \*

General Aureliano Blanquet had become Minister of War, and all the army was being mobilized under his command. He was sending his best generals to the frontier. On March 17, 1913, in the early dawn the small garrison of Nuevo Laredo was attacked by General Jesús Carranza. Unexpectedly, a group of civilians took up arms and aided the unprepared Federals. The Carrancistas advanced to the city limits. After a brisk encounter, during which the outskirts of Nuevo Laredo were strewn with wounded, Jesús Carranza ordered his men to retreat. The Constitutionalists[3] could have taken the town before the military train arrived bringing Federal reinforcements, but false news reached them that new aid was already arriving for the enemy.

Hearing the firing, the Rebel dressed quickly. She called her aunt's home in Nuevo Laredo. Getting no answer, she called several friends. There was no answer to any of her calls. Rushing out into the street, she stopped a big new car driven by a chauffeur. Directing him to drive to the offices of El Progreso, she told him to wait for her. She painted a red cross on a piece of paper and had it pasted on the windshield. Telephoning her friends, she told them her plans to go to Mexico and help take care of the wounded; she needed volunteers. With her faithful friend Jovita Idar, a writer for El Progreso, the Rebel encouraged four other young women to join them to offer immediate help.

Opening his pharmacy, Don Flavio Vargas gave her a basket of first-aid supplies. As she got in the car, he placed a towel-wrapped bundle behind her on the seat.

"You may need this," he said, patting her arm.

Told to drive to the international bridge, the chauffeur balked. He dared not take the car across the river into the battle-stricken town. Reaching behind her, the Rebel got the bundle. She felt the hard round object. Inside the towel was a long-necked bottle of whiskey. Unwrapping it, she pushed the hard bottle neck against the driver's back.

"Drive on," she ordered tersely.

---

2. Coastal city in southern Texas.
3. In addition to the revolutionists (rebels) and the Federals, the third faction in the Mexican Revolu-

tion; the members of this group—mainly middle-class urbanites, liberals, and intellectuals—wanted Mexico to have a Constitution.

As they neared the bridge at high speed, the Rebel leaned out of the car waving the white towel. The car was allowed to cross to the other side unhindered.

Leaving most of her girls at the hospital, the Rebel could be seen in the distance going south. The Rebel glanced toward a soldier. How she longed to run after him and give him the message to attack again quickly before Federal aid could arrive for the small garrison. She heard the captain's voice.

"So you are not one of us?" he said holding toward her the flag staff they had both advanced to get. "You may have this. It is yours to put your white flag on. Keep it." He handed it to her, gazing at the bronze eagle on the tip. It was not long afterward that the Rebel heard that the captain had joined the forces of Carranza.

The hospitalized Carrancistas were held prisoners in the hospital. The problem after a few days was to get them to their post at Matamoros. All the men were in good shape to join the Constitutionalists that would soon attack the town of Matamoros. Aracelito, the Rebel's young secretary, seldom left her. She was well informed of all activities concerning the White Cross. The Rebel unfolded her plan for the prisoners' escape.

"As soon as we get news of the arrival of Federal reinforcements, we will take advantage of the excitement among the people," she said.

One morning soon afterward, Aracelito rushed to the Rebel.

"The troops arrive today. There will be a huge parade. Tonight there will be a big banquet and dance on the Main Plaza." The girl's eyes danced as she told the Rebel the news. The Rebel went about her duties and daily routine. Aracelito relayed the orders to the hospital corps to clean, disinfect, and prepare the hospital for inspection. Every bed was aired and clean linens put on. Only the Rebel and Aracelito changed the beds. As they did, they placed the prisoners' clothes beneath the mattresses. Each man was told to carefully dress himself at ten minutes before midnight. There was a big clock in the ward, and the men would be told when to start. Each bed had to be camouflaged after the soldiers fled. The nurses were told to entertain the guards at the right time. Jugs of pulque and tequila with tacos would be a banquet to the men while their *jefes* were gaily celebrating in the plaza.

The Rebel left the hospital to buy provisions, but instead crossed hurriedly to Laredo. She found Pancho eating. Together they shared the simple dinner. Their talk was full of reminiscing of the dead and absent ones.

"*Mi ama*," Pancho said sadly, "it is only you and your brother Leopold now. Do as your mother always prayed: be united."

"There is no fear about that, Pancho," she replied. "He and Inés, his wife, are my guardian angels, always taking care of my children and loving them as their own."

"I am old and useless," he sobbed. "I want to go back to Mexico when this war is over."

"You shall, Pancho," she comforted him. "I will take you with me. My husband is kind. You shall live with us. Now," she said lowering her voice, "I am going to entrust a very important mission to you."

Pancho straightened up, his eyes shone. He was ready to serve his country. He looked young again.

"Please tell me what you want me to do, Little Rebel," he said smiling fondly at her.

"First of all, you must sleep this afternoon and be rested. At twelve tonight you will hear the church bells and see the fireworks in Nuevo Laredo.
The people will be celebrating. Take your skiff and row toward the cave that
is at the foot of the road leading to the hospital. Soldiers will be there, hidden. Ask them if the Rebel sent them. Then row them quietly down the
river on the Mexican side. As soon as you pass the last post of the Federals,
land them near a *jacal*. Call the sentinel; he belongs to General Pablo
González's people. Return quickly before morning, as you must not be seen."
She spoke slowly so that Pancho would remember it all.

"My Julia will help me. Her spirit will protect me." Looking out over the
waters of the river, he made the sign of the cross. The Rebel embraced
him with the firm faith in him that he had always inspired in her in her
childhood.

Buying a few things, she returned to the hospital. There was a strong smell
of disinfectant; all quarters were clean, and nurses were rushing about ready
for the Federal inspection.

It was a little before midnight. The prisoners had dressed and were
gone. Sleepy, well-fed guards looked over the wards, the dim lights helping
to conceal the secret of the vacant beds. Laughingly, they returned to their
posts. In a few minutes, there would be a changing of the guard. Hurriedly,
the Rebel and Aracelito went past the great hospital portals and asked
permission to go to the plaza for a little while. Most of the nurses had already left. The loyal nurses had taken a carriage to their homes across the
river.

Aracelito and the Rebel walked to the bridge only two blocks from the
plaza, which was ablaze with lights and crowded with newly arrived Federal
troops celebrating with the townspeople. The hospital, eight blocks away,
was in darkness and stillness. There were few people on the bridge. As the
two women passed the monument in the middle of the bridge, the Rebel
noticed that Aracelito was nervous and kept looking back. Someone was following them. The Rebel stopped as she heard the clock strike twelve. Anxiously looking toward the river bank, she thought she heard the rippling of
water and the soft paddling of oars. She stood still and prayed. A young man
had approached Aracelito and was speaking to her.

"Please believe me," he said earnestly, "ever since I first saw you, I have
loved you. I am not a Federal. I am dressed as one, but I shall escape and go
over to our people. Perhaps, tonight." He looked appealingly at the girl.

"I shall wait," she answered simply, unsmiling.

The young man disappeared in the darkness toward Mexico. The Rebel,
anxious to be safely at Pancho's cabin, took Aracelito's trembling hand and
pulled her toward the end of the bridge. Pushing open the door of Pancho's
hut, they found a heavy dark blanket on the cot and on the dying coals a pot
of coffee. They poured themselves coffee, then wrapping the blanket about
them, walked to the edge of the river bank. They waited for Pancho's return.

"The young man who followed us," Aracelito began in a tremulous voice,
"says he loves me, but I have not encouraged him. I thought he was a Federal. But he has told me that he will cross over to our people. I have promised to wait for him," she whispered, sobbing.

"Darling," the Rebel said, hugging her, "some night we will come here and
Pancho will take a message for you to him."

They sat silently watching the lights across on the Mexican side go out, one by one. The hours of the clear moonlit night passed. Sometimes dozing, sometimes making plans, they kept vigil. Finally, they heard the soft ripple of water and drip of oars. They crouched down in the river weeds. The Rebel saw Pancho swiftly plying his oars. Behind him crumpled on the floor of the boat, her head on the seat, was a girl.

Lifting her gently in his arms, Pancho ran with his precious burden. The Rebel and Aracelito followed him to the cabin. Pancho placed her on his clean bed that Julia had always taken care of. Smoothing the pillow, he went for alcohol. The Rebel stood looking amazed at the beautiful girl, one hand hanging limp off the side of the bed, the other on her breast clutching something that was hidden under her blouse. There were blood stains on the other arm. They bandaged her arm, but did not try to move her hand. Whatever was there was sacred to her. She slept, exhausted. It was daylight when Pancho finished telling his part in the daring plot.

"I left here, *mi amita*," he began as they sat drinking coffee, "just as you told me. Crossing the river, I rowed over toward the cave. I know it well; often Julia and I sat there after your mother died. I had only my skiff. I wondered what I would do if there were too many. Perhaps, I would have to make several trips. But as I was nearing the place, I noticed my *compadre's* boat tied among the bushes at the river's edge. I tied it to my boat, saying all the time, 'Compadre, I shall return it, God willing.'

"When I approached the cave, I was glad that I had taken the other boat. They all got in and helped me row. It was downstream: that made it easier. When we arrived at the hut past the last post. they left me. I rowed fast. Suddenly I heard a rustle of leaves in the shadows along the bank."

"Pancho, you are sure you took no enemy?" the Rebel asked clutching his hand.

"No, *mi amita*," he said smiling at her fear. "I got the password from every one of them. They were quiet and kind."

"Well, go on," the Rebel insisted. "What was at the water's edge?"

"I heard a woman's voice, and out of the bushes a girl rushed to the water's edge toward me. '¡*Qué bonita*! Could it be the Virgin of Guadalupe[4] herself coming to save me?' I thought to myself.

"Begging me to take her across the river she jumped into my *compadre's* boat and helped me row. We rowed a little farther and then we heard a noise. It was Federals. They cried halt and fired a shot at us.

"'It is Pancho, the *esquifero*.[5] I am going home.' I called to them and they let us pass. We were nearing my *compadre's* place. The girl had jumped into my boat as the shot had made its mark in the skiff she was in and was filling with water. We cut off the boat and I hid it where I had found it. After that, she must have fainted, as she did not speak again." Pancho finished his story and got up to put some mesquite on the low burning fire.

"Let her sleep," said the Rebel, also rising. "Do not disturb her. If she awakens and wants nourishment, prepare nice food like Julia made. I will come back as early as possible and bring you food and clothes. Tell no one of this; and let no one see her."

---

4. A *mestiza* version of the Virgin Mary; Mexico's matron saint.    5. Person in charge of a skiff; skipper.

Making their way up the embankment silently, the two women parted, promising to meet again at mid-morning. People were beginning their usual daily routine, but there was excitement caused by the little newspaper vendors calling the news of the arrival of Federal reinforcements in Nuevo Laredo, and the daring escape of forty prisoners from the hospital.

Immediately, a meeting was called of all loyal nurses that had taken part in caring for the soldiers during the days after the combat. They sent a message to General Blanquet stating their displeasure regarding the Federal treatment of prisoners. While promising to care impartially for all wounded on the battlefield, they declared themselves strictly Constitutionalist sympathizers. Accordingly, the White Cross was no longer allowed to cross the frontier, and if so under penalty of death.

It was at the time of the Huerta outbreak that the Mexican National Red Cross, organized during the last years of the Díaz regime, failed in its principles of nonpartiality and nonpartisanship. In its cause destined to aid the wounded were spies and ammunition for the Federals. It was in protest and to counteract it that the Constitutionalist White Cross was established in Laredo, Texas, serving throughout the Carranza Revolution. The Red Cross served the Federals. It was pledged that the White Cross would go with the Carranza army, organizing hospitals and replacing Federal personnel with loyal doctors and nurses. The White Cross had stayed in the hospital until every wounded Constitutionalist had escaped.

The Constitutionalists repulsed, Federal reinforcements had arrived under the command of General Quintana. Nuevo Laredo bustled with preparations against attack. Trenches were built; search towers were erected with powerful searchlights; cannons were mounted on hill tops; brush and trees were cut down to clear the horizon for miles around the surrounding country.

At the time agreed, the Rebel went to Pancho's hut. A noise among the bushes and a rapid opening and closing of the door told of Aracelito's earlier arrival. Everything within Pancho's house was still. The visitor must have been asleep.

Aracelito came to the door to greet her silently. She dared not waken the sleeping girl. Pancho came in and started the fire. The girl awoke. Slowly getting herself together, she sat up on the side of the bed, stretching both her legs as if to assure herself of her identity. Then she stretched her arms. Suddenly becoming conscious of her mission, she searched in her blouse pocket.

"How well I feel," she said in a sweet voice. "I have had a perfect rest. I know that I am among friends who fight for the same cause." Looking at each of them, she spoke confidently. "Tell me please," the girl said, looking at Pancho, "who is the Rebel? It is urgent that I get in touch with her."

The Rebel grew pale, a strange thing for her, who knew not fear. Could it be a message from her husband? She had not heard from him since the tragic death of the President. Who was this violet-eyed girl?

"I am the Rebel," Leonor answered in a quiet voice.

"Yes," said Pancho, nodding emphatically. "She is our *jefe*."

"Who are you and where do you come from?" The Rebel spoke hoarsely, sitting on the bed beside her.

Aracelito pulled up a bench and looked earnestly at the newcomer.

"I am María de Jesús González, a teacher from Monterrey. I have a friend in the telegraph office; we are both telegraph operators and Constitutionalists. Here are telegrams that we held back. They will prove our loyalty. We heard of you and your brave companions and resolved to become allied with your work. One of these messages is from General Jerónimo Villarreal in Nuevo Laredo for Secretary Blanquet, asking for reinforcements; they were expecting the second attack by General Jesús Carranza. We also heard of the Constitutionalist retreat. Two days later we had another telegram that reinforcements would arrive in Matamoros at any moment. I traveled on horseback night and day until I found this good man at the river's edge." The girl spoke rapidly as if she feared something might happen to keep her from delivering her news.

"There are messages for you from Sonora," she continued. "A companion, Marie Bringas de Carturegli; the telegraph operator, Trinidad Blanco; and her sister will be here as soon as they can travel in Coahuila. Also, a teacher from there will join you, and in Tampico, Juanita Mancha, a brave girl. There are two more in Monterrey, the Blackaller sisters, teachers." She concluded her long recital of names with relief.

María de Jesús was having a cool bath. Pancho had stretched a sheet across the back of his hut for privacy. Standing in a big wash tub, the girl poured cool water over herself from a Mexican dried-gourd dipper that had been Julia's. Her long red hair hanging down, dressed in a cool summer kimono, she sat down to a humble repast that Pancho had prepared for her.

"María de Jesús," the Rebel said, "you are fully aware of the dangers we will encounter. Will you obey orders?"

"Yes, I am ready," she replied firmly.

"Then you must leave tonight," said the Rebel, "for the nearest Constitutionalist camp. Pancho will row you there. Rest now, and we will return tonight."

That night, Aracelito and the Rebel were stealing down the hill again with more clothes and food and a little money. María de Jesús was listening. She and Pancho had their supper while they were awaiting orders.

María put on her boots. She tucked a dagger that Pancho gave her in her blouse. She wore trousers that the Rebel had brought. Her hair was neatly braided and wound around her head.

"María," the Rebel said tensely, "you will take these telegrams to General Lucio Blanco, or any of his staff. They will probably attack Matamoros before reinforcements arrive. Come back quickly. This letter is for General Pablo González. Listen for any news."

The girl jumped in the skiff with Pancho. Soon they were lost in the shadows of the mesquites along the river banks. Aracelito and the Rebel sat again by the river, alone. Pancho was not to return until the next day. They did not know whether María would return or not.

"I wish," Aracelito sighed, "I wish I was as brave as our brave companion. I would go and look for Guillermo. Perhaps he is already with General Lucio Blanco's forces."

ca. 1920/1940s                                                                1994

# CLEOFAS M. JARAMILLO
## 1878–1956

Along with Adelina "Nina" Otero-Warren and Fabiola Cabeza de Baca Gilbert, Cleofas M. Jaramillo is part of a trio that produced domestic literature about the Spanish heritage of New Mexico. Some critics have described Jaramillo's writing as unsophisticated and even naïve, but as the feminist critic Tey Diana Rebolledo has noted, Latinos in the Southwest at the time Jaramillo was writing had little education and almost no literary voice. Thus Jaramillo's depictions of bucolic life in Taos and elsewhere in the state might be seen as pioneering acts of resistance and rebellion.

Cleofas Martínez Jaramillo was born in Arroyo Hondo, in northern New Mexico. She was one of seven children in an upper-class Hispanic family; her father was a businessman who dealt in livestock, mines, and merchandise. Jaramillo was educated at the Loretto Convent School, in Taos, and the Loretto Academy, in Santa Fe. In 1898, she married her second cousin, Colonel Venceslao Jaramillo, a wealthy landowner and store proprietor who also served on Governor Miguel A. Otero's staff and who later was a state senator and a delegate to the New Mexico Constitutional Convention (1912). The couple lived in El Rito, New Mexico. The first two of their three children died in infancy.

When Colonel Jaramillo fell ill, the family moved to Denver, Colorado, then to Baltimore, Maryland, for his treatment. After his death in 1920, Jaramillo and her daughter Angélica returned to Santa Fe. Eleven years later, Angélica was murdered, leaving Jaramillo alone.

Jaramillo's literary career was inspired by the work of the New Mexico Federal Writer's Project, a government-sponsored effort after the Great Depression. To rescue the quickly vanishing Hispanic heritage of New Mexico, interviewers working for the Project talked to common folk in the hope of recording the ways of life that modernity was rapidly erasing. Jaramillo later explained that after reading a Project-related magazine article on Mexican and Spanish cooking, "It occurred to me that if we would look in our mothers' trunks we would find old costumes and jewelry which could be displayed at our Fiesta. I thought we who know the customs and styles of our region are letting them die out." Ultimately, however, the Federal Writers Project resulted in a "New Mexico Mystique," which future generations of intellectuals reacted against for being simplistic, nostalgic, and driven by a fantasy view of the past.

In 1936, Jamarillo founded the Sociedad Folkórica de Santa Fe (Santa Fe Folklore Society). The members had to be Hispanic, and all sessions were held in Spanish. Jaramillo wanted to write in Spanish to help slow down the disappearance of this tongue in New Mexico, yet she understood that only through English would she be able to reach a wide audience. Her first book was *The Genuine New Mexico Tasty Recipes: Potajes sabrosos* (the subtitle means "Delicious Stews"; 1939). *Cuentos del hogar* (Home Stories, 1939) is based on stories her mother told. *Shadows of the Past* (1941) juxtaposes folklore, customs, and personal experiences.

*Romance of a Little Village Girl* (1955) is an autobiographical tale, chronicling Jaramillo's life from childhood through courtship, marriage, motherhood, and a writer's life against the backdrop of a New Mexico transitioning from a region immersed in Hispanic customs (the values of "Old Spain") to one defined by Anglo mores. At times, it feels like a tarnished portrait of the past, meant for tourists. The two chapters included in this anthology offer a wistful view of life in New Mexico, first when Jaramillo was a child and then when she was married to an elected official in the New Mexico government. "Pleasant Outings" describes the strict differences between male and female duties and pleasures, decrying the disappearance of these activities and the overall loss of harmony. "The Territory Becomes a State" briefly explains the role Jaramillo's husband played in the Constitutional Convention, focusing on the dramatic growth Taos experienced after New Mexico achieved statehood.

"[Jaramillo's] story is one of faith, struggle, and survival," Rebolledo writes in her introduction to the 2000 edition. "At the end lies the emphasis on her involvement in the preservation of culture and tradition, and in her self-authorization to do so. She gained the courage to write and to survive from her husband, from her daughter, and from herself." Like her cookbooks and her explorations of New Mexico tradition, Jaramillo's autobiography shows, in the context of the rapid Americanization of the Southwest, the importance of defending one's culture against the assaults of assimilation.

---

### *From* Romance of a Little Village Girl

## Chapter III: Pleasant Outings

The country had adjusted itself to the new changes,[1] and prosperity had helped my father's business. His chief industries were sheep raising, farming and mercantile. But being so energetic, he touched on almost every kind of work.

Occasionally on Sundays father and mother sought relaxation from their heavy responsibilities and took the family out on the long rides and picnics. It was sheer delight to roll along in our horse-drawn buggy, gradually winding up fragrant, timbered hills, past remote villages silently drowsing on green carpet valleys. Or we rode across wide plains to the foot of high mountains and through Taos' scenic canyons.

I can still see myself, like a wild bird set free of a cage, running from one berry bush to another, filling my little play bucket, my heart beating with delight at the sight of beautiful mariposa lilies, blue bells, yellow daisies, feathery ferns—plucking some to trim the pretty sunbonnets mother made for me.

My brothers found these places a fisherman's and hunter's paradise. They caught long strings of speckled mountain trout in the streams. In lakes they found wild ducks, and on prairies they hunted wild rabbits, hen, quail and other game.

Even on these outing days, pleasure was combined with usefulness. Lupe, our cook, and Nieves, the nurse, filled flour sacks with wild hop blossoms, to be dried and kept for winter use. These were steeped in hot water and the water used to make the bread yeast. They picked berries and chock cherries for preserves.

---

1. In the previous two chapters, Jaramillo describes the arrival of Spaniards to what would eventually become New Mexico and how her ancestors settled there and became landowners. She also discusses how, after Mexico gained its independence from Spain in the early nineteenth century, rule over the area passed from Spain to Mexico to the United States.

Refreshed by the invigorating pine-fragrant air, my parents returned with renewed energy to take up their numerous tasks. Both were equally energetic. They had time for everything—work, hospitality, religion and even politics. While my father lived at Arroyo Hondo, his political party never lost their election in that precinct. He ran his combined dry goods and grocery store without help. He directed the work on his farms, and his lands produced all kinds of grain, vegetables, fruit. He raised beef, sheep, pork and race horses. These were his chief industries, but there was no limit to his ambitions. He branched out into many others. He read his Bible and kept in it a record of the births and deaths of members of his family.

In the backyard was the blacksmith shed, where wagons and farm implements were repaired and horses shod. In the carpenter shop was done all kinds of woodwork. My father, always keeping up with the times, took a notion to tear down the old-style porches and replace them with new white ones. The old ones had the best woodwork—thick round posts, carved lintels and scroll-cut corbels supported the round beams and the time-stained ceilings. The whole house was built in the best New Mexico architectural style of any old-style house I have ever seen. My grandfather, Vicente, had his wealthy father, Don Jose Manuel, to help him.

At nine years old, when I attended my Uncle Tobias' school, my father had Jose Manuel, the carpenter, make a little desk for me exactly like my teachers', but painted the brightest red. He also ordered him to make a pew to be put in the old church, where there were no seats, for our family.

My mother did her share of the work, raising her large family of five boys and two girls. She kept three, and sometimes more, servants busy. If my father was out busy with the peons and someone came who wanted something at the store, mother dropped her work and went and waited on the customer. Our store supplied the simple needs of the people, from dry goods and groceries to patent medicines, which mother would tell the people how to use.

Change of work was their relaxation. My father found it in cool eveinngs directing Erineo in planting the vegetable garden, and mother in bringing the children out to pick currants and gooseberries for jellies, and for the pies we were so fond of. Lupe and Nieves found relaxation in going out to the green bean or green pea beds to pick large dishpans full. Then fat Lupe would sit on the kitchen porch, with her legs stretched out to rest her tired feet, and called us children to help her shell the peas.

The compensation for an everyday full day's work was not material, but rather the kind that is felt in the soul. The satisfaction of having accomplished something, of doing even the small things right. For the servants it was satisfaction of doing their duty well.

Harvest time was the busiest and the happiest. I loved the loud "gid-up" and the loud cracking of the long whip that kept the herd of wild horses running around the golden wheat and oat stacks until the stacks were trampled to the ground. Then came the rumble of heavy wagons loaded with the riches of the fields to fill granaries to the ceiling. On moonlit, Indian summer evenings, it was fun to sit around the corn pile, helping to husk the corn, while listening to the witty jokes and stories of our houseservants or of neighbors who came to help. Then, later, sitting in front of a warm fireplace to watch the shelling. The corn was roasted in the large adobe oven, or boiled in lime until it peeled, then spread to dry in the sun and sent down to our log, water-run mill, to be ground into meal, and brought back to the house to be sifted and sacked.

The beeves and porks were then butchered. Hundred-pound cans were filled with the rendered pork lard. From the residue, large kettles of hard soap were made. The fruit from the big orchard that father planted across the river was picked and brought in.

The abundance of those times now are past, even out in the country. The new generation doesn't like farming. Our home was so abundantly supplied, it was always ready to receive unexpected, uninvited guests, some just passing through. Even traveling men who came to take papa's orders for the store found some excuse for stopping overnight. With that old hospitality, they were always cheerfully received. After the harvesting was over came the general housecleaning. Mattresses, blankets and carpets were washed with amole root soap suds in a long trough by the river. The walls were whitewashed inside and on the porches. Floors were smoothly plastered.

The *capilla* was treated in the same way. Religious Grandpa Vicente had built this family private chapel by the house. After the whitewash on the walls dried, the many holy pictures were hung back in their places. There were two especially beautiful ones, one of the Holy Family painted by Manuel Maceda in 1852 at Guadalajara, Mexico, and the other, also an original, of the Madonna. In it, the Virgin's face was so beautiful that I used to climb up on the altar to get a closer view at it. I loved this picture, which looked to me like a very good copy of Raphael's[2] "Madonna."

In those days the stores did not carry childrens' ready made clothes. All items of clothing, from undervests to ruffled, sailor-collared blouses for my four younger brothers, and my laced and ruffled dresses, were made at home. Mother made her babies' layettes by hand from the sheerest nainsook. She never dressed her boys in overalls, and short pants were hard on long-stocking knees; her mending basket was never empty.

She cured all our ills, from measles to tonsilitis, without aid of a doctor. Herbs have medicinal virtue, and our mountains and fields are full of them. That was all she needed. My father brought vaccine from the doctor in Taos and vaccinated all the family and some of the village children. It took so well that we never had to have it done again.

With all this work to attend to, poor mother had time to visit even her sisters only once in several months. Then it always had to be on a Sunday, though they lived near. Too busy to develop boredom, she was always cheerful and happy. There seems to be no better tonic for happiness than work. Everyone was happy in those days. The peace that laid over the land imparted to its inhabitants satisfaction and contentment. How could people be otherwise, living according to God's laws and close to the good earth and the natural beauties of nature? Beauties were there that not even the most gifted artist can copy. The real tints of a glowing sunset, when the sky seems on fire or is suffused in delicate rose and gold. Those autumn colors on trees and shrubs covering mountains, and on wooded rivers. The crystal-like sheen on the river water, and the murmur as it splashes on its way. What

---

2. Raffaello Sanzio (1483–1520), Italian painter.

sweeter music is there to soothe tired minds and nerves of hard-working people?

These good people made use of God's gifts and relaxed in their beauties, while living from the good earth's natural resources.

Children fed with simple food raised on their lands, and housed in neat little whitewashed houses with large sunny yards, were healthy and happy, too. But they were quiet and respectful, not spoiled by too much liberty and by the bold example they learn now from television and movies. Juvenile delinquency?—No one knew what it meant. People's lives radiated between church and home. Mothers stayed home taking care of their children, satisfied to live on their husbands' earnings. They were not buying new clothes all the time nor visiting beauty shops. No one was ever late for church, although some of them lived two and three miles distant and rode in slow wagons or even walked. How nice it would be if people now would live thus!

My parents were scrupulously strict in the performance of their duties, but always gentle and patient. I never heard them raise their voice to correct anyone. They lived with spiritual dignity and respect. Although never demonstrative in their affection toward their family, there was no need of display. We felt their love in everything they did for us. Mother was so refined. Once on the way to Church she noticed my gloveless hands, saying: "Bare hands?" This was enough for me not to forget my gloves again.

She often quoted from her book of *Urbanidad y Buenas Maneras.*[3] Her favorite proverb was *Nada quita al valiente lo cortez*, which meant that to be courteous even to the most humble never lowered anyone. She practiced what she preached by being kind to all. A friend said once to me: "You don't make enough distinction between yourselves and your servants." My parents were not the haughty kind of Dons; they never made their servants feel that they were inferior. There was no need, for our servants knew their place and kept it.

I loved to watch them at work. "*Comadrita*," they called me, so kindly. I answered with a silent smile. Only with my mother or someone of my own age did my tongue ever loosen. It was that reverent respect we were taught to have for our elders, more by example than by word, that made us so quiet and restrained in our outer feelings, even among brothers and sisters. "*Hermanita*"—"Little Sister"—all my brothers and my sisters call me even to this day.

Harmony existed always. If father and mother had a different idea about something, they talked it over in a nice way. If mother could not convince my father as to how a thing should be done, she dropped the subject without arguing. When father built the new store extending into the courtyard, she said it would ruin the looks of the house, and it did. It shut out the light from the inside windows. We lost the east inside porch on the court, and with it went my swing that I enjoyed so much, the locust tree and elevated adobe garden around it, where mother grew her old-fashioned marigolds and larkspurs. Around it we had played *monita siega*, blind man's buff. The porch posts we had used for bases in playing at "*las iglesias*."[4]

---

3. Urbanity and Good Manners.
4. Perhaps a softball game, but the reference is obscure.

The outside porch on the east side was also torn down and a new parlor and two bedrooms were built. The family was growing up and we must have more room, and father must have the store where it would be more handy, and not away between the house and the chapel, where my mother wanted it. She saw the attractive side rather that the convenient one. Although the change would save her all the work of having those long porches white-washed and plastered every year, still she wanted it left in its lovely old style.

We children missed our outdoor sleep. Sometime in very warm weather, mother allowed our maids to take our beds to the inside porch. What fun it was to find our beds by moonlight and to lay there looking up at the starlit heaven! We did not gaze long. After a full day of active work or play, there was no need of sleeping powders for anyone in the family. By nine o'clock every one was ready to drop into dreamland.

## Chapter XX: The Territory Becomes a State

After decades of controversy between the two political parties—one favoring statehood, the other, territorial government—the statehood party won, and on January 6, 1912, President [William] Howard Taft signed the proclamation of statehood in the presence of Congressman George Curry, and New Mexico became the forty-seventh star in the flag of the United States. A little later, one hundred elected members—my husband one of them—met at the capitol as members of the Constitutional Convention, to form the laws of the new state.

On January 15, Governor William McDonald, the first elected executive of New Mexico, was inaugurated. On the eve of the inauguration, the governor and his family arrived from their Carrizoso ranch in a Santa Fe Railroad Pullman.

Elaborate preparations had been made. The dome of the capitol was illuminated with myriads of electric lights. At the entrance to the plaza blazed a welcoming arch. White and yellow bunting formed a background to the many rows of lights that lit the front of the Palace of the Governors; above glittered a star of lights and the name of Governor McDonald, together with the names of the first three governors, Oñate, De Vargas and Bent. The reception held in one of the large rooms in the Old Palace was a very formal affair, attended only by those holding tickets or invitations. At the end, the governor and guests passed into the National Guard Armory, which had been decorated for the dance. Governor and Mrs. McDonald led the grand march, followed by Governor Mills, Lieutenant Governor E. de Baca, Adjutant General Brooks, Democratic Chairman C. C. Jones and Republican Chairman Ven Jaramillo, accompanied by their wives.

At eleven o'clock, dinner was served in the assembly room, which had been decorated, and set with small tables. Many costly gowns were seen on the guests. Silk marquisette was in style. Mrs. McDonald's gold satin one was veiled with black marquisette. I had ordered mine from the Denver Dry Goods Company, and it came in yellow marquisette with a dresden-flowered border in colors, outlined in black, with a yellow satin foundation. I still have it as a souvenir of the last great function I attended with my husband. He was still in the governor's staff and was in his full colonel's uniform.

That following summer our Denver girl friends paid us an unexpected visit. The Rev. McMenemin, rector of the Denver cathedral and an eloquent orator, was with them. They had been visiting my cousins named Burns at Tierra Amarilla, and on their way back to Denver, stopped at our house overnight.

At the dinner table Ven told the priest that I still remembered the first sermon I had heard him preach, when he had fired out: "We will build the Denver cathedral in spite of the people of Denver." "Yes," he said. "I first ask them to do something, then I plead. When that does not work, I scold." He built it, costing over one million dollars. Some people thought his sermons too flowery. For myself, I like variation, a change from the common, everyday expressions.

Next morning I joined the party to show them the way through Taos. The road through the Rio Grande canyon was steep and rough, but our reverend friend proved to be an expert driver, and we passed through Taos late in the afternoon. A little ways out of town a shower met us, and Father, not being used to the Taos sticky mud, stopped to put on chains. In the meantime I sat in the car, enraptured, watching the undescribable panorama as the shower played on the beautiful Taos Mountains. A misty white fog was rising from the foot of the mountains. The top peaks were shrouded in dark clouds, now and then lit up by zigzag lightning. Shafts of golden sun rays shot from behind dark clouds and hit green spots on the mountains, and here and there around the valley sheets of rain poured down.

In about an hour we reached Arroyo Hondo. At my old home my three brothers were batching; but they had a good cook, and our flourishing appetites were soon quenched with the simple but nourishing menu served. The girls' father owned a cattle ranch; so they knew something about ranch life, and enjoyed the visit. Because of the lack of wine and hosts, the priest could not give us mass next morning in our private chapel before leaving.

> Let the old houses their secrets keep
> Leave them alone in their quiet sleep;
> They are like old folks who nod by the fire,
> Glad with their dreams of youth and desire.

My next trip to Taos was with my friend Ruth Laughlin Barker, author of the popular book *Caballeros*. She wanted to see an old Spanish-style house to describe in her new book. On the way, I described some of the big, attractive homes I knew when I was in school at Taos. It was during the rainy month of April, and a little shower met us as we were coming into town. Next morning, when I raised the window shade in my room at the Don Fernando Hotel, another enchanting sight met my eyes. Down in the valley, the peach and apricot trees covered with pink and white blossoms, and above, the high, snow-clad mountains blinded the eyes with their brilliancy in the brightest sunshine. No wonder Taos valley has always since my childhood fascinated me like a fairyland.

After breakfast, we rode to Ranchito, but where was Aunt Piedad's attractive old home, or the new one grandpa had built for her? It was hard to believe my eyes that what I was seeing were the melting remains of these once big, fine lively homes. A sob choked in my throat.

After lunch, I thought of the Valdez home at Placita. The round *torrion*[1] always had marked this nice home for me; but now I could not find it; and we rode on to Arroyo Seco to see the fine Gonzales home. We were standing right before it, but I did not recognize it. "Where is Juanita Gonzales' home?" I asked a man in the yard. "This is the house," he answered. The whitewashed porch with the blue railing posts was gone, and the whole house was in ruins. Juanita, whom her mother always had kept so well-dressed at school, came to the door with torn hose and shabby shoes. She asked us to come in. I asked her if she had some of her mother's fine jewelry or table silver. She brought out a silver set with an exquisite design and silver grape bunches on the lids. My friend became interested right away to buy it. Juanita asked $35.00. I am sure it was worth more, but my friend continued to bargain until finally she said, "I will give you a $15.00 check." I shook my hand at the side "no," but Juanita only smiled at me, showing her pretty dimples, and answered, "Alright." This is how our rich Spanish families have been stripped of their most precious belongings. "Why did you do it?" I whispered as I was going out the door. "I need the money to fix the house," she said.

At the Don Fernando (once the Barron Hotel), Mr. Gusdorf, the proprietor, kept introducing me to the hotel guests, telling them I had been married in this hotel. Oh, how I wished the old hotel had been as fine and attractive as this new one, to accommodate our wedding guests.

1955

---

1. I.e., *torreón*, a round tower built for defense.

---

# DANIEL VENEGAS
## ca. 1880–ca. 1935

One of the first full-length novels written in Spanish in the United States dealing with U.S. themes, the picaresque *Las aventuras de Don Chipote: o, Cuando los pericos mamen* (Adventures of Don Chipote: or, When Parrots Suckle, 1928), by Daniel Venegas, paved a comedic road for Latino prose literature. (Contemporaneous newspaper columns, such as by Jorge Ulica [see p. 329], paved a similar road. Latino theatrical comedy had long been a tradition, mainly as presented by drama companies from Spain, Cuba, Puerto Rico, and Mexico that toured in the United States and performed for Latino audiences.) Little is known, though, of Venegas's life. In the early 1920s, he worked as a journalist for the Los Angeles newspaper *El Pueblo*, after which he founded the weekly satirical newspaper *El Malcriado*, which published stories, commentaries, caricatures, and send-ups of world and local news, customs, and sports. Around this time, he was the head of a theater company, La Compañía de Revistas Daniel Venegas (The Daniel Venegas Revue). Plays by him were reviewed in Spanish-language newspapers between 1924 and 1933, but all of his theatrical works have been lost.

The literary historian Nicolás Kanellos extrapolates from passages in *Adventures of Don Chipote* that Venegas "emigrated from Mexico as a laborer, traveling through Juárez, Mexico, and El Paso, Texas. He made his way to Los Angeles by working on the Santa Fe Railroad." Venegas's comic narrative is about the pleasures and disappointments of Mexican immigrants who, believing tales of "streets paved with gold," come to the United States to dig up the gold. Employing *caló*, a contemporary working-class Spanglish, well before its acceptance by Latinos and Anglos beginning in the late 1940s, Venegas presents a hilarious vanity fair of flophouses, drug dealers, pimps, quacks, and uneducated *campesinos*, who flock from the Mexican hinterlands to urban Los Angeles. While reminiscent of that other great "Don," the Spanish writer Miguel de Cervantes's novel *Don Quixote* (1605, 1615), Venegas's work is the first novel of Chicano language and sensibility. In fact, it reportedly is the first printed work that includes the word *Chicano*.

---

## *From* The Adventures of Don Chipote: or, A Sucker's Tale[1]

## Chapter One

The sun was setting. The clouds grew red like a poor man's roof, and then went from red to black, like a virgin in the night, till they looked like the oversized ears of some comical witch.

Lovebirds cuddled in their nests, pecking one another a welcome, furling their wings and preparing to snore. Bumblebees stopped buzzing. Pumpkin blossoms closed up, getting ready for the night. Bees settled into their hives to regurgitate the honey they had imbibed. The stream went on singing and watering the roots of the avocados, the *camichine*, and the *zalate*.[2]

All peace and tranquility. All the natural world beginning its rest, all except Don Chipote, who went on poking at the ox's tail, still too energized by the day's activity. He had a responsibility to his passel of kids, so he had little choice but to go on walking behind this horned beast. Every so often he would breathe in the less-than-comforting emanations of its hindquarters.

Poor Don Chipote, drowsing at noon, having wolfed down his supply of a few tacos and then sucking on a cheroot, dreamt of cornfields. But instead of ears of corn on their stalks, they were rife with brilliant Aztecs. He felt rich, the need to work had disappeared.

Dreams, just dreams. He couldn't plant much. And even then the crows ate half, while the other was divided among the passel, the dog, the cat, and the oxen.

---

1. Translated by Ilan Stavans and Harold Augenbraum. Venegas's subtitle, *Cuando los pericos mamen,* is an expression that implies the impossibility of a "natural" act, as in the English-language expressions *when hell freezes over* and *when pigs fly.* Mexican Spanish-speakers in the United States today use *si andara en bicicleta,* meaning literally "if my grandmother rode a bicycle."

Because literal renditions of the subtitle, such as "When Parrots Suckle Their Young" and "When Parrots Breast-Feed," fail to convey the idea behind it, the translators have used "A Sucker's Tale," which prefigures the foolishness of the protagonist's endeavors.
2. Fig tree. *Camichine:* rubber plant.

It had gotten dark. Don Chipote and his oxen, with the calm that comes from driving himself like an aging beast of burden, headed home as he pondered his awful lot in life.

Scrawny's bark brought him back to himself, and he realized they were in front of the hut where Doña Chipote, the chips-off-the-old-block, the cat, and Scrawny were anxiously waiting to chow down.

After he had taken off their yoke and put on the green blinders that tricked the oxen into eating sawdust instead of grain, he went into the hut and greeted his better half as he glanced sheepishly at the *gorditas*[3] and wiped the kids' runny noses. In no time at all he was stuffing his face with dinner, as if he had been tied up and starved for days, and as if you could call dinner a puddle of three little beans in water, ground chile, a jar of *atole*[4] and *gorditas*. In any case, for a while all you could hear was a gnashing of teeth and a smacking of hard-working lips.

When at last Don Chipote's belly was satisfied, he asked his consort: "How's that mule of your mother's?"

"Fine. I heard she very happily gave birth to a baby mule," she replied.

"Who would have thought it?" Don Chipote answered. "To think that she was all blocked up and now she gives birth to a mule when she was at death's door. In any case, we can probably count on a new helper if your mother offers it to us."

Doña Chipota only grunted a reply. Don Chipote, wiping the thick wires that passed for a mustache, got up to roll a cigar and await the time to say the rosary, something that as good Christians they never failed to do before stretching out on their mats to wait for the morning when they would get up and play the beast of burden again, as they did every day.

## Chapter Two

Let's leave Don Chipote and his family asleep in their underwear, legs akimbo and snoring like there's no tomorrow, and turn our eyes a few leagues away from their hut.

On the road to the *ranchería*, a local man named Pitacio is trudging along. The fact that he is travelling at night doesn't necessarily mean that he is in a hurry to get anywhere, but he surely has his reasons for getting there when everyone's still in dreamland.

Before we move on, let's introduce our new character. Pitacio first saw the light of day in the *ranchería* in which our story takes place. His parents were not only poor but drunkards. From the time he was young Pitacio developed an inordinate fear of a simple day's work. No matter how many times his father sent him to scare the crows away from the crops, he couldn't make him do it.

By the time Pitacio reached adulthood, he had become an orphan, having driven his parent to an early grave. This doesn't mean he didn't shed a tear at their funerals and feel as we do when our parents shuffle off their mortal coils, but to be honest, the main reason Pitacio mourned the loss of

3. Filled, deep-fried pockets of cornmeal dough.
4. Hot drink that includes cornmeal, water, sugar, cinnamon, vanilla, and optional chocolate or fruit.

his parents wasn't because he had ended up an orphan, but because it meant he no longer had a means of support and, as we've said, no way of supplying one.

So it wasn't until the world had been turned upside down that he thought about what he would have to do to keep his belly from growling, since it, too, had been orphaned and was feeling hunger pangs.

Idleness breeds contempt. If you'd never worked at anything, like Pitacio, had never lashed yourself to that beast of burden, had never earned your daily bread by the sweat of your brow, you too would be easily dismissed by the local ranchers. The simple fact was that Pitacio was unwilling to be that beast of burden, in any way.

So as the months passed and he tried his hand with the local croppers, one by one they sacked him until, since everyone around there was well aware of his ways, he had nothing left to do but light out for parts unknown.

That's why one day, after he had packed his bindle, though the sun set with him still on his *ranchería* it came up with him no longer there, which is how our good friend Pitacio found himself a few leagues away from where he uttered his first cry when his mother pushed him out into this Vale of Tears.

Where was Pitacio going? We don't know, and I'll bet he didn't either. He knew one thing and one thing only. He needed to work. So he eased on down the road, getting further and further from home, all the while thinking about how much he missed his parents.

Dusk fell. His dogs had begun to bark and his tummy bite when he caught sight of the village of Nacatecuaro in the distance. Seeing it meant running toward it. Despite not a penny to his name, for some strange reason he thought that when he arrived in Nacatecuaro there would be a full table with a place set just for him.

His running was soon capped by success. As the roof of these poor people's house came into focus, with the steps of that weary beast of burden he entered—what seemed to him, who had never been away from home—a teeming city.

Let's not make more of this than we should, so let's just plant our Pitacio in a small town in the United States, in a small town in Texas, where he had arrived with great serendipity and where, because of that damn belly, he found himself working and spending every penny he earned, though he paid attention to his appearance and was able to put aside a few cents to buy a secondhand suit (though who knows how may hands it had really passed through), but still it fit pretty well.

The suit wasn't of the best quality. On the other hand it was the most beautiful navy blue you've ever seen and with buttons everywhere. And our good friend Pitacio had also bought himself a pair of the wildest yellow shoes, silk socks, and a real cowboy hat.

We come across Pitacio trudging along the road, decked out and feeling like the cock of the walk, though no one saw him in the street since he didn't run into anyone and in any case they couldn't since it was nighttime, with each step getting closer to the ranch in which he had been born and where we left Don Chipote and his family fast asleep.

Okay, now that we're back at the point at which we began, since this is our story and we're in control, let's jump forward a bit and put Pitacio at the front of the ranch's corral.

It's five in the morning. Today, the sun is coming up for both the rich and the poor, just as it did yesterday. The birds that spent the night beak to beak begin to leave the nest to look for something, and someone, to peck.

The oxen are lowing, not because they are happy about a new day but because they are sad that the time is approaching when they put their heads in the yoke and they'll have to pull the plough or the cart.

The place's residents—they're animals, too, just like the oxen—take their last stretch on their padded mats and emit a last grunt before getting up and getting ready to face the task of finishing yesterday's leftover business.

It's a beautiful day. All of nature seems to have put its best foot forward to greet Pitacio, the prodigal returned when least expected.

Everyone had thrown off their covers at Don Chipote's house as well. Doña Chipota, his boon companion, was mixing the *nixtamal*[5] to have the *gorditas* to pack for lunch his lunch, while he fed the livestock. Then the dogs, led by Scrawny, began to bark like crazy at Pitacio, who had already gotten to the fence that separated the patio from the street.

To the house's owners, this meant something new was afoot. The dogs never barked when they were hungry, and they knew everyone in the neighborhood. So Don Chipote and his boon companion left off what they were doing and went out to see why the dogs were making such a racket. It was quite a surprise to come upon Pitacio, that lazy Pitacio who everyone knew intimately, but who seemed like a stranger in a gaudy suit so out of place in those parts.

Clothes make the man, they say. Before, Pitacio was never invited anywhere, but now, that getup made Don Chipote and his wife think he was an important person, and so with great pomp they invited him in.

Used as he was to handouts—but never forced to the indignity of begging—Pitacio entered the Chipote house like a *gran señor*. He went straight to the kitchen, since what mattered to him the most at that moment was to be invited for lunch given that he hadn't had a single bite since the day before.

Don Chipote right off issued the invitation, and within minutes they were both stuffing down stewed beans with, of course, chiles and warm *gorditas*.

For a long time their mouths did nothing but eat and eat and eat. So much so that Doña Chipote was afraid there wouldn't be enough *gorditas*.

Finally, when they couldn't eat another thing, they rolled cheroots and lit them on a burning stick from the fire. Taking a long drag on his cigar, Don Chipote asked his visitor how he had managed to transform himself into such a distinguished gentleman.

Everyone knows that the lazier you are the more you talk. And since he was such a champion idler, Pitacio loosened his tongue: "Well, you know full well, Don Chipote, that my father, may he rest in peace, was a well-read man and a good writer. And I, the good son that I am, take after him, maybe a bit more so. I suppose you remember that I don't exactly like prodding oxen in the butt, since it doesn't require much in the way of intelligence. And since I'm very bright, I decided to make a living by my wits. You may also remember that everyone in the *rancho* and its surroundings were

---

5. Hominy, or dried corn kernels soaked or cooked in an alkaline liquid (usually limewater) to help remove their husks and make them more palatable and easier to digest.

never able to understand me and that one by one they threw me out, until I was forced to find someplace where they would appreciate my intelligence.

"One night I was at the ranch, and the next morning I was gone, and I didn't stop until I got to the United States, where white people live. You have to see it to believe it. Don Chipote, if you could *see* how sharp these people are, distinguished and well-read, even more than the priest, who's the smartest person around these parts. I don't want to go on and on about it, because in the end you have to see it to believe it, but I will say that the gringos immediately recognized how much I was worth."

"So how much did they pay for you?" asked Don Chipote.

"Don't be an idiot," Pitacio replied. "They didn't buy me. What I'm saying is that they realized I was an intelligent person. So pretty soon I had a job for three dollars a day. The kind of dollars that are worth double."

"What kind of dollar is worth double?" inquired Don Chipote, astonished by such marvels.

"The type of dollar *they* use," Pitacio added. "You must know that their money is worth twice ours, so that earning one dollar there is like earning two here."

"You don't say," responded Don Chipote, mesmerized. "You mean that just because of who you are you made three dollars a day?"

"Exactly."

"And that's like six of ours?"

"*Seguro que* yes."

"What's '*yes*'?" asked Don Chipote, his jaw dropping further.

"Ah, *esquiusme!*" replied Pitacio. "I forgot that you don't *toquingles* and here I speaking it." He continued: "'Yes' is like saying *sí* in our language."

"Caramba," interrupted Don Chipote. "Obviously you've become a big man. All right, all right, go on. Maybe I'll learn something."

"Stop that nonsense," announced Doña Chipota, who until then had been quiet. "If you want him to tell you more, he should tell you how he got there, then maybe you could go to the white people's country and become a distinguished gentleman like him."

"That actually would be better," added Pitacio.

"You think so?" replied Don Chipote.

"You just have to put your mind to it and then you'll really be swimming in it."

And the damned Pitacio, realizing that he could swing a few days of grub from his stories, went on to spin a thousand yarns that ended up twisting Don Chipote's mind.

Of course, he didn't bother to mention how hungry he had been. Nor did he say a word about the mistreatment he had suffered at the hands of his bosses while working on a *traque*. Instead, he focused brilliantly—and solely—on his good fortune.

The United States is full of Pitacios. It's a matter of pride. No matter how many *paisanos*[6] have the bad luck to come to this country, instead of going home and telling the truth they loaf around getting everyone who listens to them all excited.

---

6. Countrymen.

Unfortunately, Chicanos are quite naïve and swallow everything they hear about El Norte whole. That's why, and not so much as a result of the miserable conditions brought along by the Mexican Revolution, everybody is leaving our country.

We don't mean to say that no *paisanos* have done well in the United States. But they're one in a million. Instead, the majority just come to dissipate their energy, be mistreated by their bosses, and be humiliated by the citizenry, until they reach old age. Then they are denied the right to work and feed their families.

I would need more space than I have here to tell the truth about Mexican life in the United States, so we'll leave it to more accomplished, more insightful scribblers than ourselves. If we've drawn out this parenthesis and interrupted our story, it's only to develop the true character of Don Chipote de Jesús María Domínguez. Therefore, with apologies and to not lose the line of our narrative, let's cut it off here and get back to the thread of our story.

## Chapter Three

It was hopeless. Don Chipote has swallowed everything Pitacio has told him, and fed him for ten days just so he could listen to his adventures in the land of Uncle Sam. During that time he neglected the parcel that made him his living.

All of this made him think that if Pitacio, who his entire life had been a layabout, had suddenly become an elegant person, then he, who had constantly played the beast of burden and spent countless hours prodding his oxen's asses, would surely make millions over there. The more he thought about it, the less interest he had in yoking the animals and tending his little parcel of land that for years had provided for him, even if it was only tacos and beans. The more he thought about it, the more he fixed on the idea of emigrating to the United States.

"I'm going," he said to his wife. "I'm gonna bring back all the gold they have. But before I come back I'll send for you so you can see it for yourself."

Doña Chipota was upset. But when she thought about all the good that would come of it, she agreed to his leaving.

The poor woman—after all, she was a woman—was also mesmerized by Pitacio's yarns. Even though she was sorry to let Don Chipote go, she encouraged him, figuring that in no time she would be wearing nice skirts and having her hair done. She could see herself arm in arm with her husband, he all decked out in a bowler hat, parading down the street in the United States.

After a great deal of cogitation and dickering, the trip was approved by majority vote in an assembly in which even the Chipote juniors were polled. Then the preparations began.

Pitacio was left in charge of managing Don Chipote's parcel of land. He also gave his word of honor that he would keep and support the family.

Since Don Chipote didn't have much by way of clothing, Doña Chipote made underwear and an undershirt from a bed sheet and fitted them to her husband's size. A pig was sold to buy a pair of pants. Everyone decked him out as well as they could.

Doña Chipota put her nose to the grindstone to prepare provisions. She made tacos and beans and quesadillas stuffed with cheese or pumpkin flower. She made lard *gorditas*. Her culinary talents emerged. Once everything was ready, the departure was set for the following morning. That night, while praying the rosary, Don Chipote entrusted himself to his patron saint and the Celestial Court. The night was spent in hugs and tears.

In the morning they hugged one another for the last time. They cried until the snot hung from their noses. Even Scrawny began to howl.

Later on, as the sun turned the clouds from black to pink, like a blushing maiden dancing the fox-trot or *zorra-trot* for the first time and feeling a bit "stimulated" by her partner—later on, on the labyrinthine roadway—Don Chipote's humble silhouette kept a steady but quick pace, loaded down by a backpack heavier in *gorditas* than clothes. Unable to decide whether to leave his owner, Scrawny trotted behind. They walked for a good many hours, until their legs began to buckle. Why? Because Don Chipote, immersed in his thoughts and sad at having left home, had no appetite. Yet when Scrawny jumped up on him, looking at him with sunken eyes, he finally decided to rest for a while and eat some of the delicacies made by his beloved wife. Thought became action. They settled down in a pleasant spot on the side of the road, and the master and his dog wolfed down their first quesadillas.

Fatigue and a full stomach made Don Chipote and his faithful dog, Scrawny, a bit drowsy and gave them the idea that since night was coming on and they had more time than energy, our travelers would stretch out and go to sleep. In no time at all they were snoring away.

How long did they sleep? Who knows! But the stars were still twinkling when Don Chipote announced it was time to go. After a good long stretch, they hit the road once again.

Don Chipote and his dog had been walking for long while without the *campesino* showing any signs of discouragement, still full of the illusions created by the words of the duplicitous Pitacio, and never wavering in his decision to leave his family behind. He was ready to make any sacrifice for the well-being of his family. The reality of his dream of making it to the United States was approaching as fast as his legs could carry him.

It was a month since the harsh pilgrimage had begun, and traces of the terrible trek had started to show on master and dog. Obviously, the provisions prepared by Doña Chipota had not lasted for that long. Since Don Chipote didn't know how far his destination was, once the food was finished he began to cut back. When he could, he would buy a large supply of tortillas and chiles. Since tortillas go more quickly, for days he would end up eating only chiles, the result being that whenever he needed to evacuate a digested meal, the act would bring tears to his eyes . . .

It was a month since they departed, as we've said, when our travelers spied the spire of the main church in Ciudad Juárez, a fact that Don Chipote found out only when another wayfarer told him so. When he realized for sure that he was close to the border, he could do no less than fall on his knees to thank his patron saint for the miracle bestowed on him. In his view, every sacrifice of his long pilgrimage was well worth it. After all, according to Pitacio he was at the gates of a country whose streets were paved with gold. Like a thirsty traveler crossing the desert who spies an oasis in the distance where he'll be able to quench his thirst, Don Chipote, despite his exhaustion, crossed the dunes that greet visitors upon arrival at Ciudad Juárez. He quickened his pace, sure as he was that the end of his travels were near.

It must have been around six in the afternoon when Don Chipote and the faithful Scrawny entered the narrow streets of the border city. Nobody even looked at him, even though he was obviously in a bad way. They were used to such things, and worse. Ciudad Juárez is destination to troopes of laborers who, forced by the dire conditions in our own Mexico, leave their homeland in search of work.

Don Chipote and his companion wandered around for a long while in search of a place to spend the night, but he had no money in a place where dollars rule and money talks. So they found a place to sleep on the railway platform.

Installed on his mat, with his dog at his side, and influenced by the warm evening air, Don Chipote began thinking about the Family Chipote. And with all the love of a father who finds himself far from his children, he sent them his blessings and then fell asleep.

1928

# ADELINA "NINA" OTERO-WARREN
## 1881–1965

With roots going back to the Spanish conquistadors, María Adelina Isabel Emilia Otero was born in La Constancia, New Mexico, 20 miles south of Albuquerque. She was educated at Maryville College of the Sacred Heart, in St. Louis, Missouri. In 1908, she married Rawson Warren, a lieutenant in the U.S. Cavalry, but the marriage lasted only a year. In 1915, Otero-Warren became state chair of the legislative committee for the Federation of Women's Clubs in New Mexico, and from 1917 to 1929 she was superintendent of schools in Santa Fe County. In 1922, she was the Republican Party of New Mexico's nominee for the U.S. House of Representatives. That same year, the New Mexican poet Felipe Maximiliano Chacón (see p. 333) dedicated a poem to her, which included these lines:

> Vástago noble de español linaje,
> y más aún, americana pura,
> pero qué importa el exterior ropaje
> del que amerita distinguida altura!

> (Noble scion of Spanish lineage,
> Yet even more, pure American light,

But how important is outward plumage
In one of such distinguished height!)

In the late 1920s, Otero-Warren and her friend Mamie Meadors purchased 1,257 acres of land outside Santa Fe, and for three years they worked the property. Drawing on these experiences, Otero-Warren wrote her book, *Old Spain in Our Southwest*, which was published in 1936 with illustrations by her cousin Aileen Nusbaum and was reprinted several times during Otero-Warren's life.

During the 1920s and 1930s, a coterie of American writers and artists had moved to New Mexico, where they developed an outsider's idea of the mystical nature of the area. In writing her book, Otero-Warren was providing a counterpoint to this idea. Like other works written in New Mexico between 1880 and 1940, such as Eusebio Chacón's "The Calm after the Storm" (see p. 336), *Old Spain in Our Southwest* shows the interplay of daily life, Iberian heritage, and native heritage in the making of the regional culture.

The book is one of the best portrayals of the Spanish customs that survived both Mexican independence from Spain in 1821 and the U.S. conquest of the region in 1848. Its many narrative voices combine to provide a broad look at the world of Spanish New Mexico. In the first section, "The Wind in the Mountains," a first-person narrator describes the harsh but beautiful landscape near the Sangre de Cristo Mountains. A storm is approaching. She sees a shepherd and his dog, solitary figures whose presence emphasizes the stark landscape. In the next section, "An Old Spanish Hacienda," which is excerpted here, the narrator contrasts the settling of the territory with the territory's earlier natural beauty. The settled community, represented by the hacienda, has its own civilized beauty, however, which allows Otero-Warren to describe some of the fashions, customs, and traditions that helped the landowners create and maintain a social contract with each other. Even the arrival of the priest becomes less a religious event than an opportunity to discuss the inhabitants' customs. In subsequent sections, Otero-Warren compiles memoirs, stories, and anecdotes, portraying the Spanish heritage and life on the *latifundios* (the grand estates that emerged from Spain's land grants to colonizers), a way of life that remained into the early part of Otero-Warren's life but no longer dominated the local culture after 1848. The book's final section is a compilation of folktales and other stories submitted to her for a contest she devised as superintendent of schools.

In the 1970s and '80s, as discussed in the "Acculturation" introduction, Chicano literary critics applied the reductive labels "Spanish fantasy heritage" and "hacienda mentality" to Otero-Warren's work and that of her southwestern contemporaries Cleofas M. Jaramillo and Fabiola Cabeza de Baca Gilbert. These women's works simply did not fit into the critics' post-1960s politics, which celebrated Aztlán (the mythical ideal of Chicano origins) and the working-class Chicano heritage. In the 1990s, however, Latina literary critics reevaluated Otero-Warren, Jaramillo, and Cabeza de Baca Gilbert in a different political light. They noted that by transmitting southwestern domestic traditions, these writers had preserved important aspects of Spanish Mexican American culture.

## FROM OLD SPAIN IN OUR SOUTHWEST

## An Old Spanish Hacienda

The Spanish descendant of the *Conquistadores* may be poor, but he takes his place in life with a noble bearing, for he can never forget that he is a descendant of the Conquerors.

In the old days the great Spanish families lived in haciendas. The hacienda was not just one house, but was actually a small community. There was the house of the *patrón*, smaller houses for the peones and a chapel. The house of the *patrón* was a one-story building with thick walls, made of adobe, a mixture of clay and straw. It was a complete square with a court-yard or *patio* in the center; on which all the rooms opened. The entrance to the house was through a large hallway which also served as a living room from which doors opened into other rooms. The rooms were large; each room had long windows opening on a balcony or porch overlooking the *patio*. From them, one could enjoy the flowers or could see the clear moon. Never did anyone but peones expose themselves to the sun. There were shutters on the windows which were closed at sundown and opened at sunrise.

The bedrooms in the house were completely carpeted; there were great high beds with feather mattresses. A gilt-framed mirror hung over the wash-stand, which had a white marble top; there were a couch and large chairs. On the papered wall hung portraits of members of the family, the frame in gold with a strip of red velvet next to the glass; a table was at the bedside with a candle-holder and a basket which was filled with fruit or cakes when the room was occupied. The reception room was most formal and was kept closed except on state occasions—a baptism, wedding or funeral. This room had a very high ceiling. A big window looked into the garden. Heavy bro-cade curtains hung at this window, and the furniture was upholstered in wine-colored velvet. Huge mirrors stood on pedestals with marble tops, made of carved wood, painted with a gold paint. A large candelabra, with glass prisms, to hold as many as two dozen candles was in the center. A marble mantelpiece with a wax bouquet on it stood at one end and over this was an oval glass.

Near the house of the *patrón* were the houses of the peones, who were not slaves, but working people who preferred submission to the *patrón* rather than an independent chance alone. Each family had a house with two or more rooms, depending upon the number in the family; a kitchen and bedrooms. Usually they received their guests in the kitchen but on formal occasions they used their bedrooms as the *patrón* used his reception room.

There was always a chapel where the mission priest celebrated Mass once a month. There the peones assembled to pray on certain days and seasons and to sing their own hymns. There, images of the Saints occupied a place on either side of a small wooden altar carved and painted white. Above the altar was a niche where the patron saint of the *patrón* stood, looking down on his large family. There were no pews; chairs were placed near the altar for the *patrones*. The servants knelt and sat on the floor. Paper flowers of all colors, in vases of china, as well as colored flowers of glass decorated the altar. The candle-holders were made of brass and the sanctuary lamp of red glass with prisms. The walls were whitewashed, the beams exposed. High windows let in the light.

For a week the people of the hacienda of Don Antonio had been preparing for the monthly visit of the priest. The chapel must be in readiness, for not only the priest but all the *señores* of the adjoining hacienda would be there. The servants had been plastering the chapel, repairing the cracks where the water had come through the mud and sand which was a part of the roof. The women did the plastering. They worked all during the day save for the afternoon siesta time. They protected their skin from the hot sun by a face powder which they made for this purpose. This face powder called *cáscara* was made of dried bones finely ground, mixed with herbs and made into a paste.

On the day the priest arrived, the hacienda took on a fiesta air. All except necessary work stopped, everyone must attend Mass. Every home heard the chapel bell, and guests from the adjoining haciendas arrived in high coaches and in straw-filled wagons. Everyone was eager to come, for the people loved pomp and ceremony whether it was a funeral procession, a wedding or a fiesta Mass. On all occasions there was time to laugh, to love and to pray. There was no great hurry, no locking of doors, for no one ever entered the home of another unless he were invited.

So the *Dons* and *Doñas* came in high coaches, drawn by prancing bays, a man on horseback behind each coach to give assistance in case of emergency. The peones came in wagons, on burro-back or on foot, the many children clinging to their mothers. They were all proud of the masters they served, proud to be part of the family. Some had traveled far, but they tried to hear Mass whenever possible, for this was part of their duty and would bring them good luck. It was always noticed if a neighbor did not come and he was considered a savage who did not know the Catholic belief or else did not abide by his Christian teaching.

The church was filled with people, the children more numerous than the grown-ups. When Mass was over, the double doors of the chapel were swung on their wooden pivots and opened wide. The *patrones* of this and adjoining haciendas left the church first. As they arose from their knees, they saw through the door a white marble statue, a gray stone image of Saint Joseph,[1] a cross of granite, for the cemetery in front of the chapel was the resting place of those members of the family who had departed. Even on a feast day they were reminded to pray for their dead.

As they left the chapel the *patrón*, Don Antonio, greeted the visiting *señores* with an invitation: "Come to my house, *señores*, the *Doña* is awaiting you. We hope to have the pleasure of your company for dinner. My house is at your disposal."

The *señores*, who had already planned to stay, accepted with a bow: "A thousand thanks—if it is not too much bother, we will appreciate it."

In Spanish homes preparation is always made for several guests. Distances are great and transportation slow, so whether a person is on a business or social visit, he is the invited guest of the *señor*. Cold lunches are

---

1. According to the New Testament of the Bible, Joseph was the husband of Mary, mother of Jesus; God was the biological father of Jesus, but Joseph served as Jesus' foster father. He is venerated as a saint by Christian Churches such as the Roman Catholic Church.

never eaten. If, on a long journey, a meal has to be eaten in the open, a stop is made, food cooked and a rest taken.

As the *señores* proceeded to the house, the servants extended invitations to their visiting friends and with bustle and chatter they went home to take off their holiday clothes.

The *Doña* of the hacienda was the dominant head of the family, for she was in complete charge of the house and the children. As she was receiving her guests, her eldest son approached her. He had to go away at once but never under any circumstances would he go without taking leave of his mother. He was sending his men to a sheep ranch. As the herders remain at each ranch six months and the camps are far away, there should be no delay in getting them started. The shepherds and provisions would go in mule- or horse-drawn carts. The *patroncito* would go in a buckboard. The young man waited—no young person ever spoke first to his elders—until his mother greeted him.

"I did not see you at Mass, Tranquilino."

"Yes, mother, I was there but thought there would not be enough chairs for our guests, so I remained in the sacristy."

"What is it that seems to make you ill at ease among our guests?" asked the *Doña* of her son.

"I am ill at ease because my herders are even now waiting for orders for their journey to the sheep camp. I have delayed too long now, because I did not wish to be abrupt, but, before leaving, I wish your blessing."

Tranquilino knelt while his mother made the sign of the cross over his bowed head. Then he kissed her hand, bowed to his guests and departed.

As the wine was passed, conversation became less formal. Eloísa, the young lady of the house, entered the room.

"Eloísa, speak to our guests," her mother said. Eloísa did so, greeting all in the customary manner, kissing the cheek of the women, her hand being kissed by the men.

"Be seated," ordered her mother. This permission to be seated was connected with a custom of the Spanish Court. When a woman was to be raised to the title of grandee, she entered the presence of the queen carrying a cushion and, after telling her reasons for seeking the title, she was ordered by the queen to "seat yourself." This meant that thereafter she belonged to the court group and could be seated in the presence of her queen.

The men then stepped to the balcony to smoke, when one of the younger sons of the house arrived. He greeted everyone with a formal "God give you a good day," and remained standing with hat in hand.

Don Antonio, with a twinkle, asked young Don Juan what had delayed him.

Don Juan answered: "I had to visit the sick with the priest."

Don Antonio then said, "Cover yourself," to his son. "Cover yourself," meaning to put on the hat, was the order the king gave to a new member of his court when raised to the rank of a social equal. So, in this country, a grandee of New Spain[2] still held court. He followed the old customs every day; his home was his court, from his family he received a courtly attention, his servants were his vassals and gave him submission.

2. From 1535 to 1821, the political unit of Spanish territories in North America and Asia-Pacific, including the present-day southwestern United States and Mexico.

The servants were preparing the dinner. The housekeeper, with her keys, had gone to the house where the food was stored. This storehouse was dark and cool, for the walls were unusually thick. It had a small window placed high which was opened only at the time the food was stored there. A store-house contained foodstuffs enough for a whole community for six months at a time. Meat was the product of the farm, also such vegetables as the fields produced. Sweet corn was not planted, but field corn, when quite tender, became a good vegetable.

For a celebration like this, special food and large quantities were neces-sary, and it was the duty of the housekeeper to give the cooks the necessary supplies. The menu was always the same: *caldo blanco*—clear soup; *pollo con arroz*—chicken with rice; *asados*—roast meat; *carne de olla*—boiled meat; *albóndigas con asafrán*—meat balls seasoned with an herb; such veg-etables as the garden produced or, in winter, pumpkins, *chili* and whatever vegetables had been dried. Canned goods were avoided as dangerous until the Americans experimented with this kind of food, bringing it with them from "the States." For dessert, there was a milk custard called *natillas*, and *arroz con leche*, rice sweetened and cooked in milk. Coffee and chocolate were the beverages.

This was served in a large dining hall at a long table covered with very large linen cloths, a candelabra in the center. The spoons and forks were of old, heavy, hammered silver. The steel knives were brought from "the States." Old Spanish silver bowls and plates were used. A servant stood at each end of the table with huge fans of peacock feathers on long handles. The servants swung these quickly at first but as the meal progressed they got sleepy, and were not so dextrous. As there were no screens, the fans served the double purpose of keeping the guests cool and the flies away. These large dining rooms were kept closed, with the dark shutters tightly shut, and the heat of the sun could not penetrate the thick walls. Only when the table was to be laid were the shutters opened.

After dinner each one went to his own room, for it was the siesta hour. For the women this was not just a rest on a couch; they went to bed as if it were night time. The men rested on lounges or large chairs. After the siesta a meal called a *merienda* was served; chocolate and cakes. These cakes were flavored with aniseed, some of them were filled with ground meat, some with dried apricots, and some were like a tart, with the meat of the piñon mixed in the stuffing.

The guests then took their departure, except Don Antonio's brother-in-law, for he had some problems to discuss with Don Antonio which must not be discussed on a feast day. The *Doñas* took their usual walk in the garden after their siesta.

While he was at the hacienda the Priest had been kept busy with his du-ties. He was first called upon to baptize a child. After he had done this the godparents of the child returned the tiny baby to the house of his parents. As the godmother handed the new little Christian to his mother, she recited a verse and then added the baptismal name:

| | |
|---|---|
| *Aquí tiene Vd. esta prenda* | I here hand you this jewel |
| *Que de la iglesia salió* | That from the church has just come |
| *Con los Santos Sacramentos* | With the most blessed sacraments |

| *Y l'agua que recibió.* | And the holy water he received. |
| *Se llama Manuel José Antonio.* | His name is *Manuel José Antonio.* |

The mother took the child in her arms and responded:

| *Te recibo prenda amada* | I receive you, beloved jewel |
| *Que de la iglesia saliste* | Who from the church has returned |
| *Con los Santos Sacramentos* | With the most blessed sacraments |
| *Y l'agua que recibiste.* | And the holy water just received. |
| *Mi hijo Manuel José Antonio.* | My son, *Manuel José Antonio.* |

The Priest then went to visit the sick. To El Cojo—the lame one, an old family servant—he administered the last Sacrament, for El Cojo was beyond cure. Then to the house of Adolfo who was ill with chills and fever. He found the room stifling, blankets were hung over the window to prevent any air reaching the patient, and he was so covered with heavy blankets that the priest had to pull back the bedclothes to make himself heard. A woman called a *curandera*, who cures with herbs, had been attending him but had not been able to do anything for him. The family had conferred in front of the patient and had decided to call the priest and the doctor. They did not want the expense of sending for the priest to administer Extreme Unction, so they had prayed to God that he might live until this day when they could get the priest's services without cost.

The local scribe was always busy on feast days. Adolfo, feeling better but still weak from fever, called him in to make a distribution of his property in case he died. He dictated as follows:

"I leave to my son, Bernabé, the north half of the house, comprising a room of seven beams. To my daughter, Cristina, the adjoining room to the north, this room having five beams. Also a cow and her calf."

If the person died, this declaration or distribution of property was always carried out in a most conscientious manner.

Adolfo then recounted his feelings of chills and fever which the scribe made into verse:

| *¡La enfermedad de los fríos* | In the illness of chills and fever |
| *No hallo cómo pueda ser!* | You hardly know what to do! |
| *¡Estos traen mil desuarios,* | This brings a thousand derangements, |
| *Son de quitar y poner!* | You take off, put on—take off, and put on! |

The scribe wrote letters not only for those who could not write, but acted as a secretary for the *patrones* on matters of importance, for they were not much given to letter writing when a scribe could be obtained to do that tedious work. The *patrón*, even though he might be annoyed at his neighbor, would always be courteous and this is the kind of letter he would send to a neighbor:

"*Muy Estimable Señor:*

"I hope that this my letter will find you and your family enjoying good health and prosperity. This I pray to Our Blessed Virgin will be the case. My family is well, thanks be to God.

"After greeting you, I desire to request that you order your servants to take from within my fence the cattle which I find have your brand, and which are doing much damage to my *temporal*—dry farming.

"This I beg you to attend to without delay. You will pardon my intrusion—
*molestia.*

"With nothing more at this time and may God grant your continued prosperity, I remain, most esteemed *señor*,"

"At your service,"

A Spaniard always has time for courtesy. He never begins his letters "Dear Sir," but "Most Esteemed and Respected *Señor*." He is never, "Yours Truly," but "At your Service" or "Most Humbly at your Feet." The signature was always followed by a scroll, *rúbrica* it was called. This was quite as important as the signature itself and was indeed considered part of the signature; the more elaborate it was, the more important the signer.

While all the extra work and additional gayety was going on in the house of the *patrón*, the servants not assigned to house duties went on with their usual tasks. After dinner, the servants had their siesta; even the work in the fields ceased. The water from the large irrigation ditch was turned into a smaller ditch and water directed on to the alfalfa fields. Rafael sat under a cottonwood tree not disturbed by the chatter of the birds; Francisco sat on the ground under the cornstalks; Ruperto, in the middle of the alfalfa field, dozed in the blazing sun, leaning on his hoe. A gust of wind stirred the air and woke the men. Slowly they continued their work. Rafael started to talk to Francisco about an incident of last year:

"Do you remember this field last spring when God must have been angry with us, for no water would come, the clouds would gather just for the winds to scatter them. How the people prayed! But the drought continued and, finally, with great religious fervor, a small statue of the Child Jesus was carried in procession through the fields that He might see the condition of the young plants. He was shown the entire fertile valley. How the people talked, prayed, how they sang to Him. We placed Him on the ground for His tiny feet to feel the dryness of the sun-baked fields; then we brought Him back into the church where we begged that He might send rain to relieve the distressed condition. I clearly remember that before the services were over, the skies were overcast, lightning was seen in all parts of the sky and thunder heard in the distance. Louder we prayed and extended our arms as if to catch the water in our cupped hands. That night the skies opened and the rain came down in torrents, the arroyos were filled with water which carried down huge bowlders and uprooted small trees by the side of these banks. How the roofs leaked! Beds were shifted while umbrellas were opened inside my house to keep my family dry! Toward morning the rain subsided, the people came to these fields to find complete destruction caused by the flood. The ditches had overflown and the silt had covered the young plants.

"The people again assembled at the church and began to pray with complaints, and formed a procession to take the statue of the Virgin through the fields. In our prayers the people pointed to the earth, as we were almost mired with Her in our arms; then She was brought back again into the church.

"A stranger asked me why it was that the Virgin was taken into the fields then, since the day before we had taken the Child Jesus and prayed for rain. I told him that we begged the Holy Child for rain. He sent us a torrent. We took the Virgin to show Her the damage Her Son had done to our crops."

So they talked then, and talk now, to the Saints, complain to them, and even scold them for the acts of nature which, in their opinion, are directly attributable to them.

As the sun began to set, Don Antonio and his brother-in-law went for a walk on the embankment of the largest irrigation ditch which offered a view of the fields. Ruperto was driving the cows from the pasture. "We must return," said the *patrón*, "for the cows will be milked and we must have our *atole* while the milk is yet warm." This gruel was made of blue corn meal to which the fresh milk was added.

As they retraced their steps, Rafael was closing the shutters, for the sun was setting and the night air bad for older people and for the children. As they neared the house the bell in the chapel was tolling. The men both hesitated for a moment, blessed themselves and prayed.

"Surely," said the *patrón*, "it cannot be the old man with the chills who has died. My son said he was much better after the priest had given him the blessing of the church."

Juanito, a young boy, came running toward the *patrón*. As he approached, he took off his hat and stood with bowed head until the *patrón* asked him his errand.

"I came to tell you, Don Antonio, that my father no longer suffers; that God, in His mercy, has taken him to the glorious heavens."

"Your mother, how is she?"

"Very sad. *Patrón*, I need money for the box and for the wake."

"Ah, yes, of course, and tell your mother that Doña Doloritas and I will accompany you tonight in your grief."

"Thank you, *patrón*."

Don Antonio went at once to his wife: "Juanito came to tell us of the death of El Cojo. May God rest his soul."

"I heard the tolling of the bells this evening."

As the sun set, a wind arose and it seemed suddenly as though winter was in the air. The cosmos were in bloom and swayed gracefully in the wind.

"See the flowers, Antonio. The flowers that El Cojo loved!"

Since every person in the hacienda had a definite duty, El Cojo, being lame, had looked after the flowers. His young son, Juanito, helped him turn the water in from the main irrigation ditch so that they could get water. He also took care of a melon patch for the children of the hacienda who came to see him often and he would see to it that only sweet and ripe melons were given them.

"We will go to the house tonight," said Don Antonio. "I have already sent candles and even now they are preparing for the wake."

"Look, Antonio! The sun has ripened the harvest. I see the yellow pumpkins in the field, and now it is beginning to rain. Rain—tears for those who mourn."

After supper, Don Antonio accompanied his wife to the house of mourning. The night was dark, the fragrance delightful, one almost forgot there could be sorrow so near at hand. Doña Doloritas was sad when one of her old servants died, for they were like part of her own life. When she was sick, many of them, refusing to go to their own homes, stayed near to pray and to get word of her condition. Sometimes, they put a veil over the face of their favorite *Nuestra Señora de los Dolores*,[3] the *patróna's* name-sake, and kept it there until she cured the *patróna*.

As they approached the house they could hear a wail in the midst of the prayer and could smell the wax from the candles. The thirteen candles for the wake had been placed in a wooden candle-holder, such as was used during Holy Week, which had been borrowed from the church and this gave most of the light for the room.

The *patrones* entered the room where Juana, El Cojo's wife, was seated. She was dressed all in black calico, a black shawl over her head. Her face was covered by the shawl and she was crying under it. Doña Doloritas and Don Antonio, in turn, shook hands with Juana, Juanito, and Ascensión, repeating the usual greeting of sympathy for bereavement.

In such families when someone died, the rest of the family did not seem to want solitude. People who were well known to the family called, most of them embraced the grieved ones and wailed with them, except, of course, the *patrones* who conducted themselves with a sympathetic dignity. The men would shake hands with the greeting, "I regret your grief"; or, "I accompany you in your sorrow." After some conversation about the deceased, as to how well he looked and seemed at peace, they would say: "Your grief is God's will."

The wake was not entirely a time of grief, since the family was completely resigned to God's will. It was an occasion for the gathering of friends. Each night (a wake lasted three nights), a big supper was served, food and drink. Frequently, a professional *Rezador*, whose business it was to lead in prayer, would sing and pray, the people responding as they went in and out of the house.

When death came to the house of the *Dons*, the women went into retirement and the grief of the family was quiet and dignified.

As the *patrones* left the house the praying and chanting continued. The air felt refreshing after the closeness of the room. The lights of the hacienda, soft as moonlight, fell across the path, welcoming them to their home.

"I quiver when I hear the wind in the trees. I believe the trees also have dead members of their family and the wind is their cry for them," said Don Antonio.

As they entered Doña Doloritas' room a servant appeared. Don Antonio gave orders: "A glass of wine, Julio, for the *señora*."

Don Antonio then went to the room of his brother-in-law where they sat and talked until the wood in the fireplace was reduced to ashes and their voices subdued with drowsiness. Most of their conversation was of politics.

The Spaniard is interested in politics because it has a dramatic climax. It is an occasion for gambling, and just as at a horse race he bets on the pinto, so he bets on his political favorite. Even the poorer people enjoy this game of chance and bet a cow and calf, a team of horses; frequently all a man has is gambled on the outcome, for he sees the result as a turn of luck. Whether he wins, or loses, God will provide him with further means of support. He accepts defeat with a dramatic flourish—a shrug of the shoulder, a wave of the hand and the statement, "It may be for the best."

---

3. Our Lady of Sorrows, a representation of the Virgin Mary as grieving mother; Catholics pray to her for strength during suffering, compassion for others in sorrow, and help with childbirth.

Don Antonio was anxious to discuss the last political campaign with his relative. The two men spoke of the ambition of the strangers who had come to live in their midst. They mentioned how well received these politicians were by their people, no matter what the circumstance of their visit; how these poor people shared their food and were not embarrassed by the kind or the lack in quantity.

"I want to relate the experience I had recently in one of our small villages," said Don Antonio.

"I visited Ojo de la Vaca to do some political work. I naturally called on the man whom I considered the most influential in the village, an old man whom the whole community respected. I was ushered into a room, large enough to be a hall, with whitewashed walls, the board floor so badly warped that I had to walk carefully to avoid catching my shoe in the knot holes. In the two far corners of the room were beds of iron, painted white; close to one of the long walls was a mattress, folded, with a blanket thrown over it. This mattress served as a seat during the day and, at night, when opened out, a full-sized bed. There was a wood stove in the center of the room. I was offered the only chair, while the old man sat on a box. Practically every person in the village, including children and two dogs, came into the room. After the preliminary greetings and a few questions about the city from the younger people, I was left with the old man.

"We talked politics; it grew late. As darkness approached, two candles were lighted. Shortly thereafter a child came in to tell her grandfather that supper was ready. I was invited, in a most cordial way, as though to a banquet. A refusal, as you well know, might indicate that the food was not good enough, an insult to their hospitality! I carried my own chair into the kitchen.

"The food on the table was not sufficient for two people much less for three grown people and five children; it consisted of *tortillas*, of which there were plenty, potatoes enough for two small servings, and beans, with a great deal of juice, undoubtedly made so the supply would 'go around,' and gruel of blue corn meal without milk. I was served first, but was allowed to serve myself. Only in this way could I have saved the food for the children. The old gentleman and his daughter kept insisting: 'Eat comfortably, sir, you do honor to my house in dining with me.'

"There was no apology for any part of this hospitality. I was welcome to whatever they had. The old gentleman presided at the table with the dignity of a *patrón*. When the meal was over, I thanked them for the excellent food.

"Politics were not discussed at the table, for it was considered more polite to speak of things that would interest the children, even though they did not speak until I spoke directly to them and the old gentleman had given them permission to answer me. The conversation was mostly on news from the city, and community interests: the teacher in the neighborhood, recent deaths and the disposition of property, how a boy of twelve was trying to take the place of his father in caring for the bequests left to his mother. The old gentleman talked about the happenings in Ojo de la Vaca when he was a boy. The mountains and he were intimate friends. He spoke of them and of his herd of goats as a child now speaks of his wooden toys. The old man has gone now. God called him and now one knows that the house is there, but not the master."

"Strangers do not understand our hospitality," said Don Antonio's brother-in-law. "A young attorney from 'the States' came to the hacienda a short time ago on business. He brought his wife. My *señora* received her guest in her usual courteous manner. The shutters of the guest room had been opened, the room well aired, the sun allowed to look through the deep windows. The high bed, with its feather mattress, was made ready. A silver basket, filled with fruit, was placed beside the candle on the bedside table. On retiring for the night, my wife told the American lady: 'My house, all that it contains, is yours.' She did not know that this phrase, perfectly sincere, is our way of making a guest feel at ease. One hardly accepts a house and its belongings! My *señora* had left a set of jewelry, a brooch, bracelet and ear-rings on the dresser of the guest room. The American lady took these away with her, thinking it was a gift to her. It was her understanding of our hospitable, 'My house is yours.'"

So they laughed and talked until a servant brought wine and cakes, a signal to the *patrón* that it was his bedtime. After the refreshments, they stood ceremoniously and bowed to each other and Don Antonio said:

"We old people, like the sun these fall days, must retire early. That forces the rest which in the fall of life we so greatly need. May your dreams be of the angels in the heavens. I leave you in your house."

The following morning there was the regular routine of the day. Everyone arose early. The *patrones*, as well as guests, were served a cup of chocolate before rising. A servant gave the usual greeting, "May God give you a good day," as he placed the tray on the table at the bedside and departed, not waiting to be answered. The shutters of the bedroom had been opened by the servant in charge of that work; the daylight came through the window, and then to arise was not such a hard task. Breakfast was a large meal served in the regular dining room. The cereal was made of sprouted wheat which had been dried in the sun and then ground. This was made into a thick paste, baked all night in the oven and thinned, at the table, with hot milk. There were eggs, always fried, pork and hominy, thin batter cakes, coffee or chocolate. Fruit, fresh if in season, or dried, was eaten last. The servants' breakfast consisted of beans, fried meat, *chili* and coffee with *tortillas*.

When the meal was over, Don Antonio gave the orders of the day to the head man who came to him at an appointed time. The sons of the family went to their mother's room where she gave them her blessing before they started on their not too difficult tasks. The *patrón*, with his brother-in-law, visited the workshops and the fields.

The work in the fields was carried on from sunup to sundown. Laborers worked slowly, stopping frequently to converse, to doze after the noon meal, to smoke. There was no need for hurry, since this occupation must continue *mañana*, and then *mañana*—tomorrow and tomorrow. Don Antonio tried to have everything possible made on the place so as to buy very little outside. Workers were building benches, chairs and tables, cupboards with sturdy outlines and carved patterns in the old designs. Art objects were being made, such as religious *Santos*, picture frames, candle sconces of decorated tin or wood. Men were doing leather work, repairing saddles, making new straps, decorating the outside leather on old chests.

There were women at work but the *señora* was in charge there. Women were grinding corn in the cool *patio* in the shade of the high adobe wall;

*chili*, too, was being ground on an ancient bread stone which was used with a stone rolling pin. Bread was being baked in outside ovens where a fire had been built. When the oven was very hot from the fire within, the wood coals were raked out and the bread, now well raised and in pans, was pushed in on a wooden shovel which had a long handle. In this way the pan could be placed deep into the oven. The oven opening was well covered with a sheep pelt and the bread remained inside for a given time. When baked, the bread was placed in earthen bowls which kept it from drying out and becoming stale. These earthern bowls were sometimes used to store coins in and, occasionally, were buried with the gold for safe keeping. This accounts for the never-ending search for hidden gold in the floors and walls of old adobe houses. Women were plastering the outside walled fence. They smoothed the plaster with their hands. Their motions were graceful, the body of the plasterer rhythmically following the movement of the hand.

Doña Doloritas, having made the rounds, followed always by a servant ready to wait on her, went under the portal of the *patio*. From the beams there hung a clay bowl, wrapped around with strips of rawhide. This bowl was filled with water, a dipper being close by it. This dipper was made from a gourd which had been cut in half, scraped clean inside and the long end left for a handle. The servant disappeared and returned with a tray on which was placed a glass; she went to the bowl, poured out the clear cold water from the gourd into the glass and handed it on a tray to her mistress. The servant then stood, as always, with folded arms, the tray held by one hand. The *Doña* dismissed the servant and seated herself in a big chair from which she could see the women at work. The Spanish *doñas* always sat with an air of great dignity, as of holding Court. This was a traditional part of their early training.

Don Antonio and his brother-in-law walked to the edge of the fields viewing the ripening grain. They turned to retrace their steps.

"I must call on my daughter-in-law," said Don Antonio. "She is still in mourning for her brother, though he has been dead now almost two years."

"Remember me to her," said his brother-in-law. Persons not members of the family must never intrude on people of the upper class who are in sorrow and social calls are not paid until the period of mourning is over.

Don Antonio approached a lovely old house with the usual flat roof, and long *portal*, with deep-set low windows.

The front door, which had glass panels on either side, was closed; the white lace curtains were drawn at the windows. Above the door was draped a black cloth which extended a foot or so on either side of the glass panel, and a straight piece of black cloth hung along the lintel of each window on the front of the house—an announcement to the community and to all passersby that that house was in mourning; that no hilarity must take place in or near the house. Passersby always lowered their voices and men raised their hats in respect as they passed the place. The black cloth was left there for the period of mourning which depended on the relationship of the deceased. Frequently, a second relative died before the period of mourning for the first was over, and so the black on black remained until it literally decayed or was torn off by the wind. White cloth was used for a young person. Within the house, the harp which was the chief musical instrument, was silenced. Mirrors were covered with a black veil, as members of the family must not display vanity during such a time.

Don Antonio was ushered into a bedroom. A lovely young woman, dressed in black silk with a black embroidered shawl over her shoulders, arose from a low chair. The Spanish people liked low chairs. The windows, too, were low and made it easy for them to look out into the garden or to see if the sun was shining.

"How do you feel, daughter?"

"I do not feel gay," she responded.

There was no laughter, nothing to indicate a feeling of happiness or joy, till the period of mourning was complete. When that period was over and music again heard in the house for the first time, there was usually a time of renewed sadness, for the music brought back memories of the deceased— "My ears hear the voice of my dear one."

1936

# WILLIAM CARLOS WILLIAMS
## 1883–1963

William Carlos Williams lived most of his life in his native New Jersey, where, as a medical doctor, he practiced obstetrics and pediatrics for many years in the small town of Rutherford. His international literary reputation comes from the 49 books he authored, in a conversational but deeply reflective style, as a poet, novelist, essayist, and playwright. In facing the wasteland produced by modern industrialization, Williams asserted the power of the creative imagination: "Men and women cannot be content any more than children," he wrote, "with the mere facts of a humdrum life—the imagination must adorn and exaggerate life, must give it splendor and grotesqueness, beauty and infinite depth."

Although he is best-known as a prominent American Modernist and an inspiration to writers such as the poet Allen Ginsberg, Williams is also part of the Latino literary tradition. Early in life, he was exposed to the Spanish language and to Caribbean culture by his mother, who was Puerto Rican, and his father, who was British but grew up in the West Indies. Williams's works frequently draw from his multicultural background. Several of his poems have Spanish titles, and he often uses Spanish terms in his writing and makes references to diverse aspects of Hispanic cultures. At points, he expresses fascination about the culturally bound behavior and eccentricities of his mother.

However, in *The Spanish American Roots of William Carlos Williams* (1994), a study of the many cultural experiences that shaped Williams's work, the critic Julio Marzán discusses Williams's ambivalence about his own Puerto Rican heritage. In fact, in his *Autobiography* (1951)—of which the chapter "Pop and Mother" is included in this anthology—Williams explains that in writing his celebrated essay collection *In the American Grain* (1925), he attempted "to find out for myself what the land of my more or less accidental birth might signify." In a July 22, 1939, letter to the poet Horace Gregory, Williams explicitly calls himself American: "Of mixed ancestry I felt from earliest childhood that America was the only home that I could ever possibly call my own." This self-designation reflects both the prevalent melting-pot ideology of his generation and his privileged status as a member of a white upper-middle-class family. But as Marzán notes, the title *In the American Grain*—of which the chapter "The Fountain of Eternal Youth" is excerpted here—refers beyond the United States to a broader hemispheric America, where for centuries many cultures have met and intermingled. In this text, Williams's dramatic statement "History begins for us with murder and enslavement, not with discovery" serves as preamble to his indictment of the rapacity of the conquistadors, represented here by Juan Ponce de León, the colonizer of Puerto Rico.

Although Williams did not believe in using art as propaganda, poems such as the ones collected here reveal his progressive views. "Apology" expresses compassion for "nonentities," the downtrodden masses. "Sub Terra" and "Libertad! Igualdad! Fraternidad!" empathize with those marginalized by race and class.

## Libertad! Igualdad! Fraternidad![1]

You sullen pig of a man
you force me into the mud
with your stinking ash-cart!

Brother!
    —if we were rich          5
we'd stick our chests out
and hold our heads high!

It is dreams that have destroyed us.

There is no more pride
in horses or in rein holding.          10
We sit hunched together brooding
our fate.

    Well—
all things turn bitter in the end
whether you choose the right or          15
the left way
        and—
dreams are not a bad thing.

1917

## Apology

Why do I write today?

The beauty of
the terrible faces

---

1. Liberty! Equality! Fraternity! (Spanish); as *Liberté, égalité, fraternité*, the national motto of France, derived from one motto of the French Revolution.

of our nonentities
stirs me to it:                                                              5

colored women
day workers—
old and experienced—
returning home at dusk
in cast off clothing                                                        10
faces like
old Florentine oak.

Also

the set pieces
of your faces stir me—                                                      15
leading citizens—
but not
in the same way.

                                                                      1917


## Sub Terra

Where shall I find you,
you my grotesque fellows
that I seek everywhere
to make up my band?
None, not one                                                                5
with the earthy tastes I require;
the burrowing pride that rises
subtly as on a bush in May.

Where are you this day,
you my seven year locusts                                                   10
with cased wings?
Ah my beauties how I long—!
That harvest
that shall be your advent—
thrusting up through the grass,                                             15
up under the weeds
answering me,
*that* shall be satisfying!
The light shall leap and snap
that day as with a million lashes!                                          20

Oh, I have you; yes
you are about me in a sense:
playing under the blue pools
that are my windows,—
but they shut you out still,                                                 25

there in the half light.
For the simple truth is
that though I see you clear enough
you are not there!

It is not that—it is you,                                    30
you I want!
—God, if I could fathom
the guts of shadows!

You to come with me
poking into negro houses                                     35
with their gloom and smell!
In among children
leaping around a dead dog!
Mimicking
onto the lawns of the rich!                                  40
You!
to go with me a-tip-toe,
head down under heaven,
nostrils lipping the wind!

1917

## *FROM* IN THE AMERICAN GRAIN

## The Fountain of Eternal Youth

History, history! We fools, what do we know or care? History begins for us
with murder and enslavement, not with discovery. No, we are not Indians
but we are men of their world. The blood means nothing; the spirit, the
ghost of the land moves in the blood, moves the blood. It is we who ran to
the shore naked, we who cried, "Heavenly Man!" These are the inhabitants
of our souls, our murdered souls that lie . . . agh. Listen! I tell you it was
lucky for Spain the first ship put its men ashore where it did. If the Italian
had landed in Florida, one twist of the helm north, or among the islands a
hair more to the south; among the Yamasses with their sharpened bones
and fishspines, or among the Caribs[1] with their poisoned darts—it might
have begun differently.

When in the later years Ponce found his plantations going under for lack
of slaves—no more to be trapped in Puerto Rico, *rico!* all ruined—he sought
and obtained a royal patent to find more in the surrounding islands. He was
granted the right to hunt out and to take the Caribs; the Caribs whom The
Great Maker had dropped through a hole in the sky among their islands; they

1. Native people of the Lesser Antilles islands; the Caribbean Sea was named after them. *Yamasses:*
American Indian people of Florida; now part of the Seminole people.

whose souls lived in their bodies, many souls in one body; they who fought their enemies, ate them; whose gods lived, Mabouya, in the forest, Oumekon, by the sea—there were other gods—

His ship came into Guadeloupe[2]—the great sulphur cone back of the water. He had arrived straight from Spain, hot foot after niggers. Having much soiled linen aboard from the long trip, he ordered his laundresses ashore, with a body of troops to guard them, where a stream could be observed coming down to the sea.

It was a paradise. A stream of splashing water, the luxuriant foliage. A gorge, a veritable tunnel led upstream between cliffwalls covered by thick vines in flower attended by ensanguined hummingbirds which darted about from cup to cup in the green light. But the soul of the Carib was on the alert among the leaves. It was too late.

Fierce and implacable we kill them but their souls dominate us. Our men, our blood, but their spirit is master. It enters us, it defeats us, it imposes itself. We are moderns—madmen at Paris—all lacking in a ground sense of cleanliness. It is the Caribs leaping out, facing the arquebuses, thinking it thunder, looking up at the sky: No rain! No clouds! Then the second volley. Their comrades bleeding, dead. Kill! Not a Spaniard but they stretched out in the streambed. Hagh, I can hear the laundresses squeal on the shore— run hither and thither. The devils had them safe. Let old Ponce sit up in his hammock on the poop of his ship. Let him send other boats ashore. The Indians have grabbed up the women. Three naked savages shot through the chest from behind before they could gain the forest rolled over and gripped the females they had been carrying by the throat with their teeth. Worth being a laundress to be carried off that way, eh? Nice psychologic study, those women. And the damned bloodhound, Berrescien.[3] Ponce had got his belly full. They outflanked him in canoes, ridiculed his strategy, took his chainshot in the chest and came back for more. They drove him off, so much so that they made him forget his dog, the precious Berrescien, of whom he thought more, that and his hidalgan pride, than—a population. The hound had been left behind in their scared flight. They saw him, they in the retreating boats, leap from the woods in pursuit of a flying Carib. Listen to this. The Indian swam out, the Spaniards in the boats turned back for the beast. The dog was steadily gaining on his victim. But, O Soul of the New World, the man had his bow and arrow with him as he swam. Tell that to Wilson.[4] He stopped, turned, raised his body half out of the water, treading it, and put a bolt into the damned hound's throat—whom sharks swallowed. Then to shore, not forgetting—leaping to safety—to turn and spit back the swallowed chainshot, a derisive yell at the Christians.

They had the women and the dog. They left what they had defeated, to—us.

If men inherit souls this is the color of mine. We are, too, the others. Think of them! The main islands were thickly populated with a peaceful folk

---

2. Archipelago in the eastern Caribbean Sea.
3. According to Williams, Ponce de León's dog.
4. Possibly the nineteenth-century physician Henry L. Wilson, who gave the name Ponce de León

Springs to a popular park on a stream in Atlanta, Georgia, based on his assertion that the water held recuperative properties.

when Christ-over[5] found them. But the orgy of blood which followed, no man has written. We are the slaughterers. It is the tortured soul of our world. Indians have no souls; that was it. That was what they said. But they knew they lied—the blood-smell proof. Ponce had been with the discoverer on his second trip. He became a planter. Sugar cane was imported from the Canaries, maize was adopted from the Indian souls. But revenues dwindled where none would work save in the traffic in girls: nine years old, reads the Italian's journal. Slaves. The Indians having no souls knew what freedom means. The Spaniards killed their kings, betrayed, raped, murdered their women and children; hounded them into the mountains. Ponce with wife and children in the *Casa Blanca*[6] was one of the bloodthirstiest. They took them in droves, forced them to labor. It was impossible to them—not having been born to baptism. How maddening it is to the spirit to hear:—Bands of them went into the forests, their forests, and hanged themselves to the trees. What else? Islands—paradise. Surrounded by seas. On all sides "heavenly man" bent on murder. Self-privilege. Two women and one man on a raft had gotten one hundred and fifty miles out to sea—such seamen were they—then luck again went against the Indian. Captured and back to slavery. Caravels crept along the shore by night. Next morning when women and children came down to the shore to fish—fine figures, straight black hair, high cheekbones, a language—they caught them, made them walk in bands, cut them down if they fainted, slashed off breasts, arms—women, children. Gut souls—

Thus the whole free population was brought into slavery or killed off. Aboujoubo, greatest chief in the island of San Ion, retreated in anguish to a rocky height. Ponce, now Governor, since he dare not economically murder every one, sallies out and is received by a native queen, girls dancing, gives one a gold crucifix, legend says. Two years later finds her under a bush, both hands hacked off. Belly-hurt he digs a shallow grave with his sword for her and shoves the gold symbol into his wallet. He exchanges names with a chief, sacred symbol of Indian faith and friendship. Hounds him out later: I am Juan Ponce de Leon! says the savage, standing before his followers— hanged nevertheless. The hound, Berrescien, gone ahead into a rocky place, comes spinning back, tumbling down, knocking against rocks, a gash in his forehead. Ponce defeated, embittered has the dog stretched upon a litter of leaves and branches and carried to the ship.

Do these things die? Men who do not know what lives, are themselves dead. In the heart there are living Indians once slaughtered and defrauded—Indians that live also in subtler ways: Ponce at fifty-two was rich, the murderous campaigns of his youth had subjugated the island— allayed his lust of common murder. The island was, in any case, mostly conquered.

An old Indian woman among his slaves, began to tell him of an island, Bimini, a paradise of fragrant groves, of all fruits. And in the center of it a fountain of clearest water of virtue to make old men young. Think of that!

---

5. I.e., Christopher Columbus (1451–1506), Spanish admiral from Genoa.
6. White House, a house in San Juan, Puerto Rico;
intended as the home of the island's governor, Ponce de León, it was not completed until 1521, the year he died.

Picture to yourself the significance of that—as revenge, as irony, as the trail of departing loveliness, *fata morgana*. Yet the real, the thing destroyed turning back with a smile. Think of the Spaniard listening. Gold. Gold. Riches. And figure to yourself the exquisite justice of it: an old woman, loose tongued—loose sword—the book, her soul already half out of her with sorrow: abandoned by a Carib who had fled back to his home having found Borequien[7] greatly overrated. Her children enslaved—

The man, fifty-two, listened. Something has escaped him. At that moment rich, idle, he was relieved of his governorship. Vessels, three. He fitted them up at his own cost. Men enough, eager to serve the old master, rushed to his banner. Let the new governor complain that he was taking away too many able soldiers. Ponce smiled. Men whose terms of service had expired do as they please.

*Por donde va la mar*
*Vayan las arenas—*[8]

They sailed north. It was March. In the wind, what? Beauty the eternal. White sands and fragrant woods, fruits, riches, truth! The sea, the home of permanence, drew them on into its endless distances. Again the new! Do you feel it? The murderer, the enslaver, the terror striker, the destroyer of beauty, drawn on by beauty across the glancing tropical seas—before Drake,[9] before the galleons. The rhythm of the waves, birds, fish, seaweed as on the first voyage. They even put in at Guanahani[1] for water—Columbus' first landfall; then populous, inviting; now desolate, defeated, murdered—unpeopled.

March! Spring! to the north. The argosy of the New World! In search of eternal youth. In search of the island of Bimini—an old woman's tale. The destroyer. Admonished that he had done enough, still there floated a third world to discover: no end—away from the beginning—tail chaser.

*A Carne de lobo*
*Diente de perro*[2]

he could not halt—no end. Curious that Amino—the boy of Palos[3] who watched Columbus prepare his vessels for the first voyage and went on the second—should be his pilot. Sea scud. The same piloted Cortez[4] to Mexico.

Let them go. They found nothing but a row of white islands called "The Martyrs," a catch of turtles, Las Tortugas,[5] a sandy coastline, a devil of a current that shoved them about and devilish Indians who drove them back from the watering places—flamingoes, pelicans, egrets, herons—Rousseau[6] has it. Thickets with striped leaves, ferns emerging from the dark, palms,

---

7. I.e., Borinquen; from *Boriquén*, the indigenous (i.e., Taíno) name for Puerto Rico.
8. Where the sea goes / Let the sand follow (Spanish).
9. Sir Francis Drake (1540 or 1543–1596), English navigator and buccaneer.
1. Native name for the Bahaman island (which one is not known) where Columbus first landed, in 1492; he called it San Salvador.
2. For wolf's meat / Dog's foot (Spanish).

3. Or Palos de la Frontera, a town and municipality in southwestern Spain; launching point for Columbus's first expedition.
4. Hernán Cortés (1485–1547), Spanish conquistador.
5. The Turtles; islands named by Columbus in 1503, on his fourth and final voyage, after the numerous sea turtles there. In 1586, Sir Francis Drake arrived and named them the Cayman Islands.
6. Henri Rousseau (1844–1910), French painter.

the heat, the moon, the stars, the sun in a pool of swampwater. Fish fly. In the water seals—back to Cuba.

Old now, heavy at heart over the death of his bloody pet, Ponce retired to his Casa Blanca and sulked for three years. Then came the news of Cortez' triumph and the wealth of Montezuma.[7]

Ponce—

*de Leon*
*en nombre y podesta*[8]

—the victor,

now defeated, must stir again. Back to Florida thinking to find on the continent, he only then found that he had discovered, another Tehuantepec.[9]

But this time the Yamasses put an arrow into his thigh at the first landing—and let out his fountain. They flocked to the beach, jeered him as he was lifted to the shoulders of his men and carried away. Dead.

1925

7. Or Moctezuma (1466–1520), last Aztec emperor of Mexico (1502–20).
8. The Lion / in name and supreme authority (Spanish).

9. Santo Domingo Tehuantepec, a town and municipality in southeastern Mexico; as a Spanish colonial port, Tehuantepec was associated with Cortés.

---

*FROM* AUTOBIOGRAPHY

## Chapter 4: Pop and Mother

My father was an Englishman who lived in America all his adult years and never became a citizen. He said it was more convenient for him to carry British than American papers on his frequent and prolonged trips to South America. He was probably right.

I'll never forget the dream I had a few days after he died, after a wasting illness, on Christmas Day, 1918. I saw him coming down a peculiar flight of exposed steps, steps I have since identified as those before the dais of Pontius Pilate[1] in some well-known painting. But this was in a New York office building, Pop's office. He was bare-headed and had some business letters in his hand on which he was concentrating as he descended. I noticed him and with joy cried out, "Pop! So, you're *not* dead!" But he only looked up at me over his right shoulder and commented severely, "You know all that poetry you're writing. Well, it's no good." I was left speechless and woke trembling. I have never dreamed of him since.

Our household always, as I remember, included guests, guests who stayed sometimes for weeks and months or even all winter, people like poor old Mrs. Forbes who got lost once between her bedroom and the bathroom in the night and yelled for help so that Mom had to rush out and rescue her.

1. Prefect of the Roman Empire's Judaea Province AD 26–ca. AD 36; according to the Bible, he ordered Jesus' crucifixion.

Our guests were either Grandma's English friends or Mother's friends and relatives from the West Indies.

Spanish and French were the languages I heard habitually while I was growing up. Mother could talk very little English when I was born, and Pop spoke Spanish better, in fact, than most Spaniards. But Pop spoke English too, and as time went on one of my happiest memories of him was when he would sometimes read to us in the evening. Those were the marvelous days!

I remember now his readings of the poems of Paul Laurence Dunbar,[2] and I can to this day repeat many of the refrains he made familiar to me then. It was he who introduced me to Shakespeare, whom I read avidly, practically from beginning to end.

Poor (or rich) Pop (he was a single-taxer) once offered me a dollar apiece if I would read. *The Origin of Species* and *The Descent of Man.*[3] I took him up. It was well-earned cash.

But I remember also the three volumes of the famous illustrated translation of Dante's *Divine Comedy.*[4] I'll never forget how I studied Gustave Doré's[5] pictures of those beautiful but damned ladies and with what profound disappointment I failed to discover from them the anatomical secrets which so fascinated me at the time. The text escaped me.

Up to then, neither Mother nor Pop had any immediate church connections, but used to meet with a few others at spiritualistic seances, sometimes at home, sometimes elsewhere around the block. A prime mover in this form of religious service was old man Demarest, a devout believer. The chief tenet of these earnest persons was that the dead did live as spirits about us and would come or could be called to us at certain times by prayer or otherwise. There were curious consequences.

One evening at the Bagellon house, where we lived, at supper, Mother, who was known among her intimates as a medium, suddenly said to my father, looking right and left at Ed and me, "So these are the boys. How they have grown. Come here, my dears," she said to us, reaching out her hands, "and let me see you!" This to her own children whom she had been caring for all day.

Pop, who was accustomed to such occasions, told us gently, bewildered as we must have been, to do as we were bid—to go to Mother, which we did, one on either side. She put her hands on each of our heads and patted us with smiles of approval and loving affection. "How well they look. I am so happy."

At this Pop said to her, to his own wife, "Who is this we have the pleasure of talking to?"

"Don't you know me?" Mother answered. "Why I'm Lou Paine." With that the seizure passed and Mother was herself again. Everything went on as before.

Pop told me many times after that that he had sent a wire forthwith to Jesse Paine, an old friend and neighbor of ours from Passaic Avenue, then residing in Los Angeles, asking what, if anything, had happened to Lou, his wife.

---

2. American poet (1872–1906).
3. Groundbreaking books on evolutionary theory, by the English naturalist Charles Darwin (1809–1882). *Single-taxer*: a subscriber to the argument that a government should not tax income, wealth, or transactions. Instead, land—especially unimproved land—should become common property, and the economic rent from it should be shared equally by members of society.
4. *Divina Commedia*, masterpiece by the Italian poet Dante Alighieri (1265–1321).
5. French artist (1832–1883).

Two weeks later he received a letter saying that Jesse was sorry not to have been able to answer the telegram sooner, the reason being that Lou had been ill; in fact at the time the telegram had arrived, she was in the hospital where, that day, she had been given up for dead, following a serious abdominal operation. Now, however, she was sufficiently recovered so that he could say that she was safe and that he could resume his regular life—and so forth.

These meetings of the spiritualists, preceding the organization of the Unitarian Church and Sunday School in Rutherford, went on for years. One night, very early in the history of the thing, when Mother was still a good deal of an outsider because of the language difficulty, she was sitting a little apart from the others, merely listening in on the proceedings, when Grandma held up her closed fist and asked to speak to whoever it was, unstated, that was represented by what she held in her hand.

Immediately Mother, insane to all appearances, went out of her head. Unable to bring her to, old man Demarest fell upon his knees to implore God to return this woman to her senses.

So intense was the appeal and so impressed were all those present by the seriousness of the situation that Mother did, after a moment, come to herself and once more act normally among them—for which Mr. Demarest gave thanks to God—and Grandma was properly reprimanded for her part in the affair.

It appears that what she had wanted was to speak to her dead daughter Rosita, whom Mother had known well, an epileptic recently dead. To achieve this, she had taken, unknown to the others, a lock of the dead girl's hair, hiding it in her fist, asking only that the spirit, unidentified, speak and say she was present. Mother, her girlhood friend, was the medium upon whom the poor girl had seized for her approaches.

Mother would be possessed at such times—and it went on for years—by an uncontrollable shaking of the head. It would happen anywhere and at any time. I even saw it happen once while she was playing the piano at Sunday School. Ed and I were horribly embarrassed. But most often it would be at home primarily under strained emotional circumstances as after the death of some friend or intimate, but not necessarily involving the appearance of that particular person.

We'd all know at once what was about to take place—Mother's look would become fixed, her face would flush, and she'd reach out her hand and grasp the hand of one of us. Sometimes she'd indicate that she wanted Ed or me or anyone. Then someone would say, Is it this one? or that one? and she would try against heavy restraints to put her hand forward, but it would be impossible for her to do it. She'd struggle to try to clasp the hand offered her, but if this were not the one she wanted, she'd recoil, violently, unable to seize it. Her face would be red, contorted, she couldn't talk, her whole body seized by some inscrutable violence.

A name would be offered. No. Then another. She would shake her head violently, her cheeks flaming, her eyes like those of a person in violent effort of any sort. Finally Pop might say, "Is it Carlos?" meaning her brother, and she'd grasp the hand offered in both hers, and the presence would leave her.

How Ed and I dreaded these occasions! Pop believed literally, I think, in their authenticity: that the spirits of the dead did materialize through her and did try to reach us. But why they should want to come I never could understand.

Once after Pop died, Mother, in one of these seizures, asked for a pencil and tried to write, but her movements were too violent. Nothing came of it.

1951

---

# BERNARDO VEGA
## 1885–1965

Bernardo Vega was from the tobacco-growing mountain town of Cayey, Puerto Rico. In Puerto Rico, he belonged to a group of self-educated working-class artisans called *tabaqueros*, cigar workers who subscribed to a form of enlightened socialism. For example, they turned their workplaces into learning halls, where hired *lectores* (readers) would read to them from daily newspapers and from classics of political thought and world literature. Vega was an active member of Puerto Rico's socialist labor movement, which since the early 1900s had been fighting for workers' rights and against the abuses and exploitative conditions in the tobacco, sugar, and needle industries. These industries were run mostly by absentee U.S. corporations and the Puerto Rican propertied class.

In the United States, Cuban, Puerto Rican and Spanish émigrés had settled in cities—such as New York, Philadelphia, Tampa, and New Orleans—where cigars were made. A Puerto Rican *colonia* had existed in the New York since the second half of the nineteenth century. By the time Vega moved to New York, in 1916, several thousand Puerto Ricans lived in the city, and more than 200 cigar-making shops or factories had been established.

In New York, Vega remained a committed labor activist and participated in the establishment of several grassroots organizations. He also contributed frequently to community newspapers. In 1927, he bought the weekly newspaper *Gráfico*, which was started by a group of tobacco workers and first edited by the Afro-Cuban actor and playwright Alberto O'Farrill. Aimed at a working-class audience and self-described as *defensor de la raza hispana* (defender of the Hispanic race), *Gráfico* was one of several Spanish-language community newspapers that promoted unity among the various Hispanic groups living in the city. Most of Vega's journalistic writings remain scattered in such publications, including the Spanish-exile newspaper *Liberación*.

In the 1940s, Vega began to write his memoirs—a meticulous account of his experiences, and those of other Puerto Rican migrants, during the years before the Great Migration, the formative decades of New York's Puerto Rican community. His narrative begins in 1857, with the story of his uncle Antonio Vega's arrival in New York. Antonio Vega, along with many other Hispanic Caribbean émigrés, moved to the United States to work and became involved in the activities of the Antillean separatist movement. Bernardo recounts in great detail what he learned from his uncle and other sources about many of the leading personalities of the nineteenth-century separatist movement and the organizations and publications they created to promote the liberation of Cuba and Puerto Rico from Spain.

In the 1950s, Bernardo moved back to Puerto Rico, where he showed the completed manuscript of his memoirs to his novelist friend and socialist comrade César Andreu Iglesias. Vega asked Andreu Iglesias to edit the manuscript for publication, but he did not accept many of his friend's initial suggestions, and the manuscript editing stopped. Twelve years after Vega's death in Puerto Rico, Andreu Iglesias edited and published the manuscript as *Memorias de Bernardo Vega* (Memoirs of Bernardo Vega).

The book's unique value as a document of the history of Puerto Rican migration and the evolution of the Puerto Rican community in New York was recognized by the Puerto Rican American critic and translator Juan Flores. In the preface to his 1984 translation, Flores writes that "the English language edition of the *Memoirs* is an event to celebrate, marking a new stage in the people's historical self-awareness. No book offers the millions of Puerto Ricans in the United States so many continuities and connections, so many recognizable and identifiable life experiences, so many incentives to recapture the buried past and to strike out against an unsatisfactory present."

# Puerto Rican Migration to the United States[1]

Many people who observe the existing antagonism against Puerto Ricans here cannot understand why thousands more Boricuas continue to arrive on these shores every month. People cannot understand how it is possible for the Borinqueños[2] to come to this country to withstand hunger, frigid weather, and to endure mistreatment, especially when it is known that the majority of the island's inhabitants support the independence of their country.

The causes of this migratory phenomenon are many. In the first place, it must be understood that this emigration of Puerto Ricans to the North is not voluntary. It is forced by the economic and social conditions that exist in Puerto Rico due to colonialism. American commercial and industrial monopolies have ruined the island's economy, forcing the cultivation of only those goods that benefit them, thereby dictating their price and obliging the natives to export them on American transports, since as the dominating nation it has a complete monopoly of the shipping fleets. It is in this way that agriculture degenerated into monocultivation, eradicating almost completely the cultivation of minor products. This change in the agricultural system forced Boricuas to supply themselves with consumer goods produced abroad and, naturally, since the United States own the shipping vessels, the products had to be bought from them. Moreover, this change completely disrupted our agriculture and created unparalleled unemployment and high cost of living.

Secondly, since there are no other methods of transportation or the means to go to any other country—and you cannot leave the island on foot or by swimming—all the dispossessed and unemployed people who want to seek refuge abroad are forced to depart for the only country for which there are already the means in place; that is, the United States.

---

1. Originally published in Spanish in *Liberación*. Translated by Edna Acosta-Belén and Susan Liberis-Hill. The footnote and the bracketed insertion are Acosta-Belén and Liberis-Hill's.
2. The terms *Boricuas* and *Borinqueños* are commonly used to identify Puerto Ricans. Both words are of indigenous (i.e., Taíno) origin and were adapted into Spanish during the colonial era to identify Puerto Rico's Creole population.

The Puerto Rican legislature and many influential Borinqueños in politics, industry, and commerce have tried to do something to alleviate unemployment and hunger, but all their efforts have clashed with the competitive stance and hostility of American monopolies. We have tested, with good intentions and patriotic fervor, a plan to create industries and provide employment to the native population so it does not have to emigrate, but these attempts have always failed or have met with an infinite number of obstacles all stemming from colonialism.

In speaking about the efforts of Boricuas to partially resolve their economic problems under colonial rule, we can cite specific cases that provide palpable evidence of the range of negative outcomes in the efforts to create more industries and employment on the island that would prevent mass emigration, for as long as the Yankees have us under their thumb.

One of these cases was the creation of a soap factory: Hispanic capital opened the John Laud factory. The product was sold in the country. Little by little it began displacing the American soaps. All of a sudden, the American monopoly inundated the island with soap, selling it at a price below the cost of production by the native company. The result: in a few months the native manufacturer failed. Another case: the cooperative that produced *gandules* [pigeon peas] was growing like a weed, especially with its sales to the New York Boricuas and throughout the island. Immediately the Texas and Florida growers started canning *gandules* and selling them for half the price of those sold by the cooperative. Result: that industry is not achieving the success that it could enjoy. And, in this manner, every new industry that Puerto Rico tries to develop is subjected to this kind of strangulation.

If Boricuas could leave for other lands, other Latin American countries, for example, they would surely not come to the North. Willingly, they would emigrate to our fellow countries on the continent, but since this seems impossible, they leave their hell of hunger and misery in order to arrive to this other hell of mistreatment and despair. This is what colonialism has made of us.

November 30, 1946

---

## *FROM* MEMOIRS OF BERNARDO VEGA[1]

### 1. From my hometown Cayey to San Juan, and how I arrived in New York without a watch

Early in the morning of August 2, 1916, I took leave of Cayey. I got on the bus at the Plaza and sat down, squeezed in between passengers and suitcases. Of my traveling companions I remember nothing. I don't think I opened my

---

1. Translated by Juan Flores.

mouth the whole way. I just stared at the landscape, sunk in deep sorrow. I was leaving a girlfriend in town . . .

But my readers are very much mistaken if they expect a sentimental love story from me. I don't write to pour my heart out—confessions of love bore me to death, especially my own. So, to make a long story short, the girl's parents, brothers, relatives, and well-wishers declared war on me. That's not exactly why I decided to leave, but that small-town drama of Montagues and Capulets[2] did have an influence. Anyway, I left Cayey that hot summer, heavy of heart, but ready to face a new life.

From an early age I had worked as a cigar-roller in a tobacco factory. I had just turned thirty, and although it was not the first time I had left my hometown, never before had I put the shores of Puerto Rico behind me. I had been to the capital a few times. But now it meant going farther, to a strange and distant world. I hadn't the slightest idea what fate awaited me.

In those days I was taller than most Puerto Ricans. I was white, a peasant from the highlands (*a jíbaro*), and there was that waxen pallor to my face so typical of country folk. I had a round face with high cheekbones, a wide, flat nose, and small blue eyes. As for my lips, well, I'd say they were rather sensual, and I had strong, straight teeth. I had a full head of light chestnut hair, and, in contrast to the roundness of my face, I had square jaws. All in all, I suppose I was rather ugly, though there were women around who thought otherwise.

I did not inspire much sympathy at first sight, I'm sure of that. I have never made friends easily. No doubt my physical appearance has a lot to do with it. I hadn't been living in New York for long before I realized how difficult it was for people to guess where I came from. Time and again I was taken for a Polish Jew, or a Tartar, or even a Japanese . . . God forgive my dear parents for my human countenance, which was after all the only thing they had bequeathed me!

I arrived in San Juan at around ten o'clock in the morning. I ordered the driver to take me to El Comercio, a cheap hotel I knew of on Calle Tetuán. I left my suitcase and went out for a walk in the city.

The sun warmed the pavements of the narrow streets. I longed for the morning chill of my native Toa valley. I decided to go for a ride in a trolley car and say goodbye to an old schoolteacher of mine. To her I owed my first stop. Her name was Elisa Rubio and I have fond memories of her to this day. In her little house in Santurce she told me glowing things about the United States and praised my decision to emigrate. I would have a chance to study there. To this day, after all these years, her exaggerated praise echoes in my mind: "You have talent and ambition. You will get ahead, I am sure. And you'll become famous" Heaven forgive my well-meaning teacher.

On my return to the old section of San Juan, I spent the afternoon taking leave of my comrades. There was Manuel F. Rojas, who had been elected secretary general of the Partido Socialista at the constituent assembly recently held in Cayey, my hometown, which I had attended as a delegate. With him were Santiago Iglesias, Prudencio Rivera Martínez, and Rafael Alonso Torres . . . They all were unhappy about my decision to leave because of the loss it would be for our newly organized workers' movement.

---

2. The feuding families in Shakespeare's *Romeo and Juliet.*

But they did not try hard to dissuade me. As socialists, we dig our trenches everywhere in the world.

I returned to the little hotel tired and sweaty. Before going up to my room I bought the daily newspapers—*La Correspondencia, El Tiempo, La Democracia.* In shirtsleeves, I threw myself onto my bed and plunged into the latest events of the day.

In those days our newspapers were not as big as they are today—none were over twelve pages. The news, especially about foreign affairs, did not take up much space. But our native writers waxed eloquent in endless polemics—original commentaries, sharp criticism, and plenty of our local humor. They reflected the life of the whole society—or rather, of its ruling class—with uneven success, but in any case they were more truthful than they are today, for sure.

Night fell, and I washed up, dressed, and went back out in the street. I had a long conversation with Benigno Fernández García, the son of a prestigious Cayey family. We talked about the European war, in which the United States was soon to be involved. Then I returned to my hotel, went to bed, and tried to sleep, but it was impossible. My mind was full of memories and my heart ached. Until then I had been acting like a robot, or a man under the influence of drugs. Now, alone in the darkness of my room, I recalled my mother's tears, the sad faces of my little brothers . . . I just couldn't get to sleep.

Once again I went back into the streets. It had rained. A pleasant breeze blew through the city. The bright moon lit up the streets. The damp pavements glistened. And I took to walking, up one street and down another, in an intimate chat with the cobblestones of that city which means so much to Puerto Ricans.

Dawn caught me by surprise, seated on one of the benches in the Plaza de Armas now and then looking up at the big clock. The cheerful rattle of the first trolley car brought me back to sad reality. Within a few minutes the bold tropical sun had taken possession of San Juan, and the streets were crowded with people. Gentlemen in jackets and hats left home to go to work. But the largest crowds were made up of people flocking in from the countryside, dealers in agricultural produce. Cornflakes had not yet replaced corn on the cob, though things were already headed in that direction.

The hours passed quickly. At around two in the afternoon I boarded the boat, the famous *Coamo* which made so many trips from San Juan to New York and back. I took a quick look at my cabin, and went right back up on deck. I did not want to lose a single breath of those final minutes in my country, perhaps the last ones I would ever have.

Soon the boat pushed off from the dock, turned, and began to move slowly toward El Morro castle at the mouth of the harbor. A nun who worked at the women's home was waving *adiós* from high up on the ramparts; I assumed she meant it for me. As soon as we were on the open sea and the boat started to pitch, the passengers went off to their cabins, most of them already half seasick. Not I. I stayed up on deck, lingering there until the island was lost from sight in the first shadows of nightfall.

The days passed peacefully. Sunrise of the first day and the passengers were already acting as though they belonged to one family. It was not long before we came to know each other's life stories. The topic of conversation, of course, was what lay ahead: life in New York. First savings would be for sending for close relatives. Years later the time would come to return home with pots of money. Everyone's mind was on that farm they'd be buying or the business they'd set up in town . . . All of us were building our own little castles in the sky.

When the fourth day dawned even those who had spent the whole trip cooped up in their cabins showed up on deck. We saw the lights of New York even before the morning mist rose. As the boat entered the harbor the sky was clear and clean. The excitement grew the closer we got to the docks. We recognized the Statue of Liberty in the distance. Countless smaller boats were sailing about in the harbor. In front of us rose the imposing sight of skyscrapers—the same skyline we had admired so often on postcards. Many of the passengers had only heard talk of New York, and stood with their mouths open, spellbound . . . Finally the *Coamo* docked at Hamilton Pier on Staten Island.

First to disembark were the passengers traveling first class—businessmen, well-to-do families, students. In second class, where I was, there were the emigrants, most of us *tabaqueras*, or cigar workers. We all boarded the ferry that crossed from Staten Island to lower Manhattan. We sighed as we set foot on solid ground. There, gaping before us, were the jaws of the iron dragon: the immense New York metropolis.

All of us new arrivals were well dressed. I mean, we had on our Sunday best. I myself was wearing a navy blue woolen suit (or *flus*, as they would say back home), a borsalino[3] hat made of Italian straw, black shoes with pointy toes, a white vest, and a red tie. I would have been sporting a shiny wrist-watch too, if a traveling companion hadn't warned me that in New York it was considered effeminate to wear things like that. So as soon as the city was in sight, and the boat was entering the harbor, I tossed my watch into the sea . . . And to think that it wasn't long before those wristwatches came into fashion and ended up being the rage!

And so I arrived in New York, without a watch.


## 2. The trials and tribulations of an emigrant in the iron Tower of Babel[4] on the eve of World War I

The Battery, which as I found out later is what they call the tip of lower Manhattan where our ferry from Staten Island docked, was also a port of call for all the elevated trains. The Second, Third, Sixth, and Ninth Avenue lines all met there. I entered the huge station with Ambrosio Fernández, who had come down to meet me at the dock. The noise of the trains was deafening, and I felt as if I was drowning in the crowd. Funny, but now that I was on land I started to feel seasick. People were rushing about every which way, not seeming to know exactly where they were headed. Now and

3. I.e., Borsalino, an Italian hat company known particularly for its fedoras.
4. In the biblical Book of Genesis, an immense tower in the city of Babel (Hebrew for "Babylon"), dedicated to the glory of man. Angered by the arrogance of the builders and inhabitants, God made them speak many conflicting languages rather than a universal one and scattered the people around the earth.

then one of them would cast a mocking glance at the funny-looking travelers with their suitcases and other baggage. Finally there I was in a subway car, crushed by the mobs of passengers, kept afloat only by the confidence I felt in the presence of my friend.

The train snaked along at breakneck speed. I pretended to take note of everything, my eyes like the golden deuce[5] in a deck of Spanish cards. The further along we moved, and as the dingy buildings filed past my view, all the visions I had of the gorgeous splendor of New York vanished. The skyscrapers seemed like tall gravestones. I wondered why, if the United States was so rich, as surely it was, did its biggest city look so grotesque? At that moment I sensed for the first time that people in New York could not possibly be as happy as we used to think they were back home in Cayey.

Ambrosio rescued me from my brooding. We were at the 23rd Street station. We got off and walked down to 22nd Street. We were on the West Side. At number 228 I took up my first lodgings. It was a boarding house run by Mrs. Arnao, the place where Ambrosio was living.

On my first day in New York I didn't go out at all. There was a lot to talk about, and Ambrosio and I had lengthy conversations. I told him the latest from Puerto Rico, about our families and friends. He talked about the city, what life was like, what the chances were of finding a job . . . To put it mildy, an utterly dismal picture.

Ambrosio himself was out of work, which led me to ask myself, "Now, if Ambrosio is out of a job, and he's been here a while and isn't just a cigar-worker but a silversmith and watchmaker to boot, then how am I ever going to find anything?" My mind began to cloud over with doubts; frightening shadows fell over my immediate future. I dreaded the thought of finding myself out in the streets of such a big, inhospitable city. I paid the landlady a few weeks' rent in advance. Then, while continuing my conversation with Ambrosio, I took the further precautionary measure of sewing the money for my return to Puerto Rico into the lining of my jacket. I knew I only had a few months to find work before winter descended on us. If I didn't, I figured I'd send New York to the devil and haul anchor.

Word was that Mrs. Arnao was married to a Puerto Rican dentist, though I never saw hide nor hair of the alleged tooth-puller around the house. She was an industrious woman and her rooming house was furnished in elegant taste. She had a flair for cooking and could prepare a delectable dinner, down to the peapods. At the time I arrived her only other boarder was Ambrosio, which led me to suspect that she wasn't doing too well financially.

But in those days you didn't need much to get by in New York. Potatoes were selling for a fraction of a cent a pound; eggs were fifteen cents a dozen; a pound of salt pork was going for twelve cents, and a prime steak for twenty cents. A nickel would buy a lot of vegetables. You could pick up a good suit for $10.00. With a nickel fare you could get anywhere in the city, and change from one line to another without having to pay more.

The next day I went out with Ambrosio to get to know New York. We headed for Fifth Avenue, where we got on a double-decker bus. It was the first time I had ever been on one of those strange contraptions! The tour was terrific. The bus went uptown, crossed over on 110th Street and made

5. I.e., flashing.

its way up Riverside Drive. At 135th Street we took Broadway up to 168th Street, and then St. Nicholas Avenue to 191st. From our comfortable seats on the upper deck we could soak in all the sights—the shiny store windows, then the mansions, and later on the gray panorama of the Hudson River.

In later years I took the same trip many times. But I was never as impressed as I was then, even though on other occasions I was often in better company. Not to say that Ambrosio wasn't good company, don't get me wrong!

At the end of our tour, where we got off the bus, was a little park. We strolled through it, reading the inscriptions commemorating the War of Independence. We couldn't help noticing the young couples kissing right there in public. At first it upset me to witness such an embarrassing scene. But I quickly realized that our presence didn't matter to them, and Ambrosio confirmed my impression. What a difference between our customs back home and the behavior of Puerto Rican men and women in New York!

We returned by the same route, but got off the bus at 110th Street. We walked up Manhattan Avenue to 116th, which is where the León brothers—Antonio, Pepín, and Abelardo—were living. They owned a small cigar factory. They were part of a family from Cayey that had emigrated to New York back in 1904. The members of that family were some of the first Puerto Ricans to settle in the Latin *barrio* of Harlem. In those days the Nadals, Matienzos, Pietris, Escalonas, and Umpierres lived there too; I also knew of a certain Julio Ortíz. In all, I'd say there were some one hundred and fifty Puerto Ricans living in that part of the city around the turn of the century.

Before our countrymen, there were other Hispanics here. There was a sizable Cuban colony in the last quarter of the nineteenth century, members of the Quesada, Arango, and Mantilla families, as well as Emilia Casanova de Villaverde. They must have been people of some means, since they lived in apartments belonging to Sephardic Jews on 110th Street facing Central Park.

As I was saying, when I took up residence in New York in 1916 the apartment buildings and stores in what came to be known as El Barrio, "our" barrio, or the Barrio Latino, all belonged to Jews. Seventh, St. Nicholas, and Manhattan avenues, and the streets in between, were all inhabited by Jewish people of means, if not great wealth. 110th Street was the professional center of the district. The classy, expensive stores were on Lenox Avenue, while the more modest ones were located east of Fifth Avenue. The ghetto of poor Jews extended along Park Avenue between 110th and 117th and on the streets east of Madison. It was in this lower class Jewish neighborhood that some Puerto Rican and Cuban families, up to about fifty of them, were living at that time. Here, too, was where a good many Puerto Rican cigarworkers, bachelors for the most part, occupied the many furnished rooms in the blocks between Madison and Park.

On Park Avenue was an open-air market where you could buy things at low prices. Early in the morning the vendors would set up their stands on the sidewalk under the elevated train, and in the afternoon they would pack up their goods for the night. The marketplace was dirty and stank to high heaven, and remained that way until the years of Mayor Fiorello La Guardia, who put the market in the condition it is in today.

Many of the Jews who lived there in those days were recent immigrants, which made the whole area seem like a Tower of Babel. There were Sephardic Jews who spoke ancient Spanish or Portuguese; there were those from the Near East and from the Mediterranean, who spoke Italian, French, Provençal, Roumanian, Turkish, Arabic, or Greek. Many of them, in fact, could get along in five or even six languages. On makeshift shelves and display cases, hanging from walls and wire hangers, all kinds of goods were on display. You could buy everything from the simplest darning needle to a complete trousseau. For a quarter you could get a used pair of shoes and for two or three cents a bag of fruit or vegetables.

At the end of our visit to this neighborhood, Ambrosio and I stopped off for dinner at a restaurant called La Luz. We were attracted by the Spanish name, though the owner was actually a Sephardic Jew. The food was not prepared in the style that was familiar to us, but we did notice that the sauces were of Spanish origin. The customers who frequented the place spoke Castilian Spanish.[6] Their heated discussions centered on the war raging in Europe. From what I could gather, most of them thought that the United States would soon be involved in the conflict, and that the Germans would be defeated in the end.

I was impressed by the restaurant because it was so hard to believe that it was located in the United States. There was something exotic about the atmosphere. The furniture and decor gave it the appearance of a café in Spain or Portugal. Even the people who gathered there, their gestures and speech mannerisms, identified them as from Galicia, Andalusia, Aragon, or some other Iberian region. I began to recognize that New York City was really a modern Babylon, the meeting point for peoples from all over the world.

At this time Harlem was a socialist stronghold. The Socialist Party had set up a large number of clubs in the neighborhood. Young working people would get together not only for political purposes but for cultural and sports activities and all kinds of parties. There were two major community centers organized by the party: the Harlem Terrace on 104th Street (a branch of the Rand School), and the Harlem Educational Center on 106th between Madison and Park. Other cultural societies and a large number of workers' cooperatives also worked out of these centers. Meetings and large indoor activities were held at the Park Palace, an auditorium with a large seating capacity. Outdoor public events were held at the corner of 110th Street and Fifth Avenue. All kinds of political, economic, social, and philosophical issues were discussed there; every night speakers aired their views, with the active participation of the public.

Housing in that growing neighborhood was for the most part owned by people who lived there. In many buildings the owners lived in one apartment and rented out the rest. There was still little or no exploitation of tenants by absentee landlords who had nothing to do with the community. The apartments were spacious and quite comfortable. They were well maintained precisely because the owners themselves lived in the buildings. Clearly, the Jewish people who lived in Harlem back then considered it

---

6. I.e., standard Spanish.

their neighborhood and felt a sentimental attachment to it. Several generations had grown up there; they had their own schools, synagogues, and theaters . . . But all of this changed rapidly during the war and in the years to follow.

It was late, almost closing time, when we reached the León brothers' little cigar factory. Antonio, the eldest, harbored vivid memories of his little hometown of Cayey, which he had left so many years ago. His younger brothers, Pepín and Abelardo, had emigrated later but felt the same kind of nostalgia. There we were, pining for our distant homeland, when Ambrosio finally brought up the problem at hand: my pressing need for work. "Work, here?" the elder brother exclaimed. "This dump hardly provides for us!" Thus, my dream of rolling cigars in the León brothers' little factory was shattered. My tribulations in the iron Tower of Babel had begun.

### 3. Proletarians extend a hand, but hunger pinches and there is no remedy but to work in a weapons factory

The following day Ambrosio and I began the challenging task of looking for work. We set out for the neighborhood where the bulk of the cigarworkers then lived: the blocks along Third Avenue, between 64th and 106th streets. Spread out over this large area were a lot of Puerto Ricans. There were also a lot in Chelsea, and up on the West Side of Manhattan, which is where the ones with money lived.

After Manhattan, the borough with the largest concentration of Puerto Ricans was Brooklyn, in the Boro Hall area, especially on Sands, Adams, and Pearl streets, and over near the Navy Yard. Puerto Rican neighborhoods in the Bronx and the outlying parts of Manhattan were still unknown.

Between 15th and 20th streets on the East Side there were the boarding houses that served as residences primarily for Puerto Rican *tabaqueros*. I especially remember the houses owned by Isidro Capdevila and Juan Crusellas. They were where Francisco Ramos, Félix Rodríguez Infanzón, Juan Cruz, Lorenzo Verdeguez, Pedro Juan Alfaro, and Alfonso Baerga were staying.

In 1916 the Puerto Rican colony in New York amounted to about six thousand people, mostly *tabaqueros* and their families. The broader Spanish-speaking population was estimated at 16,000.

There were no notable color differences between the various pockets of Puerto Ricans. Especially in the section between 99th and 106th, there were quite a few black *paisanos*.[7] Some of them, like Arturo Alfonso Schomburg,[8] Agustín Vázquez, and Isidro Manzano, later moved up to the black North American neighborhood. As a rule, people lived in harmony in the Puerto Rican neighborhoods, and racial differences were of no concern.

That day we visited a good many cigar factories. The men on the job were friendly. Many of them even said they would help us out if we needed it. That's how cigarworkers were, the same in Puerto Rico as in Cuba, the same in Tampa as in New York. They had a strong sense of *compañerismo*—we

---

7. Countrymen.                              8. See p. 371.

were all brothers. But they couldn't make a place for us at the worktable of any factory.

I spent the days that followed going around the city and visiting places of interest. A "card-carrying" socialist, I made my way down to the editors of the *New York Call*, the Socialist Party paper which back then had a circulation in the hundreds of thousands. I showed a letter of introduction given to me by Santiago Iglesias before I left San Juan, and they welcomed me like a brother. Some of the editorial staff spoke our language and showed great interest in the situation in Puerto Rico. We talked about the conditions of the workers, strikes, and the personality of Iglesias . . . They insisted that I come back that afternoon to talk to Morris Hillquit, the leader of the party.

My conversation with Comrade Hillquit centered around the question of the political sovereignty of Puerto Rico. In his opinion, our country should be constituted as a republic, while maintaining friendly relations with the United States. He told me that was what he advised Santiago Iglesias. "I do not understand," he added, "how that political position could not appear in the program of the Partido Socialista of Puerto Rico."

I left very impressed by my meetings with the North American comrades. A few days later I introduced myself to the Socialist Section of Chelsea. The secretary was an Irishman by the name of Carmichael. He attended to me in a friendly fashion and signed me up as a member, after which he introduced me to a comrade by the name of Henry Gotay. A sailor by trade, Henry was a descendant of Felipe Gotay, that celebrated Puerto Rican who commanded one of the regiments of Narciso López' army in its final and unsuccessful invasion on Cuba. Henry in turn introduced me to Ventura Mijón and Emiliano Ramos, two Puerto Rican *tabaquero* militants. They belonged to an anarchist group led by Pedro Esteves and associated with the newspaper *Cultura Proletaria*, the organ of the Spanish anarchists in New York.

In Henry's judgment, Mijón, Ramos, and Esteves were simply degrading their own intelligence and wasting their time preaching such a utopian cause. Henry was a man of deep socialist convictions. I had lunch that day with him and Carmichael at a Greek place on 27th Street and Eighth Avenue. It was an interesting experience—it was the first time I ever drank whisky. As I was not used to alcoholic beverages, I got very drunk and my two new friends had to carry me home. That was the first time I was dead drunk in New York!

Liquor in those years was dirt cheap. A hearty shot of the best brand went for a dime. All the bars had what was called "free lunch," with an endless assortment of tidbits free for the taking: cheese, ham, smoked fish, eggs, potatoes, onions, olives . . . I must admit I was a frequent client of those taverns in my needier days. I would nurse my ten-cent shot and stuff my face with free goodies. What a shame when a few years later prohibition put an end to those paradises of the poor!

My drunk cost me several days in bed. All I had to do was take a drink of water and the whisky would roll around in my stomach and I'd be drunk all over again. But once I was back on my feet I headed straight for the Socialist Club. I was there often, and Carmichael, Henry, and I became close friends. They helped me straighten out some personal problems and went to great lengths to find me a job. But times were very bad. There simply was no work, and with every passing day I saw my situation grow bleaker and bleaker . . . "As a last resort," my friend said, "when your money runs out and you can't pay your rent, bring your belongings here and sleep in the club. And as for food, don't worry about that either. There'll be some here for you. The party has an emergency fund for cases like this." Those words gave me such a lift!

In the following days I visited Local 90 of the Cigarmakers' Union, which was a local led by the "progressives" in the union. Jacob Ryan held the post of secretary. I showed him my "travel card," establishing me as a member of the Puerto Rico chapter of the International Cigarmakers' Union/A.F.L. I wasn't given much of a welcome; my meeting with the secretary was cold and formal.

I immediately started attending union meetings at the hall up on 84th Street off Second Avenue. There I met many countrymen who had been living in New York since the end of the century. The militancy of those Puerto Rican cigarmakers had been a decisive factor in the election of progressive candidates to leading positions in the local.

Despite all my efforts, after more than a month in New York I was still unemployed. If I didn't find something soon I knew I'd be in serious straits. How much longer could I stretch the little money I had? The bills I had sewn into the lining of my jacket were of course sacred, so I decided to resort to an employment agency and "buy" a job. Yes, sure, I had already been warned of all the traps set to catch the innocent. I knew how mercilessly they would swindle foreigners by "selling" them imaginary jobs. But I had to turn somewhere, and even the slightest hope was better than none. So I showed up, along with my friend Ambrosio, who was also still out of work, at one of those infamous agencies. We paid our $15.00 and set our hopes on the employment due us.

Day in, day out, we would go to the agency and be sent off to some remote "workplace." More often than not it turned out that the street number, and even the street, was completely unknown to anyone. Other times we would track down the address, only to find an abandoned building. We would of course go back to the agency and explain what had happened, but they would only treat us like idiots who couldn't even find our way around town. Finally it began to dawn on us that we were being made fools of.

One day I woke up with that *jíbaro* spirit boiling in my blood. When we got there, the agency was full of innocent new victims. I went straight up to the man in charge and raised holy hell. I yelled at him—partly in English but mostly in Spanish—and demanded my money back immediately. A few Spaniards heard the noise and joined me in a loud chorus, demanding the return of their money too. Two employees of the agency grabbed me by the arms and tried to throw me down the stairs. But the Spaniards jumped to my defense. Finally the boss of the place, afraid of a serious scandal and police involvement, gave all of us our money back.

At the next meeting of the Socialist Club I recounted my experience at the employment agency, and it was decided to make a complaint to the authorities. I later found out that they did in fact conduct an investigation, and that the agency had its license suspended. The fact is, though, that the injustices of those infamous agencies continued, and that Puerto Ricans became their most favored prey.

In those years, and for a long time to come, the Socialist Party, the Cigar-makers' Union, and the Seamen's Union were the only groups that were concerned about defending foreign workers. The other labor unions either showed no interest, or were too weak to do anything, as in the case of the Dressmakers' Union, which later became the powerful International Ladies' Garment Workers' Union. It should also be mentioned that the Fur and Leather Workers' Union showed its solidarity with the struggles of foreign workers.

Socialist influence was strong among the Jews. Many of their organizations worked with the Socialist Party and the labor unions. Most outstanding of all were the Jewish Workmen's Circle and the liberal-minded newspaper *Forward*.

I began to move in these circles and go to a lot of their activities. Truth is, though, that as far as finding work is concerned none of it did me any good. On top of that, the landlady at our rooming house, Mrs. Arnao, began to ask us every single day whether or not we had found work. Even though we would pay her religiously every week, she started to have an unpleasant look on her face.

At the same time, the warm hospitality we had enjoyed at the boarding house was cooling down. There was not such a variety of food as in our first days there. The rooms weren't cared for as carefully as they had been at the beginning. The hatchet finally fell on a Friday, after dinner. Suddenly Mrs. Arnao informed us that she was thinking of going away on a trip and that we would have to move out.

Figuring that misery makes poor company, Ambrosio and I decided to part ways. We headed off in different directions. Before long word had it that my friend had found work in a gunpowder factory. As for me, I took up lodgings at the house of a certain Rodríguez, a cigarmaker from Bayamón who had a boarding house on East 86th Street. It was actually the first floor of a modern building. The apartment was spacious and comfortable. The roomers in the house were mostly Hungarians and Czechs. The style of life in the neighborhood was strictly European, filled with traces of old Vienna, Berlin, and Prague.

Mr. Rodríguez' wife was an excellent Puerto Rican woman. To her misfortune, however, her husband drank whisky the way a camel drinks water. When he was sober he was mild-mannered and good natured, but when he took to drinking, which was usually the case, he liked to pick fights.

Several Puerto Ricans were also staying in the house, very good people to be sure. Many others of the same caliber came by to visit. Among them I got to know Paco Candelas, J. Amy Sanjurjo. J. Correa, Pablo Ortíz, and Pepe Lleras. It was a pleasant neighborhood: the atmosphere was neat and clean, the people friendly and open-minded. Everyone would express themselves in their own tongue. Most people spoke English, but poorly, and always with a foreign accent.

There were excellent restaurants in the neighborhood. You had your choice—Hungarian, German, Czech, Italian, Montenegran . . . Quite a few of them would imitate the style of cafés in Vienna and Bohemia. The area was full of good-looking women, especially Hungarian. A lot were blonde, though you'd also see dark-haired ones with that distinctive gypsy beauty. I must admit that it was those women, who looked so much like the ones from my home country, that most appealed to the romantic side of me. But what could a man do who was out of work and down to his last pennies?

But I enjoyed the neighborhood anyway. On 86th Street there were five theaters where they not only showed films but put on live shows. I loved the diversity of people. Nearby was the German colony, where the socialists were active in all community affairs. There were many meeting places there, most notably the Labor Temple. Down a little ways was the Czech area, with its center of activity being the Bohemian National Hall (*Narodni Budova*), between First and Second avenues. The followers of Beneš and Masaryk[9] used to meet there before Czechoslovakia became an independent state.

Around the time that I went to live in that part of town a good many Puerto Ricans were beginning to move in too. Many Hispanics, especially Cubans from the time of José Martí,[1] lived on those streets. Right in the heart of that area, in fact, at 235 East 75th Street, is where our illustrious countryman Sotero Figueroa[2] lived for many years.

It certainly was a good thing that I liked the neighborhood, because the truth is that my situation was desperate. Winter was near and I didn't even have adequate clothing. As fall set in I spent my days feeling the lining of my jacket and that precious return fare to Puerto Rico. But I wasn't about to give up until the eleventh hour . . .

One morning my fellow townsman Pepe Lleras invited me to go with him to Kingsland over in New Jersey. My good friend Lleras, who was also unemployed, convinced me that the only place we would be able to find work was in the munitions industry. So off we went to one of those immense plants. When asked in the personnel office if we had any experience, we said yes. I was so set on landing something that I almost went so far as to say I had grown up playing with gunpowder!

That was my first job in the United States. The war in Europe was at its height. The Germans had just suffered a setback at Verdun. In the United States, war material was being produced in enormous quantities. The work in the munitions plant was very hard. Only those hardened by rigorous labor could stand it. It really was too much for the soft hands of *tabaqueros* like ourselves. They would work us for eight hours without a break. Even to do your private business you had to get permission from the lead man of the work crew, and he would only relieve you for a few short minutes. Never before had I experienced, or even witnessed, such brutal working conditions.

Pepe and I would be out of the house at five in the morning. It took us almost two hours to get there. The work day started at seven and we would spend the whole day surrounded by all kinds of grenades and explosives. Most of the workers were Italians of peasant stock, tough as the marble of their country. There were also a lot of Norwegian, Swedish, and Polish workers, most of them as strong as oxen . . . Pepe Lleras and I, though better built than the average Puerto Rican, were beaten to a pulp after two weeks.

9. Edvard Beneš (1884–1948) and Tomáš Garrigue Masaryk (1850–1937), cofounders of the Czech National Council, a London-based organization that campaigned for an independent Czechoslovak state.
1. See p. 265.
2. See p. 260.

On the way home we would collapse onto the seat of the train like two drunks, and when we got home we hardly even felt like eating. Our hands were all beaten and bloody and felt like they were burning. After massaging each other's backs, we would throw ourselves into bed like tired beasts of burden. At the crack of dawn, feeling as though we had hardly slept more than a few minutes, we'd be up and off to another day's labor.

One day—we hadn't been there long—we met up with a stroke of hard luck. We used to get there a few minutes before work began to change into our work clothes. It so happened that one afternoon at the end of the day we couldn't find our street clothes. We complained to the man in charge, but he only responded sneeringly, "What do you think this is, a bank or something? If your clothes are stolen, that's your tough luck."

It sure was our tough luck. The clothes that were stolen were the only good clothes we had, and for me the loss was greater still—for along with my suit jacket went my passage money back to Puerto Rico. It was as though my return ship had gone up in flames.

ca. 1940s                                                                                  1977

---

# VICENTE J. BERNAL
## 1888–1915

Although his life was cut short by illness, Vicente J. Bernal wrote enough poetry to earn a place in Mexican American letters. Among his works, for example, were three poems dedicated to the college he attended, Dubuque German College (now the University of Dubuque), in Iowa; one of these, "Song to D.G.C.," is the school song. Most of what is known about his life comes from the foreword to his post-humously published work, *Las primicias* (First Fruits, 1916), edited by Bernal's brother Luis and a member of the Dubuque German College faculty, Robert N. McLean.

Until he was three years old, Bernal lived with his parents in San Pablo, Colorado, after which he was reared by his grandparents in Costilla, New Mexico, an isolated village where he tended sheep and farmed. He was educated at the Presbyterian Mission School, in Costilla, and transferred to the Menaul Presbyterian School, in Albuquerque, in 1907. In 1910, he was admitted to Dubuque German College, a mission school dedicated to the education of foreigners. Had he not died, of a brain hemorrhage on April 28, 1915, he would have entered the Dubuque Seminary that autumn.

Bernal wrote stories in English and poems in Spanish and English. Most critics have preferred the poems. Bernal's Spanish-language poems are more self-contained—less "intertextual," or referential—than his English-language poems. Though their rhyme schemes and structures are simplistic, the Spanish poems might be a lyric expression of Bernal's personality and thought. His "Spanish voice" might be less developed aesthetically because his reading and education had not ex-posed him enough to Spanish-language culture, or because he simply did not have enough time to develop that voice.

As the critic Erlinda Gonzáles-Berry has noted, Bernal's English-language poetry resembles that of the nineteenth-century English Romantics in that it is filled with romantic longing, preoccupation with death, classical allusions, and love of nature. His poems "Elvira by the Stream" and "To —————," both included here, pay homage to the Romantics. His translation into Spanish of "The Barefoot Boy," by the nineteenth-century New England poet John Greenleaf Whittier, gives evidence of his interest in the poetic culture of the eastern United States. In fact, New Mexico does not appear to have influenced his poetry, perhaps because his education immersed him so heavily in traditions and images different from the ones he grew up with.

## Elvira by the Stream

There's a valley in the mountains—
Once her Eden, ah! so fair,—
Pure and limpid are the mountains,
Vivifying is the air;
And the warbling, sweet and rare,                              5
Of the birds that tinge her sky
As from grove to grove they fly.

Lofty peaks of souls volcanic
Guard that valley from the plain.
There they stand, serene, titanic,                            10
Keeping watch o'er their domain;
None does waver nor complain,
None grows weary, nor dismay,
Tho their heads are hoary gray.

Liquid pearls on flowers sheen,                               15
When the morning clears the sky;
And kind zephyr, light, unseen.
Sings his mellow lullaby,
And the clouds of perfume fly
To caress their guardians true,                               20
As they smile from depths of blue.

Of the roses sang Porfiro;
Of the lilies sang Elvira;—
He is not a fancy's hero
Nor is she a wild chimera.                                    25
No! for this rejoicing era
Saw them prattling by the streams
And has kissed their psychic dreams.

April 1, 1915                                          1916

## To ———————

My days—what have they been?
Am I alive, or am I dead?
Am I a slave in bonds, or free?

Since I received the breath of life
And left my mother's womb,                                                5
A curse was planted in my head,
Which grows and branches as a tree—
And yields its fruitage in my life—
I near me to the tomb.

O'er craggy hills my path hath led                                       10
And sore and bleeding are my feet;
My star is veiled with clouds
Of black indiff'rence; hope hath fled
To the unknown—most wild and fleet.
My all, I count, two shrouds.                                            15

But why should I desire to scan
More thorny hills, if life's a breath
Which seeks an ampler sphere!
A flickering flame, the life of man
Extinguished by the breath of death.                                     20
Which lurks forever near.

But wilt thou listen to my plea,
For I am sick and dying, love!
My heart is in thy breast:
My love! O wilt thou set it free,                                        25
That it may coo as mateless dove,
And seek in death its rest!

O let me kiss thy brow and locks,
And draw thee to my side, my life;
Then shall I seek the blast                                              30
In deserts wild; amidst the rocks
With reptiles, share my weary life,
Till I have groaned my last.

1916

# PEDRO ALBIZU CAMPOS
## 1891–1965

Pedro Albizu Campos was one of the most charismatic, controversial, and persecuted Puerto Rican political leaders of the twentieth century. He led the Partido Nacionalista Puertorriqueño (Puerto Rican Nationalist Party) during the turbulent period from the 1930s to the 1950s. Many Puerto Ricans did not support the insurgent activities of the Nationalist Party, but to his sympathizers, Albizu Campos's life of political imprisonment and patriotic sacrifice have made him a martyr and an inspiring symbol of Puerto Rico's contemporary independence movement.

A mulatto born in the southern city of Ponce, Puerto Rico, Albizu Campos completed high school in Puerto Rico, then studied at the University of Vermont. In 1921, he received a law degree from Harvard University. In 1924, he returned to Puerto Rico and joined the Nationalist Party, which had been founded two years earlier. During the years that followed, he traveled throughout Latin America, representing the party and trying to generate support for Puerto Rico's independence.

He became president of the party in 1930 and began to shape it along the lines of Sinn Féin, the Irish nationalism movement, emphasizing Puerto Rico's Hispanic Catholic roots. Under Albizu Campos's leadership, the Nationalist Party acted upon the belief that *la patria es valor y sacrificio* (meaning "the motherland requires courage and sacrifice from its children"). Not since the revolutionary activities of nineteenth-century Puerto Rican separatists against Spain had the island's political struggle been articulated in terms of citizens giving their lives for freedom. Nationalists declared the U.S. occupation of Puerto Rico an illegal act of war. They denied the validity of the Treaty of Paris, which had ended the Spanish-American War and ceded Puerto Rico, Cuba, and other Spanish colonies to the United States. They argued, therefore, that any means, including armed struggle, were justified in the fight for national sovereignty.

This militant discourse immediately drew the attention of U.S. colonial authorities and of Puerto Rican political leaders who supported the U.S. presence on the island. Moreover, during the years of the Great Depression, Albizu Campos had supported agricultural workers' strikes against U.S. sugar corporations. Thus it did not take long for an unmerciful repressive campaign to be unleashed against him and his followers, resulting in more than two decades of violent confrontations, the deaths or woundings of U.S. authorities and local police, and the deaths, woundings, or imprisonment of many Nationalists.

Confrontations between Puerto Rican Nationalists and the authorities intensified in 1936, when the police killed four party members. In retaliation, two Nationalists assassinated the American chief of Puerto Rico's police, Colonel Francis E. Riggs. The perpetrators of the crime were in turn arrested and shot to death at police headquarters without regard to due process or their civil rights. Colonel Riggs had been a good friend of Puerto Rico's American governor, Blanton Winship, who had appointed him to his post. Despite the unlawful and arbitrary actions of the police, Governor Winship had Albizu Campos and several of his followers arrested. They were accused of conspiring to overthrow the U.S. government in Puerto Rico. After the first trial resulted in a hung jury, the second trial was held with a predominantly American jury, and the Nationalist leaders were found guilty and sent to prison. Less than a year later, in Ponce, the Puerto Rican police disrupted a Nationalist Party parade in support of the political prisoners, killing 19 people and wounding more than 200. This event is known as *la Masacre de Ponce* (the Ponce Massacre).

Albizu Campos remained in a federal prison in Atlanta, Georgia, from 1937 until 1943, when he was released after suffering a heart attack. (While a political prisoner in Atlanta, he had been subjected to radiation experiments that prompted a rapid deterioration of his health.) He was hospitalized in New York for almost two years and was not allowed to return to Puerto Rico until 1947. Immediately after his return, he began to reorganize the Nationalist Party.

In 1950, Albizu Campos masterminded an armed Nationalist revolt that involved several fronts. In the mountain town of Jayuya, Puerto Rico, a group of his followers took over police headquarters, a siege ended by the Puerto Rican National Guard air and ground troops. Several shooting incidents occurred in other towns. During a simultaneous armed Nationalist attempt to enter La Fortaleza, the San Juan residence of then governor Luis Muñoz Marín, the five perpetrators were shot. In Washington, D.C., two party followers attempted to enter Blair House, at the time the temporary residence of President Harry S. Truman, and were killed by security guards. As a result of these attempts, Albizu Campos and many of his followers were sent back to prison. Responding to pressure from several Latin American governments, Muñoz Marín pardoned Albizu Campos in 1953.

As Nationalists continued challenging U.S. colonial authority over Puerto Rico, U.S. and island officials characterized them as disillusioned fanatics or terrorists, a small group that did not represent the political views of the majority of the Puerto Rican people. The last major confrontation occurred in 1954, when four Nationalists shot their way into the U.S. House of Representatives and wounded five congressmen before being arrested by the police. (Among these Nationalists was Lolita Lebrón, now one of Puerto Rico's most revered former political prisoners.) After that shooting, Albizu Campos was sent back to prison. While there, in 1956, he suffered a stroke that ultimately left him semiparalyzed and unable to speak. He was then transferred to a San Juan hospital, where he remained confined to his sickbed in police custody. In 1964, knowing that Albizu Campos was approaching death, Muñoz Marín pardoned him again. The Nationalist leader died less than six months later.

Albizu Campos wrote scores of speeches and articles that reflect the fundamental ideological positions of the Nationalist Party. His "Observations on the Brookings Institution Report" (1930), included here, was written in response to a study commissioned by the Brookings Institution, a prominent independent think tank in Washington, D.C.

## Observations on the Brookings Institution Report[1]

Christian civilization has imposed the rule of law in the internal life and external relations of nations. There have been violent attacks on this rule but, under pain of relapsing into barbarism, it is undeniably respected.

---

1. Translated by Iris Zavala and Rafael Rodríguez. Except as indicated, all footnotes are Zavala and Rodríguez's, including this one: "Referring to the study sponsored by the Brookings Institution, by Victor S. Clark, *Porto Rico and Its Problems* (Washington, D.C., 1930). To counter the social crisis, the North American team proposed to improve governmental and administrative measures with more federal aid and industrialization. With Franklin D. Roosevelt's accession to power, the New Deal was broadly applied to Puerto Rico."

Founded in 1916, the Brookings Institution conducts social science research and makes policy recommendations on issues that would, among other goals, help strengthen democracy in the United States and promote the nation's economic and social welfare. *Victor S. Clark*: the former and first-appointed commissioner of education in Puerto Rico after the U.S. takeover; during his time as commissioner, Clark had tried to implement controversial Americanization policies in Puerto Rico's public school system. *Franklin D. Roosevelt*: Franklin Delano Roosevelt (1882–1945), U.S. president 1933–45, was instrumental in bringing about the New Deal. This legislative and administrative program of the 1930s was designed to promote the economic recovery of and social reform in the United States.

Wars of plunder themselves require justification. The aggressor country must mobilize its masses on the basis of respect for rules of a higher order. If it wants to create armed institutions capable of heroism up to the point of personal sacrifice, it cannot appeal to sordid and selfish feelings.

When a neighbor is attacked, the world must be offered explanations. Outside intervention in the struggle is a danger always taken into account, since it is to the interest of all nations to maintain an equilibrium permitting each to develop within full sovereignty.

Although the United States always planned to become master of the Antilles—to make the Caribbean a Yanqui lake and thus bring strategic influence to bear on Mexico and Central and South America—it could not disclose the real aims of conquest to the North American people; so it talked to them of making war for humanitarian reasons. Before world opinion it portrayed the case of Cuba and Puerto Rico under Spanish rule as something so intolerable to the light of civilization that a peace-loving nation was compelled to intervene so that our right to freedom should be respected.

With North American patriotism thus exalted, the concern of other powers lulled, and Antillean hopes falsely raised, war was declared.

According to the Yanquis' propaganda, their invasion of Puerto Rico in 1898 meant an end to Spanish obscurantism and oppression and the dawn of a regime of liberty, equality, fraternity, and material prosperity. All this felicity was to be ours, generously imposed by North American philanthropy and humane sentiment.

The invaders imposed the Treaty of Paris on Spain. They did not consult us in drawing it up, nor ask our approval. They forced Spain to yield Puerto Rico as war indemnity.

All of this blew the Yanquis' famous humanity into fragments, but their propaganda soothed Puerto Rican worries and international suspicions.

Puerto Ricans, irrespective of party, prepared to cooperate in this supposed dawn of liberty.

No one believed that the invaders had set themselves to profane the most sacred of human rights.

They implanted an absolutist regime enabling them to enjoy all immunities and to transfer all the wealth from native to invader hands. Thus agriculture, industry, trade, and communications became virtually theirs.

Today barely 20 percent of it remains in native hands.

Cries of alarm and of patriotism were heard, curses upon the invader. But Yanqui propaganda again put the Puerto Rican conscience to sleep. Our suspicions duly stilled, we were presented before our own and foreign eyes as a land enjoying extraordinary prosperity, due exclusively to the presence of North America's magical flag.

Workers came to believe that their good wages depended on the Yanqui government. Many intellectuals pinned their dearest hopes on occupying a high post in the North American government, especially in the diplomatic and consular services. Farmers were warned of possible labor demagogy. Businessmen were lured by the supposed advantages of free commerce between Puerto Rico and the United States. Persons of property were convinced that they must deposit their money in the invader's banks, because Yanqui propaganda hinted that we were all dishonest. The teaching profession convinced itself that everything must be taught in English. In short, the nation consented to its material and moral dismemberment, anesthetized by the vaunted good intentions.

The patriotism of a few natives went for nothing.

The workers could not believe that the Yanqui government was the fomenter of latifundism and absentee-landlordism and of the destruction of all native industry, resulting in a great rise in unemployment and cheap labor, to the enormous profit of Yanqui corporations.

Businessmen lost all sense of sane bookkeeping. They were unable to see that the free commerce under which we must sell to the Yanqui at the price he was pleased to fix, and buy from him at the price he deigned to stipulate, meant certain bankruptcy and liquidation for them.

Under the foreign propaganda spell, the ingenuous man of property believed that the branches of foreign banks were backed by mountainous millions of dollars. The money he deposited in them was used by the invader to modernize his own enterprises, withdrawing it from the market so that the interest rate rose and rehabilitation of native enterprises was impossible.

The farmer enslaved himself to the exploiting enterprises and sooner or later had to give up his farm—which for tax purposes the government appraised at the highest possible price—to the hounding creditor. At the same time invader interests were—and still are—allowed to conceal all kinds of holdings, and what they did declare was valued at a low figure; and nonpayment of those taxes that were assessed was and is tolerated, exempting them from compulsory sale of property by public auction in case of default. Meanwhile the auctioning off of Puerto Ricans' farms—often for sums not exceeding two dollars—continued year after year in the most systematic fashion.

With the excuse of teaching English, and at a cost of over $4 million a year, a public education system was maintained, using the invader's language as the only instructional medium. In fact, English was not taught, and the effect of making young people study science and Latin and other languages in English has been rather to benumb their faculties.

The invader reached the point where he no longer had to justify himself, for natives paid to do the job for him had emerged. Thus we have conspicuous "pedagogues" in the Department of Instruction approving the above barbarities.

There are plenty of lawyers to defend the invaders' interests.

A group of intellectuals has had the audacity to preach the hatching of a hybrid type, a half-Yanqui, half–Puerto Rican monster.

North American propaganda had triumphed. In spite of all this it was insisted that we had real and effective prosperity and the most advanced civilization as a special prize.

To the outside world we were portrayed as a prosperous, happy, and completely submissive people enjoying such well-being that others should follow our example.

A nationalist movement arose which did not confine itself to the colony. It sought international cooperation. It exposed the lie of North America's beneficence in Puerto Rico. Sad to tell, even abroad there were Puerto Ricans who took on the government's chore of maintaining that lie.

With Puerto Rican opinion inclining toward the nations of our own race, the colonial legislature gathered the courage to send a cable to the sixth American conference in Havana.[2]

Everyone knows the fury this evoked in the despot Coolidge.[3]

While maintaining the myth that Puerto Rico owed all its progress to North American management, his reply sketched the new-model propaganda of poverty. When Puerto Rico was supposed to be prosperous and happy under the U.S. flag, there was no reason to lower that flag. Now that the Puerto Ricans were admittedly poor and hungry, there was still no reason to lower it: the flag was necessary to help them.

Having played out the propaganda of prosperity, they began the propaganda of poverty.

Came the San Felipe hurricane,[4] and with it the colonial governor Roosevelt[5] to justify the propaganda.

This man with the style of a populist ward politico made himself out to be our great friend, and sallied forth into our hills to take photos of our nakedness and hunger. The propaganda in the United States pleaded for public and private charity, stating that we had no resources to attend to our own needs.

The unwary fell for it fast. The sycophants, as always, responded emotionally to the voice of the master. Others feared to oppose him. Everybody applauded.

The Nationalist Party raised its voice in protest against this perverse propaganda which trampled our credit and prestige underfoot.

The protest rang out in the colonial legislature itself. It said that there was no charity, public or private, for Puerto Rico in the United States. It proudly affirmed that even if there were any, we didn't want it. We only wanted justice for our nation.

The colonial governor sought special powers from the legislature to resolve the alleged crisis. He appeared in the capitol itself to give orders. No one dared protest his presence.

He wanted the whole municipal administration—which was all that remained partially in Puerto Rican hands—to submit to his absolute will. The legislature was suspicious; it wouldn't agree.

It did agree, however, to set up various agencies to function under his direct orders. They were so important that he couldn't let them come under any department.

He spoke of industrializing the country. Everyone was stunned by this delightful prospect.

He introduced the party leaders in the legislature to Davidson Bros.—as our saviors. These newcomers would, according to Roosevelt, build a great refrigeration plant for our country's crops. They had millions of dollars and could scatter many millions among us.

2. The Pan-American Union, an international organization that promoted cooperation and trade, held its sixth Conference of American States, or Pan-American Conference, in Havana from January 16 to February 20, 1928. [Anthology editors' note]
3. Calvin Coolidge (1872–1933), U.S. president 1923–29. [Anthology editors' note]
4. I.e., the Okeechobee hurricane, or Hurricane San Felipe Segundo, which struck the Leeward Islands, Puerto Rico, the Bahamas, and Florida in September 1928; the only recorded hurricane to strike Puerto Rico at Category 5 strength, and one of the ten most intense hurricanes ever recorded in the United States. [Anthology editors' note]
5. Theodore Roosevelt, Jr., governor of Puerto Rico 1929–1932.

But they needed from the legislature a gift of 6,000 square meters of land with ocean frontage in our country's chief port, San Juan, to build piers of a size to accommodate big ships. Someone investigated the financial standing of Davidson Bros. They turned out to be incorporated in Florida with a capital of *twenty-five thousand dollars.*

Now they tell us that these gentlemen are mere agents of the fearsome Yanqui octopus, the United Fruit Company. And now we understand the presence in San Juan of a United Fruit representative.[6]

We let them know that we wouldn't allow our poverty to serve as excuse for plundering our last penny. A bad start for industrialization.

Now Roosevelt wants us to believe that Puerto Rico's salvation depends on a $3 million donation from the U.S. Congress, a body notoriously reluctant to part with a cent.

And here the manifest imperial destiny triumphs. They don't need to spend money for their propaganda. We do the job and pay for it with pleasure.

*Three million!* What are three million to resolve a country's crisis? Enough of this farce.

Let us demand respect for our opinion.

Neither Roosevelt, nor his stand-in Beverly,[7] nor his subaltern Domenech,[8] dares lay a finger on the great North American interests that owe many millions to the exchequer.

At the same time they ignore the law that was supposed to ease tax payments for small proprietors.

In a word, poverty must be intensified under the guise of alleviating it.

And now we get the Brookings Institution report. Its publication coincides with Roosevelt's presence in the United States.

This is no surprise to those who know something of the Yanqui propaganda system.

The "experts" paint a gloomy picture. They recommend drastic measures to resolve the crisis. Let us look at some of them: that the colonial senate should disappear, for example.

In practice this body has still not come into existence. It has always submitted to the colonial governor's will. To keep it short, let us examine the case of the present treasurer, Domenech. His party opposed his nomination. No one wanted him in that job.

Yet his nomination was confirmed unanimously!

Since the colonial legislature is a comedy—a recognized fact up to now, according to the Institution—its acceptance of naked despotism would be nothing strange.

It is dangerous to keep a comedy running which gives serious actors the opportunity to turn it into a tragedy.

In the opinion of these "experts," the restriction of municipal power and the extension of direct centralizing power from Washington, etc., are necessary for our salvation.

The important thing is that the big-estate system should be legalized. Let the 500-acre restriction disappear, because it never existed. The colonial legislators never put it into force.

6. On the United Fruit Company, see the already classic work by Charles D. Kepner, *The Banana Empire* (1935; New York: Russell, 1967).

7. James Rumsey Beverly, governor 1932–1933.
8. Manuel V. Domenech, treasurer of Puerto Rico 1930–35. [Anthology editors' note]

Let Puerto Rico become a factory. Cheap day-laborers, foremen, and police are needed. A factory needs no legislators nor political power.

It is necessary to economize. Suppress superfluous agencies. When all of Puerto Rico's wealth shall have passed to the invaders, they will for the first time have to bear the weight of the budget. No natives will be available to cover their business deals.

The public power will frankly be a department of the factory administration.

Puerto Rico will be another Hawaii. We Puerto Ricans will be day-laborers, foremen, and policemen to guarantee to investors, against any opposition on our part that may arise, the enjoyment of our wealth.

Yet there are still those with the gall to plead tolerance for the invader. The time has come to apply sanctions to those who cooperate with him here.

There is poverty but not for lack of resources.

We must put an end to the robbery of these resources. We must distribute them among our people. The legion of small proprietors that we had in 1898 must be reborn.

For the Nationalist Party the recommendations of the Brookings Institution come as no surprise. We know the machinations of Yanqui propaganda.

We owe thanks to these "experts" for having filled the cup to the brim for many who till now have supported the invader.

We warn politicians not in our party that the Puerto Rican nation demands immediate suppression of this regime; that it will not let itself be diverted from its effort to have done with this situation.

We do not tolerate pretenses of rebellion. Is the opposition to this tremendous collective tragedy sincere, as we must hope it is? Then why not summon immediately the general assemblies of each party, and there resolve to demand recognition of our right to constitute ourselves as a free and independent country? The Puerto Rican nation demands definitive action by those who claim to represent it.

May 29, 1930

---

# MARÍA CRISTINA MENA
## 1893–1965

María Cristina Mena was born in Mexico to a Spanish mother and a Mexican father. She attended the Hijas de María (Daughters of Mary, an elite convent school in Mexico City) and later an English boarding school. She spoke four languages fluently. Her cosmopolitan background played a significant role in her short stories, particularly those that dealt with the rebellions of upper-class women against lives of privilege.

In the period just before the Mexican Revolution (i.e., before 1910), Mena moved to New York City, where she lived with various family friends. In the second and third decades of the twentieth century, mostly between 1913 and 1916, she published 11 short stories in U.S. magazines read largely by the middle class. Her magazine

publications ended abruptly in 1931, the year she married the playwright and journalist Henry K. Chambers. After Chambers's death in 1935, she wrote five children's
books and dedicated herself to working with the blind; she also learned Braille and
transcribed her work into that writing system.

Mena's literary reputation is partly based on her friendship with the English
poet and novelist D. H. Lawrence, with whom she corresponded for several years
and whom she visited at his Italian villa. In 1964, she wrote a piece for *Texas
Quarterly*, "Afternoons in Italy with D. H. Lawrence." Although Lawrence appears
to have considered Mena a true friend, he criticized her writing. In her introduction to *The Collected Stories of María Cristina Mena* (1997), Amy Doherty, the volume's editor, quotes a letter from February 18, 1928, in which Lawrence reacts to
one of Mena's stories: "The story was nearly first-rate—but the gods didn't want you
to be a writer: at least of fiction. They refuse to put the bright spark at the point of
your pen."

Once described in *Household* magazine as "the foremost interpreter of the Mexican people," and later praised for her portrayals of strong and positive female characters, Mena noted that she wanted to bring the culture of Mexico to U.S. readers,
who generally were fed a literary diet of stereotypes about low-class Mexicans. The
first of the two selections in this anthology, "The Emotions of María Concepción,"
was featured in one of the best-known periodicals of Mena's day, *Century Magazine*,
in January 1914. Reminiscent of the stories about Mexican peasants in *Flowering
Judas*, a 1930 collection by Mena's contemporary Katherine Anne Porter, it investigates the inner life of a *campesina* from a detached, paternalistic viewpoint. In the
second selection, "The Birth of the God of War," first published in *Century Magazine* in May 1914, Mena depicts the relationship between women of two generations
as they share mythologies that surround Mexican civilization.

# The Emotions of María Concepción[1]

María Concepción, having a favor to ask of her *papá* that morning, listened
at the door of his dressing-room, which adjoined her own, and tried to au-
gur an auspicious mood from the accent of the abstruse little cough with
which he punctuated every delicate task. She heard his measured pacing
to and fro, his opening and shutting of drawers, and the clash of dainty
cup and saucer as he sipped his black coffee. Her delicate nose identified
the aroma generated by *papá*'s hair under the cordial embraces of a curling-
iron, and the lilac perfume of the cosmetic with which those rampant waves
and the heavy mustache and imperial[2] were licked into lustrous immobility. At last—welcome sound!—a cough of finality, and Senator Montes de
Oca marched forth, serene in spotless, frock-coated, patent-leathered
perfection.

Not yet, however, would his daughter present herself before him. First he
must make his morning *reflexiones*,[3] a solemnity which involved his pacing
for five minutes the circuit of the gallery, with head bent, and hands clasped
behind his back, sometimes pausing to glance over the flower-decked railing
into the patio, or to order his *mozo*[4] to remove some linnet or canary whose
pipings interfered with his cerebral operations. According to domestic tradi-

---

1. Except as indicated, all footnotes are by Amy
Doherty.
2. A small part of the beard left growing beneath

the lower lip.
3. Reflections.
4. Servant.

tion, the senator, during that daily perambulation, exercised his intellect to a degree beyond the capacity of less formidable mortals to comprehend. Watching him furtively from the shelter of her room, Maria Concepción applied an extra coat of powder to her already well-whitened features, and dexterously encircled her large eyes with artificial shadows, those *ojeras*[5] which promote luster and spirituality. She found time, too, to rehearse a languid comportment, and she gave some consideration to the project of sinking at her *papá's* feet in a graceful swoon, a maneuver sometimes effective as a stimulant to the granting of special indulgences.

Intense in all things, she had an intense desire to attend a brilliant affair at the Plaza de Toros[6] on the following Sunday. All society would be there, and El Mañoso[7] was to kill—El Mañoso, the youngest and greatest swordsman of Spain, who was now to make his first bow to the cream of Mexican fashion. María Concepción had never been present at a bullfight. Before her arrival at an age for such fiestas her mother had died, and for five years the house of Montes de Oca had dragged through the successive stages of ceremonious mourning prescribed by Mexican etiquette. The senator had testified his grief *á lo gran señor*,[8] causing the finest chamber in his house to be converted into an exquisite private chapel, duly consecrated, where masses were celebrated daily in memory of the beloved. Upon his daughter, during those springtime years of hers, he had imposed the most rigid austerities. If ever a young gallant found opportunity to make "eyes of deer" at her, though he might possess all the virtues of St. Thomas, the indignant senator would suddenly discover in him all the hypocrisies of Judas.[9] María Concepción often declared with tears to her adored twin-brother, Enrique, that if it were not for her expansions of soul with him, and with the heroines of innumerable surreptitious novels, she would have perished in the bud. Soon she would be eighteen. That very morning she had discovered a wrinkle, a very little one, it was true, and possibly no deeper than the powder; but it had made her weep. *¡Qué fatalidad!*[1]

Decisive as a signal-gun was the cough with which *El Senador* Don Enrique Montes de Oca y Quintana Ruiz announced to all the world that he had concluded his *reflexiones*. The household sprang into audible activity. The great doors of the coach-house rolled open, and the senator's coupé swung into the patio. Now was the ordained moment for the bestowal of his benediction upon his daughter.

Even as the thought came to him, she approached—pale as a gardenia, her humid, dark eyes fixed upon him in a faint smile of reverence, submission, and affection. At what cost of vigilance and self-discipline she had studied to obliterate herself until the instant of need, and then to sparkle from oblivion with a smile, her *papá* never reflected, not deeming it any concern of his to discover the technique by which women compass the propri-

---

5. Rings around one's eyes.
6. Bullring.
7. The clever, the crafty one (nickname).
8. In grand style.
9. According to the Gospels, in the New Testament, one of Jesus' 12 disciples; his betrayal of Jesus led to Jesus' crucifixion. *St. Thomas*: according to the Gospels, one of Jesus' 12 disciples; after the crucifixion, Thomas reportedly helped spread Christianity in the East, perhaps as far as India. He was martyred and is venerated as a saint by Christian Churches such as the Roman Catholic Church. [Anthology editors' note]
1. What a catastrophe!

eties of their sex. But it did occur to him that she was growing every day more like her lamented mother, and that observation brought him an access of paternal tenderness as she kissed his hand.

She had brought a flower for his coat, a single violet selected from the mass which Refugio, the coachman's daughter, had placed on her dressing-table.

"But thy *papá* is too old for these fiestas," he protested indulgently as she sought to put it in his buttonhole. "Have more formality, Conchita!"

"It is so little and so pale," she pleaded—"so pale, dear *Papá*, that I think it must have grown in the moonlight."

Touched on his poetic side, he unbent so far as to permit himself to be decorated. But then—then, before she could frame the tactful phrases which were to lead up to the theme of the bull-fight, he made an announcement which swept that festival from her thoughts, and canceled every check that her imagination had ever drawn upon the bank of destiny. With an air of conferring an honor far beyond her aspirations, he said:

"Daughter of my soul, thou hast been this morning the subject of my reflections, with the consequence that God has illumined me to guide thee to happiness by making thee the companion and consolation of my remaining years on earth."

Her eyes and breathless mouth rounded in a trinity of O's. Pleased that his words had produced a palpable impression, and proud of the discretion with which he had attacked that delicate task, the making of an old maid, he coughed rhetorically and continued:

"Thou wilt rejoice that I have made thy future secure by liberating thee from the anxieties of youth and, above all, from the banalities of coquetry. Study to make thyself worthy of the consecration to which thou art elected. Invoke the sanctified spirit of thy mama, who doubtless is in heaven commending us to God. Preserve thy health, taking with diligence thine emulsion of oil of liver of codfish, that thou mayest be a comfort and not a care to thy desolate *papá*, who in a short time will have fulfilled half a century of this life, and who requires thy gentle ministrations to alleviate the dolorous path which he must follow to the tomb."

These words, pronounced in a deep and vibrating tone, affected María Concepción so piteously that, without one thought of artifice, she sank sobbing to the floor and embraced the paternal knees, entreating the senator to abandon such gloomy thoughts and to believe that she, his child, thanked Heaven for the privilege of dedicating her life to her beloved *papacito*.[2] Touched at this proof of a becoming feminine spirit, he raised her to her feet, and rewarded her with an affectionate embrace. His heart expanded, and it occurred to him that he was feeling uncommonly young and lively; nevertheless he thought it proper to utter a few pensive reflections on mortality.

When he had given her his benediction and departed for the palace María Concepción ran to change her dress. She had a habit of changing her dress under the stimulus of every new emotion, whether derived from life or from a novel. *Papá's* ministering angel! Never had she experienced an emotion

---

2. Daddy.

so difficult to fit with the psychological frock. She must design a costume, something very spiritual, with a Sarah Bernhardt[3] collar. In the meantime she would put on her habit of the Daughters of Mary, which she had worn at the College of the Sacred Heart—black silk, with a silk cord about the waist, the only touch of color being the broad ribbon of blue sackcloth by which the blessed medal of the order was suspended from the devotee's neck.

Feeling particularly angelic in that demure but bewitching costume, María Concepción sought the chapel of her mama, and earnestly invoked the Virgin to purify her heart and to make her as worthy as possible of her tender and distinguished mission. And she felt herself uplifted as on wings. Returning to her own apartments and consulting the mirrors, she was impressed by the unearthly, soft splendor of her eyes, turned upward under their sweeping lashes in this new rapture of devotion. The contemplation of her own delicate beauty moved her to tears of appreciation. *Papá* should see that he had not been mistaken in her, that she did indeed rejoice at his having set her free from—what were his words? The "anxieties of youth," yes, yes, and the "banalities of coquetry." Coquetry, with those eyes of hers! What sacrilege!

She was startled by a whistle, shrill and peremptory. It was her brother's summons to his *mozo*, and a moment later she heart Enrique's eager voice arousing the Indian from his siesta with voluble instructions for the care of his English mare, heated after a long trot through the forest roads of fashionable Chapultepec.[4] María Concepción's first impulse was to run into some ambush; then, when he had searched for her in vain, to dart out upon him, kitten-like, with a bombardment of kisses and questions—questions about his ride, and the people he had seen, and the gossip at the club, and all the agreeable variety of things constantly going on in that portion of the world exterior to the walls of the mansion of Montes de Oca. But Enrique must learn that her playing days were over.

Hearing him approach, calling her, she sank on her knees at her *prie-dieu*,[5] and hastily swept her habit into graceful folds. The outline of her classic head and delicate features was etched against the shadows as with a pencil of phosphorus.[6] So ethereal was the picture that Enrique halted in the doorway, and did not speak until his sister had signed herself with reverence and risen sedately to greet him. Then, his vivacity returning, he demanded:

"Conchita, what news? Hast thou spoken to *papá* about Sunday? Will he engage a box?[7] Shall we see El Mañoso kill, Conchita of my life?"

With a grave and beautiful gesture she thereupon proceeded to make known to him the momentous role she had been appointed to play upon the stage of life. She chose her words kindly, anxious that he should not consider her puffed up in spirit or imagine that she loved him less because she could no longer share his frivolous preoccupations. On the contrary, she assured him, she would always piously remember that he and she had been born in the same hour, and that only through the trifling accident of sex was he, Enrique, ineligible for the post of *papá*'s ministering angel.

---

3. French actress (1844–1923).
4. Park in Mexico City.
5. Kneeling desk for prayer.

6. Luminous element.
7. I.e., a box seat, an exclusive compartment from which to witness the bullfight.

Enrique was silent for some moments. Then, to her amazement and indignation, he laughed.

"By Santa Inez,[8] little sister," he exclaimed, "I am glad thou art happy over thy celibacy. Every one to his taste, as the donkey-driver said after a dinner of hay. But this is not such news to me as thou thinkest, for I always believed that *papá* would find it convenient to cause thee to remain to dress the saints."[9]

What feeling was this that dilated the fine nostrils of María Concepción, and chilled the sacrificial ardor of her heart?

"But to bad weather a good face," Enrique continued. "Old age will come soon enough without our running to meet it, little sister of my soul."

She smiled with her lips, but her eyes fled sidewise, searching among the shadows about the floor.

"All the world will be there," Enrique went on in a fume of boyish enthusiasm, "the De la Vega, the Castro, the Gorricochéa.[1] Americans are paying fabulous prices for *entradas*,[2] doubtless because El Mañoso killed before Spanish royalty, and received such rare recognition from Alfonso's angel-faced English queen. See, I have this photograph."

"The King's?"

"Bah! Who cares for a king's portrait? No, no, the great swordsman's. See his eyes, pale and distended like a cat's, as no doubt they look when he poises to deliver the fatal thrust which halts the ensanguined bull in its querulous assault and abases its proud neck beneath his conquering foot!"

María Concepción studied the face of the famous matador—a young face, as smooth as a priest's or an American's, but alight with the passion and innocent boldness of Spain. The pale, printed eyes seemed to penetrate her own. She shut hers with a frown. Enrique was saying:

"*Papá* may talk as he will about the vulgarity of Spain's great amusement, as if the Montes de Oca were of pure Indian blood; but even the proudest of unmixed Mexicans cannot be indifferent to such fame as El Mañoso has earned with his sword."

María Concepción opened her eyes and looked again at the picture. She seemed to have lived a long time since she had seen it first, and she felt astonished that it had not changed. ¡*Qué simpático!*[3] Would Enrique never stop talking?

"Are we to drop out of the world just because *papá* chooses to make a reputation as a serious man? It would serve nothing for *me* to speak to him; he would only come out with, 'Today is Thursday,' and present me with a sermon and his benediction at the end of it. But thou, Conchita, thou hast little ways of thy own with *papá*, whom thou hast trained so cleverly to have anxieties about thy health. Come, show thy invention! A timely *ataque*,[4] eh? A few fainting-fits, a day or two of hysteria—what dost thou say, my little bird?"

---

"I say," she exclaimed in a ringing voice, "and I swear, Enrique, that we go! We will not continue to be zero at the left[5] for *papá*. As surely as my name is María Concepción, we will see El Mañoso kill!"

Enrique clapped his hands; but in that very instant he received a stinging box on the ear. *¡Cáspita![6]* What did she mean? They faced each other like two angry game-chickens, exactly alike in feature, except for the crisp rigor of Enrique's chiseling, his tawnier color, and his thread of a mustache. She stormed at him. Why had he come to torment her with fiestas and with photographs at a time when she was experiencing a beautiful emotion over *papá*? How could she be a ministering angel without the emotion belonging to that role? Sustained by the appropriate emotion she could contest with pitiless tigers, yes, or with bulls; but unless so sustained, she could not live. Moreover, how dared he intimate that her *ataques* were a delusion and her fainting-fits a mockery? To all of which Enrique, of the burning ear, hissed tragically:

"*¡Hipócrita! ¡Hipócrita! ¡Hipócrita!*"[7]

And then she had an *ataque* which was anything but a delusion. It left her bathed in tears of remorse, declaring that she was good for nothing and would kill herself, since her beloved Enrique would never forgive her. Enrique forgave her, and there were kisses. But that was not sufficient. She must make atonement for the blow by procuring him some greatly desired good. Apart from getting a box at the bull-fight, which was already settled in her mind, what was his dearest present desire? *¡Ay! ¡ay!* a thing beyond her power to obtain, he assured her, a gift of jealously sought after as a trophy and decoration—nothing less than one of the blood-stained *banderillas*[8] from El Mañoso's bull.

María Concepción lowered her eyes.

The black silk habit was laid away, for María Concepción had once more changed her dress. The greatest emotion of life had come to her. She loved. How she loved! *¡Ay, Dios! ¡Qué amor!*[9] Most faintly and inadequately was the condition of her heart symbolized by her newest, loveliest, and worldliest afternoon gown, a Paris model in tea-rose *peau-de-soie*,[1] as coherent as a veneer to her fifteen-inch waist, abetted by an agitating leghorn bonnet,[2] with hand-painted streamers coaxed into an amorous bow against one cheek.

Yes, she loved El Mañoso, whom she had not yet seen. But very soon she would see him. That was her present business in the landau,[3] by Enrique's side, an hour or two after her first view of the portrait which had altered the aspect of life to her. Yet *she* had not proposed this drive. No, she had merely engineered it, and so delicately that Enrique imagined that he had tempted her out upon an escapade. He thought, poor innocent, that it was he who had instigated a certain simulated *ataque* so alarming to all the servants and the "keeper of the keys" that his hurried ordering of the carriage to give

5. Literal translation of *ser un cero a la izquierda*: to be a nobody.
6. Damn it!
7. Hypocrite!
8. Decorated darts thrust into a bull's neck or shoulders during a bullfight.
9. Oh God! What love!

1. Smooth finely-ribbed satiny fabric of silk or rayon.
2. Hat of fine plaited straw.
3. Four-wheeled, enclosed carriage with a removable front cover and a back cover that can be raised or lowered.

the sufferer some air seemed a perfectly proper proceeding. But instead of seeking the Alameda[4] or the Paseo,[5] the Montes de Oca carriage was threading the narrow business streets of the Centro, Enrique's design being to pass a certain café much frequented by bull-fighters for a glimpses—just a glimpse, he pleaded—of El Mañoso. And María Concepción played to perfection her role of fastidious reluctance, insisting on the top of the landau being closed, and keeping Enrique in a ferment of eager persuasion lest she should insist at any moment on turning back.

El Mañoso was sunning himself with other *toreros*[6] outside the Café of the Cardinal Virtues. A conspicuous group, with hats very wide and flat, jackets a little short of the waist-line, attitudes affected and graceful, faces carefully shaven and powdered, they viewed the moving spectacle with the eager frankness of children, and caused no little blushing and quick-stepping by the outspoken compliments they launched in their clipped Andalusian[7] speech at every pretty woman that met their appraising eyes. Only El Mañoso failed to avail himself of this immemorial privilege of their gild, perhaps dreaming of some bouncing Sevillana[8] who could have tossed these mincing nymphs over her shoulder, or perhaps bewildered and disheartened by the insincerity of this alien capital, with its ostentatious polish and furtive barbarism, its swarthy complexions and elaborate handshakings.

"That is he!" Enrique hissed in his sister's ear.

He! As if she were not already baptizing the object of her *gran pasión*[9] with liquid *ojitos*—those "little eyes" which confess while affecting to conceal, which invite, inflame, provoke, pacify, scorn, rebuke, and plead, all in a few instants' fall and deflection under marbled lids, perhaps to conclude in a sweet stare of unseeing indifference.

"There, the one that moved," Enrique continued out of the corner of his mouth, "the one with blue eyes, looking this way. *¡Pst! ¡Disimula!*"[1]

And, in a sudden reaction of propriety, quickened by fear of his father's wrath, should this adventure reach the paternal ears, he spoke sharply to the Indian coachman, who had pulled up his horses, partly delayed by the traffic and partly engrossed in contemplation of the bull-fighters.

El Mañoso had indeed moved. Detaching himself from his companions, he made his way toward that vehicle with the silver plaque, so distinguished, freighted with that beautiful youth and maid, the latter of whom had honored him, El Mañoso, with *ojitos* more intoxicating than any of which he had hitherto been the target, and he the idol of Spain! Enrique trembled; María Concepción was calm.

Sweeping off his hat with the flourish of a troubadour, El Mañoso addressed to the Mexican *señorita* a suite of Andalusian compliments, opening with a blessing on the mother that had given her birth, continuing with praises for various parts of her person, coupling each with the name of some charming saint, and soaring prophetically to sentiments of distinguished

---

4. Tree-lined avenue, boulevard.
5. A public walk or avenue.
6. Bullfighters.
7. From Andalusia, the southernmost region of Spain.

8. Woman from Seville, a province in southwestern Spain. [Anthology editors' note]
9. Great passion.
1. Hide!

consideration toward the numerous children of whom she would doubtless become the mother.

Enrique, blind with embarrassment and haughty rage, made a motion to strike at the respectful and breathless swordsman with his cane; but the carriage resumed its course with a suddenness which swayed him backward, almost dislodging his hat, to which he was compelled to give instant attention. Throughout the remainder of the drive he was extremely agitated, begging his sister's forgiveness for having exposed her to such an affront from a low-born *coleta* (epithet allusive to the queue in which all *toreros* proudly braid their hair), but advancing ingenious reasons why she should not permit this annoyance to revolt her against Sunday's fiesta. María Concepción fanned herself slowly and said nothing. She had seen him! *¡Simpatiquísimo!*[2] His eyes, of an intense and fiery blue—how they recalled the eyes she had adored in a certain picture of St. Michael, the archangel of the flaming sword! His voice, in that energetic patois, with its scorning of troublesome consonants, its softening of *madre* into *ma're*, and *Dios* into *Dio'*, surely she had heard it in dreams, subdued to the tender whisper, "*¡Concepcio', mi amo'!*"[3] Her eyelids fluttered, and she wondered whether El Mañoso had seen and retrieved the tightly folded morsel of paper that had shot from her fan as she opened it just before the starting of the carriage. Heaven sends it that brothers are the blindest of mortals. It was nothing, a mere entreaty, such as he doubtless received by the score, for one of the coveted *banderillas*. That was all; and yet—

That night she saw him, under the stars, wrapped in his Spanish cape, looking up at the windows of the house. What madness! He was standing beneath her father's balcony. And she—what madness!—she almost tossed him a camellia. Not yet, thou gallant youth! Soon enough thou shalt learn that María Concepción Montes de Oca y Quintana Ruiz knows how to love, that for thee she will reject every earthly allurement, including even the role of ministering angel to the most beloved and distinguished of *papás*.

A romantic elopement by the light of those Southern stars? No. Not for her that safety-valve of the Northern land, so serviceable to democratic equality in bestowing rich fathers-in-law upon young chauffeurs of comeliness and wit; not for her, or for any *señorita* of her race, her class, her unacquaintance with the barest conception of female liberty. She loved without a hope of ever touching her lover's hand; and the thought of contact with his lips would have troubled her with a sense of passion desecrated—passion all powerful, but also all delicate, immaterial, and remote compared with that which the North too confidently assumes to read in the smoldering eyes of the South.

María Concepción was suffering. Once more she changed her dress, this time for a vestal robe of white. It symbolized the virgin death to which she now resigned herself. In Mexico to die of love is something more than a dream of poets. Consumed by love—*consumida de amor*—the phrase has all the sobriety and authority of a coroner's verdict, and few families are so poor in romance, as to treasure no experience or tradition of the mortal reality

2. The most charming man ever!
3. Concepción, *mi amor* [my love].

it expresses. Thus to be consumed, María Concepción looked forward with an ardor similar to that of an evangelist on the eve of martyrdom. Her story would be an example to lovers. She thought of Héloïse, Boccaccio's Isabella,[4] and other much-loving ladies of history and legend, and her throat swelled at the daring dream that she, who had but peeped out upon life from the doors of her father's house, might prove worthy of promotion into their noble company. But her own world, the fastidious world of fashion, what would it say when the little daughter of Montes de Oca died for love of an *espada?*[5] The scandal of it! *¡Cuánta murmuración!*[6] She shuddered with delight. Before dying, she would manifest her consuming flame to him who had kindled it, and, if necessary, to all the world. And she would be a witness of his triumph and glory in the arena. Which reminded her that she had yet to work her will with *papá.*

For three days—Thursday, Friday, and Saturday—the house of Montes de Oca suffered much alarm over the health of María Concepción. "*¡La pobre niña!*"[7] the servants spoke of her in hushed tones, while tears ran down their dark faces. Never had she been the victim of *ataques* so frequent and so prostrating. Her pretty, round body seemed to lose its form and become *raquítico*[8] before one's eyes. The family doctor looked as wise as he could, and applied leeches (his art was of the old school, as befitting old families) the sanguinary extortions of which the sufferer endured with a sweet fortitude that excited Enrique to gratitude and the senator to tears. Aside, the good physician made it plain to the anxious father that the malady baffled his skill. He would strongly advise the immediate gratification of any caprice that his honored patient might manifest, and in particular he would stake his professional reputation on the excellent results to be expected from any diversion sufficiently animated to arouse her out of herself. In saying which, the excellent man believed that he was expressing his own ideas, whereas they were the ideas María Concepción instilled into his mind by suggestive processes too insidious for detection.

On Saturday afternoon Enrique, at his father's command, hastened to secure the last box available for the great occasion at the Plaza de Toros, and the senator was beguiled into believing that he was acting on his own initiative.

She chose to be exacting in her caprices, this little girl who was going to die. She did not spare her *papá*'s foibles, one of which was an abhorrence of anything conspicuous about a woman, but insisted on appearing at the bull-fight *á la española,*[9] her head and shoulders draped in a delicate *mantilla*[1] arranged over a very high comb. It was white, like the rest of her costume, and beneath it her eyes seemed of startling darkness and size, while her little face looked like mother-of-pearl. The only *mantilla* on the side of the arena called "the shade"—there were plenty on the side called "the sun," where the common people sat—it caused much *murmuración*[2] and pointing

---

4. In a story by the Italian writer Giovanni Boccaccio (1313–1375), a woman who, pining away for her murdered lover, keeps his severed head of in a pot of basil. *Héloïse*: French nun, writer, scholar, and abbess (1101–1164), best-known for her love affair and correspondence with the French philosopher, theologian, and logician Peter Abelard (1079–1142). [Anthology editors' note]

5. Sword, swordsman.
6. How much gossip there would be!
7. The poor girl!
8. Feeble.
9. In the Spanish style.
1. Lace scarf worn by Spanish women over their hair and shoulders.
2. Gossip.

of opera-glasses; and the sensitive senator perspired freely. María Concepción reflected that he would forgive her all when the end came.

That measured clamor, swelling until it drowned the strains of Bizet's[3] music, what was it? Rising from "the sun," that agitated coast of sweeping color, all a tossing confusion of fans, parasols, headdresses, scarfs, and faces, it extorted from the self-conscious occupants of "the shade" a more than indulgent echo. "¡Otro toro! ¡Otro toro!" María Concepción felt it tighten her throat and send the blood jumping to her temples. Of the six bulls dignified with a share in the entertainment, one had played his part and made his exit, dragged by four gaily decked mules, and deaf to the funeral march played jocosely in his honor; and now, this monotonous chorus, timed with a beating of multitudinous feet, "¡Otro toro! ¡Otro toro!" Imperious as a cry for bread, rhythmic as drums of war, persistent, good-humored, ferocious, that sonorous cadence proclaimed the popular exigency for "Another bull!" The chant did not vary until it lost itself in a joyous storm of acclamation for the junior *espada* of the occasion, and its supreme attraction, El Mañoso, "The Full-of-Tricks," the favored of royalty, the master-swordsman of his time.

Even the appearance of her love, princely in blue silk, overlaid with a complexity of gold embroidery, fringes, and galloons,[4] his supple legs delicately sheathed in white stockings, could not add to the emotion that possessed María Concepción. Her heart was fluttering as if preparing to escape between her lips. She scarcely breathed. So strongly was life fermenting in her that she felt as if any further excitation would expel it suddenly, leaving only a tired little body. As the time for that had not yet arrived, she concentrated the whole force of her will to prevent the tension from increasing; and by this means she brought herself to a trance-like condition, in which sights and sounds were extremely diminished, as if she were perceiving them from a great distance. El Mañoso became the graceful leader of some inexplicable fairy gambol: the *capeadores*,[5] waving their capes, were scarlet butterflies; the bull was no more than a shiny beetle, blundering and desultory, fair game for the mockery of those exquisite sprites. As for the hubbub of the crowd—the warnings, suggestions, criticisms, taunts, acclamations, upbraidings, and commands with which it assumed to direct every step of the conflict—it swept by her ears unheeded, as a gusty wind. Scarcely more attentive was she to Enrique's running fire of explanation. His gratification over the ferocity and cunning of the bull seemed to her inadequately grounded. His comments on the accuracy and iron muscle of a *picador*,[6] in holding the plunging bull from his horse with the short point of his lance planted against the beast's shoulder, seemed overdrawn praise for such child's play; and even when the second picador went down with his gored mount, necessitating hasty tactics on the part of El Mañoso and the fluttering *capeadores* to divert from him the menace of the dripping horns, it was no more to her than a fantastic frolic over a fallen chessman. She had almost a sense of detachment in a certain esthetic enjoyment of the young matador's

---

3. Georges Bizet, French composer (1838–1875), best known for the opera *Carmen*.
4. Narrow, close-woven braids of gold, silver, silk, cotton, etc., used to trim garments.

5. Amateur or novice bullfighters.
6. Mounted man with a lance who goads the bull in a bullfight.

harmony of movement, his joyous activity, and his masterly manner of directing every detail of the performance according to the exacting rules of bull-fighting, at the same time losing no opportunity to delight the crowd with some daring and insolently graceful exploit.

Without comprehension she witnessed the mortal peril of one of the *banderilleros*, those fleet-footed artists, second in popularity to the matador himself, who succeeded the *picadores* in the arena, and whose business it is to implant each his pair of beribboned darts on each side of the ridge of the victim's neck. Twice the trick had been played without fault; but the decorated monster had gained in cunning. At first he feigned a reluctance to charge his challenger—it is only while man and beast are running toward each other that the feat may be performed—then he tried to take him unaware by darting forward with short and speedy stride. The youth ran likewise, arms uplifted, and hurled his banderillas, but whirled aside an instant too late. He was rolled in the dust like a rubber ball, and lay bleeding, while the cool gallantry of El Mañoso once more averted death from a fallen comrade. There were hisses for the unlucky one as he was carried off to the infirmary; a *torero* has no more right to get himself hurt than a tenor to sing a false note.

However, the offense was wiped out by a brilliant ensemble in which every performer vied with every other in piquing and bewildering the common enemy, even to vaulting over his back with a pole, at the climax of which, all with one accord scaled nimbly from his view, leaving him to thunder against the palisade, and turn, bellowing through his foam, to attack the impartial sunshine.

A flourish from the judge's trumpet, the signal for death! A stir, a long sigh. The ladies ceased fanning themselves and leaned forward. All save María Concepción! A great pride kept her very indifferent and queenlike. El Mañoso's love must be above anxiety. With a laugh that rang silvery in that moment of suspense, she rallied Enrique on the tensity with which he started at one of the doors in the palisade. It opened for an instant, that stout door, and closed decisively behind El Mañoso. With the confidence of a knight and the elastic step of a ballet-dancer, he presented himself before the box of the president, who had risen to his feet. In a few words, with a gallant gesture, he dedicated himself to the deed he was about to perform. The president bowed. "The sun" acclaimed, expecting that the great *espada* would now favor it with his countenance for the purpose of designating the lucky beauty to whom he elected to pledge his victim, now snuffing the dust and peering at him with red eyes.

But the hero had higher aspirations. Still with his back to "the sun," he wheeled before the box of Senator Montes de Oca, and in ringing tones proffered the fruit of his valor to the lovely and virtuous daughter of that astounded dignitary. María Concepción smiled dreamily, unaware of the startled silence, and of the *murmuración* which followed it. Ages in the past, it seemed to her, this same thing had happened just thus. She raised her bouquet to throw it at the feet of her champion; but her arm was seized in a paralyzing grip. It was the senator, with face of bronze, only his congested eyes, the cording of his forehead, and the bruising power of his grasp, betraying what was passing within him. El Mañoso, bewildered, turned away without the customary "favor" from the object of his homage—turned to face a reversal of mob sentiment, which he perceived as definitely as an odor even before the populace buzzed at him like a hive of exasperated bees. Misguided man! Intoxicated by *ojitos* extraordinary, love instantaneous, dreams presumptuous, he had scandalized "the shade" and slapped the face of "the sun."

And himself betrayed to public mockery, his love scorned, his proud blood of *torero* made to boil by the slighting of the fruit of his sword! His sword— he shook it free of the enwrapping red cloth, hung flagwise on a little staff for which he had discarded his cape, and poised it in his trembling hand. A stinging taunt from "the sun" pierced him like a bullet; then another, followed by a shout of laughter; at the height of which the bull, which had sidled toward him inquisitively, gave a flirt of its tail, and ran at him from behind.

His nerves of *torero* caught, through all the clamor, the vibration of the hoofs, and unaided by a glance, goaded him to an amazing leap, which swung him just clear of that galloping death: it brushed him as it passed. In the yell that greeted his escape relief was almost submerged in censure. Sobered, bottling his rage in his heart, he addressed himself to his work of *espada*. He followed the bull, provoked it, played with it, coaxed and eluded its horns in a hundred capricious feints and maneuvers. He had changed, this El Mañoso. He had lost his belief in justice, his kinship with the people, his gaiety, his dreams—all but his skill, which was diabolical. Never had the Plaza de Toros witnesses such *atormentamiento*.[7]

María Concepción was among the stars. Her spirit soared in revolt, magnificent and comprehensive, against circumstances, society, destiny, against *papá* himself. Unfortunately, her body could neither soar nor revolt, as it was still held tightly in its seat by *papá's* grasp upon her arm, his one desperate idea being to simulate unconsciousness of the appalling disgrace which had overtaken the house of Montes de Oca. But *papá* could not pinion her soul. It was as free at that moment as it would be on the triumphant day when her body should have no more life in it. Already she felt upon her the delicious languor of death—possibly the good doctor's leeches had something to do with that—and while her swimming eyes followed each movement of El Mañoso, her imagination swiftly pictured the course of her closing days on earth. *Papá* would undoubtedly condemn her to return to her beloved College of the Sacred Heart, there to be edified by the good sisters, under durance, and with appropriate penances, until such time as the *escándolo*[8] she had caused in the world might be partly forgotten, and herself graced with sufficient *sobriedad*[9] to restrain her from a repetition of behavior fit only, in *papá's* judgment, for tourists *de los Estados Unidos*.[1] And quite unexpectedly, probably in a week or ten days, she would breathe her last. El Mañoso would hear that news, of course. She hoped that he would live on; but would her spirit have power to dissuade him from following the example of all the love-crossed matadors of romance, who in tragic immolation had presented their breasts to the devastating horns of bulls?

7. Torture.
8. Scandal.
9. Sobriety.
1. From the United States.

But, see, he kneels, El Mañoso, before her eyes! The bull charges! *¡Qué horror!*[2] She prepared in that instant to expire. But no! The monster's head struck the unresisting cloth. There arose a shout from the crowd, its resentment long since swallowed up in noisy delight. El Mañoso showed his teeth in a caustic smile. He had beaten that two-faced mob to his feet! Royally he had entertained it, far beyond its expectations or deserts, and now it clamored respectfully for the supreme act in the ritual of the bull-ring. So be it! But first he would give those pigs a lesson in manners.

María Concepción heard his voice, addressed to "the sun," to all the world. She heard the stream of Sevillan[3] scurrility, bitterly personal and shockingly frank, with which he lashed the populace who had turned against him, and then turned again. *This* her hero, this bandier of abuse with the unclean mob! Icy cold all over, she saw his sinister laugh as he tempted his victim to embark upon the charge of death. And at the moment of moments, when the bull's agitated heart at last received the sword, and four thousand human mouths gasped as one—then, in the spasm of supreme effort that transfigured his countenance as he celebrated the sacrament of his order, she divined the soul of a high priest of the abattoir. Die of love, she? Rather let her die of shame!

His triumphal march around the arena, with effeminate swagger and conceited smile, acknowledging the gifts showered upon him—cigars, money, trinkets, and what-not, to be gathered up for him by his attendants; hats and caps to be tossed back to their owners; a ceremonious bag of gold from the president—she saw it all. She looked at her *papá*. He had grown old. Her *papacito*, her handsome little *papá* of the many foibles! She saw him as an ill-used child, to whom she should have been a mother—she, far older now than he. Instead of which, what thing had she done! A trickle of discreet laughter in "the shade" made her heart leap. What if *papá* should be compelled to challenge someone, to fight a duel for the honor which *she* had exposed to mockery? With anguish she implored the Virgin to avert that peril by causing the journals and the gossips at the Jockey Club[4] to be polite and reticent about this affair! Without turning her head, she felt people's eyes playing on her skin like points of fire. She tried to rise, to escape from that abominable place and go home, where she could at least change her dress. But *papá* was exchanging diplomatic bows and smiles with neighboring friends, and pinching her to follow his example. *Papá's* pinches were of a severity to stimulate the most despairful to a renewed interest in life. Four more bulls remained to be despatched, two by the senior matador, and two by that insufferable junior. And hark! "The sun" was beginning again: "*¡Otro toro! ¡Otro toro!*"

January 1914

---

2. How horrible!
3. From Seville.

4. Meeting place for the elite in Mexico City * * *.

# The Birth of the God of War[1]

When I had been attentive and obliging, my grandmother would tell me stories of our pristine ancestors. She had many *cuentos*[2] by heart, which she told in flowery and rhythmic prose that she never varied by a word; and those epic narrations, often repeated, engraved a network of permanent channels in the memory-stuff of one small child. Indeed, the tales of *mamagrande*[3] were so precious to me that I would pray for afternoons of shade, which were the propitious ones, and I almost hated the sun, because when it baked our patio my grandmother would not occupy her favorite hammock, nor I my perch near by, on the margin of the blue-tiled fountain. And I invented a plan by which I could earn a reward.

Her cigarettes, which were very special, came from the coast once a month, packed in a cane box. Tapering at one end and large at the other, in wrappings of cornhusk, they were fastened together in cone-shaped bundles of twenty-five, and tied at apex and base with cornhusk ribbon. Now, I knew that *mamagrande* disliked to untie knots (she had often called me to unknot the waxed thread of her embroidering), so I would privately overhaul her stock of cigarettes, making five very tight knots at each end of each cone; and then at the golden hour I would watch from behind the flowerpots on the upper gallery for her tall figure in spreading black silk, with her fan in her hand and her little gold cigarette-pincers hanging at her waist. When she appeared, I would wait breathlessly for the business of her getting settled in her hammock, and suddenly calling me in a sweet, troubled voice to release a cone of cigarettes; whereupon I would run down to her and untie those bad little knots with such honeyed affability that she would proceed to recompense me from her store of Aztec mythology.

It was not mythology to me; no, indeed. I knew that *mamagrande* was marvelously old—almost as old as the world, perhaps—and although she denied, doubtless from excessive modesty, having enjoyed the personal acquaintance of any gods or heroes, I had a dim feeling that her intimate knowledge of the facts connected with such unusual events as, for instance, the birth of Huitzilopochtli,[4] was in its origin more or less neighborly and reminiscent.

Huitzilopochtli was the god of war, more honored anciently in sacrificial blood than any other deity ever set up by man. I loved him once for his mother's sake, for his gallant and wonder-stirring birth, and for the eagle light in the black eyes of my grandmother as she pronounced his name.

It is not so difficult to pronounce as might be thought. "Weet-zee-lo-potchtlee," spoken quickly and clearly with the accent on the "potch," will come somewhere near it, though it lack the relishing curl of my grandmother's square-cut lips. And the god's sweet mother, Coatlicue, may safely be called "Kwaht-lee-quay," with the accent on the "lee." But I had better begin at the beginning, as my grandmother always did, after lighting her first cigarette, and while adjusting the gold pincers in a hand like a dried leaf.

---

1. Except as indicated, all footnotes are by Amy Doherty.
2. Stories.
3. Grandmother.
4. Chief deity and god of war of the Aztecs. "He is said to have guided the Aztecs during their migration from Aztlan. . . . He was also god of the sun, and it was believed that he was born each morning from the womb of Coatlicue, goddess of the earth" (*Columbia Encyclopedia*, 1993 ed.).

"The forests have their mysteries, which are sung in their own language by the waters, the breezes, the birds."

Thus *mamagrande* would begin in a hushed voice, with a wave of the hand that would make the blue smoke of her cigarette flicker in the air like a line of handwriting.

"Nature weeps and laughs, sings and cries, and man listens to that weeping and that laughter without knowing the cause. When the branch of the tree inclines itself under the weight of the wind, it speaks, it sings, or it cries. When the water of the forest runs murmuring, it tells a story; and its voice may be accordingly either a whisper or a harsh accent.

"Listen to the legend of the forest; listen to it as sung by the birds, the breezes, the waters! The hunters have arrived. The forest is full of the thunder of their cries, and the mountain repeats from echo to echo those shouts which threaten peace and happiness. Our ancestors, the Aztecs, loved the hunt because it was the counterpart of war.

"Camatzin has given the signal to begin. His dart traverses the air and, trembling, buries itself in the heart of the stag, which falls without life. Only the great hunter Camatzin can wound in this manner; only from his bow of ebony can spring the arrows that carry certain death. At the running of the first blood the fury of the hunters is kindled. All at one time draw their bows, and a thousand arrows traverse the air, covering as a cloud of passage the brilliant face of the sun. The slaughter has begun, the fight between the irrational and man, between force and cunning."

Alas! The sonorous imagery of those well-remembered phrases loses much in my attempt to render them in sober English. Hasten we, then, to the encounter between Camatzin and the lioness, which, with its cub, the hunter has pursued to its lair.

"She raises the depressed head, she opens the mandibles, armed with white and sharp teeth. Her red tongue cleans hastily the black snout. She contracts her members of iron, and prepares to launch herself upon him who approaches.

"Camatzin is valiant. He trembles not before death, but he understands the danger of the fight with the ruler of the forest. Woe to him if he misses his aim!

"The gaze of the lioness finds that of Camatzin. Two clouds meet; they clash, and give forth a ray which strikes death. The dart sings from the bow, and nails itself in the body of the cub. Roars this for the last time—"

*"Ruge éste por la vez postrera,"* as it rolled out in my grandmother's voice, the *éste* signifying that ill-fated cub, for which I always wept. I render the construction literally because it seems to carry more of the perfume that came with those phrases as I heard them by the blue-tiled fountain.

"Roars this for the last time, and the mother roars with sorrow and anger. She sniffs at the blood that issues from the body of her young. She crouches, and so launches herself outside of the cave.

"Shines the solar ray in her red pupils! Moves *suavemente*[5] her tail, which strikes her sides! Walks her gaze all around her!"

---

5. Smoothly.

How expressive, in the mouth of *mamagrande*, was that desperate recon-
noiter, and how plainly I could see the beast's yellow gaze "walking" from
object to object!

"She straightens her members, as if to assure herself that they will not
relax. She crouches with all her weight on her rear feet, and throws herself
at Camatzin. He, without retreating, aims his bow, and the wild beast falls
with its loins to earth, wounded in the right eye.

"Roars she, and the forest trembles to her roaring. She recovers, she rises,
and so rapid is her movement that Camatzin cannot aim in time. The arrow
falls without point at the foot of the rock. The bow is useless, brave Camatzin; take the *macana*![6] He lifts his great saber of wood edged with sharp
flint, and the lion receives a well-aimed blow in the center of the forehead.
Now the attack is body against body! Falls the *macana*, but already the beast
has driven its potent claw in the muscular arm of Camatzin. He wishes to
show his force, which has made him respected by all; but the beast continually tears his flesh, and he grows weaker."

But in mercy to the reader I'll leave the end of that ferocious conflict
to the imagination, and turn to the fortunes of the beloved and blessed
Coatlicue.

"Now, Camatzin had a wife," my grandmother would continue softly, after I had supplied her with a fresh cigarette, "of noble lineage, like himself.
She was called the loving wife, the saintly woman, by the hearth and in the
temple; and her name was Coatlicue.[7]

"Coatlicue sees the night arrive and turn darker and darker. The owl sings;
the husband delays longer than usual. The wind moans in the forest, and the
branches bend as in prayer. When the hunters return at last, their arrival startles Coatlicue, as they had not announced their coming with the usual cries
of victory. On their shoulders they bring the spoils of the day—the torn body
of Camatzin! Coatlicue embraces the corpse of Camatzin, and her children
gaze with tear-blurred eyes at the relic that death has sent them."

After a moving description of that first night of bereavement—a description in which the mystic voices of nature sounded their significant notes, my
grandmother would proceed to recite in measured rhetoric the spiritual
stages by which Coatlicue found consolation in religion. For the Aztecs, apart
from and above their hero demigods, to one of whom this saintly widow was
destined to give birth, worshipped an invisible Ruler of the Universe.

"Daily, when the afternoon falls, Coatlicue burns incense in the temple to
the god of her ancestors, at the feet of whose image her beloved Camatzin
had deposited a thousand times the laurels of his victories in the hunt and
in war.[8] Religion is the consolation unique in these afflictions. When cries
the soul, only one balsam exists to cure its wound. Pray, souls that cry, if
you wish that your pains be diminished!

"Arrived the autumn, and the afternoons became painted with rich reds,
the nights tepid and clear. The first night of full moon bathed in its pale
light the temple and Coatlicue, who prayed there. That night she felt a

---

6. Ironwood club used by some indigenous
peoples.
7. The mother of Huitzilopochtli. * * * This goddess has been a central figure in Chicana litera-

ture and revisionist literary theory.
8. I.e., he offered sacrifices to the god. In ancient
Greece, laurel leaves symbolized victory.

certain pleasure in her weeping. It was no longer that which tears the heart in order to come forth; no, it was the sweet balsam that cures a wound. When her children saw her coming in, they felt themselves happy, because for the first time they saw her smile."

My grandmother would dwell significantly on that smile, which seemed to mark a vague annunciation in the legend of miraculous birth, to be followed in the morning by a miracle of conception[9] narrated with a naïve brevity which always took my breath away.

"Then came the *aurora*,[1] and it was the first day that the heavens had beautiful color and light since the first day of orphanage. Ran Coatlicue to the temple, and censed the idol and cleaned the floor carefully, according to her custom. The sun was ascending when a white cloud concealed the radiant face of the king of the heavens.

"Lifts Coatlicue her eyes, and fixes them in space. With all the colors of the rainbow appears one brilliant little cloud that, tearing itself from heaven, reaches the temple: it was a ball of plumes; not more brilliant have the birds of the earth. It rolled over the altar, and fell to the floor. Coatlicue, with respectful gesture, took the plumes and guarded them in the bosom of her white robe. She censed the idol anew, prayed, and started for home. Before descending the last step of the temple she looked in her bosom for the plumes, but they had vanished!"

Such was the conception of the Mexican god of war, and it brought strife into the home of Coatlicue. All ignorant of the miracle that had been wrought, the children of Camatzin presumed to be scandalized at the ineffable happiness that had descended upon their mother, and to conspire against her life. Her own daughter was the malignant ringleader, taunting her two brothers with cowardice, and invoking vengeance in the name of the dead father's honor. And she, with her younger brother, sealed a pact of blood. Their mother felt a change in their regard, and trembled with fear before them, and marveled greatly at the remembrance of the celestial token that had disappeared in her bosom. Meditating on her unworthiness, she deemed it impossible that she should have been chosen by the divinity to engender a god, and she went to the temple to pray for light.

In sharp whispers, with narrowed eyes, my grandmother would go on to describe how the two conspirators followed their mother furtively into the gloom of the temple. Armed with a knife, the son fell upon her as she prayed. A terrible cry filled the space.

"Son of mine, stop thy hand! Wait! Give heed!"

"Adulteress!"

She feared not death, but wished to pray for the assassin, whose fate, she knew, would be more dreadful than his crime. But now sounded a new voice, a stentorian voice which made the temple quake:

"Mother, fear not! I will save thee!"

How it thrilled, the voice of *mamagrande*, as she repeated the first words of the god! And how it thrilled the little heart of the never-wearied listener! And then:

---

9. In Christianity, the terms *miracle of conception*, *annunciation*, and *miraculous birth* refer, respectively, to God's impregnation of the Virgin Mary, Mary's receiving the news of her impending motherhood, and Mary's giving birth to Jesus. 1. Dawn.

"The hills repeat the echo of those words. All space shines with a beautiful light, which bathes directly the face of Coatlicue. The assassin remains immobile, and the sister mute with terror, as from the bosom of Coatlicue springs forth a being gigantic, strange. His head is covered with the plumage of hummingbirds; in his right hand he carries the destructive *macana*, on his left arm the shining shield. Irate the face, fierce the frown. With one blow of the *macana*, he strikes his brother lifeless, and with another his sister, the instigator of the crime. Thus was born the potent Huitzilopochtli, protector-genius of the Aztecs."

And Coatlicue, the gentle Coatlicue of my childish love? Throned in clouds of miraculously beautiful coloring, she was forthwith transported to heaven. Once I voiced the infantile view that the fate of Coatlicue was much more charming than that of the Virgin Mary, who had remained on this sad earth as the wife of a carpenter; but *mamagrande* was so distressed, and signed my forehead and her own so often, and made me repeat so many credos, and disquieted me so with a vision of a feathered Apache coming to carry me off to the mountains, that I was brought to a speedy realization of my sin, and never repeated it. Ordinarily *mamagrande* would conclude pacifically:

"Such, attentive little daughter mine, is the legend narrated to the Aztec priests by the forests, the waters, and the birds. And on Sunday, when *papacito*[2] carries thee to the cathedral, fix it in thy mind that the porch, foundation, and courtyard of that saintly edifice remain from the great temple built by our warrior ancestors for the worship of the god Huitzilopochtli. Edifice immense and majestic, it extended to what today is called the Street of the Silversmiths, and that of the Old Bishop's House, and on the north embraced the streets of the Incarnation, Santa Teresa, and Monte Alegre.[3] I am a little fatigued, *chiquita*.[4] Rock thy little old one to sleep."

May 1914

2. Your daddy.
3. Literally, Festive Mountain (Spanish). *Incarnation*: in Christianity, Jesus Christ as the union of divinity with humanity. *Santa Teresa*: Teresa of

Ávila (1515–1582), Spanish mystic, nun, and writer; venerated as a saint by the Roman Catholic Church.
4. My dear little girl.

---

# FABIOLA CABEZA DE BACA GILBERT
## ca. 1894–1991

Along with Adelina "Nina" Otero-Warren's *Old Spain in Our Southwest* (1936) and Cleofas Jaramillo's *Romance of a Little Village Girl* (1955), Fabiola Cabeza de Baca Gilbert's *We Fed Them Cactus* (1954) forms a trio of writings by women that describe the bygone era of late-colonial Spanish civilization in Arizona and New Mexico. As discussed in the "Acculturation" introduction, politicized Latino scholarship of the post-1960s generation generally rejected these works and what was seen as the "Spanish fantasy heritage" they conveyed. In the past decade, the trio has been resurrected, even termed "politically subversive," by Latina and feminist critics. And though "domestic" works such as these traditionally were not included in literary histories, literary critics now embrace them—as conveyors of domestic culture and manners akin to the family memoir and as an important element in the recovery of women's literature of the Southwest.

Fabiola Cabeza de Baca was born into an affluent ranching family in La Liendre, a town (now a ghost town) in northeastern New Mexico. The date of her birth is disputed, with various biographers stating it as anywhere between 1894—the date she gave when she entered college—and 1898. Her mother died when Fabiola was four years old, and she was raised by her highly literate father and his mother, whose stories of the Spanish past made a deep impression on Fabiola. She attended the Loretto Academy, in Las Vegas, New Mexico, and later became a teacher in a rural area before, in 1921, graduating with a teaching degree from New Mexico Normal (now Highlands) University. In 1929, she earned a second bachelor's degree, in home economics, from New Mexico State University, in Las Cruces, and entered the New Mexico Extension Service as a home demonstration agent. This career— teaching families about the topics and techniques of home economics—led Cabeza de Baca Gilbert to write about food and then to write about food preparation as a cultural signifier.

Her first book, *Los alimentos y su preparación* (Food and Its Preparation, 1934), was followed by *Boletín de Conservar* (Conservation Bulletin, 1935) and then, written in English, *Historic Cookery* (1939) and *The Good Life* (1949). *We Fed Them Cactus*, excerpted here, is probably Cabeza de Baca Gilbert's best-known work and was her third in English. The change from Spanish to English most likely gave her access to a larger market than she had enjoyed in her native tongue; it can also be seen, recent critics have noted, as undermining Anglo-American society's image of the Hispanic woman as an illiterate peasant.

---

## *FROM* WE FED THEM CACTUS

### *From* II. El Cuate

\* \* \*

#### 3. *The Rodeo*

"It was here on the Carrizito that we held the rodeo that year," El Cuate began.[1] "It was in 1886 and we had had an unusually dry spring. We held the rodeo in July."

"Don Manuel Salcedo, (may he rest in peace), was the promoter of the rodeo. He was an aristocrat if there ever was one, and he was wealthy. His herds roamed from the Salado to the Llano Estacado,[2] although by 1886 he was being pushed back by the XIT Syndicate which had moved in the year before.

---

1. The storyteller in this chapter, El Cuate (the Twin), is the ranch hand at the Spear Bar Ranch, which is owned by the narrator's father. "He was a real western character," the narrator explains in the previous chapter, "reared on the Llano." Llano County, the site of the ranch, is in central Texas.

2. A region in the southwestern United States that encompasses parts of eastern New Mexico and northwestern Texas, including the South Plains and parts of the Texas Panhandle. *The Salado*: Salado Creek, a waterway in San Antonio, Texas.

"There were two rodeos during the year. One was held in early summer and the other just before the fall, unless it was a dry year, and then there would be only one. A rodeo, in those days truly meant a roundup, not a public exhibition.

"Señor Antonio Almanzar was the cook and I was his assistant, with Santiago Estrada as the chore boy. Señor Antonio, who was as stern as he was jovial, was Don Manuel's handyman and a better man he could not have picked; honesty and loyalty towards his *patrón* were his best qualities.

"I can still hear his voice. Before daybreak, we awakened to his cry:

"'Juan, Santiago, Felipe, it is almost daylight, and you lie there as if you were gentlemen of leisure! You have no consciences to warn you that you are stealing precious time from your *patrón*. Get up, and to your duties. Juan, get the *remuda*. Santiago, start the fire for the coffee. Felipe, roll up the beds and get the saddles ready.'

"After sleeping on the hard ground, you would think that we were glad to get up, but we liked our sleep as well as you youngsters do," he said to me and Luis, winking with his white eye and looking at Papá. Papá was not an early riser but his children and the cowboys were up at dawn.

El Cuate, smiling, continued, "Santiago was bold and he answered Señor Antonio, 'If you were not so conscientious, Don Manuel would not be swimming in wealth while we drink black bitter coffee and eat black bread.'

"Felipe just turned over and growled, but when Señor Antonio's voice sounded like thunder, weakly one by one, we got up and started the morning chores, rubbing our eyes as if that would help us see in the dark.

"Juan had been gone almost an hour for the *remuda*, the string of horses.

"We had few matches in those days, but we carried candles which we lighted by striking two flint stones with a piece of cured cloth between them. Santiago lighted a small candle beside his bed, put on his boots and he was dressed. He then lighted the sticks which Señor Antonio had been gathering all the while, and soon a big bonfire was crackling and lighting the surrounding sleepers, who like white specters were seen rising from their beds as if to the sound of an alarm clock.

"The morning was as still as death, with only the hobbling of the horses heard in the distance or an occasional howl of a coyote which to the human ear sounded like a whole pack. The sound of the coffee mill furnished the music to the late risers, and not until the smell of the boiling coffee from the black can on the coals reached their nostrils, did they jump up from their happy dreams to a long day—rounding up cattle for the annual rodeo.

"Before all the men were around the breakfast circle, Juan's whistling was heard as he was approaching with the horses. *Yip! Yip!* went out from the cowboys, meaning 'Good morning and thanks for letting us sleep that extra hour.' Our breakfast was of beans, prunes, sourdough bread, jerky or fresh meat, and black coffee.

"Every cattleman who owned a thousand head of cattle or more made up a rodeo with his hired hands and as many stray men as wanted to go along. A stray man was usually the hired hand of a small cattle owner, or he might be the owner himself.

"Every rodeo had a *mayordomo*,[3] and for this one we had Don Andrés Garduño, Don Manuel Salcedo's head man. We all respected Don Andrés, a sturdy upright fellow, who knew how to give orders. When he gave them I always thought he should have been a general. I feared him more than I did Colonel Canby at Valverde during the Civil War."

El Cuate brushed away a tear as he continued:

"There were many fearless men in those days. They had to be or they would not have followed the rodeos.

"Don Andrés always mounted his horse when he gave orders, and as he started to give the command that day, he half leaned on the saddle:

"'Manuel García and Teles Urbán, follow the trail to Paloma; Andrés Guzmán and Juan Arellano, round up the cattle on the Laguna Colorada; Felipe Tafoya and Carmen Sierra, follow the old trail into San Lorenzo; Felipe Mora and Juan Peralta, your journey will be towards the Mesa Rica; Narciso Paez, Juanito Trujillo, and Rafael Baca, scour the Monte de Pajarito for cattle; Fidel Tapia and Mauricio Lucero, will go to Don Tomás Cabeza de Baca's sheep camp and tell Señor Ramón, the *caporal*,[4] to send me five fat lambs. Ride until you find the sheep, for we must feed our men well or their *patrones* will take me for a miser.'

"As the men on horseback took to different directions, Señor Antonio and I watched them until the last man disappeared over the horizon. It was our job to feed the men, so back we went to our camp. Santiago had been cleaning beans by the campfire and we were always glad to see daylight for that meant fewer pebbles in our beans. As he cleaned the beans, he kept up a weird monotonous song until Señor Antonio, out of patience, called to him in rather strong language, 'Santiago, change your tune or I shall be singing it myself.'

"Santiago was a good worker, but he was born to try men's patience. He seldom changed expression, so we never knew when he was serious or when he was trying to mortify us. He changed the tune of his song but he started another one so mournful that he drove me to desperation. To pass away the time, the cowboys would come to terms only by selling what annoyed their companions. I had to do something to stop Santiago's mournful tune, so I said, 'Sell me your tune and remember after it is paid for, it belongs to me and you cannot use it without my permission.' Santiago thought for a moment, then he replied, 'I'll sell it to you for that new quirt that you brought from Revuelto.'

"The quirt was a priceless possession, but I had to respond to the challenge so I said, 'The quirt is yours and the tune is mine.' While we waited for the return of the *vaqueros*, the cowboys, with the herds, we had to keep up our spirits with jokes and songs or tales.

"At the first sound of the *Yip! Yip!* I put wood into the fire to start the coffee boiling in the same black can which I had used at so many rodeos.

"It was toward midafternoon before all the men returned to camp with hundreds of cattle to be branded. The quiet air of the camp was soon broken by the bawling of cattle and the country became a Sodom of noise and dust from all directions with the *vaqueros* yelling and the cattle tramping.

---

3. Majordomo: the person who runs the enterprise.
4. Foreman.

"The men who remained at camp had eaten their noon meal. They saddled their horses and started out to meet the approaching herds in order to relieve these *vaqueros* who were bringing in the cattle.

"I can still see each man as he galloped into camp, sweaty and dusty. Santiago, our mascot, had the chore of unsaddling sweaty horses as the men dismounted. We watered the horses and then he turned them over to the *caballerango*[5] in charge of them.

"The men were always hungry and I felt great pride because they praised my cooking.

"While the men were eating, the branding irons were being heated to start the marking of cattle.

"Herd after herd approached the camp, until we had about a thousand head of cattle. I saw rodeos where two and three thousand head were gathered for one day's branding. Sí señores, there was almost one cow to each blade of grass in those days." (This, of course, entitled El Cuate to a fresh chew of tobacco.)

"When all was ready, Don Andrés mounted his cutting horse and, with four of his best hands, started separating the cattle with Don Manuel's brand."

"The cutting horse was swift and had plenty of sense, and when its rider spied a cow with his brand, the horse knew which cow or steer he had to follow, and he would plunge after the animal, driving it out of its herd and into the day herd with a quick rush. The cattle which had to be branded were separated, as I said, and this bunch was called the day herd.

"We had no corrals in those days, but the men on horseback made the enclosure which held the cattle together and, believe me, those longhorns were vicious-looking animals. But since they were used to being rounded up, they were no trouble, unless there were stampedes.

"I remember rodeos when it took days and days to round up the cattle. But by 1886, rodeos had taken smaller proportions as there was less territory to cover. In my youth, the rodeo boundaries were the sierras to the north, the Texas line to the east, what is now Roswell on the south and the Manzano mountains on the west.

"On that first day of the Carrizito rodeo, we only branded one hundred head of heifers and steers with Don Manuel's brand.

"The cowboys all were expert riders and ropers, but we had professionals. Teles Urbán and Carmen Sierra never missed an animal from the first throw of the lasso, and in every rodeo in which they took part they were the roping hands.

"The branding was no different from what you did today, only it seems to me that the men were more hardened and fearless than you boys.

"It seems only yesterday that we were branding, and that I saw Carmen Sierra ride through the herd, throw the rope over the calves' heads or hind feet and drag them toward the branding irons where the ground crew waited. There was Tito Lucero, ready to grab the calf and he threw the animal down. In the wink of an eye, Laureano García had taken hold of it by the front, grabbed the foreleg, and pinned the neck down with his knee while Juan Arellano (in a sitting posture) pulled the hind leg towards him—and the animal was ready for the brand and other operations. The boys on the ground

5. Ranch hand who takes care of the horses.

crew knew whose calf it was, and the roper always announced whose brand the calf's mother bore, so there were no mistakes.

"There were professional branders like your papá is today. He always followed the branding iron—but that's education for you, for those who could not read might have put the letters upside down.

"The burning hot iron was put on the proper place and the brand imprinted. Another man did the earmarking and another the castrating. The only difference from today is that in order to get through with the many herds, more men did the different chores which a small crew performs now.

"Cattle with various brands roamed all over the unfenced Llano, and the cowboys from each outfit were constantly on the watch for their stock as they rode the range all through the year. The spaciousness of the land did not permit them to know exactly how many head of each brand grazed on the plains, but the rodeos brought many surprises.

"The evening meal was the social affair of the day. Señor Antonio and I were very popular with the boys—they called us mamá, sweetheart, or honey. We fed not only the rodeo outfit, but many of the cattle owners who dropped in for meals if the rodeo grounds were within riding distance to their ranches.

"Besides the lambs which we got from nearby camps, we also butchered one or two mavericks, calves which had escaped the branding iron the previous year and belonged to the first cowboy who caught them and put his brand on them. Señor Antonio and I always picked the fattest ones to feed our men and it took a lot for a bunch of cowboys. Their work was hard and the hours were long between meals.

"After supper the boys not on night duty would gather around the campfires and sing ballads and *corridos*. Juan Arellano was a good singer, but there were many others, and we had poets, too. Our poet and storyteller on that rodeo was Fidel Tapia, and he certainly had imagination and good memory. His father and I had been *Comancheros*—Indian "traders"—and buffalo hunters together. As the darkness fell upon us, the music from the different groups around the campfire came softly, bringing cheer to the men tired from the day's labors.

"The first night, the men retired early and before the last embers died the boys were resting on their hard beds on the ground. Each man used his saddle for a pillow, wrapped himself with a blanket and took chances on lying on safe soil for the night.

"The bellowing of cattle, the bawling of calves, the sounds of hoofs stirring up dust, and the hobbling of horses were the nightly lullabies which brought sound sleep to us, for we were accustomed to it.

"The herds had to be guarded at night because it had taken almost the whole day to round up the cattle and all of them had not been separated.

"There were four shifts, with two or three men to the shift. Each shift was called a *cuarto*. The first shift was the coveted one and it usually went to the foreman's favorites, but the cowboys were good sports and, although they grumbled, they took it like men. Yet in the old days before 1886, there were even killings on account of the shifts. Nowadays the men, like the cattle, have become more tame. I felt sorry for the boys, for they had chosen a hard vocation and it was their cross to bear.

"The cattle bedded down at night and the night riders rode around and around the herd whistling or singing. The music kept the cattle aware of the riders and prevented stampedes.

"I must tell you about the stampedes. They were terrible. They could be started by a sudden peal of thunder, a large dry weed blown towards the herd, a coyote's yelp, or often a cause unknown.

"The cattle would dash together, as if driven, and run as fast as their hoofs could carry them. Woe to the man caught in their path! If his horse stumbled or if he were thrown from his seat, it was sure death.

"The stampede which remains vivid in my memory happened in 1880, just as we reached Plaza Larga with the rodeo.

"By the time we had finished supper and the first shift started, the sky had clouded and we knew the storm would reach our camp before morning. Flashes of lightning were visible even while we were eating. We knew we were in for a good soaking, but what worried the boys was the possibility of a stampede.

"There would be no sleep that night and all the boys had to be on hand if needed.

"The clouds moved faster and faster, and with them came flashes of lightning and heavy thunder. The lightning which struck in every direction made the cattle restless and the boys were on the alert.

"The storm reached its peak and down came the rain in heavy sheets. The whole camp was in confusion and all at once lightning struck close to the herd. The stampede started. The boys tried to head it off, but the wind was against them. They had to be careful that they would not be knocked down. The lightning flashes made everything visible, but just as quickly the darkness seemed more intense.

"The boys kept whistling and singing but the cattle paid no heed. They were on the run. The boys were all trying to hold them down at the risk of their lives; they whistled; they rode hard—but the cattle were beyond control.

"Señor Antonio and I had stayed in the wagon and all we could do was pray, for hardened as we were, we remembered God and we prayed. We knew there might not be one of the men left if the cattle struck their paths. In a stampede the cattle stay together; they become blinded as they run. And the cattle that night were not only blind, they were mad.

"I do not know how many miles the cattle had traveled, but at dawn, one by one the boys came back to camp exhausted. The rain had stopped and the cattle were under control, and although not a man was hurt, they were a sorry bunch. The cattle had to be guarded, so there was little rest for any of them.

"During the day's work, the *vaqueros* changed mounts as many as four times because their riding was hard. The cowmen held a high regard for their horses and would not exhaust them by riding them too long.

"There was always a *caballerango*, and for this rodeo Gabriel Anaya had the job. His duties were to drive the horses to the improvised corral which was enclosed by *reatas*, ropes. The horses were well trained, and it was seldom, if ever, that a horse tried to jump over the rope.

"Rafael Sánchez and Polo López had charge of the horses and when new mounts were wanted they roped the horses and the owner stood ready with the bridle in hand to put it on his horse. Each *vaquero* rode the horses which he claimed as his own and he usually had from seven to ten for *remuda*, change of mount. He may not have owned one, but a horse was as much a part of him as the pistol and holster which he never took off; his favorite was the cutting horse and his next best was his night horse.

"In order to have breakfast ready early, we had to start it the night before, so we buried a pot of beans and put our meat to barbecue. In the morning, we set Dutch ovens to heat while we made the dough for bread and started the coffee. We always had black coffee, as Santiago had remarked that morning.

"Some Easterner coming to New Mexico for the first time observed, 'In New Mexico there are more rivers and less water, and more cows and less milk than in any other country,' and he was right. We raise cows for beef; we cannot starve the calves in order to drink the milk.

"Before going to bed, I banked the fire and I hardly had gone to sleep when Señor Antonio's usual morning greeting started.

The second day of the rodeo followed the same pattern as the first. Señor Antonio made his daily speech and the men under him swore at him with greater strength, only to do his bidding in the same humble way once they had their boots on.

"A few of the men went out to scour the country for any stray cattle, but the other men kept on with the branding as we did not finish that day or the next. It took a whole week to brand all the calves.

"That evening as we listened to the guitars and to the discussions of the men, Don Andrés turned to the men and asked, 'Why did we have such few calves to brand for Don Manuel today? I thought we sighted a large bunch of cows with his brand on the Mesa Rica as we came along two days ago.'

"Juan Arellano replied, 'We found the cows, *patrón*, but they were without calves; their udders were bursting with milk, so we know they had calves.'

"'Thieves again,' murmured Don Andrés. 'We must look for tracks tomorrow and see if we cannot find the marauders.'

"He stood up and called, 'I want all of Don Manuel Salcedo's cowboys to come forward.'

"The word was passed on around the camp and all the men not on night duty stood before their *caporal*.

"'Boys,' he said, 'Tomorrow you are not helping with the branding, you are going hunting for cattle rustlers. They cannot be very far and since unbranded calves are their loot, you cannot miss. All of you start at Mesa Rica, divide in pairs and follow all tracks leading to the four directions.'

"'Be careful boys, I do not want any accidents, and do not shoot, unless it is in self-defense, for if the law is to be applied let it be done by the proper authorities.'

"Mauricio Sena came forward, 'I am to be *vigil*, on guard, at midnight, señor, could you send someone in my place?'

"'I shall take your place as night rider tonight. Now all of you go and get your rest, for you must be on your way before daybreak.'

"A sad bunch were Don Andrés' men as they started on a mission, which all the cowboys knew might end in tragedy, and, as they left that morning, all the men wished them good luck and Godspeed.

"Six days elapsed and the men were ready to move camp to the Rio Colorado country. Many of the cowboys had gone ahead to announce the coming of the rodeo so that other men might join the outfit.

"The camp moved slowly, traveling about twenty miles each day, for remember there were no roads and the wagons moved with difficulty over the rough beargrass (yucca) country.

"The rodeo camp consisted of two wagons and about a hundred head of horses. The chuck wagon, which Señor Antonio and I drove, carried the food and the few cooking utensils. The hoodlum's wagon,[6] which was driven by a flunky, carried the bedrolls, branding irons, ammunition and guns.

"When the men of each outfit finished branding its herds, they left the rodeo group and departed for their headquarters.

"The last night in each place was spent in bidding adieu to friends and making promises of meeting at a fiesta, *baile* (dance), or the next rodeo, so there was a great deal of merrymaking to make up for the time when work put them to bed early.

"As I said before, there were plenty of musicians and singers to make the evening gay. The storytellers were always popular and when the men tired of music, they surrounded the storytelling group.

"Tales of buffalo hunts were very popular by those having followed the trail into the Ceja and the Llano. Usually the storytellers were old men who no longer rode the range but served as cooks, *caballerangos*, or guides.

"Señor Antonio soon called to the men, 'If we can make good time, tomorrow we can reach San Hilario in time for the evening preparation for the fiesta.' 'Sí señores,' Alejo sighed. 'The lovely señoritas there are worth a day's hard ride.' 'To bed and let's dream about them,' chimed in several voices.

"Long before daybreak, Señor Antonio had the camp moving. We reached the Gallegos ranch by sunup and the men stopped there long enough to eat breakfast and to be joined by Don Jesús María's cowboys.

"To our surprise, we were met by four of Don Andrés' men who had left us four days before. One of the men had his arm in a sling, and his head bandaged.

"Señor Andrés came forward and asked, 'Did you catch up with the thieves?'

"'Yes, sir,' answered Juan Arellano. 'We followed their trail into the Mesa Rica where we surprised them at their camp on the Venado Spring. It was a hard fight, for they were well prepared, but by strategy we caught every one of them. Manuel Quintana was slightly wounded. We would have taken the law in our hands and the thieves would be hanging by their necks, but we decided that they would suffer more if we tied them up and took them on to Puerto de Luna to be tried. Rafael and Juanito are taking care of them and the other boys are driving the calves, which they had not killed, back to their mothers.'

"'Did you brand the calves?' asked Señor Andrés.

"'Yes, we did, we stopped at San Lorenzo for help.'

"The caravan continued on its way, being joined by different outfits all along the way to San Hilario."

---

6. Or hoodlum wagon, a second wagon, used to carry gear and supplies.

### 4. Fiesta at San Hilario

The first peal of thunder made us aware of the approaching rain, but the storm was still thirty miles away.

El Cuate seemed not to have heard. He was far away in the days of Spanish fiestas and as the lightning brightened the *ambiente* around us, he continued with his tale:

"In San Hilario, they were expecting the rodeo. We had made good time and arrived there on Santiago's eve, and as the last bell was ringing for Vespers in the Chapel of San Hilario, our group reached the outskirts of the village.

"This chapel was built by Don Hilario Gonzáles, who had long since passed away. Don Hilario, in his day, ran more cattle on the Llano than we had gathered in our rodeo at Carrizito; his wagons traveling from the plains to Las Vegas were counted by the hundreds. May he rest in peace!

"In San Hilario on that day ruled another *patrón*, and I reckon there must have been at least twenty families there. The *patrón* with his sons and daughters, their children and the *empleados*, employees, with their families, made up the settlement, the latter being as much a part of the family as the children of the *patrón*.

"Every man, woman, and child in the village, as well as families from the surrounding plazas, had gathered in the church for Vesper service. Bonfires were burning around the church.

"The sound of singing reached our camp and the boys who were more devout, or those who had reached the age when salvation seemed important, joined the procession which was already forming.

"While Señor Antonio and I started the meal, the boys were making preparations for the *baile* which followed Vespers. We knew there would be few boys there to eat but it was a matter of habit to prepare food.

"On stacks of bedrolls, there were men getting haircuts and shaves, for we had boys who were pretty good barbers; some were shaving themselves beside the wagon and others had gone to get a dip in the village ditch. Clean shirts, socks and underwear came out of knapsacks and *pronto*, the men were ready for the ball.

"I was not too old to enjoy whirling the pretty señoritas, and in those days, as today on the ranches, no one ever got too old to dance.

"You should have seen your papá then. It was his first dance as well as his first rodeo." (Papá only smiled as he puffed hard on his pipe. He was more interested in the rain just then.)

"By eight o'clock, the dance hall was filled and the *baile* had started.

"First came the march in which everyone took part, husbands, wives, brothers and sisters, and some daring young fellows with their sweethearts danced together.

"The musicians with their violins, guitars and accordions were seated on a platform. Ramón Atencio, Francisco Anaya, Juan Romero, Agustín Sena and Manuel Ortega had come from San Lorenzo to play for the dance.

"After the march, the *bastonero*, the master of ceremonies, took charge, and only those whom he called could get a partner for the dances that followed. As a sign of courtesy to visitors, one of our men, Felipe Tafoya, was chosen as the *bastonero*. He was partial to your papá, and were the señoritas glad! For his first dance, your papá certainly danced like a professional.

"It was the custom, when anyone danced for the first time, to take the person and carry him in arms around the hall. This was called the *amarre*. Before he was allowed to go, someone close in friendship or relationship had to redeem him. This redemption was the *desempeño*. The *desempeño* usually was a promise of a dance at a fixed date. Juan María Quintana, your grandfather's *caporal*, came to your papá's rescue by promising a dance on San Lorenzo's day, the tenth of August, as we had hoped to reach San Lorenzo with the rodeo on that date.

"There were many beautiful señoritas at the dance and good dancers as well. The girls were well chaperoned and it was not easy for lovers to have much opportunity for lovemaking, yet they managed, and after one of these *bailes*, the families of many prospective grooms went in search of brides for their sons. It was still the custom for the parents to make matches, but American influence was becoming more and more evident as the years rolled on, and the young folks were more at liberty to choose their mates.

"The dance was a beautiful sight. The señoritas in voluminous skirts, tight waists and elegant jewelry, were swung around by the cowboys of two languages, in fancy boots, bright shirts and bandannas. The tiny feet of the women were lost in the fast rhythm of the polkas, schottisches, waltzes and varsovianas, and only the boots could be seen and heard.

"The boys from our camp and others who were joining the rodeo at this point, kept assembling for the merrymaking. They were greeted and welcomed by the men of the village as they came in, with the usual greeting of how are your parents and your family, or your *patrón*, heard with every new arrival. The ever-important questions of have you had much rain down your way and how was the calf crop this year, were asked of each one.

"As the dance continued, the conversation was kept up by the older men with an occasional drink. They discussed the weather, cattle bogged down in the creeks and water holes, cattle rustling, packs of wolves attacking the stock, marriages, deaths. Such were the stories exchanged by people hungry for outside social contact in those days of limited communication.

"During the dance those who had prestige with the *bastonero*, would choose the piece to their liking and soon the *músicos* were striking a polka or waltz and putting as much fervor in it as the dancers on the floor.

"As the musicians struck the first waltz, the audience looked around to see who had requested it. The first couple on the floor was the answer: Narciso Paez had Rosa Salcedo in his arms. Every eye was upon them. The couple seemed to have been made for each other and as they waltzed and waltzed, they seemed to be in a world all of their own, quite oblivious of the crowd around them.

"Doña María Inez de Salcedo drew her rebozo to her face as if to hide for her daughter the gaze of the crowd.

"Everyone for miles around the country, knew that Narciso and Rosa were in love with each other, but the match did not please Don Manuel Salcedo, only because Narciso's father was a poor man according to Don Manuel's way of reckoning wealth. The Paezes had less money, but better blood than the Salcedos.

"This has nothing to do with my story, but I cannot help but mention it, as I can never recall that rodeo without thinking of the tragedy which happened as we wound up in Revuelto in September.

"When the dance was over, one by one the boys came back to camp to rest from the long day's travel and a night of pleasure. I watched Narciso as he lay on his bed; he had that far away look which had seemed to accompany him since he became of a marriageable age.

"In those days, dances broke up at daylight for those who came long distances had to wait for daylight to travel home. It became a custom, even when people were remaining for the feast the following day.

"By ten o'clock next morning the bells were ringing to call the people to hear Mass in honor of Santiago,[7] and every home was open to guests and prepared to feed anyone who would share its hospitality.

"Señor Antonio and I knew there was no use preparing a meal, so we joined the crowds in the village and partook of Don Juan Peña's hospitality, for there were no social lines drawn as to who should sit at the hosts' tables. Everyone was treated alike. The men were fed first; I do not know when the women ate.

"In the afternoon we had horse races, bronco riding, and the cock race.

"The boys saddled their most vicious horses and gave performances of their skill, for there were the señoritas, each watching to see how brave was the man of her heart. Often a cowboy lost his seat and landed on *tierra firme*,[8] provoking a great deal of mirth.

"The cock race was the main event, because San Hilario and San Lorenzo were competing for the *corrida*, or run. This sport, like all sports, was colorful as well as cruel. Six live roosters had been buried head down in the ground midway between the two villages. The opposite teams, on horses trained for the game, were ready to start. A shot was fired to send off the cock racers. They dug their spurs into their horses and off they went. The leader of San Hilario contestants was off before the spectators had time to focus their eyes on him. The San Lorenzo contestants pursued him and at every quarter of a mile a *mampuesto*, or guard, was ready to take the *gallo*[9] away from him. The successful rider with horse foaming at its mouth and covered with beady sweat, reached the plaza while the other contenders were struggling with the *mampuestos* all along the way. As I remember, the San Hilario team took four roosters and was declared winners.

"The excited people cheered and shouted. The men and even the women had large wagers on the *corrida*, and it was a long while before the enthusiasm broke down.

"After a night and day of merrymaking, we were ready to retire, but not a boy was fit to do any work on the morrow. The rodeo must continue and again next morning we listened to Señor Antonio's daily sermon.

"We spent ten days in San Hilario and then moved on to San Lorenzo. San Lorenzo had been the home of the López family. Don Francisco López had the most beautiful daughters I have ever seen. Those of my class could only look at them, but there were pretty girls in my class too, only we always like to touch forbidden objects to see if they are real. Don Francisco had long been dead and his family scattered throughout New Mexico, but in the village their influence still could be felt.

"This was to be your papá's dance of *desempeño* and Juan María Quintana was not one to be outdone. He had sent a messenger to Las Vegas to bring

---

7. Saint James; according to the New Testament, one of Jesus' 12 disciples; the patron saint of Spain.  8. Firm ground.  9. Cock, rooster.

the best of musicians and they were there when we arrived in San Lorenzo, but your papá can tell you about that dance."

Papá did not show any interest, as he never discussed his love affairs or youthful sprees before his children.

The first drops of rain began to be felt, so the audience quickly moved into the house, much to my chagrin. It might be years before El Cuate would be in the mood for storytelling again.

But no, El Cuate seemed to have his mind on the story which he had been telling, for as we sat in the house he remarked:

"Who would now believe that there had been gay and happy plazas on the Llano?"

I took advantage of his word, and to start him off again I asked, "What was the tragedy in Revuelto about which you spoke as you told about the *baile*?"

It was like winding a clock, and El Cuate started with greater interest.

"By September the rodeo reach Revuelto ready to wind up the season.

"We had made San Rafael, Saladito, Plaza Larga. Each of these had their chapels, but we missed the patron saints' feasts of San Rafael, Nuestro Padre Jesús, and Santo Niño. Nevertheless in each place the rodeo crowd was welcomed with a dance.

"The boys were retiring after the *baile*. I had been in bed for several hours, and although when I went to bed, I missed Narciso Paez' mount, I gave it no thought, for he had been at the dance early in the evening.

"The boys were whispering among themselves as they lay on their beds, but I thought they were telling about their conquests at the *baile*.

"In the morning before Señor Antonio's voice started, I heard galloping hoofs approaching. Tito Lucero came towards my bed. I could not see him, but I knew every boy by instinct. Because he dismounted, I knew something was not well, so I asked: 'What happened, Tito?' He and Narciso were inseparable. He could not talk, he only lay his head on my shoulder and wept. This relieved him and he spoke. 'Narciso is dead. He was shot by Don Manuel. He and Rosa were eloping.'

"I made some coffee as quickly as was possible over a campfire. The boys did not have to be awakened by Señor Antonio, for all had heard Tito's horse. Before the coffee boiled, they were getting the details from him.

"Felipe Tafoya, who was always strong tempered, cried, 'We shall lynch that old tyrant,' and he meant it. Señor Andrés came forward and said, 'Be careful boys, I know how you feel. We all loved Narciso but we cannot bring him back to life by revenge or any other means, and I know he would not have wanted any of you boys to stain your hands with blood. The law will take its course.'

"'The rodeo is breaking up, and those of you who wish to pay respects to the Paez family can move to San Rafael.'

"The whole rodeo traveled to San Rafael; we were all there to bury our pal."

"What became of Rosa?" I asked.

El Cuate, brushing a tear, replied, "Don Manuel took her home and forbade her to leave the house, but the servants said that he need not have done that, because life for Rosa was buried in the San Rafael graveyard. On the south side of the chapel a cross marks Narciso's grave. The people there told that, after dark, a ghost appeared each year on the eve of San Rafael, while the merrymakers were reveling at the *baile*. Some said it was not a ghost, but Señorita Rosa who would ride from San Hilario to cry at her lover's grave. She and Narciso had danced together for this feast since they were children.

"Don Manuel was a broken man after that, but since he was a powerful man, only his daughter knew for sure who had murdered her lover."

1954

# LUIS MUÑOZ MARÍN
## 1898–1980

The architect of the modern political state in Puerto Rico, Luis Muñoz Marín was the son of Luis Muñoz Rivera (see p. 296), a prominent public figure who advocated autonomy under Spanish rule and, in 1897, became a member of the ruling cabinet of the brief autonomist government granted to Puerto Rico by Spain. A statesman and a writer, Muñoz Marín was born in San Juan, four months before the U.S. military invasion of the island. Because of his father's position representing Puerto Rico in the U.S. Congress, he was raised in the United States, and at different points of his life he lived in Puerto Rico, Washington, D.C., and New York City. The scholar Frances Negrón-Muntaner describes Muñoz Marín's upbringing as having made him "bilingual, bicultural, and fully conversant in the ways of Washington politics, a skill that would eventually prove invaluable two decades later when he founded his own party."

But in his early adult life Muñoz Marín was not interested in a political career. Known as *El Vate* (the Bard), he cultivated a bohemian attitude and wrote poetry and journalistic essays on a wide range of social and political issues. An avid reader, he was given to passionate discussions of Marxism, Fabianism, and other freethinking ideologies. Among his major influences was the socialist philosophy of Edwin Markham, and he translated Markham's 1899 poem "The Man with the Hoe," in which Markham announces the awakening of the underclass. In New York, Muñoz Marín met Muna Lee (1895–1965), a prominent poet, feminist, and Pan-Americanist whose pieces in *The Nation* and other publications introduced Latin American literature to the English-speaking world. They married in 1919 and had two children, but their marriage ended in 1946. For a couple of years in the early 1920s, they lived in Puerto Rico, where Muñoz Marín became connected to Puerto Rican politics, especially the island's socialist labor movement. During this brief period, he developed an awareness of the conditions and struggles of the island's impoverished and exploited working masses.

Because of his many years living in the United States and his marriage to Lee, who had important connections in New York and Washington, D.C., intellectual and political circles, Muñoz Marín began to claim his father's political legacy by cultivating his connections with island political leaders and, later on, with members of U.S. president Franklin Delano Roosevelt's administration. In 1929, he was invited by the island's Legislature to serve as Puerto Rico's economic commissioner in the United States, a position he held briefly. In 1931, he returned to Puerto Rico with his family, to make it their permanent home.

Muñoz Marín immediately joined the Partido Liberal (Liberal Party), which was then led by his father's political successor, Antonio Barceló, and which largely represented the Puerto Rican propertied and professional class. Differences between the young and charismatic Muñoz Marín and the elder leader about the best course to change Puerto Rico's colonial condition eventually created a generational split within the party. Muñoz Marín won a Senate seat in the Legislature, and during these following years he began to modify some of his earlier positions regarding the United States. Less than a decade before, he had been against the U.S.'s keeping control of Puerto Rico. But the accomplishments of Roosevelt's New Deal legislation, which had been enacted to lift the United States out of the Great Depression, persuaded him that the assistance of the federal government was crucial in alleviating the widespread poverty that afflicted most of Puerto Rico's peasant population. His more radical and populist agenda for social and political change infuriated the upholders of the colonial status quo on the island, however, and he and his followers were expelled from the Liberal Party by the old guard.

His response became the material of legend. On July 22, 1938, he founded the Partido Popular Democrático (Popular Democratic Party). Its symbol was a straw hat, in the spirit of the attire used by *jíbaros* (peasants). Its slogan was ¡*Pan, tierra y libertad!* (Bread, Land, and Liberty!). Its aim was to rally the landless and politically disenfranchised peasant electorate against the exploitative practices of U.S. corporations and break the sugar monopolies and local landowners' control of the land. Driving around the island in a beat-up Ford and promoting the party through a loudspeaker, Muñoz Marín actively ran for the Senate. In 1940, he won the election. During his tenure, he worked to help the poor; advocated land redistribution, electricity, water, and health services for all; and increased educational opportunities and employment. He also fought for Puerto Ricans to have the right to choose their own governor, and in 1948 he ran for the office. He won by a landslide and served until 1964. He then returned to the Senate, where he served until 1970.

Muñoz Marín's ideological position regarding the status of Puerto Rico was controversial. He abandoned the support for independence he had defended during his younger years, but he also rejected statehood; instead, he championed the option of the island as an *Estado Libre Asociado* (Free Associated State, or commonwealth) of the United States. In his view, this status would give Puerto Rico a degree of autonomy without severing connections with the U.S., connections he viewed as essential to the island's socioeconomic development. But the new status, granted in 1952, did not significantly alter Puerto Rico's condition as a U.S. territory. Muñoz Marín's administration implemented *Operación Manos a la Obra* (Operation Put Your Hands to Work; known in English as "Operation Bootstrap"), which had a double edge: It attracted investment from abroad with generous tax exemptions, thus creating an industrial economy and modernizing the country's infrastructure; but it also displaced agricultural workers and encouraged a large portion of its labor force to migrate to the United States. In fact, over two-thirds of the Puerto Ricans in the United States trace their ancestral departure from the island to this period. Also during Muñoz Marín's governorship, the rapid pace of U.S.-led industrialization and modernization generated intellectual debates about Americanization and its detrimental effects on Puerto Rican cultural traditions and identity. To counteract the increasing American influence, the Muñoz Marín government initiated *Operación Serenidad* (Operation Serenity), a multifaceted cultural initiative that promoted Puerto Rican cultural nationalism through the founding, in 1955, of the Instituto de Cultura Puertorriqueña (Institute for Puerto Rican Culture) and through significant investments in promoting literature and the arts.

Muñoz Marín wrote the first of the following two selections, "The Sad Case of Porto Rico," when he was living in New York; it was published in the magazine *The American Mercury* in 1929. In this piece, he discusses the island—its social, political, and economic conditions—as a neglected colony of the United States. He delivered the second selection as a speech on July 17, 1951, at a public activity in Barranquitas, Puerto Rico, commemorating his father's birthday. Muñoz Marín takes this opportunity to provide a rationale for the political-status position chosen by his administration in its quest for self-government and progress for Puerto Rico. He delivered the speech almost a year before the official inauguration of the Estado Libre Asociado de Puerto Rico.

# The Sad Case of Porto Rico

*I*

Two major problems perplex the old Spanish province of Porto Rico, arising out of its enforced relationship to the United States. One deals with the consequences of American economic development, the other with cultural Americanization. Both go to the root of the drama now being acted on that gorgeous stage; both are portentous in their potentialities.

The importance of the economic problem is obvious to all, whatever their views or interests. Americanization is more insidious. The tendency works while you sleep. It changes the expression of your eyes, the form of your paunch, the tone of your voice, your hopes of Heaven, what your neighbors and your women expect of you—all without giving you a chance to fight back, without even presenting to you the dilemma of fighting back or not. Certainly no two things are more important than to have what you want and to live as spontaneously as you can manage. These two hopes are now in process of being shot to hell in my country.

The American flag found Porto Rico penniless and content. It now flies over a prosperous factory worked by slaves who have lost their land and may soon lose their guitars and their songs. In the old days most Porto Rican peasants owned a few pigs and chickens, maybe a horse or a cow, some goats, and in some way had the use of a patch of soil. Today this modest security has been replaced by a vision of opulence. There are more things that they can't get. The margin between what they have and what they can imagine has widened monstrously. While there are many more schools for their hungry children and many more roads for their bare feet, their destiny is decidedly narrower now than it was when they were part and parcel of one of the most interesting and incompetent nationalities in the world.

In 1898 Porto Rico was a semi-feudal country, typical of the old Spanish provinces in America, willing and capable of assuming with a natural grace and a natural awkwardness its position in the Spanish commonwealth of provinces, or to venture into a simple, old-fashioned Latin-American national form. Its economics were those developed by Spain in the tropical New World: fiscally rotten, socially humble and sound. Culturally, it was a slow, calm place. Racially, it shared with Costa Rica one peculiarity: a predominantly unmixed European peasantry—if Spain be Europe.

Schools were few, roads were fewer; chickens laid eggs under thatched cottages, goats cavorted outside and were corraled for a milking and sometimes killed for a stuffing, the squall of pigs and not of factory whistles woke up the countryside. Pale, wiry, moustached, sleepy-eyed men tumbled out of hammocks pulling up their trousers for the day, and barefooted women in terribly starched dresses of many colors began preparing strong coffee in iron kettles and serving it steaming in polished cocoanut shells. Although

Porto Rico was not then one of the great sugar producing centres of the world, there was usually sugar at the bottom of the cocoanut and the sleepy-eyed man stirred it lazily with a wooden spoon, tasting it with his eyes and his nose. Inside the hut the brats wailed; one of them soothed itself by finding five eggs, certified by cackles, under the floor, another by plucking from the wall the image of the Virgin, printed in screaming blue and red. The men left for the field to cut cane, to lead the oxen on their sugar grinding merry-go-round, to prune or pick the coffee bushes in the sloping shade of the tall guavas, to pick and seed the cotton or sift the tobacco leaves or spade in their master's truck field. As they wound their way along the coastal plain or twisted along the precipitous mountain paths a very few pennies jingled in their pockets.

At noon the jíbaro comforted himself, for two cents, with a tumbler of rum bought at the store under the ceiba tree, and went home to a meal of codfish with sweet potatoes and rice mixed with beans. The rice and beans were plentiful; he ate of them until he had enough, and then he slept. After the day's work he loafed in the starlight, sang fantastic songs, usually depicting a topsy-turvy grandeur of some sort, made love to one or two girls, and then went home and made love to his wife.

Of a Sunday, he might with a number of his friends eat a barbecued pig, get drunk in the shade and go to a cockfight. If there was sickness in the family, the master of the plantation would send his doctor, and the master's wife might send some quinine or rhubarb or cadillo leaves. I don't believe he ever went to bed hungry or muddled through a spell of sickness without attention.

As he could not read, it was unlikely that he would discover that Porto Rico's total production for the year came to something less than $9,000,000, and that 950,000 human beings were living, sleeping, eating, drinking, feasting, gambling, singing, and loving on that money.

His master, the feudal lord, rose out of an enormous mahogany bed, washed his hands and face in cold water out of an enamelled bowl with a design of roses, and breakfasted on a cup of coffee, rolls, butter, and cheese. Then he shouted for his horse and rode over his land, seeing that everyone was at work, inquiring after those who were sick or lazy, listening to gossip, giving advice on marriages. It was not until later in the morning that, coming upon a secluded bend of the stream where the pomarrosales[1] bent over the water, he took off his clothes and bathed.

He owned his house; his hills and ravines were lightly mortgaged or not at all; he chose out of several horses for his tours of his domain; he bred, bought or swapped roosters to uphold the honor of his judgment; he fathered his men gruffly or kindly, intelligently or stupidly. Perhaps he wanted a house in the nearest town, or, perhaps not in the nearest town but in the capital of the district. Maybe some day he would even move to San Juan. Someone had a horse or a rooster he coveted. They said that Madrid was a lively place, but it would probably bore him, so far from home, where no one would know him or greet him with deference or seek his advice. His son might be sent across to study, and might receive a visit from his parents during his last year at the university. It was a long trip though.

---

1. Aromatic fruit trees; their fruit is also known as the pink apple.

In San Juan, a city of many colors crowded within thick brown walls, occasional carriages clattered over the cobblestones; high ceilings made cool dark interiors; a rare cocoanut shell mounted in silver gave evidence in certain old houses of the time when glassware was an infrequent importation; the cafés were clubs where politics and women were discussed over ice cream, chocolate, or rum; and a bowlegged mulatto was famous as a procurer. Regional autonomy had been granted by Spain, and a native Cabinet with a native Premier ruled the green fields and polychromatic towns.

If you didn't own a house, you might own one. If you didn't have a carriage, you might have one. If you did have these goods and a little money in the bank for a trip to Madrid or Paris now and then, you were at the top, and peace, romance, or prestige were your remaining goals. Porto Rico was a land of opportunity. Opportunity in a serene Spanish sense. Opportunity within classes. All that a man of a given class could imagine himself as attaining, he could attain. His economic imagination wasn't stimulated by the brash parade of contraptions which were later to become badges of honor and tokens of social superiority. You didn't have much, and you could only want a little more. There was only one millionaire on the island, but there were many lords and masters of the soil.

## II

Presto, the flag! The one and only. The magic carpet on which Rotary,[2] benevolence, and interference fly over the crumbling liberties and inefficiencies of the earth. It found a dignified little world, bearing with an easy penury, playing the tiple,[3] and dreaming of a moon which was attainable. Its servitors set to work to transform that little world into a hasty one, pushing great iron wheels, slipping innumerable bills of lading across Grand Rapids[4] desks, and dreaming of automobiles, which are mostly unattainable. "Mother," the troubadours used to sing.

> I bought a toy
> In the market-place of love.
> How pretty it was, oh, how pretty it was,
> But what price I had to pay!

But soon they were singing:

> The automobile, oh, mother, is something
> That surprises all people, oh, mother,
> And is prodigious.

Spain had recently granted Porto Rico an autonomous form of government. The island was run by Porto Ricans under a responsible Cabinet system, and the Governor-General, barring his military command, was as purely ceremonial as his colleague of Canada. Porto Rico had control of her customs, a measure of treaty-making power, sixteen representatives in

---

2. A national and international service club; in this essay, symbolizing the importation of American cultural standards by well-meaning but ultimately self-serving members of the business-and-professional class.

3. In Puerto Rico, a small guitarlike instrument with anywhere from one to five strings.

4. City in southwestern Michigan; once a center for automobile manufacturing.

the Madrid Cortes.[5] She was empowered to develop her economic life as best suited her tastes and interests. Her statesmen and politicians had the future in their hands. Theirs was the responsibility for molding this quiet lovely place into an image of unassuming prosperity and justice. Porto Rico is small, not very complex, and the task was—and is—an easy one, if only it be undertaken in a spirit of objective statesmanship, with no axes to grind.

But there seems to be a feeling in the United States against permitting others to be responsible for their own welfare. Under American rule the native Cabinet, tolerated at first, soon found its existence made unendurable by the encroachments of the Military Governors. It resigned. A mongrel system of government, under the Foraker Act,[6] took the place of the ample autonomy established by Spain. The Lower House was elected by popular suffrage. The Cabinet was the Upper House, blithely combining legislative and executive functions. This Cabinet-Senate was composed of six Porto Ricans and five Americans, all appointed by the American authorities.

It was not difficult to find six adequate Porto Ricans. They were found. But, although a community can be ruled by a few men willing to rule it in a nice way, some kind of supporting majority is demanded by the democratic yen. So a majority was found. To be a member of this majority all you had to do was to proclaim yourself an ardent American in bad English, or in no English at all. If you were a member of the majority, you could become a street-cleaner or a health inspector, or you could recommend some poor henchman for either job.

Then the tariff wall was thrown around the island. Sugar became the chief beneficiary and cane spread over the valleys and up the hillsides like wildfire. The Spanish economy had been somewhat haphazardly predicated on small land-holding. The American economy, introduced by the Guánica, the Aguirre, the Fajardo and other great *centrales*,[7] was based on the million-dollar mill and the tight control of the surrounding countryside.

By now the development of large absentee-owned sugar estates, the rapid curtailment in the planting of coffee—the natural crop of the independent farmer—, and the concentration of cigar manufacture into the hands of the American trust, have combined to make Porto Rico a land of beggars and millionaires, of flattering statistics and distressing realities. More and more it becomes a factory worked by peons, fought over by lawyers, bossed by absent industrialists, and clerked by politicians. It is now Uncle Sam's second largest sweat-shop.

It is a sweat-shop that has a company store—the United States. Americans dollars paid to the peons are so many tokens, redeemable in the American market exclusively, at tariff-inflated prices. The same tariff that protects the prices of sugar and tobacco, controlled by the few, skyrockets the prices of commodities that must be consumed by all. Porto Rico obtains tariff prices and pays tariff prices. The appearance of justice is maintained, but the reality is a pawn-broker's reality.

The favorable trade-balances, so naively emphasized by the official reports, are therefore a choice bit of irony. During the last twenty-eight years

5. Cortes Generales, the Spanish Parliament.
6. Officially called the Organic Act of 1900; a U.S. federal law that established civilian government on Puerto Rico, which by then had been acquired by the United States as a result of the Spanish-American War (1898).
7. Sugar mills.

of American rule the island has enjoyed an unfavorable trade-balance only twice. In each of the other twenty-six years the exports have exceeded the imports in the same manner that the exports of a burglarized house exceed its imports. In brief, the renowned favorable balance is nothing but the profit of the absentee landlords and industrialists.

Here, as Al Smith[8] would say, is the lowdown. From 1901 to 1927 $228,000,000 was extracted from Porto Rico and reported as a favorable trade-balance. But if the island had been privileged to forego that flattering balance, a reasonable proportion of those millions would have gone into the development of its industrial resources. As the whole island is now valued at about $300,000,000, the effect of such reinvestment on the living standards of its overcrowded population would have been very important. To the American people, on the other hand, that money spread over that number of years, means nothing. Its ingress, even in one single year, would have no more appreciable effect on their prosperity than a bucket of water on the tides of the Great Lakes. Yet these life-giving pennies have been filched from the pocket of a pauper by the fingers of an opulent kleptomaniac.

Of course, no such gorgeous dividends could have been declared had not the influence of American enterprise and the actual investment of American capital increased Porto Rico's output of dollars so fabulously. Certainly, the imperialists could argue if they felt compelled to, those millions represent but a small percentage of the increase of wealth brought about by the American regime. In dollars, they represent a profit of 16%. In value they represent incalculably more. The operation of the tariff against the consumer and the expanding land monopoly explain the discrepancy. So far as the bulk of the population is concerned, only an eighty-cent wage paid during six months of the year to the head of each family, and redeemable only in the world's highest market, separates them from the angels.

### III

It is close contact with the United States rather than the influence of the small group of resident Americans that has given a decided, if superficial, direction to the institutional life of the island. The Y.M.C.A. has its swimming pool, its basket ball court, its inspirational talks, but I doubt that such implied notions as Christ's disapproval of cigarettes get much serious attention from the local young men. Rotary slaps backs, sings, and hears speeches in a bored and genial way, but when I gave it a somewhat fantastic talk on the culture of light ladies[9] as an index of civilization, the members really had a good time. The Elks and Odd Fellows play with their rituals, charity becomes slightly organized, evangelical preachers thunder in the villages, Holy Rollers roll in the back alleys, three or four prominent citizens become Protestants and are considered funny, women are beginning to be feared as the rolling-pin[1] follows the flag, virginity still abounds and often attains to old age, but is perceptibly on the wane.

---

8. Alfred Emanuel Smith (1873–1944), American politician.
9. Prostitutes; the "light" is related to the red lights that, in the modern world, have signaled prostitutes.
1. Comic reference to this kitchen tool as a poten-

tial weapon that was introduced to the island through Americanization. *Holy Rollers*: members of the Protestant sects whose religious services involve spontaneous expressions of faith-inspired fervor. *Elks and Odd Fellows*: two benevolent fraternal orders.

It is probably through the women that the largest doses of Americanism are being administered. The Latin-American attitude in this respect is confusing to a narrowly egalitarian world. Certainly we are wont to make a sharp nonsensical distinction between good and bad women—there is hardly any middle ground between chastity and prostitution. But this has not heretofore meant that the mere goodness of good women gave them any appreciable influence on the social point of view. Good women have been powerless and tame among us, and have grown smug in the consciousness of their hard luck. Generally speaking, there were only four things Latin women could be: old maids, wives, mistresses, or prostitutes. Now they can be girls. They can be girls for a long time.

They can also be stenographers, bookkeepers, telephone operators, shop assistants, and feminists. They may speak in public and harass legislators.

Porto Rican politicians may now be publicly accused of keeping mistresses. The charge doesn't come near defeating them, but evidently there is some suggestion in the atmosphere that makes it seem relevant. Twenty years ago it would have seemed preposterous to advance such an argument as in any way affecting a man's fitness for office.

The indications are that we may soon find ourselves adopting a subtly feminized point of view as unsatisfactory to both men and women as the one now prevailing in the United States. The change, in spite of the stupid simplicity of our traditional mores, would seem to be for the worse. We were groping toward adjustment; now we are drifting toward equality.

There are two kinds of Americanized Porto Ricans: the young men freely and spontaneously shaped into the image of whatever happens to be the Young Generation up here, just as young Germans, Italians, and Swedes are shaped in New York or Pittsburgh; and the older fellows who Americanize themselves out of a sense of their inadequacy as Porto Ricans. The former may be as charming and as innocuous as the youths who play tennis in the Saturday Evening Post.[2] The latter are a sight for the gods. Their manner is as unctuous as that of Y.M.C.A. secretaries and quite as unreal. They approve and disapprove of many things. They have Ethics and go in for Service. They emphasize the importance of their smallest actions to the working of the sacred social machinery. They need the crutch of a principle to support their conduct as it hobbles along the straight and narrow path where the primroses grow—and, of course, they always find one.

Whether as a result of American tailoring or of psycho-biological imitation, their paunches no longer grow in the reticent Spanish fashion, but rather in the aggressive, imperialistic, genial American fashion. They are gregarious and dull and oversimian, and try pathetically to find innocent amusements. They immolate the paramount heritage of Spain—individuality—in the altar of regular-fellowship. The girls don't like them, and I maliciously suggest this fact as an issue to the Porto Rican nationalists.

The tone of life in the cities has been speeded up. A certain efficiency is observable. Clerks take shorter siestas after lunch. Telephone connections are quickly achieved, although private messages may still be conveyed through the operators if they like your voice. Transportation is rapid and cheap. Good liquor is delivered within a few minutes—Scotch, $5 a quart; champagne, $7; Holland gin, $8. Soda fountains suffuse the narrow streets with

2. U.S. weekly magazine (1821–1969).

their sweet odor. Cafés are arranged to look more and more like glittering American beaneries, but conversation and not food is still the major inducement for tarrying in them.

The population is about as susceptible to nationalist emotions as to American manners. While the latter grow like a monstrous parasite on the island's Latinity, it remains a fact that whenever a politician of intelligence and prestige has taken up the issue of national independence, he has swayed the island. It is the students at the university, however, who give expression to the most conscious and complex form of nationalism, not only as a sovereign control of the jobs, but as a cultural continuity.

They don't want the local temperament violated by the bayonets of education or by the contagion imminent in close commercial relationships. They want Porto Rico to be Porto Rico, not a lame replica of Ohio or Arizona. They want its spirit to be part of the great Spanish spirit, now in process of saving itself from its political and economic ruin.

## IV

The university authorities, under the leadership of Dr. Thomas Benner, who is far from sharing the political viewpoint of the students, follow a policy that is friendly to this end. The university can boast of the most brilliant Spanish department on American territory. It is in fact among the soundest of any to be found in Spanish-speaking countries, having enjoyed at one time or another the services of such men as Vasconcelos, ex-Minister of Education of Mexico; De Onís, head of the Spanish department at Columbia; Amado Alonso, of the Centro de Estudios Históricos of Madrid; Américo Castro of Oxford, and many other first-rate men.

What effect this may have on the destiny of the island is of course doubtful. However, saving a culture, even an inferior one, from becoming the monkey of another, even a superior one, is a good in itself. And in the present case it is by no means certain that the heritage shared by Porto Rico is to be unfavourably compared with the heritage to which the blind forces of production and exchange now seek to hook it up.

The haphazard manner in which the character of the island spars for survival may influence its political future. Whether the island is to be semi-independent, like Cuba, or autonomous under some special dispensation of Congress, is a question to be determined by the interplay of politic and economic interest. But it is certain that it will never be incorporated into the Union as a State save through the operation of cultural forces: that is, not unless, and until, our manner of life and thought has been respectably Americanized.

Will this ever come about? Will the island retain its historical personality? An unqualified answer to either of these questions would necessarily fall short of the possibilities. Perhaps a more absurd fate is in store for us. Perhaps we are destined to be neither Porto Ricans nor Americans, but merely puppets of a mongrel state of mind, susceptible to American thinking and proud of Latin thought, subservient to American living and worshipful of the ancestral way of life. Perhaps we are to discuss Cervantes and eat pork and beans in the Child's restaurant[3] that must be opened sooner or later. Perhaps we will

---

3. A moderately priced eating place, part of a chain in the first half of the twentieth century. *Cervantes*: Miguel de Cervantes (1547–1616), Spanish writer; author of the novel *Don Quixote* (1605, 1615).

try not to let mother catch us reading the picaresque verses of Quevedo.[4] Perhaps we are going to a singularly fantastic and painless hell in our own sweet way. Perhaps all this is nothing but a foretaste of Pan-Americanism.

February 1929

## Speech

Language was given to man to enable him to make himself understood by his fellow man. But one of the frailties of language is that there are some words which for a time prevent understanding. In Puerto Rico *patria*—the homeland—has been such a word. At first blush this may seem strange, as there is no people of the earth who love their native land more profoundly than do the people of Puerto Rico.

To the Puerto Rican, *patria* is the colors of the landscape, the change of seasons, the smell of the earth wet with fresh rain, the voice of the streams, the crash of the ocean against the shore, the fruits, the songs, the habits of work and of leisure, the typical dishes for special occasions and the meager ones for everyday, the flowers, the valleys, and the pathways. But even more than these things, *patria* is the people: their way of life, spirit, folkways, customs, their way of getting along with each other. Without these latter things *patria* is only a name, an abstraction, a bit of scenery. But with them it is an integral whole: "the homeland *and* the people." Those who profess to love their country while taking an irresponsible attitude towards the destiny of its people suffer from spiritual confusion. The implication of their attitude is that we must save the country even though we destroy the people!

Love of country must mean love of all of the country—both the *patria* and the people. But some of us confused love of the homeland with the narrow and bitter concept of the national state. We felt that love of Puerto Rico has as a necessary corollary the desire for separate independence. We had not yet comprehended that no law, divine or human, commands that countries must be suspicious, vain, and hostile, that they must live separate from other countries whose peoples are a part of the broad equality which the Lord created on the earth. Because of the rigidity of our thinking, we could not disentangle the concept of love for our country from the fixed idea of separate independence. Anything other than independence seemed to clash with our love for Puerto Rico.

### The Dawning Light

The difficult process of clarifying these ideas began when the Tydings bill was introduced in Congress in 1936.[1] On the one hand this bill offered the

---

4. Francisco Gómez de Quevedo y Santibáñez Villegas (1580–1645), nobleman, politician, and one of the most prominent poets of the Spanish Golden Age.
1. This legislation—sponsored by Senator Millard E. Tydings, chairman of the Senate's Territories and Insular Affairs Committee—called for a U.S. referendum on the question *Should the people of Puerto Rico be sovereign and independent?* If this question had been answered affirmatively, Puerto Rico would have been granted independence in four yearly stages, during each of which tariffs on Puerto Rican products would have increased by a percentage until they equaled tariffs imposed on other countries' products. Much debated on the mainland and the island, the bill was never presented for a vote by Congress.

separate independence for which many of us had asked because of our feeling for the abstract idea of the *patria*. On the other hand, it condemned the people of our homeland to extreme poverty from which they could never hope to escape. Suddenly what had seemed to be an integral idea—the homeland and separate independence—turned out to be two conflicting ideas: one, acceptable as an abstract idea; the other, a mortal enemy of the people. The Tydings bill would have made Puerto Rico independent; but it would have shackled the people with economic misery.

It was not easy to change our views on this subject. Our minds could grasp the point that if we could have separate independence only under the economic conditions of the Tydings bill it would be not independence but a living death of hopeless poverty for Puerto Rico. Yet our emotions led us to search for other economic conditions under which independence would be possible.

At the time, our emotions were stronger than our powers of reasoning. Rationalization works where understanding is the servant, instead of the master, of emotion. Instead of using reasoning objectively to seek the truth, we used it to justify our emotions. Just as one might confuse the glittering uniform of a doorkeeper with that of a king, our powers of reasoning were led astray by rationalization induced by our emotions. We were the victims of wishful thinking in believing that separate independence would be feasible if the economic conditions in the Tydings bill came into effect over a period of ten years instead of immediately. This was also inadequate; but it served for a time to protect, in the minds of many of us, the preconceived idea of separation.

## The Untaught Wisdom

We were gripped with this emotional confusion, wanting independence but not wanting economic upheaval—when the campaign to found the Popular Democratic party was running its course between 1938 and 1940. At this point, well aware of the great economic needs of our people, and knowing our simple people well, I set out to talk with them. I learned many things from these talks.

I learned that there is a wisdom among the people in the towns and in the countryside which education may lead, but cannot improve, in its magnificent human essence. I taught many of them something, but they taught me more. I learned that the people are wise—wiser than we think. I learned that to them freedom is something deep in the heart, in the conscience, in everyday life, in personal dignity, in the furrow, the plow, and the tools. I learned that among the simple people the nationalistic concept does not exist, because in its place there is a deep understanding of freedom. I learned that in their wisdom they prefer—if they have to choose—one who governs respectfully from a distance to one who governs despotically from nearby. And that understanding is the unequaled basis and root of every great federalist concept, of great unions between countries and between men which cut across climates, races, and languages. The nationalistic concept prefers the despotic government of the nearby to the democratic government of the remote. Naturally, democratic federalism requires respect and liberty in the local as well as in the federal levels of government.

I learned many things, probably many more than I think I learned; for we learn by planting things in the mind which later bear fruit in understanding. And I learned better something I already knew: that it is unworthy of the conscience, that it is the denial of all ideals, to risk, for abstract concepts, the hope for a better life, the deep belief in the integral freedom of the good and simple people who populate the long paths, which sometimes cross the streets and squares, which are Puerto Rico. I learned all this, and I also learned that the great majority of the people of Puerto Rico prefer close association with their fellow citizens of the American Union and with all men on earth, to the bitter narrowness of separation.

I realized that with a program calling for separate independence we would never obtain the support of the people for economic development—equitable distribution and production—which the people needed so much. The profound intuition of the people was quick to point out the contradiction in a program which on the one hand talked about the struggle to reduce their extreme poverty and on the other hand talked about separate independence which would destroy any hope of ever conquering that extreme poverty—which in fact would rapidly aggravate the seriousness of that poverty.

From the instinct of the people which I observed in my journeys among them, from the doubts in my own mind and the minds of others, and from the compulsion to deal with the great economic and social problems of so many good people in Puerto Rico, there emerged the formula which made possible everything that was to come, the formula that "the political status is not in issue." The votes in favor of the Popular Democratic Party would not be counted either for separate independence or for federated statehood; they would be votes in favor of an economic and social program. Our political status would be decided by the people on another occasion, wholly apart from the regular elections—presumably in a plebiscite.

This new concept of separating the economic from the political problem of Puerto Rico liberated the Popular Democratic party from a platform which was its own worst enemy—a platform in which the political plank could destroy the economic planks with the devastating fury of a tropical hurricane. This liberated those of us who had suffered from an intolerable perplexity of spirit. It enabled us to tackle the economic problems of Puerto Rico in a way that introduced a new, large movement of reform, creation, and hope. We are still engaged in that great task; in spite of the great deal which we have accomplished, there is much more to be done.

## The Either/Or Concept Persists

However, we were free of this perplexity of the spirit for only a short period. We continued to be preoccupied as a collective group with the notion of a plebiscite in which we would be required to choose between separate independence and federated statehood—despite the fact that under either alternative the economic life of our people would be gravely threatened. It must be understood that it was not the people who were insisting on this course. This came from the political assemblies, who in this respect were not so representative of the people as they were in economic questions.

Those of us who participated in these assemblies were not insincere. With more learning and less wisdom, we continued to believe, although assailed by anguished doubts, that the choice must be between separate independence and federated statehood under economic conditions different from those in the Tydings bill and from those which existed for the states of the Union. We persisted in this view without examining closely the question of whether it would be possible to obtain these necessary economic conditions without any deviation from the two rigid alternatives. We were impaled on the horns of the dilemma which seemed to force an inexorable choice between separate independence and federated statehood. Actually, the instinct of the people used the idea of a plebiscite between these two classical forms of government to provide time for a better and autochthonous solution of the problem to appear. We can see this now. It was not easy to see it at that time.

In the 1944 campaign the promise to the people that the political status was not in issue was repeated. However, it was still imperative that we find a solution for that problem. The wisdom of the people, which I have mentioned, does not consist in a belief that the question of political status is of no importance whatsoever. Rather, recognizing that man does not live by bread alone and is in part a political being, the people have wisely refused to be bound by the intellectual straitjacket of rigid and preconceived formulas which stifle the creative will and energy of men. It was this instinct of the people, which at times their leaders must channel into action, which engendered the happy thought that the solution might well lie in some form other than the two inflexible formulas upon which the political assemblies had long focused their attention.

## A Third Possibility Recognized

We were thus one step farther along the road to reality: in a request to Congress for a plebiscite we used language which permitted consideration of solutions other than the two rigid classical alternatives. True, we committed the error, at the insistence of some of the members of the political assembly, of inserting a deadline; we asked for a solution of the problem when World War II ended. But we had freed ourselves from the tyranny of the labels, separate independence and federated statehood. We were making progress.

In 1945 I went to Washington for discussions on the question of the political status of Puerto Rico. As a result of this visit, a bill was introduced in the Senate by Senator Tydings and in the House of Representatives by Resident Commissioner Piñero. That bill presented *three* alternatives: separate independence, federated statehood, and dominion status; the economic conditions were completely different from those of the original Tydings bill and from other Tydings bills. Under either of these alternatives, free trade between the United States and Puerto Rico would continue, the internal revenue taxes which now revert to the Treasury of Puerto Rico would continue to be covered into our Treasury, and federal aid for roads, hospitals, school lunchrooms, and many other public works and services would be extended for a long period of time.

During these consultations in Washington I became aware that such a bill could not pass. However, it did serve to present graphically to Congress and to the people of Puerto Rico the minimum economic conditions we needed in order to survive, irrespective of our political status.

## The Object Lesson of the Philippines

In April 1946 I went again to Washington as a member of the Status Commission which was created by the Legislature of Puerto Rico and on which all the political parties with members in the Legislature were represented. Once more we tried to find a solution to the problem of status as we saw it. During that time hearings were being held before congressional committees on a bill to establish the economic relations which would exist between the United States and the Philippines when the latter became a republic. I read carefully the record of those hearings because of their obvious bearing on the question we were raising. It convinced me that Puerto Rico would never obtain the right to choose separate independence in a plebiscite except under economic conditions which would destroy any hope of continuing to improve their standard of living. The most important factor which led me to this conviction was the most-favored-nation clause found in trade treaties between the United States and many other countries.

The plan at the time was to give the Philippines economic treatment which would preserve for them the advantages of union with the United States for only eight years; this preference would be gradually reduced until the Philippines had no preference whatsoever in their economic relations with the United States. The principal reason for this treatment of the Philippines was the most-favored-nation clause in trade treaties to which the United States is a party. Under this clause the United States is required to give each nation with which it has a trade treaty containing the clause the most favorable economic treatment provided in a treaty with any other nation.

Obviously, the United States could not maintain its present good economic treatment of Puerto Rico, which is vital to our continued development, if we acquired a status which had all the legal paraphernalia of separate independence. It became clear that only under some form of status in association with the United States in which we retained our American citizenship could we preserve the good economic conditions which are necessary for our survival as a people. It could not be gainsaid that any status for Puerto Rico which connoted loss of American citizenship and disassociation from the American Union meant the discontinuance of our present favorable economic conditions, except perhaps for a few years on a diminishing graduated scale. The hard fact was that the present free trade between Puerto Rico and the United States could not be continued if Puerto Rico were a separate, independent nation. To provide for such free trade would require the same treatment for all the most-favored-treaty nations. And this, of course, was out of the question. Moreover, added to our economic situation was the affection and mutual respect which had developed between the peoples of Puerto Rico and the United States within our common citizenship.

We concluded that we must stop wasting time groping for a solution to the problem of political status which we knew beforehand was impossible for Puerto Rico to attain—impossible not for the American Union but for us. The Philippines with their greater territory and natural resources in relation to population, could manage under such stringent economic conditions. Our destiny lay in a different direction. It was incumbent upon us to devise creatively a realistically free form of political status which would not be at war with the solution of the economic problems of Puerto Rico and yet would protect the dignity of our people within our association with the American Union.

## The Path of Progress

Once we forthrightly faced this task in the middle of 1946, things began to happen. The political status lost its role of enemy of the solution of our economic problems; instead we considered it in the light of and in harmony with the effort to solve the great economic difficulties of our people. We moved at an unprecedentedly accelerated pace which proved beyond peradventure that the log jam on status had finally been broken.

There had been no progress in self-government for Puerto Rico since 1917. Less than two months after this new approach to the problem of status had been adopted, the President of the United States appointed Jesús Piñero,[2] who had been elected by the people of Puerto Rico as their Resident Commissioner in Washington, to the post of Governor of Puerto Rico. And it took only four years for Congress by Public Law 600[3] to offer to create a relationship between Puerto Rico and the United States based on a compact approved by the people of Puerto Rico and on a constitution written by the people of Puerto Rico themselves.

The wisdom of halting the divisive and futile debate on status, which paralyzed our progress towards self-government from 1917 until 1946, has been dramatically demonstrated by the swiftness of the events which occurred between 1946 and 1952. With this hindrance removed, the long-repressed political energy of our people soon created a new form of status, a new form of political relationship in the American Union and in all America, a new form of political harmony with the economic freedom of our people, in place of the rigid and sterile formulas which threatened the full development of Puerto Rico, which had immobilized for generations the great creative political powers of its people.

It should be made clear that what we have done has been to initiate a process of political creation in Puerto Rico, and not merely to invent just another formula. Precisely because it needs to grow in so many phases in its life as a people, Puerto Rico cannot become engaged in formulas. It must use its energy in development and continuous growth. Nothing could enslave us more than handicapping our great drive towards a happy future with a rigid, obsolescent, unprogressive, or inapplicable formula.

## Interpretation of the Constitution

Every constitution is subject to different interpretations which are made in good faith. But our thesis is that by their votes in the referenda in which Public Law 600 and the constitution were approved, the people adopted the interpretations of these documents advanced by those who campaigned for their approval. We submit then that when the time comes for judicial review

---

2. Jesús T. Piñero Jiménez (1897–1952), the first native Puerto Rican to serve as governor of Puerto Rico; appointed by the U.S. president Harry S. Truman (1884–1972).

3. Signed into law by President Truman in July 1950.

of the compact and the constitution, they should be interpreted in accordance with the understanding of the people as to their meaning and scope when they approved them. We are confident that such interpretations will prevail, and that they will yield the results which will be most favorable and liberal to Puerto Rico and which will promote fraternal understanding between Puerto Rico and the American Union.

July 17, 1951

# JESÚS COLÓN
## 1901–1974

One of the most visible community activists of the early-twentieth-century New York Puerto Rican community, Jesús Colón was born in the tobacco-growing mountain town of Cayey, Puerto Rico. Like his friend and compatriot Bernardo Vega (see p. 428), Colón was exposed at a young age to the enlightened socialist culture of the *tabaqueros* (cigar workers), although he was not an artisan as was Vega. Colón arrived in New York City in 1918, a stowaway in one of the many steamships that brought Puerto Ricans to the United States in that era. He was 17 years old, without a high school diploma, and almost penniless. He worked in several menial jobs, went to night school, and eventually began to write for the various New York Spanish-language community newspapers.

Colón developed his journalistic craft from the trenches, from daily experience—the "university of life," as he once noted. His working-class background and exposure to the socialist labor movement during his formative years in Puerto Rico, combined with his survival struggles as a black Puerto Rican migrant in New York, turned him into a dedicated activist and labor organizer. From New York in 1923, he began writing regularly for *Justicia*, the official newspaper of Puerto Rico's Federación Libre de los Trabajadores (Free Federation of Workers). In the late 1920s, he was a regular columnist for Bernardo Vega's New York newspaper, *Gráfico*. He also wrote for the New York papers *Pueblos Hispanos*, founded by the Puerto Rican nationalist poet Juan Antonio Corretjer, and *Liberación*, founded by Spanish exiles.

For over five decades, Colón's journalistic output was prolific. His early incursions turned into a full-fledged career, from the mid-1950s through 1971, as a columnist for several newspapers in addition to the ones mentioned above, particularly a long affiliation with the U.S. Communist Party newspaper, *The Daily Worker* (later to become *The Worker* and the *Daily World*). From 1957 to 1961, he also frequently contributed to the literary magazine *Mainstream*. A believer in the effectiveness of community organizing in the struggle for civil rights and social justice, Colón either cofounded or was an active member of several grassroots organizations, among them the Ateneo Obrero Hispano (Hispanic Workers' Athenaeum, founded 1926), the Liga Puertorriqueña e Hispana (Puerto Rican and Hispanic League, 1928), and the Mutualista Obrera Puertorriqueña (Puerto Rican Workers' Mutual Aid Society, 1934). During the 1950s, he was also an American Labor Party candidate for the New York State Assembly and Senate, and his writings and political activities made him the target of investigation by the House Un-American Activities Committee of the U.S. Congress.

Colón's writings reflect an incisive critical view of U.S. society. He admires the democratic foundations upon which the United States was built, but also recognizes the betrayal of those principles by a capitalist system that tends to perpetuate profound social and racial inequalities, exploits workers, and keeps power and privilege in the hands of a wealthy few. Colón is a master of the anecdotal or testimonial narrative. He used the term *sketches* to refer to his stories, which focused mostly on issues, experiences, and problems affecting the daily lives of Puerto Rican workers in U.S. society. At times, he expresses indignation or anger, and he was particularly sensitive to the stereotypes and misconceptions about the Puerto Rican people that prevailed in U.S. society. He tried to counteract some of these views and also defended African American, Jewish, and women's rights. For Colón, writing was a didactic and consciousness-raising tool in the struggles to eradicate class, racial, and gender oppression, but also the means to forge a historical record about the contributions of Puerto Rican workers to the building of their communities and to the American nation.

Colón compiled some of his writings in *A Puerto Rican in New York and Other Sketches* (1961), one of the first collections of personal short narratives written in English by a Puerto Rican migrant. This work remained mostly unknown to the Puerto Rican community until it was recovered by the U.S.-based Puerto Rican critic Juan Flores. In 1982, Flores published a new edition of *A Puerto Rican in New York*, with an insightful introduction about the significance of Colón's writings, activism, and other endeavors.

After Colón's death, his personal papers became part of a special collection at the Centro de Estudios Puertorriqueños (Center for Puerto Rican Studies) Library and Archives, at Hunter College in New York. His papers included several versions of an outline for a proposed book with the working title *The Way It Was: Puerto Ricans from Way Back*. The book manuscript, which Colón was unable to complete before his death, would have compiled many of the essays and "sketches" that he wrote throughout his long journalistic career, in addition to new, unpublished material. The scholars Edna Acosta-Belén and Virginia Sánchez Korrol have identified and collected over 400 pieces by Colón. A selection from the hundreds of articles recovered from Spanish- and English-language newspapers, along with some unpublished materials that were part of Colón's personal papers, appear in *The Way It Was and Other Writings by Jesús Colón* (1993), edited by Acosta-Belén and Sánchez Korrol. Another selection of his Spanish newspaper columns appears in *Lo que el pueblo me dice: Crónicas de la colonia puertorriqueña en Nueva York* (What the People Tell Me: Chronicles of the Puerto Rican Colonia in New York, 2001), edited by Edwin Karli Padilla.

The five selections in this anthology present Colón's views on socialism, family, race, and religion. They are written in his signature style, mixing the personal and the political. The first two pieces—"The Mother, the Young Daughter, Myself, and All of Us" and "Grandma, Please Don't Come!"—were published in English in newspapers in 1957 and later included in *A Puerto Rican in New York and Other Sketches*. Both emphasize the racism and segregation that permeated U.S. society at that time and that, as a mulatto, Colón experienced firsthand. "The Two United States" and "The Jewish People and Us" first appeared in Spanish in the newspaper *Pueblos Hispanos* in 1943. The first powerfully portrays a nation divided, with racist and neofascist forces on one side, progressive and democratic forces on the other. The second, written during World War II, denounces anti-Jewish stereotypes and blames Adolf Hitler, the German dictator and founder of Nazism, for making "hatred against Jews into a science." "My Wife Doesn't Work" was found among Colón's papers and first published in *The Way It Was and Other Writings*. It criticizes men who devalue women's work at home, expect women to serve them and tend to all their needs, and do not want their women to be "spoiled" by the independence that comes from working for a salary outside the home.

## *From* A Puerto Rican in New York and Other Sketches

## The Mother, the Young Daughter, Myself, and All of Us[1]

I was drinking a cup of coffee in one of those new places where the counter is built in a zig-zag way, like a curving long line of conga dancers. The high stools follow the wavy contours of the counter, making little bays of tall seats where the patrons seat themselves placing their feet in a sort of iron stirrup.

That day every stool was taken but one, on my right side, and another, three stools further to my left.

A mother and her young daughter about nine years old, came in evidently to have a snack.

"You sit by the gentleman," meaning me . . . the mother said to her young daughter pointing to the unoccupied stool on my right. "I will be sitting over there," the mother added, pointing to the other empty stool three seats to my left.

"I won't sit beside no nigger," said the child.

And the mother, myself, and all of us never said a word.

February 1957                                                                                        1961

## Grandma, Please Don't Come![1]

Please, grandma, don't come!

I know they have sent you the airplane ticket, and a dress just your size with black and white squares all over the beautiful taffeta silk. But please, grandma, don't come!

They have sent you the photographs of your little darling grandchildren born in New York. True, you have not seen them yet. You would like to leave your tropical sun and mountains and the little rivulet bathing the base of the fence in your backyard and the tall avocado tree right by your kitchen door, just to see and embrace those darling grandchildren. But again, I say, grandma, please don't come!

I know you are not well-to-do. But you have been living on what your sons and daughters send you every month from the states. I know there is need and poverty around you. And discrimination and economic and cultural oppression there. Something called imperialism sees to it that these things are not wiped out. But I think this is not the kind of letter in which I should go all out and try to explain to you why some people are so terribly interested in keeping other people poor and ignorant. Still I think I ought to tell you that the most important men and forces interested in keeping people poor and ignorant and fighting wars one against the other, have their offices in one short street in this New York to which your relatives are trying to bring you. The many companies with offices in that street and their counterparts in other great cities own the United States and of course, Puerto Rico.

---

1. First printed in the monthly magazine *Main-stream*, February 1957.

1. First printed in *The Daily Worker*, in Colon's column "As I See It from Here," April 1957.

Eisenhower and Muñoz Marín[2] do what they ask them to do. It might sound ridiculously amazing to you. But believe me, grandma, this is nevertheless a fact. But enough of this "deep" stuff for today. All I am asking you, grandma, today, is please don't come!

Yes, it is nice here in a way. It is nice if you are young and willing and able to go down five flights of stairs two or three times a day. If you can "take it" in a crowded subway where you are squeezed in tight twice a day as if you were a cork in a bottle. It is all right in a way—and remember—I only say in a way—for young strong people. We come to New York young and leave old and tired. All the fun and joy of life extracted from us by the hurry-up machine way of living we are forced to live here. In Puerto Rico, nobody pushes you, you walk slowly as if the day had 48 hours. Persons completely unknown to you say: "Buenos Dias," (Good morning), with a reverence and a calmness in their voices that reveals centuries of a quiescent, reposed, unhurried way of life.

No matter how many photographs they sent you of Times Square at night, or the Coney Island Boardwalk, grandma, please tell them "NO." A forceful, definite "NO." All those things you have not seen are lots of fun. Don't misunderstand me. New York has many things that are grand. But at your age you will not really be able to enjoy them. You know what snow is? What sleet and snow is? The real physical burden of 20 additional pounds of clothing on your body when you have to go out during the winter, when you have been accustomed to two pounds of calico and muslin on your old bones? Puerto Rico's climate doesn't require any more. Grandma, please don't come!

You should see hundreds of Puerto Rican grandmas like you on a wintry snowy day, standing by the window and watching the snow fall, as Ramito our folk singer[3] said when he came here: "Like coconut flakes falling from the sky." At the beginning snow is a novelty. But after you have seen it once or twice, you wish you were back in our Puerto Rico, looking out at your avocado tree and at the tall dignified royal palm piercing the deep blue Caribbean sky with its sheer beauty.

In Puerto Rico you will be chatting your head off in your own language with the other grandmothers. Nobody will shout at you: "Why don't you talk United States?" Or even threaten you with a beating because you are speaking Spanish. It has been done, you know. People have been killed because they are heard speaking Spanish. So, grandma, please, don't come!

You will be looking so sad, so despondent, so alone when everybody goes to work and you are left all by yourself in an apartment peering through a window at the passersby down below as they go back and forth splashing the grey, dirty, cold snow in the street and on the sidewalk!

All people, North Americans and Puerto Ricans alike, are looking to the day when they can spend the last years of their lives on a tropical isle—a paradise on earth surrounded by clear blue sea imprisoned in a belt of golden beaches. A land perfumed with nature's choicest fragrances. For many of us this is a dream that will never be realized. The boasted "American way of life" has taken out of us the best of our energies to reach that dream.

2. Luis Muñoz Marín; see p. 482. *Eisenhower*: Dwight David Eisenhower (1890–1969), U.S. general; U.S. president 1953–61.

3. Florencio "Flor" Morales Ramos (1915–1989), famous Puerto Rican singer and composer.

Grandma, you are there on that beautiful isle. You were born there. You have been there all your life. You now have what most people here can only dream about. Don't let sentimental letters and life-colored photographs lure you from your island, from your nation, from yourself. Grandma, please, please! DO NOT COME!

April 1957                                                                                              1961

---

## FROM THE WAY IT WAS AND OTHER WRITINGS

## The Two United States[1]

There are two United States like there are two Puerto Ricos. On the one hand, the United States of the Ku Klux Klan and the Black Legion with all its villainous followers—the Trojan horse of neofascism in this nation—; on the other, the progressive United States of Wallace and Wilkie: men who from Roosevelt to Browder[2] strove for the unification of the forces of progress and freedom for all, according to their different ways of interpreting progress and freedom.

There are also two Puerto Ricos. The Puerto Rico of the *vendepatrias* (those who sell out their country), a country where nascent capitalism is sharing a common cause with North American absenteeist capitalism, by paying measly salaries to the Puerto Rican proletariat; the Puerto Rico where police underlings massacre people during a demonstration on a Palm Sunday[3] or those who strike claiming for another piece of bread.

There is also another glorious Puerto Rico with a revolutionary tradition: the Puerto Rico of Betances and Albizu Campos, of Ruiz Belvis and Hostos;[4] the Puerto Rico that will someday astonish the world.

---

1. Translated by Edna Acosta-Belén and Susan Liberis-Hill. Acosta-Belén and Liberis-Hill's introductory footnote reads: "Translation of 'Los otros Estados Unidos,' which appeared in Colón's column, 'Lo que el pueblo me dice,' in *Pueblos Hispanos* (April 17, 1943): 3." Except as indicated, all footnotes are Acosta-Belén and Liberis-Hill's; one of their footnotes has been omitted.
2. Earl Browder (1891–1973), American Communist politician. *Ku Klux Klan*: a secret, Christian fraternal society in the United States, started after the Civil War, advocating white supremacy. *Black Legion*: in the 1930s, a paramilitary subgroup of the Ku Klux Klan. *Trojan horse*: from an episode in the Trojan War—as recounted in the *Iliad*, by the ancient Greek epic poet Homer—someone or something used deceptively to subvert from within. *Wallace*: Henry Agard Wallace (1888–1965), American agriculturalist, editor, and politician; at different points, U.S. vice-president, secretary of agriculture, and secretary of commerce under President Franklin Delano Roosevelt (1882–1945, served 1933–45); also United States Progressive Party of 1948 candidate for president. *Wilkie*:

Wendell Wilkie (1892–1944), American politician who ran for president, unsuccessfully, against Roosevelt in 1940 but whose liberal, progressive views made him one of Roosevelt's strongest allies. [Anthology editors' note]
3. A reference to the 1937 Palm Sunday police attack on a Nationalist Party demonstration held in Ponce, Puerto Rico. This event is known in Puerto Rican history as the Masacre de Ponce (Ponce Massacre).
4. Ramón Emeterio Betances (1827–1898) was a leader of the Puerto Rican separatist movement against Spanish colonial rule. Forced into exile, he directed from abroad the Grito de Lares revolt of 1868. Pedro Albizu Campos (1891–1965) became President of the Puerto Rican Nationalist Party in 1930. He was incarcerated for many years in U.S. prisons for his activities against U.S. domination of Puerto Rico. Segundo Ruiz Belvis (1829–1867) was an abolitionist and separatist advocate against Spanish colonial rule. Eugenio María de Hostos (1839–1903) was an educator, writer and separatist advocate against Spanish colonial rule.

The North Americans of the Ku Klux Klan type and Puerto Ricans who sell out their country understand each other very well. They are united, not only among themselves, but their brotherhood extends to levels representing the worst enemies of freedom all over the world. The representatives of Hitlerism, fascism, and the Spanish *falange*[5] in all countries. The Puerto Rican *vendepatrias* are internationally known and very much aware of the advantages of joining the forces of exploitation, abuse, and oppression of other countries. When they come to the United States, they are well received at the airports by the representatives of the great magnates. They lodge in the best hotels where they are wined and dined, where long conversations take place to deliberate new ways and means of extracting the last drop of energy from the emaciated bodies of the workers and peasants from the colony. The sons and daughters of the exploiters from here and back there on the island go to the same universities where they are members of the same exclusive clubs open only to a particular class of students. Their daughters and sons marry among themselves, and the offspring that come out of these unions do not receive names like Jacinta or Juana, but rather prefer Betty or Jean. There is complete unity and understanding among the exploiters.

But what kind of unity and understanding exists between the exploited here in this country and over there in Puerto Rico? Among those who have to get up every day—black and white, Protestant and Catholic, Puerto Rican or North American—to sweat in a factory? Do we Hispanics belong as much as we should to the worker unions that allow us to join with our working brothers and sisters from other nationalities residing in the United States and to know and better protect our livelihood? Do we respect or at least know what the International Labor Defense or the International Workers Order are? These powerful organizations composed mainly of North Americans, but which have done so much for Puerto Rico and the Puerto Rican people?

These powerful organizations are the true societies that continue to be guided according to the great and constructively democratic revolutionary traditions of the people of the United States. Let us learn what is not taught in the schools about Thomas Jefferson, Thomas Paine, Elijah Lovejoy,[6] Gene Debs,[7] and many other individuals that this country has produced. Let us learn where, how, and why the celebration of the first of May and International Women's Day originated, days which are known and commemorated by those all over the world who proudly call themselves workers. Let us join together in common cause in the struggles of all of those others who constitute the REAL United States. Let us respect its progressive institutions, its TRUE history and traditions, ranging from the famous words of Patrick Henry to Virginia's colonial legislature to the most recent of Marcantonio's[8] Congressional appearances claiming for justice and liberty on behalf of Puerto Rico.

---

5. The pro-Franco supporters during the Spanish Civil War. [Francisco Franco (1892–1975), Spanish general; head of Spain 1936–75.]
6. Elijah Parish Lovejoy (1802–1837), American Presbyterian minister, journalist, and editor, murdered for his abolitionist views. *Thomas Jefferson*: third U.S. president (1743–1826, served 1801–09). *Thomas Paine*: American (English-born) political philosopher (1737–1809). [Anthology editors' note]

7. Eugene Victor Debs (1855–1926) was a U.S. socialist leader.
8. Vito Anthony Marcantonio (1902–1954), American lawyer and politician; well-known for defending the rights of Italian Americans, Puerto Ricans, African Americans, and other ethnic groups in New York City. *Patrick Henry*: American statesman (1736–1799). [Anthology editors' note]

Those of us who are part of the people of Puerto Rico, let us share common cause with the PEOPLE of the United States against the exploiters from both countries.

Only then will we be able to avoid finding ourselves in a concentration camp here or in Puerto Rico four or five years from now, still arguing about whether or not we should stand when the U.S. national anthem is playing.

April 17, 1943                                                                                   1993

## The Jewish People and Us[1]

For most Hispanics a Jew means the landlord, the man who sells dresses and suits on layaway, the exploiting proprietor of the factory where we work together with the "red" or "communist" agitators. The Jew—and this word is always pronounced in a derogatory manner—is the person who sold out Christ. Wasn't this what we were told by the good and wise priest from that orange and pink colored church of our childhood where we learned catechism? Weren't our souls filled with anger and rejoicing when during the day before Easter, we would stone and carry all over town a ridiculous stuffed doll tied up and sitting straight on a coalman's horse, yelling "¡El Juá! ¡El Juá!"[2]

As we can see our emotions have been conditioned since childhood to express this scorn and hatred that, when analyzed, serves a very definite purpose. And what is that purpose? Who are the ones interested in promoting scorn and hatred toward the Jew? Let us see.

Under every system of exploitation of man by man—be it a system of barbarism or slavery, feudalism or capitalism—the exploiter needs to find, once in a while, where to displace the blame for poverty, lack of freedoms, and other survival means—conditions in which they have forced the majority of citizens to live. It is necessary to shift this hatred and resentment that the masses would logically express through action against the true oppressors and place the blame, when this understanding comes, and it will, on those truly responsible for having to wage a war every twenty years, for occasionally having to reduce the production of foods and other essential products because there is too much production, while the people die of hunger. The people themselves would take the necessary steps to get rid of the true exploiters, and, for the benefit of the majority, change the present social system.

Hitler made a new important contribution to the exploiters. He made hatred against Jews into a science. He systematized and revived all the prejudices and all the historical and scientific mistakes against this race. He made professors and academics of those who, because of money or fear, prostituted science and thought, and promoted through their "treatises" the

---

1. Translated by Edna Acosta-Belén and Susan Liberis-Hill. Acosta-Belén and Liberis-Hill's introductory footnote reads: "Translation of 'Los judíos y nosotros,' first printed in *Pueblos His-* *panos* (May 1, 1943)." The two additional footnotes are Acosta-Belén and Liberis-Hill's.
2. A shortened form of "Judas," the betrayer of Christ.

most discredited falsehoods. He constructed the most perfect propaganda machine, spreading it to every corner of the world into all languages. And through all means, Dr. Goebbels[3] and his satellites presented through a diversity of pseudoscientific articles and speeches a "theory" about the inferiority of certain races, about the unquestionable superiority of the German race over all others, and about the Jew as the cause of all evil.

We the Hispanic people, as an exploited minority group, should not fall into the trap that the exploiters have laid for us to divide the oppressed people among themselves. When we vilify a Jew, who most of the times is just another poor soul who, like most of us, has to sweat for his daily bread, we are sharing common cause with the Hitlers and Goebbelses. There are bad and exploiting Jews, we know that. Just like in our own countries and even in our colony, which is mostly proletarian, there are also Hispanics who are evil and exploiters.

We cannot make those Jewish people who have been exploited like us pay for the refugee who was able to purchase his escape from Germany and who never belonged to the exploited class. Let us not help Hitler and all his proselytizing lackeys who are trying to make the Jew the scapegoat of this war and of the . . .

We have grown. Our minds have matured. Let us not continue yelling like children "El Juá! El Juá!" and throwing stones at a silent and hollow doll that has done nothing to us.

Let us direct our anger toward the true enemy of the oppressed. You know who they are. They have neither a country nor a flag.

May 1, 1943                                                                                       1993

## My Wife Doesn't Work[1]

"My wife doesn't work." You don't know how many times I have heard these words from the lips of many married men! They pronounce these words with a certain little proudness like they were doing their wives a favor.

And what is the truth behind the resounding phrase, "My wife doesn't work"? The truth is that the woman who stays home doing house chores works as hard and many times harder than the man who goes out to work.

The saddest thing about all of this is that women's housework is hard to see or remains unacknowledged or unappreciated.

Women's work in the home never ends. There is no clock to punch in the house from the moment a woman begins to prepare breakfast or dress the kids for school, up to the time when she does the dishes and ends the day.

If the baby wakes up and cries in the middle of the night and preparation of a quick bottle is urgently needed to make the child go back to sleep, our

---

3. Adolf Hitler's Minister of Propaganda.
1. Translated by Edna Acosta-Belén and Susan Liberis-Hill. Acosta-Belén and Liberis-Hill's in-
troductory footnote reads: "Translation of 'Mi mujer no trabaja,' written for the workers' newspaper *Oye, Boricua* but unpublished."

average man continues sleeping to his heart's content. He doesn't get up, not even to rock the cradle, while the woman is in the kitchen warming up the milk.

The average man comes home from work, sits on a chair in front of the TV and takes his shoes off. With a few sweet words of endearment (*mine-grita, mi amor, mi nena linda*), he asks his wife to fetch his slippers and a cold beer from the refrigerator. When the woman yells, "Dinner is on the table," the man gets up from his chair, washes his hands and sits himself at the table to be served.

Washing dishes after dinner . . . That is left up to American husbands!

Afterwards the average man changes his clothes and goes out for a *"vuel-tecita"* (a little outing) with his buddies. And the woman, who the man says doesn't work, stays home picking up dirty laundry for the wash, imagining ways of stretching the buck so she can buy more at the *bodega*,[2] or watching one of those never-ending soap operas.

And thus, with the tiny phrase "My wife doesn't work," the average man makes a little slave of the woman, one who serves him twelve to fourteen hours a day without a salary and many times without love. There are some exceptions, but through my own experience I have encountered few.

I am very much afraid that what these kind of men truly mean when they say "My wife doesn't work" is "I don't want my wife to work outside the home because other women at the office or the factory can spoil her." (These men always emphasize the term *mi mujer* as if she were a thing or they would own her in body and soul.) "Spoil" in the sense that the average man uses this word, meaning that she would be influenced and learn about her rights as a woman and worker. The day will come when a woman may be able to make more money than her weekly allowance, which would be a mortal blow to masculine claims of superiority.

And who knows if, with the passing of time, that woman begins to read a newspaper like this, that represents her class—the working class. And from then on . . . anything goes!

1993

2. Grocery store. [Anthology editors' note]

---

# FELIPE ALFAU
## 1902–1999

Born in Barcelona, Spain, Felipe Alfau immigrated to New York City in his teens with his family during World War I. He studied music and for a short time was a music critic for *La Prensa*, a Spanish-language newspaper in Manhattan. Seeking a career in literature, he began writing in English to be in sync with his environment and because, as he put it, Shakespeare's tongue made him far more marketable. His first book, *Old Tales from Spain* (1929), consisted of stories for young adults. It was published by a major house, Doubleday, and received a modicum of attention.

The year before, he had finished writing his first book for adults, *Locos: A Comedy of Gestures*, a novel in the form of self-sufficient but loosely linked stories. This work might be seen as fitting into the Modernist tradition, which at that time was being forged by European and American writers such as Virginia Woolf and William Faulkner. Alfau was perhaps 30 years ahead of his time, however, and *Locos* employs the kinds of self-referential narrative strategies that are now associated with Postmodernism. After having trouble selling the book, he stored the manuscript until 1936, when it was published by Farrar & Reinehart in "Discoverers," a series offered exclusively to mail subscribers. A number of short notices appeared nationwide, and the eminent American novelist and critic Mary McCarthy wrote a positive review in the magazine *The Nation*.

For decades until his retirement, Alfau worked as a translator for a New York bank. In 1948, he wrote *Chromos*, a sequel of sorts to *Locos*, but again he failed to find a publisher. Nearly four decades later, an editor at Dalkey Archive Press, a small publisher of experimental literature, found a copy of *Locos* at a book sale and was wowed. When Dalkey reissued the work in 1988 with an epilogue by Mary McCarthy, Alfau achieved international recognition. When Dalkey issued *Chromos* two years later, that work was nominated for the National Book Award.

In 1992, a slim, bilingual volume of Alfau's lyrical poetry, written between 1923 and 1987 and translated by Ilan Stavans, appeared under the title *Sentimental Songs/La poesía cursi*. Critics deemed several of the poems racist, anti-Semitic, and anti-Hispanic. By that time, Alfau had become a famous recluse in a low-income retirement home in the New York City borough of Queens. In a series of interviews with Stavans in the early 1990s, he discussed topics such as his domestic life and artistic influences; his passion for European composers such as Beethoven and Wagner; his ambivalence about being perceived as a Latino; and his ambivalent feelings toward Jews, blacks, and liberals. (A staunch supporter of the Spanish dictator General Francisco Franco [1892–1975], Alfau believed that during the Spanish Civil War the government had not bombed the town of Guernica. This notorious attack, he claimed, had been invented by the artist Pablo Picasso and other prominent *izquierdistas*, or left-wingers. Cassettes containing about 20 hours of dialogue between Alfau and Stavans are available at Frost Library's Special Archives in Amherst College. Parts of those interviews, along with essays and appreciations by friends, colleagues, and critics, were included in a special issue of *The Review of Contemporary Fiction* released in 1993.)

Alfau's death nearly went unnoticed (Stavans dispatched an obituary from London to the Madrid daily *El País*). His standing in Latino literature remains uneasy. Because he was brought up in Spain, authors born in the Americas perceive him as an unwelcome alien. And his deliberately abstract art has never fit the rubric of ethnic fiction. While ahead of its time stylistically and imaginatively, it places him opposite the history-oriented trend in Latino literature. Furthermore, his conservative politics place him in a different tradition, one not attuned to categories such as colonialism, oppression, and compassion for the indigent segment of society. However, precisely because Alfau's is such a potent, unsettling "countervoice," his role is crucial: By forcing readers to approach Latino civilization unconventionally, even heretically, he helps provide a fuller, less polarized view of the entire Latino experience, a view that reflect its global range and broad ideological scope.

*Locos*, excerpted here, prefigures the aesthetic achievements of literary giants such as Luigi Pirandello, Vladimir Nabokov, and Jorge Luis Borges. The protagonists are a set of archetypes whose adventures are as implausible as they are unconventional. The fiction's extreme artificiality makes the events in it as distant from mundane reality as possible. *Chromos* takes a similar approach as it ponders a life in exile, reflecting on "what is lost forever" when a person immigrates to another culture.

## FROM LOCOS: A COMEDY OF GESTURES

## Identity

In writing this story, I am fulfilling a promise to my poor friend Fulano.[1]

My friend Fulano was the least important of men and this was the great tragedy of his life. Fulano had come to this world with the undaunted purpose of being famous and he had failed completely, developing into the most obscure person. He had tried all possible plans of acquiring importance, popularity, public acknowledgment, etc., and the world with a grim determination persistently refused to acknowledge even his existence.

It seems that about Fulano's personality, if we are to grant him a personality, hung a cloud of inattention which withstood his almost heroic assaults to break through it.

Fulano made the utmost efforts to be noticed, and people constantly missed him.

I have seen Fulano shake hands during an introduction in a vehement way, stare violently and shake his face close to the other person's, literally yelling:

*"Tanto gusto en conocerle."*[2]

And the next moment, the other individual was talking to somebody else, completely oblivious of Fulano.

I have seen Fulano at another introduction remain seated and extend two fingers in the most supercilious manner. Nothing! All in vain. A second after the other person had absolutely forgotten his existence and was blankly looking through him.

On one occasion I introduced Fulano to a friend and had to repeat three times:

"Please meet my friend Fulano." In a normal voice.

"Please meet my friend Fulano." In a louder voice.

"Please meet my friend Fulano." At the top of my voice.

The friend looked around several times and at last he perceived Fulano almost on top of him, shaking him by the shoulders with murder in his eyes. He opened his mouth and uttered in the most discouraging manner:

"Oh . . . how do you do?"

Poor Fulano's unimportance had arrived at the degree of making him almost invisible and inaudible. His name was unimportant, his face and figure were unimportant, his attire was unimportant and his whole life was unimportant. In fact, I don't know how I, myself, ever noticed him. True enough that he crushed my hand, dislocated my arm and kicked me on the shin when I met him.

Fulano had read all the pamphlets entitled: "Personal Magnetism," "Individuality and Success," etc. He had exhausted all the man-building literature, and in vain. One day he stood in the middle of La Puèrta del Sol[3] shouting:

"Fire . . . fire . . . !"

---

1. This name is the Spanish-language equivalent of "John Doe" or "So-and-so" (used later in the story).
2. A pleasure to meet you.

3. Literally, the Gate of the Sun; one of the best-known and busiest places in Madrid, and the center of the radial network of Spanish roads.

But no one seemed to hear him and at last he had to quit his post because a trolley car nearly ran him down.

Another day he threw a stone at a window of a well-known jewelry shop. At the noise of the broken glass, the owner came out. He looked at the window, and disregarding Fulano completely, muttered:

"Well, well, I wonder how that happened," and went back inside.

Not even beggars approached Fulano for alms.

All this would have been considered a blessing by a more practical person, but Fulano had no other purpose in his life except to be important, to attract attention, and these things made him only the more desperate.

Once I was at the Café de los Locos in Toledo. Bad writers were in the habit of coming to that café in quest of characters, and I came now and then among them. At that particular place one could find some very good secondhand bargains and also some fairly good, cheap, new material. As fashion has a great deal to do with market value, one could find at that place some characters who in their time had been glorious and served under famous geniuses, but who for some time had been out of a job, due to the change of literary trend toward other ideals.

I remember seeing there a poor and shabby lean fellow. He claimed to have served Cervantes.[4] Well, the poor man could interest no author at the present moment. In that manner, there was a score of good characters who had been great in their day, but were now of no earthly use.

On this particular day I had been sitting for some time at the table chatting with a friend of mine, Dr. José de los Rios, and looking around at the different faces and types. Suddenly I heard three blows struck upon my table and a hand pulled me by the collar. At the same time a voice said loudly:

"Here I am."

I turned around and saw Fulano sitting by my side.

"Well, when did you get here?"

"About half an hour ago. I have been sitting right here and trying to get into your conversation."

I apologized, saying that I had been absorbed in the contemplation of characters I expected to use in this book. After that, with no little difficulty and by applying some violent methods, I succeeded in introducing him to Dr. de los Rios. Then I observed that Fulano looked more dejected than usual.

"What is the matter? You look sad, Fulano."

"What do you expect? I have come to realize that I shall never be important, no matter how hard I try. It is no use, the world will simply ignore me."

"It is very disagreeable," I admitted. "But there are a lot of other people in the same predicament. There are, for instance, a number of husbands, preachers, dictators and . . ."

"This is no time for secondhand witty remarks. What I am telling you is serious. I know that I will never be important as a human being, and I have thought that perhaps I might gain fame and importance as a character."

" . . ."

"I don't care whether it is you or somebody else. You are my friend. You know I am willing, and perhaps you can make me a great character."

4. The Spanish writer Miguel de Cervantes (1547–1616), whose novel *Don Quixote* (1605, 1615) is about "a poor and shabby lean fellow."

I bowed under the weight of the compliment.

"If you cannot use me, then pass me along to some other writer. If you could smuggle me somewhere in this book you say you are going to write, my gratitude would know no limits. I don't care what I do, provided I gain importance."

"And . . . what are your qualifications to be a character?"

"The deuce! My very lack of importance. I shall be rated as the most unimportant character in fiction. You know that every character has more or less of a striking personality, that extraordinary things happen to all characters. Don't tell me that you will be ever able to find a character as flat and little interesting as myself."

"Well . . . you can find a lot of that in present-day literature . . . I really . . ."

Dr. José de los Rios, who had remained silent during this conversation, turned on my friend and spoke:

"Señor Fulano, although I have known you for a very short time, I can see only one way of hoping to get you out of your present condition. Señor Fulano, you must commit suicide."

"What?"

"I don't mean actually kill yourself, but commit an official suicide."

"What do you mean?"

"Just what I said. This evening as soon as it gets dark, you walk over the bridge of Alcántara and leave your coat on the ground with all your personal identification, all your credentials, your money, bankbook, etc., and a note saying that you have thrown yourself to the Tajo.[5] Then you go back to Madrid, having lost your official identity, and there we will try to make a character out of you."

Fulano looked at me questioningly. I said:

"I think that what Dr. de los Rios proposes is very logical."

Dr. de los Rios went on:

"You see? This apparent suicide will also serve as a little step toward notoriety. It is fortunate that this has taken place in this city. Toledo,[6] the Tajo, and the bridge of Alcántara have historical background and that will lend color to your action."

There was gratitude in the eyes of Fulano and he thanked Dr. de los Rios warmly, and I promised to do everything in my power to help him after he had complied with his part of the bargain.

By this time it was quite late in the afternoon. Dr. de los Rios had to go on a professional visit, and he left wishing Fulano a very successful enterprise. We remained seated at the table, and as Fulano had to wait until dark and we had nothing to do, I decided to amuse him by pointing out the characters that were gathered at the café.

"Do you see that fat, bald-headed policeman? He is Don Benito."

The policeman was unsuccessfully endeavoring to light a cigar with matches that consistently went out. Then he noticed we were speaking of him and assumed a proud air.

"Now look at that table by the window. The waitress who is laughing now is Lunarito. They call her that because of a beauty spot which cannot be

---

5. Literally, the Cut; known in English as the Tagus, and the longest river on the Iberian peninsula.

6. Municipality in central Spain, founded in the seventh century, made accessible partly by the bridge of Alcántara.

seen from here. The good-looking young man who is smoking a pipe and pinching her leg is Pepe Bejarano.

"Direct your attention toward that man whose collar is open. The one standing by the bar drinking . . . there now . . . the one that is pushing that woman away and insulting her. . . . He is El Cogote."[7]

At this moment two nuns entered the café and went from table to table seeking alms for their convent. I pointed at one of them:

"Look at that nun. The one that is interfering now between El Cogote and the woman. She is quite attractive to be a nun. She would have made a good woman of the world. Do you notice how gaily she smiles and how white her teeth are? That is Sister Carmela."

The two nuns had now approached a distant table where two priests sat, and were talking to them.

"Look at that priest, the one with the best manners who is standing talking to Sister Carmela. That is Padre Inocencio. He is supposed to do a great deal of good around here."

The two nuns went out followed by Padre Inocencio, who opened the door for them and remained there a while watching them walk across the plaza.

"Behold the bartender. See his splendid apostolic beard and the boisterous way in which he is laughing with El Cogote. He is Don Laureano Baez, an old rogue and very amusing. The old woman behind him with the sad expression who is wiping the glasses is his wife, Doña Felisa.

"Now notice that man sitting at that table. The one with the white wig and the poetic expression, who seems so distracted and aloof. His name is Garcia."

The man was smelling a flower pinned to his lapel.

At that moment a little dog, who was nosing about the café, began to paw the man's leg. Garcia gave the dog a vicious kick, then he tossed a coin over to the bartender and departed.

"Look at that pale lady dressed in black sitting at that table with a gentleman. Notice how she is going to sleep. She is Doña Micaela Valverde."

Her escort got up silently, took his hat and left the café on tiptoes. Doña Micaela, who was now fast asleep, did not see him go.

For some time I had been noticing a man standing by a table where four men sat. He was showing them small objects which he took out of his pocket and which apparently he was trying to sell them. He turned around and then I recognized him. We greeted each other and he walked toward our table holding a small object in his hand.

I said to Fulano:

"This is Don Gil, an old dealer in junk, who peddles his stuff around the cafés."

Don Gil approached us. He leaned with a hand on the wall and in the other he showed us a little Chinese figure made of porcelain.

"Here is a real bargain," he said, tossing the porcelain figure on the palm of his hand. "It is a real old work of art made in China. What do you say?"

I looked at the figure which was delicately made. It represented a herculean warrior with drooping mustache and a ferocious expression. He had a

---

7. Literally, the scruff of the neck. Like the other figures pointed out here, he is a character in other stories within *Locos*.

butterfly on his shoulder. The color of the face was not yellow but a darker color, more like bronze, and as the attire was not very representative, I suggested:

"Perhaps it is not Chinese but Indian."

Don Gil, who undoubtedly liked China better than India, looked slightly annoyed.

"No, it is Chinese," he said.

Then I could not help noticing that the hand that held the figure was quite dirty and inferred that its sister probably was in the same condition.

I said:

"Don Gil, be careful. Don Laureano is going to scold you for dirtying his walls."

Don Gil withdrew his hand, leaving a dirty mark that seemed unusually small upon the whitewashed wall, and continued to praise his merchandise:

"Yes, this is a real Chinese mandarin or warrior, I don't know which, and it is a real bargain. Perhaps your friend might be interested. . . ."

Fulano gave a jump and let out a yell. It was the first time that a stranger had noticed him of his own accord.

Poor Don Gil was so frightened that he dropped the porcelain figure, smashing it in a thousand pieces on the marble top of the table. I fancied I saw a furious look in the little porcelain head now detached from the body.

Don Gil wiped the pieces to the floor and went away, trampling over them with a chagrined expression.

"Well," I said when Don Gil had gone, "I suppose you have had enough characters for a day. It is quite dark now and you had better get ready for your suicide."

Fulano scribbled a note saying: *I have committed suicide by jumping into the Tajo*, and said:

"All my hopes depend on this." He got up and departed, promising to see me in Madrid.

Now I, as the author of this tale, can see all that Fulano did after he went away, although I am supposed to remain seated at the café table.

Fulano went to his room. He gathered all his documents and credentials and started on his fateful journey. As he walked down the stairs to the street, night had fallen, and each step he took was like dropping a century into the past, until he emerged in the midst of a hostile city which died in the Renaissance and yet lived the strangest, posthumous life. Toledo was in silence, but Toledo did not rest. As Fulano advanced hesitantly, he felt the restless and decrepit lines of buildings suddenly agitated by a wind of the past, the pavement seemed to rise, fall and revolt in its stony unevenness, like a stormy sea; he walked through streets so steep that he had to lean against the wall to keep from falling and he rushed through alleys that ran down from the top of the city like jumping torrents, to precipitate themselves down into the waters of the Tajo.

Toledo comes to life every night. It is a city of silence, but not a city of peace; at night it multiplies its interests, it becomes a city of horror, of fearful dreams of the past, of dreadful historical nightmares. At the turn of a street, this impression hit Fulano with such force that it nailed him to the spot, as if turned into one more stony specter. All the shadows of things gone came to meet him from out dark alleys, from out sad corners, to condense and take shape, to make the night blacker. He could imagine the figure of Don Pedro el Cruel, his knees rattling, trailing along the familiar alley to the house of the Jew who lent him money. He could sense the heavy atmosphere charged with the deadly breath of the Inquisition.[8]

This silence, this feeling of being left alone to share a city with the dead, suddenly revealed an idea to Fulano. Toledo, as he hoped to be soon, was a myth, Toledo did not exist. It rose at night upon its historical and aesthetic signification, forsaken among this loneliness of sterile Castilla. And thus thinking, Fulano stumbled on like a frightened, forsaken shadow after its own body. The narrow, crooked, tortuous streets fled from him, denying his path, mocking, snarling, like snakes in a jungle of bizarre structures; he staggered from one surprise into another, carried by this immense and irresistibly suggestive strength. He passed houses that were horribly worn out where they joined the ground, their stones blent together, and doors that were never opened and through whose ragged bottoms medieval cats sneaked in and out. He heard the waters of the Tajo calling and all this past splendor fading away in eternal response, all this past glory slipping down the hill, sinking into the Tajo below.

Fulano knew he had been swallowed by this maelstrom of the past, that he had sunk back centuries in history, and had already lost his identity of present existence. He was choking from this overwhelming feeling of condensed time, he was hopelessly lost in this darkness of thousands of superimposed past nights, in this labyrinth of streets that tossed him to and fro, threatening to drag him in their ominous stream and thrust him down into the Tajo, into oblivion.

His sense of direction utterly lost, Fulano let himself be ejected, cast out centrifugally, gravitationally by this semiconical city, now spinning in his dizzy mind, and he crossed one by one all the walls of Toledo, each one framing a period of history, like conquering phalanxes seen in perspective, each wall larger and lower, descending the hill, like steps, falling down into the Tajo.

And it was in this manner that the city of Toledo discarded this insignificant individual upon the bridge of Alcántara.

In the middle of the bridge, Fulano stripped himself of his coat and placed it on the ground, pinning the note on the outside.

Having done this and ascertained that no one saw him, he walked in his shirt sleeves toward the station.

Fulano did not see what happened after he left the bridge but I, of course, saw it, and if a writer had the privilege of interfering or preventing the incidents which he has the misfortune to witness, I would have prevented what took place, for the sake of my poor friend, Fulano. However, if a writer could do that, all stories would end happily and justice would prevail in all literature. As this would create a great monotony, such power has not been granted. Therefore, I had to stand by and see the happenings in a state of utter impotence and indignation.

8. The Spanish Inquisition, a notoriously harsh tribunal established in 1478 by the Spanish monarchs to punish the Jews and Muslims who had converted to Catholicism but were insincere. *Don Pedro el Cruel*: Pedro or Peter (1334–1369), sometimes called "the Cruel" or "the Lawful" (*el Jus-* *ticiero*), was the king of Castile and León—two of the kingdoms that became Spain—from 1350 to 1369. Pedro forcefully put down anti-Jewish riots inspired partly by his brother Enrique, who encouraged Castilian anti-Semitism and depicted Pedro as "King of the Jews."

A man of evil appearance walked along the bridge. By the moonlight he saw the coat on the ground and stooped and picked it up. He fumbled in the pockets and took out all the papers. He lighted a match and examined them rapidly. He then saw the note pinned to the coat and a devilish smile played over his face.

With haste he put all the papers back in the pockets, took off his own coat, pinned the note on it, and donned Fulano's coat.

In the train to Madrid, Fulano did not notice a man with a cap pulled down over his eyes and a coat that matched Fulano's trousers to perfection. Fulano sneezed furiously now and then, but his mind and heart were jumping with anticipation and happiness.

The next day a local paper of Toledo carried the following account:

> Yesterday evening So-and-so who had escaped from prison and whom the authorities were prosecuting, committed suicide by jumping into the river Tajo from the bridge of Alcántara. This has been deduced from a note pinned to his coat which was found on the bridge. It seems that after the many crimes he had committed, remorse seized him at last and he decided to end his sinful existence. R.I.P.

One day, after returning to Madrid, I was walking through the street of Sevilla when I found myself seized by the shoulders and beheld a face pale with rage at two inches from my nose.

"Hello, Fulano! But what is the matter with you?"

"What is the matter with me, you ask?"

"Yes. How did the suicide trick work?" (Of course, I had entirely forgotten what I saw at the bridge.)

"How did it work . . . ? How did it work . . . ? Infernally!!"

"What do you mean, infernally? What happened, then?"

Fulano took two steps back and stood there looking at me:

"Do you see me here?"

"A bit blurred, but I still see you."

"Well, I do not exist."

"What?"

"I do not exist."

"You do not exist?"

"No."

"But how is that possible?"

"Since I have had any use of reason, I have entertained strong doubts about my existence. No, don't look at me as if I were going to enter into a metaphysical discussion. I am talking seriously now. Yes, I had always entertained strong doubts about my own existence, but since your idiotic suggestion about suicide those doubts have abandoned me completely. Now I am sure that I do not exist."

"But explain yourself." Fulano had already spent some of his initial steam and could speak more calmly.

"Well, someone is now here in Madrid, enjoying my personality, my name, my property, my home, my wife . . . everything that belonged to me. And he is enormously famous, mind you, one of the best known politicians and businessmen, and accumulating a tremendous fortune. And I am nothing, I am absolutely lost, looking for some loose identity in order to find myself.

But every identity has its owner and I am nothing, nothing. I do not exist . . ." Fulano broke down and put a handkerchief to his eyes.

"But do you mean to say that the people who knew you cannot tell the difference? Cannot realize that this other Fulano is an impostor?"

"How can they tell the difference if they never noticed me before? I was always so unimportant, so absolutely unimportant!"

For the first time I realized in all its magnitude the tragedy of this unimportant man's life.

Fulano produced a newspaper and pointed silently but eloquently at the big headlines which said something very flattering about Fulano.

"See what they say about him. What they should be saying about me. He has taken my name, my identity, and with it all the fame and importance that should have been mine."

"No, Fulano, do not deceive yourself. It is not the name that has made him precisely. You would have never attained that success if you had remained Fulano. The man must possess the personality which you lack and he has made the name famous. Really, in a way you should be grateful to him."

"Be grateful to him . . . ! That is what you say after you got me into this mess with your idiotic suggestion!"

"It was Dr. de los Rios and not I who made the suggestion."

"Just the same, you sided with him and you are just as responsible, and now you advise me to remain nothing, while he enjoys all my possessions and glory and fame, and all that the world can offer a man. I must sit back patiently, glad to be no one and thank him to boot! Do you realize the inconvenience of being alive and not existing?"

I had to admit the inconvenience of such a strange situation:

"Yes, something must be done about it."

"Of course, something must be done about it, and it is you who must do it, you who got me into it. . . . But, my Lord! How did it happen that this man took my place in the world?"

I felt that I must confess to Fulano, that the situation compelled me to betray an author's secret. After all, to lose one's identity must be the weirdest sensation in this world. Therefore, I related all that I had seen at the bridge and mentioned the account that had been published in the paper the day after the incident.

When I finished, Fulano was foaming at the mouth and ready to spring upon me, but he was firmly seized by a hand. It was Dr. José de los Rios himself.

Fulano struggled to free himself and yelled at me:

"So you mean to say that you stood by and didn't do anything to prevent it, to save me from this horrible tragedy?"

Dr. de los Rios tried to calm him. I lowered my head.

"Fulano, my friend. If I could have done anything, I would not have hesitated to do it, but it is not in my power to interfere with the destinies of men."

"And I am supposed to be satisfied with that answer, to remain an empty body without a place in society, a supernumerary in this world. . . . To hell with you writers who can place a fellow in a situation like this and then cannot get him out of it!"

I lowered my head further.

"Forgive me, Fulano, I will see what I can do for you. . . ."

"Well, go ahead and see. I suppose you cannot make things worse than you have. Nothing could be worse."

Dr. de los Rios, who had been too busy holding Fulano, spoke now:

"Señor Fulano, I was the one who made the original suggestion about the suicide and I assume the whole responsibility."

"But I don't care who the devil is responsible. I am in trouble and want to be helped out of it."

"Very well, Señor Fulano, I admit that you are right in your demands, but I can only see one way out of it. There are no loose identities in this world which you can seize in order to regain your footing in life. There is only one superfluous identity as superfluous as yourself, and that identity is under the river Tajo. Yes, Señor Fulano, officially that identity is under that river and lately you must have realized the importance of official things. That soul upon the bed of the Tajo is craving for a body as much as you crave a soul. Go join it and end your mutual absurdity. After that I am sure that my friend will try to revive you in a story and to make a character out of you."

Again Fulano turned to me questioningly. I said:

"Yes, Fulano, I promise to do what Dr. de los Rios says."

Fulano gripped our hands firmly. Upon his features there was the determination born from despair.

"Good-by, Fulano."

"Good-by."

That night Fulano was again upon the bridge of Alcántara. He had come to look for an identity in the same place where he had gone to lose one. He looked down on the dark waters of the Tajo. Yes, there it was, his only salvation.

And once more he saw Toledo covering its hill like a petrified forest of centuries. It was absurd. With all useful justification of its existence gone, the city sat there like a dead emperor upon his wrecked throne, yet greater in his downfall than in his glory. There lay the corpse of a city draped upon a forgotten hill, history written in every deep furrow of its broken countenance, its limbs hanging down the banks to be buried under the waters of a relentless river.

Fulano looked down and then knew fate and greatness; he hesitated no more; with resolution he jumped.

And in order to fulfill my promise to that unfortunate and most unimportant of all men, I have written this story. Whether I have succeeded in making a character or even a symbol out of him, or whether he will enjoy this poor revival, I do not know. I have done my best.

1928                                                                                                    1936

# JOSÉ DÁVILA SEMPRIT
## 1902–1958

José Dávila Semprit was born in the town of Toa Baja, Puerto Rico. In the 1920s, he left Puerto Rico for New York City, where he worked as a postman. During the more than three decades that he lived in New York, he participated in several workers' and community organizations that fostered social activism, cultural activity, and solidarity among Puerto Ricans. He also advocated Puerto Rico's independence from the United States. Most of his writing remains unpublished or is scattered in the Spanish-language community newspapers and magazines to which he contributed frequently.

Dávila Semprit's only published books are the poetry collections *Brazos bronce* (Arms of Bronze, 1933) and *Poemario de la madre* (A Book of Poems for Mothers, 1958). Before his death in Puerto Rico, where he had returned in 1956, he was working on an anthology of Puerto Rican poets in New York that remains unpublished. In some of his poems, Dávila Semprit offers a critical view of the United States by exposing with an ironic tone the contradictions between, on the one hand, the American nation's claim to be a beacon of democracy and of freedom and, on the other hand, its exploitative capitalist/imperialist role in the world and the racism that still plagues its society. He is above all a nationalistic poet extremely critical of those Puerto Rican migrants who mimic American ways of life without realizing the prejudices against them that exist in U.S. society.

## The United States[1]

A sublime document that proclaims
the rights of man,
a star-spangled banner,
history that begins
with roaring rebelliousness                                    5
and ends up smelling of imperialism,
a heterogeneous people, the remains
of our old Europe turned into a Republic;
an alloy of passions, prejudices,
and entrenched arrogance,                                      10
deceit has become a God in America,
the belly laugh of the century,
the sarcasm of this era:
The United States!

In its port there is a statue                                  15
lying about liberty, insulting the cosmos.
Within there is injustice: Sacco, Vanzetti,
Mooney, the blacks of Scottsboro,[2]

1. Translated by Edna Acosta-Belén and Susan Liberis-Hill.
2. The Scottsboro Boys were nine black teenagers falsely accused of raping two white women in Scottsboro, Alabama, in the 1930s. All were repeatedly found guilty and sentenced to death by all-white southern juries, but international uproar helped free them, the last more than 20 years after the initial incident. *Sacco, Vanzetti*: Nicola Sacco (1891–1927) and Bartolomeo Vanzetti (1888–1927), Italian-born American laborers and anarchists, were executed by electrocution in 1927 for the 1920 armed robbery and murder of two pay clerks in South Braintree, Massachusetts. World-

the cry of the mothers whose sons
have died in imperialist campaigns,                                    20
the cry of the sons whose mothers
strayed into vice.
The Ku Klux Klan growling fanaticism,
the persecuted Indian in the mountains,
the black man passed over and persecuted,                             25
the Bible feeding ignorance;
mitigated pain,
with the Puritan prayer of the dead:
The United States!

Sorrow, grief that chauvinism quells!                                 30
Hatred, resentment fired by religion!
Endless smell of blood in the atmosphere,
mediocrity in a tunic made flesh,
new life in the temple of the god Janus,
Minerva's altar in ruins,[3]                                          35
a desire for power within each soul,
the word of God out on each lip:
The United States!

Reigning in Detroit, Chicago, New York
huge smoke-belching beasts                                            40
eating human flesh
baring their fangs
and pretending to rend the sky!
Detroit aspires to pollute the heavens
with the spit of its factories;                                       45
Chicago has a place in the History of crime
perpetuating itself with the shooting
and abuses of its gunmen.
New York is unique and supreme
with its Tammany Hall,[4] elegant refuge                              50
of very twentieth century robbers
and with its Wall Street tentacles,
the narrow and foul-smelling
hideout of Ginart.[5]
Continuous movement,                                                  55
huge factories that suck up
the blood of the worker;
politicians, bankers, and bandits,
Three Different People and one True Swindler:
The United States!                                                    60

1933

---

wide demonstrators argued that their trial was unfair, that contradictory evidence was ignored, and
that Sacco and Vanzetti's political beliefs had convicted them. *Mooney*: Thomas Joseph Mooney
(1882–1942), American labor leader in San Francisco, famously was sentenced to be hanged and
spent 22½ years in prison for a crime he did not
commit, the Preparedness Day Bombing of 1916.

3. Minerva was the Roman goddess of wisdom,
handicrafts, and the arts. Janus was the Roman
god of beginnings and custodian of the universe.
4. Democratic Party political machine that controlled New York City politics from 1790 to the
1960s, helping immigrants (most notably the Irish)
rise in American politics.
5. Unidentified.

## One of Many[1]

This gentleman of whom I speak, born in Puerto Rico
grew up eating mofongo and ñames and yautía[2]
forgot his past and even his own name the day
that he brought to this land his monkey humanity.
His name became Píter, it used to be Perico,                                    5
he forgot the Spanish language and only sounded
like he was quacking each time he wanted
to say in English what he was thinking, if he was thinking that chico.[3]

But one day . . . —life
goes around and comes around in big cities—                                    10
he stumbled over life and its treacheries,
felt deeply the injury
of vices and prejudices of American malice.
And cried out for his homeland in pure Spanish!

1991

1. Translated by Bethania Stewart.
2. *Mofongo* is a typical Puerto Rican dish made of mashed and seasoned plantains. Both *ñame* and *yautía* are starchy tuber edibles and also very typical side dishes in Puerto Rican cuisine.
3. I.e., if he, that boy (*chico*), was thinking at all.

---

# EUGENIO FLORIT
## 1903–1999

An introspective writer of unusual depth and complexity, Eugenio Florit is one of the most important voices in twentieth-century Cuban poetry. Born in Madrid to a Spanish father and Cuban mother, Florit spent his childhood in Spain. In 1918, his family moved to Cuba, where Florit attended secondary school and college. After receiving a law degree from the University of Havana in 1926, he entered the Cuban State Department. During the late 1920s and early 1930s, he became a well-known figure in Cuban literary circles, writing reviews and articles for the important literary magazine *Revista de Avance* and publishing his first significant collection of poems, *Trópico* (Tropic, 1930). His other books of this period are *Doble acento* (Double Accent, 1937) and *Reino* (Kingdom, 1938).

Appointed auxiliary Cuban consul in 1940, Florit moved to New York City, where he worked to promote Cuban culture. He continued to publish poems in the Cuban reviews *Orígenes*, *Nadie Parecía*, and *Espuela de Plata*. In 1942, Florit began teaching Spanish and Spanish American literature in at Columbia University. Three years later, he left the Cuban diplomatic corps and became a professor of Hispanic literature at Barnard College.

During the following decades, while living in New York City, Florit published several volumes of poetry, including *Poema mío* (My Poem, 1947), *Asonante final y otros poemas* (Final Assonance and Other Poems, 1950), and *Hábito de esperanza* (Habit of Hope, 1965), as well as critical essays, textbooks, and anthologies. After his retirement from teaching in 1969, Florit lived in New York until relocating to Miami,

Florida. He wrote and published volumes of poetry and criticism, among them *Antología penúltima* (Penultimate Anthology, 1970), *Versos pequeños* (Small Verses, 1977), *A pesar de todo* (In Spite of Everything, 1987), and *Lo que queda* (What Remains, 1995).

Although Florit considered himself Cuban rather than Latino, his poems often reflect, and reflect upon, his life in New York City, where he resided for 30 years. Calling attention to inclement weather, the crush of people, or the impersonality of a metropolis, Florit's New York poems—particularly his well-known poem "In the Big City"—evoke José Martí's writings on these subjects (see p. 265).

# In the Big City[1]

### (with Martí)

How good to take it slow
when everyone else is rushing!
What if I miss the train?
Life flashes by more quickly.

Here, among this crowd                                    5
of lost people
who walk around and about,
who walk about and back
who walk back and around
without smiling—                                          10
how good it feels to take it slow
when everyone else is rushing!

In this sunken city,
lights don't shine.
Absorbing anguish                                        15
from below, from above,
from the left and the right,
they glare at each other
as if they too were lost.
When they light our way,                                 20
they do so dimly,
afraid of being caught yawning
yellow light.

How base the world
of hurry up!
How sadly, how nervously                                 25
people walk
or run,
all to save a minute.
As if afterwards,                                        30
when our day arrives,

1. Translated by Gustavo Pérez Firmat.

we weren't going to come
to a dead stop.
As if by running
without the sun as our guide,                                    35
without the trees to give us shade,
without air or breeze,
we weren't going to be enveloped
in this fog of fumes
and wilted faces.                                                40
As if the flowers
that scream
for a breath of air
were not more beautiful
in the air above us,                                             45
where they burst out, pure,
in living colors.

How our soul
gets trapped
in the mad pace                                                  50
of hurrying!
What pulling and tugging
to tear it away
from frozen stares.
But if we succeed                                                55
in conquering hurry
and finally feel free,
how good to take it slow,
so slow,
when everyone else is rushing!                                   60

What if I miss the train?
Life flashes by more quickly!

1957

## The Lonely Poets of Manhattan[1]

The Cuban poet Alcides Iznaga visited New York in August 1959.
Upon his return to Cienfuegos, Cuba, he sent me a poem, "We're
alone in Manhattan," to which I replied with these lines:

My dear friend Alcides Iznaga:
it's true that Langston Hughes[2] wasn't home
and neither was I.
Langston, who lives with his people,
had gone downtown.                                               5

1. Translated by Gustavo Pérez Firmat.
2. African American writer (1902–1967). By 1959,
he was living in the Harlem section of Upper
Manhattan (i.e., "uptown").

And when you called
or rather stopped by,
I was far away, in the countryside,
living with my people.

The truth is that here, up here,                                           10
it doesn't matter whether you live
on 127th St.
or Park Avenue.
Here we are all alone and lost
among the roar of the subway and the fire trucks,                          15
among the sirens of ambulances
that rush to save those who kill themselves
by jumping into the river
or falling out a window
or turning on a gas stove                                                  20
or swallowing a hundred sleeping pills
because, since they haven't found themselves,
all they want to do is forget
that no one remembers them,
that they are alone, terribly alone.                                       25

I ran into Langston at the end of August
at a Pen Club[3] cocktail party.
He was solicitous and dressed in blue.
And then years go by, and perhaps we'll send
each other a book, "Inscribed for my dear friend,                          30
With best wishes . . ."
And so we grow old,
the black poet
and the white poet
and the mulatto and the Chinese poet                                       35
and every living thing.

You must be growing old too,
you and my friends from Cienfuegos
who took me, that day in 1955, to the Jagua castle
where a *vicaria* flower[4]                                                40
growing between two stones
made me tremble.
What happens here,
my dear friend Alcides Iznaga,
is that we have no *vicarias*,                                             45
or Jagua castles, or poets like you,
or palm trees,
or the blue waters of Cienfuegos bay.
The only waters here barely flow
in the lazy rivers that surround Manhattan . . .                           50

3. Writer's association.
4. Vinca, or periwinkle. *Jagua castle*: Castillo de
Nuestra Señora de los Ángeles de Jagua, a fortress
erected in the 1745 near Cienfuegos, a major sea-
port on the southern coast of Cuba.

You, my dear Alcides,
came looking for us in New York,
the city where nobody knows anybody,
where each of us is a drop of water,
a mote of dust                                                      55
like those that waft sadly from chimneys.
I say "sadly" but it's only a manner of speaking.
I'm thankful that I still have the words
with which to greet the sun that rises
—when it rises—in front of my window.                              60
And when it doesn't rise, I greet the wind,
the rain, the fog, the clouds;
I greet the world I live in
with the words I write in.
And I thank God for the day and the night                          65
and above all for letting me keep my words,
here, in this city where nobody knows me.

1959

## Portrait of a Man Alone[1]

His friends have left. Alone in the apartment, he's swimming in cigarette smoke. He opens the window so that the cold can clear the air. In the meantime, he goes about picking up coffee cups, emptying the ashtrays. Then he closes the window. He does it all calmly, as if he had all night. Besides, it's Friday, and the next day he doesn't have to get up early. Look how careless people can be . . . A scratch on the corner of the piano. What could have made it? Let's see if a moist rag will do the trick. Good, it's nothing. But oh, the book wasn't so lucky. There it is, split open, with a stain on the hand of the Gentleman with his hand on his chest. Some people are just impossible. Well, it can't be helped. (I'm thinking this as he thinks it, of course, because I'm right behind him, following his steps from the window to the table, from the table to the kitchen, from the kitchen to the piano, from the piano to the chair. He moves deliberately, as if in slow motion, from place to place.)

He takes his clothes off. In his pajamas and his brown flannel bathrobe, he sits next to the window to look outside, where the lights go out one by one, sinking into the darkness that spreads over everything. He notices a little light on the tower of a building. How high, dear God. And how alone. As if separated by many leagues from the other lights he sees here and there, also far away from one another, as if separated by many years. He had worked once on the twelfth floor of that building with the little light; yes, it was the twelfth floor. He remembered how it happened. An old friend offered him a job as a clerk in a publishing house. From nine to twelve and from one to five. A decent salary. How much was it? Something like fifty dollars a week. Enough for those days and for a man who lived alone, with few entanglements. And the truth is he enjoyed the four years he worked there. He even

1. Translated by Gustavo Pérez Firmat.

had a girlfriend, sort of. It began with the two of them eating lunch together, and then leaving their jobs at the same time each afternoon, and since there wasn't anything better to do, walking together for a few blocks, and going into a store, and having an ice cream at ten past five; and little by little their lives began to get entwined, so entwined that if the girl's mother who lived in Florida hadn't gotten ill, and if her daughter hadn't left to take care of her, it would have ended badly—with a wedding I mean. But everyone knows how that goes. There was nothing between them. Only that they liked each other and got used to being together. (But perhaps that's true of most happy marriages.) Since neither one of them had a tragic streak, the parting was relatively painless. He took her to the airport, gave her a box of chocolates, and they said goodbye a little sadly. And then they wrote to each other for a few months. And that was it. And it had all begun there, on the twelfth floor of that building, now shrouded in darkness except for the little light on the tower that the two of us were looking at through the window. (Because everything that he was seeing and thinking I was seeing and thinking also. Because I was right behind him, like his shadow. As if I had gotten inside the silhouette that the lamp made on the wall.)

He had not married. All his time for himself. Now he was glad. How things had changed. His finances had improved. He had landed an important job, and after a few years found the apartment where he now lived, very high and very bright. Away from everything and in the middle of everything. Convenient and not too expensive. But no, he had not married. That office romance left him without bitterness but also without hope. And there was so much reading to do, and so much music to listen to. But above all his reading. He never had enough time . . . Minutes, no more than minutes. And now the day had ended and night had swept into his apartment. It was time to go to sleep and he wouldn't be able to finish that page, which he bookmarked with a postcard of a river and palm trees. (I know all this as well as he does, because—as I said—I'm like his shadow.) And that's why now, at this very moment, I know that he has fallen asleep in his bed, all bundled up. And I know that he's dreaming a dream he has dreamed before, a dream of long ago when he was a boy and the river and the palm trees were so near that all he had to do was jump on the trolley and get off by the stone bridge and the river was right there. And the palm trees. And the *vicaria* flower[2] too. I know that he's dreaming all this in the bed of his apartment, way up high, after picking up the coffee cups and emptying the ash trays. And I know that he's dreaming this after having dreamed for a while with his eyes wide open, by the window, staring at the little light on the tower in the distance: The waking dream of a deliberate little man who reads and never has time to read. Who sometimes doesn't even have time to dream. Or to write what he has dreamed of writing.

1960

---

2. Vinca, or periwinkle.

## Out of the Snow[1]

Out of the melting snow,
out of the dirty newspapers on the sidewalk,
out of the fog, out of the sunken train
with its hundred hands grasping;
out of the make-believe neon lights                          5
and the roar of the fire truck,
out of the night that falls on top of us
—slabs of starless sky—,
out of every moment wasted where
the loners of the world mill about,                          10
out of the leafless tree
and the deserted trail,
once again,
like yesterday, like tomorrow,
perhaps like all the days to come,                           15
if they come,
I step into silence.

1967

1. Translated by Gustavo Pérez Firmat.

---

# JOVITA GONZÁLEZ DE MIRELES
## 1904–1983

Within the Latino literary tradition, folklorists became particularly important in the early part of the twentieth century. Through interviews with older Hispanic inhabitants of the Southwest, folklorists such as Aurelio and Gilberto Espinosa and Arturo L. Campa played significant parts in uncovering folktales and dramatic presentations that had remained relatively unchanged over hundreds of years and that, in some cases, were directly related to folktales from rural Spain. Among the subsequent folklorists who documented the disappearance of this folklore-based culture was Jovita González de Mireles. Her strength lay in the gathering and retelling, in print, of local, contemporary tales that reflected a recent past—of violence between the Mexican American minority and the dominant Anglos and of the minority's resistance to the established order.

Jovita González was born into a prominent family with roots in the early Spanish settlers of the Southwest. She was raised on her grandfather's ranch in the Rio Grande Valley, in the southernmost tip of south-central Texas. She graduated from Our Lady of the Lake College, in San Antonio, with a degree in history and Spanish and in 1930 received a master's degree in education from the University of Texas.

In 1925, she had met and begun working with J. Frank Dobie, a pioneer in the collection and interpretation of southwestern folklore (Dobie unearthed the typescript of *Memoirs*, by Jesse Pérez; see p. 327). In her articles—printed in publications such as the *Southwest Review* and various collections of Texas folklore that Dobie edited—González sought to preserve local cultures and to promote a better understanding between Mexican Americans and Anglos. For example, her 1930 article "America Invades the Border Towns" laments the changes to, and losses of, local Hispanic culture.

In 1935, González married Edmundo E. Mireles, a Mexican American who, during the next several decades, would become very influential in the promotion of bilingual education. Together they wrote textbooks for the teaching of Spanish in grade school. In Texas high schools, first in Del Rio and then in Corpus Christi, González de Mireles taught English, Spanish, and Texas history until her retirement.

In her retellings of folktales such as "The Bullet-Swallower" and "The Mescal-Drinking Horse," González de Mireles used English to convey the new legends growing on the border and to re-create the atmosphere of Mexican American storytelling. Published in J. Frank Dobie's anthology *Puro Mexicano* (1936) and reprinted here, "The Bullet-Swallower" is a romantic tale of a man who has left his upper-class environment to face the harshness of the West. González tells it with the proper awe. A few, carefully chosen Spanish words—*machete, conquistador, pelo en pecho, jacal,* and *tequila*—add authenticity to her tale but also prompt the English-language reader, especially the reader of 1936, to acknowledge both the exoticism and the alterity of the speaker.

## The Bullet-Swallower

He was a wiry little man, a bundle of nerves in perpetual motion. Quicksilver might have run through his veins instead of blood. His right arm, partly paralyzed as result of a *machete* cut he had received in a saloon brawl, terminated in stiff, claw-like, dirty-nailed fingers. One eye was partly closed—a knife cut had done that—but the other, amber in color, had the alertness and the quickness of a hawk's. Chairs were not made for him. Squatting on the floor or sitting on one heel, he told interminable stories of border feuds, bandit raids and smuggler fights as he fingered a curved, murderous knife which ended in three inches of zigzag, jagged steel. "No one has ever escaped this," he would say, caressing it. "Sticking it into a man might not have finished him, but getting it out—ah, my friend, that did the work. It's a very old one, brought from Spain, I guess," he would add in an unconcerned voice. "Here is the date, 1630."

A landowner by inheritance, a trail driver by necessity, and a smuggler and gambler by choice, he had given up the traditions of his family to be and do that which pleased him most. Through some freakish mistake he had been born three centuries too late. He might have been a fearless *conquistador,* or he might have been a chivalrous knight of the Rodrigo de Narváez[1] type, fighting the infidels along the Moorish frontier. A tireless horseman, a man of *pelo en pecho* (hair on the chest), as he braggingly called himself, he was afraid of nothing.

"The men of my time were not lily-livered, white-gizzarded creatures," he would boast. "We fought for the thrill of it, and the sight of blood maddened us as it does a bull. Did we receive a gash on the stomach? Did the guts come out? What of it? We tightened our sash and continued the fray. See

---

1. A major character, a horseman, in the anonymous Spanish narrative *El Abencerraje* (ca. 1561), which concerns Moors and Christians in Spain. In the novel *Don Quixote* (1605, 1615), by the Spanish writer Miguel de Cervantes (1547–1616), the delusional title character mistakes a peasant for Narváez and himself for a Moor.

this arm? Ah, could it but talk, it could tell you how many men it sent to the other world. To Hell perhaps, perhaps to Purgatory, but none I am sure to Heaven. The men I associated with were neither sissies nor saints. Often at night when I can not sleep because of the pain in these cursed wounds, I say a prayer, in my way, for their souls, in case my prayers should reach the good God.

"People call me Traga-Balas, Bullet-Swallower—Antonio Traga-Balas, to be more exact. *Ay*, were I as young as I was when the incident that gave me this name happened!

"We were bringing several cartloads of smuggled goods to be delivered at once and in safety to the owner. Oh, no, the freight was not ours but we would have fought for it with our life's blood. We had dodged the Mexican officials, and now we had to deal with the Texas Rangers. They must have been tipped, because they knew the exact hour we were to cross the river. We swam in safety. The pack mules, loaded with packages wrapped in tanned hides, we led by the bridle. We hid the mules in a clump of tules and were just beginning to dress when the Rangers fell upon us. Of course, we did not have a stitch of clothes on; did you think we swam fully dressed? Had we but had our guns in readiness, there might have been a different story to tell. We would have fought like wild-cats to keep the smuggled goods from falling into their hands. It was not ethical among smugglers to lose the property of a Mexican to Americans, and as to falling ourselves into their hands, we preferred death a thousand times. It's no disgrace and dishonor to die like a man, but it is to die like a rat. Only canaries sing; men never tell, however tortured they may be. I have seen the Rangers pumping water into the mouth of an innocent man because he would not confess to something he had not done. But that is another story.

"I ran to where the pack mules were to get my gun. Like a fool that I was, I kept yelling at the top of my voice, 'You so, so and so gringo cowards, why don't you attack men like men? Why do you wait until they are undressed and unarmed?' I must have said some very insulting things, for one of them shot at me right in the mouth. The bullet knocked all of my front teeth out, grazed my tongue and went right through the back of my neck. Didn't kill me, though. It takes more than bullets to kill Antonio Traga-Balas. The next thing I knew I found myself in a shepherd's hut. I had been left for dead, no doubt, and I had been found by the goatherd. The others were sent to the penitentiary. After I recovered, I remained in hiding for a year or so; and when I showed myself all thought it a miracle that I had lived through. That's how I was rechristened Traga-Balas. That confounded bullet did leave my neck a little stiff; I can't turn around as easily as I should, but outside of that I am as fit as though the accident—I like to call it that— had never happened. It takes a lot to kill a man, at least one who can swallow bullets.

"I've seen and done many strange things in my life and I can truthfully say that I have never been afraid but once. What are bullets and knife thrusts to seeing a corpse arise from its coffin? Bullets can be dodged and dagger cuts are harmless unless they hit a vital spot. But a dead man staring with lifeless, open eyes and gaping mouth is enough to make a man tremble in his boots. And, mind you, I am not a coward, never have been. Is there any one among you who thinks Antonio Traga-Balas is a coward?"

At a question like this, Traga-Balas would take the knife from its cover and finger it in a way that gave one a queer, empty spot in the stomach. Now he was launched upon a story.

"This thing happened," he went on, "years ago at Roma beside the Río Bravo. I was at home alone; my wife and children were visiting in another town. I remember it was a windy night in November. The evening was cool, and, not knowing what else to do, I decided to go to bed early. I was not asleep yet when someone began pounding at my door.

"'Open the door, Don Antonio; please let me in,' said a woman's voice. I got up and recognized in the woman before me one of our new neighbors. They had just moved into a deserted *jacal*[2] in the alley back of our house.

"'My husband is very sick,' she explained. 'He is dying and wants to see you. He says he must speak to you before he dies.'

"I dressed and went out with her, wondering all the time what this unknown man wanted to see me about. I found him in a miserable hovel, on a more miserable pallet on the floor, and I could see by his sunken cheeks and the fire that burned in his eyes that he was really dying, and of consumption, too. With mumbled words he dismissed the woman from the room and, once she had gone, he asked me to help him sit up. I propped him on the pillows the best I could. He was seized with a fit of coughing followed by a hemorrhage and I was almost sure that he would die before he could say anything. I brought him some water and poured a little *tequila* from a half empty bottle that was at the head of the pallet. After drinking it, he gave a sigh of relief.

"'I am much better now,' he whispered. His voice was already failing. 'My friend,' he went on, 'excuse my calling you, an utter stranger, but I have heard you are a man of courage and of honor and you will understand what I have to say to you. That woman you saw here is really not my wife; but I have lived with her in sin for the last twenty years. It weighs upon my conscience and I want to right the wrong I did her once.'

"As the man ended this confession, I could not help thinking what changes are brought about in the soul by the mere thought of facing eternity. I thought it very strange that after so long a time he should have qualms of conscience now. Yet I imagine death is a fearful thing, and, never having died myself nor been afraid to die, I could not judge what the dying man before me was feeling. So I decided to do what I would have expected others to do for me, and asked him if there was anything I might do for him.

"'Call a priest. I want to marry her,' he whispered.

"I did as he commanded and went to the rectory. Father José María was still saying his prayers, and when I told him that I had come to get him to marry a dying man, he looked at me in a way he had of doing whenever he doubted anyone, with one eye half closed and out of the corner of the other. As I had played him many pranks in the past, no doubt he thought I was now playing another. He hesitated at first but then got up somewhat convinced.

"'I'll take my chance with you again, you son of Barabbas,' he said. 'I'll go. Some poor soul may want to reconcile himself with his Creator.' He put on his black cape and took the little bag he always carried on such occasions.

2. Shanty.

The night was as black as the mouth of a wolf and the wind was getting colder and stronger.

"'A bad time for any one to want a priest, eh, Father?' I said in an effort to make conversation, not knowing what else to say.

"'The hour of repentance is a blessed moment at whatever time it comes,' he replied in a tone that I thought was reprimanding.

"On entering the house, we found the man alone. The woman was in the kitchen, he told us. I joined her there, and what do you suppose the shameless creature was doing? Drinking *tequila*, getting courage, she told me, for the ordeal ahead of her. After about an hour, we were called into the sick room. The man looked much better. Unburdening his soul had given him that peaceful look you sometimes see on the face of the dead who die while smiling. I was told that I was to be witness to the Holy Sacrament of Matrimony. The woman was so drunk by now she could hardly stand up; and between hiccoughs she promised to honor and love the man who was more fit to be food for the worms than for life in this valley of tears. I'd never seen a man so strong for receiving sacraments as that one was. He had received the Sacrament of Penance, then that of Matrimony—and I could see no greater penance than marrying such a woman—and now he was to receive Extreme Unction, the Sacrament for the Dying.

"The drunken woman and I held candles as Father José María anointed him with holy oil; and when we had to join him in prayer, I was ashamed that I could not repeat even the Lord's Prayer with him. That scene will always live in my mind, and when I die may I have as holy a man as Father José María to pray for me! He lingered a few moments; then, seeing there was nothing else to do, he said he would go back. I went with him under the pretext of getting something or other for the dying man, but in reality I wanted to see him safe at home. On the way back to the dying man I stopped at the saloon for another bottle of *tequila*. The dying man might need a few drops to give him courage to start on his journey to the Unknown, although from what I had seen I judged that Father José María had given him all he needed.

"When I returned, the death agony was upon him. The drunken woman was snoring in the kitchen. It was my responsibility to see that the man did not die like a dog. I wet his cracked lips with a piece of cloth moistened in *tequila*. I watched all night. The howling of the wind and the death rattle of the consumptive made the place the devil's kingdom. With the coming of dawn, the man's soul, now pure from sin, left the miserable carcass that had given it lodging during life. I folded his arms over his chest and covered his face with a cloth. There was no use in calling the woman; she lay on the dirt floor of the kitchen snoring like a trumpet. I closed the door and went out to see what could be done about arrangements for the funeral. I went home and got a little money—I did not have much—to buy some boards for the coffin, black calico for the covering and for a mourning dress for the bride, now a widow—although I felt she did not deserve it—and candles.

"I made the coffin, and when all was done and finished went back to the house. The woman was still snoring, her half-opened mouth filled with buzzing flies. The corpse was as I had left it. I called some of the neighbors to help me dress the dead man in my one black suit, but he was stiff already and we had to lay him in the coffin as he was, unwashed and dirty. If it is true that we wear white raiments in Heaven, I hope the good San Pedro[3] gave him one at the entrance before the other blessed spirits got to see the pitiful things he wore. I watched the body all day; he was to be buried early the following morning. Father José María had told me he would say Mass for him. The old woman, curse her, had gotten hold of the other bottle of *tequila* and continued bottling up courage for the ordeal that she said she had to go through.

"The wind that had started the night before did not let down; in fact, it was getting stronger. Several times the candles had blown out, and the corpse and I had been left in utter darkness. To avoid the repetition of such a thing, I went to the kitchen and got some empty fruit cans very much prized by the old woman. In truth, she did not want to let me use them at first, because, she said, the fruit on the paper wrapping looked so natural and was the only fruit she had ever owned. I got them anyway, filled them with corn, and stuck the candles there.

"Early in the evening about nine, or thereabouts, I decided to get out again and ask some people to come and watch with me part of the night. Not that I was afraid to stay alone with the corpse. One might fear the spirits of those who die in sin, but certainly not this one who had left the world the way a Christian should leave it. I left somewhat regretfully, for I was beginning to have a kindly feeling towards the dead man. I felt towards that body as I would feel towards a friend, no doubt because I had helped it to transform itself from a human being to a nice Christian corpse.

"As I went from house to house asking people to watch with me that night, I was reminded of a story that the priest had told us once, and by the time I had gone half through the town I knew very well how the man who was inviting guests to the wedding feast must have felt. All had some good excuse to give but no one could come. To make a long story short, I returned alone, to spend the last watch with my friend the corpse.

"As I neared the house, I saw it was very well lighted, and I thought perhaps some people had finally taken pity upon the poor unfortunate and had gone there with more candles to light the place. But soon I realized what was really happening. The *jacal* was on fire.

"I ran inside. The sight that met my eyes was one I shall ever see. I was nailed to the floor with terror. The corpse, its hair a flaming mass, was sitting up in the coffin where it had so peacefully lain all day. Its glassy, opaque eyes stared into space with a look that saw nothing and its mouth was convulsed into the most horrible grin. I stood there paralyzed by the horror of the scene. To make matters worse, the drunken woman reeled into the room, yelling, 'He is burning before he gets to Hell!'

"Two thoughts ran simultaneously through my mind: to get her out of the room and to extinguish the fire. I pushed the screaming woman out into the darkness and, arming myself with courage, reëntered the room. I was wearing cowboy boots, and my feet were the only part of my body well protected. Closing my eyes, I kicked the table, and I heard the thud of the burning body as it hit the floor. I became crazy then. With my booted feet I tramped upon and kicked the corpse until I thought the fire was extinguished. I dared not

---

3. Saint Peter; according to the New Testament, one of Jesus' 12 disciples. In art, he is often depicted holding the keys to Heaven.

open my eyes for fear of what I might see, and with my eyes still closed I ran out of the house. I did not stop until I reached the rectory. Like mad I pounded upon the door, and when the priest opened it and saw me standing there looking more like a ghost than a living person, he could but cross himself. It was only after I had taken a drink or two—may God forgive me for having done so in his presence—that I could tell him what had happened.

"He went back with me and, with eyes still closed, I helped him place the poor dead man in his coffin. Father José María prayed all night. As for me, I sat staring at the wall, not daring once to look at the coffin, much less upon the charred corpse. That was the longest watch I ever kept.

"At five o'clock, with no one to help us, we carried the coffin to the church, where the promised mass was said. We hired a burro cart to take the dead man to the cemetery, and, as the sun was coming up, Father José María, that man of God, and I, an unpenitent sinner, laid him in his final resting place."

1936

---

# ERNESTO GALARZA
## 1905–1984

Ernesto Galarza is credited with establishing the genre of children's literature among Latinos. He was also a writer of serious nonfictional reports for adults, a labor organizer, a pioneer in the effectiveness of bilingual education for Latinos, and a teacher at institutions such as Harvard University; the University of California, San Diego; and Notre Dame.

Galarza was born in Jalcocotán, a town in the mountains north of Puerto Vallarta, Mexico—as he once put it, "in an adobe cottage with a thatched roof that stood at one end of the only street of Jalcocotán." Following the outbreak of the Mexican Revolution, he moved with his mother (who was divorced from his father) and two uncles to Tuscon, Arizona, and then to Sacramento, California. Galarza learned English quickly and excelled in school, while working odd jobs. Even after his mother and one of his uncles had died of Spanish influenza when he was 12, leaving him and his teenaged uncle to fend for themselves, he continued to work and go to school. As a youngster, he worked as an interpreter and translator for migrant farm workers, and these services led him to organize a worker's union.

After graduating from high school, he attended Occidental College, in Los Angeles. His senior thesis became his first book, *The Roman Catholic Church as a Factor in the Political and Social History of Mexico* (1928). After earning a master's degree from Stanford University, he married Mae Taylor and moved to New York City to pursue a doctorate at Columbia University. In the 1930s, the couple ran a progressive school in the Jamaica, Queens, section of New York until, in 1936, Galarza took a job with the Pan-American Union, now the Organization of American States. By 1940, Galarza was head of the union's Division of Labor and Social Information and author of numerous publications on Latin American issues. He actively promoted workers' rights until resigning in 1947 over an internal dispute regarding possible U.S. meddling in Bolivia, with Galarza arguing that the union sheepishly promoted U.S. interests.

He moved to San Jose, California, and for the next 15 years he fought for farm workers' rights in leadership positions with the National Farm Labor Union and the National Agricultural Workers Union. Galarza recruited union members, led strikes in California and Louisiana, and testified frequently in Congress against the Bracero Program (discussed in the "Acculturation" introduction), according to which U.S. farmers could hire Mexican labor to undercut or replace domestic workers, especially ones who tried to organize. After he left the National Agricultural Workers Union in the early 1960s, Galarza devoted himself to writing books on agricultural labor, teaching at universities in the San Francisco Bay area, and organizing urban communities to advocate for better education and community services. He wrote several books and hundreds of articles and pamphlets on agriculture, labor, and Latin American history. During the 1960s, he worked with Congressman Adam Clayton Powell Jr. on the Committee of Education and Labor as chief labor counsel in an investigation into the collision, in 1963, of a bus overloaded with *braceros*. Galarza published a scathing indictment of the transport of Mexican migrant workers.

During the 1970s, Galarza published his acclaimed novel-cum-memoir, *Barrio Boy*, and 11 books for young Latino readers, written in Spanish and full of advice, humor, and clever renditions of Mother Goose rhymes. In 1982, the University of Notre Dame published a volume of his poetry, *Kodachromes in Rhyme*. Decades after its original publication, *Barrio Boy* became required reading in high schools and colleges around the country. Included here are a portion of Part One and all of Part Five. Critics have praised the book for its intimate portrayal of the evolution of Galarza's identity from Mexican to Mexican American, his embrace of the new country while holding onto the old. "The Americanization of Mexican me was no smooth matter," he writes. As the narrative progresses, the *colonia*—where he and other unskilled workers from Mexico have descended—becomes something like a large family and then gives way to the *barrio*.

An elementary school in San Jose is named for Galarza, a fitting tribute to a man who valued education equally with activism.

---

## *FROM* BARRIO BOY

## *From* Part One: In a Mountain Village

Unlike people who are born in hospitals, in an ambulance, or in a taxicab I showed up in an adobe cottage with a thatched roof that stood at one end of the only street of Jalcocotán, which everybody called Jalco for short. Like many other small villages in the wild, majestic mountains of the Sierra Madre de Nayarit, my pueblo was a hideaway. Even though you lived there, arriving in Jalco was always a surprise.

From Tepic, the nearest city to the north, you came down a steep mule track, careful not to step on the smooth round rocks that could send you spinning, or the sharp, flat ones that cut your feet. If you were traveling first class on a mule, or tourist class on a burro, you gave the beast a free rein to pick his way among the rolling stones and small boulders. The trick was to lean back slightly and ride loose so you could fall free if you had to. The trail fell away in front under a high gloomy vault of foliage that hid the sky. The trees made a stockade on both sides that gave the trail the look and feel of a winding tunnel. Loosened rocks rattled downhill, the echoes growing fainter with every bounce, until they got lost in the forest.

Unlike most tunnels, there was no patch of sunlight ahead to spot the end of the trail. It just twisted to the right, and there was Jalco, viewed from the north end of the street.

Coming in from the south end it was uphill for man or mule. The trail, called a *brecha*, climbed the mountain steadily from the pueblo next below, Tecuitata. In this direction, the forest was less dense. The palisade of pines and cedars was broken now and then where hurricanes had smashed it, leaving jagged gaps through which you could see the blue peaks of the Sierra Madre. The mule path stayed close to a stream that pell-melled its way from Jalco to the sea the year around. At the edge of the village, where the stream spread into a pond of still, hazel water, the trail broke to the left and heaved itself over the crest of the grade. You were looking at Jalcocotán from the south.

Whether you came to the pueblo from Tepic or from Tecuitata, you could surmise at once several things about the village. The Indian ancestors who had founded Jalco intended that it should be a place that would be difficult to get to. They had chosen a narrow rocky terrace parallel to a protecting gully that the arroyo had gouged out of the mountainside. Two humps of the ridge, or *cerros*, covered the flanks of the terrace. The forest fenced in the hollow, which lay under the open sky like the palm of a long, thin hand cupped to shelter the village and its people. The choice of the founding fathers had been wise. The Sierra was sometimes swept by storms that could wrench huge trees from the earth, roots and all. The sensible thing for a village to do was to squat in some natural storm cellar like the scoop in which Jalco lay, and let the hurricane pass overhead.

Shelter from the summer sun was also important. From May to October it burned, climbing the sky until it scorched, straight down, the adobe cottages and the corrals of the village. Until mid-morning the overhanging fringe of the forest filtered the hot sunlight. The arroyo, springing among the boulders in its course, pulled a cooling draft the length of the pueblo. Where the huge walnuts spread over the arroyo, children waded and men squatted until high noon had passed.

Besides providing shelter from wind and sun, the location of Jalcocotán was meant to give protection against outsiders. The old men of the pueblo told it the way it had been. And it was true, because they had heard it from the old men before them, and they in turn from the old men who had founded Jalco in the days of the Spaniards, perhaps even before that. The first settlers were refugees from the fertile river bottoms and the coast lands, taken from them by force. They had moved into the rugged mountains of the Sierra Madre, founding their villages where attack was difficult. A few hundred yards above and below Jalco, the trail squeezed through natural strong points, bottlenecks where rocks were plentiful and from which boulders could be rolled on approaching enemies.

If the invaders broke through, they would find a deserted village. A hundred footpaths, the *veredas*, unknown except to the *jalcocotecanos*, snaked away from the corrals, winding deeper into the forest and higher up the mountain. The families would wait there, watching from hidden lookouts, until the invaders left. These events had happened years—maybe centuries—before I came to live in Jalcocotán.

I also learned very early that the forest, *el monte*, was a dangerous place. Hunters told of narrow escapes from boars and mountain lions that prowled on the other side of the arroyo. The *gato montes*, the mountain cat, was a mean marauder. On the trail between Jalco and Tecuitata a five-foot rattlesnake had been killed. These were warnings for small boys, to be heeded until you became a man and learned to get along with the forest.

Jalcocotán and the forest had always been a part of each other. "El monte," the old men said, "no es de nadie y es de todos"—the forest doesn't belong to anyone and it belongs to everyone. Like those of my pueblo, the men of Tecuitata and the other villages on the mountain talked vaguely of boundary lines between their portions of the *monte*. But when anyone asked how far the village timber extended, the *jalcocotecano* would answer with a sweeping wave of the hand. The gesture could mean that it all belonged to us, even the farthest ridges of the Sierra Madre, even to Jalisco. It really didn't matter. The only part of the forest that was useful to us was the farthest point you could walk to and get home by sundown.

*El monte* was a place of wonders as well as of dangers. The pines, the huge umbrellas of the elms, and the shaggy cedars were the tallest things in the world. The pine kindling was marvelously aromatic and sticky. The woodsmen of the pueblo talked of the white tree, the black tree, the red tree, the rock tree—*palo blanco, palo negro, palo colorado* and *palo de piedra*. Under the shady canopies of the giants there were the fruit bearers—*chirimoyas, guayabas, mangos, mameyes,* and *tunas*. There were also the coffee bushes, volunteers that straggled here and there in an abandoned coffee patch.

The deep woods also gave the pueblo the songs and colors of the flocks of parakeets, macaws, and *loros* that chattered and squeaked on the fringe of the forest; in flight over our house they sounded like little rusty hinges. Springing suddenly from the tree tops into the sunlight over the village street, a flock of *loros* looked like dabs of bright green enamel streaking in formation across the blue sky.

But of all the creatures that came flying out of the *monte*—bats, doves, hawks—the most familiar were the turkey vultures, the *zopilotes*. There were always two or three of them perched on the highest limb of a tree on the edge of the pueblo. They glided in gracefully on five feet of wing spread, flapping awkwardly as they came to rest. They were about the size of a turkey, of a blackish brown color and bald-headed, their wrinkled necks spotted with red in front. Hunched on their perch, they never opened their curved beaks to make a sound. They watched the street below them with beady eyes. Sometime during the day, the *zopilotes* swooped down to scavenge in the narrow ditch that ran the length of the street, where the housewives dropped the entrails of chickens among the garbage. They gobbled what waste the dogs and pigs did not get at first. These tidbits were enough to keep the *zopilotes* interested in our town and to accustom them to the presence of people. Grim and ugly though they were, the vultures were regarded as volunteer garbage collectors who charged nothing for their services and who, like good children, were seen but not heard.

. . .

The one and only street in Jalcocotán was hardly more than an open stretch of the mule trail that disappeared into the forest north and south of the pueblo. Crosswise, it was about wide enough to park six automobiles hub to hub. Lengthwise, you could walk from one end to the other in eight minutes, without hurrying, the way people walked in the village. The dirt surface had been packed hard by hundreds of years of traffic—people barefooted or wearing the tough leather sandals called huaraches; mule trains passing through on the way to the sea or to Tepic; burros carrying firewood and other products of the forest; *zopilotes* hopping heavily here and there; pigs, dogs, and chickens foraging along the ditch.

There was a row of cottages on each side of the street, adobe boxes made of the same packed earth on which the houses stood. At one end of the street wall of every cottage there was a doorway, another in the wall standing to the back yard corral. There were no windows. The roofs were made of palm thatch, with a steep pitch, the ridge pole parallel to the street. Back of the houses were the *corrales*, fenced with stones piled about shoulder high to a man. Between the *corrales* there were narrow alleys that led uphill to the edge of the forest on the upper side of the village, and to the arroyo on the lower side. The eaves of the grass roofs hung well over the adobe walls to protect them from the battering rains. In the summer time the overhang provided shade at midday, when it seemed as if all the suffocating heat of the heavens was pouring through a funnel with the small end pointed directly at Jalco.

Since there were no sidewalks, from the front door to the street was only a step. Our pueblo was too high up the mountain, the connecting trails were too steep and narrow to allow ox carts and wagons to reach it. Like the forest, our only street belonged to everybody—a place to sort out your friends and take your bearings if you were going anywhere.

Midway down the street, on the arroyo side, there was a small chapel, also of adobe, the only building in the town that had a front yard, a patch of sun-baked clay squeezed between two cottages. Back of the patio stood the squat adobe box of the chapel, with a red tile roof and a small dome in one corner topped with a wooden cross. Once upon a time the walls of the chapel had been plastered and whitewashed, but the rains and the sun had cracked and blistered them. The adobe was exposed in jagged patches with flecks of grey straw showing like wood grain on the ancient mud. The base of the walls, pelted by the rain, was chewed as if beavers had worked on it.

Directly across the street from the chapel, the row of cottages was interrupted by the plaza. In any pueblo of some importance this would have been the *zocalo*, or the *plaza mayor*, or more grandiloquently, the *plaza de armas*. In Jalco it was a square without a name, about forty steps wide along the street and as many deep. Once, so it was said by the oldest people in the village, there had been a fountain in the center of the plaza, and a collection had been taken to buy a bust of Benito Juarez[1] for a centerpiece of the park. When I knew the drab little plaza, there was no fountain and no bust. The surface of the square was, like the street, a sheet of hardpan. Holes had been chopped in it and some trees planted. An acacia shaded one corner of the upper side of the lot. Three smaller trees lined one side of the square; in the spring they flamed with brilliant crimson blossoms like cups of fire, which is why they were called *copas de fuego*.

---

1. Mexican lawyer (1806–1872); president of Mexico 1861–65 and 1867–72.

In a village like Jalcocotán there was little use for either the chapel or the plaza. We had no resident priest; *jalcocotecanos* with serious matters to lay before their patron saints or the Virgin of Guadalupe[2] walked to Tepic, forty kilometers to the north, with its magnificent basilica. If it was a matter in which the whole village was concerned, a pilgrimage was organized to the shrine of Nuestra Señora de Talpa, where couples were married and babies baptized. Even less ever happened in the plaza than in the chapel. There was no police, no fire department, no post office, no public library. No one was ever elected mayor or sheriff or councilman. There was no jail or judge or any other sort of *Autoridades*, which explained why there was no city hall in Jalco. The shrunken, sun-beaten plaza was there nevertheless, solitary except when children played in it or passing mule drivers rested under the shade of its trees. It was a useless spot in our everyday life, but just by being there, the public square, like the chapel, gave our one and only street a touch of dignity, the mark of a proper pueblo.

Like the plaza, the street had no name. On a nameless street the houses, naturally, had no numbers. The villager was indoors and in bed after dark so there was no need for lights, of which our street had none.

Having a single gutter in the middle of the street instead of one on each side was a piece of simple and practical engineering. The shallow ditch made a slightly crooked dividing line through the center of the town. On either side of it each family took care of its frontage on the street, sprinkling it to settle the dust in the dry season, or sweeping the litter into the ditch. When it rained the trench collected the runoff, making a small torrent that scoured the gutter clean. During a downpour people stood in the doorways to watch the stuff that passed bobbing on the chocolate water—corncobs, banana peelings, twigs, an old huarache, or a dead rat drowned in the flash flood.

Whatever happened in Jalcocotán had to happen on our street because there was no other place for it to happen. Two men, drunk with tequila, fought with machetes on the upper edge of the village until they were separated and led away by the neighbors. A hundred faces peered around doorways watching the fight. When someone died people joined the funeral procession as it passed by their doors. If a stranger arrived on horseback, the clopping of horseshoes on the rocks of the trail announced his arrival before he could turn into the street. Arriving in Jalco was like stepping on a stage. The spectators were already in the doorways, watching.

The narrow lanes between the corrals on the lower side of the street led to the arroyo which ran the length of the village. The turbulent waters, even in the dry season, twisted and churned among the boulders, slapping them and breaking into spray, or dividing around them in serpentines of blue-green foam. Below the village the arroyo was checked by a natural dam of rocks and silt, over which it dropped into a quiet pond before rushing on to the sea.

On both sides the arroyo, here and there, had slammed boulders into the bank or against the trunks of trees. Downstream from these rocks the water formed small ponds over a floor of white sand and speckled pebbles. In

2. *Nuestra Señora de Guadalupe*, a sixteenth-century icon of the Virgin Mary; perhaps Mexico's most popular religious and cultural image, it has come to symbolize Catholic Mexicans and Mexico itself.

these nooks the women of the village washed clothes, kneeling waist high in the water.

On the edge of the pond, at the far side, there was an enormous walnut tree, standing like an open umbrella whose ribs extended halfway across the still water of the pool. The scars on the trunk of the mighty bole showed where the arroyo had bashed it during storms of former years. But the no-gal[3] had always won these battles. The arroyo, when the storms had passed, gave up and backed away, leaving around the trunk a small beach where the pond lapped gently on the gravel.

The arroyo was as much a part of the pueblo as the street. Like the street, it had no name; it just tumbled into town from the timber stands up the mountain that fed it the year round, and tumbled out from the pond to pick up and carry to the ocean the seepage of the forest below. It could rage dangerously in the summer freshets, called *avenidas*, pounding at the lower side of the village with boulders and ramming it with tree trunks a man could hardly circle with his two arms. Most of the year, it brought driftwood downstream and delivered it to the *jalcocotecanos* who chopped it into kindling. It supplied the pond with fish, but most important of all, it piped the sweet seepage of the forest to our town, always cold, transparent, and greenish blue. We called it *agua zarca*, good for drinking and washing.

Like the *monte* and the street, the arroyo was common property. Those who lived along the upper side of the street used the lanes between the cottages on the lower side on their way to wash, to fill their red clay *cantaros*, or to water their stock. Going to the arroyo from the street was called *bajar al agua*. Going up the lanes to the forest was called *subir al monte*. Taking the trail to Tepic was *cuesta arriba*. Taking it down to Miramar was *cuesta abajo*. These were the four points of the compass for Jalcocotán. If you followed them you could always find your way back home.

It was in the evening, when dusk was falling and supper was being prepared, that Jalco shaded itself little by little into the forest, the arroyo, the sky, and the mountain to which it belonged. Westward toward the sea, a rose and purple mist nearly always lingered after sunset.

The eastern slopes of the range became patches of black-blue. From the slant of the shadows and the signs in the sky, everyone knew when this would happen—almost to the minute. The men and the boys of working age came down or up the trail at about the right time to reach the street a few steps ahead of or a few steps behind the dusk. They walked, each man and his sons, to their cottages. On both sides of the street the doors were open. In the kitchens, the coals glowed in the adobe *pretiles* where the cooking was done, illuminated by the tin oil lamps, three inches round and two deep, the *candiles* that swung from the ceiling.

Through the doors, opened to receive the returning toilers and to freshen the air inside the cottages, came the sounds and sights of the street at sundown. There was the soft clapping of the women patting the ration of tortillas for the evening meal. The smoky light from the wicks of the *candiles* flickering through the doorways cast wobbling shadows on the threshold as people moved about. The air outside was a blend of the familiar smells of

3. I.e., tropical walnut tree.

supper time—tortillas baking, beans boiling, chile roasting, coffee steaming, and kerosene stenching. The hens were clucking in their roosts in the corrals by the time the street was dark.

After supper, if the weather was warm, the men squatted on the ground, hunched against the wall of the house and smoked. The women and the girls ate supper and put away the kitchen things, the *candiles* turned down to save kerosene. They listened to the tales of the day if the men were in a talking mood. When they pulled on their cigarettes, they made ruby dots in the dark, as if they were putting periods into the low-toned conversation. The talk just faded away, the men went indoors, the doors were shut and barred, and there was nothing on the street but the dark and the rumble of the arroyo.

Our adobe cottage was on the side of the street away from the arroyo. It was the last house if you were going to Miramar. About fifty yards behind the corral, the forest closed in.

It was like every other house in Jalco, probably larger. The adobe walls were thick, a foot or more, with patches of whitewash where the thatched overhang protected the adobe from the rain. There were no windows. The entrance doorway was at one end of the front wall, and directly opposite the door that led to the corral. The doors were made of planks axed smooth from tree trunks and joined with two cross pieces and a diagonal brace between them hammered together with large nails bent into the wood on the inside. Next to each door and always handy for instant use, there was the cross bar, the *tranca*. On both sides of the door frame there was a notched stub, mortared into the adobe bricks and about six inches long. The door was secured from the inside by dropping the *tranca* into the two notches.

All the living space for the family was in the one large room, about twelve feet wide and three times as long. Against the wall between the two doorways was the *pretil*, a bank of adobe bricks three feet high, three across, and two feet deep. In the center of the *pretil* was the main fire pit. Two smaller hollows, one on either side of the large one, made it a three-burner stove. On a row of pegs above the *pretil* hung the clay pans and other cooking utensils, bottom side out, the soot baked into the red clay. A low bench next to the *pretil*, also made of adobe, served as a table and shelf for the cups, pots, and plates.

The rest of the ground floor was divided by a curtain hung from one of the hand-hewed log beams, making two bedrooms. Above them, secured to the beams, was the *tapanco*, a platform the size of a double bed made of thin saplings tied together with pieces of rawhide. The top of a notched pole, braced against the foot of the back wall of the cottage, rested against the side of the *tapanco*, serving as a ladder. Along the wall opposite the *pretil*, in the darkest and coolest part of the house, were the big *cántaros*, the red clay jars; the *canastos*, tall baskets made of woven reeds; the rolled straw *petates* to cover the dirt floor where people walked or sat; and the hoes and other work tools.

There was no ceiling other than the underside of the thatch, which was tied to the pole rafters. On top of these, several layers of thatch were laid, making a waterproof cover thicker than the span of a man's hand. The rafters were notched and tied to the ridgepole and mortared on the lower end to the top of the walls. Between the top of the walls and the overhang there was an open space a few inches wide. Through this strip the smoke from the *pretil* went out and the fresh air came in.

It was the roof that gave space and lift to the single room that served as kitchen, bedroom, parlor, pantry, closet, storeroom, and tool shed. The slender rafters pointed upward in sharp triangles tied at the peak with bows of darkbrown rawhide that had dried as tight as steel straps. Strings of thatch hung from the ceiling like the fringe of a buggy top, making it appear that the heavy matting of grass did not rest on the rafters but tiptoed on hundreds of threads. It was always half dark up there. My cousins, Jesús and Catarino, and I slept in the *tapanco*. More than a bedroom, to us it was a half-lighted hideaway out of sight of parents, uncles, aunts, and other meddlesome people.

The corral was the other important part of a Jalco home. Ours was enclosed on three sides by stone walls and shut off from the street by the house. The only entrance to the corral was through the back door of the cottage. The ground sloped up toward the edge of the monte. A ditch along the back wall stopped the runoff water and sluiced it toward the lane between our house and our neighbor's. Close to the house, there was a corncrib built like a miniature adobe cottage with the walls sloping inward at the bottom. It was raised on stilts and covered with a grass roof.

The only landscaping of the corral was a willow tree that stood half as high as the house roof. It always looked yellowish and limp, as if it had too much sun and not enough water. For beauty it was not much, but as a hen roost it was the best there was in Jalco. During the day, especially at high noon when the willow stood deserted in the baking sunlight, the round shadow of its crown was mottled with chicken droppings continually changing in pattern.

The color and the charm of the corral were along the back wall of the house, adorned by a row of geraniums, herbs, and carnations potted in jars of many sizes and five-gallon kerosene cans. Some of the pots were on the ground, others were raised on one, two, or three adobe bricks. The thatch eaves protected the sprays of bright green and red and pink from rain and sun. When the herbs were pinched off for cooking there was a faint aroma of oregano, thyme, and mint. The herbs and carnations were on the higher bricks, to keep them out of reach of the hens.

The utensils and the furniture were matched to the cottage, as if everything had been made at the same time by the same people out of the same materials of the earth. The three-legged *metate* on which the corn for the tortillas was ground, a small, oblong sloping platform of black rock speckled with grey dots, stood on one side of the *pretil*. The *comal*, a round griddle about two feet across, hung from a peg looking like a black shield with a red rim. The beds were hewn frames of poles standing on short legs. The sides and ends of the frames were girdled to hold the loops of rawhide stretched between them, making the small squares of the bed spring. The bows where the rawhide was tied were like those that held the rafters to the thatch and the ridge pole. The straw mats were partly the color of the floor, partly the color of the thatch where it was less sooty. Who had built and designed and made all this nobody knew. We had just moved in; if we ever moved out it would all be left as it was, soaped and scrubbed to look and smell clean.

I never thought to count them, but there could have been forty such homes in Jalcocotán when I lived there. Some cottages were deeper and longer than others, some corral walls were patched with poles and adobe bricks, some roofs rested on straight-up gables and others on slanting ones. But every cottage seemed built and placed to look like every other one. There were no building codes in the pueblo about where to set the walls, or how high they must be or as to the pitch of the roof. The houses made an almost solid front on either side of the street except for the breaks of the lanes, the plaza, and the chapel.

✻ ✻ ✻

## Part Five: On the Edge of the Barrio

To make room for a growing family it was decided that we should move, and a house was found in Oak Park,[1] on the far side of town where the open country began. The men raised the first installment for the bungalow on Seventh Avenue even after Mrs. Dodson explained that if we did not keep up the monthly payments we would lose the deposit as well as the house.

The real estate broker brought the sale contract to the apartment one evening. Myself included, we sat around the table in the living room, the gringo explaining at great length the small print of the document in a torrent of words none of us could make out. Now and then he would pause and throw in the only word he knew in Spanish: "Sabee?" The men nodded slightly as if they had understood. Doña Henriqueta[2] was holding firmly to the purse which contained the down payment, watching the broker's face, not listening to his words. She had only one question. Turning to me she said: "Ask him how long it will take to pay all of it." I translated, shocked by the answer: "Twenty years." There was a long pause around the table, broken by my stepfather: "What do you say?" Around the table the heads nodded agreement. The broker passed his fountain pen to him. He signed the contract and after him Gustavo and José.[3] Doña Henriqueta opened the purse and counted out the greenbacks. The broker pocketed the money, gave us a copy of the document, and left.

The last thing I did when we moved out of 418 L was to dig a hole in the corner of the backyard for a tall carton of Quaker Oats cereal, full to the brim with the marbles I had won playing for keeps around the *barrio*. I tamped the earth over my buried treasure and laid a curse on whoever removed it without my permission.

Our new bungalow had five rooms, and porches front and back. In the way of furniture, what friends did not lend or Mrs. Dodson gave us we bought in the secondhand shops. The only new item was an elegant gas range, with a high oven and long, slender legs finished in enamel. Like the house, we would be paying for it in installments.

It was a sunny, airy spot, with a family orchard to one side and a vacant lot on the other. Back of us there was a pasture. With chicken wire we fenced the back yard, turned over the soil, and planted our first vegetable garden

1. A neighborhood in Sacramento.
2. The narrator's mother.
3. The narrator's uncles.

and fruit trees. José and I built a palatial rabbit hutch of laths and two-by-fours he gathered day by day on the waterfront. A single row of geraniums and carnations separated the vegetable garden from the house. From the vacant lots and pastures around us my mother gathered herbs and weeds which she dried and boiled the way she had in the pueblo. A thick green fluid she distilled from the mallow that grew wild around us was bottled and used as a hair lotion. On every side our windows looked out on family orchards, platinum stretches of wild oats and quiet lanes, shady and unpaved.

We could not have moved to a neighborhood less like the *barrio*. All the families around us were Americans. The grumpy retired farmer next door viewed us with alarm and never gave us the time of day, but the Harrisons across the street were cordial. Mr. Harrison loaned us his tools, and Roy, just my age but twice my weight, teamed up with me at once for an exchange of visits to his mother's kitchen and ours. I astounded him with my Mexican rice, and Mrs. Harrison baked my first waffle. Roy and I also found a common bond in the matter of sisters. He had an older one and by now I had two younger ones. It was a question between us whether they were worse as little nuisances or as big bosses. The answer didn't make much difference but it was a relief to have another man to talk with.

Some Sundays we walked to Joyland, an amusement park where my mother sat on a bench to watch the children play on the lawn and I begged as many rides as I could on the roller coaster, which we called in elegant Spanish "the Russian Mountain." José liked best the free vaudeville because of the chorus girls who danced out from the stage on a platform and kicked their heels over his head.

Since Roy had a bicycle and could get away from his sister by pedaling off on long journeys I persuaded my family to match my savings for a used one. Together we pushed beyond the boundaries of Oak Park miles out, nearly to Perkins and the Slough House. It was open country, where we could lean our wheels against a fence post and walk endlessly through carpets of golden poppies and blue lupin. With a bike I was able to sign on as a carrier of the *Sacramento Bee*, learning in due course the art of slapping folded newspapers against people's porches instead of into the bushes or on their roofs. Roy and I also became assistants to a neighbor who operated a bakery in his basement, taking our pay partly in dimes and partly in broken cookies for our families.

For the three men of the household as well as for me the bicycle became the most important means for earning a living. Oak Park was miles away from the usual places where they worked and they pedaled off, in good weather and bad, in the early morning. It was a case of saving carfare.

I transferred to the Bret Harte School, a gingerbread two-story building in which there was a notable absence of Japanese, Filipinos, Koreans, Italians, and the other nationalities of the Lincoln School. It was at Bret Harte that I learned how an English sentence could be cut up on the blackboard and the pieces placed on different lines connected by what the teacher called a diagram. The idea of operating on a sentence and rearranging its members as a skeleton of verbs, modifiers, subject, and prepositions set me off diagraming whatever I read, in Spanish and English. Spiderwebs, my mother called them, when I tried to teach her the art.

My bilingual library had grown with some copies of old magazines from Mexico, a used speller Gustavo had bought for me in Stockton, and the novels my mother discarded when she had read them. Blackstone was still the anchor of my collection and I now had a paperback dictionary called *El Inglés sin Maestro*.[4] By this time there was no problem of translating or interpreting for the family I could not tackle with confidence.

It was Gustavo, in fact, who began to give my books a vague significance. He pointed out to me that with diagrams and dictionaries I could have a choice of becoming a lawyer or a doctor or an engineer or a professor. These, he said, were far better careers than growing up to be a *camello*, as he and José always would be. *Camellos*, I knew well enough, was what the *chicanos* called themselves as the workers on every job who did the dirtiest work. And to give our home the professional touch he felt I should be acquiring, he had a telephone installed.

It came to the rest of us as a surprise. The company man arrived one day with our name and address on a card, a metal tool box and a stand-up telephone wound with a cord. It was connected and set on the counter between the dining room and the parlor. There the black marvel sat until we were gathered for dinner that evening. It was clearly explained by Gustavo that the instrument was to provide me with a quick means of reaching the important people I knew at the Y.M.C.A., the boy's band,[5] or the various public offices where I interpreted for *chicanos* in distress. Sooner or later some of our friends in the *barrio* would also have telephones and we could talk with them.

"Call somebody," my mother urged me.

With the whole family watching I tried to think of some important person I could ring for a professional conversation. A name wouldn't come. I felt miserable and hardly like a budding engineer or lawyer or doctor or professor.

Gustavo understood my predicament and let me stew in it a moment. Then he said: "Mrs. Dodson." My pride saved by this ingenious suggestion, I thumbed through the directory, lifted the earpiece from the hook, and calmly asked central for the number. My sisters, one sitting on the floor and the other in my mother's arms, never looked less significant; but they, too, had their turn saying hello to the patient Señora Dodson on the other end of the line.

Every member of the family, in his own way, missed the *barrio*. José and Gustavo could no longer join the talk of the poolrooms and the street corners by walking two blocks down the street. The sign language and simple words my mother had devised to communicate with the Americans at 418 L didn't work with the housewives on 7th Avenue. The families we had known were now too far away to exchange visits. We knew no one in Oak Park who spoke Spanish. Our street was always quiet and often lonely with little to watch from our front porch other than boys riding bicycles or Mrs. Harrison

---

4. English without a Teacher. *Blackstone*: Sir William Blackstone (1723–1780), English jurist; his *Commentaries on the Laws of England* (1765–69), a classic description of the doctrines of English law, became the basis of legal education in England and North America.

5. The previous chapter describes the boy's band, which was part of the Y.M.C.A. The narrator is its piccolo player.

hanging out her wash. Pork Chops and the Salvation Army[6] never played there.

I, too, knew that things were different. There was no corner where I could sell the *Union* and my income from running errands and doing chores around the rooming house stopped. There were no alleys I could comb for beer bottles or docks where I could gather saleable or edible things. The closest to Big Singh[7] I could find was a runty soothsayer in Joyland who sat on a rug with a feather in his turban and told your fortune.

We now had an infant boy in the family who with my two sisters made four of us. The baby was himself no inconvenience to me, but it meant that I had to mind the girls more, mostly chasing them home from the neighbors. If I had been the eldest girl in the family I would have stepped into my mother's place and taken over the management of all but the youngest. But being a boy, the female chores seemed outrageous and un-Mexican. Doña Henriqueta tried telling me that I was now the *jefe de familia* of all the juniors. But she was a gentle mother and the freedom of the house, the yard, and my personal property that she gave the two girls did nothing to make them understand that I was their *jefe*. When Nora, the oldest of the two, demolished my concertina with a hammer (no doubt to see where the notes came from) I asked for permission to strangle her. Permission was denied.

During the first year we lived at Oak Park we began to floor and partition the basement. Some day, we knew, the Lopez's[8] would come through and we would have a temporary home ready for them. With three-and-a-half men in the house earning wages, if work was steady, we were keeping up with the installments and saving for the reunion.

An epidemic erased the quiet life on 7th Avenue and the hopes we had brought with us.

I had been reading to the family stories in the *Bee* of the Spanish influenza. At first it was far off, like the war, in places such as New York and Texas. Then the stories told of people dying in California towns we knew, and finally the *Bee* began reporting the spread of the "flu" in our city.

One Sunday morning we saw Gustavo coming down the street with a suitcase in his hand, walking slowly. I ran out to meet him. By the front gate, he dropped the suitcase, leaned on the fence, and fainted. He had been working as a sandhog on the American River, and had come home weak from fever.

Gustavo was put to bed in one of the front rooms. José set out to look for a doctor, who came the next day, weary and nearly sick himself. He ordered Gustavo to the hospital. Three days later I answered the telephone call from the hospital telling us he was dead. Only José went to Gustavo's funeral. The rest of us, except my stepfather, were sick in bed with the fever.

In the dining room, near the windows where the sunlight would warm her, my mother lay on a cot, a kerosene stove at her feet. The day Gustavo

---

6. *The Salvation Army*: a musical group, related to the Christian charity organization, that raises money by playing on the street. *Pork Chops*: a street musician.
7. "A brawny Hindu" who ran a boarding house; he wore a dark turban and a white apron. The narrator helped him with his English and, in return,

was hired to work in his kitchen.
8. The Lopezes are relatives of the narrator—his aunt and uncle and some cousins—in Mexico. They try to immigrate, but authorities deny them entrance into the U.S. From Mexico, they correspond with the narrator's family.

died she was delirious. José bicycled all over the city, looking for oranges, which the doctor said were the best medicine we could give her. I sweated out the fever, nursed by José, who brought me glasses of steaming lemonade and told me my mother was getting better. The children were quarantined in another room, lightly touched by the fever, more restless than sick.

Late one afternoon José came into my room, wrapped me in blankets, pulled a cap over my ears, and carried me to my mother's bedside. My stepfather was holding a hand mirror to her lips. It didn't fog. She had stopped breathing. In the next room my sister was singing to the other children, "A birdie with a yellow bill/ hopped upon my windowsill/ cocked a shiny eye and said/ Shame on you you sleepy head."

The day we buried Doña Henriqueta, Mrs. Dodson took the oldest sister home with her. The younger children were sent to a neighbor. That night José went to the *barrio*, got drunk, borrowed a pistol, and was arrested for shooting up Second Street.

We did not find out what had happened until I bicycled the next morning to Mrs. Dodson's to report that José had not come home. By this time our friends in the *barrio* knew of José's arrest and a telephone call to a bartender who knew us supplied the details. Nothing serious, Mrs. Dodson repeated to me. Nobody had been hurt. She left me in charge of my sister and went to bail out my uncle.

They returned together. Gently, Mrs. Dodson scolded José, who sat dejectedly, his eyes closed so he would not have to look her in the eye, cracking the joints of his fingers, chewing on his tight lips, a young man compressing years of hard times and the grief of the past days in a show of manhood.

When the lecture was nearly over, Mrs. Dodson was not talking of drunkenness and gunplay, but of the future, mostly of mine, and of José's responsibility for it. She walked with us down the front stairway. Pushing my bicycle I followed him on foot the miles back to Oak Park, keeping my distance, for I knew he did not want me to see his face. As he had often told me, "Men never cry, no matter what."

A month later I made a bundle of the family keepsakes my stepfather allowed me to have, including the butterfly sarape, my books, and some family pictures. With the bundle tied to the bars of my bicycle, I pedaled to the basement room José had rented for the two of us on O Street near the corner of Fifth, on the edge of the *barrio*.

José was now working the riverboats and, in the slack season, following the round of odd jobs about the city. In our basement room, with a kitchen closet, bathroom, and laundry tub on the back porch and a woodshed for storage, I kept house. We bought two cots, one for me and the other for José when he was home.

Our landlords lived upstairs, a middle-aged brother and sister who worked and rented rooms. As part payment on our rent I kept the yard trim. They were friends of Doña Tránsito, the grandmother of a Mexican family that lived in a weather-beaten cottage on the corner. Doña Tránsito was in her sixties, round as a barrel, and she wore her gray hair in braids and smoked hand-rolled cigarettes on her rickety front porch. To her tiny parlor *chicanos* in trouble came for advice, and the firm old lady with the rasping voice and commanding ways often asked me to interpret or translate for them in their encounters with the *Autoridades*. Since her services were free, so were mine. I soon became a regular visitor and made friends with her son, Kid Felix, a prizefighter who gave free boxing lessons to the boys in the neighborhood.

Living only three houses from Doña Tránsito, saying my *saludos* to her every time I passed the corner, noticing how even the Kid was afraid to break her personal code of *barrio* manners, I lived inside a circle of security when José was away. On her front porch, summer evenings, the old Mexican dame talked about people such as I had known in the pueblo and asked how I was doing in school and where I was working.

It was Doña Tránsito who called in the *curandera* once when the child of a neighbor was dying. I had brought a doctor to the house and was in the sick room when he told the family there was nothing more he could do. Doña Tránsito ordered me at once to fetch the old crone who lived on the other side of the railroad tracks towards the river and who practiced as a healer.

With Doña Tránsito I watched the ritual from a corner of the sick room. The healer laid on a side table an assortment of bundled weeds, small glass jars, candles, and paper bags tied with strings. On the floor next to her she placed a canvas satchel. A bowl and some cups were brought to her from the kitchen. She crumpled stems of herbs into one of the cups and mixed them with oil from one of her jars. She hooked her finger into another jar and pulled out a dab of lard which she worked into a powder in another cup to make a dark paste. Two candles were lighted and placed at the head of the bed. The electric light was turned off. She opened the satchel and took out a framed picture of the Virgin of Guadalupe, which was hung on the wall over the sick child's head. The window blind was pulled down.

The little girl was uncovered. She lay naked, pale, and thin on the sheet, her arms straight down her sides. Around her the healer arranged a border of cactus leaves, which she took out of her satchel one by one, cutting them open around the edge. She warmed the cup with the powdered herbs and rubbed the concoction on the soles of the child's bare feet. With the paste, which she also warmed over the candle, the healer made a cross on the forehead of the patient and another on her chest. A blanket was then laid over her, leaving only the head uncovered.

The healer knelt before the picture of the Virgin and began to pray. The parents of the child, some relatives who were there, Doña Tránsito and I formed a circle around the room, on our knees.

We had been praying a long while when the healer arose and bent over the bed, looking intently at the wasted face. To nobody in particular she said the child was not sweating. She wrapped her black shawl around her head and shoulders, left the room, and closed the street door quietly behind her. In the morning the child died.

Through Doña Tránsito I met other characters of the *barrio*. One of them was Don Crescencio, stooped and bony, who often stopped to chat with my neighbor. He told us stories of how he had found buried treasure with two twigs cut from a weeping willow, and how he could locate an underground spring in the same way, holding the twigs just so, feeling his way on bare feet over the ground, watching until the twigs, by themselves, crossed and dipped. There were the Ortegas, who raised vegetables on a sandlot they had bought by the levee, and explained to Doña Tránsito, who knew a great deal about such matters herself, what vegetables did better when planted according to different shapes of the moon. The Kid gave us lectures and exhibitions explaining jabs and left hooks and how he planned to become the world's Mexican champion. In our basement José gathered his friends to listen to songs of love, revenge, and valor, warmed with beer and tequila.

When troubles made it necessary for the *barrio* people to deal with the Americans uptown, the *Autoridades*, I went with them to the police court, the industrial accident office, the county hospital, the draft board, the county clerk. We got lost together in the rigamarole of functionaries who sat, like *patrones*, behind desks and who demanded licenses, certificates, documents, affidavits, signatures, and witnesses. And we celebrated our successes, as when the worker for whom I interpreted in interviews that lasted many months, was awarded a thousand dollars for a disabled arm. Don Crescencio congratulated me, saying that in Mexico for a thousand American dollars you could buy the lives of many peons.

José had chosen our new home in the basement on O Street because it was close to the Hearkness Junior High School, to which I transferred from Bret Harte. As the *jefe de familia* he explained that I could help earn our living but that I was to study for a high school diploma. That being settled, my routine was clearly divided into schooltime and worktime, the second depending on when I was free from the first.

Few Mexicans of my age from the *barrio* were enrolled at the junior high school when I went there. At least, there were no other Mexican boys or girls in Mr. Everett's class in civics, or Miss Crowley's English composition, or Mrs. Stevenson's Spanish course. Mrs. Stevenson assigned me to read to the class and to recite poems by Amado Nervo,[9] because the poet was from Tepic and I was, too. Miss Crowley accepted my compositions about Jalcocotán and the buried treasure of Acaponeta while the others in the class were writing about Sir Patrick Spence and the Beautiful Lady without Mercy,[1] whom they had never met. For Mr. Everett's class, the last of the day, I clipped pieces from the *Sacramento Bee* about important events in Sacramento. From him I learned to use the ring binder in which I kept clippings to prepare oral reports. Occasionally he kept me after school to talk. He sat on his desk, one leg dangling over a corner, behind him the frame of a large window and the arching elms of the school yard, telling me he thought I could easily make the debating team at the high school next year, that Stanford University might be the place to go after graduation, and making other by-the-way comments that began to shape themselves into my future.

Afternoons, Saturdays, and summers allowed me many hours of worktime I did not need for study. José explained how things now stood. There were two funerals to pay for. More urgently than ever, Doña Esther and her family[2] must be brought to live with us. He would pay the rent and buy the food. My clothes, books, and school expenses would be up to me.

On my vacations, and when he was not on the riverboats, he found me a job as water boy on a track gang. We chopped wood together near Woodland

---

9. Mexican poet (1870–1919).
1. English translation of *La Belle Dame sans Merci*, a ballad written in 1819 by the English poet John Keats (1795–1821); Keats took the title from a fifteenth-century ballad. *Sir Patrick Spence*: or "Sir

Patrick Spens," an anonymous folk ballad, primarily of Scottish origin, first published in the nineteenth century but perhaps going back to the thirteenth century.
2. I.e., the Lopezes.

and stacked empty lug boxes in a cannery yard. Cleaning vacant houses and chopping weeds were jobs we could do as a team when better ones were not to be had. As the apprentice, I learned from him how to brace myself for a heavy lift, to lock my knee under a loaded handtruck, to dance rather than lift a ladder, and to find the weakest grain in a log. Like him I spit into my palms to get the feel of the axe handle and grunted as the blade bit into the wood. Imitating him I circled a tree several times, sizing it up, *tanteando*,[3] as he said, before pruning or felling it.

Part of one summer my uncle worked on the river while I hired out as a farmhand on a small ranch south of Sacramento. My senior on the place was Roy, a husky Oklahoman who was a part-time taxi driver and a full-time drinker of hard whiskey. He was heavy-chested, heavy-lipped and jowly, a grumbler rather than a talker and a man of great ingenuity with tools and automobile engines. Under him I learned to drive the Fordson tractor on the place, man the gasoline pump, feed the calves, check an irrigation ditch, make lug boxes for grapes and many other tasks on a small farm. Roy used Bull Durham tobacco which he rolled into the same droopy cigarettes that Doña Eduvijes smoked in Jalco and Doña Tránsito on her front porch.

Roy and I sat under the willow tree in front of the ranch house after work, I on the grass, he on a creaky wicker chair, a hulking, sour man glad for the company of a boy. He counseled me on how to avoid the indulgences he was so fond of, beginning his sentences with a phrase he repeated over and over, "as the feller says." "Don't aim to tell you your business," he explained, "but, as the feller says, get yourself a good woman, don't be no farmhand for a livin', be a lawyer or a doctor, and don't get to drinkin' nohow. And there's another thing, Ernie. If nobody won't listen to you, go on and talk to yourself and hear what a smart man has to say."

And Roy knew how to handle boys, which he showed in an episode that could have cost me my life or my self-confidence. He had taught me to drive the tractor, walking along side during the lessons as I maneuvered it, shifting gears, stopping and starting, turning and backing, raising a cloud of dust wherever we went. Between drives Roy told me about the different working parts of the machine, giving me instructions on oiling and greasing and filling the radiator. "She needs to be took care of, Ernie," he admonished me, "like a horse. And another thing, she's like to buck. She can turn clear over on you if you let 'er. If she starts to lift from the front even a mite, you turn her off. You hear?"

"Yes, sir," I said, meaning to keep his confidence in me as a good tractor man.

It was a few days after my first solo drive that it happened. I was rounding a telephone pole on the slightly sloping bank of the irrigation ditch. I swung around too fast for one of rear tracks to keep its footing. It spun and the front began to lift. Forgetting Roy's emphatic instructions I gunned the engine, trying to right us to the level ground above the ditch. The tractor's nose kept climbing in front of me. We slipped against the pole, the tractor, bucking, as Roy said it would.

Roy's warning broke through to me in my panic, and I reached up to turn off the ignition. My bronco's engine sputtered out and it settled on the ground with a thump.

---

3. Weighing up, sounding out, estimating.

I sat for a moment in my sweat. Roy was coming down the ditch in a hurry. He walked up to me and with a quick look saw that neither I nor the tractor was damaged.

"Git off," he said.

I did, feeling that I was about to be demoted, stripped of my rank, bawled out, and fired.

Roy mounted the machine, started it, and worked it off the slope to flat ground. Leaving the engine running, he said: "Git on."

I did.

"Now finish the discing,"[4] he said. Above the clatter of the machine, he said: "Like I said, she can buck. If she does, cut 'er. You hear?" And he waved me off to my work.

Except for food and a place to live, with which José provided me, I was on my own. Between farm jobs I worked in town, adding to my experience as well as to my income. As a clerk in a drug store on Second and J, in the heart of the lower part of town, I waited on *chicanos* who spoke no English and who came in search of remedies with no prescription other than a recital of their pains. I dispensed capsules, pills, liniments, and emulsions as instructed by the pharmacist, who glanced at our customers from the back of the shop and diagnosed their ills as I translated them. When I went on my shift, I placed a card in the window that said "Se habla Español." So far as my *chicano* patients were concerned it might as well have said "Dr. Ernesto Galarza."

From drugs I moved to office supplies and stationery sundries, working as delivery boy for Wahl's, several blocks uptown from skid row. Between deliveries I had no time to idle. I helped the stock clerk, took inventory, polished desks, and hopped when a clerk bawled an order down the basement steps. Mr. Wahl, our boss, a stocky man with a slight paunch, strutted a little as he constantly checked on the smallest details of his establishment, including myself. He was always pleasant and courteous, a man in whose footsteps I might possibly walk into the business world of Sacramento.

But like my uncles, I was looking for a better *chanza*, which I thought I found with Western Union, as a messenger, where I could earn tips as well as wages. Since I knew the lower part of town thoroughly, whenever the telegrams were addressed to that quarter the dispatcher gave them to me. Deliveries to the suites on the second floor of saloons paid especially well, with tips of a quarter from the ladies who worked there. My most generous customer was tall and beautiful Miss Irene, who always asked how I was doing in school. It was she who gave me an English dictionary, the first I ever possessed, a black bound volume with remarkable little scallops on the pages that made it easy to find words. Half smiling, half commanding, Miss Irene said to me more than once: "Don't you stop school without letting me know." I meant to take her advice as earnestly as I took her twenty-five cent tip.

It was in the lower town also that I nearly became a performing artist. My instructor on the violin had stopped giving me lessons after we moved to Oak Park. When we were back on O Street he sent word through José that I could work as second fiddler on Saturday nights in the dancehall where he played with a mariachi. Besides, I could resume my lessons with him. A dollar a night for two hours as a substitute was the best wages I had

4. Cultivating the soil.

ever made. Coached by my teacher, I second-fiddled for sporting *chicanos* who swung their ladies on the dance floor and sang to our music. Unfortunately I mentioned my new calling to Miss Crowley when I proposed it to her as a subject for a composition. She kept me after school and persuaded me to give it up, on the ground that I could earn more decorating Christmas cards during the vacation than at the dancehall. She gave me the first order for fifty cards and got subscriptions for me from the other teachers. I spent my Christmas vacation as an illustrator, with enough money saved to quit playing in the saloon.

It was during the summer vacation that school did not interfere with making a living, the time of the year when I went with other *barrio* people to the ranches to look for work. Still too young to shape up with the day-haul gangs, I loitered on skid row, picking up conversation and reading the chalk signs about work that was being offered. For a few days of picking fruit or pulling hops I bicycled to Folsom, Lodi, Woodland, Freeport, Walnut Grove, Marysville, Slough House, Florin, and places that had no name. Looking for work, I pedaled through a countryside blocked off, mile after mile, into orchards, vineyards, and vegetable farms. Along the ditchbanks, where the grass, the morning glory, and the wild oats made a soft mattress I unrolled my bindle and slept.

In the labor camps I shared the summertime of the lives of the *barrio* people. They gathered from barrios of faraway places like Imperial Valley, Los Angeles, Phoenix, and San Antonio. Each family traveling on its own, they came in trucks piled with household goods or packed in their second-hand *fotingos* and *chevees*. The trucks and cars were ancient models, fresh out of a used-car lot, with license tags of many states. It was into these jalopies that much of the care and a good part of the family's earnings went. In camp they were constantly being fixed, so close to scrap that when we needed a part for repairs, we first went to the nearest junkyard.

It was a world different in so many ways from the lower part of Sacramento and the residences surrounded by trim lawns and cool canopies of elms to which I had delivered packages for Wahl's. Our main street was usually an irrigation ditch, the water supply for cooking, drinking, laundering, and bathing. In the better camps there was a faucet or a hydrant, from which water was carried in buckets, pails and washtubs. If the camp belonged to a contractor, and it was used from year to year, there were permanent buildings—a shack for his office, the privies, weatherworn and sagging, and a few cabins made of secondhand lumber, patched and unpainted.

If the farmer provided housing himself, it was in tents pitched on the bare baked earth or on the rough ground of newly plowed land on the edge of a field. Those who arrived late for the work season camped under trees or raised lean-to's along a creek, roofing their trucks with canvas to make bedrooms. Such camps were always well away from the house of the ranchero, screened from the main road by an orchard or a grove of eucalyptus. I helped to pitch and take down such camps, on some spot that seemed lonely when we arrived, desolate when we left.

If they could help it, the workers with families avoided the more permanent camps, where the seasonal hired hands from skid row were more likely to be found. I lived a few days in such a camp and found out why families avoided them. On Saturday nights when the crews had a week's wages in their pockets, strangers appeared, men and women, carrying suitcases with liquor and other contraband. The police were called by the contractor only when the carousing threatened to break into fighting. Otherwise, the weekly bouts were a part of the regular business of the camp.

Like all the others, I often went to work without knowing how much I was going to be paid. I was never hired by a rancher, but by a contractor or a straw boss who picked up crews in town and handled the payroll. The important questions that were in my mind—the wages per hour or per lug box, whether the beds would have mattresses and blankets, the price of meals, how often we would be paid—were never discussed, much less answered, beforehand. Once we were in camp, owing the employer for the ride to the job, having no means to get back to town except by walking and no money for the next meal, arguments over working conditions were settled in favor of the boss. I learned firsthand the chiseling techniques of the contractors and their pushers—how they knocked off two or three lugs of grapes from the daily record for each member of the crew, or the way they had of turning the face of the scales away from you when you weighed your work in.

There was never any doubt about the contractor and his power over us. He could fire a man and his family on the spot and make them wait days for their wages. A man could be forced to quit by assigning him regularly to the thinnest pickings in the field. The worst thing one could do was to ask for fresh water on the job, regardless of the heat of the day; instead of iced water, given freely, the crews were expected to buy sodas at twice the price in town, sold by the contractor himself. He usually had a pistol—to protect the payroll, so it was said. Through the ranchers for whom he worked, we were certain that he had connections with the *Autoridades*, for they never showed up in camp to settle wage disputes or listen to our complaints or to go for a doctor when one was needed. Lord of a rag-tag labor camp of Mexicans, the contractor, a Mexican himself, knew that few men would let their anger blow, even when he stung them with curses like, "Orale, San Afabeeches huevones."[5]

As a single worker, I usually ate with some household, paying for my board. I did more work than a child but less than a man, neither the head nor the tail of a family. Unless the camp was a large one I became acquainted with most of the families. Those who could not write asked me to chalk their payroll numbers on the boxes they picked. I counted matches for a man who transferred them from the right pocket of his pants to the left as he tallied the lugs he filled throughout the day. It was his only check on the record the contractor kept of his work. As we worked the rows or the tree blocks during the day, or talked in the evenings where the men gathered in small groups to smoke and rest, I heard about *barrios* I had never seen but that must have been much like ours in Sacramento.

The only way to complain or protest was to leave, but now and then a camp would stand instead of run, and for a few hours or a few days work would slow down or stop. I saw it happen in a pear orchard in Yolo when pay rates were cut without notice to the crew. The contractor said the market for pears had dropped and the rancher could not afford to pay more. The fruit stayed on the trees, while we, a committee drafted by the camp, argued with

5. I.e., Come on, lazy sons of bitches (Mexican slang plus plays on words).

the contractor first and then with the rancher. The talks gave them time to round up other pickers. A carload of police in plain clothes drove into the camp. We were lined up for our pay, taking whatever the contractor said was on his books. That afternoon we were ordered off the ranch.

In a camp near Folsom, during hop picking, it was not wages but death that pulled the people together. Several children in the camp were sick with diarrhea; one had been taken to the hospital in town and the word came back that he had died. It was the women who guessed that the cause of the epidemic was the water. For cooking and drinking and washing it came from a ditch that went by the ranch stables upstream.

I was appointed by a camp committee to go to Sacramento to find some *Autoridad* who would send an inspector. Pedaling my bicycle, mulling over where to go and what to say, I remembered some clippings from the *Sacramento Bee* that Mr. Everett had discussed in class, and I decided the man to look for was Mr. Simon Lubin, who was in some way a state *Autoridad*.

He received me in his office at Weinstock and Lubin's. He sat, square-shouldered and natty, behind a desk with a glass top. He was half-bald, with a strong nose and a dimple in the center of his chin. To his right was a box with small levers into which Mr. Lubin talked and out of which came voices.

He heard me out, asked me questions and made notes on a pad. He promised that an inspector would come to the camp. I thanked him and thought the business of my visit was over; but Mr. Lubin did not break the handshake until he had said to tell the people in the camp to organize. Only by organizing, he told me, will they ever have decent places to live.

I reported the interview with Mr. Lubin to the camp. The part about the inspector they understood and it was voted not to go back to work until he came. The part about organizing was received in silence and I knew they understood it as little as I did. Remembering Duran in that camp meeting,[6] I made my first organizing speech.

The inspector came and a water tank pulled by mules was parked by the irrigation ditch. At the same time the contractor began to fire some of the pickers. I was one of them. I finished that summer nailing boxes on a grape ranch near Florin.

When my job ended I pedaled back to Sacramento, detouring over country lanes I knew well. Here and there I walked the bicycle over dirt roads rutted by wagons. The pastures were sunburned and the grain fields had been cut to stubble. Riding by a thicket of reeds where an irrigation ditch swamped I stopped and looked at the red-winged blackbirds riding gracefully on the tips of the canes. Now and then they streaked out of the green clump, spraying the pale sky with crimson dots in all directions.

Crossing the Y Street levee by Southside Park I rode through the *barrio* to Doña Tránsito's, leaving my bike hooked on the picket fence by the handle bar.

I knocked on the screen door that always hung tired, like the sagging porch coming unnailed. No one was at home.

It was two hours before time to cook supper. From the stoop I looked up and down the cross streets. The *barrio* seemed empty.

---

6. Unidentified.

I unhooked the bicycle, mounted it, and headed for the main high school, twenty blocks away where I would be going in a week. Pumping slowly, I wondered about the debating team and the other things Mr. Everett had mentioned

1971

# LUIS LEAL
## 1907–2010

As seen throughout this anthology, the fiction, poetry, and theater produced within the Latino literary tradition has been abundant and distinguished. However, the tradition has not yielded much criticism of the type practiced by Anglo writers such as Matthew Arnold, T. S. Eliot, Edmund Wilson, Irving Howe, Stanley Crouch, and Susan Sontag—critical work able to engage artists in their historical and aesthetic contexts while reaching audiences beyond academia. Among the most multifaceted and enduring Latino critics—certainly in Chicano literature—was Luis Leal.

Born in Linares, Nuevo León, in the northern part of Mexico, Leal immigrated to the United States in his late teens to enroll in Northwestern University. Since his first publication in 1942, he likely did more than any other writer or scholar to foster the critical appreciation of Mexican and Chicano literature and to establish Mexican literary studies in the United States. In fact, when he launched his career, Chicano studies did not have a place in American academia. Along with the Mexican American scholar Américo Paredes, Leal is deemed a pioneer who placed the discipline on solid ground. His essays on the myth of Aztlán, on the mythical figure of La Malinche, and on individual Chicano authors fastened the field and allowed others to develop it further.

Leal's earliest work was on classic Mexican writers such as José Joaquín Fernández de Lizardi (considered both the first modern novelist in the Americas and the author of the first Latin American novel, *El periquillo sarniento* [The Itching Parrot, 1816]) and Domingo Faustino Sarmiento (author of a seminal work of Latin American creative nonfiction, *Facundo: Civilización y barbarie* [Facundo: Civilization and Barbarism, 1845], and the seventh president of Argentina).

In the 1950s and early 1960s, Leal concentrated on the short story—in Spanish, *el cuento corto*—which, as a genre, was serving to introduce English-language readers to Spanish-language literature before the translation of major novels (such as by the Argentinian writer Julio Cortázar and by the Columbian writer Gabriel García Márquez). In his *Breve historia del cuento mexicano* (Short History of the Mexican Story, 1956), Leal highlights examples from pre-Columbian civilizations (Mayan, Quiché, Toltec, Aztec, and Tarasco); from the colonial era; from the Romantic, nationalist, *Modernista*, realist, positivist, and expressionist movements; and from then-contemporary authors. He followed that now-canonical scholarly study with two more: *Historia del cuento hispanoamericano* (History of the Hispanic American Story, 1966) and *Breve historia de la literatura hispanoamericana* (Short History of Hispanic American Literature, 1971). The latter—neither brief nor a single-sided history of south-of-the-border letters—appeared right on time, just as the literary movement called the "Latin American 'Boom'" was starting to make noise.

Leal did not receive his bachelor's degree until he was 33. A naturalized U.S. citizen, he served in the army during World War II. He had already enrolled in graduate school—the number of Mexican American college students at the time was insignificant—and in 1950 he received a doctorate from the University of Chicago. He then held positions at, among other schools, the University of Mississippi, Emory University, University of Illinois, and, finally, the University of California, Santa Barbara, where a Luis Leal Endowed Chair was established in 1995.

As teacher and advisor, Leal trained a battalion of professionals whose influence is felt nationwide. Among the awards he received were the Distinguished Scholarly Award from the National Association of Chicano Studies, in recognition of his lifetime achievements; the Presidential Medal of Honor, awarded to him by President Bill Clinton; and the *Orden del Águila Azteca*, the highest award granted to foreign citizens by the Mexican government. Yet is it accurate to describe Leal as a "foreign citizen" in Mexico? Perhaps his most significant contribution lay in erasing *la frontera*, the divide between Mexico and the United States. He spent 60 years of his life building a bookshelf of studies of myth, history, and culture by emphasizing a nonrestrictive, binational identity. For him, Mexico and the United States were so inextricably connected as to suggest a single, collective self. As practiced by him, criticism was almost exclusively preoccupied with community.

"Without general criticism, democracy could not survive," Leal said in an interview. "Or rather, without the liberty to criticize, democracy would be impossible." His immigrant identity, and his interest in Mexican American culture, made him sympathize with the Chicano Movement of the 1960s. But in comparison with the activist approach of many participants in the movement, Leal's worldview was less confrontational, more sedate. He exemplified the term *hispanista*—a philologist devoted to the study of Hispanic culture across geographical scopes and historical periods.

In his brief essays, dispersed in periodicals over a period of six decades and collected in *A Luis Leal Reader* (2008), Leal is at his best: ambitious in scope, wide-ranging in knowledge, succinct and crystalline in style, and methodical as well as impartial in judgment. For example, his critical appraisals of the Dominican man of letters Pedro Henríquez Ureña, the Mexican poet Amado Nervo, the Mexican American writer Rudolfo A. Anaya, and "magical realism" are maps of the often tense, fragile relations between the societies on both sides of the Rio Grande. In the essay that follows, "In Search of Aztlán" (originally published in the anthology *Aztlán: Essays on the Chicano Homeland*, 1989), Leal explores the vicissitudes of the concept of Aztlán. This utopian homeland has always been at the heart of Chicano culture, and it served as a leitmotif during the Chicano Movement.

# In Search of Aztlán[1]

One of the functions of the critic is to discover and analyze literary symbols with the object of broadening the perception that one has of a certain social or national group, or of humanity in general. In the case of Chicano literature, a literature that has emerged as a consequence of the fight for social and human rights, most of the symbols have been taken from the surrounding social environment.

For that reason, Chicano literary symbolism cannot be separated from Chicano cultural background. In order to study this symbolism, it is necessary to see it in context with the social ideas that predominate in Chicano contemporary thought. Therefore, we must consult the large bibliography that already exists and pertains to the social, racial, linguistic, and educa-

1. Translated by Gladys Leal.

tional problems that the Chicano has confronted since 1848. The social and literary symbols, as we shall see, are the same. Their origin is found in the sociopolitical struggle, from where they have passed on to literature.

The symbols that have served to give unity to the Chicano movement and that appear in literature are many: Aztlán, the black eagle of the farm-workers; the Virgin of Guadalupe; *la huelga* (the strike); the expression ¡*Viva la raza!*;[2] and the characteristic handshake, the latter, of course, being out-side of the literary field. The greatest part of these symbols, which give form to the concept of Chicanismo, are of recent origin; they were born with the political and social movement that was initiated with the strike in Delano, California, in 1965.[3] But they have their roots in Mexico's historic past. The Virgin of Guadalupe was one of the symbols that helped to create Mexican nationality and political independence, her image having been hoisted by Father Miguel Hidalgo in 1810.[4] The eagle the farmworkers used has an older origin, dating back to the foundation of Tenochtitlán by the Aztecs in 1325,[5] where the people from Aztlán found on an island an eagle sitting on a nopal devouring a serpent. César Chávez,[6] the creator of this Chicano symbol, said to *Ramparts* magazine:

> I wanted desperately to get some color into the movement, to give peo-ple something they could identify with, like a flag. I was reading some books about how various leaders discovered what colors contrasted and stood out the best. The Egyptians had found that a red field with a white circle and a black emblem in the center crashed into your eyes like nothing else. I wanted to use the Aztec eagle in the center, as on the Mexican flag. So I told my cousin Manuel, "Draw an Aztec Eagle." Manuel had a little trouble with it, so we modified the eagle to make it easier for people to draw.

According to accepted definitions, the symbol is a sensory image, which represents a concept or an emotion that cannot be expressed in its totality by any other method. The symbol expresses, with that sensory image, the significance of the spiritual. The image that we see reveals to us or makes us aware of the existence of something beyond the material. In other words, the sensory image, or symbol, is associated with a concept or an emotion (the symbolized thing). Therefore, it is necessary to interpret the symbol (the thing expressed) in terms of what is not expressed. Since the symbol can be social and not necessarily archetypal or mythical, it often has significance only for the group that has produced it and, frequently, only for the artist who has cre-ated it.

As a visual symbol, and not a literary one, the black eagle in the white cir-cle over a red background symbolized for the Chicano the triumph over eco-nomic injustice by means of the farmworkers' union, whose aim is to obtain

2. Long live the race! *The Virgin of Guadalupe*: *Nuestra Señora de Guadalupe*, a sixteenth-century icon of the Virgin Mary; perhaps Mexico's most popular religious and cultural image, it has come to symbolize Catholic Mexicans and Mexico itself.
3. A five-year-plus strike, with boycotts, led by the United Farm Workers (UFW) against table-grape growers. It led to the union's first contract with these growers.
4. The Mexican Catholic priest Father Miguel

Hidalgo y Costilla (1753–1811) helped lead the Mexican War of Independence in 1810.
5. Located on an island in Lake Texcoco, in the Valley of Mexico, Tenochtitlán was the center of the Aztec Empire. Defeated by the Spanish con-quistador Hernán Cortés and his forces, it be-came the capital of the Viceroyalty of New Spain and, subsequently, present-day Mexico City.
6. See p. 760.

a better standard of living and also cultural identity. For those who are not Chicanos, the symbol loses its significance. Nevertheless, since the colors red, black, and white have a universal symbolic meaning, the image has a broad emotional significance, although not necessarily the same for all as the one that the Chicano understands. At the same time, the use of the eagle from the Mexican flag and of the colors red and white has a symbolic meaning for the *mexicano*, since it reminds him or her of the national flag. The eagle, Aztlán, the Quinto Sol,[7] and other Chicano symbols of Mexican origin form a part of a mythic system, a characteristic often attributed to the symbol. An excellent example of the symbolic use of colors is the creation of Haiti's flag by the former slave Jean-Jacques Dessalines,[8] who ripped the white color out of the French flag and sewed together the red and blue, symbolizing the expulsion of the white people from the country.

Aztlán, which we propose to examine in this study, is as much symbol as it is myth. As a symbol, it conveys the image of the cave (or sometimes a hill) representative of the origin of man; and as a myth, it symbolizes the existence of a paradisiacal region where injustice, evil, sickness, old age, poverty, and misery do not exist. As a Chicano symbol, Aztlán has two meanings: first, it represents the geographic region known as the Southwest of the United States, composed of the territory that Mexico ceded in 1848 with the Treaty of Guadalupe Hidalgo; second, and more important, Aztlán symbolizes the spiritual union of the Chicanos, something that is carried within the heart, no matter where they may live or where they may find themselves.

As a region in mythical geography, Aztlán has a long history. According to the Nahuatlan myth,[9] the Aztecs were the last remaining tribe of seven, and they were advised by their god Huitzilopochtli to leave Aztlán in search of the Promised Land, which they would know by an eagle sitting on a nopal devouring a serpent. Later, the Aztecs, whose name is derived from Aztlán, remembered the region of their origin as an earthly paradise. During the fifteenth century, Moctezuma Ilhuicamina (1440–49)[1] sent his priests in search of Aztlán. The historian Fray Diego Durán, in his *Historia de las Indias de Nueva España e Islas de Tierra Firme*, a work finished in 1581, says that Moctezuma I, desiring to know where the Aztecs' ancestors had lived, what form those seven caves had, and the relation between the people's history and their memory of it, sent for Cuauhcóatl, the royal historian, who told him:

> O mighty lord, I, your unworthy servant, can answer you. . . . Our forebears dwelt in that blissful, happy place called Aztlán, which means "Whiteness." In that place there is a great hill in the midst of the waters, and it is called Culhuacan because its summit is twisted; this is the Twisted Hill. On its slopes were caves or grottos where our fathers and grandfathers lived for many years. There they lived in leisure, when they were called Mexitin and Azteca. There they had at their disposal great flocks of ducks of different kinds, herons, waterfowl, and cranes. Our ancestors loved the song and melody of the little birds with red and yellow heads. They also possessed many kinds of large beautiful fish.

7. The fifth sun of the Aztec calendar.
8. As Jacques I (1758?–1806), emperor of Haiti 1804–06.
9. I.e., a legend shared by speakers of the Uto-

Aztecan languages.
1. Or Moctezuma I, fifth Aztec emperor, under whose reign the empire was consolidated.

They had the freshness of groves of trees along the edge of the waters. They had springs surrounded by willows, evergreens, and alders, all of them tall and comely. Our ancestors went about in canoes and made floating gardens upon which they sowed maize, chili, tomatoes, amaranth, beans, and all kinds of seeds which we now eat and which were brought here from there.

However, after they came to the mainland and abandoned that delightful place, everything turned against them. The weeds began to bite, the stones became sharp, the fields were filled with thistles and spines. They encountered brambles and thorns that were difficult to pass through. There was no place to sit, there was no place to rest; everything became filled with vipers, snakes, poisonous little animals, jaguars, and wildcats and other ferocious beasts. And this is what our ancestors forsook. I have found it painted in our ancient books. And this, O powerful king, is the answer I can give you to what you ask of me.

Moctezuma I called for all of his sorcerers and magicians and sent them in search of Aztlán and of Coatlicue, the mother of Huitzilopochtli. The sorcerers in Coatepec, a province of Tula, transformed themselves through the art of magic into birds, tigers, lions, jackals, and wildcats, and in this way arrived at that lagoon in the middle of which is the hill of Culhuacán. They again took the form of humans and asked for Coatlicue "and the place which their ancestors left, which was called Chicomostoc [seven caves]."

The emissaries were taken in canoes to the island of Aztlán, where the hill is. "They say," relates Durán, "that the top half of the hill is made up of a very fine sand." There they found Coatlicue, who demonstrated to them that in Aztlán men never become old. She tells them:

> "Stop so that you can see how men never become old in this country! Do you see my old servant? Watch him climb down the hill! By the time he reaches you he will be a young man."
>
> The old man descended and as he ran he became younger and younger. When he reached the Aztec wizards, he appeared to be about twenty years old. Said he, "Behold, my sons, the virtue of this hill; the old man who seeks youth can climb to the point on the hill that he wishes and there he will acquire the age that he seeks."

The emissaries again transformed themselves into animals in order to make the return trip, which many of them did not succeed in completing because of having been eaten by wild beasts on the way. That is the Aztlán of the Aztec myth, the Aztlán that, like the mythical Atlantis, has never been pinpointed in geography. The search for it, like that for the fountain of youth, has never ceased. Cecilio Robelo, the Mexican historian of Nahuatlan mythology, tells us, "It's generally believed that Aztlán was located to the north of the Gulf of California." But not even that conjecture is accepted, since later he adds, "The inexorable question, then, of the place where the Mexica came from, still remains." And the inexorable question still stands, in spite of the efforts of erudite historians, whether they be Mexican, European, or American, such as Clavijero, Humboldt, Prescott, Orozco y Berra, Eustaquio Buelna, Chavero, Fernando Ramírez, Lapham, Wickersham, or

Seler.[2] There was even a book published in 1933 by S. A. Barrett titled *Ancient Aztalan*, which tried to prove that Aztlán can be found in the lakes of Wisconsin. Others have said that it was in Florida; others believe that it was in New Mexico; and still others in California. It was even said that Aztlán was to be found in China. The historian of Santa Barbara, California, Russell A. Ruíz, in a pamphlet published during the summer of 1969 that treats of the passing of the expedition of Portolá[3] through the region, tells us that when the governor arrived on August 20, 1769, at what is today Goleta, California, he baptized the land with the name Pueblos de la Isla, which Father Crespi,[4] who accompanied him, called Santa Margarita de Cortona, and to which the soldiers gave the name Mescaltitlán, believing that they had found themselves in the legendary place of origin of the Aztecs. In a few words, Ruiz says, "Mescaltitlán was another name for Aztlán, the legendary place of origin of the Aztecs or Mexican people. The Aztecs described it as a terrestrial paradise."

What interests us is not determining where Aztlán is found, but documenting the rebirth of the myth in Chicano thought. It is necessary to point out the fact that before March 1969, the date of the First National Chicano Liberation Youth Conference in Denver, no one mentioned Aztlán in writing. In fact, the first time that it was mentioned in a Chicano document was in "El plan espiritual de Aztlán" ("The Spiritual Plan of Aztlán"), which was presented in Denver at that time. Apparently, the rebirth of Aztlán owes its creation to the poet Alurista[5] who already, in autumn 1968, had spoken about Aztlán in a class about Chicano culture held at San Diego State University.

"El plan espiritual de Aztlán" is important because in it the Chicano recognizes his Aztec origins ("We, the Chicano inhabitants and civilizers of the northern land of Aztlán, from whence came our forefathers"); because it established that Aztlán is the Mexican territory ceded to the United States in 1848; and because, following one of the basic ideas of the Mexican Revolution, it recognizes that the land belongs to those who work it ("Aztlán belongs to those that plant the seeds, water the fields, and gather the crops"); and finally, it identifies the Chicano with Aztlán ("We are a nation, we are a union of free pueblos, we are *Aztlán*").

Those words were published in March 1969. Beginning with that date, Aztlán has become the symbol most used by Chicano authors who write about the history, the culture, or the destiny of their people; and the same thing occurs among those who write poetic novels or short stories. During the spring of the following year, 1970, the first number of the journal *Aztlán* was published, and in it the plan was reproduced in both English and

2. Unidentified, as are Chavero and Wickersham. *Clavijero*: Francisco Javier Clavijero Echegaray (1731–1787), Jesuit teacher, scholar, and historian in New Spain. *Humboldt*: Alexander von Humboldt (1769–1859), major German naturalist and explorer, whose voyage to the Americas helped establish the field of biogeography. *Prescott*: William Hickling Prescott (1796–1859), American historian and the author of classic epic books on the conquests of Mexico and of Peru. *Orozco y Berra*: Manuel Orozco y Berra (1816–1881), Mexican historian. *Eustaquio Buelna*: Eustaquio Buelna Pérez (1830–1907), Mexican historian and politician. *Fernando Ramírez*: José Fernando Ramírez (1804–1871), distinguished Mexican historian. *Lapham*: Increase Allen Lapham (1811–1875), American author, scientist, and naturalist.

3. Gaspar de Portolá (fl. 1734–1784), Spanish explorer in the Far West; governor of the Californias ca. 1767; founder of San Diego, 1769; governor of Puebla, Mexico, 1776–84.

4. Fray Juan Crespi (see p. 140).

5. Alberto Baltazar Heredia Urista (see p. 1657).

Spanish. The prologue consists of a poem by Alurista called "Poem in Lieu of Preface," which united the mythical Aztec past with the present:

it is said
    that MOTECUHZOMA ILHUICAMINA
    SENT
        AN expedition
        looking for the NortherN
    mYthical land
    wherefrom the AZTECS CAME
        la TIERRA
    dE
    AztlÁN
    mYthical land for those
        who dream of roses and
        swallow thorns
        or for those who swallow thorns
    in powdered milk
    feeling guilty about smelling flowers
about looking for AztlÁN

In the following year, Alurista published the anthology *El ombligo de Aztlán* (*Aztlán's Navel*), and a year later his *Nationchild Plumaroja* appeared, published in San Diego by Toltecas de Aztlán. The title *Nationchild* refers, of course, to the Chicanos of Aztlán. From here on, books in whose title the word *Aztlán* appears would multiply.

In fiction also, especially in the novel, the symbol has been utilized with advantage for artistic creation. The novels of Méndez,[6] *Peregrinos de Aztlán* (*Pilgrims of Aztlán*, 1974), and of Anaya,[7] *Heart of Aztlán* (1976), are works representative of that tendency. It is fitting to point out that both works have antecedents in Mexican narrative. Gregorio López y Fuentes[8] published in 1944 his novel *Los peregrinos inmóviles* (*Motherless Pilgrims*), and in 1949 María de Lourdes Hernández[9] printed hers, *En el nuevo Aztlán* (*In the New Aztlán*). There is no direct influence between these Mexican and Chicano novels. Nevertheless, the elements that they have in common are significant and permit us to make a comparison. The theme of *Los peregrinos inmóviles* is the search for the Promised Land; in that novel, López y Fuentes re-creates the mythical pilgrimage of the Aztecs. In *Peregrinos de Aztlán* the theme is identical, only that the pilgrimage is in reverse. We read in Méndez's novel: "My imagination got the best of me and I saw a pilgrimage of many Indian people who were being trod upon by the torture of hunger and the humiliation of despoilment, running back through ancient roads in search of their remote origin." López y Fuentes had already written: "We walked all afternoon and part of the night. . . . We were going to the land of abundance: that was the message of the eagle, and we were on the right track."

Another important incidence is that in both works the narrator is an old Indian who remembers the history of his village. For the old Yaqui Loreto

6. Miguel Méndez (b. 1930), Mexican American–Yaqui writer.
7. Rudolfo A. Anaya (see p. 1160).
8. Mexican novelist, poet, journalist, and chronicler of the Mexican Revolution (1895–1966).
9. Chicana writer (dates unknown).

Maldonado, in Tijuana, the memories of his fallen and abused people torment him; and for the old Marcos, the memory of the original pilgrimage gives him courage to guide his own people. The first part of *Los peregrinos inmóviles* is titled "Heart of the World." And years later, Rudolfo Anaya would publish his novel with the title *Heart of Aztlán*, in which there is also a pilgrimage that the protagonist makes in search of Aztlán in a vision. Here he has the help of a magic stone instead of the eagle.

A greater similarity exists between *Heart of Aztlán* and *En el nuevo Aztlán*. In both novels the theme is the search for Aztlán, the lost paradise. In the work of Hernández, a group of Aztecs, immediately after the fall of Cuauhtémoc,[1] takes refuge in a secret valley to which they can travel only by means of a mysterious river, which runs inside the grottos of Cacahuamilpa. In that valley, they founded a kind of Shangri-la, a perfect society. In the novel of Anaya, which develops in Barelas, a barrio in Albuquerque, the protagonist Clemente Chávez, not an old man but a man of some years, goes to the mountains, guided by the blind minstrel Crispín, in search of Aztlán on a truly imaginary pilgrimage: "They moved north, and there Aztlán was a woman fringed with snow and ice; they moved west, and there she was a mermaid singing by the sea. . . . They walked to the land where the sun rises, and . . . they found new signs, and the signs pointed them back to the center, back to Aztlán."

It is here where they find out that Aztlán symbolizes the center: "Time stood still, and in that enduring moment he felt the rhythm of the heart of Aztlán beat to the measure of his own heart. Dreams and visions became reality, and reality was but the thin substance of myth and legends. A joyful power coursed from the dark womb-heart of the earth into his soul and he cried out *I am Aztlán!*"

The search, for Clemente, has ended. And that is the way it must be for all Chicanos: whosoever wants to find Aztlán, let him or her look for it, not on the maps, but in the most intimate part of his being.

1989

1. Also called Guatémoc, Guatimozin, or Cuauhtemotzin; last Aztec emperor (ca. 1495–1522), killed by Cortés.

---

# FRAY ANGÉLICO CHÁVEZ
## 1910–1996

Because he liked to paint, the New Mexican–born Manuel Chávez was dubbed Fray Angélico—after Fra Angélico, the medieval Florentine painter—by his teachers at Cincinnati's Saint Francis Seraphic Seminary. Later, Chávez used the nickname as his pen name. In *My Penitente Land* (1974), which is partly his spiritual autobiography and partly a meditation on Spanish New Mexico, Fray Angélico Chávez identifies himself not as a Chicano but as a New Mexican Hispano. In this way, he emphasizes his connection with the New Mexican landscape and its indigenous people. He is *castizo,* pure-blooded, and not *mestizo,* the admixture of Spanish and Indian blood that makes up a large portion of the Mexican people.

New Mexico's first priest in the Franciscan Order, Chávez served in the U.S. Army as a chaplain in the Pacific during World War II and was stationed in Germany during the Korean War. At various times, he served the Church in different New Mexico locations: at Saint Francis Cathedral, in Santa Fe; at the parish of Peña Blanca, where he played a very active role in renovating the church; at Jémez Pueblo, where he performed a pilgrimage carrying La Conquistadora, a small statue of the Virgin Mary of great historical interest in New Mexico; as pastor of the parish of Cerrillos; and in Albuquerque. Despite such migrations, Chávez continually pursued his painting and his writing, the latter of which included poetry, short stories, historical fiction, translation, and essays. Both fields brought him favorable reviews and repeated recognition.

Among his most enduring poetry collections is *Eleven Lady-Lyrics and Other Poems* (1945), set in New Mexico but consisting of nonrealistic, schematic representations of the poet's inner life. Reminiscent of the *arrobos* (raptures) by the sixteenth-century Spanish nun and mystic Saint Teresa of Ávila, the poems strive to portray moments of intense emotion. Equally or even more successful artistically are *The Single Rose: La Rosa Única and Commentary of Fray Manuel de Santa Clara* (1948), which are poems of divine love, and *The Virgin of Port Lligat* (1959), which Chávez said was inspired by a painting by the twentieth-century Spanish artist Salvador Dalí. Among Chávez's other acknowledged influences were the seventeenth-century English poet and clergyman John Donne and the nineteenth-century English artist, poet, and mystic William Blake; his work, like theirs, considers the place and significance of humanity in the universe. In 1963, Chávez received the annual poetry award of the Catholic Poetry Society of America.

Chávez's best-known fiction is collected in *The Short Stories of Fray Angélico Chávez* (1987). In keeping with his calling, the stories deal with religious themes and settings. The following selection from his work is the third and most popular part of *New Mexico Triptych, Being Three Panels and Three Accounts: l. The Angel's New Wings; 2. The Penitente Thief; 3. Hunchback Madonna* (1940). Set in New Mexico, "Hunchback Madonna" is inspired by the miraculous appearance, in 1531, of the Virgin Mary to the Indian Juan Diego on the hilltop of Tepeyac, Mexico. The image of Mary as the Virgin of Guadalupe (*Nuestra Señora de Guadalupe*) has become central to Mexico's religious and cultural identity.

---

## *FROM* NEW MEXICO TRIPTYCH

## Hunchback Madonna

Old and crumbling, the squat-built adobe mission of El Tordo sits in a hollow high up near the snow-capped Truchas.[1] A few clay houses huddle close to it like tawny chicks about a ruffled old hen. On one of the steep slopes, which has the peaks for a background, sleeps the ancient graveyard with all its inhabitants, or what little is left of them. The town itself is quite as lifeless during the winter months, when the few folks that live there move

---

1. Mountain peaks in Rio Arriba County, northern New Mexico, halfway between Santa Fe in the south and Taos to the north.

down to warmer levels by the Rio Grande; but when the snows have gone, except for the white crusts on the peaks, they return to herd their sheep and goats, and with them comes a stream of pious pilgrims and curious sightseers which lasts throughout the spring and summer weather.

They come to see and pray before the stoop-shouldered Virgin, people from as far south as Belen[2] who from some accident or some spinal or heart affliction are shoulder-bent and want to walk straight again. Others, whose faith is not so simple or who have no faith at all, have come from many parts of the country and asked the way to El Tordo, not only to see the curiously painted Madonna in which the natives put so much stock, but to visit a single grave in a corner of the *campo santo*[3] which, they have heard, is covered in spring with a profusion of wild flowers, whereas the other sunken ones are bare altogether, or at the most sprinkled only with sagebrush and tumbleweed. And, of course, they want to hear from the lips of some old inhabitant the history of the town and the church, the painting and the grave, and particularly of Mana Seda.

No one knows, or cares to know, when the village was born. It is more thrilling to say, with the natives, that the first settlers came up from the Santa Clara valley long before the railroad came to New Mexico, when the Indians of Nambé and Taos still used bows and arrows and obsidian clubs; when it took a week to go to Santa Fé, which looked no different from the other northern towns at the time, only somewhat bigger. After the men had allotted the scant farming land among themselves, and each family raised its adobe hut of one or two rooms to begin with, they set to making adobes for a church that would shoulder above their homes as a guardian parent. On a high, untillable slope they marked out as their God's acre a plot which was to be surrounded by an adobe wall. It was not long before large pines from the forest nearby had been carved into beams and corbels and hoisted into their places on the thick walls. The women themselves mud-plastered the tall walls outside with their bare hands; within they made them a soft white with a lime mixture applied with the woolly side of sheepskins.

The Padre, whose name the people do not remember, was so pleased with the building, and with the crudely wrought reredos behind the altar, that he promised to get at his own expense a large hand-painted *Nuestra Señora de Guadalupe* to hang in the middle of the *retablo*.[4] But this had to wait until the next traders' ox-drawn caravan left Santa Fé for Chihuahua in Old Mexico and came back again. It would take years, perhaps, if there was no such painting ready and it must be made to order.

With these first settlers of El Tordo had come an old woman who had no relatives in the place they had left. For no apparent reason she had chosen to cast her lot with the emigrants, and they had willingly brought her along in one of their wooden-wheeled *carretas*,[5] had even built her a room in the protective shadow of the new church. For that had been her work before, sweeping the house of God, ringing the Angelus morning, noon and night, adorning the altar with lace cloths and flowers, when there were flowers. She even persuaded the Padre, when the first May came around, to start an ancient custom prevalent in her place of origin: that of having little girls dressed as

---

2. Town in central New Mexico.
3. Cemetery.
4. Traditional Mexican religious painting done on

a wood carving.
5. Oxcarts.

queens and their maids-in-waiting present bunches of flowers to the Virgin
Mary every evening in May. She could not wait for the day when the Guadalupe picture would arrive.

They called her *Mana Seda*, "Sister Silk." Nobody knew why; they had
known her by no other name. The women thought she had got it long ago
for being always so neat, or maybe because she embroidered so many altar-
cloths. But the men said it was because she looked so much like a silk-
spinning spider; for she was very much humpbacked—so bent forward that
she could look up only sideways and with effort. She always wore black, a
black shiny dress and black shawl with long leg-like fringes and, despite her
age and deformity, she walked about quite swiftly and noiselessly. "Yes,"
they said, "like the black widow spider."

Being the cause of the May devotions at El Tordo, she took it upon herself
to provide the happy girls with flowers for the purpose. The geraniums which
she grew in her window were used up the first day, as also those that other
women had tended in their own homes. So she scoured the slopes around the
village for wild daisies and Indian paintbrush, usually returning in the late
afternoon with a shawlful to spill at the eager children's feet. Toward the end
of May she had to push deeper into the forest, whence she came back with
her tireless, short-stepped spider-run, her arms and shawl laden with wild iris
and cosmos, verbenas and mariposa lilies from the pine shadows.

This she did year after year, even after the little "queens" of former Mays
got married and new tots grew up to wear their veils. Mana Seda's one regret was that the image of the Virgin of Guadalupe had not come, had been
lost on the way when the Comanches or Apaches attacked and destroyed
the Chihuahua–Santa Fé ox-train.

One year in May (it was two days before the close of the month), when
the people were already whispering among themselves that Mana Seda was
so old she must die soon, or else last forever, she was seen hurrying into the
forest early in the morning, to avail herself of all the daylight possible, for
she had to go far into the wooded canyons this time. At the closing services
of May there was to be, not one queen, but a number of them with their attendants. Many more flowers were needed for this, and the year had been a
bad one for flowers, since little snow had fallen the winter before.

Mana Seda found few blooms in her old haunts, here and there an aster
with half of its petals missing or drought-toasted, or a faded columbine fast
wilting in the cool but moistureless shade. But she must find enough flowers; otherwise the good heavenly Mother would have a sad and colorless
farewell this May. On and on she shuttled in between the trunks of spruce
and fir, which grew thicker and taller and closer-set as the canyon grew narrower. Further up she heard the sound of trickling water; surely the purple
iris and freckled lily flames would be rioting there, fresh and without number. She was not disappointed, and without pausing to recover her breath,
began lustily to snap off the long, luscious stems and lay them on her shawl,
spread out on the little meadow. Her haste was prompted by the darkness
closing in through the evergreens, now turning blacker and blacker, not
with approaching dusk, but with the smoky pall of thunderheads that had
swallowed up the patches of blue among the tops of the forest giants.

Far away arose rumblings that grew swiftly louder and nearer. The great
trees, which always whispered to her even on quiet, sunny days, began to

hiss and whine angrily at the unseen wind that swayed them and swung their arms like maidens unwilling to be kissed or danced with. And then a deafening sound exploded nearby with a blinding bluish light. Others followed, now on the right or on the left, now before or behind, as Mana Seda, who had thrown her flower-weighted mantle on her arched back, started to run—in which direction she knew not, for the rain was slashing down in sheets that blurred the dark boles and boulders all around her.

At last she fell, whimpering prayers to the holy Virgin with a water-filled mouth that choked her. Of a sudden, sunlight began to fall instead between the towering trees, now quiet and dripping with emeralds and sapphires. The storm had passed by, the way spring rains in the Truchas Mountains do, as suddenly as it had come. In a clearing not far ahead, Mana Seda saw a little adobe hut. On its one chimney stood a wisp of smoke, like a white feather. Still clutching her heavy, rain-soaked shawl, she ran to it and knocked at the door, which was opened by an astonished young man with a short, sharp knife in his hand.

· · ·

"I thought the mountain's bowels where the springs come from had burst," she was telling the youth, who meanwhile stirred a pot of brown beans that hung with a pail of coffee over the flames in the corner fireplace. "But our most holy Lady saved me when I prayed to her, *gracias a Dios*. The lightning and the water stopped, and I saw her flying above me. She had a piece of sky for a veil, and her skirt was like the beautiful red roses at her feet. She showed me your house."

Her host tried to hide his amusement by taking up his work again, a head he had been carving on the end of a small log. She saw that he was no different from the grown boys of El Tordo, dark and somewhat lean-bodied in his plain homespun. All about, against the wall and in niches, could be seen several other images, wooden and gaily colored *bultos*, and more *santos*[6] painted on pieces of wood or hide. Mana Seda guessed that this must be the young stranger's trade, and grew more confident because of it. As she spread out her shawl to dry before the open fire, her load of flowers rolled out soggily on the bare earth floor. Catching his questioning stare, she told him what they were for, and about the church and the people of El Tordo.

"But that makes me think of the apparition of Our Lady of Guadalupe," he said. "Remember how the Indian Juan Diego filled his blanket with roses, as Mary most holy told him to do? And how, when he let down his *tilma*[7] before the Bishop, out fell the roses, and on it was the miraculous picture of the Mother of God?"

Yes, she knew the story well; and she told him about the painting of the Guadalupe which the priest of El Tordo had ordered brought from Mexico and which was lost on the way. Perhaps, if the Padre knew of this young man's ability, he would pay him for making one. Did he ever do work for churches? And what was his name?

"My name is Esquipula," he replied. "*Si*, I have done work for the Church. I made the *retablo* of 'San Francisco' for his church in Ranchos de Taos,

---

6. Saints. *Bultos*: "image of holy person carved in the round; ghost" (Rubén Cobos, *A Dictionary of New Mexican and Southern Colorado Spanish,* 1983).

7. In New Mexican Spanish, "a kind of poncho, a short Indian saddle blanket" (Cobos).

and also the 'Cristo' for Santa Cruz. The 'Guadalupe' at San Juan, I painted it. I will gladly paint another for your chapel." He stopped all of a sudden, shut his eyes tight, and then quickly leaned toward the bent old figure who was helping herself to some coffee. "Why do you not let me paint one right now—on your shawl!"

She could not answer at first. Such a thing was unheard of. Besides, she had no other *tápalo*[8] to wear. And what would the people back home say when she returned wearing the Virgin on her back? What would She say?

"You can wear the picture turned inside where nobody can see it. Look! You will always have holy Mary with you, hovering over you, hugging your shoulders and your breast! Come," he continued, seeing her ready to yield, "it is too late for you to go back to El Tordo. I will paint it now, and tomorrow I and Mariquita will take you home."

"And who is Mariquita?" she wanted to know.

"Mariquita is my little donkey," was the reply.

Mana Seda's black shawl was duly hung and spread tight against a bare stretch of wall, and Esquipula lost no time in tracing with white chalk the outlines of the small wood-print which he held in his left hand as a model. The actual laying of the colors, however, went much slower because of the shawl's rough and unsized texture. Darkness came, and Esquipula lit an oil lamp, which he held in one hand as he applied the pigments with the other. He even declined joining his aged guest at her evening meal of beans and stale *tortillas*, because he was not hungry, he explained, and the picture must be done.

Once in a while the painter would turn from his work to look at Mana Seda, who had become quite talkative, something the people back at El Tordo would have marveled at greatly. She was recounting experiences of her girlhood which, she explained, were more vivid than many things that had happened recently.

Only once did he interrupt her, and that without thinking first. He said, almost too bluntly: "How did you become hunchbacked?"

Mana Seda hesitated, but did not seem to take the question amiss. Patting her shoulder as far as she could reach to her bulging back, she answered: "The woman who was nursing me dropped me on the hard dirt floor when I was a baby, and I grew up like a ball. But I do not remember, of course. My being bent out of shape did not hurt me until the time when other little girls of my age were chosen to be flower-maids in May. When I was older, and other big girls rejoiced at being chosen May queens, I was filled with bitter envy. God forgive me, I even cursed. I at last made up my mind never to go to the May devotions, nor to Mass either. In the place of my birth, the shores of the Rio Grande are made up of wet sand which sucks in every living creature that goes in; I would go there and return no more. But something inside told me the Lord would be most pleased if I helped the other lucky girls with their flowers. That would make me a flower-bearer every day. Esquipula, my son, I have been doing this for seventy-four Mays!"

Mana Seda stopped and reflected in deep silence. The youth who had been painting absent-mindedly and looking at her, now noticed for the first time that he had made the Virgin's shoulders rather stooped, like Mana Seda's,

8. In New Mexican Spanish, a "shawl" (Cobos).

though not quite so much. His first impulse was to run the yellow sun-rays into them and cover up the mistake, but for no reason he decided to let things stand as they were. By and by he put the last touches to his *oeuvre de caprice*,[9] offered the old lady his narrow cot in a corner, and went out to pass the night in Mariquita's humble shed.

The following morning saw a young man leading a grey burro through the forest, and on the patient animal's back swayed a round black shape, grasping her mantle with one hand while the other held tight to the small wooden saddle. Behind her, their bright heads bobbing from its wide mouth, rode a sack full of iris and tiger-lilies from the meadow where the storm had caught Mana Seda the day before. Every once in a while, Esquipula had to stop the beast and go after some new flower which the rider had spied from her perch; sometimes she made him climb up a steep rock for a crannied blossom he would have passed unnoticed.

The sun was going down when they at last trudged into El Tordo and halted before the church, where the priest stood surrounded by a bevy of inquiring, disappointed girls. He rushed forth immediately to help Mana Seda off the donkey, while the children pounced upon the flowers with shouts of glee. Asking questions and not waiting for answers, he led the stranger and his still stranger charge into his house, meanwhile giving orders that the burro be taken to his barn and fed.

Mana Seda dared not sit with the Padre at table and hied herself to the kitchen for her supper. Young Esquipula, however, felt very much at ease, answering all his host's questions intelligently, at which the pastor was agreeably surprised, but not quite so astonished as when he heard for the first time of Mana Seda's childhood disappointments.

"Young man," he said, hurriedly finishing his meal, "there is little time to lose. Tonight is the closing of May—and it will be done, although we are unworthy." Dragging his chair closer to the youth, he plotted out his plan in excited whispers which fired Esquipula with an equal enthusiasm.

• • •

The last bell was calling the folk of El Tordo in the cool of the evening. Six queens with their many white-veiled maids stood in a nervous, noisy line at the church door, a garden of flowers in their arms. The priest and the stranger stood on guard facing them, begging them to be quiet, looking anxiously at the people who streamed past them into the edifice. Mana Seda finally appeared and tried to slide quietly by, but the Padre barred her way and pressed a big basket filled with flowers and lighted candles into her brown, dry hands. At the same time Esquipula took off her black shawl and dropped over her grey head and hunched form a precious veil of Spanish lace.

In her amazement she could not protest, could not even move a step, until the Padre urged her on, whispering into her ear that it was the holy Virgin's express wish. And so Mana Seda led all the queens that evening, slowly and smoothly, not like a black widow now, folks observed, but like one of those little white moths moving over alfalfa fields in the moonlight. It was the happiest moment of her long life. She felt that she must die from pure joy, and many others observing her, thought so too.

9. Distinctive work (French).

She did not die then; for some years afterward, she wore the new black *tápalo* the Padre gave her in exchange for the old one, which Esquipula installed in the *retablo* above the altar. But toward the last she could not gather any more flowers on the slopes, much less in the forest. They buried her in a corner of the *campo santo*, and the following May disks of daisies and bunches of verbenas came up on her grave. It is said they have been doing it ever since, for curious travelers to ask about, while pious pilgrims come to pray before the hunchback Madonna.

1940

# JOSEFINA NIGGLI
## 1910–1983

Josefina (sometimes spelled Josephina) María Niggli was born in Monterrey, in the northeastern Mexican state of Nuevo León, just as *La Revolución*, the first peasant armed struggle of the twentieth century, was beginning. Her father, Frederick Ferdinand Niggli, came from a family of Swiss and Alsatians who had immigrated to Texas in 1836. Her mother, Goldie (Morgan) Niggli, was a violinist well known in the Southwest, with ancestors from Ireland, France, and Germany.

At Incarnate Word College, in San Antonio, Texas, Niggli was mentored by a professor in the English department. Her father paid for the publication of her first book, the poetry collection *Mexican Silhouettes* (1928), which employs a *costumbrista* (folkloristic) style popular at the time, particularly among Mexican émigrés. For example, in the poem "Mexico, My Beloved," the speaker reacts against clichés (the clashing of cymbals and "vermilion sails over the heart of the wind") and then talks of Mexico as "my beloved" and of the moon that "touches the silken waves" of the Lerma River. The overall impression in such early efforts, as in the narratives Niggli produced in the 1940s, is of a romanticized Mexico.

Before and after college, from which she graduated in 1931, Niggli worked for San Antonio's radio station KTSA. The approximately dozen plays she wrote in her lifetime seem suited for radio: They generally have no more than six characters, and the plotlines develop less from physical movement than from anecdotal exchanges. In the early 1930s, Niggli collaborated with the San Antonio Little Theater. She then moved to Chapel Hill and entered a playwriting program with the Carolina Playmakers, part of the University of North Carolina. Her thesis for her master's degree was the three-act historical play *Singing Valley*, written in 1937.

The next year, the University of North Carolina Press published five of her one-act pieces in a single book, *Mexican Folk Plays*. Niggli's themes in this collection echo those she pursued in college: Mexico from its pre-Columbian past to its tumultuous present. One piece is about the Aztecs, another about the female soldiers in *La Revolución*—"for whom there was no blazing patriotic fire," for "they were 'broken shells whose only desire was revenge for all they had suffered.'" The settings are mostly rural, and the characters are few. These plays are no longer staged, however, largely because they are less valuable as dramas than as cultural artifacts. They open a window of appreciation for the way Mexico has been perceived—that is, distorted—by American eyes.

Until the mid-1940s, Niggli continued exploring folklore in comedies and tragedies. Her works from this period are mostly in a historical vein. *The Cry of Dolores*

(1936) addresses the role of Father Miguel Hidalgo y Costilla in Mexico's struggle for independence in 1810. *The Fair God: Malinche* (1936) is about La Malinche, a sixteenth-century Mexican woman who aided the conquistador Hernán Cortés and became his mistress. *This Is Villa* (ca. 1936?) is about the twentieth-century Mexican revolutionary general Pancho Villa.

Around this time, Niggli collaborated with Rodolfo Usigli, one of Mexico's most important playwrights in the 1940s. Responsible for the classic drama *El gesticulador* (The Impostor, 1938), Usigli was also the author of a novel, *Ensayo de un crimen*, adapted for the screen by the Spanish filmmaker Luis Buñuel in 1955 (in English, the film is called *The Criminal Life of Archibaldo de la Cruz*). Usigli's background was similar to Niggli's—he was born in Mexico City to European parents (his father was Italian, his mother Polish)—and he longed for a national theater able to reflect the challenges of Mexico as a modern nation: "Mexican folk drama does not really exist," he once said in a comment on Niggli. "Or rather it does not exist as drama but as a casual accumulation of external, picturesque facts poorly woven into a dramatic plot. In fact drama does not seem to be, up to now, the most adequate literary expression for Mexico." He praised Niggli as a groundbreaker and saluted the cordial reception she received in U.S. theaters.

Although she felt most attached to the theater, Niggli worked, at first anonymously, for the Hollywood film studios Twentieth Century Fox and Metro-Goldwyn-Mayer. Among the movies she contributed to was Rouben Mamoulian's *The Mark of Zorro* (1940), a romanticized version of a colonial-period California hero.

In 1945, Niggli published her first novel, *Mexican Village*. As seen in the chapter excerpted here, the novel enabled her to be expansive, to flesh out her symbols and thus make them more believable. She created the community of Hidalgo, Nuevo León, populating it with almost a hundred characters that cover the wide range of classes in Mexico (and that, unfortunately, tend toward caricature). The book includes a map and a list of who's who. Niggli's alter ego of sorts is Robert Webster, a Texan interloper who moves to Hidalgo, where he is a quarry master at a mine. The novel attracted wide attention, and Niggli wrote the screenplay for the Hollywood movie based on it, Norman Foster's musical romance *Sombrero* (1953).

Niggli's second novel, *Step Down, Elder Brother* (1947), takes place in Monterrey, Saltillo, Santa Catarina, and Nuevo Laredo. Exploring the ethnic and class rivalry between *criollos* and *mestizos*—and among the aristocracy, the bourgeoisie, and the poor—the novel feels like a preview of John Steinback's *East of Eden*, published half a decade later. One of the least read of Niggli's books, it is also the most ambitious and demanding, and the one in which she came closest to realizing her artistic potential. The ample cast of characters showcases the battle for the control of power in Mexico as it emerges as a modern nation.

In 1950, Niggli worked at Dublin's Abbey Theater. In the mid-1950s, she began teaching English and drama as an instructor at Western Carolina University, where she taught until retiring in 1975. She continued writing for radio and movies and also tried her hand at television, in shows such as *The Twilight Zone* and *Have Gun—Will Travel*.

### FROM MEXICAN VILLAGE

*Rivers rise in flood and destroy,*
*Brooks water the land and sing.*
—Mexican proverb

## *From* The Quarry

The engine swung around the sharp curve between walls of packed yellow earth, travelled into open country long enough to free the rattling cars behind it, and then came to a jerking pause beside the tall wooden supports of the water tower.

A young man swung down from the last coach, his snap-brimmed felt hat pulled low over his eyes, the collar of his shabby tan raincoat standing up at the back. In one hand he held a heavy, battered suitcase that had seen hard wear in many countries. In the other was a cigarette caught between thumb and forefinger, the glowing tip protected by the cup of the narrow palm, an unconscious gesture, for there was no wind blowing.

He looked about him at the stretching fields hot under the clear yellow sun, bare of houses, with the line of mountains blue in the distance.

The conductor thrust his head through one of the open train windows and spoke jovially. "Do not be alarmed, friend. Under the slope of the hill lies the town of Hidalgo. I, personally, assure you of this."

The train, no longer thirsty, shook itself, tottered, gained speed, fled forward to meet another curve and so disappear. Its movements revealed another line of mountains, etched in gray against the dark blue sky, more cactus-studded fields, and, by the water tower, an old man standing between two saddled horses. He was slender, with a dirty blue shirt and gray trousers belted with rope. His broad-brimmed straw hat had a ragged edge, and a bushy gray mustache neatly bisected his brown face.

The stranger in the raincoat walked up to him. "Are you from the quarry?" he asked pleasantly in a deep, hard voice that clipped the words like scissors.

"As you say," the old man answered politely, but the black eyes were investigating the stranger without friendliness. "The letter that came yesterday by train, and it was read to me by Don Nacho, the alcalde, himself, said that you were a *Yanqui* with a most unpronounceable name. And yet you speak Spanish. I do not understand this. Pepe Gonzales, without doubt a boy of little worth, but with two years' schooling in Texas, taught me to say, 'Follow me, please.' It now appears that the lesson was of no necessity."

The stranger laughed, flicked his cigarette to the ground, stepped on it with the toe of his worn black shoe, grinding it to powder in the sand.

"It would also appear," continued the old man tranquilly, "that you were raised in the country, knowing well the danger of fire. That is a good thing."

"One learns."

"Yes. It is also possible that your grace knows how to mount a horse?"

"That also. Not so well, doubtless, as yourself, but that, too, can be learned. What does one do with the valise?"

The old man took the bag from him and placed it between the struts of the water tower. "Here it will be safe. You have papers in it?"

The stranger's mouth twitched in annoyance at this personal question. He answered stiffly, "No. My papers are in my pocket."

"That is good. Papers are better kept in safety. To me all papers are mysterious things, for I cannot read them, but my daughter Candelaria can read; she can also write. It is not good for a child to know more than the parent." He jerked the reins he held in his right hand. "The black horse is for you. It is one of the Castillo blacks, and the foreman of the Rancho Santo Tomás, may the good God take pity on his stupidity for he is in all things stupid save in the knowledge of horses, has assured me that it is of a complete gentleness. You understand," he added anxiously "that the letter did not state that you were learned in the matter of horses."

"I understand." The young man swung easily into the saddle, allowing his body to settle against its hardness, resting his arm across the broad pommel while the old man adjusted the stirrups.

"You are not so tall as we expected. Pepe Gonzales, who is truly a fool but has had two years' schooling in Austin, Texas, assured me that all *Yanquis* are tall, even as tall as Joaquín Castillo, may the saints watch over his soul in Paradise."

The stranger allowed the old man's chatter to flow over him like water. He reached up with a sudden gesture and pulled off his hat so that the soft, scented air could stir against his long square-chinned face. He thought, One year of this. Is it worth it for twelve God-forsaken months?

The old man had mounted the sorrel horse and was watching him, patiently waiting for the signal to move forward. But the stranger did not give it. He was looking up and down the narrow, mountain-walled valley, seeing the yellow sand broken by gray-green cactus, each leaf flaunting its crown of purple fruit, the small flowering thorn bushes covered with tiny yellow blossoms that distilled a too-sweet fragrance, and the tall *yuca* palms bent under the weight of long, purple-tipped white blossoms. Through this desolation ran the silver tracks, reflecting the sun in angry stabs of light, and curving indolently around a cement platform, which had originally been walled with red brick but was now a blackened ruin, obviously once gutted by fire. He pointed toward it.

"What was that?"

"The railroad station, and a fine building it was, presented to Hidalgo by that great good man Don Saturnino Castillo. But who is there to give buildings now that he is gone in exile from the valley? The Great Revolution was a grand thing. Don Nacho, who is alcalde, says so. Also Don Rosalío and the little Doctor, and even the priest, say so. They are all very wise. But me, I stayed safe from the battles in the hills, and now that the fighting is two years done, I say to them, 'Of what good is the Great Revolution save to hang people and to burn buildings? If it was so fine, why do they not bring people back to life and give us new buildings?' They answer me with pretty words that mean nothing. Your grace is ready?"

The stranger nodded and let the reins go lax against the silky arched neck of the black horse. With the old man in the lead, they trotted through the fields and found a trail that led them through still more fields to the line of eastern mountains. Then they came into a cañon, and the trail mounted upwards into air that grew sharper and colder. The vegetation changed, the cactus and flowering thorn disappeared, but the *yuca* remained, and lichens curved their feathery gray softness over the massive rocks. At last they reached a high mesa that hung out in space, the mountain supporting it like a placid woman carrying a tray.

In front of them was a tin-roofed wooden shack, the unpainted door fastened with a heavy chain and padlock. The old man found a key after much searching in his pockets, and with many requests for aid to various saints opened the lock and flung the door wide. "This," he said proudly, "is the office. Here much work can be done with papers."

But the stranger was paying him no attention. He had strolled to the mesa edge and was staring across the great cut in space that was the valley. The old man came to his shoulder and pointed with one gray-dirt hand toward the northeast. "There lies Monterrey. You can see the smoke from the smelters. It is a very great city. Don Nacho, who is the alcalde and should know, says it is the third largest in all the Republic. This I do not believe. Monterrey is very great. I believe it is the largest. No city could be larger. That is an impossibility. Ay, the cloud has moved. That is a good omen. The cloud wants you to see Saddle Mountain—the mountain of Monterrey. Do you not consider it beautiful?"

The young man nodded, looking at the distant purple smudge of rock with the double peak that characterized it. For a moment he was a little boy again, and a woman's voice was recounting softly in Spanish, "*So the great god of winds, Hurikán, transformed his horse into a mountain to guard his favorite valley. He smoothed down the trembling limbs. The tail he smoothed down, the fine arching neck and the proud head. But in his haste he forgot the saddle . . .*" The stranger moved his shoulders under the shabby raincoat. "Very beautiful," he agreed politely.

"And there," the old veined hand swept in a wide half circle to the southwest, "is the Peak of the Prow. Like a ship it sails the air, not so?"

"As you say. And the town at its base, that is Hidalgo?"

"No, señor, that is Mina. My daughter Candelaria, who has had, you understand, a certain schooling, says that it was named for a hero of the Revolution of 1810, one Ignacio Mina. This I do not know for truth, but only as she says. We have five towns in the Sabinas. It is a very rich valley. And there they are spread out before you."

Like toys, thought the young man. Like toys a giant has thrown down and forgotten.

The old man was saying, "Close to Saddle Mountain is Topo Grande. There is no need for you to remember the name. A collection of mud huts, a small thing of no importance. But the next town, the one with many houses and streets, that is El Carmen. The people there raise cows and sell the milk in Monterrey. Don Nacho says that many people there prefer the milk of cows to the milk of the she-goats, but this is a matter of great amazement, and I do not know it of my own knowledge."

The stranger nodded to the next town. "That one looks like a seashell, one street spiraled around to a center."

"A curious thing," agreed the old man. "My daughter Candelaria says that it is named for another hero of 1810, one Abasolo. A hero he may have been, but the name is stupid: the lonely bean!" For the first time the old man laughed, his face crinkling with mirth, like worn brown leather tortured into creases.

Another town stretched out far below them. It was oblong-shaped, with a church thrusting its belfry up from the center. The buildings were of all colors, and standing aloof was a single great house, the walls white, the roof of red tiles. This house seemed to rise out of a sea of glossy green trees, and beyond it were the sheer cliffs on which the town was built, swung out over a river that twisted through the entire length of the valley like a lazily curving shiny blue serpent. Across the river was a checkerboard of green and yellow, which the old man said were farms, and farther still was the wall of western mountains, small buildings tucked like colored dots into the folding flanks.

Looking at all this, the stranger raised his head slightly, his hazel eyes under the triangular brows filled with an almost passionate sadness. But the mouth, with the sharply cut corners jutting upwards, believed the eyes, as though the body wanted to laugh but the spirit refused the laughter. "So that's the hole I have to live in for a year," he said in English.

The old man grinned again, finding the incomprehensible sounds amusing. "If your grace will go into the office I can show you many papers. When the last *jefe* went away, he said to me, 'Anselmo'—for your grace understands that is my name, Anselmo Carvajal, your servant." He carefully wiped his palm on his trouser leg and extended it. When the stranger shook it without comment the old man seemed disappointed, as though he had expected words which had not been said. After a moment he continued, "The *jefe* said, 'Soon this Revolution will be over, and if I do not come back, another *jefe* will come, and he will want the papers; so guard them well.' That was in 1913. For seven years I have guarded the papers, and they are all in the office."

"That is a fine thing," said the young man. "I will now go and admire the papers."

Don Anselmo pattered after him into the shack. "Seven years is a long time. To God, of course, it is not even a moment, but to me, who am old, it is a long time. This office is even as the other *jefe* left it. He was a good *jefe*, not a *Yanqui* like your grace, but an Italian. He stayed here two years. He had a fine house in Hidalgo but he would not live in it. He slept on the office floor, sometimes alone but generally with one of the cave women. My woman was too old for him, and my daughter Candelaria, too young. She is, you understand, the child of my age. But many of the cave women rolled the eye at him, and then he would sleep with them. It was strange, for there were never any children. He had not in him the richness of seed. You are perhaps different, señor?"

The question was so politely put that it caught the stranger off guard. He was hardly listening to the interminable chatter while he surveyed the battered oak desk, a gaudy calendar showing a harshly colored picture of the cement plant in Monterrey, and the date, 1913, the scarred wooden filing cabinet, and the empty liquor bottles powdered with dust and linked together with strong cables of spider webs.

"How the hell should I know," he muttered with a curious sense of embarrassment.

"Precisely, señor. But then you are still young. You are perhaps twenty-four?"

The stranger's narrow face betrayed no hint of his resentment at this second invasion of his privacy. "Twenty-six," he said curtly. "Now that we have seen the office, where is the quarry?"

"But the papers, señor—all the beautiful papers in the cabinet. You do not wish to see the papers?"

To humor the old man, he pulled out a drawer of the filing case. For a moment his lips slid into a long sideways smile. The drawer was filled with French magazines devoted to displaying the beauty of nude women. "This Italian—what became of him?"

"It was a sad thing. The morning he chose to leave the safety of the mountains was the same morning that *El Rubio* captured Hidalgo and started to hang people. That blond one was very angry at not finding Don Saturnino Castillo. He would say, 'Where is Don Saturnino?' and if a man could not answer him, zas! he was hanged. Lucky for Hidalgo, all the good men were away fighting. This *Rubio* caught the Italian, and because he could not answer the question—for who was the Italian to know the secrets of such a great one as Don Saturnino—the *Rubio* hanged him. I personally went down and protested, but the *Rubio* paid me no more mind than if I had been the husband of an actress. It was a very sad thing."

The stranger shut the drawer with a quick gesture of finality. "And the quarry?"

"If your grace will follow me. It is around the slope of the mountain."

Once more in the clean open air, the young man took several deep breaths. I can't work in that place, he thought. I've got to change it. It's too small and it smells of filth. A year of this. Good God, a whole year!

He followed Don Anselmo around the curved slope, and then paused in speechless astonishment. The quarry was a deep, ugly wound in the mountain side, but above it, small ledges for walking having been carefully retained, was row after row of cave openings, so that the towering wall had a cynical resemblance to a New York apartment house sheered through the center.

People were wandering in and out of the caves, their quiet Indian poise ignoring the danger of the chasm below them, their laughter and high, shrill voices echoing in a constant flow of sound from the mountain sides. Children playing on the ledges were stepped over or pushed aside. Some of the men were squatting on their heels near a cave opening; others were stretched out at full length, their straw hats tilted over their faces, their bodies soaking up the welcome warmth of the sunlight. All of the women were working, some kneeling to pound corn into a thick white mash on porous gray-black stone, others weaving at ancient hand looms. A few were climbing the ledge, buckets of water balanced on their glossy black heads.

"This—you live in these caves?" the young man asked slowly after the scene had passed from his eyes into his mind.

"But yes, señor. The caves are very healthy. The other *jefes* wanted to build houses for us of the quarry rock, but it would not be the same. In the caves the rock still lives and gives us life. We do not sicken here as they do in the villages. Here we live to be very old, or we die from the clean stab of a knife. The living rock is very powerful."

The stranger cursed under his breath in English. Two of the children had seen him, and their shrill cries and pointing hands drew the attention of the people. They all looked at him with the blank eyes of the Indian, expecting nothing, giving nothing. He felt the blankness so strongly that he turned away, feeling as he had always felt, an outsider, a person to be tolerated but not accepted.

During the war in France, he thought, it had been different. Under the guns there are no strangers and yet there are no friends. Under the guns a man feels completely alone, completely shut off from all other men. But each man in his loneliness receives the comradeship of loneliness from those about him, so that he does not feel lost in a great void. But away from the guns and war, the people surrounding him withdrew into their private friendships, leaving him isolated, with only one friend to care for him.

When he was small he had accepted this loneliness as a part of his heritage, but later in Europe he had felt the lack to be a part of himself, and so he had come to Mexico, hoping that the nostalgia of the blood might be satisfied. Money being a necessity of living, he had posted a notice in the Foreign Club asking for a job, explaining that he was an expert with dynamite. Four years of war with the Engineers had taught him the uses of dynamite better than any school. Several offers had been made to him to work in the silver mines of Pachuca, but this northern cement quarry had attracted his fancy. He did not want the picturesque softness of the South. The blood that was in him demanded the serene austerity of the northern mountains, and although he had never seen Saddle Mountain until this morning, he could have described it minutely from stories told him in his childhood.

The blank Indian reception cut into him, for he had expected from these people the same easy response that the old man had given him, but even as he turned away he saw Don Anselmo's dark obsidian eyes hidden in the shadow of the hat brim, and he knew that the chattering tongue was only a result of politeness to a new *jefe*, and not an acceptance of him as a person.

He said quietly, "I think it is better to go into the town. I want a bath and some sleep. There was no pullman on the train, and I had to sit up all night."

"As your grace wishes."

They retraced their steps to the horses. As he started to mount the patiently waiting animal he remembered that he had left his hat in the office; so he turned and went into the shack again. The open door had freshened the dead air, but the narrow, dark room with the one small window oppressed him like a prison. He went to the window and flung it open with a savage gesture, his eyes seeing but not quickly reacting to the sight of the girl standing in a small flower bed. The soft wind tossed her blue skirt around her bare ankles. The plain white blouse was cut low and from it rose the slender column of her throat. The oval face, with arched brows and large black eyes, was proudly set. A closely woven dark-red shawl flecked with green was draped over her black hair, and in her arms was a large sheaf of pink dahlias. She looked at him without shyness and yet without boldness, in a serene confidence that he found her beautiful. Then she silently turned and moved around a corner of the shack out of his line of vision. He picked up his hat, pulled it down on his forehead, and went outside. The girl was standing by the old man, who said proudly, "This is my daughter Candelaria."

She extended her hand, murmuring, "Candelaria Carvajal, your servant, señor."

He smiled at her, wondering why, like the old man, she also seemed disappointed when he made no response. Then he was in the saddle. They left her standing at the edge of the mesa staring after them.

"Your daughter is very beautiful.'"

Don Anselmo shrugged. "Many men have found her so. Even the worthless Pepe Gonzalez has climbed the mountain side to see her. But he says, can you imagine, that the yellow-haired María—that nameless wench from the River Road—is even more beautiful. I have seen this María. She is all yellow like a grain of corn and lacks the full ripe blood. That Pepe Gonzalez is a fool."

A clever warning, the young man thought with some amusement. Not to admire the daughter is to be a fool. But to admire her too much, what then? Probably the edge of a knife. Other subjects are safer with this old man. He bent forward and petted the great black's arching neck.

"This is indeed a beautiful horse. Your sorrel is not so large, but it seems also a fine animal."

"Indeed, señor, the sorrel is of all horses the best. If one says to you, 'This morning I saw a horse flying through the air,' ask him the color, and if he answers 'sorrel,' believe him."

"And the black horse?"

"If someone says to you that he saw a horse leap from a precipice without hurt, ask him the color, and if he says, 'black,' believe him, for the black is the most energetic, the brown the most rapid, the piebald the gentlest, but the sorrel is the king of all."

The young man's mouth twisted into his slow sideways smile. His grandmother's voice sounded faintly, as though he were hearing her through water. *Always he rode a white horse. They forgot his name, but the horse they remembered.* He said, "You have no words for the white horse?"

"Blessed Heaven!" Don Anselmo gasped. He hastily crossed himself and glanced fearfully about him. "In these mountains it is not good to mention the *Caballo Blanco,* for the witches, in their laughter, might fetch his spirit before you.'"

"But surely a white horse is not the property of witches."

"Ay, you mean a horse that is white. I thought you meant . . ."

"Yes? What did you think?"

"When I was small my father told me many stories, and they were true, for my father spoke the words. But there was once a man of my people the Huachichil, who rode through all these mountains, and many times he went into Monterrey, for he was without fear. His horse was white, and from the horse came the name *El Caballo Blanco.* He stole much gold and silver and many jewels, and he buried his treasure in the hills, and he guards this treasure very fiercely, so that all who try to find it go mad from seeing him ride toward them on his white horse."

"But he is dead?"

"Executed with bullets before I was born, and I am very old."

"How old are you?"

"I was born before the plague of locusts came."

"And when did the plague come?'

"Why, after I was born, señor. That is Hidalgo in front of us."

The trail opened into a crooked, dusty road, lined on one side by limewashed varicolored houses of mud brick, and on the other by a cactus-enclosed pasture in which sat various little wooden shacks thatched with palm leaf. The stranger drew his raincoat collar closer about his face and pulled the hat lower on his nose, as though he shrank from seeing the poverty-stricken hovels. Dogs barked in mock fierceness at his horse's legs, and children peered at him through the cactus fence, but the man did not see their oriental faces as clearly as he saw the quick image in his mind of another shack and other children playing on the dirt floor, and a woman sobbing on a broken, white-painted iron bedstead.

"Is this all the town?" he asked harshly between clenched teeth. "From the mountain top it looked as though there were many houses and a church."

"So there are, señor. We call this the *Gallineros* in laughter that the poor should shut themselves off with cactus like a chicken coop. Let us turn here to the right. We are now on the Avenue of Illustrious Men."

The narrow street broadened after a block, and the stranger saw a square plaza, shaded with orange and lime trees, and a round bandstand in the center. Around the plaza ran a wide sidewalk dotted at intervals with massive cement benches. Beyond it reared the blue tower of a pink church. They turned into another street, passed the barber shop with its striped pole, a long green building with the word "Jail" written over the entrance arch, and finally stopped before a blue-painted wall, with an iron-barred window and a hand-carved door, behind which sat the dignity of the mayor of Hidalgo.

Don Anselmo led the way through a narrow hall and into a small white-washed office, which seemed filled to overflowing not by the desk but by the large-stomached man behind it. He sat very still, his black Stetson on his head, his upper chin resting on the soft fullness of the lower one so that he seemed to have a small face perpetually resting on a cushion of fat.

Don Anselmo went to the desk and carefully removed his straw hat, to hold it tight against him with both hands. "I give you good day, Don Nacho. The *Yanqui* is here."

The mayor's small eyes, cold as black glass beads, turned toward the stranger standing in the doorway. He saw a man of about five foot ten, with a slender body that could never grow stout. The straight black hair grew back at the temples, and was brushed neatly away from a side part. There were three wrinkle lines in the broad forehead, and the face was long, with well-set ears. The man was clean shaven, with no hint of beard under the skin as is common to most dark men. The wind- and sun-burned face was brown, with an undertone of red in it, and the eyes had green flecks in their hazel depths. Don Nacho's careful scrutiny did not miss the narrow, supple hands nor the shabby clothes. His penetrating glance returned to the sensitive mouth with the deep cleft in the center, the full lower lip, and the laughter-loving corners, then travelled upwards again to the somber eyes that were as unreadable as a forgotten language.

The quarry foreman spoke again, as though placidly showing off the good points of a horse. "He possesses Spanish. Some of the words are strange, and the accent is unfamiliar, but he speaks the language. I personally have heard him."

Don Nacho put his palms flat on the desk and pushed his large body upright. He held out his hand and spoke in formal tones. "Ignacio Villareal, at your orders."

As the young man moved forward to clasp the hand a vague wisp of memory returned to him in his grandmother's voice, "*When meeting strangers it is polite to speak your name.*" He said self-consciously, "Bob Webster," and for the first time the name which he knew was rightfully his sounded strange and wrong to him.

The old quarry foreman sucked in his breath; then the tobacco-stained gray mustache rolled back in a grin from the jagged teeth. "He learns quickly. This morning he knew not the politeness."

"So," Don Nacho pursed his lips. "I welcome you to Hidalgo, señor Don Bobwebster. You are doubtless tired and wish to see your house." He took a large key from a nail and opened a side door into another street. In the block across the way, its side to them, was a narrow house. A young man with a flat Indian face lounged against the wall. His stocky body was clothed in a pink shirt, grease-stained gray trousers, and leather-thonged sandals. A straw hat with a curling brim was balanced on the back of his head. He was chewing on a toothpick, and he examined Bob Webster with frank interest while speaking to Don Nacho.

"Don Alonso wants an orchestra platform in the proposed Casino large enough to hold seven men."

"Did he ask the building committee?"

"Yes. They said it was a useless expense, but an orchestra platform would be a fine thing, and I would not charge much for it."

"You would charge as much as you think they would pay you, Porfirio. You are without shame."

The young man laughed and spat out the toothpick as they left him and went around the corner.

"That Porfirio," sighed the quarry foreman. "What he would not do to gain a peso."

"I like him," said Don Nacho, and the rebuke shut the quarry foreman's half-opened mouth.

The mayor struggled to unfasten the door of the small house. "It is not large, perhaps, but the walls are good adobe, and there are five rooms."

Bob Webster looked without comment at the entrance hall, with its dead rubber plant and dusty wicker settee. Fresh air came to them from the patio, which had a cement floor save for three dirt circles where two orange trees and a pomegranate bush were planted. Somehow they had survived seven years of neglect.

Don Nacho showed off the rest of the house with an air of quiet pride. The late Italian had obviously liked wicker furniture. The narrow parlor was filled with it, and the chairs in the dining room were also wicker, although the table was a cheap imitation of American mission style. The kitchen lacked both stove and sink, but there was a very large icebox.

"Every Monday and Thursday ice comes by train from the brewery in Monterrey," said Don Anselmo. Bob Webster lifted the box lid, and four dust-shrouded beer bottles brought a sudden pathetic image of the hanged Italian. He gently closed the lid and followed his guides into the patio so that they could show him the two rooms on the opposite side of the house. The one in front was a bedroom, with a rickety washstand, an iron cot with a torn corn-husk mattress, and a pole stretched across a corner, from which dangled on rusty hangers two suits of loudly checked tweed. The three men looked at the suits, each with the uncomfortable feeling that he had invaded the privacy of the dead.

A knock on the front door came as a relief. They walked quickly into the patio, and Don Nacho bellowed, "Enter!" Two young men came in, the shorter with a head composed of circles, the round face with round eyes and round stubby nose giving him a cherubic air; the taller, handsome in a dark flashing manner, the narrow line of his black mustache unable to hide his mischievous mouth. He wore a neat blue suit with a bandana knotted around his neck in place of a tie. His hat was a worn gray felt.

He came forward with his hand outstretched, his black eyes dancing with friendly laughter. "Pepe Gonzalez, your servant," he said formally in Spanish, and then in surprisingly good English, "Now you say your name. It's an old Spanish custom."

"He speaks Spanish like an honest christian," the quarry foreman interrupted sharply. He looked at the shorter young man, who was standing in the hall arch clutching Bob's valise. His denim trousers and faded blue shirt, though of poor quality, were neat and clean. He wore thonged sandals on his bare feet, and a broad-brimmed straw hat like the foreman's.

"Andrés Treviño," he said in an agony of shyness, and quickly put down the suitcase. His brown eyes turned pleadingly to Don Nacho. "We found it beneath the water tower. Pepe said it belonged to the *Yanqui*, and that we should bring it to this house."

"Thank you," Bob mumbled, not certain whether he was supposed to tip the boy. Pepe Gonzalez winked at him.

"It is a fine thing that you can speak Spanish, for now there is no difficulty in making you a member of the Casino soon to be built behind this house. The dues are six pesos a year."

"Five," hissed Andrés Treviño.

"Porfirio said to ask for six. We need spittoons for the bar."

"Five," said Don Nacho firmly. He turned his head toward Bob. "That Porfirio, the carver of wood, watch out for him. If he can get a peso from you for nothing, he will do it."

"Porfirio is a good soul," protested the two young men in one voice. "With work he is generous, and with the spirit."

"But a peso is closer to his hand than the lines of his palm," snorted the mayor. "Pay them the five pesos so that they can leave us in peace."

Bob, who had no desire to be a member of the Casino or any other social organization in this Mexican town, but was afraid to say so for fear of giving offense, opened his overcoat and took out his worn leather wallet. From the coin compartment he extracted a ten-peso gold piece, and its shining beauty held everyone's attention for a long moment. Pepe looked at it with amusement, Andrés with longing, the quarry foreman with awe, Don Nacho with objective interest; then it dropped into Pepe's hand, and the dark young man counted out five silver pesos change.

"You have too much money for such a worthless one," Don Nacho snapped. "If I were your father, I would put you to work in the cheese factory."

Pepe grinned. "I don't like the smell of the vats."

"Such a scandal," Don Anselmo told him severely. "And your father the maker of the finest cheese on the frontier. Only yesterday I saw a goatherd from the Valley of the Three Marys . . ."

"On our side of the line?" the mayor asked quickly.

The foreman shrugged. "For lost goats there are no lines. But because he was of the Three Marys I could not let him walk Sabinas land without some punishment."

"Naturally," Andrés nodded with satisfaction.

"So I made the forked sign against the evil eye, for I am a good christian . . ."

"And he was a goatherd," Pepe Gonzalez chimed in impatiently. "Continue, old one. What did you say to him?"

"Do not hurry me, do not hurry me. I said to him, 'Would you like a taste of Don Timotéo's cheese?' And I held out a piece of it, very tempting, in my hand. You should have seen his eyes and the way his tongue touched his mouth with wetness."

"He took it?" Don Nacho demanded, scandalized.

"No. He was a good son of his valley. But how those Three Marys unmentionables miss the good cheese of Don Timotéo! And you, worthless one, are too proud to work in such a fine factory."

Pepe shrugged. "I tell you I don't like the smell."

Don Nacho patted Bob's arm. "Let me warn you. This same Pepe Gonzalez, and that fool who calls himself Andrés Treviño, and Porfirio, the carver of wood whom you saw outside, have a talent for wickedness that is beyond belief. Better for you to stay away from them."

"He can't," grinned Pepe. "Is he not now a member of the Casino, and that soon to be the finest social club between Monterrey and Torreón?"

"Such talk," Don Anselmo said, "and this poor señor tired from lack of sleep. Better we leave him to his rest."

"If you get lonesome," Pepe said mischievously, "the Saloon of the Devil's Laughter is on the next street. There we hold our committee meetings."

"Out of here," roared Don Nacho.

The two young men laughed, shook Bob's hand, and merrily departed, Andrés obviously glad to be free of the mayor's commanding presence. Bob was sorry to watch them leave. Their friendliness seemed to be free of suspicion and distrust. He forced himself to ask casually, "What is wrong with the Valley of the Three Marys that it cannot eat cheese, and where is it?"

"On the other side of the eastern mountains," said Don Nacho, and when the quarry foreman would have launched into a long explanation, he added, "Time enough for you to learn of the feud later. The water in the well is still good. You have only to pull up the bucket. The town gardener tested it for you last night. We now leave you in the peace of God."

The old men bowed formally, shook hands with the ceremony proper for strangers, and went away. Bob carried his valise into the bedroom, started to unpack it, then looked at the dirt and the two dangling suits. He gathered up some towels and soap and quickly shut the case. After he had managed a fairly competent sponge bath, he scraped dry leaves away from one corner of the patio, spread out his raincoat, and lay down on it.

Sleep was heavy on him, but when he tried to sleep, it eluded him, and his mind filled with old memories which he thrust out and away from him. As he sought desperately for release, the image of Candelaria as he had first glimpsed her that morning, the dahlias a pink beauty in her arms, swam into his consciousness, and thinking of her he sank at last into the darkness of true sleep.

By the end of the first work day, the men at the quarry discovered that they had a new type of *jefe*, a type they had never hitherto known. There had been many quarry masters in the ten years of the quarry's existence before 1913, when all work had ceased. There had been the martinet German, the casual Irishman, the homesick Englishman, the excitable Frenchman, and, of course, the drunken Italian.

With each new master came the changes. For two weeks the *jefe* would ride the mountain trails; he would set up what they called *La Sistema*, the system. There would be much writing of papers and many speeches to the quarry men, especially on the subject of living in caves. But by the end of the two weeks the system would dissolve into the endless procession of slow days and nights. Speeches would be made to the women instead of the men; and bottles of golden cognac or colorless tequila[1] would take the place of the papers. And Don Anselmo, the foreman, would see that the small red cars, fastened together by an endless chain, the rock-laden downward cars pulling up the empties, somehow reached the train tracks and that the rock was loaded on flatcars to be taken to the cement factory in Monterrey.

Sometimes the *jefes* would remember to tell Don Anselmo that he was a good foreman, and would present him with a small bottle of liquor. The Italian had even looked with soft eyes on the ripening beauty of Candelaria. On that day Don Anselmo had fastened a block of wood to a tree and had shown the Italian some tricks of knife-throwing, and after that the Italian showed no further interest in Candelaria. That Anselmo, said the Inditos,[2] was a wise one. Candelaria was worth more than a casual sleeping on an office floor. A man from the village might not be such a rich one, but he would be Candelaria's husband long after a *jefe* had forgotten the color of Hidalgo's mountains. And as for *La Sistema*, every master was entitled to his two weeks of amusement, but after that, well, the getting of stone from the quarry was a serious business and not to be entrusted to an outlander.

So the quarry men prepared themselves for the breaking in of the new *jefe*, who was, in himself, curious because he could speak Spanish, which no other quarry master had ever been able to do.

Their blank eyes hiding amusement, they watched Bob gallop up to the mesa the second morning after his arrival. He called the foreman to him.

"Good morning, Don Anselmo."

A ripple of movement passed over the waiting crowd. What manner of *jefe* was this that he should call Anselmo Carvajal "Don"? The other *jefes* in their arrogance had never bothered to bestow a title of respect on the Inditos, even though old age demanded it of politeness. New interest came to the men, and they pressed closer as Bob said, "You doubtless have a method for taking the rock to the train?"

"That is so, *jefe*."

"It is a good method?"

"There have been no complaints from the cement factory in Monterrey, señor."

"Continue it, then, in the old manner. I will watch it, and if I am not pleased we can make changes later. But now I will need five men to help me here."

---

1. A drink distilled from the sap of the maguey (agave or century plant). The sap, called "honey water," after fermentation becomes pulque. This is distilled to mescal, which in turn is distilled to tequila. All three are much prized as strong liquors. [Author's note]
2. Indians, in the sense of the simple tribespeople, like those working in the quarry. [Author's note]

Don Anselmo, as curious as the rest, waved five men aside and took the others to the quarry; but during the day many, on one pretext or another, had to make little trips to the mesa, Don Anselmo with them, and what they saw amazed them. For the new *jefe* had ordered a fire, and the precious papers which had been so carefully guarded for seven years were tossed on the blazing wood.

The empty bottles were presented to the wide-eyed audience of children. And as for the women, well, that was the impossible thing. The new *jefe* gave them not so much as a passing glance as he went about his work. Nor did the audience seem to bother him. The other *jefes* had threatened all manner of punishment to keep children and old ones from the mesa—with the old ones they had been successful, never with the children. This new *jefe* accepted their attention without comment save to warn everyone to keep out of the working area. And once when a boy leaped forward with a shout to thrust his hand into the fire and show that even at nine years he was a man and not afraid of pain, the *jefe* had merely lifted him by the back of the neck and dropped him into the ditch that carried the irrigation water to Hidalgo. The child howled as the icy water flowed over him, and the *jefe* said mockingly, "You call yourself a man, and yet you scream at a drop of water."

All the old ones and the women laughed, and after that none of the children stepped across the line the *jefe* drew in the dirt.

When the sun was well overhead, the papers had been burned, the fire extinguished with water, and the furniture moved out of the shack. Then the *jefe* squatted on the ground like anyone else and drew from his pocket the package of food he had brought from the village.

For a long time the people rested in the shade of the mesquite trees, the men eating the food the women brought them, and the *jefe* listening quietly to the talk of the wise old ones, not once interrupting to show his superior wisdom, but listening with humility and silence as the young should listen to the old. There was talk of rain and crops, for the quarry people depended on the farms of Hidalgo for their food. And after a while there was talk of the Great Revolution and what it would mean to the Inditos; if it meant anything at all, which the old ones doubted; for, as the wisest said, through all the years there had been so many promises, and so many do-nothings. Now the Great Revolution was two years finished, and it, too, seemed to end in do-nothing.

Then at last the old ones were silent, and some of the younger men began to sing. At first the *jefe* listened to the songs, but when someone started the stirring song of Morelos to which many soldiers had marched in the far-off days of 1812, the *jefe* surprised everyone by singing also, knowing both words and tune. His deep voice gave a bass to their light tenors, and he sang without effort as men sing who have known a song from childhood:

> For a corporal I'd give twenty cents,
> For a sergeant I might give fifty.
> But for General Morelos
> I'd gladly give all my heart.

At the finish he went without pause into the song of *The Flea*, the children adding their voices to the merriment:

*With all the fleas I am most angry,*
*They bite me when I am in bed.*
*Ay! How they jump! Ay! How they leap!*
*Ay! How they jump! Those wicked little fleas.*

*All these fleas fill me with terror*
*For the holes they bore into my skin.*
*Ay! How they jump! Ay! How they leap!*
*Ay! How they jump! Those wicked little fleas.*

Candelaria, watching him sing, pulled her shawl closer over her head. She had never seen eyes so somberly tragic in a man's face, and it seemed to her as though, during the music, some of the sadness left him; but it seemed also as though he went away from her into another world where she could not follow. And into her mind came the clear and bitter knowledge that all of her happiness rested in the cup of his hand, but that to him she would never be anything more than a cloud's shadow on the mountain slope.

He rose, his arms lifted for a deep stretching of his body, "More work, friends. The hour of resting is over."

Earlier that morning the men had worked in silence, obedient to his orders, but curious. Now that he had sung with them they felt a greater ease. Secret laughter trembled among them, and words flowed from one to another. One man put the large desk chair on its side and showed how he could leap over it ten times without pause. Expressionless eyes swiveled to the *jefe*'s face. Bob took a deep breath.

"After this, enough of games," he told them. Keeping his feet close together, he made twelve leaps back and forth across the chair, and there was no panting in his chest as he finished. The children mischievously sang the applause music,[3] and the women and the old ones obediently clapped.

Bob knew that the men were now ready to accept him on trial. He was their *jefe*. In all things he must be better than they were. This chair jumping was but the beginning of tests that would grow more difficult until they were satisfied that he was competent to lead them. His grandmother's wisdom flowed into his memory. *"And always the patrón, the master, must ride with the least fear, throw the longest rope, climb the highest mountain. For is he not the patrón?"* Bob's mouth lifted in the slow sideways smile, and he waved his hand towards the shack. "Amuse yourself, my children. Storm this castle with fortitude. Make it as though it had never been. The glass from the window and the tin from the roof we will keep. But the boards can be broken up and put in the cooking fires."

The men looked at each other with little curious glances. The laughter passed out of them for the *jefe* had became a stranger again. To destroy this office was a terrible thing. Was it not the symbol of authority? Surely the mind of a *jefe* was a matter not understood by common christians.

Bob felt the change in them. His fingers trembled with anger as he unfastened the door staples. Supposing they did want to keep the shack. He was the one who had to spend most of the day in it. What difference did it

---

3. The last eight bars of the *Jarabe Tapatío*, known in the United States as the "Mexican Hat Dance." This music, called the "Diana," is always played in recognition of an outstanding feat, whether it be bull-fighting, a great speech, or anything else of value. [Author's note]

make what they did or did not want? He was the *jefe,* he was the outlander, he was the stranger. For a year he would be a stranger, and then he would go away and forget them. Two hundred and fifty American dollars a month in salary. He could easily live on fifty. That left two hundred clear. Twelve times two hundred was twenty-four hundred. The letter from Tommy Eaton was very plain: "I tell you we could clean up in South America. With your Spanish and the way you understand these Latins it would be a cinch. And the whole world's going air-conscious. With me to fly the planes and you to manage the business on the ground, we'll be set. Of course we have to have capital to start with. But this flying circus I'm with now isn't bad. Besides what I can borrow, I should have about four thousand saved up by the end of the year if I can keep the wings sewn on my crate. Do you think you could swing at least two thousand by that time?"

Yes, the letter was plain, and Tommy Eaton would make a good partner. A little stupid, but the knowledge of airplanes was in his blood and his bones. And a year wasn't a long time to wait. Twelve months—three hundred and sixty-five days. Oh God, three hundred and sixty-five days of living in these mountains, of constantly proving that he was better than any quarry man, of seeing that endless cars of rocks were turned over to the care of the railroad. He'd be damned if he'd spend those days in a two-by-four shack that shut out the opalescent air and the blue arched sky. The door came loose from the jamb, and he let it fall to the ground. By evening the only reminder of the shack was a patch of hard-packed earth that marked the floor.

Don Anselmo, careful to make no reference to the desecration of the office, rode back to the village with him.

"It is in my mind," he told Bob, "that you would do well to purchase that horse. Don Fidencio, who keeps the blacksmith shop, has certain nags for hire, but they are of little value." He used the word *rocinante* for nag, and Bob looked at him curiously.

"Is it possible that Don Quixote[4] has come to these mountains?" he asked.

"Don Quixote, señor? I do not know him. He is perhaps of Monterrey?"

"No matter. But Rocinante was the name of his horse."

"Indeed, señor. Now that is a strange thing. The horse of the young Castillo, Joaquín, you comprehend, not Alejandro, was also named Rocinante. Every day he rode it along the mountain trails. How he could ride, that one! And his horse was the finest of the Castillo blacks. He called it Rocinante for a little joke. And on Sunday mornings, for the sweetheart mass at twelve o'clock, he would ride that horse to the door and make it kneel in honor of the Blessed Virgin. Ay, he took much laughter with him when he left this valley."

"Where is he now?" Bob asked idly, not really curious.

"Dead, señor." The thin lips under the gray mustache closed tightly, as though afraid of giving away too much information. This, more than the words, attracted Bob's attention. What a strange place Hidalgo was, with its minor mysteries, and its feud with the neighboring valley. Well, it was no concern of Bob Webster's. But a horse was. He really needed a horse, and perhaps

---

4. Title character of the novel (1605, 1615) by the Spanish writer Miguel de Cervantes (1547–1616).

it would be better to buy one. The money problem was an item, but he could always sell it, and if he took good care of it, he might make a little profit. And besides, there should be some compensation for this twelve months' exile. He had always wanted to own a horse . . . ever since he had been old enough to comprehend what such an animal was. And his grandmother's voice came into him again: *"It was white, with tail and mane of cream. And when its hoofs struck the ground, sparks flew. I tell you such an animal has never been seen before or since."*

Bob said lightly, "As you say, this is a fine animal. But it is in my mind to buy a white horse."

"Ay, no señor!" Don Anselmo hastily blessed himself. "To bring a white horse into these mountains is not wise. *El Caballo Blanco* would not like it."

"*El Caballo Blanco* is dead. You yourself said this yesterday."

"Dead he may be in body, but the goatherds often see him on the trails in the moonlight, his hand on his gun, his hat on the back of his head, and his white horse between his knees."

"Have you ever seen him?"

"With my own eyes, no. But it would take a very brave soul to face his jealous anger. The men like you, señor. They think you will make a good *jefe*. They would not want to see you with your mind emptied of reason and foolish laughter on your mouth."

"A brave soul," Bob repeated thoughtfully. Perhaps a white horse would solve his difficulties with the men. If they saw him riding one without harm they would set no further tests for him, for they would know he was indeed the *jefe*, afraid not even of ghosts.

But his skeptical mind could not prevent the cold touch of fear within him that was a part of his heritage. "Eh, grandmother," he whispered, "shall I buy a white horse?" And the answer came out of his memory. *"When you are grown, young one, you, too, shall own a fine white horse, and the knowledge will console him in purgatory."*

"Tomorrow I have business in Monterrey," Bob told the foreman. "See that the men do their work well, and clear me good blocks of stone for a new office. I will draw you a picture of what I have in mind."

* * *

1945

# Upheaval: 1946–1979

Militarily, politically, and economically, World War II transformed the United States from a global power to a global superpower. In Europe, the country was perceived as a liberator, having orchestrated the campaign of the Allied forces against Fascism and Nazism in Europe and Asia. The U.S. economy recovered from the Great Depression, largely as a result of the war industry. Throughout the country, a sense of pride and patriotism prevailed. As the years went by, however, racial tension in the country mounted and became more visible. For Latinos, the 1940s were defined by daily struggles and by feelings of alienation, chronicled by writers of the "Acculturation" period such as Arthur A. Schomburg (p. 371), Bernardo Vega (p. 428), and Jesús Colón (p. 497).

In the Southwest, as discussed in the "Acculturation" introduction, the Latino population included migrant laborers working the fields through the Bracero Program. Their itinerant lifestyle made it difficult for these workers to assimilate. They also faced linguistic obstacles and ingrained racism, through which *mexicano* culture was perceived as inferior to mainstream culture in the U.S. A growing Mexican middle class was located in cities such as Los Angeles, El Paso, and San Antonio. Most Mexicans lived in rural, poverty-stricken barrios.

In the Northeast, the Latino population consisted mainly of Puerto Ricans in New York, New Jersey, and a few other states. The Great Migration, which had begun in the 1940s and would extend until the 1960s, brought unprecedentedly large numbers of workers from Puerto Rico to the United States in search of employment opportunities and, they hoped, better lives. Most of them were *jíbaros*, inhabitants of the island's countryside, for whom moving to metropolitan centers on the mainland posed difficulties. For example, they had to adjust to a new climate, a faster pace of life, a higher cost of living, and the ways of working within U.S. industries.

Since the Spanish-speaking underclass had little access to political or economic power, the tenor of Latino literature from this time is primarily of frustration and endurance. Arguably, the writer within the tradition who addressed the condition of Latinos' marginality most emblematically during this time is Julia de Burgos, a Puerto Rican poet who lived in New York and who sought to establish bridges between the political status of her homeland, the struggles of the poor, and her personal ordeals. For example, in "Farewell in Welfare Island," she extends her state of mind to other sufferers:

> It has to be from here,
> right this instance,
> my cry into the world.
> My cry that is no more mine,
> but hers and his forever,
> the comrades of my silence,
> the phantoms of my grave.

Burgos wrote these lines during a hospital stay in 1953, the last year of her life.

From the start of Puerto Rican migration to the United States, New York City held the largest concentration of Puerto Ricans outside of Puerto Rico. A large number of them were gathered in two Manhattan neighborhoods: Spanish Harlem (also known as "El Barrio"), located in the northeast corner of the island, and the Lower East Side (which later came to be known locally as "Loisaida," based on Latinos' pronunciation of the name), where previously waves of Irish, Jewish, and other newcomers had settled. Dire economic conditions, high unemployment, limited education (many not finishing high school), street gangs, drug addiction, and teenage pregnancy plagued the community in both places. Evolving a new identity, the Puerto Ricans struggling in New York began to call themselves Nuyoricans.

In his memoir, *Down These Mean Streets* (1967), Piri Thomas depicts growing up in Spanish Harlem. Constantly defending himself from the surrounding violence, the adolescent Thomas finds no escape. Interviewed as an adult, Thomas described life in the United States for a Puerto Rican of African descent:

> I remember the first time I went to the South with my friend Billy. I sat in the front of the bus and when the bus got to the Mason Dixon line, our driver got off and a new driver got on. Immediately, he said: "All the colored to the back"; all the colored people got up and went back. But I just sat there. He responded: "I want all of you colored people to go to the back"; and I said: "Look, I'm *puertorriqueño*." He looked at me and said, "I don't care what kind of nigger you are"; and he put his hand into his side pocket. Using the better part of my discretion and with a great nudging on my arm from Billy, because he knew we would be killed, I grudgingly but with dignity went to the back of the bus and sat for the rest of the ride staring at the back of his head determined that I would never forget this incident.
>
> They'd call me *nigger*; and if it wasn't nigger, they'd call me *spik*. Racism was a horror to bear because most times it wasn't quite said. It was worse because they dug into your psyche with one little look of contempt or their nose would flare as you passed them as if they had smelled dirt.

Chicano literature, coming from Latinos in the Southwest, focused not on urban poverty or racism but on cultural "otherness." In his fiction, Mario Suárez described barrio life in the El Hoyo neighborhood of Tucson, Arizona, with equanimity, depicting the landscape and social types in picturesque fashion. In his novel *Bless Me, Ultima* (1972), Rudolfo A. Anaya explores the mystical, even supernatural, component of Mexican American life. The protagonist's rural environment, the New Mexican plains, has limited connection to the economic and racial disparities in the world beyond it.

During this period of upheaval, a series of historical events, most prominently the Cuban Revolution and the civil rights movement, would transform Latinos across the United States. The vocalization of grievances would empower the minority.

## The Cuban Revolution

Soon after gaining its independence from Spain in 1898, Cuba became an attractive destination for U.S. citizens, given its closeness to Florida, its tropical weather, and, during the 1920s, the availability of alcoholic beverages (which were banned in the United States during Prohibition). In the 1950s, the Cuban government, headed by General Fulgencio Batista, was perceived as a close ally of Washington. Yet the economic and social conditions on the island, especially in the countryside, were poor. The guerilla fighter Fidel Castro, a lawyer and charismatic public speaker, orchestrated an insurrection against the Batista regime, aided by a small comradeship of supporters that included his brother Raúl and Ernesto "Che" Guevara. He failed in his first attempt, an attack on the Moncada Barracks, in Santiago de Cuba, on July 26, 1953. After reorganizing the exiled remnants of his brigade under the banner of the "26th of July Movement," he succeeded in the second, a sustained operation that started in 1956 in southeastern Cuba. In January 1959, Castro entered Havana in a caravan that was enthusiastically greeted by most of the city's population. In February, he became prime minister.

During his first months as the country's leader, Castro remained ideologically independent. But he soon made a partnership with the Soviet Union. The United States reacted anxiously, fearing that Communism would spread across the hemisphere. In 1961, the administration of U.S. president John F. Kennedy provided financial and material support to a group of Cuban exiles attempting an invasion at the island's Bay of Pigs. Abandoned by the administration mid-assault, the operation was a military and political disaster for the United States and the Cuban community on the U.S. mainland. Castro used the occasion to sharpen his anti-U.S. rhetoric while strengthening his control over the Cuban people.

In the early 1960s, a wave of largely middle-class Cubans was able to leave the island, settling in Florida, New Jersey, and other northeastern states as well as in Puerto Rico, Mexico, and Spain. The term *exiliado cubano* (Cuban exile) began to describe a generalized condition. Cuban exiles had long lived in the United States, of course—Castro himself had lived in exile in Mexico before leading the successful uprising against Batista—but more people left the island after the revolution than during any previous period. By the end of the millennium, more than one million *cubanos* lived in Miami alone.

A considerable number of Cuban writers of the second half of the twentieth century wrote their oeuvres either in exile or in a state of internal siege. Those who left the island often experienced nostalgia and a sense of displacement. Through literature—as a palliative, a way of assessing life in the diaspora as temporary—they at once evoked the past and sought to reclaim the present. Guillermo Cabrera Infante, whose novel *Tres tristes tigres* (1967, translated as *Three Trapped Tigers*) is a major work in contemporary Cuban literature, lived in London for many years. Severo Sarduy, who wrote several important novels, moved to France, where he connected with the French intellectuals associated with the magazine *Tel Quel*. Another prominent writer and intellectual, Jesús Díaz, who for several decades was closely identified with the revolution, defected in the 1990s. In Madrid, he founded the magazine *Encuentro*, which seeks to build bridges, for exiles, between the Cuba within and the Cuba without. Writers such as Cabrera Infante, Sarduy, and Díaz are not "Latino," and thus not in this anthology, because they have not lived in the United States.

Disillusioned with the Castro regime, the poet José Kozer left Cuba in 1960. He has lived in the United States since then, but his work, written almost exclusively in Spanish, constantly returns to the past and the lost island. Cuban-exile writers such as María Irene Fornés switched to the English language and have focused their work on their lives in the present, eschewing nostalgia in favor of a frank, sometimes wrenching, discussion of the difficulties of finding their places in what is for them a new world. Sooner or later, however, Cuba returns, as in Fornés's play *Letters from Cuba* (2000), based on letters she received from her brother in Cuba for over three decades.

One chronicler of dissatisfaction and estrangement was the poet Lourdes Casal, who left Cuba in 1961, disappointed with Fidel Castro's Communist policies but still devoted to the spirit of the revolution. In her poem "Conversación en la estación de trenes de Bridgeport, con un anciano que habla español" (Conversation in a Train Station with an Old Man Who Speaks Spanish; published posthumously, in 1981), Casal, in the spirit of Julia de Burgos's "Farewell in Welfare Island," reflects on the influence of nostalgia on her worldview, perceiving her émigré life as "incongruous," a condition of "transplanted underdevelopment." Her work is marked by a feeling of psychological fragmentation. She devoted most of her life in the United States to *el diálogo*, a movement embraced by some in the young, second-generation exiled community in the late 1970s. *El diálogo* advocated normalization of U.S.-Cuban relations and the reconciliation between those in exile and those remaining on the island. As she writes in her poem "For Ana Veldford" (1981), however:

> . . . I will remain forever a foreigner,
> even when I return to the city of my childhood
> . . .
> too *habanera* to be *newyorkina*,
> too *newyorkina* to be
> —even to become again—
> anything else.

In the succeeding decades, Cuba became a model to emulate throughout the Americas. The terms *independencia*, *liberación*, and *revolución* (independence, liberation, and revolution) were used everywhere in an effort to bring about change in a socially unstable landscape. Throughout the Americas and beyond, the Cuban Revolution even inspired a new aesthetic in visual art, such as movies and political posters; in music, such as the genre Nueva Trova (see the section "Popular Dimensions"); and in literature. The latter was inspired by socialist realism—a style inaugurated in 1934 in the Soviet Union during Joseph Stalin's dictatorial regime (1922–53)—and it was controlled by Castro's Communist regime through the Unión de Escritores y Artistas de Cuba (UNEAC; Union of Writers and Artists of Cuba).

By the late 1960s, the repressions of the Castro regime—of freedom of speech, of freedom of religion, of political freedom—had become international news. The regime's imprisoning of homosexuals because of their "deviant behavior" caused widespread consternation in U.S. and European intellectual circles. The enthusiasm that had coalesced among intellectuals and artists of the Americas and beyond around Cuba's political approach crumbled. Spanish-language writers, many of them devotees of Castro's innovative social agenda in the initial stages of the revolution, quarreled about the lack of freedom on the island. Internally, dissident thinking was interrupted when authors officially judged dangerous were ostracized, silenced, or jailed.

In the early 1970s, the Cuban poet Heberto Padilla unwillingly ended up at the center of *El caso Padilla* (the Padilla affair). An initial supporter of Castro's ideological views, Padilla traveled through Europe representing the regime. But he grew dissatisfied with its policies. In his book *Fuera del juego* (Out of the Game, 1968), he included some verses considered subversive by the Cuban government. He and his wife, Belkis Cuza Malé, were put under house arrest. In 1971, they were imprisoned. The incident brought international attention and alarm, and pressure was put on Castro to reform. Instead, Padilla was denounced by the government-controlled media and forced to apologize in public for his supposed counterrevolutionary activities. Many writers and intellectuals in Europe and the United States signed letters of protest against his treatment; others defended the need to cleanse the revolution of fame-seeking, elitist intellectuals; still others attempted to occupy both positions.

With outside pressure at its peak, Padilla was allowed to leave Cuba in 1980. He moved to the United States, settling in Princeton, New Jersey, with his wife and their son (both of whom had been granted exit visas in 1979). Like that of Lourdes Casal, Padilla's life in the United States was marked by dislocation. Although many intellectuals had defended him and supported his release from Cuba, he did not find an easy welcome in the United States. His body of work encompassed nonpolitical subjects (love, memory, nature, poetry itself), but he was seen principally as a political writer who did not fit in any camp. Judged by the supporters of the revolution and by some in the exile community as an apostate, he was forced to confront his dilemma as the poet shamed by his enforced complicity with his oppressors yet uncomfortable in exile. Although he kept a low profile in political terms, he continued to write poetry and delved into fiction and autobiography. In many ways, however, he was broken by his experiences, and he shared the dislocation and estrangement of his fellow exiles. Nevertheless, the two decades Padilla spent as an adult in exile allowed him to connect, from the perspective of a *cubano que espera* (a Cuban in waiting), with America's cultural landscape and its language. A translator of William Blake and other English-language poets, Padilla had always felt a strong affinity for English, the language that surrounded him during the last decades of his life.

While Cuban exiles such as Padilla have waited for the political situation in Cuba to change, their intellectual activity has helped shape the ways of the Latino community and of the Latino literary tradition. They have taught at

U.S. schools, written for U.S. media, and interacted with artists of different Latino backgrounds. Are they still Cuban after decades on American shores? Although some of them may not acknowledge it, their worldviews have become Americanized, and for this reason, theirs are also Latino voices. Thus the Cuban Revolution, one of the most polarizing events in twentieth-century Latin American history, has had an enormous impact on Latinos throughout the United States.

## Chicanismo

The second half of the 1950s and most of the 1960s were the civil rights era, defined by a popular upheaval against racial discrimination. A century after the U.S. Civil War, African Americans remained segregated from whites, especially in the South. Despite breakthrough moments such as the Major League Baseball debut of the black player Jackie Robinson (1947); the U.S. Supreme Court's ruling, in Brown v. Board of Education, against "separate but equal" education (1954); and activists' bus boycott to protest the segregated transit system in Montgomery, Alabama (1955–56), the nation still perceived itself through an opposition of black and white. The movement to overturn white domination and reshape the status quo took shape nationwide, and among its guiding lights were the writings of the scholar W. E. B. DuBois (largely from the first half of the twentieth century), the civic disobedience of Rosa Parks, the Black Power rhetoric of Malcolm X, and the nonviolent campaigns of the Reverend Martin Luther King Jr.

Latinos and many other ethnic groups did not play an integral part in this drive for racial integration. For Latinos in the West and Southwest, however, the time for change had come. During the 1940s, the anxiety Mexican Americans had accumulated throughout decades of marginalization crystallized in a series of riots in California. Elsewhere, the Bracero Program had fostered a sense of ambivalence in a large number of Mexican American laborers who moved from one seasonal harvest to another without advancing economically. In California, Arizona, Texas, and Colorado, the emergence in the 1960s of a series of Chicano labor leaders committed to improving the conditions of Mexican Americans fit into the large canvas of national social unrest, but it occurred in response to Latinos' unique cultural needs. Nationalist concepts such as Aztlán and La Raza (The Race), a nativist approach to *mestizaje* as a race deemed politically, ethnically, and culturally dominant, became ubiquitous among Mexican Americans. In "La Plebe" (The Masses), his introduction to the anthology *Aztlán: An Anthology of Mexican American Literature* (1972), which he edited with Stan Steiner, Luis Valdez explains:

> We have been in America for a long time. Somewhere in the twelfth century, our Aztec ancestors left their homeland of Aztlán, and migrated south to Anáhuac, "the place of the waters," where they built their great city of México-Tenochtitlán. . . . Aztlán is now the name of our Mestizo nation, existing to the north of Mexico, within the borders of the United States.

The view that Chicanos lived as a colonized people inside one of the major world powers established the parameters for the unrest. In wanting to reclaim their past, Mexican Americans defined their collective identity as a nation within a nation. The social conditions in which they lived amounted, as the poet Abelardo "Lalo" Delgado put it, to "outright slavery under another name." Through a focus on *Chicanismo*, Chicanos sought autonomy and pride. The term *Chicano* itself became a battle cry for change.

The most significant figure in this period of upheaval was the Chicano activist César Chávez. He belongs to a time, the latter half of the twentieth century, when the United States underwent a profound demographic makeover that opened up a revaluation of the nation's collective identity. For centuries, immigrants had arrived from the Old World (Ireland, Germany, Scandinavia, Italy, France, etc.). After World War II, the newcomers began to arrive in waves from the so-called Third World. Latin Americans had been immigrating to the U.S. in force since the Spanish-American War (1898), but only in the 1950s did the shifts in the country's ethnic mix become apparent. Mexicans, Puerto Ricans, and Cubans, to name but three Spanish-speaking groups, dramatically increased their numbers from mid-century onward, as did Filipinos, Chinese, Nigerians, Senegalese, and Francophone Caribbean peoples. Chávez rose to prominence just when a leader was needed who would draw attention to the plight of the nation's heterogeneous underclass.

Guided by his deep Catholic faith, Chávez spent his adult life organizing laborers, many of them Chicanos who streamed from the tip of southeastern Texas and migrated to Michigan, Minnesota, Wisconsin, and other parts of the Midwest. From a humble beginning in Arizona to life as a migrant worker to the status of global icon, Chávez repeated his mantra: justice, equality, and the pursuit of happiness. Poverty was his prime target. Farm workers, he argued, were involved in the planting, cultivating, and harvesting of abundant food. Was it not ironic and tragic that they did not have enough food to feed themselves? To be aware of migrants' miserable labor conditions and not do anything to alleviate those conditions, Chávez said, was to become an accomplice.

His maturity as a speaker coincided with the civil rights ferment, but this did not happen by coincidence. Time and again, Chávez emphasized that the racial anxiety of the era was not exclusively about the deteriorated relations between whites and blacks, as it is still perceived today. He argued that the upper and middle classes, which were mainly white, feared the underclass: the invisible, silent, racially diverse Americans who performed menial jobs for pittances. Chávez's quest was two-pronged: to improve working conditions for the underclass, and to force the nation to recognize the variousness of its citizens' races and ethnicities.

Although Chávez was principally a labor organizer, he helped bring students, urban workers, and political activists of different backgrounds into a venture that came to be known as the Chicano Movement (also known as *El Movimiento*), a nationalist program that included marches, walkouts, hunger strikes, and other forms of unrest. The agitators came from unions, student organizations, and political parties. An important aspect of this movement was a national boycott of lettuce and grapes, in support of the farmworkers union.

Chávez was among the many leaders of the Movement who sought to connect their quest with the myths, symbols, and other iconography of the

Chicano past. In addition to Aztlán, that mythical place where Chicanos were said to have emerged from the earth, the Movement's touchstones of Mexican culture included the Virgin of Guadalupe, Mexico's matron saint; Father Miguel Hidalgo y Costilla, the priest and revolutionary who began Mexico's fight for independence in 1810; the *calavera* (skeleton), popularized by the lithographer José Guadalupe Posada at the start of the twentieth century; the revolutionary Emiliano Zapata; the modern politician and philosopher José Vasconcelos's views on the Bronze Race; and the painter Frida Kahlo. In his essay "In Search of Aztlán," the Chicano literary and cultural critic Luis Leal (see p. 551) quotes a statement Chávez made in *Ramparts* magazine:

> I wanted desperately to get some color into the movement, to give people something they could identify with, like a flag. I was reading some books about how various leaders discovered what colors contrasted and stood out the best. The Egyptians had found that a red field with a white circle and a black emblem in the center crashed into your eyes like nothing else. I wanted to use the Aztec eagle in the center, as on the Mexican flag. So I told my cousin Manuel, "Draw an Aztec eagle." Manuel had a little trouble with it, so we modified the eagle to make it easier for people to draw.

The resulting insignia, a red-and-black eagle, became a banner for Chicanos during the civil rights era. In that it was taken from Mexico but adapted to the needs of Mexican Americans, it manifests a duality—of past and present—that runs through the Latino literary tradition.

A significant aspect of *El Movimiento* were the *floricantos*, literary festivals where historically and politically conscious works (poetry, stories, and speeches) were showcased. Among the major Chicano writers featured in these venues were Abelardo "Lalo" Delgado, Oscar "Zeta" Acosta, and Ricardo Sánchez. An equally significant aspect of the Movement were the skits, known as *actos*, and other theatrical plays used to infuse a sense of awareness in the Mexican American community about the dismaying social and economic conditions. The most durable theatrical company was Luis Valdez's Teatro Campesino (Farmworkers' Theater), founded in 1965. An activist closely linked to Chávez and Chávez's union, the United Farm Workers, Valdez drew from the Marxist aesthetic of the German playwright, poet, and director Bertolt Brecht, whose Berliner Ensemble had aimed to make audiences aware of the class struggle.

The literary stage had been set for the politically oriented literature of *El Movimiento* by important antecedents: José Antonio Villarreal wrote *Pocho* (1959), believed to be the first novel published by a Chicano in English; its title is a derogatory term used to describe a Mexican raised in the United States. John Rechy, whose ancestry was Mexican and Scottish, broke ground with *City of Night* (1963), a novel about gay hustlers. Richard Vázquez depicted Mexican immigrants in his novel *Chicano* (1970).

Many works by Chicanos were influenced by but not directly related to the Movement: Rodolfo "Corky" Gonzales's manifesto *I Am Joaquín* (first published in 1967, republished for wide circulation in 1972) explored pre-Columbian myth. Oscar "Zeta" Acosta's semiautobiographical novels *The Autobiography of a Brown Buffalo* (1972) and *The Revolt of the Cockroach*

*People* (1973) portrayed a Chicano landscape infused with drugs. "Lalo" Delgado's *The Chicano Movement: Some Not Too Objective Observations* (1973) explored urban discontent.

However, not all Mexican American literature has been colored by ideological outspokenness. Throughout his career, Rolando Hinojosa has been constructing an imaginary transgenerational saga, in the mode of the novelist William Faulkner, with shifting narrative voices and perspectives. Sabine R. Ulibarrí, Tomás Rivera, and Rudolfo A. Anaya have depicted rural life and migrant labor realistically but not necessarily politically. Their talents emerged between 1970 and 1975, a period of intense Chicano literary creativity. In 1971 alone, two defining works were published: Rivera's *This Migrant Earth* and Anaya's *Bless Me, Ultima*, both of which emphasize Chicanos' connection with the land.

## Nuyorican Consciousness

The first half of the 1970s was a moment of intense creativity for Latinos in the Northeast as well. Puerto Rican writers from New York City gained increased visibility. On Manhattan's Lower East Side, in 1973, the poets Miguel Algarín, Miguel Piñero, and Pedro Pietri collaborated with others in founding the Nuyorican Poets Cafe, and the attention paid to writers from that circle validated the concept of "street poetry." The Nuyorican Poets Cafe spread the gospel of an ideologically driven oral poetry intended not for the elite but for the masses: syncopated, chaotic, free. Among the central works from the Nuyorican writers are Pietri's poetry collection *Puerto Rican Obituary* (1973) and Piñero's play *Short Eyes* (1974).

Beginning in this period, many Puerto Ricans in New York have formed what is known as a Nuyorican identity. The term *Nuyorican*, a combination of *New York* and *Puerto Rican*, was defined and propagated by Algarín in the groundbreaking anthology *Nuyorican Poetry* (1975), which he coedited with Piñero and which introduced some of these writers to the American reading public. Almost two decades later, the cultural critic Juan Flores, in his essay "'Qué assimilated, brother, yo soy asimilao': The Structuring of Puerto Rican Identity in the U.S." (1993), identified four stages of consciousness, or moments, that shape this identity. The first moment is the "here and now, the Puerto Rican's immediate perception of the New York that surrounds the person." This moment, when the Puerto Rican feels "isolated and sensationalized by the dominant culture," leads to the second moment: thinking of Puerto Rico. "The passage from the immediacy of New York to the Puerto Rican cultural background is generally less geographical than spiritual and psychological, its impetus deriving from the intimacy of family life and nostalgic reminiscences of parents and grandparents." Flores describes the first moment as a state of abandonment and the second as one of enchantment with the native homeland. The third moment, in his view, is about "return and reentry" to the U.S. setting. The fourth moment is "a branching-out, the selective connection to and interaction with North American society." Through these stages, Flores argues, "something other than assimilation or cultural separation is at work." That "something" is "a new amalgam of human experience," which allows Puerto Ricans in New York to be part of U.S. society but not become fully assimilated. The cultural critic Edna Acosta-Belén adds that the voices of Puerto Rican women and those of other Latina writers, denouncing *machismo* and expressing solidarity with women-of-color liberation movements, bring a feminist consciousness to the Nuyorican creative experience.

Since the 1970s, the number of Puerto Ricans in New York City has declined, because of the loss of manufacturing jobs. Puerto Rican migrants have been settling in large numbers not only in the Northeast, but also in the Midwest and the South. But the emergence of a Nuyorican consciousness—defined, like the *Chicanismo* consciousness, by a sense of accumulated alienation—is an integral part of the activist period in the United States. Puerto Ricans in New York and elsewhere engaged in civil rights struggles through grassroots organizations, social and political activism, and artistic movements that coincided with *El Movimiento* in the Southwest. In New York, the most active organizations included the Puerto Rican Legal Defense and Education Fund (PRLDEF), the education-focused ASPIRA, and, most prominently, the Young Lords. The latter started in the 1960s in Chicago's Lincoln Park neighborhood as a response by a group of Puerto Rican and Mexican gang members to urban-renewal evictions and police brutality. The group aimed to create programs that would improve the economic and social conditions of Latinos. At first, it tried to emulate the Black Panthers, a militant political group; years later, it transformed itself into a political party, which eventually metamorphosed into the Puerto Rican Revolutionary Workers Party. At one point, the Young Lords had chapters from California to Connecticut and even in Puerto Rico. Among the founding members of New York's Young Lords were Iris Morales, now a lawyer, filmmaker, and community activist; Pablo Yoruba Guzmán, a media and print journalist; Juan González, an author and a newspaper columnist; and Felipe Luciano, a musician, reporter, and radio and television host.

In the late 1960s and early 1970s, contacts between Nuyoricans and African Americans resulted from the similarity in their economic, racial, and political status. These contacts were especially fruitful in the poorer neighborhoods of New York's Bronx borough. There and elsewhere, they gave birth to hip-hop culture. It was an overlapping aesthetic vision—what Flores calls "the new amalgam"—with significant value not only to the community but to the nation. Through improvised spoken poetry, rap, emceeing, deejaying, and break dancing, young people—Puerto Ricans, African Americans, and others—expressed themselves and delivered ideological messages against colonialism, imperialism, racial discrimination, and socioeconomic oppression. In the tradition of Diego Rivera, José Clemente Orozco, and David Alfaro Siqueiros—politically outspoken Mexican muralists active earlier in the twentieth century—graffiti artists used public spaces for their works. The powerless became empowered by their creative imaginations.

As phrases such as *Black Power, Brown Power, Chicano Power, Boricua Power,* and *Puerto Rican Power* permeated popular culture, capturing different groups' aspirations for freedom and equality, other Latino voices joined in the chorus. Spanish-speaking immigrants continued to arrive in New York from Mexico, Central America, and the Caribbean, especially after the U.S. invasion of the Dominican Republic in 1965 crushed political efforts for democratic change and a large number of Dominicans began to seek refuge in the United States. By the late 1970s, hip-hop had spread to other Latino communities throughout the country. Poets, dancers, DJs, and visual and graffiti artists from Honduras, Guatemala, Nicaragua, Cuba, Puerto Rico, and El Salvador established *una hermandad*, a brotherhood, that blurred national differences. This bond, unnamed at the time, turned out to be the emergence of *Latinidad*, a term that became common starting in the 1980s. This feeling of commonality among Latinos from diverse backgrounds spread from New York to other U.S. cities.

At the same time, Puerto Rican writers and artists expressed a plethora of other views—unrelated to hip-hop, not about New York but about Puerto Ricanness in general. Through poems and stories, for example, Jack Agüeros and Nicholasa Mohr narrated the immigrant experience in the barrio. Such literature was mostly ignored by island Puerto Ricans, however, who questioned its cultural "authenticity." For a long time, René Marqués's play about Puerto Rican migration, *La carreta* (The Oxcart, 1952)—along with other works by his compatriots in what island critics have identified as the Generation of 1950, such as José Luis Gonzales and Pedro Juan Soto—was the islanders' main, though limited, point of reference for understanding their compatriots' lives in the United States. Subsequently, well-established island writers (such as Luis Rafael Sánchez and Rosario Ferré) who spent considerable periods living in the United States while maintaining their ties with Puerto Rico's and other Spanish-language literary circles developed a deeper understanding of the migrant experience and the American literary market. In his story "La guagua aérea" (The Airbus, 1985), Sánchez captures the transient existence of Puerto Ricans who move from the island to the mainland and back again. In her novels, short stories, and essays—some of which she has written and published in English and then rewritten and republished in Spanish—Ferré often meditates on the condition of women in the largely patriarchal society of Puerto Rico. These writers have shaped a literature celebrated by the literary establishments in Puerto Rico and other parts of the Spanish-speaking world as well as in the United States.

## The Latin American Literary "Boom"

In the late 1960s and throughout the 1970s, Latin American writers received international attention. For example, the Chilean political poet Pablo Neruda received the Nobel Prize for Literature in 1971. Like the *Modernistas* at the beginning of the twentieth century, these authors were from different countries and diverse backgrounds, but they collectively promoted a vision of Latin America defined by social inequality, political corruption, transculturation, and an exotic landscape. Known as *"el 'boom' literario latinoamericano,"* this movement was orchestrated by Carmen Balcells, a powerful literary agent in Barcelona, Spain. To a large extent, it was a commercial endeavor designed to promote and sell Spanish-language books and their subsidiary rights (such as for translations or for movie adaptations) throughout the world.

Three fiction writers were the foundational figures of *el "boom."* Jorge Luis Borges, an Argentinian author, translator, poet, and book reviewer, wrote now-canonical stories such as "Pierre Menard, autor del Quijote" (Pierre Menard, Author of the *Quixote*), "El aleph" (The Aleph), and "Emma Zunz," for the most part during and immediately after World War II. Alejo Carpentier, a Cuban novelist, wrote *El reino de este mundo* (The Kingdom of This World, 1949), an important work in the development of the style called *lo real maravilloso*, a phrase that he coined and that eventually became, through a series of mistranslations, "magical realism." Juan Rulfo, a Mexican novelist and short-story writer, set new standards of narrative economy within Latin American fiction through his spare style in *El llano en llamas* (1953; translated in 1967 as *The Burning Plain and Other Stories*) and *Pedro Páramo* (1955).

Inspired by Borges, Carpentier, and Rulfo, and dreaming of being recognized for their talents locally and internationally, were Mexico's Carlos Fuentes (*La muerte de Artemio Cruz* [The Death of Artemio Cruz, 1962]); Argentina's Julio Cortázar (*Rayuela* [Hopscotch, 1963]); Colombia's Gabriel García Márquez (*Cien años de soledad* [One Hundred Years of Solitude, 1967]); and Peru's Mario Vargas Llosa (*Conversación en La Catedral* [Conversation in The Cathedral, 1969] and *La tía Julia y el escribidor* [Aunt Julia and the Script Writer, 1977]), along with others. If modernists such as Marcel Proust, Franz Kafka, and James Joyce had brought the European novel to its zenith in the decades preceding World War II, astonishing writers of the so-called Third World, particularly from the nations of the former Spanish colonies, were reinvigorating the genre of the novel, hypnotizing readers with a novel mix of sex, myth, mystery, and social unrest. Over the years, younger figures such as Manuel Puig (*El beso de la mujer araña* [Kiss of the Spider Woman, 1976]), Isabel Allende (*La casa de los espíritus* [The House of the Spirits, 1982]), and Ariel Dorfman (*Rumbo al sur, deseando el norte: Un romance en dos lenguas* [1999; translated as *Heading South, Looking North: A Bilingual Journey*] successfully rode the waves of el *"boom."* Some eventually settled in the United States, becoming—as was the case of Heberto Padilla—part of the Latino literary tradition.

By the end of the 1970s, infatuated with the ecstatic responses from critics and the increasing sales and prestige of books such as *One Hundred Years of Solitude*, editors in the mainstream U.S. publishing industry sought narratives that resembled those works, with similar tones and with similarly magical ingredients (in García Márquez, clairvoyant prostitutes, an epidemic of insomnia, a storm of butterflies, and so on). But Latinos' experience was dramatically different from Latin Americans'. Many Latinos were children of migrant workers in the Southwest. Others came from ghettos and segregated neighborhoods. A smaller group had arrived as exiles after the Cuban Revolution. Their links with Latin America were remote and indirect. To a large extent, U.S. publishers resisted Latino work, viewing it as too noncommercial: too ethnic and incapable of satisfying what in their view was the audience's taste for exoticism.

Not surprisingly, in this period of upheaval, Latino writers felt misunderstood, even ostracized. Only a small number of Latinos were published by major houses. The Latino narratives that were presented to the general reading public—such as Villarreal's *Pocho*, Thomas's *Down These Mean Streets*, and Vázquez's *Chicano*—consistently depicted Mexicans and Puerto Ricans as alienated people on the fringes of society.

# JULIA DE BURGOS
## 1914–1953

Julia de Burgos was born Julia Constanza Burgos García in a rural part of Carolina, Puerto Rico. She was a light-skinned mulatto, with a mulatto mother and a white Puerto Rican father of German descent. The oldest child in a family of 13, she experienced the loss of six siblings and the poverty shared by many large rural families on the island. From her earliest years at school, de Burgos was a dedicated student. After graduation from high school, her academic abilities earned her a scholarship to the University of Puerto Rico in 1931. She received a normalist degree and became an elementary school teacher.

During the 1930s—in Puerto Rico, a decade of political turmoil, social destitution, poverty, and malnutrition—de Burgos became politically active. The Great Depression, a devastating hurricane, and the failed policies implemented during three decades of American occupation had become the targets of a revitalized Nationalist movement, and in 1936 de Burgos joined the Nationalist Party. Shortly thereafter, at the Ateneo Puertorriqueño (Puerto Rican Athenaeum), she gave the passionate speech "La mujer ante el dolor de la patria" (Women Facing the Pain of the Nation), rallying women to the island's struggle for independence. It was a period of intense political repression, including the incarceration of independence supporters, and de Burgos joined a committee to free nationalist political prisoners. At the time, she was employed writing scripts for a children's radio program sponsored by the island's Department of Public Instruction and was fired as a result of her political activities. She also began to publish her poems in newspapers and literary journals. Soon, her first two poetry collections, *Poema en veinte surcos* (Poem in Twenty Furrows, 1938) and *Canción de la verdad sencilla* (Song of the Simple Truth, 1939), appeared under the pen name Julia de Burgos. As a Nationalist woman writer, de Burgos challenged many of the social and political constraints that surrounded her in Puerto Rico at that time; this rebellious spirit is reflected in many of her poems, including one of her best-known works, "Pentachrome," which is among the selections in this anthology.

In 1939, de Burgos left Puerto Rico for Cuba and then New York City, where she settled in the early 1940s. She became a regular columnist for the progressive weekly *Pueblos Hispanos* in 1943, and her poems frequently appeared in this and other of the city's Spanish-language periodicals. In 1944, she moved with her second husband to Washington, D.C., where she met the Spanish writer and Nobel laureate Juan Ramón Jiménez, who once described her as one of the best poets Puerto Rico had ever produced. A year later, de Burgos returned to New York. Her life of turbulent and short-lived romantic relationships was complicated by acute health and alcohol problems, which resulted in hospitalization on several occasions. The last time she was hospitalized, in 1953, she wrote in English one of her last poems, "Farewell in Welfare Island," which is also among the selections that follow. This poem expresses the solitude and depression that characterized de Burgos's final years, and it foreshadows her approaching death. One day, at age 39, she collapsed and died on a Harlem street. Her unidentified body was buried in a common plot in New York's Potter's Field until her friends and relatives shipped her remains to Puerto Rico. Before she was buried in her hometown's cemetery, her casket was displayed at the Ateneo Puertorriqueño, and there she was honored by many prominent writers and public figures. Another collection of her poems, *El mar y tú* (The Sea and You, 1954), was published posthumously. It includes many of the poems she wrote during her years in New York.

Almost half a century after her death, Julia de Burgos is a cultural icon for women's and political liberation struggles. Her sensual, erotic, feminist, revolutionary poetry—translated into English in its entirety by the Puerto Rican poet Jack Agüeros in *Song of the Simple Truth: Obra completa poética/The Complete Poems of Julia de Burgos* (1997)—remains a powerful source of inspiration to readers and writers alike. Her poems speak to the poor and dispossessed; to people of color; to those who fight for Puerto Rican independence; and to women who love passionately, defy stifling social conventions, and forge their own lives. Collectively, her poems reveal a tormented soul, a fighter for social and political causes, and an unrestrained spirit. In the 1980s, to honor her memory and contributions, Manhattan's Public School 99, on East 100th Street, became the Julia de Burgos Junior High School. The Julia de Burgos Latino Cultural Center is on East 106th Street, which has been renamed Julia de Burgos Boulevard.

## To Julia de Burgos[1]

Already the people murmur that I am your enemy
because they say that in verse I give the world your me.

They lie, Julia de Burgos. They lie, Julia de Burgos.
Who rises in my verses is not your voice. It is my voice
because you are the dressing and the essence is me;                5
and the most profound abyss is spread between us.

You are the cold doll of social lies,
and me, the virile starburst of the human truth.

You, honey of courtesan hypocrisies; not me;
in all my poems I undress my heart.                                10

You are like your world, selfish; not me
who gambles everything betting on what I am.

You are only the ponderous lady very lady;
not me; I am life, strength, woman.

You belong to your husband, your master; not me;            15
I belong to nobody, or all, because to all, to all
I give myself in my clean feeling and in my thought.

You curl your hair and paint yourself; not me;
the wind curls my hair, the sun paints me.

You are a housewife, resigned, submissive,                    20
tied to the prejudices of men; not me;
unbridled, I am a runaway Rocinante[2]
snorting horizons of God's justice.

You in yourself have no say; everyone governs you;
your husband, your parents, your family,                      25
the priest, the dressmaker, the theatre, the dance hall,
the auto, the fine furnishings, the feast, champagne,
heaven and hell, and the social, "what will they say."

1. Translated by Jack Agüeros.
2. The title character's horse in the novel *Don*

*Quixote* (1605, 1615), by the Spanish writer Miguel de Cervantes (1547–1616).

Not in me, in me only my heart governs,
only my thought; who governs in me is me.                    30
You, flower of aristocracy; and me, flower of the people.
You in you have everything and you owe it to everyone,
while me, my nothing I owe to nobody.

You nailed to the static ancestral dividend,
and me, a one in the numerical social divider,              35
we are the duel to death who fatally approaches.

When the multitudes run rioting
leaving behind ashes of burned injustices,
and with the torch of the seven virtues,
the multitudes run after the seven sins,                    40
against you and against everything unjust and inhuman,
I will be in their midst with the torch in my hand.

                                                      1938


## Ay, Ay, Ay of the Kinky-Haired Negress[1]

Ay, ay, ay, that am kinky-haired and pure black;
kinks in my hair, Kafir[2] in my lips;
and my flat nose Mozambiques.

Black of pure tint, I cry and laugh
the vibration of being a black statue;                       5
a chunk of night, in which my white
teeth are lightning;
and to be a black vine
which entwines in the black
and curves the black nest                                   10
in which the raven lies.
Black chunk of black in which I sculpt myself,
ay, ay, ay, my statue is all black.

They tell me that my grandfather was the slave
for whom the master paid thirty coins.                      15
Ay, ay, ay, that the slave was my grandfather
is my sadness, is my sadness.
If he had been the master
it would be my shame:
that in men, as in nations,                                 20
if being the slave is having no rights
being the master is having no conscience.

Ay, ay, ay, wash the sins of the white King
in forgiveness black Queen.

---

1. Translated by Jack Agüeros.       2. A black person from southern Africa.

Ay, ay, ay, the race escapes me                                        25
and buzzes and flies toward the white race,
to sink in its clear water;
or perhaps the white will be shadowed in the black.

Ay, ay, ay, my black race flees
and with the white runs to become bronzed;                             30
to be one for the future,
fraternity of America!

## Pentachrome[1]

Today, day of the dead,[2] parade of shadows . . .
Today, shadow among shadows, I delight in the desire
to be Don Quijote, or Don Juan,[3] or a bandit
or an anarchist worker, or a great soldier.

Today I want to be a man. My longings burn me                          5
to be a bold and combative Captain[4]
fighting in the febrile Spain of Valencia,
bound to the ranks of the loyal faction.

Today I want to be a man. I would be Quijote.
I would be the true Alonso Quijano,[5]                                  10
one of the people today converting into heroes of life
the shadow heroes of the immortal madman.

Today I want to be a man. The boldest bandit
of the Seven of the City of Ecija.[6] The wildest
of those who flew on seven horses,                                     15
challenging everything with blunderbuss and dagger.

Today I want to be a man. I would be a worker,
cutting cane, sweating my shift,
with my arms up, my fists on high,
snatching from the world my piece of bread.                            20

Today I want to be a man. Climb the adobe walls,
mock the convents, be all a Don Juan;
abduct Sor Carmen and Sor Josefina,
conquer them, and rape Julia de Burgos.

                                                              1938

1. Translated by Jack Agüeros. The title means "five colors."
2. All Souls' Day, a largely Roman Catholic commemoration of the faithful departed; observed in Puerto Rico but without the elaborateness and festivity of the celebrations in Mexico.
3. Legendary male character known as a libertine, ubiquitous in literature. *Don Quijote*: Don Quixote, the title character in the novel (1605, 1615) by the Spanish writer Miguel de Cervantes (1547–1616).
4. El Cid, or Rodrigo Díaz de Vivar (ca. 1040–1099), known as El Cid Campeador, a Castilian nobleman, military leader, and diplomat.
5. One name of Don Quixote in Cervantes's novel.
6. City in the province of Seville, Spain.

# Río Grande de Loíza[1]

Río Grande de Loíza! . . . Elongate yourself in my spirit
and let my soul lose itself in your rivulets,
finding the fountain that robbed you as a child
and in a crazed impulse returned you to the path.

Coil yourself upon my lips and let me drink you,     5
to feel you mine for a brief moment,
to hide you from the world and hide you in yourself,
to hear astonished voices in the mouth of the wind.

Dismount for a moment from the loin of the earth,
and search for the intimate secret in my desires;     10
confuse yourself in the flight of my bird fantasy,
and leave a rose of water in my dreams.

Río Grande de Loíza! . . . My wellspring, my river
since the maternal petal lifted me to the world;
my pale desires came down in you from the craggy hills     15
to find new furrows;
and my childhood was all a poem in the river,
and a river in the poem of my first dreams.

Adolescence arrived. Life surprised me
pinned to the widest part of your eternal voyage;     20
and I was yours a thousand times, and in a beautiful romance
you awoke my soul and kissed my body.

Where did you take the waters that bathed
my body in a sun blossom recently opened?

Who knows on what remote Mediterranean shore     25
some faun shall be possessing me!

Who knows in what rainfall of what far land
I shall be spilling to open new furrows;
or perhaps, tired of biting hearts
I shall be freezing in icicles!     30

Río Grande de Loíza! . . . Blue. Brown. Red.
Blue mirror, fallen piece of blue sky;
naked white flesh that turns black
each time the night enters your bed;
red stripe of blood, when the rain falls     35
in torrents and the hills vomit their mud.

Man river, but man with the purity of river,
because you give your blue soul when you give your blue kiss.

---

1. Translated by Jack Agüeros. *Río Grande de Loíza*: river in northeastern Puerto Rico.

Most sovereign river mine. Man river. The only man
who has kissed my soul upon kissing my body.                    40

Río Grande de Loíza! . . . Great river. Great flood of tears.
The greatest of all our island's tears
save those greater that come from the eyes
of my soul for my enslaved people.

                                                                1938

## Song to the Hispanic People of America and the World[1]

(Dedicated with respect to
Juan Antonio Corretjer,[2]
on the first anniversay of
Pueblos Hispanos.)[3]

It is in you where my song sings, where my voice
began in mountainous screams a free scream.
It is in you where my love goes loving: in your petals,
tender flower extended from Bolívar[4] and Spain.

Towering view of the world where the moments           5
roll like pulses of the world of tomorrow.
You are a land of blood resprouting forever
in the ample universe of your own entrails.

You are a land of shelter from the sea to your name
whistling in continents through all the ravines.        10
Strengthened in a perpetual profile of palm groves,
you give your crazy love to all the words.

Explosion of horizons formed your breast,
oh Latin America, America of dawns,
America of anger burst in carnations,                   15
America of flowers converted to lances.

But your voice walks wounded on each breeze
and in each tame soil tears receive you,
a thunder of tyrants and dollars still reigns
over the spread flight of your timid countries.         20

Hispanic People, people potent like suns
braided in the orbit of America and Spain.
People gianted by roses and epic poems
that were born kissing, and kissing embrace.

1. Translated by Jack Agüeros.
2. Puerto Rican poet, journalist, proindependence
political activist, and Nationalist Party political
prisoner (1908–1985).
3. In English, "Hispanic People"; a weekly Spanish-
language newspaper in New York, launched in
1943, financed by the Communist Party, and
edited by Corretjer.
4. Simón Bolívar (1783–1830), South American
liberator.

Hispanic People, people who livid contemplate                25
the dream made blood by Martí's[5] generosity,
in Puerto Rico, a master beating freedoms
and a monster in the sanctuary of the Primal City.

Thus you break your destiny in the air, America,
between creole gods and foreign bells.                       30
Invading currents fertilize in your thirst,
and in your breast, traitors fight over your soul.

And yet you irrigate yourself in subterranean heat
wherever a thunderclap liberating infamies is heard.
On each front you launch your army in silence               35
and the new man, in you, will vanquish his disgrace.

You will break your mythical frontiers with tenderness
helped in your impulse by Bolívar in squalls.
You will be, for the future of your sons of now,
America of the world opening from Spain.                     40

1944

## Canto to the Free Federation[1]

(Motto: Workers of the World, Unite!)

Worker who lifts the world
on your pain and your laughter;
shoulder of the deaf bourgeois
and crutch of the mines:
don't let your silence                                        5
nurture the enemy's strength
nor weaken your arms
for dirty bribes.
Look, there are hard jails
awaiting your downfall:                                      10
breadless jails
between humiliating locks!
Look, there are children who wait
like toys in anger
the wind of justice                                         15
to unleash itself
on their brows!
Look, beneath your inertia
gold multiplies
and the conscience surrenders                               20
to the capitalist banquet!

5. José Martí (see p. 265).
1. Translated by Jack Agüeros. *Free Federation*:
Federación Libre de los Trabajadores (Free Federation of Workers), a socialist union federation
in Puerto Rico.

Look, in your deep misery
even night is taken from you
in coarse mental blows
that assault your living death!                              25
Look, fields refuse
to germinate your seed,
and paths stretch
through your suicidal exile!

Look, the rich are bankrolled                               30
where your suffering begins,
and justice shuts its doors
where your ruin passes!
Look, over your bed
death concentrates breezes                                  35
and there are no steel braces
to support your life!
Look, you die dying
without dying in your misfortune
because you cast your shadow                                40
and your wound keeps on bleeding!
Worker who lifts the world!
Worker who colors everything!
Hand that pushes the future
and revives progress in flesh—                              45
leave your servile wheels
and embrace your intimate wheels!
Leave your rag of a number,
and, noble, jump ranks.
Pour your arms and your energy                              50
into worthy federations,
and be one in the movement,
and one in the humane conquest!
Worker, cross the present
and advance through your justice!                           55

1944

## Farewell in Welfare Island[1]

It has to be from here,
right this instance,
my cry into the world.

Life was somewhere forgotten
and sought refuge in depths of tears                         5
and sorrows

---

1. A narrow island in the East River of New York City; formerly known as Blackwell's Island and now known as Roosevelt Island.

over this vast empire of solitude
and darkness.

Where is the voice of freedom,
freedom to laugh,                                                          10
to move
without the heavy phantom of despair?

Where is the form of beauty
unshaken in its veil simple and pure?
Where is the warmth of heaven                                              15
pouring its dreams of love in broken spirits?

It has to be from here,
right this instance,
my cry into the world.
My cry that is no more mine,                                               20
but hers and his forever,
the comrades of my silence,
the phantoms of my grave.

It has to be from here,
forgotten but unshaken,                                                    25
among comrades of silence
deep into Welfare Island
my farewell to the world.

Goldwater Memorial Hospital                                              1961
Welfare Island, NYC
Feb., 1953

---

# AMÉRICO PAREDES
## 1915–1999

Along with Luis Leal (see p. 551), the ethnographer and folklorist Américo Paredes
was one of the foremost scholars of Mexican American culture; in fact, his contributions helped develop the foundations of modern Mexican American scholarship.
From mid-century onward, his studies on border culture formed the basis of a
school of southwestern folklore studies, most of whose investigators he trained and
imbued with his strong sense of the unfairness of ethnic discrimination. At the
University of Texas, Austin, Paredes exerted an incalculable influence on two generations of border folklorists, including Tomás Rivera, Juan Gómez-Quiñones, and
Manuel Peña. His best-known contribution is the validation of border music, in
particular the tradition of the corrido (see the section "Popular Dimensions"), as an
authentic form of expression of the collective "border psyche." Paredes's work on
the folklore figure Gregorio Cortés resulted in his now-canonical volume *With His
Pistol in His Hand: A Border Ballad and Its Hero* (1958). This study—of the various

portraits of Cortés in corridos sung across the U.S.-Mexican border—has exerted enormous influence, not only on literature but in popular culture. For example, the movies of Robert Rodríguez (*El Mariachi, Desperado, Once Upon a Time in Mexico,* and the *Spy Kids* series) use Cortés as leitmotif. In interviews, Rodríguez, who studied film at Austin, has acknowledged Paredes's work as his guide. The first chapter is included in this anthology.

Paredes was born in Brownsville, Texas, and named after the sixteenth-century Italian geographer and explorer Amerigo Vespucci. His father came from a ranching family that, in the mid-1700s, settled on both sides of the lower Rio Grande Valley after nearly two centuries as part of a Sephardic Jewish colony. His mother's family had come from Spain in 1850. One of eight children, Paredes received his early education in the Brownsville public schools. He worked at various after-school jobs to help support the family. In the evenings during summer vacations he often listened to corridos, folk tales, and oral traditions recounted by border *mexicanos* around the campfire. As an adult, he recalled encountering anti-Mexican discrimination in high school. Among the more traumatic incidents was the presumption of his high school counselor that he would not to go to college. It almost deterred him. Encouraged by a more sympathetic teacher and by winning first prize in a statewide poetry contest, he enrolled in Brownsville Junior College upon graduation from high school in 1934. While attending college, he worked for *El Heraldo de Brownsville,* the Spanish daily edition of *The Brownsville Herald.* Paredes' brother-in-law was the editor. Paredes was a proofreader, translator, and staff writer. His writing also appeared in the English edition.

In 1935, Paredes began to be published in the San Antonio literary supplement of the newspaper *La Prensa.* Two years later, he published his first book of poetry, *Cantos de adolescencia* (Songs of Adolescence). In the early 1940s, Paredes married Consuelo "Chelo" Silva, a celebrated local singer. While continuing his job at the *Herald,* in 1940 he also accepted employment by Pan American Airways in work related to World War II. He resigned both jobs in 1944 to enter the U.S. Army as an infantryman. At the end of the war, he was assigned to the army journal *Stars and Stripes* and was sent to Tokyo to cover the war crimes trials. In the last year of his service, he was appointed political editor of the Pacific edition of *Stars and Stripes.* Upon taking his military discharge, Paredes worked for the International Red Cross in Tokyo as a specialist in public relations, a job that took him to Manchuria. During this time, he met his future wife, Amelia Nagamine, who also was working for the Red Cross. They married in 1950 before returning to the United States.

At Austin, Paredes completed his junior and senior work in one year, received a master's in English and folklore studies two years later, and earned his doctorate in 1956. He taught for a year at Texas Western College, now the University of Texas, El Paso, before returning to Austin to accept a tenure-track position teaching folklore and creative writing. During his first year of teaching at Austin, the University of Texas Press published *With His Pistol in His Hand.* It was an immediate success and brought Paredes widespread recognition. *Folktales of Mexico* (1970) and *A Texas-Mexican Cancionero: Folksongs of the Lower Border* (1976) assured his scholarly reputation. Paredes spent the rest of his academic career at Austin. In 1967, he helped found the Center for Intercultural Studies of Folklore and Ethnomusicology there. From 1968 to 1973, he edited the *Journal of American Folklore,* in which many of his 60-some scholarly articles were featured.

A social and cultural activist since his youthful days in Brownsville, Paredes persistently pursued his goal of validating Mexican American studies in the university. In 1970, with help from other Chicano faculty and graduate students, he succeeded and was named the first director of the Center for Mexican American Studies at the University of Texas. His struggle for Chicanos did not end there, however; he continued to fight against institutionally ingrained discrimination against *mexicanos.*

Twice in the early 1970s, Paredes tendered his resignation when he felt his suggestions were ignored or not given serious consideration by university administrators.

In 1989, for a lifetime devoted to a deeper understanding of the humanities, he became the first Mexican American to receive the Charles Frankel Prize from the National Endowment for the Humanities. The following year, he was awarded the Orden del águila azteca by the Mexican government for his work in preserving border culture and for his lifelong defense of human rights. In 1991, Mexico honored him with the Orden de José de Escandón. After his retirement, Paredes continued to research, write, and publish. In 1990, he published *George Washington Gómez: A Mexicotexan Novel*, about a *vendido* (a sellout) who buys into the American Dream. Paredes followed this publication with a book of his poems, *Between Two Worlds* (1991). Two years later, he released *Uncle Remus con chile* (1993), a compilation of *mexicano* border humor, and a scholarly collection of articles, *Folklore and Culture on the Texas-Mexican Border* (1993). His last publications were collections of his short fiction: *The Hammon and the Beans and Other Stories* (1994) and *The Shadow* (1998).

---

## *FROM* WITH HIS PISTOL IN HIS HAND

## I: The Country[1]

### *Nuevo Santander*

The Lower Rio Grande Border is the area lying along the river, from its mouth to the two Laredos.[2] A map, especially one made some thirty or forty years ago, would show a clustering of towns and villages along both river banks, with lonely gaps to the north and to the south. This was the heart of the old Spanish province of Nuevo Santander, colonized in 1749 by José de Escandón.

In the days before upriver irrigation projects, the Lower Rio Grande was a green, fertile belt, bounded on the north and south by arid plains, situated along a river which, like the Nile, irrigated and fertilized the lands close to its banks and periodically filled countless little lakes, known as *resacas* and *esteros*. Isolated by natural barriers, the country was still unexplored long after the initial wave of Spanish conquest had spent itself and Spain was struggling with the problems created by her earlier successes. Spanish colonization had gone as far north as New Mexico on the west, and to the east it had jumped overseas to Texas. The Lower Rio Grande, known as the Seno Mexicano (the Mexican Hollow or Recess), was a refuge for rebellious Indians from the Spanish *presidios*,[3] who preferred outlawry to life under Spanish rule. Thus, at its earliest period in history the Lower Rio Grande was inhabited by outlaws, whose principal offense was an independent spirit.

Toward the middle of the eighteenth century Spanish officialdom decided that better communications were needed between Texas and Mexico City,

---

1. Unless otherwise indicated, all footnotes are Paredes's.
2. Nuevo Laredo, Mexico, and Laredo, Texas, are across the Rio Grande from each other. [Anthology editors' note]
3. Garrisons. [Anthology editors' note]

routes which would cross the Seno Mexicano. José de Escandón was ordered to colonize the Lower Rio Grande. Four months after his appointment, Escandón was already on his way with parties of exploration.

Escandón was a wise and far-sighted administrator, and his methods were different from those of most Spanish colonizers. The *presidio*, symbol of military authority over settlers and Indians alike, was not part of his plans. The soldiers assigned to each settlement of Nuevo Santander were settlers too, and their captain was the colony's most prominent citizen.

The colonists came from the settled Spanish families of surrounding regions and were induced to settle on the Rio Grande by promises of free land and other government concessions. One of these concessions was freedom from interference by officialdom in the faraway centers of population. The colony of Nuevo Santander was settled much like the lands occupied by westward-pushing American pioneers, by men and their families who came overland, with their household goods and their herds.

The Indians seem to have given little trouble. They were neither exterminated in the English manner, nor enslaved according to the usual Spanish way. They lived in the same small towns as the Spanish settlers, under much the same conditions, and were given a measure of self-government.

By 1775, a bare six years after the founding of Nuevo Santander, there were only 146 soldiers still on duty among 8,993 settlers. There were 3,413 Indians in the towns, not counting those that still remained in a wild state.[4] In succeeding generations the Indians, who began as vaqueros and sheepherders for the colonists, were absorbed into the blood and the culture of the Spanish settlers. Also absorbed into the basically Spanish culture were many non-Spanish Europeans, so that on the Border one finds men who prefer Spanish to English, who sometimes talk scornfully about the "Gringos," and who bear English, Scottish, Irish, or other non-Spanish names.

By 1755 towns had been founded near the present site of Laredo—the only north-bank settlement of the time—and at Guerrero, Mier, Camargo, and Reynosa on the south bank. The colonists were pushing into the Nueces–Rio Grande area in search of pasturage for their rapidly increasing herds. Don Blas María Falcón, the founder of Camargo, established a ranch called La Petronila at the mouth of the Nueces at about this time.

By 1835 there were three million head of livestock in the Rio Grande–Nueces area, according to the assessments of the towns along the Rio Grande.[5] Matamoros, founded near the river mouth in 1765 by people from Reynosa, had grown into the metropolis of the colony with 15,000 inhabitants. The other riverbank towns, though not so large, were correspondingly prosperous. The old province of Nuevo Santander was about to emerge from almost a century of isolation and growth, when war in Texas opened the period of border strife.

4. William Curry Holden, *Fray Vicente Santa María: Historical Account of the Colony of Nuevo Santander*, Master's thesis, University of Texas, 1924, p. xi.

5. Cecil Bernard Smith, *Diplomatic Relations between the United States and Mexico*, Master's thesis, University of Texas, 1928, p. 5.

### The Rio Grande People

Most of the Border people did not live in the towns. The typical community was the ranch or the ranching village. Here lived small, tightly knit groups whose basic social structure was the family or the clan. The early settlements had begun as great ranches, but succeeding generations multiplied the number of owners of each of the original land grants. The earliest practice was to divide the grant among the original owner's children. Later many descendants simply held the land in common, grouping their houses in small villages around what had been the ancestral home. In time almost everyone in any given area came to be related to everyone else.

The cohesiveness of the Border communities owed a great deal to geography. Nuevo Santander was settled comparatively late because of its isolated location. In 1846 it took Taylor a month to move his troops the 160 miles from Corpus Christi to Brownsville.[6] In 1900 communications had improved but little, and it was not until 1904 that a railroad connected Brownsville with trans-Nueces areas, while a paved highway did not join Matamoros with the interior of Mexico until the 1940's.

The brush around Brownsville in the 1870's was so heavy that herds of stolen beef or horses could be hidden a few miles from town in perfect secrecy.[7] Even in the late 1920's the thick chaparral isolated many parts of the Border. Ranches and farms that are now within sight of each other across a flat, dusty cotton land were remote in those days of winding trails through the brush. The nearest neighbors were across the river, and most north-bank communities were in fact extensions of those on the south bank.

The simple pastoral life led by most Border people fostered a natural equality among men. Much has been written about the democratizing influence of a horse culture. More important was the fact that on the Border the landowner lived and worked upon his land. There was almost no gap between the owner and his cowhand, who often was related to him anyway. The simplicity of the life led by both employer and employee also helped make them feel that they were not different kinds of men, even if one was richer than the other.

Border economy was largely self-sufficient. Corn, beans, melons, and vegetables were planted on the fertile, easily irrigated lands at the river's edge. Sheep and goats were also raised in quantity. For these more menial, pedestrian tasks the peon was employed in earlier days. The peon was usually a *fuereño*, an "outsider" from central Mexico, but on the Border he was not a serf. *Peón* in Nuevo Santander had preserved much of its old meaning of "man on foot." The gap between the peon and the vaquero was not extreme, though the man on horseback had a job with more prestige, one which was considered to involve more danger and more skill.

The peon, however, could and did rise in the social scale. People along the Border who like to remember genealogies and study family trees can tell of instances in which a man came to the Border as a peon (today he would be called a *bracero*) and ended his life as a vaquero, while his son began life as

---

6. In March of that year, shortly before the beginning of the Mexican War, the future U.S. president General Zachary Taylor (1784–1850) established a U.S. Army fort in Brownsville. [Anthology editors' note]

7. *Informe de la Comisión Pesquisidora de la Frontera del Norte*, Mexico, 1877, p. 32.

a vaquero and ended it as a small landowner, and the grandson married into the old family that had employed his grandfather—the whole process taking place before the Madero Revolution.[8] In few parts of Greater Mexico before 1910 could people of all degrees—including landowners—have circulated and obviously enjoyed the story of Juan, the peon who knew his right, and who not only outwitted his landowning employer but gave him a good beating besides, so that the landowner afterward would never hire a peon who "walked like Juan."

This is not to say that there was democracy on the Border as Americans recognize it or that the average Borderer had been influenced by eighteenth-century ideas about the rights of man. Social conduct was regulated and formal, and men lived under a patriarchal system that made them conscious of degree. The original settlements had been made on a patriarchal basis, with the "captain" of each community playing the part of father to his people.

Town life became more complex, but in rural areas the eldest member of the family remained the final authority, exercising more real power than the church or the state. There was a domestic hierarchy in which the representative of God on earth was the father. Obedience depended on custom and training rather than on force, but a father's curse was thought to be the most terrible thing on earth.

A grown son with a family of his own could not smoke in his father's presence, much less talk back to him. Elder brothers and elder cousins received a corresponding respect, with the eldest brother having almost parental authority over the younger. It was disrespectful to address an older brother, especially the eldest, by his name. He was called "Brother" and addressed in the formal *usted*[9] used for the parents. In referring to him, one mentioned him as "My Brother So-and-So," never by his name alone. The same form of address was used toward cousins-german.

Such customs are only now disappearing among some of the old Border families. In the summer of 1954 I was present while a tough inspector of rural police questioned some suspects in a little south-bank Border town. He was sitting carelessly in his chair, smoking a cigarette, when he heard his father's voice in an outer room. The man straightened up in his chair, hurriedly threw his cigarette out the window, and fanned away the smoke with his hat before turning back to the prisoners.

If the mother was a strong character, she could very well receive the same sort of respect as the father. In his study of Juan N. Cortina,[1] Charles W. Goldfinch recounts an incident which was far from being an isolated case. After his border-raider period Cortina was forced to abandon Texas, and he became an officer in the Mexican army. At the same time his desertion of his wife set him at odds with his mother. Later Cortina returned to the Border and was reconciled with his mother. "They met just across from her ranch on the Mexican side of the river. As they met, the son handed his mother his riding crop, and, as he knelt before her, in the presence of his officers, she

---

8. I.e., the Mexican Revolution. Francisco Indalecio Madero (1873–1913) led the revolt and became president of Mexico (1911–13). [Anthology editors' note]
9. You. [Anthology editors' note]

1. Juan Nepomuceno Cortina Goseacochea (1824–1894), better known as Juan Cortina, a Mexican rancher, politician, military leader, outlaw, and folk hero. [Anthology editors' note]

whipped him across the shoulders. Then the chastised son, Brigadier General Cortina, arose and embraced his mother."[2]

These same parent-child customs formerly were applied to the community, when the community was an extended family. Decisions were made, arguments were settled, and sanctions were decided upon by the old men of the group, with the leader usually being the patriarch, the eldest son of the eldest son, so that primogeniture played its part in social organization though it did not often do so in the inheritance of property.

The patriarchal system not only made the Border community more cohesive, by emphasizing its clanlike characteristics, but it also minimized outside interference, because it allowed the community to govern itself to a great extent. If officials saw fit to appoint an *encargado*[3] to represent the state, they usually chose the patriarch, merely giving official recognition to a choice already made by custom.

Thus the Rio Grande people lived in tight little groups—usually straddling the river—surrounded by an alien world. From the north came the *gringo*, which term meant "foreigner." From the south came the *fuereño*, or outsider, as the Mexican of the interior was called. Nuevo Santander had been settled as a way station to Texas, but there was no heavy traffic over these routes, except during wartime. Even in the larger towns the inhabitants ignored strangers for the most part, while the people of the remoter communities were oblivious of them altogether. The era of border conflict was to bring greater numbers of outsiders to the Border, but most Borderers treated them either as transients or as social excrescences. During the American Civil War and the Mexican Empire, Matamoros became a cosmopolitan city without affecting appreciably the life of the villages and ranches around it. On the north bank it took several generations for the new English-speaking owners of the country to make an impression on the old mores. The Border Mexican simply ignored strangers, except when disturbed by violence or some other transgression of what he believed was "the right." In the wildest years of the Border, the swirl of events and the coming and going of strange faces was but froth on the surface of life.

In such closely knit groups most tasks and amusements were engaged in communally. Roundups and brandings were community projects, undertaken according to the advice of the old men. When the river was in flood, the patriarchal council decided whether the levees should be opened to irrigate the fields or whether they should be reinforced to keep the water out, and the work of levee-building or irrigation was carried out by the community as a whole. Planting and harvesting were individual for the most part, but the exchange of the best fruits of the harvest (though all raised the same things) was a usual practice. In the 1920's, when I used to spend my summers in one of the south-bank ranch communities, the communal provision of fresh beef was still a standard practice. Each family slaughtered in turn and distributed the meat among the rest, ensuring a supply of fresh beef every week.

Amusements were also communal, though the statement in no way should suggest the "dancing, singing throng" creating as a group. Group singing, in fact, was rare. The community got together, usually at the patriarch's house,

---

2. Charles W. Goldfinch, *Juan N. Cortina 1824–1892, a Re-Appraisal*, Brownsville (Texas), 1950, p. 67.

3. Person in charge. [Anthology editors' note]

to enjoy the performance of individuals, though sometimes all the individuals in a group might participate in turn.

The dance played but little part in Border folkways, though in the twentieth century the Mexicanized polka has become something very close to a native folk form. Native folk dances were not produced, nor were they imported from fringe areas like southern Tamaulipas, where the *huapango* was danced. Polkas, mazurkas, waltzes, lancers, *contra-danzas*, and other forms then in vogue were preferred. Many Border families had prejudices against dancing. It brought the sexes too close together and gave rise to quarrels and bloody fights among the men. There were community dances at public spots and some private dances in the homes, usually to celebrate weddings, but the dance on the Border was a modern importation, reflecting European vogues.

Horse racing was, of course, a favorite sport among the men. In the home, amusements usually took the form of singing, the presentation of religious plays at Christmas, tableaux, and the like. This material came from oral tradition. Literacy among the old Border families was relatively high, but the reading habit of the Protestant Anglo-Saxon, fostered on a veneration of the written words in the Bible, was foreign to the Borderer. His religion was oral and traditional.

On most occasions the common amusement was singing to the accompaniment of the guitar: in the informal community gatherings, where the song alternated with the tale; at weddings, which had their own special songs, the *golondrinas*; at Christmastime, with its *pastorelas* and *aguinaldos*; and even at some kinds of funerals, those of infants, at which special songs were sung to the guitar.

The Nuevo Santander people also sang ballads. Some were songs remembered from their Spanish origins, and perhaps an occasional ballad came to them from the older frontier colony of Nuevo Mexico. But chiefly they made their own. They committed their daily affairs and their history to the ballad form: the fights against the Indians, the horse races, and the domestic triumphs and tragedies—and later the border conflicts and the civil wars. The ballads, and the tradition of ballad-making as well, were handed down from father to son, and thus the people of the Lower Rio Grande developed a truly native balladry.

It was the Treaty of Guadalupe that added the final element to Rio Grande society, a border. The river, which had been a focal point, became a dividing line. Men were expected to consider their relatives and closest neighbors, the people just across the river, as foreigners in a foreign land. A restless and acquisitive people, exercising the rights of conquest, disturbed the old ways.

Out of the conflict that arose on the new border came men like Gregorio Cortez. Legends were told about these men, and ballads were sung in their memory. And this state of affairs persisted for one hundred years after Santa Anna stormed the Alamo.[4]

---

4. In 1836, during the Texas Revolution, at the now legendary chapel-fort in San Antonio called the Alamo, about 180 Texans were defeated by thousands of Mexicans led by the Mexican general Antonio López de Santa Anna (1794–1876). [Anthology editors' note]

### Mier, the Alamo, and Goliad[5]

In the conflict along the Rio Grande, the English-speaking Texan (whom we shall call the Anglo-Texan for short) disappoints us in a folkloristic sense. He produces no border balladry. His contribution to the literature of border conflict is a set of attitudes and beliefs about the Mexican which form a legend of their own and are the complement to the *corrido*, the Border-Mexican ballad of border conflict. The Anglo-Texan legend may be summarized under half a dozen points.

1. The Mexican is cruel by nature. The Texan must in self-defense treat the Mexican cruelly, since that is the only treatment the Mexican understands.

2. The Mexican is cowardly and treacherous, and no match for the Texan. He can get the better of the Texan only by stabbing him in the back or by ganging up on him with a crowd of accomplices.

3. Thievery is second nature in the Mexican, especially horse and cattle rustling, and on the whole he is about as degenerate a specimen of humanity as may be found anywhere.

4. The degeneracy of the Mexican is due to his mixed blood, though the elements in the mixture were inferior to begin with. He is descended from the Spaniard, a second-rate type of European, and from the equally substandard Indian of Mexico, who must not be confused with the noble savages of North America.

5. The Mexican has always recognized the Texan as his superior and thinks of him as belonging to a race separate from other Americans.

6. The Texan has no equal anywhere, but within Texas itself there developed a special breed of men, the Texas Rangers, in whom the Texan's qualities reached their culmination.

This legend is not found in the cowboy ballads, the play-party songs, or the folk tales of the people of Texas. Orally one finds it in the anecdote and in some sentimental verse of nonfolk origin. It is in print—in newspapers, magazines, and books—that it has been circulated most. In books it has had its greatest influence and its longest life. The earliest were the war propaganda works of the 1830's and 1840's about Mexican "atrocities" in Texas, a principal aim of which was to overcome Northern antipathy toward the approaching war with Mexico.[6] After 1848, the same attitudes were perpetuated in the works, many of them autobiographical, about the adventurers and other men of action who took part in the border conflict on the American side. A good and an early example is the following passage from *Sketches of the Campaign in Northern Mexico*, by an officer of Ohio volunteers.

> The inhabitants of the valley of the Rio Grande are chiefly occupied in raising stock. . . . But a pastoral life, generally so propitious to purity of morals and strength of constitution, does not appear to have produced its

5. Texas chapel-fort where, a few weeks after the Battle of the Alamo, Santa Anna massacred over 300 unarmed Texan prisoners. *Mier*: site of an 1840 battle between Mexican troops and invading Texan soldiers (of the Mier Expedition). In one of the most notorious episodes of his career, Santa Anna ordered the captured Texans "decimated" (each tenth man was killed); the rest were put to work on road gangs or imprisoned. As Paredes indicates, however, the "facts" here are open to interpretation. [Anthology editors' note]

6. See J. Frank Dobie, *The Flavor of Texas*, Dallas, 1936, pp. 125ff., for some of the aims and the effects of this type of work.

usually happy effect upon that people . . . vile rancheros; the majority of whom are so vicious and degraded that one can hardly believe that the light of Christianity has ever dawned upon them.[7]

In more recent years it has often been the writer of history textbooks and the author of scholarly works who have lent their prestige to the legend. This is what the most distinguished historian Texas has produced had to say about the Mexican in 1935.

> Without disparagement, it may be said that there is a cruel streak in the Mexican nature, or so the history of Texas would lead one to believe. This cruelty may be a heritage from the Spanish of the Inquisition;[8] it may, and doubtless should be attributed partly to the Indian blood. . . . The Mexican warrior . . . was, on the whole, inferior to the Comanche and wholly unequal to the Texan. The whine of the leaden slugs stirred in him an irresistible impulse to travel with rather than against the music. He won more victories over the Texans by parley than by force of arms. For making promises—and for breaking them—he had no peer.[9]

Professor Webb does not mean to be disparaging. One wonders what his opinion might have been when he was in a less scholarly mood and not looking at the Mexican from the objective point of view of the historian. In another distinguished work, *The Great Plains*, Dr. Webb develops similar aspects of the legend. The Spanish "failure" on the Great Plains is blamed partly on the Spanish character. More damaging still was miscegenation with the Mexican Indian, "whose blood, when compared with that of the Plains Indian, was as ditch water."[1] On the other hand, American success on the Great Plains was due to the "pure American stock," the "foreign element" having settled elsewhere.[2]

How can one classify the Texas legend—as fact, as folklore, or as still something else? The records of frontier life after 1848 are full of instances of cruelty and inhumanity. But by far the majority of the acts of cruelty are ascribed by American writers themselves to men of their own race. The victims, on the other hand, were very often Mexicans. There is always the implication that it was "defensive cruelty," or that the Mexicans were being punished for their inhumanity to Texans at the Alamo, Mier, and Goliad.

There probably is not an army (not excepting those of the United States) that has not been accused of "atrocities" during wartime. It is remarkable, then, that those atrocities said to have occurred in connection with the Alamo, Goliad, and the Mier expedition are universally attributed not to the Mexican army as a whole but to their commander, Santa Anna. Even more noteworthy is the fact that Santa Anna's orders were protested by his officers, who incurred the dictator's wrath by pleading for the prisoners in their charge. In at least two other cases (not celebrated in Texas history) Santa Anna's officers were successful in their pleading, and Texan lives were spared. Both Texan and Mexican accounts agree that the executions evoked horror

7. [Luther Giddings], *Sketches of the Campaign in Northern Mexico*, New York, 1853, p. 54.
8. The Spanish Inquisition was a notoriously harsh tribunal established in 1478 by the Spanish monarchs to punish the Jews and Muslims who had converted to Catholicism but were in-

sincere. [Anthology editors' note]
9. Walter Prescott Webb, *The Texas Rangers*, Cambridge, 1935, p. 14.
1. Walter Prescott Webb, *The Great Plains*, Boston, 1931, pp. 125–126.
2. *Ibid.*, p. 509.

among many Mexicans witnessing them—officers, civilians, and common soldiers.[3]

Had Santa Anna lived in the twentieth century, he would have called the atrocities with which he is charged "war crimes trials." There is a fundamental difference, though, between his executions of Texan prisoners and the hangings of Japanese army officers like General Yamashita at the end of the Pacific War. Santa Anna usually was in a rage when he ordered his victims shot. The Japanese were never hanged without the ceremony of a trial—a refinement, one must conclude, belonging to a more civilized age and a more enlightened people.

Meanwhile, Texas-Mexicans died at the Alamo and fought at San Jacinto on the Texan side.[4] The Rio Grande people, because of their Federalist and autonomist views, were sympathetic to the Texas republic until Texans began to invade their properties south of the Nueces. The truth seems to be that the old war propaganda concerning the Alamo, Goliad, and Mier later provided a convenient justification for outrages committed on the Border by Texans of certain types, so convenient an excuse that it was artificially prolonged for almost a century. And had the Alamo, Goliad, and Mier not existed, they would have been invented, as indeed they seem to have been in part.

The Texan had an undeniable superiority over the Mexican in the matter of weapons. The Texan was armed with the rifle and the revolver. The ranchero fought with the implements of his cowherding trade, the rope and the knife, counting himself lucky if he owned a rusty old musket and a charge of powder. Lead was scarce, old pieces of iron being used for bullets. Possession of even a weapon of this kind was illegal after 1835, when Santa Anna disarmed the militia, leaving the frontier at the mercy of Indians and Texans. Against them the ranchero had to depend on surprise and superior horsemanship. Until the Mexican acquired the revolver and learned how to use it, a revolver-armed Texan could indeed be worth a half-dozen Mexicans; but one may wonder whether cowards will fight under such handicaps as did the Borderers. The Rio Grande people not only defended themselves with inadequate armament; they often made incursions into hostile territory armed with lances, knives, and old swords.[5]

The belief in the Mexican's treachery was related to that of his cowardice. As with the Mexican's supposed cruelty, one finds the belief perpetuated as a justification for outrage. Long after Mexicans acquired the revolver, "peace officers" in the Nueces–Rio Grande territory continued to believe (or pretended to do so) that no Mexican unaided could best a Texan in a fair fight. The killing of innocent Mexicans as "accomplices" became standard procedure—especially with the Texas Rangers—whenever a Border Mexican shot an American. The practice had an important influence on Border balladry and on the lives of men such as Gregorio Cortez.

The picture of the Mexican as an inveterate thief, especially of horses and cattle, is of interest to the psychologist as well as to the folklorist. The

3. For a Mexican condemnation of the Alamo and Goliad, see Ramón Martínez Caro, *Verdadera idea de la primera campaña en Tejas*, Mexico, 1837, published one year after the events.
4. The final battle of the Texas Revolution occurred in 1836 at San Jacinto, near Houston. The

Texan army defeated the Mexican army and captured Santa Anna. [Anthology editors' note]
5. J. Frank Dobie in *The Mustangs*, New York, 1954, pp. 195 and 261, makes some interesting observations about the Mexican armament of the time.

cattle industry of the Southwest had its origin in the Nueces–Rio Grande area, with the stock and the ranches of the Rio Grande rancheros. The "cattle barons" built up their fortunes at the expense of the Border Mexican by means which were far from ethical. One notes that the white Southerner took his slave women as concubines and then created an image of the male Negro as a sex fiend. In the same way he appears to have taken the Mexican's property and then made him out a thief.

The story that the Mexican thought of the Texan as a being apart and distinguished him from other Americans belongs with the post cards depicting the United States as an appendage of Texas. To the Border Mexican at least, Texans are indistinguishable from other Americans, and *tejano* is used for the Texas-Mexican, except perhaps among the more sophisticated. The story that the Mexican believes he could lick the United States if it were not for Texas also must be classed as pure fiction. The Border Mexican does distinguish the Ranger from other Americans, but his belief is that if it were not for the United States Army he would have run the Rangers out of the country a long time ago.

Theories of racial purity have fallen somewhat into disrepute since the end of World War II. So has the romantic idea that Li Po and Einstein were inferior to Genghis Khan and Hitler[6] because the latter two were bloodier and therefore manlier. There is interest from a folkloristic point of view, however, in the glorification of the Plains savage at the expense of the semi-civilized, sedentary Indian of Mexico. The noble savage very early crept into American folklore in the form of tales and songs about eloquent Indian chiefs and beautiful Indian princesses. Such stories appear to have had their origin in areas where Indians had completely disappeared.[7] On the frontier the legend seems to have been dichotomized. After the 1870's, when the Indian danger was past, it was possible to idealize the Plains savage. But the "Mexican problem" remained. A distinction was drawn between the noble Plains Indian and the degenerate ancestor of the Mexican.

The legend has taken a firm grip on the American imagination. In the Southwest one finds Americans of Mexican descent attempting to hide their Indian blood by calling themselves Spanish, while Americans of other origins often boast of having Comanche, Cherokee, or other wild Indian blood, all royal of course. The belief also had its practical aspects in re-affirming Mexican racial inferiority. The Comanche did not consider Mexican blood inferior. Mexican captives were often adopted into the tribe, as were captives of other races. But the Comanche had never read the Bible or John Locke.[8] He could rob, kill, or enslave without feeling the need of racial prejudices to justify his actions.

Even a cursory analysis shows the justification value of the Texas legend and gives us a clue to one of the reasons for its survival. Goldfinch puts most Americans coming into the Brownsville-Matamoros area after the Mexican War into two categories: those who had no personal feeling against the

6. Adolf Hitler (1889–1945), Austrian-born German dictator and founder of Nazism. *Li Po*: Chinese poet (701–762). *Einstein*: Albert Einstein (1879–1955), German-born American physicist. *Genghis Khan*: Mongol conqueror (ca. 1162–1227). [Anthology editors' note]
7. See Austin E. Fife and Francesca Redden, "The Pseudo-Indian Folksongs of the Anglo-American and French-Canadian," *Journal of American Folklore*, Vol. 67, No. 265, pp. 239–251; No. 266, pp. 379–394.
8. English philosopher (1632–1704). [Anthology editors' note]

Mexicans but who were ruthless in their efforts to acquire a fortune quickly, and those who, inclined to be brutal to everyone, found in the Mexican's defenseless state after the war an easy and safe outlet for their brutality.[9] It was to the interest of these two types that the legend about the Mexican be perpetuated. As long as the majority of the population accepted it as fact, men of this kind could rob, cheat, or kill the Border Mexican without suffering sanctions either from the law or from public opinion. And if the Mexican retaliated, the law stepped in to defend or to avenge his persecutors.

In 1838 Texas "cowboys" were making expeditions down to the Rio Grande to help the Rio Grande people fight Santa Anna. In between alliances they stole their allies' cattle. McArthur states that their stealing was "condemned by some" but that it was "justified by the majority on the ground that the Mexicans belonged to a hostile nation, from whom the Texans had received and were still receiving many injuries; and that they would treat the Texans worse if it were in their power to do so."[1] In the 1850's and 1860's when the filibuster William Walker—a Tennessean—operated in Central America, he did so to the cry of "Remember the Alamo!"[2] Al Capone in the 1920's, sending his men off to take care of some German shopkeeper who had failed to kick in, might just as well have cried, "Remember Caporetto, boys! Remember the Piave!"[3] But perhaps Scarface Al lacked a sense of history.

This does not explain why the legend finds support among the literate and the educated. The explanation may lie in the paucity of Texas literature until very recent times. Other peoples have been stirred up by skillfully written war propaganda, but after the war they have usually turned to other reading, if they have a rich literature from which to draw. J. Frank Dobie has said that if he "were asked what theme of Texas life has been most movingly and dramatically recorded . . . I should name the experiences of Texans as prisoners to the Mexicans."[4] If it is true that the best writing done about Texas until recent times was ancient war propaganda directed against the Mexicans, it is not strange that the prejudices of those early days should have been preserved among the literate. The relative lack of perspective and of maturity of mind that Mr. Dobie himself deplored as late as 1952 in writers about the Southwest also played its part.[5]

Is the Texas legend folklore? The elements of folklore are there. One catches glimpses of the "false Scot" and the "cruel Moor," half-hidden among the local color. Behind the superhuman Ranger are Beowulf, Roland, and the Cid, slaying hundreds.[6] The idea that one's own clan or tribe is unique is probably inherent in certain stages of human development. Sometimes the enemy is forced to recognize the excellence of the hero. Achilles' armor and the Cid's corpse win battles; the Spanish hosts admit the valor of Brave Lord

---

9. Goldfinch, *Juan N. Cortina*, p. 40.
1. Daniel Evander McArthur, *The Cattle Industry of Texas, 1685–1918*, Master's thesis, University of Texas, 1918, p. 50.
2. Dobie, *The Flavor of Texas*, p. 5.
3. Site of a World War I battle involving Italy, Germany, and Austria-Hungary. *Caporetto*: site of a World War I battle involving Italy and Austria-Hungary. *Al Capone*: Alphonse "Scarface" Capone (1899–1947), American gangster. [Anthology editors' note]
4. *Ibid.*, p. 125.
5. J. Frank Dobie, *Guide to Life and Literature of the Southwest*, Dallas, 1952, pp. 90–91.

6. In epic story, however, the enemy is rarely cowardly. Very often it is one of the hero's own side who is the least admirable character—Thersites among the Greeks, the Counts of Carrión among the Castilians, the weeping coward among the Border raiders. [Paredes's note]
    *Beowulf*: hero of the Old English epic poem by that title (ca. eighth century–ca. tenth century). *Roland*: hero of the Old French epic poem *Chanson de Roland* (Song of Roland, ca. twelfth century–ca. fourteenth century). *The Cid*: El Cid, or Rodrigo Díaz de Vivar (ca. 1040–1099), known as El Cid Campeador, a Castilian nobleman, military leader, and diplomat. [Anthology editors' note]

Willoughby, the Englishman; and the Rangers recognize the worth of Jacinto Treviño, the Mexican.[7]

The difference, and fundamental one, between folklore and the Texas legend is that the latter is not usually found in the oral traditions of those groups of Texas people that one might consider folk. It appears in two widely dissimilar places: in the written works of the literary and the educated and orally among a class of rootless adventurers who have used the legend for very practical purposes. One must classify the Texas legend as pseudo folklore. Disguised as fact, it still plays a major role in Texas history. Under the guise of local pride, it appears in its most blatant forms in the "professional" Texan.

## The Texas Rangers

The group of men who were most responsible for putting the Texan's pseudo folklore into deeds were the Texas Rangers. They were part of the legend themselves, its apotheosis as it were. If all the books written about the Rangers were put one on top of the other, the resulting pile would be almost as tall as some of the tales that they contain. The Rangers have been pictured as a fearless, almost superhuman breed of men, capable of incredible feats. It may take a company of militia to quell a riot, but one Ranger was said to be enough for one mob. Evildoers, especially Mexican ones, were said to quail at the mere mention of the name. To the Ranger is given the credit for ending lawlessness and disorder along the Rio Grande.

The Ranger did make a name for himself along the Border. The word *rinche*, from "ranger," is an important one in Border folklore. It has been extended to cover not only the Rangers but any other Americans armed and mounted and looking for Mexicans to kill. Possemen and border patrolmen are also *rinches*, and even Pershing's cavalry is so called in Lower Border variants of ballads about the pursuit of Villa.[8] The official Texas Rangers are known as the *rinches de la Kineña* or Rangers of King Ranch, in accordance with the Borderer's belief that the Rangers were the personal strong-arm men of Richard King and the other "cattle barons."

What the Border Mexican thought about the Ranger is best illustrated by means of sayings and anecdotes. Here are a few that are typical.

1. The Texas Ranger always carries a rusty old gun in his saddlebags. This is for use when he kills an unarmed Mexican. He drops the gun beside the body and then claims he killed the Mexican in self-defense and after a furious battle.

2. When he has to kill an armed Mexican, the Ranger tries to catch him asleep, or he shoots the Mexican in the back.

3. If it weren't for the American soldiers, the Rangers wouldn't dare come to the Border. The Ranger always runs and hides behind the soldiers when real trouble starts.

4. Once an army detachment was chasing a raider, and they were led by a couple of Rangers. The Mexican went into the brush. The Rangers gal-

---

7. Hero in a widespread border corrido (early twentieth century). *Achilles*: hero in the *Iliad*, ancient Greek epic poem by Homer (ca. ninth century BC–ca. sixth century BC). *Brave Lord Willoughby*: hero of an Elizabethan ballad (1590s). [Anthology editors' note]

8. In 1916–17, the U.S. Army general John Joseph "Black Jack" Pershing (1860–1948) led a brigade on a failed expedition to capture the Mexican revolutionary general Francisco "Pancho" Villa (1878–1923). [Anthology editors' note]

loped up to the place, pointed it out, and then stepped back to let the soldiers go in first.

5. Two Rangers are out looking for a Mexican horse thief. They strike his trail, follow it for a while, and then turn at right angles and ride until they meet a half-dozen Mexican laborers walking home from the fields. These they shoot with their deadly Colts. Then they go to the nearest town and send back a report to Austin: "In pursuit of horse thieves we encountered a band of Mexicans, and though outnumbered we succeeded in killing a dozen of them after a hard fight, without loss to ourselves. It is believed that others of the band escaped and are making for the Rio Grande." And as one can see, except for a few omissions and some slight exaggeration, the report is true in its basic details. Austin is satisfied that all is well on the Border. The Rangers add to their reputation as a fearless, hard-fighting breed of men; and the real horse thief stays out of the surrounding territory for some time, for fear he may meet up with the Rangers suddenly on some lonely road one day, and they may mistake him for a laborer.

I do not claim for these little tidbits the documented authenticity that Ranger historians claim for their stories. What we have here is frankly partisan and exaggerated without a doubt, but it does throw some light on Mexican attitudes toward the Ranger which many Texans may scarcely suspect. And it may be that these attitudes are not without some basis in fact.

The Rangers have been known to exaggerate not only the numbers of Mexicans they engaged but those they actually killed and whose bodies could be produced, presumably. In 1859 Cortina was defeated by a combined force of American soldiers and Texas Rangers.[9] Army Major Heintzelman placed Cortina's losses at sixty; Ranger Captain Ford estimated them at two hundred.[1] In 1875 Ranger Captain McNelly climaxed his Red Raid on the Rio Grande by wiping out a band of alleged cattle rustlers at Palo Alto. McNelly reported fifteen dead; eight bodies were brought into Brownsville.[2] One more instance should suffice. In 1915 a band of about forty *sediciosos* (seditionists) under Aniceto Pizaña raided Norias in King Ranch. Three days later they were said to have been surrounded a mile from the Rio Grande and wiped out to the last man by a force of Rangers and deputies.[3] About ten years later, just when accounts of this Ranger exploit were getting into print, I remember seeing Aniceto Pizaña at a wedding on the south bank of the Rio Grande. He looked very much alive, and in 1954 I was told he was still living. Living too in the little towns on the south bank are a number of the Norias raiders.

It also seems a well-established fact that the Rangers often killed Mexicans who had nothing to do with the criminals they were after. Some actually were shot by mistake, according to the Ranger method of shooting first and asking questions afterwards.[4] But perhaps the majority of the innocent Mexicans who died at Ranger hands were killed much more deliberately than that. A wholesale butchery of "accomplices" was effected twice during

9. Cortina (see n. 1, p. 608) led a Mexican guerilla insurgency against the Republic of Texas, then against the United States and the Confederate States of America. In the Rio Grande Valley area in 1859–61, he fought the so-called First and Second Cortina Wars against the U.S. Army, the Texas Rangers, and the local militia of Brownsville, Texas. [Anthology editors' note]
1. Goldfinch, *Juan N. Cortina*, p. 49.

2. *Ibid.*, p. 62.
3. J. Frank Dobie, "Versos of the Texas Vaqueros," *Publications of the Texas Folklore Society*, IV, Austin, 1925, p. 32.
4. See Webb, *The Texas Rangers*, pp. 263ff., for an account of one of these "mistake" slaughters of all adult males in a peaceful ranchero community on the Mexican side, by McNelly.

Border history by the Rangers, after the Cortina uprising in 1859 and during the Pizaña uprising of 1915.[5] Professor Webb calls the retaliatory killings of 1915 an "orgy of bloodshed [in which] the Texas Rangers played a prominent part."[6] He sets the number of Mexicans killed between 500 and 5,000. This was merely an intensification of an established practice which was carried on during less troubled years on a smaller scale.

Several motives must have been involved in the Ranger practice of killing innocent Mexicans as accomplices of the wrongdoers they could not catch. The most obvious one was "revenge by proxy," as Professor Webb calls it,[7] a precedent set by Bigfoot Wallace, who as a member of Hays's Rangers in the Mexican War killed as many inoffensive Mexicans as he could to avenge his imprisonment after the Mier expedition. A more practical motive was the fact that terror makes an occupied country submissive, something the Germans knew when they executed hostages in the occupied countries of Europe during World War II. A third motive may have been the Ranger weakness for sending impressive reports to Austin about their activities on the Border. The killing of innocent persons attracted unfavorable official notice only when it was extremely overdone.

In 1954 Mrs. Josefina Flores de Garza of Brownsville gave me some idea how it felt to be on the receiving end of the Ranger "orgy of bloodshed" of 1915. At that time Mrs. Garza was a girl of eighteen, the eldest of a family that included two younger boys in their teens and several small children. The family lived on a ranch near Harlingen, north of Brownsville. When the Ranger "executions" began, other Mexican ranchers sought refuge in town. The elder Flores refused to abandon his ranch, telling his children, "El que nada debe nada teme." (He who is guilty of nothing fears nothing.)

The Rangers arrived one day, surrounded the place and searched the outbuildings. The family waited in the house. Then the Rangers called the elder Flores out. He stepped to the door, and they shot him down. His two boys ran to him when he fell, and they were shot as they bent over their father. Then the Rangers came into the house and looked around. One of them saw a new pair of chaps, liked them, and took them with him. They left immediately afterwards.[8]

From other sources I learned that the shock drove Josefina Flores temporarily insane. For two days her mother lived in the house with a brood of terrified youngsters, her deranged eldest daughter, and the corpses of her husband and her sons. Then a detachment of United States soldiers passed through, looking for raiders. They buried the bodies and got the family into town.

The daughter recovered her sanity after some time, but it still upsets her a great deal to talk about the killings. And, though forty years have passed, she still seems to be afraid that if she says something critical about the Rangers they will come and do her harm. Apparently Ranger terror did its work well, on the peaceful and the inoffensive.[9]

5. Pizaña was among the Mexicans and Mexican American *sediciosos* who planned and began an uprising intended to overthrow white rule in the Southwest and form an independent republic. In 1915–16, the resulting guerilla war, waged in Texas, resulted in much death and destruction. Texas Rangers and the U.S. Army ended the rebellion, and the Rangers and vigilantes then responded to it by harassing and killing ethnic Mexicans. [Anthology editors' note]

6. *Ibid.*, p. 478.

7. *Ibid.*, p. 87.

8. Specific data concerning sources of material obtained in interviews is found in the Bibliography [to *With His Pistol in His Hand*].

9. In *A Brief History of the Lower Rio Grande Valley*, Menasha (Wisconsin), 1917, p. 90, Frank Cushman Pierce reports: "On August 3, 1915,

Except in the movies, ruthlessness and a penchant for stretching the truth do not in themselves imply a lack of courage. The Borderer's belief that all Rangers are shooters-in-the-back is of the same stuff as the Texan belief that all Mexicans are backstabbers. There is evidence, however, that not all Rangers lived up to their reputation as a fearless breed of men. Their basic techniques of ambush, surprise, and shooting first—with the resultant "mistake" killings of innocent bystanders—made them operate at times in ways that the average city policeman would be ashamed to imitate. The "shoot first and ask questions later" method of the Rangers has been romanticized into something dashing and daring, in technicolor, on a wide screen, and with Gary Cooper in the title role.[1] Pierce's *Brief History* gives us an example of the way the method worked in actuality.

> On May 17, 1885, Sergt. B. D. Lindsay and six men from Company D frontier battalion of rangers, while scouting near the Rio Grande for escaped Mexican convicts, saw two Mexicans riding along. . . . As the horses suited the description of those alleged to be in possession of the convicts, and under the impression that these two were the men he was after, Lindsay called to them to halt, and at once opened fire on them. The elder Mexican fell to the ground with his horse, but the younger, firing from behind the dead animal, shot Private Sieker through the heart, killing him instantly. B. C. Reilly was shot through both thighs and badly wounded. The Mexicans stood their ground until the arrival of men from the ranch of a deputy-sheriff named Prudencio Herrera, who . . . insisted that the two Mexicans were well known and highly respected citizens and refused to turn them over to the rangers. . . . The citizens of Laredo . . . were indignant over the act of the rangers in shooting on Gonzalez, claiming that he was a well-known citizen of good repute, and alleging that the rangers would have killed them at the outset but for the fact that they defended themselves. The rangers, on the other hand, claimed that unless they would have proceeded as they did, should the Mexicans have been the criminals they were really after they, the rangers, would have been fired on first.[2]

There is unanswerable logic in the Ranger sergeant's argument, if one concedes him his basic premise: that a Mexican's life is of little value anyway. But this picture of seven Texas Rangers, feeling so defenseless in the face of two Mexicans that they must fire at them on sight, because the Mexicans might be mean and shoot at them first, is somewhat disillusioning to those of us who have grown up with the tradition of the lone Ranger getting off the train and telling the station hangers-on, "Of course they sent one Ranger. There's just one riot, isn't there?" Almost every week one reads of ordinary city policemen who capture desperate criminals—sometimes singlehandedly—without having to shoot first.

Sometimes the "shoot first" method led to even more serious consequences, and many a would-be Mexican-killer got his head blown off by a comrade who was eager to get in the first shot and mistook his own men for

---

rangers and deputy sheriffs attacked a ranch near Paso Real, about 32 miles north of Brownsville, and killed Desiderio Flores and his two sons, Mexicans, alleged to be bandits."

1. Paredes is referring to a metaphorical Western, not a real one, starring this iconic American actor (1901–1961). [Anthology editors' note]
2. Pierce, *A Brief History*, pp. 110–111.

Mexicans while they all waited in ambush. Perhaps "shoot first and ask questions afterwards" is not the right name for this custom. "Shoot first and then see what you're shooting at" may be a better name. As such it has not been limited to the Texas Rangers. All over the United States during the deer season, Sunday hunters go out and shoot first.

Then there is the story about Alfredo Cerda, killed on Brownsville's main street in 1902. The Cerdas were prosperous ranchers near Brownsville, but it was their misfortune to live next to one of the "cattle barons" who was not through expanding yet. One day three Texas Rangers came down from Austin and "executed" the elder Cerda and one of his sons as cattle rustlers. The youngest son fled across the river, and thus the Cerda ranch was vacated. Five months later the remaining son, Alfredo Cerda, crossed over to Brownsville. He died the same day, shot down by a Ranger's gun.

Marcelo Garza, Sr., of Brownsville is no teller of folktales. He is a respected businessman, one of Brownsville's most highly regarded citizens of Mexican descent. Mr. Garza claims to have been an eyewitness to the shooting of the youngest Cerda. In 1902, Mr. Garza says, he was a clerk at the Tomás Fernández store on Elizabeth Street. A Ranger whom Mr. Garza identifies as "Bekar" shot Alfredo, Mr. Garza relates, as Cerda sat in the doorway of the Fernández store talking to Don Tomás, the owner. The Ranger used a rifle to kill Cerda, who was unarmed, "stalking him like a wild animal." After the shooting the Ranger ran into a nearby saloon, where other Rangers awaited him, and the group went out the back way and sought refuge with the federal troops in Fort Brown, to escape a mob of indignant citizens.[3] The same story had been told to me long before by my father, now deceased. He was not a witness to the shooting but claimed to have seen the chasing of the Rangers into Fort Brown.

Professor Webb mentions the shooting in 1902 of an Alfredo Cerda in Brownsville by Ranger A. Y. Baker. He gives no details.[4] Mr. Dobie also mentions an A. Y. Baker, "a famous ranger and sheriff of the border country," as the man responsible for the "extermination" of the unexterminated raiders of Norias.[5]

The methods of the Rangers are often justified as means to an end, the stamping out of lawlessness on the Border. This coin too has another face. Many Borderers will argue that the army and local law enforcement agencies were the ones that pacified the Border, that far from pacifying the area Ranger activities stirred it up, that instead of eliminating lawlessness along the Rio Grande the Rangers were for many years a primary cause of it. It is pointed out that it was the army that defeated the major border raiders and the local authorities that took care of thieves and smugglers. The notorious Lugo brothers were captured and executed by Cortina, the border raider. Mariano Reséndez, the famous smuggler, was taken by Mexican troops. Octaviano Zapata, the Union guerrilla leader during the Civil War, was defeated and slain by Texas-Mexican Confederates under Captain Antonio Benavides. After the Civil War, when released Confederate soldiers and lawless characters were disturbing the Border, citizens did not call for Rangers

3. Letter of Marcelo Garza, Sr., to the author, dated July 7, 1955, and subsequent conversation with Mr. Garza in Brownsville, December 29, 1957.
4. Webb, *The Texas Rangers*, p. 464.
5. Dobie, "Versos of the Texas Vaqueros," p. 32.

but organized a company of Texas-Mexicans under Captain Benavides to do their own pacifying.[6]

That the Rangers stirred up more trouble than they put down is an opinion that has been expressed by less partisan sources. Goldfinch quotes a Captain Ricketts of the United States Army, who was sent by the War Department to investigate Cortina's revolt, as saying that "conditions that brought federal troops to Brownsville had been nourished but not improved by demonstrations on the part of some Rangers and citizens."[7] In 1913 State Representative Cox of Ellis attempted to eliminate the Ranger force by striking out their appropriation from the budget. Cox declared "that there is more danger from the Rangers than from the men they are supposed to hunt down; that there is no authority of law for the Ranger force; that they are the most irresponsible officers in the State."[8] John Garner, future Vice-President of the United States, was among those who early in the twentieth century advocated abolishing the Ranger force.[9]

In *The Texas Rangers* Professor Webb notes that on the Border after 1848 the Mexican was "victimized by the law," that "the old landholding families found their titles in jeopardy and if they did not lose in the courts they lost to their American lawyers," and again that "the Mexicans suffered not only in their persons but in their property."[1] What he fails to note is that this lawless law was enforced principally by the Texas Rangers. It was the Rangers who could and did furnish the fortune-making adventurer with services not rendered by the United States Army or local sheriffs. And that is why from the point of view of the makers of fortunes the Rangers were so important to the "pacification" of the Border.

The Rangers and those who imitated their methods undoubtedly exacerbated the cultural conflict on the Border rather than allayed it. The assimilation of the north-bank Border people into the American commonwealth was necessary to any effective pacification of the Border. Ranger operations did much to impede that end. They created in the Border Mexican a deep and understandable hostility for American authority; they drew Border communities even closer together than they had been, though at that time they were beginning to disintegrate under the impact of new conditions.

Terror cowed the more inoffensive Mexican, but it also added to the roll of bandits and raiders many high-spirited individuals who would have otherwise remained peaceful and useful citizens. These were the heroes of the Border folk. People sang *corridos* about these men who, in the language of the ballads, "each with his pistol defended his right."

1958

6. Annie Cowling, *The Civil War Trade of the Lower Rio Grande Valley*, Master's thesis, University of Texas, 1926, pp. 136ff.
7. Goldfinch, p. 48.

8. San Antonio *Express*, July 29, 1913, p. 3.
9. Seguin *Enterprise*, April 18, 1902, p. 2.
1. Webb, *The Texas Rangers*, pp. 175–176.

# GUILLERMO COTTO-THORNER
## 1916–1983

Born in Juncos, Puerto Rico, Guillermo Cotto-Thorner emigrated to the United States in the 1930s to pursue higher education. After receiving degrees from Columbia University, in New York City, and the University of Texas, he became a Baptist minister in 1942. He taught Spanish and Spanish-language literature at several U.S. universities, but is best-known in the Latino community for his ecclesiastic work as a Baptist minister, first in Milwaukee and later in Spanish Harlem. In addition, Cotto-Thorner was a novelist, and he published articles in various religious and literary publications. For several years, he wrote the column *Púlpito Progresista* (Progressive Pulpit) for the New York City Spanish-exile newspaper *Liberación*. This column reflected his liberal political and religious views and his commitment to the advancement of the Puerto Rican community on the mainland and to Puerto Rico's independence. He also contributed frequently to the *Revista de Artes y Letras*.

In 1951, Cotto-Thorner published his best-known work, the autobiographical novel *Trópico en Manhattan* (Tropic in Manhattan). Written during one of the periods with the highest rates of Puerto Rican migration to the United States, the novel captured the many ways in which new arrivals deal with feelings of uprootedness in the process of adapting to the boisterous and often confusing urban life in the New York metropolis. Written by an educated middle-class man who was particularly attuned to the conditions faced by a fundamentally working-class community, *Tropic in Manhattan*, one chapter of which is excerpted here, is an important antecedent to writings by subsequent generations of Puerto Rican authors on the mainland.

---

## *From* Tropic in Manhattan[1]

### Two Arrivals

"I'm telling you, you're not going to change my mind. The plane arrives at 11 a.m. and I promised Juan Marcos I'd meet him."

"But in this rain? You're going to catch a cough that'll last you for months. You know when one of those colds hits you in the summer, it hangs on till winter."

"It doesn't matter; I'll take the umbrella, the rain coat, and to please you I'll put on those damn rubbers.[2] I'll even take the old hat I've had in the closet for over a hundred years now. Anything you want, just stop nagging me 'cause I have to leave soon. . . . Anyway, I like to watch the planes landing."

Antonio was hurrying to get ready that Saturday morning to go meet a friend who was arriving from Puerto Rico. It had been raining all night, and the day had dawned black, humid, sticky, unbearable. But shining through the oppressive weather there was a ray of light: the thought of giving a welcoming embrace to a beloved countryman. Finí didn't completely share her husband's romanticism. There was a streak of pragmatism in her

---

1. Translated by Juan Flores.    2. Rubber overshoes.

thinking, the result of many years of struggle and disappointment here in New York. But Antonio went on much the same as always. New York, instead of dulling his sentimentalism, had polished it and given his spirit such a luster that, as he himself said, he felt more Puerto Rican in Harlem than in the peaceful serenity of Barranquitas.[3]

"Give me a kiss 'cause I'm leaving. As you can see I'm better equipped than an explorer. We'll be back for lunch. Don't forget to send the kid to the store. Rosendo put aside a box of guava paste for me for dessert."

"Good-bye, you stubborn mule. Give Juan Marcos a hug for me."

It was drizzling when Antonio hit the street. He bought the *News* and *La Voz*, the Spanish paper, at Lorenzano's newsstand, and in a few minutes disappeared down the stairs into the gloomy subway station. Luckily, he didn't have to wait long. A few seconds after reaching the platform he caught sight of the red eyes of the train as it made its deafening appearance to the rhythm of screeching brakes. He stepped in and found a seat in the last car. Glancing around instinctively, he noted that there were very few passengers in that part of the train. In front of him an old Jewish rabbi with a long beard and a sad look was reading a black, well-thumbed little book. From time to time he would lift his eyes to stare off into space. He was in a world of his own. He looked as though nothing in the world could distract him, or that he had suffered so much that his only solace was silent meditation. At the other end of the car Antonio spotted a woman, garishly dressed and with her legs crossed. There was a hard look on her plain, mundane face. She didn't even bother to adjust her skirt when an indiscreet breeze from the electric fan immodestly uncovered the contours of her thighs. The shocking make-up and cheap air of that woman produced in Antonio a mild sense of repugnance. At the first subway stop, an elegantly dressed black man got on. He sat down near the meditative passenger, and Antonio couldn't help noticing that he was carrying an "intellectual" magazine under his arm. He became absorbed in reading while the curious Puerto Rican observer continued his scrutiny and silent conjectures.

Antonio tried to read, but couldn't concentrate. He tried to distract himself by looking at the colorful advertisements that bordered the top of the car like a crown: ads for funeral parlors, chewing gum, whiskey, cigarettes, beer, cough remedies, films, underwear. But these didn't catch his attention either. He knew them all by heart, having seen them every day. Soon his mind turned to Juan Marcos, and couldn't help thinking about his own arrival in New York ten years earlier. The monotony of the train provided the background for his reminiscences.

He remembered his first trip underground on this exact same route: the Lexington Avenue line. He looked around him and said to himself: "the same people . . . the same indifference . . . the same types . . ." He and Finí were newlyweds when they arrived in New York on a rainy summer day just like this one. But no, he hadn't flown here, like Juan Marcos. He had come on the San Jacinto, that marvelous little steamer where you could eat well without getting sea-sick, and where it was so easy to make friends among the passengers. Suddenly his thoughts turned to that day years later, during the war, when he heard in the *Barrio* that the San Jacinto had been torpe-

---

3. A small mountain town in central Puerto Rico.

doed by a German submarine. It was as if a piece of his life, a scrap of his most precious memories, had been sunk forever beneath the dark waters of the Atlantic.

Yes, Antonio and Finí had arrived in the big city with little money and many hopes. They rented a small apartment in *El Barrio*. It was a fifth floor walk-up. The building was on the verge of being condemned by the Board of Health, but it was still considered habitable. The ceiling in the bathroom was bulging and hung overhead like a *piñata*. If some joker had pressed that plaster belly, so many cockroaches would have fallen on his hair that even ten baths wouldn't have been able to disinfect him. One of the windows in the living room was sealed shut. But there were two things in the kitchen that he (and especially Finí) had wanted for a long time: a gas stove for cooking and an electric refrigerator which, though old and cantankerous, still faithfully carried out its duty.

Antonio had gotten a job in a big hotel, helping out in the kitchen. It was the same hotel where he now worked, though by now he had moved up to a more decent and lucrative position as elevator dispatcher in the main lobby. Finí had worked for a few months in a garment sweat shop, but as soon as she became pregnant she left the job, and until just a few months ago had dedicated herself completely to taking care of her baby and home. They had had a little boy: Luis Alberto. . . .

A jolt from the train woke Antonio from his memories. Looking out the window, he realized he had to get out at that station to get the bus to the airport. The rain had ceased. Once again out in the light of day, he noticed that the sky was clearing but that the wind felt unseasonably cold.

Arriving at the airport waiting room he heard voices speaking in Spanish. There was a group of about twenty Puerto Ricans waiting for friends and family. He approached one of his countrymen, who was smoking a cigar, and asked:

"Do you know what time the plane arrives from Puerto Rico?"

"Ah, you're also from the Island. Well, they just announced that it'll be a little delayed because of bad weather." And after a pause, "Sit down, who are you waiting for?"

"I'm expecting a young friend of the family. His name is Juan Marcos Villalobos. The boy's father is a good friend of mine; we were brought up together in the interior of the Island. When I decided to get married and come to New York, I proposed that we come together. But he didn't want to leave his little business in search of adventure. He said that was alright for newlyweds, and for guys who hadn't settled down yet, but not for him."

"Well look," the other man answered, "I don't blame him for thinking that. Here I am waiting for two little kids travelling alone. My wife and I have always been very sad that we couldn't have children, and those two little ones, both boys, just lost their parents in the Lares fire,[4] so we decided to adopt them. The problem is that now we don't know where to put them, because we've got a full house. Last week my sister arrived with her two kids. She came from the Island because her husband left her and took off with a girlfriend. But you know, as the saying goes, where there's enough for two there's enough for three. . . ."

---

4. In 1945, a fire destroyed much of the town of Lares, in central-western Puerto Rico.

Just then two very lovely young girls entered, and the two new friends cut their conversation short to give them an appraising look and a smile of esthetic approval. A woman came from the information desk, shouting jubilantly to her companions: "It'll be here in ten minutes. Just ten minutes." Antonio jumped to his feet and, watching the sky through the glass, marked time with thick puffs of pale blue smoke.

1951

# RENÉ MARQUÉS
## 1919–1979

One of Puerto Rico's most accomplished and internationally known playwrights, René Marqués was among the first writers to introduce the topic of the migrant experience into Puerto Rican letters. He was part of what island critics have labeled the Generation of 1950, a group of island-born writers—including José Luis Gonzáles and Pedro Juan Soto—who lived for periods in the United States. Born in Arecibo, Puerto Rico, Marqués was trained and worked as an agronomist during the 1940s before pursuing a career as a playwright, fiction writer, journalist, and university professor. In 1946, he went to Spain to study literature and theater. His first play, *El sol y los MacDonald* (The Sun and the MacDonald Family, 1946), indicated how Marqués would combine the avant-garde experimental theater and existentialist philosophy of Europe and North America with specific circumstances and events in Puerto Rican history. After his return to Puerto Rico in 1947, he became a frequent literary contributor to newspapers and magazines and continued writing plays. His first published play, *El hombre y sus sueños* (Man and his Dreams, 1948), appeared in one of the island's leading literary journals, *Asomante*. In 1949, he received a Rockefeller Foundation fellowship to study theater in New York, at Columbia University and Erwin Piscator's Dramatic Workshop at the New School.

For one of his drama courses, Marqués wrote *Palm Sunday* (1949), an unpublished play in English that focuses on the killing of Puerto Rican Nationalists during the Ponce Massacre, on Palm Sunday, 1937. A year of living in New York had given Marqués a swift introduction to the prejudice and hardships confronted by Puerto Ricans who had moved to the U.S. during the Great Migration, and his fellow islanders' circumstances inspired *La carreta* (The Oxcart, 1952), Marqués's best-known drama. Produced in New York in 1953, the play—of which the final act is excerpted here—filled a void, in that few Puerto Rican plays were written or produced in New York during the years of the Great Migration. In 1967, the actress Miriam Colón founded the Puerto Rican Traveling Theatre in New York, and *La carreta*, its first production, proved highly popular.

*La carreta* is divided in three acts, each representing a different stage of the Puerto Rican migratory journey at a time when Puerto Rico was making its transition from an agricultural society to an industrial one. The play revolves around the lives of a displaced peasant family forced to leave its home because of the poverty and destitution that overwhelmed the island's rural areas. The family migrates first to the slums of the capital, San Juan, and later to a New York City barrio. At each stage, the family members are overpowered by economic survival issues and by a series of ill-fated events that threaten the traditional values and strong bonds that once held them together. The play presents a pessimistic view of the destiny awaiting those Puerto Ricans who migrate to the United States, and whose only salvation is to return to the abandoned homeland. In many ways, *La carreta* offers a tragic, narrow view of migrant life, failing to capture the vast range of experiences of those generations of Puerto Ricans whose lives were or became rooted in the United States. In 1979, the Nuyorican poet Tato Laviera published the poetry volume *La Carreta Made a U-Turn*, which challenged Marqués's view of migrant life.

After returning to Puerto Rico in 1950, Marqués, along with other writers and artists, worked for the División para la Educación de la Comunidad (Division for Community Education; DIVEDCO) of Puerto Rico's Departamento de Instrucción Pública (Department of Public Instruction). This government agency played an important role in strengthening cultural nationalism and popular education on the island during the U.S.-led Operation Bootstrap industrialization program, which began in the late 1940s and continued into the 1960s. From 1953 to 1958, Marqués directed DIVEDCO's editorial division. After receiving a Guggenheim fellowship to write a novel, he returned to New York in 1959 and stayed for a year. In the 1960s, he published numerous plays and played a major role in promoting theater productions and festivals in Puerto Rico, in addition to teaching at the University of Puerto Rico, from which he retired in the early 1970s. During his prolific career, Marqués published more than a dozen plays, two novels, three collections of short stories, a book of essays, and a collection of poetry.

In his controversial but influential essay "El puertorriqueño dócil (Literatura y realidad psicológica)" (The Docile Puerto Rican: Literature and Psychological Reality, 1962), featured here, Marqués attempts to define the Puerto Rican collective character. He provides a deterministic and unflattering image of the colonized Puerto Rican people and of their psychological impotence in achieving national sovereignty. As in most of his literary works, Marqués focuses on the rapid transformation of Puerto Rican society into a modern industrial one. He views this transformation negatively and as primarily the result of American colonialism and the infiltration of American values, and ways of life, that weaken the island's Hispanic values and traditions. Marqués's cultural nationalism is based, however, on an idealized view of the Spanish traditions of the landowning patriarchal society that existed before the U.S. invasion of Puerto Rico. His essay "The Function of the Puerto Rican Writer Today"—first published in Spanish in 1963 but read at the Ateneo Puertorriqueño (Puerto Rican Athenaeum), one of the main cultural institutions of Puerto Rico, less than a year before—reflects the ideology that permeates most of Marqués's creative work: an ardent denunciation of American colonialism in Puerto Rico and a historical commitment by Puerto Rican writers to the struggle for freedom and social and political emancipation. However, he also argues that these goals can be achieved more effectively when aesthetic values are not sacrificed to ideological positions.

---

## FROM THE OXCART[1]

## Act 3

*One year later. A small apartment in Morrisania, Puerto Rican area in the Bronx, New York. Sixth floor of an old, run-down building. In the foreground, extreme right, main door of the apartment. Occupying a little less than one-*

1. Translated by Charles Pildich.

*fourth of the stage, three feet behind the curtain line, there is a wall five feet long that runs parallel to the proscenium, starting almost at the frame of the front door. Along this wall there is a closed door leading to the small bathroom. In the wall to the right of the bathroom door there are three hooks for hanging up clothes. There are two woolen jackets on two of the hooks. There is a felt hat on the third. To the left of this door there is a framed print showing an ornate snowscape. This wall forms a passageway that goes from the front door to the living room. The latter occupies the rest of the stage.*

*In the right background of the living room there is a small window that looks out on a dark, inside courtyard. From the outside of the window frame to a point unseen by the audience, there extends over the courtyard a pulley line for hanging up clothes when the weather is good. At the rear, to the left of the window and next to it, there is an open door leading to the kitchen. A table and three chairs can be seen in the kitchen. The table is covered with an imitation embroidered tablecloth made of white plastic. A green pitcher, a black coffee can, and a yellow sugar bowl are on the table. On the part of the rear wall that runs from the kitchen door to the wall on the left there is a framed print of the Sacred Heart of Jesus.[2] On the wall on each side of this print there is a small, gaudy flower holder with faded and dirty artificial flowers. Beneath the print there is an old studio couch covered with cretonne. To the left of the couch, in the corner formed by the two walls, there is a small table with a shiny, aggressive radio of the latest style, in direct contrast to the rest of the furniture. On the radio is the wooden oxcart that Miguel gave to* juanita. *In the left wall of the living room there is a wide doorway covered with a curtain of flowered cretonne leading to the only bedroom.*

*In the left foreground, an upholstered chair showing unmistakable signs of age and dirt. Next to the right wall of the living room, between the rear window and the entrance passageway, another armchair similar to the one at the left. To the right of the chair there is a floor lamp with a parchment shade covered with printed flowers. To the left of the chair there is an old, rusty kerosene heater that doesn't work.*

*The living room floor is covered with worn, flowered linoleum. The passageway and the living room were painted years ago with a bright, rose colored paint. Dampness and time have faded the original color, and large whitish stains can be seen in several places. The visible part of the kitchen is painted a light green. There, too, dampness and time have faded the paint.*

*The bedroom to the left, the door to which is visible, faces the street. The noise of an electric drill can be heard tearing up the pavement. At regular intervals an elevated train can be heard passing in the distance.*

*Left and right, that of the audience.*

*It is a cold, gray autumn day with a threat of snow.*

doña gabriela *enters from the kitchen with a plastic shopping bag. She leaves the bag on the divan. She takes a woolen scarf and puts it around her head, tying it under her chin. She opens a small black purse and examines its contents as she goes to the door at the left. She stops in front of the door and says:*

da. gabriela:   Luis, I left your breakfast ready. All you have to do is heat the milk.

> [*Shuts her purse and goes to the couch. The doorbell rings.* da. ga-
> briela *hesitates. She goes to the right. The bell rings again and then*

---

2. As depicted in Christian art, Jesus' heart as the manifestation of his love for humanity. It is often flaming, shining, pierced, and/or bleeding.

*the rapping of knuckles is heard on the door.* DA. GABRIELA *opens the door.* JUANITA *enters wearing a woolen coat. She wears a silk kerchief on her head, the ends tied under her chin. She has woolen gloves and a leather handbag. For the first time we see her heavily made-up. She carries a package under one arm.*]

    Oh, it's you, child.

JUANITA: How's everythin', mamá?

    [*Kisses her.*]

    Blessing . . .

DA. GABRIELA: God bless you.

    [*Shutting the door.*]

    My heavens, what cold air comes in from those damn stairs!

JUANITA: [*Taking off her coat.*] And Luis?

DA. GABRIELA: Juanita, you oughta come live with us.

    [*Opens the door and leaves.* JUANITA *remains looking pensively toward the door. Then she goes to the sofa and sits down in the right corner, doubling her legs under her. She turns on the radio. Reaches out with her arm, takes her pocketbook, takes out a cigarette and lights it. The music of a "blues" is heard.* JUANITA *takes a deep puff on the cigarette and notices the oxcart. She looks at it, stretches out her hand and takes it. She examines it and puts it back on the radio. Her fingers are still caressing the rough from when* LUIS *enters from the left. He now appears nervous and taciturn. There is something terribly disturbing gnawing at the soul of this transplanted country-boy. He is shirtless and shoeless. He doesn't see* JUANITA *and crosses rapidly to the right.*]

JUANITA: [*Without moving.*] Hello!

LUIS: [*Stopping and turning around.*] Oh, you're here.

JUANITA: Yes, like you see.

LUIS: And the old lady?

JUANITA: At the market.

    [LUIS *makes a gesture of impatience.*]

    What's the matter, am I botherin' you?

LUIS: Heat me the milk for the coffee.

    [*Enters the bathroom and shuts the door.* JUANITA *gets up indolently. Exits rear. We hear* JUANITA's *movements in the kitchen, the water running in the bathroom basin, and the sleepy "blues" on the radio.*]

LUIS' VOICE: Change that music!

JUANITA: [*Coming to the kitchen door.*] What'd you say?

LUIS' VOICE: [*From the bathroom.*] Change that music!

JUANITA: Why? It's pretty.

LUIS' VOICE: It makes you wanna cry. Sounds like a funeral. Turn it off!

    [JUANITA *shrugs her shoulders, goes to the radio and changes the station. The "danza" Margarita by Tavárez*[3] *is heard.*]

JUANITA: There's the Spanish station for you.

    [JUANITA *goes to the kitchen. We see her putting* LUIS' *breakfast on the table.* LUIS *comes out of the bathroom, crosses rapidly and exits through the door on the left. A few seconds later he returns with his shirt half*

---

3. Manuel Gregorio Tavárez (1843–1883), Puerto Rico's first renowned composer of classical music and *danzas*. "Margarita" is intensely romantic.

*on and his shoes in his hand. He sits on the sofa and begins to put on his shoes. He stops to turn off the radio, then returns to his task.*]

JUANITA: [*From the kitchen.*]   Your breakfast's ready.

[*Comes to the rear door.*]

What happened?

LUIS:   Nothin'.

JUANITA:   You shut off the radio?

LUIS:   Yeah.

JUANITA:   What d'you got a radio for if you don't listen to it?

LUIS: [*Getting up and tucking his shirt in his pants.*]

So's I can listen to it when I feel like it.

JUANITA: [*Joking.*]   And you don't feel like it now?

LUIS:   Nope.

JUANITA:   The milk's gettin' cold.

[LUIS *enters the kitchen, sits at the table with his back to the living room, and begins to eat.* JUANITA *takes a newspaper and sits down in the armchair on the right. She glances indifferently at the front page, then looks toward the kitchen.*]

JUANITA:   You need anythin'?

[*She awaits an answer from* LUIS, *who pretends not to hear.*]

How's your job goin'?

[LUIS *continues eating and doesn't answer.* JUANITA *gets up.*]

That new radio must've cost you a pretty penny.

[*Pause.*]

Looks like you're really makin' progress.

[*Pause.*]

Of course, mamá would rather have had a new armchair.

[*Approaching the rear door, changing her tone.*]

Have you noticed how old she seems?

[*In a low voice, full of emotion.*]

Her days are numbered, Luis.

LUIS: [*Turning half-way round.*]   Shut up!

JUANITA: [*Turns around.*]   She used to be as strong as the trunk of an ausubo tree. The hurricanes couldn't blow her over. But up here she's gettin' all bent over like a dry stalk o' sugar cane. She's wrinklin' up on us like a dried fig.

LUIS: [*Getting up violently.*]   Shut up! She's better than ever.

JUANITA:   Her hair is turnin' the same color as this gray, American sky. And her hands . . . you remember her hands? When she used to grab the handle of the millstone and turn it, her hands looked like a giant's hands. And when the corn came out as yellow flour, it seemed like a miracle from her own hands and not the work of the handle and the stones. I was a little girl then and her hands were big and strong. I saw her hands today. And they were so small, and they shook so when she tried to button her sweater!

LUIS:   She's strong. She's better than ever. She's strong, I tell you!

JUANITA:   And she doesn't scold us anymore. Have you noticed how she doesn't scold us anymore? But she looks at me. She looks at me in such a way! And it's worse than a scolding.

LUIS:   She don't need nothin'. She's got everythin'. Everythin'.

JUANITA:  Are you sure, Luis?

LUIS:  I've given her what I've always wanted to give her, a decent life. She's got clothes and she's got food. And a real good bed. And she can rest whenever she wants to. And she's got all the money she needs. And I've given her all that. That's why I've been workin' so hard. That's why I work overtime. So she can live right.

JUANITA:  I know now you've gotten what you wanted.

LUIS:  And I brought her to this neighborhood from Harlem. So she can live better here. And we don't owe nothin' to nobody. Two months ago I sent Doña Isa the last cent she lent us for the plane fare. When have we ever been better off? Never!

JUANITA:  Yeah, you're makin' money all right.

LUIS:  And I'll keep on makin' it. More and more. Money. Not to be poor, understand? That's what's important.

JUANITA:  But mamá . . .

LUIS:  What d'you have to worry about the old lady for? She's all right. She don't need a thing. And I'm the one who gave it all to her! You went off to live someplace else . . .

JUANITA:  I work in Brooklyn. It's too far . . .

LUIS:  Others from here work in Long Island. And that's even further. But they live here, in their homes. Except that in their homes you can't do certain things . . .

JUANITA:  Shut up!

LUIS:  Don't make me talk, then.

JUANITA:  Okay. Talk. I'm not afraid o' what you'll say.

LUIS:  'Cause you don't have any shame.

JUANITA:  Aren't you lucky to have so much! But listen close. Those certain things you mentioned can be done anyplace. All you need is to want to do 'em. Whether it's Bronx, Brooklyn, or Long Island. If I left this house, it was for the good of all of us. 'Cause you and mamá were drivin' me crazy. You watchin' me, spyin' on me all the time like I was some criminal. And mamá lookin' at me, always lookin' at me, like she didn't know me. Like she wanted to get to know me and she couldn't.

LUIS:  It was like a stab with a dagger, you goin' away from here.

JUANITA:  Stabs can be cured. If I stayed here, it would've been like a knife always stuck in her heart. And that can't be cured. Besides, you wouldn't have gotten what you have if I stayed. I earn my own living and I don't cost you a cent. And for your information, if you've been able to pay back Doña Isa, it's cause I've been givin' mamá somethin' every month.

LUIS:  It's a lie! She never told me . . .

JUANITA:  What for? If you don't even hear what people tell you any more.

LUIS:  But where does the money go?

JUANITA:  Where does it go? You oughta know that. You buy a fancy radio and mamá has to go out in the street with a sweater.

LUIS:  I bought her a good coat. But she don't wanna wear it. She's got it put away in the closet. She says it's better to keep it like new in case somethin' happens and she has to sell it. Don't blame me for her crazy ideas.

JUANITA:  No, I know we all got our own crazy ideas.
    [*Indicating* LUIS' *wristwatch.*]
Like that gold watch. How much do you still owe on it?

LUIS: [*Furious.*]   What's it to you? Do I ask you how much you owe on that necklace, or that permanent, or all that junk you smear on your face?

JUANITA:   No, you don't ask me 'cause you know what I'll tell you. You know that *I* don't owe anythin' on all that. *Others* owe on it.

LUIS:   Well, I forbid you to give another cent o' that money to the old lady.

JUANITA:   Really? Why?

LUIS:   'Cause it's dirty money.

JUANITA:   There's no such thing as dirty money or clean money. There's just money. And in that sweatshop I earn barely enough to keep alive. Whatever else I can get to help the old lady or for the things I want, it's nobody's business what kind o' money it is.

LUIS:   Well, it does matter to me.

JUANITA:   But not to me. That's the advantage o' bein' a woman, right? We don't have to be as decent as you men.

LUIS: [*Advancing menacingly.*]   I oughta smash your face.

JUANITA: [*Without moving.*]   Go ahead.
   [*Pause.*]
But you wouldn't dare.

LUIS: [*Turning his back.*]   It's not that I wouldn't dare. It's just that you're a woman. And you're my sister.
   [*Pause.*]
Why don't you come live with us? What d' you have to work for? I can work for all of us.
   [*Turning to her.*]
You won't have to do without a thing. I work overtime. I'm gonna earn more. I'll have more money. Leave all that. Come back here, Juanita, so you can take care o' the old lady.

JUANITA:   If it was for that . . . But it's not. I know that line. Mamá'd be the one who'd be takin' care o' me. And you'd start spyin' on me again.

LUIS:   No, I promise . . . If you behave right . . .

JUANITA:   Ah, you see? If I behave right! The thing is I don't feel like behavin' right any more. And just what does behave right mean? One day we left our little farm in an oxcart 'cause we were goin' in search of freedom. The mountains were closing in on us, and we fled to the sea. But the sea closed in on us too, and we fled from the sea. Now we're closed in by buildings that look like mountains and seas of people who push us and shove us. If this is freedom, I wanna enjoy it alone. Without answerin' to anybody. You got that? I'm gonna drive my own cart and lead the oxen wherever I want.
   [*The doorbell rings.*]

LUIS:   Shut up! There's the old lady.

JUANITA:   Mamá's got a key. She don't have to ring. What's the matter with you? Why don't you open the door?
   [*She goes to the right and opens the door.* PACO *enters. He is thirty years old. He is well dressed and well groomed, like the majority of the frustrated writers from the Puerto Rican colony in New York. He is the blond type of country person descended from Canary Islanders. His voice has the unmistakable metallic, polished sound of a radio announcer. The nostalgia of his homeland in this frustrated writer has marked romantic characteristics.*]

PACO: Hi, how are you, Juanita?

JUANITA: Hi, Paco!

PACO: Caramba! I forgot your number. I thought I wasn't going to find the house.

JUANITA: Especially since here all the buildin's are the same. Come in. Come in.

[PACO *proceeds to enter and stops on seeing* LUIS.]

PACO: Hello.

JUANITA: Oh, this is my brother Luis. Luis, a friend.

PACO: [*Extending his hand, warmly.*] Pleased to meet you.

[LUIS, *with wry face, shakes hands. There is a moment of embarrassing silence.*]

JUANITA: Sit down. Mamá went out. She'll be right back. When you meet her, you'll know the rest o' the family.

[*Pause.* PACO *sits down.*]

PACO: [*For the sake of saying something.*] It's a pleasant neighborhood, isn't it?

JUANITA: At least it's better than Harlem. That's what Luis says.

[JUANITA *and* PACO *look at* LUIS *to get him to agree.* LUIS *pays no attention.*]

JUANITA: [*Insisting.*] Right, Luis?

LUIS: Huh . . . ?

JUANITA: Weren't you goin' out?

LUIS: No.

JUANITA: Oh, it seemed to me . . .

LUIS: No.

[*Annoying pause.*]

JUANITA: Why don't you bring Paco a beer?

LUIS: There isn't any beer.

JUANITA: Yes, there is. I brought some. Well, I'll go get it.

[*Gets up.*]

PACO: Please, don't bother.

JUANITA: It's no bother. But I don't think it's very cold.

[*Exits rear.* LUIS *and* PACO *look at each other out of the corners of their eyes.* PACO *takes out his cigarettes. He gets up and offers one to* LUIS.]

LUIS: Thanks, but I don't smoke.

[PACO *sits down and lights a cigarette.*]

PACO: You're lucky not to have any minor vices.

LUIS: [*Agreeing.*] Hunh . . .

PACO: What kind of work do you do?

LUIS: Factory work.

PACO: Nearby?

LUIS: Almost next door.

PACO: What kind of factory?

LUIS: Boilers.

PACO: Oh . . . !

LUIS: What about you, do you work?

PACO: [*Laughing.*] Sure! What else!

LUIS: What d' you do?

PACO: Announcer.

LUIS: What?

PACO: Radio announcer.

LUIS: Ah . . . !

PACO: [*Pointing to the radio.*]  That's a nice set.

LUIS: Yeah.

PACO: Do you listen to the Spanish station?

LUIS: Sometimes.

PACO: I have my programs from 8 to 11 in the mornings and from 2 to 5 in the afternoons. You've probably heard me.

LUIS: [*Emphasizing the fact.*]  I'm workin' at those times.

PACO: [*Laughing.*]  Well so am I.

LUIS: You get paid for that?

PACO: Yes, of course.

JUANITA: [*From the kitchen.*]  I can't find the opener, Luis.

LUIS: It's in the little drawer.

   [*To* PACO.]

Where'd you meet Juanita?

PACO: At my brother's house.

LUIS: Your brother?

PACO: Yes. My sister-in-law works with Juanita.

LUIS: Your brother's wife?

PACO: Naturally.

LUIS: Do you have any more relatives?

PACO: Not here. In Puerto Rico.

   [*Pause.*]

So? How do you like it here?

LUIS: And your wife?

PACO: My wife? Ah no, I'm a bachelor.

   [JUANITA *enters with two glasses of beer on a plate. She offers one to* PACO.]

JUANITA:  I don't know if you like it with a head on it.

PACO: That's all right, thanks.

JUANITA: [*Giving the other glass to* LUIS.]  You're really not goin' to work?

PACO: Work today? But it's a holiday!

JUANITA:  My brother works overtime. He just lives for that. For his work.

LUIS: My shift begins at eleven. I'm not in any hurry.

PACO: Aren't you having anything to drink?

JUANITA:  I don't like beer.

LUIS: How long have you known each other?

PACO: Two weeks, more or less. Isn't that so?

JUANITA:  This is the fourth time we've seen each other.

   [*Pause. The men drink.*]

LUIS: The old lady's late.

JUANITA:  Yes.

   [*Pause.*]

LUIS: I have to get goin'.

   [*He doesn't move.*]

PACO: You do?

   [*Lying.*]

I'm so sorry!

[*Pause.*]

LUIS: [*Getting up.*]   Well . . .

PACO: [*Getting up.*]   Well . . .

JUANITA:   Don't forget your jacket.

[*Takes the glass from his hand.*]

LUIS:   I don't need a jacket. I'm not goin' outside. Have you seen the dominoes?

JUANITA:   No. You probably have 'em in your room.

[LUIS *exits left.*]

PACO: [*With comic disconcertedness.*]   Is he going to invite me to play dominoes?

JUANITA:   No. He's goin' to play with a neighbor. That's the only fun he has.

PACO:   He seems worried, doesn't he?

JUANITA: [*Shrugging her shoulders.*]   He's gotten ugly. He don't even know how to treat people any more.

PACO:   Bah! It's not important. We all have our bad days.

JUANITA:   Bad days? No, it's not that. You want more beer?

PACO:   I still have some.

JUANITA:   Ah, so you do.

[LUIS *enters from the left with a box of dominoes.*]

JUANITA:   Well, are you goin' or not?

LUIS:   This is my house.

JUANITA:   So you oughta be more polite to company then.

LUIS:   He's your company, not mine.

[*Facing up to* PACO.]

You were born in the city, right? Probably in San Juan. You talk good and have a rich boy's face. We're country folk. We come from the mountains. We used to eat bananas and roots. But here we're as good as anybody else. And we live well. And we got a radio. And we're gonna have TV. 'Cause I earn enough for all that.

JUANITA:   Have you gone crazy? What does he care what you eat or what you earn?

PACO:   It doesn't matter. Leave him alone. He asked me a question. No, I wasn't born in the city. I was born in the country near Morovis. What you call my good speech is just a means of earning a living. We all do what we can.

JUANITA:   And that business about bein' as good as anybody else here is a big joke. Ha! My side's splittin' from laughin' so hard. The way we get kicked around all the time. Yeah, yeah, we're all equal. Except that everybody else here's worth more than us. But that don't bother you. You just worry about money and machines. Go on, go wait for your shift at work. Go play dominoes. But while you're playin' you'll be thinkin' about your machines. And you won't be able to enjoy yourself. 'Cause machines are eatin' your life away. They're your friends, and your family. Machines are your wife and your kids. Go on, fill yourself with 'em 'till you bust. But leave us be.

LUIS:   What're you carryin' on so about machines for? What would we do if it wasn't for them, eh? Machines give us life.

JUANITA:   God gives us life.

LUIS: I'm not talkin' about God.

[*Brusquely, turning to* PACO.]

What d' you think?

PACO: I don't know . . . For me, machines are just a good means of work. But, of course, there was work before there were machines.

LUIS: But do you know what a machine really is? No, you don't know nothin'. A machine is a tremendous thing. It's like a miracle. There's somethin' you can never completely understand in a machine. Any day it's apt to do somethin' unexpected. But people think that by knowin' about the nuts and screws it's got inside, they know what it is. But they don't know; they don't know nothin'. You really never can get to know it. You see why I say it's such a marvellous thing?

PACO: Yes . . . It seems as though you think a machine has . . . life and brains . . . a soul and a will of its own.

JUANITA: Are you goin' or stayin'? 'Cause if you stay to talk about machines, I'm the one who's goin'.

LUIS: Whenever I go in the subway, I keep thinkin': "What'll it do now? What's it gonna do now?" Yesterday a subway train in Brooklyn turned over. I bet you didn't know that!

PACO: Yes, I knew it. Those accidents aren't so rare.

LUIS: And the noise in the factory! The oven! Do you know what it's like, that enormous belly with a hunger for things you can't even guess? Like the sea. Only better . . . or worse. It's a marvel. It's a mystery you can't understand. But someday I'll find out . . . I have to find out.

[*Exits right. Pause.*]

JUANITA: Oh, please excuse all this! That brother o' mine loses his head whenever he talks about machines.

PACO: He's a strange fellow.

JUANITA: An idiot!

PACO: No. Your brother's not happy.

JUANITA: Hah, what a discovery! Do you know anyone who is happy?

PACO: Yes . . . relatively.

JUANITA: Well, either I'm happy or I'm not happy. I don't get that stuff about "relatively."

PACO: And . . . are you happy?

JUANITA: Well, the truth is I don't know if I'm happy. There was a time when I was happy. And I thought I was gonna be even more happy. But instead I was really disgraced more than ever. Now I don't know. I'm not sufferin', but I'm not content. I feel hollow like a gourd.

PACO: It's the emptiness of New York . . .

JUANITA: [*Laughing bitterly.*] Yeah. Emptiness. Eight million hollow gourds.

PACO: For that reason it's all the more terrible.

JUANITA: [*Approaching the window.*] And the summer is so short. It seems like this sky is ashamed o' bein' seen blue.

PACO: You miss your little island, don't you?

JUANITA: Although it's hard enough anyway to see the sky. Those mountains o' buildin's have no pity on anybody.

PACO: There's no room for pity when the sky is so far away.

JUANITA: It must be that the cold oppresses a person's heart.

[*Moving away from the window.*]
Grandpa used to say that the heart can dry up like an old bean. But here it don't dry up. It freezes. It freezes up like ice. And that's even worse.

PACO: They say that love can melt hearts of ice.

JUANITA: Yeah, in the soap operas. And in the movies.

PACO: Why did you invite me to come here?

JUANITA: I don't know. You make me sad. Maybe you'd better go.

PACO: Why?

JUANITA: I told you you make me sad.

PACO: You don't live here, do you?

JUANITA: No.

PACO: And why didn't you invite me to your house?

JUANITA: This is my house.

PACO: And the other?

JUANITA: A boarding house.

PACO: But do you receive visitors there?

JUANITA: Visitors? Yes.

PACO: But me, on the other hand . . .

JUANITA: Are you sorry you came?

PACO: No. I'd like to be your friend.

JUANITA: I know.

PACO: And you?

JUANITA: I don't have friends. They're just eight million hollow gourds.

PACO: I also feel lonely.

JUANITA: Lonely? Speakin' good English? With that light face? You could even pass for an American.

PACO: I'm Puerto Rican. And I feel the loneliness the way you do.

JUANITA: An American probably wouldn't feel what you feel. But there are other things an American would understand and you wouldn't.

PACO: What things?

JUANITA: I'll bring you another beer.

PACO: I thought you wanted me to go.

JUANITA: You can drink it before you go.
        [*Exits rear.*]

PACO: [*After a pause, looking towards the rear.*] How about having lunch together someplace and then going to Radio City?[4]

JUANITA: [*From the kitchen.*] Do you intend to go into debt on my account?

PACO: Don't worry. I got paid yesterday.

JUANITA: Wouldn't a neighborhood movie be better?

PACO: Well, whatever you want.

JUANITA: [*Coming in with the beer.*] I was just talkin'. I don't plan on goin' out.
        [*Hands him the glass of beer.*]

PACO: What are you up to, Juanita? What kind of game is this?

JUANITA: Game?

PACO: Why don't you answer my question?

---

4. Radio City Music Hall, an entertainment venue in midtown Manhattan.

JUANITA:   You make me sad. I don't know who you are.

PACO:   A man who offers to share his loneliness with you.

JUANITA: [*Disturbed.*]   How?

PACO:   By marrying you.

JUANITA: [*Pale, evading him.*]   You're mad.

PACO:   I'm not going to lie and say I'm madly in love. But since I met you, I knew we needed each other.

JUANITA:   You've only seen me four times.

PACO:   I see women 365 times a year. And they don't interest me.

JUANITA:   And so why do I?

PACO:   It must be because there's something in you that doesn't belong to this world of New York. Because there's something fresh in you like the fields near Morovis. Maybe a certain flavor of the land . . .

JUANITA:   The land is bitter . . .

PACO:   But it gives life. And I haven't been able to erase the sight of my land.

JUANITA:   Why did you leave it, then?

PACO:   For the same reason we all leave it. Because we believe we can only be successful far away from it.

JUANITA:   Did you also have illusions?

PACO:   Yes. I wanted to be a writer.

JUANITA:   A writer? You gotta study a lot for that.

PACO:   Not really. Anyway I couldn't. I had hardly gotten to Río Piedras to study at the University when my parents died. I couldn't continue.

JUANITA:   What did you do?

PACO:   I was a janitor in a government building. Then assistant linotypist at a printer's. I got a few minor parts in some soap operas on the radio. The main thing was just to earn something to live on. But what mattered to me were the stories I was writing and nobody wanted to publish. I did everything imaginable to get a job as a journalist, but it was impossible. In the government newspaper my ideas were too much pro-independence. In the papers backed by big business what I wrote sounded like communism. And a communist magazine rejected some articles of mine because they thought they were too bourgeois.

JUANITA:   Why was that?

PACO:   I don't know. They all made a special effort to fit me into some neat little political pigeon-hole. I couldn't think for myself. I had to belong to some group where others would think for me. That way, the others felt more at ease.

JUANITA:   I don't get it. I've always thought what I've wanted to.

PACO:   No, Juanita. You don't realize it, but the thing is others do think for you. And I got fed up with it. I decided to tell them all to go to hell. And I came here, to look for my liberty.

JUANITA:   And did you find it?

PACO: [*Laughing.*]   Yeah. At the entrance to the harbor, with a torch in one hand and a book in the other. But the torch and the book are just reinforced concrete.

JUANITA:   Ah, I've seen that too!

PACO:   Sure, that's why they have it there, so we all see it. But for me everything was the same, if not worse. Ten years ago I arrived in New York to write a novel. A hack novel that would make me famous. Then I could go back to Puerto Rico and all those who had turned me down would have to accept me and recognize their stupid mistake.

JUANITA:  What's the name o' the novel?

PACO:  I never wrote it.

JUANITA:  For God's sake! That's a fine thing!

PACO:  It's true. New York didn't give me any freedom, but it did dry up my enthusiasm. But I don't care any more! I probably would never be any good as a writer.

JUANITA:  You're an animal! Just think, if I could write I sure wouldn't give up so easy! Never! With the tremendous things I'd have to say! I'd never let anythin' get the best o' me!

PACO:  Probably what I need is your help.

JUANITA:  My help?

PACO:  Marry me, and make me write.

JUANITA:  Who, me? Hah, that's enough o' that. Nobody can make any-body do anythin'. Besides, I got no intention o' marryin' you. I don't understand you at all.

PACO:  All you have to understand is my loneliness.

JUANITA:  Don't be an idiot. If your loneliness was joined to mine, we'd just have a bigger loneliness. What do we gain by that?

PACO:  Two lonelinesses together stop being loneliness.

JUANITA:  You're talkin' now like in the soap operas. But for a long time now I don't believe in the radio. Look, you've let your beer get warm.

LIDIA'S VOICE:  [*Coming from the right.*]   Juanita! Telephone!

PACO:  Sounds like you're being called.

LIDIA:  [*Knocking at the door at the right and calling.*]   Juanita! Come to the janitor's phone!

JUANITA:  [*Shouting.*]   Coming.
        [*To* PACO.]
Well, you can go now.

PACO:  You're throwing me out now?

JUANITA:  We agreed you'd go as soon as you finished your beer. And since you're not gonna drink it . . .

PACO:  But we also agreed that you were going to invite me to lunch or that I was going to invite you.

JUANITA:  Yes, but I didn't really know you then.
        [*Gives him his hat.*]
Good-bye, Paco.

PACO:  I haven't met your mother.

JUANITA:  I'll tell her about you. It'll be the same thing.

PACO:  When will I see you again?

JUANITA:  Someday. I dunno. Good-bye.
        [PACO *opens the door and confronts* LIDIA. *She is twenty-six years old, slender and tall, with very dull hair down to her shoulders and a bang over her forehead à la Claudette Colbert.[5] Her prominent dark eyes glow against her olive complexion, giving her the look of a*

---

5. French-born American actress (1903–1996).

*gypsy.* PACO *greets her rapidly and leaves.* LIDIA *enters, looks back, and gives an admiring whistle.*]

LIDIA:  What a good-lookin' fellow! Where'd you find him?

JUANITA:  Do you know who's callin' me?

LIDIA:  Nobody. The janitor's wife told me some real handsome guy had come up here after you arrived. And I wanted to see that treasure with my own eyes.

JUANITA:  Nosey!

LIDIA:  Is he Latin?

JUANITA:  From Morovis. Well, how's everything with you?

LIDIA:  Don't change the subject. We're talkin' about your life, not mine. How come you brought him here?

JUANITA:  How do I know! Maybe 'cause he seemed different. And 'cause I liked him. But I don't like him now. And I don't like him for that reason, 'cause he is different.

LIDIA:  I don't follow you.

JUANITA:  Neither do I. But that's how it is. I just realized it here, a minute ago, while he was talkin'.

LIDIA: [*Shrugging her shoulders.*]  When we women feel like complicatin' a thing, we can't even understand ourselves.

[*Examining the glass left by* PACO.]

You got beer?

JUANITA:  Yeah, there's some in the icebox.

LIDIA: [*Going to the rear door.*]  I'm gonna take one. Your brother and my husband stayed down there playin' dominoes and drinkin' all I had left. [*Exits rear.*]

JUANITA:  How's your husband?

LIDIA: [*Out of sight, in the kitchen.*]  Okay. Still mixed up in the same business.

JUANITA:  That's dangerous. Don't your husband realize that?

LIDIA: [*Appearing with a glass of beer.*]  He knows. He knows. But he don't care.

JUANITA:  Sure, since he's a man.

LIDIA:  I'm tired o' tellin' him: "Look, Juan, with my widow's relief and a few honest bucks you could earn, we'd make out all right." But he says he'd rather go to jail than work for an American.

JUANITA:  Well just think that any day, when you least expect it . . .

LIDIA:  You think I dunno that? I don't have any kind o' life. Every time I see a cop, my heart gets stuck in my throat. I have nightmares. I hear shots, horrible shots, and then I see Juan stretched out on the floor bleedin'. Then I wake up shoutin' for him. And he gets mad 'cause I don't let him sleep in peace. No, I tell you, this is no kind o' life.

JUANITA:  I would've left him if I were you.

LIDIA:  Yeah, it's easy to say it like that. But I can't do it. And the worst part is the kid. Every day she gets more like my last husband. And every day she likes this one less. The house is gettin' to be like hell for me. If it wasn't for that poor little girl, I'd . . .

JUANITA:  Careful, Lidia. There are some things you shouldn't even think about.

LIDIA:  Well you thought about it, and you almost did it.

JUANITA: For that reason, Lidia, for that very reason. Look how I've paid for what I did. That's why I say: don't even think about it.

LIDIA: Damn it anyway! Why should I have to have this kind o' luck? Just look at the disgrace! My first husband, the one I brought from Puerto Rico, was so honest, so honest, that just 'cause he was a month without findin' work and he couldn't stand it, he threw himself off the roof. He was too proud. But he left me in the street with a kid to support. This one, on the other hand, has so little, so little shame, that he don't know how to be honest.

JUANITA: Cowards!

LIDIA: No, definitely not! My Juan is a real man.

JUANITA: A real man when it's convenient for him. But at heart, a coward. Like all o' them who come fleein' from Puerto Rico 'cause they think everythin's easier here. 'Cause they don't know how to face up to life there, in their own land. Yeah, yeah, my brother works. Your husband don't work. But they're both the same. They're our men. The manliest men in the world! The most cowardly!

[DA. CABRIELA *enters through the door at the right in time to hear* JUANITA's *last words.*]

DA. GABRIELA: Sometimes you need a lotta courage to be a coward. Hello, Lidia!

LIDIA: How are you, Doña Gabriela?

[*Takes the bag of groceries from her and carries it to the kitchen.*]

DA. GABRIELA: How's your little girl? She hasn't been here for days.

LIDIA: She started to come down with the flu.

DA. GABRIELA: You do right by takin' care o' her. These days can be fatal.

[*Takes a letter from her pocket.*]

Ah, look, Juanita. We got a letter. Read it to me.

[JUANITA *takes the letter.*]

LIDIA: Oh, how nice! A letter from Puerto Rico!

JUANITA: It's from Uncle Tomás.

[*Tears open the envelope.*]

DA. GABRIELA: He hasn't written for days . . .

LIDIA: If you want, I can go.

DA. GABRIELA: What for, child? A letter from home is no secret for anybody. Sit down.

[*To* JUANITA.]

Let's see. What does he say? What does that uncle o' yours say?

JUANITA: [*Reading.*] "Dear Sister: I hope this letter finds you all well there. Here, thank God, all are well, except the wife, who still has her aches and pains."

DA. GABRIELA: Poor thing! She always was delicate. And I always said so to my brother. "That wife o' yours is gonna be flat on her back after your first kid. She's too narrow in the hips." And I was right.

JUANITA: [*Reading.*] "About Tomasita I can tell you she has good grades in school, but since she's a young lady now, there's no livin' with her."

[*Interrupting her reading.*]

She's quite a girl! Remember the time Tomasita kissed Chaguito and he got so mad?

DA. GABRIELA: Yes, 'cause she slobbered all over him. I suppose now she's given up that habit o' kissin' boys.

[*Laughs.*]

Go on. Go on.

JUANITA: [*Reading.*] "Yesterday I sent you a few pounds of coffee from the farm and some sweet potato preserve. I was gonna send you some oranges too from the tree that the old man planted beside the well, but the post office wouldn't let me 'cause they say the oranges from here can contaminate the American oranges. I must tell you that I intend to buy four more acres of land. They belong to Miguel, Don Tello's helper."

[*Interrupting herself.*]

Miguel!

DA. GABRIELA: Must be his father's little piece o' land.

JUANITA: [*Eagerly reading again.*] "He inherited them from his father, who died two weeks ago . . ."

DA. GABRIELA: Don't tell me he died! Poor Simón!

[*Makes the sign of the cross.*]

May God have him in His Glory.

JUANITA: [*Reading.*] "Miguel wants to sell the four acres and go to New York."

[*Interrupting her reading.*]

No! Don't let him do that!

DA. GABRIELA: Go on! Go on!

JUANITA: [*Reading very slowly, with an unsteady voice.*] "For a long time Miguel has been talkin' about goin' up north to work. But he wants to go to New York, not to Michigan. I think that fellow hasn't been able to forget Juanita . . ."

DA. GABRIELA: Thank you, Blessed St. Anthony![6]

LIDIA: That Miguel, isn't he the one who gave you the model oxcart?

DA. GABRIELA: That's him, all right. But go on. What else does the letter say?

JUANITA: [*Reading with difficulty, her voice trembling from emotion.*] "He still has to straighten out a mess of papers about the inheritance . . ."

[JUANITA *interrupts herself and stands up.*]

LIDIA: What's the matter?

JUANITA: I can't read any more. My throat's dry.

DA. GABRIELA: Go get some water. Go on.

[JUANITA *exits rapidly through the rear.*]

You go on readin', Lidia.

LIDIA: [*Taking the letter.*] Lemme see where she was . . .

[*Looks. Reads to herself.*]

". . . mess o' papers about the inheritance . . ."

[*Out loud.*]

Yeah, here it is.

[*Reads.*]

"So I won't be able to buy the four acres from him for about a month. And I've been thinkin' if you people have in mind to come back, I could let you work that little plot I'm gonna buy and we could share the crops . . ."

DA. GABRIELA: [*Laughing.*] Half! Oh boy, that brother o' mine is too smart! You hear that, Juanita? Seems like they're runnin' out o' share croppers back there in the country.

---

6. Anthony of Padua (1195–1231), also known as Anthony of Lisbon, a very popular saint, invoked especially for the recovery of lost things.

LIDIA: [*Reading.*] ". . . and maybe later Luis could buy those four little acres that really are worth while."

DA. GABRIELA: Oh, well, now that's more reasonable!

LIDIA: [*Reading.*] "If you decide, let me know. Miguel asked me for your address. So when he gets to New York, he'll look you up and you can all talk about everything and everybody back here."

[*Interrupts herself, looks to the rear, and then, approaching* DOÑA GABRIELA, *asks in a low voice.*]

Listen, that Miguel, is he good-lookin?

DA. GABRIELA: [*In a low voice.*] Good-lookin'!

[*Laughing to herself.*]

He's thinner than a rail and he's got a face as serious as one carved on an Indian stone.

[*In a serious tone.*]

But he's very good, you know? And a hard worker. And Juanita likes him.

[*Looking to the rear, in a loud voice, pretending.*]

Well, what's the matter? Go on reading, go on.

LIDIA: [*Reading*] "I hope you receive the coffee and the sweet potato preserve all right. My wife sends you her best wishes. Greetings from me to all of you, and may you receive best regards from your brother who loves you, Tomás."

[LUIS *enters through the door at the right.*]

DA. GABRIELA: That's all? He don't say any more?

LIDIA: No . . .

LUIS: [*Advancing rapidly toward the living room.*] Juanita, my lunch box, I'm goin' now!

[*Entering the living room and seeing* DOÑA GABRIELA.]

Oh, you're back.

[*Looking around.*]

And the other one?

DA. GABRIELA: What other one?

LUIS: The one who came to see Juanita.

LIDIA: He left a while ago.

LUIS: Oh, listen, your husband wants you to go take care o' the kid. She's havin' another coughin' spell.

LIDIA: [*Going to the right.*] Oh, Holy Mother! Again?

DA. GABRIELA: Wait. Wait a minute. I'm gonna get you somethin' for her.

[*Exits through the left.*]

LIDIA: Here, a letter from your uncle.

[LUIS *takes the letter and sits down in the chair at the left to read it.* LIDIA *looks at him, and finally approaches him timidly.*]

Luis . . . Juan didn't say anythin' to you about lookin' for work?

LUIS: Eh?

[*Momentarily raising his eyes from the letter.*]

Your husband? No, he didn't tell me anythin'.

[*Becomes absorbed again in his reading.*]

LIDIA: I'm afraid for Juan. Every day I'm more afraid, Luis.

[DA. GABRIELA *enters from the left with a bottle of rubbing alcohol and a small jar.*]

DA. GABRIELA: Here, child. Give her a good rub-down with warm alcohol. Then rub her little chest and throat good with mentholatum.[7] And then cover her all up good and don't let her get outta bed or get cold. You'll see it'll do her good! God willing, she'll be all better in the morning.

LIDIA: Oh, thanks a lot, Doña Gabriela! May God pay you back.

[*From the stairs are heard confused shouts and the sound of running.*]

FIRST VOICE: The police! The police!

SECOND VOICE: Run, here they come! Run!

VOICE OF POLICEMAN: Stop him! Stop him!

SECOND VOICE: Let him escape. Don't be such cowards!

POLICEMAN: That damned Porto Rican!

THIRD VOICE: [*Dominating the other voices, urgently, desperately.*] Run, man, or they'll kill you!

[LIDIA *and* DA. GABRIELA, *who were heading towards the right, stop.*]

DA. GABRIELA: What's goin' on? What are they shoutin' for? What are those people sayin'?

LIDIA: [*In anguish.*] The police!

[*Frightened.*]

Good God, the police!

[*Then shouting.*]

Juan!

[*Simultaneously with* LIDIA's *scream, six terrible, deafening pistol shots which shake the building are heard.* JUANITA *appears at the rear.* LUIS *jumps up.* LIDIA *escapes from* DA. GABRIELA's *arms and gets as far as the door at the right.* DA. GABRIELA, LUIS, *and* JUANITA *run to stop her.*]

LIDIA: Juan! Juan! Juan!

[LUIS *arrives in time to lean against the door to keep it shut while* DA. GABRIELA *and* JUANITA *grab* LIDIA *and pull her back to the living room.*]

LIDIA: Lemme go! Lemme go!

DA. GABRIELA: You can't go out now, child.

JUANITA: Take it easy, Lidia, for God's sake, take it easy.

LIDIA: Juan! They've killed him on me! I told him. Don't do it, Juan, don't do it! Oh my God! They've killed him on me!

LUIS: I'll go see what's happenin'.

LIDIA: Yes, Luis, go and see. Go and see.

[LUIS *exits.* LIDIA *screams.*]

The kid, Luis, the kid!

[DA. GABRIELA *and* JUANITA *lead her to the sofa.*]

Just like my dreams! Noises and blood! What good is a man's body if it's full o'holes and bleeding? What good is a woman if she can't save her man's body?

[*Rebelling.*]

But nobody had the right to kill him. He only wanted the things that everybody wants.

[*They seat her on the sofa.* DA. GABRIELA *sits down at her right.*]

Nobody had the right to leave me alone again!

---

7. Trademarked ointment that consisted of petroleum jelly and menthol.

[*She sobs noisily, hiding her face in* DA. GABRIELA's *lap.* DA. GABRIELA *caresses her in a motherly way.*]

DA. GABRIELA: You don't know what's happened. Why would they kill your husband? You're just scared from the noise o' the shots. That's all that's the matter. You've just been over frightened. C'mon now. You'll see it wasn't anythin'. Juanita, bring me the rubbin' alcohol.

[JUANITA *brings the bottle of alcohol that* LIDIA *has dropped in the hall.* DA. GABRIELA *rubs some on* LIDIA's *neck.*]

LIDIA: [*Between sobs.*] He wasn't bad, Doña Gabriela, Juan wasn't bad at all.

[LUIS *enters through the right. He appears somber. He advances to the living room and stops.* DA. GABRIELA *and* JUANITA *straighten up instinctively and question him with anguished looks.* LIDIA *feels the weight of the anxious silence and slowly raises her head from* DA. GABRIELA's *lap. With an automatic gesture she pushes away from her face the strands of hair that cover her eyes. She begins to get up, at the same time turning her face very slowly towards* LUIS. *She looks at him for an instant. Then she throws herself at him and shakes him by the shoulders.*]

LIDIA: Say it! What're you waitin' for? Say it!

LUIS: [*Slowly.*] No. It wasn't him.

LIDIA: [*Petrified.*] What?

LUIS: [*Always somber. Without intending to console her.*] It wasn't your husband.

LIDIA: [*Not understanding.*] No? No? It wasn't him?

[*Finally realizing all the joy the news implies for her.*] It wasn't Juan! [*Moves away from* LUIS *and goes shakily to the right.*] Juan!

[*At last giving free rein to her emotions, she begins to run and exits shouting; her voice is a tremor of wild happiness.*]

Juan! Juan! Juan!

DA. GABRIELA: Who was it, Luis?

LUIS: I dunno. Some guy who stole a pocketbook from an American lady in the street.

DA. GABRIELA: But . . . did they kill him?

LUIS: He was runnin' away and he ducked into this buildin'. They filled him full o' lead on the floor upstairs.

DA. GABRIELA: May God pardon him.

[*Makes the sign of the cross and mutters a prayer as she exits through the left.*]

JUANITA: Was he . . . Puerto Rican?

LUIS: Yes.

JUANITA: The scum! To kill a man like that for stealin' . . . !

LUIS: A five-dollar bill, a lipstick, and a dirty handkerchief. That's what was in the pocketbook he robbed from the yankee. But they didn't find neither a gun or a knife on him. Only a medal of the Virgin of the Carmen.[8] And a letter from his mother postmarked in Lares, Puerto Rico. "I'm glad God has helped you and you're getting ahead," the letter said. He was just a kid, but they put six bullets in his chest. To kill him for real! To kill him once and for all!

JUANITA: And you say it so calmly!

---

8. A Roman Catholic saint.

LUIS: [*Abruptly.*]  I'm not calm. I'm not calm inside!

JUANITA: [*Furious.*]  But you *look* like you're calm. And it's the same as if you were. 'Cause a person shows what he feels. And if he don't show it, he's a coward!

LUIS:  So what the hell do you want me to do?

JUANITA:  Show you got blood in your veins. If you feel the same rage I feel, instead o' keepin' it inside, shout it out loud. This way, like me.
[*Opens the window and shouts.*]
Scum! Murderers!

LUIS:  Shut up!
[*Goes to her, pushes her brusquely away, and shuts the window.*]

JUANITA:  And if you feel like breakin' somethin', show it by breakin' it. This way, like I do.
[*Takes the glass that* LIDIA *had left and smashes it against the heater.*]
'Cause a person's gotta protest some way. Somehow you gotta say you don't agree with the things that are goin' on. Somehow you gotta show you got guts and a heart, dignity and pride.
[DA. GABRIELA *enters from the left.*]

DA. GABRIELA:  What's goin' on here, Juanita? What's all this racket?

LUIS: [*Gathering the pieces of glass together with his foot.*]  So now you shouted and you broke somethin'. What good did it do you?

JUANITA:  No good, no good at all. I raise a rumpus and that's it. 'Cause upstairs there they've killed a guy from Lares and it shocks me. It don't matter to anybody else. But it does to me. And I want them to *know* that it matters to me.

DA. GABRIELA:  It matters to all of us, child. He was a human bein'. And besides, he was one of us. But some things just can't be helped. Especially by a woman. And even less by a hysterical woman. 'Cause this is a man's world . . .

JUANITA: [*Interrupting her.*]  Well, let 'em show that it is! If it's theirs, why don't they make it any better? But they don't dare. Don't you see, ma, they're a bunch o' cowards.

LUIS:  Talk. Talk. That's all you know how to do. But it's not enough.

DA. GABRIELA:  It's hard to be a man, Juanita, it's hard!

JUANITA: [*Turning to* LUIS.]  Of course it's not enough just to talk! But at least it's better than bein' quiet and still like you were dead.

DA. GABRIELA:  All right, all right, that's enough. It can't be helped. What can be helped is this mess. Juanita, get the dustpan and pick up those pieces of glass. And the next time you come here, you bring me another glass just like the one you broke.
[JUANITA *exits rear.*]
The next time it occurs to you to shout like a crazy woman or to start breakin' things, I'm gonna beat you silly. You're both gonna see I've still got a ready hand. And you won't forget you're still my kids. My kids will always be my kids, even when their beards reach down to their belly buttons!
[*To* LUIS.]
What's wrong with you? Why're you lookin' at me like that?

LUIS: [*Smiling.*]  You haven't scolded us for so long.

DA. GABRIELA:  And since you forgot how it used to be, now you don't like it.

LUIS: On the contrary. I like it. I like it better than seein' you sad.

DA. GABRIELA: [*Grumbling.*] Sad! Sad! Who's sad? You think to be happy I gotta spend my life dancin' a cha-cha-cha? That'd sure be sad! At my age to have to be smilin' all the time like some little fifteen-year-old chicken. No, boy, no. Those things should be left for silly teen-agers like Tomás' daughter.

[*Interrupts herself.*]

Oh, now that I mention Tomás. I didn't tell you we got a letter from that brother o' mine.

[*Searching.*]

Where's that letter? Where'd Lidia put it?

[LUIS' *face grows somber again.*]

LUIS: I have it.

DA. GABRIELA: Did you read it already?

LUIS: Yes.

[*Sits down in the chair at the left.*]

DA. GABRIELA: [*Trying to hide her anxiety.*] What did you think of it?

LUIS: Well . . . !

DA. GABRIELA: Four acres to share.

LUIS: Bah! Who can live from four acres?

DA. GABRIELA: Yes, that's what I say . . . But it all depends. It's Miguel's father's farm. Good land.

LUIS: Hnnh.

[JUANITA *enters from the rear and begins to pick up the glass from the floor.*]

DA. GABRIELA: And it's got a good well.

LUIS: Yeah . . .

DA. GABRIELA: The best well in the district. The water is sweeter and purer than from Tomás' well.

[*Short pause.*]

A well right on your own farm is a great advantage.

LUIS: Half a farm . . .

DA. GABRIELA: It's true.

[*Pretending indignation.*]

No, if that's the best Tomás can think of. He's a sly one, that brother o' mine.

[*Transition.*]

Of course, he's givin' us the chance to buy the land . . . And meanwhile he'd have to supply us with seeds, and the oxen . . . and the plow . . .

[*Unable to hide her enthusiasm.*]

Tomatoes grow good there. And they bring a good price. What d' you think? It'd be a business.

[*Sitting on the floor at* LUIS' *feet.*]

Naturally I'd help you with the sowing. And you could even find somethin' you liked better to do . . . I'd take care o' the farm. Chaguito gets outta reform school soon. Between him and me we could make somethin' outta that plot o' land. The last time he wrote he said he was in charge o' the vegetable garden. So he's got experience now.

[JUANITA *has finished and has stood up. She watches, moved by her mother's enthusiasm.*]

LUIS: [*Bending down toward* DA. GABRIELA *and staring at her, unable to hide a slight trembling in his voice.*] Mamá, are you happy?

DA. GABRIELA: [*Taken by surprise.*] Eh? Me? Yes . . . Well of course I'm happy!

[JUANITA *looks sharply at* LUIS *and exits rapidly through the rear.*]

LUIS: Do you need anythin'?

DA. GABRIELA: Who me? Heavens, no!

[*Getting up.*]

What am I gonna need!

LUIS: [*Getting up, taking* DA. GABRIELA *by the shoulders and forcing her to look him in the eye.*] Are you sure?

DA. GABRIELA: Of course! Since . . . you give me everythin'. You give me all I could need.

LUIS: [*Smiling.*] I'm glad. Then get my lunch box ready, 'cause it's gettin' late and my shift at the factory starts in a little while.

DA. GABRIELA: Oh, that's right!

[*Moves away from him and goes to the rear.*]

How stupid o' me! Talkin', talkin' and forgettin' what time it is. But don't worry, I'll bring you your lunch box right away, right away.

[*Exits rapidly through the rear.* LUIS *goes to the hooks near the door, takes down a wool plaid hunting jacket and puts it on. Buttoning it, he returns to the living room.* JUANITA *enters from the rear.*]

LUIS: [*Seeing* JUANITA.] I'm glad Miguel's comin'. It's the best thing he could do.

JUANITA: [*Dryly.*] Best for who?

LUIS: For him, of course! And probably for you. I'll send Chaguito his ticket as soon as he gets out . . .

JUANITA: What are you anyway? The Department of Emigration or the Department of Tourism?

LUIS: [*Brusquely.*] I don't care about Emigration or Tourism! What I care about is my family.

JUANITA: [*Ironically.*] And machines! Machines that give life!

LUIS: Yes, I care about that too.

JUANITA: More than the family. Don't deny it. 'Cause we don't have the mystery that machines have. That mysterious thing you're lookin' for and can't ever find.

LUIS: I'll find it . . .

JUANITA: Yeah, you'll find it. Like the treasure hidden by Juan Bobo in the belly o' the iron kettle![9] In the belly o' the machine! The life-givin' machine! And what is a machine? The pistols that fired six shots upstairs a little while ago are machines. Didn't that ever occur to you? They're machines all right. And where's the life they gave?

LUIS: That's different. You don't understand my machines.

JUANITA: No, I don't understand 'em. Thank God I don't. And I hope Miguel and Chaguito never understand 'em either!

[DA. GABRIELA *enters from the rear with the lunch box.*]

DA. GABRIELA: All ready, Luis. Here it is.

---

9. In the Spanish-language cultures of the Americas, many legends feature the hero Juan Bobo, who makes many mistakes but generally has good luck.

[*Hands* LUIS *the lunch box.*]

LUIS: [*Going to the right.*]   Okay. See you this afternoon.

DA. GABRIELA:   The coffee's already got sugar in. Oh, and I put in one o' them canned meat pies for you that Juanita brought.

[LUIS *takes the felt hat that's hanging on the wall and puts it on. He opens the door and is about to go out, but he stops. He hesitates, then turns and goes toward* DA. GABRIELA. *He stops in front of her.*]

LUIS: [*With humble gentleness.*]   Blessing, ma.

DA. GABRIELA: [*Kissing him tenderly.*]   God bless you, my son.

[LUIS *hugs her tightly and exits rapidly through the right.*]

My poor boy! We shouldn't fight with him, Juanita.

JUANITA:   If I fight with him, it's for his own good, mamá.

DA. GABRIELA: [*Returning slowly to the living room.*]   We have to take care o' him. We have to take good care o' him. He's sick.

JUANITA: [*Approaching* DA. GABRIELA.]   Sick?

DA. GABRIELA:   He's sick inside.

JUANITA:   What d' you mean?

DA. GABRIELA:   Somethin' bad is happenin' to him. Haven't you noticed it?

JUANITA:   Well, I know he's changed.

DA. GABRIELA:   Some little worm of sorrow is eatin' away at his heart.

JUANITA:   I'd say it was his mind . . .

DA. GABRIELA:   No, his heart. My son is like a little orphan that's all alone, all alone. And he don't know which way to turn. Like a motherless lamb on the side of a steep rock. He can't go up. And it's a long, long way down . . .

JUANITA: [*Cautiously, with tenderness.*]   Mamá, Luis is . . . an orphan, right? He's not your son . . .

DA. GABRIELA: [*Straightening up, indignant, as if she had been struck.*]   Luis is my son! He's my son!

JUANITA:   Yes, mamá, I know. It's as if he was your son. But he's the son of my father and of . . .

DA. GABRIELA: [*Violent.*]   Quiet!

JUANITA:   Mamá, you can't hide the whole sky with one hand. Those things always get found out . . .

DA. GABRIELA:   And how did you find it out?

JUANITA:   People were talkin' back in the country . . .

DA. GABRIELA:   And they hadda tell you. People are bad, bad!

JUANITA:   What's the difference? I'm a woman, mamá. I understand these things. Anyway it doesn't matter. Luis is my brother. He's always been my brother. Even if he don't know it, I . . .

DA. GABRIELA:   But he does know!

[*Falls into a chair.*]

That's what's so awful, he knows it!

JUANITA: [*Astonished.*]   He knows it?

DA. GABRIELA:   Yes. He's never told me. Some things don't have to be said. But he knows. And for that reason he loves me more. He loves me from gratitude. And that's no good. A child's love for his parents should come from his soul, not from gratitude. And Luis has been too concerned with gratitude. Why do you think he loaded us into the oxcart to take us to La Perla? Why do you think he brought us here? Why do you think he's killin' himself workin' like an animal? 'Cause he wants me to be happy. 'Cause he wants to make me happy whether I want to or not. 'Cause he thinks I'll be happy if I have things I didn't have before. My poor son! How little he knows about happiness!

JUANITA: Mamá, you're a saint!

DA. GABRIELA: [*Getting up, indignant.*]   A saint! A saint! If I was a saint I could've made a miracle and given happiness to that son o' mine. I could've made him not feel the need for a mother. But Luis has always been an orphan. Don't you see he's lost in a world where he don't belong? Don't you realize he's always searchin', like a lost lamb that can't find its mother?

JUANITA: [*Pensively.*]   Can that be what he's lookin' for? Can that be what he's lookin' for in machines, mamá?

DA. GABRIELA:   I dunno. I dunno. I only know it's drivin' him crazy. Crazy from sorrow 'cause he don't find what he's lookin' for.
[*Sobs.*]

JUANITA:   Mamá, mamá, don't cry. We'll take care o' him, mamá. We'll be like two mothers for him.

DA. GABRIELA:   That's why I told you to come live with us. 'Cause I feel so helpless now. 'Cause I can't make him happy.

JUANITA:   Yes, mamá, I'll come and live with you. First thing tomorrow I'll bring my stuff. But now, why don't you lay down a little while and rest? I'll get lunch ready.
[*Knock at the door.* DA. GABRIELA *quickly dries her tears.*]

DA. GABRIELA:   There's somebody there.

JUANITA:   You go in the bedroom. I'll open the door.

DA. GABRIELA:   No, no. You go get the lunch. I'll see who it is.
[DA. GABRIELA *goes to the entrance hall.* JUANITA *hesitates a moment, then exits rear.* DA. GABRIELA *opens the door and* MR. PARKINGTON *enters. He is a tall, thin American about forty years old. He is dressed in black and carries a fall overcoat on his arm. He has a leather briefcase in his hand and an extremely friendly smile on his face.*]

PARKINGTON:   Good day!

DA. GABRIELA:   Good . . .

PARKINGTON:   The lady of the house, no doubt?

DA. GABRIELA:   Can I help you?

PARKINGTON:   If it's no trouble, I'd like very much to talk to you about the Lord.

DA. GABRIELA:   What lord . . . ? The landlord?

PARKINGTON:   The Lord Creator of Heaven and Earth. I have named Jehovah, my dear sister! May I come in?
[*Enters without waiting for an answer.*]
Thank you. You're very kind.
[DA. GABRIELA *looks at him in amazement, shuts the door, and follows him to the living room.*]
[*With a friendly smile.*]
May I sit down, madam?
[*Sits down before* DA. GABRIELA *can indicates for him to do so.*]
Thank you.

JUANITA: [*Out of sight in the kitchen.*]   Who is it, mamá?

DA. GABRIELA:   I dunno. Some American . . .

PARKINGTON:   My name is Parkington, sister.

JUANITA: [*Appearing in the rear doorway with a can of chopped ham in one hand and the opener in the other.*]   What does he want?

DA. GABRIELA:   I'm still waitin' for him to tell me.

PARKINGTON: [*Rising politely on seeing* JUANITA.]   Pleased to meet you, miss.

JUANITA: [*Giving him the once over as she speaks to* DA. GABRIELA.]   Mamá, I've told you not to open the door here to people you don't know.

DA. GABRIELA:   The door o' my house has always been open. If I shut it here it's on account o' the cold. Well, mister, say what you have to say.

[JUANITA *exits rear.*]

PARKINGTON:   Thank you, madam. The hospitality of you Latins is marvellous. I've always said so. Well then, here's my card.

[*Hands it to her and sits down again.*]

As you can see, I represent the Church of God, Incorporated.

DA. GABRIELA: [*Surprised.*]   God incorporated? Incorporated to what?

PARKINGTON:   No, no. God is not incorporated. What's incorporated is the Church.

DA. GABRIELA:   And What does that mean?

PARKINGTON: [*In a tight spot.*]   It means . . . Let's see . . . Incorporated is . . . a corporation.

JUANITA: [*Out of sight in the kitchen.*]   Like the sugar mills, mamá! Like the sugar mills in Puerto Rico!

DA. GABRIELA:   I don't understand. But go on . . .

PARKINGTON:   Well, you must've read about it in the papers . . . it's had magnificent publicity, front page publicity . . . the creation of the Municipal Committee for the Betterment of the Puerto Ricans. The mayor of this great democratic city of New York is terribly interested in you people.

[JUANITA *appears in the doorway and listens sceptically.*]

The mayor, following the doctrine of Jehovah, makes no discriminations between Negroes or whites, rich or poor, Puerto Ricans or Americans.

JUANITA:   Since when?

PARKINGTON: [*Interrupted.*]   What did you say, miss?

JUANITA:   The miss says since when don't the mayor make distinctions.

PARKINGTON: [*In another tight spot.*]   Well . . . Since always. Of course, errors have been made in the past . . . Errors that we all lament . . . It won't happen again! It'll be different from now on.

JUANITA:   How different?

PARKINGTON:   What?

JUANITA:   I said, how will it be different from now on?

PARKINGTON:   Well . . . the betterment of the Puerto Rican colony, miss. So it can be on the same level . . .

[*Realizes he is putting his foot in it.*]

I mean, so it can be equal . . .

[*Bites his tongue in time.*]

Well . . . so it won't be an object of discrimination.

JUANITA: [*Leaning in the kitchen doorway.*]   So they're gonna make us better. They're gonna make us as good as the Americans. That means that we're not any good now, that we're not equal to the rest o' you.

PARKINGTON:   Please, miss! You misunderstand me.

JUANITA:   [*Taking a step forward.*]   Look, mister, what you're sayin' I'd understand even in Chinese. It's as clear as daylight.
[*Looks toward the window and corrects herself.*]
Like the daylight in my country, of course.
[*Exits rear.*]

PARKINGTON:   Oh, what a shame! The girl doesn't understand. But the thing is that the Church of God, Incorporated, is going to cooperate fully with the Municipal Committee for the Betterment of the Puerto Ricans. It's a titanic job, my sister. But we'll do it! You can be sure we'll do it.
[*Takes out some leaflets and keeps handing them to* DA. GABRIELA.]
Our mission is not only religious. It's also social . . .

DA. GABRIELA:   [*Wanting to be pleasant and show an interest in something the visitor proposes.*]   Oh, you're gonna hold dances!

PARKINGTON:   [*Jumping back.*]   Dances?

DA. GABRIELA:   But didn't you say . . . ?

PARKINGTON:   We are part of the Committee for the Betterment of the Puerto Ricans. And we don't solve social problems with dances. What we hold are meetings. And problems are discussed. And orientation work is performed.
[*Takes out another series of folders.*]
The Puerto Ricans must become orientated to this mechanized civilization. They must give up superstitions and idolatry. They must become familiar with the world of machines. Look, here are some very useful folders. They're in Spanish, very well translated.
[*Keeps handing folders to* DA. GABRIELA.]
The Puerto Rican workers must recognize their responsibilities and yield the maximum labor. We orient them. In that way difficulties are avoided. And accidents are prevented. Like the one that just happened there in the boiler factory.

DA. GABRIELA:   In the boiler factory?

PARKINGTON:   Yes, madam, yes. I ran into all the commotion just minutes before coming here.
[JUANITA *appears in the doorway.*]
And all because of carelessness and clumsiness on the part of a Puerto Rican worker. That's why I say . . .

JUANITA:   [*Coming forward.*]   A Puerto Rican worker?

PARKINGTON:   Yes, miss. That's why I say the orientation of the workers is essential in a highly mechanized society.

DA. GABRIELA:   What happened in the boiler factory?

PARKINGTON:   The accident I mentioned. Because New York, as our democratic mayor strongly affirms, opens its arms to the Puerto Ricans. But . . .

JUANITA:   What accident? What accident?

PARKINGTON:   [*Annoyed by the interruptions.*]   But haven't I told you already?

DA. GABRIELA:   [*Terribly upset.*]   No, you haven't said a thing! For the love o' God, tell us what happened!

PARKINGTON:   Well, one of those frequent accidents when you're dealing with people not accustomed . . .

JUANITA: [*Going to him, violently.*]   Cut out the stupid talk and tell us once and for all what happened! What happened in the boiler factory?

PARKINGTON:   But, miss, you won't let me get a word in. It seems that a worker was examining the inside of one of the machines. The machine began to work and the man was trapped among the many steel parts that kept going full speed. The unfortunate fellow's body . . .

[*Violent knocking is heard on the door, and at the same time* LIDIA's *voice is heard calling urgently: "Juanita! Juanita! Juanita, open the door! Juanita!"* JUANITA *runs to the door at the right and opens it.* LIDIA *enters, her expression changed. She tries to speak softly to* JUANITA. DA. GABRIELA *takes a step toward the hall but stops in the living room, her eyes wide open, the fingers of both hands pressed against her lips as if she wanted to prevent something vital from escaping from her body.*]

LIDIA: [*Out of breath, in a low voice.*]   Juanita! Telephone. In the janitor's office It's urgent! Come right away. It's urgent!

[JUANITA *and* LIDIA *exit rapidly through the right.* DA. GABRIELA *goes slowly to the sofa. She stops in front of it, before the image of the Sacred Heart. She falls to her knees and sinks her face in the sofa cushion. We see only her bent back, which moves in rhythm to her difficult breathing.* MR. PARKINGTON, *disconcerted, doesn't know what to do. He finally collects his things quietly. Then he takes a step toward* DA. GABRIELA. *He stops, turns slowly, and exits through the right. Interval. Immobility. Silence.* JUANITA *enters through the right. Then* LIDIA. JUANITA *is very pale, and her movements give the impression of a momentary somnambulism. She slowly enters the living room.* LIDIA, *crying quietly, follows a short distance behind her. When she gets to the end of the hall and sees* DA. GABRIELA *kneeling,* LIDIA *stops and puts both hands to her mouth to drown her sobs. Leaning against the wall, her face between her hands, she cries silently.* JUANITA *keeps going forward. She stops beside* DA. GABRIELA, *and with a look lost in space, says.*]

JUANITA:   The orphan found what he was looking for, mother. Luis finally discovered the mystery of the machines that give life.

[DA. GABRIELA *remains still.* JUANITA *slowly lowers her eyes toward the kneeling figure.*]

Dis you hear what I said, mamá?

[DA. GABRIELA *slowly raises her head and looks at the Sacred Heart.*]

DA. GABRIELA:   Take him to your bosom, Lord. Be a good father to my son!

JUANITA:   They'll take him from the hospital to the nearest funeral parlor. Within an hour we can go see him.

[DA. GABRIELA *gets up.*]

DA. GABRIELA:   I don't want them to bury him in this land of no sunshine. Will it cost much to take him to Puerto Rico?

JUANITA:   It doesn't matter what it costs. We'll do whatever you say.

DA. GABRIELA: [*Nothing* LIDIA's *presence.*]   How's your little girl, Lidia?

[LIDIA *runs and throws herself in* DA. GABRIELA's *arms and sobs convulsively on her shoulder.* DA. GABRIELA *caresses her in a motherly fashion.*]

There. There. Don't cry. My son is happy now. The land where he was born will always be the mother who lets him sleep without toil or sorrow.

[LIDIA *leaves* DA. GABRIELA's *arms, goes more calmly to the hall, dry-ing her tears, and exits right.* DA. GABRIELA *speaks in an illumined tone.*]

Because now I know what was happening to us all. The curse of the land! The land is sacred. The land can not be abandoned. We must go back to what we left behind so that the curse of the land won't pursue us any more. And I'll return with my son to the land from where we came. And I'll sink my hands in the red earth of my village just as my father sunk his to plant the seeds. And my hands will be strong again. And my house will smell once more of patchouli and peppermint. And there'll be land outside. Four acres to share. Even though that's all! It's good land. It's land that gives life. Only four acres. Even if they're not ours!

JUANITA:   They will be ours. They'll be yours, mamá! 'Cause I'm goin' back with you to my village.

DA. GABRIELA:   [*Gently, as if waking from a dream.*]   You? You too? But you always said that from now on you were gonna drive the oxcart of your life wherever you wanted.

JUANITA:   For that very reason, mamá, for that very reason! 'Cause I do drive it wherever I want. And we'll get back before Miguel sells those acres. And if it's true that he wants me, I'll be his wife and the land will be ours. And we'll save Miguel from comin' here in search o' the mystery that killed my brother. And we'll save Chaguito. 'Cause it's not a question o' goin' back to the land to live like we were dead. Now we know the world don't change by itself. We're the ones who change the world. And we're gonna help change it. We're gonna go like people with dignity, like grandpa used to say. With our heads high. Knowin' there are things to fight for. Knowin' that all God's children are equal. And my children will learn things I didn't learn, things they don't teach in school. That's how we'll go back home back home! You and I, mamá, as firm as ausubo trees above our land, and Luis resting beneath it!

DA. GABRIELA:   Yes, just like you say. Like ausubos. As firm as ausubos.

[*Her voice begins to break.*]

Like ausubos that machines can never cut down!

[*Sobs. Her crying, so long held back, breaks forth noisily until her entire body shakes and begins to bend. Little by little* DA. GABRIELA *slips to the floor, beside* JUANITA, *and remains kneeling, then seated on her heels, then bent over herself like a small, insignificant ball, shaken by sobs and pierced by sorrow, at the feet of her daughter who stands firm and decided.*]

CURTAIN

1952

# From The Docile Puerto Rican: Literature and Psychological Reality[1]

## Definition and Demarcation

Docile, from the latin *docilis*, means "obedient" or "fulfilling the wishes of the one who commands."[2] Sainz de Robles cites, among other synonyms of the word, "meek" and "submissive," which seem to be characteristic of the most generally held meaning. For *docility* (the quality of being docile), the same scholar gives us "subordination," "meekness," "submission."[3]

In Roque Barcia's work we find that the word docility is given a broader range of meaning: "Docility is to lack the strength or even the will to put up resistance to what others demand, insinuate, or command; a propensity to obey, to follow the example, the opinion, the advice of others, which arises either from one's own weakness or failings, or from ignorance, or from lack of confidence in one's own intelligence, knowledge, or strength."[4]

From this definition, we can deduce that the submissive, meek, or docile man is necessarily a weak person ("he lacks the strength or even the will") or an ignorant one ("which arises . . . from ignorance") or the victim of a pathetic inferiority complex ("lack of confidence in one's own intelligence, knowledge, or strength").

Having clarified the term semantically, we propose to prove, throughout this essay, the docility or docile quality of the present-day Puerto Rican. Rather than attempt to discover the reasons for this docility, such as weakness, or ignorance, or complexes, or any intricate combination of these three, our purpose here is to provide the kind of data and analysis which can establish a rational proof of his docility.

Since one may explore the theme in practically any aspect of Puerto Rican society, any point of departure is possible. We have chosen contemporary literature as the springboard for an examination of psychological realities, because the literature amply reflects the diverse phenomena of the society in which it is produced.[5] Presuming that our point of departure is valid, any incident within the social structure can serve as a pretext for approaching it.

## The Sound and the Fury of a Psycho-Semantic Problem

When Alfred Kazin, the North American literary critic,[6] irritated the island society with his assertion that the Puerto Rican is docile, the intense guilt complex latent in every colonial society came spectacularly to the surface.[7]

1. Translated by Barbara Bockus Aponte. Except as indicated, all footnotes are the author's. The anthology editors have made minor, stylistic changes to the Spanish-language book titles in the text and notes. They have omitted the author's introductory note, concerning the essay's presentation history and publication history, and they have omitted one of the translator's notes.
2. V. García de Diego, *Diccionario etimológico español e hispánico*.
3. Sainz de Robles, *Diccionario de sinónimos y antónimos*.
4. Roque Barcia, *Gran diccionario de sinónimos castellanos*.

5. Since the present study is not a literary critique, it will allude to works not because of their esthetic value, but because of their theme or their psychological insight.
6. Kazin (1915–1998), part of a group known as the New York Intellectuals, often wrote about the experiences of immigrants in the United States in the early twentieth century. [Anthology editors' note]
7. Kazin's article, published originally in the magazine *Commentary*, was reproduced by the local newspaper, the *San Juan Star*, in two consecutive editions (Feb. 19 and 20, 1960), under the title "A Critical Look at Puerto Rico."

Significantly, the reaction of the North American resident in Puerto Rico was much more violent and more virulently verbalized than that of those to whom the commentary referred. The spectacle must have awakened particular interest in two specialized observers of social phenomena: the sociologist and the psychologist.[8] For the nonspecialized observer, the fact that the Puerto Rican victim should be furiously defended by those who—in the technical sense—could be blamed for his plight proved to be either pathetic or amusing, depending on the humor of the spectator.

It is curious that Alfred Kazin, a literary critic, should make such a judgment without having even been acquainted with Puerto Rican literature.[9] This is not to say that our literature exhibits, *prima facie*, characteristics that might justify a theory of docility. The reader often receives the opposite impression from a superficial or frivolous examination of contemporary literature in Puerto Rico. The amount of physical violence it contains would make the uninformed reader think that it is the expression of an aggressive people. There is no doubt, however, that had he been able to read Spanish, Alfred Kazin, an acute critic, would have found his judgment of the Puerto Rican confirmed. He had only to look beyond the surface manifestations of misspent physical energy and violence.

In any event, it is amazing to find that even today the docility of the Puerto Rican is insistently and childishly denied. The problem may be a semantic one. Sociologists, writers, educators, and even so-called "average" citizens have repeated ad nauseam, since the decade of the forties, that the Puerto Rican is *peaceful* and *tolerant*. Previously, he used to be called *fatalistic* and *resigned*. And before that, he had come to be characterized as *aplatanado*[1] and *ñangotado*.[2]

Pedreira was one of those who pointed out our touching weakness for the euphemism, which had been transformed by that time—the decade of the thirties—into the doubtful art of "sugar-coating the pill."[3] Progress, industrialization, and a high standard of living have neither eliminated nor diminished this tendency toward euphemism. Instead, the last thirty years have only intensified it. To see this, one need only look at the words mentioned above in their chronological sequence: the *aplatanado* and *ñangotado* of the twenties, became, in 1930, *resigned* and *fatalistic*; they then evolved with sly hypocrisy into *peaceful* and *tolerant*, the fashionable words today. However, it is the present-day politician in collaboration with an occasional complacent sociologist who has carried the concept to the limit of euphemistic expression: the docile Puerto Rican has come to be, for them, nothing more nor less than *democratic*.

---

8. We think it would be of great interest for the social scientist to carry out an intense and thorough study of the colony of North American residents in Puerto Rico. The ways of thinking, attitudes, and behavior of these people, who for the most part never or only precariously adapt to the Puerto Rican cultural structure, are a rich quarry for sociological exploration. Some of the so-called Puerto Rican problems, sociopolitical as well as psychological, could be clarified and better understood in the light of the results of such a study. Writers and journalists, without technical apparatus, have attempted several impressionistic studies of this type. Nevertheless, from the strictly scientific point of view, the field is virgin. It is of primary importance that it be explored, if we are to reach a complete understanding of present-day Puerto Rico.

9. The North American critic has confessed to me that he was not aware when he wrote his article that Puerto Rico had a national literature.

1. Crushed, in a moral sense; submissive.

2. Squatting, in a spiritual sense. (Both terms, linguistic inventions of the Puerto Rican when he still permitted himself the luxury of self-knowledge, are, in themselves, revealing of his psychology.)

3. Antonio S. Pedreira, *Insularismo* (1st ed.; Madrid: Tipografía Artística, 1934).

*Democracy* and *democratic*, terms which are up for grabs, can be used today to adorn almost any concept or situation, in both the Eastern and Western worlds. In Puerto Rico, they are often used by politicians as one more synonym for peaceful, tolerant, resigned, fatalistic, aplatanado, or ñangotado. Thus the Puerto Rican is praised as "democratic" when he tolerates, with asinine docility, what no civilized person would dream of tolerating in any modern democracy. If "aplatanado" was a stinging ethical barb in the stagnant colonial soul, its newest synonym—democratic—is a narcotic drug mercifully administered to quiet the conscience of the docile Puerto Rican so that he may accept, without scruple, his abject condition.

Alfred Kazin's error was to be unaware of this tendency of the present-day Puerto Rican to avoid calling things by their right names—a form of escapism. By using the term *docile* to describe in English a condition which only can be described, with precision, by this term, he forced a pill without sugar-coating into the Puerto Ricans' twisted colonial mechanism. What does the machine of the spirit (or, if one prefers, of the intellect) do when it is forced to stop and consider that what its gears assimilate as peaceful, tolerant, and democratic is nothing but the offensive word, docile? The machine of the intellect (or of the spirit, as one chooses) cannot adjust unexpectedly to assimilate such raw material. It expells the bitter foreign matter with a great grinding of gears—inoffensive belchings of every hypersensitive machine—and resumes the absorption of the usual pills coated with their precious sugar; pacific, tolerant, democratic.

There is no way that the psychosemantic conflict can obscure a fact now known and accepted, under different names and in distinct historic periods, by the subject himself: the Puerto Rican is a docile being.

There is no reason to undertake here an analysis of the causes which have produced such a condition, something already attempted in a commentary on Kazin's article.[4] Of greater importance now is to face the fact itself, independently of its causes, so as to be able to observe its repercussions in some expressions of Puerto Rican life.

### The Korean War: Myth or Reality?

Few things are more disturbing than the discussion about Puerto Rican heroism in the Korean War. What disturbs us—we should make clear—is our total ignorance about an experience which has had such important psychological, social, and perhaps even political consequences in Puerto Rican life today. No one in Puerto Rico knows what happened in Korea to the Puerto Ricans, or putting it in another way, what happened to the Puerto Ricans in the North American Army in Korea. The white paper (or the blue, red, or black) on that historic episode from the Puerto Rican point of view has not been written. Sociologists, historians, and psychologists have ignored the war as a collective Puerto Rican phenomenon. The few available statistics could perhaps give us exact figures on this or that, but they reveal nothing about the fundamental facts. What happened in Korea? What was the attitude of the "average" Puerto Rican toward his war experience? What was his reaction to the *issue* involved; to the army he was a part of; to the

---

4. The *San Juan Star*, Tuesday, March 8, 1960. * * *

citizenship for which he was contributing, without representation, his own blood; to the Korean people for whose presumed liberty he was fighting? Why was there such a high proportion of the mentally unbalanced—to use one more euphemism—among our Korean veterans? What was the consensus of the North American officers about their Puerto Rican soldiers? And that of the Puerto Rican soldiers about their North American officers? Why did the Korean War cause the permanent dissolution of the 65th Infantry Regiment, until then and for many years the only unit in the North American Army composed entirely of Puerto Ricans?

Until a thorough investigation can give us reliable answers to these questions, we will continue to find disturbing the fact that some Puerto Ricans, the majority of them now dead, mutilated, or psychopathic, received, as individuals, medals in the Korean conflict; we are even more disturbed by the monumental ignorance—better yet, tremendous indifference—of our social scientists concerning the collective phenomenon of the Puerto Rican in Korea.

Since the social sciences have shed no light on the question, we must turn to literature for a glimpse of facts which could only be documented by certain papers buried in some United States Army files in Washington, if they still exist. Fortunately, a young writer, Emilio Díaz Valcárcel, a Korean veteran, has recreated the collective experience in several of his short stories. "El Soldado Damián Sánchez,"[5] a good example of his treatment of the theme, reflects, not the myth of heroism, but the psychology of the weak and docile man, the perfect antihero. The protagonist, part of a military unit composed mainly of North Americans, has as his only friend a South Korean soldier, perhaps because he has found in him affinities to his own condition as a Puerto Rican. But Damián finds himself trapped to the point of exasperation by the prejudices, abuses, and injustices he suffers at the hands of his North American companions and officers. Instead of reacting against them, he relieves his fury, in a seemingly illogical way, by unjustly, viciously, and cruelly beating up his Korean friend, the only person who, at that moment, he can consider weaker or "inferior."

The psychological mechanism of a weak and docile man has seldom been dramatized so acutely and so accurately. The story gives us the key to why a "peaceful" and "tolerant" society like the Puerto Rican can produce a literature of violence. The violent acts of literary characters—and these abound in all the prose genres—are not, in the last analysis, the product of a revolutionary doctrine, of a heroic tradition, of a conscious and shining defiance, or of a normal and healthy aggression. Rather these acts arise from the desperation of weak and docile beings cornered in the last redoubt of human dignity.

The Nationalist movement inspired several works which better illustrate this kind of behavior. The protagonist of the short story "Lamuerte" does not take a stand, in the political-heroic sense, on the Ponce Massacre.[6] He accepts the fact of death as an existential solution, and his action, judged by common standards, could be called passive. Michel Lefranc, ex-university professor in the play by the same author, *Un niño azul para esa sombra*, is only

5. *Asomante*, no. 3 (1956).
6. René Marqués, *Otro Día Nuestro* (San Juan: Imprenta Venezuela, 1955).

a weak if not docile intellectual whom direct action—the one and only aggressive gesture in his life—leads to destruction. An exception to this rule of violence arising from exasperation is the short story, "El juramento," in which the docile personality of the Puerto Rican is carried to its furthest and most absurd consequences.[7] Here the violence of which the character is a victim does not provoke any aggressive action on his part. The protagonist—significantly unnamed—is not even a Nationalist. An innocent bystander, he nonetheless becomes a victim of the official version of the 1950 revolt and of the McCarthian[8] juridical doctrine of "guilt by association." Once trapped within the implacable mechanism of the state which devours him, he remains inert, accepting his situation with characteristic fatalism. He observes with cynical lucidity all the absurd details of the process which crushes him, incapable, nevertheless, of any initiative which might help to alter the course of his destiny. Aside from the fact that the author might have intended to dramatize or symbolize a universal problem of contemporary man, the psychology of the character and the social, political, and juridical details which set that psychology in motion are authentically Puerto Rican. Their verisimilitude only becomes clear upon studying the Puerto Rican within the context of his cultural environment at a specific moment in time.

### Nationalism and Annexationism: The Self-Destructive Impulse

In real life and in literature the Nationalist phenomenon dramatizes another psycho-social problem: the Puerto Rican's notorious self-destructive impulse, his suicidal tendency. Is repressing or inhibiting the normal aggressive impulse so as to direct it morbidly toward oneself a characteristic of docile people and nations (read ñangotados, tolerant, democratic)? The matter is perhaps debatable, but until an authority on psychology proves the contrary, we can accept it as a characteristic of the psychological picture of docility.

The literature of the last twenty years in Puerto Rico contains, as has been recently noted, an alarming number of suicides, either literal or potential.[9] It might be said that the phenomenon is a feature of contemporary Western literature. But there is an interesting statistic which can explain the fact within the island limits: Puerto Rico has the highest suicide rate of any Catholic country in the world.[1]

---

7. Ibid.
8. Related to Wisconsin senator Joseph McCarthy (1908–1957), who in the late 1940s and early 1950s investigated and attacked U.S. citizens, such as government employees, as Communists. 1950 revolt: a failed uprising by Puerto Rican Nationalists, in October of that year. [Anthology editors' note]
9. See the prologue to the anthology Cuentos puertorriqueños de Hoy (San Juan: Club del Libro de Puerto Rico, 1959).
1. United Nations, Demographic Yearbook, 1951. One can discover recent official attempts to sugar-coat this pill by assuring us that such facts are already out of date. In fact, Eric Fromm was invited last year to study suicide in Puerto Rico, and with exemplary politeness the hosts hastened to inform their future guest publically that the

situation had gotten considerably better. We do not know if Fromm accepted the invitation, but we hope that, if he agrees to do the study, he takes two facts into consideration: the decline in population growth in Puerto Rico and the emigration to the United States, a tide that carries with it a considerable number of those social classes most susceptible to expressing their self-destructive impulses in literal or physical suicide. Any contemporary study would be more truthful if it were to include the emigrant Puerto Rican population with less than five years of residence in the United States, that is to say, the group which still conserves its psychological links to the homeland. Fromm, like a good psychologist, will also be sure to examine two questions which already concern some Puerto Rican psychiatrists: Is the high and ever-growing incidence of automobile accidents

The Third Theater Festival (1960), aside from its possible dramatic merits, did reflect this circumstance, giving us at least one suicide in five of the six works presented. Earlier, the three local dramas most warmly received by the public during the last twenty years—*Tiempo Muerto, La Carreta,* and *Los Soles Truncos*—dramatized the suicidal tendency without any ambiguity. In the narrative genres, our most brilliant short story writers of the moment—José Luis González, Abelardo Díaz Alfaro, Pedro Juan Soto, and Emilio Díaz Valcárcel, among others—without even touching the Nationalist phenomenon, emphasize the suicidal impulse of the Puerto Rican. *Spiks,* a collection of stories about Puerto Ricans in New York, and *El asedio* are typical.[2]

Puerto Rican Nationalism undoubtedly reveals the suicidal psychology most clearly. One need only glance at the violence of the Nationalists in the last thirty years. Except for the political assassination of Col. Riggs[3]—the only time when they achieved their immediate objective—the Nationalists' assaults have resulted in a series of spectacular failures. What psychological flaw has made these patriotic, determined, and bold armed men fail in each one of their many attempts at political terrorism? The key must lie in the irrational suicidal impulse that dragged them into action. The real objective was not to kill or, even less, to achieve victory, but to die. Besides obvious cases like the Ponce Massacre, the assault on Blair House in Washington[4] can be seen as clearly suicidal, not because of the objective certainly, nor even because of the risks involved, but because of the way in which the Nationalists tried to reach their objective. True revolutionaries, bold but politically disciplined within a freedom-seeking movement, or professionals in political terrorism, ready to risk their lives but without the obsession or the resolute purpose of dying, would probably have achieved what turned out to be impossible for the Puerto Rican Nationalists.

Perhaps we should conclude that the cohesiveness of the Nationalist movement in its years of greatest activity was based more on a psychological condition common to its members—the suicidal impulse of the Puerto Rican carried to its greatest extreme—than on a revolutionary doctrine or on a terrorist methodology. Indeed, the Nationalist movement had no methodology. Compare the planned, methodical, and effective political terrorism of the Algerian underground or of the Cypriot liberation movement—target chosen, target hit—with the erratic terrorism, unmethodical and useless—suicidal, in short—of Puerto Rican Nationalism.[5]

---

in Puerto Rico—against which neither the sanctions of the law nor the so-called civic educational campaigns help—one more manifestation of the Puerto Rican's self-destructive impulse? Is this Puerto Rican madness at the steering wheel which so astounds and alarms the foreigner, in the last analysis, a clear symptom of a suicidal tendency? Personally, we think so. (Now, in 1966 [the year this essay was published in Marqués's collection *Ensayos* (Essays)], we can state that Eric Fromm never carried out that study under the auspices of the Puerto Rican Government.)
2. Pedro Juan Soto, *Spiks* (Mexico: Los Presentes, 1956); Emilio Díaz Valcárcel, *El asedio* (Mexico: Editorial Arrecife, 1958).
3. In San Juan in 1936, Colonel Francis E. Riggs,

of the Puerto Rico Police Department, was shot and killed by two Nationalist Party members, who were retaliating for police officers' killing of four Nationalists. [Anthology editors' note]
4. In 1950, two Nationalists attempted to enter Blair House, at the time the temporary residence of U.S. president Harry S. Truman (1884–1972), and were killed by security guards. *Ponce Massacre:* In Ponce in 1937, the Puerto Rican police disrupted a Nationalist Party parade, killing 19 people and wounding more than 200. [Anthology editors' note]
5. This analysis of the suicidal tendency in its Nationalist manifestation cannot conceal nor even detract from the importance of Nationalism in contemporary Puerto Rican political history.

The Nationalist suicidal impulse, which could be described by the euphemism "martyr complex," appears in various literary works. The theme is introduced for the first time in the short story which gives its title to the already mentioned volume *Otro día nuestro* (1955), and it is repeated successively, in the theater, with *Palm Sunday* (1956) by René Marqués, *Encrucijada* (1958) by Manuel Méndez Ballester, *El final de la calle* (1959) by Gerard Paul Marín, and *Un niño azul para esa sombra* (1960) by René Marqués; in the novel, with *La ceiba en el tiesto* (1956) by Enrique A. Laguerre, *Los derrotados* (1957) by César Andreu Iglesias, and *El gigante y el alba* (1959) by Ricardo Cordero.[6]

But the Nationalists[7] are not the only ones in the contemporary Puerto Rican political arena who dramatize the self-destructive impulse. Certainly their case is the more spectacular one since it involves physical suicide. Nevertheless, on the opposite extreme, the assimilationists, the Commonwealth partisans, and the annexationists reveal clear suicidal symptoms in varying degrees. With them, however, the irrepressible impulse toward self-destruction manifests itself not on the physical but on the moral and spiritual planes. It we take, as a pretext, two opposing ideologies, the Nationalist and the annexationist, we will find that they coincide in their urgent desire for self-destruction. The gesture of the Nationalist who attacks Blair House in search of death is as suicidal as that of the annexationist who attacks his own Puerto Rican essence in search of a moral and spiritual death. Ideologically, they appear as opposites, but psychologically they are kindred Puerto Rican souls.

---

When one views the phenomenon from a historical perspective, it can be seen that the immediate failure of Nationalism in its years of greatest activity was compensated for by its decisive and determining influence on all political activity after the decade of the thirties. As a defensive reaction, neither local colonial politics nor those of Washington failed to take into account the existence of the Nationalist movement. One can state that, in good measure, the colonial reforms granted in block under the name of the Commonwealth are the result of this reaction. One of the decisive cards played in Washington to hasten the approval of the new formula was the political threat, still latent at that time, posed by the Puerto Rican Nationalist Party. This makes one think that if Nationalist terrorism had been effective in the key years of their activity, it would have achieved the political objective which was the basis of their ideology. One can observe, as well, that in spite of the campaign of the last twenty years to defame and discredit it, of the official persecution and reprisals, of the disappearance of the Nationalists as an active political group, of the pragmatic, materialistic, and utilitarian attitudes which are fostered in our young people, and of the social atmosphere hostile to that ideology, it still holds a fascination for school and university groups. Apparently, then, one can be sure, up to a certain point, of its survival in the new generations. This is natural, since the fascination which Nationalism holds for the Puerto Rican is perhaps more psychological than ideological. There will always be Puerto Ricans, who, just because they are Puerto Ricans, will feel they must assume the collective guilt complex, thus aggravating to the hilt their self-destructive impulses.

6. The dates given in the text refer to the first staging of the plays. *Palm Sunday*, staged: not yet published. *Encrucijada*: Teatro Puertorriqueño (San Juan: Instituto de Cultura Puertorriqueña, 1959). *El final de la calle*, staged; not yet published. *Un niño azul para esa sombra* in René Marqués, *Teatro* (Mexico: Editorial Arrecife, 1959). *La ceiba en el tiesto* (San Juan: Biblioteca de Autores Puertorriqueños, 1956). *Los derrotados* (Mexico: Los Presentes, 1956). *El gigante* (Barcelona: Ediciones Rumbos, 1959).
7. Subsequent to this essay (written in 1960), Pedro Albizu Campos [see p. 445] died in San Juan on April 21, 1965. Thousands of persons of all ideologies and economic and social classes filed by his coffin lying in state in the Ateneo Puertorriqueño. According to the calculations of the North American press in San Juan, sixty thousand Puerto Ricans came to his funeral, the largest and most impressive in the history of Puerto Rico. Thus, they paid posthumous tribute to the man who dedicated and sacrificed the major part of his life to the greatest and noblest ideal a country may have; its national independence. After the funeral honors in the Cathedral and in the very old and historic Church of San José, bombarded by the North Americans in 1898, he was buried in the old Cemetery of San Juan, near the tomb of the poet and patriot José de Diego, at the foot of El Morro's centenary walls. After his death, as happens in those cases, the figure of Albizu Campos has achieved even greater stature, as a symbol of the real Puerto Rico. Today, at the end of 1965, his phrase that "one's country is courage and sacrifice" is being widely adopted as a motto by a considerable number of young Puerto Ricans.

\* \* \*

There is a difference between them. The Nationalist almost always literally accomplishes his purpose: he dies violently. The annexationist, on the other hand, is a living dead man, a never completely realized suicide, a man self-condemned to destroy himself slowly as a Puerto Rican without ever achieving his goal. He cannot totally destroy his Puerto Rican being while he still lives and breathes. The annexationist's pathetic state of eternal self-condemnation explains the degree of self-betrayal, humiliation, and servility which he can on occasion achieve in his suicidal determination to annual or destroy his Puerto Rican personality.

The phenomenon reaches its highest level of absurdity in the black annexationist. Born in a culture where racial prejudice has been kept, in this century of bloody conflicts, at a very low level, he struggles desperately and suicidally to destroy those cultural patterns of human sociability in order to merge his country into a foreign culture where prejudice against the black reaches levels of hate, cruelty, and savagery never experienced in contemporary Puerto Rican society.

Significantly, among the founders of Puerto Rican annexationism at the beginning of the century, there were several blacks who were intelligent, cultured, and proud, moreover, of their race and of their condition as Puerto Ricans. This makes the paradox even more dramatic.[8] Significantly, also, it can be stated with certainty that most blacks in Puerto Rico are annexationists. There is no doubt that in the black Puerto Rican the suicidal impulse is more acute than in the white, since today annexationism means for him an even greater degree of self-destruction than physical death signifies for the white.

How can one explain such a complex paradox? Or would it be more appropriate to ask: what psychological mechanism has the black Puerto Rican annexationist developed to reconcile his inescapable racial condition with his suicidal political ideology? The mechanism is simple and it is not, certainly, peculiar to the black, but functions equally well in the white Puerto Rican. In the former, however, the phenomenon is most obvious, which makes analysis easier.

This mechanism consists of the atrophying of the rational power of association in certain zones of the intellect. There develops a comfortable and

8. At the end of the last century the North American Constitution and its Bill of Rights (the latter incorporated as an imitation of the fundamental document of the French Revolution) were the sun which dazzled many Puerto Rican liberals: a natural reaction to the long years of authoritarian rule under Spanish domination. Their dazzlement by the democratic principles of the North American nation prevented some Puerto Ricans from clearly examining sociopolitical realities and obvious imperialist tendencies which admirers of and believers in democracy such as [José] Martí [see p. 265] and [Ramón Emeterio] Betances [p. 228] did not fail to perceive in the powerful organism of the United States of North America. It was in this way that a handful of autonomists and separatists under the Spanish regime, who did not have the vision of Martí, became, with the change in Puerto Rican sovereignty, the first proponents of annexationism or statehood-ism under the North American regime. Moreover, at the beginning of the century, the men who defended statehood believed in good faith that they were dealing with a purely political problem. The possibility of the moral, cultural, and spiritual destruction of a people by psychological means was an idea foreign to some cultured Puerto Ricans of that time. Now that the century has progressed, however, and has put two world wars behind it, the moral coercion of propaganda has been elevated to the status of a science, and the techniques of psychological aggression have been raised to their most subtle level of refinement. The brain washing and spiritual manipulation of individuals and nations are tangible realities from which man cannot escape in the atomic age. In this era of "supercivilization," unknown to the annexationists at the beginning of the century, moral, cultural, and spiritual destruction at the hands of a dominating nation is a more *real and immediate* menace for a nation than the obsolete destruction by physical means.

convenient incapacity to associate or relate intellectually certain situations, facts, and ideas. It is in this way that the black annexationist lets the tragedy of Little Rock[9] slide off his dark skin, as well as the lynchings of blacks in the South, and the racial war in certain sectors of New York and Chicago without associating, even remotely, these sociopolitical expressions of the culture of the United States with his condition as a black Puerto Rican who aspires to become a black North American.

We repeat, nevertheless, that the strange phenomenon is not peculiar to the black annexationist. The "average" Puerto Rican, whatever his race, can read a novel, see a movie, or follow a television series whose theme may be the struggle for the freedom of a country which is or was colonial (Ireland, Cyprus, Cuba, Poland, Algeria, or the thirteen American colonies, for example) without it occurring to him, even remotely, to relate what he reads, sees, or hears to the colonial condition of his own country.

It would be an error to believe that this psychological blindness afflicts the "average" citizen exclusively. Most Popular Democratic or Commonwealth intellectuals in Puerto Rico contemptuously characterize the concepts of country and freedom as *obsolete*, the believers in national sovereignty as *deluded* and *crazy*, the Nationalists as *assassins*, and as *romantics* those who place the dignity of man on a higher level than the mere digestive process. These are the same intellectuals who publicly, joyously, and noisily supported Fidel Castro and his 26th of July movement. They never stopped to observe that those revolutionary peasants were obsolete, deluded, crazy, nationalists, assassins, and romantics, in precisely the way they—the believers in the Commonwealth—had used the terms. Thanks to the mechanism we are speaking of, the Popular Democratic intellectuals could fervidly praise in Cuba what they condemned with equal fervor in Puerto Rico without being at all conscious of the flagrant contradiction in their attitude.[1] This psychological block, this notorious incapacity to associate situations, facts, and ideas intellectually, should now be considered typical of the Puerto Rican personality.

Literature spreads a strange veil of silence over the annexationist phenomenon itself. It could be argued that this is because Puerto Rican writers uphold—almost to a man—the ideal of independence or, said in another way, because virtually no Puerto Rican citizen deserving the name of writer is annexationist. The argument is perhaps valid, but it is still a little superficial. Nothing would prevent the pro-independence writer from touching on the annexationist phenomenon in order to condemn it in his work. Why, then, doesn't he do it? It is impossible to argue that the theme is not literary material since the Puerto Rican annexationist, as a human being, is a tremendously pathetic character, capable, therefore, of being transformed into a literary creation.

It seems that it is not political prejudice on the part of the creator nor the sterility of the raw material which causes the inhibition, but an ethical

9. City in Arkansas where, in 1957, U.S. federal troops had to enforce a school-desegregation order because of threats against black school-children. [Anthology editors' note]
1. It seems unnecessary to point out that as soon as the North American Department of State opened fire on the Cuban Revolutionary Government, the Fidelist enthusiasm of these Puerto Rican intellectuals rapidly faded away. Today Pan American bureaucratic planners in Washington can count on no more steadfast opponents of Fidel than they.

problem. The theme provokes a strange sensation of shyness in the writer. It is as if he felt that annexationism would contaminate his writing. Writers who have handled the most risqué themes skillfully and boldly, and who have probed with cruel objectivity, and without scruple, the miseries of the Puerto Rican and his society, hold back from the annexationist theme with something very akin to repugnance. They do not even deem it worthy of attack. The ethical man's sacred horror of such a doctrine, although comprehensible in many ways, is creating a gap in contemporary Puerto Rican literature which must be filled. The mission of the writer is always that of revealing, clarifying, and illuminating. No phenomenon is so in need of revelation, clarification, and illumination for the benefit of the very slightly illuminated Puerto Rican as the psychological phenomenon of annexationism. The writer should never refuse to pick up the glove which reality, in a mocking gesture, throws at this feet.[2]

### Synthesis of Puerto Rican Psychology: The Commonwealth Ideal

The two extreme phenomena—Nationalism and annexationism—which we have examined in the political field, have somewhat complex psychological mechanisms. Nevertheless, it is in the middle road, that of the Commonwealth, that Puerto Rican docility finds its most comfortable and natural expression, free of psychological complications. This political monster strikes us as brilliant, not for the reasons given by its eulogizers, but because it has been able, in an almost doctrinaire fashion, to mimic the psychological make-up of the people who are its raison d'être. The Commonwealth is, in fact, the authentic expression of compromise, the embodiment of euphemism, the finished product of the spurious art of sugar-coating the pill; in other words, it is the psychological synthesis of the weak, timid, and docile man.

Those who accuse its supposed creator[3] of having an Anglo-Saxon mentality do not seem to understand that only an authentic docile Puerto Rican could accommodate in a single political formula the most keenly felt psychological vices of the Puerto Rican. When the present supporter of the formula affirms, for demagogical ends, that the Commonwealth is not his creation, but that of the Puerto Rican people, he is more correct than he himself, honorably, would want to admit. On the other hand, when the Commonwealth adherents declare that this formula reflects the inescapable economic reality

2. On a non-literary level the historian Isabel Gutiérrez del Arroyo has made a very neat attempt to clarify annexationism in her *Razones de una sinrazón*, a work originally published in the newspaper *El Mundo* (1959) and then printed in the form of pamphlet under the title of *¿Puerto Rico estado federado?* (Barcelona: Imprenta Suño, 1960).

3. Supporter or present sponsor would be more exact. Already in 1922 the Union Party of Puerto Rico, oriented ideologically until his death, a few years before, by Luis Muñoz Rivera [see p. 296], had included this political compromise in its platform, and under the same name. Twenty years later, in 1942, three Puerto Ricans who were active in the Popular Democratic Party then in power (Rafael Cordero, Enrique Campos del Toro, and Miguel Guerra Mondragón) proposed to the

then North American governor of the island, Rexford G. Tugwell, the old reformist formula of the Union Party. They alleged that the Puerto Rican people were not yet ready for statehood and that the Commonwealth would serve as a preparation for future statehood. (This revelation was made by one of the guiding thinkers of annexationism today, the ex-liberal and ex-progressive Rexford G. Tugwell, in his book, *The Art of Politics* [New York: Doubleday, 1958].) In one way or another it was not until 1952 that the compromise measure, conceived by the three Puerto Ricans mentioned above as a transitional stage toward statehood, became reality under the leadership of Luis Muñoz Marín. Muñoz Rivera's political legacy, taken up by his son, was thirty years in consolidating itself as the psychological expression of the Puerto Rican people today.

of Puerto Rico, they are simply rationalizing a more inescapable, authentic, and determining reality: the psychological one. The elevation of his docility to the rank of political dogma was precisely what the Puerto Rican needed to exist spiritually and morally within his traditional ñangotamiento[4] without remorse or scruples of conscience.

The Commonwealth itself, as a political doctrine, has scarcely had a place in Puerto Rican literature. The only panegyrist of the colonial status quo has been José A. Balseiro, in his novel *En vela mientras el mundo duerme*.[5] Although it does not amount to an apologia, Enrique A. Laguerre also reveals certain Commonwealth-oriented postures or attitudes in some passages of *La ceiba en el tiesto*.[6]

On the other hand, it is not necessary for the Puerto Rican writer to focus directly on the Commonwealth in order to express its political and ethical nature. Almost all Puerto Rican literature of recent years—even that prior to 1952, the year of the latest colonial reforms—has an admonitory tone which is usually accusing and often prophetic in its comments on the present political system. In this sense it can be said that Puerto Rican literature during the last two decades—before and after the Commonwealth—has been fundamentally anti-Commonwealth. This is understandable, since the writer—rebel without a cause—will never be able to conciliate, in Puerto Rico or in any other society of the civilized world, his ethical concept of freedom and human dignity with the anti-ethical reality of colonialism under whatever name or circumstances it may be produced.

### The Authoritarian Cultural Pattern

If one undertakes a superficial examination of the world of Puerto Rican officialdom, one will soon see that beneath the epithet of "democratic" a gigantic political machine functions, docilely, without any difficulty, run entirely according to an authoritarian pattern. When our social scientist is forced to perceive the anomaly of the situation, he uses the euphemism "paternalism" to describe it. (The occasions in which he has the capacity, will, and courage to perceive it are apparently not very frequent, since he rarely informs us of it.)

Paternal or authoritarian—that, in the last analysis, is the psychosocial pattern which prevails in Puerto Rico's apparently democratic society. This fact is the daily bread of our public life, and it would be pointless to attempt a list of examples. It is enough to mention the absolute and infantile dependence of the Puerto Rican legislature on the executive power, a psychological and cultural fact which mocks in a tropical fashion the wise and serious constitutional postulates imported from other climes and other psychologies.

But whoever thinks that authoritarianism is limited to the career-politician mentality in the government ought to turn his eyes to a supposedly more intellectual and cultured environment: the University of Puerto Rico. He will note the strange submission of the faculty to the authoritarian patterns im-

4. *Translator's note*: This is the noun form of *ñangotado*. [See note 2, p. 655.]
5. José A. Balseiro, *En vela mientras el mundo duerme* (San Juan: Biblioteca de Autores Puer-

torriqueños, 1953).
6. After publication of that work in 1956, however, this author seems to have evolved ideologically toward a position favoring independence.

posed by the administration in spite of the recently established and so widely proclaimed Academic Senate. In this case a curious factor intervenes which serves to reinforce Puerto Rican docility: the total identification of most of the European and South and North American professors—a large group at present—with the authoritarian politics of the administration. This is a comprehensible reaction given the sense of insecurity which the foreigner experiences on finding himself unexpectedly thrust into a cultural structure strange to him and even, perhaps, hostile, depending on his own complexes and resentments as an exile.[7]

The authoritarian pattern is not exclusive to official spheres; it permeates all groups in Puerto Rican society. In political parties, labor unions and syndicates, professional associations, civil organizations, and cultural institutions, power tends to be concentrated and perpetuated, often in one person. The democratic process, followed externally and mechanically—with meticulous and pathetic scrupulosity on occasion—is only a polite fiction to hide the real situation: unmitigated authoritarianism. Thus it is not rare to see puppet directors and presidents in organizations in which the dictator, with sly hypocrisy, finds it expedient to hide his power "behind the throne." A de jure democracy and a de facto authoritarian government—this is an exact description not only of the Puerto Rican state but of all those groups organized more or less on the margin of direct political influence.[8]

The authoritarian pattern, in a good number of its expressions or manifestations, appears directly or indirectly, consciously or unconsciously, in almost all our contemporary literature. The short stories of Miguel Meléndez Muñoz, Emilio S. Belaval, Abelardo Díaz Alfaro, and José Luis González emphasize the theme. It concerned Laguerre in several of his novels, and especially in *La llamarada*, Méndez Ballester in one of his first dramas, *Tiempo muerto*, Pedro Juan Soto in his recent *Usmaíl*, and René Marqués in *La muerte no entrará en Palacio*, this last a tragedy where the problem is explored directly in its current manifestation: de facto authoritarianism masked by a de jure democracy.[9]

### The Matriarchal Pattern

Within the psychological panorama of Puerto Rican docility, the literature of the last twenty years reveals something of inescapable importance: the sudden appearance of women as leading characters in literary works. One author has already pointed out that it is the younger writers "who have achieved feminine characterizations of greater tragic heights and of deeper psychological

7. A similar psychological mechanism—the identification with official authoritarianism—operates in almost the entire colony of North Americans in Puerto Rico. It can be seen most clearly in the recent arrivals—technicians, experts, professionals, foremen, salesmen, hotel men, industrialists, real estate speculators, bankers, administrators, and businessmen—all of those, finally, who constitute the second and in all ways more devastating invasion.

8. It is not that this is an exclusively Puerto Rican phenomenon, but since it is Puerto Rico that concerns us, the demanding specialists will excuse us if we spare them, and ourselves, any digressions on the same situation in other contemporary societies which, if we may be pardoned, matter much less to us than our own. To express it in the picturesque argot of the Industrial Development Company: "Let every mast support its own sail."

9. *La llamarada* (1st ed.; Aguadilla, P.R.: Tipografía Ruiz, 1935). *Tiempo muerto* (1st ed.; San Juan: Publicaciones Areyto, 1940). *Usmaíl* (San Juan: Club del Libro de Puerto Rico, 1959). *La muerte no entrará en palacio*. In *Teatro* (Mexico: Ediciones Arrecife, 1959).

penetration."[1] Some might ask what relation there is between well-developed feminine characters and Puerto Rican docility, arguing that in any case the only thing this shows is a greater degree of maturity in our literature, since the bulk of the best Western literature from Euripides[2] down to the present has been achieved principally through female characters. As well as being flattering to our present literature, this observation is a valid one, as long as it is taken as a very general rule with not infrequent and notable exceptions. In accepting it as a sign of maturity, we would agree that a man of letters only obtains his "doctorate" as a writer when his analytical capacity enables him to explore objectively the psychological world of the opposite sex—an evasive, mysterious, and for him undoubtedly, poor devil, very dangerous world. But as flattering as the general or universal explanation may be, it is not, to our mind, a determining factor, though it might be a secondary one.

It seems likely that the literary fact is the result of a Puerto Rican social phenomenon: the introduction of the Anglo-Saxon-style matriarchal pattern in 1940 and its consistent and devastating development in the course of the last twenty years. Before this period the cultural pattern of paterfamilias prevailed, though our women did enjoy those legal rights to which they had laid claim, and one could find in Puerto Rican literature, after a tiresome search, only a few feminine characterizations of appreciable merit. This is not the case in the literatures of contemporary societies where the paterfamilias pattern still prevails (the French, Spanish, or Italian, for example), for they offer a wealth of female literary characters of the first rank.

Naturally, when we speak of the frequency of good female characterizations in our contemporary literature, we refer to psychological and esthetic attainments and not to any moral value. To tell the truth, the young writers seem to take a savage revenge on matriarchy—a foreign pattern recently imported into their culture—by often presenting women in the worst possible light. Apparently, the writers are the only ones in Puerto Rican society who have aggressively rebelled against the disappearance of the last cultural bulwark from which one could still combat, in part, the collective docility: *machismo*, the creole version of the fusion and adaptation of two secular concepts, Spanish *honor* and the Roman paterfamilias.

It would be difficult to present in detail the actual threat posed by the matriarchal system in Puerto Rico, because of the lack not of proof but of space. For each case of fossilized *machismo* which the social worker manages to find in a remote mountain field or in some not completely Americanized district of the city, we are sure that we can show her—if her superior, the female sociologist, provides us with the proper research tools—two or more cases of flagrant matriarchal transgression in the always growing and mighty middle class. This is the social stratum responsible for the introduction of cultural patterns in a mesocratic[3] society, which is what ours is rapidly becoming. One might add that a glance at present-day Puerto Rican public life gives the measure of the docility of the ex-paterfamilias, who presents a sad figure when faced with the aggressive advance of woman in

1. See the prologue to *Cuentos puertorriqueños de hoy* (San Juan: Club del Libro de Puerto Rico, 1959).
2. Greek dramatist (ca. 484–406 BC). [Anthology editors' note]
3. Dominated by the middle class. [Anthology editors' note]

all the spheres in which he was once, in a nostalgic past, lord and master. It is scant consolation for the native anthropologist to observe how one of the traits of Puerto Rican docility passes, unaltered, from the hands of the woman to those of the man.

Let us leave, in our turn, in the hands of the psychologist or, better yet, of the psychiatrist, the prediction as to what this new cultural reality signifies for the future Puerto Rican society. We are satisfied for the moment to refer the sociologist—who at the present could still be either male or female—to the recent population census, which yields in certain geographic sectors an alarming imbalance in the proportion of the sexes, due, it is alleged, to the masculine emigration to the United States. Political, social, cultural, economic, and psychological factors seem to coincide in the rapid solidifying of a matriarchal pattern in Puerto Rican society. As far as we know—and our information could be deficient—the credit for having given the first voice of frank alarm with respect to a problem which should be the direct incumbency of anthropologists, sociologists, and psychologists goes to the literary symbol.[4]

### Civism and Religion: Social Imposition of English [5]

A transverse cross section (even a partial one) of collective attitudes and modes of expression would necessarily reveal areas untouched by our writers. Some of these are significant if we are to obtain a clearer perspective on the national psychology.

In the following pages, given the impossibility of direct literary references, and so as to sustain the thematic unity announced in our subtitle—literature and psychological reality—we are going to permit ourselves, when we judge it opportune, to fill the literary vacuum by creating a little literature ourselves. The prudent reader, we are sure, will not let himself be thrown off the track by one or two touches of humor or flights of fancy, to the point of losing sight of the real analysis slightly concealed behind the mask of Dionysus.[6]

Without more preamble, let us introduce the theme with one of those anecdotes which North Americans so like to cultivate in their sentimental and optimistic magazines of the style of the *Readers' Digest*: A Puerto Rican writer was recently invited to speak at the Rotary Club of San Juan. What he spoke about does not matter, but since some ill-disposed person might think that the writer presented himself to the honorable members of International Rotarianism to inform them of something of fundamental interest to their membership—industrial development, for example, or methods to increase sales in ten lessons, perhaps—we must make clear that his talk of ten minutes dealt, modestly, with Puerto Rican theater and was motivated by the San Juan Drama Festival's announcement of their intention to put on a Puerto Rican work in English translation.

It was no surprise to the invited writer, nor would it be to anyone, that the Rotary Club of San Juan speaks English exclusively, both in its formal ceremonies and in its regular meetings and deliberations. This is natural—natural in our social environment, that is—since the president of the Club is

4. See the short story "En la popa hay un cuerpo reclinado" in the anthology mentioned above.
5. We make a point of the adjective *social* because we have absolutely no intention of introducing the reader to the confused field of pedagogy.
6. Ancient Greek god of wine, vegetation, and fertility. [Anthology editors' note]

North American and the membership includes a respectable number of industrialists, bankers, and businessmen who are not only North American, but also mostly monolingual. As a guest, nevertheless, the writer felt free to communicate his ideas in the language of his preference, choosing naturally the one which he had absorbed with pleasure from his mother as a child.

It is not exactly to the point, but it seems fair to make it clear as a tribute to the high degree of democratic courtesy shown by that civic group, that the individual and collective attitude was irreproachable. This violation of the linguistic dogma did not cause any disagreeable incidents. No one, it is also fair to say, accused the guest of being intellectually incompetent for having spoken, before a mixed audience, in his own language. On the contrary, the majority of the North American faces showed an expression of concentration and genuine interest as if it were important for them to try to understand what was being said in Spanish. The writer spoke, it goes without saying, slowly and correctly.

The talk and applause over, a middle-aged North American stood up and asked the president for permission to speak, after which he exclaimed in his own language: "I thank heavens that for the first time I have heard good Spanish spoken in the Rotary Club of San Juan!" The brief speech of the gentleman from North America was received with heavy and sustained applause.

Discounting the element of humor that the incident may contain, we find two points to be interesting and revealing: that it was a North American who, in the Rotary Club of Puerto Rico, expressed a veiled reproach of the linguistic policy of the civic organization to which he belonged, and that most of those who warmly applauded that reproach were Puerto Rican. We suspect that no Puerto Rican present would have said in public what the North American said. But we also suspect, to judge by the applause, that a good number of Puerto Ricans felt an underlying sense of guilt about the problem.

The language battle in local civic organizations is not always won by English, however. Very recently, another men's civic club in the metropolitan area denied the motion of one of its members to make it a bilingual organization, that is to say, to utilize English and Spanish indiscriminantly in its meetings. The proposal was defeated, by an overwhelming majority, with the official use of Spanish being conserved, except for the routine oath of allegiance to the North American flag.[7] The proposer of the motion, a Puerto Rican annexationist, indignant at and humiliated by his defeat, resigned. We do not know exactly what factors caused the triumph of the vernacular in this isolated case except, perhaps, the fact that there are only three North American members and all three—an extraordinary phenomenon—speak Spanish. This nullified the usual argument that Puerto Rican groups in which there are North American members should officially adopt English "as a courtesy." Another important factor is without a doubt a political one (the party affiliation of the majority of the membership), and this we do not know. Yet another contributing factor might be that, in this case, the club was situated on the

7. This fact—the swearing of allegiance to the North American flag by Puerto Ricans—has been reflected in our literature. It was dramatized in the already mentioned short story "El juramento" by René Marqués (1955) and more recently (1959) in a novel by the same author, *La víspera del hombre* (ch. 18).

outskirts of the city, and was smaller, more intimate, and more "provincial" than those in the center of San Juan, and in all probability more social than mercantile in character. One must take into account, nevertheless, that this area will soon undergo intensive industrial development. One can predict that, within a couple of years, English will replace Spanish even here. A motion recognizing the wisdom of the motion defeated today will be approved unanimously tomorrow and the humiliated annexationist will return triumphant to the collective bosom. His Puerto Rican companions will rise to their feet, receive him with smiles and a wave of the hand, and shout in unison: "Hi, Joe!"[8]

Having examined the problem in the civic field, let us cast a glance at the religious area. Among the diverse religious groups, it is the Catholic Church which shows the greatest persistence in imposing the social use of English.[9] With the encouragement of Monsignor James P. Davis, the present Archbishop of Puerto Rico, certain practices have become common now in the metropolitan area which are not only new but also foreign to Puerto Rican secular Catholicism. Sheets circulate, for example, with the imperious command: *Retire in English*. This does not refer, of course, as a native monolinguist might think with exemplary candor, to Federal Social Security, but, simply, to going into a Spiritual Retreat in English.[1] Similarly, the Church,

---

8. A superficial glance at the civic organizations in Puerto Rico seems to indicate that, in terms of their Americanization, the Lions are less Americanized than the Rotarians, while the Elks achieve the highest level of Americanization possible. (A curious fact: the Elks are embarassed to translate their name into Spanish. This bashfulness is inexplicable since in our language elks are simply "alces," "antas," or, as they are defined in any Spanish dictionary, "ruminant quadrupeds similar to the deer and as corpulent as the horse." We can see that being identified as "ruminant quadrupeds" is not something which would flatter the collective ego of a fraternal organization, but terms of fauna such as "alces" or "antas" are as decorous in Spanish as that of lions, and are all capable of symbolizing the noble spirit of civism and human fraternity of these North American organizations in Puerto Rico today.) The civic ladies, for their part, seem to occupy, in the Americanist scale, an intermediate place between the Lions and the Rotarians. (A curious fact: the civic ladies do not swear allegiance to the American flag in their regular ceremonies. Why in this case the civic women do not do the same as the civic men will always be difficult to determine. One might, however, ask: Are the women *less* docile than the men? Within a matriarchal society it would seem logical to suppose so.)

*Translator's note*: The greeting is in English in the original text.

9. Paradoxically, Protestantism, a recent import from North American culture, though it has contributed to the deterioration and disintegration of Puerto Rican national unity, has not had much to do, at least in its direct religious activity, with the social imposition of English. This is perhaps due to the fact that the immense majority of the Protestant heirarchy, clergy, and leadership is Puerto Rican. One must not forget, however, that in the last fifty years it has been Protestants, occupying key positions in the Department of Education and in the island legislature, who have attacked the vernacular most determinedly and have defended most fervidly linguistic North Americanization through public education in Puerto Rico.

In the general way, much the same thing can be said about Masonry, whose leaders are Puerto Rican, but whose lodges are almost all branches of the central power in the United States, from which they receive a North American nationalist orientation in open conflict with the possible survival of the Puerto Rican nationality. Even the Spiritists, whose kingdom would seem to be less of this world than that of other religious groups, cannot avoid feeling, in the Great Beyond, somewhat bewildered about Puerto Rico's political-cultural problem. Thus, Puerto Rican believers in Spiritism today have to hear their grandparents and great grandparents speak to them from beyond the grave in North American English with a Brooklyn or Middle West accent, even though they had died in the times of the Spanish rule. Perhaps this is due to the fact that often the best and most famous mediums who operate in the Puerto Rican sessions are North Americans. (The author was assured by a famous North American medium in San Juan that his maestro—a spiritual godfather or protector, we suppose—was the English writer Carlyle. The gratuitous godson was not as surprised by the fact that in a few seconds his unchosen maestro began to speak with a New York accent, as by the fact that, in spite of there being so many Spanish-speaking writers wandering in the stellar spaces, they should have to assign him in the other world one so annoying and typically British as Carlyle. This only goes to show the tremendous cultural confusion which we Puerto Ricans are condemned to suffer even beyond the frontiers of our already confused material life.)

1. *Translator's note*: The Spanish word for a retreat is *retiro*.

the guardian in every Catholic country of the secular culture, encourages confession in English in presumably "sophisticated" circles of "nouveaux américains" in Puerto Rico. Adjusting to Monsignor Davis' policy, various organizations have made praiseworthy efforts to follow the latest linguistic-religious fashion. One organization of Catholic men—a type of celestial Elks because of their advanced state of North Americanization—does everything in English: invitations, telephone calls, meetings, deliberations, confessions, and retreats. If the impartial observer did not have his sense of humor somewhat dulled, he might perhaps think that the practitioners of the new Catholicism in Puerto Rico cherish the mystic hope of a moving scene: Saint Peter[2] opening for them the gates of Heaven to the chords of the Star Spangled Banner. (A hope, we admit, which is as Christianly pious as any other that might lack celestial stereophonic sound.)

The social imposition of English, however, is not limited to civic organizations and the Catholic Church. In the School of Medicine they courteously ask the students if they wish the class in English or in Spanish. Only one need prefer it in English for the course to be taught in that language during the whole academic year. The rest of the Puerto Rican students—an absolute majority minus one—do not dare to make the slightest protest, which shows how linguistic democracy is faring in those surroundings. The picture is more or less the same in a good number of the other colleges and departments of the University.[3] Nevertheless, we will call a halt here and enter no further into the turbid field of pedagogy.[4]

Leaving religion and pedagogy aside, no one in today's world can blind himself to the reality that English is in our times the business language par excellence, as were Greek, Latin, Portuguese, French, and Spanish in different historical epochs, and perhaps as Russian may be destined to become in the future. Since the United States is still the dominating economic power in the West, the small world of commerce and banking operates and communicates in the imperial language. This is a general phenomenon which should cause no special alarm in a normally constituted society with a well-defined personality.

Nevertheless, when a colonial society of a distinct language and culture imposes English upon itself, not only as a strict necessity in the business sector, but as a political and cultural instrument disguised as a "social fashion," in order to supplant the vernacular and with it the still prevalent values of the autochthonous culture, it is worth the trouble to explore the psychological roots of the phenomenon.

It will not have escaped the notice of the objective observer that today in Puerto Rico it is not the state which officially imposes the foreign language,

2. One of Jesus' 12 apostles and a leader of the early Christian Church; typically depicted holding the keys to Heaven. [Anthology editors' note]
3. We refer to the University of Puerto Rico (a public institution subsidized and oriented by the state). In the two private universities—the Catholic one of Santa María in Ponce and the Protestant Interamerican University in San Germán—the imposition of English is carried to ridiculous extremes. Moreover, in a good number of the Catholic schools in the island, the teaching is done completely in English, thus violating the regulations of the Department of Public Education. This does not seem to bother at all the officials of this government agency charged with authorizing and regulating the operating of private schools in Puerto Rico.
4. Since docility must be considered more an acquired characteristic than a hereditary or congenital evil, a strongly anticolonialist system of public education could in two or three generations markedly change the psycho-social picture of Puerto Rican docility. Unfortunately, it is this type of education which the Puerto Rican people will never be permitted to have in their present colonial situation. The proof of this assertion can be seen in what has become of the pretentious "educational reform"—a confession of the most complete pedagogical impotence within the present colonial system.

although it does encourage it in an undercover manner. The imposition of English is principally in the hands of a series of extra-official Puerto Rican groups—professional, civic, and religious. We should consider the psychological implications of this social regimentation practiced by the upper strata of Puerto Rican society.

The motivations behind such a "fashion" must be very powerful, since the imposition itself constitutes a sacrifice for the Puerto Rican. The use of a foreign language always implies an additional intellectual effort and a tension not normal in a conversation in one's native tongue. It places the person whose language is not being spoken at an intellectual or psychological disadvantage. In addition, in this case the foreign language is fraught with mental burdens, ambivalencies, and psychological conflicts: colony–colonial power, Puerto Rican–North American, inferior–superior, weak–strong, docile–aggressive. Thus, even without his perceiving it, the Puerto Rican will experience extraordinary mental and emotional fatigue.

It is always interesting in Puerto Rico to observe a Puerto Rican and a North American communicating with each other when a business transaction is not involved. When it is, the North American's business sense may force him to use the typical salesman's approach of psychological concessions and flattery toward his client which necessarily conceal the latter's inferior position from the eyes of the casual observer. In other circumstances, however, when the conversation is not directly related to the economic advantages which the North American hopes to gain, the respective national guilt complexes come to the surface in one way or another.

The North American in Puerto Rico feels himself guilty, although never consciously, of imperialism. This guilt is translated into one of two extreme attitudes. He may exhibit the aggressive arrogance of the "superior" man who must prove to himself the validity and morality of his position, saying, in effect: "I am an imperialist because, after all, I *am* superior." On the other hand, he may become benevolently condescending in his desire to prove *to others* the legitimacy and advantages of the imperialist policy. This consists of a humanitarian concern to help the weak or "inferior" person. (He cannot, of course, be helped a lot, because this would endanger the imperialist's insecure position of "superiority.") The North American himself has called this spiritual posturing a "patronizing attitude" (while in Spanish we would call it, with greater accuracy than the term might reveal at first glance, an "attitude of patronal benevolence").

It seems opportune to point out in this respect that so-called North American humanitarianism operates almost always on the material or economic plane, very rarely on the ethical or spiritual one. A study of the process of contemporary North American Caesarism brings one to the conclusion that the North American has restricted the term freedom to a narrow economic definition: freedom from hunger.[5] In practice, this freedom can be condensed in an axiom: the nation which buys what it consumes in the United States market is "free" and "democratic." If it occurs to one of the nations under North American tutelage—and it does not have to be literally a colony like Puerto Rico—to carry the term freedom to the spiritual and ethical plane, alleging either that man does not live by bread alone or that the most tasty or most worthy bread is one's own although it may be less soft and less

5. See Amaury de Reincourt, *The Coming Caesar* (New York: Coward-McCann, 1957).

white, North American "humanitarianism" feels wounded to the core. The power of the empire moves diligently to crush that nation which dared to violate the North American dogma of "freedom." (In this respect, Cuba and Puerto Rico may not be "of one bird, two wings,"[6] but they have certainly been two very similar feathers in the ostentatious plumage of the same imperial bird.) We have, then, to realize that United States "humanitarianism" is to a great extent nothing but a rationalization of the peremptory necessities of its economic empire. Each country "freed" from hunger by the United States becomes a captive market within the complex North American economic network. Any attempt by that country to overstep the bounds in its attainment of freedom (most especially national economic freedom) constitutes a grave offense against "democracy," that is, against the United States' imperial economy. It will have to pay for this offense, if it is in the United States' power to make it do so. The punishment will be economic aggression, or a hunger siege, from which it will again be "freed" once it accepts the conditions of North American "humanitarianism" which it before had the audacity to refuse.

All of this, which is very tragic, and very real for the parties involved, forms an unexamined and unreasoned psychological sediment in the mind of the North American in Puerto Rico. Such conflicts and ambivalences become conscious material only for those North Americans who possess a great deal of sensitivity as well as culture. There are, naturally, very few of these in Puerto Rico. It is in them, nevertheless, that one can best observe all the complexities of the North American psychology. There is an undercurrent of anguish in their dealings with Puerto Ricans. The urgency to belong causes them to make a sincere and honest effort to understand the Puerto Rican and sympathize with his idiosyncrasies and his cultural patterns. But they never accomplish this completely, perhaps because their uneasiness over their "betrayal" of North American values disturbs them too much. Black sheep among the North American residents, they cannot help but see themselves as "ugly ducklings" in the Puerto Rican social group. Some, unable to stand the external tensions, arrive at the illusory compromise of pretending to be, simultaneously, North Americans among the North American residents and Puerto Ricans among the Puerto Ricans. Such psychological acrobatics in the long run cause their moral, spiritual, and intellectual deterioration. (Their sociologists and psychologists then cite the enervating tropical climate as the cause of this deterioration.)

On confronting the North American, the Puerto Rican for his part sets in motion his colonial guilt complex.[7] In order to tolerate his humiliating condition he has to find an excuse for it and admit that he is *inferior* to the North American. This motivates his obsequiousness (the traditional "courtesy," "hospitality," and "generosity") expressed in ways which closely approach servility. This unconscious admission of inferiority cannot help but hurt his ego, often provoking extreme compensatory reactions such as violent antagonism or total surrender. The most interesting from the psychological point of view

6. This is an allusion to some verses of Lola Rodríguez de Tió, a Puerto Rican poet of the past century: "Cuba and Puerto Rico are / of one bird, the two wings; / they receive flowers and bullets / in the same heart." Toward the middle of 1966 Fidel Castro, in one of his fiery speeches, made a

tremendous blunder and attributed these verses to José Martí. Is Fidel proposing to go so far as to nationalize *our* poetry?
7. The complex also operates, although to a lesser degree, when he confronts other Westerners, especially Spaniards (precisely those who occupied

is, without doubt, the latter, since by surrendering he is able to dispense with his defense mechanisms and open himself up, without resistance, to all that is North American. He hopes in this way to acquire or to incorporate the "superiority" of that feared and envied being, but, of course, he never can. In many Puerto Ricans who have some sensitivity as well as education and culture, these extreme manifestations never appear in all their brutal clarity. They develop a strange ambivalence in their social dealings with the North American, similar, in its undercurrent of anguish, to that of the sensitive North American when he tries to fraternize with the Puerto Rican.

Only in authentically bilingual individuals who believe they have resolved their ambivalence toward the politico-cultural problem into which they were born—and in Puerto Rico there are scarcely a handful of these tropical icebergs—can the painful defense mechanism be reduced to a minimum. When they communicate with a North American there appear to be no barriers. The few Puerto Ricans who, because they were raised or educated in the United States, speak English fluently but Spanish less so, are not true bilingual speakers. With them the mechanism functions inversely: they are made uneasy by Spanish. This is aggravated by the fact that, forced to use the native tongue of their compatriots in their communication with other Puerto Ricans, they develop an additional guilt complex precisely because they cannot handle it perfectly. So they avoid it, using it as little as possible. They then advocate English as the "official" language in the circles in which they move or they retire to narrow little social islands—no man's lands—where other cultural pariahs like themselves have already imposed the use of the foreign tongue.

It is becoming clear that English in Puerto Rico is not simply another foreign language, like French or Italian, but the painful site of many conflicting experiences—political, cultural, spiritual, and psychological—which exacerbate the Puerto Rican's colonial anguish.

The imposition and social acceptance of English in Puerto Rico can be viewed, then, without risk of error, as one more manifestation of Puerto Rican docility.

✳    ✳    ✳

1960                                                                                                    1962

---

at one time the place which the North American occupies today). Spaniards continue fostering in Puerto Rican artistic and cultural life certain bad habits dear to the island colonial complexes. Look at the number of Spanish mediocrities who occupy key positions among the artistic and cultural elite and in university circles. Even before the figures of those few Spanish residents of real and undeniable intellectual worth, the general attitude of the Puerto Rican is not one of dignified acknowledgement, but rather of a certain tropical servility, as if his ancestral servitude under the Conquistador had reappeared. The insulting farcical scenes put on by certain Puerto Rican circles for prestigious figures like Juan Ramón Jiménez [Spanish poet (1881–1958)] and Pablo Casals [Spanish-born Catalan cellist, conductor, and composer (1876–1973)] perhaps give an idea of what we mean. On the other hand, in the so-called social life, the Casa de España (the Spanish Club) continues to fascinate, as a supreme goal, a great number of middle-class San Juan residents. In the younger generations, better indoctrinated in North American national prejudices, the colonial complex is disguised by an air of superiority shown toward citizens of so-called "underdeveloped" countries. This arbitrary designation includes Antilleans (Puerto Ricans are apparently exempted from that category), Latin Americans, Africans, and Asiatics. The new Puerto Rican struts before these human beings classified as "inferior" by the North Americans, making an ostentatious display of his mended colonial plumage. It is an innocent and superficial attitude most of the time, but it can be truly vicious in cases of extreme North Americanization.

# The Function of the Puerto Rican Writer Today[1]

I think, or I should say, I fear that on fundamental matters there will be little or no disagreement in this forum. And I say that I fear it because it would be academic to organize a public forum to discuss a theme on which there is general agreement—in other words, to polemicize about something which does not admit or provoke or require any polemics.

I am convinced that, if this very night we were to corner any Puerto Rican citizen in the street, regardless of his social or economic condition or his academic preparation, although taking for granted, of course, that his intelligence is not yet dulled by alcohol—it is too early for that—and that he does not suffer from congenital imbecility (or imbecility acquired from the crude propaganda of the daily press); if we corner him, I repeat, and if, at close range, we put to him the question: "What do you think should be the function of the Puerto Rican writer today?" his answer, with devastating logic, would be: "To write about present-day Puerto Rico" or "To write works which reflect the present moment in Puerto Rico" or, perhaps, more succinctly, "To write Puerto Rican works," taking for granted that if they are written in the present in one way or another they will have to reflect it. This "average" man, as the anonymous citizen whom we knew before as John Doe is called today in statistics, would be saying to us, without any great intellectual effort, philosophical theories, or sociological postulations, that the function of the Puerto Rican writer is not to be alienated from the reality in which he lives, but on the contrary to face up to the reality of that time and space which was allotted to him. As a writer, he must observe its multiple contradictions so as to arrive at a profound truth.

It seems to me that neither the participants nor a substantial majority of the public present here would object to accepting in principle the validity of John Doe's opinion concerning the theme we are discussing tonight. Nevertheless, in the atmosphere of the Learned House, and unlike the man we cornered in the street, we have the mission, the obligation, and the duty—if not the function—to spin a finer thread.

I think it fitting, in the first place, to introduce some irritants into the discussion. Therefore, I am going to undertake a considerable detour before arriving at the specific theme of this evening. My friend the moderator will have the kindness to take me to task if the detour—speaking in sidereal terms—goes too far "out of orbit."

For paradoxical effect, let me begin that task of spinning more finely with a very gross platitude: The writer, be he Puerto Rican, Japanese, Russian, French, or Mexican, has as his primary function the creation of literature. If his creative gift is directed toward something other than creating literature, he will be precisely what the other thing is, but he will not be a writer.

If we accept the fact that literature is that genre among the products of human understanding which has for its goal the expression of the beautiful (or the esthetic expression of the ugly or even the horrible) by means of the

1. Translated by Barbara Bockus Aponte. Except as indicated, all footnotes are the author's. The anthology editors have omitted the author's introductory note, concerning the essay's presentation history and its use of the word *writer* to mean "creative writer," and they have omitted the translator's introductory note, about the essay's publication history.

word, we see clearly that the esthetic element is at the very root of literary creation, that is, of the function of the writer. To use a cliché, the writer is "the artist or the artificer of the word." The word in the hands of the writer is not, then, mere communication as it is for everyone else, but primarily, expression, esthetic expression.

The word thus serves two essential purposes, one utilitarian (communication) and the other esthetic (artistic expression). Any man, including the writer, naturally, *communicates* with others through daily conversation, correspondence, speeches, newspaper articles, pamphlets, the classroom, conferences, and forums. The writer as such, on the other hand, expresses himself to others through a work of literary creation. In both instances, that of communication and that of expression, the instrument is the same (the word), but the ends and the means are clearly distinct.

To what entity does this citizen whose function it is to create literature owe his first loyalty? Although it may shock many of you, I would like to affirm that, as a writer, he owes loyalty to no one but himself. And I do not make this apparently antisocial affirmation because of a childish desire to shock, but because of a firm conviction that this is so, and not in the way that many would like.

To be a writer is to undertake an agonizing and unending search for the truth. And it is not in outer space that the writer searches for the truth, but in man, in his fellow men, and in the society which surrounds him. But man, his fellow men, and society distrust or fear the truth and weave an intricate web of pseudo-truths and rigid dogmas which finally take shape in the state, and the state functions by means of a presumably miraculous cure-all which we will take the liberty of calling "the system."

The writer has to be free to be able to struggle against that web which others fashion to impede his search for the truth. And, in effect, he feels free, he knows himself to be free. This is a natural feeling, since he has the experience of creation; he knows, because he has experienced it in his own flesh and spirit, that the act of artistic creation is an act of supreme liberty, perhaps the freest of all the acts that man can execute. The writer, who knows freedom not as a political concept or as a philosophic abstraction, but as a vital experience, will love liberty for himself and, by extension, for others.

A free being who searches for the truth through esthetic expression, the writer becomes an ethical man. And, although he does not wish it and does it in spite of himself, he often becomes a moralist.

Now, what is the truth for which he anxiously searches? In the words of Ferrater Mora[2] the truth was conceived by the Greeks "as the discovery of being, that is, as the vision of the form or profile of what truly is, but which is hidden by the veil of appearance." Millennia later, Heidegger[3] returns to the Greek term of "discovery" or "unveiling" in referring to the truth. For him it becomes "an element of existence, which conceals being in its state of degradation and discovers it in its state of authenticity."

The writer, of course, does not have to be up on the different philosophical interpretations of the truth, although it wouldn't hurt him to acquaint himself with some of them. What is important to point out is that his personal

2. José Ferrater Mora (1912–1991), Spanish philosopher. [Anthology editors' note]

3. Martin Heidegger (1889–1976), German philosopher. [Anthology editors' note]

and intuitive search for truth always carries with it that dramatic element of "discovery" or "unveiling." An essential part of his labor, if not the very essence of his never-ending search, is to break through the surface appearances, to bring to light what is true, and to rip away the veils which conceal the authentic.

It is very easy for the rest of humanity to find *their* truth, or at least to hold the naive illusion that they have found it. There are even many who say they have found the absolute truth. (We use the phrase not in the rigorous philosophic sense, but in that of a presumably unquestionable truth.) The politician and the man of religion, among others, assure us that they possess it. But for the writer there are no absolute truths.[4] As soon as he learns what he believes as a writer to be the truth, he discovers that it is only a part of the truth, a half truth, or a reflection of the truth, or only a mirage. The absolute truth is not there; it is somewhere else. He must begin again his tireless search.

Do you understand now why the writer always seems to be an eternal nonconformist? Do you understand why his loyalty to governments, states, political parties, religious doctrines, institutions, and systems is almost always relative and conditional; why he so often has to feel, in reality, loyal only to himself? Do you understand why, faced with the rigid and dogmatic truths of the State, the Church, or Society, the writer almost always appears as a rebel, as a heretic, or even a subversive?[5]

It is obvious that the writer will always identify himself with libertarian causes, because freedom is a necessity for one who creates. Furthermore, his ethical sense and his moralistic inclination will cause him to identify with revolutionary causes, since he will inevitably see in them reason and justice. Still, one should not be fooled. Save for such brilliant exceptions as a José Martí,[6] the writer will never be a liberator or a revolutionary. He can, in a crucial moment in the life of his country, change his pen for a rifle, becoming a soldier or a guerrilla, or he can temporarily sacrifice expression for communication, becoming a mere pamphleteer. When the crisis is past, however, and the cause with which he has identified and for which he would fight is saved, he will again become, as a writer, faithful to himself. He will return to his uncomfortable position of eternal rebel unless, of course, he ceases being a creator, unless the man of action within him is able to destroy the

---

4. A member of the audience [when this essay was read at a forum], a young Puerto Rican priest, acutely observed that when the writer rejects all absolute truths, he is at that moment proclaiming an absolute truth. That is so. One must clarify, however, that the writer only claims to question absolute truths in relation to the act of creation. He can, as a citizen, have embraced with sincere faith an absolute truth. An example of this is the Catholic writer Graham Greene [1904–1991], who, in his novels, questions, or appears to many Catholics to be questioning, some aspects of the absolute truth in which, as an individual, he honorably believes. The profound truth which the writer brings to light in his creative work is the result of the contradictions which he observes in the world around him and even, at times, in the religious or political doctrines with which he has identified himself.

5. A Catholic group in the audience objected to this affirmation, alleging that there are cases in which the writer adapts himself or conforms, unrebelliously, to a specific ideology or doctrine. As an example of this the case of [Paul] Claudel [1868–1955] was brought up. I accept the validity of the objection—the exceptions confirm the rule—but I consider the example of Claudel a weak one. In a liberal France, where even Catholicism has achieved a degree of liberalism which shocks Rome, Claudel's act of regression in embracing and expressing in his works an almost medieval Catholicism can be interpreted to a great degree as a protest against his environment, as an act of rebellion, in fact, whether we are in agreement with him or not. The degree of rebellion of the writer and the way in which he expresses it will depend, naturally, as much on the historic circumstances of the society in which he lives, as on his own temperament and personal circumstances.

6. See p. 265. [Anthology editors' note]

writer. Barring this, he cannot avoid being in some measure a rebel within the new system, as he was within the system which he helped destroy, since in both he sees the inevitable contradictions.

He will be a rebel in the Camusian[7] sense—in disagreement with the status quo and a critic of it. If the moment arrives, he will be its declared enemy, but incapable of formulating a system to substitute for the one he condemns. The revolutionary, on the other hand, is the one who has clearly formulated the system which is to replace the one he destroys. He possesses a truth which he believes absolute. The writer is incapable of such a feat, though he may at times delude himself.

We are seeing why it is practically impossible to demand solutions from a writer. He perceives, discovers, sets forth, and denounces contradictions and problems—contradictions and problems which generally were passed unnoticed by others—but he does not give solutions. He can point out various possible solutions because he sees in each one of them a little truth, but none by itself seems to him as the absolute and true solution. If it should occur to him—and this has happened—to try to synthesize what he thinks the best of all these possibilities, the result would be an ideal impossible to put into practice in the everyday world—in short, a utopia. It falls to the man of action, to the politician, to realize the synthesis, to give the practical solution, to state the new truth with all its contradictions. These contradictions will create new problems in the future to be discovered and denounced by other writers and solved by future men of action, thus continuing, ad infinitum, the inexorable cyclical process.

In relation to what we have said, we should examine a phrase very commonly used today: "revolutionary writer." This term is applied indiscriminately to the writer who, in a given moment, has taken up arms to fight in a revolution and to the one who has incorporated in his work revolutionary episodes and events, but it is a more common practice to designate in this way the writer who inhibits his creative freedom to keep his work within the rigid ideological directives of a government party which rose to power by means of a revolution: the directives of the state, in other words.[8]

The term "revolutionary" applied to the writer in this sense is, of course, absurd. The writer, as such, is only revolutionary if he brings a "revolution"— that is, a fundamental change—to literary creation. Dante, Cervantes, Shakespeare, Pushkin, Dostoevski, Kafka, Proust, James Joyce, and Virginia Woolf were revolutionaries. Pablo Neruda[9] was a revolutionary poet long before becoming a Communist. Significantly, the more Communist he has become, the less revolutionary poet he has been. Jean Paul Sartre[1] is a

---

7. I.e., as defined by the French writer Albert Camus (1913–1960). [Anthology editors' note]

8. The danger for the creative artist in the indefinite prolongation of the subtle distinction between the revolution and the state, made by the leaders of revolutionary states, was seen very tangibly in the Soviet Union. It is clearly reasonable for a revolution to ask the writer and the artist to suspend temporarily their freedom of creation during the initial revolutionary period. But the Soviet state made the temporary suspension a permanent one, prolonging it for almost forty years—the whole lifetime of a writer or an artist—and always in the name of the revolution. Only now in the post-

Stalinist period [i.e., following the death of the Soviet leader Joseph Stalin (1879–1953)] has the Soviet state began to concede some freedom of expression to the writer, both in form and in content. This is why Soviet literature has been of such poor quality during those four decades, annulling or only precariously fulfilling both its esthetic and its social functions.

9. Chilean poet and diplomat (1904–1973). The figures listed in the previous sentence are European writers of the fourteenth through the twentieth centuries. [Anthology editors' note]

1. French philosopher, dramatist, and novelist (1905–1980). [Anthology editors' note]

revolutionary writer, in spite of his political inconstancy. His literary production is as revolutionary when he is within the Communist Party as when he is out of it, when he is praised by the Communists as when he is reviled by them. Sartre is a revolutionary writer, not because of his political activity in the French resistance, nor because of his periodic rapprochements with Communism, but because he achieves what always appeared extremely difficult, if not impossible: the writing of excellent literature with a philosophic doctrine. *The Flies, No Exit,* and *Nausea* have done more to disseminate and make understandable Sartrean existentialism than his confused and contradictory *Being and Nothingness.* That is so only because *The Flies* and *No Exit* are two excellent dramatic works and *Nausea* a good novel. It is the esthetic and human value of these literary works which sustains them as such. As a revolutionary writer Sartre has never betrayed himself, even when the citizen Jean Paul Sartre may have appeared a traitor to a revolutionary political ideology. Sartre, in my judgment, has fulfilled his function as a writer with integrity and in very difficult circumstances.

We can now, after this long detour, return to Puerto Rico and to the specific theme of this forum: the function of the Puerto Rican writer today. I imagine that we have all interpreted "function" in its social aspect. I think that that function does not escape anyone's notice. Puerto Rico has been for centuries and still is a colony. The fundamental problem of a person in a colonial situation is freedom. The writer, a lover of freedom because of his very condition as a creator, and inhabitant of a colony, will naturally identify with every movement of political emancipation. This, in our case, is not a mere theory, or an unrealized desire, but historic fact. The Puerto Rican writer was separatist in the times of Spain, as he is today a nationalist or an "independentista." His work reflects today, as it did yesterday, the colonial situation of his country. And his painful search for truth becomes one for freedom. Freedom is for the Puerto Rican writer the truth always sought and never captured. It is, therefore, the theme most repeated in Puerto Rican literature—the primary theme, I would venture to say. Whether it has a political thrust or deals with individual or metaphysical freedom, the Puerto Rican writer's desire for freedom is always present in his work. It is there not because of state imposition, nor because of party discipline, nor because of ideological directives, but because he has freely chosen this theme, one which is eternal and of the moment, for his creative work. He thus fulfills, in his free act of creation, his function as a writer in the time and space allotted to him: the colonial Puerto Rico of yesterday and today.

It only remains for me to add an observation and a warning with respect to the theme. The first is that the Puerto Rican writer, because of personal limitations, or because of the lack of a real vocation, or because he has deviated from his fundamental function, has often neglected the esthetic aspect of his craft. He has tried to be a writer using the word as his instrument, but more as a utilitarian means of communication than as a means of artistic expression. This is not a problem exclusive to Puerto Rico, but one of all Latin America. For obvious reasons, it has been the poet among us who first has been able to overcome that limitation. The problem is still visible in the prose writers, although we have to admit that, in Puerto Rico as well as in the other Latin countries of the hemisphere, there has been a great improvement in this respect over the last few decades. The Puerto Rican writer must be fully aware of this limitation, because it constitutes his major problem today. In terms of rigorous priority, the esthetic function precedes the social function. The writer has to be first an artist and then what he may choose to be or what suits his temperament best: politician, sociologist, moralist, philosopher, or metaphysician. The higher its esthetic value, the better a work will fulfill its social function; the greater its artistic values are, the wider dissemination and acceptance its content will have. Given a propagandistic work and a work of authentic literary value with the same content, the genuinely literary work will fulfill its social function more effectively and completely than the pamphlet. This is not a theory or an intellectual elaboration but a fact corroborated by millennia of literary history.

As to the warning, I feel it my responsibility to say that the Puerto Rican writer should already be preparing himself to face the not very distant time when the ideal truth so sought after by him and not yet captured will finally become reality.

Puerto Rico will be free. Because of historical imperatives the event will take place in the course of the present generation. The Puerto Rican writer, who has a long tradition of having liberty as his ultimate goal, is going to feel disconcerted before the apparently unaccustomed fact of independence. He is going to think, for a moment, that he has been able to seize hold definitively of the truth. He is even going to have the fleeting illusion that he finally finds himself before an absolute truth. But after independence there will come, in the political field, another truth to be achieved: national liberation. This will not be an absolute truth either, although it will be proclaimed as such at that time. There will never be absolute truths for the writer if he wants to fulfill, honestly and completely, not only his esthetic but his social function. He will always have a reality to examine, contradictions to discover, problems to denounce, and a more profound truth to capture. It is about this reality that I wish to caution the Puerto Rican writer of today, and of tomorrow.

1962                                                                                          1963

# SABINE R. ULIBARRÍ
## 1919–2003

Descended from one of the original Hispanic settler families of New Mexico, Sabine R. Ulibarrí was born in Santa Fe and raised in Tierra Amarilla, part of Rio Arriba County, in the northern part of the state. His mother was college educated, as was his father, a cattle rancher. In a reminiscence as an adult, Ulibarrí noted his father's love of poetry and recitation of it after a day's work at the ranch. After receiving his bachelor's degree from the University of New Mexico, in Albuquerque, Ulibarrí returned to Rio Arriba to teach. In the summer of 1941, he enrolled at Georgetown University, in Washington, D.C. When World War II began, Ulibarrí enlisted in the U.S. Army Air Corps, where he served as a gunner from 1942 until 1945. After the war, he earned his master's degree in Spanish from the University of New Mexico. He taught there for a few years before earning his doctorate, in Spanish literature, from the University of California, Los Angeles, in 1958. An early champion of bilingual education, he returned to the University of New Mexico and taught Spanish and Spanish-American literature until he retired in 1982.

In addition to garnering acclaim as an eloquent public speaker, Ulibarrí wrote literary criticism, essays, poetry, and short fiction. Although he was a master of the English language, he wrote his creative work in Spanish because of his belief that loss of the mother tongue would result in loss of the culture. Ulibarrí's poetry is *escueta* (unadorned) but with a marked Spanish Peninsular flavor. Critics have noted in it the influences of the Spanish writers Gustavo Adolfo Bécquer, Juan Ramón Jiménez (winner of the Nobel Prize, and the subject of Ulibarrí's doctoral thesis), Federico García Lorca, and the giant creative forces of what critics have labeled the Generation of 1898, Miguel de Unamuno and Antonio Machado. Ulibarrí's poetry collections—*Al cielo se sube a pie* (One Must Walk to Heaven, 1961), published first in Mexico and subsequently in Spain, and *Amor y Ecuador* (Love and Ecuador, 1966), published in Ecuador—earned him an international reputation, although his poetry is known most widely in the Latin American countries in which it was published.

Ulibarrí achieved his greatest success, however, through his fiction. While his poetry is about love, self-identification, and attempts to understand the spiritual world, his prose depicts his characters' survival in the harsh land of Tierra Amarilla. He captured in literature the land and people there, the importance of maintaining the old Latino customs, and the high value of tradition. "The land was sacred," Ulibarrí once said, "because your parents and their parents were buried there, some of your children were buried there and you would be buried there. So the sweat, blood, and tears have filtered into the land. So it is holy, it is sacred, it is sacrosanct." He avoids the label of regionalism by also presenting universal themes. The retention of *el español*, despite the incursions of the Anglo society which began during Ulibarrí's formative years, is one of his themes, though he does not necessarily portray the new Anglo settler as a villain.

*Tierra Amarilla* (1964), subtitled *Cuentos de Nuevo México* (Stories of New Mexico), was first published in Ecuador but struck a responsive chord with readers in many South American countries. The two stories presented in this anthology are translated from Ulibarrí's second short-story collection, *Mi abuela fumaba puros y otros cuentos de Tierra Amarilla* (My Grandma Smoked Cigars and Other Stories of Tierra Amarilla, 1977). In the title story, a grandmother survives the suicide of her husband and oversees the operation of their ranch. In "El Apache," the narrator innocently describes the capture of a stray horse and a subsequent clash between the horse and a blind man.

# My Grandma Smoked Cigars[1]

The way I've heard it, my grandfather was quite a guy. There are many stories about him. Some respectable, others not quite. One of the latter goes as follows. That returning from Tierra Amarilla to Las Nutrias, after cups and cards, sometimes on his buggy with its spirited trotters, sometimes on his

---

1. Translated by Thelma Campbell Nason.

*criollo* horse,[2] he would take off his hat, hang it on a fence post, pull out his six-gun and address himself to the stiff gentleman of his own invention.

"Tell me, who is the richest man in all these parts?"

Silence.

"Well then, take this."

A shot. Splinters flew out of the post or a hole appeared in the hat.

"Who's the toughest man around here?"

Silence.

"Well then, take this."

The same thing happened. He was a good shot. More questions of the same kind, punctuated with shots. When the sassy post learned his lesson and gave my grandfather the answers he wanted to hear, the ritual ended, and he went on his way, singing or humming some sentimental song of the period. The shooting was heard back in the town without it bothering anyone. Someone was sure to say with a smile, "There's don Prudencio doing his thing."

Of course my grandfather had other sides (the plural is intended) that are not relevant to this narrative. He was a civic, social and political figure and a family man twice over. What I want to do now is stress the fact that my relative was a real character: quarrelsome, daring and prankish.

He died in a mysterious way, or perhaps even shameful. I've never been able to find out exactly what streetcar my distinguished antecedent took to the other world. Maybe that wooden gentleman with his hat pulled over his eyes, the one who suffered the insults of the hidalgo[3] of Las Nutrias, gave him a woody and mortal whack. An hidalgo he was—and a father of more than four.

I never knew him. When I showed up in this world to present my Turriaga[4] credentials, he had already turned his in. I imagine that wherever he is he's making violent and passionate love to the ladies who went to heaven—or hell, depending . . . That is if my grandmother hasn't caught up with him in those worlds beyond the grave.

I don't think he and my grandmother had an idyllic marriage in the manner of sentimental novels where everything is sweetness, softness and tenderness. Those are luxuries, perhaps decadences, that didn't belong in that violent world, frequently hostile, of Río Arriba County at the end of the past century. Furthermore, the strong personalities of both would have prevented it. I do believe they were very happy. Their love was a passion that didn't have time to become a habit or just friendship. They loved each other with mutual respect and fear, something between admiration and fury, something between tenderness and toughness. Both were children of their land and their times. There was so much to do. Carve a life from an unfriendly frontier. Raise their rebellious and ferocious cubs. Their life was an affectionate and passionate sentimental war.

I say all of this as a preamble in order to enter into my subject: my grandmother. I have so many and so gratifying memories of her. But the first one of all is a portrait that hangs in a place of honor in the parlor of my memory.

---

2. Horse whose breed or strain is native to the Americas.

3. Descendant of Spanish nobility.

4. The family name.

She had her moments in which she caressed her solitude. She would go off by herself, and everyone knew it was best to leave her alone.

She always dressed in black. A blouse of lace and batiste up front. A skirt down to her ankles. All silk. A cotton apron. High shoes. Her hair parted in the middle and combed straight back, smooth and tight, with a round and hard bun in the back. I never saw her with her hair loose.

She was strong. As strong as only she could be. Through the years, in so many situations, small and big tragedies, accidents and problems, I never saw her bend or fold. Fundamentally, she was serious and formal. So a smile, a compliment or a caress from her were coins of gold that were appreciated and saved as souvenirs forever. Coins she never wasted.

The ranch was big business. The family was large and problematic. She ran her empire with a sure and firm hand. Never was there any doubt about where her affairs were going nor who held the reins.

That first memory: the portrait. I can see her at this moment as if she were before my eyes. A black silhouette on a blue background. Straight, tall and slender. The wind of the hill cleaving her clothes to her body up front, outlining her forms, one by one. Her skirt and her shawl flapping in the wind behind her. Her eyes fixed I don't know where. Her thoughts fixed on I don't know what. An animated statue. A petrified soul.

My grandfather smoked cigars. The cigar was the symbol and the badge of the feudal lord, the *patrón*. When on occasion he would give a cigar to the foreman or to one of the hands on impulse or as a reward for a task well done, the transfiguration of those fellows was something to see. To suck on that tobacco was to drink from the fountains of power. The cigar gave you class.

They say that when my grandfather died my grandmother would light cigars and place them on ashtrays all over the house. The aroma of the tobacco filled the house. This gave the widow the illusion that her husband was still around. A sentimentalism and romanticism difficult to imagine before.

As time went on, and after lighting many a cigar, a liking for the cigars seemed to sneak up on her. She began to smoke the cigars. At nightfall, every day, after dinner, when the tasks of the day were done, she would lock herself in her room, sit in her rocker and light her cigar.

She would spend a long time there. The rest of us remained in the living room playing the family role as if nothing were amiss. No one ever dared interrupt her arbitrary and sacred solitude. No one ever mentioned her unusual custom.

The cigar that had once been a symbol of authority had now become an instrument of love. I am convinced that in the solitude and in the silence, with the smell and the taste of the tobacco, there in the smoke, my grandmother established some kind of mystical communication with my grandfather. I think that there, all alone, that idyllic marriage, full of tenderness, softness and sweetness was attained, not possible while he lived. It was enough to see the soft and transfigured face of the grandmother when she returned to us from her strange communion, to see the affection and gentleness with which she treated us kids.

Right there, and in those conditions, the decisions were made, the positions were taken that ran the business, that directed the family. There in the light or in the shade of an old love, now an eternal love, the spiritual strength was forged that kept my grandmother straight, tall and slender, a throbbing woman of stone, facing the winds and storms of her full life.

When my parents married they built their home next to the old family house. I grew up on the windy hill in the center of the valley of Las Nutrias, with pine trees on all the horizons, with the stream full of beaver, trout and suckers, the sagebrush full of rabbits and coyotes, stock everywhere, squirrels and owls in the barns.

I grew up alongside my grandmother and far away from her, between tender love and reverent fear.

When I was eight years old, it was decided in the family that we should move to Tierra Amarilla so that my brothers and I could attend school. The furrows the tears left on my face still burn, and I still remember their salty taste the day we left my straight, tall and slender grandmother, waving her handkerchief, with the wind on her face on the hill in the center of the valley.

In Tierra Amarilla I was antisocial. Having grown up alone, I didn't know how to play with other children. I played with my dogs instead. In spite of this I did all right in school, and one day I was fifteen years old, more or less adapted to my circumstances.

One winter day we got ready to go to Las Nutrias. All with a great deal of anticipation. To visit my grandmother was always an event. The family would go with me in the car. My father with the sleigh and the hired hands. It was a matter of cutting fence posts.

We sang all the way. That is until we had to leave the highway. There was a lot of snow. The highway had been cleared, but the little road to Las Nutrias hadn't.

I put chains on the car, and we set out across the white sea. Now we were quiet and apprehensive. We soon got stuck. After a lot of shoveling and much pushing we continued, only to get stuck again farther on, again and again.

We were all exhausted and cold, and the day was drifting away. Finally we climbed the hill and came out of the pine grove from where we could see my grandmother's house. We got stuck again. This time there was no way of pulling the car out. My mother and the children continued on foot, opening their way through two and a half feet of soft snow. My brother Roberto pulled my sister Carmen on a small sled. It was getting dark. A trip of nine miles had taken us all day.

Juan Maes, the foreman, quickly came with a team of horses and pulled me home.

I had barely come in and was warming up. My mother had brought me dry clothes, when we saw the lights of a car in the pine grove. We saw it approach slowly, hesitating from time to time. It was easier now; the road was now open.

It was my uncle Juan Antonio. The moment he came in we all knew he had bad news. There was a frightening silence. No one said a word. Everyone silent and stiff like wooden figures in a grotesque scene.

My mother broke the silence with a heart breaking "Alejandro!"

My uncle nodded.

"What happened?" It was my grandmother.

"Alejandro. An accident."

"What happened?"

"An accidental shot. He was cleaning a rifle. The gun went off."

"How is he?"

"Not good, but he'll pull through."

We all knew he was lying, that my father was dead. We could see it in his face. My mother was crying desperately, on the verge of becoming hysterical. We put our arms around her, crying. My uncle with his hat in his hands not knowing what to do. Another man had come with him. No one had noticed him.

That is when my grandmother went into action. Not a single tear. Her voice steady. Her eyes two flashing spears. She took complete control of the situation.

She went into a holy fury against my father. She called him ungrateful, shameless, unworthy. An inexhaustible torrent of insults. A royal rage. In the meantime she took my mother in her arms and rocked her and caressed her like a baby. My mother submitted and settled down slowly. We did too. My grandmother who always spoke so little did not stop talking that night.

I didn't understand then. I felt a violent resentment. I wanted to defend my father. I didn't because no one ever dared to talk back to my grandmother. Much less me. The truth is that she understood many things.

My mother was on the verge of madness. Something had to be done.

My grandmother created a situation, so violent and dramatic, that it forced us all, my mother especially, to fix our attention on her and shift it away from the other situation until we could get used to the tragedy little by little. She didn't stop talking in order not to allow a single aperture through which despair might slip in. Talking, talking, between abuse and lullaby, she managed that my mother, in her vulnerable state, fall asleep in the wee hours of the morning. As she had done so many times in the past, my grandmother had dominated the harsh reality in which she lived.

She understood something else. That my father didn't fire a rifle accidentally. The trouble we had to bury him on sacred ground confirmed the infallible instinct of the lady and mistress of Las Nutrias. Everything confirmed the talent and substance of the mother of the Turriaga clan.

The years went by. I was now a professor. One day we returned to visit the grandmother. We were very happy. I've said it before, visiting her was an event. Things had changed a great deal. With the death of my father, my grandmother got rid of all the stock. The ranch hands disappeared with the stock. Rubel and his family were the only ones who remained to look after her.

When we left the highway and took the little used and much abused road full of the accustomed ruts, the old memories took possession of us. Suddenly we saw a column of black smoke rising beyond the hill. My sister shouted.

"Grandma's house!"

"Don't be silly. They must be burning weeds, or sage brush, or trash." I said this but apprehension gripped me. I stepped hard on the gas.

When we came out of the pine grove, we saw that only ruins remained of the house of the grandmother. I drove like a madman. We found her surrounded by the few things that were saved. Surrounded also by the neighbors of all the ranches in the region who rushed to help when they saw the smoke.

I don't know what I expected but it did not surprise me to find her directing all the activities, giving orders. No tears, no whimpers, no laments.

"God gives and God takes away, my son. Blessed be His Holy Name."

I did lament. The crystal chandeliers, wrecked. The magnificent sets of tables and washstands with marble tops. The big basins and water jars in every bedroom, destroyed. The furniture brought from Kansas, turned to ashes. The bedspreads of lace, crochet, embroidery. The portraits, the pictures, the memories of a family.

Irony of ironies. There was a jar of holy water on the window sill in the attic. The rays of the sun, shining through the water, converted into a magnifying glass. The heat and the fire concentrated on a single spot and set on fire some old papers there. And all of the saints, the relics, the shrines, the altar to the Santo Niño de Atocha, the palms of Palm Sunday,[5] all burned up. All of the celestial security went up in smoke.

That night we gathered in what had been our old home. My grandmother seemed smaller to me, a little subdued, even a little docile: "Whatever you say, my son." This saddened me.

After supper my grandmother disappeared. I looked for her apprehensively. I found her where I could very well have suspected. At the top of the hill. Profiled by the moon. The wind in her face. Her skirt flapping in the wind. I saw her grow. And she was what she had always been: straight, tall and slender.

I saw the ash of her cigar light up. She was with my grandfather, the wicked one, the bold one, the quarrelsome one. Now the decisions would be made, the positions would be taken. She was regaining her spiritual strength. Tomorrow would be another day, but my grandmother would continue being the same one. And I was happy.

1977

# El Apache[1]

Around the 25th of May the soil was soft and fluffy after having been covered with snow and frozen for months and months of intense cold. You had to step with care, on foot or on horseback, because you would sink, and in addition there were so many rat and prairie dog holes that it was very easy to twist or break a leg. Water burst out of the earth everywhere. There were swamps and mud holes everywhere, also dangerous.

The entire earth was dressed in a new green, a soft and gentle green. On the tip of every branch of every tree there was a little bomb full of life ready to explode. The robin, just arrived, paraded his dignity. The canaries and the *chichontes*,[2] in cages and on branches, filled the air with gaiety. Bold and dancing little flowers climbed the hills and looked at themselves in the crystalline water. Over everything the vital and fertile smell of the damp earth freshly plowed. In all things the pristine promise of the newborn spring, of nature, eternal always.

---

5. Palm branches that symbolize Jesus Christ's entry into Jerusalem, an event commemorated on this Christian holiday. *Santo Niño de Atocha*: Roman Catholic depiction of the infant Jesus, popular in the Hispanic cultures of Spain, Mexico, and the southwestern United States, especially New Mexico.
1. Translated by Thelma Campbell Nason.
2. Plural for a type of bird like the oriole.

The flocks of sheep returned from the winter range in this atmosphere, in this feeling. The whole family went out to meet them as far as Cuba or Tapiecitas.[3] To have a picnic. To embrace don Nicomedes and Abrán. Men who had left their homes and had watched the sheep between heaven and earth for three fourths of a year. Far from all human contact. Alone with their solitude, their loyalty and their integrity. Men of trust and judgment.

What aromas! A great bonfire of piñón and cedar, with all its crackling, until it became glowing embers. Lamb ribs roasting over the coals, the grease dripping and exploding on the coals. The bread rising, with live coals over and under. The potatoes, now they stick now they don't, on the frying pan. The pot of beans, with corn and chunks of meat, buried in the earth with live coals and stones since dawn. What a treasure of smell, hunger and taste! I now wonder with some fear whether things were really better in those days, or if I have lost in large measure the capacity to appreciate, smell and taste.

This first visit unleashed a vortex of activity that took possession of the total attention of the family for some thirty days. To say that the sheep were expecting is to say nothing. They were in a state of emergency.

The lambing season began promptly on the 25th of May. It's a mystery to me how those in charge could determine with such certainty the exact moment when three thousand ewes were going to give birth. I know that at a given moment back in the fall the ewes and the rams were brought together and they remained together for a number of days. The lambing season terminated as suddenly as it had begun. By the 24th of June it was all over. Where did all that precision come from? Caramba, every married man knows that the exact moment of the birth of his children is one big uncertainty. The doctors are wrong most of the time.

The whole family moved to the Rincón[4] de las Nutrias. We had a cabin (we called it "fort") there. Downstairs there was a big hall that served as kitchen and dining area. It had a table like the one of the second-to-the-last supper.[5] I say this because instead of sitting thirteen it sat twenty-four. There was also a bedroom for my parents. We children slept in the attic. The two cooks slept in a tent next to the fort. The sheepherders slept in a series of tents on the other side of the river.

With twenty-four men alone, married or single, and only two women alone in the middle of spring in the country, I think that the cooks gave free rein to mother nature and father indulgence. The truth is that from time to time one of the boys would show up with unexplained black eyes. I imagine that there was ferocious competition for the love and the favors of these two queens of the beans and the night. Up there in the attic we got to hear laughter and noises along with the howling of the coyotes. As I remember they were both as ugly as a goat.

After supper the sheepherders retired to their camp. There, around a big fire, with the murmur of the water in the background, they strummed the guitar, sang, told jokes and stories, they said good or bad things about their neighbor. I used to like to go visit with them every night until they called

---

3. Town in Rio Arriba County, New Mexico. *Cuba:* a village in Sandoval County, which is south of Rio Arriba.

4. Grass meadow.

5. According to the Bible, the Last Supper was eaten by Jesus and his 12 disciples.

me from home. I felt a very masculine sensation in participating in the intimate things of men. Sometimes my father came too, but when he was present everything was much more decorous. I heard there some very daring couplets addressed to Berta and Cecilia, some quite coarse jokes, some very sharp barbs. Someone would get mad and let out a bad word. I loved it. I didn't understand half of what was going on, but it didn't matter.

The sheep were divided into two flocks of fifteen hundred sheep each, a flock of five hundred year-olds and a bunch of some seventy-five goats. For reasons that I didn't understand each one of these groups had to do its thing separately.

The flocks slept in immense corrals we called *mangas* that occupied a whole hillside or gully. The sheep slept spread out, quite loosely. In the dawn the sheep were allowed to get up by themselves and leave unmolested. This was important. It was necessary not to bother the sheep that had dropped their lambs during the night, not to frighten them because they were quite nervous, and to permit the mothers to become accustomed to their children. The flock left and the recent mothers remained, licking and caressing their feeble lambs. They remained that way all day. A shepherd watched them from a distance to see that a sheep and her lamb didn't become separated, to see if there were any problems and to help a ewe to a good delivery.

At the end of the day, when the little lambs felt a little stronger, the shepherd began to ease the sheep out of the *manga* little by little and very carefully. It seems that maternity produces in animals a psychological state somewhat similar to that of humans. One has to indulge the female in both cases. The shepherd would drive the new flock to the *chiquero* (a small corral made of fallen oaks). It was imperative at nightfall to light bonfires around the *chiqueros* to frighten off the coyotes—not to light their way.

As the little lambs grew the small flocks were brought together. Little by little the large flocks were being formed once again.

Then came the shearing. A band of shearers would arrive, like gypsies, and establish their camp alongside the camp of the sheepherders. More popularity for Berta and Cecilia. Competition, sometimes violence. I remember a song they sang Cecilia that began something like this:

> I love you because you're a who . . .
> I love you because you're a who . . .
> I love you because you're a wholesome lady.

Stronger things followed.

Those shearers had the whitest and softest hands I have ever seen. The grease of the wool is the best cream there is. Much later I found out that it is called "lanolin" and that it is the most important ingredient in cosmetics.

By the 24th of June the whole excitement was over. As everyone knows, that is the day of St. John.[6] On that day the waters of the rivers are holy. All of us went to wash in the river.

The shearers left as suddenly as they had appeared. The shepherds collected their money and left. The summer shepherds and *camperos* (assistants

---

6. John the Baptist (d. ca. AD 30), a mission preacher who led a movement of baptism at the Jordan River, in southwest Asia.

to the herders) took possession of the flocks, all of the small flocks together now.

The flocks left for the mountains. The goats in front. Followed by the *primales* (year-olds). Then the mass of the herd. The kids and lambs, naughty and frolicsome. A long chain that climbed the rough hillsides and the tortuous paths slowly.

The shepherd behind with his dogs hustling the slow ones or turning points and directing them in the same direction. The *campero* followed, driving his loaded burros. Herder and *campero* astride spirited horses.

Our flocks were not the only ones. The flocks of my uncles left approximately at the same time, more or less in the same circumstances.

Once camp had been set up we had to go out and look for *el Apache*. *El Apache* was a horse with an Apache brand that consisted of a star and a half moon. It must have run away from the Indians and become attached to our mountains years before.

There was tremendous competition among the *camperos* to see who would get *el Apache*. The one who caught him first got to keep him for the rest of the summer. There were two reasons. The horse was the tamest and most useful you can imagine. Besides, it was a pleasure to beat the rest of them.

When the flocks came down in the fall *el Apache* was turned loose to make out on his own till the following summer. He would join a herd of wild horses. Who knows how he survived.

This summer I was the campero, and it was my good luck to catch *el Apache*. One day I went to take provisions to Fulgencio, the herder of the rams and bucks (he-goats). The *machos* (males) were kept away from the females until October when the flocks left for the winter range. I must mention here that the males stink, especially the *chivatos* (he-goats). They really stink. One has to situate oneself with the wind at your back so that the wind will take that masculine odor somewhere else. Anytime I meet anyone who brags about being a *macho* I think of the *chivatos*.

The tent of Fulgencio was situated at the edge of the forest. We were sitting on the ground eating, very delicious ribs. We were enjoying the solitude, silence and serenity that only sheepherders know. Before our eyes was a wide and clean hillside, covered with grass. Above us a wide and clean sky, inhabited by tranquil and white little clouds. The *machos* grazed open, loose, in total peace. The wind was on our side. All the worlds moved, or remained, in complete harmony.

*El Apache* was tied in front of the tent with the rest of the horses. Asleep as always. He would sleep asleep. He would sleep awake. Lying down or on foot. He walked, and I think he ate, sleeping. Although he was not up to those things anymore, for well known reasons, I suppose that if he had been up to them, he would have made love in sheer ecstasy, that is, fast asleep. In all cases his lower lip would hang loose as if it didn't belong to him, or as if it had come off. He was brown with white patches on his belly. He was the ideal pack horse. His load never fell off. He wasn't easily frightened. He was always there when you needed him. He accepted, asleep, all the indignities of his job.

This time he was in another world, as usual, as his tail swatted away the flies in this one. His tail was a fan, a whip and a handkerchief with which he scared off the cloud of flies that surrounded him with rhythmic and restless movements. Sometimes he shook his head. Sometimes he stamped his feet, for the same reason, without abandoning ever his animal and Apache Nirvana.

He had a belly. As round as a pot and as voluminous as an aerial balloon, and it hung on him like a wine skin. At the middle of his body it wasn't very far from the ground. The weight of this aberration, naturally, formed something like a cradle or a half-moon on top. So he looked like a thick, bizarre and sleepy hammock suspended in the air, or in time, in the most arbitrary way.

These were the circumstances in which we found ourselves when the peace of our existence went whoof and became violence. The harmony of the worlds broke and the quiet clamor of the mute was turned loose.

There was a blind ram in the herd. Blind animals live happily as long as they feel secure, surrounded by their own. Once they find themselves alone they go crazy.

This one (perhaps carried away by his gastronomical pleasures or lost in memories of his love life) became careless. Suddenly he was all alone. As was to be expected, he went berserk. He became the victim of a dreadful panic. Completely insane he began to run in the most disorderly way. Without caution. Without direction.

He kept getting farther and farther away from the herd. He kept getting closer and closer to the trees and us with reckless speed. Now and then he would bleat, half in rage, half in terror. We were fascinated, still and mute. Our hearts in our throats.

When he got to the trees what had to happen did. The first crash sounded like an explosion. It seemed that the world itself shook. The collision was so powerful that the whole back part of the animal rose in the air. The crashes continued. Sometimes he would hit a tree with such force that he bounced back, only to rise and straighten up and continue his individual mad rush, straight for us. I thought, "If he hits the tent, he'll take it with him." I forgot about the horses. We were ready to duck behind a tree at any moment. The situation was tragic, dangerous and dramatic.

I don't know if because the spectacle was so far from the normal and for that reason it began to appear unreal and fantastic to us, or because of some human perversity, we began to laugh. I know that this is cruel. Hasn't it ever happened to you sometime? The pain, the discomfort, the inconvenience of others, sometimes your own, begin to appear incongruous, they pass on to appear ridiculous and end up being laughable. We became sick with laughter. We rolled over on the ground, hit the ground with our fists, screamed as if in despair. Our tears came out in streams. Nothing else came out because God is good.

The overwhelming force of nature found us in this dementia. Only the blindness of the ram saved us. He passed in front of us like a bolt of lanolin.

This cooled us off. Our laughing spree froze. We stared stupidly as the beast ran directly toward the horses. *El Apache* was in the fifth cycle of some happy dream, sleeping happinesses and dreaming Apache paradises. I prayed fast.

Absorbed, we watched him hit the Indian horse on his motley belly with the force and velocity of a raging projectile. *El Apache* exploded like an atomic bomb. A whoosh that made the trees shake and vibrate for a mile and a half, stopped the birds in their flight, and made the fish poke their heads out to see what unheard of thing was going on. He fell with a force that made seven acres of land shake.

This time we did not get sick. This time we died. We died laughing. And being good Christians, we rose from the dead in three days.[7] *El Apache,* who wasn't a Christian, rose from the dead in three days too.

1977

7. I.e., as Jesus did.

---

# JOSÉ YGLESIAS
## 1919–1995

Born in the Ybor City section of Tampa, Florida, to Cuban Spanish parents, José Yglesias was raised in the Cuban-immigrant community. After leaving Tampa for New York City at age 17, he worked at various jobs until enlisting in the U.S. Navy during World War II. After the war, he studied at Black Mountain College, in North Carolina, and became film critic for the *Daily Worker,* a newspaper published in New York by the Communist Party USA. In 1953, Yglesias became an executive at a pharmaceutical firm. He left the company to devote himself to writing after the publication of his first novel, *A Wake in Ybor City* (1963), a groundbreaking work detailing three days in the life of a Cuban American family in Tampa. In addition to the articles, stories, and reviews he published in magazines such as *Esquire,* *The New Yorker,* and *The Nation,* he wrote seven novels, four works of nonfiction, and several translations. Over the years, he received two Guggenheim Fellowships and a National Endowment for the Humanities Award. His interest in working-class lives and his spare but lyrical style make Yglesias an important precursor of younger Latino writers.

Many of Yglesias's novels—beginning with *A Wake in Ybor City* and moving through *The Truth about Them* (1971), *Home Again* (1987), and *Tristan and the Hispanics* (1989)—chronicle the lives of Latino immigrants, most often Cubans, and their adjustment to American life. With a fine eye for detail and characterization, Yglesias charts the evolution of these families from the poverty and disorientation of their early immigrant years to their emergence into America's middle class. He writes of the close-knit warmth of the Latino family, and of the exile community's efforts to preserve its Cuban identity only to see it dissolve as new generations prosper and leave home. Yglesias's characters deal with the emptiness of leaving home and the cultural shock of returning later. Launched on a journey of self-discovery, the protagonists of his novels and stories attempt to strike a balance between their ethnic background and their political convictions and personal relationships.

In his nonfiction, Yglesias lets his subjects speak for themselves, but filters their rhetoric—of revolution and oppression, poverty and dignity—through his reportorial skepticism. In 1964, he traveled to Spain to explore the Galician village where his father was born and to which, shortly before dying, his father returned. In *The Goodbye Land* (1967), Yglesias chronicles the trip; records his reactions to the harsh province, which sent many immigrants to Cuba; and places his family's journey within the history of European immigration. In *In the Fist of the Revolution: Life in a Cuban Country Town* (1968), Yglesias explores the way Fidel Castro's revolution affected the lives of people in Mayarí, a Cuban village where he lived for three months. In *Down There* (1970), a related work, he interviews young revolutionaries in Brazil, Cuba, Chile, and Peru about their lives and the United States. Yglesias lived in Spain in 1975–76 and was there when Francisco Franco, the longtime Spanish dictator, died in 1975. In *The Franco Years* (1977), he profiles the lives under the Franco regime of Spaniards of differing ages, backgrounds, and political philosophies.

In his final book, *The Guns in the Closet* (published posthumously in 1996), a collection of stories whose settings range from New York City to Tampa, Yglesias further explores self-discovery, cultural displacement, and homecoming.

---

## *From* HOME AGAIN

## *From* Chapter One

I walked into the empty old house in Tampa and the phone was ringing. Who could it be? No one knew I had left New York. Peace, peace in my old age; that's all I wanted.

It was my cousin Tom-tom. He said, "What are you doing here?"

"Why are you calling here?" I said, hectoring like a Tampa Latin (we never called ourselves Hispanics) as if I hadn't lived my whole adult life away from that tacky, inquisitive town and family, and long ago turned into a real American, which is worse.

He made a temporizing, grumbling noise into the phone.

"You know Celia and Cuco have been dead four months," I said.

"I was at the funeral," he said. "Where were you?"

"There's nobody here now," I said, still taking his tack.

"That's why," he said softly, changing course on me. "I don't like to think of Aunt Mama's house all quiet and lonely. I call 'cause that way at least the phone rings."

"You're crazy," I said and chuckled a bit, for the first time in months.

Tom-tom laughed along for a second, and then slowly, but gathering momentum, he composed an eulogy of Aunt Mama, my mother, dead twelve years at least. He ended it with the same statement he made at every last encounter in our lives, a kind of unanswerable explanation for their closeness: "Aunt Mama and I were born the same day, November twenty-nine, you know."

"Twenty years apart," I said, denying him his claim, bastard that I am.

"I was the oldest nephew," he said. "She was my youngest aunt."

He waited me out and I finally said, "You were her favorite nephew," giving her back to him, what the hell.

"You're so smart," he said. He had said that many times. Six times, to be exact. Each time I had come visiting after I published my first book thirty years ago. More drawn out again: "You're so smart."

"Yeah," I said.

"Today is November twenty-nine," he said. Then he yelled at his wife Olivia without protecting my listening ear. "I'm talking to Pinpin, for Christ's sake, don't scratch yourself, use the salve!" To me: "She never does what the doctor tells her."

"Listen, Tom-tom, I just walked in," I said.

"How does the place look?" he said, refusing to let go.

I was standing in the doorway of the kitchen, using the wall phone there, and I looked at the dining room and the living room ahead of me and at the open front door. It framed a super-realist picture of a patch of the four-foot-deep front yard planted with coarse Florida lawn grass; beyond it the bright sun made a tarred spot in the street glisten, and beyond that Corona's front porch across the way. A young black walked on the balls of his feet on Corona's sidewalk, his face turned towards our door as if he were peering into mine. More likely, he was staking out the house.

Mother, Celia, Cuco, everyone used to say you cannot leave the screen door unlatched, the front or back door unlocked. Christ, there wasn't going to be any peace here for me either. I'd be ruled by those dead voices and the deteriorating neighborhood. You can't run away: the tritest, most worn-out wisdom of rotten movies and worse novels.

One final cliché: those dumb, wised-up heroes let you know—or their hack creators did—that they were, by God, going to start over again. Not me, I didn't want that. I was not returning, touching base, none of that. No swelling movie music for me. I was staying here for good and myself deteriorating as fast as I could. Tampa was where I came from; that's all you could say for it.

Note this: this is a fact. I'm a writer and I tend to talk fiction, but the following is fact: I am at the end of my tether, I am desperate.

Zing—standing there with the clean white phone in my hand (who kept it so clean these last months?) I got my terrifying airy feeling (it was mine alone) of total despair. My body lost its plumb, its density, its feeling of belonging to me. I had never heard of its happening to anyone, not even in literature, only to me. Coming down here, breaking all ties, holing up, that had done it—I was in outer space without an umbilical line. And no one strong enough to draw me back. I blinked and blinked and blinked: nothing took on substance. I came to on a kitchen chair, and I thought, I must not be entirely weightless: I had lowered myself into this chair.

You cannot wipe out all your knowledge and experience and then hope to start anew. You'd be an infant in an ungraspable world. You have to bring something with you, some little knowledge, a truth around which gather the barnacles of life. I didn't have it; I didn't want it.

Dixie Lee was Bing Crosby's[1] first wife. That's all I could remember and it would have to do. I took a deep breath.

The phone rang. It was Tom-tom; I must have hung up on him. He said, "Is the phone working as bad in New York with this A T and T thing?"

"Tom-tom," I began.

"Wait, wait, I'll forget. How'd you get to the house?"

"I'll call you later," I said.

---

1. American singer and actor (1903–1977). *Dixie Lee*: American actress, dancer, and singer (1911–1952).

"I mean, did you drive down or did you fly and then take a taxi or did you rent a car?"

"A taxi."

"Then I'll come pick you up."

"No, no, I got to unpack and settle in."

"Settle in?" Tom-tom said. "You here for more than a couple of days? Goddamnit, damn it, I got eleven brothers and sisters and fifteen cousins and—"

"Tom-tom," I said.

"Don't question my figures. I got nothing to do but count them up. I got fifty nieces and nephews alone. A lot of good. They didn't bother to tell me you were here. And my fifteen cousins got thirty, thirty-two kids. I'm coming right over. You got to eat. Olivia can still cook. They never tell me anything. You think you can depend on family, you can't. But you can depend on me, Pinpin—remember when I was a counterman and I got you the dishwasher job? It was much better during the Depression.[2] We saw each other, we were real cousins. I can still cook. A little. Roast beef, anyway. I'm coming over and pick you up."

"Tomorrow," I said and started to hang up but I could hear him talking fast and furious and brought the phone back to my ear.

"I have to talk to you about iron grilles for the windows. You got to have them or they'll break in and steal the furniture. Iron grilles like they put on the new Spanish restaurants. Not for fancy, for protection. And a wire mesh on the front door glass. All Cuco and Celia had was regular locks and a spotlight on the backyard. That's not enough. Not since Mariel."[3]

He was out of breath.

I quickly repeated, "Tomorrow," and hung up. What a mess.

Two steps into the living room and the phone rang again.

"Actually, I had an idea from Marina that you might be coming," he said the moment I picked it up. "Don't treat me like this. I call all my cousins and brothers and sisters all the time. Once a week. We get unlimited local calls in Tampa. But they're all too busy. Pinpin, I have to talk to you. You were always the smart one in the family. You made a living just sitting at your desk. Your own desk. In your own home. Remember, I asked you once?"

He laughed and wheezed and coughed.

"Look at me, with this apartment house. I got to look after it by myself. Olivia can't help. It takes all her energy not to scratch. Scratch! You better believe it. They got that sign says Children Playing and they don't let me take it off. I got to talk to you about that, too."

"Give me an hour," I said. "Give me an hour to unpack."

"Sure. Sure, you need time to think," he said, mollified, the anxiety in his voice disappearing like a radio turned off. "Do me a favor, think about the Children Playing. Think how I can put it nicely, humbly to the police—I always say a thing humbly the first time round. I'm not like some people come in punching. What was I saying?"

"We'll talk about it later."

2. The Great Depression, a dramatic economic downturn associated with the stock market crash on October 29, 1929.
3. The Mariel Boatlift, a mass movement of

Cubans who departed from Cuba's Mariel Harbor for the United States from April 15 to October 31, 1980.

"Oh, Children Playing. How to explain to them that it ruins my business if people think there are brats around making a lot of noise. The Police Department doesn't care. They leave it to the Traffic Department to decide. There are no children in my apartment house—Olivia wouldn't have them. I was going to take the sign off but the American wouldn't let me. It's my property, he says, my property—"

"What American?" I said and immediately regretted it.

"The one across the street. West Tampa isn't what it used to be, Pinpin— it's full of Americans."

He sighed so loudly that he would not have heard me say good-bye.

"It's not his property, it belongs to the city. The sidewalk to the curb belongs to the city. But do you think the city takes care of it? No, I got to plant the grass and then mow it the way they like. The time I was sick, those bastards from Pride came by and bothered Olivia. The weeds were too high and it didn't look good for the neighborhood. She told them a thing or two. It was better than scratching."

He laughed the low rumbling laugh that was his real laugh: it said, you made a mistake about me, buddy, I know a thing or two.

"Pride?" I said, curious like the writer I once was.

"Something they made up to clean the neighborhoods. It's a racket. They don't *pay* for anything, they just needle you, you know. And they have people of the other race to come tell you what you got to do."

Time was, and Tom-tom knew it, I would have said something angry about race prejudice.

When he got no rise from me, he hurried to explain. He needn't have—I let people be now, and everyone more or less returns the compliment.

He said, "They're just doing a job, I know that, and I'm glad colored people are getting all the jobs. But that son of a bitch doesn't own that sign and he takes no care of his yard. In fact, lousy. I was in the hospital, but I told Olivia, you look see if he don't cut his grass. He waited until I couldn't do it, then he cut his grass and called Pride about our weeds, the son of a bitch."

"Tom-tom," I said.

"OK, I'm hanging up," he said, and in his low, melodious voice, the one he always used on my mother, he added, "Oh, it's so good, man, to have you back here where you belong."

And he hung up.

I didn't unpack. He'd left me weak with irritability, he had interrupted my stride. I went out to the porch and sat claiming my territory, but I did not let my gaze stray beyond the veranda. Let the neighbors see me. But don't let them make eye contact. It won't make them less curious, but it keeps them from coming over. Some residual Spanish code of manners still operates in these Latin streets in Tampa. I believe this. That's one more reason I left New York. I was testing my block now. Could I sit on the porch whenever I wanted and not be bothered? There had once been a wooden swing at the end where I now sat. Shaded by a palm tree, and I had lain on it much of the time when I was a kid, after I gave up softball for reading. My mother and sister and grandfather spent the day at the factory (my father had died on me when I was seven) and no one bothered me then. Bother, it's a word I use a lot. But everyone on the block had seen me read. (And reach into my pants now and then to jerk off?) I know this from my first visit back years later when my mother took me round to her friends on the block and told them I wrote books and they all said, "I am not surprised—how you used to read when you were a boy!" Maybe I'll do that again. Read, not make the rounds. Dickens.[4] I could be another man who loved Dickens. I waited and still did not look up: if someone comes over, I will have to get out of Tampa. If not, I shall buy a swing, but not a wooden one: something softer for my old bones.

No one came over.

I must build a character for myself. A persona, as the phonies now say. If someone asks me, I could say I'm a former writer. A new category: former writer. I liked that kind of bitterness. No slobbering appeal for sympathy. It is a matter of fact—especially down here where everyone had retired. I looked up, ready to share the thought and, thank God, there was no one on the porch across the street. Corona, a widow and more ancient than I, lived there. My wit would be lost on her. If she had any, she would have changed her name. Former writer, I repeated to myself and a heavy stone rolled off my chest—an apt, wounding epithet always calms me.

. . .

Tom-tom woke me. My head had fallen forward willy-nilly. I slept like old people on New York park benches, and like them I came to with a start. In terror. Was I being mugged?

"I scared you," Tom-tom said.

Was he trying to provoke me?

"I'm too old for that," I said and looked him full in the face. He looked like his father, Papa Leandro, and it made me dizzy. The dizziness had nothing to do with illness, but it reminded me of my medicines.

"I have to go inside first," I said.

"Wait, wait," he said. "This ain't New York. There's time for everything. Let me look at you."

I looked at him too. Somewhere on Papa Leandro's side there must have been some peasants from the north of Spain. Asturians or Basques or maybe Galicians like my father, for he was broad and gave the impression of squat-ness, of a stone wall astride a field; his hips were as wide as his shoulders and his length was in his body not his legs. Papa Leandro could shift all that vol-ume delicately, sinuously, in a rumba danced on a dime. Not Tom-tom: his legs were only meant to hold him up, two sticks stuck wide apart into his bar-rel of a body, and he was too alert to surrender to any music.

"Can you still get it up?" he said.

He laughed and he tried to shift his green eyes about to look wicked, an old maneuver of his, ending in a misdirected Rudolph Valentino[5] amorous squint.

"You don't have to answer that," he said. "And you don't have to ask me either."

Then with a sigh of nostalgia exuding brotherly warmth and spit he grabbed my arm. "Oh, Pinpin," he exclaimed.

4. Charles Dickens (1812–1870), English novelist.     (1895–1926); known as "the Latin Lover."
5. Italian-born American actor and sex symbol

I shook my arm away. I am practically a Wasp now. All this Latin touching and importuning makes me nervous.

"I'll be right back," I said and got to the screen door before he did. I heard it slam behind me and damn if his voice didn't continue. He was talking to the neighbors, for Christ's sake. I could hear him from the second bedroom where my backpack (I was just like the kids these days about that: carry your life with you) lay on mother's old bed, filled with medicines—beta blockers, diuretics, Valiums, Dalmanes, digitalis, insulin, syringes, the whole caboodle. I could swallow any without water, but some left a bitter trail, and I went off to the kitchen hearing Tom-tom still talking to someone. They'd all be invading the old house any minute.

"Wait, wait," Tom-tom said close by and startled me again.

I said over my shoulder, "I'm just getting some water."

He held me back with his heavy grip. "Let me see. Maybe you take the same thing I do." He mauled the backpack, moving his big hands inside it, and added, "The one I take is a pink tablet. That's blue, isn't it?"

"What do you take?" I asked.

"I told you, a pink pill. It has a line down the middle, a little groove. Yours doesn't."

He was looking at the Valium. "Too yellow," he said.

I swallowed the Inderal to keep him from inspecting it. Maybe I should take a Valium. Get me through dinner with him and Olivia. Tom-tom pulled out a syringe from the backpack. I took it from him, shook out a Valium quick, and snatched the backpack from him and zippered it up.

"You're going to sleep in here?" he said unperturbed. "Why don't you take their front bedroom with the big bed?"

"I haven't decided," I said, and popped the Valium in my mouth.

"For God's sake, take some water," he said. "Go. Get some."

He followed me to the kitchen.

"Not from the faucet!" He opened the tall refrigerator. There was a plastic pitcher-container there filled with water. He knew which cabinet door to open for glasses. "Here," he said. "Marina told me she got things ready for you."

"I asked her to," I explained.

We bickered: he said, "I knew," and I replied, "Then you were aware I was coming."

"You could've asked me too," he said, "or just me only. Marina is OK in case of a funeral but otherwise she's a terrible gossip. You don't want everybody to know your business. And there are some who say that she wasn't exactly fair about how she distributed Celia and Cuco's things, you know. You coulda asked me about that too."

"Actually, she volunteered to get the house in order." Why was I explaining?

"Of course, of course," he said. "She would."

Good that I took the Valium. There are nerves that still coil up, tighter and tighter, more or less on their own, for I don't really care. No more than I cared when Cora finally died. Peace, peace. Nor did I care now about Tom-tom or what he insinuated Marina took from the old house.

"Water from the faucet can kill you," he grumbled when I didn't reply. "Did she call you or you call her?"

"I don't remember," I said.

"That's just like you," he said. "I told Olivia, Pinpin is an innocent."

"Tom-tom, I can't stay with you too long, I have to get back here and unpack."

"You said you were going to unpack. Why didn't you? I gave you time."

I took a deep breath. I did not believe in answering questions of that kind. Of any kind. That's why I was here, because I wasn't going to answer questions or even listen to them.

"What are you going to do about a car?" Tom-tom said.

"There are taxis," I said. "They'll come to the house."

"What are you trying to do—insult me? I mean, a car for your visit here. I tell you what—I'll take you around. You can't walk and take buses like the old days. You'll be mugged. They go for old men first, you know. Bang. You can't walk over to the Spanish Club or any place on Seventh Avenue. Remember old Gumersindo Gonzalez, they got him when he walked to the corner mailbox . . ."

And so on and so on.

In the car Tom-tom announced he wasn't taking the freeway. He wanted me to see what it was like now going across town from Ybor City (the old Latin section) to West Tampa (the other, almost equally old Latin section). He didn't fool me; I knew that none of my old cousins ever drove on the freeway. At first, because like good Latins they didn't take easily to new things; now, because they were old and scared of cars going fifty. Celia and Cuco were an exception and look what happened to them: squashed and killed instantly by a truck that lost its brakes on the freeway.

"I know, I know," I said when he began about the old American homes on Nebraska. "Everything has deteriorated."

"You can't know this," he said while we waited for the light at Nebraska. "Take a look, I don't want them to see me pointing."

There they were, the young black prostitutes. You know them: they're in your town too, on the worn-out old avenues, Ninth in New York, etc., sticking their shining supple legs into the street, giving the youngsters behind the wheel hardons, hooking only the aging. The young get it free now.

"Why don't you want them to see you pointing? They're no shrinking violets."

Tom-tom nudged me. "Their pimps are Marielitos, every one of them. Look."

I looked, to please him.

"You know, Cubans. They'll slit your throat."

On the porch and sidewalk at the corner rooming house were the pimps. Or were they dealers? Both, probably. They stood in poses that went with the desuetude of the house. The two-story clapboard was faded and grimy, the yard bare sand and scraggly weeds; so neglected it looked like a stage set. Down to the ersatz lace curtains at a couple of windows, near black with filth, their ends in shreds. The other windows were cavernous black holes. I could see the corner of a sheetless mattress.

"Jesus, I wish the light would change," Tom-tom said.

I had seen those guys in the Parque Central in Old Havana on my last assignment there. The park with the Jose Marti[6] statue on which some of our sailors had pissed while on a rum grand liberty. Before Fidel, of course.

6. See p. 265.

Maybe it was their brothers or cousins I'd seen. They were Cuban, in any case, and malevolent in a special Caribbean way. Slithery, a half-smile always turned on, evil male Mona Lisas.[7]

If I died at their hands, my life would be an overworked metaphor. Or a late, bad Tennessee Williams play.[8]

Tom-tom said, "That's what Fidel sent us."

You let ten years go by without publishing and nobody knows who you are and what you wrote. Tom-tom of course had read nothing I wrote, but he should've remembered I had even met Fidel. (My Cuba book was out of print, needless to say.) I had to go up to Boston two months earlier (unwillingly) to see the law firm that has been handling Cora's family's byzantine investments and trusts since . . . oh, 1776 very likely, and the young-old preppy took a glancing jab at Cuba and I let him have it for old time's sakes, for Fidel and Che and Haydée Santamaría.[9] He took a second look at my Brooks[1] suit and silk knit tie and I saw him wonder how I could so brazenly sail under false colors. Then he remembered that I had not been born into Cora's family, that every generation suffers some defection in old Massachusetts Bay Colony families, et cetera.

God, I hate those Wasps now. Jews, too, the whole lot.

"You wanted them here," I said. "Come, come, to the land of freedom—so they came."

"Me?" he said. "Never." But he kept his voice low. "How can you say that! If only in memory of my Papa Leandro."

He chuckled nostalgically. I didn't join him. I wasn't going to be sentimental about anybody.

"You know they threw red paint at our old house. Papa Leandro used to turn on the Havana station so loud when Fidel spoke that the whole block might as well have been at the meeting in Havana."

In his special adoring tone, he added, "And Aunt Mama, she was that way too."

"OK, OK," I said.

After a slight pause, for effect I swear—they're all actors in my family—he prodded me with his elbow. "Remember when we were young in New York? I was practically a Communist, right? And you weren't far behind."

"I *was* a Communist, you know that," I said. (What did he want?) "The Young Communist League."

He lowered his voice. "I didn't want to be the one to say it first."

"Why not?"

"It's very bad again. Anybody asks me, I tell them I voted for Reagan[2] both times. I can't afford to be as crazy as Papa Leandro."

"Fuck 'em."

"What?"

"Tell them to take this fucking country and stick it up their asses."

7. I.e., like distorted versions of the cryptically smiling woman in the painting by the Italian artist Leonardo da Vinci (1452–1519).
8. The lesser works of this American playwright (1911–1983) are known for their dramatic overkill.
9. Prominent political and literary figure in Fidel Castro's Communist regime; established the Cu-

ban publishing house Casa de las Américas. *Che*: Ernesto "Che" Guevara (1928–1967), Argentinian-born Latin American activist and guerrilla fighter who fought along with Castro.
1. Brooks Brothers, an upscale purveyor of men's clothing.
2. Ronald Reagan (1911–2004), U.S. president 1981–89.

He prodded me on the side again. "You're not going to talk that way around here, are you?"

"Why not? That's the way our parents and grandparents talked, remember?"

He lifted his eyebrows and moved his haunches.

"Didn't they?" I said.

"Yeah, but they're all dead."

And there's nobody to protect me. No uncle or older cousin to stand on the porch and yell at the bully who's holding me down in the dirt.

That's not true about my uncles. They watched and said nothing. Later, when the fight was over, they would say, "You don't start it, but you hit back hard. And dirty. Anywhere you can reach him and give it all you've got. If you lose, don't cry. No tears."

No tears. Reagan is no more than we deserve. It's a dumb-ass country.

Don't start it—that's what I never could learn. Chin out, I attack, I insult, I yell—the old picket-line tactics. I had to learn, after I began to meet writers and publishing types, to correct idiots only with a Century Club[3] hauteur. I stopped yelling; still, I stood my ground. But I never won. You could say I barged into things, but I spoke my piece coolly. I stayed awake nights turning the day over in my mind, rewriting the rejoinders I had made, getting ready for the next encounter, making resolutions—getting out of bed, finally, for a sleeping pill.

A couple of times a year we went up to Boston, more often as Cora grew older. (I think I grew less older than Cora and the rest of my generation.) I spent many an hour with her father or brother or cousin or old beau nodding about sailing in Maine or politely answering questions about my work as if reporting on a far-off exotic country. Then I would intentionally say something about something that I cared about—Martin Luther King, *Portnoy's Complaint*, Jules Feiffer,[4] you name it—and they would respond:

"Yes, so I've heard."

Or, "Hmnnn—you believe that?"

Or, "Well, I shall have to look into that."

Or, "Old Tonky's on the board of United Fruit.[5] It'll be fun to throw that his way and see how he gnaws on it."

Or, "How about more scotch?"

I hate scotch.

I had not counted on finding Cuban refugees in Tampa. I'd have to think about that. I asked Tom-tom if there were any on my block.

"Oooh, they're all over! They're getting welfare, they're taking over the grocery stores, the drugs, they got everything now, man. My brother-in-law Serafin is involved with them. And Serafin has never been involved with anybody good."

"So they're accepted?"

"What do you mean?"

---

3. The Century Association, a private club in Manhattan with a distinguished history. Its members include authors, artists, and professionals.
4. American cartoonist and author (b. 1929). *Portnoy's Complaint*: novel published in 1969 by the American writer Philip Roth (b. 1933). *Martin Luther King*: American clergyman and civil rights leader (1929–1968).
5. United Fruit Company, major American corporation that grew tropical fruit in the so-called Third World and sold it in the United States and Europe.

"People like them? They've made friends?"

"Me, I don't like them. Olivia won't even go into any store or restaurant they own." He laughed. "She says they make her want to scratch more."

"What's the matter with Olivia?"

"Some little thing, down there . . . women."

There was something else on his mind, and his face took on that serious air and his voice the dark tone that is sometimes genuine with him: "And then there is Papa Leandro and Aunt Mama and our Cuban grandfather and his Jose Martí this and Jose Martí that to take into consideration. It's bad luck to go against them too much."

I made a skeptical noise and wondered whether I really could live down here. Cuban refugees. *Gusanos.*[6] Worms. The ghosts of our parents.

Tom-tom misunderstood and tried to head me off. "Now, Pinpin, don't yell at me about superstition and the hereafter. I don't believe in it any more than you do, but what if they're listening and watching and know if we're making friends with those counter-revolutionaries? That's what they would call them, you know—counter-revolutionaries."

His shoulders hunched over the wheel (his was some twelve-year-old American car, a Plymouth or a Dodge or something) but he decided to chuckle. He looked out the corners of his green eyes to see what I thought. He elbowed me again and said, "I was only fooling," but he only half was.

"I don't give a shit," I said.

"What! What! Didn't you—Aunt Mama said you used to go over there to Cuba to meet all the revolutionaries and write books. You wrote a whole book about it, right?"

"Where are we?" I said.

"Where are we?" he asked. "Oh, that's the bridge, we're crossing into West Tampa. Jesus, I don't have to tell you that's the Hillsborough River, do I?"

"It's all changed," I said, but I was thinking, it's all the same.

My sons came down here for two days when my mother died. Crispin drove to the funeral home alone with me once and on the way he said, "How do you tell one street corner from the other?"

He was right, but I still feel a residual cringe at his comment. His upperclass tone too, I guess.

"Well, I guess you're retired—you're sixty-five, right?" Tom-tom asked. Then added, "But you could always go back to it."

I liked that, so I said, "Maybe."

"Come on, you may get rusty but it's like everything else, right?" he said. He slowed down. "There's a little favor you can do me. You may have guessed. Let me tell you before we get to my place."

Here it comes.

"I need you to write a letter to the Traffic Department for me. About the Children Playing sign. The police won't do anything about it until they get a request from the Traffic Department, you see." He paused. "You're a writer, even if you're retired."

"That's the favor?"

"You can write it right on the typewriter without any mistakes. I want to mail it right off. I have a typewriter—someone wasn't paying the rent, you

6. Literally, worms; derogatory term in Cuban Spanish to describe exiled Cubans in the United States.

know—and that way they won't see any difference between the signature and the writing."

He elbowed me again. "You'll do it?"

I moved a bit away from him; it's not good for me to be bruised. Hell, I forgot to transfer the insulin to the refrigerator. In Tampa it would boil and ferment in the backpack.

"That's what I was going to spend the evening doing—on my own birthday. Thinking of Aunt Mama too, of course. You were a professional, you can still zing off a letter, right? Will you do it, really?"

He lifted a hand off the wheel and poked my ribs. This time I moved to the window, and nodded. Was this all he wanted?

He slowed down even more. "Olivia has her own ideas how the letter should go. Yak, yak. A lot of boasting how we pay big taxes and that we own the apartment house. But I think we should go easy on that. Humility, that's the way to go."

"You cheating on taxes?"

"Ha, ha. But I don't want to give them ideas we should grease their palms. We gonna have to do it anyway, but there's no point raising their expectations. How do you like that—raising their expectations? That's very high-class English. You can make that letter as fancy as you like—but humble."

He speeded up again and we turned off Columbus into the dark little streets built after the war in those rattler-ridden scrub and palmettos of West Tampa. Golden real estate.

"Anyway, Olivia can't read any too well without glasses and she won't go out and get any with this scratching. So she won't put up an argument if you say you wrote what she said, more or less, right?" He chuckled. "First be humble, then if they're arrogant, knock em down."

"The police?"

"Them, never! The Traffic Department."

"What they taught us," I said and pointed at the roof of the car as he had done when talking about dead parents spying on us, "was to be polite. Humble is another matter."

"Have it your way. I'm ten years older, but you were always smarter. I got an empty apartment and that sign is a jinx. You gonna sell the old house? What do you want for it?"

So that was it.

"It's probably full of termites," he added.

I shook my head; he was bargaining.

"You're not?" He was thinking fast, speculating. "What you doing here?"

"I'm thinking . . ."

He went slower and slower, waiting for me to complete the sentence.

Finally, he said, "I didn't believe Marina. You know how she is—secretive, suspicious. You mean to live—"

"I'm thinking," I said. "I like to think in peace once in a while."

He swung the car slowly to the curb, muttered "fuck you" to the driver he cut off, and stopped altogether. There was a near-pileup of three cars, but he paid no attention to their honking.

"Tell me here now," he said. "I don't want Olivia interrupting when we get home. You say you're not selling the house, and you're thinking of living here? For good?"

Goddamnit, I had told Marina, "I'm moving into the old house," at a moment when I had hit bottom and I was sorry I didn't take it back immediately. It was a kind of expletive and she should have understood. Not that I still didn't mean to stay. But I had to hedge: I didn't want all those cousins and the hundreds of children they had spawned breathing down my neck.

"I'm a little groggy from the plane and it's getting on to evening," I said. "Let's go on."

"But Marina practically said it outright."

"I'll ask Marina," I said. "Maybe she can tell me what I'm going to do."

"You're really coming back. I knew it, I knew it! You were the only holdout. Everybody came back, you know, when you could make a living again after the war in good old Tampa."

"But not in the cigar factories," I said, which to me were the palm trees in my garden of Eden.

"So what?" he said. "Who cares about the cigar factories, so what?" He stopped abruptly and pointed up. "Shush, they might be listening—Aunt Mama, my father." Then he took a deep breath and laughed.

So what?

That's my life—so what?

My hometown—gone.

My books—out of print.

Two sons—neither looks like me or thinks like me or—

Well, they're writers, I admit. I must have influenced them somehow. A role model, as they say without cringing at the jargon. Writers, but can you call living in Hollywood and dictating to secretaries writing? The characters and ideas in their scripts are so manhandled by agents, directors, producers, studio vice-presidents, and stars that only God knows who thought up what. Neither Crispin nor Jared owns a pen, I believe, or a typewriter or a notebook. When the secretaries aren't around they tap words into a word processor and it is equipped with a screenplay software floppy disk (get that?) that makes all the proper indentations and spacings and remembers the characters' names and tells the printer how to format (get that verb?) the whole thing into what looks like a perfect, finished script. They don't even have to know how to spell correctly (and they don't, having gone to all those progressive schools)—another floppy disk does that for them. From their separate homes the computers talk to one another, hill to beach, studio to yacht, Beverly Hills restaurant to Vegas casino.

Perhaps if I owned a computer they might talk to me too.

My one pleasure in this: their writing careers gall Aunt Snooky and Aunt Lucretia and Uncles Binky, Dinky, and Boo. These Boston idiots believe that real writers are venerable in their lifetimes, like Emerson, Longfellow, and Lowell.[7] Still, the Hollywood grandnephews remain in their wills and codicils, and Cora's long last will and testament was a miracle of exclusion, adhering strictly to the royal line.

---

7. James Russell Lowell (1819–1891), American poet, essayist, and diplomat born in Cambridge, Massachusetts. *Emerson*: Ralph Waldo Emerson (1803–1882), American essayist, philosopher, and poet born in Boston. *Longfellow*: Henry Wadsworth Longfellow (1807–1882), American educator and poet born in Portland, Maine (then part of Massachusetts)

The things that Cora and I acquired together are mine for the damn little bit of life she left me to myself. (I think of myself now as having been an attendant prince. What a laugh, that flat-assed antelope a queen!) There's the furniture and paintings in the New York apartment, the books I bought on Fourth Avenue, the used linens, et cetera et cetera. But not the family silver nor the china service that they indeed ordered from China two and a half centuries ago, nor the Madeira tablecloths and the eighteen-by-thirty silk Kirman. Nor, of course, Aunt Harriet's Georgian house in Castine[8] with half a mile of deep-water frontage. Mine—my very own—is the unheated house on the treeless hill in the midst of blueberry barrens where on a windy day you can get blown down running to the outhouse. It was my own writing studio in the days when, as the therapists say, I functioned. I bought it for two thousand one hundred dollars from a debased, holy-roller descendant of the great Puritans of the Massachusetts Bay Colony.

All the stuff in the New York apartment will probably be rejected by the Salvation Army and Goodwill on my death. They will sit in a clump on a sidewalk in the Village and perhaps the world's most assiduous scavengers will shelter them for a while. The house on the blueberry barrens will fall down and the boys will sell the land without taking a last look. My surname will suffer the fate of other Iberian ones that sneaked into New England— Fenollosa, Benét[9]—no longer pronounceable in Spanish.

Mine shall end up as a game name. Computer games are all that interest my grandchildren, not stories, not books.

Anybody for Dos Passos?

Anybody for Santayana?[1]

Nobody.

Tom-tom took two turns around his block before stopping at the house. Mostly because there was a car in his drive he didn't expect. "This ruins everything," he muttered. "I got to think it over."

"Take me home," I said.

"It's my sister Lila," he said. "Ralph used to keep her home and calm and then he went and died and she started going to old folks' dances."

"Lila," I said. "I like her."

"Watch out," he warned. "Ralph had more money put away than she thought and she got herself a facelift. In our family, a facelift! Now she tries to deny it, but I remember when she told me all, in a moment of weakness. I don't forget. Anyway, watch out for her."

He parked at the far end of the short block, under an oak tree alongside his apartment building. It was only a two-story stucco structure. Eight apartments at most. Dim lights inside and out. Very small rooms, most likely. His own home stood by itself at the corner we passed twice, facing away from the

---

8. Town on Penobscot Bay, in southern Maine; one of the oldest towns in New England. *Madeira:* fine lace. *Kirman:* fine rug. *Georgian:* in most English-speaking countries, the set of architectural styles current between 1720 and 1840.
9. William Rose Benét (1886–1950), American poet, novelist, and editor; Steven Vincent Benét (1898–1943), American poet, brother of W. R.; both graduated from Yale University. *Fenollosa:*

Ernest Francisco Fenollosa (1853–1908), American professor of philosophy and political economy at Tokyo Imperial University; for a time, curator of Asian art at Boston's Museum of Fine Arts.
1. George Santayana (1863–1952), Spanish-born American poet and philosopher. *Dos Passos:* John Roderigo Dos Passos (1896–1970), American writer.

bastard-Bauhaus[2] stucco. Between his kitchen and the back entrance of the apartments a garage-utility room intervened. Tom-tom turned in his seat, as much as the steering wheel and his paunch allowed, and looked back squinting and slowly shaking his head at Lila's car.

"I want an understanding before we go in there," he said sternly, waving a hand and pointing with the thumb.

"Who're you?" I said. "A Western sheriff?"

"Now listen, and no fooling," he said. "We don't have to worry about him. It's Lila who catches on fast."

"I thought you said he was dead," I said.

"Oh, Lila married again. You really been away too long. Some American who retired here. She caught him the first dance he went to. No money. A union pension and Social Security. He's dumb, he's from New Jersey. Lila tells him everything and he does it."

"OK, I won't worry about him," I said, but he didn't laugh.

"He's always smiling. You say something and he says what can I tell you. Always. He's not asking. What can I tell you, that's all he says. It's no proper way to speak."

He lifted a hand and rubbed it over his face as if he were sopping up sweat with a towel. "I think Lila married him so she wouldn't have to mow the lawn. She lost both breasts like Mrs. Rockefeller and it was hard for her pushing the mower. Ralph wasn't a very active man—he used to sit on the porch and tell her what to do."

"Tom-tom," I said. "I've got to get back to my house."

"Your house?"

"Cuco and Celia's house, my house now."

"You're not selling, huh?"

I threw up my hands.

"I'm thinking, I'm thinking," he protested. He held my shoulder with his fleshy hand, his head with the other. "I'm trying to protect you too."

"Me?"

"First of all, not a word about Junior."

"Junior?" I said. "Who's Junior?"

"Jesus, that's a shock!" he said. "You don't remember my Junior? My only child? He used to shine your shoes in New York when you came out of the navy. You gave him money—he never forgot you and you don't remember him?"

"Sure, sure," I said. "I'm tired, that's all."

Tom-tom lowered his voice to what he considered an intimate, between-you-and-me level. "He was always a little backward, poor boy. Olivia's big worry, the cause of all her problems, though I always told her, he's all right, he's just a little backward. And I *am* right, he's OK."

A little backward? He was mentally retarded. If they had stayed in New York he might have tried for a job as a messenger, one of those you see midtown, staring at elevator push buttons trying to figure out what happened to number thirteen. Junior must be middle-aged now.

"You gave him all your navy shit—the kerchief, the little white hats, the hammock. He loved you. He still asks about you every time we go to Miami."

2. I.e., a poor imitation of this German architectural style of the 1920s.

"OK, OK, I remember him," I said. "I used to call him Jaime, not Junior. I still don't like that appellation. What's a Latin doing calling his son Junior?"

I put a hand on the car door and unlocked it and stretched a leg out towards the curb. He grabbed and pulled.

"Wait, yes, you're right. I'm sorry. You always had that craziness—I didn't mean that. I mean, you didn't want us to turn into regular Americans. Right?"

He was right; I was insane in those days. "Obsessed," I said, and nodded. Oh God.

"As if I could forget," Tom-tom said, pressing his advantage. "You and I, we're Tampa Latins. There's nothing we can do about that, but our children . . ."

"OK, OK. What about him? What's he doing in Miami?"

"Oh Pinpin, Junior is great. I think he's going to really do well with this wife. She works, she's one of those career women, women's liberation and all that and more, and he takes care of the condominium outdoors. And he does a few yards, mows lawns and things. In his neighborhood. Where he can walk over, because they won't give him a driver's license. It's very unfair."

"How come he's in Miami?"

"She got a job there in a bank and the other wife with the girls was in Tampa then, and we thought—well, I pointed out to Olivia that maybe the other marriages didn't work out because she and I were too involved, as they say. You know."

"What other marriages? Junior has been married more than once?"

"Five times," Tom-tom said, so low he was almost inaudible. Then he chuckled.

I brought my leg back into the car. "What's he got—a big wang?"

Tom-tom leaned over and put an arm around my shoulders, squeezed and chuckled some more. "Oh Pinpin, he's always been a lovable boy."

"I bet."

"I used to pry him loose from his mother," he said. "You think . . . ?"

"What are you saying?"

He pushed me away with his big meaty hands, then grabbed me back again. I felt like an uncooked hamburger.

"Jesus Christ, Pinpin," Tom-tom said. "I'm talking about psychology."

"So was I."

Tom-tom asked in his insinuating voice, "You think he's oversexed?"

I waited.

"Nowadays they say there's such a thing," he said.

I thought, maybe nature compensated down there for what it robbed him above, but said nothing.

Tom-tom grabbed me again. "Remember, say nothing about this inside. I don't mean—Jesus, Pinpin, you make me sound foolish."

I got out of the car and despite his bulk he ran around his side and caught up with me under the oak tree.

"Anyway, don't ask about Junior. And forget about his children. Yes, especially his children. OK?"

I nodded.

"And don't be surprised what you hear about the apartments. Lila don't know we own them. They think I'm the janitor, that's all. OK, let's go. On guard."

How did I get into this? I wasn't even hungry, and when I was, I was mighty finicky about what I ate.

He leaned on me as we walked and stopped me when we got to Lila's car. "I forgot, say nothing about the letter to the Traffic Department. I'll think of something to get rid of them and then you'll write the letter. We gotta wait them out, remember that. Wait them out, don't lose patience."

"Whataya talking about?" I said.

"It's Lila I worry about, not Conrad," he said and pulled me ahead as if I too were a burden.

"Conrad her husband's name?"

"Conrad Dupee. Isn't that ridiculous?" He stooped and looked at the back of Lila's car. "Dew-pee! It don't sound decent. And the dope hasn't done nothing about his muffler. He probably didn't get permission from Lila."

On the neat brick walk to his front door, Tom-tom threw his arm round me once more. It was exhausting.

"Oh Pinpin, if you only knew how glad I am that you are here. I need a real close relative like you to advise me."

The old seducer.

"I can't trust the others," he explained.

Don't trust me, I started to say, but reminded myself he didn't.

He thought of one more thing before we reached his door. "What's that word appellation? Be careful you don't make the letter too hard to read. They're a bunch of crackers at the Traffic Department. Worse, they may be Latins."

Two strange old ladies shrieked the moment Tom-tom opened the screen door and half-propelled me inside. They sprang from their seats. I halted and fell back into Tom-tom. Automatically, I brought up an arm to ward off their attack. Their faces lunged at me; enlarged, distorted, askew atop withering bodies. Deep wrinkles, blue-green mascara, painted eyebrows; agitated shrunken flesh on toothpick flailing arms; voices like the spurting, burping alarms of the emergency ambulances on the way to St. Vincent's in the Village.[3]

"Pinpin! Pinpin!"

"It's Pinpin! Pinpin, how come?"

My cousin Lila wore the heavy mascara. "Aiee!" she went on, yelling and pushing Tom-tom's Olivia out of her way. "I didn't know. They didn't tell me!"

Olivia was taller and stuck her head towards me over Lila's shoulder. "I wanted to surprise her and instead I surprised myself! Pinpin, are you hungry?"

I felt the smeary contact of lipsticked kisses.

Lila screamed. "He's eating here! Why didn't you let me know, Pinpin? How long have you been in Tampa?"

A short, red-faced, blotchy, bald man stood carefully away from the two women and smiled as if he wished to be nearer: a satellite if ever I saw one. He was all plaid—shirt, pants, windbreaker.

"That's what happens if you live in Bradenton,"[4] Lila said to him, her wide mouth stretching and puckering four inches from my face, a consider-

---

3. St. Vincent's Hospital, in the Greenwich Village neighborhood of Manhattan.

4. City in Florida, some 30 miles south of Tampa.

able feat. "Did you know I live in Bradenton? When did I last see you? Oh, oh!" She threw both arms about my shoulders and hugged me against very firm B cups. "Celia! Cuco! What a tragedy!"

"He wasn't here when they died," Tom-tom said and pulled her away. "And you weren't at the funeral either, so don't make believe you saw him there."

"That's what I mean about Bradenton, it's too far away," Lila said. "You don't hear about anything."

Olivia tapped Lila on the shoulder. "Tom-tom called Pinpin right away and was the first, the very first, to welcome him home. I told him, Tom-tom call your Aunt Mama's house, I have a feeling . . ."

"Me too, me too," Lila said. "That's why we're out—I told Conrad—oh!"

She grabbed me by the wrist and pulled me towards the funny little plaid man. "Pinpin, I want you to meet Conrad. Conrad Dupee. My husband!"

Conrad started to bring a hand forward and so did I, but we both stopped and pulled back, as if short-circuited, when we heard Lila scream. I looked at her and saw in the midst of the parallel furrows of her face that her mouth was open in delight and that her shrieks were happy ones; it did not relax me.

"Look at him, look at him!" she yelled at me and pointed at Conrad. "Imagine me married to a man named Conrad!"

She doubled up, head down, and her yelps of laughter bounced off the floor.

"I'm all right, I'm all right," she said and straightened up. "I like a good laugh."

With that Conrad and I finally shook hands. Conrad was undisturbed, for Lila immediately placed an arm around him and her face next to his as if posing for a close-up portrait.

Conrad said, "What can I tell ya," and Tom-tom slapped me on the back as if to say I told you so.

"I'm Misses Conrad Dupee," Lila said, "and no cracks about going to the bathroom. Ha-ha, I'm only fooling."

Olivia said, "Pinpin, how did you find the old house? I can come over—"

Lila interrupted. "You see, you see, that's why we have to get out of Bradenton. We can't help anybody, we don't know what's happening—"

Tom-tom said, "Pinpin's got us."

"Yes," Olivia said quickly. "You've got your daughter in Bradenton—she needs you."

Lila exhaled a sigh full of spit. "Olivia, Olivia," she pleaded, "you know the situation there." She made a grimace at me that counted on my understanding. "We have discussed and you agreed. I've discussed with all my brothers and my sisters too. They agree. Except Sarita."

With a prod, Tom-tom led me towards the couch, but Lila wheeled and took my arm again. "You can't imagine what a bitch Sarita turned out to be. You remember her and her ways, I'm sure. I bet you've got a story or two to tell about her. I never realized it until it was as plain as the nose on my face. Then everyone in the family began to tell me about her but meanwhile she still owes me—I won't tell you how much. I'm an innocent, that's the kind of person I am. Conrad says so."

Tom-tom pushed her arm away. "He's gotta sit. He just arrived." He gave her a firmer push to dislodge her and prodded me towards the sofa once more. Its fabric was nubby and its innards hard as cement. "Let him rest before he eats."

"Of course, of course," Lila said and sat sideways on the couch in order to face me. "Pinpin, you look wonderful."

"As compared to when?" I said.

"He got you there!" Olivia said, and with the forefinger and thumb of each hand she held her loose cotton dress away from her body. "Haw, haw, haw!"

Lila smiled along with her. "As compared to always. I've known him always!" she screamed and leaned forward and I saw her wrinkles stretch like a bowstring and her mouth open wide for another machine-gun laugh. It bounced off the side of my face leaving it (eyeball included) paralyzed forever, like that of a stroke victim.

Olivia stood with legs apart and fanned herself with the skirt of her dress. "I can't scratch," she explained. "That's how many years we haven't seen you." She waved the dress obscenely. "Fungus! Ever heard of it?"

Lila caressed my arm. "Years and years, but you were always the handsome one in the family, that was my belief and it still is. Let the years go by, they don't bother you."

"Olivia!" Tom-tom called impatiently.

"Everything's all prepared," Olivia replied. "Give Pinpin a drink if you can get through," and gave Lila a glare as if she were a double-parked car.

"Listen, Pinpin," Lila said as soon as Tom-tom moved away from me, "if you want to keep the old house for old times' sake—you know, as a memento—keep it. Don't deny yourself the pleasure. Conrad and me are willing to live in it and take care of it for you."

"What can I tell you," Conrad said.

Tom-tom returned fast with a drink.

"Let's not give him any advice now," Tom-tom said. Then he gave Conrad and Lila what he considered his sly, disarming smile. "Let him have a drink and take it easy. He came over here because he wanted to take it easy."

Lila gave another liquefied sigh. Olivia directed one more disgusted look her way and left for the kitchen. Who would have thought they'd be so interested in me? It was hell.

"A house has to be lived in or it runs down," Lila said, quoting from her book of life. "I told Pinpin that Conrad and me would live in his house if he wants us to, because a house runs down—"

"Depends on who lives in it. Some people are worse for them than termites," Tom-tom said and gave her no chance to answer. He grabbed my arm. "How's the drink, little cousin?"

I nodded. It was ghastly. So sweet with rum and ginger ale and sugar and a maraschino cherry that I might have to take a couple of extra units of insulin tomorrow morning.

"Another cherry?" Tom-tom asked. "Ha-ha!"

Lila didn't get it. "Yeah, yeah," she said. "Give him another, Tom-tom. Don't you love them, Pinpin?"

Olivia stood before me with a plate of deep-fried green plantains. Like the drink, it was offered only to me. I looked at them and nodded and then at her and smiled. Any hostess at the hundreds of parties I have gone to in my wasted life would have passed on and let me be. Not Olivia. She remained there holding out the Bakelite dinner plate with its brickpile of bilious green plantains.

My mother used to slice them very thin on a small wooden contraption that looked like a planer for food. She deep-fried them fast and then shook them inside a paper bag to tamp the oil off them, and with a careful flick of her wrist lightly salted them. Divine.

But that was my mother, who required no Oedipus complex to inspire admiration. Olivia obviously cut the plantain thick and then squashed the heavy slices with the heel of her hand and let them cook forever in shallow oil used for the hundredth time. *Tostones,* the Puerto Ricans call them.

(I must watch this superciliousness towards Puerto Ricans common in my family. They're no worse than anyone else and that's bad enough. No, fuck the Puerto Ricans too.)

I picked one up and felt the lard seeping through the pores of my fore-finger and thumb. Rancid. I did not have to bite into it to know, but I did and confirmed it. My palate shrank. The plantain was lukewarm and the center raw and dry. It dropped to my stomach like dead weight. And yet there was a moment—fleeting, to be sure—when my body remembered happiness.

Olivia did not move away. She wanted me to take a second one immedi-ately and I wished she would get the itch.

"Get him a napkin!" Lila said and jumped up and ran to the kitchen and back. "Here," she said and placed it on my knee and so rattled Olivia that she managed to take one of the *tostones* and bite into it before Olivia thought to move the dish out of her reach. "Delicious!" Lila shrieked and pushed my elbow and added, "Take another! Take another!"

Who would have thought there was so much agility in old Lila?

"Pinpin, don't get the idea that Lila cooked them," Tom-tom said. "Olivia made them—she's the champion of West Tampa."

Lila laughed and shrieked at that, slapping me and Tom-tom good-humoredly and waving the other arm at Olivia and Conrad as if asking them to join in on the joke.

Olivia jumped back. "Be careful," she said.

"That's right," Lila said, and not yet having withdrawn her outstretched hand took another plantain and held it out to Conrad. "Here, here, you yankee."

Conrad shrugged and took it, but did not say what can I tell you. He bit into it without changing expression.

Lila confided to me without lowering her voice that Conrad loved plan-tains, green or ripe. "But I have no time to cook them, we'd never get out of the house if I did. We have to drive far to visit—Bradenton is dead, forget it."

She turned to Olivia. "And what for? The TV dinners are better than any-thing any amateur cook can make. Right, Conrad? Don't you agree, Pinpin? And Pinpin has eaten everywhere, I bet. Why bother?"

Olivia handed the plate to Tom-tom. "Well, Pinpin, I don't have a TV din-ner for you," she said in a sarcastically apologetic tone, and signaled to me to get up. "It's only *palomillo* steak[5] and—"

"Oh, oh, I got to see this," Lila said, and headed for the kitchen ahead of everyone.

There was a formal dining table and six chairs at one end of the small living room, but you only ate there on Christmas Eve. Even the Nobel Prize

***

5. Fried marinated steak, a Cuban specialty.

would not have gotten me a place at that table on any other day of the year. I was being led to the kitchen.

I had managed to finish the first plantain, but held the other away from me.

Tom-tom said, "Eat up, there's plenty more," and like a fool I took a bite of it and felt my stomach trying to come up to meet it halfway.

"Where's the bathroom, please?" I said and headed for it, remembering that in Ybor City it is always behind the middle door of the three that give on directly to the living room. The bathroom is never demurely recessed at the end of a hallway; in fact, I didn't see a hallway in a home until I got to New York. Nor knew privacy, either.

"Right in there, right in there," Tom-tom said and didn't stop escorting me until I opened the door.

I quickly closed it behind me and sat on the edge of the bathtub next to the toilet. I threw the unfinished plantain into it and heard the others outside so clearly that I was sure the plop it made was audible to them.

Lila was saying, "You have to offer guests the bathroom. That's the first thing you do!"

I threw up into the toilet bowl as silently as I could manage, constricting my throat with an enormous effort, and then wiped the streams of oily acid at the edges of my mouth with purple toilet paper. I knew I could not survive this night.

Fourteen months since I last wrote prose. Ten years since I last published. Not a word in the last year, no journal entries, no letters, only checks to pay bills. Three months since Cora died—when I expected all my juices to start flowing again. That hope was years old, but I always suspected it would not work. You're checkmated if you're a writer: I knew the Dreiser[6] story well, the one about the man who thought he'd be *free* when his wife died and, of course, was not. Look to literature for guidance, not life.

Here in Olivia's and Tom-tom's bathroom was the first time in a year that I missed the little notebook I once always carried in my shirt pocket. (Hard to find, stitched notebooks in that size; they're all spirals now and I hate them.) I missed my Mont Blanc, too, filled with Mont Blanc black ink. I wanted to start right then and there with a list of things I needed to buy if I was to stay in the old house. Or a list of alternatives to staying in Ybor City.

Let them forget me inside. Let Lila and Conrad Dupee leave for Bradenton without my good wishes. A short whiff of nausea rose to my tonsils and I leaned forward towards the bowl and wondered if I had also vomited the medicine I had taken at the house. Should I take more? What had I taken? I peered at my bile and lost my desire to vomit but not my queasiness.

Nowhere was now-here.

In the days when I was trying to puzzle out the English language by reading the *Tampa Tribune* (a loathsome newspaper), I was stuck for days with that one. You try to make now-here take the place of nowhere in the next sentence you run across it. I was eight years old. There was no point in asking my peers, and the grown-ups' English was no better than mine. (In Ybor City and West Tampa everyone spoke Spanish, even the Sicilians.) And anyway, I

6. Theodore Dreiser (1871–1945), American editor and novelist.

wanted to figure it out for myself. I cannot remember how I solved the mystery (probably because I don't want to give anyone credit; I'm not perfect) but now-here became the magic word, my own self-discovered mantra, that broke the spell of the worst obstacles, insuperable depressions, suicidal impulses.

Now-here, I said to myself (I never shared the magic word with anyone, not even with Cora after thirty-seven years of marriage and thirty-eight of cohabitation) and a little click took place and I knew that in a moment there would be light and, finally, even some hope.

It worked when:

(1) The first girl I took to the movies in New York slowly unbuttoned my fly and reached in with cool fingers and grabbed me and for a long minute of quivering fright nothing happened.

(2) Chamberlain went to Munich and I realized, squashed in the subway on the way to work, that the Spanish Republic could not hold out until . . . [7]

(3) I had to bail out during my first gunnery training flight in Norfolk.[8]

(4) Cora came out to the back porch of Aunt Harriet's house in Maine (by then Cora's) and saw Susie leaning back against a corner post in ecstasy, breathing in rhythm to my hand under her pleated Brooks skirt.

My mantra did not always work and such days were indeed black days. And the months, torture. It did not work when the articles began to be rejected and in time the books, after many rewrites, too. It didn't work in Tom-tom's bathroom.

Now-here was nowhere and vice-versa.

*　　*　　*

1987

7. I.e., in 1938, the British prime minister Neville Chamberlain met in Munich, Germany, with the French premier Edward Daladier, the Italian dictator Benito Mussolini, and the (Austrian-born) German chancellor and founder of Nazism, Adolf Hitler. The resulting pact is now considered an attempt to appease Hitler, who never intended to abide by it and whose military actions in Europe soon led to World War II. Meanwhile, Hitler and Mussolini were providing money, weapons, and troops to the Spanish general Francisco Franco, whose military rebellion—the Spanish Civil War—would replace the liberal civilian government of the Spanish Republic with Franco's Fascist dictatorship.
8. Norfolk Naval Base, in Virginia.

---

# JOSÉ ANTONIO VILLARREAL
## b. 1924

José Antonio Villarreal was born in Mexico, where his father fought in the Mexican Revolution alongside the revolutionary general Francisco "Pancho" Villa. His family immigrated to the United States in 1921 and settled in Santa Clara, California, as migrant laborers. In 1950, Villarreal received a bachelor's degree in English from the University of California at Berkeley, where he then did graduate work toward a master's without completing a degree. He became an assistant professor in the University of Colorado at Boulder, among other institutions, and in the 1970s he worked as an editor of the tourist magazine *Now in Mexico*. Villarreal has also been a radio broadcaster, a publicist, a translator, a media relations consultant, a speech-writer for corporate executives, a counselor at juvenile correctional facilities, a delivery truck driver, and an advertising agent.

He started his literary career by publishing the stories "Some Turn to God" (1947) and "A Pot of Pink Beans Boiling" (1959) in periodicals. Until the rediscovery of Josefina Niggli's *Mexican Village* (1945), Villarreal's *Pocho* was believed to be the first Latino novel published in English by a major New York house (Doubleday printed it in 1959; Anchor reprinted it in 1971). This autobiographical best seller—it originally sold 160,000 copies—established him as an important voice.

The title is a derogatory Spanish term used to describe a Mexican who has assimilated into U.S. culture. *Pochismo* refers to an ungrammatical expression in Spanish. Richard Rubio, the novel's precocious, bookish, adolescent protagonist, does not fit in the world he moves into. He is the son of a peasant, Juan, who fought in the Mexican Revolution and who immigrates with his family to California, where English is mandatory and Spanish is looked down upon. Incidents from Juan's life are presented in the novel's first part, which is included in this anthology. In the subsequent parts, Richard's life is described in the context of the social conditions of migrants in California during the Great Depression, tense race relations, and the grinding poverty of farm labor. The narrative explores assimilation through key concepts such as fractured identity, the search for personal roots, machismo, and father/son relations. While Doubleday marketed the book for adults, Villarreal might have meant it for young adults. Critics have pointed to its lack of focus, noted that the first part is not echoed later in the book, and called the characters unconvincing, but they have admired the spare writing style and the fluid use of English seasoned with Spanish.

Villareal published one other short story, "The Conscripts," in a periodical in 1973. His second novel, *The Fifth Horseman* (1974), about the Mexican Revolution, was met with indifference. His third novel, *Clemente Chacón* (1984), released by a smaller publisher, was more accomplished but ignored by critics and the public. Two sketches, "The Last Minstrel in California" and "The Laughter of My Father," appeared in a 1992 anthology. In the 1980s, when Mexican American literature was introduced to the academic curriculum, Villarreal said in an interview that *Pocho* "isn't Chicano literature, if indeed there's such a thing." He preferred to see the book as addressing universal issues. His comments were considered apostasy by many Chicano scholars, but they have proved prophetic, as today the drive in Latino literature is to reach beyond the ethnic enclave for a larger readership.

---

## FROM POCHO

## One

### I

A light snow was falling as the train from Mexico City pulled into Ciudad Juárez. A film of ice had formed on the wooden sidewalks, and the unpaved streets were deep in mud where the wagons and automobiles had sludged through. A man got off the train and elbowed his way through the crowd that inevitably gathered at the arrival of a train from the capital. Ten years earlier, as a young man of eighteen, he had come to this same city in not so quiet a fashion. Then he had been a cavalry officer in Villa's army that took Juárez, northern lifeline to the United States, from the forces of the government. A few months later, he had returned with the great General to retake the city after it had been sold out to the enemy by the army Villa had left there to protect it.

As he walked along the crowded streets, he almost wished for the old days, and carelessly wondered how many men he had killed here. His leather pants legs showed he wore the traditional tight-fitting costume of the Mexican charro.[1] The other two-thirds of his body was encased in a huge mackinaw. On his head was a large, heavy hat, the string of which hung loosely behind, reaching down the nape of his neck. His once fair skin had been turned a ruddy color by years of outdoor life and now gave his blue-gray eyes an odd, cold mien. Although he was not an inordinately large man, the mackinaw and the sombrero made him dwarf the people around him. He walked aimlessly along the streets, carried on and directed by the crowd, until finally he turned into a cantina. He chose a corner table and hung his heavy coat on a nail behind him. He arranged himself on the chair so his gun hung loose and his arm had freedom of movement.

It was still early in the day, but the cantina was full and lively. A mariachi was playing sentimental ballads of unrequited love, and on a table across the large room a young girl was dancing a jarabe tapatío[2] to the olés of a group of men, an occasional glint of brown thigh visible as she nimbly moved her small feet around the brim of the sombrero.

A waiter approached the stranger, and he ordered the meal of the day and a bottle of mezcal. He sat there eating and drinking, seemingly oblivious to the din and gaiety about him. One or two women attempted to sit at his table, but with a shake of his head he sent them away. When he was through eating, he washed his mouth with a half tumbler of liquor and spat on the floor. The girl who had been dancing on the table went by him and disappeared in the enclosure to his left. He heard the hard, steady hiss as she relieved herself on the earthen floor. As she walked past him, he called, "Come here!"

She hesitated in mid-stride. The words, although spoken in a low voice, had been commanding. "¿Qué quieres?" She spoke in the familiar.[3] In a cantina, as in bed, courtesy was nonexistent. Outside was another thing.

"I have been watching you. You please me."

"So? I please many men," she said, very sure of herself, and made as if to leave.

"Sit down and drink with me," he said.

She knew she should go, but something about him frightened her and she lost her composure. "Even if I wanted to do so, I could not." She did not realize she was explaining to this man, a complete stranger. "My friends are waiting for me."

"Your friends? Oh, *those*?" he pointed and laughed. "No, little one, you are a woman and deserve better. Sit here."

She sat down nervously at the edge of the seat. She kept her head lowered as she spoke. "My lover is over there. He does not mind if I work when he is not here, but he is here now and I must entertain his friends." She looked up at him, sure of herself once more. She patted his hand and said very

---

1. Horseman or cowboy.
2. A folk dance known in the United States as the "Mexican Hat Dance."

3. I.e., using *tú*, the familiar form of *you* (the formal form is *usted*).

professionally, "Be good and come back tomorrow. Then I will be good to you. I am told I am very good."

"No. You are with me now. I have not had a woman in a week, and am better for you than your pimp."

The blood that came to her face erased her smile. She started to rise. He reached for her arm and easily pulled her back into the chair. He pushed his glass to her.

"I cannot drink this," she said. "It is too strong." She rubbed the four white spots on her arm where his fingers had momentarily stopped the circulation. She wondered how after six months of this life she could still blush.

He said, "Some milk, perhaps."

"He is coming now. *Please!* He is a bad one!" One of the men had detached himself from the group across the room. His friends watched with half interest. He would return with his woman.

He walked to the girl and spoke in a cultured voice. "Come, you have kept us waiting." She did not answer. It was out of her hands now.

"This one stays with me," said the stranger.

The other ignored him. "Can you not hear, deaf one? Get up!" he said to the girl.

"Do not worry, señor." The voice of the man at the table was very matter-of-fact. "I have money and you will get your share."

"Gentlemen do not speak of such things, señor. You are being insulting."

"Ah, then a gentleman procurer must never mention the fact, is that it?" His voice was still soft, almost friendly, despite the mockery of the words.

The girl's lover made an effort to control his voice. "Come," he said to her. "You are not in the country now. You need not associate with peones."[4]

"The peón has larger balls than the city-bred gachupín,"[5] said the charro. "Now go back to your friends. We are tired of you."

"Son of the great mother whore!" the other screamed. "I gave you your chance to live!" His gun was barely out of its shoulder holster when the bullet hit him above the groin. The stranger calmly shot him once more as he lay writhing on the floor; his gun had been in his hand all along. He took his coat and, without a look at the crowd, pulled the girl out of the cantina.

In the hotel he said, "You can stop crying now and take off my boots." When they were in bed, he asked, "How old are you?"

"I have fifteen years." After a moment she said, "You have not asked me my name."

"¿Qué importa?" he said.

The man was awakened a few hours later by the clatter of feet outside the door. He had his hand on his gun as the room was suddenly filled by uniformed men.

"Please do not resist, señor. You are under arrest," said a young lieutenant, who was in command. "You will dress, please, and accompany me."

"May I take my woman?"

"Why not?" The lieutenant shrugged his shoulders. He unabashedly kept his eyes on the girl as they dressed. "May I compliment your taste, señor?"

"Thank you," said the prisoner. "But you surprise me. By the manner in which you came in, I did not think you had the sense of love."

4. Peons, laborers, farmhands.
5. Derogatory term for Spaniard.

"I am not an ox. I feel deeply the intrusion, but, you know, the other died."

"But of course. It could be no other way." He was dressed now. "Do we walk or ride, Teniente?"

"We walk. It is not far."

They arrived at a stockade that covered a complete city square. A large building for administrative purposes stood in one corner. The remainder of the stockade held no buildings other than the flimsy, wooden lean-tos the prisoners used to protect them from the elements. Here and there, the prisoners' children were seen huddled together to keep warm, while their mothers cooked over their small open fires. The man and woman were taken into a room where the lieutenant seated himself behind a small desk.

"Please be seated. The mere formality of a form or two for the Commandant. It is for him to decide when you are to be shot." The young lieutenant was very businesslike.

"First, a favor, if you please."

"Yes?"

"Have a man escort the woman back to the hotel. I did not know what a pigsty you have here," said the man.

"Immediately," said the lieutenant. "We do the best we can here, señor. We will have better accommodations before long." He was still polite, but the stranger was beginning to irritate him, so he added, "By then, of course, you will not be concerned about the matter."

"You are kind, Lieutenant. Where did you make your rank?"

"At the National Academy, naturally." He became impatient and a little angry. "Come, señor. This is not exactly a social call. I will ask the questions, please. Your name?"

"Juan Rubio."

"How long have you been in Juárez?"

"I arrived today from México."

"It is obvious that you are not from the capital. Of what nature was your business there?"

"I do not see how that concerns this matter, but since you ask, I was attending the National Military Academy."

The young lieutenant smiled in disbelief. "Come, now, señor," he said complacently. "You surely do not expect me to believe that. A man of your station?" Juan Rubio said nothing, and suddenly the lieutenant said excitedly, "Wait! You cannot possibly be Juan Manuel Rubio? The Colonel Rubio?"

"The ex-Colonel Rubio, but at your service nevertheless, Teniente. You know of me?"

"Rubio of Santa Rosalía, Torreón, Zacatecas, and even here, Juárez. No one speaks more highly of you than the General. . . . But what have I done? Ah! You do not know the position in which you have put me by being who you are." He paced the narrow room nervously. "I must call the General at once. He will degrade me to the ranks, no matter that I was but following his own orders. . . . He thinks of you as his son, you know." He picked up the telephone and rang hurriedly. "¡Bueno! I wish to speak to the General, please. . . . Teniente Ramos here. . . . Yes, yes, I know, but this is highly important to the General himself. . . . No, I must speak to him personally. . . . A matter of importance, I say. . . . Yes, I assume the responsibility." He pounded his fist lightly on the table as he waited for his connection. "¡Bueno! Teniente Ramos speaking. . . . A matter of high importance, mi general. . . .

I have the prisoner whose arrest you ordered. . . . ¡No, no mi general! His name is Juan Manuel Rubio. . . . Yes. . . . Yes, your prerogative entirely, mi general. . . . Yes, sir. Thank you, sir." He slowly put the receiver down. "He says he will personally flog me for bringing you here," he said to Juan. "He will be here immediately."

Juan laughed. "Do not worry," he said. "If it is who I think it is, nothing will happen to you because of this."

"Fuentes." The young lieutenant was sad.

"Old Hermilio. I thought as much. Ah, the noise he can make, but that is all."

"Yes, but these old dogs of the Revolution—one can never tell what they will do next." He reddened suddenly. "My apologies, mi coronel. I forgot that you, too, came of the Revolution."

"Forget it," said Juan. "It was not an insult."

There was a noise in the hallway, and the General, accompanied by two officers, walked into the small room. He was short and fat, and his mustache was white. He went directly to Juan and put his arms around him. They exchanged the abrazo, the informal embrace between two close friends.

"Ah, Juan Manuel! What pleasure! It is good to see you."

"¡Quihúbole, Hermilio, quihúbole!" They spoke to each other in the provincial accent, the dialect of the peón.

"Fine, fine, but let us go, Juan Manuel. My car is outside," the General said. "And you, cabrón,[6] I will take care of you later," he said to the lieutenant.

A few minutes later, they were at the General's home. The General handed him a glass of aguardiente[7] and said:

"That was a wrong thing you did today, Juan Manuel."

"He was a Spaniard," Juan said.

"But surely you are not too stupid to realize that you cannot personally rid this world of the Spaniard!"

"I am not concerned with the world, mi general. But someday they must be driven out of México."

"My sentiments exactly, but this one, Juan Manuel—this one was a very rich one."

"Are not all of them?"

"Yes, but this one was from the other side. You know what that means now that we are friendly with the gringos."

"Ah, Hermilio! Of what good was all the fighting? The Spanish milk still flows into our women!"

"I know. We are no better off than we were before, but the problem now is how to get you away from here. Juárez has changed, and one cannot get away with such things around here now. Our proximity to the norteamericanos makes it imperative that we have an orderly city. We are so near to the other side that one errant bullet could do irreparable harm to our relationship."

"Yes, we *are* close to the other side," said Juan. "Remember the times we took this place, how we could not effectively employ our artillery because a

6. Literally, goat; here, an insult roughly equivalent to *bastard*.
7. Liquor.

slight miscalculation would have sent shells into El Paso del Norte? And remember how the gringos were all on the other side of the Bravo watching the fighting. We were like toreros those times—we had our aficionados."

"It seems like only yesterday, Juan Manuel," said the General wistfully. "But, to return to the problem at hand, the order for your arrest came from the capital. Telegraphed in less than four hours from the time of the incident. So, you see, the deceased had influence. All this trouble because you got yourself hot for a whore!"

"You did not see her, Hermilio. Even you, old as you are, would want her."

"I am still able, you crazy," said the General. "Why did you not come to me if you wanted a woman? You should see the ones that come here. Beautiful and well-bred—even gringas, if you have a taste for them."

"*Well-bred*," Juan mimicked. "You talk like a great don, old one. Did you forget the big white breeches and the huaraches when you received this command? Do you not remember that our people have better manners than this aristocracy, that our ancestors were princes in a civilization that was possibly more advanced than this one? I had enough of your high-class women in México. And as for the pale ones, they do not please me, either. No, my general with good manners, the india is still the most beautiful woman in the world."

"Forgive me, Juan Manuel," said the General. "Your rebuke was well deserved. Living in this society makes me talk like the people in it. I have not really forgotten my heritage. We are provincials, you and I, first and last. Tell me, why did you leave México?"

"I got tired of playing soldier with idiots. When that one-armed bastard Obregón offered to send the old officers to the Academy, I did not think it would be as it was. Believe me, my general, there we were, Grijalva, Orozco, López—the cross-eyed one—and other such men. You know them all, every one of them a valiant soldier. I myself campaigned almost ten years with don Pancho! And a snotty cadet sergeant with the walk of a maricón[8] would come up and say, 'Straighten up! Button up your blouse! Clean your boots!' Then, every day for two hours in the morning and two hours before dinner, it was walk, walk, walk—and me a cavalry officer—and the little fag would say, 'To the right! To the left! Attention! You are now in the National Army of México—try to look like soldiers!' Can you imagine a simple shit like that, my general? After ten years, this capón[9] tells me to look like a soldier!

"And the classes, Hermilio. You cannot imagine the number of books we had to read, books on strategy written by the same generals we defeated. The instructors were all from the old government army. Some of them I recognized from the rear, having seen them a number of times running barefaced from battle. They were teaching us tactics, and here I was practically reared by the greatest tactician of them all! We asked them to drill us on horses, and were told that was only for third-year men. I could not wait three years for a horse, so one afternoon, when the men were out drilling, I sneaked off to the stables and borrowed a horse and a reata. I did not have time to steal a saddle, so I tied the end of the rope to my waist. I rode out on the drill field, screaming and shouting, and the men broke ranks and

8. Faggot (i.e., derogatory term for gay man).
9. Castrated animal.

ran. I roped the cadet sergeant by one leg and dragged him around until he stopped screaming. Ah, what diversion, my general. The young students were frightened, certain that I had gone mad, but the old soldiers stood in one group, laughing in guffaws, and they gave me a *viva* as I left. No one tried to stop me.

"I returned that night with some tequila, and we had a fiesta in the barracks. We tied the new cadet sergeant up, until we got him drunk and he would not dare call the guard. Some of us sneaked out and smuggled some women in, and that crazy Grijalva brought back a full mariachi. Seven musicians he brought in at the point of a gun! He said he had taken the gun away from a gendarme. Ay, that crazy! The youngsters in the barracks joined in the fun, and when the guard came up, they strapped him to a bunk. Ah, what a delicious time we had, my general, until finally a platoon of armed men was sent to investigate, and I had a devil of a time getting away." Both men were laughing by the time Juan finished the narrative.

"Ah, what I would give for your youth, Juan Manuel," said the General. "And the cadet sergeant?"

"A broken arm and leg, that was all."

"Then what did you do?"

"The next day I went to see General Paz. I told him I wished to retire from the army, but he persuaded me to take a leave of absence until I decided what I wanted to do. He is a fine man and a brave one, but he is on the way out." His voice grew serious "The purge is on, my general. Villa has removed himself from active duty, but Obregón knows he must get rid of certain others before he can feel safe."

"Yes," said the General, "I know. I have already applied for my retirement, and soon will be returning to my pueblo. I think I will be left alone and in peace there. Obregón does not trust Villistas, but he fears only the General now that Felipe Angeles is dead. Every day, I wait word of the Chief's assassination."

"Don Pancho can still take care of himself."

"Not now. You know how he is living. Openly, not in the mountains. And he has but a few men with him. No," he said sadly, "I am resigned that his death is inevitable."

"But what irony," said Juan bitterly. "Villa, a man like ourselves and almost illiterate, was driven to brilliant victories by his noble illusion. With Obregón, a delusion was the driving force. Now the great one waits almost passively for an assassin's bullet while the nation he won is in the hands of the bastard opportunist."

"The destiny," said the General. "Who can go contrary to the destiny?"

Juan did not attempt to answer. He was suddenly filled with such hopelessness that he was inarticulate. His beloved general was to die—perhaps already he was dead! And all the dead in the struggle had died for nothing, and the living who had followed him would live also for nothing. But, no! He could not allow himself to believe such a thing! Such a monstrous thing should not be even thought by him! He spoke aloud with conviction. "They will not kill him. They cannot! By God! You know the man—you have seen the things he does, the risks he takes. I picture him now, calmly sitting his horse, watching the battle with his cold eyes, while twenty thousand Mausers[1] were shooting

---

1. Firearms (made by Mauser, a German arms manufacturer).

at his figure and all around him men were falling. It was die, die, die, that day—truly it was a day for dying. And I came near him, purely by accident, for I belonged on the opposite flank, but by now there was no opposite flank, and he said, 'Juan Manuelito'—he will say things like that sometimes—'they are killing too many people. It would be better if they would go over where the enemy is to die than here.' You would have thought that we were alone in that meadow, the way he talked. 'I need an example, muchacho. Go over and bring me that fieldpiece that is irritating me so much.' He was telling me to go die for him and it might help him win his battle and I knew it, but at that moment if he had asked me to turn my backside and submit to him, I would have done it without a qualm. So I rode toward the enemy, with reata in hand, but before I reached the little cannon, my horse was killed. But that was enough. Our men advanced, and the battle was won. How can they kill a man like that—a man with such balls! He walks with God, although the curates would deny it. If he wills it so, he can live forever!"

The General's voice was compassionate, and both men were unashamed of their tears. "Perhaps that is the answer, Juan Manuel," he said. "Perhaps the hour of his death is near because he wills it so."

"I will not believe it," said Juan. "It *cannot* be so." They were silent for a moment, and then Juan spoke; he addressed the old man not only as a friend but as the mature man he was. "Although I told them at the capital that I would take a year's leave of absence, within myself I have retired from the army. It is impossible for me to be a soldier for Obregón. The few weeks that I was gave me a feeling that I was not clean. I truly felt that I could better help my people if I went to the Academy, but I know differently now. I could be a general within five years, but I would have to become like the rest of them in power—be, in fact, one of them. Then I would spend so much time exploiting my people that I would have no time to help them.

"I came here because this is where the General will strike first when he returns. It is the only way to help México now. He will come back, and the people will follow him once again, and he will liberate the nation for the third time. And I wait here until he sends for me."

The old General shook his head sadly. "It is a great thing, this belief that you still have, Juan Manuel, but it is a bad thing, too, because it is futile. There has been too much war—too much blood. So much that to spill more would destroy the country completely. Yet, knowing this, I wish I could feel like you. But I am tired also of this bloodletting, and the people are sick of it. And now the biggest factor is that Obregón is recognized by the United States. Also, he is stronger, and no matter how you feel about the man, he is a soldier—indeed, you cannot deny he is a soldier."

"I would be stupid to deny that after Celaya," said Juan, but he refused to be discouraged. "Nevertheless, I know my General Villa," he said. "And I will wait as long as he sees fit. If he sends for me tonight, I am prepared to go."

"I grieve for you, my son. But you know you cannot remain here after that of this morning."

"What do you propose to do with me?" asked Juan. He had completely forgotten that a few hours ago he had killed a man.

"You can return to Zacatecas if you wish."

"I have many enemies there. There would be killing after killing, until one day I would have an unlucky day."

"Consuelo and the children, are they there?"

"I left her in Torreón with her people when I went to México."

"You have deserted her?" asked the General.

"I do not know yet," answered Juan.

The General was about to say something, then changed his mind. A man's family was his personal matter. He thought for a minute. "I think the safest place for you at present is across the bridge. Have you ever been to the other side?"

"Only to Columbus," answered Juan.

The General looked surprised and pleased. He looked at Juan with pride and respect, and there was a quality almost of possessiveness in his attitude as he spoke. "You have never told me that before. There are not many of you left."[2]

"You have never asked me before."

"There is something going on across the border that I have not told you," said the General. "Because it is a great futility and, too, because you would not be satisfied with that kind of action, or inaction, I do not wish that you become involved in it. The thing is, there are men in El Paso who are even now working to raise the funds necessary to start another offensive. When they are done with their plotting and their propaganda, they plan to contact Villa. He, meanwhile, is in Canutillo,[3] and does not even know this is going on."

"I know the breed," said Juan. "Exiled politicians seeking a soft billet. I have seen them through the years. Mysterious little people hiding in jacales, always talking, always plotting—I do not trust them."

The General laughed at him. "You are too hotheaded, Juan Manuel. I should not have worried about your becoming mixed up in their intrigues. Your anger is reassuring. And yet there is a place for the politicians in all this. They have their place. And the plotters and thinkers with the business suits—they have their place also, Madero[4] was the greatest thinker and plotter of them all. He was the one responsible for all this. Perhaps he was the one to blame."

Juan Rubio understood, and yet he was angry. "But he was for the Mexican—for the people. You may blame him for the suffering and for the killing, but that was a necessity, and the nation has been liberated and will again be liberated. Obregón[5] is not immortal you know." He stopped for a moment as an idea crossed his mind. He shook his head and continued, "The thing about little men in business suits that disturbs me is that somewhere, at this very moment perhaps, there is such a group of these animals mapping out the manner in which my general can be caught unawares. Obregón is a soldier, and a good one, but this type of thing must be done for him by civil-

2. I.e., not many men remain of those who—in March 1916, during the Mexican Revolution—crossed the border to take part in a raid on Columbus, New Mexico, during which several U.S. citizens were killed. Pancho Villa (1878–1923), formerly pro-American, planned and led the attack in retaliation for the U.S. government's support of his comrade-turned-rival Venustiano Carranza (1859–1920).

3. In August 1920, Villa negotiated a peace with the provisional Mexican government. The next month, he and several hundred of his soldiers, along with their families, "retired" to La

Purísima Concepción de El Canutillo, a former hacienda in Durango, Mexico.

4. Francisco Indalecio Madero (1873–1913), Mexican politician, elected president in 1911 after forcing President Porfirio Díaz (1830–1915) into exile. Thus Madero helped begin the Mexican Revolution. Many groups became disenchanted with his leadership, however, and revolted against him.

5. Álvaro Obregón (1880–1928), comrade-turned-rival of Villa and Carranza; president of Mexico 1920–24 and later assassinated.

ians. And, being the kind of people they are, they will undoubtedly corrupt someone near Villa with money and promises, or both, to betray him."

"Ah," sighed the General. "It is true—so true! But, tell me, did you for a minute there think of killing the President?"

Now Juan Manuel could laugh once more. "You are a sly old one," he said. "Many times I have wished that he should die. I have never until just a moment ago had the urge to do myself that favor."

"You will not be foolish . . ."

"I love life, even though you might think I do not. I could do that only if it meant that immediately everything would change. The death of Obregón is not the answer, for there are men like him, even though they are not strong in the military way, who would take his place, because now no one is opposing them. I could not die for that. And yet if my general Villa should ask that of me . . ."

The General stood up suddenly, and Juan knew he had made a decision. "Come, I will get you a change of clothing. Tonight I must secret you across the border. I have the bite on a gringo cattleman, and will give you a letter for him."

"What kind of bite?"

"Oh, I simply do not notice that he smuggles cattle across the Bravo."

"Goddamn it!" said Juan. "You too? Are there no honest people left? Is honor that worthless?"

"My hands are tied, Juan Manuel," said the General. "One might say the bribe goes with the command here. Almost a matter of courtesy on the part of the gringos. Anyway, you should be pleased, for the cattle is being stolen from the Spaniards."

"That is a point for it, but still it is very little justification for your actions. I wonder that you are helping me, for it seems that we are on opposite sides now. You have grown fat, old one."

"I have grown old, my son," said the General sadly. "You do me an injustice, and I can only grieve."

Juan looked at the old soldier, and he could not keep his contempt from showing. "Where is that courage—where has it gone? There is nothing left for you, old one. There is no need for you to retire, for you have retired already. Stay here. There is no danger that *you* might be marked for death. Only those who are yet completely men are in danger."

"Do not do this, Juan Manuel. For the memory of what I once was—what we all were. . . . But I will tell you about the courage. I left my gonads in Torreón, I left them in Zacatecas—oh, I did not know it then, but every campaign took a little from me—and I finally lost them at Celaya. Yes, at Celaya I finally recognized the fact that I was no longer young. It is a terrible thing to grow old in the midst of great futility. It was my destiny to be old when the thing started. A man should grow old strongly—old age should be a positive sort of thing, not anything like this. And yet, believe me, Juan Manuel, you too, will grow old. That is, I suppose, what makes it bearable in the end. Things have a way to equalize themselves. When I went to war, I was three times as old as you, and now I am only twice as old. Think of it, Juan Manuel, you are gaining on me. You will be me someday."

Repentant and ashamed, Juan Rubio spoke to the old soldier. "I am sorry, believe me. It is only that I remembered the old times, which are really not so old after all. Forgive me, old one, for I have loved you, and love you now. But do not think you are as soft as you make out to be. If a man has been a man, he will always be a man. I know I will be. I will never forget that which I believe is right. There must be a sense of honor or a man will have no dignity, and without the dignity a man is incomplete. I will always be a man."

"Ojalá,"[6] said the General.

"For the present," said Juan Rubio, "I will run cattle for your gringo, but only because I would rather do that than work as a farmhand. After all, I am a jinete."[7]

"Good," said the General. "Let us go in and join the others until you leave. My wife will be happy to see you again. Meanwhile, I will make a report of your escape in which I will give you a false name and a fantastic description."

"The teniente who arrested me knows my name," said Juan. "Will he not talk?"

"By noon tomorrow, he will be the youngest captain in this new National Army of México."

## II

Thus Juan Rubio became a part of the great exodus that came of the Mexican Revolution. By the hundreds they crossed the Río Grande, and then by the thousands. They came first to Juárez, where the price of the three-minute tram ride would take them into El Paso del Norte—or a short walk through the open door would deposit them in Utopia. The ever-increasing army of people swarmed across while the border remained open, fleeing from squalor and oppression. But they could not flee reality, and the Texans, who welcomed them as a blessing because there were miles of cotton to be harvested, had never really forgotten the Alamo.[8] The certain degree of dignity the Mexicans yet retained made some of them turn around and walk back into the hell they had left. Others huddled close to the international bridge and established a colony on the American side of the river, in the city of El Paso, because they could gaze at their homeland a few yards away whenever the impulse struck them. The bewildered people came on—insensitive to the fact that even though they were not stopped, they were not really wanted. It was the ancient quest for El Dorado,[9] and so they moved onward, west to New Mexico and Arizona and California, and as they moved, they planted their new seed.

In a dry creekbed under a trestle in Isleta,[1] a young boy held a lantern against the dark night while four men played at cards on an old blanket.

"Call me René," said one of the men. "It is simply René. There is no need to tell more, for to tell more may mean my death."

Juan Rubio shuffled the cards and did not speak. A second man, younger than the others, spoke.

"I know you," he said. "I have seen you before."

6. Would to God; if only.
7. Horseman.
8. In 1836, during the Texas Revolution, at the now legendary chapel-fort in San Antonio called the Alamo, about 180 Texans were defeated by thousands of Mexicans led by the Mexican gen-eral Antonio López de Santa Anna (1794–1876).
9. The legendary golden city, kingdom, and em-pire that, in 1541, inspired Spanish conquistadors to explore, famously and disastrously, the Amazon River region of South America.
1. A neighborhood in El Paso.

"You know me?" asked René, a look of fear momentarily crossing his face.

"In my village it was—in Guanajuanto—when I was but a boy," continued the young man. "But I do not know your name, for I was no bigger than the boy there at the time."

"His name is not René," said the fourth man. "And you are younger than I thought to have been a soldier, for my boy there is but twelve years old and he was born before the war."

René shifted his position, as if preparing to flee when the time came. "Why do you say that," he asked, "about René not being my name?"

"Because I have seen you many times, although you took no notice of me. I saw you in the state of Aguascalientes and in other states also, but mostly in the state of Aguascalientes. You were a civilian traveling with the army—and I especially remember you because I always meant to ask you a few questions, such as which side we were on during a particular campaign, for I could never quite figure out who I was fighting for. First I was for the people and then I was for the government, because my General Carrillo said so, and then I again was for the people, and so on. You were always with the General in those days, and I felt you could give me the answers to my questions. I took no stock in the tales of the men that you were sleeping with the General. I only felt that you had much influence and were an educated one."

"You are mistaken," said René. "It was someone else." But he was angry and his words were said in anger.

"Since you do not wish it, I will tell no one your name," said the other. "You need not fear that I will do so, but I am not mistaken, for I traveled with you, although I was but a foot soldier and you traveled with the cavalry and the General."

"I am not afraid," said René, "for I have nothing to hide. It is only that the people with whom I cast my lot are now in disfavor. It could easily have been very different, and I would be in the capital tonight, instead of here in this miserable hole."

Juan Rubio spoke up for the first time. "There is no need for you to remain here if you do not like it." He laughed, although men like René displeased him. "You know you can go to New York, or even Paris, or London. You have our permission."

René did not laugh. "You joke, Señor Rubio," he said. "But it is really no laughing matter. Here we know each other by name because we live together in common exile. But we cannot know each other's background. I know yours because it was my business to know such things. This man knows me because, in truth, he has seen me. I was a journalist—or, rather, an expert on political matters. I am also a student of the psychology of men."

"All those things," said Juan Rubio, "in so short a lifetime you were."

"All those things," said René. "And I have been to New York and Paris and London—earlier—in my student days."

"I laugh again, Gachupín," said Juan Rubio, "at the importance you give all these things."

René's tone became noticeably boastful. "And I am also a maker of generals—I, too, had a general in the palm of my hand. He was a small cacique in a remote village, and I personally made him into a leader of men. I found Juan Carrillo when he was on a drunken spree, for he had sold a cow—where he got it I do not know—but he had money that day and was drinking and whoring, and I recognized him as exactly the kind of man I was looking for. He was a born leader without a sense of direction—brave, loyal, gullible, and cruel. He was vain as an adolescent, and he loved to drink and screw. I took him and made him into a powerful man, and he did everything I asked him to do. . . . Of course, in this I had to be careful, for he would have had me shot in a minute if he suspected that I was really doing his thinking for him. And I wrote him up in newspapers and periodicals. In the end, alas, luck, which is such a necessary thing in these matters, deserted us and he died. If this had not happened, we would be in México now, Juan Carrillo and I, for I had decided that he should support Obregón."

"He was but a small shit," said Juan Rubio with contempt. "Shot by a woman—a grown man who allowed his balls to be shot clean away from his body. What a fitting end for someone like him."

"My one mistake," said René, "was to allow women to follow the troops. Women are always trouble—I myself have never really needed one—but Juan taught them to shoot, and a gun in their hand was as deadly as one in the hand of a man."

"He was nothing, and thus you are nothing," said Juan Rubio.

René looked down and away from Juan Rubio's face. Unaccountably, he had tried to impress this man and had failed. Somehow, he could now see his failure in the manner the other meant. He picked up the cards and began to deal. Preoccupied as he was with thoughts of what might have been, he was suddenly aware that the stakes had increased and that in a minute he would win everything.

The boy holding the lantern suddenly put it out. Juan Rubio reached toward the money and grasped a man's wrist strongly. A shot rang out in the dark, and it was not necessary for him to hold the wrist, for the man fell over on his face on the money. When the lamp was lighted once again, the boy was huddled against a support of the bridge and his father lay dead on the money. René put his gun away and Juan Rubio said:

"You need not have shot him."

"He was a thief," said René.

"He was that—and a fool also—but he need not have died," said Juan Rubio. "Are your fears so great that you must kill all who once knew your name? Take your money and go far; I will take him to his woman." He looked at the man who had been in the ranks of the army of Carrillo and thought of the ignobleness of death.

The man who died under the bridge that night had no name. Who he was, where he came from, how he lived—these things did not matter, for there were thousands like him at this time. This particular man had fought in the army of General Carrillo, who, in turn, was one of the many generals in the Revolution. And, like thousands of unknown soldiers before and after him, this man did not reason, did not know, had but a vague idea of his battle. Eventually there was peace, or a lull in the fighting, and he escaped with his wife and children and crossed the border to the north. Then he took his family to Pecos, far into the new country, and there, on Mr. Henderson's ranch, he shared a crop and became a cotton farmer. He had a house there in which to live, and corn and beans and occasionally meat. His cotton grew high, for cotton, and was one day thickly white. Mr. Henderson rode into the yard on horseback accompanied by a friend. He wore a star on his shirt.

"Eh, Señor Jéndeson," the sharecropper called, for it was now his custom to joke with his boss, "is it that now you are on the side of the law?" The rancher laughed also. "Yes, Mario," he answered. "All the big men around here are special deputies." He spoke to his companion for a moment, then pulled his rifle out of its scabbard and dropped it on the ground as they rode away.

The man Mario watched them ride away. He picked the gun up and inspected it, then leaned it against the house. Strange behavior, he thought. Doubtless the patrón would return for it.

It was nearly dark when Mr. Henderson returned. There were more men with him now, and one of them saw the rifle and brought it to a big man who was the sheriff. The sheriff spoke, and it amazed Mario that this man so far from his own country could speak Spanish. "Why did you forcibly take this gun from your patrón, peón?" he asked.

"I did no such thing," said Mario. "He himself threw it on the ground when he went away. I but put it aside, out of the way of the children, for I knew he must come back to get it."

"The man calls me a liar," said Mr. Henderson.

"Do not call a white man a liar, boy," said the sheriff.

"Do not call me a boy," said Mario, "for you cannot be much older than I am."

"You are leaving tonight," said the sheriff. "Get your family and your things together. Mr. Henderson will pay your train fare to El Paso. Be thankful."

Mario now wished he had kept the rifle out of sight. It was not difficult to see what was happening to him, but if he had the rifle, he would resist until death. He knew also that if he resisted he would surely die. "But my cotton," he said. "I have worked for almost a whole year for Mr. Jéndesen. Then, when we planted the cotton, he explained it to me that half of it belongs to me. The bolls are very big now and very white."

"It is because of your attack on Mr. Henderson that you forfeit your claims. You should not have done that. Now, prepare to leave," said the sheriff. "It is useless to argue."

But this man called Mario had a few gold pieces saved from a time long ago, when a pueblo had been sacked in the central part of México. With these he gambled under the trestle in Isleta. He had a plan, this man Mario, of how to get a little more money, in order to buy a piece of land in his home state. He would return to México—of that there was no doubt—but he would return with a certain amount of money, and if he did not win it fairly, he had a plan. He gave his oldest boy his orders and set out to find the trestle where it was said men would sometimes play at cards for gold.

## III

Juan Rubio worked first running cattle across the border, living with the greatest assortment of bad men he had ever known, sleeping always with one hand on his gun and the other on his knife. Whenever he had a few days free, he visited his woman in Juárez, whose name he now knew to be Dolores. She had removed herself from her old life and lived in a small white house on the river's edge. Soon she would also cross the border; but one day Juan's wife and three children arrived, making it out of the question for Dolores to come over the line. He moved his family to Isleta, and there he picked cotton and gambled and drank; occasionally, he fought. But every weekend he visited his Dolores, whom he loved until the day she told him she was pregnant.

Boredom worked its magic on the once active man. There had been no word from Canutillo, the hacienda of Francisco Villa—no word of the General, in fact—and Juan knew that it was time to do something. It was his feeling that perhaps destiny had chosen him to be a part in the changing of history.

He stood with his back against the adobe wall of the warehouse building, drawing deeply on the last of his cigarette. He held the cigarette with his fingertips, the lighted end toward his palm. He wore huaraches and the white breeches of the peasant and a large hat. His sarape was worn poncho-like and his sidearm was pulled forward, hanging near his groin. He felt a mild excitement now, after months of dissatisfaction. He had been visited at night by a total stranger and had sent him away, but now here he was, ready for an appointment with the politicians, prepared to do a thing he had believed he would never do. The door to the building was a few feet away to his right. He had been standing here, watching, for nearly an hour, making himself deliberately late. It was only a moment ago that he had lighted a cigarette, for he must be certain everything was all right outside before he entered the warehouse.

*So this was the way these things happened? In the dark of night, strangers meet and talk, and a thousand miles away a man would soon die. Strange witchcraft!*

Juan Rubio believed in witchcraft, for he had seen many times the things the art could do, but he was also a realist, and this was not really witchcraft; hence the garments of the peasant. If he was to go south tonight, he would do it as a peón. He moved to the door and knocked, as he had been directed to do. He heard movement inside, the rasp of the bolt, and a face peered out from the darkness within.

"Is it you, Colonel?"

"To serve you," said Juan Rubio. He entered, and the door was bolted once again. When the lamp was lighted, he was standing against the door and his gun was in his hand.

"There is no need for the gun, my friend," said one of the men. He wore rimless glasses and was short and slight of body. "We are friends here, and in particular there is a man here who counts himself as a friend of yours— the Señor Soto."

Juan looked at René, who sat at one end of the table around which four other men sat. "He is not my friend," he said. "And neither are you. In fact, I doubt that you are friends of each other. In all of México, you will not find two men who are truly friends." He put his gun away. "I distrust you because you are politicians and because I do not know you. I have been alone too long and must protect myself—by myself."

"I am José Luís Zamora," said the small man. "René Soto you are acquainted with, if he is not your friend. The others—I could give you names, but they are only names and unimportant. The important thing is the cause, and that is the reason we are here tonight."

"I do not know of the cause—at least in the sense you do," said Juan Rubio almost surlily. "I do not believe you and I are working toward the same end at all, but I am here because, no matter what your aim might be, the act, when accomplished, will benefit México."

"You are prepared to do it, then?" asked the small man. "Ah! You are a true patriot to agree to such a task before we quote a price."

"Did I not tell you?" said René Soto.

Juan Rubio spoke to the group, but his words were directed at René. "I want you to understand—every one of you—that I am not a man to do things in this way. I agree to do it only because I please, and not because you have convinced me to do it, nor because you control me. I follow but one man, and after him no one. You have no claims on me now, nor will you have claims on me if I live after the deed is done. I will kill you your President only because there are many reasons why he should die. But I am a soldier, and am neither a politician nor a fanatic—small difference in the two in these times—and I cannot forget that I have always faced any man openly."

The small man spoke, and there was a sharpness in his voice. "Your attitude is not what we want for a task such as this one we propose. You are too arrogant, my friend, and your arrogance constitutes a danger to our plan. Other men are involved and their blood would run free, I fear, if we were to assign this job to you. Perhaps we have made an error, or the voice of Señor Soto has been overly persuasive."

"I resent that strongly, José Luís," said René, standing suddenly. "I have told you this is the man, and I still believe he is the man. I *know* men—I have been in these things many years, and I know of what I speak. It would be suicidal to entrust this task to a zealot! The man to carry this out must be cool and calculating, and he must be allowed to proceed in this as he pleases. He must be a patriot, and I assure you Juan Manuel Rubio is a patriot—but he must also have personal reasons burning deep within him."

"I desire but one thing," said Juan Rubio, "and that is the name of a man in the capital who can find me a place in which to hide for a day or two. Other arrangements I will make myself. I want no money."

René spoke to the little man. "We have no choice, José Luís. And we are fortunate that our only choice is the best we could have made."

The little man put his face in his hands, his elbows on the table. "I do not know," he said. "I truly do not know."

"A spirited horse must be given his head," said René.

José Luís Zamora threw up his hands in a gesture of resignation. "If the other gentlemen are agreed," he said, "I accept him also."

"The analogy of the horse," said Juan Rubio to René. "It is well put. You are thinking, of course, that a spirited horse *can* be controlled."

René looked directly at Juan Rubio's face. "Yes, I am, don Juan."

"Take such ideas out of your head," said Juan Rubio, with a smile. "For to control a strong beast a man must first have a strong hand. And there is another gamble you take, René—I may die before the week is out."

"It is good we understand each other," said René, through lips that barely moved.

There was a knock on the door, and the lamp was turned down. Juan Rubio once again had his gun out as the door was opened and a man came violently into the room.

"It has happened, señores," the new voice cried excitedly before the lamp had been turned up. "The General is no more! Pancho Villa is dead!"

Juan stood with his arms hanging limply at his sides, his gun dangling from his hand. His face was pale, and he said that which he knew was not true. "You lie, son of a bitch! You lie! I do not know your motives, but you lie!"

"The details, man," said Zamora. "Quickly!"

"It was in his automobile that it happened, as his car crossed a gully. Stationary machine guns set off a crossfire, and it is a miracle if any of the men with him escaped," said the messenger. "His body is en route to the capital this minute, and will be shown to the people at the Zócalo. The news was kept from coming north, and very effectively. The atrocity was committed this morning, and we heard rumors on the other side this afternoon, but we waited to be certain."

"It is true, then?" asked René. "It cannot possibly be propaganda—I am a newspaperman and know the powers of the propaganda."

"It is true. I myself saw the marconigram[2] from Chihuahua just this moment," said the messenger.

"Then we are finished," said René. "Our work here is done, my friends, for we have lost the one man who could have taken the ragged and the hungry, the lame—and, yes, even the blind into the fight once more. The people would do for that man that which they would do for no other. And he was a brute . . . but what a magnificent one! History is replete with men like him—one to a generation—and none greater than he was."

Zamora paced back and forth. "Do not listen to this man, señores. That of the poet and the romantic within him is but showing itself. The man Villa was needed, to be sure, but he was not absolutely essential. His death will slow us a little, but he was expendable—not as expendable as most men, perhaps, but expendable nevertheless. We must search for another crude, vulgar leader for the masses. Vainglorious, dull, and malleable. We have the makings of such a man right in this room—but then we cannot send him to México."

And Juan Rubio was apart from them, rocking in his grief. He was on his knees, holding his head in his hands, and he cried unrestrainedly, as a child would cry. And as he cried he was afraid, and this was the first time; for although he had known fear, it had been momentary, and this was an intelligent fear, for himself and for humanity, but mainly for himself. The death of an immortal showed most clearly the unalterable fact that everyone must die, himself included. He had never really believed this before now. But his grief was as short as it was intense, and from now on there would be an ache and an emptiness and occasionally a dull moan, but this thing was over and in a sense he was free. He stood once again, and his dignity was noticeable, as if regenerated by the purge of his tears.

"Forgive me," he said, "but I did not hear what you were saying. But then I am not interested. I will go now, for I want nothing to do with the likes of you."

"Wait, wait!" said Zamora. "That of the trip to México is, of course, out of the question now, but we have other plans for you."

"Forget your plans," said Juan Rubio. "I want no part of them." He was impatient and was becoming visibly angry.

René Soto moved to his side. "Accept my deepest sympathies, don Juan," he said. "I know what the General was to you—what he was to your people. And, believe me, I, too, want no part of what these men will propose."

2. Radiogram; a wireless message.

"Thank you," said Juan. "Let me move."

But Zamora stood at the door, a halfsmile on his face, and began to speak almost indulgently to Juan Rubio. "Colonel," he said, "you claim to be a soldier and a fighter for the people. You loved your general and now he is dead, and those responsible for his death are ruling your people. It is not fitting that a man such as you should simply forget this and walk away."

"Forget!" shouted Juan Rubio. "Is this capón insane? Forget!" He moved toward Zamora. "You say *forget*, you stupid bastard. Of course I will not forget! But for the moment I can do nothing. A time will come when I will do that which you wanted me to do, and when I am finished, if I live I will put the gun away forever. I will do it when he is relaxed with success. It may be five years or it may be ten, but I will get him even if it is twenty years. You may be sure he will be there twenty years, for he considers the nation his. Until that day, I will live in peace. I have been a gun fighter too long—much too long—and I have been fortunate and I have killed many times. I was fifteen the first time, and now I have twenty-seven years and have had my fill for the present." His anger was checked now, and he continued, in a sarcastic mood, "Forget, you say! Can I forget while I am looking at people like you? Can I possibly forget while you speak to me as if I were a child? I do not like that, Zamora. Do not make that mistake again. You are being dishonest with me, but I was dishonest with you also. I agreed to assassinate Obregón with the hope in my heart that when Villa arose once again, he would take politicians and connivers such as you and make them dig their own graves. We did it in Torreón, you know. We took the Chinese and the Spaniards and killed them in bunches, and everyone said we were massacring chinitos and gachupines simply because of their nationality, and the truth was that we did it because we could not trust them. They would have inherited the city we liberated, and someday we would have to return and fight for it again. That is the only way to save México, by killing all leeches such as you. All this because there is no one left whom we can trust. But it was not to be so. The destiny said no to me, so I go now."

Zamora started to speak once more. "You can have power, man. And riches . . ."

René Soto grabbed him by the lapels of his jacket. "Do you not see, José Luís, this man is truly an idealist? Perhaps the first such person I have seen in my life, and I tell you his kind are dangerous! Do you want a massacre in this room? You will have just that if you insist!" He turned to Juan Rubio and said, "Let us go, Colonel. I want to go with you."

"Stop patronizing me, for Christ's sake. Call me Juan. I am not an idiot."

Outside in the darkness, René said, "To México, I suppose."

"Are you crazy, too? Juárez is full of government spies by now. I would not get two blocks into the country—in fact, I must leave El Paso as soon as possible. It is not safe for me here."

"I have always held the desire to visit the state of California," said René.

"I have never thought of California," said Juan Rubio. "But then I suppose it is as good a place as any at this time."

"You know," said René, "I have really been to Paris and London."

Juan Rubio laughed as he had not laughed for many days.

*IV*

In Los Angeles, he mourned deeply the loss of his god, but he was an active man and could not remain idle. Now he helped build the tall buildings, and was one day buried in a sand slide, but he survived, and soon his wife and children caught up with him once more. He found a new respect for this woman, who had relentlessly followed him so many miles, and his nurtured ego made him love her for the first time in his life. He stopped his drinking and gambling, and learned to be discreet in his love affairs. Two months later, their manchild, Richard, was born, and the mother believed that he was the reason her man had changed his wild way of life.

It was near Brawley, in the Imperial Valley, at a place where a dry creek met a tributary of the Canal del Alamo, that Richard was born. The Rubio family lived in a white clapboard house on a melon farm, on land that had been neardesert not too long ago. On one sidé of the habitation ran the creek, which was lined by drab mesquites and an occasional sausal. To the other side, as far as the eye could see and beyond, over the horizon, could be seen rows and rows of melons. Here and there a clump of trees shimmered, hull-down, seemingly dancing when viewed across acres of heat. The land had been reclaimed and the valley made artificially green and fertile, but the oppressive heat remained, and the people who tilled the fields, for the most part, came from the temperate climate of the central plateaus of México and found it difficult to acclimatize. Every day, one or two or three of them were carried, dehydrated and comatose, from the field, placed in some shade, and administered cold-water spongings, until, revived and more than a little nauseous, they returned to the field to close the gap in the ranks made by their departure. Indeed, there were a few that year who died before they could receive help, and were carted off to El Centro, where they ended up in a pauper's grave or on a slab in some medical school in Los Angeles or San Francisco. No one knew; and if the deceased had loved ones, they were not allowed to hold a wake, for the body belonged to the state, since there was no money to be had for a mortician, and although the people were religious, their poverty made them practical, and what little money they gathered was used to keep the living alive. So in the two or three hours it took for the authorities to arrive in the ominous gray hearse, the bereaved paid their last respects and devotion to the departed soul, worshiped the body until the hearse arrived, and the hot air was filled with anguished screams.

Then the people began to bury their own dead, in the age-old custom of people, and the only person who knew the location of the unmarked graves was an agnostic who had been a novice in a seminary in Guadalajara and who was also the only person who could lead the people in prayer in the manner in which they were accustomed. The emigrants were scattered throughout the valley, and it was a hardship to visit each other, yet they somehow formed a unit of society, and they kept its secrets well—so well, in fact, that when a witch was murdered (for there were witches in those days, as there are today), she was committed to the earth, and the English-speaking population knew nothing of her death, if, indeed, they had known of her existence.

It was here, then, near Brawley one night after she had fed her family that Consuelo Rubio felt the urge to urinate. The outhouse was near the bank of the creek under one of the willows, and she took a coal-oil lamp, for there was no wind. It was cool, as it is at night in the desert, and she wrapped her shawl around her shoulders and stepped outside. She took a few steps, and suddenly she did not know where she was going, or for what reason she was outside the house. She looked at the lamp in her hand for a long moment, then set it on the ground and wandered aimlessly. Now she walked on the creekbed, first on gravel, and the sound her shoes made on the pebbles penetrated her senses, and in her mind she was back on the hacienda in Zacatecas, walking on a dry creekbed such as this, although she did not know she was on a creekbed, on her way to a manantial[3] for water. She reached a sandy stretch and walked on, and she was dangerously near the bank of the canal. The urge to urinate, which had left her, returned with an intensity she could not resist, and she undid her cotton drawers and squatted, holding the folds of her dress under her armpits. And there on the soft sand she dropped her child. She remained in that position, draining, and did not hear her husband, who, suddenly realizing she had but a few days before her confinement, left the house to see that she did not stumble or in some way injure herself. He picked the lamp up and called to her, and he would not have found her except for the fact that somehow she got the baby to breathe and a child's cry is unmistakable. He found her then, still sitting as she had delivered, an end of her shawl around the child, her mind still distracted. Slowly he set the lamp down, and tenderly he picked his woman and child up and carried them to the house.

"Your mother has given light," he said to his oldest daughter. "Go to the creek bed and bring the lamp and cover up the mess with sand."

He was very nearly overcome by emotion, and did not question the strangeness of this as he gently laid his wife on the bed. He wiped the placenta off her ankles and feet with the shawl, while another daughter brought him warm water with which to clean the child. He had never been this close to the birth of a child, for men are usually removed from such things, but he had seen animals foal, and he took his pocketknife and severed the umbilical cord. A woman from another house came then, but before he gave her the child, he realized he did not know its sex, and now he cried, not because it was a manchild, or because its genitalia seemed enormous in proportion to the little body, but because he was relaxed and because for a moment he had caught a glimpse of the cycle of life, lucidly not penumbrally, and he knew love and he knew also that all this was good.

He took a shovel and walked to the creek to deeper bury the afterbirth, for he had a dread that a stray dog would be attracted and eat his blood.

The nomadic pace increased. Lettuce harvests in Salinas, melons in Brawley, grapes in Parlier, oranges in Ontario, cotton in Firebaugh—and, finally, Santa Clara, the prune country. And because this place was pleasing to the eye, or because they were tired of their endless migration, Juan Rubio and his wife settled here to raise their children. And, remembering his country, Juan thought that his distant cousin, the great General Zapata,[4] had been

---

3. Spring.
4. Emiliano Zapata (ca. 1879–1919), Mexican rev-
olutionary, initially a comrade of Madero, Villa, Obregón, and other leaders.

right when, in speaking of Juan, he once said to Villa, "He will go far, that relative of mine."

Now this man who had lived by the gun all his adult life would sit on his haunches under the prune trees, rubbing his sore knees, and think, *Next year we will have enough money and we will return to our country*. But deep within he knew he was one of the lost ones. And as the years passed him by and his children multiplied and grew, the chant increased in volume and rate until it became a staccato NEXT YEAR! NEXT YEAR!

And the chains were incrementally heavier on his heart.

1959

---

# MARIO SUÁREZ
## 1925–1998

Mario Suárez was born in a barrio of Tucson, Arizona, to Mexican parents who had migrated to the United States in the 1920s. After serving in the U.S. Coast Guard during World War II, he attended the University of Arizona on the G.I. Bill. Two of his literature professors suggested he submit his short stories—sketches that formed a cycle—to the *Arizona Quarterly*, and his first published story appeared there, in 1947, two years after his discharge. The pieces included in this anthology, "El Hoyo" (The Hole)" and "Señor Garza," also first appeared in that periodical. ("El Hoyo" is said to be among the first texts in the Latino literary tradition to include the word *Chicano*. It was preceded by mentions in Daniel Venegas's *The Adventures of Don Chipote* [see p. 397] and in *décimas* that circulated in the 1940s.) While attending college to earn his teaching certificate, Suárez worked as a teacher, a journalist, and a recreation supervisor for the *Los Angeles Times* Boys' Club. He later taught at Claremont College and the California State Polytechnic University at Pomona. He wrote novels, which remain unpublished.

During his formative years, Suárez considered John Steinbeck's *Tortilla Flat* (1935) his inspiration. Over time, he defined his style against this model: Whereas Steinbeck wrote about Californians as an outsider, Suárez wrote of the Chicanos or Mexican Americans of the barrio El Hoyo as an insider, someone who spoke the language, knew and lived at the heart of Chicano culture. Thus he achieved a more realistic, less romantic view of the social conditions. Indeed, by focusing unapologetically on daily life in El Hoyo, Suárez captured the customs and the fertile linguistic and ethnic mix of the barrio. In "El Hoyo"—about Mexican American veterans returning to the barrio after World War II—lines such as "Pablo Gutiérrez married the Chinese grocer's daughter and now runs a meat department; his sons are Chicanos" and "Killer Jones . . . threw a fight in Harlem and fled to El Hoyo to marry Cristina Méndez" present a microcosm of the United States' rich racial mixture rarely seen in fiction of the time. Also taking place in El Hoyo, "Señor Garza" is a character study of the barrio barber, also counselor and trusted community man, looked up to by the Chicanos who come to sit, talk, and complain of the changing world about them. The barbershop serves as a place "where men, disgruntled at the vice of the rest of the world, come to air their views. It is where they come to get things off their chests along with the hair off their heads and beard off their faces." Suárez's characters know who they are and where they came from. While life in El Hoyo is different from life in Mexico, the Mexican immigrants in this barrio do not lose self-confidence or suffer a loss of identity. Just as important, they know that in El Hoyo, Latino traditions and values continue.

## El Hoyo

From the center of downtown Tucson the ground slopes gently away to Main Street, drops a few feet, and then rolls to the banks of the Santa Cruz River. Here lies the section of the city known as El Hoyo. Why it is called El Hoyo is not very clear. In no sense is it a hole as its name would imply; it is simply the river's immediate valley. Its inhabitants are chicanos who raise hell on Saturday night and listen to Padre Estanislao on Sunday morning. While the term chicano is the short way of saying Mexicano, it is not restricted to the paisanos[1] who came from old Mexico with the territory or the last famine to work for the railroad, labor, sing, and go on relief. Chicano is the easy way of referring to everybody. Pablo Gutiérrez married the Chinese grocer's daughter and now runs a meat department; his sons are Chicanos. So are the sons of Killer Jones who threw a fight in Harlem and fled to El Hoyo to marry Cristina Méndez. And so are all of them. However, it is doubtful that all these spiritual sons of Mexico live in El Hoyo because of its scenic beauty—it is everything but beautiful. Its houses are simple affairs of unplastered adobe, wood, and abandoned car parts. Its narrow streets are mostly clearings which have, in time, acquired names. Except for some tall trees which nobody has ever cared to identify, nurse, or destroy, the main things known to grow in the general area are weeds, garbage piles, dark-eyed chavalos,[2] and dogs. And it is doubtful that the chicanos live in El Hoyo because it is safe—many times the Santa Cruz has risen and inundated the area.

In other respects living in El Hoyo has its advantages. If one is born with a weakness for acquiring bills, El Hoyo is where the collectors are less likely to find you. If one has acquired the habit of listening to Octavio Perea's Mexican Hour in the wee hours of the morning with the radio on at full blast, El Hoyo is where you are less likely to be reported to the authorities. Besides, Perea is very popular and sooner or later to everybody "Smoke In The Eyes" is dedicated between the pinto beans and white flour commercials. If one, for any reason whatever, comes on an extended period of hard times, where, if not in El Hoyo, are the neighbors more willing to offer solace? When Teófila Malacara's house burned to the ground with all her belongings and two children, a benevolent gentleman carried through the gesture that made tolerable her burden. He made a list of five hundred names and solicited from each a dollar. At the end of a month he turned over to the tearful but grateful señora one hundred dollars in cold cash and then accompanied her on a short vacation. When the new manager of a local store decided that no more chicanas were to work behind the counters, it was the chicanos of El Hoyo who, on taking their individually small but collectively great buying power elsewhere, drove the manager out and the girls returned to their jobs. When the Mexican Army was enroute to Baja California and the chicanos found out that the

1. Peasants, countrymen.
2. Boys, young men, youngsters (slang).

enlisted men ate only at infrequent intervals, it was El Hoyo's chicanos who crusaded across town with pots of beans and trays of tortillas to meet the train. When someone gets married, celebrating is not restricted to the immediate friends of the couple. Everybody is invited. Anything calls for a celebration and a celebration calls for anything. On Armistice Day[3] there are no less than half a dozen good fights at the Riverside Dance Hall. On Mexican Independence Day[4] more than one flag is sworn allegiance to amid cheers for the queen.

And El Hoyo is something more. It is this something more which brought Felipe Sánchez back from the wars after having killed a score of Germans with his body resembling a patchwork quilt to marry Julia Armijo. It brought Joe Zepeda, a gunner flying B-24's over Germany, back to compose boleros.[5] He has a metal plate for a skull. Perhaps El Hoyo is proof that those people exist, and perhaps exist best, who have as yet failed to observe the more popular modes of human conduct. Perhaps the humble appearance of El Hoyo justifies the indifferent shrug of those made aware of its existence. Perhaps El Hoyo's simplicity motivates an occasional chicano to move away from its narrow streets, babbling comadres and shrieking children to deny the bloodwell from which he springs and to claim the blood of a conquistador while his hair is straight and his face beardless. Yet El Hoyo is not an outpost of a few families against the world. It fights for no causes except those which soothe its immediate angers. It laughs and cries with the same amount of passion in times of plenty and of want.

Perhaps El Hoyo, its inhabitants, and its essence can best be explained by telling a bit about a dish called capirotada. Its origin is uncertain. But, according to the time and the circumstance, it is made of old, new or hard bread. It is softened with water and then cooked with peanuts, raisins, onions, cheese, and panocha.[6] It is fired with sherry wine. Then it is served hot, cold, or just "on the weather" as they say in El Hoyo. The Sermenos like it one way, the Garcias another, and the Ortegas still another. While it might differ greatly from one home to another, nevertheless it is still capirotada. And so it is with El Hoyo's chicanos. While being divided from within and from without, like the capirotada, they remain chicanos.

1947

## Señor Garza

Many consider Garza's Barber Shop as not truly in El Hoyo because it is on Congress Street and therefore downtown. Señor Garza, its proprietor, cashier, janitor, and Saint Francis,[1] philosophizes that since it is situated in that part of the street where the land decidedly slopes, it is in El Hoyo. Who would question it? Who contributes to every cause for which a solicitor

---

3. The anniversary of the symbolic end of World War I (November 11, 1918); in 1954, nine years after World War II, it became Veterans Day.
4. September 16; celebration of the end of Spanish rule over Mexico.
5. Music for Mexican dances.

6. A coarse sugar made in Mexico.
1. Francis of Assisi (1182?–1226), Catholic friar known for humility, love of poverty, joyousness, and love of nature; founder of the Franciscan order.

comes in with a long face and a longer relation of sadness? Who is the easiest touch for all the drunks who have to buy their daily cures? For loafers who go to look for jobs and never find them? For bullfighters on the wrong side of the border? For boxers still amateurs though punchy? For barbers without barber shops? And for the endless line of moochers who drop in to borrow anything from two bits to two dollars? Naturally, Garza.

Garza's Barber Shop is more than razors, scissors, and hair. It is where men, disgruntled at the vice of the rest of the world, come to air their views. It is where they come to get things off their chests along with the hair off their heads and beard off their faces. Garza's Barber Shop is where everybody sooner or later goes or should. This does not mean that there are no other barber shops in El Hoyo. There are. But none of them seem quite to capture the atmosphere that Garza's does. If it were not downtown it would probably have a little fighting rooster tied to a stake by the front door. If it were not rented to Señor Garza only it would perhaps smell of sherry wine all day. To Garza's Barber Shop goes all that is good and bad. The lawbreakers come in to rub elbows with the sheriff's deputies. And toward all Garza is the same. When zoot suiters come in for a very slight trim, Garza who is very versatile, puts on a bit of zoot talk and hep-cats[2] with the zootiest of them. When the boys that are not zoot suiters come in, he becomes, for the purpose of accommodating his clientele, just as big a snob as their individual personalities require. When necessity calls for a change in his character Garza can assume the proportions of a Greek, a Chinaman, a gypsy, a republican, a democrat, or if only his close friends are in the shop, plain Garza.

Perhaps Garza's pet philosophy is that a man should not work too hard. Garza tries not to. His day begins according to the humor of his wife. When Garza drives up late, conditions are perhaps good. When Garza drives up early, all is perhaps not well. Garza's Barber Shop has been known, accordingly, to stay closed for a week. It has also been known to open before the sun comes up and to remain open for three consecutive days. But on normal days and with conditions so-so, Garza comes about eight in the morning. After opening, he pulls up the green venetian blinds. He brings out two green ash cans containing the hair cut the preceding day and puts them on the edge of the sidewalk. After this he goes to a little back room in the back of the shop, brings out a long crank, and lowers the red awning that keeps out the morning sun. Lily-boy, the fat barber who through time and diligence occupies chair number two, is usually late. This does not mean that Lily-boy is lazy, but he is married and there are rumors, which he promptly denies, that state he is henpecked. Rodríguez, barber number three, usually fails to show up for five out of six workdays.

On ordinary mornings Garza sits in the shoeshine stand because it is closest to the window and nods at the pretty girls going to work and to the ugly ones, too. He works on an occasional customer. He goes to Sally and Sam's for a cup of coffee, and on returning continues to sit. At noon Garza takes off his small apron, folds it, hangs it on the arm of his chair, and after combing his hair goes to La Estrella to eat and flirt with the waitresses who, for reasons that even they cannot understand, have taken him into their confidence.

2. Acts cool (i.e., by talking the lingo of the "zoot suiters," young men dressed in a streetwise fashion of high-waisted, wide-legged, tight-cuffed pegged trousers; a long coat with wide lapels and wide, padded shoulders; a felt hat with a long feather; and pointy shoes).

They are well aware of his marital standing; but Garza has black wavy hair and picaresque charm that sends them to the kitchen giggling. After eating his usual meal of beans, rice, tortilla, and coffee, he bids all the girls good-bye and goes back to his barber shop. The afternoons are spent in much the same manner as the mornings except that on such days as Saturday, there is such a rush of business that Garza very often seeks some excuse to go away from his own business and goes for the afternoon to Nogales in Mexico or downstairs to the Tecolote Club to drink beer.

On most days, by five-thirty everybody has usually been in the shop for friendly reasons, commercial reasons, and even spiritual reasons. Loco-Chu, whose lack of brains everybody understands, has gone by and insulted the customers. Take-It-Easy, whose liquor-saturated brain everybody respects, has either made nasty signs at everybody or has come in to quote the words and poems of the immortal Antonio Plaza.[3] Cuco has come from his job at Feldman's Furniture Store to converse of the beauty of Mexico and the comfort of the United States. Procuna has come in, and being a university student with more absences than the rest of his class put together, has very politely explained his need for two dollars until the check comes in. Chonito has shined shoes and danced a dozen or so boogie pieces. There have been arguments. Fortunes made and lost. Women loved. The great Cuate Cuete has come in to talk of the glory and grandeur of zoot suitism in Los Angeles. Old customers due about that day have come. Also new ones who had to be told that all the loafers who seemingly live in Garza's Barber Shop were not waiting for haircuts. Then the venetian blinds are let down. The red awning is cranked up. The door is latched on the inside although it is continually opened on request for friends, and the remaining customers are attended to and let out.

Inside Garza opens his little National Cash Register, counts the day's money, and puts it away. He opens his small writing desk and adds and subtracts for a little while in his green record book. Meanwhile Chonito grudgingly sweeps and says very nasty words. Lily-boy phones his wife to tell her that he is about to start home and that he will not be waylaid by friends and that he will not arrive drunk. Rodríguez relates to everybody in the shop that when he was a young man getting tired was not like him. The friends who have already dropped in wait until the beer is spoken for and then Chonito is sent for it. When it is brought in and distributed, everything is talked about. Lastly, women are thoroughly insulted although their necessity is emphasized. Garza, being a man of experience and one known to say what he feels when he feels it, recalls the ditty he heard while still in the cradle and says, "To women neither all your love nor all your money." The friends, drinking Garza's beer, agree.

Not always has Señor Garza enjoyed the place of distinction if not of material achievement that he enjoys among his friends today. In his thirty-five years his life has gone through transition after transition, conquest after conquest, setback after setback. But now Señor Garza is one of those to whom most refer, whether for reasons of friendship, indebtedness, or of having never read Plato and Aristotle,[4] as an oracle pouring out his worldly knowledge during and between the course of his haircuts.

---

3. Mexican poet (1833–1882).　　　　4. Ancient Greek philosophers.

Garza was born in El Hoyo, the second of seven Garzas. He was born with so much hair that perhaps this is what later prompted him to be a barber. At five he almost burned the house down while playing with matches. At ten he was still waiting for his older brother to outgrow his clothes so that they could be handed down to him. Garza had the desire to learn, but even before he found out about school Garza had already attained a fair knowledge of everything. Especially the knowledge of want. Finally, his older brother got a new pair of overalls and Garza got his clothes. On going to school he immediately claimed having gone to school in Mexico, so Garza was tried out in the 3B. In the 4A his long legs fitted under the desk, so he had to begin his education there. In the 5B he fell in love with the teacher and was promptly promoted to avert a scandal. When Garza was sixteen and had managed to get to the eighth grade, school suddenly became a mass of equations, blocks, lines, angles, foreign names, and headaches. At seventeen it might have driven him to insanity, so Garza wisely cut his schooling short at sixteen.

On leaving school Garza tried various enterprises. He became a delivery boy for a drug store. He became a stock room clerk for a shoe store. But of all enterprises the one he found most profitable was that of shearing dogs. He advertised his business and it flourished until it became very obvious that his house and brothers were getting quite flea ridden. Garza had to give it up. The following year he was overcome with the tales of vast riches in California. Not that there was gold, but there were grapes to be picked. He went to California. But of that trip he has more than once said that the tallness of the Californian garbage cans made him come back twenty pounds lighter and without hair under his armpits. Garza then tried the CCC camp.[5] But it turned out that there were too many bosses with muscles that looked like golf balls whom Garza thought it best not to have much to do with. Garza was already one that could keep everybody laughing all day long, but this prevented almost everybody from working. At night when most boys at camp were either listening to the juke box in the canteen, or listening to the playing of sad guitars, Garza trimmed heads at fifteen cents. After three months of piling rocks, carrying logs, and of getting fed up with his bosses' perpetual desires of making him work, Garza came back to the city with the money he had saved cutting hair and through a series of deals was allowed a barber's chair in a going-establishment.

In a few years Garza came to be a barber of prominence. He had grown to love the idle conversation that is typical of barber shops, the mere idle gossip that often speaks of broken homes and forsaken women in need of friends. These Garza has always sought and in his way has done his best to put in higher spirits. Even after his marriage he continued to receive anonymous after anonymous phone call. He came to know the bigtime operators and their brand of filthy doings. He came to know the bootleggers, thieves, love merchants, and rustlers. He came to know also the smalltime operators with bigtime complex and their shallowness of human understanding. He came to know false friends that came to him and said, "We're throwing a dance. We've got a good crowd. The tickets are two dollars." And on feeling superior,

5. The Civilian Conservation Corps (CCC, 1933–42) was a national public works program for unemployed men, focused on natural-resource conservation; its members lived in camps.

once the two dollars had fattened their wallets and inflated their conceit, re-marked upon seeing him at the dance, "Damn, even the barber came." But in time Garza has seen many of these grow fat. He has seen their women go unfaithful. He has seen them get spiritually lost in trying to keep up materi-ally with the people next door. He has seen them go bankrupt buying gabar-dine to make up for their lack of style. Their hair had cooties but smelled of aqua-rosa.[6] The edges of their underwear were frilled even though they wore new suits. They gave breakfasts for half of the city to prove that "they had" and only ended up with piles of dirty dishes. Garza watched, philosophized, cut more hair, and of this has more than once said in the course of a beer or idle conversation among friends, "Damned fools, when you go, how in the hell are you going to take it with you? You are buried in your socks. Your suit is slit in the back and placed on top of you."

So in time Garza became the owner of his own barber shop. Garza's Bar-ber Shop with its three Koken barber chairs, its reception sofas, its shoe-shine stand, wash bowls, glass kits, pictures, objects to be sold and raffled, and juke box. Second to none in its colorful array of true friends and false, of drunks, loafers, bullfighters, boxers, other barbers, moochers, and occa-sional customers. Perfumed with the poetry of the immortal Antonio Plaza, and seasoned with naughty jokes told at random.

Soon the night becomes old and empty beer bottles are collected and put in the little back room. Chonito, who has swept the floor while Garza and his friends have consumed beer, asks for a fifty-cent advance or swears with the power of his fourteen years that he will never sweep the shop again, and gets it. Lily-boy phones his wife again and tells her that he is about to start home and that he is sober. Rodríguez, if he worked that day, says he has a bad cold which he must go home to cure, but asks for an advance to buy his tonic at Tom's Liquor Store. Then the lights are switched off and Garza, his barbers, his friends, and Chonito file out. Garza, not forgetting the words he heard while in the cradle, "To women neither all your love nor all your money," either goes up the street to the Royal Inn for a glass of beer or to the All States Pool Hall. Then he goes home. Garza, a philosopher. Owner of Garza's Barber Shop. But the shop will never own Garza.

1947

6. A tonic made of distilled water and rose-petal essence.

---

# JOSÉ LUIS GONZÁLEZ
## 1926–1994

José Luis González was one of the first prose fiction authors from Puerto Rico to write in Spanish about the vicissitudes of Puerto Rican migrant life in the United States. The son of a Dominican father and a Puerto Rican mother, González was born in the Dominican Republic but raised in Puerto Rico. In 1946, he earned a bachelor's degree from the University of Puerto Rico.

Three years earlier, at age 17, González published his first collection of short stories, *En la sombra* (In the Shadows). Encouraged by the Dominican author and politician Juan Bosch—whose fiction focused on the plight of his country's peasant population—González used his early fiction to present the poverty and desolation that dominated Puerto Rico during the 1930s and 1940s, and to denounce the social conditions and exploitation of peasants and urban workers by Creole landowners and U.S. corporations. This ideological outlook also reflected González's involvement in socialist organizations.

His next two short-story collections—*Cinco cuentos de sangre* (Five Blood Stories, 1945) and *El hombre en la calle* (The Man on the Street, 1948)—continued to reflect their author's populist outlook, strong social consciousness, and commitment to exposing the damaging effects of American colonialism on the lives of working-class Puerto Ricans. After traveling to New York in 1946, González wrote *Paisa* (Fellow Countryman, 1950), a novella with a tragic view of the destiny that awaited many uprooted Puerto Ricans unable to find employment in the United States and fulfill their dreams of economic prosperity. The title of González's short-story collection *En Nueva York y otras desgracias* (In New York and Other Misfortunes, 1954) sets the tone for his portrayal of the precarious conditions of Puerto Ricans in American society and the loss of their traditional cultural values. González's pessimistic and often fatalistic view of Puerto Rican migrant life would be shared by several other island writers—among them René Marqués and Pedro Juan Soto—labeled by critics the Generation of 1950.

Because of the lack of opportunities for a Marxist writer in Puerto Rico during the Cold War, González lived in Prague from 1950 to 1952. There, he married a Czech woman. When he attempted to return to Puerto Rico, his wife was unable to obtain a visa to join him. In 1953, the couple moved to Mexico, where he pursued graduate studies at the National Autonomous University of Mexico and devoted most of his time to writing, teaching, and translating. After a few years of living in Mexico, González renounced his U.S. citizenship and became a Mexican citizen. This decision, along with his socialist views and support of Puerto Rico's independence, prompted the U.S. State Department to deny him a visa to visit Puerto Rico, and this travel ban lasted for almost two decades.

In 1973, thanks to the intervention of several leading intellectuals and politicians, González returned to Puerto Rico as a visiting professor at the University of Puerto Rico's Cayey College. His visit generated numerous invitations to participate in conferences and discussions with other intellectuals and students, introducing his ideas to a new generation of Puerto Ricans both on the island and in the United States. He continued to live in Mexico and to write about Puerto Rico. González once claimed that his absence from the island gave him valuable insights about the effects of colonialism on the lives of the Puerto Rican people, on the formation of Puerto Rican identity, and on the nation's historical memory. He began to express these views in his provocative essay "El país de cuatro pisos" (1980), translated as "Puerto Rico: The Four-Storeyed Country." But as several critics have pointed out, "El país de cuatro pisos" was missing a fifth floor. González did not take into account the importance of the Puerto Rican deterritorialized nation, represented by a growing diaspora in the United States. He rectified this omission in the 1989 expanded edition of the book, to which he added "Bernardo Vega: A Fighter and His People," an insightful essay he first published in 1977, the year of the posthumous publication of Vega's memoirs (see p. 428). The essay, included in this anthology, is about the significance of Vega's memoirs in documenting the history and struggle of the Puerto Rican community in New York during the late-nineteenth and early-twentieth centuries. It also discusses González's friendship and political relationship with Vega. The story "The Night We Became People Again," also included here, takes place in Manhattan on the night of the great Northeastern blackout in November

1965. It emphasizes the courage, compassion, and humor that can bring people together when sharing adversity.

# The Night We Became People Again[1]

To Juan Sáez Burgos

Do I remember? The whole Barrio remembers, if you want to know the truth; even Crazytop won't forget, and he couldn't even tell you where they buried his mother fifteen days later. I can tell you about it better than anybody because of a coincidence you don't know about. But first let's have a couple of nice cold beers, because this damn heat is even affecting my memory.

Ah, now, *salud y pesetas*[2] . . . and plenty of strength you know where. Well, it's been four years already; I can even tell you how many months and days, because to remember all I've got to do is take a look at the chubby little fellow you saw at home when you came to get me this morning. Yeah, the oldest one, who's named after me, but if he'd been born a girl we would have had to call her Estrella, or Luz María, or something like that. Or even Milagros, because that was really . . . but if I keep on like this I'll tell you the whole thing backwards.[3]

Well, I won't mention the date, because you already know that. Turns out, that day I had told the foreman, a Jewish fellow, nice guy, knows a bit of Spanish, that I wanted some overtime, because I would need the dough for my wife's pregnancy, she was in her final months, and there were plenty of things to get. The crib, the midwife . . . ah, because she wanted to give birth at home, not in the clinic, because the doctors and the *norsas* don't speak Spanish, and anyways it's more expensive.

So at four o'clock I finished my first shift and went down to the Italian's snack bar in front of the factory. Wanted to put something into my belly, until I got home and my wife reheated the supper, you see. Well, I gulped down a couple of hot dogs with a beer while I flipped through the Spanish paper I'd bought that morning, and while I'm reading about this Latino who had cut up his girlfriend because she'd been running around with a Chinaman, I don't know if you believe in those things, but like I had a funny feeling. I felt that something big was going to happen that night. I think a person has to believe, because you might ask what's the thing about the Latino and his girlfriend and the Chinaman got to do with what I began to feel. Feel, you see, because I wasn't thinking it, which is different. Well, I stopped reading the paper and hurried back to the factory to start my overtime.

Then the other foreman, the first one had already left, he says to me, "Say, do you plan to become a millionaire and open a casino in Puerto Rico?" He's just fooling around, and then I tell him, still fooling, "No, I've already got a casino. Now I wanna open a factory." And he says, "What kinda factory?" And I tell him, "A smoke factory." So he says, "Ah, really? And what are you

---

1. Translated by Kal Wagenheim. Except as indicated, all footnotes are Wagenheim's.
2. Cheers!; literally, health and money. [Anthology editors' note]
3. The literal translations of the girls' names are Star (Estrella), Light (Luz), Miracles (Milagros).

gonna do with the smoke?" And me, real serious, deadpan, I say, "Do with it? I'm gonna can it!" Just fooling around, y'know, because that foreman was an even nicer guy than the first. That's because it's to his benefit. He puts us in a good mood and gets us to work that much harder. He thinks I don't know, but any day now I'm going to tell him that I'm not as dumb as he might think. These people think that you come from the sticks and don't know the difference between sandpaper and toilet paper, especially if you're a bit dark-skinned, and your hair is kind of kinky.

Well, anyway, that's old news, and I've got something else to tell you. That damn heat . . . and our glasses are empty. Same brand, right? Okay. Well, as I was saying, after the foreman started joking around, we got down to some serious work. Because around here goofing and work don't mix. Time is money, you know. Radios started coming at me along the assembly line and I started sticking tubes into them, bam, bam. Yeah, that was my job then, putting tubes in. Two for every radio, one in each hand, bam, bam. At first, when I was new at it, a radio would pass me right by and—oh, boy!—I had to run after it and also keep an eye on the next radio coming up; thought I would go crazy. When I left work, I felt like my whole body had St. Vitus dance. That's why I think there's so much drinking and vice in this country. Yeah, because after all that, you feel like having a shot of rum, or something, and you start getting into the habit. I think that's why women get along better in factory work, because they entertain themselves with gossip and tongue-wagging, you see, and they don't need to drink. Well, I was working along, sticking tubes into radios, and thinking silly thoughts, when the foreman comes up and says, "Say, someone's looking for you." "Who, me?" I say. "Yeah," he tells me, "you're the only one here with that name." So they got someone to take my place, because they can't stop the line, and I go to see who was looking for me. It was Crazytop. Doesn't even say hello. He spits it right out. "Hey, go home, your wife's having a baby." Just like that. You see, poor Crazytop fell out of his crib in Puerto Rico when he was little, and according to his mother, may she rest in peace, he fell on his head, and it seems that the blow softened up his brains. There was a time, when I met him here in the Barrio, that he would suddenly start spinning around, like a nut, and wouldn't stop until he was dizzy, and fell to the floor. That's where his nickname comes from. Now, nobody makes fun of him, because his mother was a good person, a spiritualist medium, you know, and she helped lots of people without charge. You gave her whatever you could, you see. And if you were broke, you didn't give her anything. So there are lots of people who kind of look after Crazytop. Because he was always an orphan on his father's side, and he had no brothers or sisters, so as they say, he's all alone in the world.

Well, Crazytop comes along and says that to me, and I say, "Ay, *mi madre*, what'll I do now?" The foreman, who was keeping an eye on us, because those people never take their eyes off you at work, comes over and asks, "What's the trouble?" And I tell him, "They came to get me because my wife is giving birth." And the foreman says, "Well, what are you waiting for?" Let me tell you, that foreman was Jewish, too, and for the Jews the family is always number one. In that sense they're not like the rest of the Americans, who between fathers and brothers and sons insult each other, even hit each other, for the slightest reason. I don't know if it's because of the kind of life people lead in this country. Always running after the dollar, like dogs at the track, after a rag rabbit. Have you seen that? They wear their lungs out and never catch the rabbit. Oh yeah, they feed them and care for them, so they'll run again another day, which is the same thing they do with people, if you really look at the way things are. In this country we're all like racing dogs.

Well, when the foreman asked me what was I waiting for, I told him, "Nothing, just to put on my coat and grab a subway before my son arrives and doesn't find me in the house." I was really happy, you see, because this was going to be my first child, and you know what that's like. And the foreman says, "Don't forget to punch out, so that you get credit for the half-hour you worked; from now on, you're going to really need money." And I tell him, "That's right," and grabbed my coat, punched my card, and I tell Crazytop, who was standing there, looking open-mouthed at all the machines, "Let's go, Crazytop, we'll be late!" And we ran down the stairs rather than wait for the elevator, and we got to the sidewalk, which was plenty crowded, because everyone was going home from work. "Damn it," I said, "I would have to get mixed up in the rush hour!" But Crazytop didn't want to run. "Wait a minute, man, wait a minute, I wanna buy a candy." Crazytop is like that, you see, just like a baby. He's good for running errands, if it's something simple, or for washing floors in a building, or anything that doesn't need thinking. But if it's a question of using the old calculator, look for someone else. So I tell him, "No, Top, the hell with candy. Buy it in the Barrio, when we get there." "No, no," he says, "they don't have the kind I want in the Barrio. You can only get them in Brooklyn." And I say to him, "Ay, you're crazy," and right away I'm sorry, because that's the one thing you can't say to Crazytop. He stops right there on the sidewalk, looking sadder than a penny's worth of cheese, and says to me, "No, no, not crazy." I tell him, "No, man, I didn't say crazy. I said silly. You didn't hear me right. C'mon! I'll get you the candy tomorrow!" And he says, "You sure you didn't call me crazy?" "Sure I am, man!" "And you'll get me the candy tomorrow?" He may be crazy, but he's pretty shrewd, too. I'm almost laughing, and I say, "Sure, I'll even get you three candies if you want." So he smiles and says, "All right, let's go, but three candies, all right?" And I'm walking towards the subway entrance with Crazytop behind me. "Sure, man, three. You tell me later which kind."

We practically ran down the stairs and found the station packed with people, you know how it gets. And I was worried about Crazytop falling behind, because with all the pushing and shoving he might get scared. When the express train pulls in, I grab him by the arm and say: "Get ready to push, or we'll be left behind." And he tells me not to worry, and when the door opened and a few people got out, we pushed in and wound up so squeezed that we couldn't even move our arms. Just as well, that way we didn't have to hold on. Crazytop looked a bit scared, because I think it was the first time he'd been on the subway at rush hour, but since I was next to him there was no problem. So we got to Columbus Circle and changed trains, because we had to go to 110th and Fifth to get home, you see, and again we were just like sardines in a can.

I was counting the minutes, wondering if my son had already been born, and how my wife was. Suddenly it occurs to me: here I am so sure it'll be a boy, and what if it winds up being a girl? You know how a fellow wants a son at first. Truth is, it's selfishness on our part, because it's better for the mother if the eldest is a girl, so she can help with the housework and raising the little ones. Well, I'm thinking about all those things, and feeling very much like a father, you see, when . . . , wham! The lights go out and the train starts to lose power, and stops right in the middle of the tunnel, between stations. Nobody got frightened right away. Lights going out in the subway isn't such a rare thing, you know: they usually come right back on, and people don't even blink. And the train stopping for a bit isn't so strange, either. They put on the emergency lights, and everyone seemed fine. But time went by, and the train didn't move. And I'm thinking, "Shit, what luck, just when I'm in a hurry." But I'm still believing it was just a question of a few minutes, you see, and about three minutes go by, and this lady next to me starts to cough. An American lady, a bit on the old side. I looked at her and saw that she was coughing, but not very hard. I thought to myself: that's no cold, she's scared. Another minute went by and the train wasn't moving and the lady says to a young fellow next to her—tall, blond, tough-looking, with like an Irish face—she says, "Young man, doesn't this seem a bit odd?" And he says, "No, don't worry, it's nothing." But the lady didn't seem satisfied with that, and she kept on with her little cough, and other passengers tried to look out the windows, but they could barely move, and anyway it was so dark you couldn't see anything. I tried to look, too, but all I got out of it was a stiff neck, which lasted quite a while.

Well, time went by and I started getting a cramp in my leg, and that's when I started feeling nervous. Not because of the cramp, but I thought I'd never get home on time. I said to myself, "Something must've happened; we've been stuck here too long." Since I had nothing else to do I started my head working, and that's when I thought about suicide. It seemed logical, right? You know that there are lot of people here who don't give a damn about themselves and they climb up the Empire State Building and jump, and by the time they reach the street they're already dead from the fall. I don't know, but that's what I've heard. And there are others who jump in front of subway cars, and you have to pick up what's left with a shovel. The ones who jump from the Empire State, I guess you'd need tissue paper to pick them up. No, but seriously, because a person shouldn't joke about such things, I figured someone had thrown himself in front of a train, and I thought: "Well, may he rest in peace, but he really screwed me up, because now I'll be late." By now, my wife must be thinking that Crazytop got lost, or that I'm drunk and don't care about what's happening at home. It's not that I'm a lush, but once in a while, you understand . . . Well, now that we're on that subject, if you want to change brands, but make sure they're plenty cold.

Ah! Where was I? Oh yeah, thinking about the suicide, when suddenly—bang!—they opened the doors. Right there in the tunnel. I'd never seen anything like that, and I thought to myself, there's gotta be trouble. Down below, in front of the door, I see a few inspectors, they're wearing uniforms, and carrying lanterns. One of them says, "Take it easy, there's no danger. Come down slowly, without pushing." Right away people start asking the mister: What's happened? What's happened? And he says, "When you're all down here, I'll tell you." I grabbed Crazytop by the arm and told him, "Did you hear? There's no danger, but don't get separated from me." He nodded. I think the fright had robbed him of his voice. He didn't say a thing, but it seemed that his eyeballs would pop right out of his head; they were shining in the dark, just like a cat's.

Well, we all got out of the train, and when we're all lined up the inspectors started walking along the line and explaining what happened. There had been a blackout in the entire city, and nobody knew when the lights would come back on. Then the lady with the little cough, who was still close to me, asked the inspector, "Say, when will we get out of here?" And he says, "We have to wait a bit, because there are other trains ahead of us, and we can't all get out at the same time." So we began to wait. And I'm thinking, "Dammit, this having to happen today," when I feel Crazytop pulling at my coat sleeve. He says to me real low, like in secret, "Say, buddy, I'm practically peeing in my pants." Imagine! That's all we needed. "Ay, Top," I say to him, "hold on. Can't you see it's impossible here?" And he says, "But I've had to go for a long time now, and I can't hold it in." So I start thinking fast, because this is an emergency, right? All I could think of was asking the inspector. "Wait right here," I say to Crazytop, "and don't move." I get out of line and walk up to the inspector. "Listen, mister, my friend wanna take a leak." And he says to me, "Goddamit to hell, can't he hold it in awhile?" I let him know that's just what I told my friend, to hold it in, but he says he can't. So he says, "Well, go ahead, but don't wander off too far." So I go back to Crazytop and tell him, "Come with me; let's see if we can find someplace there in back." We start walking, but that line of people never ended. We had already gone quite a distance when he pulls my sleeve again and says, "I really can't hold it any-more, brother." So I tell him, "Well, look, get behind me, right next to the wall, but be careful not to wet my shoes. And do it slow, so nobody hears." I hadn't even finished talking when I hear, you know how a horse sounds? Well, it was like two horses, not one. It's a wonder he hadn't ruptured his bladder. Oh, it was terrible. "Ave María," I think to myself, "he's gonna splash my coat." And I was wearing just a short coat, didn't even reach my knees, because I like to be in style, right? Well, of course, the people nearby had to notice, and I hear them whispering. I think to myself, "Just as well it's dark, and they can't see our faces. If they notice that we're Puerto Ricans . . ." You know how things are here. I'm thinking, and Crazytop still isn't finished. *Cristiano!* The things that happen to a fellow in this country! And people don't believe you. Well, Crazytop finally finished, or at least I thought he did, because I didn't hear any more noise, but he still stood there. So I say, "Hey, did you finish?" He says, "Yes." "Well," I say, "let's go." Then he says, "Wait a minute. I'm shaking it." That's when I blew my top. I ask him, "What've you got there, a garden hose? Get going, or these people are going to shake even your bones after making such a flood here." I think he finally understood the situation, and he says, "Okay, all right, let's go."

So we go back to where we were, and we're waiting for about half an hour more. I hear people around me talking English, complaining, and griping about the mayor, and everything. And suddenly I hear someone over there, in Spanish, say, "Well, it's just as well to die here as up there. At least down here the government has to pay for the funeral." Yeah, some *boricua*[4] trying to be funny. I tried to spot him, and tell him that his funeral was going to be paid for by the animal shelter, but it was too dark. His little joke affected me, be-lieve it or not. Standing there, with all my worries, you know what I thought? Imagine, I thought, if the inspector was lying, and the Third World War had

---

4. "Boricua" is another word for "Puerto Rican."

really started. No, don't laugh. I'll bet I wasn't the only one thinking it. With all the things you read in the papers, about Russians, and Chinese, and Martians in flying saucers. Why do you think there are so many nuts in this country? They don't even fit in Bellevue anymore, and I think they're going to have to build another insane asylum.

Well, just then, the inspectors come and tell us it's our turn to get out, but to stay in line and be calm. We start walking and finally reach the station, which was at 96th. We weren't too far from home, but not too close either. Imagine if we'd stopped at 28th, or something. Up shit creek, right? Well, we get to the station and I tell Crazytop, "Let's hurry." We climb the stairs with that crowd of people, it looked like when you throw hot water on an anthill, and when we reach the street, ¡ay bendito! The cars had their lights on, but there wasn't a single light on in the street, or in the buildings. A guy comes by with one of those portable radios. Since I was walking in the same direction I got close to him and started listening. Just what the inspector had told us down in the tunnel, so I stopped worrying about the war. But then I got to thinking again about my wife, and I tell Crazytop, "Well, my friend, now we use a special kind of transportation: a little on foot, and another while walking, to see who gets there first." And he says, "Let's race, let's race," laughing, as though he'd gotten over his fright.

We started walking real fast, because it was cold. When we reached 103rd, I wonder, "If there's no lights at home, how did they do the delivery? Maybe they had to call an ambulance to take her to some clinic, and I won't even know where she is." With that idea in my head, I looked like a champ in the stretch. I don't think it took us even five minutes from 103rd to home. I start running up the stairs, and they were in pitch darkness, couldn't even see the steps. Ah, but now the good part starts, because you weren't in New York that day, right? Okay. Well, let's get a couple more beers, because my throat is drier than the sand dunes of Salinas,[5] where I grew up.

Well, as I was saying, that night I broke the world record for climbing three flights of stairs in the dark. I didn't even notice if Crazytop was behind me. When I reached the apartment door I grabbed my key and shoved it right into the lock on the first try, just as though I could see it. When I open the door the first thing I see are four candles lit in the parlor, and quite a few lady neighbors sitting there, looking plenty relaxed, and gossiping away. It looked like the Olympics for tongue-wagging. Ave María, that must be the ladies' favorite sport. I think that when the day comes that they abolish gossiping, there'll be a revolution bigger than Fidel Castro's. But as soon as they spotted me, they all turned quiet. I didn't even say good evening; right away I asked, "What's happened to my wife? Where is she? Did they take her away?" One of the ladies comes over and says, "No, she's in there, and she's fine. We were just saying that for a first pregnancy . . ." And just then I hear those squeals from my son there in the room. Well, I still didn't know if it was a boy or a girl, but I'll tell you, he was shouting more than Daniel Santos in his good times.[6] So I tell the lady, "Excuse me, doña," and I rush into the room and the first thing I see is so many candles I thought it was a church altar. And the midwife there fussing with the pans, and rags, and things, and my woman in

5. Town in southern Puerto Rico, near Ponce. [Anthology editors' note]

6. Daniel Santos [was] a Puerto Rican singer of popular music.

bed, nice and still, but with her eyes wide open. When she sees me, she says, her voice very slight, "Ay, my boy, how good that you got here. I was worried about you." Imagine, she's worried about me, and she's been going through labor pains, and all that. Yeah, women are like that sometimes. I think that's why we put up with their foolishness and love them so much, right? Well, I was just going to tell her about the problem with the subway when the midwife says, "That little boy has got your identical face. Come see him, look." He was in the bed, right next to my woman, but since he was so tiny you could hardly see him. I go over and look at his little face, which is all you could see, since he was wrapped up more than a *pastel*.[7] and when I'm looking at him, my woman says, "Doesn't he resemble you?" I say, "Yes, quite a bit." But I'm thinking to myself, "No, he doesn't look like me or anybody else. Looks like a newborn mouse." But we're all like that when we come into the world, right? And my woman says to me, "He's a little boy, just what you wanted." And I, just to say something, answered, "Well, let's see if next time we can make a nice match." I didn't want her to notice how proud I felt and how happy, you see? And the midwife asks, "Well, what are you going to name him?" My woman says, "The same as his papa, so he won't forget it's his." Just joking, you see, but with her little dig. And I say, "Well, baby, if it pleases you." My son had stopped crying by then, and I start to hear like the sound of music coming from the upper part of the building. But it wasn't from a radio or phonograph, you see. It was like a combo, right there, because I heard laughing and talking. Lots of people. And I ask my woman, "Is there a party?" And she says, "I don't know, but it seems so, because we've been hearing it for quite a while. Maybe it's a birthday party." And I say, "But without any light?" And then the midwife says, "Maybe they did the same as we did, went out and bought candles." Then I hear Crazytop calling to me from the parlor, "Hey, hey, c'mere." Crazytop had gone to check. "What's happening?" I asked him. "*Muchacho*," he says, "thing's are really swell up there on the *rufo*." And I say, "Well, let's go see what's happening."

So we go up the stairs and onto the roof and I find almost the whole building there. *Doña* Lula, the widow from the first floor; Cheo, the guy from Aguadilla,[8] who had closed down his coffee shop when the lights went out; the girls from the second floor, who neither worked nor collected welfare, according to the tongue-waggers; *don* Leo, the Pentecostal minister who has four children here and seven in Puerto Rico; Pipo and *doña* Lula's boys, and one of *don* Leo's had formed a combo with a guitar, a *güiro*, some maracas, and even some drums, I don't know where they got them because I'd never seen them before. Yeah, a quartet. Say, and they were really making quite a racket! When I got there, they were playing "*Preciosa*," and the singer was Pipo, you know he's an *independentista*, and when he got to the part where it says, "*Preciosa, preciosa*, you're called by the sons of liberty," he raised his voice so much I think they heard him in Morovis.[9] And I'm standing there looking at all those people, and listening to the song, when one of the girls from the second floor comes over, a little heavyset, I think her name is Mirta, and she says to me, "Say, how good it is that you're here. Come over and have a little shot." Ah, they had bottles and paper cups atop a chair, and I don't

---

7. A meat and vegetable pie wrapped in banana leaves.
8. City in northwestern Puerto Rico. [Anthology editors' note]
9. Municipality in central Puerto Rico. [Anthology editors' note]

know if it was Bacardi or Don Q, because it was dark, but right away I tell her, "Well, if you're offering, I accept with great pleasure." She serves me the rum and I ask, "Say, can you tell me what the party's all about?" And *doña* Lula, the widow, comes over and says, "Haven't you noticed?" I look all around, but *doña* Lula says, "No, no, not there. Look *up*." And when I raise my eyes she says, "What do you see?" "Well, the moon." "And what else?" "Well, the stars."

*Ave María, muchacho!* That's when I realized! I think *doña* Lula saw it in my face, because she didn't say a thing more. She put her two hands on my shoulders and stood there looking, too, nice and still, as though I were asleep, and she didn't want to wake me. Because I don't know if you're going to believe me, but it was like a dream. The moon was this big, and yellow, yellow, as though it were made of gold, and the whole sky was full of stars, as though all the fireflies in the world had gone up there to rest in that immensity. Just like in Puerto Rico, 'most any night of the year. But it had been so long since I'd seen the sky, because of the glow of millions of electric bulbs that are turned on here every night, and we had already forgotten that the stars existed. When we stood there contemplating that miracle for I don't know how long, I hear *doña* Lula say, "It seems we're not the only ones celebrating." It was true. I can't tell you on how many rooftops in the Barrio there were parties that night, but there were quite a few, because when our combo stopped playing, we could hear music from other places, nice and clear. Then I thought of so many things. I thought of my newborn son, and what his life would be like here; I thought of Puerto Rico and my folks, and everything that we left behind, just out of need; I thought of so many things that I've already forgotten some of them, because you know that your mind is like a blackboard, and time is like an eraser that sweeps across it when it's full. But what I'll always remember is what I said then to *doña* Lula, which is what I want to tell you now, to finish my story. And that is, according to my poor way of understanding things, that was the night we became people again.

1954

## Bernardo Vega: A Fighter and His People[1]

No one could have seemed further from death, such being the force of his infectious vitality, than César Andreu Iglesias when he first spoke to me of these *Memorias de Bernardo Vega*. Neither Iglesias nor anyone else could have imagined that preparing this book for publication would be the last creative task that this veteran fighter for socialism and Puerto Rican independence would ever complete. The importance he ascribed to the job, which caused him to set aside at least two other projects that would have been first-rate contributions to our national heritage (a novel and a long essay on the national identity question), were more than justified by the intrinsic merits of Bernardo's manuscript, a text that, even beyond its claims as autobiography and as the narrative of an individual life (though that too was certainly worth the telling), constituted a quite exceptional contribution *to the history of the*

---

1. Translated by Gerald Guinness. Except as indicated, all footnotes are González's.

*Puerto Rican community in New York,* as César himself realized and as he made clear in the book's subtitle. He also understood something that his legendary modesty prevented him from admitting even to his closest friends but that I must now make public for the sake of justice, which is that no other living Puerto Rican was as qualified as he himself was to *assume* the text and unreservedly identify himself with its rich human, political and moral subject matter. The explanation for such a fortunate circumstance—fortunate both for the book itself and for its readers—lies in the profound affinity between two lives that were both dedicated with exemplary single-mindedness to the same revolutionary cause.

The ideological trenches in which Bernardo Vega and César Andreu Iglesias fought throughout their militant careers stretched across the same far-flung terrain that that nation occupies which is divided between Puerto Rico and the great emigrant community living in the United States and particularly in New York. The strong insular roots in Bernardo never lost their vigor and for his part César never succumbed to the pettiness of denying Puerto Rican identity to the great transplanted emigrant mass. Faithful sons of the working class as they were, both Vega and Iglesias knew that the fatherland isn't an inherited property, as it is for the middle class, but an attainable possibility. This was the fundamental and lasting lesson I learned from both of them in my early youth. César knew that I owed them both a debt, but in what touched him personally the only payment he extracted was an unhesitating loyalty to the principles I had learned in his company. As for the debt to Bernardo Vega, when shortly before César's unexpected and premature death he asked me to write a few pages on Bernardo for inclusion in the *Memorias,* I realized that what he was doing was giving me the opportunity to begin paying that debt off. In fact, what follows goes well beyond the mere biographical memoir that César had in mind, but I know that he would have been pleased by my overcompliance with the task that he set me. And I also know that without a doubt Bernardo too would have been pleased, because in this attempt at providing an exegesis of his book he would have recognized the best possible tribute to his life as a militant.

I first got to know Bernardo Vega in 1947, just before the period when these *Memorias* end. Our personal friendship and political collaboration—in fact two inseparable aspects of one single human relationship—began, as he himself records it in this book, the day I joined the editorial staff of *Liberación,* the weekly which for several years was the incorruptible and militant defender of the Puerto Rican, Spanish, and Hispanoamerican communities in New York, or in other words, the organ of the *Hispanic* left in that great city that the author of the *Memorias* rightly calls *our* city. And if I italicize these two words *Hispanic* and *our,* it is because this emphasis focuses attention on an ideological issue of fundamental importance for the correct understanding of this autobiography, by one of the best sons of the Puerto Rican proletariat.

Again and again in these pages Bernardo alludes to the eminently popular character of the Puerto Rican emigration to the United States. This fact (which shouldn't surprise anyone, since it is well known that mass emigrations in the modern world are invariably caused by economic hardship, although I obviously exclude the massive albeit temporary migrations caused by natural disasters and by war), is something the author repeatedly points to in the context of a class-analysis of the Puerto Rican community in New York. With the precision and clarity that only this type of analysis can provide, Bernardo establishes the fundamental difference between the forced and hazardous *emigration* of the poor, and the voluntary *exile* of the rich, the latter only honorable when it involves a sacrifice of those riches on the altars of the struggle for freedom.

Our writer tracks down this distinction to its nineteenth-century origins using the reminiscences of his uncle Antonio, an exceptionally interesting figure, whose recollections throw light on some of the least studied aspects of our history. When we Puerto Ricans decide to analyze the thoughts and actions of our nineteenth-century separatists in the light of a *social* reality that determines and conditions all *ideological* expression, not only will we discover the true historical significance of a Betances, a Ruiz Belvis, and a Hostos[2]—all anti-slavist, anti-racist, anti-monarchical, and anti-clerical, and *as a consequence* of all this, separatists—but we will also inevitably discover the essential historical difference between the revolutionary separatism last century and the conservative independentism that has impeded and objectively distorted our struggle for national emancipation this century. We will then be in a position to understand—and *must* understand, unless we wish to remain prisoners to an ideology both decrepit and unworkable—the hitherto unexplained contrast between the conservative and traditional Hispanophilia of a José de Diego or an Albizu Campos,[3] and Betances's attitude, when he distributed coins to some children on the border between France and Spain and told them to shout "Viva Cuba libre!". (José Martí,[4] whose presence is so pervasive in the *Memorias*, would surely have understood and applauded Betances for this act. On two well-known occasions he refused to enter a place where someone wanted to fly the Spanish flag. Bernardo Vega's uncle remembered one of these occasions and various biographers of The Apostle[5] have confirmed its authenticity. It happened when someone suggested that the Spanish flag should represent those Puerto Ricans present, at an event being celebrated by Antillean emigrants to New York. As for the other occasion, Martí himself refers to it in some verses from his *Versos sencillos*: "A dance! Let's go and see / The Spanish dancer. / They're right to take / The flag away; / If they had left it, / Well—I couldn't stay."[6])

The *Hispanic* left to which Bernardo adhered obviously had nothing to do with the conservative Hispanophilia, with which he never had any sympathy. The Spain he *did* admire and defend was that *other* Spain, the populist and democratic Spain that never held power here in Puerto Rico, nor alas, strictly speaking back in the home country either. What it *did* derive from—and because of what follows I want to say this unambiguously—was Bernardo's recognition of a cultural and *social* community on which the Puerto Rican, Hispanoamerican, and Spanish workers living in New York could center their existence, more than on any other aspect of their collective identity. It is (or

2. Eugenio María de Hostos (see p. 248). *Betances*: Ramón Emeterio Betances (see p. 228). *Ruiz Belvis*: Segundo Ruíz Belvis (1829–1867), Puerto Rican separatist and abolitionist; a close friend of Betances. [Anthology editors' note]
3. Pedro Albizu Campos (see p. 445). *De Diego*: José de Diego (1866–1918), Puerto Rican writer, lawyer, and politician who advocated for the

island's independence. [Anthology editors' note]
4. See p. 265. [Anthology editors' note]
5. "The Apostle" was the name by which Martí was known to his admirers. [Translator's note]
6. "Hay baile; vamos a ver / La bailerina española. / Han hecho bien en quitar / El banderón de la acera; / Porque si está la bandera, / No sé, yo no puedo entrar." [Translator's note]

should be) clear that this *populist* Hispanicism of Bernardo Vega's has nothing at all to do with the conservative Hispanophilia, which has been in the defense of a cultural patrimony denuded of all social content the reaffirmation of a link, not so much with the brother *peoples* of Spain and America, as with the hateful legacy of the Spanish colonial period. The Hispanics of New York were and continue to be a *people* and as such, as Bernardo rightly points out, are ashamed neither of their language nor of the Hispanic roots of their mestizo identity. Those who were in fact ashamed of those things were upper-class Puerto Ricans, the "respectable" Puerto Ricans who lived on Riverside Drive[7] rather than in the Barrio and didn't dare read Spanish-language newspapers in public in case people accused them of being *spiks*, people "proud" of being Puerto Ricans in the bosom of their own class but careful to call themselves "Spanish" when they were with the arrogantly racist Americans. There is a passage in these *Memorias* where the division between these two groups of Puerto Ricans—between the *two fatherlands*, as any true socialist is bound to see it—can be noted with a dramatic clarity. The passage describes the occasion when more than a thousand Puerto Rican workers protested in front of the offices of a New York newspaper that had slandered them, while the millionaire Pedro Juan Serrallés[8] *watched* the protest from the opposite sidewalk. "Yet again," as Bernardo Vega observes, "it fell to the workers to come to the defense of Puerto Rico."

"Yet again," because that is how it had been all through the nineteenth century, as Bernardo's uncle Antonio clearly remembers, when Cuban and Puerto Rican emigrant workers had supported the struggle for independence in both islands with what little money they had whereas the wealthy exiles had been niggardly to the point of meanness in their contributions to the cause. Who before Bernardo has described the cold welcome the Puerto Rican tobacco workers in New York at first gave the Puerto Rican Section of the Cuban Revolutionary party, founded by José Martí? Who has described or explained the reasons for this coolness? Of course historians of the creole bourgeoisie could not and cannot explain them, because those historians represented (and still represent) the same class interests as those who for the most part occupied positions of authority in the Section. However, Bernardo Vega *could*, because he had learned the facts from his uncle, a worker like himself, who had lived through the history *from below*. What is clear is that it needed the intervention of Sotero Figueroa,[9] the lower-class mulatto newspaper-man who enjoyed Martí's complete confidence, for the impoverished Puerto Rican workers to overcome their natural suspicion of their compatriots from the other class.

Often when I have pointed out these facts to Puerto Rican independentists, who still think in terms of an abstract fatherland ideally uncontaminated by the class struggle, I have had to listen to and find an answer for the following objection: "But were not Betances, Ruiz Belvis and Hostos all members of the socially privileged class?" What in fact they *were* members of, as I have already explained, was the revolutionary sector of that class, in a period earlier by a generation than the period of Martí, Sotero Figueroa, Pachín

---

7. A thoroughfare on Manhattan's Upper West Side, associated with upscale residences. [Anthology editors' note]
8. A major landowner in Ponce, Puerto Rico; he made his fortune in the sugar industry. [Anthology editors' note]
9. See p. 260. [Anthology editors' note]

Marín[1] and Bernardo Vega's uncle Antonio. In that earlier period, the revolutionary sector of the creole bourgeoisie that I have referred to, faced with the indifference and even opposition of the reformist and assimilationist majority of the same class, attempted to break the colonial link with Spain. In this attempt they counted not on the majority of their own class, but on the support of the peons and slaves who fought at Lares under the leadership of the insurrectionary small landowners.[2] (Betances himself more than once complained bitterly about being deserted by his class, as those who have read his correspondence will remember.) And after the defeat of this first attempt at revolution, the greater part of the Puerto Rican creole bourgeoisie opportunistically sought a *modus vivendi* with the Spanish monarchy, hoping thereby to gain a profitable role in the exploitation of their own country—which is to say, their own people. It wasn't "political skill" that this social class lacked; what it really lacked was any true sense of the nation together with a revolutionary ideology like that of the contemporary Cuban creole bourgeoisie, which is why Cuban revolutionary socialists today can see in the creole bourgeoisie's struggle against Spanish colonialism a historical antecedent for the anti-imperialism of their present-day struggle.

What lay behind the Agreement with Sagasta[3] in 1898, then, was exactly what lay behind the creation of the *Estado Libre Asociado* or Commonwealth, in 1952: the historic opportunism of the Puerto Rican creole bourgeoisie and its inveterate propensity to strike a bargain with its imperial master. It is this that our bourgeois historians, whether patriots or non-patriots, have never wanted or been able to understand, but that Bernardo Vega understood perfectly well when, three decades ago, he wrote in his diary, "What a role my old friend Muñoz Marín[4] is now playing! Every day he seems more like his father at the time of the Agreement with Sagasta!" And he understood it, not because he had the training of a professional historian, but because he had the insight of an enlightened proletarian.

It is lamentable, though no less explicable because lamentable, that many young Puerto Ricans with a revolutionary calling do not know these days the tradition of proletarian enlightenment so splendidly embodied in Bernardo Vega's thought and behavior. It is a tradition that, for all its nineteenth-century antecedents, was virtually born and grew to maturity in the first decades of this century. There are two fundamental reasons why this should have been so. The first is that under Spanish rule the limited economic development of Puerto Rico and the retrograde and oppressive character of the government prevented a modern working class from coming into being and with it an organized workers' movement, which might have influenced the country's social and political life; the second is that both these things, the relatively new working class and the organized workers' movement, were, relatively speaking, historical products of the American regime. But merely to state such a truth (no more than a commonplace for any beginning student of Marxism) has scandalized and continues to scandalize all bourgeois and petit-bourgeois patriots, who interpret it, through the warped historical

1. Francisco Gonzalo "Pachín" Marín (see p. 317). [Anthology editors' note]
2. In 1868, Puerto Rico declared its independence from Spain with the *Grito de Lares* insurrection. [Anthology editors' note]

3. González is referring to the pact made by Puerto Rican autonomists, under the leadership of Luis Muñoz Rivera (see p. 296), with Práxedes Mateo Sagasta (1825–1903), leader of Spain's Partido Liberal (Liberal Party). The agreement was that if

vision of their class, as a justification, perhaps even apology, for the colonialism imposed on them by the United States. Such misunderstandings are, alas, common among many young independentists identifying with socialism in the Puerto Rico of today.

The explanation for such misunderstandings is grounded in a straightforward historical fact, which is that these young people's identification with socialism is a *subjective* identification. By this I mean that most of these young people do not hail from the working class, but instead from those sectors of the creole bourgeoisie, or creole petite bourgeoisie, that have been marginated by the American colonial regime. From that margination stems these young people's rebelliousness toward the colonial regime, and from their recognition that their own class is both unwilling and unable to oppose that regime stems their subjective identification with the working class and with what they take to be socialism. Let me make it clear, however, that I view these young people with sympathy and with hope. On them depends, at least in part, the future of socialism in Puerto Rico, since they are the ones who are really capable of bringing about the intellectual ferment that would help make the true Puerto Rican revolution viable in our time. But for that to happen, and for the revolution not to be frustrated or deformed by the weight of ideological concepts which are out-dated and essentially alien to socialism, it is essential that these young people *objectively* make their own the historical realities facing our country and the traditions of struggle associated with our working class. So too is it vital that they discard that *other* class tradition formed this century, the tradition of bourgeois and petit-bourgeois independentism that still weighs heavily on their shoulders. What is involved here is a genuine ideological catharsis, and for such a catharsis to work, the reading of these *Memorias de Bernardo Vega* will be an enormous help. In the *Memorias* these young people would find, as an account of actual experience, what we have just expressed in the form of an historical judgment:

> The workers' movement had acquired momentum in Puerto Rico under the new [American] regime. The affluent classes, especially the industrialists and wealthy farmers, felt that their interests were now threatened, hence the notorious proceedings against Santiago Iglesias and other workers' leaders, who were accused of "conspiring to raise wages." Iglesias was condemned to three years' imprisonment and his companions to varying penalties. The news of so great an outrage enraged the workers in New York. A campaign was initiated in support of the workers' leaders and in defense of the Free Federation of Workers. . . .[5]

All the bourgeois independentists have to say about this Free Federation of Workers is that it was an instrument of colonization on behalf of American imperialism in Puerto Rico. This, although it contains a grain of truth, is certainly not the whole truth. To discover the whole truth one would first have to ask why American imperialism *could* use the Free Federation of Workers as

---

the Liberal Party came to power in Spain, it would grant an autonomy charter to Puerto Rico that would allow Creole self-government but not allow sovereignty. In 1897, Sagasta became prime minister of Spain, and autonomy was granted to both islands. [Anthology editors' note]

4. Luis Muñoz Marín (see p. 482). [Anthology editors' note]
5. Federación Libre de los Trabajadores, a socialist union federation in Puerto Rico. [Anthology editors' note]

an instrument of colonization. The judicial proceedings against Santiago Iglesias and his companions, mentioned by Bernardo Vega, can set us on the way, as few other facts can at that particular historical moment, to the discovery of an answer to this question. Iglesias and his followers were prosecuted by a Puerto Rican district attorney before a Puerto Rican judge by virtue of a Spanish law that described all strikes for better wages as "crimes of conspiracy." This was the social legislation in force in Puerto Rico under the Spanish colonial regime and this was the legislation that the Puerto Rican attorney and the Puerto Rican judge, who sent Iglesias and his companions to jail, accepted as binding after the end of Spanish sovereignty in Puerto Rico. When the case reached the Puerto Rican Supreme Court on appeal, the Attorney General of the new regime, an American named Harlan, wrote a letter to the district attorney of that court, which near the end says the following: "The right to assemble peaceably for mutual consultation and for joint endeavour in an orderly manner to better social conditions is surely fundamental. If any Spanish law in Porto Rico . . . impairs this right, in my judgment it has lost its force and become a nullity with a change of sovereignty. Such a law is contrary to the spirit of our form of government." The district attorney of the Supreme Court, now knowing what was expected of him, acceded to the petition for an acquittal, which the defending advocate had submitted. Who can be surprised, then, that Puerto Rican workers felt themselves protected and defended by the new regime? And who can be surprised that the regime, understanding this feeling, should use it to its own political advantage? What would really have been surprising would have been any other outcome.

Seeing matters in this light (and there seems to be no better light in which to see them), who can claim to find it *historically* culpable that the Puerto Rican workers' movement this century was corrupted by American influence? The bourgeois independence movement has traditionally pointed its finger at two culprits, Santiago Iglesias and American imperialism. Evidently neither of them can be wholly absolved. But then what *historical reality* made possible the success both had in working upon the feelings of the Puerto Rican working class? Neither Iglesias nor American imperialism had created that historical reality. Without a doubt, it was the Spanish colonial regime that had created it and nothing corroborates this better than what Eugenio María de Hostos wrote about the situation Puerto Rican society found itself in at the moment of the socalled "change of sovereignty."[6]

"When one looks at Puerto Rico in the dim light of a new life that is now dawning," wrote the great Puerto Rican patriot on returning to the island in 1898, "it seems as though everything in that life is hostile to the humane objectives of the *League [of Patriots]*.[7] The island's population is totally impoverished. Physiological and economic misery go hand in hand. The malarial fever that mummifies the individual is mummifying society as a whole. Those half-moving skeletons on the coastal plains and in the mountains, who give proof of how systematic the colonial regime has been in its

6. All quotations from Hostos that follow are taken from *Madre Isla*, volume V of *Obras completas* (Cultural S.A., La Habana, 1939). The page number from this edition follows each quotation.
7. The Liga de Patriotas Puertorriqueños (League of Puerto Rican Patriots), an organization founded by Hostos in New York in 1898. The League sought to exert pressure on the United States to establish a civil government on Puerto Rico and conduct a plebiscite among the Puerto Rican people to determine their future political status. [Anthology editors' note]

policy of *mass relocations*; that feeble childhood; that sunken-chested adolescence; that withered youth; that sicklied manhood; that premature old
age, in short that individual and social debility everywhere visible, seem to
have rendered our people incapable of helping themselves" (pp. 26–27). "If
for some reason [*The League of Patriots*] collapses one day, it will be because of the inertia of the Puerto Ricans, because of the terrible fact that
the Spanish domination has left them so passive that they do not even have
the energy or initiative to make themselves into a real people" (p. 24).

But it wasn't only the popular masses who were in such a state of prostra-
tion; it was also the intellectual élite, from whom so much was then to be
expected: "Because they have been so corrupted by colonialism, not even the
most educated men in Puerto Rico (and there are many more of them than
patriotism has the right to expect after so disastrous an occupation as the
Spanish), not even the most educated men in Puerto Rico can make up their
minds to take any initiative, or wholly rely on themselves, or cease to hope
that their government will solve all their problems. Since what is needed today is just the opposite . . . our society must acquire the two sources of energy colonialism has deprived it of, when it inhibited the exercise of those
rights that strengthen in the individual both his private energies and his energies in association with other people" (pp. 13–14).

Taking all this into account (and can there be any Hispanophile "patriot"
who dares accuse Hostos of falsifying the historical truth?), is it fair to accuse
Puerto Rican workers in the first half of this century, as many have done who
never knew the material and moral misery in which the Spanish colonial regime left those workers, of "lacking national feeling?" Nonetheless, twenty-
nine years after a representative of American imperialism released from jail
the strikers accused under a Spanish law of conspiracy, Pedro Albizu Campos asserted at a meeting of the Nationalist Party in Mayagüez: "In the
United States a small minority or ruling class exploits virtually the whole
country. There is no society there or nation in the strict sense of the word,
but instead a vast conglomeration, which suffers the oppression of a tiny oli-
garchical class for whom the welfare, still less the betterment, of the masses
doesn't matter in the least. By contrast, a homogeneity existed in Puerto Rico
between all the classes, together with an acute sense that people should offer
one another reciprocal help to strengthen and conserve the nation—in other
words, a rooted and unanimous sense of fatherland. As a consequence, to set
in class warfare the man who has nothing against the man who enjoys a modest income was to introduce an alien element of discord into our society."

What the nationalist leader told the Puerto Rican workers in 1931—at
the very moment when the world crisis of capitalism was intensifying the
class struggle in all four corners of our planet!—was that the creation of a
workers' movement in Puerto Rico had been unnecessary and harmful, because there had never been a class struggle on the island. According to Albizu, what *had* existed was a "homogeneity" between rich and poor, where
people offered one another "reciprocal help" to "strengthen and conserve
the nation," so that for the Puerto Rican workers to organize in defense of
their class interests constituted "an alien element of discord" and was utterly superfluous. According to this curious "sociology" of Albizu's, if a
workers' movement could be justified in the United States it was because in
that country there was neither society nor nation, but merely "a vast con-

glomeration." (How the existence of a workers' movement could be justified in all those societies and nations which *weren't* merely "conglomerations" was something that Albizu's "social science" never took the trouble to explain.) We Puerto Ricans, by contrast, were a true nation, in which all people, rich and poor, were brothers and so obliged to help one another defend the nation, of which we were all, supposedly, owners-in-common in a sort of giant co-operative or limited partnership.

But the Puerto Rican workers knew, as a result of experience and by means of a sort of elemental class instinct, that what Albizu said wasn't in fact true. They knew that Albizu's mythical and mystical fatherland had never really existed and that the real Puerto Rican society had been, and continued to be, a society divided into classes. They knew that there had been, and continued to be, Puerto Ricans who were exploited and Puerto Ricans who did the exploiting. And they rightly told themselves that the independence to which Albizu referred was an independence based on ignoring or concealing that reality. They knew that at the same time that Albizu campaigned for the expulsion of the American exploiters from Puerto Rico (exploiters whom the workers knew very well, as is obvious from the way they mounted strikes against them), he was simultaneously affirming that we should "attempt to revive that multiplicity of proprietors that we had in 1898." They knew, by virtue of an experience that no rhetoric or fantasizing "sociology" could refute, that the law by which the strikers of 1902 had been condemned as "conspirators" was a law created to defend the interests of those same proprietors. They knew that Albizu was falsifying history when he described Puerto Rican society before 1898 as "the old collective happiness." At the very moment Albizu uttered these words, there were educated workers in Puerto Rico, workers in no sense antagonistic to the idea of national independence, who had read Manuel Zeno Gandía[8] and knew that his description of that society as "a sick world" was closer to the historical truth than the description the nationalist leader was offering them.

Bernardo Vega was one of those educated workers. A tobacco worker by trade, as he often recalls with a justified pride in his *Memorias*, he belonged to the most cultivated and alert sector of the Puerto Rican proletariat. He was a member of the Free Federation of Workers and co-founder of the Socialist Party. Never deceived by the true nature of the American colonial regime in Puerto Rico, for four decades Vega struggled against it and in support of independence. But the independence he fought for was not, nor could ever be, the same independence the creole bourgeoisie, displaced from economic and political power as a result of the development of dependent capitalism in Puerto Rico, were in favor of. Men like Vega never found a place in the Nationalist Party, for the simple reason that it was never possible to fight in that party for both independence *and* the rights of the working class. (As a matter of fact, the only "leaders" the nationalists offered the Puerto Rican workers were the "men of stature"[9] they themselves had chosen!)

It was men like Bernardo Vega who in 1934 founded the Puerto Rican Communist Party—on the anniversary of the Grito de Lares, as a matter of

8. Puerto Rican novelist and independence advocate (1855–1930). [Anthology editors' note]
9. *Hombres de talla*: a class term implying a degree

of affluence and social acceptability. [Translator's note]

fact—in which it was not only possible, but mandatory, to fight simultaneously on both fronts, the nationalist and the socialist. But the nationalist movement always condemned these Puerto Rican communists as "divisionists," who "weakened" the struggle against the colonial regime by acting as the party of a separate class. The undeniable truth is that the communists always pursued a politics of alliance with *all* pro-independence groups, hoping thereby to create an alliance which would constitute an authentic national front of all classes and so unite under a single banner the entire spectrum of anti-colonial Puerto Rican society. The Nationalist Party rejected such a politics since it saw *itself* as representing the nation in its entirety (which is what the party's self-definition, as "the fatherland organized for the rescue of its sovereignty," really meant, with the implication that whoever didn't belong to the Nationalist Party didn't really belong to the fatherland either). Such an unrealistic way of seeing things not only made the creation of a nationalist anti-colonial front impossible, but led the Nationalist Party itself to an isolation that a few years later brought it to the very verge of extinction.

Bernardo Vega lived, at the heart of the Puerto Rican community in New York, through these political differences between nationalists and communists, and he gives an account of them in the *Memorias* that is particularly valuable for its frankness. The conflict, in fact, was already under way when Albizu Campos joined the Nationalist Party, which among other things proves that Albizu Campos's nationalism, far from being the creation of one man, embodied a true class ideology. Bernardo describes how in September 1923 the Workers' Alliance[1] staged a meeting during which two of those present attacked the workers' organizations as "societies without a soul" and lacking all "sense of nationality" and "love for things of the spirit." As one of these critics put it: "All they seem to want for the workers is a hunk of bread." However, it was only in the 1930s that the discord reached a new pitch of virulence. Bernardo describes it as follows:

> About this time an unhappy incident muddied the waters of fraternal accord between Puerto Rican communists and nationalists. The nationalists expected Puerto Ricans, wherever they lived, to give all their enthusiasm and support to the struggle for independence and went so far as to argue that to get involved in the immediate social struggles in New York was to divert Puerto Ricans from their primary patriotic task. In their opinion, Puerto Ricans weren't emigrants but rather "exiles," and as such their only thought should be for the redemption of their homeland and their own prompt return to Puerto Rico. The Puerto Rican workers and in particular the communists and their sympathisers, rejected this position. For them the need to fight for the independence of Puerto Rico was beyond question, but that was no reason to stand by passively when faced with the exploitation of Puerto Ricans in New York. For them, what deserved priority was the immedi-

1. The Alianza Obrera Puertorriqueña (Puerto Rican Workers' Alliance), an organization founded in New York City in 1922. Its main aims were to encourage workers to unionize, and to protect the civil rights and interests of the community. The Alliance was among the most important Puerto Rican community organizations during the 1920s. Jesús Colón, Luis Muñoz Marín, and Bernardo Vega were members. [Anthology editors' note]

ate struggle. As long as these two opposing viewpoints only met at the level of debate, there was no immediate problem. But it was now that Puerto Rican nationalists and communists began to question each other's positions at street meetings one or the other group held in the Barrio Latino. The audience interrupted speakers with questions and this gave rise to the accusation that attempts were being made to "wreck" the meeting. So it was that both sides took to street fighting, that degenerated into hand-to-hand battles. The Puerto Rican nationalist Angel María Feliú was killed in one of these scuffles and the communists were accused of the crime.[2]

When in 1946 I arrived in New York, people still remembered this tragic event, but by then relations between nationalists and communists had greatly improved—to such an extent, in fact, that collaboration in specific activities was now the order of the day. The nationalist leadership did not officially approve of this collaboration and even went so far as to expel some militants from the party for taking part in joint activities with the communists; moreover it continued to see Puerto Ricans in New York as "exiles" rather than as emigrants. But the realities of life, which bore on all with equal rigor, and the support that the communists always offered the nationalists, including Albizu Campos himself, when they were persecuted, ended by persuading most of the nationalists to take an active part in those social struggles in the community that the communists directed.

That a collaboration which couldn't yet take place in Puerto Rico took place in New York can only be explained by reference to the social composition of the emigrant community. This community, as we have already said and as everyone knows, was and continues to be overwhelmingly proletarian. The nationalism of Albizu Campos, which expressed the ideology of the marginated sector of the creole bourgeoisie and petite bourgeoisie, was for obvious reasons never to make any headway among the Puerto Rican proletariat, in either social or political terms. Any nationalist who was shackled to the ideology of the anti-American creole bourgeoisie in Puerto Rico began inevitably to become proletarianized as soon as he emigrated to the United States. Such a process made for conflicts in social, political, and psychological terms—conflicts, let it be said in passing, that comprise a quarry of topics that have yet to be exploited in our literature. The typical nationalist of the 1930s and '40s, a descendant of the ruined landowners of former times, found himself on the same social level in New York as a compatriot descended from peons and perhaps even slaves, American society showing no willingness to give him back those class privileges that had been recognized by the society back in Puerto Rico. Even those who were sufficiently well educated to see no reason why they should work in kitchens or factories often had to settle for jobs with salaries much closer to those of their proletarian compatriots than to the salaries of the better-paid sectors of the American petite bourgeoisie. On the other hand (and this is something we should in no way deny or underestimate), the nationalist emigrant, because of his intense patriotism, tended as a matter of course to live in close touch with

2. Angel María Feliú, a member of the Puerto Rican Nationalist Party, was killed in New York in 1932 during a street scuffle between Nationalists and Communists as a result of the ideological tensions between the two groups. [Anthology editors' note]

his fellow countrymen. With them he shared a basically similar cultural tradition and a basically similar national psychology, so that with them, in the long or short run, he also came to share a social conscience that had seemed to him back in Puerto Rico (to use the words of his leader) "an alien element of discord."

A proletarian with a sense of nation like Bernardo Vega knew that the situation of the Puerto Ricans in New York had a lot to do with the colonial condition of Puerto Rico, but the historical experience of his class also told him that the problem was not merely colonial but also, and fundamentally, social. The exact expression of this truth is contained in three bare but eloquent sentences in the *Memorias*:

> On May 12 1942, after the formalities of an exam, I was accepted as a low-grade clerk, something that didn't disturb me. As a Puerto Rican, I well knew that it was my destiny to be an unskilled workman. . . . Such was the fate that we suffered under the Spanish and such is the fate, unchanged to the present day, that we now have to suffer under the Yankees.

There are two phrases in this passage that we must examine more closely to extract their full and instructive significance. The menial work assigned to Bernardo (during the Second World War he worked in the censorship bureau of the American Post Office) was "something that didn't disturb me." But how that same discrimination *would* have disturbed a middle-class Puerto Rican patriot, convinced of the superiority of his "race" and "Greco-Roman heritage," over the "coarse" and "utilitarian" Anglo-Saxon conception of life! However, for a socialist proletarian like Bernardo Vega discrimination was a daily fact and the inevitable corollary of an unjust social system, something that one had to struggle against, but which there was no need to be personally, which is to say subjectively, humiliated by.

The other phrase refers to the fate of Puerto Ricans as "unskilled workmen," as much "under the Spanish" as "under the Yankees." This comparison of the *two* colonial regimes, which Bernardo advances without feeling the need to supply a gloss, is irreconcilable with the traditional Hispanophilia of the Puerto Rican bourgeois independence movement, or with Albizu Campos's description of the Spanish colonial regime as "the old collective happiness." (And I say *irreconcilable* for the benefit of those who dream there could be some "fusion" of bourgeois nationalism and proletarian socialism in the Puerto Rico of today.)

If Bernardo knew that his destiny "as a Puerto Rican" would have made him an unskilled laborer under Spanish colonialism, it was because he never belonged to the *class* of Puerto Ricans who in 1896 came to an agreement with the Spanish monarchy to share the perquisites of exploiting that *other class* of Puerto Ricans, who had never been landowners, who had never felt themselves to be "Spaniards of the New World," and whose one possible accommodation with what Betances called "the stepmother country"—oppressive, exploitative, and discriminatory like every other imperial power—could only have taken the form of outright rejection. (As for the *other* Spain—popular, democratic and revolutionary—Bernardo Vega certainly felt solidarity with *that*. Hence his insistence that we take note that three hundred Puerto Ricans had fought to defend the Spanish Republic when it was attacked by

General Franco's "nationalists" and the forces of international fascism.[3] And this at the very moment when the Puerto Rican Nationalist Party refused to take sides in the struggle, because to take sides would have been to support one of the two factions into which "the mother country," i.e. Spain, had been "divided"!)

Who, if not a Puerto Rican working man with a sense of history, could call the city of New York *our* city? A fatherland for Bernardo Vega was never an unhistorical myth, never the mystical vision of an élite, but rather a human and social reality, actual and alive. A fatherland is a community of men and women who through an extended historical process have shaped a way to live their lives that is always responsive to change and evolution. Such change and evolution never intimidated Bernardo—in fact, very much the opposite since throughout his life he lived both *with* and *in* such evolution and such change. It was this that made it possible for him to see a reality that many intellectuals of the creole bourgeoisie are still blind to: the appearance and crystallization of a distinctive way of being Puerto Rican, in certain respects similar to the insular way but in other respects different. As he says:

> The Barrio Latino was acquiring its own special characteristics. A distinctive culture began to coalesce, based on the common experience of a population that had continually survived in spite of the hostility of its surroundings. In the long run this culture would bear its own special fruits.

As I have already said, there are still those who deny Puerto Ricanness to those fruits, perhaps because they do not notice that where Puerto Ricanness is really lacking is in the cultural and moral hybridism of the *other* "emigration," that of the rich Puerto Ricans whose only real fatherland is their bank account. Bernardo knew all that perfectly well, but even more noteworthy is his perception that this phenomenon wasn't merely to be found under the American colonial regime but could also be found, and to no lesser extent, under the regime that preceded it, the regime the bourgeois and Hispanophile nationalists continued to idealize and to enshrine in myth:

> I read in the San Juan papers that wealthy Puerto Ricans are investing their money in Florida. They mention Serrallés, Roig, Ramírez de Arellano, García Méndez, and Cabassa.[4] . . . Every day I become more and more convinced that the capitalist class in Puerto Rico isn't really rooted in its native soil. The wealthy classes yesterday were Spanish. Today they are American. In the sin lies the penance!

*In the sin lies the penance.* It is the rich Puerto Ricans of yesterday and today who have committed the sin, but it is the poor Puerto Ricans who have suffered and continue to suffer the penance. Because, if the creole bourgeoisie's incapacity to fulfill its historic task still keeps our necks bowed under

---

3. Aided by Nazi Germany and Fascist Italy, the Spanish general Francisco Franco (1892–1975) led a military rebellion—the Spanish Civil War (1936–39)—that replaced the liberal civilian government of the Spanish Republic with Franco's Fascist dictatorship. [Anthology editors' note]

4. Pedro Juan Serrallés (see note 8, p. 750), Antonio Roig, Alfredo Ramírez de Arellano, Miguel A. García Méndez, and Jacobo Cabassa are considered Puerto Rico's sugar barons, since they were major landowners who made their family fortunes in the sugar industry during the first few decades of the twentieth century. [Anthology editors' note]

the colonial yoke, then strictly speaking, those who suffer the weight of that yoke are the eternally dispossessed, both those who remain on the island and those who have had to leave. It is for them—and for them only—now to lead the struggle toward the completion of this double task: our national emancipation and the destruction for good of a social regime founded on man's exploitation of man. Among all the lessons contained in this posthumous book by Bernardo Vega, none is as timely or as important as the lesson that points the way forward to our total liberation as a people.

1977                                                                                   1989

# CÉSAR CHÁVEZ
## 1927–1993

Cesario Estrada Chávez was born near Yuma, Arizona, on the small ranch that the Chávez family had owned since the 1880s. In 1937, the state took possession of the ranch. The next year, Chávez's father and several relatives found work threshing beans in Oxnard, California, a town near the coast, 30 miles northwest of Los Angeles. Chávez's mother soon followed with the children. Migrant laborers such as the Chávezes often worked 15-hour shifts under the blistering sun. They moved seasonally from field to field and from one state to another, depending on the availability of work. The pay was far below the minimum wage, and no benefits were granted. As many as eight family members might live in a single room without a toilet. Employers generally had a degrading attitude toward the workers.

Like all migrant children, Chávez attended school sporadically. Overall, he attended 67 elementary and middle schools. As an adult—in an interview with Jacques E. Levy for the authorized Chávez biography, *Autobiography of La Causa* (1975)—he said: "They always had to push me to go. It wasn't the learning I hated, but the conflicts. The teachers were very mean." Chávez spoke unschooled Spanish, and his teachers insisted migrant children learn English. Was he an American, Chávez wondered, like all the white kids in the many schools he attended? It seemed to him that his Mexicanness—*la mexicanidad*—conferred a second-class status, one intricately linked to work. In "An Organizer's Tale" (written in 1966), one of Chávez's most introspective pieces and among the selections in this anthology, he writes: "There are vivid memories from my childhood—what we had to go through because of low wages and the conditions, basically because there was no union. . . . I went through a lot of hell, and a lot of people did."

After the eighth grade, Chávez quit school and worked in the fields to help support the family. World War II was under way, and Chávez, like thousands of other *mexicanos*, readied to fight. He wanted to flee from the harsh working conditions—heat, exhaustion, boredom, and underpayment—that beat him down day after day. In the 1940s, the Chávez family was living in Delano, California, where the movie theaters were segregated, with the left side reserved for Anglo and Japanese customers. When Chávez refused to move from the left side of a theater, he was arrested and spent a night in prison. Soon after, he joined the navy.

In 1948, having returned to California after the war, Chávez married Helen Fabela, and eventually they had eight children. In San Jose, they lived in a neighborhood nicknamed Sal Si Puedes (literally, "escape if you can"), where they joined the Catholic congregation of Father Donald McDonnell. With Father McDonnell's encouragement, Chávez began to read voraciously. He studied Saint Francis, who preached absolute humility; Mahatma Gandhi's philosophy of nonviolence; the papal encyclicals. He also discovered the transcripts of the La Follette Civil Liberties Committee on Education and Labor (chaired by the Wisconsin senator Robert M. La Follette Jr.), which investigated the free-speech incursions and labor-rights violations that had occurred between 1936 and 1941. Among the committee's findings was that employers had disrupted union activities and strikes and that spy networks and secret-police systems had been formed to monitor workers: "News of organizers coming into a town, contacts the organizers make among his employees, the names of employees who join the union, all organization plans, all activities of the union—these are as readily available to the employer as though he himself were running the union." Chávez was shocked by what he found, and the evidence led him to expound an argument promoting social justice. In an essay in *Playboy* in 1970, he wrote:

> Nothing is going to happen until we, the poor, can generate our own political and economic power. Such a statement sounds radical to many middle-class Americans, but it should not. Though many of the poor have come to see the affluent middle class as its enemy, that class actually stands between the poor and the real powers in this society—the administrative octopus with its head in Washington, the conglomerates, the military complex. It's like a camel train: The herder, way up in front, leads one camel and all the other camels follow. We happen to be the last camel, trudging along through the leavings of the whole train. We see only the camel in front of us and make him the target of our anger, but that solves nothing. The lower reaches of the middle class, in turn, are convinced that Blacks, Mexican Americans, Puerto Ricans, Indians and poor Whites want to steal their jobs—a conviction that the power class cheerfully perpetuates. The truth of the matter is that, even with automation, there can still be enough good-paying jobs for *everyone* in this country. If all of us were working for decent wages, there would be a greater demand for goods and services, thus creating even more jobs and increasing the gross national product. Full and fair employment would also mean that taxes traceable to welfare and all the other hidden costs of poverty—presently borne most heavily by middle-income Whites—would inevitably go down.

In 1952, while working in an apricot orchard outside San Jose, Chávez met Fred Ross, the founder of the Community Service Organization (CSO). Ross was an outsider to migrant workers, but his calling was improving labor conditions. Aware of the substantial number of *mexicanos* working in the fields in California, Texas, Colorado, and Arizona, he wanted to recruit an insider able not only to speak Spanish but also to communicate with Mexican workers on their own terms.

In his memoir, *Conquering Goliath* (1980), Ross details his first encounters with Chávez and the early struggles before Chávez became a national figure. Chávez initially was reluctant to organize people whose communities he was not part of, but between 1952 and 1962 Ross and Chávez organized 22 CSO chapters across California. With the help of Chávez's leadership, CSO became the most effective Latino civil rights group of its day. It helped Latinos become citizens and consequently gain the right to vote. This decade was formative for Chávez. He grew to understand that the power of the working poor, properly orchestrated, was enormous. On March 31, 1962, he resigned from CSO to organize *mexicanos* full-time. His family returned to Delano, where he believed he could start building his organization. Focusing on the farmworkers posed unique challenges. In a speech at Harvard University in March 1970, Chávez announced, "Organizing farmworkers is very different from organizing any other workers in the country today. Here we don't have any rules, any regulations. We don't have any prescribed methods, no precedents."

After establishing the National Farm Workers Association (NFWA), Chávez arranged a national convention to establish the organization's mission. By emphasizing the national, not the regional, he sought to build a structure with far-reaching influence. On September 20, 1962, about 150 delegates and their families attended the convention, in an abandoned theater in Fresno, California. Members voted to organize the farmworkers and elect temporary officers. They agreed to lobby for a minimum-wage law covering farmworkers. They embraced the term *la causa* (the cause); in fact, the motto of the convention became ¡Viva La Causa! A union representing Mexican laborers in the fields had been born. In the spring of 1965, the NFWA organized its first strike, against the rose industry. On September 16—the anniversary of Mexico's independence from Spain—the NFWA joined a strike against the grape growers in the Delano area. On the first day alone, 1,200 workers joined in. The five years of the strike would become one of the most publicized periods of Chávez's career.

To his tactics of the union and the strike, Chávez soon added another one: the boycott. The NFWA started a grape boycott in November 1965. Members followed grape trucks and set up picket lines wherever grapes were sold. In a speech at New York City's Riverside Church in 1970, Chávez argued that boycotts were a potent weapon for bringing about dignity and justice. "It's difficult to get people involved, unless what we ask people to do is very simple, concrete, and painless." The largest, most renowned marches Chávez orchestrated took place in 1966. Between March and April, to make the case for the farmworkers' cause in the court of public opinion, he and strikers from the NFWA, joined by members of the Agricultural Workers' Organizing Committee (AWOC), engaged in a 340-mile pilgrimage from Delano to the steps of the California capitol, in Sacramento. NFWA organizers devised the *Plan de Delano* (Plan of Delano), in which they outlined the rights of farmworkers.

Subsequently, the NFWA organized a strike and boycott against the DiGiorgio Fruit Corporation. Lasting from the spring to the summer, the action forced the grower to hold an election so that its workers could vote on whether to unionize. The company called in the Teamsters Union to oppose the NFWA. The NFWA and the AWOC merged into the United Farm Workers of America (UFW), and the DiGiorgio workers voted in favor of joining it.

In 1967, the UFW went after Giumarra, the country's largest table-grape grower, against which farmworkers had countless grievances. Nearly all of Giumarra's workers joined in the strike, although, to Chávez's dismay, a few days later many returned to the fields. Consequently, the UFW began a boycott of Giumarra products, but this action lost effectiveness when Giumarra changed its labels. Chávez's response was categorical: He instructed the UFW to boycott *all* California table grapes. Chávez's pursuit became part of *El Movimiento*, as the civil rights–era Chicano Movement came to be known. He was joined by *mexicano* leaders such as Reies López Tijerina and Rodolfo "Corky" Gonzales (see p. 787), feminists such as Dolores Huerta, intellectuals such as Luis Valdez (p. 1244), journalists and radio broadcasters such as Rubén Salazar, muralists such as Yolanda López and Rupert García, students, teachers, housewives, and others. At rallies, Valdez's theater troupe, El Teatro Campesino (The Farmworkers' Theater), composed of farm laborers, staged both *actos*, short plays to promote political awareness, and *mitos* (myths), pieces about symbols in Mexican history. The concept of La Raza (The Race) glued people together. It was intimately linked to *mestizaje*, miscegenation between European colonizers and the New World indigenous populations.

Chávez's worldview was defined by his devout Catholicism. "I've read what Christ said," he told Jacques Levy. "He was very clear in what he meant and knew exactly what he was after. He was extremely radical, and he was for social change." But Chávez was wary of the Catholic Church as an institution. "It's common knowledge that the Catholic Church is a bloc of power in society and that the property and purchases of the Church rate second only to the government," he wrote in 1968. He challenged bishops and priests to take action:

> To build power among Mexican-Americans presents a threat to the Church; to demand reform of Anglo-controlled institutions stirs up dissension. . . . However, if representatives of the Church are immobilized and compromised into silence, the Church will not only remain irrelevant to the real needs and efforts of La Raza in the barrios; but also our young leaders of today will continue to scorn the Church and view it as an obstacle to their struggle or social, political and economic independence.

In 1984, Chávez launched a third grape boycott, but by then the labor movement had lost momentum. Two years later, to draw public awareness to the pesticide poisoning of grape workers, their families, and consumers, Chávez began the "Wrath of Grapes" campaign, calling on the American people to boycott grapes. The environmentalist movement had barely begun, and Chávez was laying the cornerstone on which to build its foundation. The response to this appeal, however, was half-hearted. In 1992, Chávez and the UFW's vice-president, his son-in-law Arturo Rodriguez, led vineyard walkouts from the spring to the summer in the Coachella and San Joaquin Valleys. With the help of these walkouts, grape workers won their first industry-wide pay hike in eight years. By this time, Chávez had become a model for younger labor leaders beyond California—in Hawaii, Oregon, Pennsylvania, New Jersey, New York, and Midwestern states. Chávez died in his sleep in San Luis, in the house of a retired Arizona farmworker. Six days later, 40,000 mourners marched behind Chávez's pine casket in Delano. He was buried in La Paz, in front of his office at the UFW's California headquarters.

The other four Chávez selections in this anthology, taken from *César Chávez: An Organizer's Tale* (2008), provide a representative sample of his opinions, illustrate his rhetorical style, and indicate his legacy. "We Shall Overcome," published on Mexican Independence Day in 1965, describes the circumstances of the Delano strike. "Jesus's Friendship" is an undated speech in which Chávez connects Christianity and the labor movement he helmed. "Rufino Contreras" (1979) is a eulogy delivered for a murdered worker. "What Is Democracy?" is a 1982 speech in which Chávez reflects on multiculturalism in the United States.

# We Shall Overcome

In a 400-square-mile area halfway between Selma and Weedpatch, California, a general strike of farm workers has been going on for six weeks. The Filipinos, under AWOC AFL-CIO, began the strike for a $1.40 per hour guarantee and a union contract. They were joined by the independent Farm Workers Association, which has a membership of several thousand Mexican Americans.

Filipino, Mexican American and Puerto Rican workers have been manning picket lines daily for 41 days in a totally nonviolent manner. Ranchers in the area, which include DiGiorgio Fruit, Schenley, and many independent growers, did not take the strike seriously at first. By the second or third week, however, they began taking another look and striking back. Mechanized agriculture began picketing the pickets, spraying them with sulfur, running tractors by them to create dust storms, building barricades of farm machinery so that scabs could not see the pickets. These actions not only increased the determination of the strikers, but convinced some of the scabs that the ranchers were, in fact, less than human. Scabs quit work and the strike grew.

The growers hired security guards for $43 a day. They began driving their Thunderbirds, equipped with police dogs and rifles, up and down the roads. The people made more picket signs, drew in their belts, and kept marching.

Production was down 30 percent and the growers began looking for more and more scabs. They went to Fresno and Bakersfield and Los Angeles to find them. They didn't tell the workers that they would be scab crews. The pickets followed them into every town and formed ad hoc strike committees to prevent scabbing. They succeeded in these towns. Within two weeks, only one bus, with half a dozen winos escorted by a pearl gray Cadillac, drove into the strike zone. A new plan was formed. The ranchers would advertise in South Texas and Old Mexico. They bring these workers in buses and the workers are held in debt to the rancher before they even arrive in town. We have a new and more difficult task ahead of us with these scabs.

As our strike has grown, workers have matured and now know why and how to fight for their rights. As the strike has grown into a movement for justice by the lowest paid workers in America, friends of farm workers have begun to rally in support of *La Causa*. Civil rights, church, student and union groups help with food and money.

We believe that this is the beginning of a significant drive to achieve equal rights for agricultural workers. In order to enlist your full support and to explain our work to you, I would like to bring some of our pickets and meet with you.

September 16, 1965

## Jesus's Friendship

The beatitudes make natural good sense to the poor. We, of course, do not analyze the words and the meanings in the way that scholars do. Jesus's words fit his life and therefore, the meaning of his words appear to be obvious to us. He spent his life with the poor, the sick, the outcasts, the powerless people. He attacked the wealthy and the powerful. He is with us! We feel that he is our friend, our advocate, our leader. (Of course it is for that reason that we expect the Church of Jesus to be with us.) It may be too simple to say that Jesus is on our side; but we tend to feel that way and perhaps his identification with the oppressed is so clear to us because we do not have to rationalize our wealth and possessions and fit Jesus's deeds and words into the world view of the powerful and the affluent.

The beatitudes make natural good sense to the poor and the oppressed. They come through to us as Good News: "Blessed are you poor," "Blessed are you who mourn," "Blessed are you meek." It is a message unlike anything we have heard from a society that sees poverty and color as signs of weakness and inferiority. Jesus turns society's standards upside down. His words point to a whole new way of looking at life. He seems to be saying: "Forget what those with earthly power have taught you. This is the way life really is: those who think they have it made have missed the point of life. The rich and the powerful will have their reward; but true happiness is reserved for those of you who are poor, who are merciful, who are peacemakers!" That is good news indeed, especially for those who have been treated with contempt by the powerful structures and the "successful" people of this world.

"Blessed are you who hunger and thirst for righteousness for you shall be satisfied." Jesus was a worker, a man of plain words. He said what was on his mind and his words were meaningful because they were drawn from the real life of the people. His listeners knew what it meant to be hungry and thirsty. They could feel the feeling because they had been there. To be hungry and thirsty was in one sense a sign of life: at least you were healthy enough to yearn for food and drink. To be hungry and thirsty also included a primitive passion for food and water that had to do with survival itself. To be hungry and thirsty was a part of life but it was also a reminder of death. In a very real way it was a matter of life and death.

In this beatitude Jesus is saying that one life-and-death matter has to do with righteousness: "Blessed are you who have an unrelenting passion for what is right and just for you shall be satisfied." Some who listened to Jesus may have concluded that the "righteousness" message was not for them since they were already poor, the victims of someone else's *un*rightousness. Others surely believed that their own rise to affluence was a clear enough sign of God's righteousness. Still others must have felt that their whole way of life was being challenged by this prophet from Galilee. For those who had ears to hear, Jesus's message was strength for their spirits, an affirmation of life as they had chosen to live it. . . . Good News!

Jesus's life and words are a *challenge* at the same time that they are Good News. They are a challenge to those of us who are poor and oppressed. By his life he is calling us to give ourselves to others, to sacrifice for those who suffer, to share our lives with our brothers and sisters who are also oppressed. He is calling us to "hunger and thirst after justice" in the same way that we hunger and thirst after food and water: that is, by putting our yearning into practice! It is not good enough to know why we are oppressed and by whom. We must join the struggle for what is right and just! Jesus does not promise that it will be an easy way to live life and his own life certainly points in a hard direction; but he does promise that we will be "satisfied" (not stuffed, but satisfied). He promises that by giving life we will find life—full, meaningful life as God meant it to be.

When I first started organizing a farm workers' union in 1962, I was looking for those farm workers who were most hungry and thirsty for justice. If we were going to have our own union we would have to pay for it so that we could control it. We set the dues at $3.50 per month with $2.00 of that amount going toward a death benefit insurance plan that was very important to the members. One of my jobs as organizer was to collect the dues. I hated it and at the same time I knew it was essential. I remember many incidents when I went to collect dues. I want to tell you just one. I went to a worker's home in McFarland, seven miles south of Delano. It was a dark, rainy night in the middle of winter. There was no work for farm workers and there would not be any for weeks. As I knocked on the door, the father of the house was going to the store with $5.00 for groceries. It was all the money he had. I told him that he was two months behind in his dues and that he would have to pay at least one month to keep his membership active. He thought a little while. I don't know what was going through his mind but he must have said to himself what we all knew in our hearts: "we have been hungry before and we are going to be hungry again; nothing will ever change unless some of us make sacrifices." He gave me the $5.00. We went to the store together and got change. I stayed with him while he bought $1.50 of groceries for his family and gave $3.50 to his union. In many of the hard days that followed I thought about that farm worker. With his kind of faith there was no person or group who could stop us from having our own union!

Since 1962, I have met many, many farm workers and friends who love justice and who are willing to sacrifice for what is right. They have a quality about them that reminds me of the beatitude. They are living examples that Jesus's promise is true: they have been hungry and thirsty for righteousness and they have been satisfied. They are determined, patient people who believe in life and who give strength to others. They have given me more love and hope and strength than they will ever know. They have also convinced me that every person has that spirit within that yearns for mercy and justice. The love for justice that is in us is not only the best part of our being but it is also the most true to our nature. The spirit of love may be thickly covered over by hurt or pride or too much money or too much power, but it is still there, yearning to be released, ready to serve the neighbor who is in need. When we respond to that yearning we release an energy for full life that is powerful and new. Life begins to make sense, to have meaning and purpose. The good that is possible comes into view and the death that is all around us loses its power to destroy. Wholeness happens because we are expressing with our body what is most true to God's nature and to our own.

It is supposed to be a very bad time in our country. There is no doubting that apathy and cynicism and boredom are around us like storm clouds. But nothing fundamental has changed. People who have lost their hunger for justice are not ultimately powerful. They are like sick people who have lost their appetite for what is truly nourishing. Such sick people should not frighten or discourage us. They should be prayed for along with the sick people who are in the hospital.

Nothing fundamental has changed! The spirit of love is still present in every person, waiting to be put to work for justice. We in the farm workers' movement see it every day in every city of the country. As we tell our story and do our work, people respond and join the boycott of grapes, head lettuce, and Gallo wines. They not only make a personal boycott pledge but they tell their friends, they join us on picket lines, they contribute money and energy and love, they write stories and make leaflets, and in thousands of other ways they add their spirits and their energy to ours. The sacrifices of the farm workers and the self-giving of the boycott supporters combine to make an unstoppable, nonviolent force for justice. These beautiful people who love justice and who are willing to put that love into practice are the reason why we will win back the grape contracts and go on to build a strong democratic union for all farm workers in our country.

Jesus is a disturbing friend to the poor. He puts into practice what it means to sacrifice for others. His words are powerful because his life is an example of what it means to hunger and thirst for righteousness. He challenges us to be different than we are, he leads us away from death and in the direction of life, and he promises us that we will discover the blessings of God if we join him in his work among the poor, the sick, the lonely, the powerless.

undated                                                                    2008

# An Organizer's Tale

It really started for me 16 years ago in San Jose, California, when I was working on an apricot farm. We figured he was just another social worker doing a study of farm conditions, and I kept refusing to meet with him. But he was persistent. Finally, I got together some of the rough element in San Jose. We were going to have a little reception for him to teach the gringo a little bit of how we felt. There were about 30 of us in the house, young guys mostly. I was supposed to give them a signal—change my cigarette from my right hand to my left—and then we were going to give him a lot of hell. But he started talking and the more he talked, the more wide-eyed I became and the less inclined I was to give the signal. A couple of guys who were pretty drunk at the time still wanted to give the gringo the business, but we got rid of them. This fellow was making a lot of sense, and I wanted to hear what he had to say.

His name was Fred Ross, and he was an organizer for the Community Service Organization (CSO) which was working with Mexican Americans in the cities. I became immediately really involved. Before long I was heading a voter registration drive. All the time I was observing the things Fred did, secretly, because I wanted to learn how to organize, to see how it was done. I was impressed with his patience and understanding of people. I thought this was a tool, one of the greatest things he had.

It was pretty rough for me at first. I was changing and had to take a lot of ridicule from the kids my age, the rough characters I worked with in the fields. They would say, "Hey, big shot. Now that you're a *politico*, why are you working here for 65 cents an hour?" I might add that our neighborhood had the highest percentage of San Quentin graduates.[1] It was a game among the *pachucos*[2] in the sense that we defended ourselves from outsiders, although inside the neighborhood there was not a lot of fighting.

After six months of working every night in San Jose, Fred assigned me to take over the CSO chapter in Decoto. It was a tough spot to fill. I would suggest something, and people would say, "No, let's wait till Fred gets back,"

1. I.e., ex-convicts who had served time in San Quentin State Prison, in Marin County, California.
2. During the 1940s and 1950s, in cities in both California and Texas, Mexican American *mestizo* adolescents who dressed flashily and spoke using their own jargon.

or "Fred wouldn't do it that way." This is pretty much a pattern with people, I discovered, whether I was put in Fred's position, or later, when someone else was put in my position. After the Decoto assignment I was sent to start a new chapter in Oakland. Before I left, Fred came to a place in San Jose called the Hole-in-the-Wall and we talked for half an hour over coffee. He was in a rush to leave, but I wanted to keep him talking; I was that scared of my assignment.

Those were hard times in Oakland. First of all, it was a big city and I'd get lost every time I went anywhere. Then I arranged a series of house meetings. I would get to the meeting early and drive back and forth past the house, too nervous to go in and face the people. Finally I would force myself to go inside and sit in a corner. I was quite thin then, and young, and most of the people were middle-aged. Someone would say, "Where's the organizer?" And I would pipe up, "Here I am." Then they would say in Spanish—these were very poor people and we hardly spoke anything but Spanish—"Ha! This *kid*?" Most of them said they were interested, but the hardest part was to get them to start pushing themselves, on their own initiative.

The idea was to set up a meeting and then get each attending person to call his own house meeting; inviting new people—a sort of chain letter effect. After a house meeting I would lie awake going over the whole thing, playing the tape back, trying to see why people laughed at one point, or why they were for one thing and against another. I was also learning to read and write, those late evenings. I had left school in the 7th grade after attending 67 different schools, and my reading wasn't the best.

At our first organizing meeting we had 368 people: I'll never forget it because it was very important to me. You eat your heart out; the meeting is called for 7 o'clock and you start to worry about 4. You wait. Will they show up? Then the first one arrives. By 7 there are only 20 people; you have everything in order, you have to look calm. But little by little they filter in and at a certain point you know it will be a success.

After four months in Oakland, I was transferred. The chapter was beginning to move on its own, so Fred assigned me to organize the San Joaquin Valley. Over the months I developed what I used to call schemes or tricks—now I call them techniques—of making initial contacts. The main thing in convincing someone is to spend time with him. It doesn't matter if he can read, write or even speak well. What is important is that he is a man and, second, that he has shown some initial interest. One good way to develop leadership is to take a man with you in your car. And it works a lot better if you're doing the driving; that way you are in charge. You drive, he sits there, and you talk. These little things were very important to me; I was caught in a big game by then, figuring out what makes people work. I found that if you work hard enough you can usually shake people into working too, those who are concerned. You work harder and they work harder still, up to a point and then they pass you. Then, of course, they're on their own.

I also learned to keep away from the established groups and so-called leaders, and to guard against philosophizing. Working with low-income people is very different from working with the professionals, who like to sit around talking about how to play politics. When you're trying to recruit a farm worker, you have to paint a little picture, and then you have to color the picture in. We found out that the harder a guy is to convince, the better leader or member he becomes. When you exert yourself to convince him, you have his confidence and he has good motivation. A lot of people who say OK right away wind up hanging around the office, taking up the workers' time.

During the McCarthy era[3] in one Valley town, I was subjected to a lot of redbaiting. We had been recruiting people for citizenship classes at the high school when we got into a quarrel with the naturalization examiner. He was rejecting people on the grounds that they were just parroting what they learned in citizenship class. One day we had a meeting about it in Fresno, and I took along some of the leaders of our local chapter. Some redbaiting official gave us a hard time, and the people got scared and took his side. They did it because it seemed easy at the moment, even though they knew that sticking with me was the right thing to do. It was disgusting. When we left the building they walked by themselves ahead of me as if I had some kind of communicable disease. I had been working with these people for three months and I was very sad to see that. It taught me a great lesson.

That night I learned that the chapter officers were holding a meeting to review my letters and printed materials to see if I really was a Communist. So I drove out there and walked right in on their meeting. I said, "I hear you've been discussing me, and I thought it would be nice if I was here to defend myself. Not that it matters that much to you or even to me, because as far as I'm concerned you are a bunch of cowards." At that they began to apologize. "Let's forget it," they said. "You're a nice guy."

But I didn't want apologies. I wanted a full discussion. I told them I didn't give a damn, but that they had to learn to distinguish fact from what appeared to be a fact because of fear. I kept them there till two in the morning. Some of the women cried. I don't know if they investigated me any further, but I stayed on another few months and things worked out.

This was not an isolated case. Often when we'd leave people to themselves they would get frightened and draw back into their shells where they had been all the years. And I learned quickly that there is no real appreciation. Whatever you do, and no matter what reasons you may give to others, you do it because you want to see it done, or maybe because you want power. And there shouldn't be any appreciation, understandably. I know good organizers who were destroyed, washed out, because they expected people to appreciate what they'd done. Anyone who comes in with the idea that farm workers are free of sin and that the growers are all bastards either has never dealt with the situation or is an idealist of the first order. Things don't work that way.

For more than 10 years I worked for the CSO. As the organization grew, we found ourselves meeting in fancier and fancier motels and holding expensive conventions. Doctors, lawyers and politicians began joining. They would get elected to some office in the organization and then, for all practi-

---

3. The period, in the late 1940s and early 1950s, during which a committee of the U.S. Congress, led by Wisconsin senator Joseph McCarthy (1908–1957), engaged in "red-baiting"—investigating and attacking U.S. citizens, such as government employees, as Communists.

cal purposes, leave. Intent on using the CSO for their own prestige purposes, these "leaders," many of them, lacked the urgency we had to have. When I became general director I began to press for a program to organize farm workers into a union, an idea most of the leadership opposed. So I started a revolt within the CSO. I refused to sit at the head table at meetings, refused to wear a suit and tie, and finally I even refused to shave and cut my hair. It used to embarrass some of the professionals.

At every meeting I got up and gave my standard speech: We shouldn't meet in fancy motels, we were getting away from the people, farm workers had to be organized. But nothing happened. In March of '62 I resigned and came to Delano to begin organizing the Valley on my own.

I drew a map of all the towns between Arvin and Stockton—86 of them, including farming camps—and decided to hit them all to get a small nucleus of people working in each. For six months I traveled around, planting an idea. We had a simple questionnaire, a little card with space for name, address and how much the worker thought he ought to be paid. My wife, Helen, mimeographed them, and we took our kids for two- or three-day jaunts to these towns, distributing the cards door-to-door and to camps and groceries.

Some 80,000 cards were sent back from eight Valley counties. I got a lot of contacts that way, but I was shocked at the wages the people were asking. The growers were paying $1 and $1.15, and maybe 95 percent of the people thought they should be getting only $1.25. Sometimes people scribbled messages on the cards: "I hope to God we win" or "Do you think we can win?" or "I'd like to know more." So I separated the cards with the pencilled notes, got in my car and went to those people.

We didn't have any money at all in those days, none for gas and hardly any for food. So I went to people and started asking for food. It turned out to be about the best thing I could have done, although at first it's hard on your pride. Some of our best members came in that way. If people give you their food, they'll give you their hearts. Several months and many meetings later we had a working organization, and this time the leaders were the people.

None of the farm workers had collective bargaining contracts, and I thought it would take ten years before we got that first contract. I wanted desperately to get some color into the movement, to give people something they could identify with, like a flag. I was reading some books about how various leaders discovered what colors contrasted and stood out the best. The Egyptians had found that a red field with a white circle and a black emblem in the center crashed into your eyes like nothing else. I wanted to use the Aztec eagle in the center, as on the Mexican flag. So I told my cousin Manuel, "Draw an Aztec eagle." Manuel had a little trouble with it, so we modified the eagle to make it easier for people to draw.

The first big meeting of what we decided to call the National Farm Workers Association was held in September 1962, at Fresno, with 287 people. We had our huge red flag on the wall, with paper tacked over it. When the time came, Manuel pulled a cord ripping the paper off the flag and all of a sudden it hit the people. Some of them wondered if it was a Communist flag, and I said it probably looked more like a neo-Nazi emblem than anything else. But they wanted an explanation, so Manuel got up and said,

"When that damn eagle flies—that's when the farm workers' problems are going to be solved."

One of the first things I decided was that outside money wasn't going to organize people, at least not in the beginning. I even turned down a grant from a private group—$50,000 to go directly to organize farm workers—for just this reason. Even when there are no strings attached, you are still compromised because you feel you have to produce immediate results. This is bad, because it takes a long time to build a movement, and your organization suffers if you get too far ahead of the people it belongs to. We set the dues at $42 a year per family, really meaningful dues, but of the 212 families we got to pay, only 12 remained by June of '63. We were discouraged at that, but not enough to make us quit.

Money was always a problem. Once we were facing a $180 gas bill on a credit card I'd got a long time ago and was about to lose. And we *had* to keep that credit card.

One day my wife and I were picking cotton, pulling bolls, to make a little money to live on. Helen said to me, "Do you put all this in the bag, or just the cotton?" I thought she was kidding and told her to throw the whole boll in so that she had nothing but a sack of bolls at the weighing.

The man said, "Whose sack is this?" I said, well, my wife's, and he told us we were fired. "Look at all that crap you brought in," he said.

Helen and I started laughing. We were going anyway. We took the $4 we had earned and spent it at a grocery store where they were giving away a $100 prize. Each time you shopped they'd give you one of the letters of M-O-N-E-Y or a flag: you had to have M-O-N-E-Y plus the flag to win. Helen had already collected the letters and just needed the flag. Anyway they gave her the ticket. She screamed, "A flag? I don't believe it," ran in and got the $100. She said, "Now we're going to eat steak." But I said no, we're going to pay the gas bill. I don't know if she cried, but I think she did.

It was rough in those early years. Helen was having babies and I was not there when she was at the hospital. But if you haven't got your wife behind you, you can't do many things. There's got to be peace at home. So I did, I think, a fairly good job of organizing her. When we were kids, she lived in Delano and I came to town as a migrant. Once on a date we had a bad experience about segregation at a movie theater, and I put up a fight. We were together then, and still are, I think I'm more of a pacifist than she is. Her father, Febela, was a colonel with Pancho Villa[4] in the Mexican Revolution. Sometimes she gets angry and tells me, "These scabs—you should deal with them sternly," and I kid her, "It must be too much of that Febela blood in you."

The Movement really caught on in '64. By August we had a thousand members. We'd had a beautiful 90-day drive in Corcoran, where they had the Battle of the Corcoran Farm Camp 30 years ago,[5] and by November we had assets of $25,000 in our credit union, which helped to stabilize the membership. I had gone without pay the whole of 1963. The next year the members voted me a $40-a-week salary, after Helen had to quit working in the fields to manage the credit union.

---

4. Francisco "Pancho" Villa (1878–1923), Mexican revolutionary general.
5. During the Corcoran Cotton Strike, in the San Joaquin Valley in 1933, a vigilante group ambushed a group of strikers, killing two Mexicans and wounding several others.

Our first strike was in May of '65, a small one but it prepared us for the big one. A farm worker from McFarland named Epifanio Camacho came to see me. He said he was sick and tired of how people working the roses were being treated, and was willing to "go the limit."

I assigned Manuel and Gilbert Padilla[6] to hold meetings at Camacho's house. The people wanted union recognition, but the real issue, as in most cases when you begin, was wages. They were promised $9 a thousand, but they were actually getting $6.50 and $7 for grafting roses. Most of them signed cards giving us the right to bargain for them. We chose the biggest company, with about 85 employees, not counting the irrigators and supervisors, and we held a series of meetings to prepare the strike and call the vote. There would be no picket line; everyone pledged on their honor not to break the strike.

Early on the first morning of the strike, we sent out 10 cars to check the people's homes. We found lights in five or six homes and knocked on the doors. The men were getting up and we'd say, "Where are you going?" They would dodge. "Oh, uh . . . I was just getting up, you know."

We'd say, "Well, you're not going to work, are you?" And they'd say no. Dolores Huerta, who was driving the green panel truck, saw a light in one house where four rose workers lived. They told her they were going to work, even after she reminded them of their pledge. So she moved the truck so it blocked their driveway, turned off the key, put in it her purse and sat there alone.

That morning the company foreman was madder than hell and refused to talk to us. None of the grafters had shown up for work. At 10:30 we started to go to the company office, but it occurred to us that maybe a woman would have a better chance. So Dolores knocked on the office door, saying, "I'm Dolores Huerta from the National Farm Workers Association."

"Get out!" the man said, "you Communist. Get out!" I guess they were expecting us, because as Dolores stood arguing with him the cops came and told her to leave. She left.

For two days the fields were idle. On Wednesday they recruited a group of Filipinos from out of town who knew nothing of the strike, maybe 35 of them. They drove through escorted by three sheriff's patrol cars, one in front, one in the middle and one at the rear with a dog. We didn't have a picket line, but we parked across the street and just watched them go through, not saying a word. All but seven stopped working after half an hour, and the rest had quit by mid-afternoon.

The company made an offer the evening of the fourth day, a package deal that amounted to a 120 percent wage increase, but no contract. We wanted to hold out for a contract and more benefits, but a majority of the rose workers wanted to accept the offer and go back. We are a democratic union so we had to support what they wanted to do. They had a meeting and voted to settle. Then we had a problem with a few militants who wanted to hold out. We had to convince them to go back to work, as a united front, because otherwise they could be canned. So we worked—Tony Oredain and I, Dolo-

---

6. Born and raised in the California migrant camps, Gilbert Padilla, a CSO staffer in Stockton, joined Chávez and became a prominent leader in organizing the farmworkers. Manuel was his brother.

res and Gilbert, Jim Drake and all the organizers—knocking on doors till two in the morning, telling people, "You have to go back or you'll lose your job."

And they did. They worked.

Our second strike, and our last before the big one at Delano, was in the grapes at Martin's Ranch. The people were getting a raw deal there, being pushed around pretty badly. Gilbert went out to the field, climbed on top of a car and took a strike vote. They voted unanimously to go out. Right away they started bringing in strikebreakers, so we launched a tough attack on the labor contractors, distributed leaflets portraying them as really low characters. We attacked one so badly that he just gave up the job, and he took 27 of his men out with him. All he asked was that we distribute another leaflet reinstating him in the community. And we did. What was unusual was that the grower would still talk to us. The grower kept saying, "I can't pay. I just haven't got the money." I guess he must have found the money somewhere, because we were asking $1.40 and we got it.

We had just finished the Martin strike when the Agricultural Workers Organizing Committee (AFL-CIO) started a strike against the grape growers, DiGiorgio, Schenley liquors and small growers, asking $1.40 an hour and 25 cents a box. There was a lot of pressure from our members for us to join the strike, but we had some misgivings. We didn't feel ready for a big strike like this one, one that was sure to last a long time. Having no money—just $87 in the strike fund—meant we'd have to depend on God knows who.

Eight days after the strike started—it takes time to get 1,200 people together from all over the Valley—we held a meeting in Delano and voted to go out. I asked the membership to release us from the pledge not to accept outside money, because we'd need it now, a lot of it. The help came. It started because of the close, and I would say even beautiful, relationship that we've had with the Migrant Ministry[7] for some years. They were the first to come to our rescue, financially and in every other way, and they spread the word to other benefactors.

We had planned, before, to start a labor school in November. It never happened, but we have the best labor school we could ever have, in the strike. The strike is only a temporary condition, however. We have over 3,000 members spread out over a wide area, and we have to service them when they have problems. We get letters from New Mexico, Colorado, Texas, California, from farm workers saying, "We're getting together and we need an organizer."

It kills you when you haven't got the personnel and resources. You feel badly about not sending an organizer because you look back and remember all the difficulty you had in getting two or three people together, and here *they're* together. Of course, we're training organizers, many of them younger than I was when I started in CSO. They can work 20 hours a day, sleep four and be ready to hit it again; when you get to be 39 it's a different story.

---

7. California Migrant Ministry, an interdisciplinary church group, supported Chávez and the farmworkers in union organizing.

The people who took part in the strike and the march have something more than their material interest going for them. If it were only material, they wouldn't have stayed on the strike long enough to win. It is difficult to explain. But it flows out in the ordinary things they say. For instance, some of the younger guys are saying, "Where do you think's going to be the next strike?"

I say, "Well, we have to win in Delano."

They say, "We'll win, but where do we go next?"

I say, "Maybe most of us will be working in the fields."

They say, "No, I don't want to go and work in the fields. I want to organize. There are a lot of people that need our help."

So I say, "You're going to be pretty poor then, because when you strike you don't have much money." They say they don't care much about that.

And others are saying, "I have friends who are working in Texas. If we could only help them."

It is bigger, certainly, than just a strike. And if this spirit grows within the farm labor movement, one day we can use the force that we have to help correct a lot of things that are wrong in this society. But that is for the future. Before you can run, you have to learn to walk.

There are vivid memories from my childhood—what we had to go through because of low wages and the conditions, basically because there was no union. I suppose if I wanted to be fair I could say that I'm trying to settle a personal score. I could dramatize it by saying that I want to bring social justice to farm workers. But the truth is that I went through a lot of hell, and a lot of people did. If we can even the score a little for the workers then we are doing something. Besides, I don't know any other work I like to do better than this. I really don't, you know.

July 1966                                                                        2008

## Rufino Contreras[1]

February 10, 1979, was a day of infamy for farm workers. It was a day without joy. The sun didn't shine. The birds didn't sing. The rain didn't fall.

Why was this such a day of evil? Because on this day greed and injustice struck down our brother Rufino Contreras.

What is the worth of a man? What is the worth of a farm worker? Rufino, his father, and brother together gave the company twenty years of their labor. They were faithful workers who helped build up the wealth of their boss, helped to build up the wealth of his ranch.

What was their reward for their service and their sacrifice? When they petitioned for a more just share of what they themselves produced, when they spoke out against the injustice they endured, the company answered them with bullets; the company sent hired guns to quiet Rufino Contreras.

---

1. A lettuce cutter who, four days before Chávez delivered this eulogy in Calexico, California, was shot to death on a picket line by a company foreman. The threat of more violence forced the union to suspend the picketing.

Capitol and labor together produce the fruit of the land. But what really counts is labor—the human beings who torture their bodies, sacrifice their youth, and numb their spirits to produce this great agricultural wealth, a wealth so vast that it feeds all of America and much of the world. And yet the men, women, and children who are the flesh and blood of this production often do not have enough to feed themselves.

But we are here today to say that true wealth is not measured in money or status or power. It is measured in the legacy that we leave behind for those we love and those we inspire.

In that sense, Rufino is not dead. Wherever farm workers organize, stand up for their rights, and strike for justice, Rufino Contreras is with them.

Rufino lives among us. It is those who have killed him and those who have conspired to kill him that have died, because the love, the compassion, the light in their hearts have been stilled.

Why do we say that Rufino still lives? Because those of us who mourn him today and bring him to his rest rededicate ourselves to the ideals for which he gave his life. Rufino built a union that will someday bring justice to all farm workers.

If Rufino were alive today, what would he tell us? He would tell us, "Don't be afraid. Don't be discouraged." He would tell us, "Don't cry for me, organize!"

This is a day of sorrow but it is also a day of hope. It is a time of sadness because our friend is dead. It is a time of hope because we are certain that Rufino today enjoys the justice in heaven that was denied him on earth.

It is our mission to finish the work Rufino has begun among us, knowing that true justice for ourselves and our opponents is only possible before God, who is the final judge.

February 14, 1979                                                                   2008


## What Is Democracy?

After thirty years organizing poor people I have become convinced that the two greatest aspirations of humankind are equality and participation.

These yearnings are indivisible because equality can only be experienced through participation and self-determination. Democracy is not an impassive system. It is sustained by people's involvement. And participation in the democratic process is a key strategy in nonviolent struggle.

Free men and women instinctively prefer democratic change to any other means. It is only the enslaved and shackled—those without hope or faith—who seek violent solutions to their problems.

It is precisely to overcome this frustration and hopelessness that we in the farm workers' movement have involved masses of people in their own struggle. Thus, demonstrations and marches, strikes and boycotts are not only weapons against the growers, but our way of avoiding the senseless violence that brings no honor to any class or community. The boycott, as Gandhi taught, is the most nearly perfect instrument for nonviolent change, allowing masses of people to participate actively in a cause.

Participation in democracy—exercising the power to control our own future—is the best hope for a nonviolent solution to the injustices we face as farm workers, minorities, or poor people. It is also the only hope our nation has of enduring and surviving in a world where the have-nots increasingly vie for ascendency against the traditional forces of wealth and influence now concentrated in Western society.

Yet, instead of recognizing these truths, our country—through its archaic immigration policies and practices—has created an underclass of exploited and ostracized men and women who are excluded from participation, which has been the key to improvement for generations of U.S. immigrants.

Instead of promoting humanity's fundamental aspirations—equality and participation—our immigration policies and the practices of many U.S. employers have endorsed the twin plagues of humanity: exploitation and discrimination. These scourges are most vividly demonstrated in America by cheap wages and wretched working conditions for immigrant workers.

For these workers such exploitation and the poverty it brings destroys their spirits, wastes their potential, and blunts their ideals. It confines them to a daily struggle for survival to simply put bread on the table.

That daily struggle for survival cheats people of the finer things in life: education, religion, and involvement in government and politics. "Primero comer que ser cristiano." You must eat before you are a Christian, goes an old Mexican saying.

America has not yet learned the lesson that in this day and age you cannot have your cake and eat it, too. Some of our basic industries—most of agriculture and segments of the garment and service industries, to name a few—have prospered in recent times by exploiting undocumented immigrants. Employers want their cheap labor and their docile acceptance of miserable working and living conditions.

Yet we as a nation don't want these same immigrants to stake a claim to the promise this country offers to people here and around the world.

When I was a child, I remember that crossing the border illegally was considered a tremendous crime. It used to be. But now many no longer think of it as a crime. People say, "No! I'm going to go the U.S. because I need to work. I need to support my kids. I need a better life."

In this age of television, films, and commercial advertising, when the poor in Third World countries are endlessly reminded of the prosperity that is always beyond their reach, the stigma of crossing borders vanishes. It is no longer a crime in the minds of many people to cross a border to feed their hungry families.

Until we recognize the powerful forces that lure so many immigrants to this land—forces that we often ignite—we can never fashion a policy that will adequately address the acute immigration problems we face.

To be sure, the only long-term solution to the dilemma of illegal immigration is improving the economies of Mexico and other nations from which the immigrants spring.

But what of the people who are here now without papers?

We need to recast our philosophy about immigrants from Third World lands; we must replace the policies that exclude people from participation in our economic and political life because of their race, language, or immigration status with policies that encourage people to participate in society. We need to get people involved.

People are now alienated; among Hispanics, this alienation affects citizens and legal residents as well as undocumented persons. We have all kinds of rules to keep people outside the process. And when you exclude people you deny the yearning for equality and participation that is so key to fulfillment and happiness.

What changes do we have to make?

Some kind of meaningful adjustment in the legal status of undocumented aliens is a critical first step. Whether this adjustment is known as amnesty or called by some other name, no workable proposal for dealing with the question of illegal immigration can succeed without it.

Resolution of their status will enable undocumented workers to rid themselves of the pervasive fear that is so paralyzing; the fear that inhibits them from dealing with their exploitation like other American workers through the process of self-organization and collective bargaining.

At the same time we reckon with the problem of undocumented persons already in the country, we should emphatically reject schemes advanced by some Republican politicians and conservative grower groups to revive the infamous Bracero Program.[1] The politicians now call it by a new name: the "guest worker program." But a fancy title cannot sugar-coat that evil system of replacing domestic farm workers with a new class of slave laborers imported from outside the U.S. to defeat unions and depress wages and working conditions.

Next, we must dramatically reform the U.S. Immigration and Naturalization Service. Perhaps it should be eliminated altogether. In our experience it is the most corrupt, most bigoted agency in our country.

The INS has a long history of dealing with noncitizens; confronting poor human beings who have no legal standing in society. So they feel they can kick them, beat them, demand money from them. They can do almost anything they want because they know these people are not citizens and can't respond.

Today many of the people who work for the INS see all Hispanics as aliens, even though we may be second-, third-, or fourth-generation Americans. In their minds, we're not citizens. It is the worst "gringo" mentality to be found anywhere in the government.

What of society's attitude towards differences in culture and language?

We all know of the so-called "melting pot" theory. It is taught in the schools, preached from the pulpit, and proclaimed by politicians.

This country is not a melting pot anymore. It used to be more of a melting pot when the bulk of the immigrants were white Europeans. But with large numbers of Third World people, particularly Asians, Latin Americans, and Africans, coming to our shores, it is no longer possible or desirable to Anglicise the waves of new immigrants.

We sometimes refer to those who oppose the struggles of minorities and people in the Third World as the "super-Americans." They claim the melting-pot theory still applies. They would like all of us to be melted, poured, and

---

1. See the "Acculturation" introduction, p. 364.

cast . . . and cloned into the all-American boy and girl. So we will all come out looking like Pat Boone and Anita Bryant.[2] They would like all of us to buy their argument that the strength of our country is in its conformity to one ethnic and cultural heritage.

But there are some of us Americans who share a different vision of what our nation is. The strength of America is not in her conformity. We believe the strength of America is in her diversity!

Our country is admired around the world not—as the "New Right" claims—because of her bombers and nuclear arsenal. We are admired for our Bill of Rights and especially for the First Amendment, which protects diversity. Let us also be admired for our cultural and linguistic pluralism.

For this country to continue to be great we need to include people, but not strip them of their cultural values in the process. I can eat tortillas and still be an American. Our country needs to understand that.

Groups of people will tolerate many things—but don't tamper with their language; don't threaten their religion. And don't meddle with their food or there's going to be a lot of problems. The greatest contribution our government and society can make is to recognize that we are all Americans, yet we are all different.

There has never really been a melting pot. As Cantinflas[3] says, "Juntos pero no revueltos," together but not together.

We need to establish a federal department of cultural affairs. A department in our government that recognizes we're all one nation but also acknowledges the differences that make us unique and valuable as individuals and as part of the society. Such an agency could handle immigration and citizenship, and be the guardian of the special cultural values each racial, ethnic, or linguistic group has to contribute.

We must also unbridle our citizenship requirements—the laborious and protracted process that often stands as an obstacle to full participation in political life for so many decent and patriotic people whose cultural or linguistic tradition has not yet fallen prey to Anglicization.

A person should not become a citizen automatically. But a man's or woman's character is what should really matter. Not whether he or she speaks English or can survive the bureaucracy. What should count is the fact that he or she has lived here and is paying taxes and is making a contribution to the country. And, of course, the person would have to say, "Yes, I want to live under this system."

We must also change the voter registration laws as they now read. For the large part they are very old and written in a time when everybody went to church on Sunday and took a bath on Tuesday. I would say we should end voter registration. Anyone who is a citizen should have the right to vote.

What I am really talking about—whether it is immigration, citizenship, cultural mores, or voting rights—is making it possible for more people to participate in the democratic process. If these changes come to pass we will witness a radical reordering—for the better—in our country. For whenever

---

2. Like Pat Boone (b. 1934), an American singer (b. 1940) known for political activism based on conservative views and on Protestant Christianity.

3. Fortino Mario Alfonso Moreno Reyes (1911–1993), Mexican comedian and actor.

new blood is transfused into our national social and political fabric our nation is enriched and strengthened.

I believe that kind of participation is the real fulfillment of democracy, a realization of humanity's greatest desires. If this country could foster those aspirations, we would not only be true to our best ideals but we would provide an example for the world.

1982                                                                                                    2008

# NASH CANDELARIA
## b. 1928

Nash Candelaria was born and raised in Los Angeles. His family moved from New Mexico to California shortly before he was born. After receiving a degree in chemistry from the University of California, Los Angeles, Candelaria took creative-writing courses at UCLA, Los Angeles City College, and the University of Southern California. He worked as a research chemist, served in the U.S. Air Force during the Korean War, and for many years worked in the advertising departments of various science companies while writing in his spare time.

In his debut novel, the autobiographical *Memories of the Alhambra* (1977)—of which the first two of 30 chapters are excerpted here—Candelaria depicts the Rafa family, part of a twentieth-century landed gentry in New Mexico that boasts of having centuries-long roots in the state. Uneasy about their background, the Rafas cling to a Spanish European past, denying their *mexicanidad* and therefore their Native American heritage. Jose Rafa travels to Mexico wanting to find his Spanish roots, but is disappointed by what he discovers. He then goes to Spain, where he realizes his Spanish heritage is tainted with Native American blood. Candelaria followed *Memories* with a sequel, *Not by the Sword* (1982), set during the Mexican-American War (1846–48) and addressing the subsequent transfer of land from Mexico to the United States. The Rafa family now keeps a tenuous hold on their land, their traditions, and their identity—namely, the persistent myth of being Spanish, although their land had belonged to Mexico with that country's declaration of independence from Spain, in 1821.

In *Inheritance of Strangers* (1985), the third book in the Rafa series, the arrival of the Americans in the West and the settlement of New Mexico as a territory of the United States continues the erosion of traditions. The grandson of Jose Rafa seeks political accommodation with an influential Anglo, while other Latinos in the book experience divided loyalties. The collapse of the indigenous Latino society in New Mexico is represented by the Rafas' move to California. In the novel *Leonor Park* (1991), Candelaria concludes the Rafa saga. Here, he focuses on a struggle over a land inheritance just before the Great Depression. Candelaria's other publications include two story collections and the novel *A Daughter's a Daughter* (2008).

### From Memories of the Alhambra

1

The patriarch was dead. But Jose Rafa had felt a vague, hovering uneasiness even before his brother had telephoned to tell him that their father had died. It was a feeling that had nothing to do with the old man's death—a feeling that he, Jose, was on the precipice of a crisis.

The feeling had intensified on the drive from Los Angeles to Albuquerque, New Mexico. Jose and his wife, Theresa, had been driven to the funeral by their son, Joe. Jose Rafa, the first of all the Rafa's to finish high school, driven by his son, the first Rafa to graduate from college, back to the country suburb of what had once been a small town. Back to Los Rafas, New Mexico, in the northwest section of Albuquerque.

The drive down Route 66 had been a blur. Albuquerque was no longer the place Jose remembered from his childhood some sixty years ago. It was a metropolis. His brothers, sisters, in-laws, cousins were familiar but slightly changed, older versions of what he remembered.

One thing had not changed. The dust. The wind was blowing the morning they rode to the cemetery. Sitting between Theresa and Joe, he trembled, watching the brown specks settle onto the shiny black surface of the limousine. The limousine ahead turned and the headlights flickered pale, bleached by the morning sun. As their limousine turned, the hearse winked into view, then disappeared. His sister, Juana, began to cry silently, while his other sister, Gregoria, sat rigid beside her. From the rear view mirror, the chauffeur's eyes looked back noncommitally. A fleeting reflection showed Jose's hair streaked with white, the dark face fleshy and ashen.

'Pobre. Pobre, papa.' Juana was building up to hysteria again. Her quiet sobs unnerved Jose. She could not forget for a moment. The fact of death was shock enough. Why must she lacerate herself and others with it?

Now, for the first time since they had left the church, Gregoria stirred. Twice she cleared her throat, then lapsed into silence. Jose turned and stared at her as if to say: All right. What is it?

After clearing her throat once more, she forced the words out. 'I should have ridden in the front car. They have no right to put me in the second car. He was my padre, too.'

'Mama and Carlos and Eufemia are in the first car,' Jose said irritably.

'There was room. Did you see that, Juana? Did you see? There was room for all of us.'

'What difference does it make?' Jose asked.

'It's not fair. We were cheated. Eufemia is up there. You don't see her in the second car. Isn't that right?' Juana sniffed her tears and nodded.

'Maybe you should have ridden in the hearse,' Jose said. 'They could have put a chair for you right alongside the casket.'

'You don't care. You weren't here all the time he was sick. You were in California getting rich. So why should you care whether or not you're in the first car?'

Jose rubbed his temples, and his face flushed. His hands closed and un-closed, a sign that he wanted a cigarette. But a funeral procession was no place to disobey doctor's orders.

'Yes,' Juana echoed. 'Why should you care? You weren't here.'

Jose looked out the window, peering vacantly at the people on the side-walk who watched the procession with disinterest. He glanced past his wife with a fleeting look of desperation, of frustrated entrapment. 'Shut up! Goddamn it! I'm tired of your nonsense. Who cares what car we ride in? Who cares if someone said the rosary too loud and another not loud enough? He's dead! How can your foolishness help that?'

Juana began to wail hysterically—like this morning at church—like the other night at the velorio.[1]

'Let's try to be a little calm,' Jose said in a quieter voice. 'Let's try to have a little respect for the dead.'

Juana's attempt to hold back her tears sounded like slurping soup. 'Please,' Jose said as he handed her a handkerchief.

Jose looked toward Theresa. They had passed the park where the sunbon-neted statue of the Madonna of the Trail looked west, then turned out of traf-fic toward the outskirts of the city. At the first dirt side road Jose closed his eyes. He knew where the limousine was going. Past a few more dirt roads to the turn onto a rutted way so covered with dust that you would not believe it was ever paved. A road one did not see. A road that one could feel and breathe.

Well, Jose thought, the family was still the same. True, his father had died. But that had been expected daily for the past ten years, so that his death was not so much a change as a realization. And—like always, after a day or two here he became jumpy. He and Theresa had left Albuquerque forty years ago, just before Joe was born, to get away from all this. Yet the place would not let them alone. It kept pulling them back to rehearse for their own time, which would be soon enough.

'We're there,' Gregoria said.

The limousine pierced through the dust into the cemetery, moving along the trimmed green lawn and the painted white crosses and engraved head-stones. 'Good,' Jose said. 'It will be a relief to get it done with.' Juana began to sniffle louder.

During the ceremony voices could be heard above the intonations of the priest—like dogs quarreling over a bone. The Widow Rafa held on to her two sons. The others were beyond, mouths still open though their whispers had faded at Jose's glance that swept back and then hesitated on his brother. There was avarice on Carlos' face. Even his feet rested tenderly on the ground so as not to despoil the precious land which seemed more valuable than life to him.

Jose became impatient as the priest droned on. He wanted to get to the limousine quickly so that they would be the first to get away. Then they would get to his mother's house before the vultures got there and picked the place clean.

When the service ended, Jose turned toward Juana and Gregoria to urge them on when a hand on his shoulder stopped him. He narrowed his eyes,

1. Wake.

leaning toward the apologetic, accented voice, trying to pierce the layer of years that covered the familiar voice with this alien flesh.

'Jose. It's Herminio. Herminio Padilla.'

Jose shook his head in bewilderment. Herminio? His cousin. His best friend from school days. No, Jose's expression seemed to say. This can't be. Not this frail, gray-haired old man. Then he remembered his own reflection in the limousine mirror, and his eyes widened in fright.

'Herminio. Herminio.' Jose clasped the stranger's bony shoulders.

'Compadre. Primo.[2] How long has it been? Twenty years? Has it been that long—to finally come to this?' Jose averted his eyes, the tears welling up—not just for his dead father, but for Herminio and for himself who one day soon would be resting in a place like this.

'Twenty years,' Jose said.

'Que lastima, su padre.'[3]

'He had a long life. May we all live to be ninety-five.'

Herminio shifted awkwardly from foot to foot, tears in his eyes as he looked sadly at Jose. 'Come see me if you have time. I'm still at the same old place. Alone now, you know. Where Indian School Road meets the river.'

Jose nodded, knowing that he would not make it, knowing that Herminio did not expect him to. They shook hands and clasped shoulders. Jose felt the touch self-consciously, seeing the rich texture of his suit in contrast to his cousin's calloused paw and threadbare sleeve. 'The same old place,' he said. Herminio nodded and disappeared into the crowd.

'There you are!' Jose turned in the direction of Juana's voice. 'Come on. The others are already gone.'

Jose muttered a curse under his breath. 'Where's Gregoria?'

'She went in the first car. They wouldn't let me go because it was too crowded. Now we'll be late.'

'Late for what?'

Juana flushed a deep purple. 'Nothing.'

'You mean they'll steal everything before you get your hands on a share.'

Juana climbed into the limousine stiffly, brushing past the chauffeur who held the door open. Jose followed, smiling, to let her know that he knew. She looked away from him. Thieves, his expression said. Goddamned Indian thieves.

The others were already there when they drove in back of the adobe house and parked under the huge cottonwood tree. Even before the handbrake had been set, Juana had leaped from the car and hurried through the screen door.

Jose opened the door with deliberation, letting Theresa and Joe in, then let the screen slam, hooking it shut to keep out the flies. As they went into the kitchen, the cacophony of voices died down. The family turned and looked silently at Jose—everyone except Widow Rafa, who sat on a straight back chair staring into space.

Carlos nodded abruptly. 'Jose. Junior. Theresa.'

Jose nodded at each in turn—at Carlos, at Eufemia and Gregoria and Juana and their husbands, Jose's brothers-in-law. Then Jose went to his

---

2. Cousin. *Compadre*: friend.      3. What a shame, your father.

mother and put a hand on her shoulder. After an awkward silence, his presence no longer seemed an intrusion, and they continued their talk.

'You'll move in with us,' Eufemia said. 'We can pack a few things now, then come back for the rest when you're ready.'

'We have more room,' Gregoria said quickly. 'Your great-granddaughters have doubled up like they've wanted to for so long. They cleaned and decorated the extra room for their favorite great-grandmother.'

Carlos nodded gravely at the old woman. 'Remember what I told you. We should keep the land in the family. Before you sell it to anyone, talk to me.'

Eufemia moved toward the closet. 'Which of your things do you want now, mama? I can start packing.'

'No, mama. We have the room. Your great-granddaughters have made it ready for you. Don't listen to her. You know her cooking. Her frijoles[4] swell you up like a balloon.'

Jose's face flushed with anger as Juana walked quietly to one wall and took down an old framed photograph of his father. Then she eased to the niche in another wall and took a small wooded statue of the Virgin Mary.

'Stop it!' Jose shouted. 'Put those things back, or I'll call the police."

The family froze in silence, focusing stonily on Juana with arms full. 'I was just going to take them for safe keeping,' she said meekly.

'Put them back.'

She rehung the photograph on the wall and replaced the statue, turning it so it faced out properly. Jose scrutinized the others—Carlos, whose avarice could be seen in the pinched squint of his eyes as he glanced through the window at the tiny apple orchard—Eufemia and Gregoria, planting their feet as if for a tug-of-war where each would grasp one of the old lady's arms and tear for the larger hunk. Once again Juana's eyes were wide with desire as they flitted from object to object. All the while the Widow Rafa sat staring, unaware of the quarrel.

'Why don't you all go home,' Jose said. Gregoria gasped. Carlos' folded arms reacted, ready to lash out, the authoritative reflex of the older brother. But that was long ago, another age, another life, and Jose looked past the now meaningless reflex as if he didn't see it.

'Well!' Eufemia said. 'Well!'

'I think mama needs to be left alone.'

'So you can take what's ours,' Juana said. 'So you can pack your car with our things and go back to California.'

Jose was infused with a calm that surprised him. As he looked at them, he spoke quietly so only Theresa and Joe could hear. 'These are not my sisters, my brother. Look at their brown, greedy faces. Listen to their accented speech. We're not members of the same family. We're not even members of the same race.' Then aloud to the others: 'Leave!'

Juana edged to the door, hesitating after each step to see if anything had changed, to see if it had all been a mistake, to see if someone would smilingly call her back. Jose stared at her darkly, and she continued through the kitchen.

Eufemia said, 'Well. Well,' then moved toward the door, Gregoria following.

4. Beans.

'You're just tired,' Carlos said. 'We're all tired. Come by the house before you go.' Jose nodded. Now they were alone with his mother who was still staring out the window, far away, all alone.

Jose put a hand on her shoulder. This was how it ended—the old widow numb and uncomprehending. Soon it would be his widow's turn. And he had never traced back to the root of things, to the beginning—back to the conquistadors—back to the hidalgos,[5] hijo de algo, son of someone. These pretenders he had thrown out of the house were not his family. Not his siblings. He was more than that. He was *someone.*

Jose looked past his mother, through the window, past the apple orchard toward the river. But his thoughts carried him farther. Across the ocean to the source, the beginnings. To a place he had never seen that was some secret, essential part of himself. And it was then that Jose knew what he must do.

## 2

The Rafas and Trujillos, Theresa's family, had lived in New Mexico for over two hundred and fifty years. Since before the founding of Albuquerque in 1706. Yet Theresa did not feel that it was home.

Over the years the trips to Albuquerque had become more odious, and it was with acute relief that she returned to Los Angeles this time. Ironically, their grown son drove them back over the same road that she and Jose had travelled on their first trip to California forty years before, when she had been carrying the unborn Joe.

Jose had headed for East Los Angeles where many refugees from the Mexican revolution of the early 1910's and 1920's had settled. It had seemed that the signs in the shop windows should have read "English spoken here" instead of "Se habla espanol.' These were not their people, these latter day migrants from below the Rio Grande River, these Chicanos who huddled protectively under the shelter of common language and common appearance in this part of the city. Yet the pull to live there, the ambivalence, had drawn them newly married to the familiarity that Spanish-speaking East Los Angeles had offered to a young couple fresh from the Albuquerque farm.

'Why do we have to rent this one?' Theresa protested in a whisper. The dark, squat, shirt-sleeved landlord held open the front door with a smile, exuding a stale aroma of beer. The little house itself was a disappointment, hidden modestly behind a larger front house like a shyly smiling young girl with a tooth missing behind a taller, more beautiful sister.

'The rent is cheap. Muy barato,'[1] the landlord said. 'It's very clean.' They stamped their shoes of yard dust on the worn mat and followed the strong smell of disinfectant into the small linoleum floored living room.

Immediately Theresa's eyes narrowed as she checked the base boards and corners for vermin. The smell reminded her of a hospital. Of disease and dirt. In the tense stillness a fly's buzz amplified into the angry whine of a squadron of airplanes. The landlord smiled weakly at the stiff and scrutinizing Theresa

5. Nobles.            1. Very cheap.

and shrugged. The rims of her eyes were red as her eyelids flickered at the welling tears.

'It's only a few dollars a month,' Jose said.

'Es muy barato,' the landlord echoed.

'No,' she said—quietly but firmly.

'Let me show you the kitchen. It's been freshly painted.'

Jose had patted Theresa's arm reassuringly. 'Freshly painted,' he echoed.

The kitchen was two strides across the linoleum to one corner where the wall color changed abruptly just in front of the tiny stove and dripping faucet.

'No,' she repeated.

The landlord turned as if he hadn't heard. 'With a little paint the bedroom would be just as nice. In fact,' he said to Jose, 'I'll buy the paint for you. All you'll have to do is put it on.'

The landlord put his arm around Jose's shoulder and led him to the other room. 'See the bedroom? It hardly needs paint, but for you, compadre—You say you're from Albuquerque? I have a cousin there. He loves it. Wonderful people, he says. I'm from Chihuahua.[2] Almost a blood brother.' Theresa stood waiting at the front door; she had not even looked into the bedroom. The two men looked at her, then at each other. 'Been married long, joven?'[3] Jose shook his head. Then the beery whisper. 'You got to let them know who's the boss. Who wears the pants in the family. Who's got the balls, hombre.'[4]

'It looks good,' Jose said aloud as if to no one in particular.

'No,' came the answer.

'Maybe I could adjust the rent. Down a dollar or two a month.'

But Theresa had left the house, and Jose followed. 'Don't forget,' the landlord said. 'Let them know who's boss.' Then a final volley. 'How about three dollars a month less?'

She sat stiffly in the Model T,[5] the hat pulled down over her bobbed hair so that the dark eyes peered out from under as if from a cave. 'Give me a cigarette,' Theresa said. Jose stood beside the car, immobilized by his emotions. He was angry at her dismissal of the little house, even more angry that she had ignored his authority in front of the landlord, and now she had brazenly asked for a cigarette—one of the many sources of criticism from his sisters and sisters-in-law. Only hussies smoked and disobeyed their husbands.

'Will you give me a cigarette?'

'No. Goddamn it! My mother doesn't like it!'

'Or your sisters,' she answered stiffly.

'Yes. All three of them.'

'They don't like me chewing gum or rolling my stocking or painting my lips red or boop-boop-te-doop.' But the words belied her true feelings, for again her eyes reddened and tears welled up. 'Give me a cigarette. Please.'

Jose took a pack of Lucky Strikes from his shirt pocket, giving it a quick forward thrust and sudden halt that popped a cigarette part way out of the torn corner of the package. With trembling hand, Theresa held it to the center of her pursed mouth while Jose fumbled for a match. The silent tears trickled down her rouged cheeks.

---

2. City and state in northern Mexico.
3. Young man.
4. Man.

5. A type of car that Ford produced from 1908 to 1927.

'You didn't want them to build us a house either,' he said. She didn't answer. 'My father and my brothers had the plans all drawn.' Still no answer. 'Goddamn it! Say something.'

She stared straight out the windshield, trying to control her tears, trying to keep from choking on the cloud of smoke that emanated from her cigarette. 'They didn't ask me,' she finally said. 'They just came over one night with the drawings. It was supposed to be my house, and I didn't have anything to say about it. It wasn't what I wanted, and it wasn't where I wanted it.'

'In the old days it had to be built before we could get married. That was the custom.'

'These are not the old days.'

'Goddamn it! What do you want? It was a free house. Built from adobe from our own land. Near the rest of the family. Right in Los Rafas.'

'That's just it. It wasn't our own house. It was the family's house. So they could walk in and out as they pleased—tell us what to do or not do. Can't you see that? Why are we in Los Angeles if it wasn't to get away from your family?'

'All right. All right.' From the corner of her eye Theresa could see the landlord close the front door of the little house and look down the dirt driveway at them. 'But what about his house?' Jose asked.

Theresa exploded into tears, her twisted mouth emitting such frightening sobs that Jose trembled. Finally the words came, disjointed, between sobs, 'I don't want . . . our child . . . to grow up . . . here. I want more!' to be dissolved again in wailing sobs.

'What child?' Jose said, looking at her abdomen. Her wailing continued. Gently he took the burning cigarette from her fingers and threw it into the gutter. 'There,' he said, patting her shoulder. 'We don't have to live here if you don't want to.'

'It's . . . got to be . . . better. Not . . . the ranchitos . . . like Albuquerque. Not . . . Frijoles Flats. But with . . . everybody else. We're as good . . . as everybody else. Better!' The landlord had passed by, shuffling his feet and whistling.

Theresa smiled now as she remembered that scene of forty years past. She looked across the seat of the car toward Jose, who had slumped down asleep. He had gotten more than he bargained for, she thought. A girl who had refused his family's gift of a house. Who talked back. A flapper[6]— a Chicana flapper, which was some kind of mutation in itself. No longer content to be a brown-skinned chula[7] of the ranchitos, but a modern woman. Whatever that meant. Jose could be so angry with her, and yet she knew he loved her. Hadn't forty years shown that? 'Till death do us part,' the words of the ceremony had gone. And it was true.

1977

6. In the decade following World War I, a term for a young woman who defied convention.

7. Woman from the back streets, low-class woman; pretty girl; girlfriend.

# RODOLFO "CORKY" GONZALES
## 1928–2005

In 1955, Rodolfo "Corky" Gonzales, a former boxer, became the first Chicano to be named district captain of the Democratic Party of Denver, Colorado. He then became chairman of a local antipoverty program, where he worked until his resignation in 1966. In 1963, in Denver, he founded the grassroots organization Los Voluntarios (The Volunteers), but he may be best-known as the founder and director of the group that sprang from it three years later, the Crusade for Justice. Until his commitment to political activism and his concentration on Chicano issues led him to resign, he also served as the regional director of the War on Poverty, a mid-1960s government program put into action by U.S. president Lyndon Johnson.

In 1967, the printing press associated with the Crusade for Justice published the book on which Gonzales's literary reputation rests: *I Am Joaquín*, a poetry collection illustrated with black-and-white photographs. No evidence supports the early, persistent rumor that Gonzales did not write the book, the full text of which is included here. In 1969, the Chicano playwright, theater director, and activist Luis Valdez directed a documentary that showed historical images from the book, together with marches, parades, and street demonstrations. Three years later, the major New York publisher Bantam released an edition, calling Gonzales's work "the most famous poem of the Chicano Movement in America." Indeed, the book came to define the Movement; Latino historians consider it a Chicano epic. In the 1970s, *I Am Joaquín* sold over 100,000 copies, becoming the first Chicano best seller. While the book's importance was mainly political, it also has influenced some contemporary writers.

The name Joaquín has been seen as a bow to Joaquín Murrieta, who began mining for gold in California in 1849 and, according to legend, became an outlaw after his wife was raped and killed when they were driven from his gold claim. The book does not deal with Murrieta, though. It is a linear history of Mexico and of the Americans of Mexican descent, the Chicanos. Because being an American with strong Mexican ties seems contradictory, Joaquín searches for meaning. He realizes that having the blood of both the Aztec prince Cuauhtémoc and the Spanish conqueror Cortés in his veins makes him the descendant of two races, at once "tyrant and slave." Joaquín embodies Chicano endurance in the face of such contradictions, despite racism and oppression. Ultimately, Gonzales's poem is an optimistic work of social protest. In his introduction, Gonzales states that

> Writing *I Am Joaquín* was a journey back through history, a painful self-evaluation, a wandering search for my peoples and, most of all, for my own identity. The totality of all social inequities and injustices had to come to the surface. All the while, the truth about our own flaws—the villains and the heroes had to ride together—in order to draw an honest, clear conclusion of who we were, who we are, and where we are going.
>
> *I Am Joaquín* became a historical essay, a social statement, a conclusion of our *mestizaje*, a welding of the oppressor (Spaniard) and the oppressed (Indian).

An anthology of Gonzales's work, *Message to Aztlán: Selected Writings of Rodolfo "Corky" Gonzales* (2001), was edited by Antonio Esquibel, with a preface by Gonzales and a foreword by Rodolfo F. Acuña.

# I AM JOAQUÍN

I am Joaquín,
   lost in a world of confusion,
   caught up in the whirl of a
         gringo society,
   confused by the rules,                                         5
   scorned by attitudes,
   suppressed by manipulation,
   and destroyed by modern society.
My fathers
     have lost the economic battle                           10
and won
     the struggle of cultural survival.

And now!
   I must choose
              between                                 15
the paradox of
victory of the spirit,
   despite physical hunger,
         or
to exist in the grasp                                                   20
of American social neurosis,
sterilization of the soul
   and a full stomach.

Yes,
I have come a long way to nowhere                                        25
unwillingly dragged by that
    monstrous, technical,
    industrial giant called
       Progress
and Anglo success. . . .                                                 30

I look at myself.
   I watch my brothers.
     I shed tears of sorrow.
      I sow seeds of hate.
I withdraw to the safety within the                                      35
circle of life—

        MY OWN PEOPLE.

I am Cuauhtémoc,[1]
proud and noble,
     leader of men,                                            40
king of an empire

---

1. Last Aztec emperor (ca. 1495–1522), reigned 1520–22. The Aztecs and this period are discussed in the "Colonization" introduction, p. 1.

civilized beyond the dreams
   of the gachupín Cortés,[2]
who also is the blood,
   the image of myself.                                                    45
I am the Maya prince.
I am Nezahualcóyotl,
great leader of the Chichimecas.[3]
I am the sword and flame of Cortés
               the despot.                          50
            And
I am the eagle and serpent of
      the Aztec civilization.[4]

I owned the land as far as the eye
could see under the crown of Spain,                                  55
and I toiled on my earth
and gave my Indian sweat and blood
     for the Spanish master
who ruled with tyranny over man and
beast and all that he could trample.                                 60
               But . . .
    THE GROUND WAS MINE.
I was both tyrant and slave.

As Christian church took its place
   in God's good name,                                               65
to take and use my virgin strength and
             trusting faith,
the priests,
     both good and bad,
             took—                                         70
but
    gave a lasting truth that
      Spaniard
        Indian
          Mestizo                                                75
were all God's children.
And
    from these words grew men
      who prayed and fought
           for                                           80
   their own worth as human beings,
      for
         that
    GOLDEN MOMENT
      of                                                            85
    FREEDOM.

2. Hernán Cortés (1485–1547), Spanish conquistador. *Gachupín*: derogatory term for Spaniard.
3. Nomadic tribes from northern Mexico. *Netzahualcóyotl*: philosopher-poet-prince (1401–1472), ruled 1418–70.

4. Legend has it that the original Aztecs settled in Tenochtitlán because they had been searching for a lake with a rock on top of which an eagle was devouring a serpent. The eagle and the serpent are now symbols in the Mexican flag.

I was part in blood and spirit
  of that
     courageous village priest
              Hidalgo        90
who in the year eighteen hundred and ten
rang the bell of independence
and gave out that lasting cry—
  el grito de Dolores:
    "Que mueran los gachupines y que viva    95
la Virgen de Guadalupe. . . ."[5]

I sentenced him
    who was me.
I excommunicated him, my blood.
I drove him from the pulpit to lead      100
  a bloody revolution for him and me. . . .
      I killed him.
His head,
  which is mine and of all those
  who have come this way,      105
I placed on that fortress wall
  to wait for independence.
Morelos!
    Matamoros!
      Guerrero![6]    110
all compañeros in the act,
STOOD AGAINST THAT WALL OF
                  INFAMY
  to feel the hot gouge of lead
    which my hands made.    115
I died with them . . .
  I lived with them . . .
    I lived to see our country free.
Free
  from Spanish rule in    120
    eighteen-hundred-twenty-one.
      Mexico was free ? ?

The crown was gone
      but
all its parasites remained    125
    and ruled
    and taught
with gun and flame and mystic power.
I worked
I sweated    130

5. Death to the Spaniards and life to the Virgin of Guadalupe. *Nuestra Señora de Guadalupe* (Our Lady of Guadalupe), a sixteenth-century icon of the Virgin Mary and perhaps Mexico's most popular religious and cultural image, has come to symbolize Catholic Mexicans and Mexico itself. *El grito de Dolores*: The cry of Dolores, Father Miguel Hidalgo y Costilla's declaration of Mexico's independence from Spain, is discussed in the "Annexations" introduction, p. 160.

6. José María Morelos (1765–1815), Mariano Matamoros y Guridi (1770–1814), and Vicente Guerrero (1783–1831), leaders of the Mexican struggle for independence.

I bled
I prayed
    and waited silently for life
        to begin again.

I fought and died
    for
Don Benito Juárez,[7]
guardian of the Constitution.
I was he
    on dusty roads
        on barren land
as he protected his archives
as Moses did his sacraments.[8]

He held his Mexico
    in his hand
      on
    the most desolate
    and remote ground
    which was his country.
And this giant
    little Zapotec[9]
        gave
not one palm's breadth
of his country's land to
    kings or monarchs or presidents
of foreign powers.

I am Joaquín.
I rode with Pancho Villa,[1]
    crude and warm,
a tornado at full strength,
nourished and inspired
    by the passion and the fire
    of all his earthy people.
I am Emiliano Zapata.[2]
    "This land,
      this earth
       is
        OURS."

The villages
    the mountains
    the streams
    belong to Zapatistas.[3]

---

7. Mexican lawyer (1806–1872), the first mestizo president of Mexico (1861–65, 1867–72).
8. According to the Old Testament, the prophet Moses received the Ten Commandments on tablets from God.
9. I.e., member of this indigenous Mexican people.
1. Francisco "Pancho" Villa (1878–1923), Mexican revolutionary leader.
2. Emiliano Zapata (ca. 1879–1919), Mexican revolutionary leader.
3. Followers of Zapata.

Our life
or yours
is the only trade for soft brown earth                                   175
and maize.
All of which is our reward,
a creed that formed a constitution
for all who dare live free!
"This land is ours . . .                                                  180
Father, I give it back to you.
Mexico must be free. . . ."

I ride with revolutionists
against myself.
I am the Rurales,[4]                                                      185
coarse and brutal,
I am the mountain Indian,
superior over all.
The thundering hoof beats are my horses.
The chattering machine guns                                               190
are death to all of me:
Yaqui
Tarahumara
Chamula
Zapotec                                                                   195
Español[5]

I have been the bloody revolution,
the victor,
the vanquished.
I have killed                                                             200
and been killed.
I am the despots Díaz
and Huerta
and the apostle of democracy,
Francisco Madero.[6]                                                      205

I am
the black-shawled
faithful women
who die with me
or live                                                                   210
depending on the time and place.
I am
faithful
humble
Juan Diego,                                                               215

---

4. Commonly used name for *Guardia Rural* (Rural Guard), a mounted police force (1861–1914) established by the Juárez regime.
5. *Yaqui . . . Español*: different national and ethnic peoples that make up the Mexican nation.
6. Francisco Indalecio Madero (1873–1913) led the Mexican Revolution and became president of Mexico (1911–13). *Díaz*: Porfirio Díaz (1830–1915), Mexican dictator. *Huerta*: General Victoriano Huerta (1854–1916), Mexican revolutionary leader and provisional president (1913–14).

the Virgin of Guadalupe,
Tonantzin, Aztec goddess, too.[7]

I rode the mountains of San Joaquín.
I rode east and north
    as far as the Rocky Mountains,           220
              and
all men feared the guns of
              Joaquín Murrieta.
I killed those men who dared
    to steal my mine,           225
       who raped and killed
               my love
               my wife.
Then
I killed to stay alive.           230
I was Elfego Baca,[8]
    living my nine lives fully.
I was the Espinoza brothers
    of the Valle de San Luis.[9]
All           235
were added to the number of heads
that
    in the name of civilization
were placed on the wall of independence,
heads of brave men           240
who died for cause or principle,
good or bad.

        Hidalgo! Zapata!
         Murrieta! Espinozas!
are but a few.           245
They
dared to face
the force of tyranny
        of men
         who rule           250
        by deception and hypocrisy.

I stand here looking back,
and now I see
        the present,
and still           255
        I am the campesino,[1]
        I am the fat political coyote—
               I,

7. Tonantzin was an Aztec goddess. *Juan Diego*: Saint Juan Diego Cuauhtlatoatzin (1474–1548), Mexican religious icon, possibly mythical.
8. Deputy sheriff of Socorro, New Mexico; a folk hero for having singlehandedly fought off a group of Texas cowboys.
9. In the San Luis Valley of Colorado in the 1860s, Vivian and José Espinoza, Mexican-born folk heroes, engaged in guerilla warfare against the Anglos.
1. Farmworker.

of the same name,
                    Joaquín,                                    260
in a country that has wiped out
all my history,
                    stifled all my pride,
in a country that has placed a
different weight of indignity upon                             265
                    my
                        age-
                            old
                                burdened back.
                    Inferiority                                 270
is the new load. . . .

    The Indian has endured and still
emerged the winner,
    the Mestizo must yet overcome,
        And the gachupín will just ignore.                      275
    I look at myself
    and see part of me
who rejects my father and my mother
and dissolves into the melting pot
    to disappear in shame.                                      280
        I sometimes
        sell my brother out
        and reclaim him
for my own when society gives me
    token leadership                                            285
            in society's own name.

I am Joaquín,
who bleeds in many ways.
The altars of Moctezuma[2]
            I stained a bloody red.                             290
    My back of Indian slavery
            was stripped crimson
        from the whips of masters
        who would lose their blood so pure
        when revolution made them pay,                          295
standing against the walls of
    retribution.

            Blood
        has flowed from
                me                                              300
on every battlefield
                between
campesino, hacendado,[3]
        slave and master
                and                                             305

2. Second-to-last Aztec emperor (1466–1520),        3. Landowner.
reigned 1502–20.

revolution.
I jumped from the tower of Chapultepec[4]
    into the sea of fame—
my country's flag
    my burial shroud—          310
with Los Niños,[5]
      whose pride and courage
could not surrender
    with indignity
      their country's flag         315
to strangers . . . in their land.
Now
    I bleed in some smelly cell
    from club
    or gun         320
    or tyranny.

I bleed as the vicious gloves of hunger
    cut my face and eyes,
as I fight my way from stinking barrios
    to the glamour of the ring        325
      and lights of fame
      or mutilated sorrow.

My blood runs pure on the ice-caked
hills of the Alaskan isles,
on the corpse-strewn beach of Normandy,    330
the foreign land of Korea
        and now
          Vietnam.[6]

Here I stand
        before the court of justice,    335
          guilty
for all the glory of my Raza
    to be sentenced to despair.
Here I stand,
    poor in money,        340
    arrogant with pride,
      bold with machismo,
      rich in courage
      and
      wealthy in spirit and faith.    345

My knees are caked with mud.
My hands calloused from the hoe.

4. Park on the outskirts of central Mexico City; Chapultepec Castle, the fortress on a hill there, was the first point of the U.S. assault on the city in 1847, in the Mexican American War (1845–48).
5. Los Niños Héroes, six military cadets who, at Chapultepec, famously gave their lives rather than surrendering during that battle.
6. During the Vietnam War, as on the Aleutian Islands (part of Alaska) during World War II; on the coast of Normandy (France), also during World II; and during the Korean War.

I have made the Anglo rich,
                yet
        equality is but a word—                                    350
                the Treaty of Hidalgo[7] has been broken
        and is but another treacherous promise.
My land is lost
                and stolen,
My culture has been raped.                                        355
                I lengthen
        the line at the welfare door
and fill the jails with crime.


                These then
are the rewards                                                    360
                this society has
for sons of chiefs
                and kings
                and bloody revolutionists,
who                                                                365
gave a foreign people
        all their skills and ingenuity
to pave the way with brains and blood
for
those hordes of gold-starved                                      370
                                strangers,
who
changed our language
and plagiarized our deeds
                                as feats of valor                 375
                                of their own.


They frowned upon our way of life
        and took what they could use.
                Our art,
                our literature,                                    380
                our music, they ignored—
so they left the real things of value
and grabbed at their own destruction
                by their greed and avarice.
They overlooked that cleansing fountain of                        385
                nature and brotherhood
        which is Joaquín.
                The art of our great señores,
                Diego Rivera,
                Siqueiros,                                         390
                Orozco,[8] is but
another act of revolution for
        the salvation of mankind.


---

7. The Treaty of Guadalupe Hidalgo (1848), which ended the Mexican American War, is discussed in the "Annexations" introduction, p. 165.

8. Diego Rivera (1886–1957), José David Alfaro Siqueiros (1896–1974), and José Clemente Orozco (1883–1949), Mexican muralists.

Mariachi music, the
    heart and soul
    of the people of the earth,
    the life of the child,
    and the happiness of love.         395

The corridos tell the tales
    of life and death,
        of tradition,         400
    legends old and new,
    of joy
        of passion and sorrow
    of the people—who I am.        405

I am in the eyes of woman,
        sheltered beneath
her shawl of black,
        deep and sorrowful
        eyes         410
that bear the pain of sons long buried
        or dying,
          dead
on the battlefield or on the barbed wire
        of social strife.        415

Her rosary she prays and fingers
endlessly
        like the family
working down a row of beets
         to turn around        420
         and work.
         and work.
         There is no end.
Her eyes a mirror of all the warmth
        and all the love for me,     425
and I am her
and she is me.
        We face life together in sorrow,
        anger, joy, faith and wishful
        thoughts.        430

I shed the tears of anguish
as I see my children disappear
behind the shroud of mediocrity,
never to look back to remember me.
I am Joaquín.        435
        I must fight
        and win this struggle
        for my sons, and they
        must know from me
        who I am.        440
Part of the blood that runs deep in me

could not be vanquished by the Moors.
I defeated them after five hundred years,
and I endured.
>           Part of the blood that is mine                           445
>           has labored endlessly four hundred
>           years under the heel of lustful
>                   Europeans.
>                   I am still here!

I have endured in the rugged mountains                               450
>   of our country.
I have survived the toils and slavery
>   of the fields.
>                   I have existed
in the barrios of the city                                           455
in the suburbs of bigotry
in the mines of social snobbery
in the prisons of dejection
in the muck of exploitation
and                                                                  460
in the fierce heat of racial hatred.


And now the trumpet sounds,
the music of the people stirs the
>                   revolution.
Like a sleeping giant it slowly                                      465
rears its head
to the sound of
>                   tramping feet
>                   clamoring voices
>                   mariachi strains                                 470
>               fiery tequila explosions
>           the smell of chile verde and
>       soft brown eyes of expectation for a
>                                   better life.

And in all the fertile farmlands,                                    475
>                   the barren plains,
the mountain villages,
smoke-smeared cities,
>                   we start to MOVE.

>   La Raza!                                                         480
Méjicano!
>   Español!
>       Latino!
>           Hispano!
>               Chicano!                                             485
or whatever I call myself,
>           I look the same
>           I feel the same

I cry
and         490
sing the same.

I am the masses of my people and
I refuse to be absorbed.
I am Joaquín.
The odds are great        495
but my spirit is strong,
         my faith unbreakable,
         my blood is pure.
I am Aztec prince and Christian Christ.
       I SHALL ENDURE!      500
       I WILL ENDURE!

               1967

---

# PEDRO JUAN SOTO
## 1928–2002

This prominent Puerto Rican author from the town of Cataño is part of a widely recognized group of island-born writers—among them René Marqués and José Luis González—who lived for periods in the United States and have been labeled by critics the Generation of 1950. These writers were among the first to pay attention to the Puerto Rican migrant experience. Soto, a supporter of Puerto Rico's independence from the United States, underscored the psychological impact of cultural dilemmas faced by working-class Puerto Rican migrants in the New York metropolis during the years of the Great Migration.

In 1946, after graduating from high school, Soto left Puerto Rico for the United States, to pursue premedical studies at Long Island University. But he abandoned his original career goal in favor of a degree in English literature. During his college years, he wrote for several of New York City's Spanish-language newspapers, but his activities were interrupted by a year of military service during the Korean War.

Upon his discharge, Soto enrolled at Teachers' College of Columbia University, where he received a master's degree in 1953. A year later, he returned to Puerto Rico to work for the División para la Educación de la Comunidad (Division for Community Education; DIVEDCO), a culture-dissemination agency of the Puerto Rican government. That same year, his short story "Los inocentes" (The Innocents) received the second prize in a literary contest sponsored by the Ateneo Puertorriqueño (Puerto Rican Athenaeum), one of the main cultural institutions of Puerto Rico. The story focuses on the dislocating effects of the migratory experience on a Puerto Rican family living in New York. It also reveals the strong influence on Soto's work of the American modernist fiction writer William Faulkner.

In 1956, Soto collected most of his short stories about the perils of Puerto Rican life in New York into the highly acclaimed volume *Spiks*. Written in Spanish, *Spiks* was widely read in Puerto Rico and other Spanish-speaking countries, but was little known in the United States until its English translation in 1973. Soto's first two novels, *Usmaíl* (1956) and *Ardiente suelo, fría estación* (Hot Land, Cold Season, 1961), powerfully indict the multiple effects of American colonialism on the lives of Puerto Ricans.

In the early 1970s, Soto was a visiting professor at the State University of New York at Buffalo, teaching in the newly established program in Puerto Rican Studies. He later returned to the island and for many years was a faculty member at the University of Puerto Rico. Until his death, Soto continued writing novels, plays, and essays, focusing primarily on political issues affecting Puerto Rico and the Caribbean region. Only his first two novels have been translated into English. In 1982, his novel *Un oscuro pueblo sonriente* (A Dark but Smiling People, 1982) won the prestigious Casa de las Américas Prize. Still unpublished is a diary Soto worked on surrounding the assassination of his son, Carlos Soto Arriví, and Soto Arriví's friend Arnaldo Darío Rosado, by the Puerto Rican police in 1978. The young men, pro-independence activists, were ambushed after being led by an undercover agent to sabotage a transmission tower at Cerro Maravilla as a symbolic protest against the long imprisonment of Puerto Rican nationalists. Soto spent his later years in a legal battle, against island and federal authorities, over the killings.

---

## FROM SPIKS[1]

### The Innocents

*Climb to the sun on that cloud with the pigeons without horses without women and not smell when they burn the tin cans in the lot without people to make fun of me*

From the window, wearing the suit made and sold to fit the man he was not, he saw the pigeons hovering under the caves across the way.

*or with doors and windows always open to have wings*

He began to flap his hands and make noises like the pigeons when he heard the voice behind him.

"Baby, baby."

The shriveled woman was seated at the table (under it was the flimsy suitcase fastened with rope, its only key), watching him with intense eyes, sunk in her chair like a hungry and abandoned cat.

"Pan," he said.

Giving it a light nudge away from the table, the woman pushed the chair out and went to the cupboard. She got the piece of bread that was lying exposed on the boxes of rice and took it to the man, who was still gesticulating and mouthing sounds.

*to be a pigeon*

"Don' make noise, Pipe."

He crumbled the piece of bread on the window sill without paying attention to her.

"Don' make noise, baby."

The men playing dominoes under the store awning were looking up.

1. Translated by Victoria Ortiz.

He stopped moving his tongue.

*without people to make fun of me*

"A pasiar a la plaza," he said.

"Yes. Hortensia's comin to take you for a walk."

"A la plaza."

"No, not to the plaza. They took it away. It flew away."

He pouted. He listened again to the fluttering of the pigeons.

"No, it wasn' the pigeons," she said. "It was the Evil One, the Devil."

"Ah."

"You have to pray to Papá Dios to bring back the plaza."

"Papá Dios," he said, looking outside. "Trai la plaza y el río . . ."

"No, no. Don' open yer mouth," she said. "Kneel down an talk to Papá Dios without openin yer mouth."

He knelt in front of the window, joined his hands and looked out over the roofs.

*want to be a pigeon*

She looked out below, at the idleness of the men on a Saturday morning and the briskness of the women hurrying to and from the market.

Slowly, sorrowfully, but erect, as if balancing a bundle on her head, she walked toward the room where her daughter, in front of the mirror, was taking the pins out of her hair and piling them on the bureau top.

"Don' take him today, Hortensia."

The younger woman glanced at her out of the corner of her eye.

"Don' start that again, mama. Nothin ain gonna happen to him. They'll take good care of him and it don' cost us nothin."

As it was freed from the pins, her hair fell over her ears in a pile of tight curls.

"But I know how to take care of him. He's my boy. Who knows better than me?"

Hortensia studied the slight and slender figure in the mirror.

"Yer old, mama."

A fleshless hand appeared in the mirror.

"I ain dead yet. I can still take care of him."

"It ain that."

The curls were still tight, despite her attempts to loosen them with the comb.

"Pipe's innocent," said the mother, her words water for a sea of grief. "He's a baby."

Hortensia put the comb down. She took a pencil from the open bag on the dresser and began to blacken her scanty brows.

"You can't cure that," she said to the mirror. "You know it. Tha's why the best thing is . . ."

"In Puerto Rico this wouldn' of happened."

"In PR it was different," said Hortensia over her shoulder. "People knew him. He could go out because people knew him. But in New York people don' care and you don' even know yer neighbors. Life's tough. Its years an years I been sewin and sewin an I ain even married yet."

Looking for the lipstick, she saw her mother's face crumble in the mirror.

"But that ain the reason either. They can take better care of him there."

"Tha's what you say," said the mother.

Hortensia tossed the makeup and comb into her bag and closed it. She turned: flimsy blouse, gleaming lips, blackened eyebrows, tight curls.

"After a year here, we deserve somethin better."

"It ain his fault what happens to us."

"But its gonna be if he stays here. Jus look."

She darted at her mother, taking her arm and pushing up the short sleeve. On the loose upper arm was a purple blotch.

"He raised his hand to you already, an me in the factory I aint easy thinkin what could be happenin with you an him. An with this already . . ."

"He didn' mean it," said the mother, pulling her sleeve down and looking at the floor as she twisted her arm so that Hortensia would let go.

"He didn' mean it, with one hand on yer throat? If I hadn' of grabbed that bottle, God only knows. We ain gotta man aroun to stand up to him, an I'm turnin into a wreck an yer scared of him."

"He's a baby," said the mother in her docile voice, drawing into her body like a snail.

Hortensia half closed her eyes.

"Don' start with that again. I'm young an I got my life in fron of me an he ain. Yer tired too an if he wasn' here you could live better fer the years you got left an you know it but you don' dare say it cause yer scared its wrong but I say it for you *yer tired* an tha's why you signed those papers cause you know that in that place they take better care of him an then you can sit an watch the people go by in the street an when you want you get up an go out an walk aroun like them but you'd rather think it's a crime an that *I'm* the criminal so you can be a martyred mother an *you bein a martyred mother* can't deny that but you gotta think of yerself an me. Cause if that horse threw him when he was ten . . ."

The mother left the room quickly, as if pushed, as if the room itself blew her out, while Hortensia was saying: ". . . an the other twenty years he lived like that, senseless . . ."

She turned to watch her leave, without following, leaning on the dresser where she now felt her fists hammering out a beat for her near scream.

". . . we lived them with him."

In the mirror she caught sight of the hysterical carnival mask that was her face.

*and there's no roosters and there's no dogs and there's no bells and there's no river wind and there's no movie buzzer and the sun doesn't come in here and I don't like*

"Enough," said the mother, bending over to brush the crumbs off the sill. The throng of kids hit and chased a rubber ball down the street.

*and the cold sleeps sits walks here inside and I don't like it*

"Enough, baby, enough. Say Amen."

"Amen."

She helped him get up and put his hat in his hand, seeing that Hortensia, serious and red-eyed, was coming toward them.

"Les go, Pipe. Give mama a kiss."

She put her bag on the table and bent down to pick up the suitcase. The mother threw herself on his neck—her hands like pliers—and kissed the burned hazelnut of a face, smoothing her fingers over the skin she had shaved that morning.

"Les go," said Hortensia, carrying bag and suitcase.

He wriggled out of his mother's arms and walked to the door, swinging the hand which carried the hat.

"Baby, put on yer hat," said the mother, and she blinked so that he would not see her tears.

Turning, he raised it and left it on top of his vaselined hair, so small it looked like a toy, as if it wanted to compensate for the waste of material in the suit.

"No, leave it here," said Hortensia.

Pipe pouted. The mother fixed her eyes on Hortensia and her chin trembled.

"Okay," said Hortensia, "carry it in yer hand."

He walked again to the door and his mother followed, hunching over a bit now and holding back the arms that wanted to stretch out toward him.

Hortensia stopped her.

"Mama, they're gonna take care of him."

"I don' want them to beat . . ."

"No. There's doctors. An you . . . every other week. I'll take you."

They both made an effort to keep their voices steady.

"Go lie down, mama."

"Tell him to stay there . . . not to make noise an to eat everythin."

"Yeah."

Hortensia opened the door and looked out to see if Pipe had stayed on the landing. He was amusing himself by spitting over the bannister and watching the saliva.

"I'll be home early, mama."

The mother stood next to the chair that was already superfluous, trying to see him through the body which blocked the entrance.

"Lie down, mama."

The mother did not answer. With her hands joined in front of her, she was rigid until her chest and her shoulders shook convulsively and the delicate and gulping sobbing began.

Hortensia pulled the door shut and went hurriedly downstairs with Pipe. Facing the immense clarity of a June midday, she longed for hurricanes and eclipses and snowfalls.

# The Champ

The cue made a last swing over the green felt, hit the cue ball and cracked it against the fifteen ball. The stubby, yellowish hands remained motionless until the ball went "clop" into the pocket and then raised the cue until it was diagonally in front of the acned, fatuous countenance: the tight little vaselined curl fell tidily over the forehead, the ear clipped a cigarette, the glance was oblique and mocking, and the mustache's scarce fuzz had been accentuated with pencil.

"Wha' happen, man?" said the sharp voice. "That was a champ shot, hey?"

Then he started to laugh. His squat, greasy body became a cheerfully quaking blob inside the tight jeans and the sweaty T-shirt.

He contemplated Gavilán—the eyes, too wise, didn't look so wise now; the three-day beard tried to camouflage the face's ill temper, but didn't make it; the long-ashed cigarette kept the lips shut tight, obscene words wading in back of them—and enjoyed the feat he had perpetrated. He had beaten him in two straight games. Gavilán had been six months in jail, sure, but that didn't matter now. What mattered was that he had lost two games with him, whom these victories placed in a privileged position. They placed him above the others, over the best players in the neighborhood and over the ones who belittled him for being nothing but a sixteen-year-old, nothing but a "baby." Now nobody could cut him out of his spot in Harlem. He was the *new one*, the successor to Gavilán and other individuals worthy of respect. He was the same as . . . no. He was better, on account of his youth: he had more time and opportunities to surpass all their feats.

He felt like running out into the street and shouting, "I won two straight games from Gavilán! Speak out now! C'mon, say something now!" He didn't do it. He only chalked his cue and told himself it wasn't worth the trouble. It was sunny out, but it was Saturday and the neighbors would be at the market place at this hour of the morning. He would have no more audience than snot-nosed kids and disinterested grannies. Anyway, a little humility suited champs well.

He picked up the quarter Gavilán threw on the felt and exchanged a conceited smile with the scorekeeper and the three spectators.

"Collect yours," he told the scorekeeper, hoping that some spectator would move to the other pool tables to spread the news, to comment how he—Puruco, the too-fat kid with the pimply face and the comic voice—had made a fool of the great Gavilán. It seemed, however, that they were waiting for another show.

He put away his fifteen cents and said to Gavilán, who was wiping his sweaty face, "Play another?"

"Let's," Gavilán said, taking from the rack another cue that he would chalk meticulously.

The scorer took down the triangular rack and shaped up the balls for the next round.

Puruco broke, and immediately began to whistle and pace around the table with a springy walk, almost on the tips of his sneakers.

Gavilán came up to the cue ball with his characteristic heaviness, and centered it, but didn't hit it yet. He simply raised his very shaggy head, his body still bent over the cue and the felt, and said, "Hey, quit the whistle."

"Okay, man," Puruco said, and twirled his cue until he heard Gavilán's shot and the balls went running around and clashed again. None of them went home.

"*Ay, bendito*," Puruco laughed. "Got this man like dead."

He hit number one, which went in and left number two lined up for the left pocket. Number two also dropped in. He could not stop smiling toward the corners of the parlor. He seemed to invite the spiders, the flies, and the numbers bookies dispersed among the bystanders at the other pool tables, to take a look at this.

He carefully studied the position of each ball. He wanted to win this other set, too, to take advantage of his recent reading of Willie Hoppe's book,[1] and all that month-after-month practicing, when he had been the butt of his opponents. Last year he was just a little pisspot; now the real life was beginning for him, the life of a champ. Once he beat Gavilán, he would lick Mamerto and Bimbo . . .

"Make way for Puruco!" the cool men would say. And he would make it with the owners of the pool parlors, gather good connections. He'd be body-guard to some, and buddy-buddy to others. Cigarettes and beer for free, he would have. And women, not the scared, stupid chicks who went no further than some squeezing at the movies. From there, right into fame: big man in the neighborhood, the one and only guy for any job—the numbers, the narco racket,[2] the broad from Riverside Drive[2] slumming in the neighborhood, this gang's rumble with that one to settle "manly things."

With a grunt, he missed the three ball and cursed. Gavilán was right behind him when he turned.

"Watch out puttin' foofoo[3] on me!" he said, ruffling up.

And Gavilán:

"Ah, stop that."

"No. Don't give me that, man, just 'cause yuh losin'?"

Gavilán did not answer. He centered the cue ball through the smoke which wrinkled his features, and pocketed two balls in opposite sides.

"See?" Puruco said, and he crossed his fingers to protect himself.

"Shaddup yuh mouth!"

Gavilán tried to ricochet the five in, but failed. Puruco studied the position of his ball and settled for the farthest but surest pocket. While aiming, he realized that he would have to uncross his fingers. He looked at Gavilán suspiciously and crossed his legs to shoot. He missed.

When he looked up, Gavilán was smiling and sucking his upper gums to spit his pyorrhea. Now he had no doubt that he was the victim of a spell.

"No foolin', man. Play it clean." Gavilán gazed at him with surprise, stepping on the cigarette distractedly.

"What's the matter?"

"No," Puruco said. "Don't you go on with that *bilongo*!"[4]

"Hey!" Gavilán laughed. "This one t'inks a lot about witches."

He put the cue behind his back, feinted once, and pocketed the ball easily. He pocketed again in the next shot, and in the next. Puruco began to get nervous. Either Gavilán was recovering his ability, or else that voodoo spell was pushing his cue. If he didn't get to raise his score, Gavilán would win this set.

---

1. William Frederick Hoppe (1887–1959), an internationally famous American billiards champion, published two books: *Thirty Years of Billiards* (1925) and *Billiards as It Should Be Played* (1941).
2. Thoroughfare on Manhattan's Upper West Side, associated with upscale residences. The

*numbers*: a kind of gambling, in which people bet on combinations of digits, such as regularly published ones. *The narco racket*: selling narcotics.
3. Putting a curse or magic spell.
4. Curse or magic spell (Afro-Caribbean religious dialect).

Chalking his cue, he touched wood three times and awaited his turn. Gavilán missed his fifth shot. Then Puruco eyed the distance. He hit, putting in the eight. He pulled a combination shot to pocket the eleven with the nine. The nine went home later. He caromed the twelve in, and then missed the ten. Gavilán also missed it. Finally Puruco managed to send it in, but for ball thirteen he almost ripped the felt. He added the score in his head. About eight more to call it quits—he could relax a little.

The cigarette went from behind his ear to his lips. When he lit it, turning his back to the table so that the fan would not blow out the match, he saw the sly smile of the scorekeeper. He turned around rapidly and caught Gavilán right in the act: feet lifted off the floor, body leaning against the table rim to make an easy shot. Before he could speak, Gavilán had pocketed the ball.

"Hey, man!"

"Wha' happen?" Gavilán said calmly, eyeing the next shot.

"Don't you pull that on me, boy! You can't beat me that way."

Gavilán raised an eyebrow at him, and bit the inside of his mouth while making a snout.

"Wha's hurtin' you?" he said.

"No, like that no!" Puruco jerked his arms open and almost hit the scorekeeper with his cue. He threw the cigarette down violently and said to the onlookers, "You seen it, right?"

"See wha'?" said Gavilán, unmoved.

"Nothin', that dirty play," squealed Puruco. "T'ink I'm stupid?"

"Aw, man," Gavilán laughed. "Don't you go askin' me, maybe I tell you."

Puruco struck the table rim with the cue.

"With me you gotta play fair. You ain't satisfied with puttin' a spell on me first, but after you put me on with cheatin'."

"Who cheatin'?" Gavilán said. He left the cue on the table and, smiling, moved closer to Puruco. "You say I'm cheatin'?"

"No," Puruco said, changing his tone, babying his voice, wavering on his feet. "But that's no way to play, man. They seen you."

Gavilán turned to the others.

"I been cheatin'?"

Only the scorekeeper shook his head. The others said nothing and looked away.

"But like he's lyin' on the table, man," Puruco said.

Gavilán clutched the T-shirt as if by chance, baring the pudgy back as he pulled him over.

"Me, nobody call me a cheatin' man."

The playing had stopped at all the other pool tables. The rest of the people watched from a distance. Nothing was heard but the buzz of the fan and the flies, and the screaming of children in the street.

"You t'ink a pile of crap like you gonna call me a cheater?" Gavilán said, forcing his fist against Puruco's chest, ripping the shirt. "I let you win two tables so you have somethin' to put on, and now you t'ink you king. Get outta here, jerk," he said between his teeth. "When you grow up we'll see ya."

The push threw Puruco against the plaster wall, where his back smashed flat. The crash filled the silence with holes. Somebody laughed, tittering. Somebody said: "He a bragger."

"An' get outta here before I kick you for good," Gavilán said.

"'Kay man," Puruco stammered, dropping the cue.

Out he went without daring to raise his eyes, hearing cues clicking again on the tables, and some giggles. On the street, he felt like crying, but held it in. That was for sissies. The blow didn't hurt; that other thing—"When you grow up we'll see ya"—hurt more. He was a full-grown man. If they beat him, if they killed him, let them do it paying no mind at all to his being a sixteen-year-old. He was a man already. He could do a lot of damage, plenty of damage, and he could also survive it.

He crossed over to the other sidewalk, furiously kicked a beer can, his hands, from inside the pockets, pinching his body nailed to the cross of adolescence.

Two sets he had let him win, Gavilán said. Dirty lie. He knew he would lose every one of them to him, from now on, to the new champ. He had pulled the voodoo stuff on account of that, on account of that the cheating, the blow on account of that. Oh, but those three other men would spread the news of Gavilán's fall. After that, Mamerto and Bimbo. Nobody could stop him now. The neighborhood, the whole world, would be his.

When the barrel hoop got trapped between his legs, he kicked it aside. He gave a slap to the kid who came to pick it up.

"Careful, man, or I knock yuh eye out," he growled.

And he went on walking, unconcerned with the mother who cursed him and ran toward the tearful kid. Lips held tight, he inhaled deeply. At his passing, he could see confetti falling and cheers pouring from the closed and deserted windows.

He was a champ. He was on the lookout only for harm.

## Scribbles

The clock said seven and he woke up for a moment. His wife wasn't in bed and the children weren't on their cot. He buried his head under the pillow to close out the racket coming from the kitchen. He didn't open his eyes again until ten, forced to by Graciela's shaking.

He rubbed his small eyes and wiped away the bleariness, only to see his wife's broad body standing firmly in front of the bed in that defiant attitude. He heard her loud voice and it seemed to be coming directly from her navel.

"So? You figured you'd spend your whole life in bed? Looks like you're the one with a bad belly, but I'm carryin the kid."

He still didn't look at her face. He fixed his eyes on the swollen stomach, on the ball of flesh that daily grew and threatened to burst the robe's belt.

"Hurry and get up, you damned good-for-nothin! Or do you want me to throw water on you?"

He shouted at the open legs and the arms akimbo, the menacing stomach, the angry face: "I get up when I want to and not when you tell me. Hell! Who do you think you are?"

He turned his face back into the sheets and smelled the Brilliantine stains on the pillow and the stale sweat on the bedspread.

She felt overpowered by the man's inert mass: the silent threat of those still arms, the enormous lizard his body was.

Biting her lips, she drowned her reproaches and went back to the kitchen, leaving the room with the sputtering candle for Saint Lazarus on the dresser, the Holy Palm from last Palm Sunday[1] and the religious prints hanging on the wall.

They lived in the basement. But even though they lived miserably, it was a roof over them. Even though overhead the other tenants stamped and swept, even though garbage rained through the cracks, she thanked her saints for having someplace to live. But Rosendo still didn't have a job. Not even the saints could find him one. Always in the clouds, more concerned with his own madness than with his family.

She felt she was going to cry. Nowadays she cried so easily. Thinking: *Holy God all I do is have kid after kid like a bitch and that man doesn't bother to look for work because he likes the government to support us by mail while he spends his time out there watching the four winds like Crazy John[2] and saying he wants to be an artist.*

She stopped her sobs by gritting her teeth, closing off the complaints which struggled to become cries, returning sobs and complaints to the well of her nerves, where they would remain until hysteria opened them a path and transformed them into insults for her husband, or a spanking for the children, or a supplication to the Virgin of Succour.[3]

She sat down at the table, watching her children run through the kitchen. Thinking of the Christmas tree they wouldn't have and the other children's toys that tomorrow hers would envy. Because tonight is Christmas Eve and tomorrow is Christmas.

"Now I shoot you and you fall down dead!"

The children were playing under the table.

"Children, don' make so much noise, *bendito*."[4]

"I'm Gene Autry!"[5] said the oldest one.

"An I'm Palong Cassidy!"[6]

"Children, I gotta headache, for God's sake . . ."

"You ain Palong Nobody! You the bad guy and I kill you!"

"No! Maaaaaaaa!"

Graciela twisted her body and put her head under the table to see them fighting.

---

1. Palm branches symbolize Jesus Christ's entry in Jerusalem, an event commemorated on this Christian holiday. *Saint Lazarus*: reputed first bishop of Marseille (d. second half of first century); in the Roman Catholic Church, he is celebrated on June 21, a few months after Palm Sunday.
2. In the original, Spanish-language version of this story, the reference is to Juan Bobo, a silly, mischievous, distracted, and simpleminded country boy in Puerto Rican rural folktales. Soto is indicating that the character's head is in the clouds.

3. The Virgen del Perpetuo Socorro (Our Lady of Perpetual Succour, or Perpetual Help), a fifteenth-century icon venerated by the Roman Catholic Church.
4. Literally, blessed; figuratively, for the love of God (shortened from the expression *bendito sea Dios*).
5. American actor and singer (1907–1998) known as the Singing Cowboy.
6. I.e., Hopalong Cassidy, an American cowboy-hero, created in 1904 and appearing in stories, novels, and movies.

"Boys, geddup from under there! *Maldita sea mi vida*. What a life. ROSENDO, HURRY AND GET UP!"

The kids were running through the room again, one of them shouting and laughing, the other crying.

"ROSENDO!"

Rosendo drank his coffee and ignored his wife's insults.

"Waddaya figure on doin today, lookin for work or goin from store to store and from bar to bar drawin all those bums?"

He drank his breakfast coffee, biting his lips distractedly, smoking his last cigarette between sips. She circled the table, rubbing her hand over her belly to calm the movement of the fetus.

"I guess you'll go with those good-for-nothin friends of yours and gamble with some borrowed money, thinkin that manna's gonna fall from the sky today."

"Lemme alone, woman . . ."

"Yeah, its always the same: lemme alone. Tomorrow's Christmas and those kids ain gonna have no presents."

"Kings Day's[7] in January . . ."

"Kings don' come to New York. Santa Claus comes to New York!"

"Well, anyhow, whoever comes, we'll see . . ."

"Holy Mother of God! What a father, my God! You only care about your scribbles. The artist! A grown man like you."

He left the table and went to the bedroom, tired of hearing the woman. He looked out the only window. All the snow that had fallen day after day was filthy. The cars had flattened and blackened it on the pavement. On the sidewalks it had been trampled and pissed on by men and dogs. The days were colder now that the snow was there, hostile, ugly, at home with misery. Denuded of all the innocence it had had the first day.

It was a murky street, under heavy air, on a grandiosely opaque day.

Rosendo went to the bureau and took a bundle of papers from the drawer. Sitting on the window sill, he began to examine them. There were all the paper bags he had collected to tear up and draw on. He drew at night, while the woman and children slept. From memory he drew the drunken faces, the anguished faces of the people of Harlem: everything seen and shared during his daytime wanderings.

Graciela said he was in his second childhood. If he spent time away from the grumbling woman and the crying children, exploring absentmindedly in his penciled sketches, the woman muttered and sneered.

Tomorrow was Christmas and she was worried because the children wouldn't have presents. She didn't know that this afternoon he would collect ten dollars for the sign he painted yesterday at the corner bar. He was saving that surprise for Graciela. Like he was saving the surprise about her present.

---

7. El Día de los Reyes, also known as Three Kings Day, a Christian holiday that celebrates the biblical story of the Magi, the three kings who followed the star of Bethlehem to bring gifts to the newborn Jesus Christ. Until the 1960s, Santa Claus did not figure prominently in island Puerto Ricans' celebrations of Christmas, and the figure's introduction into Puerto Rico was seen by some writers as a sign of Americanization.

For Graciela he would paint a picture. A picture that would summarize their life together, in the midst of deprivation and frustration. A painting with a melancholy similarity to those photographs taken at saints' day parties in Bayamón.[8] The photographs from the days of their engagement, part of the family's album of memories: they were both leaning against a high stool, on the front of which were the words "Our Love" or "Forever Together." Behind was the backdrop with palm trees and the sea and a golden paper moon.

Graciela would certainly be pleased to know that in his memory nothing had died. Maybe afterward she wouldn't sneer at his efforts anymore.

Lacking materials, he would have to do the picture on a wall, and with charcoal. But it would be his, from his hands, made for her.

Into the building's boiler went all the old and useless wood the super collected. From there Rosendo took the charcoal he needed. Then he went through the basement looking for a wall. It couldn't be in the bedroom. Graciela wouldn't let him take down her prints and palms.

The kitchen wall was too cracked and grimy.

He had no choice but to use the bathroom. It was the only room left.

"If you need to go to the bathroom," he said to his wife, "wait or use the pot. I have to fix some pipes."

He closed the door and cleaned the wall of nails and spiders' webs. He sketched out his idea: a man on horseback, naked and muscled, leaning down to embrace a woman, also naked, wrapped in a mane of black hair from which the night bloomed.

Meticulously, patiently, he repeatedly retouched the parts that didn't satisfy him. After a few hours he decided to go out and get the ten dollars he was owed and buy a tree and toys for his children. On the way he'd get colored chalks at the candy store. This picture would have the sea, and palm trees, and the moon. Tomorrow was Christmas.

Graciela was coming and going in the basement, scolding the children, putting away the laundry, watching the lighted burners on the stove.

He put on his patched coat.

"I'm gonna get a tree for the kids. Don Pedro owes me ten bucks."

She smiled, thanking the saints for the miracle of the ten dollars.

That night he returned to the basement smelling of whiskey and beer. The children had already gone to sleep. He put up the tree in a corner of the kitchen and surrounded the trunk with presents.

He ate rice and fritters, without hunger, absorbed in what he would do later. From time to time he glanced at Graciela, looking for a smile that did not appear.

He moved the chipped coffee cup, put the chalk on the table, and looked in his pocket for the cigarette he didn't have.

"I erased all those drawins."

He forgot all about the cigarette.

"So now you're paintin filth?"

---

8. Municipality in northeastern Puerto Rico.

He dropped his smile into the abyss of reality.

"You don' have no more shame . . ."

His blood became cold water.

". . . makin yer children look at that filth, that indecency . . . I erased them and that's that and I don' want it to happen again."

He wanted to strike her but the desire was paralyzed in some part of his being, without reaching his arms, without becoming uncontrolled fury in his fists.

When he rose from the chair he felt all of him emptying out through his feet. All of him had been wiped out by a wet rag and her hands had squeezed him out of the world.

He went to the bathroom. Nothing of his remained. Only the nails, bent and rusted, returned to their holes. Only the spiders, returned to their spinning.

The wall was no more than the wide and clear gravestone of his dreams.

## Bayaminiña

From the distance, if one went by its colors, it was a snappy little cart parked on the corner of 116th street. It had blue, red, and yellow stripes, and the box on top—full of cod fritters, blood sausage, and banana fritters—had glass on all four sides. From close, however, you could see that its snappiness was no more than a front that disguised the wear and tear and the rot which were consuming it from the wheels up to the push bar. On a piece of tin nailed to the front you could read in red, shaky letters: BAYAMINIÑA[1]

But no one paid attention to the cart. The crowd was watching the argument between the vendor and the policeman. The black women heading toward Lenox Avenue stopped in their rapid, ass-swinging tracks to see how it would all end. The customers in the nearby bar neglected their drinks and the TV set to follow the altercation through the glass window. And curiosity even turned heads in passing cars and busses.

"I pay no more," the vendor was saying, tense. "I pay las year other fine . . ."

The policeman only shook his head as he finished scribbling in his notebook.

"This has nothing to do with last year, buddy."

"I got no money. I no pay more."

"And the fine you'll have to pay next year will be a bigger one, if you don't get rid of that thing there."

"You're killing me," said the vendor. "Why you do this?"

"The Department of Health . . ."

"Okay, you gimme a job an I . . ."

". . . is after you guys."

"I have to eat," said the vendor. "Don't gimme no fine, gimme a job."

1. From *Vaya, mi niña,* an exclamatory phrase or flirtatious comment ("Hey, babe" or "Wow, girl") commonly used in Puerto Rico; an indication that the street vendor has not had much formal schooling but loves his colorful cart, from which he sells *cuchifritos* (literally, "fried pig"; figuratively, "Puerto Rican soul food").

"I have nothing to do with that," said the policeman. He put the summons in one of the vendor's pockets and added: "You keep that . . . And remember to go to court."

The vendor took out the summons, furious, and tried to read it. But he could understand no more than the numbers.

"All right, break it up," the policeman said to the crowd. And to the vendor: "And you get going before I lose my patience."

The vendor turned to the school kids, slight and cinnamon-colored like him.

"These bastards," he said to them in Spanish. "Sia la madre d'ehtos policías!"[2]

"C'mon," said the policeman. "Get the hell out of here."

Suddenly the vendor bent over, picked up the rock which served as the cart's brake, and stood up again with it in his fist. His face was already crumpling with a coming sob.

"Gimme a job, saramabich!"

"You'd better get your ass out of this neighborhood before I throw you in jail!" said the policeman, not raising his eyes from the threatening fist while moving his hand to his gun holster.

The vendor hesitated, grimaced angrily, turned, and threw himself on the cart. Crash! went the panes and crack! the wood. And he shrieked: "Gimme a job, saramabich, gimme a job!"

And the tin—clank! clank!—where you could still read BAYAMINIÑA, turned dirty with blood, spattered with tears, and, freed from its nails, once again became a tin can.

1956

2. Damn the mother of these policemen! (grammatical contraction of the Spanish expression *Maldita sea la madre de estos policías*).

---

# PIRI THOMAS
## b. 1928

Born Juan Pedro Tomás in New York's Spanish Harlem, where he grew up during the years of the Great Depression, Piri Thomas became the most conspicuous voice of the Puerto Rican migrant experience at a time when Puerto Rican writers on the mainland were unable to penetrate the U.S. publishing establishment or develop a mainstream readership. The publication of his autobiographical novel *Down These Mean Streets* (1967)—chapter 4 of which, "Alien Turf," is excerpted here—reflected the incipient interest of publishing houses in having ethnic writers relate their experiences of growing up in the urban ghettos of the United States, besieged by racial and social strife.

Written along the lines of African American testimonials such as Claude Brown's autobiographical novel *Manchild in the Promised Land* (1965), Malcolm X and Alex Haley's *Autobiography of Malcolm X* (1965), and Eldridge Cleaver's autobiographical essay collection *Soul on Ice* (1968), *Down These Mean Streets* is a bildungsroman, or growing-up narrative, about a life derailed by racism, poverty, social marginality, and self-destructive behavior. The book's title comes from "The Simple Art of Murder," an essay by the American crime writer Raymond Chandler about the literary tradition of the murder mystery: "Down these mean streets a man must go who is not himself mean." The narrative is built on such a premise: The protagonist is a fragile adolescent caught up in a thorny environment that pushes him to extreme behavior. In *The New York Times Book Review* (May 21, 1967), the fiction writer and critic Daniel Stern described the book as "something of a linguistic event. Gutter language, Spanish imagery and personal poetics . . . mingle into a kind of individual statement that has very much its own sound."

Thomas is the son of a light-skinned Puerto Rican mother and a dark-skinned Cuban father. As a young black Latino, he frequently felt denied an "American" identity by U.S. society. At the same time, Puerto Ricans often viewed him not as one of them but as simply a black man. He was involved with barrio gangs, became a drug addict, and landed in prison after being wounded when he participated in an attempted armed robbery at a nightclub. These experiences, as well as his difficult rehabilitation process and quest for a productive life, are at the core of most of his writings. The television documentary *The World of Piri Thomas* (1968), narrated by Thomas, dramatically renders the harsh realities of barrio life and illustrates how the author turned the mistakes of his youth into a personal triumph.

The ordeals and identity crisis that dominate *Down These Mean Streets* were followed by those narrated in *Saviour, Saviour, Hold My Hand* (1972), an account of the period after Thomas's release from prison and of his rehabilitation through love, religion, and creativity. His third novel, *Seven Long Times* (1974), chronicles the seven years the author spent in the dehumanizing environment of the New York penal system. Thomas had shown promise as a writer during his high school years. In prison, he wrote as a way of liberating his mind. As he stated in an interview:

> I promised myself not to serve time, but to have time serve me. . . . I began to tell the paper a story, and in the process I could feel memories being drawn out of me. I could feel the conversations of long ago, but instead of hearing them, I was feeling them over again. I learned to transpose those feelings into words. I had halfway failed English and my spelling was pretty lousy, but I just kept on going. If I could not spell the words, I would write them phonetically! At least I knew what the words meant and later on could check the Webster's Dictionary, but at the moment never stop the flow!

Thomas held several menial jobs until he worked for Youth Development Incorporated (YDI), an organization where he counseled young people involved in gangs. The making of the award-winning documentary about the work of YDI, *Petey and Johnny* (1961), which Thomas narrated, put him in contact with a filmmaker who encouraged him to write about his own experiences. A foundation grant gave him the time to revise the novel he had written in prison, which was published as *Down These Mean Streets* and launched his literary career.

In addition to his three novels, Thomas has published a collection of short fiction, *Stories from El Barrio* (1978), which captures the experiences of young Puerto Ricans at the fringes of U.S. society. The story "The Konk," included in this anthology, is a personal narrative about Thomas's predicament when, as a teenager, he straightened his Afro hair in an effort "not to be different" and as a reaction to the racist name-calling he often was subjected to in the barrio. Thomas also has written poetry; most of it remains unpublished, but he has released compact discs on which he performs his poems with musical accompaniment. His plays also remain unpublished, but one, *The Golden Streets*, was produced by the Puerto Rican Traveling Theatre, in New York, in 1970.

Thomas and his wife, the writer, editor, and translator Suzanne Dod Thomas, lived in Puerto Rico for a few years before settling in San Francisco. For many years, he has traveled widely, delivering motivational performances of his prose and poetry. His powerful messages about dignity and self-affirmation reflect a strong commitment to persuading at-risk groups of young adults to avoid drugs.

## *FROM* DOWN THESE MEAN STREETS

## Alien Turf

Sometimes you don't fit in. Like if you're a Puerto Rican on an Italian block. After my new baby brother, Ricardo, died of some kind of germs, Poppa moved us from 111th Street to Italian turf on 114th Street between Second and Third Avenue. I guess Poppa wanted to get Momma away from the hard memories of the old pad.

I sure missed 111th Street, where everybody acted, walked, and talked like me. But on 114th Street everything went all right for a while. There were a few dirty looks from the spaghetti-an'-sauce cats, but no big sweat. Till that one day I was on my way home from school and almost had reached my stoop when someone called: "Hey, you dirty fuckin' spic."

The words hit my ears and almost made me curse Poppa at the same time. I turned around real slow and found my face pushing in the finger of an Italian kid about my age. He had five or six of his friends with him.

"Hey, you," he said. "What nationality are ya?"

I looked at him and wondered which nationality to pick. And one of his friends said, "Ah, Rocky, he's black enuff to be a nigger. Ain't that what you is, kid?"

My voice was almost shy in its anger. "I'm Puerto Rican," I said. "I was born here." I wanted to shout it, but it came out like a whisper.

"Right here inna street?" Rocky sneered. "Ya mean right here inna middle of da street?"

They all laughed.

I hated them. I shook my head slowly from side to side. "Uh-uh," I said softly. "I was born inna hospital—inna bed."

"Umm, *paisan*[1]—born inna bed," Rocky said.

I didn't like Rocky Italiano's voice. "Inna hospital," I whispered, and all the time my eyes were trying to cut down the long distance from this trouble to my stoop. But it was no good; I was hemmed in by Rocky's friends. I couldn't help thinking about kids getting wasted for moving into a block belonging to other people.

"What hospital, *paisan*?" Bad Rocky pushed.

"Harlem Hospital," I answered, wishing like all hell that it was 5 o'clock, instead of just 3 o'clock, 'cause Poppa came home at 5. I looked around for

---

1. Brother, friend, countryman (Italian, shortened from *paisano*).

some friendly faces belonging to grown-up people, but the elders were all busy yakking away in Italian. I couldn't help thinking how much like Spanish it sounded. Shit, that should make us something like relatives.

"Harlem Hospital?" said a voice. "I knew he was a nigger."

"Yeah," said another voice from an expert on color. "That's the hospital where all them black bastards get born at."

I dug three Italian elders looking at us from across the street, and I felt saved. But that went out the window when they just smiled and went on talking. I couldn't decide whether they had smiled because this new whatever-he-was was gonna get his ass kicked or because they were pleased that their kids were welcoming a new kid to their country. An older man nodded his head at Rocky, who smiled back. I wondered if that was a signal for my funeral to begin.

"Ain't that right, kid?" Rocky pressed. "Ain't that where all black people get born?"

I dug some of Rocky's boys grinding and pushing and punching closed fists against open hands. I figured they were looking to shake me up, so I straightened up my humble voice and made like proud. "There's all kinds of people born there. Colored people, Puerto Ricans like me, an'—even spaghetti-benders like you."

"That's a dirty fuckin' lie"—*bash*, I felt Rocky's fist smack into my mouth— "you dirty fuckin' spic."

I got dizzy and then more dizzy when fists started to fly from everywhere and only toward me. I swung back, *splat, bish*—my fist hit some face and I wished I hadn't, 'cause then I started getting kicked.

I heard people yelling in Italian and English and I wondered if maybe it was 'cause I hadn't fought fair in having hit that one guy. But it wasn't. The voices were trying to help me.

"Whas'sa matta, you no-good kids, leeva da kid alone," a man said. I looked through a swelling eye and dug some Italians pushing their kids off me with slaps. One even kicked a kid in the ass. I could have loved them if I didn't hate them so fuckin' much.

"You all right, kiddo?" asked the man.

"Where you live, boy?" said another one.

"Is the *bambino* hurt?" asked a woman.

I didn't look at any of them. I felt dizzy. I didn't want to open my mouth to talk, 'cause I was fighting to keep from puking up. I just hoped my face was cool-looking. I walked away from that group of strangers. I reached my stoop and started to climb the steps.

"Hey, spic," came a shout from across the street. I started to turn to the voice and changed my mind. "Spic" wasn't my name. I knew that voice, though. It was Rocky's. "We'll see ya again, spic," he said.

I wanted to do something tough, like spitting in their direction. But you gotta have spit in your mouth in order to spit, and my mouth was hurt dry. I just stood there with my back to them.

"Hey, your old man just better be the janitor in that fuckin' building."

Another voice added, "Hey, you got any pretty sisters? We might let ya stay onna block."

Another voice mocked, "Aw, fer Chrissake, where ya ever hear of one of them black broads being pretty?"

I heard the laughter. I turned around and looked at them. Rocky made some kind of dirty sign by putting his left hand in the crook of his right arm while twisting his closed fist in the air.

Another voice said, "Fuck it, we'll just cover the bitch's face with the flag an' fuck er for old glory."

All I could think of was how I'd like to kill each of them two or three times. I found some spit in my mouth and splattered it in their direction and went inside.

Momma was cooking, and the smell of rice and beans was beating the smell of Parmesan cheese from the other apartments. I let myself into our new pad. I tried to walk fast past Momma so I could wash up, but she saw me.

"My God, Piri, what happened?" she cried.

"Just a little fight in school, Momma. You know how it is, Momma, I'm new in school an' . . ." I made myself laugh. Then I made myself say, "But Moms, I whipped the living —— outta two guys, an' one was bigger'n me."

"*Bendito*.[2] Piri, I raise this family in Christian way. Not to fight. Christ says to turn the other cheek."

"Sure, Momma." I smiled and went and showered, feeling sore at Poppa for bringing us into spaghetti country. I felt my face with easy fingers and thought about all the running back and forth from school that was in store for me.

I sat down to dinner and listened to Momma talk about Christian living without really hearing her. All I could think of was that I hadda go out in that street again. I made up my mind to go out right after I finished eating. I had to, shook up or not; cats like me had to show heart.

"Be back, Moms," I said after dinner, "I'm going out on the stoop." I got halfway to the stoop and turned and went back to our apartment. I knocked.

"Who is it?" Momma asked.

"Me, Momma."

She opened the door. "*Qué pasa?*" she asked.

"Nothing, Momma, I just forgot something," I said. I went into the bedroom and fiddled around and finally copped a funny book and walked out the door again. But this time I made sure the switch on the lock was open, just in case I had to get back real quick. I walked out on that stoop as cool as could be, feeling braver with the lock open.

There was no sign of Rocky and his killers. After awhile I saw Poppa coming down the street. He walked like beat tired. Poppa hated his pick-and-shovel job with the WPA.[3] He couldn't even hear the name WPA without getting a fever. *Funny*, I thought, *Poppa's the same like me, a stone Puerto Rican, and nobody in this block even pays him a mind. Maybe older people get along better'n us kids.*

Poppa was climbing the stoop. "Hi, Poppa," I said.

"How's it going, son? Hey, you sure look a little lumped up. What happened?"

I looked at Poppa and started to talk it outta me all at once and stopped, 'cause I heard my voice start to sound scared, and that was no good.

---

2. Literally, blessed; figuratively, for the love of God (shortened from the expression *bendito sea Dios*).
3. Work Projects Administration, originally known as the Works Progress Administration, a U.S. government agency (1935–43) that provided construction work for the unemployed.

"Slow down, son," Poppa said. "Take it easy." He sat down on the stoop and made a motion for me to do the same. He listened and I talked. I gained confidence. I went from a tone of being shook up by the Italians to a tone of being a better fighter than Joe Louis and Pedro Montanez lumped together, with Kid Chocolate[4] thrown in for extra.

"So that's what happened," I concluded. "And it looks like only the beginning. Man, I ain't scared, Poppa, but like there's nothin' but Italianos on this block and there's no me's like me except me an' our family."

Poppa looked tight. He shook his head from side to side and mumbled something about another Puerto Rican family that lived a coupla doors down from us.

I thought, *What good would that do me, unless they prayed over my dead body in Spanish?* But I said, "Man! That's great. Before ya know it, there'll be a whole bunch of us moving in, huh?"

Poppa grunted something and got up. "Staying out here, son?"

"Yeah, Poppa, for a little while longer."

From that day on I grew eyes all over my head. Anytime I hit that street for anything, I looked straight ahead, behind me and from side to side all at the same time. Sometimes I ran into Rocky and his boys—that cat was never without his boys—but they never made a move to snag me. They just grinned at me like a bunch of hungry alley cats that could get to their mouse anytime they wanted. That's what they made me feel like—a mouse. Not like a smart house mouse but like a white house pet that ain't got no business in the middle of cat country but don't know better 'cause he grew up thinking he was a cat—which wasn't far from wrong 'cause he'd end up as part of the inside of some cat.

Rocky and his fellas got to playing a way-out game with me called "One-finger-across-the-neck-inna-slicing-motion," followed by such gentle words as "It won't be long, spico." I just looked at them blank and made it to wherever I was going.

I kept wishing those cats went to the same school I went to, a school that was on the border between their country and mine, and I had *amigos* there—and there I could count on them. But I couldn't ask two or three *amigos* to break into Rocky's block and help me mess up his boys, I knew 'cause I had asked them already. They had turned me down fast, and I couldn't blame them. It would have been murder, and I guess they figured one murder would be better than four.

I got through the days trying to play it cool and walk on by Rocky and his boys like they weren't there. One day I passed them and nothing was said. I started to let out my breath. I felt great; I hadn't been seen. Then someone yelled in a high, girlish voice, "Yoo-hoo . . . Hey, *paisan* . . . we see yoo . . ." And right behind that voice came a can of evaporated milk—whoosh, clatter. I walked cool for ten steps then started running like mad.

This crap kept up for a month. They tried to shake me up. Every time they threw something at me, it was just to see me jump. I decided that the next

4. Born Eligio Sardiñas Montalvo (1910–1988); a boxer from Cuba who was very successful in the 1930s. *Joe Louis*: born Joseph Louis Barrow (1914–1981); African American boxer; world heavyweight champion 1937–49. *Pedro Montanez*: Pedro Montañez (1914–1996), also known as *El Torito de Cayey* (The Little Bull of Cayey); a boxer from Puerto Rico who was very successful in the 1930s.

fucking time they threw something at me I was gonna play bad-o and not run. That next time came about a week later. Momma sent me off the stoop to the Italian market on 115th Street and First Avenue, deep in Italian country. Man, that was stompin' territory. But I went, walking in the style which I had copped from the colored cats I had seen, a swinging and stepping down hard at every step. Those cats were so down and cool that just walking made a way-out sound.

Ten minutes later I was on my way back with Momma's stuff. I got to the corner of First Avenue and 114th Street and crushed myself right into Rocky and his fellas.

"Well-l, fellas," Rocky said. "Lookee who's here."

I didn't like the sounds coming out of Rocky's fat mouth. And I didn't like the sameness of the shitty grins spreading all over the boys' faces. But I thought, *No more! No more! I ain't gonna run no more.* Even so, I looked around, like for some kind of Jesus miracle to happen. I was always looking for miracles to happen.

"Say, *paisan*," one guy said, "you even buying from us *paisans*, eh? Man, you must wantta be Italian."

Before I could bite that dopey tongue of mine, I said, "I wouldn't be a guinea on a motherfucking bet."

"Wha-at?" said Rocky, really surprised. I didn't blame him; I was surprised myself. His finger began digging a hole in his ear, like he hadn't heard me right. "Wha-at? Say that again?"

I could feel a thin hot wetness cutting itself down my leg. I had been so ashamed of being so damned scared that I had peed on myself. And then I wasn't scared any more; I felt a fuck-it-all attitude. I looked real bad at Rocky and said, "Ya heard me. I wouldn't be a guinea on a bet."

"Ya little sonavabitch, we'll kick the shit outta ya," said one guy, Tony, who had made a habit of asking me if I had any sen-your-ritas for sisters.

"Kick the shit outta me yourself if you got any heart, you motherfuckin' fucker," I screamed at him. I felt kind of happy, the kind of feeling that you get only when you got heart.

Big mouth Tony just swung out, and I swung back and heard all of Momma's stuff plopping all over the street. My fist hit Tony smack dead in the mouth. He was so mad he threw a fist at me from about three feet away. I faked and jabbed and did fancy dance steps. Big-mouth put a stop to all that with a punch in my mouth. I heard the home cheers of "Yea, yea, bust that spic wide open!" Then I bloodied Tony's nose. He blinked and sniffed without putting his hands to his nose, and I remembered Poppa telling me, "Son, if you're ever fighting somebody an' you punch him in the nose, and he just blinks an' sniffs without holding his nose, you can do one of two things: fight like hell or run like hell—'cause that cat's a fighter."

Big-mouth came at me and we grabbed each other and pushed and pulled and shoved. *Poppa,* I thought, *I ain't gonna cop out. I'm a fighter, too.* I pulled away from Tony and blew my fist into his belly. He puffed and butted my nose with his head. I sniffed back. *Poppa, I didn't put my hands to my nose.* I hit Tony again in that same weak spot. He bent over in the middle and went down to his knees.

Big-mouth got up as fast as he could, and I was thinking how much heart he had. But I ran toward him like my life depended on it; I wanted to cool him. Too late, I saw his hand grab a fistful of ground asphalt which had been piled nearby to fix a pothole in the street. I tried to duck; I should have closed my eyes instead. The shitty-gritty stuff hit my face, and I felt the scrappy pain make itself a part of my eyes. I screamed and grabbed for two eyes with one hand, while with the other I beat some kind of helpless tune on air that just couldn't be hurt. I heard Rocky's voice shouting, "Ya scum bag, ya didn't have to fight the spic dirty; you could've fucked him up fair and square!" I couldn't see. I heard a fist hit a face, then Big-mouth's voice: "Whatta ya hittin' me for?" and then Rocky's voice: "*Puttana!*[5] I ought ta knock all your fuckin' teeth out."

I felt hands grabbing at me between my screams. I punched out. *I'm gonna get killed*, I thought. Then I heard many voices: "Hold it, kid." "We ain't gonna hurt ya." "*Je-sus*, don't rub your eyes." "Ooooohhhh, shit, his eyes is fulla that shit."

*You're fuckin' right*, I thought, *and it hurts like* coño.[6]

I heard a woman's voice now: "Take him to a hospital." And an old man asked: "How did it happen?"

"Momma, Momma," I cried.

"Comon, kid," Rocky said, taking my hand. "Lemme take ya home." I fought for the right to rub my eyes. "Grab his other hand, Vincent," Rocky said. I tried to rub my eyes with my eyelids. I could feel hurt tears cutting down my cheeks. "Come on, kid, we ain't gonna hurt ya," Rocky tried to assure me. "Swear to our mudder. We just wanna take ya home."

I made myself believe him, and trying not to make pain noises, I let myself be led home. I wondered if I was gonna be blind like Mr. Silva, who went around from door to door selling dish towels and brooms, his son leading him around.

"You okay, kid?" Rocky asked.

"Yeah," what was left of me said.

"A-huh," mumbled Big-mouth.

"He got much heart for a nigger," somebody else said.

A *spic*, I thought.

"For anybody," Rocky said. "Here we are, kid," he added. "Watch your step."

I was like carried up the steps. "What's your apartment number?" Rocky asked.

"One-B—inna back—ground floor," I said, and I was led there. Somebody knocked on Momma's door. Then I heard running feet and Rocky's voice yelling back, "Don't rat, huh, kid?" And I was alone.

I heard the door open and Momma say, "*Bueno*, Piri, come in." I didn't move. I couldn't. There was a long pause; I could hear Momma's fright. "My God," she said finally. "What's happened?" Then she took a closer look. "Ai-eeee," she screamed. "*Dios mío!*"

"I was playing with some kids, Momma," I said, "an' I got some dirt in my eyes." I tried to make my voice come out without the pain, like a man.

"*Dios eterno*—your eyes!"

"What's the matter? What's the matter?" Poppa called from the bedroom.

"*Está ciego!*" Momma screamed. "He is blind!"

I heard Poppa knocking things over as he came running. Sis began to cry. Blind, hurting tears were jumping out of my eyes. "Whattya mean, he's

---

5. Whore, bitch (Italian slang).          6. Literally, cunt; figuratively, here, shit or fuck.

blind?" Poppa said as he stormed into the kitchen. "What happened?" Poppa's voice was both scared and mad.

"Playing, Poppa."

"Whatta ya mean, 'playing'?" Poppa's English sounded different when he got warm.

"Just playing, Poppa."

"Playing? Playing got all that dirt in your eyes? I bet my ass. Them damn Ee-ta-liano kids ganged up on you again." Poppa squeezed my head between the fingers of one hand. "That settles it—we're moving outta this damn section, outta this damn block, outta this damn shit."

*Shit,* I thought, *Poppa's sure cursin' up a storm.* I could hear him slapping the side of his leg, like he always did when he got real mad.

"Son," he said, "you're gonna point them out to me."

"Point who out, Poppa? I was playin' an'—"

"Stop talkin' to him and take him to the hospital!" Momma screamed.

"*Pobrecito,* poor Piri," cooed my little sister.

"You sure, son?" Poppa asked. "You was only playing?"

"Shit, Poppa, I said I was."

*Smack*—Poppa was so scared and mad, he let it out in a slap to the side of my face.

"*Bestia!* Ani-*mul!*" Momma cried. "He's blind, and you hit him!"

"I'm sorry, son, I'm sorry," Poppa said in a voice like almost-crying. I heard him running back into the bedroom, yelling, "Where's my pants?"

Momma grabbed away fingers that were trying to wipe away the hurt in my eyes. "*Caramba,* no rub, no rub," she said, kissing me. She told Sis to get a rag and wet it with cold water.

Poppa came running back into the kitchen. "Let's go, son, let's go. Jesus! I didn't mean to smack ya, I really didn't," he said, his big hand rubbing and grabbing my hair gently.

"Here's the rag, Momma," said Sis.

"What's that for?" asked Poppa.

"To put on his eyes," Momma said.

I heard the smack of a wet rag, *blapt,* against the kitchen wall. "We can't put nothing on his eyes. It might make them worse. Come on, son," Poppa said nervously, lifting me up in his big arms. I felt like a little baby, like I didn't hurt so bad. I wanted to stay there, but I said, "Let me down, Poppa, I ain't no kid."

"Shut up," Poppa said softly. "I know you ain't, but it's faster this way."

"Which hospeetal are you taking him to?" Momma asked.

"Nearest one," Poppa answered as we went out the door. He carried me through the hall and out into the street, where the bright sunlight made a red hurting color through the crap in my eyes. I heard voices on the stoop and on the sidewalk: "Is that the boy?"

"A-huh. He's probably blinded."

"We'll get a cab, son," Poppa said. His voice loved me. I heard Rocky yelling from across the street, "We're pulling for ya, kid. Remember what we . . ." The rest was lost to Poppa's long legs running down to the corner of Third Avenue. He hailed a taxi and we zoomed off toward Harlem Hospital. I felt the cab make all kinds of sudden stops and turns.

"How do you feel, *hijo*?" Poppa asked.

"It burns like hell."

"You'll be okay," he said, and as an afterthought added, "Don't curse, son."

I heard cars honking and the Third Avenue el[7] roaring above us. I knew we were in Puerto Rican turf, 'cause I could hear our language.

"Son."

"Yeah, Poppa."

"Don't rub your eyes, fer Christ sake." He held my skinny wrists in his one hand, and everything got quiet between us.

The cab got to Harlem Hospital. I heard change being handled and the door opening and Poppa thanking the cabbie for getting here fast. "Hope the kid'll be okay," the driver said.

*I will be,* I thought. *I ain't gonna be like Mr. Silva.*

Poppa took me in his arms again and started running. "Where's emergency, mister?" he asked someone.

"To your left and straight away," said a voice.

"Thanks a lot," Poppa said, and we were running again. "Emergency?" Poppa said when we stopped.

"Yes, sir," said a girl's voice. "What's the matter?"

"My boy's got his eyes full of ground-up tar an'—"

"What's the matter?" said a man's voice.

"Youngster with ground tar in his eyes, doctor."

"We'll take him, mister. You just put him down here and go with the nurse. She'll take down the information. Uh, you the father?"

"That's right, doctor."

"Okay, just put him down here."

"Poppa, don't leave me," I cried.

"Sh, son, I ain't leaving you. I'm just going to fill out some papers, an' I'll be right back."

I nodded my head up and down and was wheeled away. When the rolling stretcher stopped, somebody stuck a needle in me and I got sleepy and started thinking about Rocky and his boys, and Poppa's slap, and how great Poppa was, and how my eyes didn't hurt no more . . .

I woke up in a room blind with darkness. The only lights were the ones inside my head. I put my fingers to my eyes and felt bandages. "Let them be, sonny," said a woman's voice.

I wanted to ask the voice if they had taken my eyes out, but I didn't. I was afraid the voice would say yes.

"Let them be, sonny," the nurse said, pulling my hand away from the bandages. "You're all right. The doctor put the bandages on to keep the light out. They'll be off real soon. Don't you worry none, sonny."

I wished she would stop calling me sonny. "Where's Poppa?" I asked cool-like.

"He's outside, sonny. Would you like me to send him in?"

I nodded, "Yeah." I heard walking-away shoes, a door opening, a whisper, and shoes walking back toward me. "How do you feel, *hijo*?" Poppa asked.

"It hurts like shit, Poppa."

"It's just for awhile, son, and then off come the bandages. Everything's gonna be all right."

I thought, *Poppa didn't tell me to stop cursing.*

"And son, I thought I told you to stop cursing," he added.

7. Elevated railway.

I smiled. Poppa hadn't forgotten. Suddenly I realized that all I had on was a hospital gown. "Poppa, where's my clothes?" I asked.

"I got them. I'm taking them home an'—"

"Whatta ya mean, Poppa?" I said, like scared. "You ain't leavin' me here? I'll be damned if I stay." I was already sitting up and feeling my way outta bed. Poppa grabbed me and pushed me back. His voice wasn't mad or scared any more. It was happy and soft, like Momma's.

"Hey," he said, "get your ass back in bed or they'll have to put a bandage there too."

"Poppa," I pleaded. "I don't care, wallop me as much as you want, just take me home."

"Hey, I thought you said you wasn't no kid. Hell, you ain't scared of being alone?"

Inside my head there was a running of *Yeah, yeah, yeah,* but I answered, "Naw, Poppa, it's just that Momma's gonna worry and she'll get sick an' everything, and—"

"Won't work, son," Poppa broke in with a laugh.

I kept quiet.

"It's only for a couple days. We'll come and see you an' everybody'll bring you things."

I got interested but played it smooth. "What kinda things, Poppa?"

Poppa shrugged his shoulders and spread his big arms apart and answered me like he was surprised that I should ask. "Uh . . . fruits and . . . candy and ice cream. And Momma will probably bring you chicken soup."

I shook my head sadly. "Poppa, you know I don't like chicken soup."

"So we won't bring chicken soup. We'll bring what you like. Goddammit, whatta ya like?"

"I'd like the first things you talked about, Poppa," I said softly. "But instead of soup I'd like"—I held my breath back, then shot it out—"some roller skates!"

Poppa let out a whistle. Roller skates were about $1.50, and that was rice and beans for more than a few days. Then he said, "All right, son, soon as you get home, you got 'em."

But he had agreed too quickly. I shook my head from side to side. Shit, I was gonna push all the way for the roller skates. It wasn't every day you'd get hurt bad enough to ask for something so little like a pair of roller skates. I wanted them right away.

"Fer Christ sakes," Poppa protested, "you can't use 'em in here. Why, some kid will probably steal 'em on you." But Poppa's voice died out slowly in a "you win" tone as I just kept shaking my head from side to side. "Bring 'em tomorrow," he finally mumbled, "but that's it."

"Thanks, Poppa."

"Don't ask for no more."

My eyes were starting to hurt like mad again. The fun was starting to go outta the game between Poppa and me. I made a face.

"Does it hurt, son?"

"Naw, Poppa. I can take it." I thought how I was like a cat in a movie about Indians, taking it like a champ, tied to a stake and getting like burned toast.

Poppa sounded relieved. "Yeah, it's only at first it hurts." His hand touched my foot. "Well, I'll be going now . . ." Poppa rubbed my foot gently and then slapped me the same gentle way on the side of my leg. "Be good, son," he said and walked away. I heard the door open and the nurse telling him about how they were gonna move me to the ward 'cause I was out of danger. "Son," Poppa called back, "you're *un hombre*."

I felt proud as hell.

"Poppa."

"Yeah, son?"

"You won't forget to bring the roller skates, huh?"

Poppa laughed. "Yeah, son."

I heard the door close.

1967

# The Konk

When I was a kid, many folks spent a lot of time, effort, and money trying to pass for white. Very few homes did not have some kind of skin-bleaching cream. If poverty prevented its purchase, raw lemon juice would suffice. Cream or juice was liberally applied to the skin with the hope of turning it yellow, which was light, if not white.

Parents were constantly pinching the noses of their children so that flat, wide nostrils could be unnaturally forced into sculptured images of white folks' noses.

Running neck and neck were hair-straightening and coloring effects. The very poor made up batches of Vaseline, lye, and harsh brown Octagon soap for their hair-straightening. For those who could afford it, there were jars of heavy white cream with "You too can have beautiful hair" advertised on the label. Even more money could buy a marcel, which straightened curly hair by pressing it out with iron-hot combs after dipping one's head in oil. The smell of burnt hair often overpowered the odors of garbage-littered alleyways. Even comic books carried ads for beauty care. One could earn a Red Ryder B.B. rifle or a bicycle if one sold enough of a particular brand of lightening cream.

By the time I was fourteen, I had grown tired of my curly hair being called "nappy," *pasas* (raisins), or *pelo malo* (bad hair). One day I decided to take the plunge. I went to a barber shop way up in the wilds of the South Bronx, recommended by some walking exponents of one hair-straightening process known as the "konk."

At Prospect Avenue station, I made my exit and headed for the barbershop, located on Westchester Avenue. A huge sign in the window advertised its specialty:

ROY'S BARBER SHOP—HAIR STRAIGHTENED

KONKS—FIVE DOLLARS—SATISFACTION GUARANTEED

Overcoming my hesitancy, I marched into that barber shop like I copped konks every day. On the walls were photographs of all kinds of celebrities, including fighters like Kid Gavilan and Ray Robinson.[1] They flashed big smiles signifying their joy at sporting straight hair via konks or marcels.

Some sad blues were being wailed by Billie Holiday[2] from an antique radio. I figured Billie was saying konking was all right too. Two young black men wearing white barbershop jackets were playing checkers. One of them looked at me with a smile and in singsong asked, "What will it be, li'l brother? A trim trip or the works?"

"Gimme a konk," I said, as if I'd invented the word.

"Sit right there, li'l brother." He pointed to a mid-Victorian barbership chair. "We'll get you straightened out in no time at all."

With cool-breeze apprehension, I lightly eased myself into the chair, which in my vivid imagination resembled the hot seat at Sing Sing.[3]

"Name's Roy, bro. What's yours?"

"Mine's Piri," I answered, my eyes glued to his own natural unprocessed hair.

Roy put on some rubber gloves like doctors use when they have to touch something they don't really want to.

"Umhh." He frowned. "This won't do . . . won't do at all."

I wondered if my Puerto Rican hair was going to be left out of konk, too. "What's the matter?"

"Too much grease, son. You got grease on your head that's been there from the year one. Gotta give you an A-1 shampoo first, okay? It's $2.00 extra."

Too deeply involved by now to say no, I agreed and Roy proceeded to do his art. After the final rinsing, he squeaked my hair between his thumb and forefinger. "It's clean now."

I had to admit my curly hair had not looked that clean in a long time. Seeing my reflection in the mirror, I grunted approval.

Roy examined my scalp carefully, arousing my anxiety.

"You got lots of good hair to work with."

I bubbled with pleasure. At last my hair pleased somebody even if it were just for a konk. Roy took out a huge jar of Dixie Peach Hair Pomade. He plunged his right hand in and came out with a gigantic blob of its thick yellow substance. I staggered under its weight as he worked close to a pound into my hair.

"Man, you sure are heavy on that grease," I protested.

"Got to, li'l man, cause without the Dixie Peach, the konk can burn your scalp right down to the bone. In fact, bro, it can cause your hair to fall right off your head or turn it red along with your scalp."

"Jesus Christ," I said, forcing my voice to stay without panic. Like I never thought it was going to be dangerous.

"A lot of bad can happen if it's not done right." My artist brother droned on, confident in his technique. "If you want white man's hair, there's a price you gotta pay. Whatcha say? Now's the time to stop or go."

I smiled bravely and said, "Go, bro. But say, man. How come you don't konk your hair, seeing as you're in the business?"

1. Sugar Ray Robinson (born Walker Smith Jr., 1921–1989), African American boxer; world welterweight champion 1946–51, world middleweight champion five times from 1951–60. Kid Gavilan: born Gerardo González (1926–2003); boxer from Cuba; world welterweight champion 1951–54.
2. African American jazz singer (born Eleanora Holiday, 1915–1959).
3. I.e., the electric chair at Sing Sing Correctional Facility, a maximum security prison in Ossining, New York.

Roy just mumbled, "No way, man. Konks or marcels ain't my stick. I just do it for others 'cause it's part of my living wages."

Convinced that my head was greased to his satisfaction, Roy unscrewed the top of a large blue jar. I observed a soft whitish cream that smelled like sulfuric acid. With a comb, he began working it into my curly, terror-stricken, cringing hairs.

"Now, li'l brother, relax and listen. Soon as you start feeling your scalp begin burning, just gimme a holler. I sure don't want to be responsible for your hair turning red, let alone dropping out. Don't get scared if you just feel your scalp warming up. That's just the konk doing its thing. Only holler when it really starts to burn. Some scalps are tender, others can . . ."

Just then a voice interrupted from the doorway. "Good morning, gentlemen. Anybody feeling lucky today?"

In the mirror, I saw a boy. He was a numbers runner[4] just a few years older than my fourteen, high yellow of color with soft reddish natural brown hair. He thoughtfully checked out my reflection, his eyes glued compassionately to the top of my head, by now a smoldering mass of plaster of Paris.

The smell of burning, agonizing hair permeated the barber shop. I strained my neck out with a grin after what seemed like hours instead of minutes. "Hey, man. My hair is starting to burn."

Damnit. I wasn't being heard. Roy the artful barber was too busy checking out the numbers game.

"Yeah, I sure feel lucky today. Gimme 50¢ on 347, 50¢ on 656, and a buck combination on 437."

"Hey, man. My head's burning."

If he refused to hear me, he should at least be able to smell the smoke. I waited as coolly as I could for a couple more suffering seconds and then without any kind of embarrassment began to let out all kinds of yells.

"Hey, man. I ain't shitting. My head's on fire."

"Listen, George," Roy went on rapping to the young numbers runner, "I guess that's all for now. No, wait, George, hold on. Gimme 50¢ on 333. I really feel lucky today."

I wished I felt that lucky. I was already heading for the faucet with my head on fire. Roy finally got hip to the seriousness of the situation and got to the sink with me.

Attempting to comfort me, he said, "It's supposed to burn a little. You want it to come out cool, don't ya?"

He brought the three-alarm fire that was my scalp under control by life-saving, cold-water rinsing. He toweled my hair dry. I stared into the mirror amazed. My short coils of curls no longer than a couple of inches around my ears were now a waterfall of hair, dead straight and hanging limply down to my shoulders.

Roy combed while I inwardly swore I looked like Cochise, if not Prince Valiant.[5]

"Now for a hair cut, bro. Do you want it long or short?"

---

4. A messenger for a kind of gambling, in which people bet on combinations of digits, such as regularly published ones.
5. In the comic strip of the same name (1938–71),

a dark-haired Nordic prince with a kind of bob haircut. *Cochise*: Apache chief (ca. 1815–1874) in Arizona, who wore his dark hair long and straight back.

"Long, man," I said. "Long enough for a pompadour in front and a duck's ass in the back."

"Gotcha."

Snip, snip, snip. Comb, comb, comb. Clip, clip, clip.

Straight razor, sweet-smelling hair lotion, some more combing, a pat here, a pat there.

"Okay, man. That's it. You got a Roy Special. Hey, man, open your eyes. Check yourself out."

Roy's voice sounded so pleased that I opened them in good faith. I ran my fingers through my hair. It was like fine silk. Roy expertly brushed away loose hairs and with a final flourish liberally splashed me with fragrant after-shave lotion. He held up a large mirror in back of me, which allowed me to see in my reflection the glory of his work.

Good God Almighty! I was sure looking good. I now had the biggest, softest, silkiest pompadour in the whole world and a duck ass style that would force vain ducks to drown themselves in sheer envy.

"Compliments of the house, li'l brother," Roy said, handing me a long slim-jim barber's comb that a short while back could only have been used to comb my eyebrows.

"Gee, thanks, man." I combed my hair in the mirror just like the cat going to the electric chair in the film *Knock On Any Door*.[6]

"What's the tab, bro?"

"Five dollars, li'l brother, plus $2.50 for the A-l Shampoo."

I gave him $9.50; the extra two was to cover some inner shame I was somehow feeling.

"Thank you, bro." Roy saluted me.

George smiled friendly at me as I walked toward the door.

"Feeling lucky today? I always pay off, so no worries."

"Yeah," I said. "Gimme a dime on 692."

I didn't check his face out. A dime is pretty cheap. But how was he to know my hair konk had damn near broken me financially?

Roy called out some last minute professional advice.

"Hey, li'l brother. Don't forget you gotta keep the treatment up or your hair will definitely return to its nappy self."

"Yeah, sure," I called back, moving fast away from Roy's Barber Shop. I began checking myself out in store windows, combing and recombing my newly reconstructed hair. I dropped my comb more than once—bending over mussed up my hair, providing another excuse to recomb it.

Going home, I purposely rode between the rumbling cars of the subway train so that the blast of air caused my new hair to rise and fly. It was no longer bound to the greasy gravity of Dixie Peach.

Leaving the train at 103rd Street, I walked into my block of 104th Street where most everybody knew me. Heads began snapping my way, and smiles grew into jeering shouts of "Hey, monkey, what's that shit on your haid?" One renamed me "Konko Pete" on the spot, followed by "Just wait until your hair turns red and your scalp drops dead."

I really felt like punching the insulters out but cooled the idea as being suicidal. I couldn't fight a whole block. As I climbed the stairs to my apartment,

6. A 1949 courtroom drama about an accused murderer named Pretty Boy Romano.

I braced myself for whatever else was ahead. I paused a long second outside my door and then strolled in, hoping no one would notice me. My two brothers were busy playing a card game of knuckles. My sister was into her Wonder Woman comics. They looked up at me vaguely, but it was enough for them to spot my new hair style. I dared them with my eyes to say anything that would put me down.

My brothers kept quiet although bursting to laugh. My sister, however, could not contain herself, blurting out, "*Mira, mira.*[7] Piri's got a wig."

"Wig, shit," I snarled. "This ain't no wig. This here is my new hair."

There was no way my brothers could contain themselves any longer. Their laughter came out roaring like wheels on a subway train. Tears of rage mixed with embarrassment jumped out of my eyes. I wished the living room floor would swallow me up.

I hit out at Ray, causing my hair to come trembling down over my face. Their laughter increased. All I could do was stand there with my new straight hair stuck like wires of black spaghetti to my angry, sweaty face.

The noise brought in Momma, followed by Poppa still chewing on his supper. Suddenly everybody was silent. I walked slowly over to the sofa and plunked down heavily on it, feeling old and tired at fourteen and wondering why my strong young legs refused to hold me up.

Poppa shook his head. He knew what my hurting was all about. Momma sat down by my side and caressed my wilted, abused hair. Then hugging me close, she allowed my tears of hurt and shame to be absorbed by her big momma breasts. She whispered to me, "*Hijo*, what have you done to your beautiful hair?"

"Oh, Moms," I whispered back. "I just didn't want to be different any more. I'm so tired of being called names. I ain't no raisinhead or nothing like that."

Momma hugged me very closely and said out loud, "Don't you ever be ashamed of being you. You want to know something, *negrito*? I wouldn't trade you for any *blanquitos*."

The next day found me playing stick ball with a red bandana around my forehead, sporting the baldest head in town.

1978

7. Look, look.

---

# RICHARD VÁZQUEZ
## 1928–1994

Information about Richard Vázquez's life is scant. After serving in the military during World War II, he became a reporter at the *Santa Monica Independent*. In 1963, while at the *San Gabriel Valley Daily Tribune*, he received a Sigma Delta Pi Award for his story on municipal corruption. Vázquez was also a feature writer for *The Los Angeles Times*. In 1970, he published his first novel, the epic saga *Chicano*. The *San Francisco Chronicle* described it as vivid, trenchant, and moving; *The New York Times* admired its vitality and honest feeling; but Mexican American critics attacked it as inhabited by stereotypes and plagued with generalizations about Mexican immigrants on the road to assimilation. Vázquez's book was not embraced by readers as was another early, equally charged precursor in Chicano letters, José Antonio Villarreal's *Pocho* (1959, 1971), yet it provided continuity to the genre of the Latino novel. Vázquez published two other novels, *The Giant Killer* (1978) and *Another Land* (1982).

## FROM CHICANO

## Chapter 1

The locomotive roared out of the narrow stone canyon and for a few moments quickly gathered speed as the tracks dropped sharply to meet the level terrain of the valley of desert stretching ahead. The men in the cab strained their eyes and briefly, just before the tracks leveled to the valley floor, they caught a glimpse of the engine and two flatcars carrying the protective troop detachment far ahead. Then, in the valley, the shimmering heatwaves cut vision to a few miles, although the tracks stretched out in an arrow-straight path for many miles.

The men glanced at one another, nodding faintly, a little of their anxiety abated at the reassuring sight of the train with soldiers ahead.

The noise of the locomotive steadied to a monotonous pounding as they settled down for the long stretch of unbroken ground before they would climb into the next low range of stone mountains.

The wheels of the fifty boxcars and cattle cars, all full of cattle, were among the first to christen this one-hundred-mile stretch of track through nothing but desert and mountains.

This was northern Mexico, where the sun rose with hideous vengefulness each day, allowing only the martyred cactus and low brush to survive on the sandy plains. One of the men pulled his head from the window into the cab, wiped away the tears caused by the torrid wind and shouted above the roar of the firebox, steam, wheels, and rushing air, "They should stay closer to us."

His companion wiped his grimy face with the sweat-soaked kerchief around his neck. "No, amigo," he hollered back, "they must have time to warn us if they run into a blockade . . . or something." It was the "or something" that made the two men's eyes hold an instant.

A third man, through shoveling coal for the moment, joined them. He was fat, wore greasy overalls, as did his companions, had an enormous mustache and his hair almost covered his ears. All wore shirts with sleeves torn off at the shoulder.

"It was a mistake, making this railway here. If the Yaquis[1] don't get us, the bandidos will. No law, no city for two hundred kilometros, no nothing. I think I quit and go to the Estados Unidos," he said.

"Don't kid me," said an engineer, "they don't let Mexicans drive locomotives in the United States. And besides, they have bandidos there, too."

---

1. An American Indian people of Sonora, Mexico.

"Not like here. Here we have fifty little generals each with his own little army, claiming to want to free Mexico, when really they just kill and steal and rob," the fireman said.

With squinted eyes, watering from the sweat and hot wind, the men passed a cloth water bag and each drank deeply, splashing some on the face and hair. Then the vigil at the windows was resumed, and the fat fireman went back to shoveling coal, and the train sprinted on into the heat waves.

More than an hour later they were stirred from their near lethargy by the slight slowing of the rhythm of the engine and tracks, and they knew the sloping climb out of the valley had begun. The engineer pushed the throttle forward a little, and the engine steadied for a while, then again started to slow its rhythm. Again the throttle was pushed forward, and soon the fireman was shoveling rapidly and the train was moving slowly, smoke trailing, as it lumbered up the incline into the mountains. They wound through a wide, low canyon, climbing, then abruptly picked up speed as they neared the summit. Over the top, the engineer put reverse steam to the driving wheels to check the train's speed, and the descent was almost as slow as the climb. For a moment coming around a curve the floor of the vast valley ahead was visible, and the tiny train carrying the troops could again be seen.

The train had almost reached the next valley floor when the engineer, looking out the window, shouted and applied the brakes. The others looked. There ahead, dust still rising, was a rockslide piled high on the tracks, small stones continuing to fall from the cliff alongside the tracks. Shouting, the men threw open the door on the cliff side and jumped, rolling over and over in the dirt by the ties, and the next moment the engine was tearing into the slide, leaving the tracks, and pulling the fifty cars behind as, miraculously, it remained upright and churned into the shallow ravine away from the cliff. The steel wheels and undercarriage bit deep into the earth as the fifty cars, like a giant hand, pushed it relentlessly along, until the wheels of all the cars, too, sank deep into softer footing, and the entire train came to a jolting stop against the far bank of the ravine.

Only the sound of the desperately bellowing cattle, some injured and dying, all frightened, could be heard. Smoke poured from the locomotive, which was tilted at a crazy angle against an earthen bank, as though it were injured also. Two of the trainmen were on their feet, looking up in fear at the crags and bluffs overhead. The third, the fat man, lay on the ground cradling his foot, moaning.

The others approached him. "Hurry! Get up. We better get out of here."

The injured man groaned. "My foot. It's broken. Don't leave me. Stay here."

"We can't stay here. Whoever caused the rockslide will be coming now. We have to start after the troop train."

"They're gone," the injured man said, gesturing. "They won't be back."

"Yes, they will. As soon as they realize we're not behind them, they'll come back to help us."

The man on the ground gave a laugh of pained irony. "As soon as they realize the bandidos wrecked this train they will go to the garrison where it is safe."

The third man spoke. "Maybe it wasn't the bandidos. Maybe the indios."

The man with the broken foot thought a moment. His voice was surprisingly calm. "You two better go. Maybe the train will wait for you. If so, maybe you can talk them into coming back for me. I can't walk. I'll have to take my chances with whoever is up there." He indicated the reaching cliffs and mountains. All three looked about, but there was no sign of life.

One of the men who was unhurt looked at the other. "We would be foolish to go on. At least here in the canyon we might find food and water."

"We might also find Indians."

"But we could only live several hours crossing that desert. The troops might have kept going."

Finally it was decided the two would walk after the train carrying the troops and see if the latter would return for the fireman.

And Hector Sandoval gently rubbed his swelling ankle as he watched his companions, each carrying a waterbag and a shovel for protection, climb the mound of rocks and start toward the shimmering valley below.

Hector Sandoval realized he was lying in the blazing sun. The cattle, still trapped in the wrecked cars, were beginning to quiet down. He crawled on his hands and knees to the ravine. He made his way down the slope to a clump of hardwood brush. Carefully, crawling along, he selected the right bough and took a pocket knife from his pocket and began cutting it. Soon he had it free. He trimmed the small branches from it, leaving the top in a large fork. He fitted the fork under his arm, whittled a little more on it, and soon had an operable crutch. He found that his injured foot could support none of his weight.

He made his way painstakingly to the locomotive. With a great deal of trouble he climbed in. The fire still burned the steam still hissed and the cattle still bawled. But the sound diminished as he waited. The long afternoon progressed slowly, the pain of his leg increased as the hours dragged by.

Presently he saw a man coming up the ravine on horseback. At first he was fearful it might be one of those responsible for the train wreck, but then he recognized the working attire of the vaquero, the chaps and pointed boots, the ancient, heavy single-shot pistol at the hip. The rider was approaching slowly, disbelief on his face as he examined the wreck.

Hector Sandoval hailed him. "Ho, amigo! Here in the cab." The rider directed his horse to the engine.

"Madre de dios,"[2] he exclaimed. "What has happened here?"

"We had a wreck. I'm hurt. My foot I think is broken. Can you help me get away from here?"

"To what? I work on a rancho ten kilometros from here. How did this happen?"

"Bandidos. Or Indians, I don't know. There are two others. They left, walking, to seek help. Do you think bandits did this? Or Indians?"

The man shrugged. "Quién sabe?[3] Such a shame. But it was a bad idea to put a railroad through here. It is too wild. Now I guess the railway will be abandoned."

Sandoval made his way to the ground with the help of the cowboy, who introduced himself as Lalo. He made himself comfortable and then examined his injured foot.

"It's badly broken. I can't walk, or ride a horse. Is there a town nearby?"

2. Mother of God.          3. Who knows?

"Yes. By the rancho where I work. I'll go send them. But what about the cattle here?"

Sandoval shrugged. "Many are injured. They should be turned loose, I guess."

"No," the other replied, "the village near here is called Agua Clara. They should have the injured cattle. And mi patrón, Señor Domínguez, he will want to keep the uninjured cattle until their rightful owner can claim them."

Sandoval gave an amused laugh. "Ha! It's my guess nobody will ever show up to claim anything. Tell you what. If you get the villagers to come and get me, tell them I will give them the injured cows. And the train, too, if they want that. The company will not risk sending another train to collect them."

Soon Lalo rose to leave. "I will carry word of the train wreck to the village. And to my patrón. Try to rest comfortably. I'm sure the villagers will care for you when they get here in the morning."

In the morning they came. Don Francisco Domínguez leading his vaqueros, and behind them the subservient villagers. The ranchero directed his men to free the cattle, shouted instructions as to how to get them out of the tilting cattle and boxcars. His delight was apparent as he counted the dozens of uninjured cattle herded together. Before noon he had what he wanted. "I will keep them safe until an owner claims them," he said in a loud voice, and he drove them to his ranch.

The men, women, and children of Agua Clara swarmed over the tilted train. Knives were unsheathed, throats of the cattle were cut, and blood was caught in earthen jugs. Fires were lighted, spits were improvised, pieces of carcasses were handed to the women. Hector Sandoval watched as an entire village ate all it wanted for the first time. Some women roasted meat, some fried, some ground it, some set to work drying meat for carne seca (beef jerky); some had brought pans and rendered fat. A festive air of a once-in-a-lifetime occasion prevailed, and the men sang and laughed as they stripped and scraped hides, sawed horns and hacked off hoofs.

"Come, taste this, taste this!" one man would shout as he cut a steaming morsel from a roasting haunch that dripped red. With perhaps a half hundred cattle left to them, they knew there was more than several times their number could eat. Almost frantically some went about preparing meat for curing.

And in the midst of the labor and gorging, a chill settled through all as they observed a large group of Indians watching, half the men mounted, women behind with babes in arms.

The villagers beckoned, addressing the newcomers in Spanish. "Come. There is plenty for all." And the Indians joined. Some wore leather leggings and no shirts, some wore the tattered remains of fine vests, many wore what had once been fine dress hats and coats; all had their hair in long braids past the shoulders, and the men were conspicuous by their lack of facial hair. The group of villagers with whom Hector Sandoval was eating was approached by one of the Indians.

"Our jefe would like to speak with the alcalde of the villagers," he said ceremoniously.

One whom Sandoval had learned was the village spokesman, Estorga, arose, stifling a pained expression at the formality of the Indian chief in sending a messenger some twenty feet to summon him. Estorga approached and shook hands with the Indian leader.

"Good afternoon, jefe," he said.

"Good afternoon, jefe," the Indian returned. "I would like it known that my people are not to blame for the train wreck," he said in perfect Spanish. "Should the federales come to punish those responsible, I know you will tell them we did not do it."

Estorga nodded politely. "Should the authorities come to the village to ask, I will say there was nobody here when we arrived, that you and your people came after we did."

"You may say we encountered the bandidos who did this as they climbed down the back of the mountain to circle around and claim these spoils. When they told me what they had done, I was angered, as were my people. Not only may we get the blame, but we wanted the railroad here, that we might develop trade with los mejicanos as other groups of poor Indians have. When the bandidos saw our anger, they left."

Estorga's face brightened. "They left? Or perhaps you killed them."

The Indian smiled broadly. "No, they saw my angry young men looking with desire at their fine horses and saddles and guns, and they left."

Estorga spread the word that the Indians had driven off a group of bandits who had derailed the train, and the feasting continued throughout the day.

Later in the afternoon the villagers prepared to go home. Burros were loaded with meat, hides, and other loot. A sled was made for the injured train man. The next morning Hector Sandoval awoke in the village of Agua Clara.

Estorga had offered his shack to Hector Sandoval, and the train man had said he planned to leave for the city as soon as his foot was well. He saw that Estorga had a crude hammer and attempted to do a little iron work, but was hampered by lack of tools.

"At the train," he told his host, "there is a fine hammer, tongs also, and bellows. You will find them in the tool box in the cab. Here, I have the key." And a few days later Sandoval suggested that the villagers take a door from a boxcar and with the burros drag it back to the village to make a roof. Within a week or so he was able to ride to the wrecked train himself, where he showed the villagers how to disassemble parts which might be useful in the village.

He noticed a girl. She was slim, dark, and typically sad-eyed. He had made no mention of his wife and children in the big city, who no doubt now thought him dead, and daily he thought about how hectic life had been in the city, how fat and demanding his wife had become, how she gave every extra little bit of money to the priest, to help heal a sick child, to bring good luck to a widowed sister looking for a husband, or to buy forgiveness for sins committed by a member of the family. Taxes, double because he couldn't pay all of last year's, rats killing the family cat in a fight over scraps of food, the cramped heat and stifling smell of the city slums. Yes . . . even though he'd been in Agua Clara only a few days, he noticed the sad-eyed girl looking at him as she passed to get water at the little stream that went by the village.

"Good morning, how is your foot today?" she asked as she went by one day, and his decision was made.

"I have decided to stay here in your village," he told a spontaneous meeting of village men one evening when his foot was almost well.

"Good."

"You will not regret it."

"We welcome you as one of us."

"And to earn my living I will catch and train wild burros. I did much of that when I was a boy near Texas. But it takes two to make a burro-catching team, as you know. Yet, I don't think the enterprise will support two men."

Straight-faced, the others agreed. What solution?

"If you could take a wife, then you could follow your chosen profession," a villager offered.

"Yes," Sandoval replied, "but there seems to be small chance of that. Unless, that girl, what's her name? Lita, I think—if she could be persuaded to be my bride . . ."

"Yes, my daughter, Lita," one villager put in. "She is getting old. Almost seventeen. She had been seeing that worthless boy Eduardo, but I stopped that. Were you and she married, she could go off with you to help."

"The priest will be here next week. He comes every month from the city. He will marry you."

Sandoval set about building a house. From the cab of the train he took the sheet metal roof, and had the finest roof in the village, with little rain gutters on each side—although it rarely rained. Boxcar doors served as walls, and from the caboose he took the little pot-bellied stove, and had the only factory-made stove in the village. Right after the marriage ceremony they left, on two borrowed donkeys, with a third loaded down with supplies and equipment.

Hector Sandoval had questioned the natives and learned the lay of the land well. By nightfall of the first day he was making his honeymoon shack beside a waterhole. The shack was mesquite boughs propped up, with a piece of canvas stretched over. And that night in the middle of a wild valley beneath a moon whose brightness hurt the eyes Lita became his wife.

The next morning he set out on a burro, leaving Lita by the waterhole. He rode fast for hours until he came to another waterhole. He built a crude fence around it and stuck poles into the ground and tied cloths to the poles, so that the fabric flapped in the breeze. Then he returned to his bride.

He explained his actions. "That one is ready. Unless the wild cows tear up my work. Sometimes they do that."

The next morning he again rode off, this time in the opposite direction, until he found the watering place he was looking for. Again he built a crude fence and erected waving banners. Again he returned to Lita.

"Now," he said, "we wait." And he moved his honeymoon cottage downwind to a small ravine where they would be out of sight.

"Too soon," he told her the next day, and he would only let her show her head above the ravine bank. "We must hide carefully. They can see a man many miles away."

She patiently waited with him in the ravine, shaking her head in wonder as he told her he now had all waterholes within burro range blocked off, and soon the animals would have to come here.

On the fifth day he saddled his burro, taking great pains to be quiet and remain out of sight. Then they sat, the two lovers, waiting, looking out over the shimmering plains.

"See?" he said quietly, looking toward the horizon. She strained her eyes and finally saw movement.

"The burros?"

"No. The wild cows, with the great horns. They too have been kept from water. They will be the first to come, as they have less fear. Then, if we are lucky, the donkeys will come to drink. Then after that maybe horses."

"Will you catch the cows or horses?"

"No. These cows are too dangerous. They will kill any man they see. To catch them requires lots of good riders, expert horsemen with lariats, and fine horses. The same with the wild horses. But I can catch the burros, I think." He crossed himself.

It took the wild longhorns two hours to make their cumbersome way to the waterhole. There were not more than a dozen, and one middle-aged bull stopped and stared suspiciously at the water as they approached. The cows leading calves brushed past him with unconcern. The animals watered at leisure and several times the bull stared in the direction of Lita and Hector. It was the first time she had ever seen these huge wild cattle up close and she was frightened by their massiveness and the size of their horns. They were crouched near the top of the little gully, heads just above the rim, peering from beneath shrubs. The bull was drinking, then suddenly he raised his head and seemingly looked right at them. Then he walked toward them, his huge blank eyes unblinking. The animal stopped within two dozen feet of the pair and stared, ears bent forward like large hearing horns. Lita and Hector held their breaths. One of their burros tethered behind them suddenly stamped its foot and brayed. Immediately the bull, satisfied it had identified the object of its suspicion, wheeled and joined the other longhorns.

"Gracias, señor burro," Hector breathed lightly.

The next day the wild burros came. Lita and Hector watched silently as they finally got up enough courage to overcome their natural suspicion and approached the waterhole. The burros drank and drank and drank, as though they might not see water for another five or six days. There were a stallion and two fine mares, each with a colt. Hector waited with his saddled and gagged burros until the wild ones were actually staggering under the weight of the water taken on. Then he mounted and spurred his donkey up over the shoulder of the gully at full speed.

The wild burros fled, but were slowed by weakness from days without water and by stomachs now sloshing like water-filled balloons. Hector's mount, bigger and stronger than the wild ones, quickly overtook one mare. His rope sang out and jerked her from her feet. The colt snorted in terror as its mother was quickly and securely tied. Then Hector went after the other mare. Even though she had a head start, he caught her within a few miles. He didn't bother with the stallion.

A few days later, when the wild mares were rope-broken, Lita and Hector rode into Agua Clara with what he announced was the embryo of his new enterprise.

Young Neftali Sandoval awoke and silently rose from the rag-stuffed mattress which served as his bed at one side of the small room. His mother and father still snored over at the other end of the room which served as a kitchen for the family. Against the opposite wall his two older sisters huddled, arms entwined, like lovers, for warmth, although there was only the smallest chill in the air. Neftali quietly crossed the room and pushed back the rough, woven blanket that was the door to the home and stepped out into the growing dawn.

The family dog raised his head on hearing Neftali emerge and wagged his tail. The mongrel stretched, yawned hugely, and got up to follow. Neftali picked up a wooden bucket with a leather thong for a handle and started for the stream: Any moment his mother would be getting up, starting breakfast by patting the cornmeal dough into round, flat tortillas, heating the boiled beans, and water would be needed to make hot chocolate, sweetened with sugar syrup squeezed from sugar cane grown nearby.

Neftali wound his way through the little village. The worn footpath took many unnecessary turns, leading by each shack, but he stayed on it, as there were fewer sharp rocks and brush stubble to hurt his bare feet. He wore white cotton trousers and a loose white cotton shirt, nothing more. In the heat of the day he would wear a wide sombrero "because the sun makes you black like an Indian."

The boy's route took him past the Rojas shack, where six girls and two sons slept in a single room made of loose stones and boards. Soon the girls would arise to begin the day's sewing. They made hand-stitched infants' and children's garments, which their father periodically took on his back to la ciudad, whence he returned after a several-days drunk, with not much more than a bolt of cloth for his daughters to begin sewing once more. The two sons labored for Estorga, the smith, or took turns watching the family's flock of chickens and driving them to fresh scratching ground daily, retrieving an egg or two a day, waiting for the young roosters to mature enough to be eaten or sold.

The next shack was that of Estorga, who had years before looted the wrecked train of items different from those taken by other members of the village. He still had the tools, the large hammer, and the bellows used to start the fires in the engine. He had taken all the metal he could pry loose or unbolt, using burros to haul load after load of metal from the wreck. As a boy Estorga had briefly been apprenticed to a blacksmith, and he recognized the value of the metal and tools. He had begun his smith shop, making hinges and iron stakes, which the ranchero Domínguez across the valley liked to buy. He could fashion iron hoops to hold barrel staves in place, and together with another villager who carved wood, they sold buckets and barrels. Yes, the train wreck had done the most good for Estorga, Neftali thought. He himself carried a knife with a razor edge which Estorga had hammered from a piece of metal from the train. Neftali had watched as Estorga heated the metal to a glowing red color and then, holding it with a pair of tongs the train had yielded, hammered it into shape, after which he made the fire intensely hot with the bellows, heated the knife until it was nearly white, and then just at the right instant, as the knife cooled, Estorga plunged it into cold water. That made the cutting edge hard, the smith had explained to the boy, so that it would not become dull easily.

Nearly all of the shacks had a dog, and as the boy wound through the helter-skelter pattern of the village homes, many mongrels came out to sniff his dog, and the animals occasionally growled at one another. Neftali passed through the village and less than fifty yards to the east he came to the stream. The inhabitants of the village had scooped out a little reservoir, which caused the water to deposit its silt and foreign matter on the bottom before resuming the journey to the valley below. Neftali went to the little pool and filled the bucket. The brook made only the tiniest of sounds, and all else was quiet. The jagged song of a meadowlark suddenly filled the air. The boy saw the sun beginning to redden the eastern sky and realized he could already feel the precious chill in the air dissipate.

He let his eyes wander up the mountainside, over the harsh rocks and shrubs which rose higher and higher. On the other side were los indios, who would come occasionally to trade or buy, their women walking silently behind the mounted men. When would they come again? High overhead large birds circled deliberately. Hawks or vultures? He could not tell from here.

He saw Doña Pura the Hag emerge from her lean-to where she lived alone, a widow for many years. She wore a burlap garment that covered her to her knees. Neftali was always uneasy in the presence of the old widow. She seldom spoke to anyone. Whenever an animal was killed, rabbit, goat or fowl, she would appear at the fortunate family's door to beg the entrails. She had no income, lived on animal entrails and beans, occasionally sewed or washed in exchange for cornmeal.

Now she came toward Neftali, bucket in hand to carry water, her steps very slow but deliberate. Neftali stood uncertainly as she approached, her eyes fastened on something out in the valley.

"I saw it hours ago," she said as she dipped her bucket.

Neftali's eyes followed hers, and he gasped as he saw a great pillar of smoke ascending from leaping flames at the Domínguez ranch house. The ranch was several miles across the valley and he could see no activity other than the flames. He stood transfixed in disbelief at the sight.

"Soon they will be arriving here," the hag continued. Neftali broke into a run as he sprinted toward his home, water forgotten, the dog yapping excitedly at his heels.

His father and mother were just rising as he burst in, out of breath. "Mama! Papa! The rancho is burning. Quick, come see."

Hector Sandoval slept in his clothes, as did his wife, and no dressing was necessary. He looked shocked as he lurched out the door and looked across the valley. Then he wheeled, looking grave, and shouted, "Ortiz! Estorga! Manuel. And you others. Hurry, come see this."

Within minutes all two hundred members of the village were gathered, watching the distant flames and smoke. A few made fearful comments. All mentioned the name Guzmán.

The old hag, who had been watching silently, raised a hand and pointed. "See. On the road from the ranch. They are coming here."

Silently, the villagers watched a little dust cloud near the burning ranch house as it moved toward them down the dirt road that bisected the vast pastures of the rancho. They watched as the dust cloud moved, seemingly inches at a time. Breakfast and children were forgotten, and soon the dust cloud took the shape of many mounted men leading spare horses and a few cattle. The group followed the dirt road out of the valley to the foothills, and began climbing the winding road to the village.

"Who will do the talking?" Estorga the smith asked, the worry in his voice as well as on his face.

"They will," the old hag said with a cackle.

Ortiz the woodcarver was nervous. "Our young men and women . . . They should run."

Señor Sandoval smiled grimly. "Why? So that they can be dragged from the hills at the end of a rope? It is best we stay here and talk."

It took nearly an hour for the mounted men to wind their way up the mountainside to the village. The last five minutes seemed the longest as they strung out around a sharp curve. Their voices could be heard as some of the riders doubled back to urge on the pack animals straggling behind. Then they rode, thirty of them, Neftali counted, into the village.

A man who was apparently the leader rode up to the villagers, who were grouped at the edge of the town. Wide-eyed, Neftali marveled at his appearance; two huge pistolas, one on each hip, two rifles in scabbards near the horn of his saddle; a wide straw sombrero added heft to his short, stocky body, but did not hide his hair, which came just below his ears and met his great mustache and full beard. Two cartridge belts crossed his chest, meeting a wide belt about his waist that was also full of fresh cartridges. A large hunting knife hung near one pistol behind one hip. His shirt was of some smooth, lustrous fabric, although dirty and smoke-stained. He wore loose cotton trousers, faded, but his boots shone like new, and Neftali recognized the handiwork of the cobbler whom the rancher Domínguez employed to make his family's footwear.

The rest of the riders reined up. All were heavily armed and unkempt, looking tired but wary. The leader dismounted and walked to the villagers. He gestured dramatically at the burning rancho.

"It is yours, what is left. We took what we need."

Neftali's father stepped up and cleared his throat before speaking. "And Domínguez? And his family? And the vaqueros?"

The man made a gesture to emphasize the insignificance of those at the rancho. "I am Guzmán. They had their choice—to stay and be killed or flee. Those who lived are by now halfway to the next state." He looked around, fierce but friendly. "Who here is a smith? Our horses need attention." Estorga came forward. Guzmán indicated the horses. "Some of these mounts need shoes. We have a long way to travel over rough roads. We must be on our way quickly." He glanced nervously across the valley where the road that ran from the village past the ranch-house disappeared into the distant mountain range. Then he barked at his followers, "Pelón! Chico! Macho! Take the barefoot horses and follow this man. All of you will behave while here. These people will have enough trouble when the federales get here tomorrow or the next day."

The rest of the riders dismounted, offering to pay for fresh tortillas and beans. The three men Guzmán had addressed led the horses to Estorga's shack, where the smith began heating and fitting horseshoes. One pack animal was brought forward and Guzmán took several bottles of liquor from the pack and opened them, offering the contents to the villagers.

"Ha!" he laughed. "I'll bet in all the years you've been here you've never had Domínguez liquor offered you."

Neftali's father accepted the bottle. "You're right, Señor Guzmán. In fact, since coming here I have never tasted strong liquor. Muchas gracias." And he drank deeply. The other men of the village came closer, talking to Guzmán and his henchmen, yet never daring to ask for more information than Guzmán offered.

The sun was rising swiftly and the heat began soaking into the mountainside as the outlaws and the villagers mingled in friendly talk in the center of the village. One of the riders took a fine guitar from a pack mule and began strumming. Before long two village men were singing, each taking a separate harmonic part without so much as discussing the songs or verses. All found seats either next to a shack or on one of the boulders strewn about, while Estorga labored mightily, shoeing the horses and mending the stirrup chains.

Those in the village center were divided into two groups; some singing with the guitarists and those gathered around Guzmán as he talked.

"The Domínguez rancho was number sixteen for us," he said laughingly, draining the remnants of one bottle and pulling another from a pack mule. He passed it to those nearest him. "But it was the first one in this state. The federales are still looking for us two hundred miles from here, where we last struck. Now with these fine horses they will never catch us."

Estorga, sweating profusely, had finished and called to Guzmán. "Señor. The horses are ready. And fine horses they are. Domínguez knew how to breed animals."

Guzmán rose heavily. "Yes," he said with an air of significance, "he took good care of animals. But not such good care of his neighbors, I think. Ha! Anyway, he now has no use for horses. He has a better method of transportation. He now has wings." All the outlaws laughed heartily and started rising to take to their mounts. Guzmán faced the villagers. "And now," he said, his voice taking an edge, "who will go with us?"

The people of the village stood still, pleading looks on many faces. Guzmán and his men looked around. For a moment nothing moved. Then a hide was pushed back from the doorway of a shack and a young girl, perhaps fifteen, pretty, flashing eyes, dressed in rags, stepped out with what was obviously her personal belongings wrapped in a shawl. All eyes traveled to her as she haltingly made her way until she stood before the bandit leader. The girl's mother rushed to her.

"No! No!" the woman screamed, embracing her daughter. "Not my baby. No. Hija, you don't know what you're doing." Guzmán gently but firmly pushed the older woman back. Her husband joined her and tried to lead her away.

"She wants to come with us. Mexico is free. Almost, anyway," Guzmán said. He strode to a nearby pack mule and untied a pack. In a moment he pulled out expensive women's garments. He sorted through them briefly and then found a lady's riding habit, which he threw to the girl. "Here," he said. "You will never regret coming with us. There is much more, waiting to be wrenched from the rich who have kept you dressed worse than an Indian."

The girl went wide-eyed as she examined the clothes. Then she hurried to the shack to change. Guzmán walked to a spare horse, already saddled in fine silver-inlaid leather. He untied the lead rope and put the bridle on the animal, and led it back to the center of the group just as the girl emerged, her face somehow changed and beaming as she looked at herself in the finery she wore.

"Here," Guzmán said, offering her the reins. "This horse will be yours as long as you ride with us." He looked around at the people again. "We need fighters," he said flatly. His eyes traveled around until they rested on Neftali. Señora Sandoval rushed to her son's side. "No!" she hissed, and then her words tumbled out, "My two brothers were conscripted by revolutionaries.

My father died by a bullet when the Mexican Army forced him to fight. It will not happen to my son. Never!" She put her arms protectively around Neftali. Her vehemence took Guzmán temporarily aback.

The outlaw leader went to his horse nearby and from the saddlebag he pulled a shiny leather holster with a silver-plated pistol in it. Neftali saw the large letter D inlaid on the leather. Guzmán tossed the holster and pistol to the boy, who caught it in involuntary reflex. He had never before held a pistol. "Let him decide for himself," Guzmán said with authority. Neftali examined the holster and pistol, looked at the agonized faces of his parents, and threw the merchandise back to Guzmán.

Guzmán shrugged, turning away. "Oh well, if he won't fight with me, within a few days he will probably be fighting against me, when the federales take him."

A slim dark youth, a little older than Neftali, stepped forward and silently reached for the holster and pistol, the while his eyes traveling in meek defiance to his parents, who stood nearby. The mother of the youth gave a choked sob and turned away, followed by her husband.

"Ah! One volunteer." Guzmán said with gusto. "Very well. Take a horse, joven.[4] Get your miserable private belongings together and let's be off, before it is too late."

A quarter of an hour later as the band rode out of the village the men, women and children of Trainwreck, as their town was now called, stood watching. The parents of the youth and of the girl who had left turned and went into their shacks, grief-stricken. The others began hurried preparations to loot the burned rancho. Señor Sandoval hurried to get his half-dozen burros, and Estorga took up his tools to dismantle whatever metal work could be salvaged from the corrals, doors, kitchen, beams and shops at the rancho.

More than a hundred made up the group that left, making its way down the winding mountain road and across the valley to the ranch houses. Neftali followed his father, who led the burros. They raised a great cloud of dust as they traveled along the valley bottom over the dirt road between the pastures. Neftali recalled that the only times he had visited the rancho were during drought, when the little stream by the village ran dry. His father each summer made a few pesos by taking his burros, laden with buckets and small barrels made in the village, to beg water from Don Francisco Domínguez, whose wells were always fresh and full. Domínguez allowed him to take water, and Hector Sandoval charged the villagers for the use of his animals and his labor. With great wonder, Neftali had watched the vaqueros go about the ranch chores. Señor Domínguez always looked elegant, in wide dress sombrero, tight clean trousers and shiny boots. His mustachio was always trimmed neatly, and only occasionally did Neftali get a glimpse of Doña Irene and her daughters, who always dressed in what Neftali thought was royal fashion. He and his father, whenever they visited the rancho, were more than aware their presence was only tolerable, as far as the rancher and his workmen were concerned. His father always bowed excessively and said "thank you" too many times, and Domínguez or his wife always dismissed him with an impatient wave of the hand.

---

4. Young man.

Now as they approached the smoldering ranch house, no dogs came out to investigate, and Neftali saw the bodies of the dogs strewn around the yard. No vaqueros came out to ask what they wanted, and he saw the bodies of those who had stayed to defend the rancho.

The villagers broke into a run as they neared the ruins. Then they were in the blackened rubble. "Ay! look here what I found!" "Look at this! A fine ax!" "This window has glass! I can put it in my house."

The remaining horses and cattle, the fine buckboards and wagons, all that could not be hidden, were left untouched. It would go hard with anyone who had identifiable loot when the federales arrived a few days hence, and harder yet when the rich relatives of Domínguez came to fall heir to the rancho.

Neftali took the handmade collars from the dead dogs. How handsome the family mongrel would be in a collar, he thought. Some of the men took the clothes from the corpses nearby: "Ho! one washing and they will be as good as new. Except for the bullet holes!"

Guzmán had chosen to leave behind the wine, but had loaded all the hard liquor he could afford to carry, and the villagers soon found the underground wine storage sanctum.

Estorga was feverishly stripping the house of the hand-wrought joining bands on the fallen beams, the hinges, many of which he had made and sold to Domínguez, the anvil in the corral area, the winch at the well, the pipings and fittings at the windmill.

Neftali found the master bedroom and in a nearly burned-out chest of drawers he discovered treasure. A compass, a jeweled belt buckle, a pair of gloves of the softest leather imaginable, a folding pocket knife and coins.

The women salvaged half-burned quilts, linen and wool blankets. A calf in the corral quickly met death and within minutes was roasting on a fire. This was a fiesta the likes of which the people of Trainwreck had not seen since the cattle train had been derailed more than a decade and a half earlier. And as night came they made their way back up the mountainside to the village, burros laden, arms full, and stomachs too.

"And you did not try to stop them!? After you saw them kill and plunder?" the lieutenant was roaring.

"How could we, teniente? We are peons, unarmed. There were forty or fifty men with Guzmán. Most had three guns."

"Now tell me this! Did any of you help them in any way?"

"No," it was Estorga, "in fact, they abducted a boy and a girl from this village. If you catch Guzmán, remember, they were taken by force and would never fight against federales."

The lieutenant spat. "We shall see about that soon. All right. You say forty or fifty men. I have thirty-five. That means I need more. Five of you had better volunteer or I will do the volunteering for you."

He looked around at the villagers gathered about him as he and his men ate tortillas and beans ravenously. Their many days on the trail had made them all lean and gaunt. His eyes traveled around as he waited for volunteers. He finished his food and wiped his mouth with a large red kerchief.

"You have waited too long. You," he pointed to a young man in his early twenties, "take the first empty horse there. Be quick about it. And you. And you." He selected those obviously young and not married. "I need one more." His eyes fell on Neftali. "How old are you, joven?"

"No, no," Neftali's mother began whimpering, "no, no, no. Not him. He is fourteen, no more, you cannot take our son."

But Teniente Ramos remained adamant. "I'm sorry. I have to catch the bandits. It is for *you*, all of you, that we are making Mexico safe. Everybody wants law and order, but no one is willing to fight for it." He looked at Neftali. "Ándale.⁵ Take a horse. You will return to the village when Guzmán and his pirates are dead, and they shall be dead by the end of the week."

With great force Hector Sandoval pushed his near-hysterical wife into the shack, clamping a hand to her mouth as she tried to scream. Then with a roar of hoofs, the detachment thundered out of the village, down the mountainside to the road leading in the direction the bandits had gone.

The group traveled at a slow, loping gallop. Neftali had never been on a horse, but found it little different from a burro. He reached down as he rode and adjusted the stirrups to his leg length. He was near the rear of the group, and the pack animals and calves were behind him. The lieutenant suddenly pulled alongside him and threw a rifle at him. Neftali had to catch it or let it strike him across the chest. The lieutenant smiled and spurred ahead to lead his troops.

Lita and Hector Sandoval stayed in their shack all day. Periodically she would begin to wail, and he would comfort her, saying their son would be back as soon as the outlaws were tracked down. But his face showed the doubt of his own words. Toward evening she went outside and looked about, exhausted from weeping. She sat on a large rock in front of the house and sobbed softly. Her daughters had huddled silently all day, glad that neither of the conscriptors had selected them.

Señora Sandoval sat quietly until darkness came. Then, "I'd like a fire here, outside," she told her husband. Without hesitation he walked out of the village, up the hillside, and gathered wood. He returned and built a small fire near her.

Hector Sandoval felt a little guilty that his grief for the loss of his son was perhaps a little outweighed by concern for his wife. He loved this woman, who still looked like a girl after sixteen years of marriage. Fate had been kind to him, he thought, again with guilt, in that he had had only three children. Others in the village had seven, eight, even ten, and he couldn't understand how such a family ate in this land of want and poverty. A thought occurred to him that had fleetingly often crossed his mind. Los Estados Unidos. Thousands, he knew, were fleeing either tyranny or poverty in Mexico. To America.

His daughters came out to sit on the ancient railroad tie that served as a bench in front of the house. "He'll be back, Mama," one of them said. Mrs. Sandoval burst into tears anew, and Hector gave his daughters a stern look. The fire crackled mockingly.

Hector silently motioned his daughters to prepare something to eat within the house. They disappeared inside. The other villagers were peculiarly absent from sight. Soon Jilda, the eldest daughter, brought her mother a plate

---

5. Let's go.

of food, but it was refused. The family sat and ate and only an occasional sob could be heard. A bright moon rose, and now and then a night animal gave its night cry. Hector Sandoval kept the fire supplied with small sticks.

Well after midnight the little fire leaped and flickered, making small popping and hissing noises in its preoccupation. Then Hector Sandoval thought he heard a sound. He raised his head and turned one ear toward the valley to the west, which at this time was a vast sea of blackness. He strained to hear. Then suddenly the sound burst upon them. A fast-approaching horse coming up the winding road. Now the hoofs clicked as they crossed stone underfooting; now they pounded as they hit soft dirt. The horse was approaching so fast the family felt terror, then horse and rider burst into the small circle of light, the animal slamming its feet into the ground to stop as the steel bit cut into its mouth, and then Neftali was running to his mother's arms.

A few minutes later when the cacaphony of reunion had abated somewhat and Señora Sandoval had momentarily ceased to praise the Mother of God, Neftali explained. "No, mamacita," it was the first time the lad had used the endearing diminutive and Hector Sandoval felt a surge go through him as he experienced a feeling of man-to-man equality toward his son, "God did not bring me back. I escaped. I am now a deserter from the Mexican Army. They'll be looking for me in the morning, to make an example of me."

Before his mother could begin wailing, Hector Sandoval took command. "All right. All of you listen. Neftali knows what we must do. He and I have talked it over before when we were alone working with the burros. We leave. Now. To go north. Quick. No talk. Pack our things. Neftali and I will go get the burros. We have six. We should be able to take everything and be a long way from here before another night."

Except for the boy, the others were stunned. "But, where . . . ?"

"To los Estados Unidos. Where there will be no more of all that makes us suffer. Hurry now. You women wrap up everything and bring it out here. We can leave within an hour. Or the lieutenant might return for Neftali."

1970

---

# ROLANDO HINOJOSA
## b. 1929

Romeo Rolando Hinojosa-Smith was born in Mercedes, in Texas's Lower Rio Grande Valley. His family traces its roots in the valley to 1748. His father fought in the Mexican Revolution while his mother, Anglo-Saxon in origin and a fluent bilingual speaker, and the rest of the family lived north of the border; Spanish and English were spoken in the household. After high school, Hinojosa joined the army and fought in the Korean War. After his military service, he earned a bachelor's degree from the University of Texas at Austin in 1953, a master's from New Mexico Highlands University in 1963, and a doctorate from the University of Illinois in 1969. His doctoral dissertation concerned the nineteenth-century Spanish novelist Benito Pérez Galdós. Like his grandmother, mother, and three of his four siblings,

Hinojosa became a teacher. Since 1981, he has been on the faculty of the English Department at the University of Texas at Austin.

Hinojosa has received many accolades, among them *el Premio Quinto Sol* (the Fifth Sun prize, 1972) for best novel, given by Quinto Sol Publications, a small press in Berkeley, California; the Casa de las Américas Prize (1976); inclusion in the Best Writing in the Southwest (1981); the Lifetime Achievement Award from the Texas Institute of Letters (1998); the Alumni Achievement Award from the University of Illinois at Urbana (1998); membership in the Texas Literary Hall of Fame (2006); and a Doctor of Letters from Texas A & M University (2007). He has been nominated for Spain's Cervantes Prize.

With a concise, experimental style marked by irony, satire, stark realism, and a cutting wit, Hinojosa incorporates into his work various genres, including sketches, reportage, epistles, journals, poetry, and, broadly speaking, detective murder mysteries. He credits the interconnected Yoknapatawpha County novels, by the American modernist writer William Faulkner, as major influences on his writing. He has published his fiction, nonfiction, and poetry primarily through Mexican American presses. Written in Spanish, English, and an often playful combination of both, the books in Hinojosa's *Klail City Death Trip* Series (*KCDTS*) have not been published chronologically in the order of the events in the series. Additionally, the Spanish and English versions differ significantly in terms of narrative sequence, with some chapters deleted, others added, and still others rearranged. Thus both language editions must be read to gain a comprehensively accurate understanding of the series.

Hinojosa's first novel, the Spanish-language *Estampas del Valle y otras obras* (1973), published in English as *The Valley* (1983), introduces a host of Texas Mexicans inhabiting the fictional Belken County, in the Lower Rio Grande Valley. Some of these characters, in particular the cousins Jehú/Jehu Malacara and Rafa/Rafe Buenrostro, are developed in subsequent novels. In the Spanish-language *Klail City y sus alrededores* (1976), published in English as *Klail City* (1987), Jehu and Rafe's lives develop, and a theme emerges that permeates the series: the historical conflict between Texas Anglos and Texas Mexicans over both land and the laws governing their lives. In the English-language *Korean Love Songs* (1978), the narrative, in verse, details Rafe's and, to a much lesser extent, Jehu's experiences in the Korean War. *The Useless Servants* (1993), also in English, uses Rafe's journal entries to extensively depict Rafe's day-to-day life in the war. One fact not escaping Rafe and other Texas Mexican soldiers in Korea is that, even while defending their country, they are still subjected to the racism of their Anglo American fellow soldiers. *Mi querido Rafa* (1981), published in English as *Dear Rafe* (1985), profiles Jehu primarily and enables readers to see, from multiple perspectives, financial, real estate, and political maneuvers enhancing the general Anglo power structure.

In *Partners in Crime* (1985), Hinojosa's first crime procedural, Rafe is a lieutenant in Belken County's homicide squad. Adverse race relations no longer dominate the valley, where the economy has become corrupted by laundered money from Mexican drug dealers. Law enforcement agencies on both sides of the border cooperate to solve gangland killings. In *Ask a Policeman* (1998), another detective murder mystery, Rafe is chief inspector of the Belken County homicide squad, again solving drug-related gangland killings. The most recent installment of the *KCDTS* is *We Happy Few* (2006), a tragicomic campus novel taking place at Belken State University, in Klail City. *Becky and Her Friends* (1990), published in Spanish as *Los amigos de Becky* (1991), is included in this anthology in its entirety. In over two dozen journalistic-style interviews, various Belken County residents tell the story of Becky Escobar, who gradually asserts her independence after divorcing her husband.

## BECKY AND HER FRIENDS

### *The Opening Shot*

What are we to do with Becky? What should we think of such a woman? A Texas Mexican who, apparently, from one day to the next, decides (that power-laden verb) that her husband is no longer going to live with her and with those two children of theirs?

And what of her mother, doña Elvira Navarrete, wife of Catarino Caldwell, Capt. U.S.A., Cav. Ret.?[1] Yes, what will doña Elvira say? with her dreams of a long, lasting alliance with the Escobar-Leguizamón-Leyva families?

And what will the world say? The world that matters: Belken County, Klail City, the Valley. This world where people talk, and talk, and talk. And despite much of the foolishness which is said, sputtered out, and, at times, hissed out, the truth comes spilling out.

The listener is no P. Galindo,[2] sad to say. P. Galindo knew people; the listener is a beginner.

The Valley, though old, is vigorous still. It has seen many rites, has produced many witnesses. In over 200 years of oral and recorded history, many generations have come and gone and taken their place in history in the cemeteries of the world: in this case, Europe, the Orient, wherever Valley men and women have died. Many lives and some miracles, but, as usual, more ordinary lives than miraculous ones.

All of this the listener knows, intuits even.

A brief prologue, then, and the listener is grateful to the Greeks for having invented the term. And, for this novel to begin, it's start with another bit of Greek, a drama. In this case, a brief one.

And, since it is brief, the reader is warned that attention is an essential. The reader must be reminded, as if in wartime, that it isn't the firing or the shrapnel one worries about. One should worry more about the holes they leave on those who don't take care and cover. As always, verbum sat sapienti.[3]

The novel begins here:

(A woman in her late thirties is standing. It's her living room; she picks up a candy wrapper and throws it a distance of some four feet and makes the basket. She smiles. While dressed nicely, she's not planning to leave the house. Not tense, not relaxed; nevertheless, she is quite sure of herself. She is waiting for someone; in this case, her husband. His name is Ira Escobar, a County Commissioner. A car's engine is heard and the closing of a door. He enters through a screened front porch and into the living room).

BECKY: "I've decided that you are not going to live with us anymore."

IRA: "What?"

BECKY: (With indescribable patience.) "I've decided that you are not going to live with us anymore."

(Exit Ira Escobar, for now.)

---

1. Cavalry Retired.
2. A fictional character; a minor poet, writer, and journalist who appears in some of the *KCDTS* novels and is mentioned in others.
3. A word to the wise (Latin).

*Cast of Characters*
(in order of appearance)

Lionel Villa
Viola Barragán
Isidro Peralta
Andrés Malacara
Emilio Tamez
Julia Ortegón
Ursula Ortegón
Martín San Esteban
E. B. Cooke
Edith Timmens
Bowly Ponder
Lucas Barrón
Otila Macías Rosales
Reina Campoy
Bill and Tippy Ochoa
Gualberto Ornelas, O.M.I.[4]
Sammie Jo Perkins
Polín Tapia
Noddy Perkins
Nora Salamanca
Matías Soto, O.M.I.
Elvira Navarrete
Raúl Santoscoy
Drinks González
Ira Escobar
Becky

*Well! some people talk of morality, and some*
*or religion, but give me a little snug property.*

Maria Edgeworth

## Lionel Villa

Let's drop in on Lionel Villa and hear what he has to say regarding Rebecca—alias Becky—Escobar. The famous Becky Escobar, wife for a certain time (in these uncertain times) of banker-politician cum horns, Ira Escobar, a native of Jonesville-on-the-Rio. This is the same Ira Escobar who graced Klail City (county seat of Belken County) and who now lives in Jonesville once again.

Now, you would think that Lionel Villa is hardly a reliable witness since he is Becky's uncle. Too, he has left her some land, some money, and much good will, but Villa is a stalwart. A bulwark his friends call him. He's a man of his word—hombre de palabra, and a man of respect, hombre de respeto. These two attributes have little to do with money Villa's case. Because he's old, his

---

4. Oblates of Mary Inmaculate, a religious order.

upper seventies, the listener would guess, and because he's never broken his word or promise, he commands respect as who wouldn't? But enough of this preamble, let's listen to what he has to say.

Right! I myself baptized that girl over to San Francisco de Paula mission on the eastern edge of the Celeste Hermoso Ranch, the Navarrete land . . . I, too, am a Navarrete, the maternal side, and so, Becky's mom and I are cousins germane, primos hermanos. She then married a Caldwell. Those are my bona fides, period.

Well now, it's no secret that my wife and I never had any kids, and that's why we decided, years ago, that whatever else happened, the land would stay in the family—en la familia, eh? And if it could be done, the money too would stay in the family, not the Church. I mean, our families built San Francisco Mission, and that's enough; probably more than enough to get some of us into God's heaven, right? So, with the Church business out of the way, the money, no matter how little it was, and the trust no matter how small it was, and the land, no matter how hard, dry, and poor it may have been, that too would stay in the family.

The listener takes a brief pause here. Lionel Villa lights up an unfiltered Camel. He then winks at me and says he's down to a pack a day. Incidentally, he says, the doctors he's continued through the years are all dead. This, of course, is by the way.

Well, when we baptized Becky, we decided then and there that she'd be the one to get the land and all. No strings. No restrictions. Outright. And that was some thirty odd years ago, and the will is still in force, yessir.

As for Becky's mom, my cousin Elvira? Two words for her: tickled and pink.

The paperwork was all done by Romeo Hinojosa, the lawyer. He was fresh out of college back then, but he knew what he was doing, all right. Everything within this country's laws, and this country sure has got some laws, don't it? A great country, but you've got to watch those laws, leave you naked if you don't.

Well, according to that last will and testament of ours, Becky was to get a good part of the trust when she hit thirty-five. And she hit them flat out, but . . . yeah, and let me point out that her divorce from Ira Escobar took place three months before she hit thirty-five and added to which, they'd had a 60-day cooling off period before that, and so let's not hear any wild talk about coincidences or anything like that. Now, if you don't take my word for it, I won't go on, won't say another word.

The truth. She divorced that jackass, but that was personal, between 'em.

Okay. Becky slams into her thirty-five years and the separation and divorce become part of history. All of this came pretty close like, but close don't count, and let me tell you this too: she—Becky, now—she didn't push the economic door on that jackass's face. Personally, I think she should have, but she didn't, and it was her money and her will to do with it what she wanted, and I have no say-so, period, period, period.

So here comes old Romeo Hinojosa, much older and much wiser, and he has some advice with him. Texas, he says, for all its damfool laws, still retains some Spanish laws regarding property—community property, see? So he, Hinojosa, he fixes it to where Becky's kids, Charlie and Sarah, are the benefactors. The heirs to the trust, see? And who's to care for the money till Charlie and Sarah come of age, when Charlie's twenty-seven and Sarah twenty-five?

The Bank. The Klail City First National with Jehu Malacara as the trust officer. As I said, I don't have a legal leg to stand on here, yo no tengo vela en este entierro, and I'm not about to get into that Becky–Jehu thing. None of my business anyways.

Now I'm going to shoot off some 180 degrees here. Talking about the late Javier Leguizamón—in the words of a famous Irishman: as fine a man as ever robbed the helpless. Now he too knew how to get the laws to serve him . . . oh, yes. All proper. Sure. But to his benefit. Double sure.

So, when he up and dies—you and I both know that he and Angelita were childless . . . well, he leaves a chunk, and that's a big chunk, to Ira Escobar. That's right, Becky's husband.

Once again Hinojosa steps in and then right back out. His advice to Becky was—not the way I'm saying it, but words to that effect—stay out. It's a mess. You've got enough to handle here. And he was right, but Romeo Hinojosa is Becky's attorney, and he added a wrinkle: He got Homer Torres, he represents Ira, see? He got Homer to add Charlie and Sarah to their father's will. Fair's fair, Romeo Hinojosa said. Becky agrees to stay out of it—free and clear, no consideration whatsoever—but the kids got to be protected by their father. Ha!

But I got to say this too. Ira did well by his kids, but as Romeo Hinojosa says: Put it on paper and let's have dates, proper signatures, and witnesses. I mean that's like looking at the traffic lights and at both sides of the street before you let the dog cross the street ahead of you. No need to take chances.

At first it looked like Becky got the short end of that stick and right away people—la gente, eh?—people said that Hinojosa'd been bought off. Couldn't resist a gift, a bribe, see? But they were wrong.

It was good advice, sound advice. Becky got to keep her money, my wife's and mine, see? There wasn't much, but what she got was all of it. And Charlie and Sarah got their father's share out of that community property.

Pretty Anglo-like, right? But that's okay. Took time for us to get used to their laws, but that's okay, too.

So that's where it stands. That land of my wife's and mine is out to Bascom. Hard by some Leguizamón holdings. And that's important 'cause Ira Escobar is a Leguizamón on his mother's side, and as I said, old Javier Leguizamón did leave that chunk to Ira, outright. Hm.

I know this don't come to much, not when you consider how much money this government has wasted away . . .

At this point Lionel Villa stops to rub his left knee. He points to it: with his chin. He says he broke his knee when he fell off a chinaberry tree. And, his father, old don Justo Villa, whipped him for it. A damfool thing Lionel says, smiling. Me falling, he says, and my father whipping me for it. (Laughing) never fell again, no sir.

But let's get a drink, and we'll talk some more.

Frosted drinks of cold limeade in hand, the listener and Lionel Villa take a seat, on the ground, facing a cedar windbreak. The Rio Grande at their backs and less than a quarter mile away as it meanders its way toward the Gulf.

It's late September. The cotton's gone now, the third and lean pick was done with ten days ago. What few stubborn stalks of cotton remain have been turned black to gray by the Valley's own soil.

As I was saying just now, my cousin Elvira Navarrete was tickled and pink with the terms of the divorce. Not happy, with, the divorce, though, since that meant that Becky, now no longer an Escobar, could not then lay claim to the name Leguizamón. Elvira is like that, poor thing. Still, time and money have a way with smoothing things out, making things come out even.

And Becky, you ask? Oh, Becky . . . Ah, Becky. She had finally got rid of that anchor, and talk about turning over new leaves here and there. First it was Spanish. She was going to learn it again after years of nothing but English. Back to grade one, you might say, and good for her, say I.

And funny? Like a kid, see? She'd say some things in Spanish that would make you laugh or cry. Ha! But mistakes or not, she'd keep at it. Sounded like those Jewish merchants in Jonesville's Gaza Strip, mixing the languages, not giving up . . . And Becky won out. It was a lack of practice, but it came back.

But the best part was about the clubs in Klail. She quit 'em. The women's, the music. That kind of shit.

And speaking of shit, while the money and the land and the kids was agreed to, Ira Escobar—on his own—well, he tried to muddy it up a bit.

How—he'd ask—how could anyone say that Becky was a good mother when everyone knew she'd tied herself to a certain someone or other. Well, that was a pile of bull.

Becky did find someone, Jehu Malacara, the banker. But tied? Living with? Arrimados?[5] No sir. Married, and in Dellis County. That's legal, isn't it? I admit Dellis is a no-count county, but it's still part of the State of Texas, ain't it?

And Jehu's a good man. I've seen him with the kids—and I see how they look to him, too. Jehu's no saint, he never said or lay claim to, and he didn't pretend to be one either in any way. He's a good man. Jehu's got a pair on him that clang when he walks. Serious, decent.

All right, take a look at this: at the Bank there, who's in charge? Noddy Perkins? Gettin' old and tough enough still, but he could hardly wait for Jehu to get back from Austin some years back. He—Noddy—he knew Jehu'd be back at the Bank. One, two, three years, was it? And Jehu did come back. Took his time getting back, but when he did, the job was still waiting for him.

And you know what Ira Escobar said back then? And he said it here, in that house where you got that drink. Said it was luck that Jehu got the job

---

5. An unmarried couple living together; at the time in which the novel takes place, this arrangement was considered immoral.

back. Luck, he said. That boy could no more read character than I could sing in the opera house. Hmph! Luck! This, he said. That, he said. Ira es poca cosa, that's right. No count.

Jehu came in through the front door of Perkins's bank. In he comes, someone tells Noddy, and out comes that old pirate, and shakes Jehu's hand like he was priming a kerosene pump.

I can imagine how Ira must've taken this. Yeah, Ira the commissioner of Place Four. But there was nothing he could do about it—so he lied to himself by calling it luck. You've got to feel sorry for a person like that. He—Ira—owed his job to Noddy and to that uncle of his, Javier Leguizamón. But he doesn't have power—el poder—ha! Money? Sure. Land? I'll go along with that. But power? No, not a bit of it.

Hate to say it, but I got to: I've always said he doesn't have what it takes to give bad news to someone or to accept the good news when it comes. He calls it luck.

But Jehu? A different story all together; he can be tough, but he knows how to be soft, tender, even. Knows how to laugh, too. And don't no one come by this farm to tell me that Jehu had it easy as a child, boy, or youngster. He didn't.

He's not Noddy's fool, and I've yet to see Jehu back down from what's right.

Remember the time with him and Martín San Esteban, the pharmacist? Olivia's brother?

And remember Olivia? Bright girl, and good. Made for Jehu. Steady. And then to die in a car wreck? Some damn drunk . . . And Jehu? At the hospital, ten days, two weeks, whatever. From there to Witwer's Mortuary and from there to holy ground.

They'd been engaged, and formally. Un noviazgo,[6] like the old days. You were there, remember? And you think Moisés San Esteban and his wife would have approved of that engagement if Jehu wasn't a serious person? That they were going to consent their one daughter, Livita, to someone without any sense? No, not by a long chalk.

Jehu, like his dad or maybe his grandfather before him, went for Livita San Esteban's hand—alone. No sponsors, nothing. Borrowed his cousin Rafe's car and drove to the San Esteban home. Like the old days, back when I was a kid. Two requests, the engagement and the right to visit, to call on her there. At home. You don't see that anymore. But he did it. And he went alone when he did.

An hour later? Back in the car and Jehu drove straight to the pharmacy. That's right, to see Martín San Esteban, his brother-in-law to be. Martín's got some Becerra blood to go along with the San Esteban mixture, and he can be dense at times. Bull headed, even.

Martín started to fuss while Jehu crossed his arms and stood there, legs apart. Just then Martín's own wife rushed in and told—that's told—told Martín not to be such a damned fool. I think that's the first time Martín San Esteban got wind who it was he'd married when he married San Juanita, old Pedro Ycaza's only daughter. This is not to say that Jehu needed help, 'cause he didn't.

---

6. Going steady; boyfriend and girlfriend.

San Juanita Ycaza knew what kind of person Jehu Malacara was—just like good cotton, a long staple and none of that middling stuff.

And I know this happened for a fact, and I know it as many others in Klail know it. I mean, how big is Klail anyway? Yeah.

Well, then what happened, happened. Some drunk Anglo came barrelin' off the old Military Highway, fails to make that curve, and he hits Olivia broadside. And just how long had she and Jehu been engaged? Seven, eight months? Something like that? In a wreck. Three blocks from her house. Son-of-a-bitch.

And then some six months go by. By now, Ira Escobar—damned fool—decides on his own to run for County Judge. Doesn't bother to ask the Bank, doesn't bother to check with Noddy Perkins . . . Well, you got to admire guts like that, but that's a very limited boy.

Now, I've got nothing against being independent, but when you go on your own after you gave your heart and your soul to someone, like Ira did, what does he expect?

The mexicanos weren't going to vote for him—he's Noddy's boy. On the other hand, they got nothing against Jehu, he works there. That's different.

County Judge. Hmph. About this time I wind up in the hospital, and things are looking bad—bad to the point where I'm going to be calling Death on a first name basis. The heart, they said. No, it's the liver, they said. Your mother! is what I said. Four doctors . . . Jesus!

So who comes to see me at the hospital, aside from family? I'll tell you. Jehu. Yeah. To talk, that's all. To laugh some. I got, I got some forty years on that boy. And he didn't come to see me on business and not 'cause we're related, which we're not. A visit. To talk.

I tell you, it's a dirty shame but damn few of Jehu's generation know what manners are all about. And my boy Ira? Sure, he was there, but because Becky came to see me and it was there as God and the forty thousand virgins are my witnesses, it was right there that I knew that Becky would be off and flying, flying away like a dove. That girl was going to leave, and if I was going to die, why, it was time for the lawyer Hinojosa to go over all my papers. One more time. Which he did.

But like I said, Becky was just too much woman for Ira Escobar. And if they lasted as long as they did—I mean, if she put up with that jackass as long as she did, it was due to that eternal stupidity, that so-called tradition. And here's another truth: Becky's mother, yes, my cousin Elvira Navarrete, kept that marriage going. Ha!

Mother, hmph. Giving birth doesn't make a woman a mother. No sir. And she's my cousin, no two ways about that. Ira—she'd say—Ira is a Leguizamón, and she'd puff up like a blow fish. A lot of that wedding and marriage was her doing. And Becky married him.

Good Lord. And of course, since it was to be the wedding of the last two centuries, they went all out. And here's poor Catarino Caldwell—the father of the bride—and who is just about nutty enough to build a new church, see what I mean? Old Catarino has always had more cents than sense, more property than brain cells. Where's my proof? Well, look who he married, my cousin!

That Becky has a spine on her, though, and a brain to go with it, and more of both than her parents, and that's not a matter of luck. I'll be the first to say that her mother can be a loose cannon at times, but she's not a bad person, you know what I mean? She's not cruel or mean, just dumb and as tiresome as a summer drought . . . And Catarino? Not a mean bone there either, I'll tell you. Now you hand him a rifle, a fishing rod, and he's off, hunting, fishing, trapping. Catarino Caldwell made himself into a mexi-cano years ago, even before the time Becky was born. Tell you what, I bet there's not a hundred people left in the Valley, farm or city folks, who've heard him say a word in English. God's truth. Just like Martín Holland, he's La Güera Fira's daddy. Yeah. You remember her, she's that good looking blondie married up with Elías Castro. Those two, Martín and Catarino Caldwell Mexicanized themselves early.

But I was saying, Becky is neither dumb nor bad looking. That she married Ira Escobar is something else again. Her mom pushed and shoved moun-tains—it was scandalous—and Becky, dutiful, young, inexperienced, gave in. She'd had four years at college and the diploma to go with them and then to end up married to that jackass. Damn!

But we all've got just one life to live and lead, and if you play your cards poorly, if you fold too soon, life and happiness—all the pleasures, yeah, and the suffering too—fly out the window. And life goes out dull as mud, too.

But then that's why friends and relatives were invented, and that's where I came in, had to.

Becky had to become independent. Economically independent, you get me? And someone else came in too: a woman, a woman with nerve and fiber, unafraid, and gutsy. And sharp, too.

The listener and Lionel Villa walked back to the farm house for some ice, for some more limeade, and for another pack of Camel cigarettes. Lionel Villa looked up at the Gulf-laden clouds and bet the listener, giving odds of four to seven, that there'd be no rain that day. The listener, with a farmer for a fa-ther, didn't take the bet. The wind was coming in from the South, the listener said. Villa's laugh cackled somewhat and this brought out a couple of dogs resting under the house. Would I bet that the Gulf hurricane would miss the Valley, he asked. The listener is much younger than Lionel Villa, but no fool.

On the way back to the windbreak, Villa said the woman he was talking about was the redoubtable Viola Barragán.

So Viola stepped in to help Becky, help her with a little boost, to make her independent. Her own person. Ha! And then, my cousin Elvira . . . did I tell you?

Ha! Not a peep out of her. Yeah. Now, way back there, when I was young— younger—around the twenties, the nineteen thirties, Viola and Elvira were a pair of good-looking beauties. Train stoppers, you know what I am talking about? Just plain, uncommon beauty, the both of them. You've got to admit that Becky is a looker, and she'll be a looker at fifty, even. Well, her mom, my cousin Elvira, didn't take a back seat to anyone—prettier than anyone of those Hollywood actresses. Oh, yeah. She'll keep, all right. You won't find any rust on Elvira and let me tell you that Viola ran just about even. Neck to neck, no daylight, just like the horse-racing, let me tell you.

And both married young, just like Becky, but younger. Becky had the col-lege and all, but marrying young just like that domineering mama of hers. 'Cause let me tell you this too: Elvira Navarrete is no weakling; she's un-afraid. But she's got a weakness, she's a climber. And that is exactly where she pushed Becky, nose first and come what may. And there Elvira went, pushing, shoving her Becky to the Leguizamón clan.

Why, a blindman can see how dumb Ira Escobar is. You won't find him hiding his light under no bushel basket. First, there's no light, and second, there's no basket either. No idea how to hold one . . . But I got to admit, limited as that boy is, he and Becky made one fine-looking couple. What they didn't make was a marriage. Simple as that. But I also got to admit that Becky worked like a slave for some ten years there so Ira'd be and stay on as a county commissioner. I now think that it was right there and right then that she saw what it was she'd married. Probably saw it before, sensed it maybe, felt it, somehow, but she wasn't the person to judge her husband. She just flat, straight out had not thought on it.

And so she married. She dressed well, ate at the best places that Klail City and the Valley have to offer. But no fool, Becky saw right away that Ira was successful in politics because of the Klail-Blanchard-Cooke Ranch. And the Bank, of course, they all being the same thing. She wised up.

So she flitted here'n there, like a butterfly. But she lived for him, not for her. She was a messenger. A flunky, for God's sake. And she lived for her mother. God!

And Elvira, her mom? Happier than a dozen clams, I'm here to tell you. And Becky again? Politicking for her husband. And what was she doing for herself, for Becky Escobar? Nothing. Not a thing.

Shoot. The Ranch and the Bank did the important things that truly mattered. Becky was a prop, visible here and there, but a prop. She was being used just like Sammie Jo Perkins who . . . hold it! Sorry. I'm on shaky ground here, but I might as well say what I think I know:

Sammie Jo's father, Noddy Perkins, used his only daughter, Sammie Jo, as a brood mare. Yes . . . Noddy married her off to a couple of absolute—total—no count losers. Talk was one of them was a fancy boy, or both of them was . . . It doesn't matter. Noddy saw his own daughter the same way he saw Becky Escobar: a tool, something to use.

I wasn't fooled a bit back then. Not for one minute, I wasn't. It was Noddy's idea and no one else's that Becky Escobar be given unanimous membership in those clubs I mentioned earlier this morning. Noddy. His idea, no one else's. And Becky? Blind, blinded by all that dazzle, by all that attention. Poor thing.

And she told me so, herself. Told me the day she first thought of a divorce. That's another story altogether, and a long one, too. But I heard it from her. And I don't blame anyone, and I won't point fingers at anyone. Not Sammie Jo, either. No one. If anything, she and Becky became good friends after the divorce.

At this point, Lionel Villa invited the listener for another light snack. Nothing special, he said. He brewed some tea, orange-leaf tea, and each of us used a cinnamon stick as a stirring spoon. Both Villa and the listener sucked the stick dry and popped it into the orange-leaf tea.

Did I mention the Spanish, I mean when she decided to use it again? Well, when she talked to me of her life as a flunky, she referred to herself as a pendeja, a fool, an asshole, really. Not angry, more of a realization, of a wasted part of her life—but I will say this as clearly as I can: Becky acted on her own. She reached and made a firm decision, and she didn't ask her mother either, no sir. Becky was going to cut loose from Ira, and she was cutting that umbilical cord from Elvira too, see?

A decision firm and personal. No crying, no hiccups, no shortness of breath, and no raising of the voice. In short, class! She told Ira that they weren't going to live together anymore. That's all she said to that jackass: that they would not be living together anymore, and that that was it.

But the people? What would they say? And the families? And society, too? Friends? And X, and Y, and Z, and every damned busybody to boot, including their bloody mother? Nothing to do with me is what that great beauty said. This is of no concern, of no business, really, to the family, the families, Klail's society, etc. It's no one's business. No one's. And Becky went on, since it doesn't matter to me—and she told me this, all smiles when she told me. . . . You seen that smile of hers?

Anyway, she said: "If it doesn't matter to me, whatever the world thinks or wants to think, is of no concern either." So, Klail, the world, everyone, could take a flying leap at the moon, the nearest lake, the Rio Grande . . .

But that was it. That union was over, and that was that.

Becky herself called Chalo Figueroa from Valley Movers, and she packed everything that belonged to Ira. Everything and by herself, too. All this according to Chalo Figueroa. And she paid for the move, too, although the lawyer Hinojosa did recover part of the expenses later on when it came to divvying up the community property.

Oh, and another thing. She got some additional money, yeah. All those years they were married and that Ira worked at the Klail Bank, and he was under a generous retirement plan? Well, she got part of that, too. For the kids, Becky said.

And she didn't do that from spite. The house and another share of the property that was coming to her, and that was it. And then, to have a friend in Viola Barragán, that was a bonus. As I said, Viola and Becky's mom had been—have been—close for years.

Anyone who's met Viola knows she's not a pushover, and if sometime back she saw Becky as willful and foolish, everyone now also admits that it was Viola—first and before anyone else—who recognized that Becky's talents had been hidden for years.

Too, that Becky, in her foolish stage, used to think that Viola Barragán was a nobody, an over-the-hill man chaser, something like that, a devil in a skirt, as we say. Anyway, Becky also saw for herself that having to depend on someone else for a living, to depend on someone else for anything, to be nothing but a kept-though-married-woman was not the way to live. She saw what being independent meant.

And they hit it off. Right away.

Viola has always been a believer of allowing people to do, to live, as they want. There are some who say Viola goes overboard on this, but what do people know, right? Now, what Viola Barragán does have is a pair of ovaries that would serve as testicles on a prize Santa Gertrudis[7] bull. Viola doesn't

7. Saint Gertrude, a breed of cattle developed in 1929.

go around begging, asking favors, etcetera. She's got a keen eye, and the world is just going to have to deal with that. She's no gossip, either. No intriguer, she doesn't go around making life hard for anyone. And she's forgiving. How 'bout that?

She'll forgive—perhaps not forget, but she's firm in compassion, I'll say that. If Viola, sometime back, said that Becky Escobar was a ninny, let's say, Viola had every right to say what she pleased, just like everybody else. And she may have been right on the money 'cause Becky was allowing herself to be used. Becky was blinder than a family of bats. She couldn't even see the tip of her own little upturned nose. She used someone else's eyes to see through, like wearing blinders.

But when she took the blinders off, threw away that blindman's cane, that's when she took a deep, deep breath and in that breath she sent Ira off, up, and away. But it didn't stop there, with her husband. Out too went those secondhand ideas and opinions she used to hang on to.

It was the change, see? A new woman, really, and that's why her mamma Elvira didn't know what to do, what to think. Whoever that woman was, it wasn't Becky, thought Elvira—who almost fainted. No. No. No. It's a devil, a ghost of some kind . . . Elvira all over.

Well, just as soon as Viola got wind of Becky's doings, Viola drove from Klail to Jonesville to see Elvira. To head her off, really. And then—just as soon as she got to Elvira's house—Viola took her aside and spoke in no uncertain, unreserved terms. Not to act the damned fool, for one. That she—Elvira—better not think, better not even think, of saying anything harsh to Becky. That Becky in her present state and sailing high, that Becky with two kids and with thirty-five years on her back, that Becky in that mood of hers now, would and could tell Elvira—mother or not—to leave her nose out of Becky's affairs. To stick to her own business, if she—Elvira—had any. And so on.

And Viola it was who could make Elvira see the light. She and Elvira, remember? Well, they've been friends through and through and friendship, after all, must stand for something; I mean, what's friendship for if one can't tell certain truths in no uncertain terms?

And my cousin didn't butt in, held her peace, and for this Becky was grateful.

Later, much later, when Becky and Viola joined up, Becky learned that it's been Viola Barragán who had held Elvira in check. And because of that . . . well, it's because of Viola that mother and daughter get on so well. Although, truth in place, Elvira looks at Becky with a bit of fear mixed with pride, somehow, because she—Becky—had the nerve to shed, be rid of, Ira Escobar as a worn out, cracked piece of luggage.

You live long enough, as the saying goes, right? And now? Becky is as enterprising as Viola. As for her life with Jehu Malacara, that's their life. They're both over twenty-one. People will talk, though, and even now, married and all, people in Klail City are still going to talk, criticize, whatnot. . . .

If Becky has one remorse it may be that she didn't jettison Ira much sooner, but that's like week-old bread, you may as well throw as much water on it as possible. Same thing, water and distance between them, oh yes. Life's shorter than a quarter-horse race and you can't afford to look back, and so on, and so forth. I'm telling you, Becky cut that growth away, and the cutting was the onliest thing that mattered, you with me?

Look, why don't we just cross the River two miles down from here, and you, my wife, and I will eat some honest-to-goodness food.


## Viola Barragán

Lionel Villa is now followed by Viola Barragán: businesswoman, world traveler and resident of Mexico, India, South Africa, the German Federal Republic, (in that order), three times a widow (Agustín Peñalosa, M.D., Karl-Heinz Schuler, Harmon Gillette), and friend-mentor-protector of Jehu Malacara, Vice President and newly-appointed Cashier at the Klail City First National Bank. Viola is called that, Viola, by her friends.

She's doña to everyone else, and that includes the listener.


Yes, it's a bit thick and bothersome too, to be called doña, but I can't deny I'm 59-years-old, and the full-length mirror is always there to remind me of it in case I forget.

That stupid bromide about the alternative to growing old is as dry as yesterday's news. But there's nothing one can do about it, age and death are the two immutables. . . .

But to the point. I've known Becky from day one; I was there at Jonesville's Mercy Hospital the day she was born. And her dad? My compadre Catarino Caldwell? Why, I've known him since he was stationed at Fort Jones, a cavalryman. This takes us back to 1938, maybe '37. By that time, well, by then—see?—me and Elvira Navarrete were friends, close friends. Closer than close. We were tight, and still are.

Fact too is that we gave people plenty to talk about in those days, and that's the truth, pure, unlacquered, and unvarnished.

Elvira and I, we liked guys and made no bones about it. It's a natural fact. Of course, there wasn't much of an opportunity to go out with them, but where there's a will, right? And we'd sneak out once in a while, not often enough, though.

Elvira's folks owned two cars in those days; *gente de posibles*,[8] see? Monied. And I knew back then, and I was in my early teens, that Elvira's father, old don Julio Navarrete, aside from owning a pharmacy, also owned two gaming houses, plus a couple of dance-cantinas where the men paid to dance. Here I'm talking about El Farolito and La Golondrina. Old don Julio owned some land, too. City lots. So, the Navarretes had money in the thirties, during the Depression. And he was also a first-class hypocrite, and like most hypocrites, he liked to brag on himself. To me, bragging's a weakness of character. Like an embryo which is half-finished, not fully developed. You know exactly what I mean.

One example ought to do it, but it needs backgrounding. No sense saying otherwise; my parents married me off to Agustín Peñalosa when I was going on sixteen. Agu was a Northerner, un norteño, from Agualeguas, Nuevo

8. Literally, a woman of possibles; a woman of means (i.e., money).

León. A north borderman, then. He was closing in on thirty-three about that time, and he was all set as a medical surgeon and all. Spoke some English, too.

In a word, he spoiled me. As for bedtime, he was steady and regular—and I never, not once, betrayed him, his trust, his confidence, or his bed. Sounds funny, self-serving even now, forty-two years later, but I didn't even think of another man. He was mine, and I was his. Simple as that.

The future? It looked and promised everything I wanted. Oh, I was a bit of a lump and foolish, but you have to remember I was a kid. Dumb and all the rest that goes with it. Life was rosy. I felt safe. Cared for.

My folks, now, they weren't out begging in the streets, either. But my dad, he was a visionary, always helping people out. That he received little or no thanks and no gratitude was of no concern to him. And he didn't preach, no sir. No sermonizing. He loved me and he loved my mother. And confidence? In me? To the fullest. And he was patience itself. Now, right now, at my age, I see that what he did should be called love. The late P. Galindo was way ahead of everyone on that score. He knew what my father was: gente decente, a good man.

But where was I? Oh—I was talking about old don Julio Navarrete . . . Well, when Agustín died that stupid death of his, I moved out of our house and went to stay with my folks again.

Rafe Buenrostro's dad, El Quieto, he took charge of the estate. For one, he got a good price for the house Agustín had had built for me. Don Jesús El Quieto also straightened out the Mexican bank accounts, some bonds, and he placed the money at the Klail City Savings and at the Bank; shares, not savings, eh? It was a right fair account, and El Quieto sat me down and showed me how to get things done. For and by myself, he always said.

Around this time, Noddy Perkins was about twenty-something years old and learning whatever there is to learn about the banking business. And it was Noddy who took time to show me what real estate meant. What it could do, more importantly, what it couldn't do. And we went to bed . . . oftener than with Agustín, but Noddy's always had a limited imagination when it comes to sex.

Well, Don Jesús El Quieto, as executor, arranged for the sale of the house, tightened up the bank accounts and invested. Conservative but safe; banks were failing all over the place. My folks? Happy and contented, and guess what I did then—I must've been nineteen then—well, I took on old Javier Leguizamón as a lover. Well, that didn't last. Didn't amount to much either, and the man was a miser . . . but what stopped that affair was something my mother said in passing. She had no idea, of course. And then again, maybe she did. Something to be said about not preaching and screaming . . .

My mom was a friend to doña Angelita, Javier's wife, and that did it for me.

Nothing doing is what I said. Fair's fair. That's how the game is played or not at all. Luckily for me, about this time Gela Maldonado came on stage, made her debut. And she didn't have to either. She liked la vida—the life. Javier Leguizamón wanted both of us, a real macho, see? But I was all set for retirement. And Gela? She was all for it. She liked the idea of three in a bed. Well, in this case, three's a crowd is not just a cliché.

I like the bed, and if I like the guy, let's go and no holds barred. I've loved, been loved, here and abroad. But there is something I won't put up with, and that's sharing the bed. I like what's mine to be mine, so, when Gela jumped into the picture it was ". . . so long, Javier," for me.

And I was ready to leave him, anyway, and what he proposed is something I just don't agree with . . . I'm not talking about hypocrisy or about me being a goody-goody. Goes beyond that, but it doesn't matter, and not now at any rate. So we broke.

And so the sun set only to rise again. It couldn't have been more than a month later when old don Julio Navarrete—Elvira's dad . . . and he was around Javier Leguizamón's age more or less—don Julio came up and blew something in my ear. As it were.

To me! His daughter's best friend! That type of thing. Happens much too much, but here I was a kid, and I got scared. That's a dangerous man, that type of person. He went after me, and then, are you ready? He went after his own daughter. Why, that's just plain monstrous. Why even thinking about it is just as bad. Isn't it?

Well, I told him to go to Hell and stay there. Straight out. I kept seeing Elvira, and though I didn't much want to, I went in and out of the house just like always. And then Elvira told me. One of the saddest days of this life of mine. Well, after that, we were always together. Protection, see?

And, too, I couldn't stop going to her house, how would that have looked?

But I would never stay alone in the same room with that man, and I never did. We never did.


A brief recess. The listener, relaxed, is sitting in V.B.'s office on what must be one of the longest sofas in the Free World. Brocade, too.

Viola Barragán had raised her hand, thus putting a stop to her story. Sitting behind the glass-topped desk, almost as large as the sofa, she pressed a button set in a plastic box full of lights and buttons.

A phone, one she doesn't have to pick up or cradle. It's business, and she calls people in her four-story office building. The conversations are short, but not cold, and the orders precise, exact. The gold-tipped Parker fountain pen is for figures, not for doodling.

An incoming call, the only one was from Becky herself. To hear her voice is to see her: attractive, bright, and the listener, who knows Becky, although not well, can tell she smiles as she talks. The listener knows many people who've tried to smile and talk at the same time. He also knows it's hard to do. Actors do it all the time, the listener knows, but it's their job; their profession calls for it.

But Becky is no actress.

And here's doña Viola Barragán again.


We're up to 1939. The Spring of. And it's rained a lot here and there since that time.

It was a bit breezy that April in the Valley. A late Easter, too. And I remember sitting at home, alone, and bored, when I left the sofa, headed for the bathroom, showered, fixed myself up and decided to go to Jonesville. Alone and by bus. But don't ask me why. It happened.

I say this because I've tried to remember why it was I wanted to go to Jonesville. I mean, why not Ruffing, going north not east, or why not Bascom, to the west? And why a bus? Of all things. Oh, sure, Elvira lived and lives in Jonesville, but I'm sure I wasn't going to see her. I would've telephoned first, see? I just did it, and I can't remember why I did so.

What happened after that is common knowledge, not to say notorious: I met up with Karl-Heinz, and I fell like a rock. I was giddy, really. And he loved me! Thanks be to God and the changes He brings. . . .

My folks? Transfixed, hypnotized, and happy for the both of us. And there was Karl-Heinz and his carroty hair, eyes like blue crystal, and speaking Spanish like a gachupín,[9] a Spaniard right off the boat. In my case, Peninsular Spanish has always made me laugh, by the way.

And if I cried for Agustín, and I did—I'm not made of iron—I cried even more for my German. A good, clear-cut diamond of the first water, that Karl-Heinz Schuler. Gente decente. At any other time in history—except this one—he would've had a brilliant career. He knew diplomacy and tact and discretion. Name it.

We suffered together and we had great, marvelous times together; and I guess that's why I still miss him so, and it's been over twenty years, now. Things, that's what we did. Things . . .

And speaking of things, this brings me right back to old don Julio Navarrete, Elvira's dad, Becky's grandfather . . . As I'd said, aside from the pharmacy and the gaming houses, and the cantina dancing houses—which most people knew nothing about—he also owned a whorehouse. Here in Klail, over by the Grand Canal. Probably Klail's only whorehouse. Later, a big one, in Flora. . . .

Well, at that time, Fira Holland entered the life. Her dad, old Martín Holland, had married a mexicana, a poor one. And Martín, although an enlisted man, was good friends with Catarino Caldwell, Becky's dad. A few years back, Estéfana Holland, maybe her name was Epifania—anyway, the Holland woman died, and left Martín a widower with little Fira. Get this: the Hollands were legally married, Church and state. So she dies, and little Fira's about eleven-years-old at this time. Twelve, top.

Martín begins to drink and Fira, a natural-born beauty if there is such a thing, was taken in by the González family. Uncles and aunts and all of them crazier than loons on or off the ground. I mean crazy-mad-insane: the men preached and the women dressed like nuns. And they sang, too. Aleluyas, rollers, is what they were.

You can imagine Fira's shame—and at that age: out on the street with them, that gaggle of silly geese. Embarrassing. No, not embarrassing, unbearable. Poor little girl. At age sixteen she left Jonesville and only looked back to check that she wasn't being followed.

So, out of Jonesville, and now she's got to eat, so she became a waitress 'cause that's where the food is. From waitressing to dancing in Navarrete's cantina, and from dancing to whoring: one-two-three.

After that? A life like a bad Mexican movie. My folks thought they'd seen her here in Klail around that time, perhaps a bit after. During World War II. Me? I was in India or in South Africa, it was a concentration camp, the South Africans invented them or the English. . . . So, I lost track of poor Firita Holland.

---

9. Mexican Spanish term for a Spaniard or one who is descended from Spaniards.

But the stars remain in place, don't they? Doesn't matter what we say or do. Anyway, a few years later, I ran into P. Galindo; on his last legs and days about that time. Dying as we spoke, he was.

Anyway, Galindo told me—and I now see him clear as anything, because he had a drink with me. He wasn't supposed to, but "It doesn't matter anymore," he said at the time. Anyhow, it seems that way back there, when Fira was a starving kid—years and years ago—that Fira ran out of Klail and fast. And scared, Galindo said. Navarrete had wanted to put her in a house—oh, she was whoring all right, but free lancing. An independent, and that way she could pick and choose. For pay, of course, and what else could she do? She had to eat. But she took care of herself. I'm not talking about rich guys here, I'm talking about hygiene.

But old man Navarrete meant to corral her. Control her, and the fear he put in her was the size of a Baldwin Grand Piano. Stuck in a whorehouse, worse than prison.

And I found out through Galindo and as reliable a person as there is, or was, in his case. How reliable? He drove Fira back to Jonesville. Yes, he did, in that little Ford he owned back then. Had a rumble seat, and maroon-colored . . . you ever see it?

So, Galindo drove Fira Holland to Jonesville and checked her into a hotel, a good one. The Belken Gardens itself, I think it was. That was a long time ago . . . and Fira eventually got married and now she's been married for years to one of the River Road Castros . . . the red heads.

Old Galindo. He was more faithful to his Paulita than he ever could be to his country, flag, or religion. And discreet? Took many a secret, many a confidence with him. Galindo knew a lot of the world and its ways . . . And I bet he never left the Valley to do so, only the once, when the U.S. Army came and took neighborhoods full of mexicanos. He knew the world by heart. Nothing surprised Galindo. And yet, he wasn't a cynic.

Galindo was one of the Chosen, and he'd been chosen to carry Fira across the desert and into Jonesville's Promised Land. He was there, available. A man whose discretion was longer than the Rio Grande. One of the Chosen. . . .

It was only when he was bout to die that he told me of the trip to Jonesville, of old don Julio Navarrete's filth. Yeah, don Julio Navarrete, a whole man they called him at the funeral. A whore man was more like it, and that's what Galindo called him. Padrote, padrotón . . . [1]

A son-of-a-bitch, and a bully add up to a coward, and that's what Julio Navarrete was.

Elvira never spoke of her father to me again. That was our secret. Never again, not a word, and you've got to remember that Elvira and I go back years and years . . . Oh, yes.

And a good part of that friendship is why I like Becky. And not to criticize here, but to me, they, Elvira and Catarino, raised her as a bolillita, an Anglo girl. Big mistake! I mean, a big mistake on Elvira's and Catarino's part. Why, the Texas Anglos looked at them, the Caldwells, as Mexicans, at least here in Klail City they did. Poor th . . . but what am I saying? Poor nothing, Becky

---

1. Gigolo, pimp (the suffix *-ón* meaning "big time").

was her own person from the start. She just hadn't found her own way. But she did, I'll say.

Lunch on Viola. She spoke into that plastic box of hers and ordered some take out: "Catfish all right with you?" she asked. "Iced tea? No dessert? You sure?"

And that was that for now. She went over some figures from several sets of books and would talk to someone or someones on the box—she just talked into it and this left both hands free to work on something else at the same time.

The rectangular shaped office measured some ten by twenty maybe more. Cream-colored; the color said nothing about the person. The usual certificates and obligatory photographs with local and state politicians. A letter from the President of the United States, but who'd signed it was anybody's guess.

On one corner an IBM-PC gathering dust on its cover. The rug was best eight-ply, easily. One could see that. The rug, too, said nothing about its owner.

The listener decided this was an indifferent office, meant to say nothing, designed to reveal nothing: the wall safes were plainly visible, nothing to hide here.

And that was it, its owner told you point blank: nothing to hide here, no need to.

But, of course, all of us have something to hide. . . .

Sharp as a needle describes Becky, nothing less. A double-edged needle is Becky, and she's made of strong fiber, too. In and out, what you see in Becky is what you'll get.

She'd been here working for me for about six months, and in that time she knew all of the help inside out. Read the suppliers and merchandisers, too. And she knew how to work, how to set an example. The first thing she sloughed off was that reticence of hers, it smacked of snobbism, somehow. But she overcame that, and she was defining herself, learning about herself, knowing just who the hell she was, and that's always a big job. Too big for some.

So . . . since she's finer than a stick pin, she began to study the business. And I came out ahead there; no question. Becky knew. She could see things, and I knew she knew. She's talented, I'm telling you. And hungry, and that always helps.

And there she is: what I can't cover, she does, and she does it and adds to it. That spells success, nothing less.

Let's go back to last summer. It had been a so-so year, profits, sure, but not much growth, so I took off for two months. I'd never done that before. A vacation, the very first one in life, since the death of my Karl-Heinz!

Since the fifties, it had been work-work-work, but Becky changed all of that for me. Yes, she did. . . .

As for Elvira, she doesn't know a thing about anything. Why, even now, when Elvira and I get together, she'll mewl and pule some—the divorce, for

Christ's sake! God in heaven knows that may be going on three years now. Oh, it's nothing to do with Catholicism or the Church. No!

Look here, the Valley's Mexican Catholic Church wears some pretty loose sleeves and garments, when it suits her to do so. Garments that would cover a multitude, know what I mean?

Does it take my money for donations here and there? Bet on it. It takes it, and I get my thanks, day and night, in rain or shine. And if the Church needs excuses to do so, all it's got to do is to look it up in some Bible or other, in some dogma, tenet. Name it. And . . .

Okay, this takes me to the late, lamented Father Pedro Zamudio—and that hook nose of his and as bald as the Americans' eagle. Don Pedro Zamudio came to the Valley as a babe in arms, same as I did. My folks carried me in from Mexico and don Pedro came in through the port at Jonesville with his Spanish parents. And landed here with those crazy gachupín ideas, that ridiculously insolent Spanish su-pe-ri-o-ri-ty, la superioridad española. Jesus . . . No matter that they came here starving to death and all they owned was one hand in front and one in back when they walked. They had two other kids, all boys, and don Pedro was the Benjamín, the baby.

So what became of the Zamudio family? The two oldest boys became Valley mexicanos, Mexicans, but from this side of the Rio. And their parents? Don Tomás and doña Cleotilde? They soon lost that lisping sound of theirs; it's almost insulting the way it's thrown at you. Dropped it—the ceceo, they call it. And they settled into good people. No better than anyone else, no worse either. They were human beings, after all, and adiós my superiority.

And a good thing, too: they weren't Spaniards anymore. Not in Texas, in the Valley. They, the Zamudios, beat us here by twenty years, and they had to make certain adjustments, just like everybody else.

Do you—just by chance—do you happen to know that gachupín uncle of Rafe Buenrostro's? He thought, the uncle did, that he was something special. He then married into the Buenrostro family, and he soon got rid of those ideas. The Buenrostros are a serious lot; they won't put up with any stuff, no sir.

I'm saying all of this because of the Navarrete family. They were old Mexicans, mexicanos viejos, but at one time they thought of themselves as Spaniards; can you beat that? Just like the Leguizamóns. Oh, sure. The Leguizamóns considered themselves Spaniards for a while there. They're a bunch of obliging shits, they are. And they're the first to spot which way the wind is blowing, too.

And get this: they'd been mexicanos on another occasion, and then they became Spaniards. How 'bout that? Talk about your turncoats!

And Becky too had similar bents, similar pretensions in that pretty head of hers. But she shook 'em out, every damned one. She's raza, she's a person. And then, when you see how bright she is . . . and lively, too. And let's not omit pretty, 'cause she is. And then when she carries all of that and turns out to be a nice kid, you can see, can't you? Can't you? I'm saying she stood on her two hind legs, straightened up her own panties, and told that Ira Escobar where to go. That's the door, cabrón.[2] Your nose is in place, isn't it? Well, follow it out that door.

2. Literally, cuckold; figuratively, here, asshole, jackass, traitor.

It'd be a comfort for me to see how that cabrón reacted when she blew up that perfect little world of his. And don't go thinking he didn't like to have Becky as a slave. Ha! The Leguizamóns are a right bunch of bastards—men and women. And then, when you add some Leyva blood to theirs? It gets worse. And worse because they turn into despots. Others come out crazier than crazy. There's Lourdes, for one, and no need to go on from there. As for those who don't come out babbling away, those turn out the worst: bullies, advantage-seekers, back stabbers . . . and see these eyes here? Yeah, these I'm pointing to, you can use 'em as witnesses.

And good for Becky, say I. Two months, as I told you. Two whole months of vacation is what I took. Two months away from this country which is out of control, like a colt that's spat out its hackamore: no way to guide it.

Two months in Bavaria, in Ulm—my Karl-Heinz's home. No, I'm not a kid anymore, I said goodbye to menopause some years back, too, but I do miss my red-headed German man. And because of him, and because of his generosity, and the kind ways of his parents—I lived with 'em, you know, my in-laws, and I did so till they died. And for all of that, I had, needed, wanted to go back.

It was for old times' sakes, sure. A sentimental journey. Me. But Ulm had changed. Noisier. And the river that goes by it was filthy, sick, oily with waste and garbage . . . But it had been home for me.

Earlier, the year I buried Günther, my father-in-law, Manfred Rommel, was the mayor in Stuttgart, and he came to the funeral. He shook my hand, stood by me. He was the son of General Rommel.[3] But what did I know about Rommel? Nothing, nothing then, and nothing now, either. . . . The one Rommel I did know was that kid, the grandson of Epigmenio Salazar, you remember Epigmenio? Didn't work a single solitary day in his life; left all of that to his wife. . . . But this Rommel, well, he must be in his forties by now.

Yes, back to Ulm. The house I lived in, the one I sold, is now an apartment house. But the neighborhood? No change to speak of: you can eat all three meals off the streets, it's that clean. But not as quiet anymore, too many cars, motorcycles . . . But the trip did me good. I even got to see people who remembered me. Me! Die Mexicane.[4] 'Cause that's what they called me.

But to tell the truth again, I never did take a liking to the language, to the way it sounded. It was probably me, in the end. Couldn't make heads or tails out of it. Oh, I could say this and that and my in-laws understood me well enough. We'd laugh, all three of us, because I'd call the things in the kitchen whatever I wanted to. At times, I'd just point, and we'd laugh again.

I swear that the man who invented that language had nothing better to do and so they drowned him in a beer vat. I could say guten morgen all right, but with kissing the old folks, sharing our coffee and tea and milk, and the quietness of it all, and love, above everything else, that, love, I lived well and happy, too.

Then, when my mother-in-law, Helga, when she and I buried Günther, we'd go to the park and take long walks. Then, on a Wednesday, every Wednesday, all of Ulm went to the cemeteries. Can you believe it? Like a day off. It was beautiful. All the cemeteries in the city, full of flowers.

---

3. Erwin Johannes Eugen Rommel (1891–1944), German field marshal.　　4. The Mexican (female; German).

And so we'd walk and sit, enjoy each other's company. Oh, and German television . . . the absolute worst. Worse than ours. I swear it is. Helga would almost die laughing at me; no, there's no future for German television. But speaking of all those good people, my Karl-Heinz died in Pretoria, of a heart attack. And to think we had been there, in that concentration camp during the War, as a German, of all things! It's like a very strange dream, all of it.

I can almost laugh about it now, but not then. And then, after the war, when the Volkswagen Werke began to open up car agencies there, in South Africa, Karl-Heinz and I went back there.

And I'll tell you this: in the four-five years we lived there, in Pretoria, we kept a sharp lookout for a familiar face, a guard, a cook, something. Never did see one. Nothing.

But I don't, I don't dwell on it. And the life was harsh, cruel even . . . but we survived to return to Germany at a time when there was no food in the cities. Those were dangerous times. And there was hunger, too. And five, six-year-old kids loaded up with firewood like little donkeys . . .

Not now, of course. Now they're fat and rich, but back then, in '45, '46, '47 . . . people would kill for a pound of potatoes. . . . Dangerous.

Karl-Heinz went right back to the diplomatic corps, but he couldn't take it; new people, he said, but no different from the Nazis. Just like them, he said, and that's what made it worse. . . . But he had connections still, and by '50, '51, Volks was off and running, and my Karl-Heinz taught me the business.

He'd say, "Viola, business is business—Geschafte ist Geschafte, algo así.[5] Business is business, cars, machines, etcetera . . . All the same. Don't drive the workers away, give the best service and even if you don't make as much, insist on the best service. The money'll come in soon enough."

Oh, he'd say other things, too, but it was the part about service, the attention to detail, that's what stuck to me.

And Becky knows. Saw it right off, she did. And she'd be in the money by now if she hadn't been such a little coward years ago and cut away from Ira. But those days are gone, and there she is: just as pretty, capable, talented, and no nonsense about her either. Able to go straight to the nub. Clear headed, cuts through the details, too. What can I say?


It's been a long day: a walk around the Barragán office building, a longish ride in Viola's car (driving at a steady clip and she waves here and there to passersby), back to the office for work and a light merienda[6] of coffee and pan de dulce, and now it's time for a frosted glass of limeade.

The listener senses—the listener feels this—that Viola is to finish up a part of Becky's life—most likely another personal side to it—and then send the listener on to other things.


And on that same note, what can I tell you about Becky and Jehu? And where to start, too? Maybe it doesn't matter where I start. . . . Yes, that's it. Maybe it doesn't matter at all, I mean about them, Becky and Jehu. . . .

---

5. Something like that.
6. An afternoon ritual, especially in Latin America: coffee with Mexican pastry.

But there's always a but, and there is one thing that matters: to me, that's of real concern, and here it is. Jehu is not a grueling bore, and he is not bored either, and that's part of his secret life. His character, personality.

And Ira? That poor devil: as bored as two pansy boys in a room full of women or real men. Worse: Ira is not only a bore, he is boring. And for me, to know this, you see, I've yet to say a word to that boy since he's lived here in Klail. So, for me to know of that dull side of his means he's got some fame going. And worse still again, and it doesn't get any better, he's heavy handed with people. Lacks the touch, and he doesn't know it. And yet, people will say, he can't be that way; why, the man's a politician.

Tell you what: county commissioner is as high as he'll get. And then, he'd not gotten that high if Noddy Perkins hadn't helped, and down he'll come if Noddy ever gets his hemorrhoids in an uproar. . . .

After Becky's decision, I've no idea how it went for Ira at the Bank. I mean, Jehu was there, and he's a great part of the Bank. It's just a good thing, though, that Ira was transferred over to the Savings and Loan.

It couldn't have been easy on Jehu either; he gets no pleasure, none at all, out of hurting people. An uncommon banker, that boy.

Of course, Noddy's no fool. That red-boned, freckle-faced son-of-a-fruit-tramp wasn't born just the other day, you know. Too, keeping Jehu at the Bank was plain good business: Jehu runs a good shop there.

That Jehu, ah, when was it? Five? Six, eight years ago, was it? When he went after Becky? That's understandable. To be expected almost. At first it was Plain Jane Sex, but as it is in everything else, he must've seen what was there, in Becky.

I don't know this. I don't discuss sex with Jehu. I don't discuss his private life with him. We're friends, that boy and I, and I've got a weakness for smart people. I just figure he saw Becky, knew, intuited maybe, guessed right, something, that Becky had *medulla*, as we say. Character. Substance. She was a person, and could be her own person, someday. See? Man was right.

About that time, Jehu was out like a cowboy, cutting and culling from the herd. But he fell off that quarterhorse of his. Livita. Livita San Esteban did it. And Jehu got serious. But we know what happened to Olivia, third-year in med school, some goddam drunk kills her. . . .

On the other side of the world, Becky sends Ira on his way, and with Jehu—a widowed-groom, really—I, yeah, me, and I admit it, too, I sort of got them, him and Becky, I sort of got them together.

I know it sounds like some play or opera the way I'm going on about it here, but it happened. Ira's line was cut off from the dock, and Becky kissed off that Music Club goodbye, too. Goodbye to all that. And goodbye to something else, too: all manner of strings.

Although Elvira Navarrete and I are friends, old friends, and we've weathered storms and hurricanes here in the Valley . . . and I'll tell you that when Becky weaned herself off her mamma's breast, she did it consciously. That was some decision, that was.

And it was, and let me tell you why: it takes a lot of damn nerve, fiber, spine, good, old-fashioned Mexican Valley guts not to knuckle to—get this—to what people will say. I'm an expert on "what people will say," that qué dirá la gente claptrap. You're talking to one of the world's biggest targets here; used to be I walked around with a target on my back. Here, hit this; yeah.

Of course, people who knew nothing, had no blood interest in any of Becky's doings, had one thing: malice and an opinion, or a set of them. Sure, and if you have the time, they'd say, I'll give it to you, here and now. It was something to do, something to get them through another hot summer. Entertainment, even.

It was the same when I married Harmon Gillette, years ago. Oh, sure. And really, who could've given a damn about that? And still, they talked. It wasn't their business, but as in business and politics, many talkers, few doers. One does deserve to go to heaven for all the chances one takes on earth, and for putting up with the Ira Escobars of the world.

Example: If I know of someone who's destined for heaven it's Blanca Rivera, the Presbyterian, Pioquinto's widow. Pioquinto and I had our motel workouts up and down the Valley. When he died, Blanca had a few pennies saved, not many. Their home? Modest but paid for. Bills? Few, nothing serious. Kids? Zero. So? Well, a year or so later, I took her on as cashier at my first Shopping Bags store. Here, in Klail.

When the business increased, I opened up another one, and Blanca handled that one, too. And now we're up to seventeen stores across Belken County, run by Blanca Rivera, widow of Reyes, and that's how she still signs for everything, bookkeeper, manager; she orders, everything, eh?

Just like Becky. I started her on the Busy Bee Burgers and from there to the three movie drive-ins, which I've just converted into flea markets. Becky it was who said to close the drive-ins. Shut 'em up, she said. Profits in the Flea Markets, she says. We can rent out three hundred stalls there, sell the speakers for scrap . . . Well, turned out we got four hundred stalls, but the decision was a right one.

And I know what you're thinking about Blanca. Did she know about Pioquinto and me. She did 'cause I told her a year after he died at the Holiday Inn we'd been at.

Blanca said then she maybe suspected something was up, but that she didn't know what it was exactly.

Now? Now she even laughs and does so because she figured out why Pioquinto went on the hunt. She kept him on short rations, and Pioquinto—forty plus years—wanted a hump at least once a day. His death over to the Holiday Inn was really something to laugh about . . .

Oh, I know that sounds cold, but mark this down: Blanca needed help, money to live on, and I took her on. I'm not talking about a guilty conscience here. Two people out of four billion doing what Pioquinto and I did? That's a sin? Making each other happy?

Sha! Blanca needed help, and guess what? Pioquinto must've taught her bookkeeping, accounting, even. I think numbers are a God-given talent, something Pro-vi-den-tial, as she says in that Presby way of hers.

That Blanca . . .

And that is Viola Barragán, one of Becky's friends. A glance at the listener's wristwatch shows it's 8:15 p.m. September, and the sun is still up there and beating down at 95 degrees Fahrenheit in the Rio Grande Valley, Belken County, Texas.

The listener dreams of a cold shower and enters the house without bothering to turn on the lights; they'd only add to the heat. There's some TV blather about a possible veering of the hurricane out in the Gulf; it just may hit the Valley. Possible and may. Words.

Tomorrow? A conversation with Isidro Peralta.

## Isidro Peralta

It's Isidro Peralta's turn at bat. The survivor of identical twins; an electrician by trade; their father, also an electrician, lives in one of the only three houses on that triple lot. The other houses belong to Eugenio Peralta's widow and to the informant. The families share one common mail box, and this calls for an explanation:

Eugenio, dead these four years now, left two surviving sons: Eugenio Jr., 20, and Isidro II, 18. For his part, Isidro also has two sons: Isidro Jr., 20, and Eugenio, 18.

The Star Route drivers who deliver the mail threw their hands in the air years ago, and hence the common rural mail box.

The listener called ahead and after the usual mix-up of names of sons and cousins, the listener made an appointment with the surviving twin.

Yep, if my brother Eugenio were alive today, he'd be forty years old, same age as me; we was twins. Got killed by a brick thrown by God Himself, yessir. That brick fell from heaven itself, wasn't a man-thrown brick at all.

He and I was working on an electrical job for Viola Barragán in that office building of hers. Started off with two and then she went on and added two more floors to make it four.

Well, it was right there where the Silva brothers, and Chago Leal, and the two of us won the first big contract to wire up the rest of that office building, and we all made a profit, you bet.

Doña Viola doesn't want shit—that's cheap wire and cheaper labor—on her property. What I'm saying is she wanted copper, not aluminum wiring. Aluminum is good and cheap but treacherous. Won't last. Copper will, though. Copper'll go through Hell itself. You can't beat copper.

The Doña is exigente. Always the best 'cause it's also the cheapest, as she sees it. And that damned brick was the best, too. That's Double-duty Fire-Up—you with me? First quality goods and made here, on this side of the Rio Grande.

Now, you're going to find a lot of Texas Anglos in the construction trades who use Mexican brick—and it's good, too—but here in Belken County, all over the Valley, there are Texas mexicanos who know how to make brick; best there is. The Munguilla brothers for starters. Or the Morales family— the ones with the funeral house and the kilns—what do you say to that?

And I do miss my bro. But he always had bad luck, you know. Born but with one testicle, just like me, a ciclán,[7] as we say. Oh, well. . . .

As for Jehu, we've known him . . . well, it's only me now, but I've known him since school. He was raised, protected by the Buenrostro family.

7. An insulting term for a person with one testicle.

They're kin, and he and Rafe Buenrostro are close, tight, always have been. You fought one, you had to fight the other, been that way since school.

Rafe's father was don Jesús Buenrostro, El Quieto. I didn't know the man, he was a grown-up, see? But he took in Jehu Malacara. What I'm telling you is what I got from my father. Yeah . . . knew don Quieto, I mean, don Jesús. And my dad, he knew the brother, too, don Julián, the father of Melchor who God keeps etcetera . . .

About Jehu—God's truth—he's always treated me fairly and more than fair sometimes. I've never been in the position of doing him a favor, but I'm ready whenever and whatever.

Sometime back, once, can't remember where or when, but once, someone told me that Jehu had bedded down Rebecca Escobar. What I'm saying here is rumor, okay? You asked and all I'm only saying is what I know or heard. . . .

Anyway. That he grabbed her by the ears and let's head for the open Gulf, the breeze is up and all that. But do I know this for a fact? For a fact? No.

But if the subject was Sammie Jo Perkins, that's a different matter. And I wasn't the only one who knew? Get me?

As for Olivia San Esteban, that was a sad piece of business. Serious, too. Here, in this case, Jehu went about it serious, formal. As my dad says: he settled down, he grew up, asentó cabeza,[8] you know? Now, Jehu didn't quit going to the Blue Bar or over to Dirty Barrón's Aquí Me Quedo Bar,[9] but he cut the rest of the stuff, the running around. Like a bullfighter, he cut off his pony tail, or like a boxer who hangs 'em up.

Got serious for once and then for what? So that some dumb pinche drunken bolillo[1] come and broadside her? So he can kill her in a second, just about? Son-of-a-bitch run a red light out at the Military turn off, and him on one of those goddam outsized pickups. Shit.

Olivia San Esteban didn't live those ten days in the hospital; she was in a coma. And Jehu? From his house to work and then to the hospital. Yessir. He was serious. When Olivia died and was buried, Jehu had to go on living; no choice. But he had his health. And he'd changed, no doubt about that.

Oh, he dated La Chacha—Irene Paredes—the one that does things with science; something. Well, she works there at the Court House, where Rafe works, you know: Jehu's cousin.

But as for Irene, Jehu didn't go out much or long either. A year? And then, de repente,[2] just like that, he marries Rebecca Escobar, living together, making or keeping a family. Why, that was like heat thunder to me, flat out of the blue and bam!

It was too fast for me to follow, I'll tell you that. La Escobar set Mr. Commissioner adrift like a shrimp trawler with no nets to drag. . . . I hear she chucked him out of the house. That's tough, right? That's what people say.

I don't know those people, the Escobars. They belong to another class of people, I'd say. But if you're talking social classes, that cuts little to no ice

---

8. The Spanish verb *asentar* has various meanings. With the noun *cabeza*, it means the person has settled down, has matured, etc.
9. I Stay Here Bar.
1. Literally, bread bun; Mexican Spanish for an

Anglo (*bolilla* for a female), but a historical reference, not an insult. *Pinche*: Mexican Spanish for a tightwad, a skinflint.
2. Suddenly.

with Jehu. For him, one standard, everyone's the same, in or out of the Bank; he's a fair one that Jehu, you got to say that for him.

Now, it can't be more than two years ago, I don't think—talking about the San Esteban girl's death. La Escobar boots her husband right in the ass, and begins her life with the kids in that house of theirs. I think Chago Leal, maybe Arnold Tucker, got the wiring contract for that one.

One thing for sure: Rebecca Escobar isn't going to starve to death, and then, all of a sudden, you just didn't see her pictures in the Enterprise-News. Yeah. And she used to be in it, a lot, with the Women's this and the Women's that, you know.

Well, on a Palm Sunday morning I think it was, there's this car parked in front of her house. And that's a No Parking zone, too. To back up just a bit, she'd got me to install two air-conditioning units, one for the kitchen and one for the glassed-in porch. I drove up that Sunday morning after Mass, and there was the car. Up front. You know what I'm saying here?

Well, it was Jehu's car. A Bank car, yeah. Can you beat that? Well, here I was, rewiring the two rooms, replacing hot plugs with a ground on 'em, one-day job. Top.

And Jehu? In shirt sleeves. Happy as a cat in a barn full of mice. That cabrón . . . No! That's just an expression; Jehu is not a cabrón. Oh no, he's far from being an asshole. No, no. That would be the last word for Jehu Malacara.

But there he was: at home. He spotted me working in the kitchen, nodded and that was it. No malice in that nod, no winking of the eye either. It was a greeting. Well, that wasn't none of my business. I mean, what did I have to do with any of that? My old man did not set out to raise idiots. Jehu was there and Jehu was there, and he sure didn't ask permission from Isidro Peralta, master electrician.

'Cause that's what I am, a master electrician, and I was hired for that, and I did the work on time. A clean house, the kids happy and laughing with their Mom, all the time I was there, and if Rebecca wasn't bothered by my comings and goings, well, I ask you: Why should I be bothered, or care?

So it's got to be two years 'cause that's when Ira was made secretary, manager, something like that, over to Klail Savings. And then, some six months after that, the same job over to Jonesville—the Escobars are originally from Jonesville. They're not from Klail. Rebecca is a Cogwell, something like that. Her father was a soldier; Anglo, and married to a monied woman, one with property. She was a Narváez or a Navarro. No, no, no, no not either one at all. She's a Navarrete; yeah. Old don Julio's daughter, 'cause there was money there . . .

Later, Chago Leal told me this was so. Years and years ago, Chago was an apprentice for an old alky named Willis here in Klail who owned another shop in Jonesville. Well, according to Chago, the Navarretes decided to rewire the entire house, top to bottom, north to south, okay? Takes money for that. Old Parr Willis got the contract, and that's how Chago Leal got inside that house. A house-and-a-half is what Chago used to say.

So, this Rebecca is part of that family. And, between you and me, I didn't know a pharmacist could make that kind of money. . . . Maybe they do, but old don Celso Villalón used to say that anything is possible, and that contraband is easier than working for a living.

That aside, that house was a well-made house. Solid. And that's why the wiring took time. No sheet rock there, no sir. Chago Leal says that after that job, that big a contract, he wasn't scared of any job, anywhere.

He earned his journeyman badge right there.

It should be pointed out that Isidro Peralta received three phone calls, gave out two estimates, and wrote a message on a pink pad. Later, one of his sons brought the mail, already sorted, no doubt.

At that time, Rebecca must've been in college, the university. Here in the state, yeah, but Up North somewhere. Near Dallas.

As for Klail City, she and Ira Escobar landed here some nine-ten years ago. Oh! About the time he became a politician real sudden like . . . well, it was about that time that Jehu was a good friend to Noddy Perkins's daughter . . . and she married for a second time, too.

I'm telling you, that Jehu was a piece of work. But there he is, married to Rebecca by a judge, so what do I know? One thing's sure, they sure as hell don't have to give me an accounting for their life together. Everyone has their one life to lead, right?

But this I got to say: there, where you see Jehu, and he's a good person, too, well anyway, like that, quiet, peaceful like, just like his cousin, Rafe. I wouldn't want to tangle with either one. Not bigmouths, either one. Goodness, when do they ever act tough? But I'd pass on some advice to anyone who doesn't know Jehu, that it's best not to crowd him.

Easy going, playful, name it, but it's like the Anglos say, "He's always holding back. Something in reserve."

And then, he doesn't hold grudges either. No grudges to hold when you don't take shit from anyone. And like I said, one standard, in or out of the Bank, and everyone's equal.

Weeeeelll, living with or married, don't matter to me which, Rebecca Escobar—or Malacara maybe—she's a person, and good at business. She runs some of Viola Barragán's Business, and I'm a witness. And Viola won't cheat you either and Rebecca's the same. Yessir.

Piece work, a big job, big contractor, little contractor—everyone gets respect. Viola's not like some—like a lot, and raza, too—that only gives the big jobs to the Anglos—Klail Electric, Belken & Co—and the little jobs to us, as if we didn't know as much as anyone. Bunch-a raza shits.

Tell you what I also like about doña Viola Barragán. She works with attorneys—contracts, deadlines, bonuses, everything. Take me, I can buy on credit or she'll give it to me: whatever I need and it's "Call me if you need anything." You listening?

I didn't mean to veer off here, but it also has to do with Jehu: If you go to the Bank on business, it doesn't matter how you're dressed. That's right. You go in there, sit in his office, explain to him what you'd like to do, and he listens. He knows how to ask questions, hard questions. Then he starts with the figures. He advises you. Yeah. That cabrón, he . . . I mean, he knows his business.

And he doesn't give a good goddammit if your name's Juan Lanas, Pepe Cabras, or Bruno Shafter of Belken & Co. or even Junior McQueen from

Klail Electric. All treated the same: courtesy, seriousness, and if you know what you're talking about, the loan is as good as yours. Right there, dammit. Right then. The man has confidence in you, yeah. And he handles big deals, yessir.

Let me tell you this. Chago Leal and I went into a temporary partnership, limited, eh? We partnered on an estimate for a job with doña Viola. Rebecca Escobar was there too.

I'm going to stop here to tell you that La Escobar is a very beautiful woman. Not bonita, pretty, but linda. Bella, even. Beautiful. And, to work with doña Viola, she's got to be sharp as good vinegar. But she better be intelligent, too, since doña Viola isn't selling newspapers on some street corner; there's money in that company. Rebecca Escobar's got to be a good one.

And you can't take her looks away, she's got 'em. You know what else? Olivia San Esteban was a beauty. And yet, they didn't look alike, did they? I mean, Rebecca Escobar's eyes are brown,[3] biggish somewhat, and round. The nose is a bit small for me, and kind-a pale, too, but that coal-tar hair helps. Her . . . her figure, ah, nice, real nice.

The San Esteban girl? Different. Pretty and a lot. But like the old days somehow. You know what I mean? I remember her eyes, sort of washed out: gray? The mouth a bit wide, but a great smile. I fell for her at Klail High, but she never knew . . . No one knew, not even my brother, I want you to know. My twin! I never told him, he never knew.

Olivia's hair was as black as Rebecca's, but longer, shiny, and then that face. That skin, like a smooth, skinned almond. Yeah. That Ollie San Esteban was special. A little on the thin side for me, but not bony, no. There's a better word for it, but what do I know?

Well, the thing was our contract—Chago Leal's and mine with doña Viola—brought us to Rebecca Escobar. She already knew who I was and said hi and shook my hand and all. Like I said, she's got to be a sharp one to work for someone like doña Viola. Well, right away she told us to leave the pick ups where they were, and she got us in her car.

And how long was the job going to take, she asked. The hot plugs this and the tubing that, the lighting and the wattage, what carpenter would we recommend; just like the owner of any other shop or store. She carried the two little green books, just like ours: how much, where, and there she'd go with that hand calculator just like Chago and me. Business, yessir.

A rosebud is what she is. And we're talking a big job here when she said right out, "Well, what do you figure you need to start? How much money are we talking about?"

Yeah. A line of credit.

Well, first off, she was going to open a special account for us at the Bank. We could draw from it, just sign for the materials. A big, fat contract all drawn up. And all the time, cool, nice, and then guess what? I realized I had my mouth hanging open . . .

And here I always thought she was a pushover you know. I mean, I'd had a few dealings with Ira Escobar at the Bank. He was like a flat tire, no air to him.

3. Note: Becky Malacara's husband, the banker Jehu, corraborates the color of his wife's eyes. This may not be important, but the listener, in going over P. Galindo's papers, read where P. Galindo says they are green. [Author's note—i.e., the listener's note]

I don't know what happens north of the Valley, like up in Austin or China and Europe, but when it comes to my craft, I can tell you chapter and verse about what I do. Ira? I never got the impression he was all there. Kind of goofy. Silly. A waste of time to talk to that guy, because I'd wind up talking to Noddy or Jehu, one. First with Noddy and then with Jehu or straight to Jehu.

Man, if I ran my shop like that, I'd've closed up by now or worse than that, my dad would've taken a stick to me, make that a BIG stick, for being so dumb.

And the guy's a county commissioner? That guy? Man, if they're all like that up at the Court House, they better change the wiring, quick.

But back to Rebecca. She wasn't out to make a big deal out of this. If there was something she didn't know, she'd pop a question. Say she'd see something different from the way we'd see it, she'd say something. But not like she was trying to show you up, not like some others.

It was negocio, man. Business.

And the way she trusted you, too, and her own ways of doing, saying things . . . I think that's why she and Jehu get along so well. Got to be.

But as I've been saying all along, I don't swim in those waters, at all. Now I'll see Jehu at the Blue Bar, like I said, 'cause he is the way he is, a natural. He doesn't claim to know everything, and you'll see him sitting and talking and listening to the old men, los viejitos. Men like Chago Leal's dad, or Garrido, or Dirty Barron himself, and old Echevarría when he used to hold court there. And sometimes he drops in with Rafe, hellos all around, one or the other will stand a round, but that's plain old friendship. We're not talking of acting like a big shot or buying rounds like politicians.

At other times, you won't see him there for weeks at a time. But he shows up, sticks around.

So he and Rebecca they both got their jobs . . . Like that one we did for doña Viola, where we came out just fine: we finished that office building, the city inspector passed on it, and then the county guy, Solís, I think his name is, he signed away on it too. It was a good job, and we guaranteed it, every time. Well, when we worked on one of the old stores and on one of the new ones, which we finished ten days ahead of schedule, and both inspectors gave their okays again, doña Viola drove up to my shop, parked her car and in she comes, handing me a five-hundred dollar check! Had one for Chago, too. So how do you think we felt? Right! And know what we did then? Passed some of the bonus money to the two apprentices. Made me feel pretty good too.

It was good business, I know that, and Rebecca Escobar—and I guess I better start calling her Rebecca Malacara, right? Anyway, she was there with doña Viola a little while later and shook our hands. Business.

Sure, good business.


## Andrés Malacara

Andrés Malacara, in his maturity. A man in his high eighties now and sitting under a chinaberry tree on a straight back chair. A terry cloth towel across his lap, a cover against the sun when he walks around and also used for shooing off blue-bottle flies. He's putting the finishing touches on some pink grapefruit wine, and he watches it drip into an aluminum vat as the listener comes up.

Been expecting you. Dirty Barron said you'd be dropping by . . . Well, let's get to it.

You and I both know that a lot of Valley people share blood kinships. Not many idiots around, though, and that's 'cause we don't mix except every three generations or so. Been going on since 1749, and here I am, eighty-two, and I heard that from my maternal grandfather, Juan Nepomuceno Vilches.

First cousins don't marry, and like I said, it's too close to the blood. Now, that some come out slow-like or dull as cast iron, it's because their folks was dumb to begin with. But idiocy, no, not from crossing the bloods.

I will say, though, that crossing and top crossing of blood is good for the breed. Same thing happens out in the pastures where I was born, the Toluca Ranch.

I'm eighty-two, on the nose; the twenty-third of March, Santo Toribio's day, and today, April fourth, Day of Santo Isidoro,[4] marks an even dozen, twelve years to the day, when we buried Esteban Echevarría. If he were here, alive, today, that'd be the man who could tell you everything. Todo. From A to Z. Yes.

I don't have the gift, and I sure don't know as much as he did, but I've got more than three-quarters of a century on me, so I must know something about the old families, las viejas familias.

When you called, you mentioned the Barragán family, but that's not an old family. Telésforo Barragán and his wife landed here around 1920 or so. An old family is a different matter.

I'll give you an example. The Leguizamón bunch got here after the end of the Civil War. They got to the border, to the southern bank of the Rio Grande, about 1857, maybe '58. But they didn't come over during the Civil War, no sir. They were across, making money: cotton, smuggling firearms, war stuff, food, you name it.

Those families are old, but they're not what we call old families or what old Echevarría called familias viejas. Now, the Cano family and the Guzmáns, and the Rincón, the Buenrostro and Malacara families, and the Vilches, the Tueros. Them. Those are the old families. Yours, see? Me, I'm a Tuero on my maternal grandmother's side, doña Esther Tuero.

The Navarrete family, to give you another instance, dropped here when this part of the world became the Republic of Texas; 1840, '42, I'd say. My grandmother Esther was becoming a señorita around that time—she was 15 or so—and she first met them then.

And Esteban Echevarría used to tell me . . . oh, Esteban's father, don Hilarión, he was a little old red-faced man about the size of a shoe tack. Had all his hair, too, and white as burro milk . . . Anyway, Esteban used to tell me that the first skirmishes, the feud, between the first Buenrostros and the Leguizamóns came about on account of the Leguizamóns allying themselves with the Anglos crowding in here way back then. The Leguizamóns also

---

4. Like Santo Toribio, a Roman Catholic saint.

sided with the army, yeah, the old Confederates. And with some raza, too, up the River . . . Laredo, those parts . . .

The governor of Texas had enough on his plate around that time and the Valley and its people suffered on account of that. He couldn't tend to us . . . Ha!

Listen, the Sedition of 1915 was a result of all that way back then. To begin with, the Rangers had lorded it over us since my century, the one I was born in, the nineteenth. Yes. They took heavy advantage after 1915 as well, and they'd go around scaring people, using boots, pistols, and shotguns, in the elections in the 1920s and the '30s, too. Shoot, in certain parts of the Valley, up to the '50s. Yeah. Can you picture that? Yesterday, you might say.

No, the seditious ones of '15 rose up and rebelled because la raza was up there with the Rangers and with their goddam guns and shootings.

But there were raza turncoats, too. Traitors. Oh, yes. And the Anglos later betrayed them. Ha, that'll teach you to leave the nest, cabrones.

So it was around there that the Buenrostro-Leguizamón bad blood first showed and flowed. Later, when don Jesús Buenrostro, El Quieto, was murdered, two Leguizamóns were taken care of, dealt with. The two Mexican nationals who murdered El Quieto, well, they were also dispatched around the same time.

Javier Leguizamón always claimed that he had nothing to do with any of that. It got to be embarrassing after a while, all that denying. He said it once and he repeated it a thousand times. Embarrassing. Got to the point where he believed it. That's really something, isn't it?

Ha! He and Angelita didn't have any kids, like me and my wife and maybe for the same reason, too. We both married good women, but we ran around a lot . . . For my part, I know I strewed four out of marriage, three boys and a girl. And I saw to them, yes I did, and all four chose my name later on. All legal.

My wife . . . I buried her over there, see that cemetery yonder, by the flume? That's our cemetery. A lot of Cano folk there, Guzmáns, too, and Malacaras, of course. Esteban Echevarría was supposed to have been buried there, but the Buenrostros said Echevarría'd be buried with them, at the Carmen Ranch.

That was young Buenrostro's doing, Rafe, and of the three Buenrostro men, Rafe took after his dad a bit more than the other two, Aaron and Mailo. We're talking of three full men here, and Rafe, the middle son, he's something else . . .

As for the Leguizamóns, what can I tell you? Back in the 1920s, like I said, the '30s, too, before some American company came and ate up every creamery and dairy farm hereabouts, they'd already had their dealings with the Leguizamón family.

And when I had to deal with the Americans, I dealt in spot cash. No checks, no thank you, sir. A bank had skinned my friends and had skinned me too like an eggshell, back in '31 and from then on I said, "No checks." It was either cash or I'd dump the milk in the garbage pails, since that's what the banks had turned my accounts to, garbage.

To this day and until tomorrow, if I die then, I'll go to my grave with one belief: those damn bankers told their friends what it was that was going to happen. Hell, yes. And us? You know what we got? We got a big fat nothing with zeroes on it. Hmph.

So as I said, they had to pay me in cash and, since there were no other mouths to feed at home except my wife Aurelia's and mine, I was all right. All smiles and cash, yessir.

Javier Leguizamón is, was, a great uncle to Ira Escobar, the county commissioner. Don't know the boy, but he can't possibly amount to much; he's got some Leyva blood on his mother's side, and that's no help.

Protected by Javier? Absolutely. Spoiled, too, I'd say. And he's a banker, I hear. As I said, I've never met him. Oh, I've seen him here and there at some farm or ranch barbecue . . . 'cause I don't go to no town barbecues. Klail or Flora, one. Won't go near any town. I'm a river man, a dairy man, and this is where you're going to find me dead tomorrow, next week, whenever.

No, I don't go into town. At all. I was well-served when I owned them two gaming houses in Klail. But when I left them, thirty years ago and more I came here, to these forty acres, and that's all anyone would want.

If I want to know what's going on, all I got to do is ask. But that's about it, 'cause if you want to find me, I'll be down by the River, fishing. So who wants to live in town, I ask you?

There's too many diseases in town. The water? On iron or plastic pipes, and then they run it through again, they reuse it. Not for me. Give me rainwater from the Gulf, the Rio Grande, and the lakes out here. And I boil it, too, and then I add half a spoonful of salt for every ten gallons, helps the digestion.

And what does one get out of living in town, anyway? Diseases! In thirty years now, this country of theirs has been in half-a-dozen wars, hasn't it? And what for? The Germans? Friends again. The Japanese? Same damn thing. And the dead? Dead.

Look, the world is no different from Belken County politics. You scratch mine, I'll scratch yours, and amen.

And there can't be anything filthier than a town, and I'm just sorry I didn't know any better when I first married. That's right. These last thirty years have been the healthiest, sanest years of my life. Absolutely.


The listener was prepared for the above. It's one of Andrés Malacara's set pieces, but he means every word of it.

He's also an expert whittler and prefers the retama tree, but the mesquite will do, he says.

Time for a walk, and Andrés Malacara, with the listener in tow, walks toward the River. The farm lies two miles from the pumping station that draws its water from the Rio Grande. Half of the land has been saved for feed grass for his jerseys and black-and-whites.

Since you're here, I'll tell you that my nephew, Manuel Avila, was here day before yesterday. You know him? He's sandy-haired. Green-eyed. Much, much older'n you; he's close to fifty, I'd say. And talking about the divorce as you were, he was the one who brought the news here two, three years ago . . .

That the Leguizamón-Leyva and the Navarrete families were all a-bother. That this was going on, that that was going on. A lot of noise, but for nothing from what I could see. And Manuel crying real tears 'cause he was laughing so hard.

Those families carried on he said. Aired a lot of clothing in public . . . Whatever happened to shame in the Valley? Manuel just laughed away and kept saying, "So what?" And he'd laugh and say, "Well? Was the Queen of Prussia pregnant? Did she give birth? Who the hell cares?"

Manuel'd say, "Nothing to it, Uncle, just one more divorce," but there they were, acting as if we'd dropped another atomic bomb somewhere. And Manuel was right. It was nothing. Ira Escobar's wife left him, pure and simple, that's all.

I can talk about that girl 'cause I know her and I know all her kind. To start off, her maternal grandfather, Julio Navarrete, was a gambler, and he also had shady businesses here and there. Half-hidden, you might say. He was also anybody's errand boy at the start of this century and later on he became a pharmacist. But I ask you, what did that piece of half-digested shit know about filling out a prescription?

First he opened up a drug store out to Flora—no, I'm wrong there. First Bascom, then Flora. Right. But a pharmacist . . . shoot, not even the Anglos had licenses back then, not in the Valley they didn't. And then again, maybe that was it. Julio Navarrete probably said to himself, "Here's where I get mine." Yeah, that was probably it.

But when he first came to the Valley, starving, he was a gambler. Now, the first gaming house I opened up was near Relámpago, and that was in 1897, and I was nineteen years old then. How do you like that?

That's right, I had my own gambling place, and I got the money from a loan made me by my uncle Daniel Estudillo.

So Julio Navarrete came here as a gambler, and he was good, the sumbitch. From gambler to part time whore-master: he ran some women here and there. After that, came the pharmacy, then the two dance hall-cantinas, and he kept them for forty years, and that's the truth.

He opened a whorehouse in Flora, and that was a big place, people said. But all undercover, except the drug store. He was a family man, decent. Ha! He was nothing of the kind; he was a hypocrite. That was dirty money, and for some sixty years or so, I think he also might've cheated when he gambled. I never caught him at it, but if I had, I'd-a broken both his hands and all his fingers and knuckles for him. He might have known what I was capable of, and maybe that's why he didn't cheat at my place . . . But who's to know, right?

Well, there it was, dirty money, made in secret. Smuggling? Why not? Smuggling's not the most difficult business in the world, and not on this border of ours; no, not when you've got relatives on both sides of the River. Easiest thing going, and you don't need any talent for that.

When Julio Navarrete died—that was out to Jonesville—I learned of it from Manuel, my nephew. As for Esteban Echevarría, all he said was, "Just one more down the chute, that's all."

Echevarría it was who told me of the dance-hall cantinas and the other stuff. Esteban knew a lot of secrets; took a lot of history with him when he died. Good person, Esteban.

Yeah . . . these forty acres of mine are in Ira Escobar's precinct, you know. And it must be going on six years now, around election time it was, some flunky of his showed up here. That the county commissioner wanted to know if I needed anything, if I needed a favor done, he said. That if there was anything that he, the commissioner, could do for me.

Like what? I asked the flunky who showed up.

He answered in a flash: that the commissioner was ready and willing to pave the road leading to my gate from the highway, see? And beyond the gate, right up to my front door if I wanted it.

"Paved?" I asked him.

Yessir.

I told him no. I thanked him all right, but no thanks.

Told him I liked the smell of dirt when the rain wets it down, and I'd just as soon keep it that way.

Do you know that old boy wouldn't believe me? So I had to insist, convince him. What I didn't tell him was that I didn't want every S.O.B. dropping in whenever he felt like it. Those paved roads smell like cities to me, brings 'em in closer.

This way, when it rains, that black Valley mud'll keep an army away. So it was no, no thank you, no, Commissioner.

He was a young guy, the boy who came over, and all he did was scratch his head. In amazement, I'd say. Probably was the first damn time someone didn't want, didn't need something, from the commissioner.

That you come here, to talk, is one thing. You're family, that's enough for me . . .

But that's about the closest I've come to dealing with that family.

My nephew Manuel Avila tells me that Jehu's back at the Bank after some sort of absence. You know, Esteban Echevarría sure was right about Jehu . . . liked him, liked what he saw in him. Jehu is one of our Malacaras, but he's also a Vilches and a Tapia to boot. Those are good people, they're from El Ranchito, just east of Relámpago, past Los Indios.

I knew Jehu's parents, both of them. Died young, both of them. She went first. Her name was Tere, and once, when there wasn't one single penny in that house, she went to town, to Klail, to work as a maid. A domestic. Those were hard times. She didn't last long though. Couldn't stand to live in a town, and she didn't like city ways either.

And Jehu? Turned out solid. His Buenrostro cousins had a hand in that. And I did too. When my wife and I still lived in Klail, I had Jehu working for me at one of my gambling places. That boy was She-Arp. Honest, too, just like all the Malacaras. Wouldn't touch a penny.

One of my sons—he first used the last name Loera from his mother—he used to say that Jehu was straighter than a cedar post. How do you like that? Oh, one can learn to be honest, but you got to have some good blood in you, for starters. Jehu was the only birth out of that Vilches-Malacara blood, but it was a good mix. Yessir.

But there's always bad luck somewhere. His novia, that girl he loved, got herself killed in a car wreck, according to Manuel. Like I been telling everybody left and right, cities are going to be the death of everyone. They're dangerous, I know what I'm talking about. You won't catch me there . . .

The listener spent two days and nights at don Andrés Malacara's farm. The man was proven correct: eight hours of hard rain made it impossible for the listener to leave, or, as don Andrés saw it, the rain also kept the townies from coming in.

## Emilio Tamez

Emilio Tamez, in the crucible. Works for the Klail-Blanchard-Cooke Ranch. Factotum says it all for this informant. Brother to the late Ernesto Tamez, killed in the bar called Aquí Me Quedo, owned and operated for years by the listener's uncle, Lucas Barrón, el Chorreao. Tamez walks with a limp, the result of a childhood accident.

I can tell you all there is to know about divorces. I'll say I can. Been through one myself, with Esthercita Monroy.

Let me tell you this: you end up with a woman like Esthercita, you better give 'em a golden bridge to walk away from you, yessir. Pave the way for 'em, give 'em distance, and then get the hell away from them.

That's what I did, followed my own prescription, yessir. She got to acting like a Ranch foreman and I just brought me some new rope. Here! I said, run with it. There's the door to this house, take off.

Ira Escobar did the very rightest thing when he got shed of Becky. Now I'm not saying Esthercita and Becky belong to the same rank in society. Becky, she comes from folks who are comfortable, she's a woman of possibles, money, eh? That aside, Becky and Esther could be twins. They both think they're independent.

I've always thought it kind-a crazy for a woman to run a man. That's a sure way to end bad!

And just like I told you, Ira was righter than right; he knew where the door was and how to open the damn thing. Sí, señor. Sí. Sí. I'd see Becky out there at the Cooke Ranch, and she'd be all decked out, nice and all, with Ira's money of course, oh sure, tailor-mades, pleats here and there.

You'd-a thought she was a queen or something. Una reina. And when I say the money belonged to Ira, I'm on target, oh, yeah. Why, even the dumbest chickens, roosters, and pullets know the Navarretes are the meanest, stingiest people anyone ever came across. Made that way, you see. Why, every President Lincoln penny they ever got has turned green by now. Yeah, that's why they got all their money. But it ain't all that much either, don't you see? Oh, they may brag they got money, but where do they ever show it off? Nah. They wouldn't spend a penny until the whole family took a vote on it.

But Ira isn't like that at all. He's a faithful husband, an honest politician, and there's damn few a-them. He's a . . . a . . . a man of honor is what he is. Sobriety, seriousness, that's what you'll find in the Escobar family flag, yessiree. And related to the Leguizamóns and to the Leyvas, too. The Leyva blood also comes from his mother's side o-things. Ira got the best of everything in that bargain.

And he's got learning, too. He and I are about the same age, but he got to go to Texas A & M University, the military school which is bettern'n the other one. And, he also got to enroll at St. Mary's, which is in the city of San Antonio. Yes. Right. That ought to tell you something, says it all, doesn't it? Are there, can there be two better colleges or universities better than those two in the entire United States and Mexico? The answer to that is no, right?

Old Ira, man, he just tightened up his belt and told Becky, straight out, that she could damn well choose: you stay, and I'm still the boss, like always, and we'll have peace around here and outside too. Otherwise, it's a divorce. Just like that. Tough.

Well, she sure thought she could play around with Ira. Ho! Couldn't read him at all, a-tall. But that's her beeswax . . .

And I did the very same thing with Esthercita Monroy. I was up to here, you understand? Whatever else you may think, or might've heard, the Monroys like to throw their weight around, and my brother-in-law, Raúl? . . . he's at the very top o' the list.

Can you even imagine that? Ha! So what happens? First male child we had, we just had to call him Raúl, nothing else but. I ask you, just what the hell kind of a name is Raúl, anyway? It's nothing, it's ordinary, it's a name like a day of the week; anybody can be named Raúl, you know that? Sure.

I wanted the first boy to be named after me, Emilio. The first born, right? And then we could call him Junior. Oh, no. Raúl, that's what the Monroys wanted, and Esthercita led the parade on that one, sure she did.

And that's where it all started. She won that fight, and I gave in, and that's what one gets for being a nice person. Let that be a lesson to all . . . and that's how one pays for one's errors. But that's water over the Falcon Dam, and the best thing you can do is to let it drift down and out to the Gulf, as the old folks say.

. . . But you see, that type of woman, and it is a type, they always run short on shame. They haven't got enough of it. Here's what I'm talking about: What did Becky Escobar turn around and do? Did she pack up and go to her folks' home in Jonesville? Did she go out there and start raising the kids? Hell, no.

I don't see how she did it, where it was she went to find all the damn nerve in the world, but she stayed in Ira's house. You ever seen nerve like that before? I bet you haven't, have you? I sure as all Hell haven't, not if I lived for a hundred years in every county in the state of Texas.

And Ira? All class that boy. The house? It's yours, he says. Keep it, keep it and raise the kids in the best there is. That's what's called a sense of honor, of doing what is right! And that's having the balls to do it. Ah, sorry. Takes guts.

To take care a-the house like God orders, yeah, and then? When bad luck follows bad, you got a heap of very big trouble there. Becky and her lawyers, that Hinojosa guy is one of them . . . he's the same one who defends those cantina killers, people who don't have a pot, 'cause that's the type of person who'll hire him for a lawyer.

Well, he got Becky to get custody of the kids. Yeah, he did. Is there justice in any of this? Tell you what, if you're looking for justice, you best wait for it in heaven, because they got none of it here in Klail City. And, yeah, the same thing happened to me with Esther. It's true.

But it must've cost the Navarretes a very pretty copper penny to pay off Judge Cantú. Sure! You can't tell me that they didn't get to Adán Cantú, got him with a bag of money, they did, and that's how Becky got the kids. Now, I ask you, how can there be justice in Klail?

What I'm about to tell you, though, is something I don't know about on a first hand basis . . . But Noddy Perkins came that close to firing Jehu Malacara, again. You talk about a lack of morality, uprightness. Hmph.

And what happens? Noddy kept him. At the Bank. But I think I know why he kept him, too: it was Ira. Ira intervened for Jehu, his behalf. Can you beat that?

Me, myself, I've told Ira that there's nothing wrong with being a good person, doing a decent turn, but I've also told him not to go around wasting favors on people who can't even spell the word gratitude. 'Cause let me tell you, every person born in this world knows that Jehu Malacara is an ungracious, ungrateful lump of clay. I'm telling you he is.

All right, let's look at this: how many times, when, how many times, has Jehu ever helped the Bank during the elections? Or helped Ira even? Not once. That's right. There's only one way to explain why Jehu is still at the Bank . . . Jehu's got, oh he's got to have, something on Noddy Perkins. Some secrets. And that's why they hired him back at the Klail First.

Yep, some guys are just born lucky, that's all. As for Ira, he's got that decent streak in him, and he can't be any other way, and what can you do?

Oh, yeah, and you know what Becky Escobar is up to now? Not much . . . a common secretary. And to Viola Barragán, of all people. So what did going to college Up North ever do for her? Nothing, college and all, and then to wind up working for that woman? Great Jesus . . . !

I can tell you that not one single solitary day of my forty years here in Belken County, not one, have I ever worked for or with Viola Barragán. And here's the sign of the cross to swear on it. Other people can go work for her if they want to. It's a free country, isn't it?

As for me, you'd have to pull a gun on me to get me to work for her.


The heat of the day drove the informant and the listener to an open air porch facing the Gulf breeze. It's a wet, humidity-laden breeze. The listener is served a tall glass of iced tea while the informant enters the house in search of cigarettes.


As you know, I work for the KBC, and I'm proud to say so. Those families know what being decent is all about. No two ways about that.

As for Viola Barragán . . . she just got here the other day, as we say. In diapers, made of discarded grocery bags, I betcha. Now, that Viola grew up to sell herself to the highest bidder is a matter for her own conscience to sort out. But everyone gets what's coming, and Viola's bound to get hers someday.

I think the first false step Viola Barragán has taken in this go-round has been to hire Becky Escobar. Take her on. That woman's going to bring down Viola Barragán's little empire, and if you don't think so, "wait for me on the corner, darling," as the song says. It's just a matter of time, that's all.

I got an idea. A theory, you might say.

Noddy Perkins—no one's slicker or sharper in the world—has already started chipping away at Viola Barragán's diamond-studded crown, oh yeah. It's a theory like I said, but see what Noddy's up to: First, Jehu no longer handles the Barragán account, and I know this from the Klail Enterprise. You got to read the paper closely: Here's what it said sometime back, that Esther Bewley, Bowly Ponder's niece, has been given a new job at the Bank, and she's to handle the bigger accounts. That's Viola's, see?

Next, people who don't know what's going on, they thought Ira'd been shipped out to Jonesville, to the Savings and Loan, because Noddy doesn't want any trouble between Ira and Jehu. And I'll come to Jehu in a minute. Well, Ira was transferred, but here's why: Now that Noddy's got Ira Escobar at the Savings in Jonesville, the Klail First National Bank is going to start calling in its loans to Viola, and then they're going to be sold, passed on, to the Savings, and there, that old biddy's going to have to give all her eggs to one Ira Escobar himself. How does that sound?

But there's more. Just wait till I light up here . . . There. Now, Noddy Perkins is going to have to retire one of these days and real soon, too. He looks tired. Okay, when he leaves, Jehu Malacara's going to be bounced out of there like a bad check. The Blanchards and the Klail family keep him on Noddy's say-so, but the first day Noddy's out of there, it's adiós, Jehu Malacara, until you're better paid. That's gospel.

The first step's already been taken: Ira is waiting in Jonesville, ready for his marching orders. I'm not saying I can see the future or anything like that, but you just think on it now. Put some of that brain power of yours to work, and you'll see I'm right; that's the play, all right. Few people in the world can measure up to Noddy Perkins, and now that he's finally seen the light, he can see Ira's merits and talent, and he's going to make full use of 'em. Not right now nor tomorrow morning, but it's only a matter of time.

And Jehu? Like I said a little while ago, that damn guy must have something on Noddy for him to keep Jehu on the job. Something big. Serious.

But Jehu'll get his too. Oh, yeah. And talk about gall, nerve, and brass . . . See these two eyes of mine? Well, they've seen him with Becky, in the street, in a shop someplace. Hell, he even parks his car, the Bank's car, in front of her house. Ira's house. Like a dog marking off trees, you know . . . But I tell you one thing, parking the car in front of the house and going in are two different things. That's right. The street's a public thing, you can park anywhere.

Oh yeah; there's some who've never shaken hands with Lady Shame. Look to this: Just how long did he keep the mourning for Olivia San Esteban? A weekend? Proof enough. That's a sizeable piece of hypocrisy to lug around. Sure and that's why I skip out of the Blue Bar, wherever, when I see Jehu Malacara come in. The best thing to do is to keep one's distance from people like that.

And Himself? Hmph? Comes in natural, like there's nothing to stop him . . . Comes in, orders a drink, pays a round for the house and then he leaves. Show off . . . Wanting to buy friends . . . just how long does he think he can count on that type of friend?

If my ex, Esthercita, and I agreed on anything it was that you had to keep an eye on Jehu . . . She'd say it all the time: "Watch him, Emilio. Keep your eye on him. Study him, Emilio."

She was right, you know, and I had to agree with her.

I don't know why, but Jehu has the reputation that he's a ladies' man. Bah Loney. He must be around thirty-something, thirty-eight or so, but he's never married as far as anybody knows. Not by the Church, and what judge would marry him, anyway? A ladies' man . . . Where? When? Who? Well? I'm listening . . . which ones?

I remember once when the Escobars first moved here. By that time, Jehu was already working at the Bank but not being able to carry his load. Just like now, eight-nine years later. Old Noddy wanted for Ira to start running the Bank, but something more important came up: County politics.

And it was here that Noddy had to come to a decision: Ira takes full charge of the Bank as my first assistant or he can use his talent to help me with the County. Ira, and listen closely, Ira himself made the decision.

As he told me later on, and more than once, too: "I walked into Noddy's office and I said to him, 'I'd like to run the Bank and do the commission thing, too. I'm sure I can. But I can see what's going on in the Commissioners' Court, it lacks leadership, and I guess I'd better tend to that for now.' Making decisions, Emilio, is not a hard job once you make up your mind . . ."

Old Ira left an out for Noddy, see? Told you he was bright . . . The out was that if Noddy wanted 'im for both jobs, then he, Ira, was available. He'd run the Bank and the Court.

It's something, isn't it? To have someone loyal like that? You know, Noddy is not an emotional man, he's very Anglo in that. Not like us. But Ira's offer caught Noddy unawares, and in order not to show how much he was touched by Ira's offer, generosity even, Noddy took to coughing, like he had a fit, and that way he didn't have to explain the tears in his eyes.

Once in a while, Ira remembers that scene and he tells me about it. But the choice and decision was Noddy's, and he chose well. Ira ran for the commissioner's post, and then he was named a high officer at the Bank.

To show you how slow some people are, there are those who say that Jehu Malacara is not interested in politics. Now, that's just not true. He wanted that commissioner's job; he even asked Noddy for it. That's right, I got this straight from Ira, and he should know.

Envy is what Jehu's got. There's a lot of raza eaten up by envy, and Jehu is one of them.

I know I talk a lot, but it's always on the side of truth, and one can't talk too much then. You got to let truth air itself out, in the sun. The hotter the better, just like cotton in midsummer.

So, when I say something, make it into a statement, it's because I know, or whoever told me knows, what he's talking about—someone like Ira, or just as good, Notary Public Polín Tapia, who knows and who is in a position to know. As for Jehu, he was born lucky, and he's still riding that lucky streak. Some got it and some don't, and Jehu's one of those who's got the luck. That's right.

Born naked just like the rest of us and it's pure dumb luck he didn't starve to death. The Buenrostro family, out of pure, unadulterated charity, 'cause they're not even blood kin, you know, they raised that boy for a while. Good thing, too, otherwise he would've wound up in Huntsville State Prison, doing time.

You bet. The State would've penned him up in his teens . . .

But luck was there, waiting for him. And then he also had the luck to join the service . . . whatever else the service has got, a person can learn a lot of things there. I didn't get to go on account of this twisted leg, otherwise, I'd-a been right there, among the first.

Yeah, the Army helped that boy, and the federal government stepped in and helped him with his schooling, you know that? They had special programs for Texas Mexicans, did you know that? So they'd learn a trade, get a job somewheres, after the Army. How the federal government picked him is a mystery, but it did.

Fair's fair, and I recognize that Jehu got himself an education and all that, but he isn't half as sharp as some people say he is. Take Ira, he'd barely started at the Bank, six months, I'd say, and he was already Jehu's boss, plus being a commissioner. How 'bout that?

And Jehu'd better not mess with Becky. Oh, I know there was that nasty story, when she was still married to Ira and that Jehu this and that and so on and so forth, but that was all talk. Becky still had pride in those days. Pride, honor, and she still knew what shame was.

Now, I'm not saying she doesn't have shame now, but Jehu'd better watch it himself. He comes fooling around that house once too often and there's going to be trouble. But who's to say? Maybe they deserve each other, eh?

And will you look at the sponsorship? No less a personage than doña Viola Barragán. Doña, hmph! That's some tree they chose for a bit of shade and protection, isn't it?

If it weren't so sad, you'd want to laugh . . . yeah.

## Julia Ortegón

Julia Ortegón, piano teacher. Has known Becky from college and before primary, middle, and high school. Hair, black; eyes, very dark. Strong, beautiful hands. Wears her hair in a chongo, a bun, and held together with a gold brooch, an antique. No rouge or eye shadow here, and no lipstick either. The listener believes Julia Ortegón doesn't need artificial help. The listener is a distant relative, a pariente; their great-grandmothers were identical twins.

Well, pariente, I'll start with high school; that's when we both decided to attend the same college. We graduated together and we settled on North Texas State; music majors, the both of us.

Becky and her mom, doña Elvira, and me and my aunt, Ursula, Dad's youngest sister. You know she raised me, us, after mom died delivering Pepe, and I've got three years on him. He'll be the regular weatherman on Channel Five starting next week, instead of substituting like he's doing now.

I remember it was a weekend; took us a couple of days to get there, but I don't remember much about the trip. We did stop at Austin the first night, at a brand new motel then, on the main highway. And from there, up to Denton.

Those four years at North Texas, and we finished there fourteen years ago, seem almost like a day now. Semesters blending in and out . . . And I liked Denton, it was small, something like Klail, at that time. But it was far from home, just the thing to become independent, at least for me it was.

Not too much for Becky, I don't think, though you've got to admire her now . . . She's always been a very sweet person, but naive, too. It was that mother of hers, and you can't learn much when someone's on top of you, handing out advice all the time. Doña Elvira's a bit *cargante*; pushy, heavy-handed, and lacks the right touch.

My dad says she draws more water than a ship full of scrap metal. Not a bad person, at all, but she likes to order people around. As for Becky, she'd go along, but she wasn't completely broken, you know. Oh, I suppose it's like everything else.

One example ought to do it, I think. In those days, the North Texas girls would pal around with the Tessies from T.S.C.W. The Tessies'd hire buses to visit College Station, a little bit like loading cattle, it seemed to me. But that Texas State College for Women was a girls' school in those days, and they had to get out of Denton.

As for us, well, there weren't many Texas mexicanos to speak of. So, you'd wind up dating some red-faced Anglo hillbilly. Too, A & M was still a stag college, so no coeds there. And both T.S.C.W. and A & M had a tradition of sorts: The Tessies'd go down to Bryan or the Aggies—mostly seniors, and those boots they wore—would come up on a special weekend . . .

Why those Aggies didn't go to Houston, or Austin even, was beyond me. I always thought it a bit idiotic.

None of this is important, but I'm just trying to go back in time here, because that's where they met, Ira and Becky. Although both were from Jonesville, Becky came to school here in Klail, to St. Ann's, not Klail High. As for Ira, he'd been sent to finish up at Central Catholic in San Antonio after his first year or two at Jonesville High.

Central Catholic. Uniforms. A little A & M, that's all. Becky once said Ira had an ear problem . . . My aunt Ursula is not a charitable person. She said the doctors had said *rear* not *ear*. And that kept him out of the real army. Not a matter of abiding interest to me, as you may imagine.

But that was Becky in those days, naive, making excuses for people, and nice to a degree. Not, a . . . a . . . a sly boots, okay? Just unwilling and unable to go out of her way to hurt or to slight anyone. And innocent in other ways too, and that's as good a point as any to start with, innocence.

I'd say we'd been four months into our first year there when we went across town to make our first trip to A & M with the Tessies. As far as Mexican guys were concerned, there couldn't have been over twenty-five at North Texas then. Our dates at A & M, and all this was prearranged, were a couple of *bolillos*—Anglos. Off the farm from the looks of them. Uncivilized would be a way to peg 'em, and so much so that they had no idea we were *raza, mexicanas*. I even spelled out my last name for them. Becky, of course, was a Caldwell on account of her father, but she's a Navarrete on her mother's side, and that's the name that rules in that house.

I'm as pale as a candle, but I'm a Texas Mexican, and if I ever forget it, people in the Valley will line up to remind me who and what I am. This too isn't important, but this is: First trip and all, this is when Becky first met Ira. It happened just minutes before the return trip to Denton; we were standing by the buses, waiting, when this mexicano, and wearing his uniform, struck a conversation with us. There were four of us, talking Spanish, except for Becky. Oh, she understood every word, just didn't speak it much, and not enough to save her soul . . . those nuns at St. Ann's were English pushers. Well, you can imagine how I got along there those four years.

Ay, Diosito[5] . . . I knew three of those nuns, and one was my Aunt Hermenegilda, and she spoke English the way I speak Greek, which I don't.

---

5. My God (diminutive used by believers).

Well, there we were, waiting to board the bus when Ira showed up. I'd never seen him before, but when he introduced himself, told us who he was, and where he was from . . . I remembered my dad saying he was a Leguizamón. Now, you and I are third or fourth cousins, right? . . . but the Buenrostros and us are much closer than that. We're Ortegón on account of my dad, but our mom was a Rincón, and Rafe Buenrostro and I call each other *primo*[6] to this day.

Bells rang right away, a Leguizamón . . . No, thank you, I said to myself.

And so, there's this uniformed type who had little to offer from what I could tell. He wasn't even homely; there was nothing there. Oh, an ingratiating manner, and somewhat charming—but unconvincingly so—and what woman wants that? There was nothing else. My dad, a man known to speak his mind in church, told me that Ira's mind was ordinary, run of the mill. When my dad says that about anyone, that's anyone, you may as well write that person off immediately.

I know, since childhood I've known, that my father has no love for the Escobars or for the Leguizamóns. To his credit, he was bang center on Ira, too.

The strange part about all this is that Becky felt the same way. Didn't talk about him on the bus at all. She talked in that la-di-da way of hers about Bobby Jack or Joe Ed, whatever the bolillos' names were, but then she called home; we all did, Sunday nights, whenever. That phone call changed her life, poor thing.

In those days getting to the Valley wasn't the easiest thing. Not from Denton anyway. The long distance calls, then, were it, as far as visits were concerned. An emergency was something else, of course.

Becky got on the phone first, and I was waiting in line. It wasn't anything startling. She may have said something like, "I met Ira Escobar or I saw Ira Escobar." Nothing, really. But, Holy Mary, Mother of God and all His Miracles! Everyone in line heard doña Elvira Navarrete's WHAT? Or something like HOW WAS THAT AGAIN? Why, you'd've thought the chance meet at A & M a favor from God Himself, for goodness' sake. Good Lo—ord.

What a mother! And poor Becky, is all I can say. From that moment on, doña Elvira, doña Elvira Navarrete de Caldwell, began her . . . her . . . her, how should I put it? . . . her instructions, like speaking to a Catholic convert, can you see that?

Absolute claptrap such as how she, Becky, should behave, respond, what Becky had to do—all right, I'm using my own words here—but what Becky had to do to snare Ira. Can you imagine that type of advice? On long distance? And for such a fool as Ira? Ira Escobar? Lo—ord.

You shouldn't take all of this to mean that Becky didn't like Ira. What was happening was that she had her mother's approval, don't you see? An entirely different matter. It put a whole different color to the thing. And then, to add to all of this, to every bit of this, Ira's mother also figured highly in this . . . this campaign. Oh, yes she did. You can forget what is being said now. I was there, in Denton, with Becky, and I could see those two women down in Jonesville. Yes, I could; across that distance and that time, they had a hand in it.

Becky is a beauty, I'll apologize for the word, but Becky is one. I'm not exactly a stuffed monkey, but I know beauty when I see it. Oh, I know we use

6. Cousin.

the word *linda*, but she went beyond that. Still does. *Bella* is what fits her, and she with two kids of her own, too. And still a beauty, despite having to live with that fool for over a decade. But you can't have everything, and poor Becky was saddled with that mother of hers . . . But don't leave Ira's mother out of it either.

Well, we couldn't make it down for Thanksgiving in those days, so we waited until the long semester break. A & M must've closed early, because by the time we got to Jonesville, Becky told me there were a dozen post cards from Ira. Mailed across town . . . Oh, well . . .

And? Doña Elvira was waiting for Becky in the driveway! Party invitations in hand, three parties, minimum, plus Christmas and New Year's. It had all been arranged. Like a fruit cake, everything piled on, don't you know.

My aunt Ursula and I still laugh when I remind her what she said after we dropped Becky off: "Elvira Navarrete is the world's biggest fool, with one exception: this diocese's bishop."

The bishop is my uncle Urbano, Aunt Ursula's oldest brother.

The rest of the story isn't history, it's a melodrama. Ira, and it's no secret to me, transferred from Bryan to San Antonio, to St. Mary's. He couldn't hack it there, either. It was a circus. Ira flunked out of A & M: three years, fifty hours. From there to San Antonio. And where would a good Catholic boy go? In San Antonio? But he forgot to read the college bulletin. Oh, you can make the hours at St. Mary's, all right, but you've also got to pass the comps, and those comprehensives are something else from what I hear. The upshot is that he took them and took them. A scandal, really. My cousin, Lupe Sosa, told me about it. He's the one with Valley Prudential, and he was at St. Mary's at the time.

It must've been fixed up somehow. Ira did graduate. And what's one more college graduate, right? But Becky must've known, had to. Most probably didn't think about it at all.

They married within the year after Becky's graduation. She majored in piano, as I had, but she didn't give piano and perhaps chose not to. Her home and her family, as the saying goes. *Su casa y su familia* . . . Lo—ord.

All this and heaven, too. And my Aunt Ursula said little on that occasion, but what she did say was enough: "One of these fine days someone's going to tear away the cobwebs off those pretty eyes and face, and when that day comes, some people'd better watch out, they'd better get out of the way."

I guess she said it because she had known doña Elvira Navarrete since childhood, and she baptized Becky, after all. And she's known the Navarretes' history, dreams, yes, and ambitions too. Oh, my aunt Ursula knew full well and quite well whose idea that marriage was. That remark about the cobwebs? There wasn't a trace of malice in it. Not in the least. It was an assessment.

Doña Elvira is not a fool, neither is Becky, for that matter. What happens, though, is that Becky is what we call *noble*, nice, kind, malleable. You can add docile to that litany. That may come from the Caldwell side, from her dad, or maybe from the Manzano side, that grandmother of hers, nobility of character there. Principles.

As for Becky, she didn't always take the best course for her. I mean, she would defer to her mother too often. You can't do that with a bully like doña Elvira. But you've got to admit that Becky, Becky Malacara, and I wish people would stop calling her Becky Escobar . . . where was . . . oh, yes, Becky is a good person, *persona decente*. If there is any malice, *mala uva*, *mala leche*,[7] as my dad says, that comes in a direct line from her mother's stark-staring blind ambition.

Too, Becky is just too loyal to her mother's wishes. And, too, she loves her mother. And of course you can ask, "Why not? Why shouldn't she? It's her mother, after all."

Well, Aunt Ursula talked about "one fine day" and that day came roaring into the Valley like one of those Gulf hurricanes.

She cut the anchor line from that . . . that oaf. She then crossed her legs, as we say, and with that, she closed that entryway to Ira. The Valley, this world of ours, almost went out of its planetary orbit.

"Why, what does that girl think she's doing?"

"What's wrong with that woman?"

"Where would someone like her get ideas like that?"

No, people aren't funny. Not here. Here, they're either dumb, drunk, dangerous, or on drugs, or all three. Or is it all four? (Laughs.) No, they're not funny, and I was just quoting Father Matías Soto who, by every account, camps out at doña Elvira's or at Ira's mother's house. Ay, Dios.

The listener watched Julia Ortegón cross the living room, and yes, she too is a Valley beauty. The listener doesn't bother to ask why La Ortegón isn't married. Come to that, why isn't the listener married?

Julia Ortegón raises the thermometer a bit. The overcast sky has blocked out the September sun; the barometer is rising a bit itself, due, as Julia's own brother, the TV weatherman, says, "due to a disturbance out in the Gulf."

And doña Elvira? Now? At this point, it's best to go to an expert: Aunt Ursula. I'll go get her, but before that, how about some more coffee? Hand me that tray there.

She doesn't like this room, by the way. I'll go into the kitchen and pass on to her room. Why don't you go on out to the porch and turn that air unit on?

The listener lights still another cigarette, and, ash tray in hand, walks to the porch.

## Ursula Ortegón

Ursula Ortegón. A woman in her fifties. An unmarried woman of the old school: prefers a life of chastity and its attendant corollary: independence.

Julia'll be back in a minute. She was telling me of Elvira Navarrete's fright and *choque*, the shock of it all. (Ursula Ortegón's laugh is a happy sound,

7. *Mala uva, mala leche*: bad faith; to act in bad faith.

not one of gloating. A sound that, to the listener, is usually the result of a particularly well-told story.)

Ursula: But I'll tell you this: such laughing will make you cry in the end, it becomes too painful to laugh. I told Elvira. Several times, too. Our friendship goes too far back to break off when harsh truths and opinions are passed on. Oh, she's touchy enough, and she's not made of wood, you know.

But, aside from Viola, I'm still the oldest friend Elvira Navarrete has. She's sloughed off dozens through the years. That's how she is, and I, for one, don't judge friends or parents. As the saying goes: have a set number of both and learn to recognize who they are.

Elvira is the way she is. Let us say she is sui generis, and enough said.

As for Becky, I am her godmother. My brother and I baptized her. My sister Gertrudis, she's been Sister John Birkman for thirty years, was in attendance at the baptism. Anyway, Becky, whether she knew it or not, had changed in the last three or four years of her marriage. I noticed it.

She was thinking for herself. Not much thinking going around, I'll grant you, but it was there. Let's call it a limited type of independence, and the slavery's got to end somewhere.

Nothing one could point to directly, but a little something. One felt this, and I made no secret of it to Elvira; for Elvira, you see, the world is unchanging, people become older, people die, but for her, the world keeps bumbling along . . . I doubt she even reads the paper, not that the *Enterprise* or the *Courier* have anything worth reading.

I have a few strange ideas myself, but that doesn't mean that I'm a bad person or a good one. They're ideas with which I've lived all of my life: it is far better, preferable, even, not to go through a divorce. (The listener was brought up short by Ursula Ortegón, who rose and said: "Don't look at me that way. What I say has nothing to do with my beliefs or with Catholicism. I attend Mass, still go to confession, and I'm a communicant, but it's become a pastime now. Oh, I donate money, of course. It wouldn't look good for that silly goose brother of mine if I didn't give to charity. He's the bishop, after all, and that should give you a fine idea of what the Roman Apostolic has come down to. So, I believe in Mary, in her Son, and in God; nothing easier. I just don't believe in the Church. I've seen too much, heard too much in this house, in this porch, in my brother's old room . . . Oh, well." Do, then, excuse the long parenthesis.)

I look upon divorces as harmful, but as in everything else, I'm sure there are special cases, and Becky's must've been one of those, I suppose. But I still don't like them, and yet, as I said, I recognize that etcetera, etcetera, etcetera . . . Now, that clap of thunder that rang down on Elvira Navarrete rang a little softer here, an ordinary thing, the closing of a door, say.

But for Elvira? Well! It was a moan the size of Texas and Northern Mexico put together . . .

"Ursula! A divorce! Those are strange steps in our family, Ursula. We don't know the way."

Well, you would've thought the *degüello*[8] had been ordered, no quarter, no prisoners. The Navarrete household was in mourning. Long faces. The

---

8. To decapitate. In military usage: When the cornet player plays *el deguello* after a warning, there will be no quarter.

end of the world. A bit of self dramatization, too. It's usually inevitable in those cases. But you can't help seeing the humor of it, really.

And Becky? Nothing. Did not utter half a word. And she wasn't angry, nor did she—is "recriminate" too strong a word? Well, she didn't. Not to her mom, or to anyone. She said she'd done what she had to do, and that that was it.

But what a family! Denser than chaparral and mesquite, yes they are. And I shouldn't say "family"; I should say Elvira . . . Why, you would've thought someone had died. It was exaggerated, and any type of exaggeration always makes me laugh. I didn't, of course . . . I'm a friend. But a small confession is in order here: I'm no good at funerals. Some of them are the greatest exaggerations on God's Green Earth.

I know you've attended funerals in your day, and you've seen wailers and fainters and mourners who carry on and on and fall on the casket, and so on. Well, no one died. It was a divorce. And maybe that's why I dislike divorces; people can then use them to excuse almost any kind of erratic behavior. One has to set limits, exhibit some self-government . . .

I told Elvira—and Becky was still there, as I said—and that accountant uncle of Becky's, the premature one, Pepe, and I said: "It's nothing, people. It's a divorce. Nothing more."

Catarino Caldwell wasn't there. Probably out fishing. Oh, and Elvira's other brother, that fool, the oldest one, Pascual, he was there too.

But I was wrong in a way. And foolish, too. In reality, there had been a tragedy of sorts. For Elvira it was the breaking of a set, a broken glass or cup. A glass of the finest, most valuable crystal. Broken, and by breaking, severing her ties with the Leguizamón family.

And you know who said all that? I'm just quoting, see? Pascual. Pascual Navarrete.

Himself, that solemn goos . . . Look, Elvira has some excellent points and some weak ones. She carries ambition tatooed on her forehead, and that is her one major fault. As big as that error is, however, she is a good wife and sister, a good mother and a good friend. I'm a friend, and she and Viola have loved each other dearly for years. Viola knows her as well as I do. And . . . I've sat in this chair here in *my* house, and in Elvira's favorite chair in *her* house, and, watched and listened as Elvira defended Viola Barragán, and Elvira's defended her in no uncertain terms. She will not tolerate the tiniest bit of criticism against Viola, by anyone. Elvira has this idée fixe regarding the Leguizamóns, but Elvira is loyal, *leal y noble, no-ble*. Her family has been in the Valley a good many years, but the Leguizamóns have become a special project for her.

She's got too much Navarrete blood for her own good. Had she had a tad more Manzano blood, Elvira would've been one of the happiest women of her generation. Believe me. Listen, God knows exactly what He's up to: Who did Elvira marry? Answer: Catarino Caldwell. Second question: Who does Catarino resemble . . . in character? Answer: his mother-in-law, doña Leola Manzano, Elvira's mother. But it's that Navarrete bloodline. Believe me. Oh yes, the blood does need tempering, now and then.

All right, who does Becky resemble? Her father: a jovial man, a bit aloof, but kindly. Sometimes serious, and above all, peaceful, one of God's own, as we say, and a die-hard enemy to ambition in any form. This is not my description, although I agree with it. This is Elvira talking and how she's always described him.

And Catarino Caldwell himself? Nothing. Quiet, pleasant, and when he does talk it's to say where he's going, and one always knows where he's going and his destination, too: fishing or hunting. Except for Elvira and Becky, there are no other women in his life. He's not a smoker or a drinker nor a skirt chaser.

He adores Becky, spoils the grandchildren, and Charlie loves to fish with his grandpa.

And where does Ira stand with his father-in-law? Catarino is courteous. But then, Catarino is that way with everyone. Now, if his daughter, who is worth both of Catarino's eyes to him, and his heart, too, if Becky is happy with Ira, fine. But if his daughter has now chosen to divorce her husband? That, too, is fine. That his daughter now says that her life with Ira is unbearable, then she has to be believed, because his daughter, Becky Caldwell, is not a liar. And there you have it.

On the Navarrete side? No need to go on . . . Becky did not divorce the late President Kennedy or anything close to that. The divorce is Elvira's via crucis.[9] She had placed every hope, all her eggs, as it were, in that bridal basket.

You'd think this was stuff of the nineteenth-century, the union of two families, and so on. Ira Escobar is an ordinary boy. Common. Run of the mill. A normality among normalities.

Let's look at him. Nose? I don't even know what size it is. Eyes? Brown? Dark? I couldn't tell you. Hair? It's either curly or it's straight, but don't go by what I say. Manners? Good, I imagine. But then, every Valley boy I've known has 'em. So?

Oh, here's Julia now. And with fresh bread, too.

(Laughs.) Do you know what Julia says about Ira? She says that Ira has no distinguishing features, that he's not even homely enough to comment on.

He is one of God's unfortunate ones. If he had ears like a bat, say . . . something, but he hasn't got a thing that'll set him off from the crowd, poor thing. Oh, he's got a bit of the Leguizamón jaw, but that's about it.

All I can say is that he may be a bit of a bore, and if he is, then there's no cure, no redemption or salvation. There can't be, in God's own world, something worse than a boy who, as a man, becomes a lethal bore . . . It's best to drown them early and young, like cats . . .


Coffee and hot rolls. Buttered pastry. The listener lights a cigarette.


And Elvira? That very afternoon. You can just imagine. She came here at a gallop. Drove straight from Jonesville. She forgot about the phone, and she loves the phone. It was about this time now. Julia here was on her way to the garage when the screen door, that one there, let in a rush of air, a cyclone.

---

9. The way of the cross (i.e., in Christianity, Jesus' walk to his death, between the fortress Antonia and Golgotha). *President Kennedy*: John Fitzgerald Kennedy (1917–1963), U.S. president 1961–63.

Elvira! Panting. Gasping. Her eyes out of focus, looking in all directions, seeing absolutely nothing, her voice rising . . .

Becky, Becky, Becky . . .

My first thought? Oh, Dear God, killed in a car wreck. I dropped whatever it was I was holding and I went to her.

Water. Limeade. *Vino tinto.*[1] Something, and then that voice again, and: Becky, oh Becky . . . what have you done?

Julia missed this part. She was in the garage looking for something, but even out there, she could hear Elvira. Well, Julia rushed in expecting holy murder at the very least. (She turns to Julia, who nods.)

And to top it, Elvira wouldn't settle down, and we couldn't get her to sit and tell us. A gasp, a pant, and: BeckyBeckyBecky . . .

Well! This had to stop. We sat down and waited her out amidst her tears and hiccups, don't you know. And then, she told us, but I'll tell you what set Elvira off and running . . . it was Becky's look of determination, resolution: One of those, "This is it, I'm not moving, and you go ahead and do what you want to."

Elvira could have saved much of her breath on that one. As for that Pascual Navarrete, that other brother, I'd've taken him with that cricket voice of his, and thrown him in the nearest lion's cage, let me tell you. He's a cloying piece of little manhood. A lap dog in a man's suit is what he is. And tiresome? He's like a barnacle on a wreck . . . Good Lo—ord.

But as I said, it was Becky's irrevocable decision, that's what Elvira saw. And, it frightened her. Resolution pure and simple, if it ever is that. And you know what else she saw in Becky's face? Elvira saw herself, and she saw Becky had had it with Ira. There was no going back. Elvira could see that Becky had considered the decision coldly, *fríamente*, and seriously.

Poor Elvira. Couldn't recognize her own daughter. Couldn't see that Becky, in spite of everything, was a person, a human being. Someone with character. Someone apart from her little daughter of eight or nine.

Becky and Julia here have known each other for years and Julia's always said that Becky, as pliable as she's been through the years, did have certain limits, limits which once crossed . . . mmmm, then it was look out! Yes.

Oh, I can imagine how much Becky must've cried alone, yes, alone, and thinking of the scandal, of her mom, and thinking of her own life with Ira . . . a life she now found unbearable. Can you imagine all of that? Oh, yes. Becky has had to put up with Ira, and that's a tall order . . . Once, about eight years ago, she paid me a visit, alone. That was eight years ago, and she sat right there, where you're sitting, and said she was in love with Jehu, and Jehu loved her . . . (Julia Ortegón is aghast. She can't believe her aunt who continues speaking.)

And why shouldn't she come to me? I'm her *madrina,*[2] I baptized her, and she lives, what? . . . a block away? Anyway, she came here and sat on that same chair.

I made a gesture of some sort, said maybe she was wrong. That she had two kids to care for, had reached a certain age, and that perhaps, just perhaps, someone can come and pay attention to her, and that she thought she

1. Red wine.
2. A diminuitive form for *madre*, a mother; here, godmother.

was in love. Hm. Becky, quietly, said she wasn't "in love," she said she loved him.

I remember quite well. She didn't cry. Not a tear. She took my hand and in that moment, she looked like a señora who will always know more about everything in the world than I will ever learn or hope to know . . .

"You're wrong, madrina." And that's all she said.

May Julia here forgive me, but there are some things, certain things one can't share, can't pass along. Can't tell anyone. It's not important now, but perhaps this may clear up some things. I just don't know anymore.

The reader may know what silence is, but with three people in a room, sixty seconds of silence seem longer, somehow. Ursula Ortegón placed her coffee cup lightly, measuring every millimeter, or so it seemed to the listener.

As for that Malacara boy, I confess ignorance. Adopted, perhaps, but blood kin to the Buenrostros. I do know Mati Buenrostro looked upon him, treated him, too, as she did Rafe, and the other two boys. I just don't know him. Oh, I see him at the Bank. At a function once in a while . . . but know him? No. One hears things . . .

A kind, relaxed, and knowing look, and then:

But Becky knows what he's made of. And I can imagine how Elvira could see herself in her only daughter's eyes. And painfully, too, for poor-dear-foolish Elvira for whom the Leguizamón union represented the sum total of her life. Dear, merciful God, what a goal to aspire to . . . And it was that exactly, a goal.

Sadder still, though, was that that was not the sum total of Becky's life. To live to be thirty-odd years for one's mother is to give her another thirty years of life. That's not doing anyone a favor of any kind . . .

The children? Charlie and Sarah? I don't know. I don't know. One never does know. I never thought of being a mother, and I raised Julia here. And I know she loves me (smiling, finally), despite my secret . . . but a secret, any secret, no more makes than breaks a love, friendship, respect.

At this point, Julia rose to turn on the six o'clock news. Her brother reported that the hurricane had settled or stalled some two-hundred miles East Southeast off Jonesville. He then gave the coordinates and said: "That's all for now. Back to you, Bill."

Julia laughed at this and explained that what we were watching was this morning's tape spliced to the six o'clock news. Julia laughed again and said it was merely another form of reality.

The listener helped with the tidying up and noticed, perhaps mistakenly, that Ursula Ortegón looked older, somehow.

# Martín San Esteban

Martín San Esteban. Pharmacist, two years older than his sister, the late Olivia San Esteban. The listener has nothing else to say about M.S.E. at this time.

Jehu and I did not get along when we were kids. I think we get along now. We speak. Too, we don't see each other very much. We run in different circles, that's all.

We were up in Austin together. And I didn't know whether he first didn't like me or whether I didn't like him. There must have been some sort of, ah, antipathy. That happens, doesn't it?

Around that time, the war in Korea was either over or winding down, and he was fresh out of the service. Jehu and his cousin, Rafe Buenrostro, showed up in Austin and registered at the University. There were very few of us Mexicans there at the time, and most of us were from the Valley, some from Laredo, El Paso, San Antonio. Not many though. There were also two other cousins of Rafe's there, Raúl Santoscoy and Cheo Campoy; they were in pharmacy with me. I had a roommate from El Paso, and he too was in pharmacy.

We all hit the beer joints pretty regularly, especially on weekends. In the Fall, during football season, that was a sure thing.

It was a strange thing between Jehu and me. We never talked about it, we didn't then, and still haven't, to any great degree . . .

I doubt if the rest of the guys ever even found out, 'cause Jehu and I never came to words, let alone a fight . . . It was strange. Of course, if Jehu ever said anything to anyone about himself, or how he felt, it would've been to his cousin, but as I say, who's to know? Besides that, who was ever going to get a word out of Rafe Buenrostro, right?

What I do know is that Jehu didn't date my sister Livvie up there, probably never even danced with her at the Newman. We were damned few raza there, and so, one turned to *bolillas*, the Anglo girls.

Our dad's family, the San Estebans, we're not related to anyone in the Valley, that we know of. My mom and dad came from Querétaro, just like the Buenrostros, but my folks came here in their twenties, during the Mexican Revolution . . . They got here yesterday, as they say in the Valley. We, my sis and I, were born on this side of the River, first born sons of foreign-born parents.

There were three of us: Merced, who was four years older than me and who drowned in Campacuás Lake during a picnic on the lake when a blue norther rolled in. Took everyone by surprise . . . The month of March . . . and then, just like that, the norther was on us, wind, cold wind, and hard rain, driving rain . . . Livvie's death . . . well, that took place a little more than two years ago. I think about her every day. It was Livvie who got me to change my mind about Jehu. He was single for years after the university, and he ran around; maybe that's not the term. It may be unfair, too. He knew a lot of girls . . .

Me, I got married to San Juanita about a year after graduation. That was the expected thing then: education, marriage, a family. It certainly worked out for San Juanita and me. I've no complaints, and especially when I look around . . .

So, Jehu's teaching at Klail High, quits, and from one day to the next, it turns out he's a banker. First, he worked at Klail Savings and Loan and then, from there, right across the street, and kitty corner from here, the Klail First National Bank. It was Jehu, in fact, who managed the loan, the loans, really, for this place, and for the pharmacy my dad, my sis, and I opened up in Ruffing.

Jehu signed every copy of the contract very carefully, neatly, not carelessly at all. He smiled when he was signing and he said to my dad, "Don Salvador, this'll teach 'em a lesson." My dad laughed too. It was like a joke between them, see?

As I recall, Livvie wasn't at the Bank. She was checking at the County Clerk's and at the title abstract company one more time.

Later on I found out why she checked so carefully. Jehu had called her on that. He told my dad, and made it a point, too, that sometimes, somehow, titles are made to disappear, changed. Anything, he said, anything can happen at the County Clerk's office.

Too, Livvie later told me, we were to be the first Mexican-owned pharmacy in the Anglo part of Ruffing . . . But somebody had to go in there first; and my dad, he'd chosen a good location, a sound location, and Jehu had sent a loan appraiser to take a measure of the traffic, the parking, the marketing end of it. All business and you sure can't say that Jehu doesn't know what he's doing. Livvie's checking off all the property titles and surveying was part of Jehu's careful checking on everything. A businessman's way . . .

He and my dad have always gotten along. When Jehu stopped his running around, his fooling around, some four or five years ago, well—I can tell you when exactly—it was the time he came back to the Bank for the second time. At any rate, he called on my folks, formally. Set a date with them, said what it was about, and he was there in a week or so. Formal, see? He and Livvie had already agreed on this, too. My parents, both of 'em, were touched by this, impressed that Jehu made it a point of formalizing it . . . ah . . .

Oh, they knew Jehu, of course, what with business and all. But he called for an appointment, *una cita*,[3] as I said. He showed up and that was it. It was very nineteenth-century, you know? 'Cause, shoot, here in the Valley now, one asks the girl and then she *tells* her folks what *she* plans to do. I mean, Jehu and Livvie dated, and he was serious . . .

And it wasn't until then . . . What I mean to say is that it wasn't until then that I could see that Jehu wasn't what I thought he was. What no one thought he was. Hmph. One time back I'd gotten angry as hell, I should say resentful, because Jehu wanted Livvie to go to med school. Yeah. Up in Galveston. I was wrong. Flat out wrong. It took me a long time, but I finally saw that I, who always thought of myself as someone on the ball, you know what I mean by that? Well, I was wrong, about a lot of things. I wanted Livvie to stay where she was, what she was, a registered pharmacist.

And Jehu? Nineteenth-century ways in some ways, he wanted Livvie to be something, to study medicine, go up in the world . . . I guess you first have to learn to read people . . .

---

3. A date.

I can swear to anyone that Livvie was never happier in her life than in those two years in med school. And Jehu? Waiting for her. That's why he came back to the Bank the second time. He had the Ph.D. to study for, but he said that was of no consequence, no importance . . .

He lied. I know he lied. If he dreamt of anything, it was to return to Austin, Texas. Oh, yeah. But he came back to Klail. He and Livvie broke off for a while, but they made up. I don't think there was ever any doubt about those two. Jehu laughed about it at the house one day; he said that lovers falling in love again always happened in bad novels.

As for me, I had to admit something that was very, very difficult for me. But I had to admit it: Jehu didn't care whether I lived or died, truly. If I was surly at him, or if I resented him and his ways, it was all the same to Jehu. The resentment, and I had to own up, came from me. I didn't like him. I didn't like his ways or the person.

And Jehu? None of this bothered him. He sure didn't show it at any rate. And then, when he fell in love with my sister, he fell in love.

Whether I or ten thousand other guys were going to be the brother-in-law didn't bother, didn't concern him in the least. He only had eyes for her. Me and my parents, other people, dead, as far as he was concerned. The one time I saw anger flash in his eyes, briefly, but enough to see the fire, he said, "Goddammit, Martín," like that, in Spanish, "You've got to think of other people." A strange guy. So I changed. I realized he wasn't a bad guy, not self-centered at all, just dead serious. And strange, yeah, strange.

So now, marrying Becky, well, that doesn't surprise me. He's serious, just like with Livvie. Jehu's not here to change the world, he takes people and the world without . . . ah . . . say . . . ah . . . preconceived notions. Right?

Took me some time to learn that much. My folks were happy when he married Becky . . . I didn't even know they'd heard of her.

As for Ira? He's all right, we get along well . . . but look at it honestly: Jehu didn't break up that marriage. He didn't take Ira's wife away from him. He didn't insult him, show him up. That's not Jehu, that's not his style. Oh, I've heard, been told, that Jehu and Becky had something going eight, nine years ago. I don't know that. It could have happened, though. He ran around a lot . . .

As for *this*, now? This is Becky's own doing. She is a divorced woman, a working woman. She's free to do, undo . . . She gives no cause for talk that I know of, and if she and Jehu reached an agreement, married, 'cause they are that, well, they're both well over twenty-one years of age.

As far as any of this concerns me, Jehu Malacara is not about to ask my permission for anything. He was faithful to Livvie, kind, considerate, and even though my sister's death was the most painful thing I've gone through, Jehu behaved as if they'd been married.

Look, it's easy to look the fool in those cases, but Jehu showed class, demonstrated it, without wanting to or without any pretension whatsoever. And what matters most, above all, and everything else, to my folks and to my wife and me, is Jehu's sincerity. No room for hypocrisy, no, not in quiet actions there isn't. He cared. Very much.

I had no idea when we started talking here what I'd say. I certainly didn't plan anything. But I must say I never thought I'd be talking about Jehu in this or in any way. But Jehu showed us, me among them, by example, that it's best not to say, "I'll drink not from that fountain."

Yes. The way things are, the way some people are . . . and yet, we're still not close. But there's respect now, and we share that. Yeah, I think we do; and that's the way it should be.

The listener has some ideas and opinions to express. The Valley is a strange place, to begin with. The speakers that follow—Valleyites to the core—are at home, at ease, both in English *and* in Spanish. They are all Texas Anglos, and they are all bicultural, to use an old term now used popularly.

There are Valley Anglos who claim they are bilingual, but aren't. It takes work to speak as a native Spanish-speaker. Then, there are also those Anglos who say they wish they were bicultural and thus bilingual, but they're neither. This also takes time. And there are those who were born to it; it had nothing to do with work, or wanting to or wishing for it. They were at home, at ease.

As the listener insists, it's a strange place.

## E. B. Cooke

E. B. Cooke. 1) A Williams College alumnus and graduate; 2) a graduate of the Harvard School of Business.

As far as I'm concerned, and from where I sit, it's live and let live, I always say. What better way is there to ensure domestic peace and tranquility?

I was born in the Valley, in February, 1910, and as many of my class, my military class, 1910, that means I learned Spanish from day one. Ranch Spanish, obviously. In college, at Williams, I spent my summers in Spain, Havana, Mexico, and so on. I'm saying this not as a brag, not entirely, but only to clear up any misconception. I'm Valley-born and I know the *gringada* just as intimately as I know *la raza*.

Well now, since I can hear and see and know the difference between right and wrong, to live and let, as I said, I don't think that Becky Escobar's leaving, abandoning, divorcing Ira is bad or good. A matter of complete indifference to me.

Regarding Ira's political career, it must be on its fifth or sixth year or term, whatever, but that's nothing to me either. Boys like Ira are in long supply and there's even more now than there were ten, twelve years ago, let's say. As for Ira, I'd say he was competent in a narrow, restrictive way.

Too, today's Becky Escobar—and I say this privately and publicly, since it doesn't matter to me, anyway—Becky is a different proposition, not the same Becky at all. At all. And I like her more, too. She's . . . she's her own person, know what I'm saying here?

Oh, she's always been nice, pleasant, tractable, let's say, but when I look at her, I see some bearing, some direction. Carriage, that's the word I was looking for . . . Sure of herself, too. Who she is, that she's aware of that, see?

If at one time she sat—and will you listen to me talk this way?—if at one time she worshipped at my niece Sammie Jo's feet, they now treat each other as equals, something which Sammie Jo likes, by the way. My niece, as Churchill used to say of Russia, is a paradox wrapped inside an etcetera . . . So what I'm saying is that Sammie Jo hated—despised, really—the way Becky, the old Becky, would abase, would efface, erase even, her own character to go around pleasing other people. And this to please those leeches in the Music Club.[4]

Well, as for Sammie Jo, she prefers for people to be themselves, not the way other people would like for them to be. You do understand that, don't you?

The listener is not hard of hearing. Informant Cooke's tic is not to be taken as a penchant for corroboration, in any way or case. The listener believes that these *huhs, rights,* etc. are breathing spaces as Cooke goes from topic to topic. A manner of speech tied, it is obvious to the listener, to Cooke's character and personality. In difference, then, to everything but his own person. In this way, not different from most egoists.

As for Sammie Jo, she's loved one man in her life, young Rafe Buenrostro. And who would've thought they'd ever marry? No one. Not here. In the Valley.

Her sad, unhappy life has been due to her father's idea of improving on an empire. That brother-in-law of mine . . . and no, it isn't an indiscretion if I speak of Noddy this way. I started it, so I'll end it here. But let's get back to Becky.

Becky, and here, above all, frankness must be brutal, home truths, then: Becky's gotten hold of an elm tree of a woman friend and protector in Viola Barragán. And even if Becky neither knows nor appreciates it yet, she's a young Viola Barragán, A seedling, let's say. She's sharp, handsome, honest, and as one must be in business, tough. She's got the future in her hands, she does. What I'm saying is not some cliché or other, these aren't set phrases; make no mistake on that score.

But aside from all this, that future that I . . . that I presage, don't you know, is being claimed here with all the confidence of one who has known, dealt with Becky at first hand. That first year after her divorce, she'd go with Viola to all the businesses in Viola's corporation.

And here we are, halfway through the second year, and what do we see? Well, there's Becky administering various of the business enterprises: the hamburger chain, the Shopping Bags, that massive trailer park which, by all accounts, holds some nine-hundred place units . . .

With that number of trailers I've already told you about, more or less indirectly, Viola's investment in that venture is substantial. You see, the average range of those mobile homes goes from nine to eleven-five when bought in

---

4. The deponent's first and only wife left him for a Brazilian, perhaps an Italian, tenor. E.B.C. has consistently laid the blame on the Music Club. [Author's note—i.e., the listener's note]

those large lots. That is a very serious amount of money. And Becky? She's the one who rules that little-wheeled kingdom. The café chain, and there's eleven of those, that's a rift of gold right there. Oh, yes. You see, Viola, with Becky's advice, has added chicken and a salad, etcetera. The Shopping Bags are frosting on the cake, let us say.

And as I just said, Becky is the director of those businesses. I'd bet dollars to doughnuts that Ira couldn't carry that load . . . *no puede con los liachos,*[5] eh? Talent's the trick, and drive, too, knowing your personnel, to show, receive common courtesies, tact . . . That's necessary; did I say necessary? Essential is the word. Well, Ira's not the one, hasn't got the knack, the talent. He's got other things going for him, and you can't deny that, but he's missing that little something, *el toque,*[6] that Becky's developed to a high degree. Learned that from Viola. Either that, or she was born to administrate—a gift.

The change, maybe it's best not to call it that. The discovery of her own persona, who she was, as a person, well, that opened up the floodgates, the whole dam, really. And it had to be opened in order to fulfill its mission, carry out its assignment . . .

The listener, attentive as ever, suspects that E.B.C. has gone off the track here. Slightly, but off. The listener has full confidence in the reader and knows the reader will get the drift.

The children? Fine, as far as I know. The oldest, a boy, is no longer enrolled at St. John's. Becky placed him in public school. The girl's no longer at Scholastics either. She's at St. Ann's, here in Klail. Becky's old school . . .

Socially, I imagine I see her and Jehu once a month, the old *rendimiento de cuentas* . . . the settling of accounts payable and receivable. It's business, but social, too.

As for Jehu, he and I've always respected each other, and that is not only a truth, it is a completely verifiable fact. If Noddy Perkins and I agree on anything, and there isn't much to hang on to, both Noddy and I recognize Jehu's talents and contributions. As Jehu says, though, praise is a great thing, but a raise is even better.

And as I said to you over the phone, I was a witness to their wedding. Jehu himself asked me to serve.

A seventy-two-year-old witness ought to count for something, don't you think? (E.B.C.'s laughter.)

Yes, Jehu is well-paid, and why shouldn't he be? By the way, Jehu took himself out of Viola's accounts, a valued account, too. Jehu said it would be improper. So, he himself went out to the main office, picked out Esther Bewley and trained her for the job. That's Esther's office, across the hall, personal office and everything as associate director of current accounts.

Jehu's been named cashier, my old job. I just come in here for coffee, something to do . . . This old office used to be the board room. I heard Jehu's name here for the first time; he was at the Savings and Loan then . . .

5. He can't carry out the assignment, he can't do the job since it's too tough for him (*liachos* is Mexican Spanish).

6. Here, the touch.

As far as the Bank, as far as I'm concerned, as one of the owners, what Jehu did in withdrawing from Viola Barragán's accounts is enough to inspire confidence in anyone. Shows you how he's grown as a banker and as a person. That's right, as a person.

Hmmm. I remember my sister Fredericka, who's no longer with us, how she resisted Jehu's hiring. It wasn't Jehu, it was the idea of what he was . . .

Jehu would've made a fine lawyer, just like that non-practicing cousin of his . . . my nephew now, right? In-law, but a nephew . . . Anyway, Jehu's grown. He asked, first me and then Noddy, if it wouldn't be better if he were transferred to Klail Savings or to our branch in Jonesville . . . soon after the Escobars' divorce . . . Well, about a week later, the three of us met in Noddy's office, a Friday, if I'm not mistaken . . . end of the week, end of the quarter . . . Anyway, Noddy mixed some highballs and after this and that, Noddy broached the subject of the transfer and said, "No, I don't want you to go out there."

Said that Jehu would stay put—you know Noddy—and that he'd talked to me—he had—and that he'd phoned Junior Klail and I don't know who else, maybe my sister Anna Faye too; that we had agreed he was to stay at the Bank.

Years back we knew he was a Buenrostro, and here we were, the Cookes, about to hire him . . . Well, there are only two Cookes left now, Anna Faye and I, since Freddie died of uterine cancer. Freddie came around though, although if anyone has ever been born a Mexican-hater, if there is such a thing as being born that way, Fredericka certainly was. Once, just once, Jehu and I talked on this, and Jehu attributed Freddie's . . . her discomfort with Mexicans, as good, old-fashioned guilt. Talking to me that way, about my own sister, but then I had brought the subject up in the first place . . . And he wasn't being flippant either; he also said it didn't matter, that the land, this land, the Valley, all of this, would be here when we were all dead. He then laughed and said, "When the state has withered away." Noddy it was who christened Jehu as The Uncommon Banker . . . he is that, all right.

Since we do get on, although just barely when he was first hired, I've learned that I'll get an honest answer; cool, perhaps, but an honest one. One day, out of the blue—well, perhaps he'd considered it deeply, but out of the blue for me—he said that Ira needed an eighteen-year-old girl. You know, someone around that age, without character. Terrible thing to say, but there it is . . .

## Edith Timmens

The listener is sitting on the east-side porch, enclosed and air-conditioned usually, of a so-called ranch style house in South Klail City. The glassed louvers have been opened widely, and the strong Gulf breeze cools the shaded porch after a driving rain earlier that morning. According to the latest weather reports, hurricane Elmer remains a hundred miles off shore, lurking, and continues to be a threat to the Valley and Northern Mexico.

The frosted pitcher of limeade looks inviting, and the listener pours two tall glasses, adding a sprig of hierba Buena, mint. The second glass is intended for the listener's hostess, Edith Timmens, widow of Ben Timmens, attorney cum public relations drum beater cum one-time state and national congressman for the KBC interests.

Edith Timmens née Bayliss is Valley-born. Strong, resolute, and with a mouth where butter doesn't stand a chance. The listener has always found Edith Timmens discreet at times, outspoken at others, to lean toward the truth, although it must also be admitted that euphemisms and circumlocutions may be employed when the informant deals with her own family. The KBC and its families, however, are presented as she, Edith Timmens, sees them. Not a gossip then, but she has heard and participated in too many of the KBC lives and doings for her to have to succumb to niceties and shadings in this regard.

My Ben never did learn Spanish, astonishing as that may be. Couldn't get the hang of it, he claimed. A poor head for languages was another of his excuses. I never, for one minute, believed him.

He didn't want to, and that was plain enough to me. You can lie to almost anyone and get away with it, but you can't lie to your wife. Not convincingly, at any rate. Oh, she'll go along, pretend to believe, perhaps, but taken in? No, that's not the same thing. For his part, his lying about why he didn't learn Spanish was stupid, but Ben was also a bit of a racist. And don't look at that admission as a betrayal of his memory or as the lack of loyalty of a widow. Ben was a racist, and he had little reason and no excuse for it. His mother was Mexican, and one who didn't speak English, and how do you like that?

The Timmenses came here by way of San Luis Potosí. Ben's great-grandfather served in the Confederacy. He married into a Southern family which had settled in San Luis after the Civil War. Ben was brought here this century by his father, Big Ben Timmens, the one who married a Mexican from Potosí. At that time, my father was the chief KBC veterinarian for the Klail Division of the Ranch, the Atticus Klail *potrero.*[7] And, it was he who saw to it that Big Ben was made a *caporal* right off. That's right, foreman of the K Division . . . His wife was named Petra Cedillo, and she died of dysentery when my Ben was eleven or so. About the time of the Spanish influenza epidemic of 1919 or so. Anyway, Big Ben then married Laura Pennington when my Ben was thirteen. Laura was his mother. He called her that, and she reared him, cared for him, but that didn't make her his blood mother, *su mamá.*

And speaking of my father, now there was a piece of work. Raised on cactus milk, as we say. Not originally from here, but he might as well have been born here. This was home, he said. Virginia? That was just a place to be born in. As for Spanish, not once did he insist we learn it or that we had to, we just did. Never a question of if or when. Made use of the maids who raised us, of course . . . simple as that.

I was raised as a KBC-er, and my Ben was too. The KBC paid for our schooling, all of it, Austin, Georgetown Law, wherever we chose.

---

7. A pen for colts as a corral is a pen for horses.

I loved Austin, Washington, too. Happy years in Washington, but I'm a Texan, through and through. And don't take this talk of mine as a smoke-screen to hide anything about my brother Hap. He was always a delicate child. I'm no psychiatrist, and I can't begin to tell you why he turned out the way he did, but he did, and I'm not here to whitewash anything or anyone. I'm already a hypocrite in my own eyes, so I certainly don't need to cover up for anyone. Every family has its own rarities, and happily, for us, Hap knew how to be discreet. He didn't accost anyone in a man's bathroom in some restaurant or library, and he didn't approach any young accordion players or whatever . . . You and I know what I mean, and that's the end of that.

As for the KBC, they're sharp as red pepper, but they're odd, too. To my mind, they've never enjoyed their money. Have never known how to and that's a sad truth, a truth as big as Texas, as big as the Ranch. They lack something; a taste for life in some strange way. And they're skinflintish, too. In a phrase: they've not been able to find pleasure in each other as a family. I'm not talking of one or two nor will I spew out names for you, but as a whole, an unhappy bunch. And you can forget about taste. Everyone took a separate road there, although the roads all lead to the same point. And Klail City itself? The town would've died if it hadn't been for enterprising Mexi-cans and Anglos, believe me. The KBC wanted an enclave and discouraged whatever looked like growth . . . But this was a Mexican town, had been since the 1700s . . . The Valley's history is no secret, after all.

And I'm not opening any old sores here; that sore is very much alive, and the KBC knows it. And they're lucky, and smart, at the same time . . . They've made huge blunders, but they've been written off . . . my Ben saw to that many times.

Of all of them, I prefer Noddy and Sammie Jo, and their company and friendship. They laugh, smile, and they're a pleasure to be with. And Noddy's wife, Blanche? The very devil herself, and I mean that in a nice way: she's a wit. And she drinks, and she knows it. She doesn't lie to herself.

Sammie Jo? Adored by both of them. They're a lively damned bunch and both mother and daughter love and suffer together, and who wouldn't? Af-ter all, living with Noddy wouldn't make for one continuous barrel of fun and laughter, would it? Still, the three are a team. As for Noddy marrying off Sammie Jo, a crime. Two, really, since he pushed her into two horrible disasters . . . And Sammie Jo? She understands her father's weaknesses and insecurities. Do you actually believe it is easy to marry into the KBC?

As for Blanche's drinking, it was a serious problem and remains so. I'm not here to defend her, even as a friend. Alcoholism is not to be defended or excused, you've got to admit it, your friends have to admit it, everyone. Blanche is much better, and I think seeing Sammie Jo happy has helped her. But let's not blame Noddy Perkins for Blanche's drinking. That's the easy way out.

As for Noddy, red-faced, that irritating nasal twang, and that cool, chilling side of his at times—all of that, when it comes to his wife and daughter he is the picture of consideration and sensivity. He knew he was wrong when he engineered those weddings . . . And now? Some people laugh and say Noddy is stuck for a third time, and this time with a Mexican for a son-in-law . . . The only thing cheaper than talk is people's bad breath, and I would suggest they save it and their saliva, too.

I go on like this because when my Ben was down with pancreatic cancer the Perkinses were the only ones from the KBC who came to visit him. Noddy, most of all, and Sammie Jo and Blanche would send flowers every other day. They would do the arranging, too. And Noddy was there, in the room. I knew we were friends and we visited, but this is Mexican *cumplir*, isn't it? . . . *ser cumplidor*[8] . . . I once heard your cousin Jehu say that about Noddy . . . It wasn't until my Ben fell ill that the true meaning of the word came to me . . . Hit me full-face. And E.B.? Not once. Not ever. Anna Faye. Not her.

Poor Ben, was he ever wrong about who'd stand by him, and he was even wrong about Becky Escobar . . .


The listener was offered several drinking choices: iced-tea, iced-coffee, or limeade. The listener was also offered a cigarette from a box of Delicados. The listener chose limeade and a Delicado as did Edith Timmens.


No doubt about it, my Ben was a fine lawyer, and always well-prepared, too. But he lacked the human touch; he worked for the KBC all of his professional life, and he never represented anyone else in court. Not that Ben spent much time in court, anyway.

My father, years ago, had passed on some sound advice to me: don't you ever fall in love with institutions of any kind. He said it to Ben, too. My father knew full well who he worked for and he wanted Ben to understand. I understood. Perfectly. Poor Ben, he was loyal and he expected loyalty. Good thing he didn't ask for it. He loved the KBC, lived for it. And he a lawyer . . .

And here I was, protected by this Ranch and its power, having to remind myself of what my father said, and having to remind myself that the KBC did put the food on the table and the clothing on my back . . . But also remembering that this wasn't charity, that work was performed, that the food and clothing were earned, not given. One has time to think in a hospital. One can only read so much . . . And Ben, Ben was in pain, and so I cried for both of us.

The day before he died, Jehu Malacara walked in. After shaking hands with me, he walked to Ben and shook his. It wasn't much, his only visit, but it set me to thinking of the first time I saw him at the Bank years ago. I didn't like what I saw; I was frightened, I think. He carried about him a whiff of independence, something the KBC considers dangerous. "He won't last," I remembered thinking.

Just a whiff of it, but enough to recognize it. I had been independent when I was his age, perhaps. Later, when I saw him, and I was in my fifties then, I also understood there was a difference between that kid—Jehu—and me. And between him and Ira, too, later on. Sammie Jo was a big help in this case. She once said that Jehu was prepared to leave the bank at any time; nothing to it, he'd told her.

---

8. *Ser cumplidor*: one who sees things through, one who comes through on a job. *Cumplir*: to fulfill, to perform.

Oh, yes. He hadn't fallen in love with the institution. And? . . . Well, he did leave. Oh, he came back, but it took three years, and when he came back, the look of independence was still there. Not a defiant look, that one used by people who feel inferior and who adopt a pose or something. Not that at all. A self-assurance, a nice way with people. Warm, courteous. The way he behaved with Ben at the hospital, with me.

No, he wasn't about to go under the way Ben did and the way Ira did when he came on board . . . Ira sank, disappeared without a trace, didn't he? Who is Ira? Is a fair question.

I've seen and talked with him since the divorce, since Jehu married Becky. Ira has yet to see, to understand the connection between Becky's disaffection, the divorce, and the direction their life had taken, was being led.

As for Becky, she finally met a man who loved her, one who knew how to love, to care. Jehu needs no instructions from me, he can distinguish between a person and an institution, to get back to that again. But it was true, Jehu saw her as a person, as an individual, as a woman full-blown and grown. And Becky had changed, oh yes . . .

And it happened, one afternoon, about a year after the divorce, Jehu—and this comes from Becky—Jehu called on the phone. Thirty minutes later they sat on the front porch overlooking Klail Boulevard. In the daytime, nothing to hide. A chat, brief, to the purpose. I can only imagine what was said—Becky didn't go into that—but it's common knowledge from that day on Jehu called on her and they went out. Nothing secretive about that.

That Ira was subsequently transferred to Jonesville gave people a lot to talk about, but Noddy told me, in person and as a friend, that it was he who had Ira transferred . . . His decision to make, with the KBC agreeing, of course. And Noddy doesn't run away from decisions. But here's the clincher: If Noddy hadn't acted on it, then Ibby Cooke would have. That's right, E.B. himself, even if not for the same reasons as Noddy. But do let's get one thing straight up here: Ira is still very useful to the KBC in county politics. Too, it could well be that Ira likes that kind of life. Takes all kinds, as you know. Life still smiles on him, as Ira sees it; some of that "it was great to be alive, but to be young was really heaven." That's Ira all over. Well, Becky wasn't getting any younger. Now you see?

A break. The postman comes by to the porch door needing Edith Timmens's signature. The listener, meanwhile, takes a walk around the living room. No expert on furniture as to period or style, the listener does recognize fine workmanship: wooden pegs, hand carving, old brocade which looks better with age. The listener also counted six cigarette ash trays; nothing fancy, merely serviceable.

Where were we? Oh, yes. Well, the last time I talked with Becky was last year sometime. She was leaving the Camelot, we said hello and talked without sitting down. Less than a minute, I'd say. And then, and I couldn't tell you why, but I reached out and gave her a peck. She grinned at me. You know, I truly believe she knew what the kiss was for. Funny. A slight raise of the hand, the slightest tilt of the head. She said it all without saying a word.

We talked about a lunch date, but you know how that goes. I keep up with her through Sammie Jo; they see a lot of each other.

And Sammie Jo? Forty, last month, and every time I see her, I remember the day she was born. I was there, at Klail General . . . Blanche Perkins almost died giving birth and it took her over a year to recover. Her health even before the birth was never the best. But there was Blanche, sickly, weak, nursing her and she did so for more than a year. Blanche's own life hasn't been the healthiest either in every sense. But we're the way God and the world and life itself fashions us. Blanche is special, what Rafe Buenrostro calls *una persona*, right?

And as for Sammie Jo, well! Headstrong and wild as a kid, and then those two horrible marriages that . . . Well, the past belongs to the past and that's what cemeteries are for, anyway. She's always loved Rafe. The opposition at seventeen was formidable: the whole of the KBC, and Noddy, and I, oh yes, and her so-called friends, and Mexicans and Anglos alike. But if you live long enough . . . right?

Beyond that, a long life is useless unless you grab happiness by the throat and hang on to it. Sammie Jo did; Rafe was happiness for her, and she never let go; not even when he married soon after high school, before the Army and all that . . .

Oh, I know everything about Rafe going to the Bank and all that followed. Yes, and Sammie Jo going to live in the house El Quieto built years ago. I would've given both eyes to be able to've gotten inside Noddy's mind when Rafe walked in, even with an appointment, which he had requested . . . A tough, tough rock, that Rafe.

And that too is what Becky saw in Jehu: a rock, one which wouldn't crack; a diamond, one which couldn't be bought, could never wear out . . . Someone in whom Becky could confide, say things to. Something. Anything. Life!

Becky. I saw myself in her years ago, in that little climber, as she was then. A trimmer of sails for any occasion, one who wanted all of everything. Until she learned that what she was going after was what her mother wanted . . . had wanted all along. Poor Elvira Navarrete, and poor Edith Timmens, too, who also wanted it all . . .

No, not a matter of luck, of drawing lots . . . Becky merely found a second mother, Viola Barragán. And if Viola was not the *madrina*, the sponsor, when Becky was born, that was due to Elvira Navarrete's weakness, poor thing.

Viola Barragán remained her friend. For life, in it for the long pull, as friends must be, are. Viola has not only seen a great part of the world, she also knows the world. Why do you think she and Noddy get on so well? Ha, they've both taken this world on its terms and reached the same conclusions. It's there, take it, oh yes, but don't fall in love with it, don't be surprised by anything that's in it . . . I got mine from books, which is a silly way to live. But not those two, not Viola, not Noddy . . .

Viola had a hand in Jehu and Becky getting together, but it wasn't her doing. Jehu, who can zip up his own pants, thank you, went to Becky. This new Becky I'm talking about, this Becky who has the intelligence to see things clearly, who saw in Jehu what she needed to see. He went to her, but only because she couldn't come to him. And who knows? The new Becky would have gone to him in time.

It's called love. And that's all there is, but it's enough, isn't it?

And now, what do you say to lunch? On me . . . well (laughs) . . . on the KBC.

## Bowly Ponder

The informant Bowly Ponder is a police officer assigned to the Belken County Sheriff's Office. A native of Klail City, and uncle to the just mentioned Esther Bewley, the bank administrator. Ponder, although the listener has no direct knowledge, is said to be in one of Noddy Perkins's hip pockets.

If the listener had been given to choose one, and only one, word to describe the informant, the chosen word would be elliptical.

I know Rafe Buenrostro much better than I know his cousin Jehu Malacara. But it also happens that I got to know Ira Escobar through Jehu himself. It was all a big coincidence. It happened that Noddy Perkins had sent for me, to the Bank, not to the Ranch; you see, around that time, I was still on patrol here in Klail.

Noddy needed my help, he wanted me to help out in a couple of things dealing with the county elections. And since these were not city elections, I had no conflict of . . . ah . . . ah . . . no . . . ah . . . conflict of interests according to lawyer Ben Timmens. Aside from that, to render some sort of service to Mr. Perkins is only right, smart, and proper . . . One should always take the opportunity.

Mr. Perkins and I were talking about what he needed me for when Jehu Malacara walked right into Mr. Perkins's office, no knocking or anything. I remember he nodded at me, and I also remember, and quite clearly, too, that Noddy Perkins didn't act surprised. He didn't introduce us either. I knew who Jehu Malacara was, of course. My niece Esther Bewley was Jehu's secretary at the time, and she always spoke well of him. And too, the way Esther talked of him and of Ira Escobar, you could tell right off who was her favorite.

But to tell the truth here, Ira and I have always gotten along well. Real well. He treats me with respect, consideration, and I've always been ready to help him in any way. And why not admit it, right?

Both of them, Ira and Jehu, work for Noddy, and as for me, I've said it twenty times over that Noddy Perkins has always been one of my strongest supporters. Always, and I'm proud to say it.

Ira Escobar, I'm sure, will say the same. He's still the County Commissioner, and one needs all the friends one can get.

So . . . given my current post with the County Patrol, you might say I've also had the opportunity to know Ira's wife, Becky Caldwell. And I know the kids, too. They usually ride around with their mother, and it's obvious she's a good mother . . . As far as the separation business and the divorce, that's their business, and I see no reason why I should cut through that briar patch . . .

Too . . . ah, and how big is Belken County anyway, right? As a County police officer, I get to know about people's lives. Part of the job. One sees and knows things . . . No need for me to explain, is there?

And things being the way they are, and they are that way . . . Well, I can assure you that Becky Escobar is not mixed up in drugs or in smuggling of any kind. She is a businesswoman, and there's her office to prove it in that company owned by Viola Barragán.

Don't take what I've just said to mean that Becky Caldwell, ah, Escobar, I mean, Malacara now, right? It's not to be taken to mean that she's been under surveillance. What happened was that Ira Escobar had once asked me to look out for her, for her well-being, but that was it. They hadn't gone through the divorce at that time, see? . . . and he, Ira, just wanted to be sure that Becky was all right, that no one would come by to pester her, you know. A precaution on his part, that's what it was.

I didn't see then, nor now, anything wrong with doing a friend a favor. They're divorced now, and since Becky got custody of Charlie and Sarah, Ira again asked me to look out for them. A continuation of the favor, let's say. Being divorced, of course, doesn't mean that Ira is going to abandon her . . . the kids . . . I mean you have . . . you know. And Ira's a man of morals, ethics, and as he's explained it to me, he wouldn't want for someone to come and dirty up his name, or Becky's either. And he was also looking out for the ki—the children, too, as I said . . .

And . . . ah . . . we . . . ah . . . and things have now changed somewhat. I mean, well, Becky has remarried, hasn't she? And this, of course, has put or puts, rather, a different color on things, to be sure. I mean, her life, the one she leads, is respectable, right?

It also happens that . . . that Mr. Perkins had called me in some days ago, that there'd been some sort of complaint . . . Not against me, not that. But a sort of complaint from someone who . . . that Becky was bothered, ah, didn't want to see a car, or county cars . . . parked by her house, you know? Or patrolling . . .

This was a favor to Ira, right? And Mr. Perkins let me know that he, ah, understood perfectly . . . Why this arrangement . . . And that County Patrol cars could be put to better use elsewhere. And I agreed . . . As he said . . .

And it's now been a while that my niece Esther Bewley told her mom, my sister Sally, that Ira'd been transferred to Jonesville. Esther said this for a purpose. Oh, yes. She told her mom to let me know about the transfer . . . let me tell you, I didn't like the way Esther said it, but those are Mr. Perkins's orders, so that puts another light on the subject. Know what I mean? But it's Esther's way of putting things . . . She said, "And Mom, tell Uncle Bowly to lay off. He'll understand what I mean." That's how she put it.

I, ah, I couldn't've said it any clearer myself . . . So I called my brother Dempsey and told him to let the Commissioner know of the new arrangement.

As I said just now, I agree with Mr. Perkins, although I was also very careful to point out to him that I was just doing Ira a favor, nothing more.

For his part, Mr. Perkins said he understood perfectly well I was just rendering a favor, but as he then pointed out, there was no further need for the patrol car. He went on to point out that Becky was a married woman and, as such, did not need, ah . . . require is what he said, did not require County protection. Yes . . .

And as I've just been saying, I agree with Mr. Perkins one hundred percent. Well, that's where we were when Jehu came into the office and nodded to me, like I said. I . . . ah . . . I tried to read his face, maybe some sort of something, like a gesture, you know? He and Mr. Perkins talked for a minute or so, then both of them signed a whole bunch of papers and in the middle of the signing, Mr. Perkins he let out a big laugh and then went back to signing. But don't ask me what that was all about.

Not two minutes later, my niece Esther pops in and Mr. Perkins got up, said "thanks" to me and handed me a Cuban cigar. And I left, got out of there. An hour later, a call is patched through while I'm driving around. It's my niece Esther, and she says Mr. Perkins was very happy, very satisfied with the way I carried out my official duties. And like I say, Mr. Perkins is a considerate man, and one ought to be helpful and considerate right back, isn't that the truth?

## Lucas Barrón

Lucas Barrón, aka Dirty. Bar owner and thirty-third degree Mason, (York) and uncle to the listener. Corpulent, as we say in Spanish, congenitally red-faced, in his mid-sixties and, to quote him, "No, not quite as strong as an ox, anymore, but more intelligent, at this stage." The listener was baptized at Our Lady of Mercy Church by the informant and by the woman who shared everything with him for over forty years of marriage, the listener's aunt: Doña Socorro. The informant, and not as a by the way, is a staunch supporter to Jehu Malacara.

Friends, you say? Which ones? Look here, you're old enough to know better: friends disappear, they die off, they move on and away, and as sometimes happens, they're no longer friends. You sure you got all that? And if you're talking about those women, forget it. For-get-it.

Listen, Becky knew those women in those clubs, but did she have friends there? No. Friends are something else. I happen to think that it's difficult for a woman to have men friends and I certainly think it's hard for certain women to form strong friendships with other women. There are exceptions to everything, got to be. Hell, what kind of a world would this be without exceptions?

But those women, those clubby types, they may have been friends to each other, but the question remains: where was Becky in all of this? Where did she fit in? Mexican girls have other problems . . .

Ha! Listen, that one of our girls, *una chica nuestra*, wants to go to college, to a university, what usually happens? First off, who and what does she think she is? She must be one of those who don't like men. What kind of a father, a mother, allows a daughter to go off, away from the Valley? They'll say she's crazy, some screw loose somewhere. How many times have I heard people say that? In this bar? Jesus . . .

No, I admit it isn't as bad as all that now, today, Thank God, but even today, right now, you can still hear it. God, yes. There's a lot of ass-holish *raza*, out there. Oh, and wait a minute, let me add that she damn well better not try to be anything else other than a grade-school teacher. She better not go earn a living at the Klail Enterprise as a reporter or at the Jonesville Courier or something like that. A pissant teacher, you slut, 'cause that's where you belong . . . Sure. And some of their own brothers say that. Maybe not slut or whore, but it's the idea. So, too often, even if just once, too, some women will never forgive other women. Why, they're just like men, yeah. Sure, it's sad, but it's the damned truth, too.

Oh, and you know what they also say? It's because we were raised that way, to think that way. Well, that's not the whole damned truth, no sireee. In Becky's case it was an entirely different matter, and that was the best stroke of luck ever. An only daughter, somewhat well-off by Valley standards, and since her mother, Elvira Navarrete, was a bit pushy, it was she who saw to it that Becky went off to college. To get married up there . . .

Enough to make you stop drinking . . . But what a drubbing Elvira took on that one. Becky wised up a bit, didn't she? Oh, sure she married, was almost forced to. The usual, you know . . . Although, in her case, she was married off to a perfect idiot. She married that son of Angustias Leyva and Nemesio Escobar. Poor quality semen on both sides, and that's for starters.

That marriage was nothing, you understand? Nothing special. A common, ordinary marriage: money was spent, pictures taken and posed for all over the place, newspaper stories, and from there, to raise a family. Like I said, common, everyday. But then, not only common and everyday, it was sad, too.

But look at how things stand now. That drop of water falls hard and steady, long enough, that rock's gonna crack eventually. Got to. And in this case, the divorce had nothing to do with money, or the lack of it, no. Not at all. Nothing on that account. Becky sharpened up, and she got the living scare of her life to see herself at her age anchored to that Fat Zero. Jesus . . .

And remember the pharmacist, Olivia San Esteban? Applies to medical school? Why, even her own brother, Martín, yeah . . . bad-mouthed her, and maybe not directly, but to be sure, he was against the idea. What a crock! But typical, typical.

And you remember Socorro Tuero? Named for your aunt . . . What did she do? Studied to be a vet, graduated from Up North, and God Almighty, she almost starved to death here, in the Valley, 'cause those jackasses didn't know what to do with a woman who could treat cows and horses. Poor kid left the Valley at a hundred miles an hour. Had to. Moved Up North. Houston, some place. Took Socorro some twelve damned years to get back here. Toughened her up, too.

Made her better than tough, 'cause toughness wears out with time. Made her independent, and that's harder to get rid of than live-in in-laws. God, yes. Impossible. Okay, say she'd've stayed here? What then? Oh, sure: go to work for the KBC. She'd done that, she would've sunk like a shrimper in a hurricane . . . Gone, and to the bottom, too. Became, made herself independent. And that's exactly what Olivia San Esteban wanted to do.

No, no doubt about it. This Valley of ours can be a pure-dee-mean sonofabitch, like your Dad used to say. Remember? And the Valley's unforgiving, too. And forget the Anglos on that score; the *raza* itself can stick it to you like a choya cactus patch.

All right, try this one: there's Angela Vielma; she lives with Rafe Buenrostro's sister-in-law. What do you say to that? Angela has talent, brains, and she's no stranger to party politics. She's been a lawyer, for what? Ten years? Fifteen?

And she's a Vielma, all right: high forehead, eyes darker than the ace of spades, and a good, loyal, smile. And she paid for her own education, too. That was a hard-working family, and money didn't rain down on them. The U.S. Army money for Pepe Vielma's death in Korea was something Angela didn't touch. That's right. She didn't think the money was dirty, no. She just thought the money should go to her mom and dad. That's what Angela is made of.

Well, it took her longer to finish than most, but when she made herself a lawyer up at Austin, the Vielmas gave her the money from the Army insurance. They'd saved it. That's what Pepito Vielma would have done, they said.

Did you know that your cousin Jehu was over there? Jehu Malacara once told me that his cousin Rafe was right there when Pepe Vielma died in Korea. Artillery fire, according to Jehu. This is some country we live in, isn't it? Jesus.

So . . . don Prudencio Vielma and his wife had saved the insurance money, and that's how Angela got her start. About five years after Angela had been practicing the law and living with her folks, she bought herself a house and that's when Rafe's sister-in-law moved in.

Ha! Did those two give enough reasons for people to talk? But the talk didn't last long. Two unmarried women, oh, yes, and people who'll talk on anything and for no reason, well, they talked. Opened fire on them, they did. Then they got bored. Jesus . . .

First of all, whose business was it? Bunch-a-goddam snoops, that's what. Put-your-nose-up-somebody's-ass type of people, that's who. Got nothing better to do.

Well, the very same damn thing happened in Becky's case when she drop-kicked that damfool Ira Escobar. Right away: it was this, that, the same old crap. Why, to hear people talk, a stranger to the Valley would think we were a population of saints here. Jesus . . .

And then, Becky went to work for Viola Barragán. To earn a living, for Christ's sake. And let me ask you this: Who the hell's business was that? What did people want, anyway? Did they want her to stay at home all day long? Was that it? Well, they're crazy as hell is all I got to say. She's a doer, she's educated . . . she's active. Is it crime to earn a living, dammit?

And what about Viola and her business? Drugs? Smuggling? Viola is tough in business, and so am I, 'cause there's no second place in the business. That's right. And this too is the truth: Viola's got a couple of things up her sleeve: she's honest, and she'll drive the hardest bargain ever, but her checks don't bounce. And when it comes to *honradez*, honor, I'll stick by her up until the day someone can prove she's otherwise. Up to that time, my word stands.

I've known Viola's father since the '20s, when they got here, one hand in front and one in back, as we say. That's all they could call their own. Teléfforo Barragán, without one word of English in his head, without knowing even one person in all of Klail, he came here with his wife, Felícitas Surís de Barragán, and Viola, a baby in her father's arms . . . And to work, goddammit.

Telésforo kept books and accounts, he taught at the Mexican schools we built, and he farmed, too. And he worked in the worst job there is: uprooting mesquite trees. Try that for exercise . . . Whatever there was, there he'd go. The thing to do was to work, to bring food home. And how did Viola come out from all that? Ha!

You and I are related, we're family; so, family aside, I'm willing to beat the living shit out of any mortal who says, dare says it, I swear, a single, solitary word against the Barragáns. If Viola hired Becky it was based on Becky's talents, and that's a freezing fact. Oh, she'd've kept Becky out of friendship to Elvira, but without responsibilities . . . that kind of thing. We all do that, to help somebody out . . . But she earns her keep, she does.

Now here, in this *cantina* of mine, people talk, and that's why God invented *cantinas*. That some double-barreled jackass like Emilio Tamez comes and says what he says, or some C.P.A., some Certified Political Asshole like Polín Tapia comes here and talks, that's okay, too. A place is a place and your uncle runs a bar here, not a church.

But there's a limit, you can't cross a certain line, and all of us know it when we reach drinking age in a *cantina*. That line gets crossed, and I take over. That's why I own this place, by God.

They want to bad mouth Jehu, and they do so, that's one thing. But for them to say it to Jehu's face, that's something different. No sir. Something like that can cause a fight in here. Jehu's got an education, but he won't run.

But why worry? There's no more than two balls hanging between Tapia and Tamez; they wouldn't dare . . .

As for Jehu, he'll put up with a lot, but let's face it, he's not Jesus Christ. I mean, he doesn't have all the patience in the world. So, those who talk can go right ahead, but they got to remember what they're in for . . .

Jehu doesn't give a damn if someone says something about him. They just better not say it to his face. Think about that. He has a very good idea of who he is and gossip or rumor are just that and nothing more to him. But, as I said, people better not get the idea that he's going to spend his life crossing and uncrossing his arms. That he won't act. Oh, no. The biggest water tower in the world gets filled up and spills over, and that's a big truth.

Let me put it this other way, why do you think that neither Emilio Tamez nor Polín Tapia come in here when Jehu's at the bar or having a beer in that booth there? Or look to this: Why do they settle up, pay, and get the hell out when he comes in? Well? I said they were assholes, I didn't say they were fools.

If they were fools, they'd be picking some of their teeth off the sawdust, 'cause that's where they'd land after Jehu got through with them. Jehu likes a good joke, and he'll put up with a bunch-a-shit just like anybody else, but there is a limit.

Now that he's married, he won't fight, I mean, he's got to set an example for Becky's kids, his kids . . . It doesn't look right, does it? Made himself into a man, that boy. Fearless, and that's the frightening kind . . .

You don't know this story. Once, and Jehu was just a kid of eleven or twelve, no more than that, he killed a rabid dog. By himself. Went out in the middle of Klail Boulevard, a .22 in hand, and bam! A little later, but this you do know, when the late Baldemar Cordero killed Ernesto Tamez? It happened right here, in my place. This place. Well, right there, not two feet from that table there.

Around that time, Jehu was working at his uncle Andrés's gaming house. And Andrés used to rent the back of my place here, and that's where the gambling took place, right by that unpaved alley back there.

Young Cordero knifed Neto Tamez, but after long provocation and to hell with what Judge Phelps said then or says now. Right here, look. See? Neto Tamez fell right there, and he fell screaming like a newborn. A minute or two later, here comes Jehu by the back way with a bag full of money he'd carried over from the gaming house and told me to keep it for his Uncle Andy.

Jehu didn't say a word then . . . He saw Balde, knife in hand, who was walking toward the door, and then Jehu threw a glance at Ernesto Tamez.

It's too goddam bad to be a kid and to have to see that kind-a shit, but he didn't say a word, like I said. He looked at me for a while and then a few seconds later he lifted the bag and said: "Dirty, here's a bag of money from Uncle Andy."

You beat that? Tough little piece-a shit . . . But he's been like that ever since he was a kid. A good kid, too, and so much so that when don Manuel Guzmán went for him to don Celso Villalón's ranch . . . what? You didn't know this? Well, he did; Manuel went to pick up Jehu at the goat ranch so he'd register in school, and Jehu lived with don Manuel and doña Josefa for some time. He sure did. Manuel, in peace now resting, used to burst out laughing when he'd talk about it. He'd say: "That so-and-so will never be president of this country 'cause he's a *mexicano*, but he sure as hell isn't going to die of hunger either. Not him. He ever gets an education in him, people would do well to bet on him. There's some good blood there."

And Manuel was right, wasn't he? And now, Jehu married to Becky Escobar, well, not Escobar anymore, she's a Malacara now. One of us . . . And Jehu did get a little money when don Víctor Peláez died years back, two hundred dollars, a gold watch with fob, and a Stetson.

I took the money and straight into the bank during the four years of high school, Jehu's army service, and then four years up at the University. The money grew some, not much; I then borrowed money against it, and bought him two lots with it. As Jehu says, "I work at the Bank so I can keep my eye on the money Dirty put there in my name." He's a good *cabrón* . . .

But Jehu's always been respectful, and helpful, but he won't come up to you walking with his hat in his hand. He's very Malacara . . . My father, you know, got to know Jehu's great-great-grandfather, don Braulio Tapia. Balls? Like a bull's, a man among men and the poorest of the poor. *Hombría*, manliness. All of the Malacaras have been fine husbands with one exception, my compadre Andrés Malacara, who was a chaser. Jehu chased, too, but he was single. But, when they settle down, they settle down, and they won't set eyes on another woman.

Yes. He did the right thing in marrying Becky Navarrete-Caldwell. Jehu will know how to be a good father to Becky's children. You'll see.

Becky *es persona* according to Viola Barragán and Viola's not the type to go around throwing away money, words, or compliments. And she knows what she's talking about.

This bar and the two lots on either side and the one across the street, the one Urban Renewal came and leveled all to Hell . . . all of that property belonged to me. It belongs to Viola now. And the day I die, the I.R.S. is going to get Ned-shit from me. Damned people've diddled me enough during my lifetime . . . Sure. Becky took care of the paper work. Ha! Leave it to Becky is what Viola said. How about that? That damfool Escobar had no idea who he'd married. No idea. Damfool thought he was riding some broken-down mare . . . Wrong as always, that boy.

Now. When I die, it's adiós to the Aquí Me Quedo. This *cantina*, which I owned and operated in four, five places in town, but always with the same name, will die and the name with it, when I die. That's right. Just as soon as Ramón Rosales loads me up on one of his hearses, Viola's going to put up a big brick building on all three lots. An old folks home. Air conditioning. Heat. Lights. Three or four floors or more, whatever the money I'm leaving gives for that. A well-made building is what Viola wants. Brick, not no goddam hollow cement crap. Brick, and with air conditioning, like I said. And heat. Yeah.

It's a good idea, and people will live with dignity, *con dignidad*. Oh, I know there's some Anglos who stick their old folks in homes, and shoot, some Anglo folk in Klail don't even know where their kids live. But the Anglos will live there, too. They're going to live in my monument, 'cause that's what Becky calls it. So those old Anglos, abandoned some of them, are going to have to live with *la raza* under the same roof. That, too, is Becky's idea. She's got some idea, she has . . .

Well, I say it's time for a Buddy Watson. What? No, no, it's still my bar, and in my bar, I pay; family or not. Well, is a Budweiser okay or do you like Ess-litz?

After the one beer, my uncle Lucas went behind the counter and pulled several Closed notices; he passed two of them for me to hang outside of the Aquí Me Quedo cantina: Closed. Death in the Family.

After this, Lucas Barrón took the listener by the elbow, out the door, and to dinner.

## Otila Macías Rosales

Otila Macías Rosales. Wife to Alfredo Ramón Rosales, owner of Morales Funerales, "At Your Service." Otila stands four-feet-ten to the listener's five-nine. Otila does not wear heels, an affectation, she says. She never has, and assures the listener that she, Otila, does not suffer "the short person syndrome." The listener understands all of this perfectly well. The listener and Otila graduated from Klail High eighteen years ago.

Good to see you! (She laughs.) Mrs. Rosales, at your service, and married these fifteen years. (More laughter.) Macías, as you know, on my father's side. Old don Cayetano, known to all as don Tano, the Tight-Rope Walker, and Morales on my mother's side. She was the daughter of the famous third baseman, Down Town Morales, who was the best infielder Klail City has ever produced. I'm also a Parás, on my mother's side, and she, then, was a younger sister to don Orfalindo Buitureyra y Parás, pharmacist and propietor of The Herb Shop, El Porvenir. What they now call a *Botánica* . . .

We are from Klail, Klail-ites or Klail-ilians. Just like you. I heard you been going around talking to people, and I thought I'd give you the family facts, ha!

You may not know that my uncle don Orfalindo, despite his age, knew Jehu very well, and closer when Jehu first went to work at the Bank. Bright, well-educated, is how my uncle described him. And he would say that drunk or sober, and that is saying something.

It is well-known, as Reverend Mora says, all of us as God's children are as fragile pieces of crystal. It is also well-known, I say, that my uncle used to go off on some serious *parrandas*; those drinking bouts were long and prolonged. Why, his fame and theirs, the *parrandas*, covered all of Belken County, extending to Dellis County. This is hardly something to brag about, but then there's no reason to deny an incontrovertible fact, is there? I don't put on airs about anything, and my husband, Alfredo Ramón, always says this about me. We're fragile, and my late uncle don Orfalindo stood at the head of the line.

My Alfredo Ramón, born and raised in Flora, where the hardy people come from, as he says, hired, some while back, a *sepulturero*, a burier, that some people called Ecce Homo. Did you ever hear of him? That isn't his name, you understand. His name is Damián Lucero.

Well, now, this Damián was a farm hand from Up River, and he worked as a gravedigger, like I said, a burier, but he could also embalm, if called upon. He's still alive, and he's older than the Holy Mother Church of Rome . . . As old as he is, he works at the same bank Jehu Malacara works, the Bank.

Ecce Homo is a man of discretion, judgment, and also a man of few words. He says he owes his job to Jehu. Jehu, though, says and tells him otherwise. Jehu says that Damián Lucero works at the Bank because he's a good mechanic and that's why he's paid. I happen to know that Ecce Homo was a friend of Jehu's father, out in Relámpago, and that's a truth the size of a whale.

And I can tell you this, too. Ecce Homo buried Jehu's parents, first the mother, then the father, and Ecce Homo groomed and watered the two small plots for years. And for free. That's the truth.

After a lifetime of work here and there, and in and out of the farm fields, Ecce, I mean Damián . . . Damián did not have enough quarters for Social Security. So now, with his job in Noddy Perkins's bank, Damián Lucero receives his social security, and he works, too. I swear that I am not the smartest person in Klail, but I think I can see Jehu's hand in all of this. Back when you and I were kids, there was a line in a *tango* by Gardel[9] which ran, ". . . si precisás un amigo . . . ," if you should need a helping hand . . .

So let me tell you, that Jehu Malacara married that divorced girl is a good thing, a great thing. My husband says she's a fine person, despite the divorce, and why shouldn't she be, right? Is a divorce the worst thing that can happen to a woman? You can forget that. There are worse things in life, many-many worse things. My husband, Alfredo Ramón, also says she works for a living, and is employed by doña Viola, that she went to college like you, and that she's nice, and that people say she is.

---

9. Carlos Gardel (1887 or 1890–1935), Uruguayan-born Argentinian tango singer.

As far as I'm concerned, all of that, to me, is as fine a recommendation as you can get. On that account, and from what one hears and sees, the divorce matter means absolutely nothing. If the Church has a worry, let the Church worry about it, if it wants to. Better yet, the Church's priests who come to the Valley should come prepared to speak Spanish, YESSIR. I say this with some heat, because once in too many whiles they'll send us some Irishman or a French guy, and worst of all, one of the damned Spaniards whose tongues, I swear on St. Elmo, Patron Saint of Sailors, I swear those Spaniards have tongues that just don't seem to fit in their mouths. So they send that type, old Church, old Church, old Church. Irish, French, Spaniards, whatever. Divorce is bad, yes, it is terrible, but it is also human, isn't it? I mean, animals don't divorce . . . so what do they recommend? Prayer and reconciliation. That's what comes from not being married, don't you think? *Que recen ellos, nosotros a trabajar.* That's what my father used to say: Let them pray, as for us, we got to work . . .

Anyway . . . who understands those *gachupines*? I bet even they don't understand each other. As for the French, well! And the Irish? They can say what they wish, but that's not English, is it?

May God forgive me, but I only go to Mass to go. I lost my religion along the way, and I like what Jehu said one day when he brought Damián Lucero for a visit.

"All you have to do is believe, have faith. Everything else, what they demand, that has nothing to do with believing."

How about that? That's the type of advice I can live with.

My Alfredo Ramón says Jehu is right. I do too, and that's why I think that he must be something special. Got to be.

He's firm; *firme.* He's there at baptisms, marriages, and burials. He knows a lot of people, and they know him back. And now that he's married, his wife's kids go out with him from time to time.

I was raised in the old-fashioned way, and I think that people who come through in a pinch are special people. When my uncle don Orfalindo passed on some two years ago, Viola Barragán and Jehu attended the funeral and brought wreaths, flowers, and I'm talking about fresh-cut flowers, none of that paper stuff or those plastic ones, either.

Of course, everybody in the world knew that my uncle was madly in love with Viola, but one of those far-away loves, nothing to it. A theoretical love, you know? It was one-sided, and yet Viola, not once, laughed or said a word. That would've hurt my uncle. Oh, I know he was a sad, ridiculous figure and all that, and who knows? Maybe in his old age he began to believe that he had poisoned Viola's first husband on purpose . . . He didn't; he was an apprentice pharmacist at the time, and he had no business concocting anything for anybody . . .

You know, he would've died of happiness had he known that Viola had come to his funeral, but that water has gone out to the Gulf and back since that time.

As you know, my husband and I work together. Not in the body business, but in tailoring. I'm a tailor. A tailoress? Whatever; I design, cut and sew dresses, blouses, all kinds of skirts, and I can fix up coats and such. I can do anything. And, because of the tailoring, that's how I came to know Becky Malacara. And I also got to know her tastes, her preferences.

She knows material, too. Knows what it's all about. Cashmere this, or Indian wool that, or cotton, Egyptian and Pima, she knows. Better than that, she knows what she wants. First class in clothes. Buys only what's necessary, not a waster but not a haggler, either. Judges quality, can distinguish. And she knows how to treat a person.

As for shoes, well, I don't know the first or the last thing, and that's the truth. She does. And as I said, when it comes to quality goods, she knows what that's about. Well, when she sent that shrimp trawler called the Ira Escobar to the bottom of the boat basin, and then turned around and married Jehu, that should've shown that she was no fool.

And listen to this: Her mother, doña Elvira, for years, has come by car, from Jonesville, so I can fit her up. Her tastes are somewhat exotic, know what I mean? I was learning the trade then; you remember doña Elenita? Now there was a seamstress . . . Anyway, Becky would show up with her mom, and she must've picked up her knowledge then.

There's some raza in the Valley with more money and time, but they lack the *mesura* . . . the touch and feel. Why, not even Sammie Jo can beat her, and that red-head's no cow, right?

Take silk. It's a delicate fabric. A treacherous piece of material, and Becky can wear it. That comes from knowing what goes with a body . . . she's something like doña Viola, who can wear a box suit better than anyone I know or have seen on the television.


The listener had heard, from other sources, that Becky Malacara was a spendthrift. Otila Macías Rosales's words give the lie to that report. What the informant also stated, "Her children dress nicely, but not tailor-mades; that's silly," is also revelatory.


## Reina Campoy

Reina Campoy (baptismal font name: María de los Reyes), the oldest woman, Mexican or Anglo, in the whole of the Valley, from the westernmost parts of Dellis County to Belken County's eastern reaches on the Mexican Gulf. The Campoys came to the northern bank of the Rio Grande, this part of Texas also called Nuevo Santander (originally Nueva, with an *a*, Santander), in 1749, with the Escandón colonists. Reina's great-grandmother, doña Mauricia Puig, was born a Spanish subject in 1814; at age ten she was a Mexican citizen; by the summer of 1836, she was a Texan. Later, in 1845, an American when Texas was annexed that December 21st; *aquel día, 21 de diciembre*, as the old *corrido* says.

A citizen of the Confederacy in the 1860s, and an American citizen again after being duly Reconstructed to the lights and likes of General Sherman.[1] Doña Mauricia's son, Jaume (and that is Jaume with a *u* and not Jaime with an *i*), fought for the Union in the 1860s.

---

1. William Tecumseh Sherman (1820–1891), American general; Union military leader during the Civil War.

Jaume's sister, Montserrat, married the first Rafael Buenrostro in the Campacuás Mission in the mid 1870s. (Reina, who does not like the appellation doña—an idiosyncrasy—is a memorialist.)

That piece of noise that a woman marries more than once carries no weight with me; it isn't a novelty, in other words. I've buried three husbands, and the second one wasn't even my husband because I had divorced him, and that was years before I married Julio César Campoy. But! To leave a man, to abandon and desert him, and then to tell him to-get-the-hell-out, that is something special, very special.

At my age, it's hard to pull any kind of surprise on me. Nothing surprises me anymore; from the assassination of President McKinley when I was a child, to that bomb in Japan,[2] or that some time ago an Anglo from Up North made himself into a capon so he could be a woman from one day to the next . . . Nothing. I'm old, I'm over ninety years of age, and if I've learned anything in the Valley, it's that there are people around this world who are capable of anything. *Sí, señor, sí,* as the kids say.

And Valley people are like that, too. Valley people can work hard, get drunk, and they can die in France like my first husband, leaving me a widow at twenty-eight. That's right: we've got people for everything in this place.

That the one and only daughter of Elvira Navarrete sent Young Escobar on his way—*lo mandó de paseo,* right?—well, all I can say is Good For Her. That she remarried, that's just dandy, too. Life's no better than a widowed bitch-dog. Life won't forgive or forget; you'll die anyhow and it's a fool who deserves to die with his face to the bedroom wall.

Is this too fast for you? Here's what I mean:

My father was born in 1860, and he was thirty when I was born, and then he died thirty years later on account of the Spanish influenza, something you certainly never knew about, *a Dios gracias.*

Now. When I became a widow in 1918, my father said something like this: See here, María de los Reyes, this damned country has already buried one husband, and now you're thinking of marrying a Pulido. As far as I'm concerned, Odón Pulido isn't worth the price of one cumin seed; two, tops. But that's up to you. You're a grown woman once married.

But, I'm still your father, and I'm saying this because I know how much you're worth. You've got good blood in you, mine and Santoscoy blood on your mother's side. The Santoscoys live for centuries, and you will too. So, you decide, María de los Reyes, if you marry, and you live a long time, is it to be with Odón Pulido? You're what? Thirty something? Okay. Will you put yourself underground with that Odón Pulido? The world's got more than its quota of shiftless, idling sons-of-bitches, you know.

My dad was right. Well, when my brother-in-law Macedonio Campoy first came around here from out Toluca Ranch way, he came with one purpose in mind: to marry me. I was married to Odón at the time, you follow?

---

2. I.e., the two atomic bombs dropped by the United States on Japanese cities during World War II. *President McKinley:* William McKinley (1843–1901), U.S. president 1897–1901.

Macedonio proposed to me, in person. Right in my face, as we say. And, as I said, me a married woman . . . Right then, right there.

Well! Poor Odón Pulido shrugged his shoulders, and adios, *Reina de mi vida*.[3] But he was a good man, Odón, and years later Macedonio and I went to his funeral by Media Luna lake. A nice, clear day . . .

Panic? Gossip? Noise? All and more, and then what happened? What usually happens: people conveniently forgot what they said . . . My family? They said it was no one's business. Now, I had no brothers, and given the way things were then, maybe that was a good thing. But my father ruled, and chances are he would've told them not to be damned fools. Odón and I divorced through the Court House in Klail. Mace and I married here, in Relámpago.

To live and to learn is what people say . . . Well, Elvira Navarrete came running in here two years ago, hiccuping and mewling and puling and saying, "What will people say . . . the family" and every foolish thing she could think of in that holey head of hers.

I put a stop to that. "Sit," I said.

I then lighted two cigarettes and handed her one of them, making sure the lit part faced me, given her state of mind . . . After this, a jigger of mezcal with anise seed, some of that unleavened bread I'd made that morning, and I always add anise to that too. Anise is healthy for you, you know.

I was the first person in God's own Rio Grande Valley to tell Elvira that she was making a fool of herself. Now, if there is one thing that Elvira Navarrete is afraid of in this life—I mean, that woman will face snakes and fires, okay?—if there's anything she's afraid of in this life it's being thought of, looked on, as a fool. I said: That she was to love Becky's kids as she always has and then I saved the best for last: that she was not going to give Becky any advice at all, today, tomorrow, next year. Elvira was to hush up.

Poor Elvira couldn't keep her eyes off me. Three Pall Mall cigarettes later, and two more jiggers of mezcal to go with them, made the hiccups disappear. Best of all, her voice lost that hysterical squeal she'd brought with her. Not stupid, just high strung.

One has to understand Elvira Navarrete. Some common sense and a little mezcal. But before that? All week long just about everyone was agreeing with her. Not the Ortegóns, of course; others . . .

I'm too old not to recognize pride when I see it; Elvira also likes to play the martyr. Hasn't had much reason to, not being married to a womanizer . . . All I wanted was to remind her not to listen to everyone, in fact not even to me. To listen to herself, to look at herself. Yes. What was she doing? And for whom? There are too many set phrases in Spanish and English, and they're there ready to come out of some idiotic mouth full of teeth: a poor wife and a worse mother, to begin with. A messy housekeeper; you know the rest. I told Elvira, right here in this porch, she was always welcome, and that she'd bring flowers to my funeral, but until then, she was to cross herself every morning. And, she was to remember her own mother. That brought her up a bit, I'll say. I then said: "We get enough *caca*-shit-*mierda*-*cuacha* as it is. And now? You're piling it up and worry about what people will say. What people? Anglos? Hang 'em from a mesquite. Mexicans? Right along with them, I say. Family?

3. Literally, Queen of my life; figuratively, my dear, dearest, darling.

What family? Those slave traders, the Leguizamóns? For you, Elvira, there are only five people that matter: Charlie and Sarah, you and Catarino, and Becky. That, Elvirita—and I called her that too—is family."

That's as sharply as I'll ever speak. But Elvira is important in spite of her ridiculous ideas about family and society and such. And then; now? Becky made the right choice, the proper one: she remarried, as I did, as anyone with sense would, if she wanted to marry. She just chose to marry, that's all.

You're related to Jehu, I know that. But where was that boy born? On this land, here, in Relámpago. When his father died, all Jehu had was both parents dead. Try that one on, Elvira, I told her. And that's who Becky chose, decided on.

No, I didn't go back and say Elvira nudged Becky toward Ira, and what for? Now? Elvira wanted comfort, but she didn't know what kind of comfort. Facts are best. No need to change them . . . facts and family . . . Sometimes the first brings disasters, and the second causes them . . . All the time I'm thinking of Macedonio and my father . . . Macedonio came here, to this house . . . in those days . . . that was no easy thing. He had no guarantee how my father would react. *Esos son hombres.*[4] And that Jehu has something of that . . . raised differently, but gritty enough.

And that Becky . . . came here years ago, with the kids. They're out playing around the house and Becky, looking straight at me, says, "I gave myself to Jehu." Married still, of course.

She looked for some sign from me. I didn't say a word. Don't misunderstand, it wasn't that I didn't care, I just wasn't surprised, that's all. I'm too old for surprises, remember? And I won't condone that type of behavior, no matter how old I am. Just that I'm not surprised . . . one divorce, a thousand. They're not the end of the world. We've got us a hurricane out in the Gulf right this minute . . . so? We had one hit here last year. That one dropped 23 inches of rain. The end of the world? No.

What I told Becky was this: One can't do that, one doesn't go to bed with just anyone. Leave your husband or stay. Don't lie to him. Don't lie to yourself, either. And no confessions, to him or to the Church. Choose, Becky. And she did.

Oh, that Becky . . . very Mexican in spite of those Anglo ways of hers . . . and her Spanish is a riot. What she says, though, does come from the heart, and I love her for it. And here we sat, on this porch; and I? I was looking at our family's cemetery, wondering who would sit here looking at my headstone . . .

I finally shook that off and told her, reminded her, really, that a divorce is just another divorce, that's all that it was. It isn't fatal, it is the reverse: Becky was buying her ransom. She was to be saved, rescued, and with enough love for the kids and for that new husband of hers. A new life for a new woman.

'Cause that's what her Uncle Lionel Villa calls her: *una mujer nueva.* And he, Lionel Villa, he too is a good person; old Valley people, those Villas. They've seen the sun rise out of that Mexican Gulf for many years now . . .

As for the Anglos, not many understand us, even now. Only way to do so is to marry us, live with us, die with us. But even then, they most likely wouldn't understand us. No, they like to change things around, change the forms of

---

4. Literally, these men; figuratively, a standup guy, not a quitter.

things, and the names of things and places. They're . . . they're unstable somehow. *Gente descontenta,*[5] oh, yes.

The listener, a smoker, enjoyed lighting another unfiltered Pall Mall for María de los Reyes Campoy. The listener also drank two thimblefuls of San Carlos mezcal, "The Best There Is." The listener, from experience, remembers what Un Tal Lucas once said, "There ain't such a thing as good mezcal."

## Bill and Tippy Ochoa

Bill and Tippy Ochoa. Friends to Becky before the divorce. He speaks, she nods assent: head, eyes, and mouth all move in union and in approbation. Almost a rehearsal speech it seems. Set phrases. Pauses for emphasis. Brief silence. Etc. The Ochoas are well-known to the listener; Klail City, after all, is Klail City.

I couldn't believe it; let's say I didn't want to believe it. And with all of that education, right. Incredible. Why, I ask you? Why did she do it? To go live with . . . with him. Not the same social class, not at all . . . I must say that at one time neither Tippy nor I were in Becky's class either, but through hard work and dedication one forms friendships, one is invited here, there . . . One can't possibly remain where one starts out. A matter of natural progress, that's all.

Oh, Becky would still be accepted in our circle, no doubt about that, but to marry like that, and to leave Ira? Unwise, wouldn't you say, Tippy? (Eager assent of the head.)

And to think that a Navarrete married to an Escobar blooded to Leguizamón-Leyvas would divorce him and thus lose hundreds of friends? Hundreds of connections? That's quite impossible to understand, am I right, Tippy? (T. nods; Bill Ochoa is then rewarded with a smile.)

I have always said, and I've given it some thought, too, if there is no structure, there can't be any form. In brief, society can't exist, the world as we know it would crumble. Society, respect for institutions, for good manners, the right touch, you understand? That's how people should live. One's people, you understand. Am I not right, Tippy? (A wink from T.)

Let's see. What kind of a married life can Becky and . . . and? her new husband expect? I happen to know that he has been known to go into one of those cantinas now and then, those neighborhood cantinas. This is not to say he's a drunkard, by any means . . . But, why doesn't he drop in at Chip's or at Cap'n Easy's? A lounge is not a cantina; everyone knows that.

I happen to know that Becky's husband owes a certain loyalty to the Buenrostro family, and that he drinks at those places because his cousin, the

---

5. Unhappy people; those who gripe.

policeman, invites him, asks him there. But that doesn't make it right, either. It looks bad.

Mr. Apolinar Tapia, the Notary Public, is absolutely right when he says that to frequent those places is bad form, is to cause a break in the situation of things. The Notary, that's one of his official duties, goes in those places to witness depositions and such. It's part of his job, and it's through him that we learned that Becky's husband goes there. Tippy and I happen to believe firmly that a banker of that rank and status shouldn't be seen in those places. Isn't that true, Love? (Moue and smile from T.)

It must be painful for doña Elvira Navarrete de Caldwell having to hear, having to learn this at second hand. Thank the Lord she doesn't have to witness her new son-in-law going to those places . . .

But then, having to know and making comparisons between Ira and him must be a fate worse than Hell itself.

What vice is that? Why the desire and penchant to return to those places? When he was poor, that was understandable. Is it that he is uncomfortable in nice places? No, that can't be it, can it? I mean, not if he's a banker who can go anywhere he likes . . . If I was in banking, people would sit up and take notice, I'd make sure of that . . . But who am I to complain? Tippy and I own and operate three gift shops, plus the flower shop and some rentals, right, Dear? (The cutest smile followed by the sunniest grin imaginable; a brunette Doris Day,[6] say.)

The listener is not a censor, by any means or stretch. The conversation was brought short by business and by a delivery boy who needed help in the loading and unloading of stock items bearing the "B and T Enterprises" logo.

## Gualberto Ornelas, O.M.I.

Gualberto Ornelas, O.M.I. A year before his graduation from Klail High, this future Oblate of Mary Immaculate enrolled in a seminary and began his long study for the priesthood. To date, he is the one young Texas Mexican serving in the Valley. His bishop, Urbano Ortegón, brother to doña Ursula and uncle to Julia Ortegón, was the very first Valley Mexican to enter the priesthood; both are Klail City natives.

The listener knows of a third, a native of Jonesville, who is a Jesuit, a serious young man some five years older than Becky's husband, Jehu.

The listener thinks this is a sorry record, given the number of Mexican Catholics in Belken County. The listener, however, sets down facts; some Valley Mexicans find this a disturbing, disgraceful fact.

As the tailoress Otila Macías Rosales says, "This is a truth as big as a whale."

6. American singer and actress (b. Doris Mary Anne von Kappelhoff, 1922).

I don't agree with Father Eloy, although this should not be taken to mean—nor do I wish to be misunderstood that it mean—that I approve of the divorce. I'm looking for a reconciliation, and if the search, or if the road to it takes time, then, time is what the Mother Church offers all of us as an arm and support against adversity and during times of weakness.

No, I most assuredly do not believe in divorce. I, however, don't hold that divorce is a passport to Hell eternal; I know Father Eloy believes it to be so . . . and he preaches it; you yourself must have heard him on occasion.

A divorce is harmful to society, and that's where one should start; closer to home. Too, a divorce harms, even torments, the children, if there are any. In Becky's and Ira's case, there are two. There's more to say in this regard, but from what I take it you're interested in, and do stop me if I'm wrong, you're a friend to Jehu, as I am. Unlike you, of course, we're not blood relations, but we are friends, and have been since childhood.

That he subsequently married Becky is not only an inconvenience to our friendship, it is also an obstacle. But one must work to overcome inconveniences and obstacles. The Church does not see their living together as constituting a marriage. Living in sin, as Father Eloy would say. . . . But as for Jehu and me, we're long-time friends. And I'm grateful to him. My late father was a candy maker and he'd lost a leg to diabetes . . . My mother had to carry on as best as she could, and Jehu, a teenager as I was, worked for them and for free. *Eso no se olvida*[7] . . . And how could I forget that, when I wasn't there, myself, to help? Oh, there's some guilt in me still, but the priesthood is what I had to do, wanted to do . . .

Aside from the present bishop, who did not request I come to Klail City by the way, and as far as I know, I may be the only Klail Texas Mexican who's become a priest, an Oblate. That's unfortunate, and I must say this does not reflect well on Holy Mother Church. Don't be offended, but I ask you not to take this as an attack on the Institution. God has His mysteries, and it could very well be that the scarcity of raza in the priesthood to date is a plan to which I'm not privy.

The simple faith I had at seventeen is not the same one twenty-years later; it is, however, as powerful now as it was then.

Jehu and I have truly known each other since infancy, and we were friends, *amigos de amistad*,[8] and we're still friends. I insist on this, because as a priest, I have no enemies, save Satan and unforgiveable sins. Friendship is not a sin nor should one forsake one's friends or neighbors.

I won't be the one to speak of changing the Church, that is to say, to attack it or disagree with it. The day I do, the day I disagree with the determinations and findings of the Church will be the day I hang up the cassock for good . . .

But I have faith; I believe in justice, and I also believe that one must work for it, for justice, and one must work in favor of those who are defenseless . . . The Church, the Bishop, and I, in my role here, all of us agree in this, although we're not always in agreement as to how to defend people in need.

---

7. That's something not to be forgotten; meaning, as here, I won't forget this, I'll have my revenge someday.

8. Literally, friends of friendship; bosom buddies, friends to be trusted no matter what.

Father Eloy, and I recognize his kindness, and let there be no doubt about that, counsels that prayers remain the most . . . efficacious remedy in these cases.

For my part, I maintain otherwise, and so I try to have our parishioners help themselves. This is also counseled by the Holy Bible. However, since people are not always prepared to help themselves, I see that as a fault which must be corrected. It's no mystery that they must help themselves, but this doesn't mean that I'm to stay in the rectory waiting for them to come to see me. And so, because of what I feel and believe, I go to their meetings, and that's how I use whatever time I have available.

I did the very same things in Houston and in Laredo, and now, more than twenty years since I entered the seminary, I now find myself with two years in the Valley, and the last two months of them in Klail.

As for Becky, I hold her in the highest esteem, and for her part, she assists the Church financially. Her actions, to me, are some of the Lord's mysteries, and as long as she lives, she will still be able to change her opinion and return to her husband. This is a fervent hope of mine, and it should be, after all, but I do not keep after Becky on this. She will see and take for herself the proper road, make the correct decision, and she wouldn't be, nor will she be, the first to admit a mistake. It's a transitory lapse.

Her money is both welcomed and accepted, because it's of benefit to all of those who need its benefits. Her children take Mass and to any way of looking at things, this is the first step toward some sort of reconciliation. As for Jehu, and I can't stress enough how long we've been friends, he picks up the boy and the girl as soon as Mass is over. If he doesn't come by, then it's Becky who'll do so. I attach no degree of importance to it, but Jehu doesn't come into the church itself. That's not uncommon in many Valleyites either.

But, when it's monetary matters and we deal with the Klail City First National, Jehu is the one who talks to Father Eloy or with Monsignor Quick. The Monsignor, by the way, isn't unaware of the Escobar family; I mean, the Escobars, particularly in Jonesville, were not only the pillars but also the base of St. Boniface's for years. The bank business is business, it's nothing personal. And really, President Perkins almost always assigns Jehu to these negotiations. They're most delicate, of course, and Jehu possesses marked talents in these regards. And here's something, Jehu himself is a magnet of contradictions. And no, this is neither an attack upon him nor on his methods or his beliefs in any way, and I want that to be understood as well. All it means is that Jehu, nothing more, nothing less, is human.

As for Ira, I'm convinced that he too will return to the Church. He is still on the rolls of this parish, and is one of its assiduous parishioners for over a decade, according to Father Eloy. It's only lately that he hasn't been coming to Mass. It's quite possible, of course, that he is now a parishioner at Jonesville's Sacred Heart, the Leguizamón family parish. Entirely possible.

The listener knows some facts at first hand. The listener also read of and verified the community organizational work of Father Ornelas. Never a pastor with his own church, and always an assistant in the poorest of the poor, this remarkably thin priest, younger in age than his old, tired face betrays, has a talent for being disobliging and for organizing the unorganized. The listener also knows that Father Ornelas has proved an embarrassment to his two past bishops. The first one, in no less a city of consequence than Houston, removed him, exiled is a more proper term, from Houston's notorious Navigation District to a solidly middle class, well-fed, comfortable Mexican American parish in Houston, where he languished. The next assignment, Laredo, was a trial for Church authorities: Father Ornelas insisted on working to organize the poor and the needy, unwed mothers, and other so-called social undesirables. The charges against him were that he neglected his religious duties.

His health can't be the best is the listener's opinion. Still, he's a human who does seem to survive by faith alone.

## Sammie Jo Perkins

Sammie Jo Perkins, a special item. As tall as the listener, auburn-haired, a ridge of faint freckles dots the nose below some light, light green eyes. Cheek bones? High, as if a Scandinavian's. Thin upper lip, a full-bodied lower one set in an easy smile. Beige silk blouse, long sleeves, no rings on any finger. A gold anchor pendant pinned below a flowing beige silk bow tie.

The listener is fully aware of having given a fairly long description of the persona and the attire. The voice and intonation are Valley products: more U.S. Midwestern than West Texas twang or East Texas drawl.

The Spanish, though, is Northern Mexican-ranch Spanish, smoothed out a bit first at Hollins and later at Smith. An alumna but not a graduate of either; not, as those who know her say, not that she needed to graduate.

The listener has been served a tall, frosted glass of the inevitable Valley limeade. The informant begins.

Spanish was my first language both in the house and of course out in the Ranch. My Daddy, whom I call Noddy more often than not when we get together, speaks Spanish almost as well as I do, but is not at ease in it. For instance, he and I don't speak Spanish to each other as I do, say, with Mamma or with Edith Timmens.

I learned it at home, first from the maids, their kids, the cowboys, Anglos some but mostly Mexican, and later on in Mexico, Spain, and one summer at Smith's summer program in the Baleares . . . So, it isn't a matter of talent or a special flair for it; a matter of circumstance. Of the kids I grew up with, Rafe's and my generation, I must be one of the few Texas Anglos who still speaks Spanish. In my mom's generation and Uncle Ibby's too, they spoke it and retained it since it was common practice. But as I said, those of my generation didn't speak it much, but that was their choice, and a poor one at that. Some even bragged about it and now they complain they can't understand a word. Or so they say. In my view, a case of wholesale stupidity. But let's not omit racism since we're dealing known Valley facts, you and I.

And we understand each other, you and I. We both know that Spanish has always been a ticklish affair in the Valley. And so much so that Becky and other mexicanas her age preferred English to Spanish; some were coerced, but this is hard to enforce . . . I mean, were the teachers going to follow the kids home? Watch them? Report them? No such thing. Many kids preferred to in many instances, and as a consequence, lost their Spanish, even though their folks spoke little to no English.

In Becky's case, her mother, Elvira, seldom uses English, even now. When Captain Caldwell went native, Mexicanized himself, Elvira saw no reason to change. But she made damned sure Becky spoke English, pushed her toward the language. Becky did what most, many, kids did: lost the ability to speak it. Perhaps not the understanding of it . . . not when she heard her folks all the time . . . Becky preferred English. It's not a crime, but it is a damned shame to lose something which doesn't need to be, but as Rafe says, "You can charge people with stupidity, but they'd be no-billed, there'd be no indictment."

What Elvira did, though, was what numerous Mexican families did, rich and poor alike; they pushed English on the kids. And I see nothing wrong with trying to get on in English, but at the risk and cost of not learning Spanish? That's worse than stupid, that's wrong! Becky herself, and she's a perfect example and product of this, Becky had to make a very special effort to re-learn her Spanish. It wasn't impossible, but she did have to work for it.

I'm on this because I've come to believe that Becky's decision, her changes, let's say, came when she decided to do away with that ridiculous mask. When she did it, she showed us her own sweet face, to put it that way. Using Spanish was part of the restoration . . .

And why did she cast Ira off? Who knows? Why does one do anything? I can tell you what I think, but that's not direct knowledge, not at all.

I think she became tired with that cored-shell of a life she was living. And she grew tired of Ira; why not? He is a bore, you know. Duller than battleship gray. Now, that Becky put up with him as long as she did is one of the miracles of the twentieth century. As for Ira, the poor man possesses no sense of humor. There's not a whit of it anywhere in his body. In Spanish or English. Nothing. Nada. Un cero . . . A zero. *That's* dull.

What also happened to the younger Becky is that she fell in love with him, Ira, and worse, her mother nudged and pushed them up and down the aisle. That's not what I think; I know . . .

Yes, it's irony of the purest kind. Here I am, talking about Becky being pushed into a disaster of a marriage, when I had two disasters of my own. And there is certainly no excuse for either of mine. And I was old too, and one whole hell of a lot more experienced than Becky . . . But I was a fool. I allowed Noddy to push me around. And the fault was all mine; I'm supposed to have a mind, a will of my own, and I didn't use either one.

What kept me from winding up at Flora is that through both horrors I didn't forget who I was, wouldn't dream of forgetting who I was. Oh, I swore like a trooper, in public, anywhere. I was a very sick person. Oh, yes. Sick enough to be interned in Flora's asylum.

I got myself into those messes, and it was up to me to get myself out and away from those two damned leeching drones . . . What also helps me too is that I'm allergic to alcohol in any form, and since smoking has never been a source of fascination for me, I remained healthy, physically, at any rate.

My life with Rafe, our life, should be no one's concern. Not yours, Noddy's, Mamma's, anybody's. I first saw him when he was fourteen; I'm two years older . . . We courted, nothing serious . . . but I felt something. Kid stuff, but

I also knew it was crazy . . . I was crazy. Years later, your cousin Jehu and I had an understanding . . . but it wasn't love. We fit; we liked each other.

That Rafe and I didn't marry until twenty years later ranks at the very top of the thousand and one dumb things I've done. I was another Becky too. I didn't have the nerve . . . And now I realize I never showed Rafe I loved him. I thought he'd just know.

And now I'm forty and we live together, with a license to prove it . . . We're not kids . . . living in El Quieto's house, Rafe's house now, and built by his father. That I have a very good part of the money in Belken County comes as no fault of mine, and through no talent, obviously. And no, no more ironies, no coincidences, no soap opera plot by a third-rate writer . . . (Laughs.) make that second-rate. And it's no accident that an heiress—what a word!—of the KBC would marry a Buenrostro. In one of Rafe's books I read where it said that God was funny, that He had a sense of humor . . . And you know what? Valley people say the same thing, I've heard it many times . . . And so, it's Rafe and I. I'm a born sucker for honorable people. And I married him because he proposed, although I was about to ask him, anyway. It happened there, at the Court House; I'd gone to see him at work, a Friday. I couldn't have been there five minutes when he said he was going to see Noddy.

No phony confrontation, just two men, and Rafe with that even, flat voice of his, saying it was time for him to go see Noddy. Well, I told Becky this, same as I'm telling you . . . And then it happened two weeks later, certainly no more than that. She salvaged what remains of her life here in Klail. She lanced that carbuncle called Ira Escobar.

And she also left the clubs, those same clubs she would've killed for at one time. I'd left them too . . . And what happened to them? Dried up, disappeared. Now there was a lovely piece of sisterhood. And my friends? Which ones? Very few . . .

But Becky's decision was a different affair . . . and I called her. That's when I began to like her too. And we talked, and talked. Like we'd never done before . . . straight, honest talk. Good, earnest talk. But there was a lot of learning, new realizations when the Clubs broke up . . .

Look at Heidi Simpson, she divorced Hollis, took little Kimmy or Tiffany, whatever. Returned to school, to earn her own living. And Polly Baxter? Pinkston Baxter never knew what hit him, and Polly took all five kids and left for Lake Charles or some place on the coast. Then there was Nell . . . Nell Blankenship. Married for years. Used to not working or having to work . . . worse, working like crazy to have a good time. So, there were a few . . . and they too changed their lives, as Becky did, as I did . . .

The rest? The others? Here, buried alive in Klail City . . . where would they go if the Camelot Restaurant closed its doors?

Well . . . Becky fooled me too. Fooled herself in the process . . . But when she kicked Mr. Commissioner out that door, she removed all doubt. That pretty face was held up by some spine . . .

In my case, the easiest thing . . . but not in Becky's case. I didn't have to, don't have to answer to anyone . . . She did, and she did so, too. You can't help but like someone like that . . . And to jump off here, Jehu has always been lucky; and (Laughs.) I told him so at the wedding . . .

Rafe and I waited until Mamma returned from Vail . . . her life has been hellish, you know. I think Aunt Anna Faye had called her about the Clubs . . .

Mamma could hardly care if all the clubs in all the world blew up. But Aunt Nellie, Kirpatrick, she, oh, she was not best pleased. And she said some things. Not to my face, of course. But aunt or no aunt, she knows what I'm about . . . Meddle in my life? Not a bit of it, but no direct criticism, and not to Noddy either. At least she's learned that.

The one thing Daddy said was that it would be to Aunt Nellie's profit to invest her time and serious efforts in other enterprises than in thinking overlong on her niece. And goodness, when Aunt Nellie learned of Rafe and me . . . the end of the world. *El fin del mundo.* But she came to the wedding. See?

And Jehu stood by Rafe, Mamma was my bridesmaid. Wasn't that sweet?

Lunch consisted of a light chicken salad and a phone call from Rafe.

## Polín Tapia

Polín Tapia, born Apolinar. He is the Notary Public mentioned by the florist Bill Ochoa. Tapia is a Belken County Court House fixture. Part of the plumbing, as the raza says. Never out of politics, even in off-election years; the listener has been told for years that Noddy Perkins keeps Tapia on some payroll or other. And, as always in those cases, on a short leash. Of course.

Tapia holds himself responsible for Ira Escobar's initial and subsequent elections to the County Commissioner's post (now the gerrymandered Precinct 3), and he also holds himself to blame (though he most certainly shouldn't) for not having Ira in Washington lined up at the federal trough as the Valley's Congressman.

The listener finds Polín entertaining, interesting, even. Biased people usually are an interesting species. And, as most egotists, entertaining, although not for long.

Let me begin by stating in the strongest terms possible that Becky Escobar committed a grave error in divorcing Ira. Her inability to see the man's qualities, in my way of thinking, denotes a lack of foresight, a lack of judgment, and a marked inability in the most important realm there is, the ability to read people. To think that after some eleven years of marriage she didn't acquire, couldn't focus on the type of person Ira was and is, is to set her off apart. Yes, that says it all for Becky Escobar, or rather, Malacara now . . . This last really tears it for me; beyond belief, is how I put it.

Yes. Incredible, inconceivable that that girl who appeared to have everything going for her, that she lost her head, stumbled, and then only to fall into Jehu's arms and hands.

No. It's witchery of some kind. A thing of magic dust and powder to blind that poor girl somehow.

Yes. It's easy for one to believe that, easier still to accept such a supposition. I'm not saying Jehu is a warlock or something like that, but there's something there. I don't know what, though. An intrigue of some sort. Something sinister; got to be.

It must be that, otherwise, how can you or I or anyone explain why she left Ira? Hmph . . . Ira Escobar is a model, a prototype. No, no, no, no! Becky lost her head; a moment of transitory madness, no two ways about it. I can't find any other reasonable explanation.

And for what, I ask you? So she could then go live with Jehu Malacara? I mean, really now . . . I certainly thought her to be a sensible girl . . . I thought of her as someone serious, yes. Jehu Malacara! Well, as for me, I rise at six every morning, and as soon as my feet hit the floor, I ask myself how is it that God hasn't found out about that guy. Because that's what Jehu Malacara is, a guy.

And then, to see, year after year, how Noddy Perkins puts up with him at the Bank. . . . Oh, no, there's got to be something there. Got to be some big, fat, thick mystery. Worse than that, for all I know. What I fail to see is that so-called talent of his. Where is it? I'm open-minded, and if someone can prove it to me that Jehu has a spark of talent, then I'll be a convert too. But I've yet to see it, no matter how many people say he has it.

What talent, Dearest Lord? Which one? Where? How? No, no. It's a myth, a mystery. Talent? I'd gladly hand over all the riches of the Orient if I could ever see his so-called talent.

Talent? I'll give you talent: Ira, he's the one. Upstanding young man, good family background, educated, proper, efficient. Someone who has served this County precinct in his political duties and obligations.

I taught him what I know about politics, but I soon saw that he wasn't merely a good learner; Ira Escobar could be a teacher of it in some college. And I tell him so, repeatedly: "Ira, you are one of the chosen. To be a commissioner in the County Commissioner's Court, in Belken County, is not just anything. No sir."

If one, quite objectively now, compares Belken with Dellis County, we'll use Dellis as an example, then there's no comparison. And there he is, Ira Escobar, governing the important business of the County. Belken, as St. Paul[9] would say, is no mean city. We are talking here of one of the most important counties in the whole of South Texas. Yes, without a doubt.

All right. Fine. What can you tell me about Becky? Hmph. There she is. Sweeping the Escobar name as if through a dirt floor in the poorest farm. And worse, oh yes. Dragging and hauling the kids wherever she goes . . . Really, now. She takes them here, she takes them there. I ask you, seriously: What kind of a mother is that?

Can Jehu Malacara pass out advice? No, no, no. I'm telling you: the world is breaking up, coming unraveled. There's no structure anymore. That's right. The divorce is but one hint among many of what's happening in the world today . . .

What more can one say, right? Now, one would suppose that Sammie Jo could well help Becky, to guide her, let's say. And maybe she did, and maybe she was turned away, right? And seeing how the world is nowadays, and Becky's perverse state of mind, why, anything is possible.

In a pragmatic way, let us say, I don't believe the divorce has hurt Ira. The elections are looming in the very near future, almost like that hurricane out in the Gulf right now. Looming. Threatening . . . Where was I? Ira, yes.

---

9. Early Christian missionary (d. ca. 64–65); author of epistles in the New Testament.

Well, Ira remains faithful to his political ideals, and I've just devised—paraphrased—a new slogan for him, and you should hear Ira, in that natural, loose, but controlled way of his when he speaks to his Spanish-speaking constituency: "Effective voting, down with corruption!"

How's that, eh? From my own pen and ink, and with echoes of the heroes of the Mexican Revolution.

But life is long, not short, and carries with it its consequences. True enough, and you hold on to that. That girl will meet a sad, unhappy ending, although I certainly wish her nothing mean or evil, and I want that to be shouted from the top of Our Lady of Mercy or even downtown, from the third floor of the Klail First National. I wish Becky only the best . . .

But a bad ending is inevitable, and it's sad because I admire some of her qualities. But I'm a realist, and one has to be a realist. All you have to do is see what company she keeps: Viola and Jehu. And then what does she do? She resigns from her duties in important women's clubs. Klail Society. That can't possibly lead to any good for anyone. Just wait and see.

And, I should very much wish to point out that Ira won't lose any ground because of those resignations two years ago. The divorce wasn't his idea; everyone knows that, takes it into account. So, as a result, Ira came out unharmed, let's say . . . it was Becky's disaster, not his.

In personal matters, that is an entirely different subject . . . let it also be said that I am Courtesy Itself in all my dealings with Becky. I harbor no rancor. You like the phrase? My behavior is that which the Tapias have always maintained: rectitude, honesty, and loyalty to all institutions. As for Becky, I give her all of my counsel and advice. To date, I've no evidence she has ever followed anything I've ever said. But one does what one can. Yessir. One fulfills one's duties and obligations. Do we understand ourselves here?

That she chooses to follow her own counsel and advice, as poor or harmful as they may subsequently prove to be, that, unfortunate as it maybe, is not an immediate concern of mine. But if it were, if . . . it were, I would be the first to offer my services and my advice as to how she should proceed.

But no, this won't come to pass. It's impossible for me to help her as long as she lives with Jehu. And married, some say.

Well, say what they may, say whatever it is they wish to say, how can anyone believe such a union is marriage?

She'll learn, poor Becky. She'll learn of his eccentricities, his inconstancy. Yes, she'll see Jehu Malacara for what he is.

In a word, there is no comparison between Ira and Jehu. None. No sir.

What Becky does have, unquestionably, unhesitatingly, and close at hand, at any time, is the unconditional, disinterested friendship of one Apolinar Tapia.

Yessir.


The eye of the storm, no, no, Apolinar Tapia is not the eye of the storm . . . Rather, the real eye of the storm, in the words of Julia Ortegón's brother, the weatherman, is "calm, but the area outside the eye is packing winds of 125 miles an hour." The weatherman also reports that tornadoes are to be expected when the hurricane hits land. It is not known, however, where or when this last will occur.

# Noddy Perkins

The listener has an appointment with Noddy Perkins. Powerful personality, restless, edgy, inclined to make nervous those around him. Pure upmanship.

Proud and loving father to Sammie Jo, and husband to Blanche Cooke.

The red face and its red scalp with a shock of white hair remain in place.

The listener may, perhaps not, but the listener may have omitted to point out the strong chin and slight but deep scar above the right side of his upper lip. The listener has not found anyone who knows how the scar came about. It's an old scar, the only piece of non-red tissue in his face.

Fine restorative dental work there, by the upper lip. Eyes, a soft, royal blue. They appear incongruous, given that strong nose and the stronger chin, but the penetrating look of the eyes attests power; the listener has formed the opinion that Perkins has decided, perhaps trained himself, to blink as little as possible.

The listener intrudes and explains here because the elections are "looming" (Cf. Tapia) and the listener wishes to hear, learn, at first hand what Noddy Perkins has to say about the Commissioner.

Ira Escobar is a fine young man. He does good work as a County Commissioner, and I've no objection at all regarding his private life, either.

I know there are people who say we run him like a sheep dog, but I don't see it that way.

I'm a businessman, and I want the Valley to prosper. If a Mexican can be helped on his way to occupy a local political post, the county is a good example; that's what we're here for.

Ira's transfer to our branch in Jonesville was most convenient. We're in the same precinct after the last reapportionment and his residency in Jonesville suits him. He's in no danger of losing his seat. The *Enterprise-News* certainly holds that view.

Ira is a serious young man and carries out his duties. To add to this, he has some sensible ideas which help him see his duties clearly.

My policy is not to meddle in my employees' private lives; I've nothing more to say on this. I'm not cutting you off here exactly, it's that my chief concern is running the Bank. I've three or four appointments this afternoon also . . .

Now, if you have some time, let's go across to El Fénix for some coffee. I'll flip you for it.

The listener prefers the Perkins Treatment than to being hustled by easy language. Note: the listener won the coin toss for coffee but lost the pastry toss. To quote Jehu Malacara: When going against Noddy, in anything, a tie tastes as good as a win.

## Nora Salamanca

Next, the formidable Nora Salamanca. Eyes? Blue black. Hair, graying and with a bluish tint. Height: 5' 4" and weighing in at 125 lbs. By Valley Mexican and Anglo standards, not an old family, but old enough. Gaspar Nieto and María de la Concepción Hirsch (de Nieto) say that the first Salamancas came to the Valley around the time of the War of '98. The Salamancas, to a man and woman, came to the Valley as members of the merchant class; this is still the case. N.S. is married to Pascual Navarrete.

It seems quite impossible for such a well-educated girl as my niece, Becky Escobar, certainly is, to have thrown away her life just like that; out the window, as we say. Too, I'm convinced that she was in the wrong, and that someone handed her some bad advice; otherwise, how can anyone explain to me that rash, abrupt decision of hers?

Notary Public Polín Tapia, by the way, calls on us once in a while. Always respectful towards all members of this household, Polín speaks and says many truths. As I say, if that man had been afforded a formal university education, no telling where he'd be by now.

At any rate, getting back to Becky. I see a sinister hand here. That decision could not have come out of Becky's mouth alone, unless, of course, a something or a someone or some nefarious spirit entered her mind and soul . . .

What she did, to rid herself of as good a man as Ira Escobar, is not the decision made by a woman who's in control of her senses, a woman so created by the Lord.

I have no earthly idea what got into that girl's head. I'm not saying that she should have been a slave, no, not at all; however, her actions may lead, influence, other girls to consider the same thing with their lives. And what if we do come to that pretty pass? What then? I ask you.

Why bother having *familias directoras*, being the leading families? I ask you. How are we to serve as an example to others? What will the Anglos think? I ask you. And, who will we have to lead in the future?

Women can vote, can't they? And they can own property, right? Well? What else do they want? Becky is and was raised spoiled, whatever she wanted was always handed her. And now? Well, now she has to earn a living, but at what cost to her position? And, she's going to have to learn what it means to work. To have to compete. What it means to bring food to the table. And, do you honestly think a woman, so raised, can actually earn a living? I ask you.

I truly hope she can avoid the suffering, but what she did isn't right at all. And how can it be right when by her own selfish actions, she just did away with one of the most important social laws: to remain at the side of a man who could provide for her, who could stand guard over her, as society has been observing for saecula saeculorum?[1]

It's a bad piece of business is what it is. An enterprise which will end badly, and I say this sadly, even if, at the same time, I recognize I'm right.

---

1. Usually *in saecula saeculorum*: forever, through the centuries.

First of all: the children need their father. And just what is it that those two poor innocents have to see, day after day? What a perfectly lovely example, isn't it? Seeing their mother living with your relative, cousin is it? Well, relative anyway . . . with that not-quite-right-in-the-head Jehu Malacara. From all I hear, about your cousin, it's an everlasting miracle he's not been run off from the Bank for a second time. That's right, a miracle.

Jehu Malacara, and you must excuse my bluntness and my frankness, I'm just built that way, is not the proper person to raise children, and less still, to raise someone else's children.

Now you see why I'm convinced that there's something sinister about all this? Witchcraft, even? And don't you doubt that for a minute, either. There's something hiding near the woodpile . . . And I'll tell you this, too: time will tell, it always does.

I've known Ira for years and years, and his family before that, and let me stress and underline that there's excellent blood in that lineage, a good, healthy breed. The Leguizamóns—and Ira is one on his maternal grandmother's side—are steadfastly honest and honorable. Exactly.

I know, I know there are some who would and do try to discredit their blood names. Those are the words of pernicious rumormongers. The Leguizamóns have always behaved as the gentlemen they are. Generous, unstinting in the charitable projects, freehanded in their contributions to Holy Mother Church . . . a sense of honor that thrills all believers to witness such probity, such openhandedness in giving away their earthly goods. There's a long line of people who'd love to measure up to those standards, oh yes.

And if one must swear on the Bible, I swear I saw that Caldwell-Navarrete union with the Escobar-Leguizamón-Leyva as something designed by heaven. I swear it. Anyone who could have foreseen that marriage would have forecast nothing but the very best for that young couple. Exactly.

But now? And with that war in China? wherever . . . And the few Mexicans in college acting up? What's this country coming to? What's this world coming to? And now Becky divorcing . . . the end of all the good things on earth is close at hand. We, thank the Lord, have no relatives fighting in that country. But what kind of an example are the present mexicanos presenting to the Anglos? Long hair, longer than some of the girls. And the girls, the way they dress in college? Whatever happened to modesty, to clean hands and clothes, I ask you? They're supposed to been school to learn!

And now, Becky in a divorced state. Now, if what I'm about to say isn't too out of place, I would repeat what I said earlier, since, surely, others are saying it now. Becky's actions are not those of someone who is mentally balanced.

I do not mean to say that she's deranged, or that she's one of those who doesn't care about what people say. Not at all. What I do mean, however, is that I am not entirely convinced that Becky wasn't drugged or influenced by something, a someone, by that nefarious force I spoke of. In times such as these and that war and all, no one who understands these things could possibly disagree with me.

I would be the last person to claim to know the exact reason, but is it possible that Jehu Malacara drilled a hole in her head and sucked out every bit of sense she ever had? Your cousin isn't a monster, nor do I suggest that, but it's all beyond me.

Oh, I know that talking this way sounds just as crazy or like someone who is still living in the past century . . .

As for Jehu . . . I'm just saying and say what our friend Polín Tapia says. He knows him far better than I do, of course, and all I do is quote; you mustn't hold it against me. He asks what other people ask: who is Jehu Malacara? Better still, he says, what is Jehu Malacara? And the answer is nothing, a Mr. Nothing. I won't go that far, but that's what Polín Tapia says.

But he asks just what many of us ask. And then, to have him at the Bank! At the KBC Ranch's own Klail First! What possible talents could he have been born with? And if he does possess some talents, where does he keep them, hide them?

On the other hand, Ira Escobar is a talent. That my nice Becky is blind to it is a different matter altogether. Ira not only worked at the Bank, he's now at the Savings and Loan, and then, when you add that fine public service, you'll see exactly what I mean. There's a wide gap between the two men.

And frankly, it's the children I feel for. Thank goodness that Dalia is here. It's not because she's my sister's daughter, but at times I wish Ira would've had more luck in his choice of partners in his twenties . . . Dalia Ramos-Botín would have been my choice, and still is. There's her picture: as nice and as beautiful as ever, and she's two years younger than Becky, too.

I won't be the one to get those two together, but in all truth, aside from being my niece, as is Becky, I don't see anyone else who belongs to the same social category. Do you?

Poor Ira. That boy never knew what hit him. Elvira Navarrete herself paved the road, laid the tracks, and engineered the entire affair. I've never seen the equal to that sister-in-law of mine. She moved half the world to get her way so that Becky would marry Ira.

I'm not criticizing Elvira; she did what she had to do and what she thought was right as a mother. And I'll be the first to say so. What is a bother, though, is that Elvira herself was blinded, yes, even she didn't see all of Ira's merits, all his good points.

This is not to say that Becky is entirely without her own plusses, or that Ira was better or even too good for Becky. Not at all. What Becky failed to see back then, though, was that Ira's brilliant future lay before them, call-ing to them. She'd set her sights too low, from the beginning. In a word, she didn't strive hard enough toward Ira's success.

Oh, she had those two darling kids, she joined some clubs and all, and that's beyond reproach, obviously. But anyone could see that what she wanted was independence. A bit selfish, she just didn't do more for Ira.

And how did she wind up? Well, see for yourself. Working for that Se-ñora, that, that, that Viola Barragán. As I've always heard repeatedly, one cannot be too careful in choosing one's friends . . . Anybody who is any-body knows and admits that Elvira and the Barragán woman became great friends years and years ago. As to how Elvira has remained close to her, even now, is the mystery of mysteries. And poor Becky? With that woman as a model for her? But it just so happens that Becky doesn't have to work. And if she has to work, and she's working now and has been almost since that tragic day, why must it be with that woman? Of all people. I ask you.

Yes, oh, yes. And talking of a poor choice of friends, Jehu, your cousin, as so well you know, travels in that same Barragán orbit. No doubt on that at all. Everybody knows how that woman has taken him under her wing, for years now. And maybe that's what accounts for Becky's downfall: The

Barragán woman pushed and shoved and schemed to get your cousin and Becky together. I ask you.

Let all of us pray that Becky's affair doesn't give rise to some unfortunate incident, that something bad awaits her. Although you must admit that a large part of Becky's fault in all of this is due to her insistence to work. Well? Doesn't she have enough work at home? No one required her to resign from the clubs.

A family grows, is nurtured in the hearth with the man defending the family home and its honor, and the woman, as always, reigning as his faithful partner. Exactly. My Pascual and I must be an example of what I'm talking about.

When my sister Norma died, I raised Dalia, and favorite niece or not, she knows what keeping and maintaining a house is all about. She's also respectful, highly modest, and very good looking, too.

Ira Escobar would have to travel to China and back before he could hope to find someone as suitable as Dalia. As regular as the sun, she is a devout believer, and that too is essential and thus a requirement for a Christian household. Hardworking, industrious, she's also respectful, highly modest, and very good looking, too. My nice is not, as we say in Spanish, *una pelagatos*, someone who skins cats for a living. She's graceful, she carries herself well, and you're hearing from one who knows. Blood kin or not, my assessment doesn't enter into this. She has her own very good points, as I never tire of telling anyone.

But as far as Becky is concerned, nothing good comes for those who behave as she did. Yes, straying off morality's well-paved high road is bound to bring something ill, something dangerous . . . But as I said, God forbid . . .

What's galling, though, is to have to see Becky lowering herself. You know, I think we women are our worst enemies sometimes . . . and tell me this, is Becky working for what some people call progress? God help us!

The listener lost some notion of time and thought. It was time for a final cigarette and a drink. The listener, tired and all, found that food, not drink, was called for. Food was not offered at the Salamanca home; the listener ate shortly after and felt rejuvenated, if not in a spiritual sense.

## Matías Soto, O.M.I.

Matías Soto, O.M.I. Native of Boiro, in Spanish Galicia.[2] Living, praying and saving some selected souls in the Valley for over twenty years. A high-pitched, almost hysterical, raspy voice accompanies a perennial five'o clock shadow on a very white, very pale face.

No, I agree, one divorce more or less does not mean or signal the end of the world, nor will the world lose its place in the galaxy, but you must admit

---

2. Autonomous community in northeast Spain.

that a divorce may very well destroy the welfare of any family which has enjoyed the Church's blessing.

The unsettling part in this serious affair, however, is that Becky didn't ask or seek for a way to have prevented what she did. At the first sign of trouble, she could have come here for solace and counsel. That's what we're here for, after all. She committed an error of judgment, a fault, let us say. She acted poorly.

Didn't she trust me? The Church? As a mother, Becky's first thoughts should have been as they should always be, for the family's welfare. Ira isn't blameless, either, you know, but women are the first bastion, the principal base and foundation of the Church family. That is not a debatable point. But, Ira, as a man and father, had his obligations, goodness knows. Oh, I can well understand his error and his willful pride, another error, of trying to resolve everything alone and without advice from any quarter. But it so happens I know both of them, and in spite of the fact that they changed to the Anglo parish when they moved from here to Klail, I was always, as I am now, ready to listen and to help them resolve their problems.

The Sisters now tell me that the children are no longer enrolled in their school, and that is an error. Why are they to bear any blame for any of this? But I guess that's what always happens in these cases, one precipitous ill-conceived action that . . .

As for Becky, I fail to see the reason why she disenrolled the children. And even less now, when they are in more need than ever of spiritual guidance. Yes, now, when the children need the help and support of our institutions, the Church's institutions.

But all of this was done on the spur of the moment, surely; it came upon as sure as that hurricane out in the Gulf will land here tonight, or tomorrow. Happy as larks one moment and then unhappy in the twinkling of a bird's eye. It's the times, these times! The Church sees herself threatened on all sides. And don't you remember, not too long ago, that assassination attempt in the Philippines on His Holiness Pope Paul? And then that horrible war in French Ind—in Viet Nam? A Catholic country soon to be in the deadly grip of Communists and Communism? The Church has every right to feel threatened, beset. Lord, Lord, it's the times.

To give you an idea, I am the last Spanish Peninsular priest in the Valley . . .

That's right; the Irish are returning to the Valley, and now the Texas Mexican faithful will be left to shift for themselves all over again. But as I've said, it's these times . . . Listen to this, how many new churches have been erected in Klail or Bascom, let's say, or in Jonesville, the largest city in the Valley? The number is zero plus zero.

And now? What? Well, two very important mexicanos divorced! What an example on their part! Bad business, bad, bad . . .

But what is to be done? As for me, I'm no longer either surprised or shocked by anything. Just as soon as we dispensed with Latin, that signaled the inevitable crumbling of forms, believe me. This is an institution, and more than that, a holy institution with special rites, forms, and its special history.

Oh, yes. Holy days, fasting before communion, the confession as a private sacrament, and more . . . all of this heaved as so much trash on some country road. Well, we still have our doctrine, but if catechism classes are suspended, we may as well close the doors and turn our churches into museums, I say.

That's right, and while young and socially influential couples like the Escobars do not take the reins of moral leadership, what can we expect from the rest of the parishioners? Oh, yes, Know that the majority of our parishioners make up the very foundations of the Church, but they still need the models such as those provided by the sons and daughters of the *clases directions*.

And now? To begin with, one less acolyte, since Charlie is no longer a member of this parish, and worse, Father Thomas now tells me that Charlie is not serving at masses in his parish in Klail.

That may just be another signal that Baby Sarah will no longer be helping the Dames of the Perpetual Candle Society . . . I must say that Becky probably didn't even stop to consider as to what would take place on account of her precipitous action.

The parish certainly will not close its doors to her when and if she repents with all her heart and after she's undergone an examination of conscience with cleansed, sane thoughts proving, too, that everything is in place. We're not living in the era of the Inquisition,[3] goodness knows; we're flexible and ever ready to embrace the fallen. We live and work with human beings who are, after all, imperfect because of their humanity. It's because of this knowledge in mind that we are always disposed to help those who've suffered some transient, momentary lapse. It all has to do, let there be no doubt, with saving souls and with praying that they attain a personal conviction of the Holy Faith. And, too, how is one to know that this is just one test on the part of the Lord? Anything is possible. There exist many mysteries in this world, and let's all pray that Becky take measure of herself and her actions, and that she direct her feet on the road to righteousness. And do please forgive my having to leave at this moment, but I've some parish affairs I must attend to.

The listener thanked Father Soto for his time. The listener plans to wait two days before driving to Jonesville. Mrs. Elvira Navarrete de Caldwell has kindly consented to talk to the listener.

## Elvira Navarrete

Elvira Navarrete (de Caldwell). Becky's mother.

Thanks be to God and to all His Angels, and the consolation they bring, but I see Becky's divorce as the Lord's punishment. God Himself knows why He's inflicting this pain on me, and that's why I've resigned myself to see this as further proof of my faith. And, I can't possibly be in better hands in this travail! Father Soto has brought consistent consolation and advice during

3. A former tribunal of the Roman Catholic Church, charged with suppressing heresy.

this tragic occasion. Although it's been over two years since the divorce, I manage to live my life from day to day . . .

As you so well know, Becky has gone off and married that, that Jehu person, and then? In a civil ceremony! Yes, yes, and yes, I know perfectly well who he is, and I most assuredly do not need Viola's reassurances and details as to his background.

And Viola is my oldest and my very best friend, and now she talks to me of "your son-in-law, Elvira," and she wants me to convince myself to accept him. It's been difficult, don't you see? Viola and I are friends, but despite that, I'm not going to fully accept that man or even follow, let alone take, Viola's advice. But whatever else you may have heard to the contrary, I do talk to him.

Father Soto let me know that my acceptance of this second husband could well occasion the most gravest consequences. That's what he said. I, I, I didn't even stop to ask him what they could be . . . but the Church is all powerful and she knows the answer. And what am I supposed to do? He brings Charlie and Sarah here . . . they can't very well walk here from Klail, can they?

And Catarino? You could well have asked me, yes. That husband of mine is blind, since birth, I would say, blind to any fault of Becky's. His baby is always right! Can you imagine? Why, if it hadn't been for me, Becky and Ira would have never married, believe me. To wait, to have to depend on Catarino to make a move in that direction, would have been to wait for a snowfall in the Valley . . . To wait for a miracle, to put it that way.

Catarino knows a lot about a lot of things, but he doesn't have the slightest notion of how to go about engagements, marriages . . . Not the slightest. He is a good man, as decent as you'll ever find, but it's almost impossible to introduce anything like this into that head of his.

Of course, since he was raised as a Protestant, what does he understand of a Catholic conscience? Oh, he reads that Bible there, but what's that to me? That has absolutely nothing to do with me, I'm no Bible-thumper; I'm a Catholic woman and very Catholic, and yet, for two years now, I stand here, watching the world go to pieces all around me. But my faith and Father Soto's advice see me through during these difficult events . . .

And Becky? My, my darling little girl, my baby, has fallen in error, and she won't let me cry to my heart's content and relief.

"None of that, Mama," she says. "You can cry in front of your friends, and all you want, too."

Can you believe that from her?

And now trying to talk in Spanish, yes. She, who speaks English just like the Anglos; identically. And she still speaks it, of course, but she says that Spanish is important to her. Is that true? Where did she get that idea?

Well now, I'm a mexicana, and my husband an americano, and our household is also mexicano. Becky attended the Catholic school, and the Sisters taught her English just like the Anglos, but you must know we never stopped using Spanish. But as far as I'm concerned, and Father Soto, too, it's that love of money which is at the root of all this . . . this corruption. Well, not corruption, really, but at the heart of the end of that marriage. Oh, what God has united, what God has united . . .

You see, Ira calls on me, faithfully. He behaves as what he is, a gentleman. As for Becky, she'll lose those blinders, she'll see the light.

And I can tell you, as I'd tell the world, too, that that second marriage is not a legal act. It could very well be annulled, as Father Soto assures me. The Church would do it for us, for the family . . . Father Soto says the proceedings would probably take some time, and perhaps some financial resources by way of a gift to the parish, but I tell you, whatever would be given would be as nothing for their eventual reconciliation.

And what does Becky say to this? "What a hope!" Dear God, at times she says some things that'll rattle your teeth. But all of this is perfectly understandable in an unstable state, as Father Soto says. At times, too, Becky says that Jehu, Jehu Malacara, that Jehu is a man, and you should hear how she says it, "A man!" As if that were something special, right? Well, isn't Ira a man, too? And isn't her own father a man? There's no way to understand young people today.

And the children? What can I possibly tell you? Happy as they can be with their Mom, oh, yes. And, since this house is the one place Ira can call on them, that's where you'll see them . . .

Charlie? You'll find his nose stuck in a book somewhere, and you can't get a word out of him. Baby Sarah? She listens to what her Dad says with as much attention as I pay to the wind outside. Oh, she sits close to him, but she could well be in the next county. She'll wander into the kitchen, helps me make some chocolate, sets the table and all, and she does it smiling and humming, but I don't think her heart is in kitchen work at all. But when it comes to respect, she, and Charlie, too, they are respectful as can be to their father. But when Ira leaves, why, it's like he's never been here at all.

I think that's strange. And me? Well, I'm Grandma, Mamá Grande, and Catarino is Grandpa . . . I know they love their father and all, but you should see them when they talk about Jehu. And how can I even think of stopping them from talking of Jehu in this house? That isn't done, and I will not be the one to put a stop to that. One has one's religion, true, but there's social courtesy too, you know.

Don't think of me as a crazy person, but I fail to see or understand what it is that Becky sees in Jehu Malacara. You can't say he's good-looking. That rather smallish nose has a decidedly Jewish hook to it. Eyes? A light green, I think. A sort of erased look about them, gray, perhaps. As for the rest, regular features, nothing outstanding, to speak of. A bit taller than Ira, thin-like, while Ira has the Leguizamón look with that cute little stomach bulge which suits him quite well. Gives him an air of respectability, don't you think? Jehu is nondescript. Period.

And Becky says Jehu is a first-rate banker, although, in the very few times I've spoken to him, I don't find him smart at all . . . I don't know . . . I have a very good idea what a banker should look like, be like . . . like Ira, for instance. And as far as I'm concerned, Jehu Malacara doesn't even look like a banker. He's just like Noddy Perkins.

That Noddy Perkins looks like something plucked from a cotton field not fifteen minutes ago: red-faced, red-necked . . . He looks like a field hand to me, and yet Becky says that according to Jehu, Noddy Perkins knows banking from the ground up. Well, you could've fooled me . . . Oh, and Noddy speaks Spanish, yes he does. I've not one clue as to his family background, where he came from, but since he married someone from the Ranch, he must have some lineage to him. In those affairs, the Ranch crowd is mighty cautious, you know.

It may sound strange to you, but Becky doesn't care one whit about any of that. She says that for her, people are people, and that's it. For example, her friendship with Sammie Jo Perkins is as strong as ever, stronger perhaps. That americanita is a bit, no, not a bit, she's very, actually, too independent for my likes. She scares me at times . . . But she and Becky get along just fine, thank you. And even more and better now. Becky also assures me they get along so well because of a solid friendship, and because of, of that, ah, that new life of Becky's.

A life, let me tell you, that I do not understand. But I will say this too, if the kids are happy, and I certainly see them that way, and as long as Becky isn't hurt, I'm her mother after all, I'll be happy and at peace, and I'll just wait until she sees the light. I'll have you know Becky won't allow me to talk this way, about seeing the light. And she says, the little devil, that she *has* seen the light. Can you imagine? That she saw the light, and that she likes it, and I don't just know what all she does say. But, in spite of everything, and I do mean everything, Becky is not a bad person, thanks be to God.


The phone rings, and the listener makes for another room, only to be stopped by a wave of the hand. Doña Elvira Navarrete points to the television set and signals it be turned on; cupping the mouthpiece, doña Elvira wants to listen to a weather report. The phone call, from a neighbor, perhaps, is a short one, and both the listener and Becky's mother listen to the most recent stalling of the hurricane some eighty-five miles southwest of Jonesville.


After this, strong coffee and some homemade *empanadas de calabaza.*[4]


## Raúl Santoscoy

Raúl Santoscoy. A cousin of Jehu; also Jehu's fellow university student; currently a pharmacist and rancher/farmer.


### i

Jehu? For years? Since we were kids. As for Becky, only since she and Ira first came to Klail, and what facts I picked up at the time, and that was common knowledge. That's all changed, of course.

In all truth, I didn't care for her when they first blew in here from Jonesville. I met him first, and I sure didn't like him from the get-go. And then, I went ahead and just thought she'd be cut from the same cloth. And I held on to that until I had a long talk with Viola Barragán. That's been years, though, and by then Jehu'd left the Bank and the Escobars were cutting that wide,

4. Pumpkin empanadas, or turnovers (empanadas can also be filled with sweet potatoes, pineapple, etc.).

loud swath of theirs. It was about then, I think, that Viola'd come over to see me and my dad about leasing some land for a couple of seasons. As you know, I don't farm much on this side of the River; my cousin Rafe and I farm some together, but mostly, we farm on the Mexican side. Our families been doing that for years, so what's new? . . . and now you got Anglos farming on the other side, too. I guess they'll always be with us, like St. John says[5] . . .

Well, as it usually turns out on those visits from town, we had some supper, a few drinks, and as always, too, a lot of politics. The usual. Well, Viola isn't much of a drinker to speak of, and though the talk happened a long time ago, and I can't remember what my uncle Blas said, but I'm sure it had to do with County politics, all of a sudden Viola cut in. She said something like this: ". . . it seems to me that Elvira Navarrete's little girl is the one with the brains in that marriage."

She said it again after supper, and what impressed me was that Viola felt very sure of what she was saying. And that from a woman who doesn't like to hear herself talk.

I sure hadn't thought or remembered that dinner years ago until the Escobars separated. But that was then, and now, Becky's married to my cousin Jehu. I was a *padrino*; I stood for him, and I made most of the arrangements too. I called Judge Treviño, the restaurant, and so on. I also got to see Becky a heck of a lot and certainly more than I had in the past eight to nine or however many years it was.

So I changed my mind about her; I liked what I saw: a serious woman and her two kids at the right side next to Jehu. She kissed him and then the kids right after the ceremony. She shook my hand, firmly too, then she hugged Viola and Mr. and Mrs. Caldwell. We'd all crowded into Ramón Treviño's chambers, and then she hugged old Hinojosa, the attorney. From there, straight to the restaurant for a smallish reception.

My wife was already there, and she'd brought her sister, Julia, and Aunt Ursula. Casa Cordoba, of course. And first thing, Jehu opened some double doors and Charlie and Sarah went off somewhere, like the three had planned it ahead somehow. At any rate, the rest of us sat down for breakfast and everything.

As Rafe says, and this is worth noting: Judge Treviño didn't make a fool of himself. I remember Jehu laughing and saying that there hadn't been enough time for that. Anyway, after the last toast, Jehu and Becky and the kids drove out to the beach.

Oh, one thing. Right before they all left, Jehu handed me a sealed envelope. No idea how he got 'em, but inside there were four tickets for the season's top bullfight. Eloy Cavazos, no less. There were some lottery tickets too, and Jehu'd hit the last numbers twice, so I got some forty bucks back! Ese Jehu . . .

Well, my dad died some six months after the wedding, and I sold my dad's part of the pharmacy to my cousin, Beto Chayres. And then before the year was out, Beto's kids moved to Houston, away from the Valley, Beto himself retired, and then turned around and sold the drug store to Viola. Well, I happen to know for a fact that Becky also runs that end of the business, because Viola again drove out to see me and to ask whether or not that was a solid enough investment.

5. One of Jesus' 12 apostles; author of the fourth Book, or Gospel, of the New Testament.

I said it was and added that I'd sell her my twenty percent . . . it all fit like a handmade glove. Old Hinojosa is Viola's favorite lawyer, and since he represented Becky in the divorce . . . Old Romeo told me to keep the deed to the building, to which Viola agreed, then I just rented it out to her and it worked out well for all.

Now, Jehu's no lawyer, but he had a big hand in that transaction. He then asked me to work at the pharmacy on salary, say twenty hours a week, part time, and Viola saw that I made out all right. A fine arrangement, and the Bank, you can't escape that, made some money, but that's part of Jehu's job, too.

And now Martín San Esteban is talking about wholesale pharmaceuticals. Told him to go ahead, I'm no competition to him. With what Rafe and I farm and now me working for myself and for Viola under the arrangement, those twenty hours in town are enough. I can do them any which way I want to: a weekend, two days in a row, three . . . it doesn't matter. After farming, it's nice to get inside a place. Sure is.


The listener and Raúl Santoscoy went across the street for afternoon coffee and rolls. That took half an hour.


*ii*

As for Jehu, it's about time he had some luck . . . There he was, thirty-something, and he finally meets and falls in love with Olivia San Esteban, and then to have her die that stupid death . . . Man! But good luck had to come his way, sometime. Becky saw in him what Viola and Noddy both had seen right from the start, a man without a price. Hmph. Damned Noddy finally gave up trying to get my cousin into County politics . . .

And that's a major difference. Ira lapped it up. Talk about limitations. Talk about not knowing one's own limitations. He doesn't quite have the reach, you know. He's got some things going for him, but my wife says he lacks something. I married one of those Ortegón women and there's not much they don't know . . .

Now that we're on Ira, maybe there isn't a word to describe or to sort him out with. Maybe that's why Carmen says to let it go. And of course there isn't a drop of Anglo blood in him, and yet he's not a mexicano. Explain that.

Let me tell you a story: during his first election, I didn't let the political workers staple Ira's flyers on our fence posts. That's not much, just a couple of miles on the Military Highway give or take. Now, you and I know Noddy Perkins isn't going to get into chicken feed like that. But someone called my dad, said something like your son Raúl won't let us use his posts on the highway there. My dad, and he was fuming, too, asked just who the hell was on the line. Some name. Raza, too. And the guy was hiding behind Perkins's name, using it.

My dad's fuse was shorter than a midget's pencil, know what I mean? Anyway, my dad swore that the guy on the line was a Texas Mexican, and he told him, nicely, too, since he recognized that the guy was just doing his job, earning his pay, but that it would be best to call Ira and have Ira call don Diego Santoscoy. Well, Ira was new in town, and he wouldn't know my dad from a pile of books, and he never did call. Well, after that, I didn't allow political bills anywhere, and then my dad followed suit. Nothing important, nothing major, but just to show you how some people are.

After he got into office . . . tell you when it was, just two weeks after P. Galindo left us. Old P. was here with my dad, had his wife Paulita with him, driving him around, making his goodbyes, he said, and either I or my dad, one, asked him about the new County Commissioner; that's important, since my dad's land is on that precinct. P. Galindo, kindly, too, said he was a nice boy.

And though there didn't seem to be any malice in that dying man's voice, I hope no one ever calls me that, thinks of me in those terms. A nice boy.

But Ira's got friends, a wide circle from what I hear. They're just not our friends. I think it's St. James[6] who asks if you can draw sweet and bitter water from the same place . . . That apostle just didn't make it down to the Valley, did he?

## Drinks González

Drinks González, baptized Saúl. Sexton.

People such as Becky Escobar, NO! not Escobar, Becky Malacara, belonged to a class and category with old money, but not too old. For instance, I knew don Julio Navarrete, her grandfather. The money is sixty years old, let's say, and then, some sixty years ago, I had convinced myself that social classes were necessary for order and for one's well-being. But that was a long time ago.

But let me tell you this, too. In that give and take we call life, one runs into people who earn all kinds of livings. Business, they call it. Making a living. To earn it, then, one needs the proper touch. You hear this in the Valley all the time, *el tacto*. And know what? Becky Malacara has it, and she uses it by being respectful, but truly respectful. That's important. She has what that husband of hers has, what a man you never knew called Jesús Buenrostro had. The one called El Quieto by his family, although everyone uses that name for him now, and him dead after too brief a life . . . One standard. And she's no actress, no put on. Here, let me serve my nephew Henry González, the veteran, as an example.

One fine day, Viola Barragán came by, and Viola is a power, right? And I bet I've got some twenty years on her. Maybe more. Sure. I've known her since she married Dr. Peñalosa, and that was a little before the second World War. At least six hurricanes since then, you know that? Well, she was just a kid then and her folks, the Barragán-Surís, married her off to Peñalosa. She must've been a kid of seventeen at the time . . . You're much too young to know of these affairs and things. Much too young.

6. Author of an epistle in the New Testament; possibly one of Jesus' 12 apostles.

The listener lights a cigarette and hands it to Sexton González, who's settled down for talk cum digressions; the best way.

You're much too young to even know of these things, but the Doctor, that's Doctor Peñalosa, and I knew him well, he was from Agualeguas; the Doctor, he died, poisoned to death. Not a suicide, though, but more of an accident. Oh, you can still hear some tart tongues running on and on that it was murder. No such thing.

Homicide by poison, but accidental, and done by a pharmacist. An apprentice pharmacist. But he's dead, too. Orfalindo Buitureyra, the King of the Parrandas.[7] It's possible it was murder, the Valley's part of the world, isn't it? You live long enough, and with patience on your side, you'll see a million things. For my money, and that's just a saying, it wasn't murder.

Viola became a widow . . . and now? A person of business, a handsome woman who walks and talks like a field general and who dresses in the best from top to bottom. Good for her!

But as I was saying, one Sunday Viola came by some time after High Mass, the last one. I'd finished with the sweeping and wiping of the church and benches. I'd checked the candles, the votaries too, and then polished the altar till I made that white marble shine and sparkle, just like the day they brought it in here all the way from a place really Up North. One of those cold states. So, I was doing what I always do: work.

Finished with that, a glass of wine. After this, a sign of the cross and I went out the side door, lit a cigarette and stood ready for my cup of hot chocolate, when this big old car pulled up. I haven't been able to tell a car or its make since the thirties. But, that car was A CAR AND A HALF. *Un carrazo.*[8]

Air, four doors, dark-colored, and maybe even a television set if there is such a thing now that the Japanese have begun to eat the world feet first . . . And there came Viola, a cigarette in hand, and holding a hot cup of coffee for me . . . Yeah!

I must stop here to let you know that Viola Barragán has always treated me with respect. Although just about everyone, and that includes those saints and devils of God, the kids, they all call me Drinks, Viola has always called me Saúl.

So as not to surprise me, so as to bring me up to date, she told me of my father's old property. My father, don Antonio, died in '22, and that property'd been lost on account of taxes. Well, she just bought it, she told me. That she wanted to open one of her businesses on that lot, and that she knew that my nephew Henry González had just retired from the U.S. Army after some twenty or thirty years in there. You follow?

And that she, Viola, wanted to know if Henry had any plans. Was he just going to laze around for the rest of his life, playing dominoes and shootin' pool? Was he going to take a drink every day or was he planning to take up some job so as not to break the routine. Or what?

Didn't even let me answer. That's her style, though. That she was thinking of opening up a corner store business, some neighborhood place. That

---

7. Parties, drinking binges, etc.                    8. A big, luxurious car.

she needed someone she could trust, rely on. Well, we'd been at this some 10 or 15 minutes, and me without my hot chocolate, when I asked her to come into the rectory. She took my coffee and put it in some tray in that big old hearse of hers.

Viola Barragán is not one of our parishioners here at Sacred Heart. Me? I'm a believer, all right, but I don't stink up the place by going to every Mass every day. I just go to daily Mass and you'll find me there at five ayem, seven days a week, 'cause it's my duty and obligation since Mass is a sacrament. BUT! When it comes to converting folks, I leave that to other people.

Well, once in the rectory, Viola offered me one of her cigarettes, and I lit her fresh one and mine. Here, with this Zippo. A present from Father Ornelas, a Klail City boy.

And there went Viola again: "Someone reliable, Saúl. And I'll see to Henry's kids' education, if they haven't finished it yet." Like that, see? Said she remembered Emma Zepulveda, Henry's wife, and that she always saw her as a woman of sense, and that's why she, Viola, had come to see me on this.

And this wasn't just talk either. Henry's folks are dead, been dead. For years. That boy joined the army at fifteen; yes, he did. The Army people came here, to Pérez's Pool Hall, and signed him up at twenty-one dollars a month with uniforms, room and board for three years, five if he wanted them. That boy got drunk on all that money and stayed drunk for two weeks until the U.S. Army sent two soldiers for him. Henry, he wanted to go, but he had lost the time and the date, and the place. They, the soldiers, put him on the Missouri Pacific nine-fifteen and from there to Fort William Barret to start a new life. Loved the Army. Never ate so much and so well. Came back like a balloon, well, almost, 'cause the U.S. Army don't like you fat, but he, Henry, said he never met a meal he didn't like. And you know, like he said, years later, too, and he wasn't a kid then, a prisoner in Korea, the war many of the boys were in, a prisoner, and he ate everything. Lost weight, but he wasn't skin and bone. He was one of those big sergeants. You can't get no more stripes on him, see? Fills up the sleeves, both of 'em. That's my nephew Henry.

But like I said, Viola wasn't just talking. I told her Henry was ready to work, anytime. And he was. Well, not six months later, that corner store grows out of the ground there, and it's open for business. And there they were, Henry and Emma running the place . . . Becky, she runs those stores, and now Henry and Emma own part of it. Becky worked it out this way.

Henry, he was a baker in the U.S. Army, and Becky says why doesn't he open up a bakery on the same lot. Emma runs the store, Henry runs the bakery, and the bakery is theirs. Just like that. Becky says the store will make business because people will come in for both on the way home. That girl was right. And Henry's no drinker, by the way. Ever since he went on that *parranda* on the Army money, he swore never again. Not even a beer.

So, Becky runs the Shopping Bags and that agency of small cafes, the hamburger places. Busy Bees? The Busy Bees, right?

We're not a rich parish, not like others I could name . . . but Father Ornelas—he's not the pastor, that's Father Eloy—but Father Ornelas—and I always call him that even if I had known his folks before they even married— anyway, Father Ornelas talks to both Jehu and Becky; and let me tell you, she's business and at the same time, nice. But nice. And with Mexican courtesy for all. There are some people who wouldn't know courtesy if it hit 'em in the face like a water-filled balloon. Anyway, Father Ornelas talks to them. They bring the kids here, to this church, this parish, and they don't live here, in this area. But Jehu grew up with Father Ornelas, see? Now, this is a secret, and I don't have to explain to you what that means. Becky says that Jehu would like to be told if Father Ornelas is . . . is threatened with a transfer. Yes.

Old Juvencio Ornelas the Candyman died as a result of the many sugars in his body, and now it's only Petronila Ornelas, and she lives with some old folks. Folks like me, but folks who need more help. Me? I can work. I'm like that man who used to bury people, he now works at the big Bank, *el banco del rancho* . . .

Well, Jehu and Becky keep up with people like that. Jehu knew and knows and remembers what being poor means . . . Becky? She had money from that old grandfather of hers and from her own father too. But she says that doesn't matter. What matters, and here she sounds a lot like Viola, what matters is what you do. What you do . . . I am me, I told her. I explained it in Spanish. *Yo soy yo.*

And now? Everytime she sees me, she says, "*Yo soy yo, don Saúl. ¿Y usted?*" I tell her who I am, *quién soy yo* . . . Ha!

*Esa*[9] Becky is independent, and married too. Reminds me of the late Enriqueta Farías. An old woman when I knew her, and that means going back in God's time. She was Jehu Malacara's great-aunt. Well, Rafe Buenrostro's too, of course. A Relámpago woman. Born there, died there. Religious, but fierce, too. Generous. Lived to be a hundred, maybe more. They live long in that family, unless God calls them early or some man decides . . .

As for Becky, well, I've known the Navarretes since 1893, '94. And I let her know who she is, where she comes from . . . she likes to know things like that. Respects the past but won't live in it.

Me? Married the once and that was it. Hmmm. St. Paul says it's better to marry than to burn. What did he know? He ever marry? Always traveling, giving advice in that hysterical voice of his. But Dr. Luke?[1] Ah. Remember the crumbs which fell from the rich man's table? It's what you do with them, as Father Ornelas says. And Jehu doesn't hand out crumbs. Money and jobs are far from crumbs . . .

Can't say much about Becky's first husband. I never met the City Councilman. Belonged to one of the other parishes. Yes.


## Ira Escobar

Now, how could she have come up with such ideas, I ask you. To throw me out of the house. Me! Sounds incredible, doesn't it? My God, who would've thought she'd do something like that?

I park the car, come into the house after a hard day's work with the County Commissioners' Court, and that was it, picked up and dumped like an old dish rag, right to the trash barrel. Just like that.

---

9. She, that one.
1. Author of the third Gospel of the New Testa-
ment; possibly one of Jesus' 12 apostles and, if so, possibly a physician.

I asked her three times, four, maybe more, and the answer was the same in each case: "I've decided etcetera, etcetera, etcetera." And I couldn't get her to say anything else. Like a cracked record, "I've decided . . ."

The bitch had been changing all along, sure she was, and I bet she didn't even know that I was noticing something new about her. Han![2] To throw me out of the house; and out of the bed, too. But that was our secret. And the kids? What could they have been thinking about my sleeping in the spare bedroom?

The bitch planned it real good, too. Oh, yeah . . . here comes that jackass and there we were, in the living room. The kids by her side. She planned it right down to the last detail. And then? To choose Romeo Hinojosa to represent her? No, whatever anybody says, choosing him was no accident.

God . . . every time something happens on the County level, there he is. Jesus. Aren't there any other lawyers in town? Han! All I can say about him is that he's got nothing else to do but get in the County's hair. Buttinsky! Know-it-all! And nosey? All those rolled up in one . . . And let's see? Why isn't he rich if he's such a hotshot? Why, he hasn't got a pot to put a flower in . . .

Someone, somewhere, helped him in our divorce every step of the way. What does he know about the law? Someone helped him out, had to. I know I've asked Polín Tapia a thousand times, but even he hasn't been able to find out anything . . . Han!

But she sure showed a lack of consideration, and of shame, too. Imagine getting married just eighteen months later? What was the bitch's rush, anyway? Jehu Malacara! You'd swear she'd done it on purpose, to make me look the fool . . . Well, all I can say is she's going to learn, and see and know, that Jehu Malacara isn't the bargain she thought he was when they married.

But Jehu too didn't exactly strike oil there; I look upon that marriage as a case of private punishment for Jehu. He'll learn. He'll see just what size pants she wears. Oh, yeah. He who is so sure of himself. He who walks around as if he were bullet-proof or something. He'll see.

And that ought to teach him. Her, too. That Jehu is a regular hell on wheels, and my wi . . . well, all I can say is that she better watch out. And I'll say this too: They deserve each other. Yessir.

And will you look at them? That's a lovely role they're acting out, isn't it? As if they were worthy of respect. Han! Why, she's a divorced woman, what my mother calls a woman of the world. A divorced woman turned around and married a Mr. Nothing. A relative of the Buenrostros. Who says so? And what do I care if he is or not? My uncle don Javier said that the Buenrostros, all of them and their relatives, too, that the Buenrostros were, are, and will continue to be a big bunch of hypocrites. That's right! Did you know that the Buenrostros own 200 hectares in Soliseño? Part of the Llano Grande grant? Rafe owns and farms that in Mexico! Right across from the El Carmen Ranch. Is that legal? Probably bribed Mexican officials to farm there!

Yessir. The Buenrostros are not a band of angels. You mean that just because the oldest brother and Rafael were in the service that gives 'em a special place somewhere? I didn't go to Korea 'cause I took and passed a deferment exam when I was up at St. Mary's. And Jehu? What did he do in

2. A honking sound made by someone seeking corroboration for a statement or anything; equivalent in English to *Eh?*

the Army? Yeah. He himself says he worked as a chaplain's assistant; as if chaplains were in any sort of danger. Han!

But the marriage won't last. How can it? And, neither one knows how to spend money; they lack the talent. Worse, they can't even satisfy the kids when it comes to buying presents, as I can . . . and do. But Becky'll see for herself, she'll see what kind of person Jehu is. Yessir.

To begin with, he's not generous, he is one of the most conservative bankers there is and so much so, there's a smell of tight-waddishness there.

It's funny. And her? Becky? Does she think that just because she works with Viola—and how much can she earn, anyway?—does she think she can buy all the clothes she wants? She's the world's leading spendthrift. And him? Why, that man is the original Mr. Skinflint, I've never seen a man so tightfisted, and he uses all four fingers and a thumb, too. He thinks he'll keep her happy being the way he is and just because, right? Han!

They'll see, they'll see . . .

And Becky too will learn something else, if she hasn't already. Let me ask you this: How many friends does she have? The very few Anglos she knew at the Music Club moved away from Klail City, yeah. And those who stayed, and I can bet you on this, they probably don't even know or care if she's alive. That's right, let me remind you she's no longer The Commissioner's Wife. She's never had less friends than now.

And that's it; goodbye to whatever social life she had, and forever, too, because Jehu lacks the grace and savvy as to how to make new friends. If Becky isn't careful, the bitch'll be like a cloistered nun because that guy is a stay-at-home. For days, weeks even. He's like a hermit, you know. But Becky will see just what kind of trouble she bought when she married Mr. Jehu Malacara. Han!

And that town! Nothing like Jonesville. Everywhere you turn around, so and so is related to so and so, and it doesn't matter if you're first, second or third cousins. They'll fit you in. Why, talk about inferiority complexes where they have to hide behind relatives and such . . .

And what does she know about sacrifices? I'm the one who told, pointed out to Noddy Perkins, when that job opened up in Jonesville.

The job at the Klail Bank was taking too much time from County business. And now that I'm here at the Jonesville Savings and Loan, I'm better off by two hundred percent. Jonesville is a bigger town; it's a city, really. And Noddy's very happy with my performance and my work both here at the S. and L. and in the County.

One has to live one's life, right? There's no reason why I should give up my freedom, is there? My Mom and I have talked on this a thousand times, and we see eye to eye on this.

And look, when Jehu brings the kids to my mother-in-law's, I say it isn't necessary that he wait in the car until he sees them walking through the door. I've told Charlie and Sarah to tell him how I feel about that, but you think he cares? It's not that important, I know, but it's like throwing dirt in my face that he's the one who brings the kids here.

It's a good thing the kids are sweet kids; otherwise they would've insulted Jehu by now. But they weren't raised that way. They should treat everyone with the same respect. This house was established with social responsibilities; it's our form and function.

But those two don't have to worry about me. She's the one who wanted the divorce, and now she's stuck with it. She's the one who wanted to marry Jehu Malacara, and that was a door she opened for and by herself, yessir. She made the decision, well, she's got to hold on to it now, and may God and His Holy Church forgive me, but I wouldn't go back to her even for the kids' sake.

This is not overweening pride; not at all. I look at it as a great favor that's been given me, a boon, something for which I'll be forever grateful when I was rid of her.

No, I'm not coming back for seconds, thank you, no. Here I am, closing in on forty, and I sure won't be the one who's going to cry for someone who doesn't deserve crying for. Oh, no! And doña Elvira better not even think of coming to this house. My mother has never cared for her. In her life. Never.

But there's no danger from that front and so, why worry? I'm the happiest I've ever been, and I, for one, certainly don't wish them any ill-fortune of any kind. And why would I, anyway? What would be the use? Me? I'm content enough to say that they deserve each other, one and the other, and that's nothing less than the Truth itself.

But that's up to them, that life of theirs. They're each going to have a handful putting up with one another. And that's as sure as rain falls somewhere every day, just like it's falling out in the Gulf right now. And they're just like the rain, inconsistent.

And you know what she said? What she had the nerve to say? I heard she was talking to Sammie Jo or to Viola, to somebody, anybody who'd listen to her most likely . . . Someone had asked her why, why the divorce? Know what the little bitch said? Han! Listen to this and tell me if she isn't going out of her head: "I saved myself. That's all that happened between Ira and me. I saved myself, and I'll let it go at that."

The listener, too, will let it go at that.


## Becky

Becky. The listener has nothing to add here. Nor does the listener intend to add a colophone, a coda. Becky, and it's high time, too, should speak for herself.


Years ago, Daddy decided to Mexicanize himself, and so much so that he's not an Anglo anymore, a *bolillo* as Jehu says.

As a kid, when I was with the Scholastics[3] and later on at St. Ann's, we used English and nothing but . . . I spoke English to Mama, and she'd answer me in Spanish. That's pretty normal for Valley mexicanos. Besides, Mama prefers Spanish, and that's it.

---

3. One of the many Catholic nun-directed schools for girls.

Daddy is the sweetest, dearest thing there is. He's a good man in the good sense of the word. Oh, I know what people say, and I've heard it all my life: "All he does is hunt and fish." That's just talk. And Mama? She adores him, and I do too. He is something that people wish they were: kind, giving, and—a word not much in currency—virtuous.

People. People say Mama pushed me into marrying Ira. That's partly true, but I'm the one who made that mistake. I thought I loved Ira, convinced myself I did, and for a long time, too.

And what's the big to-do? Is there a mother who doesn't want her daughter well off? Comfortable? But it happens that I let myself, had placed myself there. I wanted to marry Ira. That I don't love him as a husband now, or that I don't want him to live with me and the kids, that is something I decided as well. I made a mistake a long time ago, and it was up to me to correct it.

Can't I be allowed to make a decision? Must I always accommodate myself, every time?

And I certainly didn't talk the divorce over with Mama and Dad beforehand. The difficulty, but difficult only in broaching the subject, was in talking to the kids. Sarah was eight at the time, and Charlie going on eleven. They love their Father, as they should. I insist on it. But they can also see that this is another life, that their Mom has remarried. That Mom works, and that there's nothing wrong in it. As far as I know, the kids have not had the divorce thrown in their faces. If someone were to, old or young, the kids know what to say to that. Now then, that Jehu and I married a year and a half after the divorce is as much our business as it is Charlie's and Sarah's, but no one else's.

Jehu prefers straight talk. I do too, although I had to learn that for myself. It was hard going, but that wasn't Jehu's fault.

And this is what people must understand: Jehu is not the kids' Father; he's their Dad. There shouldn't be any mistake on that score, I don't think. They both love and respect Jehu, and he loves them. When they're not with me or when I can't take them to work with me, Jehu leaves the bank, takes them to the park, to Mom's house, or to see Rafe or Rafe's nephews out at the farm.

The first visits to Mom's house were strained. And why shouldn't they have been? But Time's a great leveler; it's like money, says Jehu. And he laughs when he says it; I do too. And in time, Mom's learned to come around. Mama is a snob, but is that a high crime? Aren't there worse things?

It seems almost a hundred years ago that Ira and I moved to Klail. And then, straight away, Noddy decided that Ira was to run for the Commissioner's post . . . even before we left Jonesville for Klail. Many things happened back then. Personal things.

Among them, I lied for Jehu. I lied to Mr. Galindo. To Noddy. To myself. But I didn't know Jehu then, and I had no way of knowing that Jehu was, is, capable of defending himself, from any quarter. But I lied because I already loved him, and so I sought to protect him from Ira, from Noddy. *That's* funny.

Ollie San Esteban. I do not, nor will I ever, speak ill of Ollie San Esteban or her memory. Never. I was a spoiled, silly, nattering little fool, but with all of that, I sensed somehow that changes had to be made. I knew I wanted Jehu. That's a difference. And we made love; he wanted to, and I wanted to.

I wanted to see him, be with him, hold him. I was indiscreet, of course, but I wasn't a fool. All he saw in me was a pretty face. I knew that. But he had to know who I was, what I was.

As for those changes, I didn't have the nerve, the courage, or even the imagination to figure them out. But I learned. Now, alone or with Jehu, here, in our home, I think about what held me back from seeing the changes. It was fear. Finally, one day, I asked myself what it was I feared. The answers came tumbling out, hundreds of them. But then, at that time, I hadn't learned about ultimate questions . . . oh, yes. When I asked myself the ulti- mate question, and I answered yes to myself, and I knew I was dead serious, fear, or whatever it was, flew out that front door, through the porch, and away from this house . . .

That day, the kids came in from school, and I prepared some limeade for the three of us. Sarah brought the cookies, I remember, and Charlie set the table . . . He was about to go upstairs for his shorts and sneakers, ready to go out and play, but I asked them to sit. For a talk. I had no idea what they'd say, how long I would talk, but talk I did and all of us cried, too. And then we waited for Ira . . .

I sat there, I thought I'd done a selfish thing, that I was the same old Becky. And I cried. Just then, Sarah moved over and told me not to cry. And she was just eight years old, you understand. Charlie then ran upstairs and put on some long pants and a shirt. We waited. The car, the door, the front porch . . .

We were a long way from the first day we'd moved to Klail . . . I cut a ridicu- lous figure. And for a while there, I even pretended to myself that I wasn't Elvira Navarrete's daughter, as if Ira's mother had raised me. Denial, of course; nothing else but.

I had made myself into another person, and, too, I was such a fool I couldn't see Sammie Jo's friendship when it was offered.

And Sammie Jo and I are friends. She's something. *Es persona.* And that is how she saw me. As a person, but I couldn't see myself.

But getting back to Jehu. I was just one more conquest, but hardly that, since there'd been no resistance on my part. I went to him, even when I knew he loved Ollie San Esteban. And why shouldn't he love her, and yes, I also knew about him and Sammie Jo . . . And well, was I any better?

But I didn't love Ira. And there were the kids. And people. And Mom . . . And then the ultimate question . . . what would I do for Jehu to know me so that he would then love me. And so I told Ira that I'd decided he was not to live with us anymore.

That man Jehu . . . He called on the San Esteban family for over a year af- ter Ollie's death. A man of responsibilities, you see. And then, twelve months to the very day of the decision, on a day like today, a bit gray and overcast, somewhat windy, hurricane weather, he showed up. There, on the porch.

We sat, and I couldn't stop talking. Poor Jehu. But I didn't care what he thought of me then and there. What I wanted to know, all I wanted to know, was did he love me, did he love me as I loved him? But thank God Jehu is the way he is. He nodded and looked at me for the longest time. I couldn't know, of course, but I felt it.

I don't know about you, but have you ever had someone look at you, up close, eye to eye? A clear, unclouded, an almost unblinking look at you? Jehu looked at me that way that afternoon.

I didn't ask him to say he loved me, I wasn't a kid. But he said it anyhow. One surprise after another, that man.

And then? He said to call the kids, to go out, for a walk, on the sidewalk, around the block. And Sarah, who'd never seen him, took his hand, hugged him. Sarah! Yes. And kissed him. Even the weather helped; the wind calmed down, as calm as the kids.

Charlie? Charlie ran up to his room and brought back a sketch he'd drawn at the Scholastics. When Jehu smiled, Charlie gave it to him: a present. I don't think they said a word between them.

Since much Spanish common property law prevails in Texas, the management and apportionment of property took time. It was Jehu who suggested that Romeo Hinojosa represent me. Jehu then said it would be better if he didn't call on me until after the divorce. He then explained this to the kids: clearly, simply, no embellishment. Well, Mr. Hinojosa made an excellent case for me and the kids, although I must say that Ira behaved like a pig in this. Kept bringing up the fact, his lawyer did, that Jehu had called on me. Poor Ira! He still doesn't understand a thing.

That's been two years now, and the trouble with Ira is that he can't see beyond tomorrow. The kids are growing up, and they may wind up not loving Ira because of Ira's behavior. Jehu, now, he will not allow the baby, Sarah, or Charlie either, for that matter, he won't allow them to speak disrespectfully about Ira. Jehu says that isn't done. He, too, never says a word against Ira, and so, the kids follow his example: no criticism.

Don't mistake what I say, though. Jehu knows Ira for the fool he is. And he knows that Noddy controls Ira, who doesn't know the first word about banking or little else. Jehu says Noddy knows this, and since Ira likes the easy way out of things, Noddy keeps him under wraps.

As for Noddy, he can throw both Jehu and Ira out of the banking business and into the streets any time he wants to. It's his bank. But Jehu doesn't care, and poor Ira does care. That's the difference.

And this is my new life, and it's the best one I could have chosen. There's no set routine to our lives . . . As I said earlier, Jehu comes home at noon, on a Wednesday, say, he'll call the bank and say he won't be back that afternoon. He'll drive to Klail Mid-School, sign out for the kids, and if I've got nothing pressing at the moment, we'll drive out to El Carmen Ranch and visit a while.

That's Jehu, impromptu. It's the same with the few parties we give at home. A few people we know, mostly family.

For Jehu it's always the family. Me. The children, that's the first family. And then the other family, Rafe, who's more than just a cousin. They're like kids, they call each other on the phone.

And speaking of Rafe, Jehu wanted to postpone the wedding, and I was for it. Rafe was recuperating from his eye trouble again, but Rafe wouldn't hear of it. Got me on the phone, "*No lo dejes*,"[4] is what he said.

---

4. Don't leave him, don't quit on him, he'll come through.

People who don't know Rafe think he's reserved; that's the word I always hear. He's quiet, sure, and he's certainly that way in public. He's funny, though. Like Jehu, he laughs, he can tell a joke . . .

To me, Jehu is the reserved one. And patient? I think that's why the kids also love him. He's incredibly patient . . . and you know, it takes a good business head and sense to be patient. I learned that on my own.

I won't talk about my work or what I do at Barragán Enterprises. It's boring to talk about it, but it's something else to live it. It's my professional life; that's all there is to that.

Viola? I was wrong about her as I was wrong about many things. She loves me as if I were her own daughter, had she had one . . . I learned the business by watching her, by being there . . . and I remember my first important lesson in business: *Yes* means *yes*, and *no* means *no*. Negotiations are always preliminaries, but the yeas and nays are the finalities . . .

I talked to few people about what I wanted to do . . . I talked to Mrs. Campoy, a hundred if she's a year, and bright and lucid . . . I also talked to Viola. Before I talked to Mama. See? And Viola? She cried. But do you see? We're talking about a fearless woman here. And she was the first to see what was in me, before I could even see for myself. Saw it before Jehu, too.

And that's it. I'm not a woman who was saved, redeemed. I saved myself. With help, of course. With love and good will, too, and all the rest. But if I couldn't save myself, if I couldn't save me from myself . . . But why go on?

Let's say I saved myself, and let it go at that.


Yes, the listener will also let it go at that.


### End Note

*. . . what a strange accident the truth is.*
George Santayana[5]

1990

5. Spanish philosopher, essayist, poet, and novelist (1863–1952), associated with the United States, where he was educated and lived several decades.

---

# MARÍA IRENE FORNÉS
## b. 1930

One of the most prolific and influential Latino playwrights, María Irene Fornés was born and raised in Havana, Cuba. After her father died, her mother moved with Fornés and her sister to New York City. There Fornés, then a teenager, worked in a factory to help support the family. In her 20s, she took up painting and went to Europe to pursue a career as an artist. In 1957, she returned to New York, where she began working as a textile designer. As her interest in painting faded, she discovered that her vocation lay in writing, and she wrote her first play, *La viuda* (The Widow), in 19 days. It was published in an anthology of Cuban plays in 1961. Later that year, Fornés won a Whitney Foundation fellowship. In 1963, *There! You Died* was presented in San Francisco, becoming the first of her works to be produced on stage. In the play, two male lovers—portrayed as both a father and son, a teacher and pupil—perform a seemingly endless tango, until one murders the other. In 1965, *There! You Died*, retitled *Tango Palace*, was staged in Minneapolis along with her next important play, *The Successful Life of 3*, in which He, She, and 3 become entangled in a love triangle; the action is presented through vignettes in which time and space are blurred. In the same year, her musical comedy *Promenade* became an Off-Broadway hit. This work, about two escaped prisoners who return to prison after their experiences in the outside world, satirizes a cruel, materialistic society.

A Yale University fellowship (1967–68), a Cintas Foundation fellowship (1967), and a Boston University Tanglewood fellowship (1968) enabled Fornés to write several plays: *A Vietnamese Wedding* protested U.S. involvement in Vietnam, as did *The Red Burning Light: or Mission XQ*. In *Dr. Kheal*, the lone character gives eccentric, philosophical lectures. In *Molly's Dream*, movie stars fill the daydreams of a saloon waitress, only to prevent her from finding love in the "real world." Aided by Rockefeller and Guggenheim fellowships, Fornés wrote eight more plays during the 1970s and 14 during the 1980s. *The Curse of the Langston House* was produced in Cincinnati in 1972. *Aurora* premiered in New York in 1974. *Cap-a-Pie*, a musical written in Spanish, was produced in 1975 by INTAR (International Arts Relations), a Latino theater group in New York that has since produced many of Fornés's plays. *Washing* appeared Off-Broadway in 1976. In 1977, both *Lolita in the Garden*, written in Spanish, and *Fefu and Her Friends* were produced in New York. The latter—the winner of two Obie Awards and included here in its entirety—consists of a gathering of eight friends in the home of Fefu in 1935. The characters come together to make plans for a fundraiser, and in plotless vignettes they discuss their past and their hopes for the future. During the second act, the audience follows the characters through four rooms of Fefu's house, sharing the intimate space and the lives of the characters.

In 1979, Fornés won another Obie, for *Eyes on the Harem*, a collection of feminist stories based on ancient Turkish legends. In 1980 and 1981, she produced *Evelyn Brown (A Diary)* in New York and adapted two plays: *Bodas de sangre* (Blood Wedding), by the twentieth-century Spanish poet and playwright Federico García Lorca, and *La vida es sueño* (Life Is Dream), by the seventeenth-century Spanish playwright Pedro Calderón de la Barca. *A Visit*, the story of a seductive young girl in 1910 Michigan, and *The Danube*, in which a couple's failure to communicate destroys their relationship, are also from this period. In 1983, *Mud*, about a violent love triangle, was produced in California. In 1984, Fornés won Obies for *The Danube*, *Mud*, and *Sarita*, the story of a young girl obsessed with a man.

In 1985, *The Conduct of Life*, an ambitious study of the relationship between a torturer and his victim, received an Obie for best new play. Fornés won a Playwrights USA award for her translation of *Cold Air*, by the contemporary Cuban playwright Virgilio Piñera. In 1986, *The Trial of Joan of Arc in a Matter of Faith* and *Lovers and Keepers*, a collection of three one-act musicals, were produced in New York. In 1987, *Abingdon Square* won an Obie, and Fornés directed adaptations of *Uncle Vanya*, by the nineteenth-century Russian playwright Anton Chekhov, and *Hedda Gabler*, by the nineteenth-century Norwegian playwright Henrik Ibsen. Two years later, her short plays *Hunger*, *Charlie*, *Springtime*, and *Lust* were produced together in New York as *And What of the Night*. In 1996, Fornés directed a revised, one-set version of *Fefu and Her Friends*. In 1997, *Balseros*, a play about Cuban rafters (refugees who fled by raft to the United States in the 1990s), was produced in Miami by the Florida Grand Opera. *The Summer in Gossensass* was produced in

New York in 1998, and the following year a season-long retrospective of Fornés's work was produced by the Signature Theater Company in New York. In 2000, *Letters from Cuba*, written and directed by Fornés, premiered in New York. Based on the more than 200 letters she received over 30 years from her older brother Rafael, who remained in Cuba, it is the first play in which she deals directly with her Cuban heritage. A young dancer serves as Fornés's alter ego, living in a spare New York apartment and receiving letter after letter from her brother in Cuba. The set depicts a starlit Havana rooftop, emblematic of the place beloved by both siblings. Onstage, their lives proceed in parallel, connected spiritually by their letters but forever spatially disconnected. Fornés received an Obie Special Citation for the play.

Throughout her career, Fornés's work has defied classification. Although many of her plays, especially *Fefu and Her Friends*, *Eyes on the Harem*, and *Mud*, deal with feminist themes, Fornés avoids pronouncements and obvious messages, preferring instead to let the characters reveal themselves by their words, slowly and intimately. Many of her plays, while ostensibly protesting U.S. involvement in Vietnam, or satirizing problems of gender, poverty, and society, reveal emotional complexity as well as a lyrical romanticism. She has often combined comedy, song, and dance with serious drama. The exuberance of the music, humor, and playfulness in Fornés's plays is balanced by the quiet tableaux of her staging, which suggests her visual artist's sensitivity to composition. While her work is often called realistic, it can also be surreal and absurd, using discontinuities of language, of time, and of space. In staging her plays, Fornés aims to let spectators see the characters and spaces free from outside impressions and preconceived opinions. She seeks to involve the audience both emotionally in the dramatic situations and as participants in the theatrical spectacles. Many of her plays are simply successions of short episodes, with seemingly pointless dialogue, interruptions, and silences. As Fornés's characters arrange and rearrange their thoughts, emotions, and perceptions, so too her audiences must revise their understandings of the plays' complex unpredictability.

---

# Fefu and Her Friends

*Author's Note:* Fefu is pronounced Feh-foo.

---

New England, Spring 1935.

*Part I: Noon. The living room. The entire audience watches from the main auditorium.*

*Part II: Afternoon. The lawn, the study, the bedroom, the kitchen. The audience is divided into four groups. Each group is led to the spaces. These scenes are performed simultaneously. When the scenes are completed the audience moves to the next space and the scenes are performed again. This is repeated four times until each group has seen all four scenes. Then the audience is led back to the main auditorium.*

*Part III: Evening. The living room. The entire audience watches from the main auditorium.*

## Part I

[*The living room of a country house in New England. The décor is a tasteful mixture of styles. To the right is the foyer and the main door. To the left, French doors leading to a terrace, the lawn and a pond. At the rear, there are stairs that lead to the upper floor, the entrance to the kitchen, and the entrance to other rooms on the ground floor. A couch faces the audience. There is a coffee table, two chairs on each side of the table. Upstage right there is a piano. Against the right wall there is an open liquor cabinet. Besides bottles of liquor there are glasses, an ice bucket, and a seltzer bottle. A double barrel shotgun leans on the wall near the French doors. On the table there is a dish with chocolates. On the couch there is a throw.* FEFU *stands on the landing.* CINDY *lies on the couch.* CHRISTINA *sits on the chair to the right.*]

FEFU: My husband married me to have a constant reminder of how loathsome women are.
CINDY: What?
FEFU: Yup.
CINDY: That's just awful.
FEFU: No, it isn't.
CINDY: It isn't awful?
FEFU: No.
CINDY: I don't think anyone would marry for that reason.
FEFU: He did.
CINDY: Did he say so?
FEFU: He tells me constantly.
CINDY: Oh, dear.
FEFU: I don't mind. I laugh when he tells me.
CINDY: You laugh?
FEFU: I do.
CINDY: How can you?
FEFU: It's funny.—And it's true. That's why I laugh.
CINDY: What is true?
FEFU: That women are loathsome.
CINDY: . . . Fefu!
FEFU: That shocks you.
CINDY: It does. I don't feel loathsome.
FEFU: I don't mean that you are loathsome.
CINDY: You don't mean that I'm loathsome.
FEFU: No . . . It's something to think about. It's a thought.
CINDY: It's a hideous thought.
FEFU: I take it all back.
CINDY: Isn't she incredible?
FEFU: Cindy, I'm not talking about anyone in particular. It's something to think about.
CINDY: No one in particular, just women.
FEFU: Yes.
CINDY: In that case I am relieved. I thought you were referring to us.
FEFU: [*Affectionately.*] You are being stupid.

CINDY: Stupid and loathsome. [*To* CHRISTINA.] Have you ever heard anything so outrageous.

CHRISTINA: I am speechless.

FEFU: Why are you speechless?

CHRISTINA: I think you are outrageous.

FEFU: Don't be offended. I don't take enough care to be tactful. I know I don't. But don't be offended. Cindy is not offended. She pretends to be, but she isn't really. She understands what I mean.

CINDY: I do not.

FEFU: Yes, you do.—I like exciting ideas. They give me energy.

CHRISTINA: And how is women being loathsome an exciting idea?

FEFU: [*With mischief.*] It revolts me.

CHRISTINA: You find revulsion exciting?

FEFU: Don't you?

CHRISTINA: No.

FEFU: I do. It's something to grapple with.—What do you do with revulsion?

CHRISTINA: I avoid anything that's revolting to me.

FEFU: Hmmm. [*To* CINDY.] You too?

CINDY: Yes.

FEFU: Hmm. Have you ever turned a stone over in damp soil?

CHRISTINA: Ahm.

FEFU: And when you turn it there are worms crawling on it?

CHRISTINA: Ahm.

FEFU: And it's damp and full of fungus?

CHRISTINA: Ahm.

FEFU: Were you revolted?

CHRISTINA: Yes.

FEFU: Were you fascinated?

CHRISTINA: I was.

FEFU: There you have it! You too are fascinated with revulsion.

CHRISTINA: Hmm.

FEFU: You see, that which is exposed to the exterior . . . is smooth and dry and clean. That which is not . . . underneath, is slimy and filled with fungus and crawling with worms. It is another life that is parallel to the one we manifest. It's there. The way worms are underneath the stone. If you don't recognize it . . . [*Whispering.*] it eats you. That is my opinion. Well, who is ready for lunch?

CINDY: I'll have some fried worms with lots of pepper.

FEFU: [*To* CHRISTINA.] You?

CHRISTINA: I'll have mine in a sandwich with mayonnaise.

FEFU: And to drink?

CHRISTINA: Just some dirty dishwater in a tall glass with ice.
       [FEFU *looks at* CINDY.]

CINDY: That sounds fine.

FEFU: I'll go dig them up. [FEFU *walks to the French doors. Beckoning* CHRISTINA.] Pst! [FEFU *gets the gun as* CHRISTINA *goes to the French doors.*] You haven't met Phillip. Have you?

CHRISTINA: No.

FEFU: That's him.

CHRISTINA: Which one?

FEFU: [*Aims and shoots.*] That one!

> [CHRISTINA *and* CINDY *scream.* FEFU *smiles proudly. She blows on the mouth of the barrel. She puts down the gun and looks out again.*]

CINDY: Christ, Fefu.

FEFU: There he goes. He's up. It's a game we play. I shoot and he falls. Whenever he hears the blast he falls. No matter where he is, he falls. One time he fell in a puddle of mud and his clothes were a mess. [*She looks out.*] It's not too bad. He's just dusting off some stuff. [*She waves to Phillip and starts to go upstairs.*] He's all right. Look.

CINDY: A drink?

CHRISTINA: Yes.

> [CINDY *goes to the liquor cabinet.*]

CINDY: What would you like?

CHRISTINA: Bourbon and soda . . . [CINDY *puts ice and bourbon in a glass. As she starts to squirt the soda . . .* ] lots of soda. Just soda. [CINDY *starts with a fresh glass. She starts to squirt soda just as* CHRISTINA *speaks.*] Wait. [CINDY *stops squirting, but not soon enough.*] I'll have an ice cube with a few drops of bourbon. [CINDY *starts with a fresh glass.*]

CINDY: One or two ice cubes?

CHRISTINA: One. Something to suck on.

CINDY: She's unique. There's no one like her.

CHRISTINA: Thank God.

> [CINDY *gives the drink to* CHRISTINA.]

CINDY: But she is lovely you know. She really is.

CHRISTINA: She's crazy.

CINDY: A little. She has a strange marriage.

CHRISTINA: Strange? It's revolting.—What is he like?

CINDY: He's crazy too. They drive each other crazy. They are not crazy really. They drive each other crazy.

CHRISTINA: Why do they stay together?

CINDY: They love each other.

CHRISTINA: Love?

CINDY: It's love.

CHRISTINA: Who are the other two men?

CINDY: Fefu's younger brother, John. And the gardener. His name is Tom.—The gun is not loaded.

CHRISTINA: How do you know?

CINDY: It's not. Why should it be loaded?

CHRISTINA: It seemed to be loaded a moment ago.

CINDY: That was just a blank.

CHRISTINA: It sounded like a cannon shot.

CINDY: That was just gun powder. There's no bullet in a blank.

CHRISTINA: The blast alone could kill you. One can die of fright, you know.

CINDY: True.

CHRISTINA: My heart is still beating.

CINDY: That's just fright. You're being a scaredy cat.

CHRISTINA: Of course it's just fright. It's fright.

CINDY: I mean, you were just scared. You didn't get hurt.

CHRISTINA: Just scared. I guess I was lucky I didn't get shot.

CINDY: Fefu won't shoot you. She only shoots Phillip.

CHRISTINA: That's nice of her. Put the gun away, I don't like looking at it.

FEFU: [As she appears on the landing.] I just fixed the toilet in your bathroom.

CINDY: You did?

FEFU: I did. The water stopper didn't work. It drained. I adjusted it. I'm waiting for the tank to fill up. Make sure it all works.

CHRISTINA: You do your own plumbing?

FEFU: I just had to bend the metal that supports the rubber stopper so it falls right over the hole. What happened was it fell to the side so the water wouldn't stop running into the bowl. [FEFU sits near CINDY.] He scared me this time, you know. He looked like he was really hurt.

CINDY: I thought the guns were not loaded.

FEFU: I'm never sure.

CHRISTINA: What?

CINDY: Fefu, what do you mean?

FEFU: He told me one day he'll put real bullets in the guns. He likes to make me nervous. [There is a moment's silence.] I have upset you . . . I don't mean to upset you. That's the way we are with each other. We always go to extremes but it's not anything to be upset about.

CHRISTINA: You scare me.

FEFU: That's all right. I scare myself too, sometimes. But there's nothing wrong with being scared . . . it makes you stronger.—It does me.—He won't put real bullets in the guns.—It suits our relationship . . . the game, I mean. If I didn't shoot him with blanks, I might shoot him for real. Do you see the sense of it?

CHRISTINA: I think you're crazy.

FEFU: I'm not. I'm sane.

CHRISTINA: [Gently.] You're very stupid.

FEFU: I'm not. I'm very bright.

CHRISTINA: [Gently.] You depress me.

FEFU: Don't be depressed. Laugh at me if you don't agree with me. Say I'm ridiculous. I know I'm ridiculous. Come on, laugh. I hate to think I'm depressing to you.

CHRISTINA: All right. I'll laugh.

FEFU: I'll make you a drink.

CHRISTINA: No, I'm just sucking on the ice.

FEFU: Don't you feel well?

CHRISTINA: I'm all right.

FEFU: What are you drinking?

CHRISTINA: Bourbon.

FEFU: [Getting CHRISTINA's glass and going to the liquor cabinet.] Would you like some more? I'll get you some.

CHRISTINA: Just a drop.

FEFU: [With great care pours a single drop of bourbon on the ice cube.] Like that?

CHRISTINA: Yes, thank you.

FEFU: [Gives CHRISTINA the drink and watches her put the cube to her lips.] That's the cutest thing I've ever seen. It's cold. [CHRISTINA nods.]

You need a stick in the ice, like a popsicle stick. You hold the stick and your fingers won't get cold. I have some sticks. I'll do some for you.

CHRISTINA: Don't trouble yourself.

FEFU: It won't be any trouble. You might want some later.—I'm strange, Christina. But I am fortunate in that I don't mind being strange. It's hard on others sometimes. But not that hard. Is it, Cindy? Those who love me, love me precisely because I am the way I am. [To CINDY.] Isn't that so? [CINDY smiles and nods.]

CINDY: I would love you even if you weren't the way you are.

FEFU: You wouldn't know it was me if I weren't the way I am.

CINDY: I would still know it was you underneath.

FEFU: [To CHRISTINA.] You see?—There are some good things about me.— I'm never angry, for example.

CHRISTINA: But you make everyone else angry.

[FEFU thinks a moment.]

FEFU: No.

CHRISTINA: You've made me furious.

FEFU: I know. And I might make you angry again. Still I would like it if you liked me.—You think it's unlikely.

CHRISTINA: I don't know.

FEFU: . . . We'll see. [FEFU goes to the doors. She stands there briefly and speaks reflectively.] I still like men better than women.—I envy them. I like being like a man. Thinking like a man. Feeling like a man.—They are well together. Women are not. Look at them. They are checking the new grass mower. . . . Out in the fresh air and the sun, while we sit here in the dark. . . . Men have natural strength. Women have to find their strength, and when they do find it, it comes forth with bitterness and it's erratic. . . . Women are restless with each other. They are like live wires . . . either chattering to keep themselves from making contact, or else, if they don't chatter, they avert their eyes . . . like Orpheus[1] . . . as if a god once said "and if they shall recognize each other, the world will be blown apart." They are always eager for the men to arrive. When they do, they can put themselves at rest, tranquilized and in a mild stupor. With the men they feel safe. The danger is gone. That's the closest they can be to feeling wholesome. Men are muscle that cover the raw nerve. They are the insulators. The danger is gone, but the price is the mind and the spirit. . . . High price.—I've never understood it. Why?—What is feared?—Hmm. Well . . . —Do you know? Perhaps the heavens would fall.—Have I offended you again?

CHRISTINA: No. I too have wished for that trust men have for each other. The faith the world puts in them and they in turn put in the world. I know I don't have it.

FEFU: Hmm. Well, I have to see how my toilet is doing. [FEFU goes to the landing and exits. She puts her head out. She smiles.] Plumbing is more important than you think.

[CHRISTINA falls off her chair in a mock faint. CINDY goes to her.]

---

1. In ancient Greek mythology, the poet and musician Orpheus ventured into Hades, the Underworld, to bring his wife, Eurydice, back from the dead. Eurydice could return to life with him as long as, on their way back from Hades, he did not turn around to look at her. When he did turn around, he lost her forever.

CINDY:   What do you think?

CHRISTINA:   Think? I hurt. I'm all shreds inside.

CINDY:   Anything I can do?

CHRISTINA:   Sing.

> [CINDY *sings "Winter Wonderland."* CHRISTINA *harmonizes. There is the sound of a horn.* FEFU *enters.*]

FEFU:   It's Julia. [*To* CHRISTINA, *who is on the floor.*] Are you all right?

CHRISTINA:   Yes. [FEFU *exits through the foyer.*] Darn it! [CHRISTINA *starts to stand.*]

FEFU:   [*Off-stage.*]   Julia . . . let me help you.

JULIA:   I can manage. I'm much stronger now.

FEFU:   There you go.

JULIA:   You have my bag.

FEFU:   Yes.

> [JULIA *and* FEFU *enter.* JULIA *is in a wheelchair.*]

JULIA:   Hello Cindy.

CINDY:   Hello darling. How are you?

JULIA:   I'm very well now. I'm driving now. You must see my car. It's very clever the way they worked it all out. You might want to drive it. It's not hard at all. [*Turning to* CHRISTINA.] Christina.

CHRISTINA:   Hello Julia.

JULIA:   I'm glad to see you.

FEFU:   I'll take this to your room. You're down here, if you want to wash up.

> [FEFU *exits through the upstage exit.* JULIA *follows her.*]

CINDY:   I can't get used to it.

CHRISTINA:   She's better. Isn't she?

CINDY:   Not really.

CHRISTINA:   Was she actually hit by the bullet?

CINDY:   No . . . I was with her.

CHRISTINA:   I know.

CINDY:   I thought the bullet hit her, but it didn't.—How do you know if a person is hit by a bullet?

CHRISTINA:   Cindy . . . there's a wound and . . . there's a bullet.

CINDY:   Well, the hunter aimed . . . at the deer. He shot.

CHRISTINA:   He?

CINDY:   Yes.

CHRISTINA:   [*Pointing in the direction of* FEFU.]   It wasn't . . . ?

CINDY:   Fefu? . . . No. She wasn't even there. She used to hunt but she doesn't hunt any more. She loves animals.

CHRISTINA:   Go on.

CINDY:   He shot. Julia and the deer fell. The deer was dead . . . dying. Julia was unconscious. She had convulsions . . . like the deer. He died and she didn't. I screamed for help and the hunter came and examined Julia. He said, "She is not hurt." Julia's forehead was bleeding. He said, "It is a surface wound. I didn't hurt her." I know it wasn't he who hurt her. It was someone else. He went for help and Julia started talking. She was delirious.—Apparently there was a spinal nerve injury. She hit her head and she suffered a concussion. She blanks out and that is caused by the blow on the head. It's a scar in the brain. It's called the petit mal.

> [FEFU *enters.*]

CHRISTINA:  What was it she said?

CINDY:  Hmm? . . .

CHRISTINA:  When she was delirious.

CINDY:  When she was delirious? That she was persecuted.—That they tortured her. . . . That they had tried her and that the shot was her execution. That she recanted because she wanted to live. . . . That if she talked about it . . . to anyone . . . she would be tortured further and killed. And I have not mentioned this before because . . . I fear for her.

CHRISTINA:  It doesn't make any sense, Cindy.

CINDY:  It makes sense to me. You heard? [FEFU *goes to* CINDY *and holds her.*]

FEFU:  Who hurt her?

CINDY:  I don't know.

FEFU:  [*To* CHRISTINA.]  Did you know her?

CHRISTINA:  I met her once years ago.

FEFU:  You remember her then as she was. . . . She was afraid of nothing. . . . Have you ever met anyone like that? . . . She knew so much. She was so young and yet she knew so much. . . . How did she learn all that? . . . [*To* CINDY.] Did you ever wonder? Well, I still haven't checked my toilet. Can you believe that. I still haven't checked it. [FEFU *goes upstairs.*]

CHRISTINA:  How long ago was the accident?

CINDY:  A year . . . a little over a year.

CHRISTINA:  Is she in pain?

CINDY:  I don't think so.

CHRISTINA:  We are made of putty. Aren't we?
    [*There is the sound of a car. Car doors opening and closing. A house window opening.*]

FEFU:  [*Off-stage.*]  Emma! What is that you're wearing. You look marvelous.

EMMA:  [*Off-stage.*]  I got it in Turkey.

FEFU:  Hi Paula, Sue.

PAULA:  Hi.

SUE:  Hi.
    [CINDY *goes out to greet them.* JULIA *enters. She wheels herself to the downstage area.*]

FEFU:  I'll be right down! Hey, my toilet works.

EMMA:  Stephany. Mine does too.

FEFU:  Don't be funny.

EMMA:  Come down.
    [FEFU *enters as* EMMA, SUE, *and* PAULA *enter.* EMMA *and* FEFU *embrace.*]

FEFU:  How are you?

EMMA:  Good . . . good . . . good . . . [*Still embracing* FEFU, EMMA *sees* JULIA.] Julia! [*She runs to* JULIA *and sits on her lap.*]

FEFU:  Emma!

JULIA:  It's all right.

EMMA:  Take me for a ride. [JULIA *wheels the chair in a circle.* EMMA *waves as they ride.*] Hi, Cindy, Paula, Sue, Fefu.

JULIA:  Do you know Christina?

EMMA:   How do you do.

CHRISTINA:   How do you do.

EMMA: [*Pointing.*]   Sue . . . Paula . . .

SUE:   Hello.

PAULA:   Hello.

CHRISTINA:   Hello.

PAULA: [*To* FEFU.]   I liked your talk at Flossie Crit.

FEFU:   Oh god, don't remind me. I thought I was awful. Come, I'll show you your rooms. [*She starts to go up.*]

PAULA:   I thought you weren't. I found it very stimulating.

EMMA:   When was that? . . . What was it on?

FEFU:   Aviation.

PAULA:   It wasn't on aviation. It was on Voltairine de Cleyre.[2]

JULIA:   I wish I had known.

FEFU:   It wasn't important.

JULIA:   I would have gone, Fefu.

FEFU:   Really, it wasn't worth the trouble.

EMMA:   Now you'll have to tell Julia and me all about Voltairine de Cleyre.

FEFU:   You know all about Voltairine de Cleyre.

EMMA:   I don't.

FEFU:   I'll tell you at lunch.

EMMA:   I had lunch.

JULIA:   You can sit and listen while we eat.

EMMA:   I will. When do we start our meeting?

FEFU:   After lunch. We'll have something to eat and then we'll have our meeting. Who's ready for lunch?

[*The following lines are said almost simultaneously.*]

CINDY:   I am.

JULIA:   I'm not really hungry.

CHRISTINA:   I could eat now.

PAULA:   I'm ready.

SUE:   I'd rather wait.

EMMA:   I'll have coffee.

FEFU:   . . . Well . . . we'll take a vote later.

CINDY:   What are we doing exactly?

FEFU:   About lunch?

CINDY:   That too, but I meant the agenda.

SUE:   Well, I thought we should first discuss what each of us is going to talk about, so we don't duplicate what someone else is saying, and then we have a review of it, a sort of rehearsal, so we know in what order we should speak and how long it's going to take.

EMMA:   We should do a rehearsal in costume. What color should each wear. It matters. Do you know what you're wearing?

PAULA:   I haven't thought about it. What color should I wear?

EMMA:   Red.

PAULA:   Red!

EMMA:   Cherry red or white.

2. American anarchist activist (1866–1912).

SUE:  And I?

EMMA:  Dark green.

CINDY:  The treasurer should wear green.

EMMA:  It suits her too.

SUE:  And then we'll speak in order of color.

EMMA:  Right. Who else wants to know? [CINDY *and* JULIA *raise their hands. To* CINDY.] For you lavender. [*To* JULIA.] Purpurra. [FEFU *raises her hand.*] For you, all the gold in Persia.

FEFU:  There is no gold in Persia.

EMMA:  In Peru. I brought my costume. I'll put it on later.

FEFU:  You're not in costume?

EMMA:  No. This is just a dress. My costume is . . . dramatic. I won't tell you any more about it. You'll see it.

SUE:  I had no idea we were going to do theatre.

EMMA:  Life is theatre. Theatre is life. If we're showing what life is, can be, we must do theatre.

SUE:  Will I have to act?

EMMA:  It's not acting. It's being. It's springing forth with the powers of the spirit. It's breathing.

JULIA:  I'll do a dance.

EMMA:  I'll stage a dance for you.

JULIA:  Sitting?

EMMA:  On a settee.

JULIA:  I'm game.

EMMA:  [*Takes a deep breath and walks through the French doors.*]  Phillip! What are you doing?—Hello.—Hello, John.—What? I'm staging a dance for Julia!

FEFU:  We'll never see her again.—Come.
[FEFU, PAULA, *and* SUE *go upstairs.* JULIA *goes to the gun, takes it and smells the mouth of the barrel. She looks at* CINDY.]

CINDY:  It's a blank.
[JULIA *takes the remaining slug out of the gun. She lets it fall on the floor.*]

JULIA:  She's hurting herself. [JULIA *looks blank and is motionless.* CINDY *picks up the slug. She notices* JULIA's *condition.*]

CINDY:  Julia. [*To* CHRISTINA.] She's absent.

CHRISTINA:  What do we do?

CINDY:  Nothing, she'll be all right in a moment. [*She takes the gun from* JULIA. JULIA *comes to.*]

JULIA:  It's a blank . . .

CINDY:  It is.

JULIA:  She's hurting herself. [JULIA *lets out a strange whimper. She goes to the coffee table, takes a piece of chocolate, puts it in her mouth and goes toward her room. After she crosses the threshold, she stops.*] I must lie down a while.

CINDY:  Call me if you need anything.

JULIA:  I will. [*She exits.* CINDY *tries to put the slug in the rifle. There is the sound of a car, a car door opening, closing.*]

CINDY:  Do you know how to do this?

CHRISTINA:  Of course not.

[CINDY *succeeds in putting the slug in the gun.* CECILIA *stands in the threshold of the foyer.*]

CECILIA:  I am Cecilia Johnson. Do I have the right place?

CINDY:  Yes.

[CINDY *locks the gun. Lights fade all around Cecilia. Only her head is lit. The light fades.*]

## Part II

### On the Lawn

[*There is a bench or a tree stump.* FEFU *and* EMMA *bring boxes of potatoes, carrots, beets, winter squash, and other vegetables from a root cellar and put them in a small wagon.* FEFU *wears a hat and gardening gloves.*]

EMMA: [*Re-enters carrying a box as* FEFU *exits.*]  Do you think about genitals all the time?

FEFU:  Genitals? No, I don't think about genitals all the time.

EMMA: [*Starting to exit.*]  I do, and it drives me crazy. Each person I see in the street, anywhere at all . . . I keep thinking of their genitals, what they look like, what position they are in. I think it's odd that everyone has them. Don't you?

FEFU: [*Crossing Emma.*]  No, I think it'd be odder if they didn't have them.
  [EMMA *laughs.* FEFU *re-enters.*]

EMMA:  I mean, people act as if they don't have genitals.

FEFU:  How do people with genitals act?

EMMA:  I mean, how can business men and women stand in a room and discuss business without even one reference to their genitals. I mean everybody has them. They just pretend they don't.

FEFU:  I see. [*Shifting her glance from left to right with a fiendish look.*] You mean they should do this all the time.
  [EMMA *laughs.*]

EMMA:  No, I don't mean that. Think of it. Don't you think I'm right?

FEFU:  Yes, I think you're right. [FEFU *sits.*] Oh, Emma, EmmaEmmaEmma.

EMMA:  That's m'name.—Well, you see, it's generally believed that you go to heaven if you are good. If you are bad you go to hell. That is correct. However, in heaven they don't judge goodness the way we think. They don't. They have a divine registry of sexual performance. In that registry they mark down every little sexual activity in your life. If your faith is not entirely in it, if you just perform as an obligation and you don't feel the most profound devotion, if your spirit, your heart, and your flesh is not religiously delivered to it, you are condemned. They put you down in the black list and you don't go to heaven. Heaven is populated with divine lovers. And in hell live the duds.

FEFU:  That's probably true.

EMMA:  I knew you'd see it that way.

FEFU:  Oh, I do. I do. You see, on earth we are judged by public acts, and sex is a private act. The partner cannot be said to be the public, since both partners are engaged. So naturally, it stands to reason that it's angels who judge our sexual life.

EMMA: Naturally.
[*Pause.*]
FEFU: You always bring joy to me.
EMMA: Thank you.
FEFU: I thank you. [FEFU *becomes distressed. She sits.*] I am in constant pain. I don't want to give in to it. If I do I am afraid I will never recover. . . . It's not physical, and it's not sorrow. It's very strange, Emma, I can't describe it, and it's very frightening. . . . It is as if normally there is a lubricant . . . not in the body . . . a spiritual lubricant . . . it's hard to describe . . . and without it, life is a nightmare, and everything is distorted.—A black cat started coming to my kitchen. He's awfully mangled and big. He is missing an eye and his skin is diseased. At first I was repelled by him, but then, I thought, this is a monster that has been sent to me and I must feed him. And I fed him. One day he came and shat all over my kitchen. Foul diarrhea. He still comes and I still feed him.—I am afraid of him. [EMMA *kisses* FEFU.] How about a little lemonade?
EMMA: Yes.
FEFU: How about a game of croquet?
EMMA: Fine.
[FEFU *exits.* EMMA *improvises an effigy of* FEFU. *She puts* FEFU's *hat and gloves on it.*]

> Not from the stars do I my judgment pluck.
> And yet methinks I have astronomy;
> But not to tell of good or evil luck,
> Of plagues, of dearths, or seasons' quality;
> Nor can I fortune to brief minutes tell,
> Pointing to each his thunder, rain, and wind,
> Or say with princes if it shall go well
> By oft predict that I in heaven find.
> But from thine eyes my knowledge I derive.
> And, constant stars, in them I read such art
> As truth and beauty shall together thrive
> If from thyself to store thou wouldst convert:
> > Or else of thee this I prognosticate,
> > Thy end is truth's and beauty's doom and date.

[*If* FEFU's *entrance is delayed,* EMMA *will sing a popular song of the period.* FEFU *re-enters with a pitcher and two glasses.*]

### In the Study

[*There are books on the walls, a desk, Victorian chairs, a rug on the floor.* CHRISTINA *sits behind the desk. She reads a French text book. She mumbles French sentences.* CINDY *sits to the left of the desk with her feet up on a chair. She looks at a magazine. A few moments pass.*]

CHRISTINA: [*Practicing.*] Etes-vous externe ou demi-pensionnaire? La cuisine de votre cantine est-elle bonne, passable ou mauvaise? [*She continues reading almost inaudibly. A moment passes.*]
CINDY: [*Reading.*] A lady in Africa divorced her husband because he was a cheetah.

CHRISTINA: Oh, dear. [*They laugh. They go back to their reading. A moment passes.*] Est-ce que votre professeur interroger souvant les élèves? [*They go back to their reading. A moment passes.*]

CINDY: I suppose . . . when a person is swept off their feet . . . the feet remain and the person goes off . . . with the broom.

CHRISTINA: No . . . when a person is swept off their feet . . . there is no broom.

CINDY: What does the sweeping?

CHRISTINA: An emotion . . . a feeling.

CINDY: Then emotions have bristles?

CHRISTINA: Yes.

CINDY: Now I understand. Do the feet remain?

CHRISTINA: No, the feet fly also . . . but separate from the body. At the end of the leap, just before the landing, they join the ankles and one is complete again.

CINDY: Oh, that sounds nice.

CHRISTINA: It is. Being swept off your feet is nice. Anything else?

CINDY: Not for now. [*They go back to their reading. A moment passes.*] Are you having a good time?

CHRISTINA: Yes, I'm very glad I came.

CINDY: Do you like everybody?

CHRISTINA: Yes.

CINDY: Do you like Fefu?

CHRISTINA: I do . . . She confuses me a little.—I try to be honest . . . and I wonder if she is . . . I don't mean that she doesn't tell the truth. I know she does. I mean a kind of integrity. I know she has integrity too. . . . But I don't know if she's careful with life . . . something bigger than the self . . . I suppose I don't mean with life but more with convention. I think she is an adventurer in a way. Her mind is adventurous. I don't know if there is dishonesty in that. But in adventure there is taking chances and risks, and then one has to, somehow, have less regard or respect for things as they are. That is, regard for a kind of convention, I suppose. I am probably ultimately a conformist, I think. And I suppose I do hold back for fear of being disrespectful or destroying something— and I admire those who are not. But I also feel they are dangerous to me. I don't think they are dangerous to the world; they are more useful than I am, more important, but I feel some of my life is endangered by their way of thinking. Do you understand?

CINDY: Yes, I do.

CHRISTINA: I guess I am proud and I don't like thinking that I am thoughtful of things that have no value.—I like her.

CINDY: I had a terrible dream last night.

CHRISTINA: What was it?

CINDY: I was at a dance. And there was a young doctor I had seen in connection with my health. We all danced in a circle and he identified himself and said that he had spoken to Mike about me, but that it was all right, that he had put it so that it was all right. I was puzzled as to why Mike would mind and why he had spoken to him. Then, suddenly everybody sat down on the floor and pretended they were having singing lessons and one person was practicing Italian. The singing professor was being tested by two secret policemen. They were having him correct the voice of someone they had brought. He apparently didn't know how to do it. Then, one of the policemen put his hands on his vocal cords and kicked him out the door. Then he grabbed me and felt my throat from behind with his thumbs while he rubbed my nipples with his pinkies. Then, he pushed me out the door. Then, the young doctor started cursing me. His mouth moved like the mouth of a horse. I was on an upper level with a railing and I said to him, "Stop and listen to me." I said it so strongly that he stopped. Everybody turned to me in admiration because I had made him stop. Then, I said to him, "Restrain yourself." I wanted to say respect me. I wasn't sure whether the words coming out of my mouth were what I wanted to say. I turned to ask my sister. The young man was bending over and trembling in mad rage. Another man told me to run before the young man tried to kill me. Meg and I ran downstairs. She asked me if I wanted to go to her place. We grabbed a taxi, but before the taxi got enough speed he came out and ran to the taxi and was on the verge of opening the door when I woke up.

> [*The door opens.* FEFU *looks in. Her entrance may interrupt* CINDY's *speech at any point according to how long it takes her to reach the kitchen.*]

FEFU: Who's for a game of croquet?

CINDY: In a little while.

FEFU: See you outside.

CHRISTINA: That was quite a dream.

CINDY: What do you think it means?

CHRISTINA: I think it means you should go to a different doctor.

CINDY: He's not my doctor. I never saw him before.

CHRISTINA: Well good. I'm sure he's not a good doctor.

> [*At the end of the fourth repeat, when* FEFU *invites them for croquet,* CINDY *says, "Oh let's play croquet" and they follow* FEFU.]

### In the Bedroom

[*A plain unpainted room. Perhaps a room that was used for storage and was set up as a sleeping place for* JULIA. *There is a mattress on the floor. To the right of the mattress there is a small table, to the left is* JULIA's *wheelchair. There is a sink on the wall. There are dry leaves on the floor although the time is not fall. The sheets are linen.* JULIA *lies in bed covered to her shoulders. She wears a white hospital gown. Julia hallucinates. However, her behavior should not be the usual behavior attributed to a mad person. It should be rather still and luminous. There will be aspects of her hallucination that frighten her, but hallucinating itself does not.*]

JULIA: They clubbed me. They broke my head. They broke my will. They broke my hands. They tore my eyes out. They took my voice away. They didn't do anything to my heart because I didn't bring my heart with me. They clubbed me again, but my head did not fall off in pieces. That was because they were so good and they felt sorry for me. The judges. You didn't know the judges?—I was good and quiet. I never dropped my smile. I smiled to everyone. If I stopped smiling I would get clubbed

because they love me. They say they love me. I go along with that because if I don't . . .

[*With her finger she indicates her throat being cut and makes the
sound that usually accompanies that gesture.*]

I told them the stinking parts of the body are the important ones: the
genitals, the anus, the mouth, the armpit. All important parts except the
armpits. And who knows, maybe the armpits are important too. That's
what I said. [*Her voice becomes gravelly and tight in imitation of the
judges.*] He said that all those parts must be kept clean and put away.
He said that women's entrails are heavier than anything on earth and
to see a woman running creates a disparate and incongruous image
in the mind. It's anti-aesthetic. Therefore women should not run. Instead
they should strike positions that take into account the weight of their
entrails. Only if they do, can they be aesthetic. He said, for example,
Goya's Maja. He said Rubens' women are not aesthetic.[3] Flesh. He said
that a woman's bottom should be in a cushion, otherwise it's revolting.
He said there are exceptions. Ballet dancers are exceptions. They can
run and lift their legs because they have no entrails. Isadora Duncan[4]
had entrails, that's why she should not have danced. But she danced
and for this reason became crazy. [*Her voice is back to normal.*] She
wasn't crazy.

[*She moves her hand as if guarding from a blow.*]

She was. He said that I had to be punished because I was getting too
smart. I'm not smart. I never was. Neither is Fefu smart. They are after
her too. Well, she's still walking!

[*She guards from a blow. Her eyes close.*]

Wait! I'll say my prayers. I'm saying it.

[*She mumbles. She opens her eyes with caution.*]

You don't think I'm going to argue with them, do you? I repented. I told
them exactly what they wanted to hear. They killed me. I was dead. The
bullet didn't hit me. It hit the deer. But I died. He didn't. Then I repented and the deer died and I lived. [*With a gravelly voice.*] They said,
"Live but crippled. And if you tell . . ."

[*She repeats the throat cutting gesture.*]

Why do you have to kill Fefu, for she's only a joker? [*With a gravelly
voice.*] "Not kill, cure. Cure her." Will it hurt?

[*She whimpers.*]

Oh, dear, dear, my dear, they want your light. Your light my dear. Your
precious light. Oh dear, my dear.

[*Her head moves as if slapped.*]

Not cry. I'll say my prayer. I'll say it. Right now. Look.

[*She sits up as if pulled by an invisible force.*]

The human being is of the masculine gender. The human being is a
boy as a child and grown up he is a man. Everything on earth is for the
human being, which is man. To nourish him.—There are evil things

---

3. The Flemish painter Peter Paul Rubens (1577–
1640) is known for his portraits of fleshy women.
*Goya's Maja*: Among the most famous works of
the Spanish painter Francisco José de Goya y
Lucientes (1746–1828) are *La maja vestida* (Maja

Clothed) and *La maja desnuda* (Maja Nude), portraits of a reclining woman with her hands behind her head.
4. American dancer (1877–1927).

on earth, and noxious things. Evil and noxious things are on earth for man also. For him to fight with, and conquer and turn its evil into good. So that it too can nourish him.—There are Evil Plants, Evil Animals, Evil Minerals, and Women are Evil.—Woman is not a human being. She is: 1—A mystery. 2—Another species. 3—As yet undefined. 4—Unpredictable; therefore wicked and gentle and evil and good which is evil.—If a man commits an evil act, he must be pitied. The evil comes from outside him, through him and into the act. Woman generates the evil herself.—God gave man no other mate but woman. The oxen is good but it is not a mate for man. The sheep is good but it is not a mate for man. The mate for man is woman and that is the cross man must bear.—Man is not spiritually sexual, he therefore can enjoy sexuality. His sexuality is physical which means his spirit is pure. Women's spirit is sexual. That is why after coitus they dwell in nefarious feelings. Because that is their natural habitat. That is why it is difficult for them to return to the human world. Their sexual feelings remain with them till they die. And they take those feelings with them to the afterlife where they corrupt the heavens, and they are sent to hell where through suffering they may shed those feelings and return to earth as man.

[*Her head moves as if slapped.*]

Don't hit me. Didn't I just say my prayer?

[*A smaller slap.*]

I believe it.

[*She lies back.*]

They say when I believe the prayer I will forget the judges. And when I forget the judges I will believe the prayer. They say both happen at once. And all women have done it. Why can't I?

[SUE *enters with a bowl of soup on a tray.*]

SUE:   Julia, are you asleep?

[*Short pause.*]

JULIA:   No.

SUE:   I brought your soup.

JULIA:   Put it down. I'm getting up in a moment.

[SUE *puts the soup down.*]

SUE:   Do you want me to help you?

JULIA:   No, I can manage. Thank you, Sue.

[SUE *goes to the door.*]

SUE:   You're all right?

JULIA:   Yes.

SUE:   I'll see you later.

JULIA:   Thank you, Sue.

[SUE *exits.* JULIA *closes her eyes. As soon as each audience group leaves, the tray is removed, if possible through a back door.*]

### In the Kitchen

[*A fully equipped kitchen. There is a table and chairs and a high cutting table. On a counter next to the stove there is a tray with a soup dish and a spoon. There is also a ladle. On the cutting table there are two empty glasses.*

*Soup is heating on a burner. A kettle with water sits on an unlit burner. In the refrigerator there is an ice tray with wooden sticks in each cube. The sticks should rest on the edge of the tray forming two parallel rows, like a caterpillar lying on its back. In the refrigerator there are also two pitchers, one with wa-ter, one with lemonade. PAULA sits at the table. She is writing on a pad. SUE waits for the soup to heat.]*

PAULA: I have it all figured out.

SUE: What?

PAULA: A love affair lasts seven years and three months.

SUE: It does?

PAULA: [*Reading.*] 3 months of love. 1 year saying: It's all right. This is just a passing disturbance. 1 year trying to understand what's wrong. 2 years knowing the end had come. 1 year finding the way to end it. After the separation, 2 years trying to understand what happened. 7 years, 3 months. [*No longer reading.*] At any point the sequence might be inter-rupted by another love affair that has the same sequence. That is, it's not really interrupted, the new love affair relegates the first one to a second plane and both continue their sequence at the same time.
   [SUE *looks over* PAULA's *shoulder.*]

SUE: You really added it up.

PAULA: Sure.

SUE: What do you want to drink?

PAULA: Water. The old love affair may fade, so you are not aware the pro-cess goes on. A year later it may surface and you might find yourself figuring out what's wrong with the new one while trying to end the old one.

SUE: So how do you solve the problem?

PAULA: Celibacy?

SUE: [*Going to the refrigerator.*] Celibacy doesn't solve anything.

PAULA: That's true.

SUE: [*Taking out the ice tray with the sticks.*] What's this? [PAULA *shakes her head.*] Dessert. [PAULA *shrugs her shoulders.* SUE *takes an ice cube and places it against her forehead.*] For a headache. [*She takes another cube and moves her arms in a Judo style.*] Eskimo wrestling. [*She places one stick behind her ear.*] Brain cooler. That's when you're thinking too much. You could use one. [*She tries to put the ice cube behind* PAULA's *ear. They wrestle and laugh. She puts the stick in her own mouth. She takes it out to speak.*] This is when you want to keep chaste. No one will kiss you. [*She puts it back in to demonstrate. Then takes it out.*] That's good for celibacy. If you walk around with one of these in your mouth for seven years you can keep all your sequences straight. Finish one before you start the other. [*She puts the ice cube in the tray and looks at it.*] A frozen caterpillar. [*She puts the tray away.*]

PAULA: You're leaving that ice cube in there?

SUE: I'm clean. [*Looking at the soup.*] So what else do you have on love? [SUE *places a bowl and spoon on the table and sits as she waits for the soup to heat.*]

PAULA: Well, the break-up takes place in parts. The brain, the heart, the body, mutual things, shared things. The mind leaves but the heart is still there. The heart has left but the body wants to stay. The body leaves but the things are still at the apartment. You must come back. You move everything out of the apartment but the mind stays behind. Memory lingers in the place. Seven years later, perhaps seven years later, it doesn't matter any more. Perhaps it takes longer. Perhaps it never ends.

SUE: It depends.

PAULA: Yup. It depends.

SUE: [*Pouring soup in the bowl.*] Something's bothering you.

PAULA: No.

SUE: [*Taking the tray.*] I'm going to take this to Julia.

PAULA: Go ahead.

[*As* SUE *exits,* CECILIA *enters.*]

CECILIA: May I come in?

PAULA: Yes . . . Would you like something to eat?

CECILIA: No, I ate lunch.

PAULA: I didn't eat lunch. I wasn't very hungry.

CECILIA: I know.

PAULA: Would you like some coffee?

CECILIA: I'll have tea.

PAULA: I'll make some.

CECILIA: No, you sit. I'll make it. [CECILIA *looks for tea.*]

PAULA: Here it is. [*She gets the tea and gives it to* CECILIA.]

CECILIA: [*As she lights the burner.*] I've been meaning to call you.

PAULA: It doesn't matter. I know you're busy.

CECILIA: Still I would have called you but I really didn't find the time.

PAULA: Don't worry.

CECILIA: I wanted to see you again. I want to see you often.

PAULA: There's no hurry. Now we know we can see each other.

CECILIA: Yes, I'm glad we can.

PAULA: I have thought a great deal about my life since I saw you. I have questioned my life. I can't help doing that. It's been many years and I wondered how you see me now.

CECILIA: You're the same.

PAULA: I felt small in your presence . . . I haven't done all that I could have. All I wanted to do. Our lives have gone in such different directions I cannot help but review what those years have been for me. I gave up, almost gave up. I have missed you in my life. . . . I became lazy. I lost the drive. You abandoned me and I kept going. But after a while I didn't know how to. I didn't know how to go on. I knew why when I was with you. To give you pleasure. So we could laugh together. So we could rejoice together. To bring beauty to the world. . . . Now we look at each other like strangers. We are guarded. I speak and you don't understand my words. I remember every day.

[FEFU *enters. She takes the lemonade pitcher from the refrigerator and two glasses from the top of the refrigerator.*]

FEFU: Emma and I are going to play croquet. You want to join us? . . . No. You're having a serious conversation.

PAULA: Very serious. [PAULA *smiles at* CECILIA *in a conciliatory manner.*] Too serious.

FEFU: [*As she exits.*] Come.

PAULA: I'm sorry. Let's go play croquet.—I'm not reproaching you.
CECILIA: [*Reaching for* PAULA's *hand.*] I know. I've missed you too.
    [*They exit. As soon as the audience leaves the props are reset.*]


# Part III

[*The living room. It is dusk. As the audience enters, two or three of the women are around the piano playing and singing Schubert's "Who Is Silvia."*[5] *They exit.* EMMA *enters, checks the lights in the room on her hand, looks around the room and goes upstairs. The rest enter through the rear.* CECILIA *enters speaking.*]

CECILIA: Well, we each have our own system of receiving information, placing it, responding to it. [*She sits in the center of the couch; the rest sit around her.*] That system can function with such a bias that it could take any situation and translate it into one formula. That is, I think, the main reason for stupidity or even madness, not being able to tell the difference between things.

SUE: Like?

CECILIA: Like . . . this person is screaming at me. He's a bully. I don't like being screamed at. Another person or the same person screams in a different situation. But you know you have done something that provokes him to scream. He has a good reason. They are two different things, the screaming of one and the screaming of the other. Often that distinction is not made. We cannot survive in a vacuum. We must be part of a community, perhaps 10, 100, 1000. It depends on how strong you are. But even the strongest will need a dozen, three, even one who sees, thinks, and feels as he does. The greater the need for that kind of reassurance, the greater the number that he needs to identify with. Some need to identify with the whole nation. Then, the greater the number the more limited the number of responses and thoughts. A common denominator must be reached. Thoughts, emotions that fit all, have to be limited to a small number. That is, I feel, the concern of the educator—to teach how to be sensitive to the differences in ourselves as well as outside ourselves, not to supervise the memorization of facts. [EMMA's *head appears in the doorway to the stairs.*] Otherwise the unusual in us will perish. As we grow we feel we are strange and fear any thought that is not shared with everyone.

JULIA: As I feel I am perishing. My hallucinations are madness, of course, but I wish I could be with others who hallucinate also. I would still know I am mad but I would not feel so isolated.—Hallucinations are real, you know. They are not like dreams. They are as real as all of you here. I have actually asked to be hospitalized so I could be with other nuts. But the doctors don't want to. They can't diagnose me. That makes me even more isolated. [*There is a moment's silence.*] You see, right now, it's an awful moment because you don't know what to say or

5. A song that is among the best-known works of the Austrian composer Franz Peter Schubert (1797–1828).

do. If I were with other people who hallucinate, they would say, "Oh yeah. Sure. It's awful. Those dummies, they don't see anything." [*The others begin to relax.*] It's not so bad, really. I can laugh at it. . . . Emma is ready. We should start. [*The others are hesitant.* JULIA *speaks to* FEFU.] Come on.

FEFU: Sure. [FEFU *begins to move the table. Others help move the table and enough furniture to clear a space in the center. They sit in a semicircle downstage on the floor facing upstage.* CECILIA *sits on a chair to the left of the semicircle.*] All right. I start. Right?

CINDY: Right.

[FEFU *goes to center and faces the others.* EMMA *sits on the steps. Only her head and legs are visible.*]

FEFU: I talk about the stifling conditions of primary school education, etc. . . . etc. . . . The project . . . I know what I'm going to say but I don't want to bore you with it. We all know it by heart. Blah blah blah blah. And so on and so on. And so on and so on. Then I introduce Emma . . . And now Miss Emma Blake. [*They applaud.* EMMA *shakes her head.*] What.

EMMA: Paula goes next.

FEFU: Does it matter?

EMMA: Of course it matters. Dra-ma-tics. It has to build. I'm in costume.

FEFU: Oh. And now, ladies and gentlemen, Miss Paula Cori will speak on Art as a Tool for Learning. And I tell them the work you have done at the Institute, community centers, essays, etc. Miss Paula Cori.

[*They applaud.* PAULA *goes to center.*]

PAULA: Ladies and gentlemen, I, like my fellow educator and colleague, Stephany Beckmann . . .

FEFU: I am not an educator.

PAULA: What are you?

FEFU: . . . a do gooder, a girl scout.

PAULA: Well, I, like my fellow girl scout Stephany Beckmann say blah blah blah blah, blah blah blah and I offer the jewels of my wisdom and experience, which I will write down and memorize, otherwise I would just stand there and stammer and go blank. And even after I memorize it I'm sure I will just stand there and stammer and go blank.

EMMA: I'll work with you on it.

PAULA: However, after our other colleague Miss Emma Blake works with me on it . . . [*In imitation of* EMMA *she brings her hands together and opens her arms as she moves her head back and speaks.*] My impulses will burst forth through a symphony of eloquence.

EMMA: Breathe . . . in . . . [PAULA *inhales slowly.*] And bow. [PAULA *bows. They applaud.*]

PAULA: [*Coming up from the bow.*] Oh, I liked that. [*She sits.*]

EMMA: Good . . .

[*They applaud.*]

FEFU: And now, ladies and gentlemen, the one and only, the incomparable, our precious, dear Emma Blake.

[EMMA *walks to center. She wears a robe which hangs from her arms to the floor.*]

EMMA: From the prologue to "The Science of Educational Dramatics" by Emma Sheridan Fry.[6] [*She takes a dramatic pose and starts. The whole speech is dramatized by interpretive gestures and movements that cover the stage area.*]

Environment knocks at the gateway of the senses. A rain of summons beats upon us day and night. . . . We do not answer. Everything around us shouts against our deafness, struggles with our unwillingness, batters our walls, flashes into our blindness, strives to sieve through us at every pore, begging, fighting, insisting. It shouts, "Where are you? Where are you?" But we are deaf. The signals do not reach us.

Society restricts us, school straight jackets us, civilization submerges us, privation wrings us, luxury feather-beds us. The Divine Urge is checked. The Winged Horse balks on the road, and we, discouraged, defeated, dismount and burrow into ourselves. The gates are closed and Divine Urge is imprisoned at Center. Thus we are taken by indifference that is death.

Environment finding the gates closed tries to break in. Turned away, it comes another way. Kept back, it stretches its hands to us. Always scheming to reach us. Never was suitor more insistent than Environment, seeking admission, claiming recognition, signaling to be seen, shouting to be heard. And through the ages we sit inside ourselves deaf, dumb and blind, and will not stir. . . .

. . . Maybe you are not deaf. . . . Perhaps signals reach you. Maybe you stir. . . . The gates give. . . . Eternal Urge pushes through the stupor of our senses, making paths to meet the challenging suitor, windows through which to see him, ears through which to hear him. Environment shouting, "Where are you?" and Center battering at the inner side of the wall crying, "Here I am," and dragging down bars, wrenching gates, prying at port-holes. Listening at cracks, reaching everywhere, and demanding that sense gates be flung open. The gates are open! Eternal Urge stands at the threshold signaling with venturous flag. An imperious instinct lets us know that "all" is ours, and that whatever anyone has ever known, or may ever have or know, we will call and claim. A sense of life universal surges through our life individual. We attack the feast of this table with an insatiable appetite that cries for all.

What are we? A creation of God's consciousness coming now slowly and painfully into recognition of ourselves.

What is Personality? A small part of us. The whole of us is behind that hungry rush at the gates of Senses.

What is Civilization? A circumscribed order in which the whole has not entered.

6. Emma Sheridan Fry taught acting to children at The Educational Alliance in New York from 1903 to 1909. In 1917, her book *Educational* *Dramatics* was published by Lloyd Adams Noble. The text of Emma's speech is taken from the prologue. [Author's note]

What is Environment? Our mate, our true mate that clamors for our reunion.

We will meet him. We will seize all, learn all, know all here, that we may fare further on the great quest! The task of Now is only a step toward the task of the Whole! Let us then seek the laws governing real life forces, that coming into their own, they may create, develop and reconstruct. Let us awaken life dormant! Let us, boldly, seizing the star of our intent, lift it as the lantern of our necessity, and let it shine over the darkness of our compliance. Come! The light shines. Come! It brightens our way. Come! Don't let its glorious light pass you by! Come! The day has come!

> [EMMA *throws herself on the couch.* PAULA *embraces her.*] Oh, it's so beautiful.

JULIA:    It is, Emma. It is.
> [*They applaud.*]
CINDY:    Encore! Encore!
> [EMMA *stands.*]
EMMA:    Environment knocks at the gateway . . . [*She laughs and joins the others in the semi-circle.* PAULA *remains seated on the couch.*] What's next.
FEFU: [*Going center.*]    I introduce Cecilia. I don't think I should introduce Cecilia. She should just come after Emma. Now things don't need introduction. [*Imitating* EMMA *as she goes to her seat.*] They are happening.
EMMA:    Right!
> [CECILIA *goes to center.*]
CECILIA:    Well, as we say in the business, that's a very hard act to follow.
EMMA:    Not *very* hard. It's a hard act to follow.
CECILIA:    Right. I should say my name first.
FEFU:    Yes.
CECILIA:    I should breathe too. [*She takes a breath. All except* PAULA *start singing "*CECILIA.*"* CECILIA *is perplexed and walks backwards till she sits on the couch. She is next to* PAULA. *Unaware of who she is next to, she puts her hand on* PAULA's *leg. At the end of the song* CECILIA *realizes she is next to* PAULA *and stands.*] I should go before Emma. I don't think anyone should speak after Emma.
CINDY:    Right. It should be Fefu, Paula, Cecilia, then Emma, and then Sue explaining the finances and asking for pledges. And the money should roll in. It's very good. [*They applaud.*] Sue . . . [SUE *goes to center.*]
SUE:    Yes, blahblahblahblah, pledges and money. [*She does a few balletic moves and bows. They applaud.*]
FEFU: [*As* SUE *returns to her seat.*]    Who's ready for coffee?
CINDY: [*As she stands.*]    And dishes.
CHRISTINA: [*As she stands.*]    I'll help.
EMMA: [*As she stands.*]    Me too.
FEFU:    Don't all come. Sit. Sit. You have done enough, relax.
> [*They put the furniture back as* EMMA *and* SUE *jump over the couch making loud warlike sounds. As they exit to the kitchen,* SUE *tries to get ahead of* EMMA. EMMA *speeds ahead of her. All except* JULIA *jump over the couch. All except* CINDY *and* JULIA *exit.*]
JULIA:    I should go do the dishes. I haven't done anything.

CINDY: You can do them tomorrow.
JULIA: True.—So how have you been?
CINDY: Hmm.
JULIA: Let me see. I can tell by looking at your face. Not so bad.
CINDY: Not so bad.
> [*There is the sound of laughter from the kitchen.* CHRISTINA *runs in.*]
CHRISTINA: They're having a water fight over who's going to do the dishes.
CINDY: Emma?
CHRISTINA: And Paula, and Sue, all of them. Fefu was getting into it when I left. Cecilia got out the back door.
> [CHRISTINA *walks back to the kitchen with some caution. She runs back and lies on the couch covering her head with the throw.* EMMA *enters with a pan of water in her hand. She is wet.* CINDY *and* JULIA *point to the lawn.* EMMA *runs to the lawn. There is the sound of knocking from upstairs. While the following conversation goes on,* EMMA, SUE, CINDY, *and* JULIA *engage in water fights in and out of the living room. The screams, laughter, and water splashing may drown the words.*]
PAULA: Open up.
FEFU: There's no one here.
PAULA: Open up, you coward.
FEFU: I can't. I'm busy.
PAULA: What are you doing?
FEFU: I have a man here. Ah ah ah ah ah.
PAULA: O.K. I'll wait. Take your time.
FEFU: It's going to take quite a while.
PAULA: It's all right. I'll wait.
FEFU: Do me a favor?
PAULA: Sure. Open up and I'll do you a favor.
> [*There is the sound of a pot falling, a door slamming.*]
FEFU: Fill it up for me.
PAULA: O.K.
FEFU: Thank you.
PAULA: Here's water. Open up.
FEFU: Leave it there. I'll come out in a minute.
PAULA: O.K. Here it is. I'm leaving now.
> [*Loud steps.* PAULA *comes down with a filled pan.* EMMA *hides by the entrance to the steps.* EMMA *splashes water on* PAULA. PAULA *splashes water on* EMMA. SUE *appears with a full pan.*]
PAULA: Truce!
SUE: Who's the winner?
PAULA: You are. You do the dishes.
SUE: I'm the winner. You do the dishes.
FEFU: [*From the landing.*] Line up!
SUE: Psst. [PAULA *and* EMMA *look.* SUE *splashes water on them.*] Gotcha!
EMMA: Please don't.
PAULA: Truce. Truce.
FEFU: O.K. Line up. [*Pointing to the kitchen.*] Get in there! [*They all go to the kitchen.*] Start doing those dishes. [*There is a moment's pause.*]
JULIA: It's over.

CINDY: We're safe.

JULIA: [*To* CHRISTINA.] You can come up now. [CHRISTINA *stays down.*] You rather wait a while. [CHRISTINA *nods.*]

CHRISTINA: [*Playful.*] I feel danger lurking.

CINDY: She's been hiding all day.

[FEFU *enters. She is wet.*]

FEFU: I won. I got them working.

JULIA: I thought the fight was over who'd do the dishes.

FEFU: Yes. [*Starting to go.*] I have to change. I'm soaked.

CHRISTINA: They forgot what the fight was about.

FEFU: We did?

JULIA: That's usually the way it is.

FEFU: [*Going to* CHRISTINA *and lifting the cover from her face.*] Are you ready for an ice cube?

[FEFU *exits upstairs.* CHRISTINA *runs upstairs. There is silence.*]

CINDY: So.—And how have you been?

JULIA: All right. I've been taking care of myself.

CINDY: You look well.

JULIA: I do not. . . . Have you seen Mike?

CINDY: No, not since Christmas.

JULIA: I'm sorry.

CINDY: I'm O.K.—And how's your love life?

JULIA: Far away. . . . I have no need for it.

CINDY: I'm sorry.

JULIA: Don't be. I'm very morbid these days. I think of death all the time.

PAULA: [*Standing in the doorway.*] Anyone for coffee? [*They raise their hands.*] Anyone take milk? [*They raise their hands.*]

JULIA: Should we go in?

PAULA: I'll bring it out. [PAULA *exits.*]

JULIA: I feel we are constantly threatened by death, every second, every instant, it's there. And every moment something rescues us. Something rescues us from death every moment of our lives. For every moment we live we have to thank something. We have to be grateful to something that fights for us and saves us. I have felt lifeless and in the face of death. Death is not anything. It's being lifeless and I have felt lifeless sometimes for a brief moment, but I have been rescued by these . . . guardians. I am not sure who these guardians are. I only know they exist because I have felt their absence. I think we have come to know them as life, and we have become familiar with certain forms they take. Our sight is a form they take. That is why we take pleasure in seeing things, and we find some things beautiful. The sun is a guardian. Those things we take pleasure in are usually guardians. We enjoy looking at the sunlight when it comes through the window. Don't we? We, as people, are guardians to each other when we give love. And then of course we have white cells and antibodies protecting us. Those moments when I feel lifeless have occurred, and I am afraid one day the guardians won't come in time and I will be defenseless. I will die . . . for no apparent reason.

[*Pause.* PAULA *stands in the doorway with a bottle of milk.*]

PAULA: [*In a low-keyed manner.*] Anyone take rotten milk? [*Pause.*] I'm kidding. This one is no good but there's more in there . . . [*Remaining in good spirits.*] Forget it. It's not a good joke.

JULIA: It's good.

PAULA: In there it seemed funny but here it isn't. [*As she exits and shrugging her shoulders.*] It's a kitchen joke. Bye.

JULIA: [*After her.*] It is funny, Paula. [*To* CINDY.] It was funny.

CINDY: It's all right, Paula doesn't mind.

JULIA: I'm sure she minds. I'll go see . . . [JULIA *starts to go.* PAULA *appears in the doorway.*]

PAULA: [*In a low-keyed manner.*] Hey, who was that lady I saw you with?—That was no lady. That was my rotten wife. That one wasn't good either, was it? [*Exiting.*] Emma. . . . That one was no good either.

> [SUE *starts to enter carrying a tray with sugar, milk, and two cups of coffee. She stops at the doorway to look at* PAULA *and* EMMA, *who are behind the wall.*]

SUE: [*Whispering.*] What are you doing?—What?—O.K., O.K. [*She enters whispering. Sue puts the tray down.*] They're plotting something.

> [PAULA *appears in the doorway.*]

PAULA: [*In a low-keyed manner.*] Ladies and gentlemen. Ladies, since our material is too shocking and avant-garde, we have decided to uplift our subject matter so it's more palatable to the sensitive public. [PAULA *takes a pose.* EMMA *enters. She lifts an imaginary camera to her face.*]

EMMA: Say cheese.

PAULA: Cheese. [*They both turn front and smile. The others applaud.*] Ah, success, success. Make it clean and you'll succeed.—Coffee's in the kitchen.

SUE: Oh, I brought theirs out.

PAULA: Oh, shall we have it here?

JULIA: We can all go in the kitchen. [*They each take their coffee and go to the kitchen. Sue takes the tray to the kitchen. The sugar remains on the table.*]

PAULA: Either here or there. [*She sits on the couch.*] I'm exhausted.

> [CECILIA *enters from the lawn.*]

CECILIA: Is the war over?

PAULA: Yes.

CECILIA: It's nice out. [PAULA *nods in agreement.*] Where's everybody?

PAULA: In the kitchen, having coffee.

CECILIA: We must talk. [PAULA *starts to speak.*] Not now. I'll call you. [CECILIA *starts to go.*]

PAULA: When?

CECILIA: I don't know.

PAULA: I don't want you, you know.

CECILIA: I know.

PAULA: No, you don't. I'm not lusting after you.

CECILIA: I know that. [*She starts to go.*] I'll call you.

PAULA: When?

CECILIA: As soon as I can.

PAULA: I won't be home then.

CECILIA: When will you be home?

PAULA: I'll check my book and let you know.

CECILIA: Do that.—I'll be leaving after coffee. I'll say goodbye now.

PAULA: Goodbye. [CECILIA *goes towards the kitchen.* PAULA *starts towards the steps,* FEFU *comes down the steps.*]

FEFU: You're still wet.

PAULA: I'm going to change now.

FEFU: Do you need anything?

PAULA: No, I have something I can change to. Thank you.

> [PAULA *goes upstairs.* FEFU *stands by the steps. She is downcast. As the lights shift to an eerie tone,* JULIA *enters in slow motion, walking. She goes to the coffee table, gets the sugar bowl, lifts it in* FEFU's *direction, takes the cover off, puts it back on and walks to the kitchen. As soon as* JULIA *exits,* SUE's *voice is heard speaking the following lines. Immediately after,* JULIA *re-enters wheeled by* SUE. CINDY, CHRISTINA, EMMA, *and* CECILIA *are with them. On the arms of the wheelchair rests a tray with a coffee pot and cups. As they reach the couch and chairs they sit.* SUE *puts the tray on the table.* FEFU *stares at* JULIA.]

SUE: I was terribly exhausted and run down. I lived on coffee so I could stay up all night and do my work. And they used to give us these medical check-ups all the time. But all they did was ask how we felt and we'd say "Fine," and they'd check us out. In the meantime I looked like a ghost. I was all bones. Remember Susan Austin? She was very naive and when they asked her how she felt, she said she was nervous and she wasn't sleeping well. So she had to see a psychiatrist from then on.

EMMA: Well, she was crazy.

> [FEFU *exits.*]

SUE: No, she wasn't.—Oh god, those were awful days. . . . Remember Julie Brooks?

EMMA: Sure.

SUE: She was a beautiful girl.

EMMA: Ah yes, she was gorgeous.

> [PAULA *comes down the stairs as soon as she has changed. She sits on the steps half way down.*]

SUE: At the end of the first semester they called her in because she had been out with 28 men and they thought that was awful. And the worst thing was that after that, she thought there was something wrong with her.

CINDY: [*Jokingly.*] She was a nymphomaniac, that's all.

SUE: She was not. She was just very beautiful so all the boys wanted to go out with her. And if a boy asked her to go have a cup of coffee she'd sign out and write in the name of the boy. None of us did, of course. All she did was go for coffee or go to a movie. She was really very innocent.

EMMA: And Gloria Schuman? She wrote a psychology paper the faculty decided she didn't write and they called her in to try to make her admit she hadn't written it. She insisted she wrote it and they sent her to a psychiatrist also.

JULIA: Everybody ended up going to the psychiatrist.

> [FEFU *enters through the foyer.*]

EMMA: After a few visits the psychiatrist said: Don't you think you know me well enough now that you can tell me the truth about the paper? He almost drove her crazy. They just couldn't believe she was so smart.

SUE: Those were difficult times.

PAULA:  We were young. That's why it was difficult. On my first year I
thought you were all very happy. I had been so deprived in my childhood
that I believed the rich were all happy. During the summer you spent
your vacations in Europe or the Orient. I went to work and I resented
that. But then I realized that many lives are ruined by poverty and many
lives are ruined by wealth. I was always able to manage. And I think I
enjoyed myself as much when I went to Revere Beach on my day off as
you did when you visited the Taj Mahal.[7] [CECILIA *enters from the foyer.*
*She stands there and listens.* PAULA *doesn't acknowledge her.*] Then, when
I stopped feeling envy, I started noticing the waste. I began feeling contempt for those who, having everything a person can ask for, make such
a mess of it. I resented them because they were not better than the poor.
If you have all you need you should be generous. If you can afford to go
to school your mind should be better. If you didn't have to fight for your
place on earth you should be nobler. But I saw them cheating and grabbing like the kids in the slums, or wasting away with self-indulgence.
And I saw them be plain stupid. If there is a reason why some are rich
while others starve it must be so they put everything they have at the
service of others. They should take the responsibility of everything that
happens in the world. They are the only ones who can influence things.
The poor don't have the power to change things. I think we should teach
the poor and let the rich take care of themselves. I'm sorry, I know that's
what we're doing. That's what Emma has been doing. I'm sorry . . . I
guess I feel it's not enough. [PAULA *sobs.*] I'll wash my face. I'll be right
back. [*She starts to go towards the kitchen.*] I think highly of all of you.
[CECILIA *follows her,* PAULA *turns.* CECILIA *opens her arms and puts them*
*around* PAULA, *engulfing her. She kisses* PAULA *on the lips.* PAULA *steps*
*back. She is fearful.* CECILIA *follows her.* FEFU *enters from the lawn.*]

FEFU:  Have you been out? The sky is full of stars.

  [EMMA, SUE, CHRISTINA, *and* CINDY *exit.*]

JULIA:  What's the matter?

  [FEFU *shakes her head.* JULIA *starts to go toward the door.*]

FEFU:  Stay a moment, will you?

JULIA:  Of course.

FEFU:  Did you have enough coffee?

JULIA:  Yes.

FEFU:  Did you find the sugar?

JULIA:  Yes. There was sugar in the kitchen. What's the matter?

FEFU:  Can you walk? [JULIA *is hurt. She opens her arms implying she hides*
*nothing.*] I am sorry, my dear.

JULIA:  What is the matter?

FEFU:  I don't know, Julia. Every breath is painful for me. I don't know.
[FEFU *turns* JULIA's *head to look into her eyes.*] I think you know.

  [JULIA *breaks away from* FEFU.]

JULIA:  [*Avoiding* FEFU's *glance.*]  No, I don't know. I haven't seen much of
you lately. I have thought of you a great deal. I always think of you.

---

7. A grand and elaborately decorated mausoleum
and surrounding structures in Agra, India; one
of the world's architectural masterpieces, built

1630–48. *Revere Beach:* a public beach just
north of Boston, Massachusetts; the first public
beach in the United States, established 1896.

CINDY tells me how you are. I always ask her. How is Phillip? Things are not well with Phillip?

FEFU: No.

JULIA: What's wrong?

FEFU: A lot is wrong.

JULIA: He loves you.

FEFU: He can't stand me.

JULIA: He loves you.

FEFU: He's left me. His body is here but the rest is gone. I exhaust him. I torment him and I torment myself. I need him, Julia.

JULIA: I know you do.

FEFU: I need his touch. I need his kiss. I need the person he is. I can't give him up. [*She looks into* JULIA's *eyes.*] I look into your eyes and I know what you see. [JULIA *closes her eyes.*] It's death. [JULIA *shakes her head.*] Fight!

JULIA: I can't.

FEFU: I saw you walking.

JULIA: No. I can't walk.

FEFU: You came for sugar, Julia. You came for sugar. Walk!

JULIA: You know I can't walk.

FEFU: Why not? Try! Get up! Stand up!

JULIA: What is wrong with you?

FEFU: You have given up!

JULIA: I get tired! I get exhausted! I am exhausted!

FEFU: What is it you see? [JULIA *doesn't answer.*] What is it you see! Where is it you go that tires you so?

JULIA: I can't spend time with others! I get tired!

FEFU: What is it you see!

JULIA: You want to see it too?

FEFU: No, I don't. You're nuts, and willingly so.

JULIA: You know I'm not.

FEFU: And you're contagious. I'm going mad too.

JULIA: I try to keep away from you.

FEFU: Why?

JULIA: I might be harmful to you.

FEFU: Why?

JULIA: I am contagious. I can't be what I used to be.

FEFU: You have no courage.

JULIA: You're being cruel.

FEFU: I want to rest, Julia. How does a person rest. I want to put my mind at rest. I am frightened. [JULIA *looks at* FEFU.] Don't look at me. [*She covers* JULIA's *eyes with her hand.*] I lose my courage when you look at me.

JULIA: May no harm come to your head.

FEFU: Fight!

JULIA: May no harm come to your will.

FEFU: Fight, Julia!

[FEFU *starts shaking the wheelchair and pulling* JULIA *off the wheelchair.*]

JULIA: I have no life left.

FEFU: Fight, Julia!

JULIA: May no harm come to your hands.

FEFU: I need you to fight.

JULIA: May no harm come to your eyes.

FEFU: Fight with me!

JULIA: May no harm come to your voice.

FEFU: Fight with me!

JULIA: May no harm come to your heart.

[CHRISTINA *enters.* FEFU *sees* CHRISTINA, *releases* JULIA. *To* CHRISTINA.]

FEFU: Now I have done it. Haven't I. You think I'm a monster. [*She turns to* JULIA *and speaks to her with kindness.*] Forgive me if you can. [JULIA *nods.*]

JULIA: I forgive you.

[FEFU *gets the gun.*]

CHRISTINA: What in the world are you doing with that gun!

FEFU: I'm going to clean it!

CHRISTINA: I think you better not!

FEFU: You're silly!

[CECILIA *appears on the landing.*]

CHRISTINA: I don't care if you shoot yourself! I just don't like the mess you're making!

[FEFU *starts to go to the lawn and turns.*]

FEFU: I enjoy betting it won't be a real bullet! You want to bet!

CHRISTINA: No! [FEFU *exits.* CHRISTINA *goes to* JULIA.] Are you all right?

JULIA: Yes.

CHRISTINA: Can I get you anything?

JULIA: Water. [CECILIA *goes to the liquor cabinet for water.*] Put some sugar in it. Could I have a damp cloth for my forehead? [CHRISTINA *goes toward the kitchen.* JULIA *speaks front.*] I didn't tell her anything. Did I? I didn't.

CECILIA: [*Going to* JULIA *with the water.*] About what?

JULIA: She knew.

[*There is the sound of a shot.* CHRISTINA *and* CECILIA *run out.* JULIA *puts her hand to her forehead. Her hand goes down slowly. There is blood on her forehead. Her head falls back.* FEFU *enters holding a dead rabbit.*]

FEFU: I killed it . . . I just shot . . . and killed it. . . . Julia . . .

[*Dropping the rabbit,* FEFU *walks to* JULIA *and stands behind the chair as she looks at* JULIA. SUE *and* CINDY *enter from the foyer,* EMMA *and* PAULA *from the kitchen,* CHRISTINA *and* CECILIA *from the lawn. They surround* JULIA. *The lights fade.*]

1977

# ROSARIO MORALES and AURORA LEVINS MORALES
## b. 1930 and b. 1954

Rosario Morales grew up in Spanish Harlem and the Bronx, a New York City borough north of Manhattan. She and her husband, Aaron Levins, a Jewish American, moved to the mountains of Indiera Baja, Puerto Rico. A few years after the birth of their daughter Aurora Levins Morales, the Moraleses returned to the United States and lived in several cities, including New York and Chicago. Rosario Morales holds a master's degree in anthropology from the University of Chicago.

She and Aurora Levins Morales first became known within feminist and ethnic literary circles when a sample of their collaborative writing was included in the groundbreaking collection *This Bridge Called My Back: Writings by Radical Women of Color* (1981), edited by the Chicana writers Cherríe Moraga and Gloria Anzaldúa. A few years later, mother and daughter coauthored *Getting Home Alive* (1986), a collection interweaving poems and prose testimonials. Morales and Levins Morales wrote some of these pieces individually and some jointly. Throughout, their commanding voices define the historical and racial terms of their hybrid identity and, by implication, the identity of their homelands. The book is not only a labor of love and mutual respect, but also a political expression of feminist collective work and a reflection of a strong social and historical consciousness.

Her progressive parents instilled in Aurora Levins Morales a love for reading and writing as well as a strong sense of social justice. In 1976, she moved to Berkeley, California, and began publishing her work and reading it in public appearances. She holds a doctoral degree in history and women's studies and continues an active career in creative writing and documenting community history. In her book *Remedios: Stories of Earth and Iron from the History of Puertorriqueñas* (1998), she links her feminism to a keen sense of the history of the Americas viewed through the oppression of women and of colonized Indian and African cultures. Her essay collection *Medicine Stories: History, Culture, and the Politics of Integrity* (1998) has been described by the scholar Cynthia Enloe as offering "the paradigm of integrity as a political model to people who hunger for a world of justice, health and love." For several years, Levins Morales has been researching the history of Puerto Ricans in California; a traveling exhibit she created documents the presence and experiences of this migrant population. She is also collecting narratives about the experiences of Puerto Ricans living in other U.S. localities besides New York City.

In the selections included in this anthology, both poets, individually and together, define and celebrate their Puerto Rican and panethnic Latina/o experience in the United States and elsewhere in the Americas.

---

## *From* Getting Home Alive

## I Am What I Am[1]

I am what I am and I am U.S. American   I haven't wanted to say it because if I did you'd take away the Puerto Rican   but now I say go to hell   I am what I

1. By Rosario Morales.

am and you can't take it away with all the words and sneers at your command   I am what I am   I am Puerto Rican   I am U.S. American   I am New York Manhattan and the Bronx   I am what I am   I'm not hiding under no stoop   behind no curtain   I am what I am   I am Boricua as Boricuas[2] come from the isle of Manhattan and I croon sentimental tangos in my sleep and Afro-Cuban beats in my blood and Xavier Cugat's[3] lukewarm latin is so familiar and dear   sneer dear but he's familiar and dear   but not Carmen Miranda[4] who's a joke because I never was a joke   I was a bit of a sensation   See! here's a real true honest-to-god Puerto Rican girl and she's in college   Hey! Mary   come   here   and look she's from right here   a South Bronx girl and she's honest-to-god in college now   Ain't that something   who wouda believed it   Ain't science wonderful or some such thing   a wonder a wonder.

And someone who did languages for a living stopped me in the subway because how I spoke was a linguist's treat   I mean there it was yiddish and spanish and fine refined college educated english   and irish which I mainly keep in my prayers   It's dusty now   I haven't said my prayers in decades but try my Hail Marrrry full of grrrace with the nun's burr with the nun's disdain   it's all true and it's all me   do you know I got an English accent from the BBC[5]   For years in the mountains of Puerto Rico when I was twenty-two and twenty-four and twenty-six   all those young years   I listened to the BBC and Radio Moscow's English english announcers announce and denounce and then I read Dickens[6] all the way through three or four times at least and then later I read Dickens aloud in voices and when I came back to the U.S. I spoke mockDickens and mockBritish especially when I want to be crisp efficient I know what I'm doing and you can't scare me   tough   that kind   I am what I am and I'm a bit of a snob too   Shit! why am I calling myself names   I really really dig the funny way the British speak   and it's real it's true   and I love too the singing of yiddish sentences that go with shrugs and hands and arms doing melancholy or lively dances   I love the sound and look of yiddish in the air   in the body   in the streets   in the English language   nooo   so what's new   so go by the grocer and buy some fruit   oye vey   gevalt   gefilte fish   raiseleh[7]   oh and those words   hundreds of them dotting the english language like raisins in the bread   shnook and shlemiel   zoftik   tush   shmata[8]   all those soft sweet sounds saying sharp sharp things   I am what I am and I'm naturalized Jewish-American   wasp is foreign and new but Jewish-American is old shoe familiar   shmata familiar and it's me dears it's me   bagels blintzes and all   I am what I am   Take it or leave me alone.

2. I am Puerto Rican as Puerto Ricans; in what is now Puerto Rico, the pre-Columbian indigenous Taíno people called the island Boriquén and themselves Boricuas.

3. Spanish (Catalan) Cuban American bandleader (born Francesc d'Asís Xavier Cugat Mingall de Bru i Deulofeu, 1900–1990).

4. Portuguese-born Brazilian singer and actress (1909–1955) who often performed wearing a hat topped with tropical fruit.

5. British Broadcasting Corporation, here presenting programs on the radio.

6. Charles Dickens (1812–1870), English novelist.

7. Rose. Oye vey: or oy vey, also just oy, an expression of dismay. Gevalt: or oy gevalt, an expression related to oy vey.

8. Rag; old, worn clothing. Shnook: patsy, sucker. Schlemiel: clumsy bungler. Zoftik: fat, juicy, shapely.

# Child of the Americas[1]

I am a child of the Americas,
a light-skinned mestiza of the Caribbean,
a child of many diaspora, born into this continent at a crossroads.

I am a U.S. Puerto Rican Jew,
a product of the ghettos of New York I have never known.          5
An immigrant and the daughter and granddaughter of immigrants.
I speak English with passion: it's the tongue of my consciousness,
a flashing knife blade of crystal, my tool, my craft.

I am Caribeña, island grown. Spanish is in my flesh,
ripples from my tongue, lodges in my hips:                        10
the language of garlic and mangoes,
the singing in my poetry, the flying gestures of my hands.
I am of Latinoamerica, rooted in the history of my continent:
I speak from that body.

I am not african. Africa is in me, but I cannot return.           15
I am not taína. Taíno[2] is in me, but there is no way back.
I am not european. Europe lives in me, but I have no home there.

I am new. History made me. My first language was spanglish.
I was born at the crossroads
and I am whole.                                                   20

# Puertoricanness[1]

It was Puerto Rico waking up inside her. Puerto Rico waking her up at 6:00 a.m., remembering the rooster that used to crow over on 59th Street and the neighbors all cursed "that damn rooster," but she loved him, waited to hear his harsh voice carving up the Oakland sky and eating it like chopped corn, so obliviously sure of himself, crowing all alone with miles of houses around him. She was like that rooster.

Often she could hear them in her dreams. Not the lone rooster of 59th Street (or some street nearby . . . she had never found the exact yard though she had tried), but the wild careening hysterical roosters of 3:00 a.m. in Bartolo, screaming at the night and screaming again at the day.

It was Puerto Rico waking up inside her, uncurling and shoving open the door she had kept neatly shut for years and years. Maybe since the first time she was an immigrant, when she refused to speak Spanish in nursery school. Certainly since the last time, when at thirteen she found herself between

1. By Aurora Levins Morales.
2. The Taíno peoples were the pre-Columbian inhabitants of the Bahamas and the Greater and Lesser Antilles. *Taína* is the female form of the name.
1. By Aurora Levins Morales.

languages, between countries, with no land feeling at all solid under her feet. The mulberry trees of Chicago, that first summer, had looked so utterly pitiful beside her memory of flamboyan and banana and. . . . No, not even the individual trees and bushes but the mass of them, the overwhelming profusion of green life that was the home of her comfort and nest of her dreams.

The door was opening. She could no longer keep her accent under lock and key. It seeped out, masquerading as dyslexia, stuttering halting unable to speak the word which will surely come out in the wrong language, wearing the wrong clothes. Doesn't that girl know how to dress? Doesn't she know how to date, what to say to a professor, how to behave at a dinner table laid with silver and crystal and too many forks?

Yesterday she answered her husband's request that she listen to the whole of his thoughts before commenting by screaming, "This is how we talk. I will not wait sedately for you to finish. Interrupt me back!" She drank pineapple juice three or four times a day. Not Lotus, just Co-op brand, but it was piña, and it was sweet and yellow. And she was letting the clock slip away from her into a world of morning and afternoon and night, instead of "five-forty-one-and-twenty seconds—beep."

There were things she noticed about herself, the Puertoricanness of which she had kept hidden all these years, but which had persisted as habits, as idiosyncracies of her nature. The way she left a pot of food on the stove all day, eating out of it whenever hunger struck her, liking to have something ready. The way she had lacked food to offer Elena in the old days and had stamped on the desire to do so because it *was* Puerto Rican: *Come, mija . . . ¿quieres café?*[2] The way she was embarrassed and irritated by Ana's unannounced visits, just dropping by, keeping the country habits after a generation of city life. So unlike the cluttered datebooks of all her friends, making appointments to speak to each other on the phone days in advance. Now she yearned for that clocklessness, for the perpetual food pots of her childhood. Even in the poorest houses a plate of white rice and brown beans with calabaza or green bananas and oil.

She had told Sally that Puerto Ricans lived as if they were all in a small town still, a small town of six million spread out over tens of thousands of square miles, and that the small town that was her country needed to include Manila Avenue in Oakland now, because she was moving back into it. She would not fight the waking early anymore, or the eating all day, or the desire to let time slip between her fingers and allow her work to shape it. Work, eating, sleep, lovemaking, play—to let them shape the day instead of letting the day shape them. Since she could not right now, in the endless bartering of a woman with two countries, bring herself to trade in one-half of her heart for the other, exchange this loneliness for another perhaps harsher one, she would live as a Puerto Rican lives en la isla, right here in north Oakland,[3]

2. Eat, girl . . . want coffee? (*Mija*, a contraction of *mi hija*, literally means "daughter" but is used colloquially to mean "girl.")

3. I.e., the northern part of Oakland, a city in northern California, east of San Francisco and, south of Berkeley. *En la isla*: on the island.

plant the bananales and cafetales of her heart around her bedroom door, sleep under the shadow of their bloom and the carving hoarseness of the roosters, wake to blue-rimmed white enamel cups of jugo de piña and plates of guineo verde,[4] and heat pots of rice with bits of meat in them on the stove all day.

There was a woman in her who had never had the chance to move through this house the way she wanted to, a woman raised to be like those women of her childhood, hardworking and humorous and clear. That woman was yawning up out of sleep and into this cluttered daily routine of a Northern California writer living at the edges of Berkeley. She was taking over, putting doilies on the word processor, not bothering to make appointments, talking to the neighbors, riding miles on the bus to buy bacalao,[5] making her presence felt . . . and she was all Puerto Rican, every bit of her.

# Ending Poem[1]

I am what I am.
*A child of the Americas.*
A light-skinned mestiza of the Caribbean.
*A child of many diaspora, born into this continent at a crossroads.*
I am Puerto Rican. I am U.S. American.                                    5
*I am New York Manhattan and the Bronx.*
A mountain-born, country-bred, homegrown jíbara[2] child,
*up from the shtetl, a California Puerto Rican Jew.*
A product of the New York ghettos I have never known.
*I am an immigrant*                                                       10
and the daughter and granddaughter of immigrants.
*We didn't know our forbears' names with a certainty.*
They aren't written anywhere.
*First names only, or mija, negra, ne,[3] honey, sugar, dear.*

I come from the dirt where the cane was grown.                           15
*My people didn't go to dinner parties. They weren't invited.*
I am caribeña, island grown.
*Spanish is in my flesh, ripples from my tongue, lodges in my hips,*
the language of garlic and mangoes.
*Boricua.[4] As Boricuas come from the isle of Manhattan.*               20
I am of latinoamerica, rooted in the history of my continent.
*I speak from that body. Just brown and pink and full of drums inside.*

---

4. Green bananas, used in many Puerto Rican dishes. *Jugo*: juice.
5. Codfish.
1. By Rosario Morales and Aurora Levins Morales.
2. Puerto Rican peasant.
3. Shortened form of *negra*, literally "black girl"
or "black woman" but commonly used by Puerto Ricans as a term of endearment equivalent to *sweetheart* or *sweetie*. *Mija*: my daughter (contraction of *mi hija*), used colloquially to mean "girl."
4. See note 2, p. 982, and note 2, p. 983.

I am not African.
*Africa waters the roots of my tree, but I cannot return.*

I am not Taína.                                                                25
*I am a late leaf of that ancient tree.*
and my roots reach into the soil of two Americas.
*Taíno is in me, but there is no way back.*

I am not European, though I have dreamt of those cities.
*Each plate is different,*                                                     30
wood, clay, papier mâché, metal, basketry, a leaf, a coconut shell.
*Europe lives in me but I have no home there.*

The table has a cloth woven by one, dyed by another,
*embroidered by another still.*
I am a child of many mothers.                                                  35
*They have kept it all going*
All the civilizations erected on their backs.
*All the dinner parties given with their labor.*

We are new.
*They gave us life, kept us going,*                                            40
brought us to where we are.
*Born at a crossroads.*
Come, lay that dishcloth down. Eat, dear, eat.
*History made us.*
We will not eat ourselves up inside anymore.                                   45

*And we are whole.*

1986

---

# JAIME CARRERO
## b. 1931

Born in the city of Mayagüez, Puerto Rico, Jaime Carrero earned a degree in fine arts from Pratt Institute, in New York City, where he lived for many years. His frequent moves between Puerto Rico and New York partly explain why his understanding of the migrant experience is more sympathetic than those of other island writers of his generation. After returning to Puerto Rico in the late 1970s, Carrero for many years directed the art department at the Interamerican University in San Germán, Puerto Rico, and his paintings have been part of many international exhibitions. Although he is known primarily as a painter, some of Carrero's literary contributions are an important addition to island-based Puerto Rican writers' interpretations of the migrant experience.

Carrero's poetry collection, *Jet neorriqueño* (Neo-Rican Jetliner, published in Puerto Rico in 1964), introduced the term *neorriqueño*, referring to mainland

Puerto Ricans. Almost a decade later, a group of Puerto Ricans—poets, writers, artists, musicians, and others—born or raised in the barrios of New York coined and propagated their own term, *Nuyorican*, to underscore the uniqueness of their bicultural experiences as an ethno-racial minority in U.S. society. Island Puerto Ricans now commonly use the Spanish terms *neorriqueño* or *nuyorriqueño* (Nuyorican) to refer to mainland Puerto Ricans. As the critic Juan Flores noted in 1993, *Jet neorriqueño* "directly foreshadowed the onset of Nuyorican literature in New York." Written two years after the publication of this pioneering collection, Carrero's poem "Neo Rican Lesson," included here, reiterates the theme of a Puerto Rican identity's being reshaped by diasporic experience and besieged by the prejudices of American society. Some of Carrero's plays, such as *Flag Inside, Captain F4C*, and *Pipo Subway no sabe reír* (Pipo Subway Doesn't Know How to Laugh, 1973) also deal with issues of Puerto Rican identity and with the influence of U.S. culture on the lives of island and mainland Puerto Ricans.

In addition to being a poet and playwright, Carrero is an accomplished novelist. Among his several novels is *Raquelo tiene un mensaje* (Raquelo has a Message, 1967), which received an award from the Ateneo Puertorriqueño (Puerto Rican Atheneum), one of Puerto Rico's main cultural institutions.

## Neo Rican Lesson

### I. Primera Lección en Inglés

*Primera lección en inglés*
         *escucha bien—*
*cuando vayas a caminar:*
         Never say Puerto Rican again.
         Never say that the island is in:                    5
                  within yourself
         Just say   French
                  Peruvian
                  Chilean
                  Czech                                       10
         anything  else
         anything  else
                  but never, never,
                  open that chest
                  and say Puerto Rican again.                 15
Tell me, Sir, tell me something about myself:
         I've met a man
         just like you—a gentleman—
         who said to me in Mayagüez—
                  loud and clear—                             20
                  a gentleman, Sir—
                  just like you—
                  polite English—
                  not French—
         the smile on the ground,                            25
         a fragile smile—
         like from the corner of the mouth:
         'I bet Puerto Ricans are to the intellect,

I bet, I bet,
What the Jews to the Nazis are—                    30
. . . . . . . . . . . . . . . . . . . . . . . . .
that I bet . . .'

## II. Segunda Lección en Inglés

*Segunda lección en inglés,*
*escucha bien—*
*cuando vayas a caminar:*                           35
Never say to the next door man
that your white Puerto Rican skin
is Puerto Rican
because like the bee
you may die from the sting.                        40

*Cuando vayas a caminar*
*escucha bien:*
Never say that your kinky hair
with the flat nose on the side
is fair.                                            45

Tell me, Sir, tell me something about myself:
*No me atrevo a decirlo en inglés*
*por temor a sentirme al revés.*
. . . . . . . . . . . . . . . . . . . . . . . . .
But in this corner, Sir                             50
a man was kicked to death.
You want to know why, Sir?
Because the man spoke in Spanish
and the cop came
and asked—                                          55
point blank:
'Anyone speak' Puerto Rican right?'

In that very moment, Sir
with the neon in my eyes
I was hoping for my skin                            60
to fall by my side.

June, 1966

# ABELARDO "LALO" DELGADO
## 1931–2004

Abelardo Delgado was born in La Boquilla de Conchos, in Chihuahua, Mexico. In 1943, he and his mother migrated to El Paso, Texas, where they settled in Voting Precinct Number Two, a heavily populated Mexican American neighborhood known locally as *El Segundo Barrio* (The Second Barrio). Delgado grew up in a tenement packed with 23 families who shared three bathrooms. His lack of English held him back at first, but in 1950 he graduated from high school in the top 10 percent of his class. After graduation, he worked in restaurants and construction. In 1955, he became the special-activities director at Our Lady's Parish Youth Center, where for 10 years he worked with underprivileged youngsters. As he acknowledged later, the period prepared him for "my formative years in the Chicano Movement," leaving him with a lifetime commitment "to struggle for those afflicted with the social illness of poverty." In 1962, he earned a degree in secondary education from the University of Texas at El Paso. He then worked in the health and social-services sector for public schools, colleges, and universities, in Colorado, Texas, Utah, and Washington, primarily on behalf of young, undocumented farm laborers.

Although *El Movimiento*, as the Chicano Movement became known in Spanish, was concerned primarily with civil rights, equitable education, and fair employment practices, it also attracted artists and intellectuals. In the early 1960s, Delgado worked with César Chávez and the farmworkers, and he later became the executive director of the Colorado Migrant Council. Through his poetry, he helped promote Chávez's cause. His best-known collection of poetry is *Chicano: 25 Pieces of a Chicano Mind* (1969), and among his most controversial pieces is "Stupid America," inspired by educators who blamed Chicanos for failing to succeed academically. In 1971, Delgado collaborated with the Chicano poets Ricardo Sánchez, Raymundo "Tigre" Pérez, and Magdaleno Ávila (aka Juan Valdez) on *Los cuatro* (The Four). Focused on social protest, these four volumes were not distributed widely, but they made their way into Chicano consciousness. Employing literature as an instrument for change, Delgado's verses here reflect on racism and police brutality, condemn mainstream U.S. society's ignorance of Chicanos, and seek to sensitize Anglo society to Chicanos' changing consciousnesses.

Delgado's next book, arguably his most significant, was the nonfiction prose work *The Chicano Movement: Some Not Too Objective Observations* (1973), which was privately distributed in typed form but became a manifesto for the Mexican American activism of the late 1960s and mid-1970s. In 24 brief chapters, 10 of which are presented in this anthology, Delgado addresses issues relating to justice, economics, education, and housing; declares what *El Movimiento* ought to accomplish; explores the weaknesses of the Movement's leaders and examines their strategies. Yet Delgado's central concern remains the poor, a topic he tackled again in his next book, *El niño del migrante* (The Migrant's Child, 1979). If Chicanos suffer in the world's richest nation, he asks, what should one expect from countries where democracy is an elusive dream?

Over the years, Delgado wrote poems for "special occasions"—in Spanish, English, and Spanglish—and he read in multiple cities and at many universities. He presented poems to couples being married, and every year he composed a new poem for Mother's Day, which he read to fellow worshipers at church. It is said that when Delgado was courting Lola Estrada, his future wife, he sent her a dollar bill every day from California, where he worked in a hotel, so she could buy a wedding dress. On each bill, Delgado wrote a poem. His verses became more personal in the undated volumes *Mortal Sin Kit* and *Reflexiones*, in both of which the focus is his quest as an artist. Ideological concerns reappear in *It's Cold: 52 Cold-Thought*

*Poems of Abelardo* (1974). Here, Delgado indicts the U.S. government for ignoring the marginalized groups in its population (particularly blacks and Chicanos) at the time of the Vietnam War and during the Watergate scandal. *Cold* is the operative term: Delgado accuses the country of replacing its humanity with indifference.

By the mid-1970s, Delgado's concerns had become international. In *A Thermos Bottle Full of Self Pity: 25 Bottles by Abelardo* (1975), he cries out against world hunger in plain language, asking readers to eradicate inequality by "breaking bread" collectively. Taking a Christian tone, Delgado embraces a message of love, peace, understanding, and compassion, while condemning those who thwart humanitarian effort. In 1978, he won *el premio Quinto Sol* (Fifth Sun prize) for best novel—given by Quinto Sol Publications, a small press in Berkeley, California—for his novel *Letters to Louise*. As a result, the novel was disseminated widely in the Mexican American community. In *Totoncaxihuitle, a Laxative: 25 Laxatives of Abelardo* (1981), Delgado prescribed a cosmic—and comic—laxative to cleanse the world.

For 17 years, Delgado taught Chicano studies at Metropolitan State College of Denver, in Colorado. He helped develop many Chicano Studies programs in universities throughout the western United States, including at the University of Colorado. He also taught Spanish and helped educate Mexican immigrants on obtaining U.S. citizenship. Two months after Delgado's death, Denver mayor John Hickenlooper made the one-year, posthumous appointment of Delgado as the city's first poet laureate.

# *From* The Chicano Movement: Some Not Too Objective Observations

## *Background*

We can say that the Chicano movement has recently been confined, exposed, structured, and felt, particularly in the Southwest, but to say that the Chicano movement began not too long ago is our error. The Chicano community in the United States has been in a constant state of rebellion against the economic and foreign mode of life that has been cruelly imposed on them, ever since the first day a white man and a brown man crossed paths. This refusal to acculturate or to be absorbed, or assimilated, into the dominant and larger society is the heart of the Chicano movement, and it has been ticking away, quite healthy, without a need for a transplant. Among our abuelos there were many quiet heroes of the scope of Jacinto Treviño, who never got a corrido written[1] but whose feats of sheer defiance at life's risks surpass our present demonstrations.

Hanging on to the language and values treasured much more than the alluring plushness of materialistic wealth was perhaps the most meaningful contribution and base in the Chicano movement. We now criticize our ancestors for taking so much abuse at the hands of the powerful gringo, but fail to see with what meticulous care they managed to protect the family and the children for a later day, our day, today. While it is true that they took some literal kicks from despotic patrones and back seats here and there and right out omission of this and that and were subject to the derogatory remark and

---

1. I.e., written about them, the way Jacinto Treviño became the hero in a widespread border corrido (early twentieth century).

the stern look-down, the pioneers in the Chicano movement managed to survive, and what is best, their and our dignity, though roughed and bent, was never destroyed.

The Pachuco movement[2] was a more manifest way of expressing a desire to remain autonomous, but unfortunately the movement was too much of a retreat into drugs rather than a direct confrontation with the oppressors. We became infested with a blind desire to strike out and did so through gang wars at our own carnales.[3] This was in the early forties and continued to the fifties and was perhaps a close predecessor of a combined effort emulated throughout the Southwest, but in particular in El Chuco (El Paso, Texas, and (Los Angeles, California). The peg pants gave way to khakis, and the oxblood shoes with triple soles and horse-shoe taps to combat boots, but the "calo" (slang) way of communication remains even now a strong influence on our language, i.e., ese, bato, carnal, jefe,[4] etc. It was at the beginning not necessarily a youth thing with us, but quite mature men were involved. While the duck tail hair cut and the fancy zoot suit (sharkskin) were trademarks and the gang the ambassadors of this movement, almost a million Chicanos through the Southwest were part of the movement, in that they dared in their dress and walk and way of talking chose to be identified with the Pachuco, daring school officials, employers, and others who scorned them.

It can be said that while a war was going on and ended and a vast majority of Chicanos returned as veterans, exposed to a forced equality in the army structure, they came to demand that equality in their own communities. This new breed of exposed Chicanos returning had seen the high price paid during World War II by la raza and brought back the bill to America. While this was a healthy experience, a sad mentality accompanied many of those Chicano brothers. The bug that bit them to make them claim a better way of life had the mortal ill effect that it could only be done la gringo way. Most of those ex-G.I.'s, realizing their own short-comings, language, and education, wisely decided their children would only speak English and that education was indeed the salvation of the Chicano. Most of us in the movement are direct descendants or second generation of that Chicano and that mentality.

### The Chicano Movement Identified

Is there a Chicano movement because a few of us go around saying there is, or do some of us go around saying there is a Chicano movement because we see it and can now identify it? It is possible that as movements go, ours is highly obscured by the many movements which force their way to national attention. This can be to our advantage since definitely we cannot expect to gain much by mere publicity. Since I am one who claims very strongly and loudly that there is a Chicano movement in our country, the burden of proof rests on my shoulders.

A movement of national significance has to have national common denominators and visible signs of identification. The first of these common denominators is that as a movement of national scope it is very much at the

2. Mexican American style in the 1940s (discussed in the "Acculturation" introduction, p. 366).

3. Bros (as in slang for "brothers").
4. Chief. *Ese*: dude. *Bato*: dude.

hands of the Chicano youth and therefore the Chicano student, in particular in the Western states where the heaviest Chicano population exists. We must associate with the youth not only in that it is primarily at their control but that they have taken the initiative in establishing such a movement. Because of the cultural overtones of Chicanismo the youth have not attempted to divorce themselves from their parents and do their own thing and even fight their own parents or leave them as in the case of the "beautiful people." The movement then has gone into the Chicano home and has in fact become a family affair. The wisdom of the movement is not to start from scratch but to acknowledge the progress Chicanos have made up to now and take off from there, acknowledging and accepting all Chicanos regardless of social status or meagerness of contribution into the movement. Major common denominators of course have always been the evident neglect which Chicanos suffer in their work, education, and political arena. The injured and abused Chicano cannot help but find companionship and a spirit of protest from any other Chicano anywhere in the nation.

As to visible signs of the movement, we can start with the very word "chicano," a word coined in the barrio to impose itself in our lingo and for the first time forge itself upward, gathering respectability as it climbs into the very sacredness of churches and schools because there is no shame to the name as many would wish to make us believe. The Chicano handshake, which although a borrowed sign from the black movement, has its peculiar Chicano flavor as it is seldom given without an abrazo (embrace), the Chicano power yell with its hypnotic significance of a people hungry to experience the power (economic and social) that we have merely observed others use for the last one hundred years. There is a brand new type of movement art and poetry and a rebirth of desire to wear our bright colored zarapes, chalecos or mañanitas[5] and frankly and honestly a basic desire to be seen and heard and acknowledged, similar to a newly born baby giving out its first cry.

There is too in the new symbolism a hatred for the force that has made us forget our language, our customs, and our values in return for nothing. But the outstanding common denominator and most visible sign of the Chicano in the movement is pride. "Orgullo"[6] borders on the cocky side, but it is this which if respected can alone end any racism. Now the Chicano no longer whispers when he talks to the anglo, and what is best, stares with his brown or dark eyes directly into the blue or hazel eyes of a man his equal.

### National Jefes

If the movement has so much structure and direction by now, it cannot all be attributed to mere chance; somebody must be offering both. There are various figures of national prominence who have gained such stature at much personal loss and damage. It is not easy, as we have found out, to confront even on the local level, but to confront on the national level can spell suicide and often does. It is not enough to anger the power structure to gain a leadership spot, but those that do must have the respect and support of those in the

---

5. Traditional songs that Mexicans sing early in the morning or on special occasions, such as birthdays. *Zarapes*: or serapes, Mexican blankets.

*Chalecos*: vests.
6. Pride.

movement who alone determine who will lead. The movement is wise enough not to be diverted by the imposed and often bought leadership that the power structure waves in front of us. Among some of the national figures which have the most following and respect for their views are César Chávez, Corky Gonzalez, Reyes López Tijerina, and José Angel Gutiérrez.[7] To know these four personalities may be quite disturbing for people outside the movement, for while they crisscross their powers and loyalties, they are very much, each one of them, individuals living their own roles to a "t." Again the fact is evident that while each one may claim a different ideal, the advocacy is always on behalf of the deprived Chicano. Chávez, through unionization, fair wages for the farmworker; Corky, through the plan de Aztlan, the uplifting of the Chicano youth through meaningful education; Tijerina, reclaiming the land stolen from us in New Mexico; and José Angel, political self-determination through the newly formed Raza Unida party.

These four national figures have managed to provoke a national awareness, even concern, for the plight of Chicanos and have done much in arousing even among us Chicanos a response to involve ourselves in their struggle, which is of course our own struggle.

While those of us that merely follow may have a preference for which leader to follow and what line suits us best, the Causa is one and the same, a more adequate place in our communities, in our own country.

It is obvious that there are many other national leaders in more restrictive fields, government, O.E.O., H.E.W., V.B.A.,[8] colleges and arts and letters. These leaders too influence the national chicano mind, and their decisions have an effect on the barrio and the campos,[9] but as I said, their leadership is confined to the field of work they have chosen, and they have little if any real following in the movement people.

Each of the four national leaders I have mentioned is naturally under heavy scrutiny by the larger dominant white society and by us. What the white views as charismatic in our leaders we may view as weaknesses and visa versa. Their leadership has one basic thing in common in that more than being leaders, these four men have taken upon themselves to guide the Chicanos where they wish to go and at the pace they set rather than impose themselves on the people that follow; they sensitively feel the "riendas"[1] and obey.

These leaders have proven to possess a high balance of measured qualities which compare if not surpass those of other creditated national figures: wisdom, endurance, expression, and every unique attribute which other national leaders at times lack. Each of them, regardless of the hardness or softness of his line, continues to speak of hope and work constructively to prove himself, and not to the gringo. While high overtones of nationalism are expressed by

7. Attorney and professor; founding member of the Mexican American Youth Organization (MAYO), a civil rights group, in 1967; founding member and past president of the Raza Unida Party, a Mexican American political party in the Southwest and Midwest. *César Chávez*: see p. 760. *Corky Gonzalez*: see p. 787. *Reies López Tijerina*: community activist, spokesman for the rights of Hispanics and Mexican Americans, and a major figure of the early Chicano Movement (b. 1926).

8. These three sets of initials represent offices and agencies of the U.S. federal government: Office of Economic Activity (agency that administered most War on Poverty programs under the Great Society legislation of the 1960s); Department of Health, Education, and Welfare (1953–79—now the Department of Health and Human Services); Veterans Benefits Administration (established 1930).
9. Fields.
1. Reins.

all four at various degrees, it is a positive kind of nationalism, which is neither un-American nor racist.

## Regional and Local Jefes

No attempt will be made here to identify the total range of local and regional leaders, because no matter how objective the intention or how thorough, I would wind up omitting some who in their own right are of prominant importance to the movement.

As mobile as I have been in the last four years, it never fails to amaze me how little I know of the true size of our movement. I go to the farthest corners in any direction and am surprised to find a group of MAYOS, Brown or Black Berets, UMAS, MECHAS, G. I. forum,[2] or an already organized and functioning group of Chicanos taking on the responsibility of holding their own ground against bigotry or injustice.

\* \* \* Even in our own capital of Washington, D.C., a group now exist who openly claim their Chicanismo and carry on strategy during their many coffee breaks. For sure the states of Oregon, Washington, Utah, Montana, Nevada, Oklahoma, Kansas, and Idaho are very much up to date on the movement and very much a part of it. I have to mention Michigan and Illinois in a separate breath, for the strength of the movement there will not take a back seat even to Colorado, Texas, and California. It is staggering the number of Chicanos involved. Someone said long ago that the basic strategy of the movement was to encircle the U.S. with latinos, and while he was somewhat facetiously playing with an anglo audience, the jest is now on him, for it is surely happening.

New Mexico and Arizona comprise the other two fronts of major significance in the movement. There are Chicanos in Florida, drop-outs of the migrant stream who are organized, as well as Chicano students in Minnesota, and Nebraska is also heavily populated by Chicanos.

It is not out of place to speculate that if it were possible to measure the strength of the various Chicano organizations existing today, you would need a directory of the size of a New York phone book. These organizations express already a desire to communicate with other existing and neighboring groups with the hope of sharing issues, seeking or offering support. These efforts to communicate and link are evident in the two or three hundred underground Chicano newspaper publications that have emerged.

Since I'm not pinpointing any names for the sake of not omitting others, let me at least pinpoint where these leaders operate and something about their range of activity. First of all, in the barrio where the old gang used to exist, a chartered organization has come up, and they no longer knife each other but take up school and housing, health, or employment issues and even recently a strong fight against drugs. These leaders by and large are

---

2. American G.I. Forum (AGIF), a Congressionally chartered Hispanic veterans and civil rights organization. *Brown or Black berets*: The Brown Berets, a Chicano nationalist organization of the late 1960s and the 1970s, was modeled on the Black Panther Party, an African American militant organization of the mid-1960s whose members often wore black berets. *UMAS*: United Mexican-American Students, a group of the late 1960s that sought to increase Chicano enrollment in college. *MECHAS*: i.e., members of ME-ChA, or Movimiento Estudiantil Chicano de Aztlán (Chicano Student Movement of Aztlán), an organization that promotes Chicano unity and empowerment through education and political action.

young barrio batos, not yet sophisticated with the complexities of a larger society which has failed to engage them. In the jails too, organizations of Chicanos keep up with what is going on in the outside world and contribute with their art or writings while still inside, and many pledge to involve themselves in the movement rather than continue a most likely career of crime. In the fields where a great number of our Chicano brothers work, organization takes the shape of la huelga[3] and the fight becomes more lasting and more bitter. The colleges, high schools, and even grammar schools are another of the arenas for the Chicanos grouping themselves and daring to ask for change in a system that is shocked at the very audacity of a Chicano to speak when not called on to do so.

### Goals

The goals of the Chicano movement are various, and most of them are justifiable. In El Paso, decent housing; in Denver, community patrol; in California, educational opportunities; in Tierra Amarilla and El Valle de Tejas, economic survival; in San Antonio, political justice; and all over, the refusal to serve in a war that serves only to eliminate our youth; in the college scene, admittance, Chicano studies, Chicano recognition; in the jobs, supervisory, managerial, and administrative positions; in the courts, a voice; in the jails and in the hospitals, a recognition of la raza and what makes it so vividly different.

What is of importance in discussing goals is to view them very objectively and see if first of all they are feasible and secondly if they are justifiable. It is here that the movement and its goals become almost disproportionately comical in that there are at least two million Chicanos who cannot even be acknowledged in any of the social status of our country. For these Chicanos, then, it is reasonable to have as an objective the basic necessities for living—home, food, a job, medicines—a basic education, and some basic necessities such as clothes and furniture. For these Chicanos, the movement is sometimes a mirage with which they cannot truly identify, as those of us in the movement are so involved in fighting the racism of a cultural ghost that we forget that the real movement is to get these carnales liberated from the misery in which they live.

A primary goal of the movement is then that of abolishing the extreme poverty under which the huge population of Chicanos do live. It is because this goal is so sacred that we put our emphasis on the scenario and the leader who struggles there. The people who were well aware how the perimeter where the war on poverty is taking place. The people who are, in fact, looked down on even by us, their own.

Many of us still mistake goals in terms of range and importance and claim foolishly to arrive at a quick solution for a devious century of deprivation. Yes, if we pay a man a decent wage, he can take care of his needs. If we build him a home, if we help him get a G.E.D., if we help him through college, if we train him for a job, if we make him a U.S. citizen, if we organize him, if we teach him to speak English, and on and on we go drafting solutions; if we register him to vote, if we put him in business, if, if, if, and

---

3. The strike.

we ignore that the movement is in fact a combination of making all those ifs possible. Better yet, the movement is shaking each other up so that we realize our state and decide to shed both the real and the imaginary shackles that have us where we are and prevent us from saying the beautiful movement words—Ya Basta[4]—the rest is easy.

Truthfully speaking, one of the most promising of the goals of the Chicano movement is to salvage the youth so that they can at least be free of the burdens we have endured. But how, and here is where the movement turns into a gallinero[5] with all the chickens plucking grains wherever they can. Instead of an intelligent work plan which can, in fact, give the Chicano movement the national input it needs, we continue to shadow box. Yes, goals we can agree to without too much hassle, but the means of reaching them and the speed with which we may reach them are very much subject to debate even among ourselves.

### Methods—Strategy

Let us discuss strategy and methods openly, as we are accustomed to do within our movement. We hold no secrets from the dominant society and certainly not from one another. Why I used two different words for this chapter is because at least in my mind, they are two. Looking about, we see that all our lives are dominated by very strong institutions, with even the barrio and the campos here being considered an institution. La iglesia, la escuela,[6] la familia, the police, the welfare, the employment office, the credit bureau, the local, state, and federal government, social security, the army, and so on, are but some of the mass institutions that, in fact, govern our lives. The movement is trying to do several things with these institutions, from mild discreditment to total elimination; trying to achieve from partial to total control. We can say, then, the goal, or one of the goals, of the movement is that of institutional change. Institutional change to have these institutions more accessible to Chicanos, more responsive to the needs of the Chicano, more effective in carrying out their own objectives. The method to do this is our thing, and strategy within the movement to arrive at this method is another thing altogether.

In methods we have now a full file of information on how to deal with institutions; we ridicule them, we confront them, we make demands on them, we boycott them, we picket them, we, at times, burn them down. Thus, the Chicano and the institution, through the movement, go a few rounds almost daily in different arenas.

As to strategy, we have learned that to confront, we must be busy and do our homework; research the enemy who controls the institutions, what did they promise to do, where are their strong and weak points, what is it that they respond to, and then we seek the injured or abused people at the hands of such institutions, or they seek us who have been more successful in coping with them, as the case may be, and we speak, we educate, and we agitate. We admit this with no shame, because whites, at the same time they give the word a negative connotation, indulge themselves in the most vicious form of

4. Ya Basta: Enough!
5. Rooster.

6. The school. La iglesia: where the roosters are kept on a farm.

agitation and distortion of truth. When we use the word agitate, we mean reminding ourselves about the many screwings we have been dealt and getting enough "huevos"[7] to say enough.

There are both millions of dollars and millions of talented people betting that much of the movement can, in fact, be financed by the government through O.E.O. and H.E.W. and other related programs and that some good can come of playing the O.E.O. game. Much also exists to the contrary arguing that all that government programs do is retard any real progress for Chicanos. There is no evident sign that Washington wishes to abolish poverty, or else it would launch a war against the causes of poverty rather than poverty itself. Don't tell me poverty comes about from lack of education. Whether we agree or not, some of us are involved in creating change and educating the community with poverty funds and consider it very much a method, if not a strategy. Others in the movement have launched an open war on poverty programs. Time alone will prove us right or wrong.

The question of militancy must be entertained in discussing methods and strategy within the movement, and to that all I can say is that while we can answer yes to the charge of being ill-educated, we must answer no to the one of being stupid. Few advocate militancy associated with violence, but most of us advocate militancy in exposing our problems and demanding change and naturally protection and self-defense at all costs.

### The Movement Handicaps

Almost across the board, the number one handicap of the Chicano movement is the way in which it is misunderstood. It is not only misunderstood by those Chicanos outside and apathetic, but what is even stranger is that it is at times misunderstood by movement people themselves. To be plain, let me cite some basic misconceptions first by those sitting on the sidelines.

The charge against the movement is that it is only a small group of malcontent troublemakers who do not want to study or work as the case may be. Those "mitoteros"[8] are charged with the mere function of agitating their communities and challenging the old established ways. This mentality serves to close the mind and eyes to the issues behind, which in most cases merit serious looking into. When, in fact, small groups tend to march, picket, speak, shout, confront, and challenge, it is obvious that the job doesn't end there, but if those community members of the minority with positions of power do not endorse the issue or step in the legal and more sophisticated level of fighting on behalf of those who raise issues, the isolation and ostracizing of groups can be fatal and a detriment even to those who claim they are secure in the anglo community—income or possession wise.

Those in the movement at times misjudge their power to go beyond raising questions and meeting the establishment head on, and what is more, take on issues and fail to point out the real ultimate causes. In reacting to injustices, which obviously do exist in many of our communities, we fail to do our homework and identify well those injustices and their consequences. Ill-prepared

7. Literally, eggs; i.e., balls.
8. Fussy or finicky people; rowdy or boisterous people.

and ill-informed, we sometimes move in on sheer emotion and lose much ground every time we do this.

Perhaps along these same lines, another huge handicap is the inability to interpret the movement in positive terms. Being against poor education, bad housing and bad wages, police brutality, and shitty services are all valid arenas, but carry a negative air. Hating the white oppressor indiscriminately and hating gringos per se are negative forces which only show to what extent we have been brainwashed, for now we react accordingly to those we dislike the most and are ourselves indeed racists and narrow-minded brown people. I'm not saying forgive or love the gringo either, for that takes effort and all effort needs to be focused into our own communities. The gringo, in fact, is not important in our movement, and making him the object just weakens our movement. In our sentence of positive flavor, our movement simply says, we have not had our share of the prosperity of this country, even though we have contributed much—how do we improve our lot as of now, in all that affects our lives. Also, we, it is not true, do not wish merely to criticize and attack, we want to correct and defend that which is good. We do not yet see ourselves declaring war on all systems and America in general, although some members of the movement, who suffer the most and who are on the receiving end of a very despotic society, certainly see the futility of continuing to work within the system. Were we to go that route, it could only be a sheer reaction to a very apathetic nation to our pleas to share in the resources we continue to build.

Of lesser impact, but very much considered movement handicaps, are the regionalistic views we continue to share, for this is a national movement and regions must take a second place. Our petty jealousies of our own leadership and a persistent failure to sit down and talk goals and strategy instead of crying on each other's shoulders. Failure from the middle-class-oriented Chicano to recognize values of the movement for himself and his family, and finally the failure of many of us to be honest with one another about our own strengths and weaknesses.

### Movement Strong Points

I like to relate the mood and situation that I am in when I write these papers, giving the reader a greater grasp on the full meaning of the words, and so I write this afternoon aboard a Texas International plane on my way to the opening of the first all-Chicano college in history. As for the mood, I am my usual happy/sad self, but since this particular chapter deals with strong points of the movement, I would like to start out by pointing out the obvious communication and mobility most Chicanos now enjoy. This is, perhaps, the one asset which has contributed to the growth and prosperity of the movement. Chicanos no longer feel isolated; they now know other Chicanos far away care about and are also working to alleviate the situation.

The way we talk at times, those not knowing first-hand the lot of many Chicanos would think we had nothing but starving, oppressed, ill-housed, ill-paid, ill-fed Chicanos everywhere, and that we content ourselves with bellyaching all over the nation at the drop of a hat. While a majority of the Chicanos are socially and economically—not to mention educationally— deprived, it is true a great many also enjoy the comforts and luxuries this country offers; but the battle against attitudes of right-out racist discrimination affect even those who think themselves a salvo.

* * *

I believe the strongest point in the Chicano movement is that it is in the hands of our youth and not us viejitos.[9] For youth, thank God, will not take promises or be embobada[1] so easily any longer. Their view as to how life should be is still unspoiled by the many disappointments we of the older generations have endured.

A second strong point in the movement is that the majority of the movement people in key positions where policy is made are by and large what we now call "cool heads"; they are not about to blow it all foolishly, and they weigh heavily the course and strategy and maintain activities within the course of self-determination without having to use other channels than those we have learned from both cultures and which may be summarized best in one of our leader's own words, "El respeto al derecho ajeno es la paz" (to respect someone else's right is peace).

A third strong point of the movement, but of no less importance than the other two, is the fact that the time is ripe world-wide to challenge the old establishment (which obviously cannot stand the challenge) and to build a freer world with not necessarily new value systems, but with an honest living-up to the old ones we never quite got around to understanding, let alone trying. This world-wide mood makes for the Chicano movement to fit in a greater perspective of man's struggle to be truly free of the bondage that most times we set on one another.

It is obvious that I abuse my privilege of objectively presenting the movement, and get quite philosophically preachy, but that is me and I cannot objectively divorce myself from what I am writing.

Fourthly and finally, another strong point in which we take much pride is that ours is a family movement. A greater example of this I cannot give than the Crusade for Justice,[2] where from the very young to the very old, they not only live Chicanismo but can so vividly and apostolically spread it. For the last nine years, thanks to that fact and the ability of the full-time leadership offered by Gonzalez, much success in the way of focusing on injustices in the state of Colorado and gaining much in the way of institutional change has been had. In El Paso, Texas, where housing and education continue to be inflammatory issues, the youth (MAYA) and the parents (MACHOS)[3] have endured already five years of side-by-side combat against well-rooted prejudices. And so it may be in your own community, where, with good reason and good pride, you may disagree with these points and point to some of your very own.

### Aztlán

Of a confusing nature, even to movement Chicanos, is the concept of Aztlán. It is a concept unknown, revered, feared, and at times very much disliked and

---

9. Old guard.
1. Stupefied.
2. Grassroots organization founded by Rodolfo

"Corky" Gonzales (see note 7, p. 993).
3. Unidentified organization. MAYA: Mexican American Youth Association.

unaccepted. First, it is considered foreign; when merely looking at the word or hearing it, one fights it mentally. Its authoritative or academic source is vague, in that being an Indian concept (Aztec), it was merely an abstract at the time. Aztecs had their empire. It has a mere reference to the territories north of their empire, which now can be said to be the western United States (south-, mid-, and northwest). It was then a name to refer to what lay north of Mexico, their empire. Now we know what lies north of that empire—our homes, our cities, our states—and since there is a definite relationship linking us to that civilization, we, in fact, merely wish to acknowledge that we know where we are.

California and Colorado, the first to wise up to this fact, capitalized immediately on this idea, making it a definite movement concept, a pillar. Because these two states were alert to use the idea, certainly a bit of natural jealousy and regionalism crept up, and the concept was not that readily embraced, understood, or accepted in the other western states and to the east. Thanks to the excellent network of communication, most Chicanos in the movement now know of the Aztlan concept.

Aztlán became, in fact, a plan of work within the movement in Denver and became known as "El plan espiritual de Aztlan." In my earlier paper, "1970—The Year of the Chicano," I made more detailed reference to this plan. Let it suffice to recall that the plan speaks strongly of a Chicano nationalism which is a prerequisite to assert our proper role in our communities and be given the respect we deserve. It is based on a strong carnalismo, which is the spiritualism strength of the movement.

Interpreted in general terms for most of us Chicanos, it is another attack on those who stole the lands that belonged to our abuelos and a serious attempt to reclaim those lands; and since the land issue is always more vividly alive in New Mexico, Aztlán has a flavor of its own in that state. Most Chicanos in the movement have, by now, gotten into the habit of introducing themselves, por ejemplo,[4] Lalo Delgado from El Paso, Aztlán. So, do not look for this Aztlán on gringo maps, because it will not be there. As a point of departure: a friend and I were hitchhiking, and we were picked up by a nice anglo couple, who proceeded to make conversation and asked us where we were from. When we said Aztlan, they did not say anything, but went on to ask us how it was "over there," thinking all the while we had said "Iceland." We must do something about our pronunciation!

The Aztlan concept benefits the movement in precisely the last point. I have tried to make. It combats the regionalism which has caused us so much harm in keeping us divided. If we are from Califa, Tejas, Colorado, Nuevo Mejico or Arizona or Utah and we are Chicanos, then let us reinforce that fact by also having in common being residents of Aztlan—a concept which knows no state lines or fronteras, just whatever lies beyond the reach of my eye.

Aztlan confuses the post office somewhat because most of us who are writing Aztlan on our letters are educating the United States Post Office at the same time. Again the word Aztlán, like the word Chicano, does not set too well with some of our more educated brothers, who dismiss both as nonsense or tools we invent to make boobs of the many Chicanos who swallow

4. For example.

the terms blindly and thereby being in fact as cruel as gringo historians in dispensing lies. Chicano and Aztlán are both words which are hijas legíti-mas[5] del barrio y de la raza and therefore true and a strong source of pride.

## Nationalism

The Chicano movement is, in fact, an effort to nationalize the second largest minority in the United States. Manifestations of this nationalization process are now evident. This grouping of Chicanos doesn't necessarily mean we are the only ones pushing for it, or that we are the initiators. Examine, if you will, any city in which Chicanos live; the barrio is a very marked, isolated, geo-graphic means of economically corraling Chicanos and therefore nationaliz-ing the city. If it is the school, the peers of Chicano children will band to survive the stifling experience. If it is job-wise, we see the Chicano truckers, sanitation men, mail clerks continuing this process. If at the social level, we see the circle of compadres y comadres[6] attending a series of showers, wed-dings, baptisms, quince añeras,[7] birthdays, and plain groupings to share a parranda, our equivalent of the cocktail hour. Naturally, the isolation im-posed on us for years by our lighter blond brothers has made the nationaliza-tion process now only a mere awareness of what we have had all along.

Nationalism in our case is a matter of culture, values, and language, plus, in most cases, the common denominator of economic deprivations. We have come, then, through the movement not only to recognize and acknowledge this separatism, but to call it by its proper name, rather than accept the socio-logical garble that has labeled us unique and slow in assimilation. We now take full pride in our isolation, which is responsible for our very survival.

It is not a mere case of being different and wishing to remain different, but now we have also realized that nationalism is the very force we must use to regain control of our communities, of our lives, of our destinies.

The Raza Chicana has today the following manifestations to indicate that nationalization is not only essential to the movement, but is the very vehicle for positive lawful action:

1. Colegio Jacinto Treviño, Centro Educativo Chicano in Mercedes, Texas—a college by Chicanos, for Chicanos, staffed by Chicanos. The same educational efforts were launched by the Crusade for Justice in Denver, Col-orado, in their Plaza de las Tres Culturas, Tlatelolco * * *. Where it is not possible to have our own educational system provided to the conventional school, we have it in school organizations such as UMAS, MAPA,[8] MECHA, Brown and Black Berets as well as MAYOS and MAYAS. Most colleges have made big strides in correcting their deficiencies by devising Chicano cultural and curricular improvements plus enriching their faculties with knowledge-able and committed movement teachers.

La Raza Unida, our own political party, has made a bid for existence that has already shaken our two twin parties. The bid is serious, as now for the first time Chicano candidates and Chicano issues relate directly to our situ-ation. This, plus the evident neglect of Republicans and Democrats, has

---

5. *Hijas legítimas*: biological daughters.
6. *Compadres y comadres*: male and female pals.
7. Sweet fifteens.
8. Mexican American Political Association.

assisted in making La Raza Unida one of the significant and attractive pieces of nationalization.

What about economic nationalization? Our efforts in that direction, though less impressive, continue to amaze some of us who were pessimistic that we might succeed in this area given the scant exposure we have suffered historically. CEDA and ULABA,[9] again of Denver, stand out as very sturdy pioneers in setting the Chicano up to run his own businesses. From construction companies to a bank of our own, our own radio stations, our own newspapers, our own restaurants and stores, barbershops and cleaners, and why not?

I had hoped to spend some words defending against, or counterattacking, the criticisms expressed against our nationalistic efforts, but I will not do so. Instead, may I re-direct those criticisms to the most successful nationalists within our country, the Jews, the Italians, the Orientals, for I am very sure that whatever motives they have had all along to remain very much unique groups are the same motives that we could express. Anyway, let me just quote my Joseph W. Barr dollar bill—E Pluribus Unum.[1]

\* \* \*

1973

---

9. An economic movement in states such as Oregon, Washington, and Michigan. *CEDA*: Community and Economic Development Association.
1. Out of many, one (Latin); motto that appears on U.S. coins. *Joseph W. Barr dollar bill*: Joseph Walker Barr (1918–1996), American businessman and politician, served as undersecretary of the U.S. Treasury 1965–68 and secretary of the Treasury 1968–69 (and thus had his "signature" on U.S. dollar bills printed during this latter two-year period).

---

# HEBERTO PADILLA
## 1932–2000

Regarded by many as Cuba's leading contemporary poet, Heberto Padilla was born into a family of Spanish immigrants in Pinar del Río, Cuba. During the dictatorship of Fulgencio Batista, Padilla and his parents lived in exile in the United States, where from 1955 to 1959 he worked as a journalist and language instructor. In 1959, after the Batista regime fell to the rebel forces of Fidel Castro, Padilla spent several months as the New York correspondent for *Prensa Latina*, the new Cuban government's information agency. He soon returned to Cuba, but for the next few years he spent much time away from the island, reporting as foreign correspondent from London and Moscow. With the Cuban writer Guillermo Cabrera Infante, he founded and edited the important literary weekly *Lunes de Revolución* and helped establish the UNEAC (Unión de Escritores y Artistas de Cuba), the Cuban union for artists and writers.

During his travels through Europe, Padilla worried about the repression of writers and intellectuals under the Marxist regime in Cuba. His close relations with high officials in Castro's government led him to believe that many of them were hostile to intellectual freedom. In his second poetry collection, *El justo tiempo humano* (Just

Human Time, 1962), Padilla expressed his continuing support for the revolution, but voiced misgivings about its increasing authoritarianism. When *Lunes de Revolución* was shut down by the government and Cabrera Infante went into exile, Padilla defended his colleague, a gesture that was interpreted as support for counterrevolutionary elitism and resulted in Padilla's dismissal from his foreign posts.

In 1968, Padilla submitted a new manuscript, *Fuera del juego* (Out of the Game), to a poetry contest sponsored by the UNEAC. The poems in this collection were full of anger and disillusionment, expressing sympathy for the victims of oppression throughout the world. The jury, which included distinguished Cuban and non-Cuban writers, faced intense pressure from the Ministry of Culture to deny Padilla the prize, which included publication of the book and a trip abroad. The poems were denounced by government officials as decadent and antisocial, and hence unworthy of such distinction. Still, Padilla won the contest. The UNEAC reluctantly published Padilla's poems, but added a preface denouncing him for his lack of revolutionary zeal. After the publication of *Fuera del juego*, the attacks on Padilla increased, and he was condemned as a traitor to the revolution. Padilla's difficulties with the Castro regime had begun to attract notice outside Cuba, however, and international pressure from writers and intellectuals helped ensure his freedom. His personal appeal to Castro, with whom he had been friends for many years, brought him a teaching post at the University of Havana in 1969.

Padilla continued to write, working on a novel and sending his poems to friends abroad to be published. Early in 1971, a reading to his colleagues at the UNEAC from the manuscript of his new poetry collection, *Provocaciones* (Provocations), unleashed a new storm of attacks from the regime. In March, Padilla and his wife, the writer Belkis Cuza Malé, were arrested for conspiracy against the revolution. While in prison, Padilla was beaten and terrorized. Castro visited him in the hospital, where Padilla was recovering from his wounds, and repeated his denunciation of writers and literature. Once again, writers and intellectuals throughout the world protested Padilla's ill treatment. Padilla and his wife were released, though not before he was forced to appear before another meeting of the writers' union and confess to counterrevolutionary actions and sentiments. Padilla and his wife lived through much of the 1970s in Cuba as social pariahs. He was allowed to work as a translator, but not to publish his work or leave the country. A few poems were smuggled out and published in the United States. *Sent Off the Field*, a selection in English of poems from *Fuera del juego* and *El justo tiempo humano*, was published in London in 1972, and *Provocaciones* was published in Spain in 1973.

The international outcry that followed Padilla's public humiliation led many intellectuals who had previously supported the Cuban Revolution—among them the Mexican writer, diplomat, and Nobel Prize–winner Octavio Paz and the Peruvian writer and politician Mario Vargas Llosa—to distance themselves from Castro, who accused Padilla's supporters of being bourgeois elitists and libeling the revolution. Vargas Llosa wrote that "to force comrades, with methods repugnant to human dignity, to accuse themselves of imaginary betrayals and sign letters in which even the syntax seems to be that of the police, is the negation of everything that made me embrace, from the first day, the cause of the Cuban revolution: its decision to fight for justice without losing respect for individuals."

The incident came to be known as *El caso Padilla* (the Padilla affair). A campaign by the French philosophers Jean-Paul Sartre and Simone de Beauvoir; the American critic and writer Susan Sontag; Robert B. Silvers, editor of *The New York Review of Books*; and others put pressure on the Cuban government to free the poet and let him leave the island. Padilla's departure finally took place in 1980, thanks to U.S. senator Edward Kennedy, who secured his release to the United States. Padilla was hailed as a hero by President Ronald Reagan. (In 1971, Lourdes Casal wrote an incisive book on the topic: *El caso Padilla: Literatura y revolución en Cuba*.)

Padilla began his second exile at Princeton University, the first of many visiting appointments he would hold at American universities during the next 20 years. He and Cuza Malé founded *Linden Lane Magazine*, an outlet for Cuban and Cuban American writers. In 1981, he published a new book of poems, *El hombre junto al mar* (The Man by the Sea, translated and published in English in the United States as *Legacies* that same year), and the novel, *En mi jardín pastan los heroes* (translated and published in English as *Heroes Are Grazing in My Garden*), that he had begun years earlier in Cuba. In the novel, the lives of two despairing intellectuals chart the Cuban Revolution's evolution from idealism to oppression. In his 1988 memoir, *La mala memoria* (published in English in 1989 as *Self-Portrait of the Other*), Padilla tells his story and the stories of other Cuban writers who suffered prison or exile under the Castro regime. Inescapably, the "other" at the center of the book is Castro, the friend turned nemesis.

Padilla died in Auburn, Alabama, where he held a teaching position.

# The Gift[1]

I have bought these strawberries for you.
I wanted to bring you flowers,
but I saw a girl biting into
strawberries in the street
and the thick sweet juice                                                5
ran over her lips so that
I felt that her avid warmth
was like yours,
the very image of love.
We have lived out years                                                 10
struggling with sharp winds,
the ancient stench of ruins,
but always there was fruit,
the very simplest,
and there was always a flower.                                          15
So that even though these strawberries
are not the most important thing in the universe,
I know that they will swell your joy
like the glee of falling snow.
Our son smiling melts it in his hands                                   20
as God must do with our lives.
We have put on overcoats and boots,
and our numb red skin
is another image of the resurrection.[2]
Creatures of the disapora of our time.                                  25
Oh, give us, God, the strength to go on!

1982

---

1. Translated by Alistair Reid and Andrew Hurley.

2. In Christianity, the return to life of Jesus Christ after his crucifixion.

## A Remembrance of Wallace Stevens in Florida[1]

At this moment the sea is at full boil,
and if you were with me you, I know, would say
that what boils is only the image of the sea.
In a language where abstracting is a curse,
you grasped the abstraction in those sun-drenched worlds          5
almost impossible to seize and hold.
I have seen unkempt gardens, the leftover shapes
of harried flowers.
There is a continuum, an order in this landscape
where a tree is ghost of the idea of tree.                       10
Leafless triptych, lines of stone, wave on wave
repeating their questions; the only reply is the mass
of an underwater rock, the rusted cans
in the sand, the glug-glug in shadows.

The boats have put to sea, all of a sudden                       15
turning to mathematics
lazily, numbers in air—
abandoned parasols.
Here, no ghost-notions argue with the weather.
No body of light disperses in the sea                            20
better than in your poem.

If anyone spoke the language of survivors
it was you, who fused the snow-touched ferns
of New Hampshire with the shimmering expanses of the South.
You are not the unwelcome guest, driving us mad.                 25
Rather, you are the sea's own form, the shiver of that wave
becoming a wave in your words.

1991

## Man on the Edge[1]

He is not the man who goes over the wall,
feeling himself enclosed by his times,
nor is he the fugitive breathing hard
hidden in the back of a truck
fleeing from the terrorists,                                      5
nor is he the poor guy with the canceled passport
who is always trying to cross a new border.
He lives on this side of heroics
—in that dark part—
but never gets rattled or surprised.                             10

1. Translated by Alistair Reid and Alexander
Coleman. *Wallace Stevens*: American poet (1879–
1955).

1. Translated by Alistair Reid and Alexander
Coleman.

He does not want to be a hero,
not even a romantic
around whom we might
weave a legend.
He is sentenced to this life, and, what terrifies him more,          15
condemned irretrievably to his own time.
He is headless at two in the morning,
going from one room to another
like an enormous wind
which barely survives in the wind outside.          20
Every morning he begins again
as if he were an Italian actor.
He stops dead
as if someone had just stolen his being.
No looking glass would dare reflect          25
this fallen mouth, this wisdom gone bankrupt.

1991

## Princeton Cemetery[1]

A town can be a fortunate assembly of many souls,
but it is also a steady contemplation of death.
Suddenly the lights go on in a house,
someone moves the curtains,
you hear the sound of someone hurrying up the stairs,          5
and we have another casualty, an empty algebra.
The tilted tombstones
coexist with our workdays.
The routine of our lives
skips over this thin grass          10
where a rake scrapes up the fallen leaves.
None of this is reason for insomnia.
Our wakefulness comes only from hassles or money worries.
No one feels they must attend these dead,
not even that young gravedigger,          15
or the other, who casually wields his clippers
around the tombstones.
O God, tell us where, tell us why.
There is not just one Ash Wednesday[2] in our lives.
Toward that cemetery          20
everyone travels with the same fear,
the same eyes, the same feet.

1991

1. Translated by Alistair Reid and Alexander Coleman.
2. *Ash Wednesday*: in Christianity, a day of repentance before God, the seventh Wednesday before Easter.

## Song of the Prodigal Son[1]

Give me back the sun's din
the schoolroom door
In the end, let the summer blaze
into my stubborn eyes

I've walked so much                                     5
that zeal and snow
singe my traveler's eye
Wet my lips now
with my bathtub sponge
Give back to me                                         10
the rustle of green trees
and the sea of always.

1991

1. Translated by Alistair Reid and Alexander Coleman. In the Bible, the prodigal son returns to his
parental home and begs for his father's forgiveness after living a disreputable life in a distant
country.

# JACK AGÜEROS
## b. 1934

Born in East Harlem to Puerto Rican parents, Jack Agüeros grew up in New York
City. He studied literature and theater at Brooklyn College, where in 1964 he earned
a bachelor's degree. Later he earned a master's in urban studies from Occidental College, in Los Angeles. Agüeros's involvement in New York's artistic circles began in the
early 1950s, with his participation in Los Amigos de Puerto Rico, a group that promoted the work of Puerto Rican artists living on the mainland. Two decades later, he
cofounded Caymán Gallery, in Manhattan's SoHo neighborhood. From 1976 to 1986,
he directed New York's El Museo del Barrio, an institution committed to bringing the
work of Puerto Rican and other Latino artists to the greater community.

Although he is known for his fiction, poetry, and drama, Agüeros's first publication
was the personal narrative "Halfway to Dick and Jane: A Puerto Rican Pilgrimage,"
included here. Originally presented in the anthology *The Immigrant Experience: The
Anguish of Becoming American* (1971), it reveals his family's struggles to earn a living
in the U.S. and his efforts to feel at home in the land where he was born. Most of
Agüeros's stories depict barrio life realistically and demonstrate his ability to capture
the speech patterns and local color of the community. His first collection of short fiction was *Dominoes and Other Stories from the Puerto Rican* (1993). After placing
many of his poems in literary journals, Agüeros published his first poetry collection,
*Correspondence between the Stonehaulers* (1991). In *Sonnets from the Puerto Rican*
(1996), he uses the sonnet, a classical fourteen-line poetic form, to deal with social

and political concerns and street themes. His play *Dream Star Cafe* was produced in New York City in 2002.

Agüeros is also a literary critic and translator. In 1997, he compiled and translated into English the most complete collection of the Puerto Rican poet Julia de Burgos's works, *Song of the Simple Truth*. Ten years later, he compiled and translated the Cuban poet José Martí's works in *Come, Come, My Boiling Blood: The Complete Poems of José Martí*.

# Halfway to Dick and Jane: A Puerto Rican Pilgrimage

My father arrived in America in 1920, a stowaway on a steamer that shuttled between San Juan and New York. At sixteen, he was through with school and had been since thirteen or fourteen when he left the eighth grade. Between dropout and migrant, the picture is not totally clear, but three themes dominate: baseball, cockfighting, and cars. At sixteen, my father had lived in every town of Puerto Rico, had driven every road there in Ford Models A and T, had played basketball, baseball, studied English and American History, hustled tourists, and had heard the popular and classical music of two cultures.

With a superficial knowledge of America, wholly aware that the streets were not paved in gold, interested specifically in neither employment nor education, my father visited New York in the same spirit in which a family might drive out in the country on a Sunday afternoon. But it was winter 1920, and my father's romantic picture of snow was shattered. His clothes were inadequate for cold weather, and he himself was not prepared either physically or emotionally for cold. The light English patter he had charmed the tourists with was no match for the rapid-fire slurred English of New York's streets. His school English, with its carefully pronounced "water" and "squirrel," seemed like another language compared to "wudder" and "squaral."

It was a three-day winter for my father. In seventy-two hours, he thought he understood New York: the flatness of its geography and humanity, the extreme cold of climate and character, the toe to toe aloneness. On the fourth day, Joaquin Agueros went back to San Juan.

He came back "north" again in his early twenties, but again there is an unclear time span. There appears to have been a short hitch in the Puerto Rican National Guard, and during this time, there was an upheaval in island and mainland politics. Governors of Puerto Rico were appointed by the White House and had considerable powers over the island's economy and politics. The new governor began a thorough shake-up of the civil service, and as a result, my father left the National Guard and my grandfather, Ramon Agueros, was relieved of his title and duties of police captain. My father's family, composed of my grandparents, three brothers, a sister, and one or two *hermanos de crianza* (literally, "brothers of upbringing," or children brought up as if brothers), was plunged into total poverty. My grandfather was not and had never been a landowner. His policeman's pay was the only source of income. Joaquin was the oldest son, and unemployed. The family was spared starvation by the Order of the Masons, which delivered trucks full of food once or twice a month (Grandpa was a master).

The tyranny of the new gringo governor was causing serious repercussions on the island. Puerto Rico was an extraordinarily underdeveloped country, very poor and depressed, without a unanimity of affection for America. There was a massacre of civilians at Ponce by the police. This was blamed on the new governor, as were all the island's problems. My father has told me that talk and rumors of assassination were common. Many people expected to hear of the governor's death. Nevertheless, the governor was not assassinated, and there were no more Ponce massacres. Capitan Ramon Agueros was readmitted to the force but not reinstated in rank. Soon thereafter, his eldest son Joaquin also became a policeman.

In my youth, I loved to look at the pictures of Father and Grandfather in their police uniforms. Of Ramon, bald and clean shaven in his *capitan's* jacket, I remember a large chest, a strong jaw, and tough eyes. Set in a gilded oval frame with an American eagle at the top, it hung under glass in my parents' bedroom. Of my father, I remember a patched-up photo, probably torn up by my mother after a spat. In it a tall, very handsome young man was standing full length with hat and riding boots. Face not stern like Ramon's, but with a look of forced seriousness. Joaquin bore a resemblance to Rudolph Valentino[1] and to Carlos Gardel, the Argentinian singer and film star.

"Are you still a policeman?"

"No," my father says. He is sitting in a rocking chair, stroking his mustache idly, enjoying the nightingale in the cage hanging between rooms. "No, I am not a cop." He pauses, strokes, rocks, gives a big smile as if enjoying some inside joke, and says, "I had a bad revolver. Used to chew up the bullets, chack, chack, chack; finally, bang." Then he stops smiling.

"Why did you have such funny shoes?"

"Your father was a mounted police," my mother tells me from the kitchen. (One day I told a cop on a horse in Central Park,[2] "My father was a mounted policeman." "So what?" shot back the cop.) "He was very skinny, but very tall in the saddle, and a good rider."

"Those are riding boots. I had a big red, sixteen hands, so alive he couldn't walk." (Furious rocking.) "I'd take him down to the beach and let him go. It was illegal, but we both loved it, and we'd wash down in the ocean. . . ."

My father, once animated, would and does go on telling stories. Most of high adventure, with chase-escape climaxes, and every one peppered with mischief.

I was told that my father left the police force because he had shot and wounded a moonshiner in a raid on a still. (Not very unlikely, for such raids were common: there is a photo, sepiaed by time, Grandpa and Father, guns pointing at a group of desperados with hands held high up against a wall of vats, jugs, and plumbing.) The wounded moonshiner turned out to be a member of high society, and my father was accused of misconduct and promiscuous use of a firearm—the chack chack story had its undivulged point.

Joaquin, like many Puerto Ricans, has always been proud to a fault. Standing departmental hearings, he was exonerated of the charges. But the exoneration was meaningless; outraged that his integrity had been questioned at all, he resigned from the force.

This pride and value of integrity is ancient. You can find it in *El Cid*, in the plays of Lope de Vega, in *Don Quixote*.[3] And you find it among the Puerto

---

1. Italian-born American actor and sex symbol (1895–1926); known as "the Latin Lover."

2. Grand public park in Manhattan.

3. Novel (1605, 1615) by the Spanish writer

Ricans today. In America it debilitates them, it keeps them from filing complaints of violation of human and civil rights, from contesting employers' decisions before state referees, and it keeps them from insisting upon full service from city and state agencies.

That's what I know about my old man's early life—he was a picaresque character from a Spanish novel. It is a collage of information, some of it concrete and verifiable, most of it gathered haphazardly and connected by conjecture. Does it matter what the governor's name is? Does it matter whether any or all of it is fact or fiction? What matters is that I thought my old man enjoyed life, let no grass grow under his feet, and it also matters that he came back to New York.

I was born in Harlem in 1934. We lived on 111th Street off Fifth Avenue. It was a block of mainly three-story buildings—with brick fronts, or brownstone, or limestone imitations of brownstone. Our apartment was a three-room first-floor walk-up. It faced north and had three windows on the street, none in back. There was a master bedroom, a living room, a kitchen–dining room, a foyer with a short hall, and a bathroom. In the kitchen there was an air shaft to evacuate cooking odors and grease—we converted it to a chimney for Santa Claus.

The kitchen was dominated by a large Victorian china closet, and the built-in wall shelves were lined with oilcloth, trimmed with ruffle, both decorated by brilliant and miniature fruits. Prominent on a wall of the kitchen was a large reproduction of a still life, a harvest table full of produce, framed and under glass. From it, I learned to identify apples, pumpkins, bananas, pears, grapes, and melons, and "peaches without worms." A joke between my mother and me. (A peach we had bought in the city market, under the New Haven's elevated tracks, bore, like the trains above, passengers.)

On one shelf of the kitchen, over the stove, there was a lineup of ceramic cannisters that carried words like "nutmeg," "ginger," and "basil." I did not know what those words meant and I don't know if my mother did either. "Spices," she would say, and that was that. They were of a yellow color that was not unlike the yellow of the stove. The kitchen was itself painted yellow, I think, very pale. But I am sure of one thing, it was not "Mickey Moused." "Mickey Mousing" was a technique used by house painters to decorate the areas of the walls that were contained by wood molding. Outside the molding they might paint a solid green. Inside the wood mold, the same solid green. Then with a twisted-up rag dipped in a lighter green they would trace random patterns.

We never used wallpaper or rugs. Our floors were covered with linoleum in every room. My father painted the apartment every year before Christmas, and in addition, he did all the maintenance, doing his own plastering and plumbing. No sooner would we move into an apartment than my father would repair holes or cracks, and if there were bulges in the plaster, he would break them open and redo the area—sometimes a whole wall. He would immediately modify the bathrooms to add a shower with separate valves, and usually as a routine matter, he cleaned out all the elbow traps, and

---

Miguel de Cervantes (1547–1616). *El Cid*: historical epic film (1961) based loosely on the life of Rodrigo Díaz de Vivar (ca. 1040–1099), known as El Cid Campeador, a Castilian nobleman, military leader, and diplomat. *Lope de Vega*: Spanish playwright and poet (1562–1635).

changed all the washers on faucets. This was true of the other families in the buildings where I lived. Not a December came without a painting of the apartment.

We had Louis XIV furniture[4] in the living room, reflected in the curved glass door and curved glass sides of the china closet. On the walls of the living room hung two prints that I loved. I would spend hours playing games with my mother based on the pictures making up stories, etc. One day at Brooklyn College, a slide projector slammed, and I awoke after having dozed off during a dull lecture to see Van Gogh's "The Gleaners"[5] on the screen. I almost cried. Another time I came across the other print in a book. A scene of Venice by Canaletto.[6]

The important pieces of the living room, for me, were a Detrola radio with magic-eye tuning and the nightingale, Keero. The nightingale and the radio went back before my recollection. The bird could not stop singing, and people listened on the sidewalk below and came upstairs offering to buy Keero.

The Detrola, shaped like a Gothic arch with inlaid woodwork, was a great source of entertainment for the family. I memorized all the hit songs sung by Libertad Lamarque and Carlos Gardel.[7] Sundays I listened to the Canary Hour presented by Hartz Mountain Seed Company. Puppy, a white Spitz, was my constant companion. Puppy slept at the foot of my bed from the first day he came to our house till the day he died, when I was eleven or twelve and he was seven or eight.

My *madrina* lived on the third floor of our building, and for all practical purposes, her apartment and ours formed a duplex. My godmother really was my second mother. Rocking me to sleep, playing her guitar, and singing me little songs, she used to say, "I'm your real mother, 'cause I love you more." But I knew that wasn't so.

Carmen Diaz, my mother, came to New York in 1931. Her brother, a career soldier, had sent for her with the intention of taking her up to Plattsburgh,[8] where he was stationed. Like my father, she arrived in New York on a steamer. My uncle had planned to show his kid sister the big city before leaving for Plattsburgh, but during a week in New York my mother was convinced to stay. More opportunities, and other Spanish-speaking people, were the reasons that changed her mind.

Carmen had had a tough time all her life in Puerto Rico. Her mother had died when she was only two. Her father, a wealthy farmer and veterinarian, remarried and began paying less and less attention to his business affairs. The stepmother was not very fond of the children. Thus, when her older sister married a policeman, Carmen accepted the invitation to live with the newlyweds, acting as a sort of housekeeper-governess. After many years in this role, which my mother describes as "rewarding, but not a life for a young girl," came the offer to "go north."

On the island, my mother had had two serious suitors. One was a schoolteacher who had an ailing mother and could not afford to marry on his salary. The other was a rookie cop who had arrested her brother-in-law for carrying

4. I.e., of the Baroque style associated with this French king (1638–1715).
5. The painting *Des glaneuses* (The Gleaners, 1857) is by the French artist Jean-François Millet (1814–1875). In 1885, the Dutch artist Vincent van Gogh (1853–1890) sketched a peasant woman gleaning (picking up grain after the harvest).
6. Italian painter (1697–1768).
7. Uruguayan-born Argentinian tango singer (1887 or 1890–1935). *Libertad Lamarque*: Argentinian actress and singer (1908–2000).
8. A city in upstate New York.

a concealed weapon. The brother-in-law took the arrest in good humor, and after proving that he was an off-duty cop, invited the rookie home for dinner. The rookie became a frequent visitor, twirling apples for Carmen's delight, but one day he came to visit and said he was going north, to find a good job. He said he would write, but no letter ever came from Joaquin.

Carmen had big plans for her life in America, intending to go to school and study interior decorating. But the Puerto Ricans who came to New York at that time found life in the city tough. It was the Depression, and work was hard to come by. My mother went from job to job for about six months and finally landed a job in the garment district as a seamstress. Twenty years later, she retired from the ILGWU,[9] her dream of becoming a decorator waylaid by bumping into my father on a Manhattan street and reviving the old romance. My father had been back in America since the mid-twenties. In America he remembers working a long day to earn $1.25. After a time, he found a job in a restaurant that paid nine dollars a week and provided two meals a day. That was a good deal, even at a six-day week, twelve to fifteen hours a day.

I am an only child. My parents and I always talked about my becoming a doctor. The law and politics were not highly regarded in my house. Lawyers, my mother would explain, had to defend people whether they were guilty or not, while politicians, my father would say, were all crooks. A doctor helped everybody, rich and poor, white and black. If I became a doctor, I could study hay fever and find a cure for it, my godmother would say. Also, I could take care of my parents when they were old. I liked the idea of helping, and for nineteen years my sole ambition was to study medicine.

My house had books, not many, but my parents encouraged me to read. As I became a good reader they bought books for me and never refused me money for their purchase. My father once built a bookcase for me. It was an important moment, for I had always believed that my father was not too happy about my being a bookworm. The atmosphere at home was always warm. We seemed to be a popular family. We entertained frequently, with two standing parties a year—at Christmas and for my birthday. Parties were always large. My father would dismantle the beds and move all the furniture so that the full two rooms could be used for dancing. My mother would cook up a storm, particularly at Christmas. *Pasteles, lechon asado, arroz con gandules*, and a lot of *coquito* to drink (meat-stuffed plantain, roast pork, rice with pigeon peas, and coconut nog). My father always brought in a band. They played without compensation and were guests at the party. They ate and drank and danced while a victrola covered the intermissions. One year my father brought home a whole pig and hung it in the foyer doorway. He and my mother prepared it by rubbing it down with oil, oregano, and garlic. After preparation, the pig was taken down and carried over to a local bakery where it was cooked and returned home. Parties always went on till daybreak, and in addition to the band, there were always volunteers to sing and declaim poetry.

My mother kept an immaculate household. Bedspreads (chenille seemed to be very in) and lace curtains, washed at home like everything else, were hung up on huge racks with rows of tight nails. The racks were assembled in

---

9. International Ladies' Garment Workers Union.

the living room, and the moisture from the wet bedspreads would fill the apartment. In a sense, that seems to be the lasting image of that period of my life. The house was clean. The neighbors were clean. The streets, with few cars, were clean. The buildings were clean and uncluttered with people on the stoops. The park was clean. The visitors to my house were clean, and the relationships that my family had with other Puerto Rican families, and the Italian families that my father had met through baseball and my mother through the garment center, were clean. Second Avenue was clean and most of the apartment windows had awnings. There was always music, there seemed to be no rain, and snow did not become slush. School was fun, we wrote essays about how grand America was, we put up hunchbacked cats at Halloween, we believed Santa Claus visited everyone. I believed everyone was Catholic. I grew up with dogs, nightingales, my godmother's guitar, rocking chair, cat, guppies, my father's occasional roosters, kept in a cage on the fire escape. Laundry delivered and collected by horse and wagon, fruits and vegetables sold the same way, windowsill refrigeration in winter, iceman and box in summer. The police my friends, likewise the teachers.

In short, the first seven or so years of my life were not too great a variation on Dick and Jane, the school book figures who, if my memory serves me correctly, were blond Anglo-Saxons, not immigrants, not migrants like the Puerto Ricans, and not the children of either immigrants or migrants.

My family moved in 1941 to Lexington Avenue into a larger apartment where I could have my own room. It was a light, sunny, railroad flat on the top floor of a well-kept building. I transferred to a new school, and whereas before my classmates had been mostly black, the new school had few blacks. The classes were made up of Italians, Irish, Jews, and a sprinkling of Puerto Ricans. My block was populated by Jews, Italians, and Puerto Ricans.

And then a whole series of different events began. I went to junior high school. We played in the backyards, where we tore down fences to build fires to cook stolen potatoes. We tore up whole hedges, because the green tender limbs would not burn when they were peeled, and thus made perfect skewers for our stolen "mickies." We played tag in the abandoned buildings, tearing the plaster off the walls, tearing the wire lath off the wooden slats, tearing the wooden slats themselves, good for fires, for kites, for sword fighting. We ran up and down the fire escapes playing tag and over and across many rooftops. The war ended and the heavy Puerto Rican migration began. The Irish and the Jews disappeared from the neighborhood. The Italians tried to consolidate east of Third Avenue.

What caused the clean and open world to end? Many things. Into an ancient neighborhood came pouring four to five times more people than it had been designed to hold. Men who came running at the promise of jobs were jobless as the war ended. They were confused. They could not see the economic forces that ruled their lives as they drank beer on the corners, reassuring themselves of good times to come while they were hell-bent toward alcoholism. The sudden surge in numbers caused new resentments, and prejudice was intensified. Some were forced to live in cellars, and were then characterized as cave dwellers. Kids came who were confused by the new surroundings; their Puerto Ricanness forced us against a mirror asking, "If they are Puerto Ricans, what are we?" and thus they confused us. In our confusion we were sometimes pathetically reaching out, sometimes pathologically

striking out. Gangs. Drugs. Wine. Smoking. Girls. Dances and slow-drag music. Mambo. Spics, Spooks, and Wops. Territories, brother gangs, and war
councils establishing rules for right of way on blocks and avenues and for seating in the local theater. Pegged pants and zip guns. Slang.

Dick and Jane were dead, man. Education collapsed. Every classroom had
ten kids who spoke no English. Black, Italian, Puerto Rican relations in the
classroom were good, but we all knew we couldn't visit one another's neighborhoods. Sometimes we could not move too freely within our own blocks. On
109th, from the lamp post west, the Latin Aces, and from the lamp post
east, the Senecas, the "club" I belonged to. The kids who spoke no English
became known as Marine Tigers, picked up from a popular Spanish song.
(The *Marine Tiger* and the *Marine Shark* were two ships that sailed from
San Juan to New York and brought over many, many migrants from the
island.)

The neighborhood had its boundaries. Third Avenue and east, Italian. Fifth
Avenue and west, black. South, there was a hill on 103rd Street known locally as Cooney's Hill. When you got to the top of the hill, something strange
happened: America began, because from the hill south was where the "Americans" lived. Dick and Jane were not dead; they were alive and well in a better
neighborhood.

When, as a group of Puerto Rican kids, we decided to go swimming to Jefferson Park Pool, we knew we risked a fight and a beating from the Italians.
And when we went to La Milagrosa Church in Harlem, we knew we risked a
fight and a beating from the blacks. But when we went over Cooney's Hill, we
risked dirty looks, disapproving looks, and questions from the police like,
"What are you doing in this neighborhood?" and "Why don't you kids go back
where you belong?"

Where we belonged! Man, I had written compositions about America.
Didn't I belong on the Central Park tennis courts, even if I didn't know how
to play? Couldn't I watch Dick play? Weren't these policemen working for
me too?

Junior high school was a waste. I can say with 90 per cent accuracy that I
learned nothing. The woodshop was used to manufacture stocks for "home-
mades" after Macy's stopped selling zip guns. We went from classroom to
classroom answering "here," and trying to be "good." The math class was
generally permitted to go to the gym after roll call. English was still a good
class. Partly because of a damn good, tough teacher named Miss Beck, and
partly because of the grade-number system (7-1 the smartest seventh grade
and 7-12, the dumbest). Books were left in school, there was little or no homework, and the whole thing seemed to be a holding operation until high school.
Somehow or other, I passed the entrance exam to Brooklyn Technical High
School. But I couldn't cut the mustard, either academically or with the
"American" kids. After one semester, I came back to PS 83, waited a semester, and went on to Benjamin Franklin High School.

I still wanted to study medicine and excelled in biology. English was always an interesting subject, and I still enjoyed writing compositions and
reading. In the neighborhood it was becoming a problem being categorized
as a bookworm and as one who used "Sunday words," or "big words." I dug
school, but I wanted to be one of the boys more. I think the boys respected
my intelligence, despite their ribbing. Besides which, I belonged to a club

with a number of members who were interested in going to college, and so I wasn't so far out.

My introduction to marijuana was in junior high school in 1948. A kid named Dixie from 124th Street brought a pack of joints to school and taught about twelve guys to smoke. He told us we could buy joints at a quarter each or five for a dollar. Bombers, or thicker cigarettes, were thirty-five cents each or three for a dollar. There were a lot of experimenters, but not too many buyers. Actually, among the boys there was a strong taboo on drugs, and the Spanish word *"motto"* was a term of disparagement. Many clubs would kick out members who were known to use drugs. Heroin was easily available, and in those days came packaged in capsules or "caps" which sold for fifty cents each. Method of use was inhalation through the nose, or "sniffing," or "snorting."

I still remember vividly the first kid I ever saw who was mainlining. Prior to this encounter, I had known of "skin-popping," or subcutaneous injection, but not of mainlining. Most of the sniffers were afraid of skin-popping because they knew of the danger of addiction. They seemed to think that you could not become addicted by sniffing.

I went over to 108th Street and Madison where we played softball on an empty lot. This kid came over who was maybe sixteen or seventeen and asked us if we wanted to buy Horse. He started telling us about shooting up and showed me his arms. He had tracks, big black marks on the inside of his arm from the inner joint of the elbow down to his wrist and then over onto the back of his hand. I was stunned. Then he said, "That's nothing, man. I ain't hooked, and I ain't no junky. I can stop anytime I want to." I believe that he believed what he was saying. Invariably the kids talking about their drug experiences would say over and over, "I ain't hooked. I can stop anytime."

But they didn't stop; and the drug traffic grew greater and more open. Kids were smoking on the corners and on the stoops. Deals were made on the street, and you knew fifteen places within a block radius where you could buy anything you wanted. Cocaine never seemed to catch on although it was readily available. In the beginning, the kids seemed to be able to get the money for stuff easily. As the number of shooters grew and the prices went up, the kids got more desperate and apartment robbing became a real problem.

More of the boys began to leave school. We didn't use the term drop out; rather, a guy would say one day, after forty-three truancies, "I'm quitting school." And so he would. It was an irony, for what was really happening was that after many years of being rejected, ignored, and shuffled around by the school, the kid wanted to quit. Only you can't quit something you were never a part of, nor can you drop out if you were never in.

Some kids lied about their age and joined the army. Most just hung around. Not drifting to drugs or crime or to work either. They used to talk about going back at night and getting the diploma. I believe that they did not believe they could get their diplomas. They knew that the schools had abandoned them a long time ago—that to get the diploma meant starting all over again and that was impossible. Besides, day or night, it was the same school, the same staff, the same shit. But what do you say when you are powerless to get what you want, and what do you say when the other side has all the cards and writes all the rules? You say, "Tennis is for fags," and "School is for fags."

My mother leads me by the hand and carries a plain brown shopping bag. We enter an immense airplane hangar. Structural steel crisscrosses on the ceiling and walls: large round and square rivets look like buttons or bubbles of air trapped in the girders. There are long metallic counters with people bustling behind them. It smells of C.N. disinfectant. Many people stand on many lines up to these counters; there are many conversations going on simultaneously. The huge space plays tricks with voices and a very eerie combination of sounds results. A white cabbage is rolled down a counter at us. We retaliate by throwing down stamps.

For years I thought that sequence happened in a dream. The rolling cabbage rolled in my head, and little unrelated incidents seemed to bring it to the surface of my mind. I could not understand why I remembered a once-dreamt dream so vividly. I was sixteen when I picked up and read Freud's *The Interpretation of Dreams*.[1] One part I understood immediately and well, sex and symbolism. In no time, I had hung my shingle: Streetcorner Analyst. My friends would tell me their dreams and with the most outrageous sexual explanations we laughed whole evenings away. But the rolling cabbage could not be stopped and neither quack analysis nor serious thought could explain it away. One day I asked my mother if she knew anything about it.

"That was home relief, 1937 or 1938. You were no more than four years old then. Your father had been working at a restaurant and I had a job downtown. I used to take you every morning to Dona Eduvije who cared for you all day. She loved you very much, and she was very clean and neat, but I used to cry on my way to work, wishing I could stay home with my son and bring him up like a proper mother would. But I guess I was fated to be a workhorse. When I was pregnant, I would get on the crowded subway and go to work. I would get on a crowded elevator up. Then down. Then back on the subway. Every day I was afraid that the crowd would hurt me, that I would lose my baby. But I had to work. I worked for the WPA[2] right into my ninth month."

My mother was telling it "like it was," and I sat stupefied, for I could not believe that what she said applied to the time I thought of as open and clean. I had been existing in my life like a small plant in a bell jar, my parents defining my awareness. There were things all around me I could not see.

"When you were born we had been living as boarders. It was hard to find an apartment, even in Harlem. You saw signs that said 'No Renting to Colored or Spanish.' That meant Puerto Ricans. We used to say, 'This is supposed to be such a great country?' But with a new baby we were determined not to be boarders and we took an apartment on 111th Street. Soon after we moved, I lost my job because my factory closed down. Your father was making seven or eight dollars a week in a terrible job in a carpet factory. They used to clean rugs, and your father's hands were always in strong chemicals. You know how funny some of his fingernails are? It was from that factory. He came home one night and he was looking at his fingers, and he started saying that he didn't come to this country to lose his hands. He wanted to hold a bat and play ball and he wanted to work—but he didn't want to lose his hands. So he quit the job and went to a restaurant for less pay. With me out of work, a

---

1. Book (1899) in which the Austrian psychiatrist Sigmund Freud (1856–1939) laid out his theories of dream analysis.
2. Work Projects Administration, originally known as the Works Progress Administration, a U.S. government agency (1935–43) that provided construction work for the unemployed.

new apartment and therefore higher rent, we couldn't manage. Your father was furious when I mentioned home relief. He said he would rather starve than go on relief. But I went and filled out the papers and answered all the questions and swallowed my pride when they treated me like an intruder. I used to say to them, 'Find me a job—get my husband a better job—we don't want home relief.' But we had to take it. And all that mess with the stamps in exchange for food. And they used to have weekly 'specials' sort of—but a lot of things were useless—because they were American food. I don't remember if we went once a week or once every two weeks. You were so small I don't know how you remember that place and the long lines. It didn't last long because your father had everybody trying to find him a better job and finally somebody did. Pretty soon I went into the WPA and thank God, we never had to deal with those people again. I don't know how you remember that place, but I wish you didn't. I wish I could forget that home relief thing myself. It was the worst time for your father and me. He still hates it.

(He still hates it and so do many people. The expression, "I'd rather starve than go on welfare" is common in the Puerto Rican community. This characteristic pride is well chronicled throughout Spanish literature. For example, one episode of *Lazarillo del Tormes,* the sixteenth-century picaresque novel, tells of a squire who struts around all day with his shiny sword and pressed cape. At night the squire takes food from the boy, Lazarillo—who has begged or stolen it—explaining that it is not proper for a squire to beg or steal, or even to work! Without Lazarillo to feed him, the squire would probably starve.)

"You don't know how hard it was being married to your father then. He was young and very strong and very active and he wanted to work. Welfare deeply disturbed him, and I was afraid that he would actually get very violent if an investigator came to the house. They had a terrible way with people, like throwing that cabbage, that was the way they gave you everything, the way we used to throw the kitchen slop to the pigs in Puerto Rico. Some giving! Your father was, is, *muy macho,* and I used to worry if anybody says anything or gives him that why-do-you-people-come-here-to-ruin-things look he'll be in jail for thirty years. He almost got arrested once when you were just a baby. We went to a hospital clinic—I don't remember now if it was Sydenham or Harlem Hospital—you had a swelling around your throat—and the doctor told me, 'Put on cold compresses.' I said I did that and it didn't help. The doctor said, 'Then put hot compresses.' Your father blew up. In his broken English, he asked the doctor to do that to his mother, and then invited him to transfer over to the stable on 104th Street. 'You do better with horses—maybe they don't care what kind of compresses they get.'

"One morning your father tells me, 'I got a new job. I start today driving a truck delivering soft drinks.' That night I ask him about the job—he says, 'I quit—bunch of Mafia—I went to the first four places on my list and each storeowner said, "I didn't order any soda." So I got the idea real fast. The Mafia was going to leave soda in each place and then make the guys buy from them only. As soon as I figured it out, I took the truck back, left it parked where I got it, and didn't even say good-bye.' The restaurant took him back. They liked him. The chef used to give him eggs and meats; it was very important to us. Your father never could keep still (still can't), so he was loved wherever he worked. I feel sorry for people on welfare—forget about the cabbage—I never should have taken you there."

Pity was not a universal emotion provoked by welfare recipients in Harlem—East Harlem—residents. One old man on whom I used to gingerly test my developing notions despised welfare and people on it. Don Pedro had pure white hair, his back was rounded into a slight hump, and he was not very tall—at sixteen I was taller than he. He had come to America looking for something he did not find. He was bitter about people who did not work, and he did not work. He was for me the local wiseman, historian of Harlem and American commentator, willing to discuss anything with me—so long as I remembered my place—*los niños hablan cuando las gallinas mean* (the Puerto Rican version of children should be seen and not heard, literally, "children speak when chickens urinate"). That small saw quickly ended conversations, for it indicated annoyance—and I was taught never to be disrespectful in any way to an elder.

Don Pedro never said whether he had been on welfare, but everything about it was mind-bending for him. His pride would have prohibited him from accepting welfare, and if life had been cruel enough to force him to it, his pride would have kept him from such an admission. He was the contemporary starving squire. And the racist and conservative arguments that I came to hear as an adult from White America, I first heard as a teenager from Don Pedro. "Lazy bastards. I see them every day playing dominoes, drinking beer. Late in the afternoons going off to buy parts for their cars. Healthy as me. Have two or three women pregnant, children running around like savages, no discipline, no education [meaning in Spanish not school, but manners and morals]. And the other ones, you think they like to answer so many questions? You think they like to buy on credit, wait for checks? Why shouldn't they have a TV? What government has the right to tell me I can't give a person a TV as a gift? [Welfare families were not allowed to buy or receive as gifts TV sets. On the day the investigator was due, the tenements were like a scene from a Beatles movie[3]—many doors open—out come people with TVs, carrying them all into one door. End of day back go people with their TV sets.] And what about those investigators? Where do they find people who take such jobs? They don't ask so many questions if you work out an 'agreement.' A few bucks from your miserable check to them every month and they won't look under the bed. Bastards! But they all deserve what they get. You know what—I have more respect for a thief than any of them. A thief has—well I don't mean I would be a thief—I mean if it came to welfare or stealing—I'd steal. I'd steal before I would become an investigator, let alone a client."

And welfare was not the only thing Don Pedro was turned off on. He didn't believe in voting. "Fixed, the whole thing is fixed. First they decide who they want for anything. Take the judges. All of a sudden you have a bunch of names for a judge. Their names on all the parties. Well hell, if the guy is both a Republican and a Democrat, what's the sense of voting? He is an automatic winner! Then, I've seen them take the machines and turn them around. Or else somebody conveniently forgets to turn the little key,

---

3. Probably a reference to the movie *A Hard Day's Night* (1964), in which the Beatles play comic versions of themselves—a hugely popular rock group being pursued by crazed fans.

so no votes register. Or else they get you on technicalities. You changed your address. You gotta take the literacy test again. You can't vote—you got two last names. [In Puerto Rico, children assume the father's surname followed by a hyphen and then the mother's maiden name, but this causes so much confusion in New York that most Puerto Ricans eventually drop the usage.] Then they get you the other way. You sit and read about the candidates and what they stand for. You go down and vote for what you think is right. Meanwhile they take a truck up to the Bowery[4] and pick up fifteen or twenty guys, tell them how to vote, and then give 'em a pint of whiskey for their troubles. I've seen them buy a whole family with a bag of groceries, and I've seen dead men vote, if you know what I mean."

If there was one thing that Don Pedro believed about America, it was that it was a thoroughly corrupt nation. There was not one bureaucracy, not one establishment that he dealt with, that didn't have somebody on the make. The problem for the poor, he said, "is that they didn't have any money to bribe people."

"You know how many jobs, how many apartments I lost because I couldn't fix somebody? Some goddamned Irish could go to a super and give him twenty-five dollars for an apartment, but if you were Puerto Rican you had to give fifty dollars for the same apartment."

Why shouldn't I believe him? By sixteen I had my own collection of anecdotes supporting discrimination. Police telling me to "move on" for no reason, to get off the stoop of the building where I lived, being called fag and spic, stopped and searched on the streets, in hallways, in candy stores, and anywhere that we congregated. Called fag because in a time of crew cuts the Puerto Rican male took pride in his long hair. With the postwar movies of American heroes in Germany, Gestapo and Nazi were familiar figures, and for me they were our police. Who could you complain to about police? Hitler?[5]

In school, Mr. Miller, goddamn him to hell forever, took a Puerto Rican boy named Luis and kept him under the teacher's desk during class periods. When Luis would moan, Miller would kick him. Between periods, Miller walked Luis around the school, keeping him in a painful armlock. Mr. Flax, the principal, laughed. And Diamond, the algebra teacher, either sent us to play basketball or asked us to lay our heads on our desks while he checked the stock market reports in the *New York Times*. To whom did you complain about a teacher—a laughing principal?

But in the process of discrimination, different attitudes are produced. Don Pedro, prejudged in housing, employment, and health services, hated the Puerto Ricans who made slums, the Puerto Ricans who would not work, the Puerto Ricans who did not respect the Gestapo. And he hated Luis under the desk as much as Mr. Miller. And when I tried to tell Don Pedro, "Baby, who you really hate is you," he would say, "When chickens urinate."

My father and I are walking through East Harlem, south down Lexington from 112th toward 110th, in 1952. Saturday in late spring, I am eighteen

---

4. A thoroughfare and small neighborhood in Lower Manhattan, once associated with poverty and "Bowery bums" (alcoholics and homeless people).

5. Adolf Hitler (1889–1945), Austrian-born German dictator and founder of Nazism. *Gestapo:* secret police in Nazi Germany.

years old, sun brilliant on the streets, people running back and forth on household errands. My father is telling me a story about how back in nineteen thirty something, we were very poor and Con Ed[6] light meters were in every apartment. "The Puerto Ricans, maybe everybody else, would hook up a shunt wire around the meter, specially in the evenings when the use was heavy—that way you didn't pay for all the electric you used. We called it 'pillo' (thief)."

We arrive at 110th Street and all the cart vendors are there peddling plantains, avocados, yams, various subtropical roots. I make a casual remark about how foolish it all seemed, and my father catches that I am looking down on them. "Are they stealing?" he asks. "Are they selling people colored water? Aren't they working honestly? Are they any different from a bank president? Aren't they hung like you and me? They are *machos*, and to be respected. Don't let college go to your head. You think a Ph.D. is automatically better than a peddler? Remember where you come from—poor people. I mopped floors for people and I wasn't ashamed, but I never let them look down on me. Don't you look down on anybody."

We walk for a way in silence, I am mortified, but he is not angry. "One day I decide to play a joke on your mother. I come home a little early and knock. When she says 'Who?' I say 'Edison man.' Well, there is this long silence and then a scream. I open the door and run in. Your mother's on a chair, in tears, her right arm black from pinky to elbow. She ran to take the *pillo* out, but in her nervousness she got a very slight shock, the black from the spark. She never has forgiven me. After that, I always thought through my jokes."

We walk some more and he says, "I'll tell you another story. This one on me. I was twenty-five years old and was married to your mother. I took her down to Puerto Rico to meet Papa and Mama. We were sitting in the living room, and I remember it like it happened this morning. The room had rattan furniture very popular in that time. Papa had climbed in rank back to captain and had a new house. The living room had double doors which opened onto a large *balcon*. At the other end of the room you could see the dining table with a beautiful white handmade needlework cloth. We were sitting and talking and I took out a cigarette. I was smoking Chesterfields then. No sooner had I lit up than Papa got up, came over, and smacked me in the face. 'You haven't received my permission to smoke,' he said. Can you imagine how I felt?" So my father dealt with his love for me through lateral actions: building bookcases, and through tales of how he got his wounds, he anointed mine.

What is a migration? What does it happen to? Why are the Eskimos still dark after living in that snow all these centuries? Why don't they have a word for snow? What things are around me with such high saturation that I have not named them? What is a migration? If you rob my purse, are you really a fool? Can a poor boy really be president? In America? Of anything? If he is not white? Should one man's achievement fulfill one million people? Will you let us come near your new machine: after all, there is no more ditch digging? What is a migration? What does it happen to?

The most closely watched migrants of this world are birds. Birds migrate because they get bored singing in the same place to the same people. And

---

6. Consolidated Edison, New York City's utilities company.

they see that the environment gets hostile. Men move for the same reasons. When a Puerto Rican comes to America, he comes looking for a job. He takes the cold as one of a negative series of givens. The mad hustle, the filthy city, filthy air, filthy housing, sardine transportation, are in the series. He knows life will be tough and dangerous. But he thinks he can make a buck. And in his mind, there is only one tableau: himself retired, owner of his home in Puerto Rico, chickens cackling in the back yard.

It startles me still, though it has been five years since my parents went back to the island. I never believed them. My father, driving around New York for the Housing Authority, knowing more streets in more boroughs than I do, and my mother, curious in her later years about museums and theaters, and reading my books as fast as I would put them down, then giving me cryptic reviews. Salinger is really silly (*Catcher in the Rye*), but entertaining. That evil man deserved to die (*Moby Dick*). He's too much (Dostoevski in *Crime and Punishment*). I read this when I was a little girl in school (*Hamlet* and *Macbeth*). It's too sad for me (*Cry, the Beloved Country*).[7]

My father, intrigued by the thought of passing the foreman's exam, sitting down with a couple of arithmetic books, and teaching himself at age fifty-five to do work problems and mixture problems and fractions and decimals, and going into the civil service exam and scoring a seventy-four and waiting up one night for me to show me three poems he had written. These two cosmopolites, gladiators without skills or language, battling hostile environments and prejudiced people and systems, had graduated from Harlem to the Bronx,[8] had risen into America's dream-cherished lower middle class, and then put it down for Puerto Rico after thirty plus years.

What is a migration, when is it not just a long visit?

I was born in Harlem, and I live downtown. And I am a migrant, for if a migration is anything, it is a state of mind. I have known those Eskimos who lived in America twenty and thirty years and never voted, never attended a community meeting, never filed a complaint against a landlord, never informed the police when they were robbed or swindled, or when their daughters were molested. Never appeared at the State or City Commission on Human Rights, never reported a business fraud, never, in other words, saw the snow.

And I am very much a migrant because I am still not quite at home in America. Always there are hills; on the other side—people inclined to throwing cabbages. I cannot "earn and return"—there is no position for me in my father's tableau.

However, I approach the future with optimism. Fewer Puerto Ricans like Eskimos, a larger number of leaders like myself, trained in the university, tempered in the ghetto, and with a vision of America moving from its unexecuted policy to a society open and clean, accessible to anyone.

Dick and Jane? They, too, were tripped by the society, and in our several ways, we are all still migrating.

1971

7. This list refers to two plays by William Shakespeare and novels by the American writer J. D. Salinger (b. 1919), the American writer Herman Melville (1819–1891), the Russian writer Fyodor Dostoyevsky (1821–1881), and the South African writer Alan Paton (1903–1988).

8. A New York City borough north of Manhattan, parts of which were (and still are) more upscale than Harlem.

## Sonnet for 1950

All the kids came rumbling down the wood tenement
Shaky stairs, sneakers slapping against the worn
Tin tread edges, downhall came Pepo, Chino, Cojo,
Curly bursting from the door like shells exploding
Singing "I'm a Rican Doodle Dandy" and "What shall          5
We be today, Doctors or Junkies, Soldiers or Winos?"

Pepo put a milk crate on a Spanish Harlem johnny pump[1]
And drops opened like paratroopers carrying war news.

Then Urban Renewal[2] attacked the pump, cleared the slums
Blamed Puerto Rico and dispersed the Spics, blasting          10
Them into the Army or Anywhere Avenue in the Bronx.[3]

And nobody, but nobody, came back from that summer.

Just as Korea was death in service to the warring Nation[4]
The Bronx was death in service to the negligent Nation.

1996

## Sonnet: The History of Puerto Rico

Puerto Rico was created when the pumpkin on top of
The turtle burst and its teeming waters poured out
With all mankind and beastkind riding on the waves
Until the water drained leaving a tropical paradise.

Puerto Rico was stumbled on by lost vampires bearing          5
Crucifix in one hand, arquebus in the other, sucking
The veins of land and men, tossing the pulp into the
Compost heap which they used as the foundation for
Their fortifications and other vainglorious temples.

Puerto Rico was arrested just as it broke out of the          10
Spanish jail and, renamed a trusty, it was put in an
American cell. When the prisoner hollered, "Yankee, Go
Home," Puerto Rico was referred to the United Nations.

Puerto Rico, to get to paradise now, you have to ride blood.

1996

1. *Johnny pump*: New York City slang for fire
hydrant.
2. Government-sponsored redevelopment program in cities such as New York.
3. A New York City borough north of Manhattan,
long associated with waves of immigrants to the
United States; after 1945, newcomers included
African Americans, Hispanic Americans, and
immigrants from the Caribbean, especially from
Puerto Rico and the Dominican Republic. While
sections of the Bronx are upscale, immigrants
tend to land in the poverty-stricken areas.
4. I.e., during the Korean War.

# JOHN RECHY
## b. 1934

John Rechy was born in El Paso, Texas, to a tender and caring Mexican mother and an authoritarian and abusive Scottish father. In his memoir, *About My Life and the Kept Woman* (2008), Rechy comes across as a ferocious fighter for a libertine existence. He offers stringent comments about Mexican hypocrisy. He also explores his dual identity without subterfuges. In a country where *la hispanidad* is often seen as shameful, Rechy's passing as Anglo (he has lighter skin and "was considered *güero*, a Mexican who didn't look Mexican by entrenched standards") was his ticket into American society. He states:

> I had always been assumed by strangers to be Anglo. As a kid, before I learned English, I would necessarily respond in Spanish to whatever might be asked, in a store, at the barber college we went to for the cheapest cuts, at the library, the bus. Then, someone would often protest, saying something like, "Oh, you must be Spanish, you're too fair to be Mexican, don't say you're Mexican."

Rechy's autobiographical debut novel, *City of Night* (1963), was released by Grove Press, a publisher of controversial literature (such as Henry Miller's *Tropic of Cancer* and William Burroughs's *Naked Lunch*) and erotica. Chronicling the sexual adventures of a hustler who moves from Times Square, in New York, to the French Quarter, in New Orleans, the book became an overnight sensation. It was denounced and embraced, and its novice author (who shied away from the limelight at the time) became the target of innuendoes. Seen as part of the canon of Beat literature, the novel was translated into numerous languages and contributed to the atmosphere of experimentation—sexual and literary—in vogue at the time. Rechy followed it with provocative books such as *Numbers* (1967) and *The Sexual Outlaw: A Documentary* (1985). For a Mexican to have been at the forefront of the Age of Aquarius is impressive. This success, based on a topic shied away from and condemned by macho Latino culture, was unacceptable to Chicano critics writing about traditional Mexican American lives.

Rechy, whose first language was Spanish, began writing in high school. During this period, he also translated the twentieth-century Spanish poet Federico García Lorca into English. During the Korean War, he served in the military and was stationed in Germany, and his experiences as a U.S. citizen abroad shaped his identity as an outsider. When he returned to the United States, he applied to Columbia University, where the Nobel Prize–winning writer Pearl S. Buck was teaching. Buck read a piece by Rechy and disliked it; Columbia rejected him. Rechy moved to New York City anyway, and there he discovered nightlife and made his living as a hustler. After publishing a piece in a magazine, Rechy sold the as-yet-unfinished *City of Night* to Grove.

In addition to portraying a peripatetic male prostitute, *City of Night* is a study of a mother's possessiveness and its tragic consequences, of restlessness, and of a lack of satisfaction and solace despite numerous sexual relationships. The book employs black humor, and it may be the only existentialist novel in Chicano letters. Eventually, the Publishing Triangle, an association of lesbians and gays in publishing in New York, named *City of Night* one of the 25 all-time "best gay novels." For decades, Rechy has lived in Los Angeles, where he teaches literature and film courses for writers in the graduate division of the University of Southern California. He has received the PEN-USA-West's 1997 Lifetime Achievement Award as well as the Publishing Triangle's William Whitehead Award for Lifetime Achievement. Charles Casillo wrote a biography, *Outlaw: The Lives and Careers of John Rechy* (2002).

## *From* City of Night

## City of Night

Later I would think of America as one vast City of Night stretching gaudily from Times Square to Hollywood Boulevard—jukebox-winking, rock-n-roll-moaning: America at night fusing its darkcities into the unmistakable shape of loneliness.

Remember Pershing Square[1] and the apathetic palmtrees. Central Park[2] and the frantic shadows. Movie theaters in the angry morning-hours. And wounded Chicago streets. . . . Horrormovie courtyards in the French Quarter—tawdry Mardi Gras floats with clowns tossing out glass beads, passing dumbly like life itself. . . . Remember rock-n-roll sexmusic blasting from jukeboxes leering obscenely, blinking manycolored along the streets of American strung like a cheap necklace from 42nd Street[3] to Market Street, San Francisco. . . .

One-night sex and cigarette smoke and rooms squashed in by loneliness. . . .

And I would remember lives lived out darkly in that vast City of Night, from all-night movies to Beverly Hills mansions.

But it should begin in El Paso, that journey through the cities of night. Should begin in El Paso, in Texas. And it begins in the Wind. . . . In a Southwest windstorm with the gray clouds like steel doors locking you in the world from Heaven.

I cant remember now how long that windstorm lasted—it might have been days—but perhaps it was only hours—because it was in that timeless time of my boyhood, ages six through eight.

My dog Winnie was dying. I would bring her water and food and place them near her, stand watching intently—but she doesnt move. The saliva kept coming from the edges of her mouth. She had always been fat, and she had a crazy crooked grin—but she was usually sick: Once her eyes turned over, so that they were almost completely white and she couldnt see—just lay down, and didnt try to get up for a day. Then she was well, briefly, smiling again, wobbling lopsidedly.

Now she was lying out there dying.

At first the day was beautiful, with the sky blue as it gets only in memories of Texas childhood. Nowhere else in the world, I will think later, is there a sky as clear, as blue, as Deep as that. I will remember other skies: like inverted cups, this shade of blue or gray or black, with limits, like painted rooms. But in the Southwest, the sky was millions and millions of miles deep of blue—clear, magic, electric blue. (I would stare at it sometimes, inexplicably racked with excitement, thinking: If I get a stick miles long and stand on a mountain, I'll puncture Heaven—which I thought of then as an island somewhere in the vast sky—and then Heaven will come tumbling down to earth. . . . Then, that day, standing watching Winnie, I see the gray

---

1. Public park in downtown Los Angeles.    3. In Manhattan.
2. Grand public park in Manhattan.

clouds massing and rolling in the horizon, sweeping suddenly terrifyingly across the sky as if to battle, giant mushrooms exploding, blending into that steely blanket. *Now youre locked down here so Lonesome suddenly youre cold.* The wind sweeps up the dust, tumbleweeds claw their way across the dirt. . . .

I moved Winnie against the wall of the house, to shelter her from the needlepointed dust. The clouds have shut out the sky completely, the wind is howling violently, and it is Awesomely dark. My mother keeps calling me to come in. . . . From the porch, I look back at my dog. The water in the bowl beside her has turned into mud. . . . Inside now, I rushed to the window. And the wind is shrieking into the house—the curtains thrashing at the furniture like giant lost birds, flapping against the walls, and my two brothers and two sisters are running about the beat-up house closing the windows, removing the sticks we propped them open with. I hear my father banging on the frames with a hammer, patching the broken panes with cardboard.

Inside, the house was suddenly serene, safe from the wind; but staring out the window in cold terror, I see boxes and weeds crashing against the walls outside, almost tumbling over my sick dog. I long for something miraculous to draw across the sky to stop the wind. . . . I squeezed against the pane as close as I could get to Winnie: *If I keep looking at her, she cant possibly die!* A tumbleweed rolled over her.

I ran out. I stood over Winnie, shielding my eyes from the slashing wind, knelt over her to see if her stomach was still moving, breathing. And her eyes open looking at me. I listen to her heart (as I used to listen to my mother's heart when she was sick so often and I would think she had died, leaving me Alone—because my father for me then existed only as someone who was around somehow; taking furious shape later, fiercely).

Winnie is dead.

It seemed the windstorm lasted for days, weeks. But it must have been over, as usual, the next day, when Im standing next to my mother in the kitchen. (Strangely, I loved to sit and look at her as she fixed the food—or did the laundry: She washed our clothes outside in an aluminum tub, and I would watch her hanging up the clean sheets flapping in the wind. Later I would empty the water for her, and I stared intrigued as it made unpredictable patterns on the dirt. . . . ) I said: "If Winnie dies—" (She had of course already died, but I didnt want to say it; her body was still outside, and I kept going to her to see if miraculously she is breathing again.) "—if she dies, I wont be sad because she'll go to Heaven and I'll see her there." My mother said: "Dogs dont go to Heaven, they havent got souls." She didnt say that brutally. There is nothing brutal about my mother: only a crushing tenderness, as powerful as the hatred I would discover later in my father. "What will happen to Winnie, then?" I asked. "Shes dead, thats all," my mother answers, "the body just disappears, becomes dirt."

I stand by the window, thinking: It isn't fair. . . .

Then my brother, the younger of the two—I am the youngest in the family—had to bury Winnie.

I was very religious then. I went to Mass regularly, to Confession. I prayed nightly. And I prayed now for my dead dog: God would make an exception. He would let her into Heaven.

I stand watching my brother dig that hole in the backyard. He put the dead dog in and covered it. I made a cross and brought flowers. Knelt. Made the sign of the cross: "Let her into Heaven. . . ."

In the days that followed—I dont know exactly how much later—we could smell the body rotting. . . . The day was a ferocious Texas summerday with the threat of rain: thunder—but no rain. The sky lit up through the cracked clouds, and lightning snapped at the world like a whip. My older brother said we hadnt buried Winnie deep enough.

So he dug up the body, and I stand by him as he shovels the dirt in our backyard (littered with papers and bottles covering the weeds which occasionally we pulled, trying several times to grow grass—but it never grew). Finally the body appeared. I turned away quickly. I had seen the decaying face of death. My mother was right. Soon Winnie will blend into the dirt. There was no soul, the body would rot, and there would be Nothing left of Winnie.

That is the incident of my early childhood that I remember most often. And that is why I say it begins in the wind. Because somewhere in that plain of childhood time must have been planted the seeds of the restlessness.

Before the death of Winnie, there are other memories of loss.

We were going to plant flowers in the front yard of the house we lived in before we moved to the house where Winnie died. I was digging a ledge along the sidewalk, and my mother was at the store getting the seeds. A man came and asked for my father, but my father isnt home. "Youre going to have to move very soon," he tells me. I had heard the house was being sold, and we couldnt buy it, but it hadnt meant much to me. I continue shoveling the dirt. After my mother came and spoke to the man, she told me to stop making the holes. Almost snatching the seeds from her—and understanding now—I began burying them frantically as if that way we will have to stay to see them grow.

And so we moved. We moved from that clean house with the white walls and into the house where Winnie will die.

I stand looking at the house in child panic. It was the other half of a duplex, the wooden porch decayed, almost on the verge of toppling down; it slanted like a slide. A dried-up vine, dead from lack of water, still clung to the base of the porch like a skeleton, and the bricks were disintegrating in places into thin streaks of orangy power. The sun was brazenly bright; it elongates each splinter on the wood, each broken twig on the skeleton vine. . . . I rushed inside. Huge brown cockroaches scurried into the crevices. One fell from the wall, spreading its wings—almost two inches wide—as if to lunge at me—and it splashes like a miniature plane on the floor—*splut!* The paper was peeling off the walls over at least four more layers, all different graycolors. (We would put up the sixth, or begin to—and then stop, leaving the house even more patched as that layer peeled too: an unfinished jigsaw puzzle which would fascinate me at night: its ragged patterns making angryfaces, angry animalshapes—but I could quickly alter them into less angry figures by ripping off the jagged edges. . . . ) Where the ceiling had leaked, there are spidery brown outlines.

I flick the cockroaches off the walls, stamping angrily on them.

The house smells of Rot. I went to the bathroom. The tub was full of dirty water, and it had stagnated. It was brown, bubbly. In wild dreadful panic,

I thrust my hand into the rancid water, found the stopper, pulled it out holding my breath, and looked at my arm, which is covered with the filthy brown crud.

Winters in El Paso for me later would never again seem as bitter cold as they were then. Then I thought of El Paso as the coldest place in the world. We had an old iron stove with a round belly which heated up the whole house; and when we opened the small door to feed it more coal or wood, the glowing pieces inside created a miniature of Hell: the cinders crushed against the edges, smoking. . . . The metal flues that carried the smoke from the stove to the chimney collapsed occasionally and filled the house with soot. This happened especially during the windy days, and the wind would whoosh grimespecked down the chimney. At night my mother piled coats on us to keep us warm.

Later, I would be sent out to ask one of our neighbors for a dime—"until my father comes home from work." Being the youngest and most soulful looking in the family, then, I was the one who went. . . .

Around that time my father plunged into my life with a vengeance.

To expiate some guilt now for what I'll tell you about him later, I'll say that that strange, moody, angry man—my father—had once experienced a flashy grandeur in music. At the age of eight he had played a piano concert before the President of Mexico. Years later, still a youngman, he directed a symphony orchestra. Unaccountably, since I never really knew that man, he sank quickly lower and lower, and when I came along, when he was almost 50 years old, he found himself Trapped in the memories of that grandeur and in the reality of a series of jobs teaching music to sadly untalented children; selling pianos, sheet music—and soon even that bastard relationship to the world of music he loved was gone, and he became a caretaker for public parks. Then he worked in a hospital cleaning out trash. (*I remember him, already a defeated old man, getting up before dawn to face the unmusical reality of soiled bloody dressings.*) He would cling to stacks and stacks of symphonic music which he had played, orchestrated—still working on them at night, drumming his fingers on the table feverishly: stacks of music now piled in the narrow hallway in that house, completely unwanted by anyone but himself, gathering dust which annoyed us, so that we wanted to put them outside in the leaky aluminum garage: but he clung to those precious dust-pilling manuscripts—and to newspaper clippings of his once-glory—clung to them like a dream now a nightmare. . . . And somehow I became the reluctant inheritor of his hatred for the world that had coldly knocked him down without even glancing back.

Once, yes, there had been a warmth toward that strange red-faced man—and there were still the sudden flashes of tenderness which I will tell you about later: that man who alternately claimed French, English, Scottish descent—depending on his imaginative moods—that strange man who had traveled from Mexico to California spreading his seed—that turbulent man, married and divorced, who then married my Mother, a beautiful Mexican woman who loves me fiercely and never once understood about the terror between me and my father.

Even now in my mother's living room there is a glasscase which has been with us as long as I can remember. It is full of glass objects: figurines of angels, Virgins of Guadalupe,[4] dolls; tissue-thin imitation flowers, swans; and a small glass, reverently covered with a rotting piece of silk, tied tightly with a faded-pink ribbon, containing some mysterious memento of one of my father's dead children. . . . When I think of that glasscase, I think of my Mother . . . a ghost image that will haunt me—Always.

When I was about eight years old, my father taught me this:

He would say to me: "Give me a thousand," and I knew this meant I should hop on his lap and then he would fondle me—intimately—and he'd give me a penny, sometimes a nickel. At times when his friends—old gray men—came to our house, they would ask for "a thousand." And I would jump on their laps too. And I would get nickel after nickel, going around the table.

And later, a gift from my father would become a token of a truce from the soon-to-blaze hatred between us.

I loathed Christmas.

Each year, my father put up a Nacimiento—an elaborate Christmas scene, with houses, the wisemen on their way to the manger, angels on angel-hair clouds. (On Christmas Eve, after my mother said a rosary while we knelt before the Nacimiento, we placed the Christchild in the crib.) Weeks before Christmas my father began constructing it, and each day, when I came home from school, he would have me stand by him while he worked building the boxlike structure, the miniature houses, the artificial lake; hanging the angels from the elaborate simulated sky, replete with moon, clouds, stars. Sometimes hours passed before he would ask me to help him, but I had to remain there, not talking. Sometimes my mother would have to stand there too, sometimes my younger sister. When anything went wrong—if anything fell—he was in a rage, hurling hammers, cursing.

My father's violence erupted unpredictably over anything. In an instant he overturns the table—food and plates thrust to the floor. He would smash bottles, menacing us with the sharp-fanged edges. He had an old sword which he kept hidden threateningly about the house.

And even so there were those moments of tenderness—even more brutal because they didnt last: times in which, when he got paid, he would fill the house with presents—flowers for my mother (incongruous in that patched-up house, until they withered and blended with the drabness), toys for us. Even during the poorest Christmas we went through when we were kids—and after the fearful times of putting up the Nacimiento—he would make sure we all had presents—not clothes, which we needed but didnt want, but toys, which we wanted but didnt need. And Sundays he would take us to Juarez[5] to dinner, leaving an exorbitant tip for the suddenly attentive waiter. . . . But in the ocean of his hatred, those times of kindness were mere islands. He burned with an anger at life, which had chewed him up callously: an anger which blazed more fiercely as he sank further beneath the surface of his once almost-realized dream of musical glory.

One of the last touches on the Nacimiento was two pieces of craggy wood, which looked very heavy, like rocks (very much like the piece of pet-

---

4. Figures representing *Nuestra Señora de Gua-dalupe*, a sixteenth-century icon of the Virgin Mary; perhaps Mexico's most popular religious and cultural image, it has come to symbolize Catholic Mexicans and Mexico itself.
5. City in Mexico, across the border from El Paso.

rified wood which my father kept on his desk, to warn us that once it had been the hand of a child who had struck his father, and God had turned the child's hand into stone). The pieces of rocklike wood were located on either side of the manager, like hills. On top of one, my father placed a small statue of a red-tailed, horned Devil, drinking out of a bottle.

Around that time I had a dream which still recurs (and later, in New Orleans, I will experience it awake). We would get colds often in that drafty house, and fever, and during such times I dreamt this: Those pieces of rock-like wood on the sides of the manager are descending on me, to crush me. When I brace for the smashing terrible impact, they become soft, and instead of crushing me they envelop me like melted wax. Sometimes I will dream theyre draped with something like cheesecloth, a tenebrous, thin tissue touching my face like spiderwebs, gluing itself to me although I struggle to tear it away. . . .

When my brothers and sisters all got married and left home—to Escape, I would think—I remained, and my father's anger was aimed even more savagely at me.

He sat playing solitaire for hours. He calls me over, begins to talk in a very low, deceptively friendly tone. When my mother and I fell asleep, he told me, he would set fire to the house and we would burn inside while he looked on. Then he would change that story: Instead of setting fire to the house, he will kill my mother in bed, and in the morning, when I go wake her, she'll be dead, and I'll be left alone with him.

Some nights I would change beds with my mother after he went to sleep—they didnt sleep in the same room—and I surrounded the bed with sticks, chairs. The slightest noise, and I would reach for a stick to beat him away. In the early morning, before he woke, my mother would change beds with me again.

Once—without him, because he was working on his music—we were going to take a trip to Carlsbad Caverns, in New Mexico: my mother, my sister and her husband, my older brother and his wife, and I. My mother prepared food that night.

In the morning, before dawn, I woke my mother and went to my sister's house to wake her. When I returned, I saw my mother in our backyard (under the paradoxically serene star-splashed sky). "Dont go in!" she yells at me. I ran inside, and my father is standing menacingly over the table where the food we were taking is. Swiftly I reached for the food, and he lunges at me with a knife, slicing past me only inches short of my stomach. By then, my sister's husband was there holding him back. . . .

There was a wine-red ring my father wore. As a tie-pin, before being set into the gold ring-frame, it had belonged to his father, and before that to his father's father—and it was a ruby, my father told me—a ruby so precious that it was his most treasured possession, which he clung to. As he sat moodily staring at his music on one particularly poor day, he called me over. Quickly, he gave me the ring. The red stone in the gold frame glowed for me more brilliantly than anything has ever since. A few days later he took it back.

During one of those rare, rare times when there was a kind of determined truce between us—an unspoken, smoldering hatred—I was crossing the street with him. He was quite old then, and he carried a cane. As we crossed, he stumbled on the cane, fell to the street. Without waiting an instant, I run to the opposite side, and I stand hoping for some miraculous avenging car to plunge over him.

But it didnt come.

I went back to him, helped him up, and we walked the rest of the way in thundering silence.

And then, when I was older, possibly 13 or 14, I was sitting one afternoon on the porch loathing him. My hatred for him by then had become a thing which overwhelmed me, which obsessed me the length of the day. He stood behind me, and he put his hand on me, softly, and said—gently: "Youre my son, and I love you." But those longed-for words, delayed until the waves of my hatred for him had smothered their meaning, made me pull away from him: "I hate you!—youre a failure—as a man, as a father!" And later those words would ring painfully in my mind when I remembered him as a slouched oldman getting up before dawn to face the hospital trash. . . .

Soon, I stopped going to Mass. I stopped praying. The God that would allow this vast unhappiness was a God I would rebel against. The seeds of that rebellion—planted that ugly afternoon when I saw my dog's body beginning to decay, the soul shut out by Heaven—were beginning to germinate.

When my brother was a kid and I wasnt even born (but I'll hear the story often), he would stand moodily looking out the window; and when, once, my grandmother asked him, "Little boy, what are you doing by the window staring at so hard?"—he answered, "I am occupied with life." Im convinced that if my brother hadnt said that—or if I hadnt been told about it—I would have said it.

I liked to sit inside the house and look out the hall-window—beyond the cactus garden in the vacant lot next door. I would sit by that window looking at the people that passed. I felt miraculously separated from the world outside: separated by the pane, the screen, through which, nevertheless— uninvolved—I could see that world.

I read many books, I saw many, many movies.

I watched other lives, only through a window.

Sundays during summer especially I would hike outside the city, along the usually waterless strait of sand called the Rio Grande, up the mountain of Cristo Rey, dominated at the top by the coarse, weed-surrounded statue of a primitive-faced Christ. I would lie on the dirt of that mountain staring at the breathtaking Texas sky.

I was usually alone. I had only one friend: a wild-eyed girl who sometimes would climb the mountain with me. We were both 17, and I felt in her the same wordless unhappiness I felt within myself. We would walk and climb for hours without speaking. For a brief time I liked her intensely—without ever telling her. Yet I was beginning to feel, too, a remoteness toward people—more and more a craving for attention which I could not reciprocate: one-sided, as if the need in me was so hungry that it couldnt share or give back in kind. Perhaps sensing this—one afternoon in a boarded-up cabin at the base of the mountain—she maneuvered, successfully, to make me. But the discovery of sex with her, releasing as it had been, merely turned me strangely further within myself.

Mutually, we withdrew from each other.

And it was somewhere about that time that the narcissistic pattern of my life began.

From my father's inexplicable hatred of me and my mother's blind carnivorous love, I fled to the Mirror. I would stand before it, thinking: I have only Me! . . . I became obsessed with age. At 17, I dreaded growing old. Old age is something that must never happen to me. The image of myself in the mirror must never fade into someone I cant look at.

And even after a series of after-school jobs, my feeling of isolation from others only increased.

Then the army came, and for months I hadnt spoken to my father. (We would sit at the table eating silently, ignoring each other.) And when I left, that terrible morning, I kissed my mother. And briefly I looked at my father. His eyes were watering. Mutely he held out the ruby-ring which once, long ago, he had given me and then taken back. And I took it wordlessly. And in that instant I wanted to hold him—*because he was crying*, because he did feel something for me, because, I was sure, he was overwhelmed at that moment by the Loss I felt too. I wanted to hold him then as I had wanted to so many, many times as a child, and if I could have spoken, I know I would have said at last: "I love you." But that sense of loss choked me—and I walked out without speaking to him. . . . Only a few weeks later, in Camp Breckenridge,[6] Kentucky, I received a telegram that he was very sick.

And I came back to El Paso.

I felt certain that this time it would be different.

I reached our house, in the government projects we had moved into from that house with the winged cockroaches, and I got in with the key I had kept. There is no one home. I called my brother. My father was dead.

I hang up the telephone and I know that now Forever I will have no father, that he had been unfound, that as long as he had been alive there was a chance, and that we would be, Always now, strangers, and that is when I knew what Death really is—not in the physical discovery of the Nothingness which the death of my dog Winnie had brought me (in the decayed body which would turn into dirt, rejected by Heaven) but in the knowledge that *my Father* was gone, *for me*—that there was no way to reach him now—that his Death would exist only for me, who am living.

And throughout the days that followed—and will follow forever—I will discover him in my memories, and hopelessly—through the infinite miles that separate life from death—try to understand his torture: in searching out the shape of my own.

The army passed like something unreal, and I returned to my Mother and her hungry love. And left her, standing that morning by the kitchen door crying, as she always would be in my mind, and I was on my way now to Chicago, briefly—from where I would go to freedom: New York!—embarking on that journey through nightcities and nightlives—looking for I dont know what—perhaps some substitute for salvation.

6. Training camp for infantry units during World War II and the Korean War.

# Mr King: Between Two Lions

## 1

34th Street in New York City hurries urgently from river to river, and on that street, east, is the soul-squashing building where a few days later (not yet) I will add to the shadows in that cavern of halls, rooms, community kitchens, yellow-mirrored bathrooms (*and whatever light entered the maze from outside squeezed in reluctantly through grimecoated windows at the ends of each hall*), and at one corner was the Armory like an Errol Flynn[1] movie, and on the next Lexington Avenue rushes determinedly past bars and stores and checkertabled Italian restaurants; and everywhere, gray steel buildings stab the sky—and beyond the Armory, past technicolor Kress's,[2] is the goodbye Greyhound station, where I arrived from Chicago one weepy day in September, welcomed by banner headlines warning of a female hurricane—and I think suddenly for the first time:

*My God! Im on an island!*

From El Paso, I had gone to Evanston outside Chicago—a serene green campus city—where I saw a friend I had met in El Paso when he was in the army. Sensing the anarchic restlessness in me, he tried to persuade me not to go to New York yet. (And through him—because I had given most of my separation money to my mother and what I had was running out—I got a job cleaning autumn yards.) In the afternoons, in that quiet city—especially quiet now that summer was over for the University students and the fall term hadnt yet begun—my friend and I would walk through the campus, along the lake. . . . And at the same time that I felt myself being lulled by the serenity of the lake and the soon-to-fade green of the scenery, the craving for a certain life drew me away from them. Because even before I got there, New York had become a symbol of my liberated self, and I knew that it was in a kind of turbulence that that self must attempt to find itself.

After my separation from the army, I had come into my first contact with the alluring anarchic world which promised such turbulence. On my way to El Paso, I had stopped in Dallas for about a week, to postpone facing my mother with my decision to leave El Paso. In Dallas—*suddenly!*—with the excitement of someone exploring a new country I discovered that world. As abruptly as that, it happened; that sudden, that immediate: One day, nothing, and the next it was there . . . as if a trapdoor had Opened.

Those days in Dallas, without entering it then, I explored the surface of that seething world; and from the isolation of my early years and the equally isolated time in the army—purposely apart from everyone—I resolved to free myself swiftly, to leave my place by the Window, uninvolved with life, and hurl myself into its boiling midst. But it had to be after I had faced my mother again.

I couldnt tell why I was determinedly taking that journey. Perhaps in part it was because of the obsessive ravenous narcissism craving attention. Whatever it was, it was a compulsion for which I didnt have clear-cut reasons. I only knew that in the world I had discovered and not yet entered there was a

---

1. Australian-born actor (1909–1959) known for playing romantic swashbucklers in Hollywood movies.
2. A "five-and-dime" department store.

desperation which somehow matched—and justified—my own. . . . And although, now, to you, this sounds unclear, I'll clarify it very soon. This is only by way of saying that when I reached New York, that world was waiting for me. I required no slow initiation.

2

Times Square, New York, is an electric island floating on a larger island of lonesome parks and lonesome apartment houses and knifepointed buildings stretching Up. (I will think dazedly one night: Someday this city will tear its wharf-lined fringes from the ocean and soar in desperation to the Sky. . . . )

Times Square is the magnet for all the lonesome exiles jammed into this city. . . . And this is how I found that world of Times Square.

In the incessantly running showers of the Sloane House YMCA the day I arrived in New York, the big hairy man made conversation with me; where am I from and what am I doing and am I working yet ("No? Good. I mean good that you dont have to be anywhere at a set time."), and will I come to his room and he'll buy hamburgers. Hes a merchant marine, tanned from a recent Voyage to somefarwhere—on his way now to Boston with I imagine a roll of money big enough to make me greedy. Unfairly, Im almost broke—$20.00 when I left Chicago, and one phone number who said nervously we must have lunch sometime. And no prospect of a job which will pay me before the money runs out.

In the tiny cubicle-room facing the courtyard across which a lonesome youngman, also undoubtedly just arrived in the City, played a doleful guitar by his window, we sit eating oniony greaseburgers and ignoring the persistent sound of the running showers. For a moment, I think it's the hurricane.

Outside, in the hallway, doors open and close. The sound of feet walking up and down never stops. A hurried conversation outside, a door closes.

Even before this man speaks it, I know that something of what Ive come to find in this city will soon be revealed in this room.

"They dont call this Y the French Embassy for nothing," the merchant marine laughs. He has sized me up slyly: broke and green in the big city—and he said: "You wouldnt be broke if youd been at Mary's last night—thats a place in the Village[3] and everything goes." He watches me evenly for some reaction, determining, Im sure, how far he can go how quickly. "So I spot this cute kid there—" Hes still studying me carefully, and when I dont say anything, he continues with more assurance: "So I spot him and I want him—yeah, sure, Im queer—whatya expect?" he challenges. He pauses longer this time, watching me still calculatingly. He goes on: "And the kid's looking for maybe a pad to flop in and breakfast—hes not queer himself, I dont like em queer: If I did, I'd go with a woman—why fuck around with substitutes? . . . So this kid goes with me—Im feeling Good, just off the ship, flush—I lay 50 bucks on him."

A strange new excitement wells inside me.

He adds slyly, confident now that hes got me interested: "If youda been there I woulda preferred you. . . ." He places his hairy hand on my leg. "Unfortunately, Im almost broke now," he says, "but I got some more pay coming soon."

I stand up quickly; pause only for a moment at the door.

3. Greenwich Village, a Manhattan neighborhood traditionally associated with bohemian life.

He calls after me:

"Hell, if you decide to make that scene later, try Times Square—always good for a score. . . . And play it dumb—they dig that."

I stand on 42nd Street and Broadway looking at the sign flashing the news from the Times Tower like a scoreboard: The World is losing. The hurricane still menaces—the sky ashen with night rainclouds, and looking at it, which is suddenly like a shroud, I panic, I think about this wailing concrete island, and I cant even swim: an island—and the shrouded sky makes it a Cage.

Along this street, I see the young masculine men milling idly. Sometimes they walk up to older men and stand talking in soft tones—going off together, or, if not, moving to talk to someone else.

The subway crowds surged in periodic waves, blank newyork faces, as if, for air, they had just crawled out of the little boxes in the automat for say a quarter and two nickels.

I feel explosively excited to be on this street—at the sight of the people and the lights, sensing the anarchy. . . . The merchant marine's story about the youngman he had picked up—and the implied offer of sexmoney to me—have acted on me like a narcotic that makes me crave it.

Predictably (and the life I have come to find is unfolding swiftly before me) the newyork cop comes by, to Welcome me, I will think later. He was shaped appropriately like a zero. Watching his approach, the other aimless youngmen leave their stands along the street. Stopping before me, the cop says to me in a bored, automatic, knowing tone: "Why dont you go to the movies, kid? . . . I aint seen you before—so I dont feel like running you in."

I take his advice. Two Sexy foreign movies at the Apollo theater: I surrender to the giant cavernous mouth with decaying brown seats for teeth—gobble!—where youll see me often, later, in the balcony. But I kept thinking about the hurricane. Im nervous.

Outside, the rain is coming furiously. I stand under the marquee wondering where to go. Im reacting instinctively to this world, studying the stances of other obviously drifting youngmen.

Then he walks by me, hat slouched to one side, dont-give-a-damn walk: a grayhaired middle-aged man—and says—exactly how he came on: verbatim: "I'll give you ten, and I dont give a damn for you." I follow the man, who has paused a few feet from me.

"What did you say?" I asked.

He looks at me steadily: "Was I wrong?" he asks me, but hes looking at me smiling confidently.

"I just asked what you said."

"You heard me," he says, without looking at me now, completely sure now. . . . "Well, for chrissake, you wanna come or not?"

"Yes."

"Then come on, we're getting wet."

That world has opened its door, and I walk in.

In the taxi he asked me have I eaten—and I have but I say no because I might as well make up for the greaseburgers earlier—you would too, as a citizen of the grubby world. "All right, we'll go eat," he said. This reminded him of A Funny Story. "I was in this Swank place once," he says, "and at the table next to me is this old woman, see, and shes with this great big beautiful blond boy, probably she picked him off the docks, hes uncomfortable as hell in a tie—he says to the waiter, 'I want wiver and onions.' The woman's embarrassed, see, she says in a low voice, 'Dear, why dont we have some Chateaubriand?—it's wonderful here.' 'Wiver and onions,' he insists. 'Some lobster?' she says. 'Wiver and onions! Wiver and onions!' he kept repeating. It broke me up."

At the restaurant he isnt sure theyll let me in dressed in levis. "But it aint so swank," he says, "and they know me here." Inside, I ask for the most expensive steak, still remembering the greaseburgers. . . . He peers at me, half-smiling: "No wiver and onions for you, huh?"

Later, in his apartment, he said, "Why are you so nervous, aint you been with a cocksucker before?—thats what I am, pal and I aint ashamed of it." He got into a purple robe, and I lay back and fix my eyes on a picture on the wall: rainclouds, a sad tree draped in something like moss—a skeleton vine, I think. If I squint, the tree looks like a shawled Mexican woman. I stop looking at the picture immediately. I try to stop thinking. . . . I feel him touch my body—hesitantly at first, despite his bravado; then more freely, intimately. For one wild instant I want to run out. . . . Then I heard his voice; indignant: "Why are you holding it, for chrissake?"

"So you wont bite." I wish instantly I hadnt said that.

He laughs, and Im relieved strangely. "Jesus!" he said. "You *are* green! . . . Where are you from?—the backward South somewhere?"

I purposely didnt answer, trying to forget El Paso. I listen to the rain, to the Wind lashing at the windows. And I feel a mixture of panic and excitement—one moment as if somehow Im being liberated, at last; another moment as if Ive entered a world for which Im not really prepared.

I move away from him.

"Christ, what now?" he says, and he sat up abruptly. He wrapped the purple robe modestly about himself. "Hell," he says, "you dont have to look at me." He handed me a cigarette. "Whats your name, pal?"

I told him my first name.

Hes annoyed. "My name is Ed King," he said precisely. "K-i-n-g. What the hell are people afraid of giving their last names for? . . ." Then almost gently: "Was that your first time on 42nd Street?"

I told him yes.

"It aint good," I heard him say through the sound of the rain. (It reminds me of the showers at the YMCA earlier—except that eventually the rain would stop, but the showers will go on Forever. . . . Crazily Im remembering a Mexican kid song: "Let it rain, let it rain, Virgin of the Cave. . . .") He moves away, sits on a chair a few feet from me, looking at me. "No," he repeats, "it aint no good—whattaya wanna hang around the streets for? Youre a nicelooking kid," he goes on, "not what I would call Handsome," he says indifferently, "but—umm—youll do—"

He lost points.

"—but kinda Sexy, maybe, if you like your type—"

He gained the lost points, plus a few.

"—maybe a little new—but Available—" He hurled the last word at me.

And he lost the points hopelessly.

"—so, cummon, whattaya wanna hang around the streets for?" he went on. "Go on back Home and marry your girlfriend—you gotta girlfriend?—and raise lots of snottynosed little bastards, and I'll tell you what: Keepem away from New York—all those fuckin cities—are you from L.A.? No? Keepem

away from there too—you look like you could be—I was there once, L.A.—
too many creeps for me, though: like a nuthouse. . . . That Pershing
Square!—it's a loony asylum! . . . 42nd Street, thats the lowest, though. All
those lights, sure you think theyre Pretty—Im tellinya, listena-me, they aint:
It's bullshit—got the same fuckin lights in New Orleans—are you really
from the South? New Orleans maybe—no, you wouldnt be so nervous if you
were—12 years old there and youd know Everything: hell, I know a
12-year-old boy there, hustles. But all this shit aint worth knowing, like I
say. It was Chicago for me," he said. He squashes the cigarette into a butt-
crammed ashtray; the butts squirm like gutted white worms.

"You still wanna make the ten bucks?" he asked me abruptly.

I panic. I think hes lost interest; and I realize uncomfortably how important it is, to me, that he still want me. "Yeah, sure," I said, trying to sound
casual.

"Yeah!—say yes *sir*, punk!—aint you got Respect for your elders?—hell, Im
twice as old as you are, dont forget that. . . . Greedy bastards—allasame. . . .
Well, then, for chrissake, I aint even got a quarter's worth from you," he says,
coming back to the bed. "Now stop squirming and dont hold it—relax, if
youre gonna go along with it—at least pretend you enjoy it—what the hell, I
should pay and you act like you dont give a damn?—punks, allasame. I was
like you once—you believe it?" he says, "and now look at me, playing the
other side of this goddam game. What the hell, pal, people change, remember that, dont forget it for a moment, remember that and dont be so fuckin
cocky. Now lay back, close your goddam eyes and stop staring at me like Im a
goddam creep—hell, I aint ashamed of nothing. Pretend Im some milkfed
chick back in—wherever the hell youre from. . . . Thats it, thats better. . . .
Relax. . . . Thats it. . . ."

Later, he adjusted his robe modestly again, reached for his pants, handed
me a $10.00 bill. "Thats what you came for, aint it?—so take it," he said
looking at me very long.

I take the bill, crush it quickly into my pocket. Suddenly the room is
explodingly hot. I want to leave quickly.

"And say thankyou, cantcha?" he adds, looking away now.

The roles we have just played for each other seem to materialize harshly
now that it's over.

"And heres three more bucks for cabfare," he said. "It's always goodluck to
give cabfare," he added. "You-wanna-come-back-sometime? . . . Hell, I dont
care. I can pick up a different punk any night, see?—and no skinny wiseass
punk pulls any shit on me, pal, I know judo like the best of em. . . . But youre
kinda new, I like that. Available, but kinda new. . . . Take my advice, I know
what Im tellinya, go Home and get Married," he says guiltily, "that streetll
swallow you so deep you wont know where you got sucked in, and it wont
even throw you up like bad beer, itll digestya—" He gnashed his teeth
harshly. "Hell, youll become a part of the 42nd Street army of punks—
sleeping in movies, cant make it; everybody's had you: the dayll come nobody
wants you—then what? . . . Bad scene, bad scene. . . . So you wanna see me
again or not? Tellyawot, we'll have dinner again, wanna have dinner?—how
about Friday?"

"All right—Friday," I say quickly, I want to get out. Im sure I wont be
there.

"You know where the public library is?" he asked me. "Fifth Avenue and 42nd—here, I'll write it down so you wont forget. I'll meet you there on the steps, between the two statues, the two lions—Friday, seven oclock, if you want to—and dont go fuckin around 42nd Street, you got ten bucks—dont be greedy. Is it a date? If you dont show, hell, I'll know you took my advice: went Home, got married—put down this fuckin life. I'd prefer that, for your sake, pal—but if you dont take that advice, be there, punk. . . . Shit, I might as well take advantage of you if youre gonna stick anyway—someone else will. . . ."

The hurricane hadnt come, and it was a cool night, like those Texas winter-nights when my mother piled coats on us to keep us warm and the heating stove glowed orange at the stomach like a grotesque ironman. . . .

I did show up. I stand between the statues of the two lions on the steps of the public library.

Hes disappointed that I didnt dress up. Im wearing a black turtleneck sweater thinking cornily he'll like it. He didnt. "I wanted to show you the nightclubs, pal," he said. "Cant go in that circus outfit—now we'll have to go where theyll let you in." Himself, hes carefully dressed, youll notice. He just got a haircut, he smells of cologne. . . . "You shoulda worn a suit," he said. "Whats the matter?—dont you have any other clothes?"

Again in his apartment—later (after dinner and an expensive movie during which, at least five times, he asked me if I wanted popcorn)—it was much easier than before. "Youre learning," he said, "now youll never go back home—" and adds cautiously, "Can I take your picture like that?" I said no. "Suit yourself," he said aloofly, "no difference to me, Ive had better, you be-lieve it—and bigger." Then he asked me, coughing between words, if I wanted to move in with him. Not now, I said, maybe later. "Thanks, Ed," I said.

"*Ed!*" he shouted indignantly, although I had called him that all night. "*Mister* King to you, punk!—respect me a little, cantcha? . . . Hell, if you dont wanna move in, suit yourself. But think about it," he said, "better than the all-night movies, and thats where youll end up—hell, you can sleep on another bed, I'll get one for you, I wont bother you—except sometimes, maybe—when I feel like it—I aint no wolf, pal."

We agreed to meet again, again, between the two lions.

"I—uh—kinda—like you," he said hesitantly as Im leaving. "But dont get no ideas," he added quickly, "theres dozens just like you—all of you even get to look alike—pictures in a fuckedup album. What the hell, I dont give a damn for you or all the others like you, like I toldya: dime a fuckin dozen, no fuckin good. . . . If youre there to meet me, okay. If not, theres someone else around the corner—just as good, maybe better. . . . But be there, punk—between the two lions."

3

In the morning of the day I was to meet him again, I moved out of the Y—away from the never-stopping showers and the fixed looks along the hall-ways; the doors opening and closing all night.

And I moved into that building on 34th Street known as The Casbah for its menagerie of Twilight people, and I added to the shadows in one of those thousands of hallways in New York City in immense apartment houses erected in the large American cities before buildings grew tall and skinny rather than short and fat. They squat self-consciously in the midst of slick skyscrapers waiting sullenly to be bought, torn down, replaced: And this one has four cagelike elevators corresponding to each of the building's wings; moving up and down grudgingly like tired old ladies constantly grumbling about their present, unmerited station of life. . . .

As I stand in the hallway opening the door to the room I had rented, a woman with burningly demented eyes just seems to appear. "Im Gene de Lancey, sweetie," she said. "I live down the hall with my husband—his name's Steve. And I want you to consider us your Best Friends." Then she disappeared, leaving behind her the odor of strong perfume and wine. . . .

At night, on my way to meet Mr King, I walk through Times Square. And along that street—outside the Italian restaurant featuring squirming spaghetti for 40¢ a plate; before the racks of magazines with photographs of almost-naked youngmen like an advertisement for this street; along the moviehouses, the subway entrances; along that fourth-of-july colored street: I saw the army of youngmen he knew so well—like photographs in a strange exhibition: slouched invitingly, or moving back and forth restlessly; pretending to be reading the headlines flashing across the Tower—but oblivious, really, of the world those headlines represent (but an integral part of it); concerned only with the frantic needs of Inside—*Now!!*

I move on, that cold, autumnal newyork night, and this time the sky was dotted with sad cold stars—and I walk through Bryant Park behind the library, the fallen leaves crunching beneath my feet like spilled popcorn—I walk past the shadows of staring lonesome men along the ledges, suddenly astonishingly real in the instant flickering light of a struck match—then shadows again, faceless—*and I get the feeling in the park now that silence is a person listening to Me, watching.* . . . I walked into the library, from 42nd Street, through the echoing halls, toward the Fifth Avenue entrance.

Through the door, I see him standing on the steps, between the two lions, waiting for me. He is even more neatly dressed than before. Smoking. He looks at his watch, looks toward either side of the street. I can almost smell the sweet cologne. Carefully dressed and talcumed, clothes freshly pressed, his grayish hair combed neatly. . . .

*Frantically trying to look good for me!*

Suddenly I turned back, away from him, down the hall and the stairs, out the 42nd Street entrance, through the park waiting somehow like a Trap—through the popcorn-crunching leaves, the shadows of the trees grotesque in the faint autumn moon like in a witchstory . . . the stars hugely unconcerned.

And I take the subway back to 34th Street, to that giant spider building I had moved into. . . .

And days later I saw him again, on Times Square, as he crossed the street cockily with a hoodylooking black-haired boy to get into a cab. He glanced at me, turned away quickly.

His hat still slouched defiantly to one side.

1963

# OSCAR "ZETA" ACOSTA
## 1935–1974

Best-known popularly as the 300-pound Samoan in the American writer Hunter S. Thompson's classic nonfiction novel *Fear and Loathing in Las Vegas* (1972), Oscar "Zeta" Acosta was a legendary Chicano lawyer and activist. Acosta chronicled his own turbulent career in two rowdy, controversial volumes—part autobiography, part fiction—written in the style of Thompson's "gonzo journalism": *The Autobiography of a Brown Buffalo* (1972) and *The Revolt of the Cockroach People* (1973).

Acosta was born in El Paso, Texas. Five years later, he moved with his family to Riverbank, now a part of Modesto, California. At the time, the area experienced much racial strife and social unrest surrounding Mexican immigrants; as discussed in the "Acculturation" introduction, the Sleepy Lagoon incident and the Zoot Suit Riots took place in 1942 and 1943, respectively. Acosta would respond to his feelings about this period by becoming politically involved during the civil rights era. In high school, he used drugs and alcohol. After graduating from high school but being rejected for a music scholarship at the University of Southern California, he enlisted in the U.S. Air Force and was stationed in Panama, where he preached as a Baptist missionary in a leper colony. Honorably discharged, he attempted suicide in New Orleans, married Betty Daves in 1956, and soon after began an unsuccessful 10-year-long psychiatric treatment. In 1959, the same year his son, Marco, was born, Acosta suffered another of several mental breakdowns.

From 1962 to 1967, Acosta aimed for a literary career, including the writing of plays and poetry. The manuscripts he sent to New York publishers were rejected, but one of his stories, "Perla Is a Pig," which focuses on discrimination, was included in an anthology. He then studied at San Francisco Law School, passed the bar exam on his second attempt, and became a lawyer for the East Oakland Legal Aid Society, an antipoverty agency near Modesto. Unhappy with his job, he quit, took a road trip around the Southwest, and was temporarily jailed in Juárez, Mexico. In 1968, Acosta returned to California and acquired a new identity. He took the nom de guerre "Zeta," which invokes the mission of Zorro, a mythical figure said to have defended the indigent California population during the colonial period. He also described himself as a buffalo and Chicanos as cockroaches, taking the color brown as a political banner of sorts. He put the name "Buffalo Z. Brown" on his business cards. Acosta represented poor Chicanos in East Los Angeles and became an ardent defense lawyer and activist. Having divorced Betty Daves, he married Socorro Aguinaga in 1968.

Acosta acted as the lead attorney for two landmark civil rights cases. The first was Salvador Castro et al. v. the Superior Court of Los Angeles County. Salvador Castro and other public school teachers were indicted for disturbing the peace during walkout demonstrations. The California State Court of Appeals quashed the felony charges, ruling that stricter standards of proof were required under the Constitution's First Amendment. In Acosta's second case, Carlos Móntez et al. v. the Superior Court of Los Angeles County, he proved that Spanish-surnamed citizens had been systematically excluded from Los Angeles grand juries. Acosta had found his calling. He later defended Mexican Americans charged with setting fires at the Biltmore Hotel, in Los Angeles, when Ronald Reagan, then the governor of California, delivered a speech. Soon after, Acosta declared his candidacy for sheriff of Los Angeles County as a La Raza Unida Party independent. Running on an anarchist, apocalyptic platform that promised to abolish the police force, Acosta lost decisively.

In the 1960s, Acosta became addicted to drugs and alcohol; he was also diagnosed with a stomach ulcer. He lost legal cases, was disbarred, and was arrested on charges of drug possession. In 1967, he met Hunter S. Thompson, and four years later they traveled to Las Vegas on a psychedelic trip that became the source of myth. Thompson's chronicle of the events—in *Fear and Loathing in Las Vegas*, first published in *Rolling Stone* magazine—angered Acosta, who felt exploited as a Chicano by an "abusive, lying" Anglo. Acosta's versions of the same events appeared in *The Autobiography of a Brown Buffalo* (excerpted in this anthology) and *The Revolt of the Cockroach People*, both published by an imprint connected with *Rolling Stone*. Structurally chaotic and using a personal "I" that at once denounces oppression and is trapped in an inferiority complex, the volumes have become cult classics. After Acosta's son, a musician, brought them back into print in 1989, they became widely read.

Acosta last spent time with his family on Thanksgiving in 1973. In 1974, he was hospitalized for ulcers in San Francisco. In June of that year, he disappeared mysteriously in Mazatlán, Mexico. Ilan Stavans's biography, *Bandido: The Death and Resurrection of Oscar "Zeta" Acosta* (1995), focuses on Acosta's career as a lawyer, his activism and literature, his drug abuse and family life. Stavans also edited *Oscar "Zeta" Acosta: The Uncollected Works* (1996), which includes "Perla Is a Pig" and unfinished material from the Oscar "Zeta" Acosta archive at the University of California in Santa Barbara. Acosta's standing in Latino culture is that of an underground hero with sympathies for the underdog. His antiestablishmentarianism was a perfect fit for the 1960s, an era of social and ideological disturbance. His obese body and larger-than-life personality have been depicted in two Hollywood movies based on Thompson's writing: Art Linson's *Where the Buffalo Roam* (1980), with Peter Boyle playing "Carl Lazlo," and Terry Gilliam's *Fear and Loathing in Las Vegas* (1998), with Benicio del Toro playing "Dr. Gonzo."

# FROM THE AUTOBIOGRAPHY OF A BROWN BUFFALO

## Chapter 6[1]

With thundering hoofbeats hammering and kicking whirlwinds of dust to my rear, I eat up the burning sands and concentrate on the white line, my only guide. Sacramento, Lake Tahoe and Shell stations. I pass up long-haired hitchhikers. I discard empty Budweisers along the trail just in case I lose my direction now that I am without my shrink, my guru and their magic. Tall buildings and rectangular slabs of pavement sink behind me as I dig my claws into the gas pedal of my green '65 Plymouth. With a head full of speed, a wilted penis and a can in my hand, my knuckles redden as I hold tightly to the wheel and plunge headlong over the mountains and into the desert in search of my past . . .

Although I was born in El Paso, Texas, I am actually a small-town kid. A hick from the sticks, a Mexican boy from the other side of the tracks. I grew up in Riverbank, California; post office box 303; population 3,969. It's the only town in the entire state whose essential numbers have remained un-

---

1. In the preceding chapters, Acosta reflects on his ambivalent identity as a Chicano ("I stand naked before the mirror. Every morning of my life I have seen that brown belly from every angle"). He discusses his obesity ("What value is a life without booze and Mexican food?"), his strained relationship with a psychologist, his difficulty attracting women, his fast life, and his ancestry ("All my life strangers have been interested in my ancestry. There is something about my bearing that cries out for history").

changed. The sign that welcomes you as you round the curve coming in from Modesto says, "The City Of Action."

Manuel Mercado Acosta is an *indio* from the mountains of Durango. His father operated a mescal distillery before the revolutionaries drove him out. He met my mother while riding a motorcycle in El Paso.

Juana Fierro Acosta is my mother. She could have been a singer in a Juárez cantina but instead decided to be Manuel's wife because he had a slick mustache, a fast bike, and promised to take her out of the slums across from the Rio Grande. She had only one demand in return for the two sons and three daughters she would bear him: "No handouts. No relief. I never want to be on welfare."

I doubt he really promised her anything in a very loud, clear voice. My father was a horsetrader, even though he got rid of both the mustache and the bike when FDR[2] drafted him, a wetback, into the U.S. Navy on June 22, 1943. He tried to get into the Marines, but when they found out he was a good swimmer and a noncitizen, they put him in a sailor suit and made him drive a barge in Okinawa.[3]

We lived in a two-room shack without a floor. We had to pump our water and use kerosene if we wanted to read at night. But we never went hungry. My old man always bought the pinto beans and the white flour for the tortillas in one-hundred-pound sacks which my mother used to make dresses, sheets and curtains. We had two acres of land which we planted every year with corn, tomatoes and yellow chiles for the hot sauce. Even before my father woke us, my old ma was busy at work making the tortillas at 5 A.M. while he chopped the logs we'd hauled up from the river on the weekends.

Reveille was at 6 A.M. sharp for me and my older brother, Bob. Radio station KTRB came on the air each morning with "The Star-Spangled Banner." A shrill, foggy whistle woke us to the odors of crackling wood in the cast-iron stove cooking the perfectly rounded, soft, warm tortillas.

"All right, boys. Up and at 'em," the wiry *indio* calls out to me and Bob. Sleep is for the lazy, those whom my parents detest, the slow-minded types afraid of the sunlight. And so to prove my worth I'm always the first one to jump up, stand on the bed and place my hand respectfully over my heart— I'm only a civilian—to show my allegiance to my father's madness for a country that has given him a barge and a badge at Okinawa in exchange for an honorable discharge. And made him a citizen of the United States of America to boot.

After the salute we scramble to dress while on KTRB one of the Maddox brothers says to Rose, "Give us a great big smile, Rose."[4] She giggles and they stomp away to an Okie beat. Roll call comes on the Acosta ship at exactly 6:10 on the button. My father waits for his crew outside. We stand in line, my brother, myself and my mother, who is trying to lose weight.

She has been on a diet all my life. She has a definite concern about people being overweight. She has nagged me and my sisters—my brother Bob was always skinny—until we all ended up with some doctor or another; but I stayed fat and she has always had a fine body, even sexy you might say.

---

2. Franklin Delano Roosevelt (1882–1945), U.S. president 1933–45.
3. Japanese island.

4. The Maddox Brothers and Rose—five siblings— were an American "hillbilly band" (1930s–50s).

After we eat our scrambled eggs and chorizo guzzled down with Mexican chocolate, we trudged through the well-worn paths across empty lots with wild wheat to Riverbank Grammar School, where I learned my *p*'s and *q*'s from Miss Anderson. At noon we ran down Patterson Road for lunch. Two miles in fifteen minutes flat. My mother was of the strict opinion that you cannot learn without a hot lunch in your stomach. So we were permitted exactly thirty minutes to finish up our daily fights at the old black oak tree. A tree with gnarled branches with small, corklike, burnt balls we used for floaters when we waited for catfish down at the river near the Catholic church, where the sisters taught us about sin and social politics.

Bob and I had to chop wood for the evening meal. We had to pump the water into tin tubs for our nightly bath. And unless we bathed and washed the dishes, we couldn't turn on the little brown radio to listen to *The Whistler*, *The Shadow*, or *The Saturday Night Hit Parade* with Andy Russell, the only Mexican I ever heard on the radio as a kid. We would sit and listen while we shined our shoes. During the commercials my mother would sing beautiful Mexican songs, which I then thought were corny, while she dried the dishes. "When you grow up, you'll like this music too," my ma always prophesied. In the summer of '67, as a buffalo on the run, I still thought Mexican music was corny.

Usually, my old man would wait until we got in bed before he gave us our nightly lectures. Then he'd pull out a blue-covered book they'd given him in the navy called *The Seabee's Manual*. It was the only book I ever saw him read. He used to say, "If you boys memorize this book, you'll be able to do anything you want." It showed you how to do things like tie fantastic knots, fix boilers on steamships and survive without food and water when lost at sea. Admittedly, it helped when I took my entrance exams into Boy Scout Troop 42, but it didn't offer any advice on how to get rid of ulcers or the ants in my stomach. Its primary wisdom was its advice against waste. The horsetrader was so hung up on this principal sin that once he made me go to bed without supper because I'd filled a glass with water when I required only half the precious liquid.

"Why can't you fill it halfway? Then if you want more, fill it about one fourth . . . et cetera," he'd tell us in total seriousness. To this day I get a twinge of guilt when I throw away water, leftovers and old clothes that I can't possibly use.

We used to go to the garbage dump down by the old aluminum plant, which to my knowledge never produced aluminum. Immediately after its construction Tojo[5] and FDR got into it and the place was converted into a shell-casing plant. That event, along with the Riverbank Canning Company, placed Riverbank on the map. We had one of the three shell-casing plants in the country during the Second World War and the largest tomato paste cannery in the world.

We'd take a truckful of junk to the dump and spend the entire morning searching through the rotting, burning piles of trash, broken furniture, old clothes, busted tools and old family items, all of us in search of things that the horsetrader thought could still be saved under the rules of *The Seabee's Manual*. By the time we got done, the truck was as full as when we left.

---

5. Hideki Tojo (1884–1948), Japanese general and politician.

Then the singer and the *indio* would get into it. And when he'd turn his back to her, shake his head and say "You just don't understand," she'd start in on me and Bob. But she never contradicted him in our presence.

"You'd better do what your dad tells you, hijo,"[6] she'd warn us. Even when she knew it was madness, when she suspected he was suffering from shell shock, still she never disagreed with his instructions to his sons. She'd simply take another aspirin and sing Mexican songs, dreaming maybe of what might have been had she not become a captain's wife.

Even the time he gave us the ultimate lesson on becoming "a man," she didn't say a word. We were all at the supper table. I was wolfing down hot, fresh corn with huge glasses of milk. I'd eat so fast that even when I dropped a piece of meat on the adobe floor or spilled the Kool-Aid, I wouldn't miss a stroke. He warned me of the effect it would have on both my character and my stomach. Every single night of my childhood, my folks bugged me about my speed. It got to where I even tried eating with my left hand to slow me down, but after three weeks I became ambidextrous and it wouldn't work anymore. I consoled myself with the idea that even though it didn't help my diet any, it would still be of use in case I ever got my right hand chopped off by the Japs.

That night my old man said, "If you can eat a spoonful of your mother's chile, I'll give you a penny."

I looked at my brother. He wasn't about to take up the challenge. He didn't pay as much attention to my dad as I did. For some reason, he wasn't that interested in becoming a man.

"Right away? A penny for every spoonful?" The six-year-old kid said.

"Don't you trust me?"

My brother merely laughed when he saw the tears running down my fat, brown cheeks after the third spoonful. But I proved my point. I never backed off from any challenge.

My mother just shook her head. She disapproved of his madness. She even tried to imagine there might be some mystery that she, as a mere woman, couldn't understand.

Frugality and competition were their lot. The truth of it was they both conspired to make men out of two innocent Mexican boys. It seemed that the sole purpose of childhood was to train boys how to be men. Not men of the future, but *now*. We had to get up early, run home from school, work on weekends, holidays and during vacations, all for the purpose of being men. We were supposed to talk like *un hombre*, walk like a man, act like a man and think like a man. When they called us from the corner lot to play keep-away, we couldn't go until we finished pulling weeds from the garden. And while the gang gathered behind the grocery store to smoke cigarette butts, we had to shine our shoes and read *The Seabee's Manual*. In fact, the only times we could read funny books was when my father was in the navy. Nothing would infuriate him more than to catch us browsing through *Captain Marvel* or *Plastic Man*. Men, after all, didn't waste their time reading funny books. Men, he'd tell us, took life seriously. Nothing could be learned from books that were funny.

6. Son.

I used to think that only my father was mad. I doubted that the fathers of my friends in the barrio taught them the same things. But one day I learned differently. Walking home from school on a Tuesday afternoon, I spit on the picture of an American flag. It was Victory Stamp Day. We used to save them the way some people collect green stamps.

We had been lectured by Miss Anderson on the art of self-preservation in case of an enemy attack. Although she spoke strictly about the Japanese, I always pictured the real enemy as not only a kamikaze with the red rising sun on his wings, but also some old man with an enormous fountain pen who sent printed letters to the poor families living in small towns. FDR was as much my enemy as were the Japs. After all, it was he, not Tojo, who drafted my old man. He's the one who made my mother and my brother cry for a whole month after we drove my dad down to the post office. He's the one who took a razor blade and cut out entire sentences from the little letters that looked like telegrams that my father wrote us from Okinawa, Iwo Jima and Tarawa.[7] And when my father said *they* hadn't told him how much longer he'd have to drive the barge, we knew he referred to FDR, not Tojo.

So you have eight ragtag ten-year-old brown-baked Mexican boys marching single file along the curb in front of the old PT&T.[8] Oscar sees a leaflet with the picture of the American flag. He spits!

"Hey, look what Oscar did," Johnny Gomez tells the others. He stands back, points to the leaflet as if it were some snake. The others circle around and shake their heads.

"What'd you do that for?" his brother David demands of me.

"Why not? It's just a picture," I explain.

"That's the American flag, stupid!"

"So what?"

"So don't do it no more."

"Why? You gonna make me?"

David beat the shit out of me. While I dusted my pants off and wiped the blood from my elbows, they all laughed at me.

"You ain't so tough," the short little Indian said to me.

"Oh, yeh?" He got on top of me and pinned my arms to the ground with his knees. I had to give up . . . but only to start again with Alfonso when he said I was a chicken. As things turned out, I had to fight each of them that afternoon. I lost every single fight.

The seven whipped my ass on that day that I spit on the picture of my father's flag. I have never, to this day, had any respect for that flag or that country. You can blame it on my childhood experiences. Politics has nothing to do with it. I have no ideology. I've been an outlaw out of practical necessity ever since. And I have never backed off from a fight.

My old man taught me to fight dirty. He said, "Don't start anything. But if you have to fight, don't fool around. Pick up a stick, a rock or anything that's hard. You hit them on the head a few times and they'll never pick on you again."

He bought us boxing gloves and a punching bag for Christmas. After a while, none of the guys in the neighborhood my age wanted to come over

---

7. Pacific island. *Iwo Jima*: Japanese island in the Pacific.   8. Now AT&T.

and work out. Years later, as a senior in high school, I won the heavyweight boxing championship by hitting Harry Greene below the belt until he couldn't stand up. When his manager ran into the ring to protest, I punched him too. Some of his followers chased me into the locker room after they gave me the medal. I picked up a track shoe with spikes and held them at bay until my football coach, Joe Sigfried, ordered them out.

Living in Riverbank was no different from living in a strange, foreign town. I was an outsider then as much as I am now. Particularly during the first three years, Bob and I had to defend ourselves against the meanest and toughest boys on the list because we were considered "easterners." They said we weren't *real* Mexicans because we wore long, black patent leather boots and short pants, which my mother bought for us in Juárez just before we boarded the Greyhound bus to join up with my father, who'd left the year before to seek the riches of California's golden peach orchards.

California, then, was a land of *pochos*.[9] These California Mexicans were not much higher than the Okies[1] with whom they lived. They spoke English most of the time, while we looked upon life "out west" simply as a temporary respite from the Depression. The five bucks a week my old man earned as a mechanic in El Paso hadn't been quite enough to satisfy my mother's dreams. She wanted a sewing machine, a house with electricity and running water. She never dreamed of actually owning a house; she just wanted to live in one with all the modern conveniences she read about in the Sears, Roebuck catalogue. So, when we left El Segundo Barrio across the street from the international border, we didn't expect the Mexicans in California to act like *gringos*.

But they did. We were outsiders because of geography, and outcasts because we didn't speak English and wore short pants. And so we had to fight every single day. Until the day Bob beat up Jimmy Pacheco, the youngest of a bunch of Apaches who lived on the edge of the barrio with ten brothers and about seven dogs. They were the only ones in the entire neighborhood that had a wire fence around their property. They were always slaughtering pigs and goats and young bulls, getting drunk on tequila and drinking raw blood with fresh onions. But one day Bob grabbed Jimmy by the wrist and flung him against the trunk of an old black oak tree, and that was that. Jimmy didn't fool anyone with the long-sleeved shirts he wore for weeks after the incident. We all knew he had a cast underneath. Generally, the *pochos* quit picking on us after that. Not that they accepted us as part of their tribe, but they simply quit fucking with us. I never had to fight a Mexican again until I joined the revolution some thirty years later.

The fight with Pacheco didn't end the war, however. Our biggest battle-front opened at seven-thirty in the morning at the railroad tracks which marked the edge of Okie Town. At night and on weekends we fought the Mexicans in the neighborhood, but during the day and at school we had to fight off the Okies. We had an unspoken rule that you never fought one of your own kind in front of others. In the battle for group survival you simply don't weaken your defenses by getting involved in family squabbles in front of the real enemy.

---

9. Derogatory term for Americanized Mexicans.
1. Derogatory term for destitute, mostly white people who, in the 1930s, moved from the so-called Dust Bowl (states such as Oklahoma and Texas) to California in search of jobs and a fresh start.

We had to fight the Okies because we were Mexicans! It didn't matter to them that my brother and I were outcasts on our own turf. They'd have laughed if we'd told them that we were easterners. To them we were greasers, spics and niggers. If you lived on the West Side, across from the tracks, and had brown skin, you were a Mexican.

Riverbank is divided into three parts, and in my corner of the world there were only three kinds of people: Mexicans, Okies and Americans. Catholics, Holy Rollers and Protestants. Peach pickers, cannery workers and clerks.

We lived on the West Side, within smelling distance of the world's largest tomato paste cannery. With its hordes of flies and the ugly stench of rotting waste on hot summer days, the West Side was tucked a safe distance from the center of town, where the Americans lived. Every home had a garden, at least a rosebush or two, and if nothing else a couple of chickens. We grew vegetables not for victory but for survival during the frosted, tully-fogged winter months after the peaches, walnuts, tomatoes, grapes and olives had been picked. And long before it became fashionable for the American women to plant flowers and lemon trees in cute little bonnets and white gloves, the Mexican women were watering their roses and chile plants on Saturday mornings while we went to our catechism classes at the Lady of Guadalupe.

The West Side is still enclosed by the Santa Fe Railroad tracks to the east, the Modesto–Oakdale highway to the north and the irrigation canal to the south. Within that concentration only Mexicans were safe from the neighborhood dogs, who responded only to Spanish commands. Except for Bob Whitt and Emitt Brown, both friends of mine who could cuss in better Spanish than I, I never saw a white person walking the dirt roads of our neighborhood.

If you climb the water tower next to the railroad depot, you can see Okie Town to the east. Riverbank is flat, farming country. Except for the bank and the Masonic lodge, there are no three-story dwellings or structures for miles around. I always wanted to climb that aluminum-colored, ten-thousand-gallon water storage tank, but Harry March, who owned the five-and-dime, always warned against it. He looked like John L. Lewis[2] and sold us cigarettes if we scribbled a note and pretended it was from our parents. I used to ask for Wings[3] and sign my father's name, even though we both knew he was away in the navy. "If they catch you, they'll put you in the hoosegow," he'd tell us when we stopped by on the way home from school for our afternoon ice cream cone.

One day I couldn't wait anymore to do my part for the war effort Miss Anderson kept talking about. I wanted my father home because my mother was going crazy. She ate nothing but aspirins and oranges, drank black coffee and beat us with belts, rubber hoses, ice hooks. Even though I'd sort of taken over the family at the age of ten, got to zip up my mother's dresses when she dressed for the cannery and had the final word on whether my sisters could go to the movies, still I wanted the sailor back home.

The headlines of the *Modesto Bee* made us cry every day, even when Mr. McClatchy said we'd pounded the daylights out of the Japs. The constant flow of mile-long troop trains with soldiers herded in like cattle was a daily reminder of my uselessness as a civilian. We'd go down to the railroad and

2. American labor leader (1880–1969).
3. During the Great Depression, a popular economy brand of cigarette.

wave at the brave men headed for San Francisco on their way to fight the Japs. They'd give us pennies and nickels and once in a while ask us to bring our sisters to say hello. Mine was practically still in diapers, so I couldn't offer much of that.

I had even taken to looking for the red cellophane strips from Lucky Strike packs, which Harry March had told us could be exchanged for German shepherd Seeing Eye dogs for the crippled veterans. After a year I had only two hundred of them. I'd had enough arithmetic to know that at that rate I'd be picking up dirty, empty cigarette packs for five more years. We tried to save newspapers, but it didn't amount to much. And I knew it would take the rest of my life to save ten pounds of tinfoil from Juicy Fruit and the insides of the cigarette packs.

So one day I finally made my decision to join the resistance. I climbed to the top of the lily tree in our backyard. This tree with the purple blossoms and little green balls the size of steelies—the best marble you can pick for playing fish—this was my own personal, private place. Bob was the owner of the eucalyptus tree, and we all shared the fruits of the plum, the fig and the almond trees; but no one could climb my lily tree without my permission.

I carry my pump-action .22 strapped to my shoulder as I carefully and quietly climb the thirty-foot-tall sniper post. The enemy planes fly day and night over this land. I just have to wait. Gary Cooper[4] didn't complain when he had to sit in that tree with the Japs marching underneath, the flies and gnats driving him crazy in that hot, steaming jungle, did he? . . . I hear the drone in the distance. I close my eyes. You can tell by the hum of the motor whose side he's on. And when it is overhead I take careful aim. I know it *looks* like a P-38, but that's a disguise . . . I shoot.

I wait for it to fall, but somehow it keeps flying toward the aluminum plant . . . I wipe the sweat from my brow and think it through again. What would Coop do in this situation? I have only one bullet left. One shot. Do I wait for another plane? Of course they heard the blast from my rifle. Soon they'll be here. I'm not afraid of the torture. I can take anything, remember? But a man has to destroy any target, any supply of war material, do anything that will hurt the Nips.[5] It doesn't have to be a moving target. It doesn't have to be a human . . .

And there it sits, big as day. No more than one block from my scope is the infamous water tower. The whole town depends upon it. Cut off their water supply and you'll have them in the palm of your hand in a week. Does the Geneva Convention[6] actually prohibit sniper action against the civilian population? What would Miss Anderson say about this? Fuck it! I've got to help my father get home any way that I can. After all, *this is war!* Surely God will understand even if the sisters don't. Look at Humphrey Bogart.[7] He's still alive, isn't he? And how many has he snuffed out? I squeeze the trigger and close my eyes.

Two days later I take a casual stroll to the railroad depot. Just going down to say hello to the troops, I tell my ma. For two whole days and nights I've not even dared to look toward the east. It's bad luck to look for death and

---

4. American movie actor (1901–1961), here representing a type of war hero.
5. Derogatory term for Japanese, from *Nipponese*.
6. One of a series of international agreements

concerning the treatment of prisoners of war and of the sick, wounded, and dead in battle.
7. American movie actor (1899–1957), here representing a type of efficient killer.

destruction. No one's mentioned it, but I've been certain all weekend that the entire population will soon be dying of thirst. The fact that our faucet keeps pumping clear water doesn't throw me; I know they're on the spare tank now. By tomorrow it'll be all over with.

Without looking up, I stand under the palm trees in the little park behind the Santa Fe depot. When I'm certain no one is watching, I look up toward the water tank. I squint my eyes to see the damage. I look for evidence of a flood. Something. It's possible, of course, that they already dried it out, sucked the water up with some huge pump. Good soldiers always hide their true battle conditions. Besides, how can I really be sure? I haven't binoculars to be positive. I'll merely report it as an "attempt." I didn't do it for any goddamn Purple Heart[8] anyway! The old man will simply have to take my word for it. He knows I never lie to him. He knows perfectly well I've never lied to him since that day he hung me from a rafter in the chicken coop.

We had been pulling weeds from the tomatoes. My young uncle Hector started it all. He threw the first rock at Bob. My brother thought it was me and threw a clod the size of a pumpkin. The captain warned us twice. The third time he ordered us inside. Before he found a belt, some Americans stopped by to purchase some corn. We sold it for fifty cents a dozen, and put in an extra one in case you found one with worms. While the horsetrader picked the corn from the stalks, Hector talked us into stuffing newspapers under our V-8's.[9] "Don't forget to pretend when he hits us," my uncle said . . . Well, I blew it. I forgot. I should have rubbed onions in my eyes.

When the captain discovered the sports pages of the *Modesto Bee* under my shorts, he asked, "Okay, you cheaters, whose idea was it?"

Shit, not even my old man can make me talk once I've made up my mind. I am loyal to the core. Even when he marched us to the chicken coop under the plum tree, did you see me cry? When he made the three of us stand on that four-by-four, tied the rope around our necks, did you hear me beg for mercy?

"When you're ready to talk, I'll cut you down," he said.

Even when he walked out, leaving us there to die, I said nothing. Despite the fact I was the youngest of the three, you didn't see me holding up any white flag of surrender. Though as the blood curdled in my legs, even cramps of electrical shocks up my spine didn't do a thing. I knew my mother would find us with our tongues hanging out when she came for the eggs in the morning. And when that mean bantam rooster pecked at my feet, when we could no longer hear my father's voice outside, you still didn't hear me cry, did you?

It was Hector who chickened out and called for help. "Manuel, you better cut me down or I'll tell 'Ama." Who knows how long the captain would have let us hang if Hector hadn't been his kid brother? Whatever influence or authority Hector had over me because he was my uncle and five years older, he lost it that afternoon in the chicken coop. And but for his lack of character, I'd probably have never started on those nasty habits in the shower.

During the summers we used to pick peaches. My father would challenge the three of us to a race. If Bob, Hector and me could pick more lugs of peaches than the captain, he'd buy us a watermelon and take us to the canal

---

8. U.S. military decoration awarded to a member of the armed forces wounded or killed in action.

9. A kind of underpants (briefs).

after work. We always lost because we took an hour for lunch while the old man kept picking away, but he took us to swim anyway. The sweltering heat and the itching peach fuzz didn't bother Indians like him. But laggards and sissies such as we were had to plunge and dip and show off in front of girls at the canal during the lunch hour to feel better.

If it hadn't been for my fatness, I'd probably have been able to do those fancy-assed jackknifes and swan dives as well as the rest of you. But my mother had me convinced I was obese, ugly as a pig and without any redeeming qualities whatsoever. How then could I run around with just my Jockey shorts? V-8's don't hide fat, you know. That's why I finally started wearing boxers. But by then it was too late. Everyone knew I had the smallest prick in the world. With the girls watching and giggling, the guys used to sing my private song to the tune of "Little Bo Peep": "Oh, where, oh where can my little boy be? Oh, where, oh where can he be? He's so chubby, panson,[1] that he can't move along. Oh, where, oh where can he be?"

I tried like hell to stop eating ice cream and tortillas with mayonnaise, but I still always stayed five or ten pounds overweight. And no matter what I did or what I thought, even when I asked the Virgin Mary to make me a man and give me at least a bit of pubic hair, still my prick was an inch or two smaller than all the rest.

In fact, if it hadn't been for Vernon Knecht, I might have remained the deformed freak that I was to this day. He was a big, red-headed German kid who taught me how to leave markings on trees and traffic arrows made of rocks when I studied for my merit badges with Troop 42. When I was twelve, we went on a hiking and camping weekend with our fag Boy Scout leader out at the Oakdale Reservoir, and I was instructed to be Vernon's *buddy*. In case you drowned, got lost or were attacked by Indians, you were supposed to have a buddy. Since Vernon was a First Class Scout and about three years older, the Tenderfoot that I was leaned on his every word. So that night, under the pup tent while the summer rain kept us all inside, I asked him how to make the bugger grow.

"Shit, you mean you don't know how to jack off?"

"You mean pull it?" I asked my guide.

He whipped out his long, white dick and said, "Yeh, man. Push and pull . . . just like this."

When Hector, brother Bob and cousin Manuel used to make fun of my obesity and little penis, I would yell through my teeth, "At least I don't pull it." They always got a kick out of that and called me a liar. I had to show them the palms of both my hands to prove that I didn't masturbate.

"You see any warts?" I'd ask.

So that weekend at the Oakdale Reservoir, I told Vernon Knecht, "I don't want to do anything dirty. I haven't made my confirmation yet."

"What do you mean?" the German infidel asked.

"Shit, man, how would you confess that to a priest? You think he'd believe me if I told him I did it to make it grow?"

"Well, fuck, man. Just don't tell him."

I lost most of my religion the same night I learned about sex from old Vernon. When I saw the white, foamy suds come from under his foreskin, I

---

1. Spanish slang for fat.

thought he had wounded himself from yanking on it too hard with those huge farmer hands of his. And when I saw his green eyes fall back into his head, I thought he was having some sort of a seizure like I'd seen Toto, the village idiot, have out in his father's fig orchard after he fucked a chicken.

I didn't much like the sounds of romance the first time I saw jizz.

I knew that Vernon was as tough as they came. Nothing frightened or threatened him. He'd cuss right in front of John Hazard, our fag Boy Scout leader, as well as Miss Anderson. But when I heard him oooh and aaah as the soapsuds spit at his chest while we lay on our backs inside the pup tent, I wondered for a minute if sex wasn't actually for sissies. I tried to follow his example, but nothing would come out. With him cheering me on, saying, "Harder, man. Pull on that son of a bitch. Faster, faster!" it just made matters worse. The thing went limp before the soapsuds came out.

He advised me to try it more often. "Don't worry, man. It'll grow if you work on it."

When I got home the next day, my mother wouldn't let me in the kitchen until I cleaned up. I was starving from being on pork and beans all weekend, so I hurried into the shower.

Maybe if I put soap on it, just to warm up, I said to myself.

Sure enough, the bugger's big spit jumped in my eyes for the first time in my life. Every time I've heard the saying about cleanliness being next to godliness, I really get a bang.

1972

---

# NICHOLASA MOHR
## b. 1935

In the 1970s, Nicholasa Mohr became one of the pioneers and most notable voices among a growing group of Puerto Rican writers born or raised in the United States. Her first novel, *Nilda* (1973), gained her immediate critical attention at a time when Piri Thomas was the only other widely recognized mainland Puerto Rican fiction writer. Mohr's novel received the Jane Addams Book Award and was selected Best Book of the Year by *School Library Journal* and Outstanding Book of the Year by *The New York Times*. *Nilda*—a chapter of which is included in this anthology—belongs to the genre of the bildungsroman, which is now commonplace within Latino literature. The novel focuses on the life of a Puerto Rican girl growing up in New York's El Barrio (Spanish Harlem) during the 1940s, as she discovers the complexities of her environment and shares with her family the poverty and racial discrimination endured by many Puerto Ricans in American society. Mohr describes the work as "autobiographical in feeling, but not necessarily in fact."

Like her protagonist and many New York Puerto Rican writers, Mohr was born and raised in El Barrio. She studied graphic arts at New York's Art Students League, the Brooklyn Museum Art School, the New School for Social Research, and the Pratt Institute, and her artwork appeared in many exhibits in New York and Puerto Rico. She noted in a 1980 interview with the cultural critic Edna Acosta-Belén that the transition from graphic art to writing was not difficult. She described herself simply as "an artist learning a new craft," translating some of her visual images into writing. However, being a woman in the male-dominated emerging market of Puerto Rican literature on the mainland was not easy:

> The major problem for me has been exposure of my books. Recognition is given more to those books that are great escapades: a little bit of robbing, shooting, swearing; men going around like Puerto Rican John Waynes, and women who are either morons or prostitutes devoid of any real depth or substance. Those books for some reason get an enormous amount of play and recognition.

Compared with the male-focused narratives that preceded it, *Nilda* more subtly depicts the Puerto Rican experience in New York. Hardships and discrimination faced by the community remain central, as does anger at injustice, but the tapestry of characters represents a celebration of communal solidarity, a shared sense of humanity, and a strong determination to endure and prevail. In referring to her body of work, Mohr has noted that "Our traditions—who we are, our language, gender battles, survival skills, and our place in society—have been handed down from generation to generation, primarily as oral history. In my stories, I attempt to carry on this venerable tradition using the written word."

After the success of *Nilda*, Mohr gradually adopted writing as her primary means of artistic expression, though most of her publications, including *Nilda*, display some of her graphic work either on their jackets or in accompanying original illustrations. *Nilda* was followed by *El Bronx Remembered: A Novella and Stories* (1975), a *Time* Outstanding Book and a National Book Award finalist, and *In Nueva York* (1977), an American Library Association Best Book for Young Adults and a *School Library Journal* Best Book for Young Adults. In the latter collection, stories such as "The Wrong Lunch Line: Early Spring 1946" (included here) focus on issues of interethnic friendship among schoolchildren—and children's obliviousness to the prejudices shared by the adults around them—at a time when forced segregation was common. The story makes clear why Mohr's short fiction is appealing to younger readers and used widely in school curricula at the elementary, secondary, and college levels. The apparent simplicity of the prose is balanced by the moving tales, the rich galleries of characters, and an engaging narrative style. Quite often, Mohr tells her stories through the voices of young characters.

Mohr's success in the young adult literature market and her recognition of the lack of children's books by Latino authors led her to write *Felita* (1979), her first novel aimed at younger readers, and its sequel, *Going Home* (1986). She has also written two illustrated books for children, including *The Song of El Coquí/La canción del coquí* (1995), a joint venture with the Puerto Rican graphic artist Antonio Martorell. Mohr's autobiographical narrative *In My Own Words: Growing Up inside the Sanctuary of My Imagination* (1994) was also marketed for a young adult readership. This inspiring memoir of Mohr's coming-of-age in American society ends with an account of her last conversation with her dying mother at the age of 14. Her mother's last words encourage young Nicholasa to follow her artistic dreams to become a successful professional. In turn, Mohr passes this message along to her young readers, encouraging them to fulfill their dreams by exploring their imaginations and creative spirits.

One of Mohr's most acclaimed works for adult readers is the collection *Rituals of Survival: A Woman's Portfolio* (1985). In these stories—such as "Aunt Rosana's Rocker (Zoraida)," included here—Mohr presents a vivid group of Puerto Rican women characters against the background of urban poverty, racism, and gender subordination. These are feminist stories of self-discovery and individual and collective liberation that defy stereotypes and bring to the forefront those aspects of Puerto Rican culture that are oppressive to women. Mohr also celebrates the resilience of women in some of her subsequent work.

In addition to novels, stories, essays, and memoir, Mohr has written plays and film and television scripts. She has been a writer-in-residence at several American universities and writers' colonies. She is the recipient of an honorary doctorate from the University at Albany, SUNY (1989) and a commendation from New York's State Legislature (1986). Mohr presented the essay "A Journey toward a Common Ground: Struggles and Identity of Hispanics in the U.S.A." in 1999 at the Hispanic Media Conference, in San Juan, Puerto Rico. In it, she describes the historical journey of Latinos in becoming part of what she describes as "a new American ethnic consciousness."

## FROM NILDA

### May, 1945

Nilda waited in the corridor outside the ward, standing next to Victor, who was in uniform. He was to be discharged from the service in three weeks, but had arrived last night on special leave. Frankie walked back and forth nervously; once in a while he whispered something to Victor.

Everyone had been informed; telegrams had been sent to Jimmy and to Paul. Aunt Rosario had been at the hospital most of the night and, after going to the apartment briefly, had returned early this morning to summon a priest for Nilda's mother. Aunt Delia had not been allowed to come to the hospital this past week. Despite her persistent questioning, everyone had reassured the old woman that all was going well at the hospital.

Aunt Rosario stepped out of the ward, wiping her eyes. She looked at Nilda. "Nilda . . . go on inside now . . . but remember your mama is very, very sick, and I want you to try to compose yourself so that you don't make her too nervous." Aunt Rosario waited and Nilda did not move. "Go on . . . for heaven's sake," she said impatiently. "Lydia wants to see you alone for a little while . . . hurry up." Nilda nodded and slowly walked inside the ward and over to her mother's bed. This time the heavy green cloth curtains were pulled around the sides and front of the bed. Nilda extended her arm and pushed a section of the curtains aside, looking in. Recognizing her mother, she stepped in all the way, closing the curtains behind her.

Her mother was lying back with her eyes shut, her head slightly tilted forward. For an instant she felt her insides jump. Is Mama dead? she thought. But then she looked up and saw a metal stand supporting a bottle which hung upside down. An invisible liquid flowed out of the bottle and into a long thin tube; the tube was attached to a needle that was taped into her mother's right forearm. She went closer to her mother and heard her breathing. Then raising her hand, she lightly touched her mother's arm.

Opening her eyes, she looked at Nilda and smiled faintly. "Nilda?" Her voice was very hoarse and just above a whisper.

"Mama, how are you?" Nilda said shyly. She had not been to see her mother for a few days.

"Nilda . . . I'm very sick, nena."[1] She paused and breathed heavily. Looking down, Nilda began to cry. Her mother watched her and slowly shook her head. Nilda buried her face next to her mother's on the pillow and cried uncontrollably for what seemed a long time. After a while she raised her head. "Take a tissue," her mother said. Nilda picked up a tissue, blew her nose, and wiped her eyes. "How's school?" her mother asked.

"Fine, Mama."

"You still drawing those wonderful pictures?"

"Yes."

"You are gonna stay in school . . . like a good girl and finish?" Her mother spoke very slowly. "You are not gonna be foolish and quit?"

"No, Mama." Nilda sat on a chair and was very still, her eyes fixed on her mother.

"Nilda, you have to promise me that you will stay in school, and that you will listen to Rosario." Nilda nodded. "You eating all right?"

"Yes." There was a long silence. This morning, at home, Nilda had planned to ask her mother about a whole lot of things, and to talk about some of the things that bothered her. Now, as she sat close to her mother, she was very frightened and felt almost like a stranger. She did not know what to say or what to do. "Mama?" Her mother looked at her. "Petra had a baby girl last Sunday." Her mother smiled. "She had a little girl; she named her Marianne."

"Marianne? Do you know, Nilda, that was my mother's name. Mariana. Yes, your grandmother. That's a pretty name. Have you seen the baby yet?"

"No, I just heard about it. Maybe I'll go visit them next week."

"What about Indio? Nilda, did they get in touch with that boy?"

"Well, I heard he is coming home on leave, and that his father already gave Mr. López his word that Indio would marry Petra. Even though they are Lutheran, they said he will marry Petra in the Catholic Church. Anyway, that's what I heard."

"Nilda, you must never do anything foolish like that. Never. Don't have a bunch of babies and lose your life."

"You had children, Mama, and you love them and—"

"Nilda," her mother interrupted, and reaching out with her free hand, took both of Nilda's hands and held them tightly. "Listen to what I say. I love you, Nilda, and I love your brothers, all of you, regardless who the father was, I don't care . . . you are all . . . still mine." She paused and closed her eyes, remaining silent for a while. Nilda wondered if she had fallen asleep, but she opened her eyes again. "You are a woman, Nilda. You will have to bear the child; regardless of who planted the seed, they will be your children and no one else's. If a man is good, you are lucky; if he leaves you, or is cruel, so much the worse for you. . . . And then, if you have no money and little education, who will help you, Nilda? Another man? Yes, and another pregnancy. Welfare? Yes, and they will kill you in the process, slowly robbing you of your home, so that after a while it is no longer yours." She stopped speaking, and pushing her head back against the pillow, she stared at the ceiling, but continued to hold Nilda's hands.

1. Dear girl.

"Mami?" Nilda whispered. "Aren't you happy? I love you, Mama. Aren't you happy with us? I want to be with you all the time, Mama."

Tightening her grip on Nilda's hands, and without looking away from the ceiling, her mother said, "I have no life of my own, Nilda." Her voice was very low and hoarse; Nilda had to lean closer to hear what she said. "I have never had a life of my own . . . yes, that's true, isn't it? No life, Nilda . . . nothing that is really only mine . . . that's not fair, is it? That's not right . . . I don't know what I want even. . . ."

She paused, and Nilda felt her mother's body shaking; she was laughing without making any sound. "Do you know if I were to get well tomorrow . . . what I would do? Nilda? . . . I would live for the children I bore . . . I guess . . . and nothing more. You see, I don't remember any more what I did want. . . . Sometimes when I am alone, here in the hospital, I remember a feeling I used to have when I was very young . . . it had only to do with me. Nobody else was included . . . just me, and I did exist so joyfully in that feeling; I was so nourished . . . thinking about it would make me so excited about life. . . . You know something? I don't even know what it was now. How is that possible? That there is this life I have made, Nilda, and I have nothing to do with it? How did it all happen anyway?

"Do you have that feeling, honey? That you have something all yours . . . you must . . . like when I see you drawing sometimes, I know you have something all yours. Keep it . . . hold on, guard it. Never give it to nobody . . . not to your lover, not to your kids . . . it don't belong to them . . . and . . . they have no right . . . no right to take it. We are all born alone . . . and we die all alone. And when I die, Nilda, I know I take nothing with me that is only mine." She paused and said, "You asked me something, didn't you? . . . oh yes. . . . Am I happy? . . . I don't know. . . . But if I cannot see who I am beyond the eyes of the children I bore . . . then . . ." turning her head, she looked directly at Nilda for a moment ". . . it was not worth the journey . . . and I might as well not have bothered at all." Shutting her eyes once more, she lay back against the pillow.

Nilda began to cry again, this time quietly. After a bit, she said, "Mama, I don't understand you."

"Someday you will, you know . . . yes. Hold on to yourself, even if at times you have to let go some . . . but not all! No . . . Nilda . . . not ever. A little piece inside has to remain yours always; it's your right, you know. To give it all up . . . entonces, mi hijita[2] . . . you will lose what is real inside you."

Opening her eyes, she turned and, smiling at Nilda, released her hands and stroked her hair. "My poor Nilda. I have nothing to leave you, nothing. I only know that you have a little more than I ever had, and that will have to be enough." Nilda watched as her mother breathed heavily; closing her eyes, she began to snore softly and evenly.

Nilda felt very confused. She had wanted to say so many things and had forgotten what they were. Watching her mother sleep, she remembered that she had wanted to ask permission to go to Leo's for a while. They had invited her, and Concha had said that she would be happy to have her the entire summer. She did not dare to wake her mother or ask her anything. She watched the bottle as it gulped bubbles of the invisible liquid into her

---

2. Then, my little daughter.

mother, then glanced again at her mother, who seemed to sleep so peacefully. Nilda stood up and very carefully kissed her on the forehead, then walked past the curtains and out into the corridor, joining Aunt Rosario and her two brothers. They all looked at her anxiously.

"She's asleep . . . she . . ." Nilda hesitated and shrugged.

"O.K. Good, honey," Aunt Rosario said. "Did she talk long to you, honey? She wanted very badly to talk to you." Nilda nodded her head. "Good. Victor, the priest has already been here; now, do you want to stay, and shall I take Frankie and Nilda home for now? What do you think?"

"That's a good idea, Tía.[3] Go on ahead. I will stay and find out what's happening. I don't think she should be alone now."

Aunt Rosario nodded and asked, "Will you come home for a bite to eat, Victor?"

"No, I'll grab something down in the hospital cafeteria. Go on, it's fine . . . now, if anything develops, I'll call Jacinto's grocery store. So don't worry . . . go ahead . . . you look tired, Titi Rosario, why don't you go on back and take a little nap yourself?"

"No, Victor. I'm O.K., and today is Thursday, so Willie is bringing Claudia and Roberto tomorrow. He has been a very big help to us." Victor nodded his head. "I'll see you this evening, Victor."

Nilda followed behind Aunt Rosario and Frankie. Outside it was hot and muggy; the streets were crowded with people.

"Let's walk to the subway, kids; it's faster," said Aunt Rosario. They walked along and Nilda glanced at the newspaper headlines as they passed the newsstand.

GERMANY TO SURRENDER
HITLER FLEES!
AXIS RETREATS
WAR TO END WITHIN 24 HOURS

A radio was blaring from an open lunch stand, and Nilda heard the newscaster talking about the end of the war and the signing of a peace treaty. She stepped down a stairway quickly, and all three headed for the subway train.

That night Nilda had a feeling of emptiness, making her exhausted. She felt that she would never see her mother again and that today was the last time they would ever speak. She had her window open and a cool breeze swept through the room. It had cooled down some, she thought, and remembered that tomorrow was school; she had an English test and she had not prepared for it. Too tired to really care, she fell asleep and dreamed she heard her mother calling her in a whisper.

"Nilda! . . . Nilda!"

She opened her eyes and felt someone's hand on her shoulder, gently shaking her. It was Victor. Sitting up, she looked at him.

"Nilda, wake up, honey," he said. "Mama is dead; she died this morning at two A.M."

1973

---

3. Aunt.

# The Wrong Lunch Line: Early Spring 1946

The morning dragged on for Yvette and Mildred. They were anxiously waiting for the bell to ring. Last Thursday the school had announced that free Passover lunches would be provided for the Jewish children during this week. Yvette ate the free lunch provided by the school and Mildred brought her lunch from home in a brown paper bag. Because of school rules, free-lunch children and bag-lunch children could not sit in the same section, and the two girls always ate separately. This week, however, they had planned to eat together.

Finally the bell sounded and all the children left the classroom for lunch. As they had already planned, Yvette and Mildred went right up to the line where the Jewish children were filing up for lunch trays. I hope no one asks me nothing, Yvette said to herself. They stood close to each other and held hands. Every once in a while one would squeeze the other's hand in a gesture of reassurance, and they would giggle softly.

The two girls lived just a few houses away from one another. Yvette lived on the top floor of a tenement, in a four-room apartment which she shared with her parents, grandmother, three older sisters, two younger brothers, and baby sister. Mildred was an only child. She lived with her parents in the three small rooms in back of the candy store they owned.

During this school year, the two girls had become good friends. Every day after public school, Mildred went to a Hebrew school. Yvette went to catechism twice a week, preparing for her First Communion and Confirmation. Most evenings after supper, they played together in front of the candy store. Yvette was a frequent visitor in Mildred's apartment. They listened to their favorite radio programs together. Yvette looked forward to the Hershey's chocolate bar that Mr. Fox, Mildred's father, would give her.

The two girls waited patiently on the lunch line as they slowly moved along toward the food counter. Yvette was delighted when she saw what was placed on the trays: a hard-boiled egg, a bowl of soup that looked like vegetable, a large piece of cracker, milk, and an apple. She stretched over to see what the regular free lunch was, and it was the usual: a bowl of watery stew, two slices of dark bread, milk, and cooked prunes in a thick syrup. She was really glad to be standing with Mildred.

"Hey Yvette!" She heard someone call her name. It was Elba Cruz, one of her classmates. "What's happening? Why are you standing there?"

"I'm having lunch with Mildred today," she answered, and looked at Mildred, who nodded.

"Oh yeah?" Elba said. "Why are they getting a different lunch from us?"

"It's their special holiday and they gotta eat that special food, that's all," Yvette answered.

"But why?" persisted Elba.

"Else it's a sin, that's why. Just like we can't have no meat on Friday," Yvette said.

"A sin. . . . Why—why is it a sin?" This time, she looked at Mildred.

"It's a special lunch for Passover," Mildred said.

"Passover? What is that?" asked Elba.

"It's a Jewish holiday. Like you got Easter, so we have Passover. We can't eat no bread."

"Oh. . . ."

"You better get in your line before the teacher comes," Yvette said quickly.

"You're here!" said Elba.

"I'm only here because Mildred invited me," Yvette answered. Elba shrugged her shoulders and walked away.

"They gonna kick you outta there. . . . I bet you are not supposed to be on that line," she called back to Yvette.

"Dumbbell!" Yvette answered. She turned to Mildred and asked, "Why can't you eat bread, Mildred?"

"We just can't. We are only supposed to eat matzo. What you see there." Mildred pointed to the large cracker on the tray.

"Oh," said Yvette. "Do you have to eat an egg too?"

"No . . . but you can't have no meat, because you can't have meat and milk together . . . like at the same time."

"Why?"

"Because it's against our religion. Besides, it's very bad. It's not supposed to be good for you."

"It's not?" asked Yvette.

"No," Mildred said. "You might get sick. You see, you are better off waiting like a few hours until you digest your food, and then you can have meat or the milk. But not together."

"Wow," said Yvette. "You know, I have meat and milk together all the time. I wonder if my mother knows it's not good for you."

By this time the girls were at the counter. Mildred took one tray and Yvette quickly took another.

"I hope no one notices me," Yvette whispered to Mildred. As the two girls walked toward a long lunch table, they heard giggling and Yvette saw Elba and some of the kids she usually ate lunch with pointing and laughing at her. Stupids, thought Yvette, ignoring them and following Mildred. The two girls sat down with the special lunch group.

Yvette whispered to Mildred, "This looks good!" and started to crack the eggshell.

Yvette felt Mildred's elbow digging in her side. "Watch out!" Mildred said.

"What is going on here?" It was the voice of one of the teachers who monitored them during lunch. Yvette looked up and saw the teacher coming toward her.

"You! You there!" the teacher said, pointing to Yvette. "What are you doing over there?" Yvette looked at the woman and was unable to speak.

"What are you doing over there?" she repeated.

"I went to get some lunch," Yvette said softly.

"What? Speak up! I can't hear you."

"I said . . . I went to get some lunch," she said a little louder.

"Are you entitled to a free lunch?"

"Yes."

"Well . . . and are you Jewish?"

Yvette stared at her and she could feel her face getting hot and flushed.

"I asked you a question. Are you Jewish?" Another teacher Yvette knew came over and the lunchroom became quiet. Everyone was looking at Yvette, waiting to hear what was said. She turned to look at Mildred, who looked just as frightened as she felt. Please don't let me cry, thought Yvette.

"What's the trouble?" asked the other teacher.

"This child," the woman pointed to Yvette, "is eating lunch here with the Jewish children, and I don't think she's Jewish. She doesn't—I've seen her before; she gets free lunch, all right. But she looks like one of the—" Hesitating, the woman went on, "She looks Spanish."

"I'm sure she's not Jewish," said the other teacher.

"All right now," said the first teacher, "what are you doing here? Are you Spanish?"

"Yes."

"Why did you come over here and get in that line? You went on the wrong lunch line!"

Yvette looked down at the tray in front of her.

"Get up and come with me. Right now!" Getting up, she dared not look around her. She felt her face was going to burn up. Some of the children were laughing; she could hear the suppressed giggles and an occasional "Ooooh." As she started to walk behind the teacher, she heard her say, "Go back and bring that tray." Yvette felt slightly weak at the knees but managed to turn around, and going back to the table, she returned the tray to the counter. A kitchen worker smiled nonchalantly and removed the tray full of food.

"Come on over to Mrs. Ralston's office," the teacher said, and gestured to Yvette that she walk in front of her this time.

Inside the vice-principal's office, Yvette stood, not daring to look at Mrs. Rachel Ralston while she spoke.

"You have no right to take someone else's place." Mrs. Ralston continued to speak in an even-tempered, almost pleasant voice. "This time we'll let it go, but next time we will notify your parents and you won't get off so easily. You have to learn, Yvette, right from wrong. Don't go where you don't belong. . . ."

Yvette left the office and heard the bell. Lunchtime was over.

Yvette and Mildred met after school in the street. It was late in the afternoon. Yvette was returning from the corner grocery with a food package, and Mildred was coming home from Hebrew school.

"How was Hebrew school?" asked Yvette.

"O.K." Mildred smiled and nodded. "Are you coming over tonight to listen to the radio? 'Mr. Keene, Tracer of Lost Persons' is on."

"O.K.," said Yvette. "I gotta bring this up and eat. Then I'll come by."

Yvette finished supper and was given permission to visit her friend.

"Boy, that was a good program, wasn't it, Mildred?" Yvette ate her candy with delight.

Mildred nodded and looked at Yvette, not speaking. There was a long moment of silence. They wanted to talk about it, but it was as if this afternoon's incident could not be mentioned. Somehow each girl was afraid of disturbing that feeling of closeness they felt for one another. And yet when their eyes met they looked away with an embarrassed smile.

"I wonder what's on the radio next," Yvette said, breaking the silence.

"Nothing good for another half hour," Mildred answered. Impulsively, she asked quickly, "Yvette, you wanna have some matzo? We got some for the holidays."

"Is that the cracker they gave you this afternoon?"

"Yeah. We can have some."

"All right." Yvette smiled.

Mildred left the room and returned holding a large square cracker. Breaking off a piece, she handed it to Yvette.

"It don't taste like much, does it?" said Yvette.

"Only if you put something good on it," Mildred agreed, smiling.

"Boy, that Mrs. Ralston sure is dumb," Yvette said, giggling. They looked at each other and began to laugh loudly.

"Old dumb Mrs. Ralston," said Mildred, laughing convulsively. "She's scre . . . screwy."

"Yeah," Yvette said, laughing so hard tears began to roll down her cheeks. "Dop . . . dopey . . . M . . . Mi . . . Mrs. Ra . . . Ral . . . ston. . . ."

1975

## Aunt Rosana's Rocker (Zoraida)

Casto paced nervously, but softly, the full length of the small kitchen, then quietly, he tiptoed across the kitchen threshhold into the living room. After going a few feet, he stopped to listen. The sounds were getting louder. Casto returned to the kitchen, switched on the light, and sat down trying to ignore what he heard. But the familiar sounds were coming directly from their bedroom where Zoraida was. They grew louder as they traveled past the tiny foyer, the living room and into the kitchen, which was the room furthest away from her.

Leaning forward, Casto stretched his hands out palms down on the kitchen table. Slowly he made two fists, squeezing tightly, and watched as his knuckles popped out tensely under his skin. He could almost feel her presence there, next to him, panting and breathing heavily. The panting developed into moans of sensual pleasure, disrupting the silence of the apartment.

"If only I could beat someone!" Casto whispered hoarsely, banging his fists against the table and upsetting the sugar bowl. The cover slipped off the bowl, landed on its side and rolled toward the edge of the table. Casto waited for it to drop to the floor, anticipating a loud crash, but the cover stopped right at the very edge and fell quietly and flatly on the table, barely making a sound.

He looked up at the electric clock on the wall over the refrigerator; it was two-thirty in the morning.

Again, Casto tried not to listen and concentrated instead on the night noises outside in the street. Traffic on the avenue had almost completely disappeared. Occasionally, a car sped by; someone's footsteps echoed against the pavement, and off at a distance, he heard a popular tune being whistled. Casto instinctively hummed along until the sound slipped away, and he then realized he was shivering. The old radiators had stopped clanking and hissing earlier; they were now ice cold. He remembered that the landlord never sent up heat after ten at night. He wished he had thought to bring a sweater or blanket with him; he was afraid of catching a cold. But he would not go back inside; instead, he opened his special section of the cupboard and searched among his countless bottles of vitamins and nutrient supplements until he found the jar of natural vitamin C tablets. He popped several tablets into his mouth and sat down, resigned to the fact that he would rather stay here, where he felt safe, even at the risk of getting a chill. This was as far away as he could get from her, without leaving the apartment.

The sounds had now become louder and more intense. Casto raised his hands and covered his ears. He shut his eyes trying not to imagine what she was doing now. But with each sound, he could clearly see her in her ecstasy. Casto recalled how he had jumped out of bed in a fright the first time it had happened. Positive that she had gone into convulsions, he had stood almost paralyzed at a safe distance looking down at her. He didn't know what to do. And, as he helplessly watched her, his stomach had suddenly turned ice-cold with fear. Zoraida seemed to be another person. She was stretched out on the bed pulling at the covers; turning, twisting her body and rocking her buttocks sensually. Her knees had been bent upward with her legs far apart and she had thrust her pelvis forward forcefully and rhythmically. Zoraida's head was pushed back and her mouth open, as she licked her lips, moaning and gasping with excitement. Casto remembered Zoraida's eyes when she had opened them for brief moments. They had been fixed on someone or something, as if beckoning; but there was no one and certainly nothing he could see in the darkness of the room. She had rolled back the pupils and only the whites of her eyes were visible. She had blinked rapidly, shutting her eyes and twitching her nose and mouth. Then, a smile had passed her lips and a stream of saliva had run down her chin, neck and chest.

Now, as he heard low moans filled with pleasure, interrupted by short painful yelps that pierced right through him, Casto could also imagine her every gesture.

Putting down his hands, Casto opened his eyes. All he could do was wait patiently, as he always did, wait for her to finish. Maybe tonight won't be a long one; Casto swallowed anxiously.

He remembered about the meeting he had arranged earlier in the evening without Zoraida's knowledge, and felt better. After work, he had gone to see his mother; then they had both gone to see Zoraida's parents. It had been difficult for him to speak about it, but he had managed somehow to tell them everything. At first they had reacted with disbelief, but after he had explained carefully and in detail what was happening, they had understood his embarrassment and his reluctance to discuss this with anyone. He told them that when it all had begun, he was positive Zoraida was reacting to a high fever and was simply dreaming, perhaps even hallucinating. But, it kept happening, and it soon developed into something that occurred frequently, almost every night.

He finally realized something or someone had taken a hold of her. He was sure she was not alone in that room and in that bed!

It was all bizarre and, unless one actually saw her, he explained, it was truly beyond belief. Why, her actions were lewd and vulgar, and if they were sexual, as it seemed, then this was not the kind of sex a decent husband and wife engage in. What was even harder for him to bear was her enjoyment. Yes, this was difficult, watching her total enjoyment of this whole disgusting business! And, to make matters more complicated, the next day, Zoraida seemed to remember nothing. In fact, during the day, she was normal again.

Perhaps a bit more tired than usual, but then, who wouldn't be after such an exhausting ordeal? And, lately she had become even less talkative with him, almost silent. But, make no mistake, Casto assured them, Zoraida remained a wonderful housekeeper and devoted mother. Supper was served on time, chores were done without fuss, the apartment was immaculate, and the kids were attended to without any problems. This happened only at night, or rather early in the morning, at about two or two-thirty. He had not slept properly since this whole affair started. After all, he had to drive out to New Jersey to earn his living and his strength and sleep were being sapped away. He had even considered sleeping on the living room couch, but he would not be driven out of his own bed. He was still a man after all, a macho, master of his home, someone to be reckoned with, not be pushed out!

Trying to control his anger, Casto had confessed that it had been a period of almost two months since he had normal and natural relations with his wife. He reminded them that he, as a man, had his needs, and this would surely make him ill, if it continued. Of course, he would not touch her . . . not as she was right now. After all, he reasoned, who knows what he could catch from her? As long as she was under the control of something—whatever it might be—he would keep his distance. No, Casto told them, he wanted no part of their daughter as a woman, not as long as she remained in this condition.

When her parents had asked him what Zoraida had to say about all of this, Casto had laughed, answering that she knew even less about it than he did. In fact, at one point she did not believe him and had sworn on the children's souls, claiming her innocence. But Casto had persisted and now Zoraida had finally believed him. She felt that she might be the victim of something, perhaps a phenomenon. Who knows? When Zoraida's parents and his mother suggested a consultation with Doña Digna, the spiritualist, he had quickly agreed.

Casto jumped slightly in his chair as he heard loud passionate moans and deep groans emanate from the bedroom and fill the kitchen.

"Stop it . . . stop, you bitch!" Casto clenched his teeth, spitting out the words. But he took care not to raise his voice. "Stop it! What a happy victim you are! Puta! Whore! Some phenomenon . . . I don't believe you and your story." But, even as he said these words, Casto knew he was not quite sure what to believe.

The first loud thump startled Casto and he braced himself and waited, anticipating what was to come. He heard the legs on their large double bed pounding the floor as the thumping became louder and faster.

Casto shuddered and folded his arms, digging his fingers into the flesh of his forearms. After a few moments, he finally heard her release, one long cry followed by several grunts, and then silence. He relaxed and sighed deeply with relief; it was all over.

"Animal . . . she's just like an animal, no better than an alley cat in heat." Casto was wet with cold perspiration. He was most frightened of this last part. "Little hypocrite!"

Casto rememberd how she always urged him to hurry, be quiet, and get it over with, on account of the children. A lot she cares about him tonight! Never in all their years of marriage had she ever uttered such sounds—he shook his head—or shown any passion or much interest in doing it.

Casto looked up at the clock; it was two minutes to three. He thought about the noise, almost afraid to move, fearful that his downstairs neighbor Roberto might knock on the door any moment. He recalled how Roberto had called him aside one morning and spoken to him, "Two and three in the morning, my friend; can't you and your wife control your passions at such an ungodly hour? My God . . . such goings on! Man, and to tell you the truth, you people up there get me all worked up and horny. Then, when I touch my old lady, she won't cooperate at that time, eh?" He had poked Casto playfully and winked, "Hey, what am I gonna do? Have a heart, friend." Casto shook his head, how humiliating and so damned condescending. They were behaving like the most common, vulgar people. Soon the whole fucking building would know! Roberto Thomas and his big mouth! Yes, and what will that sucker say to me next time? Casto trembled with anger. He wanted to rush in and shake Zoraida, wake her, beat her; he wanted to demand an explanation or else! But, he knew it wouldn't do any good. Twice he had tried. The first time, he had spoken to her the following day. The second time, he had tried to wake her up and she had only become wilder with him, almost violent, scaring him out of the bedroom. Afterwards, things had only become worse. During the day she withdrew, practically not speaking one word to him. The next few nights she had become wilder and the ordeal lasted even longer. No, he could not confront her.

Casto realized all was quiet again. He shut off the light, then stood and slowly, with trepidation, walked through the living room and entered the small foyer leading to their bedroom. He stopped before the children's bedroom, and carefully turned the knob partially opening the door. All three were fast asleep. He was grateful they never woke up. What could he say to them? That their mother was sick? But sick with what?

As he stood at the entrance of their bedroom, Casto squinted scrutinizing every corner of the room before entering. The street lights seeping through the venetian blinds dimly illuminated the overcrowded bedroom. All was peaceful and quiet; nothing was disturbed or changed in any visible way. Satisfied, he walked in and looked down at Zoraida. She was fast asleep, breathing deeply and evenly, a look of serene contentment covered her face. Her long dark hair was spread over the pillow and spilled out onto the covers. Casto was struck by her radiant appearance each time it was all over. She had an air of glamour, so strange in a woman as plain as Zoraida. He realized, as he continued to stare at her, that he was frightened of Zoraida. He wanted to laugh at himself, but when Zoraida turned her head slightly, Casto found himself backing out of the room.

Casto stood at the entrance and whispered, "Zoraida, nena[1] . . . are . . . are you awake?" She did not stir. Casto waited perfectly still and kept his eyes on her. After a few moments, Casto composed himself. He was sure she would remain sleeping; she had never woken up after it was all over. Slowly, he entered the room and inched his way past the bulky bureau, the triple dresser and the rocking chair near the window, finally reaching his side of the bed.

Casto rapidly made the sign of the cross before he lay down beside Zoraida. He was not very religious, he could take it or leave it; but, now, he reasoned that by crossing himself he was on God's side.

1. Dear.

Casto glanced at the alarm clock; there were only two-and-a-half hours of sleep left before starting the long trip out to the docks of Bayonne, New Jersey. God, he was damned tired; he hardly ever got enough sleep anymore. This shit had to stop! Never mind, wait until the meeting. He remembered that they were all going to see Doña Digna, the spiritualist. That ought to change things. He smiled and felt some comfort knowing that this burden would soon be lifted. Seconds later he shut his eyes and fell fast asleep.

Everyone finished supper. Except for the children's chatter and Junior's protests about finishing his food, it had been a silent meal.

Casto got up and opened his special section of the cupboard. The children watched the familiar ritual without much interest as their father set out several jars of vitamins, two bottles of iron and liver tonic and a small plastic box containing therapeutic tablets. Casto carefully counted out and popped an assortment of twenty-four vitamin tablets into his mouth and then took several spoonfuls of tonic. He carefully examined the contents of the plastic box and decided not to take any of those tablets.

"Okay, Clarita, today you take vitamin C . . . and two multivitamin supplements. You, too, Eddie and Junior, you might as well . . ."

The children accepted the vitamins he gave them without resistance or fuss. They knew by now that no one could be excused from the table until Casto had finished taking and dispensing vitamins and tonic.

"Okay, kids, that's it. You can all have dessert later when your grandparents get here."

Quickly the children left.

Although Casto often suggested that Zoraida should eat properly, he had never asked her to take any of his vitamins or tonic, and she had never expressed either a desire or interest to do so.

He looked at Zoraida as she worked clearing the table and putting things away. Zoraida felt her heart pounding fiercely and she found it difficult to breathe. She wanted him to stop staring at her like that. Lately she found his staring unbearable. Zoraida's shyness had always determined her behavior in life. Ever since she could remember, any attempt that others made at intimate conversations or long discussions created feelings of constraint, developing into such anxiety that when she spoke, her voice had a tendency to fade. This was a constant problem for her; people often asked, "What was that?" or "Did you say something?" These feelings extended even into her family life. When her children asked impertinent questions, she would blush, unable to answer. Zoraida was ashamed of her own nakedness with Casto and would only undress when he was not present. When her children chanced to see her undressed at an unguarded moment, she would be distraught for several days.

It had been Casto's self assurance and his ability to be aggressive and determined with others that had attracted her to him.

Casto looked at Zoraida as she worked. "I'll put my things back and get the coffee started for when they get here," he said. She nodded and continued swiftly and silently with her chores.

Zoraida was twenty-eight, and although she had borne four children (three living, one still-born) and had suffered several miscarriages, she was of slight build and thin, with narrow hips. She had a broad face and her smile revealed a wide space between her two front teeth. As a result, she appeared frail and childlike, much younger than her years. Whenever she was tired, dark circles formed under her eyes, contrasting against the paleness of her skin. This evening, she seemed to look even paler than ever to Casto; almost ghostlike.

Casto was, by nature, hypochondriacal and preoccupied with avoiding all sorts of diseases. He was tall and robust, with a broad frame; in fact, he was the picture of good health. He became furious when others laughed at him for taking so many vitamins and health foods. Most people ignored his pronouncements of ill health and even commented behind his back. "Casto'll live to be one hundred if he lives a day . . . why, he's as fit as an ox! It's Zoraida who should take all them vitamins and then complain some. She looks like a toothpick, una flaca![2] That woman has nothing to show. I wonder what Casto ever saw in her, eh?"

Yet, it was her frail and sickly appearance that had attracted him the first time he saw her. He was visiting his married sister, Purencia, when Zoraida had walked in with her friend, Anna. Anna was a beautiful, voluptuous young woman with an olive tone to her skin that glowed; and when she smiled, her white teeth and full lips made her appear radiant. Zoraida, thin and pale by contrast, looked ill. In Casto's presence, she had smiled sheepishly, blushing from time to time. Anna had flirted openly, and commented on Purencia's brother, "You didn't tell me you had such a gorgeous macho in your family. Trying to keep him a secret, girl?" But it had been Zoraida that he was immediately drawn to. Casto had been so taken with her that he had confided in a friend that very day, "She really got to me, you know? Not loud or vulgar like that other girl, who was acting like a man, making remarks about me and all. No, she was a real lady. And, she's like, well, like a little sick sparrow flirting with death and having the upper hand. Quietly stubborn, you know? Not at all submissive like it might seem to just anybody looking at Zoraida. It's more as if nobody's gonna make the sparrow healthy, but it ain't gonna die either . . . like it's got the best of both worlds, see?"

Yet, in all their nine years of marriage, Zoraida had never become seriously ill. Her pregnancies and miscarriages were the only time that she had been unable to attend to her family. After the last pregnancy, in an attempt to prevent children, Casto had decided on the rhythm system, where abstention is practiced during certain days of the month. It was, he reasoned, not only sanctioned by the Catholic Church, but there were no drugs or foreign objects put into one's body, and he did not have to be afraid of catching something nor getting sick.

Even after this recent miscarriage, Zoraida appeared to recover quickly, and with her usual amazing resiliency, managed the household chores and the children all by herself. She even found time to assuage Casto's fears of sickness and prepare special foods for him.

Casto could feel his frustration building inside as he watched her. What the hell was the matter with this wife of his? Quickly he reached into his cupboard and took out some Maalox; God, the last thing he wanted was an ulcer on account of all of this.

"I think I'll coat my stomach." Casto chewed several Maalox tablets vigorously, then swallowed. "This way, I can have coffee later and it won't affect

---

2. A skinny one.

me badly." He waited for a response, but she remained silent. Casto sighed, she don't even talk to me no more . . . well, that's why I invited everybody here tonight, so they could see for themselves! He waited, staring at her, and then asked, "You got the cakes ready? I mean, you got them out of the boxes and everything?"

Zoraida nodded, not looking in his direction.

"Hey! Coño,[3] I'm talking to you! Answer!"

"Yes," Zoraida whispered.

"And the cups and plates, you got them for the coffee and cake?"

"Yes," Zoraida repeated.

"I don't know, you know? It's been almost three months since Doña Digna did her job and cured you. I didn't figure you were gonna get so . . . so depressed." Zoraida continued to work silently. "Wait. Stop a minute. Why don't you answer me, eh? Will you look at me, for God's sake!"

Zoraida stopped and faced Casto with her eyes lowered.

"Look, I'm trying to talk to you, understand? Can't you talk to me?" Zoraida kept perfectly still. "Say something, will you?"

"What do you want me to say?" Zoraida spoke softly, without looking at him.

"Can't you look at me when you talk?"

Swiftly and furtively, Zoraida glanced at Casto, then lowered her eyes once more.

"Coño, man, what do you think I do all day out there to make a living? Play? Working my butt off in those docks in all kinds of weather . . . yeah. And for what? To come home to a woman that won't even look at me?" Casto's voice was loud and angry. He stopped, controlled himself, then continued, lowering his voice. "I get up every morning before six. Every freaking morning! I risk pneumonia, rheumatism, arthritis, all kinds of sickness. Working that fork-lift, eight, ten hours a day, until my kidneys feel like they're gonna split out of my sides. And then, to make it worse, I gotta take orders from that stupid foreman who hates Puerto Ricans. Calling me a spic. In fact, they all hate Puerto Ricans out there. They call me spic, and they get away with it because I'm the only P.R. there, you know? Lousy Micks and Dagos! Listen, you know what they . . . ah, what's the use, I can't talk to you. Sure, why should you care? All you do is stay in a nice apartment, all warm and cozy. Damn it! I can't even have my woman like a normal man. First you had a phantom lover, right? Then, ever since Doña Digna took him away, you have that lousy chair you sit in and do your disappearing act. That's all you're good for lately. I can't even come near you. The minute I approach you like a human being for normal sex, you go and sit in that . . . that chair! I seen you fade out. Don't think I'm blind. You sit in that freaking thing, rocking away. You look . . . you . . . I don't even think you're breathing when you sit there! You should see yourself. What you look like is enough to scare anybody. Staring into space like some God damned zombie! You know what I should do with it? Throw it out, or better yet, bust that piece of crap into a thousand splinters! Yeah, that's what I ought to do. Only thing is, you'll find something else, right? Another lover, is that what you want, so you can become an animal? Because with me, let me tell you, you ain't no

3. Literally, cunt; figuratively, damn it.

animal. With me you're nothing. Mira,[4] you know something, I'm not taking no more of this. Never mind, when they get here they can see your whole bullshit act for themselves. Especially after I tell them . . ."

Zoraida barely heard him. The steady sound of the television program and the children's voices coming from their bedroom filled her with a pleasant feeling. How nice, she thought, all the children playing and happy. All fed and clean; yes, it's nice and peaceful.

The front doorbell rang.

"There they are." Casto had finished preparing the coffee. "I'll answer the door, you go on and get things ready."

Zoraida heard voices and trembled as she remembered Casto's threats and the fury he directed at her. Now he was going to tell them all sorts of things about her . . . untruths.

"Zoraida, where are you?" She heard her mother's voice, and then the voices of her father, mother-in-law and sister-in-law.

"Mommy, Mommy," Clarita ran into the kitchen, "Nana and Granpa, and Abuelita and Titi[5] Purencia are here. Can we have the cake now?"

"In a little while, Clarita." Zoraida followed her daughter out into the living room and greeted everybody.

"Mommy, Mommy!" Junior shouted, "Tell Eddie to stop it, he's hitting me!"

"I was not, it was Clarita!" Eddie walked over to his little brother and pushed him. Junior began to cry and Clarita ran over and smacked Eddie.

"See?" Casto shouted, "Stop it! Clarita, you get back inside." He jumped up, grabbing his daughter by an elbow and lifting her off the ground. "Demonia,[6] why are you hitting him? Zoraida, can't you control these kids?" He shook Clarita forcefully and she began to whine.

"Casto," Zoraida's thin shriek whistled through the room. "Don't be rough with her, please!"

"See that, Doña Clara, your daughter can't even control her own kids no more." He turned to the children, "Now, all of you, get back inside your room and watch television; and be quiet or you go right to bed and nobody gets any cake. You hear? That means all three, Clarita, Eddie and you too Junior."

"Can we have the cake now?" Eddie asked.

"I'll call you when it's time. Now go on, go on, all of you." Quickly, the children left.

"Calm yourself, son." Doña Elvira, Casto's mother, walked over to him. "You know how children are, they don't know about patience or waiting; you were no angel yourself, you and your sister."

"Let's go inside and have coffee, everybody." Casto led them into the kitchen. There were six chairs set around the kitchen table. Doña Clara and her husband, Don Isidro, Doña Elvira and her daughter, Purencia, squeezed in and sat down.

"Cut some cake for the kids and I'll bring it in to them," Casto spoke to Zoraida, who quickly began to cut up the chocolate cake and place the pieces on a plate. Everyone watched in silence. "Milk," snapped Casto. Zoraida set out three glasses of milk. Casto put everything on a tray and left.

"So, mi hijita,[7] how are you?" Doña Clara asked her daughter.

---

4. Look.
5. A derivative of *tía* (Spanish for aunt); it shows special affection and love.

6. Demon, devil.
7. My little daughter.

"I'm okay." Zoraida sat down.

"You look pale to me, very pale. Don't she, Papa?" Doña Clara turned for a moment to Don Isidro, then continued without waiting for an answer. "You're probably not eating right. Zoraida, you have to take better care of yourself."

"All right." Casto returned and sat down with the others. "They're happy now."

"Son," Doña Elvira spoke to Casto. "You look tired, aren't you getting enough rest?"

"I'm all right, Ma. Here, everybody, have some cake and coffee."

Everyone began to help themselves.

"It's that job of his. He works so hard," Doña Elvira reached over and placed an extra large piece of chocolate cake on Casto's plate before continuing, "He should have stayed in school and become an accountant, like I wanted. Casto was so good at math, but . . . instead, he . . ."

"Pass the sugar, please," Doña Clara interrupted, "and a little bit of that rum cake, yes. Thank you."

They all ate in silence.

Doña Elvira looked at Zoraida and sighed, trying to hide her annoyance. What a sickly looking woman, bendito.[8] She looks like a mouse. To think my handsome, healthy son, who could have had any girl he wanted, picked this one. Doña Elvira could hardly swallow her cake. Duped by her phony innocence is what it was! And how could he be happy and satisfied with such a woman? Look at her, she's pathetic. Now, oh yes, now, he's finding out who she really is: not the sweet innocent one, after all! Ha! First a phantom lover and now . . . who knows what! Well, we'll see how far she can go on with this, because now he's getting wise. With a sense of smug satisfaction, Doña Elvira half-smiled as she looked at her daughter-in-law, then ate her cake and drank her coffee.

Purencia saw her mother's look of contempt directed at Zoraida. She's jealous of Zoraida, Purencia smiled. Nobody was ever good enough for Casto. For her precious baby boy, well, and there you have it! Casto finally wanted Zoraida. Purencia smiled, serves Ma right. She looked at her sister-in-law who sat with her head bowed. God, she looks sicker than ever, but she never complains. She won't say nothing, even now, when he's putting her through this whole number. Poor goody-two-shoes Zoraida, she's not gonna get on Casto's case for nothing; like, why is he jiving her? I wonder what it is she's doing now? After that whole scene with Doña Digna, I thought she cured her of whatever that was. Purencia shrugged, who knows how it is with these quiet ones. They're the kind that hide the action. Maybe she's doing something nobody knows about . . . well, let's just see.

Doña Clara looked at her son-in-law, Casto, with anger and a scowl on her face. Bestia . . . brute of a man! He doesn't deserve anyone as delicate as Zoraida. She has to wait on that huge monster hand and foot. With all his stupid medicines and vitamins when he's as fit as a horse! Ungrateful man. He got an innocent girl, pure as the day she was born, that's what. Protected and brought up right by us. Never went out by herself. We always watched out who her friends were. She was guarded by us practically up until the

8. Literally, blessed; figuratively, poor thing (shortened from the expression *bendito sea Dios*).

moment she took her vows. Any man would have been proud to have her. Canalla! Sinvergüenza![9] She's clean, hardworking and obedient. Never complains. All he wants to do is humiliate her. We already went to Doña Digna, and Casto said Zoraida was cured. What now, for pity's sake? Doña Clara forced herself to turn away from Casto because the anger fomenting within her was beginning to upset her nerves.

Don Isidro sat uneasily. He wished his wife would not drag him into these things. Domestic disputes should be a private matter, he maintained emphatically, between man and wife. But, his wife's nerves were not always what they should be, and so he had to be here. He looked at his daughter and was struck by her girlish appearance. Don Isidro sighed, the mother of three children and she hasn't filled out . . . she still has the body of a twelve-year old. Well, after all, she was born premature, weighing only two pounds at birth. Don Isidro smiled, remembering what the doctors had called her. "The miracle baby," they had said, "Mr. Cuesta, your daughter is a miracle. She should not be alive." That's when he and Clara had decided to give her the middle name of Milagros.[1] He had wanted a son, but after Zoraida's birth, his wife could bear no children, and so he had to be satisfied with what he had. Of course, he had two grandsons, but they wouldn't carry on his last name, so, in a way it was not the same. Well, she's lucky to be married at all. Don Isidro nodded slightly, and Casto is a good, honest, hardworking man, totally devoted. Don't drink or gamble; he don't even look at other women. But, he too was lucky to get our Zoraida. After all, we brung her up proper and right. Catholic schools. Decent friends. Don Isidro looked around him at the silent table and felt a stiffness in his chest. He took a deep breath; what had she done? This whole business confused him. He thought Doña Digna had made the situation right once more.

"So, Casto, how are you? How's work?" Don Isidro asked.

"Pretty good. The weather gets to me, though. I have to guard against colds and sitting in that fork-lift gives me a sore back. But, I'm lucky to have work, the way things are going."

"You're right, they're laying off people everywhere. You read about it in the news every day."

"Zoraida, eat something," Doña Clara spoke to her daughter.

"I'm not hungry, Mami," Zoraida's voice was just above a whisper.

"Casto, you should see to it that she eats!" Doña Clara looked at her son-in-law, trying to control her annoyance. "Whatever this problem is, I'm sure part of it is that your wife never eats."

"Why should he see that she eats or not?" Doña Elvira interjected, "He has to go to work every day to support his family . . . he hasn't got time to . . ."

"Wait a minute, Ma," Casto interrupted, "the problem here ain't food. That's not gonna solve what's going on."

"It seems to solve all your problems, eh?" Doña Clara looked at Casto with anger.

"Just hold on now . . . wait," Don Isidro raised his hand. Now, we are all arguing here with each other and we don't even know what the problem is. Why don't we find out what's going on?" Don Isidro turned to Casto and waited.

9. Scoundrel! Shameless person!     1. Miracles.

Everyone fell silent. Don Isidro continued, "I thought that Doña Digna's treatment worked. After all, you told us that yourself."

"It's not that no more," Casto looked around him, "it's something else now."

"What?" Doña Elvira asked.

Casto looked at Zoraida who sat with her hands folded on her lap and her eyes downcast.

"Weren't things going good for you two?" Don Isidro asked. "I mean, things were back to normal relations between you, yes?"

"Yes and no," Casto said. "Yes for a while and then . . ."

"Then what?" Doña Elvira asked. "What?"

Casto looked at Zoraida. "You want to say something, Zoraida?" She shook her head without looking at anyone.

"All right, then like usual, I gotta speak. You know that rocking chair Zoraida has? The one she brought with her when we got married?"

"You mean the one she's had ever since she was little? Why, we had that since Puerto Rico, it belonged to my titi Rosana." Doña Clara looked perplexed. "What about the rocker?"

"Well, she just sits in it, when . . . when she shouldn't." Casto could feel the blood rushing to his face.

"What do you mean she sits in it?" Doña Clara asked. "What is she supposed to do? Stand in it?"

"I said *when she shouldn't.*"

"Shouldn't what?" Doña Clara turned to Don Isidro, "Papa, what is this man talking about?"

"Look," Casto continued, "this here chair is in the bedroom. That's where she keeps it. All right? Now when, when I . . . when we . . ." Casto hesitated, "you know what I mean. Then, instead of acting like a wife, she leaves the bed and sits in the chair. She sits and she rocks back and forth."

"Does she stay there all night?" Doña Elvira asked.

"Pretty much."

Everyone looked at Zoraida, who remained motionless without lifting her eyes. A few moments passed before Don Isidro broke the silence.

"This is a delicate subject, I don't know if it's a good thing to have this kind of discussion here, like this."

"What do you want me to do, Isidro?" First she has those fits in bed driving me nuts. Then we call in Doña Digna, who decides she knows what's wrong, and puts me through a whole freakin rigamarole of prayers and buying all kinds of crap. After all of that pendejá,[2] which costs me money that I frankly don't have, then she tells me my wife is cured. Now it starts again, except in another way. Look, I'm only human, you know? And she," Casto pointed to Zoraida, "is denying me what is my right as a man and as her husband. And I don't know why she's doing this. But I do know this time you're gonna be here to know what's going on. I ain't going through this alone. No way. And get myself sick? No!"

"Just a moment, now," Doña Clara said, "you say Zoraida sits in the rocker when you . . . approach her. Does she ever sit there at other times? Or only at that time?"

2. Foolishness (from *pendejada*).

"Once in a while, at other times, but always . . . always, you know, at that time!"

"Ay . . . Dios mio!"[3] Doña Elvira stood up. "I don't know how my son puts up with this, if you ask me." She put her hands to her head. "Casto has the patience of a saint, any other man would do . . . do worse!"

"What do you mean, the patience of a saint?" Doña Clara glared at Doña Elvira. "And do worse what? Your son might be the whole cause of this, for all I know . . ."

"Now, wait." Don Isidro stood up. "Again, we are fighting and blaming this one or that one. This will get us nowhere. Doña Elvira, please sit down." Doña Elvira sat, and then Don Isidro sat down also. "Between a man and wife, it's best not to interfere."

"Okay then, Papa, what are we here for?" Doña Clara asked.

"To help, if we can," Purencia spoke. Everyone listened; she had not spoken a word before this. "I think that's what my brother wants. Right, Casto?" Casto nodded, and then shrugged. "Let Zoraida say something," Purencia continued. "She never gets a chance to say one word."

"Nobody's stopping her." Casto looked at Zoraida. "Didn't I ask her to say something? In fact, maybe she can tell us what's going on. Like, I would like to know too, you know."

"Zoraida," Doña Clara spoke firmly to her daughter, "mira, you better tell us what all of this is about."

Zoraida looked up, meeting her mother's angry stare. "I don't know what Casto means about the chair."

"Do you sit in the rocker or do you not sit there, like he says?" Her mother asked.

"Sometimes."

"Sometimes? What times? Is it like the way he says it is? Because, if this is so, we want to know why. Doña Digna told me, you and all of us, that there was an evil spirit in you that was turning your thoughts away from your husband, so that you could not be a wife to him. After she finished her treatment, she said the evil spirit or force was gone, and that you would go back to a normal husband-and-wife relationship. We have to accept that. She is a woman of honor that has been doing this work for many years, and that she is telling us the truth, yes?" Doña Clara took a deep breath. "But, if you feel anything is wrong, then it could be that Doña Digna did not succeed." She turned to Casto. "That's possible too, you know. These things sometimes get very complicated. I remember when the Alvarez household was having the worst kind of luck. Don Pablo had lost his job, his wife was sick, and one of their boys had an accident; all kinds of problems, remember? You remember, Papa? Well, Doña Digna had to go back, and it took her a long time to discover the exact cause and then to make things straight again." She turned to Zoraida, "Bueno, mi hija, you have to tell us what you feel, and if you are doing this to your husband, why." Doña Clara waited for her daughter's response. "Go ahead. Answer, por Dios!"[4]

"I . . ." Zoraida cleared her throat in an effort to speak louder. "I just sit in the rocker sometimes. Because I feel relaxed there."

---

3. My God!  4. By God!

"Yeah!" Casto said, "Every time I go near her at night, or at two or three in the morning, she relaxes." He raised his hand and slammed the table, "God damned chair!"

"Calmate, mi hijito, calm yourself." Doña Elvira put her hand over her eyes. "I don't know how long my son can put up with all of this. Now she's got an obsession with a chair. Virgen, purisima![5] Somebody has to tell me what is going on here!"

"Listen to me," Don Isidro spoke in a firm voice, "if it's the chair that bothers you, then we'll take it back home with us. Right, Mama?" He turned to Doña Clara who nodded emphatically. "There should be no objection to that, eh?"

Everyone looked at Casto who shrugged, and then at Zoraida who opened her mouth and shook her head, but was unable to speak.

"Very good." Don Isidro clasped his hands and smiled. "There, that ought to take care of the problems pretty much."

"Except, she might find something else," Casto said. "Who knows with her."

"Well, but we don't know that for sure, do we?" Don Isidro replied, "and in the meantime, we gotta start somewhere."

"I feel we can always call Doña Digna in again if we have to." Doña Clara poured herself a cup of coffee. "After all, she was the one that told us Zoraida was cured."

"I agree," Doña Elvira said, "and even though she don't ask for money, I know my Casto was very generous with her."

"That's right, they don't charge, but after all, one has to give these people something, or else how can they live?" agreed Doña Clara.

"Isn't the weather funny this Spring?" Doña Elvira spoke amiably. "One minute it's cold and the next it's like summer. One never knows how to dress these . . ."

They continued speaking about the weather and about television programs. Purencia spoke about her favorite movie.

"That one about the professional hit-man, who has a contract out to kill the President of England . . . no, France, I think. Anyway, remember when he goes into that woman's house and kills her? I was so scared, I loved that movie."

Everyone agreed, the best kinds of movies were mysteries and thrillers.

Zoraida half-listened to them. They were going to take away the rocker. She had always had it, ever since she could remember. When she was a little girl, her parents told her it was a part of their history. Part of Puerto Rico and her great Aunt Rosana who was very beautiful and had countless suitors. The chair was made of oak with intricate carving and delicate caning. As a little girl, Zoraida used to rub her hands against the caning and woodwork admiringly, while she rocked, dreamed and pretended to her heart's content. Lately it had become the one place where she felt she could be herself, where she could really be free.

"Bueno, we have to go. It's late."

"That's right, me too."

"Wait," Casto told them, "I'll drive you people home."

5. An invocation of the Virgin Mary.

"You don't have to . . ." Don Isidro protested. "We know you are tired."

"No, I'm not. Besides, I gotta drive ma and Purencia home anyway."

"That's right," Purencia said, "my old man doesn't like me going out at night. It's only because of Mami that he let me. So, Casto has to take me home."

"I gotta get you the chair, wait," Casto said. "And, you don't wanna carry that all the way home. It's not very big, but still, it's a lot to lug around."

"All right then, very good."

Everyone got up and Zoraida began to clear away the dishes.

"Let me help you," Doña Clara said as she stood up.

"Me too," Doña Elvira said, without rising.

"No, no thanks. That's all right. I can do it myself," Zoraida said. "Besides, I have to put the kids to bed and give them their milk and all."

"I don't know how she does it. Three little ones and this place is always immaculate." Doña Clara turned to Doña Elvira. "It's really too much for her, and she has no help at all."

Doña Elvira stood. "She keeps a very clean house," she said and walked out with Purencia following after Casto and Don Isidro.

Doña Clara looked at her daughter, who worked silently and efficiently. "Mira, mi hija, I better talk to you." She stood close to Zoraida and began to speak in a friendly manner keeping her voice low. "You have to humor men; you must know that by now. After all, you are no longer a little girl. All women go through this difficulty, eh? You are not the only one. Why, do you know how many times your father wants . . . well, you know, wants it? But I, that is, if I don't want to do it, well I find a way not to. But diplomatically, you know? All right, he's older now and he bothers me less; still, what I mean is, you have to learn that men are like babies and they feel rejected unless you handle the situation just right. Now, we'll take the rocker back home with us because it will make him feel better. But you must do your part too. Tell him you have a headache, or a backache, or you can even pretend to be asleep. However, once in a while you have to please him, you know. After all, he does support you and the children and he needs it to relax. What's the harm in it? It's a small sacrifice. Listen, I'll give you some good advice; make believe you are enjoying it and then get it over with real quick, eh? So, once in a while you have to, whether you like it or not; that's just the way it is for us. Okay? Do you understand?" Zoraida turned away and, without responding, continued with her work. "Did you hear what I just told you?" Doña Clara grabbed Zoraida's shoulder firmly, squeezing her fingers against the flesh. "You didn't even hear what I said to you!"

Zoraida pulled away and turned quickly facing her mother. She looked directly at Doña Clara, "I heard you . . ." Zoraida stopped and a smile passed her lips. "I heard every word you said, Mami."

"Oh, all right then . . ." Doña Clara said, somewhat startled by her daughter's smile. "I only wanted to . . ."

"Mama! Come on, it's time to go," Don Isidro's voice interrupted her.

Doña Clara and Zoraida went into the living room. Casto carried the rocking chair and waited by the door. The children had come out of their room and were happily jumping about.

"Look, Mommy, Granpa gave me a quarter," Clarita said.

"Me too," said Eddie. "He even gave Junior one."

"All right, get to bed!" Casto shouted. "Zoraida, put them down, will you?"
Everybody said goodbye and, in a moment, Casto and the others left.
"Mommy, where is Daddy taking your chair?" Clarita asked.
"To Nana's."
"Why?"
"Because they want it now?"
"Don't you want it no more?"
"I already had it for a long time, now they need to have it for a while."
Zoraida gave the children their milk, bathed them and put them to bed.
Then, she finished rapidly in the kitchen and went to bed herself. She looked
over at the empty space near the window. It was gone. She wouldn't be able to
sit there anymore and meet all her suitors and be beautiful. The last time . . .
the last time she was dancing to a very slow number, a ballad. But she
couldn't remember the words. And she was with, with . . . which one? She
just couldn't remember him anymore. If she had the rocker, she could remember; it would all come back to her as soon as she sat down. In fact, she
was always able to pick up exactly where she had left off the time before. She
shut her eyes, deciding not to think about the rocker, about Casto, Doña
Digna or her mother. Instead, Zoraida remembered her children who were
safe and asleep in their own beds. In a short while, she heard the front door
open and recognized Casto's footsteps. She shut her eyes, turned over, facing
away from his side of the bed. Casto found the apartment silent and dark,
except for the night light.

In the bedroom, Casto looked at Zoraida, who seemed fast asleep, then at
the empty space near the window where the rocker usually stood. Their bedroom seemed larger and his burden lighter. Casto sighed, feeling better. He
reached over and lightly touched Zoraida; this was a safe time of the month,
maybe she would wake up. He waited and, after a moment, decided to go to
sleep. After all, he could always try again tomorrow.

1985

## A Journey toward a Common Ground: The Struggle and Identity of Hispanics in the U.S.A.

As a daughter of a Puerto Rican diaspora, I was born and raised in an urban
village nestled in the heart of New York City. I grew up unaware that
throughout the United States there existed many barrios similar to Manhattan's Spanish Harlem. I had no idea that I had an extended Hispanic family
living in Chicago, Tampa, Los Angeles, and in a multitude of towns and cities all across this nation, or that we shared a common culture. Just like my
family, who lived in Spanish Harlem, they spoke both Spanish and English,
shopped in the bodegas, ate plantains with rice and beans, listened to Spanish radio programs, attended mass in Spanish, and perhaps the children,
like myself, might have even attempted to read our parents' copy of the
Spanish daily newspapers. Back then, in the 1940s and 1950s, most Hispanics stayed in their neighborhoods. The only way to achieve acceptance and a
chance to be in the mainstream of this society was to not only embrace the

local American culture, but also to reject one's own Hispanic culture. This attempt at assimilation, this frustrating struggle to fit in, was encouraged. It was reinforced in the schools by social workers and most authority figures outside our community. For most of us growing up then, it was a time when success meant acceptance into that European culture that dominated these United States. All too often, the price of this success was paid by discarding our own history and never seeking the truth of our past. Anglo-American values demanded that we had to reject our parents' language and change our way of thinking. Even our clothes and food were seen to be foreign.

Going as far as changing our name from Rivera to Rivers wasn't such a bad idea either. In fact it made it easier when you went looking for an apartment in a better Anglo neighborhood. Assimilation as defined by the Anglo society was a primary focus—the aspiration and the ultimate goal of an Hispanic child who expected to make it in the dominant system. And in the movies and television, newspapers and magazines, and on the radio, it was validated that this was the only way to be a true American. Hispanics, along with blacks, were seen in menial roles or depicted as crude stereotypes such as Frito Bandito and the lazy Mexican. Spanish was never heard; our people were never seen as we really were; our stories were never told. There was a rhyme that many of us kids in the streets of New York recited. To my knowledge, it was originated by African Americans in the South. Our variation follows:

> If you're white, you're right;
> If you're yellow, you're mellow;
> If you're brown, hang around;
> If you're black, step back;
> If you're just Spanish, you'll be banished.

This rhyme rang true for those of us who fit these descriptions.

Schools provided either nothing or a distorted sense of our own history. As Puerto Ricans we knew we were not only different from Anglos, but we were also different from other Latinos. First we were born citizens. Even the island of Puerto Rico which was owned by the United States was not a real country, we were informed. I learned in the public schools in New York City that it was the benevolent Americans who saved us from the cruel Spaniards and in a sense adopted us. We, in turn, should be grateful, speak only English and strive toward total acceptance.

There were no positive role models for me out there in the Great Society when I was growing up. When I searched with a need to emulate a living person—preferably a woman with whom I could identify—my efforts were futile. As a Puerto Rican female in the U.S., my legacy was one of either a negative image or invisibility. My knowledge of myself, of the history of the Puerto Rican people, and of the Hispanic contribution to the United States were to come later when I would seek and find those works and books that held the truth. From the outset, first as a visual artist early in my career and later as I began to write, I understood that the source of my output had to come from within my community. As a female Puerto Rican coming from a long line of strong, determined women, I was not going to be a party to the stereotyping that existed—in particular the stereotype of the Spanish woman that I call the Maria syndrome. Maria the Virgin, or Maria the Magdalena.[1]

The Maria syndrome was even immortalized in that great American classic *West Side Story*: beautiful music, exquisite dancing, the entire production conceived, arranged, choreographed, and presented by successful white males—not one of them Hispanic. Here we have Maria the Virgin ready to sacrifice all. On the other side, the Latino Anita, a loose one who said, "I want to live in America, not in Puerto Rico. That ain't America. It ain't good enough." In the old black and white movies, we had the famous Carmen Miranda[2] dancing on mountains of tropical fruits, and there was always the prostitute—sometimes disguised as a dancer or sexy performer— and the virgin offering, often the sacrificing mother.

Where were the rest of us? Where were my mother and aunt and all those valiant women who had left Puerto Rico out of necessity, for the most part, by themselves, bringing small children to a cold and hostile city? They came with thousands of others driven out by poverty, ill-equipped, with little education, and no knowledge of English. But they were determined to give their children a better life and hope for the future. This is where I had come from, and it was these women who became my heroes. When I look for subjects to paint and stories to write, and I look for role models that symbolize strength, I have only to look at my own and my source is boundless—my folklore is rich and the work to be done consumes an eternity. It was that sense of being invisible in society that I felt while growing up, that has compelled me to produce a body of work that will confront the reader with the truth of my existence and my communities' impact on the larger society.

Much of this awakening began as we entered the 1960s as the black social revolution swept the rest of the ethnic minorities into confronting political and racial issues—issues that for generations had been ignored or rejected by our government and elected officials. And with these confrontations came the trials of self-examination. The question of whether Puerto Ricans and other Spanish-speaking Americans were black or white was posed. For the first time, Mexican Americans, Puerto Ricans, Cuban Americans—in fact, any persons coming in from Spanish-speaking countries—were all classified as Hispanic Americans. Being black or white created a dilemma for many Hispanic families, where one child was white and the other brown, such as my own, or where the pigmentation of one's skin was academic. We were now—whether blond, brown or black, whether immigrant or migrant— all Hispanics. As Puerto Ricans we had an identity across this vast nation that would unite us with other Hispanics in numbers and geography, and thus this new status gave us greater political clout and began to establish cultural bonds with our Hispanic family throughout the U.S. Out of this new awareness came frustration, anger, marches, demonstrations, and sit-ins. The results of these efforts helped to create such opportunities as open enrollment, affirmative action, and bilingual education. Puerto Rican history began to be taught in the schools and colleges. Sadly, we know that

1. I.e., the virgin or the whore; Mary Magadalene, identified in the New Testament as a disciple of Jesus, venerated as a saint by branches of Christianity such as the Roman Catholic Church, has for centuries been misidentified as an adulteress and repentant prostitute.

2. Portuguese-born Brazilian samba singer and actress (1909–1955), most popular in the 1940s–50s; she often performed wearing a hat topped with tropical fruit.

some of these programs have been discontinued and others are being threatened, but the impact and awareness remain.

Inevitably we began to question who we were and how similar we were, coming from such a variety of Spanish-speaking countries. Classifying people with so many different nationalities as one group can cause confusion. After all, outside the United States we were Cuban, Mexican, Chilean, but here, whether one came from the sophisticated metropolis of Buenos Aires, Argentina, or the village of Mocha in the highlands of the Dominican Republic, we were now classified as members of one Hispanic community.

Invariably, it is and will be easier for the children who are born and raised in the United States to accept and understand what it means to be an Hispanic American and to belong to that particular ethnic group. It is from this rich and varied Latino culture that we now share, that a new American ethnic consciousness has erupted. Its manifestations are becoming visible and evident, and it is because of this that we have writers, musicians, and film makers who began out of necessity to create an informal hegemony in arts and letters. We now have dance and theater companies, magazines, and small presses. An example is Arte Publico Press. Arte Publico is the press that publishes Latino writers who would otherwise be ignored by the American literary establishment. The results in terms of works produced reflect our common ground which is indeed an Hispanic experience. And it is mostly ours. It is from this peculiar position in American history that my work has evolved.

I would like briefly to share my role as a writer. Back in 1972, I was asked to write a novel based on a short number of vignettes that I had completed. It was then that I decided that if I as a woman in my ethnic community did not exist in North American letters, I would now. In 1973, Harper & Row published my first novel, *Nilda*. Although much of this story comes from the realms of my imagination, nonetheless, like so many writers' first books, it contains a great deal of autobiographical material. In this book I was able to unlock the memories and sensibilities of my early years. I was able to document what it was to be poor, female, and Puerto Rican in an alien environment. Survival, after all, must not be all our children should strive for. They must be allowed to thrive and to continue to explore their God-given talents. I felt the need to continue and write about my community—women, the children, the heart of my culture. And I'm still at it, exploring and never ceasing to be amazed at the human capacity for endurance and peoples' ability to surprise and disarm.

The challenge to work and document events that unfold within my community with its varied players, its complex and ever-changing position, fires me on to work with a gusto that I could only feel in writing about what I really know and truly care about. Today as I work I no longer feel that sense of isolation I did growing up, and when I'm invited to a conference honoring and recognizing someone like Virginia Hamilton[3] it makes me proud. I'm also very pleased to be here sharing this time with my other co-workers and artists, writers here who are women of color. I know there are some of us out there doing something right—working and producing for our children, trying

---

3. Writer of children's books (1936–2002); a leader in the field of African American children's literature.

to make significant changes, providing positive role models for our young people.

I leave you with this final thought. Our children deserve to have that pride in themselves and their community that was missing from many of our own lives as youngsters. Those that follow us do not have to be outcasts in their own lands. All of us go forward. Let's take that responsibility and run with it. Let's validate and celebrate not only what we have managed to accomplish, but all that we must do and build in the years ahead. Let us continue to fight in order to insure our rightful place in society and commit to a positive legacy for all of our children.

April 21, 1999

# TOMÁS RIVERA
## 1935–1984

In 1970, the fledgling ethnic publisher Quinto Sol, in Berkeley, California, awarded the house's first *premio Quinto Sol* (Fifth Sun prize) for best novel to Tomás Rivera for . . . *y no se lo tragó la tierra*. This novel, a series of interrelated vignettes, relates migrant life from a child's viewpoint, employing a stream of consciousness that recalls textually challenging works by the American modernist writer William Faulkner. Published in bilingual form as . . . *And the Earth Did Not Part*, the book has become a classic of the Latino literary tradition.

Tomás Rivera was born in Crystal City, Texas. In his youth, he accompanied his parents as they migrated throughout the Midwest in search of farm work. Still, he was able to graduate from Crystal City High School. He earned a bachelor's degree from Southwest Texas State University at San Marcos (now Texas State University) in 1958 and a master's in education administration from the same institution in 1964. After teaching in public schools and at Southwest Texas Junior College (in Uvalde), he attended the University of Oklahoma, earning a master's degree in Spanish literature and a doctorate in Romance languages and literature in 1969. He taught at Sam Houston State University and was one of the planners of the University of Texas at San Antonio, where he filled several positions until he became the chief executive officer of the University of Texas at El Paso in 1978. In 1979, he left to become chancellor of the University of California at Riverside, a position he held until the year of his death. The first—and so far only—Mexican American to serve as a chancellor in the University of California system, Rivera championed education for all, fought for inclusion of Chicano literature in the Modern Language Association (i.e., for recognition of the tradition's value by the academic establishment), and served on numerous national boards, such as the Carnegie Foundation, the Corporation for Public Broadcasting, and the Educational Testing Service. Rivera was appointed to commissions on higher education by U.S. presidents Jimmy Carter and Ronald Reagan. After his death, the Tomás Rivera Policy Institute was created at Pomona College; it is now at the University of Southern California.

Rivera's literary reputation rests on . . . *y no se lo tragó la tierra*, but his writing there is straightforward, unembellished, tender yet spare; the multiple plots are simple; and in many scenes the characters, most of them nameless, are present only as voices. The novel's power comes from its unrelenting, realistic presentation of the brutish way of life imposed on migrant farm laborers in the Midwest by racism and by their powerlessness. Readers witness the grinding work, the chicken coops serving as homes, the cheating of the migrant farm laborers by other Mexican Americans, the distintegration of families due to illness and death, the unhelpful rituals and rigidity of the Catholic Church, and the Korean War's effects on the migrants. In one episode, a truck driver abandons workers in Minnesota. In another, a homicidal couple psychologically marks a child. And yet the novel is optimistic and subtly humorous. Even under the most trying conditions, Rivera's characters refuse to knuckle under. Early reviewers criticized the work's lack of condemnation of the planters/growers/owners, but Rivera explained that he did not want to preach or write a political tract. The politics of poverty, he said, were there for all to see.

The history of Rivera's novel is fascinating. As the book manuscript (available at the Rivera archives at the University of California, Riverside) makes clear, the publisher, Quinto Sol, reorganized the chapters of *. . . y no se lo tragó la tierra*. It also eliminated a chapter (about a pachuco character named Pete Fonseca) it deemed anti-Chicano. The original translator remains a mystery. Rivera once credited Hermenio Ríos C., a Quinto Sol publisher, and once credited a student, a woman at the University of Texas in San Antonio. Another plausible candidate is Gustavo Valadez, the language director in the Spanish and Portugues Department at the University of California, Santa Barbara, in 1978–79. At UCLA in 1981, Rivera revealed to Rolando Hinojosa that he was unhappy with the available translation and asked if Hinojosa would try his hand at a new one. Hinojosa began rereading and teaching the novel after Rivera's death, at which point he decided to undertake his rendition. Working from the original manuscript, Hinojosa rendered the text in English as *This Migrant Earth* (1985), included in its entirety in this anthology. The result begins, as Rivera's original does, with seven chapters. After a break of short, untitled pieces, seven more chapters follow. Throughout, Hinojosa aims to make the original's idiosyncratic style come alive in English, providing the omniscient narrator and Rivera's cast of characters a channel into the reader's consciousness. Among the changes Hinojosa made were to the work's title and chapter titles.

The most established English-language version is Evangelina Piñon-Vigil's *And the Earth Did Not Devour Him* (1987), which follows Quinto Sol's amended table of contents but also changes the chapter titles. For example, the chapter that Quinto Sol titled "The Night of the Blackout" is titled "Love and Darkness" in Hinojosa's version and "The Night the Lights Went Out" in Piñon-Vigil's. Vigil-Piñón also gives titles to the short pieces with the unnamed and unidentified narrators, although Rivera deliberately left some characters unnamed because they were "the invisible people," meaning that those who pick the crops are seldom identified. As he said, "When we're driving at seventy miles an hour, we don't look at the field hands who are picking the fruit and vegetables."

Rivera's slender book *Always and Other Poems* (1973) is about his experiences as a migrant farm laborer, the early death of his father, and the enduring power of love. A separate and longer poem, *The Searchers* (1990), presents the stark lives of people who endure deplorable working and living conditions. Rivera's many essays remain uncollected and unpublished. An early curriculum vita presents a second novel, *La casa grande*, as forthcoming from a Mexican American publisher. A subsequent vita calls it a work in progress. A third one lists it as a tentative work. The chapters "Eva y Daniel" and "El Pete Fonseca," which appeared in literary journals, might have been part of *La casa grande*, which Rivera probably did not complete. He intended the work to be not a sequel to *This Migrant Earth* but a further exploration of the lives of migrant farm laborers.

## This Migrant Earth[1]

Bowed by the weight of centuries he leans
Upon his hoe and gazes on the ground
The emptiness of ages in his face,
And on his back the burden of the world.

Edwin Markham

## The Paling Time and the Fading Year

Lost, that was what that year was to him. Lost. And though he tried—time and again—to remember and to recover that lost year (for that's what he called it), he found it would melt away. The words, too, had failed him, and how he needed words to find that lost, wandering year.

It would usually begin within—or, as if in—a dream where he imagined himself wide awake only to find he was dreaming still. How could this be?

And then, as time went on, he couldn't decide—admit, perhaps—tell, even—whether those things he thought on were real or not. Nor, could he swear that he had merely dreamt them.

And the pattern was always the same, too. He'd turn in a rush, hoping to catch whoever it was that called to him by name. He'd make a complete turn, too, but it was useless. There was never anyone there. No one to see, no one for him to discover. Come to that, he'd also forget the name used by the voice when it called him.

But one thing he did know, was sure of: it was he who was being called. He. No one else.

And one day he broke the pattern; he stopped at mid-circle. He had broken the pattern, and fear had set in, but as it did so—and at that moment— he also realized that it was he who had been calling himself all along. Yes, and this is how (through his own voice), how he found both himself and that pale, fading, childhood year.

This done, he then tried to pinpoint the time he referred to—identified, really—as a *year*.

And, in the midst of all this, he also realized that he thought. That is, that he thought about thinking, about memory, and of time. But further than this, he couldn't go until . . . until his mind would become a blank. No thoughts to be held there, and then, peace, and from peace: sleep. And, it was here, at this point, awake, asleep, and awake again just before dropping off to sleep, that he would hear things, and see them, too . . .

In his sleep, in that wandering year.

## Water, Water Everywhere

Texas Winter Garden area heat, remorseless and humid. But a strange heat since it was only the beginning of April. Why, heat like this doesn't come

1. Rendered into English by Rolando Hinojosa.

on . . . doesn't settle to wear you down until the end of the month, begin-
ning-a May, or later. But the heat had come on so that the owner . . . the
planter . . . couldn't keep up the water supply.

It was hot, and he knew it, too. But where was he then? He'd made two
trips that morning, and that was it. And it wasn't enough, not nearly enough,
let me tell you that.

The field hands—what else could they do?—they took to going over to a
water tank; it was meant for the stock, see? And that's what the planter
meant it for, too. He'd said that. So, when the hands went there (you got to
understand that it was hot, see?), he'd get angry. Yeah.

Get away from there!

We were getting paid by the hour, all of us was. No piece work, nossir.
And he looked at those water trips we took as a waste-a time. And money.
But it was hot out in those field rows. What did he know?

Know what he did then? Threatened to fire us, he did.

No more water drinking, hear? Get away from that tank!

But it was the little kids, see? They couldn't do the work, and him not
bringing enough water for us. Only made those two trips in the morning,
see? So, the kids'd go out to the stock tank.

"Thirsty, Pa . . . That old guy coming over any time soon?"

"Yeah, that's what he said. You hurtin'? For water?"

"Mmmmm. M'throat's full-a dust, Pa. Think he'll be here soon? You
think I ought-a go to that tank there?"

"Better not. Can you wait a bit? 'Member what he said? About firing us?"

"I know what he said, but . . . It's just that I'm . . . I wish I didn't have to
wait."

"That's a good boy. You'll be all right in a while, okay? He'll be here,
really."

"Hmmmm. I'll try, Pa. You know, Pa, why ah, why doesn't he just let us
bring our own water? We can, you know. And Up North, we always . . ."

"Why? I'll tell you why: 'cause he's no damned good, and he's lazy, and he
doesn't care, and that's the way he is."

"We, ah, we can hide the water jugs under the car seat, right? I mean, Up
North we can get all the water we want, any time. Right? How, ah, how
about if I make like I'm going off the field, to take a leak, see? But near the
tank, all the same."

And that was it. Came that afternoon, the field hands'd sneak off—just like
the kid said—away from the crops, but near enough the tank.

But the old guy found out right off. He just didn't make out like he had,
is all. He was waiting for his chance, see? A chance to grab a whole bunch
together, and that way, why, he'd find a way to come up with less wages.
Thing is, most of the work would-a been done by late afternoon, but he had
the leverage: he could always say no one was working as hard as he'd
wanted us to.

What really set him off was a kid. The little guy couldn't wait. He was
thirsty, see, but that grower, he, ah, he got angry.

Angry at a kid, can you imagine that? Angry at a kid? Well, he was going
to teach that boy a lesson, he was.

Hmph. What he did and what he said he planned to do were two different things, let me tell you that. Fired off a shot is what he did. To scare him off, he said. Can you beat that? A kid . . .

Shot that boy right in the head. Dead's dead, and he dropped him on the spot. Blood all over the place, the kid's shirt, pants, in the tank water.

Didn't mean to, he said. Hmph. That *didn't mean to* won't bring the boy back, I'll tell you that.

"Well now, I hear that old boy almost went crazy."

"Almost."

"Yeah, he did, and he lost part-a the land, too; and then he took to drinking quite a bit. You know there was a trial . . . or hearing, right? Got off okay, but then he tried to kill himself, he did. Yeah. He, ah, jumped off a tree."

"That kill him?"

"No . . . but he tried to."

"Ah-hah."

"But, look, Compadre, I hear he's gone nearly crazy over this. You seen him lately? Did-ja see the way he was dressed?"

"Look: he dresses that way 'cause he's run out-a cash, that's all."

"Yeah, but still, Compadre . . . you know what I mean?"

"Hmph."


## Burnt Offerings

In all, there were five Garcías: Don Efraín and his wife, Doña Chona, and their five-, six- and seven-year-old kids: María, Juan, and the oldest, Raulito. They'd just returned from the Sunday night picture show—about a prizefighter—and it'd been a lot of fun for everybody.

Don Efraín had liked the show so much that he was barely inside the chicken coop when he made straight for the old boxing gloves and then went ahead and put them on the two boys. First he stripped them down to their shorts, then he rubbed alcohol on them—he'd seen the trainers do this—and then he had the two kids go at it. Doña Chona she tried to stop this on the spot; she knew exactly what the outcome would be: one or both of the kids would wind up mad, crying, hurt and whatnot.

"Look, Efra, why in the world would you want them hitting each other? It just isn't worth it; Juan's going to end up with a bloody nose—he always does, you know—and you also know how hard it is to stop it. And besides that, it's been a long day for everyone and they should all be in bed by now."

"Man, Chona, you ought-a . . ."

"And don't *man* me, Efraín."

"They're playing, that's all. And look, maybe they'll learn how to defend themselves."

"We're not home now, remember? This is a chicken coop. We can hardly move around here, the five of us. And there *you* go making 'em run around, as if we had all the room in the world here."

"Oh, yeah? Well what do you think they do when you and I are out working in the fields? I just wish they were a little older and that way we'd be
able to take 'em to the fields with us. And if we could do that, then maybe
they'd help us out, or we could keep an eye on them."

"Oh, sure. You really think so, do you? Look, the older they get, the row-
dier they're gonna get. It's part of growing up, Efra. What I don't like is
having to leave them here, alone."

"You know, wouldn't it be something if one of the kids was real good at
this? Boxing. We'd be in clover, Chona. You know just how much money
some of those champs make? Thousands. Yeah, thousands. And this gives
me an idea: I'm going to order a punching bag from the catalogue house
next week, just as soon as we get paid."

"Well, it's worth a try . . . you never know, you know."

"Right. That's what I've been saying all along."

One of the grower's standing orders was: no children allowed. They'd get in
some mischief or other, he'd say. Or they'd take time from their folks, if they
had to tend to them. So this meant the nonworking kids had to stay home, in
the coops. They'd brought the kids out and kept them in the car once, but
the weather had turned brutally hot and humid and they'd all taken sick.
So that took care of that. And now the kids stayed home, but this sure didn't
take away the worry.

And then Don Efraín and Doña Chona came up with a partial solution:
instead of packing a lunch, Don Efraín and Doña Chona would come home
at noon. Eat with the kids. Be with them a while.

Came Monday morning, and after a while with each other, off to work.
The kids slept on, but this wasn't anything new.

"Efra . . . Efra, you really look happy this morning."

"Ho! And you're the reason, right?"

"Oh, I don't mean that. It's more than that. What is it?"

"I guess it's the kids, Chona. I love them, and I love you, and I know you
feel the same way I do. And I was thinking about how they play with you and
me, how they like to play with us."

Around ten or so, the two of them looked up in time to see some smoke.
Heavy, dark smoke. From the settlement, no doubt about that now. And then:
the chicken coops. Don Efraín and Doña Chona dropped their hoes, ran to
the car, and then the rest of the fieldhands did the same and followed them
out there, fast, out where they lived. But when they got there, all of them saw
it'd been the García chicken coop; and it was going and gone up in smoke.

The seven-year old, that's Raulito, he was the sole survivor.

"The word is that the seven-year old made the other two put the gloves on.
They were fooling around—y'know how that goes. But then the boy went
ahead and rubbed alcohol on 'em, on María and Juan. And he probably
rubbed other junk on 'em, too, for all I know. Just like in the movie, see? But
they were playing, that's all. Fooling around, see?"

"Yeah, but how could they just burn up, like that?"

"Well, what happened was that the oldest—Raulito—he started to fry himself some eggs at the same time the other two were goin' at it, and I think

something must've happened, and then the little guys burned up; caught fire, see?"

"Maybe he put too much alcohol on them, you think that's it?"

"Who's to know? Those coops we live in are so damned small, and you know how much stuff we have to keep in there. I don't know, but it could've been the kerosene tank atop the stove. Exploded or something; maybe that's what set them on fire, and the coop, too."

"Yeah, it could've happened that way. Sure."

"And you know what else?"

"What's that?"

"Well, did you notice how the gloves didn't burn up at all? What's the little girl's name? María? Well, she was all burned up, but the gloves sure weren't."

"Well, that's the manufacturers, the people who make 'em. They know what they're doing."

"But what about the Garcías? How're they doing now?"

"They came around; had to. But this ain't something you forget, y'know, and it's going to take time, too. But, I mean, what *can* you do? It's there, waiting for you, but you never know when. Or how . . ."

"God's truth, all right."

## Love and Darkness

The lights failed, that's all, went out, but no one knew what could have caused them to go out so fast, just like that, see? And some of the people were really scared; lights off, all over town. No warning, no storm, nothing. And no lightning, either. They were on, and then they were off. Poof! And there'd been a dance on, see?

Now, the people at the dance saw the lights go out first, right away. But some people who'd stayed home, gone to bed early, well, for them it wasn't till morning when they first heard about it. Some a-them must've wondered what was going on, 'cause the lights went out and then the music stopped, flat. But like I said, it wasn't till morning when they found out what had really happened.

"Ramón, he really liked that girl of his; loved her. A lot. And he was a good buddy of mine, too; we were close. And he's the one who told me about her, see? And he was sort-a secretive, but not with me he wasn't; we were friends, see? And he told me he loved her, and he told me more'n once, too. They'd been going steady for about a year, and they'd gone over to the Kress[2] and got themselves some nice engagement rings from there. But don't think it was all his doing, see? She loved him back. It's just that something happened between them last summer. And then, when they met up again, and it had been four months, see, well, when they met up again . . . look: nobody knows for sure, okay?"

2. A "five-and-dime" department store.

RAMÓN: "A promise is a promise, and I promise I won't even look at another girl. And we both want to get married, right? Okay, now. We *can* run away, elope, if that's what you want. Or we can wait till school's over. How's that? But you're the only one for me. And like I just said, we can run away, if that's what you want. And I can work, for both of us. I know the folks'll get mad and all, but they'll get over it. Would you run away? Now?"

JUANITA: "I think we better wait. It'd be better, wouldn't it? I mean, we better do it right. Proper. And I'll cross *my* heart: I love you. Trust me. Y'see, m'dad wants me to finish school, that's all. And I can't go against him, you can see that, can't you? And I do love, a lot. There. I trust you, and I sure won't see anyone either, Ramón. A promise."

"Who says it's a mystery? *Everybody* knows . . . ha. Don't you tell *me* nobody knows. Listen to this: I heard she ran around when she was up in Minnesota, during the migrant season. But you want to know what else she was doing at the same time? Well, running around and all, she was still writing letters to Ramón. Yeah, at the same time. Lying to him, of course; and she kept writing those letters to him just the same.

"But Ramón he found out right quick; some friends of his told him all about it, and all about her, too. And I'll tell you how the friends found out. They were working at the same place where Juanita and her folks were staying. So, as soon as everybody came back home—to Texas—they went up and told Ramón right away. First thing, don't you know. Now, *he* was faithful. She was the *one*, see?

"And it was some guy from San Antonio, yeah. That's who she was running around with up in Minnesota. And he was a bag-full-of-wind, he was. One of those sharp dressers, right? Oh, yeah. Orange leather shoes, and he wore one a-them long, drawn out sport coats, and then he walked around with his shirt collar turned up. Cute. Hmph.

"But she liked that, the fooling around part of it. Bound to. What she should've done, but didn't, was to break off with Ramón first. Right? She could've, if she wanted to. When the picking season was over, Ramón and his folks and all the other crews out there, they got back to Texas before Juanita and her folks and their group.

"Ramón, he started getting drunk just about every night. I ran into him a couple of times, you know. And we got to talking. A sliver is what he called it. A splinter or something like that. It's in my heart, he said. That's what women leave there, that's all the're good for. Hurting a guy; taking his heart. Giving it back, full of splinters . . ."

RAMÓN in Iowa: "Well, I'm through waiting. Soon's I get back to Texas, I'm not putting up with this anymore. We'll just do it, get married. And she'll come, she'll run away with me.

"Every time I pick up this hoe and plunk it down, I can hear her name. Over and over. And why does one feel this way? When one's in love? And then, after work and supper, I sit and stare at her picture till nighttime, but something strange happens . . . The more I look at her—at the picture—the less I remember what she really looks like. I mean, it's her picture all right, but it doesn't look like her. I mean, it's her, but it's not her. At the same time. Yeah, that's it. She doesn't look like the picture, or maybe the other way 'round, the picture doesn't look like her. And the guys rag me about it all the time, but that's okay: I usually go off into the woods anyway to look at the picture. But it's the same thing there: I look at the picture, I stare at it, and then I forget what she looks like. I don't know; maybe I shouldn't look at it so much.

"Faith and trust, she said. And I believe her. Her eyes, that smile; it's the truth, I can remember them all right.

"But I'll be home soon; Texas. And every morning, dawn comes, those old roosters get the day up, and it's just one more day closer to home. And I can see her there, on the streets of home. Pretty soon now."

JUANITA to a friend: "It isn't as if I'm not in love with Ramón anymore. It isn't the same thing at all. I still love him, it's just that I happen to like the way this new guy carries on, that's all. But I don't mean nothing by it, it's just that I like the way he talks. But that's all, okay?

"And then, have you noticed how the other girls stare at him too? Sure they do. And he dresses nice. And what do you mean I don't love Ramón? Of course I do. Where do you get off? I do. All I said was that this guy's nice to me. That's all. He's a nice guy with a nice smile, and he's here . . . Why should I break up with Ramón?

"And what's so bad about my talking with this guy? We talk, that's all. It's nothing serious, see? Besides, I promised Ramón. And that's it. The new guy? Oh, he follows me around; but that's all. It's not that I'm the one doing the chasing. And break up with Ramón? Why? Why should I? I'm not going out with this guy. Like I said, I talk to him, and how about the other girls? You know how they feel? They're jealous, that's all. And that's why I talk to him. But it's Ramón I love, and I happen to love him very much. Look, Ramón and I are going to be together in a few weeks; we'll all be going home soon . . .

"What did you say? What do you mean this new guy is seeing Petra? Is he? Yeah? Well why does he keep tagging after me, then? And not only that, I also get notes from him. Sure. He gets Don José's little boy to give 'em to me."

A note from Ramiro, the new guy:

"I know you're going with somebody else now, but what's that to me? I like talking to you, being with you. Let's meet at Saturday's dance, the two of us. Love you, Ramiro."

"Well, she started dancing with Ramiro that Saturday, and he's the only one she danced with, too. And know what? All her girl friends told her it was wrong, pointed it out to her, but do you think she *cared*? And you know what else? When the last dance came on, they made a date to see each other at home; yeah, Texas. It's hard to see how she could have been thinking of Ramón then and there like she was saying she was. But Ramón, see, he'd already got the word by then. Had to know. The first time she and Ramón met again, and this was after four months, right?, well, he walked up to her, told her off, to her face. Well . . . no. Not at first. I was with him then, and he was happy to see her and what anger he might have had just melted away. But then the more they talked, see? Something happened, all of a sudden, and this really set him off, and so he was angry all over again. And then they broke right there, on the spot; yeah."

The argument:

    JUANITA:   "You sure you know what you're doing?"

    RAMÓN:   "Of course I do."

    JUANITA:   "And you want to break it off; our understanding?"

    RAMÓN:   "That's right. And you want to know something? You dance with somebody else—anybody else—and you're going to be sorry. So don't you do it."

    JUANITA:   "Says who? You just said we're not going together anymore. We're through, you said. And besides, you haven't got any say-so on who I dance or don't dance with."

    RAMÓN:   "Look, whether or not we broke up doesn't mean a thing to me. You got that? I'm getting even. Period. And listen to this: from now, on you're going to do what I tell you to do, and for as long as I tell you. You got that? Nobody makes a fool out of me. You hang on to that. So I'm going to make you pay for everything you've done to me, and I'm going to do it one way or another. It doesn't matter which way, either."

    JUANITA:   "You stop that. You got no hold on me."

    RAMÓN:   "I'm telling you, Juanita. You do what I say, and if you get up on that dance floor, you dance with me or you're not dancing with anyone else, and that's final. You got that, too?"

"But listen to this, though. I heard Juanita had asked her folks for permission to go to the dance, but she asked to go earlier than usual. And she and her girlfriends got there before the band showed up, before they started warming up. And you know why? Hmph: So she and her friends could all stand by the main door. In that way, the guys coming in would see them first. Talk to them; and pick 'em out when the dance started; get it?

"Well, Juanita'd been dancing with just one guy by the time Ramón showed up. First thing he did was to go start looking for her. He found her a-course, but when he did, the dance tune was about over when he walked over to cut in."

"No, I don't know who her partner was or anything; some guy, okay? At any rate, the music starts up again, but Juanita says no; she won't dance with him, Ramón. And I mean they were right in the middle of the dance floor, too. And they stood there, the music playing, the dance going on, people dancing all around them, and there they stood.

"And then they had some words. Know what she did then? She slapped him! Yeah. And then he called *her* a name, and after that, he stomped out, walked on out. With this, she made for one of the benches lining the sides and sat down, just like that. Well, that same dance tune was still playing when all-of-a-sudden-and-just-like-that, the lights went out. Well, people tried to turn them, on, but how? Right? And everyone milled around in the dark, a lot of loud talk, nervous laughter, you know. But no lights came on, no sir. And then someone said the lights had gone out all over town, and that was it for the dance.

"The next day it was, some employees working for the city's utility plant found Ramón; he was dead. The power plant was just a block away from the dance floor. Yeah, they found him, all right: stuck to one of the transformers his hand was. Burned to a crisp, they say. Him, all over. And that's why the lights went out, see?

"But like I said, the people at the dance knew the lights had gone out, but that's all they knew. And you know what else? Some of the people standing by Juanita and Ramón—during the argument—well, they said he told her he was going to kill himself. Can you beat that?

"The folks at home had no idea what was going on. All they knew was that the lights went out. But they didn't find out what happened to Ramón until later; after mass I think it was.

"But it's really a case of love, don't you understand? I mean, those two really and truly loved each other, y'know."

"Well, yeah, if you say so. Hard to tell, though."


## With Storms of Prayer

My dear God, and most holy Jesus, it's me again—my third Sunday here, and I come with the same request again—please: Won't you please tell me where my son is? I haven't heard from him—is he hurt? Don't let him, please don't. Save and keep him for me—tell me he's all right, please. I don't want him dead, no, no, not like Doña Virginia's boy—he was killed, and he's with You now. But my boy: Save and keep him for me, dear Sweet Jesus, protect him from bullets and wounds and shooting. He's a good boy, yes he is—he's always been a good son and gracious, too. And when I nursed him, a good boy, not once, no, never, not once did he bite or chew or gnaw on me. A good, innocent child. He means no harm—he's good and kind—please keep and save his heart from harm. He's a loving son, yes. Please, please keep and save his heart from harm.

Please, Sweet Mother of God, you tend to him, too. Cover him, and cover his head, and blind the communists, those Koreans and Chinese, please. Protect him from them. Please.

I still have his toys, yes. All his toy cars and trucks, and a kite, yes, I found it the other day, under his old baby clothes. And I've got his school report cards and the comic books he used to read. Everything, see? I've saved everything for him.

Jesus, Son of God, save him, don't let them take him away from me. No: I've made a promise—yes, I have—a promise to the Virgin to visit the Shrines of Our Lady of San Juan de los Lagos in Jalisco, and to Our Lady of Guadalupe, and my boy carries a medal, yes, he made a vow to Our Lady of San Juan down in the Valley.[3] He wants to live: Do take care of him. Take your Hand, take it, and cover his heart—no bullets can enter then . . . he's good and kind, a nice boy.

Oh, he didn't want to go . . . no, he told me so. He was afraid, he said, and yet he was taken away from me. And he cried in my arms, just before he left, and I could feel his heart, and it was like when he was a child and I'd nurse him . . . and then he'd be happy and I was happy, with him.

---

3. In expectation of or thanks for divine aid, Catholics sometimes pray or offer devotional rites to Jesus Christ, the Virgin Mary, and/or saints. In Mexico, major subjects of such veneration include two incarnations of the Virgin: *Nuestra Señora de* *San Juan de los Lagos* (Our Lady of St. John of the Lakes), in Jalisco, and Mexico's matron saint, *Nuestra Señora de Guadalupe*, near Mexico City. *Nuestra Señora de San Juan del Valle* is a shrine in San Juan, Texas, devoted to Our Lady of St. John.

So care for him, tend to him, cover him. I promise, I promise my life for his. Yes: Bring him back from Korea for me, bring him back safely, unharmed, and do cover his heart, do. God, Sweet Jesus, and Our Lady of Guadalupe, all of You, together, bring him back to me, his mother. Why have you taken him from me? Where is my boy? He's done nothing bad; he's innocent, and he's obedient and humble, yes, he is. He wouldn't harm a soul; not him, no, he wouldn't . . . Please, please: Bring him back to me, alive, alive—I don't want him dead, to die, no.

Look, look: Here's my heart. Go on! Take it! Here, see? Take it—now! Blood? You want blood? Here's mine, if that's what you want. My heart? Is that it? My heart for his? Yes! Now! Here, here's my heart, mine for his, it's the same blood, don't you see?

Yes, that's it; bring him back, bring him back to me, and I'll give you my heart. Please!

## Picture of His Father's Face

Nothing to it; all the picture salesmen from San Antonio had to do was to sit and wait, like turkey buzzards, my Pa said, 'cause it was the same every year when the people came back home after some seven months on the migrant trail. There'd be money in their pockets, so, right behind them, the picture salesmen. Nothing to it.

And they brought sample cases of pictures, frames, and black and white and color proofs, too. Here's how they dressed: white shirt first of all, and a tie to go with it. Sure. Respectable, see? And that's why *la raza*, the people, would open their doors to them. I mean, a shirt and a tie represented honesty and respectability. Nothing to it. Easier than stealing, right? . . . and that's what I'm talking about here, see?

You know how people are, how we all of us are wanting our kids to get ahead and be somebody? Wear a white shirt. And a tie. Sure.

And there they came down those dusty streets, sample cases handy, and they were ready to work the town and the people . . .

Once (and I remember it well, too) I'd gone with Pa on a visit; a call to a compadre's house, when one of the sales types shows up. And he looked hesitant at first, kind of timid. Pa's compadre, Don Mateo, he asked the salesman to come on in, sit, make yourself at home.

"Afternoon (he said), you-all doing all right? We got something new to show you this year. Sí, señor."

"Oh, yeah? And what's that?"

"Let me explain what I'm talking about. You give us a photograph, a picture, right?, and what we do is to amplify it, we make it larger, and that's what amplify means. And then, after that, here's what we do: put that picture on wood. Yes. Sort of rounded off, see? What we call three dimensional."

"And what's the reason for that?"

"Realism. Makes the person come alive, you might say. It-a, it sort of jumps out at you, see? Three dimensional. Here, let me show you this one here . . . This is part of what we do. How about that, eh? Like he's alive, right? It sure looks it, don't it?"

"Yeah, that's pretty good. Hold on a minute, I'm going to show it to my wife . . . (Will you look at this? Isn't that something. Come over here, will you?) . . . You know, we were talking, the wife and me, thinking of sending off some snapshots this year, making them bigger. Enlarging them, right? Ah . . . but this ought to cost quite a bit, am I right?"

"Not as much as you'd think. The problem is *the process*, do you know what I mean by that?"

"Ah-hah. How much money we talking about here?"

"Well, not as much as you'd think, like I said. How does thirty dollars sound? But first-class, rounded off, see? Three dimensional . . ."

"Well, thirty dollars does sound kind of steep to me. I thought I heard you say it wouldn't go much more than the old ones. And this is on the installment plan, you say?"

"Well, if it was up to me . . . but it happens that we got us a new sales supervisor this year, and with him, it's cash; cash on the barrelhead, I'm afraid. You know how it is, but he's also right in a way, see? It's good, first class, quality workmanship. It'd make a great picture for that table, see? Realer than real. Rounded off, like this one here. Here, hold it youself. Fine work, right? And we can do it in a month, too. Everything. But what we need from you is to tell us what color clothing, hair, and like that; and then, before you know it, the month's gone by, and you got yourselves the genuine article here. For a lifetime. And listen to this: we'll throw in the frame, too. Free, gratis. And it'll take a month. Tops. And I wish we could do business, but this new supervisor, he wants to get paid on the nail. And he pushes us, see?"

"Oh, I like the work, all right. But it's the money; it's kind-a high."

"I know what you mean. But you got to agree that that's what we call first-class goods, substantial, see? . . . and that's what we're looking at here. You never seen work like this in your life, am I right? On wood? Like that?"

"No, I sure haven't, but . . . here, I'll ask the wife again . . . What do you think, eh?"

"It's nice. I like it. A lot. Look, why don't we try one? See how it comes out. We like it, we get some more. Let's start off with Chuy's picture. That's the only one we got of him, though, God rest him . . ."

"She's right. We took it right here before he left for Korea; and he died there. See? Here's the picture we're talking about. You, ah, you think you can do that rounding off with this one? Like you say? Like he looks alive, kind of?"

"Absolutely. We do a lot of servicemen, yes ma'am. You see, in this rounding that we do, they're better than photographs or snapshots. A whole lot. Now, all I need's the size, but you got to tell me that; the size you want. Oh, and that free frame I talked about, you want it in a square shape? Round, maybe? What d'you say? What should I write down here?"

(Don Mateo looked at his wife) "What d'you think? Can we order the one?"

"Well, I already told you what I think. I'd like to have my boy looking like that. Rounded off, in color."

"Okay, write it up like that, but like I said: that's the only picture we got of the boy. So, you got to take good care of it. He was supposed to send us one in uniform, all fitted out, see? And with the Mexican and the United

States flags around him. You seen 'em, right? But we never got that picture. What happened was that as soon as he got to Korea, we then heard from the government. Missing in action, they said. Missing. So you best take good care a-that photo there."

"We'll take good care of it, yessir. You can count on it. The company knows you all are making a sacrifice here; oh, yes. We don't want you to worry none. And you just wait when you get it back, cleaned up and everything. What's it gonna be? We put on a navy-blue uniform on 'im?"

"Can you really do that? He's not even wearing a uniform on this one."

"Nothing to it. We just kind of fix it in; what we call an *inlay* job. You know about that? On the wood, see? Here, let me show you these over here . . . See this one here? Well, that boy there didn't have no uniform on when they took his picture. Our company was the one that put it on him. How about that, eh? Blue is it? Navy-blue?"

"Oh yeah, sure."

"And don't you worry none about your boy's picture, okay?"

"How long till we get those pictures, you think?"

"Can't be too long, right? But it takes time on account of *the process*. It's good work. And these people sure know what they're doing, too. You notice? The people in the samples looked alive, real."

"Oh, yeah, I know they do good work, no denying that. It's just that it's been over a month, or more."

"Yeah, but don't forget: how many towns between here and San Antonio? They must've gone through every one, see? It'll probably take 'em more'n a month on account of all the business they did."

"Yeah, that's got to be it, then. Sure."

And then, two weeks after that last exchange, something happened. There'd been some hard rains in the region, and some kids fooling around near the city dump, over by those big drain pipes there, well, that's where the kids found the photographs! Wet, and most beyond recognition, worn out, through and through, and full of holes some of them. But they were the snapshots and the pictures, all right. You could see they were; most of them were the same size, and you could still make out some of the faces on them, too.

Sold! They'd been taken in, and that sure didn't take long to sink in. Taken. Like babies. And Pa's compadre, Don Mateo, he got so mad, so mad, he just took off to San Antonio; went after that guy who'd conned them good, who'd taken their money, who'd taken his Chuy's last picture.

"Well, Compadre, I'll tell you what I did; how I went about it. First off, I stayed with Esteban. Every morning I'd go out with him, to that stall of his, where he sells vegetables; the San Antonio *mercado*, that open-air veg market. Worked with him, loading and unloading, helping out, you know. But I had me a plan, a hunch; a hope, maybe. And I just knew I was going to run across that big city con man, yeah.

"Anyway, every morning after helping Esteban set up that stand of his, I'd walk around some of the barrios there, by the market. Got to see a lot, see? But by now, it wasn't the money so much. That mad kind-of wore off.

It was the wife's crying, see? And that'd been Chuy's one and only picture, and we'd told the guy, too. The only one we had of him, and the wife crying all the time. So it wasn't the money so much, now. Oh, we'd found them all there in the sewers, but that snapshot was ruined. Nothing left, see?"

"But in San Antonio, Compadre? How would anyone go about finding a guy like that?"

"I'll make it short, Compadre. He himself showed up at Esteban's stall one day. Just like that! Bought himself some vegetables, he did, right there. And I saw him face to face. He saw me too, but he made out like he didn't know me, know who I was. Never seen me before, see? Oh, I made him right away, and then you know what happened? Let me say this, Compadre, when you're angry, really angry, but I mean really angry now, you don't forget a face or anything. It all comes clear somehow.

"Well, I came up to him, grabbed him, yeah I did, and he went *white* on me, scared. You bet, he was. And I said: 'I want my boy's picture. And I want it rounded off, like you said. Three di—mension. You got that?'

"And then I told him I'd eat him up and spit him out if he didn't come through with that portrait of his. Hmph. He didn't know what to do, where to start. But he did it. From memory, you understand? But he did it."

"Yeah? Well how did he do that, Compadre?"

"Well, that's a mystery, but with fear working overtime, I guess you might say you can remember *anything*, everything. And there it was, three days later, and I didn't have to go after him this time. There he was at Esteban's stall, picture and everything. Well, there it is, see it? Right behind you. Good piece of work, right?"

"Tell you the truth, Compadre, I can't remember what young Chuy looked like anymore . . . But he, ah, he was beginning to look like you, wasn't he?"

"He sure was, Compadre. And you know what people say when they see the picture? They say the same thing. Yeah. That Chuy, had my boy lived, he'd look a lot like me, they say. And there's the picture, here, let me get it for you. I—dentical, eh, Compadre? Him and me, right?"

## And All through the House . . .

Christmas Eve was almost on them, but it was the same old story: the advertising sound truck hired by the Ideal Theater blared out songs of the season, mixing business and heaping blessing on one and all, and now, three days till Christmas Eve, Doña María had made up her mind: *this year* she was going to buy the kids some store-bought toys.

There was always a first time, she'd said, and that decision was firm; final. Nothing new on the promise, however; she'd said the same thing the year before. And the year before that. But it was always the same: no, we can't afford it. And her husband would then bring the same things to the kids: Valley oranges and Texas pecans. But no toys. In that way, her husband would say, and he'd convinced himself by now, they'd each have something; they wouldn't do without.

Nothing new: the kids would ask for *their* toys, her husband would say the same thing: the sixth of January, that's our day. Just hold on till then, okay? The sixth. Epiphany. The Magi.[4] So, every year, Christmas would come, go, the sixth of January would arrive, but by then the kids would either forget or get over their disappointment. But Doña María had noticed something that last Christmas.

About that time, Don Chon, an old family friend, would come over on Christmas night, and he'd bring the sack full of Valley oranges and Texas pecans. Always the same, and Doña María knew it was time for a change . . .

"Why? Why is it that Santa Claus doesn't come to this house, Ma? Why doesn't he bring us something?"

And Doña María: "Of course he comes to see us. Who do you suppose brings us the oranges and the pecans?"

"Oh, Ma, that's not Santa Claus. That's Don Chon."

"Oh, I'm not talking about that, I'm talking about what's under the sewing machine. What you find there."

"That? That's Pa who puts the fruit there. You think we don't know that? And what's wrong with *us*? Aren't we as good as anybody else?"

"Sure you are! Of *course*, you are . . . All we have to do is wait for the Three Wise Men, and that's when the toys and the presents really come. In Mexico, Santa Claus won't come until the Night of the Magi, the sixth of January. And that's because that's the right *day*."

"Well, maybe, Ma. But what happens is that you and Pa always forget; it goes right by. 'Cause as far as we're concerned, it's been nothing. Nothing on the sixth and nothing on Christmas Eve."

"Well, maybe it'll be different this year."

"Well, yeah . . . maybe. We sure hope so, Ma."

And that's when she decided she'd buy them something. But it was the same old problem for them: they didn't have any cash for the toys. As for her husband, he worked two shifts down at the cafe, worked more than two shifts sometimes, as a cook and dish-washer. And *he* didn't have the time to go Christmas shopping for the kids' toys . . .

And then, what pay they'd have left over at the end of the week, that would go to their savings: the money was needed to pay for their trip to Iowa; the truck driver charged the kids a full fare and even a full fare meant having to stand up from Texas all the way to the Midwest. So, it was him, his wife, and the three boys; that came to a lot of money. But Doña María had made up her mind, and she was going to talk with her husband, that very night, just as soon as he came in from work. She hated to do it since he was so tired, but she had to; she'd made up her mind.

"You know, the boys would like a little something for Christmas."

"Why? What's wrong with the oranges, the pecans?"

"Nothing, really. It's just that they want some toys now. It isn't food they want. They're bigger now, see? They know more."

"They don't need toys."

"Ah, didn't you have toys when you were a kid yourself?"

4. Epiphany, a Christian feast traditionally occurring on January 6 following the 12 days of Christmas, commemorates three biblical events: the visit of the Magi (or Three Wise Men) to the stable of Bethlehem following the birth of Jesus, Jesus' baptism, and Jesus' first miracle.

"It was different then. I made 'em myself: toy soldiers and toy horses. Out of clay, but you know that."

"Of course I do, but it's not the same here; here, they see things and they want them. What d'you say? Why don't we look? Let's buy them something, for once. I'll go to the Kress, myself, really."

"You would?"

"I really would." Resolute.

"I thought you were afraid of going downtown? Remember when we were Up North? In Wilmar, Minnesota? Remember how you got lost there? You sure you'll be okay? You're not afraid or anything?"

"Oh, I remember when I got lost, confused; sure. But I'm okay now; I've been preparing myself all day for this, you'll see. And I won't get lost; listen to this: I go out on the street, right? From there, I can make out the ice house. And that's a matter of four blocks; that's what Doña Regina says. All right: then, when I get to the ice house, I take another right and downtown's right there, two blocks from the ice house, and then there's Kress. After that, from the Kress to the ice house, turn to this street here, and I'm home. How's that?"

"Sounds good to me. I'll go ahead and leave some money on top of the table on my way to work tomorrow morning. But do try to be careful, will you? It's Christmas time, and the streets and stores are both jammed and crowded, and noisy . . . Okay?"

The thing was that Doña María was housebound, and had been for years. The few times she'd venture out it would be to the cemetery, but never alone, or she'd visit her sister and their father a block away, or her own backyard, *el solar*. As for church, she'd go there to the occasional wedding, funeral, but always with her husband and seldom looked to where she was going.

To add to this, her husband had always bought the groceries and what clothes were needed. And so, although downtown was but six blocks away, she'd never been, at all.

She'd seen it, from the back of a truck, as she rode by on her way Up North or back from another migrant season, and once in a while, on a family trip to San Antonio; but other than that, no. As for the long trips, these were normally made late at night; less traffic that way, everybody said.

But this time; this time she meant to walk there alone. She was ready. And so, she arose early, as she always did, served breakfast, as she always did, and she saw to the kids, too; the money was on the table. She started planning her big trip then and there; a smallish shopping district, six blocks away . . . It didn't take her long to get ready.

"I really have no idea why I'm such a scaredy cat; I really don't. My God! Downtown's only six blocks away, and all I have to do is go straight ahead and take a right at the railroad tracks. Then, it's two more blocks and that's it: Kress is right there. To come back from there, it's the two blocks back, take a turn to the left, and that'll put me on this street, and home! I just hope to God I don't meet up with some dog or something else. Or something worse, like when I have to cross the railroad tracks, and maybe some train'll be coming along about the time I have to cross over . . . I hope to God I won't run into no dogs, and no trains, either."

No incident from her house to the railroad tracks, and she'd taken to walking in the middle of the street, too. On the yellow line. No sidewalks for me, she'd said. Some dog could come darting out and then?

Worse: someone might just reach out and grab her. The fact was there was but one dog on the way, but it wasn't there that day. And as far as people are concerned, who'd notice her?

But she hewed to the yellow line, and lucky for her no cars appeared on her way to the ice house. In any case, had there been a car, she wouldn't have known what to do, anyway.

She was now coming up to those railroads tracks and she began to lose her nerve; she could hear the train's engine, the whistle, the deafening noise, and her agitation increased. And now, she couldn't bring herself to cross the tracks; she just couldn't. She'd grit her teeth and head straight for them, head bent low, but she'd come to a dead stop when the train's whistle, blocks away, would blow now and again.

But in the end, she was game. Made up her mind (and closed her eyes) and she made it across the tracks. Courage took over again, and she made the turn to the right; on her way again.

The crowded sidewalks frightened her, but she couldn't walk on the street, not downtown she couldn't. And the noise: dull, incessant, grating. Too, she didn't know or recognize a soul either walking toward her or alongside. And she'd just about decided to give it up, return to the safety of home, but she was bumped ahead by the crowd, and this kept her going toward the center of town.

The noise continued unabated and Doña María heard more than actually saw the people milling about, window shopping, laughing. Fear set in again and a question came to her: Why had she come here? Downtown? With all these *people*? She glanced at a gap between two department stores and dashed in for a breather. It was quieter here; she stared hard at the people walking by and was now steeling herself to go out there, among the crowd.

"Oh, my God, what in the world is the matter with me? It's . . . it's like Wilmar, Minnesota. All over again. I hope to God I won't get sick here; that everything'll turn out all right.

"Let's see: the ice house lies that way. No! The other way . . . Oh, Dear God, what's *wrong* with me? Now, now . . . All right: I was walking from that way there, and then I got here . . . so that means the ice house is over *there*. No, no, no! Good God, I should've stayed home. What am I doing here, *here*?

"Excuse me. Pardon me. ¿Dónde está el Kress, por favor? Ah, Gracias."

She headed where she was told and walked into the Five and Dime . . . But that crowd! And the noise! It was worse here, inside the store.

And now fear bordering on terror, hysteria. What she wanted, needed to do, was to leave, get out, away from this place, from these people, the noise . . . But, but, where was the door? All she could see were shapes and things. And people. Things piled atop of things, and people piled atop of people, crushing each other, pushing, shoving . . .

And the objects talked to her, she felt. And then she stopped; stood there, eyes vacant, staring but unseeing. Some of the shapes—the people!—were beginning to stare at her, too. Others merely pushed her out of their way, but

she stood firm, remaining in place, dull-eyed, unfocusing. Blinking and focusing now, she made for the toy sections, and she walked to that counter.

She opened her grocery bag and began stuffing it with toys; a billfold?
She took that and put it in the bag as well. At this point the noise stopped:
she could see the crowds now, and she could see herself walking, her legs
moving, and her arms and mouth moving as well. But the noise had stopped.
Yes. And then she stopped, turned around, and asked someone for the door,
for the exit sign. Someone pointed to it, and she headed that way, but now
she was pushing, shoving the people out of her way. When she got to the
door, she pushed that, too, and now she was outside, out of that store, away
from the noise, and away from the people . . .

She stood on the sidewalk for a moment, trying to get her bearings again
when suddenly a hand reached out and grabbed her by the arm, forcibly.
The suddenness and the strength of the grasp shocked her.

"Here she is . . . these damn people, always stealing something, stealing.
I've been watching you all along. Let's have that bag."

"Bu . . . . . . ?"

And now she couldn't hear a thing again, and the next moment the cement sidewalk came rushing at her; a bit of a pebble lodged in her eye, and
the pain was awful.

Her arms were grabbed here and there and now she was flat on her back.
People looked down on her; they looked misshapen, elongated somehow.
And now she could see herself lying on the sidewalk. She *thought* she was
talking to someone, but what did those words mean? And yet, there she
was: flat on her back and she could see herself, and her mouth, it was moving, talking to someone. A man appeared. Who was she talking to? A man
and a holstered gun. Bending over her. I'm out of my mind, she thought.

The kids; the kids! The tears came and she began to cry again. And this
was the last thing she remembered.

A sea of people, she could see this; I'm walking through a sea of people;
their arms, like waves.

"Lucky for us our Compadre was at the store; he's the one who came running over to the cafe; he told me all about it. How do you feel now? A little
better?"

"No . . . I think I've gone mad . . ."

"Well, I was afraid you'd get sick or something, like back in Wilmar,
Minnesota."

"Oh, yes . . . and the kids, how're the kids? What's going to happen to
them now? What're they going to do now? What's going to happen to them
now? What're they going to do with a madwoman on their hands? A woman
who can't talk, who can't even go downtown, who . . ."

"So the first thing I did was to get the Notary Public, see? And then he
and I ran over here, to the jailhouse. He's the one who talked to the desk
man. Told him how you got confused, nervous. That you got scared, outside
the house, that crowds made you nervous, right?"

"And what if I'm to be put away? In some madhouse? And then? I don't want
to leave the kids, our kids . . . promise me—whatever you do—promise me
you won't let them send me away. *Promise* they won't take me away. Ohhhhhh,
I should have stayed home! What was I doing downtown, anyway?"

"But you're home now. You're safe here, and you don't have to go out if you don't want to. And if you do go out, why, stay close to home, in the patio, in the backyard. There's no need for you to go out. Look: it'll be like always; I'll bring everything we need, like I always do.

"And go ahead and cry, okay? It's all right . . . probably the best thing for you right now. And listen: I'll talk to the kids; I don't want them pestering you, fretting you, about no Santa Claus ever again. I'll go ahead and tell 'em the truth: 'Look, kids, there's no such thing as Santa Claus, and that's the end of that.'"

"Oh, no, don't do that! Tell 'em about the sixth; tell them that if Santa doesn't bring them something for Christmas, that he'll make it up to them on the sixth, that the Magi'll bring them something, anything."

"Are you sure? That's what you want, is it? . . . . . . Well, I guess you're right; maybe in the long run that's the best thing; give them some kind of hope."

The kids, huddled and hiding behind a door, heard their mom and dad. They heard them clearly enough, even if they weren't sure they understood.

And so, it was back to waiting for the Three Wise Men, just like before. January sixth came, but no presents came with it. By now, the kids didn't bother to ask for any, either.

. . .

It happened almost immediately. She first went rigid for a moment, just-like-that, and then she was in a trance. Everyone there looked at her closely, intently. They then checked to see if anyone had crossed his legs, arms, hands, anything; to see if there was anything that even looked like a cross. Another look around by everyone, and once satisfied, all were assured that the all-seeing spirit was now in her.

"Who . . . Who among you needs help tonight, brothers and sisters?"

"I'm first. It's about my boy—he's in the service—and I haven't heard from him for about two months now. And then, just yesterday, I got a notice from the Government . . . what does that mean? They say he's missing . . . been missing . . . in action. But what I want to know is: is my boy alive? Is he? I'm going half crazy over this."

"But Julianito is doing well, sister. Yes, he is. Don't worry now—and there's no need to—he'll be home soon, next month. Yes, next month; he'll be here then . . . yours to hold again."

"Thank you . . . oh, thank you so much."

What his mother never knew—she used to set a glass of water under his bed; for the spirits, she'd say—but like I said, what his mother never knew was that it was he who drank the water. Every night. She'd go ahead and place that waterglass under his bed—part of her duty, she said—but he'd drink it right down. She thought it was the spirits, of course, and he never did tell her. He planned to, as soon as he grew up, but he just never got around to it.

The boy needed a haircut, bad; and since the movie house wouldn't open up for another hour, he crossed the street, walked into that barbershop and sat down. And when he did, one-a the barbers, he said something to him. The barber he came up to him again and said he wasn't going to cut his hair.

The kid looked up and thought that the barber meant it'd be a long wait. With this, he then waits for the other barber. And then, as soon as that chair was empty, up he climbs, waits for his turn, but this second barber, he says the same thing: Can't cut your hair. And then the barber went on to say that the best thing for him was to leave the shop. Once and for all; just like that. So, he went back across the street, looked at the movie billboards a while, but here comes that first barber. And he told him to go away, to get away from there.

It was then—finally—that the kid got the message, and he headed for home. To get Pa, he said.

"Hey! Why do you guys go to school so much for, anyway? What's the use?"

"My old man, my dad, he says we got to be ready. 'Cause someday there just might be an opportunity, a chance, see, and we may be the ones to get it."

"What are you talking about? Look, if I was you, that'd be the last thing I'd worry about. Let me tell you something: we're in a hole—all of us, see?—and we ain't getting out of it. Got that? There's just no getting out-a that hole . . . so why worry about it? Now, you know who's got to hump it? *They* do; the ones on top . . . they got more to lose, they got to be careful they don't fall in the hole with us. You understand? You see, if they're not on their toes, they're going to wind up down here, with us. But as for us? Shoot! We're about as low as we can get. Yeah."

That schoolteacher didn't know what to do, what to think, what to say . . . Here they all were, by the classroom bulletin board, when all of a sudden, this Mexican kid pops a button from his shirt and hands it to her. Here. Take it.

Sure, the class needed something to set off the town's button factory, but . . . And it was probably his only shirt, too. Had to be.

Questions. But who's to answer whywhywhy? Did he, did he mean to help? Be part of the group? Did he do it for *her*?

Why?

He did it because he had to, he wanted to. She felt this. A desire, that's what it must have been. An overwhelming urge, the intensity of it all. She sensed this. Felt it. The intense feeling of wanting to give, of giving.

But she couldn't explain it; not to anyone; not to herself.

Migrating time again, and just before *la raza*—the people—headed Up North, the priest'd come over and start blessing the cars and trucks: five bucks a shot. And one time, he made out pretty good . . . good enough to go to Barcelona—that's in Spain—to see his folks.

Well—as a token of thanks, I guess—he brought back some picture post-cards; one-a them showed this big old church. A cathedral, *he* called it. And then the priest, he tacked up those postcards at the front, right where you come in. People'd admire the cards, look hard at that *cath*-edral, see; and then—just maybe—then they'd get to working for one just like it, is what he thought.

Well, sir, wasn't long before someone or somebody takes to writing on them cards he put up. Started marking them, too, with crosses and everything, a line here, another there and writing *con safos*[5]—with a *s*, yeah— *con safos*, ha! Better you than me, right?

The priest, he just couldn't understand it; called it a sin and a shame, a *sacrilege*, yeah, that's what he called it.

Oh, and it was such a lovely day for a wedding! All week long, the groom-to-be (and his father, too) worked on his future wife's backlawn—mowing, cutting back, setting up the truck tarp for the reception line, and like that. That backyard was all worked over; decked out in Texas pecan branches, Indian paint brush, wild lilies, hollyhock; and then—careful, now—the tamping down all around the tarp; smooth as glass it was.

And water. They watered the dancing area first of all, and then they watered it down some more. There. Hard; smooth, there, that'll hold the dust in time for the dance.

After the wedding ceremony, the couple walked the length of main street toward home amid cheers and laughter. The groomsmen and bridesmaids trailed right behind them, but up front: the neighborhood kids: yelling, and whooping and hollering—Here they come, everybody! Here come the bride and groom!

Yes, a beautiful day; just a great day for a wedding.

"Comadre, what's this I hear about you-all going to Utah?"

"No, Compadre, where'd you hear that? Besides, we just don't believe that new labor contractor . . . He says he's taking people to, to . . . what's the name-a that place, again?"

"They call it Utah, Comadre. But what is it . . . you don't trust the contractor?"

"Well, what if he's just making up the name-a that state? Have you ever heard-a that Utah, Compadre?"

"Well, no, but there's a lot of states out there, you know; and, well, it's just that this is the first time they're hiring people to go there, and that's why it sounds strange."

"Yeah, sure . . . but . . . all right, tell me this: You yourself ever heard-a that place?"

"No . . . not really; not having been there before, see? But I hear tell it's by Japan, or close to it."

Here was a chance to quit working in the fields as stoop labor . . . One of those Protestant preachermen from town had driven over to the migrant farm shacks: A man was coming, the preacher said. A man who was going to teach them the trades: carpentry, and such. This'd get them out of the hot sun.

Most of the grownups thought it a fine idea . . . an opportunity.

About two weeks later, a man showed up, just like the preacher said he would. Came in driving a pickup and the pickup, it had a trailer house in the back.

5. An expression that means "May the evil eye not touch this person or artifact."

The preacher's wife showed up, too; she was going to help; pitch in as a translator.

So, what happened? Well, those two they went into that air conditioned trailer house and stayed there that whole day. Stayed there the week, inside that trailer house, and then one day they pulled out. Took off.

Word was that the woman had left her preacher-husband for the carpenter or whatever he was . . .

It was just a few minutes before six, about the time the spinach cutters usually come in from the fields. The first thing we heard right off was the siren atop the water tower; this was followed by the siren on the firetrucks, and then the ambulance, last of all. Some of the other fieldhands filled us in:

That one of the trucks, one loaded with-a bunch of people, had been in a wreck. With a car, they said. That the truck was on fire, and burning real hot. One-a them new pickups—a van, they call it—all sealed up, and only a few made it out in time.

The witnesses—'cause they saw it—they said that that van just about blew up then and there and burned everybody in it; it-just-caught-fire, they said. And-a those who jumped out in time, well, some-a them was on fire themselves, hair and everything.

The Anglo woman—she was driving the car—well . . . she was drunk-drivin'.

They say she lives in one-a them dry counties around here, but the reason she got drunk was on account-a her husband: ran out on her, they say. Yeah.

How many dead? About sixteen, I think; that's what I hear.

"I hear Figueroa's out on parole; is that right?"

"Yeah, but he's a sick man. I hear tell that up to Huntsville—that state prison there—they'll give you shots; vaccinations, if they take a disliking to you. Them things are meant to do you in."

"Nah . . . where'd you hear stuff like that, anyway? . . . Any idea who turned him in?"

"Some Anglo guy, more'n likely. Way I figure it, he must-a seen Figueroa walking downtown with that little blond thing; the one Figueroa brought down from Wisconsin . . . And where was Figueroa gonna get himself an attorney, eh? And then, to pile bad on top-a worse, they say that little old blond thing was underage. Seventeen, and that's against the law."

"Tell you what: five bucks says he won't last a year here."

"I dunno as I'll take that bet. He's got something in him. A rare disease, they call it."

Bartolo, he was the town poet, and he'd show up about the time he figured the people'd be coming back home . . . home from Up North after all the work, around December. And he'd localize the poems, and this'd then give the people a chance to see their names in print; yeah.

And he usually would sell out everything on that first day back. Just about.

Oh, and then he'd read the poems. He'd read 'em serious like. Emotional, and solemn, too. And this is true, too: I remember he told the people—*la raza*—to read his poems aloud . . . where they could *hear* them, he said.

And then he'd say this: the human voice seeds love in the dark, or, the voice is love's own seed in the dark. Something like that; real pretty.

The old man—his grandfather—was felled by a stroke; left him paralyzed. He spent his days sitting on a big oak chair, thinking. And then one day, a grandson of his came in for a visit . . . to *platicar*, he said; chat a bit.

That old man asked the boy how old he was, and what was it—above all else, now—what was it he wanted the most, if he could have it. The youngster said he was twenty. Twenty years old, but what he wanted—really wanted, and most of all—was for time to go by, in a flash. And in this way, he said, he would then know what his life would be like, ten years from now.

The old man looked at him and then looked far, far away.

"Why, that's the stupidest thing I heard yet." He said that, the old man, and then he didn't say another word; wouldn't even look at the boy.

The grandson was stunned . . . stung, too, I'll bet. What does he mean *stupid*?

Took him ten years, but when he hit thirty, some of the answers started coming to him.

## And When We Get There

On the road, four in the morning, and that's when the truck broke down. The sudden stop brought a halt to the whining of tires on pavement and this roused some of the fieldhands. Most were still stupefied, hypnotized almost, by the steady whine and woke up with a start when the truck came to a dead stop by the side of the road.

Silence. Something must've happened; the motor had been acting up lately, heating up; that must've been it.

The driver did make one more try to rev it up again, but he did it more out of habit than from anything else.

And this would have to be home for what was left of the night, where this place was, at four in the morning. One had to wait, and then, at daylight, someone would hitch a ride to the nearest town. Wherever that was.

Awake now, a few of the fieldhands—men, women, and youngsters—talked in low tones. Most of them went back to sleep and desultory conversations opened up only to close again. The two sounds, their hushed tones and the chirping of the crickets, mixed in the open air, as the ten-tire truck rested on the shoulder of the two-laned blacktop. There was talk here and there amid the light snoring; others, awake, too, but not talking, looked dully into the night, thinking . . .

". . . good thing it stopped *here*. I had to go; bad. Good thing the truck died when it did. Shoot, I'd have had to wake up half the truck cutting through the people and thumping on the window of the cab to get them to stop.

"It's still kind-a dark, though. Wonder what time it is? It doesn't matter; I'm getting off this thing, and I've got to find me a place to *go*. A ditch somewhere; anything.

"Must have been the picante sauce that did it; it might have gone bad on me. But then I went ahead and ate all of it. Yeah, waste not, want not. . . . But I can't see where I'm walking.

"Hope the wife's okay and her having to hold on to that boy of ours. Can't be helped, though, she's got to hold on to him in this crush. . . ."

"I think we're in luck. We drew us a good driver this season; steady, goes at a good clip, and he won't stop unless absolutely necessary. Take on some gas and there we go again.

"Let's see, we took off yesterday morning about this time. Yeah, I'd say we've been on the road some twenty-four hours. That means we're closing in on Des Moines.

"But I'm kind-a stiff. Sure wish I could sit down somewhere for a bit. I'd just as soon get off, too, lie down on the road, but . . . you never know what's going to be down there. A snake or something.

"I, ah, I fell asleep standing up, but I woke up a couple of times when I felt my knees giving way. Funny what the body can do, put up with. Sleep a little, wake up, and like that.

"But it's the kids, see? They got to stand up, too. Now, they really get tired, no two ways on that.

"Poor little guys. And they can't even grab-a hold of something, like those two by fours which hold the tarp in place.

"That driver must've loaded forty of us on this trip, but I remember the time we had some wetbacks with us and there was some sixty of us then. Sixty's quite a bit, and I could hardly light a cigarette in that mob.

"You seen a dumber woman in the world? In your entire life? What was she doing? I mean, what was the thinking about? Here this diaper loaded full and *she* throws it *forward*! Damn thing came right back, slid on that tarp, and damn!

"Good thing I had them glasses on, man, otherwise I'd-a got shit in my eyes, know what I'm saying? Dumb? No, there's got to be another word for her.

"Jesus! What in hell was she thinking about . . . it's cause and effect, man. Couldn't she see what the hell was going to happen? Shit flying every which way? Jesus! And she could've waited, right? Bound to be some gas stop or something, and then she could leave that shit there. . . ."

"You should've seen that black man. 'I want fifty-four hamburgers, partner.'

"At two in the morning. I walked in that little place, and he couldn't have seen the truck 'cause I walked a good piece before I got to that hamburger joint a-his.

"I said, 'fifty-four hamburgers' and his old eyes bulged out. Two in the morning, fifty-four.

"And he said, 'Man you must eat one hell of a lot.' The thing was that the people hadn't eaten all day and the driver, he said the best thing to do was to save time, to avoid stopping, and that the best thing too was to have one person go get something to eat for everybody.

"That black man, though . . . surprised? You wouldn't believe how surprised he was. 'Fifty-four? Is that right?'

"You know what I think? I think that at two in the morning, and hungry, I think you could put a good dent into fifty-four-a them Wimpy's. . . ."

"Listen to this, and *listen* to what I'm saying: This is the very last time I'm coming up here. We get to that farmland we're going to this year, and I'm walking. Walking the hell out and heading for Minneapolis. Get me a damn job there. Anything.

"Me back to Texas? Up yours! Say what you want, but you get to earn a living here, Up North. I'll go hunt for that uncle of mine, and he'll get me something. Maybe a job in some hotel or something. Be a bellboy, yeah. Maybe I can come up with something in that hotel; get some kind-a break, see? There or at some other hotel, I don't care.

"And now about those Viking girls? They're going to have to stand in line . . ."

". . . and with that money Mr. Thompson loaned to me, I figure we can make do, eat and live on for something like two months. By then, see, we'll be drawing our pay for the sugar beet season.

"Sure hope we don't get too much in debt, though. Y'see, with these two hundred he come up with, I had to spend about half on the trip 'cause now I got to pay for the kids, too. Half price, sure, but I still got to pay for them. And when we get back, it's four hundred I got to pay back. And that's double, right? But what's the choice? So, I got to come up with four hundred. I know it's a big interest, but when you need the money, you got to get it from somewhere.

"Now, some people've come up and told me to turn him in to the law for him charging too much . . . Well, he's already got the deed to our house, see?

"Sure hope that sugar beet season's a good one, otherwise . . . otherwise, we start eating air, and that's a hell of a diet.

"And we got to come up with that four hundred. After that, we'll see how much we can come up with . . . and these little guys, they got to go to school and all. And that'll take a chunk, right?

"But, ah, but it's always chancy with us, isn't it? I mean, we *hope* everything turns out for us, but if it don't, well, if it don't, we're up against it again. And so what's new, right? About the only thing I want from God is a place for us to work in."

"Fucking fucked-up life! That's what it is . . . a crazy, worthless, fucked-up fucking life. And you know why it is we live this way? 'Cause we're assholes, that's why. Every damn one of us: fucking assholes.

"And it's a fucking assholish life, too. But no less than we deserve for being the assholes that we are, right?

"Goddammit to hell, and I'm the one leading the way. But this is it! This is the very last goddam time I'm coming up here like some fucking pack mule, standing every inch, foot, and mile in every state-a the goddam way.

"The last time! Anybody got ears 'round here? You just wait: just as soon as we get there, it's Minneapolis here I come!

"And what do you mean work at what? Hmph, don't you worry about *that*. I'll *make* something, goddammit.

"One-a these days, I'm going to take my pecker out and let the world blow on it. And this life? Well, it's my fault, my own goddam fault 'cause I'm a dumbass, and I'm the one who let 'em *do it* to me, and that's why I'm an asshole!"

". . . I know my husband's tired. Been on his feet since we started out on the trip. Saw him nodding off, I did. I'd help him if I only could, but . . . but I'm carrying these two.

"I wish we were there now; that hardwood floor be soft enough after this. And the babies . . . they'll beat you down, work you to death.

"I just hope I can help him, somehow, out in the fields this year. But with these two? And I have to be with them all the time. And nurse? Every five minutes, it seems like. But they're so little, they just tie you down. Wish they were older.

"Still, I'm going to give it a try. I'm going to try my best to help him out on the hoeing and the chopping . . . but not on the picking, though. I'll follow him, keep him company in the beet rows; that'll help, he won't get so tired then.

"I know what; I'll do it in bits and pieces, a little at a time.

"And he's so funny, they're babies and he's talking about them going off to school already. I hope to God I can help, be of help to him. And I will, God willing."

"And will you look at those stars? From out here they look like they're touching the tarp, coming down to it. And so quiet you'd swear there wasn't a soul in the truck over there. And there's hardly any traffic, not at this hour. A trailer once in a while, but that's about it. And the silence at this hour. A soft silence is what dawn is. Soft as silk.

"One thing'd be nice, though . . . what if it were always like this: a nice, soft dawn; quiet, like silk.

"But I bet we're still here at noon. By the time they get to town, find help in town, and by the time they get around to fixing the engine or whatever . . .

"But if it were always like this, dawn . . . who'd complain then? I'm going to look at the sky, the last star. And I wonder how many people in the world are looking at the same star right now? And how many others are thinking about those who are thinking about keeping an eye on that last star? And it's so quiet, too; quiet enough to imagine, to hear, maybe, that the crickets are talking to the stars."

"This damn truck! Nothing but a damn nuisance, that's what it is. A nuisance and a damned botheration. Yeah. I know what I'm going to do just as soon as we get there. I'm chucking this old heap, yeah, and these damned people can damn well look out for themselves.

"I'll drive them out to those farmlands, leave 'em there like I told 'em I would, and then to hell with it. I'm gone!

"And I didn't make no contract with them. They paid me, I brought them here, and how they're going to make it back to Texas is up to them. And besides, someone'll come by, pick 'em up, take them back to where they came from.

"And I'll say this about that sugar beet crop: the money's just about played out, it ain't the paying proposition it once was. Not like it used to be, not like in other years.

"Best thing for me to do now is to get right back to Texas, yeah, and I will just as soon as I get rid of them back there. And then I'm going to try the watermelon business, I'll truck me some. And it's close to watermelon time now, too.

"Damn! All I need now is not to be able to find someone who can work on this damn thing. And if I don't? What then? And those damned cops better not come 'round here, telling me to move on like they did in that other town; bunch-a shits.

"And who was stopping, goddammit! We was passing through, that's all. But that big-ass cop he caught up with us, and gave me one-a those 'Okay buddy, keep it moving, just follow the highway, and keep your nose straight ahead.'

"Show-off shit, grandstanding for the town folks he was. And who the hell was stopping? Goddammit!

"You just wait; just as soon as we get there, I'll deliver 'em, sort 'em out, and I'm gone! After that, why, it's every man for himself."

". . . and when we get there, I'm going to see about a bed, a soft one, for my wife. Her kidneys are giving out on her. A bed, 'cause last year . . . and what if this year's chicken coops have cement floors, just like the ones last year? *Then* what?

"And that floor was *cold*; it didn't matter how much hay we'd spread or pile around it. Nothing. Cold is cold, and that's what the floor was.

"She can't take it, and she shouldn't. And I bet that's why the rheumatism flared up on me last year. Sure as shooting' . . ."

". . . just as soon as we get there. Sure. Just as soon as we get there. But here's the plain truth of that. I'm tired of getting there. Gettin' there's just like leaving . . . Yeah. Sure.

"What's the difference? Coming and going, going and coming. Right? And the truth is . . . the truth is I'm tired of *getting there*. Hmph. Probably be better if I said, just as soon as we *don't* get there, 'cause that's closer to the truth: We *never* get there.

". . . just as soon as we get there, just as soon as we get there. . . ."

The crickets didn't stop their chirping all at once; they'd chirp here and there and now and again. Maybe getting tired of it themselves. And dawn wasn't holding back either, but it was more subtle than the crickets.

A light here and then one over there; a clump of something became a wild apple tree, for instance. Little by little as if afraid people'd find out what it—dawn—was up to.

A light would then spring up over there and some rounded objects would become people and not dark, slow-moving shapeless things.

And when the light did come, *la gente*, the people, alit from the truck and gathered 'round it and each other. And what did they talk about?

They talked about what people always talk about, about what to do, about what they'd do just as soon as they got there. Someplace.

· · ·

## This Migrant Earth

It was his mother's crying that set him off. And worse, his mother wasn't crying for herself alone, and so, he felt anger. And hatred. Ma was crying for his uncle, and his uncle's wife, Auntie. T.B., the doctors said. T.B.

Each was carted off to a different sanatorium. This meant that the other aunts and uncles took in the kids; family's family, they said. True, it had been hard on everyone, but family's family, and that's what family means.

And then his aunt died, and it wasn't long before his uncle was brought home. Too late, they said; spitting up blood, they said.

And that was the morning he saw his mother—Ma—crying. The anger he felt was real enough, but what could *he* do?

And then? His own Pa! So the anger that had not gone away renewed itself, and then hatred came with it. *This* time, this time it was Pa—*his* Pa.

"Oh, sonny, you, ah, you should've brought him in earlier, sonny. Earlier. He was sick, sonny; you couldn't see this? It's that sun, sonny, it beat him down. Beat him to the ground. You shouldn't . . . and the kids, too."

"I couldn't tell, Ma. I mean, we were all of us sopping wet, sweatin', and you don't feel the heat then, right? But . . . but you're right, Ma. It's different when the sun gets to you, isn't it? I mean, Pa'd been struck, right? Only we didn't see it, didn't know it. Beat by the sun. And it's different in his case, isn't it? I mean, I'd told him to go on in and rest, 'Go to that tree yonder,' I'd said. But he wouldn't. Didn't want to. And when he began to throw up then . . . get sick, like that. And then we saw he couldn't hold on to the hoe, and that's when the other kids 'n me dragged him over to the trees. And he didn't fight us off, either; he really did let us carry him. Didn't say a word or anything."

"That poor suffering man. And you know he didn't sleep at all last night, don't you? Could you hear him last night, when he went outside? He was in pain, bent over he was. Like he had the cramps all over his body. God rest him, I hope he comes around soon; you see, all morning I've been giving him some lemonade, trying to cool him down somehow. You see his eyes, sonny? Watery and glassy, they look. I shouldn't have let him go out to the fields with you-all . . . Nothing would've have happened then; nothing. And he's such a good man, your Pa. And he'll suffer with these cramps for three days and nights, 'cause that's how long those things last. And you-all better watch it, too. And don't you work so hard, you hear? That landowner he tries to hurry you, don't pay him no mind. You understand? He says 'hurry it up,' you-all throw down those hoes, you kids hear me? I mean it, sonny. He finds it easy work, does he? Let him try it; he doesn't have his rump and tail sticking out to the sun all day long. Every day . . . What does he know? What does he care?"

And this time Ma did mean it, but the boy was still angry, angrier if anything. And even more when he'd hear his dad—his Pa—moaning and groaning out by the chicken coops. Where they slept. His Pa couldn't stay inside the coops, though. He just couldn't. He'd choke, suffocate, he said. Now, outside, he said, outside the air would get to him, and he could breathe. And on the grass. Yes, he could stretch out there. And then when the cramps'd come and him being out on the grass there, that helped some. He could roll there, when the cramps bit into him and doubled him over.

And suddenly this thought came to him: would his dad die? Could his *Pa* die? From the sun? A moan, and the boy turned to his Pa. Pa was praying! Pa, praying to God, wanting God to help him, somehow.

He thought his dad would get better the next day. And when he didn't, the boy became angry. Angrier. And angrier still when his mother—not angry at her, no—but angrier when he'd hear both of them begging for God's help.

Begging God to help *them*? What had *they* ever done to anybody?

His Ma had gotten up then. She removed the scapularies (they were supposed to *help* him) and she washed them. She then lighted some votary candles.[6] Nothing. It was his uncle and aunt, all over again.

Alone:

"Why does Ma waste her time washing that stuff, lighting those candles there; that sure didn't help Unc or Auntie, either. Why does Ma keep *doing* that?

"And how is it *we're* the ones? Like we've been buried alive here, on top of the earth? And when it isn't TB, it's something else. The sun! Always sick, somebody is. Why *is* that?

"And there's my dad . . . no one can say he's a loafer. He works hard. He was born working. There he was, he says, five years old, barely five years old, and he was already working out there . . . with *his* Pa, planting corn.

"What's the use? Why? Here we are: feeding this *earth*, feeding *it* and feeding the sun, too. And *then* what? That sun just beats you down, to the ground . . . on your knees.

"And what can *we* do? Nothing. That's what; nothing. And then Ma and Pa pray to God, of all things. God doesn't care. He doesn't even know we're *here*.

"Shoot! I don't think there's such a thing as G . . . Hmph. What if I say it? What if Pa gets worse? *Then* what? I don't know, maybe praying's good for them, if it makes 'em feel better."

His mother could see how angry he was—raging almost. So she tried to get him to calm down; it's in God hands, she'd say. Pa'll be all right, you'll see, with God's help.

With his mother:

"God's help? What? God doesn't care, Ma. He doesn't. Not about us, He doesn't. God's help. All right, all right, tell me this, then: what kind of man is my Pa? A bad man? A good man? Mean-hearted, is he? My Pa? When's he *ever* hurt anyone? Taken advantage of anyone? Well, Ma? Tell me that."

"No, your Pa's a good man, but that's not the point, sonny. No . . ."

"No, Ma. That *is* the point. He's a good person, Pa is . . . And Unc? And Auntie? Dead, both of them. And my cousins? Why, they're going to grow up never having known their parents; yeah. Ha! God doesn't care, not about us, at any rate . . . And not about the poor. No.

"And listen to this, too, Ma: tell me this. You ready? Why is it we have to live this way? Suffer like this? Why us? Who have *we* ever harmed? Ah? And you? You're a good person, Ma. A *good* person."

---

6. Candles lit, especially by Roman Catholics, as a token of devotion in a time of crisis or to commemorate such a time. *Scapularies*: or devotional scapulars, sacaramental ornaments worn primarily by Roman Catholics, typically consisting of two rectangular pieces of fabric connected by bands.

"No, no, no, sonny. You mustn't talk that way. You mustn't say that. Don't you *ever* talk that way again, not about God, not against God. His word! Please, please, sonny. Please. I'm scared already, and then you go ahead and scare me some more with that kind of talk . . . You . . . I mean, I know that you don't . . . but it's like the Devil's got into you somehow. In your blood, somehow."

"Maybe, Ma. And why not? I'll probably be better off that way; yeah. And then maybe the anger'd go away. But it's got to where I can't think anymore, Ma. Why us, Ma? Whywhywhy? And why *you*? Pa? M'uncle? And my aunt, too, why? Why her? And their kids? Why them? Why should they be made to suffer? Tell me that. *You* tell *me*, okay?"

"Why *us*, Ma? Why should we be treated like animals, yeah. Animals . . . without hope. And here's what really kills me, Ma. You know what kind-a hope we got? Do you, Ma? *Our* hope is that *we* make it back here, to this place, next year. That's some hope, that is. And, and, and like you say, we'll rest when we die. But who wants *that*? Rest when we die . . . hmph. But that's what happened to Auntie and Unc, Ma! Does Pa feel that way? Believe that? Does he?"

"Yes. Yes, sonny, that's how it is. Death. Death will give us peace. And rest."

"No! Why us, Ma? Us!"

"You have to believe . . . I mean, it's written that . . ."

"Allrightallrightallrightallright. All right, okay, Ma? I know what you're going to say. I know exactly what you're going to say: 'The Poor Are Going to Heaven.' Right?"

The next morning started off as a cool one; cooler, anyway. And cloudy. A slight cool northern breeze; he felt it skim by, fluttering his eyelashes. He and his two kid brothers started the day's work. Hoe up, hoe down. Chopping weeds.

His mother stayed at the chicken coops. Had to, she was taking care of Pa . . . this meant the boy was in charge of the kids, and he began to urge them to work, hurry them up, like his Pa.

Most of the morning had stayed cool, and cloudy, and the sun had let up somewhat, but it wouldn't stay cool for ever. An hour later, the sun broke through the clouds, swept them away, and the heat of the day settled in to stay, to keep them company, they said.

They worked well enough, but the heat would make them slow down a bit, and because of the heat, they tired faster. But it was the sun that was working against them. So, whenever they tried to hurry, to catch up, to do more work, the heat beat them back. And, it was a clammy, sticky heat; sweat would run into their eyes, and when they rubbed, the sweat crept in their eyes, made them cry and, at the same time, this caused their eyesight to blur. It was the blurring; this was the danger sign. They knew.

To the kids:

"Listen now: you start getting dizzy, blurry-eyed, you slow it down some; take it easy, okay? And, when we get to the edge of the rows, stop. Rest a bit. It was nice this morning for a while, but it's going near to noon now, and it looks like a hot one from now on in. Be different if it was cool, cloudy. But it ain't, okay? So don't hurry none. It's the sun that's scaring all those clouds away. But that ain't the worst of it, compared to what's coming up.

"I figure we'll get through here 'round two or so, and *then* we go to that patch across the way. And that's gonna be the hard part. It's the hills, the rises, see? Up and down, just like the hoe, see? Now, it's okay on the up part, 'cause there's some breeze there; it's the coming down, see? In the gullies down there, there's not a bit-a air, let me tell you. That air just can't make it down there. You hold on to that. Okay?"

"Yeah . . . sure."

Half an hour later:

"All right, since we're gonna catch the hottest part of the day hoeing up and down on the chop by those knolls there, don't forget to drink the water. You drink as much as you can, got that? Every now and then, okay? Don't go too long without it. And listen, it doesn't matter what the grower says if he comes over. If you're thirsty, you stop work and get yourself a drink. And *do* it! Never mind the grower; you get yourself some water.

"I don't want you coming down sick, now. You start feeling bad, you stop right there and do it! You just let me know . . . and as soon as you do, we go straight home. Okay? You remember what happened to Papa? Huh? You saw him, right? He overdid it, see? That sun'll eat you right up . . . it will."

It was just like he said. They'd moved over to the new patch, and it was hot. By three o'clock, they were wetting up again, parts of the sweat coming through the clothing. And they found they had to stop more often now, just as their brother had said. They had trouble breathing, and once in a while, one of them would get blurry-eyed, and he'd stop. A bad sign, just like Pa.

At the other patch, the grower:

"How's it going, guys? Working hard? Kind of hot, eh?"

"Whew. It's just too hot to work sometimes. But we'll go on till six here."

To the older brother:

"We've been drinking water like you said, but it won't cut the kind-a thirst we got. We were talking, Older Brother, sure wish we had some good-old-well water. Fresh. Cool. Yeah. Or maybe a Coke. Yeah, a Coke'd do it . . . real cold . . ."

"What are you kids talking about? You drink something that cold and then you'll really come down with something serious. Yeah, you will. Look. Just slow it down, that's all. The grower knows how hot it is; we just go on till six, like we told him. What d'you say? Six? Can we make it?"

But they didn't make it till six o'clock. Along about four or so, the youngest kid got sick on 'em. And here he was, his youngest brother, barely nine years old and drawing adult wages. Yeah, he was. And that's why he was pushing himself, trying to do as much as the others, the older guys. His own kid brother doing that. The first thing he did was to throw up; and then he sat down, for a bit he said. But then he rolled over, flat, out.

The older brother saw this, and the youngest standing by him got scared. What's the matter with him? And now the nine year old had his eyes shut, tight.

So now the older boy had to pry his brother's eyes open, and when he did, all he could see was the white part; at this point, the youngest started to cry.

Here, the boy said, let's get him out of here. C'mon. The two of them began to carry the nine year old; and the kid, in a dead faint, got the shakes, like he was cramping up on them. The older boy began to carry his kid brother by himself, and as he did so, he started off again: whywhywhy.

"First my dad, now him, my kid brother. Why? He's nine years old! Why? Look at him: a nine year old boy sweating like he was a work animal! Why? What's my Pa ever done to anyone? In his life? And my Ma? Well? And now him, my kid brother. Why?"

And with every step he took there was that whywhywhy. On their way home now, and he's becoming angrier and angrier still. Halfway home now, and here's when he burst out crying!

But there was anger, resentment, in that cry. And then the other, smaller brother began to cry; out of fear, mostly, but what could *he* do?

And now the boy carrying his brother, and caring for all, began to swear. Swear and say things that had been stored up, welled up for a long, long time. And he said them. And they needed to be said, he felt. No time to stop and think *when* he started saying those things. They flat needed to be said, yeah.

So, he swore at God himself. Right at Him. Cursed Him up and down, up and down, like the hoe. And then he became fearful; there had been too many years of training, advice, whatever, from his parents and family. He had to be scared.

But then he looked to the ground. And the anger returned: whywhywhy. This earth, he said. And if it opens up for swearing at God just like Ma said? And if it eats me up for calling God a . . . and he looked down again, for a moment there he was, sure that the earth was ready to swallow him whole. Gobble him up, whole . . . But no. The ground was harder, if anything. Yeah, if anything, it was harder now than ever before. And the stored anger came right back.

After this, he began cursing God again. He then looked at his kid brother— the one he was carrying—he *looked* better, he thought. But was he? And then he thought on what he'd *said*. Did the little kids know, understand what he'd said? He'd yelled out some terrible things, screamed out some horrible things, yes, but did they understand what it meant?

And now they were home, but tired as he was, he wasn't about to go to sleep or rest, just yet. Instead, he stayed up late, alone; and he then found he was at peace, at rest. And that peace was like nothing he'd ever known before. He felt apart, removed from everything around him; isolated like. But at peace in that isolation. And he was no longer worried about his dad or about his kid brother or about what he'd said, either. He now looked toward the new day, that very next day. The cool morning, its fresh breeze.

He got up at first light and found his dad—his Pa—doing well. Much better, in fact, and getting stronger, too. Coming around. And the kid brother, he too was doing better. A cold shiver, a minor cramp now and again, but doing better, cured almost.

But yesterday lingered on his mind, and what he'd *said*. Himself surprised, awed, too, and shocked at times by what he'd said. He was about to tell his mother but he stopped: no. He decided against telling her almost as soon as he thought about it. He was also about to tell her that the earth didn't open up, didn't swallow people whole. She'd said this to him sometime back, and she believed it. But he didn't. She believed that the earth would open up and eat those who cursed God. But not me, he said. No.

Well? He'd done it, and here he was on top of the earth. He'd cursed God, and yet here he was, walking up and down on this migrant earth. No, that earth wasn't going to eat anybody, and not *him*. And that went for the sun, too. No sun was going to eat *him*. No sir.

Wide awake, past surprise, awe, shock, he got up; up and off to the fields as before. As always, a cool fresh-aired morning. Nothing new. With clouds, too. But it wasn't yesterday any longer. He felt, he knew now that he could do what he wanted to. That he could do anything, could undo anything. Anything on this earth he wanted to. Yeah.

He looked at the plowed land, its dirt, that earth around him, and then—suddenly—he kicked it! Hard. As hard as he could now. And he said:

"No; not yet you don't. Not yet. You won't eat me, no. You're not getting *me* yet! Someday, but not today. No. And when you *do*, ha! I won't *care*; I won't even *know* . . ."

## With This Ring

Do you remember a man called Don Laíto? Do you? You remember his wife? Doña Bonny? You do? Those weren't their real names, right? I mean, people called them that, but those weren't their names at all. Hilario was his name, and her's was Bonifacia. And I remember them, too; I'll say.

Well, one time, a long time ago, and I was just a kid then, I stayed with them at that place of theirs; and I stayed with them for three weeks, too. Enough for me to finish school that spring term, and it wasn't bad being with them; at first. Later on, well, later on, it wasn't so hot, let me tell you.

Oh, I know you used to hear all kinds of stuff about them, and about how they made bread, right? It was true, every word. A-course, people wouldn't mention the bread making to their faces, but d'you also remember how people'd say those two would rob you blind, and steal things? Well, that part was true, too. And I saw it all. First hand.

But they weren't exactly bad, see? I can't explain it, but let me say this: after I'd been there a while, about the same time school let out, I was getting kind of scared, see? Scared to ride around with them in that old car of theirs, afraid to stay one more night in that place where they lived, and afraid to eat their food, too. Know what I'd do then? I'd sneak off to some corner candy store, yeah, and stuff myself on candy. And I did this till my folks showed up—thank God they came by—till they came by to pick me up when they did.

As I said, the stay there started off pretty good: they were real nice to me that first day. Don Laíto'd laugh a lot, showing off the gold teeth, but I could make out the rotten ones, too. And his wife, Doña Bonny? Was she fat? Fatter'n fat, she was. And always hugging me until it got to be a pain after a while.

Boy, was she fat!

Well, that first meal was supper, but I was the only one who ate anything. They did without, or at least I think they did. Come to think, I don't know when they ate. I never saw them eating, anytime.

Anyway, she puts this piece of meat in the frying pan, and that meat looked kind-a green. Yeah. And smelled some, too. At first it smelled bad, really bad, but then the smell kind of wore off, okay? Maybe I got used to it; at any rate, Don Laíto he opened a window when she was cooking; had to. But I was hungry, and most of it tasted pretty good, so I ate it. Ate the whole thing, the smelly parts, too. Didn't want to hurt their feelings, see?

It seemed like everybody liked them, and that went for the Texas Anglos, too. The Texas Anglos'd give 'em canned goods and clothes, toys, too. Now, Don Laíto and Doña Bonny, they'd usually sell that stuff to us, but to show you what kind of folks they were, they'd give the stuff away, too, provided they couldn't sell it.

Sometimes you'd see them out in the fields, selling that bread they'd make, and they'd also sell thread, needles, stuff like that. Sometimes cans of this or that, sweet cactus, the kind you can eat with eggs, right? . . . and shoes, yeah. And coats, if they had them. Lots of stuff, and some of it was good. Not all, sure, but you know what I mean . . .

They'd say: "Look at this. Here's a nice pair of work shoes for you. They're a good buy, eh? A-course they're used, but so what? They're in good shape; here, look for yourself. This is quality footwear, this is. Wear like iron. You want a guarantee? Okay: these shoes here'll last you till they wear out. No kiddin'."

Like I said, I didn't want to hurt their feelings, so I wound up eating all the meat that first meal. All of it, but it must've not settled right 'cause I spent a lot of time in and out of the bathroom that first night. But that's not the best part: I hadn't seen my bedroom yet!

And you should've seen it! Well, you couldn't, there being no light, see? It was jam-packed, tight and close, on account of the smell. Full of all kinds of stuff, boxes of God-knows-what, and empty bottles; old calendars, piles of clothes. And there was just the one door to the place. Windows? Sure, but you couldn't see them or out of them, either. I mean, with all that junk piled there? And piled higher'n high. Might as well have had no windows, for all the good they did.

That first night I slept off and on, but mostly I didn't sleep; mostly I dozed off and off, instead of off and on. You see, I was worried about a hole in the ceiling. Well, I was sure—that hole was like a sky light, okay?—anyway, I was sure that a spider'd drop on me from up there. And then there was that smell again. Everywhere. Whew! Rancid like. And dark? Hmmmmmmmmmmm. Once, that first night, I must've woken up 'round midnight, but I must've gone back to sleep; like that, off and off, see? And, when I was awake, all I could see was that hole up there. Why, I even thought I could see faces up there; my imagination, sure, but what could I do?

But I was scared, whatever it was that was up there. So that did it as far as sound sleep was concerned. But I guess I must've slept some, and when I did, it was beginning to get light outside. At times, in my sleep, I guess, I thought I could see them, Don Laíto and Doña Bonny, sitting there 'round the bed, staring at me. I even reached out a couple of times, just to make sure. I don't mind telling you, I wanted to go home, I wanted Pa to come for me, now, right away. Something in my bones, in my heart. Like something was bound to happen. But don't get me wrong. It's not that they weren't nice to me, they *were*. But like people said: You got to watch 'em. Close like.

School was something else entirely. I was getting along all right; the classes were going pretty good, but it was the going home, to those two.

Say, ah, say I'd come home of an afternoon and that little house'd be quiet. Spooky. Not a sound, uh-huh. But Doña Bonny, well, she'd choose the quietest time, see? And then: She'd scare me half to death. And she'd *laugh*? Shoot. Me, jumping about ten feet down the line, and you know what she'd do then? She'd laugh harder. Yeah. She'd laugh herself silly sometimes. Oh, I'd laugh, too, at first. Later on, though, I didn't think it was so durn funny. Later on it got to where I hated it; but you think she'd stop? Ha!

And then, about a week later, been there a week, they started dropping hints. Hints about what they did when they went on into town. In the stores there. Know what? They'd steal! What? Most anything, anything that wasn't nailed down: food, liquor, clothing, cigarettes. Meat. Yeah. And then they'd go out and sell the stuff, but again—and that's why it's hard to make them out—what they couldn't sell, they'd give away. They'd even deliver the stuff to somebody's door for 'em. See?

But this next part is really awful. They told me I could come watch 'em bake pan de dulce, that Mexican bread; store-bought type. Pan de dulce. And old Don Laíto, he'd first take off his shirt, and he always looked sticky to me, somehow. And when he worked the dough, a big pile of it, he'd run up a sweat. And, while he worked the dough—while he was at it—he'd bring both his hands up to those hairy, sweaty armpits of his. Yeah, and *then* (and he didn't wipe them or anything) and then he'd bring both hands right into the dough. Aagh! But it was true, what people said about them. So he'd be watching me, see? He knew what he was doing, and there I was, rolling my eyes and I'd get kind of nauseous. He'd laugh, that's all. Yeah. And smiling right at me, the whole time. And he'd say, "*All* the bakers do that." Ugh.

I'm here to tell you I didn't take bite one out-a that pan de dulce he made. No sir. And there'd be piles of it, all over the house. Well, thank-you-kindly-but-no-thanks.

And then, one day, right after school, they wouldn't let me in the house. Know what they did instead? They put me to work in their backyard. Now, the work wasn't all that hard, but it was the *idea* of it: workworkwork. Do this, do that; *you* know. And at all hours, too. Kind of screwy. But what the heck, my Pa'd paid them! Pa paid 'em my room and board. I don't have to work, I'd say to myself. I was going to school, that was my *job*, Pa'd said. But that didn't matter to them. It just got worse when they took me to town.

Ha! Grab that five-pound sack of flour, they'd say. Is that crazy? Stealing? But I wouldn't do it, and I didn't. It wasn't right; no sir. Well, Don Laíto he'd laugh: "You ain't cut out for this; you ain't got the guts for it. Man needs balls for that," he'd say.

And it didn't get any better; I was more than ready to leave. Run away. Yeah, I considered that too. But what could I do? Pa'd left me there with those two, and he'd already paid them his hard-earned money. Yeah.

And let's not talk about the food again. The work? Oh, they kept me at it. And then . . .

Look. I'm about to tell you something, but this story stays here. You 'n me? Okay? Shake on it, now.

It started off with the Wetback. A wetback, see? No, I don't know his name. I started noticing a pattern of some kind. The Wetback he'd come calling but only when Don Laíto wasn't home. Now, how did the Wet know that? Anyway, whatever it was, say I was inside the house doing some work for them, okay? Well, Doña Bonny she'd sort of push me out and then she'd *bolt* the door. But say I was already outside, well, then she'd just lock me out. Just like that, and out I'd stay, too. Oh, yeah.

Doña Bonny once started to tell me what it was she did, what was going on between her and the Wet, but, I . . . I . . . I didn't want to hear about that. I was embarrassed, see? But she went ahead and talked about it anyway, but I sure let my mind wander when she did. I just flat didn't want to know about such things.

But the Wet, he'd pass her money, I learned. The Wet was an old looking guy. But he'd smarten up some and use after shave stuff. And when he'd leave, you could still smell whatever it was he was using.

And then, one night, I heard something . . . Don Laíto first. And then Doña Bonny. They were whispering. Talking in that quiet house.

"I know what I'm telling you, this guy's got money holed up somewhere. What relatives? What-are-you-talking-about? He ain't got any relatives. Not here anyway. Look, Laíto, it'd be easy. Like taking candy, you get me? And who's he got here? Nobody."

"You sure, Bonny?"

"That man he works for doesn't know what's going on, and you think he cares about the Wetback? Ha! That's why he hired him in the first place. So *what* if something happened to him? Who's to know? You really think that grower's gonna worry about one more wetback? About a *mojado*, a wetback?"

"Yeah, I guess you're right . . . No one knows he comes around here, right?"

"Who's to know? Look, you just leave all of this to me, Laíto."

"Like taking candy, eh?"

"You just leave that to me."

So, that very next day, right after school again, I went out . . . was sent out to the backyard. They laid out some lines on the ground and marked 'em off. A square. Dig, they said. It's going to be a root cellar, they said. Take your time, but don't dawdle, they said. Preserves, they said. Doña Bonny's gonna jar-up some stuff for us.

Hmmmmmmph. I went at it, though. Three days straight of that digging, and then they told me to stop, to hold it right there. I thought the pit was kind of shallow for a cellar.

Changed their minds, they said.

But now listen to this: and I want you to know I remember it like it was just this morning. No kidding. I really do. That old man he showed up that afternoon; he'd got himself a haircut and he smelled up the place like he always did. So, I was locked out again, right? That Wet he stayed there a long time; the sun started going down by the time Doña Bonny called me in.

For supper, she says. And then guess what? Don Laíto he was already there! Inside! Now, how did he do that?

Well, I ate my supper and they said: "Off to bed you go. Hurry, now." It was early, but into that smelly old bedroom I went.

Talk about a fright! A fright to end 'em all. I was in bed, and I thought it was a snake! In the bed, hear? Know what it was? The Wetback! His arm! I thought he was drunk then, passed out. I jumped out-a that bed and lit out through that door, and from there, to the *kitchen*.

That old couple was fit to be tied. Laugh? I thought they'd never stop. And then? Well, that's when I saw the blood. The Wet's blood! On my shirt front. Sopping red. Man-oh-man, I didn't know *what* to say, think . . . And then I saw Don Laíto's teeth, he was smiling at me . . . And I saw the gold. And the rot, too. Oh, I remember that . . .

So they waited until it got dark, and me with them. Nothing to do but to help them drag out the body. Can you imagine that? Me? A kid? Well, they made me do it, forced me, made me help them. And you know where we took him to? Hmph. To that hole I'd started, that's where!

I didn't much want to, right? But you got to know what it was that those two told me: "We'll tell the cops *you* did it."

You beat that? All I thought about was my dad's money—how he'd paid these two—and then I thought about the Anglos—how much they liked these two. And then what all my dad had wanted me to do was to finish school someday. Finish school and get myself a nice little job somewhere. Nothing like their job out in the field and in the sun all day, see? And here I was, with these two.

But, I went ahead and helped them; laid the Wet in that hole and then the three of us began to cover him up. I didn't even see his face; ever. All I wanted now was to get out of there, to finish school, have my folks come for me . . . That was all I wanted, and I wanted it now.

Two weeks to go, and those were the longest in anybody's history. But I also thought I'd forget this somehow. In time. I'd forget, I kept saying. But no; no such thing. The next day, Don Laíto was already wearing the Wet's wristwatch, right where I could see it. And out in the backyard? Well, there was this hump of dirt, see?

Finally. When my folks drove in, the first thing they said was, "You look kind-a skinny, boy. You sick or something?"

And I lied. Naw, I'm all right, I said. I just play a lot here and at school . . .

So, right before I left, Don Laíto and Doña Bonny both came up and gave me a hug, yeah. And then they made a big to-do and all. And then, in a whisper (but loud enough for Pa to hear) they said I'd better not say a word to anyone, 'cause if I did, they'd call the police. Like a game we were all playing, see? And they laughed and laughed, like I told you.

And my dad? Oh, he thought it was a great-big-huge joke, see?

So we drove off, Pa, Ma, my two kid brothers and me; back to where my Pa worked, and he and Ma talked about Don Laíto and Doña Bonny, and about how everybody liked them.

All I did was to look out the window of the pickup truck. Oh, I'd nod in agreement once in a while. Yeah. Nice folks.

Two months'd gone by, and I was well on the way to forgetting parts of what had happened back there when both of them showed up. For a visit. They'd come all the way out here, to this farmland Pa was working then. And they'd brought me a present, they said.

A ring.

And then there was nothing I could do *but* take it. Try it on, they said. Put it on, they said. Hmph. I knew whose ring it was, right away. The Wet's.

And then, just as soon as they left, I wanted to get rid of it; bury it; dump it somewhere . . .

But I didn't. I couldn't. I can't even tell you myself why I didn't, couldn't. Fear, most likely, right? The fear that someone would find it, right?

But that's not the worse of it. It goes on, see? 'Cause then, for a long time after that, I'd look up, see a stranger somewhere, and the first thing I'd do was to run the ring hand down my front pants pocket. And I'd keep it there; keep it there long after the stranger had gone, disappeared . . .

And that was a habit that stayed, lived with me for a long time. A long time. Yeah.

## Devil with Devil Damn'd

There was this full moon out, see? . . . and he'd decided by then to call out the Devil. Dare him, sort of. And it was clear; star-studded. Silvery, almost. One of those bright nights you can almost read by. You know the kind. And there was a whiff of daylight about it, it was so bright.

Now, going out at night to call the Devil, well, that was something he'd been thinking about for a long time, but he'd just decided on it that day. Naturally enough, he had a fear on, but this soon gave way to fear's sister: curiosity. And there was some doubt, too: what would happen if he went through with this idea of his? *Could* something happen if he went through with it?

Eventually, though, curiosity shoved fear aside, and that was that.

When night came and his father turned off the light in that one-room chicken coop they were staying in, he knew he was going out. That night, at midnight. The best time, he said. Now, he'd just inch over to that door there, sliding and gliding, and then right up to the door with nobody feeling or hearing or seeing him. Had to be tonight.

"Pa, aren't you going to leave the door open for us? There's no mosquitos out, right?"

"I know that, but I'm thinking about the animals, son. A rat or something. You remember what happened over to the Flores's coop that time? One-a them coons, a ring tail, it snuck up in there with them, 'member?"

"Sure, but that was a couple of seasons ago, Pa. C'mon, what do y'say? Leave it open just a bit, okay? It's still kind-a hot, Pa. Besides, what could come in here? There's a clump-a trees out there, but that's for grackles, and they sure won't come in no chicken coop, right? The rest of the people with us leave theirs open . . ."

"Yeah, and they do that 'cause *they* got screen doors aside from the wooden ones, see? We don't."

"Not all-a them, they don't. Go on, Pa . . . look at that moon! Isn't it pretty? Peaceful looking, ain't it?"

"All right, all right."

"What's the boy going on about now?"

"Nothing; he's all right. He just wants the door open, that's all. I'll go ahead and open it a crack."

"You going to leave the door open?"

"Just a tad, okay? Don't *you* start worrying; nothing's going to happen."

The Devil—the very idea of a *Devil*—this had fascinated him for a long time; he couldn't even remember when he didn't think about the Devil.

And recently, it had been on his mind even more, and way before Aunt Pana's Christmas *pastorelas*, those Christmas plays with Baby Jesus, the Devil, and the shepherds, and everything. Before that, yeah. And before something else, too: before he'd discovered Old Man Lightning's—Don Rayos', remember him?—well, before he discovered that costume of his. The Devil's own with that big, black cape, and the smoky tin mask he wore, and the horns, too. The boy had stumbled across the whole outfit under Don Rayos's house a time he was playing there. He saw that mask, the cape; everything. You see, he'd dropped a shooter, an aggie or a taw,[7] and it'd rolled under the house, and there they were for all the world to see: the horns, that shiny black cape and mask . . . the whole shebang, yeah! And then he'd dragged it out from under the house. Full-a dust it was; him, too. The boy then shook off the dust, and then he went ahead and put on the mask; yeah.

"The way I look at it, Compadre, Man just wasn't meant to fool around with the Devil or with the Devil's things, either. I've even heard of men who've called out to him, oh yes. I can tell you that right now. A-course, some go out in a group, see?

"Try to lessen the fear that way, but the Devil's not about to show his face then. No sir. Know what he does? He waits. Yeah, sure; waits until he gets 'em one-by-one, all alone. And *that's* how the Devil works it. And you know what? He doesn't always *look* like the Devil, that's right.

"I know what I'm talking about here. No, sir, a man can't afford to get mixed up with the Devil no way . . . And here's something else, too: say you do meet up with him. Ha! He's got your soul right then and there, ah-hah. And then comes the shock and fright, and people die-a that. No, not all of 'em, but some. First off, they get kind-a sad-like, and then they stop talking all together, yessir. Why, it's like their very soul has left them . . . flown away, you might say."

The boy, lying on the floor as he was, could make out the clock easily enough; he was just waiting for his chance. The two kid brothers were the first to go to sleep, and all he was waiting for was his folks to drop off.

On either side of him stood the chicken coops where the other fieldhands slept, entire families, just like his. And he could hear the snoring coming across the way, but it was the time which dragged by. For that clock to move from eleven to 11:55 was like a year to him. And as he lay there—with that clock ticking away—he'd change his mind, but then he'd look outside again, and it was nice, quiet, and clear. The moon saw to that.

---

7. I.e., a marble.

And he thought:

"Now. Say I leave here at ten to midnight, that'll give me time enough to reach that clump-a trees there, the grove. Be right in the middle of 'em. Mmmmmmmmm; it's a good thing there's no snakes hereabouts . . . I'd sure hate to run into *them* out there in the middle-a that grove there . . . And in those *weeds*, too.

"Here's what I'll do: I'll call him at twelve on the dot. Right at twelve. But I'd better take that clock with me just to make sure-a the time, 'cause you got to call him at the right time. If you don't, he won't show up, and that's it. Twelve midnight, and it's got to be at twelve sharp, right on the nose, or there's nothing doing . . . not eleven fifty-nine, no sir. Twelve. On the button."

First thing he did was to get his hands on that table clock. Slow and easy now. And he was outside. Didn't make a sound. From this, he placed the clock in his pants pocket, and he could hear the ticking. Loud. He started walking away from the chicken coops as carefully and as quietly as he could. And then, all of a sudden, he stopped. Just checking. It was nothing, but he thought someone was watching him all the same. Yeah, but who?

And on he went, and just as quiet, too. Past the outdoor privies and beyond them now. Looking back, he could see he was a good distance away from the chicken coops where his folks slept. He figured he was far enough away now, and talking softly to himself, he said:

"And how does it go, now? Right. I'll call and, but what if he appears there, sudden-like? No; no, I don't think he'd do *that*, just like that.

"But what if he does? Well, so what? What can he do to me? I'm not dead yet . . . So, just as long as I'm alive, there's nothing he *can* do. It's just that . . . I just want to know, for myself. That's all. *Is* there a Devil or not?

"Okay. Say there's *no* Devil. *And* if there's no Devil, maybe there's no G . . . uh-huh . . . better not say *that*. I mean, I could be punished, right? Let me put it this way: if there's no Devil, then maybe there's no punishment either. No, that can't be right 'cause you gotta have punishment and suffering.

"Okay, now how am I going to call him? Do I just say *Devil*, is that it? How about if I call him Old Hornie? Or Ketch . . . *Jack* Ketch. Old Nick. Clootie. Lucifer. Satan . . . Well, whatever comes out first, that's what I'll use."

And he arrived at the grove and walked deeper into it. And then he stood there. The words wouldn't come out, see? There was fear there, but then, just-like-that, accidental-like, the words popped out. But nothing happened. And he wasn't whispering either. So, he called him again, and he used all those names: Ned. Nick. Clootie. Old Hornie.

Nothing. At all. Why, everything looked the same, *was* the same. Just like it'd been a few minutes before. Peace and quiet.

But he wasn't through yet. Next thing to do was to swear, yeah, cuss him out. And then he did this, too. Nothing happened. So up he came with all the cuss words he knew, and he'd even use different tones of voice, too. Nothing.

He then cursed the Devil's mother, yeah, that'll bring him out. Cussed her, *then* cussed *him*. Nothing. Not-a-thing, see?

And nothing had changed, no one had appeared. Everything was the same. Just like an hour ago; thirty minutes ago; *now*.

He made for home, to bed.

What a disappointment; and after all-a that, too. Ah, but now he felt like a man: tough, mean. Brave, too; yeah, he did. The wind went right through the leaves, shaking them, making them dance some, sounding off some. And he could feel the faint breeze now.

No such thing as the Devil. Nope. Nothing. The wind was the only thing with him here, and he headed for the coops. . . .

"Okay, if there's no Devil, does that mean that there's no . . . but what am I saying? I better watch that kind-a talk. I could be punished for it. Yeah, I could. But one thing's sure: there's no such thing as a Devil anywhere.

"Maybe, and I mean just *maybe*, like in it-could-be-just-perhaps-maybe . . . Nah! If there was a Devil, he would've come out by now. Sure he would've; it's just that there's no such thing, that's all.

"I mean, like tonight, right? That was the perfect time. Right? So what happened? Nothing. Midnight. Me. All alone. Calling him. Hah! There's no Devil. No sir."

A couple of times there he thought he heard his name being called out. But he wouldn't turn around. Wouldn't look back. What for? Why should I, he'd say. There's nothing there—and it wasn't 'cause he was afraid, either. It was nothing. Nobody.

And then he was there, home; the chicken coops. Quietly, he got down on the floor, and the Devil wasn't there either. Lying on the floor, eyes open, and then came a slight shiver, and he felt queasy-like. Must've been the strain of it all, don't you see? Something he ate.

But he didn't even try to go to sleep just yet. He wanted to think some. Needed to.

"There's no Devil. Nothing. There's no Devil and no nothing to go with it. No sir."

His voice—*that*—that was the only thing out there, in that clump a-trees. Nothing else. And then he thought about how right the people had been! Sure. They were right when they said you just didn't go around playing with the Devil—the devil.

Clear as anything. Those people who called out to him; to the devil, those who sought him out and went crazy. Well, they went crazy not because he appeared, but because there's no such thing. No devil. None.

They went crazy because the devil didn't appear. To them. To anybody. That's why, and that's why he didn't appear, he *couldn't*. Hmph.

Hardest thing to remember, to know, even, is that moment when one falls asleep. Can't be done. The boy looked out into the night; clear, bright. And there was the moon again. Beaming. Happy about something; skipping, sliding, and gliding right through the clouds it was.

## The Hurt

It's the hurt; that's why I hit him back and just as hard as I could, too. But what am I going to do now?

Maybe—just maybe, now—maybe I wasn't really kicked out of school. I mean, maybe it didn't happen; maybe I misheard the principal. Right?

Naw, they kicked me out, all right. I'll say they did. But . . . but what am I going to *do*? About home?

I think I know when it all started. I was shamed, and ashamed, too, but mostly, mostly I was just angry. Both, together, at the same time . . . Oh me, I sure don't want to go home now. And what am I going to say to Ma, anyway? And then? Well, Pa'll come in from the cropfield, and I'll catch it from both of them then. And a good belting into the bargain. But—well, you just get fighting mad, and there's the shame, and anger, too. It's the hurt.

Durn! Happens every time we come Up North to these schools. Yeah. They just stare at you. Up and down. And then they laugh; and right to your face, too. And that school teacher . . . In she comes with that Eskimo Pie stick-a hers. Looking for lice and cooties, she says.

Shoot! Anyone'd be embarrassed at that. Right there: in front of everybody else. But that's not all of it, 'cause then they turn their noses up at you, and that brings on the anger. It's bound to; can't they see that?

Best thing for me to do is to stay out in the fields; out-a everybody's way. Out by that grove there, the one near the chicken coops. Yeah, the fields, that's where. But anywhere'll do me, really. Anywhere; free.

"Look alive, son; we're almost there."

"And you'll come in with me this time, Pa? To register?"

"Nah. You don't need me. Really. I mean, you speaking English and all, right? See that door, that must be the main entrance. Now, if you don't know where to go exactly, just ask somebody, anybody. Right. Don't hang back now; you go in and ask somebody. Nothing to it, boy; and there's nothing to be afraid of, either."

"Yeah . . . but why won't you . . . why don't you come in with me, Pa?"

"You don't need *me*, son. Hey? You're not scared, are you? Good . . . Go on; that's got to be the main door. See it? Look, there's someone coming up there now—a man, see? Now: best behavior, okay?"

"Sure, Pa . . . But can't you . . . can't you help me out, Pa? Register with me?"

"Oh, you'll do right well without me; I'd only be in your way. Go on—nothing to be afraid of. Right?"

It's the same thing every time. First they take you to see the nurse, and right off she starts checking you for lice. Yeah, and it's all those old ladies' fault too. A-course it is. Come a Sunday, and there they go, out in the sun, right by the chicken coops where everybody'll see them. And what do they *do*? They start combing their hair, checking for lice. Out in the open! But what about the Anglo men and their wives, huh? What do they do? Well, come-a Sunday they drive out there where we're staying. They drive up and they point their fingers at us, at those old ladies.

Pa's right; Pa says that when those old ladies start delousing themselves, they begin to look like monkeys out in a zoo somewheres. But what the heck, they give us chicken coops to live in, and who wants to live with lice, anyway?

"Here, Ma, hold it, let me tell you this: I was barely in the classroom, okay? Just sat down and then I was sent back out again: Go see the nurse, they said. And there *she* was, all in white.

"First off, she made me take my clothes off; all of them. Stripped naked I was, and she looked at my behind. Yeah. But it was my head she was really interested in. Sure she was; but I was all cleaned up, right? You think that mattered to that nurse? Hmph! Know what she did? I'll tell you: she brought herself one-a those jars full a-vaseline, it looked like. And it stunk! Worm killer it smelled like . . . can you still smell it on me, Ma?

"Well, she rubbed it in—clean head or not. And it itched, too. Then she picked up a pencil, yeah she did. And she began parting my hair with it. Hmph. And then? Get dressed, she says, and I do, and I go right back to class.

"But I felt bad; ashamed, Ma. Of myself, see? And, and . . . And they made me *strip*, Ma. Shirt, pants, and my shorts, too. Yes'm, right in front of that old nurse."

And now? What am I going to tell my folks when I get home? That I was kicked out? Expelled? No . . . But . . . but it wasn't all my fault. Not all of it; not entirely. That Anglo boy, he looked like trouble, right off. He just stared, but no laughter out-a him; staring, looking right at me, and then I was sent off—to sit by myself, yeah. Away from everybody else . . . and that Anglo boy? He kept his eyes on me; shot me the finger, too. Yes, he did.

But the hurt was something else; being set apart like that. Why, everybody had a clear shot at me. And they stared, and then *I* felt like a monkey in the zoo. A-course I was angry, but I was embarrassed; embarrassed by being set apart, away from the rest of the class.

And then, when it came to my turn to read, I didn't. Or I couldn't. It felt funny, though: I could *hear* myself all right, but the words, the words weren't coming out at all. Strange . . .

Hmmm. This is a nice cemetery . . . nothing scary about this one; not a bit. It's pretty. Go right across it every day, to and from school. Green. And nice. The grass is leveled off, too, why, parts of it are paved! Looks like a golf course or something . . .

But I won't be playing here today; no rolling down that little hill there; no somersaulting, either; and, I won't have a chance to lie down on the grass today; not for long, anyway. Lie down, listen, try to count the different sounds I hear . . . counted up to twenty-six of them the last time I was here . . .

Now, if I hurry, I might just be able to run into Doña Cuquita, maybe go on to the City Dump with her. Yeah, that's what I'll do. She usually starts out about this time when the sun's cooling down some.

"Careful, kids . . . watch your step now; some of this stuff's on fire, even if you can't see it. And you can't tell just by looking. Careful, I said. Might be some coals smouldering down there. I know what I'm talking about: I got me a good burn once, and I got the scar to prove it . . . Here, kids. Here, look, each one of you grabs a long pole and you poke it about, okay? But you got to poke hard. There.

"Now, that old dump Inspector shows up, you just tell him you came to *leave* stuff. He's all right—most of the time—he mostly looks for those little books, the dirty kind. Never mind him now.

"Oh, and keep an eye out when we're up on that trestle there . . . Man was run over last year some time. Got caught right in the middle of the trestle there, and he tried to outrun the train."

"Do all you kids have your folks' permission to be out here with me? Do you? Now, don't be eating anything less you wash it first, okay?"

Okay. Let's say Doña Cuquita shows up, then what? If I do go with her—and without permission—that's a belting, for sure. But what am I going to tell 'em at home about school? Well, maybe they really didn't go through with it, maybe they didn't kick me out.

What am I saying? *A-course they did.*

But what *can* I say? That it wasn't *all* my fault? And that I just had to go real bad, and then when I did, that same Anglo boy was right there, right by that urinal—that same Anglo boy, giving me looks and stares, and a hard time, too. Yeah.

"Hey, Mex . . . I don't like Mexicans because they steal. You hear me?"
"Yes."
"I don't like Mexicans. You hear, Mex?"
"Yes."
"I don't like Mexicans because they steal. You hear me?"
"Yes."

I remember the first fight I had in school. Back home. And I was scared, too, and it had all been arranged, planned out ahead of time by the big guys. Why, some-a those second graders were big enough to grow a mustache, yeah, they were. And the fight was all their doing, too. They kept shoving me and that other boy together, against each other. Yeah. I guess we fought more out-a fear than anything else. The fight started just a block away from school; those older boys started pushing Ramiro and me, and like I said, we fought each other, too. Real hard. Lucky for us two neighbor ladies came out and separated the both of us. And *then*, after the fight, I thought I was pretty tough. Humph . . . but I was plenty scared right up to the time of the fight, though.

But it was different this time around. No warning; nothing. That boy just hauled off and whacked me one behind the ear. Hard, too. Things sounded kind-a hollow for me, like at the beach, when you bring a shell up to your ear or something . . . I don't even remember hitting that guy, but I must've 'cause someone went for the principal: There's a fight in the boys' room!

It wasn't all my fault, so . . . maybe I didn't get kicked out, after all.

*Fat chance-a that.* I was kicked out. Period.

And how'd that principal hear about the fight, anyhow? I mean, who went and told him? That janitor . . . eyes popping out-a his head. *He* was scared, all right, and him holding that broom ready to whack me one . . . sure he was. Ready to give me what-for, he was; ready and willing, he was.

"The Mexican kid just got in a fight and beat up a couple of our boys . . . No, not bad . . . but what do I do?"

. . . . . . . . . . . . . . . . . . . . . . . . . . . . . . . . . . . . . . . . . . .

"No, I guess not, they could care less if I expel him . . . They need him in the fields."

. . . . . . . . . . . . . . . . . . . . . . . . . . . . . . . . . . . . . . . . . . .

"Well, I just hope our boys don't make too much about it to their parents. I guess I'll just throw him out."

. . . . . . . . . . . . . . . . . . . . . . . . . . . . . . . . . . . . . . . . . . .

"Yeah, I guess you're right."

. . . . . . . . . . . . . . . . . . . . . . . . . . . . . . . . . . . . . . . . . . .

"I know you warned me. I know . . . I know . . . but . . . yeah, okay."

And where did that janitor think I was going to run off to, anyway? Everyone at home wants me, *expects* me to stay in school . . . and besides, that janitor, he kept waving that big old broom at me. He just stood there, watching, ready for anything. . . . And then, it was over, kicked out, they said. Leave, they said. Go on home.

Home!

This part of the cemetery puts me halfway to home. It's sure a pretty one, though. Nothing like the one back home, in Texas. That one'll really scare you. I just can't get used to it. And you know what really scares me about the cemetery at home? It's the funerals, or after the funerals, anyway. I look up and there's an old archway with writing on it. *Forget Me Not*, it says. Yeah. It's like I can hear the dead. Talking. Saying those words to me. And the words stay—stick—yeah. Why, even I don't look up at the archway, the words just come right at me. It doesn't matter, you don't even have to look at them, the words. They're there.

But not here; this is a nice cemetery—grass, trees, real nice. And I guess that's why the people here don't cry much at funerals. Too pretty to cry in. And I can play in it, too. Be great if we could fish here, though; be easy, too. But I, we, can't fish here; need a license for that, and besides, they wouldn't sell fishing licenses to *us*; we're from out of state.

And now, I won't be able to go to school anymore. And what is it I'm going to tell them at home? I can't remember how many times I've been told that the teachers are our second parents . . . And *now* what?

And, and, and when we all get back to Texas? What then? Why, everybody'll know. Sure they will. Ma and Pa're going to get angry—I know they are. I'll get that belting sure, now. Maybe more than just the belt, too.

And to top it off, my uncle—and my grandfather, too—they're *all* going to find out. If I'm not careful, why, I could maybe land in one-a those state schools they're always talking about. They'll sure straighten you out there, in those places. Quick. Take the starch right out-a one, there. Go in like a lion, come out like a lamb. Yessir.

But . . . it's possible, kind-a; maybe they *didn't* kick me out. Maybe, I left too soon . . .

Who'm I kidding? Still, it's just poss . . . forget it: I'm *out*.

Now, I could make out like I went to school every day. Sure. But instead, I'd stay here, in the cemetery. Yeah. I could do that. But how about later on? What *then*? Well, I *could* say that I lost my report card. Sure, that's it.

But that's the least of it; what really hurts is that I won't ever get to be a telephone operator, like my Dad wants, 'cause that's what Pa wants me to study for . . . but . . . but, ah, you got to finish school for that job.

"Hon! *Vieja*—woman—call the boy out . . . Compadre, ask the boy here what it is he wants to do—what he wants to be—when he grows up and is out of school."

"Well, what's it going to be, godson?"

"I'm not sure."

"Sure you are! Go on! Tell him! Don't hang back, the man's your god-father, after all."

"What's it going to be, *ahijado*?[8] What do *you* want to do?"

"I want to be a telephone operator."

"Do you, now?"

"Yes, he does. Compadre, he has his heart set on it; he really does. Every time we talk about this, he says he wants to be a telephone operator. And I imagine the pay's pretty good, don't you? And just the other day, I told my Boss himself about this, but all he did was laugh. Hmph. Probably figures my boy's not up to it—well, he's wrong there, I'll tell you; he doesn't know my boy like I do, and that's a fact. The boy's smart as a whip. And that's why he goes to school. I don't ask God for much, but this I do, I want my boy to finish school; I want him to make something out of himself. Know what I mean, Compadre? Make something out of himself: a telephone operator."

That was some movie, that was. And the telephone operator, why, he had the most important job of all . . . I think that's why Pa's so set on it once I finish school . . .

But, you know . . . it's still possible; maybe I wasn't expelled just like that. I mean, what if it didn't happen?

What am I going to *do*? Well, one thing's sure: no one'll have to ask me what it is I'm going to do when I grow up now.

But, you know, it just could be. An outside chance. NO! What am I say-ing? I was there. A fact's a fact, and the fact is I was booted out. But the hurt!

The hurt, the shame; both, together. Best thing for me is to stay put right here. But then, what about Ma? She'll be scared, stiff; scared just like when there's lightning and thunder and all. She gets scared to death . . .

No, no, no . . . I've just *got* to tell them. Got to. And now, when Godfather comes calling, I, I, I guess I'm going to have to hide off somewheres. But then I won't get a change to read for him any more, the way Pa always likes me to. I know what I'll do on Godfather's next visit: I'll run and hide behind the cedar chest; maybe under the bed, even. And *that'll* avoid embarrass-ment all around . . . Yeah.

But won't it be something? If they didn't really kick me out? I mean, maybe it's all been a big mistake. Won't it be something, though? I mean, who can tell? Right? Maybe I haven't been kicked out, after all.

Hmph . . . *A-course I have* . . .

---

8. Godson.

# First Fruits

Midspring meant first communion,[9] and that was the priest's, the Father's, doing, his schedule.

First communion day, mine; can anyone not remember their first?

I remember what we all wore (white) and what I had for late breakfast: hot chocolate and pan de dulce, that sweet bakery-bought bread. This last was also a rite, for after communion.

And I also remember the tailor shop, and what I saw there. The tailor shop stood to the side and across the street from the parish church, and I saw what I saw because I got to church early. Earlier than anybody else, in fact. And I got there early because I couldn't sleep; and I couldn't sleep because of the sins; I mean because of the exact number of sins I had to confess to. All of us had to remember each and every sin and then to keep track of how many we'd committed and what kind, too, so we'd come up with the right total.

And I'll tell you why else I couldn't sleep. There was a scary picture Ma'd placed on the wall at the foot of the bed. And too, the room had been re-papered, and I could see ghosts in that new pattern. And then that picture Ma'd hung up was a picture of Hell; the real thing; yeah. So there I was: first communion and how many sins was it? And Hell. And the ghosts on the wall paper. Everything jumbled up together.

"Now, boys and girls, you must please stop that squirming. Quiet now. Ready? One: you've all got your prayers down, and this is good. Two: you know which sins are mortal and which are not. Fine. Three: you know what a sacrilege is. Right? Four: we're all of us God's own children. Yes. And, five: although we're in God's grace, we can always lose it, and when this happens, the Devil will then claim us as his children—pay attention. And we don't want this."

"Next. When it's your turn at the confessional, you must account for your sins—mortal or venial—and you must account for all of them. And you know why? Well, because if you don't confess all . . . if you leave one out and then go ahead and take *la hostia*, the host, what will that be? A sacri-lege. Right! And when one commits a sacrilege, what happens? Well? Right, we're Hell bound. And don't forget: God knows everything. Everything we do, everything we think.

"You can lie to me, the Sister, and get away with it; why, you can even lie to Father, but you can't lie to God. God knows everything. Everything . . .

"And another thing: you have to be pure in spirit and cleansed of sins; if not, then there's no communion for you. You shouldn't go up to the railing and take communion. That's a sacrilege.

---

9. First Communion, or First Holy Communion, is the colloquial name for a Roman Catholic cer-emony (also practiced, somewhat differently, in some Protestant Churches) undergone when the practitioners are eight or nine years old. It is the first time that the practitioners receive or cele-brate the Eucharist, a Christian sacrament com-memorating the Last Supper, Jesus' final meal before his crucifixion. To be purified before this ritual, the practitioner must confess to a priest his or her sins, which can be mortal (major, knowing, willful) or venial (slight). Having con-fessed, the practioner then receives sacramental bread, sometimes called the Lamb, the Host, or Communion Bread.

"And one thing more: You must start thinking on your sins now. Each-and-every-one-of-them. How would you feel if you took communion and then remembered you had left one out, forgot one of them?

"Fine, fine . . . Let's run over the sins again. And we'll start with the sins of the flesh, the things we do when we touch ourselves, our bodies. Who's going to go first?"

I remember that Sister always started off on sins of the flesh, but the truth is I didn't understand what she really meant then. And besides that, we practiced the part about the sins of the flesh all the time. For me, Hell was the scary part. I'd stumbled into a brazier a short while back and got a good burn from that, so I knew all about Hell. And I also knew what Sister meant when she talked about Hell Everlasting. But I didn't know the other part: the part she liked, the sins of the flesh part."

So there I was, the night before my first communion, counting all my sins: each-and-every-one-of-them. But that wasn't the hard part. The hard part was coming up with an actual number of them.

Dawn rolled by and I finally settled on something: I reckoned some one hundred and fifty sins, but to be on the safe side, I was going to claim two hundred; that would do it.

"The way I figure it, if I go ahead and confess to the one fifty, and then say I've left out some, by mistake, then I'll be in the wrong. Same as a sin. But if I say two hundred, even if I ain't done that many, it's more than one fifty, and that's not a sacrilege, right? Okay, so here's what I'm going to say: Bless me, Father, for I have sinned. 'How many sins?' 'Two hundred, Father. All kinds.' 'Anything else, the Commandments?' 'Them? Yes, Father. All ten, Father.'

"Sure, I'll just say all ten and in that way, I'm safe from sacrilege again. It's the best way, the more you claim, the cleaner you are. Yeah."

And I remember I got up early like I said, and earlier than usual, even for me. And Ma sure wasn't ready for that. Godfather was going to be waiting for me over at the church, and I sure didn't want to be late, not for a second.

"C'mon, Ma, hurry it up . . . you got to iron my pants, okay? I . . . I thought you did that last night."

"No, I couldn't see a thing last night. There's something wrong with my eyes, they're getting weaker. I decided to do the ironing in the morning . . . but what's your hurry? You've got plenty of time. Confession's not till eight o'clock, isn't it? And what's it now? Six? Besides, your godfather won't get there until eight o'clock, that's the hour."

"Yeah, yeah, I know, but I couldn't sleep at all, Ma. Will you please hurry it up? I want to get going."

"All right, but tell me this: what're you going to be doing as early as all this?"

"It's just that I'm afraid I'm going to forget some sins, and I got to say 'em all to Father; I think it'll be easier if I'm inside the church. It's a help, see?"

"I'll be through here in a minute. You know, sonny, once my eyes start to clear up, I can go like sixty here."

So I headed for church, counting the sins one by one, keeping the sacraments in order, and like that. But there was hardly anybody around; the day was beginning to clear up and light was coming first here and then over there, but where was everybody? Maybe I *was* early, maybe Father slept late; maybe he was busy.

I then walked around just to be doing something, and I went by the side of the church and across the street to the tailor shop. Well! That's when I heard what sounded like people laughing, having a good time. But then I also heard some groans coming out of that tailor shop. Sounded like a neighborhood dog or something. But there went the voices again. And since I was sure it was voices, I peeked in, just for a second or so.

Two people, and I could see them clearly, but they hadn't seen me just yet. A man and a woman, and they weren't wearing clothes; and I saw them holding on to each other and rolling around some sheets and dresses, lying on the floor. I couldn't keep my eyes off them, and I remember I didn't move away.

And then they saw me! They began to go after their clothes, yelling at me, telling me to get away from there. The woman must've been sick though; her hair was all mussed, and she didn't look too good. I started to run right then. To church I ran, but I kept thinking of them back there, and then that was all I could think of. And then it hit me: why, those must be the sins of the flesh Sister was always going on about, when we touch ourselves. Yeah.

And then it was back to thinking about those two back there; I could see them again even when I had my eyes closed. There they were, rolling on the floor. Naked.

The rest of the kids began to show up, gather around the church, and it was then I planned to tell them what I'd seen. Well, I planned to, but I didn't. I then decided to tell them later, after communion and everything. So, I didn't say a thing to 'em then. Or to anyone else, right? But I felt a kind of guilt. Guilty, like I'd done the sin of the flesh myself.

Too late to do anything about it now. And I sure couldn't tell the others, right? And I didn't. I didn't because if I had, why, they'd become sinners too, wouldn't they? Just like me. Yeah. (So . . . . . . . . . Got it! I won't take communion, I won't take the host. And I won't go to confession either. But that's not right! I know about the sins of the flesh. I *know*, see? And I know what they mean. What Sister was going on and on about.)

But what if I don't go up front for communion? Well, both Pa and Ma'll know and everybody'll know. And Godfather, too. And I sure as shooting ain't going to leave Godfather at church, mouth hanging open, egg on his face like that. One choice and that's it: I got to confess what I just saw.

(And you know what? I got an itch to go back outside, to see those two again. To see if they were still there. On the floor.)

Hold it! I got the one choice: I got to go straight to confession. But what if I lie, just a little bit? Or, what if I forget about what I saw, between now and confession time? Yeah, that's it. Better still, maybe I didn't see anything after all. Yeah. Sure. What I mean is, what if I didn't see anything? Well?

But there was no choice, was there? I *had* to go to confession, and I did. And I walked into that booth, I told Father I'd committed two hundred sins, all kinds, too. I just left one out. I kept that one aside. I ate it. And then? And then I walked out of that confessional, and there was nothing to it.

Walked home with Godfather, and it was just like everything had changed somehow. But it looked smaller somehow. Less important, unimportant, it seemed to me.

And when we got home, there was Pa. And Ma, too. And I could see them on the floor. I really could. And then I looked around; all the grownups were naked. And they were all on the floor. And they were making all kinds of faces, too. Why, I could even hear them laughing. Oh, and then I saw Sister, too. Yeah. And she was on the floor . . .

But who could drink hot chocolate now? Or, eat the pan de dulce? But I had to, and I did, in a gulp, and then I rushed outside. Running hard. Away from the house, away from there, and away from them. I was choking and out of breath.

"Hey, what's wrong with that boy anyway? Running off like that? Where did he leave the manners we taught him, eh?"

"Aw, don't pay him no mind, Compadre, and don't worry about me. I know kids; I got some of my own, remember? I'll tell you something about kids nowadays: play is all they think about. All day long. But let him be: it's his first big day: Communion."

"Yeah, I guess you're right, Compadre. And it isn't as if I'm against him playing and all, but . . . well, you know how it is: they got to have some manners. Respectful, right? And they got to respect their elders 'cause we know better. And manners and respect to you as his godfather."

"No argument there about respect, Compadre. But you know how kids are."

I stopped running when I got to the *monte*, the boonies. And I was away from everybody, finally. Alone. By myself. Got me some rocks for target practice and I started on the cactus, and then I went after some of the bottles lying around. Broke them, too. I then shinnied up a pin oak, and stayed there a while till I got bored, and I'd climbed all the way to the top, too.

And then I thought back on the tailor shop. Yeah. And I liked it. Liked thinking about it. Oh, yeah. Heckfire, I even forgot I'd lied to Father at confession. Ha! And then? Then I remembered that traveling preacher, missionary I guess, and what he'd said about the grace of God and all.

And then, all of a sudden, I wanted to learn things. And I wanted to learn, period. More and more. A lot. And as I thought on this, it hit me that maybe everything was the same. Even after you did something, saw something. Everything. The same.

## The Burden of the World

The fleas, that's what made him move around, squirm. Under a house is where he was; and he'd been there for hours it seemed. And he was in hiding. Early that morning, he'd been on his way to school when, out of nowhere, the thought struck him: skip. Skip school today. Now.

And he had. That old schoolteacher would take it out of his hide, anyway; he hadn't learned the day's word list. From this to going under the house was but a short, easy step.

But there was also a need, an urge to hide. Be off by himself. Where? Anywhere. And for how long? It didn't matter. So, it was settled: he'd go off and hide somewhere, and hang the time.

It was the dark that he liked, enjoyed it, in fact. But those fleas! Bound to be spiders down here, too, but he went ahead and crawled under the house, and there he stayed: alone, comfortably alone and in secret.

Under the house. What daylight there was came off on a straight line, about a foot from the ground. Face down, now, his shoulders rubbing against the under boards, and these gave him security somehow. But then the fleas got to him, they forced him to move about, crawl about on his stomach; it was that tight down there.

"If it weren't for the fleas. It's nice down here, and I bet kids who play hookey regularly do this all the time; hide out under some old house somewhere. No, not bad at all, and I can think here. I mean, who's going to bother me down here?"

Deep in thought, the fleas forgotten, and forgotten too that he was under a house. It was dark, safe, and he could think here; alone. Dark. The dark was necessary, to think in; and that's what he needed to do.

The first thought was that of his Pa telling him stories of witches and things. About how his Pa said he could charm owls off the trees; and he could too, with special prayers and with the seven knots to go with them. *That* would do it.

"Well, at that time we had some land of our own, and we had the watering rights to go with it. So, coming home and darkening some, it wasn't uncommon to see electric sparks, but more than sparks, they were round-shaped balls of fire. And these little balls would bounce up and down, around the telephone wires. From the city of Morelos down in Michoacan;[1] that's where their home base was, that's where the witches lived. And one time, I almost got me one. Almost knocked one of those witches down.

"Old Don Remigio it was who taught me the prayers and the way to tie those special knots, too. First a prayer, then a knot, see? But you got to know what you're doing. Well, that time I almost got me one, I'd gone through all seven prayers and was working on the seventh knot. But you know what? I couldn't tie it. No different from the other knots, but I just couldn't tie it. I couldn't come up with it, but I was that close, see? And so close that the witch fell off the wire, landed at my feet, but it got up sudden-like. I just didn't have the last knot, see?"

". . . And that kid was so little, so young, you know they don't understand so well at that age. And he couldn't hold off any longer; he was thirsty, and the water tank was there, at the edge of the row. Hmph. But I hear the guy's going scot free; he's got a lot of pull 'round here. But listen to this: how would it have been had we been the ones who shot one of their kids? What do you think would've have happened *then*? One of the things I heard was that the little kid's father had gone after a rifle, to even it up, see? But nothing came of it. Never could run into the guy, he said."

1. State in south-central Mexico.

". . . That old lady? Sure, as soon as she'd set foot in the church, she'd start to cry, and then she'd be off into her prayers. And then, before she knows herself what she's doing, there she'd be, praying out loud, talking out loud. And then she'd start to wail, and scream, yeah, and moan some more. It was that son, don't you know. And if you didn't know her, you'd think she was having a fit or something . . ."

". . . You know who I think is still alive? Old Doña Cuquita; yeah. Been years since I've seen her, of course. She took good care of us out at that old dump. I really liked her. You know, I didn't get to know either of my grandmothers and neither did Pa, and maybe that's why he looked at her as a grandma . . . But like I said, I really liked Doña Cuquita, and I really liked it when she hugged me. Know what she'd say then? She'd say I was bright; brighter than the moon, she'd say."

"Get out of there, get away from that goddam window. Go away. Go away . . ."

". . . Nothing I can do, but you can't come home with me anymore. Look, I like to play with you, but some old ladies told Mama that Mexicans steal, and now Mama says not to bring you home anymore. You got to turn back. But we can still play at school. Okay? I'll choose you and you choose me."

". . . Listen to what I'm saying here: there's no getting out of this damn hole. I'm right! And what's more, you know I'm right. Look, come another war, we ain't the ones who're going to suffer, uh-huh. And don't be such a damn jackass! You know who tends to lose if there's another war? *They* do; they got more to lose, too. Hell, we're already down in the pits. It could be, now, it just might, that we'll do right well if another war does come along."

". . . And you know what I went and did? Well, I walked in to town to buy myself a new hammer. Yeah; I was going to be ready to go to work just as soon as that carpenter or whatever he was, came in to teach us something. And you know what people are now saying? They're saying that the preacher, as soon as he heard about his wife and that other guy, that he went into that house of theirs, grabbed himself an ax, and broke every stitch and piece of furniture they had there. And then he piled everything outside, and once he'd done that, he set the damn thing on fire. Watched it, too; stood there watching that fire until all there was left was the ashes . . ."

"No, I don't see how my husband's going to be able to work out in the sun anymore. And when we told the grower that my husband had been beat down by the sun, know what he did then? He shrugged. Walked away. That man had other things on his mind. Rain, for one; the crop, for another. So, it was the rain and the crop he was on about. And listen to this: his wife came down with a cancer and was operated on. And even that didn't worry him as much as the crop. So, you tell me how much he cared when we told him about my man, my husband."

". . . No such thing. There's no such thing as a devil or anything like it, either. The only devil around here is Don Rayos—Old Man Lightning—and that's because he dresses with that cape and he wears those horns during the Christmas plays. Devil? What devil you talking about?"

". . . You blind? What the hell's wrong with you? We almost hit that damn truck! Couldn't you see it? 'Ta hell's wrong with you?"

". . . That youngish teacher, she started to cry. Why'd she cry for? For that Mexican kid? When they took him away?

"Young and inexperienced, not like those in Texas; back home, they're old and born with a stick in their hands ready to whack you one if you lost your place on the reading. And if you lose it, it's bend over and whack! No less than five licks, yeah.

". . . And you think that's why they broke up? It's hard to believe, that's all. Hard to believe they broke up that fast."

". . . It was a hot flame and then once the clothing catches fire, that's it, you can just forget it.

"Yeah, I guess. You remember that other family? Burned up around Christmas time, I think it was. They burned up in their sleep. And then the firemen cried like babies when they carried the little bodies out. Those hot flames had rendered the kids' fatty tissue, and this splattered all over and inside the firefighters' boots . . ."

". . . Free citizens! This is an important, nay, a glorious day for all of us. Eighteen-sixty-two it was, when the troops of the great Napoleon went down in defeat as they faced the brave Mexican forces who so gallantly . . . Well, that's the way I'd start all my speeches, my oratory. And the term *free citizens*, sovereign people, see?, that was something I always used. A-course, I was younger then, m'boy, but then this stroke came and there went my legs, my boy . . . And it's even affected my thinking, too. . . . I can't seem to remember what else I'd say to the people in those days . . . And then? Well, the 1910 Revolution came rumbling through and our side lost; we lost at the end, but losing is the same everywhere. Pancho Villa?[2] Oh, he did all right for himself; he's one of the ones who came out ahead. Not me. I had to come to this side of the Rio Grande. But there's no one here who knows what I did over *there*. What it was I did during the Revolution. And now, I try to remember myself what it was I did, but I can't. Memory's all gone, boy. But let's leave that. Now, I want you to tell me what it is you really and truly want, more than anything else. At this time and moment, boy, at this time in your life, right now. What is it you really want?"

". . . We came up with 50 pounds of copper wire yesterday. Enrique found himself one of those big magnets to locate metals with. Easier, see? People throw away a lot of stuff, but that magnet goes right to the iron metals. We do okay sometimes. But, most of the time, well, most of the time we come up empty; it's a waste of time. Can't even come up with enough to eat a snack somewhere. What are they paying for tin foil these days? Say, why don't you all come with us the next time we go out?

2. Francisco "Pancho" Villa (1878–1923), Mexican revolutionary general.

". . . That cold weather is coming on. We'll get us a hard freeze tonight. I bet it covers the ground. And the high flying cranes, you seen 'em? They're flying south about as fast as you'll ever see 'em . . ."

"Sunday? There's a wedding on then, and I can tell you right now what they're going to feed us. *Cabrito en mole.* That good old roasted kid goat, and rice to go with it. A bed of rice, yeah. And then there's the dance, right? And how about that groom? Ha! Antsy as hell for night time to come, ha!"

". . . Did you say fright? I'll say we had one, Comadre. There we were, talking, watching the kids, when out of the blue, the lights go out. And dark? Hooo! And you know what else, Comadre? We didn't have a single, solitary candle anywhere in the house. But that didn't scare us as much as what happened next. That Juan of ours, and he can be such a little rat sometimes, he—and don't ask me how—but he shoved an orange seed up his nose. In that dark. Yes, he did. So he cried, and *how* he cried. And my husband? Well, all we had was matches, like I told you, and there he was lighting matches while we tried to get that seed out. He'd light one, he'd light two, and like that.

"Well, what was it happened that night anyway? We heard the whole town was dark, that right?"

". . . The way I hear it, Doña Amada's boy was found by the irrigation canal, but Don Tiburcio's boy, he burned right inside that van. Now I don't really know, but I heard Don Jesús is going to be sued plenty over this thing; him and his van and carrying people while that back door was locked from the outside. It trapped them, see? As for Don Tiburcio's boy, well, some people went inside the van to get the boy out. The people they tried to stretch the body out to take him outside, but when they tried to stretch him, a leg dropped off . . ."

". . . The picture guys? Nah, they don't show up here anymore. And they won't, not after Don Mateo gave 'em what for."

". . . Ma? Yeah, she almost went out of her mind for a while there. And then she'd cry up a storm every time she'd talk about what happened to her when she went downtown that time . . ."

(I wish I could see all those good people at once, together, at the same time. And then, if my arms were long enough, I'd reach out to embrace 'em all. Give 'em a warm hug. And I wish I could talk with them again; see them all here, together; the only way I could—can—do that is in a dream. Somehow.)

It's a good place, under this house. I can think about anything I want to. But you have to go off by yourself to do that, to be alone. And then, when you do that, you can get all the people together. Gather them in one place, in one thought.

And I needed to get away. Needed to hide, be off by myself to learn, know, to understand, finally. From here on out, all I've got to do is to come here, in the dark, and then I can go back in time and think about those fine people. But there's never enough time, it seems. I've so much to think about and so little time. I think that today's the one day I wanted to remember all of last year. But that's only last year, and what I want, need to do, is to come back to this place, to remember all the other years . . .

A child's cry and then a painful sensation down the leg. Rocks! They're throwing rocks at me. Why?

"Mamma, Mamma, there's some old guy there, under the house. Come quick, Mamma. Hurry, will you? It's some old man down there . . . some old guy."

"Where did you say? Where is he? Oh . . . Here, I'll go get some long sticks, switches; and tell you what: you go get Doña Luz's dog. Go!"

Looking up in the clear daylight, he could see eyes looking at him. Then it got darker under the house as more people blocked out the daylight; and the kids kept throwing rocks at him, and then they brought the dog and it started barking. And here was this woman trying to switch him, trying to get him.

"Who is it down there?"

In the end he had to get out; nothing else he could do. Why, that's no old man at all, they said. They knew him. Sure they did.

And he walked away, slowly. As he did so, he heard this old lady say: "What a family . . . and such a shame, too. First their ma, and now this boy of theirs. Maybe he's going crazy, too. Got a screw loose somewhere, rattling around in that head of his. He's . . . he's lost some years, some time. Know what I mean?"

But he wasn't crazy. He smiled and pointed toward home with head held high through that chuck-hole ridden street he lived on. And he was happy; oh, he'd heard that woman say those things, but so what? What did she know?

He hadn't lost a *thing*. A year? He hadn't even lost a day! He'd found! Refound, recovered, you might say, and as a result he could connect things, weld them together.

Yes, to connect things, to make relationships, and to discover patterns: this goes with this, and that with that over there, and this with this, and all with all . . . That's what it was all about. And that was a lot. It was everything.

And he became happier still over this find, this personal discovery of his. First thing he did once he was home was to head straight for that shade tree of theirs. Up he went, shinnying up he went, and when he stopped, he looked some distance away, and there was that old, familiar palm tree.

Was there someone there, in that old palm tree, he thought to himself? It seemed as if there were. He kept this eyes on the palm tree. And it seemed he could make out someone over there, waving at him. Yes. Saw him raise his arm, waving to him, waving to let him know that he knew he was *there*.

1970                                                                                        1985

# LUIS RAFAEL SÁNCHEZ
## b. 1936

Born in Humacao, Puerto Rico, Luis Rafael Sánchez, aka "Wico," is a prolific fiction writer, essayist, and playwright. In his celebrated text "La guagua aérea" (1985; translated into English as "The Airbus" in 1987), an ingenious mixture of essay and fiction, he introduced the term *la guagua aérea*, which immediately provided a metaphor for describing Puerto Ricans' airborne commutation between the island and the mainland. In fact, this term has replaced René Marqués's symbolic "oxcart," of the 1950s, becoming the definitive metaphor for describing the back-and-forth pattern of Puerto Rican migration and the vital connections that Puerto Ricans on the mainland maintain with their homeland. In high school, Sánchez became interested in theater, participating in some school productions and acting in radio programs. In 1955, he left Puerto Rico to pursue theater studies in Mexico, where he won an acting award. The next year, he returned to Puerto Rico, and as a theater student at the University of Puerto Rico, he joined the Comedieta Universitaria (University Comedy Company). During this time, he began to publish short stories and poetry in literary journals, and several of his stories received literary awards.

Sánchez left Puerto Rico with a scholarship to study playwriting at Columbia University, in New York City. He later earned a master's degree in Hispanic literature at New York University. Upon his return to Puerto Rico, he joined the faculty at the University of Puerto Rico. In 1976, he received a doctoral degree from the Complutense University of Madrid. Sánchez's first published book, *Sol 13, interior* (1960), included his plays *Los ángeles se han fatigado* (The Angels Have Become Tired) and *Farsa del amor compradito* (Farce about a Love That Is Bought). These plays were included a year later in the Institute for Puerto Rican Culture's prominent annual theater festival, as would be most of his subsequent dramatic works. Sánchez did not publish major works of prose fiction until the short-story collection *En cuerpo de camisa* (In Shirt Sleeves, 1966). In this volume, he moved beyond the conventional narrative styles and techniques of Puerto Rican prose fiction and began giving voice to the island's popular culture. Few authors have been able to match Sánchez's verbal virtuosity or his ear for the language of the Puerto Rican masses. During the 1960s, he also became a regular cultural columnist for the island newspaper *El Mundo*.

Sánchez's reputation as a playwright was further enhanced by his play *La pasión según Antígona Pérez* (The Passion According to Antígona Pérez, 1968), but outside Puerto Rico, his novel *La guaracha del macho Camacho* (Macho Camacho's Beat, 1976) made Sánchez a household name among critics and readers. He was awarded a Guggenheim Fellowship in 1979. The next year, the publication of the acclaimed translator Gregory Rabassa's English translation of *La guaracha* placed Sánchez's name among the best-known contemporary Puerto Rican writers in Latin America and the Caribbean and outside the Spanish-speaking world. In 1983, he was a guest scholar at the Woodrow Wilson Center, in Washington, D.C. In the early 1990s, he held the position of writer-in-residence at New York University.

*La guagua aérea* (1994), a collection of essays that often read like short stories, was the basis for a 1995 film of the same title, initially shown in Puerto Rico, the United States, and Latin America. Among Sánchez's other acclaimed works are the play *Quíntuples* (Quintuplets, 1985; translated into English in 1989), another example of the author's masterly linguistic experimentation, and the novel *La importancia de llamarse Daniel Santos* (The Importance of Being Named Daniel Santos, 1988), based on the life of the popular Puerto Rican *guaracha* and *bolero* singer. Among Sánchez's most recent works is the novel *Indiscreciones de un perro gringo* (Indiscretions of a Gringo Dog, 2007), in which, with his characteristic satirical humor, the author provides a critical view of the United States.

"The Airbus," the first of this anthology's two Sánchez selections, humorously depicts cultural translocations of a Puerto Rican nation constantly "on the move," migrating between "two ports." The essay "El cuarteto nuevayorkés" (1993), here translated as "The New Yorkian Quartet," reflects on colonialism, Americanization, cultural nationalism, and the preservation of the Spanish language among Puerto Ricans. This piece dates from one of Sánchez's winter stays in New York, a place the author sees as being transformed by the convergence of Spanish American nationalities and by inventive Spanish linguistic regionalisms.

# The Airbus[1]

A startled cry releases the furled silences, one by one. The stewardess slowly backs away, angelic, innocent, like a character out of a short story by Horacio Quiroga,[2] a blonde of a frozen intensity that would heighten the libidinous drives of the easily smitten King Kong. The passengers' anxious faces share exaggerated premonitions, as they turn, ready to encounter a hand grasping a gun, a knife, or a homemade bomb. For the startled cry must surely be either the unrestrained and historical denunciation of one more airplane hijacker or the cry of a menacing lunatic. An "Our Father"[3] pinches and bursts the released silence. The stewardess continues her backward movement. The stewardess has seen her reflection in her pool of fear and fear has not avoided her gaze, marking her instead with a pallor that is conclusive promise of a faint. But the airplane hijacker or the menacing lunatic are nowhere in sight. Humble and contrite "Our Fathers" burst forth on various levels of faith and orality. Lights flash on, violating retinas and exposing the full gallop of heartbeats. The airbus becomes a mammoth, dissected by indiscrete fluorescence at 31,000 feet above sea level. The captain or chauffeur of the airbus appears, together with the official engineer or mechanic, and their studied nonchalance elicits a stir of discomfort and caution, the rest of the crew is alerted, hysteria's attempt ignites a spark that grows threatening; the stewardess is just an inch away from being consumed by horror. But the airplane hijacker or the menacing lunatic is nowhere in sight.

Suddenly, with incomparable license and surprise, a peal of laughter corrupts in equal measure both the silence and the "Our Fathers" that had advanced, on some lips, as far as the Amen. Pure in its offense, the parenthesis cut by it so perfect that it could be glued to a page, the peal of laughter infects the hundreds of passengers on an airbus that makes nightly trips between Puerto Rico and New York's airports. Peals of laughter, delightful because of the disorder and ferocity of their emergence, a disorder that prefaces automatic convergence, a ferocity that reveals secret and unforgotten resentments. A nervous Nellie might assert at this point that all the shimmying and shaking caused by the widespread hilarity endangers the safety of the airbus, and low-flying angels with a penchant for prying might sacrifice

1. Translated by Diana L. Vélez.
2. Horacio Silvestre Quiroga Forteza (1878–1937), *Modernismo*-influenced Uruguayan writer whose stories feature supernatural elements and sur-

real effects.
3. The Lord's Prayer, or paternoster, the best-known Christian prayer.

the sacred sheen of their golden locks just to know what the devil is making that mestizo bunch laugh so loudly, traveling so un-self-consciously in their midst. Only the crew, uniformly gringo as it is this evening, seems immune to the laughter, immune to the infectious laughter, immune to the mockery aimed at the fear that so unhinged the blonde stewardess's angelic and innocent countenance just a minute ago.

Gales of laughter threaten to depressurize the cabin and slow down the airbus. Laughter threatens, for the incredible cause of the commotion is right there for all to see. There on the thickly carpeted aisle of the airbus, swaggering like a couple of gangsters, strolling like a pair of bullies, indifferent to the uproar and fear engendered by their presence, are a pair of self-satisfied, pompous, and healthy-looking crabs.

Paradoxically, their healthy glow is the very harbinger of their imminent fate—tomorrow they will be crab stew on Prospect Avenue or fritter filling in the South Bronx or baked crab with drawn butter in Sunset Park or crab marinated in picante sauce on the Lower East Side or temporary inhabitants of a crab colony in the cultivated recesses of a darkened basement, hidden from the inspecting gaze of a super or a landlord.[4]

But tonight, their healthy glow and their unexpected use of the airbus as a makeshift stepping stone, their acquisition of an informal right of way, are the subject of lively comments and vivid chitchat, precipitating the generalized disorder that now reigns, a disorder that reigns by means of a loosening of spirits and widespread recourse to agitated prose, the anarchic choreography of bodies straining, bending, straightening, twisting in the imprisonment of their seats, a generalized disorder spurred on by unadulteratedly patriotic discourses and assimilationist cross-examinations, by off-color jokes of every hue, by womanizing glances eliciting man-baiting winks, by detailed true confessions—we just can't resist the autobiographical—by the irate testimony of repeated humiliations on the crosstown bus, the elevator, the damned job, the liberal university, the Jewish junkshop; the generalized disorder suddenly extends a dividing line, invisible but palpable, between them, the gringos, and us, the Puerto Ricans, a line whose contours are heightened by the unprovable assertion of a brown-skinned woman who, while making the precious offering of nutritious liquid from her calid[5] and radiant breast to her newborn child, states: the blonder they are, the dumber; a disorder that inspires fear, or so it seems, in the crew, uniformly gringo as it is tonight.

Taken aback by the unexpected collapse of modern technology, amazed that the rigor of the security devices could have missed that unmentionable contraband, the crew demands that the crabs' owner identify himself immediately. They do this with gestures befitting an overly German-Expressionistic comedy, softened only by the bantering and playful reminiscence of a Buster Keaton or a Charlie Chaplin.[6] These insistent demands made with vigorous gestures and the insistent offers made by potential crab executioners are headed off by the dramatic mouthings of a wiry fiftyish man who, ambling up to the front, half-asleep and slightly annoyed, exhibiting

4. I.e., as in all the examples above, they will be put to use somewhere in New York City, where the airbus is headed.
5. Hot; burning.
6. As masterly actors in silent films, Charles Chaplin (1889–1977) and Buster Keaton (1895–1966) used expressive gestures more subtle than those associated with the often wildly exaggerated early-twentieth-century aesthetic style known as German Expressionism.

an impressive manual dexterity which some, in their ignorance, have referred to as primitive, immobilizes the fugitive pair, scolding them with a mixture of crankiness and pride, "I send you off to crab heaven with a nice shot of valium and this is what I get for it."

Euphoria triumphs, becomes widespread; laughter, the element that can brighten a cloudy day and unstop nasal passages, laughter, now, by its sheer abundance, manages merely to congest. Someone who had been eyeing the dismembered bodies lavishly illustrated in the newspaper El Vocero declares "I almost choked" and another person, who had been praising the country singer from Manatí's[7] variety show, declares "I almost wet my pants" and a shrewd observer notes "this is what you might call a gas," to which a few other shrewd observers add "put me on that bubble, my man," and another observer philosophizes in rhymed couplets to the effect that we sure are cooking now. The airbus effervesces, swayed between tumultuous motion and the pull of a chimera,[8] swaying between the forward thrust of assertiveness and that secular cross called ay bendito[9] or wellwhatcanyoudo; a well-dressed woman who hides the well-kept secret of her curlers under a floral kerchief announces that she regularly jumps back and forth across the creek on the average of once a month, so she has forgotten what side of it she does live on; an adolescent girl, worried to distraction, made up to perfection though a bit heavily rouged, lists among her woes the change in Rene's voice that forced him to give up his job at the Mincemeat nightclub while she listens distractedly to the tale of an adolescent boy on edge and on the edge of hysteria because he is off to Newark[1] but he doesn't know why. Another lady of a gregarious and un-self-conscious nature pulls out and starts to unfold a crocheted bedspread made for a king size bed while under the protection of the bedspread's craftsmanship, a spontaneous and somewhat atonal quartet merrily plays the ballad "En mi viejo San Juan." A well-dressed and well-mannered old gent with studied charm asks the brown-skinned woman with the calid and radiant breast haven't they met somewhere before, perhaps in the carnival celebrated in honor of the patron saint Monserrat in the town of Hormigueros.[2] The brown-skinned woman with the calid and radiant breast replies that she has never been to the town of Hormigueros. The same well-dressed and well-mannered old gent with the studied charm turns to the woman wearing a pumpkin-colored shift and asks haven't they met somewhere before, perhaps in the carnival celebrated in honor of the guardian angel of the town of Yabucoa.[3] The woman wearing the pumpkin-colored shift replies that she has never been to the town of Yabucoa, adding by the way of clarification that what she is into is Bocaccio, Topaz, Bachelor, and other gay watering holes. A choral ensemble, purposely annoying and loud, calls from the airbus' kitchen that it is all set to do an encore and "If they don't give me something to drink soon, I'll start crying," a man deeply immersed in his righteous indignation refers to his son's imprisonment for

7. Municipality in northern Puerto Rico.
8. A monster made of incongruous parts; an illusion or dream.
9. Literally, oh blessed; figuratively, oh my God (shortened from the expression bendito sea Dios), dear Lord, that's too bad, poor thing, or what a shame.
1. Presumably the city in northeast New Jersey.
2. Municipality in western Puerto Rico. Monser-

rat: the Virgin of Montserrat, a statue in Catalonia, Spain, of the Virgin Mary as black; venerated as the patron saint of Catalonia and of Hormigueros. Thousands of pilgrims visit the church in Hormigueros that dates back to the sixteenth century, after a miraculous event there was attributed to the Virgin's intervention.
3. Small town in southeastern Puerto Rico.

refusing to cooperate with a federal grand jury while his listener holds that being a nationalist in Puerto Rico entails hidden prestige while in New York it entails merely official hostility.

Ushered in by resonant outbursts, the anecdotes begin to weave their pattern, anguish laden and laughable, heartrending and superficial, lovably heroic in their formulation of a resistance to the indignities, the exposed prejudices, the hidden prejudices, an infinite string of anecdotes which the Puerto Rican passengers fill to bursting with elements of the cunning, the courageous, and the picaresque, with the suspicion that attends their lives, anecdotes whose narrative montage delights the listener, anecdotes whose more occurrence moves the listener, anecdotes told in a surprisingly round-about and spicy prose, the most familiar and easily recognizable rice-and-beans style, anecdotes that a sharp-witted country bumpkin listens to with interest, a *jíbaro*[4] who does not use highflown, hillbilly vernacular, no air, but uses instead sly street speech and proper English if the occasion should call for it and just plain old common sense talk whenever that's needed, anecdotes told by Puerto Ricans who on one fine day had visited upon them the compound evils of unemployment, hunger, and the desire to eat, pathetic anecdotes told by a subject people who refuse to submit though they will apologize for the naked sin of being born Puerto Rican, anecdotes told by the Puerto Ricans who get hot under the collar and curse aloud if anyone should question their being Puerto Rican, anecdotes of a life ill-lived, of a life sung out of tune, phrases, anecdotes of thick-skinned survivors whose hearts are free of debts, anecdotes told in a charming sputter of Puerto Rican Spanish, bubbling in its perfect rhythm and tone, a Puerto Rican Spanish exact and compact, broad and baroque, a Puerto Rican Spanish as invigoratingly corrupt as Argentine Spanish, as Mexican Spanish, as Venezuelan Spanish, as Spanish Spanish, anecdotes told by a thousand and one travelers moving between that precarious and discredited paradise that is New York and that eroded an uninhabitable paradise that is Puerto Rico.

A nervous Nellie might predict—a nervous Nellie a bit like Jeane Dixon[5] but a zodiac without a cosmic temple and without her mystical thinking cap, in short, like a second-hand Jeane Dixon—that the airbus might burst tonight because the subversive laughter and human energy that it carries tonight is a dangerous explosive. And low-flying angels with a penchant for prying would willingly sacrifice the sacred tinsel of tiny eucharistic wings just to know what the hell that mestizo bunch is jabbering about, flying so un-self-consciously in their midst.

Only the crew, uniformly gringo as it is tonight, seems immune to the laughter, resolute in its desire to overcome it with the rapid distribution of insipid-tasting turkey sandwiches, tiny bags of peanuts, Coca Cola by the gallon, playing cards, and the plastic interjections of the captain, who tries to put out the growing conflagration with his own tiny sparklers that cannot and will not take off—"Ladies and gentlemen, this is the captain speaking. Now that the dangerous kidnappers are back in their bags, now that it is really sure that we are not going to be taken to an unexpected meeting with that *poco simpático señor* Fidel Castro I invite all of you to look through the

4. Peasant.
5. Famous American psychic (1904–1997), author of a syndicated newspaper astrology column.

windows and catch the splash of the Milky Way. In a few minutes we will be showing, without charge tonight, a movie starring that funny man Richard Pryor."[6]

The woman to my left turns to me and with calm hostility asks "What that man say?" But I don't get to answer because the man who claims to travel with no luggage and who repeats: "I live with one leg in New York and the other one in Puerto Rico" and who states: "I make my bucks in Manhattan, but I spend them in Santurce"[7] and who claims: "I'm everybody's friend but nobody's buddy, the only buddy you ever have in life is your balls, they're always on hand," beats me to the punch as he belts out a response, turns me into an unsuspecting ally as he unravels a long answer in a monotone made bearable only by a hint of sarcasm: "The captain wants to bring us down by making us watch a movie with that colored guy who almost burned himself to a crisp getting stoned,[8] he wants us down so he can be on top," pulling together the scattered chords of his utterance, he murmurs in a low voice, using an orgasmic dialect, the most ascerbic of inferences about the captain and the blonde stewardess, inferences that, if written, would be immediately published in the pages of *Penthouse* or *Playboy*. The woman to my left misses the inferences for she has again picked up her two simultaneous conversations about the strike at the insane asylum: "I hear they're threatening to get sane," and about the unrelenting stubbornness of President Reagan: "I hear that fiend will be the end of El Salvador."[9]

The peal of, laughter that originally opened the door to a seditious, almost unanimous hilarity now fertilizes the raucous friendliness that begins to spread out over the tourist cabin, a raucous friendliness that finds expression in the noisy tolerance with which a harsh opinion is extended or withheld or in the noisy gratitude with which someone accepts a compliment about the paper flowers they're bringing as a gift for an aunt who moved into some housing project in New Jersey, or in the noisy distribution and sharing befitting those who suffer alike and love alike—love guava-filled pastries, love fresh-baked sweets packed in a shoe box, love a dozen fruit-shaped candy bars, love homemade sausage and draughts of raisin-cured cane liquor made in a home still, a liquor that is swallowed without neurotic sipping or fastidious holding back, a raucous, passionate friendliness, one whose fullness, intimacy of feeling, whose clatter, whose raw gusto and willingness to be sociable right at the outset and for no particular reason is simply indifferent to the disapproval it now elicits from those who, from the shelter of the first-class compartment, those who, between sips of California champagne and a tit-à-tête[1] with a reasonably nosed and subtly mannered stewardess, venture a rationalized "They are my people but" or venture a resentful "Wish they'd learn how to behave" or venture a final judgment: "They will never make it because they are trash"; a raucous, passionate friendliness that sputters, bubbles up and spills over the edge as the wiry fiftyish man recites his self-explanatory agenda: "If I can't live in Puerto Rico because I just can't make it

---

6. African American comedian and actor (1940–2005).
7. District in San Juan, northeastern Puerto Rico.
8. In 1980, Pryor severely injured himself when he caught fire while freebasing (heating and smoking) cocaine and drinking rum.
9. During the administration of Ronald Wilson Reagan (1911–2004), U.S. president 1981–89, the United States supported the right-wing government of El Salvador despite that government's well-documented human-rights abuses, including the use of "death squads" against its citizens.
1. A pun on *tête-a-tête*, or private conversation.

there I'll take it all with me bit by bit; this time I've got four crabs from Vacia Talega,[2] last time I brought over a pure bred fighting cock and next time it will be every single ever recorded by Cortijo."[3]

And he follows up with a list of items he defends with the tender mercies of a smile; he's governed by the savory memories of other happy travels, other attempts to reduce the distance, other intimate possessions salvaged, utterances that if analyzed by a deformed or myopic spirit might amount to nothing more than a cheap naturalism, a mediocre slice of life, trivia, the elements of a merely folksy *lelolai*[4] syndrome. But when their none-too-imposing appearance, eroded prestige and poor taste are transcended, they manifest their true nature as the useful, reiterated and undeniable revelations of a temperament that, day after day, modulates its uniqueness and secures permanence despite, in spite of, in the face of, let alone and all the same, still, yet, even, perhaps and other stutterings and dialectical and dialectal babblings born of superlatively grammatical attempts at speech, attempts conjugated by our devasting and inexorable yanquification, a unique, different, permanent, and integral temperament with which our militant, familiar, and neighborhood ties of warmth lay the foundations of our sacrosanct state of dependency: just one person leaves for New York, but five come along to see him off and two people come back from New York but they're met by eight; a temperament that keeps our reserves of humor flowing—just because we love to laugh wholeheartedly and with irreverence, we love a joke with a little bite; a temperament that is the mainstay of our emotional dominion—just because we suffer and weep lavishly, operatically, cine Mexicanly; for ours is the laughter, ours the tears, barely distinguishable one from the other just as they are fused right now in the airbus.

For at this moment the wiry fiftyish man is busy establishing his reputation as a lover of chitchat and ruckus, totally oblivious to the mysterious overarching shadow be is casting on the screen the purser has rolled out. He shares his asides with a certain Cayo from Cayey[5] who is on his way to hug his two grandsons whom he hasn't seen since September and with a certain Soledad Romero who charges off to Puerto Rico whenever her soul's battery needs a recharge and with a certain Isidro from El Yunque[6] who came down to sell some lots because his son got in trouble and he doesn't want him to get ruined in jail, and with a certain Laura Serrano who can't take the winters but refuses to give up what destiny has prefigured for her in New York and with a certain Yacoco Calderón from Loíza[7] who is moving to Spanish Harlem for a few months as he puts it to make a quick bundle and get out, and with a certain Gloria Fragoso who is off to New York to keep her dying son Vitín from dying and with a certain Bob Márquez who introduces himself with a fervent and somewhat overly familiar: "Black Puerto Rican and proud of it, my friend" and with another who hems and haws over his name, saying: "I'm only on loan in New York"; they jump into rhythmic giddiness in the aisles, sharing hopes they have just dusted off, repeating their "Where are you from's" with the urgency of a demographic counter, chiming in "If you're

2. Beach close to Piñones, a community near San Juan.
3. Rafael Cortijo (1928–1982), Puerto Rican composer, musician, and bandleader.
4. Nonsense syllables typically used in Puerto Rican folk music.
5. Mountain town in central Puerto Rico.
6. Rain forest in Río Grande, northeastern Puerto Rico.
7. Small town in northeastern Puerto Rico.

from Río Grande, then you must know Mister Pagán who teaches industrial arts and if you're from Aguadilla[8] you probably know Tata Barradas."

On the airbus Puerto Ricans expound once more on the difficulties and delights of provincial airs, the delights of a country that never grew to be more than a big village, or a nation that dabbled in becoming a small country, Puerto Ricans who glorify the uneasy illusion that they're traveling to New York strictly on a temporary basis, Puerto Ricans who swear on the holy memory of their dead relatives that they'll just stay in New York long enough to get out from under, and just until things straighten out in Puerto Rico, or just till the time when they've saved enough for a decent down payment on a house in the seventh subdivision of San Juan's Levittown,[9] Puerto Ricans who on any given night of the week might climb aboard an airbus provided they've got with them an open return round trip ticket, a ticket that guarantees their return, a ticket that makes an urgent return possible at a moment's notice when Grandma's on her deathbed or when the Old Man dies suddenly, a ticket that instantly satisfies the urgent hunger for an island whose memory is nestled like a treasure gently distorted by reminiscences, tenderly reworked by the imagination at a distance, the island once described as having reefs gently billowing in a golden blue-green warmth of sand and sea, an open return round trip ticket that puts an end to the sudden joy experienced while walking around mountains and beaches on the island, taking a spin around the plaza, meandering around the familiar streets that are so beautiful despite or maybe because of their ugliness, recovering friendships through desultory conversations that stretch out over a savanna of days or weeks or going on a binge that lasts for several days, a momentary return to that certain something that never changes despite failure, inertia, erosion, that certain something that lacks even the trappings of magical realism or the lyrical vibrations of nostalgia, a ticket that attests to the fact that no roots will go down in New York nor will there be burials in a foreign land; Puerto Ricans who can't breathe freely in Puerto Rico but who breathe new life into their souls in New York, Puerto Ricans who can't score a hit in Puerto Rico while in New York they can bat a thousand, Puerto Ricans in whom the rhythmic swaying of the island bravoes produces a certain psychic vertigo while the constant struggle for survival in New York produces a certain tranquillity, Puerto Ricans who are confused, annoyed and disturbed by their inability to live uninterruptedly in Puerto Rico and who become needlessly irritated and needlessly uncomfortable, become captives of their own needless explanations? "Listen pal, the only thing people are into on the island is drinking and joking, having a good time; listen old buddy, everything's a big hassle in Puerto Rico and I tell you, in Puerto Rico the lack of mental rigor and the glorification of speech for its own sake entertains me but it leaves me bewildared, my friend; folks down there will break their word and stay as cool as a cucumber, I'll tell you; I've cast my fate over here and, I find myself lost down there except maybe I'll try it down there for a while and then if I don't like it I'll just slip back up here again." Puerto Ricans who want to be down there but must be up here, Puerto Ricans who must be down there but can't stay put down

---

8. City on the northwestern tip of Puerto Rico.
9. I.e., the Puerto Rican equivalent of Levittown, a Long Island community often seen as the prototypical cookie-cutter suburb.

there, Puerto Ricans who are there but dream of being here, Puerto Ricans whose lives are spread out between the question marks that burst from the two adverbs like knife stabs, Puerto Ricans who are permanently installed in the wanderground between here and there and who must therefore informalize the trip, making it little more than a hop on a bus, though airborne, that floats over the creek to which the Atlantic Ocean has been reduced by the Puerto Ricans. A crossing over the Atlantic made simpler so as to return, go, return once more, a return fervently and loudly applauded whenever the airbus lands anew.

My neighbor brings up once more the incident turned accident involving the crabs and aims the inevitable. "And where are you from?" at me as soon as they announce "In a few minutes we are going to land in the John F. Kennedy International Airport." I reply "I'm from Puerto Rico" only to hear her respond with a surprisingly psychic "That's written all over your face." "From Humacao"[1] I add, no doubt pleasing her for she agreeably states "I've been to Humacao" but she looks at me as if I've shortchanged her, as if I've thoughtlessly forgotten that the vestiges of a tribal community impose their authority on the airbus, where dialogues lose their loincloths and the opening between speakers is broadened by the belief that an apparent equality and solidarity between Puerto Ricans is made possible by chance and fate. "Where are you from?" I ask though I know full well what the answer will be. With a coquettish twinkle in her eye and a shameless blush in her cheek she replies "I'm from Puerto Rico" forcing me to say, just slightly psychic, "Even the blind can see that much," adding "From which town in Puerto Rico?" And she specifies "From New York."

It might be a tired cliché or an unfortunate geographical slip or a joke vibrating with sarcasm, or a new drawing of the boundaries or the silent but sweet revenge of the invaded invading the invader. It is, of course, all of that and more. It is the story that history books find to tell. It is the obverse of the rhetorical twist that slips out of politics' reach. It is the datum missed by statistical counts. It is the translucent statement that confirms once more the utility of poetry. It is the overdue and just payment to those souls who watched in worry and doubt from the decks of the steamship *Borinquen* or *Coamo* as the outline of their beloved island disappeared forever into the horizon; it is the perindication of those who emerged from the stupor of 14 hours of travel in the narrow and uncomfortable flying machines of Pan American.[2] It is reality's current, leveling and deciding in its pursuit of a new space, furiously conquered. It is the course of a nation about between two parts where the contributed is hope.

1985

1994

---

1. City on the eastern coast.
2. Pan American World Airways, the major U.S. international airline from the 1930s until its collapse, in 1991.

# The New Yorkian Quartet[1]

*To Silvia and Carlos Fuentes,[2] for the pleasure of their friendship.*

*1*

Besides illuminating the front page of the paper that I am reading, the photograph soothes the ravages of this winter I am spending in New York like so many other Puerto Ricans. How many? There is no way of knowing. We travel here without the necessity of producing any documentation whatsoever, legalized by a North American citizenship which negated Puerto Rican citizenship since 1917. We return to Puerto Rico at the slightest provocation, possessed of a certainty that the poet turns to stone—*"Nothing changes in my beloved corner of the world."* We come and go with such regularity, this hopeful promenade among the states of the Union, that the moving about has become destiny; a destiny that has become symbolic of the Wandering Puerto Rican. No, there is no way of knowing how many of us are around in New York, either transient or resident. However, statistics take a stab at a number—around one million.

New York would be the other capital of Puerto Rico, if were not already the capital of all of Hispanic America. In New York the foundations are laid for the capital envisioned by Bolívar,[3] one which accommodates all nationalities of Spanish-speaking America. And Fourteenth Street in Manhattan is the marketplace where all converge in a rendezvous of meetings and appointments.

Meetings to conduct business transactions, most of them poorly compensated, most situated on that Apache territory of the sidewalk: fruit stands tended by Mexicans, alpaca sweaters being sold by Ecuadorans with jet-black braids, costume jewelry of synthetic amber hustled by Dominican María Montez[4] look-alikes, Colombian psychics who will draw back the curtain of the future, the big, cardboard arrow pointing toward the basement window that announces—*Learn to dance the tango with a real Argentinian*, folding tables jammed with who knows how many cassettes—all of Carlos Gardel, Pedro Infante, Felipe Rodríguez, Juan Luis Guerra,[5] all the representative singers of this ethnicity, of that musical style. And, from time to time, above that sidewalk-turned-Apache territory, winding its way to the umbrella sky over Fourteenth Street, rises a mini Afro-carnival interpretation of the *Inka Jazz Fusion Band*.[6]

---

1. Translated by Susan P. Liberis-Hill. Unless otherwise indicated, all footnotes are Liberis-Hill's, as are the bracketed insertions in the text.
2. Mexican writer (b. 1928). The Spanish journalist and television host Silvia Lemus de Fuentes is his wife. [Anthology editors' note]
3. Simón Bolívar (1783–1830), South American liberator. [Anthology editors' note]
4. Dominican-born actress (1912–1951), best-known for playing exotic beauties in colorful Hollywood adventure movies of the 1940s. [Anthology editors' note]
5. Dominican singer and songwriter (b. 1957).

*Carlos Gardel*: Uruguayan-born Argentinian tango singer (1887 or 1890–1935). *Pedro Infante*: José Pedro Infante Cruz (1917–1957), Mexican actor and singer of mariachi and ranchera music. *Felipe Rodríguez*: Luis Felipe Rodriguez (1926–1999), known as "La Voz" (The Voice), Puerto Rican bolero singer. [Anthology editors' note]
6. I.e., not an interpretation of the Inka Jazz Fusion Band, but perhaps a street performance by the band, a recording of its music, or a similar interpretation of Caribbean and Brazilian-Afro carnival music. [Anthology editors' note]

Meetings taking place near the words beloved by Hispanic-Americans; earthy and transcendent words never lacking on the shelves of *Macondo* and *Lectorum*, the Spanish-language bookstores of Fourteenth Street—Rómulo's words from the Venezuelan plains, hypnotic words of Gabriel, restless words of Julia, prophetic words of Octavio, harsh words of Nicanor, denouncing words of Miguel Angel.[7]

Meetings being conducted with intensity—someone looking for a Latino priest to Christianize a moorish infidel, somebody needing to find the forms to apply for a green card, another sending a money order to the sister who lost her husband to guerrillas, yet another begging a fellow countryman to let him know if a *chiripa*, an odd job or a fluke of fortune, might turn up for him.

This confluence of Hispanic American nationalities, in this unplanned Bolivarian cosmopolis, is a melding of tongues: the mellifluous tones of Central Americans, the shouting of Caribbeans, the filtered affectations of South Americans. To hear them harmonize such diversity *within the belly of the beast*, to hear them replace the fascist ideal of idiomatic purity with a respect for verbal creativity and the infusion of regionalisms, pleases the ear and delights the intellect. A language that demonstrates its capability to transform itself demonstrates its capacity for permanence.

When I tell you that the photo published in the North American paper moves me, you haven't heard the least of it. That photo impassions me. Why wouldn't the fascinating image of a parade of unfurled Puerto Rican flags not arouse my passion? Like a ship's figurehead or parade vanguard, the street banner proclaims, *Our Language Is Spanish!* It blares, rather than declares, with letters of threatening size. And, according to the caption, one hundred and fifty thousand marching compatriots agree, proclaiming it with hearts and minds.

On the eve of the one hundredth anniversary of the North American invasion, Spanish continues to be the language of the Puerto Rican motherland. A nation of minor epic tradition and perpetual melodrama. For it is true that the practice of over-animated gesticulation, which the Hispanic character often dissolves into, is cultivated in its purest form in Puerto Rico.

The habits of jesting, making witty comebacks, and fooling around provide cover for the melodrama. So much so that the stranger might very well label Puerto Ricans as superficial people devoid of tragedy because they approach everything with delight or dying with laughter. The stranger's perception would be missing the point. The Puerto Rican nation produces nothing that is more dramatic than laughter and nothing more serious. And it is this laughter which consumes a substantial portion of its emotional

---

7. These are all literary allusions to the works of several well-known Latin American writers. The first is an allusion to Venezuelan Rómulo Gallego's novel *Doña Bárbara*; the second to the writings of Columbian Gabriel García Márquez; the third to those of Puerto Rican poet Julia de Burgos; the fourth to those of Mexican poet Octavio Paz; the fifth to those of Chilean poet Nicanor Parra; and the last to Guatemalan writer Miguel Angel Asturias's novel *El señor presidente*.

budget. A laughter which expresses nonconformity rather than complacency, fury rather than feast. A laughter which periodically assumes the responsibility of masquerade.

This nation of minor epic traditions and perpetual melodrama forces those who try to find it on a world map to employ visual effort, given the fact that its graphic depiction is no larger than a pinpoint. Gabriela Mistral,[8] whose poetry is like the very essence of an endless embrace, defines Puerto Rico with finesse as *"Barely reposing on the waters."* The diminutive forms *terruño* [wee land] and *islita* [tiny island] reoccur in popular songs as if comforting, with sweet pity, a country lacking in mass. Puerto Rico is one hundred miles long and thirty-six miles wide, according to the *History* by Silvestrini and Luque.[9]

Other epithets and praises to the tiny island result in a circular rhetoric whose goal is to overcompensate for the helplessness of its size. In fact, these epithets and praises exceed the bounds of exaggeration: Pearl of the Caribbean, Daughter of the Sea and Sun, Land of Eden, Reflection of the Lost Paradise on Earth, the House of All that Is Good.

Above all epithets and praise is the most often performed serenade to Puerto Rico, the beautiful song *Preciosa* [Precious Island] by the great bard Rafael Hernández.[1] It occupies an elevated place in patriotic music together with *Bello Amanecer* [Beautiful Dawn] by Tito Enríquez, *En mi viejo San Juan* [In My Old San Juan] by Noel Estrada and *Verde Luz* [Green Light] by Antonio Cabán Vale.[2] Well-known to Puerto Ricans, the exquisite art song *Preciosa* enumerates the harmonic attributes of Borinquen[3] beauty. A synthesized beauty obtained from the mixture of Taino and Spanish heritage. On the one hand, the savage refrain of the valiant native. On the other, the noble hidalgo of the motherland.

One verse is lacking in *Preciosa*, a verse giving tribute to that sweet blackness, a verse in the style of *Y de ti prende el salero de la tía Africa* [From you sprinkles the salt of Sister Africa]; a salting more manifest among the children of Borinquen, the Boricuas, than Taino ferocity or Iberian noblesse.

The noticeable exclusion of Mother Africa, rooted in our character, our moral fiber, our physical characteristics and advanced spirituality, from *Preciosa*, that enchanting ode to paradise, invites puzzlement and causes wonder. Puzzlement, because blackness sweeps like a wave throughout the Antilles. A wave that is vital, salty, and abundant. Wonderment because the

8. Gabriela Mistral (b. Lucila de María del Perpetuo Socorro Godoy Alcayaga, 1889–1957) was a Chilean poet, educator, and diplomat. She was the first Latin American author to win the Nobel Prize in Literature (1945).
9. A reference to the book *Historia de Puerto Rico: Trayectoria de un pueblo* by Blanca G. Silvestrini and María Dolores de Luque Sánchez.
1. Puerto Rican composer (1892–1965); the song "Preciosa" is considered his masterpiece. [Anthology editors' note]

2. Also known as "El Topo"; Puerto Rican guitarist, singer, and composer of folklore themes (b. 1942). *Tito Enríquez*: Mexican keyboardist and composer (birth date unknown). *Noel Estrada*: Puerto Rican bolero composer (1918–1979). [Anthology editors' note]
3. Puerto Rican; Puerto Rico's indigenous people, the Taínos, called the island Boriquén and themselves Borinqueños or, as below, Boricuas. [Anthology editors' note]

great bard Rafael Hernández was the legitimate relative of Sister Africa. As am I, dark of skin, thick of lip, wide of nose, and nearly kinky-haired. Like half of the Puerto Rican people. Half, if counted quickly, and one omits the towns of Loíza, Arroyo, Dorado, and Carolina.

Could the omission be motivated by the fact that, until recently, the catalogue of western beauty ignored black or negroid features? Could it be that, only recently, Africa was decolonialized and had just acquired the reputation of being beautiful and civilized? Or has the exclusion confirmed that this African parentage continues to embarrass and confound, on this greater Antillean island, what has been painstakingly cleansed with an illusory whitewashing?

Nor do the graphic representations of neighboring lands that surround Puerto Rico exceed the size of a pinpoint. Storyteller, soothsayer, and student of history, a great poet and collector of verse asked himself if the Antilles were not another Pleiades or the remains of the lost Atlantis.[4]

Indeed, the Caribbean is a fragmented whole. The Caribbean is a bouquet of seas kissed by the sun, as we read in trite promotional blurbs. The Caribbean is a postcard torn into four pieces and eleven thousand bits. A postcard encased by bars of salt blocking your way. A postcard that swells with songs of praise, say the tourists who visit the Caribbean. A postcard that swells with intonations of hell, say the natives who leave it behind.

2

Despite its small stature, its insularity, its contemptuous treatment by Imperial Spain, reducing it to a mere footnote in the diary of unknown clerics en route to Peru; despite the irregularity or scarcity of communications with the other fragments of the Caribbean totality; despite the dissociated creoles, Puerto Rico devises, prematurely, a coherent and distinct idea of its national identity. This national identity does not dwell in the house of independence, a dream that eludes the Puerto Rican dreamer as often as it promises itself. The Puerto Rican national identity resides and defines itself, matures and grows, makes friends and finds respect in the adventurous zones of the Spanish language.

A language to be admired for its American impurity. A language that absorbs the clamor that waited for it in the Indies: flights of language flavored by *guanábana*, *mamey*, *guava*; colloquialisms such as *conuco*, *batey*, *canoa*, picked up through dealings with the natives; a riot of Africanisms.[5] A language with a proclivity toward onomatopoeia, toward a music that pulsates with sounds. A language, as a result, deeply rooted in the masses, and which automatically Puerto-Ricanizes, one could say, the many linguistic

4. This a reference to the poem "Canción de las Antillas" [Song of the Antilles] by Puerto Rican Modernist poet and politician Luis Lloréns Torres (1876–1944). *Pleiades*: *Hespérides* in Spanish; star cluster known in astronomy as the Seven Sisters. *Atlantis*: According to Greek mythology, Atlantis was a city in the middle of the Atlantic that sank into the ocean.
5. All of these Spanish words are of Taíno Indian origin. See Luis Hernández Aquino, *Diccionario de voces indígenas en Puerto Rico* (Bilbao, España: Editorial Vasco Americana, 1969).

interferences of English. The gringo says "watchman," the Puerto Rican says "*guachimán.*" The gringo says "hold-up" and the Puerto Rican says "*jolope.*" The gringo says "big shot" and the Puerto Rican says "*bichote.*" A language with ebullient flourishes and cosmoramic synthesis, that doesn't give a damn about norms and keeps language academies in perpetual debate.

Since time immemorial, this Spanish language transformed by natives, Africans and creoles serves each Puerto Rican every time he wishes to whisper a prayer, hurl an insult, write a letter of condolence, or when he feels the urge to send somebody to the smelly nooks of hell. Don't even ask about transcending loneliness or bad company. How well it serves to pray to Mary in the morning, to the Médico Chino[6] in the afternoon, to the Seven African Powers at night and, at who knows what hours, to consult with Walter Mercado and Anita Cassandra for what the stars can foretell.[7]

Above all, this Spanish touched by Indians, this Spanish touched by Africans, this Spanish touched by creoles serves the Puerto Rican by allowing him to unleash a passion anointed by words.

The photograph that relieves the ravages of this winter I spend in New York, like so many other Puerto Ricans, depicts a sign whose words testify *I do it in Spanish.* Raised in the air by the muscular arm of a man whose thirty-something years well agree with him, and accompanied by an attractive woman pointing to the words with her finger, the sign refers to the outcome of love. It refers to the love for a romantic language which gives voice to the shouts and cries of newborns, clamorings, and supplications, flaming moans of sensuality, flames that want everything but to be extinguished. The sign refers to a joyous linguistic voice that proclaims a masculine release of semen. And, to the other, to the feminine voice that counts, quavering, the sixth, the seventh orgasm. This sign refers to the language that elevates this love, the language which is the medium by which the spirit becomes one with matter. And makes it flesh. And demands flesh.

To say languages, says it better.

One language which, during moments of restless love, arises from the mouth of the beloved with a mission to urge forth the heavens, to liberate its less mystic petitions, to call bread, bread and wine, wine. Yes, in moments of sexual intimacy, besides revealing an honesty which eludes social settings, this language harmonizes with the sins of Platonism,[8] with the evaporation of distances between modesty and obscenity, between the permissible and the taboo. Indeed, from time to time, a good ravaging, a getting down to brass tacks without mincing words, beautifies physical love. As is the case during sexual intimacy, so does language disrobe.

6. The expression "el Médico Chino" (literally, the Chinese Doctor) is used in Puerto Rico to express lack of understanding or the difficulty of communicating with someone.
7. Walter Mercado and Anita Cassandra are two popular Puerto Rican astrologists with their own

TV and radio programs, and newspaper columns.
8. The ideas of the ancient Greek philosopher Plato, who considered worldly things to be copies of transcendent ideal forms. [Anthology editors' note]

The other language, during the moments of love's quietude, the moments of sleep following sweet exhaustion, recites the verse of Pablo, of Miguel, of Peache,[9] close to the lips which understand how to listen, beautifully.

## 3

It will soon be nearly one hundred years that the Spanish language has been a border of Puerto Rico. A border confirming its difference to the other side: the gringo and the English language which was to be imposed once and for all. The North American army invaded through Guánica, and through San Juan Dr. Victor Clark invaded with his linguistic North Americaniza-tion crash-course-in-a-briefcase.[1] They were expected to fail, this and subse-quent incidental Mister Clarks. The imposition of English, ludicrous by any stretch of the imagination, was attacked by the protests of all sane journal-ists, the harangues of all conscious politicians, and the half-hearted struggle of those people of minor epic tradition so many times accused of superficial-ity and lack of tragedy because they undertake every task dying of laughter and enjoying it.

Our laughter, how many artificial analyses have been undertaken in its name. Our laughter, cleansed by tears, how often attacked by serious pro-fessionals. Our laughter, laughter as teacher, how little does the Pharisee deny you and misunderstand you.

Why wouldn't the whole country die laughing when the most recalcitrant defenders of the English language express terror, to the point of panic, when faced with the prospect of having to speak it! How is the country not going to enjoy laughing at this perpetual drama when the majority of defenders of *el Difícil* [the Difficult Thing] speak it as if their mouths are filled with tacks, as if spraying gunshot!

*El Difícil?*

Sancho, we've stumbled into *el Difícil.*[2]

As a way of distancing ourselves, swearing oaths at the strangeness, Puerto Ricans have christened the English language with a wonderful alias, *el Difícil.* Such distancing, such swearing of oaths, tear to bits the laughable notion that English finds its way around Puerto Rico as *the* other language. The notion, with its initial demagoguery, reaches an outrageous lie when it claims that Puerto Ricans can maneuver *indiscriminately* back and forth between English and Spanish. If this was indeed the case, these same Puerto Ricans would not argue, as they often gleefully jest, that they chew on *el Difícil* rather than speak it. They chew on it when the imposition of an official language leaves them no other choice but to communicate via gestures. They chew on it when a neighbor, Mister Whoever, who has lived in Puerto Rico since the

---

9. This is a literary allusion to three poets: Pablo Neruda from Chile, Miguel de Unamuno from Spain, and P. H. Hernández from Puerto Rico.
1. Victor Clark was a North American who served as president of Puerto Rico's Education Board during the early years of the U.S. colonial regime. He is known for using the public school system to propagate the Americanization policies of the new government. He wrote the book *Porto Rico and Its Problems* (Washington, D.C.: Brookings Institution, 1930). [See p. 446.]
2. This line is presented as though a present-day Don Quixote, the delusional title character of the novel (1605, 1615) by the Spanish writer Miguel de Cervantes (1547–1616), is speaking to his man-servant, Sancho Panza. [Anthology editors' note]

year of the Kennedy assassination,[3] doesn't struggle a damn bit with speaking Spanish and you have to lend him a hand.

You don't know how many misunderstandings are drawn by the term *el Difícil*! How much semiotic inventiveness! How much, how very much *jaibería* [popular wisdom] shows through! Although it pales in comparison to the *jaibería* and *malamaña* [con artistry] that is condemned as follows.

One obstacle faces the movement to incorporate Puerto Rico as the fifty-first state. This obstacle, in all its suffocating beauty, impossible to disguise or hide, is none other than the everyday Puerto Rican language, the Spanish language.

The sudden invasion by a million relatives of Sister Africa into the North American union would provoke a minor disturbance compared to the mayhem that would be created by the sudden invasion of a million Spanish-speaking Caribbean people. To a country where, at this moment, under the slogan of *English Only*, a battle is being waged against the recognition of any language which would threaten or upset linguistic *unity*. The problem, the irresolute problem with the movement toward the incorporation of Puerto Rico as the fifty-first state, is rooted in the Spanish language; that language which has served the Puerto Rican personality as a home where it can reside and define itself, mature and grow, make friends with itself and find respect.

Like the turn of a screw, the movement to incorporate Puerto Rico as the fifty-first state, like the trick which an able wizard is accustomed to performing, a sleight of hand, a duplicitous con; a decree, of Macondian[4] inspiration, signed and sealed by Governor Don Pedro Roselló González,[5] transforms Puerto Ricans into impeccable bilinguals: beautiful speakers of Spanish and facile users of *el Difícil*.

It is folly not to recognize the importance of the English language in every strata of contemporary life. It is associated with one of the most important, influential and studied cultures of the century. It puts at the disposal of those who are interested a headstrong press, eager to challenge the usurpation of authority, answer duplicity, and question political nonfulfillment. In English, a literature with daring content is expressed, a literature of polished artistry and depth clothed in the many guises of the human condition. Its wide-ranging technical baggage does not stop renewing itself, since electronics, information science and the rest of the sciences of the century use English as their principle means of communication. Those who make the effort to master it possess the key that opens all that the modern world has to offer.

But one cannot cover the sky with one's hand.

3. U.S. president John Fitzgerald Kennedy (b. 1917) was assassinated in 1963. [Anthology editors' note]
4. A reference to the magical town of Macondo in Gabriel García Márquez's novel *One Hundred Years of Solitude*.
5. Pedro Roselló González was a prostatehood governor of Puerto Rico from 1992 to 2000.

Puerto Ricans deal with English from the limited perspective of the foreigner. When required by circumstance, Puerto Ricans employ English as
an instrument of survival. In contrast, the Spanish language is preserved
and valued as an instrument of life.

4

The newspaper photograph I was contemplating still disturbs me. The sea
of Puerto Rican flags unfurled shown in the photo still leaves a lump in my
throat. Still, the banner which exclaims *Our Language Is Spanish!* grips me.

Can so much emotion be a symptom of illness or is it an indication of
health?

I always tell myself that the least harmful kind of nationalism makes villages. And I tell myself that the most harmful kind of nationalism makes
tribes. They both compete in order to triumph or achieve primacy for the
statistic which is only of interest to demographic record-keepers: place of
birth. No, there is no genetic superiority or mysterious touch of the divine
in being part of anything. Although, from the time a Puerto Rican begins to
crawl, he is indoctrinated into believing that to be a North American guarantees genetic superiority and the mysterious touch of the divine, a grace
granted by heaven and revered on earth.

This nationalism, a spurious substitute, barely ever discussed or condemned, prepares to find the nation beyond its borders. This nationalism,
practiced by the most blind reactionary armies, leads to historic irresponsi-
bility, better suited to masquerade theater than the politics of morality—the
Puerto Rican legislature enjoys the perverse distinction of being the only
decision-making body that endorsed the Vietnam War because *the future of
our country* was at stake. Not one legislative assembly in North America
displayed behavior more foolishly pro-American than this!

The Puerto Rican brand of nationalism, as in the observation of Albert
Camus[6]—*to arrive at human society, one has to go through nationality*, the
type that claims its sovereignty among varied voltages of expression—
pragmatics, superflamboyants, radicals, closes ranks behind a single watchword, one standing for permanent, spiritual unyieldingness. But it does not
incite the village nor raise up the tribal dust.

In Puerto Rico, which throughout the centuries has served as a convenient stopping-off point for foreign travelers passing through or in need of
aid, nationalist sentiment has never had an exclusionary character that is
found in other latitudes, other developed First World countries. This nation,
conceived surreptitiously as a dream which eludes the Puerto Rican dreamer
as often as it promises itself, has fashioned itself as a house with open doors,
a house where generosity is in style.
One recent example comes to mind.

---

6. French writer (1913–1960). [Anthology editors' note]

During the last thirty years, this house of open doors has seen itself bombarded, practically speaking, by some of those pieces of that torn postcard that is the Caribbean. Hoards of Cubans and masses of Dominicans have installed themselves there and established a firm, admirably impudent foothold, to the extent that some of the rooms in this house, like Isla Verde and Capetillo,[7] have become, respectively, cubanized and dominicanized. A few of these elements have displayed rather blemished behavior. Others have shown themselves to be all out discourteous. In response, thankfully, Puerto Ricans have not neglected the norms of generosity which had been forged throughout the centuries. They have seen past some of this disrespect, some of this ingratitude. Generously, they have facilitated the exchange of customs and traditions, arrived at a productive coexistence with one another as hosts, as friends, as neighbors, as brothers.

Neither provincial nor tribal nor irresponsible, but another distinct feeling and ineffable manifestation of the soul is *the natural love of homeland*. This is what the Inca Garcilaso[8] called the torrent of affection that is unleashed in the spirit when you listen again to the voices who rocked you in your infancy, the voices of your heritage, the voices of the place where you belong. They are the voices with names like country, birthplace, the name spoken from the lips of a mother. They are the voices of things: the parlor of home, the rough-hewn seesaw, the make-believe horse made from the handle of a broom. They are the voices of aromas—rice cooking, oatmeal drinks. They are the voices of color—dawn's light through the blinds, the flowering mango on the way to school, a cinnamon-colored dog. They are the voices that speak of *places in the memory*, as they are called by today's most daring and lyrical Puerto Rican poet, Aurea Sotomayor.[9] They are the voices that occupy territory in our memory until death or madness disengage them.

*The motherland defends itself against the ruins of exile*, according to the carefully weighed words of Edward Said.[1] It defends itself against the homelessness expressed by loneliness. And against the wretchedness that the emigrant endures. Country defends itself against solitude in the world— the *world* always invites the distance, always lives in the distance.

I confess that this natural love of homeland, whose manifestation and feeling varies from person to person, has been expressed barely by me in the same epic and eloquent proportions as expressed in the anguish that defines the poetry of Luis Palés Matos.[2] Or when fragrance transforms into a voice like that of Carmen Delia Dipiní and carries a song by Sylvia Rexach.[3] What soulful lament is seen in these poems, what melancholy I feel which is translated by these songs, I cannot even begin to understand. Even less does my

7. City in northeastern Puerto Rico. *Isla Verde*: a district of the city of Carolina, northeastern Puerto Rico. [Anthology editors' note]
8. See p. 61. [Anthology editors' note]
9. Aurea María Sotomayor Miletti (birth date unknown), writer and professor at the University of Puerto Rico. [Anthology editors' note]
1. Palestinian American literary theorist and cultural critic (1935–2003). [Anthology editors' note]
2. Puerto Rican poet (1898–1959). [Anthology editors' note]
3. Puerto Rican poet, singer, and composer of boleros (1922–1961). *Carmen Delia Dipiní*: Puerto Rican bolero singer (1927–1998). [Anthology editors' note]

reason fathom what memory is stirred in the tombs of time, what imagery is awakened in the subconscious by these voices. In like manner, I am moved when I contemplate a canvas by Carlos Raquel Rivera[4] that rises with the flames of a Puerto Rican sunset, flames that will be conquered by imminent nightfall. What apostrophe to my heart is released by that masterful canvas, I do not even know. What I do know is that it sears me. Just as I am seared by the photograph of the sea of Puerto Rican flags unfurled behind the banner that declares *Our language Is Spanish!*

I confess, then, that this natural love of homeland is concentrated within me silently, soporiferously,[5] pleasantly. I confess, then, that Puerto Rico envelopes my heart like a perpetual blessing.

This New Yorkian February afternoon that I spend, like so many thousands of other Puerto Ricans, has a certain dying splendor, more conducive to tarnishing things than to displaying them. Now, the splendor ceases, like Bécquer[6]-like sighs, unnoticed. Out with the old, in with the new: electricity rushes through the streetlights and announces nightfall. This bedraggled winter afternoon has mournful shadows, shadows which gore and tear apart the street where I live; it is an afternoon with baneful cavern-like light. And to think that it is five o'clock in the afternoon on all the clocks! To think that it is exactly five o'clock![7]

1993                                                                                          1994

4. Puerto Rican painter and printmaker (b. 1923). [Anthology editors' note]
5. I.e., soporifically; inducing or tending to induce sleep. [Anthology editors' note]
6. Gustavo Adolfo Domínguez Bastida, better known as Gustavo Adolfo Bécquer (1836–1870), Spanish writer. [Anthology editors' note]

7. This refers to a verse in the poem "Elegía a la muerte de Ignacio Sánchez Mejía" [Eulogy to the Death of Ignacio Sánchez Mejía] by Spanish writer Federico García Lorca. Sánchez Mejías was a famous bullfighter who was mortally wounded during a bullfight at five o'clock in the afternoon.

---

# ESTELA PORTILLO TRAMBLEY
## 1936–1999

An early Chicana writer, Estela Portillo Trambley took a sensitive, universal approach to female characters whose freedom is persistently curtailed in a patriarchal society. Her work asks readers to rebel against gender stereotypes, and Portillo Trambley frequently complained that, because she was a woman, she was denied the recognition received by male Chicano authors such as Tomás Rivera, Rudolfo A. Anaya, and Rolando Hinojosa. She was born in El Paso, Texas, and spent most of her life there. From the College of Mines (now part of the University of Texas), in El Paso, she earned a master's degree in English literature. She taught high school, wrote and directed plays, wrote fiction and poetry (notably haiku), and hosted a radio talk show and a Hispanic cultural-affairs TV program, before becoming resident dramatist at El Paso Community College in 1970. In 1995, she held the Presidential Chair in Creative Writing at the University of California, Davis.

Portillo Trambley is best-known for *Rain of Scorpions and Other Writings* (1975), which includes the story anthologized here, "The Paris Gown." In this cautionary tale, the protagonist, Clotilde, is a strong-willed and free-spirited young woman from an upper-class Spanish family in northern Mexico. Her father is trying to force her to marry an old, rich man, and a gown ordered for the engagement announcement becomes an important element in the surprise ending. Portillo Trambley also published a novel, *Trini* (1986), about a Mexican woman's fight for survival. In her play *The Day of the Swallows*, published in 1970 in the journal *El Grito*, a woman trapped by societal disapproval of her lesbian relationship commits a horrific act of violence and later commits suicide. Also notable among her seven other plays is *Sor Juana* (1983), about the victimization by the male establishment of the seventeenth-century Mexican nun Sor Juana Inés de la Cruz. Known as "The Tenth Muse," Sor Juana became a touchstone of Chicana feminists, in part thanks to Portillo Trambley's appreciation.

# The Paris Gown

"Cognac with your coffee, Teresa?"

"No, thank you, Gran—Clo." Somehow the word "grandmother" did not suit Clotilde Romero de Traske, sophisticated, chic, and existentially fluent. Teresa had awaited with excitement this after-dinner tête à tête. She knew so little about this woman who had left her home in Mexico so long ago. The young girl curiously searched her grandmother's face for signs of age. There were few. They were indistinguishable in the grace and youthful confidence exuded by this woman. Her gestures, eyes, flexible body, and above all her quick, discerning mind spoke of the joy of living.

Clotilde was an art dealer at the Rue Auber. Back home she was more than that. She was a legend. Tongues wagged incessantly recounting her numerous marriages, her travels, her artistic ventures, her lovers, and the rich and famous that frequented her salon. Then there was the hushed up scandal concerning her departure from Mexico so long ago. No one was willing to tell an innocent girl like Teresa how her grandmother had come to live in Paris. Back home, the wealthy women cushioned in static, affluent, stagnant lives had clacked tongues in furious gossip about the infamous Clotilde. Infamous or not, Clotilde Romero de Traske was to be admired.

"How do you like Paris, child?" There was a daring in her grandmother's eyes.

"Oh, I love it. It's so old-world—so rich in history and culture."

The older woman laughed. "Above all, Paris is a flesh and blood city, the City of Lights. Here the soul blossoms like a flower opening to the sun."

"Yes, I felt it. But I'm not clever enough to put it the way you did."

"You are most clever and lucky. Everybody should see Paris before they are twenty-five. I heard that somewhere. Can't remember where. But, there is no place like it in the world."

You should know, Grandmother, Teresa reminded herself. You've been everywhere, but you never returned. It was time to ask.

"You never returned home, Clo. Why?"

"Does anyone ever really go back home? We change so with time, but home remains the same, and so it's no longer home. Home to me is the pieces of my life that have fitted the puzzle called 'me.' Good or bad—ugly or beautiful. I guess I'm home."

"Were you always so wise?"

The grandmother laughed. "My dear, if you knew the idiotic things I've done. Wisdom is what you learn from the mountain of mistakes you make in life."

It was amazing, the beautiful clear depth of the "legend." Teresa felt a rush of admiration for the emberlike quality of her grandmother's spirit. It filled the room. She knows who she is, thought Teresa. How wonderful to have reached that comprehension of one's place in the universe. Teresa looked about the room and decided that it too was a piece of Clotilde, of what she had become in the life process. The art, the furniture, the flowers were all impressions of a great ferocity for living. Teresa caught herself. Why am I doing this? Analyzing rooms? My grandmother? Yet the feeling of the room could not be ignored. The colors were wonderful. They seemed to awaken feelings she could not really define. Maybe it's all a mystery beyond me.

"So—you are traveling with a university group?" Clotilde's expressive eyes searched her granddaughter's face.

She thinks I'm uncomfortable, thought Teresa. "I escaped."

"Escaped?"

"You know what I mean."

Clotilde laughed. "Assuredly, not in the same way."

"I can't believe the attitudes back home. They all live in the seventeenth century where I must not be exposed to the evils of the world." Teresa realized the petulance of her words.

"You really believe that?" Clo seemed amused.

"They're all stifling, sometimes my mother, my father, my aunts, you name it! Everybody back home is so—so proper."

Clo reflected, "Some moles, some eagles. I don't mean to judge, but you know what they say, 'different strokes'—"

Teresa laughed. "—'for different folks'. Of course. But *you* don't think 'old'!" Teresa saw the fairness in Clo's words.

"What is 'old'? Don't you think it's a knack for seeing what's real?" Clotilde put down her cup and walked to the mantelpiece over the fireplace as if she wanted to observe her granddaughter from a new perspective. Teresa also saw something new. A convex reflection of mood. Clo was the focal point in front of the wild, unkempt order of her art, a form liberated from civilized order. Teresa felt more than knew it, for she knew little about art.

"I love your paintings, your sculpture. The old mixed in with the new . . . I know very little about art, but this excites me."

"How discerning! Your feel for art is more important than knowing about it, art without doctrinaire implications."

"What does that mean?"

"You felt something. It left an impression perhaps relating to your experiences. You do not need rules or labels to understand."

Teresa felt inadequate. But it spurred her, so she asked, "Are you an artist yourself, Clo?"

"A very bad one, I'm afraid. When I was your age, I thought I had great talent. I was foolish."

"So you became a dealer in art?"

"It amounted to that after so many years." The collector went up to a massive piece of sculpture and touched its outline reverently. "Have you ever heard of Gaudier-Brzeska?"[1]

"Heavens no." Teresa confessed her ignorance, knowing that she was about to be enlightened.

"Gaudier was a man of great passion, a primitive; he plunged into the world of feeling, and instinct, and energy. Free of barbarism."

This puzzled Teresa. "Primitive—barbarism—don't these go together?"

"Primitives? People of instinct and intuition—free—like children in their thinking, like animals when in fear—brutal. Savages, you might say, but savages do less harm than barbarians. Barbarians are a product of civilization. Artists attempt to preserve our humanity. Civilization destroys it, little by little."

Teresa was intrigued. "Artists are not barbarians?"

Clo checked herself. "*Some* artists cannot be barbarians if they are artists. Remember, barbarians are associated with crudeness of taste, excessive greed, excessive cruelty, and a fondness to be on top. What does that sound like to you?" She did not wait for an answer but continued. "Politicians, big business, warmongers for great gain. All these are creatures of civilization."

"That's not what I learned in history books." Teresa was bewildered.

Clotilde looked apologetic. "I talk too much. I think too much for my own good. Gaudier made out of stone and metal what I have tried to make out of my life—to leave the field of invention open, to step out of apathetic and pathetic comforts."

"You're free . . ." Why had she said that? She didn't even know why the people back home considered Clotilde so infamous. If the result of infamy led to the kind of woman standing next to her, then it must have redeeming virtues. She touched the figure by Gaudier as if to add a part to herself, to understand what made her grandmother who she was. "I know now why you never went back to Mexico, Clo . . ."

"I may go back one of these days, if the fancy strikes me."

"Why? If I had a choice I would stay in Paris."

"Ah! But you do have a choice."

"No, no, my father would forbid it. You know how fathers are. They're so archaic." But no matter how archaic, I'll always obey him, do what he says, think what he thinks, Teresa realized. She asked Clo, "How old were you when you ran away from home?"

"I didn't exactly run away." Clotilde's eyes were full of memories.

Teresa did not want to press. She got up and walked around the room, looking at paintings, vases, bronze figures. She pondered aloud, "I can't imagine my father being comfortable in this room. It is too primitive and wild and free, without rules . . ."

Clotilde concluded, ". . . and fathers love rules."

"More than they love us?" Teresa looked at her grandmother intently.

"You want to know how I felt about my father's love?"

"Yes . . ." Teresa's voice anticipated.

---

1. Henri Gaudier-Brzeska (1891–1915), French sculptor.

"He was proud of me because I was pretty, because I was modest. But he was foremost a businessman and a very rich man. I'm not condemning him. He tried to be fair, but all the rules were his rules. I was a commodity to him, an investment. He could marry me off to a man of property. That was good business."

"That was not love. My father didn't want me to go to the university in Mexico City—but he gave in."

"It's a different time from my time, Teresa. Each generation has its dead ends for women." The grandmother's words were the words of experience.

"Did he try to marry you off to a rich man?" Teresa remembered that part of the story from back home.

"Oh, yes, he had decided to marry me to Don Ignacio, our neighbor, a widower about my father's age."

"I'm glad I live in this generation." Teresa felt a tinge of relief.

Clo's eyes were back in time. "It was something that rich fathers did. Quite commonplace. Then there were the alternatives: If you refused to marry your father's choice, there was the nunnery. Or—remaining single, an old maid, totally dependent on the charity of others, unwanted and ignored. There were times I considered running away with the stable boy. He was beautiful, so young and strong. But that choice led to poverty, sacrifice, discomforts. That's all there was until the day Tío Gaspar came to visit.

"He had squandered his inheritance living the life of a bohemian. I liked him; he treated my brother and me like people. He didn't talk down to us. Spent hours talking about his gypsy life and the freedom of artists. He painted—badly, but with heart. He bought some easels for my brother and me so we could try our hand at watercolors. When my brother showed his first picture to my father, my father was so proud he fooled himself into thinking that Manolo had great talent. But that was to be expected. He always raved about anything my brother did. The sun rose and set around my brother; after all, he was a boy, a varón, a macho, his future heir. I was only a girl."

"It's still like that with many families."

"Oh yes, traditions do not die easy. For thousands of years men have believed themselves superior to women. They do not mean to be cruel. They are just overwhelmed with this self-given image." Clotilde paused, then asked, "Do you have a young man?"

"I've fallen in love several times. Most men want to possess you. So I run away."

"Are you running away now?"

"In a way. The word 'love' confuses me," Teresa confessed.

"Your instinct is pure. You sense that love can destroy you when it is not love but the illusion of love. I myself have been so careful. I hear the wisdom of the prophet and use it to measure the quality of love. It's a good test."

"What prophet?" Teresa was intrigued.

"Khalil Gibran.[2] His words—'But let there be spaces in your togetherness . . .' Real love respects separateness. I have chosen well."

2. Lebanese American artist and writer (1883–1931), best-known for *The Prophet* (1923), a book of philosophical essays.

Clotilde made her way to the French windows leading to her garden and opened them. She did not go outside but looked out from the doorway as Teresa came up behind her. Teresa was amazed. The garden was like the room—lacking neat symmetry, with a cobblestone path leading to nowhere in particular and trailing vines snaking up cypress trees. Here and there flowers grew like surprises. A storybook garden—the secret garden—a garden found in dreams. What was that fragrance? Teresa inhaled it slowly, deliberately. "What is it?"

"Italian jasmine, a gift from a man who knows the pricelessness of our aloneness. That is a must: to find the heights of oneself, a solitary journey."

"Where is he now?"

"I don't know. He had a calling to walk the silence among pyramids. But he'll be back. He always surprises me."

"All those alternatives you talked about back home you didn't take any of them, Grandmother." She dared to use the word now. Clotilde's ember eyes accepted.

"My father bought my brother expensive artist's palettes and gave him lessons. But then, Manolo took advantage. He had no talent. His work was awkward and miserable. But he told my father he wanted to study art seriously; would my father finance a stay in Paris? He didn't want to study art, just have a good time. Tío Gaspar knew I was a much better artist. He bought me books on art and told me I must give it my full dedication if I were ever to go to Paris. An open door! My father could send me to an artists' colony, I could travel. When my father heard these plans, he was enraged. How dare I presume I could have such freedoms! I was only a girl! I should dedicate myself to learning the social graces, to embroidering, practicing meekness, to readying myself for a worthy husband. But I did just the opposite. I spent my days reading all the art books I could get my hands on. Mostly I took Manolo's, for he merely threw them aside and never bothered to read one. I worked and worked on landscapes and painting with charcoal. I was truly convinced I had a talent. I had always competed with Manolo—to dare my father. I needed his approval so badly. My brother and I rode horses, and we loved to ride. I would ride my horse into the hills, without a saddle, my hair wild and unkempt. Again, all this angered my father. Nevertheless, one summer he bought a pair of stallions, beautiful horses, for Manolo and me. Every morning I would race Manolo and beat him every time. My father would watch, and after the race I would run to him, throw back my head, and look him in the eye, hoping for some word of praise. He was oblivious to me, his eyes on my brother, though he chided, 'A man must never allow a woman to outdo him. A varón can ride better than a mere girl. A man must master all things!' Funny, Manolo never mastered anything. I did all things well, but I never heard a word of praise from my father."

They walked into the garden in silence, watching a bird hop along a branch. The cypress looked silver in the slant of shadows and sun. From outside the garden walls came the sounds of moving traffic, whistles, muffled conversations, the splashing of rain puddles left from the night before, a wonderful cacophony touching only the edge of a life. Clotilde led her visitor along the cobblestone path that rambled to nowhere in particular. They came to a low stone bench facing an arched terrace lined with colored earthen pots full of flowers. How Mexican! thought Teresa. They sat absorbing sounds until her grandmother picked up the threads of her thoughts and feelings of long ago.

"Well, my brother did not want to go into the banking business, so he talked my father into sending him to Europe with Tío Gaspar to study art! He, of course, had no intentions of doing so; he wanted the good times of the idle rich. He would write letters to me from here, from Montmartre,[3] about the great life, making new friends. He claimed people were alive in Paris. The phrase echoed again and again in my thoughts—where people were alive, where people were alive . . . I went to my father and asked him if I could go live with Manolo and Tío Gaspar to study art. I reminded him how much more talent I had than my brother. Papá thought I was insane. 'What! You're only a girl! It's time you thought about marriage.' That's when he told me about his plans for marrying me off to Don Ignacio; a great dream of his life—to merge two great estates. I had to pay the price for being *bien gentille!*[4] I argued with him, told him I deserved better than the fates imposed on women in the town. I demanded equality with Manolo; I wanted the same trust and freedom. My mother accused me of wanting to drive my father to his grave. He was close to a nervous breakdown because of my selfish and willful behavior. Why couldn't I behave like a good daughter? Like a good woman?"

Teresa understood. "All choices were dead ends."

Clotilde rose and walked among the earthen pots, feeling the twinges of pain in the memory of a sad experience. Then she stood tall, looked at the blue-hazed sky and smiled down at her granddaughter, continuing her story:

"Dead ends, yes. I had to think of something, something to free myself from a prison that made me a lesser being. I took my horse and ran away into the hills. No, it was not running away, really. When I raced my horse I felt the only freedom I knew. I rode and rode, my mind, my body, my spirit melting in the wind, the wild nature of the hills. I stopped racing my horse when I could go no more! My poor little horse was so tired. It was dark and I realized I was lost. I heard the scurrying of some animal in the dark; it terrified me, so I huddled against a clump of bushes and cried myself into a numbness. Then I decided to die with the night's cold.

"I didn't die with the night's cold, but I almost died after three days of thirst, hunger, and exposure to the heat of the days and the cold of the nights. I had given up when my father's search party found me. He had been looking for two days. I remember how he picked me up in his arms. There were tears in his eyes. Poor dear father. In his blind way he loved me . . . Well, I came down with pneumonia and was delirious for a long time. There were no miracle drugs then. I awoke one afternoon to see my father hovering over me. He was so gentle and concerned. My first thought was to take advantage of that concern. In a weakened voice I begged him not to force me to marry old Don Ignacio, to let me go to Paris. I remember his eyes widening in angry surprise, a look of disbelief on his face. He gave me a long lecture on the consequences of my rebellion, my unloving manner toward my family, my ingratitude, and on and on . . . He stormed out of my room and refused to come visit me during my recovery. In a way, it was a blessing in disguise. I had time to think."

3. A section of Paris traditionally associated with artists and bohemian life.    4. Really nice (French).

It was time to gather thoughts and feelings and to put them in perspective. Clotilde surveyed her garden as if it were some part of a triumphal memory. "Look around. This garden is so different from the garden in my father's house. It was an impressive garden, manicured to perfection. It had a pond with swans and flowers, all in symmetry, according to color and species. I remember hedge after hedge after hedge. I looked out my window during my recovery and saw some of my little cousins playing hide-and-seek just as I had when I was a child, running from one hedge to another. Two children around four years old were happily playing when a toddler ran toward them. They walked him over to the pond to play. When the child saw the water, he took off his clothes and went in. The water came up to his knees. I saw the nurse running to him, picking him up, shaking him in reprimand. She turned him around and spanked his little bottom. A curious episode of innocence. But the whole day the scene kept coming back into my mind. I was trying to find a solution to my life, and this scene kept intruding. Suddenly I had an answer, a real solution to escape my father's tyranny."

Teresa's eyes awaited the wonderful solution, but Clotilde merely motioned for them to return to the house. Teresa followed Clotilde back into the room where light and shadows played in whispered silences. Clotilde walked to the Gaudier sculpture and touched flowing curves that mated. She kept her hand on the figure as if transferring some unknown energy from the figure to herself. Then she went on with her story.

"After that I became the daughter that my parents wanted. I didn't argue or beg. I simply accepted their plans for my marriage. It was all a feigned acceptance, of course. I pretended great interest in an engagement party they were planning to announce my marriage to Don Ignacio. I was to have the best and most exclusive ball any young girl had ever had. Money was no object. My father, overwhelmed by my docility, told me I could have whatever my heart desired. My heart's desire! He had already forgotten what it was. He meant something he could buy for me.

"So I played his game. 'Papa,' I said, 'I would like a beautiful gown from Paris, by the best designer, elegant, expensive . . .' I remember how his eyes lighted up. To parade me around in finery that would show off his money, he liked that. 'Of course,' he said, the most expensive gown he could buy. Right away my mother and he set about getting hold of the best Paris couturier and ordering a gown to my specifications. In the following weeks I corresponded with a French designer and told him exactly what I had in mind. At the dinner table I would talk of nothing else, like some frivolous fool! My father was so pleased that I had finally fallen into the routine pattern of genteel women.

"Finally the gown arrived. It was a beautiful gown, with masses of tulle and lace and pearl insets, all done by hand. The French designer assured my father there was no other gown like it in the world. Then my life became a whirl of parties with the fawning Don Ignacio by my side. How I hated the man! What makes old, rich, doddering fools think they deserve a young wife? But I went through all the social rituals and pretended gaity. At night I would lock the door of my room and put on my Paris gown. I would stare at the image in the mirror, at the beautiful gown, at the face wanting courage, wanting enough valor to carry out the plan. I knew that what I intended to do would assure my freedom."

The afternoon sun had lost its full ardor. The pale coolness of early dusk came through the opened doors. On a line of light, pieces of shadows touched the coming night with a gentle sobriety. It was a time suitable for sadness, part of the long ago and part of the present. Clotilde picked up the threads of her design from so long ago. "I spent a lot of time after that planning a grand entrance at the ball. My father decided that at a precise moment he would make a champagne toast and direct the guests' attention to my entrance, down the long staircase. I would come down wearing my Paris gown. Both my father and Don Ignacio were looking forward to the occasion with great pride. How appropriate! My father would show off the precious possession he was turning over to his very rich friend!

"The night of the banquet I stayed in my room, making myself beautiful, but my thoughts were with my racing horse, the wind, and the taste of freedom. I could hear the music from downstairs, people talking and laughing. The gown was laid out on my bed in full glory. It was really a beautiful thing. But then, my plan was a beautiful plan. Close to the appointed time for my descent, I put the finishing touches to my face, my hair; then, I was ready. I had to be brave. When I opened the door, the orchestra had just begun playing the music for my entrance. My father's voice rose above the music for the toast, making some remark about the long friendship of the two families that were to be united, then the voice of Don Ignacio toasting our future happiness. In my mind's eye I could see all the glasses raised.

"I swallowed hard and slipped silently down the hall to the staircase. I could feel my whole body trembling, but I knew I could not falter. I was at the top of the staircase. I remember how cold the banisters were. My throat was tight and my head high. I did not look down. I guided my footing on each step as I counted. That was what was important, counting the steps to my freedom. There would be no marriage, no convent, no old maid existence for me. I remember the next words that came out of my father's mouth: 'May I present . . .' Then I heard the cries of disbelief and horror, yes, among all present. Still, I held my head high and looked directly into their faces, all frozen by shock. I saw my mother fall into a faint. And poor Don Ignacio, his face was purple, his mouth gaping. He flung his glass to the floor and left the room without ceremony. But no one noticed because all eyes were on me. After all, how often had they seen a girl of my upbringing, betrothed to the richest man in town, come down a staircase—stark naked . . ."

Clotilde's hands played with the buttons of her blouse, lost in the memory of her truimph. There was a sudden flurry of curtains touched by wind. Teresa went up to her and kissed her cheek. "You were so brave, so brave . . ."

Clotilde smiled as she talked about the consequences of her act. "My poor darling father! I will really never know the full extent of his distress, his shame. He couldn't abandon an insane daughter rejected by his best friend. But she couldn't remain in his house as a constant reminder of the scandal she had caused. He had the solution. He would send her away forever with enough funds to stay away. Poor darling father!"

"Were you lonely leaving everything behind?"

"Of course I was lonely, but I've never had any regrets."

"It was all worth it, then . . . the solitary journey."

"Oh, yes, it's all that matters, my child."

Both women looked out of the window and caught the last full colors of the day.

1975

# RUDOLFO A. ANAYA
## b. 1937

Rudolfo Alfonso Anaya is one of the foremost Mexican American writers. Having grown up listening to family members tell *cuentos*, traditional stories involving witches and mysterious events, Anaya firmly believes in the preservation of New Mexico's *mexicano* culture. In his novels, plays, children's books, nonfiction explorations, and folktale anthologies, he connects the oral traditions of New Mexico with modernist literary exploration, Native American culture with environmentalism.

He was born in Las Pasturas, a rural village in New Mexico. The fifth of seven children, he also had three half-siblings from his parents' previous marriages. With his family, he moved to Santa Rosa, on the eastern New Mexico plains. In their isolation, Santa Rosa and the surrounding villages would become Anaya's literary locus. His best-selling and best-known novel, *Bless Me, Ultima* (1972), is defined by their landscapes. And Anaya's love for the desert is on display everywhere in his work, including in *Jalamanta: A Message from the Desert* (1996). As a teenager, Anaya moved with his family to Albuquerque. In 1963, he received his bachelor's degree from the University of New Mexico, where he began writing poetry and fiction. He worked as a public school teacher in Albuquerque from 1963 to 1970, and during that period he married Patricia Lawless. Anaya then worked as the director of counseling for the University of Albuquerque before accepting a position as an associate professor at the University of New Mexico. He received one master's degree from that institution in 1968 and another in 1973.

*Bless Me, Ultima*, Anaya's breakthrough novel (the first two chapters of which are excerpted here), took him seven years to write. After it was rejected by various New York publishing houses, he sent it to Quinto Sol Publications, a small press in Berkeley, California, and in 1971 it received *el premio Quinto Sol* (the Fifth Sun prize) for best novel. (The previous year, Tomás Rivera's *. . . y no se lo tragó la tierra* [ . . . and the Earth Did Not Part] received the first such prize.) Dealing with faith and the loss of faith, *Bless Me, Ultima* presents the New Mexico *llanos* (plains) through local legends and a stark realism that contrasts with, but does not destroy, the mystical sense felt by the protagonist, young Antonio Márez. Highly sensitive and impressionable, Antonio witnesses murder, witchcraft, and the gathering of the Márez and Luna clans as his mentor, Ultima, a *curandera* (wise healer), imparts knowledge to him. Anaya writes lovingly of the Márez family's hardscrabble existence, then of its breakup when Antonio's three brothers return as World War II veterans ready to move beyond the plains. Through the changes then facing New Mexico's countless villages and the cities they overshadow, Anaya subtly presents the changes facing the United States.

In his next novel, *Heart of Aztlán* (1976), Anaya continues to record the changes in New Mexico. Showing New Mexican Chicanos in both rural and urban settings was a first for Mexican American writers from that part of the Southwest. Anaya's use of the word *Aztlán*, the mythical homeland of Chicanos much mentioned within the Chicano Movement of the 1960s and early 1970s, awakened political sensibilities among younger Mexican Americans in New Mexico. Anaya's third novel, *Tortuga* (1979), the third part of a loose trilogy with *Bless Me, Ultima* and *Heart of Aztlán*, is about the rites of passage undergone by a youngster in a hospital ward during the polio epidemics of the early 1950s. The plot is partly autobiographical; in his youth, Anaya survived a life-threatening spinal injury. The enchanting, risky story "The Apple Orchard" (1980), included here, also deals with youth, depicting schoolboys' sexual curiosity and the path toward "becoming a man."

The nonfictional *A Chicano in China* (1986) displays Anaya's talents as an observer and commentator. His four detective novels—*Zia Summer* (1995), *Rio Grande Fall*

(1996), *Shaman Winter* (1999), and *Jemez Spring* (2005)—address the ongoing accul-turation, urbanization, assimilation, and racism in New Mexico. In each book, the Chicano sleuth Sonny Baca solves a mystery amidst Albuquerque's *mexicano* and Native American communities. "Bendíceme, América," also included here, is a lecture Anaya delivered in 1992 at the Mercantile Library, in New York City. The occasion was a national gathering of Latino writers to mark the (controversial) quin-centennial, or 500th anniversary, of the Genoa-born Spanish admiral Christopher Columbus's first voyage across the Atlantic Ocean and his exploration of the lands that would come to be known as the Americas. In this piece, Anaya calls for a new awareness of social, political, and environmental issues as the Old World and the New World become increasingly intertwined.

In 1993, Anaya retired from the University of New Mexico, where he held the Regents Professorship and received the Regents Meritorious Service Medal. Among his awards are various honorary degrees, a City of Los Angeles Award, and the Mexican Medal of Friendship from the Mexican Consulate. Anaya has twice won New Mexico's Governor Public Service Award. In 1980, he was invited by U.S. president Jimmy Carter to read at the White House in a Salute to American Poets and Writers. In 2002, he received from U.S. president George W. Bush the National Medal of Arts.

# The Apple Orchard

The last week of school and the warm spring weather made us restless. Pico and Chueco ditched every chance they got, and when they came to school it was only to bother the girls and upset the teachers, otherwise they played hooky in Durán's apple orchard, the large orchard which lay between the school and our small neighborhood. They smoked cigarettes and looked at *Playboy* magazines, which they stole from their older brothers.

I had stayed with them once, but my father had found out about it and he had been very angry. "It costs money to send you to school," he had said, "so go! Go and learn everything there is to learn! That's the only way to get ahead in this world! Don't play hooky with those tontos,[1] they will never amount to anything!" So I dragged myself to school, which, in spite of the warm spring weather, had one consolation: Miss Brighton. She was the young substitute teacher who had come to replace Mr. Portales, who had had a nervous breakdown. I had her for first-period English and last-period study hall. The day she arrived I helped her move her supplies and books, so we formed a good friendship. I think I fell in love with her, because I looked forward to her class, and I was sad when she told me she would be with us only these few days until the end of school. Next year she would have a regular job in Santa Fe.

So for a few weeks I was happy, and my fascination with Miss Brighton grew. During study hall I would pretend to read, but most often I would sit and stare over my book at her. When she happened to glance up she would smile at me, and sometimes she came to my desk and asked me what I was reading. She loaned me a few books, and after I read them and told her what I had found in them she was very pleased. Her lips curled in a smile

---

1. Fools, dolts.

which almost laughed and her bright eyes shone with light. I began to memorize her features, and at night I began to dream of her.

Then on the last day of school Pico and Chueco came up with their crazy idea. It didn't interest me at first, but the truth is I was also filled with curiosity. So I gave in reluctantly.

"It's the only way to become a man," Pico said, as if he really knew what he was talking about.

"Yeah," Chueco agreed, "we've seen it in pictures, but you gotta see the real thing to know what it's like."

"Okay, okay," I said finally, "I'll do it."

That night I stole into my parents' bedroom. I had never done that before. Their bedroom was a place where they could go for privacy, and I was never to interrupt them when they were in there. My father had only told me that once. We were washing his car when unexpectedly he turned to me and said, "When your mother and me are in the bedroom you should never disturb us, understand?" I nodded. I knew that part of their life was shut off to me, and it was to remain a mystery.

Now I felt like a thief as I stood in the dark and saw their dark forms on the bed. My father's arm rested over my mother's hip. I heard his low, peaceful snore and I was relieved that he was asleep. I hurried quickly to her bureau and opened her small vanity box. I knew the small mirror we needed for our purpose lay among the bottles of perfume and nail polish. My hands trembled when I found it. I slipped it into my pocket and left the room quickly.

"Did you get it?" Pico asked the next morning.

We met in the apple orchard where we always met on the way to school. The flowering trees buzzed with honeybees as they swarmed over the thick clusters of white petals. The fragrance reminded me of my mother's vanity case, and for a moment I wondered if I should surrender the mirror to Pico. I had never stolen anything from her before. But it was too late to back out. I took the mirror from my pocket and held it out. For a moment it reflected the light which filtered through the canopy of apple blossoms, then Pico howled and we ran to school.

Miss Brighton was the kindest teacher we knew, so we decided to steal the glue from her room.

"Besides, she likes you," Pico said. "You keep her busy, I'll steal the glue." So we pushed our way past the mob which filled the hallway to her room.

"Isador," she smiled when she saw me at the door, "what are you doing at school so early?" She looked at Pico and Chueco, and a slight frown crossed her face.

"I came for the book," I reminded her. She was dressed in bright spring yellow, and the light which shone through the windows glistened on her dress and her soft hair.

"Of course . . . I have it ready." I walked with her to the desk and she handed me the book. I glanced at the title, *The Arabian Nights*. I shivered because out of the corner of my eye I saw Pico grab a bottle of glue and stick it under his shirt.

"Thank you," I mumbled. We turned and raced out of the room to the bathroom. A couple of eighth graders stood by the windows, looking out and smoking cigarettes. They usually paid little attention to us seventh graders, so we slipped unnoticed into one of the stalls. Pico closed the door. Even in the early morning the stall was already warm and the odor very bad.

"Okay, break the mirror," Pico whispered.

"Seven years bad luck," Chueco reminded me.

"Don't pay attention to him, break it!" Pico commanded.

I took the mirror from my pocket, recalled for a moment the warm, sweet fragrance which filled my parents' bedroom, the aroma of the vanity case, the sweet scent of the orchard, like Miss Brighton's cologne, and then I looked at Pico and Chueco's sweating faces and smelled the bad odor of the crowded stall and my hands broke out in a sweat.

"Break it!" Pico said sharply.

I looked at the mirror, briefly saw my face in it, saw my eyes which I knew would give everything away if we were caught, and I thought of the disgrace I would bring my father if he knew what I was about to do.

I can't, I said, but there was no sound. There was only the rancid odor which rose from the toilet stool, Chueco's heavy breathing, and Pico's eyes glued to the mirror as I turned my hand and let it fall. It fell slowly, as if in slow motion, reflecting us, changing our sense of time, which had moved so fast that morning, into a time which moved so slowly I thought the mirror would never hit the floor and break. But it did. The sound exploded, the mirror broke and splintered, and each piece seemed to bounce up to reflect our dark, sweating faces again.

"Shhhhhhhh," Pico whispered, finger to lips.

We held our breath and waited. Nobody moved outside the stall. No one had heard the breaking of the mirror which for me had been like the sound of thunder.

Then Pico reached down and picked up three well-shaped pieces, about the size of silver dollars. "Just right!" He grinned and handed each of us a piece. Then he put his right foot on the toilet seat, opened the bottle of glue and smeared the white, sticky glue on the tip of his shoe. He placed the piece of mirror on the glue, looked down and saw his sharp, weasel face reflected in it and smiled. "Fits just right!"

We followed suit, first Chueco, then me.

"This is going to be fun!" Chueco giggled.

"Hot bloomers! Hot bloomers!" Pico slapped my back.

"Now what?"

"Wait for it to dry."

We stood with our feet on the toilet seat, pant legs up, waiting for the glue to dry.

"Whose panties are you going to see first?" Chueco asked Pico.

"Concha Panocha's," Pico leered. "She's got the biggest boobs!"

"If they have big boobs, does that mean they have it big downstairs?" Chueco asked.

"Damn right!"

"Zow-ee!" Chueco exclaimed, and spit all over me.

"Shhhh!" Pico whispered. Two boys had come in. They talked while they used the urinals, then they left.

"Ninth graders," Pico said.

"Those guys know everything," Chueco said.

"Yeah, they know how to get it, but after today we'll know too."

"Yeah," Chueco smiled.

I turned away to escape another shower and his bad breath. The wall of the bathroom stall was covered with drawings of naked men and women. Old Plácido, the janitor, worked hard to keep the walls clean, but the minute he finished scrubbing off the drawings in one stall, others appeared next door. The drawings were crude, hastily done diagrams. The one in front of me showed two legs spread apart. A swollen tool hung down from two giant balloons. Everything was always dripping. I wondered why. And why had I joined Pico and Chueco in this crazy plan?

Last year the girls didn't seem to matter to us. We played freely with them. But the summer seemed to change everything. When we came back to school the girls had changed. They had grown bigger. Some of them began to wear lipstick and nail polish. They carried their bodies differently, and I couldn't help but notice for the first time their small, swollen breasts. Pico explained about brassieres to me. An air of mystery began to surround the girls we had once known so well.

I began to listen closely to the stories the ninth-grade boys told about girls. They gathered in the bathroom to smoke before class and during lunch break, and they talked about cars or sports or girls. Some of them already dated girls, and a few bragged about girls they had gotten naked. I guessed those were the ones who drew the pictures on the bathroom walls. They knew.

But their stories were incomplete, half whispered, and the crude drawings only aroused more curiosity. The more I thought about the change which was coming over us, the more troubled I became, and at night my sweaty dreams were filled with the images of women, phantasmal creatures who danced in a mist and removed their veils as they swirled around me. But always I awoke before the last veil was removed. I knew nothing. That's why I gave in to Pico's idea. I wanted to know.

He had said that if we glued a small piece of mirror to our shoes, we could push our feet between the girls' legs when they weren't watching, then we could see everything.

"And they don't wear panties in the spring," he said. "Everybody knows that. So you can see everything!"

"Eehola!" Chueco whistled.

"And sometimes there's a little cherry there—"

"Really?" Chueco exclaimed. "Like a cherry from a cherry tree?"

"Sure," Pico said. "Watch for it, it's good luck." He reached down and tested the mirror on his shoe. "Hey, it's dry! Let's go!"

We piled out of the dirty stall and followed Pico toward the water fountain at the end of the hall. That's where the girls usually gathered, because it was right outside their bathroom.

"Watch me," he said daringly, then he worked his way carefully behind Concha Panocha, who stood talking to her friends. She wore a very loose skirt, perfect for Pico's plan. She was a big girl, and she wasn't very pretty, but Pico liked her. Now we watched as he slowly worked his foot between her feet until the mirror was in position. Then he looked down and we saw his eyes light up. He turned and looked at us and grinned. He had seen everything!

"Perfect! Perfect!" he shouted when he came back to us. "I could see everything! Panties! Nalgas! The spot!"

"Eee-heee-heeee," Chueco moaned. "Now it's my turn!"

They ran off to try Concha again, and I followed them. I felt the blood pounding in my head and a strange excitement ran through my body. If Pico could see everything, then I could too! I could solve the terrible mystery which had pulled me back and forth all year long. I slipped up behind a girl, not even knowing who she was, and with my heart pounding madly, I carefully pushed my foot between her feet. I worked cautiously, afraid to get caught, afraid of what I was about to see. Then I peered into the mirror, saw in a flash my guilty eyes, moved my foot to see more, but all I could see was darkness. I leaned closer to her, looked closely into the mirror, but there was nothing except the brief glimpse of her white panties and then the darkness.

I moved closer, accidentally bumped her, and she turned and looked puzzled and I said excuse me and pulled back and ran away. There was nothing to see; Pico had lied. I felt disappointed. So was Chueco when we met again at lunchtime.

"They all wear panties, you liar!" Chueco accused Pico.

"And most of them wear dirty panties," I added. That had been my only discovery.

"One girl caught me looking at her and she hit me with her purse," Chueco complained. His left eye was red. "What do we do now?" he asked.

"Let's forget the whole thing," I suggested. The excitement was gone, there was nothing to discover. The mystery which was changing the girls into women would remain unexplained. And not being responsible for the answer was even a relief. I reached down to pull the mirror from my foot. My leg was stiff from holding it between the girls' legs.

"No!" Pico exclaimed and grabbed my arm. "Let's try one more thing!"

"What?"

He looked at me and grinned. "Let's look at one of the teachers."

"What? You're crazy!"

"No I'm not! The teachers are more grown up than the girls! They're really women!"

"Bah, they're old hags," Chueco frowned.

"Not Miss Brighton!" Pico smiled.

"Yeah," Chueco's eyes lit up and he wiped the white spittle that gathered at the edges of his mouth. "She reminds me of Wonder Woman!" He laughed and made a big curve with his hands.

"And she doesn't wear a bra. I know, I've seen her," Pico said.

"No." I shook my head. No, it was crazy. It would be as bad as looking at my mother. Again I reached down to tear the mirror from my shoe and again Pico stopped me.

"You can't back out now!" he hissed.

"Yeah," Chueco agreed, "we're in this together."

"If you back out now, you're out of the gang," Pico warned me. He held my arm tightly, hard enough for it to hurt. Chueco nodded. I looked from one to the other, and I knew they meant it. I had grown up with them, known them even before we started school.

"This summer we'll be the kings of the apple orchard, and you won't be able to come in," Pico added to his threat.

"But I don't want to do it," I insisted.

"Who then?" Chueco asked, and looked at Pico. "We can't all do it, she'd know."

"So let's draw," Pico said, and drew three toothpicks out of his pocket. He always carried toothpicks and usually had one hanging from his lips. "Short man does it. Fair?"

Chueco nodded. "Fair." They looked at me. I nodded. Pico broke one toothpick in half, then he put one half with two whole ones in his hand, made a fist and held it out for us to draw. I lost.

"Eho, Isador, you're lucky," Chueco said.

"I, I can't," I mumbled.

"You have to!" Pico said. "That was the deal!"

"Yeah, and we never break our deals," Chueco reminded me, "as long as we've been playing together we never broke a deal."

"If you back out now, that's the end . . . no more gang," Pico said seriously. Then he added, "Look, I'll help you. It's the last day of school, right, so there's going to be a lot of noise during last period. I'll call her to my desk, and when she bends over it'll be easy! She won't know!" He slapped my back.

"Yeah, she won't know!" Chueco repeated.

I finally nodded. Why argue with them, I thought. I'll just put my foot out and fake it, and later I'll make up a big story to tell them in the apple orchard. I'll tell them I saw everything. I'll say it was like the drawing in the bathroom. But it wasn't that easy. The rest of the day my thoughts crashed into each other like wild goats. Fake it, one side said. Look and solve the mystery, others shouted. Now's your chance!

By the time I got to last period study hall I was very nervous. I slipped into my seat across the aisle from Pico and buried my head in the book Miss Brighton had lent me. I sat with my feet drawn in beneath my desk so the mirror wouldn't show. After a while my foot grew numb in its cramped position. I flipped through the pages and tried to read, but it was no use, my thoughts were on Miss Brighton. I wondered if she was the woman who danced in my dreams. And why did I always blush when I looked into her clear blue eyes, those eyes which even now seemed to be looking at me and waiting for me to dare to learn their secret.

"Ready," Pico whispered, and raised his hand. I felt my throat tighten and go dry. My hands broke out in a sweat. I slipped lower into my desk to try to hide as I heard her walk toward Pico's desk.

"I want to know this word," Pico pointed.

"Contradictory," she said. "Con-tra-dic-to-ry . . ."

"Cunt-try-dick-tory," Pico repeated.

I turned and looked at her. Beyond her, through the window, I could see the apple orchard. The buzz of the bees swarming over the blossoms filled my ears.

"It means 'to contradict.' Like if one thing is true, then the other is false," I heard her say.

I would have to confess, I thought . . . Forgive me, Father, but I have contradicted you. I stole from my mother. I looked in the mirror and saw the secret of the woman . . . And why shouldn't you, something screamed in my head. You have to know! It's the only way to become a man! Look now! See! Learn everything you can!

I took a deep breath and slipped my foot from beneath my desk. I looked down, saw my eyes reflected in the small mirror. I slid it quietly between her feet. I could almost touch her skirt, smell her perfume. Behind her the light of the window and the glow from the orchard were blinding. I will pull back now, won't go all the way, I thought.

"Con-tra . . ." she repeated.

"Cunt-ra . . ." Pico stuttered.

Then I looked, saw in a flash her long, tanned legs, leaned to get a better image, saw the white frill, then nothing. Nothing. The swirl of darkness and the secret. The mystery remained hidden in darkness.

I gasped as she turned. She saw me pull my leg back, caught my eyes before I could bury myself in the book again, and in that brief instant I knew she had seen me. A frown crossed her face. She started to say something, then she stood up very straight.

"Get your books ready, the bell's about to ring," was all she said. Then she walked quickly to her desk and sat down.

"Did you see?" Pico whispered. I said nothing, but stared at pages of the book, which were a blur. The last few minutes of the class ticked by very slowly. I thought I could even hear the clock ticking, and each stroke was like a bell.

Then seconds before the bell rang I heard her say, "Isador, I want you to stay after school."

My heart sank. She knew my crime. I felt sick in the pit of my stomach. I cursed Pico and Chueco for talking me into the awful thing. Better to have let everything remain as it was. Let them keep their secret. Whatever it was, it wasn't worth the love I knew would end between me and Miss Brighton. She would tell my parents, everyone would know. I wished that I could reach down and rip the cursed mirror from my shoe, undo everything and set it right again.

But I couldn't. The bell rang. The room quickly emptied. I remained sitting at my desk. Long after the noise had cleared on the school grounds, she called me to her desk. I got up slowly, my legs weak and trembling, and I went to her desk. The room felt very big and empty, bigger than I could ever remember it. And it was very quiet.

She stood and came around her desk. Then she reached down, grabbed the small mirror on my shoe and jerked it. It splintered when she pulled and cut her thumb, but she didn't cry out. She was trembling with anger. She let the pieces drop on the floor; I saw the blood as it smeared her skirt and formed red balls on the tip of her thumb.

"Why did you do it?" she asked. Her voice was angry. "I know that Pico and Chueco would do things like that, but not you, Isador, not you!"

I shook my head. "I wanted to know," I heard myself say, "I wanted to know . . ."

"To know what?" she asked.

"About women . . ."

"But what's there to know?" she said. "You saw the film the coach showed you . . . and later we talked in class when the nurse came. She showed you the diagrams, pictures!"

I could only shake my head. "It's not the same. I wanted to know how women are . . . why different? How?"

She stopped trembling. Her breathing became regular. She took my chin in her hand and made me look at her. Her eyes were clear, not angry, and the frown had left her face. I felt the blood wet my chin.

"There's stories . . . and drawings, everywhere . . . and at night I dream, but I still don't know, I don't know anything!" I cried.

She looked at me while my frustrations came pouring out, then she drew me close and put her arms around me and smoothed my hair. "I understand," she said, "I understand . . . but you don't need to hide and see through the mirror. That makes it dirty. There is no secret to hide . . . nothing to hide . . ."

She held me tight and I could hear her heart pounding, and I heard her sigh, as if she too was troubled by the same questions which hounded me. Then she let me go and went to the window and pulled shut all the venetian blinds. Except for a ray of light streaming through the top, the room grew dark. Then she went to the door and locked it. She turned and looked at me, smiled with a look I had never seen before, then she walked gracefully to the small elevated platform in the back of the room.

She stood in the center and very slowly and carefully she unbuttoned her blouse. She let it drop to her feet, then she undid her bra and let it fall. I held my breath and felt my heart pounding wildly. Never had I seen such beauty as I saw then in the pale light which bathed her naked shoulders and her small breasts. She unfastened her skirt and let it drop, then she lowered her panties and stepped out of them. When she was completely naked she called me.

"Come and see what a woman is like." She smiled.

I walked very slowly to the platform. Beneath me my legs trembled, and in my ears I began to hear a buzzing sound, the kind of sound the bees make when they are swarming around the new blossoms of the apple trees. I stood looking at her for a long time, and she stood very still, like a statue. Then I began to walk around the platform, still looking at her, noting every feature and every curve of her long, firm legs, her flat stomach with its dot of a navel, the small round behind that curved down between her legs then rose along her spine to her hair which fell over her shoulders . . . I walked around and I began to feel a swirling sensation, a very pleasant feeling, as if I was slowly getting drunk. And I continued to hear the humming sound, perhaps she was singing, or it was the sound of the bees in the orchard, I didn't know. But she was smiling, a distant, pleasant smile.

The glowing light of the afternoon slipped through the top of the blinds and rested on her hair. It was the color of honey, spun so fine I wanted to reach out and touch it. But I didn't. A part of her secret she would have to keep, I was content to look at the beauty of her soft curves. Once I had gone hunting with my uncles and I had seen a golden aspen forest which had entranced me with its beauty, but even it was not as beautiful as this. Not even the summer nights when I slept outside and watched the swirl of the Milky Way in the dark sky could compare to the soft curves of her body. Not even the brilliant sunsets of the summer when the light seemed painted on the glowing clouds could be as full of wonder as the light which fell on her naked body. I looked until I thought I had memorized every curve, every nook and shadow, the color of her hair, the flesh tone of her skin . . . and I breathed in, deep, to inhale the aroma of her body. Then when I could no longer stand the beauty of the mystery unraveling itself before my eyes, I turned and ran.

I ran out the door into the bright *setting sun,* a cry of joy exploded at my lips. I ran as hard as I *could, and I felt* I was turning and leaping in the air like a ballet *dancer.*

"Now I know!" I shouted to myself. "Now I know the secret and I'll keep it forever!"

I ran through the orchard, laughing with joy. All around me the bright white blossoms of the trees shimmered in the spring light. I heard music in the radiance which exploded around me; I thought I was dreaming.

I ran around the trees and then stopped to caress them, and the smooth trunks and branches reminded me of her body. Each curve developed a slope and shadow of its own, each twist was rich with the secret we now shared. The flowers smelled like her hair and reminded me of her smile. Then gasping for breath and still trembling with excitement, I fell exhausted on the ground.

It's a dream, I thought, and I'll soon wake. No, it had happened. For a few brief moments I had shared the secret of her body, her mystery. But even now as I tried to remember how she looked, her image was fading like a dream. I sat up straight and looked toward the school, tried to picture the room and the light which had fallen on her bare shoulders, but it was fuzzy, like a dream which fades as one awakens. Her smile, her golden hair and the soft curves of her body were already fading into the sunset light, dissolving into the graceful curves of the trees. The image of her body, which just a short time ago had been so vivid, was working itself into the apple orchard, becoming the shape of trunks and branches . . . and her sweet fragrance blended into the damp earth smell of the orchard and its nettles and wild alfalfa.

For a moment I reached out to keep it from fading away, and that's when I realized that this was the real mystery. That she should fade and grow softer in my memory was the real beauty! That's why she told me to look! It was like the mystery of the apple orchard, changing before my eyes even as the sun set. All the curves and shadows, the sounds and smells, were changing form! In a few days the flowers would wilt and drop, then I would have to wait until next spring to see them again, but the memory would linger, parts of it would keep turning in my mind. Then next spring I would come back to the apple orchard to see the blossoms again. I would always keep coming back, to rediscover, to feel the smoothness of flesh and bark, to smell hair and flower, to linger as I bathed in beauty . . . The mystery would always be there, and I would be exploring its form forever.

1979                                                                                          1980

---

## From BLESS ME, ULTIMA

## Uno

Ultima came to stay with us the summer I was almost seven. When she came the beauty of the llano unfolded before my eyes, and the gurgling waters of the river sang to the hum of the turning earth. The magical time of childhood stood still, and the pulse of the living earth pressed its mystery into my living blood. She took my hand, and the silent, magic powers she

possessed made beauty from the raw, sun-baked llano, the green river valley, and the blue bowl which was the white sun's home. My bare feet felt the
throbbing earth and my body trembled with excitement. Time stood still,
and it shared with me all that had been, and all that was to come. . . .

Let me begin at the beginning. I do not mean the beginning that was in my
dreams and the stories they whispered to me about my birth, and the people
of my father and mother, and my three brothers—but the beginning that
came with Ultima.

The attic of our home was partitioned into two small rooms. My sisters,
Deborah and Theresa, slept in one and I slept in the small cubicle by the
door. The wooden steps creaked down into a small hallway that led into the
kitchen. From the top of the stairs I had a vantage point into the heart of our
home, my mother's kitchen. From there I was to see the terrified face of
Chávez when he brought the terrible news of the murder of the sheriff; I was
to see the rebellion of my brothers against my father; and many times late at
night I was to see Ultima returning from the llano where she gathered the
herbs that can be harvested only in the light of the full moon by the careful
hands of a curandera.

That night I lay very quietly in my bed, and I heard my father and mother
speak of Ultima.

"Está sola," my father said, "ya no queda gente en el pueblito de Las
Pasturas—"[1]

He spoke in Spanish, and the village he mentioned was his home. My
father had been a vaquero[2] all his life, a calling as ancient as the coming of
the Spaniard to Nuevo Méjico. Even after the big rancheros and the tejanos
came and fenced the beautiful llano, he and those like him continued to
work there, I guess because only in that wide expanse of land and sky could
they feel the freedom their spirits needed.

"¡Qué lástima,"[3] my mother answered, and I knew her nimble fingers
worked the pattern on the doily she crocheted for the big chair in the sala.

I heard her sigh, and she must have shuddered too when she thought of
Ultima living alone in the loneliness of the wide llano. My mother was not a
woman of the llano, she was the daughter of a farmer. She could not see
beauty in the llano and she could not understand the coarse men who lived
half their lifetimes on horseback. After I was born in Las Pasturas she persuaded my father to leave the llano and bring her family to the town of Guadalupe where she said there would be opportunity and school for us. The
move lowered my father in the esteem of his compadres, the other vaqueros
of the llano who clung tenaciously to their way of life and freedom. There
was no room to keep animals in town so my father had to sell his small herd,
but he would not sell his horse so he gave it to a good friend, Benito Campos. But Campos could not keep the animal penned up because somehow
the horse was very close to the spirit of the man, and so the horse was
allowed to roam free and no vaquero on that llano would throw a lazo on
that horse. It was as if someone had died, and they turned their gaze from
the spirit that walked the earth.

---

1. She is alone. She no longer belongs to the
people of the small town of Las Pasturas.

2. Cowhand, cowboy.
3. What a shame!

It hurt my father's pride. He saw less and less of his old compadres. He went to work on the highway and on Saturdays after they collected their pay he drank with his crew at the Longhorn, but he was never close to the men of the town. Some weekends the llaneros would come into town for supplies and old amigos like Bonney or Campos or the Gonzales brothers would come by to visit. Then my father's eyes lit up as they drank and talked of the old days and told the old stories. But when the western sun touched the clouds with orange and gold the vaqueros got in their trucks and headed home, and my father was left to drink alone in the long night. Sunday morning he would get up very crudo[4] and complain about having to go to early mass.

"—She served the people all her life, and now the people are scattered, driven like tumbleweeds by the winds of war. The war sucks everything dry," my father said solemnly, "it takes the young boys overseas, and their families move to California where there is work—"

"Ave María Purísima," my mother made the sign of the cross for my three brothers who were away at war. "Gabriel," she said to my father, "it is not right that la Grande be alone in her old age—"

"No," my father agreed.

"When I married you and went to the llano to live with you and raise your family, I could not have survived without la Grande's help. Oh, those were hard years—"

"Those were good years," my father countered. But my mother would not argue.

"There isn't a family she did not help," she continued, "no road was too long for her to walk to its end to snatch somebody from the jaws of death, and not even the blizzards of the llano could keep her from the appointed place where a baby was to be delivered—"

"Es verdad," my father nodded.

"She tended me at the birth of my sons—" And then I knew her eyes glanced briefly at my father. "Gabriel, we cannot let her live her last days in loneliness—"

"No," my father agreed, "it is not the way of our people."

"It would be a great honor to provide a home for la Grande," my mother murmured. My mother called Ultima la Grande out of respect. It meant the woman was old and wise.

"I have already sent word with Campos that Ultima is to come and live with us," my father said with some satisfaction. He knew it would please my mother.

"I am grateful," my mother said tenderly, "perhaps we can repay a little of the kindness la Grande has given to so many."

"And the children?" my father asked. I knew why he expressed concern for me and my sisters. It was because Ultima was a curandera, a woman who knew the herbs and remedies of the ancients, a miracle-worker who could heal the sick. And I had heard that Ultima could lift the curses laid by brujas, that she could exorcise the evil the witches planted in people to make them sick. And because a curandera had this power she was misunderstood and often suspected of practicing witchcraft herself.

4. Hungover.

I shuddered and my heart turned cold at the thought. The cuentos of the people were full of the tales of evil done by brujas.

"She helped bring them into the world, she cannot be but good for the children," my mother answered.

"Está bien," my father yawned, "I will go for her in the morning."

So it was decided that Ultima should come and live with us. I knew that my father and mother did good by providing a home for Ultima. It was the custom to provide for the old and the sick. There was always room in the safety and warmth of la familia for one more person, be that person stranger or friend.

It was warm in the attic, and as I lay quietly listening to the sounds of the house falling asleep and repeating a Hail Mary over and over in my thoughts, I drifted into the time of dreams. Once I had told my mother about my dreams and she said they were visions from God and she was happy, because her own dream was that I should grow up and become a priest. After that I did not tell her about my dreams, and they remained in me forever and ever . . .

*In my dream I flew over the rolling hills of the llano. My soul wandered over the dark plain until it came to a cluster of adobe huts. I recognized the village of Las Pasturas and my heart grew happy. One mud hut had a lighted window, and the vision of my dream swept me towards it to be witness at the birth of a baby.*

*I could not make out the face of the mother who rested from the pains of birth, but I could see the old woman in black who tended the just-arrived, steaming baby. She nimbly tied a knot on the cord that had connected the baby to its mother's blood, then quickly she bent and with her teeth she bit off the loose end. She wrapped the squirming baby and laid it at the mother's side, then she returned to cleaning the bed. All linen was swept aside to be washed, but she carefully wrapped the useless cord and the afterbirth and laid the package at the feet of the Virgin on the small altar. I sensed that these things were yet to be delivered to someone.*

*Now the people who had waited patiently in the dark were allowed to come in and speak to the mother and deliver their gifts to the baby. I recognized my mother's brothers, my uncles from El Puerto de los Lunas. They entered ceremoniously. A patient hope stirred in their dark, brooding eyes.*

*This one will be a Luna, the old man said, he will be a farmer and keep our customs and traditions. Perhaps God will bless our family and make the baby a priest.*

*And to show their hope they rubbed the dark earth of the river valley on the baby's forehead, and they surrounded the bed with the fruits of their harvest so the small room smelled of fresh green chile and corn, ripe apples and peaches, pumpkins and green beans.*

*Then the silence was shattered with the thunder of hoofbeats; vaqueros surrounded the small house with shouts and gunshots, and when they entered the room they were laughing and singing and drinking.*

*Gabriel, they shouted, you have a fine son! He will make a fine vaquero! And they smashed the fruits and vegetables that surrounded the bed and replaced them with a saddle, horse blankets, bottles of whiskey, a new rope, bridles, chapas, and an old guitar. And they rubbed the stain of earth from the baby's forehead because man was not to be tied to the earth but free upon it.*

*These were the people of my father, the vaqueros of the llano. They were an exuberant, restless people, wandering across the ocean of the plain.*

*We must return to our valley, the old man who led the farmers spoke. We must take with us the blood that comes after the birth. We will bury it in our fields to renew their fertility and to assure that the baby will follow our ways. He nodded for the old woman to deliver the package at the altar.*

*No! the llaneros protested, it will stay here! We will burn it and let the winds of the llano scatter the ashes.*

*It is blasphemy to scatter a man's blood on unholy ground, the farmers chanted. The new son must fulfill his mother's dream. He must come to El Puerto and rule over the Lunas of the valley. The blood of the Lunas is strong in him.*

*He is a Márez, the vaqueros shouted. His forefathers were conquistadores, men as restless as the seas they sailed and as free as the land they conquered. He is his father's blood!*

*Curses and threats filled the air, pistols were drawn, and the opposing sides made ready for battle. But the clash was stopped by the old woman who delivered the baby.*

*Cease! she cried, and the men were quiet. I pulled this baby into the light of life, so I will bury the afterbirth and the cord that once linked him to eternity. Only I will know his destiny.*

The dream began to dissolve. When I opened my eyes I heard my father cranking the truck outside. I wanted to go with him, I wanted to see Las Pasturas, I wanted to see Ultima. I dressed hurriedly, but I was too late. The truck was bouncing down the goat path that led to the bridge and the highway.

I turned, as I always did, and looked down the slope of our hill to the green of the river, and I raised my eyes and saw the town of Guadalupe. Towering above the housetops and the trees of the town was the church tower. I made the sign of the cross on my lips. The only other building that rose above the housetops to compete with the church tower was the yellow top of the schoolhouse. This fall I would be going to school.

My heart sank. When I thought of leaving my mother and going to school a warm, sick feeling came to my stomach. To get rid of it I ran to the pens we kept by the molino[5] to feed the animals. I had fed the rabbits that night and they had had alfalfa and so I only changed their water. I scattered some grain for the hungry chickens and watched their mad scramble as the rooster called them to peck. I milked the cow and turned her loose. During the day she would forage along the highway where the grass was thick and green, then she would return at nightfall. She was a good cow and there were very few times when I had to run and bring her back in the evening. Then I dreaded it, because she might wander into the hills where the bats flew at dusk and there was only the sound of my heart beating as I ran and it made me sad and frightened to be alone.

I collected three eggs in the chicken house and returned for breakfast.

"Antonio," my mother smiled and took the eggs and milk, "come and eat your breakfast."

I sat across the table from Deborah and Theresa and ate my atole[6] and the hot tortilla with butter. I said very little. I usually spoke very little to my two sisters. They were older than I and they were very close. They usually

5. Mill.
6. Cornmeal-based gruel.

spent the entire day in the attic, playing dolls and giggling. I did not concern myself with those things.

"Your father has gone to Las Pasturas," my mother chattered, "he has gone to bring la Grande." Her hands were white with the flour of the dough. I watched carefully. "—And when he returns, I want you children to show your manners. You must not shame your father or your mother—"

"Isn't her real name Ultima?" Deborah asked. She was like that, always asking grown-up questions.

"You will address her as la Grande," my mother said flatly. I looked at her and wondered if this woman with the black hair and laughing eyes was the woman who gave birth in my dream.

"Grande," Theresa repeated.

"Is it true she is a witch?" Deborah asked. Oh, she was in for it. I saw my mother whirl then pause and control herself.

"No!" she scolded. "You must not speak of such things! Oh, I don't know where you learn such ways—" Her eyes flooded with tears. She always cried when she thought we were learning the ways of my father, the ways of the Márez. "She is a woman of learning," she went on and I knew she didn't have time to stop and cry, "she has worked hard for all the people of the village. Oh, I would never have survived those hard years if it had not been for her—so show her respect. We are honored that she comes to live with us, understand?"

"Sí, mamá," Deborah said half willingly.

"Sí, mamá," Theresa repeated.

"Now run and sweep the room at the end of the hall. Eugene's room—" I heard her voice choke. She breathed a prayer and crossed her forehead. The flour left white stains on her, the four points of the cross. I knew it was because my three brothers were at war that she was sad, and Eugene was the youngest.

"Mamá." I wanted to speak to her. I wanted to know who the old woman was who cut the baby's cord.

"Sí." She turned and looked at me.

"Was Ultima at my birth?" I asked.

"¡Ay Dios mío!"[7] my mother cried. She came to where I sat and ran her hand through my hair. She smelled warm, like bread. "Where do you get such questions, my son. Yes," she smiled, "la Grande was there to help me. She was there to help at the birth of all of my children—"

"And my uncles from El Puerto were there?"

"Of course," she answered, "my brothers have always been at my side when I needed them. They have always prayed that I would bless them with a—"

I did not hear what she said because I was hearing the sounds of the dream, and I was seeing the dream again. The warm cereal in my stomach made me feel sick.

"And my father's brother was there, the Márez and their friends, the vaqueros—"

"Ay!" she cried out, "Don't speak to me of those worthless Márez and their friends!"

"There was a fight?" I asked.

7. Oh my God!

"No," she said, "a silly argument. They wanted to start a fight with my brothers—that is all they are good for. Vaqueros, they call themselves, they are worthless drunks! Thieves! Always on the move, like gypsies, always dragging their families around the country like vagabonds—"

As long as I could remember she always raged about the Márez family and their friends. She called the village of Las Pasturas beautiful; she had gotten used to the loneliness, but she had never accepted its people. She was the daughter of farmers.

But the dream was true. It was as I had seen it. Ultima knew.

"But you will not be like them." She caught her breath and stopped. She kissed my forehead. "You will be like my brothers. You will be a Luna, Antonio. You will be a man of the people, and perhaps a priest." She smiled.

A priest, I thought, that was her dream. I was to hold mass on Sundays like Father Byrnes did in the church in town. I was to hear the confessions of the silent people of the valley, and I was to administer the holy Sacrament to them.

"Perhaps," I said.

"Yes," my mother smiled. She held me tenderly. The fragrance of her body was sweet.

"But then," I whispered, "who will hear my confession?"

"What?"

"Nothing," I answered. I felt a cool sweat on my forehead and I knew I had to run, I had to clear my mind of the dream. "I am going to Jasón's house," I said hurriedly and slid past my mother. I ran out the kitchen door, past the animal pens, towards Jasón's house. The white sun and the fresh air cleansed me.

On this side of the river there were only three houses. The slope of the hill rose gradually into the hills of juniper and mesquite and cedar clumps. Jasón's house was farther away from the river than our house. On the path that led to the bridge lived huge, fat Fío and his beautiful wife. Fío and my father worked together on the highway. They were good drinking friends.

"¡Jasón!" I called at the kitchen door. I had run hard and was panting. His mother appeared at the door.

"Jasón no está aquí," she said. All of the older people spoke only in Spanish, and I myself understood only Spanish. It was only after one went to school that one learned English.

"¿Dónde está?" I asked.

She pointed towards the river, northwest, past the railroad tracks to the dark hills. The river came through those hills and there were old Indian grounds there, holy burial grounds Jasón told me. There in an old cave lived his Indian. At least everybody called him Jasón's Indian. He was the only Indian of the town, and he talked only to Jasón. Jasón's father had forbidden Jasón to talk to the Indian, he had beaten him, he had tried in every way to keep Jasón from the Indian.

But Jasón persisted. Jasón was not a bad boy, he was just Jasón. He was quiet and moody, and sometimes for no reason at all wild, loud sounds came exploding from his throat and lungs. Sometimes I felt like Jasón, like I wanted to shout and cry, but I never did.

I looked at his mother's eyes and I saw they were sad. "Thank you," I said, and returned home. While I waited for my father to return with Ultima

I worked in the garden. Every day I had to work in the garden. Every day I reclaimed from the rocky soil of the hill a few more feet of earth to cultivate. The land of the llano was not good for farming, the good land was along the river. But my mother wanted a garden and I worked to make her happy. Already we had a few chile and tomato plants growing. It was hard work. My fingers bled from scraping out the rocks and it seemed that a square yard of ground produced a wheelbarrow full of rocks which I had to push down to the retaining wall.

The sun was white in the bright blue sky. The shade of the clouds would not come until the afternoon. The sweat was sticky on my brown body. I heard the truck and turned to see it chugging up the dusty goat path. My father was returning with Ultima.

"¡Mamá!" I called. My mother came running out, Deborah and Theresa trailed after her.

"I'm afraid," I heard Theresa whimper.

"There's nothing to be afraid of," Deborah said confidently. My mother said there was too much Márez blood in Deborah. Her eyes and hair were very dark, and she was always running. She had been to school two years and she spoke only English. She was teaching Theresa and half the time I didn't understand what they were saying.

"Madre de Dios, but mind your manners!" my mother scolded. The truck stopped and she ran to greet Ultima. "Buenos días le de Dios, Grande," my mother cried. She smiled and hugged and kissed the old woman.

"Ay, María Luna," Ultima smiled, "Buenos días te de Dios, a ti y a tu familia." She wrapped the black shawl around her hair and shoulders. Her face was brown and very wrinkled. When she smiled her teeth were brown. I remembered the dream.

"Come, come!" my mother urged us forward. It was the custom to greet the old. "Deborah!" my mother urged. Deborah stepped forward and took Ultima's withered hand.

"Buenos días, Grande," she smiled. She even bowed slightly. Then she pulled Theresa forward and told her to greet la Grande. My mother beamed. Deborah's good manners surprised her, but they made her happy, because a family was judged by its manners.

"What beautiful daughters you have raised," Ultima nodded to my mother. Nothing could have pleased my mother more. She looked proudly at my father who stood leaning against the truck, watching and judging the introductions.

"Antonio," he said simply. I stepped forward and took Ultima's hand. I looked up into her clear brown eyes and shivered. Her face was old and wrinkled, but her eyes were clear and sparkling, like the eyes of a young child.

"Antonio," she smiled. She took my hand and I felt the power of a whirlwind sweep around me. Her eyes swept the surrounding hills and through them I saw for the first time the wild beauty of our hills and the magic of the green river. My nostrils quivered as I felt the song of the mockingbirds and the drone of the grasshoppers mingle with the pulse of the earth. The four directions of the llano met in me, and the white sun shone on my soul. The granules of sand at my feet and the sun and sky above me seemed to dissolve into one strange, complete being.

A cry came to my throat, and I wanted to shout it and run in the beauty I had found.

"Antonio." I felt my mother prod me. Deborah giggled because she had made the right greeting, and I who was to be my mother's hope and joy stood voiceless.

"Buenos días le de Dios, Ultima," I muttered. I saw in her eyes my dream. I saw the old woman who had delivered me from my mother's womb. I knew she held the secret of my destiny.

"¡Antonio!" My mother was shocked I had used her name instead of calling her Grande. But Ultima held up her hand.

"Let it be," she smiled. "This was the last child I pulled from your womb, María. I knew there would be something between us."

My mother who had started to mumble apologies was quiet. "As you wish, Grande," she nodded.

"I have come to spend the last days of my life here, Antonio," Ultima said to me.

"You will never die, Ultima," I answered. "I will take care of you—" She let go of my hand and laughed. Then my father said, "pase, Grande, pase. Nuestra casa es su casa. It is too hot to stand and visit in the sun—"

"Sí, sí," my mother urged. I watched them go in. My father carried on his shoulders the large blue-tin trunk which later I learned contained all of Ultima's earthly possessions, the black dresses and shawls she wore, and the magic of her sweet smelling herbs.

As Ultima walked past me I smelled for the first time a trace of the sweet fragrance of herbs that always lingered in her wake. Many years later, long after Ultima was gone and I had grown to be a man, I would awaken sometimes at night and think I caught a scent of her fragrance in the cool-night breeze.

And with Ultima came the owl. I heard it that night for the first time in the juniper tree outside of Ultima's window. I knew it was her owl because the other owls of the llano did not come that near the house. At first it disturbed me, and Deborah and Theresa too. I heard them whispering through the partition. I heard Deborah reassuring Theresa that she would take care of her, and then she took Theresa in her arms and rocked her until they were both asleep.

I waited. I was sure my father would get up and shoot the owl with the old rifle he kept on the kitchen wall. But he didn't, and I accepted his understanding. In many cuentos I had heard the owl was one of the disguises a bruja took, and so it struck a chord of fear in the heart to hear them hooting at night. But not Ultima's owl. Its soft hooting was like a song, and as it grew rhythmic it calmed the moonlit hills and lulled us to sleep. Its song seemed to say that it had come to watch over us.

I dreamed about the owl that night, and my dream was good. La Virgen de Guadalupe was the patron saint of our town. The town was named after her. In my dream I saw Ultima's owl lift la Virgen on her wide wings and fly her to heaven. Then the owl returned and gathered up all the babes of Limbo and flew them up to the clouds of heaven.

The Virgin smiled at the goodness of the owl.

## Dos

Ultima slipped easily into the routine of our daily life. The first day she put on her apron and helped my mother with breakfast, later she swept the house and then helped my mother wash our clothes in the old washing machine they pulled outside where it was cooler under the shade of the young elm trees. It was as if she had always been here. My mother was very happy because now she had someone to talk to and she didn't have to wait until Sunday when her women friends from the town came up the dusty path to sit in the sala and visit.

Deborah and Theresa were happy because Ultima did many of the household chores they normally did, and they had more time to spend in the attic and cut out an interminable train of paper dolls which they dressed, gave names to, and most miraculously, made talk.

My father was also pleased. Now he had one more person to tell his dream to. My father's dream was to gather his sons around him and move westward to the land of the setting sun, to the vineyards of California. But the war had taken his three sons and it had made him bitter. He often got drunk on Saturday afternoons and then he would rave against old age, he would rage against the town on the opposite side of the river which drained a man of his freedom, and he would cry because the war had ruined his dream. It was very sad to see my father cry, but I understood it, because sometimes a man has to cry. Even if he is a man.

And I was happy with Ultima. We walked together in the llano and along the river banks to gather herbs and roots for her medicines. She taught me the names of plants and flowers, of trees and bushes, of birds and animals; but most important, I learned from her that there was a beauty in the time of day and in the time of night, and that there was peace in the river and in the hills. She taught me to listen to the mystery of the groaning earth and to feel complete in the fulfillment of its time. My soul grew under her careful guidance.

I had been afraid of the awful *presence* of the river, which was the soul of the river, but through her I learned that my spirit shared in the spirit of all things. But the innocence which our isolation sheltered could not last forever, and the affairs of the town began to reach across our bridge and enter my life. Ultima's owl gave the warning that the time of peace on our hill was drawing to an end.

It was Saturday night. My mother had laid out our clean clothes for Sunday mass, and we had gone to bed early because we always went to early mass. The house was quiet, and I was in the mist of some dream when I heard the owl cry its warning. I was up instantly, looking through the small window at the dark figure that ran madly towards the house. He hurled himself at the door and began pounding.

"¡Márez!" he shouted, "¡Márez! ¡Ándale, hombre!"[1]

I was frightened, but I recognized the voice. It was Jasón's father.

"¡Un momento!" I heard my father call. He fumbled with the farol.

---

1. Come on, man!

"¡Ándale, hombre, ándale!" Chávez cried pitifully, "mataron a mi hermano—"[2]

"Ya vengo—"[3] My father opened the door and the frightened man burst in. In the kitchen I heard my mother moan, "Ave María Purísima, mis hijos—"[4] She had not heard Chávez' last words, and so she assumed the aviso was one that brought bad news about her sons.

"Chávez, ¿qué pasa?" My father held the trembling man.

"¡Mi hermano, mi hermano!" Chávez sobbed, "He has killed my brother!"

"¿Pero qué dices,[5] hombre?" my father exclaimed. He pulled Chávez into the hall and held up the farol. The light cast by the farol revealed the wild, frightened eyes of Chávez.

"¡Gabriel!" my mother cried and came forward, but my father pushed her back. He did not want her to see the monstrous mask of fear on the man's face.

"It is not our sons, it is something in town—get him some water."

"Lo mató,[6] lo mató—" Chávez repeated.

"Get hold of yourself, hombre, tell me what as happened!" My father shook Chávez and the man's sobbing subsided. He took the glass of water and drank, then he could talk.

"Reynaldo has just brought the news, my brother is dead," he sighed and slumped against the wall. Chávez' brother was the sheriff of the town. The man would have fallen if my father had not held him up.

"¡Madre de Dios! Who? How?"

"¡Lupito!" Chávez cried out. His face corded with thick veins. For the first time his left arm came up and I saw the rifle he held.

"Jesús, María y José,"[7] my mother prayed.

My father groaned and slumped against the wall. "Ay que Lupito," he shook his head, "the war made him crazy—"

Chávez regained part of his composure. "Get your rifle, we must go to the bridge—"

"The bridge?"

"Reynaldo said to meet him there—The crazy bastard has taken to the river—"

My father nodded silently. He went to the bedroom and returned with his coat. While he loaded his rifle in the kitchen Chávez related what he knew.

"My brother had just finished his rounds," he gasped, "he was at the bus depot cafe, having coffee, sitting without a care in the world—and the bastard came up to where he sat and without warning shot him in the head—" His body shook as he retold the story.

"Perhaps it is better if you wait here, hombre," my father said with consolation.

"No!" Chávez shouted. "I must go. He was my brother!"

My father nodded. I saw him stand beside Chávez and put his arm around his shoulders. Now he too was armed. I had only seen him shoot the rifle when we slaughtered pigs in the fall. Now they were going armed for a man.

---

2. They killed my brother.
3. I'm coming.
4. Hail Mary Immaculate, my sons; i.e., an invocation of the Virgin Mary for protection.

5. But what are you saying.
6. He killed him.
7. Jesus, Mary, and Joseph [i.e., Saint Joseph, Mary's husband and Jesus' adoptive father].

"Gabriel, be careful," my mother called as my father and Chávez slipped out into the dark.

"Sí," I heard him answer, then the screen door banged. "Keep the doors locked—" My mother went to the door and shut the latch. We never locked our doors, but tonight there was something strange and fearful in the air.

Perhaps this is what drew me out into the night to follow my father and Chávez down to the bridge, or perhaps it was some concern I had for my father. I do not know. I waited until my mother was in the sala then dressed and slipped downstairs. I glanced down the hall and saw candlelight flickering from the sala. That room was never entered unless there were Sunday visitors, or unless my mother took us in to pray novenas and rosaries for my brothers at war. I knew she was kneeling at her altar now, praying. I knew she would pray until my father returned.

I slipped out the kitchen door and into the night. It was cool. I sniffed the air, there was a tinge of autumn in it. I ran up the goat path until I caught sight of two dark shadows ahead of me. Chávez and my father.

We passed Fío's dark house and then the tall juniper tree that stood where the hill sloped down to the bridge. Even from this distance I could hear the commotion on the bridge. As we neared the bridge I was afraid of being discovered as I had no reason for being there. My father would be very angry. To escape detection I cut to the right and was swallowed up by the dark brush of the river. I pushed through the dense bosque until I came to the bank of the river. From where I stood I could look up into the flooding beams of light that were pointed down by the excited men. I could hear them giving frenzied, shouted instructions. I looked to my left where the bridge started and saw my father and Chávez running towards the excitement at the center of the bridge.

My eyes were now accustomed to the dark, but it was a glint of light that made me turn and look at a clump of bullrushes in the sweeping water of the river just a few yards away. What I saw made my blood run cold. Crouched in the reeds and half submerged in the muddy waters lay the figure of Lupito, the man who had killed the sheriff. The glint of light was from the pistol he held in his hand.

It was frightening enough to come upon him so suddenly, but as I dropped to my knees in fright I must have uttered a cry because he turned and looked directly at me. At that same moment a beam of light found him and illuminated a face twisted with madness. I do not know if he saw me, or if the light cut off his vision, but I saw his bitter, contorted grin. As long as I live I will never forget those wild eyes, like the eyes of a trapped, savage animal.

At the same time someone shouted from the bridge, "There!" Then all the lights found the crouched figure. He jumped and I saw him as clear as if it were daylight.

"Ayeeeeee!" He screamed a blood curdling cry that echoed down the river. The men on the bridge didn't know what to do. They stood transfixed, looking down at the mad man waving the pistol in the air. "Ayeeeeeeee!" He cried again. It was a cry of rage and pain, and it made my soul sick. The cry of a tormented man had come to the peaceful green mystery of my river, and the great *presence* of the river watched from the shadows and deep recesses, as I watched from where I crouched at the bank.

"Japanese sol'jer, Japanese sol'jer!" he cried, "I am wounded. Come help me—" he called to the men on the bridge. The rising mist of the river swirled in the beams of spotlights. It was like a horrible nightmare.

Suddenly he leaped up and ran splashing through the water towards me. The lights followed him. He grew bigger, I heard his panting, the water his feet kicked up splashed on my face, and I thought he would run over me. Then as quickly as he had sprinted in my direction he turned and disappeared again into the dark clumps of reeds in the river. The lights moved in all directions, but they couldn't find him. Some of the lights swept over me and I trembled with fear that I would be found out, or worse, that I would be mistaken for Lupito and shot.

"The crazy bastard got away!" someone shouted on the bridge.

"Ayeeeeee!" the scream sounded again. It was a cry that I did not understand, and I am sure the men on the bridge did not either. The man they hunted had slipped away from human understanding; he had become a wild animal, and they were afraid.

"Damn!" I heard them cursing themselves. Then a car with a siren and flashing red light came on the bridge. It was Vigil, the state policeman who patrolled our town.

"Chávez is dead!" I heard him shout. "He never had a chance. His brains blown out—" There was silence.

"We have to kill him!" Jasón's father shouted. His voice was full of anger, rage and desperation.

"I have to deputize you—" Vigil started to say.

"The hell with deputizing!" Chávez shouted. "He killed my brother! ¡Está loco!" The men agreed with their silence.

"Have you spotted him?" Vigil asked.

"Just now we saw him, but we lost him—"

"He's down there," someone added.

"He is an animal! He has to be shot!" Chávez cried out.

"¡Sí!" the men agreed.

"Now wait a moment—" It was my father who spoke. I do not know what he said because of the shouting. In the meantime I searched the dark of the river for Lupito. I finally saw him. He was about forty feet away, crouched in the reeds as before. The muddy waters of the river lapped and gurgled savagely around him. Before the night had been only cool, now it turned cold and I shivered. I was torn between a fear that made my body tremble, and a desire to help the poor man. But I could not move, I could only watch like a chained spectator.

"Márez is right!" I heard a booming voice on the bridge. In the lights I could make out the figure of Narciso. There was only one man that big and with that voice in town. I knew that Narciso was one of the old people from Las Pasturas, and that he was a good friend to my father. I knew they often drank together on Saturdays, and once or twice he had been to our house.

"¡Por Dios, hombres!" he shouted, "let us act like men! That is not an animal down there, that is a man. Lupito. You all know Lupito. You know that the war made him sick—" But the men would not listen to Narciso. I guess it was because he was the town drunk, and they said he never did anything useful.

"Go back to your drinking and leave this job to men," one of them jeered at him.

"He killed the sheriff in cold blood," another added. I knew that the sheriff had been greatly admired.

"I am not drinking," Narciso persisted, "it is you men who are drunk for blood. You have lost your reason—"

"Reason!" Chávez countered. "What reason did he have for killing my brother. You know," he addressed the men, "my brother did no one harm. Tonight a mad animal crawled behind him and took his life. You call that reason! That animal has to be destroyed!"

"¡Sí! ¡Sí!" the men shouted in unison.

"At least let us try to talk to him," Narciso begged. I knew that it was hard for a man of the llano to beg.

"Yes," Vigil added, "perhaps he will give himself up—"

"Do you think he'll listen to talk!" Chávez jumped forward. "He's down there, and he still has the pistol that killed my brother! Go down and talk to him!" I could see Chávez shouting in Vigil's face, and Vigil said nothing. Chávez laughed. "This is the only talk he will understand—" he turned and fired over the railing of the bridge. His shots roared then whined away down the river. I could hear the bullets make splashing noises in the water.

"Wait!" Narciso shouted. He took Chávez' rifle and with one hand held it up. Chávez struggled against him but Narciso was too big and strong. "I will talk to him," Narciso said. He pushed Chávez back. "I understand your sorrow, Chávez," he said, "but one killing is enough for tonight—" The men must have been impressed by his sincerity because they stood back and waited.

Narciso leaned over the concrete railing and shouted down into the darkness. "Hey Lupito! It is me, Narciso. It is me, hombre, your compadre. Listen, my friend, a very bad business has happened tonight, but if we act like men we can settle it—Let me come down and talk to you, Lupito. Let me help you—"

I looked at Lupito. He had been watching the action on the bridge, but now as Narciso talked to him I saw his head slump on his chest. He seemed to be thinking. I prayed that he would listen to Narciso and that the angry and frustrated men on the bridge would not commit mortal sin. The night was very quiet. The men on the bridge awaited an answer. Only the lapping water of the river made a sound.

"¡Amigo!" Narciso shouted, "You know I am your friend, I want to help you, hombre—" He laughed softly. "Hey, Lupito, you remember just a few years ago, before you went to the war, you remember the first time you came into the Eight Ball to gamble a little. Remember how I taught you how Juan Botas marked the aces with a little tobacco juice, and he thought you were green, but you beat him!" He laughed again. "Those were good times, Lupito, before the war came. Now we have this bad business to settle. But we are friends who will help you—"

I saw Lupito's tense body shake. A low, sad mournful cry tore itself from his throat and mixed into the lapping sound of the waters of the river. His head shook slowly, and I guess he must have been thinking and fighting between surrendering or remaining free, and hunted. Then like a coiled spring he jumped up, his pistol aimed straight up. There was a flash of fire and the loud report of the pistol. But he had not fired at Narciso or at any of the men on the bridge! The spotlights found him.

"There's your answer!" Chávez shouted.

"He's firing! He's firing!" Another voice shouted. "He's crazy!"

Lupito's pistol sounded again. Still he was not aiming at the men on the bridge. He was shooting to draw their fire!

"Shoot! Shoot!" someone on the bridge called.

"No, no," I whispered through clenched lips. But it was too late for anything. The frightened men responded by aiming their rifles over the side of the bridge. One single shot sounded then a barrage followed it like the roar of a canon, like the rumble thunder in a summer thunderstorm.

Many shots found their mark. I saw Lupito lifted off his fee and hurled backward by the bullets. But he got up and ran limping and crying towards the bank where I lay.

"Bless me—" I thought he cried, and the second volley of shots from the bridge sounded, but this time they sounded like a great whirling of wings, like pigeons swirling to roost on the church top. He fell forward then clawed and crawled out of the holy water of the river onto the bank in front of me. I wanted to reach out and help him, but I was frozen by my fear. He looked up at me and his face was bathed in water and flowing, hot blood, but it was also dark and peaceful as it slumped into the sand of the riverbank. He made a strange gurgling sound in his throat, then he was still. Up on the bridge a great shout went up. The men were already running to the end of the bridge to come down and claim the man whose dead hands dug into the soft, wet sand in front of me.

I turned and ran. The dark shadows of the river enveloped me as I raced for the safety of home. Branches whipped at my face and cut it, and vines and tree trunks caught at my feet and tripped me. In my headlong rush I disturbed sleeping birds and their shrill cries and slapping wings hit at my face. The horror of darkness had never been so complete as it was for me that night.

I had started praying to myself from the moment I heard the first shot and I never stopped praying until I reached home. Over and over through my mind ran the words of the Act of Contrition. I had not yet been to catechism nor had I made my first holy communion, but my mother had taught me the Act of Contrition. It was to be said after one made his confession to the priest, and as the last prayer before death.

Did God listen? Would he hear? Had he seen my father on the bridge? And where was Lupito's soul winging to, or was it washing down the river to the fertile valley of my uncles' farms?

A priest could have saved Lupito. Oh why did my mother dream for me to be a priest! How would I ever wash away the stain of blood from the sweet waters of my river! I think at that time I began to cry because as I left the river brush and headed up the hills I heard my sobs for the first time.

It was also then that I heard the owl. Between my gasps for air and my sobs I stopped and listened for its song. My heart was pounding and my lungs hurt, but a calmness had come over the moonlit night when I heard the hooting of Ultima's owl. I stood still for a long time. I realized that the owl had been with me throughout the night. It had watched over all that had happened on the bridge. Suddenly the terrible, dark fear that had possessed me was gone.

I looked at the house that my father and my brothers had built on the juniper-patched hill; it was quiet and peaceful in the blue night. The sky sparkled with a million stars and the Virgin's horned moon, the moon of my mother's people, the moon of the Lunas. My mother would be praying for the soul of Lupito.

Again the owl sang. Ultima's spirit bathed me with its strong resolution. I turned and looked across the river. Some lights shone in the town. In the moonlight I could make out the tower of the church, the school house top, and way beyond the glistening of the town's water tank. I heard the soft wail of a siren and I knew the men would be pulling Lupito from the river.

The river's brown waters would be stained with blood, forever and ever and ever . . .

In the autumn I would have to go to the school in the town, and in a few years I would go to catechism lessons in the church. I shivered. My body began to hurt from the beating it had taken from the brush of the river. But what hurt more was that I had witnessed for the first time the death of a man.

My father did not like the town or its way. When we had first moved from Las Pasturas we had lived in a rented house in the town. But every evening after work he had looked across the river to these barren, empty hills, and finally he had bought a couple of acres and began building our house. Everyone told him he was crazy, that the rocky, wild hill could sustain no life, and my mother was more than upset. She wanted to buy along the river where the land was fertile and there was water for the plants and trees. But my father won the fight to be close to his llano, because truthfully our hill was the beginning of the llano, from here it stretched away as far as the eye could see, to Las Pasturas and beyond.

The men of the town had murdered Lupito. But he had murdered the sheriff. They said the war had made him crazy. The prayers for Lupito mixed into prayers for my brothers. So many different thoughts raced through my mind that I felt dizzy, and very weary and sick. I ran the last of the way and slipped quietly into the house. I groped for the stair railing in the dark and felt a warm hand take mine. Startled, I looked up into Ultima's brown, wrinkled face.

"You knew!" I whispered. I understood that she did not want my mother to hear.

"Sí," she replied.

"And the owl—" I gasped. My mind searched for answers, but my body was so tired that my knees buckled and I fell forward. As small and thin as Ultima was she had the strength to lift me in her arms and carry me into her room. She placed me on her bed and then by the light of a small, flickering candle she mixed one of her herbs in a tin cup, held it over the flame to warm, then gave it to me to drink.

"They killed Lupito," I said as I gulped the medicine.

"I know," she nodded. She prepared a new potion and with this she washed the cuts on my face and feet.

"Will he go to hell?" I asked.

"That is not for us to say, Antonio. The war-sickness was not taken out of him, he did not know what he was doing—"

"And the men on the bridge, my father!"

"Men will do what they must do," she answered. She sat on the bed by my side. Her voice was soothing, and the drink she had given me made me sleepy. The wild, frightening excitement in my body began to die.

"The ways of men are strange, and hard to learn," I heard her say.

"Will I learn them?" I asked. I felt the weight on my eyelids.

"You will learn much, you will see much," I heard her faraway voice. I felt a blanket cover me. I felt safe in the warm sweetness of the room. Outside the owl sang its dark questioning to the night, and I slept.

But even into my deep sleep my dreams came. In my dream I saw my three brothers. I saw them as I remembered them before they went away to war, which seemed so very long ago. They stood by the house that we rented in town and they looked across the river at the hills of the llano.

*Father says that the town steals our freedom; he says that we must build a castle across the river, on the lonely hill of the mockingbirds. I think it was León who spoke first, he was the eldest, and his voice always had a sad note to it. But in the dark mist of the dream I could not be sure.*

*His heart has been heavy since we came to the town, the second figure spoke, his forefathers were men of the sea, the Márez people, they were conquistadores, men whose freedom was unbounded.*

*It was Andrew who said that! It was Andrew! I was sure because his voice was husky like his thick and sturdy body.*

*Father says the freedom of the wild horse is in the Márez blood, and his gaze is always westward. His fathers before him were vaqueros, and so he expects us to be men of the llano. I was sure the third voice belonged to Eugene.*

*I longed to touch them. I was hungry for their company. Instead I spoke.*

*We must all gather around our father, I heard myself say. His dream is to ride westward in search of new adventure. He builds highways that stretch into the sun, and we must travel that road with him.*

*My brothers frowned. You are a Luna, they chanted in unison, you are to be a farmer-priest for mother!*

*The doves came to drink in the still pools of the river and their cry was mournful in the darkness of my dream.*

*My brothers laughed. You are but a baby, Tony, you are our mother's dream. Stay and sleep to the doves cou-rou while we cross the mighty River of the Carp to build our father's castle in the hills.*

*I must go! I cried to the three dark figures. I must lift the muddy waters of the river in blessing to our new home!*

*Along the river the tormented cry of a lonely goddess filled the valley. The winding wail made the blood of men run cold.*

*It is la llorona, my brothers cried in fear, the old witch who cries along the river banks and seeks the blood of boys and men to drink!*

*La llorona seeks the soul of Antonioooooooooo . . .*

*It is the soul of Lupito, they cried in fear, doomed to wander the river at night because the waters washed his soul away!*

*Lupito seeks his blessinggggggggg . . .*

*It is neither! I shouted. I swung the dark robe of the priest over my shoulders then lifted my hands in the air. The mist swirled around me and sparks flew when I spoke. It is the presence of the river!*

*Save us, my brothers cried and cowered at my words.*

*I spoke to the presence of the river and it allowed my brothers to cross with
their carpenter tools to build our castle on the hill.*

*Behind us I heard my mother moan and cry because with each turning of
the sun her son was growing old . . .*

1972

# Bendíceme, América

May the spirit of our ancestors watch over us as we enter the new century.
May we walk in the path of beauty. Now it is our turn as poets and writers
to take the breath of life, these words which are our gift, and bless the
earth and people of the Americas. In the midst of the pain and the atrocities we commit on one another, in the enslavement of the worst oppression,
we must remember the blessing. As long as we can draw breath to bless one
another, we are still human.

Bendíceme, América. We ask the blessing of the earth, in return. Oh ravaged earth, oh Eden we have trampled, oh paradise we have filled with greed
and hate and murder, bless us. Forests we have burned and llanos we have
plowed, bless us. Oh sky we have polluted, bless us with your rain and kind
breezes. It is the earth that nurtures us. Our mother, Las Américas, bless us.

Let us resolve with this blessing that we will commit our hearts and souls
to the earth and the people of these continents. To the guardian spirit of the
Americas, to the grandfather and all the deities of our people, to the sacred
directions, we turn and ask for blessing. Center us in joy, in harmony, so we
may act with purpose this day and during the difficult years ahead.

The history of the Americas tells us many things. We know that in 1492,
the Old World met the New. And at once began the exploitation and colonization of these lands, which became a battle ground for the souls and
bodies of the Native Americans. We know, too, that the Eurocentric view
has always been challenged by the indigenous cultures on which it was
imposed—as it is being challenged today. And by those who have not had a
voice in shaping their own destinies, the Quincentennial is being celebrated
as 500 years of resistance. We, the many communities of the Americas, are
the heirs of that long legacy. Today we must raise our voices to proclaim our
various identities. We must demand an active role in determining the direction this hemisphere will take in our generation and in the future.

What should the Quincentennial mean to us? There are fundamental issues
facing the citizens of the Americas today: We must protect basic human
rights. We must help formulate the hemisphere's economic policies. And we
must champion the cause of democracy. We need to take part, as well, in the
new age of technology and information, and understand how this new age
affects our children. And yet we need to protect the resources of the earth.

In this sector of the globe, a very small percentage of the population
consumes the majority of the products, while many suffer in poverty. This
year can be a time of activism during which all groups work at better
understanding one another. The walls of separation must come down. The
hermandad of the Americas must be proclaimed. Let us seek to establish

fellowship and peace. Let us help instill a new pride in our children so they can face the coming millennium with confidence.

For 500 years, another people's way of seeing the world became the dominant interpretation of history throughout North and South America. Indigenous histories were destroyed, and educational systems were remodeled on those of Europe. That Eurocentric view failed to portray the essence of our diverse civilizations. Now is the time for us to acknowledge and proclaim the true multicultural nature of the Americas. To listen to the many voices of the Americas.

Eduardo Galeano, in *The Book of Embraces*,[1] reminds us of an African proverb: Until lions have their own historians, histories of the hunt will glorify the hunter. The hunters who wrote the histories of the Americas have glorified the European perspective. And in the meantime, the chronicles of our peoples have been neglected, lost, even systematically obliterated. Now we must be the lions who rediscover right and redress the balance. Now we must restore and take pride in our own histories.

Each cultural group of the Americas must tell and write its stories and inform the world of its many accomplishments. One often hears that those who do not know their history are doomed to repeat it. Lest we subject our children to the oppression endured by their ancestors, we must teach them to be lions who are familiar with their past and who can wisely chart a course through the decades ahead.

Such knowledge will help foster a spirit of liberation. All of our communities have played a role in building the Americas, yet the efforts of many have not been acknowledged. When people recount their achievements, they create and inspire pride. That is why our children need to hear our voices. That is why our histories need to be read in the schools. Only in this way will our offspring be empowered to introduce a new vision of the Americas— one that transcends the offenses of the past.

At a gathering of writers in Managua, Nicaragua, during the summer of 1989, I heard Eduardo Galeano tell a story. A child is being born on an isolated ranch. By the time the doctor arrives, the mother is near death. It is a breech delivery, and the baby's body lies twisted in its mother's womb. The doctor does not think the child is alive, until its hand reaches out and grabs his fingers. The baby wants to live. And so the doctor goes to work and completes the delivery.

This, Galeano tells us, represents the birth of the Americas, a birth that took place in the midst of the cataclysm of 1492. Born into the exploitation, poverty and pain of workers, that child nevertheless showed a tenacity for life. Against all odds, the Americas were born, survived and became the mother we know.

From Tierra del Fuego to the Arctic Circle, our mother is known by many names, and she has herself given birth to many nations. Our mother, the Americas, has a history—or rather, many histories, which we are obliged to celebrate. And I am not speaking only of the past 500 years, but also of the time before Columbus's crossing. For the roots of our own histories lie in those of the indigenous people of the Americas. Each one of us can help

---

1. *El libro de los abrazos* (1991), a book by this Uruguayan writer (b. 1940) that combines genres such as poetry, fiction, memoir, documentary, and fantasy.

write a new and complete account of our past. And the more we learn from one another, the more encompassing our vision of the future will become.

This willingness to learn the multicultural story of our land and cultures will help us deal with the real issues of life. As we know ourselves, we recognize our beauty. The old class and color distinctions must be eradicated. We cannot liberate one another if we do not first liberate ourselves.

Many of the voices of the Americas have been repressed. But there is change in the air. New songs are being sung, new stories told. New battles for human decency are daily being fought. During our own time, writers from many oppressed nations have spoken out. Mothers have marched in the streets against unjust governments. They are the lions, pointing the way for us to follow. Together, then, let us take command of our destinies and make our voices heard.

1992

---

# LOURDES CASAL
## 1938–1981

Lourdes Casal was born and raised in Cuba. As a young woman, she actively fought against the dictatorship of Fulgencio Batista. In 1961, disillusioned with the Marxist ideology of the Castro government, she left Cuba and went into exile. Once in the United States, she earned a doctorate in social psychology, taught at several universities, and wrote and edited books and articles on political and social subjects related to Cuba and Cuban Americans. Among her scholarly works, particularly noteworthy is her volume on the persecution and jailing of the Cuban poet Heberto Padilla, *El caso Padilla: literatura y revolución en Cuba* (The Padilla Case: Literature and Revolution in Cuba, 1971). In the early 1970s, Casal became active in Cuban and Cuban American organizations, and in 1974 she cofounded the journal *Areíto*, which promoted dialogue between the revolutionary society on the island and the exile community in the United States.

In 1973, Casal published *Los fundadores: Alfonso y otros cuentos* (The Founders: Alfonso and Other Stories, 1973). The seven stories in the book include many references to her childhood, her exile in New York, Cuban customs and traditions, and Cuban national history. Casal's poems appeared posthumously in *Palabras juntan revolución* (Words Make Revolution, 1981), one of the first books by a Cuban exile to be published on the island. The collection consists of four parts: "El barrio regresa en sus sonidos" (The Barrio Returns to Its Sounds), a nostalgic evocation of the author's Cuban past; "Tanto más vulnerable que la piedra" (A Little More Vulnerable than Stone), poems full of allusions to Casal's exile in the cold winters of New York City; "Tigre con una herida en el costado" ("Tiger with a Wounded Side"), which records the passing of the years and the loss of youth; and "Palabras juntan revolución," which revisits and reconsiders the 1959 Revolution.

The dislocations in Casal's work perhaps found their counterpart in her lifelong refusal to condemn the Castro regime's persecution of homosexuals and her silence about her lesbianism, unacceptable in one who desired to remain "within the Revolution." After returning to Cuba in 1979, Casal died there two years later and was buried with great ceremony in the Pantheon of Revolutionary Exiles, in Havana.

## Hudson in Winter[1]

This unreal landscape
trees dancing
a church that turns into a castle
in the mist
and the river that refuses to flow                                    5
with the stiffness and sparkle of a grenadier.

Everything here reminds me
of the sky, gray and gray,
the trees, the stones,
water and steel.                                                      10
A world that languishes because you haven't smiled,
that mournfully awaits you.

Now I know
that distance has three dimensions.
Now I know that the space between us                                  15
can't be measured in meters or inches
as if streets could be crossed with impunity
as if it were easy to extend a hand.

This distance is solid, robust,
and your absence is total,                                            20
impregnable:
in spite of the illusory reach
of a telephone,
it has depth and length and breadth.

1981

## For Ana Veldford[1]

Never a summertime in Provincetown[2]
and even on this limpid afternoon
(so out of the ordinary for New York)
it is from the window of a bus that I contemplate
the serenity of the grass up and down Riverside Park[3]          5
and the easy freedom of vacationers resting on rumpled blankets,
fooling around on bicycles along the paths.
I remain as foreign behind this protective glass
as I was that winter
—that unexpected weekend—                                          10

1. Translated by Gustavo Pérez Firmat. *Hudson*: the Hudson River, which runs through eastern New York State and, along its southern terminus, marks the border between the states of New York and New Jersey.

1. Translated by David Frye.
2. A beach community on Cape Cod, in Massachusetts.
3. On the Upper West Side of Manhattan.

when I first confronted Vermont's snow.
And still New York is my home.
I am ferociously loyal to this acquired *patria chica*.[4]
Because of New York I am a foreigner anywhere else,
fierce pride in the scents that assault us along any West Side street,     15
marijuana and the smell of beer
and the odor of dog urine
and the savage vitality of Santana[5]
descending upon us
from a speaker that thunders, improbably balanced on a fire escape,     20
the raucous glory of New York in summer,
Central Park[6] and us,
the poor,
who have inherited the lake of the north side,
and Harlem sails through the slackness of this sluggish afternoon.     25
The bus slips lazily,
down, along Fifth Avenue;
and facing me, the young bearded man
carrying a heap of books from the Public Library,
and it seems as if you could touch summer in the sweaty brow of the     30
    cyclist
who rides holding onto my window.
But New York wasn't the city of my childhood,
it was not here that I acquired my first convictions,
not here the spot where I took my first fall,
nor the piercing whistle that marked the night.     35
This is why I will always remain on the margins,
a stranger among the stones,
even beneath the friendly sun of this summer's day,
just as I will remain forever a foreigner,
even when I return to the city of my childhood     40
I carry this marginality, immune to all turning back,
too *habanera* to be *newyorkina*,[7]
too *newyorkina* to be
—even to become again—
anything else.     45

                                                          1981


# Conversation in a Train Station with an Old Man
# Who Speaks Spanish[1]

A frayed coat,
dirty shoes,
sparse white hair.
An incongruous lordly air.

---

4. Hometown or home province.
5. A Latin-jazz-influenced rock band led by the Mexican-born American guitarist Carlos Santana (b. 1947).
6. Grand public park in Manhattan.
7. New Yorker. *Habanera*: from Havana.
1. Translated by Gustavo Pérez Firmat.

I think: "This old man reminds me of Unamuno."[2]
The creases on his olive-skinned face:
trenches rather than wrinkles.
He speaks slowly.
He moves his hands slowly.
"Sixteen years," he says.
Bridgeport[3] and sixteen years of his life.
Sixteen years
without sun,
for this pair of pants of a dubious color
and this bitter tiredness
that gives his smile a leaden pallor.

This transplanted underdevelopment,
conspicuous, incongruous,
here,
on the shores of the Hudson,[4]
hits us hard.

This underdevelopment that our families flaunt
on Kennedy Boulevard,
that turns into superkitsch on Bergenline . . . [5]
This underdevelopment mindful of appearances,
of a narrow and obsessive
sexuality . . .
The archeology of an extinct society,
one thousand and six hundred miles from its place of origin.

1981

2. Miguel de Unamuno y Jugo (1864–1936), Spanish writer and philosopher.
3. City on the southern coast of Connecticut.
4. See note 1, p. 1189.
5. Bergenline Avenue, a thoroughfare, major commercial district, and largely Cuban neighborhood in the North Hudson section of Hudson County, New Jersey, across the river from Manhattan. *Kennedy Boulevard*: an adjacent thoroughfare.

---

# ROSARIO FERRÉ
## b. 1938

Rosario Ferré is one of Puerto Rico's leading authors and the island Puerto Rican writer who has most successfully crossed over into the English-speaking market. Although Spanish is her dominant language, Ferré's fluency in English enables her to move with ease between the cultures and languages of her homeland and the mainland.

She was born in Ponce, Puerto Rico, into one of the islands' most prominent political families. Her father, Luis A. Ferré, was a wealthy industrialist, political leader, and, from 1968 to 1972, the governor of Puerto Rico. While over time Rosario Ferré's political views have become akin to those of her family, in the past she often disagreed with the family's support of statehood for Puerto Rico. In the early 1970s, she publicly advocated Puerto Rico's independence from the United States. Ferré received her primary education in Puerto Rico and her secondary education at Dana Hall School, in Wellesley, Massachusetts. After attending Wellesley College for a year, she earned her undergraduate degree from Manhattanville College, in Purchase, New York. She entered Puerto Rico's literary scene in the early 1970s, when she founded and coedited the literary magazine *Zona de Carga y Descarga*, an influential publication that represented the avant-garde of Puerto Rican letters. *Zona* broke new ground in Puerto Rican aesthetics by rejecting the constraints and exclusions of the conventional, patriarchal canon and seeking to validate alternative modes of expression.

Ferré's short-story collection *Papeles de Pandora* (Pandora's Papers, 1976) introduced both an innovative female voice into the male-dominated literary canon and a feminist perspective into Puerto Rican prose fiction. Before long, Ferré's writings caught the attention of feminist critics in Latin America and the United States, and she is one of a handful of Latin American women writers whose work has consistently been promoted among English-speaking audiences. Her fascination with the art of translation began when she translated her first novel, *Maldito Amor* (1987), from its original Spanish into English as *Sweet Diamond Dust* (1988). In 1991, she translated *Papeles de Pandora* into English under the title *The Youngest Doll*.

With *The House on the Lagoon* (1995), her first novel written in English, Ferré took on the challenge of inventively transferring the historical context and cultural signs and codes of her native Puerto Rican culture. Instead of simply translating this critically acclaimed novel—a finalist for the National Book Award—into Spanish, she rewrote it as *La casa de la laguna* (1997). In both versions, the novel is an intergenerational family saga that blurs the lines between history and storytelling in its attempts to capture the class, gender, racial, and identity conflicts that dominate a patriarchal Puerto Rican society at different historical moments. As shown in the chapter presented in this anthology, what makes the novel so intensely original is Ferré's powerful evocations of the past, her audacious challenging of social conventions, her mastery of irony and the subtleties of language, and the confluence in her narratives of the real and surreal. Linking Puerto Rico's social and political struggles to the conditions that contribute to women's subordination, Ferré captures historical class conflicts and contradictions of island society, and the banal and pretentious lives of the old patriarchal ruling class and the urban bourgeoisie.

In her essay "Writing in Between" (1997), also included here, Ferré reflects on her crossover writing and issues of national identity. She has repeated her crossover writing endeavors in her second English-language novel, *Eccentric Neighborhoods* (1998), published in Spanish as *Vecindarios excéntricos* (1998). Although Ferré's most-acclaimed works are prose fiction, she has also authored the poetry collection *Fábulas de la garza desangrada* (Fables of a Bleeding Heron, 1980); a volume of feminist essays about women's writing, *Sitio a Eros* (Eros Under Siege, 1980); and several children's books. She believes that "the secrets of writing, like the secrets of good cooking, absolutely do not have anything to do with gender, but rather with the wisdom behind the mixing of the ingredients." And whether one reads her works in the original language in which they were written or in her rewritten translations, the unconventional trademarks of Ferré's style rarely get lost.

Ferré lives in Puerto Rico, but has lived intermittently in the United States while pursuing her graduate education and other professional activities. She holds a degree in Hispanic studies from the University of Puerto Rico, a doctoral degree in comparative literature from the University of Maryland, and an honorary degree from Brown University. Among the awards Ferré has received is a Guggenheim Fellowship. She has also been a faculty member at the University of Puerto Rico and a visiting writer at various U.S. universities.

FROM THE HOUSE ON THE LAGOON

# Thanksgiving Day, 1936

He was seven years old. Quintín remembered it clearly. Don Esteban Rosich was still alive, and he enjoyed having the family over for turkey. Don Esteban must have been almost ninety, but he was very sociable, and Quintín was his favorite grandson.[1] He insisted that Quintín was a big boy now, and when dinner was over, he told him he could sit with them out on the terrace. Madeleine[2] served him his apple pie à la mode, and Quintín sat down in his grandfather's white Thonet[3] rocking chair to eat contentedly.

Quintín loved his grandmother's pies; nobody made them like that; the crust was so light it melted on your tongue before you closed your mouth. It was one of the reasons he liked to visit the country house in Guaynabo,[4] another being the grass-covered slope behind the house, where he could slide as fast as lightning on his red sled all the way to the fern-shadowed creek at the bottom of the hill. His grandparents' house was the only one he knew where people celebrated Thanksgiving. None of his friends had heard of it or understood what the word meant. They pronounced it "San Gibin," as if in honor of an obscure Catholic saint. They knew nothing about the Puritans, Plymouth Rock, or the four wild turkeys of President Washington.[5] In fact, as there were very few turkeys on the island and no one ate them on that day, Madeleine's fowl was a large hen, fattened especially for the feast.

Quintín finished his apple pie and began slowly swaying to and fro, leaning as far back as he could in the rocking chair that reminded him of a bicycle with huge wheels on its sides. He liked to listen to grownup talk, and the family forgot all about him.

Don Esteban, Quintín's great-grandfather, never saw eye to eye with Buenaventura,[6] and there were always fireworks when they got together for cigars and after-dinner drinks. Usually they ended up talking about the island's disquieting political events. "Autonomists are all Independentistas in disguise," Don Esteban said to Buenaventura. "They'll argue about the moral virtues of being an independent nation, while they profit shamelessly from the wealth of the United States. Let's see what they do after Senator Millard Tydings presents his bill calling for immediate sovereignty for the island."[7]

"A barking dog never bites!" said Arístides,[8] with a reassuring smile at Madeleine. "I don't believe anything serious will come of it. The Nationalists are trying to intimidate the United States into giving up the island, and Senator Tydings has fallen into their trap. But it's just a lot of propaganda, and the other senators know better!"

---

1. I.e., great-grandson.
2. Don Esteban's daughter; Quintín's maternal grandmother.
3. A brand of designer furniture.
4. A municipality in northern Puerto Rico.
5. George Washington (1732–1799), U.S. president 1789–97, declared November 26, 1789, a national holiday called Thanksgiving Day. This day commemorated the first thanksgiving, a feast in 1621 celebrating the bountiful harvest of the Puritan colony near Plymouth Rock, in Massachusetts. Thanksgiving Day became a yearly holiday in 1863, and the turkey dinner traditionally served on Thanksgiving was inspired by the four wild turkeys eaten at the Puritans' feast.
6. Buenaventura Mendizabal, Quintín's father.
7. See note 1, p. 491.
8. Arístides Arrigoitia, Quintín's maternal grandfather (Madeleine's husband).

They were talking about Millard Tydings, a senator from Maryland who was a personal friend of Governor Blanton Winship.[9] Tydings had introduced a bill in Congress which proposed independence for Puerto Rico in a matter of months, freeing the United States from the official guardianship of a possibly mutinous island.

Governor Winship was incensed by the latest shootout of the Nationalist Liberation forces of Pedro Albizu Campos, during which several police agents had been murdered. Pedro Albizu Campos was the son of an *hacendado*[1] from Ponce and of a mulatto woman; he had studied law at Harvard, where he became friendly with Irish nationalists. He believed the Irish had won their independence through the "blood sacrifice" of the martyred Catholic rebels executed after the Easter Rebellion of 1916,[2] and he thought Puerto Ricans could do the same. He came back to the island, founded the Nationalist Party in 1932,[3] and began a frontal assault on what he termed "American Imperialism." Albizu maintained that Puerto Rico had been illegally ceded to the United States by Spain at the end of the Spanish-American War, since in 1897 we had been granted autonomy by the Spanish courts. He named himself President of the Republic of Puerto Rico and began publicly to harangue the masses, encouraging them to fight the "invader" by every violent means possible. Four years later, in 1936, he was arrested and tried for sedition.

"*Nombrare il Diabolo e vederli venire sono due cose molti diversie:* Calling the Devil and watching him come are two very different things," said Don Esteban, shaking his head. "People on this island were given a great gift when they were made American citizens nineteen years ago. They should be going to Washington on their knees, to persuade the Senate that Puerto Rico should be made a state as soon as possible, instead of bickering about when or even if they should ask for statehood. Now we'll see what happens with the Tydings Bill!"

"I'm not as afraid of Pedro Albizu Campos as of Luis Muñoz Marín,"[4] said Arístides. "That young politician is a smart one: he wants us to achieve the maximum degree of independence through negotiation, using autonomy as a stepping-stone to a Nationalist Republic. It was all done in Ireland fourteen years ago; there's nothing new under the sun."

Buenaventura blamed President Franklin Delano Roosevelt's supposedly socialist measures for the divided opinions on the status of the island. "That man is a turncoat," Buenaventura said. "He betrayed his own class when he made us pay income tax,[5] and no one who's anybody in Puerto Rico is going

---

9. For Winship and Pedro Albizu Campos, discussed below, see p. 445.
1. Landowner.
2. Also called the Easter Rising of 1916; on Easter Monday of that year and for the following six days, Irish nationalists proclaimed an Irish Republic and revolted against the British government. After putting down the revolt, the British executed 15 of its leaders.
3. Albizu Campos did not found the Nationalist Party in 1932; it was founded by others a decade earlier. Albizu Campos became active in the Party in 1924 and was elected its president in 1930.
4. See p. 482.
5. Roosevelt (1882–1945), U.S. president 1933–45, did not create the U.S. income tax, which has

a long and complicated history. During his administration, especially in response to the Great Depression, the government spent more money on programs and projects than ever before in U.S. history, and the income tax rates were raised accordingly. To fund the Social Security program, which Roosevelt initiated, the government instituted payroll taxes in 1936. Ferré is being ironic here, showing the political differences that can exist among family members. *His own class*: the upper class, the monied and propertied class. During this period, most members of Puerto Rico's propertied class tended to support statehood or autonomy as a way of maintaining the island's economic relationship with the United States.

to want the island to be part of the Union as long as he's President. We might as well stay as we are now, don't you think?"

Don Esteban didn't reply. His father had been an anarchist laborer in one of the marble quarries of Bergamo, in northern Italy, and he felt a great admiration for President Roosevelt, precisely because he had passed a law that made everybody pay taxes on their income. He didn't want to discuss President Roosevelt with Buenaventura.

"Taxation is a mistake. In Valdeverdeja[6] no one ever paid taxes and the town always had enough money for public works," Buenaventura went on morosely. Whenever he mentioned his hometown, he became nostalgic and pulled more deeply on his cigar. Don Esteban looked at him disapprovingly. He knew that, in spite of his complaints, Buenaventura hardly paid taxes at all, because he charged cash for most of his merchandise and never declared his real income. "I don't see why we should give those lazy representatives in our local legislature a third of our hard-earned money," Buenaventura added, extending his arm to flick a sliver of red ash into a flowerpot.

"Well, there's no need to worry about independence for now," said Arístides. "I'm a friend of several Statehood Republican Party leaders, and they assure me the Tydings Bill isn't going anywhere. Taking our citizenship away from us would raise an outcry and make the United States look like a bully. They are in a difficult position—they're not sure they want us, but they can't let us go."

Rebecca[7] sat demurely in the chair next to Buenaventura, drinking iced lemonade and listening absentmindedly to all that was said. Madeleine, however, was all pins and needles when she heard this kind of talk. She took out a handkerchief from her sleeve and began to dab at her forehead with eau de cologne. "God have pity on the people of this island if they ever take away their American citizenship!" she said to Buenaventura in English. "Chaos will reign and no one will know what to do. I was born in Boston; I could never live in a foreign country."

Don Esteban looked despondently at his daughter. He had to admit she was right. If the island were ever made a republic, they would have to sell the Taurus Line and go back to Boston.[8] Still, there was very little they could do to prevent it. Politics on the island were a complicated affair: it was better to keep a low profile and not get mixed up in any of it. In any case, they didn't really have to get involved. Don Esteban's son-in-law, Arístides, was an officer in the police force, even though only part-time, and he took care of them very effectively. He saw to it that their businesses were never unduly investigated for back taxes by the Departmento de Hacienda and that their homes were under adequate police protection.

Don Esteban had been very upset when he found out Buenaventura had beaten Rebecca because she had danced for her friends in a risqué evening gown.[9] He went to visit her and he was shocked: Rebecca had a blue ring

6. A municipality in Toledo, Spain.
7. Rebecca Arrigoitia Mendizabal, Quintín's mother (Buenaventura's wife; Madeleine and Arístides's daughter).
8. Don Esteban was born in Italy and immigrated to the United States. He settled in Boston, became a U.S. citizen, and made a fortune importing Italian shoes to the U.S. He also owns the Taurus commercial shipping line, which does

business in Boston, New York, and San Juan. His business interests are linked to the U.S. economic and political control of Puerto Rico; hence his decision to live on the island.
9. Rebecca had dreamed of becoming a poet and ballet dancer, but her parents discouraged her from pursuing an artistic career. She maintains a circle of artistic friends, and with them she once performed at her home—the house on the

around her right eye and several cuts on her brow. He insisted Rebecca leave Buenaventura and come to live with her own family again. But this time Rebecca didn't go back to her parents as she had when they went to live in Atlanta. Instead, she became pregnant with Ignacio.[1]

It was almost as if, taking her penance to heart, Rebecca was determined to prove she had more willpower than anyone else. One can be a rebel by being obedient; in fact, absolute obedience can be the most perfect kind of rebellion, as saints who embraced the hairshirt under silk garments discovered long ago. Rebecca's metamorphosis was something of the kind. Before, she admired Oscar Wilde and Isadora Duncan.[2] Now she went to Mass and to Communion daily. She was one of those people who, if told by the Pope they should be poor to save their souls, the next day give everything away and go barefoot to attain their goal. But it was also as if she were acting out a role onstage. In the thirty-seven years she had lived, she had given several very intense performances.[3] Now she was set on being the perfect wife.

The house on the lagoon was always spotlessly clean. Industriousness became the Mendizabal family's supreme virtue, and no one was ever supposed to be sad. Order and discipline were very important. One day Rebecca went down to the cellar, where the servants lived, and made inquiries as to who was married and who was not. She found out Petra and Brambon had been living in sin for years, and she was horrified. Rebecca made them dress up as bride and groom, got them a marriage license, and took them to see the judge. Petra and Brambon did everything she told them, as if it were all a game. They thanked her for the wedding gifts, drank champagne, and ate a slice of wedding cake, but the next morning they secretly went back to the civil court and asked the judge to divorce them. They had been married a long time ago, in a voodoo ceremony in Guayama, and were afraid the legal marriage might put a hex on them.

When Ignacio was born, Rebecca took care of him herself. She was almost fanatical about it: she bathed him, fed him, and wouldn't let anyone else near him. On the other hand, she began to neglect Quintín again. He was born in the old house, and his mere presence reminded her of a different time. In Pavel's time[4] she often went down to the cellar to drink water at the spring or to take long baths. She wrote poetry and her house had been full of her friends. But since Buenaventura's beating, she hadn't gone down there once. Precisely because she didn't want to remember, she hardly ever asked to see poor Quintín. Petra and Eulodia kept Quintín with them in the kitchen. They would sit him down on a red stool and give him a bowl of green beans to snap, or in front of revolving ice-cream maker and let him pour the rock salt on the crushed ice.

That Thanksgiving Day in 1936, as Quintín remembered it, did not have a peaceful ending. After Don Esteban's speech on the blessings of Ameri-

---

lagoon—the play *Salomé* (1891, 1894). This tragedy, by the Irish writer Oscar Wilde (1854–1900), retells the biblical story of Salomé, famous for her dance of the seven veils. Rebecca played Salomé, and when Buenaventura arrived to find his wife dancing naked for her friends, he beat her up.
1. Quintín's brother.
2. American dancer (1877–1927); like Wilde, she represents creativity, bohemianism, and modernity.

3. I.e., at the terrace of the house on the lagoon, together with her friends.
4. I.e., the time during which Rebecca was close friends with Pavel, a Czech-born American architect with whom she shared artistic interests but who died in an accident. Pavel had designed and built the first house on the lagoon, which Buenaventura ordered to be destroyed and replaced because he considered Pavel a bad influence on Rebecca.

can citizenship, Buenaventura kept a hostile silence. Just before he left the house, however, he decided to get even. "I heard that the Taurus Line had a very good year, Don Esteban," he said as he was going out the door. "I want to congratulate you. Profits are much higher here than in Boston, thanks to our new coastal trade laws, which force the island to ship everything through the mainland. Before, we could ship directly to Spain, and Mendizabal & Company was doing good business. Now things have changed and it's *your* turn. American, Spanish, who knows! At this rate, we're never going to make up our minds what we'd like to be!"

Arístides was furious. He was sure Buenaventura had meant to insult Don Esteban and the United States. He took hold of him by the lapels of his jacket and pushed him unceremoniously out the door.

1995

# Writing in Between

Puerto Ricans are always asking existential questions. Are we Latins or North Americans? Do we want our island to be independent, or do we want to become a state of the Union? Can our Hispanic culture and language survive within an Anglo-Saxon framework? How Hispanic *is* our culture? Fully, half, or only slightly? Why is it that when we travel to the States, we feel as Latin as the *salsero* Rubén Blades, but when we visit Latin America, we feel more American than John Wayne?[1]

Are we poor, or are we rich? Should we use the United States or South America as a measure? Could we subsist on our own, at the standard of living we are used to? If Puerto Rico became a state, could it live with a stifled heart, or would internal strife break out?

How safe is our American citizenship? Can our American passports be recalled? We were not consulted in 1917 when we were made citizens, and some politicians have argued that our citizenship could be revoked.[2] The Supreme Court affirmed in 1980 (*Harris v. Rosario*) that the Commonwealth of Puerto Rico was subject to the territorial clause. Our citizenship was given to us by law and therefore is not a constitutional right; it could be repealed by Congress on the basis of a reasonable argument. Furthermore, Puerto Rico's ambiguous political status puts the United States in an awkward position in the United Nations vis-à-vis colonialism, which means that someday the United States might unilaterally grant us independence. Puerto Ricans who wished to retain their American citizenship could do so, but those born under the new republic would not be U.S. citizens. These are some of the issues we have faced for nearly a century.

Because of our difficulties with self-definition, we are passionately involved in the political process. Almost 90 percent of our adult population votes every four years, as compared to about 50 percent in the United States. We are well informed and conscious of the need for honesty in public office. In fact,

---

1. American movie actor (Marion Robert Morrison, 1907–1979), associated with Westerns, war movies, and a conservative patriotism. *Rubén Blades*: Panamanian singer/songwriter and actor (b. 1948).

2. See the discussion of the Jones Act in the "Acculturation" introduction (p. 361). For the text of the act, see Appendix 2: Treaties, Acts, and Propositions (p. A15).

our precarious fence sitting since the United States gave us citizenship has developed in us an acute awareness of the democratic process and the importance of participating in it.

Yet the conundrum of our identity has made us profoundly insecure. First and foremost is the problem of language. Both the statehood and the commonwealth parties have declared that we will never give up the Spanish language; Spanish will have to be an official language for us, together with English, if we become a state. In Spain, Spanish is the main official language, but the Spanish constitution provides for secondary official languages in regions like Catalonia and the Basque provinces. Can the United States do the same? Can it rise to the challenge of not only allowing but encouraging immigrants to keep their languages while ensuring the permanence of English?

Come what may, Puerto Ricans will not voluntarily give up their American citizenship. Like the Spanish language, it is not negotiable; it represents for us economic stability and the assurance of civil liberties and democracy. Thus Puerto Rico's status is a paradox: We refuse to give up mutually exclusive things. How will we deal with this catch-22, in view of the growing insularity of the United States today? The English-only debate and the struggle for more stringent immigration laws are only two examples of this radicalization. As a writer who is proud to be a Puerto Rican and at the same time cherishes her American citizenship, I am very much aware of the conflict. We are people in perpetual search of ourselves.

Some time ago I read that newborn babies suck faster at the breast if they hear someone speak their mother's language, which they have learned to recognize in the womb. I did not learn to speak English until I was seven, and I learned most of it from books. At ten I had read *Wuthering Heights, Jane Eyre, The Three Musketeers,* and *The Thousand and One Nights*[3] by sneaking into my father's library. I still speak English with a Spanish accent; "canary" and "cannery," "sheet" and "shit" make me tremble when I have to say them, because my pronunciation often gets me in trouble. Spanish still makes me suck faster at life's breast.

I write Spanish the way I speak it, fast. For me, Spanish is *la lengua escrita;*[4] English is "the written word." That's why it's impossible for me to write in English the way I write in Spanish. English makes me slow down. I have to think about what I'm going to say two or three times—which may be a good habit, because I can't put my foot, or rather my pen, in it so easily. I can't be trigger-happy in English, because shaping the words takes so much effort.

Spanish literature has an oral quality to it, and Caribbean literature especially so, since it comes directly from an oral tradition. Perhaps that is why it does not translate well. Caribbean stories can be like incantations that lead to alternate realities; their meaning often cannot be discerned until they are read aloud. English has Milton,[5] Shakespeare, and the King James Version of the Bible standing behind it, swords drawn. Spanish doesn't have to be taken

---

3. A collection of folktales from the Middle East and North Africa (ca. ninth century–ca. fourteenth century), often known in English as the *Arabian Nights.* The other literary classics listed here are nineteenth-century novels by, respectively, the English writer Emily Brontë (1818–

1848); her sister, Charlotte Brontë (1816–1855); and the French writer Alexandre Dumas, père (1802–1870).
4. The written language.
5. John Milton (1608–1674), English poet.

so seriously; there's more room in it for *bachata* and *relajo*,[6] for irreverent humor.

To say it in plain English, I love to write in Spanish. Spanish is like a luxuriant jungle I love to get lost in, meandering down paths of words that may lead only to the rustle of their own foliage. Like Rocinante, Don Quixote's horse,[7] I can roll on the ground and frolic in Spanish free of worry, because the words always mean exactly what they say. I love to make love in Spanish; I've never been able to make love in English. In English I get puritanical; I could never do a belly dance, a flamenco, or a zapateado[8] in English.

Writing in English is like looking at the world through a different pair of binoculars; it imposes a different mind-set. When I write in Spanish, my sentences are often as convoluted as a baroque *retablo*.[9] When I write in English, Locke[1] is locked into every sentence; each paragraph has to be like a beam placed across a ceiling, bearing the weight of meaning erected on it. In English I have to be precise as well as practical. I feel like Emily Dickinson holding a loaded gun;[2] if I shoot, I must bring down my target.

Yet beneath my Puerto Rican English a Latin passion throbs, a salsa rhythm swings. I'm always coming and going from English to Spanish, from the conga drums to the violins. Language has become *la guaga aérea*[3] for me; it keeps me flying *entre* Puerto Rico and New York. When I was a child, I used to love asking friends "¿Cómo se dice 'Entre, entre que va a caer un aguacero!' en inglés?" "Between, between the water zero is dropping in!" I'd answer, laughing my head off. Now I know why I liked that silly joke so much. It was a prophecy of what my life as a writer would be like.

Puerto Rican writers write mostly in Spanish. Our books are seldom translated into English, and few of us are known in the United States. Nor does our literature commonly reach Latin American countries, in spite of the shared language. For almost a hundred years we have inhabited a cultural no-man's-land. In Latin America we are seen as gringos, in North America as *latinoamericanos*. This fact has contributed greatly to our isolation and to the limited distribution of our books off the island.

Eighty-two years ago, with the Jones Act, education in English was made mandatory on our island, even though our vernacular was Spanish. It wasn't a matter of learning a second language; it was a matter of giving up one first language for another. Of course it didn't work. From the moment Puerto Ricans were forced to speak English, they refused to learn it. People laughed at English; it was the language of those who saw themselves as superior to us when they weren't. They came from places like Chicago, which had "shit" trapped inside it twice, both in "chit" and in "cago," or like Florida, *espiritismo con bay rum*.[4] It wasn't until the forties, when hundreds of thousands of Puerto Ricans emigrated to the States and, as soon as they got there, tried to go back home and couldn't (but swore they would one day), that English began to trickle into our collective unconscious. Today 2.5 million Puerto Ricans live in the States, always coming from and going to the island, and

---

6. Joking, jesting; debauchery. *Bachata*: partying, dancing, playing a musical instrument.
7. In the novel *Don Quixote* (1605, 1615), by the Spanish writer Miguel de Cervantes (1547–1616).
8. An old Spanish heel-tapping dance.
9. Altarpiece.
1. John Locke (1632–1704), English philosopher.

2. A playful reference to the first line of a poem written in 1863 by the American poet Emily Dickinson (1830–1886): "My Life had stood - a Loaded Gun - ."
3. See the opening paragraph of the Luis Rafael Sánchez headnote (p. 1133).
4. Spiritualism with bay rum.

3.8 million live on the island, continually traveling to the States. The trickle of English has become a flood.

To speak more than one language is typical of the Caribbean. Taking over a language is a cannibalistic activity, and speaking your neighbors' language is a way of becoming them: *Veni, vidi, edi.*[5] Puerto Ricans are typically Caribbean: We are 65 percent bilingual; we speak English *and* Spanish. Each time we return from the States, we bring back a crumb, a flake, a nugget of gold from its citadels. Bilingualism is a tremendous advantage; I see no reason to give up a language if I can help it. Having two different languages, two different views of the world, is profoundly enriching.

Latinos are the fastest-growing minority in the United States; by 2010 their numbers there are expected to reach 39 million—more than the population of most republics in Latin America today. So bilingualism, at home as well as in school, will inevitably become a part of American culture. But we will not be alone: Many European and Asian countries—Spain, Belgium, and India, for example—have more than one official language. Speaking other languages helps us understand each other better, and understanding is the basis for progress and peace. Language must be the electric current that propels us out, rather than the electrified fence that keeps us in.

In September 1996 newspapers on the mainland—the *New York Times*, the *Washington Post*—were full of photographs of Puerto Rico flooded by Hurricane Hortense. What made me cringe when I saw them were the miserable zinc-roofed wooden shacks reflected on the muddy waters of lagoons and rivers. Most of the people photographed were from the poorer barrios, barefoot, half naked. Even the middle-class barrios like Puerto Nuevo and Levittown looked desperately poor by mainland standards.

My first thought was, "There goes the publicity campaign the Department of Tourism has spent millions on this year!" But then I realized that those photographs *were* Puerto Rico—the hidden island, the reality I tried to portray in my novel *The House on the Lagoon*. Las Minas, the terrible slum on the shores of Morass Lagoon, is connected by a labyrinth of mangroves to Alamares Lagoon, where the well-to-do reside. One lagoon is the reflection of the other, its direct result. This situation is not exclusive to Puerto Rico. I lived in Washington, D.C., from 1983 to 1992 and drove by Anacostia and then Arlington many times. Whether in Puerto Rico or in the United States, we have to look at our reflections in our lagoons and try to change what we see for the better. This is what I wanted readers in the United States to understand when I wrote my novel in English.

My voluntary exile in D.C. had its advantages. My own age was invisible; I hardly noticed it when I looked at myself in the mirror. Since I was never with people of my generation, I was sure I looked as young as I felt, so I took the liberty of saying that I was four years younger than I really was. Every time I traveled to the island, however, I was shocked at how much my friends had aged. I pitied them for their wrinkles, gray hairs, and nervous ticks, which I ascribed to the fear of having to outrun carjackers and bumper locks in a *tapón*—traffic jam—an ill I had miraculously escaped in D.C. This mirage, alas, vanished when I moved back to the island. Age and vandalism

5. We came, we saw, we ate (Latin); a play on the famous phrase *Veni, vidi, vici* (We came, we saw, we conquered).

caught up to me with a vengeance. My car was broken into twice and then stolen and destroyed; my house was burglarized while my husband and I slept in our bed; and now I could no longer knock four years off my vita, since it might land in the hands of a cousin or friend five years younger than I was.

During my visits to the island I had always looked for signs of modernization, improvements that permitted Puerto Ricans to live in consonance with the modern age. Today, however, people who return to the island after living on the mainland for a number of years have a different reaction. It's as if they had been caught in a time warp, dreaming of an island that had long since disappeared.

I've met people who miss terribly the Puerto Rico of the seventies and eighties, when you could drive lazily down a half-distorted Ashford Avenue,[6] walk in the streets at night without feeling terrified, go for a drive in mountains still covered with vegetation. There were only a few Kentucky Fried Chickens and no Hooterses, Ponderosas, or Hard Rock Cafés; the residents smiled often, knew nothing about angel dust, often traveled by *público*,[7] had no cellular phones or television. Many today cling to a vision of this Puerto Rico long gone—a bucolic paradise, an Arcadia—where the hunger and TB they ran away from have dimmed with time but the beauties of nature are more vivid than ever. And they blame us, the ones who weren't forced to emigrate to survive, for not having taken care of the island, for not having preserved it in its "pristine" state.

Puerto Ricans living in the States resent that the island is "too Americanized." But if you ask them whether they would want to come back if it became an independent nation or a free associated state, they say no, except to vacation. They have very good jobs in the States, thank you, and would like to see those changes take place on their island homeland from over there.

What do our exiled compatriots mean by "Americanized"? Do they mean that we should not learn to speak English? Puerto Ricans are certainly not speaking less Spanish; our language is as healthy and alive as ever. Do they mean that drug use, crime, AIDS, and traffic jams are on the rise? These ills are part of every modern society. Do they mean a higher standard of living, better living conditions, Medicare and Medicaid? These changes are due to our modernization, achieved by our own efforts, and to our economic association with the United States.

Many Puerto Ricans on the mainland also believe that they should be allowed to participate in the next plebiscite held on the island. I can't agree with them. A ballot is like a gun: You have to be responsible for what you aim at. Voting for a political status when you don't have to endure the consequences in the flesh seems to me unfair.

I believe in globalization, in which Puerto Rico has an enormous advantage over Latin America. For almost a hundred years we have been at the vanguard of cross-culturalization and bilingualism. We have an American passport—and are not willing to give it up. But most Puerto Ricans would probably also be glad to have a Puerto Rican passport and Puerto Rican citizenship, if they could have it both ways. This is a distinct possibility, considering the way global politics is developing in other countries. Sometime

6. Avenida Ashford, a thoroughfare in a coastal area of San Juan, Puerto Rico, and one of the capital's main tourist areas, devoted to dining, shopping, nightlife, and high-end style.
7. Public transportation.

in the future the United States might change its laws and grant double citizenship to Puerto Ricans, indigenous Hawaiians, and Navajos.

As a bilingual, technologically advanced community, we can set the pace for our neighboring Latin American countries, help them enter the modern world, and at the same time help the United States become more cosmopolitan. We can help Anglo-Americans deal with the Latino "problem," for example, by setting their minds at ease when, like peoples of every age before them, they hear in the unfamiliar languages spoken around them the sounds of barbarians at the gates.

Puerto Ricans are heroes of modernity; in spite of our poverty of resources and limited land, our "passivity," "indecision," and "plasticity"—our bending over to please the powerful, as those envious of us like to say—we have achieved what some of our richer and more powerful neighbors have not. I believe in our future as a community inseparable from our culture and our language, because we are so passionately committed to the modern world.

During a recent book tour on the mainland I was asked, again and again, why I had written *The House on the Lagoon* in English. It didn't matter to my listeners that I wrote a Spanish version of it a few months later or that it would soon be published in Spain and later in the United States. The question remained: Why had I written the book in English *first*?

I know I should have been prepared for this, but every time I heard it, I trembled. "You're a nincompoop!" my husband told me, when I called him from Chicago in tears. "Have a pat answer ready! Tell them you're like Sir Edmund Hillary:[8] You did it because it was there! Writing that novel in English was like climbing Mount Everest, I can attest to that!" When I called a friend, looking for comfort, she said, "Tell them you did it as an experiment, because you love to do bizarre things! And promise you'll never do it again!"

I couldn't follow either piece of advice. I had thoroughly enjoyed writing the novel in English, even if it *had* been difficult, and I meant to go on writing books in English and Spanish, no matter what anyone said.

Not long ago I was convinced that language and culture were like Cuba and Puerto Rico, two wings of the same bird. This has long been an axiom of Puerto Rican intellectuals, who have been deeply concerned about our losing our identity as a people. Now I am not so sure that the axiom is true. After seeing how Puerto Ricans on the mainland have lost their Spanish while firmly holding on to their culture, I feel that it must be reevaluated. Language is an important part of culture, but its exclusivity is not fundamental to culture's survival.

Some suspected that I had "done it" to sell more books. This was nonsense. All writers want their books to sell and be read as much as possible. Others asked if I believed English a richer and more universal language than Spanish and expressed myself better in it. This blow dart hurt. I like to write in English, but for me there's something sacred about writing in Spanish, the language of my dreams. Spanish has no reason to envy English; its own capacity to convey the impact of human emotions is enormous. The truth was, I had "done it" for none of these reasons.

---

8. New Zealand mountaineer and explorer (1919–2008). The English mountaineer and explorer George Mallory (1886–1924) famously replied, "Because it's there," to the question *Why do you want to climb Mount Everest?*

As I stood at the lectern, trying to think of answers, I came up with an improbable explanation: I wrote the novel in English *and* Spanish because I'm ambidextrous. When I was a little girl, I wrote with my left hand, but when I turned seven, Mother made me use my right. I couldn't be left-handed, she told me. Left-handed people were impaired. There were no left-handed desks at school; when you ate at the table, you were constantly nudging your neighbors in the ribs and making them spill their soup; doorknobs and faucets always turned to the right. So at seven I became "right-handed" *obligada*; I had to assimilate my left self to my right self. Today I write with both hands, be it with a pen or (thankfully) with a computer, and also in both languages.

Learning to speak a second language in the United States has a lot to do with learning how to live with *el otro*, the other that lurks inside us: our neighbor to the north if we come from Latin America, our neighbor to the south if we come from North America. It still surprises me that the Anglo-Saxon majority in the United States is so indifferent to learning a second language. Speaking more than one language has always been not only a practical necessity but a status symbol in Europe; in our communication-oriented society it is also an effective way to get ahead. Given that North and South America are mainly divided between Spanish and English speakers, and that by 2050 Latinos will be the largest ethnic group in the United States, it would be reasonable for Spanish to be taught in American schools as a second language and for English to be part of the regular curriculum in countries like Mexico, Argentina, and Colombia. In Puerto Rico, after all, English has been taught as a second official language for almost a hundred years.

Puerto Rico has always been afraid of being swallowed up by *el otro*. We were a colony of Spain for three hundred years. Then, in 1898, we became a colony of the United States. In 1917 we were given American citizenship, which the majority of us cherish. But we suffered from an inferiority complex. We were poor and undernourished, short and frail, mulatto *and* mestizo. We died young of dozens of illnesses that didn't exist on the mainland. A very important part of our difference was that we spoke Spanish. We began to flaunt our singularities as weapons against assimilation by *el otro*, *el americano del norte*, even though we had a common citizenship.

As the century progressed, our struggle for self-definition intensified. Our dilemma made us feel like Hamlet, lost in the marshes of Elsinore.[9] But as we argued with ourselves, something extraordinary happened. Our differences with *el otro* began to ebb. Puerto Ricans were no longer so poor. In 1997 the per capita income was $8,500, compared to $5,000 in Latin America. We were no longer undernourished, frail, or short. Today we are a mulatto-mestizo nation and proud of it. We eat Kentucky Fried Chicken, tacos from Taco Bell, and Whoppers from Burger King as well as *arroz con pollo*, *pasteles* and *lechón asao*.[1] Many of us access the Internet and practically live inside our computers. With the arrival of the modern age, the other faded more and more from our screens, except in one respect: language. That hasn't changed. We love Spanish. It sits well on our tongues.

9. The English name for the Danish city Helsingør and for the royal castle there, in which Shakespeare's *Hamlet* takes place. In the play, Prince Hamlet struggles with himself, pondering existence and his life, as he attempts to take action.

1. Barbecued pork. *Arroz con pollo*: literally, rice with chicken. *Pasteles*: similar to tamales but wrapped in banana leaves; the doughlike mass is made of green bananas or starchy roots.

When we discovered that we could learn English without losing our Spanish and that our Spanish gave us an edge in the world, we became less afraid of *el otro*. Maybe we could teach him a thing or two—make our neighbors to the north better American citizens by making them resemble *us*. Our second language is the ace up our sleeve. Growing up ambidextrous has been an unexpected blessing.

This is what I tried to explain to people whenever they asked me, perplexed, why I wrote the novel in English. I wasn't betraying them or myself; *they* would have written it in Spanish if they could have, if they hadn't lost their language. I "did it" in English and in Spanish and will go on doing it because I believe in freedom of speech.

1997

---

# ARTURO ISLAS
## 1938–1991

Arturo Islas was born in El Paso, Texas, and grew up in a desert, on the U.S.-Mexico border, that served as an inspiration for his fiction. He received his bachelor's degree (1960), master's (1963), and doctorate (1971) from Stanford University, where he subsequently was a professor of English. In "On the Bridge, At the Border: Migrants and Immigrants," which Islas delivered as the "Ernesto Galarza Commemorative Lecture" in 1990, he stated:

> I was educated in the public schools that my parents had attended before my brothers and I were born. People of Mexican ancestry in what was then a thriving military town did not enjoy the privilege of a college education. They were working so that their children could enjoy it. My father thinks his sacrifices have paid off. He likes to say that his youngest son, a lawyer, will defend him on earth, that his middle son, a priest, will defend him in heaven, and that his oldest son is at a "big deal" college in California teaching the gringos how to express themselves in their own language.

Islas's primary literary themes are race and homosexuality. His first novel, *The Rain God: A Desert Tale* (1984), from which one of the six chapters is excerpted in this anthology, is considered a classic in the Latino literary tradition. It describes the cultural conflict at the heart of the Angels, an extended Mexican American family struggling to accept their Chicano and Indian heritages and rejecting their Mexican past. Through the interweaving of various characters' paths, Islas demystifies the concept of family unity while addressing racial discrimination, religion, machismo, homosexuality, and physical handicaps. *Migrant Souls* (1990), Islas's second novel, continues the saga of the Angel family as its members become consumed by the tensions between their Spanish and Mexican heritages. In depicting the assimilation of Latinos into U.S. society, Islas avoids didacticism by presenting complex, multifaceted characters for whom migration involves internal and external rupture.

Islas also wrote poetry, and he left behind diaries and a hefty correspondence that narrate his battles with drugs, the racial discrimination he faced, and his experiences as a professor predating Latino studies. His odyssey is chronicled in Frederick

Luis Aldama's *Dancing with Ghosts: A Critical Biography of Arturo Islas* (2006). Almada also published a collection of essays, *Critical Mappings of Arturo Islas's Fiction* (2005), which includes appreciations by Erlinda Gonzales-Berry, José David Saldívar, and Rosaura Sánchez. After Islas's death, from AIDS, the scholar Paul Skenazy shaped Islas's unfinished manuscript for publication as *La Mollie and the King of Tears* (1996). This novel began as a creative writing assignment Islas posed to his class at the University of Texas in El Paso, where he was a visiting professor, in which he asked the students to write in a voice most unlike their own. The novel's protagonist, Louie Mendoza, is a hipster and saxophonist in San Francisco.

## *FROM* THE RAIN GOD

## Judgment Day[1]

A photograph of Mama Chona and her grandson Miguel Angel—Miguel Chico or Mickie to his family—hovers above his head on the study wall beside the glass doors that open out into the garden. When Miguel Chico sits at his desk, he glances up at it occasionally without noticing it, looking through it rather than at it. It was taken in the early years of World War II by an old Mexican photographer who wandered up and down the border town's main street on the American side. No one knows how it found its way back to them, for Miguel Chico's grandmother never spoke to strangers. She and the child are walking hand in hand. Mama Chona is wearing a black ankle-length dress with a white lace collar and he is in a short-sleeved light-colored summer suit with short pants. In the middle of the street life around them, they are looking straight ahead, intensely preoccupied, almost worried. They seem in a great hurry. Each has a foot off the ground, and Mama Chona's black hat with the three white daisies, their yellow centers like eyes that always out-stared him, is tilting backward just enough to be noticeable. Because of the look on his face, the child seems as old as the woman. The camera has captured them in flight from this world to the next.

Uncle Felix, Mama Chona's oldest surviving son, began calling the boy "Mickie" to distinguish him from his father, Miguel Grande, a big man whose presence dominated all family gatherings even though he was Mama Chona's youngest son. Her name was Encarnacion Olmeca de Angel and she instructed everyone in the family to call her "Mama Grande" or "Mama Chona" and never, ever to address her as *abuelita*, the Spanish equivalent to granny. She was the only grandparent Miguel Chico knew. The others had died many years before he was born on the north side of the river, a second generation American citizen.

Thirty years later and far from the place of his birth, on his own deathbed at the university hospital, Miguel Chico, who had been away from it for twelve years, thought about his family and especially its sinners. Felix, his

---

1. According to various religions, the day of God's judgment at the end of the world.

great-aunt Cuca, his cousin Antony on his mother's side—all dead. Only his aunt Mema, the pariah of the family after it initially refused to accept her illegitimate son, was still alive. And so was his father, Miguel Grande, whose sins the family chose to ignore because it relied on him during all crises.

Miguel Chico knew that Mama Chona's family held contradictory feelings toward him. Because he was still not married and seldom visited them in the desert, they suspected that he, too, belonged on the list of sinners. Still, they were proud of his academic achievements. He had been the first in his generation to leave home immediately following high school after being admitted to a private and prestigious university before it was fashionable or expedient to accept students from his background.

Mama Chona did not live to see him receive his doctorate and fulfill her dream that a member of the Angel family become a university professor. On her deathbed, surrounded by her family, she recognized Miguel Chico and said, *la familia*, in an attempt to bring him back into the fold. Her look and her words gave him that lost, uneasy feeling he had whenever any of his younger cousins asked him why he had not married. Self-consciously, he would say, "Well, I had this operation," stop there, and let them guess at the rest.

Miguel Chico, after he survived, decided that others believed the thoughts and feelings of the dying to be more melodramatic than they were. In his own case, he had been too drugged to be fully aware of his condition. In the three-month decline before the operation that would save his life, and as he grew thirstier every day, he longed to return to the desert of his childhood, not to the family but to the place. Without knowing it, he had been ill for a very long time. After suffering from a common bladder infection, he was treated with a medication that cured it but aggravated a deadly illness dormant since childhood though surfacing now and again in fits of fatigue and nausea.

"You didn't tell me you had a history of intestinal problems," the doctor said, leafing back through his chart.

"You didn't ask me," Miguel Chico replied. "And anyway, isn't it right there on the record?" He had lost ten pounds in two weeks and was beginning to throw up everything he ate.

"Well, I can't treat you for this now. I've cured your urinary infection. You'll have to go to a specialist at the clinic for the other. And stop taking the medication I prescribed for you." Later Mickie learned that no one with his history of intestinal illness ought to take the medication the doctor had prescribed. By then, it was too late.

He was allowed only spoonfuls of ice once every two hours and the desert was very much in his mouth, which was already parched by the drugs. Not at the time, but since, he has felt his godmother Nina's fear of being buried in the desert. Those chips of ice fed to him by his brother Raphael were grains of sand scratching down his throat. In the last weeks before surgery, as he lost control over his body, he floated in a perpetual dusk and, had it happened, would have died without knowing it, or would have thought it was happening to someone else.

There was one moment when he sensed he might not live. As the surgeon and anesthetist lifted him off of the gurney and onto the hard, cold table, each spoke quietly about what they were going to do. Mickie heard their voices, tender and kind, and was impressed by the way they touched him—as if he were a person in pain. He thought in those seconds that if theirs were the last voices he was to hear, that would be fine with him, for he longed to escape from the drugged and disembodied state of twilight in which he had lived for weeks. His uncle Felix had been murdered in such a twilight.

The doctors set him down and uncovered him. He weighed ninety-eight pounds and looked pregnant.

"Your mother is waiting just outside," said the surgeon's voice at his right ear.

"I'm going to relax you a little bit so that this tube won't hurt your nose or throat," said the anesthetist at his left.

Someone began shaving his abdomen and loins. "God, is he hairy," said a nurse loudly.

Miguel Chico did not care whether or not he survived the operation they planned for him. When they described it to him and told him he would have to wear a plastic appliance at his side for the rest of his life—a life, they were quick to assure him, which would be perfectly "normal"—they grinned and added, "It's better than the alternative."

"How would you know?" he asked. "Let me die."

Thus, at first he was considered a difficult patient. Later on, the drugs seeped through, drop by drop, and conquered his rebelliousness. When the nurses came in to check on him every twenty minutes and to ask him how he felt, "Just fine," he would answer, even as he watched himself piss, shit, and throw up blood. Only later, when he survived ("It's a miracle," the surgeon told his mother, "his intestine was like tissue paper"), forever a slave to plastic appliances, did he see how carefully he had been schooled by Mama Chona to suffer and, if necessary, to die.

Lying on a gurney in the recovery room, Miguel Chico came to life for the second time. Tubes protruded from every opening of his body except his ears, and before he was able to open his eyes, he heard a woman's voice calling his name over and over again in the way that made him wince: "Mee-gwell, Mee-gwell, wake up, Mee-gwell." Another voice from inside his head kept saying, "You cannot escape from your body, you cannot escape from your body."

He opened his eyes. In the gurney next to his there appeared a fat, strawberry blonde on all fours screaming for something to kill the pain inside her head. "Nurse, give me something for my head!" she yelled without stopping. The nurse, this time a delicate Polynesian dressed in bright green and wearing a mask, glided in and out of his vision.

"Now, now, sweetheart," she said to the fat woman in a lovely, lilting voice, "you're going to be all right, and I'll bring you something in just a minute." She disappeared with a lithe, dreamy motion.

The fat woman was not appeased and she screamed more loudly than before. He wondered why she was on all fours if she had just come from surgery. Only later did it occur to him that he might have imagined her. At the time, she awakened him to his own pain.

Looking down at himself, he saw that his body was being held together by a network of tubes and syringes. On his left side, by the groin, the head of a safety pin gleamed. He could not move his lips to ask for water, and from neck to crotch his body felt like dry ice, the desert on a cold, clear day after a snowfall. If he had been able to move his arms, he would have pulled out the tubes in his nose and down his throat so that he, too, might shout

out his horror and sense of violation. All of his needs were being taken care of by plastic devices and he was nothing but eyes and ears and a constant, vague pain that connected him to his flesh. Without this pain, he would have possessed for the first time in his life that consciousness his grandmother and the Catholic church he had renounced had taught him was the highest form of existence: pure, bodiless intellect. No shit, no piss, no blood—a perfect astronaut.

"I'm an angel," he said inside his mouth to Mama Chona, already dead and buried. "At last, I am what you taught us to be."

"Mee-gwell," sang the nurse, "wake up, Mee-gwell."

"It's Miguel," he wanted to tell her pointedly, angrily, "it's Miguel," but he was unable to speak. He was a child again.

· · ·

They took him to the cemetery for three years before Miguel Chico understood what it was. At first, he was held closely by his nursemaid Maria or his uncle Felix. Later, he walked alongside his mother and godmother, Nina, or sometimes, when Miguel Grande was not working, with his father, holding onto their hands or standing behind them as they knelt on the ground before the stones. No grass grew in the poor peoples' cemetery, and the trees were too far apart to give much shade. The desert wind tore the leaves from them and Miguel Chico asked if anyone ever watered these trees. His elders laughed and patted him on the head to be still.

Mama Chona never accompanied them to the cemetery. "Campo Santo" she called it, and for a long time Miguel Chico thought it was a place for the saints to go camping. His grandmother taught him and his cousins that they must respect the dead, especially on the Day of the Dead when they wandered about the earth until they were remembered by the living.[2] Telling the family that the dead she cared about were buried too far away for her to visit their graves, Mama Chona shut herself up in her bedroom on the last day of October and the first day of November every year for as long as she lived. Alone, she said in that high-pitched tone of voice she used for all important statements, she would pray for their souls and for herself that she might soon escape from this world of brutes and fools and join them. In that time her favorite word was "brute," and in conversation, when she forgot the point she wanted to make, she would close her eyes, fold her hands in prayer, and say, "Oh, dear God, I am becoming like the brutes."

At the cemetery, Miguel Chico encountered no saints but saw only stones set in the sand with names and numbers on them. The grownups told him that people who loved him were there. He knew that many people loved him and that he was related to everyone, living and dead. When his parents, Miguel Grande and Juanita, were married, his godmother, Nina, told him, all the people in the Church, but especially her, became his mothers and fathers and would take care of him if his parents died. Miguel Chico did not want them to die if it meant they would become stones in the desert.

---

2. On *El Día de los Muertos*, also known as All Souls' Day, a holiday celebrated in Mexico and by Latinos, family members and friends gather to remember and pray for people they have known who have died.

They bought flowers that smelled sour like Mama Chona and her sister, his great-aunt Cuca, to put in front of the stones. Sometimes they cried and he did not understand that they wept for the dead in the sand.

"Why are you crying?" he asked.

"Because she was my sister" or "because she was my mother" or "because he was my father," they answered. He looked at the stones and tried to see these people. He wanted to cry too, but was able to make only funny faces. His heart was not in it. He wanted to ask them what the people looked like but was afraid they would become angry with him. He was five years old.

There were other people walking and standing and kneeling and weeping quietly in front of the stones. Most of them were old like his parents, some of them were as old as Mama Chona, a few were his own age. They bought the yellow and white flowers from a dark, toothless old man who set them out in pails in front of a wagon. Miguel shied away when the ugly little man tried to give him some flowers.

"Take them, Mickie," said his godmother, "the nice man is giving them to you."

"I don't want them." He felt like crying and running away, but his father had told him to be a man and protect his mother from the dead. They did not scare him as much as the flower man did.

A year later, he found out about the dead. His friend Leonardo, who was eight years old and lived in the corner house across the street, tied a belt around his neck. He put one end of the belt on a hook in the back porch, stood on a chair, and knocked it over. Nardo's sister thought he was playing one of his games on her and walked back into the house.

The next morning Miguel's mother asked if he wanted to go to the mortuary and see Leonardo. He knew his friend was dead because all the neighborhood was talking about it, about whether or not the boy had done it on purpose. But he did not know what a mortuary was and he wanted to find out.

When they arrived there, Miguel saw that everything was white, black, or brown. The flowers, like the kind they bought from the old man only much bigger and set up in pretty ways, were mostly white. The place was cold and all the people wore dark, heavy clothes. They were saying the rosary in a large room that was like the inside of the church but not so big. It was brightly lit and had no altar, but there were a few statues, which Miguel recognized. A long, shiny metal box stood at the end of the room. It was open, but Miguel was not able to see inside because it was too far away and he was too small to see over people's heads, even though they were kneeling.

Maria and his mother said that he must be quiet and pray like the others in the room. He became bored and sleepy and felt a great longing to look into the box. After the praying was over, they stood in line and moved slowly toward the box. At last he would be able to see. When the people in front of them got out of the way, he saw himself, his mother, and Maria reflected in the brightly polished metal. They told him it was all right to stand so that his head was level with theirs as they knelt. The three of them looked in.

Leonardo was sleeping, but he was a funny color and he was very still. "Touch him," his mother said, "it's all right. Don't be afraid." Maria took his hand and guided it to Nardo's face. It was cold and waxy. Miguel looked at the candles and flowers behind the box as he touched the face. He was not afraid. He felt something but did not know what it was.

"He looks just like he did when he was alive, doesn't he, Mickie?" his mother said solemnly.

"Yes," he nodded, but he did not mean it. The feeling was circling around his heart and it had to do with the stillness of the flowers and the color of Nardo's face.

"Look at him one more time before we go," Maria said to him in Spanish. "He's dead now and you will not see him again until Judgment Day."

That was very impressive and Miguel Chico looked very hard at his friend and wondered where he was going. As they drove home, he asked what they were going to do with Leonardo.

His mother, surprised, looked at Maria before she answered. "They are going to bury him in the cemetery. He's dead, Mickie. We'll visit him on the Day of the Dead. *Pobrecito, el inocente*," she said, and Maria repeated the words after her. The feeling was now in his stomach and he felt that he wanted to be sick. He was very quiet.

"Are you sad, Mickie?" his mother asked before saying goodnight to him. "No."

"Is anything wrong? Don't you feel well?" She put her hand on his forehead. Miguelito thought of his hand on Nardo's face.

"I'm scared," he said, but that was not what he wanted to say.

"Don't be afraid of the dead," his mother said. "They can't hurt you."

"I'm not afraid of the dead." He saw the sand and stones for what they were now.

"What are you afraid of, then?"

The feeling and the words came in a rush like the wind tearing the leaves from the trees. "Of what's going to happen tomorrow," he said.

The next day, Miguel Chico watched Maria comb her long beautiful black and white hair in the sun. She had just washed it, and the two of them sat on the backstairs in the early morning light, his head in her lap. Her face was wide, with skin the color and texture of dark parchment, and her eyes, which he could not see because as he looked up her cheekbones were in the way, he knew were small and the color of blond raisins. When he was very young, Maria made him laugh by putting her eyes very close to his face and saying in her uneducated Spanish, "Do you want to eat my raisin eyes?" He pretended to take bites out of her eyelids. She drew back and said, "Now it's my turn. I like your chocolate eyes. They look very tasty and I'm going to eat them!" She licked the lashes of his deeply set eyes and Miguel Chico screamed with pleasure.

Maria was one of hundreds of Mexican women from across the border who worked illegally as servants and nursemaids for families on the American side. Of all ages, even as young as thirteen or fourteen, they supported their own families and helped to rear the children of strangers with the care and devotion they would have given their own relatives had they been able to live with them. One saw these women standing at the bus stops on Monday mornings and late Saturday nights. Sunday was their only day off and most of them returned to spend it on the other side of the river. In addition to giving her half of her weekly salary of twenty-five dollars, Juanita helped Maria pack leftover food, used clothing, old newspapers—anything Maria would not let her throw away—into paper bags that Maria would take to her own family. Years later, wandering the streets of New York, his own bag glued to his side, Miguel Chico saw Maria in all the old bag ladies waiting on street corners in Chelsea or walking crookedly through the Village,[3] stopping to pick through garbage, unable to bear the waste of the more privileged.

"Now, Maria," Juanita said, "if the immigration officials ask you where you got these things, tell them you went to bargain stores."

"Si, señora."

"And if they ask you where you have been staying during the week, tell them you've been visiting friends and relatives. Only in emergencies are you to use our name and we'll come to help you no matter what it is."

"Si, señora."

The conversation was a weekly ritual and unnecessary because Miguel Grande through his police duties was known by immigration officials, who, when it came to these domestics, looked the other way or forgot to stamp cards properly. Only during political campaigns on both sides of the river were immigration laws strictly enforced. Then Maria and all women like her took involuntary vacations without pay.

Mama Chona did not approve of any of the Mexican women her sons and daughters hired to care for her grandchildren. They were ill educated and she thought them very bad influences, particularly when they were allowed to spend much time with her favorites. Mama Chona wanted Miguel Chico to be brought up in the best traditions of the Angel family. Juanita scoffed at those traditions. "They've eaten beans all their lives. They're no better than anyone else," she said to her sister Nina. "I'm not going to let my kids grow up to be snobs. The Angels! If they're so great, why do I have to work to help take care of them?"

Miguel Chico could not remember a time when Maria was not part of his family and even though Mama Chona disapproved of the way she spoke Spanish, she was happy to know that Maria was a devout Roman Catholic. She remained so the first six years of his life, taking him to daily mass and holding him in her arms throughout the services until he was four. After mass during the week and before he was old enough to be instructed by Mama Chona, Maria took him to the five-and-ten stores downtown. If she had saved money from the allowance Juanita gave her, she would buy him paper doll books. He and Maria spent long afternoons cutting out dolls and dressing them. When he got home from the police station, Miguel Grande would scold Maria for allowing his son to play with dolls. "I don't want my son brought up like a girl," he said to Juanita in Maria's presence. He did not like to speak directly to the Mexican women Juanita and his sisters took on to help them with the household chores. Miguel Chico's aunts Jesus Maria and Eduviges left notes for the "domestics" (the Spanish word criadas is harsher) and spoke to them only when they had not done their chores properly. Mama Chona had taught all her children that the Angels were better than the illiterate riffraff from across the river.

"Maria does more good for people than all of them put together," Juanita complained to her sister and to her favorite brother-in-law, Felix, who shared her opinion of his sisters. "They're so holier than thou. Just because they can read and write doesn't make them saints. I'd like to see them do half the

---

3. Greenwich Village, a neighborhood in Lower Manhattan, is bordered to the north by the neighborhood of Chelsea.

work Maria does." Juanita knew that Jesus Maria and Eduviges considered Felix's wife an illiterate and not worthy of their brother, who, after all, was an Angel.

"Apologize to your father for playing with dolls," Juanita said to Miguel Chico. He did but did not understand why he needed to say he was sorry. When his father was not there, his mother permitted him to play with them. She even laughed when Maria made him a skirt and they watched him dance to the jitterbug music on the radio. "Yitty-bog," Maria called it. Miguel Grande had caught them at that once and made a terrible scene. Again, Miguel Chico was asked to apologize and to promise that he would never do it again. His father said nothing to him but looked at Juanita and accused her of turning their son into a *joto*. Miguel Chico did not find out until much later that the word meant "queer." Maria remained silent throughout these scenes; she knew enough not to interfere.

After Miguel Chico's birthday, several months after his friend Leonardo "accidentally" hanged himself, Maria stopped taking him to mass. Instead, she spent the afternoons when he got home from school talking to him about God and reading to him from the Bible, always with the stipulation that he not tell his parents or Mama Chona. She especially liked to talk to him about Adam and Eve and the loss of paradise.[4] He loved hearing about Satan's pride and rebelliousness and secretly admired him. Before he was expelled from the heavenly kingdom, Maria told him, Satan was an angel, the most favored of God's creatures, and his name was *Bella Luz*.

"Why did he turn bad, Maria?"

"Out of pride. He wanted to be God."

"Did God make pride?"

Miguel Chico learned that when he asked Maria a difficult question she would remain silent, then choose a biblical passage that illustrated the terrible power of God the Father's wrath. She loved to talk to him about the end of the world.

Maria began braiding her hair and tying it up in a knot that lay flat on her neck. It gave her a severe look he did not like, and he missed those mornings when she let her hair hang loosely to her waist and brushed or dried it in the sun, with his head on her lap. She did not allow him into her room any more and asked him to leave if he opened the door and caught her with her hair still unbraided. The word "vice" occurred frequently now in her talks with him; everything, it seemed, was becoming a vice to Maria. She had become a Seventh Day Adventist.

His mother and Maria got involved in long, loud, and tearful arguments about the nature of God and about the Catholic church as opposed to Maria's new religion. They excluded him from these discussions and refused to let him into the kitchen where they wrangled with each other and reached no conclusions. Miguel Chico hid in his mother's closet in order not to hear their shouting.

"The Pope is the anti-Christ!" Maria said loudly, hoping he would hear. And before Juanita could object, Maria cited a passage from the Bible as irrefutable proof.

---

4. See the Old Testament, Genesis 1–5.

"It's not true," Juanita said just as strongly, but she was not at ease with the holy book, and there was no priest at hand to back her up. She wept out of frustration and tried to remember what she had learned by rote in her first communion classes.

In the closet, Miguel Chico hugged his mother's clothes in terror. The familiar odors in the darkness kept him company and faintly reassured him. In the distance, the strident voices arguing about God continued. What would happen if he told his mother and father that Maria was sneaking him off to the Seventh Day Adventist services while they were away at work or having a good time? His father had said to his mother that he would kill Maria if she did that.

The services—which were not so frightening as his father's threats and the arguments between his mother and Maria—were held in a place that did not seem like a church at all it was so brightly lit up, even in the middle of the day. There were no statues and the air did not smell of incense and burning candles. The singing was in Spanish, not Latin, and it was not the sort he enjoyed because it reminded him of the music played in the newsreels about the war. The people at these services were very friendly and looked at him as if they all shared a wonderful secret. "You are saved," they would say to him happily. He did not know what they meant, but he sensed that to be saved was to be special. The more he smiled, the more they smiled back; they spent most of the time smiling, though they talked about things that scared him a great deal, such as the end of the world and how sinful the flesh was. He could not rid himself of the guilt he felt for being there, as no matter how much they smiled, he knew he was betraying his mother and father and Mama Chona in some deep, incomprehensible way.

The voices of the women he loved were farther away now, which meant they were almost finished for the time being and would soon resume their household chores. His mother had just given birth to a second son and was staying home from work to nurse him. They named him Gabriel and Miguel Chico was extremely jealous of him.

Opening the closet door after the voices had stopped altogether, Miguelito stumbled over the clothes hamper and some of his mother's things spilled out into the light. He saw an undergarment with a bloody stain on it. Quickly, he threw the clothes back into the basket and shoved it into the closet. He was careful not to touch the garment. Its scent held him captive.

Maria swept him up from behind, forcing him to laugh out of surprise, and trotted him into the kitchen. Together they stood looking out into the backyard through the screen door. It was a hot day and the sun made the screen shimmer. Miguel saw his mother bending over the verbena and snapdragons that she and Maria took great pains to make grow out of the desert. The flowers were at their peak, and already he knew that the verbena, bright red, small, and close to the ground, would outlast the more exotic snapdragons he liked better. The canna lilies, which formed the border behind them, were colorful, but they had no fragrance and were interesting only when an occasional hummingbird dipped its beak into their red-orange cups. In the corner of that bed grew a small peach tree that he had planted at Maria's suggestion from a pit he had licked clean two summers earlier. It was now a foot high and had branched. His mother was approaching it. Leaning over him and with her hand on his face directing his gaze toward the tree, Maria whispered hypnotically. "Look at the little tree," she said very softly in Spanish so that his mother could not hear. "When it blooms and bears fruit that means that the end of the world is near. Now look at your mother. You must respect and love her because she is going to die." In front of him, in the gauzy brightness of the screen, the red of the flowers merged with the red stain he had seen a few moments before. He believed Maria. In that instant, smelling her hair and feeling her voice of truth moist on his ear, love and death came together for Miguel Chico and he was not from then on able to think of one apart from the other.

Two years later, in a fit of terror because he knew the world was going to end soon, he told his parents that Maria had been taking him to her church. His father threw her out of the house but allowed her to return a few weeks later on the condition that she say nothing about her religion to anyone while she lived in his house. The arguments stopped, and she no longer read to him from the Bible.

Maria treated him nicely, but she hardly spoke to him and spent more time caring for his brother. Once or twice Miguel Chico caught her looking at him sadly and shaking her head as if he were lost to her forever. One day after school, when he was feeling bold, he said, "If God knew that Satan and Adam and Eve were going to commit a sin, why did He create them?"

"You must not ask me such things," she replied, "I'm not allowed to talk to you about them."

It was a lame answer and he knew that in some important way, he had defeated her. He hated her now and hoped that she would leave them soon and return to Mexico. When, several months later, she did go away, he stayed at Mama Chona's house all day and did not say goodbye to her. Juanita was upset with him when he got home.

"Maria wanted to tell you goodbye. Why didn't you come home before she left?"

"I don't like her any more," he said. "I'm glad she's gone." But later that night he felt an awful loneliness when he thought about her hair and eyes.

•  •  •

Long after Miguel Chico had completed his education and given up all forms of organized religion, a few years after his operation and his decision to live alone in San Francisco, his mother wrote him a long letter about Maria's visit to the desert. It was her first and only one, for she had moved to California and joined a congregation there. Except for her hair, which was now completely white, his mother said that she looked exactly the same. Miguel Chico reread the last paragraphs of the letter while sitting at his desk, occasionally looking out to the garden. The fog had not yet burned away and the ferns and lobelia were a neon green and blue. "She took me back to the years when I was young and you were a little boy," his mother wrote.

> She remembers all the things you did, even the long white dress she made for you and how you would dance and swirl around while she and I played your audience. She even got up and showed me how you danced! That surprised me because she still is very religious and I thought her church prohibited dancing.

She eats raw cabbage "for her mind," she says, carrots for her eyes, and turnips for her arthritis. She looks healthy enough to me, but according to her she has diabetes, arthritis, varicose veins, and bad eyesight.

One afternoon while I was resting, she cleaned all my flower beds. She still loves gardening. We took her across the river where she stayed a few days with a niece. Your father and I picked her up the following Tuesday on Seventh St. where she had called from a phone booth. She had walked through the worst parts of town completely unafraid, at least three miles.

She left on Thursday because it snowed on Wednesday, and I didn't want to let her go. I was very sad to see her leave because I thought as I saw her get on the bus that I might never see her again.

I hope she comes back, Mickie, so that I can take her to visit all the family. She remembered every one of the Angels but only talked to some of them and to your godmother on the phone. I wasn't driving or getting out much. She told me it was all right because she had come to be with me anyway.

Your brother Gabriel came over several times during her visit when he was able to get away from his duties at the parish. Would you believe that the first time he came and even though she knows he is a priest, Maria asked him when he was going to get married. I thought this was rude but I didn't say anything. Gabriel replied quite strongly, though, "No, thanks. I've seen what marriage does to many people in my parish."

She promised to come and see us later in the year. I hope so.

Later, on his birthday, he received a letter from Maria herself. It was written in the kind of Spanish his grandmother deplored and was sent from Los Angeles.

My Dear Miguelito,

With all my love I write you this letter to greet you and offer my congratulations. I have wanted for a long time to find out your address so that I might write to you. Your little mother told me that you had been very ill with a terrible sickness but that you are now well. I'm very glad.

Your *mamita* is very beautiful still and I love her very much because she is very friendly and does not look down on anyone. Your father and brother were also very kind to me so that I must tell you that a week with them seemed like a day.

In three days, you will celebrate your birthday. I am going toward old age, 79, and I plan to walk into my eighties. I wish you long life and good health. May God bless you and keep you well, so that when the Father comes in the clouds of the sky, He will take you and me with Him to live in paradise and joy in the kingdom He is preparing for those who love Him, think in His name and keep His commandments.

I send you a hug.

Maria L. v. de Sanchez

Write me.

He meant to respond to her note right away, believing himself to be free of her influence and her distortions of religion and vice. He put it off, telling himself he would write as soon as his academic duties were finished for the year. She visited him in dreams, her hair loose and white and streaming to the floor, her immense jaw frozen in a perpetual smile that was alternately loving and terrifying.

A month later, Juanita phoned him from the desert to tell him that Maria was dead. She had been knocked down by a car as she was leaving her church service in Los Angeles. The driver was drunk. A child by her side had been killed outright. Maria survived a night and a day in the hospital, surrounded by members of her congregation, talking with them until she fell into a coma. She had died on the anniversary of his operation.

"Well, the end of the world finally came for her," he said.

"Oh, Mickie, don't be so heartless," his mother said quietly.

"I'm not being heartless, Mother. She lived for the end of the world. Of course, it had to be some poor vice-ridden slob who caught up with her." In trying to joke about death with Juanita, he sensed that he was only making it worse for her.

"Well, anyway, I thought you would want to know," she said.

"Sure, Mom, and I'm sorry I sounded cold about it. I'm just tired of death and everything associated with it."

"Well, I'm going to have your brother celebrate a mass in her name. I know you don't believe in it, but I'm going to pray for her even if she did think we were all going to hell for being Catholics."

"You do what you need to, Mom. I'm going to look for peach trees in Golden Gate Park for her."

"What are you talking about? Are you trying to be funny again?"

"No, Mom. I'm dead serious. I'll tell you that story sometime."

He did not go to the park that day and did not think very much about Maria or the family in general. He and his therapist had decided that Sundays made him even more melancholy than usual because they were "family" days and he knew that though the park would be filled with all kinds of people, he would find himself drawn to the family groups, especially if there were old people among them.

Instead, he did his laundry in the washeteria around the corner where he knew he would be in the company of those people who lived alone in the neighborhood. They would not disturb each other except to ask for change and would read their Sunday papers in peace and isolation like that of the islands in the Baltic he loved visiting every summer. When he got back, he put away his clothes and began to prepare supper for himself. He chopped mushrooms, onions, garlic, and tomatoes for the spaghetti sauce he had perfected over the years. His secret was to add sugar, marsala, onion soup mix, and finally, one of the red chiles from the wreath his godmother gave him every Christmas and to let the concoction simmer off and on for two or three hours. Its flavor would improve throughout the week.

While the sauce was bubbling, he put on his favorite records and went to the bathroom to change his appliance. It was a weekly ritual which took him an hour, or a little more if the skin around the piece of intestine sticking out from his right side was irritated. Without the appliance and the bags he attached to it and changed periodically throughout each day, he knew he could not live. He had forgotten what it was like to be able to hold someone, naked, without having a plastic device between them. He wanted to ask Maria if, on Judgment Day, his body would rise from the grave in its condition before or after the operation. He was still feeling bitterness toward her and all people who thought like her because they seemed so literal and simpleminded. This time, the skin around the stoma looked all right and he finished the process before all the records had played out.

After supper, he tried to read in his study and found that he kept looking at the photograph in which he and Mama Chona are walking downtown. He had no photograph of Maria. In some vastly significant way, he felt he was still the child of these women, an extension of them, the way a seed continues to be a part of a plant after it has assumed its own form which does not at all resemble its origin, but which, nevertheless, is determined by it. He had survived severe pruning and wondered if human beings, unlike plants, can water themselves.

He was also beginning to see in his day-to-day life with the bag at his side that too many false notions surrounded people like him who have been given a reprieve. He did not automatically or necessarily see life more or less positively for almost having lost it. Nor did he come bearing insights from the other side of the grave to comfort and reassure those who have not yet been threatened.

He was still seeing people, including himself, as books. He wanted to edit them, correct them, make them behave differently. And so he continued to read them as if they were invented by someone else, and he failed to take into account their separate realities, their differences from himself. When people told him of their lives, or when he thought about his own in the way that is not thinking but a kind of reverie outside time, a part of him listened with care. Another part fidgeted, thought about something else or went blank, and wondered why once again he was being offered such secrets to examine. Later he found himself retelling what he had heard, arranging various facts, adding others, reordering time schemes, putting himself in situations and places he had never been in, removing himself from conversations or moments that didn't fit.

Most of the time his versions were happier than their "real" counterparts, and in making them so he was indulging in one of Mama Chona's traits that as a very young child—the child who was holding her hand forever in a snapshot—he loved most. Mama Chona was never able to talk about the ugly sides of life or people, even though she was surrounded by them. For her grandchildren she dressed up the unpleasant in sugary tales and convinced them that she believed what she was saying. Later, in his adolescence and while she still retained her wits, Miguel Chico hated her for this very trait, seeing it as part of the Spanish conquistador snobbery that refused to associate itself with anything Mexican or Indian because it was somehow impure. What, Miguel Chico asked himself, did she see when she looked in the mirror? As much as she protected herself from it, the sun still darkened her complexion and no surgery could efface the Indian cheekbones, those small very dark eyes and aquiline nose. By then, his cousins and he smiled at each other when she began telling her tales of family incidents and relatives long since dead and buried. By then, in their young adulthood, they knew the "truth" and were too self-involved in their educations away from her and the family to give her credit for trying to spare them the knowledge that she, too, knew it. Slowly, she slipped into her fairy-tale world—at least outwardly. "Oh, my dear Miguelito," she said to him just after his first year at the university, "you are going to be the best-educated member of this family."

Sitting at his desk, gazing at the garden, fixing that old photograph forever outside of time and far from where it was taken, he knew she had not called him "dear." Mama Chona did not use endearments with anyone in the family. How silent she had been even when she talked—silent like those pyramids he had finally seen in Teotihuacan[5] built to pay tribute to the sun and moon. He had felt the presence of the civilizations that had constructed them and, as he climbed the steep, stone steps so conceived as to give him the impression that he was indeed walking into the sky, he had seen why those people, his ancestors, thought themselves gods and had been willing to tear out the hearts of others to maintain that belief. The feeling horrified him still.

And Mama Chona was still very much a part of him. Perhaps, he told himself, watching the first wisps of fog drift in over his garden, perhaps he had survived—albeit in an altered form, like a plant onto which has been grafted an altogether different strain of which the smelly rose at his side, that tip of gut that would always require his care and attention, was only a symbol—perhaps he had survived to tell others about Mama Chona and people like Maria. He could then go on to shape himself, if not completely free of their influence and distortions, at least with some knowledge of them. He believed in the power of knowledge.

His need to give meaning to the accidents of life had become even more intense, and he had not yet begun to laugh at that need. Years earlier, he had started out to be a brain surgeon but had found his pre-med courses lifeless and impossible. Literature had given him another way to examine the mind. He knew he was no poet like his cousin JoEl, the most sensitive member of the family. He, Miguel Chico, was the family analyst, interested in the past for psychological, not historical, reasons. Like Mama Chona, he preferred to ignore facts in favor of motives, which were always and endlessly open to question and interpretation. Yet unlike his grandmother and Maria, Miguel Chico wanted to look at motives and at people from an earthly, rather than otherworldly, point of view. He sensed he had a long way to go.

He walked out into the garden. The fog was in and thicker than usual in his part of the City. He knew that during the early hours of the day it would moisten and freshen all he had planted there. In the morning, before going to teach his classes, he would get rid of the petunias. Their purple velvet color was fading and they were now rangy and going to seed. Like a god, he would uproot them and discard them even after having loved and enjoyed them so much.

He felt Maria's hand on his face, her hair smelling of desert sage and lightly touching the back of his neck as she whispered in his ear. Every moment is Judgment Day and to those who live on earth, humility is a given and not a virtue that will buy one's way into heaven.

Miguel Chico left the garden, changed his bag, undressed and went to bed.

1984

---

5. An enormous archeological site in central Mexico; once the largest city in the pre-Columbian Americas.

# MARY HELEN PONCE
## b. 1938

Mary Helen Ponce was born in Pacoima, California. At California State University, Northridge, she earned bachelor's and master's degrees. From 1982 to 1984, she studied at the University of California at Los Angeles, and in 1988 she worked toward her Ph.D. at the University of New Mexico. Ponce writes in Spanish and English, often about biculturalism and bilingualism and their impacts on Latinos' daily lives. Her autobiography, *Hoyt Street: Memories of a Chicana Childhood* (1993), captures the 1940s and 1950s in the San Fernando Valley; the following selection is the first chapter, from "Part I: Innocence." Ponce is also the author of the story collections *Recuerdo: Short Stories of the Barrio* (1983) and *Taking Control* (1987) and the novel *The Wedding* (1989).

---

## *FROM* HOYT STREET

## 13011 Hoyt Street

The town of Pacoima lay to the northeast of Los Angeles, about three miles south of the city of San Fernando. The blue-grey San Gabriel Mountains rose toward the east; toward the west other small towns dotted the area. Farther west lay the blue Pacific and the rest of the world. The barrio, as I knew it, extended from San Fernando Road to Glenoaks Boulevard on the east and from Filmore and Pierce streets on the north. We lived in the shadow of Los Angeles, twenty odd miles to the south.

Most of the townspeople were Mexican immigrants, as were my parents, who had moved to Pacoima in the 1920s. Across the tracks lived the white folks, many of them Okies. There were few blacks in the area up until the early fifties, when the Joe Louis[1] housing tract near Glenoaks Boulevard allowed black ex-GIs to buy there.

Many men in the barrio worked in agriculture, en el fil,[2] weeding, pruning, or watering various crops. Others worked as troqueros,[3] as did Rocky, my father's compadre, who each fall drove workers in his truck to the walnut orchards of Camarillo. Men who owned their own trucks worked for themselves. They lugged fertilizer from poultry farms to nearby ranches or trucked produce into Los Angeles. Still others took the bus to the union hall in San Fernando, where they hired out as "casual laborers" or found work in the packinghouse in that same town. A neighbor, el Señor Flores, owned a flower nursery; Don Jesús, a kind, rotund man, had his own grocery store. For the most part men either hired out as unskilled laborers or worked for themselves, as did my father, who sold used wood from our backyard.

Pacoima streets were unpaved, full of holes and rocks. During a rain the rich, brown mud clung to our shoes. Van Nuys Boulevard, the main street,

---

1. African American boxer (Joseph Louis Barrow, 1914–1981).

2. In the field (Spanglish).
3. Truck drivers (Spanglish).

was paved and lit with lamps that burned till late at night; that was where most stores and businesses were located. The boulevard cut through the middle of the barrio, then continued west to Van Nuys, North Hollywood, and other towns.

San Fernando Road, which ran north and south, was the main artery to Los Angeles; it connected Pacoima with Roscoe (later renamed Sun Valley), Burbank, and Glendale, then curved west to the Hill Street overpass that led to downtown Los Angeles, called "Elay" or "Los" by the locals. To the north this highway went over the mountains to become Highway 99. It cut through the town of Gorman, a truckers' stop with a huge restaurant and one motel, and on to the "Grapevine," a long, lonely section constantly filled with huge trucks: Once past the highest mountain peak, the road no longer curved but shot into the fertile San Joaquin Valley in an endless straight line.

The barrio was laid out like a huge square. The streets ran up and down with nary a curve or dead end. Streets that ran north and south started at Filmore Street and came to a screeching halt en la Pierce, where the Pacoima airport, known as Whiteman Airport, stood. The airstrip was more like a weed-infested field with cracked pavement. Small shedlike buildings stood at one end. At one time this area was an empty space where students playing hookey from school would hide out. During Easter vacation and in the summer, kids used the unpaved road along the airport as a shortcut to the nearby hills that dipped and rolled toward Hansen Dam. In spring they came alive with scrub bushes and other plants, none of which grew very tall. From the highest peak you could see Guardian Angel Church and the Pacoima General Store, the two tallest buildings in town. When later a chain link fence and gates with padlocks went up, hiking to the Pacoima hills became less fun.

Homes in Pacas, as we called Pacoima, were modest, ranging from a one-room shack where people slept in the "front room," to the more elegant homes such as Rocky's, which boasted an ample living room, a bathroom with tile and chrome faucets, and a separate bedroom for each child. On our street, and in the immediate neighborhood, houses were one story high except for that of the Torres family; theirs had upstairs bedrooms with tall windows. In the next block was the quasi-Victorian structure belonging to Doña Mercedes. It sat back from the street, as if ashamed to be seen next to older, shabbier homes.

On Hoyt Street the houses were neither fancy nor ugly, but like the houses of poor folks everywhere. While some were constructed of stucco, the majority were of wood, madera. Wood was plentiful and cheaper than cement, so wood it was. The houses, while not uniform, had some similarities: a window on each side and a door smack in the middle. Others appeared lopsided because of the many additions tacked on as a family grew. Still others were of different types of wood bought for price and not appearance. From afar it was easy to spot the short boards nailed next to the smooth planks of polished wood bought at the lumberyard. People were innovative, too, and sometimes built houses of rock and cement.

On Filmore Street sat two stone houses made of the white and gray rocks that filled the Pacoima Wash, a small stream to the east. The sturdy-looking homes, so unlike any others in the barrio, were fascinating. Unlike

Rapunzel's castle,[4] they were not surrounded by trees, nor did they have a large tower. Still they were quaint, like the stone huts in the dark German forests where Hansel and Gretel lived. Along the front were large windows embedded in the round stones, with a wooden door in the middle. One rock house even had a fireplace, an anomaly in our town, where few homes even had a spacious living room.

Not all homes had electricity or indoor plumbing. Many casitas on Hoyt Street still had an outhouse somewhere in the back, hidden behind a nopalera or standing blatantly in the middle of the yard. Once the electrical lines reached Van Nuys Boulevard, and local residents were allowed to connect, my father was among the first to do so. After he wired our house, he did that of Doña Luisa, our adopted grandmother, who lived next door. She, like others in our town, continued to use la lámpara de petroleo, which had a long wick and gave only a faint light. She felt that electricity was terribly expensive, and insisted that every time el foco was turned on, it cost a penny! Each time I yanked the string hanging from the light bulb on the ceiling, Doña Luisa pursed her thin lips and reminded me I was wasting electricity—and pennies. She then lit the kerosene lamp and set it next to the trunk alongside her bed.

Mejicanos in our town took pride in their homes and, when money allowed, repaired a dilapidated roof or painted their casitas a bright color. They took special pride in having a yard full of plants and flowers, and these grew well in the rich California soil. La familia Santos had a pretty front yard with bright red geraniums growing in old cans and fruit trees along the side. Like other women in our street, each morning Mrs. Santos raked the front yard, sprinkled water on it to keep the dust down, then trimmed her geraniums. In the Lopez family's yarda was a birdbath made of crude cement, rocks, and pipes. It was pretty and the pride of Mr. Lopez, who had designed and made it himself. People said he was un artista. Each day the birdbath was filled with clean water for the many birds that congregated there. In other gardens, bird cages bought at the five and dime in San Fernando hung from the various trees. Still other casitas sported a porch swing where, on warm summer evenings, adults gossiped or told stories of la llorona[5] to pesky children, the soft Spanish words drifting down Hoyt Street and dissolving into the night. While the homes on our street were different in color, shape, and size, they had one thing in common: each had a junk pile somewhere in the back yard.

El yonque was important for folks who were short on money but full of ingenuity. The junk pile held the necessary parts to wire a car together or replace rusted pipes, and it helped keep folks from spending hard-earned cash at the hardware store in town. The Morenos had not one but several junk piles in their huge yard. On one side la Señora Moreno grew flowers and vegetables. On the other were two piles of junk that included automobile parts: engines, carburetors, dented fenders, old batteries, and flat tires. Except for la familia Soto, whose backyard held only a crude table and benches and a row of apricot trees, the junk pile was an accepted part of a Mexican household.

---

4. Like Hansel and Gretel (below), part of a German fairy tale for children, recorded in the nineteenth century by the Brothers Grimm.
5. The weeping woman; a popular legend in Spanish-speaking cultures in the Americas, generally about a beautiful woman who kills her children to be with a man, is rejected by him, and then wanders, weeping, searching for children and, in some versions of the tale, ready to kidnap wandering children. For a text of the legend, see p. 2452. For a variation on the legend, see p. 2454.

My father, too, clung to junk, a thing that bothered my mother, who functioned best in a clean and orderly household. The yonque, or clutter as I thought of it, was of value to my father as it was to other pobres.[6] Pipes, rusty tin tubs, old tires, wood, wire, and car radios lay scattered here and there. My father was certain that at some point, good use could be made of the stuff. Neighbors and friends would come by for a piece of pipe, a strip of tar paper, or some two-by-fours, all from the junk pile and all freely given to someone in need.

People in Pacoima, I often thought, needed more space than did those in upwardly mobile San Fernando, where homes had sidewalks and paved streets, but sat close together, as if afraid to breathe too much of their neighbor's air. On Hoyt Street most residents had once lived in Mexican ranchitos and had a greater need for land. In the large double lots, they planted fruit trees, vegetable and flower gardens, and assorted hierbas that also grew in Mexico. The Garcias had a nopalera, a wall of prickly pear cactus in the back that served two purposes: it was a fence that kept out errant dogs and kids, and it also provided food. The succulent cactus, nopalitos, were popular during Lent[7] along with deep-fried camarones, shrimp; the prickly pear fruits, or tunas, fell off when ripe and were quickly gobbled up.

We lived at 13011 Hoyt Street, a block from church and the Pacoima General Store (called la tienda blanca),[8] and two blocks from Pacoima Elementary School. Our house sat in the middle of a double lot. The front door, which was rarely used, faced Hoyt Street. The back gate led to the alley and an open field, el llano,[9] which faced Van Nuys Boulevard. To our right lived Doña Luisa. Next to her, in a house that extended the length of the lot, lived the Morenos. To our left was a roomy yellow house with a big garage, occupied on and off by different families. I remember best the Montalvos, a handsome family with light hair and eyes; their daughter Margarita was close to my age.

Our house was built by my father when he and my mother and their three older children moved from Ventura to the San Fernando Valley, sometime in the 1920s. Originally our house had three rooms: a kitchen and two bedrooms. The large kitchen extended the length of the house. Later, as his family grew, my father added on to the house, with some interesting results—our kitchen had a window that opened into the living room! The kitchen floor was covered with dark green linoleum. On one wall was el trastero, the pantry, where flour, sugar, and beans were stored. On the other wall were two large cabinets in which sat assorted dishes and the blue-willow plates that came in a soap box and were used for company. A double sink faced the west wall, and in one corner was the white gas stove with a big griddle. A large window hung with dotted-swiss curtains trimmed in rickrack faced the driveway and framed a huge eucalyptus tree. In the summer my sisters moved the kitchen table next to the window; from there we looked out at the wild birds in the tree branches. In the summer too, my sisters served our dinner outdoors on the cement patio with the roof of palm fronds that my father had also built.

6. Paupers.
7. In Roman Catholicism and other branches of Christianity, the 40 days from Ash Wednesday to Easter; generally a period of penitence and ab- staining from some foods.
8. The white store.
9. The plain.

My first memories are of the kitchen with the window, the small room where my parents slept, and the large living room with a bed where my sisters slept. Nora, the eldest of the bunch, was said to have "good taste." She kept after my father until he put up a wall to separate their bed from the living room. Although the bed against the wall was covered with a pretty bedspread bought at J.C. Penney, Nora did not care to have her friends see a bed en la sala. That was much too ranchero, too low class for her taste. She never could do anything about the kitchen window in the living room, though.

As we grew older, my father built los cuartitos. The men's rooms, as we called them, were separate from the main house, with windows that looked out on the front and back yards, and had room for several beds. My two older brothers slept there. Later, when my mother had her own bedroom, my father too slept there. Josey, the youngest, slept in my mother's room. From the age of three, I slept with Doña Luisa. Later my uncles, who emigrated as braceros, also slept in the men's rooms. As was the custom, they first stayed with a close relative, in this case my father. Much later their sons laid claim to the beds used earlier by their fathers.

My friends found it strange that my father slept in the cuartitos and my mother in her room; I thought it perfectly natural, until I grew older and learned otherwise. After my mother gave birth to my younger brother, Josey (at age forty or so), she decided that in order not to have more children, she and my father should sleep apart. She often said (a bit smugly, I thought) that *her* mother's children were born three years apart, and that when my grandmother turned forty (after giving birth to thirteen children) she and my grandfather slept apart. This ended the possibility of continual pregnancies, considered muy ranchero even out on the ranch. On our street women often grew sick and worn out from having children year after year; they would die, leaving behind large, motherless families. Having separate beds was, for most couples, the prudent thing to do. No one else thought otherwise, except perhaps my father.

I often think my father agreed to sleep in the men's rooms because by the time my mother was forty, she had already given birth to eleven children and was often sick. She never recovered from the death of Rosalie, her firstborn, who died when I was an infant, nor from that of Socorro, who died in Ventura. The death of Rito, my older brother, depressed her more. Still my father, a healthy man in his forties, often sneaked into my mother's bedroom. I once saw him near her bed. I heard him say the word "tetas," but did not understand this Spanish word. When I lingered to talk with my mother, he quickly left the room. My mother, who was taking her afternoon nap, appeared relieved.

By the time I was in school, my father had remodeled our house more than once. He drew up a simple plan, then hired two carpenters to help him build the new additions. Down came the embarrassing kitchen window and up went a bedroom. The old front room became two bedrooms and a hall. A sunny living room with large, pretty windows that looked out on the lawn and picket fence was added with money earned en la nuez, when our family harvested walnuts in Camarillo. A maroon sofa and stuffed chair sat against one wall. Two scatter rugs lay on the living-room floor. Later we had a coffee table, lamps, and a small bookcase. We were not allowed in la sala, but sneaked in there anyway, being careful not to slide on the rugs. The front door led to a half-porch that faced the street; this was swept clean each morning. Last of all, our house, formerly a sick green, was painted a creamy white. Sometimes, though, I thought I detected the slimy green trying to seep through.

As our house grew, so did our extended family of relatives who arrived from Mexico to find work. Andrés, a handsome cousin with blue-green eyes, and José, or Joe as he was soon called, stayed with us. Still later two brothers, also cousins, moved into the men's rooms. When they first came they spoke only Spanish and would answer "what?" to any and all questions; we nick-named them "Los Whats." Although they learned to speak English within a year, we still called them "Los Whats."

The kitchen was the heart of our home, the place where my mother cooked, ironed, and bathed her many children. Everyone congregated there to eat, and when relatives visited, they sat there as my mother bustled around the stove. A huge wooden table built by my father dominated the room. Against the wall sat a large bench where we, the youngest children, sat to eat. In our family it was the custom to wait until everyone finished eating before leaving the table. Josey and I were forced to sit while our elders finished supper. Often we tired of the wait (our father chewed so slow) and taking care not to pass within reach of our older sister Trina's foot, we slid from the bench. But Trina was quick and often sent us flying with a swift kick.

"Trina kicked me."

"Liar."

"Owwwwwwwww!"

Josey and I would come out wailing and rubbing a bruised elbow; we often bumped heads too! In her moderate voice my mother would caution us not to fight. My father would say nothing, merely fixing us with a stare that ended all arguments.

In our backyard grew an abundance of trees: pepper, eucalyptus, walnut, and a small fig tree, called la higuera, that never gave fruit. The two eucalyptus trees grew next to the garage and were the tallest trees in the yard. They had come with the property; my father built around them. Their branches appeared to reach to the sky and were much too high for us to climb. They gave some shade and in fall shed fragrant gray leaves. One year my father put one of the branches to good use; he hung a thick rope with a tire on it to make a swing. Later he built a wooden seat from pieces of lumber from the wood pile. The seat was wide enough for two, and only we youngest kids got to swing in it. The rest were too old—and heavy. On summer days Josey and I climbed on the swing, kicked to get going, pumped hard, then drifted to and fro. It was fun to lean back and gaze at the blue California sky between the branches.

In the front yard, to the left of the driveway, grew los pirules. The two pepper trees grew close together and were my favorite trees. My father, who had good instincts about what made us children happy, nailed a wide board across the two trees to make a bench. My friends and I sat there all the time, because it was close to the street. Later mi papá fastened wide boards across the branches to make something similar to a tree house. It was here, among the pungent branches thick with red berries, that Josey and I would whisper to each other, while below us Doña Luisa, who helped our mother with our care, pretended not to know where we had disappeared to.

From the treehouse Josey and I had fun throwing rocks at cars and dogs. First we stashed small pebbles on the boards, then we picked a target. As a car went past, we aimed for the rear fender. When we heard a *ping*, we scampered to the top branches, afraid the driver might spot us and turn around. On hot summer days we sat atop the boards, playing until a car came by. We planted our feet, let fly with the rocks, then disappeared inside the trees.

Facing the street was a garden with rambling roses and yellow and white daisies. In spring and summer, Shasta daisies, called margaritas, bloomed next to healthy weeds. In the middle of the lawn, toward the right, grew an orange tree with glossy green leaves; in the summer the intoxicating, sweet smell of orange blossoms attracted hordes of bees, but it never gave oranges. Near the front porch was una rosa de castilla, a bush of roses with velvet petals and huge thorns. A wisteria vine grew alongside my mother's bedroom window; its branches, like tentacles, reached to the corner, where they met the rambling roses growing on the opposite wall.

To the right of the front yard, facing Doña Luisa's house, my father planted a variety of trees. First came the willow tree bought home by my brother Norbert. It was beautiful and exotic but soon died, leaving a huge hole that was filled by a stumpy palm tree that gave little shade. I hated this tree, although I knew palm trees did well in California.

Close to Doña Luisa's yard, my father planted tomatoes and chiles. Later either he or my mother planted sweet peas, called chícharos, with glossy leaves similar to those of tomato vines. The flowers were a bright pink, delicate, but when cut, never lasted long. At one time my father planted peanuts given him by my Uncle Nasario, but like the willow tree, they too died. I was not surprised, because Uncle Nasario, a handsome, pompous man, claimed only he knew how to cultivate peanuts.

Toward the rear of the house, near Doña Luisa's property, were the clotheslines that separated our two yards. These were in addition to those facing the alley, which because of the eucalyptus trees were always in the shade. Near the cement pole that held the lines grew a thick-trunked walnut tree where I hid out when in trouble. Next to it stood the solitary fig tree with a large white trunk and round holes that resembled eyes. When at night I went to the outhouse, I avoided looking at that tree.

Beneath the walnut tree and next to the fig tree were the stacks of used lumber my father sold to make a living. Josey and I liked to play atop the wood. It was an easy climb to the top of the boards but another thing to get safely down the woodpile, because the wood shifted under our weight. More than once Josey and I got our feet caught between the boards and our knees scratched by nails; however, no one thought of rushing us to a doctor for a shot. Either our parents did not know the dangers of a rusty nail, or they could not afford the doctor. My mother or Doña Luisa would put alcohol on cuts; we would put mud, lodo, on all insect bites. Somehow we survived.

In the back, next to the eucalyptus trees, was the garage. Here my father and older brothers Berney and Norbert piled old bike and automobile tires; rubbery tubes hung along the walls. On a shelf sat coffee cans chock full of nails, nuts, and bolts. Below this was a vise and assorted pliers and ball peen hammers. A lone light bulb hung from the middle of the ceiling. Near the door was the leather punching bag with which Berney and Norbert worked out. Each evening Norbert, the huskier of the two, used both the punching bag and barbells, following the instructions sent him by Charles Atlas,[1] who guaranteed that Norbert need not be a ninety-nine-pound weakling. Norbert knew that if he exercized each day he would become muscular. Once finished with the barbells and weights, Norbert went another round with the punching bag. I liked to watch him work out, amazed at the perfect rhythm of the punches: *ba boom, boom, boom. Ba boom, boom, boom.* Norbert danced on his feet, moving around the punching bag with ease, leaning in and out with each punch. *Boom, ba-boom, boom, boom.* He rarely varied from this pattern. He once offered to teach me how to hit a "right to the jaw," just like Joe Louis, but I was too clumsy. He grew bored with my efforts and politely told me to go back to my dolls.

In the back, near the alley, was the outhouse made of old, old wood with a rickety door and two seats, or holes. I hated to use it, scared stiff of falling into the bigger hole. I refused to use Doña Luisa's outhouse, as it was too close to the alley, and was relieved when my father, who wanted the best for his family, built our first bathroom. He left the outhouse for emergencies. Although I had to wait my turn for the bathroom, I refused to use el excuzado[2] after that.

My father had a thing about fences. We had many different ones! One year I counted eight different fences on our property. A picket fence on cement faced Hoyt Street. The wall facing the Montalvos' was made of chicken wire, and cement slabs on a cement foundation. Alongside the men's rooms was a wooden fence that connected with the garage. The back fence next to the alley was made of wood overgrown with cactus. The side fence behind which the goats and chickens were kept was part of the cactus wall. No fence was to be found between Doña Luisa's house and ours, only my mother's flowers and my father's chiles and tomatoes. Doña Luisa, though not a blood relative, was considered family; *entre familia* there was no need for fences.

My father's pride and joy was the white picket fence. It faced Hoyt Street and was his original design, or so he liked to think. The wooden spikes were set in cement; the bottom half was of wood and cement slabs set in concrete. Each picket was exactly the same size; each was nailed to a thin crosspiece. When finished it was sanded and then painted white. We were not allowed to hang onto this fence, which was the only one of its kind on our street. I hated el cerco[3] that faced the Montalvos; it looked like a huge cement wall and was out of place next to the pretty picket fence. But this too was my father's original design.

On the summer day on which he poured the concrete for this wall, my father allowed Josey and me to scratch our names on the still-wet cement. Josey, acting like the brat he was, insisted on putting his handprint on the cement too! When I tried to do the same he pushed me; I fell on the cement, and left two knee holes on the smooth finish! My father became angry, but just for a minute. After that he no longer let Josey and me help him but told us to go play on the tree swing. For years I could still make out the names on the wall. Josey. Mary Helen. June, 1945.

---

1. American bodybuilder (1892–1972), born Angelo Siciliano in Italy), whose company, Charles Atlas Ltd., has since 1929 marketed, for the "97-pound weakling," a combination bodybuilding method and exercise program.
2. The toilet.
3. The fence

While studying the many fences I often thought that perhaps my father's family had not owned property in Mexico. It was important for him to fence, to secure the right of ownership. Or perhaps, unknown to us, my father was an artist who liked to express himself in works of cement, wire, and wood. Probably he liked to keep busy. Like most men of his generation, my father hated to be de oquis, with nothing to do.

Josey and I were always alert for the sound of cement being mixed in the big wheelbarrow. This meant a new wall would soon go up at 13011 Hoyt Street, where we might record our names for posterity.

1993

# JOSÉ ANTONIO BURCIAGA
## 1940–1996

An accomplished painter, José Antonio "Tony" Burciaga is best-known for his humorous essays, stories, and poems. Using a playful, elastic combination of Spanish, English, and Spanglish, he reflects on stereotypes and gives a sense of the fluidity of identities in the United States. Spanglish was his particular passion, and he has traced its roots to the Mexican stand-up comedians and movie actors Mario Moreno, aka "Cantinflas," and Germán Valdéz, aka "Tin Tan," who became extraordinarily popular during the Golden Age of Mexican cinema, in the 1940s.

Burciaga was born in El Paso, Texas. His family lived in the basement of a synagogue, an experience that inspired him to write *The Temple Gang*, a novel left unfinished at the time of his death, from cancer. (An excerpt appears in *The Last Supper of Chicano Heroes: Selected Works of José Antonio Burciaga* [2008], edited by Mimi R. Gladstein and Daniel Chacón.) In 1960, Burciaga joined the air force. He was stationed in Iceland and Spain, where in Zaragoza he came across the work of the Spanish poet and dramatist Federico García Lorca, a major influence on him.

Burciaga studied at the University of Texas at El Paso and the San Francisco Art Institute. In 1966, he became a graphic illustrator in the town of Mineral Wells, Texas. He then moved to Washington, D.C., where he met Cecilia Preciado. They married in 1974 and soon returned to California, where Preciado worked as a vice provost for Chicano Affairs at Stanford University. She was instrumental in the formation of the student center, El Centro Chicano. By then, Burciaga was writing newspaper columns and trying his hand at other genres. His first book of poetry and short pieces, *Restless Serpents* (1976), written with Beatriz Zamora, reveals a penchant for linguistic wordplay.

For the next two decades, Burciaga's material appeared in periodicals ranging from the ethnically oriented *Revista Chicano-Riqueña* to the upscale *Texas Monthly*. In response to the American bicentennial celebrations of 1976, Burciaga took a satirical look at Paul Revere's ride in the short story "El corrido de Pablo Ramírez" (1980). In "Españotli Titlan Englishic" (1980), he humorously analyzes the connection between pre-Columbian tongues in contemporary Latino slang. *Weedee Peepo: A Collection of Essays* (1988) consists of comic meditations on U.S. culture that turn linguistic playfulness into a literary style. The collection *Drink Cultura: Chicanismo* (1993) lightheartedly ponders the intersection of advertising and Mexican American culture.

A founding member of the theater troupe Culture Clash, Burciaga performed with the group from 1984 to 1988. From 1985 until 1994, he and Preciado were resident fellows at Casa Zapata, a Chicano-themed dormitory at Stanford, where in the dining hall Burciaga painted one of his most popular murals: *Last Supper of Chicano Heroes* invokes the imagery of Jesus Christ and the Apostles as it portrays figures such as César Chávez, Robert Kennedy, Ernesto "Ché" Guevara, and the Reverend Martin Luther King Jr. Among Burciaga's most popular and enduring pictorial sketches are the Christmas cards he devised in 1979. One of them displays the Magi, the Three Wise Men, dressed as *charros* (Mexican horsemen in traditional costumes) and standing in front of the fence marking the U.S.-Mexico border. The fence has been ripped open from the Mexican side. The light of the Star of Bethlehem shines on the fence and the three figures.

The following four selections are from Burciaga's collection *Spilling the Beans* (1995). The title piece reflects on the gastronomic and symbolic value of *frijoles*, beans, in Mexican American culture. "The Honorable Senator Ralph W. Yarborough" is both an autobiographical look at a writer's beginnings and a profile of a deft member of the U.S. Senate. "What's in a Spanish Name?" looks humorously at bilingual speakers' formation and pronunciation of words. "Bilingual Cognates" delves further into the type of Spanglish word games pioneered by Tin Tan. Among Burciaga's other works are *Undocumented Love* (1992) and the posthumously published bilingual anthology *In Few Words: A Compendium of Latino Folk Wit and Wisdom* (1997).

---

## *FROM* SPILLING THE BEANS

## Spilling the Beans

"Eat your beans!" I hated beans, I ate them all the time. We had beans in the morning, at noon and at night.

"Eat your beans!" "Finish your beans!" We ate them freshly made *frijoles de la olla*, we ate them in different recipes: *frijoles borrachos, frijoles charros, frijoles sencillos*[1] . . . We ate *enfrijoladas*, like enchiladas but soaked in beans instead of chile, we had *tacos de frijoles*, bean burritos, tostadas de burritos, refried bean sandwiches and even matzohs or bagels smothered with refried beans. We scrambled them with eggs, we ate them with diced jalapeños, nopalitos, chorizo, melted cheese . . . You name it. We ate *frijoles* when its soup thickened. We ate them when the refried beans had just about dried up.

Enter any Mexican home and you can tell by the smell if there is a fresh pot of beans on the stove. The aroma is unmistakable. A pot of freshly made beans is a delectable dish. Well cooked, beans will just about melt in your mouth. Immediately after cooking, add oregano, cilantro, onions, or even Parmesan cheese to individual servings for an exquisite culinary experience. For many of us, it is our invariable soup du jour. Some people will add a can of beer when the beans are cooking. And the second time they are warmed up some people add milk or cream or cheese.

But somehow, grandmother's beans always tasted better, and my Mother's were also good but different from my aunts' and my mother-in-law's. It

---

1. Basic beans (i.e., fried in oil). *De la olla*: a pot of (i.e., boiled in water). *Borrachos*: drunken (i.e., cooked in beer). *Charros*: cowboy (i.e., long-simmered, stewed).

was the water! Or a mystery that will forever remain a *secreto*. And there were times when my Mexican aunts would open up a quart of beans the way you opened a glass liter of milk. Some entrepreneur began marketing it as an indispensable common staple like milk.

And once in a while my mother made them my favorite way, as a dessert, as a sweet pudding, similar to chocolate. Gently cooking them with sugar instead of salt, she blended them and added cinnamon and a touch of vanilla, sometimes raisins. It was better than chocolate pudding. Beans were not only economical but versatile. However, we did have a choice at mealtime: It was eat them or *nada!*

We also feasted on many other kinds of legumes such as *lentejas,* which my mother called *frijolitos del niño Dios,* because Baby Jesus was supposed to have eaten them. How could we refuse? There were navy beans, garbanzos, lima beans, kidney beans, black beans and pinto beans. Whether we liked them or not, we ate them all.

Easy to prepare—the most essential and critical part was to thoroughly clean them of hard little rocks that could easily demolish your molars, incisors or front teeth. But beans also had fun uses. Small bean bags were fun to throw and play catch with. Pea shooters had their season. Beans were what we played Lotería with, the Mexican bingo game. "*¡El Cazo!*" And we would put a pinto bean on that picture.

Beans could also be dangerous. Little kids would put a dry pinto bean up their nose. Sometimes they said nothing until the bean softened, grew and sprouted like a sponge, then had to be extracted by the family doctor.

While I was being forced to eat my beans, little Johnny and Susie were being forced to eat their spinach. As the All-American vegetable, it was supposed to make them strong like Popeye the Sailor Man. In Crystal City, Texas, the supposed spinach capitol of the world and a stronghold of Chicano activism in the late sixties, they even erected a statue of Popeye.

I liked spinach, but no one ever told us that beans packed more power than spinach. We should have brought out Freddy Frijol, who would have whipped Popeye. The difference at the Battle of the Alamo[2] was the difference between *espinacas* and frijoles. Mexico won! Remember the Alamo!

High in iron, beans form an essential part of the mechanism in the blood that helps supply oxygen to body cells, aids in respiration and energy production. It's also an excellent source of fiber, and rich in minerals, including calcium, phosphorus, magnesium, niacin, thiamine, riboflavin, B vitamins and zinc. It helps in blood clotting. Beans, *frijoles,* legumes, those dehydrated pods of edible food that turn soft and nutritious when cooked go back to the Bronze Age, thus the reason for our color. A couple of thousand years before Christ, they were already grown by Egyptians who claimed they had a mystical power and offered them in their rituals to the deceased.

The Romans determined the guilt or innocence of a man on trial with beans. Jurors would cast a white bean for innocence and a black or red bean for guilt. The status of beans among Romans is found in the names of a prominent ancient family: Fabius was named after the Faba bean, Lentulus

2. In 1836, during the Texas Revolution, at the now legendary chapel-fort in San Antonio called the Alamo, about 180 Texans were defeated by thousands of Mexicans led by the Mexican general Antonio López de Santa Anna (1794–1876).

was named after the lentil, Piso from the pea and the most distinguished Cicero was named after the chick pea.

Then there was Judge Roy Bean (1825?–1904) a West Texas saloon keeper, coroner and justice of the peace on the West Texas frontier. He had his hands full with his six guns and a town filled with gamblers, rustlers and thieves. He was the "Law West of the Pecos," who once fined a corpse $40 for carrying a concealed weapon. In more modern times, another Texan, U.S. astronaut Alan Lavern Bean, piloted the lunar module Intrepid on the Apollo 12 mission and in November of '69 made man's second moon landing. Last but not least is my friend Frijol, who has yet to do anything of such magnitude, but his life isn't over.

One historical dish stands out: *Moros y Cristianos*, Moors and Christians. That's what you call a plate of white rice and black beans, referring to the African Moors who occupied white Spain for close to 800 years until they were expelled in 1492. In Nicaragua, a similar dish is called *Gallo Pinto*.

Other Spanish names for frijoles abound: *frejoles, judias de león, habichuelas, alubias*, and *habas*. As kids we would change frijoles to a more Chicano sounding *firoles* or *balas; un plato de balas* was a deadly "plate of bullets." Beans are rich in nutrition, but many people shy away from them because of their gas producing properties, something that can easily be remedied. (One way is to repeatedly discard the water. First, let the beans soak temporarily or overnight and then throw out the water. Boil them and throw out the water again. When adding new water, boil it first if you want your pinto beans to retain a pink color, otherwise they turn dark. Another remedy is to use a commercial food additive known as Beano and follow their directions. *Muy importante!*)

Long thought to be the staple of peasants—who would have thought they would be served in fancy restaurants or banquets? Imagine a *maitre d'* reciting the soup du jour as *frijoles de la olla* or a *pate de refritos*. But there are very exclusive restaurants that serve these dishes. Between San Francisco and San Diego it has become part of the new California cuisine.

Some people eat chicken and burp beans, so goes the Mexican proverb, *Comen pollo y erutan frijoles!* From the children's story about Jack and the Beanstalk to Miguel de Cervantes Saavedra's immortal *Don Quixote de la Mancha*,[3] beans have risen to the highest levels of the literary classics.

Native to North and South America, many beans were domesticated by the Incas of Peru. Easier to cultivate in poorer soil than corn, they can be dried and stored for long periods of time.

But the beans that will spill from this book are beans that have boiled for over 500 years. Not a melting pot but a kettle filled with black beans, white beans, red kidney beans, cranberry beans, coffee beans, navy beans and pinto beans.

Spilling the beans is about disclosing, divulging, revealing, confessing and publishing pods of truth, facts of integrity, humor and pathos. Spilling them, hell! We are throwing them up in the air.

---

3. Novel (1605, 1615) by this Spanish writer (1547–1616).

# The Honorable Senator Ralph W. Yarborough

Wrtiers always remember the first time their work is published. The thrill of seeing one's own printed name beneath the title of an essay, poem or story is unforgettable. Quite by chance, my first publication was in the U.S. Congressional Record for September 2, 1964, although I didn't find out about it until a year later.

In 1964 after four years in the military I continued my studies at Texas Western College, now the University of Texas at El Paso, but it was difficult. In those days there was no financial assistance for minorities or Cold War veterans. I had heard about Texas Senator Ralph W. Yarborough's proposal for a Cold War G.I. Bill. Since the Korean War, millions of military servicemen had served in the Cold War without benefits.[1]

So I wrote Texas Senator Ralph W. Yarborough, a Democrat and populist of the first order:

El Paso, Texas
August 19, 1964

Dear Senator Yarborough: I am writing you in reference to the proposed Cold War G.I. bill which you introduced. My deep interest in this bill is shared by thousands of other young men for the following reasons:

I am now 23 years of age and have just completed a four-year tour of duty with the U.S. Air Force.

Since my return to civilian life I have found myself in a precarious situation. My future is not very bright without a college education. I consider myself young and ambitious but cannot afford to continue my education without help. I have not been able to find a suitable full-time or part-time job. Many ex-servicemen have returned home and found nothing awaiting them. Such is the position I find myself in. Unless this new G.I. bill is soon passed a lot of us will have to settle for second-rate jobs and no education.

In the near future the draft will be eliminated. Thus a new generation of young men will not be obliged to serve, nor will they have to live through years of uncertainty waiting to be drafted, not knowing what course to take. At such a young age men should be forming and shaping their lives.

The Cold War has produced innumerable tensions, anxieties, and hazards upon today's servicemen. They have played the greatest role in the development of what the United States is so rightly proud of—guarding the peace and maintaining the strongest power on earth. Vietnam, Guantánamo, Berlin, Korea, Panama, Turkey and hundreds of other unheard of and isolated places are the homes of the servicemen. Some die in Vietnam, others suffer hardships, and quite a few are separated from their loved ones. The soldier, sailor and airman are quite underrated in this country and sometimes taken for granted.

---

1. The Korean War lasted from June 1950 until July 1953. The political, military, and economic tensions of the Cold War, between the Soviet Union and (primarily) the United States, began at the end of World War II (i.e., after 1945) and lasted until 1991.

The last two military pay raises should not be considered as a benefit to the military. That is to say that such a raise was approved basically because of the previous low wages.

For these reasons I urge you to expedite this bill, not only for my personal benefit but for my former comrades in arms and the nation. Further, I would deeply appreciate it if you could advise me of its present and future status.

José Antonio Burciaga
*Airman First Class, U.S. Air Force Inactive Reserve*

The good Senator Yarborough liked the letter enough to take it to the Senate Floor one day, read it aloud and requested that it be published in *The Congressional Record*. There being no objection, my letter was published.

But it was not until a year later that I found out. In 1965 I took a summer trip to Washington D.C. looking for work. In D.C. I had a friend, Tom Dunigan, who worked as a college intern at Senator Yarborough's office. I mentioned the Cold War G.I. Bill and he handed me a green covered government book on the Cold War G.I. Bill Hearings. I reached for the book and began leafing through the pages until my name jumped out at me. I couldn't believe it; there it was, published in the distinguished and historical Congressional Record, thus giving me some form of immortality.

The Cold War G.I. Bill was passed in 1966 and I was able to reap its educational fruits for three years of college, and a year of study at The San Francisco Art Institute.

I never forgot the good senator and briefly shook his hand one time in the Nation's capitol. But the Cold War G.I. Bill was not the sole reason for my admiration for this man. In Texas, a state with a notoriously racist history against Mexicanos, Ralph W. Yarborough was championing their causes. It was amazing, long before the Chicano Movement, this man was helping. Besides the Cold War G.I. Bill, the senator also introduced two other major pieces of legislation that had great significance and beneficial impacts on Latinos everywhere: one was the Bilingual Education Act and the second was the Minimum Wage Law.

On a 1991 trip to the University of Texas at Austin I arranged for a one hour interview with the Senator at his home through Marta Cotera, a friend and long-time activist. I not only wanted to thank him for starting me off on my writing career and for the G.I. Bill, but I was also curious about his life long commitment to helping the Mexican-American community in Texas when it was not popular, long before any Anglo politician found it politically safe.

So it was one Friday afternoon in November of 1991 that I rang the doorbell to the very charming but unpretentious Yarborough home in an upper middle-class Austin neighborhood. The Senator himself opened the door and momentarily startled me. Despite his eighty-eight years I hardly noticed a wrinkle on his face and his long silver hair gave him a more liberal appearance than I had imagined.

With a firm handshake he invited me in, introduced me to his wife, Opal, and led me into his beautifully furnished living room. The Senator walked slowly as he apologized for a bad back and wearing a brace. He sat in a straight chair with arm rests and next to him was a small table piled with a few books, pamphlets and papers pertaining to his Senate career. I wanted to delve into a more personal side of him, his early life and association with the Mexican-American community. But the Senator was prepared with his own agenda and out of respect, I listened to his fascinating stories of struggles, victories and defeats. His voice was soft and twanged with an East Texas accent. A recorder helped me double check his words.

"One of my greatest victories was the passage of the Cold War G.I. Bill," the Senator said, "despite opposition by President Eisenhower, President Kennedy, it finally passed through President Johnson in 1966."[2] Basic opposition had come from the Pentagon but Senator Yarborough had kept the bill alive in every session. "It passed," he claims, "because the war in Vietnam[3] got so unpopular President Johnson couldn't hold the tide any longer."

By the mid 1970's more than 8,200,000 veterans had been affected by the Cold War G.I. Bill. It covered widows of soldiers killed in combat and enabled wives of permanently disabled veterans and their children to get an education. Its benefits were not only for education but also for agriculture, home buying and building. Like the former G.I. Bills, the country reaped its investment through a greater tax base from educated and home owner veterans. That bill, he claims, "was the longest, hardest fight of my senatorial career."

In 1994, the first G.I. bill, for World War II veterans, celebrated its 50th anniversary. More than a benefit, these G.I. Bills were a just compensation for the service of individuals who had not been able to afford college. To this day the country has reaped greatly through the higher income and property taxes these veterans paid.

Seating next to a pile of books and pamphlets, Senator Yarborough handed me a monograph listing his accomplishments. In 1991, Senator Yarborough was honored with a Humanitarian Award by the Texas Democratic Women for ". . . his many significant contributions to the cause of human rights by legislation while serving in the United States Senate." In twelve years, Senator Ralph Yarborough had accomplished more than most legislators hope to in a lifetime. The few bills mentioned here are but milestones in a long list of other legislation he helped pass.

Of significant focus in this award was his 1966 Minimum Wage Increase and Expansion Bill. "For the first time, the minimum wage was extended to employees in retailing, laundries, restaurants, hotels, hospitals and agricultural workers. It was called the Widows amendment because it covered so many low-paying jobs which women usually held."

He helped co-sponsor the Higher Education Act of 1965 to assist qualified high school graduates to attend college through scholarships, graduate fellowships, low interest loans to students and work-study programs.

In 1966 he also introduced the first Bilingual Education Bill that became law. This legislation grew out of several education conferences in the Southwest that focused attention on the language learning barrier affecting over 1.7 million Spanish-speaking children.

"I not only attended meetings and studied the problem of Spanish-speaking children, but I had seen the language barriers and resulting poverty first hand."

---

2. Dwight David Eisenhower (1890–1969), U.S. president 1953–61; John Fitzgerald Kennedy (1917–1963), U.S. president 1961–63; Lyndon Baines Johnson (1908–1973), U.S. president 1963–69.
3. The Vietnam War lasted from 1959 until 1973.

In 1919 he graduated from Tyler High School and received an appointment to the U.S. Military Academy at West Point. After one year, he had firmly decided that a career in the Army was not what he wanted. At seventeen, Yarborough taught in one-room schools around his hometown and continued his college education at Sam Houston State College in Huntsville. At eighteen he was ready to see the world and worked his way across the Atlantic on a cattleboat from New Orleans, wound up in Berlin, hired as Assistant Secretary of the American Chamber of Commerce, learned German and entered the Stendhal Academy. By 1923 he was back in Texas to enroll at the University of Texas Law School. In 1927 he graduated with highest honors and set out to distinguish himself as a recognized authority in land and water rights law. At the University of Texas Law School he lectured on land law.

Senator Yarborough explained, "In 1927, as a fresh law graduate from the University of Texas at Austin I joined a large El Paso law firm representing corporations, not people. Nonetheless, being a people-oriented young man I came to know and love the Mexican and Mexican-American people." On Saturdays and Sundays Mr. Yarborough would cross the border to Juarez to enjoy a good dinner. "When you could catch quail along the Río Grande," he recalled.

In 1928, the young attorney married his childhood sweetheart, Opal Warren, and brought her to El Paso. She became ill and for awhile needed the daily care and help of two Mexican women. "They were just wonderful, taking care of my wife." When Opal got well, the Yarboroughs decided to register in a Spanish class, two nights a week, at a local high school. This lasted two months before he was offered the position of Assistant Attorney General of Texas. "That ended my chance to learn conversational Spanish. Had it not been for that offer I would've stayed in El Paso and learned Spanish. But my real interest was aroused during my four years as Assistant Attorney General, that was when I became became acquainted with the Mexican-American educational problems." Following his tenure as Assistant Attorney General, he was appointed a District Judge for five years and those educational problems became even more apparent.

By 1938 Ralph Webster Yarborough had established a distinguished background that included an East Texas political heritage, in a region well known for its populist politicians. Yarborough became the most prominent.

How he got into politics is almost due to the generous permission of his future wife, Opal, who warned him about running for County Attorney in his native Henderson County. "If you run, the wedding is off. I won't marry a man in politics." Ralph loved her enough to set his ambitions aside and joined the El Paso law firm. By 1938, Opal had changed her mind and found no objection to Yarborough running for Texas Attorney General on a shoe-string budget and using the old family car. "In that year driving through West Texas and seeing the migratory laborers and children pulling the cotton sacks, I first saw the terrible shape they were in and the few rights they had. I decided then that if the opportunity ever came I would do something about that."

He lost that first campaign, but his taste for public life had set in so well that it survived through six unsuccessful statewide campaigns for Governor and Senator. Or as he puts it, "I ran for statewide office nine times: Won three, lost three and had three stolen from me. Texas percentages."

It was through these campaigns that Ralph Yarborough refined his populist method of meeting people on a personal basis, the handshake and look in the eye. He totally mistrusts the modern media hype of managed public relations with pseudo-images of candidates.

With the Pearl Harbor attack in 1941[4] he volunteered for the Army as a Captain and served as a Judge Advocate at the Pentagon before requesting combat service. He served with the 97th Division under General George Patton's[5] Third Army and saw action in the drive to liberate Czechoslovakia. After the war, Lt. Colonel Yarborough continued his military service under General Douglas MacArthur's[6] command as a military government officer in Japan.

His return to Texas after World War II provided new opportunities with a background bound to impress any voter. But Texas politics is a whole different animal in the U.S. political arena. Just the names of some of the populist characters that have risen from that state are fascinating: "Cactus Jack" Garner served two terms as Vice President of the United States under President Franklin D. Roosevelt[7] and was a former Speaker of the House. There was "Pa" and "Ma" Ferguson, "Pappy" O'Daniel, and of course, Lyndon Baines Johnson, to name a few.

Yarborough lost Texas political races in '52, '54 and '56 which included a volley of mudslinging and character assassinations during Senator McCarthy's era.[8] But Senator Yarborough never gave in to personal slander. When asked if he and President Lyndon Baines Johnson were ever at odds he answers no. "Sometimes he said some things about me but I didn't answer or pay any attention because we both had people back home who supported the both of us."

His opportunity to serve in the U.S. Senate came as a result of a special Texas election called for when the seat was made vacant by the November election of Price Daniel as Governor.[9] Once in the Senate, Lyndon Johnson and Ralph Yarborough became a formidable pair, but oftentimes it was Johnson who stole the limelight as Senate Majority Leader and later as Vice President and President.

Nonetheless, Senator Yarborough gives much credit to Johnson for his accomplishments. When Johnson was Senate Majority Leader he helped select Yarborough for the Senate Labor and Public Welfare Committee. A senator on the Labor and Public Welfare Committee died, and it became a very controversial decision as to who would inherit that position. Liberals wanted Senator Joseph Clark, an outstanding liberal from Pennsylvania, and the Conservatives wanted Senator Strom Thurmond,[1] who was a Democrat at that time. Senator Yarborough recalls, "Lyndon didn't want to offend

4. This surprise aerial attack by the Japanese on the U.S. naval base in Pearl Harbor, Hawaii, brought about the U.S. entrance into World War II.
5. George Smith Patton (1885–1945), American general.
6. Douglas MacArthur (1880–1964), American general.
7. Franklin Delano Roosevelt (1882–1945), U.S. president 1933–45.
8. The period, in the late 1940s and early 1950s, during which a committee of the U.S. Congress, led by Senator Joseph McCarthy, engaged in "red-baiting"—investigating and attacking U.S. citizens, such as government employees, as Communists.

9. Marion Price Daniel Sr. (1910–1988) was a U.S. senator from 1952 until 1957, following his election as governor of Texas in 1956; William A. Blakely was appointed to replace him as senator. In 1957, Yarborough won a special election for the Senate seat. The next year, Daniel was reelected as governor, and he served until 1963.
1. James Strom Thurmond (1902–2003), American politician from South Carolina; he switched from the Democratic Party to the Republican Party in 1964. *Senator Joseph Clark*: Joseph Sill Clark Jr. (1901–1990), American lawyer and Democratic Party politician.

either side, so he said, 'Well, I got somebody from my native state I need to show a favor'." Senator Yarborough's entrance into the committee was unopposed after he promised both sides he wasn't necessarily a liberal or a conservative. "I didn't want to get beat before I started." No one knew how this fresh young senator was going to vote. Soon after that, he was able to get on the Education Subcommittee, which is what he was really aiming for. As a former one-room school teacher, his priority was education.

A national health care plan is nothing new. Senator Yarborough advocated it back in the sixties. He tried to make it a national goal when he said, "I want to tackle what I believe to be the biggest domestic problem in this country today." Close to thirty years later the problem is even more critical.

Senator Yarborough was one of the last of the great populist *políticos* from the South. While Governor Bill Clinton's populist approach to his presidential campaign was commendable, it is mild compared to populists of twenty plus years ago.

Because of the bills he helped pass, employers who now had to pay fair "minimum wages" raised the necessary opposition to oust him in 1970. Senator Yarborough lost reelection. He had been able to unify Texas' fiercely independent progressive elements through the force of his personality and vigorous leadership. But there were people who didn't want to pay for what they called "the big spending ways." Nonetheless, Yarborough's legacy as a people's politician is secure.

I asked him which state, Texas or California, was more progressive for Mexican Americans. He responded by recalling a march he had made with César Chávez[2] and farmworkers in California's Central Valley, ". . . I've never seen farmers look as mad. The look of hate from the deputy sheriffs and special constables . . . I think the only reason they didn't shoot at us is because we had some senators with us, Fritz Mondale and Ted Kennedy[3] . . . I just got a little smell of that . . ."

"What Mexican American stands out that you admire the most as a hero?"

"That would have to be Dr. Hector García of Corpus Christi. You know he did so much and founded the G.I. Forum."[4]

Senator Yarborough was unspoiled by big business. In a 1958 Senatorial Campaign, the ultra-conservative *Dallas Morning News* accused Yarborough of receiving some $25,000 in campaign contributions from labor unions. Yarborough's opponents gleefully thought this would be the "kiss of death." This was the trump card at the crucial moment of the campaign. Yarborough came back with a correction. The Dallas paper had actually understated the amount of labor's contributions to his campaign. Yarborough pointed out that his opponent, Bill Blakely, was a well-known millionaire, and so he appealed for even more campaign contributions from the "little people" for whom he was fighting. This dramatic political turnaround confounded his opponents and helped produce a grand victory. For the next five

---

2. See p. 760.
3. Edward Moore Kennedy (1932–2009), American politician from Massachusetts. *Fritz Mondale*: Walter Frederick Mondale (b. 1928), American politician from Minnesota.
4. The American G.I. Forum (AGIF), a Congressionally-chartered Hispanic veterans and

civil rights organization founded by Hector P. García (1914–1996), Mexican American physician, surgeon, World War II veteran, civil rights advocate, alternate ambassador to the United Nations (1967), and recipient of the Presidential Medal of Freedom (1984).

years, he became a strong supporter of the progressive Kennedy–Johnson program.

The Senator won't delve into old campaign wounds. Perhaps out of pain, or letting them be. It is well-known that President John F. Kennedy's fatal trip to Texas[5] was to help heal the political factions in that state.

As I prepared to leave, the Senator acknowledged the love and support he had received from his wife, Opal, of sixty-three years. She was close by, gracious but also aware of her husband's frail condition at that moment.

Will we ever see a Senator like Yarborough from Texas or any other state? He was a true populist, who cared and voted for all people, but especially for the downtrodden.

# What's in a Spanish Name?

The first time I ever ran across a Spanish word in Anglo-American literature was in grade school when we were assigned to read Mark Twain's "The Celebrated Jumping Frog of Calaveras County." It was a fun-filled, humorous story.[1] Despite my home-honed fluency in *Español*, I did not recognize the Spanish word in the title and story.

I knew what a *calavera* was. It was a skull. For *el Día de los Muertos* in México,[2] they were made into little skulls out of sugar and eaten like candy. In the Mexican game *Lotería*,[3] *La Calavera* was illustrated with the crossed bones under the skull.

But within the context of an Anglo-American English class, in a school where Spanish was strictly forbidden and punishable by paddling, ridicule, and writing "I shall not speak Spanish in school" a hundred times, *calaveras* was pronounced anglo-phonetically "*kel-awe-ver-rahs.*" The Spanish word Ca-la-ve-ras was hidden, disguised, nothing more than the name of a county. It was the mysterious name of an unknown person, place or thing. Innocently or naively, I took the word to be just another eccentric English word pronounced with a suave Anglo-American accent.

It took me a few years to discover that Calaveras County in California had been named for *Río Calaveras*, where a great number of skulls and skeletons had been discovered by early Spanish explorers.

Like Calaveras, hundreds of Spanish words remained in this country, changed, unchanged and disguised due to loss of meaning, evolution of misspellings, and mispronunciations. After 1848, when the U.S. took over the Southwest, Spanish had to survive on its own.

There's a town in Texas named Buda. With a Texas accent it is pronounced Bew-da. On the highway from Austin (pronounced Awe-stn or *Ostin* in Spanish) to San Marcos, pronounced Sanmar-cuss, there's a sign announcing Buda. That shouldn't have been odd, but being from Texas it just didn't seem right. I could have understood Buddha or even Buttocks, Texas, but Buda?

5. Kennedy was assassinated while riding in a presidential motorcade through Dealey Plaza, in Dallas, Texas, on November 22, 1963.
1. Authored in 1865 by the American writer Samuel Clemens (1835–1910), aka Mark Twain.
2. On the Day of the Dead, also known as All Souls' Day, a holiday celebrated in Mexico and by Latinos, family members and friends gather to remember and pray for people they have known who have died.
3. See Burciaga's discussion in "Spilling the Beans" (p. 1228).

It didn't take much ask'n before learning that the name was originally *Viuda*, which is Spanish for widow. Some monolingual Texan just didn't know any better and wrote it down just the way he heard it. That's how we got lariat from *la rieta*, hoosegow from *juzgado*, and buckaroo from *vaquero*.

What's Polamas? That's a street in San José, California. It's actually supposed to be Palomas, pigeons, but the person doing the lettering on street signs just didn't know better.

The Bank of America put out some cute little refrigerator magnets the size of a business card for its Spanish speaking clients where they could write important telephone "Numberos." Numberos? That's neither English, Spanish nor Caló. The biggest bank in the U.S. of A. meant *números*. Even though it may have been an innocent billingual typo, would you trust them with your *dinero*?

The one that has always troubled me is the English "tamale" pronounced tamalee. The Spanish singular for this food item is *tamal*, plural tamales. Don't go to the English language experts because Meriam-Webster's New Collegiate Dictionary also misspells tamale and its etymological rationale is that it comes from the Aztec Nahuatl *tamallí*.

Sarape is another such word. Webster says it's *serape*, but in the Spanish speaking world everyone pronounces it and spells it as sarape. Look it up in an English-Spanish dictionary or a Spanish-English dictionary and it's "sarape" in Spanish and "serape" in English. Why?

Throughout the last century and a half Spanish has had free rein, running wild, with complete freedom to produce some mighty interesting words and sounds, not only from Gringos but from Mexicans themselves. Murrieta is now spelled Murieta, Monterrey is now spelled Monterey and Arrastradero is now spelled arastradero. Why anyone decided to take away the rolling "r" from so many of the Spanish words is beyond *moi*. Did someone find the extra "r" unnecessary, were they in short supply of r's, or was it just too difficult to roll their r's in Spanish?

In addition, words from 16th-century Spanish still roam throughout the Southwest, along with Caló, the Chicano dialect. These words have flourished and even emigrated back to Mexico where they have become part of the popular vernacular of the masses. The opposite also happens in Mexico and France and the rest of the world for that matter.

Though there may be many innocent reasons for this evolution of language, the isolation and syncretism, fusion of two cultures in language is fascinating.

I ran across a word in Mexico that is related to this argument but couldn't find in any dictionary, much less a synonym. It was *resemanticización*—resemanticization, also absent from any English dictionary.

Resemanticization was not defined, but it was derived from the word "semantics"—the historical and psychological study and classification of changes in the meaning of words or objects. In politics and cross cultural situations, words, ideas and objects constantly assimilate, "transculturate," or adapt for the sake of survival.

Thus the anglicization or hispanization of words in this country. The word "Chicano" was a resemanticized term that was once pejorative. Alurista,[4] an

4. See p. 1657.

early Chicano poet, resemanticized many words such as Aztlán, the ancient place of origin for the Aztecs that was and is the Southwest. Amerindio came to describe not only an "American" Indian but all Indigenous peoples across the continent.

Chicano film, art and literature constantly redefines, resemanticizes, an experience that is part Anglo, part Español, part Mexicano. Resemanticization is also the exploitation of connotation and ambiguity in propaganda. Resemanticization deals not only with words but with ideas, and symbols, that cross borders and languages to take different meanings.

We become chameleons, we are chameleons. As we move from one world to the other, we exchange colors, ideas, symbols and words in order to fit, to relate and to survive. The result is a prismatic iridescence when the different colors play on each other, like a rainbow after a rainstorm in the desert. We are chameleons.

## Bilingual Cognates

*Bilingual Love Poem*

Your sonrisa is a sunrise
that was reaped from your smile
sowed from a semilla
into the sol of your soul
with an ardent pasión,
passion ardiente,
sizzling in a mar de amar
where more is amor,
in a sea of sí
filled with the sal of salt
in the saliva of the saliva
that gives sed but is never sad.

Two tongues that come together
is not a French kiss
but bilingual love.

A cognate is a word related to another through derivation, borrowing or descent. From one language to another, I suppose they become bilingual cognates if not bloopers. Like in the poem above, there are Spanish and English words that look alike or sound alike:

—Vincent Price[1] has been known as "beans and rice" or vice versa.

—El Benny Lechero was actually a short serial movie character in the fifties known as "The Vanishing Shadow."

—Somewhere in the Southwest there was a teacher who thought his Chicano kids were calling him "Cool Arrow" when in reality they were calling him a *"culero,"* an insult.

—Two Chicanos were dining at a fashionable restaurant and one of them says to the other, "This is the best *gabacho* (*gazpacho*) soup I've ever tasted.

—My mother once called her comadre and her German born husband answered. "Lucina is not in," he said in perfect Spanish, "she is out buying 'grocerías.'" (*Grocerías* are coarse, vulgar statements and acts.)

1. American actor (1911–1993).

—One morning our friend Muggins called and my Mother answered. Trying to be courteous, he asked my Mother in Spanish how she was born instead of how she had awakened: *"Buenos dias, Señora, ¿Como nació?"* instead of *"¿Como amaneció?"*

Some are not necessarily cognates, but the mental mistranslations some-time result in funny situations. My friend Rana has forever confused his Spanish with his English. As a high schooler, he was dazzled by a beautiful young woman and greeted her with "How are you going?" from *"¿Como te va?"* Even in English he had trouble. Lone Star Beer became Long Star, humble became noble, and misconstrue became misconstrew. In the con-text of a serious conversation the result is laughter.

Jokes abound about Latinos who come to this country and read English signs in Spanish. Back when Cokes were only a dime, a Mexicano put a ten cent coin in the machine but did not receive a bottle of Coke. He waited, hit it and nothing. Finally he read just above the coin slot where it said "Dime" (which translates to "tell me" in Spanish}. So he bent down to the slot and whispered into it, *"Dame una Coca Cola."*

We have all seen real estate signs that say "For Sale, No Lease." A newly arrived immigrant looking for housing, read the sign and kicked the door open. If you read that in Spanish and run the first two words together it reads, "force it, it's alright."

Introducing someone in Spanish is not the same as introducing someone in English. *Introducir* in Spanish means to put in, to infiltrate. The correct term is *presentar*. Yet *introducir* is used so often that people don't even catch it. Many bilingual cognates have returned to Mexico to become part of what is known as Mexican caló. *Chansa* comes from chance, for *oportuni-dades. Trakes* for tracks, *mechas* for matches, *chutear* for shooting, *raides* from rides. Mexican film actor Tin Tan and singer Juan Gabriel[2] have been very influential in "introducing" Chicano terms to Mexico.

Most of the Spanish terminology for baseball comes from the English. *Ni ketcha, ni pitcha, ni deja batear* is a well known proverb for someone who won't do anything and won't let anyone else do anything—He/she won't catch, doesn't pitch and won't let anyone bat.

One of my favorite anecdotes is the one about my good friend and ex-roommate Darío Prieto. Though it has little to do with cognates, it shows how our bilingual minds sometimes work. In a Washington, D.C., recep-tion, he was once asked by our other roommate Ed Gutierrez, "Hey Darío, where does the Lone Ranger take his trash?" Darío didn't know, so Ed sang him the answer to the tune of the television show's theme, "to the dump, to the dump, to the dump! dump! dump! . . ."

Darío laughed heartily and then went to ask a couple the same question. But Darío always had to polish his English. He cleared his throat, some-thing he always did, and asked, "Where does the Lone Ranger dispose of his debris?" The couple didn't know, so Darío sang the answer, "Ta-da-da, ta-da-da, ta-da-da,da,da . . ." The couple just stared at him.

1995

2. Mexican singer and songwriter (Alberto Agu-ilera Valadez, b. 1950), associated with *ranchera*, mariachi, and pop music. Tin Tan catered to the Pachuco population in Los Angeles and other ma-jor cities of the American Southwest; his idiosyn-cratic Spanish hilariously juxtaposed Mexican-isms, Anglicisms, and Chicano street language.

# JOSÉ KOZER
## b. 1940

Born to Jewish parents in Havana, José Kozer is one of the most distinctive poetic voices to have emerged from the Cuban diaspora. Kozer first left Cuba in early 1958 to study at New York University, in New York City. He returned to the island in 1959, a supporter of the Castro revolution. Disillusioned, he left Cuba again for New York the following year, and he worked at odd jobs while writing poetry and earning his bachelor's degree, which he received from NYU in 1965. In 1967, he began teaching at Queens College, in New York. Kozer married in 1962, but the years following were unhappy, rife with arguments, alcohol, drugs, and depression; in 1968, Kozer and his wife divorced. In 1970, after not writing for almost a decade, he returned to poetry. He also began to spend summers in Spain, where he met Guadalupe Barranechea, whom he married in 1974. He and Guadalupe raised his daughter, Mía, and their daughter, Susana, while he taught and immersed himself again in Spanish.

His first book of poetry, *Padres y otras profesiones* (Fathers and other professions), was published in 1972, and since then Kozer has produced more than 40 books and chapbooks. His work has appeared in over 250 literary magazines and anthologies. With *Bajo este cien* (Under this hundred, 1983), a generous selection of his work published by the prestigious Mexican publishing house Fondo de Cultura Económica, his work acquired a visibility and prestige in Latin America that have continued to increase during the last 20 years. His most noteworthy collections are *Este judío de números y letras* (This Jew of Numbers and Letters, 1975), *Jarrón de las abreviaturas* (The Vase of Abbreviations, 1980), *La garza sin sombras* (The Heron without Shadows, 1985), *El carillón de los muertos* (Carillon for the Dead, 1987), *Dípticos* (Diptychs, 1998), and *Un caso llamado FK* (A Case Called FK, 2002). His poetry collection *No buscan reflejarse* (Not Looking for Reflections), published in Havana in 2002, was the first book published in Cuba by a living exiled Cuban writer since the 1970s. Of his many volumes of personal diaries, several have been published in *Una huella destartalada: Diarios* (A Crumbling Footprint: Diaries, 2003).

Kozer remained at Queens College until his retirement, in 1995; he and Barranechea then lived briefly in Spain, but currently reside in South Florida. In light of his many years in New York, Kozer could be considered, like the contemporary novelist Oscar Hijuelos, a Latino writer from New York, but his work makes this identification almost impossible, for someone who comes to Kozer's poems without knowing anything about the author would be hard-pressed to locate this poet in that city or even in the United States. Although his writing makes clear that he is a Cuban Jewish exile, Kozer, like other exiled writers, tends to write not about the world that surrounds him but about the one he left. His poetry and its almost exclusive use of Spanish—a Spanish so rich, capacious, and cosmopolitan that perhaps only an exile could have written it—are an effort to build a verbal edifice that will isolate the poet from the realities of exile. The poems' collages of words—containing the terms of the everyday, of the household, of fantasy and memory—baroque and difficult, suggest the myriad displacing experiences of exile, the fixed points being only the poet's family, his Cubanness, and his Jewishness.

Kozer constantly returns to the past, to prerevolutionary Cuba, and to the Eastern European Jewish tradition of his parents and grandparents. He has written that "the notion of language . . . links individual and family with a tradition, a community. That community, with its history, its memory, its archetypal quality, and respiratory movement, sometimes finds a meeting point, a convergence, in creation." For Kozer, that meeting point occurs in poetry. Recently, however, the predominantly nostalgic and escapist impetus of his poetry has begun to change, and Kozer has composed short, playful poems in English. He has described the language of his poems, where Cuban slang abides side by side with Peruvianisms, Colombianisms, anglicisms, and expressions in Spanglish, as follows: "We live outside, speaking and thinking and writing in this marginal language, made of remnants and of grease spots, surrounded by strange enclaves of foreign languages."

In the following selections—all but one translated from the Spanish by Mark Weiss—Kozer describes various locations, both geographic and spiritual. "Nimia," written in English, is an impression of a metropolitan train station. In "Diaspora," as the poet mourns the water and flowers he has never seen, the dullness and gray rigidity of his family home in Cuba stand out in contrast to the fluid possibilities of the city outside. "First & last" deals with the fleeting presence of his family in Cuba—fleeting because the only traces are sterile vistas of dusty furniture and memories of rooms and of faces. The soaring bird of "Diaspora," erased by flame and water, reappears—but as Nothing. In "The final journey," the poet emerges from the house into an ecstasy of detail, vivid fruit, and scattered petals. He then attempts to force open the boundaries of his home.

## Diaspora

The shop in Havana is dust
and the Irish cotton is dust
and my father, a dusty Jew,
day after day comes home with a loaf of bread beneath his arm.
Day after day, each day alike,                                                  5
his eyes oblique as striped gabardine,
not like the restless eyes of a captain searching the shallows
he returns to the house, a rough and bubbling crater.
Papa arrives: we eat lunch, our eyes fixed on the ceiling's ornate
    molding,
I have never seen the water come in, have seen neither fish nor           10
    flowerpot.
My mother enters and polishes the furniture's heavy carving,
changes Thursday's sheets,
no flower ever to be seen in any bedroom.
All of the shops in Havana have closed,
the workers, in a noisy fever, file through the streets,                    15
and my father, a dusty Jew,
carries once more the Ark of the Law[1]
when he leaves Cuba.

1975                                                                    2006

## Nimia

### IN A STATION OF THE METRO: NEW YORK, 5 O'CLOCK[1]

RUSH HOUR, brush hour.

                                                                         1999

---

1. In a Jewish synagogue, an ornate cabinet that holds the sacred scrolls of the Torah (the first five books of the Hebrew Scriptures), which are used during religious services.

1. "In a Station of the Metro" (1913, 1916), by the American poet Ezra Pound (1885–1972), reads in its entirety: "The apparition of these faces in the crowd; / Petals on a wet, black bough."

## First & last

1. My parents came from Poland and Czechoslovakia, at twenty I ousted myself from my country, foreseeing that the nation would take on something like the air of a general prison; that wasn't to my taste (I would come to learn that the whole planet is a general prison): I was born in Cuba, where I left no progeny, and I will not return: I am the first and last Cuban generation.

2. Here at home we have a dinner table for eight that cost us a fortune over fifteen years ago, its legs carved with grapes and crabs, a flat surface that to touch made one tremble. I doubt we've dined at that table ten times. I was always aware that at home we had nothing to celebrate. It was the first and last time that I ever wasted money like that.

3. In the Cuban version I read that the first was called Adam; in the Hebrew version that the last was called Nothing. In the Cuban version I read that the first was called Eve; in the Hebrew version that the last is called Bird, that flies towards the edge where Nothing will be quickened. We are all the dead Mother.

1999

2006

## The final journey

We live in a more-or-less middle-class neighborhood.

Uniform housefronts, painted (the same) my own included, within (in
    the hidden space where things tremble) could use
    some sprucing-up.

Let's go outside anyway, let's go outside: it's the violet season of aca-     5
    cias in bloom, an acacia in bloom in each garden of
    each house, the lemon trees in bloom, mine resplen-
    dent yellow, bearing fruit, perfect lemons, and shad-
    ows of (two pots of) sour geraniums in bloom tremble
    at the front door, I'll slice a lemon later, a scattering    10
    of ants and sour shadows the geranium's petals.

One house and the next: in all the houses the law of the mother, this
    Law in every case.

I'm leaving, life here has become intolerable to me. Intolerable any-
    where, of course, but I won't tolerate the intolerable    15
    in my house.

I set it ablaze, everything in flames. Let's proceed to the burning of our
    things, shadows and housefront, that is this violet
    season: where is the hawk, where the fountain and
    where the ruddy outline of the bird that floating rode    20
    the air, and shivers now in flaming water.

Cloth becomes burning coals, a simple apron trimmed with gold be-
    comes embers: and the masonry (impermanent foun-
    tain of durability) has blackened.

I fall now, my little virtues were sour, I couldn't evade the law that      25
    never leaves: that death sustains everything, and I
    journey from coming and going to a fixed, stony
    euphoria, I journey to the edge, I cast my eyes (in
    passing?) from neighborhood to neighborhood, from
    housefront to housefront: the moment of this violet      30
    season will not lengthen.

2002                                      2006

---

# LUIS VALDEZ
## b. 1940

Luis Valdez is the son of migrant farmworkers, and at the age of six he started working with his parents in the fields. In 1964, he earned a bachelor's degree in English from San Jose State University, where he developed a lasting interest in theater. After graduation, he remained in the Bay Area to gain additional dramatic training with the San Francisco Mime Troupe, known for its activism against the Vietnam War. Focusing his skills on the plight of Mexican migrant workers, Valdez formed El Teatro Campesino (The Farmworkers' Theater), a controversial agitprop theatrical group composed of farm laborers. As discussed in the "Upheaval" introduction, this group's activism was an essential component of the Chicano Movement, led by César Chávez, Dolores Huerta, and others. "If *la raza* will not come to the theater," he claimed once, "then the theater must go to *la raza*. This, in the long run, will determine the shape, style, concept, spirit, and form of *el teatro chicano.*"

The central method used by El Teatro Campesino was improvisation, then in fashion among socially conscious directors in Europe and Latin America. As improvisors, actors created their material around stereotypes, news pieces, and past events. El Teatro Campesino explored the life of the farmworkers, exposed the labor and living conditions of many Mexican Americans, and thus aimed to be a tool for change, to help make its predominantly Mexican audiences historically informed and politically aware. Its themes included discrimination and racial prejudice, political corruption, and the need to improve labor, educational, and economic opportunities. Using a minimum of stage props and employing a variety of didactic techniques (masks, signs, and role reversals) adapted from the work of the German playwright Bertolt Brecht (1898–1965), Valdez created *actos*, Spanish medieval–type stage skits, to enhance the ideological battles of *El Movimiento*. They were connected with *las huelgas*, strikes organized by the United Farmworkers Union. The *actos* were performed on streets and dirt roads, in schools, in community centers, and wherever migrant workers congregated. Valdez was at once the orchestrator of El Teatro Campesino and its connection with the larger regional and national political forces and groups equally committed to social theater. In "Notes on Chicano Theater," a section of his book *Luis Valdez: Early Works* (1990), Valdez argues, in part, that "Chicanos must be seen as a nation with geographical, religious, cultural, and racial roots in Aztlán, the mythic homeland of the Aztecs." He adds: "The organizational support of the national theater should be from within, because *'el corazón de la raza'* (the heart of Chicanos) cannot be revolutionized on a grant from Uncle Sam."

Among the *actos* are *Las dos caras del patroncito* (The Two Faces of the Grower, 1965) and *La quinta temporada* (The Fifth Season, 1966). The former used role reversals to show the owner/planter's vulnerability when stripped of his power over the farmworkers. The latter is an allegorical and optimistic piece prophesying that—in keeping with "Jesus's Friendship," César Chávez's essay on the perfect compatibility of union activisim and Christianity—the worker will enjoy a season of social justice and of pay commensurate with the demanding work in the fields. In 1967, Valdez and El Teatro Campesino broadened their concerns from the need to unionize toward a more inclusive social commentary. Belonging to this period are *actos* such as *Los vendidos* (The Sellouts, 1967), which skewers Chicanos who profit at the expense of the poor and the uneducated, and *No saco nada de la escuela* (I Don't Learn Anything at School, 1969). In *Vietnam Campesino* (1970) and *Soldado razo* (The Buck Private, 1971), Valdez juxtaposes the suffering of Vietnamese farmers with the injustice and oppression suffered by Mexican Americans.

In 1972, a television adaptation of *Los vendidos* aired on PBS and received an Emmy Award. Two years later, when *La gran carpa de la familia Rascuachi* (The Great Tent Show of the Rascuachi Family) was staged in Mexico City during an international theater festival, Chicano and Latin American theater companies reacted negatively to the play's religious ending. The uproar shook Valdez, who subsequently broke ties with other Mexican American intellectuals, playwrights, and theater troupes. The play was eventually shown on PBS and toured Europe to much acclaim. As the energy surrounding the Chicano Movement dwindled from the late 1970s through the 1980s, Valdez's style matured in its use of satire, music, and humor. He took a more traditional (i.e., individualistic rather than collective) approach to authorship without betraying his activist roots. He also embarked on more-conventional performances, staging his plays of this period—*Zoot Suit* (1978), *Corridos* (1982), and *I Don't Have to Show You No Stinkin' Badges* (1986)—in standard theaters. Valdez's work in television and movies generated criticism, including accusations of his being a *vendido* who had abandoned his grassroots theatrical formation. He adapted *Zoot Suit* into an experimental movie released in 1981. He then directed *La Bamba* (1987), a biographical movie about the Mexican American rock and roll singer Ritchie Valens (aka Richard Steven Valenzuela), who died in a plane crash in 1959. Most recently, he directed *The Cisco Kid* (1994), starring Jimmy Smits.

By far the most prominent of his works has been *Zoot Suit*, a play in two acts. It was partly a response to *West Side Story* (1957), a highly successful Broadway musical about rival Puerto Rican and Anglo teenage gangs in New York City. After a long run in Los Angeles, *Zoot Suit* moved to Broadway, becoming the first Mexican American play to be staged in New York. As discussed in the "Acculturation" introduction, the play—included in its entirety in this anthology—is based on an incident that culminated in the so-called Zoot Suit Riots of 1943. It explores the inner life of a pachuco. A Los Angeles subculture during the World War II era, pachucos were young Mexican American men who wore *zoot suits*, which included high-waisted, wide-legged, tight-cuffed pegged trousers (*tramos*) and a long coat (*carlango*) with wide lapels and wide, padded shoulders. Young men of other ethnic groups, among them Italian Americans, African Americans, and Filipino Americans, also wore zoot suits, but Mexican Americans added a felt hat (*tando*) with a long feather and pointy, French-style shoes (*calcos*). Valdez's play emphasizes this fashion while meditating on marginality, resistance, rebellion, and archetypes, the latter represented by an emblematic figure called El Pachuco. Dances of the period—mambo, danzón, swing, bolero, beguín—are invoked to re-create the effervescence of the scene.

Valdez connected the quest for legitimacy among pachucos in the 1940s with the search for recognition among Chicanos in the 1960s. He perceived himself as an unapologetically defiant speaker for *la raza* and thus a conduit for social change. Although the result was well received critically, Valdez has been attacked for twisting the historical facts. Some critics argue that the play romanticizes zoot suiters as antecedents of the Chicano Movement, while others counter that pachucos prefigured the Chicano Movement as rebels with a cause who refused to assimilate. As a theatrical experience, *Zoot Suit* is directed, first and foremost, at a broad bilingual Mexican American audience. However, even that target audience will not be able to enter fully into the linguistic world of the play. Much of the dialogue, especially lines spoken by Pachuco, consists of an argot, known as caló or Pachuco, spoken by Chicano youths in cities of the Southwest during the 1940s. This idiosyncratic jargon existed almost exclusively in those places at that time. Even then, Latinos elsewhere would not have used it or necessarily understood it; they might have had their own brands of Spanglish. Many of these words and expressions are certain to evade the understanding of most people, speakers of Spanish and nonspeakers of Spanish alike. As a result, in making everyone but pachucos of the period feel alienated, left out, ignored, the play successfully builds a ghetto within a ghetto. So as not to infringe on Valdez's artistic strategy, the editors of this anthology have annotated only broader contextual items, some slang in Spanish or English, and the lyrics of popular songs.

# ZOOT SUIT

## Characters

EL PACHUCO
HENRY REYNA

His Family:
ENRIQUE REYNA
DOLORES REYNA
LUPE REYNA
RUDY REYNA

His Friends:
GEORGE SHEARER
ALICE BLOOMFIELD

His Gang:
DELLA BARRIOS
SMILEY TORRES
JOEY CASTRO
TOMMY ROBERTS
ELENA TORRES
BERTHA VILLARREAL

The Downey Gang:
RAFAS
RAGMAN

HOBO
CHOLO
ZOOTER
GÜERA
HOBA
BLONDIE
LITTLE BLUE

Detectives:
LIEUTENANT EDWARDS
SERGEANT SMITH

The Press:
PRESS
CUB REPORTER
NEWSBOY

The Court:
JUDGE F.W. CHARLES
BAILIFF

The Prison:
GUARD

The Military:
BOSUN'S MATE
SAILORS
MARINE
SWABBIE
MANCHUKA

SHORE PATROLMAN

Others:
GIRLS
PIMP
CHOLO

## Setting

*The giant facsimile of a newspaper front page serves as a drop curtain.*

*The huge masthead reads: LOS ANGELES HERALD EXPRESS Thursday, June 3, 1943.*

*A headline cries out: ZOOT-SUITER HORDES INVADE LOS ANGELES. US NAVY AND MARINES ARE CALLED IN.*

*Behind this are black drapes creating a place of haunting shadows larger than life. The somber shapes and outlines of pachuco images hang subtly, black on black, against a back-ground of heavy fabric evoking memories and feelings like an old suit hanging forgotten in the depths of a closet some- where, sometime . . . Below this is a sweeping, curving place of levels and rounded corners with the hard, ingrained brilliance of countless spit shines, like the memory of a dance hall.*

## Act One

### Prologue

*A switchblade plunges through the newspaper. It slowly cuts a rip to the bot- tom of the drop. To the sounds of "Perdido" by Duke Ellington,[1] EL PACHUCO emerges from the slit. HE adjusts his clothing, meticulously fussing with his collar, suspenders, cuffs. HE tends to his hair, combing back every strand into a long luxurious ducktail, with infinite loving pains. Then HE reaches into the slit and pulls out his coat and hat. HE dons them. His fantastic costume is complete. It is a zoot suit. HE is transformed into the very image of the pachuco myth, from his pork-pie hat to the tip of his four foot watch chain. Now HE turns to the audience. His three-soled shoes with metal taps click- clack as HE proudly, slovenly, defiantly makes his way downstage. HE stops and assumes a pachuco stance.*

PACHUCO:
  ¿Qué le watcha a mis trapos, ése?[2]
  ¿Sabe qué, carnal?
  Estas garras me las planté porque
  vamos a dejarnos caer un play, ¿sabe?
    [HE *crosses to center stage, models his clothes.*]

---

1. American jazz composer and bandleader, born Edward Kennedy Ellington (1899–1974).
2. Pachuco's first line introduces the kind of Spanglish that makes *Zoot Suit*, linguistically, so evocative and provocative. *Watcha*, for example, is the English verb *watch* given a Spanish spin. *Ése* is a Chicano expression meaning dude, guy, man, as in *Órale, ése* (hey, man). *Carnal*, at the end of the next line, means bro (brother).

Watcha mi tacuche, ése. Aliviánese con mis calcos, tando, lisa, tramos,
y carlango, ése.
  [*Pause.*]
Nel, sabe qué, usted está muy verdolaga. Como se me hace que es puro
square.
[EL PACHUCO *breaks character and addresses the audience in perfect
English.*]
Ladies and gentlemen
the play you are about to see
is a construct of fact and fantasy.
The Pachuco style was an act in life
and his language a new creation.
His will to be was an awesome force
eluding all documentation . . .
A mythical, quizzical, frightening being
precursor of revolution
Or a piteous, hideous heroic joke
deserving of absolution?
I speak as an actor on the stage.
The Pachuco was existential
for he was an actor in the streets
both profane and reverential.
It was the secret fantasy of every bato
in or out of the Chicanada
to put on a Zoot Suit and play the Myth
más chucote que la chingada.
  [*Puts hat back on and turns.*]
¡Pos órale!
  [*Music. The newspaper drop flies.* EL PACHUCO *begins his chuco stroll
  upstage, swinging his watch chain.*]

### 1. ZOOT SUIT

*The scene is a barrio dance in the forties.* PACHUCOS *and* PACHUCAS *in zoot
suits and pompadours.*

*They are members of the* 38TH STREET GANG, *led by* HENRY REYNA, *21,
dark, Indian-looking, older than his years, and* DELLA BARRIOS, *20, his girlfriend, in miniskirt and fingertip coat. A* SAILOR *called* SWABBIE *dances with
his girlfriend* MANCHUKA *among the* COUPLES. *Movement. Animation.* EL
PACHUCO *sings.*

PACHUCO:

PUT ON A ZOOT SUIT, MAKES YOU FEEL REAL ROOT
LOOK LIKE A DIAMOND, SPARKLING, SHINING
READY FOR DANCING
READY FOR THE BOOGIE TONIGHT!
  [*The* COUPLES, *dancing, join the* PACHUCO *in exclaiming the last
  term of each line in the next verse.*]

THE HEPCATS UP IN HARLEM WEAR THAT DRAPE SHAPE
COMO LOS PACHUCONES DOWN IN L.A.
WHERE HUISAS IN THEIR POMPADOURS LOOK REAL
KEEN ON THE DANCE FLOOR OF THE BALLROOMS
DONDE BAILAN SWING.

YOU BETTER GET HEP TONIGHT
AND PUT ON THAT ZOOT SUIT!

[*The* DOWNEY GANG, *a rival group of pachucos, enters upstage left.
Their quick dance step becomes a challenge to* 38TH STREET.]
DOWNEY GANG:    Downey . . . ¡Rifá!
HENRY:  [*Gesturing back.*]  ¡Toma! [*The music is hot.* EL PACHUCO *slides
across the floor and momentarily breaks the tension.* HENRY *warns* RAFAS,
*the leader of the* DOWNEY GANG, *when* HE *sees him push his brother* RUDY.]
¡Rafas!
PACHUCO:  [*Sings.*]

TRUCHA, ESE LOCO, VAMOS AL BORLO
WEAR THAT CARLANGO, TRAMOS Y TANDO
DANCE WITH YOUR HUISA
DANCE TO THE BOOGIE TONIGHT!

'CAUSE THE ZOOT SUIT IS THE STYLE IN CALIFORNIA
TAMBIÉN EN COLORADO Y ARIZONA
THEY'RE WEARING THAT TACUCHE EN EL PASO
Y EN TODOS LOS SALONES DE CHICAGO

YOU BETTER GET HEP TONIGHT
AND PUT ON THAT ZOOT SUIT!

### 2. THE MASS ARRESTS

*We hear a siren, then another, and another. It sounds like gangbusters. The
dance is interrupted.* COUPLES *pause on the dance floor.*

PACHUCO:    Trucha, la jura. ¡Pélenle! [PACHUCOS *start to run out, but* DETEC-
TIVES *leap onstage with drawn guns. A* CUB REPORTER *takes flash pictures.*]
SGT. SMITH:    Hold it right there, kids!
LT. EDWARDS:    Everybody get your hands up!
RUDY:    Watcha! This way! [RUDY *escapes with some others.*]
LT. EDWARDS:    Stop or I'll shoot! [EDWARDS *fires his revolver into the air. A
number of pachucos and their girlfriends freeze. The cops round them
up.* SWABBIE, *an American sailor, and* MANCHUKA, *a Japanese-American
dancer, are among them.*]
SGT. SMITH:    ¡Ándale! [*Sees* SWABBIE.] You! Get out of here.
SWABBIE:    What about my girl?
SGT. SMITH:    Take her with you. [SWABBIE *and* MANCHUKA *exit.*]
HENRY:    What about my girl?

LT. EDWARDS: No dice, Henry. Not this time. Back in line.

SGT. SMITH: Close it up!

LT. EDWARDS: Spread! [*The* PACHUCOS *turn upstage in a line with their hands up. The sirens fade and give way to the sound of a teletype. The* PACHUCOS *turn and form a lineup, and the* PRESS *starts shooting pictures as* HE *speaks.*]

PRESS: The City of the Angels, Monday, August 2, 1942. The *Los Angeles Examiner* Headline:

THE LINEUP: [*In chorus.*] Death Awakens Sleepy Lagoon [*Breath.*] LA Shaken by Lurid "Kid" Murder.

PRESS: The City of the Angels, Monday, August 2, 1942. The *Los Angeles Times* Headline:

THE LINEUP: One Killed, Ten Hurt in Boy Wars: [*Breath.*] Mexican Boy Gangs Operating Within City.

PRESS: The City of the Angels, August 2, 1942. *Los Angeles Herald-Express* Headline:

THE LINEUP: Police Arrest Mexican Youths. Black Widow Girls in Boy Gangs.

PRESS: The City of the Angels . . .

PACHUCO: [*Sharply.*] El Pueblo de Nuestra Señora la Reina de los Ángeles de Porciúncula, pendejo.

PRESS: [*Eyeing the* PACHUCO *cautiously.*] *The Los Angeles Daily News* Headline:

BOYS IN THE LINEUP: Police Nab 300 in Roundup.

GIRLS IN THE LINEUP: Mexican Girls Picked Up in Arrests.

LT. EDWARDS: Press Release, Los Angeles Police Department: A huge showup of nearly 300 boys and girls rounded up by the police and sheriff's deputies will be held tonight at eight o'clock in Central Jail at First and Hill Street. Victims of assault, robbery, purse snatching, and similar crimes are asked to be present for the identification of suspects.

PRESS: Lieutenant . . . ? [EDWARDS *poses as the* PRESS *snaps a picture.*]

LT. EDWARDS: Thank you.

PRESS: Thank you. [SMITH *gives a signal, and the lineup moves back, forming a straight line in the rear, leaving* HENRY *upfront by himself.*]

LT. EDWARDS: Move! Turn! Out! [As *the rear line moves off to the left following* EDWARDS, SMITH *takes* HENRY *by the arm and pulls him downstage, shoving him to the floor.*]

### 3. PACHUCO YO

SGT. SMITH: Okay, kid, you wait here till I get back. Think you can do that? Sure you can. You pachucos are regular tough guys. [SMITH *exits.* HENRY *sits up on the floor.* EL PACHUCO *comes forward.*]

HENRY: Bastards. [HE *gets up and paces nervously. Pause.*] ¿Ése? ¿Ése?

PACHUCO: [*Behind him.*] ¿Qué pues, nuez?

HENRY: [*Turning.*] Where the hell you been, ése?

PACHUCO: Checking out the barrio. Qué desmadre, ¿no?

HENRY: What's going on, ése? This thing is big.

PACHUCO: The city's cracking down on pachucos, carnal. Don't you read the newspapers? They're screaming for blood.

HENRY:   All I know is they got nothing on me. I didn't do anything.

PACHUCO:   You're Henry Reyna, ése—Hank Reyna! The snarling juvenile delinquent. The zoot-suiter. The bitter young pachuco gang leader of 38th Street. That's what they got on you.

HENRY:   I don't like this, ése. [*Suddenly intense.*] I DON'T LIKE BEING LOCKED UP!

PACHUCO:   Calmantes montes, chicas patas. Haven't I taught you to survive? Play it cool.

HENRY:   They're going to do it again, ése! They're going to charge me with some phony rap and keep me until they make something stick.

PACHUCO:   So what's new?

HENRY:   [*Pause.*] I'm supposed to report for the Navy tomorrow. [EL PACHUCO *looks at him with silent disdain.*] You don't want me to go, do you?

PACHUCO:   Stupid move, carnal.

HENRY:   [*Hurt and angered by* PACHUCO's *disapproval.*] I've got to do something.

PACHUCO:   Then hang tough. Nobody's forcing you to do shit.

HENRY:   I'm forcing me, ése—ME, you understand?

PACHUCO:   Muy patriotic, eh?

HENRY:   Yeah.

PACHUCO:   Off to fight for your country.

HENRY:   Why not?

PACHUCO:   Because this ain't your country. Look what's happening all around you. The Japs have sewed up the Pacific. Rommel[3] is kicking ass in Egypt but the mayor of L.A. has declared all-out war on Chicanos. On you! ¿Te curas?

HENRY:   Órale.

PACHUCO:   Qué mamada, ¿no? Is that what you want to go out and die for? Wise up. These bastard paddy cops have it in for you. You're a marked man. They think you're the enemy.

HENRY:   [*Refusing to accept it.*] Screw them bastard cops!

PACHUCO:   And as soon as the Navy finds out you're in jail again, ya estuvo, carnal. Unfit for military duty because of your record. Think about it.

HENRY:   [*Pause.*] You got a frajo?

PACHUCO:   Simón. [HE pulls *out a cigarette, hands it to* HENRY, *lights it for him.* HENRY *is pensive.*]

HENRY:   [*Smokes, laughs ironically.*] I was all set to come back a hero, see? Me la rayo. For the first time in my life I really thought Hank Reyna was going someplace.

PACHUCO:   Forget the war overseas, carnal. Your war is on the homefront.

HENRY:   [*With new resolve.*] What do you mean?

PACHUCO:   The barrio needs you, carnal. Fight back! Stand up to them with some style. Show the world a Chicano has balls. Hang tough. You can take it. Remember, Pachuco Yo!

HENRY:   [*Assuming the style.*] Con safos, carnal.

---

3. Erwin Johannes Eugen Rommel (1891–1944), German field marshall.

## 4. THE INTERROGATION

*The* PRESS *enters, followed by* EDWARDS *and* SMITH.

PRESS: [*To the audience.*]    Final Edition; The *Los Angeles Daily News.* The police have arrested twenty-two members of the 38th Street Gang, pending further investigation of various charges.

LT. EDWARDS:    Well, son, I was hoping I wouldn't see you in here again.

HENRY:    Then why did you arrest me?

LT. EDWARDS:    Come on, Hank, you know why you're here.

HENRY:    Yeah. I'm a Mexican.

LT. EDWARDS:    Don't give me that. How long have I known you? Since '39?

HENRY:    Yeah, when you got me for stealing a car, remember?

LT. EDWARDS:    All right. That was a mistake. I didn't know it was your father's car. I tried to make it up to you. Didn't I help you set up the youth club?

SGT. SMITH:    They turned it into a gang, lieutenant. Everything they touch turns to shit.

LT. EDWARDS:    I remember a kid just a couple of years back. Head boy at the Catholic Youth Center. His idea of fun was going to the movies. What happened to that nice kid, Henry?

PRESS:    He's "Gone With The Wind," trying to look like Clark Gable.[4]

SGT. SMITH:    Now he thinks he's Humphrey Bogart.[5]

PACHUCO:    So who are you, puto? Pat O'Brien?[6]

LT. EDWARDS:    This is the wrong time to be anti-social, son. This country's at war, and we're under strict orders to crack down on all malcontents.

SGT. SMITH:    Starting with all pachucos and draft dodgers.

HENRY:    I ain't no draft dodger.

LT. EDWARDS:    I know you're not. I heard you got accepted by the Navy. Congratulations. When do you report?

HENRY:    Tomorrow?

SGT. SMITH:    Tough break!

LT. EDWARDS:    It's still not too late, you know. I could still release you in time to get sworn in.

HENRY:    If I do what?

LT. EDWARDS:    Tell me, Henry, what do you know about a big gang fight last Saturday night, out at Sleepy Lagoon?

PACHUCO:    Don't tell 'em shit.

HENRY:    Which Sleepy Lagoon?

LT. EDWARDS:    You mean there's more than one? Come on, Hank, I know you were out there. I've got a statement from your friends that says you were beaten up. Is that true? Were you and your girl attacked?

HENRY:    I don't know anything about it. Nobody's ever beat me up.

SGT. SMITH:    That's a lie and you know it. Thanks to your squealer friends, we've got enough dope on you to indict for murder right now.

---

4. American movie actor (1901–1960) best-known as the handsome leading man in *Gone with the Wind* (1939).
5. American movie actor (1899–1957) best-known at the time for playing tough guys, such as the crooked lawyer in *Angels with Dirty Faces* (1938).
6. American movie actor (1899–1983); in *Angels with Dirty Faces*, he played a priest who was a criminal as a child.

HENRY: Murder?

SGT. SMITH: Yeah, murder. Another greaser named José Williams.

HENRY: I never heard of the bato.

SGT. SMITH: Yeah, sure.

LT. EDWARDS: I've been looking at your record, Hank. Petty theft, assault, burglary, and now murder. Is that what you want? The gas chamber? Play square with me. Give me a statement as to what happened at the Lagoon, and I'll go to bat for you with the Navy. I promise you.

PACHUCO: If that ain't a line of gabacho bullshit, I don't know what is.

LT. EDWARDS: Well?

PACHUCO: Spit in his pinche face.

SGT. SMITH: Forget it, lieutenant. You can't treat these animals like people.

LT. EDWARDS: Shut up! I'm thinking of your family, Hank. Your old man would be proud to see you in the Navy. One last chance, son. What do you say?

HENRY: I ain't your son, cop.

LT. EDWARDS: All right, Reyna, have it your way. [EDWARDS and PRESS exit.]

PACHUCO: You don't deserve it, ése, but you're going to get it anyway.

SGT. SMITH: All right, muchacho, it's just me and you now. I hear you pachucos wear these monkey suits as a kind of armor. Is that right? How's it work? This is what you zooters need—a little old-fashioned discipline.

HENRY: Screw you, flatfoot.

SGT. SMITH: You greasy son of a bitch. What happened at the Sleepy Lagoon? Talk! Talk! Talk! [SMITH beats HENRY with a rubber sap.[7] HENRY passes out and falls to the floor, with his hands still handcuffed behind his back. DOLORES, his mother, appears in a spot upstage as he falls.]

DOLORES: Henry! [Lights change. Four PACHUCO COUPLES enter, dancing a 40's pasodoble (two-step) around HENRY on the floor, as they swing in a clothesline of newspaper sheets. Music.]

PACHUCO:
Get up and escape, Henry . . .
leave reality behind
with your buenas garras
muy chamberlain
escape through the barrio streets of your mind
through a neighborhood of memories
all chuckhole lined
and the love
and the pain
as fine as wine . . .

     [HENRY sits up, seeing his mother DOLORES folding newspaper sheets like clothes on a clothesline.]

DOLORES: Henry?

PACHUCO: It's a lifetime ago, last Saturday night . . . before Sleepy Lagoon and the big bad fight.

DOLORES: Henry!

---

7. Blackjack, a clublike weapon.

PACHUCO: Tu mamá, carnal. [HE *recedes into the background.*]

DOLORES: [*At the clothesline.*] Henry, ¿hijo? Ven a cenar.

HENRY: [*Gets up off the floor.*] Sorry, jefita, I'm not hungry. Besides, I got to pick up Della. We're late for the dance.

DOLORES: Dance? In this heat? Don't you muchachos ever think of anything else? God knows I suffer la pena negra seeing you go out every night.

HENRY: This isn't just any night, jefa. It's my last chance to use my tacuche.

DOLORES: ¿Tacuche? Pero tu padre . . .

HENRY: [*Revealing a stubborn streak.*] I know what mi 'apá said, 'amá. I'm going to wear it anyway.

DOLORES: [*Sighs, resigns herself.*] Mira, hijo. I know you work hard for your clothes. And I know how much they mean to you. Pero por Diosito santo, I just don't know what you see en esa cochinada de "soot zoot."

HENRY: [*Smiling.*] Drapes, 'amá, we call them drapes.

DOLORES: [*Scolding playfully.*] Ay sí, drapes, muy funny, ¿verdad? And what do the police call them, eh? They've put you in jail so many times. ¿Sabes qué? I'm going to send them all your clothes!

HENRY: A qué mi 'amá. Don't worry. By this time next week, I'll be wearing my Navy blues. Okay?

DOLORES: Bendito sea Dios. I still can't believe you're going off to war. I almost wish you were going back to jail.

HENRY: ¡Órale! [LUPE REYNA, 16, *enters dressed in a short skirt and baggy coat. She is followed by* DELLA BARRIOS, 17, *dressed more modestly.* LUPE *hides behind a newspaper sheet on the line.*]

LUPE: Hank! Let's go, carnal. Della's here.

HENRY: Della . . . Órale, ésa. What are you doing here? I told you I was going to pick you up at your house.

DELLA: You know how my father gets.

HENRY: What happened?

DELLA: He treats me like a nun sometimes.

DOLORES: Della, hija, buenas noches. How pretty you look.

DELLA: Buenas noches. [DOLORES *hugs* DELLA, *then spots* LUPE *hiding behind the clothesline.*]

DOLORES: [*To* LUPE.] Oye y ¿tú? What's wrong with you? What are you doing back there.

LUPE: Nothing, 'amá.

DOLORES: Well, come out then.

LUPE: We're late, 'amá.

DOLORES: Come out, te digo. [LUPE *comes out exposing her extremely short skirt.* DOLORES *gasps.*] ¡Válgame Dios! Guadalupe, are you crazy? Why bother to wear anything?

LUPE: Ay, 'amá, it's the style. Short skirt and fingertip coat. Huh, Hank?

HENRY: Uh, yeah, 'amá.

DOLORES: ¿Oh sí? And how come Della doesn't get to wear the same style?

HENRY: No . . . that's different. No, chale.

ENRIQUE: [*Off.*] ¡Vieja!

DOLORES:    Ándale. Go change before your father sees you.

ENRIQUE:    I'm home. [*Coming into the scene.*] Buenas noches, everybody. [*All respond.* ENRIQUE *sees* LUPE.] ¡Ay, jijo! Where's the skirt?!

LUPE:    It's here.

ENRIQUE:    Where's the rest of it?

DOLORES:    She's going to the dance.

ENRIQUE:    ¿Y a mí qué me importa? Go and change those clothes. Ándalè.

LUPE:    Please, 'apá?

ENRIQUE:    No, señorita.

LUPE:    Chihuahua, I don't want to look like a square.

ENRIQUE:    ¡Te digo que no! I will not have my daughter looking like a . . .

DOLORES:    Like a puta . . . I mean, a pachuca.

LUPE: [*Pleading for help.*]    Hank . . .

HENRY:    Do what they say, sis.

LUPE:    But you let Henry wear his drapes.

ENRIQUE:    That's different. He's a man. Es hombre.

DOLORES:    Sí, that's different. You men are all alike. From such a stick, such a splinter. De tal palo, tal astillota.

ENRIQUE:    Natural, muy natural, and look how he came out. ¡Bien macho! Like his father. ¿Verdad, m'ijo?

HENRY:    If you say so, jefito.

ENRIQUE: [*To* DELLA.]    Buenas noches.

DELLA:    Buenas noches.

HENRY:    'Apá, this is Della Barrios.

ENRIQUE:    Mira, mira . . . So this is your new girlfriend, eh? Muy bonita. Quite a change from the last one.

DOLORES:    Ay, señor.

ENRIQUE:    It's true. What was her name?

DELLA:    Bertha?

ENRIQUE:    That's the one. The one with the tattoo.

DOLORES:    Este hombre. We have company.

ENRIQUE:    That reminds me. I invited the compadres to the house mañana.

DOLORES:    ¿Que qué?

ENRIQUE:    I'm buying a big keg of cerveza to go along with the menudo.

DOLORES:    Oye, ¿cuál menudo?

ENRIQUE: [*Cutting him off.*]    ¡Qué caray, mujer! It isn't every day a man's son goes off to fight for his country. I should know. Della, m'ija, when I was in the Mexican Revolution, I was not even as old as my son is.

DOLORES:    N'ombre, don't start with your revolution. We'll be here all night.

HENRY:    Yeah, jefe, we've got to go.

LUPE: [*Comes forward. She has rolled down her skirt.*]    'Apá, is this better?

ENRIQUE:    Bueno. And you leave it that way.

HENRY:    Órale, pues. It's getting late. Where's Rudy?

LUPE:    He's still getting ready. Rudy! [RUDY REYNA, 19, *comes downstage in an old suit made into a tacuche.*]

RUDY:    Let's go, everybody. I'm ready.

ENRIQUE:   Oye, oye, ¿y tú? What are you doing with my coat?

RUDY:   It's my tacuche, 'apá.

ENRIQUE:   ¡Me lleva la chingada!

DOLORES:   Enrique . . . ¡por el amor de Dios!

ENRIQUE: [*To* HENRY.]   You see what you're doing? First that one and now this one. [*To* RUDY.] Hijo, don't go out like that. Por favor. You look like an idiot, pendejo.

RUDY:   Órale, Hank. Don't I look all right?

HENRY:   Nel, ése, you look fine. Watcha. Once I leave for the service, you can have my tachuche. Then you can really be in style. ¿Cómo la ves?

RUDY:   Chale. Thanks, carnal, but if I don't join the service myself, I'm gonna get my own tacuche.

HENRY:   You sure? I'm not going to need it where I'm going. ¿Tú sabes?

RUDY:   Are you serious?

HENRY:   Simón.

RUDY:   I'll think about it.

HENRY:   Pos, no hay pedo, ése.

ENRIQUE:   ¿Cómo que pedo? ¿Nel? ¿Simón? Since when did we stop speaking Spanish in this house? Have you no respect?

DOLORES:   Muchachos, muchachos, go to your dance. [HENRY *starts upstage.*]

ENRIQUE:   When I was your age, I had to kiss my father's hand.

HENRY:   Buenas noches . . . [ENRIQUE *holds out his hand.* HENRY *stops, looks, and then returns to kiss his father's hand. Then* HE *moves to kiss his* MOTHER *and* RUDY *licks* ENRIQUE's *hand.*]

ENRIQUE:   ¡Ah, jijo!

HENRY:   Órale, we'd better get going . . . [General *"goodbyes" from everybody.*]

ENRIQUE: [*As* RUDY *goes past him.*]   Henry! Don't let your brother drink beer.

RUDY:   Ay, 'apá. I can take care of myself.

DOLORES:   I'll believe that when I see it. [SHE *kisses him on the nose.*]

LUPE:   Ahí to watcho, 'amá.

ENRIQUE:   ¿Que qué?

LUPE:   I mean, I'll see you later. [HENRY, DELLA, LUPE *and* RUDY *turn upstage. Music starts.*]

ENRIQUE:   Mujer, why didn't you let me talk?

DOLORES: [*Sighing.*]   Talk, señor, talk all you want. I'm listening. [ENRIQUE *and* DOLORES *exit up right.* RUDY *and* LUPE *exit up left. Lights change. We hear hot dance music.* HENRY *and* DELLA *dance at center stage.* EL PACHUCO *sings.*]

PACHUCO:

CADA SÁBADO EN LA NOCHE
YO ME VOY A BORLOTEAR
CON MI LINDA PACHUCONA
LAS CADERAS A MENEAR

ELLA LE HACE MUY DE AQUÉLLAS
CUANDO EMPIEZA A GUARACHAR

AL COMPÁS DE LOS TIMBALES
YO ME SIENTO PETATEAR[8]

[*From upstage right, three pachucos now enter in a line, moving to the beat. They are* JOEY CASTRO, *17;* SMILEY TORRES, *23; and* TOMMY ROBERTS, *19, Anglo. They all come downstage left in a diagonal.*]

LOS CHUCOS SUAVES BAILAN RUMBA
BAILAN LA RUMBA Y LE ZUMBAN
BAILAN GUARACHA SABROSÓN
EL BOTECITO Y EL DANZÓN![9]

[*Chorus repeats, the music fades.* HENRY *laughs and happily embraces* DELLA.]

### 5. THE PRESS

*Lights change.* EL PACHUCO *escorts* DELLA *off right.* THE PRESS *appears at upstage center.*

PRESS: *Los Angeles Times:* August 8, 1942.
[*A* NEWSBOY *enters, lugging in two more bundles of newspapers, hawking them as he goes.* PEOPLE *of various walks of life enter at intervals and buy newspapers. They arrange themselves in the background reading.*]
NEWSBOY: EXTRA! EXTRAAA! READ ALL ABOUT IT. SPECIAL SESSION OF L.A. COUNTY GRAND JURY CONVENES. D.A. CHARGES CONSPIRACY IN SLEEPY LAGOON MURDER. EXTRAAA! [*A* CUB REPORTER *emerges and goes to the* PRESS, *as* LIEUTENANT EDWARDS *enters.*]
CUB REPORTER: Hey, here comes Edwards! [EDWARDS *is besieged by the* PRESS, *joined by* ALICE BLOOMFIELD, *26, a woman reporter.*]
PRESS: How about it, lieutenant? What's the real scoop on the Sleepy Lagoon? Sex, violence . . .
CUB REPORTER: Marijuana?
NEWSBOY: Read all about it! Mexican Crime Wave Engulfs L.A.
LT. EDWARDS: Slums breed crime, fellas. That's your story.
ALICE: Lieutenant, what exactly is the Sleepy Lagoon?
CUB REPORTER: A great tune by Harry James,[1] doll. Wanna dance? [ALICE *ignores the* CUB.]
LT. EDWARDS: It's a reservoir. An old abandoned gravel pit, really. It's on a ranch between here and Long Beach. Serves as a swimming hole for the younger Mexican kids.
ALICE: Because they're not allowed to swim in the public plunges?
PRESS: What paper are you with, lady? *The Daily Worker?*[2]

8. These lyrics are for a rumba, a ballroom dance of Cuban origin. They can be translated as "Each Saturday night, I go dancing with my beautiful pachuca girl. We move our asses rhythmically. She's legendary in her movement when she starts to dance, following the timba beats, and I feel I'm about to die."
9. "Cool pachucos dance the rhumba, they dance the rumba and get the beat, they dance the guara-cha with delight, the botecito and the danzón." *Guaracha*: a style of fast-paced Cuban dance music. *Botecito*: the title of a cumbia, an often fast-paced Colombian and Panamanian folk dance. *Danzón*: a Cuban dance.
1. American trumpeter and bandleader (1916–1983).
2. A newspaper published in New York by the Communist Party USA.

LT. EDWARDS: It also doubles as a sort of lovers' lane at night, which is why the gangs fight over it. Now they've finally murdered somebody.

NEWSBOY: EXTRA! EXTRA! ZOOT-SUITED GOONS OF SLEEPY LAGOON!

LT. EDWARDS: But we're not going to mollycoddle these youngsters any more. And you can quote me on that.

PRESS: One final question, lieutenant. What about the 38th Street Gang— weren't you the first to arrest Henry Reyna?

LT. EDWARDS: I was. And I noticed right away the kid had great leadership potential. However . . .

PRESS: Yes?

LT. EDWARDS: You can't change the spots on a leopard.

PRESS: Thank you, sir. [PEOPLE *with newspapers crush them and throw them down as they exit.* EDWARDS *turns and exits.* ALICE *turns towards* HENRY *for a moment.*]

NEWSBOY: EXTRA, EXTRA. READ ALL ABOUT THE MEXICAN BABY GANGSTERS. EXTRA! EXTRA!

[THE PRESS *and* CUB REPORTER *rush out happily to file their stories. The* NEWSBOY *leaves, hawking his papers.* ALICE *exits, with determination. Far upstage,* ENRIQUE *enters with a rolling garbage can.* HE *is a street sweeper. During the next scene* HE *silently sweeps up the newspapers, pausing at the last to read one of the news stories.*]

### 6. THE PEOPLE'S LAWYER

JOEY: ¡Chale, ése, chale! Qué pinche agüite.

SMILEY: Mexican Baby Gangsters?!

TOMMY: Zoot-suited goons! I knew it was coming. Every time the D.A. farts, they throw us in the can.

SMILEY: Pos, qué chingados, Hank. I can't believe this. Are they really going to pin us with a murder rap? I've got a wife and kid, man!

JOEY: Well, there's one good thing anyway. I bet you know that we've made the headlines. Everybody knows we got the toughest gang in town.

TOMMY: Listen to this, pip squeak. The biggest heist he ever pulled was a Tootsie Roll.

JOEY: [*Grabbing his privates.*] Here's your Tootsie Roll, ése.

TOMMY: What, that? Get my microscope, Smiley.

JOEY: Why don't you come here and take a little bite, joto.

TOMMY: Joto? Who you calling a joto, maricón?

JOEY: You, white boy. Did I ever tell you, you got the finest little duck ass in the world.

TOMMY: No, you didn't tell me that, culero. [JOEY *and* TOMMY *start sparring.*]

SMILEY: [*Furious.*] Why don't you batos knock it off?

HENRY: [*Cool.*] Cálmenla.

SMILEY: ¡Pinches chavalos! [*The batos stop.*]

JOEY: We're just cabuliando, ése.

TOMMY: Simón, ése. Horsing around. [HE *gives* JOEY *a final punch.*]

SMILEY: [*With deep self-pity.*] I'm getting too old for this pedo, Hank. All this farting around con esos chavalillos.

HENRY:   Relax, carnal. No to agüites.

SMILEY:   You and me have been through a lot, Hank. Parties, chingazos, jail. When you said let's join the pachucada, I joined the pachucada. You and me started the 38th, bato. I followed you even after my kid was born, but what now, carnal? This pinche pedo is serious.

TOMMY:   He's right, Hank. They indicted the whole gang.

JOEY:   Yeah, you know the only one who ain't here is Rudy [HENRY *turns sharply.*] He was at the Sleepy Lagoon too, ése Throwing chingazos.

HENRY:   Yeah, but the cops don't know that, do they? Unless one of us turned stoolie.

JOEY:   Hey, ése, don't look at me. They beat the shit out of me, but that's all they got. Shit.

TOMMY:   That's all you got to give. [*Laughs.*]

HENRY:   Okay! Let's keep it that way. I don't want my carnalillo pulled into this. And if anybody asks about him, you batos don't know nothing. You get me?

SMILEY:   Simón.

TOMMY:   Crazy.

JOEY: [*Throwing his palms out.*]   Say, Jackson, I'm cool. You know that.

HENRY:   There's not a single paddy we can trust.

TOMMY:   Hey, ése, what about me?

HENRY:   You know what I mean.

TOMMY:   No, I don't know what you mean. I'm here with the rest of you.

JOEY:   Yeah, but you'll be the first one out, cabrón.

TOMMY:   Gimme a break, maniaco. ¡Yo soy pachuco!

HENRY:   Relax, ése. Nobody's getting personal with you. Don't I let you take out my carnala? Well, don't I?

TOMMY:   Simón.

HENRY:   That's because you respect my family. The rest of them paddies are after our ass.

PACHUCO:   Talk about paddies, ése, you got company. [GEORGE SHEARER *enters upstage right and comes down.* HE *is a middle-aged lawyer, strong and athletic, but with the slightly frazzled look of a people's lawyer.*]

GEORGE:   Hi, boys.

HENRY:   Trucha!

GEORGE:   My name is George Shearer. I've been retained by your parents to handle your case. Can we sit and talk for a little bit?
[*Pause. The* BOYS *eye* GEORGE *suspiciously.* HE *slides a newspaper bundle a few feet upstage.*]

PACHUCO:   Better check him out, ése. He looks like a cop.

HENRY: [*To the* GUYS, *sotto voce.*]   Pónganse al alba. Éste me huele a chota.

GEORGE:   What was that? Did you say I could sit down? Thank you. [HE *pulls a bundle upstage.* HE *sits.*] Okay, let me get your names straight first. Who's José Castro?

JOEY:   Right here, ése. What do you want to know?

GEORGE:   We'll get to that. Ismael Torres?

SMILEY: [*Deadpan.*]   That's me. But they call me Smiley.

GEORGE: [*A wide grin.*]   Smiley? I see. You must be Thomas Roberts.

TOMMY:   I ain't Zoot Suit Yokum.

GEORGE:   Which means you must be Henry Reyna.

HENRY: What if I am. Who are you?

GEORGE: I already told you, my name's George Shearer. Your parents asked me to come.

HENRY: Oh yeah? Where did they get the money for a lawyer?

GEORGE: I'm a People's Lawyer, Henry.

SMILEY: People's Lawyer?

JOEY: Simón, we're people.

TOMMY: At least they didn't send no animal's lawyer.

HENRY: So what does that mean? You doing this for free or what?

GEORGE: [*Surprise turning to amusement.*] I try not to work for free, if I can help it, but I do sometimes. In this case, I expect to be paid for my services.

HENRY: So who's paying you? For what? And how much?

GEORGE: Hey, hey, hold on there. I'm supposed to ask the questions. You're the one going on trial, not me.

PACHUCO: Don't let him throw you, ése.

GEORGE: I sat in on part of the Grand Jury. It was quite a farce, wasn't it? Murder one indictment and all.

SMILEY: You think we stand a chance?

GEORGE: There's always a chance, Smiley. That's what trials are for.

PACHUCO: He didn't answer your question, ése.

HENRY: You still didn't answer my question, mister. Who's paying you? And how much?

GEORGE: [*Getting slightly peeved.*] Well, Henry, it's really none of your damned business. [*The* BOYS *react.*] But for whatever it's worth, I'll tell you a little story. The first murder case I ever tried, and won incidentally, was for a Filipino. I was paid exactly three dollars and fifty cents plus a pack of Lucky Strike cigarettes, and a note for a thousand dollars—never redeemed. Does that answer your question?

HENRY: How do we know you're really a lawyer?

GEORGE: How do I know you're Henry Reyna? What do you really mean, son? Do you think I'm a cop?

HENRY: Maybe.

GEORGE: What are you trying to hide from the cops? Murder? [*The* BOYS *react.*] All right! Aside from your parents, I've been called into this case by a citizens committee that's forming in your behalf, Henry. In spite of evidence to the contrary, there are some people out there who don't want to see you get the shaft.

HENRY: ¿Sabes qué, mister? Don't do us any favors.

GEORGE: [*Starting to leave.*] All right, you want another lawyer? I'll talk to the Public Defender's office.

JOEY: [*Grabbing his briefcase.*] Hey, wait a minute, ése. Where are you going?

TOMMY: De cincho se le va a volar la tapa.

JOEY: Nel, este bolillo no sabe nada.

GEORGE: [*Exploding.*] All right, kids, cut the crap!

SMILEY: [*Grabs his briefcase and crosses to* HENRY] Let's give him a break, Hank. [SMILEY *hands the briefcase to* GEORGE.]

GEORGE: Thank you. [HE *starts to exit. Stops.*] You know, you're making a big mistake. I wonder if you know who your friends are. You boys are about to get a mass trial. You know what that is? Well, it's a new one on me too. The Grand Jury has indicted you all on the same identical crime. Not just you four. The whole so-called 38th Street Gang. And you know who the main target is? You, Henry, because they're saying you're the ringleader. [*Looks around at the* GUYS.] And I suppose you are. But you're leading your buddies here down a dead-end street. The D.A.'s coming after you, son, and he's going to put you and your whole gang right into the gas chamber. [GEORGE *turns to leave.* SMILEY *panics.* JOEY *and* TOMMY *react with him.*]

SMILEY/JOEY/TOMMY: [*All together.*]   Gas chamber! But we didn't do nothing! We're innocent!

HENRY:   ¡Cálmenla! [*The batos stop in their tracks.*] Okay. Say we believe you're a lawyer, what does that prove? The press has already tried and convicted us. Think you can change that?

GEORGE:   Probably not. But then, public opinion comes and goes, Henry. What matters is our system of justice. I believe it works, however slowly the wheels may grind. It could be a long uphill fight, fellas, but we can make it. I know we can. I've promised your parents the best defense I'm capable of. The question is, Henry, will you trust me?

HENRY:   Why should I? You're a gringo.

GEORGE: [*Calmly, deliberately*]   ¿Cómo sabes?

TOMMY: [*Shocked.*]   Hey, you speak Spanish?

GEORGE:   Más o menos.

JOEY:   You mean you understood us a while ago?

GEORGE:   More or less.

JOEY: [*Embarrassed.*]   ¡Híjole, qué gacho, ése!

GEORGE:   Don't worry. I'm not much on your pachuco slang. The problem seems to be that I look like an Anglo to you. What if I were to tell you that I had Spanish blood in my veins? That my roots go back to Spain, just like yours? What if I'm an Arab? What if I'm a Jew? What difference does it make? The question is, will you let me help you? [*Pause.* HENRY *glances at the* PACHUCO.]

PACHUCO:   ¡Chale!

HENRY: [*Pause.*]   Okay!

SMILEY:   Me too!

JOEY:   Same here!

TOMMY:   ¡Órale!

GEORGE: [*Eagerly.*]   Okay! Let's go to work. I want to know exactly what happened right from the beginning. [GEORGE *sits down and opens his briefcase.*]

HENRY:   Well, I think the pedo really started at the dance last Saturday night . . . [EL PACHUCO *snaps his fingers and we hear dance music. Lights change.* GEORGE *exits.*]


### 7. THE SATURDAY NIGHT DANCE

SWABBIE *and* MANCHUKA *come running onstage as the barrio dance begins to take shape.* HENRY *and the batos move upstage to join other* PACHUCOS *and* PACHUCAS *coming in.* HENRY *joins* DELLA BARRIOS; JOEY *teams up with* BERTHA VILLARREAL, TOMMY *picks up* LUPE REYNA; *and* SMILEY *escorts his wife,*

ELENA TORRES. *They represent the* 38TH STREET *neighborhood. Also entering the dance comes the* DOWNEY GANG, *looking mean.* RUDY *stands upstage, in the background, drinking a bottle of beer.* EL PACHUCO *sings.*

PACHUCO:
CUANDO SALGO YO A BAILAR
YO ME PONGO MUY CATRÍN
LAS BOLSITAS TODAS GRITAN, DADDY
VAMOS A BAILAR EL SWING![3]

[*The* COUPLES *dance. A lively swing number. The music comes to a natural break and shifts into a slow number.* BERTHA *approaches* HENRY *and* DELLA *downstage on the dance foor.*]

BERTHA: Ése, ¡surote! How about a dance for old time's sake? No te hagas gacho.
HENRY: [*Slow dancing with* DELLA.] Sorry, Bertha.
BERTHA: Is this your new huisa? This little fly chick?
DELLA: Listen, Bertha . . .
HENRY: [*Stops her.*] Chale. She's just jealous. Beat it, Bertha.
BERTHA: Beat it yourself. Mira. You got no hold on me, cabrón. Not any more. I'm as free as a bird.
SMILEY: [*Coming up.*] Ése, Hank, that's the Downey Gang in the corner. You think they're looking for trouble?
HENRY: There's only a couple of them.
BERTHA: That's all we need.
SMILEY: Want me to alert the batos?
HENRY: Nel, be cool.
BERTHA: Be cool? Huy, yu, yui. Forget it, Smiley. Since he joined the Navy, this bato forgot the difference between being cool and being cool-O.[4] [SHE *laughs and turns but* HENRY *grabs her angrily by the arm.* BERTHA *pulls free and walks away cool and tough. The music changes and the beat picks up.* EL PACHUCO *sings as the* COUPLES *dance.*]

PACHUCO:
CUANDO VOY AL VACILÓN
Y ME METO YO A UN SALÓN
LAS CHAVALAS GRITAN, PAPI VENTE
¡VAMOS A BAILAR DANZÓN![5]

[*The dance turns Latin. The music comes to another natural break and holds.* LUPE *approaches* HENRY *on the dance foor.*]

LUPE: Hank. Rudy's at it again. He's been drinking since we got here.
HENRY: [*Glancing over at* RUDY.] He's okay, sis, let the carnal enjoy himself.
RUDY: [*Staggering over.*] ¡Ése, carnal!
HENRY: What you say, brother?

---

3. "When I go out dancing, I become quite amazing. All the bag-carrying girls scream, 'Daddy, let's dance the swing!'" *Swing:* a group of dances generally related to the swing jazz music of the 1920s–50s.

4. Pun on *culo,* Spanish for butt or ass.
5. "When I go to a party and I enter a dancehall, the girls scream, 'Papi, come, let's dance a danzón!'"

RUDY: I'm flying high, Jackson. Feeling good.

LUPE: Rudy, if you go home drunk again, mi 'apá's going to use you for a punching bag. [RUDY *kisses her on the cheek and moves on.*]

DELLA: How are you feeling?

HENRY: Okay.

DELLA: Still thinking about Bertha?

HENRY: Chale, ¿qué traes? Listen, you want to go out to the Sleepy Lagoon? I've got something to tell you.

DELLA: What?

HENRY: Later, later.

LUPE: You better tell Rudy to stop drinking.

HENRY: Relax, sis. If he gets too drunk, I'll carry him home. [*Music picks up again.* EL PACHUCO *sings a third verse.*]

PACHUCO:

TOCAN MAMBO SABROSÓN
SE ALBOROTA EL CORAZÓN
Y CON UNA CHAVALONA VAMOS
VAMOS A BAILAR EL MAMBO[6]

[*The* COUPLES *do the mambo. In the background,* RUDY *gets into an argument with* RAFAS, *the leader of the* DOWNEY GANG. *A fight breaks out as the music comes to a natural break.* RAFAS *pushes* RUDY, *half drunk, onto the foor.*]

RAFAS: ¡Y a ti qué te importa, puto!

RUDY: [HE *falls.*] ¡Cabrón!

HENRY: [*Reacting immediately.*] Hey! [*The whole dance crowd tenses up immediately, splitting into separate camps. Batos from* 38TH *clearly outnumber the* GUYS *from* DOWNEY.]

RAFAS: He started it, ése. Él comenzó a chingar conmigo.

RUDY: You chicken shit, ése! Tú me haces la puñeta, ¡pirujo!

RAFAS: Come over here and say that, puto!

HENRY: [*Pulling* RUDY *behind him.*] ¡Agüítala, carnal! [*Faces* RAFAS.] You're a little out of your territory, ¿qué no Rafas?

RAFAS: It's a barrio dance, ése. We're from the barrio.

HENRY: You're from Downey.

RAFAS: Vale madre. ¡Downey Rifa!

DOWNEY GANG: ¡SIMÓN!

RAFAS: What are you going to do about it?

HENRY: I'm going to kick your ass. [*The* TWO SIDES *start to attack each other.*] ¡Cálmenla! [*All stop.*]

RAFAS: [*Pulls out a switchblade.*] You and how many batos?

HENRY: Just me and you, cabrón. That's my carnalillo you started pushing around, see? And nobody chinga con mi familia without answering to me, ése! Hank Reyna! [HE *pulls out another switchblade.*]

BERTHA: All-right!

---

6. "A wonderful mambo is played, making the heart go crazy. With a gorgeous girl we go to dance a mambo!" *Mambo:* a Cuban ballroom dance that resembles the rumba.

HENRY: Let's see if you can push me around like you did my little brother, ése. Come on . . . Come on! [*They knife fight.* HENRY *moves in fast. Recoiling,* RAFAS *falls to the foor.* HENRY's *blade is at his throat.* EL PACHUCO *snaps his fingers. Everyone freezes.*]

PACHUCO: Qué mamada, Hank. That's exactly what the play needs right now. Two more Mexicans killing each other. Watcha . . . Everybody's looking at you.

HENRY: [*Looks out at the audience.*] Don't give me that bullshit. Either I kill him or he kills me.

PACHUCO: That's exactly what they paid to see. Think about it. [EL PACHUCO *snaps again. Everybody unfreezes.*]

HENRY: [*Kicks* RAFAS.] Get out of here. ¡Píntate!

BERTHA: What?

GÜERA: [RAFAS' *girlfriend runs forward.*] Rafas. ¡Vámonos! [SHE *is stopped by other* DOWNEY *batos.*]

RAFAS: Está suave. I'll see you later.

HENRY: Whenever you want, cabrón. [*The* DOWNEY GANG *retreats, as the* 38TH *razzes them all the way out. Insults are exchanged.* BERTHA *shouts "¡Chinga te madre!" and they are gone. The* 38TH *whoops in victory.*]

SMILEY: Órale, you did it, ése! ¡Se escamaron todos!

TOMMY: We sure chased those jotos out of here.

BERTHA: I could have beat the shit out of those two rucas.

JOEY: That pinche Rafas is yellow without his gang, ése.

LUPE: So why didn't you jump out there?

JOEY: Chale, Rudy ain't my baby brother.

RUDY: [*Drunk.*] Who you calling a baby, pendejo? I'll show you who's a baby!

JOEY: Be cool, ése.

TOMMY: Man, you're lucky your brother was here.

BERTHA: Why? He didn't do nothing. The old Hank would have slit Rafas' belly like a fat pig.

HENRY: Shut your mouth, Bertha!

RUDY: ¿Por qué, carnal? You backed down, ése. I could have taken that sucker on by myself.

HENRY: That's enough, Rudy. You're drunk.

DELLA: Hank, what if Rafas comes back with all his gang?

HENRY: [*Reclaiming his leadership.*] We'll kill the sons of bitches.

JOEY: ¡Órale! ¡La 38th rifa! [*Music. Everybody gets back with furious energy.* EL PACHUCO *sings.*]

PACHUCO:

DE LOS BAILES QUE MENTÉ
Y EL BOLERO Y EL BEGUÍN
DE TODOS LOS BAILES JUNTOS
¡ME GUSTA BAILAR EL SWING! HEY![7]

[*The dance ends with a group exclamation: HEY!*]

---

7. "Of the dance rhythms I've listed, as well as the bolero and the beguín, among all of these, the one I like most is the swing—hey!" *Bolero:* a dramatic Spanish dance. *Beguín:* a Caribbean dance that resembles the rumba.

### 8. EL DÍA DE LA RAZA

*The* PRESS *enters upstage level, pushing a small hand truck piled high with newspaper bundles. The batos and rucas on the dance floor freeze in their final dance positions.* EL PACHUCO *is the only one who relaxes and moves.*

PRESS:   October 12, 1942: Columbus Day. Four Hundred and Fiftieth Anniversary of the Discovery of America.[8] Headlines!
> [*In their places, the* COUPLES *now stand straight and recite a headline before exiting. As they do so, the* PRESS *moves the bundles of newspapers on the floor to outline the four corners of a jail cell.*]

SMILEY/ELENA:   President Roosevelt[9] Salutes Good Neighbors in Latin America. [SMILEY *and* ELENA *exit.*]

TOMMY/LUPE:   British Begin Drive to Oust Rommel From North Africa. [TOMMY *and* LUPE *exit.*]

RUDY/CHOLO:   Japs in Death Grip on Pacific Isles. [RUDY *and* CHOLO *exit.* PRESS *tosses another bundle.*]

ZOOTER/LITTLE BLUE:   Web of Zoot Crime Spreads. [ZOOTER *and* LITTLE BLUE *exit.*]

MANCHUKA/SWABBIE:   U.S. Marines Land Bridgehead on Guadalcanal.[1] [MANCHUKA *and* SWABBIE *exit.*]

JOEY/BERTHA:   First Mexican Braceros Arrive in U.S.A. [JOEY *and* BERTHA *exit.*]

DELLA:   Sleepy Lagoon Murder Trial Opens Tomorrow. [DELLA *and the* PRESS *exit. As they exit,* GEORGE *and* ALICE *enter upstage left.* HENRY *is center, in a "cell" outlined by four newspaper bundles left by the* PRESS.]

GEORGE:   Henry? How you doing, son? Listen, I've brought somebody with me that wants very much to meet you. I thought you wouldn't mind. [ALICE *crosses to* HENRY.]

ALICE:   Hello! My name is Alice Bloomfield and I'm a reporter from the *Daily People's World*.[2]

GEORGE:   And . . . And, I might add, a red hot member of the ad hoc committee that's fighting for you guys.

ALICE:   Oh, George! I'd hardly call it fighting, for Pete's sake. This struggle has just barely begun. But we're sure going to win it, aren't we, Henry?

HENRY:   I doubt it.

GEORGE:   Oh come on, Henry. How about it, son? You all set for tomorrow? Anything you need, anything I can get for you?

HENRY:   Yeah. What about the clean clothes you promised me? I can't go to court looking like this.

GEORGE:   You mean they didn't give them to you?

HENRY:   What?

GEORGE:   Your mother dropped them off two days ago. Clean pants, shirt, socks, underwear, the works. I cleared it with the sheriff last week.

HENRY:   They haven't given me nothing.

GEORGE:   I'm beginning to smell something around here.

HENRY:   Look, George, I don't like being like this. I ain't dirty. Go do something, man!

---

8. I.e., of the first voyage from Spain to the New World, in 1492, of Christopher Columbus (1451–1506), Spanish admiral from Genoa.
9. Franklin Delano Roosevelt (1882–1945), U.S.

president 1933–45.
1. Island in the western Pacific.
2. A newspaper published in California by the Communist Party USA.

GEORGE:   Calm down. Take it easy, son. I'll check on it right now. Oh! Uh, Alice?

ALICE:   I'll be okay, George.

GEORGE:   I'll be right back. [HE *exits*.]

ALICE: [*Pulling out a pad and pencil*.]   Now that I have you all to myself, mind if I ask you a couple of questions?

HENRY:   I got nothing to say.

ALICE:   How do you know? I haven't asked you anything yet. Relax. I'm from the progressive press. Okay? [HENRY *stares at her, not quite knowing how to react.* ALICE *sits on a bundle and crosses her goodlooking legs.* HENRY *concentrates on that.*] Now. The regular press is saying the Pachuco Crime Wave is fascist inspired—any thoughts about that?

HENRY: [*Bluntly*.]   No.

ALICE:   What about the American Japanese? Is it true they are directing the subversive activities of the pachucos from inside the relocation camps?[3] [HENRY *turns to the* PACHUCO *with a questioning look*.]

PACHUCO:   This one's all yours, ése.

HENRY:   Look, lady, I don't know what the hell you're talking about.

ALICE:   I'm talking about you, Henry Reyna. And what the regular press has been saying. Are you aware you're in here just because some bigshot up in San Simeon[4] wants to sell more papers? It's true.

HENRY:   So?

ALICE:   So, he's the man who started this Pachuco Crime Wave stuff. Then the police got into the act. Get the picture? Somebody is using you as a patsy.

HENRY: [*His machismo insulted*.]   Who you calling a patsy?

ALICE:   I'm sorry, but it's true.

HENRY: [*Backing her up*.]   What makes you so goddamned smart?

ALICE: [*Starting to get scared and trying not to show it*.]   I'm a reporter. It's my business to know.

PACHUCO:   Puro pedo. She's just a dumb broad only good for you know what.

HENRY:   Look, Miss Bloomfield, just leave me alone, all right? [HENRY *moves away*. ALICE *takes a deep breath*.]

ALICE:   Look, let's back up and start all over, okay? Hello. My name is Alice Bloomfield, and I'm not a reporter. I'm just somebody that wants very much to be your friend. [*Pause. With sincere feeling*.] Can you believe that?

HENRY:   Why should I?

ALICE:   Because I'm with you.

HENRY:   Oh, yeah? Then how come you ain't in jail with me?

ALICE: [*Holding her head up*.]   We are all in jail, Henry. Some of us just don't know it.

PACHUCO:   Mmm, pues. No comment. [*Pause*. HENRY *stares at her, trying to figure her out*. ALICE *tries a softer approach*.]

---

3. In February 1942, President Roosevelt authorized the forcible relocation and internment of approximately 110,000 Japanese nationals and Japanese Americans, most of them on the West Coast.

4. Location, on the central California coast, of Hearst Castle, at that time the estate of the very powerful newspaper publisher William Randolph Hearst (1863–1951).

ALICE: Believe it or not, I was born in Los Angeles just like you. But for some strange reason I grew up here, not knowing very much about Mexicans at all. I'm just trying to learn.

HENRY: [*Intrigued, but cynical.*]  What?

ALICE: Little details. Like that tattooed cross on your hand. Is that the sign of the pachuco? [HENRY covers his right hand with an automatic reflex, then HE realizes what he has done.]

HENRY: [*Smiles to himself, embarrassed.*]  Órale.

ALICE: Did I embarrass you? I'm sorry. Your mother happened to mention it.

HENRY: [*Surprised.*]  My mother? You talked to my jefita?

ALICE: [*With enthusiasm.*] Yes! And your father and Lupe and Rudy. The whole family gave me a helluva interview. But your mother was sensational. I especially liked her story about the midnight raid. How the police rushed into your house with drawn guns, looking for you on some trumped up charge, and how your father told them you were already in jail . . . God, I would have paid to have seen the cops' faces.

HENRY: [*Hiding his sentiment.*]  Don't believe anything my jefa tells you. [*Then quickly.*] There's a lot she doesn't know. I'm no angel.

ALICE: I'll just bet you're not. But you have been taken in for suspicion a dozen times, kept in jail for a few days, then released for lack of evidence. And it's all stayed on your juvenile record.

HENRY: Yeah, well I ain't no punk, see.

ALICE: I know. You're an excellent mechanic. And you fix all the guys' cars. Well, at least you're not one of the lumpen proletariat.

HENRY: The lumpen what?

ALICE: Skip it. Let's just say you're a classic social victim.

HENRY: Bullshit.

ALICE: [*Pause. A serious question.*]  Are you saying you're guilty?

HENRY: Of what?

ALICE: The Sleepy Lagoon Murder.

HENRY: What if I am?

ALICE: Are you?

HENRY: [*Pause, a serious answer.*]  Chale. I've pulled a lot of shit in my time, but I didn't do that. [GEORGE re-enters flushed and angry, trying to conceal his frustration.]

GEORGE: Henry, I'm sorry, but dammit, something's coming off here, and the clothes have been withheld. I'll have to bring it up in court.

HENRY: In court?

GEORGE: They've left me no choice.

ALICE: What's going on?

HENRY: It's a set up, George. Another lousy set up!

GEORGE: It's just the beginning, son. Nobody said this was going to be a fair fight. Well, if they're going to fight dirty, so am I. Legally, but dirty. Trust me.

ALICE: [*Passionately.*]  Henry, no matter what happens in the trial, I want you to know I believe you're innocent. Remember that when you look out, and it looks like some sort of lynch mob. Some of us . . . a lot of us . . . are right there with you.

GEORGE: Okay, Alice, let's scram. I've got a million things to do. Henry, see you tomorrow under the big top, son. Good luck, son.

ALICE: Thumbs up, Henry, we're going to beat this rap! [ALICE *and* GEORGE *exit.* EL PACHUCO *watches them go, then turns to* HENRY.]
PACHUCO: "Thumbs up, Henry, we're going to beat this rap." You really think you're going to beat this one, ése?
HENRY: I don't want to think about it.
PACHUCO: You've got to think about it, Hank. Everybody's playing you for a sucker. Wake up, carnal!
HENRY: Look, bato, what the hell do you expect me to do?
PACHUCO: Hang tough. [*Grabs his scrotum.*] Stop going soft.
HENRY: Who's going soft?
PACHUCO: [*Incisively.*] You're hoping for something that isn't going to happen, ése. These paddies are leading you by the nose. Do you really believe you stand a chance?
HENRY: [*Stubborn all the more.*] Yeah. I think I got a chance.
PACHUCO: Just because that white broad says so?
HENRY: Nel, ése, just because Hank Reyna says so.
PACHUCO: The classic social victim, eh?
HENRY: [*Furious but keeping his cool.*] Mira, ése. Hank Reyna's no loser. I'm coming out of this on top. ¿Me entiendes, Mendez? [HE *walks away with a pachuco gait.*]
PACHUCO: [*Forcefully.*] Don't try to out-pachuco ME, ése! We'll see who comes out on top. [HE *picks up a bundle of newspapers and throws it upstage center. It lands with a thud.*] Let's go to court!

### 9. OPENING OF THE TRIAL

*Music. The* JUDGE's *bench, made up of more newpaper bundles piled squarely on a four-wheeled hand truck, is pushed in by the batos. The* PRESS *rides it in, holding the state and federal flags. A* BAILIFF *puts in place a hand cart: the* JUDGE's *throne.*

*Simultaneous with this set up,* EL PACHUCO *steps downstage, accompanied by* THREE PACHUCAS *who join him singing backup.* EL PACHUCO *lights a reefer and sings:*

PACHUCO:
MARI-MARI-JUANA
MARI-MARI-JUANA BOOGIE
MARI-MARI-JUANA
MARI-MARI-JUANA BOOGIE
MARI-MARI-JUANA
THAT'S MY BABY'S NAME

[HENRY *comes downstage, into a tight spot.*][5]

PUT ON YOUR DRAPES, ESE BATO
MAKE THOSE CALCOS SHINE
PUT ON YOUR DRAPES, ESE BATO

5. I.e., a spotlight focused tightly on him.

MAKE THOSE CALCOS SHINE
THEY'RE HOLDING COURT ON THE CORNER
IT'S MARIJUANA BOOGIETIME!

[MUSIC *continues under, as* PACHUCO *takes a hit on the joint.*]

PACHUCO: Still feeling patriotic, ése?

HENRY: [*Stubbornly.*] What do you mean? The trial hasn't even started.

PACHUCO: Let's cut the shit and get to the verdict, Hank. This is 1942. Or is it 1492?

HENRY: [*Suddenly fearful.*] You're doing this to me, bato.

PACHUCO: Something inside you craves the punishment, ése. The public humiliation. And the human sacrifice. Only there's no more pyramids,[6] carnal. Only the gas chamber.

HENRY: [*Panicking.*] But I didn't do it, ése. I didn't kill anybody! [HENRY's FAMILY *enters with* ALICE, DELLA *and* BERTHA. *Carrying their own folding chairs, they sit to one side.*]

PACHUCO:

I'VE GOT A WOMAN NAMED JUANA
JUANA, JUANA, JUANA
BUT ALL THE MEN SHE'S MADE LOVE TO
THEY CALL HER MARI-JUANA
MARI-MARI-JUANA
THAT'S MY BABY'S NAME!

[HENRY *turns and goes upstage, where he joins the batos in line, sitting on newspaper bundles. The* PRESS *enters.*]

PRESS: The largest mass trial in the history of Los Angeles County opens this morning in the Superior Court at ten A.M. The infamous Sleepy Lagoon Murder case involves sixty-six charges against twenty-two defendants, with seven lawyers pleading for the defense, two for the prosecution. The District Attorney estimates that over a hundred witnesses will be called and has sworn—I quote—"to put an end to Mexican baby gangsterism." End quote.

BAILIFF: [*Bangs a gavel on the bench.*] The Superior Court of the State of California. In and For the County of Los Angeles. Department forty-three. The honorable E.W. Charles, presiding. All rise! [JUDGE CHARLES *enters. All rise.* EL PACHUCO *squats. The* JUDGE *is played by the same actor that portrays* EDWARDS.]

JUDGE: Please be seated. [*All sit.* PACHUCO *stands.*] Call this case, bailiff.

BAILIFF: [*Reading from a sheet.*] The people of the State of California versus Henry Reyna, Ismael Torres, Thomas Roberts, Jose Castro and eighteen other . . . [*Slight hesitation.*] . . . Pa-coo-cos.

JUDGE: Is Counsel for the Defense present?

GEORGE: [*Rises.*] Yes, Your Honor.

JUDGE: Please proceed. [*Signals the* PRESS.]

PRESS: Your Honor . . .

---

6. I.e., where the Aztecs performed human sacrifice.

GEORGE: [*Moving in immediately.*]   If the Court please, it was reported to me on Friday that the District Attorney has absolutely forbidden the Sheriff's Office to permit these boys to have clean clothes or haircuts. Now, it's been three months since the boys were arrested . . .

PRESS: [*Jumping in.*]   Your Honor, there is testimony we expect to develop that the 38th Street Gang are characterized by their style of haircuts . . .

GEORGE:   Three months, Your Honor.

PRESS:   . . . the thick heavy heads of hair, the ducktail comb, the pachuco pants . . .

GEORGE:   Your Honor, I can only infer that the Prosecution . . . is trying to make these boys look disreputable, like mobsters.

PRESS:   Their appearance is distinctive, Your Honor. Essential to the case.

GEORGE:   You are trying to exploit the fact that these boys look foreign in appearance! Yet clothes like these are being worn by kids all over America.

PRESS:   Your Honor . . .

JUDGE: [*Bangs the gavel.*]   I don't believe we will have any difficulty if their clothing becomes dirty.

GEORGE:   What about the haircuts, Your Honor?

JUDGE: [*Ruling.*]   The zoot haircuts will be retained throughout the trial for purposes of identification of defendants by witnesses.

PACHUCO:   You hear that one, ése? Listen to it again. [*Snaps.* JUDGE *repeats automatically.*]

JUDGE:   The zoot haircuts will be retained throughout the trial for purposes of identification of defendants by witnesses.

PACHUCO:   He wants to be sure we know who you are.

JUDGE:   It has been brought to my attention the Jury is having trouble telling one boy from another, so I am going to rule the defendants stand each time their names are mentioned.

GEORGE:   I object. If the Prosecution makes an accusation, it will mean self-incrimination.

JUDGE: [*Pause.*]   Not necessarily. [*To* PRESS.] Please proceed.

GEORGE: [*Still trying to set the stage.*]   Then if the Court please, might I request that my clients be allowed to sit with me during the trial so that I might consult with them?

JUDGE:   Request denied.

GEORGE:   May I inquire of Your Honor, if the defendant Thomas Roberts might rise from his seat and walk over to counsel table so as to consult with me during the trial?

JUDGE:   I certainly will not permit it.

GEORGE:   You will not?

JUDGE:   No. This is a small courtroom, Mr. Shearer. We can't have twenty-two defendants all over the place.

GEORGE:   Then I object. On the grounds that that is a denial of the rights guaranteed all defendants by both the Federal and State constitutions.

JUDGE:   Well, that is your opinion. [*Gavel.*] Call your first witness.

PRESS:   The prosecution calls Lieutenant Sam Edwards of the Los Angeles Police Department.

PACHUCO: [*Snaps. Does double take on* JUDGE.] You know what. We've already heard from that bato. Let's get on with the defense. [*Snaps.* PRESS *sits.* GEORGE *stands.*]

GEORGE: The defense calls Adela Barrios.

BAILIFF: [*Calling out.*] Adeela Barreeos to the stand. [DELLA BARRIOS *comes forth out of the spectators.* BERTHA *leans forward.*]

BERTHA: [*Among the spectators.*] Don't tell 'em nothing. [*The* BAILIFF *swears in* DELLA *silently.*]

PACHUCO: Look at your gang. They do look like mobsters. Se watchan bien gachos. [HENRY *looks at the batos, who are sprawled out in their places.*]

HENRY: [*Under his breath.*] Come on, Batos, sit up.

SMILEY: We're tired, Hank.

JOEY: My butt is sore.

TOMMY: Yeah, look at the soft chairs the jury's got.

HENRY: What did you expect? They're trying to make us look bad. Come on! Straighten up.

SMILEY: Simón, batos, Hank is right.

JOEY: ¡Más alba, nalga!

TOMMY: Put some class on your ass.

HENRY: Sit up! [*They all sit up.*]

GEORGE: State your name please.

DELLA: Adela Barrios. [*She sits.*]

GEORGE: Miss Barrios, were you with Henry Reyna on the night of August 1, 1942?

DELLA: Yes.

JUDGE: [*To* HENRY.] Please stand. [HENRY *stands.*]

GEORGE: Please tell the court what transpired that night.

DELLA: [*Pause. Takes a breath.*] Well, after the dance that Saturday night, Henry and I drove out to the Sleepy Lagoon about eleven-thirty.

### 10. SLEEPY LAGOON

*Music: "The Harry James theme."* EL PACHUCO *creates the scene. The light changes. We see a shimmering pattern of light on the floor growing to the music. It becomes the image of the Lagoon. As the music soars to a trumpet solo,* HENRY *reaches out to* DELLA, *and* SHE *glides to her feet.*

DELLA: There was a full moon that night, and as we drove up to the Lagoon we noticed right away the place was empty . . . [*A pair of headlights silently pulls in from the black background upstage center.*] Henry parked the car on the bank of the reservoir and we relaxed. [*Headlights go off.*] It was such a warm, beautiful night, and the sky was so full of stars, we couldn't just sit in the car. So we got out, and Henry took my hand . . . [HENRY *stands and takes* DELLA's *hand.*] We went for a walk around the Lagoon. Neither of us said anything at first, so the only sounds we could hear were the crickets and the frogs . . . [*Sounds of crickets and frogs, then music faintly in the background.*] When we got to the other side of the reservoir, we began to hear music, so I asked Henry, what's that?

HENRY: Sounds like they're having a party.

DELLA: Where?

HENRY: Over at the Williams' Ranch. See the house lights.

DELLA: Who lives there?

HENRY: A couple of families. Mexicanos. I think they work on the ranch. You know, their name used to be González, but they changed it to Williams.

DELLA: Why?

HENRY: I don't know. Maybe they think it gives 'em more class. [*We hear Mexican music.*] Ay, jijo. They're probably celebrating a wedding or something.

DELLA: As soon as he said wedding, he stopped talking and we both knew why. He had something on his mind, something he was trying to tell me without sounding like a square.

HENRY: Della . . . what are you going to do if I don't come back from the war?

DELLA: That wasn't the question I was expecting, so I answered something dumb, like I don't know, what's going to keep you from coming back?

HENRY: Maybe wanting too much out of life, see? Ever since I was a kid, I've had this feeling like there's a big party going on someplace, and I'm invited, but I don't know how to get there. And I want to get there so bad, I'll even risk my life to make it. Sounds crazy, huh? [DELLA *and* HENRY *kiss. They embrace and then* HENRY *speaks haltingly.*] If I get back from the war . . . will you marry me?

DELLA: Yes! [SHE *embraces him and almost causes them to topple over.*]

HENRY: ¡Órale! You'll knock us into the Lagoon. Listen, what about your old man? He ain't going to like you marrying me.

DELLA: I know. But I don't care. I'll go to hell with you if you want me to.

HENRY: ¿Sabes qué? I'm going to give you the biggest Pachuco wedding L.A. has ever seen. [*Another pair of headlights comes in from the left.* DELLA *goes back to her narration.*]

DELLA: Just then another car pulled up to the Lagoon. It was Rafas and some drunk guys in a gang from Downey. They got out and started to bust the windows on Henry's car. Henry yelled at them, and they started cussing at us. I told Henry not to say anything, but he cussed them back!

HENRY: You stay here, Della.

DELLA: Henry, no! Don't go down there! Please don't go down there!

HENRY: Can't you hear what they're doing to my car?

DELLA: There's too many of them. They'll kill you!

HENRY: ¡Chale! [HENRY *turns and runs upstage, where* HE *stops in a freeze.*]

DELLA: Henry! Henry ran down the back of the Lagoon and attacked the gang by himself. Rafas had about ten guys with him and they jumped on Henry like a pack of dogs. He fought them off as long as he could, then they threw him on the ground hard and kicked him until he passed out . . . [*Headlights pull off.*] After they left, I ran down to Henry and held him in my arms until he came to. And I could tell he was hurt, but the first thing he said was . . .

PACHUCO: Let's go into town and get the guys. [*Music: Glenn Miller's*[7] *"In the Mood."* HENRY *turns to the batos and they stand.* SMILEY, JOEY *and*

---

7. American jazz/swing musician, composer, and bandleader (1904–1944).

TOMMY *are joined by* RUDY, BERTHA, LUPE *and* ELENA, *who enter from the side. They turn downstage in a body and freeze.*]

DELLA:   It took us about an hour to go into town and come back. We got to the Lagoon with about eight cars, but the Downey gang wasn't there.

JOEY:   Órale, ?pos qué pasó? Nobody here.

SMILEY:   Then let's go to Downey.

THE BOYS:   [*Ad lib.*]   Let's go!

HENRY:   ¡Chale! ¡Chale! [*Pause. They all stop.*] Ya estuvo. Everybody go home. [*A collective groan from* THE BOYS.] Go home!

DELLA:   That's when we heard music coming from the Williams' Ranch again. We didn't know Rafas and his gang had been there too, causing trouble. So when Joey said . . .

JOEY:   Hey, there's a party! Bertha, let's crash it.

DELLA:   We all went there yelling and laughing. [*The group of batos turns upstage in a mimetic freeze.*] At the Williams' Ranch they saw us coming and thought we were the Downey Gang coming back again . . . They attacked us. [*The group now mimes a series of tableaus showing the fight.*] An old man ran out of the house with a kitchen knife and Henry had to hit him. Then a girl grabbed me by the hair and in a second everybody was fighting! People were grabbing sticks from the fence, bottles, anything! It all happened so fast, we didn't know what hit us, but Henry said let's go!

HENRY:   ¡Vámonos! Let's get out of here.

DELLA:   And we started to back off . . . Before we got to the cars, I saw something out of the corner of my eye . . . It was a guy. He was hitting a man on the ground with a big stick. [EL PACHUCO *mimes this action.*] Henry called to him, but he wouldn't stop. He wouldn't stop . . . He wouldn't stop . . . He wouldn't stop . . . [DELLA *in tears, holds* HENRY *in her arms. The batos and rucas start moving back to their places, quietly.*] Driving back in the car, everybody was quiet, like nothing had happened. We didn't know José Williams had died at the party that night and that the guys would be arrested the next day for murder. [HENRY *separates from her and goes back to stand in his place.* DELLA *resumes the witness stand.*]

## 11. THE CONCLUSION OF THE TRIAL

*Lights change back to courtroom, as* JUDGE CHARLES *bangs his gavel. Everyone is seated back in place.*

GEORGE:   Your witness.

PRESS:   [*Springing to the attack.*]   You say Henry Reyna hit the man with his fist. [*Indicates* HENRY *standing.*] Is this the Henry Reyna?

DELLA:   Yes. I mean, no. He's Henry, but he didn't . . .

PRESS:   Please be seated. [HENRY *sits.*] Now, after Henry Reyna hit the old man with his closed fist, is that when he pulled the knife?

DELLA:   The old man had the knife.

PRESS:   So Henry pulled one out, too?

GEORGE:   [*Rises.*]   Your Honor, I object to counsel leading the witness.

PRESS:   I am not leading the witness.

GEORGE: You are.

PRESS: I certainly am not.

GEORGE: Yes, you are.

JUDGE: I would suggest, Mr. Shearer, that you look up during the noon hour just what a leading question is?

GEORGE: If the Court please, I am going to assign that remark of Your Honor as misconduct.

JUDGE: [*To* PRESS.] Proceed. [GEORGE *crosses back to his chair.*]

PRESS: Where was Smiley Torres during all this? Is it not true that Smiley Torres grabbed a woman by the hair and kicked her to the ground? Will Smiley Torres please stand? [SMILEY *stands.*] Is this the man?

DELLA: Yes, it's Smiley, but he . . .

PRESS: Please be seated. [SMILEY *sits.* PRESS *picks up a two-by-four.*] Wasn't José Castro carrying a club of some kind?

GEORGE: [*On his feet again.*] Your Honor, I object! No such club was ever found. The Prosecution is implying that this two-by-four is associated with my client in some way.

PRESS: I'm not implying anything, Your Honor, I'm merely using this stick as an illustration.

JUDGE: Objection overruled.

PRESS: Will José Castro please stand? [JOEY *stands.*] Is this the man who was carrying a club? [DELLA *refuses to answer.*] Answer the question please.

DELLA: I refuse.

PRESS: You are under oath. You can't refuse.

JUDGE: Answer the question, young lady.

DELLA: I refuse.

PRESS: Is this the man you saw hitting another man with a two-by-four? Your Honor . . .

JUDGE: I order you to answer the question.

GEORGE: Your Honor, I object. The witness is obviously afraid her testimony will be manipulated by the Prosecution.

PRESS: May I remind the court that we have a signed confession from one José Castro taken while in jail . . .

GEORGE: I object. Those were not confessions! Those are statements. They are false and untrue, Your Honor, obtained through beatings and coercion of the defendants by the police!

JUDGE: I believe the technical term is admissions, Mr. Prosecutor. Objection sustained. [*Applause from spectators.*] At the next outburst, I will clear this courtroom. Go on, Mr. Prosecutor.

PRESS: Sit down please. [JOEY *sits.* GEORGE *goes back to his seat.*] Is Henry Reyna the leader of the 38th Street Gang? [HENRY *stands.*]

DELLA: Not in the sense that you mean.

PRESS: Did Henry Reyna, pachuco ringleader of the 38th Street Gang, willfully murder José Williams?

DELLA: No. They attacked us first.

PRESS: I didn't ask for your comment.

DELLA: But they did, they thought we were the Downey Gang.

PRESS: Just answer my questions.

DELLA: We were just defending ourselves so we could get out of there.

PRESS: Your Honor, will you instruct the witness to be cooperative?

JUDGE: I must caution you, young lady, answer the questions or I'll hold you in contempt.

PRESS: Was this the Henry Reyna who was carrying a three-foot lead pipe?

GEORGE: I object!

JUDGE: Overruled.

DELLA: No.

PRESS: Was it a two-foot lead pipe?

GEORGE: Objection!

JUDGE: Overruled.

DELLA: No!

PRESS: Did he kick a women to the ground?

DELLA: No, he was hurt from the beating.

PRESS: Sit down. [HENRY *sits.*] Did Tommy Roberts rip stakes from a fence and hit a man on the ground?

GEORGE: Objection!

JUDGE: Overruled.

DELLA: I never saw him do anything.

PRESS: Did Joey Castro have a gun?

GEORGE: Objection!

JUDGE: Overruled. [JOEY *stands.*]

PRESS: Sit down. [JOEY *sits.*] Did Henry Reyna have a blackjack in his hand? [HENRY *stands.*]

DELLA: No.

PRESS: A switchblade knife?

DELLA: No.

PRESS: A two-by-four?

DELLA: No.

PRESS: Did he run over to José Williams, hit him on the head and kill him?

DELLA: He could barely walk, how could he run to any place?

PRESS: [*Moving in for the kill.*] Did Smiley Torres? [*The batos stand and sit as their names are mentioned.*] Did Joey Castro? Did Tommy Roberts? Did Henry Reyna? Did Smiley Torres? Did Henry Reyna? Did Henry Reyna? Did Henry Reyna kill José Williams?!

DELLA: No, no, no!

GEORGE: [*On his feet again.*] Your Honor, I object! The Prosecution is pulling out objects from all over the place, none of which were found at Sleepy Lagoon, and none of which have been proven to be associated with my clients in any way.

JUDGE: Overruled.

GEORGE: If Your Honor please, I wish to make an assignment of misconduct!

JUDGE: We have only had one this morning. We might as well have another now.

GEORGE: You have it, Your Honor.

JUDGE: One more remark like that and I'll hold you in contempt. Quite frankly, Mr. Shearer, I am getting rather tired of your repeated useless objections.

GEORGE:  I have not made useless objections.

JUDGE:  I am sorry. Somebody is using ventriloquism. We have a Charlie McCarthy[8] using Mr. Shearer's voice.

GEORGE:  I am going to assign that remark of Your Honor as misconduct.

JUDGE:  Fine. I would feel rather bad if you did not make an assignment of misconduct at least three times every session. [*Gavel.*] Witness is excused. [DELLA *stands.*] However, I am going to remand her to the custody of the Ventura State School for Girls for a period of one year . . .

HENRY:  What?

JUDGE:  . . . to be held there as a juvenile ward of the State. Bailiff?

GEORGE:  If the court please . . . If the court please . . . [BAILIFF *crosses to* DELLA *and takes her off left.*]

JUDGE:  Court is in recess until tomorrow morning. [JUDGE *retires.* PRESS *exits.* HENRY *meets* GEORGE *halfway across center stage. The rest of the batos stand and stretch in the background.*]

GEORGE:  Now, Henry, I want you to listen to me, please. You've got to remember he's the judge, Hank. And this is his courtroom.

HENRY:  But he's making jokes, George, and we're getting screwed!

GEORGE:  I know. I can't blame you for being bitter, but believe me, we'll get him.

HENRY:  I thought you said we had a chance.

GEORGE: [*Passionately.*]  We do! This case is going to be won on appeal.

HENRY:  Appeal? You mean you already know we're going to lose?

PACHUCO:  So what's new?

GEORGE:  Don't you see, Henry, Judge Charles is hanging himself as we go. I've cited over a hundred separate cases of misconduct by the bench, and it's all gone into the record. Prejudicial error, denial of due process, inadmissible evidence, hearsay . . .

HENRY:  ¿Sabes qué, George? Don't tell me any more. [HENRY *turns.* ALICE *and* ENRIQUE *approach him.*]

ALICE:  Henry . . . ?

HENRY: [*Turns furiously*]  I don't want to hear it, Alice! [HENRY *sees* ENRIQUE, *but neither father nor son can think of anything to say.* HENRY *goes back upstage.*]

ALICE:  George, is there anything we can do?

GEORGE:  No. He's bitter, and he has a right to be. [JUDGE CHARLES *pounds his gavel. All go back to their places and sit.*]

JUDGE:  We'll now hear the Prosecution's concluding statement.

PRESS:  Your Honor, ladies and gentlemen of the jury. What you have before you is a dilemma of our times. The City of Los Angeles is caught in the midst of the biggest, most terrifying crime wave in its history. A crime wave that threatens to engulf the very foundations of our civic well-being. We are not only dealing with the violent death of one José Williams in a drunken barrio brawl. We are dealing with a threat and danger to our children, our families, our homes. Set these pachucos free, and you shall unleash the forces of anarchy and destruction in our society. Set these pachucos free and you will turn them into heroes. Others just like them must be watching us at this very moment. What

8. The famous dummy used by the American ventriloquist Edgar Bergen (1903–1978).

nefarious schemes can they be hatching in their twisted minds? Rape, drugs, assault, more violence? Who shall be their next innocent victim in some dark alleyway, on some lonely street? You? You? Your loved ones? No! Henry Reyna and his Latin juvenile cohorts are not heroes. They are criminals, and they must be stopped. The specific details of this murder are irrelevant before the overwhelming danger of the pachuco in our midst. I ask you to find these zoot-suited gangsters guilty of murder and to put them in the gas chamber where they belong. [*The* PRESS *sits down.* GEORGE *rises and takes center stage.*]

GEORGE:  Ladies and gentlemen of the jury, you have heard me object to the conduct of this trial. I have tried my best to defend what is most precious in our American society—a society now at war against the forces of racial intolerance and totalitarian injustice. The prosecution has not provided one witness that actually saw, with his own eyes, who actually murdered José Williams. These boys are not the Downey Gang, yet the evidence suggests that they were attacked because the people at the ranch thought they were. Henry Reyna and Della Barrios were victims of the same bunch. Yes, they might have been spoiling for a revenge—who wouldn't under the circumstances—but not with the intent to conspire to commit murder. So how did José Williams die? Was it an accident? Was it manslaughter? Was it murder? Perhaps we may never know. All the prosecution has been able to prove is that these boys wear long hair and zoot suits. And all the rest has been circumstantial evidence, hearsay and war hysteria. The prosecution has tried to lead you to believe that they are some kind of inhuman gangsters. Yet they are Americans. Find them guilty of anything more serious than a juvenile bout of fisticuffs, and you will condemn all American youth. Find them guilty of murder, and you will murder the spirit of racial justice in America. [GEORGE sits *down.*]

JUDGE:  The jury will retire to consider its verdict. [*The* PRESS *stands and starts to exit with the* BAILIFF. EL PACHUCO *snaps. All freeze.*]

PACHUCO:  Chale. Let's have it. [*Snaps again. The* PRESS *turns and comes back again.*]

JUDGE:  Has the jury reached a verdict?

PRESS:  We have, Your Honor.

JUDGE:  How say you?

PRESS:  We find the defendants guilty of murder in the first and second degrees.

JUDGE:  The defendants will rise. [*The batos come to their feet.*] Henry Reyna, José Castro, Thomas Roberts, Ismael Torres, and so forth. You have been tried by a jury of your peers and found guilty of murder in the first and second degrees. The Law prescribes the capital punishment for this offense. However, in view of your youth and in consideration of your families, it is hereby the judgement of this court that you be sentenced to life imprisonment . . .

RUDY:  No!

JUDGE:  . . . and sent to the State Penitentiary at San Quentin. Court adjourned. [*Gavel.* JUDGE *exits.* DOLORES, ENRIQUE *and family go to* HENRY. BERTHA *crosses to* JOEY; LUPE *goes to* TOMMY. ELENA *crosses to* SMILEY. GEORGE *and* ALICE *talk.*]

DOLORES:  ¡Hijo mío! ¡Hijo de mi alma! [BAILIFF *comes down with a pair of handcuffs.*]

BAILIFF:  Okay, boys. [HE *puts the cuffs on* HENRY. RUDY *comes* up.]

RUDY:  ¿Carnal? [HENRY *looks at the* BAILIFF, *who gives him a nod of permission to spend a moment with* RUDY. HENRY *embraces him with the cuffs on.* GEORGE *and* ALICE *approach.*]

GEORGE:  Henry? I can't pretend to know how you feel, son. I just want you to know that our fight has just begun.

ALICE:  We may have lost this decision, but we're going to appeal immediately. We're going to stand behind you until your name is absolutely clear. I swear it!

PACHUCO:  What the hell are they going to do, ése? They just sent you to prison for life. Once a Mexican goes in, he never comes out.

BAILIFF:  Boys? [*The* BOYS *exit with the* BAILIFF. *As they go* ENRIQUE *calls after them.*]

ENRIQUE: [*Holding back tears.*]  Hijo. Be a man, hijo. [*Then to his family.*] Vámonos . . . ¡Vámonos! [*The family leaves and* EL PACHUCO *slowly walks to center stage.*]

PACHUCO:  We're going to take a short break right now, so you can all go out and take a leak, smoke a frajo. Ahí los watcho. [HE *exits up center and the newspaper backdrop comes down.*]


## Act Two

### Prologue

*Lights up and* EL PACHUCO *emerges from the shadows. The newspaper drop is still down. Music.*

PACHUCO:
Watchamos pachucos
los batos
the dudes
street-corner warriors who fought and moved
like unknown soldiers in wars of their own
El pueblo de Los was the battle zone
from Sleepy Lagoon to the Zoot Suit wars
when Marines and Sailors made their scores
stomping like Nazis on East L.A. . . .
pero, ¿saben qué?
That's later in the play. Let's pick it up in prison.
We'll begin this scene inside the walls of San Quintín.


#### 1. SAN QUENTIN

*A bell rings as the drop rises.* HENRY, JOEY, SMILEY *and* TOMMY *enter accompanied by* GUARD.

GUARD:  All right, people, lock up. [BOYS *move downstage in four directions. They step into "cells" simply marked by shadows of bars on the floor in their separate places. Newspaper handcarts rest on the floor as cots. Sound of cell doors closing. The* GUARD *paces back and forth upstage level.*]

HENRY:

San Quentin, California
March 3, 1943
Dear Family:
Coming in from the yard in the evening, we are quickly locked up in our cells. Then the clank and locking of the doors leaves one with a rather empty feeling. You are standing up to the iron door, waiting for the guard to come along and take the count, listening as his footsteps fade away in the distance. By this time there is a tense stillness that seems to crawl over the cellblock. You realize you are alone, so all alone.

PACHUCO:    This all sounds rather tragic, doesn't it?

HENRY:    But here comes the guard again, and he calls out your number in a loud voice . . .

GUARD: [*Calls numbers;* BOYS *call name.*]    24-545

HENRY:    Reyna!

GUARD:    24-546

JOEY:    Castro!

GUARD:    24-547

TOMMY:    Roberts!

GUARD:    24-548

SMILEY:    Torres! [GUARD *passes through dropping letters and exits up left.*]

HENRY:    You jump to your feet, stooping to pick up the letter . . .

JOEY: [*Excited.*]    Or perhaps several letters . . .

TOMMY:    You are really excited as you take the letters from the envelope.

SMILEY:    The censor has already broken the seal when he reads it.

HENRY:    You make a mental observation to see if you recognize the handwriting on the envelope.

SMILEY: [*Anxious.*]    It's always nice to hear from home . . .

JOEY:    Or a close comrade . . .

TOMMY:    Friends that you know on the outside . . .

HENRY:    Or perhaps it's from a stranger. [*Pause. Spotlight at upstage center.* ALICE *walks in with casual clothes on. Her hair is in pigtails, and* SHE *wears a pair of drapes.* SHE *is cheerful.*]

### 2. THE LETTERS

ALICE:

Dear Boys,
Announcing the publication (mimeograph) of the *Appeal News,* your very own newsletter, to be sent to you twice a month for the purpose of keeping you reliably informed of everything—the progress of the Sleeping Lagoon Defense Committee (We have a name now) and, of course, the matter of your appeal.

Signed,
Your editor
Alice Bloomfield

[*Music. "Perdido" by Duke Ellington.* ALICE *steps down and sits on the lip of the upstage level. The* BOYS *start swinging the bat, dribbling the basketball, shadow-boxing and exercising.* ALICE *mimes typing movements and we hear the sounds of a typewriter. Music fades.* ALICE *rises.*]

ALICE:    The *Appeal News* Volume I, Number I.
  April 7, 1943.
  Boys,
  You can, you must, and you will help us on the outside by what you do on the inside. Don't forget, what you do affects others. You have no control over that. When the time comes, let us be proud to show the record.

Signed,
Your editor

[*Music up again. The* BOYS *go through their activities.* ALICE *moves downstage center and the music fades.*]

SMILEY:    [*Stepping toward her.*]
  April 10, 1943
  Dear Miss Bloomfield,
  I have discovered from my wife that you are conducting door-to-door fundraising campaigns in Los Angeles. She doesn't want to tell you, but she feels bad about doing such a thing. It's not our custom to go around the neighborhoods asking for money.
ALICE:    [*Turning toward* SMILEY.]
  Dear Smiley,
  Of course, I understand your feelings . . .
SMILEY: [*Adamant.*]    I don't want my wife going around begging.
ALICE:    It isn't begging—it's fund-raising.
SMILEY:    I don't care what you call it. If that's what it's going to take, count me out.
ALICE:    All right. I won't bother your wife if she really doesn't want me to. Okay? [SMILEY *looks at her and turns back to his upstage position. Music. The batos move again.* TOMMY *crosses to* ALICE. *Another fade.*]
TOMMY:
  April 18, 1943
  Dear Alice,
  Trying to find the words and expression to thank you for your efforts in behalf of myself and the rest of the batos makes me realize what a meager vocabulary I possess . . .
ALICE:
  Dear Tommy,
  Your vocabulary is just fine. Better than most.
TOMMY:    Most what?
ALICE:    People.
TOMMY: [*Glances at* HENRY.]    Uh, listen, Alice. I don't want to be treated any different than the rest of the batos, see? And don't expect me to talk to you like some square Anglo, some pinche gabacho. You just better find out what it means to be Chicano, and it better be pretty damn quick.

ALICE: Look, Tommy, I didn't . . .

TOMMY: I know what you're trying to do for us and that's reet,[9] see? Shit. Most paddies would probably like to see us locked up for good. I've been in jail a couple of times before, but never nothing this deep. Strange, ain't it, the trial in Los? I don't really know what happened or why. I don't give a shit what the papers said. We didn't do half the things I read about. I also know that I'm in here just because I hung around with Mexicans . . . or pachucos. Well, just remember this, Alicia . . . I grew up right alongside most of these batos, and I'm pachuco too. Simón, ésa, you better believe it! [*Music up. Movement.* TOMMY *returns to his position.* HENRY *stands.* ALICE *turns toward him, but* HE *walks over to* EL PACHUCO, *giving her his back.*]

JOEY: [*Stepping forward anxiously.*]
May 1, 1943
Dear Alice . . . Darling!
I can't help but spend my time thinking about you. How about sending us your retra—that is, your photograph? Even though Tommy would like one of Rita Hayworth[1]—he's always chasing Mexican skirts (Ha! Ha!)—I'd prefer to see your sweet face any day.

ALICE: [*Directly to him.*]
Dear Joey,
Thank you so much. I really appreciated receiving your letter.

JOEY: That's all reet, Grandma! You mind if I call you Grandma?

ALICE: Oh, no.

JOEY: Eres una ruca de aquéllas.

ALICE: I'm a what?

JOEY: Ruca. A fine chick.

ALICE: [*Pronounces the word.*] Ruca?

JOEY: De aquéllas. [*Makes a cool gesture, palms out at hip level.*]

ALICE: [*Imitating him.*] De aquéllas.

JOEY: All reet! You got it. [*Pause.*] P.S. Did you forget the photograph?

ALICE: [SHE *hands it to him.*]
Dearest Joey,
Of course not. Here it is, attached to a copy of the *Appeal News.* I'm afraid it's not exactly a pin-up.

JOEY: [*Kissing the photo.*] Alice, honey, you're a doll! [JOEY *shows the photo to* TOMMY *then* SMILEY, *who is curious enough to come into the circle.* ALICE *looks at* HENRY, *but* HE *continues to ignore her.*]

ALICE: [*Back at center.*] The *Appeal News,* Volume I, Number III
May 5, 1943
Dear Boys,
Feeling that el Cinco de Mayo is a very appropriate day—the CIO[2] radio program, "Our Daily Bread," is devoting the entire time this evening to a discussion of discrimination against Mexicans in general and against you guys in particular.

---

9. Slang for right or all right.
1. American actress (1918–1987); photographs of her were famous pinups in the 1940s.

2. The Congress of Industrial Organizations (1938–55), a federation of unions; it officially supported the Sleepy Lagoon case defendants.

[*Music up. The repartee between* ALICE *and the batos is now friendly and warm. Even* SMILEY *is smiling with* ALICE. *They check out her "drapes."*]

### 3. THE INCORRIGIBLE PACHUCO

HENRY *stands at downstage left, looks at the group, then decides to speak.*

HENRY:
May 17, 1943
Dear Miss Bloomfield,
I understand you're coming up to Q this weekend, and I would like to talk to you—in private. Can you arrange it? [*The batos turn away, taking a hint.*]

ALICE: [*Eagerly.*]   Yes, yes, I can. What can I do for you, Henry? [HENRY *and* ALICE *step forward each other.* EL PACHUCO *moves in.*]

HENRY:   For me? ¡Ni madre!

ALICE: [*Puzzled.*]   I don't understand.

HENRY:   I wanted you to be the first to know, Alice. I'm dropping out of the appeal.

ALICE: [*Unbelieving.*]   You're what?

HENRY:   I'm bailing out, ésa. Dropping out of the case, see?

ALICE:   Henry, you can't!

HENRY:   Why can't I?

ALICE:   Because you'll destroy our whole case! If we don't present a united front, how can we ask the public to support us?

HENRY:   That's your problem. I never asked for their support. Just count me out.

ALICE: [*Getting nervous, anxious.*]   Henry, please, think about what you're saying. If you drop out, the rest of the boys will probably go with you. How can you even think of dropping out of the appeal? What about George and all the people that have contributed their time and money in the past few months? You just can't quit on them!

HENRY:   Oh no? Just watch me.

ALICE:   If you felt this way, why didn't you tell me before?

HENRY:   Why didn't you ask me? You think you can just move in and defend anybody you feel like? When did I ever ask you to start a defense committee for me? Or a newspaper? Or a fundraising drive and all that other shit? I don't need defending, ésa. I can take care of myself.

ALICE:   But what about the trial, the sentence? They gave you life imprisonment.

HENRY:   It's my life!

ALICE:   Henry, honestly—are you kidding me?

HENRY:   You think so?

ALICE:   But you've seen me coming and going. Writing to you, speaking for you, traveling up and down the state. You must have known I was doing it for you. Nothing has come before my involvement, my attachment, my passion for this case. My boys have been everything to me.

HENRY:   My boys? My boys! What the hell are we—your personal property? Well, let me set you straight, lady, I ain't your boy.

ALICE: You know I never meant it that way.

HENRY: You think I haven't seen through your bullshit? Always so concerned. Come on, boys. Speak out, boys. Stand up for your people. Well, you leave my people out of this! Can't you understand that?

ALICE: No, I can't understand that.

HENRY: You're just using Mexicans to play politics.

ALICE: Henry, that's the worst thing anyone has ever said to me.

HENRY: Who are you going to help next—the Colored People?

ALICE: No, as a matter of fact, I've already helped the Colored People. What are you going to do next—go to the gas chamber?

HENRY: What the hell do you care?

ALICE: I don't!

HENRY: Then get the hell out of here!

ALICE: [*Furious.*]   You think you're the only one who doesn't want to be bothered? You ought to try working in the Sleepy Lagoon defense office for a few months. All the haggling, the petty arguments, the lack of cooperation. I've wanted to quit a thousand times. What the hell am I doing here? They're coming at me from all sides. "You're too sentimental and emotional about this, Alice. You're too cold hearted, Alice. You're collecting money and turning it over to the lawyers, while the families are going hungry. They're saying you can't be trusted because you're a Communist, because you're a Jew." Okay! If that's the way they feel about me, then to hell with them! I hate them too. I hate their language, I hate their enchiladas, and I hate their goddamned mariachi music! [*Pause. They look at each other.* HENRY *smiles, then* ALICE— *feeling foolish—and they both break out laughing.*]

HENRY: All right! Now you sound like you mean it.

ALICE: I do.

HENRY: Okay! Now we're talking straight.

ALICE: I guess I have been sounding like some square paddy chick. But, you haven't exactly been Mister Cool yourself . . . ése.

HENRY: So, let's say we're even Steven.

ALICE: Fair enough. What now?

HENRY: Why don't we bury the hatchet, you know what I mean?

ALICE: Can I tell George you'll go on with the appeal?

HENRY: Yeah. I know there's a lot of people out there who are willing and trying to help us. People who feel that our conviction was an injustice. People like George . . . and you. Well, the next time you see them, tell them Hank Reyna sends his thanks.

ALICE: Why don't you tell them?

HENRY: You getting wise with me again?

ALICE: If you write an article—and I know you can—we'll publish it in the *People's World*. What do you say?

PACHUCO: Article! Pos, who told you you could write, ése?

HENRY: [*Laughs.*]   Chale.

ALICE: I'm serious. Why don't you give it a try?

HENRY: I'll think about it. [*Pause.*] Listen, you think you and I could write each other . . . outside the newsletter?

ALICE: Sure.

HENRY: Then it's a deal. [*They shake hands.*]

ALICE: I'm glad we're going to be communicating. I think we're going to be very good friends. [ALICE *lifts her hands to* HENRY's *shoulder in a gesture of comradeship.* HENRY *follows her hand, putting his on top of hers.*]

HENRY: You think so?

ALICE: I know so.

GUARD: Time, miss.

ALICE: I gotta go. Think about the article, okay? [SHE *turns to the* BOYS.] I gotta go, boys.

JOEY: Goodbye, Grandma! Say hello to Bertha.

SMILEY: And to my wife!

TOMMY: Give my love to Lupe!

GUARD: Time!

ALICE: I've got to go. Goodbye, goodbye. [ALICE *exits, escorted by the* GUARD *upstage left. As* SHE *goes,* JOEY *calls after her.*]

JOEY: See you, Grandma.

TOMMY: [*Turning to* JOEY *and* SMILEY.] She loves me.

PACHUCO: Have you forgotten what happened at the trial? You think the Appeals Court is any different? Some paddy judge sitting in the same fat-ass judgment of your fate.

HENRY: Come on, ése, give me a break!

PACHUCO: One break, coming up! [HE *snaps his fingers. The* GUARD *blows his whistle.*]

GUARD: Rec time! [*The batos move upstage to the upper level. Music. The* BOYS *mime a game of handball against the backdrop. During the game,* GEORGE *enters at stage right and comes downstage carrying his briefcase. The* GUARD *blows a whistle and stops the game.*]

GUARD: Reyna, Castro, Roberts, Torres! You got a visitor.

### 4. MAJOR GEORGE

The BOYS *turn and see* GEORGE. *They come down enthusiastically.*

JOEY: ¡Óra-leh! ¡Ése, Cheer!

SMILEY: George!

GEORGE: Hi, guys! [*The* BOYS *shake his hand, pat him on the back.* HENRY *comes to him last.*] How are you all doing? You boys staying in shape?

JOEY: Ése, you're looking at the hero of the San Quentin athletic program. Right, batos? [HE *shadowboxes a little.*]

TOMMY: Ten rounds with a busted ankle.

JOEY: ¡Simón! And I won the bout, too. I'm the terror of the flyweights, ése. The killer fly!

TOMMY: They got us doing everything, Cheer. Baseball, basketball.

SMILEY: Watch repairing.

GEORGE: [*Impressed.*] Watch repairing?

SMILEY: I'm also learning to improve my English and arithmetic.

GEORGE: Warden Duffy has quite a program. I hear he's a good man?

JOEY: Simón, he's a good man. We've learned our lesson . . . Well, anyway, I've learned my lesson, boy. No more pachuquismo for me. Too many people depending on us to help out. The raza here in Los. The whole Southwest. Mexico, South America! Like you and Grandma say, this is the people's world. If you get us out of here, I figure the only thing I could do is become a union organizer. Or go into major league baseball.

GEORGE: Baseball?

JOEY: Simón, ése. You're looking at the first Mexican Babe Ruth.[3] Or maybe, "Babe Root." Root! You get it?

TOMMY: How about "Baby Zoot"?

JOEY: Solid, Jackson.

GEORGE: Babe Zooter!

JOEY: Solid tudee, that's all reet, ése.

GEORGE: What about you, Henry? What have you been doing?

HENRY: Time, George, I've been doing time.

TOMMY: Ain't it the truth?

SMILEY: Yeah, George! When you going to spring us out of here, ése?

HENRY: How's the appeal coming?

GEORGE: [Getting serious.]   Not bad. There's been a development I have to talk to you about. But other than that . . .

HENRY: Other than what?

SMILEY: [Pause.]   Bad news?

GEORGE: [Hedging.]   It all depends on how you look at it, Smiley. It really doesn't change anything. Work on the brief is going on practically day and night. The thing is, even with several lawyers on the case now, it'll still be several months before we file. I want to be honest about that.

HENRY: [Suspiciously.]   Is that the bad news?

GEORGE: Not exactly. Sit down, boys. [Pause. HE laughs to himself.] I really don't mean to make such a big deal out of this thing. Fact is I'm still not quite used to the idea myself. [Pause.] You see . . . I've been drafted.

JOEY: Drafted?

TOMMY: Into the Army?

SMILEY: You?

GEORGE: That's right. I'm off to war.

JOEY: But . . . you're old, Cheer.

HENRY: [A bitter edge.]   Why you, George? Why did they pick on you?

GEORGE: Well, Henry, I wouldn't say they "picked" on me. There's lots of men my age overseas. After all, it is war time and . . .

HENRY: And you're handling our appeal.

GEORGE: [Pause.]   We have other lawyers.

HENRY: But you're the one who knows the case!

GEORGE: [Pause.]   I knew you were going to take this hard. Believe me, Henry, my being drafted has nothing to do with your case. It's just a coincidence.

HENRY: Like our being in here for life is a coincidence?

GEORGE: No, that's another . . .

HENRY: Like our being hounded every goddam day of our life is a coincidence?

GEORGE: Henry . . . [HENRY turns away furiously. There is a pause.] It's useless anger, son, believe me. Actually, I'm quite flattered by your concern, but I'm hardly indispensable.

---

3. George Herman "Babe" Ruth (1895–1948), American baseball player.

HENRY: [*Deeply disturbed.*]   What the hell are you talking about, George?

GEORGE:   I'm talking about all the people trying to get you out. Hundreds, perhaps thousands. Alice and I aren't the only ones. We've got a heck of a fine team of lawyers working on the brief. With or without me, the appeal will be won. I promise you that.

HENRY:   It's no use, George.

GEORGE:   I realize all that sounds pretty unconvincing under the circumstances, but it's true.

HENRY:   Those bastard cops are never going to let us out of here. We're here for life and that's it.

GEORGE:   You really believe that?

HENRY:   What do you expect me to believe?

GEORGE:   I wish I could answer that, son, but that's really for you to say.

GUARD:   Time, counselor.

GEORGE:   Coming. [*Turns to the other* BOYS.] Listen, boys, I don't know where in the world I'll be the day your appeal is won—and it will be won—whether it's in the Pacific somewhere or in Europe or in a hole in the ground . . . Take care of yourselves.

TOMMY:   See you around, George.

SMILEY:   So long, George.

JOEY:   'Bye, Cheer.

GEORGE:   Yeah. See you around. [*Pause.*] Goodbye, Henry. Good luck and God bless you.

HENRY:   God bless you, too, George. Take care of yourself.

TOMMY:   Say, George, when you come back from the war, we're going to take you outa town and blast some weed.

JOEY:   We'll get you a pair of buns you can hold in your hands!

GEORGE:   I may just take you up on that. [*The* GUARD *escorts* GEORGE *out, then turns back to the* BOYS.]

GUARD:   All right, new work assignments. Everybody report to the jute mill. Let's go. [SMILEY, JOEY *and* TOMMY *start to exit.* HENRY *hangs back.*] What's the matter with you, Reyna? You got lead in your pants? I said let's go.

HENRY:   We're supposed to work in the mess hall.

GUARD:   You got a new assignment.

HENRY:   Since when?

GUARD:   Since right now. Get going!

HENRY: [*Hanging back.*]   The warden know about this?

GUARD:   What the hell do you care? You think you're something special? Come on, greaseball. Move!

HENRY:   Make me, you bastard!

GUARD:   Oh yeah. [*The* GUARD *pushes* HENRY. HENRY *pushes back. The* batos *react, as the* GUARD *traps* HENRY *with his club around the chest. The* BOYS *move to* HENRY's *defense.*] Back!

HENRY: [*To the* batos.]   Back off! BACK OFF! Don't be stupid.

GUARD:   Okay, Reyna, you got solitary! Bastard, huh? Into the hole! [HE *pushes* HENRY *onto center stage. Lights down. A single spot.*] Line, greaseballs. Move out! [*As they march.*] Quickly, quickly. You're too slow. Move, move, move. [*The* BOYS *exit with the* GUARD.]

5. SOLITARY

*A lone saxophone sets the mood.*

PACHUCO:  Too bad, ése. He set you up again.

HENRY:  [*Long pause.* HE looks *around.*]  Solitary, ése . . . they gave me solitary. [HE *sits down on the floor, a forlorn figure.*]

PACHUCO:  Better get used to it, carnal. That's what this stretch is going to be about, see? You're in here for life, bato.

HENRY:  I can't accept it, ése.

PACHUCO:
You've got to, Hank . . .
only this reality is real now,
only this place is real,
sitting in the lonely cell of your will . . .

HENRY:  I can't see my hands.

PACHUCO:
Then tell your eyes to forget the light, ése
Only the hard floor is there, carnal
Only the cold hard edge of this reality
and there is no time . . .
Each second is a raw drop of blood from your brain
that you must swallow
drop by drop
and don't even start counting
or you'll lose your mind . . .

HENRY:  I've got to know why I'm here, ése! I've got to have a reason for being here.

PACHUCO:  You're here, Hank, because you chose to be—because you protected your brother and your family. And nobody knows the worth of that effort better than you, ése.

HENRY:  I miss them, ése . . . my jefitos, my carnalillo, my sis . . . I miss Della.

PACHUCO:  [*A spot illuminates* HENRY's *family standing upstage;* EL PACHUCO *snaps it off.*]
Forget them!
Forget them all.
Forget your family and the barrio
beyond the wall.

HENRY:  There's still a chance I'll get out.

PACHUCO:  Fat chance.

HENRY:  I'm talking about the appeal!

PACHUCO:  And I'm talking about what's real! ¿Qué traes, Hank? Haven't you learned yet?

HENRY:  Learned what?

PACHUCO:
Not to expect justice when it isn't there.
No court in the land's going to set you free.
Learn to protect your loves by binding them
in hate, ése! Stop hanging on to false hopes.

The moment those hopes come crashing down,
you'll find yourself on the ground foaming at
the mouth. ¡Como loco!

HENRY: [*Turning on him furiously.*]   ¿Sabes qué? Don't tell me any more.
I don't need you to tell me what to do. Fuck off! FUCK OFF! [HENRY
*turns away from* EL PACHUCO. *Long pause. An anxious, intense moment.*
EL PACHUCO *shifts gears and breaks the tension with a satirical twist.* HE
*throws his arms out and laughs.*]

PACHUCO:
¡Órale pues!
Don't take the pinche play so seriously! Jesús!
¡Es puro vacilón!
Watcha.
   [HE *snaps his fingers. Lights change. We hear the sounds of the city.*]
This is Los, carnal.
You want to see some justice for pachucos?
Check out what's happening back home today.
The Navy has landed, ése—
on leave with full pay
and war's breaking out in the streets of L.A.!

### 6. ZOOT SUIT RIOTS

*We hear music: the bugle call from "Bugle Call Rag." Suddenly the stage is
awash in colored lights. The city of Los Angeles appears in the background in
a panoramic vista of lights tapering into the night horizon.* SAILORS *and* GIRLS
*jitterbug on the dance floor. It is the Avalon Ballroom. The music is hot, the
dancing hotter.* EL PACHUCO *and* HENRY *stand to the side.*

*The scene is in dance and mostly pantomime. Occasionally words are heard
over the music, which is quite loud. On the floor are two* SAILORS (SWABBIE *is
one) and a* MARINE *dancing with the* GIRLS. A SHORE PATROLMAN *speaks to the*
CIGARETTE GIRL. A PIMP *comes on and watches the action.* LITTLE BLUE *and*
ZOOTER *are also on the floor.* RUDY *enters wearing* HENRY'S *zoot suit with* BER-
THA *and* LUPE. LUPE *takes their picture, then all three move up center to the
rear of the ballroom.* CHOLO *comes in down center, sees them and moves up
stage. All four make an entrance onto the dance floor.*

*The* MARINE *takes his girl aside after paying her.* SHE *passes the money to
the* PIMP. *The* SAILORS *try to pick up on* LUPE *and* BERTHA, *and* CHOLO *pushes
one back. The* SAILORS *complain to the* SHORE PATROL, *who throws* CHOLO *out
the door down center. There is an argument that* RUDY *joins. The* SAILORS *go
back to* BERTHA *and* LUPE, *who resist.* CHOLO *and* RUDY *go to their defense and
a fight develops.* ZOOTER *and* LITTLE BLUE *split.* CHOLO *takes the* GIRLS *out and*
RUDY *pulls a knife. He is facing the three* SAILORS *and the* MARINE, *when* EL
PACHUCO *freezes the action.*

PACHUCO: [*Forcefully.*]   Órale, that's enough! [EL PACHUCO *takes* RUDY'S
*knife and with a tap sends him off-stage.* RUDY *exits with the* GIRLS. EL
PACHUCO *is now facing the angry* SERVICEMEN. *He snaps his fingers. The*
PRESS *enters quickly to the beeping sound of a radio broadcast.*]

PRESS: Good evening, Mr. and Mrs. North and South America and all the ships at sea. Let's go to press. FLASH.[4] Los Angeles, California, June 3, 1943. Serious rioting broke out here today as flying squadrons of Marines and soldiers joined the Navy in a new assault on zooter-infested districts. A fleet of twenty taxicabs carrying some two hundred servicemen pulled out of the Naval Armory in Chavez Ravine[5] tonight and assembled a task force that invaded the eastside barrio. [*Unfreeze. The following speeches happen simultaneously.*]

MATE: You got any balls in them funny pants, boy?

SAILOR: He thinks he's tough . . .

SWABBIE: How about it, lardhead? You a tough guy or just a draft dodger?

PRESS: The Zoot Suiters, those gamin' dandies . . .

PACHUCO: [*Cutting them off.*] Why don't you tell them what I really am, ése, or how you've been forbidden to use the very word . . .

PRESS: We are complying in the interest of the war.

PACHUCO: How have you complied?

PRESS: We're using other terms.

PACHUCO: Like "pachuco" and "zoot suiter?"

PRESS: What's wrong with that? The Zoot Suit Crime Wave is even beginning to push the war news off the front page.

PACHUCO:
The Press distorted the very meaning of the word "zoot suit."
All it is for you guys is another way to say Mexican.
But the ideal of the original chuco
was to look like a diamond
to look sharp
hip
bonaroo[6]
finding a style of urban survival
in the rural skirts and outskirts
of the brown metropolis of Los, cabrón.

PRESS: It's an afront to good taste.

PACHUCO: Like the Mexicans, Filipinos and blacks who wear them.

PRESS: Yes!

PACHUCO: Even the white kids and the Wops and the Jews are putting on the drape shape.

PRESS: You are trying to outdo the white man in exaggerated white man's clothes!

PACHUCO:
Because everybody knows
that Mexicans, Filipinos and Blacks
belong to the huarache
the straw
hat and the dirty overall.

PRESS: You savages weren't even wearing clothes when the white man pulled you out of the jungle.

---

4. I.e, news flash.
5. A Los Angeles neighborhood that in the 1940s was home to thousands of Mexican Americans; the site of Sleepy Lagoon; now the site of Dodger Stadium.
6. Slang for great or best.

MARINE:  My parents are going without collars and cuffs so you can wear that shit.

PRESS:  That's going too far, too goddamned far, and it's got to be stopped!

PACHUCO:  Why?

PRESS:  Don't you know there's a war on? Don't you fucking well know you can't get away with that shit? What are we fighting for if not to annihilate the enemies of the American way of life?

MATE:  Let's tear it off his back!

SAILORS / MARINE:  Let's strip him! Get him! [*Etc.*]

PRESS:  KILL THE PACHUCO BASTARD!! [*Music: "American Patrol" by Glenn Miller. The* PRESS *gets a searchlight from upstage center while the* FOUR SERVICEMEN *stalk* EL PACHUCO.]

SAILOR:  Heh, zooter. Come on, zooter!

SWABBIE:  You think you're more important than the war, zooter?

MATE:  Let's see if you got any balls in them funny pants, boy.

SWABBIE:  Watch out for the knife.

SAILOR:  That's a real chango monkey suit he's got on.

MATE:  I bet he's half monkey just like the Filipinos and Niggers that wear them.

SWABBIE:  You trying to outdo the white man in them glad rags, Mex? [*They fight now to the finish.* EL PACHUCO *is overpowered and stripped as* HENRY *watches helplessly from his position. The* PRESS *and* SERVICEMEN *exit with pieces of* EL PACHUCO'S *zoot suit.* EL PACHUCO *stands. The only item of clothing on his body is a small loincloth.* HE *turns and looks at* HENRY, *with mystic intensity.* HE *opens his arms as an Aztec conch blows, and* HE *slowly exits backward with powerful calm into the shadows. Silence.* HENRY *comes downstage.* HE *absorbs the impact of what* HE *has seen and falls to his knees at center stage, spent and exhausted. Lights down.*]

## 7. ALICE

*The* GUARD *and* ALICE *enter from opposite sides of the stage. The* GUARD *carries a handful of letters and is reading one of them.*

GUARD:  July 2, 1943.

ALICE:
Dear Henry,
I hope this letter finds you in good health and good spirits—but I have to assume you've heard about the riots in Los Angeles. It was a nightmare, and it lasted for a week. The city is still in a state of shock.

GUARD:  [*Folds the letter back into the envelope, then opens another.*] August 5, 1943.

ALICE:
Dear Henry,

The riots here in L.A. have touched off race riots all over the country— Chicago, Detroit, even little Beaumont, Texas, for Christ's sake. But the one in Harlem was the worst. Millions of dollars worth of property damage. 500 people were hospitalized, and five Negroes were killed.

GUARD:  Things are rough all over.

ALICE:  Please write to me and tell me how you feel.

GUARD: [*The* GUARD *folds up the second letter, stuffs it back into its envelope and opens a third.*]   August 20, 1943.

ALICE:
Dear Henry,
Although I am disappointed not to have heard from you, I thought I would send you some good news for a change. Did you know we had a gala fundraiser at the Mocambo?[7]

GUARD:   The Mocambo . . . Hotcha![8]

ALICE:   . . . and Rita Hayworth lent your sister Lupe a ball gown for the occasion. She got dressed at Cecil B. DeMille's house, and she looked terrific. Her escort was Anthony Quinn, and Orson Welles[9] said . . .

GUARD:   Orson Welles! Well! Sounds like Louella Parsons.[1] [HE *folds up the letter.*] September 1, 1943.

ALICE:   Henry, why aren't you answering my letters?

GUARD:   He's busy. [HE *continues to stuff the envelope.*]

ALICE:   Henry, if there's something I've said or done . . . [*The* GUARD *shuffles the envelopes.*] Henry . . . [*Lights change.* GUARD *crosses to center stage, where* HENRY *is still doubled up on the floor.*]

GUARD:   Welcome back to the living, Reyna. It's been a long hot summer. Here's your mail. [*The* GUARD *tosses the letters to the floor directly in front of* HENRY'S *head.* HENRY *looks up slowly and grabs one of the letters.* HE *opens it, trying to focus. The* GUARD *exits.*]

ALICE:   Henry, I just found out you did ninety days in solitary. I'm furious at the rest of the guys for keeping it from me. I talked to Warden Duffy, and he said you struck a guard. Did something happen I should know about? I wouldn't ask if it wasn't so important, but a clean record . . . [HENRY *rips up the letter* HE *has been reading and scatters the others. Alarmed.*] Henry? [HENRY *pauses, his instant fury spent and under control.* HE *sounds almost weary, but the anger is still there.*]

HENRY:   You still don't understand, Alice.

ALICE: [*Softly, compassionate.*]   But I do! I'm not accusing you of anything. I don't care what happened or why they sent you there. I'm sure you had your reasons. But you know the public is watching you.

HENRY: [*Frustrated, a deep question.*]   Why do you do this, Alice?

ALICE:   What?

HENRY:   The appeal, the case, all the shit you do. You think the public gives a goddamn?

ALICE: [*With conviction.*]   Yes! We are going to get you out of here, Henry Reyna. We are going to win!

HENRY: [*Probing.*]   What if we lose?

ALICE: [*Surprised but moving on.*]   We're not going to lose.

HENRY: [*Forcefully, insistent, meaning more than* HE *is saying.*]   What if we do? What if we get another crooked judge, and he nixes the appeal?

ALICE:   Then we'll appeal again. We'll take it to the Supreme *Court.* [*A forced laugh.*] Hell, we'll take it all the way to President Roosevelt!

---

7. Glamorous, Latin American–themed nightclub (1941–59) on the Sunset Strip, in West Hollywood, California.
8. Slang expressing approval or delight.
9. American actor, writer, and director (1915–1985); married Rita Hayworth on September 8, 1943. *Cecil B. DeMille*: American movie director (1881–1959). *Anthony Quinn*: Mexican-born American actor (1915–2001).
1. American gossip columnist (1881–1972) whose radio show featured interviews with Hollywood celebrities.

HENRY: [*Backing her up—emotionally.*]   What if we still lose?

ALICE: [*Bracing herself against his aggression.*]   We can't.

HENRY:   Why can't we?

ALICE: [*Giving a political response in spite of herself.*]   Because we've got too much support. You should see the kinds of people responding to us. Unions, Mexicans, Negroes, Oakies. It's fantastic.

HENRY: [*Driving harder.*]   Why can't we lose, Alice?

ALICE:   I'm telling you.

HENRY:   No, you're not.

ALICE: [*Starting to feel vulnerable.*]   I don't know what to tell you.

HENRY:   Yes, you do!

ALICE: [*Frightened.*]   Henry . . . ?

HENRY:   Tell me why we can't lose, Alice!

ALICE: [*Forced to fight back, with characteristic passion.*]   Stop it, Henry! Please stop it! I won't have you treat me this way. I never have been able to accept one person pushing another around . . . pushing me around! Can't you see that's why I'm here? Because I can't stand it happening to you. Because I'm a Jew, goddammit! I have been there . . . I have been there! If you lose, I lose. [*Pause. The emotional tension is immense.* ALICE *fights to hold back tears.* SHE *turns away.*]

HENRY:   I'm sorry . . .

ALICE: [*Pause.*]   It's stupid for us to fight like this. I look forward to coming here for weeks. Just to talk to you, to be with you, to see your eyes.

HENRY: [*Pause.*]   I thought a lot about you when I was in the hole. Sometimes . . . sometimes I'd even see you walk in, in the dark, and talk to me. Just like you are right now. Same look, same smile, same perfume . . . [HE *pauses.*] Only the other one never gave me so much lip. She just listened. She did say one thing. She said . . .

ALICE: [*Trying to make light of it. Then more gently.*]   I can't say that to you, Henry. Not the way you want it.

HENRY:   Why not?

ALICE: [SHE *means it.*]   Because I can't allow myself to be used to fill in for all the love you've always felt and always received from all your women.

HENRY: [*With no self-pity.*]   Give it a chance, Alice.

ALICE: [*Beside herself.*]   Give it a chance? You crazy idiot. If I thought making love to you would solve all your problems, I'd do it in a second. Don't you know that? But it won't. It'll only complicate things. I'm trying to help you, goddammit. And to do that, I have to be your friend, not your white woman.

HENRY: [*Getting angry.*]   What makes you think I want to go to bed with you. Because you're white? I've had more white pieces of ass than you can count, ¿sabes? Who do you think you are? God's gift to us brown animals.

ALICE: [ALICE *slaps him and stops, horrified. A whirlpool of emotions.*]   Oh, Hank. All the love and hate it's taken to get us together in this lousy prison room. Do you realize only Hitler[2] and the Second World War could have accomplished that? I don't know whether to laugh or cry.

---

2. Adolf Hitler (1889–1945), Austrian-born German dictator and founder of Nazism.

[ALICE *folds into her emotional spin, her body shaking. Suddenly* SHE *turns, whipping herself out of it with a cry, both laughing and weeping. They come to each other and embrace. Then they kiss—passionately. The* GUARD *enters.* HE *frowns.*]

GUARD: Time, miss.

ALICE: [*Turning.*] Already? Oh, my God, Henry, there's so many messages I was going to give you. Your mother and father send their love, of course. And Lupe and . . . Della. And . . . oh, yes. They want you to know Rudy's in the Marines.

HENRY: The Marines?

ALICE: I'll write you all about it. Will you write me?

HENRY: [*A glance at the* GUARD.] Yes.

GUARD: [*His tone getting harsher.*] Let's go, lady.

HENRY: Goodbye, Licha.

ALICE: I'll see you on the outside . . . Hank. [ALICE *gives* HENRY *a thumb up gesture, and the* GUARD *escorts her out.* HENRY *turns downstage, full of thoughts.* HE *addresses* EL PACHUCO, *who is nowhere to be seen.*]

HENRY: You were wrong, ése . . . There's is something to hope for. I know now we're going to win the appeal. Do you hear me, ése? Ése! [*Pause.*] Are you even there any more? [*The* GUARD *reenters at a clip.*]

GUARD: Okay, Reyna, come on.

HENRY: Where to?

GUARD: We're letting you go . . . [HENRY *looks at him incredulously. The* GUARD *smiles.*] . . . to Folsom Prison[3] with all the rest of the hardcore cons. You really didn't expect to walk out of here a free man, did you? Listen, kid, your appeal stands about as much chance as the Japs and Krauts of winning the war. Personally, I don't see what that broad sees in you. I wouldn't give you the sweat off my balls. Come on! [HENRY *and the* GUARD *turn upstage to leave. Lights change.* EL PACHUCO *appears halfway up the backdrop, fully dressed again and clearly visible.* HENRY *stops with a jolt as* HE *sees him.* EL PACHUCO *lifts his arms. Lights go down as we hear the high sound of a bomb falling to earth.*]

### 8. THE WINNING OF THE WAR

*The aerial bomb explodes with a reverberating sound and a white flash that illuminates the form of pachuco images in the black backdrop. Other bombs fall, and all hell breaks loose. Red flashes, artillery, gunfire, ack-ack.* HENRY *and the* GUARD *exit. The* FOUR SERVICEMEN *enter as an honor guard. Music: Glen Miller's "Saint Louis Blues March." As the* SERVICEMEN *march on we see* RUDY *down left in his marine uniform, belt undone.* ENRIQUE, DOLORES *and* LUPE *join him.* DOLORES *has his hat,* LUPE *her camera.* ENRIQUE *fastens two buttons on the uniform as* RUDY *does up his belt.* DOLORES *inspects his collar and gives him his hat.* RUDY *puts on his hat and all pose for* LUPE. *She snaps the picture and* RUDY *kisses them all and is off.* HE *picks up the giant switchblade from behind a newspaper bundle and joins the* SERVICEMEN *as they march down in drill formation. The family marches off, looking back sadly. The drill ends, and* RUDY *and the* SHORE PATROL *move to one side. As* RUDY'S

---

3. State prison in the city of Folsom, California; northeast of San Quentin.

*interrogation goes on,* PEOPLE *in the barrio come on with newspapers to mime daily tasks. The* PRESS *enters.*

PRESS: The *Los Angeles Examiner,* July 1, 1943. Headline: WORLD WAR II REACHES TURNING POINT If the late summer of 1942 was the low point, a year later the war for the Allies[4] is pounding its way to certain victory.

SHORE PATROL: July 10!

RUDY: U.S., British and Canadian troops invade Sicily, sir!

SHORE PATROL: August 6!

RUDY: U.S. troops occupy Solomon Islands, sir!

SHORE PATROL: September 5!

RUDY: MacArthur's forces land on New Guinea, sir!

SHORE PATROL: October 1!

RUDY: U.S. Fifth Army enters Naples, sir!

PRESS: On and on it goes. From Corsica to Kiev, from Tarawa to Anzio. The relentless advance of the Allied armies cannot be checked. [*One by one,* HENRY's *family and friends enter, carrying newspapers. They tear the papers into small pieces.*] The *Los Angeles Times,* June 6, 1944. Headline: Allied forces under General Eisenhower land in Normandy.

SHORE PATROL: August 19!

RUDY: American First Army reaches Germany, sir!

SHORE PATROL: October 17!

RUDY: MacArthur returns to the Philippines, sir!

PRESS: On the homefront, Americans go on with their daily lives with growing confidence and relief, as the war pushes on toward inevitable triumph. [*Pause.*] The *Los Angeles Daily News,* Wednesday, November 8, 1944. Headline: District Court of Appeals decides in Sleepy Lagoon murder case . . . boys in pachuco murder given . . .

PEOPLE: FREEDOM!!! [*Music bursts forth as the joyous crowd tosses the shredded newspaper into the air like confetti. The* BOYS *enter upstage center, and the crowd rushes to them, weeping and cheering. There are kisses and hugs and tears of joy.* HENRY *is swept forward by the triumphal procession.*]

### 9. RETURN TO THE BARRIO

*The music builds and people start dancing. Others just embrace. The tune is "Soldado Razo"[5] played to a lively corrido beat. It ends with joyous applause, laughter and tears.*

RUDY: ¡Ese carnal!

HENRY: Rudy!!

4. The Allied Forces (including the United States, Britain, and Canada), who fought the Axis powers (including Japan, Germany, and Italy) during World War II. The following lines refer to important points in the Pacific theater of operations, where the American general Douglas MacArthur (1880–1964) played a prominent role, and the European theater of operations, where the American general and future president Dwight David Eisenhower (1890–1969) was supreme commander of the Allied Forces. The Allied Forces landed in Normandy on June 6, 1944, but the American First Army did not reach Germany until September.

5. Buck Private; a farewell song about a young man who joins the Mexican army to prove his manhood; among the recordings are one done in 1943 by the Mexican singer and actor Pedro Infante (1917–1957).

DOLORES: ¡Bendito sea Dios! Who would believe this day would ever come? Look at you—you're all home!

LUPE: I still can't believe it. We won! We won the appeal! [*Cheers.*]

ENRIQUE: I haven't felt like this since Villa took Zacatecas.[6] [*Laughter, cheers.*] ¡Pero, mira! Look who's here. Mis hijos. [*Puts his arm around* HENRY *and* RUDY.] It isn't every day a man has two grown sons come home from so far away—one from the war, the other from . . . bueno, who cares? The Sleepy Lagoon is history, hombre. For a change, los Mexicanos have won! [*Cheers.*]

GEORGE: Well, Henry. I don't want to say I told you so, but we sure taught Judge Charles a lesson in misconduct, didn't we? [*More cheers.*] Do you realize this is the greatest victory the Mexican-American community has ever had in the history of this whole blasted country?

DOLORES: Yes, but if it wasn't for the unselfish thoughtfulness of people like you and this beautiful lady—and all the people who helped out, Mexicanos, Negros, all Americanos—our boys would not be home today.

GEORGE: I only hope you boys realize how important you are now.

JOEY: Pos, I realize it, ése. [*Laughter.*]

RUDY: I came all the way from Hawaii just to get here, carnal. I only got a few days, but I'm going to get you drunk.

HENRY: Pos, we'll see who gets who drunk, ése. [*Laughter and hoots.* HENRY *spots* EL PACHUCO *entering from stage right.*]

DOLORES: Jorge, Licha, todos. Let's go into the house, eh? I've made a big pot of menudo, and it's for everybody.

ENRIQUE: There's ice-cold beer too. Vénganse, vamos todos.

GEORGE: [*To* ALICE.] Alice . . . Menudo, that's Mexican chicken *soup?* [*Everybody exits, leaving* HENRY *behind with* EL PACHUCO.]

HENRY: It's good to see you again, ése. I thought I'd lost you.

PACHUCO: H'm pues, it'd take more than the U.S. Navy to wipe me out.

HENRY: Where you been?

PACHUCO: Pos, here in the barrio. Welcome back.

HENRY: It's good to be home.

PACHUCO: No hard feelings?

HENRY: Chale—we won, didn't we?

PACHUCO: Simón.

HENRY: Me and the batos have been in a lot of fights together, ése. But we won this one, because we learned to fight in a new way.

PACHUCO: And that's the perfect way to end this play—happy ending y todo. [PACHUCO *makes a sweeping gesture. Lights come down.* HE *looks up at the lights, realizing something is wrong.* HE *flicks his wrist, and the lights go back up again.*]
But life ain't that way, Hank.
The barrio's still out there, waiting and wanting.
The cops are still tracking us down like dogs.
The gangs are still killing each other,
Families are barely surviving,

---

6. City in central Mexico; the *Toma de Zacatecas* (Taking of Zacatecas) occurred in 1914, during the Mexican Revolution, when the Constitutionalist troops led by General Francisco "Pancho" Villa (1878–1923) defeated the Federal army of General Victoriano Huerta (1854–1916), ending Huerta's provisional presidency of Mexico.

And there in your own backyard . . . life goes on.

[*Soft music.* DELLA *enters.*]

DELLA: Hank? [HENRY *goes to her and they embrace.*]

HENRY: Where were you? Why didn't you come to the Hall of Justice to see us get out?

DELLA: I guess I was a little afraid things had changed. So much has happened to both of us.

PACHUCO: Simón. She's living in your house.

DELLA: After I got back from Ventura, my parents gave me a choice. Forget about you or get out.

HENRY: Why didn't you write to me?

DELLA: You had your own problems. Your jefitos took care of me. Hey, you know what, Hank, I think they expect us to get married.

PACHUCO: How about it, ése? You still going to give her that big pachuco wedding you promised?

HENRY: I have to think about it.

ALICE: [*Off-stage.*] Henry?

PACHUCO: [*Snaps fingers.*] Wish you had the time. But here comes Licha.

ALICE: [*Entering.*] Henry, I've just come to say good night. [DELLA *freezes, and* HENRY *turns to* ALICE.]

HENRY: Good night? Why are you leaving so soon?

ALICE: Soon? I've been here all afternoon. There'll be other times, Henry. You're home now, with your family, that's what matters.

HENRY: Don't patronize me, Alice.

ALICE: [*Surprised.*] Patronize you?

HENRY: Yeah. I learned a few words in the joint.

ALICE: Yo también, Hank. Te quiero. [PACHUCO *snaps.* ALICE *freezes, and* RUDY *enters.*]

RUDY: Ese carnal, congratulations, the jefita just told me about you and Della. That's great, ése. But if you want me to be best man, you better do it in the next three days.

HENRY: Wait a minute, Rudy, don't push me.

RUDY: Qué pues, getting cold feet already? [HENRY *is beginning to be surrounded by separate conversations.*]

DELLA: If you don't want me here, I can move out.

RUDY: Watcha. I'll let you and Della have our room tonight, bato. I'll sleep on the couch.

ALICE: You aren't expecting me to sleep here, are you?

HENRY: I'm not asking you to.

PACHUCO/ALICE/RUDY/DELLA: Why not?

RUDY: The jefitos will never know, ése.

ALICE: Be honest, Henry.

DELLA: What do you want me to do?

HENRY: Give me a chance to think about it. Give me a second!

PACHUCO: One second! [PACHUCO *snaps.* ENRIQUE *enters.*]

ENRIQUE: Bueno, bueno, pues, what are you doing out here, hijo? Aren't you coming in for menudo?

HENRY: I'm just thinking, jefito.

ENRIQUE: ¿De qué, hombre? Didn't you do enough of that in prison? Ándale, this is your house. Come in and live again.

HENRY: 'Apá, did you tell Della I was going to marry her?

ENRIQUE:  Yes, but only after you did.

RUDY:  ¿Qué traes, carnal? Don't you care about Della anymore?

ALICE:  If it was just me and you, Henry, it might be different. But you have to think of your family.

HENRY:  I don't need you to tell me my responsibilities.

ALICE:  I'm sorry.

RUDY:  Sorry, carnal.

DELLA:  I don't need anybody to feel sorry for me. I did what I did because I wanted to. All I want to know is what's going to happen now. If you still want me, órale, suave. If you don't, that's okay, too. But I'm not going to hang around like a pendeja all my life.

RUDY:  Your huisa's looking finer than ever, carnal.

ALICE:  You're acting as if nothing has happened.

ENRIQUE:  You have your whole life ahead of you.

ALICE:  You belong here, Henry. I'm the one that's out of place.

RUDY:  If you don't pick up on her, I'm going to have to step in.

HENRY:  That's bullshit. What about what we shared in prison? I've never been that close to anybody.

ALICE:  That was in prison.

HENRY:  What the hell do you think the barrio is?

RUDY:  It's not bullshit!

HENRY:  Shut up, carnalillo!

RUDY:  Carnalillo? How can you still call me that? I'm not your pinche little brother no more.

GEORGE:  [*Entering.*]  You guys have got to stop fighting, Henry, or the barrio will never change. Don't you realize you men represent the hope of your people?

ALICE:  Della was in prison too. You know you had thousands of people clamoring for your release, but you were Della's only hope.

HENRY:  Look, ésa, I know you did a year in Ventura. I know you stood up for me when it counted. I wish I could make it up to you.

DELLA:  Don't give me your bullshit, Henry. Give it to Alice.

ALICE:  I think it's time for Alice Bloomfield to go home.

HENRY:  Don't be jealous, ésa.

DELLA:  Jealous? Mira, cabrón, I know I'm not the only one you ever took to the Sleepy Lagoon.

RUDY:  The Sleepy Lagoon ain't shit. I saw real lagoons in those islands, ése—killing Japs! I saw some pachucos go out there that are never coming back.

DELLA:  But I was always there when you came back, wasn't I?

DOLORES: [*Entering.*]  Henry? Come back inside, hijo. Everybody's waiting for you.

RUDY:  Why didn't you tell them I was there, carnal? I was at the Sleepy Lagoon. Throwing chingazos with everybody!

HENRY:  Don't you understand, Rudy? I was trying to keep you from getting a record. Those bastard cops are never going to leave us alone.

GEORGE:  You've got to forget what happened, Henry.

HENRY:  What can I give you, Della? I'm an ex-con.

DELLA:  So am I!

SMILEY: [*Entering.*]  Let's face it, Hank. There's no future for us in this town. I'm taking my wife and kid and moving to Arizona.

DOLORES: [*Simultaneously.*] I know what you are feeling, hijo, it's home again. I know inside you are afraid that nothing has changed. That the police will never leave you in peace. Pero no le hace. Everything is going to be fine now. Marry Della and fill this house with children. Just do one thing for me—forget the zoot suit clothes.

ENRIQUE: If there's one thing that will keep a man off the streets it's his own familia.

GEORGE: Don't let this thing eat your heart out for the rest of your . . .

ALICE: Sometimes the best thing you can do for someone you love is walk away.

DELLA: What do you want, Hank?

RUDY: It cost me more than it did you.

SMILEY: We started the 38th, and I'll never forget you, carnal. But I got to think about my family.

HENRY: Wait a minute! I don't know if I'll be back in prison tomorrow or not! I have nothing to give you, Della. Not even a piece of myself.

DELLA: I have my life to live, too, Hank. I love you. I would even die for you. Pero me chingan la madre if I'm going to throw away my life for nothing.

HENRY: But I love you . . . [*Both* GIRLS *turn.* HENRY *looks at* ALICE, *then to the whole group upstage of him. Still turning,* HE *looks at* DELLA *and goes to embrace her. The freeze ends and other people enter.*]

LUPE: ¡Órale, Hank! Watcha Joey. The crazy bato went all the way to his house and put on his drapes.

JOEY: ¡Esos, batoooooosss! ¡Esas, huisaaaaaass!

TOMMY: Look at this cat! He looks all reet.

LUPE: Yeah, like a parakeet!

HENRY: ¿Y tú, ése? How come you put on your tacuche? Where's the party?

JOEY: Pos, ain't the party here?

RUDY: Yeah, ése, but this ain't the Avalon Ballroom.[7] The zoot suit died under fire here in Los. Don't you know that, cabrón?

ENRIQUE: Rudolfo!

LUPE: And he was supposed to get Henry drunk.

RUDY: Shut up, ésa!

ENRIQUE: ¡Ya pues! Didn't you have any menudo? Vieja, fix him a great big bowl of menudo and put plenty of chile in it. We're going to sweat it out of him.

RUDY: I don't need no pinche menudo.

HENRY: Watch your language, carnal.

RUDY: And I don't need you! I'm a man. I can take care of myself!

JOEY: Muy marine el bato . . .

ENRIQUE: Rudy, hijo. Are you going to walk into the kitchen or do I have to drag you.

RUDY: Whatever you say, jefito.

GEORGE: Well, Alice. This looks like the place where we came in. I think it's about time we left.

___

7. In San Francisco; at the time, a dancehall and site for big-band music.

ALICE:    Say the word, George, just say the word.

DOLORES:    No, no. You can't leave so soon.

JOEY:    Chale, chale, chale. You can't take our Grandma. ¿Qué se trae, carnal? Póngase más abusado, ése. No se haga tan square.

GEORGE:    Okay, square I got. What was the rest of it?

JOEY:    Pos, le estoy hablando en chicas patas, ése. Es puro chicano.

RUDY:    ¿Qué chicano? Ni que madre, cabrón. Why don't you grow up?

JOEY:    Grow up, ése?

RUDY:    Try walking downtown looking like that. See if the sailors don't skin your ass alive.

JOEY:    So what? It's no skin off your ass. Come on, Bertha.

RUDY:    She's staying with me.

JOEY:    She's mine.

RUDY:    Prove it, punk. [RUDY *attacks* JOEY *and they fight. The* BATOS *and* RUCAS *take out* JOEY. HENRY *pacifies* RUDY, *who bursts out crying.* ENRIQUE, DELLA, DOLORES, ALICE, LUPE *and* GEORGE *are the only ones left.* RUDY *in a flush of emotion.*] Cabrones, se amontonaron. They ganged up on me, carnal. You left me and they ganged up on me. You shouldn't have done it, carnal. Why didn't you take me with you? For the jefitos? The jefitos lost me anyway.

HENRY:    Come on in the house, Rudy . . .

RUDY:    No! I joined the Marines. I didn't have to join, but I went. ¿Sabes por qué? Because they got me, carnal. Me chingaron, ése. [*Sobs.*] I went to the pinche show with Bertha, all chingón in your tachuche, ése. I was wearing your zoot suit, and they got me. Twenty sailors, Marines. We were up in the balcony. They came down from behind. They grabbed me by the neck and dragged me down the stairs, kicking and punching and pulling my greña. They dragged me out into the streets . . . and all the people watched while they stripped me. [*Sobs.*] They stripped me, carnal. Bertha saw them strip me. Hijos de la chingada, they stripped me. [HENRY *goes to* RUDY *and embraces him with fierce love and desperation. Pause.* TOMMY *comes running in.*]

TOMMY:    ¡Órale! There's cops outside. They're trying to arrest Joey. [GEORGE *crosses to* TOMMY.]

GEORGE: [*Bursting out.*]    Joey?

TOMMY:    They got him up against your car. They're trying to say he stole it!

GEORGE:    Oh, God. I'll take care of this.

ALICE:    I'll go with you. [GEORGE, TOMMY *and* ALICE *exit.*]

HENRY:    Those fucking bastards! [HE *starts to exit.*]

DELLA:    Henry, no!

HENRY:    What the hell do you mean no? Don't you see what's going on outside?

DELLA:    They'll get you again! That's what they want.

HENRY:    Get out of my way! [HE *pushes her out of the way, toward* DOLORES.]

ENRIQUE: [*Stands up before Henry.*]    ¡Hijo!

HENRY:    Get out of my way, jefe!

ENRIQUE:    You will stay here!

HENRY:    Get out of my way! [ENRIQUE *powerfully pushes him back and throws* HENRY *to the door and holds.*]

ENRIQUE: ¡TE DIGO QUE NO! [*Silent moment,* HENRY *stands up and offers to strike* ENRIQUE. *But something stops him. The realization that if* HE *strikes back or even if* HE *walks out the door, the family bond is irreparably broken.* HENRY *tenses for a moment, then relaxes and embraces his father.* DELLA *goes to them and joins the embrace. Then* DOLORES, *then* LUPE, *then* RUDY. *All embrace in a tight little group.* PRESS *enters right and comes down.*]

PRESS: Henry Reyna went back to prison in 1947 for robbery and assault with a deadly weapon. While incarcerated, he killed another inmate and he wasn't released until 1955, when he got into hard drugs. He died of the trauma of his life in 1972.

PACHUCO: That's the way you see it, ése. But there's other ways to end this story.

RUDY: Henry Reyna went to Korea in 1950. He was shipped across in a destroyer and defended the 38th Parallel until he was killed at Inchon in 1952, being posthumously awarded the Congressional Medal of Honor.

ALICE: Henry Reyna married Della in 1948 and they have five kids, three of them now going to the university, speaking caló and calling themselves Chicanos.

GEORGE: Henry Reyna, the born leader . . .

JUDGE: Henry Reyna, the social victim . . .

BERTHA: Henry Reyna, the street corner warrior . . .

SMILEY: Henry Reyna, el carnal de aquéllas . . .

JOEY: Henry Reyna, the zoot suiter . . .

TOMMY: Henry Reyna, my friend . . .

LUPE: Henry Reyna, my brother . . .

ENRIQUE: Henry Reyna . . .

DOLORES: Our son . . .

DELLA: Henry Reyna, my love . . .

PACHUCO: Henry Reyna . . . El Pachuco . . . The man . . . the myth . . . still lives. [*Lights down and fade out.*]

1978

---

# VICTOR VILLASEÑOR
## b. 1940

Victor Villaseñor was born in Carlsbad, California, to Mexican parents, and grew up on a ranch four miles north, in Oceanside. After dropping out of high school, he moved to Mexico, then returned to the United States in 1960. A self-taught writer, he credits his artistic awakening to reading the autobiographical novel *A Portrait of the Artist as a Young Man* (1916), by the Irish writer James Joyce (1882–1941). "It awakened a desire to confront through literature the problems associated with [my] cultural heritage," he has explained. None of Villaseñor's first nine novels or first 65 short stories was accepted for publication—he claims to have received 265 rejections. His first publication, the novel *Macho!* (1973), tells the inspirational story

of Roberto García, who emigrates to the United States from the state of Michoacán, in southwestern Mexico, and becomes a migrant laborer. Villaseñor's next
book, *Jury: The People vs. Juan Corona* (1977), is a documentary account, written in
the freewheeling style of New Journalism and based on his interviews with the
jurors on the case, of the arrest and trial of a California labor contractor convicted
of being a serial killer who murdered two dozen people.

*Rain of Gold* (1991) narrates, often with high melodrama, the saga of Villaseñor's
family from the Mexican Revolution to life in Carlsbad. It describes his father's
escape from the armed struggle and subsequent imprisonment in an Arizona penitentiary for stealing six dollars' worth of ore, and his mother's birth in a gold mine.
An established New York publishing house acquired the manuscript, but rejected it
when Villaseñor refused to turn the book into a novel; he accused his editor of
offenses ranging from cultural insensitivity to censorship. A small Latino publisher
in Houston, Arte Público Press, released the book as Villaseñor wrote it, and it
went on to become a best seller. It now forms a trilogy with the memoirs *Wild Steps
of Heaven* (1996) and *Thirteen Senses* (2001).

In the collection *Walking Stars: Stories of Magic and Power* (1998) and in *Burro
Genius* (2004), a memoir about his dyslexia, Villaseñor displays the New Age philosophy that has become his trademark, emphasizing the value of serendipity in life and a
connection with higher powers. The story "The Greatest Christmas Gift," part of
*Walking Stars* and included in this anthology, is about a boy—based on Villaseñor's
father—who encounters the town witch and comes to terms with her "magic." Among
the children's books Villaseñor has written are *The Frog and His friends Save Humanity* and *Little Crow to the Rescue* (both 2005). In 1982, Villaseñor collaborated on the
screenplay for the PBS movie *The Ballad of Gregorio Cortez* with the movie's director,
Robert M. Young; it is a drama based on Américo Paredes's ethnographic study *With
His Pistol in His Hand: A Border Ballad and Its Hero* (1958).

# The Greatest Christmas Gift

It was the week before Christmas, and everyone was going crazy around the
house. Juan's older sister, Luisa, was going to get married right after Christmas, and much had to get done. So many things had to be accomplished for
the holy day of Christ's birthday and then, also, for the wedding. Oh, it was
an exciting time at the Villaseñor household in Los Atlos de Jalisco.[1]

And this night, right after dinner, Domingo got up and went out the back
door, signaling for his younger brother Juan to follow him. But Juan didn't
want to go outside with Domingo. No, he wanted to stay indoors with *la
familia*. So, Domingo made a face at Juan that said, "You better get out here
quick or you're going to get it later when nobody's around to protect you."

Juan took a big breath, glanced around at everyone, and decided that there
was no way to escape this. So, he got up and went out the back door, too.

Immediately, Domingo grabbed Juan once they were out of sight from the
adults and gave him a sharp knock on the head with his middle knuckle.
"Come on, *cabezón*![2] They're waiting for us by the creek behind the pig pen!"

Getting to the creek, they met Lucha.

"Where have you two been?" she said. "I slipped out the front door when
no one was watching, and I've been waiting for you."

"Is Emilia coming?" asked Domingo.

1. Region in the state of Jalisco, in central-western Mexico (just north of Michoacán).
2. A term of endearment for children who act impulsively.

"No, you know how she is. She's a coward."

"Yes, just like chicken here," said Domingo. "I had to knock him on the head to straighten him out."

Saying this, Domingo went to hit Juan on the head for good measure again, but Juan ducked away.

"Stop hitting me," he said, "or I'll just run home and tell José or Emilia!"

"Oh, you think we're afraid of them?" said Lucha. "I'll show you!" And she took a swing at Juan's large head, but he dodged, knocking her hand away.

Suddenly, a pig squealed an ear-piercing screech right behind them, taking them all by surprise. Lucha and Domingo stopped picking on Juan, and they turned to see the whole pen come alive with squealing, grunting pigs. The dogs at the house yelped and the neighbor's dogs began to bark; a coyote family answered in the distance. The full moon slipped behind a soft, white-laced cloud, giving the whole night an eerie feeling.

"What is it?" whispered Lucha.

"Probably nothing," said Domingo, "or it could mean that those coyotes are a lot closer than they sound."

"Oh, I don't like this," said Juan, glancing around at the night. "Couldn't we wait and do it some other night?"

"No!" said Domingo. "You know that this is the last night of the full moon, so you must do it tonight!"

Juan gulped. "But why?" he asked. What they wanted him to do was go to José-Luis' house and summon the Devil, because they all thought that Luis' mother was a witch. "Wouldn't it make more sense to wait until La Bruja's powers weakened so that I'll have a better chance of doing it for sure?"

"Eh, he has a point there," said Lucha. "We don't want to fail. Our entire family's future depends on this, so maybe it would be best to wait."

"Lucha!" said Domingo, becoming as indignant as an enraged priest, "have you forgotten everything we've been taught at church? The Devil is strong, remember? At one time he was God's most glorious angel, and if we expect to show him that we are not afraid of him, then we can't do it when a witch is at her weakest. No, we must do it when La Bruja's power is at its greatest! Then, and only then—like the good priest says—do we break the evil spell that has been put upon our family."

"Oh, I see. I remember now," said Lucha. "So," she added, shrugging her shoulders, "there is no other way, Juan. You must do it tonight."

Juan's whole body shivered with fear as he glanced up at the bright, full moon and then across the little creek to the far side of the valley. In the distance he could see the tiny light of José-Luis' house and his mother's orchard of peach trees over to one side. His little heart was pounding. He took a big breath. "Look," he said, "maybe the whole wedding will be called off and then we don't even have to worry about having a witch in our family."

"Oh, no, you don't! You started that whole business last night," said Domingo. "And you heard what Luisa said tonight. She and Luis are in love, and the date is set for their wedding. This is the last full moon in which we can save our immortal souls," added Domingo, sounding just like the priest who came to their village once a month.

Juan and Lucha made the sign of the cross over themselves. Domingo really had a way about him.

"Look," said Lucha, drawing close to Juan, "if I could do it for you, little brother, you know I would. But I can't. I'm older than you and not pure of heart anymore, and so it would mean nothing for me to go and confront La Bruja."

Juan brushed Lucha's hand away. Of all his sisters, Lucha was the one who Juan trusted the least. She had big beautiful eyes and was always flirting and acting all lovey-dovey to get her way. He knew that she would no more do for him what had to be done than a fat pig give up his food for another fat pig.

"So, why aren't you pure of heart anymore?" asked Juan.

"Oh," she said, acting like some great lady. "What kind of a man are you to ask a lady a question like that?"

"A boy," said Juan. "A very scared boy who doesn't want to go to the witch's house for all the money in the world. And you're older, Lucha, stronger, faster, and so I want to know why you can't do it."

"Well, if you must know," said Lucha, playing with a long strand of her hair, "Last summer I . . . but you must swear to never tell a soul!"

"We wouldn't!" said Domingo excitedly. "I swear it! So come on, tell us," he added quickly.

"Well, ah," she said, smiling and looking at them from the corner of her eyes, "you know our cousin Agustín. Well, when he stayed with us, he and I, well . . ." she turned all red. ". . . we kissed."

"You kissed Agustín?!" said Domingo. "But he's our first cousin! How could you do such a thing?"

"Well, we just kissed. It's not like we're going to get married or have a baby."

"You better not!" said Domingo. "It would have a long pointed tail, because it would be a baby conceived of the Devil!"

"I know. That's why we only kissed, but by the hours," she added, laughing.

"You . . . enjoyed it?" asked Juan.

"Yes, very much," said Lucha.

"Eeeuuuuu!" said Juan, making a face of pure repulsion.

Lucha went to hit Juan, but Juan only laughed and dodged away. "I'm going to brain you!" she said.

"Enough! Stop that! Both of you!" said Domingo. "What we have here tonight is VERY serious. It's about saving the immortal soul of our entire Villaseñor family."

Juan and Lucha immediately settled down, because they both knew that Domingo was right. Ever since José-Luis had come to their home and asked for their sister Luisa's hand in marriage, the other kids in the village had been telling Juan and the other younger kids of his family that they were now all destined to go to hell. For everyone knew that Luis' mother was a witch of the highest power. And when her son married into the Villaseñor family, then Luis' mother would also be part of the Villaseñor family. They'd all be condemned to burn in the fires of hell for all eternity.

"All right now, do you remember what you're supposed to do?" asked Domingo of Juan.

Juan nodded. "Yes, I remember."

"Well then, repeat it. I don't want any screw-up."

Juan lowered his head, feeling like he might cry. "I'm supposed to go up to her house and . . ."

"I can't hear you! Talk louder! And look at me in the eyes, like a man!"

Juan lifted his face. His eyes were brimming with tears. He was just a scared little boy, but he straightened up the best he could, trying to look like a man. "I'm supposed to go up to her house," he repeated, "then say aloud that I don't fear her powers or the Devil's, either, then . . . then . . ."

"Then what?"

Juan's eyes became huge. "I'm supposed to make the sign of the cross and yell 'We walk in God's love and we fear no evil!'"

"Exactly," said Domingo, "exactly."

"But—but—but what if her five big dogs wake up?" asked Juan. "Maybe I should just whisper it and not say it out loud." He had to squeeze his legs together so he wouldn't pee. "That huge black dog, the one called El Diablo. Oh, my God, if they wake up, they'll kill me and eat me! You saw what they did to that stranger last year. They took him down, with his horse, too, and half-ate him before she could call them off."

"We've been over that!" snapped Domingo impatiently. "That's why you circle her house, coming in through the peach orchard. Her dogs sleep on the other side of her house. They won't even hear you, if you do it right."

"Oh, Domingo," said Juan, his little heart going crazy, "why can't you do it for me? I'm scared and not as fast or as strong as you."

"Look, *cabezón*, we've been over this a dozen times! I'm older than you and not pure of heart anymore! You know that! I'm mean to you and kick dogs and torture ants and swear all the time!"

"Look," said Juan, "I'm not so pure, either. I've kicked goats and tortured bugs, too. And last year when the priest came and found the poor box empty at the church, it was me who took the money."

"You took that money?!" yelled Lucha. "How awful! And you never spoke up when the priest kept accusing us all of stealing! That was terrible!"

Domingo looked at his little brother with new respect. "You really did that?" he asked.

"Oh, yes," said Juan, "and I've done other bad things, too!"

"Like what?" asked Lucha.

"Well, I've sneaked up and watched how you girls have to squat down to pee, and we don't."

"You've watched us?!" yelled Lucha. "Oh, you're dirty!"

"No, I stand up to pee," he said proudly.

"I'm going to hit you and tell Mamá!" yelled Lucha, grabbing Juan and trying to hit him on the head. But he kept ducking. Domingo separated them.

Just then, some other kids came running up. It was Mateo, Domingo's best friend, and his two smaller brothers, Alfonso and Pelón, and their sister Carmelita. Immediately, Mateo wanted to know what was going on. He and Domingo were the two best fighters with rocks or their bare hands in all the region. They were so feared that even some adult men wouldn't go against them in an all-out rock fight.

"My little brother is ready to do it," Domingo announced proudly.

Mateo took a good, long look at Juan. "He doesn't look ready to me. He looks scared, and everyone knows if you show fear to the Devil, then the ground will open up and swallow you down, down, down! Into the very depths of hell itself!" Mateo laughed, truly enjoying himself.

Domingo whirled on Juan. "Are you scared?" he yelled. "Ah, tell me right now! Are you scared? Ah, what's wrong with you? Don't you love your mother? Don't you love your father? I'll thrash you good if you're scared, you stupid *cabezón*!"

ed Domingo's righteous anger, so he hit each of his brothers, too. "You see, *burros*, what happens to you it you're
not to be brave at all times so that the Devil doesn't come in
Mateo a coy̌ul."

and little Pelón lowered their heads and took their older
, just like Juan accepted Domingo's. After all, this was the
here in the mountains of Jalisco. A boy had to endure much
come a proper Christina. As the good priest explained to them
came to their village, God's only Son, Jesus Christ, had come
he Earth to suffer for man's sins. So, the least a good Christian
is to suffer along with Jesus in God's ongoing battle against the
f *El Diablo*.

n, Emilia came running up. She was almost fifteen years old and
n all of them. "Stop hitting him!" she told Domingo. Emilia had
n-brown hair just like Domingo and bright blue eyes like their father.
ne was tall and slender and very beautiful. Her skin was so white that it
hurt her to spend much time in the sun.

"I thought I'd catch you out here bullying Juan again." She turned Juan
around by the shoulders to face her. "You don't have to do this, you know.
When the priest marries them, he is going to bless their wedding and so all
this will be . . ."

"But the priest won't dare mention that Luis' mother is *una bruja*!" said
Domingo, cutting her off. "You know very well that ever since the witch sent
that basket of peaches and the fine fat chicken to the old priest in town, and
he choked to death on that chicken bone, no one—but no one—dares to even
bring up her name for fear of her putting a spell of death on them, too!"

"That's true," said Lucha. "You have to admit that, Emilia. This new young
priest is never going to even mention her name." She made the sign of the
cross over herself. "May the soul of the old priest rest in Heaven, dear God,"
she added.

Emilia looked from Domingo to Juan. Her eyes filled with tears as she took
her little brother in her arms. "Oh, Juan, Juan, my little baby brother, Juan.
I just don't know what to do. Maybe we should just go ask Mamá or Luisa.
They always know what to do."

"No!" shouted Domingo. "That would be the worst thing we could do! Luisa
can't possibly speak out against her future mother-in-law. And our mother—
what can she do except tell us to pray? Or worse still, have us go talk with the
priest, and we all know that he's deathly afraid of La Bruja. Remember, he's
the one who heard the old priest's last words, 'Josefina, Josefina,' just before
he . . ."

"Oh, my Lord God!" said Lucha. "You just said her name, Domingo!"

Instantly, Domingo dropped to his knees, quickly making the sign of the
cross over himself and asking as fast as he could for God to protect him.
Everyone else fell to their knees, too, crossing themselves and praying . . .
except Juan, who remained on his feet.

"Eh, wait," said Juan, deep in thought. "Just how could the old priest's last
words have been . . ." Everyone stared at him. He stopped himself. "I mean,
when someone is choking on a chicken bone, they can't talk, can they? Every
time I've almost choked, I couldn't talk. So how could the old priest have said
La Bruja's name if he was choking to death, eh?"

"Are you questioning the good priest's word?" snapped D
his knees.

"Well, no," said Juan, "I'm not. But I was only thinking that

"Stop thinking!" exploded Domingo, getting to his feet. "You on
well that 'thinking' is one of the cardinal sins that caused our fal
Garden of Eden!"

"Yes, I know," said Juan, "but I was only trying to say that . . ."

"Stop it, Juan!" demanded Domingo. "No more of this! It's time for y
stand up like a proper Christian and do what you have to do to save
family! Don't you love your mother? Eh, answer me! Don't you love o
dear, beloved mother?"

"Well, yes, I do, of course," said Juan.

"And don't you love our father?"

Juan wanted to think about this one. At times he wasn't quite sure if he
did. His father was always so mean to him, hitting him on the head and
calling him 'cabezón.'

"Well, answer me!" ordered Domingo. "You love your father, don't you?"

Juan glanced up at his brother. At times like this, Domingo looked so
much like their father that it was scary. His whole face was red with rage
and his blue eyes were all glassed over, looking almost white.

"Yes," said Juan, not wanting to get hit anymore.

"Good," said Domingo, "then go do it right now!"

"But how are we to know if he really goes all the way to La Bruja's house
and does it?" asked Mateo. "He could just go halfway across the valley and
we'd never know. The way the moon is going in and out of those clouds, it's
going to be hard to see him after he crosses that first fence."

"That's true," said Lucha, looking across the valley into the darkness.
"After that first fence, we won't be able to see what he does if the moon goes
behind the clouds."

"Oh, just leave him alone!" said Emilia, tears coming to her eyes once more.
"It's enough that he's even attempting to do it! If you bigger ones are so doubtful, then why don't you just go along with him or, better still, do it yourself?"

"Well, no, we can't do that," said Lucha defensively. "We'd, ah, well, be
sure to wake up her dogs because there'd be too many of us and then we'd all
be killed."

Domingo shoved Lucha. "That was really a dumb thing to say," he said.
"We're trying to give him reassurance, not scare him." He turned to Juan.
"Look, Juan, it's not her dogs that we're afraid of. Right, Mateo?"

"Yeah, sure, right," said Mateo.

"The reason that we don't go along with you, little brother, and protect
you is that then you wouldn't have the chance to prove how brave you are.
And, after all, that's the only thing that defeats the Devil . . . when a man is
willing to meet El Diablo all by himself with nothing between him and eternal damnation but the faith he has in Almighty God."

"That's true!" said Mateo, making the sign of the cross over himself and
kissing the back of his thumb, which was folded over his index finger in the
form of the cross. "The only weapon a true Christian needs against all evil
is the faith he carries here, inside of his chest! Oh, I envy you, Juan. When
you succeed doing this tonight, not only will you be saving all your family,
but you'll be saving the whole world, too. For, remember what the good
priest says, 'One man's battle in overcoming the Devil's way is all mankind's

⟩ smiled, feeling proud of how well he'd repeated the words
⟩'d learned in church.

*salvation*
*of God*  ⟩eo's straight white teeth smiling across his wide, handsome
⟩d he felt a sudden strength come shooting up into his chest.
*Ju*⟩olutely right. He just hadn't looked at it like that. This was,
*In*⟩ance for Juan to prove—not just to his family but to all the
⟩ much he loved them, just as Christ Himself had done on the
⟩o as long as he kept faith here inside his heart and soul, then no
⟩d possibly come to him.

⟩ore Juan could speak, telling them about his newly-found cour-
⟩ia spoke. "No! This is wrong! What if he fails?!" she said. "If you
⟩is is so grand, Mateo, then why don't you and Domingo—who are
⟩ with rocks—go do it. At least you'll have a chance if her killer dogs
⟩en to wake up!"

Then, right then, was when it happened. It came up out of Juan before he
even realized that he'd spoken. "No!" he said to Emilia, whom he knew truly
loved him and only wanted the best for him. "I will not fail!" he shouted. "I
will not fail! And the Earth will not open up and swallow me, for I love my
mother, I truly do. And I will save us all. I don't want us burning in the
fires of hell for all damnation!" His eyes began to cry, but his heart held
strong. He turned and started for the creek.

Quickly, Pelón rushed after Juan. The two boys were friends. Over the
years, their older brothers had forced them to fight each other many times,
but their hearts had never really been in it. "Here," said Pelón, giving Juan
his special rock. "I found this little rock inside the church one day. I think
it came from Jesus' feet when they were repairing the walls."

"*Gracias*," said Juan, taking the well-worn, smooth little stone.

Pelón gave Juan a quick *abrazo*[3] and then watched him go down the slope
to the creek and hop from rock to rock so he wouldn't get wet.

"But how will we know if he goes all the way?" asked Mateo again.

"That's right," said Lucha. "How will we know?"

Domingo thought a moment, then shouted after Juan, who was quickly
disappearing into the night. "Bring back a peach!"

Juan just kept walking.

"Maybe he didn't hear you," said Lucha, so she screamed out, "Bring back
a peach so we'll know you went all the way!"

"Quiet!" said Emilia. "What do you want to do? Wake up the dogs so
they'll be sure to kill him?"

"But he didn't answer," said Lucha.

"He heard us," said Domingo, smiling. "No more shouting. Emilia is right.
We don't want to wake up the dogs. My little brother needs a fair chance." He
took a big breath. "Look at him go. He really is a brave little kid, isn't he?"

"Yes," said Pelón quietly, tears running down his wide cheeks. "Very, very
brave."

•  •  •

"'Bring back a peach!' they yell after me," said Juan in disgust to himself as he
kept walking. "What do they think I am, one of the wise men[4] to bring them

3. Embrace, hug.
4. The Magi.

Christmas presents? My God, the last person who tried to steal off her trees she hit on the head so hard with a club that it's said old man lost his memory and now thinks he belongs to her, and him like a slave from sun to sun.

"Oh, yes, I'll bring you back a peach—six of them wrapped in cho so you'll see once and for all that I did it and our Mamá isn't going t to burn in hell for all eternity."

Juan wiped the tears that came to his eyes and continued talking to h self as he walked across the valley, rubbing the little stone that Pelón ha given him. "Oh, Lord God, why does it always have to happen to me? Ah? Why me? If I'm not getting hit for losing a goat to the coyote, then I'm getting hit because the pigs ate the chayote plant. Oh, I pray for the day that it isn't me that needs to get hit on the head, dear God.

"By the way," Juan continued, getting a twinkle in his eyes as he came to the first fence made of stone, "next week is Your Beloved Son's birthday, right?" He put his right hand on the rock fence and looked up at the heavens. The moon was smiling down on him between two great white clouds. "Well, then, Dear God, I'd like to dedicate what I'm about to do tonight as a Christmas gift to Your Most Beloved Son for His birthday. How about that? Pretty good, eh, dear God?"

And having said this, Juan laughed and climbed over the first rock fence on his way to the witch's house. He felt pretty good now. He liked the way he'd slipped this one in on God. After all, by offering to dedicate what he was about to do tonight to God's only Son, then God couldn't very well let him fail, could He? No, of course not. So now it was in the bag, because God had to make sure that he, Juan, succeeded so that His Most Beloved Son, Jesus Christ, wouldn't be disappointed on His birthday.

Feeling much better, Juan continued at a brisk pace across the valley. With God indebted to him, what could possibly go wrong? Nothing, absolutely nothing. The five big dogs would be sound asleep, and the biggest, juiciest peaches would be down on the lower branches so he could just pick them as easy as he pleased.

He stopped. He could now make out the individual peach trees by the side of La Bruja's house. He took a big breath. It was said that the reason her trees were so big and green and had the biggest, sweetest peaches in all the region was because she fed the trees the blood and guts of her chickens.

And once, long ago when Domingo and Mateo were little, they said that they'd actually witnessed her feeding her trees. It had just been dusk when Mateo and Domingo had sneaked up to her place to steal some of her fine peaches. She'd come out of her house, singing, with a big fat chicken under her arm. She was petting the chicken with such love when she'd suddenly taken a little knife from under her dress and slit the chicken's throat so quickly that they could hardly believe that she'd done it. Then she began to dance around her beloved trees, holding the big chicken upside down by its feet, singing with gusto as she fed the chicken's dripping blood to her trees. She raised the dead chicken to the sky, and they'd heard her summon the powers of the Devil to give her the greatest peaches. Domingo and Mateo *had barely* crawled away with their lives intact. She'd been as quick as lightning with that chicken-killing knife.

Remembering this story, Juan took a few deep breaths. "Oh, Dear God," he said, "remember, we got a deal. So no matter how quick she is with that knife of hers, You got to keep brave and stay by my side ready to help me out. Or, remember, Your Most Beloved Son might not find a present waiting for Him on His birthday, and then He'll be so, so sad. And you don't want to see Your Beloved Son all sad and red-eyed, do You? Of course, You don't. The poor Boy, His eyes are so red all the time, hanging on that cross. So let's be sure He gets a good birthday, ah, God?"

Having said this, Juan laughed and looked out across the valley to the witch's house. He figured that it was best to keep working God as he went along. That way, God wouldn't get distracted with the other jobs that he had going across the universe, and He'd remember to keep Juan in mind.

He could now see that La Bruja's house wasn't very far. He'd have to keep his wits about him and make sure that her dogs weren't out hunting in the fields around her house. Because if he came upon her dogs out in the open fields, then they'd get him for sure. It was said that she had the meanest dogs in all the region, because she deliberately kept them half-starved.

It made Juan's skin want to crawl when he remembered what happened to that poor stranger who'd been caught by her dogs last year. He'd been riding this horse across the valley when he'd caught the scent of her wonderful-smelling peaches. So he'd reined in his horse and followed the scent. With his nose in the breeze, he'd ridden into her orchard thinking he'd found Heaven. But when he'd reached up to pick a big juicy peach, the dog called El Diablo had leaped out of nowhere, roaring like death itself as he'd caught the horse by the head. The other dogs bit at the horse's legs and flank and the horse went bucking, kicking through the orchard, falling over backwards.

The man was thrown off his horse and his pistol was ripped out of his hands before he could defend himself. The five big starving dogs started tearing at him and his horse in a frenzy of wild hunger. Kicking and whinnying, the horse was finally able to get to his feet and take off, but the man couldn't get up and kept screaming cries of agony until the witch came out of her house, calling off her dogs.

Getting to the second stone wall, Juan stopped to catch his breath. Her house was right ahead of him now, and her orchard of peach trees started just on the other side of that last rock wall. He glanced up at the full moon and then back across the valley to where he'd left Domingo and the others. But he couldn't see them anymore. In fact, he could barely make out the dark outline of the pig pens and the horse corrals behind them. He could see his parents' house easily. The bright light from the kitchen could be seen through the window. He wondered if he couldn't just turn around now and go back home. After all, to have come this far in the dark, he'd already shown the Devil that he was pretty darn brave.

"Look, God," he said out loud, "people ride their horses clear around this side of the valley so they don't have to come near her orchard. I've already come closer to her place in the night than few mortals would dare. So what do You think, eh, God? Do I really have to go any further? The Devil can already see that I'm pretty brave."

Suddenly, the moon went behind some dark clouds and the night darkened and turned cold. Instantly, Juan's eyes got big.

"All right, all right, God!" he said quickly. "I'll go all the way. Just don't take my moonlight away. I need all the light I can get."

The moon came out from behind the clouds and the night was bright with light once more.

He took a big breath and made the sign of the cross over himself, kissing the back of his thumb, which was folded over his index finger in the form of a cross, just like he'd seen Mateo do. He blew out and continued across the open field toward the witch's home—this woman, this person who grew the finest peaches in all the region.

Suddenly, Juan thought he heard something and he stopped dead. Slowly, carefully, he glanced around, hoping to God that it wasn't her dogs that had sneaked up on him. But he saw nothing. And the moon was now out from between the clouds, and it was so huge and bright and big around that it illuminated the whole area around him almost as bright as day. He could see her house clearly, too. Why, he could actually begin to make out the individual stones of the rock fence around her home.

Then, as he was studying her place carefully, he spotted the huge dog. His heart stopped. Good God, it was the famous dog, El Diablo, and there he was up on her porch, stretching and yawning with his open mouth so gigantic— reaching up toward the moon—that Juan was sure that his whole leg could fit inside.

Juan swallowed, not moving a muscle. The huge dog continued yawning and stretching. If the monster dog El Diablo was up and about, then Juan figured that her other four dogs were up and about, too. Without moving his head, Juan quickly rolled his eyes about, carefully searching for the other dogs around the house. For Juan well knew that the most dangerous dog for him this night wasn't El Diablo, her biggest dog, but Cara Chata, her smallest dog. For in this area of Mexico, every ranch kept a pack of dogs, and among their pack they always had a nervous little dog that was a light sleeper so it would start barking at the slightest sound and wake up the larger dogs.

Juan searched her porch with his eyes, examining every potted plant, then carefully looked around her famous mango tree. It was said that mango trees couldn't live up in this mountainous region of Jalisco, Mexico, that mangoes were strictly tropical fruit trees, so they could only grow big and strong and bear fruit further south in the regions of Guerrero and Oaxaca. And yet, there stood Josefina's mango tree alongside her house, as big and as strong as a fully-grown oak and full of fruit as huge around as bull's . . .

Juan stopped his thoughts. "Good God," he said to himself. "I just thought of her name inside my head! I wonder if she also knows when people think about her?" Just then, as he had this thought, the door flew open with a bang and out came the witch herself. She was a tall, well-built woman with big, strong hands and large calloused feet. It was said that she always worked barefooted and she was never without a shovel or hoe in her hand. She'd always done all her own work—building fences, planting trees, hauling dirt— until she'd hit that poor old man on the head a few years back. And now she had him working with her from sun to sun.

"¡*Perrrros!*" she said to the dogs. "Here are a few scraps, but I'm not feeding you too much tonight."

Quickly, all the dogs got to their feet and she threw them the scraps. Juan crouched down into a little ball, holding as still as he could. He was out in midfield with nothing between him and the terrible witch. The rock fence that he'd just climbed over was quite a ways behind him.

"Oh, dear God," he prayed, "please don't let her see me."

"I want all of you dogs staying alert tonight," she said, petting her pack of hungry beasts. "It's a full moon, a good night for some no-good, lazy so-and-so to try and steal some fruit off my trees. So you keep alert or I'll cut your guts out and feed them to my trees, too!

"Here, Diablito," she said to her huge black dog, calling him Little Devil, "you be extra ready tonight. I got this strange feeling that something very, very strange is going to happen tonight." Then she suddenly turned and looked straight out at Juan. "What is that funny little clump I see out in my field? Ah, answer me! Are you a rock that fell off my stone fence, or what?"

Juan squeezed his eyes closed, hoping he could just disappear. "Dear Lord God," he said to himself, "what are You doing? I thought we had a deal! Oh, please, dear God, help me! Help me! I'm just a little boy!"

"Oh, so you won't answer me!" yelled the witch at the clump that she thought might be a rock. "All right, then, take this!" And she picked up a stone from the pile of rocks she kept on her porch and threw it with all her strength at the clump, almost hitting Juan. "I can see you, you no-good thief! Don't you dare think I can't see in the dark! The full moon is my friend, and you come any closer to my winter peaches and I'll have my dogs on you in a second! Do you hear me? IN A SECOND!!" And then she lifted her mighty arms and screamed up toward the Heavens. "The full moon is my friend! And the old woman who lives up there looks out after me and my trees! Because we're both women! Do you hear me? Because we're both women all alone in the night! And we have our special ways!"

Juan didn't dare move a muscle. He was rolled up in a little ball, rooted to the ground. His eyes wouldn't even open. They were transfixed, staring into the eternal darkness of his own forgotten soul. Then he heard her door close with another big bang, and he figured she'd gone back inside. He could hear her dogs gnawing at their bones and lapping up the scraps. He figured that this was maybe his last chance to escape with his life. But he didn't dare get up and run, so he began to crawl backwards as fast as he could.

Just then the little dog called Cara Chata began barking.

"Oh, dear God," said Juan, "she's spotted me. I don't have a chance now. Good God, I was a fool to have let them talk me into doing this."

Then Juan heard the roar, the huge howling ROAR of El Diablo, and here came the pack of dogs flying off the porch straight toward him.

"Oh, dear God!" said Juan, almost peeing in his pants. "Now what am I to do? If I stay here, I'm sure to be ripped to pieces and eaten alive. But if I get up to run, they're sure to catch me, or . . . wait, what if I can make it to her peach trees over there and climb up a tree? Yes, that's it!" he said excitedly.

Juan tried to get to his feet so he could run as fast as he could to her peach trees, but he couldn't get up. Something was holding him down to the ground like a gigantic magnet. The pack of howling dogs was getting closer and closer, bellowing sounds of hell as they came, but Juan just couldn't get to his feet no matter how much he pushed against the Earth, trying to right himself so he could take off running. Carefully, he placed both of his hands against the ground in front of him and he pushed and pushed with all his might. But for the life of him, he just couldn't move himself even one inch. A gigantic hand-like force was holding him down tight to the Mother Earth.

Finally, he gave up. And in that instant when he gave up and relaxed, he saw it. A female coyote was over there not far from him, sniffing in his direction.

He looked at the coyote and she looked at him, and their eyes held on to each other for a long, long, heart-in-your-throat, timeless moment. Then the coyote smiled—actually smiled—at him, glanced at the pack of howling dogs, gave a yelping howl, and leaped over the rock fence, passing over the moon as graceful as a dream.

Juan couldn't believe what his eyes had just seen: a smiling female coyote leaping over the full moon. And so he relaxed, feeling the warmth of the gigantic hand that was holding him down against the rich, good-smelling earth. Suddenly he felt much better; he was safe now. All he had to do was stay still and the dogs would follow the coyote.

The pack of dogs came racing up, hollering as they came. Juan watched each one of them jump up on the fence, gather their feet under themselves and leap past the full moon, too. But not nearly as gracefully as the she-coyote had done.

Then all the big dogs were gone, giving chase to the coyote. Juan now thought that he was perfectly safe . . . until he realized that Cara Chata was staring at him, eyeball-to-eyeball. The little dog hadn't been able to make it over the fence, and her long tongue was hanging out as she now tried to catch her breath. Juan swallowed, not moving a muscle. "Oh, dear God," he said to himself, "I've been caught dead."

• • •

Back across the valley, Domingo and the others heard La Bruja's door open with a bang and then they heard her shout into the night.

"Do you think she saw him?" asked Emilia. "Oh, Lord God, we should never have allowed him to go!"

"Quiet!" said Domingo. "Let us hear!"

They heard another shout, even louder than the first, and then the door slammed shut.

"What do you think, Mateo?" asked Domingo. "Did she spot him?"

"No, I don't think so," said Mateo, "or we'd hear her dogs."

They listened to the silence of the night, wondering what was happening to Juan. Then suddenly they heard the high-pitched barking of the witch's little dog, and then came that huge, devastating ROAR of El Diablo, filling the whole valley with sound.

"Oh, good God!" yelled Emilia. "They're killing Juanito! Quick, let's go tell Mamá!"

"No!" said Domingo: "Do you want us all to get in trouble?"

"Besides," added Mateo, "they don't have him yet. Those barks are of dogs giving chase, not of dogs ripping and killing."

"That's true," said Lucha. "Dogs sound very different when they got their prey down on the ground. They're just chasing right now. Listen to them; our little brother must be really running," she said, smiling proudly. "He really went all the way. Wow, I wouldn't have ever REALLY gone all the way. Would you, Domingo?"

"Quiet!" he said. "We need to hear! Those dogs are going crazy! Just listen to them. He must be in the orchard, climbing a tree or something."

"See, Mateo," continued Domingo, turning to his friend. "All these years I've been telling you that my little brother is brave. You're going to have to push Alfonso and Pelón a long way for them to match my little brother."

"We'll see, we'll see," said Mateo. "How do we know that the dogs aren't just chasing a coyote or something? For all we know, your brother could just be laying down by some rocks, hiding."

An adult voice suddenly startled them all. "What's going on?" asked José Villaseñor, coming up behind them. All six kids turned around and came face to face with José. And beside José stood Luis, as tall and wide as a giant.

"Eh?" continued José, glancing them over. "Why are those dogs barking? What mischief have you kids come to do behind the pig's pen? Come on, answer me. Mamá sent us down here, thinking you might be up to something."

His voice was calm. He always spoke very calmly. "Domingo," he said, "hear me good. Don't glance like that at Emilia again, or I'll take you down to size in front of everyone. Now talk. Quickly. What's going on?"

Mateo didn't dare do anything, either. The giant Luis had come in close to him and was ready to snatch him up by the throat if he so much as breathed. They were trapped. There was no getting around it, and Emilia was dying to talk.

"José," said Emilia, "they sent Juan to La Bruj—I mean to Don Luis' mother's house, and I told them not to, but Domingo kept insisting that . . ."

"Oh, no!" said Luis.

But José never said a word. He'd already turned and was racing toward the horse corrals. In a matter of seconds, he caught a horse, jumped on it bareback, and was racing off at a full gallop, leaping across the little creek.

Luis got a horse, too, and took off after José. Domingo and the other kids watched as both men disappeared into the night, horses' hooves pounding the good Earth with sound. The dogs continued howling in the distance, filling the night with terrible sound.

• • •

The short little dog called Cara Chata caught her breath and started barking into Juan's face, calling the pack of howling dogs back.

"Oh, my God!" said Juan to himself. He leaped to his feet. "I'll run to La Bruja's house and summon the Devil. Then I'll race to her orchard, pick a bunch of peaches, and take off back across the valley before her dogs return!"

Thinking that he had it easy now, Juan laughed at the barking little dog and dodged left, then right, then leaped over the short-legged little dog and took off racing toward the witch's house. But he hadn't gone more than ten feet before the stout little dog caught him by his leg, dragging him to the ground.

"You fool!" screamed Juan, kicking at her. "Don't you know I'm about God's business?!" But the little dog didn't seem to care, and she kept hold of Juan, growling and biting and snapping.

Juan finally broke loose and took off running with Cara Chata in fast pursuit, grabbing him and knocking him down every few feet.

"Now, what are You doing, God? Having fun? Well, it's not funny to get past a pack of killer dogs only to have my feet chewed off by this little nothing-dog!"

Then Juan heard laughter, a great ROAR of huge laughter. He glanced up at the moon, thinking that God was now openly laughing at him. But then he realized that the laughter came from behind him. He turned, and there was the witch herself no more than twenty feet away. And she had a shovel in her hand, holding it like a club to do him in. His heart leaped into his throat.

"What have we here? A baby thief?" she yelled viciously.

Juan swallowed. "No!" he yelled, leaping to his feet and standing up as tall as he could. "I'm here to . . . to summon the Devil and all the forces of evil that you have in your great powers, and . . . and say that I don't fear you, or your witchcraft, for our familia walks in the love of Almighty God!

"DO YOU HEAR ME?" Juan added with all the power of his little seven-year-old heart and soul. "We do not fear you, for WE FOLLOW GOD'S PATH OF LOVE!!"

The large woman stopped dead in her tracks, not expecting this—especially not from such a small child. The little female dog, Cara Chata, also stopped yapping at Juan and stood there in the moonlight with her head cocked at an odd angle, looking at him in a strange way, too.

Juan made the sign of the cross over himself, kissed the back of his thumb that was folded over his index finger in the form of a cross and said, "The Earth shall not swallow me, and no harm shall ever come to my mother and my family, for I can truly say to you that I carry God's love here inside my heart and soul, and you are powerless before me."

Hearing these last words, La Bruja came out of her momentary surprise and said, "Powerless, am I? You little piece of chicken caca! We'll see! We'll see!" And she charged Juan, swinging at him with her shovel.

But from so many years of getting hit on the head, Juan was pretty agile. So he ducked her blows and took off running toward her orchard, heart pounding so fast that he was sure that it was going to come up his throat and jump out of his mouth. He swallowed again and again, trying to keep his pounding heart down in his chest as he ran. But here came Cara Chata again, trying to grab his legs. Juan jumped and jumped, hopped and hopped, dodged and kicked, and managed to keep going until he got to her peach trees.

Quickly, he glanced around for some fruit, but none was hanging from the lower branches; all the peaches were up high in the trees. It was strange, nobody in all the region had winter peaches except La Bruja. Juan was just deciding which tree to climb when he heard that huge, devastating roar of El Diablo. The pack of dogs was headed back his way.

Instantly, Juan climbed the tree nearest him as fast as a squirrel and picked one, two, three, four, five, six big peaches, swung down from the tree, gathered up his fruit and put it in his pouch, then took off racing as fast as he could. But the pack of dogs was on his tail. The witch, too.

"Good, God!" said Juan to himself as he ran, "I did it, God! I really did it! Even right to her face! So please don't let her killer dogs get me now!" He was racing across the open field as fast as he could go, hoping to get to the first rock fence, scramble over it, and then . . . oh, he just didn't know what to do. The big woman was going crazy, yelling at her dogs to hurry up and get the boy. "He's a thief! A thief! Get him, Diablo! Get him and tear his no-good heart from his chest and eat it for your DINNER!!"

The moon was going in and out of clouds, giving the whole valley an eerie feeling. Juan got to the first fence and climbed up on top of it so he could look around. There came the pack of dogs, no more than a hundred yards away, hollering to the Heavens as they closed in on him. Right behind him came the witch, no more than fifty feet away.

Juan quickly glanced around and spotted a pile of big rocks not far out in the next field. "If I can get to those rocks, I'll have a fighting chance," he said. "But I'll need a club to fight the dogs off with. Oh, God, please help me!" he said, glancing up to the heavens.

Just then, as he asked for help, he saw the witch stop thirty feet away from him and raise the shovel above her head, whirling it around like a lariat. She sent it flying at him with all the power of her body, the whole while screaming, "May you burn in hell, you little no-good thief!"

Calmly, carefully, Juan watched the shovel coming right at him, long wooden handle following large spoon-like metal in a spinning circle of air-swishing noise. Smiling, Juan ducked, jumping off the rock fence, and the shovel passed right over him like a great ocean-sailing vessel.

"*Gracias!*" yelled Juan to the old witch, and he ran over and picked up the shovel and took off for the pile of big boulders out in midfield.

"Don't give me '*gracias*'!" screamed La Bruja, getting to the fence. "May your thieving soul burn in hell for all eternity! I've worked hard for what I got! Do you hear me?!" She kept yelling after Juan as she stood there by the fence she'd built with her own two hands. "I worked hard! And you have no right to enjoy the fruits of my labor! May you choke on the seed of my peaches! Choke! Choke! Choke! TO DEATH!!"

Hearing the words "Choke! Choke! Choke! TO DEATH!" as he ran, Juan thought it had been pretty stupid of him to have stolen so many peaches, because how could they really enjoy eating them, realizing that they came from the witch's trees and that an old priest had, indeed, choked to death while eating one of her fat chickens? He dropped the peaches. The big rocks were getting closer and closer as he ran, but her dogs were almost on top of him.

"Oh, dear God," said Juan, leaping over the grass and rough terrain as he went. "I did do wrong to steal her peaches because she does work hard to grow them. I see that now; I really do. So, could You please forgive me for my trespasses, like I forgive others for their trespasses? And from now on, I'm the biggest forgiver of trespasses You've ever seen! No kidding, dear God! The biggest!"

He could hear the dogs getting closer and closer. He turned and saw that the huge black dog was leading the pack. They were no more than thirty yards away from him, howling to the heavens with vengeance. "Oh, MAMÁ! MAMÁ! Help me!" yelled Juan. "I think God has forgotten me!"

He pumped his little legs as hard as he could, trying to get to the boulders before the pack overtook him. He figured that if he could just get to the rocks and scramble up, then he could maybe fight them off with the shovel. The rocks were getting bigger and bigger as his little legs went flying.

"You won't make it to those rocks!" the witch yelled at him. "And if you do, my dog El Diablo will pull you off of them and eat you alive!"

She began to laugh and shout and sing. "Ha, ha, ha! You're going to get yours! Ha, ha, ha! All of you thieving men are going to get yours. This is judgment day FOR ALL OF YOU!"

"Boy, she's not very forgiving of other's trespasses," said Juan to himself as he ran. "I wonder if she's dancing, too?"

He was tempted to turn around and take a quick look at her, but he knew he couldn't. The dogs were almost on top of him. He could feel their breathing, and they smelled awful.

Then he reached the big rocks and was just scrambling up when he felt a sharp, tearing pain in his left foot as he was being dragged down off the rocks. He turned and saw that El Diablo had him by the foot and was trying to get his whole leg into his huge mouth, growling and biting and yanking and ripping. Juan kicked and jerked and SCREAMED at the top of his lungs, and tried hitting the monstrous dog with the shovel. But then the other dogs came, leaping on him from all sides, ready to devour him, too.

The last thing Juan saw before he passed out was the form of a huge horse-like creature with wings come flying out of the Heavens, smashing into the pack of dogs. Then a mighty angel was swinging a club with a head of steel, lashing dogs left and right, cutting them to pieces as they yelped in pain. Then a larger angel also appeared, and this angel grabbed El Diablo by the throat, strangling him.

All this time, La Bruja was weeping hysterically, and yelling, "No, no, no! Please, no, no, no!" The larger angel turned and took La Bruja into his arms with such tenderness, calling her "Mamá." Juan thought that was so, so, so funny. He'd never for the life of him thought that witches could also be loving mothers, especially not of angels. And that was the last thing Juan remembered. Then he was gone, done, no more.

. . .

Waking up, Juan found that he was in bed under the covers in his parents' bedroom. His whole body was in pain. Why, it hurt his head to just move his eyes to look around the room. He tried to lick his lips, but his mouth was so dry that he had trouble moving his tongue. He swallowed a few times. He was so thirsty that he didn't know what to do. Water. He needed lots of water, right now. He tried to get up to go get some water, but when he moved, his whole body screamed out in terrible pain.

"Oh, my God!" he said. "What happened to me?"

"Mamá, he's woken up," Juan heard Emilia yell in the distance.

"About time!" Juan heard his mother answer from another room. "It's been nearly three days!" Then he heard his mother's feet come rushing over the tile floor, with sister Emilia right behind her.

"So, you've finally come back from the dead," said his mother, smiling at him. "Oh, *mi hijito*,[5] you gave us an awful scare. But what ever possessed you to do such a crazy thing? You know very well how Domingo and those wild boys are about everything. Did you really think that their interpretation of God's wishes would be any different than what they think of the rest of the world?" Gently, she took the back of his head with her right hand and lifted him up just a little so she could spoon-feed the watery fluid that she'd prepared for him.

"Oh, *mi hijito*, I'm so surprised at you. You're my last-born son, and all these years I've been raising you to realize down deep inside yourself that the things of men aren't necessarily true. Especially not when they hurt you or cause harm to others."

Juan heard his mother's words as in a far-away dream, and he felt the warm, watery liquid go slowly down his throat. Then he was sound asleep once more, dreaming, dreaming, seeing that flying horse and angel come

5. My little son.

swooping down out of the Heavens and once more scattering the pack of mad dogs. The female coyote came to him again, and she smiled. Juan felt so warm and good all over with the female coyote at his side. Then his head was being raised up again and he was spoon-fed some more warm, watery liquid. When he opened his eyes, he saw that his mother was, indeed, the female coyote and she was smiling down on him as she fed him. Now he realized why that female coyote had been so willing to lead the pack of dogs away from him. Why, the female coyote had been his own beloved mother.

"Drink up," his mother was now saying as she fed him with the smooth-feeling wooden spoon. "And keep in mind as you grow stronger that, all these years, I've been raising you to be a gentle man—not a lost male who destroys all he lays his hands on because he feels so left out of the joy of giving birth.

"Oh, *mi hijito*, I love you, I love you so much. And you must promise me to never do such a thing without consulting me first. You've become a little man, *mi hijito*, and a man always needs a woman's opinion in order to round out his decisions—like the broken rocks need the river waters to smooth out their rough edges and make the rocks smooth and round and whole. Believe me, no man's decisions are complete without a woman's influence. And no woman's garden can give life without a man's participation.

"Which leads me to another point, *mi hijito*. I want you to realize that Doña Josefina is no witch. I don't care what all the people say about her. She isn't a *bruja*. She's just a lonely, bitter woman who has tilled her garden alone all these years, because she was wronged by a man in her youth—as so many women have been wronged by men since the beginning of time. And so she has strange ways and doesn't trust any man, especially not since that old mule driver abused her, too. But she's basically a good woman, *mi hijito*—a little crazy and scared like so many of us when we lose our faith in God. But, believe me, she's no witch. That's just the rumor that people like to pass around, especially men who can't stand to see a woman doing well all on her own.

"Here, drink up. We've got to get you strong again. Christmas is only a few days away, and then a week later we have the wedding. That poor woman, she works so hard for her peaches and she'd have none to sell if she didn't have you boys intimidated by her wild ways."

As he sipped the liquid from the smooth-feeling spoon, Juan could see that his mother really liked this woman who'd he'd always known as a witch. He could also see that, yes, indeed, his mother was a coyote. She really was. Her eyes, her mouth, her kind loving touch. She was absolutely a wonderful, loving female-coyote, and she'd been the one who'd come to his rescue when the pack of dogs had been upon him.

Then Juan heard heavy footsteps, and into the room came José and Luis.

"Juan," said José. "Luis is here to see you. He's been coming to see you every day since the accident."

"That was no accident," said Luis with power. "That was a message sent to Luisa and me straight from God! Now we can go into our marriage with open hearts! Juanito, you saved the day for us by bringing everything out into the open that everyone has been talking about for years all over the valley, but has never had the guts to come and say to my face or to my beloved mother's face!"

"Are you two the ones, the . . . the angels who got the dogs off me?" asked Juan, not quite able to fully see yet.

José grinned. "Yes, Luis and I are those angels."

Luis came close and took Juan's hand gently. "We destroyed all the dogs. Now you can come by our home without fear any time you please. I swear, *en el otro mundo no hay mal, pero en este mundo ¿quién sabe con todo los miedos y celos que la gente esconde en sus corazones?*" In the other world there is no evil, Luis had said, but in this world, who can know with all the fears and jealousy that people hide in their hearts?

"You are *mi amo*," continued Luis, "you are my soul, my hero, my savior. And my poor mother will come around to saying the same thing once she gets over mourning for her dogs. Yes, we had to kill them all, except for Cara Chata. She wasn't biting you when we ran up. No, like the proper little lady she is, she'd figured that she'd done her job of calling in the pack, and so she was just sitting back and watching with that head of hers tilted at that funny little angle she always gets." Luis laughed. "You are *mi amo*, my hero, and I give you homage!" Then he kissed Juan on the forehead ever so gently.

"All right, no more now," said Doña Margarita. "That's enough for today. He needs to sleep so he can regain his strength. Oh, I knew those wild boys were up to no good when I sent you two to go check on them. I could feel it in my bones."

"And you were right, Mamá," said José. "We just barely got there in time."

"Yes," said Luis, "and if José wasn't the greatest horseman in all the region, he wouldn't have been able to clear those rock fences with such ease riding bareback and get there before the dogs did even more damage."

Juan heard no more. He was off in dream once again and the smiling coyote was by his side, keeping watch over him. He smiled back at the coyote, feeling so happy, and Luis' words *"en el otro mundo no hay mal,"* continued singing in his brain. Then he realized that yes, indeed, his own beloved mother could turn herself into a she-coyote at will, but this didn't make her a witch, either. No, she was simply a powerful woman who was wild of heart. There were no witches. There was no evil on the other side. That was all just a rumor coming out of the fear and jealousy that people hide in their hearts.

•  •  •

It was Christmas day. The whole house smelled of cooking and baking, and there was much activity in the front of the house. All the family was present: thirty-some cousins and their fathers and mothers. Don Pío, Juan's grandfather on his mother's side, had also come up the mountain from the town of Piedra Gorda, Fat Rock, with his young bride.

Emilia and José came into the bedroom where Juan was staying. Emilia said, "Come on, lazy bones! Mamá has said to bring you into the living room where we've set up a special chair for you!" She was so happy. It made Juan feel all warm inside.

José picked up Juan in his arms, being careful not to touch the leg that El Diablo had almost eaten, and carried him across the house. All the children came rushing to Juan. He was the talk of the whole valley. In fact, it was now said that Juan was a boy so brave that the blood ran backwards from his heart.

Domingo watched all the cousins give Juan greeting and ask him if it was true that he'd faced the witch eye-to-eye in midfield and had single-handedly fought her pack of dogs to a standstill. Seeing all the cousins speak to Juan with such adoration, Domingo's face filled with rage and jealousy.

Suddenly, out of nowhere, Domingo felt a powerful hand grip his shoulder. It was José. "If you want people to look at you like that, little brother," José said, "then next time you do your own dirty work and don't push people littler than you to do it for you."

"But he's the youngest!" snapped Domingo. "The purest of heart! And the priest has always told us that . . ."

"Don't give me that," said José calmly. "We both know that you can always take the words of the Bible or the words of the priest and twist them into any sneaky act you want to do. Remember what our beloved mother always adds to the Bible or the priest's words: Does it harm anyone? Does it cause more pain and darkness? Or does it bring a little more peace and understanding among all of us lost mortals?

"Look at me in the eyes. You're no fool, Domingo. You're smart and could be a good leader, but—and I say this with all sincerity—you've got to stop sneaking off behind pig pens to do your glorious deeds." Eye-to-eye, both brothers held. One was small and dark and older. The other was fair-headed, large-boned and younger.

The tension was so great that Domingo was ready to explode. But just then the front door opened, and in came Luis with his mother. The woman was all dressed up and had a basket covered with a cloth in her hand. In all these years, no one had ever seen La Bruja dressed up like a lady. The room went silent. Even Don Juan, the children's father, who'd been talking loudly and drinking tequila with a couple of his fair-skinned relatives, stopped his words. No one moved. Everyone stared in complete silence—adults and children alike. It was Doña Margarita, who had been talking to Don Pío and his beautiful young bride, who finally got up and went across the room. She walked right up to the tall, handsome woman and her son, who both towered over her.

"Welcome to our humble home, Doña Josefina," said Doña Margarita. "This is, indeed, a glorious day for us to finally have you here with us under our roof. Merry Christmas!"

"Merry Christmas," said the tall, powerful woman. Cautiously, she glanced around the room at the dozens and dozens of faces that she'd seen at a distance over the years, but never up this close. "The honor is mine, Doña Margarita. I feel . . . well, most happy that you've invited me and my son to spend this most holy day of Jesus Christ's birthday with you and your family."

Some people were heard to inhale sharply, being taken aback by the fact that the witch had dared pass God's Most Sacred Son's name through her lips.

But Doña Margarita wasn't surprised at all, and said, "From now on, you and your son will always be invited to pass the holy days of Christmas with us. For let it be known," she added, taking La Bruja by the hand and turning to everyone in the room, "that from now on, Doña Josefina and her son Luis are part of *nuestra familia* and they are both to be loved and respected as our family members here on Earth and afterwards in Heaven, too!"

A couple of the younger cousins giggled. "Here on Earth, maybe yes," one whispered, "but how is a witch supposed to ever get into Heaven?" All the kids giggled.

Juan's mother turned toward Juan and the children, saw them giggling, and came flying toward them, bringing the witch with her by the hand. "And, children, I want you each to meet Doña Josefina personally and shake hands with her."

The kids froze in terror. Domingo and a few others quickly tried to crouch down and sneak away, but there was José on one side of them, and here came Luis on the other side. Domingo froze, and so did the others who'd been thinking of getting away.

"Come on, step forward one at a time and shake hands with Doña Josefina," said Doña Margarita once again. But no child would dare come forward. They all held back in dreaded terror. They didn't care what Doña Margarita said; they knew that this woman was evil to the bottom of her heart.

Seeing how terrified the children were of her, Doña Josefina took a big breath and then said, "They don't have to shake my hand, Doña Margarita." Tears came to her eyes. "Children, after all, really do no more . . . than what their parents would truly like to do themselves, but . . . don't have the guts . . . to come forward and do it!"

A hush of whispers went through the room.

Wiping her eyes, Doña Josefina turned to her son Luis. "Come, let's go. I'd told you it was a mistake for you to bring me here today. These fine people will never accept me in a million years!"

"But Mamá," said Luis helplessly, "we've got to try and . . ."

"Then stay if you like!" she snapped. "But I'm leaving!" And she turned with all the dignity she could muster and started to go when a voice behind her said, "I'd like to shake your hand, señora."

It was a child's voice, and La Bruja stopped dead in her tracks. She and everyone else turned to see who had spoken. The group of children opened up, and there sat Juan in the big chair that had been prepared for him. He swallowed, then repeated himself. "I'd like to shake your hand, señora."

"Eh, aren't you the one who . . ." the big woman stopped her words. Juan's hands and arms and legs were still all covered with swollen bruises and large reddish-black wounds.

"Yes," said Juan, "I'm the one and, well, I want to say that I'm sorry for . . . for . . ." Tears came to his eyes and he had to swallow several times before he could go on. The room was silent. "I mean, I know you work real hard to grow your peaches, señora, and I had no right to steal them, even if I think you are a witch."

People gasped. Others choked. The whole room was filled with a nervous hush of coughing and breathing. Some people began to fan themselves, trying to get air.

"Juan, you must apologize for what you said," said Doña Margarita.

"No, señora," said Doña Josefina, "please don't have him apologize for simply saying what he really thinks. For the truth is that half of the good people in this room think the same thing but do not have the nerve to say it to my face." She glanced around the room, looking from face to face. The room was absolutely still. Then she turned back to Juan. "Thank you, child, for acknowledging that I do work hard to grow my peaches. I accept your apology. And about your thinking I'm a witch, well, what can I say, except that . . ."

"You don't have to explain yourself, Mamá!" bellowed Luis, standing up tall, the cords of his powerful neck coming up like ropes, he was so mad.

"But I want to explain," said his mother. "I don't want you having to run away from this valley like your brother had to do."

She took a deep breath. "I'm no witch," she said to everyone—men, women and children. "Do you hear me? I'm no bruja. Yes, maybe I've acted like one over the years, being over-protective of my trees. And using manure and animals' guts and blood to feed my trees has, I'm sure, caused much talk, too, but . . . but that doesn't make me a witch! That just makes me a woman who doesn't have much trust in people—especially men—and shows that I know what I'm doing when it comes to growing plants and trees.

"My mango tree, my winter peaches, they aren't the accomplishments of witchcraft. No, they are the accomplishments of, well . . ." Tears came to her eyes. ". . . of science, which the old priest in town taught me along with so many other wonders of life." She stopped her words and began to cry. Luis took his mother in his arms, holding her tenderly. Luisa also came up and hugged her mother-in-law-to-be.

A few people began to whisper, but no one spoke aloud. They were stunned. They were shocked. They'd never expected in a hundred million years to see this big, powerful, wild woman—whom they'd all considered to be a witch— to be crying like this, so tenderly, on her son's massive shoulder.

"All right," said Doña Margarita, stepping forward after a proper quiet moment. "As I was saying, I want each of the children to meet you, Doña Josefina, and Juan here has volunteered to be the first."

"Oh, yes, excuse me," said the large woman, "just let me dry my eyes, please."

And so everyone watched as this powerful woman dried her eyes and then stepped forward to meet little Juan. "I'm so glad to meet you," she said, smiling. "In the last few days, my son Luis has told me so much about you."

She reached out, giving Juan her huge, hard hand. Juan looked at the big fingers and calloused palm and then took it. It felt as heavy as a large stone.

"Merry Christmas," she said, eyes full of merriment. "And look, I've brought you a basket of peaches." They were the largest, prettiest peaches anyone had ever seen. "And from now on," she continued saying to Juan, "whenever you want some, just come by the house and we'll pick them together. That way, you won't get green ones like you did the other night."

"Those were green?" asked Juan, astonished.

"Yes," she said, laughing. "Green-green!"

"Oh, no!" said Juan, laughing, too. Then, looking at the basket full of peaches and smelling the rich aroma, Juan took one and bit into it. "Oh, my God, this is heaven!" he said.

"Exactly!" said the tall woman. "And those were the exact same words the poor old priest always used to tell me, too," she said, tears coming to her eyes again. "Oh, he was a good man, a very good man, God rest his soul in heaven," she added, making the sign of the cross over herself. "I loved him; I truly loved him. He was my everything good and bad here on Earth, all wrapped up in one blessed human being, so help me God!"

And in that instant, all the people in the room realized who José-Luis' father was. Why, this large, tall woman and the old priest had loved each other as a man and a woman.

Quickly, others started making the sign of the cross over themselves, too. For this was, indeed, a special moment, a holy moment. God had come down upon the Earth and visited them, His people, in all His power and mystery and miraculous wonders of love.

Then a child spoke—the smallest child in the room who could speak. "If I shake your hand and let you hug me and kiss me," said the child, "will you give me a peach, too?"

People started laughing, melting, relaxing.

"Why, yes," said Doña Josefina, "certainly."

"Oh, good, Señora Witch!" shouted the little girl, throwing open her tiny arms for a big hug and kiss.

The whole room exploded with laughter. Even Domingo was finally caught up in the whole spirit of the moment.

So the child and Josefina hugged each other, and the rest of the day went beautifully. People were so filled with happiness that they just couldn't stop from smiling and laughing as they ate all the special foods and drank all the special drinks that had been prepared all week long. The much-feared woman of their valley wasn't a witch, after all. No, she was just a poor lost soul, like each one of them when they were alone and scared.

Juan sat there on his throne-like chair like a little king, rejoicing in God's Only Beloved Son's birthday. And when the time came to sing to Jesus for His birthday, Juan would swear that he actually saw Jesus stop looking so sad hanging there on the cross over the doorway. And He straightened up and cast a big smile at Juan winking His left eye.

· · ·

## Author's Note

My father always explained to me the story that made him into the man that he later became. "When you bully people and lie and cheat, you do it because you're scared," he told me, "and you become a small, frightened person. But when you stand up to the truth with all your love and heart and soul, no matter what, you become brave and strong and develop guts!"

Remembering my father's words, years later when a large picture window was broken at our home, I called my boys and their ten cousins together and asked who did it. No one would talk. I demanded for them to have the guts to be truthful. One little cousin finally spoke up and said that he'd thrown the rock, but that my son had ducked and so that's why the window was broken.

"So are you saying that my son broke it because he ducked?"

"Well, yes, in a way."

"Look," I said, "stop passing the buck. You're not a politician. Have some guts and tell me who's responsible."

He was scared. Really scared. But finally he said, "I did it. I broke the window."

"Great," I said, and I pulled out a twenty-dollar bill and gave it to him. He was shocked and now everyone wanted to tell me what they'd done wrong, too. One little kid even offered to break another window for me.

1998

# RICARDO SÁNCHEZ
## 1941–1995

His *New York Times* obituary called Ricardo Sánchez the "poet who voiced Chicano anger." A pioneer of Spanglish as a tool of change, Sánchez was committed to social action and linguistic experimentation. "The genesis of Chicano literature," he explained in a preface to his collection *Hechizospells* (1976),

> can be traced back to our poverty strickened barrios and oppressive pinta [jail] conditions. . . . In the main, literature has always been born within the reality of the people—folklore—and not in academia. . . . Art is a process of flux not to be contained nor constricted, ever seeking spontaneity and multiavenues for its expression.

His family had roots in New Mexico, but Sánchez was born and raised in El Paso, Texas, in a neighborhood called El Barrio del Diablo. After dropping out of high school, he enlisted in the U.S. Army. Upon his return from the service, he committed armed robberies, for which he served prison sentences in California and Texas. During his incarceration, he discovered literature. After being paroled, Sánchez earned a high school degree. In 1969, he received a Ford Foundation sponsorship as a Frederick Douglass Fellow in Journalism in Richmond, Virginia. Soon after, he was hired by the University of Massachusetts, Amherst, as a humanities instructor. His book *Canto y grito mi liberación* (I Sing and Shout My Liberation) was published by a small house, Mictla Publications, in 1971, then reprinted two years later by a major house, Anchor Books. The volume's thematic concerns can be seen in the poem "In Exile," a literary manifesto not too distant from the work of the nineteenth-century American poet Walt Whitman:

> i write of my people—LA RAZA!—
> with pride, love, and out of need . . . for
> i am indelibly CHICANO.
> to justice, freedom, and humanity.

According to the critic Luis Leal (see p. 551), the most striking formal characteristic of the volume is

> the use of prose and poetry in both English and Spanish. This mestizo structure lends itself well to the expression of the social and political ideas of the Chicano writer. There is also an echo of pre-Hispanic poetry in the book's repetition in verse of the images and concepts previously expressed in prose. This parallelism gives the book an aesthetic dimension.

In 1974, Sánchez received a doctorate in American Studies and Cultural Linguistic Theory at the Union Graduate School, in Cincinnati, Ohio. He then taught at universities such as the University of Wisconsin, Milwaukee, and the University of Alaska before finding a tenure-track position at the University of Utah. In addition to his academic work, he wrote columns for the *San Antonio Express-News* (1985–88) and the *El Paso Herald-Post* (1988–91).

The five poems included in this anthology display Sánchez's talents for pyrotechnic linguistic invention and his relentless fight to improve social conditions for Chicanos. "Indict Amerika"—from an anthology, *Los cuatro* (1971), of his work and that of the poets Raymundo "Tigre" Pérez, Abelardo "Lalo" Delgado (included in this anthology), and Juan Valdez (aka Magdaleno Ávila)—condemns the United States for its political abuses. A similar message appears in "Stream," from *Canto y grito mi liberación*. And "Fridays Belong to Friends, Sometimes" and "Teresa, last night," both from *Hechizospells*, celebrate friendship and Sánchez's wife, Maria Teresa

Silva, respectively. In "And Would That I Could," from *Brown Bear Honey Madnesses* (1982), the poet sings to "the real" Mexico "songs / that might waft / on mariachi strains, / that I could feel comfort / in all that you should be."

Among his later books are *Eagle-Visioned/Feathered Adobes: Manito Sojourns and Pachuco Ramblings* (1990) and *Amerikan Journeys/Jornadas americanas* (1994). *Selected Poems* appeared in 1985, followed by another collection, *The Loves of Ricardo* (1997). In the last years of his life, Sánchez returned to El Paso. The last column he wrote celebrates the place:

> These sands—where my parents, brothers and son are entombed—are sacred to my sentiments, as are memories of frontera experiences within the burning power of salsa and other condiments. . . . The blaring horns of mariachis and the strains of passion steeped guitars accompanying Chicano voices rapturously harmonize *baladas* that celebrate a visceral, romantic understanding of our mutual humanity—sensuously shared as loving people create a greater sense of this borderland.

## Indict Amerika[1]

        porque mi alma lamenta
            desmadres y duelos,
        porque he vivido
            bajo tinieblas y soledades,
        porque de mi ser ha brotado                                5
            el suero hecho de crueldades[2]
            he llegado al momento
            cuando nomás puedo gritar
            mi última y penumbrosa protesta . . . [3]

        AMERIKA,                                                   10
            hechizo racista de ojos azules—
                ojos  mentirosos,
                ojos  del vacío cruel,
                ojos  imperialistas,
                ojos  desgraciados,                                15
                ojos  hipócritas,
                ojos  moribundos y mórbidos . . . [4]

        AMERIKA,
            mad, genocidic lecher
            drinking our blood,                                    20
            feasting on our carcasses;

        AMERIKA,
            suckler of life and love,
            murderer of brown-flecked children . . .

1. The German spelling of *America* has been adopted by radical political commentators to reflect their view of the United States as racist, repressive, and even fascist.
2. Because my soul laments / disorder and sorrow, / because I have lived / under darkness and solitudes, / because from my being has welled up / the whey made of cruelties.
3. I have reached the point / Where I can only shout / My final, darkening protest . . .
4. Racist spell with blue eyes— / lying eyes, / eyes of cruel emptiness, / imperialist eyes, / disgraceful eyes, / hypocritical eyes, / dying, morbid eyes . . .

venomous putain[5] nation,                                                    25
genuflector to dollar signs,
adulator of sordid rapes and mafiosi enterprises,

#### AMERIKA-THE-DESECRATOR,
the world sits
                    tribunally indicting you                                  30
                    with anger reminiscent
                              of Dachau, Buchenwald[6]

but out there
in my haunted, hungry barrio—
                    in   east/south el paso burnished bowels,                 35
                    in   denver by the crusade,[7]
                    in   migrant stream hovel,
                    in   texas tragic valley dispossession,[8]
                    in   east l.a. desmadrazgo,[9]
                    in   east texas prison hatred,                            40
                    in   barelas albuquerque,[1]
                    in   all those hard-core centers of pobreza[2]
                    WHEREVER WE LIVE, HAVE LIVED,
          yes,
          you puta[3]-kind-of-nation,                                         45
          you pillaging insult to the human race,

          OUT THERE, AMERIKA,
                              ever patiently we await you . . .

THERE—OUT THERE—
                    AMERIKA-THE-DESECRATOR,                                   50

we stand
in bronzed anger
with clenched fist
          and feisty spirits,
con cojones[4] stemming out,                                                 55
desmadrazgo in our souls,
while harsh reality has a field day
snuffing out our children's lives . . .

we now declare
in the midst of hungered growls and furious poverty                          60
that we mean      NOW!      what we say . . .

courthouse of la gente,
oigan hoy la verdad desgraciada . . .

---

5. Whore (French).
6. Nazi concentration camps, in Germany before
and during World War II.
7. A reference to Rodolfo "Corky" Gonzales and
his Crusade for Justice (see p. 787).
8. A reference to the Rio Grande Valley.

9. East Los Angeles overturned.
1. *Barelas*: the old section of Albuquerque, New
Mexico; at the time, a poverty-stricken barrio.
2. Poverty.
3. Whore.
4. With balls (nerve); bravely.

escuchen y demanden
que AMERIKA sea desmadrada . . .[5]                                    65

indictment in the people's court,
true bill     must be made,
there can be no other out,
no excuse can be forthcoming . . .

indictment,     indictment     INDICTMENT OF AMERIKA???     70
yes, yes, yes,     YES!!!!!!

AMERIKA    land of el hijo de la chingada,[6]
land of landed gentry gorging on gringoismo,
land of exploitation, creator of pollution,

LA RAZA no longer asks—we shall take                                  75
our reparations
and in the process
do more
than hope
for land/freedom . . .                           80

now     here     this very place
is our viet-nam,[7]
from tierra amarilla
to court house steps,
denver, September 16, 1970 . . .                                      85
to el paso and California,
el valle y las colonias . . .[8]

SOMOS
espiritu de tizoc,
hijos de joaquín,                                    90
carnales espinosa,
NEO-ZAPATISTAS MERGING WITH VILLAISMO. . . .[9]

AMERIKA,
irrelevant malcreance,[1]
screwed-up money grubber,                          95

the streets puke out
the morbid resin of your perversity,

---

5. People, / listen today to the painful truth . . . / listen and demand / that AMERIKA be overturned . . .
6. *El hijo de la chingada*: bastard.
7. I.e., our war.
8. Lines 83–87 refer to "Corky" Gonzales's Crusade for Justice.
9. WE ARE / Tizoc's spirit, / Joaquín's children, / Espinosa's siblings. . . . *Tizoc*: seventh Aztec ruler of Tenochtitlán (today's Mexico City). *Joaquín*: reference to the mythical protagonist of "Corky" Gonzales's poem *I Am Joaquín* (see p. 788). *Espinosa*: Aurelio M. Espinosa (1880–1958), a leading folklorist and ethnomusicologist; see the "Popular Dimensions" introduction, p. 2429. *NEO-ZAPATISTAS*: the Chicano followers of Emiliano Zapata (ca. 1879–1919), a leader of the Mexican Revolution. *VILLAISMO*: reference to the ideology of the followers of Francisco "Pancho" Villa (1878–1923), another leader of the Mexican Revolution.
1. Possibly a play on *malcriado* (bad-mannered, ill-bred); or possibly Sánchez's coinage, based on the English word *miscreant* (infidel, heretic, one who behaves viciously or criminally).

and you sit smugly at Washington desk
pavlovianly expecting
    grovelling, muted responses              100
    from those that you oppress.

blind, bigoted amerika,
klanish genociders
        mucking/fucking up the world,
while mouthing wishy-washy sentiments        105
      prefacing racist onslaughts
        on "the wretched of the earth . . ."

let our gongs ring out
clarion calls to real involvement,
creating out of muck and mire          110

     a new world social order.
let our voices swell,
our minds, souls, and bodies becoming
unidad humana color de bronce
with a final acclamation:          115

    THIS LAND IS OURS
      and
    WE ARE FREE OF U.S. IMPOSITIONS.

if our blood must flow,
let it become an engulfing ocean        120
drowning our oppressors;
if we must fight,
the enemy is here,
not in asian jungles . . .

Carnales,     look now lovingly, long, and analytically    125
        at the children of la raza . . .
let their visceral yearnings
        and their hurt-filled eyes
make this decision.
padres y madres   que somos,        130
carnales y carnalas that we are,
let us answer the hollow-eyed plea of our children,
let moral indignation
        couple with deliberate action. . . .
no longer         135
can we permit
        rampaging gringoismo to defile us,

the time for action is NOW!
indict Amerika,
       AMERIKA-THE-DESECRATOR. . . .    140

    —R.S.—

1971

tenth month,
el año del chicano[1]

## Stream

Middle america . . . middle amerika[2] it all is the same
when hate becomes the calling card and out of stream of

consciousness, out of migrant stream patterns, the same

crappy situation evolves time after time, and everything is run together like
crazy quilt pattern, and people live, die, and somehow nothing is ever          5
resolved in their lifetime       and does it—or anything—ever come to matter somewhere, now, a child is dying for lack of certain       things, and no
one seems to give a damn—other than the child's parents, and they are
helpless parents, while society or what passes for the elite ruling class
attends groovy party and nice, rounded fanny gets pinched and broad mar-     10
ried to one fat-cat winds up in hay with her husband's friend, but her hubby
won't mind, for they both can share his friend in as many different combinations as are possible—for this is amerika, land of pubic liberty as long as
you don't get caught, and nothing is truly immoral, except being poor and/
or helpless . . . so that immoral child and its parents better get on the ball     15
and learn the name of the game and how to play it . . .

y duelos leídos
en sermones religiosos
son paradojas
señalando
sonidos huecos,                                                                                  20
tres biblias
cambiadas por los terrenos
del afamado rancho king
bajo los rezos inútiles
de sacerdotes ciegos y racistas                                                             25
a la cama los enfermos
mientras aclaramos
cuestiones vanas[3]

creo en un dios verdadero                                                                   30
cerca del basurero,
ahí en el atascadero,
un solo dios verdadero
la gente en el humidero,[4]

un solo dios verdadero . . . [5]                                                             35

1. The year of the Chicano.
2. See note 1, p. 1324.
3. And the mourning read aloud / in religious
sermons / is a paradox / signaling / empty sounds,
/ three Bibles / traded for land / on the infamous
King Ranch / under the useless prayers / of blind,
racist priests / the sick to their beds / while we

clarify / useless questions. *King Ranch*: the largest ranch in the United States at that time.
4. I believe in one true god / near the dump, /
there in the muck, / one true god— / the people
in a smoker.
5. One true god . . .

y los rinches
como casi-dioses
y al cabo el dios
amerikano es racista,
borracho y pirujo,                                        40
una pantalla
con cara de payaso
y alma de baboso,
       aún lo cuentan
       los gavachos                               45
       un solo dios verdadero,
       el barrio un quemadero,
       la muerte ya mero-mero,
       un solo dios verdadero.[6]

and the subway ride continues on from lexington avenue to becoming the el     50
in bronx by 125th and the night air chills the body, while 5th avenue[7] satiny
broads promenade ailing aimlessly in their loneliness . . . nearby in Massachusetts with its many empty universities, more

    desecrated assaults on the spirit is the name of the game

    around fireside chatter about bahai folklore and wishful               55

    thinking, conversion of ex-militant blacks . . . a new toy

    for middle amerika, this of persian religious order and

    ritualistic rhetoric of brotherhood as long as niggers

remember that their place is near enough to hear them but not to touch
them, except during humanistic education                                      60

workshops (purely experimental to see if their kinks are springy and their
smell pungent with musk and gringos turn up their noses even then), and
that goes for all minority people . . . and a porty-rican (un boricua de man-

hattan), quien se llama johnny cabrón, he believes he has white brethren . . . and they'll smite him and they'll smite him, til he learns that he's     65
not white . . .

            oda de fé sonora
            miel amarga

---

6. And the rangers [rinches] / like demigods / in the end / Amerika's god is a racist, / a drunk and a fag, / a screen / with the face of a clown / and the soul of a village idiot, / and still he matters / to whitey / one true god / the barrio a crematorium / where death means so little / one true god.

7. In Manhattan, as is Lexington. The 125th St./ Harlem stop is just after the point at which the underground Metro North rail line (not the sub-way) becomes "the el," or an elevated line, that then continues into the Bronx, the New York City borough north of Manhattan.

crujía sepultosa
cautivadora del alma                                          70

un grito por mi hombresa
gimiendo bajo la presa

verdad que grité en mi sueño,
la busca un boringqueño

oda de triste verano                                          75
dentro el desmadre chicano

el existir pa' la raza
es duelo que en vida pasa.[8]

and his sugra- (like nigra) -dripping illusions of nirvana cum míctla[9] via
panacea become the mandible spewed out honey madness of racist resin in      80
amerika—and he like other confundidos,[1] dies a man without a soul . . . it
is sad that there exist those who in trying to sell themselves have found no
one to buy them and they can only become

regalados[2] . . . their souls cast away in hope of acceptance,

and never are they accepted . . . gift horses looked in the                  85

mouth by a system bent on cruel oppression, repression, and human suppression . . . and some fight for medals for

decorum, only to lose their sanity in the end and wind up in v.a. hospitals,
hopped up, loaded to the gills on

nembutal and stimulants, cruising labyrinths and empty rooms, their souls     90
hanging limply . . . eyes hollow and lusting, mind plotting, and inside an insidious need

for self-affirmation.

el vacío derrama
la voz angustiosa                                             95
del alma; es mejor
vivir o morir como hombre
que besarle los huevos
al boss / rinche,
ese pinche desgraciado.[3]                                    100

---

8. Ode to a sounding faith / sour honey // buried /
which captivates the soul // a shriek for my manhood / howling by the dam // it's true I screamed
in my dream, / in search of a Borinqueño // ode of
a sad summer / part of the Chicano upheaval / the
act of existence for *la raza* / is a duel that passes by
in life.

9. Mictla Publications, in El Paso.
1. Confused.
2. Given away.
3. Emptiness spills / the soul's / anguished voice;
it's better / to live or die like a man / than to kiss
the stupid boss's balls, / the fucking bastard.

i phantasmagorize about the stream of my life, wending its way—como un
duelo penumbroso y al mismo tiempo como canto ilustroso[4]—from the madness of east el paso pachuquísmo en el barrio del diablo, out there by the

coliseum—between hammett and boone streets, from paisano

drive south to el río grande . . . and i ran streets in the            105
anguished futility of a chavalón encabronado y encojonado,[5]

with a yearning itch in my hands for a filero[6] to use against the hated unknown force(s) that seemed to control us through school systems geared to
disparage us, shopping areas designed to make us hunger for that which we
could not afford; and time passed and i grew up with anger and confusion    110
reigning side by side in my being . . . one moment, jefferson high seemed
the avenue for my salvation, until racist teachers (mcbride, willis, travis &
co.) and vendidos (i.e., mares, mendoza, & peña, inc.) turned me off, while
beguiling (or trying to) the carnales to pursue a materialistic, roboticized
life (si, you young kids can get those new cars & fancy duds, etc., just by   115
bartering your souls to mad-eee-son-of-a-bitch-avenue!). i was youth at the
crossroads without a map or turn signal. the army finished the job begun by
the schools; i became flame of need for mine liberation—and i vented my
furious

desperation with gun and madness, that monstrous bitch            120

residing in the gut lining of my soul/mind . . . and sunny

California gave me from one to 25 years in prison, and i

mulled over and over in my mind, between el desmadrazgo,

eviscerations, the canards handed me by a bigoted/unsane

society; the cloister of soledad prison[7] steadfastly demanded my capitula-   125
tion; i could only retreat into a world of dreams and hopes—while reality
assailed me to conform    conform    CONFORM!    and all about me i saw
humanity deform itself . . . years passed in the space of a hope born, nurtured, and then wantonly killed. eternity became the blinking of my eyes,
and i stepped out of prison with turmoil defining the drive in my soul . . .   130

          the chirping of birds,
          even that is cold-blooded;

          two years
          and you sent me four letters;

          the steel of the bars,            135
          cement of the floor,

---

4. Like a darkening duel and at the same time like
an illustrating chant.
5. Young man angry as hell.

6. Knife.
7. I.e., Salinas Valley State Prison, near Soledad,
in southwestern California.

stripes sear my soul,
cold sttriiiips my being . . .

la pinta is death,
ay by day you pay out,                                              140

the price is your sanity,
the hurt is reality,

escape from rejection
leads one to nowhere,

the chirping of birds,                                             145
even that is cold-blooded . . .

streets of el paso, you received me with frigidity and indifference. i no longer had youthful trust. my life was turbulent—the see/saw machinations of
hunger/lust stemming from deprived ansiedad de la pinta . . . pinto viejo[8] at
age 22 as if mockery were to instigate a coup-d'état sobre mi vida[9] . . . came       150
out breathing decadence and hope,

weird merger, paradoxical and wanting change for the better (i had read and
believed all the jive bullshit about rehabilitation that prisons are notorious for

disseminating) . . . lonely, hurting, needing, and my mind

kept churning out razones filosóficas a través de mi                155

existencia[1]—and i continued being el pobre de ricardo's kind of sartre,
camús, platón,[2] et al—while sensing the

perversity of juárez nights, sojourns midst el gran putismo[3] . . . y yo gritaba
aún sin saber profundamente el por qué de mi vivir tal como vivía dentro
tiniebla, como                                                       160

refugiado de la ansiosa absurdidad.[4] noches i spent

enloqueciéndome momento por momento dentro el putismo de la calle
mariscal—de club a club[5] . . . hasta que llegué a conocer muchas putas por
nombre,[6] and i was numb with

despair—and in my now numb anomie i sought nothing, yet anger and an-        165
gustia[7] assailed me until i ran from the

---

8. Old browny. *Ansiedad*: anxiety.
9. About my life.
1. Philosophical reasons through my // existence.
2. I.e., the ancient Greek philosopher Plato. *Sar-tre*: Jean-Paul Sartre (1905–1980), French philos-opher, dramatist, and novelist associated with existentialism. *Camús*: Albert Camus (1913–1960), French novelist, essayist, and dramatist associ-ated with existentialism.
3. The great fucking thing.

4. And I screamed without knowing still, in my depth, the reasons for my being alive as it took shape in darkness, like // a refugee of anxious absurdity.
5. Going crazy one moment after another inside the fucking thing of Mariscal Street—from one club to the next.
6. Until I ended up knowing many whores by first name.
7. Anguish.

putismo into the purifying arms of a woman who gave me her nourishing love and purity of spirit and being . . . a woman both sensuous and real, one who could uplift my soul while enflaming my visceral body and we became

an earthy fusing of body and emotion . . . we wed and even then it all seemed confusing, this of fusing, when all about us the world was topsy-turvy, universal scurvy . . . Teresa, esposa, you with trust in heart, hope in your bosom, passion in the way we kissed and embraced, yet a way of life that had never known other than the shelter of your parents' home, i came rampagingly into your life with a million angers and a will to either change society or destroy it, and you visibly trembled at the strange, strong way i assailed an unyeilding world, and you stood by me . . . i frightened you, yet our love se enfloreció,[8] & our son, Rik-Ser, came into being. Teresa, i watched anxiously the swelling of you with our son, and i never realized that i would come to know him only after he was four years old, for once more i went to prison— two days before his birth, i stood alone in my mind indicted for robbery, you meanwhile suffering the pangs of birth

deliverance, also alone . . . aloneness, the condemnation of humanity— aloneness! robbery committed in anxiety and desperation; joblessness so i pulled jobs—and you both waited while i spent tumultous years pent up in

texas—ramsey prison farm no. 1[9]—years of quasi-college courses at alvin jr. college, working first in the fields

picking white gold, later in education department, ever

striving to jive the man to grant me a parole, and my jive worked, for i got out . . . only to find i still was

imprisoned within the horrendousness of a social structure

predicated on stricture and desecration . . . but i got out march of 1969, this time more dedicated and devoted to transform the gelatinous globulin of society . . . and el paso again stood on my horizon . . .

> horizonte paseño,
> duelo de juventud,
> calles corridas
> hambrientamente,
> mi alma un peñasco
> mi vida un poema[1]

> el chuco, ciudad furiosa
> nacimiento del chicanismo,
> cuna del carnalismo,
> creadora ciudad de llanto
> de medianoche[2]

8. It bloomed.
9. In Otey, Texas, on the Gulf Coast.
1. El Pado horizon / youthful mourning, / streets crossed-over / hungrily, / my soul on the cliff / my life a poem.
2. El Chuco, furious city / birth of Chicanismo, /

el paso, conociste mi tristeza
mi locura y mi desmadrazgo,
corrí tus calles y callejones
gritando ansiedad y buscando liberación;[3]

volví a encontrar amor                                    210
en los besos apasionados,
en los brazos cautivadores,
en los ojos como norias de cariño
de mi amada y querida señora,[4] Teresa . . .
Teresa, hembra complementando                            215
mi hombreduría,
somos fuego y rigor,
amor y lumbre estética,
somos existencia,
somos paradoja,                                          220
somos lo que somos,
y seremos
el vuelo
de nuestra propia trayectoria;[5]

hijo,                                                    225
hechizo de amor y enloquecimiento,
de la experiencia chicana,
del aprecio vital que vivimos;
Rick, fibra de mi ser y
extención de tu madre, mi esposa,                        230
eres
llanto del alma
y grito de alegria . . . [6]

rik        rik        rik
como el timbál sonando                               235
y la canción gemiendo . . . [7]
la realidad

se desarrolla
cuando la vida es valerosa . . . [8]

rik        hijo                                          240
te
quiero . . .

---

el paso streets . . . the southside, VISTA M.M.P. work and

MACHOS,[9] where i rapped about liberation and in between words, i wrote
out past and present, knowing that tomorrow is a finite concept ending with     245
the sunset . . . and never had i had a sunset . . . other than the closing of all

doors, so it seemed, and being sum and total of social

brutalization (i am chicano!), sheer idiocy gnawed at me . . . demanding that
i rip off a world belonging to my people, but controlled by middle amerika.
nights that ate out my innards became days that dazed me with the cruelty     250
of too much light—light that burnt and cauterized,

congealing the hurts in my soul. el paso, you insatiable bastard thing, cold
and unrelenting, conniver and deliberate obfuscator, era miseria otra vez
hasta que chacha

gardea, y otros carnales destendieron las manos con apoyo y ayuda[1]—and     255
my stream elongated and expanded . . . from the

mired-up madness of amerika's hateful south (virginny) to washington, d.c.,
baltimore, new york, and massachusetts . . .

then on to chicago, harvard, yale, northwestern, columbia,

etc., all for rapping and more and awareness . . . then to     260

denver, oregon, michigan, the mid-west, and on and on . . . and i lived in the
jungle of lalo's pad, mi compa abelardo[2] a fat-gut chicano who lurks in my
unconscious like a

neo-buddhist cristo, wonder of wonders, the martyr of south el paso, bato/
carnal,[3] there in denver with the colorado migrant council co-directing itin-     265
erant health program with juan coyotero gilll-eeesss-pie, el mucho malo kid
when it comes to coyote killing on king ranch grounds enroute to the valle
from houston . . . denver, abject

city of chicanos who no longer pueden hablar nuestro idioma[4]

(mestizaje), y les digo,[5] carnales, que duele al oír mi     270

raza periquiar en inglés o que ellos pidan poesía chicaha escrita en el idioma
del gringo . . . y no puedo traducir ciertas cosas, pues siento mi alma brotar
cantos del

espiritu chicano . . . y mi ser demanda la verdad de nuestro

carnalismo escrita con sangre apasionada . . . [6]     275

9. Unidentified organization. *VISTA M.M.P.*:
unidentified.
1. It was misery again until Cha-Cha // Gardea,
and other bros opened their hands with support
and help.

2. Abelardo "Lalo" Delgado (see p. 989).
3. Bro (brother)/dude.
4. Can speak our language.
5. And I say.
6. And feels pain when hearing my // race that

        denver denver denver
en el lanno[7] rojo
de enojo[8]
en colorado
con cruzada por la justicia,[9]            280
donde carnales
como corky, gurulé,
ken luján, narciso,[1]
y especialmente
abelardo (que no es) delgado brotan;[2]     285
lugar del ya natalizando chicanismo
donde gorillas águila y tigre cantan[3]

oficina del concilio pa' migrantes,
calle grant numero 665,[4]

denver, ft. lupton, alamosa,         290
pueblo, springs, las ánimas,
tienen parte de mi alma[5]

t. rotole con señal de paz,
tú que eras sacerdote,
hoy buscas paz en mis palabras      295
      y hallas el pésame hecho del desmadre,
tal ha sido mi existencia.[6]

salí de denver hacia el valle mágico (más bien trágico), en tejas . . . y mi
raza es bella y hecha de bronce; soy orgulloso y penumbroso viendo
la confusion, la paradoja de mi existir . . . marchas, gritos, protestas,  300
demandas . . . [7]

ubicando mi mente
es el grito de:
GRINGOS, MÁTENLOS . . .
eco de mi pasado            305
y lo grité
con furia y realidad
corriendo por mis venas.[8]

---

parrots in English or they should ask for Chicano poetry written in the Gringo's tongue . . . and I cannot translate certain things, that I feel erupting from my soul songs of // the Chicano spirit . . . and my being demands the truth about our // brotherhood written with passionate blood.
7. llano as pronounced by a denver carnal. [Sánchez's note]
8. In the red, furious / sobbing.
9. See note 7, p. 1325.
1. Chicano activists.
2. Erupt.
3. Place of the already-native-made Chicanismo / where gorilla singers like Ávila and Tigre sing.
4. Office of the Council for Immigrants, / 665 Grant Street.
5. Ft. lupton, alamosa, / people, springs, the souls, / have a portion of my soul. [Fort Lupton, Alamosa, Pueblo, Springs, and Las Ánimas are places in Colorado.]
6. T. rootle with a peace sign, / you're a priest, / today you look for peace in my words / and find the condolence that results from chaos, / such has been my existence.
7. I left Denver; toward the magical (or better, tragic) valley, in Texas . . . and my race was beautiful and bronze-made; I'm proud and melancholic looking at the confusion, the paradox of my existence . . . marches, screams, protests, demands . . .
8. Locating my mind / is the scream of: / GRINGOS, KILL THEM . . . / echo of my past / and I screamed / with fury and reality / running through my veins.

sitting here in my shorts, in magic valley court no. 2, highway 83 east, pharr,
tejas, i write in sketches the never ending sensations of my life streaming      310
in and out. early today, a march in McAllen[9] about and around the need for
chícanismo in the schools, and a chicanito was

dispossessed by the principal . . . a few weeks ago, ranted and raved in denver, front of capitol bldg, read poem (INDICT AMERIKA) and felt hollow
yet real, fulfilled and needy, and i made hectic love with my wife in Califor-      315
nia street hotel in denver later than night . . . still trying to bring about a
redress for the emptiness of prison (nine years of my life, and i am only 29
yrs old); my new born daughter, Libertad-Yvonne, is now gurgling out her
need of my arms to embrace her . . . y la adoro con todo el alma, she, born in
northampton, massachusetts, strange place for a chicano to be born in, part      320
of my escapade as staff writer/lecturer for school of education, u of mass
at amherst . . . part of me died there mid the vacuousness of new england.

> hijita linda,
> es bellisimo ser chicano,
> casado con chicana,      325
>
> tener hijos hechos
> del hierro de la raza
> de bronce . . . [1]
>
> grito ¡VIVA AZTLAN!
>
> siento orgullo      330
> en el pecho
> miro tu rostro
> y sé vida mía,
> que embelleces mi existir.[2]

the stream wends on and on and on . . . never a surcease, tal es la vida.[3]      335

1971

JANUARY 1, 1974
E. P. T.

## Teresa, last night

Teresa, last night
we drank, danced,
y gritamos[1]
as mariachis sang
joyous songs;      5

9. Like Pharr, a large city at the southern tip of
Texas, specifically in the Lower Rio Grande
Valley.
1. It's gorgeous to be a Chicano, / married to a
Chicana, / have children made / of the iron / of
the bronze race.

2. I feel pride / in my chest / I see your face / and
I know my dear one, / that you embellish my
existence.
3. Such is life
1. We yell.

                              the músicos
                              serenaded us,
                              love songs
                                  that moved our spirits
                              years ago                               10
                              when in our need to know
                              each other's life
                              we clung
                                  to fragile moments
                              and saw new worlds beckoning     15
                              in our words;
            years later,
                    two children and a
            four year separation & prison
                    sentence later,                           20
            we've once more
            sought out ternura y cariño,[2]
            expressing them again
            within
            the worlds—of música, palabras,[3]              25
            and searching hands/lips/realities—
            we lovingly create & re-create
            within the delicate balance
                of our separate realities
                    as we coincide through time/space        30
            and mutually give shape
            to naturaleza in its universal sense
                    of duality as it creates oneness of life;

            having refound you
            so many times,                                   35
            in moods, moments, caresses, and sharing,
            reconozco que solamente
                te quiero,
            tal como quiero/aprecio
                el poder vivir,                               40
                    vibrantemente. . . . [4]

1974                                                        1976

                                        May 10, 1974
                                        trío de locos
                                        in juárez bistros,
                                        drinking/listening
                                        to mariachis.


## Fridays Belong to Friends, Sometimes

            fridays belong to friends, sometimes,
            when Horacio "Chacho" Minjárez,
            Rafa "Chafa" Aguirre and I

2. Tenderness and affection.        4. I recognize that I only / love you, / just like I love/
3. Words.                           appreciate / being able to be alive, / vibratingly. . . .

can galavant all night
from cantina to cantina, 5
jiving with the pimps
as they shout:
    "Say, can you spare a messican minute, fellows,

    and i'll take you to see the girls,"

and his mouth opens in surprise 10
as one of us shouts back jivingly,

    "No, ese, we want to see the boys,

    damn the girls,"

and we walk/saunter laughingly
up different streets, 15
stopping
with don cojón-chon,[1]
buy little french rolls,
        sliced in half and stuffed
        with avocado, mexican cheese, 20
        jalapeños and a dash of salt,
and we continue
in our camaraderie
walking up juárez avenue
to carlos or the manhattan or the san luis 25
to hear mariachis and shout,
all the time eating tortas,
winking at the women,
alluding to ourselves
as being non-tourists 30
in this city on the border.

we enter the manhattan,
and mariachis serenade us,
and the tourist trade is thick,
aguirre squirms and says 35
let's go to another place
as young horacio bolts about,
splashing his tequila doble on his shirt,
and we walk down and cross the tracks,
get in the car and drive 40
across that stretch
of supertourist traps.

swarming streets
filled with hungers of amérika,[2]
seekers of sexual bliss, 45

---

1. A play on rhyming words. *Cojón:* someone who is brave. *Chon:* a cuckold.
2. See note 1, p. 1324.

we laugh,
for we just came to drink
and shout and pay mariachis
for their art . . .
we enter the san francisco bar,                           50
expecting music to blare out,
we drink and wait for them,
and then realize
that may 10th
is always                                                 55
Mexican Mother's Day,
and good mariachis
make more money
        serenading
home to home                                              60
than in bars,
and these mariachis are the best,
so they'll play
out on the streets,
and we mope and start to talk.                            65

Chacho is a youth who
wants to write
and film
and live
a legendary life                                          70
while creating sketches
of reality
on the canvas of our souls.
he is a poet,
        young and strong,                                 75
and full of vision,
and he reminds me
of garcía lorca and whitman
and rimbaud
and baudelaire                                            80
and lalo
and salinas[3]
and more especially of himself,
and his quick mind
pounces on every word;                                    85
all night long rafa and i revel
in the magic
of the word worlds Chacho gives us,
he wants to go to yale
to whip it,                                               90
and he will,
and rafa is moved to tears
by Chacho's words,

3. Raúl R. Salinas (1934–2008), pioneering Chicano poet from Texas. *García Lorca*: Federico García Lorca (1898–1936), Spanish poet and dramatist. *Rimbaud*: Arthur Rimbaud (1854–1891), French poet. *Baudelaire*: Charles Baudelaire (1821–1867), French poet.

and i feel strong/good
in meeting such a delicate/virile/affirmative mind/soul 95

as this young bato[4]
who speaks of years at Jefferson high
and the projects and the fact that he and his mother
survive somehow on about $1000, yes one thousand dollars, a year,
yet, he believes in himself, in raza, in the struggle, 100
and
we sense him puffing out his chest,
he's gonna tell us something,
aguirre in his forty years of life
has learned patience and he listens, 105

and i, in 33, have learned
how to bob/weave/and jive,
so i jive,
and we three laugh,
rap on 110
'til we tire
of the blandness
of music-less bars,
and walk out into the street
and as we rave and jive and galavant 115
we hear the far off strains
of inebriated music-makers,
over there
in that club on the corner,
yes, tontos,[5] there, 120
sí, at the forum,
we enter, sit, order
bohemias for rafa and me,
a tequila doble for horacio,
he's beginning to get high, 125
        "I really don't drink, I, ah er . . ."
we let it go at that and smile,
mariachis come on over,
toquen,[6] we say, something
for our friend Chacho here 130
it's mother's day, and for his age
he's a hell of a mothuh, he is,
so it's his day,
now play "Las Mañanitas,"
or something to that effect, 135
we laugh and jive,
and $23 later
we walk out of that joint,
drive over to max-fim's
and look at ballroom waltzers, 140

4. Dude.
5. Fools.

6. Play (music).

and drink a round or two
and drive back to el paso . . .

1974                                                          1976

it is late, México, DF,[1]
waddles in heat, humidity,
unlike glacial realities
awaiting my return . . .
Hotel del Paseo
16 de julio de 1979

# And Would That I Could

and would
         that I could
sing you, Mexico,
songs
that might waft                                               5
on mariachi strains,
that I could feel comfort
in all that you should be.
your beggars cry out
               for bread                                      10
to feed distended stomachs,
while Chicanos cry and lament
over a distorted history
               the severing
of all that could bind us                                     15
one to the other,
that horrid loss of meaning,
sovereignty
               was sepulchred
               in San Jacinto,[2]                             20
               afterward
it was unceremoniously
               disinterred
in New Mexico, Arizona,
California and other places                                   25
only
to be dismembered : : we became
shards of clay figurines,
and now

here                                                          30
at Tlatelolco,
         Plaza de Las Tres (singrifa) Culturas[3]
I stoke my mind

1. Distrito Federal, i.e., Mexico City
2. In the Battle of San Jacinto, 1836.
3. Tlatelolco Square, in Mexico City, and in particular La Plaza de las Tres Culturas, was the site
of a student massacre in 1968. *Singrifa*: without
marijuana.

playing v.i.p.
    in the entourage of writers                    35
invited to the Mexico City
    Metropolitan Book Fair
which el presidente of this república
    officiously inaugurated.
I much preferred cursi mariachi songs             40
to discolandia[4]
or other anti-mejicano doings
in this ancient capital
of the Nahuatl peoples. . . .

1979                                                                      1982

---

4. Disco land, a pejorative term for the U.S.

# The Nuyorican Poets

No other artistic movement has drawn as much attention to the Puerto Rican experience in the United States than the Nuyorican Poets Cafe, in New York City. Cofounded in 1973 by Miguel Algarín, the Cafe originated from frequent *tertulias*, gatherings of poets, at his home. Located in the Manhattan neighborhood called the Lower East Side (promptly baptized in Spanglish by these poets as *Loisaida*), the Cafe provided a performance space that was an alternative to mainstream literary and theatrical culture. On the Cafe's stage, unknown writers could share their poems and plays with public audiences. In fact, most of the Nuyorican poets became accomplished performance artists and playwrights. Their experiences at the Cafe proved formative for the writers, and their writing served important communal functions.

Most of the Nuyorican poets were raised in the Lower East Side or other New York City neighborhoods: Spanish Harlem, the South Bronx, or *Los sures* (the souths), a Puerto Rican barrio in south Williamsburg, Brooklyn. Before the founding of the Nuyorican Poets Cafe, literary activity by Puerto Ricans born or raised in the United States was limited and little known outside New York. Only a handful of writers had published works concerning the migrant experience. American mainstream publishers were indifferent to Latino literature, claiming that this material did not appeal to mainstream readers and that no significant readership existed among the underclass. In the meantime, many of these writers were reading and performing in public places (cafes, schools and universities, community centers, political demonstrations, the streets), bringing an unprecedented cultural vitality to the civil rights' struggles, and ethnic revitalization movements, that took place from the late sixties through the early seventies among Puerto Ricans and other ethnoracial minorities in the United States. For example, many writers affiliated with the Cafe were inspired by the Puerto Rican street poet Jorge Brandon, who for many years read his poetry at Union Square Park, a public park in Manhattan with a long history of public assembly and protest. In fact, Brandon is often considered the father of Nuyorican poetry.

Before the word *Nuyorican* began to be used by the Nuyorican poets to identify themselves, it was mostly a derogative term used by island Puerto Ricans to distance themselves from their migrant compatriots, who were marginalized in U.S. society and commonly stereotyped as welfare dependent; politically disenfranchised; burdened with high unemployment rates, gang violence, and large school-dropout rates; and with few prospects for overcoming their underprivileged status. Because *Nuyorican* indicated that Puerto Ricans were mostly from New York, the term was not adopted by all Puerto Rican writers on the mainland. Critics and the general public often applied it to all Puerto Ricans, however, and particularly to all the writers and artists who happened to be Puerto Rican.

Algarín and his fellow Nuyorican poet Miguel Piñero proudly adopted and popularized the term as a way of bringing legitimacy and attention to a different way of being Puerto Rican: a Puerto Ricanness born out of migration and out of survival experiences in a racist, Anglocentric U.S. society; a Puerto Ricanness that had as many differences as shared commonalities with the island culture. According to the critic Efraín Barradas, the Nuyorican poets tended to mythicize island culture and traditions, criticize aspects of them, or reject them.

Through their readings and performances at the Cafe, Algarín, Piñero, Pedro Pietri, José Angel Figueroa, Sandra María Esteves, Tato Laviera, and Jesús "Papoleto" Meléndez became the best-known names of the Nuyorican poetic movement. The publication of *Nuyorican Poetry: An Anthology of Words and Feelings* (1975), edited by Algarín and Piñero, was a significant step in bringing the Nuyorican experience to a wider audience. "The power of Nuyorican talk is that it is street-rooted," Algarín stresses in the book's introduction.

> The experience of Puerto Ricans on the streets has caused a new language to grow: Nuyorican. Nuyoricans are a special experience in the immigration history of the city of New York. We come to the city as citizens and can retain the use of Spanish and include English. . . . The interchange between both yields new verbal possibilities, new images to deal with the stresses of living on tar and cement.

Algarín reiterates some of these ideas in his essay "Nuyorican Literature" (1981), included in this anthology. Many of the Nuyorican writers learned Spanish at home without formal instruction and English in the public schools or the streets. They wrote primarily in English but also in Spanish or Spanglish, a mixture that includes frequent code-switching between English and Spanish or adapting English words to Spanish morphological (word-formation) structures. The poet, Algarín argued, "is responsible for inventing the newness. The newness needs words, words never heard before or used before. The poet has to invent a new language, a new tradition of communication."

The Nuyorican poets viewed themselves as the voices of the people, representatives of those generations of Puerto Ricans born or raised in the United States who grew up straddling two cultures and languages and experiencing racism and poverty. The concepts of "street poetry" and "outlaw poetry" were frequently used to describe an artistic movement that came from the margins to challenge the conventions, myths, and exclusions of the white Anglo-Saxon tradition. The Nuyoricans wanted not only to capture their community's social and racial marginality, but also to bring their creative work to the masses and use it as a consciousness-raising tool. Their poetry was meant to be read aloud or performed. By vocalizing, the poets would appeal to their audiences' emotions and provoke responses. So successful was this movement that the Cafe is now a New York artistic institution, a gathering place for new artists to receive audience approval or be booed in its (in)famous "poetry slams."

# MIGUEL ALGARÍN
## b. 1941

Considered the main promoter of the Nuyorican movement, Miguel Algarín was born in Santurce, Puerto Rico. Both his mother and her sister wrote poetry. In Puerto Rico, Algarín's family often experienced racial prejudice, because his maternal grandmother was black but had several children from a relationship with a white man; among them were his mother and his aunt, who were light-skinned. He moved with his family to the Lower East Side in 1950.

Algarín holds a bachelor's degree from the University of Wisconsin, a master's from Pennsylvania State University, and a doctorate from Rutgers University in Romance languages, English, and comparative literature. He is currently an emeritus professor of English at Rutgers and combines his academic career with his work as a poet, playwright, and translator. In a 1997 interview with Carmen Dolores Hernández, a cultural columnist in Puerto Rico, he describes significant changes in the styles and themes of his poetry collections, including *Mongo Affair* (1974), *On Call* (1980), *Body Bee Calling from the 21st Century* (1982), *The Time Is Now/Ya es tiempo* (1984), and *Love Is Hard Work: Memorias de Loisaida/Poems* (1997):

> The *persona* that speaks in *Mongo Affair* is a Nuyorican who is not yet free to understand the political and emotional relationship between a place—which is the tar and concrete jungle of Manhattan—and the cosmos, which is where that tiny little speck of tar and concrete-covered land is in relation to, first, the state, then the nation and the hemisphere, and then the globe. By the time I hit *Body Bee Calling from the 21st Century*, I create a persona that has lifted himself out of locality and has made a trip into the future from where he looks back. . . . But if by *Body Bee Calling from the 21st Century*, I'm in the future looking back, by the time I hit *Time's Now* I'm looking at the whole world.

Algarín and the poet Bob Holman coedited *Aloud: Voices from the Nuyorican Poets Cafe* (1994), an extensive collection of the work of poets from many nationalities who had performed at the Cafe. The volume received a 1994 American Book Award. An accomplished director, producer, and actor, Algarín is the creative force behind the Puerto Rican Playwrights'/Actors' Workshop and the Nuyorican Theater Festival, venues for aspiring playwrights and performers to develop their crafts. He also coedited the volume *Action: The Nuyorican Poets Cafe Theater Festival* (1997). Several of his plays have been produced but not published. Among those published is *Olú Clemente, the Philosopher of Baseball* (1973), coauthored with Tato Laviera and celebrating the memory of Roberto Clemente, the Afro–Puerto Rican Hall of Fame baseball player.

"A Mongo Affair," included in this anthology, is the signature poem of Algarín's first published collection. It addresses the social, racial, and existential conditions of Puerto Rican migrants. The other three poems included here are from *Love Is Hard Work*, which presents personal experiences and depicts life on the Lower East Side. "Nuyorican Angel of Despair" is one of several "Nuyorican Angel" poems in the collection, and Algarín's angels can be creative or destructive, individuals or nationalities, emotions or attributes. Algarín has described them as "human interactions with the incorporeal world. . . . Angels are sometimes people, objects, or simply live-wire ideas." "Nuyorican Angel of Despair" extends its sympathies and solidarities beyond the confines of Loisaida to make a poignant statement about the consequences of misguided U.S. foreign policies and uninformed notions about distant, impoverished countries. In "forGet," the poetic voice appears to command the reader to not remember the names of some of the immortal composers and performers of Latin American popular music, but means the complete opposite. "Hiram Morales," inspired by the death of one of Algarín's cousins, captures the different ways in which family members deal with the shock and anguish of losing a loved one.

The volume *Survival Supervivencia* (2009) is a selection, by T. Marc Newell, of the poetry and essays Algarín has written since 1974.

# A Mongo Affair

On the corner by the plaza
in front of
the entrance to González-Padín[1]
in old San Juan
a black Puerto Rican talks                                    5
about "the race"
he talks of Boricuas
who are in New York on welfare
and on lines waiting for food stamps,
"yes, it's true, they've been taken out                      10
and sent abroad and those that
went over tell me that they're
doing better over there than here
they tell me they get money
and medical aid                                              15
that their rent is paid
that their clothes get bought
that their teeth get fixed
is that true?"
on the corner by                                            20
the entrance to Gonzalez-Padín
I have to admit that he has been
lied to, misled,
that I know that all the goodies
he named humiliate the receiver,                            25
that a man is demoralized
when his woman and children
beg for weekly checks
that even the fucking a man does
on a government bought mattress                             30
draws the blood from his cock
cockless, sin espina dorsal,[2]
mongo—that's it!
a welfare fuck is a mongo affair!
mongo means flojo[3]                                        35
mongo means bloodless
mongo means soft
mongo can not penetrate
mongo can only tease
but it can't tickle                                         40
the juice of the earth-vagina
mongo es el bicho Taino
porque murió[4]
mongo es el borinqueño
who's been moved                                            45
to the inner-eity jungles
of north american cities

1. A building erected in 1923, long the home of a       3. Lazy.
famous department store by that name.                    4. The Taíno penis that died.
2. Spine.

mongo is the rican who survives
in the tar jungle of Chicago
who cleans, weeps, crawls,                          50
gets ripped off,
sucks the eighty dollars a week
from the syphilitic
down deep frustrated
northern man—                                  55
viejo[5] negro africano,
Africa Puerto Rico
sitting on department store entrances
don't believe the deadly game
of Northern cities paved with gold and plenty      60
don't believe the fetching dream
of life improvement in New York
the only thing you'll find in Boston
is a soft leather shoe up your ass,
viejo, anciano africano, Washington           65
will send you in your old age
to clean the battlefields
in Korea and Vietnam
you'll be carrying a sack
and into that canvas                          70
you'll pitch las uñas[6]
los intestinos
las piernas[7]
los bichos mongos
of Puerto Rican soldiers                     75
put at the front to face
sí!
to face the bullets, bombs, missiles,
sí! the artillery
sí!                                       80
to face the violent hatred of Nazi Germany
to confront the hungry anger of the world
viejo negro
viejo puertorriqueno
the north offers us pain                     85
and everlasting humiliation
IT DOES NOT COUGH UP
THE EASY LIFE: THAT IS A LIE
viejo que has visto la isla
perder sus hijos[8]                         90
are there guns to deal with
genocide, expatriation?
are there arms to hold
the exodus of borinqueños
from Borinquen?                         95
we have been moved

---

5. Old man.
6. The nails.
7. The legs.
8. Who has seen the island lose its children.

we have been shipped
we have been parcel posted
first by water then by air
el correo[9] has special prices                          .100
for the "low island element" to be
removed, then dumped
into the inner-city ghettos
Viejo, Viejo, Viejo
we are the minority                                      105
here in Borinquen
we, the Puerto Rican,
the original man of this island
is in the minority
I writhe with pain                                       110
I jump with anger
I know
I see
I am "la minoría de la isla"
viejo, viejo anciano                                     115
do you hear me?
there are no more Puerto Ricans
in Borinquen
I am the minority everywhere
I am among the few in all societies                      120
I belong to a tribe of nomads
that roam the world without
a place to call a home,
there is no place that is ALL MINE
there is no place that I can                             125
call mi casa,
I, yo, Miguel ¡Me oyes[1] viejo!
I, yo, Miguel
el hijo de Maria Socorro y Miguel
is homeless, has been homeless                           130
will be homeless
in the to be
and the to come
Miguelito, Lucky, Bimbo
you like me have lost                                    135
your home
and to the first idealist
I meet
I'll say
don't lie to me                                          140
don't fill me full of vain
disturbing love for an island
filled with Burger Kings
for I know
there are no cuchifritos[2]                              145

9. The mail.                           2. Small pieces of pork dipped in batter and deep-
1. Can you hear me.                     fried.

in Borinquen
I remember last night
viejito lindo[3]
when your eyes fired me
with trust                                                    150
do you hear that?
with trust
and when you said
that you would stand by me
should any danger threaten                                    155
I halfway threw myself
into your arms to weep
mis gracias
I loved you
viejo negro                                                   160
I would have slept
in your arms
I would have caressed
your curly gray hair
I wanted to touch                                             165
your wrinkled face
when your eyes fired me
with trust
viejo corazón puertorriqueño
your feelings cocinan                                         170
en mi sangre
el poder de realizarme[4]
and when you whispered
your anger into my ears
when you spoke of                                             175
"nosotros los que estamos
preparados con las armas"[5]
it was talk of future
happiness
my ears had not till                                          180
that moment heard such
words of promise and of guts
in all of Puerto Rico
old man with the golden chain
and the medallion with an indian                              185
on your chest
I love you
I see in you
what has been
what is coming                                                190
and will be
and over your grave
I will write
HERE SLEEPS

---

3. Endearing old man.                          5. "We who are ready to take up arms."
4. Cook in my blood the power to be fulfilled.

A MAN                                                    195
WHO SEES ALL OF
WHAT EXISTS
AND THAT WHICH WILL EXIST.

1975


# Nuyorican Literature

The four-hundred-year plus history of Puerto Rico is really a very simple story of greed and amorality. The men who ventured to cross the great Atlantic arrived greedy for gold and the acquisition of land, and in their wake, they left whole generations of people, whole tribes of people, dead and without any semblance of a history because all historical records were destroyed. And then, in 1917, we were all made United States citizens by Jones Law.[1] By 1946 Puerto Rico was allowed to have its first Puerto Rican-born governor, and there are reforms in the Jones Law that make it possible for Puerto Ricans from the lower classes to come to America looking for bread, land, and liberty. This maxim really is the thing under which the idealized trip up North is sold, and so, in 1948, the Department of Labor initiated the migration to the North that was to result in a mass evacuation of the island of Puerto Rico.

What does it mean, then, to the New York Puerto Rican to have been moved to the North and to find once he gets to the North that there is no real hot opportunity going on—that the dollars are really hard to get to, that the jobs are demeaning, and that historical continuity has been totally severed? It means that only a heroic act can save what becomes the Nuyorican—the Puerto Rican caught in the urban ghettos, where the population that is economically mobile is evacuated and where businesses have long left, and where housing is falling apart, and where all semblance of hope seems to be in the direction of Uncle Sam's welfare check. What that leaves us with is a situation where what we must do is to perpetuate rituals and habits that are the remnants of an already badly weakened historical consciousness or historical self.

What happens is that the first generation of Puerto Ricans in the 1930s and 1940s boldly and heroically maintained the family traditions as intact as they could, with as much fervor as they could. However, the economic situation made it very difficult for the family to hold together, and the dissolution of the family seems to be the actual living threat we now face. At the heart of all of that, there is a loss of trust that leaves us aimless and looking for love in empty spaces. The generations have been very badly stripped of all historical consciousness, and, as I say, what's left is an heroic attempt at a continuity which is really pale in comparison to what it could have been.

What are the roots of the New York Puerto Rican or of the Northern Puerto Rican? Those roots are really the debris of the ghettos, the tar and

1. Passed by the U.S. Congress, the Jones Act made Puerto Ricans U.S. citizens and increased their participation in their own government by adding an elective Senate to the island's legisla-ture. On the history of the period discussed here, see the "Acculturation" introduction (p. 359). For the text of the Jones Act, see Appendix 2: Treaties, Acts, and Propositions (p. A15).

concrete that covers the land, the dependence on manual labor that is merely brute force, the force feeding of the young in schools that kill their initiative rather than nourish it, and the loss of trust. I know that that's not fair to say that the lost of trust is a root, but it is, and if you know that it's your root, you might do something about it.

On the more positive side, we have maintained our music, we have put down in New York something that is called *salsa*, and we have carried forward into the 1980s the Black man's religion, a mixture of Catholicism and African religions, and most importantly, we carry on the oral tradition—the tradition of expressing self in front of the tribe, in front of the family. The holding force in that expression is a feeling and commitment that becomes the deepest bond of trust that we have going at the moment. The conflicts are very many. Languages are struggling to possess us; English wants to own us completely; Spanish wants to own us completely. We, in fact, have mixed them both.

The acculturation is happening very, very quickly, but the bilingualism is helping curb it, so I hope we don't end up like the Polish-Americans. We create poems for ourselves; poverty keeps us away from the space and time that composing long prose pieces require, but that is changing too. So what does the future hold? The future will be procured by what we do that is cultural in the present, so that we are not so much chasing the tradition of a culture as we are putting it down. We do not so much look to the historical development of Puerto Rican literature as much as we just lay down the poem on the page. Our usage and our new content is going to struggle with the forms and the old meanings, but that is again nothing new, and we will continue to fight that struggle.

Puerto Rican literature is alive and well in New York. Its vibrancy stems from Point Zero. When you have nothing and can expect nothing, anything you do is something, so that our experience makes it possible for us to write poems that describe our actual conditions without fearing that they might be too personal or too lost in the detail of the day and not metaphysical enough. The consequence of having that content freed of standards that kept white American writers enslaved for so many years brings with it a blessing, and the blessing is that language can be worn again and it can be worn as feeling; you can feel it all over again, since it is something you have just learned.

The persistence of Spanish as a live form of expression makes it even richer because like all European tongues, this mixing of Spanish and English is an old phenomenon, and at the edges of the Latin Empire, French, Portuguese, Rumanian, Italian were all considered the vulgar languages—at the edges of the Empire, and they were really just reflecting constant and daily usage, so that their irregular verbs or irregular usages became dialects which in the ultimate passage of time made the formal respected languages of today. We expect to be able to do the same by mixing Spanish and English and not fearing the present insistence on the part of those who fear it—they claim that if we go the route of mixing languages, we will be ignorant in both and control neither. That's nonsense—language is serviceable on the streets, not in compositions for expository writing, and everyone knows that. If language functions on the street and is useful in conducting the economy of the tribe, it will grow. So the roots of the Puerto Rican literature are in the New World in the urban centers now being evacuated by the white part of the society, and we are inheriting dead cities with no industry and no money to rehabilitate them or to start business again. So the attitude must be something about the future, something about establishing patterns of survival all over again. I don't know that we will have enough time to do it or that there will be my need for it, if, in fact, there is nuclear aggression.

I would say that the Nuyorican esthetic has three elements to it. The first is the expression of the self orally and the domination of either language or both languages together to a degree that makes it possible for you to be accurate about your present condition—psychic, economic, or historical, and I think that the first steps are always oral. The second reality of the New Nuyorican esthetic is that if we are to procure the future, we have to create a discourse between ourselves about setting up systems of protection and mutual benefices, and those in the urban centers of the Northeast are very hard and very difficult things to do, but if we don't, we will find that in the next ten to fifteen years, there will be roving bands of young women and of young men in numbers of fifteen to twenty, all serf-dependent, but mutually aggressive, aggressive against any other band of kids, and those are what you call the gangs inside of the urban centers. We need to be making a discourse that procures our future by realizing that we must establish a constitution for survival on top of tar and concrete, so we must put it down, or we make beer can roses. The second part has a little (a) to it, which is something to do with prosody—the ways in which we use the languages. English has a stress on stress system; Spanish has a syllabic system. I think that Nuyorican verse is a combination of both and it is also doing something that Charles Olson[2] took great pains in his essay on projective verse to clarify, which is that the kingpin of English written verse is the syllable. I don't know why he decided to say that in the '50s, but he did, and it is accurate, and we can prove it by our poems and the black man in America can prove it, because the more he depends on the syllable, the more the language can become his, he having the problem of having lost all other traces of ethnicity.

The last thing about the Nuyorican esthetic is something I counsel for anybody looking for art or looking to art to relieve him or her, and that is the transformations before the public eye are a very important way of psychic cure. In other words, create spaces where people can express themselves and create that space expressly for that purpose, and you open it three to four times a week, and you wait, and your public will come, and they will bring their writings. And if you, as guide of the space, have a generosity of spirit, you will find that you will have created a center for the expression of self and for people to transform themselves before the public eye.

1981

---

2. American poet (1910–1970).

# Nuyorican Angel of Despair

(December 31, at the End of the Millennium)

So free that liberty weighs 'round my neck,
so without restraint that ropes tie my mind to Somalia,
so world-wide-bright-eyed gone wild
that Africa is the brilliant white-and-black
of an opaque 1934 Tarzan flick,                                         5
a dream that rides me to the burial grounds
so I couldn't leave my house till Ted Koppel[1]
showed me how valiantly the U.S. Somalian
relief operation yields the best
Channel 7 Eyewitness Nightline News[2]                                  10
foreign occupation television special.
I couldn't leave my house, so I didn't get to find out
if my date was a he or a she
cross-dressed either way.
You see, I've already seen The Crying Game[3]                           15
and I'm not taking bets on who's a she or he,
but forget that,
do you know what surprised the Marines,
it wasn't Somalians,
it was a sea of extra-terrestrial lights                                20
and television pre-occupation news teams,
"It's an eerie sight," said a two-star general
as he arranged his would-be-presidential hair
for a 2000 run for the White House T.V. shot.
It isn't that the Somalians need food and relief,                       25
you see, we also need great T.V. viewing
and Allah knows that we have to have it,
and Allah delivers,
the warlords perform in the theater of operations,
yes, Allah is great,                                                    30
so during the morning talk shows we're dismayed
by how our kids are traumatized
by skeletal two-, three-, ten-year-old Somalian children—
what counseling should we do for them?
Well maybe the good samaritan thing to do                               35
is turn the T.V. off and let your child eat,
then turn it on again
when you want to see the great moral
imperative of our armed nation
dump Marines on a lit beach                                             40
with a civilian army of world correspondents
eagerly waiting with microphones in hands
while our Marines crawl on their bellies
up to the microphones to say,

---

1. Edward James Koppel (b. 1940), English-born
American television journalist; best-known as the
anchor for the ABC News program Nightline from
1980 until 2005.

2. In New York, ABC is broadcast on Channel 7,
whose local news program is called Eyewitness
News.

3. Movie (1992) involving transvestism.

"Hey, these Africans don't have bullets,      45
they're just hungry."

1997

## forGet

forget Tito Puente riffing on his timbales,
forget Ray Barretto,
forget Rubén Blades,
forget Chano Pozo,
forget Pérez Prado,      5
forget the best of Xavier Cugat,
forget Celia Cruz and her basso profundo voice,
forget Agustín Lara,
forget Sylvia Rexach,
forget Bobby Capó,      10
forget Ismael Rivera,
forget Cortijo,[1]
forget it, just for get it.

1997

## Hiram Morales

The day's light blasting a bouquet
of white, yellow, red flowers
accompany my solo drive to mother in Queens,[1]
trying to remember who they are;
my aunt Carmen, her son now dead,      5
Ruthie, my cousin, attending my father's last days,
Elba, crying out as she spots her brother Johnny,
Hiram, Jr., grappling with his father's death,
Hersilia, now in college, newly returned home to mourn,
Joshua, Hiram's last son, too young to make it all out,      10
family, all of them family,
and I knitting with the thinnest thread

1. Rafael Cortijo (1928–1982), island Puerto Rican percussionist, composer, and bandleader. *Tito Puente*: Ernest Anthony Puente Jr. (1923–2000), mainland Puerto Rican Latin jazz composer and bandleader, known as *el rey del timbal* (the King of the Kettledrums). *Ray Barretto*: mainland Puerto Rican conga player and bandleader (b. 1929). *Rubén Blades*: Panamanian singer/songwriter and actor (b. 1948). *Chano Pozo*: Luciano "Chano" Pozo (1915–1948), Cuban percussionist, singer, dancer, and composer. *Pérez Prado*: Dámaso Pérez Prado (1916–1989), Cuban bandleader and composer, associated with Mexico and New York City; known as "the King of Mambo." *Xavier Cugat*: Francesc d'Asís Xavier Cugat Mingall de Bru i Deulofeu (1900–1990), Spanish Catalan Cuban American bandleader, originally from Havana; very popular in the United States during the 1930s–60s. *Celia Cruz*: Cuban American singer (1925–2003). *Agustín Lara*: Ángel Agustín María Carlos Fausto Mariano Alfonso del Sagrado Corazón de Jesús Lara y Aguirre del Pino (1897–1970), Mexican composer. *Sylvia Rexach*: island Puerto Rican singer and ballad composer (1922–1961). *Bobby Capó*: Félix Manuel Rodríguez Capó (1922–1989), island Puerto Rican singer/songwriter. *Ismael Rivera*: island Puerto Rican singer (1931–1987), who generally worked with Cortijo.

1. A New York City borough east of Manhattan.

of recognition who is who,
what is what,
how he died.                                                           15
A perfunctory priest solemnly pushes
the commencement prayers on the ailing widow
with pious fast-food-blessings.
Hiram's mother is not yet here
for the incantations to his spirit.                                   20
It all ends mysteriously,
tears, shouts, deep guttural,
wrenching, throaty screams,
wounds gaping at the breathless
corpse,          "dejame al ladito de él,[2]                          25
                 al ladito de él,
                 Ay Dios mio,
                 al ladito de él
                 I can't believe it,
                 I can't believe it."                                 30
Dante's hell[3] descends sweeter than this,
no molten steel melts flesh
faster than Tia Carmen's breath
wanting to breathe life into Hiram,
                 "I can't believe it,                                 35
                 I can't believe it."
Wailing cries about staying,
                 "by your side Hiram,"
your mother's by your side,
and sirens blare from her breast,                                     40
                 "I can't believe it,
                 ay Dios mio,
                 I can't believe it."
Death's impatient hand grips hard,
steady, compelling Hiram's soul                                       45
to part,
to move away from flesh,
Tia Carmen can't believe it,
not her Hiram, not her boy,
                 "I can't believe it,                                 50
                 Socorro[4] dejame al ladito de él,
                 al ladito de él,
                 I can't believe it."

                                                            1997

---

2. Leave me at his little side.
3. In *Divine Comedy* (*Divina Commedia*), by the

Italian poet Dante Alighieri (1265–1321).
4. Help!

# PEDRO PIETRI
## 1944–2004

Pedro Pietri was born in Puerto Rico. When he was four years old, he moved with his parents to Spanish Harlem, where he was raised by his grandmother after his parents died. His poetry first began to be noticed through his eccentric performances in public spaces and at the Nuyorican Poets Cafe. He usually appeared on stage dressed in a black suit, wearing a black beret, and carrying a shopping bag, or a worn-out suitcase with the label "Coffin for Rent," in which he carried his poems. He also gave himself the title "Reverend." His book *Puerto Rican Obituary* (1973), one of the first and most original Nuyorican poetry collections published by a major mainstream house, was reprinted many times. Among his best-known poems are the title poem of that collection and another poem in it, "A Broken English Dream." Both poems, included in this anthology, make powerful statements about the survival struggles of Puerto Ricans on the mainland and their potential to overcome the brutal forces of poverty and racial prejudice. On his long-playing recording of some of his *Puerto Rican Obituary* poems, Pietri, who was also an actor and a performing poet, emphasizes the oral and dramatic aspects of his poetry. But a few of his poems in subsequent collections consist of unintelligible orthographic characters, a noticeable contrast with the social and political bent of his most successful works.

*Obituario puertorriqueño*, one of the first Spanish translations of a book by a mainland Puerto Rican writer, was published in Puerto Rico in 1977. However, Pietri's second collection of poetry, *Traffic Violations* (1983), did not achieve the success of *Puerto Rican Obituary*. In a 1997 interview with Carmen Dolores Hernández, Pietri described himself as "a poet who writes plays through the eye of the poet and the ear of the poet." Many of his plays were produced Off-Broadway in New York, among them his first published play, *The Masses Are Asses* (1984). The poem-play *Illusions of a Revolving Door* provided the title for a seven-play collection (1992). In the foreword to *Illusions*, the literary critic Alfredo Matilla Rivas, Pietri's Spanish translator, writes that "the circular and in-motion character of his dramas, indeed of all of his literature, is transposed to the metaphor of the revolving door: circular movement locked in seemingly static and separate compartments (realities) carrying their own structural order within a larger body." While Pietri's plays sometimes experiment heavily with dramatic and linguistic forms, they never sacrifice their social or historical contexts. These works are about how Puerto Ricans live and survive in the problem-ridden environment of New York City.

In 1994, Pietri and the graphic artist Adal Maldonado developed the Web site *El Puerto Rican Embassy* (elpuertoricanembassy.org). For this project, described as "a sovereign state of mind," they created a Puerto Rican passport, named ambassadors to the arts, and composed a national anthem in Spanglish. Conceived in a colonial metropolis by a poet and visual artist from the diaspora, *El Puerto Rican Embassy* is an anticolonial political statement. It proclaims artistic liberation, creating an imaginary space that affirms the survival of Puerto Rican national identity and subverts the confines of Puerto Rico's colonial condition.

## Puerto Rican Obituary

They worked
They were always on time
They were never late

They never spoke back
when they were insulted                                        5
They worked
They never took days off
that were not on the calendar
They never went on strike
without permission                                           10
They worked
ten days a week
and were only paid for five
They worked
They worked                                                  15
They worked
and they died
They died broke
They died owing
They died never knowing                                      20
what the front entrance
of the first national city bank looks like

Juan
Miguel
Milagros                                                     25
Olga
Manuel
All died yesterday today
and will die again tomorrow
passing their bill collectors                                30
on to the next of kin
All died
waiting for the garden of eden
to open up again
under a new management                                       35
All died
dreaming about america
waking them up in the middle of the night
screaming: Mira Mira[1]
your name is on the winning lottery ticket                   40
for one hundred thousand dollars
All died
hating the grocery stores
that sold them make-believe steak
and bullet-proof rice and beans                              45
All died waiting dreaming and hating

Dead Puerto Ricans
Who never knew they were Puerto Ricans
Who never took a coffee break
from the ten commandments                                    50
to KILL KILL KILL

1. Look! Look!

the landlords of their cracked skulls
and communicate with their latino souls

Juan
Miguel                                                              55
Milagros
Olga
Manuel
From the nervous breakdown streets
where the mice live like millionaires                               60
and the people do not live at all
are dead and were never alive

Juan
died waiting for his number to hit
Miguel                                                             65
died waiting for the welfare check
to come and go and come again
Milagros
died waiting for her ten children
to grow up and work                                                70
so she could quit working
Olga
died waiting for a five dollar raise
Manuel
died waiting for his supervisor to drop dead                       75
so he could get a promotion

Is a long ride
from Spanish Harlem
to long island[2] cemetery
where they were buried                                             80
First the train
and then the bus
and the cold cuts for lunch
and the flowers
that will be stolen                                                85
when visiting hours are over
Is very expensive
Is very expensive
But they understand
Their parents understood                                           90
Is a long non-profit ride
from Spanish Harlem
to long island cemetery

Juan
Miguel                                                             95
Milagros
Olga
Manuel

2. Long Island, which extends east from Manhattan.

All died yesterday today
and will die again tomorrow                                    100
Dreaming
Dreaming about queens[3]
Clean-cut lily-white neighborhood
Puerto Ricanless scene
Thirty-thousand-dollar home                                    105
The first spics on the block
Proud to belong to a community
of gringos who want them lynched
Proud to be a long distance away
from the sacred phrase: Que Pasa                               110

These dreams
These empty dreams
from the make-believe bedrooms
their parents left them
are the after-effects                                          115
of television programs
about the ideal
white american family
with black maids
and latino janitors                                            120
who are well train
to make everyone
and their bill collectors
laugh at them
and the people they represent                                  125

Juan
died dreaming about a new car
Miguel
died dreaming about new anti-poverty programs
Milagros                                                       130
died dreaming about a trip to Puerto Rico
Olga
died dreaming about real jewelry
Manuel
died dreaming about the irish sweepstakes                      135

They all died
like a hero sandwich dies
in the garment district
at twelve o'clock in the afternoon
social security number to ashes                                140
union dues to dust

They knew
they were born to weep
and keep the morticians employed
as long as they pledge allegiance                              145

---

3. Queens, a New York City borough east of Manhattan, on the western tip of Long Island.

to the flag that wants them destroyed
They saw their names listed
in the telephone directory of destruction
They were train to turn
the other cheek by newspapers                                    150
that mispelled mispronounced
and misunderstood their names
and celebrated when death came
and stole their final laundry ticket

They were born dead                                              155
and they died dead

Is time
to visit sister lopez again
the number one healer
and fortune card dealer                                          160
in Spanish Harlem
She can communicate
with your late relatives
for a reasonable fee
Good news is guaranteed                                          165

Rise Table Rise Table
death is not dumb and disable
Those who love you want to know
the correct number to play
Let them know this right away                                    170
Rise Table Rise Table
death is not dumb and disable
Now that your problems are over
and the world is off your shoulders
help those who you left behind                                   175
find financial peace of mind
Rise Table Rise Table
death is not dumb and disable
If the right number we hit
all our problems will split                                      180
and we will visit your grave
on every legal holiday
Those who love you want to know
the correct number to play
Let them know this right away                                    185
We know your spirit is able
Death is not dumb and disable
RISE TABLE RISE TABLE

Juan
Miguel                                                           190
Milagros
Olga
Manuel

All died yesterday today
and will die again tomorrow                                          195
Hating fighting and stealing
broken windows from each other
Practicing a religion without a roof
The old testament
The new testament                                                    200
according to the gospel
of the internal revenue
the judge and jury and executioner
protector and eternal bill collector

Secondhand shit for sale                                             205
Learn how to say Como Esta Usted
and you will make a fortune
They are dead
They are dead
and will not return from the dead                                    210
until they stop neglecting
the art of their dialogue
for broken english lessons
to impress the mister goldsteins
who keep them employed                                               215
as lavaplatos[4] porters messenger boys
factory workers maids stock clerks
shipping clerks assistant mailroom
assistant, assistant assistant
to the assistant's assistant                                         220
assistant lavaplatos and automatic
artificial smiling doormen
for the lowest wages of the ages
and rages when you demand a raise
because is against the company policy                                225
to promote SPICS SPICS SPICS

Juan
died hating Miguel because Miguel's
used car was in better running condition
than his used car                                                    230
Miguel
died hating Milagros because Milagros
had a color television set
and he could not afford one yet
Milagros                                                             235
died hating Olga because Olga
made five dollars more on the same job
Olga
died hating Manuel because Manuel
had hit the numbers more times                                       240
than she had hit the numbers
Manuel

4. Dishwashers.

died hating all of them
Juan
Miguel                                                          245
Milagros
and Olga
because they all spoke broken english
more fluently than he did

And now they are together                                      250
in the main lobby of the void
Addicted to silence
Off limits to the wind
Confine to worm supremacy
in long island cemetery                                        255
This is the groovy hereafter
the protestant collection box
was talking so loud and proud about

Here lies Juan
Here lies Miguel                                               260
Here lies Milagros
Here lies Olga
Here lies Manuel
who died yesterday today
and will die again tomorrow                                    265
Always broke
Always owing
Never knowing
that they are beautiful people
Never knowing                                                  270
the geography of their complexion

PUERTO RICO IS A BEAUTIFUL PLACE
PUERTORRIQUENOS ARE A BEAUTIFUL RACE

If only they
had turned off the television                                  275
and tune into their own imaginations
If only they
had used the white supremacy bibles
for toilet paper purpose
and make their latino souls                                    280
the only religion of their race
If only they
had return to the definition of the sun
after the first mental snowstorm
on the summer of their senses                                  285
If only they
had kept their eyes open
at the funeral of their fellow employees
who came to this country to make a fortune
and were buried without underwears                             290

Juan
Miguel
Milagros
Olga
Manuel                                                    295
will right now be doing their own thing
where beautiful people sing
and dance and work together
where the wind is a stranger
to miserable weather conditions                          300
where you do not need a dictionary
to communicate with your people
Aqui Se Habla Espanol all the time
Aqui you salute your flag first
Aqui there are no dial soap commericals                  305
Aqui everybody smells good
Aqui tv dinners do not have a future
Aqui the men and women admire desire
and never get tired of each other
Aqui Que Pasa Power is what's happening                  310
Aqui to be called negrito
means to be called LOVE

Negrito = Love                                           1973


## The Broken English Dream

It was the night
before the welfare check
and everybody sat around the table
hungry heartbroken cold confused
and unable to heal the wounds                            5
on the dead calendar of our eyes
Old newspapers and empty beer cans
and jesus is the master of this house
Picture frames made in japan by the u.s.
was hanging out in the kitchen                           10
which was also the livingroom
the bedroom and the linen closet
Wall to wall bad news was playing
over the radio that last week was stolen
by dying dope addicts looking for a fix                  15
to forget that they were ever born
The slumlord came with hand grenades
in his bad breath to collect the rent
we were unable to pay six month ago
and inform us and all the empty                          20
shopping bags we own that unless
we pay we will be evicted immediately
And the streets where the night lives

and the temperature is below zero
three hundred sixty-five days a year                    25
will become our next home address
All the lightbulbs of our apartment
were left and forgotten at the pawnshop
across the street from the heart attack
the broken back buildings were having                   30
Infants not born yet played hide n seek
in the cemetery of their imagination
Blind in the mind tenants were praying
for numbers to hit so they can move out
and wake up with new birth certificates                 35
The grocery stores were outnumbered by
funeral parlors with neon signs that said
Customers wanted No experience necessary
A liquor store here and a liquor store
everywhere you looked filled the polluted               40
air with on the job training prostitutes
pimps and winos and thieves and abortions
White business store owners from clean-cut
plush push-button neat neighborhoods
who learn how to speak spanish in six weeks             45
wrote love letters to their cash registers
Vote for me! said the undertaker: I am
the man with the solution to your problems

To the united states we came
To learn how to mispell our name                        50
To lose the definition of pride
To have misfortune on our side
To live where rats and roaches roam
in a house that is definitely not a home
To be trained to turn on television sets                55
To dream about jobs you will never get
To fill out welfare applications
To graduate from school without an education
To be drafted distorted and destroyed
To work full time and still be unemployed               60
To wait for income tax returns
and stay drunk and lose concern
for the heart and soul of our race
and the climate that produce our face

To pledge allegiance                                    65
to the flag
of the united states
of installment plans
One nation
under discrimination                                    70
for which it stands
and which it falls
with poverty injustice

and televised
firing squads                                         75
for everyone who has
the sun on the side
of their complexion

Lapiz: Pencil
Pluma: Pen                                            80
Cocina: Kitchen
Gallina: Hen

Everyone who learns this
will receive a high school equivalency diploma
a lifetime supply of employment agencies             85
a different bill collector for every day of the week
the right to vote for the executioner of your choice
and two hamburgers for thirty-five cents in times square

We got off
the two-engine airplane                              90
at idlewild airport[1]
(re-named kennedy airport
twenty years later)
with all our furniture
and personal belongings                              95
in our back pockets

We follow the sign
that says welcome to america
but keep your hands
off the property                                     100
violators will be electrocuted
follow the garbage truck
to the welfare department
if you cannot speak english

So this is america                                   105
land of the free
for everybody
but our family
So this is america
where you wake up                                    110
in the morning
to brush your teeth
with the home relief
the leading toothpaste
operation bootstrap[2]                               115

---

1. In Queens, a New York City borough east of Manhattan.
2. *Operación Manos a la Obra* (Operation Put Your Hands to Work; known in English as "Operation Bootstrap"), a 1950s-era U.S.-led mass-industrialization and -modernization program in Puerto Rico. On this program and related patterns of Puerto Rican migration, see the "Acculturation" introduction (p. 359).

promise you you will get
every time you buy
a box of cornflakes
on the lay-away plan
So this is america                                        120
land of the free
to watch the
adventures of superman
on tv if you know
somebody who owns a set                                   125
that works properly
So this is america
exploited by columbus
in fourteen ninety-two
with captain video                                        130
and lady bird johnson
the first miss subways[3]
in the new testament
So this is america
where they keep you                                       135
busy singing
en mi casa toman bustelo[4]
en mi casa toman bustelo

1973

---

3. *Miss Subways*: a New York City contest (1941–76) by which a woman who lived in the city and rode the subway was given this title and depicted on posters in the trains. *Columbus in fourteen ninety-two*: i.e., the first voyage to the New World of Christopher Columbus (1451–1506), a Spanish admiral from Genoa. *Captain Video*: main character on *Captain Video and His Video Rangers*, a pioneering American science fiction television series (1949–55). *Lady Bird Johnson*: Claudia Alta "Lady Bird" Taylor Johnson (1912–2007); wife of Lyndon Baines Johnson (1908–1973), U.S. president 1963–69.

4. *En mi casa, toman Bustelo, pues sabemos de café* (At my house, we drink Bustelo, because we know about coffee) is a line from a jingle, played on Spanish-language television and radio stations, for Café Bustelo. This brand of ground coffee, made for espresso, was originally manufactured by a Latino company and aimed at the Latino market.

---

# JOSÉ ANGEL FIGUEROA
## b. 1946

José Angel Figueroa was born in Mayagüez, Puerto Rico, but grew up in the Bronx. He holds a bachelor's degree in English literature from New York University and a master's from the State University of New York at Buffalo. One of the poets associated with the early years of the Nuyorican Poets Cafe, he was also one of the first to introduce his poetry to island readers, when, in 1981, the Institute for Puerto Rican Culture published a Spanish translation of his best-known collection, *Noo Jork* (1978). Previously, he had published the collection *East 110th Street* (1973) and edited the volume *Unknown Poets from the Full-Time Jungle* (1975). Figueroa has edited numerous anthologies of children's poetry selected from the Poems in the School program; has taught creative writing, literature, and drama at several American

universities; and has written and directed for Joseph Papp's Public Theater and Miriam Colón's Puerto Rican Traveling Theatre, both in New York. As a performing artist, he also has been involved in numerous theater and musical productions.

"Boricua," the first of two Figueroa selections in this anthology, is from *Noo Jork*.
Its title is a term commonly used to identify Puerto Ricans, and its verses are a call to
Puerto Rican youths to learn from the suffering that their forbears endured. "Cow-
boynomics," the second selection, is from *Hypocrisy Held Hostage* (2007), a collection
of older and new poems. Written in 1991, when U.S. president Ronald Reagan was in
office, this piece portrays a United States that, in exercising its world power, has lost
its way and needs to patrol its heart.

# Boricua

*Boricua*: you were
born somewhere
between American Airlines
near San Juan
and Kennedy Airport[1]                                          5
near The Bronx
   and I have seen
   your grim face
   listening to bleeding
   in the distance                                  10
   as your mind walks
B A C K W A R D S
B A C K w a r d s
b a c k w a r d s
   and sees Lincoln Hospital[2]                      15
having a field day
with your mother because
she had labor pains
with a Spanish accent
remember, *prieto?*[3]                                          20

Schools wanted
to cave in your
Puerto Rican accent
and because you
wanted to make it                                              25
you had to pledge
allegiance lefthanded
when you had lost your soul
during some English exam
report cards fed you                                           30
with counterfeit dreams
dictionaries carved fear
into your skin and had
a warrant for your accent

1. In Queens, a New York City borough east of     2. In the Bronx.
Manhattan, southeast of the Bronx.               3. Dark person.

because they said you were                                35
always culturally deprived
remember, *Negra*?

And I often wondered why
they kept smirking their lips
when they called you *Perro* Rican[4]                     40
instead of Puerto Rican
        but who am I talking
        about, Negro?

We're really the same
youngblood, except I have                                 45
seen you drown in multicultural
hangouts in Central Park[5] where
hypertensed congas make
unemployed crowds freak out
on people trying to become                                50
a part of one crowd or another;

And your spirit looks back
for an island, and
        She said:
I am not all paradise, *Boricua*                          55
Remove your eyes and plant them
inside my soul; flirt with me
but glance deeper now.
See infants not yet born crumble
and fire will grow on your lap once                       60
knowing the distance our people
have suffered, my child.
        But never let your mind
        eat silence or wait
        for *mañanas* to dust off                         65
        your anger.

Help her! this island says:
        Help me to silence
        slum poetry by giving
        the self to your people                           70
        so we could eat away all
        those fatty acids making
        it difficult to recognize you
        anymore in airports, stand-by
        airplanes, in The Bronx                           75

    *Y los callejones*[6] *de Puerto Rico.*

                                                        1978

---

4. Dog Rican.                        6. Alleys.
5. Grand public park in Manhattan.

# Cowboynomics

## I

Go home, America
but it may never know exactly where
and home is now a foreign affair;
an alliance with hideous tyrants
and oligarchic dictators                                      5
holding peace ransom by treachery
with purple hearts
that seduce the filthy rich
marching with the saints
to resurrect the profiteers                                   10
by brutally impoverishing the noble poor
who worship bold-faced liberation
as these pot-bellied autocrats
ambush the assassinated dead
by ripping off the tongues and prayers                        15
of widowed mothers or stolen wives
who sleepwalk to sniff and kiss those demised
then embrace to heal their own wounds
when there could be no question
the doves that prey by day                                    20
do turn into bats at night
to play with vultures in early morning
and rape virginity before it's born
so they could all withstand
the wild stench of freedom!                                   25

## II

Come home, America
shift winds or hit the road
and get off the next exit
but it may never know exactly where
nor perhaps be that aware                                     30
home is now a foreign affair;
it is a flea-market
where mice and rat patrols turn amok
after rushing from church to pray for justice
if not to plea-bargain                                        35
with the flies and the insects
for chopped off genitals or mutilated breasts
and the rampaged eyes
torn out of children's faces
when diehard cynics                                           40
trade aspirations with rightwing maggots
while kids who play with revolution
grow old much too fast much too soon
and will no longer be born as children
but downhill soldiers or restless vaqueros                    45

dying at their best like scattered shadows
under a drunken moon
so they could all bankroll
the pride and pomp of the elite!

### III

Return home, America                                      50
and remain to patrol your own heart
but America's an outward-bound backyard broker
set adrift from dusk to dawn
between bamboo skies and plantain trees
passed all these roadblocks                                55
and sideroads of genocide
mounting its flag on uprooted winds
with rattlesnake eyes
that bewitch the drumbeat of wardogs
before sucking Death from its anus                         60
so they could all scrounge The Heartland
to kidnap or pacify the doubtful
and dance passionately
the tango delta with ravaged nuns
to engender immaculate traitors and renegades             65
who get unscrupulously drunk on amnesia
before asking the neurotic fascist
for his daughter's hand with prick diplomacy
when the last shoot-out is final
in the name of national security!                          70

### IV

Stay home, America
come and shift winds or hit the road
and get off the next exit:
return to yourself and remain
to patrol your own heart                                   75
but America may never know exactly where
nor perhaps be that aware
home is now a foreign affair
where American
is no longer spoken anymore!                               80

1991

# MIGUEL PIÑERO
## 1946–1988

Miguel Piñero was a close friend and collaborator of Miguel Algarín. Born in Puerto Rico but raised on the Lower East Side, he was a gang leader in his youth, and he went to prison for theft when he was 13 years old. A severe drug and alcohol dependency contributed to his return to prison for armed robbery at age 24. In Sing Sing Correctional Facility, just north of New York City, Piñero became interested in theater and acting and began writing his play *Short Eyes* (1974), a harsh portrait of the brutality of American prison life. After Piñero's release from jail, the play was produced by a theater group made up of ex-convicts. A subsequent production of the play received the New York Drama Critics' Circle Award and an Obie for Best Off-Broadway Production of 1973–74; the play was made into a movie (1977). Subsequently, Piñero wrote plays and acted in television series, among them *Kojak* and *Miami Vice*, as well as in some feature films. He also was a consultant and script writer for crime shows.

In 1982, Piñero was awarded a Guggenheim Fellowship in drama. Two years later, his plays *The Sun Always Shines for the Cool, Midnight Moon at the Greasy Spoon*, and *Eulogy for a Small Time Thief* were published in one volume, followed two years later by the volume *Outrageous One Act Plays*. As their titles suggest, the plays center around the violent street life of New York City, and his mostly male characters are always walking at the edge of an abyss. The marginalized inhabitants of this coarse and dark world are often homosexuals or members of the criminal underworld such as prostitutes and pimps. Piñero's plays develop an aesthetic of life seen from below—from the vantage point of the "outlaw," the individual who lives outside established society and its rules. The raw language, sexual situations, and proud display of a code of honor among outlaws represent a troubled creative mind taking aim, sometimes humorously and sometimes ironically, at conventional worldviews.

Included in this anthology are two of Piñero's best-known poems, both from his first poetry collection, *La Bodega Sold Dreams* (1980). "This Is Not the Place Where I Was Born" reflects the feelings of rejection and estrangement often felt by Puerto Ricans on the mainland when they visit Puerto Rico, feeling that arise from their cultural "in-betweenness" and their straddling two cultures and two languages. "A Lower East Side Poem" emphasizes the poet's strong connection with the only place he calls home: Loisaida. Within the confines of his beloved barrio, the author's identity was formed and he learned the survival skills that set the course of his life. When Piñero died, of cirrhosis of the liver, Algarín and many other friends, relatives, and admirers of Piñero's work honored the wish he expresses in "A Lower East Side Poem": "so please when I die . . . / don't take me far away / keep me near by / take my ashes and scatter them thru out / the Lower East Side. . . ."

# Short Eyes[1]

Dedicated to the power of Adelina Piñero-Rivera[2]

> Adelina de Gurabo
> es una mujer que le
> dió diez potencias a la
> nación puertorriqueña.[3]
> Adelina, Adelina
> Adelina, Adelina
> brought out to
> the world the
> true energy
> she creates Dusmic Energy[4]
> she does not sell a bill
> of lies to bring about
> a revolution: no she dances
> beyond that: Nuyorican is a
> state of mind,
> it is a metaphysics
> of being
> and Adelina
> brought ten beauties
> to the world of pain.
> She put muscles on the planet
> freedom of the world
> she used no
> ploys
> she used a truth that
> creates men of feelings
> and power & aggression
> it is a noble mind
> it is a full, giving
> powerful loving mind
> that Adelina gives
> New York.

*Excerpt from "El Cumpleaños de Adelina," a poem by Miguel Algarín*

## The People

JUAN    *A Puerto Rican in his early thirties*
CUPCAKES    *A Puerto Rican pretty boy of twenty-one who looks younger*

1. The published play includes a glossary of slang, from which pertinent entries have been inserted here as footnotes. The glossary's entry for the phrase *short eyes* reads: "Child molester; according to prisoners, the lowest, most despicable kind of criminal."
2. Miguel Piñero's mother. She was from the town of Gurabo, in northeastern Puerto Rico.
3. These four lines are hyperbolic praise for Adelina Piñero-Rivera's human attributes (such as lovingness, honesty, and generosity) and her gifts to the world, including her children. The *Siete*, or seven, *potencias* are the main African Orishas (deities) in the religion Santería; this woman had the power of *diez*, or ten.
4. A force related to *Dusmic Poetry*; Miguel Algarín introduced this latter term in *Nuyorican Poets: An Anthology of Words and Feelings* (1975), referring to love poems "that transform aggression being directed at you by another person into your strength."

PACO    *A Puerto Rican in his early thirties with the look of a dope fiend*
ICE    *A black man in his late twenties who looks older*
OMAR    *A black amateur boxer in his mid-twenties, virile*
EL RAHEEM    *A black man in his mid-twenties with regal look and militant bearing*
LONGSHOE[5]    *A hip, tough Irishman in his mid-twenties*
CLARK DAVIS    *A handsome, frightened white man in his early twenties*
MR. NETT    *An old-line white prison guard in his late forties*
CAPTAIN ALLARD    *Officer in House of Detention. Straight and gung-ho*
MR. BROWN    *An officer in the House of Detention*
SERGEANT MORRISON    *Another officer*
BLANCA and GYPSY    *Walk-on, nonspeaking parts*

*The entire play takes place in the dayroom on one of the floors in the House of Detention.*
ACT I:    *Early morning, lock-in after breakfast*

* * *

# Act One

*Dayroom in the House of Detention. Upstage right is entrance gate. Upstage left is gate leading to shower room and slop sink. Upstage center is a toilet and drinking fountain. Above is a catwalk. Stage left is a table and chairs. Downstage right is a garbage can. Upstage right is a TV set on a stand. Early-morning lock-in after the morning meal.*

*Early-morning light.*

INMATES' VOICES *can be heard: various ad-libs, calling out to each other, asking questions, exchanging prison gossip, etc.*

MORRISON:    All right, listen up . . . I said listen up.
     [*Whistle.*]
When I call your names, give me your cell location.
     [*Catcalls.*]
Off the fucking noise. Now if I have to call out your name more than once, pray—cause your soul may belong to God, but your ass is mine.
     [*More catcalls. House lights go out.*]
Williams, D.
VOICE RESPONSE:    Upper D 14.
MORRISON:    Homer, J.
VOICE RESPONSE:    Lower D 7.
MORRISON:    Stone, F.
VOICE RESPONSE:    Lower D 5.
MORRISON:    Miller, G.
VOICE RESPONSE:    Upper D 3.

---

5. [Nickname] for someone who's hip, slick, and "has his act together." [Glossary of slang]

MORRISON: Lockout for criminal court . . .
[*Whistle.*]
"A" side dayroom. All right, already! . . . knock it off. Supreme Court.
[*Whistle.*]
Johnson.
INMATE VOICE: Who?
MORRISON: Johnson.
TWO INMATE VOICES: Who?
MORRISON: Johnson.
A LOT OF VOICES: Who? . . . who? . . . who? . . . who? . . .
MORRISON: Aw, come on, fellas, give me a break.
INMATE VOICE: Your brains may belong to the state, but your sanity belongs to me.
INMATE VOICE: Aw, come on, fellas, give the fella a break.
INMATE VOICE: Break . . .
[*Bronx cheer.*]
MORRISON: Johnson.
INMATE VOICE: Upper D 15.
MORRISON: *Corree*-a.
INMATE VOICE: *Can't you say my name right?*
[*Giving proper pronunciation.*]
Correa . . . Correa . . . Correa.
MORRISON: You guys go to the "C" side dayroom
[*Whistle.*]
Sing Sing reception center. Gomez, A.
VOICE RESPONSE: Lower D 9.
MORRISON: Shit-can-do.
[*Catcalls.*]
VOICE RESPONSE: Scicando . . . Lower D 11.
MORRISON: Bring all your personal belongings and go to the "B" side dayroom.
[*Catcalls.*]
All right, you guys want to play games, you guys don't let up that noise, you guys ain't locking[6] out this morning.
INMATE VOICE: You got it.
[*Ad-libs continue until* OMAR *speaks.*]
ICE: Fuck you, sucker.
[*Silence. Sound of prison gate opening is heard.*]
MORRISON:
[*Whistle—dayroom lights come on.*]
All right, on the lockout.
[*Enter* OMAR, LONGSHOE, EL RAHEEM, PACO, *and* ICE. *Each runs toward his respective position. Ad-libs.*
Then JUAN *walks slowly toward his position.*
CUPCAKES *is the last to come in. The* MEN *accompany him with simple scat singing to the tune of "The Stripper." Ad-libs.*]
JUAN: Why don't you cut that loose? Man, don't you think that kid get tired of hearing that every morning?

6. As in "Where are you locking?", meaning "Where's your cell?" [Glossary of slang]

PACO:   Oh, man, we just jiving.

ICE:   Hey, Cupcake, you ain't got no plexes[7] behind that, do you?

CUPCAKES:   I mean . . . like no . . . but . . .

PACO:   You see, Juan, Cupcake don't mind.

CUPCAKES:   No, really, Juan. Like I don't mind . . . But that doesn't mean
that I like to listen to it. I mean . . . like . . . hey . . . I call you guys by your
name. Why don't you call me by mine? My name ain't Cupcakes, it's Julio.

EL RAHEEM:   If you would acknowledge that you are God, your name
wouldn't be Cupcake or Julio or anything else. You would be Dahoo.

LONGSHOE:   All ready! Can't you spare us that shit early in the a.m.?

EL RAHEEM:   No . . . one . . . is . . . talking . . . to . . . you . . . Yacoub.

LONGSHOE:   The name is Longshoe Charlie Murphy . . . *Mister* Murphy
to you.

EL RAHEEM:   Yacoub . . . maker and creator of the devil . . . swine merchant. Your time is near at hand. Fuck around and your time will be now.
Soon all devils' heads will roll and now rivers shall flow through the
city—created by the blood of Whitey . . . Devil . . . beast.

OMAR:   Salaam Alaikum.[8]

PACO:   Salami with bacons.

ICE:   Power to the people.

LONGSHOE:   Free the Watergate 500.[9]

JUAN:   Pa'lante.[1]

CUPCAKES:   Tippecanoe and Tyler too.[2]

PACO:
   [*On table, overly feminine.*]
A la lucha . . . a la lucha . . . que somo mucha . . .[3]

OMAR:   Hey! Hey . . . you know the Panthers[4] say "Power to the people."

MR. NETT:   On the gate.[5]

OMAR:
   [*Strong voice.*]
Power to the people. And gay liberators say . . .
   [*High voice, limp wrist in fist.*]
Power to the people.
   [*Enter* NETT.]

MR. NETT:   How about police power?

JUAN:   How about it? Oink, oink.

MR. NETT:   Wise guy. Paco, you got a counsel visit.

PACO: Vaya.[6]

OMAR:   Mr. Nett?

---

7. Psychological complexes. [Glossary of slang]
8. (From the Arabic) Peace be with you. [Glos-
sary of slang]
9. Ironic reference to the then-current scandal surrounding the Watergate office complex, in Washington, D.C., where in June 1972, five (not 500)
men were arrested for breaking and entering into
the Democratic National Committee headquarters. The five turned out to have been hired for the
job by advisors to Richard M. Nixon (1913–1994),
U.S. president 1969–74. Some of Nixon's advisors
were convicted; Nixon resigned on August 9, 1974.
1. (Short for [the Spanish phrase] *para adelante*)

Forward and onward. [Glossary of slang]
2. Slogan from the 1840 U.S. presidential election, used in a popular and influential campaign
song promoting the ticket of William Henry
Harrison (1773–1841, hero of the 1811 Battle of
Tippecanoe) and John Tyler (1790–1862).
3. To the fight . . . to the fight . . . because we're
many . . . (*que somo mucha* is slang).
4. The Black Panthers, a militant political group
of the 1960s–70s.
5. Mr. Nett is on the other side of the gate and
wanting to be let in to the dayroom.
6. Literally, go; figuratively, O.K.

MR. NETT:   Yeah, what is it?

OMAR:   Mr. Nett, you know like I've been here over ten months—and I'd like to know why I can't get on the help.[7] Like I've asked a dozen times . . . and guys that just come in are shot over me . . . and I get shot down . . . Like why? Have I done something to you? Is there something about me that you don't like?

MR. NETT:   Why, no. I don't have anything against you. But since you ask me I'll tell you. One is that when you first came in here you had the clap.

OMAR:   But I don't have it any more. That was ten months ago.

MR. NETT:   How many fights have you had since the first day you came on the floor?

OMAR:   But I haven't had a fight in a long time.

MR. NETT:   How many?

OMAR:   Seven.

MR. NETT:   Seven? Close to ten would be my estimation. No, if I put you on the help, there would be trouble in no time. Now if you give me your word that you won't fight and stay cool, I'll give it some deep consideration.

OMAR:   I can't give you my word on something like that. You know I don't stand for no lame coming out the side of his neck[8] with me. Not my word . . . My word is bond.

EL RAHEEM:   Bond is life.

OMAR:   That's why I can't give you my word. My word is my bond. Man in prison ain't got nothing but his word, and he's got to be careful who and how and for what he give it for. But I'll tell you this, I'll try to be cool.

MR. NETT:   Well, you're honest about it anyway. I'll think it over.

[PACO *and* MR. NETT *exit.*]

EL RAHEEM:   Try is a failure.

OMAR:   Fuck you.

EL RAHEEM:   Try is a failure. Do.

OMAR:   Fuck you.

EL RAHEEM:   Fuck yourself, it's cheaper.

CUPCAKES:   Hey, Mr. Nett—put on the power.

MR. NETT:

[*From outside the gate.*]

The power is on.

CUPCAKES:   The box ain't on.

MR. NETT:   Might be broken. I'll call the repairman.

JUAN:   Might as well listen to the radio.

ICE:   The radio ain't workin' either, Juan. I tried to get BLS[9] a little while ago and got nothin' but static, Jack.

CUPCAKES:   Anyone wants to play Dirty Hearts? I ain't got no money, but I'll have cigarettes later on this week.

OMAR:   Money on the wood makes bettin' good.

---

7. Prison job. To be "on the help" means to get a prison job. [Glossary of slang]
8. *Coming out the side of your neck*: bullshitting; saying stupid things. *Lame*: sucker; chump. [Glos-sary of slang]
9. WBLS, an FM station that plays R&B (rhythm and blues) and classic soul.

ICE:  Right on.
      [LONGSHOE *gives* CUPCAKES *cigarettes.*]
JUAN:  Hey, Julio.
      [*Throws* CUPCAKES *cigarettes.*
          BROWN *appears outside entrance gate.*]
BROWN:  On the gate.
      [*Gate opens and* PACO *enters. Gate closes and* BROWN *exits.*]
CUPCAKES:  Shit. That was a real fast visit.
PACO:  Not fast enough.
LONGSHOE:  What the man say about your case?
PACO:  The bitch wants me to cop out to a D[1]—she must think my dick is
      made of sponge rubber. I told her to tell the D.A. to rub the offer on his
      chest.[2] Not to come to court on my behalf—shit, the bitch must have
      made a deal with the D.A. on one of her paying customers. Man, if I
      wait I could get a misdemeanor by my motherfucking self. What the
      fuck I need with a Legal Aid? Guess who's on the bench?
ICE:  Who they got out there?
PACO:  Cop-out Levine.
ICE:  Wow! He give me a pound for a frown.
PACO:  First they give me a student, and now a double-crossin' bitch.
LONGSHOE:  We all got to make a living.
PACO:  On my expense? No fucking good.
EL RAHEEM:  You still expect the white man to give you a fair trial in his
      court? Don't you know what justice really means? Justice . . . "just
      us" . . . white folks.
PACO:  Look here, man. I don't expect nothing from nobody—especially
      the Yankees. Man, this ain't my first time before them people behind
      these walls, cause I ain't got the money for bail. And you can bet that it
      won't be my last time—not as long as I'm poor and Puerto Rican.
CUPCAKES:  Come on, let's play . . . for push-ups.
JUAN:  How many?
CUPCAKES:  Ten if you got just one book, fifteen if you got two.
PACO:  I ain't playing for no goddamn push-ups.
ICE:  Hey—come on, don't be like that.
PACO:  Said ain't playing for no push-ups. Tell you what, let's play for
      coochie-coochies.
ICE:  What the hell is coochie-coochies?
JUAN:  It's a game they play in Puerto Rico. You ever see a flick about
      Hawaii? Them girls with the grass skirts moving their butts dancing?
      That's coochie-coochies.
ICE:  I thought that was the hula-jack.
PACO:  Put your shirt on your hips like this and move your ass. Coochie-
      coochie-coochie . . .
CUPCAKES:  That's out.
PACO:  You got a plexes?
CUPCAKES:  Told you before that I don't have no complexes.
JUAN:  You got no plexes at all?

---

1. I.e., plead guilty to a class D felony.
2. *Rub it on your chest*: forget about it. [Glossary of slang]

CUPCAKES: No.

JUAN: Then why not let me fuck you?

CUPCAKES: That's definitely out.

JUAN: People without complexes might as well turn stuff.[3]

OMAR: Thinking of joining the ranks? Cruising the tearooms?[4]

EL RAHEEM: What kind of black original man talk is that? Cupcakes puts the wisdom before the knowledge because that's his nature. He can't help that. But you are deliberately acting and thinking out of your nature . . . thinking like the white devil, Yacoub. Your presence infects the minds of my people like a fever. You, Yacoub, are the bearer of three thousand nine hundred and ninety-nine diseases . . . corrupt . . . evil . . . pork-chop-eating brain . . .

LONGSHOE: Look.

EL RAHEEM: Where?

LONGSHOE: I'm sick and . . .

EL RAHEEM: See, brothers, he admits he is sick with corruption.

LONGSHOE: Who?

EL RAHEEM: You're not only the devil, you're also an owl?

LONGSHOE: Why?

EL RAHEEM: "Y"—why? Why is "Y" the twenty-fifth letter of the alphabet?

LONGSHOE: You . . . son of . . .

EL RAHEEM: You . . . me . . . they . . . them. This . . . those . . . that . . . "U" for the unknown.

LONGSHOE: I . . . I . . .

EL RAHEEM: Eye . . . I . . . Aye . . . Aye . . . Aiiii . . . hi . . .

LONGSHOE: Games, huh?

EL RAHEEM: The way of life is no game. Lame.

LONGSHOE: G . . . O . . . D . . . D . . . O . . . G . . . God spelled backward is dog . . . dog spelled backward is God . . . If Allah is God, Allah is a dog.

EL RAHEEM: Allah Akbar.[5]

[*Screams, jumps on him.*]

Allah Akbar.

[MR. NETT *and* BROWN *appear outside entrance gate.*]

MR. NETT: On the gate.

[BROWN *opens gate.* MR. NETT *and* BROWN *enter.* MR. NETT *breaks them apart.*]

MR. NETT: What the hell is going on here?

OMAR: Mr. Nett, let these two git it off, else we's gonna have mucho static around here.

ICE: Yeah . . . Mr. Nett . . . they got a personality thing going on for weeks.

MR. NETT: Fair fight, Murphy?

LONGSHOE: That's what I want.

MR. NETT: Johnson?

EL RAHEEM: El Raheem. Johnson is a slave name.

[*Nods.*]

May your Christian God have mercy on your soul, Yacoub.

---

3. *Stuff*: a male homosexual. [Glossary of slang]
4. *Tearoom*: men's room, especially in subways, where [some] homosexuals seek sexual contact with each other. To "cruise the tearoom" is to go into a men's room for homosexual purposes. [Glossary of slang]
5. God is great (Arabic).

[BROWN *closes gate.*
EL RAHEEM *and* LONGSHOE *square off and begin to fight . . . boxing . . . some wrestling.*
EL RAHEEM *is knocked clean across the room.*]

LONGSHOE:   Guess you say that left hook is Whitey trickology?

EL RAHEEM:   No, honky, you knocked me down. My sister hits harder than that. She's only eight.

[*They wrestle until* EL RAHEEM *is on top. Then* NETT *breaks them apart.*]

OMAR:   Why didn't you break it up while Whitey was on top?

MR. NETT:   Listen, why don't you two guys call it quits—ain't none of you really gonna end up the winner . . . Give it up . . . be friends . . . shake hands . . . Come, break it up, you both got your shit off . . . break it up. Go out and clean yourselves up. Make this the last time I see either of you fighting. On the gate. Next time I turn on the water.

[BROWN *and* NETT *exit, gate closes.*
The RICANS *go to their table and begin to play on the table as if it were bongos.*]

ICE:   You two got it together.

EL RAHEEM:   I am God . . . master and ruler of my universe . . . I am always together.

OMAR:   Let me ask you one question, God.

EL RAHEEM:   You have permission to ask two.

OMAR:   Thank you . . . If you're God, why are you in jail? God can do anything, right? Melt these walls down, then create a stairway of light to the streets below . . . God. If you're God, then you can do these things. If you can't, tell me why God can't do a simple thing like that.

EL RAHEEM:   I am God . . . I am a poor righteous teacher of almighty Allah and by his will I am here to awaken the original lost in these prisons . . . Black original man is asleep . . . This is your school of self-awareness. Wake up, black man, melt these walls? You ask me, a tangible god, to do an intangible feat? Mysterious intangible gods do mysterious intangible deeds. There is nothing mysterious about me. Tangible gods do tangible deeds.

[PUERTO RICAN GROUP *goes back to playing. "Toca, si vas a tocar."*[6]]

CUPCAKES

[*On table, M.C.-style.*]
That's right, ladies and gentlemen . . . damas y caballeros . . . every night is Latin night at the House of Detention. Tonight for the first time . . . direct from his record-breaking counsel visit . . . on congas is Paco Pasqual . . . yeaaaaaa. With a all-star band . . . for your listening enjoyment . . . Juan Bobo Otero on timbales . . . On mouth organ Charles Murphy . . . To show you the latest dancing are Iceman, John Wicker . . . and his equally talented partner, Omar Blinker . . . yeaaaaaa. While tapping his toes for you all . . . moving his head to the rhythm of the band is the mighty El Raheem, yeaaaaaa. Boooooooo. Yes, brothers and sisters, especially you sisters, don't miss this musical extravaganza. I'll be there, too . . . to say hello to all my friends . . . So be there . . . Don't

---

6. Play already, if you're going to play.

be the one to say "Gee, I missed it" . . . This is your cha-cha jockey, Julio . . .

ALL: Cupcakes . . .

CUPCAKES: Mercado . . . Be sure to be there . . . Catch this act . . . this show of shows before they leave on a long extended touring engagement with state . . .

[PACO *pinches* CUPCAKES'*s ass.*]

Keep your hands off my ass, man.

[CUPCAKES *moves stage left, sits pouting. Ad-libs.*]

PACO: Hey, kid, do one of those prison toasts . . .

[*They urge him on with various ad-libs.*]

CUPCAKES: All right, dig . . . You guys gotta give me background . . . Clap your hands and say . . . Mambo tu le pop . . . It was the night before Christmas . . . and all through the pad . . . cocaine and heroin was all the cats had. One cat in the corner . . . copping a nod[7] . . . Another scratching thought he was God . . . I jumps on the phone . . . and dial with care . . . hoping my reefer . . . would soon be there . . . After a while . . . crowding my style . . . I ran to the door . . . see what's the matter . . . And to my surprise . . . I saw five police badges . . . staring . . . glaring in my eyes . . . A couple of studs . . . starts to get tough, so I ran to the bathroom . . . get rid of the stuff . . . narc[8] bang . . . bang . . . but they banged in vain . . . cause you see . . . what didn't go in my veins went down the drain . . . Broke down the door . . . knock me to the floor . . . and took me away, that's the way I spent my last Christmas Day . . . like a dirty dog . . . in a dark and dingy cell . . . But I didn't care cause I was high as hell . . . But I was cool . . . I was cool . . . I was cool . . . You people are the fools . . . cream of the top . . . cause I got you say something as stupid as Mambo tu le pop.

[GROUP *chases* CUPCAKES *around stage.*

BROWN *and* CLARK DAVIS *appear outside entrance gate.*]

BROWN: On the gate.

[*Gate opens and* CLARK DAVIS *enters, goes to stage center.* BROWN *closes gate and exits.*]

CUPCAKES: Hey, Longshoe . . . one of your kin . . . look-a-like sin just walked in . . .

EL RAHEEM: Another devil.

LONGSHOE: Hey . . . hey, whatdayasay . . . My name's Longshoe Charlie Murphy. Call me Longshoe. What's your name?

CLARK: Davis . . . Clark . . . Ah . . . Clark Davis . . . Clark is my first name.

PACO: Clark Kent.

CUPCAKES: Mild-mannered, too.

OMAR: No, no, Superman.

[*Other ad-libs: "Faster than a speeding bullet," etc.*][9]

PACO: Oye . . . Shoe . . . Está bueno . . . Pa' rajarlo . . .[1]

---

7. Nodding, an involuntary response as someone high on an opiate drifts in and out of consciousness.
8. I.e., narcotics officers.
9. In the spoken-word introduction to the television series *Adventures of Superman* (1952–58),

*faster than a speeding bullet* described Superman and *mild-mannered* described his alter ego, Clark Kent.
1. Hey, listen . . . Shoe . . . He is good-looking . . . To be fucked ("Pa' rajarlo" is a contraction for *para rajarlo*).

LONGSHOE: Back . . . back . . . boy . . . no está bueno . . . anyway, no mucho . . . como[2] Cupcake.

PACO: Vaya.

LONGSHOE: Pay them no mind . . . crazy spics . . . where you locking?

CLARK: Upper D 15.

LONGSHOE: Siberia,[3] huh? . . . Tough.

CLARK: First time in the joint.

LONGSHOE: Yeah? Well, I better hip you to what's happening fast.

ICE: Look out for your homey, Shoe.

OMAR: Second.

LONGSHOE: Look here, this is our section . . . white . . . dig? That's the Rican table, you can sit there if they give you permission . . . Same goes with the black section.

ICE: Say it loud.

OMAR: I'm black and proud.

ICE: Vaya!

LONGSHOE: Most of the fellas are in court. I'm the Don Gee[4] here. You know what that mean, right? Good . . . Niggers and the spics don't give us honkies much trouble. We're cool half ass. This is a good floor. Dynamite hack[5] on all shifts. Stay away from the black gods . . .

[NETT *appears outside gate.*]

NETT: On the gate.

LONGSHOE: You know them when you see them.

[NETT *opens gate and enters.*]

NETT: On the chow.

ICE: What we got, Mr. Nett?

NETT: Baloney à la carte.

ICE: Shit, welfare steaks again.

[*All exit except* CLARK *and* LONGSHOE. *Gate stays open. The men reenter with sandwiches and return to their respective places.*

NETT *closes gate and exits*]

LONGSHOE: Black go on the front of the line, we stay in the back . . . It's okay to rap with the blacks, but don't get too close with any of them. Ricans too. We're the minority here, so be cool. If you hate yams,[6] keep it to yourself. Don't show it. But also don't let them run over you. Ricans are funny people. Took me a long time to figure them out, and you know something, I found out that I still have a lot to learn about them. I rap spic talk. They get a big-brother attitude about the whites in jail. But they also back the niggers to the T.

ICE

[*Throws* LONGSHOE *a sandwich.*]

Hey, Shoe.

LONGSHOE: If a spic pulls a razor blade on you and you don't have a mop wringer in your hands . . . run . . . If you have static with a nigger and

---

2. Like.

3. Ironic reference to an area of northern Asia in Russia; i.e., a remote, isolated place.

4. A big shot; "gee" is short for "gun." [Glossary of slang]

5. *Hack*: a guard. [Glossary of slang]

6. A popular food item among blacks and Puerto Ricans; however, *yams* is also street slang for cocaine and for female breasts.

they ain't no white people around . . . get a spic to watch your back,[7] you may have a chance . . . That ain't no guarantee . . . If you have static with a spic, don't get no nigger to watch your back cause you ain't gonna have none.

OMAR:   You can say that again.

ICE:   Two times.

LONGSHOE:   You're a good-looking kid . . . You ain't stuff and you don't want to be stuff. Stay away from the bandidos.[8] Paco is one of them . . . Take no gifts from no one.

[NETT *appears outside entrance gate.*]

NETT:   Clark Davis . . . Davis.

CLARK:   Yes, that's me.

NETT:   On the gate.

[NETT *opens gate, enters with* CLARK's *belongings, leaves gate open.*] Come here . . . come here . . . white trash . . . filth . . . Let me tell you something and you better listen good cause I'm only going to say it one time . . . and one time only. This is a nice floor . . . a quiet floor . . . There has never been too much trouble on this floor . . . With you, I smell trouble . . . I don't question the warden's or the captain's motive for putting you on this floor . . . But for once I'm gonna ask why they put a sick fucking degenerate like you on my floor . . . If you just talk out the side of your mouth one time . . . if you look at me sideways one time . . . if you mispronounce my name once, if you pick up more food than you can eat . . . if you call me for something I think is unnecessary . . . if you oversleep, undersleep . . . if . . . if . . . if . . . you give me just one little reason . . . I'm gonna break your face up so bad your own mother won't know you . . .

LONGSHOE:   Mr. Nett is being kinda hard . . .

NETT:   Shut up . . . I got a eight-year-old daughter who was molested by one of those bastards . . . stinking sons of bitches and I just as well pretend that he was you, Davis, do you understand that . . .

PACO:   Short eyes.

LONGSHOE:   Short eyes? Short eyes . . . Clark, are you one of those short-eyes freaks . . . are you a short-eyes freak?

NETT:   Sit down, Murphy . . . I'm talking to this . . . this scumbag . . . yeah, he's a child rapist . . . a baby rapist, how old was she? How old? . . . Eight . . . seven . . . Disgusting bastard . . . Stay out of my sight . . . cause if you get in my face just one time . . . don't forget what I told you . . . I'll take a night stick and ram it clean up your asshole . . . I hope to God that they take you off this floor, or send you to Sing Sing . . . The men up there know what to do with degenerates like you.

CLARK:   I . . . I . . .

NETT:   All right, let's go . . . Lock in . . . lock in . . . for the count[9] . . . Clark, the captain outside on the bridge wants to see you. I hope he takes you off this floor . . .

---

7. *Back:* as in "watch your back," meaning someone may attack you (usually with a knife) when you aren't looking. Prisoners attack each other from the front ("fronting") when they have some respect for their adversaries or when the attack constitutes some kind of showdown. Stabbing someone in the back either is an act of cowardice or signifies that the target isn't worth "fronting." [Glossary of slang]

8. *Bandido (or bandit):* someone who chases attractive young prisoners for sexual purposes. [Glossary of slang]

9. The roll call of prisoners. A convict is "on the count" if he is present and accounted for; hence the expression "off the count," which means (since escapes from Sing Sing and other

LONGSHOE: Hey, Davis . . .
  [*Walks up to him and spits in his face.*
  *Men exit*]
NETT: Juan, stay out and clean the dayroom. Omar, take the tier.
  [CAPTAIN ALLARD *appears on the catwalk above.* CLARK *joins* ALLARD
  *and they carry on inaudible conversation.*
    *Crossing from stage right to stage left on the catwalk are* CUP-
  CAKES, ICE, *and* LONGSHOE, *followed by* MR. BROWN. *As* LONGSHOE
  *passes, he bumps* CLARK.
    MR. BROWN *stops beside* CLARK, *and* CAPTAIN ALLARD *chases after*
  LONGSHOE *to catwalk above left*]
ALLARD: Hey, just a minute, you. That's just the kind of stuff that's going
  to cease.
  [BROWN *and* CLARK *exit catwalk above right and appear at entrance*
  *gate stage right.*]
BROWN: On the gate.
  [BROWN *opens gate,* CLARK *enters dayroom,* BROWN *closes gate.*
  CLARK *says something inaudible to* BROWN.]
You're lucky if you get a call before Christmas.
  [BROWN *exits.* CLARK *leans on gate.*]
LONGSHOE: Get off that fuckin' gate.
  [*While the above was going on,* JUAN *has taken his cleaning equip-*
  *ment from the shower upstage left and placed can of Ajax and rag*
  *on the toilet area upstage center, and broom, mop, bucket, dustpan,*
  *dust broom, dust box in downstage left corner.* JUAN *sits at table,*
  CLARK *at window.* JUAN *pours coffee, offers* CLARK *a sandwich.*
  CLARK *crosses to table and sits.*]
JUAN: Hey, man, did you really do it?
  [OMAR *starts chant offstage.*]
CLARK: I don't know.
JUAN: What do you mean, you don't know? What you think I am, a fool,
  or something out of a comic book.
CLARK: No . . . I don't mean to sound like that, I . . . I . . .
JUAN: Look, man, either you did it or you didn't.
  [JUAN *stands.*]
That all there is to it . . .
CLARK: I don't know if I did it or not.
JUAN: You better break that down[1] to me
  [*Sits.*]
cause you lost me.
CLARK: What I mean is that I may have done it or I may not have . . . I
  just don't remember . . . I remember seeing that little girl that morn-
  ing . . . I sat in Bellevue[2] thirty-three days and I don't remember doing
  anything like that to that little girl.
JUAN: You done something like that before, haven't you?
CLARK: I . . . ye . . . yes . . . I have . . . How did you know?
JUAN: Your guilt flies off your tongue, man.

---

maximum-security prisons are so rare) that a prisoner is dead, usually murdered by fellow inmates.
[Glossary of slang]

1. *Break it down*: Explain it. [Glossary of slang]
2. Municipal hospital in Manhattan with a well-
known psychiatric unit.

[*Stands.*]
Sound like one of those guys in an encounter session
[*Starts to sweep.*]
looking to dump their shit off on someone . . . You need help . . . The
bad part about it is that you know it . . .

CLARK: Help? I need help? Yes . . . yes, I do need help . . . But I'm afraid to
find it . . . Why? . . . Fear . . . just fear . . . Perhaps fear of knowing that I
may be put away forever . . . I have a wife and kid I love very much . . .
and I want to be with them. I don't ever want to be away from them . . .
ever. But now this thing has happened . . . I don't know what to do . . . I
don't know . . . If I fight it in court, they'll end up getting hurt . . . If I
don't, it'll be the same thing . . . Jesus help me . . . God forgive me.

JUAN: Cause man won't.
[JUAN *at downstage left corner sweeping up dust.*]

CLARK: No, man won't . . . Society will never forgive me . . . or accept
me back once this is openly known.
[JUAN *begins to stack chairs stage right.* CLARK *hands* JUAN *a chair.*]
I think about it sometimes and . . . funny, I don't really feel disgusted . . .
just ashamed . . . You wanna . . .

JUAN: Listen to you? It's up to you . . . You got a half hour before the
floor locks out unless you wanna go public like A.A.
[JUAN *picks up stool.*]

CLARK: No . . . no . . . no . . . I can't . . . I didn't even talk with the psychiatrist in the bughouse.

JUAN: Run it . . . [3]
[JUAN *puts down stool.*]

CLARK: You know, somehow it seems like there's no beginning. Seems
like I've always been in there all my life. I have like little picture incidents running across my mind . . . I remember being . . . fifteen or sixteen years old
[JUAN *crosses upstage center to clean toilet.*]
or something around that age, waking up to the sound of voices coming
from the living room . . . cartoons on the TV . . . They were watching
cartoons on the TV, two little girls. One was my sister, and her friend . . .
And you know how it is when you get up in the morning, the inevitable
hard-on is getting up with you. I draped the sheet around my shoulders . . . Everyone else was sleeping . . . The girl watching TV with my
sister . . . yes . . . Hispanic . . . pale-looking skin . . . She was eight . . .
nine . . . ten . . . what the difference, she was a child . . . She was very
pretty—high cheekbones, flashing black eyes . . . She was wearing blue
short pants . . . tight-fitting . . . a white blouse, or shirt . . . My sister . . .
she left to do number two . . .
[JUAN *returns to stage right.*]
She told her friend wait for me, I'm going to do number two, and they
laughed about it. I sneaked in standing a little behind her . . . She felt me
standing there and turned to me . . . She smiled such a pretty little smile . . .
I told her I was a vampire and she laughed . . . I spread the sheets apart and
she suddenly stopped laughing . . . She just stood there staring at me . . .

3. Go ahead and tell your story. [Glossary of slang]

Shocked? surprised? intrigued? Don't know . . . don't know . . . She just stood and stared . . .

[JUAN *crosses to downstage left.*]

I came closer like a vampire . . . She started backing away . . . ran toward the door . . . stopped, looked at me again. Never at my face . . . my body . . . I couldn't really tell whether or not the look on her face was one of fear . . . but I'll never forget that look.

[BROWN *crosses on catwalk from left to right with a banana. Stands at right.*]

I was really scared that she'd tell her parents. Weeks passed without confrontation . . . and I was feeling less and less afraid . . . But that's not my thing, showing myself naked to little girls in schoolyards.

[JUAN *crosses to downstage right corner and begins to mop from downstage right to downstage left.*]

One time . . . no, it was the first time . . . the very first time. I was alone watching TV . . . Was I in school or out . . . And there was this little Puerto Rican girl from next door . . . Her father was the new janitor . . . I had seen her before . . . many times . . . sliding down the banister . . . Always her panties looked dirty . . . She was . . . oh, why do I always try to make their age higher than it really was . . . even to myself. She was young, much too young . . . Why did she come there? For who? Hundred questions. Not one small answer . . . not even a lie flickers across my brain.

OFFSTAGE VOICE:   All right, listen up. The following inmates report for sanitation duty: Smalls, Gary; Medena, James; Pfeifer, Willis; Martinez, Raul. Report to C.O. grounds for sanitation duty.

CLARK:   How did I get to the bathroom with her? Don't know. I was standing there with her, I was combing her hair. I was combing her hair. Her curly reddish hair . . .

[JUAN *crosses upstage right, starts to mop upstage right to upstage left.*]

I was naked . . . naked . . . except for these flower-printed cotton underwears . . . No slippers, barefooted . . . Suddenly I get this feeling over me . . . like a flash fever . . . and I'm hard . . . I placed my hands on her small shoulders . . . and pressed her hand and placed it on my penis . . . Did she know what to do? Or did I coerce her? I pulled down my drawers . . . But then I felt too naked, so I put them back on . . . My eyes were closed . . . but I felt as if there was this giant eye off in space staring at me . . .

[JUAN *stops upstage left and listens to* CLARK, *who is unaware* JUAN *is in back of him.*]

I opened them and saw her staring at me in the cabinet mirror. I pulled her back away from the view of the mirror . . . My hands up her dress, feeling her underdeveloped body . . . I . . . I . . . I began pulling her underwear down on the bowl . . . She resisted . . . slightly, just a moment . . . I sat on the bowl . . . She turned and threw her arms around my neck and kissed me on the lips . . . She gave a small nervous giggle . . . I couldn't look at her . . . I closed my eyes . . . turned her body . . . to face away from me . . . I lubricated myself . . . and . . . I hear a scream, my own . . . there was a spot of blood on my drawers . . . I took them off right then and there . . . ripped them up and flushed them down the toilet . . . She had dressed herself up and asked me if we could do it again tomorrow . . . and was I her boyfriend now . . . I said yes, yes . . .

> [JUAN *goes to center stage, starts mopping center stage right to stage left.*
>
> BROWN *exits from catwalk above right.*]

I couldn't sit still that whole morning, I just couldn't relax. I dressed and took a walk . . . Next thing I know I was running—out of breath . . . I had run over twenty blocks . . . twenty blocks blind . . . without knowing . . . I was running . . . Juan, was it my conscious or subconscious that my rest stop was a children's playground . . . Coincidence perhaps . . . But why did I run in that direction, no, better still, why did I start walking in that direction . . . Coincidence? Why didn't my breath give out elsewhere . . . Coincidence?

> [JUAN *moves to downstage left,* CLARK *moves to upstage center and sits on window ledge.*]

I sat on the park bench and watched the little girls swing . . . slide . . . run . . . jump rope . . . Fat . . . skinny . . . black . . . white . . . Chinese . . . I sat there until the next morning . . . The next day I went home and met the little Puerto Rican girl again . . . Almost three times a week . . . The rest of the time I would be in the playground or in the children's section of the movies . . . But you know something? Er, er . . .

> [CLARK *moves toward* JUAN, *who is in downstage left corner.*]

JUAN: Juan.

CLARK: Yes, Juan . . . Juan the listener . . . the compassionate . . . you know something, Juan . . . I soon became . . . became . . . what? A pro? A professional degenerate?

> [*The sound of garbage can banging together is heard offstage.*]

I don't know if you can call it a second insight on children. But . . . I would go to the park . . . and sit there for hours and talk with a little girl and know if I would do it or not with her . . . Just a few words was all I needed . . . Talk stupid things they consider grownup talk . . . Soon my hand would hold hers, then I would caress her face . . . Next her thighs . . . under their dress . . . I never took any of them home or drove away with them in my car . . . I always told them to meet me in the very same building they lived in . . .

OFFSTAGE VOICE: On the sanitation gate.

> [*Sound of gate opening.*]

CLARK: On the roof or their basements under the stairs . . . Sometimes in their own home if the parents were out . . . The easiest ones were the Puerto Ricans and the black girls . . . Little white ones would masturbate you right there in the park for a dollar or a quarter . . . depending on how much emphasis their parents put in their heads on making money . . . I felt ashamed at first . . . But then I would rehearse at nights what to do the next time . . . planning . . . I

> [JUAN *starts moving slowly from downstage left to upstage left.*]

couldn't help myself . . . I couldn't help myself . . . Something drove me to it . . . I thought of killing myself . . . but I just couldn't go through with it . . . I don't really wanna die . . . I wanted to stop, really I did . . . I just didn't know how. I thought maybe I was crazy . . . but I read all types of psychology books . . . I heard or read somewhere that crazy people can't distinguish right from wrong . . . Yet I can . . . I know what's right and I know what I'm doing is wrong, yet I can't stop myself . . .

JUAN:  Why didn't you go to the police or a psychiatrist . . .

> [JUAN *crosses to shower room upstage left.*]

CLARK:  I wanted to many a time . . . But I know that the police would find some pretext to kill me . . . And a psychiatrist . . . well, if he thought he couldn't help me he'd turn me over to them or commit me to some nut ward . . . Juan, try to understand me.

> [JUAN *comes out of shower room and starts putting away his cleaning equipment.*]

JUAN:  Motherfucker, try to understand you . . . if I wasn't trying to, I would have killed you . . . stone dead, punk . . .

> [JUAN, *at downstage left corner, picks up broom and bucket.*]

The minute you said that thing about the Rican girls . . . . If I was you I'd ask transfer to protection . . . cause

> [JUAN *returns to shower room.*]

if you remain on this floor you're asking to die . . . You'll be committing involuntary suicide . . .

> [JUAN *again crosses to downstage left corner, picks up remaining equipment, crosses to toilet, picks up Ajax and rag, and crosses to shower room.*]

Shit, why the fuck did you have to tell me all of it . . . You don't know me from Adam . . .

> [JUAN *comes out of shower room and crosses to* CLARK, *stage center.*]

Why the hell did you have to make me your father confessor? Why? Why didn't you stop, why?

CLARK:  Cause you asked. Cause you . . . What I told you I didn't even tell the doctors at the observation ward . . . Everything is coming down on me so fast . . . I needed to tell it all . . . to someone . . . Juan, you were willing to listen.

> [*Whistle blows.*]

MR. NETT

> [*Offstage.*]

All right, on the lookout . . .

> [*Whistle.*]

OTHER VOICES:  On the lookout.

> [BROWN *appears outside the gate.*]

BROWN:  On the gate.

> [*Enter* EL RAHEEM, PACO, OMAR, ICE, CUPCAKES, *and* LONGSHOE. BROWN *closes gate and exits.* ICE *and* OMAR *get one chair and cross to table.* OMAR *starts playing cards.*
> LONGSHOE *gets his stool and crosses to behind table.*
> CUPCAKES *does push-ups on chair stage right.*]

ICE:  You're gonna be on the help for good, Omar.

OMAR:  No, the man said just for today . . . But he put me on top of the list.

ICE:  You gonna look out for me, heavy homeeeeey?[4]

---

4. *Homey:* a fellow prisoner from one's neighborhood or home town. [Glossary of slang]

OMAR: Since when did we become homeeeeeys? Shit, man—you're way out there in Coney Island somewhere . . . and I'm way in Bed-Stuy.[5]

ICE: How you gonna show, brother man? It's the same borough, ain't it?

OMAR: It's the same borough, Iceman . . . but it's a different world.

ICE: Ain't this a bitch? I comes on this here floor with this man . . . There was nothing but Whiteys on the floor. It was me and him against the world . . . I come out every night and stand by his side, ready to die . . . to die . . .

PACO: Yeah, cause you no wanna die alone.

ICE: That has nothing to do with nothing.

OMAR: It has everything to do with everything.

ICE: How you going to show? How you do this to me, Omar, homey.

OMAR: Being how you mentioned it, perhaps it's not a bad idea. Save me some money when you go to the store.

ICE: I ain't gonna argue that . . . cause this is me, the Iceman, talking— my hand don't call for this type of talking, man. Your main mellow-man, this is too strong . . . Contracts . . . [6]

OMAR: Who said anything about contract? I didn't say anything about contract . . . Anybody here said anything about a contract? . . .

CUPCAKES: I didn't hear anybody say anything . . . I didn't say it.

PACO: Me neither . . .

LONGSHOE: Who could say anything with a swollen lip.

JUAN: I mind my own business.

OMAR: See, you must be hearing things.

ICE: You didn't say it . . . but you implied it . . . You was leading right up to it.

OMAR: Well, now that you mentioned it . . . perhaps it's not a bad idea . . .

ICE: How you gonna do this to me? Omarrrrr . . . homeeey . . .

OMAR: Did it to yourself . . . You knew I'd always look out . . . but now you put these ideas into my head . . . and it sounds kinda . . .

ICE: Omar . . . my pretty nigger . . . even if you get no bigger, you'll always be my main nigger . . . And if you get any bigger, you'll just be my bigger nigger . . .

OMAR: Better run that shit on the judge . . . You know what you can do for me . . . give me a softshoe.

ICE: Yes sir, boss, captain, your honor, mister, sir.
  [*Fast softshoe.*]

OMAR: Hey, freak.
  [*To* CLARK.]
You're sittin' on my Chinese handball court . . .
  [CLARK *moves to upstage right.*]

ICE: That there is where I hangs my wet clean clothes . . . and I don't wanna have them sprayed. Move . . . creep.[7]

---

5. Bedford-Stuyvesant, a neighborhood in central Brooklyn; Coney Island is a beachfront neighborhood on Brooklyn's south shore.
6. *Contract*: an agreement between prisoners, such as a "contract" to wash another prisoner's clothes in exchange for a sandwich sneaked out of the kitchen by a prisoner who works there. Prison authorities tolerate such violations because this kind of crude barter helps make prison life more tolerable for inmates. *Mellow-man*: close friend. [Glossary of slang]
7. Sexual offender; the lowest rung of the prison hierarchy. Creeps never "get a hang-out card" (command enough respect to mingle and converse freely with other prisoners). [Glossary of slang]

[CLARK *moves to stage center.*]

EL RAHEEM: You're in God's walking space.

[CLARK *moves to lower stage right.*]

PACO: That's Paco's walking space.

CUPCAKES: Hey, Clark . . . that spot's not taken . . . Right over there . . . Yeah, that's right . . . The whole toilet bowl and you go well together.

CLARK: I'm not going to stand for this treatment.

PACO: Did you say something out of your mouth, creep . . .

OMAR: You talking to everyone, or to someone in particular?

LONGSHOE: I know you ain't talking to me.

ICE: You got something you wanna say to someone in this room, faggot?

CLARK: I was talking to myself.

EL RAHEEM: Well, don't talk to yourself too loud.

CUPCAKES: Talk to the shitbowl . . . You'll find you got a lot in common with each other . . .

JUAN: Drop it . . . Cut it loose . . .

PACO: ¿Donde está La Mancha? . . . or did Sancho go to another floor? . . . [8]

JUAN: Paco . . . one of these days you gonna get me very very angry.

PACO: I'm trembling, man . . . whooo, I'm scared . . . Can't you smell it, I'm shitting bricks . . .

ICE: Juan . . . be cool . . . don't know why you wanna put front for that freak . . . But, man . . . if you don't wanna vamp[9] . . . don't go against your own people . . . You be wrong, man . . .

JUAN: Ain't going against my own brother man . . . But if the dude is a sicky . . . cut him loose . . . All that ain't necessary . . . Ice.

ICE: It ain't your place, Juan, and you know it . . . You're out of time . . .

PACO: I think he has a special interest.

ICE: Don't come out of your face wrong, Paco.

PACO: Ice.

ICE: You're interrupting me, Paco . . . Me and you both know where you're coming from . . . Don't make me put your shit in the streets . . . And, Juan, you know you're out of order. This ain't your turn, man . . .

CUPCAKES: Let's go do up them clothes, Juan.

JUAN: Yeah. O.K., kid . . . go get the buckets . . . I'll be down the tier.

[BROWN *appears outside gate.*]

CUPCAKES: On the gate.

BROWN: On the gate.

[BROWN *opens gate and* CUPCAKES *and* JUAN *exit.* BROWN *closes gate and exits.*]

PACO: Man thinks he El grande Pingú[1] . . .

ICE: Squash it . . .

LONGSHOE

[*Goes over to toilet, where* CLARK *is.*]

Hey, man . . . don't leave. I want you to hold it for me . . . while I pee.

---

8. An ironic reference to the novel *Don Quixote* (1605, 1615), by the Spanish writer Miguel de Cervantes (1547–1616). The title character delusionally believes he is a knight. He lives in La Mancha, an arid plateau in central Spain, and is accompanied by his "squire," Sancho Panza. 9. Attack someone. [Glossary of slang] 1. *Pingú:* big shot; literally, "big dick." [Glossary of slang]

CLARK: What . . . wha . . .

LONGSHOE: I want you to hold my motherfucking dick while I pee, sucker, so I don't get my hands wet . . .

    *[Laughter.]*

    Well?

CLARK: No . . . no . . . I can't do that . . .

LONGSHOE: Oh. You can't do that . . . but you can rape seven-year-old girls.

CLARK: I didn't rape anybody. I didn't do anything.

LONGSHOE: Shut up, punk.

    *[Pushes CLARK's chest.]*

    What's this—smokes.

CLARK: They're all I have . . . but you're welcome to some.

LONGSHOE: Some? I'm welcome to all of them, creep.

CLARK: What about me?

LONGSHOE: What about you?

CLARK: They're all I have.

LONGSHOE: Kick.[2]

CLARK: But . . .

ICE: Kick, motherfucker, kick.

LONGSHOE: Kick . . . hey, let me see that chain . . . gold . . .

CLARK: Yes.

LONGSHOE: How many carats?

CLARK: Fourteen.

ICE: Damn, Shoe . . . if you gonna take the chain, take the chain.

LONGSHOE: I . . . me . . . take . . . Who said anything about taking anything. That would be stealing and that's dishonest, ain't it, Clarky baby . . . You wanna give that chain, don't you . . . After all, we're both white and we got to look out for one another. Ain't that true, Clarky baby . . . You gonna be real white about the whole thing, aren't you, Clarky baby.

CLARK: It's a gift from my mother.

ALL: Ohhh.

LONGSHOE: I didn't know you had a mother . . . I didn't think human beings gave birth to dogs, too.

OMAR: Looks like the freak ain't upping the chain, Shoe.

LONGSHOE: Oh man, Clarky baby, how you gonna show in front of these people? You want them to think we're that untogether? What are you trying to say, man? You mean to stand there in your nice cheap summer suit looking very white and deny my whiteness by refusing to share a gift with me? That totally uncool . . . You're insulting me, man.

OMAR: Man's trying to say that you're not white enough.

LONGSHOE: You're trying to put a wire[3] out on me, creep?

OMAR: Man saying you're a nigger-lover.

LONGSHOE: You saying that I'm a quadroon?

EL RAHEEM: What? Freak, did you say that devil has some royal Congo blood in his veins?

ICE: I ain't got nothin' to do with it, Shoe, but I swore I heard the freak say that you were passing, Shoe.

---

2. Kick the habit. [Glossary of slang]
3. A false rumor or untrue story. [Glossary of slang]

CLARK:   I didn't say that . . . I didn't say anything.

ICE:   You calling me a liar.

CLARK:   No, no . . . no.

LONGSHOE:   Then you did say it?

> [*They all push* CLARK *around.*]

CLARK:   Please, please, here, take this chain, leave me alone.

ICE:

> [*Yanks chain from around neck.*]
> Pick the motherfucking chain up, freak.

EL RAHEEM:   That's right . . . You tell that man he ain't good enough to talk to.

LONGSHOE:   First I'm a nigger-lover . . . then a quadroon . . . Now I'm not even good enough to talk to.

EL RAHEEM:   Boy, I told you about being in God's walking space, didn't I?

ICE:   You better answer God when he speaks, boy.

LONGSHOE:   Don't you turn your back on me, motherfucker.

> [*Strikes* CLARK. *He falls against* EL RAHEEM, *who hits him too.*
> OMAR *begins kicking him.*
> MR. NETT *appears outside gate.*]

MR. NETT:   On the gate.

> [NETT *opens gate, enters.*]

OMAR:   Mr. Nett.

EL RAHEEM:   Mr. Nett, Mr. Nett, the man started a fight with Omar and we just broke it up.

ICE:   That's right, Mr. Nett.

MR. NETT:   You guys shouldn't whip his face. Omar, you are on the help permanently. The Torres brothers beat their case this morning.

OMAR:   Right on . . . Bet them two are high as all hell by now.

MR. NETT.:   Yeah, and they'll be back, mark my words . . . Listen, get this man off the floor . . . You guys know the rules . . . No sleeping on the floor.

> [MR. NETT *closes gate and exists.*]

ICE:   You guys oughta learn how to touch up a dude.

OMAR:   I'll get a bucket of water.

LONGSHOE:   Fuck the bucket of water, Omar. Put the sucker's head in the toilet bowl. There's water there.

EL RAHEEM:   He's still a devil . . . I won't do that to no man.

LONGSHOE:   We could get it on again.

EL RAHEEM:   That don't present me no problems . . .

ICE:   Squash it, man . . . both of you . . .

LONGSHOE:   Come on, Omar, grab his other side . . .

OMAR:   Hey, there's still piss in there.

LONGSHOE:   Put his head in and I'll flush it.

EL RAHEEM:   Omar . . . let me put his head in there and you flush it.

LONGSHOE:   Makes me no difference . . . flush the motherfucker, Omar.

> [OMAR, LONGSHOE, PACO *pick up* CLARK *to put his head in toilet bowl. They use him as a ramrod, making three runs at the toilet,* CLARK *screaming. On third ram, toilet is flushed, and lights fade.*]

1974

# A Lower East Side Poem

Just once before I die
I want to climb up on a
tenement sky
to dream my lungs out till
I cry                                                              5
then scatter my ashes thru
the Lower East Side.

So let me sing my song tonight
let me feel out of sight
and let all eyes be dry                                            10
when they scatter my ashes thru
the Lower East Side.

From Houston to 14th Street
from Second Avenue to the mighty D[1]
here the hustlers & suckers meet                                   15
the faggots & freaks will all get
high
on the ashes that have been scattered
thru the Lower East Side.

There's no other place for me to be                               20
there's no other place that I can see
there's no other town around that
brings you up or keeps you down
no food little heat sweeps by
fancy cars & pimps' bars & juke saloons                           25
& greasy spoons make my spirits fly
with my ashes scattered thru the
Lower East Side . . .

A thief, a junkie I've been
committed every known sin                                         30
Jews and Gentiles . . . Bums and Men
of style . . . run away child
police shooting wild . . .
mother's futile wails . . . pushers
making sales . . . dope wheelers                                  35
& cocaine dealers . . . smoking pot
streets are hot & feed off those who bleed to death . . .

all that's true
all that's true
all that is true                                                  40
but this ain't no lie

1. Avenue D, which marks the eastern side of a
geographical box with Houston Street on the
southern end, 14th Street on the north, and Second Avenue on the west. The Lower East Side
was once broadly defined as including this area.
The Lower East Side extends far below Houston
Street, however, and the area above Houston is
now generally called the East Village.

when I ask that my ashes be scattered thru
the Lower East Side.

So here I am, look at me
I stand proud as you can see                                        45
pleased to be from the Lower East
a street fighting man
a problem of this land
I am the Philosopher of the Criminal Mind
a dweller of prison time                                           50
a cancer of Rockefeller's ghettocide[2]
this concrete tomb is my home
to belong to survive you gotta be strong
you can't be shy less without request
someone will scatter your ashes thru                              55
the Lower East Side.

I don't wanna be buried in Puerto Rico
I don't wanna rest in long island[3] cemetery
I wanna be near the stabbing shooting
gambling fighting & unnatural dying                               60
& new birth crying
so please when I die . . .
don't take me far away
keep me near by
take my ashes and scatter them thru out                          65
the Lower East Side . . .

                                                                1980

# This Is Not the Place Where I Was Born

puerto rico 1974
this is not the place where i was born
remember—as a child the fantasizing images my mother planted
within my head—
the shadows of her childhood recounted to me many times          5
over welfare loan on crédito food from el bodeguero[1]
i tasted mango many years before the skin of the fruit
ever reached my teeth
i was born on an island about 35 miles wide 100 miles long
a small island with a rainforest somewhere in the central
regions of itself                                                 10
where spanish was a dominant word
& signs read by themselves
i was born in a village of that island where the police

---

2. I.e., the controversial "urban development"—
construction and modernization—carried out
during the administration of Nelson Aldrich
Rockefeller (1908–1979), governor of New York

1959–73.
3. Long Island, which extends east from Manhattan.
1. The grocer. Crédito: credit.

who frequented your place of business—hangout or home—came as 15
servant or friend & not as a terror in slogan clothing
i was born in a barrio of the village on the island
where people left their doors open at night
where respect for elders was exhibited with pride
where courting for loved ones was not treated over confidentially 20
where children's laughter did not sound empty & savagely alive
with self destruction . . .
i was born on an island where to be puerto rican meant to be
part of the land & soul & puertorriqueños were not the
minority 25
puerto ricans were first, none were second
no, i was not born here . . .
no, i was not born in the attitude & time of this place
this sun drenched soil
this green faced piece of earth 30
this slave blessed land
where the caribbean seas pound angrily on the shores
of pre-fabricated house/hotel redcap hustling people gypsy taxi cab
fighters for fares to fajardo² 
& the hot wind is broken by fiberglass palmtrees 35
& highrise plátanos marianos³ on leave & color t.v.
looneytune cartoon comicbook characters with badges
in their jockstraps
& foreigners scream that puertorriqueños are foreigners
& have no right to claim any benefit on the birthport 40
this sun drenched soil
this green faced piece of earth
this slave blessed land
where nuyoricans come in search of spiritual identity
are greeted with profanity 45
this is insanity that americanos are showered
with shoe shine kisses
police in stocking caps cover carry out john wayne
television cowboy law road models of new york city detective
french connection/death wish instigation ku-klux-klan mind⁴ 50
panorama screen seems
in modern medicine is in confusion needs a transfusion quantity
treatment if you're not on the plan the new stand
of blue cross blue shield blue uniform master charge
what religion you are 55
blood fills the waiting room of death
stale air & qué pasa stares are nowhere
in sight & night neon light shines bright
in el condado area⁵ puerto rican under cover cop

2. Small, popular, beachfront city on the eastern tip of Puerto Rico.
3. *Plátanos marianos*: a shorter and now less common variety of the regular plátanos, or plantains. Like "fiberglass palmtrees," "highrise plátanos marianos" alludes to modern, urbanized Puerto Rico.
4. Here, the Ku Klux Klan (a secret, Christian fraternal society in the United States, advocating white supremacy), the American actor John Wayne (Marion Robert Morrison, 1907–1979), and the movies *The French Connection* (1971) and *Death Wish* (1974) represent aspects of a racist, right-wing, militaristic police force.
5. El Condado is one of the major hotel areas catering to American tourists in San Juan.

stop & arrest on the spot puerto ricans who shop for the flag    60
that waves on the left—in souvenir stores—
puertorriqueños cannot assemble displaying the emblem
nuyoricans are fighting & dying for in newark,[6] lower east side
south bronx where the fervor of being
puertorriqueños is not just rafael hernández[7]    65
viet vet protest with rifle shots that dig into four pigs
& sociable friday professional persons rush to the
golf course & martini glasses work for the masses
& the island is left unattended because the middle class
bureaucratic cuban has arrived spitting blue eyed justice    70
at brown skinned boys in military khaki
compromise to survive is hairline length
moustache trimmed face looking grim like a soldier
on furlough further cannot exhibit contempt for what is
not cacique[8] born this poem will receive a burning    75
stomach turning scorn nullified classified racist
from this pan am eastern first national chase manhattan
puerto rico . . .

    1980

6. Newark, New Jersey, a city about eight miles
west of Manhattan.
7. Puerto Rican composer (1892–1965), who
wrote the popular patriotic song "Preciosa" (Precious Island or Precious Homeland), considered
his masterpiece, while living in New York.
8. A chief or leader of a tribe.

---

# SANDRA MARÍA ESTEVES
## b. 1948

Few female voices emerged from the Nuyorican poetic movement, and Sandra María Esteves was the only one to sustain a long career as a performing poet and visual artist. Perhaps that is why her fellow poets regard her as the godmother of Nuyorican poety. Born in the South Bronx to a Puerto Rican father and Dominican mother who separated before she was born, Esteves was raised by her mother and a paternal aunt. Esteves's mother, like many migrant women of her generation, worked in needlework factories; trying to insulate her daughter from the problems of life in the inner city, she sent Esteves to Catholic boarding school for her elementary and secondary education. After Esteves graduated from high school, she earned a bachelor's degree in fine arts from Pratt Institute, in New York, in 1978. A graphic artist as well as a poet and playwright, she illustrates her poetry collections and is affiliated with the Taller Boricua, a community-oriented Puerto Rican graphic artists' collective in the city. In a 1997 interview with Camen Dolores Hernández, Esteves described the transforming effect of and inner relationship between writing and painting in her early work:

> The artist began writing as a different way of painting. But what I was writing about—the themes—had to do with the process of self-discovery. And even though you do that with painting, you don't do it in the same way because in

painting I was just recording things that I saw around me and painting from life. I didn't need to have an identity in order to be able to do that; I just had to have a photographic view of whatever I was looking at. But when I began writing I had to define, to name things. And that's when the process of discovering my Puerto Rican side started happening. And that's where the self-transformation began.

Esteves's first poetry collection, *Yerba Buena: Dibujos y poemas* (The Good Herb: Drawings and Poems, 1980), reflects her involvement in the civil rights movement and in various political causes. It was among the first poetry books published by a Latina in the United States, and *Library Journal* named it the best small-press publication of the year. Her second collection, *Tropical Rains: A Bilingual Downpour* (1984), did not enjoy the success of her first, perhaps because of its more limited circulation as a self-published book. *Bluestown Mockingbird Mambo* (1990) conjures up the spiritual world of *santería* and *espiritismo* to the tune of Afro-Caribbean rhythms and in the voice of a familiar bilingual vernacular. Esteves's subsequent works include *Contrapunto in the Open Field* (1998) and *Portal, A Journey in Poetry* (2007).

From 1983 to 1985, Esteves was a producer and director for the African Caribbean Poetry Theatre, in New York, an experience that enhanced her writing and performing. In addition to performing her poetry at the Nuyorican Poets Cafe, she has been a member of the consciousness-raising socialist musical ensemble El Grupo. Accompanying the performances of several of the Nuyorican poets, the group introduced audiences to a poetry that spoke of personal and political issues such as Puerto Rico's colonial condition, the oppression of people of color, and women's subordination. Esteves once noted that "the poet is absolutely an advocate for the people, whether or not he or she chooses to be," and her poems reflect a touching personal quest for defining and embracing a Puerto Rican/Dominican identity battered by racial prejudice and social injustice. The poems included in this anthology, "Here" and "Puerto Rican Discovery #3: Not Neither," explore the cultural identity dilemmas that characterize Nuyorican and Latino poetry generally.

# Here

I am two parts/a person
boricua/spic
past and present
alive and oppressed
given a cultural beauty                                          5
. . . and robbed of a cultural identity

I speak the alien tongue
in sweet boriqueño thoughts
know love mixed with pain
have tasted spit on ghetto stairways                             10
. . . here, it must be changed
we must change it

I may never overcome
the theft of my isla heritage
dulce palmas de coco on Luquillo                                 15
sway in windy recesses I can only imagine
and remember how it was

But that reality now a dream
teaches me to see, and will
bring me back to me.                                    20

1980

## Puerto Rican Discovery #3: Not Neither

Being Puertorriqueña-Dominicana
Borinqueña-Quisqueyana
Taina-Africana
Born in the Bronx.[1] Not really jíbara
Not really hablando bien[2]                              5
But yet, not gringa either
Pero ni portorra[3]
Pero sí, portorra too
Pero ni qué what am I? Y qué soy?
Pero con what voice do my lips move?                     10
Rhythms of rosa wood feet dancing bomba
Not even here. But here. Y conga
Yet not being. Pero soy
And not really. Y somos
Y como somos—bueno,                                      15
Eso sí es algo lindo. Algo muy lindo.[4]

We defy translation
Ni tengo nombre. Nameless
We are a whole culture once removed
Lolita[5] alive for twenty-five years                    20
Ni soy, pero soy Puertorriqueña cómo ella
Giving blood to the independent star
Daily transfusions
Into the river
Of la sangre viva.[6]                                    25

1984

---

1. A borough of New York City, north of Manhattan. *Borinqueña-Quisqueyana / Taina*: The Taíno peoples were the indigenous tribes in what are now Puerto Rico (where they called the island Boriquén and themselves Boricuas) and the Dominican Republic (where they called the island Quisqueya and themselves Quisqueyanos).
2. Speaking well. *Jíbara*: female peasant.

3. But neither portorra (slang word for Puerto Rican). The commonly used form in Puerto Rico and the United States is *puertorro/a*.
4. And we are / And how we are—well, / That is something nice. Something very nice.
5. A reference to the Puerto Rican Nationalist political prisoner Lolita Lebrón (b. 1919).
6. Passionate blood.

# TATO LAVIERA
## b. 1950

The affirmation and transformation of the Puerto Rican identity in the United States is at the center of most of Tato Laviera's poetry. Born in Santurce, Puerto Rico, Jesús "Tato" Laviera Sánchez arrived in New York's Lower East Side when he was nine years old. Before his mother migrated with her children to the United States, Laviera had studied under Juan Boria, a well-known black Puerto Rican performer of Afro-Antillean poetry. At Catholic school in New York, one of his teachers decided that the name Jesús was not suitable for a mulatto child who at the time did not speak English, and the school immediately changed his name to Abraham. Laviera wanted to become a writer, in part, to reclaim his proper name; but when he began writing, he used the nickname "Tato," which his brother had given him.

Laviera attended Cornell University, in upstate New York, and Brooklyn College, but he does not hold a college degree. For several years, he did community work and social services work until he focused on a full-time writing career. His first poetry collection, *La Carreta Made a U-Turn* (1979), disputes the tragic view of the migrant experience presented by René Marqués in his classic drama *La carreta* (The Oxcart, 1952). Laviera's work argues that Marques's play neglects the multifaceted reality of those Puerto Rican migrants who never return to the island or whose offspring are born in the United States. In that sense, Laviera represents the voice of a new generation of Puerto Ricans, unwilling to relinquish their Puerto Ricanness in a United States that is no longer the exclusive domain of white Anglo-Saxon culture.

From 1979 to 1981, Laviera taught courses in the Puerto Rican Studies Department at Rutgers University's Livingston College. In 1980, he was invited by U.S. president Jimmy Carter to a White House gathering of American poets. He followed *La Carreta Made a U-Turn* with the poetry collection *Enclave* (1981), which celebrated his Afro-Caribbean heritage and won the Before Columbus Foundation's American Book Award. In the collection *AmeRícan* (1985), Laviera redefines himself as both Puerto Rican and American, an individual straddling two cultures. But he conceives the United States as a vibrant converging point for the many peoples of the Americas. In the volume's title poem, the pun on "AmeRícan" and "I'm a Rican" synthesizes a new way of being American without renouncing one's ethnic heritage. In "Lady Liberty," written in 1986, the year of the centennial commemoration of the Statue of Liberty, Laviera celebrates freedom while broadening the meaning of American identity. In *Mainstream Ethics* (*Etica corriente*; 1988), he once again stresses the impact of Latino culture on mainstream U.S. culture and portrays an Anglocentric society being transformed by multiculturalism. The poems "my graduation speech" and "asimilao" are good examples of how he uses code switching, colloquial speech, and humor to convey the linguistic and cultural hybridity of the Nuyorican experience. Laviera's latest collection is *Mixturado and Other Poems* (2008).

In a 1997 interview with Carmen Dolores Hernández, Laviera called himself "a Puerto Rican of multidimensional definitions. I have five hats, all Puerto Rican: the Latino hat, the urban hat, the black hat, the Boricua hat, and the hemispheric hat." The interplay between the Spanish and English languages and between his native and adoptive cultures are an essential aspect of Laviera's poetry. His bilingualism allows him to play with words, coin new terms, and convey different cultural and affective meanings. Laviera also acknowledges the powerful influence of Afro-Caribbean poetry and musical rhythms on his work. Through irony, parody, and wordplay, Laviera has become one of the most powerful poetic voices in denouncing the consequences of American domination in Puerto Rico and in linking the Puerto Rican migratory exodus to the island's colonial condition. And in his frequent public performances, he brings to his poetry the dramatic and humorous qualities that have served him well as an actor and playwright. (Many of his plays have been produced, but most remain unpublished.)

## my graduation speech

i think in spanish
i write in english

i want to go back to puerto rico,
but i wonder if my kink could live
in ponce, mayagüez and carolina[1]                          5

tengo las venas aculturadas[2]
escribo[3] en spanglish
abraham in español
abraham in english
tato in spanish                                              10
"taro" in english
tonto[4] in both languages

how are you?
¿cómo estás?
i don't know if i'm coming                                   15
or si me fui ya[5]

si me dicen barranquitas,[6] yo reply,
"con qué se come eso?"[7]
si me dicen caviar, i digo,[8]
"a new pair of converse sneakers."                           20

ahí supe que estoy jodío
ahí supe que estamos jodíos[9]

english or spanish
spanish or english
spanenglish                                                  25
now, dig this:

hablo lo inglés matao
hablo lo españñol matao
no sé leer ninguno bien[1]

1. City in northern Puerto Rico. *Ponce*: city in southern Puerto Rico. *Mayagüez*: city in western Puerto Rico. *My kink*: his kinky hair.
2. I have acculturated veins.
3. I write.
4. Fool, dolt.
5. Or if I left already.
6. If someone mentions Barranquitas [a mountain town in Puerto Rico].

7. Literally, "How do you eat that?"; figuratively, "What the heck is that?"
8. I say.
9. That's how I learned I'm screwed / That's how I learned we're screwed.
1. When I speak I kill the English language / When I speak I kill the Spanish language / I can't read either well.

so it is, spanglish to matao                                        30
what i digo
                        ¡ay, virgen, yo no sé hablar!²

                                                    1981


## asimilao

assimilated? qué assimilated,
brother, yo soy asimilao,
así mi la o sí es verdad
tengo un lado asimilao.¹
you see, they went deep . . . . Ass                               5
oh . . . . . . . . they went deeper . . . SEE
oh, oh, . . . they went deeper . . . ME
but the sound LAO was too black
for LATED, LAO could not be
trans*lated*, assimilated,                                         10
no, asimilao, melao,²
it became a black
spanish word but
we do have asimilados
perfumados and by the                                              15
last count even they
were becoming asimilao
how can it be analyzed
as american? así que se
chavaron                                                           20
trataron
pero no
pudieron
con el AO
de la palabra                                                      25
principal, déles gracias a los prietos
que cambiaron asimilado al popular asimilao.³

                                                    1985


## AmeRícan

we gave birth to a new generation,
AmeRícan, broader than lost gold
never touched, hidden inside the
puerto rican mountains.

---

2. Oh my God, I don't know what I speak!
1. I am assimilate', / ass-ee-mee-laah / I have an
assimilated side.
2. The syrup extracted from sugarcane.

3. Thus / they took / hooked / but no / they
couldn't / with the AO / in the principal / word,
give thanks to the brownees / who changed assimilated for the popular assimilate'.

we gave birth to a new generation,                                                    5
AmeRícan, it includes everything
imaginable you-name-it-we-got-it
society.

we gave birth to a new generation,
AmeRícan salutes all folklores,                                                      10
european, indian, black, spanish,
and anything else compatible:

AmeRícan,    singing to composer pedro flores'[1] palm
             trees high up in the universal sky!

AmeRícan,    sweet soft spanish danzas gypsies                                       15
             moving lyrics la española cascabelling[2]
             presence always singing at our side!

AmeRícan,    beating jíbaro[3] modern troubadours
             crying guitars romantic continental
             bolero love songs!                                                      20

AmeRícan,    across forth and across back
             back across and forth back
             forth across and back and forth
             our trips are walking bridges!

             it all dissolved into itself, the attempt                              25
             was truly made, the attempt was truly
             absorbed, digested, we spit out
             the poison, we spit out the malice,
             we stand, affirmative in action,
             to reproduce a broader answer to the                                    30
             marginality that gobbled us up abruptly!

AmeRícan,    walking plena[4]-rhythms in new york,
             strutting beautifully alert, alive,
             many turning eyes wondering,
             admiring!                                                               35

AmeRícan,    defining myself my own way any way many
             ways Am e Rícan, with the big R and the
             accent on the í!

AmeRícan,    like the soul gliding talk of gospel
             boogie music!                                                           40

AmeRícan,    speaking new words in spanglish tenements,
             fast tongue moving street corner "que

1. Puerto Rican composer of ballads and boleros          a pellet; figuratively, playing the castanets.
(1894–1979).                                             3. Peasant.
2. Literally, making a percussive noise with a          4. A folkloric music native to Puerto Rico, influ-
cascabel, a small, hollow, spherical bell holding       enced by African music and Spanish music.

corta"[5] talk being invented at the insistence
of a smile!

AmeRícan,   aboundng inside so many ethnic english    45
people, and out of humanity, we blend
and mix all that is good!

AmeRícan,   integrating in new york and defining our
own destino, our own way of life,

AmeRícan,   defining the new america, humane america,    50
admired america, loved america, harmonious
america, the world in peace, our energies
collectively invested to find other civilizations, to touch God, further and further,
to dwell in the spirit of divinity!    55

AmeRícan,   yes, for now, for i love this, my second
land, and i dream to take the accent from
the altercation, and be proud to call
myself american, in the u.s. sense of the
word, AmeRícan, America!    60

1985

## lady liberty

for liberty, your day filled in splendor,
july fourth, new york harbor, nineteen eighty six, 1986
midnight sky, fireworks splashing,
heaven exploding
into radiant bouquets,    5
wall street a backdrop of centennial adulation,
computerized capital angling cameras
celebrating the international symbol of freedom
stretched across micro-chips,
awacs[1] surveillance,    10
wall-to-wall people, sailing ships,
gliding armies ferried
in pursuit of happiness, constitution adoration,
packaged television channels for liberty,
immigrant illusions    15
celebrated in the name of democratic principles,
god bless america, land of the star
spangled banner
that we love.

5. Play on words: "biting."
1. Airborne Warning and Control System.

but the symbol suffered                                          20
one hundred years of decay
climbing up to the spined crown,
the fractured torch hand,
the ruptured intestines,
palms blistered and calloused,                                   25
feet embroidered in rust,
centennial decay,
the lady's eyes,
cataract filled, exposed
to sun and snow, a salty wind,                                   30
discolored verses staining her robe.

she needed re-molding, re-designing,[2]
the decomposed body
now melted down for souveniers,
lungs and limbs jailed                                           35
in scaffolding of ugly cubicles
incarcerating the body
as she prepared to receive
her twentieth-century transplant
paid for by pitching pennies,                                    40
hometown chicken barbecues,
marathons on america's main streets.

she heard the speeches:
the president's
the french and american partners,                                45
the nation believed in her, rooted for the queen,
and lady liberty decided to reflect
on lincoln's emancipatory resoluteness,
on washington's patriotism,
on jefferson's lucidity,                                         50
on william jennings bryan's socialism,
on woodrow wilson's league of nations,
on roosevelt's new deal,
on kennedy's ecumenical postures,
and on martin luther king's non-violence.[3]                     55

lady liberty decided to reflect
on lillian wald's settlements,
on helen keller's sixth sense,

2. The statue was cleaned and restored for its centennial.
3. Abraham Lincoln (1809–1865), U.S. president 1861–65, freed the slaves in the southern states by issuing the Emancipation Proclamation. Thomas Jefferson (1743–1826), U.S. president 1801–09, is known for the quality of his writing, particularly in documents such as the U.S. Declaration of Independence. William Jennings Bryan (1860–1925), American lawyer and politician, was a Christian socialist. (Thomas) Woodrow Wilson (1856–1924), U.S. president 1913–21, was instrumental in founding the League of Nations, an association that prefigured the United Nations. Franklin Delano Roosevelt (1882–1945), U.S. president 1933–45, was the driving force behind the New Deal, a legislative and administrative program during the Great Depression, designed to promote the economic recovery of and social reform in the United States. John Fitzgerald Kennedy (1917–1963), U.S. president 1961–63, made all-embracing, liberal pronouncements about the spread of freedom and democracy around the world. The Reverend Martin Luther King Jr. (1929–1968), American clergyman and civil rights leader, preached nonviolent resistance to injustice.

on susan b. anthony's suffrage movement,
on mother cabrini's giving soul,                                    60
on harriet tubman's stubborn pursuit of freedom.[4]

just before she was touched,
just before she was dismantled,
lady liberty spoke,
she spoke for the principles,                                      65
for the preamble,
for the bill of rights,
and thirty-nine peaceful
presidential transitions,
and, just before she was touched,                                  70
lady liberty wanted to convey
her own resolutions,
her own bi-centennial goals,
so that in twenty eighty-six,
she would be smiling and she would be proud.                       75
and then, just before she was touched,
and then, while she was being re-constructed,
and then, while she was being celebrated,
she spoke.

if you touch me, touch ALL of my people                            80
who need attention and societal repair,
give the tired and the poor
the same attention, AMERICA,
touch us ALL with liberty,
touch us ALL with liberty.                                         85

hunger abounds, our soil is plentiful,
our technology advanced enough
to feed the world,
to feed humanity's hunger . . .
but let's celebrate not our wealth,                                90
not our sophisticated defense,
not our scientific advancements,
not our intellectual adventures.
let us concentrate on our weaknesses,
on our societal needs,                                             95
for we will never be free
if indeed freedom is subjugated
to trampling upon people's needs.

4. Lillian D. Wald (1867–1940), American social worker, founded various pioneering settlement houses, institutions providing community services, in New York City. Helen Adams Keller (1880–1968), American lecturer for the deaf and blind, was herself deaf and blind and thus had a "sixth sense" that enabled her to accomplish far more than had been expected of her as a child. Susan Brownell Anthony (1820–1906), American civil rights leader, helped introduce women's suffrage in the U.S. Mother Cabrini, or Saint Francis Xavier Cabrini (1850–1917), Italian-born American nun, founded over 60 institutions—orphanages, schools, hospitals—in the U.S. and other countries. Harriet Tubman (ca. 1820–1913), African American abolitionist and suffragist, escaped from slavery and subsequently helped many other slaves escape.

this is a warning,
my beloved america.                                   100

so touch me,
and in touching me
touch all our people.
do not single me out,
touch all our people,                                 105
touch all our people,
all our people
    our people
        people.

and then i shall truly enjoy                          110
my day, filled in splendor,
july fourth, new york harbor,
nineteen eighty six, midnight sky,
fireworks splashing,
heaven exploding                                      115
into radiant bouquets,
celebrating in the name of equality,
in the pursuit of happiness,
god bless america,
land of star                                          120
spangled banner
that we love.

        1985

---

# JESÚS "PAPOLETO" MELÉNDEZ
## b. 1951

Jesús "Papoleto" Meléndez, born in El Barrio, was one of the first Nuyorican performance poets to publish individually authored books: *Casting Long Shadows* (1970) and *Street Poetry and Other Poems* (1972). He also wrote the play *The Junkies Stole the Clock* (1974). *Street Poetry* reflected the attempt of male Nuyorican poets to recreate the vicissitudes and hardships of growing up surrounded by both poverty and the interethnic and racial strife and violence that often plague U.S. inner-city life. Meléndez was a founding member of El Grupo (discussed in the Sandra María Esteves headnote, above) and can be heard on its recording *El Grupo: Canciones y poesías de la lucha de los pueblos latinoamericanos* (El Grupo: Songs and Poems about the Struggles of Latin American Peoples, 1974). He also directed the South Bronx theater collective the Latin Insomniacs, founded by Pedro Pietri in 1973. While continuing to perform and write poetry and plays, Meléndez has worked as an educator and "poetry facilitator" in public school programs such as New York City's Poets in the Schools and San Diego's Young at Art. Among his later works is the collection *Concertos on Market Street: Poems* (1993). In 2001, he received a fellowship in poetry from the New York Foundation for the Arts (NYFA).

## of a butterfly in el barrio
## or a stranger in paradise

    Home;
a place to rest your feet,
a place where you can sleep,
    Man,
a place where you can shit,               5
and no one can complain.

    My Home/    *el barrio*
where people rest their feet;
outside on the fire escapes,
where i have a place to sleep           10
with my brothers, sisters, cousins,
    oh yes, and Rover
all in the same bed.
                /where no one can smell shit
                'cause we've been living in it    15
                all our lives
(we're immune to its stink)

    My home;
where on hot summer days
people gather on the grandstands/        20
                   the fire escapes
and in the box seats/
            the stoops
and cheer our home gang's stickball team
    (they call themselves "the new york junkies"),   25

and on those cool summer evenings
we hang our legs from the windows/
the roofs/   the fire excapes
while eating pop corn and sippin coke
/or snorting it/shooting it           30
and watch the saturday evening gang flights.

    yes, this is home/     our paradise
and you're always welcomed
as long as you're poor.

and it was here    /in my home         35
that a butterfly happened to wing by

he was easily spotted as a *UFO*
because of all his beautiful colors

    he flew over the buildings/
    through the lots/           40
    around home plate    a sewer top
    in the middle of the street

he flew
in his dance about manner,

and i almost cried when i saw children reaching                    45
reaching out for him        reaching for hope
for love/
for that lost dream

and he continued dancing/        or maybe flying
away                                                                50
away to save his beauty from these love-hungry
children

he flew        he flew
and i cried
when he fell down the sewer/                                        55
                              now he was part of us.

                                                          1972

# San Antonio Women Poets

San Antonio, Texas, is a thriving cultural center with a sizable Mexican American population. Partly in response to the upheaval generated by the Chicano Movement, San Antonio garnered a poetic voice of its own, in large part thanks to women writers. Three of the major women poets from San Antonio—Angela de Hoyos, Evangelina Vigil-Piñón, and Carmen Tafolla—are or were from working-class backgrounds and were greatly inspired by the Chicano Movement. The three were involved in the social revolution of the late 1960s and 1970s and spoke out against racism and social oppression. Their work switches among English, Spanish, and Spanglish.

Born in Mexico, de Hoyos moved to San Antonio with her parents after World War II. De Hoyos's work became more complex and experimental as she developed from a feisty, socially conscious poet to a more introspective one. Her first period is openly political, as is evident in *Arise, Chicano: and Other Poems* (1975) and *Chicano Poems for the Barrio* (1976). In the 1980s, de Hoyos widened her poetic scope to include satire. In the 1990s, while still focusing on the role of women and the oppressed, she switched gears, coediting *Daughters of the Fifth Sun: A Collection of Latina Fiction and Poetry* (1995) and *Floricanto, Sí!: A Collection of Latina Poetry* (1998). The two poems by de Hoyos included in this anthology showcase her view of women as centers of gravity in the Latino community. "La Malinche to Cortés and Vice Versa" imagines a dialogue between the famous conquistador and his mistress, a canonical figure in Mexican culture. De Hoyos highlights the gender tension between them and explores its historical implications. "La Vie: I Never Said It Was Simple" reflects playfully on the passing of wisdom among historical, mythical, and literary figures.

Evangelina Vigil-Piñón, like Carmen Tafolla, was raised in U.S. government housing on San Antonio's West Side. In 1974, Vigil-Piñón earned a bachelor's degree from the University of Houston. Her activities as an undergraduate included work for the Mexican American Youth Organization (MAYO), which, with other campus entities, helped establish Mexican American Studies at the university. Vigil-Piñón has also studied at San Antonio's Witte Museum, the San Antonio Art Institute, and the University of Texas at San Antonio. She names as influences contemporary African American writers such as James Baldwin, Nikki Giovanni, and Ntozake Shange; countercultural American poets and writers; and Latin American writers from "*el 'boom'*," among them the novelists Julio Cortázar, Gabriel García Márquez, and Carlos Fuentes. Married to the artist Mark Piñón, she is a noted photographer.

Vigil-Piñón writes lyrical poetry about childhood, aging, and life on the West Side, while also launching ironic attacks against machismo. Although not a regionalist, she was among the first poets to capture the sounds and characters of the urban Chicano scene. In her early books, *Nade y nade* (Swimming and Swimming, 1978) and *Thirty an' Seen a Lot* (1982), she describes—vigorously but not always optimistically—women who hold their own in male worlds and the ambivalence of dead-end jobs.

Upon completing *Thirty an' Seen a Lot*, Vigil-Piñón returned to the University of Houston as a guest lecturer in English. Within a year, she compiled *Woman of Her Word: Hispanic Women Write* (1983), an anthology of Latina critics and creative writers that was the first of its kind and was deemed an important contribution to

Mexican American letters. However, Vigil-Piñón's work does not focus exclusively on Mexican Americans. *The Computer Is Down* (1987) virulently attacks the environmental wreckage around Houston. Its title is a popular expression used to cover up mistakes or laziness. She has translated Tomás Rivera's classic novel . . . *y no se lo tragó la tierra* as *And the Earth Did Not Devour Him* (1987; see pp. 1077–78).

Two of the three Vigil-Piñón poems in this anthology, "apprenticeship" and "corazón en la palma" (the palm's heart), are about the role of memory, in life and art, as it passes from one generation of women to the next. The third poem, "crimson the color," explores brownness in lyrical terms.

Carmen Tafolla began writing as a teenager. After six years of schooling at a predominantly Chicano school, Tafolla won a scholarship to a private school. She went on to earn a bachelor's degree in 1972 from Austin College and a master's from the same institution the following year. She earned a doctorate in bilingual education at the University of Texas at Austin in 1981.

After teaching high school, Tafolla served as the director of the Mexican American Studies Center at Texas Lutheran College in the late 1970s. She gained notice at a reading at the Festival de Floricanto in Austin, Texas. Tafolla won the Chicano Literary Prize in Poetry, given by the University of California at Irvine. She made her mark in feminist circles with *To Split a Human: Mitos, machos y la mujer chicana* (Myths, Machos and the Chicana Woman, 1985). Among her subsequent publications are the poetry collections *Sonnets to Human Beings and Other Selected Works* (1995) and *Sonnets and Salsa* (2004), the children's books *Baby Coyote and the Old Woman* (2000) and *Fiesta Babies* (2010), and the story collection *The Holy Tortilla and a Pot of Beans* (2008).

This anthology includes three of Tafolla's poems and a chapter from *To Split a Human*. The poem "Letter to Ti" imagines the impressions of a 15-year-old Vietnamese immigrant in the United States. "Marked" is advice from a mother to a daughter on how to find her place in the world. The third poem, "Compliments," is about both types and stereotypes of Mexicans. In the chapter "Myths, Machos and the Movies," Tafolla analyzes both Chicanos' roles in U.S. culture and U.S. cultural perceptions of Chicanos.

---

# ANGELA DE HOYOS
## 1940–2009

### La Malinche to Cortés and Vice Versa[1]
*(or, "Love Does Not Forgive, Not Even for Love")*

SHE:   Give me your name, my lord and master,
       so it shall adorn me. How I long
       to carve it here, beside my own in the sand.
       . . . because I am yours. Yours! and I want the
       whole world to know about it.       5

1. Translated by Angela de Hoyos. *La Malinche*: also known as Malintzin and Doña Marina (ca. 1496 or 1505–ca. 1529), aboriginal mistress of and translator for the Spanish conquistador Hernán Cortés (1485–1547), who led the conquest of the Aztecs. In Mexico, *malinchista* means both traitor and a person ungrateful for what Mexico offers.

HE:   The whole world
knows about it already,
my dear Marina. You do not need
superfluous adornments.
I love you and that is enough.      10

*And in parentheses HE says to himself:*

Besides, hrrrmmmppp!!! It is unseemly
for a white man of *my*
noble standing to marry a
simple slave, hrrmmpp! . . . Although it's true,      15
as women go, she's a ten . . . but no.
This little barefoot social climber is letting
her ambitions run away with her, hrrmmpp!!!

SHE:   Yes, O lord and master, you are *so* right.
I know full well that you love me, and      20
forgive my foolishness. It's that we silly
women always dream of things impossible . . .

*And in parentheses SHE tells herself:*

Huh! And for that I gave you
*my* blood and *my* people! O yes, I      25
see it now . . . you the white, the bland,
the utterly tasteless man
love me . . . you love me so much
that you plan to marry me off
to your subordinate Don Juan,[2]      30
snap! like that! just as if I
were a pound of meat
—well, it's not as though you were *my* father
to sell me when and where you will,
my arrogant-cavalier-greedy-gringo friend . . . !!!      35

Etcetera, etcetera.      1995

## La Vie: I Never Said It Was Simple

*for Alicia Z. Galván—3/27/96*

She reminds me of that painting by
Velázquez: *La Infanta Margarita,*[1]
in a pink and silver gown . . .

except that here, she is sentadita muy
atenta,[2] listening to my incantations,      5

2. Don Juan Jaramillo, a Castilian lieutenant.
1. Portrait of Margarita Teresa de España (1651–1673), infanta of Spain, by the Spanish painter

Diego Rodríguez de Silva y Velázquez (1599–1660).
2. Sitting very attentively.

listening as I command the heavens,
cutting the clouds con mi cuchillito;[3]

eyes round with hope in breathless
expectation, she wants simple clear-cut
answers to her square-root questions;                    10

little does she know I can barely—just
barely—hew my own antidotal sword
from the selfsame tree that grows the
nightmare dragons. (. . . Ay, if only I had
the wisdom of Sor Juana!)[4]                             15

. . . An oracle? Listen, I am nowhere *near*
Delphi.[5] Ni soy curandera, con polvitos y
milagros, con monitos de aserrín[6]

. . . not a wonder-woman-shaman who
paints a mystic mandala, who wraps up the              20
world in a huge tortilla de maíz, with a
    *Here it is, take it, it's all yours.*

. . . She is, let us say, a captive voyeur
witnessing the secret dragline of my
voice. My voice that comes and goes like               25
the wail of La Llorona[7] . . . Llora que llora

La Llorona . . . ¿Por sus hijos?[8] . . . Ay, no . . .
Llora porque *nunca* tuvo hijos. Pobrecita,
es yerma. Qué pena.[9] So she cries and cries.
Llora que llora La Llorona por los callejones           30
de San Cuilmas.[1] Finally, por fin, she comes
to her favorite stomping ground: the river.
She finds her spic & span spot on a rock,
sits down and dries her eyes con una pata.[2]
A sigh, and she twists her thorax to the right,         35
reaches down to open the tiny silver door of
her spinneret. Out comes the moonlight magic.
The magic moonlight thread. The moonlight
thread with which she weaves her stories. Her
brain-children. Her bambinos. Los muñecos y            40
las monadas:[3]

---

3. With my little knife.
4. Sor Juana Inés de la Cruz (1648 or 1651–
1695), Mexican nun, scholar, writer, and poet.
5. Site of an ancient Greek oracle, or shrine in
which, through a designated person known as an
oracle, a deity revealed hidden knowledge or a
divine purpose.
6. I'm neither a healer, with small powders and /
Miracles with saw-dust-made voodoo figures.
7. The weeping woman; a popular legend in
Spanish-speaking cultures in the Americas, generally about a beautiful woman who kills her

children to be with a man, is rejected by him, and
then wanders, weeping, searching for children
and, in some versions of the tale, ready to kidnap
wandering children. For a text of the legend, see
p. 2452. For a variation on the legend, see p. 2454.
8. For your children?
9. She cries because she *never* had children. Poor
little one, / she's barren.
1. Through the narrow streets of San Cuilmas.
2. With a monkey paw.
3. The handsome and the gorgeous.

*Míos. Re-te-míos. Re-que-te-míos!*[4] *Just*
*think! Such beautiful 8-legged people. . . .*

And she thinks and thinks and thinks about it,
until she imagines they are in truth her very                    45
own. (The people, that is—and well yes, the
stories too. . . . Why, everyone knows she puts
them to bed every night, singing a soft
    *Coo-coo-roo-coo-coo paloma*[5]
. . . all dressed up in pink & blue & yellow                     50
pajamas. Pink for girls. Blue for boys. And yellow
for those undecided.)

. . . But let's not talk about chiquilladas.[6] Let's talk
instead about that sword—yeah, sure, why not—
that Huitzilopochtli[7] sword of lightning. If we                55
follow the *HOW-TO* instructions carefully, I'm
sure we can construct one. . . . Oh, yes, of course,
someone is *bound* to discover our upstart
"Wishing Well" machinations. Our Mad Hatter;
our Crazy Coyotl[8] notions. . . .                               60

But by then, it will be too late. I will have given
you the sword. You will have given it to the Queen.[9]
The Queen has called a meeting of the deck. The
deck has counted the ayes and the nays. Meeting
adjourned!!! The order has been submitted in                     65
triplicate. Sealed and delivered by hand. At 10 A.M.,
the Queen accepts and *HO!* . . . A deft swing, a
ringing whooooooosh . . . and there!!! She has klopt
off the eeny meany, what a greedy Medusa head. . . .

¿Ya ves?[1] Like I said, it's not simple . . .                  70

1996

---

4. Mine. My own. My precious.
5. A line from and the title of a famous Mexican song.
6. Silly things.
7. In Aztec mythology, a god of war, a sun god, and the patron of the city of Tenochtitlan.
8. *Coyotl*: Nahuátl word for coyote. *Mad Hatter*: eccentric character in *Alice's Adventures in Won-*

*derland* (1865) and *Through the Looking-Glass, and What Alice Found There* (1871), children's fiction by the English writer Lewis Carroll (Charles Lutwidge Dodgson, 1832–1898).
9. The Queen of Hearts, one of several playing cards who serve as characters in *Alice's Adventures in Wonderland*.
1. You see?

# EVANGELINA VIGIL-PIÑÓN
## b. 1949

### apprenticeship

I hunt for things
that will color my life
with brilliant memories
because I do believe
lo que nos dice                                      5
la mano del escritor:[1]
that life is remembering

when I join my grandmother
for a tasa de café[2]
and I listen to the stories                          10
de su antepasado[3]
her words paint masterpieces
and these I hang
in the galleries of my mind:

I want to be an artist like her.                     15

1978

### crimson the color

crimson is the color
of a dream:

beam from fierce ball of fire
pierces the frigid darkness of the universe

tender is the touch of a child                       5

pierce through your thoughts
mind streams in explosive directions

conceive in black ink
what you've made of your life
day in and day out                                   10
who will, if you won't
tell of the secrets
buried so deeply?

crimson is the color of a dream
peer through the window                              15

1. What the writer's hand tells us.          3. Of her ancestor.
2. Cup of coffee.

ivory roses in full bloom in the backyard
the shocking orange-reds of granada blossoms
the fragile fragrance of nostalgia
dreams and dreams away:

a gold bracelet from a sweetheart                    20
the words inscribed
*amorcito consentido*[1]
    distant planets with no names
       flicker and blink red and blue
    in deep vast space                           25

crimson is the color of a dream
delicate the fragrance
fine the bracelet of white gold
soft the touch
rapturous the kiss                                   30
distant the dreams

                      1995

## corazón en la palma

is it the same muse
whose song
stirred mine—

life was young
even as leaves swirled                               5
I, dizzy
time turning golden

is it the same song
just sung a different way
the melody without its words                         10
how far, far in time
its sadness reaches

*bien me dijo mi abuela*
*nunca sabe uno*
*lo que viene atrás de los años*[1]                  15

                      1996

1. Spoiled little love.
1. My grandmother told me well / one never knows / what comes with the years.

# CARMEN TAFOLLA
## b. 1951

## Compliments

They say I don't look thirty
They also say
I don't look Mexican.
They mean them, I guess,
as compliments.                                      5

If that is so,
then it must be
complimentary
to not be
thirty                                               10
or
Mexican.

Therefore,
I guess,
they don't                                           15
(as much)
like people
who are over
thirty
or too                                               20
Mexican.

But now they know
and therefore, I guess
it means
that now                                             25
they don't
(as much)
like me.

1980                                                 1992

## Marked

Never write with pencil,
m'ija.[1]
It is for those

---

1. *M'ija* or *mija*, a contraction of *mi hija*, literally means "daughter" but is used colloquially to mean "girl."

who would
  erase.            5
Make your mark proud
    and open,
Brave,
      beauty folded into
  its imperfection,       10
Like a piece of turquoise
    marked.

Never write
with pencil,
m'ija.            15
Write with ink
    or mud,
or berries grown in
gardens never owned,
  or, sometimes,      20
    if necessary,
    blood.

1984                        1992


## Letter to Ti

*—From Le Van Minh, 15 and Amerasian, after arriving in the
U.S. from Viet Nam, having spent the last four years surviving
being fed by and carried on the back of a friend called "Ti."*

It is strange being here
like yellow fog wrapped softly around a dream.
The wrapping paper comes undone
and inside I see my face
reflected.           5
Now, I do not try to look less American.
I should try to look less Vietnamese.
But most times, I just rest,
and don't try anything at all.
The time to close one's eyes is good here    10
Except that I see you,
the stiff hairs on the back of your neck
laying flatter
with the sweat,
your hard breathing and your bony shoulders    15
body-friends to my riding body.
As much as I loved your eyes,
the back of your neck was just as dear to me,
the straining neck smiled just as much,
the light shone from around your ears    20

like the gentle friendship of your face
looking at me.
I knew your neck better than anyone.

Many carry me here.
There will be a chair too                                               25
in which I can carry myself.
I eat every meal.
I am in a bed at night.
People do not laugh at me
for my features,                                                        30
my spine or legs.
I no longer make paper flowers.

I unwrap gifts from people I do not know.
The wrapping paper falls aside.
Sometimes I pick it up and fold it curve it                             35
lay my cheek against it.
"Are you making flowers?" they ask me.
"No.
A neck.
The back of a neck,                                                     40
Four years my home . . .
and still."

1990                                                                    1992

---

## From To Split a Human: Mitos, Machos y la Mujer Chicana

## Chapter III: Myths, Machos and the Movies: Will the Real Chicana Please Stand Up?[1]

> . . . "Let me tell you about these Mexicans—their chili and their women are hot."
> —old cowhand in western.

Chicanos tell us what Chicanas are like. Anglos tell us what Chicanas are like. Even the cowboys in old westerns add their warnings. Norman Rockwell paints shy, fan-waving señoritas on phone book covers, while Louie L'Amour[2] thrives on bare-shouldered, loose-moraled cantina "girls." We feel like asking "Will the *real* Chicana please stand up?" but when she does, we can't see her, because the room is already packed with a standing mob of stereotyped impersonators.

---

1. Except as indicated, all footnotes are Carmen Tafolla's.
2. Louis L'Amour (1908–1988), American writer, primarily of Western fiction. *Norman Rockwell*: American artist (1894–1978). [Anthology editors' note]

### The Stereotypes

Despite the assertive and astute actions perpetrated by Chicanas year after year, the stereotypes still persist. Chicanas are submissive, happy, rather dumb creatures who enjoy doing business as prostitutes. In the popular sphere, examples of this stereotyping abound. A recent issue of a flight magazine carries a classic example. The story begins with the usual "American Cowboy riding into Small Mexican Town" scene. He dismounts, handing a few coins to a small boy to bring water. (Somehow the classic cowboy scene always seems to conveniently place a tall "Americano" on *horseback* next to a very small Mexican child [or doting barefoot woman] to emphasize his fantasized stature and to fit with a theme of not-so-subtle racism and sexism.) It continues:

> . . . *to a clay-baked structure. He walked toward it, mindful of dark eyes that might be watching. Inside . . . he noticed first the table of silent men to his left and then, in a way he tried not to show, the woman with the bare shoulders leaning next to the rough hewn bar. A brief, grudging smile of introduction crossed his lips as he proceeded across the dirt floor. "Cerveza," he said hoarsely. The barman grinned nervously and reached for a dark brown bottle. Dark and brown as the woman's skin above the white blouse, as her almond eyes, not nearly so dark as her ebony hair. He drained the bottle at the first swallow and wiped his lips. She watched steadily. He looked at the men and at her and gestured for the barman to bring another, then extracted a brass watch from his pocket and flipped up the cover. Four p.m. The men from the north would be here by six. The woman smiled at him as if she had suddenly realized something. He put the watch back in his pocket. For the time being, the train could wait.*[3]

There is more than one stereotype blaring at us in this classic script. The Anglo man is subjected to hero expectations that he care and yet not show he cares. He tries not to show he notices *anything*. Even his smile is done grudgingly. He is to be a work machine and satisfy the clock, and yet he must prove his animal lust to be a "*real*" man. To be "cool" (ironically enough, what is now called "macho" in contemporary youth slang of the U.S.), he must be interested in only what he can "get out of" a woman. But our main interest in this passage is in its scant, well-repeated reflection of the dark brown woman. The image of the fiery-eyed, bare-shouldered Mexican woman passionately attracted to the first "Americano" male to walk in the door is not a new image. The distinct odor wafting across the page is of a loose woman, pleasant, accommodating, and interested. The image has 150-year-old roots.

George Kendall, in 1841, describes the Mexican women of the Southwest from a perspective that is to become the traditional Anglo-American stereotype of Chicanas.

> *They are joyous, sociable, kind-hearted creatures almost universally liberal to a fault, easy and naturally graceful in their manners, and really appear to have more understanding than the men. Had we fallen into the*

---

3. Rod Davis, "¿Cerveza?" *The Texas Flyer* (Austin: Texas Parade, Inc., June 1977) p. 38.

> *hands of the women, instead of the men, our treatment would have been*
> *far different while in New Mexico.*[4]

Kendall is shocked at the way the women dress, in clothing which allows their natural "gracefully-curving lines of beauty" to be seen instead of compressing their bodies in the tight-laced corsets worn by proper Anglo-American women of the time. He correctly predicts the attitudes and reactions of Anglo men to "the indelicacy or . . . brazen impudence to appear before him in dishabille so immodest." (At the time, the women of New Mexico wore "only" a blouse and skirt, or a blouse and skirt with a dress over it all.) While Kendall, with time, accepts this as a difference of social custom, and eventually even begins to question how the women of his own native land can "compress . . . and contort themselves out of all proportions, causing . . . the exquisite undulations of the natural form to become flat or angular, or conical, or jutting . . .", many of his contemporaries do not reach this level of cultural objectivity, and the stereotype of the passionate and "loose" Mexican woman begins to engrave itself on Anglo-American literature and folklore.

The two most common stereotypes which the Chicana encounters are seemingly opposites. The first and by far the most common is that of "a spicy Mexican dish," a seductive flashy-eyed cantina "working-girl," good- (or at least warm-) hearted but flighty and simple minded. She is the perfect hot-blooded receptacle-object for her stereotyped counterpart, the "Macho" bandido/desperado or Latin lover *patrón*. This particular flashy-eyed "model" is also seen as especially and magnetically attracted to tall, good-looking "Americanos," or basically *any* "Americano" she is exposed to. The hot-blooded *cantinera* is usually pictured as fascinated, amazed, and impressed by the strength, intelligence, and (especially) manliness of the "Americano." It usually takes one flash of his smile (and in extreme cases, a snap of his fingers) to make her arrive at these conclusions. (It is curious to note that in most racist contact, the stereotype lanced at the male of the "threat" or oppressed population is lack of manliness, with the "oppressed" female being seen as unusually attracted [hence submissive] to the men of the dominant group.)[5]

The second stereotype commonly encountered is that of the fervent, feverishly-religious "Spanish" noblewoman, attending early mass daily and devoting her life solely to the one man she loves or loved, be he daring, dastardly, or dead. This woman is pictured as having the capacity for only one love in all her life. She is as faithful (and as one-track minded) as a dog.

There is also a visible overlap between stereotypes for the three major Hispanic ethnic groups. Stereotypes are not concerned with precision; those assigned to one Hispanic group are often confused and extended to other Hispanic groups. Chicanas, Puertorriqueñas, and Cubanas all begin to "look alike" in the stereotypes, with minor variations. Puerto Rican and Cuban women are stereotyped as tropical bombshells—sexy, sexed, and interested. Year after year we see resurrected recurrences of the same image—a sexy dancer singing "Chiquita Banana" and rolling her hips and eyes. A sexual version of the "luscious dessert with fruit topping," this banana-toting teaser

---

4. George Kendall, *Narrative of the Texas Sante Fe Expedition* (Chicago: The Lake Side Press, 1929) pp. 432–433.
5. Note especially the treatment in the media of

Asians, Mexican peasants, and people from India. A significant exception to this is seen in stereotypes of Blacks where both men and women are reduced to an animal level as sex objects.

sways her hips into your heart (or reasonable sexual facsimile thereof). She simply perpetrates the image of a sexy, Latin pleaser.

To those readers perplexedly wondering "But what's the matter with the Chiquita Banana commercial? I *like* the way she dances!" and maybe even mumbling, "I even thought the Frito Bandito was cute. What's the big deal?", a small explanation. A Frito Bandito, in a different context and different world, could be perfectly harmless. By *himself*, Frito-Lay's miniature bandido would not have stirred a single social ruffle. *But he is not by himself!* He is surrounded by a social reality of countless other Mexican bandido images: Mexican bandidos ride across the badlands using Arrid Extra Dry because "if it works for *him*, it'll work for you"; Mexican bandidos ride across the badlands to discover the latest model of Frigidaire; Mexican bandidos ride across the badlands to be defeated by John Wayne.[6] We are almost braced to see Mexican bandidos ride into the middle of a Japanese science fiction movie, to serve as greasy prey for Godzilla, until we remind ourselves that these "bandido" images are U.S. illusions, *not* universal realities. In essence, what we must protest is that in the dearth of representative or even frequent images of Chicanos *or* Chicanas, we find only one or sometimes two images of that group, repeated over and over until they become the very heart of caricatured undesirability. If the public has seen only cantina maids or Chiquita Bananas dance across the screen, then any Chicana they come into contact with— be she scientist, computer programmer, playwright, or (heaven forbid) grade school student, will be expected to fit in some way this distinct image which the media has portrayed of "what Chicanas are like."

### Modern Science to the Rescue

Even in the realm of "scientific" studies and professional académe, stereotypes abound. According to much of the social science literature, Chicanos dwell in a backward land where machismo and masochism reign. "Machismo" is by far the greatest field day which ethnocentric social scientists have enjoyed. Ignoring their own sexist attitudes, many social scientists accuse Chicano males of being ruthless oppressors and the sole power in Chicano families. The consequences of this attitude, as Martha Cotera has described, are that "As the role of the man is laden with terribly oppressive characteristics, the woman's role within the family is proportionately described as weak and totally valueless."[7] The Machismo myth ignores the power which the Chicana has traditionally held in the familial structure, thought by some to be the single most important social unit in Chicano culture. As Octavio Romano states, in criticism of William Madsen:[8]

> *In Madsen's world, not only are Mexican-Americans passively fatalistic, their women are super passively-fatalistic with a touch of sadomasochism thrown in for good measure . . .*"[9]

6. Iconic American actor (Marion Robert Morrison, 1907–1979) associated with Westerns. *Frigidaire*: i.e., refrigerator. [Anthology editors' note]
7. Cotera, *Diosa y Hembra: The History and Heritage of Chicanas in the U.S.* (Austin, Information Systems Development: 1976) p. 152.
8. American professor of anthropology and writer (1920–2003) who specialized in the society and religious practices of Mexico. [Anthology editors' note]
9. Octavio Ignacio Romano-V., "The Anthropology and Sociology of the Mexican Americans," *El Grito* (Vol. II, No. 1) p. 19.

Let Madsen speak for himself: "Some wives assert that they are grateful for punishment at the hands of their husbands, for such concern with short-comings indicates profound love."[1] Countless Chicanas disagree.

Yet within Chicano culture, the feminine image is one of strength. Where she has been portrayed negatively, "voluntary" self-denials is a more specifically pronounced theme than passivity.[2] The passive image does not seem as pronounced in Chicano culture as it seems in general Anglo-American litera-ture. In the realm of modern Chicano folk literature, the more popular women appear as active and aggressive. "La Camelia" in popular song, the "pachuca" in Chicano poetry, and Ultima in the Chicano novel[3] epitomize defiance, aggressive action, and wisdom, respectively.

But negative images do exist within the culture. The three most pro-nounced themes of folk wisdom center around three women—a Virgen de Guadalupe (powerful, revered virgin), La Llorona (weeping spirit of the night, who killed her children), and La Chingada (common curse word for the debased, tricked or screwed). In classic sexist approach, women would be given a choice only between extremes. Compared to many cultures, Mexican culture has been somewhat liberal in its recognition of women's intellectual capacity, but not so liberal in its recognition of a single moral standard for men and women. In its most extreme version, woman is either Goddess, Mother, or Chingada. Chicano culture, like other cultures, has not been exempt from underlying currents of sexism.

### The Destruction of Two Illusions

Two of the most popular and most harmful of public illusions about the Chi-cana are so common that they frequently go unquestioned and unnoticed. The first is an external illusion (i.e., a belief about an ethnic group that comes from *outside* that ethnic group). The second is an internal illusion, arising from within our own culture. Stereotypes from within are no less dangerous than those from without; if anything, we lend them more credence, and propagate the illusion under the banner of "The Inside Truth." Saddest of all, we finally begin to believe them ourselves. They become honored as tradi-tion, and passed on as heirlooms of cultural wisdom or "human nature." With a critical review of our own assumption, we can sort out what we have observed from what we have been told is true. We can destroy those illusions which are neither factual nor beneficial to us.

### Feminism as Anglicism

In a time-bound provincialism and a nearsightedness which lets us see only the 30 miles and 30 years immediately around us, we "modern," "well-educated" citizens of the 20th century sometimes judge customs and cul-tures by the two or three examples we choose to notice. Very frequently,

1. Ibid.
2. Ann M. Pescatello. *Power and Pawn: The Female in Iberian Families, Societies, and Cultures* (West-port, Connecticut/London, England: Greenwood Press, 1976) p. 200. "La mujer abnegada," the self-renounced woman, is a theme frequently encountered in Mexican culture.

3. Rudolfo A. Anaya's *Bless Me, Ultima* (see p. 1160). "La Camelia" in popular song: the arche-type of the woman capable of controlling her lover. The "Pachuca" in Chicano poetry: the ar-chetype of Mexican American women in the 1940s. [Anthology editors' note]

Chicanas are confronted by the belief that "Women's Lib" was invented by Anglo women in the 1970's. Therefore, it is concluded, a Chicana who is concerned with matters of sexism is probably on the road to becoming "acculturated" by Anglo society, and hence, is a form of traitor to our people and "our ways."

This is perhaps an expectable reaction from those who are concerned with an ever-present fear of being "swallowed up" by Anglo-American culture. This fear, however, can be transformed into a fear of all change, and the inherent danger in that transformation is the inevitable truth that that which does not change, dies.

The argument that feminism is a form of Anglicism is not rare. Chicano men have often used it when threatened by Chicanas' demands for equal male-female responsibilities and decision-making in parenting, financial decisions, and other family concerns. They may charge that feminism is "another gringo plot," or a way to deteriorate the strength of our family unit. The actual fear (like that of men from other cultures) is that the woman's growing power would decrease or diminish in some way the man's power. That is, "If you 'let' your wife do that, you will be less of a man." There are many fallacies in this style of logic. First of all, the wording reveals a basic attitude toward the power and freedom of each individual. If a man "*lets*" his wife or "*doesn't let*" his wife do something, then it is *he* who owns the power and prerogative for all decisions, while *she* is merely under his guardianship, much as a child is under a parent's guardianship. Obviously, in most cases, she is not chained or physically bound by him—and she *has*, in most cases, the power to do what she wants. But the unspoken rule is that the husband's word carries the absolute authority, which she dare not transgress. Hence, he "*lets*" her or "*doesn't let*" her and she holds no power of her own. (She must then, in order to get what she wants, resort to undercover or manipulative tactics, a more socially accepted "behavior" for women.)

Secondly, the "increase of power—decrease of power" juxtaposition reflects a competitive "economy" of power, which *can* be viewed as more inherently an acculturation to Anglo values than any charge of feminism. It is a "If you become more, I become less" view of human growth, based on a competition model, which does not allow for two winners. If we carry this to its logical conclusion, then every person should prevent his or her friends and companions from getting a better education, a better job position, a more secure personal attitude, or a more peaceful spiritual approach to life, because that growth or improvement in our companions would represent a *relative* decrease or shrinking of our own powers. "If you become smarter, I become dumber."

Yet a competitive model of human growth is not the mode in many cultures, among them Chicano culture. Cooperation is highly praised, team efforts are encouraged, and the belief that "If one of us gets ahead, that's a boost for all of us" is constantly reiterated. Perhaps then, Chicano culture is not being consistent or "authentic" *to its own values* where the question of sex roles is concerned. The man who believes that "letting" his wife get more power reduces his own masculinity is falling victim to a superstition which is *not consistent* with his culture's professed values.

The accusation that feminism is an Anglo phenomenon is also heard from the mouths of Chicanas, who may also feel *threatened* or confused by the changes in sex role expectations. She may conclude that feminism is inherently Anglo-introduced "because, after all, my mother never felt that way." And her mother, in her mind, may be her usual model of what a good Chicana should be. Yet what is ignored in this argument is the generational changes common to both cultures. The mother of her feminist Anglo friend may be just as opposed to the current trends in feminism as her own mother.

What cannot be denied is that cultures, naturally and from within, are in a constant process of change. Without this, they would never progress but would stagnate and die. Chicano culture's growing concerns with equal rights and shared responsibilities between the sexes is not simply a reflection of acculturation to an Anglo model, but is instead a natural growth of our own awareness of human oppression.

Finally, the illusion that feminism is an Anglo innovation can also be seen in the perspectives of some Anglo women (as also with the men). Many self-labeled feminists are surprised to find an organized and substantive women's movement in other parts of the world, or to find that many third world women are among the more advanced innovators in feminist thought. This is often an extension of a national chauvinism that states flatly "We're the best and the most advanced nation in the world, while most other countries are rather primitive." This kind of racist feminism often results in a condescending use of and exploitation of minority women, as if "they" could never fully understand feminism. When leadership is chosen for government or business positions in "women's concerns," Anglo women are given the positions. Minority women are called in, if at all, to "assist in reaching other populations." The U.S. Women's Movement, however, has made a much more concerted effort toward multicultural awareness and unity than have the existing structures and organizations of the male-dominated society.

An excellent rejection of the stereotype of Chicanas as inherently "non-feminist" lies in the film *Salt of the Earth*, produced by blacklisted filmmakers and Mexican American workers in 1954. It presents the struggle of striking Mexican American mineworkers and does not shrink from the problem of oppressed men, in turn, oppressing women. The women are shown in their developing boldness, until finally they take the lead in fighting the oppression, with or without their husbands' approval. The story is a factual one.

It is not a contradiction to be a Chicana and a feminist. We can be both and, in doing so, be more consistent with our own professed opposition to human oppression.

### Mrs. Macho Man

Many Chicanas have good reason for feeling ill at ease with Anglo Women's groups. They have too often been stuck with the left-over stereotypes from old cowboy movies. If their men are indeed the desperado "machos" that are portrayed, then they themselves must be the counterpart "bare-shouldered cantina girl" or "Spanish noblewoman," two roles which are not usually comfortable *or* satisfying. In addition, what kind of dummies must they be to have married such blatantly evil bandidos in the first place? Few Chicanas want to wear the name tag "Mrs. Macho Man."

Most importantly, the concept of *macho* portrayed in the bandido movies and the sociology textbooks *is not the concept of macho existent in Chicano culture.* There are indeed, at *least* two different definitions to the word *macho.* While the U.S. mainstream has come to use macho to mean male chauvinist, Mexican culture *and* Chicano culture have traditionally utilized the term macho in praise of "a good man." The macho is the man *"quien cumple."* who fulfills his responsibilities, who is brave, who stands up for his beliefs. The popular Mexican song "El Rey" is the assertion of a macho that his word is firm and that he does not shrink from what needs to be done. "Hay que saber llegar"[4] he asserts, not shrinking from what needs to be done, but refusing to compete on someone *else's* standards.

The man who is "muy macho" is a man who is "very masculine," and this is not defined in *physical* terms, but in terms of *character.* Granted it is a definition of a sex role, and as such, it more narrowly defines an individual's options; however, it is not a cognate for "male chauvinist" and this usage in the United States is largely an extension of the stereotype for Latinos.

In addition, the most current usage of the term *macho* in the U.S. is, in a praising, idealized tone, a new form of the old word "cool." The description given in the former #1 hit "Macho Man" is almost exclusively on physical characteristics (". . . Big thick moustache," "see the hair on my chest?," "works out at the health spa," "to have the kind of body always in demand," etc. . . . ) except for two expected behaviors ("wanna thrill my body" and "ready to get down with anyone he can."). The word *macho* has become so lost in the translation that the English word would best be considered a totally different one from the Spanish.

### Sex-Defined Roles

Although Chicano culture has made much internal progress toward the liberation of and respect for all its human members, one theme surfaces repeatedly, usually in the mouth of the male: "In order to better our situation and simultaneously preserve our culture, perhaps the Chicano should work on the first task, and the Chicana should guard the culture." This suggestion, which would have Chicanas tend primarily to the "cultural" rearing of the children, is a sexist view of woman as divine *preserver* of the culture and man as the *liver* of that culture. It reveals a restricted "Guadalupe complex," for as the Virgin of Guadalupe is officially "Protectoress of the Mexican People," woman is expected in like form to be "protectoress of the culture." This shifts the moral and "human" responsibilities to the woman, and again, leaves business and power to the man, an unsatisfying and an unhealthy division of tasks.

Yet this symbol of Guadalupe, the protectoress, can also be one of great power. It holds the potential to symbolize active justice, compassion, and strength simultaneously. Within Chicano culture, this symbol is often utilized as a source of thought and *love*, of doing *and* feeling, and as such represents the whole human being and not simply a sex-defined half.

Of all the myths, "Mr. Machos" and other stereotypes abounding, in the final analysis, Chicanas are still as varied and as limitless as any group of people. There are many common problems which confront us, but there are also many talents which lay hidden, unrecognized, or undeveloped, and these talents are our hope for the future.

1985

4. One needs to know how to make it.

# Puerto Rican Young Lords

In 1969, the Young Lords Organization (YLO) was created to pursue a militant civil rights agenda. The organization emerged from the Young Lords, a Puerto Rican and Mexican gang in Chicago, then the U.S. city with the second-largest Puerto Rican population. The YLO's main goal was to demand that the city's government be more responsive to the dire living conditions of the Latino communities. A year before, José "Cha-Cha" Jiménez, one of the gang's founders, had been incarcerated for drug possession, and in prison he was encouraged by a Black Muslim fellow inmate to read the works of the African American civil rights leaders Martin Luther King Jr. (1929–1968) and Malcolm X (Malcolm Little, 1925–1965), and of socialist revolutionary leaders such as Russia's Vladimir Lenin (1870–1924) and China's Mao Tse-tung (1893–1976). These readings awakened Jiménez's interest in civil rights and social justice. After his release from prison, and following the advice of the militant African American group the Black Panthers, Jiménez turned the Young Lords into a political group. At the time, the Black Panthers were attempting to forge a coalition of minority groups victimized by racial and socioeconomic oppression, to join in the struggles for equality and for liberation. The YLO began to denounce police brutality, the deplorable and segregated living conditions of Puerto Ricans and other Latinos in Chicago, and the unfair practices and neglect of various city agencies regarding minority communities. To draw public attention to their efforts, the YLO interrupted a meeting of the city's Urban Renewal and Community Preservation Council, demanding representation in the discussions for any projects that would affect Latino communities. When this demand was not met, some of the organization's members trashed the place. Cha Cha Jiménez was blamed for the incident and arrested a few days later. In response, over 200 people started a protest for his release that culminated in their taking over the Chicago Avenue Police Station. Incidents such as these brought the YLO media attention and inspired many young Latinos to join the organization and support its struggles for change.

In New York, the U.S. city with the largest number of Puerto Ricans, a group of Puerto Rican college and high school students had organized in 1968 the Sociedad de Albizu Campos (Albizu Campos Society), an organization named after the prominent Puerto Rican nationalist leader and that promoted Puerto Rico's struggle for independence. Wanting to join the movements for social and political change that characterized the civil rights era, and that engaged many groups of color in U.S. society, members of the Sociedad learned about Jiménez and the YLO, visited them, and shortly thereafter requested permission to form their own branch of the organization. Less than a year later, the New York branch of the YLO had become the most active and visible. The New York group then split from the Chicago group and became the Young Lords Party. Among the founders and leaders of the New York Young Lords were Gloria González, Juan González, Pablo "Yoruba" Guzmán, Felipe Luciano, Miguel "Mickey" Meléndez, Iris Morales, Denise Oliver, and Richie Pérez. Other branches of the Young Lords were later initiated in Philadelphia, at the time the third largest mainland Puerto Rican community; and in Bridgeport, Connecticut; Newark-Hoboken, New Jersey; and Ponce, Puerto Rico.

With the slogan *Tengo Puerto Rico en mi corazón* (a slightly incorrect way of saying in Spanish "I carry Puerto Rico in my heart"), the Young Lords Party articulated an ambitious and idealistic revolutionary agenda that went beyond pride in their cultural roots and was also aimed at inspiring and engaging working-class Puerto Rican urban youth in seeking solutions to some of the everyday problems of the impoverished inner city barrios. The organization was effective in mobilizing youth for many campaigns, including creating free health clinics for the detection of lead poisoning, tuberculosis, diabetes, and other diseases. Additionally, they fought for the improvement of hospital services, housing, and prison conditions, and pressed to make inner city schools more responsive to the educational needs of migrant children with limited English proficiency. They supported bilingual education and curricular reforms that took into consideration a student's cultural and linguistic heritage.

One of their earliest, most visible, and more mundane undertakings was mobilizing the community to help in cleaning up the garbage on the streets of the barrios and forcing the city's municipal government to improve its garbage collection. Actions such as taking over an underutilized Spanish First Methodist Church and turning it into the People's Church to sponsor a daily breakfast program for the children of the community, forcing city authorities to build a new Lincoln Hospital to replace the decaying facility that was not offering adequate services to the South Bronx, and drawing attention to the dismal conditions of state prisons made the Young Lords one of the most prominent groups of the Puerto Rican civil rights movement.

The Young Lords' newspaper, *Pa'lante* (Moving Forward), was an important vehicle for denouncing injustices against Puerto Rican and other Latino communities, as well as a consciousness-raising tool. The group also sponsored a weekly radio program on a New York radio station, WBAI-FM. The party platform condemned capitalism and racism as the major sources of workers' oppression, and it embraced socialism. The party denounced U.S. imperialism and colonial domination of Puerto Rico and supported the island's quest for independence. In their organizing efforts, the Young Lords tried to reach not only those living in the urban barrios, but also others who could help them advance the organization's social and political goals—students on college campuses, community professionals, and other activists. In addition to their efforts to improve the quality of basic government services in the barrios, one issue that resonated with many Puerto Ricans was seeking the release of Nationalist political prisoners, some incarcerated in federal prisons since the 1950s. This particular cause was dramatized in 1977, when the Puerto Rican flag was hung on the forehead of the Statue of Liberty by a group of activists demanding the prisoners' freedom. In 1979, some of the prisoners were pardoned by U.S. president Jimmy Carter.

The media-savvy tactics of the Young Lords not only drew attention to their many audacious activities; they also captured the hearts of and empowered a young generation of Puerto Ricans in their struggles for equality, social justice, and their share of the American dream. Although their community activism gained them a large degree of visibility and support, the Young Lords' radical politics had less mass appeal and made them the target of surveillance and abuses by federal and local authorities. Some of the former Young Lords partly blame FBI infiltration and the agency's counterintelligence program (COINTELPRO) for creating the mistrust and factionalism that ultimately led to the disbanding of the organization in 1975.

Roughly four decades after their emergence, the Young Lords have become a symbol of hope for change and of the civil rights struggles that have transformed the United States into a more tolerant and just society, one more aware of its racial and social divisions and more inclusive of the richness and potential of its diverse population. Two former Young Lords have recorded the history of their organization: Iris Morales, in the documentary *¡Palante, Siempre Palante!: The Young Lords* (1996), and Miguel "Mickey" Meléndez, in the book *We Took the Streets: Fighting for Latino Rights with the Young Lords* (2003).

Morales was one of a handful of women in the early years of the organization. She served as the Party's deputy minister of education and, along with other women, confronted male chauvinism and sexism within the group and made the group more responsive to women's issues and rights. Some years later, after the organization disbanded, she received a law degree from New York University, became an educator, and worked for the Puerto Rican Legal Defense and Education Fund (PRLDEF). Directing ¡Palante, Siempre Palante! led Morales to create the Latino/a Education Network Service (LENS), a community empowerment nonprofit organization that uses visual media to foster dialogue on social and political issues relevant to the Latino community. She is currently the executive director of the Union Square Awards program, a philanthropic initiative in New York City aimed at supporting groundbreaking grassroots projects or organizations that address pressing social issues.

In "¡PALANTE, SIEMPRE PALANTE!: The Young Lords," the selection that follows, Morales addresses her working-class background and role as a U.S.-born Puerto Rican who eventually became a translator between her migrant parents and English-speaking society. She describes some of her experiences growing up Puerto Rican in New York City, discusses what led her to join the Young Lords, provides an insider's view of the organizations achievements and weaknesses, and notes its place in the history of Puerto Ricans in the United States.

The former Young Lord Pablo "Yoruba" Guzmán is a media journalist and, like most former members of the Young Lords' leadership, still active in consciousness-raising community-oriented projects. The son of a U.S.-born Cuban mother and a Puerto Rican father, Guzmán was born in Spanish Harlem and raised in the South Bronx. He was eighteen years old and a college student at the State University of New York at Old Westbury when he joined the Sociedad de Albizu Campos and later the Young Lords, eventually becoming the Party's minister of information. A semester in Mexico during his first year in college helped connect Guzmán with his Latino roots. As a black Puerto Rican growing up in New York City, Guzmán also identified with the civil rights struggles of African Americans. He once stated that "Before people called me a spic, they called me a nigger."

During his post–Young Lords years, Guzmán worked for WBAI-FM and was briefly its programming director. He published numerous articles in the Village Voice and in Latin New York, a magazine geared to the Latino community and that focused on music and performance. He has won Emmy Awards as a television reporter, working for WNBC and later for CBS News in New York. Guzmán shared his early experiences as a member of the Young Lords in the volume Palante: Young Lords Party (1971), where in a sentence he attempted to capture the essence of the organization: "We're trying to make a society where opportunity is the rule for everybody." More than two decades later, he recounts the history and activities of the Young Lords and summarizes the organization's main accomplishments in "La Vida Pura: A Lord of the Barrio." This essay, which appears below, was originally published in the Village Voice in 1995 and was reprinted in The Puerto Rican Movement: Voices from the Diaspora.

# IRIS MORALES
## b. 1948

## ¡PALANTE, SIEMPRE PALANTE!: The Young Lords

### A Childhood as "Go-Between"

My parents came to the United States during the Puerto Rican migration of the late 1940s. My mother came from the northwest town of Aguadilla to work in the garment industry as a sewing-machine operator. My father, a sugarcane cutter from Sabana Grande, worked as an elevator operator in several New York City hotels. They met and married in the United States and raised four daughters. As the oldest child, I became the translator for my parents, serving as the bridge between the Puerto Rican culture and the American way of life. Other family members would bring letters they received from North American institutions asking me to translate from English into Spanish and write any required English response. Neighbors would regularly ask my mother's permission for me to accompany them to the Social Security office, the worker's compensation or welfare office, or any other place where English only was spoken. Often when on a translating trip at the hospital or local school with my mother or a neighbor, another person— a Spanish-speaking stranger—would also require and request translating assistance.

The role as "go-between" helped in my later radicalization because I got to see institutional practices up close. I got to feel the disdain and injustices with which people, bureaucrats, and institutions responded to Puerto Ricans. I experienced the mistreatment and humiliation. It seemed that all the institutions—from the local school to the Social Security office to the hospital emergency room—were willing to experiment with and throw away our lives. I felt the disrespect and the lack of understanding of people who are poor, who speak another language, and who are of a different skin color. These experiences with institutional racism were imprinted somewhere in my consciousness. Later when I read about the racist practices of U.S. institutions in other communities or countries, I connected with it and thought, yes, I have seen them do that. Yes, I know how the holders of power exploit poor communities. Those early experiences were invaluable in becoming a political person and being able to maneuver the system to survive.

### Leading Up to the Young Lords Experience

My political awakening began while I was in high school. I learned that the U.S. government forced Native Americans to live on reservations and interned Japanese Americans in concentration camps during World War II. Through some school friends, I attended youth meetings of the Student Non-Violent Coordinating Committee (SNCC) and the NAACP (National Association for the Advancement of Colored People), and I marched in demonstrations against the Vietnam War.

After graduating from high school, I became a tenant organizer with the West Side Block Association, a neighborhood storefront set up by a group of Columbia University students. We went knocking door-to-door, talking to people about housing problems—everything from lack of heat and hot water to vermin infestation. We represented tenants in court and conducted rent strikes, organizing people to fight for decent and humane living conditions.

Later when I entered City College, I joined ONYX, the African American student organization; there were no Puerto Rican or Latino organizations on campus. I studied African American history and especially the teachings of Malcolm X. As the number of Puerto Rican students increased on campus, we organized the first Puerto Rican group, called Puerto Ricans in Student Activities (PRISA).

During this time, I was also working as a teacher in the Academy for Black and Latin Education (ABLE), a storefront school on 105th Street and Columbus Avenue. Several African American men from the neighborhood created the school; we had attended school together and knew the neglect of the public school system first hand. ABLE was an alternative way for young people to complete their high-school equivalency diploma. But as we taught our classes, many of our students, who were addicted to heroin, nodded out in class and were unable to learn. When we searched for treatment services, we found none. St. Luke's, the local hospital, was completely unresponsive to our concerns. As a result, ABLE organized a takeover of the hospital administrative offices demanding services. Out of the takeover, ABLE successfully negotiated the first thirteen hospital beds in the city to specifically treat drug addiction among adolescents.

Around this time I participated in cultural activities at the East Wind in Harlem and at the Gut Theater in *El Barrio* where I met many emerging poets, writers, and political leaders of the day. Although impressed with the artistic and intellectual vibrancy of the cultural movement, I was disappointed with those who justified the second-class position of women of color as a positive cultural legacy. Also in *El Barrio*, I connected with the Real Great Society[1] and joined a bus load of Latinos and Latinas and African Americans on a trip through the Midwest to the Crusade for Justice Conference in Denver, Colorado, in 1968.[2] It was there that I first met Jose "Cha Cha" Jiménez and other members of the Chicago Young Lords.

Cha Cha, a soft-spoken and unassuming leader, told us that the Young Lords were originally a street gang that developed in Chicago during the 1950s to protect neighborhood territory. Cha Cha, a member since 1959, had been in and out of jail for petty offenses. In jail, he met Fred Hampton, the leader of the Chicago Black Panther Party, who introduced him to political ideas. They talked about the movement for Black liberation and discussed building unity between Blacks and Puerto Ricans. When Cha Cha got out of jail, he returned to his neighborhood and organized the Young Lords to protest the city's urban renewal plans that would have uprooted the Puerto Rican/Latino community. It was 1968, and the gang, while protesting urban removal, was transformed into the Young Lords Organization (later the Young Lords Party). They designed a button with a map of Puerto

---

1. An antipoverty advocacy group founded on the Lower East Side of Manhattan in 1964 by former gang leaders. The East Harlem branch, dedicated to "total environmental control," was formed in 1967.

2. The group Crusade for Justice was founded and directed by Rodolfo "Corky" Gonzales (see p. 787).

Rico and the slogan, *"Tengo Puerto Rico En Mi Corazón"* ("I have Puerto Rico in my heart"). They went door-to-door promoting community control and self-determination for Puerto Ricans and pressured institutions to respond to the concerns of the surrounding Latino community. The Young Lords Organization set up "serve the people" programs and united with the Black Panthers and the Young Patriots (a radical hillbilly group) to organize the Rainbow Coalition. From the streets of the second-largest Puerto Rican community in the United States, the Young Lords Organization was becoming known as fighters for the equality of Puerto Ricans.

The winter after the Denver conference, I traveled to Cuba where supporters from every country in the world gathered to participate in the tenth anniversary celebration of the Cuban Revolution. While I was in Cuba, my fellow Latino and Latina and African American students at City College took over the university demanding open admissions and African American and Latino/Latina studies. From the Cuba trip, I returned to Harlem University where the takeover was still in progress.

Within six months, I was working with the Young Lords in *El Barrio*. Joining the Young Lords was a natural progression of the activism I had been involved in and the ideology for liberation that I was developing.

## THE YOUNG LORDS' ACHIEVEMENTS AND CONTRIBUTIONS

### Puerto Rican Pride, Political Militancy

At a significant historical moment, Puerto Rican youth entered a national and worldwide movement that said, in no uncertain terms, the status quo must change. Inspired by liberation struggles worldwide, in the United States, and in Puerto Rico, the Young Lords militantly and proudly stood up for the Puerto Rican community. It was a stand against economic exploitation, social injustice, and colonial dependency that resonated throughout the communities in the United States. It was a call for revolution!

The Young Lords said, "We're tired of injustice, and we're not going to take it lying down." That was the first step toward a very simple, popular appeal, reflected in the garbage offensive. The squalor of the barrio was the most visible and physical manifestation of oppression and neglect. Streets overflowed with garbage because the people of *El Barrio* were not a high priority for New York City sanitation services. When the Young Lords swept the streets and set fire to the garbage throughout the summer of 1969, they pressured the sanitation department to clean up the barrio streets. From East 110th Street, the garbage offensive spread to other blocks in the neighborhood and established the Young Lords as street fighters willing to confront the police and government authority to get results.

On another level, we reclaimed our identity, our heritage, our place in society. Although we were living in the United States, we declared, "We're Puerto Rican and proud." We were now here in mass numbers, and our generation asked, "Where do we go next? Our mothers have worked in sweatshops; our fathers have been dish washers. We want better jobs and doors opened to quality educational opportunities." We were trying to figure out our situation without too many role models.

### SERVE THE PEOPLE: THE BASIC IDEOLOGY

In the fall of 1969, the Young Lords began to work with welfare mothers and expanded activities to provide free breakfast for children and free clothing programs. As the programs grew, they required more space. Looking around *El Barrio*, the Young Lords assumed that the local churches would want to help. Since the First Spanish Methodist Church on 111th Street was not used during the week, the Young Lords approached the pastor requesting space. Not knowing that the reverend was a Cuban refugee, the Young Lords tried to convince him to open the basement facilities for the free breakfast program. He adamantly refused. One Sunday, the Lords went to church to address the congregation directly. When they got up to speak, a signal was given to the police, who were stationed throughout the church. Bedlam broke out as police attacked, beat, and arrested members. The incident gained strong media attention—"Young Puerto Ricans ask Church for Food Program for Children. Thirteen Arrested" read the headlines.

About three weeks later, the Young Lords occupied the church, named it the People's Church, and set up "serve the people" programs. We ran free breakfast and clothing programs, provided health services and community dinners, set up a liberation school, and on New Year's Eve held a revolutionary service to herald the "People's Decade." We proved that programs to serve the barrio community were possible when there was political will. Thousands of people passed through the doors of the People's Church, attracted by the spirit and clarity of purpose. We explained our programs and recruited hundreds of supporters. But the church's pastor continued to deny the use of space. The Central Committee of the YLO negotiated with the police, and at the end of eleven days, the police moved in. They arrested 106 Young Lords and supporters who, with raised fists and singing "*Que Bonita Bandera*," filed out of the church into the waiting police wagons.

Puerto Ricans watched closely. Some were frightened by the militant rhetoric, but the Young Lords won the hearts of the barrio community. The People's Church drew national media attention to the miserable living conditions of the Puerto Rican people in this country. It became a political landmark proclaiming the dissatisfaction of the growing Puerto Rican population in the United States. A new generation of young Latinos and Latinas challenged the system, boldly demanded respect, and popularized the idea of "serve the people."

### THE MEMBERS WERE THE STRENGTH OF THE ORGANIZATION

The militant spirit and commitment to work directly in the community attracted many of the best organizers. Activists who had participated in the Civil Rights, Black liberation and cultural Nationalists movements joined. Others were community organizers with experience fighting for education, jobs, housing, and health issues. Some united from the student protest movements including the Columbia University and City College takeovers.

We were convinced that we could make the world a better place for all of humanity. After all, the richest country in the world had resources to provide food, clothing, housing, and health care for everyone. It was unconscionable to have so few with so much and so many people with so little. We believed that the most disenfranchised segment of our community, the most oppressed—the street people—would play a revolutionary role because they had nothing to lose. For us, "community" included these people, who today are considered part of the "underclass." We identified completely with the most oppressed sectors because we came from those sectors.

The Young Lords had popular appeal because the issues that we were talking about were issues that we had lived. Most members were Puerto Ricans born and/or raised in the United States in working-class and Spanish-speaking homes. The majority had attended U.S. public schools and were very familiar with other U.S. institutions. Young African Americans also joined and made up about 25 percent of the membership. Other Latinos— Cubans, Dominicans, Mexicans, Panamanians, and Colombians—also joined. One member was Japanese-Hawaiian. Young Lords were veterans of the street fights in the 1950s, former prison inmates, recovering heroin addicts and alcoholics. We were college students and high-school youth no longer in school. Young Lords were also young factory and hospital workers and mothers. Some were veterans from Puerto Rico and the United States who had fought in Vietnam. The Young Lords were committed men and women in their late teens and early twenties who had experienced racism and exploitation in the United States. We learned to work together and developed bonds that have lasted a lifetime.

The strength of the Young Lords Organization was in transcending our differences and understanding the power of collective action. The Young Lords raised consciousness through bold public actions that focused on the exploitation suffered by our community. Even those who disagreed with our tactics had to agree the injustices we pointed to were clear. The Lords' Information Ministry skillfully used the mainstream media to get our message out beyond our communities and across the United States. Through the *Pa'lante* newspaper, first published in 1970, and the "Palante" radio program on WBAI, young Latinos and Latinas also discussed the major political events of the day—not just those taking place in the local community but about national and international current events as well.

The organization touched people of conscience in our community. Not many organizations do that. Often people vehemently disagreed with the Young Lords. Today we could identify a dozen organizations that have put out position papers on this or that. Who knows, who cares? The Young Lords engaged a generation, and from that a movement and people were inspired to do other things. That was a tremendous contribution.

### PEOPLE'S HEALTH: A POLITICAL PRIORITY

People's health was a political priority for the Young Lords right from the beginning. "How can children go hungry in the richest country in the world? Children cannot learn in school if they do not have breakfast," we said. The breakfast program was about the nutrition of children, about having a healthy body in order to have a healthy mind. Subsequently, the Young Lords created a comprehensive health program advocating for preventive care and developing innovative programs around drug addition, lead poisoning, tuberculosis, and anemia.

Every Saturday, Young Lords, accompanied by a group of medical students, went knocking door-to-door talking to families and collecting urine samples from their children. The testing exposed the high incidence of lead poisoning in our community. Landlords used cheap lead-based paint for tenement walls, and young children unknowingly put the chipping paint in their mouths and suffered brain damage. Journalists wrote about it, and officials passed legislation requiring the removal of the paint.

Similarly, the Young Lords exposed high levels of tuberculosis when conducting door-to-door testing in the Bronx[3] and *El Barrio*. We tried to get city administrators to bring a tuberculosis detection X-ray truck into our communities, but they refused. One day in June 1970, we liberated the X-ray truck, named it the "Ramón Emeterio Betances[4] Free X-ray Truck," and brought it into East Harlem. The driver and technician stayed in the truck and helped us take X-rays. Over the next three days, we tested hundreds of people.

We believed that institutions in a community have a responsibility to that community. Lincoln Hospital in the South Bronx was a dilapidated building that had been condemned twenty-five years earlier. The community called it the "butcher shop." Although the city kept promising a new facility, they never got to its construction. With the Health Revolutionary Unity Movement (a group of hospital workers, doctors, and community members), the Young Lords rallied for community-worker control of Lincoln and formed the Think Lincoln committee. When a young Puerto Rican woman, Carmen Rodríguez, died from a botched abortion, the Young Lords organized protests that brought attention to the deplorable hospital care for Puerto Rican and African American women.

In July 1970, the Young Lords occupied Lincoln Hospital for one day. The demands to the hospital included immediate funding to build a new hospital; door-to-door preventive health programs in the community; no personnel cutbacks, and child care for workers and patients. A second Lincoln Hospital takeover took place later that year, and fifteen people were arrested. It resulted in the hospital administrators agreeing to the creation of the Lincoln Detox Program, which would serve hundreds of people addicted to heroin. We believed in community control of institutions; and in spite of the personalities and big egos, we understood the importance of collective action. In 1976, the city built the Lincoln Hospital that now stands at 149th Street in the South Bronx.

### FREE PUERTO RICO NOW!

While working in local communities, we raised consciousness about the United States' colonial domination and exploitation of Puerto Rico. Uniting with the Puerto Rican Socialist Party, El Comité, the Puerto Rican Student Union and other groups, we made sure that the colonial status of Puerto Rico got on the agenda of progressive movements across the United States. In 1970, the Young Lords and the Puerto Rican Student Union organized a student conference at Columbia University specifically to create "Free Puerto Rico Now!" committees in every school and college campus. A thousand students from throughout the major northeastern cities attended. As

---

3. A New York City borough north of Manhattan.
4. See p. 228.

a result of that work, we also mobilized ten thousand people in 1970 to march to the United Nations calling for the liberation of Puerto Rico and an end to police brutality.

### PRISONERS' RIGHTS

Also, from the beginning, the Young Lords made a commitment to work with brothers and sisters in prison. We communicated regularly with Latinos in prisons who wrote us describing inhumane living conditions, and we set up the Inmates' Liberation Front. More than once, brothers showed up straight out of jail to the Young Lords office "reporting for duty."

When the Attica rebellion took place in 1971, the inmates specifically requested that the Young Lords participate as one of the prisoners' representatives negotiating with authorities.[5] A former Attica inmate, José "G. I." Paris, and seventeen-year-old Central Committee member Juan "Fí" Ortiz represented the organization in the historic negotiations. With other progressive organizations, the Young Lords organized support demonstrations in communities throughout the city.

Young Lords also participated in organized campaigns to free political prisoners Martin Sostre, Eduardo Pancho Cruz, Carlos Feliciano, the five Nationalist prisoners, and the Black Panthers.

### WOMEN'S LIBERATION

The Young Lords Organization raised consciousness about feminism and women's rights. The initial Central Committee was all-male, including Felípe Luciano as chairman, David Pérez as minister of defense, Juan González as minister of education, Pablo "Yoruba" Guzmán as minister of information, and Juan "Fí" Ortiz as minister of finance. With the consent of the Central Committee, women members organized a caucus to discuss "women's issues" and study the thirteen-point program of the organization.

To us, point thirteen, "We want a socialist society," meant the liberation of both women and men. As we met and talked, our indignation at our second-class status grew. We worked just as hard as the men; we also put our lives on the line, and we wanted our voices as women reflected in the ideology and activities of the organization. The Young Lords would have to concretely address the oppression of Latinas and machismo. We prepared a list of demands that were presented to the Central Committee.

First, we wanted women represented in the top leadership. The Central Committee appointed Denise Oliver as the first woman to the Central Committee in 1969; with her participation, we gained a strong feminist advocate in the leadership. A year later the Central Committee added another woman, Gloria Fontáñez, to the top leadership. We also wanted all other leadership levels and all ministries to include women. The Central Committee responded by appointing women to the national and central staffs and to the defense ministry. Some brothers said, "The women are not as politically developed

---

5. In September 1971, almost half of the prisoners at the Attica Correctional Facility, in Attica, New York, rioted and seized control of the prison. For four days, authorities negotiated with the prisoners over demands for better living conditions. When negotiations failed, state police regained control of the prison. Among the 39 people killed were prisoners, correction officers, and civilian employees.

as the men." Our response was, "Women will develop within struggle. Put women in leadership."

We also demanded that the thirteen-point program and platform of the Young Lords be changed. Point ten read, "Machismo must be revolutionary and not oppressive." We responded that machismo could never be revolutionary. That is like saying, "Let's have revolutionary racism." It is a contradiction in terms. The Central Committee rewrote point ten and moved its position to number five. It said, "We want equality for women. Down with machismo and male chauvinism." This point was the only change that the Young Lords ever made to the program.

The Young Lord women won an important victory. However, we knew that it was not enough to say, "We want equality for women." We were not interested in just a paper victory. Significantly, the Central Committee agreed that machismo or abuses of women would be grounds for discipline, suspension from leadership, or even expulsion from the organization. Most of the leaders were disciplined or suspended for machismo at one time or another.

Accountability was extremely important because many organizations practiced only lip service when it came to feminist ideas. We insisted on child care so that women could attend meetings and be politically involved in the movement. It is still the case, and it most definitely was then, that women are the primary child-care providers.

We insisted that every issue of the *Pa'lante* newspaper reflect the struggles of women and include articles written by women. Women wrote articles about women's oppression and machismo, about workers' struggles in hospitals and factories. We also wrote an initial article exposing the mass sterilization of Puerto Rican women. We reported on a conference in Canada, which we attended to express solidarity with the women of Vietnam.

With these principles in place, more women joined the organization. The internal struggle strengthened the participation of women and gave voice to Latinas across the movement. We considered ourselves feminists but distinct from the White women's liberation movement, which believed that men were the principal enemy. We were critical of that movement for purporting to speak for all women when it represented primarily White, middle-class women. It never successfully addressed the concerns of women of color and poor women. In fact over time, the demand for affirmative action in some industries became synonymous with creating job opportunities for White women but leaving people of color behind.

We organized the Woman's Union, a mass organization for Latinas, working directly around women's issues, such as child-care and health concerns. In *El Barrio*, the union tried to establish a much-needed childcare center, but the project got mired in New York City regulations and bureaucracy. The Women's Union published its own newspaper, *La Luchadora*. It wrote about the three levels of oppression faced by Latinas—as women, as workers, and as Latinas. The paper reached out to all Latinas—homemakers, factory and hospital workers, students, and also women who made a living on the streets as prostitutes. *La Luchadora* also provided information and took positions on such critical health issues as the need for birth control information, the right to an abortion, and the battle against the forced sterilization of women. The Woman's Union held meetings and conducted political education classes and activities with Latinas throughout communities and schools and led the way for other Latina organizations that subsequently developed.

### DEALING WITH INTERNALIZED RACISM

The Young Lords believed that to create a new society, we had to deal with internal contradictions among the people, such as domination based on gender or race. The organization unmasked and exposed the existing racism among Puerto Ricans and Latinos. There was much denial about the existence of racism in Puerto Rico, even in the independence movement. Yet examining the economic and social structure of Puerto Rico or Latin America showed that White, European descendants held the upper positions of power and privilege. Further, they excluded and systematically exploited people of African and indigenous descent.

The Young Lords also challenged the hypocrisy in our culture that accepted the racist ideology inherent in such sayings as "*hay que mejorar la raza*" ("to better the race") and "*pelo bueno, pelo malo*" ("good hair, bad hair"). The organization opposed white supremacy and cultural genocide— the devaluation and destruction of our culture. Instead we celebrated our African ancestry and culture; members wore large Afros, and some assumed African names. We fought "colonized mentality," the psyche of inferiority resulting from U.S. colonial domination of Puerto Ricans and consistently presented these ideas in the *Pa'lante* newspaper and other publications, such as the pamphlet entitled "The Ideology of the Young Lords."

### YOUNG LORDS OUTSIDE NEW YORK

Outside New York, Latinos and Latinas were inspired by the ideology and actions of the Young Lords and sought to connect with the organization. Defense Minister David Pérez was in charge of visiting interested groups. He traveled to other cities, assessed the groups' work, conducted political education classes, and developed relationships. In this way, the organization established solid branches in Newark, Philadelphia, and Bridgeport and developed close political ties with groups in Boston, New Haven, Jersey City, Hoboken, Cleveland, Detroit, and other cities. The branches followed the thirteen-point program, conducted "serve the people" programs, and organized at the community level for Puerto Rican/Latino concerns in their city. They all faced direct police harassment, firebombings, and repression—often more severe than what was experienced in New York.

## SHORTCOMINGS AND WEAKNESSES

### *Youthfulness*

Though the youthfulness of the organization was a strength, it was also a major limitation. Certain mistakes made by the Young Lords were simply the result of lack of life experience and perspective. Also, with initial successes and growing recognition, a youthful arrogance and failure to understand organizational vulnerabilities developed. Accordingly, destructive forces were able to capitalize on this lack of experience and maturity.

The organization's rules of discipline required that members work "twenty-five hours a day, eight days a week." Membership on this basis could not be sustained over the long term. Because of the full-time commitment, people with full-time jobs and/or families could not easily participate. Therefore, the membership base remained primarily youth, students, and the unemployed. Yet, the organization paid little attention to personal development issues of the youth members, such as getting a formal education or job, developing relationships, childbearing, and parenting.

## Centralism and Democracy

A more serious problem had to do with a faulty decision-making process, and this was related to our militarist structure. We followed the theory of "democratic centralism," attempting to balance centralized decision-making with democratic participation by the membership. Centralism was necessary to discuss the strategy and tactics involved in various takeover actions and activities that required maximum security and trust. However, at other times there was little democracy. In practice, the Central Committee made all decisions and set the direction of the organization. The first leaders founded the organization, and they decided who else would join leadership. There were no elections. Emphasis on strict adherence to Central Committee directives frequently stifled member creativity and initiative. Charismatic leadership sustained the organization initially but not over the long term.

At different points in the organization's history and as early as 1970, there were various internal crises expressed as conflict against a particular leader or the struggle for the inclusion of women. These were really part of a broader struggle to democratize the organization, to have members' voices and by extension, the community, really heard in the decision-making process.

Unfortunately, the organization never achieved a balance between democracy, individual freedom, and collective accountability. As the organization evolved from the Young Lords to the Puerto Rican Revolutionary Workers Organization in 1972, there was a deceiving appearance of democracy; but the opposite was true. There was a total lack of democracy. A few individuals decided and established the politics of the organization expecting all members to follow.

When members raised differences of opinion with ideology or tactics or leaders, they were often subjected to name-calling and labeled "opportunists." The Central Committee even falsely accused some members of being police agents. During the Puerto Rican Revolutionary Workers' phase, the ruling group maintained control by accusing everyone who disagreed with them of being agents and collaborators. The accusations lost credibility and allowed real agents to continue to operate in the movement unexposed.

## The Move to Puerto Rico

The Young Lords sought to define the relationship between Puerto Ricans in the United States and Puerto Rico. Initially, the Young Lords promoted the "Divided Nation" theory. This was the position that Puerto Rico was a divided nation with one-third of Puerto Ricans living in the United States and two-thirds living in Puerto Rico. From that position flowed several political consequences. Among them was the decision that the primary struggle of Puerto Ricans in the United States was the liberation of Puerto Rico. In March 1971, the Young Lords launched "*Ofensiva Rompecadenas*" ("Break-the-Chains Offensive") directing resources and attention to Puerto Rico. The U.S. branches were considered the base area necessary to keep the Puerto Rico branches in El Caño and in Aguadilla operating. The military slogan was, "Prepare the base, to defend the front."

As "*Ofensiva Rompecadenas*" unfolded, members both in Puerto Rico and the United States questioned the expansion. In April 1972, all the members in the Aguadilla branch resigned and the Central Committee accused them of factionalism. In the United States, many of us concerned about the decreasing attention to local community organizing activities were at a loss about what to do. When Minister of Information Pablo Guzmán, after returning from a trip to China, wrote a paper outlining how to get the organization back on track, we supported it. The paper argued that the move to Puerto Rico was a mistake and that we had to get back to organizing poor and working Latinos in the United States. It rejected the divided nation theory, concluding that Puerto Ricans in the United States are an "oppressed national minority" and that Puerto Rico is the nation. Several Central Committee members and some national staff members, such as Richie Pérez and myself, supported the paper, and we all agreed to launch a rectification movement. We were excited about the possibility of revitalizing the organization and took advantage of the fact that the Central Committee members who would object were out of town. When they returned to New York, they were furious.

After a critical meeting, the Central Committee adopted the position paper. However, they also agreed to discipline the supporters of the rectification movement for "violating democratic centralism." As a result, some of us were sent to branches outside New York, a move to divide the dissenting group. That is how I got to Philadelphia in 1972.

The move to Puerto Rico was a disaster for the organization and the biggest mistake it ever made. The group lost its relationship to the Puerto Rican community in the United States. Simultaneously, the organization became increasingly dogmatic as members spent most of their days in endless debates about Marxist-Leninist-Maoist philosophy. Isolated from reality of the Puerto Rican/Latino community, the organization became irrelevant.

### Leaving the Organization

I resigned from the Central Committee of the Puerto Rican Revolutionary Workers Organization in 1975. By then it had disintegrated into a small group run by Gloria Fontañez, a self-proclaimed "proletarian leader." She surrounded herself with an unthinking clique who did her bidding, including intimidation and violence against those members who disagreed with her.

I was back in New York after having spent two years in Philadelphia. As part of the branch there, I first worked as a sewing-machine operator in several men's clothing factories. Later I was a hospital worker and organizer. Gloria Rodríguez, a dedicated organizer from New York, was also a leader of the branch. Most of the brothers were from the North Philly streets. Although the branch was in decline by 1972, we organized against the rampant police brutality and racism for which Philly and so many other urban cities are well known. We united with other groups, especially the Black Panther Party and I Wor Kuen, an organization of Chinese-American activists. We produced a newsletter, *Abuso,* and organized students at Temple University and women in the community.

The year in New York before I resigned, there was little community work taking place, no "serve the people" programs, no more door-to-door health testing, no community education classes, no more Women's Union. Most of the early Central Committee members were gone. Membership had dwindled. A few organizers were abandoned in factories and other workplaces. The passion, commitment, and hard work of the Young Lords was replaced with ideological squabbling. I was totally demoralized. The organization I joined five years earlier was dead.

### The Role of Government Repression

COINTELPRO, the FBI's counterintelligence program, was set up to destroy the African American liberation movement, the Black Panther Party, and progressive organizations, such as the Young Lords. Police agents within the organization worked to intensify the differences and natural contradictions that existed among us. Using Nationalism and disagreements about political strategies, they sharpened divisions and created factions. Intimidation tactics and beatings silenced opposition. They replicated this scenario across the United States.

The U.S. government's surveillance and repression against the independence movement started with the invasion of Puerto Rico in 1898. For decades after, the government launched jailings and massacres of proindependence activists, including the Nationalist Party and its leader, Don Pedro Albizu Campos.[6] As the Puerto Rican community grew in the United States, the government extended its repressive activities to activists living in the United States. In 1960, the New York FBI field office circulated a memo to its San Juan and Washington, D.C., offices instructing agents to initiate a counterintelligence program against proindependence activists in New York. The FBI's articulated goals were clear. Create disruption and discord, demoralize activists, and cause defections from the movement. The explicit strategy was to exploit factionalism—a fault that they identified as endemic within proindependence groups. Those marching orders were given to FBI agents who also played that role within the Young Lords. Unfortunately, the full story of police and government involvement within the Puerto Rican movement in the United States has yet to be told and documented.

### PUERTO RICO'S FUTURE

In 1998, the United States marks one hundred years of colonial domination of Puerto Rico. I continue to believe that Puerto Rico should be independent, a free country, and I support the right of the Puerto Rican people to self-determination. Within the United States, we have a special responsibility to continue to struggle for Puerto Rico's independence and for the

6. See p. 445.

freedom of political prisoners who are still in prisons for fighting for a free Puerto Rico.

## Models of Leadership

Not everyone who commits to progressive movements as a young person necessarily sustains commitment for a lifetime. Leadership is determined by practice, by what a person does. Many leaders separate their politics from their personal lives. Yet politics has to translate into one's life in order to truly transform society. "Leaders" who work with youth and who have children must provide for them—financially, emotionally, and with time spent with their children. Leaders have to set an example.

We must reevaluate our notions of leadership. Unfortunately, today's ideas of leadership are still quite patriarchal and elitist. The definition of a leader is still the lone charismatic male heading a hierarchal organization. Collective leadership models to include working people, women, youth, gays, and those who are most marginalized need to be developed.

## MAKING THE DOCUMENTARY

### ¡PALANTE, SIEMPRE PALANTE! THE YOUNG LORDS

In 1988, a group of former Young Lords met. Some of us had not seen each other since the disintegration of the organization in the mid-seventies. As we reflected on our experience, we expressed concerns about what we saw happening with Latino and Latina youth—the internal violence, the deep sense of hopelessness, and the lack of purpose. We talked about how important the study of our history had been to our development and planned various activities to connect with young people. I volunteered to work on a committee to produce a video about the Young Lords experience, and as often happens, I inherited the project.

The initial work consisted of proposal writing. Fund raising was difficult because grant makers were not interested in political projects or Latino/Latina history. Also I was committed to telling the Young Lords' story the way that we experienced it. History books are generally written by those in power, and I knew it was important that we be the protagonists of this story. As I conducted interviews with former members, I looked for consensus about facts, beliefs, activities, and lessons learned. This approach made fund raising more difficult because many funders wanted a traditional "objective" documentary with the expert outsider commentary.

Over a six year period, the project received research and production grants from the New York State Council for the Humanities, the Paul Robeson Fund, and the Aaron Diamond Foundation. In 1996, POV/Point of View, the public television documentary series, granted funds and technical assistance to complete the project and set a broadcast date.

An important funding source was the Latino/Latina youth community. For more than two years, I screened and presented a work-in-progress to student and community groups. Those presentations gave me the opportunity to engage in discussions with Latino/Latina youth across the United States, and the feedback was invaluable to the finished work. Also many young activists joined me to complete the project doing everything from research to original music. Among them Vanessa Roman continues as the distribution coordinator of the documentary. Through these exchanges, we successfully established relationships with the documentary's intended audience.

In the fall of 1996, ¡PALANTE, SIEMPRE PALANTE! The Young Lords was broadcast nationally on public television. That night, 750 people gathered together to watch the broadcast and celebrated the screening with poetry, hip hop and *bomba* music, and *plena* performances at the Borough of Manhattan Community College in New York.

## DIALOGING WITH TODAY'S YOUTH

### History and Identity

Young Latinos and Latinas today face a complicated world of poverty, single-parent homes, segregated and low-quality public schools, drugs, violence, prison, and lack of jobs. They have grown up familiar with AIDS, homelessness, police brutality, and the criminalization of Latino/Latina and African American youth. Subjects of a fast-paced, highly consumer-oriented society, they buy and wear fashion styles that advertise the logos of companies that often do not employ people of color. Increasing numbers of Latino/Latina youth struggle to hold down jobs while attending college, knowing an education is important to a future in a globalized economy. Latino and Latina young people are major consumers of television and film, yet they rarely find positive representations. The Latino/Latina community continues to be marginalized.

A cultural and political renaissance is happening among Latino/Latina youth, and they are engaged in renewed interest and exploration. Young Latinos and Latinas are seeking information about history and the role that Latinos have played in this country. Books are still scarce; videos are almost nonexistent. Youth are also interested in the activism of Latinos in the 1960s and 1970s. The Young Lords experience, especially the early period— very dramatic, militant, defiant—is appealing to young people who are rebellious.

Young Latino/Latinas are struggling with issues of identity, class, and race. Second-, third-, and fourth-generation Puerto Ricans in the United States, many who do not speak Spanish, ask, "Am I Puerto Rican? Am I American?" When one parent is Puerto Rican and the other African American or Dominican or Irish, they ask, "Where do I belong?"

There are questions that interface with class. In the 1960s, we were primarily working class, all of us. Today the children of a middle-class sector ask, "Am I really Puerto Rican? My parents are Puerto Rican. We ate rice and beans, but we were not poor," assuming that to be Puerto Rican or Latino means only to be economically disadvantaged.

Latino and Latina youth are insecure about the future. Will there be jobs? Many are setting up small businesses for economic survival, others because they want creative independence. Health and environmental concerns also raise the level of insecurity about the future.

Color issues persist. A portion of the documentary addresses the struggle against racism within the Latino community, and it resonates deeply with youth who experience racism as a continuing major internal problem. Studying our African ancestry and promoting our culture is very important to young Latinos and Latinas.

Latino/Latina youth are also grappling with what it means to be Latino as the community grows to include people from all Latin America and the Caribbean. Young people struggle with maintaining national identity while simultaneously developing Latino unity. There are bonds of affinity as well as tension and conflict. Clearly, we need varied organizational forms and multiple tactics to build a mass Latino movement for social and economic justice.

Finally, young people ask many questions about what motivated individuals or what motivated a generation to take the actions taken in the 1960s and 1970s. Of course the related question is, how to motivate people to take political action today.

### BUILDING LENS: THE LATINO/LATINA EDUCATION NETWORK SERVICE

¡PALANTE, SIEMPRE PALANTE! The Young Lords led to the creation of LENS—the Latino/Latina Education Network Service, a nonprofit organization that owns and distributes the documentary throughout the United States. It has been enthusiastically received by youth, community organizations, and educational institutions. The reception confirms the importance that young people assign to documenting our history and disseminating our stories.

LENS is dedicated to using the visual medium as a positive way to open dialogues about social and political issues. With ¡PALANTE, SIEMPRE PALANTE! as an educational and outreach tool, LENS works directly with Latino and Latina youth. The focus is to motivate young people to develop their talents for social justice and community empowerment.

### THE STRUGGLE CONTINUES

I am pleased to see the resurgence of activism and organization-building that is underway in our community. We have to use our knowledge and resources to continue to struggle for economic, political, and social justice. We need to organize for universal health care, food, clothing, and shelter for everyone, for quality education and jobs. We have to create conditions to allow the full artistic, spiritual, and intellectual development of all of us. Learning from our past to continue toward the liberation of humanity, our struggle continues.

1996

# PABLO GUZMÁN
b. 1951

## La Vida Pura: A Lord of the Barrio

I had never done anything like this before. Twelve other guys, one woman, myself, and a small handful of people who until moments before had been spectators, were about to set a barricade of garbage on fire. Garbage in the ghetto sense: rusted refrigerators from empty lots, the untowed carcasses of abandoned vehicles, mattresses, furniture, and appliances off the sidewalk as well as the stuff normally found in what few trash cans the city saw fit to place in *El Barrio*. We were taking on the sanitation department, although it wouldn't be long before firefighters and police became involved—not to mention John Lindsay's[1] city hall.

It was a late Sunday afternoon. Somehow, after gathering the material on the corners of Third Avenue and 110th Street, we had managed to pile it across the wide avenue between green lights, catching the uptown traffic before it moved again. Many drivers cursed, a few were just curious. But though Juan tried explaining through a bullhorn, and though Sonia, Voodoo, David, Mauricio, and a couple of others began waving their purple berets to warn the first drivers to slow down, none of them were prepared when this instant barrier suddenly got torched. I was helping to flip a junked car into the blockade when I saw the gasoline being poured. It was ignited and more gasoline was poured as the flames shot upward. A couple of bystanders I didn't know amazed me with how quickly and professionally they stoked the fire.

When the fire trucks arrived, I should not have been surprised that they were met with bottles and bricks. But it was still unsettling. We had been trying for weeks to rally a crowd and could never draw one, though the week before we had some success on the steps of a church at 111th and Lexington Avenue when David unfurled a Puerto Rican flag. Now, however, this blazing protest had done more than get people's attention. We needed to control what was becoming a mob. Through his bullhorn, Juan González shouted: "The firemen are not our enemy! They're not the problem!" But the firefighters had already gone into reverse.

When the cops arrived minutes later, we had wanted to talk, to explain. That we were making a point, and now we'd clean the mess up. All we had been trying to do after sweeping up the streets on previous Sundays was talk with sanitation about once-a-week pickups and nonexistent trash cans, and about how to decently treat people asking for help instead of blowing them off with "You spics get the fuck outta here, this space is off-limits. You gotta problem, talk to the mayor." But the cops came out of their cars swinging. We whipped off our berets and tried melting into the crowd. What really saved us, though, was the people on the rooftops, who instantly started hurling missiles from above. As we had prearranged in case of such an emergency, we ran in twos and threes to a spot outside *El Barrio* in Black Harlem. There, we sized up our first battle. I couldn't believe how my chest was pounding from

1. American politician (1921–2000), mayor of New York City 1966–73.

the run. And the rush. About a dozen "civilian" participants had taken off with us, following the purple berets. This took us by surprise. Still, it was an opportunity. So in a playground we explained what we were about and enlisted our first recruits. It was the summer of 1969, and the first stateside organization of radical young Puerto Ricans was announcing itself—we hoped—as a political force.

### Raíces/Roots

We called ourselves the Young Lords Organization. In June 1969, two small groupings from Spanish Harlem and one from the Lower East Side, consisting overwhelmingly of guys between seventeen and twenty-two, decided to merge. I was in the Sociedad de Albizu Campos, named for the leader of the old Nationalist Party of Puerto Rico. Primarily college students, we had begun meeting three months before. I had just returned from a semester of study in Cuernavaca, Mexico, completing the required "in-the-field" half of my freshman year at the State University at the brand-new Old Westbury. I left as Paul Guzman, a nervous only child of a Puerto Rican–Cuban mother and a Puerto Rican father, both of whom were born "here"—stateside. I came back to the states as Pablo Guzmán. The other East Harlem group consisted mostly of high-school dudes who met in an after-school photo workshop run by Hiram Maristany. The Lower East Side group was a mix of college and high-school aged guys who we later found out had already been penetrated by two or three NYPD Red Squad[2] agents.

   Immediately after the merger, Mickey, David, and I drove in Mickey's Volkswagen Beetle to Chicago. We didn't know at the time about the Brown Berets or La Raza Unida[3] among the Chicanos and the Mexicans of the West and Southwest. But Mauricio and I had read in that week's *Guardian* about what the Chicago Panthers called a "Rainbow Coalition" they had put together. The Panthers had turned (or were trying to turn) two Chicago gangs, the Young Patriots (poor Whites with Appalachian roots) and the Young Lords (Puerto Ricans and Mexicans), away from 'banging[4] and toward something more constructive. If there was already a Latino group in action, we reasoned, why not throw in together? The Lords' chairman, Cha Cha Jiménez, breezily gave us permission to organize as the New York chapter of the YLO. The affiliation with Chicago was where we got our purple berets—even though they claimed to be moving away from street life, the Lords weren't giving up their colors.

   This whole gang thing was fairly jolting. Although to this day people think the New York group was a gang because of that name, we never were, and except for Felipe Luciano (one of the few New Yorkers who had been in a gang himself), we walked lightly around the Chicago boys. Nevertheless, it was a Mexican member of the Chicago Lords, Omar López, who came up with our slogan, *"Tengo Puerto Rico en Mi Corazón"*—"I Have Puerto Rico in My Heart." We loved it, and it soon spread through out Puerto Rican circles. Only years later did we learn that it contained a slight grammatical

---

2. I.e., the New York Police Department's agency for monitoring political activity; known in the 1960s–70s as the Bureau of Special Services (BOSS).

3. A Mexican American political party established in 1970. *Brown Berets*: a Chicano nationalist organization of the late 1960s and the 1970s.
4. I.e., gangbanging, engaging in gang activity.

error, a testimonial to the bad Spanish most of us "spoke." We were truly examples of Ricans raised in the states.

I wasn't yet nineteen. My folks would have freaked if they'd known what their only child—the altar boy from Our Lady of Pity who was supposed to use his Bronx science diploma[5] and college scholarship to bust out of the ghetto—was really doing on his summer vacation. But it didn't come from nowhere—my parents and my grandparents, after all, had first instilled in me a sense that there was far too long a history of injustice in this society. "Only," as my father would say later at my trial, "your mother and I never thought you would actually try to do something about it. Not on such a scale, anyhow."

By the time of that trial, the Young Lords Party—we split from Chicago in April 1970 because we felt they hadn't overcome being a gang—had been targeted by Hoover's FBI as the Latino version of the Panthers and the Weather Underground.[6] Although we never kept a roster, I tallied our New York membership at the end of 1970, and we had grown to more than a thousand, with storefront offices in *El Barrio,* the Lower East Side, and the South Bronx. We had branches in Newark-Hoboken, Bridgeport, Philadelphia, and Puerto Rico, active supporters in Detroit, Boston, Hawaii, in the military and in the prisons. We published a weekly newspaper, *Pa'lante.* We had organized workers, including medical professionals, in the city's hospitals and had a sizeable following on campuses across the country, where we often spoke.

Links with artists and rising entrepreneurs had broken the grip of two White DJs on what was beginning to be called "salsa" music and inspired a cultural boom reflected in songs by musicians like Ray Barretto and Eddie Palmieri[7] with a vision beyond "Hey Mami you look so fine." Unlike some on the New Left who specialized in trying to out-argue each other, we had a community base, leading ten thousand people in October 1970 on a march from Spanish Harlem to the United Nations demanding Puerto Rico's independence. We also had a reputation for taking the best the police threw at us and hitting 'em right back: pitched battles from rooftops and street corners that spanned days and nights were common through 1971. It may be hard for some to understand now, but back then, petitioning for change often meant the cops got turned loose on you.

By our sixth year, it was over. Partly because of destabilization by arrest and government infiltration but mainly because we were young and prone to mistakes—mistakes of leadership, of vulnerability to betrayal, and of the same movement infighting that we had once so despised. But before we dissolved, the Young Lords Party had left its mark:

- A new Lincoln Hospital was built in the South Bronx after we seized a facility that the city had run out of a condemned building for twenty-five years.
- We forced the city to use the lead-poisoning and tuberculosis detection tests gathering dust in some agency's basement after we liberated

5. I.e., from the Bronx High School of Science, a highly regarded public school. The Bronx is a New York City borough north of Manhattan.
6. Weatherman, also known as the Weathermen and the Weather Underground Organization, an American radical-left organization of the late 1960s and early 1970s. *Hoover's FBI*:

From 1924 to 1972, the U.S. Federal Bureau of Investigation was directed by J(ohn) Edgar Hoover (1895–1972).
7. Mainland Puerto Rican pianist and bandleader (b. 1936). *Ray Barretto*: mainland Puerto Rican conga player and bandleader (b. 1929).

them and exposed epidemics in both diseases—which are now making comebacks.

- We pushed the Board of Corrections into reforming prison conditions just before the Attica uprising—which our sixteen-year-old chief of staff, Juan "Fi" Ortiz, witnessed as our representative on the negotiation team.[8]
- We encouraged schools to teach Puerto Rican history. Some, at least, now do.
- We created a climate for the start of bilingual education. Never intended as a parallel track, but as a way of mainstreaming Spanish-dominant kids to English proficiency, it has since been sabotaged by educators who were against it from the beginning.
- We produced the first radio show by a New York–born Latino (myself, over WBAI).
- Ask any Latino professional in Nueva York who advanced in government or the corporate world between, say, 1969 and 1984, and you'll be told they owe part of their opportunity to the sea change in perception that the Young Lords inspired.
- We helped raise the understanding, first among Latinos and then the society at large, that Puerto Ricans possessed a culture on a par with anyone's.

Try to understand what all this meant to a generation of Latinos and others we came in touch with. Even Rudolph Giuliani's special adviser and running mate Herman Badillo,[9] one of our early targets, has said, "A measure of just how significant the Lords were is that in the years since, no group has come along to provide that kind of leadership for our people." Of course, in 1969, when the Lords were coming up, "our people" were barely a step beyond neo-colonialism. There were no "Kiss me, I'm Puerto Rican" buttons. Salsa concerts did not sell out Madison Square Garden. No borough had a Puerto Rican plurality. There was no Hostos Community College.[1] WCBS's Gloria Rojas and J. J. González were the only Latinos reporting local news on TV. White racists had only recently been forced (by sheer numbers, sometimes reinforced by fists) to drop a "tradition" at Orchard Beach[2] that "restricted" Puerto Ricans to two sections. Santana had not yet electrified Tito Puente's music.[3] Al Narvaez was the only Latino with a regular byline at the *Times*. It was not taken for granted that there would soon be a Puerto Rican mayor of New York.[4] That Oscar de la Renta and José Ferrer[5] were Latino was over-

8. See note 5, p. 1435.
9. Island-born Puerto Rican (b. 1929), now a Bronx-based politician, who in 1993, while still a Democrat, ran unsuccessfully for comptroller of New York City on a "fusion" ticket with the Republican mayoral candidate, Rudolph "Rudy" Giuliani (b. 1944), who was elected. Badillo held a series of positions in Giuliani's administration.
1. Eugenio María de Hostos Community College, a community college in the City University of New York system, located in the Bronx. Created in 1968 by the Board of Higher Education in response to demands from the Hispanic/Puerto Rican community for higher-educational service, the college is named after the Puerto Rican writer, educator, and patriot Eugenio María de Hostos (see p. 248).

2. A public beach in the Bronx.
3. The rock music of the Mexican-born American guitarist Carlos Santana (b. 1947) and the band that bears his surname has roots in the Latin jazz of Tito Puente (Ernest Anthony Puente Jr., 1923–2000), mainland Puerto Rican percussionist, composer, and bandleader. Santana has recorded some of Puente's songs.
4. In fact, New York City has not yet had a Puerto Rican mayor.
5. Island-born Puerto Rican Oscar-winning actor and director (José Vicente Ferrer de Otero y Cintrón, 1912–1992). *Oscar de la Renta*: American fashion designer (Oscar Aristides Renta Fiallo, b. 1932), originally from the Dominican Republic; his mother was Dominican, his father Puerto Rican.

looked by almost everyone but themselves. The idea of Goya foods[6] as a "gourmet" product was unimaginable. There was no Puerto Rican legislative caucus in Albany.[7] Freddie Prinze[8] had not yet broken through.

Though there was a small Latino middle class, it was unknown to the "outside" world. Puerto Ricans were still classified on official documents as "other" or "White." Most of us in the states did not know who or what we were. We tended to identify, according to our skin color, with "being White" or "being Black"—and more than a few misguided souls ID'd with "being White" even when Mama Nature had us looking more like Aunt Jemima's baby. Certainly the organization stamped everyone involved. In almost everything I do today, be it compassion and discipline as a father or my fairness as a journalist, I am incorporating what I learned as a Young Lord. They were five and a half of the most exhilarating years of my life. Even the brief stretch in prison. You learn from every experience. Or you die. Some snapshots follow.

### JANE FONDA AND THE PEOPLE'S CHURCH

In September 1969, we had picked up on the Panthers' example of serving free breakfast to ghetto kids to illustrate yet another priority "the system" somehow missed. By November, the demand for the program was booming; we needed space. After scouting several locations, we found a Methodist church under our noses at 111th Street and Lexington Avenue.

What we didn't know at the time was that the church was empty six days a week because most of the congregation had fled to the suburbs, and that the pastor, who had escaped from Castro's Cuba, viewed us as his worst nightmare. But we found out that in December the church was having a "Testimonial Sunday," where anyone could stand and, uh, testify. Felipe, who had been vacillating about whether or not to commit to the Lords, finally gave in to our idea that he'd be the ideal chairman. He testified on behalf of the breakfast program, with eight or so other Lords present. But church officials had alerted the police, who were hiding in a nearby room and sitting in the pews in plain clothes, and when Felipe rose to speak, a melee erupted. At one point, a choir member in robes cracked a brass candelabra over a Lord's head. Everyone was arrested, and Felipe's arm was broken.

In the immortal words of Bugs Bunny, "Of course, you know this means war." We waited a couple of weeks for the heat to die down—and then, the Sunday after Christmas, barricaded the building, renamed it the "People's Church," and quickly set up our programs: free breakfast, health services, clothing drives, cultural events, Puerto Rican history classes. The cops posted hundreds of blue coats and helmets around the area, but by then Spanish Harlem was loyal to the Lords, and the cops couldn't stop the flow of supporters. For ten days, the church became a mecca for Latinas and Latinos who had been looking for just this. That's how the Philly branch got started—the word traveled that far. As Minister of Information, I soon figured out that the takeover was a godsend to the media, coming at the slowest time of the news

---

6. Goya Foods, founded in 1936 in Lower Manhattan, calls itself "the premier source for authentic Latino cuisine." It is well known for its packaged seasonings, canned beans, rice, and so on.

7. The capital of New York State.
8. American actor and comedian (Frederick Karl Pruetzel, 1954–1977), born in New York City to a Puerto Rican mother and a Hungarian father.

year. Coverage was so massive that I decided to change my style—rejecting the bad Panther imitation[9] of the first day of the takeover, I switched to clear glasses instead of shades, a more collegiate sweater, a touch of wit in the give-and-take. Ultimately, Ted Kheel[1] and Herman Badillo, of all people, mediated a settlement that wiped out the symbolic arrests of early January that ended the takeover. The National Council of Churches[2] made other space available. But not before Jane Fonda and her *Klute* costar Donald Sutherland[3] showed up. Still in costume, they were stopped and frisked at the door like everyone else—I got to the door in time to catch Donald Sutherland "in the position," spread-eagled against a wall and getting patted down. It was a goof to see people from the neighborhood nudging each other for stardust ("Look, Jane Fonda!"). Absurd, and sweet. And Fonda surprised us with some on-the-mark questions ("Just what do you stand for? Who are you allied with?"). Later, as that night's activities ended and three hundred or so people were leaving, Fonda and Pia Lindstrom enjoyed a warm reunion ("Jane!" "Pia!") complete with *mucho* air kisses and hugs. Lindstrom, one of Ingrid Bergman's daughters, was a general-assignment reporter for WNBC,[4] and the two obviously knew each other from way back. I loved watching but wasn't ready for Fonda coming over and asking—she was cool though, she made sure it was away from Lindstrom—if I could give Pia an interview. It was the second week of the takeover, and I had frozen media requests not wanting to burn us out. But . . . "Pia!" "Jane!"

### THE MOB COVERS OUR CONTRACT

During the first half of 1970, after repeated demands from folks in *El Barrio*, we tried moving out the drug dealers. Not the small-time, nickel-bag-of-pot guys but the bigger heroin pushers. Frankly, we didn't have the resources to tackle it. But it was the neighborhood's number-one quality-of-life complaint. We couldn't ignore it.

Needless to say, many cops were part of the problem, and working with a few movement documentarians from Newsreel,[5] we surreptitiously shot footage of cops doing business with dealers—shaking hands, putting goods in the trunks of squad cars, transferring the goods to their own cars. We brought the film to WCBS, WNBC, and WABC, and I got a lesson. They all refused to air it. Said they didn't use outside camera crews. When we offered to take their crews to the same spots, they also refused. That's when I first learned TV news bosses could be cardboard cutouts.

We told the dealers that maybe it would be in their interest to take their business elsewhere. They laughed. We started a campaign of getting loud around their favorite spots, blasting their cover with bullhorns, hassling their foot soldiers, leafleting, and generally being a pain. Then somebody in the neighborhood took it upon themselves to escalate matters. A couple of

9. The Black Panthers, cultivating a tough image, often wore black sunglasses, black leather jackets, and black berets.
1. Theodore Woodrow Kheel (b. 1914), New York City lawyer and labor mediator.
2. The National Council of the Churches of Christ in the USA (NCC), an ecumenical fellowship of 35 Christian groups in the United States.
3. Canadian American movie actor (b. 1935). *Jane Fonda*: American movie actress and politi-

cal activist (b. 1937). *Klute*: 1971 thriller.
4. Lindström (b. 1938), an American television anchorperson and arts critic, was born in Sweden to the famous Swedish movie actress Ingrid Bergman (1915–1982) and Dr. Aron Petter Lindström.
5. Originally California Newsreel, a highly political group of documentary filmmakers associated with sociopolitical movements of the late 1960s and early 1970s.

dope dealers slipped off a couple of rooftops, and at least one "business-man" was found early one morning swinging from a lamppost. Lynched. All this could have been because of some turf battle among drug factions, but given the timing, we obviously got the "credit." The good people in the neighborhood patted us on the backs when we walked down the street, and if we tried to demur, we met "knowing" nudges and a conspiratorial wink.

Other interested parties were less amused. A few of us soon got the word that the Mafia had put out a contract: five thousand dollars on four of the five Central Committee members and ten thousand dollars on Felipe. We decided that the best defense would be to go public. At a news conference we called to expose the contract, Chris Borgen of WCBS-TV asked whether we were saying "the Italian mob is after" us. "The Mafia," I answered, "is an equal opportunity employer. They work with every ethnic group in the drug business. The Italians are not necessarily the ones putting out the hit."

The next day, I got feedback from a highly unexpected source: my father. He was at the door of our storefront on Madison between 111th and 112th. My mother had helped out with our clothing drives, but my father never came by, though he had reluctantly given his support. We went for a walk through *El Barrio*. Two of the security detail assigned to the Central Committee in the wake of the contract started walking a bit behind; my father stopped and looked back somewhat scornfully. I waved them off, knowing he wanted privacy. "Those two are supposed to come between you and a mob hit?" he said sarcastically. "Including the woman?" "Hey, she kicks ass. You'd be surprised. There's women throughout the organization." There would have been a woman on the Central Committee if Sonia hadn't left because of family problems. By November, two women would be added to the top leadership. Now, if my old man knew about the Gay Caucus . . .

My father wanted to turn the corner in more ways than one. "About that business you were talking about on TV—I got a call from Pete." Pete and Orlando Moreno were two of my father's brothers. As kids Pete and Orlando had thrown in with the toughest elements in an East Harlem that was then more ethnically mixed. With Pete as the "brains" and Orlando as the "enforcer," they had become associates of one of the Five Families, subcontracting a numbers-and-coke[6] operation in Spanish Harlem and the South Bronx. "Pete says his partners want to have a meeting with your boys to discuss this contract business. I suggest you do it. But I don't want you there."

"What, I'm not afraid—"

"That's the deal." His tone had changed. He cut me off sharply. "We're arranging the sit-down. But I told Pete to tell them that you're not to be there. If Felipe's there, they'll feel like they're talking to a boss. That's very important to these people. But I want you out." He looked straight at me. "Paulie . . . you're all I've got."

I let out a frustrated breath. We started walking again. My father's voice grew softer. "So, this is where you're living now?" "Yeah on 111th." He laughed. "This is what your mother and I left. And now you're back in the tenements. Remember when I would take you here for a visit? You would keep close to my leg, afraid. 'When are we going to go home?' I wanted you to

---

6. Cocaine dealing. *Numbers:* a kind of gambling, in which people bet on combinations of digits, such as regularly published ones.

see how tough it was out here, so you wouldn't come back. And now . . . we stopped again. He took my shoulders. "Paulie, your mother and I worry about you. But we love you. And we're proud of you, *coño*.[7] You're doing what my generation never did. And should have." He gave me a hug. I felt damn good.

The deal that went down was that the Cuban dealers who had put out the contract would withdraw in return for the Lords backing off. This was just as well. In response to our war on heroin, the cops were squeezing us from the other end, sending all complaints about robberies, muggings, and rapes to the Lords. We had to deal with the more serious of these crimes or lose standing in the community, but the burden was too much—the neighborhood needed police even if the worst of them demanded a piece of the action. We passed word through the mob that dealers had to stop hustling near schools and conducting street bazaars, claimed a small victory, and moved from our own Vietnam-style quagmire[8] on to projects we could win.

My father called upon my uncles one other time. Just before I began my prison sentence, the word went out to Mafiosos in every federal prison to look out for "the Marino kid." It was weird, in places like Lewisburg, Atlanta, and the old West Side House of D in Manhattan,[9] to have wise guys seek me out and ask if I needed anything. Weird but admittedly welcome.

### YORUBA MEETS THE SPIRITS

Soon after we opened our first office, the Madison Avenue storefront, in September 1969, a Lord came up to me with a mysterious smile on her face. "Some people up front want to see you. They say they'll only talk to Yoruba." A few of us had taken nicknames, and mine came from the name of a mostly Nigerian tribe. Since I had been getting a sizable number of kook calls, I was leery: "Have they been screened?" But when I parted the curtain, all I saw was eight or ten people in African finery, a few carrying percussion instruments. The tallest man in the group approached me. "Yoruba?" he asked me. I nodded. "*Somos un círculo Santero*.[1] We have come to honor you, to thank you for taking our name, and to give this place a blessing." *Un limpio*. A cleansing. It made sense. When the Yoruba were "brought" to the Americas, they carried with them their ancient religion, Ife, which took different forms on different soil: in Haiti, Vodun; in Brazil, macumba; down South, particularly in the Louisiana bayou country, one worked roots or saw the monkey lady; and in Cuba and Puerto Rico, the followers of the seven powers practiced Santería. Before any of us could really say anything, the chanting and drumming had begun. I was completely caught off guard. There was nothing in Mao's *Red Book*[2] to cover this.

A woman in the group came up to me. In a near whisper, she said, "We knew your grandmother." Talk about a small world. My father's deceased mother was a Santería priestess—and her mother's mother was an African slave. "You have the same aura around you. We can see it." She gave me a warm feeling.

---

7. Literally, cunt; figuratively, man.
8. I.e., an "unwinnable" war like the Vietnam War.
9. I.e., the House of Detention on Manhattan's West Side. *Lewisburg*: Lewisburg Federal Penitentiary, in Lewisburg, Pennsylvania. *Atlanta*: Atlanta Federal Penitentiary, in Atlanta, Georgia.

1. We are a Santero circle (Spanish); i.e., they are practitioners of Santería.
2. *Quotations from Chairman Mao Tse-tung*, better known in the West as *The Little Red Book* (1964–76).

A couple of other Lords came to the office and were taken aback. "*Un limpio*?" one said. "What kind of metaphysical bullshit is this?" Calling something metaphysical was one of the harsher slams we revolutionary materialists could deliver. "Watch your language," I scolded. "Metaphysics had nothing to do with it. This is a legitimate part of our people's culture. And besides, it's got a good rhythm!"

### "WHERE ARE THE DAMN GUNS!"

In early October 1970, two of our members, Bobby Lemus and Julio Roldán, were arrested basically for drinking beer and hanging out with some guys on a stoop one night. This was 1970, remember. The next morning, Julio was found hung in his cell at the "Tombs" (Manhattan House of Detention), the latest in a series of controversial "suicides" in jails and police precincts, often with autopsies returned that did not indicate unassisted death. We had been covering the issue in *Pa'lante*. Julio was a quiet, unassuming little guy of about thirty who joined mainly because he believed in independence. His main contribution was cooking at one of our communal apartments at East Harlem.

Surrounded by five thousand demonstrators, we carried his casket from the González Funeral Home on Madison Avenue and marched to the church on 111th that we had taken over a year before. We took it over again, suddenly, posting armed guards at the entrance and at either side of the casket. The standoff would continue, we said, until conditions in the prisons changed. It was the first time we had ever been connected with weapons. We caught even most of our own organization by surprise. Given the risk involved, and the infiltration we took as a given, we had to. The police, already at war with the "soft" Lindsay administration, were furious, but the mayor did not want a confrontation, and so he negotiated. The cops vented their frustration in other ways.

Very soon after the takeover, the Central Committee received reports from inmates in cells next to Julio indicating that he may have taken his own life. This created a debate that split the leadership. My view was that we should admit to doubts and cut our losses immediately. By this time Felipe was not part of the leadership, and indeed, soon he would be gone altogether. Meanwhile, a hard-liner named Gloria Fontanez, recruited from Gouverneur Hospital in the Lower East Side, had risen rapidly through the ranks. She argued that we should stick with our issue regardless of its actual truth, and the majority went along so as not to undermine the months of work we'd put into the UN march scheduled for October 1970. Because I continued to argue, I was suspended. In five and a half years of hard work, that is the only episode of which I am not proud—that and not doing more to get Gloria tossed out.

The march to the UN came off spectacularly, as it probably would have had we left the church earlier. But when the march was over with, we were still there. Negotiations were ongoing, however, and by God they budged: The Board of Corrections would institute sweeping reforms, and José Torres[3] would get a seat on the board.

---

3. José Torres (1936–2009), aka "Chegui," Puerto Rican professional boxer; light heavyweight champion 1965–67; later a journalist and author. He was a friend and ardent supporter of the Young Lords Party.

So now there was the matter of getting out of the church. Past the ring of cops waiting to bust us for the guns. The deal with the city included an amnesty clause that the city was sure would backfire on us. The cops would be allowed in to make sure there were no guns, and only upon their OK could we walk with no charges against us. Because the police had the place surrounded and had infiltrators inside, they were sure they were going to catch us sneaking guns out. And then, all bets would be off. On the appointed day, the police arrived, and at the front door I had the captain and his escort put up against the wall and frisked. "Sorry, Captain," I said, "but we agreed: no weapons. And that includes you. We don't want to say anybody planted anything, right?" The captain acquiesced, and because this occurred within view of reporters covering the "surrender," the image of the Young Lords telling a police captain to assume the position spread. The PBA (Policemen's Benevolent Association) and indignant editorialists called for his head, on a stake right next to ours.

The cops searched thoroughly and found nothing. To this day, I have had police veterans ask me how we pulled it off. Later that day, I had to break policy and get the story from the Lord in charge, David Pérez. "Never underestimate the power of the people," he said laughing. "The cops stopped everybody they thought looked like a Young Lord a block from the church. 'Where are the damn guns?!' one cop yelled at me. But we've spent the last year and change organizing this whole community, not just a part of it. They've been stopping everyone under thirty-five. We broke the weapons down and hid them under the coats of *las viejitas*, the little old ladies who look like your grandmother. Hey, those little old ladies were down."

#### GERALDO RIVERA SAVES MY ASS

In April 1970, a seven-month effort by Juan González was to culminate in the takeover of Lincoln Hospital. Juan and his team had organized doctors, nurses, other health-care providers, and patients in Manhattan and the Bronx in revealing exposés of just how poorly the system works for poor folks. From lead poisoning and tuberculosis, we had gone on to report the wave of unnecessary hysterectomies performed on Latin women, organized disgruntled rank-and-file workers within 1199,[4] "liberated" an X-ray truck, promoted preventive medicine, and tried to show the links between the pharmaceutical companies, the AMA[5] establishment, hospitals, and insurance outfits that made up the multibillion-dollar health-care industry. But our immediate plan was to take over Lincoln Hospital in the South Bronx and run it with the help of staff who were fed up with rats in the emergency room, antiquated equipment, meager supplies, and chronic personnel shortages.

Lincoln was a mess. For twenty-five years it awaited demolition, and for twenty- five years the city never funded the construction of its replacement. Getting spics a better hospital was the last thing on their agenda. I was from the South Bronx, and growing up I had heard the stories of a stabbing victim crawling two blocks to the catchment zone where the ambulance would take him to Morrisania[6] (which would eventually be shut down as well). Apocryphal, perhaps, but it reflected Lincoln's street rep.

---

4. The National Health Care Workers' Union.  
5. American Medical Association.  

6. Hospital in the South Bronx.

At dawn, we moved in, sneaking through windows and doors opened by doctors and nurses working with us. From inside, we told the guards they could go on a "lo-o-o-ong" break. A huge Puerto Rican flag was flown from the roof. The city was notified, and acute-care patients were transferred, but all other patients were treated by a reenergized staff. A phalanx of cops in riot gear sealed off the area outside, and the standoff was on. We held a news conference in the hospital auditorium, me in an Afro and white lab coat, and made our case against the city. Deputy Mayor Aurelio sent Sid Davidoff and Barry Gottehrer and their Latino "liaison," Arnie Segarra (who went on to become Dinkins's[7] appointment aide). Negotiations began. By late afternoon, we had won: A new Lincoln would be built. And, of course, the participants would receive amnesty.

The cops were not going for this amnesty bullshit. And they could give a fuck that Lindsay was their boss—he was as hated as Dinkins. So a few blocks from the hospital, I was chased by four detectives in an unmarked car. I thought I had given them the slip, but a dog, a goddamn dog, came nipping after me and slowed me down, and I was collared. Just before they got the cuffs on, I pulled my beret from my back pocket and waved it to the onlookers. "Call the Young Lords!" I vainly cried out. Then my wrists got pinched tight, and my head was slammed on the car roof before I was thrown inside.

They gave me a few more shots, but I knew I was in for a serious beating back at the precinct. As spokesmen, Felipe and I were the biggest targets. On two occasions, cops arrested guys they mistook for me, breaking one's leg and another's arm. In Chicago, I spoke at a rally at the start of the Chicago 7 trial,[8] and as I was finishing, word came that the cops were going to bust me. I managed to escape but learned later that once again the cops grabbed a look-alike and beat the shit out of him. I had been shot at by cops and nearly run over by a squad car in both Chicago and New York. And now my charmed existence had come to an end.

At the 40th Precinct, I was put in a "bing," or holding cell. Louie Perez, who had been assigned as my security when he left Lincoln, was already there. This Negro detective put on a show for his White comrades. They had taken Louie's nunchakus, the "karate sticks" many Lords used. "So, this is what you use against cops, huh?" the lackey said. "Well, let's see how it stands up against this"—and he patted one of the three guns he was visibly packing. His boys laughed, and I knew we were goners. "This is America, cocksucker." He was leaning in close through the bars. His hand was at the lock. "And you oughta be taught what happens to punks who want to mess it up for the rest of us." He was going for the key. Louie and I braced ourselves.

Suddenly, there was a commotion. Bustling sounds from below. Shouting, growing louder. Gerry Rivera materialized, with what seemed like half the precinct coming up the stairs behind him, Keystone Kops–style.[9] He dodged a cop, leaped over a railing, dodged another, and got to our cell. "You OK?"

7. David Norman Dinkins (b. 1927), African American politician, mayor of New York City 1990–93. *Deputy Mayor Aurelio*: Richard Aurelio served in this position during the Lindsay administration; Sidney Davidoff was the mayor's administrative assistant, and Barry Gottehrer was a special assistant to the mayor.
8. In September 1969, seven defendants—known as the Chicago Seven or the Conspiracy Seven—went on trial for conspiracy, inciting to riot, and other charges related to protests at the 1968 Democratic National Convention, in Chicago, Illinois.
9. I.e., like this brigade of bumbling police officers who were the main characters in a series of silent movies (1912–17).

he asked. I was ready to kiss his feet. "Yeah, yeah," I panted. "You just made it. Behind you, watch out!" He turned just before the first cop could grab him. "I'malawyerthesearemyclientsyoutouchanyoneofusI'lltakeallyourbadges." Cops froze in mid air.

From an office, a supervisor emerged looking down at some paper. "Jesus! I just got off the phone with headquarters. Do we have some Young Lord here for the hospital thing, they're getting all kinds of calls from the media—" He finally looked up and took the scene in. "What the fuck is all this?" Gerry wadded through fifty or so cops and glibly explained. I had to laugh; he was a piece of work.

Gerry burst into our collective lives soon after we had opened the first office, interrupting a meeting with our lawyers to charge that we had no Latino representation, like, for instance, him, even though one of our attorneys was a Puerto Rican he knew personally. Appalled though we were, we admired his chutzpah. But when he tried to join we drew the line. "This is an adventure for you, bro," he was told. "You're not really into the ideology." Still, he had a lot of heart, and he loved the street battles—and the press conferences. Eventually he took advantage of a scholarship to the Columbia School of Journalism that I had turned down because it would have meant leaving the Lords. We wished him well. Once out of Columbia, he got a gig with WABC-TV and hit the ground running. And that's how the Young Lords Party unleashed Geraldo Rivera[1] on an unsuspecting universe.

### When the Music's Over

The Young Lords Party began a couple of years after the Panthers, and while they were an inspiration, we also learned from their negative examples—one of which was, avoid going to jail because of stupid shit. So we never got wrapped up in legal battles that consumed precious resources, and most of our leadership remained intact—until my Selective Service case came up. When I had to report to the draft board, I did it with a flourish, in full regalia—beret festooned with various movement buttons, safari field jacket, combat boots, shades—accompanied by one male and one female Lord. Tore up my draft card and gave the requisite speech. The whole thing was silly, and the Central Committee would never have approved my Abbie Hoffman–style[2] gesture. But a year later, when the government moved to prosecute, it got serious.

While I was out on a personal recognizance bond for my pending case, the Central Committee allowed me one last "present." I would be the group's representative at a celebration of the Chinese Revolution. In the People's Republic of China. This meant slipping out of the country when I wasn't even supposed to be in Brooklyn. I arrived in Shanghai in late August 1971 and left in early November. Traveling through China's cities was eye-popping, just a wondrous oversaturation in a completely different culture . . . and it also strengthened me for one last shot, when I returned, at returning the organization to its community base. By the time I went to China, the

1. American lawyer, journalist, and former television talk-show host (b. 1943); his father was Puerto Rican, his mother Jewish.
2. I.e., like the sometimes outrageously theatrical

Abbot Howard "Abbie" Hoffman (1936–1989), American social and political activist; Hoffman was one of the Chicago Seven.

group that had been so welcomed by so many Latinos had taken a narrow, "movement" path of dogmatic "correctness." We were on the verge of acting like . . . a gang—of beating down anyone in our ranks who disagreed. This change was mostly because of Gloria and the clique around her—and those of us they were able to browbeat. Gloria "exiled" Juan González to Philadelphia, where I would be a year later.

While the organization was rightly grappling with how to advance toward an older, working-class base (and in the process maturing), Gloria & Co.'s definition of "working class" became, in practice, paradoxically elitist. When I came back from China, I was alarmed by the number of resignations. I had talked with many who had left and kept hearing the same thing: "Gloria . . . there's no democracy . . . too much bullshit . . . we've gotten away from the people." Juan "Fí" Ortíz and I tried to lead an internal campaign to open things up again without forcing a split. We saw what the fed-encouraged Huey Newton–Eldridge Cleaver break[3] had done to the Panthers. The rank and file rallied to our proposals. But Gloria & Co. called our hand. Fí said, "In this case, bro, a split would be progressive. Fuck 'em." And even though we would have lost in the Central Committee, an overwhelming majority of Lords would have left with us. Many more would have returned. But I was haunted by the corpses of factionalism that littered the Left. Reluctantly, miserably, I abdicated my leadership of the internal democratic campaign and accepted yet another suspension for insubordination. Fí became the latest veteran to resign. Soon Juan would be demoted. And in February 1972, I was "banished" to Philadelphia.

### "How Many Ping-Pong Balls Can You Put Up Your Ass?"

I was charged with two counts of Selective Service violation. We decided to fight, to see whether we could set a precedent with a hung jury, which had never happened in a draft case. I was opposed to the Vietnam War and to the double system of justice based upon race, class, and sex in this country. But I was no draft "dodger"; I didn't go to Canada or accept China's invitation of asylum. Apparently, the government began to wonder about its chances. As the trial approached, they began offering deals: Just go to the induction center at Whitehall,[4] we'll see you flunk the physical. No? How's this: We'll accept conscientious objector status. (Sorry. That should be reserved for genuine pacifists and others. As I said at the trial from the witness stand, I wasn't opposed to war. I would have fought in World War II. I was opposed to *this* war.) After a three-day trial, the jury deliberated for about forty minutes. When a juror cried during my testimony, I thought we had the holdout we needed. But the judge's instructions echoed the prosecutor's summation: "Did Mr. Guzmán report for induction or not?" Guilty.

Appeals took about another year. Then on May 30, 1973, I was brought in for sentencing. Similar defendants were getting six months or community service. But it was payback time. "Two years. Concurrent. Be grateful, young man. It could have been more."

3. In 1971, the Black Panther cofounder and leader Huey Percy Newton (1942–1989) expelled Cleaver (1935–1998), a novelist and one of the Party's leaders, from the group.
4. On Whitehall Street, in Manhattan.

Nevertheless, I was lucky. Going in, my biggest fear was getting raped—and somehow, not showing that my biggest fear was getting raped. But prison was a wild pecking order. When you first come in, you get classified by other prisoners according to what got you busted. When the word got out that I was in for being a Young Lord, most guys steered clear. Some, out of respect for what groups like the Lords and Panthers represented. But many others because they were sure I was goddamn crazy.

Tallahassee[5] was somewhere between maximum and minimum security. After six months in prison, where I observed my twenty-third birthday, my body was in the best shape it would ever be. There was nothing else to do. And, as with most places, you make friends. One day, one of the Cubans from Miami came up to me. "Hey man, I hear you're getting a visit this week. That's great man, me too. *Mira*—she's bringing me some stuff. *Perico. Me entiendes?*"[6] Coke. The antenna went up. He went on, lowering his voice like we were going to be in on something together. "I'm bringing it in to sell, *entiendes*, but I figure there'll be enough to give the guys a taste. You know, *para nosotros*."[7] He took my silence as a sign to continue. "The stuff's gonna be wrapped in bags. Now how many Ping-Pong balls can you get up your ass?"

"Wha—*QUE FUE?!*"[8]

"I figure I can do six—"

"Whoa, *'perate*,[9] back up. I'm out."

"What? How can you be like that, man?"

"It's easy. Forget it. Ain't nothin' goin' up back there, you dig it?"

"Come on man, it's for the brothers!"

"Yo, fuck the brothers."

Word got around fast. Cats were coming up to me on the chow line. One guy just materialized next to me with a downcast look: "Come on, man. I'd do it for you." "*Pa'carajo*."[1] Another guy: "Yo, home, I thought you was down."

Practically every Latin shut me out of the crowd—not a good deal long term. Don't get this wrong: Back then, I got high. But this was stupid. And the perpetrator of this BS was one of the more unstable guys in a population not noted for Cool Hand Lukes.[2]

Visiting day came. Also in the big loungelike room was a lower-level Colombo associate from Queens[3] who made the trip down South with me. Call him Vinnie.

Vinnie sashayed over to where I was sitting. He thought this was a cool walk. He pointed over to the Ping-Pong champion.

"What the fuck is he doin'?"

"I know this is his, like, fifth trip to the bathroom."

"Guy's fuckin' obvious. You did the right thing."

"Yeah, but now, only two of the Latinos will talk to me."

"Fuck 'em."

He cruised back to his spot. Once the visitors had gone, they lined us up to reenter. And then it was announced. "Strip search!" The Ping-Pong champ

5. A Federal correction institution in Tallahassee, Florida.
6. *Me entiendes*: Understand? *Perico*: Keep it quiet; don't talk like a parakeet. *Mira*: Look.
7. For us.
8. What did you say?
9. Short for *espérate*, or hold it.

1. Short for *vete pal' carajo*, or go to hell.
2. A reference to the Paul Newman character in the movie *Cool Hand Luke* (1967).
3. A New York City borough east of Manhattan. *Colombo*: a famous New York City crime family; one of the "Five Families" of the Mafia, mentioned above.

was dead. With what he had up his butt, he was going to be firing bullets when they bent him over. Ping-Pong was coming up soon. He was sweating.

I whispered to Vinnie, "Come on, let's help this schmuck out."

"How?"

"We start a fight."

"Are you serious?"

And before I could answer, Vinnie shouted, "Are you serious!" and shoved me back several feet. "Damn right I'm serious!" And I knocked him back. We "grappled," knocking over a lamp and moving some furniture, before the guards came and grabbed us, whistling everyone else back into general population. Vinnie and I were questioned and held for about an hour and then released to a warm welcome. Ping-Pong was at the front of a crowd of Latinos and New Yorkers. "My man!" Guys cheered. "You too!" he told Vinnie. "You all right with the Latin brothers, amigo."

"Fuck that," Vinnie said. "Where's the blow?"

## Punto / *But Not the End*

I was paroled on Valentine's Day 1974, after nine months. You need a job to qualify for parole. My old man used his garment-center contacts to get me into the warehouse of a Philadelphia dye factory. Had to join the Teamsters.[4] With overtime, it was the most money I had ever made. I was still with what was now called the Puerto Rican Revolutionary Workers Organization, heading its Philadelphia branch. Before my sentence, my suspension had been lifted, and I was a member of Gloria's "expanded" (read "packed") Central Committee. It was obvious that the organization was spinning its wheels. Not even a rectification movement would turn things around; there wasn't much left.

In September, Gloria ordered me to move back to New York. The only job I could get on short notice was as an assistant dishwasher at a day-care center in the Bronx, and I lost it within a month. Some serious bills were due, and I decided to bite the bullet and go for some "nonproletarian" labor. I sold an article to the *Voice*. By late December, there was no getting around it: We weren't the Young Lords anymore. I still wanted to organize but not with this crowd. I left. A week or so later, I returned home from another wasted day trying to find work—whenever I came close, the FBI would scare employers off. Somebody was already inside my apartment, a cop who had once been assigned to surveil us. "They think your leaving is a front," he told me. "That you're really heading up the underground wing. That you're going to run the FALN."[5] I threw my keys on a table and laughed as I fell into a chair. Most Lords figured the FALN was either a COINTELPRO operation or close to it, because their targets were purely terroristic, organizing no one and scaring everybody; the month before, they'd set off a bomb at Fraunces Tavern.[6] I think I convinced the cop I had genuinely left the organization.

---

4. International Brotherhood of Teamsters (IBT), a union.

5. Fuerzas Armadas de Liberación Nacional (Armed Forces of National Liberation, FALN), a Puerto Rican clandestine paramilitary group, considered a terrorist organization by the FBI. In fighting for Puerto Rican independence, the FALN members who called themselves Los Macheteros (the Machete Wielders) set off bombs in the United States between 1974 and 1983; in 1983, they masterminded one of the largest bank robberies in U.S. history.

6. A Revolutionary War–era restaurant (now also museum) in Lower Manhattan.

A few days later, there was a knock on the door. The voice on the other side was a sister from the organization who I thought was cool. When I opened the door, two of my former buddies sprung on me, one with a gun to my head. The young woman ran down the stairs crying. "I'm sorry, Yoruba." They were all sorry. Said they were ordered by Gloria to get some books I had "stolen." "This is bullshit," I told them. "She's trying to play us against each other." It was like talking to zombies. But I got off light. By the spring of 1975, there were people being held and tortured. In a weird reunion, many of the original members got together at the new Lincoln hospital and sent Gloria & Co. a message that we'd put her lights out if the violence persisted. It was our last act. But more important, it got some of us talking to each other again. We had become quite estranged. Gloria had taken an organization that had captured the imagination of a large chunk of Latin New York with more than one thousand members and reduced it to about fifteen dangerous wackos.

So: Was it worth it?

Yeah. We were kids who succeeded wildly, raising ideas that have lasted. More college groups are asking us to speak about the Lords than ever. Sure, I wish we had overcome the dogmatic tendency within us that Gloria fed off. I wish I had helped Fí split the organization. It didn't happen. Many of us went into a funk about how it all ended. We didn't even speak to each other for a long time. But for too long we let that cloud over all the good we accomplished.

The main reason why so many kids, and quite a few adults, are asking about the Lords today is because they took a look around the current landscape. They see nearly three times as many Latinos in the New York area and even more of a middle class than there was in the Lords heyday. Yet they see that as a group we have not advanced. Politically. Economically. In education, housing, business, ownership, family stability, prison rate, mortality rate—by any yardstick we are getting clobbered. There is no independent Latino voice setting our agenda or holding the government, media, or corporate structure accountable. So what people are asking is, what would today's Lords do? Because they know that one way or another they'd be kicking ass. I have faith that this question will be answered. After all, when we started in 1969, there had been no precedent. Only a raging need. So— *Que viva*[7] *los* Young Lords of tomorrow.

1995

7. Long live.

# Into the Mainstream:
# 1980–Present

In the United States, the civil rights era generally led Anglos to display energetic good will toward both blacks and ethnic minorities. Still, the era's ideological motifs ran along racial lines that were primarily white and black. Efforts to end segregation for African Americans affected Latinos, Asians, and Native Americans—but tenuously and without providing the historical contexts in which to understand these groups' particular situations. For Latinos, the racism, xenophobia, and anti-Hispanism widely evident in the United States since the mid-nineteenth century remained ingrained. The upheaval of the late 1960s and the 1970s—connected with, for example, *El Movimiento*, the Brown Berets, and the Puerto Rican Young Lords— received sporadic media attention. Changes in Latino life were slow in coming.

Thus it came as a surprise when in 1978 *Time* magazine declared the 1980s "the decade of Hispanics." (As stated in the general introduction, "The Search for Wholeness," the term *Hispanic* was adopted by the U.S. government when, on September 12, 1969, President Richard M. Nixon signed into law the celebration of a Hispanic Heritage Week. The term was then consistently used in government documents as an umbrella category for Spanish-speakers, regardless of their ethnic and national backgrounds.) Other media outlets quickly followed suit, publishing an assortment of reports on different aspects of the Latino minority, including its literature. This journalistic attention—the media's search for "the new Americans"—came in response to the demographic growth of Latinos in the United States. According to the U.S. Census Bureau, in 1980 there were approximately 14,600,000 Latinos in the country. That number increased by 53 percent in the 1980s to some 22,300,000 by 1990, and the growth continued unabated in the 1990s. By the early years of the twenty-first century, Latinos had become the largest ethnic group in the country, surpassing African Americans. In 2003, the Census Bureau predicted that by 2050 one of every four U.S. citizens would have a Latino ancestor. By 2006, the Latino population had reached 43,168,000. By 2009, it had surpassed 45 million, and more people of Puerto Rican descent lived on the mainland than in Puerto Rico!

While Latinos had lived on the North American continent since the Spanish colonial period, and they had been part of the United States since the nation's founding, U.S. society transformed during the 1980s, when fresh attention was focused on the nation's ethnic and racial diversity. Latinos were at the forefront of that multicultural awakening. Consequently, the media's focus became immigration. Unlike the waves of newcomers who had arrived at the end of the nineteenth century and the first half of the twentieth and whose place of origin was Europe, the majority of arrivals in the 1980s came from the so-called Third World, including Latin America and the Caribbean. According to the Census Bureau, in this decade the increase in the number of Latinos born outside the United States was the largest in any period up to that time.

The arrival of these numerous immigrants increased the demographic visibility of Latinos and thus increased their power within U.S. society. The newfound power of the growing Latino minority, however, highlighted the national, ethnic, racial, and social differences among the many groups lumped under this collective label. Obvious generational differences existed between second- and third-generation Latinos and, to an even greater extent, between the newly arrived Latinos and those with deeper roots in the land. Factions sometimes questioned both each other's patriotism toward the United States and other expressions of loyalty. Individual national groups' positions about immigration, U.S. foreign policy, domestic priorities, and political affiliations were far from homogenous. In other words, as Latinos became more visible, the idiosyncrasies of and differences among Mexicans, Puerto Ricans, Cubans, and other national groups provoked waves of discontent. It was indicative of the differences in outlooks among Latinos that the majority of foreign-born Latinos, and a substantial number of those born in the United States (on the mainland, in the case of Puerto Ricans), identified themselves by nationality rather than ethnicity. For the most part, they called themselves Colombians, Puerto Ricans, Mexicans, and so on, rather than Latinos. To understand the Latino minority, markers of nationality were often at least as important as markers of ethnicity—and thus the term *Latino* was regarded by some as more of a statistical convenience than a reality. Nonetheless, although it does not stand for a unified sense of identity, the panethnic label *Latino* serves important cultural and political functions within the United States.

The increase in the number of Latino immigrants entering the United States came as a consequence of global events. The Cold War (from the end of World War II until 1991) created a series of confrontations between the United States and the U.S.S.R.: over the rise of Fidel Castro's socialist government, after the successful 1959 Cuban Revolution; over the Nicaraguan Revolution and the subsequent, U.S.-funded war of the Contras against the Sandinista socialist regime (1979–90); and so on. In Cuba, political repression and a feeling of asphyxia culminated in 1980 in the storming of the Peruvian Embassy in Havana by thousands of people wanting exit visas. The consequent boatlift at the port in Mariel, northern Cuba, orchestrated by the Castro regime under pressure from the administration of U.S. president Jimmy Carter, allowed many dissidents to leave the island and enter the United States. (In the same massive immigration, Castro's government deliberately included hundreds of inmates from Cuba's jails.) In the 1980s and 1990s, civil wars and military repression in Guatemala and El Salvador forced many Central Americans to seek refuge in the United States, Mexico, and Canada. The resulting influx of refugees from affected counties redrew the ethnic, economic, and political map of major cities such as Los Angeles, Dallas, and Houston. Moreover, the 1980s is known in Latin America as *la década perdida* (the lost decade), because of the major foreign debt crisis and rampant inflation rates that afflicted most nations in the region, exacerbating poverty among their respective populations and increasing Latino immigration to the United States and other countries.

Over the decades, *El español* gradually became the second language of the United States, ubiquitous in streets, schools, restaurants, and so on. The endurance of this immigrant tongue puzzled linguists and cultural commentators. When other languages had entered the United States, they largely disappeared among acculturated schoolchildren, but Spanish refused to vanish among the Latino youth. Instead, it acquired immense force, partly thanks to television, radio, and other media, but also because of the continuous influx of first-generation Latino immigrants. For a time, Spanish was used as a vehicle of classroom instruction, as Bilingual Education programs started in Florida in the 1960s and, with federal support, spread from coast to coast. As the country recognized its linguistic diversity, however, conservative forces pointed to the perseverance of Spanish as proof that Latinos were not entering the melting pot. Some Latinos sensed that Spanish was too easily accessible and was an obstacle on the road to cultural immersion, and thus that bilingualism was not the best course to integration into U.S. society. Presenting the position of some non-Latinos, the liberal American historian Arthur Schlesinger argued that promoting bilingualism and multiculturalism would contribute to, as the title of his 1992 book put it, *The Disuniting of America*.

In the 1990s, the various national groups within the Latino minority articulated a message of unity grounded in diversity. Rather than viewing themselves as disparate entities with little in common, Mexicans, Cubans, Puerto Ricans, and other national groups sought to gain social, political, and economic power by stressing the elements they shared: a common language albeit with variants, a vibrant and diverse popular culture with music at the forefront, and a similar colonial heritage. The minority's strength began to materialize at the local, state, and federal levels, with an increasing number of Latino politicians being elected for office in parts of the country with growing Latino populations, among them California, Texas, New Mexico, Arizona, Illinois, New York, Connecticut, and Florida. Likewise, power became clear in the consumer index, as Latinos became a favorite target of advertising agencies representing major corporations. The Latino "taste" became desirable.

During the years of the Reagan administration (1981–89), young Latinos tended to view the militants of the previous generation as role models but not to adopt their radical rhetoric. The new strategy was not to revolt and promote secession, as some revolutionary figures in the 1960s and 1970s had done, but rather to work through existing Latino organizations, increase lobbying efforts, and seek consensus on issues. As new laws granted both civil rights and equal opportunity, activism decreased noticeably. More Latinos became lawyers, doctors, entrepreneurs, and so on, as federal programs such as Affirmative Action made it possible for ethnic students from lower-income families to attend colleges and universities. The minority was joining the middle class in larger numbers. These advances helped foster an era of multiculturalism.

## A Literary Renaissance

Despite the general curiosity aroused by *Time* magazine's declaration, mainstream publishing houses released few Latino titles in "the decade of Hispanics." Several small, ethnically oriented publishers, such as Arte Público Press and Bilingual Review Press, had started in the 1970s, often with grants from government agencies. In the 1980s, these presses sought to satisfy the small but palpable demand for the novels, stories, poems, and dramas of Latinos.

In the late 1980s and early 1990s, authors such as Oscar Hijuelos and Julia Alvarez signed contracts with major publishers. Consequently, the mainstream media paid increasing attention to Latino writers. Hijuelos's novel *The Mambo Kings Play Songs of Love*, about two Cuban brothers in the New York music scene of the 1950s who achieve momentary fame when they appear in an episode of the real-life television sitcom *I Love Lucy*, was published by Farrar, Straus and Giroux in 1989 and was awarded the Pulitzer Prize for that year. Other publishers began seeking manuscripts treating Latino lives in the United States. Along with this drive, now known as the Latino literary renaissance, came the recognition that Spanish was capable of turning a profit as a literary language in the United States. Some New York publishers, big and small, released particular books simultaneously in English and Spanish.

Translation became a sticky issue, though. Manuscripts were not always sent to professional translators and often were improperly rendered. More important than grammar problems were the unsynchronized connections with authors' national backgrounds. For instance, Junot Díaz's *Drown* (1996), a collection of English-language short stories about Dominican Americans in New Jersey, was translated awkwardly into Spanish by an Iberian.

As discussed in the "Upheaval" introduction, *el "boom" literario latino-americano* had established a readership eager to connect with Hispanic civilization. Among that readership were Latino writers inspired by Julio Cortázar, Gabriel García Márquez, Mario Vargas Llosa, and others from south of the border. The Latinos felt a closer kinship, however, with other ethnic authors in the United States. For instance, Julia Alvarez, in a 1998 conversation published at the Web site *Salon*, described the way she recognized her responsibility as a storyteller:

> I come from a culture in which women were not encouraged to speak up. [The Chinese American writer] Maxine Hong Kingston was helpful to me. She begins *The Woman Warrior* [a groundbreaking 1975 combination of memoir, fiction, and nonfiction] by saying: "My mother told me never, ever to repeat this story." That was such an eye-opener, because that's the way with many of my stories. No "once upon a time" or any of those catch phrases. . . . Here I am—a woman with a voice in another language, one that we're supposed to keep things from, the gringos and the Americans. . . . I'm saying things about women and women's experience which are not nice.

A favorite genre within the Latino literary renaissance was the coming-of-age story, delivered either as a straightforward memoir or as thinly disguised autobiographical fiction. Richard Rodriguez, Edward Rivera, Esmeralda Santiago, and, later, Denise Chávez, Ariel Dorfman, Gustavo Pérez Firmat, and Ilan Stavans would use the genre to reflect on the trials and tribulations of Latino life in the United States. Autobiographical narratives had been an essential component of the Latino literary canon since the nineteenth century; in the twentieth century, authors such as Bernardo Vega, Jovita González de Mireles, Ernesto Galarza, Piri Thomas, John Rechy, and Oscar "Zeta" Acosta opened windows into their personal affairs, writing about immigration, sexism, drug addiction, and political activism. In the 1990s, U.S. culture's growing obsession with self-revelations gave the genre a boost, and works such as Rodriguez's *Hunger of Memory: The Education of Richard Rodriguez* (1982) and Santiago's *When I Was Puerto Rican* (1993) were reprinted frequently.

An important element of the Latino literary renaissance was the consistent emergence of women writers. Julia Alvarez, Denise Chávez, Ana Castillo, and Sandra Cisneros (the first three of whom are included in this anthology) came to be known as *Las Girlfriends*, as a result of a media-manufactured drive to promote their works as a kind of movement. Alma Luz Villanueva, Judith Ortiz Cofer, Helena María Viramontes, and Cristina García also drew attention. From the Spanish colonial period on, women writers—María Amparo Ruiz de Burton, Josefina Niggli, and Julia de Burgos being prime among them—were minorities within the predominantly male Latino literary tradition. One oft-cited reason is the machismo inherent in many Latino cultures, where women are considered second-class citizens, sexual objects rather than free agents. Grounded in the feminist ideologies of previous decades (as formulated by writers and activists such as Simone de Beauvoir, Betty Friedan, and Gloria Steinem), the new voices of the 1980s challenged the "macho" perspective, often by reinterpreting stereotypical female spaces, including the kitchen, the closet, and the bedroom. Latina thinkers and writers such as Gloria Anzaldúa and Cherríe Moraga, in essays and anthologies that meditated on the roles women play and have played in Latino history, asserted their positions at the forefront of change within the minority and in the nation as a whole.

Another important feature of the renaissance was a new openness in addressing gay and lesbian themes through literature. Lesbian authors such as Anzaldúa and Moraga and gay ones such as Arturo Islas (who appears in the "Upheaval" section of this anthology) and Jaime Manrique tackled Latino homosexuality, a previously taboo topic, in stylistically accomplished books. Still, the controversies engendered by these discussions signaled that the struggles for free expression would continue.

# Spanglish

Throughout its history in the United States, the Spanish language was in constant flux, adapting to new conditions. In the 1980s and 1990s, the mixing of Spanish and English into Spanglish became an increasingly important device in the Latino writer's arsenal of expressive resources. The use of Spanglish was even more widespread in media such as television, radio, and music.

The roots of Spanglish extend back to the colonization period, when Iberian civilization left its imprint in the South and the Southwest, as is indicated by the countless place names of Spanish origin: Florida, Arizona, Montana, San Diego, and so on. Up until the signing of the Treaty of Guadalupe Hidalgo, in 1848, in these regions Spanish was the tongue of business and education. As such, it became mixed with aboriginal languages. With the subsequent arrival of Anglos, Spanish began to be hybridized with English. At the end of the nineteenth century, this process was reinforced by the Spanish-American War, when American citizens arrived in the Caribbean Basin and brought English. (The British had brought the language to Cuba when they occupied Havana in 1762.)

Spanglish has since existed in various parts of the Spanish-speaking world, from Madrid to the Argentine Pampas, but it has thrived most among Latinos in the United States in the last decades of the twentieth century. The mixture—a natural linguistic process—has occurred in rural areas, but it has taken off most rapidly and pervasively in the major urban centers, such as Los Angeles, San Antonio, Houston, Chicago, Miami, and New York. Instead of one single Spanglish, there are varieties: Chicano, Cuban, Puerto Rican, Dominican, and so on. Usage varies from one place to another and from generation to generation, and it is also influenced by social status and levels of education. A Mexican immigrant in El Paso, Texas, is likely to use elements that distinguish her from a second-generation Colombian American in Victory Gardens, New Jersey.

In general, Spanglish speakers employ three strategies: code switching, whereby elements of Spanish and of English alternate within the same sentence; simultaneous translation; and the coining of new terms, ones that do not appear in either the *Oxford English Dictionary* or the *Diccionario de la Lengua Española*, such as *wáchale* (watch out) and *rufo* (roof). Like the myriad other "border" languages around the globe, among them *franglais* (French and English), *portuñol* (Spanish and Portuguese), and *hibriya* (Hebrew and Arabic), Spanglish is controversial, due to the contact between a dominant tongue and a minority one. Some have perceived Spanglish as a half-cooked verbal effort spoken by the lazy or uneducated, an utterance fitting neither here nor there. Others have applauded the inventiveness behind it. Opponents of Spanglish have argued that it proves Latinos have not integrated into U.S. culture as previous immigrants did. Those more sympathetic to it have countered that since Latinos were already the largest minority in the country and their immigration pattern differed from those of previous immigrant groups, acculturation could not have happened in the usual way. Latinos often came from just next door, on the other side of the U.S.-Mexico border, and they have arrived continuously, whereas other groups tended to arrive in waves during defined periods. In addition, Spanglish may have been an unintended byproduct of Bilingual Education. Latinos who had gone through the program as children retained connections, however tenuous, with both Spanish and English.

As noted in the "Upheaval" section of this anthology, the linguistic feature that would come to be known as Spanglish made substantial inroads after the civil rights era. See, for example, the playfulness of Rodolfo "Corky" Gonzales's epic poem *I Am Joaquín* (first published in 1967; p. 787), the hybrid verbal code in the poetry of Ricardo Sánchez (p. 1323), and the Pachuco dialect throughout Luis Valdez's play *Zoot Suit* (1978; p. 1244). The word *Spanglish* was first used by Nuyoricans in the 1970s, and Spanglish was an essential part of spoken-word poetry of the type promoted by the Nuyorican Poets Cafe (p. 1344). The Nuyorican poet Tato Laviera's volume *AmeRícan* (1985) illustrates, starting with its title, the hybridity of Spanglish.

In the "Into the Mainstream" period, pioneers of written forms of Spanglish include the Mexican American poet Alurista, in works such as *Spik in Glyph?* (1981), and the Cuban American novelist Roberto G. Fernández, author of *La vida es un special*. Gloria Anzaldúa's *Borderlands/La Frontera: The New Mestiza* (1987) includes inspired sections connecting Spanglish and *mestizaje*. The use of written Spanglish accelerated with Giannina Braschi's *Yo-Yo Boing!* (1998), the first bilingual novel in a free-flowing style that edged back and forth between Spanish and English. In her manifesto, "Pelos en la lengua" (2001), Braschi explains her position in aesthetic and existential terms, referencing Shakespeare: "El bilingüismo es una estética bound to double business. O, 'tis most sweet when in one line two crafts directly meet. To be and not to be." In 2002, Ilan Stavans angered linguistic purists by translating into Spanglish the first chapter of *Don Quixote de La Mancha*, the seventeenth-century novel by the Spanish writer Miguel de Cervantes. A year later, Susana Chávez-Silverman released her memoir *Killer Crónicas: Bilingual Memories*, another full-fledged Spanglish volume. As an aesthetic motif, Spanglish has become identified with the duality of Latino life in the United States, what the cultural critic Gustavo Pérez Firmat has called "life on the hyphen."

# Latinidad

The period that followed the civil rights era also carried to the forefront the concept of *Latinidad*, an idealistic wish for unity and harmony among Latinos in the United States, inspired by nineteenth-century intellectuals such as José Martí (see p. 265). The concept was largely a by-product of the emergence of Latino Studies as a legitimate field of academic study, a field that played a crucial role in the dissemination of the Latino literary tradition.

In the 1960s, there were no Latino Studies programs, because a pan-Latino label encompassing all national groups from the Americas was then inconceivable. The notion of unity among different Latino nationalities in the United States had been promoted in the past, by organizations such as the League of United Latin American Citizens (founded in 1929) and the Congress of Spanish-Speaking Peoples (founded in 1938). Before the 1970s, however, the Hispanic/Latino population consisted mainly of Chicanos, Puerto Ricans, and Cubans, groups identified primarily by their individual nationalities. Only particular national groups had succeeded in promoting their academic agendas. Through marches, sit-ins, building takeovers, and protests, Chicanos, by then already the largest subgroup within the Latino minority, forced administrators to implement programs to better the social and intellectual support of Mexican American students. From the University of California, Los Angeles, to the University of New Mexico, in Albuquerque, programs echoed the patterns of life at home and on the street.

Similarly, Puerto Ricans in New York struggled at several institutions affiliated with the city and state university systems to open up the classroom to the experiences of both Nuyoricans and migrant pioneers such as Bernardo Vega (p. 428) and Jesús Colón (p. 497). But Latino Studies did not emerge until the exponential demographic growth of the minority began in the 1980s, when the need became evident to look beyond the national prism to a more continental one. The experiences of not only Chicanos but also Guatemalans, Salvadorans, and Nicaraguans needed to be addressed. Cuban Studies and Dominican Studies made their way from the University of Miami to City College of New York. Institutions in states such as New York, New Jersey, Connecticut, Massachusetts, and Illinois initially focused on Puerto Ricans and then gradually encompassed other Latino groups. Latino Studies soon became a staple in institutions in the Northeast and Midwest and are now spreading to institutions throughout the country. (In California, Arizona, New Mexico, Texas, and Colorado, the focus remains on Chicano/ Mexican American Studies.)

Professors, students, and administrators recognized Latino Studies as an exciting new area of inquiry, though administrators were not always convinced of its necessity. It followed the interdisciplinary model of African American Studies, employing the multiple tools used by anthropologists, historians, sociologists, political scientists, literary critics, educators, and cultural studies specialists. None of these disciplines alone would yield the necessarily wide perspective on and deep understanding of the culture.

The emergence of Latino Studies was tied to the teaching of the Spanish language in the United States. Although the academic study of Spanish in the United States goes back to the beginning of the nineteenth century (for example, the American poet Henry Wadsworth Longfellow taught Spanish at Harvard), foreign languages such as French, German, and Italian were regarded as more important and therefore more deserving of study. In addition, until well into the twentieth century, in American universities "Spanish" referred only to Iberian Spanish.

The Spanish language got off to a poor start in the academy largely due to the sensationalist journalism relating to the Spanish-American War (the war is discussed in the "Annexations" and "Acculturation" introductions). This writing fostered negative stereotypes of Spaniards (and by extension of Latinos), who were often seen as an awkward, primitive people. The atrocities committed by Spanish soldiers in Cuba and monitored by the media that followed Theodore Roosevelt's Rough Riders had a lasting impact on the U.S. imagination. The result was an understanding of Spaniards as cruel and barbaric. This perception contributed to making the study of Iberian culture a not-quite-genuine field of intellectual inquiry in comparison with Italian, French, and German, all of whose literary traditions—from the thirteenth- and fourteenth-century Italian poet Dante Alighieri to the eighteenth-century French encyclopedist Denis Diderot to the eighteenth- and nineteenth-century German poet and dramatist Johann Wolfgang von Goethe—were considered sophisticated.

As a topic of instruction, Spanish crept in after World War II, as part of the package of "Romance languages." Teaching Cervantes's tongue (rather than that of any Latin American or U.S. Latino) stressed the past of Spanish, not its present. During the upheaval years of the 1960s, revolutionary movements initiated by disenfranchised *campesinos* spread south of the border, while on the northern side a struggle for civil rights took place on campuses and beyond. The Chicano Movement made Spanish the recognizable language of the indigent, especially the farmworkers in the Southwest. Thanks to the Latin American literary "boom," the study of Spanish American literature began to enjoy equal footing with that of its Iberian counterpart.

In the late 1990s, contemporary, U.S.-based Latino literature began to be studied in undergraduate courses nationwide. Books by Richard Rodriguez, Julia Alvarez, Oscar Hijuelos, Sandra Cisneros, Esmeralda Santiago, and Cristina García were read alongside those of other "people of color." Contexts in which to understand their contributions were offered by the growing army of Latino faculty members, who, like these authors, were born or grew up in the United States and felt American.

At the dawn of the twenty-first century, the Latino literary renaissance, along with television, radio, the Internet, music, and politics, promoted "a fusion," a mix of diverse, heterogeneous voices, a call for unity under the rubric of *Latinidad*, an invitation to be part of an imagined community of Latinos. The minority in the United States now consists of over 45 million people, who hail from every corner of the Spanish-speaking world. What do they all have in common? Generally, language. More abstractly, a shared ethos based on their minority status and on their history of struggles for equality and social justice. Some critics see this ethos as an artificial, manufactured idea. They argue that just as there is not a Latino person per se but, instead, a person of Mexican, Puerto Rican, Cuban, or Dominican background, the concept of *Latinidad* is nothing but wishful thinking, political opportunism, or simply a mistake—the need for power masked as a cultural search for unity. Yet *America* and its national motto, *E pluribus unum* (Out of many, one), are also invented ideas, abstract concepts that have inspired and continue to inspire people to partake in a shared sense of history.

# TINO VILLANUEVA
## b. 1941

Tino Villanueva was born in San Marcos, Texas, to a family of migrant workers. Although unable to attend school regularly, he graduated from San Marcos High School in 1960. He then began working on an assembly line at a local furniture factory. In 1963, Villanueva was drafted into the U.S. Army. He spent two years in the Panama Canal Zone, where he became immersed in Latin American literature, especially in the works of *Modernistas* such as Rubén Darío (discussed on pp. 168–69) and José Martí (p. 265). Upon returning to San Marcos, he took advantage of the GI Bill to study English and Spanish at South West Texas State University (now Texas State University), in San Marcos. He completed his bachelor's degree in three years and then attended the State University of New York at Buffalo, from which he received his master's in Hispanic Studies in 1971. Ten years later, he received his doctorate in the same discipline from Boston University. He has taught at that institution and held a full-time faculty post at Wellesley College. He lives in Boston but regularly travels to Paris, where he stays during the summer.

Villanueva's first book was *Hay otra voz: Poems, 1968–1971* (1972); it includes the lyrical poem "Cycle Bound," included in this anthology. In 1980, he edited the most authoritative literary anthology on the Mexican American literary tradition thus far, *Chicanos: Antología histórica y literaria.* Published by the prestigious Fondo de la Cultura Económica, in Mexico City, it stressed the period of *El Movimiento* and proved an auspicious eye-opener to Mexican readers, who generally are uninterested in the social, political, and cultural conditions of *mexicanos* north of the Rio Grande. Villanueva subsequently authored the poetry collections *Shaking Off the Dark* (1984, rev. 1998), *Chronicle of My Worst Years* (1994), and *Primera causa/First Cause* (1999). He is the most outward-looking Chicano poet, with Europe as his source of inspiration; the twentieth-century Welsh poet Dylan Thomas and the twentieth-century Spanish poet and dramatist Federico García Lorca are among his earliest and enduring influences. Villanueva's strongest poetry focuses on his family life and the friends who toiled in the searing Texas farmfields. Racial prejudice remains a constant theme in his work. He also decries the indifference of Anglos toward migrant laborers, as is evident in three of the poems included in this anthology: "My Certain Burn toward Pale Ashes" and "Catharsis," both from *Chronicle of My Worst Years*, and "Voice over Time," the seventh part of the ten-part sequence that makes up *Primera causa.*

Villanueva won the American Book Award for his book-length poem, *Scene from the Movie* Giant (1993). The title poem, included in this anthology, was inspired by Villanueva's boyhood. In San Marcos, he first viewed, at a segregated theater, the now-classic American movie *Giant* (1956), starring James Dean, Elizabeth Taylor, and Rock Hudson and based on the novel by Edna Ferber. Villanueva's famous poem "At the Holocaust Museum: Washington, D.C." (2000), also included here, resulted from a visit to the museum of the title. Villanueva connects his suffering, and memories of his Chicano upbringing, with the disaster that befell European Jews in the mid-1940s. In 1995, he received the Distinguished Alumnus Award from Texas State University. *Il canto del cronista: Antologia poetica*, an anthology of his poetry in Spanish, English, and Italian, was published in Florence, Italy, in 2002.

# Cycle Bound

We,
    the moon lovers, a waxed
    multitude of breaths personified
    into existence,

make                                                            5
    all gestures of a cycle on the
    turning surface, moving matter
    kindled by life's rays—
    within us, gray and slanted goes
    the waning light . . . light carrying              10
    metaphors of reality.

                                                    1972


## Scene from the Movie *Giant*

What I have from 1956 is one instant at the Holiday
Theater, where a small dimension of a film, as in
A dream, became the feature of the whole. It
Comes toward the end . . . the café scene, which
Reels off a slow spread of light, a stark desire          5

To see itself once more, though there is, at times,
No joy in old time movies. It begins with the
Jingling of bells and the plainer truth of it:
That the front door to a roadside café opens and
Shuts as the Benedicts (Rock Hudson and Elizabeth        10

Taylor), their daughter Luz, and daughter-in-law
Juana and grandson Jordy, pass through it not
Unobserved. Nothing sweeps up into an actual act
Of kindness into the eyes of Sarge, who owns this
Joint and has it out for dark-eyed Juana, weary          15

Of too much longing that comes with rejection.
Juana, from barely inside the door, and Sarge,
Stout and unpleased from behind his counter, clash
Eye-to-eye, as time stands like heat. Silence is
Everywhere, acquiring the name of hatred and Juana       20

Cannot bear the dread—the dark-jowl gaze of Sarge
Against her skin. Suddenly: bells go off again.
By the quiet effort of walking, three Mexican-
Types step in, whom Sarge refuses to serve . . .
Those gestures of his, those looks that could kill       25

A heart you carry in memory for years. A scene from
The past has caught me in the act of living: even
To myself I cannot say except with worried phrases
Upon a paper, how I withstood arrogance in a gruff
Voice coming with the deep-dyed colors of the screen;    30

How in the beginning I experienced almost nothing to
Say and now wonder if I can ever live enough to tell

The after-tale. I remember this and I remember myself
Locked into a back-row seat—I am a thin, flickering,
Helpless light, local-looking, unthought of at fourteen.          35

1993


## My Certain Burn toward Pale Ashes

My certain burn
 toward pale ashes, is told by the
 hand that whirls the sun; each
 driving breath beats with the quick
 pulsing face.                                          5

My falling stride
 like sand toward decision,
 drains heavy with fixed age; each
 ghostly grain a step in time that
 measures tongues.                                       10

My ruddy sea
 that streams to dryness, bares
 bewildered its clay bone; each
 vessel's roar at God's speed drowns
 by force.                                               15

My waking light
 began when the fertile lips spun
 my pulse; and I, with muted tongue,
 was drawn destroyed from the making-
 mouth into this mass.                                    20

And held below
 by nature, the sweeping hand now
 turns my dust-bound youth; tell the
 world that I was struck by the
 sun's grave plot.                                        25

1994


## Catharsis

Into the page-stuffed night
in Pavlovian-like[1] response at
semester's end,


1. Automatic (as in research by the Russian physiologist Ivan Pavlov [1849–1936]).

I go groping through
    Lorca's New York surrealism,              5
    Whitman's symbology,[2]
        greenboard formulas,
    and untangling dangling participles by
    midnight tick-tock alarm clock.

In late Fall and Spring comes this        10
    ritual of grotesque notebooks,
thoughts surrounded by underlined
    paragraphs of future.
And shortly,
        early rays come solid through the    15
curtains in my cram . . . cram . . . cramming for a
final classroom catharsis-
with only the morning sun for breakfast,
        turning the pages in habitual
syndrome with cigarette,        20
        I yield to nausea.

1994

## Voice over Time[1]

I wanted to write so badly it hurt.
All afternoon tied to a desk,
to a page flat out on a table—
I was getting nowhere,
just fending off failure and the darkening light.    5

I want to say hours passed,
then days: and how to grasp the essence
that came shimmering in air and the obscuring shade?
How exactly to say it, to get it laid out on paper
with my pencil or pen?    10
Slow, so slow, this process of clear recollection,
of sifting back through the shadows of memory—
there, too, is life.

Oh memory, my memory,
give me back what is mine and guide me    15
in the very telling of everything that stayed behind
—may my voice win out over time.

1999

2. The American poet Walt Whitman (1819–1892) lived part of his life in New York City, where Lorca spent 1929–30, a period Lorca chronicled in his experimental volume *Poeta en Nueva York* (1940).
1. Translated by Lisa Horowitz.

# At the Holocaust Museum: Washington, D.C.

### I. Before Our Eyes

We've had it told to us before;
we've seen annihilation, *Vernichtung*[1]
at the movie house in town.
Videos reveal the same declensions of rage,
speech acts crowds shall act upon—      5
no principles governing reflection,
words shattering glass, building up the
circumstances of the fire,
the same conclusion mortality demands.

Now before our eyes: how darkly different      10
when a deep terrain of text persists with artifacts;
and photographs, each one a cell of time made real.
We turn, and make our way on cobblestones
pounded out from Mauthausen,[2]
and through a freight car walk along once more,      15
fitting facts in place—:
what led up to what; how a people lived
keeping at their tasks which came to be their lives
with the etched impression of their
history taking place,      20
until one day: were seized
and carted off in trains like perishable goods
squeezed into the mind-dark of enclosure,
breath coming hard.

Great god,      25
what geography of pain we are walking through.
What a season of convincing clouds that
hang like smoke, as when the soul,
unassailable,
has found release through manumission.      30
And what indecent will of those who
saw no cause to care, foreshadowing, therefore,
the concentric rush of time running out.

This is fact: the harsh articulation
of someone's life that, in the end,      35
will end too soon.

### II. The Freight Car

We move on, affirming the proximity of everything,
eyes breaking open to the light: installations here,
photographs and objects there, the visual details of

---

1. Destruction (German).
2. Mauthausen-Gusen, a concentration/labor-  camp complex in Upper Austria run by the Nazis
during World War II.

time-kept dying. Suddenly: an intractable fragment                    40
of truth—a freight car brought, finally, to a halt

on the same illicit logic of rails. No stench now;
human grime gone, washed away by water and soap
and the varnish of time. Still it affronts: the tight
seal of steel and wood, a prisonhouse suffocatingly                   45
small, nonsequent, disconnected from the event.

If steel and scarred wood could recount their story
from memory, could beg forgiveness or bring back
the dead, then my hand might not flinch at their
touch as I enter, enter the past: One evening                         50
a cantor was singing before a full congregation,

true worship known by heart. Peacefulness in
the infinite, and the lightness of candlelight
breathlessly still when: a muster of men from a
shadow realm broke forth, cutting off the prayer.                     55
Cantor, families and friends by the thousands,

hundreds of thousands, were led to the station,
rabid soldiers barking out orders, firing pistols
in the air, dogs bringing up the right flank. So
many helpless immortals so far from their dwelling,                   60

clutching their garments, huddled like the bundles
they carried, unable to run away from their names.
To think they leaned where I'm standing, squatted
or kneeled, dark-stricken, their children driven
to tantrums; or stood where they could against                        65

steel-dug-into-wood, no heaven above them, no earth
below. Some in their places fell mute, were confused,
riddled with fright when the train screeched, jolted
forth, shimmied and swayed and pulled out. Others
kept faith, and for them the summit of sky remained                   70

whole; still others felt death beginning to sink
into them—everyone drawing a breath: breath in,
breath out, holding their breath, sighing, inhaling-
exhaling full breaths, half-breaths, gasping with
all complexities of thirst. Long after Treblinka,[3]                  75

"Water," I hear them cry. "Water, air." I step
out, looking back as I move away with the crowd.
One freight car at a standstill, uncoupled from its
long concatenation of steel dissolved into this
artifact: the summation of all that advances no more.                 80

---

3. A Nazi concentration/extermination camp in Poland.

*III. The Photographs*

To look
into devastated eyes is not enough; to touch
the photographs is not enough.
Even if their breath could reach me,
I could utter nothing among the ruins                                        85
written with light.
But someone such as I, a nobody in all of this,
has come to see (this much the heart allows):
what man has done to man, human acts of the profane,
and the defeated countryside.                                                90

Led to camps
by the uniform substance of hate,
one by one they held
still enough to be caught in the strict regulation
of natural or flat light. I read it in their eyes:                          95
reluctance seeking its own landscape
with so much night to come. To myself I say:
this face, or that face had a name:
Joseph, Daniel, or Hannah,
but oh, you are a number—                                                   100
sharp alchemy scored on skin.
I pray your soul remained intact until the end.

(Print after print: I am carried away by destruction
exhausted into fact, forgetting
the persecuted who escaped; who from the                                    105
edges of the battlefield were saved, here by a
timely neighbor, a benevolent baker; there by a
factory owner, a farmer, or by decent Catholic nuns
—reflexive acts of the unsung.)

Then there was Ejszyszki (A-shish-key), 1941:                               110
a village of 4,000[4] that could not find the
doors to exodus—slaughtered in two days.
I touch the photographs of how it was
before it ended in a great field of darkness . . .
and my body shrieks.                                                        115
Five decades, and in another country,
I am too late in a blazing nightmare
where I reach out,
but cannot save you, cannot save you.
Sarah, Rachel, Benjamin, in this light you have risen,                      120
where the past is construed as present.
For all that is in me: Let the dead go on living,
let these words become human.

I am your memory now.

2000

---

4. In what was then eastern Poland and is now Lithuania.

# ISABEL ALLENDE
## b. 1942

Isabel Allende Llona, a best-selling Chilean writer whose novel *The House of the Spirits* (1985) provided the Latin American literary "boom" with a leading female voice, lives in San Francisco, California. While Allende sees herself as an exile, and while she writes her books in Spanish (and they are later translated into English), she became a U.S. citizen in 2003, and since the 1990s she has addressed themes such as the California Gold Rush (1848–55) and multiculturalism north of the Rio Grande. Chile continues to play a role in her narratives, however, through figures such as the nineteenth-century outlaw Joaquín Murrieta (see "Corrido de Joaquín Murrieta" in the "Popular Dimensions" section, p. 2466; a legend suggests he was Chilean by origin) and Doña Isabel de Quiroga (the only woman to actively participate as a soldier in the Spanish conquest of Chile).

Isabel Allende was born in Lima, Peru. Her father, Tomás, was Chile's ambassador to Peru and a cousin of Salvador Allende, the future elected Socialist president of Chile, deposed in a coup d'état by General Augusto Pinochet on September 11, 1973. After Isabel's father left the family in 1945, her mother and the three children returned to Chile, where they lived until 1953, with brief stays in Bolivia and Lebanon. They returned to Chile in 1959 for Isabel to complete her secondary education.

After she married in 1962, Allende was, by her own account, a devoted housewife and mother of two. As a representative for the Food and Agriculture Organization of the United Nations, she often traveled to Europe, mainly to Brussels. She translated romance novels from English to Spanish (although she was fired for making up dialogue and giving different twists to mechanical plots). She also hosted a comedic television show, wrote for a feminist magazine, and published two children's books (she has disavowed them and an early collection of columns). As a journalist, she once sought an interview with the Nobel Prize–winning Chilean poet Pablo Neruda, who declined after telling Allende she was too imaginative to be a journalist. He recommended that she publish her volume of satirical poems, and she did so.

In 1973, Allende's play *El embajador* (The Ambassador) played in Santiago, Chile. A few months later, the military coup occurred. After Allende's name was put on a "wanted" list and she received death threats, she fled to Venezuela, where she stayed for 13 years. In 1981, when Allende learned that her grandfather, aged 99, was on his deathbed, she started writing him a letter. It became her first novel, *The House of the Spirits*. The literary agent Carmen Balcells, in Barcelona, Spain, immediately sold the world rights, and in the mid-1980s the book became an international sensation. In this multigenerational saga about a family in Chile, Allende combines exoticism and extreme passion with important moments in the nation's history, especially the 1973 coup. Neruda makes a cameo appearance. In 1993, the book was turned into a Hollywood movie.

Allende met her second husband in 1988 and moved to San Francisco. Her novel *The Infinite Plan* (1993) deals with immigration from Chile to the United States. *Daughter of Fortune* (1999) is about the wave of Chileans to California in the mid-nineteenth century. *Zorro* (2005) is a mock biography of the pulp hero, set in Alta California at the end of the eighteenth century and inspired by Johnston McCulley's novella *The Curse of Capistrano* (1919). *Inés of My Soul* (2006) is structured in the form of a *crónica* and is loosely inspired by the masterpiece of Latin American epic poetry, Alonso de Ercilla's *La araucana* (1569), in which Chile is described as a "fertile, majestic province . . . strong, paramount, and powerful." While Allende has described her fiction as "a work of intuition," loosely engaging with the past to reinterpret it, some critics have accused her of revisionism. Her stated purpose is to look for "the other facet" of history: its feminine side.

Aside from fiction, Allende has written the young adult fantasy narratives *City of the Beasts* (2002), *The Kingdom of the Golden Dragon* (2003), and *Forest of the Pygmies* (2005); a culinary book about exotic food and its connection to spiritual matters, *Aphrodite: A Memoir of the Senses* (1998); and a travel book, *The Invented Country: A Nostalgic Journey through Chile* (2003). Her memoir *Paula* (1994), excerpted in this anthology, is about her daughter Paula Frías Allende's struggle with the fatal disease porphyria. Allende began the book as a letter to Paula, who died on December 6, 1992.

---

## *From* Paula[1]

## *From* Part One: December 1991 to May 1992

Listen, Paula. I am going to tell you a story, so that when you wake up you will not feel so lost. The legend of our family begins at the end of the last century, when a robust Basque sailor disembarked on the coast of Chile with his mother's reliquary strung around his neck and his head swimming with plans for greatness. But why start so far back? It is enough to say that those who came after him were a breed of impetuous women and men with sentimental hearts and strong arms fit for hard work. Some few irascible types died frothing at the mouth, although the cause may not have been rage, as evil tongues had it, but, rather, some local pestilence. The Basque's descendants bought fertile land on the outskirts of the capital, which with time increased in value; they became more refined and constructed lordly mansions with great parks and groves; they wed their daughters to rich young men from established families; they educated their children in rigorous religious schools; and thus over the course of the years they were integrated into a proud aristocracy of landowners that prevailed for more than a century—until the whirlwind of modern times replaced them with technocrats and businessmen. My grandfather was one of the former, the good old families, but his father died young of an unexplained shotgun wound. The details of what happened that fateful night were never revealed, but it could have been a duel, or revenge, or some accident of love. In any case, his family was left without means and, because he was the oldest, my grandfather had to drop out of school and look for work to support his mother and educate his younger brothers. Much later, when he had become a wealthy man to whom others doffed their hats, he confessed to me that genteel poverty is the worst of all because it must be concealed. He was always well turned out—in his father's clothes, altered to fit, the collars starched stiff and suits well pressed to disguise the threadbare cloth. Those years of penury tempered

1. Translated by Margaret Sayers Peden. [Anthology editors' note]

In December 1991 my daughter, Paula, fell gravely ill and soon thereafter sank into a coma. These pages were written during the interminable hours spent in the corridors of a Madrid hospital and in the hotel room where I lived for several months, as well as beside her bed in our home in California during the summer and fall of 1992. [Allende's note]

his character; in his credo, life was strife and hard work, and an honorable man should not pass through this world without helping his neighbor. Still young, he already exhibited the concentration and integrity that were his characteristics; he was made of the same hard stone as his ancestors and, like many of them, had his feet firmly on the ground. Even so, some small part of his soul drifted toward the abyss of dreams. Which was what allowed him to fall in love with my grandmother, the youngest of a family of twelve, all eccentrically and deliciously bizarre—like Teresa, who at the end of her life began to sprout the wings of a saint and at whose death all the roses in the Parque Japonés[2] withered overnight. Or Ambrosio, a dedicated carouser and fornicator, who was known at moments of rare generosity to remove all his clothing in the street and hand it to the poor. I grew up listening to stories about my grandmother's ability to foretell the future, read minds, converse with animals, and move objects with her gaze. Everyone says that once she moved a billiard table across a room, but the only thing I ever saw move in her presence was an insignificant sugar bowl that used to skitter erratically across the table at tea time. These gifts aroused certain misgivings, and many eligible suitors were intimidated by her, despite her charms. My grandfather, however, regarded telepathy and telekinesis as innocent diversions and in no way a serious obstacle to marriage. The only thing that concerned him was the difference in their ages. My grandmother was much younger than he, and when he first met her she was still playing with dolls and walking around clutching a grimy little pillow. Because he was so used to seeing her as a young girl, he was unaware of his passion for her until one day she appeared in a long dress and with her hair up, and then the revelation of a love that had been gestating for years threw him into such a fit of shyness that he stopped calling. My grandmother divined his state of mind before he himself was able to undo the tangle of his own feelings and sent him a letter, the first of many she was to write him at decisive moments in their lives. This was not a perfumed billet-doux testing the waters of their relationship, but a brief note penciled on lined paper asking him straight out whether he wanted to marry her and, if so, when. Several months later they were wed. Standing before the altar, the bride was a vision from another era, adorned in ivory lace and a riot of wax orange blossoms threaded through her chignon. When my grandfather saw her, he knew he would love her obstinately till the end of his days.

To me, they were always Tata and Memé. Of their children, only my mother will figure in this story, because if I begin to tell you about all the rest of the tribe we shall never be finished, and besides, the ones who are still living are very far away. That's what happens to exiles; they are scattered to the four winds and then find it extremely difficult to get back together again. My mother was born between the two world wars, on a fine spring day in the 1920s. She was a sensitive girl, temperamentally unsuited to joining her brothers in their sweeps through the attic to catch mice they preserved in bottles of Formol.[3] She led a sheltered life within the walls of her home and her school; she amused herself with charitable works and romantic novels, and had the reputation of being the most beautiful girl

2. Japanese Park/Gardens; in Santiago.
3. Formaldehyde, a temporary preservative of remains.

ever seen in this family of enigmatic women. From the time of puberty, she had lovesick admirers buzzing around like flies, young men her father held at bay and her mother analyzed with her tarot cards; these innocent flirtations were cut short when a talented and equivocal young man appeared and effortlessly dislodged his rivals, fulfilling his destiny and filling my mother's heart with uneasy emotions. That was your grandfather Tomás, who disappeared in a fog, and the only reason I mention him, Paula, is because some of his blood flows in your veins. This clever man with a quick mind and merciless tongue was too intelligent and free of prejudice for that provincial society, a rara avis in the Santiago of his time. It was said that he had a murky past; rumors flew that he belonged to the Masonic sect, and so was an enemy of the Church, and that he had a bastard son hidden away somewhere, but Tata could not put forward any of these arguments to dissuade his daughter because he lacked proof, and my grandfather was not a man to stain another's reputation without good reason. In those days Chile was like a mille-feuille pastry. It had more castes than India, and there was a pejorative term to set every person in his or her rightful place: *roto, pije, arribista, siútico,*[4] and many more, working upward toward the comfortable plateau of "people like ourselves." Birth determined status. It was easy to descend in the social hierarchy, but money, fame, or talent was not sufficient to allow one to rise; that required the sustained effort of several generations. Tomás's honorable lineage was in his favor, even though in Tata's eyes he had questionable political ties. By then the name Salvador Allende, the founder of Chile's Socialist Party, was being bruited about; he preached against private property, conservative morality, and the power of the large landowners. Tomás was the cousin of that young deputy.

Look, Paula, this is Tata's picture. This man with the severe features, clear eyes, rimless eyeglasses, and black beret is your great-grandfather. In the picture he is seated, hands on his cane, and beside him, leaning against his right knee, is a little girl of three in her party dress, a pint-size charmer staring into the camera with liquid eyes. That's *you.* My mother and I are standing behind you, the chair masking the fact that I was carrying your brother Nicolás. The old man is facing the camera, and you can see his proud bearing, the calm dignity of the self-made man who has marched straight down the road of life and expects nothing more. I remember him as always being old—although almost without wrinkles except for the two deep furrows at the corners of his mouth—with a lion's mane of snow-white hair and an abrupt laugh filled with yellow teeth. At the end of his days it was painful for him to move, but he always struggled to his feet to say hello and goodbye to the ladies and, hobbling along on his cane, escort them to the garden gate as they left. I loved his hands, twisted oak branches, strong and gnarled, his inevitable silk neckerchief, and his odor of English Creolin-and-lavender soap. With inexhaustible good humor, he tried to instill in his descendants his stoic philosophy: he believed discomfort was healthful and that central heating sapped the strength; he insisted on simple food—no

---

4. Presumptuous person whose mannerisms imitate French or other foreign styles. *Roto*: poor but honest and courageous person; also a vulgar person. *Pije*: member of the aristocratic class who dresses in an exaggerated way that emphasizes his or her status and might call attention to his or her right-wing views. *Arribista*: person who pretends to be what he or she is not or spends according to the standards of a different social class; also a person who wants to progress quickly and by any means necessary.

sauces or pot-au-feu—and he thought it bad taste to have too good a time. Every morning he took a cold shower, a custom no one in the family imitated, and one that when he resembled nothing more than a geriatric beetle he fulfilled, old but undaunted, seated in a chair beneath the icy blast. He spoke in ringing aphorisms and answered direct questions with a different question, so that even though I knew his character to the core, I know very little about his ideology. Look carefully at Mother, Paula. In this picture she is in her early forties, and at the peak of her beauty. That short skirt and beehive hair were all the rage. She's laughing, and her large eyes are two green lines punctuated by the sharp arch of black eyebrows. That was the happiest period of her life, when she had finished raising her children, was still in love, and the world seemed secure.

I wish I could show you a photograph of my father, but they were all burned more than forty years ago.

Where are you wandering, Paula? How will you be when you wake up? Will you be the same woman, or will we be like strangers and have to learn to know one another all over again? Will you have your memory, or will I need to sit patiently and relate the entire story of your twenty-eight years and my forty-nine?

"May God watch over your daughter," don Manuel told me, barely able to whisper. He's the one in the bed next to yours, an elderly peasant who has undergone several operations on his stomach but has not given up fighting for health and life. "May God watch over your daughter" was also what a young woman with a baby in her arms said yesterday. She had heard about you and come to the hospital to offer me hope. She suffered an attack of porphyria two years ago and was in a coma for more than a month. It was a year before she was normal again and she will have to be careful for the rest of her life, but she is working now, and she married and had a baby. She assured me that being in a coma is like a sleep without dreams, a mysterious parenthesis. "Don't cry anymore, Señora," she said, "your daughter doesn't feel a thing; she will walk out of here and never remember what happened." Every morning I prowl the corridors of the sixth floor looking for the specialist, in hopes of learning something new. He holds your life in his hands, and I don't trust him. He wafts through like a breeze, distracted and rushed, offering me worrisome explanations about enzymes and copies of articles about your illness that I try to read but do not understand. He seems more interested in the statistics from his computer and formulas from his laboratory than in your poor body lying crucified on this bed. He tells me—without meeting my eyes—"That's how it is with this condition; some recover quickly after the crisis, while others spend weeks in intensive therapy. It used to be that the patients simply died, but now we can keep them alive until their metabolism resumes functioning." Well, if that's how it is, all we can do is wait and be strong. If you can take it, Paula, so can I.

When you wake up we will have months, maybe years, to piece together the broken fragments of your past; better yet, we can invent memories that fit your fantasies. For the time being, I will tell you about myself and the other members of this family we both belong to, but don't ask me to be precise, because inevitably errors will creep in. I have forgotten a lot, and some of the facts are twisted. There are places, dates, and names I don't remember;

on the other hand, I never forget a good story. Sitting here by your side, watching the screen with the luminous lines measuring your heartbeats, I try to use my grandmother's magic to communicate with you. If she were here she could carry my messages to you and help me hold you in this world. Have you begun some strange trek through the sand dunes of the unconscious? What good are all these words if you can't hear me? Or these pages you may never read? My life is created as I narrate, and my memory grows stronger with writing; what I do not put in words on a page will be erased by time.

Today is January 8, 1992. On a day like today, eleven years ago in Caracas,[5] I began a letter that would be my goodbye to my grandfather, who was dying, leaving a hard-fought century behind him. His strong body had not failed, but long ago he had made his preparations to follow Memé, who was beckoning to him from the other side. I could not return to Chile, and he so detested the telephone that it didn't seem right to call, but I wanted to tell him not to worry, that nothing would be lost of the treasury of anecdotes he had told me through the years of our comradeship; I had forgotten nothing. Soon he died, but the story I had begun to tell had enmeshed me, and I couldn't stop. Other voices were speaking through me; I was writing in a trance, with the sensation of unwinding a ball of yarn, driven by the same urgency I feel as I write now. At the end of a year the pages had grown to five hundred, filling a canvas bag, and I realized that this was no longer a letter. Timidly, I announced to my family that I had written a book. "What's the title?" my mother asked. We made a list of possibilities but could not agree on any, and finally it was you, Paula, who tossed a coin in the air to decide it. Thus was born and baptized my first novel, *The House of the Spirits*, and I was initiated into the ineradicable vice of telling stories. That book saved my life. Writing is a long process of introspection; it is a voyage toward the darkest caverns of consciousness, a long, slow meditation. I write feeling my way in silence, and along the way discover particles of truth, small crystals that fit in the palm of one hand and justify my passage through this world. I also began my second novel on an eighth of January, and since have not dared change that auspicious date, partly out of superstition, but also for reasons of discipline. I have begun all my books on a January 8.

When some months ago I finished my most recent novel, *The Infinite Plan*, I began preparing for today. I had everything in my mind—theme, title, first sentence—but I shall not write that story yet. Since you fell ill I have had no strength for anything but you, Paula. You have been sleeping for a month now. I don't know how to reach you; I call and call but your name is lost in the nooks and crannies of this hospital. My soul is choking in sand. Sadness is a sterile desert. I don't know how to pray. I cannot string together two thoughts, much less immerse myself in creating a new book. I plunge into these pages in an irrational attempt to overcome my terror. I think that perhaps if I give form to this devastation I shall be able to help you, and myself, and that the meticulous exercise of writing can be our salvation. Eleven years ago I wrote a letter to my grandfather to say goodbye to him in death. On this January 8, 1992, I am writing you, Paula, to bring you back to life.

---

5. Capital and largest city of Venezuala.

My mother was a radiant young woman of eighteen when Tata took the family to Europe on a monumental journey that in those days was made only once in a lifetime: Chile lies at the bottom of the world. He intended to place his daughter in an English school to be "finished," hoping that in the process she would forget her love for Tomás, but Hitler wrecked those plans; the Second World War burst out with cataclysmic force, surprising them on the Côte d'Azur.[6] With incredible difficulty, moving against the streams of people escaping on foot, horseback, or any available vehicle, they managed to reach Antwerp[7] and board the last Chilean ship to set sail from the docks. The decks and lifeboats had been commandeered by dozens of families of fleeing Jews who had left their belongings—in some cases, fortunes—in the hands of unscrupulous consuls who sold them visas in exchange for gold. Unable to obtain staterooms, they traveled like cattle, sleeping in the open and going hungry because of food rationing. Through that arduous crossing, Memé consoled women weeping over the loss of their homes and the uncertainty of the future, while Tata negotiated food from the kitchen and blankets from the sailors to distribute among the refugees. In appreciation, one of them, a furrier by trade, gave Memé a luxurious coat of gray astrakhan. For several weeks they sailed through waters infested with enemy submarines, blacking out lights by night and praying by day, until they had left the Atlantic behind and safely reached Chile. As the boat docked in the port of Valparaíso,[8] the first sight that met their eyes was the unmistakable figure of Tomás in a white linen suit and Panama hat. At that moment, Tata realized the futility of opposing the mysterious dictates of destiny and so, grudgingly, gave his consent for the wedding. The ceremony was held at home, with the participation of the papal nuncio and various personages from the official world. The bride wore a sober satin gown and a defiant expression. I don't know how the groom looked, because the photograph has been cropped; we can see nothing of him but one arm. As he led his daughter to the large room where an altar of cascading roses had been erected, Tata paused at the foot of the stairway.

"There is still time to change your mind," he said. "Don't marry him, Daughter, think better of it. Just give me a sign and I will run this mob out of here and send the banquet to the orphanage." My mother replied with an icy stare.

Just as my grandmother had been warned by the spirits in one of her sessions, my parents' marriage was a disaster from the very beginning. Once again, my mother boarded a ship, this time for Peru, where Tomás had been named secretary at the Chilean embassy. She took with her a collection of heavy trunks containing her bridal trousseau and a mountain of gifts, so much china, crystal, and silver that even now, a half-century later, we keep running into them in unexpected corners. Fifty years of diplomatic assignments in many latitudes, divorce, and long exile have not rid the family of this flotsam. I greatly fear, Paula, that among other ghastly prizes you will inherit a lamp that is still in my mother's possession, a baroque chaos of nymphs and plump cherubs. Your house is monastically spare, and your meager closet contains nothing but four blouses and two pairs of slacks. I wonder

6. The coast of southeast France, on the Mediterranean Sea. *Hitler:* Adolf Hitler (1889–1945), Austrian-born German dictator and founder of Nazism.
7. City in Belgium.
8. City in central Chile.

what you do with the things I keep giving you? You're like Memé, whose feet had scarcely touched solid ground before she removed the astrakhan coat and draped it over a beggarwoman's shoulders. My mother spent the first two days of her honeymoon so nauseated by the tossing Pacific Ocean that she was unable to leave her stateroom; then, just as she felt a little better and could go outside to drink in the fresh air, her husband was felled by a toothache. While she strolled around the decks, indifferent to the covetous stares of officers and sailors, he lay moaning in his bunk. At sunset the vast horizon was flooded with shades of orange and at night a scandal of stars invited love, but suffering was more powerful than romance. Three interminable days had to pass before the patient allowed the ship's physician to intervene with his forceps and ease the torment. Only then did the swelling subside, and husband and wife could begin married life. The next night they appeared together in the dining room as guests at the captain's table. After a formal toast to the newlyweds, the appetizer was served: prawns arranged in goblets carved of ice. In a gesture of flirtatious intimacy, my mother reached across and speared a bit of seafood from her husband's plate, unfortunately flicking a minute drop of cocktail sauce onto his necktie. Tomás seized a knife to scrape away the offensive spot, but merely spread the stain. To the astonishment of his fellow guests and the mortification of his wife, the diplomat dipped his fingers into his dish, scooped up a handful of crustaceans, and smeared them over his chest, desecrating shirt, suit, and the unsoiled portion of his tie; then, after passing his hands over his slicked-down hair, he rose to his feet, bowed slightly, and strode off to his stateroom, where he stayed for the remainder of the voyage, deep in a sullen silence. Despite these mishaps, I was conceived on that sea voyage.

Nothing had prepared my mother for motherhood. In those days, such matters were discussed in whispers before unwed girls, and Memé had given no thought to advising her about the libidinous preoccupations of the birds and the flowers because her soul floated on different planes, more intrigued with the translucence of apparitions than the gross realities of this world. Nevertheless, as soon as my mother sensed she was pregnant, she knew it would be a girl. She named her Isabel and established a dialogue that continues to the present day. Clinging to the creature developing in her womb, she tried to compensate for the loneliness of a woman who has chosen badly in love. She talked to me aloud, startling everyone who saw her carrying on as if hallucinating, and I suppose that I heard her and answered, although I have no memory of the intrauterine phase of my life.

My father had a taste for splendor. Ostentation had always been looked upon as a vice in Chile, where sobriety is a sign of refinement. In contrast, in Lima,[9] the city of viceroys, swagger and swash is considered stylish. Tomás installed himself in a house incommensurate with his position as second secretary in the embassy, surrounded himself with Indian servants, ordered a luxurious automobile from Detroit, and squandered money on parties, gaming, and yacht clubs, without anyone's being able to explain how he could afford such extravagances. In a short time he had managed to establish relations with the most illustrious members of Lima's political and social circles, had discovered the weaknesses of each, and, through his

9. Capital and largest city of Peru.

contacts, heard a number of indiscreet confidences, even a few state secrets. He became the indispensable element in Lima's revels. At the height of the war, he obtained the best whiskey, the purest cocaine, and the most obliging party girls; all doors opened to him. While he climbed the ladder of his career, his wife felt as if she was a prisoner with no hope for escape, joined at twenty to an evasive man on whom she was totally dependent. She languished in the humid summer heat, writing interminable pages to her mother; their correspondence was a conversation between the deaf, crossing at sea and buried in the bottom of mailbags. Nevertheless, as melancholy letters stacked up on her desk, Memé became convinced of her daughter's disenchantment. She interrupted the spiritist sessions with her three esoteric friends from the White Sisterhood, packed her prophetic deck of cards in her suitcase, and set off for Lima in a light biplane, one of the few that carried passengers, since during times of war planes were reserved for military purposes. She arrived just in time for my birth. As her own children had been born at home with the aid of her husband and a midwife, she was bewildered by the modern methods of the clinic. With one jab of a needle, they rendered her daughter senseless, depriving her of any chance to participate in events, and as soon as the baby was born transferred it to an aseptic nursery. Much later, when the fog of the anesthesia had lifted, they informed my mother that she had given birth to a baby girl, but that in accord with regulations she could have her only during the time she was nursing.

"She's a freak, that's why they won't let me see her!"

"She's a precious little thing!" my grandmother replied, trying to sound a note of conviction, although she herself had not yet actually seen me: through the glass, she had spied a blanket-wrapped bundle, something that to her eyes did not look entirely human.

While I screamed with hunger on a different floor, my mother thrashed about, prepared to reclaim her daughter by force, should that be necessary. A doctor came, diagnosed hysteria, and administered a second injection that knocked her out for another twelve hours. By then my grandmother was convinced that they were in the anteroom to hell, and as soon as her daughter was conscious, she splashed cold water on her face and helped her get dressed.

"We have to get out of here. Put on your clothes and we'll stroll out arm in arm like two ladies who've come to visit."

"For God's sake, Mama, we can't go without the baby!"

"Of course we can't!" exclaimed my grandmother, who probably had overlooked that detail.

The two women walked purposefully into the room where the newborn babies were sequestered, picked one out, and hastily exited, without raising an alarm. They could tell the sex, because the infant had a rose-colored ribbon around its wrist, and though there wasn't enough time to be certain that it was theirs, that wasn't vital anyway; all babies are more or less alike at that age. It is possible that in their haste they traded me for another baby, and that somewhere there is a woman with spinach-colored eyes and a gift for clairvoyance who is taking my place. Once safely home, they stripped me bare to be sure I was whole, and discovered a small birthmark in the shape of a sun at the base of my spine. "That's a good sign," Memé assured my mother. "We won't have to worry about her; she'll grow up healthy and blessed with good fortune." I was born in August, under the sign of Leo, sex, female, and, if I was not switched in the clinic, I have three-quarters Spanish-Basque blood, one-quarter French, and a tot of Araucan or Mapuche Indian, like everyone else in my land. Despite my birth in Lima, I am Chilean. I come from a "long petal of sea and wine and snow," as Pablo Neruda described my country, and you're from there, too, Paula, even though you bear the indelible stamp of the Caribbean, where you spent the years of your childhood. It may be difficult for you to understand the mentality of those of us from the south. In Chile we are influenced by the eternal presence of the mountains that separate us from the rest of the continent, and by a sense of precariousness inevitable in a region of geological and political catastrophes. Everything trembles beneath our feet; we know no security. If anyone asks us how we are, we answer, "About the same," or "All right, I guess." We move from one uncertainty to another; we pick our way through a twilight region. Nothing is precise. We do not like confrontations; we prefer to negotiate. When circumstances push us to extremes, our worst instincts are awakened and history takes a tragic turn, because the same men who seem mild-mannered in their everyday lives can, if offered impunity and the right pretext, turn into bloodthirsty beasts. In normal times, however, Chileans are sober, circumspect, and formal, and suffer an acute fear of attracting attention, which to them is synonymous with looking ridiculous. For that very reason, I have been an embarrassment to my family.

And where was Tomás while his wife was giving birth and his mother-in-law effecting the discreet kidnapping of her first grandchild? I have no idea. My father is a great lacuna in my life. He went away so early, and vanished so completely, that I have no memory of him at all. My mother lived with him for four years, including two long separations—but sufficient time to bring three children into the world. She was so fertile that she became pregnant if a pair of men's undershorts was waved anywhere within a radius of a half kilometer, a predisposition I inherited, although, to my good fortune, the age of The Pill arrived in time for me. With each birth her husband disappeared—as he did at the sign of any major difficulty—and then, once the emergency was over, returned, beaming, with some extravagant present. She watched the proliferation of paintings on the walls and Chinese porcelains on the shelves, totally mystified at where all the money was coming from. It was impossible to explain such luxuries when others at the consulate could scarcely make ends meet, but when she asked him, my father gave her the runaround—just as he did when she asked about his nocturnal absences, his mysterious trips, and his shady friendships. My mother had two children, and was about to give birth to the third, when the whole house of cards of her innocence came tumbling down. Lima awoke one morning to rumors of a scandal that escaped the newspapers but filtered into every salon. It had to do with an elderly millionaire who used to lend his apartment to special friends for clandestine trysts. In the bedroom, lost among pieces of antique furniture and Persian tapestries, hung a false mirror in a heavy baroque frame—actually, a window. On the other side, the master of the house liked to sit with a select group of guests, well supplied with liquor and drugs, eager to enjoy the antics of the current, usually unsuspecting, couple in the bed. That night a high-ranking politician was among the invited. When the curtain was drawn for the voyeurs to spy on the unwary lovers, the first surprise was that they were two males; the second was that one of them, decked out in a corset and lace garters, was the eldest son of the politician, a young lawyer destined for a brilliant career. In his humiliation, the father lost control; he kicked out the mirror, threw himself on his son to tear off the women's frippery, and, had he not been restrained, might have murdered him. A few hours later every circle in Lima was humming with the particulars of the event, adding more and more scabrous details with each telling. It was suspected that it was not a chance incident, that someone had planned the scene out of pure malice. Frightened, Tomás disappeared without a word. My mother did not hear of the scandal until several days later; she was isolated by the demands of her series of pregnancies, and also by a desire to escape the creditors who were clamoring for payment. Tired of waiting for their wages, the servants had deserted; only Margara remained, a Chilean employee with a hermetic face and heart of stone who had served the family since the beginning of time. It was in these straits that my mother felt the pangs of imminent birth. She gritted her teeth and prepared to have the baby under the most primitive circumstances. I was almost three, and my brother Pancho was barely walking. That night, huddled together in the corridor, we heard my mother's moans and witnessed Margara scurrying back and forth with towels and kettles of hot water. Juan came into the world at midnight, tiny and wrinkled, a hairless wisp of a mouse, barely breathing. It was soon obvious that he couldn't swallow; he had some knot in his throat that wouldn't let food pass. Although my mother's breasts were bursting with milk, he was destined to perish of hunger, but Margara was determined to keep him alive, at first by squeezing drops from milk-soaked cotton, then later using a wooden spoon to force a thick pap down his throat.

For years, morbid explanations for my father's disappearance rattled around in my head. I asked about him until finally I gave up, recognizing that there is a conspiracy of silence around him. Those who knew him describe him to me as a very intelligent man, and stop there. When I was young, I imagined him as a criminal, and later, when I learned about sexual perversions, I attributed all of them to him, but the facts suggest that nothing so dramatic colored his past; he merely had a cowardly soul. One day he found himself trapped by his lies; events were out of control, so he ran away. He left the Foreign Service and never again saw my mother or any of his family or friends. He simply vanished in smoke. I visualized him—partly in jest, of course—fleeing toward Machu Picchu[1] disguised as a Peruvian Indian woman, wearing a wig with long black braids and layers of many-colored skirts. "Don't ever say that again!" my mother screamed when I told her my fantasy. "Where do you get such crazy ideas?" Whatever happened, he disappeared without a trace, although obviously he did not hie himself off to the thin, clear air of the Andes to live unnoticed in some Aymara village;[2] he just descended a rung in the immutable scale of Chile's social classes and became invisible. He must have returned to Santiago and walked the streets of the city center but as he did not frequent the same social milieu it was as if he had died. I never again saw my paternal grandmother or any of my father's family—except for Salvador Allende, who out of a strong sense of loyalty kept

1. A pre-Columbian Inca site in Peru.
2. The Aymara, or Aimara, are an indigenous people in the Andes and Altiplano regions of South America.

in close touch with us. Nor did I see my father again, or hear his name spoken aloud. I know absolutely nothing about his physical appearance, so it is ironic that one day I was called to identify his body in the morgue—but that came much later. I'm sorry, Paula, that this character must disappear at this point, because villains always are the most delicious part of a story.

My mother, who had been brought up in a world of privilege in which women were excluded from money matters, entrenched herself in her house, wiped away the tears of abandonment, and found consolation in the fact that for a time, at least, she would not starve; she had the treasure of the silver trays, which she could pawn one by one to pay the bills. She was alone in a strange land with three children, surrounded by the trappings of wealth but without a cent in her pocketbook and too proud to ask for help. The embassy, nonetheless, was alert, and learned immediately that Tomás had disappeared, leaving his family in bankruptcy. The honor of the nation was at stake; they could not allow the name of a Chilean official to be dragged through the mud, much less permit his wife and children to be put out into the street by creditors. So the consul was sent to call on the family, with instructions to help them return to Chile with the greatest possible discretion. You guessed right, Paula, that man was your Tío Ramón, your grandfather, a prince, and the direct descendant of Jesus Christ. He himself tells that he was one of the ugliest men of his generation, but I think he is exaggerating. We can't call him handsome, but what he lacks in good looks he more than makes up for in intelligence and charm. Besides, the years have lent him an air of great dignity. At the time he was sent to our aid, Tío Ramón was bone thin, had a greenish tint to his skin, a walrus mustache, and Mephistophelian eyebrows; he was the father of four children and a practicing Catholic, and not a spot on the mythic character he would become after he had shed his skin like a snake. Margara opened the door to this visitor and led him to the bedroom of her señora, who received him lying in bed surrounded by her children, still slightly battered by the youngest's birth but glowing with striking beauty and youthful ebullience. The consul, who had scarcely known his colleague's wife—he had always seen her pregnant, and with a remote air that did not invite closer contact—stood near the door, sinking into a swamp of emotions. As he questioned her about the intricacies of her situation and explained the plan to send her back to Chile, he was tormented by a stampede of wild bulls in the area of his chest. Calculating that there was no more fascinating woman alive, and failing to understand how her husband could have abandoned her—he would give his life for her—he sighed at the crushing injustice of having met her too late. She looked at him for a long moment, and finally agreed:

"All right, I will return to my father's house."

"In a few days a ship is leaving Callao[3] for Vuh-Valparaíso. I'll try to obtain passages," he stammered.

"I shall be traveling with my three children, Margara, and the dog. I don't know whether my baby will survive the trip; this little one is very weak," and although her eyes were shining with tears, she refused to allow herself to cry.

---

3. Port city in Peru.

In a flash, Ramón's wife and his children filed before his eyes, followed by his father pointing an accusing finger, and his uncle, the bishop, holding a crucifix shooting rays of damnation. He saw himself excommunicated from the Church and disgraced in the Foreign Service, but he could think of nothing but this woman's perfect face. He felt as if he had been blown off his feet by a hurricane. He took two steps toward the bed. In those two steps, his future was decided.

"From now on, I will look after you and your children. . . . Forever."

\* \* \*

1994

# GLORIA ANZALDÚA
## 1942–2004

Gloria Anzaldúa was a major theoretician of *mestizaje*, and her intellectual explorations of lesbianism, inequality, and racism have been widely influential in the U.S. academy. Through stylistic experimentation—in the books she authored by combining insightful, provocative arguments with quotations and marginalia, in the anthologies she edited, and in the interviews she gave—Anzaldúa created a distinctive place for herself in the Latino literary tradition. She has enormously influenced several generations of scholars.

A sixth-generation *tejana*, Anzaldúa was born in the Lower Rio Grande Valley of Texas. At age 11, she moved with her family to the village of Hargill, Texas, within the Valley but some 30 minutes from Mexico. Early in life, she discovered her lesbian identity and rebelled against the conservatism of her parents and of Hargill generally. Her mother, appalled, refused to accept Anzaldúa's sexual orientation; she wanted both of her daughters to be feminine, subservient, and mindful of their manners. Her mother's attitude, combined with racism, anti-Mexicanism, sexism, and the death of her father when she was 12, marked Anzaldúa's adolescent years and helped shape her creative and intellectual life. Anzaldúa earned her bachelor's degree in English from the University of Texas–Pan American, in the Valley, and her master's in English from the University of Texas at Austin. She completed the course work for a doctorate in comparative literature, but failed to write the dissertation needed for the degree. She worked as a school teacher before moving in 1977 to California, where she supported herself through lecturing and writing. She also taught at San Francisco State University; the University of California, Santa Cruz; and Florida Atlantic University.

She became known with the anthology *This Bridge Called My Back: Writings by Radical Women of Color* (1981), edited with Cherríe Moraga. Other anthologies by Anzaldúa are *Making Face, Making Soul/Haciendo Caras: Creative and Critical Perspectives by Feminists of Color* (1990) and, with AnaLouise Keating, *This Bridge We Call Home: Radical Visions for Transformation* (2002). Anzaldúa's central theoretical volume is *Borderlands/La Frontera: The New Mestiza* (1987), named one of the 38 best books of the year by *Library Journal* and 100 Best Books of the Century by *Hungry Mind Review* and *Utne Reader*. In this work, two chapters of which are included here, Anzaldúa defines *mestizaje* not as an either/or but as a multisided identity with a forceful presence in the global world. For her, the concept conveys a juxtaposition of cultures that never diminishes its various ingredients. She also explores the concept of the borderland as a spiritual idea carried by mestizos everywhere they travel. These views made Anzaldúa a central thinker in ethnic, border, and Latino studies. As a feminist arguing against a bipolar vision of gender, meanwhile, she was at odds with some of the macho tenets of the Chicano Movement of the late 1960s and early 1970s.

José Vasconcelos's book *The Cosmic Race* (1925; discussed on pp. 162–63; for an excerpt, see Appendix 3: Influential Essays by Latin American Writers, p. A65) inspired Anzaldúa to shape her concept of "the new mestiza" into a fresh way of viewing local, national, and world events. She called on Latinas to take the lead in shaping a more equitable future. Arguing for spiritual activism, she developed the idea of *Nepantleras* (women from Nepantla, the latter being a Nahuatl word connoting in-between or a space in the middle) to describe the ways contemporary social agents ought to combine spirituality with politics. People who have been subjected to invasion, conquest, and marginalization, she argued, need to decolonize their mindsets by embracing what she called the Coatlicue State, a reference to the Aztec goddess who, as she put it in *Borderlands/La Frontera*, "is the consuming internal whirlwind, the symbol of the underground aspects of the psyche."

Anzaldúa wrote about Mexican female icons such as the Virgin of Guadalupe, La Malinche, Sor Juana Inéz de la Cruz, and Frida Kahlo. She also wrote about Nahuatl/Toltec divinities and Yoruba orishas such as Yemayá and Oshún. Anzaldúa's interest in language encouraged her to reflect on the role Nahuatl and Spanish played during the conquest and colonial periods in Mexico. Her writing often employs Spanglish as a strategy for creating a more comprehensive collective identity among Latinos, and in fact anthologizers are contractually forbidden from translating or annotating her work. Anzaldúa's books for children are *Prietita Has a Friend* (1991), *Friends from the Other Side/Amigos del otro lado* (1993), and *Prietita y La Llorona* (1996). Among the honors she received were the Before Columbus Foundation American Book Award (1986), a National Endowment for the Arts Award (1991), the Lesbian Rights Award (1991), Sappho Award of Distinction (1992), and the American Studies Association Lifetime Achievement Award (2001). Anzaldúa died at her home in Santa Cruz, California, from complications of diabetes. She was within weeks of completing her dissertation and receiving her doctorate from the University of California, Santa Cruz.

---

## *From* Borderlands/La Frontera: The New Mestiza[1]

### 1: The Homeland, Aztlán: *El otro México*

*El otro México que acá hemos construído*
*el espacio es lo que ha sido*
*territorio nacional.*
*Este es el esfuerzo de todos nuestros hermanos*
*y latinoamericanos que han sabido*
*progressar.*
—Los Tigres del Norte[2]

---

1. All footnotes are Anzaldúa's.    2. Los Tigres del Norte is a *conjunto* band.

"The *Aztecas del norte* . . . compose the largest single tribe or nation of Anishinabeg (Indians) found in the United States today. . . . Some call themselves Chicanos and see themselves as people whose true homeland is Aztlán [the U.S. Southwest]."[3]

Wind tugging at my sleeve
feet sinking into the sand
I stand at the edge where earth touches ocean
where the two overlap
a gentle coming together
at other times and places a violent clash.

Across the border in Mexico
stark silhouette of houses gutted by waves,
cliffs crumbling into the sea,
silver waves marbled with spume
gashing a hole under the border fence.

*Miro el mar atacar*
*la cerca en* Border Field Park
*con sus buchones de agua,*
an Easter Sunday resurrection
of the brown blood in my veins.

*Oigo el llorido del mar, el respiro del aire,*
my heart surges to the beat of the sea.
In the gray haze of the sun
the gulls' shrill cry of hunger,
the tangy smell of the sea seeping into me.

I walk   through the hole in the fence
to the other side.
Under my fingers I feel the gritty wire
rusted by 139 years
of the salty breath of the sea.

Beneath the iron sky
Mexican children kick their soccer ball across,
run after it, entering the U.S.

I press my hand to the steel curtain—
chainlink fence crowned with rolled barbed wire—
rippling from the sea where Tijuana touches San Diego
unrolling over mountains
and plains
and deserts,
this "Tortilla Curtain" turning into *el río Grande*
flowing down to the flatlands

---

3. Jack D. Forbes, *Aztecas del Norte: The Chicanos of Aztlán.* (Greenwich, CT: Fawcett Publications, Premier Books, 1973), 13, 183; Eric R. Wolf, *Sons of Shaking Earth* (Chicago, IL: University of Chicago Press, Phoenix Books, 1959), 32.

of the Magic Valley of South Texas
its mouth emptying into the Gulf.

1,950 mile-long open wound
   dividing a *pueblo*, a culture,
   running down the length of my body,
    staking fence rods in my flesh,
   splits me  splits me
     *me raja  me raja*

  This is my home
  this thin edge of
   barbwire.

  But the skin of the earth is seamless.
  The sea cannot be fenced,
*el mar* does not stop at borders.
To show the white man what she thought of his
    arrogance,
  *Yemayá* blew that wire fence down.

   This land was Mexican once,
   was Indian always
   and is.
   And  will be again.

*Yo soy un puente tendido*
 *del mundo gabacho at del mojado,*
*lo pasado me estira pa' 'trás*
  *y lo presente pa' 'delante,*
*Que la Virgen de Guadalupe me cuide*
*Ar ay ay, soy mexicana de este lado.*

  The U.S.-Mexican border *es una herida abierta* where the Third World grates against the first and bleeds. And before a scab forms it hemorrhages again, the lifeblood of two worlds merging to form a third country—a border culture. Borders are set up to define the places that are safe and unsafe, to distinguish *us* from *them*. A border is a dividing line, a narrow strip along a steep edge. A borderland is a vague and undetermined place created by the emotional residue of an unnatural boundary. It is in a constant state of transition. The prohibited and forbidden are its inhabitants. *Los atravesados* live here: the squint-eyed, the perverse, the queer, the troublesome, the mongrel, the mulato, the half-breed, the half dead; in short, those who cross over, pass over, or go through the confined of the "normal." Gringos in the U.S. Southwest consider the inhabitants of the borderlands transgressors, aliens— whether they possess documents or not, whether they're Chicanos, Indians or Blacks. Do not enter, trespassers will be raped, maimed, strangled, gassed, shot. The only "legitimate" inhabitants are those in power, the whites and those who align themselves with whites. Tension grips the inhabitants of the borderlands like a virus. Ambivalence and unrest reside there and death is no stranger.

In the fields, *la migra*. My aunt saying, "*No corran*, don't run. They'll think you're *del otro lao*." In the confusion, Pedro ran, terrified of being caught. He couldn't speak English, couldn't tell them he was fifth generation American. *Sin papeles*—he did not carry his birth certificate to work in the fields. *La migra* took him away while we watched. *Se lo llevaron*. He tried to smile when he looked back at us, to raise his fist. But I saw the shame pushing his head down, I saw the terrible weight of shame hunch his shoulders. They deported him to Guadalajara by plane. The furthest he'd ever been to Mexico was Reynosa, a small border town opposite Hidalgo, Texas, not far from McAllen. Pedro walked all the way to the Valley. *Se lo llevaron sin un centavo al pobre. Se vino andando desde Guadalajara.*

During the original peopling of the Americas, the first inhabitants migrated across the Bering Straits and walked south across the continent. The oldest evidence of humankind in the U.S.—the Chicanos' ancient Indian ancestors—was found in Texas and has been dated to 35000 B.C.[4] In the Southwest United States archeologists have found 20,000-year-old campsites of the Indians who migrated through, or permanently occupied, the Southwest, Aztlán—land of the herons, land of whiteness, the Edenic place of origin of the Azteca.

In 1000 B.C., descendants of the original Cochise people migrated into what is now Mexico and Central America and became the direct ancestors of many of the Mexican people. (The Cochise culture of the Southwest is the parent culture of the Aztecs. The Uto-Aztecan languages stemmed from the language of the Cochise people.)[5] The Aztecs (the Nahuatl word for people of Aztlán) left the Southwest in 1168 A.D.

> Now let us go.
>> *Tihueque, tihueque,*
> *Vámonos, vámonos.*
>> *Un pájaro cantó.*
>
> *Con sus ocho tribus salieron*
>> *de la "cueva del origen."*
> *los aztecas siguieron al dios*
>> *Huitzilopochtli.*

*Huitzilopochtli*, the God of War, guided them to the place (that later became Mexico City) where an eagle with a writhing serpent in its beak perched on a cactus. The eagle symbolizes the spirit (as the sun, the father); the serpent symbolizes the soul (as the earth, the mother). Together, they symbolize the struggle between the spiritual/celestial/male and the underworld/earth/ feminine. The symbolic sacrifice of the serpent to the "higher" masculine powers indicates that the patriarchal order had already vanquished the feminine and matriarchal order in pre-Columbian America.

---

4. John R. Chávez, *The Lost Land: The Chicano Images of the Southwest* (Albuquerque, NM: University of New Mexico Press, 1984), 9.
5. Chávez, 9. Besides the Aztecs, the Ute, Gabrillino of California, Pima of Arizona, some Pueblo of New Mexico, Comanche of Texas, Opata of Sonora, Tarahumara of Sinaloa and Durango, and the Huichol of Jalisco speak Uto-Aztecan languages and are descended from the Cochise people.

At the beginning of the 16th century, the Spaniards and Hernán Cortés invaded Mexico and, with the help of tribes that the Aztecs had subjugated, conquered it. Before the Conquest, there were twenty-five million Indian people in Mexico and the Yucatán. Immediately after the Conquest, the Indian population had been reduced to under seven million. By 1650, only one-and-a-half-million pure-blooded Indians remained. The *mestizos* who were genetically equipped to survive small pox, measles, and typhus (Old World diseases to which the natives had no immunity), founded a new hybrid race and inherited Central and South America.[6] *En 1521 nació una nueva raza, el mestizo, el mexicano* (people of mixed Indian and Spanish blood), a race that had never existed before. Chicanos, Mexican-Americans, are the offspring of those first matings.

Our Spanish, Indian, and *mestizo* ancestors explored and settled parts of the U.S. Southwest as early as the sixteenth century. For every gold-hungry *conquistador* and soul-hungry missionary who came north from Mexico, ten to twenty Indians and *mestizos* went along as porters or in other capacities.[7] For the Indians, this constituted a return to the place of origin, Aztlán, thus making Chicanos originally and secondarily indigenous to the Southwest. Indians and *mestizos* from central Mexico intermarried with North American Indians. The continual intermarriage between Mexican and American Indians and Spaniards formed an even greater *mestizaje*.

*El destierro*/The Lost Land

> *Entonces corre la sangre*
> *No sabe el indio que hacer,*
> *le van a quitar su tierra,*
> *la tiene que defender,*
> *el indio se cae muerto,*
> *y el afuerino de pie.*
> *Levántate, Manquilef.*
>
> *Arauco tiene una pena*
> *más negra que su chamal,*
> *ya no son los españoles*
> *los que le hacen llorar,*
> *hoy son los propios chilenos*
> *los que le quitan su pan.*
> *Levántate, Pailahuan.*
> —Violeta Parra, *"Arauco tiene una pena"*[8]

In the 1800s, Anglos migrated illegally into Texas, which was then part of Mexico, in greater and greater numbers and gradually drove the *tejanos* (native Texans of Mexican descent) from their lands, committing all manner of atrocities against them. Their illegal invasion forced Mexico to fight a war to keep its Texas territory. The Battle of the Alamo, in which the Mexican

---

6. Reay Tannahill, *Sex in History* (Briarcliff Manor, NY: Stein and Day/Publishers/Scarborough House, 1980), 308.
7. Chávez, 21.

8. Isabel Parra, *El Libro Mayor de Violeta Parra* (Madrid, España: Ediciones Michay, S.A., 1985), 156–7.

forces vanquished the whites, became, for the whites, the symbol for the cowardly and villainous character of the Mexicans. It became (and still is) a symbol that legitimized the white imperialist takeover. With the capture of Santa Anna later in 1836, Texas became a republic. *Tejanos* lost their land and, overnight, became the foreigners.

> *Ya la mitad del terreno*
> *les vendió el traidor Santa Anna,*
> *con lo que se ha hecho muy rica*
> *la nación americana.*
>
> *¿Qué acaso no se conforman*
> *con el oro de las minas?*
> *Ustedes muy elegantes*
> *y aquí nosotros en ruinas.*
> —from the Mexican corrido,
> *"Del peligro de la Intervención"*[9]

In 1846, the U.S. incited Mexico to war. U.S. troops invaded and occupied Mexico, forcing her to give up almost half of her nation, what is now Texas, New Mexico, Arizona, Colorado and California.

With the victory of the U.S. forces over the Mexican in the U.S.-Mexican War, *los norteamericanos* pushed the Texas border down 100 miles, from *el río Nueces* to *el río Grande*. South Texas ceased to be part of the Mexican state of Tamaulipas. Separated from Mexico, the Native Mexican-Texan no longer looked toward Mexico as home; the Southwest became our homeland once more. The border fence that divides the Mexican people was born on February 2, 1848 with the signing of the Treaty of Guadalupe-Hidalgo. It left 100,000 Mexican citizens on this side, annexed by conquest along with the land. The land established by the treaty as belonging to Mexicans was soon swindled away from its owners. The treaty was never honored and restitution, to this day, has never been made.

> The justice and benevolence of God
> will forbid that . . . Texas should again
> become a howling wilderness
> trod only by savages, or . . . benighted
> by the ignorance and superstition,
> the anarchy and rapine of Mexican misrule.
> The Anglo-American race are destined
> to be forever the proprietors of
> this land of promise and fulfillment.
> Their laws will govern it,
> their learning will enlighten it,
> their enterprise will improve it.
> Their flocks range its boundless pastures,
> for them its fertile lands will yield . . .
> luxuriant harvests . . .

9. From the Mexican *corrido*, "Del peligro de la Intervención." Vicente T. Mendoza, *El Corrido Mexicano* (México, D.F.: Fondo de Cultura Económica, 1954), 42.

> The wilderness of Texas has been redeemed
> by Anglo-American blood & enterprise.
> —William H. Wharton[1]

The Gringo, locked into the fiction of white superiority, seized complete political power, stripping Indians and Mexicans of their land while their feet were still rooted in it. *Con el destierro y el exilio fuimos desuñados, destroncados, destripados*—we were jerked out by the roots, truncated, disemboweled, dispossessed, and separated from our identity and our history. Many, under the threat of Anglo terrorism, abandoned homes and ranches and went to Mexico. Some stayed and protested. But as the courts, law enforcement officials, and government officials not only ignored their pleas but penalized them for their efforts, *tejanos* had no other recourse but armed retaliation.

After Mexican-American resisters robbed a train in Brownsville, Texas on October 18, 1915, Anglo vigilante groups began lynching Chicanos. Texas Rangers would take them into the brush and shoot them. One hundred Chicanos were killed in a matter of months, whole families lynched. Seven thousand fled to Mexico, leaving their small ranches and farms. The Anglos, afraid that the *mexicanos*[2] would seek independence from the U.S., brought in 20,000 army troops to put an end to the social protest movement in South Texas. Race hatred had finally fomented into an all our war.[3]

> My grandmother lost all her cattle,
> they stole her land.

"Drought hit South Texas," my mother tells me. "*La tierra se puso bien seca y los animals comenzaron a morirse de se'. Mi papá se murió de un* heart attack *dejando a maamá* pregnant *y con ocho huercos,* with eight kids and one on the way. *Yo fui la mayor, tenía diez años.* The next year the drought continued *y el ganado* got hoof and mouth. *Se cayeron* in droves *en las pastas y el* brushland, *panzas blancas* ballooning to the skies. *El siguiente año* still no rain. *Mi pobre madre viuda perdió* two-thirds of her *ganado.* A smart *gabacho* lawyer took the land away; *mamá* hadn't paid taxes. *No hablaba inglés,* she didn't know how to ask for time to raise the money." My father's mother, Mama Locha, also lost her *terreno.* For a while we got $12.50 a year for the "mineral rights" of six acres of cemetery, all that was left of the ancestral lands. Mama Locha had asked that we bury her there beside her husband. *El cementerio estaba cercado.* But there was a fence around the cemetery, chained and padlocked by the ranch owners of the surrounding land. We couldn't even get in to visit the graves, much less bury her there. Today, it is still padlocked. The sign reads: "Keep out. Trespassers will be shot."

In the 1930s, after Anglo agribusiness corporations cheated the small Chicano landowners of their land, the corporations hired gangs of *mexicanos* to pull out the brush, chaparral and cactus and to irrigate the desert.

---

1. Arnoldo De León, *They Called Them Greasers: Anglo Attitudes Toward Mexicans in Texas, 1821–1900* (Austin, TX: University of Texas Press, 1983), 2–3.
2. The Plan of San Diego, Texas, drawn up on January 6, 1915, called for the independence and segregation of the states bordering Mexico: Texas, New Mexico, Arizona, Colorado, and California. Indians would get their land back, Blacks would get six states from the south and form their own independent republic. Chávez, 79.
3. Jesús Mena, "Violence in the Rio Grande Valley," *Nuestro* (Jan/Feb. 1983), 41–42.

The land they toiled over had once belonged to many of them, or had been used communally by them. Later the Anglos brought in huge machines and root plows and had the Mexicans scrape the land clean of natural vegetation. In my childhood I saw the end of dryland farming. I witnessed the land cleared; saw the huge pipes connected to underwater sources sticking up in the air. As children, we'd go fishing in some of those canals when they were full and hunt for snakes in them when they were dry. In the 1950s I saw the land, cut up into thousands of neat rectangles and squares, constantly being irrigated. In the 340-day growth season, the seeds of any kind of fruit or vegetable had only to be stuck in the ground in order to grow. More big land corporations came in and bought up the remaining land.

To make a living my father became a sharecropper. Rio Farms Incorporated loaned him seed money and living expenses. At harvest time, my father repaid the loan and forked over 40% of the earnings. Sometimes we earned less than we owed; but always the corporations fared well. Some had major holdings in vegetable trucking, livestock auctions and cotton gins. Altogether we lived on three successive Rio farms; the second was adjacent to the King Ranch and included a dairy farm; the third was a chicken farm. I remember the white feathers of three thousand Leghorn chickens blanketing the land for acres around. My sister, mother and I cleaned, weighed and packaged eggs. (For years afterwards I couldn't stomach the sight of an egg.) I remember my mother attending some of the meetings sponsored by well-meaning whites from Rio Farms. They talked about good nutrition, health, and held huge barbecues. The only thing salvaged for my family from those years are modern techniques of food canning and a food-stained book they printed made up of recipes from Rio Farms' Mexican women. How proud my mother was to have her recipe for *enchiladas coloradas* in a book.

### El cruzar del mojado/Illegal Crossing

> *"Ahora si ya tengo una tumba para llorar,"*
> *dice Conchita,* upon being reunited with
> her unknown mother just before the mother dies.
> —from Ismael Rodriguez' film,
> *Nosotros los pobres*[4]

*La crisis.* *Los gringos* had not stopped at the border. By the end of the nineteenth century, powerful landowners in Mexico, in partnership with U.S. colonizing companies, had dispossessed millions of Indians of their lands. Currently, Mexico and her eighty million citizens are almost completely dependent on the U.S. market. The Mexican government and wealthy growers are in partnership with such American conglomerates as American Motors, IT&T and Du Pont which own factories called *maquiladoras*. One-fourth of all Mexicans work at *maquiladoras*; most are young women. Next to oil, *maquiladoras* are Mexico's second greatest source of U.S. dollars.

---

4. *Nosotros los pobres* was the first Mexican film that was truly Mexican and not an imitation European film. It stressed the devotion and love that children should have for their mother and how its lack would lead to the dissipation of their character. This film spawned a generation of mother-devotion/ungrateful-sons films.

Working eight to twelve hours a day to wire in backup lights of U.S. autos or solder minuscule wires in TV sets is not the Mexican way. While the women are in the *maquiladoras*, the children are left on their own. Many roam the street, become part of *cholo* gangs. The infusion of the values of the white culture, coupled with the exploitation by that culture, is changing the Mexican way of life.

The devaluation of the *peso* and Mexico's dependency on the U.S. have brought on what the Mexicans call *la crisis. No hay trabajo.* Half of the Mexican people are unemployed. In the U.S. a man or woman can make eight times what they can in Mexico. By March, 1987, 1,088 *pesos* were worth one U.S. dollar. I remember when I was growing up in Texas how we'd cross the border at Reynosa or Progreso to buy sugar or medicines when the dollar was worth eight *pesos* and fifty *centavos*.

*La travesía.* For many *mexicanos del otro lado*, the choice is to stay in Mexico and starve or move north and live. *Dicen que cada mexicano siempre sueña de la conquista en los brazos de cuatro gringas rubies, la conquista del país poderoso del norte, los Estados Unidos. En cada Chicano y mexicano vive el mito del tessro territorial perdido.* North Americans call this return to the homeland the silent invasion.

> *"A la cueva volverán"*
> —El Puma *en la canción "Amalia"*

South of the border, called North America's rubbish dump by Chicanos, *mexicanos* congregate in the plazas to talk about the best way to cross. Smugglers, *coyotes, pasadores, enganchadores* approach these people or are sought out by them. *"¿Qué dicen muchachos a echársela de mojado?"*

> "Now among the alien gods with
> weapons of magic am I."
> —Navajo protection song,
> sung when going into battle.[5]

We have a tradition of migration, a tradition of long walks. Today we are witnessing *la migración de los pueblos mexicanos*, the return odyssey to the historical/mythological Aztlán. This time, the traffic is from south to north.

*El retorno* to the promised land first began with the Indians from the interior of Mexico and the *mestizos* that came with the *conquistadores* in the 1500s. Immigration continued in the next three centuries, and, in this century, it continued with the *braceros* who helped to build our railroads and who picked our fruit. Today thousands of Mexicans are crossing the border legally and illegally; ten million people without documents have returned to the Southwest.

Faceless, nameless, invisible, taunted with "Hey cucaracho" (cockroach). Trembling with fear, yet filled with courage, a courage born of desperation. Barefoot and uneducated, Mexicans with hands like boot soles gather at

5. From the Navajo "Protection Song" (to be sung upon going into battle). George W. Gronyn, ed., *American Indian Poetry: The Standard Anthology* *of Songs and Chants* (New York, NY: Liveright, 1934), 97.

night by the river where two worlds merge creating what Reagan calls a frontline, a war zone. The convergence has created a shock culture, a border culture, a third country, a closed country.

Without benefit of bridges, the "*mojados*" (wetbacks) float on inflatable rafts across *el río Grande*, or wade or swim across naked, clutching their clothes over their heads. Holding onto the grass, they pull themselves along the banks with a prayer to *Virgen de Guadalupe* on their lips: *Ay virgencita morena, mi madrecita, dame tu bendición.*

The Border Patrol hides behind the local McDonalds on the outskirts of Brownsville, Texas or some other border town. They set traps around the river beds beneath the bridge.[6] Hunters in army-green uniforms stalk and track these economic refugees by the powerful nightvision of electronic sensing devices planted in the ground or mounted on Border Patrol vans. Cornered by flashlights, frisked while their arms stretch over their heads, *los mojados* are handcuffed, locked in jeeps, and then kicked back across the border.

One out of every three is caught. Some return to enact their rite of passage as many as three times a day. Some of those who make it across undetected fall prey to Mexican robbers such as those in Smugglers' Canyon on the American side of the border near Tijuana. As refugees in a homeland that does not want them, many find a welcome hand holding out only suffering, pain, and ignoble death.

Those who make it past the checking points of the Border Patrol find themselves in the midst of 150 years of racism in Chicano *barrios* in the Southwest and in big northern cities. Living in a no-man's-borderland, caught between being treated as criminals and being able to eat, between resistance and deportation, the illegal refugees are some of the poorest and the most exploited of any people in the U.S. It is illegal for Mexicans to work without green cards. But big farming combines, farm bosses and smugglers who bring them in make money off the "wetbacks'" labor—they don't have to pay federal minimum wages, or ensure adequate housing or sanitary conditions.

The Mexican woman is especially at risk. Often the *coyote* (smuggler) doesn't feed her for days or let her go to the bathroom. Often he rapes her or sells her into prostitution. She cannot call on county or state health or economic resources because she doesn't know English and she fears deportation. American employers are quick to take advantage of her helplessness. She can't go home. She's sold her house, her furniture, borrowed from friends in order to pay the *coyote* who charges her four or five thousand dollars to smuggle her to Chicago. She may work as a live-in maid for white, Chicano or Latino households for as little as $15 a week. Or work in the garment industry, do hotel work. Isolated and worried about her family back home, afraid of getting caught and deported, living with as many as fifteen people in one room, the *mexicana* suffers serious health problems. *Se enferma de los nervios, de alta presión.*[7]

*La mojada, la mujer indocumentada*, is doubly threatened in this country. Not only does she have to contend with sexual violence, but like all women,

---

6. Grace Halsell, *Los ilegales*, trans. Mayo Antonio Sánchez (Editorial Diana Mexica, 1979).
7. Margarita B. Melville, "Mexican Women Adapt to Migration," *International Migration Review*, 1978.

she is prey to a sense of physical helplessness. As a refugee, she leaves the familiar and safe homeground to venture into unknown and possibly dangerous terrain.

> This is her home
> this thin edge of
> barbwire.

## 2: *Movimientos de rebeldía y las culturas que traicionan*

*Esos movimientos de rebeldía que tenemos en la sangre nosotros los mexicanos surgen como ríos desbocanados en mis venas. Y como mi raza que cada en cuando deja caer esa esclavitud de obedecer, de callarse y aceptar, en mi está la rebeldía encimita de mi carne. Debajo de mi humillada mirada está una cara insolente lista para explotar. Me costó muy caro mi rebeldía—acalambrada con desvelos y dudas, sintiéndome inútil, estúpida, e impotente.*

*Me entra una rabia cuando alguien—sea mi mamá, la Iglesia, la cultura de los anglos—me dice haz esto, haz eso sin considerar mis deseos.*

*Repele. Hable pa' 'tras. Fui muy hocicona. Era indiferente a muchos valores de mi culture. No me dejé de los hombres. No fui buena ni obediente.*

*Pero he crecido. Ya no sólo paso toda mi vida botando las costumbres y los valores de mi cultura que me traicionan. También recojo las costumbres que por el tiempo se han probado y las costumbres de respeto a las mujeres.* But despite my growing tolerance, for this Chicana *la guerra de independencia* is a constant.

### The Strength of My Rebellion

I have a vivid memory of an old photograph: I am six years old. I stand between my father and mother, head cocked to the right, the toes of my flat feet gripping the ground. I hold my mother's hand.

To this day I'm not sure where I found the strength to leave the source, the mother, disengage from my family, *mi tierra, mi gente,* and all that picture stood for. I had to leave home so I could find myself, find my own intrinsic nature buried under the personality that had been imposed on me.

I was the first in six generations to leave the Valley, the only one in my family to ever leave home. But I didn't leave all the parts of me: I kept the ground of my own being. On it I walked away, taking with me the land, the Valley, Texas. *Gané mi camino y me largué. Muy andariega mi hija.* Because I left of my own accord *me dicen, "¿Cómo te gusta la mala vida?"*

At a very early age I had a strong sense of who I was and what I was about and what was fair. I had a stubborn will. It tried constantly to mobilize my soul under my own regime, to live life on my own terms no matter how unsuitable to others they were. *Terca.* Even as a child I would not obey. I was "lazy." Instead of ironing my younger brothers' shirts or cleaning the cupboards,

I would pass many hours studying, reading, painting, writing. Every bit of self-faith I'd painstakingly gathered took a beating daily. Nothing in my culture approved of me. *Había agarrado malos pasos.* Something was "wrong" with me. *Estaba más allá de la tradición.*

There is a rebel in me—the Shadow-Beast. It is a part of me that refuses to take orders from outside authorities. It refuses to take orders from my conscious will, it threatens the sovereignty of my rulership. It is that part of me that hates constraints of any kind, even those self-imposed. At the least hint of limitations on my time or space by others, it kicks out with both feet. Bolts.

### Cultural Tyranny

Culture forms our beliefs. We perceive the version of reality that it communicates. Dominant paradigms, predefined concepts that exist as unquestionable, unchallengeable, are transmitted to us through the culture. Culture is made by those in power—men. Males make the rules and laws; women transmit them. How many times have I heard mothers and mothers-in-law tell their sons to beat their wives for not obeying them, for being *hociconas* (big mouths), for being *callejeras* (going to visit and gossip with neighbors), for expecting their husbands to help with the rearing of children and the housework, for wanting to be something other than housewives?

The culture expects women to show greater acceptance of, and commitment to, the value system than men. The culture and the Church insist that women are subservient to males. If a woman rebels she is a *mujer mala*. If a woman doesn't renounce herself in favor of the male, she is selfish. If a woman remains a *virgen* until she marries, she is a good woman. For a woman of my culture there used to be only three directions she could turn: to the Church as a nun, to the streets as a prostitute, or to the home as a mother. Today some of us have a fourth choice: entering the world by way of education and career and becoming self-autonomous persons. A very few of us. As a working class people our chief activity is to put food in our mouths, a roof over our heads and clothes on our backs. Educating our children is out of reach for most of us. Educated or not, the onus is still on woman to be a wife/mother—only the nun can escape motherhood. Women are made to feel total failures if they don't marry and have children. *"¿Y cuándo te casas, Gloria? Se te va a pasar el tren."* Y yo les digo, *"Pos si me caso, no va ser con un hombre."* Se quedan calladitas. *Sí, soy hija de la Chingada.* I've always been her daughter. *No 'tés chingando.*

Humans fear the supernatural, both the undivine (the animal impulses such as sexuality, the unconscious, the unknown, the alien) and the divine (the superhuman, the god in us). Culture and religion seek to protect us from these two forces. The female, by virtue of creating entities of flesh and blood in her stomach (she bleeds every month but does not die), by virtue of being in tune with nature's cycles, is feared. Because, according to Christianity and most other major religions, woman is carnal, animal, and closer to the undivine, she must be protected. Protected from herself. Woman is the stranger, the other. She is man's recognized nightmarish pieces, his Shadow-Beast. The sight of her sends him into a frenzy of anger and fear.

*La gorra, el rebozo, la mantilla* are symbols of my culture's "protection" of women. Culture (read males) professes to protect women. Actually it keeps women in rigidly defined roles. It keeps the girlchild from other men—don't poach on my preserves, only I can touch my child's body. Our mothers taught us well, "*Los hombres nomás quieren una cosa*'; men aren't to be trusted, they are selfish and are like children. Mothers made sure we didn't walk into a room of brothers or fathers or uncles in nightgowns or shorts. We were never alone with men, not even those of our own family.

Through our mothers, the culture gave us mixed messages: *No voy a dejar que ningún pelado desgraciado maltrate a mis hijos.* And in the next breath it would say, *La mujer tiene que hacer lo que le diga el hombre.* Which was it to be—strong, or submissive, rebellious or conforming?

Tribal rights over those of the individual insured the survival of the tribe and were necessary then, and, as in the case of all indigenous peoples in the world who are still fighting off intentional, premeditated murder (genocide), they are still necessary.

Much of what the culture condemns focuses on kinship relationships. The welfare of the family, the community, and the tribe is more important than the welfare of the individual. The individual exists first as kin—as sister, as father, as *padrino*—and last as self.

In my culture, selfishness is condemned, especially in women; humility and selflessness, the absence of selfishness, is considered a virtue. In the past, acting humble with members outside the family ensured that you would make no one *envidioso* (envious); therefore he or she would not use witchcraft against you. If you get above yourself, you're an *envidiosa*. If you don't behave like everyone else, *la gente* will say that you think you're better than others, *que te crees grande*. With ambition (condemned in the Mexican culture and valued in the Anglo) comes envy. *Respeto* carries with it a set of rules so that social categories and hierarchies will be kept in order: respect is reserved for *la abuela, papá, el patrón*, those with power in the community. Women are at the bottom of the ladder, one rung above the deviants. The Chicano, *mexicano*, and some Indian cultures have no tolerance for deviance. Deviance is whatever is condemned by the community. Most societies try to get rid of their deviants. Most cultures have burned and beaten their homosexuals and others who deviate from the sexual common.[1] The queer are the mirror reflecting the heterosexual tribe's fear: being different, being other and therefore lesser, therefore sub-human, in-human, non-human.

### Half and Half

There was a *muchacha* who lived near my house. *La gente del pueblo* talked about her being *una de las otras*, "of the Others." They said that for six months she was a woman who had a vagina that bled once a month, and that for the other six months she was a man, had a penis and she peed standing up. They called her half and half, *mita' y mita'*, neither one nor the other but a strange doubling, a deviation of nature that horrified, a work of nature inverted. But there is a magic aspect in abnormality and so-called

1. Francisco Guerra, *The Pre-Columbian Mind: A study into the aberrant nature of sexual drives, drugs affecting behaviour, and the attitude towards* life and death, with a survey of psychotherapy in pre-Columbian America (New York, NY: Seminar Press, 1971).

deformity. Maimed, mad, and sexually different people were believed to possess supernatural powers by primal cultures' magico-religious thinking. For them, abnormality was the price a person had to pay for her or his inborn extraordinary gift.

There is something compelling about being both male and female, about having an entry into both worlds. Contrary to some psychiatric tenets, half and halfs are not suffering from a confusion of sexual identity, or even from a confusion of gender. What we are suffering from is an absolute despot duality that says we are able to be only one or the other. It claims that human nature is limited and cannot evolve into something better. But I, like other queer people, am two in one body, both male and female. I am the embodiment of the *hieros gamos*: the coming together of opposite qualities within.

### Fear of Going Home: Homophobia

For the lesbian of color, the ultimate rebellion she can make against her native culture is through her sexual behavior. She goes against two moral prohibitions: sexuality and homosexuality. Being lesbian and raised Catholic, indoctrinated as straight, I *made the choice to be queer* (for some it is genetically inherent). It's an interesting path, one that continually slips in and out of the white, the Catholic, the Mexican, the indigenous, the instincts. In and out of my head. It makes for *loquería*, the crazies. It is a path of knowledge— one of knowing (and of learning) the history of oppression of our *raza*. It is a way of balancing, of mitigating duality.

In a New England college where I taught, the presence of a few lesbians threw the more conservative heterosexual students and faculty into a panic. The two lesbian students and we two lesbian instructors met with them to discuss their fears. One of the students said, "I thought homophobia meant fear of going home after a residency."

And I thought, how apt. Fear of going home. And of not being taken in. We're afraid of being abandoned by the mother, the culture, *la Raza*, for being unacceptable, faulty, damaged. Most of us unconsciously believe that if we reveal this unacceptable aspect of the self our mother/culture/race will totally reject us. To avoid rejection, some of us conform to the values of the culture, push the unacceptable parts into the shadows. Which leaves only one fear—that we will be found out and that the Shadow-Beast will break out of its cage. Some of us take another route. We try to make ourselves conscious of the Shadow-Beast, stare at the sexual lust and lust for power and destruction we see on its face, discern among its features the undershadow that the reigning order of heterosexual males project on our Beast. Yet still others of us take it another step: we try to waken the Shadow-Beast inside us. Not many jump at the chance to confront the Shadow-Beast in the mirror without flinching at her lidless serpent eyes, her cold clammy moist hand dragging us underground, fangs bared and hissing. How does one put feathers on this particular serpent? But a few of us have been lucky—on the face of the Shadow-Beast we have seen not lust but tenderness; on its face we have uncovered the lie.

### Intimate Terrorism: Life in the Borderlands

The world is not a safe place to live in. We shiver in separate cells in enclosed cities, shoulders hunched, barely keeping the panic below the surface of the skin, daily drinking shock along with our morning coffee, fearing the torches being set to our buildings, the attacks in the streets. Shutting down. Woman does not feel safe when her own culture, and white culture, are critical of her; when the males of all races hunt her as prey.

Alienated from her mother culture, "alien" in the dominant culture, the woman of color does not feel safe within the inner life of her Self. Petrified, she can't respond, her face caught between *los intersticios*, the spaces between the different worlds she inhabits.

The ability to respond is what is meant by responsibility, yet our cultures take away our ability to act—shackle us in the name of protection. Blocked, immobilized, we can't move forward, can't move backwards. That writhing serpent movement, the very movement of life, swifter than lightning, frozen.

We do not engage fully. We do not make full use of our faculties. We abnegate. And there in front of us is the crossroads and choice: to feel a victim where someone else is in control and therefore responsible and to blame (being a victim and transferring the blame on culture, mother, father, ex-lover, friend, absolves me of responsibility), or to feel strong, and, for the most part, in control.

My Chicana identity is grounded in the Indian woman's history of resistance. The Aztec female rites of mourning were rites of defiance protesting the cultural changes which disrupted the equality and balance between female and male, and protesting their demotion to a lesser status, their denigration. Like *la Llorona*, the Indian woman's only means of protest was wailing.

So *mamá, Raza*, how wonderful, *no tener que rendir cuentas a nadie*. I feel perfectly free to rebel and to rail against my culture. I fear no betrayal on my part because, unlike Chicanas and other women of color who grew up white or who have only recently returned to their native cultural roots, I was totally immersed in mine. It wasn't until I went to high school that I "saw" whites. Until I worked on my master's degree I had not gotten within an arm's distance of them. I was totally immersed *en lo mexicano*, a rural, peasant, isolated, *mexicanismo*. To separate from my culture (as from my family) I had to feel competent enough on the outside and secure enough inside to live life on my own. Yet in leaving home I did not lose touch with my origins because *lo mexicano* is in my system. I am a turtle, wherever I go I carry "home" on my back.

Not me sold out my people but they me. So yes, though "home" permeates every sinew and cartilage in my body, I too am afraid of going home. Though I'll defend my race and culture when they are attacked by non-*mexicanos*, *conozco el malestar de mi cultura*. I abhor some of my culture's ways, how it cripples its women, *como burras*, our strengths used against us, lowly *burras* bearing humility with dignity. The ability to serve, claim the males, is our highest virtue. I abhor how my culture makes *macho* caricatures of its men.

No, I do not buy all the myths of the tribe into which I was born. I can understand why the more tinged with Anglo blood, the more adamantly my colored and colorless sisters glorify their colored culture's values—to offset the extreme devaluation of it by the white culture. It's a legitimate reaction. But I will not glorify those aspects of my culture which have injured me and which have injured me in the name of protecting me.

So, don't give me your tenets and your laws. Don't give me your lukewarm gods. What I want is an accounting with all three cultures—white, Mexican, Indian. I want the freedom to carve and chisel my own face, to staunch the bleeding with ashes, to fashion my own gods out of my entrails. And if going home is denied me then I will have to stand and claim my space, making a new culture—*una cultura mestiza*—with my own lumber, my own bricks and mortar and my own feminist architecture.

## The Wounding of the *india*-Mestiza

*Estas carnes indias que despreciamos nosotros los mexicanos asi como despreciamos condenamos a nuestra madre, Malinali. Nos condenamos a nosotros mismos. Esta raza vencida, enemigo cuerpo.*

Not me sold out my people but they me. *Malinali Tenepat*, or *Malintzín*, has become known as *la Chingada*—the fucked one. She has become the bad word that passes a dozen times a day from the lips of Chicanos. Whore, prostitute, the woman who sold out her people to the Spaniards are epithets Chicanos spit out with contempt.

The worst kind of betrayal lies in making us believe that the Indian woman in us is the betrayer. We, *indias y mestizas*, police the Indian in us, brutalize and condemn her. Male culture has done a good job on us. *Son las costumbres que traicionan. La india en mí es la sombra: La Chingada, Tlazolteotl, Coatlicue. Son ellas que oyemos lamentando a sus hijas perdidas.*

Not me sold out my people but they me. Because of the color of my skin they betrayed me. The dark-skinned woman has been silenced, gagged, caged, bound into servitude with marriage, bludgeoned for 300 years, sterilized and castrated in the twentieth century. For 300 years she has been a slave, a force of cheap labor, colonized by the Spaniard, the Anglo, by her own people (and in Mesoamerica her lot under the Indian patriarchs was not free of wounding). For 300 years she was invisible, she was not heard. Many times she wished to speak, to act, to protest, to challenge. The odds were heavily against her. She hid her feelings; she hid her truths; she concealed her fire; but she kept stoking the inner flame. She remained faceless and voiceless, but a light shone through her veil of silence. And though she was unable to spread her limbs and though for her right now the sun has sunk under the earth and there is no moon, she continues to tend the flame. The spirit of the fire spurs her to fight for her own skin and a piece of ground to stand on, a ground from which to view the world—a perspective, a home-ground where she can plumb the rich ancestral roots into her own ample *mestiza* heart. She waits till the waters are not so turbulent and the mountains not so slippery with sleet. Battered and bruised she waits, her bruises throwing her back upon herself and the rhythmic pulse of the feminine. *Coatlalopeuh* waits with her.

> *Aquí en la soledad prospera su rebeldía.*
> *En la soledad Ella prospera.*

1987

---

# ARIEL DORFMAN
## b. 1942

Born in Argentina to Eastern European Jews, Vladimiro Ariel Dorfman lived in New York City in the early years of his life, after his father, an economist, accepted a job with the United Nations. The middle-class family lived in the United States for a decade, then relocated in 1954 to Chile, where in 1967 Dorfman became a naturalized citizen. He earned his bachelor's degree from the University of Chile, in Santiago, where he later became a faculty member. As a graduate student at the University of California, Berkeley, he wrote a thesis on the absurdist plays of the English writer Harold Pinter. Two decades later, Dorfman was an active left-wing intellectual connected to the government of the elected Socialist president Salvador Allende. On September 11, 1973, General Augusto Pinochet led a coup d'état against Allende, and Dorfman was then briefly forced to live clandestinely. His books were burned in the country's capital, Santiago. He received death threats. Eventually, he went into exile, living in France and Holland until he and his family settled in Durham, North Carolina, where as a Distinguished Professor at Duke University he teaches principally about Latin American cultures.

In his early writing, Dorfman studied popular culture in Latin America. He became famous for *Cómo leer al Pato Donald* (How to Read Donald Duck, 1975), a critique of Walt Disney's characters, coauthored with Armand Mattelart. His first novel, the avant-garde *Moros en la costa* (translated as *Hard Rain*, 1990), addresses questions of good and evil. It was followed by a dozen others, including *La última canción de Manuel Sendero* (The Last Song of Manuel Sendero, 1982), *Konfidenz* (1994), and *La nana y el iceberg* (The Nanny and the Iceberg, 1999). Among his volumes of poetry are *In Case of Fire in a Foreign Land: New and Collected Poems from Two Languages* (2002). Dorfman is best-known internationally for his play *La muerte y la doncella* (*Death and the Maiden*, 1991), staged on Broadway in 1992 and adapted for the screen in 1994. The play is a meditation on truth, reconciliation, and remembrance in a fictitious Latin American country—much like Chile—that has returned to democracy but is struggling to evaluate its moral standing. Dorfman's cinematic work includes, in collaboration with his son Rodrigo, writing and directing an adaptation of his book *My House Is on Fire* (1997), about the fear and confusion of two children growing up under the Chilean dictatorship.

In his memoir *Heading South, Looking North* (1998), of which the second of sixteen chapters (plus an epilogue) is included here, Dorfman addresses both his journey into exile and his loyalty to and ambivalence about Anglo and Hispanic cultures. He also focuses on his Jewish identity, which has become increasingly relevant to him in his later years. Although he has lived in the United States longer than anywhere else and has been shaped by Latino culture, Dorfman finds inspiration not in other Latino writers but in Latin American figures such as Jorge Luis Borges and Julio Cortázar. He is at once a Latin American writer in exile and a Latino writer in the United States. His first language was English, he then became fluent in Spanish, and only in his late adolescence did he return to English. In fact, much as Rosario Ferré does with her work, Dorfman writes his fiction, nonfiction, and opinion pieces (in, for example, Madrid's *El País*, London's *The Guardian*, *The Washington Post*, and the *Los Angeles Times*) in Spanish or English and then rewrites them in the other language—not just translating his thoughts but redesigning them. His linguistic choice varies not by genre but by the audience he has in mind for a piece. In a 1999 interview with Ilan Stavans in *Michigan Quarterly Review*, Dorfman explained: "For me the perfect audience would be one made of 40 to 60 million people like I am. I honestly think that if I had an audience, I would write in an entirely different way: switching languages, going in and out, like the Nuyoricans and Chicanos."

---

### FROM HEADING SOUTH, LOOKING NORTH

### Two: A Chapter Dealing with the Discovery of Life and Language at an Early Age

I was falling.

It was May 6, 1942, and the city was Buenos Aires and I had only just been born a few seconds ago and I was already in danger.

I did not need to be told. I knew it before I knew anything else. But my mother warned me anyway that I was falling, the first words I ever heard in my life, even if I could not have registered them in my brain, the first words my mother remembers being pronounced in my presence. Strange and foreboding that of all the many words attending the scattered chaos and delirium of my birth, the only shrapnels of sense my mother snatched from extinction and later froze into family legend should have been that warning.

It was not intended as a metaphysical statement. My mother had been dosed with a snap of gas to ease her pain as she labored, and when her newborn baby had been placed on a nearby table to be cleaned, she thought in her daze that it was slanted and the boy was about to roll off, and that was when she cried out. "*Doctor*," she called, and my uncomprehending ears must have absorbed the meaningless sound. "*Doctor, se cae el niño, se cae el niño*," she told the doctor that I was falling, the boy was about to fall.

She was wrong about my body and right about my mind, my life, my soul. I was falling, like every child who was ever born, I was falling into solitude and nothingness, headlong and headfirst, and my mother, by her very words, by the mere act of formulating her fear in a human language, inadvertently stopped my descent by introducing me to Spanish, by sending Spanish out to catch me, cradle me, pull me back from the abyss.

I was a baby: a pad upon which any stranger could scrawl a signature. A passive little bastard, shipwrecked, no ticket back, not even sure that a smile, a scream, my only weapons, could help me to surface. And then Spanish slid to the rescue, in my mother's first cry, and soon in her murmurs and lullabies and in my father's deep voice of protection and in his jokes and in the hum of love that would soon envelop me from an extended family. Maybe that was my first exile: I had not asked to be born, had not chosen anything, not my face, not the face of my parents, not this extreme sensitivity that has always boiled out of me, not the early rash on my skin, not my remote asthma, not my nearby country, not my unpronounceable name. But Spanish was there at the beginning of my body or perhaps where my body ended and the world began, coaxing that body into life as only a lover can, convincing me slowly, sound by sound, that life was worth living, that together we could tame the fiends of the outer bounds and bend them to our will. That everything can be named and therefore, in theory, at least in desire, the world belongs to us. That if we cannot own the world, nobody can stop us from imagining everything in it, everything it can be, everything it ever was.

It promised, my Spanish, that it would take care of me.

And for a while it delivered on its promise.

It did not tell me that at the very moment it was promising the world to me, that world was being disputed by others, by men in shadows who had other plans for me, new banishments planned for me, men who were just as desperate not to fall as I had been at birth, desperate to rise, rise to power.

Nor did Spanish report that on its boundaries other languages roamed, waiting for me, greedy languages, eager to penetrate my territory and establish a foothold, ready to take over at the slightest hint of weakness. It did not whisper a word to me of its own imperial history, how it had subjugated and absorbed so many people born into other linguistic systems, first during the centuries of its triumphant ascendancy in the Iberian peninsula and then in the Americas after the so-called Discovery, converting natives and later domesticating slaves, merely because the men who happened to carry Spanish in their cortex were more ruthless and cunning and technologically practical than the men who carried Catalán or Basque or Aymará or Quechua or Swahili inside them. It did not hint that English was to the North, smiling to itself, certain that it would father the mind that is writing these words even now, that I would have to surrender to its charms eventually, it did not suggest that English was ready to do to me what Spanish itself had done to others so many times during its evolution, what it had done, in fact, to my own parents: wrenched them from the arms of their original language.

And yet I am being unfair to Spanish—and also, therefore, to English. Languages do not only expand through conquest: they also grow by offering a safe haven to those who come to them in danger, those who are falling from some place far less safe than a mother's womb, those who, like my own parents, were forced to flee their native land.

After all, I would not be alive today if Spanish had not generously offered my parents a way of connecting with each other. I was conceived in Spanish, literally imagined into being by that language, flirted, courted, coupled into existence by my parents in a Spanish that had not been there at their birth.

Spanish was able to catch me as I fell because it had many years before caught my mother and my father just as gently and with many of the same promises.

Both my parents had come to their new language from Eastern Europe in the early years of the twentieth century, the children of Jewish émigrés to Argentina—but that is as far as the parallel goes, because the process of their seduction by Spanish could not have been more different.

And therein lies a story. More than one.

I'll start with my mother. Hers is the more traditional, almost archetypical, migratory experience.

Fanny Zelicovich Vaisman was born in 1909 in Kishinev. Her birthplace, like her life itself, was subject to the arbitrary fluctuations of history: at that time, Kishinev belonged to Greater Russia, but from 1918 was incorporated into Romania and then in 1940 into the Soviet Union—only to become, after the breakup of that country, the capital of the republic of Moldavia. If my mother had stayed there, she would have been able to change nationalities four times without moving from the street on which she had seen the first light of this world. Though if she had remained there she would probably not have lived long enough to make all those changes in citizenship.

Her maternal grandfather, a cattle dealer, was murdered in the pogrom of 1903. Many years later, I heard the story from my mother's uncle Karl, in Los Angeles, of all places. It was 1969 and he must have been well over eighty years old but he cried like a child as he told us, tears streaming down his face, speaking in broken English and lapsing into Yiddish and being semi-translated by my mother into Spanish so Angélica and I would understand, his pain imploding like a storm into the mix of languages, unrelieved by the passing of time: how his mother had hid with him and his sisters and brothers in a church, how they had listened for hours while the Cossacks raged outside—those screams in Russian, those cries for help in Yiddish, the horses, the horses, my great-uncle Karl whispered—and how he had emerged who knows how many centuries later and found his father dead, his father's throat slit, how he had held his father in his arms.

It was that experience, it seems, that had led the family, after aeons of persecution, to finally emigrate. Australia was considered, and the United States, but Argentina was selected: Baron Maurice de Hirsch's Jewish Colonization Association had helped to open the pampas to Jews anxious to own land and cultivate the prairies. Two brothers of my grandmother Clara set out, and when they wrote back that the streets of Buenos Aires were paved with gold, the rest of the family started making plans to leave as well. Only Clara's mother was unable to emigrate: her youngest daughter would not have passed the tests of the health authorities in Argentina, apparently because she had had meningitis, which had left her seriously retarded. Which meant that both of them, mother and daughter, lived their lives out in Kishinev until they were killed by the Nazis. According to my mother, the old woman went out into the streets the day the blackshirts drove into town and insulted them and was shot on the spot; and though I would love this story to be true, love to have a great-grandmother who did not let herself be carted off to a concentration camp and forced her foes to kill her on the same streets where her husband had been slaughtered, I have often wondered if this version is a fantasy devised more to inspire the living than to honor the dead.

What is certain is that my mother was saved from such a fate by departing with her parents. At the age of three months, she found herself on a boat from Hamburg[1] bound for an Argentina that, devoid as it might be of pogroms, nevertheless had enough Nazis and Nazi-lovers to force her, thirty-six years later, into her next exile. The ambivalent attitude of the host

---

1. City in northern Germany.

country toward the Jews was presaged in two run-ins my mother had with the Spanish language at an early age.

When she was six years old, my mother recalls, she had been sent to her first school. In the afternoons, private piano lessons were offered and my grandmother Clara insisted that her child take these, perhaps as a way of proving how genteel and civilized the family had become. On one of the first afternoons, my mother was by herself in the music room waiting for the teacher, when the door slammed shut. From the other side, a mocking chorus of Argentine children started shouting at her in Spanish. She tried to open the door but they were holding it tight. '*No podés*,' they taunted her. You can't open the door, because you're a Jew, "*porque sos judía*." Definitely not the first words she ever heard in Spanish, but the first words she ever remembers having heard, the words that have remained in her memory like a scar. You talk funny, they said to her. You talk funny because you're a Jew.

She probably did talk funny. Yiddish had been the only language her family spoke in Argentina for years. It is true that my mom's father, Zeide, forced himself to learn some rudimentary Spanish: a week after arriving in Argentina, he was peddling blankets house-to-house in Buenos Aires, starting with the Jewish community, and was soon knocking at the doors of Spanish-speaking goyim as well, prospering enough to eventually start a small shop. But his wife, at least during those first years, was inclined to stay away from the new life, from the new language: almost as if Clara feared, clutching her baby daughter to her, that out there the Cossacks were still lurking, ready to attack.

Instead of the dreaded Cossacks, another military man passed briefly through the family's life and inadvertently convinced my Baba Clara, several years before those anti-Semitic school brats refused my mother entry into the community, that Argentina was truly willing to welcome the immigrants.

One day, an Argentine colonel emerged from his brother's residence, next door to the Zelicovich house. He stepped into the torrid heat of the Buenos Aires summer and there, on the sidewalk, he saw his little niece playing with a pretty, blond-haired, foreign-looking girl—my mother, who was probably three years old, maybe four, who had by then picked up a smattering of Spanish from the neighborhood kids. The colonel advanced, reached out with one hand toward his Argentine niece and with the other did not take out a gun and shoot my mother but clasped her small hand and trundled both of them off to the corner for some ice cream. An irrelevant incident, but not to Baba Clara: my mother's mother, upon seeing the colonel go off with the children so amiably and then return with prodigal ice-cream cones, was amazed beyond belief. She said she lifted her hands to heaven to thank the Lord. An Army officer, any member of any Army, was a devil, a potential Jew-killer: that such a man should invite a child from the Tribe of Israel to share sweets with his niece was as miraculous as the Czar quoting the Torah.

My mother does not remember the colonel or the little friend or the ice cream. What she has consigned to memory is the reaction of her mother. What she remembers is her mother's voice that very night, recounting in Yiddish the marvels of Argentina and its love of the Jews to her skeptical sister Rosa. Or was it on a later occasion? Because Clara repeated the same story over and over again through the years. Paradoxical that it should have been in Yiddish, because the story registers and foretells the defeat of Yiddish, how kindness forced it to retreat, her offspring's first tentative, independent steps into a world where Yiddish was not necessary. A world that would demand of my mother, as it demands of all immigrant children, that she abandon the language of her ancestors if she wanted to pass through that door those children would soon be trying to slam shut. I believe this story has abided in the family memory so many years because it is foundational: the prophetic story of how my mother would leave home and assimilate, escaping from that ghost language of the past into the Spanish-echoing streets.

Streets where my father, many years down the road, was waiting for her.

By then, fortunately for me, they both spoke Spanish. I can almost hear him now convincing her to marry him in the one language they both shared, I try to eavesdrop so many years later on the mirror of their lovemaking, listening to how they conceived me, how their language coupled me out of nothingness, made me out of the nakedness of night, *la desnudez de la noche.*

My father's trail to the wonders of the sleek Spanish he murmured in her ears had not been as direct and simple as my mother's. Rather than the normal relay race of one language replacing the other, it had been a more convoluted bilingual journey that he had taken.

To begin with, he had emigrated not once but twice to Argentina; though perhaps more crucial was that he came from a family sophisticated in the arts of language, a sophistication that would end up saving his life several times over.

Adolfo was born in 1907 in Odessa, now Ukraine, then Greater Russia, to a well-to-do Jewish family that had been in the region for at least a century and probably longer. As well as Russian, his father, David Dorfman, spoke English and French fluently, as did his mother, Raissa Libovich, who also happened to be conversant in German after three years of studying in Vienna. All those languages, but no Yiddish: they considered themselves assimilated, cosmopolitan, definitively European. If David and Raissa ended up in Argentina, it was not due to any pogrom. In fact, the 1903 pogrom where my mother's grandfather died had been beaten back in Odessa by the Jewish riffraff and gangsters immortalized later in Isaac Babel's[2] writings. Their expatriation derived from a more trite and middle-class problem: in 1909, at about the time my mother was being born across the Black Sea, David Dorfman's soap factory had gone bankrupt and he had been forced to flee abroad to escape his creditors. Of that venture, only a seal, used to stamp certain particularly fragrant epitomes of soap, remains in my father's possession: "Cairo[3] Aromas," it grandly proclaims in Russian. But my grandfather, rather than heading for the mythical Cairo of the seal, set off for the more distant and promising Buenos Aires of history. And one year later his wife and three-year-old Adolfo followed him.

Some years later—it was 1914 by then and the child was six—Raissa and her son were headed back to Russia, purportedly on a visit to the family, though persistent rumors mention another woman, whom David might have been scandalously visiting. Whether or not the gossip is true, what is certain is that my grandmother and my father picked the worst time to go back: they

2. Russian Jewish journalist, playwright, and short-story writer (1894–1940).
3. Capital of Egypt.

were caught in the eruption of the First World War and then in the Russian Revolution. The reasons for their staying on have always been nebulous. "We were going to beat those Prussians in a matter of months, it was going to be a picnic," my baba Pizzi told me half a century later, when she and the world knew that it had been anything but a picnic. "And," she added, "you always think it's about to end and then it doesn't and you wait a bit more and you've invested so much hope in believing that it'll all finish tomorrow that you don't want to give up that easily." Pizzi would tell me this in English on my visits to Buenos Aires, before I myself would experience what it is to believe that something terrible will end soon, before my own exile would teach me that we spend a good part of our lives believing things will get better because there is no way we can imagine them, wish to imagine them, getting worse. My exile—when I fled Buenos Aires after fleeing Chile; my exile—when the phone rang in Amsterdam with the news that Pizzi had died and I learned that banishment does not take from you only the living but takes their death from you as well. Pizzi had died and I had not been there, I would never sit by her side again and ask her about the past, the steps of Odessa and the *Potemkin*,[4] the Russian secret police raiding the house, never again be able to ask her about the day my father had brought my mother home to be introduced as his future wife, never again discuss with my favorite grandparent the difficulties of being a woman journalist in Buenos Aires, never again hear her painstakingly translate into English for my benefit the stories for children she wrote for the Argentine Sunday papers and had herself translated from Russian into Spanish, as she had translated *Anna Karenina*[5] for the first time into Spanish, never again hear from her lips the tales of how they had survived the hardships of the war, how she had spent those years alone with her son, preparing to return to the land where her husband awaited them.

And then the Revolution had come. Like so many Jews at the time, she fervently supported it. But how to make a living with everything in turmoil? While her son went to school with the bullets flying and the walls splattered with red slogans and the city changing hands overnight—she kept a home for him, and food on the table, and managed to put him through school, and it was all due to her languages; that's what kept them alive. And she was so proficient at them that she started working with Litvinov and ended up serving the most prominent Bolshevik Jew of them all, Trotsky, acting as one of his interpreters at the peace talks with the Germans at Brest Litovsk,[6] where the fate of the Soviet Union was decided. She remembered how he had paced up and down on the train as it sped through the Ukraine to the meeting: how much to give up, how much to concede, how much to pay for peace and the time to build a new Army, a new society?

And while she was translating German into Russian in order to survive, her husband, half the world away, was patiently translating from Russian into

---

4. Russian battleship whose crew, during the Russian Revolution of 1905, mutinied against their officers, who were members of the country's Czarist regime. The ship then docked in Odessa, where a funeral for one slain crewman became a demonstration against the regime. On the steps from the port area to the center of the city, dismounted cavalry officers fired on the demonstrators.
5. Novel by the Russian writer Leo Tolstoy (1828–1910), published in installments from 1873 to

1877.
6. City in Russia (now in Belarus) where, in March 1918, Russia exited World War I by signing a treaty with the Central Powers (the German Empire, the Austrian-Hungarian Empire, the Ottoman Empire, and the Kingdom of Bulgaria). *Litvinov*: Maksim Maksimovich Litvinov (1876–1951), Russian Jewish revolutionary and Soviet diplomat. *Trotsky*: Leon Trotsky (1879–1940), Russian revolutionary and Communist leader.

Spanish in order to bring her and the boy safely to Argentina. When the Revolution broke out,[7] it became almost impossible to get people safely out of the newly formed Soviet Union, but my grandfather had hit on a plan: there was a flood of immigrants streaming into Argentina and the police needed people who could interpret for them and help streamline the process, and David found a job with them, hoping that his new post would strengthen his assertion that his faraway wife and son were de facto Argentine citizens and should be helped to exit from Ukraine. Incredibly, he managed to convince some official in the Argentine government to intervene, and more incredibly, somebody in the frenzied Soviet Foreign Minstry listened, and that is how Raissa and Adolfo managed to take the last ship—at least so goes the family legend—to leave Odessa at the end of 1920. My father remembers a stow-away: the Red Army soldiers coming on board and the young man's fearful eyes when he was discovered, the stubble on his face, the look of someone who knew he would die—and then they hauled him away, dragged him back to that glorious Odessa of my father's youth, that Odessa now of danger and death.

It's hard to be sure, but there's a good chance, my father says, that he and his mother would not have outlived the terrible year of 1921. The civil war, the famine, the plague, decimated Odessa and so many other cities in the country: most of Raissa's family, left behind, died. And among the dead was Ilyusha, Adolfo's older cousin. To the fatherless boy, Ilyusha had been a protector, an angel, a brother for seven lonely years. That cousin of his had let my father tag along as he plunged into the turmoil and romance of the Revolution. My father's participation had not gone beyond carrying a mys-terious black bag that Ilyusha always wanted near him, a bag that contained nothing more dangerous, it seems, than poems and pamphlets, but it was the first social activism of my father's life and he was never to forget it. Ilyu-sha's memory was to haunt him through the turbulent twenties and into the thirties as Argentina itself began to head for what seemed a revolution of its own.

Spanish received my father with open arms, a smoother welcome than my mother's. Either because he had already had previous experience with the language as a child or because his parents were polylingual themselves, he was soon speaking and writing Spanish brilliantly, so well that, soon after graduating from the university, the Russian émigré Dorfman wrote and had published the first history of Argentine industry, becoming his country's leading expert on the subject. More books, many articles and essays followed, all of them focusing on Argentina and its tomorrow, all of them in Spanish: apparently an absolute commitment to his new land and language.

My father was bilingual and remains so to this day. That he kept his Rus-sian intact can be attributed to his having spent his formative years in Odessa, to the fact that Russian contained within its words the full force of its nationhood and literature and vast expanses—unlike the language that my mother discarded, a Yiddish that occupied no territory, possessed no name on the map of nations, had never been officially promoted by a state. But my father's retention of Russian may signal something else: a double-ness that did not plague my mother. She rid herself of Yiddish as a way of

---

7. I.e., the Russian Revolution of 1917 led by the Bolsheviks.

breaking with the past, bonding forever with the Argentina that had taken her by the hand the day when she was three and offered her an ice cream in Spanish. She could easily segregate her first, her original, language, relegate it to the nostalgia of yesteryear, a gateway to a land that no longer existed except in the shards of hazy family anecdotes. Her monolingualism was a way of stating that Yiddish had become irrelevant to the present, to her present.

My father could never have said that of Russian. The language of his youth, the language his parents spoke with him at home, was to embody, for many in my father's generation—in Argentina and all over the world— the language in which the future was being built: the first socialist revolution in history, the first socialist state, the first place on the planet where men would not exploit men. Always vaguely leftist and rebellious, by the early 1930s my father had joined the Communist Party and embraced Marxism. Like many men and women his age, he saw no alternative to what he was sure were the death throes of capitalism reeling from the Depression. It is one of the ironies of history that those ardent internationalists who were so suspicious of nations and chauvinism and proclaimed that only the brotherhood of the proletariat of all countries would free mankind should have ended up subjecting their lives, ideas, and desires to the policies and dictates of one country, the Soviet Union. They perceived no contradiction: to defend real socialism in the one territory where it had taken power would mean sustaining a state that, by its shining example—and later by armed force— would help bring freedom and equality and justice to every corner of the globe.

And the Moscow trials? And Stalin's purges? And the famine and destruction of the peasantry? And the Kronstadt massacre?[8] And the gathering bureaucratic power of a new elite speaking in the name of the vast masses?

Few Communists at the time protested or even seemed to care. My father was no exception. Though I have wondered whether my father's love affair with the Soviet Union was not also buttressed and even hardened by his romance with Russian, the circumstance that the language that had caught him as he fell into the abyss of birth happened to be the very language that he believed was destined to redeem the whole of fallen humanity. The language of his dead cousin, the language of the streets of Odessa, the language of the Revolution: my father's past was not something to be thrown away, as my mother threw away her Yiddish. It could coexist with his Argentine present and inseminate it and bring together the two sides and periods of his life, Russia and Latin America, to create a nationless future, socialism in Argentina.

But there is, in fact, no need for this sort of pop psychology, no need to resort to linguistic explanations for my father's blind adoration of the Soviet

8. In March 1921, at Kronstad, a Soviet naval fortress on Kotlin Island (in the Gulf of Finland), sailors, soldiers, and civilians rose up against the Bolshevik government. The government's forces put down the rebellion; thousands were killed on both sides. *Moscow trials*: a series of trials (1937–38), during which supposed political opponents of the Soviet leader Joseph Stalin (1879–1953) were arrested. Many were executed, including Bolshevik leaders of the Revolution. *Stalin's purges*: or the Great Purge, a series of campaigns (1936–38), including the Moscow trials, during which Stalin instituted political repression and persecuted government officials, army officers, and civilians. Millions were arrested and at least 680,000 (perhaps many more) were killed.

Union. History was furnishing reasons enough: the consolidation of Mussolini and the rise of Hitler and then the Civil War in Spain[9] convinced innumerable revolutionaries to swallow their doubts (if they had any) and embrace
the one power ready to stand up to the Nazis. And even after my father was
expelled from the Party at the end of the 1930s—but not, I am sad to report,
because of ideological or political differences, but due to a slight divergence
about some abstruse question of internal democracy—even then, even after
the Hitler-Stalin Pact of 1939, he adhered steadfastly to Marxist philosophy
and politics.

Up to the point that when I was born in 1942 my father gave me a name
I would disclaim when I was nine years old, for reasons that will be revealed:
the flaming moniker of Vladimiro. In honor of Vladimir Ilyich Lenin[1] and
the Bolshevik Revolution, which, my father felt, was fast approaching the
pampas.

What was really approaching those pampas was Fascism—at least, a
deformed and mild criollo version of it. A year after my birth, in June 1943,
the military headed by General Ramírez toppled the conservative government of Ramón Castillo.[2] It was a pro-Axis coup and behind it was the enigmatic figure of then Colonel Juan Domingo Perón.[3]

My father would soon run afoul of these men. When the new military government took over the Universidad de la Plata, where my father taught, he
resigned indignantly, sending them a letter of protest, à la Emile Zola.[4] A
copy, unfortunately, does not exist: but I have been told that in it my father
insulted the military, their repressiveness, ignorance, clericalism, extreme
nationalism, and, above all their infatuation with Franco, Hitler, and Mussolini. The authorities reacted by expelling him from his position (a first in
the history of Argentina) and then decided to put him on trial, demanding
that his citizenship be revoked. I have taken out the old boxes in my parents'
Buenos Aires apartment and leafed through the yellowed pro-government
tabloids of the day, and there they are, the headlines calling for the "dirty
Jew-dog Dorfman" to be shipped back to Russia, "where he belonged."

History does repeat itself, first as tragedy and then as farce: almost half a
century later, ultra-conservative anti-Semitic right-wingers in the United
States would suggest that I do the same thing, following me around with
signs screeching VLADIMIRO ZELICOVICH (sic) GO HOME TO RUSSIA whenever
I gave a lecture about Chile at a university, waving copies of a twenty-
minute speech Jesse Helms[5] had delivered against me on the Senate floor,

9. In 1936–39, the Spanish general Francisco
Franco (1892–1975) led this military rebellion,
which replaced the liberal civilian government of
the Spanish Republic with Franco's Fascist dictatorship. The Italian Fascist leader Benito Mussolini (1883–1945) and the Austrian-born German
Nazi leader Adolf Hitler (1889–1945) had formed
the Axis, a political and military alliance—later
including Japan—that supported Franco, subjugated many countries in a push toward world
domination, and eventually led to World War II.
1. Russian Communist leader (1870–1924).
2. Ramón S. Castillo Barrionuevo (1873–1944),
president of Argentina from June 27, 1942, to
June 4, 1943. Castillo had maintained Argentina's neutrality during World War II. His minister
of war, General Pedro Pablo Ramírez Machuca

(1884–1962), founded and led a Fascist militia,
was fired by Castillo, helped oust Castillo, and
was president of Argentina from June 7, 1943, to
February 24, 1944.
3. Argentine general and politician (1895–1974);
president of Argentina 1946–52, 1952–55, and
1973–74.
4. French writer (1840–1902); in 1898, he famously published "J'accuse" (French for "I Accuse"), an open letter to the president of France
that accused the leaders of the French Army of
anti-Semitism and obstruction of justice for their
conviction of a Jewish artillery officer, Alfred
Dreyfus (1859–1935), of espionage.
5. Jesse Alexander Helms Jr. (1921–2008), Republican politician; U.S. senator from North Carolina 1973–2003.

brimming with information provided to him by the Chilean Secret Police. But those people in America in the 1980s couldn't do anything to me. The men who threatened my father in Argentina in 1943 were somewhat more powerful.

Again, my father was falling.

But this time it wouldn't be Russian that would catch him, save him. Or the Russians, for that matter. It would be their arch-rivals.

Before he could be jailed, my father skipped the country on an already granted Guggenheim Fellowship. My anti-imperialist father fled in December of 1943, to the United States, the most powerful capitalist country in the world, protected by a foundation built with money that had come out of one of the world's largest consortiums. Money that had come from tin mines in Bolivia and nitrate in Chile and rubber plantations in the Congo and diamonds in Africa saved my Leninist dad.

But the Americans were preparing Normandy and Stalingrad was raging and Auschwitz was burning Jews and homosexuals and Gypsies and Roosevelt had created the New Deal[6] and anyway, even if my father had not been able to offer himself all these expediently progressive reasons for journeying to the center of the empire, there was a more practical one: he had to escape. And America was the only place he could go.

And therefore the place where, over a year later, in February of 1945, the rest of the family joined him.

First, we hopped across Latin America, Santiago and Lima and Cali and Barranquilla, and then finally Miami,[7] each flight delayed for a day or two because of the war, as if Spanish was saying goodbye to me very slowly, as if it were reluctant to let me depart on what would end up being a bilingual journey. Though what may have been most significant about that initial trip North was that the first night of my first exile was spent in the neighboring country just across the Andes,[8] the place that still symbolizes the South for me, there, in that city of Santiago de Chile which was to become my home so many years later. *Wondrous* may be a better word than *significant*: that my first night in that city should have been in a hotel, the Carrera, facing the Presidential Palace of La Moneda, where I was to spend so many nights in the last days of the Allende revolution, looking out onto the plaza, catching a glimpse of men behind the windows of that hotel looking back at me, perhaps from the very room where I had slept as an infant. A mysterious symmetry which would have been even more amazing if I had died at La Moneda—because, in that case, my first childhood voyage to Santiago could have been construed as truly premonitory, that two-and-a-half-year-old child visiting the site of the murder that awaited him twenty-eight years in the future.

6. Franklin Delano Roosevelt (1882–1945), U.S. president 1933–45, was the driving force behind the New Deal, a legislative and administrative program during the Great Depression, designed to promote the economic recovery of and social reform in the United States. *Normandy*: the Battle of Normandy (June–July 1944); in the Normandy region of northern France, the U.S. military (as part of the Allied forces) landed and fought to liberate Europe from the Axis. *Stalingrad*: the Battle of

Stalingrad (July 1942–February 1943); Nazi Germany and other Axis forces fought the Soviet Union for control of the city of Stalingrad, southwestern Russia. *Auschwitz*: Nazi concentration/extermination camp in Poland.
7. I.e., from Chile to Peru to Colombia to southeastern Colombia to northeastern Colombia to the United States, specifically Florida.
8. Mountain system in South America.

If the gods existed and if they were inclined to literary pastimes, they would have organized precisely that sort of ending for their enjoyment, they would have taken my life and harvested one hell of a metaphor. Fortunately, in this case at least, nobody powerful enough to intervene was playing a sick practical joke on me.

Instead, I was the one playing jokes—on my mother and older sister, who spent most of the one afternoon they had for sightseeing shut up in that hotel room searching for the baby shoes, my only pair, that I had mischievously hidden in a pillowcase. With such skill and malevolence, according to my mother, that we almost missed the chance to tour the city before it grew dark. I like to think that the boy I used to be knew what he was doing, that he was in fact trying to intercept my innocent eyes from seeing Santiago for the first innocent time, from crossing the path of Angélica, the woman of my life, who was that same afternoon breathing those very molecules of air under those same mountains. I like to think he recognized Santiago, he had heard the city or its future calling quietly to him to wait, to hold himself in reserve, to hide the shoes. Or maybe it was the city that recognized him.

New York, however, did not recognize me at all. Or maybe sickness is a form of making love, tact, contact, the winter of New York seeping into the lungs of the child still immersed in mind, if not body, in the sultry heat of the Buenos Aires summer, New York blasting that child inside his simulacrum of a snowsuit, inside the garments that had been hastily sewn together by his mother in the remote southern tip of the hemisphere to simulate a snowsuit, New York claiming that child, telling him that things were not going to be easy, no hiding shoes in this city, no guided tours: in this city we play for keeps, kid.

Our family descended from the train onto the platform in Grand Central Station, and there was no one there to greet us but the cold. We had crossed the South of the United States during the night. I have no memory, again, of that trip, except that years later, when I read Thomas Wolfe and his long, shattering train ride to the home toward which the angel was fruitlessly looking,[9] the home he said you could never return to, I felt a shudder of acknowledgment—I had been on that train, I had crossed that U.S. South leaving my own Latino South. So I do not remember the moment when I stepped for the first time in my life onto the concrete of the North, there in New York, holding my mother's hand.

My father was not there waiting for us.

He appeared fifteen minutes later, explained that he had made a mistake or the train had arrived at a different platform, but my mother felt something else was wrong, she felt the mix-up was ominous, because my dad was distant, unfamiliar, his eyes avoiding hers. What my father could not bring himself to tell her was that just before our arrival, at around the time I was hiding my shoes in a Chilean pillow, he had been conscripted into the U.S. Army, and unless he could get a deferment or change his 4A classification,[1]

9. In *Look Homeward, Angel: A Story of the Buried Life* (1929), a novel by the American writer Thomas Wolfe (1900–1938).
1. Dorfman probably means 1A classification, or "available for military service." At different times, IV-A and 4A have meant "registrant with sufficient military service or who is a sole surviving son," "unfit for military service," or "registrant who has completed military service."

he would be off to the European Front and my mother, who didn't know a word of English, would be stranded in a foreign city with two small children, forced to live on a fifty-dollar-a-month GI salary. Four days later, still without telling his wife the truth, my father departed early from the hotel where we were lodged and reported for duty in downtown Manhattan, fully expecting to return in uniform to break the news to my mother; the uniform would tell the news he dared not utter himself. He showered with dozens of other conscripts, he slipped into the Army clothes and then, at the very last moment, was informed that he had been reclassified because the sort of work he was doing at the newly established office of Inter-American Affairs had been deemed "essential." Nelson Rockefeller, who had created that office in the State Department to fight the advance of fascism in Latin America, had intervened.[2] Again, the tricks and treats of history: a Republican saved my philo-Communist father from being sent to war against the allies of the fascists he had just escaped from back home. The point is that my father was able to make a cheerful trip back uptown and tell my mother the reason why he had seemed so remote since our arrival, assure her there was nothing to worry about, from now on happy days would be here again.

But they wouldn't, at least not for me, at least not immediately.

The first order of business was to move out of our prohibitively expensive hotel, not easy in a New York where no new housing had been built since the start of the war. A savvy Uruguayan friend suggested my parents read the obituaries in the newspapers and nab a vacated apartment. Implausibly, that stratagem worked. They rented what in the folklore of the family would always be called *la casa del muerto*, the Dead Man's House. It was, according to my mother, the most depressing, run-down joint she had ever inhabited: a two-room dump, airless under a weak dim bulb hanging like a noose from the ceiling, with small slits of windows gaping onto a gray desolate inner courtyard, three beds in each room, as if several people had died there, not just one.

That was the place, the house of death. That's where I caught pneumonia one Saturday night in February of 1945, when my parents had gone out by themselves for the first time since we had arrived in the States—and I carefully use that verb, to catch, aware of its wild ambiguity, still unsure, even now, if that sickness invaded me or if I was the one who invited it in. But more of that later. To save his life, that boy was interned in a hospital, isolated in a ward where nobody spoke a word of Spanish. For three weeks, he saw his parents only on visiting days and then only from behind a glass partition.

My parents have told me the story so often that sometimes I have the illusion that I am the one remembering, but that hope quickly fades, as when you arrive at a movie theater late and never discover what really happened, are forever at the mercy of those who have witnessed the beginning: *te internaron en ese hospital*, my mother says slowly, picking out the words as if for the first time, *no nos acordamos del nombre*, there is a large glass wall, it

---

2. The American businessman and politician Nelson Aldrich Rockefeller (1908–1979) was named the Coordinator of Inter-American Affairs by Franklin Delano Roosevelt (1882–1945), U.S. president 1933–45. The Office of Inter-American Affairs was a U.S. agency that, during the 1940s, promoted inter-American cooperation.

is a cold bare white hospital ward, my parents have told me that every time they came to see me, tears streamed down my face, that I tried to touch them, I watch myself watching my parents so near and so far away behind the glass, mouthing words in Spanish I can't hear. Then my mother and my father are gone and I turn and I am alone and my lungs hurt and I realize then, as I realize now, that I am very fragile, that life can snap like a twig. I realize this in Spanish and I look up and the only adults I see are nurses and doctors. They speak to me in a language I don't know. A language that I will later learn is called English. In what language do I respond? In what language can I respond?

Three weeks later, when my parents came to collect their son, now sound in body but in all probability slightly insane in mind, I disconcerted them by refusing to answer their Spanish questions, by speaking only English. "I don't understand," my mother says that I said—and from that moment onward I stubbornly, steadfastly, adamantly refused to speak a word in the tongue I had been born into.

I did not speak another word of Spanish for ten years.

1998

---

# REINALDO ARENAS
## 1943–1990

One of the more than 120,000 Cubans who left the island during the Mariel boat-lift in the summer of 1980, Reinaldo Arenas arrived in the United States with nothing but pajamas and a spare shirt. His manuscripts had been confiscated by the Cuban authorities before he left. During the next 10 years, while living in a small walk-up apartment in New York City, Arenas re-created the novels he had written in Cuba and created new works that reflected his life in exile. His highly original fiction and his eloquent criticisms of the Cuban Revolution make Arenas one of the most engaging and controversial figures in contemporary Cuban literature.

Arenas was born in Perronales, a rural village in the province of Oriente, Cuba. After his father abandoned the family, Arenas spent his childhood in poverty and neglect. His early schooling was sketchy, but in 1955 he moved with his mother to the town of Holguín, where he was able to attend a secondary school. In 1958, he joined Fidel Castro's guerrilla forces. Arenas then studied agricultural business and later took courses at the University of Havana. Thanks to the still-developing socialist government's support for cultural activities, Arenas began working at the National Library, where he met two homosexual writers who would strongly influence him, José Lezama Lima and Virgilio Piñera. In 1967, Arenas's literary career was launched when he received an honorable mention in the Cirilo Villaverde National Novel Contest for his first novel, *Celestino antes del alba* (Celestino before Dawn), which was published in Havana. It was published in Argentina the following year, in France (as *Le puits*) in 1973, in Spain (as *Cantando en el pozo*) in 1982, and in English (as *Singing from the Well*) in 1987. Semiautobiographical, the book explores the fantasies of a small boy raised in Cuba's rural poverty. The child creates an alter ego, Celestino, a poet-cousin who escapes persecution by carving poems into the bark of trees. This novel, the only one of Arenas's works published in Cuba during his lifetime, became the first part of a projected trilogy dealing with the history of Cuba and the protagonist's desperate search for freedom. This series eventually developed into five novels, which Arenas termed his "Pentagony."

Arenas's second novel, *El mundo alucinante* (1969), translated in 1971 as *Hallucinations* and in 1987 as *The Ill-Fated Peregrinations of Fray Servando*, also received honorable mention in the same competition, but its publication was forbidden by the Cuban government. The manuscript of *El mundo alucinante* was smuggled out of Cuba and published in 1968 in a French translation that won a prize for the best foreign book of the year. The original was published in Mexico in 1969. *El mundo alucinante* is the fantastic re-creation of the life and adventures of Fray Servando Teresa de Mier (1763–1827), a Mexican priest who endured imprisonment and torture in Spain. Although not part of Arenas's Pentagony, this novel also deals with the suppression of the individual and a miraculous escape from persecution. The Castro government banned *El mundo alucinante* for its openly homosexual and antirevolutionary implications, and it accused Arenas of being a "counterrevolutionary sexual deviant."

Persecuted for his subversive writing and homosexuality, Arenas spent the early 1970s on a sugar plantation in the Pinar del Rio province. He continued to write, narrating his experiences of forced labor in a long epic poem, *El Central* (The Sugar Mill), which was not published until 1981. In 1973, Arenas smuggled out of the country the second novel of his Pentagony, *El palacio de la blanquísimas mofetas* (The Palace of the Whitest Skunks); it was published in French in 1975, in Spanish in 1980. This blend of fantasy and reality calls on the reader to provide a resolution based on the *agonía* of the characters. The adolescent Fortunato—an extension of Celestino, from *Celestino antes del alba*—leaves his home to fight with the revolutionary forces. Tortured and executed by the government soldiers, Fortunato dies in a moment that is part memory and part hallucination.

In 1974, Arenas was arrested—for, he said, "contempt of the public order" and "ideological divergence." He escaped and lived as a fugitive in Havana's Lenin Park, until he was caught and sent to El Morro, a medieval fortress outside Havana that was then being used as a an extremely harsh prison. After being tortured, he pleaded guilty to the charges against him and was sent to a "reeducation" camp. The manuscript of his novel *Otra vez el mar* (Farewell to the Sea), which he had rewritten after losing the original while he was a fugitive, was confiscated. From 1976 to 1980, Arenas was allowed no employment, but he continued to write, attempting to re-create his twice-lost novel. The Cuban government prevented his works from being published on the island, but they were published outside Cuba and acclaimed by critics. Admirers abroad sought his release from prison and permission to emigrate, but Arenas was not able to leave the country until the Mariel boatlift. Once in the United States, he settled in New York City, cofounded the journal *Mariel* (with his friend the Cuban-exile poet Roberto Valero), and lectured at many U.S universities. His political essays were published in 1986 as *Necesidad de libertad: Testimonios de un intelectual disidente* (The Necessity of Liberty: Testimonies of a Dissident Intellectual). Arenas found life in American university circles difficult, because there he met supporters of the Castro government who, in his view, chose to ignore the suffering and oppression caused by the revolution. In addition, his haphazard education made him unsuited for academic positions, so he was forced to squeeze out a living from his writing.

In 1980, Arenas published a novella written ten years earlier, *La vieja Rosa* (Old Rosa), about an old woman who becomes a victim of the revolution but escapes through suicide. The novella also includes the story of Rosa's son, who is killed when he attempts to escape a work camp for homosexuals, but who finds release in telling his story. This tale was published independently in 1984 as *Arturo, la estrella más brillante* (Arthur, the Brightest Star). Having written the third volume of the Pentagony twice in Cuba, Arenas finally wrote it for the third time, and it appeared in 1982 as *Otra vez el mar*. The novel contrasts the corruption of the Castro regime with the hopes of the once idealized revolution. The main character, Héctor, experiences an exile both internal and fantastic, as he is forced into his imagination by political and sexual repression.

Diagnosed with AIDS in 1983, Arenas spent the last years of his life gathering his scattered works and overseeing their publication. He published a dazzling array of works in different genres: an experimental play, *Persecución* (1986), which once again denounces the Castro regime; *La loma del ángel* (Graveyard of the Angels, 1987), a parodic rewriting of a classic Cuban antislavery novel, Cirilo Villaverde's *Cecilia Valdés* (1882), poking fun at nineteenth-century realism and the socialist realism promoted by the Cuban revolution; the novella *El portero* (The Doorman, 1989) and *Viaje a la Habana* (Voyage to Havana, 1990); and two books of poems, *Leprosorio* (Leper Colony, 1990) and *Voluntad de vivir manifestándose* (The Will to Live Openly, 1989). But his principal interest during these years was the completion of his Pentagony. In the fourth volume, *El color del verano o nuevo jardín de las delicias* (The Color of Summer or the New Garden of Delights, 1991), Arenas experiments with science fiction in apocalyptic fragments that prophesy the end of the Castro dictatorship; in *El asalto* (The Assault, 1991), the fifth and final volume, he presents a hallucinatory meditation on power, centering on the composite Oedipal figure of the mother/dictator who, in the climactic scene of all of Arenas's work, is bludgeoned to death with the son's engorged phallus.

When Arenas committed suicide, in New York City, he left a letter in which he blamed Fidel Castro for his miseries and asked his friends to scatter his ashes on a Caribbean beach. Shortly before his death, he completed his memoir, *Antes que anochezca* (Before Night Falls, 1992), which was turned into an award-winning movie (2000) by the artist and director Julian Schnabel. The title refers both to the author's imminent death and to the days he spent hiding in Lenin Park, when his only escape from reality was reading and writing during the daylight hours. Arenas vividly describes scenes from his childhood up through his last days in the United States. He exposes the banal corruption and evil of the Castro regime. Linking sexual and literary freedom, he writes frankly about his many sexual encounters. In the chapter included here, he describes the Mariel boatlift, using his subversive, lyrical voice—strangely innocent despite his life of risk and violence—to expose human cruelty and history's persecution of outsiders. In the first selection here—the short story "Mona," from *Viaje a la Habana*—the narrator describes a Cuban exile's arrest, imprisonment, and death. The narrative's fantastic events are rendered ambiguous by fictional explanatory notes, which follow several timelines.

In his life as in his writing, Arenas remained staunchly opposed to any ideological attempt to control the body and suppress the imagination. Surveying Arenas's career, the critic Michael Wood has noted that Arenas "sought to give voices to the voiceless, and not only the obviously voiceless, the visibly suppressed, but also those victims and sufferers whose distress eludes us, perhaps because they are too many or because we can't read their mute style. In Arenas's fiction even the most cramped or muffled minds are lent a fabulous fluency; no sorrow is left unturned."

# Mona[1]

## Foreword

A Peculiar bit of news appeared in the international press in October of 1986. Ramón Fernández, twenty-seven, who had come to the United States

---

1. Translated by Dolores M. Koch. Except as indicated, all footnotes are part of Arenas's fictional story.

in the Mariel exodus from Cuba, was arrested at the Metropolitan Museum of Art[2] as he "attempted to knife" the Mona Lisa, Leonardo da Vinci's famous painting, valued at a hundred million dollars.

Most of the newspaper reports offered basic information on the artist and his masterpiece, then speculated that Mr. Fernández was one of the many mental patients who were expelled from Cuba in the 1980 Mariel boatlift. The museum's exhibit of the famous painting would be extended until the fifteenth of November, 1986, by special permission from the Louvre.[3] That was all they said, and whether it was for reasons of diplomacy or out of ignorance, they omitted a minor detail: Mitterrand's[4] French government would pocket five million dollars for the "courtesy" of having allowed the Mona Lisa to cross the Atlantic. It is interesting to note that the press—especially that in the U.S.—emphasized the fact that the suspect, a presumed mental case, was a *marielito*. Also of interest is the media's reference to an attempt to knife the painting, when according to all the evidence, including the suspect's confession, the assault weapon was a hammer. . . . A few days later, on October 17, the *New York Times*, deep in one of its back pages, printed a brief account of the strange death of the detainee Ramón Fernández: "The young man from Cuba who attempted to destroy Leonardo da Vinci's masterpiece was found strangled in his prison cell this morning. He had been waiting to make his first court appearance. Oddly," the reported added, "the suicide weapon is still a mystery." Aware of the detainee's mental condition, the authorities had deprived him of his belt and shoelaces. The prisoner seemed to have strangled himself with his bare hands. No one from the outside had visited Mr. Fernández who, according to the warden, had spent his six days of incarceration in a highly agitated state, writing what appeared to be a long letter—which he subsequently mailed to one of his Cuban friends in exile. The warden declared that because this was a special case, he had taken the precaution of reading this document (obtained through a policeman who had pretended to befriend Mr. Fernández), and it confirmed the inmate's state of extreme mental disturbance. After photocopying the letter, he had it mailed to its addressee, "since it added nothing (sic) to the evidence." Two days later, while the front pages gave coverage to Mother Teresa's suicide,[5] only a few newspapers reported that Ramón Fernández's body had mysteriously disappeared from the morgue, where it was awaiting the arrival of the forensic physician and the district attorney. Thus ends the more or less hard news regarding the case, news that began with a confused bit of information (the so-called knifing of the Mona Lisa) and ended similarly (with the apparent suicide of the suspect). In the confident wisdom so characteristic of ignorance, the yellow press sniffed a crime of passion behind all this. . . . Needless to say, a flock of magazines and New York tabloids—those called liberal because they are ready to defend any enemy empire against the American empire—headed by the *Village Voice*, reported the events differently: Ramón

---

2. In Manhattan. [Anthology editors' note]
3. Major French museum, in Paris. [Anthology editors' note]
4. François Mitterand (1916–1999), president of France 1981–95. [Anthology editors' note]

5. Mother Teresa (b. Agnes Gonxha Bojaxhiu, 1910–1997), an Albanian Roman Catholic nun who founded the Missions of Charity in Calcutta, India, died of heart failure. She did not commit suicide. [Anthology editors' note]

Fernández was an anti-Castro Cuban terrorist who, in clear opposition to the socialist French government, had attempted to destroy that country's most treasured work of art. And as if this were not enough to grant us Cubans the status of troglodytes, a libelous Hispanic rag published in New Jersey and funded by a Cuban extremist, Luis P. Suardíaz, wrote a blazing editorial in praise of Fernández's "patriotic deed," saying that his "action" had served to draw the French government's attention to the case of Roberto Bofill, a Cuban who had gained political asylum in the French embassy in Havana and had repeatedly been denied an exit permit by Fidel Castro.

Six months have passed since the mysterious death of Ramón Fernández. *La Gioconda* has returned to her home in the Louvre. The case appears to be closed.

There is someone, however, who won't easily accept the hasty closing of this case, particularly after twice having had the privilege of gracing the pages of the *New York Times*, as well as being published in several other journals. That person is none other than the author of these lines, Daniel Sakuntala, the recipient of the long testimony produced by Ramón Fernández. The police handed it to me, a week after Ramón's death, in an attempt to find out if there had been any compromising or murky dealings between the "suicide suspect" and myself. They intended to watch my reactions and follow my every step, and I am sure they did.

As soon as I received the manuscript from my friend Ramoncito, whom I had met in Cuba, I tried to publish it in a serious newspaper or magazine, but all the editors agreed with the dull-witted police, saying that this testimony was the product of a hallucinating or deranged mind and that anyone who dared publish it would be ridiculed. Since I found no serious publication willing to make the text known, I contacted Reinaldo Arenas, as a last resort, to see if he would print it in his magazine, *Mariel*. But Arenas, with his proverbial frivolity* and in spite of the fact that he was already very sick with AIDS, the cause of his recent death, laughed at my suggestion, saying that *Mariel* was a modern magazine in which there was no room for this "nineteenth-century tale." To compound the insult, he told me to take it to the director of *Linden Lane Magazine*, Carilda Oliver Labra. . . . My guess is that Reinaldo had met Ramoncito in Cuba, and Ramoncito, who was attracted only to real women, had completely ignored Reinaldo. But that is another story, which reminds me of the time when Ramoncito, my friend and brother, slapped Delfín Proust[6] in a crowded bus in Havana because Delfín had suddenly grabbed at his fly. . . . Well, no respectable publication was willing to print my friend's desperate testimony. Perhaps if it had been taken seriously from the start, his life would have been saved.

Since I hope it will save the lives of many other young and handsome men, such as he was, I am taking it upon myself to promulgate this document, using all the means at my disposal. Here is the text, with only a few

---

*Besides being frivolous, Arenas was a real ignoramus. As evidence of this, let me point out that in his short story "End of a Story," he mentions a statue of Jupiter atop the Chamber of Commerce in Havana, when everybody knows that crowning the cupola of that building is a statue of the god Mercury. —D.S.
6. A character in Arenas's novel *El color del verano* (The Color of Summer, 1982). [Anthology editors' note]

clarifying notes added. I sincerely hope that someone, someday, will take it seriously.

DANIEL SAKUNTALA

*New York, 1987*

### EDITORS' NOTE

Before presenting this testimony by Ramón Fernández, it seems advisable to clarify a few points. Daniel Sakuntala was unable to publish this document during his lifetime in spite of tenacious efforts. In the end, it seems that his economic situation prevented him. We have a copy of a letter from Editorial Playor, asking two thousand dollars in advance for the "printing of the booklet." The text was published in New Jersey more than twenty-five years ago, in November 1999, after Mr. Sakuntala's mysterious disappearance (the body was never found) near Lake Ontario. The publishers were Ismaele Lorenzo and Vicente Echurre, the editors then of the magazine *Unveiling Cuba*—who themselves have recently also disappeared, together with most of the copies of the book. (Unconfirmed rumors indicate that these senior citizens returned to Cuba after the invasion of Havana by Jamaica in alliance with other Caribbean islands and, of course, Great Britain.) As for Reinaldo Arenas, mentioned by Mr. Sakuntala, he was a writer of the 1960s generation, justly forgotten in our century. He died of AIDS in the summer of 1987 in New York.

Because of the number of printing errors in the first edition of this document and then its near disappearance, we are proud to present this edition as the true first edition. For that reason, we have left unchanged Ramón Fernández's idiosyncratic expressions, as well as Daniel Sakuntala's notes and those of Messrs. Lorenzo and Echurre, even though by now they may seem (or be) anachronistic or irrelevant.

*Monterey, California, May 2025*

### Ramón Fernández's Testimony

This report is being written in a rush, and even so, I am afraid I won't be able to finish it. She knows where I am and any moment now will come to destroy me. I am saying *she*, and perhaps I should say *he*; though I don't know what to call *that thing*. From the beginning, she (or he?) ensnared me, confused me, and now is even trying to prevent me from writing this statement. But I must do it; I must do it, and in the clearest way possible. If I can finish it and someone reads it and believes it, perhaps I could still be saved. The authorities in this prison are certainly not going to do anything for me. That I know very well. When I told them that I needed not to be left alone, that I wanted them to lock me up and have someone watch over me day and night, they broke up laughing. "You're not important enough to deserve special security," they said. "But don't you worry, you won't be able to get out of this place anyway." "My problem is not that I want to get out," I told them. "What worries me is that someone might be able to get in. . . ." "Get in? Here no one gets in of his own free will, and you better be quiet unless you want us to put you to sleep right now. I was going to insist, but before opening my mouth again, I looked at one of the officers and saw in his eyes that sneering attitude of a free human being who looks down upon a madman, an imprisoned one at that. And I realized they were not going to listen to me.

The only thing left for me to do is to write, to describe the events, to write the whole thing up quickly and in a logical manner, as logical as my situation allows, and see if someone finally believes me and I am saved though that is very unlikely.

Since I came to New York—and that was more than six years ago—I have worked as a security guard at the Wendy's on Broadway between 42nd and 43rd streets. It is open twenty-four hours a day, and since I had the night shift, my job was always very lively, dealing with many different kinds of people. Without overlooking my responsibilities, I had the opportunity to meet many women who came in for a snack or who just passed by, and from my post behind the glass wall and in my well-pressed and gold-braided uniform, I beckoned them in. Of course, not all of them took the bait, but many did. I want to make very clear that I am not bragging. One night, in just one shift, I managed to have three women (not including the Wendy's cashier, a very solid black woman I made it with in the ladies' room). The trouble came at quitting time: the three of them were waiting for me. I managed somehow, but this is no time to go into it. I left with the one I liked best, though I was really sorry I had to give up the other two. I have no family in this country, and all my lovers and even friends have been these nameless women whom I spotted while at my post at Wendy's or who (and I say this without any false modesty) spotted me and came in with the pretext of having a cup of tea or something.

One night I was on the alert, watching the street and looking for a woman worthy of a wink, when a truly extraordinary female specimen stopped outside. Long reddish hair, ample forehead, perfect nose, fine lips, and honey-colored eyes that looked me over openly (a bit shamelessly) through long false eyelashes. I must confess, she struck me instantly. I straightened my uniform jacket and took a good look at her body, which even under bulky winter clothes promised to be as extraordinary as her face. I was fascinated. Meanwhile, she came in, took off the stole or cape she had around her shoulders and uncovered part of her breasts. That same night we agreed to meet at three o'clock in the morning, when I finished my shift.

She told me her name was Elisa, that she was of Greek ancestry, and that she was in New York for just a few weeks. This was enough for me to invite her to my room on 43rd Street, on the West Side, only three blocks away. Elisa accepted without hesitation, which pleased me enormously because I don't like women who play hard-to-get before going to bed with you. These are the ones who later, when you want to get rid of them, make your life unbearable. Since I didn't want to have that kind of trouble at Wendy's, I stayed away from this kind of "difficult" women, who later, when you are not interested anymore, become quite a nuisance, capable of following you all the way to Siberia[7] if necessary.

---

7. Area of northern Asia in Russia; i.e., a remote, isolated place. [Anthology editors' note]

But with Elisa—let's keep calling her Elisa—that was no problem. From the start, she laid her cards on the table. She obviously liked me and wanted to go to bed with me often before returning to Europe. So I did not ask her any more personal questions (if you want to have a good time with a woman, never ask her about her life). We went to bed, and I must confess that in spite of all my experience, Elisa surprised me. She possessed not only the imagination of a real pleasure-seeker and the skills of a woman of the world but also a kind of motherly charm mixed with youthful mischief and the airs of a grand lady, which made her irresistible. Never had I enjoyed a woman so much.

I noted nothing strange in her that night, except for a peculiar pronunciation of certain words and phrases. For instance, she would begin a word in a very soft, feminine tone and end it in a heavy voice, almost masculine. I supposed it was due to her lack of knowledge of the Spanish language, which she adamantly insisted on speaking after I told her I was Cuban, though I had proposed, for her convenience, that we speak English. I could not help but laugh when she told me (perhaps to empathize with my Caribbean origins) that she had been born near the Mediterranean. I laughed not because being born there was funnier than having come into this world somewhere else but because she pronounced each syllable of the word *Mediterráneo* in a different voice. It seemed you were listening not to one woman but to five, each different from the other. When I pointed this out, I noticed that her beautiful forehead wrinkled.

Next day was my day off, and at dinnertime she suggested going to Plum's, an elegant restaurant that did not concur with the state of my wallet. I informed her of that fact, and she, looking at me intently but with a bit of mockery, invited me to be her guest. I accepted.

At the restaurant that evening, Elisa did something that puzzled me. The waiter, in this fancy place, forgot to bring us water. I signaled him several times. The man would promise it right away, but the water was not forthcoming. Unexpectedly, Elisa grabbed the vase adorning our table, removed the flowers, and drank the water. She quickly replaced the flowers and continued our conversation. She did this so naturally that anyone would have thought that drinking the water from a flower vase was the normal thing to do. . . . After dinner we went back to my room, and I enjoyed again, even more than before, the pleasures of her incredible body. At dawn, half asleep, we were still kissing. I remember at one point the strange sensation of having close to my lips the thick underlip of some animal and quickly turned the light on. Next to mine, fortunately, I had only the lips of the most beautiful woman I had ever met. So fascinated was I with Elisa that I accepted her idea of my not going to Wendy's that night, which was a Monday. She claimed that it was the only day in the week that she could spend with me, and proposed taking a ride on my motorcycle (a 1981 Yamaha) out of the city. Across the Hudson,[8] on the New Jersey side, Elisa asked me to stop for a look at the New York skyline. I knew that for a foreigner (and a tourist, given her carefree manner), the panoramic view of Manhattan, its towers like sierras, today mysteriously disappearing in fog, had to be impressive. Even I, so used to this panorama that I seldom took

8. The Hudson River, which runs along the west side of Manhattan. [Anthology editors' note]

the time to look at it anymore, felt the enchantment of the view and seemed to perceive an intense glow radiating from the tallest buildings. This was rather strange, since at that time, close to eleven in the morning, the skyscrapers had no reason to be lit. I turned to tell Elisa, but she, leaning on the railing, facing the river, was not listening to me. She was as if transported, looking at the strange luminosity and muttering unintelligible words that I assumed were in her mother tongue. To bring her back from her soliloquy, I approached her from behind and put my hands on her shoulders, which were covered by a heavy woolen stole. A chill ran down my spine. One of her shoulders seemed to bulge out sharply, as if the bone was out of joint and in the shape of a hook. To make sure there was a deformity that inexplicably I had not discovered until then, I felt her shoulder again. There was no deformity, however, and through the fabric my hand caressed her warm, smooth skin. Then I thought that surely I must have touched a safety pin or a shoulder pad, now back in place. At that moment Elisa turned to me and said that we could go on whenever I wished.

We got on the motorcycle, but I couldn't get it to start. I inspected it carefully and finally told Elisa that I thought we could not continue our trip. My cycle had finally given out, and it would be better if we left it right there and took a taxi back to Manhattan. Elisa wanted to examine the motor herself. "I know about these things," she explained with a smile. "In my country I have a Lambretta"[9]—that's what she said—"which is similar to this." Mistrusting her mechanical skills, I stepped aside to the lookout on the Hudson and lit a cigarette. I had no time to finish it. Giving its characteristic explosion, the starting motor began to roar.

Elated, we dashed off. Elisa suggested we take I95 North to a little mountain town near the route to Buffalo.[1] The higher we climbed, the more radiant the autumn noon became. The trees, deep crimson, appeared to be on fire. The fog had dissipated, and a warmish glow seemed to envelop everything. I kept glancing at Elisa in the rearview mirror; she had an expression of sweet serenity. It gave me such pleasure to see her like this, with her look of mysterious abandon, her face against the forest background, that I kept watching her in the little mirror, spellbound. Once, instead of her face, I thought I saw the face of a horrible old man, but I attributed this to our speed, which distorted images. . . . During the afternoon, we reached the mountains, and before dark we stopped at a town on a hill, with one- and two-story houses. More than a town, it looked like a promontory of whitewashed stones, above which rose a pure white church steeple so old that it did not seem to belong in America. Elisa cleared up the mystery for me. The town had been founded in the eighteenth century by a group of European immigrants (Spaniards and Italians), who chose such a remote location in order to be able to hold on to their old traditions. They were peasant folk, and according to Elisa, though they had arrived in 1760, they were still living as if in the Middle Ages. And it was indeed a small medieval city, despite its electricity and running water, and its location on the foothills of a New York mountain.*

---

9. Brand of motor scooter. [Anthology editors' note]
1. City in New York State. [Anthology editors' note]
*Obviously the city Ramoncito refers to is Syracuse, in northern New York State. It's named for

Siracusa, port and province of Italy, the land of Archimedes and Theocritus, and location of a famous Greek theater. —D.S.
We strongly disagree with Mr. Sakuntala.

I was not surprised at Elisa's knowledge of architecture and history. I have always thought that Europeans, simply by being Europeans, know more about the past than Americans do. Up to a point, if you allow me, they *are* the past.

• • •

The prison bell is ringing; it's dinnertime, and I run. There, among the inmates and their shouting, and in the midst of all the clatter of dishes and silver, I feel more secure than here, alone in my cell. To urge myself on, I vow that right after dinner I will continue writing this report.

• • •

Now I am in the prison library. It is eleven P.M. I am thinking that if nothing had happened, I would now be at Wendy's in my blue uniform with gold braid, behind the glass wall, protected from the cold and inspecting with my clinical eye every woman who passes by. But I have no time for women now. I am imprisoned here for a crime I have not committed, but given my status as a *marielito*, it is the same as if I had. I am waiting here not for my sentence, which by now obviously does not worry me much, but for Elisa, who, as soon as she can, will come and kill me.

But let's go back a few days to the night we spent in that old mountain town so dear to Elisa. After walking around for a while, we entered a restaurant that looked like a Spanish inn, something like La Bodeguita del Medio—The Little Inn in the Middle of the Block—a popular restaurant in Havana, which I, as a native, was not allowed to visit, except once, when a tourist, a Frenchwoman, invited me. . . . Elisa knew the place well. She knew how to choose the best table and the best dishes on the menu. It was clear she felt completely at home. And her beauty seemed to grow by the minute. She also knew how to pick a hotel; small and comfortable, it looked like a guesthouse. We retired early and made love passionately. I confess that in spite of all my enthusiasm, Elisa was hard to please (What woman isn't!), but I have my ways, and in these matters I always have the last word—even if my companion is a great conversationalist. Yes, I think that by daybreak I had managed to satisfy her completely. She was resting peacefully by my side. Before turning off the light, I wanted to get my fill of that quiet serenity of hers. She had fallen asleep, but her eyes did not remain closed for long. Suddenly I saw them disappear. I screamed in order to wake myself up—I had to have been dreaming—and immediately I could see her eyes, looking at me intently. "I think I had a nightmare," I told her in apology, and embracing her, I said good night. But afterward I was barely able to sleep at all.

Before dawn, Elisa got up and, without making a sound, left the room. I stood behind the window curtains and watched her vanish in the glow of

---

After traveling throughout New York State, we have concluded that the city visited by Ramón Fernández and Elisa must have been Albany. Only that city has houses that look like "whitewashed stone" and is located on the foothills of a mountain. There is also an old church with an all-white steeple. —Ismaele Lorenzo and Vicente Echurre, 1999

We reject both Daniel Sakuntala's and Messrs. Lorenzo and Echurre's theories. The city must be no other than Ithaca, located on a mountain north of New York City. Notice that in his testimony, Mr. Fernández states: "More than a town, it looked like a promontory of whitewashed stones." That is what Ithaca is. The stones are the famous Cornell University, and the white tower that looks like a church is the gigantic pillar that supports the library clock. —Editors, 2025

the morning mist, following a yellow path that disappeared among the trees. I decided to stay awake and wait for her, even though I tried to calm myself by thinking that it was natural for someone to get up before dawn and take a walk: a European custom, maybe. I remembered the French-woman who took me to La Bodeguita del Medio: she used to get up at dawn, take a shower, and, still wet, throw herself into bed. . . . About an hour later, I heard Elisa push the door open—I pretended to be asleep. She seemed out of breath. She sat next to me at the edge of the bed and turned off the light. Protected by darkness, I opened my eyes slightly. Facing the early light, her back to me, was a beautiful naked woman who would, any minute now, snuggle into bed with me. Her bottom, her back, her shoulders, her neck, everything was perfect. Except that her perfect body had no head.

Since in the face of the most outlandish circumstances we always search for logical explanations, I rationalized what I had seen as purely an effect produced by the heavy fog usual in that place. Anyway, my instinct told me it was better to keep silent and close my eyes. I felt Elisa sliding into bed next to me. Her hand, with unerring skill, caressed my genitals. "Are you asleep?" she asked. I opened my eyes as if waking up from a deep sleep and saw, next to me, her perfectly serene, smiling face. The color of her hair seemed to have grown even more intense. She kept caressing me, and even though I could not dismiss my misgivings, we embraced until we were totally fulfilled.

* * *

I have already been imprisoned for three days, and I believe I don't have three more days to live. So I must hurry. . . . This morning I was again shouting that I didn't want to be left alone. By noon the prison psychiatrist was sent to see me. I let him know I was not interested and answered his questions curtly. Not only because I knew he would do nothing for me, since, unfortunately, I am not crazy, but also because his interview, his stupid questions, were a waste of time, a waste of the precious little time I have left and that I must use to finish this story, send it to a friend, and see if he can do anything. Though I doubt it, I must go on.

* * *

We were back in New York City by nine-thirty in the morning, truly record time. Elisa had kept asking me to go very fast because, she claimed, she had to be at the Greek consulate at ten. At a red light on Fifth Avenue, she suddenly leaped off and began to run, saying that she would come to see me the next day at Wendy's. And she did. She came around nine P.M. to tell me she would be waiting for me when I left work—that is, at three in the morning. This was our agreement. But with all I had seen, or thought I had seen, plus the attraction Elisa exerted on me (or should I call it love?), I concluded that, as a matter of life and death, I had to find out who this woman really was.

On the pretext of sharp stomach pains, I left Wendy's without bothering to take off my uniform, and cautiously began to follow Elisa rather closely. At Broadway and 44th, she made a phone call, then started walking toward the theater district. On 47th Street, someone, who evidently was waiting for her, opened the door of a limousine, and Elisa got in. I was only able to see a masculine hand helping her in. It was easy to get a taxi and follow the limo, which stopped at 172 East 89th Street. The chauffeur opened the door, and Elisa and her companion went into the apartment building. To keep warm, I waited inside a telephone booth. An hour later, that is, around ten-thirty, Elisa came out. With my experience, I could tell that she had enjoyed a long and satisfying sexual encounter. She looked at her watch and started walking toward Central Park. She reached 79th and approached a bench where a young man was sitting, obviously waiting for her. I thought (I am sure of it) that he was the person Elisa had phoned from Broadway. The dialogue now was as short as the phone call had been. Without any fuss, they disappeared into the shrubbery. Unseen, I was able to watch how quickly and easily the pair coupled. Dry leaves crackled under their bodies, and their panting scared away the squirrels, which clambered up the trees, screeching loudly. The whole thing lasted about an hour and a half, since by twelve-thirty Elisa was taking a leisurely walk in the 42nd Street porno district. Boldly, without any shame, she would ogle the men who passed obviously looking for a woman or something like that. Farther down the street, Elisa stopped in front of a towering, handsome black man standing by the door of a peep show. I was not able to hear their conversation, of course, but it seemed that Elisa got straight to the point: in less than five minutes they were inside one of the booths at the peep show. They stayed locked up in there for more than half an hour. When they came out, the young black man seemed exhausted; Elisa was radiant. It was now two o'clock in the morning, and she was still cruising around the area. A few seconds later I saw her, accompanied by three jocks who looked like hillbillies, enter a booth at the Black Jack peep show. Fifteen minutes later, the door slammed open and she came out, looking quite pleased. I did not wait to see the men's faces. . . . When I saw Elisa (now with a Puerto Rican who looked very much like a pimp) go into another peep show, the one on Eighth Avenue between 43rd and 44th, I realized that my "fiancée" would not come to me late that night, as she had promised. And in spite of what I had been witnessing, I could not but feel a sense of total loss. Elisa was the woman with whom I had fallen in love, for the first time. . . . But at quarter to three, she came out of the peep show and started walking toward Wendy's. To be with her once more, I obliterated everything I had seen and started running, so I'd be there, waiting, when she came. The cashier and the other employees were puzzled to see me taking my post behind the glass wall. Elisa was there in no time, and together we went to my room.

That night in bed she was extraordinarily demanding, more so than ever, which is saying a lot. In spite of my desire and my extensive experience, it was not easy to satisfy her. . . . Though after the encounter I pretended to fall asleep, I did not sleep a wink. What I had seen had left me totally perplexed. Of course, I could not tell her I had spied on her, could not appear jealous, though in all truth I was. Actually, I did not think I had the right to demand fidelity from her, since at no point had we vowed to be faithful to each other.

It was close to nine o'clock in the morning when, while I pretended to be asleep, she woke up, dressed in silence, and went out without saying goodbye. But I was obsessed (though now I regret it) with following that woman and finding out where she lived, who she really was. . . . At 43rd and Eighth she took a taxi. I took another. While following her, nodding in my seat, I wondered if it was possible for Elisa to be on her way to another tryst. She was not. After such a turbulent night, Elisa seemed to want to find inner peace by looking at works of art. At least that is what I thought when I saw her get out of the taxi and hurriedly enter the Metropolitan Museum, just at the moment it was opening its doors. After paying for admission, I rushed inside the building and went up to the second floor, following the route she had taken. I watched her go in one of those large galleries, and right there, in front of my eyes, she disappeared. I looked for her for hours throughout the immense building, without any success. I did not skip any possible corner. I looked behind every statue, went around every amphora (there are some enormous ones) and even searched inside them. On one occasion I got lost among countless sarcophagi and centuries-old mummies, while calling Elisa's name out loud. Once out of that labyrinth, I found myself in a temple of the time of the Ptolemies (according to a placard),* seemingly floating in a pool. I searched everywhere in that enormous pile of stones, but Elisa was not there either. About three in the afternoon I went back to my room and threw myself on the bed.

I woke up at two in the morning. In a rush, I put on my uniform and left for Wendy's. My boss, who had always been pretty decent to me, told me that this was no time to start working; it was almost time to leave. I detected a tinge of sadness in his voice when he informed me that next time this happened I would be fired. I assured him there would be no next time, and I went back to my room. Elisa was waiting by the door. I was not even surprised that she had been able to enter my building, though the front door is always locked and only the tenants have keys. She said she had been at Wendy's several times and I was not there, so she decided to wait for me in my house. We went into my room, and perhaps because I had slept for hours or because I was afraid I would never see her again, I made love to her with renewed passion. Yes, that night, I believe, I was the clear victor. But how many duels—I sadly asked myself—had she fought today before coming to me? . . . At dawn, when I again started an attack, sliding over her naked body, I saw that Elisa had no breasts. I jumped to the edge of the bed, wondering whether this woman was driving me insane. As if sensing my anguish, she immediately pulled me over with her arms to her beautiful breasts.

---

*It is only natural that Ramoncito, who is not used to museums, mixes themes, styles, and periods. The temple he refers to must be that of Ramses II, built at the height of his reign during the nineteenth dynasty, in 1305 B.C., to be exact. It is an enormous red granite mound, where anyone who is not an expert can get lost. —D.S.

The only portion of that temple in the Metropolitan Museum was a stone about six feet tall, impossible for Ramón Fernández to have entered. He must have entered the temple of Debot, which is in fact set in an artificial lake to re-create the original natural setting on the Nile.
—Vicente Echurre, 1999

I disagree with my colleague, Mr. Echurre. The temple he is referring to exists, but it is in Madrid. It has surely escaped his memory, and I have tried to refresh it but in vain. Since obviously I must dissent, we have decided to express our opinions individually, no matter how absurd that of my associate

might seem. Mine, specifically, is this: the area Mr. Fernández reached in the Metropolitan Museum was the temple, supposedly, of Kantur, which once belonged to Queen Cleopatra and which in 1965, thanks to the efforts of President John F. Kennedy, UNESCO sold to the United States for twenty million dollars. It was discovered later that this transaction had been a fraudulent one (one of many) carried out in collusion with Mr. Kennedy. UNESCO had sent the original temples to their headquarters in the Soviet Union and a plastic replica to the United States. This highly flammable copy was the cause of the big fire in the Metropolitan Museum. It seems that someone had carelessly dropped a lighted cigarette butt on it. —Ismaele Lorenzo, 1999

The only Egyptian temple then in the Metropolitan Museum was that of Pernaabi, from the fifth dynasty, circa 2400 before the Common Era. —Editors, 2025

As on the previous day, Elisa got up around nine, dressed quickly, and went out. Her destination was the same, the Metropolitan Museum. And again she disappeared in front of my eyes.

She did not come to see me at work Thursday or Friday. On Saturday I got up early, determined to find her. I must add that, independent of all the mystery surrounding her person, which fascinated me, I felt the urge to go to bed with her immediately.

I took a taxi to the Metropolitan. Evidently there was a relationship between Elisa and that building, and I thought it was sort of stupid of me not to have realized before that she must be a museum employee, which explained why she was so interested in getting there at ten o'clock, when the doors opened to the public. My mistake had been to search for her among the visitors instead of in the offices.

I searched for her everywhere. I inquired at the information desk and in the staff office. There was no employee named Elisa. Of course, the fact that she told me her name was Elisa did not mean that was really her name; quite the contrary, perhaps. Anyone who worked among so many valuable objects (which for me, by the way, didn't mean a thing) and carried on sexually as she did, had to take precautions.

So I tried to find her physically among the numerous women who worked at the museum. While I was looking over the female guards, I noticed in one room a large group representing many nationalities (Japanese, South Americans, Chinese, Indians, Germans) gathered around a painting, while several guards, almost shouting, were trying to prevent the taking of photographs. Maybe I can find Elisa among them, I thought, and pushed my way into the crowd. And in fact, there she was. Not among those taking the photos, nor among the guards warning that this was not permitted, but inside the very painting everyone was looking at. I got as close as the red cord that served as barrier between painting and public would allow. That woman, with her straight, dark-reddish hair and perfect features, with one hand placed delicately over the other wrist, was smiling almost impudently, against a background that seemed to be a road leading to a misty lake. The woman was, without any doubt, Elisa. . . . I thought then that the mystery had been solved: Elisa was a famous, exclusive artists' model. That was why it was so difficult to find her. At that moment she was probably posing for another painter, perhaps as good as the one who had made this perfect portrait of her.

Before asking one of the guards where I could find the model for the painting that so many people wanted to photograph, I got closer in order to see it in greater detail. Next to the frame, a small placard stated that it was painted in 1505 by one Leonardo da Vinci. Stunned, I backed up to take a good look at the canvas. My eyes then met Elisa's intense gaze in the painting. I held her gaze and discovered that Elisa's eyes had no eyelashes; she had the eyes of a serpent.

• • •

The prison bell is again announcing it is bedtime. I will have to continue this report tomorrow. I must rush, since I believe I have no more than two days left to live.

• • •

Of course, no matter how much the woman in the painting resembled Elisa, it was impossible for her to have been the model. So I quickly tried to find a reasonable explanation for the phenomenon. According to the small catalog at the gallery's entrance, the painting was valued at many millions of dollars (more than eighty million, the catalog read).* The woman in the picture (according to the same catalog) was European. And so was Elisa. The woman in the picture then could be one of Elisa's remote ancestors. Therefore Elisa could be the owner of that painting. And since it was so valuable, Elisa could travel with it for security reasons and would come and inspect it every morning. Then, after checking that nothing had happened to it during the night, which is the time when most thieves choose to operate, she would withdraw to another area of the museum. Now her pains to hide her identity seemed clear to me. She was a nymphomaniac millionaire who, for obvious reasons, had to keep her sexual relationships anonymous.

I have to admit I enjoyed the idea of being associated with a woman who had so many millions. Perhaps, if I played my cards right and pleased her in every way (and this was my heart's desire), Elisa would help me out and I could someday open my own Wendy's. In my enthusiasm I was forgetting the eccentricities and the imperfections, the defects, anomalies, or whatever you want to call them, that at certain moments I detected in her.

Now the only thing I had to do was to be pleasant, to show no interest in money, and not to bother her with indiscreet questions. I bought a bunch of roses from a stand that, being on Fifth Avenue, charged me fifteen dollars, and I went to wait for Elisa at the front entrance of the museum, because if she was inside—and I was sure she was—sooner or later she would have to come out. But she did not. With my bunch of roses, I remained at my post, under a New York drizzle, until ten o'clock, when the museum closed on Fridays.†

When I got to Wendy's it was eleven P.M. I was three hours late. I was fired then and there. Before leaving, I gave the roses to the cashier.

After walking around Broadway until very late, I returned to my room in a state of depression. Elisa was there, waiting for me. As usual, she was elegantly dressed, and this time she was carrying a camera, a very expensive professional one. I invited her in and told her about my being fired. "Don't worry," she said. "With me on your side, you won't have any problem." And I believed her, thinking of her fortune, and so I asked her to get into bed with me. Because the first thing a man must do to keep on good terms with a woman is to invite her to his bed; even though she may not accept at the beginning, or maybe ever, she will always be grateful. . . . Strangely enough, she did not accept. She asked me to go to bed alone

---

*It is interesting to note that the value of the painting according to the *New York Times* was about $100 million, while the catalog quoted $80 million. We believe this was a government trick to raise taxes for the right to exhibit that famous masterpiece in this country. This suspicion was almost absolutely confirmed in 1992 when it was disclosed, on the opening of former President Ronald Reagan's will, that he had owned the *New York Times* since 1944. The anti-Republican sentiment of that newspaper (which after this scandal was forced to cease publication) was nothing but a political tactic to prevent suspicion. —Lorenzo and Echurre, 1999

†There must have been a special event that day at the museum, since it usually closes at ten only on Wednesdays. —D.S.

The Metropolitan Museum in New York closed at ten o'clock on Wednesdays and Fridays. Mr. Sakuntala's knowledge of these matters is negligible. —Lorenzo and Echurre, 1999

Before the big fire, the Metropolitan Museum was open Tuesdays and Sundays until ten o'clock. We hope that as soon as repairs are completed and the museum reopens, it will have the same schedule. —Editors, 2025

because she had to meditate ("concentrate," I remember now, is the word she used) on a project she had to work on the following day, Saturday—though since the sun was almost out, it was already Saturday.

I thought it was best to obey my future boss, and I went to bed alone though, of course, I did not intend to sleep. Awake but snoring lightly, I observed her discreetly. She walked back and forth in my studio for over two hours while mumbling unintelligible gibberish. I could make out "the inventors . . . the interpreters" at one point. Though I am not even sure of that, for Elisa was talking faster and faster, and her pace seemed to keep rhythm with her words. Finally she took off her splendid dress and went out the window, naked, onto the fire escape. With her hands uplifted and her head tilted back, as if in position to receive an extraordinary gift from the skies (now gray and overcast), she remained outside on the landing for hours, indifferent to the cold and even to a freezing drizzle, which was getting heavier. About one in the afternoon she came back in and, "waking me," said she needed to go do some work in the mountain town we had visited. It seemed she had to take some photos representing the region.

Soon on our way, we got there before dusk. The streets were deserted or, rather, filled with mounds of purple leaves, which moved in eddies from place to place. We stayed at the same hotel (or motel) as before; it was so quiet, we seemed to be its only guests. Before dark we went out into town, and she began to take some photos of houses still in the light. (If I appear in some of those photos, it's because she asked me to pose for her.) We went to the restaurant that reminded me of La Bodeguita del Medio. I noticed that Elisa had a ravenous appetite. Without losing her elegant composure, she downed several portions of soup, pasta, cream sauce, roast, bread, and dessert, besides two bottles of wine. Then she asked me to take her for a walk. The streets were narrow and badly lit, and after coming out of a place that so resembled La Bodeguita del Medio, it seemed as if I were back in Havana during my last years there. But what most brought me back to those days was a sensation of fear, of terror, even, which seemed to emanate from every corner and every object, including our own bodies. Night had fallen, and though there was no moon, there was a radiant luminosity in the sky. The usual evening fog enveloped everything, even ourselves, in a gray mist that blurred all silhouettes. Finally we reached a yellowish esplanade, which no car seemed to have crossed ever before. Elisa was walking ahead with all her equipment. The road narrowed and disappeared between dim promontories that looked like tapering, greenish rocks. Or like withered cypresses linked by a strange viscosity. On the other side of the promontories we came upon a lake, also greenish and covered by the same nebulous vegetation. Elisa deposited her expensive equipment on the ground and looked at me. As she talked, her face, her hair, and her hands seemed to glow.

"*Il veleno de la conoscenza é una della tante calamità di cui soffre l'essere umano*," she said, her eyes fixed on me. "*Il veleno della conoscenza o al meno quello della curiosità.*"*

"I don't understand a word," I blurted out in all sincerity.

---

*Poor Ramoncito only wrote the phonetic representation of these phrases. With my extensive knowledge of the Italian language (I studied with Giolio B. Blanc), I was able to make the necessary corrections. I must clarify that this is the only correction I have made in the manuscript. The translation into English would read like this: "The poison of knowledge is one of the many calamities

"Well, I want you to understand. I have never killed anybody without first telling him why."

"Who are you going to kill?" I asked her with a smile, to let her know I was not taking her words seriously.

"Listen to me, you fool," she said, stepping away from me while I, pretending not to understand, tried to embrace her. "I know everything you did. Your trips to the museum, your incessant surveillance, your detective work. Your pretended snoring did not fool me either. Of course, until now your stupidity and your cowardice have prevented you from seeing things as they are. Let me help you. There is no difference between what you saw in the painting at the museum and me. We are one and the same thing."

I must confess that it was impossible for me then to assimilate Elisa's words. I asked her to explain in "simpler language," still hoping it was all a joke or the effect of the two bottles of wine.

After she repeated the same explanation several times, I finally got an idea of what she meant. The woman in the painting and Elisa *were* one and the same. As long as the painting existed, she, Elisa, would exist too. But for the picture to exist, she had, of course, to be there. That is, whenever the museum was open, she had to remain there inside the picture— "smiling, impassive, and radiant," as she put it, with a tinge of irony. Once the museum was closed, she could get out and have her amorous escapades like the ones I had participated in. "Encounters with men, the handsomest men I can find," she explained, looking at me, and in spite of my dangerous situation, I could not help but experience some feelings of vanity. . . . "But all those men," continued Elisa, "cannot simply *enjoy*, they want to *know*, and they end up like you, with a vague idea of my peculiar condition. Then the persecution begins. They want to know who I am, no matter what the cost, they want to know everything. And in the end, I have to eliminate them. . . ." Elisa paused for a moment and, glaring at me, continued: "Yes, I like men, and very much, because I am also a man, as well as a genius!" She said this looking at me, and I could see that her anger was mounting; realizing I was facing a dangerous madwoman, I decided it was best to "go with her flow" (as we used to say in Havana), and begging her to control herself, I asked her to tell me about her sex change. "After all," I tried to console her, "New York is full of transvestites, and they don't look so unhappy. . . ." She, completely ignoring my words, explained to me: Not only was Elisa the woman in the painting, but the woman in the painting was also the painter, who had done his self-portrait as he wished to be (the way he was in his mind): a lusty, fascinating woman. But his real triumph was not that he portrayed himself as an alluring woman. "That," she said with scorn, "had already been done by most painters." His true achievement was that through a mustering of energy, genius, and mental concentration— which, she claimed, were unknown in our century—the woman he painted had the ability to become the painter himself and to outlive him. This person

humans suffer. The poison of knowledge or, at least, that of curiosity." —D.S.

Even though his translation is correct, we doubt very much that Mr. Sakuntala ever studied with Baron Giolio B. Blanc. The high social status of this nobleman would not have permitted him to rub elbows with people like Mr. Sakuntala, let

alone accept him as his tutee, unless there were *highly* personal motives. —Lorenzo and Echurre, 1999

Giolio B. Blanc was for many years the editor of the magazine *Noticias de Arte de Nueva York* and therefore had probably met Daniel Sakuntala, who had literary pretensions. —Editors, 2025

(she? he?) would then exist as long as the painting existed, and had the power, when nobody was present, to step out of the painting and escape into the crowds. And in this way she was able to find sexual gratification with the kind of men that the painter, as a man not graced by beauty, had never been able to get. *"But the power of concentration I must muster to achieve all that does not come easily. And now, after almost five hundred years, I sometimes lose the perfection of my physical attributes or even one of my parts, as you on several occasions were astonished to see but could not believe."*

In brief, I was facing a man over five hundred years old who had transformed himself into a woman and also existed as a painting. The situation would have been truly hilarious were it not for the fact that, at that point, Elisa drew from her bodice an ancient dagger, sharp and glimmering nonetheless.

I tried to disarm her, but in vain. With only one hand she overpowered me, and in an instant I was on the ground, the dagger before my eyes. Crouching, and imprisoned under Elisa's legs, I still was able to identify the landscape around us. It was exactly the same as in the famous (and now, for me, accursed) painting at the museum. Something sinister was indeed going on, though I could not determine its extent. Elisa—I will keep calling her Elisa until the end of this report—made me move along in my crouched position until we reached the lakeshore. Once there, I saw it was not a lake but a swamp. This was obviously the place, I thought, where she sacrifices her surely numerous indiscreet lovers.

The alternatives Elisa seemed to be offering me were equally frightful: to die either drowned in that swamp or pierced by the dagger. Or perhaps she had both in mind. Again she fixed her gaze on me, and I understood that my end was near. I started to cry. Elisa took off her clothes. I continued crying. It was not my family in Cuba that I remembered at that moment but the enormous salad bar at Wendy's. To me it was like a vision of my life these last few years (fresh, pleasant, surrounded by people, and problem-free), before Elisa came into it. Meanwhile she lay naked in the mud.

"Let it not be said," she muttered, barely moving her lips, "that we are not parting on the best of terms."

And beckoning me to join her, she kept smiling in her peculiar way, lips almost closed.

I couldn't stop crying, but I came closer. Still holding the dagger, she placed her hand behind my head, quickly aligning her naked body with mine. She did this with such speed, professionalism, and violence that I realized it would be very difficult for me to come out of that embrace alive. . . . I am sure that in all my long erotic experience, never has my performance been so lustful and tender, so skillful and passionate—because in all truth, even knowing she intended to kill me, I still lusted for her. By her third orgasm, while she was still panting and uttering the most obscene words, Elisa had not only forgotten the dagger but become oblivious of herself. I noticed she apparently was losing the concentration and energy that, as she said, enabled her to become a real woman. Her eyes were becoming opaque, her face was losing its color, her cheekbones were melting away. Suddenly her luscious hair dropped from her head, and I found myself in the arms of a very old, bald man, toothless and foul-smelling, who kept whimpering while slobbering my penis. Quickly he sat on it, riding it as if he were a true demon. I quickly put him on all fours and, in spite of my revulsion, tried to give him as much pleasure as I could, hoping he would be so exhausted he would let me go. Since I had never practiced sodomy, I wanted to keep the illusion, even remotely, that this horrible thing, this sack of bones with the ugliest of beards, was still Elisa. So while I possessed him, I kept calling him by that name. But he, in the middle of his paroxysm, turned and looked at me; his eyes were two empty reddish sockets.

"Call me Leonardo, damn it! Call me Leonardo!" he shouted, while writhing and groaning with such pleasure as I have never seen in a human being.

"Leonardo!" I began repeating, then, while I possessed him, "Leonardo!" I repeated as I kept penetrating that pestiferous mound. "Leonardo," I kept whispering tenderly, while with a quick jump I got hold of the dagger, then flailing my arms, I escaped as fast as I could through the yellow esplanade. "Leonardo! Leonardo!" I was still shouting when I jumped onto my motorcycle and dashed away at full speed. "Leonardo! Leonardo! Leonardo!" I think I kept saying, still in a panic, all the way back to New York, as if repeating the name might serve as an incantation to appease that lecherous old man still writhing at the edge of the swamp he himself had painted.

I was sure that Leonardo, Elisa, or "that thing" was not dead.

What's more, I think I'd managed to do no harm at all to it. And if I did, would a single stab be enough to destroy all the horror that had managed to prevail for over five hundred years and included not only Elisa but the swamp, the sandy road, the rocks, the town, and even the ghostly mist that covered it all?

That night I slept in the home of my friend the Cuban writer Daniel Sakuntala.[*] I told him I had problems with a woman and did not want to sleep with her in my apartment. Without giving him any more details, I presented him with the dagger, which he was able to appreciate as the precious jewel it was. Would it solve any problem, I wondered, if I told him of my predicament? Would he believe me?[†] Right now, only two days away from my imminent demise, when there is no way out for me, I am telling my story mainly as an act of pure desperation and as my last hope, because nothing else is left for me to do. At least for now, I realize how very difficult it is for anyone to believe all this. Anyway, before the little time I have left runs out, let me continue.

Of course I did not, even remotely, consider going back to my room, terrified as I was by the possibility of finding Elisa there. I was sure of only one thing: she was looking for me, and still is, in order to kill me. This is what my own instinct, my experience of fear and persecution, are telling me (and don't forget I lived twenty years in Cuba).

---

[*]"Cuban writer Daniel Sakuntala" (!): We question this statement, obviously the product of friendship. Not even the lengthiest of directories register that name. —Lorenzo and Echurre, 1999

[†]A serious error of appreciation on the part of my friend Ramoncito. After studying for more than twenty years and with the superior knowledge I acquired of alchemy, astrology, metempsychosis, and the occult sciences, I would have believed him and could have helped him to conjure away this evil. Had he trusted me, Ramoncito would be alive today. By the way, the dagger he gave me (pure gold, with an ivory handle) has disappeared from my room. I am sure it was taken by a black man from the Dominican Republic who accompanied Renecito Cifuentes when he visited me a few days ago. —D.S.

For three days I roamed the streets without knowing what to do and, naturally, without being able to sleep. On Wednesday night I showed up again at Daniel's. I was shaking, not only out of fear but because I was running a fever. Maybe I had caught the flu, or something worse, during the time I was out on the streets.

Daniel behaved like a real friend, perhaps the only one I had and, I believe, still have. He prepared something for me to eat and hot tea, made me take two aspirins, and even gave me some syrupy potion.* Finally, after so many nights of insomnia, I fell asleep. I dreamed, of course, of Elisa. Her cold eyes were looking at me from a corner of the room. Suddenly that corner became the strange landscape with the promontories of greenish rocks around a swamp. By the swamp, Elisa was waiting for me. Her eyes were fixed on mine, her hands elegantly entwined below her chest. She kept looking at me with detached perversity, and her look was a command to get closer and embrace her right at the edge of the swamp. . . . I dragged myself there. She placed her hands on my head and pulled me down close to her. As I possessed her, I sensed that I was penetrating not even an old man but a mound of mud. The enormous and pestiferous mass slowly engulfed me while it kept expanding, splattering heavily and becoming more foul-smelling. I screamed as this viscous thing swallowed me, but my screams only produced a dull gurgling sound. I felt my skin and my bones being sucked away by the mass of mud, and once inside it, I became mud, finally sinking into the swamp.

My own screams woke me up so suddenly that I still had time to see Daniel sucking my member. He pretended it wasn't so and withdrew to the opposite side of the bed, making believe he was asleep, but I understood I could not stay there either. I got up, made some coffee, thanked Daniel for his hospitality and allowing me to sleep in his apartment, borrowed twenty dollars from him, and left.†

It was Thursday. I had decided to leave New York before Monday. But with only twenty dollars, where could I go? I saw several acquaintances (Reinaldo García Remos, among them) and offered the key to my room, and everything in it, in exchange for some money. I got a lot of excuses but no cash. Late on Sunday I went to Wendy's, where, as a security guard, I had spent the best part of my life. At the cash register I talked to the stout black woman who had been so good to me (in every sense of the word). She let me have a salad, a quart of milk, and a hamburger, all for free. About five o'clock in the morning, the establishment was deserted and I dozed off on my seat. Another employee who was mopping the second floor called the cashier to pass on some piece of gossip. While they chatted, I took advantage of the situation and grabbed all the money from the cash register.

*The "syrupy potion" I gave him was just Riopan, a stomach relief medication against diarrhea. —D.S.

†Out of pure intellectual honesty, I am leaving this passage as it appears in the manuscript by my friend Ramoncito. I want the text to be published in its entirety. But the lascivious abuse he refers to can only be a product of his psychological state and of the nightmare he was having. It is true we slept that night on the same bed; it's the only one I have. I heard him scream, and to bring him out of his delirium, I shook him several times. Naturally, when he woke up, it was logical for him to

find my hands on his body. —D.S.

We are of the opinion that Ramón Fernández was sexually harassed, as he indicates, by Mr. Sakuntala. The moral history of this character, who disappeared naked into Lake Erie in the midst of a communal orgy, proves our point. —Lorenzo and Echurre, 1999

We have already indicated that Daniel Sakuntala disappeared close to the shore of Lake Ontario, where his clothes were found. We have not been able to confirm reports about a supposed orgy. —Editors, 2025

Without counting it, I ran to Grand Central. I wanted to take a train and go as far as possible. But the three long-distance trains would not leave until nine in the morning. I sat on a bench and, while waiting, began to count the money. There was twelve hundred dollars. I thought this was salvation. By eight A.M. the station was swarming with people—or rather with beasts: thousands of people who pushed and shoved mercilessly to make it to work on time. By nine, I hoped, I would be sitting on a train, fleeing from all those people and, above all, from that thing.

· · ·

But it didn't turn out that way. I was standing in line to buy my ticket when I saw Elisa. She was below the big terminal clock, oblivious to the crowd but with her eyes fixed on me, with her enigmatic smile and her folded hands. I saw her coming my way and started to run toward the tracks. But since I did not have a ticket, I could not get in. Pushing people, and trying to find a place to hide, I went across the room again. But she was everywhere. I remember dashing through the Oyster Bar, colliding with a waiter and upsetting a table on which a number of lobsters were arrayed. At the back door of the restaurant, Elisa was waiting for me, I knew, or sensed, that I could not stay alone with that "woman" a second longer, that the larger the crowd around me, the harder it would be for her to kill me or drag me into her swamp. I began screaming in English and in Spanish, begging for help, while I pointed at her. But the people, the masses of people, rushed by without looking at me. One more madman shouting in the most crowded train station in the world could not alarm anyone. Besides, my clothes were dirty and I had not shaved for a week. On the other hand, the woman I was accusing of attempted assault was a grand lady, serene, elegant, expertly made up and attired. I realized that I was not going to attract anybody's attention by shouting, so I rushed to the very center of the main hall, where it was most crowded, and quickly took off my clothes and stood there, naked. Then I began to jump about in the crowd. Evidently that was more than even a madman is allowed to do in the very center of the city of New York. I heard some police whistles. Arrested, I felt relieved and peaceful, for the first time in many days, as they handcuffed me and shoved me roughly into the patrol car.

Unfortunately, I only stayed overnight at the police station. There was no evidence on which to hold me as a criminal of any sort, and if I was insane—and I quote the officer in charge—"luckily, that would not be a matter for the New York police; otherwise, we would have to arrest almost everybody." As for the money, it had disappeared into the hands of the arresting officers when they searched my clothes. So there was no evidence that I had committed any crime. Of course, among other things, I confessed to being a thief, which was nothing but the truth, and mentioned the money that had been stolen from me. Apparently the police found no computer record of any accusation by the Wendy's management or any report of the loss of that money.*

*It seems that Ramoncito Fernández had, without being aware of it, a woman who really loved him: Wendy's cashier. From my investigation I learned that out of her salary she had, little by little, covered the so-called embezzlement that occurred while she was in charge, without ever disclosing the name of the thief. Obviously that woman was another person, besides me, whom Ramoncito could have asked for help, had he been more trusting and less obstinate. —D.S.

On Tuesday I was again roaming the streets of Manhattan. The drizzle and strong winds were unbearable, and I had no money at all and no umbrella either, of course. It was eleven A.M. I knew the Metropolitan Museum would be open until seven that evening, so for the moment, at least, I was in no danger. Inside the picture frame, she would now be smiling at all her admirers. It was then (I recall I was crossing 42nd Street) that I had a sort of epiphany. An idea that could really save me. Why hadn't I thought of it before? I blamed myself for being such a fool, particularly when I pride myself on not being a complete idiot. The painting! The painting, of course! There she was, and the swamp, the rocks, the yellow esplanade. . . . Everything the painter had conceived, including even himself, was now in the museum, fulfilling its destiny as a work of art and at the mercy of whoever dared to destroy it.

Back in my room, I took a hammer I use for my occasional carpentry,* and hiding it under my jacket, I rushed to the Metropolitan Museum. There I met with another little inconvenience: I had no money to pay for admission. Of course I could force my way in, but I didn't want to be arrested before doing my work. Finally someone coming out of the building agreed to give me the metal badge that indicates you have paid for admission. I clipped it on my jacket and entered the building. Running to the second floor, I went into the most visited gallery in the museum. There she was, captive inside the flame, smiling at her audience. Pushing the stupid crowd away, I rushed in, brandishing my hammer. I was finally going to do away with the monstrosity that had destroyed so many men and that very soon would destroy me too. But then, just as I was ready to hit the first blow, one of Elisa's hands moved away from the other, and with incredible speed (while her expression remained impassive), she pressed the alarm button on the wall next to her painting. Suddenly a steel curtain dropped from the ceiling, covering the painting completely.† And I, hammer in hand, was restrained by the museum security guards, by the police (who materialized instantly), and by the fanatic crowd that had come to worship that painting. The same crowd that in Grand Central had done nothing for me when I screamed for help because my life was in danger was the one that now shoved me angrily into the patrol car.

Today, Friday, after being under arrest for four days, I am coming to the end of my story, which I will try to send to Daniel as soon as possible. I may be able to do it. Quite unexpectedly, I have become a notorious character.

---

*It is true that Ramoncito knew about carpentry. He built me an excellent bookcase once. The hammer in question was not his but mine. I had lent it to him when he installed the air-conditioning in his studio with the help of Miguel Correa. —D.S.

†This protection system is the most efficient ever devised. At the same time the alarm goes off, the metal curtain drops over the wall where the piece of art is being exhibited. It is very expensive to install. There are only three masterpieces in the world that have this protection. According to the research carried out by my friend Kokó Salás, the curator, the three works are *La Joconde*, by Leonardo da Vinci; *Guernica*, by Pablo Picasso; and *The Burial of Count Orgaz*, by Doménikos Theotokópoulos, El Greco. —D.S.

Daniel Sakuntala is completely misguided when he calls Kokó Salása "curator." In all truth, he is a common criminal† dedicated to the illegal traffic of works of art in Madrid, under the protection of the Cuban government in Havana. —Lorenzo and Echurre, 1999

†To label Kokó Salás as a common criminal is to underestimate his character and historic significance. Kokó Salás was a sophisticated, gifted person (it is now impossible to determine whether he was a man or a woman) who worked for an international spy ring in service to the Kremlin. Under the secretary for mineral rights, Victorio Garrati, he conspired indefatigably and took part in intrigues until he finally achieved the annexation of Italy and Greece to the Soviet Union in the year 2011. For more information, see *La Matahari* [sic] *de Holguin*, by Teodoro Tapia. —Editors, 2025

There are two police officers here who seem to admire me because I am a strange case they cannot figure out. It was my intention not to steal a painting worth millions of dollars but to destroy it. One of the officers (I am withholding his name) has promised to get this manuscript out and give it to my friend Daniel. If this testimony reaches his hands soon enough, I do not know what he will be able to do, but I am sure he will do something. Maybe some influential person will read it; maybe it will be taken seriously and I will be granted personal protection, efficient full-time vigilance. Understand this: the fact is I don't want to get out of this prison cell; what I need is for Elisa not to get in. The ideal situation would be to install here the same metal curtain that protects her. But all that would have to be done before Monday. The museum closes that day, and she will be totally free and with time to accumulate all the energy and develop all the stratagems she needs in order to get to me here, to destroy me. Please, help me! Or else I will soon become another of her countless victims, those buried under that greenish swamp that you can see in the background of her famous painting, from which she is still watching, with those eyes without lashes, while she keeps smiling.

1990

## *From* BEFORE NIGHT FALLS[1]

### Mariel

Around the beginning of April 1980, a driver on the number 32 bus route drove a bus full of passengers through the doors of the Peruvian embassy asking for political asylum. Strangely enough, all the passengers on the bus also decided to ask for political asylum. Not one of them wanted to leave the embassy.

Fidel Castro demanded that all the people be returned, but the ambassador from Perú stated that they were on Peruvian territory, and according to international law, they had the right to political asylum. Days later, during one of his fits of anger, Fidel Castro decided to withdraw the Cuban guards from the embassy, perhaps trying in this way to pressure the ambassador to give in and force the people out of the embassy.

This time he miscalculated. When it became known that the Peruvian embassy was no longer guarded, thousands upon thousands of people, young and old, entered the grounds asking for political asylum. One of the first to do so was my friend Lázaro. I did not believe in the possibility of asylum because the news was even published in *Granma*;[2] I thought it was a trap, and that once all the people were inside the embassy, Castro would arrest them. As soon as he knew who his enemies were—that is, all those who wanted to leave—he could then easily put them in jail.

1. Translated by Dolores M. Koch.
2. The official daily publication of the Central Committee of the Communist Party of Cuba.

Lázaro said good-bye to me before going to the embassy. The following day the embassy doors were closed again, but there were 10,800 people inside and 100,000 more outside, trying to get in. From all over the country, trucks were arriving full of young people who wanted to get in, but at that point Fidel Castro knew he had made a big mistake by withdrawing the guard from the Peruvian embassy. Not only was the embassy closed but only people living in Miramar[3] were allowed near the site.

Electricity and water to the embassy were cut off, and for 10,800 people, 800 food rations were delivered. In addition, State Security smuggled in numerous undercover agents who went as far as to murder former high government officials requesting asylum. The area surrounding the embassy was scattered with Communist Youth Organization and Communist Party IDs, discarded by the people inside.

All the world press agencies were wiring the news, but the Cuban government tried to play down the incident. Even Julio Cortázar and Pablo Armando Fernández,[4] stalwart champions of Castro who were in New York at the time, declared that there were only six or seven hundred people inside the embassy.

One taxi driver drove his car at full speed trying to break into the embassy, and was machine-gunned down by State Security; wounded, he still tried to get out of his car and into the embassy, but he was carried away in a patrol car.

The events at the Peruvian embassy were the first mass rebellion by the Cuban people against the Castro dictatorship. After that, people tried to enter the U.S. Interest Section office in Havana. Everybody was seeking an embassy to get into, and police persecution reached alarming proportions. In the end, the Soviet Union sent a high official of the KGB to Cuba, to hold a number of meetings with Fidel Castro.

Fidel and Raúl Castro[5] had personally taken a look at the Peruvian embassy. There, for the first time, Castro heard the people insulting him, calling him a coward, a criminal, and demanding freedom.

It was then that Fidel ordered that they be gunned down, and those people—who had gone for fifteen days with almost no food, sleeping on their feet because there was no space to lie down, trying to survive amid the filth of their own excrement—faced up to the bullets by singing the old national anthem. Many were wounded.

To avoid the danger of a popular uprising, Fidel and the Soviet Union decided that a breach must be opened to allow a number of those nonconformists to leave; it was like curing sickness by bleeding.

During a desperate and angry speech, accompanied and applauded by Gabriel García Márquez and Juan Bosch,[6] Castro accused those poor people in the embassy of being antisocial and sexually depraved. I'll never forget that speech—Castro looked like a cornered, furious rat—nor will I forget the

---

3. An upscale district in Havana where many embassies are located.
4. Cuban writer (b. 1930), who lived in the United States between 1945 and 1959. Julio Cortázar: Belgian-born Argentinian writer (1914–1984), who lived in Paris after 1951.
5. Fidel's brother (b. 1931); at the time, Cuba's vice-president, minister of the Revolutionary

Armed Forces, and highest ranking general.
6. Juan Emilio Bosch Gaviño (1909–2001), Dominican politician, historian, writer, and educator; president of the Dominican Republic February–September 1963. Gabriel García Márquez: Colombian writer and Nobel Prize–winner (b. 1928).

hypocritical applause of García Márquez and Juan Bosch, giving their support to such a crime against the unfortunate captives.

The port of Mariel was then opened, and Castro, after stressing that all those people were antisocial, said that precisely what he wanted was to have that riffraff out of Cuba. Posters immediately started to appear with the slogans LET THEM GO, LET THE RIFFRAFF GO. The Party and State Security organized a "voluntary" march against the refugees at the embassy. People had no choice but to take part in the march; many went with the hope of perhaps being able to jump the fence and get inside. But the marchers could not get close, not with three rows of cops between them and the fence.

Thousands of boats full of people started to leave for the United States from the port of Mariel. Of course, not all those at the embassy who wanted to leave were able to do so, but only those whom Fidel Castro wanted to get rid of: common prisoners and criminals from Cuban jails; undercover agents whom he wanted to infiltrate in Miami; the mentally ill. And all this was paid for by the Cuban exiles who sent boats to get their relatives out. The majority of those families in Miami spent all their resources renting boats to rescue their loved ones, and when they arrived at Mariel, Castro would often fill their boats with criminals and insane people, and they could not get their relatives out. But thousands of honest people also managed to escape.

Of course, to be able to depart from the Port of Mariel, people had to leave the Peruvian embassy with a safe-conduct issued by State Security, and had to return to their homes and wait until the Castro government gave them the order to leave. From that moment on, State Security, not the Peruvian embassy, was making the decisions as to who could leave the country and who could not. Many resisted, not wanting to abandon the embassy, especially those most involved with the Castro regime.

The mobs organized by State Security waited outside the embassy for those leaving with safe-conducts and in many instances tore up their permits. Besides losing their right to exile, they were beaten up by the rabble.

Lots of people were physically attacked, not only for being at the Peruvian embassy but merely for sending telegrams asking their relatives in Miami to come for them at the Port of Mariel. I saw a young man beaten unconscious and left on the street just as he was coming out of the post office after sending one of those telegrams. This happened daily, everywhere, during the months of April and May 1980.

Twenty days later, Lázaro returned from the embassy and was hardly recognizable; he weighed less than ninety pounds. He had gone to a lot of trouble to avoid being beaten, but he was starving. Now all he could do was wait for his exit permit. The day it came, I accompanied him in a taxi to where the documents were being issued, and he said to me: "Don't worry, Reinaldo, I am going to get you out of here." When he left the taxi, I saw the mob attack him and hit him on the back with steel bars as he ran under a shower of rocks and rotten fruit; in the midst of all that, I saw him disappear toward freedom, while I remained behind, alone. But in my building almost everyone wanted to leave the country, so it felt like a sort of refuge.

During that civil strife, terrible things were happening. To escape being beaten by the mob, one man got in his car and drove it into some of the people who were attacking him. An agent of State Security immediately shot him in the head, killing him. The incidents were even published in *Granma*; to have killed such an antisocial person was considered a heroic act.

The homes of those waiting for exit permits were surrounded by mobs and stoned; in the Vedado,[7] several people were stoned to death. All the terrors suffered for twenty years were now reaching their peak. Anyone who was not Castro's agent was in danger.

Opposite my room someone had put up various posters reading: HOMOSEXUALS, GET OUT; SCUM OF THE EARTH, GET OUT. To get out was exactly what I wanted, but how? Ironically, the Cuban government hurled insults at us and demanded that we leave, but at the same time prevented us from leaving. At no point did Fidel Castro open the Port of Mariel to all who wanted to leave; his trick was simply to let go the ones who posed no danger to the image of his government. Professionals with university degrees could not leave, nor could writers who had published abroad, such as myself.

However, since the order of the day was to allow all undesirables to go, and in that category homosexuals were in first place, a large number of gays were able to leave the Island in 1980. People who were not even homosexual pretended to be gay in order to obtain permission to leave from the Port of Mariel.

The best way to obtain an exit permit was to provide any documentary proof of being a homosexual. I did not have such a document, but I had my ID, which stated that I had been in jail because of a public disturbance; that was good enough proof; and I went to the police.

At the police station they asked me if I was a homosexual and I said yes; then they asked me if I was active or passive and I took the precaution of saying that I was passive. A friend of mine who said he played the active role was not allowed to leave; he had told the truth, but the Cuban government did not look upon those who took the active male role as real homosexuals. There were also some women psychologists there. They made me walk in front of them to see if I was queer.

I passed the test, and a lieutenant yelled to another officer, "Send this one directly." This meant that I did not have to go through any further police investigation. They made me sign a document stating that I was leaving Cuba for purely personal reasons, because I was unworthy to live within the marvelous Cuban Revolution. They gave me a number and told me not to leave my home. The cop filling out my papers said: "Listen carefully, if you are going to have a 'clotheshanger party' you must have it at home, because if you are not there when the exit permit arrives, you'll miss your chance." I think that cop would have been delighted to go to the imaginary nude party that he said I would have at home.

My exit permit had been negotiated at the neighborhood level, the police station. The mechanisms of persecution in Cuba were not yet technically sophisticated; for that reason, I could leave without State Security finding out about it; I was leaving as just another queer, not as a writer; in the middle of that pandemonium, none of the cops who authorized my exit knew anything about literature or had any reason to know my books, almost none of which, in any case, had ever been published in Cuba.

---

7. Downtown Havana.

When I had finally dozed off one night, after a sleepless week locked up in my unbearably hot room, there was a knock at my door. It was Marta Carriles and Lázaro's father calling out: "Get up, your exit permit is here! We knew Saint Lazarus[8] would help you!" I ran downstairs in my pajamas and right there at the building's entrance, holding a sheet of paper, was a cop who asked me if I was Reinaldo Arenas. I answered affirmatively, in as low a voice as I could, and he told me I had thirty minutes to get ready and show up at a place called Cuatro Ruedas to leave the country.

Rushing up the stairs I ran into Pepe Malas, who was always on the watch, and he said: "There is a cop down there looking for you. What does he want?" With panic in my face I told him that they had come to take me in again, that there was going to be another trial. I was so terrified at the thought that he could discover my real reasons, that he believed me.

In those days it was very difficult to get to Cuatro Ruedas in thirty minutes. When the bus came, I told the driver I had an exit permit, and that I would give him a gold chain if he got there in less than half an hour. The driver stepped on the gas and drove at full speed, without making any stops, and I made it on time. I quickly said good-bye to Fernando, Lázaro's father, and ran to the place where a soldier was waiting. I surrendered my ration booklet and the document I had received from the police officer at home, and was immediately given a passport and a safe-conduct stating that I was one of the exiles from the Peruvian embassy. I left for Mariel on the first bus of the day. To cap it all, the bus broke down on the way and we had to wait about two hours for another bus to pick us up and take us to our destination.

We arrived at El Mosquito, the concentration camp near Mariel; it was aptly named because of the swarms of mosquitoes there. We had to wait two or three days for our turn to leave Mariel. During this time I met some friends, and also many who I knew were undercover agents; I tried to stay out of their way so they would not notice me. We were searched, since we were not allowed to take any letters, not even the telephone number of someone in the United States. I had memorized the number of my aunt in Miami.

Before entering the area for people already authorized to leave the country, we had to wait in a long line and submit our passports to an agent of State Security who checked our names against those listed in a huge book; they were the names of people not authorized to leave the country. I was terrified. I quickly asked someone for a pen and since my passport was handwritten and the *e* of *Arenas* was closed, I changed it to *i* and became Reinaldo Arinas. The officer looked up my new name, and of course never found it.

Before we boarded the buses for the Port of Mariel, another officer told us that we were all leaving "clean," that is, that no passport contained any criminal records, and that, therefore, when we arrived in the United States all we had to say was that we were exiles from the Peruvian embassy. There was, no doubt, a dirty and sinister game behind these procedures; the Revolutionary government purposefully intended to create an enormous confusion so that

---

8. Lazarus of Bethany, also known as Lazarus of the Four Days; according to the Gospel of John, in the New Testament, Lazarus died and was miraculously brought back to life by Jesus four days later. *Marta Carriles*: like Pepe Malas, in the next paragraph, a friend who lives in either the same house or the same neighborhood in Havana.

authorities in the United States would not know who were the actual exiles and who were not.

Before boarding the boats, we were sorted into categories and sent to empty warehouses: one for the insane, one for murderers and hard-core criminals, another for prostitutes and homosexuals, and one for the young men who were undercover agents of State Security to be infiltrated in the United States. The boats were filled with people taken from each of these different groups.

It should be remembered that there were 135,500 people in that exodus; the majority were people like myself; all they wanted was to live in a free world, to work and regain their lost humanity.

Finally, at one in the morning of May 4, my turn came. The name of my boat was *San Lázaro* and I remembered Marta Carriles's words. A soldier took several pictures of us and minutes later we were under way. We were escorted by two Cuban police launches; it was a precaution to prevent people who had not received exit permits from illegally boarding those boats.

Something horrendous happened just then. As we were leaving, a member of the coast guard threw his rifle into the water and quickly started to swim toward us. The other coast guard launches approached the swimmer, and the men killed him, while he was still in the water, with their bayonets.

The *San Lázaro* continued sailing away from the coast. The Island turned into a jumble of blinking lights, and then everything became a deep shadow. We were now on the open sea.

For me, who for so many years had wanted nothing more than to abandon that land of horrors, it was easy not to cry. But there was a youth, perhaps seventeen years old, forced on board in Mariel having to leave all his family behind, who was crying disconsolately. There were some women with children who, like me, had not eaten in five days. There were also several mental patients.

The captain of the boat was an exile who had left Cuba for the United States twenty years ago, and had now returned just to get his family out. Instead, he was carrying a ship full of strangers, with the promise that, on his next trip, he would be allowed to take his family with him. He was the navigator because he had no other choice. He told me he knew nothing about navigation, and had chartered that boat in order to rescue his family. There was, to make the situation even worse, nothing to eat on board.

The trip from Havana to Key West[9] is only seven hours. However, we had been sailing for more than a day without seeing that blessed Key West. Finally the captain confessed that he was completely off course and did not know where we were. He did have a radio and was trying to contact other vessels, but to no avail.

On the second day, the boat ran out of gas, and we began drifting in the powerful current of the Gulf Stream. We had not eaten for so many days that we couldn't even throw up; we only vomited bile. One of the mental patients tried to jump overboard several times and had to be held down while some of the ex-convicts yelled at him to control himself, telling him that he was going to "Yuma."[1] The poor man shouted back, "To hell with

9. U.S. island in the Straits of Florida, at the southernmost tip of the Florida Keys.
1. In Cuban street slang, code for the United States. The origin of the term is mysterious; the term does not refer to the city of Yuma, in Yuma County, Arizona.

Yuma, I want to go home." He had no idea that we were going to the United States of America. Sharks were circling around us, waiting to devour anyone unlucky enough to fall overboard.

At last the captain was able to raise another boat, which then called the U.S. Coast Guard, who in turn ordered a helicopter search. Three days later the U.S. helicopter appeared; it dropped almost to water level, shot some photos, and left. It radioed rescue orders to the coast guard and that very night a coast guard vessel came by. They threw us lines and brought us aboard, tied our boat to their stern, and we were soon on our way. They fed us, and little by little, we recovered our strength and began to feel a great joy. At last we reached Key West.

1990                                                                                                    1992

# DOLORES PRIDA

## b. 1943

"I don't need to be discovered," Dolores Prida once said. "I've never been lost." This quote indicates the way Prida, a playwright and newspaper columnist, approaches her material: distinctively, with pride and self-confidence. A native of Cuba, Prida left the island for New York City with her family in 1961. During the 1960s, she attended Hunter College and worked as an international correspondent for Collier-McMillan. She has been director of Information Services for the National Puerto Rican Forum, assistant editor of *Simon and Schuster's International Dictionary*, editor of the New York Spanish-language daily *El Tiempo*, and columnist for the magazine *Latina*. The recipient of a Cintas Fellowship Award for Literature (1976) and the Creative Artistic Public Service Award (CAPS) for playwriting for 1979–80, Prida also has been active in Cuban American groups that have sought to promote dialogue with the government and people of Cuba. For the New York newspaper *The Daily News*, she writes columns about politics, art, and society.

Prida's first two books were poetry collections: *Treinta y un poemas* (Thirty-One Poems, 1967) and *Women of the Hour* (1971). Her first play, *Beautiful Señoritas* (1977), was originally produced in New York. Within the motif of a beauty pageant, it uses music, dance, and humor to dramatize the demands and values that traditionally have been imposed on Hispanic women. In 1979, Prida wrote *The Beggars Soap Opera*, a musical comedy based on *Die Dreigroschenoper* (The Threepenny Opera, 1928), a musical by the German dramatist Bertolt Brecht and the composer Kurt Weill. In 1981, three of her plays were produced in New York: *Coser y cantar* (Sewing and Singing); *Crisp!*, based on *Los intereses creados* (The Bonds of Interest, 1907), a comedy by the Spanish dramatist Jacinto Benavente; and *Juan Bobo* (John the Fool), about a silly, mischievous, distracted, and simpleminded country boy who appears in Puerto Rican rural folktales. Her later plays are *Savings* (1985), a musical comedy in English about a close-knit New York neighborhood fighting the forces of gentrification; *Pantallas* (Screens, 1986), a black comedy in Spanish about nuclear Armageddon threatening the characters of a Hispanic *telenovela*, or soap opera; and *Botánica* (1990), in which Hispanic characters express their ambivalence about their roots as well as toward their new culture. Like these plays, *Coser y cantar* and

*Beautiful Señoritas* have been produced throughout the United States and broadcast on radio.

To express the problems endured by the Hispanic population in the United States, Prida's theatrical productions skillfully blend elements of popular culture, American and Hispanic, within a frame of musical comedy or the theater of protest. Her characters embody the uprootedness of immigrant life, the sense of not belonging "here" while no longer living "there." Frequently they struggle to assimilate into a new culture without "crossing over" and abandoning their traditions, community, and identity. In *Coser y Cantar*, featured in full in this anthology, two roommates, one living in English and one in Spanish, personify the two elements of one female Cuban immigrant's split cultural personality.

## Coser y cantar: A One-Act Bilingual Fantasy for Two Women

### Characters

ELLA, una mujer
SHE, the same woman
The action takes place in an apartment in New York City in the present/past.

### Set

*A couch, a chair, and a dressing table with an imaginary mirror facing the audience is on each side of the stage. A low table with a telephone on it is upstage center. In the back, a low shelf or cabinet holds a recordplayer, records and books. There are back exits on stage right and stage left.*

*Stage right is* ELLA's *area. Stage left is* SHE's. *Piles of books, magazines and newspapers surround* SHE's *area. A pair of ice skates and a tennis racket are visible somewhere. Her dressing table has a glass with pens and pencils and various bottles of vitamin pills.* SHE *wears jogging shorts and sneakers.*

ELLA's *area is somewhat untidy. Copies of* Cosmopolitan, Vanidades *and* TV Guías *are seen around her bed.* ELLA's *table is crowded with cosmetics, a figurine of the Virgen de la Caridad[1] and a candle. A large conch and a pair of maracas are visible.* ELLA *is dressed in a short red kimono.*

### Important Note from the Author

*This piece is really one long monologue. The two women are one and are playing a verbal, emotional game of ping pong. Throughout the action, except in the final confrontation,* ELLA *and* SHE *never look at each other, acting independently, pretending the other one does not really exist, although each continuously trespasses on each other's thoughts, feelings and behavior.*

*This play must* NEVER *be performed in just one language.*

---

1. *Nuestra Señora de la Caridad del Cobre* (Our Lady of Charity of Cobre), or *La Caridad del Cobre*, the patron saint of Cuba.

*In the dark we hear "Qué sabes tú", a recording by Olga Guillot.[2] As lights go up slowly on ELLA's couch we see a naked leg up in the air, then a hand slides up the leg and begins to apply cream to it. ELLA puts cream on both legs, sensually, while singing along with the record. ELLA sits up in bed, takes a hairbrush, brushes her hair, then using the brush as a microphone continues to sing along. Carried away by the song, ELLA gets out of bed and "performs" in front of the imaginary mirror by her dressing table. At some point during the previous scene, lights will go up slowly on the other couch. SHE is reading Psychology Today magazine. We don't see her face at the beginning. As ELLA is doing her act by the mirror, SHE's eyes are seen above the magazine. SHE stares ahead for a while. Then shows impatience. SHE gets up and turns off the recordplayer, cutting off ELLA's singing in mid-sentence. SHE begins to pick up newspapers and magazines from the floor and to stack them up neatly.*

ELLA: [*With contained exasperation.*]   ¿Por qué haces eso? ¡Sabes que no me gusta que hagas eso! Detesto que me interrumpas así. ¡Yo no te interrumpo cuando tú te imaginas que eres Barbra Streisand!

SHE: [*To herself, looking for her watch.*]   What time is it? [*Finds watch.*] My God, twelve thirty! The day half-gone and I haven't done a thing. . . . And so much to be done. So much to be done. [*Looks at one of the newspapers she has picked up.*] . . . Three people have been shot already. For no reason at all. No one is safe out there. No one. Not even those who speak good English. Not even those who know who they are . . .

ELLA: [*Licking her lips.*]   Revoltillo de huevos, tostadas, queso blanco, café con leche. Hmmm, eso es lo que me pide el estómago. Anoche soñé con ese desayuno.

> [ELLA *goes backstage singing "Es mi vivir una linda guajirita". We hear the sound of pots and pans over her singing. At the same time,* SHE *puts on the Jane Fonda exercise record[3] and begins to do exercises in the middle of the room. Still singing,* ELLA *returns with a tray loaded with breakfast food and turns off the record player.* ELLA *sits on the floor, Japanese-style, and begins to eat.* SHE *sits also and takes a glass of orange juice.*]

SHE:   Do you have to eat so much? You eat all day, then lie there like a dead octopus.

ELLA:   Y tú me lo recuerdas todo el día, pero si no fuera por todo lo que yo como, ya tú te hubieras muerto de hambre. [ELLA *eats.* SHE *sips her orange juice.*]

SHE: [*Distracted.*]   What shall I do today? There's so much to do.

ELLA: [*With her mouth full.*]   Sí, mucho. El problema siempre es, por dónde empezar.

SHE:   I should go out and jog a couple of miles.

ELLA: [*Taking a bite of food.*]   Sí. Debía salir a correr. Es bueno para la figura. [*Takes another bite.*] Y el corazón. [*Takes another bite.*] Y la circulación. [*Another bite.*] A correr se ha dicho. [ELLA *continues eating.* SHE

---

2. Cuban singer (b. 1922), considered the queen of bolero. "*Qué sabes tú*": a classic bolero about forlorn love.
3. *Jane Fonda's Workout Tape* (1981), part of a

hugely successful series of workout materials created by the American movie actress and political activist Jane Fonda (b. 1937).

gets up and opens an imaginary window facing the audience. SHE looks
out, breathes deeply, stretches.]

SHE: Aaah, what a beautiful day! It makes you so . . . so happy to be
alive!

ELLA: [From the table, without much enthusiasm.] No es para tanto.

SHE: [SHE goes to her dressing table, sits down, takes pen and paper.] I'll
make a list of all the things I must do. Let's see. I should start from the
inside. . . . Number one, clean the house . . .

ELLA: [Still eating.] Uno, limpiar la casa.

SHE: Two, take the garbage out.

ELLA: Dos, sacar la basura.

SHE: Then, do outside things. After running, I have to do something
about El Salvador.

ELLA: Salvar a El Salvador.

SHE: Go to the march at the U.N.

ELLA: [Has finished eating, picks up tray, gets enthusiasitc about the planning.] Escribir una carta el editor del New York Times.

SHE: Aha, that too. [Adds it to the list.] How about peace in the Middle
East?

ELLA: La cuestión del aborto.

SHE: Should that come after or before the budget cuts?

ELLA: [With relish.] Comprar chorizos mexicanos para unos burritos.

SHE: [Writing.] See that new Fassbinder[4] film. [ELLA makes a "boring"
face.] Find the map . . . [SHE writes.]

ELLA: [Serious.] Ver a mi madrina. Tengo algo que preguntarle a los caracoles. [Splashes Florida Water[5] around her head.]

SHE: [Exasperated.] Not again! . . . [Thinks.] Buy a fish tank. [Writes it
down.]

ELLA: ¿Una pecera?

SHE: I want to buy a fish tank, and some fish. I read in Psychology Today
that it is supposed to calm your nerves to watch fish swimming in a
tank.

ELLA: [Background music begins.] Peceras. [Sits at her dressing table. Stares
into the mirror. Gets lost in memories.] Las peceras me recuerdan el aero-
puerto cuando me fui . . . los que se iban, dentro de la pecera. Esperando.
Esperando dentro de aquel cuarto transparente. Al otro lado del cristal,
los otros, los que se quedaban: los padres, los hermanos, los tíos. . . . Allí
estábamos, en la pecera, nadando en el mar que nos salía por los ojos . . .
Y los que estaban dentro y los que estaban afuera solo podían mirarse.
Mirarse las caras distorcionadas por las lágrimas y el cristal sucio—lleno
de huellas de manos que se querían tocar, empañado por el aliento de
bocas que trataban de besarse a través del cristal. . . . Una pecera llena de
peces asustados, que no sabían nadar, que no sabían de las aguas hela-
das . . . donde los tiburones andan con pistolas . . .

SHE: [Scratches item off the list forcefully.] Dwelling in the past takes
energies away.

---

4. Rainer Werner Fassbinder (1945–1982), German dramatist and filmmaker.
5. A citrus-oil-based perfume used in Santería rituals.

ELLA: [ELLA *looks for the map among objects on her table. Lifts the Virgen de la Caridad statue.*] ¿Dónde habré puesto el mapa? Juraría que estaba debajo de la Santa . . . [ELLA *looks under the bed. Finds one old and dirty tennis shoe. It seems to bring back memories.*] Lo primerito que yo pensaba hacer al llegar aquí era comprarme unos tenis bien cómodos y caminar todo Nueva York. Cuadra por cuadra. Para saber dónde estaba todo.

SHE: I got the tennis shoes—actually, they were basketball shoes . . . But I didn't get to walk every block as I had planned. I wasn't aware of how big the city was. I wasn't aware of muggers either . . . I did get to walk a lot, though . . . in marches and demonstrations. But by then, I had given up wearing tennis shoes. I was into boots. . . .

ELLA: . . . Pero nunca me perdí en el subway . . .

SHE: Somehow I always knew where I was going. Sometimes the place I got to was the wrong place, to be sure. But that's different. All I had to do was choose another place . . . and go to it. I have gotten to a lot of right places too.

ELLA: [*With satisfaction.*] Da gusto llegar al lugar que se va sin perder el camino.

[*Loud gunshots are heard outside, then police sirens, loud noises, screams, screeches. Both women get very nervous and upset. They run to the window and back, not knowing what to do.*]

SHE: There they go again! Now they are shooting the birds on the trees!

ELLA: ¡Están matando las viejitas en el parque . . .

SHE: Oh, my God! Let's get out of here!

ELLA: . . . Y los perros que orinan en los hidrantes!

SHE: No, no. Let's stay here! Look! They've shot a woman riding a bicycle . . . and now somebody is stealing it!

ELLA: ¡La gente corre, pero nadie hace nada!

SHE: Are we safe? Yes, we are safe. We're safe here . . . No, we're not! They can shoot through the window!

ELLA: ¡La gente grita pero nadie hace nada!

SHE: Get away from the window!

ELLA: [*Pause.*] Pero, ¿y todo lo que hay que hacer?

[*They look around undecided, then begin to do several things around the room, but then drop them immediately.* SHE *picks up a book.* ELLA *goes to the kitchen. We hear the rattling of pots and pans.* ELLA *returns eating leftovers straight from a large pot.* ELLA *sits in front of the mirror, catches sight of herself. Puts pot down, touches her face, tries different smiles, none of which is a happy smile.* SHE *is lying on the couch staring at the ceiling.*]

ELLA: Si pudiera sonreír como la Mona Lisa me tomarían por misteriosa en vez de antipática porque no enseño los dientes . . .

SHE: [*From the couch, still staring at the ceiling.*] That's because your face is an open book. You wear your emotions all over, like a suntan . . . You are emotionally naive . . . or rather, emotionally primitive . . . perhaps even emotionally retarded. What you need is a . . . a certain emotional sophistication . . .

ELLA: . . . sí, claro, eso . . . sofisticación emocional . . . [*Thinks about it.*] . . . sofisticación emocional . . . ¿Y qué carajo es sofisticación emocional? ¿Ser como tú? ¡Tú, que ya ni te acuerdas como huele tu propio sudor, que no reconoces el sonido de tu propia voz! ¡No me jodas!

SHE: See what I mean! [SHE *gets up, goes to her dressing table, looks for the map.*]

ELLA: [*Exasperated.*]   ¡Ay, Dios mío, ¿qué habré hecho yo para merecérmela? Es como tener un . . . un pingüino colgado del cuello!

SHE: An albatross . . . you mean like an albatross around your neck. Okay, Okay . . . I'll make myself light, light as a feather . . . light as an albatross feather. I promise. [SHE *continues to look for the map.*] Where did I put that map? I thought it was with the passport, the postcards . . . the traveling mementos . . . [*Continues looking among papers kept in a small box. Finds her worry beads. That brings memories. She plays with the beads for a while.*] . . . I never really learned how to use them . . . [ELLA *continues searching elsewhere.*] Do you know what regret means?

ELLA: [*Absentmindedly.*]   Es una canción de Edith Piaf.[6]

SHE: Regret means that time in Athens, many years ago . . . at a cafe where they played bouzuki music. The men got up and danced and broke glasses and small dishes against the tiled floor. The women did not get up to dance. They just watched and tapped their feet under the table . . . now and then shaking their shoulders to the music. One Greek man danced more than the others. He broke more glasses and dishes than the others. His name was Nikos. It was his birthday. He cut his hand with one of the broken glasses. But he didn't stop, he didn't pay any attention to his wound. He kept on dancing. He danced by my table. I took a gardenia from the vase on the table and gave it to him. He took it, rubbed it on the blood dripping from his hand and gave it back to me with a smile. He danced away to other tables. . . . I wanted to get up and break some dishes and dance with him. Dance away, out the door, into the street, all the way to some cheap hotel by the harbor, where next morning I would hang the bedsheet stained with my blood out the window. But I didn't get up. Like the Greek women, I stayed on my seat, tapping my feet under the table, now and then shaking my shoulders to the music . . . a bloodied gardenia wilting in my glass of retsina . . .

ELLA: No haber roto ni un plato. That's regret for sure.

[*The clock strikes the hour. Alarmed, they get up quickly and look for their shoes.*]

SHE: [*Putting boots on. Rushed, alarmed.*]   I have to practice the speech!

ELLA: [*Puts on high heels.*]   Sí, tienes que aprender a hablar más alto. Sin micrófono no se te oye. Y nunca se sabe si habrá micrófono. Es mejor depender de los pulmones que de los aparatos. Los aparatos a veces fallan en el momento más inoportuno.

[*They stand back to back, each facing stage left and stage right respectively. They speak at the same time.*]

SHE: [*In English.*]   A E I O U.

ELLA: [*In Spanish.*]   A E I O U.

ELLA: Pirámides.

---

6. French singer and cultural icon (b. Edith Giovanna Gassion, 1915–1963); among her most famous songs was "Non, je ne regrette rien" (No, I Regret Nothing, 1960). Piaf and Olga Guillot performed a concert together in Cannes in 1958.

SHE: Pyramids.
ELLA: Orquídeas.
SHE: Orchids.
ELLA: Sudor.
SHE: Sweat.
ELLA: Luz.
SHE: Light.
ELLA: Blood.
SHE: Sangre.
ELLA: Dolphins.
SHE: Delfines.
ELLA: Mountains.
SHE: Montañas.
ELLA: Sed.
SHE: Thirst.

> [*Freeze. Two beats. They snap out of their concentration.*]

ELLA: Tengo sed.
SHE: I think I'll have a Diet Pepsi.
ELLA: Yo me tomaría un guarapo de caña. [SHE *goes to the kitchen.*]
ELLA: [*Looking for the map. Stops before the mirror and looks at her body, passes hand by hips, sings a few lines of "Macorina"[7] and continues to look for the map behind furniture, along the walls, etc. Suddenly, it seems as if* ELLA *hears something from the apartment next door.* ELLA *puts her ear to the wall and listens more carefully. Her face shows confusion.* ELLA *asks herself, deeply, seriously intrigued.*] ¿Por qué sería que Songo le dió a Borondongo? ¿Sería porque Borondongo le dió a Bernabé? ¿O porque Bernabé le pegó a Muchilanga? ¿O en realidad sería porque Muchilanga le echó burundanga? [Pause.] . . . ¿Y Monina? ¿Quién es Monina? ¡Ay, nunca lo he entendido . . . el gran misterio de nuestra cultura! [SHE *returns drinking a Diet Pepsi. Sits on the bed and drinks slowly, watching the telephone with intense concentration.* ELLA's *attention is also drawn to the telephone. Both watch it hypnotically.*] El teléfono no ha sonado hoy.
SHE: I must call mother. She's always complaining.
ELLA: Llamadas. Llamadas. ¿Por qué no llamará? Voy a concentrarme para que llame. [*Concentrates.*] El teléfono sonará en cualquier momento. Ya. Ya viene. Suena. Sí. Suena. Va a sonar.
SHE: [*Sitting in the lotus position, meditating.*] Ayer is not the same as yesterday.
ELLA: Estás loca.
SHE: I think I'm going crazy. Talking to myself all day.
ELLA: It must be. It's too soon for menopause.
SHE: Maybe what I need is a good fuck after all.
ELLA: Eres una enferma.
SHE: At least let's talk about something important—exercise our intellects.
ELLA: ¿Como qué?

---

7. A song made famous by the Cuban salsa singer Celia Cruz (1925–2003), based on a folktale that includes the characters named below.

SHE:  We could talk about . . . about . . . the meaning of life.

ELLA:  Mi mamá me dijo una vez que la vida, sobre todo la vida de una mujer, era coser y cantar. Y yo me lo creí. Pero ahora me doy cuenta que la vida, la de todo el mundo: hombre, mujer, perro, gato, jicotea, es, en realidad, comer y cagar . . . ¡en otras palabras, la misma mierda!

SHE:  Puke! So much for philosophy.

> [*Both look among the books and magazines.* ELLA *picks up* Vanidades *magazine, flips through the pages.* SHE *starts reading* Self *magazine.*]

ELLA:  No sé que le ha pasado a *Corín Tellado.* Ya sus novelas no son tan románticas como antes. Me gustaban más cuando ella, la del sedoso cabello castaño y los brazos torneados y los ojos color violeta, no se entregaba así, tan fácilmente, a él, el hombre, que aunque más viejo, y a veces cojo, pero siempre millonario, la deseaba con locura, pero la respetaba hasta el día de la boda . . .

SHE:  I can't believe you're reading that crap.

ELLA:  [*Flipping through the pages some more.*]  Mira, esto es interesante: ¡un test! "Usted y sus Fantasías". A ver, lo voy hacer. [*Gets a pencil from the table.*] Pregunta número uno: ¿Tienes fantasías a menudo? [*Piensa.*]

SHE:  Yes. [ELLA *writes down answer.*]

ELLA:  ¿Cuán a menudo? [*Thinks.*]

SHE:  Every night . . . and day.

ELLA:  [*Writes down answer.*]  ¿Cuál es el tema recurrente de tus fantasías?

SHE:  [*Sensually mischievous.*]  I am lying naked. Totally, fully, wonderfully naked. Feeling good and relaxed. Suddenly, I feel something warm and moist between my toes. It is a tongue! A huge, wide, live tongue! The most extraordinary thing about this tongue is that it changes. It takes different shapes . . . It wraps itself around my big toe . . . then goes in between and around each toe . . . then it moves up my leg, up my thigh . . . and into my . . .

ELLA:  ¡Vulgar! No se trata de esas fantasías. Se trata de . . . de . . . de ¡Juana de Arco![8]

SHE:  I didn't know that Joan of Arc was into . . .

ELLA:  Ay, chica, no hablaba de fantasías eróticas, sino de fantasías *heróicas* . . . a lo Juana de Arco. A mí Juana de Arco me parece tan dramática, tan patriótica, tan sacrificada . . .

SHE:  I don't care for Joan of Arc—too hot to handle! . . . ha, ha, ha. [*Both laugh at the bad joke.*]

ELLA:  [*Picking up the chair and lifting it above her head.*]  Mi fantasía es ser una superwoman: ¡Maravilla, la mujer maravilla! [*Puts chair down and lies across it, arms and legs kicking in the air, as if swimming.*] . . . Y salvar a una niña que se ahoga en el Canal de la Mancha, y nadar, como Esther Williams, hasta los blancos farallones de Dover[9] . . . [*Gets up, then rides astride the chair.*] ¡Ser una heroína que cabalgando siempre adelante,

8. Joan of Arc, or Jeanne d'Arc (1412–1431), martyr (executed by burning), Catholic saint, and French national heroine.
9. And to save a girl who is drowning in the English Channel and swim, like Esther Williams, to the white cliffs of Dover. *Esther Williams:* competitive swimmer and movie star (b. 1921 or 1922). *White cliffs of Dover:* possibly a reference to "(There'll Be Bluebirds Over) The White Cliffs of Dover," a World War II–era hit performed by the English singer Vera Lynn (b. Vera Margaret Welch, 1917).

hacia el sol, inspirada por una fe ciega, una pasión visionaria, arrastre a las multitudes para juntos salvar al mundo de sus errores!

SHE: Or else, a rock singer! They move crowds, all right. And make more money. How about, La Pasionaria and her Passionate Punk Rockers!

ELLA: [*Disappointed.*]  Tú nunca me tomas en serio.

SHE: My fantasy is to make people happy. Make them laugh. I'd rather be a clown. When times are as bad as these, it is better to keep the gathering gloom at bay by laughing and dancing. The Greeks do it, you know. They dance when they are sad. Yes, what I really would like to be is a dancer. And dance depression . . . inflation . . . and the NUCLEAR THREAT . . . AWAY!

ELLA: [*To herself, disheartened.*]  Pero tienes las piernas muy flacas y el culo muy grande.

SHE: [*Ignoring* ELLA's *remarks.*]  Dancing is what life is all about. The tap-tapping of a hundred feet on Forty-Second Street[1] is more exciting than an army marching off to kill the enemy. . . . Yes! My fantasy is to be a great dancer . . . like Fred Astaire and Ginger Rogers![2]

ELLA: ¿Cuál de ellos, Fred Astaire o Ginger Rogers?

SHE: Why can't I be both?

ELLA: ¿Será que eres bisexual?

SHE: [*Puts her head between her legs, as if exercising.*]  No. I checked out. Just one.

ELLA: ¿Nunca has querido ser hombre?

SHE: Not really. Men are such jerks.

ELLA: Pero se divierten más. ¿De veras que nunca te has sentido como ese poema?: ". . . Hoy, quiero ser hombre. Subir por las tapias, burlar los conventos, ser todo un Don Juan; raptar a Sor Carmen y a Sor Josefina, rendirlas, y a Julia de Burgos violar . . ."[3]

SHE: You are too romantic, that's your problem.

ELLA: ¡Y tú eres muy promiscua! Te acuestas con demasiada gente que ni siquiera te cae bien, que no tiene nada que ver contigo.

SHE: [*Flexing her muscles.*]  It keeps me in shape. [*Bitchy.*] And besides, it isn't as corny as masturbating, listening to boleros.

ELLA: [*Covering her ears.*]  ¡Cállate! ¡Cállate! ¡Cállate! [*Goes to the window and looks out.*] [*Pause.*] Está nevando. No se ve nada allá afuera. Y aquí, estas cuatro paredes me están volviendo . . . ¡bananas! [ELLA *goes to the table, takes a banana and begins to eat it.* SHE *plays with an old tennis racket.*] Si por lo menos tuviera el televisor, podría ver una película o algo . . . pero, no . . .

SHE: Forget about the TV set.

ELLA: ¡Tuviste que tirarlo por la ventana! Y lo peor no es que me quedé sin televisor. No. Lo peor es el caso por daños y perjuicios que tengo pendiente.

SHE: I don't regret a thing.

---

1. I.e., on Broadway.
2. Astaire (1899–1987) and Rogers (1911–1995), American dancers and movie actors, appeared as a team in a series of classic Hollywood musicals.
3. ". . . Today I want to be a man. Climb over walls, sneak into convents, become a complete Don Juan; kidnap Sister Carmen and Sister Josefina, seduce them, and rape Julia de Burgos," a quotation from "Pentacromía," a well-known poem by Julia de Burgos (see p. 595).

ELLA:   La mala suerte que el maldito televisor le cayera encima al carro de los Moonies[4] que viven al lado. ¿Te das cuenta? ¡Yo, acusada de terrorista por el Reverendo Sun Myung Moon! ¡A nadie le pasa esto! ¡A nadie más que a mí! ¡Te digo que estoy cagada de aura tiñosa!

SHE:   You are exaggerating. Calm down.

ELLA:   Cada vez que me acuerdo me hierve la sangre. Yo, yo, ¡acusada de terrorista! ¡Yo! ¡Cuando la víctima he sido yo! ¡No se puede negar que yo soy una víctima del terrorismo!

SHE:   Don't start with your paranoia again.

ELLA:   ¡Paranoia! ¿Tú llamas paranoia a todo lo que ha pasado? ¿A lo que pasó con los gatos? ¡Mis tres gatos, secuestrados, descuartizados, y luego dejados en la puerta, envueltos en papel de regalo, con una tarjeta de Navidad!

SHE:   You know very well it didn't happen like that.

ELLA:   ¿Y la cobra entre las cartas? How about that snake in the mail box? Who put it there? Who? Who? Why?

SHE:   Forget all that. Mira como te pones por gusto . . . Shit! We should have never come here.

ELLA: [*Calming down.*]   Bueno, es mejor que New Jersey. Además, ¿cuál es la diferencia? El mismo tiroteo, el mismo cucaracheo, la misma mierda . . . coser y cantar, you know.

SHE:   At least in Miami there was sunshine . . .

ELLA:   Había sol, sí, pero demasiadas nubes negras. Era el humo que salía de tantos cerebros tratando de pensar. Además, aquí hay más cosas que hacer.

SHE:   Yes. Más cosas que hacer. And I must do them. I have to stop contemplating my navel and wallowing in all this . . . this . . . Yes, one day soon I have to get my caca together and get out THERE and DO something. Definitely. Seriously. [*Silent pause. Both are lost in thought.*]

ELLA:   I remember when I first met you . . . there was a shimmer in your eyes . . .

SHE:   Y tú tenías una sonrisa . . .

ELLA:   And with that shimmering look in your eyes and that smile . . .

SHE:   . . . pensamos que íbamos a conquistar el mundo . . .

ELLA:   . . . But . . .

SHE:   . . . I don't know . . . [SHE *goes to her table and picks up a bottle of vitamins.*] Did I take my pills today?

ELLA:   Sí.

SHE:   Vitamin C?

ELLA:   Sí.

SHE:   Iron?

ELLA:   Sí.

SHE:   Painkiller?

ELLA:   Of course . . . because camarón que se duerme se lo lleva la corriente.

SHE:   A shrimp that falls asleep is carried away by the current?

ELLA:   No . . . that doesn't make any sense.

---

4. Members of the Unification Church; an informal term derived from the name of the Church founder, the Reverend Sun Myung Moon (b. 1920). Church members prefer to be called "Unificationists."

SHE: Between the devil and the deep blue sea?

ELLA: . . . No es lo mismo que entre la espada y la pared, porque del dicho al hecho hay un gran trecho.

SHE: Betwixt the cup and the lip you should not look a gift horse in the mouth.

ELLA: A caballo regalado no se le mira el colmillo, pero tanto va el cántaro a la fuente, hasta que se rompe.

SHE: An eye for an eye and a tooth for a tooth.

ELLA: Y no hay peor ciego que el que no quiere ver. [*Both are lethargic, about to fall asleep.*]

SHE: [*Yawning.*] I have to be more competitive.

ELLA: [*Yawning.*] Despues de la siesta.

[*They fall asleep. Lights dim out. In the background, music box music comes on and remains through* ELLA's *entire monologue.*]

ELLA: [*Upset voice of a young child.*] Pero, ¿por qué tengo que esperar tres horas para bañarme? ¡No me va a pasar nada! . . . ¡Los peces comen y hacen la digestión en el agua y no les pasa nada! . . . Sí, tengo muchas leyes. ¡Debía ser abogada! ¡Debía ser piloto! ¡Debía ser capitán! ¡Debía ser una tonina y nadar al otro lado de la red, sin temer a los tiburones! [*Pause. Now as a rebellious teenager.*] ¡Y no voy a caminar bajo el sol con ese paraguas! ¡No me importa que la piel blanca sea mas elegante! . . . ¡No se puede tapar el sol con una sombrilla! ¡No se puede esperar que la marea baje cuando tiene que subir! [*As an adult.*] . . . No se puede ser un delfín en las pirámides. No se le puede cortar la cabeza al delfín y guardarla en la gaveta, entre las prendas más íntimas y olvidar el delfín. Y olvidar que se quiso ser el delfín. Olvidar que se quiso ser la niña desnuda, cabalgando sobre el delfín . . .

SHE: [*Lights up on* SHE. *Needling.*] So, you don't have dreams. So, you can't remember your dreams. So, you never talk about your dreams. I think you *don't want* to remember your dreams. You always want to be going somewhere, but now you are stuck here with me, because outside it's raining blood and you have been to all the places you can possibly ever go to! No, you have nowhere to go! Nowhere! Nowhere! [ELLA *slaps* SHE *with force. The clock strikes twice. They awaken. Lights come up fully.* SHE *slaps herself softly on both cheeks.*] A nightmare in the middle of the day!

ELLA: Tengo que encontrar ese mapa. [*They look for the map.*]

SHE: [*Picks up a book, fans the pages. Finds a marker in one page. Reads silently, then reads aloud.*] "Picasso's[5] gaze was so absorbing one was surprised to find anything left on the paper after he looked at it . . ." [*Thinks about this image. Then softly.*] Think about that . . .

ELLA: Sí. Claro. Así siento mis ojos en la primavera. Después de ver tanto árbol desnudo durante el invierno, cuando salen las primeras hojas, esas hojitas de un verde tan tierno, me da miedo mirarlas mucho porque temo que mis ojos le vayan a chupar todo el color.

SHE: I miss all that green. Sometimes I wish I could do like Dorothy in "The Wizard of Oz" . . . close my eyes, click my heels and repeat three times, "there's no place like home" . . . and, puff! be there.[6]

5. Pablo Picasso (1881–1973), Spanish artist who lived in France.
6. I.e., return to her home in Kansas, as the character Dorothy does in the movie musical *The Wizard of Oz* (1939).

ELLA: El peligro de eso es que una pueda terminar en una finca en Kansas.

SHE: . . . I remember that trip back home . . . I'd never seen such a blue sea. It was an alive, happy blue. You know what I mean?

ELLA: A mí no se me había olvidado. Es el mar más azul, el más verde . . . el más chévere del mundo. No hay comparación con estos mares de por aquí.

SHE: . . . It sort of slapped you in the eyes, got into them and massaged your eyeballs . . .

ELLA: Es un mar tan sexy, tan tibio. Como que te abraza. Dan ganas de quitarse el traje de baño y nadar desnuda . . . lo cual, por supuesto, hiciste a la primera oportunidad . . .

SHE: . . . I wanted to see everything, do everything in a week . . .

ELLA: [*Laughing.*] . . . No sé si lo viste todo, pero en cuanto a hacer . . . ¡el trópico te alborotó, chiquitica! ¡Hasta en el Malecón! ¡Qué escándalo!

SHE: [*Laughing.*] I sure let my hair down! It must have been all that rum. Everywhere we went, there was rum and "La Guantanamera"[7] . . . And that feeling of belonging, of being home despite . . .

ELLA: [*Nostalgic.*] ¡Aaay!

SHE: ¿Qué pasa?

ELLA: ¡Ay, siento que me viene un ataque de nostalgia!

SHE: Let's wallow!

ELLA: ¡Ay, sí, un disquito!

[SHE *puts a record on. It is "Nostalgia habanera" sung by Olga Gui-llot. Both sing and dance along with the record for a while. The music stays on throughout the scene.*]

BOTH: [*Singing.*]

"Siento la nostalgia de volver a ti
más el destino manda y no puede ser
Mi Habana, mi tierra querida
cuándo yo te volveré a ver
Habana, como extraño el sol indiano de tus calles
Habana etc. . . ."

ELLA: ¡Aaay, esta nostalgia me ha dado un hambre!

SHE: That's the problem with nostalgia—it is usually loaded with calo-ries! How about some steamed broccoli . . .

ELLA: Arroz . . .

SHE: Yogurt . . .

ELLA: Frijoles negros . . .

SHE: Bean sprouts . . .

ELLA: Plátanos fritos . . .

SHE: Wheat germ . . .

ELLA: Ensalada de aguacate . . .

SHE: Raw carrots . . .

ELLA: ¡Flan!

SHE: Granola!

---

7. The Girl from Guantánamo; a famous Cuban song with music by Joseíto Fernández (José Fernández Diaz, 1908–1979) and lyrics taken from *Versos sencillos*, by José Martí (see p. 265).

ELLA:    ¿Qué tal un arroz con pollo, o un ajiaco?

SHE:    Let's go!

[They exit out to the kitchen. Lights out. Record plays to the end. We hear rattling of pots and pans. When lights go up again, they lie on their respective beds.]

ELLA:    ¡Qué bien! ¡Qué rico! Esa comida me ha puesto erótica. I feel sexy. Romántica.

SHE:    [With bloated feeling.] How can you feel sexy after rice and beans? . . . I feel violent, wild. I feel like . . . chains, leather, whips. Whish! Whish!

ELLA:    No, no, no! Yo me siento como rosas y besos bajo la luna, recostada a una palmera mecida por el viento . . .

SHE:    Such tropical, romantic tackiness, ay, ay, ay.

ELLA:    Sí, . . . y un olor a jasmines que se cuela por la ventana . . .

SHE:    I thought you were leaning on a swaying coconut tree.

ELLA:    . . . Olor a jasmines, mezclado con brisas de salitre. A lo lejos se escucha un bolero: [Sings.]

> "Te acuerdas de la noche de la playa
> Te acuerdas que te di mi amor primero . . ."

SHE:    . . . I feel the smell of two bodies together, the heat of the flesh so close to mine, the sweat and the saliva trickling down my spine . . . [Both get progressively excited.]

ELLA:    . . . y unas manos expertas me abren la blusa, me sueltan el ajustador, y con mucho cuidado, como si fueran dos mangos maduros, me sacan los senos al aire . . .

SHE:    . . . And ten fingernails dig into my flesh and I hear drums beating faster and faster and faster!

[They stop, exhaling a deep sigh of contentment. They get up from bed at different speeds and go to their dressing tables. ELLA lights up a cigarette sensually. SHE puts cold cream on her face, slowly and sensually. They sing in a sexy, relaxed manner.]

ELLA:    "Fumar es un placer . . .

SHE:    . . . Genial, sensual . . .

ELLA:    . . . Fumando espero . . .

SHE:    . . . Al hombre que yo quiero . . .

ELLA:    . . . Tras los cristales . . .

SHE:    . . . De alegres ventanales . . .

ELLA:    . . . Y mientras fumo . . ."

SHE:    [Half laughs.]    . . . I remember the first time . . .

ELLA:    Ja ja . . . a mí me preguntaron si yo había tenido un orgasmo alguna vez. Yo dije que no. No porque no lo había tenido, sino porque no sabía lo que era . . . Pensé que orgasmo era una tela.

SHE:    I looked it up in the dictionary: orgasm. Read the definition, and still didn't know what it meant.

ELLA:    A pesar del diccionario, hasta que no tuve el primero, en realidad no supe lo que quería decir . . .

SHE:    It felt wonderful. But all the new feelings scared me . . .

ELLA:    [Kneeling on the chair.]    . . . Fui a la iglesia al otro día . . . me arrodillé, me persigné, alcé los ojos al cielo—es decir al techo—muy devotamente, pero cuando empecé a pensar la oración . . . me di cuenta de que, en vez de pedir perdón, estaba pidiendo . . . aprobación! . . . permiso para hacerlo otra vez!

SHE:    . . . Oh God, please, give me a sign! Tell me it is all right! Send an angel, una paloma, a flash of green light to give me the go ahead! Stamp upon me the Good Housekeeping Seal of Approval,[8] to let me know that fucking is okay!

ELLA:    ¡Ay, Virgen del Cobre! Yo tenía un miedo que se enterara la familia. ¡Me parecía que me lo leían en la cara!

[*They fall back laughing. The telephone rings three times. They stop laughing abruptly, look at the telephone with fear and expectation. After each ring each one in turn extends the hand to pick it up, but stops midway. Finally, after the third ring,* SHE *picks it up.*]

SHE:    Hello? . . . Oh, hiii, how are you? . . . I am glad you called . . . I wanted to . . . Yes. Okay. Well, go ahead . . . [*Listens.*] Yes, I know . . . but I didn't think it was serious. [*Listens.*] . . . You said our relationship was special, untouchable . . . [*Whimpering.*] then how can you end it just like this . . . I can't believe that all the things we shared don't mean anything to you anymore . . . [*Listens.*] What do you mean, it was meaningful while it lasted?! . . . Yes, I remember you warned me you didn't want to get involved . . . but, all I said was that I love you . . . Okay. I shouldn't have said that . . . Oh, please, let's try again! . . . Look . . . I'll . . . I'll come over Saturday night . . . Sunday morning we'll make love . . . have brunch: eggs, croissants, Bloody Marys . . . we'll read the *Times* in bed and . . . please, don't . . . how can you? . . .

ELLA:    [*Having been quietly reacting to the conversation, and getting angrier and angrier* ELLA *grabs the phone away from* SHE.]    ¿Pero quién carajo tú te crees que eres para venir a tirarme así, como si yo fuera una chancleta vieja? ¡Qué huevos fritos ni ocho cuartos, viejo! ¡Después de tanta hambre que te maté, los buenos vinos que te compré! ¡A ver si esa putica que te has conseguido cocina tan bien como yo! ¡A ver si esa peluá te va a dar todo lo que yo te daba! ¡A ver si esa guaricandilla . . . [*Suddenly desperate.*] Ay, ¿cómo puedes hacerme esto a mí? ¡A mí que te adoro ciegamente, a mí, que te quiero tanto, que me muero por ti! . . . Mi amor . . . ay, mi amor, no me dejes. Haré lo que tú quieras. ¡Miénteme, pégame, traicióname, patéame, arrástrame por el fango, pero no me dejes! [*Sobs. Listens. Calms down. Now stoically melodramatic and resigned.*] Está bien. Me clavas un puñal. Me dejas con un puñal clavado en el centro del corazón. Ya nunca podré volver a amar. Mi corazón se desangra, siento que me desvanezco . . . Me iré a una playa solitaria y triste, y a media noche, como Alfonsina, echaré a andar hacia las olas y . . . [*Listens for three beats. Gets angry.*] ¡Así es como respondes cuando vuelco mi corazón, mis sentimientos en tu oído? ¿Cuando mis lágrimas casi crean un corto circuito en el teléfono?! ¡Ay, infeliz! ¡Tú no sabes nada de la vida! Adiós, y que te vaya bien. De veras . . . honestamente, no te guardo rencor . . . te deseo lo mejor . . . ¿Yo? . . . yo seguiré mi viaje. Seré bien recibida en

---

8. Popular name for the "Good Housekeeping Seal," which is bestowed on products meeting standards established by the Good Housekeeping Institute and *Good Housekeeping* magazine.

otros puertos. Ja, ja, ja . . . De veras, te deseo de todo corazón que esa tipa, por lo menos, ¡sea tan BUENA EN LA CAMA COMO YO! [*Bangs the phone down. Both sit on the floor back to back. Long pause.* ELLA *fumes.* SHE *is contrite.*]

SHE: You shouldn't have said all those things.

ELLA: ¿Por qué no? Todo no se puede intelectualizar. You can't dance everything away, you know.

SHE: You can't eat yourself to numbness either.

ELLA: Yeah.

SHE: You know what's wrong with me? I can't relate any more. I have been moving away from people. I stay here and look at the ceiling. And talk to you. I don't know how to talk to people anymore. I don't know if I want to talk to people anymore!

ELLA: Tu problema es que ves demasiadas películas de Woody Allen,[9] y ya te crees una neoyorquina neurótica. Yo no. Yo sé como tener una fiesta conmigo misma. Yo me divierto sola. Y me acompaño y me entretengo. Yo tengo mis recuerdos. Y mis plantas en la ventana. Yo tengo una solidez. Tengo unas raíces, algo de que agarrarme. Pero tú . . . ¿tú de qué te agarras?

SHE: I hold on to you. I couldn't exist without you.

ELLA: But I wonder if I need you. Me pregunto si te necesito . . . robándome la mitad de mis pensamientos, de mi tiempo, de mi sentir, de mis palabras . . . como una sanguijuela!

SHE: I was unavoidable. You spawned me while you swam in that fish tank. It would take a long time to make me go away!

ELLA: Tú no eres tan importante. Ni tan fuerte. Unos meses, tal vez unos años, bajo el sol, y, ¡presto! . . . desaparecerías. No quedaría ni rastro de ti. Yo soy la que existo. Yo soy la que soy. Tú . . . no sé lo que eres.

SHE: But, if it weren't for me you would not be the one you are now. No serías la que eres. I gave yourself back to you. If I had not opened some doors and some windows for you, you would still be sitting in the dark, with your recuerdos, the idealized beaches of your childhood, and your rice and beans and the rest of your goddam obsolete memories! [*For the first time they face each other, furiously.*]

ELLA: Pero soy la más fuerte!

SHE: I am as strong as you are! [*With each line, they throw something at each other—pillows, books, papers, etc.*]

ELLA: ¡Soy la más fuerte!

SHE: I am the strongest!

ELLA: ¡Te robaste parte de mí!

SHE: You wanted to be me once!

ELLA: ¡Estoy harta de ti!

SHE: Now you are!

ELLA: ¡Ojalá no estuvieras!

SHE: You can't get rid of me!

ELLA: ¡Alguien tiene que ganar!

SHE: No one shall win!

---

9. American comedian and filmmaker (b. Allen Stewart Konigsberg, 1935), whose characters are often neurotic New Yorkers.

[*Loud sounds of sirens, shots, screams are heard outside. They run towards the window, then walk backwards in fear, speaking simultaneously.*]

SHE: They are shooting again!

ELLA: ¡Y están cortando los árboles!

SHE: They're poisoning the children in the schoolyard!

ELLA: ¡Y echando la basura y los muertos al río!

SHE: We're next! We're next!

ELLA: ¡Yo no salgo de aquí!

SHE: Let's get out of here! [*Another shot is heard. They look at each other.*]

ELLA: El mapa . . .

SHE: Where's the map?
[*Black out.*]

1981

# EDWARD RIVERA
## 1944–2001

Born in the mountain town of Orocovis, Puerto Rico, Edward Rivera moved to New York City with his family when he was seven years old. He went to Catholic school for his primary and secondary education and completed an undergraduate degree at City College, City University of New York, and a master of fine arts degree in English at Columbia University. Rivera pursued his literary career while holding a teaching position in the English Department at City College. He was a mentor to young Latino writers such as Junot Díaz and Abraham Rodriguez. In the mid-1970s, Rivera began publishing his short stories in literary journals. Some of these stories later appeared in the volume *Family Installments: Memories of Growing Up Hispanic* (1983), which largely employs sharp, satiric humor to re-create incidents from Rivera's formative years, when he lived in the conflictful and often humiliating multiethnic environment of New York. Rivera's inventive style enables him to avoid replicating the bleak realism of other U.S. Puerto Rican male growing-up narratives.

The American writer, critic, and scholar Philip Lopate, in reviewing *Family Installments* in *The New York Times Book Review*, described the book as "noisily beaming with life" and praised its "graceful, lyrical language." Rivera's brother, Richard, in an interview, said his brother had taken a decade to write this memoir and that it was "a way of documenting the importance of our family in his life, and the pain of acculturation." A fragment of the book was dramatized in the documentary *Birthwrite: Growing Up Latino* (1989), in which the author was also interviewed. Rivera wrote many essays and stories for journals and magazines, but never published another book. In the autobiographical essay "Stable Manners: or, How the Publication of *Family Installments* was Stalled for Three Years and $3,000," published in a special issue of *The Massachusetts Review* edited by Ilan Stavans in 1996, he described his ordeal in finding a publisher for *Family Installments* because it did not fit preconceived notions of what he called "Underclass Lit." Rivera's life was cut short when he died of a heart attack. His story "In Black Turf," chapter 7 of *Family Installments* and included here, presents a poignant account of how Puerto Ricans of different racial backgrounds often internalize and reproduce in their behavior the prejudices and racist norms prevalent in U.S. society.

---

## FROM FAMILY INSTALLMENTS

## 7: In Black Turf

The day before, I had made up my mind to cut Sunday Mass for the fourth straight week. In parochial school, the Christian Brothers[1] gave you no choice about religious matters. But I was out of their clutches now, and there was no punishment to worry about if I got to Mass late, or if I didn't get there at all. Giving up the Holy Ghost[2] and the rest of the religious business was a serious decision, the most serious I'd made to date. I was beginning to feel like a real grown-up. But because it was a critical decision, I couldn't bring myself to make it all at once; growing up, I knew, was a slow process, and I was in no hurry to become a full-grown man before my time. I decided to spend Sunday morning strolling with my buddy Panna in the wilds of Central Park.

At 9:45, fifteen minutes before the young people's Mass began, I came down and found Panna sitting on the steps of my stoop. His real name was Teodoro, but to his friends he was Panna because he called everyone he liked "Partner." He'd picked up the word from cowboy movies. He was small, undernourished, and about as black a Puerto Rican as I'd ever known. I don't think he had a drop of white blood in him. Half his ancestors must have been shipped to the Caribbean from Africa, and the other half, the Indian side of his family tree, must have been waiting for them on the island long before Ponce de León got there.[3] He had an immense head topped with an abundance of thick, unwashed, kinky hair, and tiny, rotting teeth. People sometimes took him for an American black, but he was as Puerto Rican as I was. Maybe more so, because at least he didn't try to deny his origins by getting rid of his East Harlem accent.

My own accent was closer, though not really close, to the speech of American disc jockeys and TV-radio detergent pushers. This was a result of having spent eight submissive years under the influence of the hard-driving Christian Brothers, who subscribed as faithfully to the myth of the American melting pot as they did to their vows of poverty, chastity, and obedience. Nobody had ever taken me for someone whose veins might contain Negro or Arab or Caribbean Indian blood. I was too light-skinned for that. On various occasions I had been mistaken for a Jew, an Italian, a

---

1. Or the Congregation of Christian Brothers (Latin: *Congregatio Fratrum Christianorum*), a worldwide religious community within the Catholic Church, devoted chiefly to the evangelization and education of youth.
2. Along with God and the Son, the third person in the Christian Trinity (Godhead).
3. The Spanish conquistador Juan Ponce de León (1460–1521) might have explored Puerto Rico in 1506, but he began its colonization in 1508, after which the Spanish Crown appointed him governor of the island.

Greek, even a Hungarian; and each time I had come away feeling secretly proud of myself for having disguised my Spik accent, and with it my lineage. I could almost feel myself melting smoothly and evenly into the great Pot.

The north end of Central Park was right across from our block. We went there to scout around for girls who might be willing to join us in the bushes. This was a favorite fantasy of ours. It gave our excursions in the park a specific purpose, and it satisfied one part of a favorite daydream of mine: saving a nice-looking girl from rape. She could be a Puerto Rican dusky, or an American blonde, it didn't matter, as long as she was equipped with big, plump boobs and a nice round rump.

The time would be early evening, just as the sun was about to drop between the tall tenements of Central Park West; the place, a clump of bushes near the baseball diamonds. I would arrive on the scene just as the pervert, a big, muscular black man with a shaved head, was tearing off her pink polka-dot panties with one hand and unzipping his fly with the other. With a baseball bat or a sawed-off broomstick I just happened to be carrying, I would splinter the lecher's skull. By risking my life for the poor girl's chastity, I'd be putting her in my debt. To remind her of this would be crude; but she'd know it, and she would want to repay me in kind. At this juncture I would stoop to pick up her panties, and when I offered them to her, she would take my hand and lead me into the bushes for a satisfactory settlement. Afterward, holding hands, we would walk off toward Loui's Luncheonette on the corner of 108th and Fifth. After a thick malted (two straws, one glass), she'd leave me her name, address, and phone number, and an open invitation to come and see her whenever I had time.

What usually happened, whenever a girl saw Panna and me approaching her with a look of undisguised lust in our eyes, was that she would clutch her purse to her chest, turn abruptly, and scamper off for the nearest exit. Copping a girl's drawers in that park was even more difficult than stealing a squirrel's hoard of nuts, but we liked to pretend it was easy.

The only people in the park at ten on a Sunday morning were mounted cops on their big, brown, huge-assed horses, perverts like ourselves, and members of the Puerto Rican Baseball League. At the baseball diamonds we watched one inning that lasted over a half hour (the beer-bellied pitchers couldn't get the ball over the plate, which wouldn't have mattered much, since catcher and batters were too sleepy to see the ball; and the fielders, undernourished and weighted down with heavy, loose-fitting uniforms, couldn't catch up with flyballs and groundballs), and when we decided that Puerto Rican baseball had no future as a national pastime, we headed north toward the black people's section of Central Park.

Across the bicycle path, on a grassy area where Puerto Rican families picnicked on sunny weekends, we looked for empty beer and soda bottles. If we found enough empties, we could get them "changed" at Miguel's *bodega* on Madison and head for the movies or Loui's Luncenoette. All we found was a bag of dried chicken bones crawling with ants, and a used condom. Panna picked up the condom with a crooked stick and came at me, swishing it like a secondhand sword inches from my face. I tore off down the sloped picnic grounds and stumbled to a halt in front of a marshy stream that divided "our" section of the park from the black people's section.

Like a scrawny, scraggly blackbird, Panna stumbled after me and jabbed playfully at my chest with his stick and condom.

I stooped and picked up a wet, scummy stone. "Don't touch me with that thing, mother-fo!" I warned him, taking a full windup.

Thrown off guard by my unexpected counterattack, he halted. He was a few inches smaller than me and about half as strong. His head, with its thick tangle of kinky hair, was attached to his thin neck like a bowling ball to a skinny long finger; it swayed uneasily from side to side on its precarious stem. His round, coarse face, dotted here and there with pimples, looked about five years older than his actual age. He was fourteen, my age, but already half his teeth were hopelessly rotting. No amount of dental work could save them. One had been knocked out in a fight with his older brother. I don't think he'd ever seen a dentist. Maybe that was why girls took off when they saw us coming.

"All right," he said, thrusting his head forward and closing in on me with quick little hops, like a starling advancing on a worm. "Drop the rock or I'll plug you with my fuckin' scumbag."

Stabbed helpless with laughter, I lurched backward. He opened his mouth wide and grinned at me, the evil guy stalking his helpless victim. The sight of his putrid teeth, with the black, blank gap in the middle, disarmed me completely. I slipped on the slimy grass, dropped the rock, and tried to fall forward. But I splashed into the stream, flat on my ass.

Panna hurled himself to the ground in convulsions.

"See what the fuck you did?" I screamed, already worrying about what Mami would say when she saw what I'd done to my best pair of pants. Panna was too busy laughing to hear me.

"You black fuck!" I snapped. "You think it's funny?"

He suddenly became silent. He hurled the stick into the stream while I got to my feet. I was completely soaked from the waist down. Green slime dripped from my Sunday pants and clung to my recently polished shoes.

"Don't call me that shit, Santos."

I stood up and slapped at my pants. "You asked for it, shit. Look what the hell you did."

"Just don't call me that," he said, biting his big lower lip. "I don't like nobody calling me a black fuck, understand?"

"Just watch it next time," I said, half sorry I had insulted him.

He bent his head a little and stared at my throat, as if readying himself for a savage fight. "You better say you're sorry, Santos."

I was sure I could take him if he wanted a fight, but the thought of fighting him was as repulsive to me as the condom he had just threatened to stick in my face. He was my "panna."

"All right, forget it, okay?" I had to raise my voice so he wouldn't think I was backing down.

He raised his dark eyes to my face. "So say you're sorry."

"All right, shit. I'm sorry. You satisfied?"

He jerked his shoulders and started to walk off alongside the shallow stream, kicking at the grass with his sneakers.

I followed him.

"Hey, man," I said, "you heard me say I'm sorry, right?"

"Yeah, I heard you." He was staring at the ground.

I walked in front of him and faced him. He stopped abruptly, tilted his large head, and scowled. His hands were clenched tight at his sides.

"I don't wanna fight witchu, Panna."

"So whatchu want, then?"

"Say you're sorry."

"For what?"

I slapped my pants. "You made me fall in the filthy water."

He stepped to the side and shrugged his shoulders. If we got into a fight, the only thing I'd have to guard against was his head. He could crack my jaw with one butt of that bowling ball.

He raised his voice: "I didn't touch you, Santos."

"You stuck that scumbag in my face."

He shook his head and smirked slow-motion. "I don't wanna argue, Santos."

"So say it and I'll call it evens."

He hesitated, squinting at the stream. An apology was a confession of weakness, but so was not asking for one when you felt insulted. So I kept him on the hook. Let him learn better than to humiliate his own friend.

"Okay, muh man," he said. It came out weak. "So I'm sorry you got wet. Next time watch your balance—otherwise, tough shit."

That was all. Take it or leave it. I pretended to be fully satisfied.

"Forget it, Panna. That stream was out to get me."

We continued walking, quietly, keeping the distance between us a little wider than usual. I was afraid he'd hold a lifetime grudge against me for the insult. What I couldn't understand was that he and his older brother, who was a little lighter than he was, were always calling each other names like "nigger" and "spook" whenever they got into an argument, and never thought anything about it. With them it was a game.

What the hell was he being so sensitive about all of a sudden? We spoke the same language, lived in the same block, and shared the same friends. Maybe he'd had another fight with his brother earlier that morning and was taking it out on me. I should have kicked his ass when he poked the condom in my face.

The stream dipped and disappeared under a rise of large, jagged rocks which formed a natural bridge to the "black" part of the park. People got killed there, I'd heard, women raped. It was a hilly area where the vegetation grew thicker than anywhere else in the park and was, for that reason, darker. People from our side of the park, from our neighborhood, stayed away from that section. It was strictly for blacks. I seldom ventured there, never on my own.

When we got to within a few feet of the stone bridge, Panna broke into a quick run and leaped onto a rock.

"Where you going?" I asked.

"Thataway, partnuh." He pointed to the other side of the stream.

I was pleased at his rapid change of mood. "Whatchu going there for?"

"Whatchu mean what I'm going there for? Ain't you coming?"

I stared at a dragonfly hovering over the little stream below the rocks. "What for, man?"

He dropped his hands and shrugged. "I don't know. Maybe we can find some empties."

I grinned. "Or some broad."

He grinned back. "Or some scumbags."

The dragonfly was swooping and circling less than an inch over the water, searching for insects.

"Whatsa matter, Santos, you scared?"

"Whatchu mean, scared?" I leaped up on the rock next to him.

"So let's go."

I let him lead the way.

On the other side of the stream, we had to climb a steep hill on all fours; the ground was damp and loose, even though it hadn't rained in over a week. Every time I grabbed a small plant for support, it came up by the roots and I would slide back a foot or more. I was wearing my Sunday shoes, leather-soled and tight-fitting. Panna was wearing sneakers and had less trouble climbing. As long as he didn't tilt his huge head backward, he was all right.

When I got to the top, minutes after he did, he was staring at an old fortress a short way off to our left.

"Hey, Santos, you know"—he was shielding his eyes with one hand and pointing with the other—"old George Washington fought in there."[4] He sounded like any one of the Brothers of Saint Misericordia's[5] driving home a startling fact. ("And after old Judas Iscariot betrays Our Lord, boys, the sap goes and hangs himself! He didn't even get to spend those thirty denaras of silver.")[6]

"Bullshit, Panna."

"No, I ain't lying to you, Santos. I'm just saying what I know. He whipped them Redcoats right there in that focken fort."

"Who told you that?"

"Whatchu mean, who told me? You ignorant? I been here before, lots of times. I grew up in this park."

He picked up a small stone and pitched it hard at the fortress. "So don't tell me what I know and don't know. Everybody knows it, except you. Where you been at, stud?"

"You're jiving me, Panna. You lie."

"Okay, I'll betchu."

"Who, you? You ain't got no money."

"That's fine with me," he said. "I can pay you back tomorrow. But I ain't gonna lose. *You* is. I'll leave you broke you bet with me."

"Forget it, Panna. I don't wanna take your money."

He was always broke. His spending money came mostly from empty bottles and from tips he got delivering groceries on Saturdays. But he always managed to spend it all on candy and the movies by the end of the day, because if he didn't, he had told me, his big brother would go through his pockets at night and steal it. "He steal me blind when I'm sleeping, Santos."

He turned his head toward the fortress. "You *know* I'm right."

"Go ahead, Panna, prove it."

4. George Washington (1732–1799), first U.S. president (1789–97), commanded the Continental Army against the English Army (Redcoats) in the American Revolutionary War (1775–1783).
5. The narrator attends the Catholic parochial school Saint Misericordia, run by the Christian Brothers.
6. According to the New Testament, Judas Iscariot betrayed Jesus to the Roman authorities for 30 pieces of silver. *Denaras*: The *denarius* (plural *denarii*) was a small silver Roman coin first struck in 211 BC.

"Come on, I'll show you. Just follow Panna the leader." He trotted off toward the old fort.

I hesitated. "I ain't going in there, Panna. Smells fishy to me."

"What the hell you scared of?" he said. "You turning into a lame or something?"

So I followed him down some rocks and onto a narrow dirt path thick with weeds. Below I could hear the traffic going in both directions along 110th Street, and smell the gasoline fumes.

We squeezed through a small opening that had been knocked into the stone wall, like the holes in playground fences, only this one must have been smashed with a sledgehammer. Inside there was nothing but tall grass, more weeds, a few commonplace bushes, and a strong smell of human shit. Not far from where I stood, close to the wall, someone had relieved himself and left it at that, uncovered. Now flies, hundreds of them, buzzed around the mess like Ancient Romans at a banquet. In the center of the fortress, rising from a jungle of grass, a shredded, faded flag with only forty-eight stars flapped on a thin white pole, like a pigeon flyer's bandanna tied to the end of a bamboo stick.

"C'mon," Panna called. He was several feet ahead of me, up to his neck in grass.

"Fuck you," I said. "I'm staying right here. There ain't nothing in there but shit."

"There's an old, whatchamacallit, plaque, around here someplace."

I could just about make out his head now, a huge, black, kinky-haired ball rolling slowly along the grass, like an immense sunflower minus petals.

"That's where it says George Washington whipped the Redcoats right here in this spot."

"All you're gonna find in there is a big lump of shit," I called. "There ain't no plaque. You'll fall in a hole and break your leg. Come on, let's go back."

I was getting hungry. The Mass I'd missed should have been over long ago, and I was anxious to change into dry clothes.

I leaned against the stone wall and waited for him to emerge. "Panna," I yelled, "let's go, man. Forget the fuckin' plaque. George Washington never came near this place, you jerk."

A pebble bounced off my head. I looked up and saw one, two, then four black faces. Their owners were standing and sitting on the ledge of the wall, staring down at me. The sun was almost directly overhead now, and I had to squint and shield my eyes to see them clearly.

"Whatchu doin' in there, white boy?" the tallest of the four said. He was about six feet, and he was tapping the wall with the heels of his sneakers and cracking his knuckles. I moved back a few steps for a better look. They were all very black, blacker than Panna even; the noon sun gave their faces a smooth, rubbery look.

"I'm waiting for my friend," I said. My legs began to sag slightly below the knees. I couldn't have run more than a few yards before they caught me. But even a speed-runner didn't stand a chance in that trap.

"Where your friend at?" another one asked. He wasn't much taller than me, but he had the arm muscles of a professional athlete or a truck loader in the garment district. His pants were the color of orange soda; he was holding a stickball bat out in front of him like a fishing pole.

I pointed toward the tall grass. "He's in there." I realized my mistake immediately. Panna had probably spotted them before I did; that was why he hadn't answered when I called him.

When I squinted up again, only one of them was sitting on the wall. He was the smallest, an inch or two smaller than Panna. A blue beret, spattered with dust, was tilted dramatically to one side of his head.

"Don't move, motherfucker," he said.

I pressed my back to the wall and looked for a possible way out. The hole I'd come in through was impassable; they would be coming in any second. There was nothing but grass, the long white flagpole, and the pile of human shit with its frantic flies. If there was an exit, it would have to be across the field, on the other side. If Panna had found it, he must have escaped. That bastard, I thought. It was all his fault, and now he had copped out on me.

The three came in through the hole in the wall one at a time and surrounded me. I stared at the ground, waiting stiffly for the first blow and regretting that I didn't have a gun on me and that I had never taken Karate lessons.

The six-foot one stepped up to me and looked down for a few seconds. I listened to the roar of a crosstown bus far away.

"Where your buddy, stud?"

"I told you," I said. "He's in there somewhere."

"What he doin' there?"

"He's looking for a plaque."

The one with orange-colored pants stroked the grass with his stickball bat. "A what?"

"A plaque," I said. "My friend says there's this plaque in here that says George Washington fought the Redcoats here during the Ci-Ci-Civil War."

They looked at each other, shook their heads, smiled, and broke into laughter. One of them slapped the side of his head and came down on his knees, almost touching the ground. He had on a sleeveless white sweat shirt with CLINTON HIGH SCHOOL lettered across the chest.

"Man, you must be outa your fuckin' skull," he said when he straightened out. "Old Georgie never came near this fuckin' place."

"He puttin' us on," the tall one said.

"I ain't puttin' you on," I insisted. I didn't see what was so funny. "That's what my friend said."

The one in orange pants snapped his fingers. "Maybe he mean *Booker T. Washington*."[7] He stepped up to me and tapped me on the shoulder with his stick. "You tell your friend to come on out here 'fore I go in there and get him out myself."

I hesitated.

"You better do like he say, son," the one from Clinton said. "He ain't playing witchu."

I cleared my throat. The strong sun was beginning to give me a headache. "Hey, Panna," I called. "C'mere, man."

No answer.

They all frowned. They thought I had lied to them about Panna and the plaque.

7. African American educator (1856–1915).

I called again. "Hey, Panna, man, come on out, you *lame!*"

Nothing. I was sure he was back on the block, or in his house stuffing himself with peanut butter sandwiches and very likely enjoying the thought that I was getting just what I deserved for having called him a black fuck.

The one with the stick started off in the direction of the flagpole. "Man," he said, "if I don't find your friend in there, I'm gonna crack your hea-ud with this stick, dig?" In a few seconds he disappeared. I could hear his stick stroking the grass.

"I didn't do nothing," I said to the tall one.

"Nobody say you did, Jack."

"How much brea-ud you got, son?" the one with the sleeveless sweatshirt asked me. He was flexing the muscle of his right arm and staring at it as if it were some abnormal growth that had suddenly emerged into full view. It resembled a large sweet potato. I didn't stand a chance.

"'Scuse me?"

"I said how much brea-ud you got? You know, *mmmoneh, honeh.*"

Before I left the house that morning, Mami had given me a quarter for the church collection. I had planned on treating Panna to a soda at Loui's Luncheonette, but now he could go screw himself.

"I ain't got nothin' on me," I said.

"Put your hands behind your head," the tall one commanded.

I inched away from him. "For what?"

He grabbed my shirt collar and pushed me hard against the stone wall. A shock of pain shot through my spine. My legs felt like two pieces of lumber.

"Put your hands behind your hea-ud," the Clinton student said. He was standing so close now that I could smell his bad breath.

I lifted my arms and clasped my hands behind my head, the way I'd seen it done on the block whenever the cops were frisking a suspect.

The big one stuck his hand in one of my pockets, then in the other, and came up with the quarter.

His mouth spread in a thick-lipped smile. "Dig," he told his friends. He pinched the shiny quarter between two long fingers and held it up for the others to see. The solemn silver face of George Washington flashed in the sun.

"Maybe he got a wallet on him," the one sitting on the wall called down.

The tall one slipped the quarter in his pocket and patted my head. "Turn around, cracker."

I turned quickly and raised both arms high over my head, the palms flat against the warm wall, while he slapped my back pockets. Where was Panna? I refused to believe he had run off. Not that it made any difference. He was too small to defend himself against one of them, let alone all four. Only the gang from the block could pull me out of this mess, and they were all far away, ignorant of the trap I had walked into. This was strange turf for me; I was used to dealing only with Spiks like myself. On the block my name stood for something among my friends; here it was less than shit. It was useless to tell these black guys that I had many friends who would descend on them in an all-out war if they didn't release me unharmed. That kind of threat might only get me a busted head.

"Sheeet, he ain't got nothin' on him," the tall one told his friends after he had gone through my pockets. "Turn around."

I dropped my hands and turned slowly.

The Clinton student grabbed my right arm and jerked it upwards. A pain shot down my shoulder. "Nobody say to drop your hands."

I raised them again, stretching them to their limits, to show that I hadn't meant any harm.

"And keep them up, mother," the lookout man on the wall yelled down.

Suddenly the six-foot one stuck his long leg between my legs and rammed the heel of his hand against my shoulder. I stumbled, scraped my back on the wall, and collapsed with a squeal on something soft. A swarm of flies, thousands it seemed, exploded around me, and in seconds I was immersed in the odor of human shit. I sat there, too overcome with disgust and rage to move. And the flies swarmed and buzzed around me, as if they had discovered a newly laid mass of human excrement and had gone into delirium.

Not because I had been pushed around and robbed of a quarter, which had not been mine to begin with, nor even because I had been smeared in shit, which could be washed off, but because I had been humiliated without any possibility of fighting back, of standing up for myself—for that reason I began to cry. I didn't cry loudly or hysterically; only girls and women had the right to that kind of display. I cried softly, missing my breath once in a while and sucking in the thin, fibrous liquid that spilled like egg white from my nostrils. A slow accumulation of pain, brought on by the strong noon sun, began to tighten around my forehead. I dropped my head and waited for them to kick my face in.

But they just stood there, silently staring down at me.

From the grassy area, where Panna and his pursuer had disappeared, I could hear voices and a stick slashing grass. I waited, resigned to the stink of the shit I was sitting on and the sting and buzz of frenzied flies. The voices had the sound of calm conversation rather than conflict.

In a few moments, Panna and his captor emerged. I watched them through half-closed eyes. They were still talking. Panna was smiling.

When he saw me he stopped, clapped a hand to his mouth, and whispered: "Holy shit! Oh, lordie."

I rubbed two fists in my eyes.

"Who you got there?" the tall one asked the one who had found Panna.

"This here's Ramírez, my friend," he said, slapping Panna on the back. "We went to junior high. He all right. Foo! Whatchu-all been doin' to whitey here?"

"He pushed me in," I said.

The one with the Clinton sweatshirt kicked some dirt in front of me. "I make you eat that shit, too, if you don't shut your big mouth."

"He's my friend," Panna told him. "Right, Santos?"

The tall one sucked his teeth and looked him up and down. "So whatchu be hangin' out with him for? He ain't none o' your kind."

"We live in the same block," Panna explained.

His school friend held out the stickball bat to me. "Here, man, grab on to this."

I shook my head, suspecting a trick.

"Go on, Santos," Panna said. "Get up, man."

I grabbed the stick cautiously and pulled myself up quickly, in case he might decide to release his hold on it.

The seat of my pants felt wet. Repulsed by the stink, the others backed up a few steps.

"Man, you full of shit," the kid on the wall said. He was holding his nose.

The tall one stuck his hand in his pocket and brought out my quarter. "Here," he told me, "take your fuckin' George Washington back. I don't want your quarter."

I put out my hand suspiciously and let him slap the shiny quarter in the palm.

"Let me tell you somethin', white boy," he began. "This here's our turf, understand?"

I nodded, biting my lip.

"And it don't make no difference to me who your friend is, even if he black as an asshole. You stick to your side of the park."

I kept nodding.

"Otherwise I make you eat that shit. Just keep that in mind."

Then he turned to Panna. "And you, shorty with the big hea-ud, don't think cause you black all over and ugly as sin you can bring who you wants around here."

Panna nodded. "Okay, man, I keep him off of here."

A long silence followed. I stared at the flagpole and longed to be back on my small block, where there were no territorial divisions, no white and black bullshit.

"You better get on home, Ramírez," the school friend said to Panna.

I let Panna go on ahead and tried to remain calm during the few seconds it took to squeeze through the hole in the wall of the fort. And just as I was about to emerge on the other side, I heard a voice behind me: "Man, you full of sheeet," followed by a fit of laughter.

We walked slowly side by side until we reached the top of the hill, from where we could see part of the baseball diamonds, and beyond them the mansions of Fifth Avenue. I started down in a half-run, then broke into an awkward, stumbling rush down the steep hill until I was on the safe side of the little stream.

From somewhere behind me I could hear Panna calling. "Hey, Santos, man. Slow down. Whatchu scared of?"

I ignored him and picked up speed. Near the baseball diamonds, I heard the reassuring sounds of Spanish and slowed down. "Nothing," I said to myself. "I ain't scared of nothing." I stopped and looked back for Panna. He was nowhere in sight. I continued walking at a steady, brisk pace, leaving a strong stench behind me.

1983

# RICHARD RODRIGUEZ
## b. 1944

Like Gloria Anzaldúa, Richard Rodriguez is a seminal thinker in the Latino literary tradition. He stands out in the tradition for his contrarian political stances and his complicated approach to Mexican American identity.

Rodriguez was born into a Mexican immigrant family in San Francisco and spoke Spanish at home, but he attended an otherwise all-white Catholic school. His family then moved to Sacramento, where Rodriguez delivered newspapers and worked as a gardener. As a child, he became preoccupied with the need to overcome his ethnic "handicap." While white rich kids abandoned their wealthy environs to embrace the culture of the slums, he moved in the opposite direction, desiring the white kids' roots. Throughout his writing, Rodriguez has offered stories about his thriving in an environment he was not expected, by mainstream society or his barrio family, to be in.

Rodriguez earned his bachelor's degree in English from Stanford University and a master's in philosophy from Columbia University, then worked toward a doctorate in Renaissance English literature at the University of California, Berkeley. He also attended the Warburg Institute, in London, on a Fulbright fellowship. As a journalist, he has written for publications such as *Harper's, Mother Jones, The American Scholar,* and *Time,* and he regularly contributes to the PBS show *The NewsHour with Jim Lehrer,* for which he received a George Foster Peabody Award in 1997. His first book, *Hunger of Memory: The Education of Richard Rodriguez* (1982), began a trilogy that includes *Days of Obligation: An Argument with My Mexican Father* (1992) and concludes with *Brown: The Last Discovery of America* (2002).

Taking as his model the personal essays of the sixteenth-century French writer Michel de Montaigne, Rodriguez writes autobiographically, inserting himself in his works as a case study to understand social, cultural, and ideological issues affecting the United States. Yet his trilogy is not about history, sociology, or politics. It is a sustained meditation on Latino life in the United States, filled with labyrinthine philosophical and moral reflections. The two major questions that run through the trilogy are *What do Hispanics mean to the life of America?* and *How did Hispanics become brown?* He believes that brown, as a metaphor for mixture, is the essential quality of Latinos. "Brown is impurity," he writes in *Brown.* "I write of a color that is not a singular color, not a strict recipe, not an expected result, but a color produced by careless desire, even by accident." Brown is the color of *mestizaje,* that is, the miscegenation that has shaped the Americas since Christopher Columbus's first expedition, in 1492. It is the juxtaposition of white European and dark aboriginal, as in the Spanish conquistador Hernán Cortés and his mistress and translator La Malinche. And it is also the so-called *raza cósmica* that the Mexican philosopher José Vasconcelos wrote about in the early twentieth century, a master race that, capitalizing on its own impurity, would rise to conquer the entire hemisphere, if not the globe.

In *Hunger of Memory* (from which this anthology includes the first part, "Aria"), Rodriguez denounces a stagnant society—the United States on the verge of the Reagan era—interested in the politics of superficial compassion more than in the politics of equality, a society with little patience for Mexicans. He portrays himself as a "scholarship boy" who benefited from a racially based decision that left him with an unending feeling of reproach. In his eyes, only individual talent, aptitude, should be considered in a person's application for school or work—not skin color, last name, and country of origin. He sees programs such as Affirmative Action and Bilingual Education—traditionally considered aids to Latinos—as having only balkanized families, neighborhoods, and cities. This view has made him a target in the Latino academic and intellectual communities. That Rodriguez did not acknowledge his homosexuality until *Days of Obligation* (from which this anthology includes the chapter "Late Victorians"), as the first Bush presidency was approaching its end, angered many gay rights activists.

Reading the trilogy chronologically shows Rodriguez's maturation. He started as an antisegregationist, interested in the assimilation of Mexicans to the larger landscape of America. His tortured feelings about Mexico and about his homosexuality became clear, or at least clearer, in the second installment, which includes both a painfully explored argument with *mexicanidad*, personified by his father, and a picture of San Francisco desolated by AIDS. Assimilation was still a priority at that time, but by the 1990s Rodriguez had turned his attention to his condition as a publicly gay Latino man. His goal of capturing what surrounds him is now matched by an intellectual obsession with his stream of consciousness, and his book is at once a tape recorder and a mirror.

Another interpretation of Rodriguez's three volumes can be summed up in the words *class, ethnicity,* and *race*. In this take, which he introduces in the preface to *Brown* (included here), the first installment is about a low-income family whose child moves up in the hierarchy; the second about the awakening of his across-the-border roots; and the third about "a tragic noun, a synonym for conflict and isolation": race. But Rodriguez adds:

> Race is not such a terrible word for me. Maybe because I am skeptical by nature. Maybe because my nature is already mixed. The word race encourages me to remember the influence of eroticism on history. For that is what race memorializes. Within any discussion of race, there lurks the possibility of romance.

*Mestizaje,* Rodriguez argues, is no longer the domain of Latinos. We are all brown. "This is not the same as saying 'the poor shall inherit the earth' but is possibly related," Rodriguez states in *Brown*. "The poor shall overrun the earth. Or the brown shall." In his view, the United States is about to become the *United* States—everyone in it a Latino, if not physically, at least metaphorically. For an interesting comparison with Rodriguez's work, see Octavio Paz's "The *Pachuco* and Other Extremes" (in Appendix 3: Influential Essays by Latin American Writers, p. A65), in which Paz focuses on a subculture of Latino youth in Los Angeles in the 1940s.

---

## *FROM* HUNGER OF MEMORY: THE EDUCATION OF RICHARD RODRIGUEZ

## Aria

### *1*

I remember to start with that day in Sacramento—a California now nearly thirty years past—when I first entered a classroom, able to understand some fifty stray English words.

The third of four children, I had been preceded to a neighborhood Roman Catholic school by an older brother and sister. But neither of them had revealed very much about their classroom experiences. Each afternoon they returned, as they left in the morning, always together, speaking in Spanish as they climbed the five steps of the porch. And their mysterious books, wrapped in shopping-bag paper, remained on the table next to the door, closed firmly behind them.

An accident of geography sent me to a school where all my classmates were white, many the children of doctors and lawyers and business executives. All my classmates certainly must have been uneasy on that first day of school—as most children are uneasy—to find themselves apart from their families in the first institution of their lives. But I was astonished.

The nun said, in a friendly but oddly impersonal voice, 'Boys and girls, this is Richard Rodriguez.' (I heard her sound out: *Rich-heard Road-ree-guess*.) It was the first time I had heard anyone name me in English. 'Richard,' the nun repeated more slowly, writing my name down in her black leather book. Quickly I turned to see my mother's face dissolve in a watery blur behind the pebbled glass door.

Many years later there is something called bilingual education—a scheme proposed in the late 1960s by Hispanic-American social activists, later endorsed by a congressional vote. It is a program that seeks to permit non-English-speaking children, many from lower-class homes, to use their family language as the language of school. (Such is the goal its supporters announce.) I hear them and am forced to say no: It is not possible for a child—any child—ever to use his family's language in school. Not to understand this is to misunderstand the public uses of schooling and to trivialize the nature of intimate life—a family's 'language.'

Memory teaches me what I know of these matters; the boy reminds the adult. I was a bilingual child, a certain kind—socially disadvantaged—the son of working-class parents, both Mexican immigrants.

In the early years of my boyhood, my parents coped very well in America. My father had steady work. My mother managed at home. They were nobody's victims. Optimism and ambition led them to a house (our home) many blocks from the Mexican south side of town. We lived among *gringos* and only a block from the biggest, whitest houses. It never occurred to my parents that they couldn't live wherever they chose. Nor was the Sacramento of the fifties bent on teaching them a contrary lesson. My mother and father were more annoyed than intimidated by those two or three neighbors who tried initially to make us unwelcome. ('Keep your brats away from my sidewalk!') But despite all they achieved, perhaps because they had so much to achieve, any deep feeling of ease, the confidence of 'belonging' in public was withheld from them both. They regarded the people at work, the faces in crowds, as very distant from us. They were the others, *los gringos*. That term was interchangeable in their speech with another, even more telling, *los americanos*.

I grew up in a house where the only regular guests were my relations. For one day, enormous families of relatives would visit and there would be so many people that the noise and the bodies would spill out to the backyard and front porch. Then, for weeks, no one came by. (It was usually a salesman who rang the doorbell.) Our house stood apart. A gaudy yellow in a row of white bungalows. We were the people with the noisy dog. The people who raised pigeons and chickens. We were the foreigners on the block. A few neighbors smiled and waved. We waved back. But no one in the family knew the names of the old couple who lived next door; until I was seven years old, I did not know the names of the kids who lived across the street.

In public, my father and mother spoke a hesitant, accented, not always grammatical English. And they would have to strain—their bodies tense—to catch the sense of what was rapidly said by *los gringos*. At home they spoke Spanish. The language of their Mexican past sounded in counterpoint to the English of public society. The words would come quickly, with ease. Conveyed through those sounds was the pleasing, soothing, consoling reminder of being at home.

During those years when I was first conscious of hearing, my mother and father addressed me only in Spanish; in Spanish I learned to reply. By contrast, English (*inglés*), rarely heard in the house, was the language I came to associate with *gringos*. I learned my first words of English overhearing my parents speak to strangers. At five years of age, I knew just enough English for my mother to trust me on errands to stores one block away. No more.

I was a listening child, careful to hear the very different sounds of Spanish and English. Wide-eyed with hearing, I'd listen to sounds more than words. First, there were English (*gringo*) sounds. So many words were still unknown that when the butcher or the lady at the drugstore said something to me, exotic polysyllabic sounds would bloom in the midst of their sentences. Often, the speech of people in public seemed to me very loud, booming with confidence. The man behind the counter would literally ask, 'What can I do for you?' But by being so firm and so clear, the sound of his voice said that he was a *gringo*; he belonged in public society.

I would also hear then the high nasal notes of middle-class American speech. The air stirred with sound. Sometimes, even now, when I have been traveling abroad for several weeks, I will hear what I heard as a boy. In hotel lobbies or airports, in Turkey or Brazil, some Americans will pass, and suddenly I will hear it again—the high sound of American voices. For a few seconds I will hear it with pleasure, for it is now the sound of *my* society—a reminder of home. But inevitably—already on the flight headed for home—the sound fades with repetition. I will be unable to hear it anymore.

When I was a boy, things were different. The accent of *los gringos* was never pleasing nor was it hard to hear. Crowds at Safeway or at bus stops would be noisy with sound. And I would be forced to edge away from the chirping chatter above me.

I was unable to hear my own sounds, but I knew very well that I spoke English poorly. My words could not stretch far enough to form complete thoughts. And the words I did speak I didn't know well enough to make into distinct sounds. (Listeners would usually lower their heads, better to hear what I was trying to say.) But it was one thing for *me* to speak English with difficulty. It was more troubling for me to hear my parents speak in public: their high-whining vowels and guttural consonants; their sentences that got stuck with 'eh' and 'ah' sounds; the confused syntax; the hesitant rhythm of sounds so different from the way *gringos* spoke. I'd notice, moreover, that my parents' voices were softer than those of *gringos* we'd meet.

I am tempted now to say that none of this mattered. In adulthood I am embarrassed by childhood fears. And, in a way, it didn't matter very much that my parents could not speak English with ease. Their linguistic difficulties had no serious consequences. My mother and father made themselves understood at the county hospital clinic and at government offices. And yet, in another way, it mattered very much—it was unsettling to hear my parents struggle with English. Hearing them, I'd grow nervous, my clutching trust in their protection and power weakened.

There were many times like the night at a brightly lit gasoline station (a blaring white memory) when I stood uneasily, hearing my father. He was talking to a teenaged attendant. I do not recall what they were saying, but I cannot forget the sounds my father made as he spoke. At one point his words slid together to form one word—sounds as confused as the threads of blue and green oil in the puddle next to my shoes. His voice rushed through what he had left to say. And, toward the end, reached falsetto notes, appealing to his listener's understanding. I looked away to the lights of passing automobiles. I tried not to hear anymore. But I heard only too well the calm, easy tones in the attendant's reply. Shortly afterward, walking toward home with my father, I shivered when he put his hand on my shoulder. The very first chance that I got, I evaded his grasp and ran on ahead into the dark, skipping with feigned boyish exuberance.

But then there was Spanish. *Español*: my family's language. *Español*: the language that seemed to me a private language. I'd hear strangers on the radio and in the Mexican Catholic church across town speaking in Spanish, but I couldn't really believe that Spanish was a public language, like English. Spanish speakers, rather, seemed related to me, for I sensed that we shared—through our language—the experience of feeling apart from *los gringos*. It was thus a ghetto Spanish that I heard and I spoke. Like those whose lives are bound by a barrio, I was reminded by Spanish of my separateness from *los otros, los gringos* in power. But more intensely than for most barrio children—because I did not live in a barrio—Spanish seemed to me the language of home. (Most days it was only at home that I'd hear it.) It became the language of joyful return.

A family member would say something to me and I would feel myself specially recognized. My parents would say something to me and I would feel embraced by the sounds of their words. Those sounds said: *I am speaking with ease in Spanish. I am addressing you in words I never use with los gringos. I recognize you as someone special, close, like no one outside. You belong with us. In the family.*

(*Ricardo.*)

At the age of five, six, well past the time when most other children no longer easily notice the difference between sounds uttered at home and words spoken in public, I had a different experience. I lived in a world magically compounded of sounds. I remained a child longer than most; I lingered too long, poised at the edge of language—often frightened by the sounds of *los gringos*, delighted by the sounds of Spanish at home. I shared with my family a language that was startlingly different from that used in the great city around us.

For me there were none of the gradations between public and private society so normal to a maturing child. Outside the house was public society; inside the house was private. Just opening or closing the screen door behind me was an important experience. I'd rarely leave home all alone or without reluctance. Walking down the sidewalk, under the canopy of tall trees, I'd warily notice the—suddenly—silent neighborhood kids who stood warily watching me. Nervously, I'd arrive at the grocery store to hear there the sounds of the *gringo*—foreign to me—reminding me that in this world so big, I was a foreigner. But then I'd return. Walking back toward our house, climbing the steps from the sidewalk, when the front door was open in summer, I'd hear voices beyond the screen door talking in Spanish. For a second or two, I'd stay, linger there, listening. Smiling, I'd hear my mother call out, saying in Spanish (words): 'Is that you, Richard?' All the while her sounds would assure me: *You are home now; come closer; inside. With us.*

'*Sí*,' I'd reply.

Once more inside the house I would resume (assume) my place in the family. The sounds would dim, grow harder to hear. Once more at home, I would grow less aware of that fact. It required, however, no more than the blurt of the doorbell to alert me to listen to sounds all over again. The house would turn instantly still while my mother went to the door. I'd hear her hard English sounds. I'd wait to hear her voice return to soft-sounding Spanish, which assured me, as surely as did the clicking tongue of the lock on the door, that the stranger was gone.

Plainly, it is not healthy to hear such sounds so often. It is not healthy to distinguish public words from private sounds so easily. I remained cloistered by sounds, timid and shy in public, too dependent on voices at home. And yet it needs to be emphasized: I was an extremely happy child at home. I remember many nights when my father would come back from work, and I'd hear him call out to my mother in Spanish, sounding relieved. In Spanish, he'd sound light and free notes he never could manage in English. Some nights I'd jump up just at hearing his voice. With *mis hermanos* I would come running into the room where he was with my mother. Our laughing (so deep was the pleasure!) became screaming. Like others who know the pain of public alienation, we transformed the knowledge of our public separateness and made it consoling—the reminder of intimacy. Excited, we joined our voices in a celebration of sounds. *We are speaking now the way we never speak out in public. We are alone—together*, voices sounded, surrounded to tell me. Some nights, no one seemed willing to loosen the hold sounds had on us. At dinner, we invented new words. (Ours sounded Spanish, but made sense only to us.) We pieced together new words by taking, say, an English verb and giving it Spanish endings. My mother's instructions at bedtime would be lacquered with mock-urgent tones. Or a word like *sí* would become, in several notes, able to convey added measures of feeling. Tongues explored the edges of words, especially the fat vowels. And we happily sounded that military drum roll, the twirling roar of the Spanish *r*. Family language: my family's sounds. The voices of my parents and sisters and brother. Their voices insisting: *You belong here. We are family members. Related. Special to one another. Listen!* Voices singing and sighing, rising, straining, then surging, teeming with pleasure that burst syllables into fragments of laughter. At times it seemed there was steady quiet only when, from another room, the rustling whispers of my parents faded and I moved closer to sleep.

2

Supporters of bilingual education today imply that students like me miss a great deal by not being taught in their family's language. What they seem not to recognize is that, as a socially disadvantaged child, I considered Spanish to be a private language. What I needed to learn in school was that I had the right—and the obligation—to speak the public language of *los gringos*. The odd truth is that my first-grade classmates could have become bilingual, in the conventional sense of that word, more easily than I. Had they been taught (as upper-middle-class children are often taught early) a second language like Spanish or French, they could have regarded it simply as that: another public language. In my case such bilingualism could not have been so quickly achieved. What I did not believe was that I could speak a single public language.

Without question, it would have pleased me to hear my teachers address me in Spanish when I entered the classroom. I would have felt much less afraid. I would have trusted them and responded with ease. But I would have delayed—for how long postponed?—having to learn the language of public society. I would have evaded—and for how long could I have afforded to delay?—learning the great lesson of school, that I had a public identity.

Fortunately, my teachers were unsentimental about their responsibility. What they understood was that I needed to speak a public language. So their voices would search me out, asking me questions. Each time I'd hear them, I'd look up in surprise to see a nun's face frowning at me. I'd mumble, not really meaning to answer. The nun would persist, 'Richard, stand up. Don't look at the floor. Speak up. Speak to the entire class, not just to me!' But I couldn't believe that the English language was mine to use. (In part, I did not want to believe it.) I continued to mumble. I resisted the teacher's demands. (Did I somehow suspect that once I learned public language my pleasing family life would be changed?) Silent, waiting for the bell to sound, I remained dazed, diffident, afraid.

Because I wrongly imagined that English was intrinsically a public language and Spanish an intrinsically private one, I easily noted the difference between classroom language and the language of home. At school, words were directed to a general audience of listeners. ('Boys and girls.') Words were meaningfully ordered. And the point was not self-expression alone but to make oneself understood by many others. The teacher quizzed: 'Boys and girls, why do we use that word in this sentence? Could we think of a better word to use there? Would the sentence change its meaning if the words were differently arranged? And wasn't there a better way of saying much the same thing?' (I couldn't say. I wouldn't try to say.)

Three months. Five. Half a year passed. Unsmiling, ever watchful, my teachers noted my silence. They began to connect my behavior with the difficult progress my older sister and brother were making. Until one Saturday morning three nuns arrived at the house to talk to our parents. Stiffly, they sat on the blue living room sofa. From the doorway of another room, spying the visitors, I noted the incongruity—the clash of two worlds, the faces and voices of school intruding upon the familiar setting of home. I overheard one voice gently wondering, 'Do your children speak only Spanish at home, Mrs. Rodriguez?' While another voice added, 'That Richard especially seems so timid and shy.'

*That Rich-heard!*

With great tact the visitors continued, 'Is it possible for you and your husband to encourage your children to practice their English when they are home?' Of course, my parents complied. What would they not do for their children's well-being? And how could they have questioned the Church's authority which those women represented? In an instant, they agreed to give up the language (the sounds) that had revealed and accentuated our family's closeness. The moment after the visitors left, the change was observed. 'Ahora, speak to us *en inglés*,' my father and mother united to tell us.

At first, it seemed a kind of game. After dinner each night, the family gathered to practice 'our' English. (It was still then *inglés*, a language foreign to us, so we felt drawn as strangers to it.) Laughing, we would try to define words we could not pronounce. We played with strange English sounds, often overanglicizing our pronunciations. And we filled the smiling gaps of our sentences with familiar Spanish sounds. But that was cheating, somebody shouted. Everyone laughed. In school, meanwhile, like my brother and sister, I was required to attend a daily tutoring session. I needed a full year of special attention. I also needed my teachers to keep my attention from straying in class by calling out, *Rich-heard*—their English voices slowly prying loose my ties to my other name, its three notes, *Ri-car-do*. Most of all I needed to hear my mother and father speak to me in a moment of seriousness in broken—suddenly heartbreaking—English. The scene was inevitable: One Saturday morning I entered the kitchen, where my parents were talking in Spanish. I did not realize that they were talking in Spanish however until, at the moment they saw me, I heard their voices change to speak English. Those *gringo* sounds they uttered startled me. Pushed me away. In that moment of trivial misunderstanding and profound insight, I felt my throat twisted by unsounded grief. I turned quickly and left the room. But I had no place to escape to with Spanish. (The spell was broken.) My brother and sisters were speaking English in another part of the house.

Again and again in the days following, increasingly angry, I was obliged to hear my mother and father: 'Speak to us *en inglés*.' (*Speak*.) Only then did I determine to learn classroom English. Weeks after, it happened: One day in school I raised my hand to volunteer an answer. I spoke out in a loud voice. And I did not think it remarkable when the entire class understood. That day, I moved very far from the disadvantaged child I had been only days earlier. The belief, the calming assurance that I belonged in public, had at last taken hold.

Shortly after, I stopped hearing the high and loud sounds of *los gringos*. A more and more confident speaker of English, I didn't trouble to listen to *how* strangers sounded, speaking to me. And there simply were too many English-speaking people in my day for me to hear American accents anymore. Conversations quickened. Listening to persons who sounded eccentrically pitched voices, I usually noted their sounds for an initial few seconds before I concentrated on *what* they were saying. Conversations became content-full. Transparent. Hearing someone's *tone* of voice—angry or questioning or sarcastic or happy or sad—I didn't distinguish it from the words it expressed. Sound and word were thus tightly wedded. At the end of a day, I was often bemused, always relieved, to realize how 'silent,' though crowded with words, my day in public had been. (This public silence measured and quickened the change in my life.)

At last, seven years old, I came to believe what had been technically true since my birth: I was an American citizen.

But the special feeling of closeness at home was diminished by then. Gone was the desperate, urgent, intense feeling of being at home; rare was the experience of feeling myself individualized by family intimates. We remained a loving family, but one greatly changed. No longer so close; no longer bound tight by the pleasing and troubling knowledge of our public separateness. Neither my older brother nor sister rushed home after school anymore. Nor did I. When I arrived home there would often be neighborhood kids in the house. Or the house would be empty of sounds.

Following the dramatic Americanization of their children, even my parents grew more publicly confident. Especially my mother. She learned the names of all the people on our block. And she decided we needed to have a telephone installed in the house. My father continued to use the word *gringo*. But it was no longer charged with the old bitterness or distrust. (Stripped of any emotional content, the word simply became a name for those Americans not of Hispanic descent.) Hearing him, sometimes, I wasn't sure if he was pronouncing the Spanish word *gringo* or saying gringo in English.

Matching the silence I started hearing in public was a new quiet at home. The family's quiet was partly due to the fact that, as we children learned more and more English, we shared fewer and fewer words with our parents. Sentences needed to be spoken slowly when a child addressed his mother or father. (Often the parent wouldn't understand.) The child would need to repeat himself. (Still the parent misunderstood.) The young voice, frustrated, would end up saying, 'Never mind'—the subject was closed. Dinners would be noisy with the clinking of knives and forks against dishes. My mother would smile softly between her remarks; my father at the other end of the table would chew and chew at his food, while he stared over the heads of his children.

My *mother*! My *father*! After English became my primary language, I no longer knew what words to use in addressing my parents. The old Spanish words (those tender accents of sound) I had used earlier—*mamá* and *papá*—I couldn't use anymore. They would have been too painful reminders of how much had changed in my life. On the other hand, the words I heard neighborhood kids call *their* parents seemed equally unsatisfactory. *Mother* and *Father*; *Ma*, *Papa*, *Pa*, *Dad*, *Pop* (how I hated the all-American sound of that last word especially)—all these terms I felt were unsuitable, not really terms of address for *my* parents. As a result, I never used them at home. Whenever I'd speak to my parents, I would try to get their attention with eye contact alone. In public conversations, I'd refer to 'my parents' or 'my mother and father.'

My mother and father, for their part, responded differently, as their children spoke to them less. She grew restless, seemed troubled and anxious at the scarcity of words exchanged in the house. It was she who would question me about my day when I came home from school. She smiled at small talk. She pried at the edges of my sentences to get me to say something more. (What?) She'd join conversations she overheard, but her intrusions often stopped her children's talking. By contrast, my father seemed reconciled to the new quiet. Though his English improved somewhat, he retired into silence. At dinner he spoke very little. One night his children and even his wife helplessly giggled at his garbled English pronunciation of the

Catholic Grace before Meals. Thereafter he made his wife recite the prayer at the start of each meal, even on formal occasions, when there were guests in the house. Hers became the public voice of the family. On official business, it was she, not my father, one would usually hear on the phone or in stores, talking to strangers. His children grew so accustomed to his silence that, years later, they would speak routinely of his shyness. (My mother would often try to explain: Both his parents died when he was eight. He was raised by an uncle who treated him like little more than a menial servant. He was never encouraged to speak. He grew up alone. A man of few words.) But my father was not shy, I realized, when I'd watch him speaking Spanish with relatives. Using Spanish, he was quickly effusive. Especially when talking with other men, his voice would spark, flicker, flare alive with sounds. In Spanish, he expressed ideas and feelings he rarely revealed in English. With firm Spanish sounds, he conveyed confidence and authority English would never allow him.

The silence at home, however, was finally more than a literal silence. Fewer words passed between parent and child, but more profound was the silence that resulted from my inattention to sounds. At about the time I no longer bothered to listen with care to the sounds of English in public, I grew careless about listening to the sounds family members made when they spoke. Most of the time I heard someone speaking at home and didn't distinguish his sounds from the words people uttered in public. I didn't even pay much attention to my parents' accented and ungrammatical speech. At least not at home. Only when I was with them in public would I grow alert to their accents. Though, even then, their sounds caused me less and less concern. For I was increasingly confident of my own public identity.

I would have been happier about my public success had I not sometimes recalled what it had been like earlier, when my family had conveyed its intimacy through a set of conveniently private sounds. Sometimes in public, hearing a stranger, I'd hark back to my past. A Mexican farmworker approached me downtown to ask directions to somewhere. '¿Hijito . . . ?' he said. And his voice summoned deep longing. Another time, standing beside my mother in the visiting room of a Carmelite convent, before the dense screen which rendered the nuns shadowy figures, I heard several Spanish-speaking nuns—their busy, singsong overlapping voices—assure us that yes, yes, we were remembered, all our family was remembered in their prayers. (Their voices echoed faraway family sounds.) Another day, a dark-faced old woman—her hand light on my shoulder—steadied herself against me as she boarded a bus. She murmured something I couldn't quite comprehend. Her Spanish voice came near, like the face of a never-before-seen relative in the instant before I was kissed. Her voice, like so many of the Spanish voices I'd hear in public, recalled the golden age of my youth. Hearing Spanish then, I continued to be a careful, if sad, listener to sounds. Hearing a Spanish-speaking family walking behind me, I turned to look. I smiled for an instant, before my glance found the Hispanic-looking faces of strangers in the crowd going by.

Today I hear bilingual educators say that children lose a degree of 'individuality' by becoming assimilated into public society. (Bilingual schooling was popularized in the seventies, that decade when middle-class ethnics began to resist the process of assimilation—the American melting pot.) But the bilingualists simplistically scorn the value and necessity of assimilation. They do not seem to realize that there are *two* ways a person is individualized. So they do not realize that while one suffers a diminished sense of *private* individuality by becoming assimilated into public society, such assimilation makes possible the achievement of *public* individuality.

The bilingualists insist that a student should be reminded of his difference from others in mass society, his heritage. But they equate mere separateness with individuality. The fact is that only in private—with intimates—is separateness from the crowd a prerequisite for individuality. (An intimate draws me apart, tells me that I am unique, unlike all others.) In public, by contrast, full individuality is achieved, paradoxically, by those who are able to consider themselves members of the crowd. Thus it happened for me: Only when I was able to think of myself as an American, no longer an alien in *gringo* society, could I seek the rights and opportunities necessary for full public individuality. The social and political advantages I enjoy as a man result from the day that I came to believe that my name, indeed, is *Rich-heard Road-ree-guess*. It is true that my public society today is often impersonal. (My public society is usually mass society.) Yet despite the anonymity of the crowd and despite the fact that the individuality I achieve in public is often tenuous—because it depends on my being one in a crowd—I celebrate the day I acquired my new name. Those middle-class ethnics who scorn assimilation seem to me filled with decadent self-pity, obsessed by the burden of public life. Dangerously, they romanticize public separateness and they trivialize the dilemma of the socially disadvantaged.

My awkward childhood does not prove the necessity of bilingual education. My story discloses instead an essential myth of childhood—inevitable pain. If I rehearse here the changes in my private life after my Americanization, it is finally to emphasize the public gain. The loss implies the gain: The house I returned to each afternoon was quiet. Intimate sounds no longer rushed to the door to greet me. There were other noises inside. The telephone rang. Neighborhood kids ran past the door of the bedroom where I was reading my schoolbooks—covered with shopping-bag paper. Once I learned public language, it would never again be easy for me to hear intimate family voices. More and more of my day was spent hearing words. But that may only be a way of saying that the day I raised my hand in class and spoke loudly to an entire roomful of faces, my childhood started to end.

3

I grew up victim to a disabling confusion. As I grew fluent in English, I no longer could speak Spanish with confidence. I continued to understand spoken Spanish. And in high school, I learned how to read and write Spanish. But for many years I could not pronounce it. A powerful guilt blocked my spoken words; an essential glue was missing whenever I'd try to connect words to form sentences. I would be unable to break a barrier of sound, to speak freely. I would speak, or try to speak, Spanish, and I would manage to utter halting, hiccuping sounds that betrayed my unease.

When relatives and Spanish-speaking friends of my parents came to the house, my brother and sisters seemed reticent to use Spanish, but at least they managed to say a few necessary words before being excused. I never managed so gracefully. I was cursed with guilt. Each time I'd hear myself addressed in Spanish, I would be unable to respond with any success. I'd know the words I wanted to say, but I couldn't manage to say them. I would try to speak, but everything I said seemed to me horribly anglicized. My mouth would not form the words right. My jaw would tremble. After a phrase or two, I'd cough up a warm, silvery sound. And stop.

It surprised my listeners to hear me. They'd lower their heads, better to grasp what I was trying to say. They would repeat their questions in gentle, affectionate voices. But by then I would answer in English. No, no, they would say, we want you to speak to us in Spanish. ('... en español.') But I couldn't do it. *Pocho* then they called me. Sometimes playfully, teasingly, using the tender diminutive—*mi pochito*. Sometimes not so playfully, mockingly, *Pocho*. (A Spanish dictionary defines that word as an adjective meaning 'colorless' or 'bland.' But I heard it as a noun, naming the Mexican-American who, in becoming an American, forgets his native society.) '¡*Pocho!*' the lady in the Mexican food store muttered, shaking her head. I looked up to the counter, where red and green peppers were strung like Christmas tree lights and saw the frowning face of the stranger. My mother laughed somewhere behind me. (She said that her children didn't want to practice 'our Spanish' after they started going to school.) My mother's smiling voice made me suspect that the lady who faced me was not really angry at me. But, searching her face, I couldn't find the hint of a smile.

Embarrassed, my parents would regularly need to explain their children's inability to speak flowing Spanish during those years. My mother met the wrath of her brother, her only brother, when he came up from Mexico one summer with his family. He saw his nieces and nephews for the very first time. After listening to me, he looked away and said what a disgrace it was that I couldn't speak Spanish, '*su proprio idioma*.' He made that remark to my mother; I noticed, however, that he stared at my father.

I clearly remember one other visitor from those years. A long-time friend of my father from San Francisco would come to stay with us for several days in late August. He took great interest in me after he realized that I couldn't answer his questions in Spanish. He would grab me as I started to leave the kitchen. He would ask me something. Usually he wouldn't bother to wait for my mumbled response. Knowingly, he'd murmur: '¿*Ay Pocho, Pocho, adónde vas?*' And he would press his thumbs into the upper part of my arms, making me squirm with currents of pain. Dumbly, I'd stand there, waiting for his wife to notice us, for her to call him off with a benign smile. I'd giggle, hoping to deflate the tension between us, pretending that I hadn't seen the glittering scorn in his glance.

I remember that man now, but seek no revenge in this telling. I recount such incidents only because they suggest the fierce power Spanish had for many people I met at home; the way Spanish was associated with closeness. Most of those people who called me a *pocho* could have spoken English to me. But they would not. They seemed to think that Spanish was the only language we could use, that Spanish alone permitted our close association. (Such persons are vulnerable always to the ghetto merchant and the politician who have learned the value of speaking their clients' family language to gain immediate trust.) For my part, I felt that I had somehow committed a sin of betrayal by learning English. But betrayal against whom? Not against visitors to the house exactly. No, I felt that I had betrayed my immediate family. I *knew* that my parents had encouraged me to learn English. I *knew* that I had turned to English only with angry reluctance. But once I spoke English with ease, I came to *feel* guilty. (This guilt defied logic.) I felt that I had shattered the intimate bond that had once held the family close. This original sin against my family told whenever anyone addressed me in Spanish and I responded, confounded.

But even during those years of guilt, I was coming to sense certain consoling truths about language and intimacy. I remember playing with a friend in the backyard one day, when my grandmother appeared at the window. Her face was stern with suspicion when she saw the boy (the *gringo*) I was with. In Spanish she called out to me, sounding the whistle of her ancient breath. My companion looked up and watched her intently as she lowered the window and moved, still visible, behind the light curtain, watching us both. He wanted to know what she had said. I started to tell him, to say—to translate her Spanish words into English. The problem was, however, that though I knew how to translate exactly *what* she had told me, I realized that any translation would distort the deepest meaning of her message: It had been directed only to me. This message of intimacy could never be translated because it was not *in* the words she had used but passed *through* them. So any translation would have seemed wrong; her words would have been stripped of an essential meaning. Finally, I decided not to tell my friend anything. I told him that I didn't hear all she had said.

This insight unfolded in time. Making more and more friends outside my house, I began to distinguish intimate voices speaking through *English*. I'd listen at times to a close friend's confidential tone or secretive whisper. Even more remarkable were those instances when, for no special reason apparently, I'd become conscious of the fact that my companion was speaking only to me. I'd marvel just hearing his voice. It was a stunning event: to be able to break through his words, to be able to hear this voice of the other, to realize that it was directed only to me. After such moments of intimacy outside the house, I began to trust hearing intimacy conveyed through my family's English. Voices at home at last punctured sad confusion. I'd hear myself addressed as an intimate at home once again. Such moments were never as raucous with sound as past times had been when we had had 'private' Spanish to use. (Our English-sounding house was never to be as noisy as our Spanish-speaking house had been.) Intimate moments were usually soft moments of sound. My mother was in the dining room while I did my homework nearby. And she looked over at me. Smiled. Said something—her words said nothing very important. But her voice sounded to tell me (*We are together*) I was her son.

(*Richard!*)

Intimacy thus continued at home; intimacy was not stilled by English. It is true that I would never forget the great change of my life, the diminished occasions of intimacy. But there would also be times when I sensed the deepest truth about language and intimacy: *Intimacy is not created by a particular language; it is created by intimates.* The great change in my life was not linguistic but social. If, after becoming a successful student, I no longer heard intimate voices as often as I had earlier, it was not because I spoke

English rather than Spanish. It was because I used public language for most of the day. I moved easily at last, a citizen in a crowded city of words.

4

This boy became a man. In private now, alone, I brood over language and intimacy—the great themes of my past. In public I expect most of the faces I meet to be the faces of strangers. (How do you do?) If meetings are quick and impersonal, they have been efficiently managed. I rush past the sounds of voices attending only to the words addressed to me. Voices seem planed to an even surface of sound, soundless. A business associate speaks in a deep baritone, but I pass through the timbre to attend to his words. The crazy man who sells me a newspaper every night mumbles something crazy, but I have time only to pretend that I have heard him say hello. Accented versions of English make little impression on me. In the rush-hour crowd a Japanese tourist asks me a question, and I inch past his accent to concentrate on what he is saying. The Eastern European immigrant in a neighborhood delicatessen speaks to me through a marinade of sounds, but I respond to his words. I note for only a second the Texas accent of the telephone operator or the Mississippi accent of the man who lives in the apartment below me.

My city seems silent until some ghetto black teenagers board the bus I am on. Because I do not take their presence for granted, I listen to the sounds of their voices. Of all the accented versions of English I hear in a day, I hear theirs most intently. They are *the* sounds of the outsider. They annoy me for being loud—so self-sufficient and unconcerned by my presence. Yet for the same reason they seem to me glamorous. (A romantic gesture against public acceptance.) Listening to their shouted laughter, I realize my own quiet. Their voices enclose my isolation. I feel envious, envious of their brazen intimacy.

I warn myself away from such envy, however. I remember the black political activists who have argued in favor of using black English in schools. (Their argument varies only slightly from that made by foreign-language bilingualists.) I have heard 'radical' linguists make the point that black English is a complex and intricate version of English. And I do not doubt it. But neither do I think that black English should be a language of public instruction. What makes black English inappropriate in classrooms is not something *in* the language. It is rather what lower-class speakers make of it. Just as Spanish would have been a dangerous language for me to have used at the start of my education, so black English would be a dangerous language to use in the schooling of teenagers for whom it reenforces feelings of public separateness.

This seems to me an obvious point. But one that needs to be made. In recent years there have been attempts to make the language of the alien public language. 'Bilingual education, two ways to understand . . . ,' television and radio commercials glibly announce. Proponents of bilingual education are careful to say that they want students to acquire good schooling. Their argument goes something like this: Children permitted to use their family language in school will not be so alienated and will be better able to match the progress of English-speaking children in the crucial first months of instruction. (Increasingly confident of their abilities, such children will be more inclined to apply themselves to their studies in the future.) But then the bilingualists claim another, very different goal. They say that children who use their family language in school will retain a sense of their individuality—their ethnic heritage and cultural ties. Supporters of bilingual education thus want it both ways. They propose bilingual schooling as a way of helping students acquire the skills of the classroom crucial for public success. But they likewise insist that bilingual instruction will give students a sense of their identity apart from the public.

Behind this screen there gleams an astonishing promise: One can become a public person while still remaining a private person. At the very same time one can be both! There need be no tension between the self in the crowd and the self apart from the crowd! Who would not want to believe such an idea? Who can be surprised that the scheme has won the support of many middle-class Americans? If the barrio or ghetto child can retain his separateness even while being publicly educated, then it is almost possible to believe that there is no private cost to be paid for public success. Such is the consolation offered by any of the current bilingual schemes. Consider, for example, the bilingual voters' ballot. In some American cities one can cast a ballot printed in several languages. Such a document implies that a person can exercise that most public of rights—the right to vote—while still keeping apart, unassimilated from public life.

It is not enough to say that these schemes are foolish and certainly doomed. Middle-class supporters of public bilingualism toy with the confusion of those Americans who cannot speak standard English as well as they can. Bilingual enthusiasts, moreover, sin against intimacy. An Hispanic-American writer tells me, 'I will never give up my family language; I would as soon give up my soul.' Thus he holds to his chest a skein of words, as though it were the source of his family ties. He credits to language what he should credit to family members. A convenient mistake. For as long as he holds on to words, he can ignore how much else has changed in his life.

It has happened before. In earlier decades, persons newly successful and ambitious for social mobility similarly seized upon certain 'family words.' Working-class men attempting political power took to calling one another 'brother.' By so doing they escaped oppressive public isolation and were able to unite with many others like themselves. But they paid a price for this union. It was a public union they forged. The word they coined to address one another could never be the sound (*brother*) exchanged by two in intimate greeting. In the union hall the word 'brother' became a vague metaphor; with repetition a weak echo of the intimate sound. Context forced the change. Context could not be overruled. Context will always guard the realm of the intimate from public misuse.

Today nonwhite Americans call 'brother' to strangers. And white feminists refer to their mass union of 'sisters.' And white middle-class teenagers continue to prove the importance of context as they try to ignore it. They seize upon the idioms of the black ghetto. But their attempt to appropriate such expressions invariably changes the words. As it becomes a public expression, the ghetto idiom loses its sound—its message of public separateness and strident intimacy. It becomes with public repetition a series of words, increasingly lifeless.

The mystery remains: intimate utterance. The communication of intimacy passes through the word to enliven its sound. But it cannot be held by the word. Cannot be clutched or ever quoted. It is too fluid. It depends not on word but on person.

My grandmother!

She stood among my other relations mocking me when I no longer spoke Spanish. '*Pocho*,' she said. But then it made no difference. (She'd laugh.) Our relationship continued. Language was never its source. She was a woman in her eighties during the first decade of my life. A mysterious woman to me, my only living grandparent. A woman of Mexico. The woman in long black dresses that reached down to her shoes. My one relative who spoke no word of English. She had no interest in *gringo* society. She remained completely aloof from the public. Protected by her daughters. Protected even by me when we went to Safeway together and I acted as her translator. Eccentric woman. Soft. Hard.

When my family visited my aunt's house in San Francisco, my grandmother searched for me among my many cousins. She'd chase them away. Pinching her granddaughters, she'd warn them all away from me. Then she'd take me to her room, where she had prepared for my coming. There would be a chair next to the bed. A dusty jellied candy nearby. And a copy of *Life en Español* for me to examine. 'There,' she'd say. I'd sit there content. A boy of eight. *Pocho*. Her favorite. I'd sift through the pictures of earthquake-destroyed Latin American cities and blond-wigged Mexican movie stars. And all the while I'd listen to the sound of my grandmother's voice. She'd pace round the room, searching through closets and drawers, telling me stories of her life. Her past. They were stories so familiar to me that I couldn't remember the first time I'd heard them. I'd look up sometimes to listen. Other times she'd look over at me. But she never seemed to expect a response. Sometimes I'd smile or nod. (I understood exactly what she was saying.) But it never seemed to matter to her one way or another. It was enough I was there. The words she spoke were almost irrelevant to that fact—the sounds she made. Content.

The mystery remained: intimate utterance.

I learn little about language and intimacy listening to those social activists who propose using one's family language in public life. Listening to songs on the radio, or hearing a great voice at the opera, or overhearing the woman downstairs singing to herself at an open window, I learn much more. Singers celebrate the human voice. Their lyrics are words. But animated by voice those words are subsumed into sounds. I listen with excitement as the words yield their enormous power to sound—though the words are never totally obliterated. In most songs the drama or tension results from the fact that the singer moves between word (sense) and note (song). At one moment the song simply 'says' something. At another moment the voice stretches out the words—the heart cannot contain!—and the voice moves toward pure sound. Words take flight.

Singing out words, the singer suggests an experience of sound most intensely mine at intimate moments. Literally, most songs are about love. (Lost love; celebrations of loving; pleas.) By simply being occasions when sound escapes word, however, songs put me in mind of the most intimate moments of my life.

Finally, among all types of song, it is the song created by lyric poets that I find most compelling. There is no other public occasion of sound so important for me. Written poems exist on a page, at first glance, as a mere collection of words. And yet, despite this, without musical accompaniment, the poet leads me to hear the sounds of the words that I read. As song, the poem passes between sound and sense, never belonging for long to one realm or the other. As public artifact, the poem can never duplicate intimate sound. But by imitating such sound, the poem helps me recall the intimate times of my life. I read in my room—alone—and grow conscious of being alone, sounding my voice, in search of another. The poem serves then as a memory device. It forces remembrance. And refreshes. It reminds me of the possibility of escaping public words, the possibility that awaits me in meeting the intimate.

The poems I read are not nonsense poems. But I read them for reasons which, I imagine, are similar to those that make children play with meaningless rhyme. I have watched them before: I have noticed the way children create private languages to keep away the adult; I have heard their chanting riddles that go nowhere in logic but harken back to some kingdom of sound; I have watched them listen to intricate nonsense rhymes, and I have noted their wonder. I was never such a child. Until I was six years old, I remained in a magical realm of sound. I didn't need to remember that realm because it was present to me. But then the screen door shut behind me as I left home for school. At last I began my movement toward words. On the other side of initial sadness would come the realization that intimacy cannot be held. With time would come the knowledge that intimacy must finally pass.

I would dishonor those I have loved and those I love now to claim anything else. I would dishonor our closeness by holding on to a particular language and calling it my family language. Intimacy is not trapped within words. It passes through words. It passes. The truth is that intimates leave the room. Doors close. Faces move away from the window. Time passes. Voices recede into the dark. Death finally quiets the voice. And there is no way to deny it. No way to stand in the crowd, uttering one's family language.

The last time I saw my grandmother I was nine years old. I can tell you some of the things she said to me as I stood by her bed. I cannot, however, quote the message of intimacy she conveyed with her voice. She laughed, holding my hand. Her voice illumined disjointed memories as it passed them again. She remembered her husband, his green eyes, the magic name of Narciso. His early death. She remembered the farm in Mexico. The eucalyptus nearby. (Its scent, she remembered, like incense.) She remembered the family cow, the bell round its neck heard miles away. A dog. She remembered working as a seamstress. How she'd leave her daughters and son for long hours to go into Guadalajara to work. And how my mother would come running toward her in the sun—her bright yellow dress—to see her return. 'Mmmaaammmmmááááá,' the old lady mimicked her daughter (my mother) to her son. She laughed. There was the snap of a cough. An aunt came into the room and told me it was time I should leave. 'You can see her tomorrow,' she promised. And so I kissed my grandmother's cracked face. And the last thing I saw was her thin, oddly youthful thigh, as my aunt rearranged the sheet on the bed.

At the funeral parlor a few days after, I knelt with my relatives during the rosary. Among their voices but silent, I traced, then lost, the sounds of individual aunts in the surge of the common prayer. And I heard at that moment what I have since heard often again—the sounds the women in my family make when they are praying in sadness. When I went up to look at my grandmother, I saw her through the haze of a veil draped over the open lid of the casket. Her face appeared calm—but distant and unyielding to love. It was not the face I remembered seeing most often. It was the face she made in public when the clerk at Safeway asked her some question and I would have to respond. It was her public face the mortician had designed with his dubious art.

1982

---

## FROM DAYS OF OBLIGATION: AN ARGUMENT WITH MY MEXICAN FATHER

### Chapter Two: Late Victorians

St. Augustine[1] writes from his cope of dust that we are restless hearts, for earth is not our true home. Human unhappiness is evidence of our immortality. Intuition tells us we are meant for some other city.

Elizabeth Taylor, quoted in a magazine article of twenty years ago, spoke of cerulean Richard Burton days[2] on her yacht, days that were nevertheless undermined by the elemental private reflection: This must end.

• • •

On a Sunday in summer, ten years ago, I was walking home from the Latin mass at St. Patrick's, the old Irish parish downtown, when I saw thousands of people on Market Street. It was the Gay Freedom Day parade—not the first, but the first I ever saw. Private lives were becoming public. There were marching bands. There were floats. Banners blocked single lives thematically into a processional mass, not unlike the consortiums of the blessed in Renaissance paintings, each saint cherishing the apparatus of his martyrdom: GAY DENTISTS. BLACK AND WHITE LOVERS. GAYS FROM BAKERSFIELD. LATINA LESBIANS. From the foot of Market Street they marched, east to west, following the mythic American path toward optimism.

I followed the parade to Civic Center Plaza, where flags of routine nations yielded sovereignty to a multitude. Pastel billows flowed over all.

Five years later, another parade. Politicians waved from white convertibles. "Dykes on Bikes" revved up, thumbs-upped. But now banners bore the acronyms of death. AIDS. ARC.[3] Drums were muffled as passing, plum-spotted young men slid by on motorized cable cars.

1. Augustine of Hippo (AD 354–430), bishop of Hippo Regius, Berber philosopher and theologian; Christian Church father.
2. I.e., Taylor (b. 1932), English-born British American actress, fondly recalled times spent with Burton (1925–1984), Welsh actor. They were married twice (1964–74, 1975–76), and both marriages ended in divorce.
3. As in the AIDS/ARC [American Red Cross] Blood Fund for people with AIDS.

Though I am alive now, I do not believe an old man's pessimism is necessarily truer than a young man's optimism simply because it comes after. There are things a young man knows that are true and are not yet in the old man's power to recollect. Spring has its sappy wisdom. Lonely teenagers still arrive in San Francisco aboard Greyhound buses. The city can still seem, by comparison with where they came from, paradise.

. . .

Four years ago on a Sunday in winter—a brilliant spring afternoon—I was jogging near Fort Point while overhead a young woman was, with difficulty, climbing over the railing of the Golden Gate Bridge. Holding down her skirt with one hand, with the other she waved to a startled spectator (the newspaper next day quoted a workman who was painting the bridge) before she stepped onto the sky.

To land like a spilled purse at my feet.

Serendipity has an eschatological tang here. Always has. Few American cities have had the experience, as we have had, of watching the civic body burn even as we stood, out of body, on a hillside, in a movie theater. Jeanette MacDonald's loony scatting of "San Francisco" has become our go-to-hell anthem.[4] San Francisco has taken some heightened pleasure from the circus of final things. To Atlantis, to Pompeii, to the Pillar of Salt,[5] we add the Golden Gate Bridge, not golden at all, but rust red. San Francisco toys with the tragic conclusion.

For most of its brief life, San Francisco has entertained an idea of itself as heaven on earth, whether as Gold Town or City Beautiful or the Haight-Ashbury.[6]

San Francisco can support both comic and tragic conclusions because the city is geographically in extremis, a metaphor for the farthest-flung possibility, a metaphor for the end of the line. Land's end.

To speak of San Francisco as land's end is to read the map from one direction only—as Europeans would read it or as the East Coast has always read. In my lifetime San Francisco has become an Asian city. To speak, therefore, of San Francisco as land's end is to betray parochialism. My parents came here from Mexico. They saw San Francisco as the North. The West was not west for them. They did not share the Eastern traveler's sense of running before the past—the darkening time zone, the lowering curtain.

I cannot claim for myself the memory of a skyline such as the one César saw. César came to San Francisco in middle age; César came here as to some final place. He was born in South America; he had grown up in Paris; he had been everywhere, done everything; he assumed the world. Yet César

---

4. In the Hollywood drama/adventure movie San Francisco (1936), MacDonald (1903–1965), American singer and actress, performs the now-classic title song numerous times, and it becomes an anthem for earthquake survivors.
5. According to the biblical Book of Genesis, God turned Lot's wife into a pillar of salt because she looked back at the city of Sodom. She, Lot, and their daughters were fleeing Sodom (its name is the source of the word sodomy) because God was about to destroy it and other cities as punishment for their citizens' sins. Atlantis: according to legend, an ancient island and naval power that sank into the sea. Pompeii: ancient Roman city de-

stroyed, and completely buried, by the eruption of the volcano Mount Vesuvius in AD 79.
6. San Francisco district named for the intersection of Haight and Ashbury streets; famous as a center of the hippie movement in the mid- to late 1960s. Gold Town: a reference to San Francisco's prominent role in the California gold rush of 1849. City Beautiful: San Francisco's Civic Center and the City Hall (1915) that stands on it are products of the City Beautiful Movement, a program in the 1890s and early 1900s of beautifying and supplying monumental grandeur to North American cities.

was not condescending toward San Francisco, not at all. Here César saw revolution, and he embraced it.

Whereas I live here because I was born here. I grew up ninety miles away, in Sacramento. San Francisco was the nearest, the easiest, the inevitable city, since I needed a city. And yet I live here surrounded by people for whom San Francisco is the end of quest.

I have never looked for utopia on a map. Of course I believe in human advancement. I believe in medicine, in astrophysics, in washing machines. But my compass takes its cardinal point from tragedy. If I respond to the metaphor of spring, I nevertheless learned, years ago, from my Mexican father, from my Irish nuns, to count on winter. The point of Eden for me, for us, is not approach but expulsion.

After I met César in 1984, our friendly debate concerning the halcyon properties of San Francisco ranged from restaurant to restaurant. I spoke of limits. César boasted of freedoms.

It was César's conceit to add to the gates of Jerusalem, to add to the soccer fields of Tijuana, one other dreamscape hoped for the world over. It was the view from a hill, through a mesh of tram wires, of an urban neighborhood in a valley. The vision took its name from the protruding wedge of a theater marquee. Here César raised his glass without discretion: To the Castro.[7]

. . .

There were times, dear César, when you tried to switch sides, if only to scorn American optimism, which, I remind you, had already become your own. At the high school where César taught, teachers and parents had organized a campaign to keep kids from driving themselves to the junior prom, in an attempt to forestall liquor and death. Such a scheme momentarily reawakened César's Latin skepticism.

Didn't the Americans know? (His tone exaggerated incredulity.) Teenagers will crash into lampposts on their way home from proms, and there is nothing to be done about it. You cannot forbid tragedy.

. . .

By California standards I live in an old house. But not haunted. There are too many tall windows, there is too much salty light, especially in winter, though the windows rattle, rattle in summer when the fog flies overhead, and the house creaks and prowls at night. I feel myself immune to any confidence it seeks to tell.

To grow up homosexual is to live with secrets and within secrets. In no other place are those secrets more closely guarded than within the family home. The grammar of the gay city borrows metaphors from the nineteenth-century house. "Coming out of the closet" is predicated upon family laundry, dirty linen, skeletons.

I live in a tall Victorian house that has been converted to four apartments; four single men.

7. The Castro District, commonly known as The Castro, is a San Francisco neighborhood that has long been associated with gay life. It runs along Castro Street—named for José Castro (1808– 1860), a leader of Mexican opposition to U.S. rule in California in the nineteenth century, governor of Alta California 1835–36—and the Castro Theatre is a 1922 movie palace on that street.

Neighborhood streets are named to honor nineteenth-century men of action, men of distant fame. Clay. Jackson. Scott. Pierce. Many Victorians in the neighborhood date from before the 1906 earthquake and fire.

Architectural historians credit the gay movement of the 1970s with the urban restoration of San Francisco. Twenty years ago this was a borderline neighborhood. This room, like all the rooms of the house, was painted headache green, apple green, boardinghouse green. In the 1970s, homosexuals moved into black and working-class parts of the city, where they were perceived as pioneers or as block-busters, depending.

Two decades ago, some of the least expensive sections of San Francisco were wooden Victorian sections. It was thus a coincidence of the market that gay men found themselves living within the architectural metaphor for family. No other architecture in the American imagination is more evocative of family than the Victorian house. In those same years—the 1970s—and within those same Victorian houses, homosexuals were living rebellious lives to challenge the foundations of domesticity.

Was "queer-bashing" as much a manifestation of homophobia as a reaction against gentrification? One heard the complaint, often enough, that gay men were as promiscuous with their capital as otherwise, buying, fixing up, then selling and moving on. Two incomes, no children, described an unfair advantage. No sooner would flower boxes begin to appear than an anonymous reply was smeared on the sidewalk out front: KILL FAGGOTS.

The three- or four-story Victorian house, like the Victorian novel, was built to contain several generations and several classes under one roof, behind a single oaken door. What strikes me at odd moments is the confidence of Victorian architecture. Stairs, connecting one story with another, describe the confidence that bound generations together through time—confidence that the family would inherit the earth. The other day I noticed for the first time the vestige of a hinge on the topmost newel of the staircase. This must have been the hinge of a gate that kept infants upstairs so many years ago.

If Victorian houses assert a sturdy optimism by day, they are also associated in our imaginations with the Gothic—with shadows and cobwebby gimcrack, long corridors. The nineteenth century was remarkable for escalating optimism even as it excavated the backstairs, the descending architecture of nightmare—Freud's labor and Engels's.[8]

I live on the second story, in rooms that have been rendered as empty as Yorick's skull[9]—gutted, unrattled, in various ways unlocked—added skylights and new windows, new doors. The hallway remains the darkest part of the house.

This winter the hallway and lobby are being repainted to resemble an eighteenth-century French foyer. Of late we had walls and carpet of Sienese red; a baroque mirror hung in an alcove by the stairwell. Now we are to have enlightened austerity—black-and-white marble floors and faux masonry. A man comes in the afternoons to texture the walls with a sponge and a rag

---

8. Playful reference to the influential theories of Sigmund Freud (1856–1939), Austrian neurologist whose subjects included dreams and the unconscious, and Friedrich Engels (1820–1895), German socialist who cowrote *The Communist Manifesto* (1848) with Karl Marx.

9. Unearthed in Act 5, Scene 1, of Shakespeare's *Hamlet*; Yorick was the king's jester, and his skull prompts Prince Hamlet, who knew him, to ponder the decay brought on by death: "to what base uses we may return" (line 187).

and to paint white mortar lines that create an illusion of permanence, of stone.

The renovation of Victorian San Francisco into dollhouses for libertines may have seemed, in the 1970s, an evasion of what the city was actually becoming. San Francisco's rows of storied houses proclaimed a multi-generational orthodoxy, all the while masking the city's unconventional soul. Elsewhere, meanwhile, domestic America was coming undone.

Suburban Los Angeles, the prototype for a new America, was character-ized by a more apparently radical residential architecture. There was, for example, the work of Frank Gehry.[1] In the 1970s, Gehry exploded the nuclear-family house, turning it inside out intellectually and in fact. Though, in a way, Gehry merely completed the logic of the postwar suburban tract house—with its one story, its sliding glass doors, Formica kitchen, two-car garage. The tract house exchanged privacy for mobility. Heterosexuals opted for the one-lifetime house, the freeway, the birth-control pill, minimalist fiction.

· · ·

The age-old description of homosexuality is of a sin against nature. Moral-istic society has always judged emotion literally. The homosexual was sin-ful because he had no kosher place to stick it. In attempting to drape the architecture of sodomy with art, homosexuals have lived for thousands of years against the expectations of nature. Barren as Shakers and, interest-ingly, as concerned with the small effect, homosexuals have made a cove-nant against nature. Homosexual survival lay in artifice, in plumage, in lampshades, sonnets, musical comedy, couture, syntax, religious ceremony, opera, lacquer, irony.

I once asked Byron, an interior decorator, if he had many homosexual cli-ents. "Mais non,"[2] said he, flexing his eyelids. "Queers don't need decorators. They were born knowing how. All this ASID[3] stuff—tests and regulations—as if you can confer a homosexual diploma on a suburban housewife by granting her a discount card."

A knack? The genius, we are beginning to fear in an age of AIDS, is irreplaceable—but does it exist? The question is whether the darling affini-ties are innate to homosexuality or whether they are compensatory. Why have so many homosexuals retired into the small effect, the ineffectual career, the stereotype, the card shop, the florist? Be gentle with me? Or do homosexuals know things others do not?

This way power lay. Once upon a time, the homosexual appropriated to himself a mystical province, that of taste. Taste, which is, after all, the inse-curity of the middle class, became the homosexual's licentiate to challenge the rule of nature. (The fairy in his blood, he intimated.)

Deciding how best to stick it may be only an architectural problem or a question of physics or of engineering or of cabinetry. Nevertheless, society's condemnation forced the homosexual to find his redemption outside nature. We'll put a little skirt here. The impulse is not to create but to re-create, to sham, to convert, to sauce, to rouge, to fragrance, to prettify. No effect is

1. Canadian architect (b. Ephraim Owen Gold-berg, 1929), based in Los Angeles.
2. Of course not (French).

3. American Society of Interior Designers, a pro-fessional association.

too small or too ephemeral to be snatched away from nature, to be ushered toward the perfection of artificiality. *We'll bring out the highlights there.* The homosexual has marshaled the architecture of the straight world to the very gates of Versailles—that great Vatican of fairyland[4]—beyond which power is tyrannized by leisure.

In San Francisco in the 1980s, the highest form of art became interior decoration. The glory hole[5] was thus converted to an eighteenth-century foyer.

• • •

I live away from the street, in a back apartment, in two rooms. I use my bedroom as a visitor's room—the sleigh bed tricked up with shams into a sofa—whereas I rarely invite anyone into my library, the public room, where I write, the public gesture.

I read in my bedroom in the afternoon because the light is good there, especially now, in winter, when the sun recedes from the earth.

There is a door in the south wall that leads to a balcony. The door was once a window. Inside the door, inside my bedroom, are twin green shutters. They are false shutters, of no function beyond wit. The shutters open into the room; they have the effect of turning my apartment inside out.

A few months ago I hired a man to paint the shutters green. I wanted the green shutters of Manet[6]—you know the ones I mean—I wanted a weathered look, as of verdigris. For several days the painter labored, rubbing his paints into the wood and then wiping them off again. In this way he rehearsed for me decades of the ravages of weather. Yellow enough? Black?

The painter left one afternoon, saying he would return the next, leaving behind his tubes, his brushes, his sponges and rags. He never returned. Someone told me he has AIDS.

• • •

A black woman haunts California Street between the donut shop and the cheese store. She talks to herself—a debate, wandering, never advancing. Pedestrians who do not know her give her a wide berth. Somebody told me her story; I don't know whether it's true. Neighborhood merchants tolerate her presence as a vestige of dispirited humanity clinging to an otherwise dispiriting progress of "better" shops and restaurants.

Repainted façades extend now from Jackson Street south into what was once the heart of the "Mo"—black Fillmore Street. Today there are watercress sandwiches at three o'clock where recently there had been loudmouthed kids, hole-in-the-wall bars, pimps. Now there are tweeds and perambulators, matrons and nannies. Yuppies. And gays.

The gay-male revolution had greater influence on San Francisco in the 1970s than did the feminist revolution. Feminists, with whom I include lesbians—such was the inclusiveness of the feminist movement—were preoccupied with career, with escape from the house in order to create a sexually

4. I.e., the ultra-elaborate decoration of the Château de Versailles, the royal palace in Versailles, France, has become a kind of ultimate style authority for gays, as the State of the Vatican City, where the pope resides and rules, is the center of the Roman Catholic Church.

5. A hole in a wall or other partition, often between the stalls in public bathrooms, through which people engage in anonymous sexual activity or observe sexual activity.

6. As in the work of Édouard Manet (1832–1883), French painter.

democratic city. Homosexual men sought to reclaim the house, the house that traditionally had been the reward for heterosexuality, with all its selfless tasks and burdens.

Leisure defined the gay-male revolution. The gay political movement began, by most accounts, in 1969 with the Stonewall riots in New York City,[7] whereby gay men fought to defend the nonconformity of their leisure.

It was no coincidence that homosexuals migrated to San Francisco in the 1970s, for the city was famed as a playful place, more Catholic than Protestant in its eschatological intuition. In 1975, the state of California legalized consensual homosexuality, and about that same time Castro Street, southwest of downtown, began to eclipse Polk Street as the homosexual address in San Francisco. Polk Street was a string of bars. The Castro was an entire district. The Castro had Victorian houses and churches, bookstores and restaurants, gyms, dry cleaners, supermarkets, and an elected member of the Board of Supervisors. The Castro supported baths and bars, but there was nothing furtive about them. On Castro Street the light of day penetrated gay life through clear plate-glass windows. The light of day discovered a new confidence, a new politics. Also a new look—a noncosmopolitan, Burt Reynolds,[8] butch-kid style: beer, ball games, Levi's, short hair, muscles.

Gay men who lived elsewhere in the city, in Pacific Heights or in the Richmond, often spoke with derision of "Castro Street clones," describing the look, or scorned what they called the ghettoization of homosexuality. To an older generation of homosexuals, the blatancy of Castro Street threatened the discreet compromise they had negotiated with a tolerant city.

As the Castro district thrived, Folsom Street, south of Market, also began to thrive, as if in contradistinction to the utopian Castro. Folsom Street was a warehouse district of puddled alleys and deserted corners. Folsom Street offered an assortment of leather bars—an evening's regress to the outlaw sexuality of the fifties, the forties, the nineteenth century, and so on—an eroticism of the dark, of the Reeperbahn,[9] or of the guardsman's barracks.

The Castro district implied that sexuality was more crucial, that homosexuality was the central fact of identity. The Castro district, with its ice-cream parlors and hardware stores, was the revolutionary place.

Into which carloads of vacant-eyed teenagers from other districts or from middle-class suburbs would drive after dark, cruising the neighborhood for solitary victims.

The ultimate gay-basher was a city supervisor named Dan White, ex-cop, ex-boxer, ex-fireman, ex-altar boy. Dan White had grown up in the Castro district; he recognized the Castro revolution for what it was. Gays had achieved power over him. He murdered the mayor and he murdered the homosexual member of the Board of Supervisors.[1]

• • •

7. Now-legendary violent demonstrations by gays against the police raid of the Stonewall Inn, in downtown Manhattan's Greenwich Village neighborhood.
8. American movie actor (b. 1936), generally associated with machismo.

9. Street in Hamburg, Germany; a center of that city's nightlife and red-light district.
1. At San Francisco's City Hall, Supervisor Daniel James "Dan" White (1946–1985) assassinated Mayor George Moscone (1929–1978) and Supervisor Harvey Milk (1930–1978).

Katherine, a sophisticate if ever there was one, nevertheless dismisses two men descending the aisle at the Opera House: "All so sleek and smooth-jowled and silver-haired—they don't seem real, poor darlings. It must be because they don't have children."

Lodged within Katherine's complaint is the perennial heterosexual annoyance with the homosexual's freedom from childrearing, which does not so much place the homosexual beyond the pale as it relegates the homosexual outside "responsible" life.

It was the glamour of gay life, after all, as much as it was the feminist call to career, that encouraged heterosexuals in the 1970s to excuse themselves from nature, to swallow the birth-control pill. Who needs children? The gay bar became the paradigm for the singles bar. The gay couple became the paradigm for the selfish couple—all dressed up and everywhere to go. And there was the example of the gay house in illustrated life-style magazines. At the same time that suburban housewives were looking outside the home for fulfillment, gay men were reintroducing a new generation in the city—heterosexual men and women—to the complaisancies of the barren house.

Puritanical America dismissed gay camp followers as yuppies; the term means to suggest infantility. Yuppies were obsessive and awkward in their materialism. Whereas gays arranged a decorative life against a barren state, yuppies sought early returns—lives that were not to be all toil and spin. Yuppies, trained to careerism from the cradle, wavered in their pursuit of the Northern European ethic—indeed, we might now call it the pan-Pacific ethic—in favor of the Mediterranean, the Latin, the Catholic, the Castro, the Gay.

* * *

The international architectural idioms of Skidmore, Owings & Merrill,[2] which defined the skyline of the 1970s, betrayed no awareness of any street-level debate concerning the primacy of play in San Francisco or of any human dramas resulting from urban redevelopment. The repellent office tower was a fortress raised against the sky, against the street, against the idea of a city. Offices were hives where money was made, and damn all.

In the 1970s, San Francisco divided between the interests of downtown and the pleasures of the neighborhoods. Neighborhoods asserted idiosyncrasy, human scale, light. San Francisco neighborhoods perceived downtown as working against their influence in determining what the city should be. Thus neighborhoods seceded from the idea of a city.

The gay movement rejected downtown as representing "straight" conformity. But was it possible that heterosexual Union Street was related to Castro Street? Was it possible that either was related to the Latino Mission district? Or to the Sino-Russian Richmond? San Francisco, though complimented worldwide for holding its center, was in fact without a vision of itself entire.

In the 1980s, in deference to the neighborhoods, City Hall would attempt a counterreformation of downtown, forbidding "Manhattanization." Shadows were legislated away from parks and playgrounds. Height restrictions

---

2. Chicago-based architectural, urban design and planning, and engineering firm.

were lowered beneath an existing skyline. Design, too, fell under the retro-jurisdiction of the city planner's office. The Victorian house was presented to architects as a model of what the city wanted to uphold and to become. In heterosexual neighborhoods, one saw newly built Victorians. Downtown, postmodernist prescriptions for playfulness advised skyscrapers to wear party hats, buttons, comic mustaches. Philip Johnson[3] yielded to the doll-house impulse to perch angels atop one of his skyscrapers.

. . .

I can see downtown from my bedroom window. But days pass and I do not leave the foreground for the city. Most days my public impression of San Francisco is taken from Fillmore Street, from the anchorhold of the Lady of the Donut Shop.

She now often parades with her arms crossed over her breasts in an "X," the posture emblematic of prophecy. And yet gather her madness where she sits on the curb, chain-smoking, hugging her knees, while I disappear down Fillmore Street to make Xerox copies, to mail letters, to rent a video, to shop for dinner. I am soon pleased by the faint breeze from the city, the slight agitation of the homing crowds of singles, so intent upon the path of least resistance. I admire the prosperity of the corridor, the shop windows that beckon inward toward the perfected life-style, the little way of the City of St. Francis.

Turning down Pine Street, I am recalled by the prickly silhouette of St. Dominic's Church against the scrim of the western sky. I turn, instead, into the Pacific Heights Health Club.

In the 1970s, like a lot of men and women in this city, I joined a gym. My club, I've even caught myself calling it.

In the gay city of the 1970s, bodybuilding became an architectural preoc-cupation of the upper middle class. Bodybuilding is a parody of labor, a useless accumulation of the laborer's bulk and strength. No useful task is accomplished. And yet there is something businesslike about habitués, and the gym is filled with the punch-clock logic of the workplace. Machines clank and hum. Needles on gauges toll spent calories.

The gym is at once a closet of privacy and an exhibition gallery. All four walls are mirrored.

I study my body in the mirror. Physical revelation—nakedness—is no longer possible, cannot be desired, for the body is shrouded in meat and wears itself.

The intent is some merciless press of body against a standard, perfect mold. Bodies are "cut" or "pumped" or "buffed" as on an assembly line in Turin.[4] A body becomes so many extrovert parts. Delts, pecs, lats, traps.

I harness myself in a Nautilus cage.

Lats become wings. For the gym is nothing if not the occasion for tran-scendence. From homosexual to autosexual . . .

I lift weights over my head, baring my teeth like an animal with the strain.

3. American architect (1906–2005).
4. Industrial city in northwestern Italy; home to the auto manufacturer Fiat.

. . . to nonsexual. The effect of the overdeveloped body is the miniaturization of the sexual organs—of no function beyond wit. Behold the ape become Blakean angel,[5] revolving in an empyrean of mirrors.

. . .

The nineteenth-century mirror over the fireplace in my bedroom was purchased by a decorator from the estate of a man who died last year of AIDS. It is a top-heavy piece, confusing styles. Two ebony-painted columns support a frieze of painted glass above the mirror. The frieze depicts three bourgeois graces and a couple of free-range cherubs. The lake of the mirror has formed a cataract, and at its edges it is beginning to corrode.

Thus the mirror that now draws upon my room owns some bright curse, maybe—some memory not mine.

As I regard this mirror, I imagine St. Augustine's meditation slowly hardening into syllogism, passing down through centuries to confound us: evil is the absence of good.

We have become accustomed to figures disappearing from our landscape. Does this not lead us to interrogate the landscape?

With reason do we invest mirrors with the superstition of memory, for they, though glass, though liquid captured in a bay, are so often less fragile than we are. They—bright ovals, or rectangles, or rounds—bump down unscathed, unspilled through centuries, whereas we . . .

The man in the red baseball cap used to jog so religiously on Marina Green. By the time it occurs to me that I have not seen him for months, I realize he may be dead—not lapsed, not moved away. People come and go in the city, it's true. But in San Francisco death has become as routine an explanation for disappearance as Mayflower Van Lines.

AIDS, it has been discovered, is a plague of absence. Absence opened in the blood. Absence condensed into the fluid of passing emotion. Absence shot through opalescent tugs of semen to deflower the city.

And then AIDS, it was discovered, is a nonmetaphorical disease, a disease like any other. Absence sprang from substance—a virus, a hairy bubble perched upon a needle, a platter of no intention served round: fever, blisters, a death sentence.

At first I heard only a few names—names connected, perhaps, with the right faces, perhaps not. People vaguely remembered, as through the cataract of this mirror, from dinner parties or from intermissions. A few articles in the press. The rumored celebrities. But within months the slow beating of the blood had found its bay.

One of San Francisco's gay newspapers, the *Bay Area Reporter*, began to accept advertisements from funeral parlors and casket makers, inserting them between the randy ads for leather bars and tanning salons. The *Reporter* invited homemade obituaries—lovers writing of lovers, friends remembering friends and the blessings of unexceptional life.

*Peter. Carlos. Gary. Asel. Perry. Nikos.*

Healthy snapshots accompany each annal. At the Russian River. By the Christmas tree. Lifting a beer. In uniform. A dinner jacket. A satin gown.

*He was born in Puerto La Libertad, El Salvador.*

---

5. As depicted in the works of William Blake (1757–1827), English artist, poet, and mystic.

*He attended Apple Valley High School, where he was their first male cheerleader.*

*From El Paso. From Medford. From Germany. From Long Island.*

I moved back to San Francisco in 1979. Oh, I had had some salad days elsewhere, but by 1979 I was a wintry man. I came here in order not to be distracted by the ambitions or, for that matter, the pleasures of others but to pursue my own ambition. Once here, though, I found the company of men who pursued an earthly paradise charming. Skepticism became my demeanor toward them—I was the dinner-party skeptic, a firm believer in Original Sin and in the limits of possibility.

Which charmed them.

*He was a dancer.*

*He settled into the interior-design department of Gump's, where he worked until his illness.*

*He was a teacher.*

César, for example.

César had an excellent mind. César could shave the rind from any assertion to expose its pulp and jelly. But César was otherwise ruled by pulp. César loved everything that ripened in time. Freshmen. Bordeaux. César could fashion liturgy from an artichoke. Yesterday it was not ready (cocking his head, rotating the artichoke in his hand over a pot of cold water). Tomorrow will be too late (Yorick's skull). Today it is perfect (as he lit the fire beneath the pot). We will eat it now.

If he's lucky, he's got a year, a doctor told me. If not, he's got two.

The phone rang. AIDS had tagged a friend. And then the phone rang again. And then the phone rang again. Michael had tested positive. Adrian, well, what he had assumed were shingles . . . Paul was back in the hospital. And César, dammit, César, even César, especially César.

That winter before his death, César traveled back to South America. On his return to San Francisco, he described to me how he had walked with his mother in her garden—his mother chafing her hands as if she were cold. But it was not cold, he said. They moved slowly. Her summer garden was prolonging itself this year, she said. The cicadas will not stop singing.

When he lay on his deathbed, César said everyone else he knew might get AIDS and die. He said I would be the only one spared—"spared" was supposed to have been chased with irony, I knew, but his voice was too weak to do the job. "You are too circumspect," he said then, wagging his finger upon the coverlet.

So I was going to live to see that the garden of earthly delights[6] was, after all, only wallpaper—was that it, César? Hadn't I always said so? It was then I saw that the greater sin against heaven was my unwillingness to embrace life.

• • •

César said he found paradise at the baths. He said I didn't understand. He said if I had to ask about it, I might as well ask if a wife will spend eternity with Husband #1 or Husband #2.

---

6. Allusion to *The Garden of Earthly Delights* (or *The Millennium*), a triptych by Hieronymus Bosch (ca. 1450–1516), Dutch painter.

The baths were places of good humor, that was Number One; there was nothing demeaning about them. From within cubicles men would nod at one another or not, but there was no sting of rejection, because one had at last entered a region of complete acceptance. César spoke of floating from body to body, open arms yielding to open arms in an angelic round.

The best night. That's easy, he said, the best night was spent in the pool with an antiques dealer—up to their necks in warm water—their two heads bobbing on an ocean of chlorine green, bawling Noël Coward[7] songs.

But each went home alone?

Each satisfied, dear, César corrected. And all the way home San Francisco seemed to him balmed and merciful, he said. He felt weightlessness of being, the pavement under his step as light as air.

• • •

It was not as in some Victorian novel—the curtains drawn, the pillows plumped, the streets strewn with sawdust. It was not to be a matter of custards in covered dishes, steaming possets, *Try a little of this, my dear.* Or gathering up the issues of *Architectural Digest* strewn about the bed. Closing the biography of Diana Cooper[8] and marking its place. Or the unfolding of discretionary screens, morphine, parrots, pavilions.

César experienced agony.

Four of his high-school students sawed through a Vivaldi[9] quartet in the corridor outside his hospital room, prolonging the hideous garden.

*In the presence of his lover Gregory and friends, Scott passed from this life. . . .*

*He died peacefully at home in his lover Ron's arms.*

*Immediately after a friend led a prayer for him to be taken home and while his dear mother was reciting the 23rd Psalm,[1] Bill peacefully took his last breath.*

I stood aloof at César's memorial, the kind of party he would enjoy, everyone said. And so for a time César lay improperly buried, unconvincingly resurrected in the conditional: would enjoy. What else could they say? César had no religion beyond aesthetic bravery.

Sunlight remains. Traffic remains. Nocturnal chic attaches to some discovered restaurant. A new novel is reviewed in *The New York Times.* And the mirror rasps on its hook. The mirror is lifted down.

A priest friend, a good friend, who out of naïveté plays the cynic, tells me—this is on a bright, billowy day; we are standing outside—"It's not as sad as you may think. There is at least spectacle in the death of the young. Come to the funeral of an old lady sometime if you want to feel an empty church."

I will grant my priest friend this much: that it is easier, easier on me, to sit with gay men in hospitals than with the staring old. Young men talk as much as they are able.

---

7. English dramatist, composer, actor, and singer (1899–1973).
8. Diana Olivia Winifred Maud Cooper, Viscountess Norwich (1892–1986), English socialite and actress.

9. Antonio Lucio Vivaldi (1678–1741), Italian composer.
1. Biblical poem that describes God as a protector and provider.

But those who gather around the young man's bed do not see Chatterton.[2] This doll is Death. I have seen people caressing it, staring Death down. I have seen people wipe its tears, wipe its ass; I have seen people kiss Death on his lips, where once there were lips.

*Chris was inspired after his own diagnosis in July 1987 with the truth and reality of how such a terrible disease could bring out the love, warmth, and support of so many friends and family.*

Sometimes no family came. If there was family, it was usually Mother. Mom. With her suitcase and with the torn flap of an envelope in her hand.

*Brenda. Pat. Connie. Toni. Soledad.*

Or parents came but then left without reconciliation, some preferring to say "cancer."

But others came. They walked Death's dog. They washed his dishes. They bought his groceries. They massaged his poor back. They changed his bandages. They emptied his bedpan.

Men who sought the aesthetic ordering of existence were recalled to nature. Men who aspired to the mock-angelic settled for the shirt of hair. The gay community of San Francisco, having found freedom, consented to necessity—to all that the proud world had for so long held up to them, withheld from them, as "real humanity."

And if gays took care of their own, they were not alone. AIDS was a disease of the entire city. Nor were Charity and Mercy only male, only gay. Others came. There were nurses and nuns and the couple from next door, co-workers, strangers, teenagers, corporations, pensioners. A community was forming over the city.

*Cary and Rick's friends and family wish to thank the many people who provided both small and great kindnesses.*

*He was attended to and lovingly cared for by the staff at Coming Home Hospice.*

And the saints of this city have names listed in the phone book, names I heard called through a microphone one cold Sunday in Advent[3] as I sat in Most Holy Redeemer Church. It might have been any of the churches or community centers in the Castro district, but it happened at Most Holy Redeemer at a time in the history of the world when the Roman Catholic Church pronounced the homosexual a sinner.

A woman at the microphone called upon volunteers from the AIDS Support Group to come forward. Throughout the church, people stood up, young men and women, and middle-aged and old, straight, gay, and all of them shy at being called. Yet they came forward and assembled in the sanctuary, facing the congregation, grinning self-consciously at one another, their hands hidden behind them.

I am preoccupied by the fussing of a man sitting in the pew directly in front of me—in his seventies, frail, his iodine-colored hair combed forward and pasted upon his forehead. Fingers of porcelain clutch the pearly beads of what must have been his mother's rosary. He is not the sort of man any gay man would have chosen to become in the 1970s. He is probably not what he

2. English poet (1752–1770); his fatal arsenic poisoning might have been suicide, or it might have resulted from attempted self-medication for a venereal disease.

3. In Christianity, the period from the fourth Sunday before Christmas up to Christmas; a time of expectation, sometimes of prayer and fasting.

himself expected to become. Something of the old dear about him, wizened butterfly, powdered old pouf. Certainly he is what I fear becoming. And then he rises, this old monkey, with the most beatific dignity, in answer to the microphone, and he strides into the sanctuary to take his place in the company of the Blessed.

So this is it—this, what looks like a Christmas party in an insurance office, and not as in Renaissance paintings, and not as we had always thought, not some flower-strewn, some sequined curtain call of greasepainted heroes gesturing to the stalls. A lady with a plastic candy cane pinned to her lapel. A Castro clone with a red bandana exploding from his hip pocket. A perfume-counter lady with an Hermès scarf mantled upon her shoulder. A black man in a checkered sports coat. The pink-haired punkess with a jewel in her nose. Here, too, is the gay couple in middle age; interchangeable plaid shirts and corduroy pants. Blood and shit and Mr. Happy Face. These know the weight of bodies.

*Bill died.*

*. . . Passed on to heaven.*

*. . . Turning over in his bed one night and then gone.*

These learned to love what is corruptible, while I, barren skeptic, reader of St. Augustine, curator of the earthly paradise, inheritor of the empty mirror, I shift my tailbone upon the cold, hard pew.

1992

---

## *FROM* BROWN: THE LAST DISCOVERY OF AMERICA

### Preface

Brown as impurity.

I write of a color that is not a singular color, not a strict recipe, not an expected result, but a color produced by careless desire, even by accident; by two or several. I write of blood that is blended. I write of brown as complete freedom of substance and narrative. I extol impurity.

I eulogize a literature that is suffused with brown, with allusion, irony, paradox—ha!—pleasure.

I write about race in America in hopes of undermining the notion of race in America.

Brown bleeds through the straight line, unstaunchable—the line separating black from white, for example. Brown confuses. Brown forms at the border of contradiction (the ability of language to express two or several things at once, the ability of bodies to experience two or several things at once).

It is that brown faculty I uphold by attempting to write brownly. And I defy anyone who tries to unblend me or to say what is appropriate to my voice.

You will often find brown in this book as the cement between leaves of paradox.

You may not want paradox in a book. In which case, you had better seek a pure author.

Brown is the color most people in the United States associate with Latin America.

Apart from stool sample, there is no browner smear in the American imagination than the Rio Grande. No adjective has attached itself more often to the Mexican in America than "dirty"—which I assume gropes toward the simile "dirt-like," indicating dense concentrations of melanin.

I am dirty, all right. In Latin America, what makes me brown is that I am made of the conquistador and the Indian. My brown is a reminder of conflict.

And of reconciliation.

In my own mind, what makes me brown in the United States is that I am Richard Rodriguez. My baptismal name and my surname marry England and Spain, Renaissance rivals.

North of the U.S.-Mexico border, brown appears as the color of the future. The adjective accelerates, becomes a verb: "America is browning." South of the border, brown sinks back into time. Brown is time.

In middle chapters, I discuss the ways Hispanics brown an America that traditionally has chosen to describe itself as black-and-white. I salute Richard Nixon, the dark father of Hispanicity.[1] But my Hispanic chapters, as I think of them—the chapters I originally supposed were going to appear first in this book—gave way to more elementary considerations. I mean the meeting of the Indian, the African, and the European in colonial America. Red. Black. White. The founding palette.

Some months ago, a renowned American sociologist predicted to me that Hispanics will become "the new Italians" of the United States. (What the Sicilian had been for nineteenth-century America, the Colombian would become for the twenty-first century.)

His prediction seems to me insufficient because it does not account for the influence of Hispanics on the geography of the American imagination. Because of Hispanics, Americans are coming to see the United States in terms of a latitudinal vector, in terms of south-north, hot-cold; a new way of placing ourselves in the twenty-first century.

America has traditionally chosen to describe itself as an east-west country. I grew up on the east-west map of America, facing east. I no longer find myself so easily on that map. In middle age (also brown, its mixture of loss and capture), I end up on the shore where Sir Francis Drake[2] first stepped onto California. I look toward Asia.

As much as I celebrate the browning of America (and I do), I do not propose an easy optimism. The book's last chapter was completed before the events of September 11, 2001, and now will never be complete. The chapter describes the combustible dangers of brown; the chapter annotates the tragedies it anticipated.

I think brown marks a reunion of peoples, an end to ancient wanderings. Rival cultures and creeds conspire with Spring to create children of a beauty, perhaps of a harmony, previously unknown. Or long forgotten. Even so, the terrorist and the skinhead dream in solitude of purity and of the straight line

---

1. On the use of the word *Hispanic* by the administration of Richard Milhous Nixon (1913–1994), U.S. president 1969–74, see the "Into the Main-

stream" introduction, p. 1461.
2. English navigator and buccaneer (1540 or 1543–1596).

because they fear a future that does not isolate them. In a brown future, the most dangerous actor might likely be the cosmopolite, conversant in alternate currents, literatures, computer programs. The cosmopolite may come to hate his brownness, his facility, his indistinction, his mixture; the cosmopolite may yearn for a thorough religion, ideology, or tribe.

Many days, I left my book to wander the city, to discover the city outside my book was comically browning. Walking down Fillmore Street one afternoon, I was enjoying the smell of salt, the brindled pigeons, brindled light, when a conversation overtook me, parted around me, just as I passed the bird-store window: Two girls. Perhaps sixteen. White, Anglo, whatever. Tottering on their silly shoes. Talking of boys. The one girl saying to the other: . . . *His complexion is so cool, this sort of light—well, not that light* . . .

I realized my book will never be equal to the play of the young.

. . . *Sort of reddish brown, you know* . . . The other girl nodded, readily indicated that she did know. But still Connoisseur Number One sought to bag her simile. . . . *Like a Sugar Daddy bar—you know that candy bar?*

Two decades ago, I wrote *Hunger of Memory*, the autobiography of a scholarship boy. Ten years later, in *Days of Obligation*, I wrote about the influence of Mexican ethnicity on my American life. This volume completes a trilogy on American public life and my private life. *Brown* returns me to years I have earlier described. I believe it is possible to describe a single life thrice, if from three isolations: *Class. Ethnicity. Race.*

When I began this book, I knew some readers would take "race" for a tragic noun, a synonym for conflict and isolation. Race is not such a terrible word for me. Maybe because I am skeptical by nature. Maybe because my nature is already mixed. The word race encourages me to remember the influence of eroticism on history. For that is what race memorializes. Within any discussion of race, there lurks the possibility of romance.

2002

---

# ALMA LUZ VILLANUEVA
## b. 1944

Alma Luz Villanueva was born in Lompoc, California, and raised in San Francisco's Mission District by her grandmother with the assistance of Villanueva's mother and aunt. She never knew her father. Villanueva dropped out of tenth grade to have her first child and had a second child at 17. She was married to a violent man and lived on welfare in public housing. "That period of my life was an early drama," Villanueva stated later, "quite a challenge to survive." She began writing before the age of 13, but interrupted her work to raise her children and cope with the immediate needs. She did not return to her poems until the 1970s. Villanueva completed her postsecondary education at City College of San Francisco and Norwich University, in Vermont, and earned her master of fine arts degree from Vermont College in 1984. She has held writer-in-residence positions at various colleges and universities in California: Cabrillo College, in Aptos; the University of California, Irvine;

Stanford University; San Francisco State College; and the University of California, Santa Cruz.

Her early work, especially the collection *La Chingada* (Screwed-Up Woman, 1985), is concerned with poverty and the mistreatment of women. The poems in *La Chingada* focus on the Chicano male hierarchy and the female quest to find a voice. The feminist novel *Ultraviolet Sky* (1988), arguably Villanueva's most popular work, is about a woman who struggles with and against her husband, son, and female best friend to make changes in her life. The novel *Naked Ladies* (1994) is set in the San Francisco Bay area and focuses on the female protagonist's quest for fulfillment in relationships with her husband and three female friends.

Villanueva's short fiction in *Weeping Woman: La Llorona and Other Stories* (1994) deals with controversial issues in the Chicano community and painful issues in women's lives, such as drug abuse, rape, incest, prostitution, and murder. The poems in *Desire* (1998), intertwining the personal and the political, offer a vision of reconciliation among people of different ethnic backgrounds. Written in the form of a diary, *Luna's California Poppies* (2002) has a protagonist that serves as the author's alter ego: Her name is Luna Luz Villalobos, and she uses literature both as a therapeutic device to face her personal challenges and as a more universal channel of expression. The poetry collection *Vida* (2002) returns to Villanueva's interest in pre-Columbian civilization to further explore her feminist themes. Despite Villanueva's reputation and traditional style, literary historians have paid scant attention to her work, but she has won the University of California, Irvine's Third Chicano Literary Prize (1977); the American Book Award (1989); and the Latino Literature Prize (1994). She lives in San Miguel de Allende, Mexico, and teaches in the Master of Fine Arts in Creative Writing Program at Antioch University, Los Angeles.

The four Villanueva selections in this anthology display the breadth of her poetry. "Bitch bitch bitch bitch" seeks empowerment by injecting new political meaning into a demeaning word. "Delicious Death," in the form of a letter, passes along a vision to the poet's son. "Warrior in the Sand," a spiritual call to action, equates the poet's life quest with her environment. And "Even the Eagles Must Gather" meditates on the tension between opposites, concluding "to love the enemy is to love the self."


bitch                                    bitch
                    bitch
                                                            bitch

    I kind of like the sound
    of bitch—   such a word.
    seems to leap right
    off the tongue:
       reminds me of a woman looking        5
         directly at a man
           (and he doesn't like it)
       of a woman fighting with her kids
         (but they need it)
       of a woman needing something real    10
        and swearing at the world
           (and the world doesn't have it)

reminds me of when I have to
reach right down
inside me, right into                                     15
the fleshy hurt and let it
come inching out—then bursting out
by way of laugh/cry, and cry
being the best of all because then
the ocean that lives within                               20
me shatters the seawall
of my reason
and washes over my sandyface and
I catch them on my tongue
and replenish the salt that evaporates                    25
between tidal waves;
and maybe when I'm
reaching down to
fathoms of this sea
I never dreamed existed,                                  30
and the pull of the moon is
stronger than usual,
　　　maybe I look like a bitch, probably
because that's what
I am.                                                     35

1985

## Delicious Death

*To my son, Marc Jason*

Memory: You were fifteen in the mountains,
your friends were going hunting,
you wanted to go.

Cold, autumn day-sky of steel
and rifles, the shades of bullets. We                      5
fought. I didn't want to let you go.

And you stood up to me, "My friends are
going, their parents let them hunt; like
am I some kind of wimp or what, Mom . . ."

We walked into Thrifty's to buy the bullets,              10
you would use one of their rifles—I imagined
you being shot or shooting another eager boy/man

"What you kill you eat, do you understand?"
I stared each word into your eyes. As you
walked away, I said to the Spirits, "Guard                15

this human who goes
in search of
lives."

           •  •  •

You brought home four small quail.
I took them, saying, "Dinner." I stuffed              20
them with rice, apples, baked them in garlic,

onions, wine. "Tonight, Mom?" "Yes, tonight."
I plucked the softest tail feathers and as you
showered, I placed them in your pillowcase:

"May the hunter and                           25
the prey be
one.

May the hunter truly
be a human
being.                                       30

May the hunter eat
and be eaten in
time.

May the boy always
be alive in the                              35
man."

           •  •  •

We ate, mostly, in silence—
I felt you thinking, I just
killed this, what I'm chewing . . .

On the highest peaks the first          40
powder shines like the moon—
winter comes so quickly.

On your face soft blond hair (yes, this
son is a gringo) shines like manhood—
childhood leaves so quickly.          45

The wonder of the hunt is on my tongue,
I taste it—wild, tangy, reluctant—
this flesh feeds me well.

I light the candles and thank the quail
in a clear voice—I thank them for their          50
small bodies, their immense, winged souls.

"God, Mom, you're making me feel like a
killer." "Well, you are and so am I."
Swallowing, swallowing this delicious death.

1988

## Warrior in the Sand

I want to be a black belt in
Kung Fu at fifty—

I want to fall in love at fifty,
sixty, seventy, eighty—

I want to wear my bikini (or be                         5
naked) until I die—

I want to dance and sweat at
my pre-death party,

and get drunk on champagne
with my exuberant guests—                               10

and when I've achieved transformation,
I want no crying.

I want laughter. I want someone
to recite my poetry in a loud,
clear voice. I want babies and                          15
children to be in the room, and

I want the poems to mean nothing
to them. I want to peek through
their eyes once before my long,
dangerous journey home. Home                            20

to the spiral that burns with
its terrible, pulsing love.
And let the children laugh with
that recognition before they forget.

It's so easy to forget—                                 25
making love, cooking food,
finding shelter, giving birth,
fighting pain, seeking joy.

Will my own children be there—
grandparents by that time—                              30

will I look through my
great-great-grandchildren's

eyes—who knows. I've
insisted they take their freedom
so that I may have mine. Freedom                    35
demands nothing, and love

gives everything. I have
wandered between these
extremes—mountain to ocean,
silence to shout, poet to                           40

woman, counting the stones,
the shells, the feathers in
my pockets, fingering my solitude
as a child runs ahead, singing.

At the edge of the tide, in the                     45
twilight, is a human figure
with arms and legs, a body, a
head, with no particular gender—

a woman/man. Spirals edge its
body, and a spiral is drawn down                    50
the center, where the throat, heart,
lungs, and genitals should be.

Feathers grow from its head.
I laugh with recognition and,
kneeling, plant mine. I place                       55
a perfect, white shell in its

dream-eye. Now I see I was
saving everything for the warrior
in the sand, who will be washed
away by morning.                                    60

1990


## Even the Eagles Must Gather

I lay with an acupuncture needle
at the top of my head
and the Berlin Wall[1] goes down—

---

1. The multifaceted barrier, erected in 1961 by the Communist government of East Germany, that completely cut off East Berlin from the non-Communist part, West Berlin. Until its destruction in 1989, the Wall thus symbolized the Cold War (post–World War II) division of Europe.

I lay with an acupuncture needle
in my left hand pulse                                         5
and Prague[2] is free—

I lay with an acupuncture needle
in my right hand pulse
and Mandela[3] walks into sunlight—

I lay with an acupuncture needle                             10
in my left foot pulse
and Russia yearns for commercialism—

I lay with an acupuncture needle
in my right foot pulse
and Chile leans toward democracy—                           15

I send my best energy through my body
in spite of the usual human obstacles—
my spirit is too pure for me, as my body
struggles toward its light-streaked path—

but then, my spirit is all I truly trust                     20
and so I entice it back, I say, "Fill me
up with your pure potential—freedom before
death is what I want, the circle—"

It's afternoon, after a storm, wind
that clears dead branches from trees—                        25
the sun sets—the world seeks its freedom
in its own slow way—we kill the enemy,

make love to the enemy, again and again—
it's the way of transcendence. I look out
the window and despise the cars, the circling                30
traffic and realize, peace in my body;

Even the eagles must gather (to love
the spirit is to love the body—to love
the earth is to love the world—to love
the enemy is to love the self).                              35

1992

2. Since 1993, the capital of the non-Communist Czech Republic; for decades preceding that, the capital of Czechoslovakia, which was controlled by the Soviet Union. In 1989, the nonviolent Velvet Revolution led to social and political reforms similar to the ones then occurring in Berlin.

3. Nelson Mandela (b. 1918), South African political leader; after being imprisoned for 27 years as a result of his anti-apartheid activism, he was released in 1990 and served as president of the country from 1994 to 1999.

# LUCHA CORPI
## b. 1945

Lucha Corpi was born in Jáltipan, a small town in the state of Veracruz, Mexico. She moved to the city of San Luis Potosí with her immediate family, which still resides there. In San Luis Potosí, she married Guillermo Hernández, who later became a professor at the University of California, Los Angeles. As a young couple, they relocated to the San Francisco Bay area, where Corpi earned bachelor's and master's degrees in comparative literature at the University of California, Berkeley. Her divorce from Hernández and her duties as the mother of a young child curtailed her studies. In 1977, she began working as an English-as-a-Second-Language teacher in the Oakland Unified School District. Corpi worked as an ESL teacher until her retirement in 2006. She lives in Oakland with her second husband, Carlos M. Gonzales.

Corpi has distinguished herself in poetry, the short story, the novel, and children's literature. Her poetry collections, written in Spanish and translated into English by Catherine Rodríguez-Nieto, are *Palabras de mediodía/Noon Words* (1980) and *Variaciones sobre una tempestad/Variations on a Storm* (1990). Through abundant metaphors and similes, the lyrics in these books demonstrate a rich sensuality. They also address feminist concerns and the miserable working conditions of unskilled laborers in industrialized countries. The four Corpi poems in this anthology are from *Variaciones sobre una tempestad*: "Winter Song" is a bucolic meditation on the passage of time. "Day's Work" establishes a counterpoint between nature and death. "Undocumented Anguish" imagines the disquiet of a worker thrown into an environment that may rightfully be his but where he remains an alien. And "Sonata in Two Voices" reflects the marginalization of the self in a society driven by consumerism.

Corpi's first novel, *Delia's Song* (1989), is a semiautobiographical bildungsroman. Set in the 1960s at the University of California, Berkeley, this coming-of-age narrative describes the Chicano Student Movement, confrontations over free speech, and other political episodes. Three years later, Corpi published *Eulogy for a Brown Angel*, the first detective novel by a Chicana. In it, the private investigator Gloria Damasco looks into the mysterious murder of a child in the Los Angeles area in 1970 during a Chicano political demonstration. Corpi develops the character further—and further exhibits her commitment to social issues—in the novels *Cactus Blood* (1995), *Black Widow's Wardrobe* (1999), *Crimson Moon* (2004), and *Death at Solstice* (2009).

## Winter Song

*To Magdalena Mora*
*(1952–1981)*

In the opening
and shutting of an eye
full
of magic
clocks                                                          5
and old dreams
winter comes:

The wind murmurs melancholy
as the all's well of the night watchman

who looked after my parents' house 10
—I go back every winter
lest I forget who I am
or where I come from.

The rain comes down singing
toward its destiny of mineral and seed. 15
Between the hollow of an opening wing
and the lowering of eyelids in repose
we learn to love in instants and surrenders
and between the intimate question posed by night
and the darksweet reply given by dawn 20
we engender in pain a new life.

Nothing is fixed or perpetual
not rain
or seed
or you 25
or I
or our grief
in this world that is bleeding
because we're forever cutting paths
opening our way along unfamiliar roads 30
conquering the fury of oblivion verse by verse.

1985–89                                                    1990

# Day's Work

## 1.

Death is reincarnated in every flower
one city rises on top of another
and in an ordinary street
in the town square
in a gateway 5
or among flowers and birds
at the edge of the marketplace
two old men look through the garbage
for their daily bread,
a child roams in search of tenderness, 10
a dark-skinned mother
widowed early of her love
waits in a silent queue
at the factory door.

In an ordinary city 15
of the old world or of the new
two pairs of dark eyes
share one history.

2.

There are nights when the rose hides its thorns
and light goes to find its cause at voice's edge.                    20
These are nights of murmuring, of anxieties repressed,
and though the head on the pillow has forgotten
that tonight the doves flew
buffeted by the wind
and the lilies on the altar fell                                     25
riddled with fear,
the spirit toils alone,
even under hardship conditions,
twenty-four hours a day: Our exhausted heart
and weathered kidneys can be transplanted                           30
but our spirit we have always with us
and the tolling bell reminds us at each stroke
that in matters of conscience there are no teachers
and we cannot digest our bread
in someone else's stomach.                                          35


3.

Death is reincarnated in every flower . . .

On an ordinary street,
on an ordinary day
time is shot over the sea,
the missile hits the target                                         40
with mathematical precision
and the guerrilla fighter falls,
his vision dissolving
slowly
on the indifferent cement.                                          45

The morning does not restrain
its desire for the day
that's true
but something in us flutters,
plasma floods                                                       50
into the arteries of the soul,
a new voice takes up residence
in our own
and we realize that we can no longer
like a snake                                                        55
in the humid heat of August
slough off the fighter's skin
for it has become our own.

1985–89                                                            1990

## Undocumented Anguish

Insatiable harpies
    the skyscrapers
    devour the stars
    eating their fill of the moon
    caging the wind                  5
    which in turn wreaks vengeance
    on flowers and umbrellas
    appeased only
    when its great, transparent tongue
    savors again                 10
    the smooth skin of the water.

The fog rolls in then
    full of countless wandering
    hands and birds,
    flowing among the trodden leaves     15
    muting groans and the crack of whips,
    quieting the undocumented anguish
    of the man living illegally in his own land,
    plunging its fingers into the moon
    and into the distance without harbors,     20
    without beacons.

1985–89                                                     1990

## Sonata in Two Voices

*To Mark Greenside*

### 1. Largo frenetico

It's hard to realize I'm alive
in the improbable rush
of these days.

Weeks accumulate in droves
    Sundays full of numbers     5
    chimerical Thursdays
    when time
    betrays itself
    and returns to zero hour.

So many fronts to fight on:     10
    messages at the door
    meetings
    dates
    names submerged

in a sea of sweat                                            15
shopping lists
soup
fresh lima beans
and dirty clothes

Schemes to straighten out                                    20
shirts to mend
absences to unravel
bureaucratic bugs to neutralize
before we can recover the dreams
we left in the pawnshop                                      25
when our budget got tighter
and a friend left without a word,
when the time came to plant hyacinths
on the graves of our dead.

### 2. *Adagio*

A silence is embedded in my throat                           30
a clot of voice stubbornly blocking
any desire to sing.

My eyes drink the dusk
in slow green draughts
and words linger between my lips                              35
like the fading scent of dead jasmine.

In the street
someone is whistling a quiet tune
stopping to gather the last clover
of the season                                                40
for a little daughter at home
who still likes
these small wonders
and shares the centipede's dream
of roaming the world on frantic feet                         45
one day.

In the patio
amid a thousand bullets of rain
and violent wind
the lemon tree has bloomed and borne fruit.                  50

In the distance
a train rumbles southward
the fog moving with it at full gallop.

Stupefied
the city gazes at its profile                                55
in the faithless mirror of the water
while

in El Salvador children die quickly
and in Africa the blood dries slowly
and there is no word that can avert                    60
the long, shadowed kiss of death
if no friendly hand reaches out
if the heart remains a stranger
because
when all is said and done                             65
only love will save us.

1985–89                                              1990

---

# OCTAVIO ARMAND
## b. 1946

Octavio Armand was born in Guantánamo, Cuba, and has been exiled twice from his native country: in 1958, when his family fled the dictatorship of Fulgencio Batista; and in 1960, when his family fled the dictatorship of Fidel Castro. Like his fellow exile José Kozer, Armand writes primarily in Spanish and has turned the language into a second homeland. His poetry and prose are characterized by delight in the contours of words, combined with an intellectual grappling with issues such as exile, identity, and perception.

Having settled in the United States, Armand earned a doctorate from Rutgers University (1975), in New Jersey, and has taught at Bennington College, in Vermont, and at universities. In 1978, he founded the Spanish-language journal *Escandalar*, which he edited until 1984. His poetry collections include *Horizonte no es siempre lejanía* (Horizon Is Not Always Distance, 1970), *Cosas pasan* (Things Happen, 1975), *Origami* (1987), *El pez volador* (The Flying Fish, 1997), and *Son de ausencia* (Song of Absence, 1999). He has also published the essay collections *Piel menos mía* (Skin Hardly Mine, 1976), *Superficies* (Surfaces, 1980), *Hacer la tradición* (To Make a Tradition, 1984), and *El aliento del dragon* (The Breath of the Dragon, 2005). His translations into Spanish of twenty poems by the American poet Mark Strand were published in Venezuela as *Mark Strand: Veinte poemas* (1979). Carol Maier has translated into English some of Armand's work: his poetry in *With Dusk* (1984), from which this anthology's selections "Braille for Left Hand" and "Poem with Dusk" have been taken, and his essays in *Refractions* (1994), the source of the selection "Poetry as *Eruv*."

Armand's poetry and prose demonstrate a playfully eccentric use of language. In the essay "Poetry as *Eruv*"—first presented at the Festival of New Latin American Poetry, in Durango, Colorado, in 1985, and subsequently published in Spanish and in translation—Armand discusses the importance of language to someone separated from his people and homeland. He offers poetry as a means of transcending this breach. For Armand, puns, allusions, fantasies, and wordplay construct and encircle the world of the exile's past, keeping its remnants while appropriating the new.

## Braille for Left Hand

*To Carol Maier*

### 1

The world does not close in your eyes; there
you are born, with the weight of one lip on another.
There everything fits, as in a room that grows emptier
and emptier.

You are not in your eyes. You are here,                          5
hinting at presence. Irresistible. As if
trapped in a statue.

Someone buries you, forgets you behind
awkwardness.

### 2

Yes, the shadow is astute. The statue                           10
knows a lot. But once again you touch walls,
faces; and the warmth of a cup creates
order.

### 3

Beside you, brewing words. Braising them.
Since you have not stayed on your eyelid. You are             15
here, in palms no gypsy will read.

Touch them. Tunnel between these
lines, mole; make your little space; read.

1984

## Poem with Dusk

Wind, just wind
in the elm's pliant bark.
The quiet question of the birds
—which are small, round—
is a seed, leaf among leaves.                                    5

There are few colors now: one, none.
Things lack size.
I look more, see less. My eyes are teeming.
The window, open, is out of place.
Caught in the night of a lung,                                  10
distance teems, is lacking.

Seeing is enough, or looking.
Wind is my erased body,
my scattered name,
my expanding breath.                                    15
Wind, just wind.

I look less, see more. My eyes are teeming.

1984

## Poetry as *Eruv*[1]

*Ruins are better for defense than intact buildings.*

—General Frido von Senger und Etterlin[2]

### 1

There is one dossier I will never forget. It belonged to a Latin American who
applied for a teaching position in a Venezuelan university. Among his professional qualifications he had included two that were totally, absolutely new to
me: Torture, Exile. Their presence seemed to offer my vision a physical challenge, daring me to join the blackness of a few letters and form those two
words on a predictable, boring page. My eyes slid on the letters and could not
connect with them, as if the words had been left there like the banana skin
that turns up in so many sitcoms. But this was not a case of carelessness; this
was a serious joke. The two words blazed like the colophon of a carefully
prepared document. I felt sad, amused, sick to my stomach.

For me, exile had always been a decentering experience. I looked desperately for an elusive center that perhaps had been hopelessly lost. As if they
were pieces of a puzzle, I joined bits of landscape, tastes, phrases, instants
that might permit a semblance of continuity. A possible history. I was determined to construct ruins, and I looked for everything, saw everything in the
rearview mirror that was Cuba. People who know me well know that those
efforts—those failures—were part of an increasing bitterness.

Exile isolated me not only from the island but from the isolated Cuba-in-
exile, and the cowardly aggression and pettiness I encountered increased my
solitude. There were, and there are, people who persecute those exiles who
do not fit easily into their particular image of the American diaspora. I have
a *curriculum* too, of course. Wasn't it Darío[3] who said that everyone among
the living has a *vita*? Mine, however, excluded me automatically, because it
indicated my date and place of birth. As a Cuban exile, the only discipline
available to me was bitterness. Others did not suffer what for many years
I have been calling a double exile. This is why some people underline the supposed condition of "tortured," "exiled" when they apply for jobs. But how can
a decentered being dare to approach the center so boldly? The torture victims

---

1. Mixture (Hebrew).
2. German general (1891–1963) during World
War II.
3. Rubén Darío (b. Félix Rubéen García Sarmiento,

1867–1916), Nicaraguan diplomat and poet who
initiated the late-nineteenth-century Latin American literary movement *Modernismo* (discussed in
the "Annexations" introduction, p. 168).

I have known do not usually talk about their tortures. Maybe they never learned how to capitalize on them? We are certainly living in pathetic times if to the profession of torturer we can add the no-less-terrible profession of tortured. Exile has also become a profession. After all, here I am, momentarily but absolutely centered, to repeat once again *et campos ubi Troja fuit, etiam periere ruinae, et in Arcadia ego!*[4] I will not do it. I am probably going to disappoint you, but today I want to speak of an appealing illusion: the adventures and advantages of exile. Exile as Arcadia.

## 2

When I speak of poetry as *eruv*, I realize that I am building castles in the air, for it would certainly be no easy task to undo the work of heavenly bodies and politicians with a poetics. Nevertheless, this must be tried. Poetry could be a cure for some of the ills that afflict our planet. And since we are talking about castles, even though they are in the air, I want to recall a curious therapy whose roots go back to the days when castles were built. This so-called cure was healing by sympathy, also known as magnetic transfer, transplanting, or translation. It was only applicable to movable diseases. Movable or transplantable. Some years ago I spoke to several groups of translators about the five types of cure by *translatio*, since I believed and I still believe, that language—being a movable disease—is susceptible to this treatment. Evidently exile is an even more *movable disease* than language. Consequently I feel obliged to list once more the various types of sympathetic therapies, all of which involve the transference or transportation of an illness from the affected body to another body: *inseminatio, implantatio, impositio, inoratio, inescatio.* According to this doctrine, it is believed that a patient will be cured if the body used as the object of transference falls ill or dies. On the other hand, if the body rejects the illness, there is no hope. For example, in the treatment by *inseminatio*, a seed is sown and watered with a liquid distilled from *magnes mumia*, the remains of a mummy; its growth determines whether or not a cure will be possible. Healing by *impositio* is no less dramatic: a piece of skin from the affected part of the body or some of the patient's excrement is inserted between the bark and the trunk of a tree and then covered with mud. In *inescatio*, a third type of healing by *traslatio*, *magnes mumia* is fed to an animal. A variation of *inescatio* is of particular interest with respect to the theme of exile, of transposition: nail clippings from the patient are tied to a crab that is then thrown to the current. In this case, there is a literal effort to distance the illness. Perhaps we exiles are crustaceans thrown to the current by the millions in order to cure or remove the ailments of our peoples. If this is true, the sacrifice may well be worthwhile.

---

4. And the fields where Troy once was, its very ruins are gone, and I too once lived in Arcadia (Latin). By "once again," Armand means that the longing of exile for the lost homeland often leads to repeated lamentations of mourning and of nostalgia, not that he is repeating a phrase spoken earlier.

3

To read Valle-Inclán's *esperpentos* and Joyce's[5] English after he put so much English on it is to consider the possibility of a tribal revenge: the use of intense caricature, a billiard prose to counter the linguistic models imposed by the metropolis. Grimaces, deformations, defects as effects produced by a rigorous sequence of disrespectful caroms all throw language out of whack, provoking an eccentricity that can sneak Galician into Castilian and Gaelic into English. Exiles are very sensitive to this kind of eccentricity. The distance and time that gradually separate them from their landscapes and their people threaten to ruin their languages, rip their last ties away from them. Language is seen, felt, and traversed as territory. Excess and word play are methods for keeping it alive. The fascination awakened by the mechanisms and mysteries of a language reveal a fear of losing it. Exiles turn into Champollions[6] not to interpret hieroglyphics but to create them. Every day they risk burying or disinterring their own tongues. Finally, there comes a moment when they themselves do not know if they are speaking a dead tongue, since exile is a shadowy zone where languages can die, become petrified, pulverized. Exiles fight, play with their languages to keep them from turning into Latin in the hands—and handling—of power. This gives them the advantage of knowing danger in the flesh, of feeling the immediacy of its painful reality. People who have not experienced such an apprenticeship live in a hypnotic state: ideological and commercial propagandas are the poetics of pawnbrokers and jailers. In truth there is no longer a free world.

4

Recently, we have seen literature, language itself as a living image of human experience, become a clandestine activity. Through the erasures of censorship and self-censorship, which are very routine phenomena for a large part of humanity, we are made aware that what gets expressed barely hints at expression itself, and that expression, which is at times hidden, oblique, latent, is based on simulation, on silence, and on an emphasis dismantled and dissolved by discreet irony. The abyss between what we say we mean and what we mean to say, between the meaning of a particular expression and the meaning it expresses, has perhaps never been greater. That abyss reveals one of the state's most radical encroachments, perpetuated on behalf of a new man who has already been duly mummified. As an added insult, the same state that strips words imposes abundant and monstrous catchwords. You must learn to silence what you feel and you must also learn to proclaim what you do not feel.

Exiles enjoy a freedom inconceivable in the landscapes they left behind. They are trapped like the rest of their compatriots, but they are outside the cage and can therefore take notes for an unofficial, heterodox history. This is one of the decided advantages of exile. People in exile are living documents, their very language is a document. Thus the obsession, which grips

5. James Joyce (1882–1941), Irish writer who lived in various European countries. *Valle-Inclán*: Ramón María del Valle-Inclán y de la Peña (1866–1936), Spanish dramatist and novelist whose *esperpentos* (literally, frights or absurdities) satirized the classical heroes of Spanish history and literature.

6. Versions of Jean-François Champollion (1790–1832), French classical scholar and decipherer of Egyptian hieroglyphs.

some as if they were notaries, with fixing an image, a moment. Certain aspects of things Cuban, even of Cuban speech, have been frozen in Miami, Paris, London, New York: as living fossils, they may survive mutations, mutilations, and many deaths. In this sense the literature of exile has the ghostly, poignant presence of a daguerreotype. Remember, for example, how Spain has been remembered in the Sephardic tradition, which is still alive. Archaic, conservative like the earth, like language and motherhood, the tradition of the diaspora recovers what history and time itself erase, forget. In 1981 a collection of ballads by Spanish Jews living in New York was published in the United States. Recited in New York and published in Los Angeles, these ballads carry us back from both coasts of English America to the Spain of the Catholic Kings. When we hear or read them, we are in 1492 and Spain is descending on America.[7] Perhaps those of us now in exile were then conquistadors, *encomenderos*,[8] and slaves. Or Jews. History repeats itself.

We no longer enjoy an easy homeland. The millions of Latin Americans in exile are the Sephardics of Spanish America. I recognize the exaggeration: it is hard to compare an experience of years or decades with one of centuries. Nevertheless, I feel as though we were living in 1492, a year of discovery and expulsion. The discovery of America proved that Earth was not a dish. But we twentieth-century Americans have insisted on refuting geography with history, which is certainly not round. We are falling from our landscapes into the abyss of exile. At least for us the Earth is a dish. Which is why some of us are gathered here in Colorado, an English-speaking land with a Spanish name. A new language, a new world.

We have repeatedly emphasized the tragedy of expulsion, but we have not dared to throw ourselves into the adventure of discovery, because we are so weighed down by an intense, painful fidelity to the past. In a radical way, however, exile forces us to espouse a difficult but rich and unexpected new humanism. When we encounter new languages, we have no choice but to discover new worlds. A chain of changes and transpositions, the deepest meaning of *uprooting*, recalls translation and its original sense of transfer or removal. For us, the word *translation* still has that flavor, which is why some of us are bilingual, why most of us are a bit schizophrenic. Whether we like it or not, expulsion has made us cosmopolitan in the stoic sense of the word, that is, in the best sense. We can testify to the fragility of borders between peoples and nations; we can testify to the traitorous expiration of documents and papers, those friends of fire; we must submit to laws that are infinitely more human, since at times we are undocumented and we are always outcasts; we know that language itself, the only territory we have left, permits no complacency, that language has meaning only if we are willing to grant it meaning, if necessary placing it again and again on the stone of Sisyphus.[9] After it falls a thousand times, maybe everyone will be able to glimpse the stereotype of the absurd in the lapidary cooing of dogmas.

---

7. I.e., through the first voyage of Christopher Columbus (1451–1506), Spanish admiral from Genoa.
8. Literally, commissioners; historically, Spanish colonists in charge of Indian laborers.

9. In Greek mythology, King Sisyphus was punished after death by being forced, over and over for eternity, to roll a huge stone up a hill and then watch it roll back down.

5

Exile is not only alienation. It can also be a cosmopolitanism, albeit an involuntary and painful one. The experience of transposition, which is deeply related to translation, implies the possible convergence of two unpaired spheres, that of the exile and that of the host. People in exile are never completely dispossessed; like snails, they always carry along their homes: the languages, customs, traditions of their countries. They transpose and translate: they live between two shores. Their homes and landscapes live within them, although they are no longer places of physical dwelling. Seen in this way, exile becomes a staggering enlargement of a landscape's four walls. When people are uprooted, those walls become windows. The exile's very existence represents an endless challenge to immensity and formlessness. A permanent construction and reconstruction of what has been lost, and at the same time a cautious, laborious appropriation of what is discovered, in other words, what is different. Because of the very circumstances of this uprooting, the pressing need to overcome or sublimate helplessness, the poetry of exile could take on, and perhaps fully carry out, a task that Heidegger set for poetry in his essay about Hölderlin:[1] the creation of poetic dwelling.

Heidegger bases his thoughts on the expression *dichtersich wohnet der Mensch*: man dwells poetically. I suggest a different one: *eruv*. In the Mishnah there is a list of the thirty-nine principal types of chores affected by ritual restrictions that absolutely forbid any kind of work on the Sabbath. For example, tying a knot, untying a knot, twisting two threads, separating two threads, sewing two stitches, making a tear so as to sew two stitches, lighting a fire, putting out a fire, writing two letters, erasing in order to write two letters. Another restriction that is perhaps no less surprising to Gentiles forbids the transportation or conveyance of things from one sphere to another, in other words from the private sphere to the public sphere or vice versa. Among Orthodox Jews there is a legal fiction—denoted by the word *eruv*—that permits the conveyance of certain things—a house key, for example—without breaking the laws of the Sabbath. On Saturdays, Orthodox Jews designate an area of their neighborhood as a private sphere by encircling it with a piece of wire. An *eruv* is this wire rampart that enlarges the house and suspends the Sabbath restriction by converting the house into a walled city, into Jerusalem. When I return to Cuba, that is if I return to Cuba, I will ask Christo[2] to surround the entire island with an *eruv*. I want him to wrap it like a present so that it finally belongs to everyone. In the meantime, the poetry of exile could serve as a rampart. Wire, architecture, dwelling, walled city: Jeruvsalem. Perhaps we can make a sphere of translation itself. At least we can try.

1994

---

1. Johann Christian Friedrich Hölderlin (1770–1843), German poet. *Heidegger*: Martin Heidegger (1889–1976), German philosopher.
2. Bulgarian-born artist (Christo Vladimirov Javacheff, b. 1935); with his wife, the Moroccan-born French artist Jeanne-Claude (Jeanne-Claude Denat de Guillebon, 1935–2009), he has created environmental works, such as by wrapping with polypropylene and fabric the Reichstag, in Berlin, and the Pont-Neuf bridge, in Paris.

# RENÉ ALOMÁ
## 1947–1986

A native of Cuba, René Alomá settled in Canada in 1962. At Wayne State University, in Detroit, Michigan, he trained as a theater apprentice at the Bonstelle Theatre and, in 1969, earned his bachelor's degree. He then toured the Midwest as actor/director of the Migrant Theatre Force. He began the master's program in modern languages at the University of Windsor, Canada, but left in 1970 for England, where he studied theater design while teaching at the London City Literary Institute. In England, he toured with the Argyle Theatre Company as road manager. In 1971, Alomá returned to Canada and completed his master's at the University of Windsor, while freelancing as a costume designer. During the early 1970s, Alomá taught at De La Salle College, in Toronto, and directed a number of popular musical plays. His play *Once a Family* was produced in Toronto at the Tarragon Theatre, where he was playwright-in-residence in 1974–75. It was produced again in 1977 by the Memphis Repertory Company, under the direction of the Scottish novelist Muriel Spark. He continued to direct stage productions in Canada and in various university and "little" theaters in the United States while studying directing and acting in New York.

In 1979, his play *The Exile* received the Smile Company Playwriting Award (Southampton University); retitled *A Little Something to Ease the Pain*, the play was produced in 1980 by Toronto Arts Productions at the St. Lawrence Centre for the Arts. Alomá's radio adaptation of the play was produced in 1981 by the Canadian Broadcasting Company. While directing other plays in Canada, Alomá joined the Playwright's Workshop at INTAR (International Arts Relations), a Latino theater group in New York. At INTAR, he wrote and directed *A Flight of Angels* (1983) and the one-act *Mountain Road* (1984). Alomá continued to direct and produce plays in Canadian theater while writing his play *Secretos de Amor* (Secrets of Love). In collaboration with his wife, the Canadian actress Zoey Adams, he also wrote several musical plays for children, which have become popular favorites in the United States and Canada. In 1986, during the last weeks of his life, Alomá completed the definitive versions of *A Little Something to Ease the Pain* and *Secretos de Amor*. After his death, English and Spanish productions of *A Little Something to Ease the Pain/Alguna cosita que alivie el sufrir* were staged by the New York Puerto Rican Traveling Theater and two companies in Florida: Teatro Avante, in Miami, and the Coral Gables Theater. Loosely based on the author's life, *A Little Something*, included here in its entirety, traces the voyages of exile and return in the lives and relationships of two cousins, one a revolutionary in Cuba and the other an exiled playwright who returns to his homeland after a 17-year absence.

---

## A LITTLE SOMETHING TO EASE THE PAIN

### *Characters*

CARLOS RABEL (PAYE), a visiting exile
NELSON RABEL (TATÍN)
DONA CACHA (ABUELA), their grandmother
DILIA (TÍA), their aunt

CLARA (TÍA), their grand-aunt
ANA, Tatín's wife
AMELIA, a student
JULIO RABEL, a cousin
FR. EPHRAIM*
PACO*

*The roles of FR. EPHRAIM and PACO can be played by the actors who play TATÍN and JULIO.

## Place

The action takes place in and around the Rabels' house in Santiago de Cuba during one week in July, 1979

*Spanish Words*:
Abuela, Abue: Grandmother
Tía: Aunt
Natilla: a custard dessert
Ay: all-purpose exclamation
Mar Verde: Green Sea, the name of a beach
Dulce Coco: coconut sweet
Mantilla: lace shawl
Compañera: Comrade
Doña: Madam, title of respect to elderly matrons
Señor: Mister, sir
Tío: Uncle

## Prologue

> *Stage in complete darkness. At the stage right hand corner we see a light that looks like the light that would be cast by a round stained glass window of an old church in the noonday sun. In the shadow there is a wooden chair in which FR. EPHRAIM sits wearing a white cassock. We should not see him clearly, but we should realize that he is an old man and he seems to be asleep. PAYE enters and puts down a suitcase and shoulder-strap tape recorder. He looks at the darkness, steps into the light. He sees the old priest, but is afraid to wake him, so he waits.*

EPHRAIM: [*Clearing his throat as he speaks.*]   What is it?
PAYE:   [*Startled.*] What?
EPHRAIM:   What can I do for you?
PAYE:   I'm looking for the priest.
EPHRAIM:   You have found him.
PAYE:   Father Ephraim?
EPHRAIM:   Yes?
PAYE:   It's Carlos. Carlos Rabel. The one they called Paye. Carmela Santos and I were the ones who printed those fliers against the banning of sermons . . . ?

EPHRAIM: My sister Carmela wanted to marry a colored man, but mother would not allow it. Later when Mama was blind she married him. Darkness is a great equalizer. [*Pause.*]

PAYE: I used to be an altar boy.

EPHRAIM: [*Remembering suddenly.*] Once you were trying to light the top candles last and you set your sleeves on fire . . . !

PAYE: [*Delighted by the recognition.*] Yes, that was me!

EPHRAIM: I'm sorry. I fell asleep on my meditation.

PAYE: I thought the church was empty.

EPHRAIM: I was dreaming of dust. Everyone was dust and the wind was blowing us away. I was supposed to be meditating on the five glorious mysteries. [*Sighs.*] I fell asleep.

PAYE: Maybe I could come back another . . .

EPHRAIM: You're back?

PAYE: For a visit.

EPHRAIM: Ah!

PAYE: I live in Toronto. Canada.

EPHRAIM: Canada! [PAYE *nods.*] The church hasn't changed any, has it?!

PAYE: It's too dark, Father. I can't really see.

EPHRAIM: It hasn't changed. La Placita has changed. It's changed a lot since you left.

PAYE: Yes, and the new monument is . . .

EPHRAIM: I say Mass on that monument every thirtieth of November in memory of your uncle. It's the most attended Mass . . . next to Palm Sunday.[1]

PAYE: Palm Sunday is still a favorite?

EPHRAIM: Everyone wants palms to hang behind their door. It's more of a superstition than a holy rite, but it's nice to have church full.

PAYE: Not many people come to church anymore?

EPHRAIM: Not many people come to church ever. It's the perpetual malady of Catholicism in Latin America; devotion without participation. [*Off on a tangent.*] When the Cardinal was here from Spain we had the altar covered in jasmines. The smell of jasmines goes well with mantillas and incense. I can't stand up anymore, you know. My knees are too weak to hold me up.

PAYE: There's no priest to assist you?

EPHRAIM: I was praying you'd have a vocation, no? What do you do?

PAYE: I'm a playwright, but . . ,

EPHRAIM: A playwright. Pity. I thought you might have had a calling.

PAYE: To the priesthood?

EPHRAIM: You might have been a Cardinal. Are you famous?

PAYE: No. Not at all. Not yet.

EPHRAIM: Carlos . . . Carlos Rabel. A Cuban writing plays in Canada. [*Laughs.*] Canada, right?

PAYE: Yes, Father.

EPHRAIM: Tell me, Paye, have you written a play about us?

PAYE: No. I . . . I haven't.

---

1. A Christian holiday that commemorates Jesus Christ's entry into Jerusalem, an event represented by palm branches.

EPHRAIM:   You should. You should write a play about an old priest who's resigned to the fact that his church will be dark and dusty forever. I would like to be in your play. [*Quotes.*] "The whole world is a stage and the people are the players." Shakespeare, the bard of Avon.[2] [*Coughs.*] Is your mother still as beautiful?

PAYE:   Yes.

EPHRAIM:   Raphael is a good painter. You like Raphael?[3]

PAYE:   Yes.

EPHRAIM:   Your mother was a convert, you know. [*Silence.* PAYE *comes close to the priest and looks closely into his eyes.* EPHRAIM *does not see him.*]

PAYE:   Father?

EPHRAIM:   Yes.

PAYE:   Do they still censor your sermons?

EPHRAIM: [*As if not hearing.*]   Tell me Paye, when you become famous, will you be a famous foreign playwright or a famous Cuban in exile?

PAYE:   I don't know.

EPHRAIM: [*Slowly.*]   You must resign yourself to being either foreign or at best a Cuban "*in exile.*" It is a title you will have to bear just as I wear my robes.

PACO: [*Entering.*]   Father! Who's there? [*He stays out of the light.*]

EPHRAIM:   Ah, Paco. I have a visitor. From Canada. Carlos Rabel. Paco Gómez. [PACO *and* PAYE *shake hands.*]

PACO:   Julio's cousin?

PAYE:   Yes.

EPHRAIM:   Paco is the caretaker cum sacristan. But he thinks he is my guardian angel.

PACO:   It's dark in here.

EPHRAIM:   My friend will understand. You see, Carlos, my eyes have become sensitive to the light.

PACO:   The truth is he prefers the darkness.

EPHRAIM:   Darkness is a great equalizer.

PACO:   You must excuse Father Ephraim, but he must take his siesta now.

PAYE:   Yes, I . . . [PACO *picks up the priest in his arms.*]

EPHRAIM:   Tell your mother that I still remember her as one of Raphael's madonnas.

PACO:   Pleased to meet you, Rabel.

EPHRAIM:   And put me in one of your plays. I would like that. [PACO *begins to exit with* EPHRAIM.]

PAYE:   Yes, I will.

EPHRAIM:   Thank you for coming to see me. God bless you, Carlos.

PAYE:   Yes, Father, goodbye. [*Looks around at the dimly lit stage, genuflects and exits.*]

---

2. In Shakespeare's comedy *As You Like It*, but the lines are "All the world's a stage, / And all the men and women merely players" (lines 138–39).

3. Italian painter (Raffaelo Sanzio, 1483–1520).

# Act I

*From the black after* PAYE *has exited, the stage lights come up to reveal some pillars and railings to indicate a verandah, and four large archways through which we see a kitchen,* AMELIA's *bedroom,* CACHA's *bedroom and the rest of the house beyond. The stage floor should be painted so that these rooms seem to be around a small square patio. There are steps leading from the corner stage right onto the verandah. There we see a suggestion of a door which leads into the house.* PAYE *comes up the steps, feeling the heat, carrying the suitcase and shoulder-strap tape recorder. He looks through the open door, but does not go in. Instead he comes around to the corner of the verandah which will be down stage center. He looks to the left, to the rest of the verandah which stretches to the stage left corner. The walls between the verandah and house through which we see the patio and the rooms surrounding it are non-existent, but must be respected as walls and therefore there is another entrance at the stage left side of the verandah, which can be indicated by a hanging piece of tiled roof.* PAYE *looks at the house and speaks directly to the audience from the corner of the verandah center stage.*

PAYE: [*Addressing the audience.*]  My grandparents' house is a big square house which they rented until the Revolutionary Government passed a law giving the deed to the property to tenants who had paid rent for a period longer than twenty years. It is an old house, a Spanish colonial house, one of the oldest in the city of Santiago de Cuba. I was born in this house and I spent my childhood riding a tricycle on this verandah with assorted cousins—all boys! My grandparents' house has seen weddings and wakes, nine children, twenty-six grandchildren, fires, earthquakes, hurricanes, revolutions, departures and reunions. Now behind the door there is a little plaque stating the ownership of the occupants with the headline "Thank You, Fidel." [*He picks up the suitcase and enters the house through the stage right door.*]

PAYE:  Abue! Good morning! Abuela! [PAYE *moves into the patio. There are clothes on the line. A towel has fallen. He picks it up and is about to hang it when* AMELIA *enters. Alarmed by his presence, she grabs a mop and cocks it in mid air.*]

AMELIA:  Drop it!

PAYE: [*Startled.*]  What?!

AMELIA: [*Calling.*]  Dilia! Cacha!

PAYE:  I . . .

AMELIA:  Somebody! Quick!

PAYE:  Wait a minute!

AMELIA:  Thief! Thief!

PAYE:  No. You got it all wrong!

AMELIA:  Dilia! [*Swings the mop at him.*]

PAYE:  Wait! [AMELIA *throws the mop at him and as* PAYE *ducks, she grabs him from behind in a bear hug.*]

AMELIA:  I got him! [DILIA *enters.*] I got him!!

DILIA: Amelia, let him go, he'll hurt you.

AMELIA: I'll kill 'im first!

PAYE: It's me.

AMELIA: Call somebody! [*Begins calling out "thief" repeatedly. From this point on everyone speaks at once, saying their respective lines without waiting for any cue. The effect should be a jumble of everyone screaming and shouting until* CACHA *screams "shut up." At that point everyone stops.*]

DILIA: Amelia, don't be crazy, let him go!

PAYE: I sent a cable . . . [AMELIA *bites him on the neck.*] Ouch!!

CACHA: [*Entering.*] What in the world . . .

ANA: [*Enters.*] What is it?!

DILIA: A thief!

PAYE: Abuela. [*Breaks loose.*]

DILIA: Look out!

ANA: Amelia, are you sure he's a thief?

PAYE: It's me, Tía!

ANA: Let the man get out!

DILIA: Look out, Mama.

ANA: Here, Amelia. [*Gives* AMELIA *the bat.*]

PAYE: Listen, it's me, Paye. Abuela!

AMELIA: I'll knock 'im out!

ANA: [*Taking up* AMELIA's *repeated cry of "thief."*] Thief! . . .

PAYE: It's me. Paye!

CACHA: Paye? Shut up all of you! It's Paye!

DILIA: Paye? [*Rushes over to turn off the radio.*]

CACHA: It's Paye! [*Opens her arms to him.*] Paye, my Paye. [*They embrace.*]

AMELIA: [*After a long pause.*] Jesus, I nearly bashed his head in! [*Picks up her mop and exits.*]

VOICE: [*Off.*] Is everything okay, Doña Cacha?

CACHA: Yes, Beto. It's Tato's son, Paye; he's come home. [*Blackout. Afro-Cuban drums are heard. People chattering as they get into places. Laughter. As the lights come up we find* CACHA *seated in one of the rocking chairs.* PAYE *is seated on the arm of* CACHA's *chair with his arm around her.* DILIA *and* ANA *are gathering the clothes off the line as they speak.*]

DILIA: But the carnival is not till next week!

ANA: You haven't changed a bit!

CACHA: Ay, Paye, what a surprise!

DILIA: The last we heard, you were coming for the carnival!

PAYE: They just changed my flight!

ANA: I would have picked you out in a minute!

DILIA: We weren't expecting you till next week.

CACHA: It doesn't matter. The main thing is that you're here. I thought that I would have to close my eyes for good and never see you again, Paye. [PAYE *kisses her.*] I've missed you and Tato and . . . all of you.

DILIA: You didn't recognize us, eh, Paye?

PAYE: Sure I did.

CACHA: Older. Much older!

PAYE: Abue, you look terrific.

DILIA: Huh, don't let her fool you.

CACHA: What are you trying to do, make me out an invalid? [*To* PAYE.] I'm over eighty years old, and I have my own teeth, I cut my own food, I bathe and dress myself, and I haven't lost control of my bowels. [PAYE *laughs.*]

DILIA: Ah, Mama, Paye's come hundreds of miles, he doesn't want to hear about your bowels! Ay, Paye, how long has it been?

PAYE: Seventeen years?

DILIA: I bet you miss it plenty.

PAYE: Yes.

DILIA: What's Canada like? Not like here, is it?

PAYE: No.

ANA: Nothing's like here, they say. Perucho's son, you remember Perucho?

DILIA: Who?

ANA: Long time ago. Perucho.

PAYE: I remember.

ANA: [*To* DILIA.] He used to sell corn fritters at La Placita.

PAYE: Greasy little blobs! He had a glass eye and wore a raincoat regardless.

CACHA: Ay, what a memory!

PAYE: It's hard to forget a man with a glass eye.

DILIA: I did.

ANA: Well, his sister is a good friend of Gaetana, the lady that used to sew for Mirta, next door to my sister Somalia. Anyway, Perucho's son left for New York, and he had a terrible time with English and the cold. He *hated* it there. So he moved to Miami because everyone told him it was just like Cuba. But no. The place was crawling with Cubans, sure enough, all pretending they were still in Havana. But Havana's not Santiago, and it wasn't the same, not at all.

DILIA: Ay, Ana, this is taking too long.

ANA: Wait, I'm just getting to it. Paye knows what I'm talking about, don't you, Paye?

PAYE: Yes. I guess.

ANA: Anyway, Paye, he moved from Miami to Puerto Rico because they say that San Juan is *just* like here. But, no sir. His father got a letter from him just last New Year's . . . he said that *nothing* was like Santiago! Now he wants to come back!

DILIA: [*Totally disinterested in* ANA's *story.*] I wonder where Tatín's got to?

ANA: He said he'd be home before lunch.

CACHA: Oh, he's going to be surprised!

ANA: He'll be glad we came to Santiago early this year.

DILIA: Ay, Ana, are the boys going to get here before Paye leaves?

ANA: I don't think so . . . we made arrangements for them to be here next week . . . we thought that . . .

DILIA: Ay, Tatín'll be so disappointed.

'NA: So will the boys.

'E: Where are they?

Ernesto's got a scholarship to a special course . . .

One of the best schools on the island!

ANA: And Adrián's at a boys' camp near Havana. It's on a farm. We arranged for them to come for the carnival. They've asked a lot about you and the rest of the family abroad.

CACHA: Adrián looks a lot like you when you were that age!

AMELIA: [*Enters more groomed.*] I hope I didn't miss anything important.

DILIA: Ay, here's the one who nearly broke his skull! [*Laughs.*]

CACHA: This is my grandson, Carlos. Paye, this is Amelia. [*They shake hands.*]

AMELIA: Pleased to meet you.

CACHA: Amelia's living here with us while she goes to school in Santiago.

PAYE: Where are you from?

AMELIA: Oh, you never heard of it. It's up in the hills. Near Baracoa. It's a village called Alan.

PAYE: Alan?

AMELIA: It used to be a coffee plantation and the American who owned it named the village after himself.

CACHA: It's *way* up in the hills.

AMELIA: You can see the coast line when the clouds lift. Maybe you would like to go?!

DILIA: Ay, Amelia, Paye's not a tourist. He's here to see us!

CACHA: Ay, yes! And we want to see him. Wait till Clara sees you!

DILIA: You better run down to Tía Clara's or she'll accuse us of keeping him all to ourselves!

CACHA: Clara's waited seventeen years, a few more minutes won't hurt.

DILIA: You forget how Tía Clara is when it comes to Paye?

ANA: [*To* PAYE.] Your Godmother, no?

PAYE: Yes.

DILIA: Clara has two gods, Jesus and this one! [AMELIA *laughs.*]

PAYE: I should go and see her . . .

ANA: Why don't I go and tell her he's here . . . she'll come . . .

DILIA: Ana, tell her that he just arrived. This very second.

VOICE: [*Off stage.*] Hello, Doña Cacha.

CACHA: Hello, Graciela.

DILIA: [*Under her breath.*] You should see Graciela. The girl's a cow!

CACHA: Alpidio's daughter, you remember her, Paye? I think she went out with Tatín.

DILIA: Only one, Mama. Tatín was going out with Ana when Paye left.

CACHA: Dilia doesn't like her because she went out with Tatín.

DILIA: The girl was vulgar. She would cough and spit like a lizard.

PAYE: I'm glad Tatín married Ana.

CACHA: Oh, yes.

DILIA: She's all right.

CACHA: It's not easy being married to Tatín. Mr. Perfect!

DILIA: He has high standards, and that's good.

CACHA: Too high. Ernesto and Adrián are terrified of him. And Ana, she lives trying to keep things smooth.

DILIA: Tatín hasn't been given everything on a silver platter, and he expects everyone to strive just as hard . . .

CACHA: See, Paye, no one can say a word about Tatín in front of your Aunt Dilia.

PAYE: Has he . . . ? [*Gets up.*] It's hot, isn't it?

CACHA: Paye, you all right?

DILIA: You want some water? [DILIA *motions to* AMELIA, *who goes but looks puzzled.*] It's the heat. He's not accustomed to this heat.

CACHA: Paye?

DILIA: You hungry? I bet you haven't eaten.

PAYE: I'm fine, Tía.

DILIA: I'll go get lunch ready, right away! [*Exits.*]

AMELIA: [*Hands* PAYE *a glass of water.*]   Here.

PAYE: Thanks. [*Drinks.*]

DILIA: [*Shouting from the kitchen.*]   Amelia, will you give me a hand in here!

AMELIA: Coming!

PAYE: [*Giving* AMELIA *the glass.*]   Thank you, Amelia. [AMELIA *exits.*]

CACHA: You all right, Paye?

PAYE: Abue, I'm not sure if I have forgotten my feeling against Tatín. He hurt me.

CACHA: You hurt him a lot too. You refused to speak to him—even to say goodbye.

PAYE: Abue, you think that Tatín, that he still . . .

CACHA: [*Taking* PAYE'*s hand.*]   When I was a little girl, Paye, my mother had a friend, Nenita. She was a beautiful lady; always powdered and combed. She used to visit us often. Then suddenly she stopped coming, and I asked why. My mother told me that Nenita had been in a fire and that she had been badly scarred. I cried, and I burst into tears on the spot! But as time went on, one day she came to visit us again. I heard her voice from the other room and I knew it was Nenita. I got nervous. I was afraid to come out. But they called. When I walked into the room and I saw her, I burst into tears again. She looked so lovely, just as lovely as ever, though her dress was cut high around her throat and her sleeves were long. I felt like such a fool. You see, Paye, Nenita had learned to cover her scars for her friends. [*Pause.*] Tatín is your brother, and if he has scars, he's learned to conceal them. You must do the same, Paye. You see?

PAYE: [*Almost in tears.*]   Yes, Abue, I see. [*They sit in a long silence.* CLARA *enters followed by* ANA.]

CLARA: Where is he? Where's . . . ay, my Paye.

PAYE: [*Meeting her.*]   Tía!

CLARA: Oh, look at you. Oh, my Paye. [*Covers* PAYE'*s face with kisses.*] Let me look at you. [*Stands back.*] Oh, God in Heaven! [*Throws herself at* PAYE *again.*]

PAYE: Tía, please. [*Comforts her.*]

CLARA: Isn't he beautiful, Cacha?

CACHA: All my grandchildren are beautiful.

CLARA: And look at me. I must be a fright!

PAYE: You look fine, Tía. Pretty as ever!

CLARA: Go on. I don't even have any face powder, and I'm all sweaty. And my hair! I was going to tint it this evening. I'm all grey, you know, almost white! Ay, there was a time when I couldn't get a bottle of dye even for American money. Everyone thinks I'm too vain for my age, but I say they

can all go fart into the wind. But, look at me now. I'm not even dressed
and here you are! Oh, Paye. My little Paye, all grown up! [*Cries.*]

DILIA: [*Entering.*] Ay, Tía, let him breathe!

CLARA: You shut up, you've had Tatín all these years. My Paye's here
now, and I . . . [*Cries.*]

PAYE: Tía.

ANA: I wonder what's keeping Tatín?

CLARA: [*Blowing her nose on the hem of her dress.*] I'm so proud of you.
Your father, he keeps us up to date on your plays and . . . things.

PAYE: Papa tends to brag a little . . .

CLARA: I've always known you were the one in the family with the real
sentiment . . . [*Kisses* PAYE.]

DILIA: Did you know Tatín got a medal from the Hispanic Academy?[4]

PAYE: Yes, yes.

CLARA: A writer needs real sentiment!

DILIA: First prize!

CACHA: First time a Cuban's held that honor since 1948.

DILIA: [*Correcting her.*] '38, Mama. He's been published in Mexico and
Chile and . . .

CLARA: Will you stop talking abut Tatín! I want to hear about Paye!

CACHA: How's lunch coming?

DILIA: The rice is on.

CACHA: Tell me about Sylvia; how's your mother?

PAYE: Fine.

DILIA: Mama, if you want to bathe, you better go do it now before the
water shuts off for the day.

CACHA: I'll bathe later.

DILIA: There won't be enough in the tanks later. If Amelia does the dishes!
That girl refuses to realize that on the days the water shuts off, whatever
is in those tanks is all we have for the rest of the day. I'm always running
out.

CACHA: Well, talk to her.

DILIA: I can't talk to her. You invited her here.

CACHA: I'm not the one who keeps running out of water.

DILIA: Never mind. I'll see about getting the tanks fixed myself.

CLARA: What's the matter with them now?

DILIA: They don't fill up properly.

CLARA: They never did. Ever since I can remember, those tanks . . .

DILIA: And what am I supposed to do, climb up on the roof myself?! I
asked Fito to have a look at them, and Roberto was supposed to have fixed
them, and he couldn't be bothered to look at them again! And Nando's
useless! Sometimes my brothers make me sick. They live only a few
blocks away and they only come here to tell me what I'm doing wrong in
the caring of their mother!

CLARA: Dilia, please!

DILIA: And Mama thinks they're all saints!

ANA: All right, Tía.

---

4. The National Hispanic Academy of Media Arts and Sciences, an association of performing artists.

CLARA: Ay, Dilia, we don't want Paye to think that the whole family's falling apart.

DILIA: Who said anything about falling apart?!

CLARA: It's the way you complain about everyone.

DILIA: I have reason to complain, Tía.

CACHA: Enough!

DILIA: I don't know what Tía Clara's accusing me of. Paye knows the family. What are we supposed to do, pretend we always get along like nuns on a bus ride? [PAYE *laughs.*]

CACHA: [*Getting up.*] I'll go take my shower . . .

DILIA: [*Exiting.*] Luck will be another twenty minutes. Hurry up, Mama! [CACHA *follows* DILIA *off to the interior of the house.*]

CLARA: You musn't pay your Aunt Dilia any attention. Age doesn't agree with her. [*Looks around to see if they're alone.*]

ANA: I'll go give Tía a hand with lunch. [*Exits.*]

CLARA: Come, let's sit and talk for a minute. [CLARA *leads* PAYE *to the rocking chairs.*] When I heard you were here, I couldn't believe it. My heart jumped to my throat. Ana couldn't keep up with me running up the hill. I kept walking out of my shoes. These lousy things! [*Shows them.*] Come from Rumania, or something. They melt in the heat!! Soles come right off on the sidewalk!! Ay, Paye, if we had only known back then that it would turn out like this. Everyone here at the house still thinks that Fidel is Christ our Saviour! If I open my mouth in front of anyone here, they'd have my head on a skewer! I don't say a word up here. Out of respect for Cacha. I'm not afraid of anyone! I've put Tatín in his place a few times and good! Once I made a reference to the day he slapped you during lunch, and he said that he would do it again. And I said to him, "Thank God, Paye's not here because, if you did it again, I would slap you silly, Señor Tatín." I gave him such a piece of my mind . . . He's never said another word to me since.

PAYE: You and Tatín don't speak to one another?

CLARA: Yes, we do. But he knows just where to draw the line. In front of me, he doesn't even praise Fidel! But, Paye, don't you open your mouth, please! God in Heaven! If anything happened to you on this trip your mother would never forgive us.

PAYE: Nothing is going to happen, Tía.

CLARA: You remember Niko the Turk? [PAYE *nods.*] They picked him up about a month ago. He was saying atrocities about the committee!

PAYE: He's half mad anyway, no?

CLARA: Exactly! He's even worse since you left! Half the time he runs around with a load of shit in his pants! Ay, Paye, you have no idea what it's like! Imagine a shortage of oranges in Cuba!

PAYE: Well, that's because of the trade with Russia.

CLARA: Oh yes, that's what they say, but all I know is that during capitalism we had oranges!

PAYE: [*Laughs.*] You haven't changed a bit, Tía!

CLARA: Now tell me, tell me all about Canada and . . . Oh your postcards! I got your postcards from all over Europe. I keep them in an album. I feel as if I've been to all those places! But you're so thin, Paye. Don't you have anyone to cook for you? We'll have to fatten you up. You'll have to come down to my house. I'll make some natilla[5] for you. But, here I'm talking and talking and you should be the one who should be talking.

PAYE: I'd rather hear about you.

CLARA: Me?! What's there to tell. I go from my house to church and from church to my house and that's it. A widow's life can be pretty desolate sometimes. Especially when she doesn't have any children. Your uncle and I . . . [Makes the sign of the cross.] . . . we never had any children. Of course you knew that. It would have been good to have a few children. But . . . I couldn't.

PAYE: Tía, I didn't know . . .

CLARA: Naturally no one speaks of it anymore. It doesn't come up in conversation or anything, but there was a time when everyone in the family felt sorry for your uncle for having married a barren woman. Oh, but that was before donkeys learned to bray! Beside I have my Paye here with me again! Oh, we're going to have such fun! It'll be like the old days. Like when I used to celebrate your birthdays! You remember? [PAYE nods. TATÍN enters from the street.]

TATÍN: Ey, Tía!

CLARA: Tatín! [TATÍN advances in their direction, eyeing PAYE.] You'll never guess . . .

TATÍN: Paye? [PAYE stands up.]

CLARA: That's right! [They stare at one another in silence.]

TATÍN: Paye? Are you speaking to me now? [PAYE advances tentatively. TATÍN wipes his sweat.]

PAYE: [Locked in TATÍN's embrace.] Tatín . . . [DILIA and ANA enter from inside and stand watching.]

DILIA: He didn't recognize him!?

CLARA: He did. Right away!

TATÍN: Paye, you remember Ana.

ANA: Yes. He did.

DILIA: He got here by surprise!

PAYE: They got my visa all mixed up.

CACHA: [Entering.] Is Tatín here yet?

DILIA: Yes, Mama.

CACHA: Well, our Paye's here early!

CLARA: My Paye! [PAYE and TATÍN try to speak at once. They laugh.]

TATÍN: Paye-Paye!

PAYE: It's nice to be called Paye again!

DILIA: What do they call you . . . ?

PAYE: My friends, Carlos.

CACHA: Ay!

TATÍN: Should we call you Carlos?

PAYE: No! No! Paye's fine. It's just fine. It's just that no one's called me Paye in so long. Even the family in Jamaica. Once when I was there for Christmas, Papa called me Paye by mistake and Alexandra nearly choked on her milk. She thought it was the funniest thing since Aunt Sophie fell

---

5. A creamy custard.

into Uncle Solomon's grave. [TATÍN *looks puzzled*.] They were lowering him in. Oh, you should've been there! She had been wailing: "Solomon, take me with you! Don't leave me, Solomon!" Then as she fell, she started screaming, "Draw me out! Will you get me outta here!" [*Everyone bursts into laughter but* TATÍN.] Everyone was laughing so hard they didn't have the strength to get her out of the hole. And Uncle Elías, he slipped in the mud and fell in too! [*More laughter.*]

TATÍN: Why do you still make up these lies? [*A moment of tension.*]

CACHA: [*To* DILIA.] How's lunch coming?

PAYE: [*Softly.*] It's the truth, I swear.

DILIA: I was waiting for you to start frying. [*Exits.*]

PAYE: Ay, Tatín, I brought a tape recorder for you. [*Looks around for his suitcases.*]

CACHA: Amelia put your things in your room. Your old room.

PAYE: I brought something for you too, Abue, and for you, Tía. [*Starts to exit.*]

CLARA: [*Following him.*] What is it?

PAYE: [*Off.*] Your favorite! Yardley's Violets.[6]

CLARA: [*Off.*] Ay!

ANA: [*To* TATÍN.] Don't be so hard on him.

TATÍN: [*Looking toward* CACHA *to see if she heard.*] Ana, please!

CACHA: Go see what Paye brought for you. [CLARA *gasps with delight.*] You've been wanting a recorder for a long time, no?

TATÍN: Yes. Don't you want to see what he brought for you?

CACHA: I'm old. I can wait. Go. Go on! [ANA *and* TATÍN *start off.*] Tatín. [*They stop.*] He's here for one week . . . I want everything to be nice for him . . .

TATÍN: Yes, Abue.

CACHA: Paye. [ANA *and* TATÍN *exit to* PAYE's *room.* CACHA *sits in her rocking chair and fans herself. She speaks to the audience.*] It's a funny thing with names! Take Tatín; when he was born Tato did not want to name him Carlos after himself. That was too much like everybody else. So he named him Nelson after the Englishman.[7] [*Smiles and shakes her head.*] Well, since he didn't inherit his father's name, he ended up inheriting even worse, his father's nickname, and from Tato he got Tatín. [PAYE *and* TATÍN *laugh off.*] When Paye was born the whole family was expecting a girl. Well, imagine, I already had . . . [*Counts.*] . . . five grandchildren, and all of them boys. Tato had an armful of girls' names picked out. All of them foreign; after some duchess in Sweden or a lady writer from France. None that I would be able to pronounce. But when the midwife put him in my arms and said, "It's another boy," we were all stumped. So I named him Carlos, like his father and my husband. That's a sensible name. How he got to be called Paye is really quite a simple story. As a baby, Sylvia took him to visit her family in Jamaica, and there he learned to say "Bye-bye" and wave his little hand; in English! It was real cute. But his cousins who had no idea of what he was saying, started calling him "Paye-paye"

---

6. Brand of soap or perfume.
7. Famous British admiral in the Royal Navy

(Horatio Nelson, 1st Viscount Nelson, 1st Duke of Bronté, 1758–1805).

and it stuck. [*Laughs.*] The third one was named Aramis after the Three Musketeers,[8] [*Raises an eyebrow.*] and no nick-names were allowed. Well, Ari for short. [*Smiles.*] Tato's always been one for foreign airs! I believe he named his daughter after a Russian princess. Alexandra.[9] [*Pause.*] I never met Alexandra. I never held her in my arms. I've held all my grandchildren at birth. They were all born in this house and the midwife passed them directly into my arms. All my grandchildren, except one. Tato sent us a cable when Sylvia had Alexandra, and I held it, the little piece of paper . . . I held it next to my cheek and I cried. [*Rocks gently in her chair, fans herself and is silent. After a long pause,* AMELIA *calls from the kitchen.*]

AMELIA: Lunch! Doña Cacha! Tatín, Paye. [TATÍN, PAYE *and* CLARA *laugh offstage.*] Lunch! [*Lights fade as* CACHA *gets up and exits. Lights up on* TATÍN. *The inside of the house is in darkness. He sits on the downstage railing.* PAYE *enters from the interior of the house wearing jogging shorts and an open shirt, bare feet, stands behind* TATÍN *and yawns.*]

TATÍN: Where do you think you are? Miami Beach? You don't wear things like that in Santiago.

PAYE: I couldn't sleep. [*Pause.*]

TATÍN: Me neither. [*Pause.*] The heat?

PAYE: Yea, the heat. [*Pause.*] Ana sleep?

TATÍN: I guess. [*Pause.*] Time?

PAYE: Almost five. Tatín . . . ? [*Pause.*] Want to talk some more?

TATÍN: Sure. What did I say?

PAYE: You told her I was a "noteworthy Cuban playwright" and . . .

TATÍN: Aren't you?

PAYE: I was surprised at the adjective.

TATÍN: Noteworthy?

PAYE: No, Cuban. [*Silence.*]

TATÍN: An orange is an orange because it comes from an orange tree. [*They look at one another.*] They get oranges in Canada, no? [PAYE *smiles. Silence.*] Very few of our writers write for the theater. At the last writer's conference I met a young woman who wrote plays, but they were really for television. I myself have a few scenarios that might be best served by dialogue, but between my radio broadcast and lecturing I hardly have enough time to write all the things I want. [*Smokes.*] Besides. I really felt more at home in prose. I don't have a flair for the dramatic. I'm working on a story about a man who's on trial because his neighbors accuse him of manufacturing butterflies out of thin air. I want to finish it for an anthology. I'm really quite excited about it. [*Pause.*] And you, are you working on anything?

PAYE: [*Shaking his head.*] I try. I sit at the typewriter with my finger perched . . . and nothing. I haven't written anything in nearly two years.

TATÍN: You're wasting time.

8. In *Les trois mousquetaires* (The Three Musketeers, 1844), a novel by the French writer Alexandre Dumas, père (1802–1870), the title characters are named Athos, Porthos, and Aramis.
9. Perhaps Alexandra Feodorovna (1872–1918), czarina of Russia; she was born Viktoria Alix Helena Luise Beatrice of Hesse and by Rhine, princess of a Grand Duchy that was part of the German Empire.

PAYE:   You remember that poem I wrote when I was eleven? "Ode to the Triumphant Revolution." [TATÍN *nods.* PAYE *smiles.*] I remember when it came out in the paper, Tía Clara read it out loud, and everyone was so proud, even Tía Dilia . . . everyone. I remember, you took the newspaper, glanced at my poem, and without even looking up went on to read the news of the day. Why must you always put me down?

TATÍN:   I don't always put you down.

PAYE:   Yes, you do. You call me a liar. Because I'm having difficulty writing, you say I'm wasting time.

TATÍN:   You are wasting time. The first act of the play you sent was light weight.

PAYE:   I was trying to come up with a comedy. Serious plays don't sell. [*They are beginning to raise their voices.*]

TATÍN:   Serious plays become literature.

PAYE: [*Shouts.*]   I know the people in that play. I write about people I know.

TATÍN:   Then you should denounce the people you know.

PAYE: [*Shouts.*]   I don't want to write propaganda. [DILIA *enters wearing a light housecoat.*]

DILIA: [*To* PAYE.]   Shhh! Do you want to wake up your grandmother? [PAYE *turns brusquely and walks into the house.* DILIA *walks to* TATÍN *and caresses his head.*] What's the matter? There's something the matter, isn't there?

TATÍN:   No.

DILIA:   I know you well. Tatín. There's something brewing inside of you. I'm hurt that you won't talk to me. [TATÍN *doesn't answer. Pause. She kisses him on the cheek.*] Come on. You should get some sleep. [*Lights fade as they enter the house. Cuban music comes up. Daylight comes up on* ANA *seated at the table. She cleans stones from a bowl of beans. The Rabel household is occupied by* DILIA *in the kitchen.* PAYE *and* CACHA *getting up from their respective beds.* CACHA *and* PAYE *go through the archway that goes to the interior of the house.* PAYE *is carrying a towel.* CACHA *is still in her nightgown. While* ANA *speaks,* DILIA *fixes a tray comprised of a large expresso coffee pot and a pot of hot milk. She enters the interior of the house shortly after* PAYE *and* CACHA *pass by. Music volume cuts to half.*]

ANA:   The Rabel family is quite the important family. Cacha's youngest son died fighting for Fidel. The whole family was up to their eyeballs in the fight against Batista,[1] and when Fidel took power, naturally the Rabels took their place in the ranks of the revolutionary government. [*Music fades to nearly nothing.*] Paye turned against the revolution with a vengeance. The Jesuits really had their claws in him. But still, imagine what a shock it was when Tato Rabel, the eldest of the Rabels, decided to leave Cuba. No, no, no, it was unbelievable. [*Music has faded . . . Pause.*] I've heard a hundred times how in 1942, Tato Rabel came back from Jamaica married to Sylvia. He had been working in the consular office in the island, that's where he learned to speak English; and he came back married to a fifteen-year-old English Jewess, with the face of an angel! Sylvia

---

1. Fulgencio Batista y Zaldívar (1901–1973), Cuban soldier; president of Cuba 1940–44, 1952–59.

had to convert to everything. To Catholicism. To Spanish. To pesos. To the Rabel family. She gave up everything for her husband and for twenty years she was more Cuban than sugar cane. But in '62, Tato and Sylvia took Paye and Aramis and went back to Jamaica. Tatín refused to leave. Paye was delighted to take his father away. [*Blackout. We hear a radio playing Cuban music. Lights come up on* PAYE *and* TATÍN *sitting on the patio in rocking chairs. No one else is seen. As lights come up, music fades to background.*]

PAYE:   I was so surprised when your letter came, the first one. What made you sit down and actually write to me?

TATÍN:   I don't know. [*Offers* PAYE *a cigarette.*]

PAYE:   No, thanks.

TATÍN: [*Lighting up.*]   I think it was a letter Papa wrote to Abue saying he was concerned with your involvement in the Anti-Vietnam movement in university.

PAYE: [*Smiling.*]   And you figured there was hope for me yet?!

TATÍN:   Something like that. [*They chuckle.*] And you, why did you write back?

PAYE:   I don't know. But when your letters would come talking about your work and the family and the carnival . . . [*Sighs.*] You know, I have your letters all filed by date and once in a while I go through them. My favorite is one you wrote around the time Adrián was born. You talked about every one of the cousins, what they were like, what they were doing . . . I read that one often. I've wanted to be here so many times. [*Looks up the street.*] I was really hoping to be here for the carnival.

TATÍN:   That would have been nice.

PAYE:   Tatín . . . ? [*Pause.*] You ever think about going abroad?

TATÍN:   Why? Should I want to?

PAYE:   No. I suppose not. [*A persistent jeep's horn is heard from the street.* JULIO *enters from the jeep.*]

TATÍN:   You remember your cousin Julio?

PAYE:   Not looking like that.

JULIO: [*Shouting.*]   Paye!

DILIA: [*Rushing out.*]   What's going on?

JULIO:   Paye, put it there!

DILIA:   It's only Julio, Mama.

CACHA: [*Joining them.*]   At this hour . . . ?!

PAYE:   Julio! Jesus, look at you!

JULIO: [*Flexing his arm.*]   Just a little exercise. You look good for an old man your age! Whiter than salt pork! I got the jeep to take you to the beach.

PAYE:   The beach?

TATÍN:   We haven't been to bed yet.

JULIO:   *You* go to bed. Who invited you?

DILIA:   Don't say hello to us.

JULIO:   Ooops! [*Kisses* DILIA.] Abuela. [*Kisses* CACHA.]

CACHA:   How's the baby?

DILIA:   Julio's wife just had a baby.

CACHA:   A month ago.

JULIO:   A boy.

CACHA:   Eduardo.

JULIO: What about you? You married yet?

PAYE: No, not yet.

JULIO: Christ, I'm on my third.

CACHA: It's nothing to brag about.

JULIO: Why not? Not many men can get a really good looking woman, let alone three.

DILIA: Not many men can get two women to divorce him in such a hurry!

PAYE: You've been divorced twice?

JULIO: Sure, we're a modern nation.

AMELIA: [*Enters, still dressing herself.*] Julio!

JULIO: Hey big mama! [JULIO *takes* AMELIA's *face in his hands and shows it to* PAYE.] You ever seen anything as ugly as this anywhere?

AMELIA: Get out! [AMELIA *slaps* JULIO *around.*]

JULIO: [*Trying to pat her ass.*] Well, at least you have something to fall back on. [*Pats her.*]

AMELIA: Get your hands off.

JULIO: Only teasing.

AMELIA: See what I have to put up with at every rehearsal?

JULIO: See what Abuela saddled me with?

CACHA: And I intend you to watch out for her.

JULIO: You kidding! With that face who'd bother her?

CACHA: Ther're a lot of drunks in the carnival and . . . ?

JULIO: They'd have to be plastered! [AMELIA *hits* JULIO.]

DILIA: Did you hear? Paye can't stay for the carnival.

JULIO: That's what he thinks. You think you're getting on a plane before July 25th, you're even stupider than me!

PAYE: Well, the main thing was to see the family.

JULIO: This year's dance is going to knock the judges on their asses. It's the best La Placita has ever done. One of the guys playing the bongos just came back from Angola.

AMELIA: And he's got some rhythms that are going to make the conga *hot!*

PAYE: I wish I could, Julio.

JULIO: Well?

DILIA: His visa's only for one week.

JULIO: What the hell does he need a visa for?!

PAYE: Next time, Julio.

JULIO: So, you'll miss the carnival. We'll have to have a party AT LEAST. How about it, Tía? Let's roast a pig!

DILIA: Where are we supposed to get a pig from?

JULIO: I'll get a pig. How about Saturday?!

CACHA: [*Lowering her voice.*] Julio, I don't want you getting into any trouble . . .

JULIO: Don't worry, Abue. The pig's as good as roasted.

AMELIA: Ay, a party!

JULIO: Okay! Them that's going to the beach, let's go. I only got the jeep for a few hours.

DILIA: Before you go, Julio, I want you to look at the water tanks.

JULIO: Right now?

DILIA: Just look at them now; it'll only take a second . . . [JULIO *begins to exit with* DILIA.]

JULIO: Get your towels and wait for me in the jeep. These old women are going to drive me crazy!

AMELIA: That Julio!

PAYE: He's certainly changed. I remember Julio as a skinny little shrimp with no teeth and always scratching himself! [AMELIA *laughs and exits.*]

CACHA: I guess you all grow up. Are you going to the beach?

TATÍN: I don't know, I . . .

CACHA: Why not? You're young! [*Exiting.*] I'll get your towels and things. Ana!

PAYE: The beach! A party! A roast pig! This pig Julio's talking about; where's he going to get it?

TATÍN: I don't know. He probably knows a man who raises pigs.

PAYE: Is that allowed?

TATÍN: Raising pigs?

PAYE: No. Knowing a man.

TATÍN: This is still Cuba, Paye. Sure you're not tired?

PAYE: Of course I'm tired, but I couldn't sleep now.

ANA: [*Enters.*] Paye, Abue can't find your bathing suit.

PAYE: Oh, it's still in my duffle bag. I'll find it. [*Exits.*]

ANA: Are you really going to the beach?

TATÍN: Yes, why?

ANA: No, nothing. Remember you have to prepare two radio broadcasts for when you get back.

TATÍN: Have I ever needed reminding?

ANA: No . . . How are things going with you and Paye?

TATÍN: Fine.

ANA: You know, he reminds me of Adrián. [TATÍN *laughs cynically.*] What's the matter?

TATÍN: Nothing.

ANA: What did I say?

TATÍN: Now I know why I lose patience with Adrián. He is like Paye.

ANA: You didn't lose patience with Adrián until recently.

TATÍN: Well, he gets so vehement when anyone in the house complains about shortages or anything like that. He doesn't respect me anymore. He talks back.

ANA: That's true maybe. But it's also you. You have been in a foul mood for months. And when I ask you what's the matter, you always say nothing. Is it me? [*Moves after him.*] Are you unhappy with me?

TATÍN: [*Sharply.*] It's not you! It has nothing to do with you!

JULIO: [*Offstage.*] No sweat. I'll fix it Saturday. [TATÍN *moves away from* ANA. *She stares at him silently.*] Here we go! Abue's packing us breakfast, we better get outta here before she decides to pack a bed!

CACHA: Here! [*To* JULIO.] Make sure they're back before lunch.

JULIO: [*Shouting over* CACHA's *line.*] To the beach! And don't anyone fart in the jeep, the floor boards are real loose! [*They exit noisily.* CACHA *waves.* ANA *stands perfectly still.*]

CACHA: You all right, Ana?

ANA: Yes. I just didn't sleep well. I worry when Tatín isn't in bed with me.

CACHA: There's nothing to worry about. They'll get some sleep later on. Now he's too excited to sleep. You can't imagine what Paye's visits means to him, to all of us.

ANA: I don't know what to imagine, what to expect.

CACHA: There's nothing to worry about, you'll see. [*Exits. Blackout. Music from the radio is heard.* DILIA *is busy in the kitchen stirring in a double boiler.* PAYE *enters from the street, shouting.*]

PAYE: [*Entering.*] Abue!

DILIA: [*In lowered voice.*] She's resting.

PAYE: Oh. [*Stands there for a moment with nothing to say.*]

DILIA: I'm making something special for you. Natilla.

PAYE: For me?

DILIA: Don't you like it anymore?

PAYE: Yes, I love it.

DILIA: Used to be your favorite.

PAYE: Oh, yes!

DILIA: Good! I've been skimming the top of the milk every day when I scald it. I wasn't going to say anything until I was sure I had enough.

PAYE: For the party?

DILIA: No, it's for you. I didn't want you to go back without something to remember me by. [*Silence.*] Where's Tatín?

PAYE: He went over to La Placita; someone called him over . . .

DILIA: He has quite a following here in Santiago; never comes often enough. [*Silence.*] How about something cold to drink? [*Pours him a glass of lemonade.*]

PAYE: It's hot, isn't it?

DILIA: Yes, unbearable.

PAYE: Doña Rosario said it was earthquake weather.

DILIA: Tch! What the hell does she know? Some people always have something to add to the confusion. As if it wasn't enough with the heat. [DILIA *watches* PAYE *drink.*] Tell me if it needs more sugar.

PAYE: It's fine, Tía.

DILIA: We haven't had a chance to talk, you and me. I know you probably haven't thought kindly of me . . . [PAYE *tries to speak.*] No, no. It's only natural, I . . .

PAYE: Tía . . .

DILIA: I never had much time for anyone else but Tatín. [*Pause. The radio D.J. blurts out the word "carnival."*] It's a pity you couldn't stay for the carnival.

PAYE: Do you still go out, Tía?

DILIA: Me? No! I'm too old for that. I like to watch . . . see them go by and wave and clap. There has to be someone to watch! [*Silence. Turns the radio down to almost nothing. Looking down.*] I don't know you've noticed on this trip . . . Tatín and I aren't like we used to be. I find out things about Tatín's life by reading them in the papers. I'm . . . another aunt. Mama always said that I was a stupid, selfish woman. Sometimes when the stakes are very high, you have a good hand, but you end up playing the wrong card and losing everything. Why do you live all the way up in Toronto?

PAYE: Because in Jamaica, there's very little theater.

DILIA: Yes, but you see your family only once a year.

PAYE: That's as much as I can afford. And Papa pays half.

DILIA: Is there anything else you would do instead?

PAYE: Than playwriting? I've thought about it often.

DILIA: Why don't you get married and have children?

PAYE: [*Laughs.*] I couldn't support a wife, let alone have children. Besides, knowing a playwright's income, no woman would marry me.

DILIA: I still think that you should move to Kingstown.

PAYE: If I could live under communism, I would live in Santiago.

DILIA: I am not a communist, Paye. I'm too old and too stupid to understand socialism. I'm a Fidelista because I am a Rabel. I'd never heard of Karl Marx.[2] The fact of the matter is that my life hasn't changed that much one way or the other. I still get up at six-thirty every morning to scald the milk, make the coffee, butter the bread, fry the bacon. The revolution was not for me. It was for Tatín. He and his sons will see the Cuba that Fidel is building . . . I'm not campaigning. But that is why Tatín had to stay. Tato couldn't take him. I begged him. Tatín's place was here. He *understands* the revolution. He had a right to stay?! He was all I had.

PAYE: [*Putting his hand on* DILIA'S *shoulder.*] Tía . . .

DILIA: Tatín's life here . . . is a good life. He's *someone.*

PAYE: Oh yes, Tía. Tatín has everything. I envy him, Tía, if you want to know the truth.

DILIA: Do you? Really?

PAYE: Yes. Yes, I do. [*They stare at one another.* DILIA *smiles.*]

DILIA: [*Stirring her mix.*] You have to keep stirring or it'll separate. [*Tastes it.*] I think it needs more vanilla.

PAYE: [*Handing her the bottle.*] Here. You know, I love natilla!

DILIA: Good! I'll warn you, it's not as good as Mama's, but she's my teacher, so it can't be too bad. [*Offers him a taste off the mixing spoon.*]

PAYE: Hmmmmmmmm! It's delicious.

DILIA: [*Smiles.*] Stay, I'll let you lick the bowl. [*Music swells. Blackout. Exit. Lights come up on* PAYE *in his room changing shirts.* AMELIA *stands by the dresser dressed in a militia uniform. She reaches into the bottom drawer and takes out a belt-holster.*]

PAYE: Thank you for giving me your room, Amelia.

AMELIA: It's your room.

PAYE: [*Laughs.*] Yea. [AMELIA *has put on the holster.*]

AMELIA: It's a good thing you got some sun.

PAYE: Why?

AMELIA: When you arrived you looked whiter than a Polish sailor. [*Slight pause.* AMELIA *sits at the edge of the bed.*] Doña Cacha is so happy since you arrived. She seems younger somehow. She doesn't even seem tired. [PAYE *sits down, takes off his running shoes and socks.*]

PAYE: You are very good to her, Amelia. I've noticed.

AMELIA: Doña Cacha has been good to me. I was only little when the revolution built the first schoolhouse in my village. It was named Tony Rabel after your uncle. Doña Cacha came up and I was chosen to present her with a bunch of flowers. She said that the future of Cuba was in the hands of us children. She didn't let got of my hand. I was so proud. I wrote to her often. I told her about the monument to her son and how I polished the plaque. When I graduated, I wrote her that I had been

2. German political philosopher and socialist (1818–1883).

offered a scholarship to study in Santiago but that my father didn't have the money to send me. Doña Cacha wrote to my father and told him that she would take me into her home while I studied in Santiago. [*She stands up.*] Doña Cacha has been good to me. The revolution has been very good to me and my family. I work hard and I study hard because I want to reflect the values of the revolution. I know first hand that these values are good and true for our people. [*They are standing at either side of the bed.*]

PAYE: [*Bursting into a rage.*]    Bullshit! We've traded one tyrant for another. [TATÍN *stands within earshot.*]

AMELIA: [*Shouting.*]    Things have improved!

PAYE:    Improved?! Improved from what? All we needed was an honest government—and a market for our sugar, coffee, tobacco and rum!

AMELIA:    How about the literacy program?

PAYE:    Yeah, sure, learn to read so that we can better indoctrinate you! Read the news! It tells you how great Fidel is.

AMELIA:    He is great! I would lay down my life for him.

PAYE:    Well, I hate him, and I would gladly see him dead! [*Pause.*]

PAYE:    When I left Cuba, I never dreamed it would be for good—an exile. I thought Fidel wouldn't last. But he closed the borders. He decides who can go and who has to stay. He stole my birthright to *my* country. He set up a dictatorship and taught you to say "Thank you, Fidel." [*Pause.*] For what?! He sold us to the Russians for a chance to stay in power forever.

AMELIA:    Doña Cacha warned us not to discuss politics with you. She was right.

PAYE:    I'm sorry I blew up at you—it's not you I'm angry with.

AMELIA: [*Changing the topic abruptly.*]    Is it true they have penguins in Toronto?

PAYE:    Sure. They have them as pets; walk them around on leads—a friend of mine has one; bit me here, once. See!

AMELIA:    I don't think I could live in a place that had penguins!

PAYE:    No.

AMELIA:    I've got to run now—or I'll be late! [*She exits.*]

PAYE: [*Angry at himself.*]    Jesus Christ! [*He flops on the bed crying. Blackout—slow fade on* TATÍN. *Lights up as* TATÍN *is dragging both rocking chairs onto the verandah.* CACHA *follows him slowly. A newspaper is on one of the rocking chairs.* TATÍN *places the chairs near the railing and he sits on the stage right chair.* CACHA *sits in the stage left chair. She is carrying her fan.* TATÍN *opens the newspaper and begins to read.*]

CACHA:    Paye's quite the young man! [*Silence.*] It's nice to see you two, you and Paye. [*Silence.*]

TATÍN: [*Reporting from the paper.*]    They're going to make it easier for exiled Cubans to return for a visit. They are no longer being considered as traitors. Fidel is urging everyone to treat the visitors with "greatest respect" . . .

CACHA:    Yes. I'm glad you spoke highly of Paye's work in front of Amelia. Paye needed to hear you say all that. He's waited a long time for it. [*Sighs.*] Now, whether you mean it or not . . . Paye will only be home a few more days. [*Silence.* CACHA *rocks and fans herself.* TATÍN *reads the paper.*] I miss your father. Don't you?

TATÍN: Yes. [*Silence.*]

CACHA: When your Uncle Tony died, I thought that I would never recover. But death is very final and . . . in time . . . [*Pause.*] Having a son in exile never ends. A son. A father. A brother. Paye's missed too much. Exile is a terrible punishment. For everyone. [*Pause.*]

VOICE: [*Off.*] Good evening, Doña Cacha.

CELIA: [*Off.*] Yes, I know. They say he weighs sixty-eight pounds!

CACHA: Paye?!

CELIA: No, the pig! [CLARA *and* PAYE *enter laughing.* TATÍN *gives his seat to* CLARA *and sits on the railing reading.*]

CACHA: What's so funny?

CLARA: [*Controlling her laughter.*] Just as we were walking up the hill, the Chinese couple that moved into Dr. Pera's house come running out into the street. The man came out followed by the wife beating him over the head with a half-plucked chicken and screaming in Chinese. And a herd of children running behind like Chinese New Year's. [CLARA *and* PAYE *laugh again.*]

TATÍN: Tía, in the first place, they're not Chinese. They're Korean. Remember Korea? Where the war took place in the fifties?

CLARA: Ay, no wonder there's war in the world. There was a time when a Chinaman was a Chinaman no matter where he came from! This heat! [*Fans herself.*] It doesn't get this hot in Canada, eh Paye?

PAYE: No.

CACHA: [*Under her breath.*] It snows.

PAYE: In winter.

CLARA: Don't stand there like a flag pole. I'll fan you. Come. [PAYE *moves next to her.*] Come, Paye, sit on my lap like when you were my little boy.

PAYE: Tía, I'm too heavy! [*He does.*]

CLARA: Ay, snow! What's in Canada, Paye? Is that where Canada Dry comes from? [*She fans* PAYE. PAYE *and* TATÍN *laugh.* TATÍN *closes the paper and gives it to* CACHA, *who opens it.*]

TATÍN: I've always had a rather picturesque image of Canada. Sort of like Peyton Place;[3] leaves on the sidewalk, picket fences and always a neighbor named Billy, with freckles.

PAYE: Leaves on the sidewalk gets a definite yes, the picket fence is iffy and the neighbor kid is more likely to be called Enzio or Pasquale.

TATÍN: What do you like about Toronto?

PAYE: In twenty words or less?! Oh . . . Toronto is like a pubescent girl. It's got everything, but it doesn't know what to do with it. [CLARA *laughs.*]

CACHA: [*Putting the paper aside.*] Well, that's that.

CLARA: She can only read the headlines without her glasses.

PAYE: Can I get you your glasses, Abuela?

CACHA: No, no. I really don't need them. I only read the headlines anyway. If something is important enough, it'll come up in conversation.

CLARA: [*Whispering.*] She's too vain to wear her glasses.

---

3. Fictional New England town in the 1956 novel of that title by the American writer Grace Metalious (1924–1964); the novel, a best seller, inspired a 1957 movie and a 1964–69 television soap opera. The town has come to represent small towns in the United States (generally ones in which the inhabitants have secrets).

CACHA: Nonsense! I don't like to wear them because they distort everything. I can see. I don't see as well as I used to, but it's gone gradually and I've become accustomed to how I see things. I know my world. Then they gave me those glasses and I didn't know what was what. One minute the wall's over there, the next minute it's closer. If I look up I see you, if I look down I see only your nose!

TATÍN: They're bifocals.

CACHA: They're infuriating! I like to see things equally. If I have to give up reading little letters, it's a small price to pay to keep my world in perspective. [CLARA *fans* PAYE.] I see you got a little color. [PAYE *looks at his forearms.*] Maybe Julio can take you to Mar Verde again. I hear it's really beautiful.

PAYE: It is. You've never been?

CACHA: [*Laughing.*] Me?! Your grandfather used to take me to the beach. He used to go to Ciudamar on Saturday afternoons.

CLARA: Ay, yes!

CACHA: In those days, the beaches were not all public and there was a section, fenced off so that Batista's military men could swim. A diving board, a pavilion, lawn chairs and umbrellas. They had everything. The rest of us had to share two showers and a stretch of sand no bigger than a sandbox. In the private part there were always matrons looking like Eva Perón,[4] covering their porcelain skin from the sun. No negroes were allowed there. [*Laughs.*] But they say that when a black man takes revenge, he does it with style. [*Giggles.*] You know what they used to do? They used to wait for the current to be flowing from the public section to the military and they'd swim over to the rope fence that divided even the water, and they'd shit and wave their load goodbye to the other side! [*Laughs.*] Once your grandfather was floating on his back out in the deep water, when the current suddenly reversed and all the turd kept coming back. He felt something bobbing by his feet; a shark?! No! It was a turd the size of a sausage. [*They're all laughing. The lights start to change slowly into a sunset effect.*] He never went to the beach again. That was in nineteen . . . forty-four. I haven't been to the beach since.

PAYE: You should come with us next time. The sea air will do you good!

CACHA: I'm afraid Mar Verde's not for me.

PAYE: Mar Verde's for everybody. It is paradise! It's beautiful. Abue, it's *so* beautiful. [*He stands at the edge of the verandah. Silence.*]

CACHA: They say that when Columbus landed in Cuba[5] he said: "This is the most beautiful . . ."

PAYE: [*Finishing the quote.*] ". . . beautiful land that human eyes ever beheld."

CACHA: No one is quite certain where Columbus landed, but wherever it was, he certainly summed it up quite nicely. [*The sunset glows for a few seconds. Blackout.*]

---

4. María Eva Duarte de Perón (1919–1952); as the second wife of Juan Domingo Perón (1895–1974), multiterm president of Argentina, she served as the first lady of Argentina from 1946 until her death.

5. Christopher Columbus (1451–1506), Spanish admiral from Genoa, arrived at the island in 1492.

# Act II

*Lights come up on a barrel in the middle of the patio.* JULIO *sings "Quiéreme Mucho" from inside the barrel. He stands up and reveals his bare chest.* PAYE *enters.* JULIO *sings to him . . .*

JULIO:  Remember that one?

PAYE: [*Applauding.*]   I'm surprised *you* remember it.

JULIO:  I always think of you when I hear that song. You sang it at Abuelo's sixtieth birthday. [PAYE *smiles, embarrassed.* JULIO *climbs out of the barrel.*]

PAYE:  Is that it? Fixed?

JULIO: [*Wiping his chest and flexing his muscles.*]   Yes. The outgoing pipe was jammed with dirt. Well, that ought to hold it for a while. Now, you gotta help me get this sucker back up on the roof!

PAYE:  Okay, let's go.

JULIO:  Wait a minute! Let me cool off a second at least. Where's Tatín?

PAYE:  He's writing something for his radio broadcast. I'll get 'im.

JULIO:  No, no. Leave him be. He doesn't have to get sweat on his back. Neither do you, really.

PAYE:  In this heat you can't help but sweat.

JULIO:  Not like this. You guys have brains. You guys don't ever have to exert your muscles. Not like me. All I got is muscles. [*Flexes with pride.*] Nice, no? It drives the women crazy. [*Flexes into another pose.*] I don't have any brains.

PAYE:  I'm sure you do.

JULIO:  No. None to speak of. You guys, you got the brains in the family. I'll cut sugar cane every season and work out with the militia, and that'll be it for the rest of my life.

PAYE:  What would you rather do?

JULIO:  You really want to know.

PAYE:  Yeah, tell me.

JULIO:  What I'd really like to do? I'd like to have a steady sit-down job in an office with a big window to stare out of, like in Havana. And drive a car; one of those little sports cars. Red.

PAYE:  Julio, you're an aspiring playboy.

JULIO:  What's that?

PAYE:  A playboy? It's like a gigolo, but independent.

JULIO:  Oh, yes, I could live with that.

PAYE:  Have you ever thought of leaving . . . ?

JULIO:  No. If you don't have brains, no matter where you go, you still end up shoveling shit. [PAYE *laughs.*] You make lots of money?

PAYE:  Me? No.

JULIO: [*Surprised.*]   How come?

PAYE:  Playwrights don't get to make lots of money.

JULIO:  Is that right? [*Stretches his back muscles. Dries himself off once more.*] You don't mind not making lots of money?

PAYE:  Me? Yeah, I mind. I'm miserable about it.

JULIO:  You didn't want to be a doctor like Ari?

PAYE: No.

JULIO: And you're still outside?

PAYE: What do you mean?

JULIO: Well, if I was going to be something that didn't make lots of money . . . if I was going to be miserable and broke, I'd rather do it in Cuba. Now, you, you got brains. You could be rich! If I had brains, I might consider going abroad and getting rich . . . but then I'd only be miserable outside of Cuba. Twice as miserable. [*Thinks a moment.*] I would have to be *very* rich. I can't understand being abroad and not being rich. There isn't much consolation in that! [*Silence.*] You remember the time you set Tatín's bed on fire?

PAYE: And I threw a bucket of water on him! [*They laugh.*] I locked myself in the bathroom, and when I thought it was quiet enough and everyone was back in bed, I came out . . . Papa was there, with the belt. [*They laugh. Music. Blackout. Lights come up on* AMELIA *on the verandah.*]

AMELIA: [*Shouting.*] Rosario! Ah, compañera. Doña Cacha wants to know if we could borrow some of your chairs for the party?

VOICE: Ay, yes, of course. I have six cane-back ones, four with the chrome legs, the one from my vanity and . . .

AMELIA: How about the long bench?

VOICE: Ay, that's so tough!

AMELIA: It's tougher standing up! There's going to be such a crowd!

VOICE: I've been thinking about the pig all day!

AMELIA: [*Trying to exit.*] I got to run now, I got to run down to Clara to borrow her tablecloths!

VOICE: Ay, Amelia! I only have five cane-backs. I forgot. Graciela busted the other one last week!

AMELIA: She can stand up! [*Blackout. Lights come up on* TATÍN *sitting on the railing center. Smoking. There are party noises in the background. Dance music. Voices. He addresses the audience.*]

TATÍN: Paye's letters were always full of all the wonderful things that are out there. He'd mention steaks he had when there were real shortages here. He'd bring up his trip to Europe and things he'd seen there, and remark too bad you couldn't see this or that. It was as if he wanted to hurt me.

ANA: [*Enters.*] So here you are. [TATÍN *looks.*] It's cooler out here. [*Sits beside him.*] The pork was good, wasn't it? [TATÍN *nods.*] I'm sorry Tía Cuca put sauce all over your rice. I know you don't like it that way. [*There is a burst of laughter from inside.*] Listen to that! Too bad the boys didn't get to come. They should have come, you know. [*Pause.*] I suppose it would have made it harder for you and Paye to talk.

TATÍN: [*Butting a cigarette.*] You were dancing with Paye.

ANA: Yes. He was telling me about seeing Baryshnikov[6] at an open air amphitheater. [*Pause.*] Did he tell you he was unhappy living in Toronto?

TATÍN: Why? Why do you ask?

ANA: I don't know. I always thought that . . . you know . . . but from the way he speaks, I get the feeling he feels . . . dissatisfied.

TATÍN: He's having a bad time of it right now.

ANA: Did he tell you that?

---

6. Mikhail Nikolaevich Baryshnikov (b. 1948), Russian American dancer, choreographer, and actor.

TATÍN:  In dribs and drabs.

ANA:  He still manages pretty well.

TATÍN:  He works at a lot of other things.

ANA:  Ahh! [TATÍN *looks at* ANA.] You know the shirt he's wearing. It's silk.
Bought it in India. He spent three months in India.

TATÍN:  Yes, I know.

ANA:  He's been everywhere.

TATÍN:  Yes, I know. He gets the Sunday *New York Times* and he's met Lillian Hellman. He has an electric typewriter, a private phone and everything Paul Simon[7] ever recorded. [*Pause.*]

ANA:  You wish you were in his shoes?

TATÍN:  I wish I were in anybody else's shoes.

ANA:  Tatín . . .

TATÍN:  What about you? Whose shoes do you wish you were in?

ANA:  I . . . I don't know . . .

TATÍN:  Come on, just off the top of your head.

ANA:  [*Thinks.*]  I guess I still wish that I was Kim Novak.[8]

TATÍN:  Kim Novak?

ANA:  When I was a little girl I always wanted to look like Kim Novak.
Now, Paye tells me she's not even a star anymore.

TATÍN:  You asked Paye about Kim Novak? [*Laughs.*]

ANA:  Well, why not? [TATÍN *laughs heartily.*] You're making me feel stupid. [*Starts to smile.*]

TATÍN:  Kim Novak!!! [*They both burst out laughing.*]

ANA:  [*As laughter subsides.*]  Tatín . . . I know what's the matter . . . why
you've been acting like you've been acting. [TATÍN *looks at her attentively.*] I thought it had to do with Paye . . . His visit and memories
and . . . but, it really has to do with the radio broadcasts, doesn't it? It
does, doesn't it? [*Applause from inside. Voices. As* DILIA *and* CACHA *enter*
TATÍN *jumps to attention as if he'd been discovered.*]

DILIA:  C'mon you two, the party's inside!

TATÍN:  Abue! Tía! [*They walk up stage but sit at the patio.*]

CACHA:  You should be inside dancing!

TATÍN:  We were getting some air.

CACHA:  Ah, yes, it's cooler out here.

DILIA:  You should see Tía Clara!

TATÍN:  She must be boiling over in that dress.

DILIA:  [*To* TATÍN *as if gossiping.*]  She's been trying to match up Amelia
with one of the Moreno boys. Manolo.

TATÍN:  Is he the one with the gold tooth?

DILIA:  No, he's the one with the warts. [*Points to her chin, her cheek, and
her eyebrow. Laughs.*] I think Tía Clara's had too much to drink.

TATÍN:  You're not too sober yourself, Tía.

DILIA:  Drunk? Me?!

TATÍN:  I saw you swig back Tío Nando's beer at the table. More than
once!

7. American singer/songwriter (b. 1941). *Lillian Hellman*: American playwright (1905–1984).
8. American actress (b. 1933).

DILIA:   Tch! That much won't even take the itch from a bee sting! [*Laughter and cheers from inside.*]

CACHA:   Listen to that! [CLARA *enters. She is wearing an overly fancy 50's cocktail dress.*]

CLARA:   Ay! The queen of the carnival is here! I've been dancing and dancing . . .

CACHA:   You better sit . . .

CLARA:   And I'm still in one piece! I'm putting the young girls to shame. [*She sits.*] Ay, to be eighteen again!

CACHA:   Or fifty. [*All laugh.*]

CLARA:   Ay, no! No, Cacha, not me; if I'm going to dream, I want it all beautiful: eighteen, technicolor, violins and blonde hair! I'm glad I got all dressed up! [*Blows down the front of her dress.*]

ANA:   Can I get you a drink, Tía?

CLARA:   Ay, Anita, you know I don't drink. But be an angel and get me my fan. It's on the table by the gramophone. [ANA *exits.*] I'm just a little hot, but as soon as I cool off . . . Ay Cacha, I didn't take a break! [*Laughs.*]

CACHA:   Clara, remember Monday's wash day.

CLARA:   I may not even wash this Monday. [*Music changes to a conga.*]

DILIA:   Conga! [DILIA *exits dancing.*]

ANA: [*Entering.*]   I think Julio's drunk, he keeps trying to lift Tía Carmen. [*Gives* CLARA *her fan and ice water.*]

CLARA:   You'll know he's drunk when he tries to lift Graciela! [TATÍN *laughs.*]

CACHA:   You should laugh, you used to go out with her.

ANA:   Before he was married.

CLARA:   Before she was fat!

PAYE: [*Off.*]   Tía Clara! Conga!

CLARA:   Ay, a request! A request!

CACHA:   Slow down, Clara . . .

CLARA: [*Hurriedly trying to put on shoes.*]   I'm fine, Cacha . . . [*Suddenly screams.*] Anhhh! My bunion! I can't get my shoes back on! [*All laugh.*]

ANA:   Sit this one out, Tía.

CLARA:   Not on your life! I'll have to dance barefoot.

CACHA:   Clara, tomorrow, you'll . . .

CLARA: [*Getting up.*]   Tomorrow, I don't care if they amputate! [*Hobbles off, waving her shoes in the air.*]

ANA:   She's crazy!

CACHA:   Ay, no, Anita. Clara's wearing her party dress, that's all. I'm glad Julio got the pig—and that we've all made it like the carnival for Paye. [DILIA *laughs from inside.*] When your grandfather was alive, there'd be parties in this house till noon the next day. Your uncles . . . when they were young, they used to dance like they had an itch in their groins from the inside out. Your Uncle Pucho used to spend the three days of the carnival dancing. Even when he came by for a clean shirt in the afternoons, he'd be congaing through the house singing, "If I don't dance, I lose the beat, if I don't dance, I lose the beat," over and over and over.

DILIA: [*Entering.*] You should see Paye dancing. He hasn't forgotten that he's Cuban! And Tía Clara! You know she's dancing barefoot? [*Takes* CLARA's *fan.*]

ANA: I've never seen Tía Clara like this.

DILIA: Two weeks ago, all she could talk about was her hemorrhoids! Poor Tía Clara! Having to do without Paye all these years.

CLARA: [*Enters.*] The room's spinning in there.

DILIA: Tired, Tía?

CLARA: No! I just wanted the young girls to have a crack at Paye. Give me my fan. [*Sits.*]

DILIA: You're going to have to give away that dress after tonight.

CLARA: It'll wash.

ANA: Tía, you should get a new one.

CLARA: And where is one supposed to get this kinda material in . . .

DILIA: Don't get her started, please. [*Cheers are heard from inside.*]

CLARA: Listen to that! It sounds like the old days. Ay, if Sylvia and Tato could only be here tonight. [*To* ANA.] Sylvia used to have such a good time at these things. Once she had two drinks in her, she didn't know if she was talking English, Spanish or Jew. [*To* DILIA.] You remember the time she was trying to tell Father Ephraim that he hit the nail on the head and she wound up telling him that he really knew how to screw! [*All laugh.*]

PAYE: [*Enters holding a beer.*] So the party's out here.

DILIA: Look at him, he's soaking wet!

CACHA: Isn't he beautiful! Why don't you change your shirt, you'll . . .

PAYE: I just have the shirt I'm leaving with tomorrow.

CACHA: What did you do with the others?

TATÍN: He's leaving some to me.

PAYE: And Julio, and Roberto and so on and so on.

CACHA: What are you going to do, run around Canada naked?

PAYE: How's everybody doing out here? [*All mumble "fine" or "all right," except* CLARA, *who is staring into space.* PAYE *stumbles.*]

DILIA: You're drunk, Paye.

CLARA: Everybody's drunk to you, Dilia. It's a pity you never had a husband, then you'd know what drunk really was.

DILIA: Let's not start on that one!

AMELIA: [*Enters wearing her full carnival costume.*] Where's Paye?

CACHA: Ay, Amelia!

DILIA: See, Tía, Amelia couldn't stand to see you the only one all dressed up.

CLARA: Turn around, let's see.

AMELIA: I promised Paye I'd try it on before he left.

PAYE: It's superb!

AMELIA: La Placita's going to take first prize this year.

DILIA: As always! [AMELIA *exits.*]

CACHA: Having a good time, Paye?

PAYE: The time of my life. [*Raises his drink.*] To La Placita!

CACHA: Tonight we're all happy, Paye.

DILIA: You'll have a lot to tell them when you get back.

CACHA: Ay, yes, look at him; he's even got some color. [CLARA *fans* PAYE, *who has put himself within reach of the breeze.*]

DILIA: A few more days at Mar Verde and he'd really start looking like a Cuban again!

PAYE: [*Suddenly standing up.*] I have something to say. [*A shrill scream from inside.*]

DILIA: I better go see . . .

PAYE: No, no, Tía, sit down. I want everyone to hear. [*Kisses her.*] You know, I used to be afraid of you. [*To all.*] Now I find out that Tía loves me after all.

DILIA: Ay, Paye, you're drunk!

PAYE: [*Raising his beer.*] To my Tía Dilia! [*Tries to stand on a chair.*]

ANA: [*To* TATÍN.] I think he's had too much to . . .

CLARA: Ay, yes, Paye, sit down.

PAYE: [*Kissing* CLARA.] No, no, Tía. Now that everyone is here. [*Looks around.*] Well, the main ones . . . my family [*Pause.*] I want to return to Cuba for good! [*There is a momentary silence.*]

TATÍN: He's drunk!

PAYE: No, I'm not. I want to come home. If you'll have me?!

TATÍN: You're crazy! [*There are voices rasied from inside. A girl screams.* PAYE *and* TATÍN *shout over the voices.*]

PAYE: What's so crazy about it? It happens . . .

AMELIA: [*In a panic.*] Dilia, come quick. It's Julio; he's drunk!

TATÍN: You don't know what the hell you're saying! You couldn't live here!

VOICE: [*Off.*] Julio!

VOICE: [*Off.*] Get somebody, quick, get Dilia! [DILIA *exits.*]

TATÍN: It's not as simple as that!

VOICE: [*Off.*] What the hell is he doing?!

PAYE: What's the matter, don't you want me here?!

TATÍN: No!

PAYE: It's my home!

AMELIA: Dilia, hurry!

VOICE: [*Off.*] Don't let 'im! Grab him!

VOICE: [*Off.*] Go around!

VOICE: [*Off.*] Stop him!

TATÍN: You're thinking of no one but yourself! Well I got news for you. Life in Cuba isn't like you've seen here this week. There isn't always a party.

VOICE: [*Off.*] He's had too much to drink!

PAYE: And you think I have everything given to me on a silver platter!

VOICE: [*Off.*] Don't, Julio!

AMELIA: Dilia, he's taking off everything!

VOICE: [*Off.*] Stop it, Julio! [*The voices from inside have increased in urgency. Screams.* JULIO *appears stark naked.* AMELIA *and* DILIA *run after him.* DILIA *stops at upstage door.*]

JULIO: Adiós, Abuela! [PAYE *and* TATÍN *ignore the chase and get into a screaming match of their own.*]

TATÍN: You wouldn't be happy here!

PAYE: Julio is!

TATÍN: You're not Julio!!! [TATÍN *climbs on the table.*] I have an announcement too. I'm leaving Cuba for good!

ANA: On what boat?

DILIA: That is the most preposterous . . .

ANA: What about us, your wife and your kids?

TATÍN: Why is it with the goddamned Cubans that they won't listen and they all want to speak at once?

PAYE: Well, you'll have to put up with me because I intend to apply to come back.

TATÍN: I will do everything in my power to stop you.

PAYE: You hateful son of a bitch, what power do you have?!

TATÍN: You don't think I heard what you said to Amelia! I'll report that . . .

PAYE: You stinking commie bastard—you'd betray your brother to get your way . . . You hate me that much.

TATÍN: Bullshit!

PAYE: Yes, it's hate—and I hate you back. You have the heart of a cockroach. [PAYE goes wild screaming.] I hate you! I hate you! I hate you!!! [TATÍN slaps PAYE. PAYE slaps him back. Silence. PAYE bursts into tears and falls into TATÍN's arms. DILIA notices that CACHA is having difficulty breathing.]

DILIA: Mama! [To ANA.] Water!

CLARA: Take mine. [She does.]

PAYE: Abuela?

CACHA: I'm okay. I'm okay.

DILIA: [To ANA and CLARA.] Help me get her to bed. [PAYE goes to help.]

TATÍN: No. Stay. [Trying not to be heard.] I don't hate you, Paye. I don't want you here because if I could I'd leave myself.

PAYE: [Loudly.] You! You want to leave Cuba! [ANA and DILIA turn to look at TATÍN. PAYE sits.]

TATÍN: If I could get my wife and my sons out—all at once—I'd take the next plane, boat, raft out of here.

PAYE: What?

TATÍN: This is a mess. We're sending troops to Angola, we're buying arms from Russia. My radio show is being censored. My writing is being questioned . . .

PAYE: In the six days that I've been here, you've been leading me to believe . . .

TATÍN: You believed what you wanted to believe. [ANA enters.]

ANA: Is that what it is, Tatín?

TATÍN: Yes. [ANA crosses to him and puts her arms around him in support.]

PAYE: How is she?

ANA: All right. The shock, her age. She's breathing fine now.

TATÍN: Do you want to leave, Ana?

ANA: I'm not the one who's being censored.

TATÍN: Could you leave?

ANA: My needs are simple. A ballet bar and a bunch of kids doing demipliés—anywhere. But if we leave, Tatín, we all leave together. You, me, the boys. All four of us. Paye, you have a plane to catch tomorrow. I'm glad you came. It doesn't take much to live in Cuba. Just blind faith. Either you have it or you don't. [She hugs PAYE.]

PAYE: [Returning the embrace.] Thank you, Ana. [ANA exits. To TATÍN.] What are you going to do?

TATÍN:   Leaving Cuba is a slow, tedious process at best.

PAYE:   You know, Tatín, I never felt like I belonged anywhere as much as I do here. I have been living in exile all these years. And you're right, I'm not writing. And I don't care if I ever write again.

TATÍN:   You don't mean that.

PAYE:   Yes, I do. I only write because I'm lonely. Because I'm seeking approval from total strangers in the dark, because . . .

TATÍN:   You have something to say. You have imagination.

PAYE:   Up there, in the winter, people bundle up and cast their eyes on the sidewalk. Ice is slippery. It's a way of life. You don't look up. You don't see who you're passing on the street.

TATÍN:   Here, the committees are becoming more powerful. Now that my work is getting noticed abroad, what I write becomes scrutinized. I'm asked what things mean by people who learned to read ten years ago.

PAYE:   Surely you knew there'd be censorship?

TATÍN:   Of course. It is understood that until stability is reached, censorship is necessary, and that under siege, the militia must be armed to the teeth. Our neighbors must be watched. Our people must be indoctrinated so that they can learn to cope with the new way of life. [He lights up a cigarette.] But, that has become the new way of life. You see, Paye, I am a disillusioned man. And it makes me sad.

PAYE:   So what will you do?

TATÍN:   I have two sons who know nothing but this and who believe fervently the lessons they've been taught. And in a few years, they'll be of military age and won't be allowed to leave. [There is a long silence.] Paye, stay abroad. And write.

AMELIA: [Enters.]   We found Julio! [Giggles.]

TATÍN:   Shhh! Abuela's in bed.

AMELIA: [Suppressing her laughter.]   He was sitting on the pitcher's mound on a nest of red ants. [She laughs.]

TATÍN:   It's not funny.

AMELIA:   His balls are swollen like pineapples! [She exits.]

PAYE:   I'll envy you the carnival.

TATÍN: [Shrugging his shoulders.]   Euphoria for the masses, a little something to ease the pain. What time is your plane? [Before PAYE can reply, DILIA enters.]

DILIA:   Paye, Mama wants to see you. She is afraid she'll fall asleep and you'll leave without seeing her. Tatín, you wouldn't leave, would you? [Almost in tears.] When Mama dies, what will I do? [TATÍN bursts into tears in DILIA's arms. Lights fade. Lights come up in CACHA's room. PAYE is sitting on the edge of the bed under the mosquito net.]

PAYE:   Abuela?

CACHA:   Paye?

PAYE:   Tía said . . .

CACHA:   I've been waiting for you. They gave me something, I think to make me sleep, but I've been waiting . . . I must talk to you, Paye.

PAYE:   Yes, Abue.

CACHA:   Here, sit close to me. [PAYE moves closer.]

CACHA:   I'm not going to die, Paye. Not yet. I . . . I'm waiting for everyone to come home. They have to come. Because I'm waiting. [Touches PAYE's *hand lovingly.*] Tomorrow . . . I will have to speak to Julio. And Tatín! Tell them. I will speak to them tomorrow.

PAYE: Yes, Abue. Now rest . . . [*Starts to get up.*]

CACHA: [*Holding him back.*] Tato is my son. You are my grandson. You were born in my arms! [*SILENCE.*] This is your home, Paye. No one can turn you away. You understand, Paye?

PAYE: Yes, Abue.

CACHA: Even after I'm dead . . . this is your home. You were born in my arms, Paye. In this house.

PAYE: Abue . . .

CACHA: You will come back, Paye. I know it. Maybe not soon, but you will come back. You will all come back. [*Reaches out for him.*] My little Paye.

PAYE: [*Controlling his emotions.*] Sleep now, Abuela, tomorrow . . .

CACHA: Yes. Tomorrow. Tell Tato I'm fine. I'm not going to die. Tomorrow, Paye . . . Paye-Paye. [CACHA *is asleep.* PAYE *kisses her. Music comes up softly. Blackout. Lights come up on* DILIA, ANA *and* TATÍN *facing front on the verandah.* CACHA *joins them. They clap and wave as though the carnival were passing by. There is carnival music. On the stage right corner, a light comes up on* PAYE. *He is speaking into a tape recorder.*]

PAYE: It is coming around to winter again real soon. The trees all over the city are a carnival of color; though in my mind they'll never compare to the carnival I missed that time. I shall never stop missing it. It and everything else I left behind. No matter where I am, I guess a part of me will always be there. My home. [*Pause.*] I miss you, Tatín. I think of you all the time. I think of what we said to one another and what we left still unsaid. [*Pause.*] I never quite managed to tell you that . . . that I love you, and that neither miles, nor long silences, will ever alter that. It's a pleasant thought that makes my exile less cruel, easier to bear. Enough said and not enough. Mama and Papa are trying all they can through the Jamaican Embassy. Mama knows the counsel well and she seems hopeful that he'll get you and your family out. A million warm and gentle kisses for you and the whole family . . . from your brother who awaits you, Paye. P.S. I am enclosing a copy of my play. I hope you like it. [*As he speaks the last few words, everything goes wild with color and light. The music swells and confetti pours from the sky. Suddenly the music stops and all freeze in a tableau as the confetti falls slowly as in a glass-enclosed souvenir shaker. As the last of the confetti falls, lights fade to black.*]

1986                                                                              1991

# ALBERTO BALTAZAR HEREDIA
# URISTA aka ALURISTA
# b. 1947

Alberto Baltazar Heredia Urista, better known as "Alurista," began publishing poetry as a teenager. His presence at the forefront of Chicano letters dates to the establishment of some of the earliest Chicano publishing houses, such as Quinto Sol, in Berkeley, California, and Pajarito, in Albuquerque, New Mexico. He was among the first Chicano writers to develop a bilingual voice, introducing linguistic code switching as a fundamental component of Chicano poetry.

Alurista was born in Mexico City and attended primary school in the Mexican state of Morelos. With his family, he moved to the United States at age 13 and settled in San Diego. In addition to his public-school assignments, his readings included in-depth studies of the history, literature, and folklore of the Aztecs and the Mayas. These studies influenced his first publications, in the 1960s, when he began to take poetry seriously and became fluent in Spanish, English, and pre-Columbian languages. After graduating from high school in 1965, he became a business administration major at Chapman University, in Orange County, California. He later transferred to San Diego State University to study religion, but earned his bachelor's degree in psychology in 1970 and a master's degree in 1978. He cofounded the Chicano Studies Department at San Diego State, and in the mid-1970s he taught in the fledgling Center for Mexican American Studies at the University of Texas at Austin. In 1983, Alurista earned his doctorate in literature from the University of California, San Diego, with a dissertation on the work of Oscar "Zeta" Acosta (see p. 1039). Since then, he has taught at California Polytechnic State University, in San Luis Obispo, and Escuela Tlatelolco, in Denver, Colorado.

An activist in and out of the classroom, Alurista became involved with César Chávez's farmworkers' strike in Delano in the 1960s. In addition, he is credited as one of the earliest proponents of Aztlán as the Chicano homeland, a physical and mental territory to be reclaimed by Mexican Americans. In 1969, Alurista collaborated with political figures in the writing of *El plan espiritual de Aztlán* (The Spiritual Plan of Aztlán) and read it at the first Chicano Youth Liberation Conference, held in Denver, Colorado, and sponsored by Rodolfo "Corky" Gonzales and his Crusade for Justice organization (p. 787).

The experience with Chávez and the farmworkers made Alurista aware of the labor conditions of Mexican migrants on the fields and thus helped define his artistic vision. Beginning in 1967, he embraced the collective voice of Chicano workers. In the late 1960s, Alurista was a member of the Brown Berets, a Chicano nationalist activist group. In San Diego, he worked for the Volunteers in Service for America (VISTA), an antipoverty program created by U.S. president Lyndon Johnson's Economic Opportunity Act of 1964 as a domestic version of the Peace Corps. Alurista's first poetry collection, the groundbreaking *Floricanto en Aztlán* (*Flor y canto*, Flower and Song, in Aztlán, 1971), displays his affinities. He uses the sarape, a colorful woolen shawl that is typically a working-class garment, as the symbol of *la raza de bronce*, itself derived from the modern politician and philosopher José Vasconcelos's concept of the Bronze Race. (See Appendix 3: Influential Essays by Latin American Writers, p. A65.) Also typical is Alurista's mingling of Spanish and English and his embrace of Spanglish.

His interest in religion, particularly in Catholicism, dates to his teenage years, when he became interested in serving the Church and entered a school for aspirants to the priesthood. He left three months later because he came to see the Church as a business. The break with the Church is revealed in his second book, *Nationchild Plumaroja* [Red feather], *1969–1972* (1972), in which he decries parishioners' kneeling in church and their subservience to an institution that disregards their frailties. *Floricanto en Aztlán* and *Nationchild Plumaroja* became foundational texts of the Chicano canon. In 1973, Alurista cofounded the first, and most successful, Floricanto festival, which brought Chicano writers to the campus of the University of Southern California, among them Oscar "Zeta" Acosta, Rolando Hinojosa (p. 842), and Tomás Rivera (see p. 1077). Floricantos became a tradition among Mexican American writers, with annual gatherings on campuses in Milwaukee, Wisconsin; Corpus Christi, Texas; and Austin, Texas. (When a festival scheduled for Pueblo, Colorado, failed to materialize, the tradition ended.)

In a 1976 review, the critic Tomás Ybarra-Frausto called Alurista's *Timespace Huracán: Poems, 1972–1975* "a synthesis of previous thematic concerns and a new departure." Ybarra-Frausto was among the readers who saw Alurista's use of lowercase letters as displaying the influence of the American poet E. E. Cummings. Among those who disagreed was Gary D. Keller, founder of the Bilingual Review Press, who argued that Alurista's "intention is usually to undermine the oppressive status of English, to put it on a par with Spanish, which rarely uses capitals." In *Spik in Glyph?* (1981), Alurista celebrated the Chicano working class, decried oppression and the Vietnam War, and attacked the policies of the Reagan administration, but his writing emphasized linguistic experimentation, especially the use of puns. Some critics reacted negatively to his focus on language. Others believed Alurista and other Chicano poets of his generation romanticized the Amerindian past. In 1986, the scholar Cordelia Candelaria argued that the declining quality of Alurista's poetry merely "reconfirms the greatness" of *Floricanto en Aztlán* and *Nationchild Plumaroja*.

Alurista's subsequent publications include *Z Eros* (1995), *Et tu . . . Raza?* (1996), and the compilation *Chorizo Tonguefire* (1999). With his then wife, Xelina Rojas, he edited the short-lived literary journal *Maize* and two anthologies: *Festival de flor y canto: An Anthology of Chicano Literature* (1976) and *Southwest Tales: A Contemporary Collection* (1986). Along with Juan Felipe Herrera and Mario Aguilar, between 1973 and 1975, he was part of the music and theater ensemble Servidores del Arbol de la Vida (Guardians of the Tree of Life). During the mid-1990s, Alurista traveled and performed with the Taco Shop Poets, a spoken-word initiative that began in 1994 as a poetry series at the Centro Cultural de la Raza in San Diego's Balboa Park. However, he disapproved of the use of hip-hop style in Chicano poetry, stating that hip-hop was not part of the Chicano literary tradition. After spending the period from 1995 to 1998 in a "spiritual meandering," Alurista moved to San Jose, California.

The three Alurista poems in this anthology—"a bone," "sometime war," and "labyrinth of scarred hearts"—are a representative sample of his aesthetic and his Chicano consciousness. The fourth selection, "juan," is the first chapter of Alurista's somewhat plotless novel, *as our barrio turns . . . who the yoke b on?* (2000), which offers snapshots of his activist years, his youthful travels in Mexico, his criticism of Catholicism, and his role in building the Chicano Movement. The material is delivered in an idiosyncratic Spanglish, emphasized through anarchic spelling in English. The seven chapters are named after the Spanish mispronunciations of the first seven Arabic numbers (*juan, tú, tree, for, fi, seek, se ven*), and the book opens with a disclaimer:

> resemblance to any actual person is deliberate. the historical timespace b real. based in the bellybutton of Aztlán: san Diego. inspired by a real character: emiliano Zapata del ejido de Anenecuilco, morelos. all other characters' names have been changed to protect the guilty.

"Juan" is about adolescent sex and rebellion and is set against a political background in the Mexican state of Zacatecas, known for its sugar production.

## a bone

time
it shines with
a bone in one
hand
strange jate                                    5
dusty dreams
of immortality
of power
omnipotent
delusions                                      10
test waves
rippled waters
trickling blood
hemorrhage
and death                                      15
killing time
it shines with
a bone
in one hand

1972


## labyrinth of scarred hearts

labyrinth of scarred hearts
    wounded in the sown struggle
    sproutings in the making of a
        historical leaf of radical movement
a people powered in red clad faith               5
en penitencia guerrera
en revolución morena[1] grasp
    serene hands on the earth
plowing, plowing
    watering in tears for torn backs            10
and burning perspiration in the fields
a few paths lead, follow and walk
    alone, to the light out the cueva
out the solitude caverna de miedo[2]
on                                               15
to the path that has a heart
a nomad drinking agua de barro
cortando la maleza
    con machete voluntad,[3] cutting the earth
healing the wounds planting barro[4]            20

1. A warrior penitence / in brown revolution.    machete of will.
2. Cavern of fear. *Cueva*: cave.                4. Mud.
3. Water of mud / cutting the weeds / with a

planting paths with heart
and clarity

                                                    1972

## sometime war

sometime war
of hollow hearts
well wedded to the wind
blowing blitz of propaganda
down the throats                                     5
of iks / yank iks[1]

          people without love
          agitating nightmares
          off the shore of dreams
          professorial chatterboxes    10
          chatter day
          and chatter night

many moonglooms full of wrath
running down the mazes
labyrinths of fear                                   15
heroin's full blossom
minds addicted, crucified
to the broken lines

          thought flows freely
          towards death               20
          nightmares wallow deep
          drunken lies of "progress"
          dying empires!
          dawn is near!

                                                    1976

---

### FROM AS OUR BARRIO TURNS . . . WHO THE YOKE B ON?[1]

#### juan

i first met her at the ingenio azucarero[2] de Zacatepec, the heart of the sugar
cane monopoly in the great state of morelos; zuzana. Our eyes locked. i was

1. Possibly a play on "icks / yank-icks (i.e.,
yankees)."
1. The first part of the title is a playful reference

to the long-running soap opera *As the World
Turns.*
2. *Ingenio azucarero:* sugar mill.

leading a pack of ocelotl from the cristóbal colón, a military catholic school in cuernavaca.[3] her school, too, was on a field trip. the nuns guarded them like jewels off the pope's crown. we managed to stumble into each other behind one of the thrashers where the paper-to-be refuse of the cut and cleaned sugar canes were machine-deposited after extracting all the sugar from them. zuzana was also on scholarship at the sor juana inés de la cruz catholic school for girls.[4] i knew the school well, it was across from ours. we were both in the fourth grade. the little jaguars were looking for me while zuzanita y yo nos abrazábamos, nos besábamos.[5] we kissed and hugged, kiss 'n' hugged 'n' hugged 'n' kissed. we belonged to the same class across the street where sexuality palpitated in each of us. quique and vic found us conversing, dialoguing, laughing, holding hands . . . everyone was lining up by the buses. the left hands on shoulder were going up.

—you're tarde! the discipline sticks 'r' being readied.

—vamos or the palo de membrillo[6] will slice our calves!

—i'll get there in time jaguares! let's go, zuzi

. . . the motors of the buses are warming up. i make it in, just before the gate slams shut.

—we almost got fried, xandro. my spinal column revertebrates, reverberates, i am in love . . .

the bus ride back to cuernavaca snakes us back through rolling hills of maize fields receeding to the onslaught of the sugar caña, cash crop in the world market. the people ate maize and chewed caña and used its strands to floss. refined sugar had not scoured the jewels off their jaws. el quique wants to be a dentist and vic has all his dice in law school. not one of the jaguars want to pursue a military career at the capital in el colegio militar de México. we are feline, they are canine. the upperclassman riding with us today stands in front of the aisle and commences his tirade of praises for the mexican army—at the time hunting for rubén jaramillo, a campesino from Cuauhtla[7] who has taken up arms against the hacendados[8] and the sugar mill company.

what is our school?!
cristóbal colón! in chorus all dogs howl.
what is our tradition?!
cristóbal colón! catholic!
what is our honor?!
cristóbal colón! méxico!
what is our discipline?!

3. A town south of Mexico City. *Ocelotl*: ocelots (medium-sized wildcats). *Cristóbal Colón*: Spanish name of Christopher Columbus (1451–1506), Spanish admiral and explorer from Genoa.
4. *Sor Juana Inés de la Cruz*: Mexican nun, scholar, and writer (1648/51–1695).

5. And we hugged, we kissed.
6. A reference to the quince, an apple-like fruit.
7. Farmworker from the town of San Gabriel Cuauhtla, southern-central Mexico.
8. Hacienda owners.

cristóbal colón! military!
what is our excellence?!
cristóbal colón! the arts and sciences.
crastíbol culón[9] . . . the jaguares mutter.

you know there is that bandido out there in our state roads. rubén jaramillo
and his band of thugs are stopping the sugar cane trucks and burning them.
jaramillo is a terrorist. he has kidnapped citizens from the capital. the fingers of these people have been cut off to take their rings. ladies have lost
emeralds and pearls off their necks, yanked by the paws of this misguided
rabble who think castro and guevara[1] a worthy example and sign of the
times. rubén jaramillo must be infomed that the zapatista[2] days are over. we
have to inform him that zapata is dead and history! jaramillo must and will
be brought to justice. military lieutenants trained in this our treasured cristóbal colón, true men, who, from here, went on to the colegio militar de
México in Tenoxtitlan,[3] are now amongst the principal strategists plotting
to capture and execute rubén once and for all.

—this dude is waco,[4] xandro, like we got ourselves a rising little adolfo
here.

—yeah, just what we need, another hitler,[5] a mexican hitler.

—hey, let's throw a cuete out the window. audy murphy[6] here will think
we're being shot at!

—hey cat, that can be dangerous . . .

—all the better, this ride is boring me.

—here they go!

—stop the bus! cadets! hit the floor! camilo, you come with me. bring your
forty-five. where the hell is the mausser?[7] open the door . . . slowly . . .

there is a magnificent mockingbird symphony on the edge of the cornfield.
finches and cardinals criss-cross the road chirping snappy tunes. eagles
swoop and sway high above the low hills to the west. the sun races with
them, seeking the coolness of the guerrero[8] state coast. dopey hitler and
our bus driver camilo go into the milpa.[9] the cornfields are tall, and the

9. *Crastíbol*: a play on Cristóbal. *Culón*: scaredy
cat.
1. The Cuban revolutionary leaders Fidel Castro
(b. 1926) and Ernesto "Che" Guevara (1928–
1967).
2. Follower of the Mexican revolutionary leader
Emiliano Zapata (1879–1919).
3. Also spelled Tenochtitlán; the original Nahuatl
name of Mexico City.
4. A play on "wacko" and the city of Waco, Texas.
In 1993, a ranch north of Waco became the site
of the Waco Siege, a deadly confrontation between the U.S. Bureau of Alcohol, Tobacco, and
Firearms and the Branch Davidian cult.
5. I.e., another Adolf Hitler (1889–1945),
Austrian-born founder of Nazism, leader of Germany 1933–45.
6. Audie Murphy (1926?–1971), a U.S. soldier
and real-life war hero, plays himself in the movie
version of his autobiography, *To Hell and Back*
(1955). *Cuete*: firework.
7. Rifle or pistol made by Mauser, a German arms
manufacturer. *Forty-five*: a .45-caliber pistol.
8. Warrior.
9. A small corn field owned by a campesino.

stalks stand heavy with ears ready to pluck ripe, crowned with the golden hairs of maturity and full flavor. we hear a couple of shots: no doubt into the air. dopey returns to the bus. camilo sits smoking by the road, squatting as only Mixtecas[1] know how, holding his cigarette with both hands, as in prayer.

—it's all right now, cadets! you may rise to your feet. the vandals ran at the shot of my mausser and the sight of our full regalia. our uniform is feared, you know. we are the military school in morelos.

—ah pu's qué![2] you are the military in morelos, not us, quique mumbles.

—pinchi[3] liar! i'm telling you . . . i bet he believes what he is barking.

—let's suggest an elote cookout before we get back and let's have a séance at dusk.

—sir, lieutenant pedroza, sir—clicking boots and saluting with garb—some of the cadets would like to suggest an elote[4] cookout by the field, in order to let these vandals know that we, from cristóbal colón, will hold ground against any guerrilleros.[5]

—identify yourself when you address me, dog!

—underclassman vic, at your command sir!

—who knows how to handle detail for this operation, dog?!

—xandro, sir! underclassman xandro.

—you may leave, dog. xandro!

—at your command sir, lieutenant pedroza, sir!

—do you know how to handle an elote cookout detail, dog?

—yes sir!

—what are you waiting for? on the double! you got two hours!

—may i have two men, sir?!

—choose your puppies, dog!

—vic, you get the wood, get two perros[6] to help you. quique, you get the rocks. you'll need at least four perros. i'll clear the ground for the fire. rest of you dogs come with me, half of you go into the milpa and gather fifty two

1. Those from Mixteca, a region in Mexico.
2. Or *pues qué*: so what?
3. Or *pinche*: fucking.

4. Corn.
5. Guerilla fighters.
6. Dogs.

ears, the biggest ones. the other half come with me. let's clear a circle, get branches everyone! this is sweeping duty, compañeros. who knows we may even get to spend the night here. quique, wait. i got to talk to you. look . . . i'll distract camilo and dopey while you get the tires deflated. use the pencil, the eraser side. just push it into the tire valves.

—you're nuts, xandro. they'll have our heads if we get caught!

—they'll have yours if you don't synchronize with me. in ten minutes i'll call them to approve the fire site. by then your perros should be bringing down the rocks. hang to the rear and do it! or do i have to do everything? do you want to distract them while i do it? what the heck are you going to talk to them about? i'm the one with the gab, remember?

i haven't done this for two moons. this is february's waning moon with mars inside the lunar slice rising on the east. it is more fun at compadre cheno's ranchito. his field is near, up on the hills and often guarded by rattlesnakes which feed on the mice and even blackbirds that come looking for seed at planting time. by the time we had our first elote, the milpas towered above us and we had to pick the half-stalk ears.

first it is necessary to surround the milpa and walk in one direction making noise with wooden rattles and drums to shoo the snakes out the west side of the field. the best sling shooters try their best at a snake head which is the only way to kill one and claim its rattle as a prize. this is a low field, and the mice stay away from the trained ocelotes Tata Xieu keeps as pets. the rattle-snakes take to the milpa alta, the high ground away from the stream and the people. they like the rocks.

—lieutenant pedroza, the site is clear and ready for approval, sir!

—very well, cadet! i'll draw the circle. bring in the rocks, the wood.

—we'll need camilo to start the fire, sir.

—camilo! get your indian ass down here! pero, ya! on the double!

sssssshhhhh. sssssshhhhhh. two tires flat. quique stealthily blends with the other rock-carrying perros. vic is coming back with enough wood for two fogatas[7] and then some. the corn plucking perros have been piling the ears of maize by the now well-drawn one-meter-in-diameter circle. dopey hitler barks out orders to set the rock circle, pile the wood and ready some dry husks of maize for firing. camilo has gotten a spark going with his ronson . . . i do wonder where he got that silver-cased lighter. he says he won it in a game of cubilete dice.[8] we now have to wait about an hour for the fire to settle into embers so that we can position the corn ears, husks and all, to roast on the cinders. vic, quique and i make our disappearing act

7. Bonfires.
8. *Cubilete*: tumbler, goblet; i.e., a holder used in throwing dice.

to the west side of the field. our séance is about to begin. the yellow-white sun is flaming orange-red. the fire crackles yellow-red with blue-white tips. the three of us assume the Mixteca squat with our palms hanging loosely on our knees. we can feel our own pulse that way and tune it with our breathing to dance with the gentle breeze that brings the frog song to the lowlands. i'm in love.

—zapatavive, vic whispers, enunciating clearly . . . zapatalives, zapatavive, jaguares, zapatavive.

—'n' we gonna stay here all night, felinos, quique duskdreams.

i try to visualize hita on the face of the smirking february moon with mars glowing on her forehead. Huitzilopoxtli[9] scintillates its red seeds as our irises expand, focusing on its light.

—camilo! what is the meaning of this!? here i come to get my poncho, and the tires are flat!!?

camilo circles the bus three times and concludes.

—the sun, the heat, the road, the wind is out of them. we will need to fill them up tomorrow morning, dawn: when the sugar cane trucks pass this road.

—que la chingada![1] of all freaking times. the senior cadets ball is tomorrow night. i have trillions of things to do! mierda!

—we better get more wood, patroncito teniente[2] . . . the cadets . . .

camilo walks away smirking like the slivered moon and sparkling light off his third red eye. his eyebrows arch like a hawk in full swoop to capture prey, walking toward the campfire.

—o'nta xandro? i need to speak to him, joven[3] perro, i sit here and wait.

squat palms hanging five off his knees, feeling his pulse, controlling his breath to dance with the dusk.

—xandro! camilo's looking for your face, and his looks are death incarnate. you better come now!

the sun had glowed out of our western gaze. guerrero ocean waters would quench his thirst.

—a'i voy! brothers. the séance is over. for all our relatives, our feline mind, amén! vámonos![4]

9. An Aztec god.
1. What the fuck!
2. Lieutenant boss.

3. Young (man). O'nta: Where is it? (¿Adónde está?).
4. Let's go! A'i voy!: There I go!

we raced back through the milpa high-stepping our knees to the height of our waist. it was easier and faster to go through the field the way Xieu had taught us. vic and henry ran up to the edge of the fogata and warmed their hands and behinds. i walked right up to camilo. i had no choice except die.

—hear you looking for me, milo.

—el dopey is fuming. you better pray to our lord and lady that the caña trucks don't get intercepted. lieutenant pedroza will fry me before he fries any of you.

—you know the so-called "balazos"[5] were not gunshots, camilo. you know better. the trucks will show up at the brake of dawn. this is Tata Xieu land, que nó? well . . . then . . . as napoleón said to this coachman: "slowdown, i'm in a hurry!" as cantinflas[6] would have it, camilo: "reeelax, reelax, relax." the elotes are ready. quieres unos?[7] muchachos! al maize! call little hitler camilo, he's probably hungry.

—you best pray, little jaguar. best pray.

adolfito walks into the camp. strutting like an angry peacock while turning his eyelids into snake squints. we offer him two of the best roasted ears. he barks.

—hay agua?!, he howls! we got water?!

—hay ron,[8] camilo whispers to his chest.

—cadets! chowtime! kill it! get water from the stream. camilo, leave me the rum.

we gather more wood and ears of corn. we have to post guard for Tata Xieu's ocelotes; though domestic cat size they bear the hearts of ancient jaguars, pumas, and mountain lions. ocelotes can be very mean if provoked. they normally do not bother with big game like humans. they are worse than pit dogs if you cross them. camilo returns with lard cans filled with water. Tata Xieu keeps them by the stream for occasions like this one. this is a pilgrimage stop to Xochicalco,[9] in cuernavaca. lieutenant pedroza is getting bored . . . and drunk. he's not allowed to fraternize with the underclassmen. i know what's coming.

—camilo! organize a boxing match between the feistiest perritos here present. now let's have a sixth grader and a puppy. a feisty . . . little dog. camilo! let's have us some fun. here, have a swig . . . indio de tu madre! have a swig!

5. Gunshots.
6. Mexican comedian and actor (Fortino Mario Alfonso Moreno Reyes, 1911–1993). *Napoleón*: Napoleón Bonaparte (1769–1821), emperor of France 1804–15.
7. Do you want some?
8. There's rum.
9. A Nahuatl site.

—'ta bien, patroncito, as you say, it will be done. gorila ponce. take your shoes and your shirt off!

—right on! give me a perrito to slaughter!

—now what? nobody in the fifth grade has the huevos![1] it'd be really pinchi to let a third grader take the pounding. vic? quique? you know i can't do it. i wear glasses and can't see a thing without them, quique quickly adds.

—why don't you try to talk him into a boxing exhibit, vic? he wins hands down. i'll take a few punches. down on seven.

—you're crazy, xandro. you know this guy has wanted your blood since he joined the school in the middle of the year.

—negotiate it. Xingao! do it!

—hey, gorila man. xandro will take you on for an exhibition, "de a mentis"[2] you know, like not-for-real match. he'll take some punches in the seventh round and give you a k.o. hands down. he'll give a good show, you'll look good.

—i'm gonna cream him and put him in my coffee. i want to see him cringe and say "uncle."

—mierda,[3] xandro. don't do it. maybe one of the perros in our class will take him on.

—this is an ocelot challenge. we can't afford to lose the respect of third, second and first. let the fifth graders fry. it's up to us cats.

—get some water ready 'n' tell camilo to save some rum for cuts.

—this fight is yours, ponce, i don't want it, i mumble to his face as our hands are joined by camilo.

—there will be no hits below the waist or above the shoulders. a count of five is a knockout. no fall can last more than a five count. only three falls allowed for a technical decision.

—va por ti zuzana! this one is for you, zuzi!, i mumble to myself.

—come over here, runt, let me quarter you in two chingazos![4]

i know that ponce's strategy will be to keep me away from his thorax with his skinny and wiry arms. he reminds me of my spider monkey. ponce b

---

1. Eggs, i.e., balls.
2. Lying.
3. Shit.
4. Hits.

eager to establish himself as a cadet before graduation, and i am his rite of passage. so b it. my only hope is to work under him right into his skinny gut.

—mocos![5] the dogs howl out. i am on the ground with a bleeding nose. camilo rushes in and tries to stop the bout as i leap into ponce's stomach doing a one, two, three, to raise the dead, wake up the owls, and keep myself alive. the gorila falls windless. i am exhausted. my face hurts. i'm grinning and clenching my teeth.

—get up perro, and i'll have you roasted behind the palacio de cortez[6] in cuernavaca! ponce says nothing and takes the count. uno, dos, tres, cuatro. victoria!

—victoria! perro xandro wins! knockout. limpio, clean fight.

lieutenant pedroza has dozed off leaning against the truck's flat tire where he had a balcony view of our growing pains.

—get me some water, vic, quique. jaguares! agua!

i fall to the ground on my knees and grab ponce's hand in a solid two-handed shake. i rise and hit my heart with open right-handed paw and tell him:

—my heart is yours. buenas noches.

mierda! just because i'm the smallest and on scholarship, all these spoiled pretty boys want my blood. i lie by the fire now. zuzanita's face is shaping out of the smoke. the frog song and cicada orchestra are into full swing. bats and owls flapping around. mierda! i'm in pain and i'm in love. i fall on my back clutching the piloncillo de panocha[7] which zuzana gave me in exchange for one of my poems. i clutch it tight to my chest, smirking, mirroring the slivered moon. mars has moved out of its grin. the Ahuehute[8] branches sway.

—brown sugar for life! zapatalives! excellence: cristóbal colón: arts and sciences

. . . so what?! i sink into the meandering of Nezahualcoyotl Acomixtli[9]

　　　　　　where is your heart?

"if you give your heart to
each and everything,
you lead it nowhere:
you destroy your heart.
can any truth be found on earth?"

our lady's skirted darkness gleams in a blue-black cape filled with the diamonds of a morelos slivered moon. venus rises to square off the trinity of light. grandmother moon smirks back, mars and venus stand side to side. if you put your ear to the moist earth, you can hear the slithering water snakes. the ocelotes should be stalking just now. i hear a purr-growl. they're here: Ome and Teo.[1] the earth rumbles caress my tired bones. my navel has connected to a warm spot on the periphery of the fogata. the night hawks swoop down and fly off with chicotera[2] water snakes.

—iaa, iaa. perros! camilo! they're killing me! dopey shrieks in pain, agony, and fear.

we all rush to the scene. Ome and Teo have jumped him, not without provocation for sure. little hitler's thigh and nalga[3] have been pawed into bleeding. he's lucky they didn't go for his throat, sinking their jaws into his jugular.

—you should have seen the size of these mountains lions, twice my size each one!

—everyone back to your petates.[4] i'll take care of lieutenant pedroza! it's a good thing you didn't drink all the rum, patroncito, you're gonna need it now. xandro! bring some water over here! we got to clean his wounds and dress him. get some ashes and a sheath of that aloe plant.

dopey moaned and groaned for a while until he got drunk again and passed out babbling inanities and self-deprecations for his bad star. he's never going to make it to the cadet's ball now, at least not in one piece. morpheus calls. i fall asleep stalking the smile of dawn.

2000

1. The term *teotl* is a frequent part of the Spanish pronuniations of the names of Aztec deities, such as Ometeotl.

2. An instrument used to beat something.
3. Butt.
4. Small mat made of palm.

# LUZ MARÍA UMPIERRE-HERRERA
## b. 1947

Luz María "Luzma" Umpierre-Herrera was born and educated in Puerto Rico, where she earned her bachelor's degree at the University of Sagrado Corazón. She moved to the United States in 1974 to embark on her graduate education. After earning her doctorate from Bryn Mawr College, in Pennsylvania, Umpierre-Herrera taught at Rutgers University, in New Jersey; Western Kentucky University, in Bowling Green; the State University of New York at Brockport; and Bates College, in Lewiston, Maine. Actively involved in the educational struggles of Puerto Ricans and other minority students, she participated in the founding of the Pennsylvania Association for Bilingual Education (PABE) and became a strong advocate for Puerto Rican Studies and the inclusion of cultural diversity in the curriculum. She also has contributed to various human rights projects sponsored by Amnesty International and the Red Cross, focused on support services for emotionally challenged individuals and those afflicted by AIDS, and pursued studies in health science administration. Among the awards she has received for her human rights advocacy are a Lifetime Achievement Award from the Coalition of Gay and Lesbian Organizations in New Jersey.

Umpierre-Herrera writes in Spanish and English. Her work has been widely recognized among Latina poets in the United States and is also known in Puerto Rico. Her collection *Una puertorriqueña en Penna* (1979) is about both Umpierre-Herrera's early experiences with discrimination and her adaptation to U.S. society. The title is intended to have two meanings: "A Puerto Rican Woman in Pain" and "A Puerto Rican Woman in Pennsylvania" (*Penna* referring to both the Spanish word *pena* and the abbreviation for the state name). Subsequent collections include *En el país de las maravillas* (In Wonderland, 1982), *Y otras desgracias/And Other Misfortunes* (1985), and *For Christine* (1995). *The Margarita Poems* (1987) became a particularly important text in the expanding world of Latina writing, since, as Umpierre-Herrera puts it at her Web site, the book represents "the coming out period" of her writing at a time of few lesbian or gay voices within Latino literature. In a 2002 interview with the scholar Maria DiFrancesco, Umpierre-Herrera mentioned that becoming the victim of sexual abuse at age 13 brought about her initiation in the art of writing but that she did not fully dedicate herself to writing until her years at Bryn Mawr. In the same interview, she acknowledged suffering from anorexia at a young age, a condition that remained undiagnosed until she was 30 years old.

As a scholar, Umpierre-Herrera has published two volumes of literary criticism: *Ideología y novela en Puerto Rico* (Ideology and the Novel in Puerto Rico, 1982) and *Nuevas aproximaciones críticas a la literatura puertorriqueña contemporánea* (New Critical Approaches to Contemporary Puerto Rican Literature, 1983). In the aforementioned interview, Umpierre-Herrera notes that American writers such as Audre Lorde and Margie Piercy were important in her "development of a Lesbian conscience." "Immanence," one of the two Umpierre-Herrera poems included in this anthology (both from *The Margarita Poems*), is a courageous and explicit affirmation of love among women, and it expresses the author's outrage toward sexual prejudice. "No Hatchet Job" presents an obstinate defiance of social and patriarchal restraints.

# Immanence

*for Gail*

I am crossing
the MAD river in Ohio,[1]
looking for Julia
who is carrying me away
in this desire.                                                5

I am crossing
the river, MAD,
afflicted by the rabies

1. The Mad River is a stream in west-central Ohio.

for those who'll call me
sinful, insane and senseless,                    10
a prostitute, a whore,
a lesbian, a dyke
because I'll fall,
I'll drop,
I'll catapult                                    15
    my Self
into this frantic
excitement for your
    SEX
my Margarita,                                    20
my yellow margarita,
my glorious daisy.

I am traversing
this river MAD,
crossing myself                                  25
against the evil eye,
hectic, in movement,
my narrow body
covered with pictures
of women I adore or I desire,                    30
armies of Amazons
that I invoke
in this transubstantiation
or arousal
that will bring my Julia forth.                  35

Julia
who'll lose her mind
over your glorious vulva,
my Margarita,
my yellow margarita,                             40
my luminous daisy.

I am traversing
this body full of water,
    MAD,
cursing all Hopkinses,[2]                        45
incestuous writers,
who fucked your head and mine
in spring and summer
with images of death and sin
when all we wanted                               50
was to touch the yellow leaves,
the fall under our skirts.

I am transferring my Self,
changing my clothes,

2. Presumably such as Gerard Manley Hopkins (1844–1889), English poet and Jesuit priest.

spitting three times,                                    55
clicking my heels,[3]
repeating all enchantments:
   Come, Julia, come,
come unrestrained,
wild woman,                                              60
hilarious Julia,
come Julia come forth
to march the streets
at winter time,
to walk my body,                                         65
to proclaim
over the radio waves
the coming of the lustful
kingdom,
in sexual lubrication                                    70
and arousal
over my Margarita,
my yellow margarita,
my brilliant daisy.

I am crossing                                            75
the MAD river in Ohio,
leaving possessions and positions,
shedding my clothes,
forgetting, oh, my name,
putting life on the line,                                80
to bring my Julia forth,
lesbian woman,
who'll masturbate and rule
over my body, Earth,
parting the waters                                       85
of my clitoral Queendom,
woman in lust,
who'll lose her mind
and gain her Self
in want,                                                 90
in wish,
in pure desire and lust
for the rosy colored lips
covered with hair
of Margarita,                                            95
my yellow margarita.

    (pause)

I am Julia,
I have crossed the river
   MAD,                                    100

---

3. In the movie *The Wizard of Oz* (1939), the main character, Dorothy, clicks her heels three times to return home.

I have come forth,
new lady lazarus[4]
to unfold my margarita,
my carnal daisy
that buds between                                                      105
my spread out legs.

I touch my petals:
"I love me,
I love me not,
I love me,                                                              110
I love me not,
I love me!"

1987

## No Hatchet Job

*for Marge Piercy*[1]

They would like
to put the tick and flea collar
around her neck and
take her for walks on sunny afternoons
in order to say to the neighbors:                                       5
"We have domesticated this unruly woman."

They would like
to see her curled up on the corner,
fetal position, hungry, un-nursed
so that they can enter the scene,                                       10
rock-a-bye her to health
to advertise in the *Woman News* or *Psychology Today*:
"We have saved, we have cured this vulnerable woman."

They would like
to see her unclean,                                                     15
10 days without showers,
in filth and foul urine,
frizzled hair and all,
her business in ruins,
her reputation in shambles,                                            20
her body repeatedly raped on a billiard board
so that they can say in their minds:
"We have finally reduced this superior woman."

4. Cf. "Lady Lazarus" (1965), by the American poet Sylvia Plath (1932–1963). According to the Gospel of John, in the New Testament, Lazarus (of Bethany, also known as Lazarus of the Four Days) died and was miraculously brought back to life by Jesus four days later.

1. American poet, novelist, and social activist (b. 1936).

They would like
to have her OD on the carpet,                                           25
anorexic, bulimic and stiff on her bed
so that they can collect a percentage for burial
from the deadly mortician:
"We have found you this cadaverous woman."

They would like                                                        30
to spread her ashes at sea,
arrange *pompas fúnebres*,[2]
dedicate a wing or a statue in her name
so that their consciences
can finally rest in saying:                                            35
"We have glorified this poet woman."

But headstrong she is unleashed,
intractable she nourishes her mind,
defiantly she lives on in unity,
obstinately she refused the limelight, the pomp and the glory.         40
Eternally she breathes
one line after next,
unrestrained, unshielded
    willfully
    WRITER
    WOMAN                                                              45

                                                                     1987

2. A funeral.

---

# DENISE CHÁVEZ
## b. 1948

Denise Chávez was born in Las Cruces, New Mexico. Her father was absent through much of her childhood, but Chávez was influenced by her mother, a schoolteacher, and by her two sisters. Because the oral storytelling tradition was an important part of her upbringing, Chávez calls herself a performance artist. Her success in writing, she said in an interview with the scholar Marie-Elise Wheatwind, "comes from loving a good story, from having heard from the very best storytellers that one could possibly hear stories from."

At Madonna High School, in Mesilla, New Mexico, Chávez was involved in theater. Awarded a drama scholarship to New Mexico State University, in Las Cruces, she studied there with Mark Medoff, author of the play *Children of a Lesser God* (1980), but she earned her bachelor's and master's degrees in dramatic arts at Trinity University, in San Antonio. While in college, Chávez started writing plays. Upon graduation, she worked at the Dallas Theater Center. In 1984, she received her Master of Fine Arts degree in writing from the University of New Mexico, in Albuquerque. Her plays include *Novitiates* (1973), *The Mask of November* (1975), *The*

*Flying Tortilla Man* (1975), *Elevators* (1977), *The Adobe Rabbit* (1980), *Nacimiento* (1980), *Santa Fe Charm* (1980), *An Evening of Theater* (1981), *How Junior Got Throwed in the Joint* (1981), *Sí, Hay Posada* (Yes, There's Lodging, 1981), *El Santero de Cordova* (The Saintmaker from Cordova, 1981), *The Green Madonna* (1982), *Hecho en Mexico* (Made in Mexico, 1983), *La Morenita* (The Brown Girls, 1983), *Francis!* (1983), *Plaza* (1984), *Plague-Time* (1985), *Novena Narrative* (1987), *The Step* (1987), *Language of Vision* (1988), and *Women in the State of Grace* (1989).

In 1986, Chávez published a collection of stories, *The Last of the Menu Girls*, with Arte Público Press, in Houston, Texas. It received the Premio Aztlán Literary Award and the Mesilla Valley Author of the Year Award. This autobiographical volume deals with the roles of women, of motherhood, and of religion in the Chicano community. Her first novel, *Face of an Angel* (1994)—three chapters of which are included here—was published by Farrar, Straus and Giroux and received the American Book Award. The protagonist, Soveida Dosamantes, is a waitress in Agua Oscura, a town in New Mexico. In her journal, Dosamantes reflects on professional issues such as uniforms and the proper handling of a waitress's challenges. The language employs slang, especially Spanglish from New Mexico, and at times defies Standard English. Intertwining different literary genres, Chávez's narrative charts the character's inner world as she develops from vulnerability to decisiveness. The central motif is the crossroads of womanhood and the service industry, especially in relation to men, the community, and the country:

> In our family, men usually come first. Then God and Country. Country was last. Should be last. When you grow up in the Southwest, your state is your country. There exists no other country outside that which you know. Likewise, neighborhood is a country. As your family is a country. As your house is a country. As you are a country.

In the late 1990s, during her professorship in creative writing at the University of New Mexico, Chávez wrote her second novel, *Loving Pedro Infante* (2001), about a married man, the teacher's aide that he loves, and the aide's infatuation with the 1950s Mexican movie icon Pedro Infante. Chávez's memoir-cum-recipe book, *A Taco Testimony: Meditations on Family, Food and Culture* (2006), draws on her vast experience in restaurants, as both waitress and customer, and includes tips for Southwestern cooking and serving.

---

## FROM FACE OF AN ANGEL

## 1. A Long Story

Luardo my father. Dolores my mother. Hector my brother. Mara my cousin. Fathers. Mothers. Brothers. Sisters. Cousins. The concept of naming gets in the way. Now that I am older I can allow myself to look at my family as people. People like myself with hunger and hope. People with failings.

Luardo was once Dad, and as I grew older Dolores became Dolly. I was always Soveida. The Soveida who sat in other rooms.

What kind of name is that?

It's the name of a dead woman. The other Soveida was a pregnant woman with two small children. She was only twenty-seven years old when she was killed instantly in a car accident. Dolores read about it in the obituary column. She liked the name. It stuck. I, Soveida Dosamantes, am her name-sake. Husbandless. Childless. Daughter of. Sister of. Wife of. Mother of no one except herself. A helpless child who would never have chosen that name.

I am also almost parentless. My mother, Dolly, is more like a sister to me now than a mother. My father, Luardo, was never a real father, more like an unpleasant uncle. My real family is my grandmother, Mamá Lupita, and my cousin, Mara.

I never knew the face of the real Soveida, but I have imagined her often in my dreams. I see her proud fertile nakedness, a vision of life dancing in a nearby room, her long dark hair flowing. In my dreams she is forever young, not as she would be now: seventy-two years old, white-haired, belly-bloated, a babysitter sucking on the past like a mint.

I don't want to call them by those names. Mother. Father. Brother. Sister. Cousin.

The longer I live, the more I see that it is the same life, the same story, the same characters. All of them with the same face.

The more I think about it, it had to happen.

My grandmother Lupita says, "Soveida, you like to read. What you're read-ing is the story of the world. Everyone has a story, your mamá has a story, your daddy has a story, even *you* have a story to tell. Tell it while you can, while you have the strength, because when you get to be my age, the telling gets harder. The memories are the clothes in your closet that you never wear and are afraid to throw out because you'll hurt someone. But then you realize one long day, m'jita,[1] that there's no one left to hurt except yourself. All of a sudden you get old. You love your life. You sing. You dance. You laugh. You love. You cry. It had to happen. Don't you see? You lie down. And then you wake up suddenly with a mouthful of cenizas, nothing but ash. A memory of sweetness buried in the ground. M'jita, everyone has to die."

I speak for them now. Mother. Father. Brother. Sister. Cousin. Uncle. Aunt. Husband. Lover.

Their memories are mine. That sweet telling mine. Mine the ash.

It's a long story.

## 2. The Sleepwalker

Manuel Dosamantes Iturbide, my great-grandfather on my father's side, was born in Guanajuato, México. He came to the U.S. through Nuevo Laredo and worked for a while in Texas. His destination was California, but he never made it.

Manuel was a jack-of-all-trades, working at times as a carpenter, farmer, and cowboy. A man of natural talent, keen ingenuity, and cleverness, he was good at whatever he did. He was a hard worker as well, honest and forthright. Wherever he went, his bosses begged him to stay on, promising him a home, and good pay.

At the last job in Fort Davis, he was offered a partnership in a cattle ranch. The ranch came with a price tag, however: the owner's dark-skinned,

---

1. A contraction of *mi hijita*: dear daughter.

flat-chested daughter, Tobarda Acosta. Tobarda was well past her prime, like a piece of meat with all its natural juices gone. Manuel knew it was time to move on when Tobarda herself sought him out, flowers in her wispy hair, offering herself to him in the long summer darkness, no moon to be seen. Manuel wished that Tobarda was a woman he could love, for already that magic, soul-sinking pull of West Texas had affected him. He longed to stay awhile, maybe a long time, in that place that had almost brought him peace. Damn! If it weren't for that woman sidling up to him like a hungry cat, the one that was always ignored. He could not look at her without feeling some kind of pity, and that was very bad. So he turned away, leaving everything behind: his clothes, his horse, his gear.

Walking away from Tobarda that immense, still night was one of the hardest things he ever did, he told his son Profetario years later. Manuel knew that he could never love Tobarda the way he wanted to love a woman, and he was mad at himself for not wanting to love her. He was mad at himself as well for abandoning Don Severio, her father, an old man with a bad stomach who knew he didn't have long to live. Don Severio had offered Manuel his beloved children: Tobarda and the ranch, La Esperanza, named after his mother.

Manuel knew he would break the old man's heart, as well as the daughter's. He'd done it already, as he walked into that solid night: no stars, no light, no prayers. Nothing but a desperate, almost hopeful darkness, the darkness of a sleepwalker who must and will get away. His actions that night were just as automatic and deep-rooted.

Earlier, Tobarda had come to him in the small room near the stables, "his room." It was full of the smell of horse and man. Leather harnesses and saddles hung on the walls. Manuel's small bed faced an open window that looked out onto an exercise yard where he gently broke the new horses, asking only as much as the horse could give. Likewise, he took Tobarda that night. What else could he do? He felt sorry for her.

She came in brazenly, as he was reading by the kerosene lamp. He felt a presence, took his gun out, then lowered it, seeing the once shy woman standing there, in a dark robe, with her stringy, longish hair draped over her bony shoulders. He stood there as she took off the robe, then the nightgown, and lay on top of his bed. Her body was like that of a fifteen-year-old boy's: very thin, with no muscle tone, her legs long as a newborn calf's. Her arms were crossed over her breasts, which were more like a cow's reddish teats.

Manuel Dosamantes approached her, sat on the edge of the bed, and embraced her nakedness. She cried softly, and then with a deep breath placed her arms around him and drew him near. He felt like running but he was unable to. She had him, a demon lover, and she pulled him to her. And he, a mere man, caressed her as he would a dying tree, with outstretched hands, feeling a deep compassion, an overwhelming, nostalgic emptiness. Dry, bumpy, uncharted, her body lay there, unmoving, as he took off his clothes and got on top of her. His actions were heavy, like an underwater swimmer, and when she opened her legs, he awoke. She was dry, and nothing could unloosen her. He struggled, she was silent; he moaned, she bit her lip. Exhausted, he slid off her, his own sweat the only wetness he'd felt. Dios mío, what have I done, what am I doing, he thought to himself as he arose, startled from his nocturnal walk toward hell, or freedom, he didn't know which. What have I done? What am I trying to do?

Tobarda lay there stiffly, hands clenched, eyes closed.

Quickly, Manuel moved away from her and threw on his clothes. It was then that Tobarda opened her eyes and stared at him, wide-eyed, slightly sad. He looked at her, and again a wave of pity and unrest came upon him. But before it washed over him completely, he was gone from the room.

He left behind all his memories: the picture of his mother, Galardita, in her high-collared dress, her braided hair wrapped around her head like a halo; his father, Pacífico, with his white beard, seated next to his mother, she standing over him, ever watchful, stern; his brothers, Juan María and Evaristo, as children, in long, white dresses; and himself, as a boy, standing next to a dried tree, in a nowhere land on the outskirts of his colonial hometown, Guanajuato. He had lived in poverty and hope there, full of parched dreams from all the heat. Now that hope for water, for green, for lushness was dead. It had died in the mountains near Fort Davis with a thirsty woman whom he could not love. Ever.

Manuel ran toward the heat and the desert, toward the mesquite and the scrub brush. When he tired of running, he found a town of five hundred in Natividad county, New Mexico. Agua Oscura—dark water—it was called.

He would work here and make his money here. He knew how to farm, to build, to handle animals. He had all the experience anyone needed to survive in this harsh land. Its severity suited him. He responded to this land as a hearty, hungry woman does to lovemaking. He found it gave him what he needed: a response. He was able to see the change, dramatically. Water was this land's lover, and this love affair, the push and pull of nature with man, a man with his spirit, was what drew him to Agua Oscura. It allowed him to feel, at last, at home.

Tobarda was a parched memory. If Don Severio had ever looked for him, he never knew. What became of Tobarda and his photographs, he didn't know either. After he lost his photographs, he lost contact with the world of his birth: Guanajuato, that celebrated place where the clay in the earth preserved its buried corpses. Yes, he was far away from those human mummies that were later dug up and displayed for the tourists: leering men, defiled women, and pathetic children, with leathery, caked limbs, dusty, sparse hair, flaccid breasts and crumbling penises that reminded him of who he was, where he was always going.

He would never again see those mountains, those valleys. The view was now of another land, a land where his children would grow and flourish.

When he first moved to Agua Oscura, Manuel had nightmares, of walking down a long dark tunnel leading to a large room where the walls were cluttered with glass-enclosed coffins. Wandering through that unpleasant maze, he would stop and come up to someone familiar. He peered through the dusty glass, where he saw the naked form of the long-dead Tobarda. He tried to get away, and he would wake with a small cry, engulfed in a lingering mustiness and the scent of decay. Even as an old man, he could summon up that smell at will; it had pervaded his life and permeated his clothes. It was the smell of resentment from the dead, a bitter scent of the spirits who were angry at what had been done to them. It was the smell of Tobarda.

Sometimes it caught him unawares, and he would be back again in Guanajuato or Fort Davis, or in the grave, or all those places at once, with all those he'd loved, the living and the dead.

It was enough to make a man go mad.

But Manuel Dosamantes was not weak; he was convinced he could overcome the haunting aroma of the past. And so, when he got to Agua Oscura, he found a job, right off, on a farm belonging to Jorge Campos. In time he became the foreman, and then the manager. But Jorge died and so did his wife, quickly, of a broken heart. Manuel bought the farm, named it De los Campos in memory of Jorge, and determined it was time to find a wife. But who?

In Agua Oscura, there was no one he could love. If he was to love anyone, it would have to be someone from far away, someone who would come to him out of the vast unknown. Someone sent by God.

He could either go searching for that person or wait until she came to him. Manuel was tired of always running, so this time he decided the woman he would love would come along, eventually.

He waited ten years. At age thirty-five Manuel Dosamantes was in the prime of his manhood. He was tall, with a large chest and slim hips. A quiet man, he worked hard and ran a successful farm with various employees. He owned a great deal of land in Agua Oscura as well, and could have retired at his young age, if he had so wished. Everyone wondered why he had not married or moved someplace else, to a larger city.

Agua Oscura now had a population of nearly two thousand. There were years of drought, some years of abundance, and Manuel Dosamantes had held firm and prospered. He still looked out of the corner of his eye for that woman he'd always waited for: someone to ease his tormented dreams, someone to give him children and make him feel as if all his expended energy and sweat hadn't been for nothing.

In the summer of 1885, Elena Harrell came from Chihuahua to Agua Oscura to visit her father's sister, Jewel Harrell. She was eighteen years old, a radiant young woman with blond hair, blue eyes, and a lovely face. She was tall, stately, thin, but substantial. Her father, Bartel Harrell, was a miner and speculator and spoke impeccable Spanish. He had married Estrella de las Casas, daughter of Enrique Palomar de las Casas, from Chihuahua, México, scion of one of the wealthiest families in the state of Chihuahua. Their daughter, Elena, had grown up in luxury but, despite that, was a simple, selfless girl. She taught in a small community school for people who couldn't afford private schooling. This caused her father, Bartel, and her mother much consternation.

The summer of 1885 was hot and dry. The year before, Agua Oscura had witnessed devastating floods: the Río Grande jumped its banks and caused the town to shift its boundaries. Manuel Dosamantes lost most of his crops, but was able to sell what he was able to salvage at a premium price. No matter what—floods, droughts, earthquakes, influenza outbreaks—Manuel survived them all.

Jewel Harrell welcomed her niece, Elena, with open arms. It was time, Bartel had told her, for his daughter to learn her father's language. Perhaps while she was away her notions of running the charitable school would dissipate. Possible, thought her father. Probable, thought her mother. Doubtful, thought Elena.

Once Elena Harrell came to Agua Oscura in the summer of 1885, she never left. She did learn some English: that had been her father's real concern. Her mother got her wish, as well: she never went back to the dusty adobe classroom on the outskirts of Chihuahua. Instead, she became Mrs. Manuel Dosamantes.

It was inevitable that Manuel and Elena should be drawn to each other: both were Mexicans hungry for a preservation of language and custom. Both were loners with keen intellects. Both were young, hard-working, physically rooted people in full flower. Both had eyes that constantly looked inward.

They met at la tía Harrell's, at a welcoming party for Elena in early June. It was a delicious night, a slight breeze fanning Jewel's long patio.

"Mr. Dosamantes, I want you to meet my niece, Elena Harrell. Elena, dear, this is Mr. Dosamantes."

"Good evening, Señorita Harrell."

"Buenas noches, I mean, good evening, Mr. Dosamantes. Tía, do you mind if I speak Spanish?"

"Now, Elena, remember what your father said!"

"Sí, tía, I remember. But please, tía, I'm sure Mr. Dosamantes won't mind, will you? Oh, all right, now you go on, I promise to speak only English."

"Very well, Elena. Mr. Dosamantes, I'll leave you now, as I see Reverend Prithley coming this way. Excuse me, won't you?"

Manuel and Elena talked all night long, in Spanish. She felt as if she'd known Manuel all her life. She felt so comfortable with him she didn't have to be Elena Harrell, American citizen. In her heart, she was Elena Harrell, a Mexican whose father was an Anglo. He was a good man; it wasn't his fault he was a güero.[2] Everyone loved Bartel Harrell—her mother, especially. It was Estrella who had taught him his beautiful Spanish. She had taught it to him lovingly, carefully, not at all with any sign of impatience, so common among relatives or married people who try to teach something to each other.

Manuel taught Elena what correct English he knew in the same patient way. It did not matter—not then or later—that Elena never mastered English fully; she spoke in a delightfully broken, colorful way.

The night of tía Jewel's party was the beginning of a new life for Manuel Dosamantes. He knew that evening that he had, at last, met the woman for whom he had waited so many years. He began a committed courtship the very next day. Elena, for her part, reciprocated his attention. She was taken with this gentleman farmer she'd met in this small, out-of-the-way town. When he asked her to marry him, she said yes.

The night they were married, his nightmares stopped.

Manuel told Elena everything about himself, save the story of Tobarda Acosta, the woman whose husband he felt he should have been. Elena would have understood, he thought, but why tell her, what for? To deepen his guilt? Besides, he had only now begun to live. Why stunt himself further with the retelling of what might have been?

They married in August. It was a big wedding. Everyone came from Chihuahua; no one from Guanajuato. Manuel had lost or forgotten all the addresses of his family. He could not remember his brothers' faces; no doubt his parents were long dead, Don Severio too. Tobarda was probably still alone, childless, with a womb tight as a walnut, her once red teats now brown, small dry outcroppings on a dying cottonwood—far away in a forgotten field.

Manuel and Elena named their first child Teodelfiño. Elena made up the name Teodelfiño—she liked to do that—as she made up the names of their

2. Blond.

other children: Clotildora, Amparinata, Ismindalia, and Profetario. If they were real names, she'd never heard them. Elena Harrell de Dosamantes would give her children a fighting chance with names like that, names even the demons would have trouble pronouncing, names like Reina María del Cielo, Rosa Elena Perfecta, María del Carmen Graciela, or Canutino Jesús Salvador, names with a ring to them of paradise. Manuel, too, had never seen or heard of names like these in his many wanderings, or in his dreams of that large room off the long tunnel, names that had been tacked on the bottoms of glass-covered coffins.

Manuel was very happy. All the rest of his life, until he died at the age of eighty-five, he thanked God he had awakened in time to leave that darkened room in Fort Davis, Texas, Tobarda Acosta burning there, in her private, inextinguishable hell. With Elena, he had long, light nights of liquid dreams.

I never knew my great-grandfather Manuel Dosamantes. Nor did I really know my grandfather Profetario very well. To me he was a blustery man, big as the sky, always yelling at my grandmother Lupe. He was a man who lived under the yoke of his father Manuel's perfectly balanced life. Profetario was a rascal, living with two wives, two families. The Dosamantes name fit him, eternally split between two lovers. My father, Luardo, was like his own father, a divided man, unable to ever come together within himself.

What stories I know about these people I will share with you. The stories begin with the men and always end with the women; that's the way it is in our family.


## 4. Are You Wearing a Bra?

Dolores Loera, my mother, grew up harnessed. As a child, she'd been swaddled in rags; as a young girl, she was confined to dark Victorian blouses with high necklines and long sleeves; as a young woman, she was bound in softened cloth. Her mother, Doña Trancha, was old-fashioned. She thought that every respectable young woman should have her breasts taped down. But it was a losing battle and finally Doña Trancha had to acquiesce when Dolores turned twelve. It was hopeless. Dolores needed a brassiere.

Every few months Dolores had increased a notch: from an AA to an A, from a 34 to a 36, from a B to a C, from 38 to 40, and on to a D. "My harness," that's what she always called her brassiere. She wouldn't call it a bra. The diminutive wasn't for her. What she wore was a *brassière*, with a harsh z sound. She was large-busted, uncomfortable. The straps cut into her shoulders, leaving reddened, indented areas. She was prone to headaches, as well as back and neck problems. Sleep was a dilemma. Dolores could never rest on her chest or sides. From the age of twelve, she slept fully on her back, without a pillow.

Luardo liked her from the beginning. She was thirteen when he met her, thin, but with the breasts of a mature woman. He liked women with what he called "two strong points." That was his joke, anyway. "She's a *sharp* woman, get it?"

But what a man thinks and a woman knows is another matter.

Dolores often talked to me about breasts. Hers and mine.

"My breasts have been like misbehaving children, unmanageable and in the way. I've never wished my curse on any other living woman. Now you, Soveida, you have a good-sized bust, with the promise of getting larger, just let you have a child. You've always had the nipples of a married woman. I hate to think why. First they were silver-dollar size. Then small-pancake size. It isn't nice to have nipples so large."

Dolores was not happy with the way I turned out. Physically, I was a pre-cocious girl, just as she had been. By age fifteen I was eager and ready for some man to come along. But no one did, Dolores saw to that.

"No dating until you're eighteen, Soveida!"

"Eighteen!!" I screeched. "But Mara got to go out when she was seventeen."

"Well, Mara. It must have been a mistake on Mamá's part. You know as well as I do that Mamá wouldn't let her date at all. She must have sneaked out at seventeen, maybe even before that. But that was Mara, Soveida, that isn't you. You may look like a woman, you may have the *nipples* of a woman, but you aren't a woman. Breasts doesn't mean you have brains. I was hoping you wouldn't grow up so fast. God knows I know what it's like having some man pinching and punching away at your breasts and wanting to get inside your blouse and your skirt. I was just hoping you'd stay a little girl longer, without having to worry about all that stuff."

When Dolores spoke about "all that stuff," she meant anything having to do with the bodily functions or necessities of being female—from top to bot-tom and back around. There was a lot of ground to cover in that phrase, "all that stuff."

"Dolores, who ever thought of that phrase 'sanitary napkin'? It had to have been a man, because no woman in her right mind would refer to them as 'sanitary.' They aren't a bandage to swab up something dirty. The blood that comes out of me is beautiful! Have you ever tasted it?"

"Ay, Soveida! Cochina, you dirty thing! Shut your mouth!"

"Only a man with his head in the dirt would think of calling them 'sanitary napkins,' thank you, wipe up your mess. Once I was in these sand dunes, and it was during my period. It got so I had trained myself to go bleed only when I went to the bathroom, and there I was, alone, on some high windswept dune, when I had the urge. I just dug a hole in the sand. I squatted there and the blood came out of me. Clean, pure. That's the way it should be, a good bleeding outdoors, natural, unfettered, in full moonlight. But no, we have 'sanitary napkins,' and worse yet, little deodorized pellets to plug us up, keep the dirty stuff inside. Later we pull out the pellet and flush it away."

"Escandalosa![3] Soveida, don't talk about all that stuff! They're things we shouldn't talk about, not now, not ever. Don't even think about them."

"Maybe we'll forget we have bodies that bleed. I don't want to forget I have a body, maybe you do. I don't!"

"Oh, Soveida! I know I have a body. Wait until you're older. Then you'll want to forget when your man's still stuck to your nipples and you gave up nursing thirty years before."

"Dolores! You're talking about all that stuff again!"

---

3. Scandalous, shocking.

"No, I'm not. I'm just talking about life. How about when you just want to go to sleep and your entire backside is wet and your man is angry with you and won't talk to you during the day but at night he's all smiles and 'let me rub your legs.' Just wait, Soveida. Someday my words will come back to haunt you. You'll remember. You're young still, even if you have the nipples of a married woman."

"Dolores!"

"You can't lie to me. You never could. All those cuchispetes,[4] as Mamá Lupita calls them, aren't the same thing as being married to the same man for forty years. And I am *still* married to your father even if we *are* divorced. When you take a man on, you take a man on. Mark my words. After all these years, I still have to answer to others for your father."

"You do *not* have to answer for Luardo. When are you going to remember that?"

"Soveida, you never lived with a man a full number of years. And him not altered in the place that matters. Imagine how it is when all a man wants to do is stay in bed and he's almost retirement age. If I'd known I was going to eventually divorce your father, I would have done it a lot sooner. Learn from my mistakes."

"Is that true? Would you really have divorced Luardo?"

"Why can't you just call us Mom and Dad?"

"I just can't. You know that."

"I tried to keep you a girl as long as I could, just as my mother, Trancha, did with me. May she rest in peace. I wouldn't listen to her. I started having dreams about what I thought love was when I was only thirteen. Your dad had already been sniffing around me. Three years later we were married. Yes, I was happy with him in the beginning. Maybe if it weren't for all the other women. But it wasn't only the women. When he was with those women, at least there was peace and rest. It was too many other things."

"Do you still love Luardo?"

"Why do you ask? No. Yes. Sometimes. Not often."

"Is this what you meant by 'all that stuff,' Dolores?"

"I'm trying to talk to you, Soveida, but you're not listening to me."

"I'm listening."

"You got your breasts from me. No one else. Your grandmother had teats like a dog's. Maybe that's why she lost all her children when they were still little. Pobrecita[5] mamá, she didn't have any nourishment to give any of us. I never felt bad about Dad being gone all the time. I could never blame him. She was so hard to live with. That's why I married your dad."

"You were sixteen? It's hard to believe."

"I loved him, Soveida. I did love him! When I loved him, the nights were never long enough. Your brother, Hector, looks so much like Luardo. Maybe that's why they hate each other so much. Why don't you make up with your brother, Soveida? You never talk about him, you never see him. He just became the assistant manager at that car-parts place, Dyno-Car."

"Let's not talk about Hector. Or Luardo. Have you ever noticed that when we start talking about ourselves we always end up talking about them?"

---

4. Shameless people (male or female), without morals or good sense; the word is used in El Polvo, now Redford, Texas, across from Ojinaga, Mexico (where the author's mother came from).
5. Poor.

"I can truthfully say that the happiest times of my life have been when I've been sleeping. And here all those years I thought *I* was the problem. But it was your father, Soveida. He'd leave the house early and would come back later, smelling of another woman or his own vomit. I should have locked the door and never let him come back in. His absences got longer and my tears got harder until one day they just dried up. It's a good story. Somebody should write about it. But it won't be me. I'd rather write about mi tía Adelaida and the day she got paralyzed. I could never tell all the stories even if I tried. And I don't want to try. Who would believe them? You just tell me who. And if I've gone on too long about all that stuff, Soveida, it's because I wanted you to have a different life."

Dolores dabbed the inside of her wrist with cologne and then behind her ears. She then patted the front of her bra straps, discolored by countless applications of cologne. "My harness," she said out loud as she carefully tapped the cologne under each armpit and then in the cleavage between her ponderous breasts and then lifted the finger to her nose. "My Sin."

1994

---

# JUAN FELIPE HERRERA
## b. 1948

Juan Felipe Herrera was born in Fowler, California. His parents were migrant workers in the San Joaquin and Salinas Valleys, and the family's experiences in the fields have informed Herrera's work as a writer, an actor, a performer, a musician, and a cartoonist.

After attending elementary and high schools in various small towns as well as in San Francisco and San Diego, Herrera earned a bachelor's degree in social anthropology from the University of California, Los Angeles, where he became involved in student activism and Teatro Tolteca, a Chicano theater troupe that incorporated jazz forms, spoken word, multimedia, and dance into its performances. A major contribution during this period was his groundbreaking film and photographic work on endangered indigenous communities in the Lacandón jungle of Chiapas, Mexico, and in the Huichol communities in Nayarit, Mexico. He also wrote protest songs as part of *El Movimiento*. Along with Mario Aguilar and Alberto Baltazar Heredia Urista, aka "Alurista," he was part of the music and theater ensemble Servidores del Arbol de la Vida (Guardians of the Tree of Life) from 1973 to 1975. The group specialized in mixing Mexican, U.S., and pre-Columbian material.

In 1980, Herrera earned his master's degree in social anthropology from Stanford University, where he was a key participant in the *Vórtice Journal of Art, Literature and Criticism*. Three years later, he founded Troka, a spoken-word and percussion ensemble, and in the late 1980s he and Margarita Robles, a poet and performance artist, cofounded Manikrudo-Raw Essence, a poetry-into-performance workshop. In 1990, Herrera earned his Master of Fine Arts degree in poetry from the Writers' Workshop at the University of Iowa, in Iowa City. Plays that he helped create, based on poetry and collage, were featured at the University of Iowa Playwrights Festival.

Herrera has written Latino musicals for young audiences and published poems, stories, children's books, and novels for young adults and adults. His more recent publications include *Border-Crosser with a Lamborghini Dream* (1999), *Notebooks of a Chile Verde Smuggler* (2002), and *Half the World in Light: New and Selected Poems* (2008). *187 Reasons Mexicanos Can't Cross the Border: Undocuments 1970–2007* (2007) is a selection of his work. Influenced by cubism, surrealism, the Latin American literary "Boom," the postwar poets of Eastern Europe, and hip-hop, Herrera's writing is jazzy and irreverent. Some of his poetry is based on the spoken word, some of it on the meditative lyric. In his readings, he engages and provokes the audience. The three poems in this anthology are among his most famous: "Exiles," from *Exiles of Desire* (1985), is a meditation on the condition of exile. "Literary Asylums," from the same volume, looks at writing and audience, power and class. "Quentino," first published in *Akrílica* (1989), explores the passing of time and the ways in which people cope with adversity.

Herrera's awards include National Endowment for the Arts fellowships (1979, 1985), the Smithsonian Notable Children's Book (1996), the Latino Hall of Fame Award (2000, 2002), the Americas Book Award (2000, 2006), the Tomás Rivera Mexican American Award for Children's Literature (2007), the National Book Critics Circle Award (2008), the PEN Oakland/Josephine Miles Award in Poetry (2008), and the Latino International Award in Poetry in English (2008). He lives with Margarita Robles in Redlands, California, and holds the Tomás Rivera Endowed Chair at the University of California, Riverside.

## Exiles

> and I heard an unending scream piercing nature.
>
> —FROM THE DIARY OF EDVARD MUNCH,[1] 1892

At the Greyhound bus stations, at airports, at silent wharfs
the bodies exit the crafts. Women, men, children; cast out
from the new paradise.

They are not there in the homeland, in Argentina, not there
in Santiago, Chile; never there no more in Montevideo, Uruguay,      5
and they are not here

in *America*

They are in exile: a slow scream across a yellow bridge
the jaws stretched, widening, the eyes multiplied into blood
orbits, torn, whirling, spilling between two slopes; the sea, black,      10
swallowing all prayers, shadeless. Only tall faceless figures
of pain flutter across the bridge. They pace in charred suits,
the hands lift, point and ache and fly at sunset as cold dark
birds. They will hover over the dead ones: a family shattered
by military, buried by hunger, asleep now with the eyes burning      15
echoes calling *Joaquín, María, Andrea, Joaquín, Joaquín, Andrea,*

*en exilio*

From here we see them, we the ones from here, not there or across,
only here, without the bridge, without the arms as blue liquid

---

1. Norwegian painter and printmaker (1863–1944), best-known for *The Scream*.

quenching the secret thirst of unmarked graves, without                    20
our flesh journeying refuge or pilgrimage; not passengers
on imaginary ships sailing between reef and sky, we that die
here awake on Harrison Street, on Excelsior Avenue[2] clutching
the tenderness of chrome radios, whispering to the saints
in supermarkets, motionless in the chasms of playgrounds,                   25
searching at 9 A.M. from our third-floor cells, bowing mute,
shoving the curtains with trembling speckled brown hands.
     Alone,
we look out to the wires, the summer, to the newspapers wound
in knots as matches for tenements. We that look out from                    30
our miniature vestibules, peering out from our old clothes,
the father's well-sewn plaid shirt pocket, an old woman's
oversized wool sweater peering out from the makeshift kitchen.
We peer out to the streets, to the parades, we the ones from here
not there or across, from here, only here. Where is our exile?              35
Who has taken it?

                                                                      1985


## Literary Asylums

*for Francisco X. Alarcón & Alfred Arteaga*[1]

### Writing

(Writing is richman's work, therefore richman's history. Lately, the
unrich are growing accustomed to the forbidden pleasure of writing.)

R-writers live in immense warehouses. There they write at ease; all quarters
are at their disposal, anytime. They will summon the workers, the maids.
They will call upon the ushers, the watchmen at the snap of a button, the     5
tone of a finger, a casual flutter of an eyebrow or even with a rhythmic
twitch of a torso. They are to be served with imagination, magazines,
graphic suffering, light-tables, ribbons, rare inks, tall quills. They can
dictate, murmur, jump glottal stops, gargle, spit, jam the jaw out, point
with the cornea, pin down figures with an opaque thin triangle of elbow       10
for the ecstasy of a thought, a fancy, a dream, a vision (especially a
vision) for an ether, a helium space, an infinite image of a new warehouse:
a turquoise clinic spinning in the future filled with flasks of dormant
immortal replicas, unmixed serums and hexagons: crystals awaiting a
genealogy of R-words.                                                         15

No one needs to hear the sage of the R-writer that rejects the kingdom,
that undergoes a series of initiations, that confesses and casts out the
jewels from the family's purse heralding verses from the colony of the
beasts.

---

2. Thoroughfares in San Francisco.
1. Chicano poet, writer, and scholar (1950–2008). *Francisco X. Alarcón*: Chicano poet, writer, and educator (b. 1954).

There is always an element of suspicion in the claims of all converts.  20
It is said that the beast obeys the master's wish. Even if we grant that
animals engage in rational deliberation, a beast must follow the command
or meet its death. Perhaps the beast can rehearse loyalty, disguise
allegiance while conjuring plans to overtake the household. Perhaps after
the overthrow a celebration will mark a new age.  25

Will they still obey an invisible voice? Will the creatures be able to
pronounce the new language?
What words? What signs? What writing?

Obviously, unrich writers are not animals, not reptiles. It does not
matter.  30
They are prowling at the master's gate. Most are feasting, many have
repainted the walls, remodeled the furniture, provided extra exits, taken
the mahogany bedroom headboards out, shaken the ivory tusk carved
woman away from the staircase entrance, stripped the floors, thrown out
the serfs (in most instances).  35
After changing their names they will gather in the same rectangles: the
kitchen, the family room, the porch, next to the vegetable gardens
admiring native art.
Somewhere,

in one of the studios, tablets of the ancestors are being placed openly  40
over velvet cushions. There is quiet laughter amidst the ferns.

### Reading

There are no audiences. No readers. An audience is an assumption, an
image: silent flesh block of absorbing membrane. An idea.

Faces have the same diameter of cells across the forehead. Everyone wears
shoes, socks, stockings, underwear, shirts, blouses, shoulder pads, cuffs,  45
brassieres, earrings, watches, zippers, buttons, wallets, hats, caps, scarfs,
lotions, spray, has 10 fingers, 1 hand folded over the husband's knee, the
wife's thigh, the child's neck sitting, the eyes sitting, sitting, the ears,
sitting, sitting the belly sitting, the sitting throat, open, listening across
the tiers, the warehouse, listening across the floors, wet, clean, listening  50
to the writer read, write, words, reading.

Another idea of audience: the conquered, the unkempt, the wounded, the
forgotten, the dreaming, spread over a mat, the boards under blue light,
they lay over assemblages of coats, razors. No sofas. They fall back, back
to back.  55

Does it matter?
The idea of an audience, the idea itself cuts into all descriptions, tears
into all experience. The assumption of an audience: *they are listening*.
That is it.
Who listens, if they cannot gain power, if they cannot prevent power from  60
being taken? There are only guards.

No one is talking about handcuffs, wardens, stripes, breaking rock with
long hammers. Remember? No one was talking about fangs, claws or
foaming fur.
It is a simple angle. If you think there is an audience, you don't see guards,    65
the eyes tracking your lips, taking your oxygen away into a hearse, tearing
the spine, the skin, off, making splintered bone shoot out with veins as
ribbons, as petals for a funeral bouquet. The body lays cut behind
camouflaged watchtowers, nude. You don't see their lapels stained with
fluids from your syllables.    70
You see an audience only. You don't listen to the iron gates closing, locking
slow around you at every vowel; only audience.

You are only reading.

### Being

Who wants air?
Explosions disturb the quiet talk in the garden, the dining room.    75
Gas jets of flesh perturb the remote chatter of assemblies in the south
quarters.
At best, the galleries will stage a false burst of bodies from a cell; a
delirium of actors will escape from a gray frame of papier-mâché.

The theater of the unrich will emerge. Applause.    80

Who wants air?
Who will destroy?

Not hurt, not mutilate, not even assassinate, but, destroy.
Can individuals perform this maneuver? Must there be group consensus?
Has the world ever known destruction or only change?    85

We are busy at the museums. We are going over and over and over the
archives of our own bandages. There are no R-writers. There are no
unrich. Even guards really do not exist. There are only bleeding asylums
for those that cannot breathe.

Outside beasts and jagged strokes of color blur.    90

1985

### Quentino[1]

I'm writing you on this ocean table/a paragraph between the sand
tablets/a pilgrimage of eyes/from the chasm to the voice/here
outside/when someone screams the branches moisten with gray lips and
veils/words fly up from the beams of shoulders/and bellies like startled

1. Translated from the Spanish by Stephen Kessler.

gulls/bellies of prisoner thunder/slave salt/it's Friday Quentino/your 18      5
years/beat in the cell/like littleboyfists/here too there is an iron
tuberculosis/the spider's smile/daggers springing from the nipples of the
administrators/secretaries naked in a chainlink shorthand/it's Friday/
when the old men are rocking in big dark armchairs and/now and
then gaze at their trembling hands/the jawbones groaning in the      10
pasture/and then/your eyebrows remembered/and your guitarfists that
used to play sun and moon when/we asked only for earth/we're in
June/somewhere between the first and the/thirtieth/Quentino/an
infinite petal between two imaginary padlocks/Quentino/and the iodine
flag in the soldiers' barracks and the perfume in your hands and the      15
assemblage of an M-16 stuck in Somoza's[2] face?/45 years of smoke and
blood exploded in the street/what changes?/Quentino/yesterday your father
died under the insecure hospital makeup/today

I walk the streets/I look for eyes/and look for them/I look when it is
lighter but the people get used to the eternal/bars/between their eyes and      20
summer

1989

2. Anastasio "Tachito" Somoza Debayle (1925–1980), president of Nicaragua 1967–72, 1974–79; the
country's ruler, as head of its National Guard, 1967–79. *M-16*: an assault rifle.

---

# PABLO MEDINA
## b. 1948

Born in Cuba but a resident of the United States since 1961, Pablo Medina is a poet
and novelist whose work focuses on his complicated ties to Cuban culture and North
American culture. After attending schools in New York City, Medina earned his
bachelor's degree in Spanish and his master's degree in English from Georgetown
University, in Washington, D.C. He taught at Mercer County Community College, in
New Jersey, and has been writer-in-residence at several academic institutions, includ-
ing New York University; the New School for Social Research, in New York; and the
University of Nevada, Reno.

Medina's first book, *Pork Rinds and Cuban Songs* (1975), was the first poetry volume
written and published in English by a Cuban-born writer in the United States. The
poems explore his relationships with family and homeland, and they include a long
narrative, "Miguel Medina," that chronicles a hundred years of family exile, from
Spain to Cuba and then from Cuba to the United States. In 1976, Medina won the
William Carlos Williams Poetry Award. During the next decade, his poetry, essays,
and translations appeared in numerous anthologies and periodicals. Medina's subsequent poetry collections, from which some of the selections in this anthology are
taken, include *Arching into the Afterlife* (1991), *The Floating Island* (1999), and the
bilingual *Points of Balance/Puntos de apoyo* (2005). These books combine lyrical recollections of Cuba with often sardonic commentaries on life in contemporary America.

*Exiled Memories: A Cuban Childhood* (1990)—a sensitively evocative memoir, one
chapter of which is included in this anthology—anticipates Medina's first novel, *The
Marks of Birth* (1994), in which the protagonist, Anton, and his family flee an

unnamed Latin American island after a dictator comes to power. Anton grows up in New York City and ends up in another kind of exile: unhappily married to an American woman in suburban New Jersey.

Medina's second novel, *The Return of Felix Nogara* (2000)—one chapter of which is excerpted in this anthology—describes the title character's return to a phantasmagoric Cuba after many years of exile. His third novel, *The Cigar Roller* (2005), is about Amadeo Terra, a Cuban immigrant who, having suffered a stroke that left him paralyzed in a Catholic nursing home in Tampa, Florida, reminisces about his life as a cigar roller in Cuba and his move to Ybor City, a Tampa neighborhood historically populated by cigar rollers.

An equally important facet of Medina's career is his work as a translator. With Carolina Hospital, he translated *Everyone Will Have to Listen* (1990), a collection of writings by the Cuban dissident Tania Díaz Castro. With Mark Statman, Medina translated the Spanish poet Federico García Lorca's *Poeta en Nueva York* (Poet in New York, 1940; 2008). Medina and Statman's version of this experimental classic is more sensitive to the encounter between Spanish and English in New York than are other English translations.

Medina has received grants from the Cintas Foundation, the Pennsylvania Council for the Arts, the New Jersey State Council of the Arts, the National Endowment for the Humanities, and the Lila Wallace–Reader's Digest Foundation.

---

## *From* EXILED MEMORIES: A CUBAN CHILDHOOD

### Arrival: 1960

Snow. Everywhere the snow and air so cold it cracks and my words hang stiffly in the air like cartoons. After that first stunning welcome of the New York winter, I rush down the steps of the plane and sink my bare hands into the snow, press it into a ball, and throw it at my sister. I miss by a few yards. The snowball puffs on the ground. I make another and miss again. Then I can make no more, for my hands are numb. I look down at them: red and wet, they seem disembodied, no longer mine. A few flakes land on them, but these flakes are not the ones I know from *Little LuLu* or *Archie*;[1] they are big lumpy things that melt soon after landing. On closer look. I can make out the intricate crystals, small and furry and short lived. As if from a great distance, I hear my mother calling. Her voice seems changed by the cold and the words come quicker, in shorter bursts, as if there might be a limited supply of them. I follow the family into the airport building. It is early February. It is El Norte.[2]

The drive into Manhattan is a blur. We piled into a cab and took a wide and busy highway in, most probably the Grand Central Parkway. Once over the East River, my first impression was of riding down into a canyon, much of it shadowy and forbidding, where the sky, steel gray at the time, was a straight path like the street we were on, except bumpier and softer: old cotton swabbed in mercury. It seemed odd that out of that ominous ceiling came the pure white snow I had just touched.

---

1. Comic books.          2. The North.

But the snow on the ground did not stay white very long. Nothing does in New York. It started graying at the edges four days after our arrival, when my father took my sister and me to school, Robert F. Wagner Junior High, on East 72nd Street. It was a long brick building that ran the length of the block. Inauspicious, blank, with shades half-raised on the windows, it could have been a factory or a prison. Piled to the side of the entrance steps was a huge mound of snow packed with children like fruit on supermarket ice. J.H.S. 167 was a typical New York school, a microcosm of the city where all races mingled and fought and, on occasion, learned. The halls were crowded, the classes were crowded, even the bathroom during recess was packed to capacity.

On that first day I was witness to a scene that was to totally alter my image of what school was. On my way from one class to the next, I saw a teacher—who, I later learned, was the prefect of discipline—dragging a girl away by the arm. The girl, trying to tug herself free, was screaming, "Mother fucker, mother fucker." He slapped her across the face several times. Most students, already practicing the indifference that is the keynote of survival in New York, barely turned their heads. I, however, stared, frozen by violence in a place previous experience had deluded me into thinking ought to be quiet and genteel and orderly. It was the loud ring of the bell directly overhead that woke me. I was late for English class.

When I entered the room, the teacher, a slightly pudgy lady with silver white hair, asked if I had a pass. I did not know what a pass was but I answered no anyway. It was my first day and I had gotten lost in the halls.

"Well, in that case, young man, you may come in."

She spoke with rounded vowels and smooth, slightly slurred r's rolling out of her mouth from deep in the throat. Years later I was to learn to identify this manner of speech as an affectation of the educated.

"Next time, however, you must have a pass."

Not that it mattered if one was late to English class. Much of the time was spent doing reading or writing assignments while Mrs. Gall, whose appearance belied that she was close to retirement, did crossword puzzles. A few days later, in fact, something happened that endeared me to her for the rest of the term. Speaking to herself, not expecting any of the students to help her, she said, "A nine letter word for camel." Almost instantaneously, as if by magic, I responded, "Dromedary."

She looked up at me. "That's very good. You have a nice complexion. Where are you from?"

"Complexion?" I asked.

"Yes, skin."

Skin? What does skin have to do with any of this? I had never thought of my skin, let alone considered it a mark of foreignness.

"Cuba."

"Ah, I was there once."

Then she went off on a monologue of beaches and nightlife and weather.

Home for now was a two-bedroom apartment in a residential hotel on East 86th Street, which we would not have been able to afford were it not for the graces of the company my father worked for. We had few clothes, little money, and no possessions to speak of, yet I do not remember ever lacking anything, except perhaps good food, as my mother, who as a middle-class housewife had always relied on maids in Cuba, was just beginning to learn how to cook.

If there was no money for expensive restaurants or theater tickets, I always had thirty cents for the subway fare. From this building that glossed our poverty, I set out into the city that lay open like a geometric flower of concrete and steel. Its nectar was bittersweet, but it kept me, us, from wallowing in the self-pity and stagnation that I have seen among so many exiles. After a few months, realizing that a return to the island was not forthcoming, we looked on a future where the sun was rising again. Not the fierce tropical sun that made everything jump with life and set over the palm trees as quickly as it had risen, but a gentler, slower sun that yielded reluctantly to night and promised to renew itself. Constancy. It was blonde.

The New York sun is not ubiquitous. It hides behind buildings until well after eleven, then appears and disappears for a few hours in the grid sky. Eventually one does not see it at all, only its afterglow diffused by smog and its reflection on the windows of the tallest buildings. Manhattan is an island without sunrise or sunset. If you want to witness the former, you go to the Long Island shore and look toward Europe; if you want the latter, you move west.

And so it was. I could go nowhere but into the city. Sometimes alone, sometimes with Sam, the one friend I made at school, I traveled from one end of the city to the other. At first boredom was the motivator, but soon an intense curiosity that my parents not only tolerated but encouraged became the fire that fueled me.

Thus I discovered Washington Square, the source of Fifth Avenue. Elegant, restrained, neo-Parisian, and ebbing southward from it, Greenwich Village, already in decadence but nevertheless glowing with an odd sort of peripheral, rebellious energy. Some seed had sprouted there I sensed, but it was years before I saw its vines spread throughout the land.

North I went, too, to find the Avenue's mouth and realized that this was no river of gold, but a snake that devoured its own and spewed them back to a place beyond light or hope or future. When one sees Harlem at 125th Street and Fifth Avenue, one comes face to face with the worst despair. The people there are fixed in a defeat not of their making, but rather the result of the color of their skins and a heritage imposed on them from the outside. Black you are and poor you shall remain; black you are and damned you shall be. The Avenue begins in Paris and ends in hell.

In six months we moved to 236th Street in the Upper Bronx,[3] this time to a modest apartment in a modest building. The trees on the streets actually looked like trees, not like stunted saplings. They gave shade; there was enough room on their trunks to carve initials and love notes; the streets were not forever clogged with traffic; the sun was more visible, and from our sixth-floor windows the red blood of the sunset spilled over the Hudson[4] a mile away.

Discovering the installment plan, my parents bought furniture and china and pictures to put on the walls. We even got a stereo. We met other families in the building, formed friendships. We were, suddenly, in middle-class mainstream America, Bronx style, and the past released its grip and ebbed far enough away so that only memory could reach it. Somehow luck had graced us: we had circumvented the snake.

1990

3. The Bronx is a New York City borough north of Manhattan.

4. The Hudson River, which runs south along the west side of Manhattan and of the Bronx.

## Calle de la Amargura

*In Havana there is a street called Calle
de la Amargura or Street of Bitterness.*

On the Street of Bitterness
a man runs from the rain
arms raised into the next imagination.

A woman sits head down
on the stoop of a house                                            5
where her indiscretions
fly about like butterflies.

All songs end,
memories soar over rooftops,
an eyelid swells with desire.                                      10

On the Street of Bitterness,
Calle de la Amargura, there are boys
scratching their tongues,
they dare not speak, they await
their turn in the line of understanding.                          15

On that street
a daughter is dying.
Her father searches for a cure
and finds instead the pillar of his wife,
covered with lizard scales,                                        20
melting with the rain.

On the Street of Bitterness,
Calle de la Amargura, no one is surprised
at the awful taste of Paradise.

1999

## Nothing Nietzsche[1]

*. . . by excess of history life becomes maimed . . .*

There is nothing, Nietzsche,
in this night but the fallen moon
and the carcasses of deer
by the side of the road.

1. Friedrich Wilhelm Nietzsche (1844–1900), German philosopher. The epigraph below is from Nietzsche's essay "Vom Nutzen und Nachteil der Historie für das Leben" (The Use and Abuse of History for Life, 1874): "For by excess of history life becomes maimed and degenerate, and is followed by the degeneration of history as well" (translated by Adrian Collins).

Nothing but cold and the bare trees,                                    5
a meteor in the sky and the long
ride home to the empty house.

Even memories are limping,
Nietzsche, old Friedrich, old specter,
the country lost, the whole world lost                                  10
and too little time to recover.

Once in a woods I thought I saw
deep water, but it was only my need
hobbling into autumn.

There is nothing but watching                                           15
Virtue end her abstinence and God walk away
through steeple-stern landscapes.

There is a noise outside
and someone parking illegally,
a handkerchief waving                                                   20
and willows dropping their leaves,
a phone ringing
and no one, Nietzsche, answering.

There is the country of kindness
into which I am moving,                                                  25
abandoning all umbilicals—
my mother's arms, my father's voice,
the glue of name—until there is
no other way but her whom I love
calling me like a flute or a bird                                       30
out of the wilderness
and the storm of history
dying east of my body.

1999

---

## *From* The Return of Felix Nogara

### *From* Seven

On the last day of his life Nicolás Campión was at his desk by five in the
morning, opening for the tenth time the file state security had compiled on
General Chelo Wences. It was all there: reports of Chelo's secret agreements with opposition leaders in Africa; memoranda of meetings in Miami
with the Baratan underworld in exile; and signed affidavits from three convicted drug barons implicating the great hero of the revolution in their
nefarious traffic. Put together over the last three years after Campión

began to suspect that Chelo was conspiring against him, the file contained enough evidence to execute the general twenty times over.

This time Campión skipped over the reports on the general's illegal activities and came to the section that included family photographs: Chelo with his wife, Chelo with his parents, Chelo at one of his daughters' birthday parties dressed in a clown costume. Following the family photos were somber official ones: General Wences inspecting his troops, General Wences in fatigues aiming an AK-47[1] somewhere in the jungles of the Amazon, General Wences surrounded by an idolatrous group of elite troops on the banks of the lower Congo,[2] General Wences executing a deserter with a short weapon.

The last photograph of the group was cracked and yellowed with age. It showed Wences and Campión as fourteen-year-old boys posing with carbines in the midst of a general strike during the rule of Fuentes Llorens. Somebody had given them the guns on the street and they had run home with them, where Chelo's sister had taken their picture with her box camera. They had played with the guns for a few hours, pointing them at each other and, when they couldn't resist the urge any longer, firing them against the wall in the backyard. Chelo's grandmother had screamed at them to stop, the noise was making her crazy, and Chelo had screamed back at her some obscenity. When they tired of the play, they wrapped the guns in burlap and buried them, hoping to dig them out at some future time. On the reverse of the photograph the sister's handwriting was still visible: "¡Viva Barata Libre! Two rebels ready for the struggle!"

Campión smacked his lips and closed the file. He rose from his desk, pulling up his pants and his underwear and walked to the bathroom. His left testicle felt inflamed and tender. He could feel that it had slipped out from under the elastic of his jockey shorts, which seemed unexpectedly baggy. He balanced himself over the toilet bowl, pulled down the zipper, and pushed his testicle carefully back under the elastic. He closed his eyes and released the stream, easy and thick and warm this morning, not like the last few weeks when he'd had to force the urine out of himself and it had dribbled out without enthusiasm and made him think enviously of horses with their jets like yellow rivers and their penises like firehoses. Today his bladder was strong and the liquid flowed hot and thick, as it had when he was young. When the last drop plopped out of him, he opened his eyes and looked down to find the water in the bowl tainted a dark red. For a moment he held his breath; then he composed himself. He had given up panic long ago, when as a young revolutionary he had held a companion whose jaw had been blown off by a police bullet and heard him gurgle his last unintelligible words. He knew then instinctively that no amount of uncontrolled emotion and no release of tears was going to save his friend from certain death. Panic led nowhere but to paralysis, and a revolutionary could not afford paralysis. Mierda,[3] he allowed himself to think, and he flushed.

Campión walked slowly back to his desk and called his secretary through the intercom. Thinking that it would help no one to delay the matter any longer than absolutely necessary, he had signed Chelo Wences's order of execution and had written in his own hand the time to be dawn of the next

---

1. An assault rifle.
2. River in central Africa.

3. Shit.

day. Nothing would save Chelo now. And for those who would question the decision, let them look at the record. Chelo Wences had been given a fair trial, and at no point had he denied any of the charges against him. In addition, there was little question that he was, by mere egotism and arrogance, a clear and palpable danger to the revolutionary government. The worst thing for Barata at this point in its history was for someone to usurp the popular will, not because he had any idea what do with the country and how to solve its problems, but because he was too vain to turn down the attention of a few sycophants and idolaters. It was Campión's responsibility, as leader of the nation, not to allow a small mind to achieve any degree of power, even if Chelo Wences was his best and most trusted friend and the most courageous soldier Campión had ever known.

Already three doctors had told the dictator of the cancer that was gnawing at his bladder and had spread to his prostate and his testicles. Death was the thing he was used to dispensing—true, with increasing reluctance in his later years—but not receiving. He buzzed the secretary a second time. Still she did not come to take the file away, and he had to sit and stare at the loose-leaf folder, black and solid like an anvil on his desk.

With the effort of a man whose every cell weighs a pound, he stood once again, walked over to the mahogany double doors that Leandro Sotelo had stolen from a monastery in the Once-Sacred Mountains and had installed in the inner office, and opened them. They were so well hung they moved like parchment leaves. Outside the doors, to the right, was the secretary's empty desk. Just beyond the desk on the far wall was a large window through which the sun was shining, the fierce Baratan sun of September that was bathing the world in urine yellow. The guard at the other end of the hallway crossed his weapon and stood at attention. Campión had never seen him before, and he eyed him suspiciously. From his stiff eagerness it was obvious that the guard was a new recruit. He was perhaps nineteen years old, perhaps not even that. It was not long ago that the palace guard was made up of the most loyal veterans, but after Chelo Wences's trial, they could no longer be trusted. Loyalty was a rare quality these days.

"Where is Commander Albizu?" Campión asked him. He never used his secretary's first name in public, although they had once been intimate.

"I don't know, my general," the guard answered, speaking to the wall in the stiff artificial tones of the enlisted man. "She is due in at oh-seven-thirty, my general."

"What time is it now?" Campión asked, unaware that he was wearing his watch.

The guard brought his gun down at ease, lifted his arm in front of his face, and yelled out, "Oh-seven-fifteen, my general."

"Tell Luis to bring me my coffee."

"At your orders, my general," the guard barked. He sounded like a scared dog.

The old dictator glared for a moment, wanting to strike fear in the boy, but with his hair disheveled, his shirt half outside his pants and fly undone, Campión looked more ludicrous than threatening. In the old days he would have sent the recruit to Corrientes to guard the lunatics. Moving quickly for once, the dictator turned on his heels and slammed the doors behind him.

In a few minutes a slight man wearing a white smock, younger even than the guard, brought a tray bearing a thermos of coffee and a glass of ice water. The black folder lay on the desk, threatening to cave it in. Campión had gone to the bathroom again and bled some more, though he took some comfort that the liquid had not been as red or as hot.

"Luis, where is Silvia?" Campión asked the servant. "I've been calling her all morning."

"How should I know?" the boy said. There was an effeminate air about him and he moved like a wild creature. He unloaded the water and coffee onto the desk, placing the thermos, the glass, and the demitasse carefully around the stacks of papers and the heavy black folder.

Campión watched him silently. Delicate as he looked, Luis Avellaneda was ten times more a man than the guard outside. With a hundred more like him, Campión thought he could be another Hernán Cortés.[4] The boy had soft black eyes and thick lips that he had the habit of moistening with his tongue. His dark copper skin exuded an odor like tanned pelt and dry anise, the smell of night just before dawn. Campión had found Luis at a technical school in the outskirts of the capital. As he was passing the student line, he had noticed the unusual smell, and when he looked at the source, the boy did not avert his sight, instead offering a wry, knowing smile. At that moment, Nicolás Campión fell in love for the first time in his life, though he did not know it then.

For days the dictator could not sleep, haunted as he was by Luis Avellaneda, by his eyes somewhere between a man and a woman's, and by his descaro, the gall to stare and smile brazenly at the Liberator himself, whose mere presence made the strongest men quiver. In the ensuing days, Campión visited each of his six mistresses, bedding them down at all hours of the day and night in a futile attempt to rid himself of the memory of those eyes and that scent. When that did not work, he joined his troops for a week of military exercises, hoping that the camaraderie of soldiers in the field would erase the feeling of weakness he was experiencing. Nothing helped. The truth was that Luis had breached the old tyrant's heart, and the ineluctable fact that he was in love came to Nicolás Campión as he was in a rubber raft, attempting a commando landing at midnight, one mile off the northern coast of the island. Once he and the commandos were safely on the beach, Campión radioed his secretary and made her leave the warmth of her bed to find Luis Avellaneda. That same morning at six, Campión received the boy in his office and told him that he needed a valet. Luis would start his job immediately.

The boy stared at him with the same wild-dog look as before and said, "Bien. You can call me Luisito now," as if he had known all along how the story would evolve. Campión had had men killed for such insolence, but instead of rage he felt an immense tenderness and had to use all of his fortitude to keep from kissing him. That was two years ago.

"Luisito," he said to the valet. "I need you to rub my back."

Luis went around the back of the chair and began to work Campión's shoulders, tickling his neck occasionally, calling him Papi, and making the dictator feel like a lover and a father at the same time.

"What is that?" Luis asked, meaning the black folder.

4. Spanish conquistador (1485–1547).

"Nothing important to you," said the dictator. He was being short out of habit.

For forty years he had had to keep people's noses out of the business of government, usually by force, for despite the popular wisdom about democracy and cooperation, principles he had on more than one occasion invoked, he was convinced that you couldn't rule by consensus.

"Ay, mi amor," said Luis. "I was only asking. It looks so big and heavy. Like somebody's life story. Maybe yours. Take off your shirt."

Campión did as he was told. How easy it was to be docile! Then he folded his arms on the desk and rested his head on them so that Luis could move further down his back.

At that moment the secretary opened the double doors, called out a good morning to don Nicolás, using the title as a public formality, and went straight to the desk.

"You are late," Campión said to her, this time not out of habit but because he felt like it. Authority was in his blood. He was born telling people what to do. He felt a sudden pain in his testicles as if a horse had kicked him. It made his body tense, but he said nothing and stayed with his head on his arms. The pain passed quickly.

"Two minutes," she responded, and then to Luis, coldly: "What time was he up this morning?"

She disliked Luis and thought it absurd that a man of Campión's stature should take up with a young boy. But then, no one had ever stopped the dictator from doing whatever he pleased, and by now she was well used to his caprices. At least this little bird wasn't running around bragging about his conquest.

Luis shrugged.

"How was your urine this morning?" she asked Campión with a sisterly air. After forty-five years at his side, doing everything from reloading his gun to hiding him in her apartment after the March massacre, she had a right to ask questions.

"Clean," he answered as always. "Como un caballo."[5]

Silvia knew it was a lie. Everything he ever said to her was a lie. She reached over the desk and pulled Chelo Wences's file toward her. Campión sat up and put on his glasses, gently removing Luis's hand from his shoulder.

Silvia opened the flap and looked at the order. "Tomorrow morning," she said. Though she intervened in the dictator's personal life—his health, eating habits, even his drinking—she had not once questioned his decisions in matters of state. Chelo might have been his best friend, but he was first and foremost a matter of state.

"I have a request from him on my desk," she said closing the flap. "He wants to see you."

"I will see him."

Campión stood up and felt the pain again. This time the testicles kicked him. The pain shot through his bowels, up his spine, and settled in his chest. It took all of his strength to catch his breath. Silvia had noticed, and Luis might have sensed something too.

---

5. Like a horse.

"Papi, you want some breakfast?" Luis asked. His voice was suddenly officious and worried.

"Breakfast is for cowards," the dictator said, filling out his chest with bravado as he did in the old days when no one, not even death, was his equal.

"Shall I give La Roca word to bring the general?" she asked.

"No. I will go to him."

"But Nicolás, you are in no condition." She was genuinely worried. It was her job to worry. It was her passion to worry.

Campión went into the bedroom and dressed with difficulty. His lower abdomen felt heavy and distended, as if it were holding up a large rock. The urge to urinate was constant now, but he had seen enough of his blood flowing into the toilet bowl. He decided against bathing and tried on several undershorts until he found a pair that fit. He'd wear his fatigues and the Rolex watch Chelo had given him ten years ago to celebrate the glorious Thirtieth Anniversary. When he looked at himself in the mirror, he noticed he was stooping. He tried to push his chest out and straighten his back, but that only made his bowels feel heavier, as if they had somehow stopped being a part of him. Then another stroke of pain shot through him so intensely that his whole body trembled and for a moment he saw three green lines across his field of vision, which were three successive shores. Behind them, close to the horizon, was an island with a tree out of which spread seven branches with a cluster of lanceolate leaves at each tip. Campión shook his head clear of the pain and shuffled over to the bed.

He knew the place of his vision existed, but he didn't know where, or if he had ever been there to begin with, or if it was a place he was going to soon, or if the place was inside of him or out, or if it was a chimera and thinking about it was also a chimera and he and all of his life, too, a chimera. His body began to shiver uncontrollably and sweat profusely as if all of the fluids of his body were seeping out of him. He sat carefully on the bed so as not to disturb the stone in his gut and he called Silvia in.

Thinking he had summoned her about the next case, the one about the dissident whose release from prison was being negotiated by two U.S. congressmen, Silvia brought that folder with her. It had a green cover and was not nearly as thick as Chelo Wences's.

"I want to see Padre Eusebio," Campión said to her.

Silvia stared at him incredulously. In the old days she had always been taken in by his jokes, but he hadn't played a trick on her for fifteen years.

"I want him to hear my confession." His tone of voice told her that he wasn't joking.

Feeling a great terror spilling onto a great sadness, Silvia walked over and looked down at him. She spoke as if to a child.

"Padre Eusebio was executed six months ago."

"I have no friends left in this world," he said without irony. He had killed many of them, jailed others, exiled the rest.

She thought of saying, you have me, but she had long ago stopped being his friend. She had been his lover when they were both young and her flesh was firm on her body. She had been his confidante after that, the one person with whom he could share the most inviolable state secrets, and she had wound up as his secretary and caretaker. She loved him though, more than she loved her husband or her children, and she was ready to do anything for him. That love, unconditional and ardent, had kept her from being his friend and had kept her alive.

"I will call the archbishop," she said.

\* \* \*

2000

## A Dictionary of Guatemalan Bird Calls

In the market a young girl
is selling entrails (boreal,

membranous). The ambiguities
are singing in my ear:

Sunset means a crow. City                                    5
means Quetzaltenango[1] drowning.

2001                                                                                    2005

1. More commonly known as Xela; city in southwestern Guatemala.

---

# ESMERALDA SANTIAGO
## b. 1948

Born in Santurce, Puerto Rico, Esmeralda Santiago grew up in the rural barrio of Macún, in the town of Toa Baja, and was part of a large, poor family. When she was 13 years old, she moved with her mother and siblings to Brooklyn, New York. Because of her academic achievements in junior high school, Santiago was admitted to New York City's Performing Arts High School, where she studied acting. Seven years after graduating from high school, at age 25, she began studying at Harvard University, where she earned her bachelor's degree in film production. She also holds a Master of Fine Arts degree from Sarah Lawrence College, in Bronxville, New York, and Doctor of Letters honorary degrees from Trinity College, in Hartford, Connecticut; Pace University, in New York; and the University of Puerto Rico, in Mayagüez.

Santiago's writing career took a while to develop. Soon after graduating from Harvard, she went back to Puerto Rico to work after many years of absence. There she was confronted with severe underemployment, a situation faced by many other educated women on the island. But more hurtful was the rejection she felt from those island Puerto Ricans who questioned her Puerto Ricanness or viewed her as too Americanized. These personal dilemmas compelled her to return to the United States after a few months. She moved to Boston and worked as a grant proposal writer for a Hispanic community agency and for the Massachusetts district attorney's office. During this period, she started publishing personal essays and articles in newspapers and magazines, and these pieces captured the attention of a book editor who encouraged her to write an autobiographical narrative. The publication of *When*

*I Was Puerto Rican* (1993), a chapter of which is included in this anthology, immediately gained Santiago critical attention as a narrator of women's, especially Puerto Rican women's, oppressive experiences in often sexist cultural environments on the island and on the mainland. In a 1997 interview with Carmen Dolores Hernández, a cultural columnist in Puerto Rico, Santiago called herself a women's writer in the full sense of the term: "I write for women. I don't care if men read my work; it doesn't matter to me. I'm very deliberate about that. It's women's lives I'm interested in."

*When I Was Puerto Rican* is not a rejection of Santiago's Puerto Rican identity, as the title may suggest, but an engaging account of her life and that of her family during her growing-up years in Puerto Rico. Only a small portion of the book deals with her school years in New York. Her second book, the novel *America's Dream* (1996), records the displacement and self-discovery of a young Puerto Rican woman seeking a new life in the United States. Santiago's third book, *Almost a Woman* (1998), a sequel to *When I was Puerto Rican*—adapted by Santiago in 2001 for the PBS television show *Masterpiece Theater*—expands on the author's adult life in the United States and her artistic development.

In *The Turkish Lover* (2004), the third installment in her autobiographical series, Santiago addresses her relationship with the Turkish filmmaker Ulvi Dogan, who spotted her in a phone booth when she was 18 years old and immediately wanted to use her as an actress. The book follows their relationship, in which Santiago was controlled by her abusive lover and devoted most of her time to his endeavors, and which ended when Santiago entered Harvard and began her passage to self-realization.

With several other Latino writers, Santiago coedited the essay volumes *Las Christmas* (1998) and *Las Mamis* (2000). She is also runs the film production company Campomedia. Santiago writes primarily in English, but most of her novels have been translated into Spanish. She is well-known in Puerto Rico and other Spanish-speaking countries. The second Santiago selection in this anthology, "Island of Lost Causes," is a remembrance of the tragic death of Santiago's Nationalist uncle and a reflection on Puerto Rico's unresolved status as part of the United States. It was first published in *The New York Times* in 1993; two years later, it was included in the anthology *Boricuas: Influential Puerto Rican Writings.*

---

### FROM WHEN I WAS PUERTO RICAN

## The American Invasion of Macún

*Lo que no mata, engorda.*

•

*What doesn't kill you, makes you fat.*

> *Pollito*, chicken
> *Gallina*, hen
> *Lápiz*, pencil
> *y Pluma*, pen.
> *Ventana*, window
> *Puerta*, door
> *Maestra*, teacher
> *y Piso*, floor.

Miss Jiménez stood in front of the class as we sang and, with her ruler, pointed at the chicks scratching the dirt outside the classroom, at the hen leading them, at the pencil on Juanita's desk, at the pen on her own desk, at the window that looked out into the playground, at the door leading to the yard, at herself, and at the shiny tile floor. We sang along, pointing as she did with our sharpened pencils, rubber end out.

"¡Muy bien!" She pulled down the map rolled into a tube at the front of the room. In English she told us, "Now gwee estody about de Jun-ited Estates gee-o-graphee."

It was the daily English class. Miss Jiménez, the second- and third-grade teacher, was new to the school in Macún. She looked like a grown-up doll, with high rounded cheekbones, a freckled café con leche complexion, black lashes, black curly hair pulled into a bun at the nape of her neck, and the prettiest legs in the whole barrio. Doña Ana[1] said Miss Jiménez had the most beautiful legs she'd ever seen, and the next day, while Miss Jiménez wrote the multiplication table on the blackboard, I stared at them.

She wore skirts to just below the knees, but from there down, her legs were shaped like chicken drumsticks, rounded and full at the top, narrow at the bottom. She had long straight hair on her legs, which everyone said made them even prettier, and small feet encased in plain brown shoes with a low square heel. That night I wished on a star that someday my scrawny legs would fill out into that lovely shape and that the hair on them would be as long and straight and black.

Miss Jiménez came to Macún at the same time as the community center. She told us that starting the following week, we were all to go to the centro comunal before school to get breakfast, provided by the Estado Libre Asociado, or Free Associated State, which was the official name for Puerto Rico in the Estados Unidos, or in English, the Jun-ited Estates of America. Our parents, Miss Jiménez told us, should come to a meeting that Saturday, where experts from San Juan and the Jun-ited Estates would teach our mothers all about proper nutrition and hygiene, so that we would grow up as tall and strong as Dick, Jane, and Sally, the Americanitos in our primers.

"And Mami," I said as I sipped my afternoon café con leche, "Miss Jiménez said the experts will give us free food and toothbrushes and things . . . and we can get breakfast every day except Sunday . . ."

"Calm down," she told me. "We'll go, don't worry."

On Saturday morning the yard in front of the centro comunal filled with parents and their children. You could tell the experts from San Juan from the ones that came from the Junited Estates because the Americanos wore ties with their white shirts and tugged at their collars and wiped their foreheads with crumpled handkerchiefs. They hadn't planned for children, and the men from San Juan convinced a few older girls to watch the little ones outside so that the meeting could proceed with the least amount of disruption. Small children refused to leave their mothers' sides and screeched the minute one of the white-shirted men came near them. Some women sat on the folding chairs at the rear of the room nursing, a cloth draped over their baby's face so that the experts would not be upset at the sight of a bare

---

1. The family's next-door neighbor in Macún.

breast. There were no fathers. Most of them worked seven days a week, and anyway, children and food were woman's work.

"Negi,[2] take the kids outside and keep them busy until this is over."

"But Mami . . ."

"Do as I say."

She pressed her way to a chair in the middle of the room and sat facing the experts. I hoisted Edna on my shoulder and grabbed Alicia's hand. Delsa pushed Norma out in front of her. They ran into the yard and within minutes had blended into a group of children their age. Héctor found a boy to chase him around a tree, and Alicia crawled to a sand puddle, where she and other toddlers smeared one another with the fine red dirt. I sat at the door, Edna on my lap, and tried to keep one eye on my sisters and brother and another on what went on inside.

The experts had colorful charts on portable easels. They introduced each other to the group, thanked the Estado Libre Asociado for the privilege of being there, and then took turns speaking. The first expert opened a large suitcase. Inside there was a huge set of teeth with pink gums.

"*Ay Dios Santo, qué cosa tan fea*," said a woman as she crossed herself. The mothers laughed and mumbled among themselves that yes, it was ugly. The expert stretched his lips into a smile and pulled a large toothbrush from under the table. He used ornate Spanish words that we assumed were scientific talk for teeth, gums, and tongue. With his giant brush, he polished each tooth on the model, pointing out the proper path of the bristles on the teeth.

"If I have to spend that much time on my teeth," a woman whispered loud enough for everyone to hear, "I won't get anything done around the house." The room buzzed with giggles, and the expert again spread his lips, took a breath, and continued his demonstration.

"At the conclusion of the meeting," he said, "you will each receive a toothbrush and a tube of paste for every member of your family."

"*¿Hasta pa' los mellaos?*" a woman in the back of the room asked, and everyone laughed.

"If they have no teeth, it's too late for them, isn't it," the expert said through his own clenched teeth. The mothers shrieked with laughter, and the expert sat down so that an *Americano* with red hair and thick glasses could tell us about food.

He wiped his forehead and upper lip as he pulled up the cloth covering one of the easels to reveal a colorful chart of the major food groups.

"*La buena* nutrition is *muy importante para los niños*." In heavily accented, hard to understand Castilian Spanish he described the necessity of eating portions of each of the foods on his chart every day. There were carrots and broccoli, iceberg lettuce, apples, pears, and peaches. The bread was sliced into a perfect square, unlike the long loaves Papi brought home from a bakery in San Juan, or the round *pan de manteca* Mami bought at Vitín's store. There was no rice on the chart, no beans, no salted codfish. There were big white eggs, not at all like the small round ones our hens gave us. There was a tall glass of milk, but no coffee. There were wedges of yellow cheese, but no balls of cheese like the white *queso del país* wrapped in banana leaves sold in

2. A nickname for Negrita, which her father called her when she was born, because of her dark skin.

bakeries all over Puerto Rico. There were bananas but no plantains, potatoes but no *batatas*, cereal flakes but no oatmeal, bacon but no sausages.

"But, *señor*," said Doña Lola from the back of the room, "none of the fruits or vegetables on your chart grow in Puerto Rico."

"Then you must substitute our recommendations with your native foods."

"Is an apple the same as a mango?" asked Cirila, whose yard was shaded by mango trees.

"*Sí*," said the expert, "a mango can be substituted for an apple."

"What about breadfruit?"

"I'm not sure . . ." The *Americano* looked at an expert from San Juan, who stood up, pulled the front of his *guayabera* down over his ample stomach, and spoke in a voice as deep and resonant as a radio announcer's.

"Breadfruit," he said, "would be equivalent to potatoes."

"Even the ones with seeds?" asked Doña Lola, who roasted them on the coals of her *fogón*.[3]

"Well, I believe so," he said, "but it is best not to make substitutions for the recommended foods. That would throw the whole thing off."

He sat down and stared at the ceiling, his hands crossed under his belly as if he had to hold it up. The mothers asked each other where they could get carrots and broccoli, iceberg lettuce, apples, peaches, or pears.

"At the conclusion of the meeting," the *Americano* said, "you will all receive a sack full of groceries with samples from the major food groups." He flipped the chart closed and moved his chair near the window, amid the hum of women asking one another what he'd just said.

The next expert uncovered another easel on which there was a picture of a big black bug. A child screamed, and a woman got the hiccups.

"This," the expert said scratching the top of his head, "is the magnified image of a head louse."

Following him, another *Americano* who spoke good Spanish discussed intestinal parasites. He told all the mothers to boil their water several times and to wash their hands frequently.

"Children love to put their hands in their mouths," he said, making it sound like fun, "but each time they do, they run the risk of infection." He flipped the chart to show an enlargement of a dirty hand, the tips of the fingernails encrusted with dirt.

"Ugh! That's disgusting!" whispered Mami to the woman next to her. I curled my fingers inside my palms.

"When children play outside," the expert continued, "their hands pick up dirt, and with it, hundreds of microscopic parasites that enter their bodies through their mouths to live and thrive in their intestinal tract."

He flipped the chart again. A long flat snake curled from the corner at the top of the chart to the opposite corner at the bottom. Mami shivered and rubbed her arms to keep the goose bumps down.

"This," the *Americano* said, "is a tapeworm, and it is not uncommon in this part of the world."

Mami had joked many times that the reason I was so skinny was that I had a *solitaria*, a tapeworm, in my belly. But I don't think she ever knew what a tapeworm looked like, nor did I. I imagined something like the earthworms

3. An indoor open-hearth grill that uses charcoal. Up to the 1950s, it was commonly used in the kitchens of rural Puerto Rican houses without electricity.

that crawled out of the ground when it rained, but never anything so ugly as the snake on the chart, its flat body like a deck of cards strung together.

"Tapeworms," the expert continued, "can reach lengths of nine feet." I rubbed my belly, trying to imagine how long nine feet was and whether I had that much room in me. Just thinking about it made my insides itchy.

When they finished their speeches, the experts had all the mothers line up and come to the side of the room, where each was given samples according to the number of people in their household. Mami got two sacks of groceries, so Delsa had to carry Edna all the way home while I dragged one of the bags full of cans, jars, and bright cartons.

At home Mami gave each of us a toothbrush and told us we were to clean our teeth every morning and every evening. She set a tube of paste and a cup by the door, next to Papi's shaving things. Then she emptied the bags.

"I don't understand why they didn't just give us a sack of rice and a bag of beans. It would keep this family fed for a month."

She took out a five-pound tin of peanut butter, two boxes of cornflakes, cans of fruit cocktail, peaches in heavy syrup, beets, and tuna fish, jars of grape jelly and pickles and put everything on a high shelf.

"We'll save this," she said, "so that we can eat like *Americanos cuando el hambre apriete*." She kept them there for a long time but took them down one by one so that, as she promised, we ate like Americans when hunger cramped our bellies.

. . .

One morning I woke up with something wiggling inside my panties. When I looked, there was a long worm inside. I screamed, and Mami came running. I pointed to my bottom, and she pulled down my panties and saw. She sat me in a basin of warm water with salt, because she thought that might draw more worms out. I squatted, my bottom half in, half out, expecting that a *solitaria* would crawl out of my body and swim around and when it realized it had come out, try to bite me down there and crawl back in. I kept looking into the basin, but nothing happened, and after a long time, Mami let me get up. That night she gave us only a thin broth for supper.

"Tonight you all get a *purgante*," she said.

"But why," Delsa whined. "I'm not the one with worms."

"If one of you has worms, you all have worms," Mami said, and we knew better than to argue with her logic. "Now go wash up, and come get your medicine."

The *purgante* was her own concoction, a mixture of cod-liver oil and mugwort, milk of magnesia, and green papaya juice, sweetened to disguise the fishy, bitter, chalky taste. It worked on our bellies overnight, and in the morning, Delsa, Norma, Héctor, and I woke up with cramps and took turns at the latrine, joining the end of the line almost as soon as we'd finished. Mami fed us broths, and in the evening, a bland, watery boiled rice that at least stuck to our bellies and calmed the roiling inside.

"Today," Miss Jiménez said, "you will be vaccinated by the school nurse."

There had never been a school nurse at Macún Elementary School, but lately a woman dressed in white, with a tall, stiff cap atop her short cropped hair, had set up an infirmary in a corner of the lunchroom. Forms had been sent home, and Mami had told me and Delsa that we would be receiving polio vaccines.

"What's polio?" I asked, imagining another parasite in my belly.

"It's a very bad disease that makes you crippled," she said.

"Is it like meningitis?" Delsa asked. A brother of one of her friends had that disease; his arms and hands were twisted into his body, his legs splayed out at the knees, so that he walked as if he were about to kneel.

"No," Mami said, "it's worse. If you get polio, you die, or you spend the rest of your life in a wheelchair or inside an iron lung."

"An iron lung!?!?" It was impossible. There could not be such a thing.

"It's not like a real lung, silly," Mami laughed. "It's a machine that breathes for you."

"¡Ay Dios Mío!" Polio was worse than *solitaria*.

"But how can it do that?" Delsa's eyes opened and shut as if she were testing to see whether she was asleep or awake.

"I don't know how it works," Mami said. "Ask your father."

Delsa and I puzzled over how you could have an iron lung, and that night, when Papi came home from work, we made him draw one for us and show us how a machine could do what people couldn't. He drew a long tube and at one end made a stick figure face.

"It looks like a can," Delsa said, and Papi laughed.

"Yes," he said, "it does. Just like a can."

Miss Jiménez sent us out to see the nurse two at a time, in alphabetical order. By the time she got to the S's, I was shaky, because every one of the children who had gone before me had come back crying, pressing a wad of cotton against their arm. Ignacio Sepúlveda walked next to me, and even though he was as scared as I was, he pretended he wasn't.

"What crybabies!" he said. "I've had shots before and they don't hurt that much."

"When?"

"Last year. They gave us shots for tuberculosis." We were nearing the lunchroom, and Ignacio slowed down, tugged on my arm, and whispered, "It's all because of politics."

"What are you talking about? Politics isn't a disease like polio. It's something men talk about at the bus stop." I'd heard Papi tell Mami when he was late that he'd missed the bus because he'd been discussing politics.

Ignacio kept his voice to a whisper, as if he were telling me something no one else knew. "My Papá says the government's doing all this stuff for us because it's an election year."

"What does that have to do with it?"

"They give kids shots and free breakfast, stuff like that, so that our dads will vote for them."

"So?"

"Don't you know anything?"

"I know a lot of things."

"You don't know anything about politics."

"Do so."

"Do not."

"Do so."

"Who's the governor of Puerto Rico, then?"

"Oh, you could have asked something really hard! . . . Everyone knows it's Don Luis Muñoz Marín."[4]

"Yeah, well, who's *el presidente* of the Jun-ited Estates?"

"Ay-sen-hou-err."[5]

"I bet you don't know his first name."

I knew then I had him. I scanned Papi's newspaper daily, and I had seen pictures of *el presidente* on the golf course, and of his wife's funny hairdo.

"His first name is Eekeh," I said, puffed with knowledge. "And his wife's name is Mami."[6]

"Well, he's an imperialist, just like all the other *gringos*!" Ignacio said, and I was speechless because Mami and Papi never let us say things like that about grown-ups, even if they were true.

When we came into the lunchroom, Ignacio presented his arm to the nurse as if instead of a shot he were getting a medal. He winced as the nurse stuck the needle into him and blinked a few times to push back tears. But he didn't cry, and I didn't either, though I wanted to. There was no way I'd have Ignacio Sepúlveda calling me a crybaby.

"Papi, what's an imperialist?"

He stopped the hammer in midstrike and looked at me. "Where did you hear that word?"

"Ignacio Sepúlveda said Eekeh Aysenhouerr is an imperialist. He said all *gringos* are."

Papi looked around as if someone were hiding behind a bush and listening in. "I don't want you repeating those words to anybody . . ."

"I know that Papi. . . . I just want to know what it means. Are *gringos* the same as *Americanos*?"

"You should never call an *Americano* a gringo. It's a very bad insult."

"But why?"

"It just is." It wasn't like Papi not to give a real answer to my questions. "Besides, *el presidente*'s name is pronounced Ayk, not Eekeh." He went back to his hammering.

I handed him a nail from the can at his feet. "How come it's a bad insult?"

He stopped banging the wall and looked at me. I stared back, and he put his hammer down, took off his hat, brushed his hand across his forehead, wiped it on his pants, sat on the stoop, and leaned his elbows back, stretching his legs out in front of him. This was the response I expected. Now I would hear all about *gringos* and imperialists.

"Puerto Rico was a colony of Spain after Columbus landed here,"[7] he began, like a schoolteacher.

"I know that."

"Don't interrupt."

"Sorry."

"In 1898, *los Estados Unidos* invaded Puerto Rico, and we became their colony. A lot of Puerto Ricans don't think that's right. They call *Americanos*

---

4. See p. 482.
5. I.e., Dwight David Eisenhower (1890–1969), U.S. president 1953–61; commonly known as "Ike."
6. I.e., Mamie Geneva Doud Eisenhower (1896–

1979), U.S. first lady 1953–61.
7. I.e., during the first voyage of Christopher Columbus (1451–1506), Spanish admiral and explorer from Genoa.

imperialists, which means they want to change our country and our culture to be like theirs."

"Is that why they teach us English in school, so we can speak like them?"

"Yes."

"Well, I'm not going to learn English so I don't become American."

He chuckled. "Being American is not just a language, *Negrita*, it's a lot of other things."

"Like what?"

He scratched his head. "Like the food you eat . . . the music you listen to . . . the things you believe in."

"Do they believe in God?"

"Some of them do."

"Do they believe in phantasms and witches?"

"Yes, some Americans believe in that."

"Mami doesn't believe any of that stuff."

"I know. I don't either."

"Why not?"

"I just . . . I believe in things I can see."

"Why do people call *Americanos gringos*?"

"We call them *gringos*, they call us spiks."

"What does that mean?"

"Well," he sat up, leaned his elbows on his knees and looked at the ground, as if he were embarrassed. "There are many Puerto Ricans in New York, and when someone asks them a question they say, 'I don spik inglish' instead of 'I don't speak English.' They make fun of our accent."

"*Americanos* talk funny when they speak Spanish."

"Yes, they do. The ones who don't take the trouble to learn it well." He pushed his hat back, and the sun burned into his already brown face, making him squint. "That's part of being an imperialist. They expect us to do things their way, even in our country."

"That's not fair."

"No, it isn't." He stood up and picked up his hammer. "Well, I'd better get back to work, *Negrita*. Do you want to help?"

"Okay." I followed him, holding the can of nails up so he wouldn't have to bend over to pick them up. "Papi?"

"Yes."

"If we eat all that American food they give us at the *centro comunal*, will we become *Americanos*?"

He banged a nail hard into the wall then turned to me, and, with a broad smile on his face said, "Only if you like it better than our Puerto Rican food."

The yard in front of the *centro comunal* teemed with children. Mrs. García, the school lunch matron, opened the door and stepped out, a bell in her hand. We quieted before she rang it. She beamed.

"Good." There was whispering and shoving as we crowded the door to be the first in for breakfast. Mrs. García lifted the bell in warning. We settled down again.

"Now," she said in her gruff voice, "line up by age, youngest first."

The smaller children, who had been pushed to the back of the crowd by bigger ones, scurried to the front. I took my place halfway between the younger and the older ones, who scowled at us and jammed the line forward with rough shoves.

"Stop pushing!" Mrs. García yelled. "There's enough for everyone."

She opened the double doors and we rushed ahead in a wave, goaded from behind by boys who crushed against us with their chests and knees.

The *centro comunal* had been decorated with posters. Dick and Jane, Sally and Spot, Mother and Father, the Mailman, the Milkman, and the Policeman smiled their way through tableau after tableau, their clean, healthy, primary-colored world flat and shadowless.

"Wow!" Juanita Marín whispered, her lips shaped into a perfect O.

People who looked like Mother and Father held up tubes of Colgate toothpaste or bars of Palmolive soap. A giant chart of the four basic food groups was tacked up between the back windows. In a corner, the Puerto Rican seal, flanked by our flag and the Stars and Stripes, looked like a lamb on a platter. Above it, Ike and Don Luis Muñoz Marín faced each other smiling.

"What's that smell?" I said to Juanita as we shuffled closer to the counter lined with steaming pots.

"It's the food, silly," she giggled.

It was a sweet-salty smell, bland but strong, warm but not comforting, lacking herbs and spices.

"It's disgusting!"

"I think it smells good." She pouted and took a tray, a pale green paper napkin, and a spoon.

The server picked a blue enamel tin plate from a stack behind her and scooped out a bright yellow blob from the pot in front of her. She dumped a ladleful on Juanita's plate and slid it onto the tray.

"You'd like some eggs too, wouldn't you?" she asked me with a smile.

"Those are eggs?"

"Of course they're eggs!" she laughed. "What else could they be?" She heaped a mound of it in the middle of my plate, where it quivered, its watery edges green where they met the blue.

"They don't look like eggs."

Ignacio Sepúlveda poked his tray into my ribs. "You're holding up the line!"

"They're *huevos Americanos*," said the next server, whose job it was to spear two brown sausages with a fork and slip them onto the plate. "They're powdered, so all we do is add water and fry them." She arranged my sausages to flank the eggs. "And here are some *salchichas Americanas*, so you can put some meat on those bones." She laughed, and I gave her a dirty look. That only made her laugh harder.

The next server slapped margarine on two bread squares, which he laid like a pyramid over the eggs. Next, a girl not much older than the kids behind us poured canned juice into a bottom-heavy glass, which she put on our trays so carelessly it splashed out and made watery orange puddles that ran to the corners of our trays.

We sat on long benches attached to plastic tables, Juanita and I across from one another.

"This is great!" she chirruped in her reedy voice, lips wet with anticipation. Her black eyes took in the colors of our American breakfast: maroon tray, blue plate, yellow eggs, brown sausages, milky white bread with a thin beige crust, the hueless shimmer of margarine, orange juice, pastel green paper napkin, silvery spoon. "Wow!" she oohed again.

I rearranged the food so that none of it touched and dipped my spoon into the gelatinous hill, which was firmer than I expected. It was warm and gave off that peculiar odor I'd smelled coming in. It tasted like the cardboard covers of our primers, salty, dry, fibrous, but not as satisfyingly chewy. If these were once eggs, it had been a long time since they'd been inside a hen. I nicked the tip of the sausage with the spoon and tongued it around before crushing it between my teeth. Its grease-bathed pepperiness had a strong bitter aftertaste like anise, but not sweet. The bread formed moist balls inside my mouth, no matter how much I chewed it. The juice might have had oranges in it once, but only a faint citrus smell remained.

I was glad the food wasn't tasty and played it around the blue plate, creating yellow mountains through which shimmering rivers of grease flowed, their edges green, the rolled up balls of white bread perfect stones along strips of brown earth studded with tiny black flecks, ants perhaps, or, better yet, microscopic people.

. . .

> Are ju slippin? Are ju slippin?
> Bruder John, Bruder John.
> Mornin bel sar rin ging.
> Mornin bel sar rin ging.
> Deen deen don. Deen deen don.

Miss Jiménez liked to teach us English through song, and we learned all our songs phonetically, having no idea of what the words meant. She tried to teach us "America the Beautiful" but had to give up when we stumbled on "for spacious skies" (4 espé chosk ¡Ay!) and "amber waves of grain" (am burr gueys oh gren).

At the same time she taught us the Puerto Rican national anthem, which said Borinquén[8] was the daughter of the ocean and the sun. I liked thinking of our island as a woman whose body was a garden of flowers, whose feet were caressed by waves, a land whose sky was never cloudy. I especially liked the part when Christopher Columbus lands on her shores and sighs: "¡Ay! This is the beautiful and I've been searching for!"

But my favorite patriotic song was "En mi viejo San Juan," in which a poet says good-bye to Old San Juan and calls Puerto Rico a "sea goddess, queen of the coconut groves."

"Papi . . ." He was on his knees, smoothing the cement floor of the new kitchen he was attaching to the house.

"Sí. . . ." He put his trowel down and squeezed his waist as he stretched his back. I squatted against the wall near him.

"Where was Noel Estrada going when he was saying good-bye to Old San Juan?"

Papi reached over and turned the radio down. "I think he was sailing from San Juan Harbor to New York."

"It's such a sad song, don't you think?"

---

8. The indigenous Taíno people's name for Puerto Rico.

"At the end he says he'll come back someday."

"Did he?"

"The last verse says he's old and hasn't been able to return."

"That makes it even sadder."

"Why?"

"Because he says he's coming back to be happy. Doesn't that sound like he wasn't happy in New York?"

"Yes, I guess it does."

"Maybe he didn't want to go."

"Maybe." He picked up his trowel, slid a thin layer of cement on it, and levelled it on the floor, smoothing and stretching it in arcs that formed half circles, like grey rainbows.

"Look how pretty this is!"

Mami held a yellow blouse with a ruffled collar against her bosom, patted the neckline into shape, and stretched it across her shoulders to check the fit. It was a wonderful color against her skin, making the freckles on her nose look like gold specks.

"I'll put it away for now. It's a little small." She was pregnant again, and her belly pressed against the fabric of her dress and strained the seams that zigzagged down the sides, where bits of flesh showed pale and soft between the stitches. She folded the blouse and pulled a dress out of the box. Delsa and I both grabbed for it, but Mami yanked it out of reach and crossed her arms, crushing it against her.

"Stop that! Let me see what size it is." She held it up. It was perfect for me. It had red dots on white puffy sleeves, a white bodice, a white skirt with a stripe of red dots at the hem, and two dotted heart-shaped pockets.

"Negi, I think this one is for you."

I grabbed it and ran to the other end of the room, where Norma was already trying on pink shorts with a matching tee shirt. I stuck my tongue out at Delsa, who sent daggers with her eyes, but only until Mami pulled out a sky-blue dress with ruffles and lace on the collar. Perfect for Delsa.

Tata, Mami's mother, had sent us a box from New York full of clothes that Mami's cousins no longer wore. Clothes that were almost new, with no stains or tears or mended seams. Héctor, the boy in our family, was the only one to get new pants and shirts, because none of Mami's New York relatives had boys his age. But for us girls there were shiny patent-leather shoes with the heels hardly worn, saddle shoes that had already been broken in, a red sweater with a bow at the neck and only one button missing, pleated skirts with matching blouses, high heels for Mami, a few nightgowns, and a pair of pajamas that I claimed, because I loved the cowboys and Indians chasing each other across my body, down my arms and legs.

"Our cousins must be rich to give up these things!" Norma said as she tried on a girl's cotton slip with embroidered flowers across the chest.

"Things like these are not that expensive in New York," Mami said. "Anyone can afford them."

She sat on the edge of the bed and unfolded a letter that had been taped to the inside of the box. A crisp ten dollar bill fell out. Héctor and Alicia dove for it and wrestled one another to be the first to get it. While they fought, Delsa calmly picked it up and handed it to Mami.

"What does the letter say, Mami?" I asked.

"It says she hopes we like the presents." She looked up at me, her eyes shiny. "Maybe you could write Tata a letter and tell her we love them."

"Sure!" I liked writing letters. Especially if they were going far away. I had often written things for Mami, like addresses on envelopes she sent to Tata in New York, or notes for my teachers, which I wrote and she signed.

That night I wrote Tata a letter. It took me a long time, because we were just learning cursive in school, and I had to look up the shapes of some letters on the back of the book Miss Jiménez had given us for penmanship practice. I found it difficult to form the capital *E* of my first name, with its top and bottom curlicues and uneven-size bulges that faced in what seemed like the wrong direction no matter how many times I wrote it. So I signed it Negi, which I considered to be my real name. When I finished the letter, Mami read it out loud.

"'Dear Tata, We liked the presents you sent us. The dress with the polka dots fits me and Delsa looks pretty in the blue dress. Mami is saving the yellow blouse for after the baby. We love you and thank you for the things you sent. Love, Negi.'... You made a mistake...."

"What?"

"You didn't start with a salutation."

"Yes I did. See? Dear Tata."

"I know, but you also have to write, 'I hope when you receive this letter you are feeling well. We are all well here, thank God.' You can abbreviate 'A Dios Gracias' by writing 'A.D.G.' if you want to."

"Why does it have to start that way?"

"All letters start that way."

"But why?"

"I don't know!" she said, exasperated. "That's how I learned it. And every letter I get starts that way. If you don't have a salutation at the beginning, it's not a real letter.... Besides, it's rude not to wish the reader good health, and God has to be thanked first thing.... You'd better write it again."

"I don't want to write it again."

"You have to." She set it down on the table. "Finish it and I can take it to the post office tomorrow." She walked away.

"I'm not doing this stupid letter over," I mumbled.

"What was that?" She'd whirled in her tracks and was at me before I could blink my eyes, her left hand gripping my arm.

"Nothing! I didn't say anything."

Mami stood over me, crushing my arm, right hand at her side, the fingers trembling. I wanted to grab her fingers, to bite into them, to make them hurt, those fingers that sometimes soothed but so many times splayed against my skin in smacks, or, fisted, knuckled my head in *cocotazos*[9] that echoed inside my brain. She slammed me against the chair. The rungs dug into my bony back.

"Finish it." I could almost touch the heat she gave off, the faint sweaty smell of her anger. Hot, quiet tears dribbled down my cheeks in a steady flow, like the faucet at the public fountain. The drone inside my head was louder, my ears felt warm, red, too big for my head. Mami stood there watching, as I

9. Puerto Rican term for a rap on the head with the knuckles; formerly a common practice on the island for punishing children (at home and in school) when they were misbehaving.

picked up the pencil, carefully tore a sheet from my notebook, and, in labored script, wrote, "Dear Tata, I hope when you receive this letter . . ."

> My bonee lie sober de o chan,
> My bonee lie sober de sí,
> My bonee lie sober de o chan,
> O breen back my bonee 2 mí, 2 mí . . .

"What's that smell?" The breakfasts at the *centro comunal* had fallen into a pattern of *huevos Americanos* alternating with hot oatmeal, which at least tasted like oatmeal, except it was not as smooth, sweet, and cinnamony as the oatmeal Mami made.

"They must be giving us something new today," said Juanita Marín.

The steaming pots were gone. Instead, there was a giant urn in the middle of the table and a five-pound tin of peanut butter. One of the servers scooped a dollop of peanut butter into the bottom-heavy glasses, and another filled them with warm milk from the urn.

"Here's a spoon so you can stir it," she said as she put the glasses on our trays.

I carried my tray to the usual table Juanita and I shared. Even she, who loved the breakfasts, had a suspicious expression on her face. We faced each other, looked down at the glass full of milk with the brown blob on the bottom, looked at each other again, then at the milk.

"Are you going to taste it?" I asked her.

"Sure," she said, unconvinced. "Are you?"

"Sure." I stirred the milk, and beige pellets floated up from the bottom, like sand encased in a shimmery oil that skimmed the top and bubbled around the whirlpool I made with my spoon. Juanita stirred hers too. I took a sip from the spoon but couldn't really taste much except the milk. Juanita spooned a dribble into her mouth. She smiled.

"Yum!" But it wasn't her usual happy "Yum!" It was more of an "I'm going to pretend to like this in case it's good" kind of "Yum!"

I wrapped my hands around the glass, lifted it to my lips, and drank. A consoling warmth compensated for the milky smell, and the gritty, salty-sweet taste. The peanut butter, which was supposed to dissolve in the milk, broke off into clumps, like soft pebbles.

I gagged, and the glass fell out of my hand, spilled over my uniform, and crashed to the tile floor where it broke into large chunks that gleamed in the pebbly milk. I threw up what little I'd swallowed, and children around me jumped and receded into a tittery circle of faces with milky mustaches. Mrs. García pushed through the crowd and pulled me away from the mess, while one of the servers dragged a dirty mop across it.

"*Now* look what you've done!" she said, as if this were something I did every day of the week to annoy her.

"I couldn't help it!" I cried. "That milk tastes sour!"

"How can it taste sour?" she yelled as she wiped me down with a rag. "It's powdered milk. We made it fresh this morning. It can't get sour."

I remembered a word Mami used for food that made her gag. "It's . . . *repugnante!*"

"I suppose you'd find it less repugnant to go hungry every morning!"

"I've never gone hungry!" I screamed. "My Mami and Papi can feed us without your disgusting *gringo* imperialist food!"

The children gasped. Even Ignacio Sepúlveda. Mrs. García's mouth dropped open and stayed that way. From the back, a loud whisper broke the silence: "Close it, or you'll trap flies!" My face burned, but I couldn't stifle a giggle. Mrs. García closed her mouth and forgot about me for a moment.

"Who said that?" Everyone looked innocent, eyes cast down, lips fighting laughter. She grabbed me by the arm and dragged me to the door. "Get out! And tell your mother I need to speak to her."

Before she could push me, I pulled my arm from her grip and ran, not sure where I should go because the last thing I wanted to do was go home and tell Mami I'd been disrespectful to an adult. I dragged my feet down the dirt road, leaving my body behind, burying it in dust, while I floated in the tree-tops and watched myself from above, an insignificant creature that looked like a praying mantis in a green and yellow uniform. By the time I got home, I had decided to lie to Mami. If I told her the truth, she was sure to hit me, and I couldn't bear that humiliation on top of the other. When I came into the yard, my sisters and brother surrounded me, their curiosity comforting, as they pulled on my dirty clothes with remarks that I smelled bad.

"What happened to you?" Mami asked, all eyes. And all of a sudden I felt very sick. "I threw up in the lunchroom," I said, before falling into a faint that lasted so long that by the time I woke up from it, she had taken off my soiled uniform and washed me down with *alcoholado*.

For days I lay sick in bed, throwing up, racked by chills and sweats that left the bedcovers soaked and sent Delsa to sleep with Norma and Héctor, swearing that I was peeing on her. If Mrs. García ever talked to her, Mami never said anything. After what seemed like weeks, I went back to school, by which time the elections had been won, the breakfasts ceased, and my classmates had found someone else to tease.

1993

## Island of Lost Causes

On Oct. 30, 1950, 15 policemen and 25 National Guardsmen surrounded the Salón Boricua in Villa Palmeras, Puerto Rico, a barbershop owned by the nationalist leader Vidal Santiago Diaz. The windows of the shop were shuttered, but every once in a while gunfire erupted through the slats and was returned by the police and guards armed with pistols, machine guns, rifles and tear gas.

The siege lasted more than four hours. When the police were finally able to ax their way into the shop, they found a man slumped in a corner, his torso ripped by a grenade, his head bleeding. Two policemen dragged him out to the street and threw him on a stretcher.

Vidal Santiago Diaz was my uncle. As a child, I sat on his lap and stuck my index finger into the soft hole in the middle of his forehead, the scar left from a bullet.

In the 32 years since I left Puerto Rico for the United States, I haven't told many people about Tío Vidal. No one has ever asked me much about the island other than the location of the most charming hotels and whether we cook with hot chili peppers.

Lately, however, I've been grilled politely about the plebiscite taking place there today: Should Puerto Rico become the 51st state? Should it be an independent nation? Should it remain a commonwealth?[1]

The vote is nonbinding—not much more than a recommendation to the U.S. Congress. But as the first referendum since 1967, it has excited intense interest, on the island as well as among Puerto Ricans now living in the U.S.

As a Puerto Rican born in San Juan but now living in New York, I'm not eligible to vote on these questions. If I could, however, I would be filled with ambivalence.

Puerto Rico has been a colony for 500 years, first of Spain, then, since 1898, the U.S. Today's plebiscite gives Puerto Ricans only the illusion of self-determination—an illusion that deflects attention from the basic problems on the island.

The reality of Puerto Rico is an unemployment rate of 17.3 percent; 862 murders in 1992—a number that is expected to rise in 1993; a language so quickly becoming Spanglish that we have an inferiority complex about the purity of our spoken tongue; rampant urbanization that has destroyed thousands of acres of farmland; American businesses that set up shop for as long as they can get tax breaks, then move on to another part of the world where there is no minimum wage and the workers don't expect as much.

Puerto Rico's unsettled political status is symptomatic of the internal conflicts its people struggle with every day, whether we live on the island or in the U.S. We are born American citizens but harbor an intense Latin American identity.

Yet we are looked down upon by some Latin American neighbors because our culture is a hodge-podge of American influences grafted onto 400 years of Spanish traditions. We are told that our island doesn't have the rich heritage of bloody struggles for independence that other countries do.

The truth is, we do have a history of struggle for independence, but the opposition has always won. The failure of our best hopes for independence through centuries of failed insurrections has caused many Puerto Ricans to simply give up.

To some, statehood seems a clear solution to the island's ambiguous commonwealth status and a way of making the U.S. accountable for our future. After all, many Americans already refer to Puerto Rico as "part of the United States," as if the island were attached to the North American continent, like Kansas or Nebraska.

We are taken for granted by the U.S., and that sharpens in us a stubborn nationalist streak—yet we don't demonstrate it at the ballot box. In our hearts, we want to believe independence is the right choice, but our history forces us to see it as a lost cause. Still, we are not willing to give up so completely as to vote for statehood. It would be the ultimate statement of surrender.

---

1. For more information on the history referred to in the following paragraphs, see the discus- sions in the "Annexations" and "Acculturation" introductions (e.g., pp. 171 and 360–64).

This is why so many Puerto Ricans will vote for the status quo. It fosters the illusion of choosing a destiny, neither capitulating nor fighting. But it continues to evade the question of who we are as a people.

An elusive cultural identity lies at the heart of our unwillingness to declare ourselves either a nation or a state. A vote for the commonwealth insures that we don't have to commit one way or the other.

Ironically, neither violent insurrection nor the democratic process seems able to solve that question. Tío Vidal had a belief in nationhood that drove him to risk his life. How many of us Puerto Ricans would go that far? We need to look at ourselves hard and to stop hiding behind the status quo. It is not a choice. It is a refusal to choose.

1993                                                                                                        1995

---

# SHEREZADA "CHIQUI" VICIOSO
## b. 1948

Born in Santo Domingo, Dominican Republic, Sherezada Vicioso earned a bachelor's degree in sociology and Latin American history from Brooklyn College and a master's degree in the design of educational programs from Columbia University. She has published almost two dozen books. Vicioso's poetry collections are are *Viaje desde el agua* (Voyage from the Water, 1981), *Un extraño ulular traía el viento* (A Strange Howling in the Wind, 1985), and *Internamiento* (Internment, 1992). Her essay collections include *Volver a vivir: ensayos sobre Nicaragua* (1985) and *Julia de Burgos la nuestra* (1992).

Because Vicioso writes mainly in Spanish and her work is rarely translated, her readership has been mainly Dominican. Thanks to that audience and other Spanish speakers, her poetry and essays have helped draw attention to socially and politically charged issues of race in the Dominican Republic and to the plights of Dominican women. Since 1844, the island of Hispaniola has been divided between the Dominican Republic on the east and Haiti on the west. Haiti is the poorest country in the Caribbean, and Haitians often cross the border to work in the Dominican Republic, despite that country's own crushing poverty. Because of racial and linguistic differences, Haitians thus become "the other." Likewise, by entering the United States, Dominicans become "the other." "Perspectives," the first of two Vicioso poems in this anthology, addresses such concerns by looking at the daily routines of Latino laborers in New York City. "Haiti," the second selection, pays homage to that country's history while acknowledging the ambivalence of a Dominican observer.

## Perspectives[1]

One looks around to see
Eudocia, always hard-working, convinced
that for Reginaldo and her children
Alfonso and Rita there's no going back.

---

1. Translated by Ilan Stavans.

One looks around to find                                        5
Rosa, with her faith in the lottery:
"these dreams are better than the movies,
they cost one peso and last a week."

One looks at María Luisa sighing
from the exaltation of telenovelas,[2]                          10
to hear her say again, like an excuse:
"in this loneliness, they're my joy."

One looks at working-class women
on the subway, hiding their mistreated hands,
the unkempt nails, behind the glasses                           15
bags permanent beneath their eyes.

One looks at workers during *rush hour*[3]
deafened by a noise equal,
compares the Daily News,[4]
to jets about to land.                                          20

One looks at young Latino men,
*loose pants, acid*, and single cigarettes,
children short in years who've lost
their original humanity on these streets.

One also looks at young women                                   25
of brief, fragile adolescence, gone;
devoid of illusion at twenty,
born from Mondays and diapers.

One looks at the garbage, the ruins
of 103rd Street, the drunks;                                    30
people looking for *specials*
in revamped thrift shops.
And one begins to sense
this fetid air; like walking on the dead,
fighting against one's own death,                               35
while attempting to make a new life.

New York,                                                       1981
July 19, 1978


## Haiti[1]

Haiti
I imagine you a virgin
before earlier pirates
took off your mahogany clothes

---

2. Spanish-language soap operas.
3. Italicized words appear in English in the original.
4. New York tabloid newspaper.
1. Translated by Ilan Stavans.

and left you this way:                                          5
your round breasts exposed
and a disheveled grass skirt,
barely green,
timid brown girl.

Haiti                                                          10
I imagine you an adolescent
redolent of vetiver, tender from the dew,
no multitude of scars
to integrate you into the market of maps
and offer you in multicolor                                    15
on the sidewalks of Port-au-Prince,
of Jacmel, of San Marcos, and in Artibonite,
in a huge sale of scrap.

Haiti
like a stroller eagerly smiling at me                          20
interrupting siestas on the path
softening stones, asphalting the dust
with your sweaty bare feet.
Haiti, you, who weaves art in a thousand ways
and paints the stars with your hands—                          25
I've discovered that love and hatred
bear your name.

New York,                                                    1981
September 9, 1978

---

# VÍCTOR HERNÁNDEZ CRUZ
## b. 1949

Víctor Hernández Cruz is a pioneer among Puerto Rican poets in the United States. He is so prolific and widely read that in 1981 *Life* magazine included him in its list of best American poets.

Born in the mountain town of Aguas Buenas, Puerto Rico, Hernández Cruz moved with his family to New York in 1954. He was educated in New York City's public schools, and after graduating from high school took courses at Lehman College, in the city's Bronx borough, during the early days of that institution's Puerto Rican Studies Program. His first poetry collection, the chapbook *Papo Got His Gun*, was published in 1966. Two years later, Hernández Cruz left New York for Berkeley, California, to work in a program that promoted art in public schools. His second collection, the full-length volume *Snaps* (1969), was published by Random House, at the time an unusual accomplishment for a relatively unknown Latino poet.

After coediting the volume *Stuff: A Collection of Poems, Visions & Imaginative Happenings from Young Writers in Schools—Opened & Closed* (1970), Hernández Cruz became during the early 1970s, in the words of the literary critic Nicolás Kanellos, a "traveling troubadour" throughout the United States, Puerto Rico, and other countries. He has frequently incorporated his travel experiences into his poetry, which often explores cultural differences; draws on Spanish, African, and Taíno cultural and historical references; and re-creates a wide range of Caribbean musical forms. In a 1997 interview with the Puerto Rican cultural columnist Carmen Dolores Hernández, the poet addressed the bilingual/bicultural nature of his work:

> I consider myself an American writer because I write in English and not Spanish. . . . My poetry is in English and thus part of the North American literary landscape. . . . I live in Puerto Rico and lead a total personal and cultural life in Puerto Rican Spanish. I write in Spanish also, so that I am a Latin American writer as well, but I have published a lot more in English.

Quite often, Hernández Cruz's poetry purposely challenges the grammatical and syntactical structures of the two languages. The often surrealistic quality of Cruz's poetic vision and his intricate, elusive, and inventive use of musical rhythms, bilingual sounds, and cultural images immediately appealed to Latino and mainstream readers, explaining why he has become one of the most anthologized mainland Puerto Rican writers.

His subsequent poetry collections include *Mainland* (1973), *Tropicalization* (1976), *By-Lingual Wholes* (1982), *Rhythm, Content & Flavor* (1998), *Maraca: New and Selected Poems, 1966–2000* (2001), and *The Mountain in the Sea* (2006), the latter of which reflects his travels to North Africa and his interest in the contact between Spanish and Arab cultures. In 1988, Hernández Cruz moved back to Aguas Buenas, though he has not given up his life of travel. In 1991, he received a Guggenheim creative writing fellowship.

In "The Latest Latin Dance Craze," the first of five Hernández Cruz selections in this anthology, Latino rhythms in music, dancing, and even walking become a form of poetry. In "Lunequisticos," the sounds and structures of Spanish and English collide to produce a downpour of rhythmic code switching, chaotically defying the notion of linguistic purity. "Poema Chicano," an expression of panethnic solidarity, illustrates Hernández Cruz's close contact with Chicano culture, history, and language during his years in California. "Cantinflas" pays tribute to the Mexican comedian Mario Moreno (1911–1993), whose wit and clowning in numerous films over decades made him one of the most legendary and beloved actors in Latin America. "Is It Certain or Is It Not Certain: Caso Maravilla" refers to the televised Puerto Rican Senate hearings on the police cover-up of the assassination, in 1978, of two Puerto Rican proindependence students (one of them the son of the writer Pedro Juan Soto; see p. 799) at the Cerro Maravilla, a mountain peak located near the town of Jayuya, Puerto Rico. The question "Is it certain or is it not certain?" was asked repeatedly by the Puerto Rican Senate investigator as he interrogated witnesses; soon after, it became a catchphrase in popular discourse.

## The Latest Latin Dance Craze

First
You throw your head back twice
Jump out onto the floor like a
Kangaroo
Circle the floor once                                    5
Doing fast scissor work with your
Legs
Next
Dash towards the door

Walking in a double cha cha cha 10
Open the door and glide down
The stairs like a swan
Hit the street
Run at least ten blocks
Come back in through the same 15
Door
Doing a mambo-minuet
Being careful that you don't fall
And break your head on that one
You have just completed your first 20
Step.

1976

## Lunequisticos

In what language do you jump off one boat
to get to another one to buy something cold
to drink while at the same time you contemplate
The shapes and curves of the eyes the various
family trees have produced in all the people 5
present buying something cold to drink
The shades of minds each beaming glaze of their
spirit all being here for a second of my questions
I am in the young woman's tenor her lips drum
pictures of thin Spanish fans waving 10
Ships sailing in pictures hanging on living
room walls    Chaotic room of thirsty tongues
Moving my whistle sounds to investigate
Each glassy eyes my windows
Their fires in the cold drinks 15
So if I ask you my creature friends in what language
do I ask the question to come in: Do I take my
Oye/lo/que/one/time/eva/or/iva/decir/que/uno/una
ves/sepuso/la/cosa/de bullets/peor que/one guerra
en/the/escuela/corner/de/maestros/ya/con/lisencia 20
y/todo/una/mes/mass/de/masas/tambien/con/masa/cuando
ella/pasaba/lo/profesores/le/cantaban/siquere/gozar
ben/a/bailar/tengo/libros/de/to/colores/estudiaremos
el/at/most/fear/el/turn/de/una/language/como/hace/in
side/the/mind/calculate/while/it/separates/words/in/two 25
languages/sounds/spellings/systems/whole/tone/latitude
and/altitude/altiduego of voces/in/gas/communications/gets
filtered/and/ironed/tambien/the/two/musics/through/one/breath
Para/
    Or do I spray it around in straight talk 30
Filtar: Presuming you tailored the rough edges of your
tenor    dress it up with my wave of syllables say to me
What is your idea what flavor did you ask for

In what tense does it remain the same color when it
laughs in your cup.                                              35
Pure orange juice.
Pure ginger root-boiled.
Pure grapefruit—the ones with freckles.
Pure Spanish/Pure English
Pure tunes tos tono tos tones                                   40
When is exactly Saturday and Sabado two different nights
Do you say in one aspect of the night your deep feelings
to whoever might be involved in a need to hear them from
you or do you avoid what's really going on and talk other
heavens go over to the jukebox before ordering a cold          45
drink put on Tito Rodriquez's[1] "Double Talk" put the boat
In reverse and relax you have just given birth to twins
The tongue figures out how not to jump from one boat to
another and takes a dash out onto the street where the
wrong speed can brake anybody's record.                        50

1978–90                                                        2001


## Poema Chicano

Los Angeles de mi Chihuahua Mama
Su carrucho de burgundy.
Ciudad que empieza y no acaba
Hay más calles que estrellas.
José Montoya poeta de Sacras-Califas,                          5
El del Royal Chicano Air Force—
El del Highway 99
El higuey—
El de aquellas ese
De la balada ranchera                                          10
Lo dijo bien:
"Los Angeles es un desmadre, una pinche perdida allí y te
Lleva la chingada."

Rucas de amanecer-mole poblano-chile verde besos
La china poblana-sarape panries-jalapeño miradas             15
Las Lupitas que salsita down Pico Avenue
Que crucigrama con Sunset Boulevard
Más largo que Cuba,
Sus malinches lenguas de la poesía
El guachupín Cortez padre de las voladas                      20
Bilingües.

L.A. del cielo químico
Se vive en el carro—
Se pasan paredes de murales aztecas

---

1. Puerto Rican singer and bandleader (1923–1973) popular in the 1950s and 1960s.

Máscaras de Chichimecas ojos                                    25
Cachetes yaquis enchinaos
Harina de maíz en metate de colores
Sueños de mescal—por sorpresas
De Olivera Street—ciudad en medio
De un desierto.                                                 30
Maravilla Housing Projects
Vatos locos
Pandilleros, cocos pelaos
Tatuajes como is fueran
Lienzos para Frida Kahlo.                                       35
Homegirls rucas
Bonitas doncellas con el
Tatuaje de la cruz azul
En sus manos—
Hablan palomitas de caló                                        40
Al lado de carruchos
Pintados como is fuesen
Pirámides—
Olor de carnitas y frijoles
Bajan en alas de águilas.                                       45
Desde las ventanas
El acappella de los oldies
El Little Joe y la Familia.

Ahora en esta antillana isla
Me recuerdo tus panes dulces—                                   50
Y tus picantes Serranos.
Aquel East Los
Infinito Barrio
Echo Park
Frogtown                                                        55
El Mercado
Como is estuvieses en México
Grande como liga de fútbol
Mariachi por todo aire—
Braceros con sus botas de cuero                                 60
Tequilazos de Simón ese,
Bigotes que llegavan a la frontera—
Su español volado tejiendo
Por aquéllos otros Chicanos
Más pachucados pochos                                           65
Creando un tráfico de polka
Y emplumado mescalito hip-hop
Por todo el San Bernardino.

Órale, pues—
A la chingada el español                                        70
Y el inglés:
"Hey vato, where's Chuey ese."
"Está en la chante con su ruca, trais fralo, dame trola.
Buena yeska—Tijuana mama—tus ojos llegan a Jalisco,
Jalisquéate ya."                                                75

Virgen Guadalupeña—Ponte trucha
Por todo Aztlán
Estrella Mística.

La Virgen como tatuaje
En la espalda de aquél 80
Que le dicen el Chino—
El que era pinto
Allá en Soledad
También en San Quin—
El más chingón 85
Carnal del Fredy Mejías
De Santa Ana
Llegaba como la breeza.
Se conocieron en la pinta,
Estaba todo el East Side 90
Y el Valley también
Hijos de Pachucos
Generaciones de low riders
Esa vena que se va por Arizona
En el Interstate 10 95
Y llega a Albuquerque
Nuevo México—
Las Sandía Mountains
Huevos rancheros
Las Cruces 100
Llano Quemado—
Ojo Caliente
El Río Grande gorge
Mirar pa'abajo
Es ver el infierno— 105
Esos páramos de Juan Rulfo
En el norte
Mariachi y turquesa
Pueblo Taos ancestro collares—
Huercas con ojos de pura plata 110
Llenos del firmamento Oaxaca
Como oyen todo el metote
Las sultanas—
Oigo los caracoles danzantes
De Andrés Segura— 115
La fragancia del copal
El órale pues—los híjoles
Descienden por la montaña
Borincana de Jagüeyes.

El Californow de retratos 120
Los zoot suits
Sombreros de aquéllas
Estás qualifi—
Saludos Juan Felipe Herrera
". . . show me the way to San José" 125
Y tus cantos de paya papaya va paya.

Alejandro Murguía y las perdidas
Que nos dimos buscando a la tamalera
Callejera y la tortillera casera—
Y el Alurista que se inventó Aztlán                    130
De la mitología—
Como cruzábamos la frontera—
Empezabamos en Chicano Park/San Diego
Y llegabamos pistiando hasta Ensenada
Casi sin feria                                          135
Donde en la playa
Taquitos de sesos y madres—
Aquel viejo que dijo:
"Ponle limón a todo para evitar
La cruda de estas son las mañanitas."                  140

Ah, California, mi segundo país
Hoy suenas con el Suavecito de Malo
Y el jingo pop de Santana.
Y los bellos terremotos
Porque allí hasta la misma                             145
Tierra bailaba.
California el poppy de oro,
Rascacielos de redwoods
Califorica
Californow                                             150
Califas
C/S
Con Safos.

1996–99                                                          2001


## Cantinflas

Montezuma's court jester
Quetzalcoatl's[1] mime.
he is everything in us that laughs
The smallest bones
aligned with the verses of necessity                    5
He walks upside down,
it's not his pants falling
It's a pyramid rising,
Coatlicue was at the formation,
Ollin[2] movement gave his joints flex.                 10

Even in terror I have seen
the charm of grace.

1. Aztec god. *Montezuma*: or Moctezuma (1466–1520), next-to-last Aztec emperor (1502–20).
2. The Aztecs' word for movement; an influential concept among Mesoamerican cultures. *Coatli-*
*cue*: Aztec goddess who gave birth to the moon, stars, and Huitzilopochtli, the god of the sun and war.

Lord of movement
dismantling the bourgeoisie,
A tortilla in its face.                                             15
Aztec counterculture
going up an elevator
In the squares of buildings
on la Avenida Reforma,[3]
Cantinflas struts on                                               20
the shining marble floors,
His feet talking
the language of riddles,
The syntax—the grammar
arrive as if to rescue                                             25
The poet exiled from the
dictionary.

Sense sensulet,
Cantinflas is the only
man who doesn't                                                    30
Have to move
to travel the cosmicos
Cómicos
Our mestizo jaws
go from grin to cracklin                                           35
Peeling in the spreading
and even then swelling.

Without motion
he makes murals of flowers
Jaguars and skulls                                                 40
he pulls out of a clay pot.
Egyptian and Toltec theater,
alive of humanness humeros
Humoros
He gives Charlie Chaplin[4]                                        45
the Americas conquered ridicule
Ridículos back
in a flaming heart of laughter
upon the altar of sacrifice,
For we were born for joy,                                          50
Cantinflas brings the teeth out,
to overcome the hacienda
Son of a bitch,
We are the earth
He takes for gyrations                                             55
orbits which expose the king,
one pivotal turn in any scene,
Spread feathers
Wind which strips

---

3. Major thoroughfare in Mexico City.
4. Charles Spencer Chaplin (1889–1977), English
comedian, actor, and director. Cantinflas is generally considered the Charlie Chaplin of the Hispanic world.

the Patron's tuxedo                                    60
Exposing us all
as cookies
In the shape of skeletons.

1996–2000                                              2001

## Is It Certain or Is It Not Certain
## Caso Maravilla

Note: In which two young independentistas
      are brutally beaten and killed
      by members of the intelligence division
      who claimed that they were on their way
      to sabotage a tower which controlled          5
      the electrical power for the San Juan
      area.[1]

Cover up like mascara
Helena Rubenstein[2]
Not even Paris in its glory                           10
A man has to follow with a sack
To collect objects falling
Given that all objectivity has fallen
The backache is a confusion even
To the Chinese doctor                                 15

We're moving with legs down a hill of
what
Listening to a policeman present in the
jam
How he lost his memory                                20
Remembered only that he had a coffee
Two witnesses down another officer
With an I didn't do it kind of face
Said
They had a trail of pork chops                        25
Possibly some rice
And that everyone ate
And the previous police officer
who only recalled coffee
Had seconds according to this                          30
witness
So much for digestion

1. The students were accompanied by an undercover agent, who had given advance notice to the
officers who arrived on the scene. The officers
claimed to have shot the students in self-defense,
and the Puerto Rican government and the FBI
agreed with the police's version of the events.
Later investigations by the Puerto Rican legislature, the press, and the U.S. Department of Justice led to the 1983–84 Senate hearings, which
showed that the students had been murdered
in cold blood. Several police subsequently were
found guilty of second-degree murder.
2. Brand of cosmetics.

We are walking up a hill
which is walking down us

Walk in front of Christ                                    35
carrying the cross
Pursued by maladies
Chasing the thoughts in your
Mucus head
This is the church people                                  40
Of decency repute
The bad people in this case
Are Satanás[3] themselves
Mercy means the opposite
In the dictionary of the lard                              45

Be careful
Cause look what is loose
And possessive of power

If a psychiatrist saw such fantasy
Him make for airport                                       50

Christians
Of the kind that sold themselves to Rome[4]
Who maintain the language of the killers
Of Christ
As the ceremonial language of the very                     55
Church of Christ

Condemn them
For they might know what they
are doing
And know no better[5]                                      60

Police set them up like dinner table
For Queen Elizabeth[6]
Every knife in its proper place
Saucers and plates at measured angles

Now that you have seen the beauty parlor                   65
imagine the wig

Colonial Spanish language
was directional
Monolingual
A one way street                                           70
A question was also an answer

---

3. Satan.
4. According to the New Testament, Judas Iscariot betrayed Jesus to the Roman authorities for 30 pieces of silver.
5. According to the New Testament, among Jesus'

last words on the Cross were "Father forgive them, for they know not what they do" (Luke 23.34).
6. Elizabeth II (b. 1926), British queen from 1952 to the present, here represents propriety.

A mind which has nothing to give
Gives it vigorously
Force is what it has learned
From the monarchs                                                    75
From the priest
Who made a generation of Tainos
transform into biology
to school teachers who teach
you the rules with the very rulers                                  80
The plan is to take over
what has been made
While you destroy those
who made it

They kill you one day                                               85
The next day they want to know
why you are dead
The Aztecs
The Romans
The armies                                                          90
The police
Missionaries
who forever want to change beings
Obsessed with others doing something
wrong                                                               95
This has created a knot
Which not even seven Houdinis⁷
A place in which the devil
screams three times

The search light of the scrambled head                             100
Veins where cheese travels
Watch tower eye head
Those who cannot live life will not
allow anyone else to live it
The plan is to put things in order                                 105
To balance the Libras
To put in place
To set straight
To cut to size
To sharpen up                                                       110
To move out the way
To eliminate
To kill
To invade

Look what a small door                                             115
A bull is trying to push
Through dressed as justice
Caso Maravilla the tall

7. Reference to the Hungarian-born American magician Harry Houdini (b. Ehrich Weiss, 1874–1926).

hill from which everyone must
Run                                                                    120
Senators
Judges
Governor
Desks
Police                                                                 125
Agents
Neckties
Microphones
Nails
Television                                                             130
and all

Run into the
Rhythm of justice
Played by the drums of consciousness
Of original mountain rock                                              135

We know the proverb well:
You cannot cover the sky with your hands,
Especially if the sky is blood red

So be careful
and be cool                                                           140
Even though
Caguax[8] is hot.

2001

8. One of Puerto Rican's Taíno chieftains at the time of the Spanish conquest.

# JAIME MANRIQUE
## b. 1949

Jaime Manrique was born in Barranquilla, Colombia, an out-of-wedlock child of Gustavo Manrique, a member of the most powerful banana-plantation family, and Soledad Ardila, a peasant of African descent. In 1967, he and his mother immigrated to Lakeland, Florida, where his mother found work as a domestic servant.

Manrique narrates his upbringing in the last section of his book *Eminent Maricones* (Eminent Faggots, 1999), a series of four portraits of Latin homosexuals (the Argentine novelist Manuel Puig, the Cuban fiction writer and memoirist Reinaldo Arenas, the Spanish poet and dramatist Federico García Lorca, and himself), structured as an homage to the English critic Lytton Strachey's *Eminent Victorians* (1918) but with an added component of kitsch. Although Manrique acknowledged his homosexuality early in life, when he began having gay relationships, the machismo of Colombian society was a tall psychological obstacle. "Guilt ran my life from adolescence on," Manrique writes.

He decided to become a writer after watching Ken Hughes's movie *The Trials of Oscar Wilde* (1960) and falling in love with the defiant, ostentatious style of Wilde, a late-nineteenth-century Irish writer whose homosexuality was an open secret during his lifetime. While still in high school, Manrique wrote a play, *¿En las manos de quién?* (In Whose Hands?), which was produced in Barranquilla's Teatro de Bellas Artes. In 1972, he earned his bachelor's degree from the University of South Florida, in Tampa.

Manrique's first book of poetry, *Los adoradores de la luna* (Those Who Adore the Moon, 1976), received Colombia's National Poetry Award. The next year, Manrique was accepted into a fiction workshop taught at Columbia University by Manuel Puig. Manrique's debut as a fiction writer was the novella *El cadáver de Papá* (My Father's Corpse, 1978), which dealt with the assassination of a wealthy father by his young son and the subsequent attempt at seducing his father-in-law. It became a best seller in Colombia thanks to its controversial nature. Manrique then wrote a political thriller, *Colombian Gold: A Novel of Power and Corruption* (1983). *Latin Moon in Manhattan* (1992), the first chapter of which is included here, is a picaresque novel about Santiago Martínez Ardila, a Colombian gay man in New York. *Twilight at the Equator* (1997) presents Ardila's further adventures in Colombia, Spain, and New York. *Our Lives Are the Rivers* (2006) is about Manuela Sáenz, the mistress of the nineteenth-century South American liberator Simón Bolívar who became a colonel in Bolívar's army.

Manrique's other poetry collections are *Scarecrow* (1990), *My Night with Federico García Lorca* (1997), *Mi cuerpo y otros poemas* (My Body and Other Poems, 1999), and *Tarzan / My Body / Christopher Columbus* (2001). With Joan Larkin, Manrique translated the poetry of the seventeenth-century Mexican nun and scholar Sor Juana Inés de la Cruz in *Sor Juana's Love Poems/Poemas de amor de Sor Juana* (1997). With Jesse Dorris, he edited an anthology of gay Latino literature, *Bésame Mucho* (Kiss Me Much, 1999). After teaching at Mount Holyoke College, in Massachusetts; New York University; and New School University, in New York City, Manrique became a professor in the Master of Fine Arts program at Columbia University. He has received a Guggenheim Fellowship, among other honors.

---

## *From* LATIN MOON IN MANHATTAN

## 1. Little Colombia, Jackson Heights[1]

After it leaves Manhattan, the number seven train becomes an elevated,[2] and crosses a landscape of abandoned railroad tracks, dilapidated buildings and, later, a conglomerate of ugly factories that blow serpentine plumes of gaudy poisonous smoke. As the train journeys deeper into Queens, the Manhattan skyscrapers in the distance resemble monuments of an enchanted place—ancient Baghdad, or even the Land of Oz. The sun, setting behind the towers of the World Trade Center, burnishes the sky with a warm orange glow and the windows of the towers look like gold-leafed entrances to huge hives bursting with honey.

---

1. Little Columbia is a neighborhood in the Jackson Heights section of Queens, a New York City borough east of Manhattan.

2. I.e., the 7, a subway line in Manhattan, becomes an elevated railway.

Riding the number seven train to Jackson Heights, I thought of our immigration to the United States eighteen years ago. But "immigration" is too big a word to describe what happened. Let's just say we moved from Bogotá, Colombia, to Jackson Heights, Queens—from one cocaine capital to another, the main difference being that the former sits ten thousand feet up in the Andes,[3] while the latter is a mere twenty-minute train ride from Manhattan.

I finished high school and college in Queens and it wasn't until years later, when I settled in Times Square, that I finally felt I was living in a foreign country. What I had observed through the years was that while Queens became more prosperous and upscale, the city of New York more and more resembled a third world capital; there was a wide—and ever widening—gap between rich and poor, and the streets teemed with crazies, junkies, homeless people, street urchins, hustlers, hookers, and pickpockets, just like in Bogotá. Since I had arrived in America, the human traffic on the number seven train had also changed; there were still a few blacks going to Queens, but now the Asians were just as numerous as the South Americans. The nicely dressed, well-scrubbed people riding in my car looked like solid, hardworking, law-abiding Republicans. That, plus the lack of graffiti, made the Queens-bound trains different from the Brooklyn and Bronx lines.[4]

I was so engrossed in my observations that I almost missed my stop. Ninetieth Street, with its garish shops, vegetable and root stands, and South American eateries—everything in a small, Lilliputian scale—looks unreal, like a movie set. All the signs are in Spanish, and the pedestrians talk in the various regional accents of Colombia.

I walked under the elevated, and turned right at Eighty-seventh Street. I began to metamorphose; the closer I got to my mother's house, the more Colombian I became. Intense cravings for foods that were unavailable to me in the city—such as *ajiaco, arepa de huevo, morcillas, chicharrones*[5]— awoke in me. The tree-shaded street was getting dark and, although this was hardly the country, I felt light-years away from the overheated cement of Forty-second Street. I passed pretty two-story houses with attics and gabled roofs, cypresses on their lawns, rose gardens in bloom, and sidewalks spattered with dog shit. It was hard to believe that just a few blocks away there was a world of drugs and crime in which coke-crazed Colombians iced each other in the most vicious, post-modern ways.

My mother's house was in darkness, except for the light above the side entrance that led to the kitchen. This was the house that Victor, my mother's present husband, gave her as a wedding present. Victor, a Sicilian who worked all his life for the mob and Queens politicians, had supported my mother nicely by running numbers[6] until he developed Alzheimer's disease and was put in an institution. Now my mother lives alone, except for the periods when my nephew Eugene runs away from my sister's apartment.

I climbed the steps to the landing outside the kitchen and was about to open the door—which my mother still left open after all these years—when

3. Mountain system of South America.
4. At the time, many parts of these boroughs were associated with newly arrived immigrants, racial and ethnic minorities, and the poor.
5. Fried pork skin with the fat still attached to it. *Ajiaco*: a traditional Colombian soup made in the Andean region; its main ingredientes are shred-

ded chicken, potatoes, cilantro, onions, and cream. *Arepa de huevo*: a fried arepa (a kind of round empanada) with an egg inside it. *Morcillas*: blood sausage.
6. *Numbers*: a kind of gambling, in which people bet on combinations of digits, such as regularly published ones.

I felt something rubbing against my ankles. It was Puss, one of Mother's cats. Since her cats were not allowed inside the house, I sat on the steps to play with him. Puss was old and had lost a lot of his thick, tawny coat, but his tail was still beautiful and soft, like an ostrich feather.

"Hi, Puss. How're you doing, you old cat? Where is Me-shu?" I said, looking around for Mother's other cat, who was shy. Although Puss had lived all his life outside—maybe because of it—he craved human affection. He purred and purred, lying at my feet, while I scratched him behind the ears. He was wearing the flea collar I had given him a couple of months ago, but he had fleas, and his hair was so matted in places that he looked like a Rastafarian.

It was dark now, and the pertinacious mosquitoes were determined to get their evening meal. I got up, and as I turned the doorknob, I could hear Simón Bolívar screeching inside, "Who is it?" I tensed up; I intensely dislike my mother's parrot. Turning on the kitchen light, I saw to my relief that Simón Bolívar was caged. "Hello, hello, hello," he shrieked stupidly.

"Hi, Simón," I acknowledged him so he would shut up.

On the kitchen table Mother had left me a note: "I went to play bingo. Will be back late. Your dinner is on the stove. Love, Mother."

I was hungry so I uncovered the pans: Mother had cooked tongue stew, coconut rice with raisins, and fried ripe plantains. Everything was still warm. Serving myself, I sat down to eat. I picked up *El Espectador*, a Bogotá newspaper Mother bought every day, and began to peruse the headlines. Although I no longer feel very connected to Colombian life, I still read the newspapers and magazines Mother buys because, invariably, the first question I'm always asked by people I meet is, "How are things in Colombia?" Consequently, even though I'm an American citizen now, I keep abreast of the latest developments in the war against drugs and guerrilla insurgency down home.

There was a pitcher full of *peto* on the table, a Colombian corn drink; I poured myself a glass and started sipping it, tasting the cinnamon and nutmeg with which my mother peppered the drink. Suddenly Simón Bolívar said in Spanish, "Long live the Liberal party!" He sat on his perch, staring at me uncannily with his bright yellow eyes.

"Shut up," I said, and threatened to fling the remnants of my *peto* at him. This created pandemonium. Thinking he was about to get a bath, Simón started flapping his brightly colored wings.

At my grandmother's death, my mother had inherited two ancestral avocado trees and a parrot. Simón had thus immigrated to the States ten years ago and I used to tease my mother that he was the only Colombian in Jackson Heights with a green card.

Imitating Flaubert's Felicité,[7] my mother fell in love with the parrot. Some years back, in early spring, she placed his cage out in the backyard to give the bird some sun, and somehow Simón Bolívar managed to escape. Mother was sure he had been stolen, though why anyone would have wanted to steal such an obstreperous animal is beyond my understanding. Mother cried and cried and stopped eating and when these measures didn't bring Simón back, she built a shrine to San Martín de Porres in her living room and prayed to the

---

7. The main character in *Un coeur simple* (A Simple Heart, 1877), a tale by the French writer Gustave Flaubert (1821–1880); at her death, Félicité has a vision of her pet parrot as the Holy Ghost (the third part of the Christian trinity, or Godhead).

Peruvian saint for the return of her parrot. Months later, a storm awakened her late at night. She claims she saw light streaming through the curtains of her bedroom window. She knew San Martín had answered her prayer, and when she opened the windows she found Simón Bolívar seeking shelter from the rain in the cypress tree. Since that time, Mother has declared him a holy parrot who has been to heaven and back. It was hard for me to believe that this was God's envoy as he sat on his perch screaming the sickeningly hackneyed words of some Julio Iglesias[8] song.

I looked away, ignoring his nonsense. I had lost my appetite; it was too warm in the kitchen to eat. I set aside the newspaper. Simón Bolívar had quieted down, but suddenly I heard him screech, "Who's there?" I heard noises outside. The doorknob turned, the door opened, and a pair of huge decomposing Reeboks burst into the kitchen.

"Sammy, dude, what's happening?" my nephew Gene greeted me.

"Hi, Gene," I replied.

Gene sat at the table, lit a Marlboro and started whiffing clouds of smoke. He was seventeen and already six foot two, with the face of a baby Gulliver. Gene glanced suspiciously at the food on my plate. "Is that tongue?" He indicated the stew on my plate, making a face.

"It's better than hamburger, which is probably all you eat."

"Look, Sammy, I'm an American, not a Colombian, and Americans don't eat tongue."

"That just shows what a hick you are. In French cuisine tongue is considered a great delicacy."

"Oh, yeah? But we're in America not in France."

"We're in Jackson Heights, Colombia," I said.

"But don't let me spoil your chow," he added magnanimously. "It's cool with me, man. If you want to eat tongue, go right ahead."

"I've had enough. So you're living here now?"

"I guess so. School's out."

"Are you getting along with Wilbrajan?"

"Oh yeah, everything's cool."

"Is she working?"

"She's singing tangos at the Rose Saigon. The Japanese love tangos."

"But Saigon is not in Japan."

Gene shrugged. "What do I know; I just finished the tenth grade. I like to come here to keep grandma company. She's lonely, and she's getting old."

Guiltily, I said, "That's really nice of you."

"She nags like hell, though."

"You know what the French say: 'If you can't send them the devil, send them an old woman.'"

Gene smiled. "You're so mean."

I got up to turn on the air conditioner.

"Better not," Gene warned. "Grandma doesn't like it on unless it's above one hundred degrees. She's pretty nuts about conserving energy."

"You want to go outside and sit in the garden?"

As we were getting ready to leave the kitchen, Simón Bolívar, pissed off that were leaving him behind, started a racket.

8. Spanish singer (b. 1943).

"Shut up, asshole," Gene ordered him.

"Asshole, asshole, asshole," Simón Bolívar echoed as we stepped outside.

"Maybe I should leave the door open and let the cats in. I'm sure they'd love him for dinner. What do you think?" I asked, grinning.

"The cats are scared shitless of him. That parrot could scare a Colombian pusher away. He's the meanest mother I know."

We walked to the back of the house, where Mother had her vegetable and flower gardens and sat down on the wooden chairs next to the barbecue grill. Above us was a patch of open sky. The night was clear and cool, and we could see a spattering of stars and a crescent moon. Pointing to the sky, I said, "That's the North Star over there, see it? If you ever get lost at sea just follow it and you'll reach land."

"You know the weirdest shit," Gene snorted. "Thanks for the tip, but I hate the sea. All that activity makes me crazy." There was a pause, which Gene broke by saying, "I haven't seen you in a long time. What's up?"

"Everything's okay," I said, not wanting to sound too pessimistic in front of a teenager. "I've been thinking about going back to school to finish my Ph.D."

Gene chortled. "Sammy, you have more degrees than a thermometer. Why don't you finish your book? That'd make you feel better." He referred to my Christopher Columbus[9] epic, which I had been writing for some years.

"I haven't written anything new in some time. You know, one day it occurred to me that I couldn't go on writing it until I saw one of the caravels in which Columbus traveled."

"What's that?"

"You know, one of the ships he sailed to the New World in. There's a replica of one in the Barcelona[1] harbor and somehow I feel I have to go see it before I can finish the poem," I concluded.

"And when are you going?"

"Soon," I said cryptically.

"Sammy, why don't you write something good?"

I bristled at his criticism. "What do you mean 'something good?' I want to write a great epic poem."

"That's what I mean. When was the last time there was a best-seller epic poem? Write something like . . . like . . . a story about teenagers. In English. You know, I could help you with it. What you have to do is write something that English teachers like so that they recommend it to the students. I'll guarantee you it'll make a million bucks."

"You write the teenager story, okay, and I'll write whatever I want to write."

"No need to get sore, man. I'm not gonna write anything. I just want to be an actor."

"Like Rocky Rambo, I suppose."

"Fuck no. Like Marlon Brando. Man, he's neat as shit. Did you see him in *The Wild One*?[2] You haven't? I've seen it thirty-seven times. The way he rides that motorcycle all dressed up in black leather and chains. He's so cool, so radical—a real bad dude. He's awesome," Gene sighed, his face glowing in the dark. "I'm gonna buy me a motorcycle," he vowed.

9. Spanish admiral and explorer from Genoa (1451–1506).
1. City in northeastern Spain.

2. American movie (1953) about motorcycle gangs, starring Brando (1924–2004).

"I wish you wouldn't; motorcycles are extremely dangerous. People get killed on those things all the time."

"You're so uncool; you don't know anything. More people get killed going to the post office, at least here in Jackson Heights."

"Who's giving you the money to buy a motorcycle?"

"I got a summer job. I'm going to save all the money I make, and in the fall I'll buy it."

"What kind of a job?"

"Making . . . deliveries . . . here in Queens. Hey, you want to get high?" Gene pulled a fat joint from his pack of Marlboros.

"I quit smoking," I said. Recently I had come to the sudden realization that it was because of drugs and alcohol that I had dropped out of graduate school and the reason why in the past ten years I had accomplished so little.

Gene lit the joint and inhaled deeply. "You want to smoke this," he said melodramatically, holding the smoke in his lungs. "This is great Colombian shit; this kind of thing never hits the streets of Manhattan. The Colombians smoke it all as soon as it comes in."

"Well, a puff won't do me any harm, I suppose."

Gene was right; this was great pot. It was like pouring hot water in a glass full of ice—I melted right away. Yet the sense of guilt gnawed at my conscience. I said, "Gene, I hope you're not into heavy drugs."

"No, man. Rusty and the Boners—you've got to meet them sometime; they're my best friends—do all kinds of shit. I just smoke pot, and drink beer on the weekends and do a line of coke once in a while."

I was horrified. "Gene, I didn't start doing anything until I was twenty-one."

"Yeah, well, that was a long time ago, right? You're old, Sammy; you know that."

"If you're lucky, some day you'll be my age," I said, pissed off, as if I were putting a curse on him. "Promise me you'll never do crack."

"You think I'm fucking crazy? I don't wanna get fucked up; I wanna be a famous actor."

Let's hope his thespian instincts will win out in the long run, I thought. We finished smoking the joint; I felt as if I were tripping.

"What are you doing tonight?" Gene asked.

"Nothing; just hanging out. Want to go see a movie?"

"Maybe tomorrow. I'm going to a party. Want to come along?"

"What's the occasion?" I asked, although I had no intention of going to a party with a bunch of drug-addicted teenagers.

"You know, girls, beer. We smoke jays and listen to Sinead O'Connor."[3] Gene stood up. "Okay, Sammy, I've got to go. I promised the Boners I'd be there by now."

"What kind of name is that—the Boners?"

"They're twins. You have to meet them. They're real sleaze balls, but I know you'll like them. They're cool and neat as hell. They've done so many drugs they're all skin and bones. The Boners, you got it now?"

"I got it."

---

3. Irish singer/songwriter (b. 1966).

"If you get bored, just go by the Rose Saigon. Mom goes on around midnight. Okay, catch you later."

"Have a nice time and don't get too wasted," I said, feeling old. Gene disappeared into the darkness, and I was left by myself, pleasantly stoned. I thought about uncles and nephews, and, specifically, I thought about my Uncle Hernán, whom I worshiped in my adolescence. Twelve years before, he had died in a plane accident. In the sixties, he became mixed up with radical politics in Colombia and fled to Venezuela when the military got on his case. There, he go a job working in the diamond mines near Ciudad Bolívar. One Christmas, he was on his way to visit my grandparents when a bomb went off in the plane, blowing it to pieces and all that they could find of him was his arm.

The last time I had seen Uncle Hernán I was around Gene's age. That was the year my mother came to New York to see about settling here. She had dismantled our home in Bogotá and my sister and I were sent to stay with our maternal grandparents in the country. Uncle Hernán was twenty-two then, the youngest of my uncles. Although I had many cousins, he felt a special kinship for me. Every day after lunch he'd pack his rifle and I my fishing gear and we'd ride to Las Marías, my grandfather's farm a few miles outside of town. Uncle Hernán taught me to ride horses, burros and mules, to lasso cows and milk them, to fish and swim in the ponds of the Magdalena and César rivers. He read books about Marxism and the Cuban and Russian revolutions and was passionate about radical politics. Yet hunting was his favorite occupation. Every afternoon, he'd hunt ducks and other birds, and each night after supper he'd drive the jeep down to the savannah, where enormous termite colonies loomed, spectral and lunar in the darkness. There he'd hunt deer, tigers, armadillos, and wild boar.

My male cousins made fun of how clumsy I was at all the country activities for boys, but Uncle Hernán was patient. Sometimes, he'd take a break from tracking prey and, finding a shady tree on the plain, he'd read to me about Lenin or Trotsky.[4] But that December, I had turned sixteen, and he informed me that the time had come for me to visit the town's whorehouse. The particular afternoon I remember so vividly, he had been looking for game without success and we had wandered far away from the farmhouse, arriving at the foothills of the Sierra Nevada.[5] It was getting late, and in the mountains it was much cooler than in the town. The brooks and streams we waded through were cold and clear, and their sandy beds glittered with gold. In my grandfather's youth, this had been a gold-mining region and there was still gold to be found, but not in quantities sufficient to exploit commercially. The hills we ascended were paved with the palest green grass; the mango and ciruela trees, upon which fed flocks of parrots, macaws, and parakeets, and bands of boisterous monkeys, were now below us in the plain surrounding the river. Occasionally we ran into stray cows and menacing bulls and shy wild horses, but Uncle Hernán seemed pretty sure of the direction in which we were heading.

I was beginning to get tired of carrying his heavy rifle, as I always did, but I felt it would be unmanly to complain. Now we had an unobstructed view of

---

4. Leon Trotsky (1879–1940), Russian Communist leader. *Lenin*: Vladimir Ilyich Lenin (b. V. I. Ulyanov, 1870–1924), Russian Communist leader.

5. Sierra Nevada de Santa Marta, mountain range in northern Colombia.

the snowy peaks of the Sierra Nevada as they caught the reflection of the setting sun. The world was growing still, hushed. We started descending into an open *potrero*[6] of verdant pastures with high hills on all sides fencing it in. At its center was a shallow pond where scores of burros were drinking and playing in the water. Above them, rainbow-colored dragonflies darted about. The burros seemed young, but tame and friendly. Uncle Hernán approached them cautiously, talking to them in low, silky tones, patting their backs and stroking their long ears. "*Burra, burrita,*" he said, separating two of them and patting their behinds until they had wandered meters away from the rest of the herd. Then Uncle Hernán stood behind one of the burras and lifted her tail, putting his fingers inside her vulva. He motioned me to do the same with the other donkey which stood still, expectantly. When I lifted her tail, little white gnats flew into the saffron light of sunset. It was smelly down there. The rims of the vulva were pinkish and ivory, and the tips of my fingers felt warm and gluey. A few inches inside the vagina a flexible but resistant membrane stopped my fingers from exploring further. Even though the animal seemed to enjoy it, I was afraid of pursuing this activity. I saw Uncle Hernán unzip his pants. With his huge dick sticking out, he approached me. Not understanding what was happening, I was seized with terror and started to shake. He motioned for me to move aside, and penetrated the burra once, twice, rocking back and forth. The burra stamped one of her hind hoofs on the ground and grunted, as if she were pleased. Uncle Hernán grinned. "Okay, Sammy, she's all yours: a virgin no more."

He hurried over to the other burra, which had stood motionless, waiting for him, and penetrated her. I imitated his bumping motions and was about to get an erection when several male burros with their black, baseball-bat-sized members, began circling the herd at a gallop and braying hysterically. I was afraid that they were angry and were getting ready to attack us. My cock kept falling out of the enormous vagina. Soon, Uncle Hernán was in a frenzy, eyes closed, his buttocks pushing in and out, in and out; he moaned and cried in pleasure when he finished. Then he rested his head on the burra's rump and embraced her around her haunches. He remained that way, panting, until he stepped backward and collapsed on the grass, his penis limp but still large, his pants tangled around his boots. I walked over to the burra he had just fucked, and what seemed like large quantities of semen oozed out of her vagina. Becoming aroused, I put my hard cock inside her.

A car door slamming brought me back to reality. Mother was back home from her bingo game.

"*Buenas noches, mi amor*" Mother called out to her friend as the car pulled away.

1992

---

6. Pasturing place.

# JULIA ALVAREZ
## b. 1950

In "Entre Lucas y Juan Mejía," an essay included in this anthology, Julia Alvarez ponders the title expression. In her native Dominican culture, a person might answer the question *How are you?* by saying, "Between Lucas and Juan Mejía," though these names mean nothing beyond the expression. This intriguing linguistic tic leads Alvarez to explain why "you have to go on and tell the tale of why you feel the way you do."

Alvarez, a chronicler of in-between-ness, was born in New York City but raised by her extended upper-class family in the Dominican Republic. There, she attended an American school, dressed like an American girl, and spoke English. Her father's opposition to General Rafael Leónidas Trujillo Molina (1891–1961), who ruled the Dominican Republic as a dictator from 1930 until his assassination, resulted in the family's exile and return to the United States in 1960. In her novel *How the García Girls Lost Their Accents* (1991), a best seller that was quickly adopted at schools across the United States, Alvarez chronicles her transformation from a Dominican infatuated with U.S. culture to an immigrant. The García sisters—Sofía, Sandra, Carla, and Alvarez's fictional stand-in, Yolanda—explore Americanness from different perspectives, reinventing themselves through fashion, food, and ideas. The chapter included here focuses on Yolanda (or Yoyo, or simply Yo), the family chronicler, as she experiences life in New York and, with her parents' encouragement, embraces her new language.

Upon arriving in the United States, Alvarez sought refuge in the world of books. She went to Connecticut College, in New London; but after attending the Breadloaf Writers' Conference, at Vermont's Middlebury College, she transferred to Middlebury, where in 1971 she received her bachelor's degree in English and creative writing. In 1974, she received her master's degree in creative writing from Syracuse University, in New York State. After teaching at various universities, she returned to Middlebury in 1988 and became a full professor of English there in 1996. In her debut collection of poetry, *Homecoming* (1984), Alvarez dealt with her search for place at a time when she had neither a specific career direction nor a family of her own. In *¡Yo!* (1997), Alvarez presented further adventures and assimilation of the García family. Each section of the book is narrated by a different person—a maid's daughter, a college professor, and so on. The section presented here, "The Sisters," is narrated by Sofía, the youngest, once seen as a maverick and now reacting to the fame and notoriety Yo has achieved with her novel about the Garcías.

Among Alvarez's most important works is *In the Time of the Butterflies* (1995), a novel based on a tragic event in Dominican history. On November 25, 1960, the three Mirabal sisters—active opponents of the Trujillo dictatorship—were found dead near their wrecked Jeep, at the bottom of a 15-foot cliff in the northern part of the country. Today the Mirabal sisters are known throughout the Caribbean Basin as *las mariposas* (The Butterflies). Others in the Dominican Republic have used this episode as a springboard to discuss the quest for freedom on the island. While Alvarez uses the story to meditate on the roles of gender and repression in the Dominican Republic, she also attempts to insert the Latino literary tradition into what south of the Rio Grande and in the Caribbean is known as *la novela del dictador*, fiction about tyrants.

In her historical novel *In the Name of Salomé* (2000), Alvarez explores the life of Salomé Ureña, a nineteenth-century Dominican anticolonialist who became well-known at a very young age for her patriotic poetry; started a school for women; and was the mother of Pedro, Max, and Camila Henríquez Ureña, a trio of distinguished intellectuals. Alvarez focuses on Salomé and Camila, depicting their struggles to make their places in the male-dominated world of Latino intellectuals.

In the historical novel *Saving the World* (2006), Alvarez creates two parallel narratives about epidemics: the tale of a modern doctor with a humanitarian bent who goes to the Dominican Republic to fight AIDS, and of his wife, a Latina writer; and the story of an ill-fated nineteenth-century expedition by a spinster doctor of a Spanish orphanage eager to vaccinate almost two dozen of her charges with cowpox and bring them from Spain to Central America to prevent future smallpox epidemics.

Aside from her fiction, Alvarez has published half a dozen other volumes of poetry and nonfiction, including *El otro lado/The Other Side* (1995) and *Something to Declare* (1998). She has also authored children's books, such as *The Secret Footprint* (2000), which is based on a Dominican fable; *A Cafecito Story/El Cuento del Cafecito* (2001), an environmental fable inspired by the organic coffee farm Alvarez owns in the Dominican Republic with her husband, Bill Eichner, and an onsite school that teaches basic reading and writing (Alvarez and Eichner live both at the farm and in their house in Vermont); *Before We Were Free* (2002); *The Gift of Gracias: The Legend of Altagracia* (2005); and *The Best Gift of All: The Legend of La Vieja Belen* (2008). Her books for young adults include *How Tía Lola Came to Stay* (2001), about the effect of divorce on a child, who is supported emotionally by a flamboyant aunt; *Return to Sender* (2009), about the raid operations that the Department of Homeland Security conducted in 2006 on undocumented immigrant workers; and *How Tía Lola Learned to Teach* (2010).

In her poem "Bilingual Sestina," also included here, Alvarez explores the double-consciousness of speaking two languages and, therefore, existing in parallel universes. She luxuriates in the sensuous sounds of Spanish and "an intimacy I now yearn for in English— / words so close to what I mean that I almost hear my Spanish / heart beating."

---

## *From* How the García Girls Lost Their Accents

## Daughter of Invention

For a period after they arrived in this country, Laura García tried to invent something. Her ideas always came after the sightseeing visits she took with her daughters to department stores to see the wonders of this new country. On his free Sundays, Carlos carted the girls off to the Statue of Liberty or the Brooklyn Bridge or Rockefeller Center, but as far as Laura was concerned, these were men's wonders. Down in housewares were the true treasures women were after.

Laura and her daughters would take the escalator, marveling at the moving staircase, she teasing them that this might be the ladder Jacob saw with angels moving up and down to heaven. The moment they lingered by a display, a perky saleslady approached, no doubt thinking a young mother with four girls in tow fit the perfect profile for the new refrigerator with automatic defrost or the heavy duty washing machine with the prewash soak cycle. Laura paid close attention during the demonstrations, asking intelligent questions, but at the last minute saying she would talk it over with her husband. On the drive home, try as they might, her daughters could not engage their mother in conversation, for inspired by what she had just seen, Laura had begun inventing.

She never put anything actual on paper until she had settled her house down at night. On his side of the bed her husband would be conked out for an hour already, his Spanish newspapers draped over his chest, his glasses propped up on his bedside table, looking out eerily at the darkened room like a disembodied bodyguard. In her lighted corner, pillows propped behind her, Laura sat up inventing. On her lap lay one of those innumerable pads of paper her husband brought home from his office, compliments of some pharmaceutical company, advertising tranquilizers or antibiotics or skin cream. She would be working on a sketch of something familiar but drawn at such close range so she could attach a special nozzle or handier handle, the thing looked peculiar. Her daughters would giggle over the odd doodles they found in kitchen drawers or on the back shelf of the downstairs toilet. Once Yoyo was sure her mother had drawn a picture of a man's you-know-what; she showed her sisters her find, and with coy, posed faces they inquired of their mother what she was up to. *Ay,* that was one of her failures, she explained to them, a child's double-compartment drinking glass with an outsized, built-in straw.

Her daughters would seek her out at night when she seemed to have a moment to talk to them: they were having trouble at school or they wanted her to persuade their father to give them permission to go into the city or to a shopping mall or a movie—in broad daylight, Mami! Laura would wave them out of her room. "The problem with you girls . . ." The problem boiled down to the fact that they wanted to become Americans and their father—and their mother, too, at first—would have none of it.

"You girls are going to drive me crazy!" she threatened, if they kept nagging. "When I end up in Bellevue,[1] you'll be safely sorry!"

She spoke in English when she argued with them. And her English was a mishmash of mixed-up idioms and sayings that showed she was "green behind the ears," as she called it.

If her husband insisted she speak in Spanish to the girls so they wouldn't forget their native tongue, she'd snap, "When in Rome, do unto the Romans."

Yoyo, the Big Mouth, had become the spokesman for her sisters, and she stood her ground in that bedroom. "We're not going to that school anymore, Mami!"

"You have to." Her eyes would widen with worry. "In this country, it is against the law not to go to school. You want us to get thrown out?"

"You want us to get killed? Those kids were throwing stones today!"

"Sticks and stones don't break bones," she chanted. Yoyo could tell, though, by the look on her face, it was as if one of those stones the kids had aimed at her daughters had hit her. But she always pretended they were at fault. "What did you do to provoke them? It takes two to tangle, you know."

"Thanks, thanks a lot, Mom!" Yoyo stormed out of that room and into her own. Her daughters never called her *Mom* except when they wanted her to feel how much she had failed them in this country. She was a good enough Mami, fussing and scolding and giving advice, but a terrible girlfriend parent, a real failure of a Mom.

Back she went to her pencil and pad, scribbling and tsking and tearing off sheets, finally giving up, and taking up her *New York Times.* Some nights, though, if she got a good idea, she rushed into Yoyo's room, a flushed look on her face, her tablet of paper in her hand, a cursory knock on the door she'd just thrown open. "Do I have something to show you, Cuquita!"

1. Municipal hospital in Manhattan that includes a well-known psychiatric facility.

This was Yoyo's time to herself, after she finished her homework, while her sisters were still downstairs watching TV in the basement. Hunched over her small desk, the overhead light turned off, her desk lamp poignantly lighting only her paper, the rest of the room in warm, soft, uncreated darkness, she wrote her secret poems in her new language.

"You're going to ruin your eyes!" Laura began, snapping on the overly bright overhead light, scaring off whatever shy passion Yoyo, with the blue thread of her writing, had just begun coaxing out of a labyrinth of feelings.

"Oh, Mami!" Yoyo cried out, her eyes blinking up at her mother. "I'm writing."

"Ay, Cuquita." That was her communal pet name for whoever was in her favor. "Cuquita, when I make a million, I'll buy you your very own typewriter." (Yoyo had been nagging her mother for one just like the one her father had bought to do his order forms at home.) "Gravy on the turkey" was what she called it when someone was buttering her up. She buttered and poured. "I'll hire you your very own typist."

Down she plopped on the bed and held out her pad. "Take a guess, Cuquita?" Yoyo studied the rough sketch a moment. Soap sprayed from the nozzle head of a shower when you turned the knob a certain way? Instant coffee with creamer already mixed in? Time-released water capsules for your potted plants when you were away? A keychain with a timer that would go off when your parking meter was about to expire? (The ticking would help you find your keys easily if you mislaid them.) The famous one, famous only in hindsight, was the stick person dragging a square by a rope—a suitcase with wheels? "Oh, of course," Yoyo said, humoring her. "What every household needs: a shower like a car wash, keys ticking like a bomb, luggage on a leash!" By now, it had become something of a family joke, their Thomas Edison Mami[2], their Benjamin Franklin Mom.

Her face fell. "Come on now! Use your head." One more wrong guess, and she'd show Yoyo, pointing with her pencil to the different highlights of this incredible new wonder. "Remember that time we took the car to Bear Mountain,[3] and we re-ah-lized that we had forgotten to pack an opener with our pick-a-nick?" (Her daughters kept correcting her, but she insisted this was how it should be said.) "When we were ready to eat we didn't have any way to open the refreshments cans?" (This before fliptop lids, which she claimed had crossed her mind.) "You know what this is now?" Yoyo shook her head. "Is a car bumper, but see this part is a removable can opener. So simple and yet so necessary, eh?"

"Yeah, Mami. You should patent it." Yoyo shrugged as her mother tore off the scratch paper and folded it, carefully, corner to corner, as if she were going to save it. But then, she tossed it in the wastebasket on her way out of the room and gave a little laugh like a disclaimer. "It's half of one or two dozen of another."

None of her daughters was very encouraging. They resented her spending time on those dumb inventions. Here they were trying to fit in America among Americans; they needed help figuring out who they were, why the Irish kids whose grandparents had been micks were calling them spics.

---

2. Franklin (1706–1790) and Edison (1847–1931)     3. State park north of New York City.
here represent famous American inventors.

Why had they come to this country in the first place? Important, crucial, final things, and here was their own mother, who didn't have a second to help them puzzle any of this out, inventing gadgets to make life easier for the American Moms.

Sometimes Yoyo challenged her. "Why, Mami? Why do it? You're never going to make money. The Americans have already thought of everything, you know that."

"Maybe not. Maybe, just maybe, there's something they've missed that's important. With patience and calm, even a burro can climb a palm." This last was one of her many Dominican sayings she had imported into her scrambled English.

"But what's the point?" Yoyo persisted.

"Point, point, does everything need a point? Why do you write poems?"

Yoyo had to admit it was her mother who had the point there. Still, in the hierarchy of things, a poem seemed much more important than a potty that played music when a toilet-training toddler went in its bowl.

They talked about it among themselves, the four girls, as they often did now about the many puzzling things in this new country.

"Better she reinvents the wheel than be on our cases all the time," the oldest, Carla, observed. In the close quarters of an American nuclear family, their mother's prodigious energy was becoming a real drain on their self-determination. Let her have a project. What harm could she do, and besides, she needed that acknowledgement. It had come to her automatically in the old country from being a de la Torre.[4] "García de la Torre," Laura would enunciate carefully, giving her maiden as well as married name when they first arrived. But the blank smiles had never heard of her name. She would show them. She would prove to these Americans what a smart woman could do with a pencil and pad.

She had a near miss once. Every night, she liked to read *The New York Times* in bed before turning off her light, to see what the Americans were up to. One night, she let out a yelp to wake up her husband beside her. He sat bolt upright, reaching for his glasses which in his haste, he knocked across the room. "*¿Qué pasa? ¿Qué pasa?*" What is wrong? There was terror in his voice, the same fear she'd heard in the Dominican Republic before they left. They had been watched there; he was followed. They could not talk, of course, though they had whispered to each other in fear at night in the dark bed. Now in America, he was safe, a success even; his Centro de Medicina in the Bronx[5] was thronged with the sick and the homesick yearning to go home again. But in dreams, he went back to those awful days and long nights, and his wife's screams confirmed his secret fear: they had not gotten away after all; the SIM[6] had come for them at last.

"*Ay*, Cuco! Remember how I showed you that suitcase with little wheels so we should not have to carry those heavy bags when we traveled? Someone stole my idea and made a million!" She shook the paper in his face. "See, see! This man was no *bobo*![7] He didn't put all his pokers on a back burner. I kept telling you, one of these days my ship would pass me by in the night!"

---

4. Literally, of the tower; signifying "the upper crust."
5. New York City borough, north of Manhattan. *Centro de Medicina*: medical center.

6. Servicio de Inteligencia Militar, the Dominican secret police under Trujillo.
7. Fool.

She wagged her finger at her husband and daughters, laughing all the while, one of those eerie laughs crazy people in movies laugh. The four girls had congregated in her room. They eyed their mother and each other. Perhaps they were all thinking the same thing, wouldn't it be weird and sad if Mami did end up in Bellevue?

"*¡Ya, ya!*" She waved them out of her room at last. "There is no use trying to drink spilt milk, that's for sure."

It was the suitcase rollers that stopped Laura's hand; she had weathervaned a minor brainstorm. And yet, this plagiarist had gotten all the credit, and the money. What use was it trying to compete with the Americans: they would always have the head start. It was their country, after all. Best stick close to home. She cast her sights about—her daughters ducked—and found her husband's office in need. Several days a week, dressed professionally in a white smock with a little name tag pinned on the lapel, a shopping bag full of cleaning materials and rags, she rode with her husband in his car to the Bronx. On the way, she organized the glove compartment or took off the address stickers from the magazines for the waiting room because she had read somewhere how by means of these stickers drug addict patients found out where doctors lived and burglarized their homes looking for syringes. At night, she did the books, filling in columns with how much money they had made that day. Who had time to be inventing silly things!

She did take up her pencil and pad one last time. But it was to help one of her daughters out. In ninth grade, Yoyo was chosen by her English teacher, Sister Mary Joseph, to deliver the Teacher's Day address at the school assembly. Back in the Dominican Republic growing up, Yoyo had been a terrible student. No one could ever get her to sit down to a book. But in New York, she needed to settle somewhere, and since the natives were unfriendly, and the country inhospitable, she took root in the language. By high school, the nuns were reading her stories and compositions out loud in English class.

But the spectre of delivering a speech brown-nosing the teachers jammed her imagination. At first she didn't want to and then she couldn't seem to write that speech. She should have thought of it as "a great honor," as her father called it. But she was mortified. She still had a slight accent, and she did not like to speak in public, subjecting herself to her classmates' ridicule. It also took no great figuring to see that to deliver a eulogy for a convent full of crazy, old, overweight nuns was no way to endear herself to her peers.

But she didn't know how to get out of it. Night after night, she sat at her desk, hoping to polish off some quick, noncommittal little speech. But she couldn't get anything down.

The weekend before the assembly Monday morning Yoyo went into a panic. Her mother would just have to call in tomorrow and say Yoyo was in the hospital, in a coma.

Laura tried to calm her down. "Just remember how Mister Lincoln couldn't think of anything to say at the Gettysburg, but then, bang! *Four score and once upon a time ago*,"[8] she began reciting. "Something is going to come if

---

8. The Gettysburg Address (1863)—delivered at the dedication of the Soldiers' National Cemetery in Gettysburg, Pennsylvania, by U.S. president Abraham Lincoln (1809–1865)—begins "Four score and seven years ago."

you just relax. You'll see, like the Americans say, *Necessity is the daughter of invention.* I'll help you."

That weekend, her mother turned all her energy towards helping Yoyo write her speech. "Please, Mami, just leave me alone, please," Yoyo pleaded with her. But Yoyo would get rid of the goose only to have to contend with the gander. Her father kept poking his head in the door just to see if Yoyo had "fulfilled your obligations," a phrase he had used when the girls were younger and he'd check to see whether they had gone to the bathroom before a car trip. Several times that weekend around the supper table, he recited his own high school valedictorian speech. He gave Yoyo pointers on delivery, notes on the great orators and their tricks. (Humbleness and praise and falling silent with great emotion were his favorites.)

Laura sat across the table, the only one who seemed to be listening to him. Yoyo and her sisters were forgetting a lot of their Spanish, and their father's formal, florid diction was hard to understand. But Laura smiled softly to herself, and turned the lazy Susan at the center of the table around and around as if it were the prime mover, the first gear of her attention.

That Sunday evening, Yoyo was reading some poetry to get herself inspired: Whitman's poems in an old book[9] with an engraved cover her father had picked up in a thrift shop next to his office. *I celebrate myself and sing myself. . . . He most honors my style who learns under it to destroy the teacher.* The poet's words shocked and thrilled her. She had gotten used to the nuns, a literature of appropriate sentiments, poems with a message, expurgated texts. But here was a flesh and blood man, belching and laughing and sweating in poems. *Who touches this book touches a man.*

That night, at last, she started to write, recklessly, three, five pages, looking up once only to see her father passing by the hall on tiptoe. When Yoyo was done, she read over her words, and her eyes filled. She finally sounded like herself in English!

As soon as she had finished that first draft, she called her mother to her room. Laura listened attentively while Yoyo read the speech out loud, and in the end, her eyes were glistening too. Her face was soft and warm and proud. "Ay, Yoyo, you are going to be the one to bring our name to the headlights in this country! That is a beautiful, beautiful speech. I want for your father to hear it before he goes to sleep. Then I will type it for you, all right?"

Down the hall they went, mother and daughter, faces flushed with accomplishment. Into the master bedroom where Carlos was propped up on his pillows, still awake, reading the Dominican papers, already days old. Now that the dictatorship had been toppled, he had become interested in his country's fate again. The interim government was going to hold the first free elections in thirty years. History was in the making, freedom and hope were in the air again! There was still some question in his mind whether or not he might move his family back. But Laura had gotten used to the life here. She did not want to go back to the old country, where, de la Torre or not, she was only a wife and a mother and a failed one at that, since she had never provided the required son). Better an independent nobody than a high-class houseslave. She did not come straight out and disagree with her husband's plans. Instead, she fussed with him about reading the papers in bed, soiling

9. Probably *Leaves of Grass* (1855), the major work of the American poet Walt Whitman (1819–1892).

their sheets with those poorly printed, foreign tabloids. "*The Times* is not that bad!" she'd claim if her husband tried to humor her by saying they shared the same dirty habit.

The minute Carlos saw his wife and daughter filing in, he put his paper down, and his face brightened as if at long last his wife had delivered the son, and that was the news she was bringing him. His teeth were already grinning from the glass of water next to his bedside lamp, so he lisped when he said, "Eh-speech, eh-speech!"

"It is so beautiful, Cuco," Laura coached him, turning the sound on his TV off. She sat down at the foot of the bed. Yoyo stood before both of them, blocking their view of the soldiers in helicopters landing amid silenced gun reports and explosions. A few weeks ago it had been the shores of the Dominican Republic. Now it was the jungles of Southeast Asia they were saving.[1] Her mother gave her the nod to begin reading.

Yoyo didn't need much encouragement. She put her nose to the fire, as her mother would have said, and read from start to finish without looking up. When she concluded, she was a little embarrassed at the pride she took in her own words. She pretended to quibble with a phrase or two, then looked questioningly to her mother. Laura's face was radiant. Yoyo turned to share her pride with her father.

The expression on his face shocked both mother and daughter. Carlos's toothless mouth had collapsed into a dark zero. His eyes bored into Yoyo, then shifted to Laura. In barely audible Spanish, as if secret microphones or informers were all about, he whispered to his wife, "You will permit her to read *that*?"

Laura's eyebrows shot up, her mouth fell open. In the old country, any whisper of a challenge to authority could bring the secret police in their black V.W.'s. But this was America. People could say what they thought. "What is wrong with her speech?" Laura questioned him.

"What ees wrrrong with her eh-speech?" Carlos wagged his head at her. His anger was always more frightening in his broken English. As if he had mutilated the language in his fury—and now there was nothing to stand between them and his raw, dumb anger. "What is wrong? I will tell you what is wrong. It show no gratitude. It is boastful. *I celebrate myself? The best student learns to destroy the teacher?*" He mocked Yoyo's plagiarized words. "That is insubordinate. It is improper. It is disrespecting of her teachers—" In his anger he had forgotten his fear of lurking spies: each wrong he voiced was a decibel higher than the last outrage. Finally, he shouted at Yoyo, "As your father, I forbid you to make that eh-speech!"

Laura leapt to her feet, a sign that *she* was about to deliver her own speech. She was a small woman, and she spoke all her pronouncements standing up, either for more projection or as a carry-over from her girlhood in convent schools where one asked for, and literally, took the floor in order to speak. She stood by Yoyo's side, shoulder to shoulder. They looked down at Carlos. "That is no tone of voice—" she began.

But now, Carlos was truly furious. It was bad enough that his daughter was rebelling, but here was his own wife joining forces with her. Soon he

---

1. This sentence refers to U.S. involvement in the Vietnam War (1959–75); the previous one, to the U.S. invasion of the Dominican Republic (1965).

would be surrounded by a houseful of independent American women. He too leapt from the bed, throwing off his covers. The Spanish newspapers flew across the room. He snatched the speech out of Yoyo's hands, held it before the girl's wide eyes, a vengeful, mad look in his own, and then once, twice, three, four, countless times, he tore the speech into shreds.

"Are you crazy?" Laura lunged at him. "Have you gone mad? That is her speech for tomorrow you have torn up!"

"Have *you* gone mad?" He shook her away. "You were going to let her read that . . . that insult to her teachers?"

"Insult to her teachers!" Laura's face had crumpled up like a piece of paper. On it was written a love note to her husband, an unhappy, haunted man. "This is America, Papi, America! You are not in a savage country anymore!"

Meanwhile, Yoyo was on her knees, weeping wildly, collecting all the little pieces of her speech, hoping that she could put it back together before the assembly tomorrow morning. But not even a sibyl could have made sense of those tiny scraps of paper. All hope was lost. "He broke it, he broke it," Yoyo moaned as she picked up a handful of pieces.

Probably, if she had thought a moment about it, she would not have done what she did next. She would have realized her father had lost brothers and friends to the dictator Trujillo. For the rest of his life, he would be haunted by blood in the streets and late night disappearances. Even after all these years, he cringed if a black Volkswagen passed him on the street. He feared anyone in uniform: the meter maid giving out parking tickets, a museum guard approaching to tell him not to get too close to his favorite Goya.[2]

On her knees, Yoyo thought of the worst thing she could say to her father. She gathered a handful of scraps, stood up, and hurled them in his face. In a low, ugly whisper, she pronounced Trujillo's hated nickname: "Chapita! You're just another Chapita!"

It took Yoyo's father only a moment to register the loathsome nickname before he came after her. Down the halls they raced, but Yoyo was quicker than he and made it into her room just in time to lock the door as her father threw his weight against it. He called down curses on her head, ordered her on his authority as her father to open that door! He throttled that doorknob, but all to no avail. Her mother's love of gadgets saved Yoyo's hide that night. Laura had hired a locksmith to install good locks on all the bedroom doors after the house had been broken into once while they were away. Now if burglars broke in again, and the family were at home, there would be a second round of locks for the thieves to contend with.

"Lolo," she said, trying to calm him down. "Don't you ruin my new locks."

Finally he did calm down, his anger spent. Yoyo heard their footsteps retreating down the hall. Their door clicked shut. Then, muffled voices, her mother's rising in anger, in persuasion, her father's deeper murmurs of explanation and self-defense. The house fell silent a moment, before Yoyo heard, far off, the gun blasts and explosions, the serious, self-important voices of newscasters reporting their TV war.

A little while later, there was a quiet knock at Yoyo's door, followed by a tentative attempt at the door knob. "Cuquita?" her mother whispered. "Open up, Cuquita."

---

2. I.e., a work by the Spanish painter Francisco José de Goya y Lucientes (1746–1828).

"Go away," Yoyo wailed, but they both knew she was glad her mother was there, and needed only a moment's protest to save face.

Together they concocted a speech: two brief pages of stale compliments and the polite commonplaces on teachers, a speech wrought by necessity and without much invention by mother and daughter late into the night on one of the pads of paper Laura had once used for her own inventions. After it was drafted, Laura typed it up while Yoyo stood by, correcting her mother's misnomers and mis-sayings.

Yoyo came home the next day with the success story of the assembly. The nuns had been flattered, the audience had stood up and given "our devoted teachers a standing ovation," what Laura had suggested they do at the end of the speech.

She clapped her hands together as Yoyo recreated the moment. "I stole that from your father's speech, remember? Remember how he put that in at the end?" She quoted him in Spanish, then translated for Yoyo into English.

That night, Yoyo watched him from the upstairs hall window, where she'd retreated the minute she heard his car pull up in front of the house. Slowly, her father came up the driveway, a grim expression on his face as he grappled with a large, heavy cardboard box. At the front door, he set the package down carefully and patted all his pockets for his house keys. (If only he'd had Laura's ticking key chain!) Yoyo heard the snapping open of locks downstairs. She listened as he struggled to maneuver the box through the narrow doorway. He called her name several times, but she did not answer him.

"My daughter, your father, he love you very much," he explained from the bottom of the stairs. "He just want to protect you." Finally, her mother came up and pleaded with Yoyo to go down and reconcile with him. "Your father did not mean to harm. You must pardon him. Always it is better to let bygones be forgotten, no?"

Downstairs, Yoyo found her father setting up a brand new electric typewriter on the kitchen table. It was even better than her mother's. He had outdone himself with all the extra features: a plastic carrying case with Yoyo's initials decaled below the handle, a brace to lift the paper upright while she typed, an erase cartridge, an automatic margin tab, a plastic hood like a toaster cover to keep the dust away. Not even her mother could have invented such a machine!

But Laura's inventing days were over just as Yoyo's were starting up with her school-wide success. Rather than the rolling suitcase everyone else in the family remembers, Yoyo thinks of the speech her mother wrote as her last invention. It was as if, after that, her mother had passed on to Yoyo her pencil and pad and said, "Okay, Cuquita, here's the buck. You give it a shot."

1991

## Entre Lucas y Juan Mejía

There's an expression in the Dominican Republic, hard to translate into English. If you ask a Dominican how he is, and he doesn't have a simple answer to give you, he might say "Entre Lucas y Juan Mejía" if he's doing well. Or, if he's doing poorly, "Entre Lucas y Juan Mejía."

"I'm fine." "I'm not feeling so good." These are straightforward responses, the black and white world of fact. And out of these two states of being, straightforward explanations usually follow. "I'm flying high because I just won the lottery." Or, "I'm in the pits because my man left me." But in that third, in-between space, where you cannot easily get at what you feel, you need a story to render full justice to your emotions.

Let's go back to the saying for a minute. What does it actually mean, "entre Lucas y Juan Mejía"? "Between the devil and the deep blue sea" isn't right, because you're not describing the sensation of being caught between a pair of bad alternatives—"a rock and a hard place." No. "So-so" isn't the meaning either, because the Dominican expression isn't at all meant to suggest bland stasis, mediocrity. It's much more intriguing than that. "How are you doing?" "I'm between Lucas and Juan Mejía."

But who are these two guys? Who knows? The very story that inspired the saying is gone. So of course, what happens is, you have to go on and tell the tale of why you feel the way you do. What are the forces you're caught between? How did you get there? And how does it feel to be there? For me, that moment of crisis, that being-in-the-middle, is always the nexus of a story.

So what does all this have to do with Hispanic writers living in the United States? Or rather, since I don't like to speak for all of the others, what does it have to do with me, a Dominican-American novelist?

Already that description of myself tells you something. I am a Dominican, hyphen, American. As a fiction writer, I find that the most exciting things happen in the realm of that hyphen—the place where two worlds collide or blend together. In fact, if it hadn't been for my coming to the United States at the age of ten, if I'd just grown up Dominican with no hyphen, I don't think I'd be doing what I'm doing today. I'm definitely not one of those born writers. I was an active little kid, not bookish, not solitary in the least. Although I did always love a good story.

My parents sent me to the local American school, Carol Morgan, so I could learn my English. (That's how everyone spoke of it. It was always "your English." "You have to learn your English.") And I did a poor job of it. I flunked the subject in every grade and kept having to go to summer school. I played hookey by hiding under the bed when all the cousins would gather in the morning to be driven off to school so they could go learn their English. I wasn't interested in Dick and Jane and Spot and Puff. No one could sit me down to those dull pastel puppets when, all around me, the women who cooked and cleaned—Gladys, Rosario, Altagracia y Iluminada—were full of stories about the witch that scared Juanita, who went out after dark one night and gave birth, and the baby had an extra finger. Or about the boy with warts all over his arms, Porfirio, who made Ignacio count those warts one afternoon and, next morning, Porfirio's arms were smooth as an infant's but Ignacio had twenty-seven warts on his. Or about how Fulanita was seen going into Arturo's room when Ana-Flor was out of the house and she wasn't carrying her cleaning bucket, no señor.

Those first ten years on the island, we were living in the bloody Trujillo dictatorship. My father, already exiled once, was now back home and had again become involved in the underground. Our house was under constant surveillance.

In the way of children, I didn't think anything adults did could go wrong. Then suddenly one day we were on a plane to New York, because the SIM, the secret police,[1] were after my father. In a sense, I felt lucky. After all, I had heard from Rosario and Altagracia and Gladys about Nueva York. Now I would get to see the miracle of the snow . . . stores full of anything you could think of to buy . . . buildings that pricked the sky with their roofs . . . and a host of other marvels that, up till then, had existed only in the province of story.

We arrived in New York City in August. Nothing I'd been told prepared me for the shock of America. I was silenced with astonishment. The doors of huge edifices swung open when you approached them. Elevators carried you up into the sky like a ride at la féria.[2] And all around me, people were speaking English. But not the slow, carefully enunciated English of my Dominican classroom. This was gibberish—or at best, talk I had to strain to understand. It was like finding yourself at the foot of the Tower of Babel.[3] And as the months went by, the most frightening thing of all happened. I began losing my Spanish before getting a foothold in English. I was without a language, without any way to fend for myself, without solid ground to stand on.

Determined to make myself understood, I began reading. I began studying words in a precise, self-conscious, intentional way, which is perfect training for a writer. And I began writing. In self-imposed solitude, I started making sense of my new life in this country. I discovered that the act of writing was a way of bringing together those two worlds that would often clash in my own head, driving me in different directions. A way of reconciling two cultures that mixed together in such odd combinations. At my desk, I could sort out and understand those combinations.

I grew older and made my life here. Not here in the United States, and not allá[4] in Santo Domingo, but here in the world of words. They gave me ground to stand on as I pushed away from my family and their Old World ideas of what my role as a female should be. They gave me ground to stand on as I resisted being labeled in the New World as an "other," an outsider who had better assimilate if she expected to share in the goodies.

In a sense, I was in no man's land. No woman's land. But that land is any writer's blank page. Or as Czeslaw Milosz, the Polish poet and immigrant,[5] once put it, language is the only homeland.

What I've discovered, then, is that this in-between place is not just one of friction and tension but one that offers unique perspectives, visions, energy, choices. And our stories chart these. And our poems name them. And this naming and charting are crucial for understanding ourselves, for validating ourselves as individuals and as members of communities that happen to be of neither one world nor another . . . that happen to be entre Lucas y Juan Mejía.

1992

---

1. See note 6, p. 1742.
2. The fair, the carnival.
3. In the biblical Book of Genesis, an immense tower in the city of Babel (Hebrew for "Babylon"), dedicated to the glory of humanity. Angered by the arrogance of the builders and inhabitants, God made them speak many conflicting languages rather than a universal one and scattered the people around the earth.
4. Over there.
5. Miłosz (1911–2004) emigrated to the United States in 1960.

# Bilingual Sestina

Some things I have to say aren't getting said
in this snowy, blond, blue-eyed, gum-chewing English:
dawn's early light sifting through *persianas* closed
the night before by dark-skinned girls whose words
evoke *cama, aposento, sueños* in *nombres*                    5
from that first world I can't translate from Spanish.

Gladys, Rosario, Altagracia[1]—the sounds of Spanish
wash over me like warm island waters as I say
your soothing names: a child again learning the *nombres*
of things you point to in the world before English            10
turned *sol, tierra, cielo, luna* to vocabulary words—
*sun, earth, sky, moon.* Language closed

like the touch-sensitive *morivivi* whose leaves closed
when we kids poked them, astonished. Even Spanish
failed us back then when we saw how frail a word is           15
when faced with the thing it names. How saying
its name won't always summon up in Spanish or English
the full blown genie from the bottled *nombre*.

Gladys, I summon you back by saying your *nombre*.
Open up again the house of slatted windows closed             20
since childhood, where *palabras* left behind for English
stand dusty and awkward in neglected Spanish.
Rosario, muse of *el patio*, sing in me and through me say
that world again, begin first with those first words

you put in my mouth as you pointed to the world—             25
not Adam, not God, but a country girl numbering
the stars, the blades of grass, warming the sun by saying,
*¡Qué calor!* as you opened up the morning closed
inside the night until you sang in Spanish,
*Estas son las mañanitas*, and listening in bed, no English   30

yet in my head to confuse me with translations, no English
doubling the world with synonyms, no dizzying array of words
—the world was simple and intact in Spanish—
*luna, so, casa, luz, flor*, as if the *nombres*
were the outer skin of things, as if words were so close      35
one left a mist of breath on things by saying

their names, an intimacy I now yearn for in English—
words so close to what I mean that I almost hear my Spanish
heart beating, beating inside what I say *en inglés.*

1995

---

1. In Alvarez's essay "Entre Lucas y Juan Mejía," among the names of "the women who cooked and cleaned" (see p. 1748).

## FROM ¡YO!

## The Sisters

Suddenly her face is all over the place in a promo picture that makes her look prettier than she is. I'm driving downtown for groceries with the kids in the back seat and there she is on *Fresh Air*[1] talking about our family like everyone is some made-up character she can do with as she wants. I'm mad as anything, so I U-turn the car and drive back home and call her up and I get her long-winded machine that says she can't come to the phone right now, please call her agent. Like hell I'm going to call her agent to give her a piece of my mind. Instead, I call up one of the other sisters.

's now on to Papi in the Laurentians,[2] imagine."

us! Doesn't she have any sense?"

as this whole spiel about art and life mirroring each other and how to write about what you know. I couldn't listen to it, it was mak-

running around, screaming, knowing it's a heyday because d at somebody else. And then little Carlos comes up and I really in Auntie Yoyo's book? Am I going to have my ?" And then he's begging to bring his auntie's book to that the whole third grade of little Christians can a crisp with the doctored-up family story.

e that book to school!" I snap at him. And then more weet chocolate-kisses eyes are blinking back tears,

" the eighth grader chimes in. She has started wearout like her aunt's.

drive me crazy. When I end up at Bellevue—"[3] And elf because that sounds more than vaguely familiar— he book always says. "Are you still there?" I say to my rangely silent. Now I'm the one blinking back tears. s into my personal stuff, I'm going to . . ."

Pile o? Mami's saying she's going to sue her."

was g s just pulling her usual. Remember when she used to ber? ids and drive over to the Carmelite nuns and say she suppose the convent unless we'd promise to behave? Rememwas goin by the car and all these Carmelite nuns, who weren't We're b ir faces, were at the windows wondering what the hell better abou

ory these day g over that old story. I don't know if we actually feel ctional characters or if it's just so nice to have a mem-That night I lk ve haven't seen already worked over in print. him in on the d how, usband—after the kids are off to their rooms. I fill how, the phone call with my sister, our mother's temper

1. A talk show on Nona Public Radio.
2. Mountain ran southern Quebec, Canada;
the name also appli to the Laurentides, a region in Quebec that includes some of the Laurentians.
3. Municipal hospital in Manhattan that includes a psychiatric facility.

tantrums out there for the whole world to know about. "What are we going to do about this?"

"About what?" he says.

I am not going to act like our mother and blow my temper. At least, not right away. "This . . . this exposure," I say, because suddenly I don't know what to call it myself. "I don't think it's good for the kids."

My husband looks over his shoulder as if to assure himself there are no hidden cameras or reporters around. "We seem quite cozy here," he says. He has a quaint way of saying things in his German accent that makes it hard to get angry at him. It's as if you were to yell at someone in an ESL class who needs all the help he can get. I don't know why he calls up this tender tolerance in me when I'm just as much a foreigner as he is. "There is no need to get upset. Soon she will write another book and this one will be forgotten."

"Yeah, right. She was on the radio today talking away about Papi skiing topless in the Laurentians with all his French-Canadian girlfriends. Mami's going to hit the roof!"

"Your mother will hit the roof anyway," he says nonchalantly until he sees the look on my face. "But this is true," he says lamely, scratching his balding head, something he does when he's nervous that usually blunts the sharp edge of my anger. Tonight, it's not really anger I'm feeling. I'm in and out flabbergasted that he would say such a thing even if it is true, which it is. I know for a fact that before he read the book and had lines that plopped into his mouth, he would never have said so of his own accord. He used to be more polite. I feel like my whole life is losing ground to fiction.

"I just won't have everyone criticizing the family," I say in a teary voice that goes dry on me before I can wring any sympathy from him. So I go to the kitchen to fix the kids' lunches and settle my nerves. The last thing I want to do tonight is not be able to go to sleep and have to come down and lie on the couch till all hours reading some stupid novel. I always was a reader, but now, whenever I open a book, even if it's something historical and dead, all I can do is shake my head and think, oh my god, I wonder what their family thought of this story?

I'm in there cutting up the bread into little space-food squares the way my third-grader likes his sandwich and leaving out mayonnaise the way my eighth grader likes hers when the phone rings and it's my other sister. "The victimized sister," or so she introduces herself in a grim voice. I don't go in for all this labeling but my two sisters are psychologists. It's the way they get a handle on things. Me, I just get mad.

"People have been coming up to me at work asking, so what happened next? My therapist says this is a kind of abuse!" She goes quiet and then adds, "How are you doing? It sounds like you're hitting something."

"Just making the kids' lunches."

My sisters, I love them all, but sometimes they get on my nerves. This one is always seeing trauma and sadness. Around her, I go shallow, hoping I'll get her to smile. "Oh, we'll survive," I say. "But I'll tell you one thing, I'm glad my husband has calmed me down.

"Oh, come on," I say.

"I mean it. I'm glad this is all happening around my birthday. Because when she calls me, I'm just going to let her have it."

"I know," I say instead of pointing out that if she's not talking to our sister, she can't let her have it. "So how are things?" I say in a bright voice, hoping to get her talking about something happy. Why is it that with all my sisters I always feel like I'm the therapist?

"Well, actually, there is something else. But you've got to promise me that you're not going to tell her—"

"Hey, I'm not talking to her either," I lie. I'm not sure why. It's as if I'm caught up in some family melodrama that I don't necessarily like. "So what is it?"

A coy pause, and then a jubilant, "I'm pregnant."

"Ay-ay!!!" I cry out, and here comes my husband, rushing into the room, the paper still in his hand. "Good? Bad?" he mouths. Recently, he observed—one of his new insights—how it's hard to tell what's really going on in my family with so much overreaction. Anyhow, I tell him my sister is pregnant and he gets on the phone and says he is delighted. Delighted?! I grab the phone back, and we gab for half an hour, the book forgotten, all those fictional doubles sent packing, my sister remarking on all the errors our mother made with us that she is not going to make with her child, and I kind of defending our mother because actually, though I don't say so, I've repeated all those sins with my own kids—except the one with the nuns and that's probably because there are no Carmelite convents that I know of in Rockford, Illinois. My sister concludes with the reminder that I am not to breathe a word of this to you-know-who.

"It seems kind of mean," I even surprise myself by saying so. I guess I'm feeling expansive, like there are really only a few big things in this world, LOVE and DEATH and LITTLE BABIES. Forget fame and fortune and whether or not someone plagiarized you into a fictional character. "I think you should tell her."

"You promised!" she says with such fury that even our mother could take lessons from her.

"Hey, I'm not going to say a word, it's not that. But I think *you* should tell her. After all, she is going to be an aunt."

"I can't believe you're saying this! I'm going to be a mother!"

"But why not tell her?"

"I just don't want my baby to become fictional fodder."

I get this crazy picture in my head—a cartoon really more than a picture—of this tiny baby being put through a big roller and coming out the other end as one of those small books that reviewers like to call a *slim volume*. But I also kind of see my sister's point—it's not just the baby, but the rest of the story will probably find its way into that slim novel: single motherhood, artificial insemination, sperm brought up from the D.R. from an area of the country where hopefully there aren't many first cousins. Just thinking about it I get goosebumps up and down my arm.

"What are you doing? It sounds like you're crying."

"No, no, I'm so happy," I reassure her, and then she makes me swear on my own children, which makes me very uneasy, that I won't mention a word of this to our sister.

Well, I no sooner put the phone down and finish wrapping up the sandwiches and putting in an applesauce for the dieter and a jellybean cookie for the little Christian when the phone rings and it's you-know-who.

"What's going on?" she says all weepy like it just occurred to her that everyone isn't ecstatic over her being famous.

"What do you mean?" I say, because if I've learned one thing in this family it's you better not let on that anyone has gotten to you first with another version of the story.

And she tells me. Mami is going to sue her. Papi has to call her from a public phone. Our eldest sister has her husband say that she's not available. "And I just called Sandi, and she hung up on me." There is a wrenching sob, and though I myself was going to kill her six hours ago, all I want to do is ease that mournful sound. I keep remembering how when we first got to this country the only way she'd go to sleep was if I held her hand across the space between our beds and told her something I remembered from being back on the island.

"Hey," I say, putting the best face on this messy situation, "I bet there were a lot of people mad at Shakespeare, too, but aren't we all glad he wrote *Hamlet*?" I don't know why I'm saying this since I dropped out of college in part because I just couldn't pass the Renaissance. "But still," I go on, getting everyone's point of view in, "imagine how you'd feel if you were his mother."

"What do you mean? What's art going to mirror if it isn't life? Everybody, I mean everybody, writes out of his or her own experience!" And she's off into all the stuff I already heard her say on *Fresh Air*. But I let her say it. For one thing, my head is going a mile a minute, all that clunky, outdated emotional machinery from childhood that should have been replaced years ago with the trim, cutting-edge technology of feeling is chugging away, and nothing short of a handful of sleeping pills is going to shut it off. I might as well stay up on the phone instead of sitting in the living room shaking my head at some dead novelist.

"It really hurts, you know, that my family can't share this with me. I mean I haven't done anything wrong. I could have been an axe murderer. I could have gotten up on some roof in a shopping mall and mowed down a bunch of people."

I sure am glad it's me she's talking to and not one of the psychologist sisters.

"All I did was write a book," she wails.

"Everyone's feeling a little exposed, that's all."

"But it's fiction!" she starts in.

Oh yeah? I want to say. I don't care what it says on that page up front about any resemblance is entirely coincidental, you know when you spot yourself in some paragraph of description. "But it's fiction based on your own experience! Like all fiction," I add, quoting her from the radio. "I know, I know, what else are you going to write about?" But to myself, I'm thinking, why can't she write about axe murderers or law-firm scams or extraterrestrials and make a million and divide it four ways, which by the way is what the other sisters suggest she should do with this book since we provided the raw material.

"So you do understand, ay, it means so much you understand."

### FROM ¡YO!

## The Sisters

Suddenly her face is all over the place in a promo picture that makes her look prettier than she is. I'm driving downtown for groceries with the kids in the back seat and there she is on *Fresh Air*[1] talking about our family like everyone is some made-up character she can do with as she wants. I'm mad as anything, so I U-turn the car and drive back home and call her up and I get her long-winded machine that says she can't come to the phone right now, to please call her agent. Like hell I'm going to call her agent to give her a piece of my mind. Instead, I call up one of the other sisters.

"She's now on to Papi in the Laurentians,[2] imagine."

"Jesus! Doesn't she have any sense?"

"She has this whole spiel about art and life mirroring each other and how you've got to write about what you know. I couldn't listen to it, it was making me sick."

The kids are running around, screaming, knowing it's a heyday because their mother's mad at somebody else. And then little Carlos comes up and says, "Mamma, am I really in Auntie Yoyo's book? Am I going to have my picture in the paper?" And then he's begging to bring his auntie's book to Easter show-and-tell so that the whole third grade of little Christians can get their ears burned to a crisp with the doctored-up family story.

"No! You cannot take that book to school!" I snap at him. And then more gently because those sweet chocolate-kisses eyes are blinking back tears, "It's a grown-up book."

"So can *I* take it in?" the eighth grader chimes in. She has started wearing her hair all fluffed out like her aunt's.

"You kids are going to drive me crazy. When I end up at Bellevue—"[3] And then I have to stop myself because that sounds more than vaguely familiar— it's what the mami in the book always says. "Are you still there?" I say to my sister, who has gone strangely silent. Now I'm the one blinking back tears.

"I tell you, if she gets into my personal stuff, I'm going to . . ."

"But what can we do? Mami's saying she's going to sue her."

"Ay, come on, Mami's just pulling her usual. Remember when she used to pile us in the car as kids and drive over to the Carmelite nuns and say she was going to leave us in the convent unless we'd promise to behave? Remember? We'd be kneeling by the car and all these Carmelite nuns, who weren't supposed to show their faces, were at the windows wondering what the hell was going on!"

We're both laughing over that old story. I don't know if we actually feel better about being fictional characters or if it's just so nice to have a memory these days that we haven't seen already worked over in print.

That night I talk to my husband—after the kids are off to their rooms. I fill him in on the radio show, the phone call with my sister, our mother's temper

1. A talk show on National Public Radio.
2. Mountain range in southern Quebec, Canada; the name is also applied to the Laurentides, a region in Quebec that includes some of the Laurentians.
3. Municipal hospital in Manhattan that includes a psychiatric facility.

tantrums out there for the whole world to know about. "What are we going to do about this?"

"About what?" he says.

I am not going to act like our mother and blow my temper. At least, not right away. "This . . . this exposure," I say, because suddenly I don't know what to call it myself. "I don't think it's good for the kids."

My husband looks over his shoulder as if to assure himself there are no hidden cameras or reporters around. "We seem quite cozy here," he says. He has a quaint way of saying things in his German accent that makes it hard to get angry at him. It's as if you were to yell at someone in an ESL class who needs all the help he can get. I don't know why he calls up this tender tolerance in me when I'm just as much a foreigner as he is. "There is no need to get upset. Soon she will write another book and this one will be forgotten."

"Yeah, right. She was on the radio today talking away about Papi skiing topless in the Laurentians with all his French-Canadian girlfriends. Mami's going to hit the roof!"

"Your mother will hit the roof anyway," he says nonchalantly until he sees the look on my face. "But this is true," he says lamely, scratching his balding head, something he does when he's nervous that usually blunts the sharp edge of my anger. Tonight, it's not really anger I'm feeling. I'm out and out flabbergasted that he would say such a thing even if it is true, which it is. I know for a fact that before he read the book and had lines like that plopped into his mouth, he would never have said so of his own accord. He used to be more polite. I feel like my whole life is losing ground to fiction.

"I just won't have everyone criticizing the family," I say in a teary voice that goes dry on me before I can wring any sympathy from him. So off I go to the kitchen to fix the kids' lunches and settle my nerves. The last thing I want to do tonight is not be able to go to sleep and have to come out here and lie on the couch till all hours reading some stupid novel. I always was a reader, but now, whenever I open a book, even if it's something by someone dead, all I can do is shake my head and think, oh my god, I wonder what their family thought of this story?

I'm in there cutting up the bread into little space-food squares the way my third-grader likes his sandwich and leaving out mayonnaise the way my eighth grader likes hers when the phone rings and it's my other "fictionally victimized sister," or so she introduces herself in a grim voice. I can't say I go in for all this labeling but my two sisters are psychologists and that's the way they get a handle on things. Me, I just get mad.

"People have been coming up to me at work asking, so which one are you. My therapist says this is a kind of abuse!" She goes quiet a moment. "What are you doing? It sounds like you're hitting something."

"Just making the kids' lunches."

My sisters, I love them all, but sometimes they get on my nerves. This one is always seeing trauma and sadness. Around her, I purposely go shallow, hoping I'll get her to smile. "Oh, we'll survive," I say. Maybe talking to my husband has calmed me down.

"Speak for yourself," she says gloomily. "But I'll tell you one thing, I'm never going to talk to her again."

"Oh, come on," I say.

"I mean it. I'm glad this is all happening around my birthday. Because when she calls me, I'm just going to let her have it."

"I know," I say instead of pointing out that if she's not talking to our sister, she can't let her have it. "So how are things?" I say in a bright voice, hoping to get her talking about something happy. Why is it that with all my sisters I always feel like I'm the therapist?

"Well, actually, there is something else. But you've got to promise me that you're not going to tell her—"

"Hey, I'm not talking to her either," I lie. I'm not sure why. It's as if I'm caught up in some family melodrama that I don't necessarily like. "So what is it?"

A coy pause, and then a jubilant, "I'm pregnant."

"Ay-ay!!!" I cry out, and here comes my husband, rushing into the room, the paper still in his hand. "Good? Bad?" he mouths. Recently, he observed—one of his new insights—how it's hard to tell what's really going on in my family with so much overreaction. Anyhow, I tell him my sister is pregnant and he gets on the phone and says he is delighted. Delighted?! I grab the phone back, and we gab for half an hour, the book forgotten, all those fictional doubles sent packing, my sister remarking on all the errors our mother made with us that she is not going to make with her child, and I kind of defending our mother because actually, though I don't say so, I've repeated all those sins with my own kids—except the one with the nuns and that's probably because there are no Carmelite convents that I know of in Rockford, Illinois. My sister concludes with the reminder that I am not to breathe a word of this to you-know-who.

"It seems kind of mean," I even surprise myself by saying so. I guess I'm feeling expansive, like there are really only a few big things in this world, LOVE and DEATH and LITTLE BABIES. Forget fame and fortune and whether or not someone plagiarized you into a fictional character. "I think you should tell her."

"You promised!" she says with such fury that even our mother could take lessons from her.

"Hey, I'm not going to say a word, it's not that. But I think *you* should tell her. After all, she is going to be an aunt."

"I can't believe you're saying this! I'm going to be a mother!"

"But why not tell her?"

"I just don't want my baby to become fictional fodder."

I get this crazy picture in my head—a cartoon really more than a picture—of this tiny baby being put through a big roller and coming out the other end as one of those small books that reviewers like to call a *slim volume*. But I also kind of see my sister's point—it's not just the baby, but the rest of the story will probably find its way into that slim novel: single motherhood, artificial insemination, sperm brought up from the D.R. from an area of the country where hopefully there aren't many first cousins. Just thinking about it I get goosebumps up and down my arm.

"What are you doing? It sounds like you're crying."

"No, no, I'm so happy," I reassure her, and then she makes me swear on my own children, which makes me very uneasy, that I won't mention a word of this to our sister.

Well, I no sooner put the phone down and finish wrapping up the sandwiches and putting in an applesauce for the dieter and a jellybean cookie for the little Christian when the phone rings and it's you-know-who.

"What's going on?" she says all weepy like it just occurred to her that everyone isn't ecstatic over her being famous.

"What do you mean?" I say, because if I've learned one thing in this family it's you better not let on that anyone has gotten to you first with another version of the story.

And she tells me. Mami is going to sue her. Papi has to call her from a public phone. Our eldest sister has her husband say that she's not available. "And I just called Sandi, and she hung up on me." There is a wrenching sob, and though I myself was going to kill her six hours ago, all I want to do is ease that mournful sound. I keep remembering how when we first got to this country the only way she'd go to sleep was if I held her hand across the space between our beds and told her something I remembered from being back on the island.

"Hey," I say, putting the best face on this messy situation, "I bet there were a lot of people mad at Shakespeare, too, but aren't we all glad he wrote *Hamlet*?" I don't know why I'm saying this since I dropped out of college in part because I just couldn't pass the Renaissance. "But still," I go on, getting everyone's point of view in, "imagine how you'd feel if you were his mother."

"What do you mean? What's art going to mirror if it isn't life? Everybody, I mean everybody, writes out of his or her own experience!" And she's off into all the stuff I already heard her say on *Fresh Air*. But I let her say it. For one thing, my head is going a mile a minute, all that clunky, outdated emotional machinery from childhood that should have been replaced years ago with the trim, cutting-edge technology of feeling is chugging away, and nothing short of a handful of sleeping pills is going to shut it off. I might as well stay up on the phone instead of sitting in the living room shaking my head at some dead novelist.

"It really hurts, you know, that my family can't share this with me. I mean I haven't done anything wrong. I could have been an axe murderer. I could have gotten up on some roof in a shopping mall and mowed down a bunch of people."

I sure am glad it's me she's talking to and not one of the psychologist sisters.

"All I did was write a book," she wails.

"Everyone's feeling a little exposed, that's all."

"But it's fiction!" she starts in.

Oh yeah? I want to say. I don't care what it says on that page up front about any resemblance is entirely coincidental, you know when you spot yourself in some paragraph of description. "But it's fiction based on your own experience! Like all fiction," I add, quoting her from the radio. "I know, I know, what else are you going to write about?" But to myself, I'm thinking, why can't she write about axe murderers or law-firm scams or extraterrestrials and make a million and divide it four ways, which by the way is what the other sisters suggest she should do with this book since we provided the raw material.

"So you do understand, ay, it means so much you understand."

Oh dear, I'm thinking, if this gets out to the rest of the family! And before I know it I've opened one of the lunchboxes and I'm nibbling away on the space rations.

"Mamma, why are you eating my lunch?" It's my boy coming in to say good night. He has stopped in the doorway, hands on his hips, striking a righteous pose. He fancies himself part of The Force policing the galaxy. Catching me snacking is right up his alley.

"I'm talking to your auntie Yoyo," I say as if that's a reason to eat his lunch. Oh boy! Those little galactic-fighter eyes light up.

"I want to talk to Auntie Yoyo!" he cries out. I hand him the phone, but suddenly, the Milky Way's motor-mouth is totally stagestruck. All he can manage are little earthling grunts and murmurs. "Uh huh. Nah. Um um, yeah." His face is pink with terror and delight.

"Love ya, too," he whispers at the end and hands me the phone with such a radiant look on his face you'd think he'd gotten the baby Jesus Himself in his Easter basket.

"You got one fan here," I tell my sister.

"Only one?" she asks, straining for a light tone, but I can hear those tears just ready to rain down if I say the wrong thing.

It strikes me that what my sister wants is that look of adoration on every one of our faces. The best I can do is, "Well, you *are* a big hit with all the nieces and nephews." And then, I can't help myself, even if my own two precious babes are hanging in the bargain of my silence, I tell her that she's going to be a new aunt, that our sister is pregnant, and that she better not write about it or all my little sticks are going to fall, too.

"I have to pretend I don't know a thing?" She sounds so sad like she's just been kicked out of our gene pool or something. But I know what hurts her most is to be left out of a family story.

So, I tell her that I'm going to talk to the others because no matter what, we're sisters, and we're always going to be sisters, even though I was pissed as hell to hear her talking our stuff on *Fresh Air*, but I love her and that's the bottom line, and she's all subdued and listening and saying, well thanks, thanks, and it's like we're ten and nine again, our arms swinging in the dark as we hold on tight to each other's hands.

"Have you talked to your sister?" my mother wants to know, as if *my* sister is only related to me, not her. She's already gone off the phone twice to see who's on the other line. Mami, the gadget lover—that part the book got right. She's got every conceivable option on that phone of hers. I've teased her that if the extraterrestrials finally get through to planet Earth, it's going to be on her phone number.

"What sister?" I hedge, and then because I don't want to wimp out on my promise, I say, "She sends everyone her love." I don't know why I'm making up this stuff except I'm figuring that with a few touches here and there, surely we can get back together as a family.

"Humpf!" Mami scoffs. "Her love?! What does her love mean? She didn't even send me a Mother's Day card."

And I'm thinking, but you were going to sue her. What's she going to say? Dear Mami, happy Mother's Day from your plaintiff daughter. Or wait a minute, is the plaintiff the accused or the other way around? I should know with all that O.J. stuff[4] on TV all the time. "It probably just slipped her mind," I explain. "She's on the road a lot these days."

"Oh?" she says, curiosity peeking out from her voice like the toe of a lover's shoe under a bedskirt. "Where's she been? Your Tía Mirta saw her on live TV. Mirta says she looked terrible like maybe her conscience was bothering her. It was one of those programs where you can call in with a question, but your aunt couldn't get through. I tell you, I want my equal time. I want my chance to tell the world how she's always lied like the truth is just something you make up. Remember the time she ran away to the Carmelite convent and told them she was an orphan?"

For the first time in my life that I can remember my jaw drops of its own accord, not in some pantomined gesture of shock. I'm pacing up and down the little stretch of kitchen promising myself that I'm going to get one of those cordless phones so I can walk off steam while talking to my family. At the very least, get some of my housework done. "You're the one who used to drive us over there, Mami, don't you remember?"

"Why would I do something like that, mi'ja?[5] You can't visit Carmelites, silly. They take this vow of leaving the world and you can only talk to them in an emergency through a grate. But of course, if a little orphan girl is pounding on the door, they're going to open it. Thank God your cousin Rosita, who had joined not long before, recognized Yoyo right away and called me."

How can you argue with such good details? I start thinking that maybe my sister and I made up this memory of Mami threatening to dump us at the convent to make ourselves feel better about a mother suing a daughter. Anyhow, I want to hear the end of her crazy story. "So, what happened?"

"What happened? We pile in the car and go pick her up and bring her back and I'm ready to give her the spanking of her life but first I ask her why, why would she do something like this. Imagine, it's like giving her an invitation. So she says she was just missing Cousin Rosita so much, she slipped out of the playground to the grounds of the convent, knocked on the door, and told the head nun that she's an orphan come to see her only living family, Rosita García!" Now even Mami is laughing. "Can you believe it?"

And I'm shaking my head, no, no, because I don't know what to believe anymore except that everyone in our family is lying.

A few months pass, and things quiet down like my husband said they would. Mami drops her suit, though she's still not talking to Yoyo except through me, and poor Papi gets mugged while emptying his pocket change on the little metal shelf in a phone booth near his old office in the Bronx.[6] The other sisters exchange a couple of stiff birthday cards and calls with Yoyo, everything very cool like we're a New England family or something.

And week by week, the photos pour in that I've got to keep from the kids. They show a naked Sandi in profile from shoulder to living-color crotch, and on back in very neat handwriting like she's tidying up her act for this baby,

---

4. The 1995 murder trial of Orenthal James "O. J." Simpson (b. 1947), retired American football player and actor.
5. M'ija, mi'ja, or mija, a contraction of mi hija,

literally means "daughter" but is used colloquially to mean "girl."
6. A New York City borough north of Manhattan.

she writes, four weeks and two days, five weeks, and so on, and then in parenthesis, *Eyes have formed! Differentiation of fingers going on!* And then I turn
the photo over and stare and stare because it really takes an act of faith to
believe that a secret life is growing in that bikini-flat belly.

"And Yoyo doesn't know a thing about it," Sandi gloats over the phone.
My knees go weak beneath me so I have to go sit down in the living room.
Thank God for this cordless phone I got as an anniversary gift from my
husband although the beautiful gold pendant would have been more than
enough. But he says this phone might save him a heart attack from always
having to run into the kitchen to see if I'm yelling because I cut off my fingers or I'm just talking to my family.

Finally, about the twelfth week I get an irate call from Sandi. Some friend
of hers just called her from Florida and told her there is a story in *USA
Weekend* by Yoyo about a single mother. "You didn't say anything to her, did
you?" Sandi is breathing so heavy that I tell her to go sit down, to think of
the baby. But she won't be placated, and though I'd like to think of myself as
having more character, I take the easy way out. "Of course, I didn't tell her."

Soon as I hang up with her, I call Yoyo. I'm all set to say a few choice
things on her machine, since I haven't reached a live person at her house for
months. But she answers and is so obviously happy at hearing my voice that
it's as if someone let a few decibels out of my anger. Still, I'm mad enough to
practically yell at her that I really think she's purposely trying to piss off
everybody.

"What are you talking about?" she says in this truly shocked voice. I just
wish I could see her face because I can always tell from her eyes if she's
making up something.

"I mean writing about Sandi in this *USA Weekend* story!"

"Sandi?" She's rifling through her memory, I can hear it in her voice, as if
she were looking for something of mine in her drawer. And then she finds
it. "Oh, *that* story. What makes you think it's about Sandi?"

"There's a single mother in it, isn't there?"

"And that makes it about Sandi?!" There is the sound of laughter on the
phone, not real laughter but the kind of backslapping laughter that has a
dagger in its other hand. "First off, I'd have you know, Sandi isn't the only
single mother I know. And number two, for your information—"

There is something fearsome about Yoyo when she knows she is right.
She's not just going to tell you you're wrong. She's going to take it to the
Supreme Court.

"In actual fact, I wrote that story about two and a half years ago, no,
three, three years ago, that's right. I didn't have my new printer yet so I can
prove it."

"Okay, okay," I say.

"But let's explore this further."

Do we have to? I'm thinking. I've unfolded the ironing board so at least I
can get everything smoothed out on cloth if not in the family.

"Maybe Sandi got the idea of being a single mother from my story, you
think? I used to send you guys my stories back then, so she probably read it,
and said, Gee, that's a swell idea. I think I'm going to go kidnap a baby, too.
You think?"

"Sandi isn't kidnapping a baby. She's pregnant."

"Precisely. *My* single mother kidnaps her baby because she doesn't want to pass down her crazy family's genes to some poor kid. Now that part isn't fiction."

Laid out in front of me on the board is my husband's favorite blue and lavender striped shirt. I put down the iron. I button it up as tenderly as if he were inside it. What would happen if we couldn't imagine each other, I wonder. Maybe that's why crazies shoot people in shopping malls: all they see are aliens instead of mamis and papis and sisters and precious babies. "You're right," I admit. "I'm sorry." To make it up to her I fill her in on everything going on in the family, including the new baby just getting his full-fledged sex organs this week. Then I can't help myself. I've got to know. "So what happened to the woman who kidnapped her baby?"

There is a pause in which I can just imagine the look of delight on Yo's face at being asked. And I know what's coming as if I had peeked ahead in a thick book to the last page. "Read my story," she says.

It isn't until that real baby is born on a bright December day that the family gathers face to face at St. Luke's.[7] We pore over that little guy like we've got to pass a test on what he looks like if we want to keep him. He's a dark olive that Papi keeps saying is just a suntan until Sandi shuts him up by saying well the kinky hair must be a perm. "Dr. Puello screened the sperm," Mami assures him, and again one of my loony cartoons pops in my head. Some old guy in a sombrero with a droopy mustache is sieving sperm like he's separating egg whites into this bowl-like vagina.

Anyhow the aunties are delighted with their new nephew. I should say two of the aunts, because Yoyo isn't here. Even though Sandi later read the kidnapping story I sent her and felt pretty foolish, the grudge is on. I suppose Yo's absence is why I'm feeling blue even though a healthy baby's birth is right up there with True Love and Mami's guava flan on my scale of happiness. And something else, though I would never breathe this out loud, I feel bad that there's no father here. Call me old-fashioned, but it seems like a baby should have a *set* of parents. Look at my family. What would we do if we didn't have Papi to call us from a public phone when Mami sues us? Or when Papi disowns us, who but Mami is going to assure us that he'll get over it?

But even this considerable sadness melts away when I look into that honey-drop face, uncurl those little fists to convince him that he doesn't really have to fight the love that's pouring into him from his mamma and aunts. I know his genes are only half ours, but I've already traced every one of his features to some relation. When I put him back together again and try to figure out who he looks like as a whole, it just pops out of my mouth. "He looks like Yo's baby pictures, you know."

Sandi scowls into the baby blanket. "In the whites of his eyes, you mean?"

But Carla agrees, especially when the baby lets out a peal of angry crying, his little mouth opening so wide as if he doesn't know how to work it yet. "Same big mouth, see?" Carla points out.

We burst out laughing, and suddenly we can feel her absence in the room as if there were a caption above the bed, along with all those blue *It's-a-boy* balloons: *What is missing from this picture?*

---

7. St. Luke's Hospital, in upper Manhattan.

For the umpteenth time, I tell Sandi, "I think you should call her." Carla nods. Sandi bites her lip, but I can tell she is being swayed. Her eyes have this soft-boiled look as if the room were wallpapered with pictures of her beautiful baby. Suddenly, she cocks her head at us. "I can't believe you haven't told her!"

Both Carla and I look down to hide the guilty look in our eyes.

"I see, I see," she says. "No one in your family can keep a promise," she tells her little boy. As she picks up the phone, she adds, "I guess that includes me."

And then, I could kill Yoyo, because I can tell from the look on Sandi's face that she's getting that stupid machine that says to call Yoyo's agent. Sandi rolls her eyes, and as if on cue that baby starts to cry with the big mouth of his aunt.

"Ya, ya," she coos to the baby and then in this prepared voice you use for machines, she begins. "Yo! It's me, your *real* sister number two, and I know you know you've got a new nephew who everyone says looks like you, god forbid, but I personally think he looks like our handsome Tío Max on Mami's side, though if he turns out to be as big a womanizer, I'll cut off his baboodles, just kidding, just kidding, did you hear those lungs? He's got the cutest toes without a nail on the little toe which he gets from Papi, and you know what they say about why the Garcías don't have a little toenail—"

I take that baby from her because I can just tell she's settling into a long one. It's as if Sandi is filled with nine months' worth of news that she's going to deliver now that she's finished giving birth to her son. And she's talking to a machine, for heaven's sake! I suppose it's her one chance to say all she wants without someone in the family cutting in with their version of the story.

1997

---

# DAGOBERTO GILB
## b. 1950

Dagoberto Gilb was born in Los Angeles, California, to a Mexican mother and a father of German descent. "That's the future of this country," he said in a 2001 interview in *The Los Angeles Times*. "This kind of mestizaje is what we have, the culture we're creating." Gilb's parents divorced when he was a toddler, and he was raised by his mother. After high school, Gilb enrolled in junior college. In 1973, he earned a bachelor's degree from the University of California, Santa Barbara, with a double major in philosophy and religious studies, and in 1976 he earned a master's in religion from the same institution.

For 16 years, while writing in his free time, Gilb worked in high-rise construction as a journeyman carpenter and member of the United Brotherhood of Carpenters. Through the 1980s, he went back and forth between Los Angeles and El Paso, Texas. In El Paso, he met the fiction writer Raymond Carver, who offered to help him land a spot in the prestigious University of Iowa Writer's Workshop. Gilb disregarded the suggestion, unaware that admission was tantamount to entrance into what he came to call this country's literary "system."

In 1982, Gilb published a story in the *The Threepenny Review*. Soon after, his chapbook collection, *Winners on the Pass Line* (1985), became the first publication of Cinco Puntos Press. In 1988, Gilb received a Dobie-Paisano Fellowship from the Texas Institute of Letters. Four years later, he received a National Endowment for the Arts fellowship for creative writing.

His first book, the story collection *The Magic of Blood* (1993), published by the University of New Mexico Press, observes characters, as Annie Proulx put it, "in an American Southwest of bills and debts and being laid off, difficult bosses, color of skin, language games, and a hunger for work." The volume sold well and brought Gilb national recognition and literary prizes such as the Ernest Hemingway Foundation/ PEN Award. Since then, he has become a leading Latino voice, contributing fiction and essays to publications such as *The New Yorker, Harper's, The Nation, The Washington Post, The New York Times,* and *Texas Observer.* In the novel *The Last Known Residence of Mickey Acuña* (1994), Gilb explores the life of a drifter stuck in a border-town YMCA. *Woodcuts of Women* (2002), his best-selling story collection, is about men obsessed with women. In *Gritos* (2003), which was a National Book Critics Circle Award finalist, he collects a decade's worth of nonfiction about, among other topics, the writing life and the family and his journey from working construction to spending time with Al Gore. In his novel *The Flowers* (2008), Gilb offers a coming-of-age story as a riot—the Watts Riots, in 1965, an event he lived through—looms in the background. He is also the author of *Before the End, After the Beginning* (2011).

About his own status as a Tejano, Gilb said in the aforementioned interview: "It's hard to be a writer when you are treated as a foreigner, not really part of the American landscape." To fill a literary void and to counteract the "offensive ignorance of the huge national population" regarding *mexicano* life in Texas, Gilb edited *Hecho en Tejas: An Anthology of Texas-Mexican Literature* (2006).

Since 2009, Gilb has been writer-in-residence at the University of Houston, Victoria. He has also taught at myriad other institutions, including the University of Arizona and Vassar. He has received a Guggenheim Fellowship, a Whiting Writers' Award, and the PEN Southwest Book Award in Nonfiction, and has been a PEN/ Faulkner Award finalist.

Both of the Gilb stories included in this anthology are studies of class and male identity. "Look on the Bright Side" is a tragicomic tale of a working-class family in hard economic times, with the father trying to maintain dignity as he becomes homeless for lack of work. "Down in the West Texas Town" vividly presents the interactions, racial views, and drug taking of a group of construction workers.

# Look on the Bright Side

The way I see it, a man can have all the money in the world but if he can't keep his self-respect, he don't have shit. A man has to stand up for things even when it may not be very practical. A man can't have pride and give up his rights.

This is exactly what I told my wife when Mrs. Kevovian raised our rent illegally. I say illegally because, well aside from it being obviously unfriendly and greedy whenever a landlord or lady wants money above the exceptional amount she wanted when you moved in not so long ago, here in this enlightened city of Los Angeles it's against the law to raise it above a certain percentage and then only once every twelve months, which is often enough. Now the wife argued that since Mrs. Kevovian was a little ignorant, nasty, and hard to communicate with, we should have gone ahead and paid the increase— added up it was only sixty some-odd bones, a figure the landlady'd come up with getting the percentage right, but this time she tried to get it two months too early. My wife told me to pay it and not have the hassle. She knew me better than this. We'd already put up with the cucarachas[1] and rodents, I fixed the plumbing myself, and our back porch was screaming to become dust and probably would just when one of our little why nots—we have three of them—snuck onto it. People don't turn into dust on the way down, they splat first. One time I tried to explain this to Mrs. Kevovian, without success. You think I was going to pay more rent when I shouldn't have to?

My wife offered the check for the right amount to the landlady when she came to our door for her money and wouldn't take it. My wife tried to explain how there was a mistake, but when I got home from work the check was still on the mantle where it sat waiting. Should I have called her and talked it over? Not me. This was her problem and she could call. In the meantime, I could leave the money in the bank and feel that much richer for that much longer, and if she was so stupid I could leave it in the savings and let it earn interest. And the truth was that she was stupid enough, and stubborn, and mean. I'd talked to the other tenants, and I'd talked to tenants that'd left before us, so I wasn't at all surprised about the Pay or Quit notice we finally got. To me, it all seemed kind of fun. This lady wasn't nice, as God Himself would witness, and maybe, since I learned it would take about three months before we'd go to court, maybe we'd get three free months. We hadn't stopped talking about moving out since we unpacked.

You'd probably say that this is how things always go, and you'd probably be right. Yeah, about this same time I got laid off. I'd been laid off lots of times so it was no big deal, but the circumstances—well, the company I was working for went bankrupt and a couple of my paychecks bounced and it wasn't the best season of the year in what were not the best years for working people. Which could have really set me off, made me pretty unhappy, but that's not the kind of man I am. I believe in making whatever you have the right situation for you at the right moment for you. And look, besides the extra money from not paying rent, I was going to get a big tax return, and we also get unemployment compensation in this great country. It was a good time for a vacation, so I bunched the kids in the car with the old lady and drove to Baja.[2] I deserved it, we all did.

Like my wife said, I should have figured how things were when we crossed back to come home. I think we were in the slowest line on the border. Cars next to us would pull up and within minutes be at that red-light green-light signal. You know how it is when you pick the worst line to wait in. I was going nuts. A poor dude in front of us idled so long that his radiator overheated and he had to push the old heap forward by himself. My wife told me to settle down and wait because if we changed lanes then it would stop moving. I turned the ignition off then on again when we moved a spot. When we did get there I felt a lot better, cheerful even. There's no prettier place for a vacation than Baja and we really had a good time. I smiled forgivingly at the customs guy who looked as kind as Captain Stubing on the TV show "Love Boat."

"I'm American," I said, prepared like the sign told us to be. My wife said the same thing. I said, "The kids are American too. Though I haven't checked out the backseat for a while."

Captain Stubing didn't think that was very funny. "What do you have to declare?"

1. Cockroaches.
2. Baja California, Pacific peninsula in northwestern Mexico.

"Let's see. A six-pack of Bohemia beer. A blanket. Some shells we found. A couple holy pictures. Puppets for the kids. Well, two blankets."

"No other liquor? No fruits? Vegetables? No animal life?"

I shook my head to each of them.

"So what were you doing in Mexico?"

"Sleeping on the beach, swimming in the ocean. Eating the rich folks's lobster." It seemed like he didn't understand what I meant. "Vacation. We took a vacation."

"How long were you in Mexico?" He made himself comfortable on the stool outside his booth after he'd run a license plate check through the computer.

"Just a few days," I said, starting to lose my good humor.

"How many days?"

"You mean exactly?"

"Exactly."

"Five days. Six. Five nights and six days."

"Did you spend a lot of money in Mexico?"

I couldn't believe this, and someone else in a car behind us couldn't either because he blasted the horn. Captain Stubing made a mental note of him. "We spent some good money there. Not that much though. Why?" My wife grabbed my knee.

"Where exactly did you stay?"

"On the beach. Near Estero Beach."

"Don't you work?"

I looked at my wife. She was telling me to go along with it without saying so. "Of course I work."

"Why aren't you at work now?"

"Cuz I got laid off, man!"

"Did you do something wrong?"

"I said I got *laid off*, not *fired*!"

"What do you do?"

"Laborer!"

"What kind of laborer?"

"Construction!"

"And there's no other work? Where do you live?"

"No! Los Angeles!"

"Shouldn't you be looking for a job? Isn't that more important than taking a vacation?"

I was so hot I think my hair was turning red. I just glared at this guy.

"Are you receiving unemployment benefits?"

"Yeah I am."

"You're receiving unemployment and you took a vacation?"

"That's it! I ain't listening to this shit no more!"

"You watch your language, sir." He filled out a slip of paper and slid it under my windshield wiper. "Pull over there."

My wife was a little worried about the two smokes I never did and still had stashed in my wallet. She was wanting to tell me to take it easy as they went through the car, but that was hard for her because our oldest baby was crying. All I wanted to do was put in a complaint about that jerk to somebody higher up. As a matter of fact I wanted him fired, but anything to make him some trouble. I felt like they would've listened better if they hadn't found those four bottles of rum I was trying to sneak over. At that point I lost some confidence, though not my sense of being right. When this other customs man suggested that I might be detained further if I pressed the situation, I paid the penalty charges for the confiscated liquor and shut up. It wasn't worth a strip search, or finding out what kind of crime it was crossing the border with some B-grade marijuana.

·

Time passed back home and there was still nothing coming out of the union hall. There were a lot of men worried but at least I felt like I had the unpaid rent money to wait it out. I was fortunate to have a landlady like Mrs. Kevovian helping us through these bad times. She'd gotten a real smart lawyer for me too. He'd attached papers on his Unlawful Detainer to prove *my* case, which seemed so ridiculous that I called the city housing department just to make sure I couldn't be wrong about it all. I wasn't. I rested a lot easier without a rent payment, even took some guys out for some cold ones when I got the document with the official court date stamped on it, still more than a month away.

I really hadn't started out with any plan. But now that I was unemployed there were all these complications. I didn't have all the money it took to get into another place, and our rent, as much as it had been, was in comparison to lots still cheap, and rodents and roaches weren't that bad a problem to me. Still, I took a few ugly pictures like I was told to and had the city inspect the hazardous back porch and went to court on the assigned day hoping for something to ease our bills.

Her lawyer was Yassir Arafat without the bedsheet.[3] He wore this suit with a vest that was supposed to make him look cool, but I've seen enough Ziedler & Ziedler[4] commercials to recognize discount fashion. Mrs. Kevovian sat on that hard varnished bench with that wrinkled forehead of hers. Her daughter translated whatever she didn't understand when the lawyer discussed the process. I could hear every word even though there were all these other people because the lawyer's voice carried in the long white hall and polished floor of justice. He talked as confidently as a dude with a sharp blade.

"You're the defendant?" he asked five minutes before court was to be in session.

"That's me, and that's my wife," I pointed. "We're both defendants."

"I'm Mr. Villalobos, attorney representing the plaintiff."

"All right! Law school, huh? You did the people proud, eh? So how come you're working for the wrong side? That ain't a nice lady you're helping to evict us, man."

"You're the one who refuses to pay the rent."

"I'm disappointed in you, compa.[5] You should know I been trying to pay the rent. You think I should beg her to take it? She wants more money than she's supposed to get, and because I wanna pay her what's right, she's trying to throw us onto the streets."

---

3. For much of his life, the Palestinian leader Mohammed Abdel Rahman Abdel Raouf Arafat al-Qudwa al-Husseini (1929–2004), known as Yasser or Yassir or Yasir Arafat, wore and was as-sociated with the kaffiyeh, or traditional desert head scarf.
4. Zeidler & Zeidler Ltd., a men's clothing store.
5. Short for *compadre*: friend, pal.

Yassir Villalobos scowled over my defense papers while I gloated. I swore it was the first time he saw them or the ones he turned in. "Well, I'll do this. Reimburse Mrs. Kevovian for the back rent and I'll drop the charges."

"You'll drop the charges? Are you making a joke, man? You talk like I'm the one who done something wrong. I'm *here* now. Unless you wanna say drop what I owe her, something like that, then I won't let the judge see how you people tried to harrass me unlawfully."

Villalobos didn't like what I was saying, and he didn't like my attitude one bit.

"I'm the one who's right," I emphasized. "I know it, and you know it too." He was squirming mad. I figured he was worried about looking like a fool in the court. "Unless you offer me something better, I'd just as soon see what that judge has to say."

"There's no free rent," he said finally. "I'll just drop these charges and reserve you." He said that as an ultimatum, real pissed.

I smiled. "You think I can't wait another three months?"

That did it. He stiff-armed the swinging door and made arrangements with the court secretary, and my old lady and me picked the kids up from the babysitter's a lot earlier than we'd planned. The truth was I was relieved. I did have the money, but now that I'd been out of work so long it was getting close. If I didn't get some work soon we wouldn't have enough to pay it all. I'd been counting on that big income tax check, and when the government decided to take all of it except nine dollars and some change, what remained of a debt from some other year and the penalties it included, I was almost worried. I wasn't happy with the US Govt and I tried to explain to it on the phone how hard I worked and how it was only that I didn't understand those letters they sent me and couldn't they show some kindness to the unemployed, to a family that obviously hadn't planned to run with that tax advantage down to Costa Rica and hire bodyguards to watch over an estate. The thing is, it's no use being right when the US Govt thinks it's not wrong.

Fortunately, we still had Mrs. Kevovian as our landlady. I don't know how we'd have lived without her. Unemployment money covers things when you don't have to pay rent. And I didn't want to for as long as possible. The business agent at the union hall said there was supposed to be a lot of work breaking soon, but in the meantime I told everyone in our home who talked and didn't crawl to lay low and not answer any doors to strangers with summonses. My wife didn't like peeking around corners when she walked the oldest to school, though the oldest liked it a mess. We waited and waited but nobody came. Instead it got nailed to the front door very impolitely.

So another few months had passed and what fool would complain about that? Not this one. Still, I wanted justice. I wanted The Law to hand down fair punishment to these evil people who were conspiring to take away my family's home. Man, I wanted that judge to be so pissed that he'd pound that gavel and it'd ring in my ears like a Vegas jackpot. I didn't want to pay any money back. And not because I didn't have the money, or I didn't have a job, or that pretty soon they'd be cutting off my unemployment. I'm not denying their influence on my thinking, but mostly it was the principle of the thing. It seemed to me if I had so much to lose for being wrong, I should have something equal to win for being right.

"There's no free rent," Villalobos told me again five minutes before we were supposed to swing through those doors and please rise. "You don't have the money, do you?"

"Of course I have the money. But I don't see why I should settle this with you now and get nothing out of it. Seems like I had to go outa my way to come down here. It ain't easy finding a babysitter for our kids, who you wanna throw on the streets, and we didn't, and we had to pay that expensive parking across the street. This has been a mess of trouble for me to go, sure, I'll pay what I owe without the mistaken rent increase, no problem."

"The judge isn't going to offer you free rent."

"I'd rather hear what he has to say."

Villalobos was some brother, but I guess that's what happens with some education and a couple of cheap suits and ties. I swore right then that if I ever worked again I wasn't paying for my kids' college education.

The judge turned out to be a sister whose people hadn't gotten much justice either and that gave me hope. And I was real pleased we were the first case because the kids were fidgeting like crazy and my wife was miserable trying to keep them settled down. I wanted the judge to see what a big happy family we were so I brought them right up to our assigned "defendant" table.

"I think it would be much easier if your wife took your children out to the corridor," the judge told me.

"She's one of the named defendants, your honor."

"I'm sure you can represent your case adequately without the baby crying in your wife's arms."

"Yes ma'am, your honor."

The first witness for the plaintiff was this black guy who looked like they pulled a bottle away from the night before, who claimed to have come by my place to serve me all these times but I wouldn't answer the door. The sleaze was all lie up until when he said he attached it to my door, which was a generous exaggeration. Then Mrs. Kevovian took the witness stand. Villalobos asked her a couple of unimportant questions, and then I got to ask questions. I've watched enough lawyer shows and I was ready.

I heard the gavel but it didn't tinkle like a line of cherries.

"You can state your case in the witness stand at the proper moment," the judge said.

"But your honor, I just wanna show how this landlady . . ."

"You don't have to try your case through this witness."

"Yes ma'am, your honor."

So when that moment came all I could do was show her those polaroids of how bad things got and tell her about roaches and rats and fire hazards and answer oh yes, your honor, I've been putting that money away, something which concerned the judge more than anything else did.

I suppose that's the way of swift justice. Back at home, my wife, pessimistic as always, started packing the valuable stuff into the best boxes. She couldn't believe that anything good was going to come from the verdict in the mail. The business agent at the hall was still telling us about all the work about to break any day now, but I went ahead and started reading the help wanted ads in the newspaper.

A couple of weeks later the judgment came in an envelope. We won. The judge figured up all the debt and then cut it by twenty percent. Victory is sweet, probably, when there's a lot of coins clinking around the pants' pockets, but I couldn't let up. Now that I was proven right I figured we could do some serious negotiating over payment. A little now and a little later and a little bit now and again. That's what I'd offer when Mrs. Kevovian came for the money, which she was supposed to do the next night by 5 p.m., according to the legal document. "The money to be collected by the usual procedure," were the words, which meant Mrs. Kevovian was supposed to knock on the door and, knowing her, at five o'clock exactly.

Maybe I was a tiny bit worried. What if she wouldn't take anything less than all of it? Then I'd threaten to give her nothing and to disappear into the mounds of other uncollected debts. Mrs. Kevovian needed this money, I knew that. Better all of it over a long period than none of it over a longer one, right? That's what I'd tell her, and I'd be standing there with my self-confidence more muscled-up than ever.

Except she never came. There was no knock on the door. A touch nervous, I started calling lawyers. I had a stack of junk-mail letters from all these legal experts advising me that for a small fee they'd help me with my eviction procedure. None of them seemed to understand my problem over the phone, though maybe if I came by their office. One of them did seem to catch enough though. He said if the money wasn't collected by that time then the plaintiff had the right to reclaim the premises. Actually the lawyer didn't say that, the judgment paper did, and I'd read it to him over the phone. All the lawyer said was, "The marshall will physically evict you in ten days." He didn't charge a fee for the information.

We had a garage sale. You know, miscellaneous things, things easy to replace, that you could buy anywhere when the time was right again, like beds and lamps and furniture. We stashed the valuables in the trunk of the car—a perfect fit—and Greyhound was having a special sale, which made it an ideal moment for a visit to the abuelitos back home, who hadn't been able to see their grandkids and daughter in such a long time. You have to look on the bright side. I wouldn't have to pay any of that money back, and there was the chance to start a new career, just like they say, and I'd been finding lots of opportunities from reading the newspaper. Probably any day I'd be going back to work at one of those jobs about to break. Meanwhile, we left a mattress in the apartment for me to sleep on so I could have the place until a marshal beat on the door. Or soon I'd send back for the family from a house with a front and backyard I promised I'd find and rent. However it worked out. Or there was always the car with that big backseat.

·

One of those jobs I read about in the want ads was as a painter for the city. I applied, listed all this made-up experience I had, but I still had to pass some test. So I went down to the library to look over one of those books on the subject. I guess I didn't think much about the hours libraries keep, and I guess I was a few hours early, and so I took a seat next to this pile of newspapers on this cement bench not that far from the front doors. The bench smelled like piss, but since I was feeling pretty open-minded about things I didn't let it bother me. I wanted to enjoy all the scenery, which was nice for the big city, with all the trees and dewy grass, though the other early risers weren't so involved with the love of nature. One guy not so far away was rolling from one side of his body to the other, back and forth like that, from under a tree. He just went on and on. This other man, or maybe woman—wearing a sweater on top that was too baggy to make chest impressions on and another sweater below that, wrapped around like a skirt, and pants under that, cords, and unisex homemade sandals made out of old tennis shoes and leather, and finally, on the head, long braided hair which wasn't braided too good—this person was foraging off the cement path, digging through the trash for something. I thought aluminum too but there were about five empty beer cans nearby and the person kicked those away. It was something that this person knew by smell, because that's how he or she tested whether it was the right thing or not. I figured this was someone to keep my eye on.

Then without warning came a monster howl, and those pigeons bundled-up on the lawn scattered to the trees. I swore somebody took a shot at me. "Traitor! You can't get away with it!" Those were the words I got out of the tail end of the loud speech from this dude who came out of nowhere, who looked pretty normal, hip even if it weren't for the clothes. He had one of those great, long graying beards and hair, like some wise man, some Einstein.[6] I was sure a photographer would be along to take his picture if they hadn't already. You know how Indians and winos make the most interesting photographs. His clothes were bad though, took away from his cool. Like he'd done caca and spilled his spaghetti and rolled around in the slime for a lot of years since mama'd washed a bagful of the dirties. The guy really had some voice, and just when it seemed like he'd settled back into a stroll like anyone else, just when those pigeons trickled back down onto the lawn into a coo-cooing lump, he cut loose again. It was pretty hard to understand, even with his volume so high, but I figured it out to be about patriotism, justice, and fidelity.

"That guy's gone," John said when he came up to me with a bag of groceries he dropped next to me. He'd told me his name right off. "John. John. The name's John, they call me John." He pulled out a loaf of white bread and started tearing up the slices into big and little chunks and throwing them onto the grass. The pigeons picked up on this quick. "Look at 'em, they act like they ain't eaten in weeks, they're eatin like vultures, like they're starvin, like vultures, good thing I bought three loafs of bread, they're so hungry, but they'll calm down, they'll calm down after they eat some." John was blond and could almost claim to have a perm if you'd asked me. He'd shaven some days ago so the stubble on his face wasn't so bad. He'd never have much of a beard anyway. "They can't get enough, look at 'em, look at 'em, good thing I bought three loafs, I usually buy two." He moved like he talked—nervously, in jerks, and without pausing—and, when someone passed by, his conversation didn't break up. "Hey good morning, got any spare change for some food? No? So how ya gonna get to Heaven?" A man in a business suit turned his head with a smile, but didn't change direction. "I'll bury you deeper in Hell then, I'll dig ya deeper!" John went back to feeding the birds, who couldn't get enough. "That's how ya gotta talk to 'em," he told me. "Ya gotta talk to 'em like that and like ya can back it up, like ya can back it up."

6. Albert Einstein, German-born American physicist (1879–1955) often photographed with long, wild hair.

I sort of got to liking John. He reminded me of a hippie, and it was sort of nice to see hippies again. He had his problems, of course, and he told me about them too, about how a dude at the hotel he stayed at kept his SSI check, how he called the police but they wouldn't pay attention, that his hotel was just a hangout for winos and hypes and pimps and he was gonna move out, turn that guy in and go to court and testify or maybe he'd get a gun and blow the fucker away, surprise him. He had those kind of troubles but seemed pretty intelligent otherwise to me. Even if he was a little wired, he wasn't like the guy who was still rolling around under the tree or the one screaming at the top of his lungs.

While we both sat at the bench watching those pigeons clean up what became only visible to them in the grass, one of the things John said before he took off was this: "Animals are good people. They're not like people, people are no good, they don't care about nobody. People won't do nothing for ya. That's the age we live in, that's how it is. Hitler had that plan.[7] I think it was Hitler, maybe it was somebody else, it coulda been somebody else." We were both staring at this pigeon with only one foot, the other foot being a balled-up red stump, hopping around, pecking at the lawn. "I didn't think much of him gettin rid of the cripples and the mentals and the old people. That was no good, that was no good. It musta been Hitler, or Preacher Jobe. It was him, or it musta been somebody else I heard. Who was I thinkin of? Hey you got any change? How ya gonna get to Heaven? I wish I could remember who it was I was thinkin of."

I sure didn't know, but I promised John that if I thought of it, or if something else came up, I'd look him up at the address he gave me and filed in my pocket. I had to show him a couple of times it was still there. I was getting a little tired from such a long morning already, and I wished that library would hurry up and open so I could study for the test. I didn't have the slightest idea what they could ask me on a test for painting either. But then jobs at the hall were bound to break and probably I wouldn't have to worry too much anyway.

I was really sleepy by now, and I was getting used to the bench, even when I did catch that whiff of piss. I leaned back and closed the tired eyes and it wasn't so bad. I thought I'd give it a try—you know, why not?—and I scooted over and nuzzled my head into that stack of newspapers and tucked my legs into my chest. I shut them good this time and yawned. I didn't see why I should fight it, and it was just until the library opened.

1993

## Down in the West Texas Town

The sun was sucking up the thin juices of this desert earth until a lazy effluvium floated above the motionless river named the Rio Grande, sucking until the naked mountains named the Franklins seemed to scream out in

---

7. Adolf Hitler (1889–1945), Austrian-born founder of Nazism and leader of Germany, planned to conquer the world and purify it by re-moving "undesirables." "The Final Solution" was his plan to exterminate the Jewish people.

silence, sucking until the back side of the man named Danny had become a cracking hide. The sun burned; the heat was all, consumed all—even the whacks of a twenty-eight ounce framing hammer swatting a sixteen penny nail one time two times and three through the ridge board and into the peak end of a rafter, even the rippling buzz of an electric saw chewing through woodflesh, even they fell short of cutting through this insatiable heat.

"Alfuckinmost!" the Texan was yelling at no one in particular.

Danny was dropping his hammer back into the sling at his side and was slipping off a red bandana he had tied around his forehead to wipe away the sweat that still clung to his face. He'd nailed his last two-by into this skeleton roof; the half-inch sheeting was all that was left and Peppy, who preferred the English mispronunciation of the Spanish, was pulling that up, though not without a strain and a gripe. Danny didn't move to help him. He liked this moment too much, liked standing there, watching, his arms looped around rafters, his boots bent over joist. He liked it because it felt dangerous but safe, and being closer to the sun, to the heat, being still in it, quieted something within himself.

At the other end of the roof, not too far from where Peppy began tacking in the plywood, the Texan unhooked his bags and threw them below into the dirt—it was breaktime.

"All right!" Peppy wailed, fidgeting with happiness. "It's time to go home!"

"You been fuckin home all day, Peppy!" moaned the Texan. "The resta us are jus gonna cool down some. You can stay up here, maybe work more on your suntan."

"Pinche culero!"[1] Peppy laughed.

Danny climbed down where he was and walked around to the shady area off to a side of this house they were framing and headed for the five-gallon water jug. He waited for Nigger, who got his name because he was so prieto, so dark, to get his fill of water as it trickled down from a spout and into his open mouth. Impatient, Danny grabbed a coke bottle that was lying nearby, lifted the lid of the cooler and listened to it bubble full after he submerged it into the icy water.

"I can do better than that," Nigger boasted, and he lifted the cooler like it was an over-sized mug and drank from the rim while water splashed and drooled down his face and chest and into the dirt.

"Git your face outa that water!" the Texan yelled. "God only knows what kinda things been sloppin between those lips, and *shit*, you don't *never* brush your teeth!"

Danny joined the Texan and Peppy. Then Nigger came and sat, making it a circle.

"Ernie's got some really good stuff," Peppy was saying to the Texan. "I mean really good, ese.[2] Dark brown. It gets you really high. . . . Just a little bit"—he took a pinch of sandy brown dirt from the circle's middle—"just about this much"—about an eye drop full in the palm of his other hand—"and about five of water"—he pinched up some more of the dirt—"like this"—and mixed it with what was already lining the wrinkles of his dark, chapped palm—"and you get off real good."

1. Fucking asshole.
2. *Ese* is a Chicano expression meaning dude,    guy, man, as in *Órale, ése* (hey, man).

Peppy sat there in the silence, growing big with the thought that he'd had it, that he could tell about it now, could draw interest in it, growing yearnful enough that a few rays of wishfulness radiated from his smirk and warmed up the shady area they sat under.

Danny took a couple more cold swallows from his bottle of water. The water tasted good, he thought. It was nice to be away from the heat too, to feel cool inside. Sometimes it was better to avoid the heat. Sometimes it felt very good.

"It was *so* good," Peppy went on, "that Ernie had to cut it down because these dudes OD'd on it. But even cut you can get off like. . . ."

"Quit talking about that," Nigger whined plaintively, stretched out on a dusty patch of desert. "It makes me feel sick."

"Well, here," replied Peppy, sprinkling the dirt over Nigger's chest. "Stick this shit in your arm!" He cackled at Nigger and looked over at the Texan, who grinned unenthusiastically. "You know," he added, still giggling, "one time Nigger bought a half of dirt. Dark brown dirt, just a little darker than this." Another handful from the inner circle, only a little wet.

Nigger rolled his head.

"How'd that happen?" the Texan asked Nigger. "Didn't you even look at it?"

"No," he muttered.

"Why the fuck not?"

"I just didn't."

The Texan's wince was a blend of disgust and understanding.

"Let's hump this bullshit. It's only gittin hotter."

Danny and Peppy were squeezed between sticks of lumber and beer cans and electrical cords in back of Texan's dented up '62 Chevy pick-up. They'd finished the job and were headed out in the direction of the place the Texan called home.

Peppy, who liked to complain whenever possible, fumbled for a comfortable seat in the back of the pick-up and grumbled to himself, until finally he bitched out loud. "That gabacho is a real judío."[3]

"Whadaya mean?" Danny chuckled.

"The fucker's only gonna pay us sixteen dollars."

"He told you that?" Danny expected low wages—it was hard to get a job, and he had trouble keeping them—but not this low.

"That's what he says, ese." Peppy stood and banged arrogantly on the back window and then leaned himself around to the driver's window and barked about something to the Texan.

"That sure isn't much, man. You sure?"

"Well . . . he's gonna get us something else too."

Danny understood. He'd ask for his payment in coin.

They turned off Dyer Street and onto another street. Peppy yelled at the Texan and pointed to an auto-parts store, and the Texan skidded up against the curb on the street opposite it. Peppy hopped out of the car anxiously, with a belligerent smirk. Danny waited on the business alone in the back; the Texan and Nigger, both smoking cigarettes in the front seat, quietly lis-

---

3. That gringo is a real Jew.

tened to a country music station until suddenly Nigger opened his door and puked on the curb—about three retching convulsions. Moments passed, then Peppy came scampering into the street from the parts store in his way, a kind of flat-footed, short-stepped, stiff-legged, stooped-over prance. Nigger, his door locked open in wait, shoved his head into the gutter again.

Peppy kept coming and as he just about reached the Texan's door, he threw his feet high in the air toward it and farted. "God*damn*, you're a disgustin mexikin!" the Texan yelped sincerely. Giggling, Peppy dashed around the front of the truck to Nigger's open door. "Here, hold this," he said, handing him the brown paper bag from the store jauntily, unconcerned about Nigger's condition. Peppy pulled out a bright blue bandana from his pocket and snatched back the paper bag from Nigger, whose face was wrenched with anticipation and sickness, then joining bag to rag, looked around nervously, but also with that smirk, and let the hissing within the bag soak the rag throughout. The Texan barked out something from the driver's side, and Peppy sneered with a chuckling contempt. Then he mashed his face into the rag and wheezed in the fumes. When Peppy'd finished, Nigger imitated Peppy's performance. They all drove off for a bar and few beers.

They bounced into the front yard of the Texan's rented house about five pitchers and a dozen games of pool later. Driving into his front yard was not a show of disrespect; the curb was recessed just for this. And the yard—the rocky dirt lot with large chunks of gravel driven in here and left undisturbed there, keeping the dirt turned mud after a rain from being an undriveable slop—the yard seemed more suited to the days when horses were hitched to a post and boots were scraped on a mud-sling before vittles. The house, the shack, was a simple job—a narrow rectangle with a left-to-right lean-to roof, the paint on the wood-siding so ancient that it made it hard to guess what the faded rust color once really was.

Inside it was cramped, the swap-meet furnishings stuffed or crammed into a corner or against a wall, and the remaining path through it cluttered with baby toys and needs. The three non-belongers took a seat after they said their hellos to the Texan's old lady, who was spoon-feeding her baby boy. Texan was already on the phone.

"Do you think you could do another whole for forty?" he asked with abject concern, sort of squinting down at the colorless telephone dial and speaking with a calm determination. "I can't do it all myself. Could you do half? . . . No, I'm ten dollars short. . . ."—the Texan seemed emaciated or anemic, his eyes a droopy and saddened blue-green—". . . Okay. Orale." He hung up the phone dispassionately. He kept a distant gaze in those eyes, a look of distant time and place.

"So wha'd Ernie say?" Nigger wanted to know.

"He's gonna call back."

"Another whole?" The three of them had agreed to divide up a whole and a half. Danny had to sit it out—he had to resist.

"He's gonna see if he can do a half."

Peppy and Nigger sat nervously. The Texan's old lady sat wordlessly at the kitchen table, with her legs crossed, her baby fed. She never said much, and when she did say something it took the form of a private conversation that only she and the Texan could make absolute sense of.

The Texan paced evenly, in a way that didn't resemble pacing exactly, but which nonetheless was. The baby, who had just learned to walk, danced across a dingy cord rug from one man to another until one would pick him up or tease him or make a ridiculous face which would convince the baby to momentarily stay.

The heat hung in the room. Danny was uncomfortable. He felt parched, like his flesh was a tight fitting jacket. He felt dizzy, felt like he was still up on that roof pounding nails.

"Anyone ready for another beer?" the Texan asked, looking inside the refrigerator. "There's only three, but maybe if we all spit a mouthful Peppy'll get a glass." He laughed and took out three cans of beer. Then he got out a glass from the cupboard and put a share of each can into it until it was full. The phone rang.

The Texan listened, grunting his presence to the other end of the line. "I'll be back," he said dropping the receiver hard, and before the jarred bell inside the telephone had stilled, the screen door slammed once and again on a rebound and the Texan was opening the door of his pick-up.

"Is there mota?"[4] Peppy asked the Texan's old lady.

"On top of the television there should be a tray with some."

Nigger played with the baby. He played affectionately and the baby squealed with happiness.

Peppy and Danny shared a joint. Nigger didn't want any. Neither did the Texan's old lady.

"You don't like chiva?" Nigger asked Danny. Nigger was subtle about it. If Peppy would have asked, which he had already a couple of times, it would have been why can't you do some heroin with us, ese? You're a man, aren't you? You can handle it, can't you?

"I don't do it."

"You never do it?"

"I already been in the joint for a while."

Nigger considered that. "You shouldn't mess with it no more, dude."

"You don't like it no more?"

"Shit yeah I like it. It's just expensive. A dude shouldn't never get started, you know?"

"How long you been into it?"

"A few years. It's that I'm used to putting it in my vein." He paused, unhappily. "It just fucks you up too much. It fucks everything up too much." He thought this over. "But it feels good." And he no longer seemed unhappy.

Danny let the heat take him over. He let it lift him, send him back to the roof, closer to the sun. It was so hot that he could barely stand it. He could barely stand it.

The air snapped as the Texan burst through the door hurrying to the kitchen table where the gleaming silver object was dropped. Peppy and Nigger flung themselves by him to be by it. Danny's heart pumped thunderously. He felt himself backing away, then approaching, awed, fascinated,

4. Marijuana.

scared, tempted. His heart raged. He saw the room through a dizziness which tested his equilibrium. He tried to watch, he wanted to watch, but for him it was as dangerous as staring at that sun.

Nigger and Peppy waited. The Texan organized. A glass of water appeared upon the table. Then the foil was unwrapped, and a soup spoon received brownish dust.

"It looks good, man," Peppy said more seriously than necessary as he eye-dropped the water into the spoon.

"Just git it in there!" the Texan sniffed irritably.

The baby played behind Danny. The Texan's old lady stood near the men, vibrating as imperceptibly as a rattler's tongue. Danny's heart pounded on. He considered: he felt an unmistakable rush. The very air resonated.

Peppy struck a kitchen match against the box it came in and guided its sulphur smelling flame to the burner on the stove.

"Willya quit the fuckin around!" screeched the Texan. "Light the damn thing!" He was waiting, prepared, a bandana tied still loosely around his bicep.

"I can't get it, ese. It won't light."

"Let me see them matches," he said more calmly, but then exploding— "son of a *bitch!*" He snatched the matches away from Peppy, lighting one match then a second. The burner came on, its tiny choreographed flames rolling into a circle, and the mixture was readied.

The Texan sucked the juice up into the syringe and put out his arm. His face was twisted in nervous anticipation. His arm reached out starvingly, angrily, and his eyes took aim. The needle roamed around a purplish vein that swelled up, stalking it muscularly. And then it struck, and the syringe purled toward emptiness. The Texan responded as in reflex: his eyelids cascaded shut, tranquility flooded his desert baked face.

Serene, he yanked the bandanna from his arm and walked toward Danny. "Let's go check on that other job," he said.

"The other job?"

"A remodel on the eastside."

"Vámonos pues."[5]

He threw a glance at his old lady which said see you in a while. Danny followed him out the screen door while Peppy and Nigger took their turns. The baby cried to go with his daddy but the screen door slammed and the Texan's old lady latched it to the door jamb and consoled the child. The two of them watched the Texan and Danny drive away.

Danny had the window down on his side of the truck. He let the cool air pour in and dry the perspiration that had beaded up on his forehead and around his scalp. Relieved, he relaxed his arm on the window's frame, but it was burning hot, as hot as the noon sun, so he quickly took it away, though not before he let out a little yip of pain.

The Texan shook his head sympathetically. "I hate this fuckin heat. I hate to do anything in this fuckin heat."

But Danny liked the heat. He preferred the heat. Danny needed the heat.

He rolled his window up, telling the Texan that it was to keep himself from burning his arm again.

1993

5. Let's go, then.

# CARLOS M. N. EIRE
## b. 1951

Born in Cuba, Carlos M. N. Eire is a child of the Cuban Revolution. At age 11, his parents sent him away from the island, with 14,000 other Cuban children, in an airlift that brought him to Florida. Now the T. Lawrason Riggs Professor of History and Religious Studies at Yale University, he has written several scholarly books, among them *War against the Idols: The Reformation of Worship from Erasmus to Calvin* (1986); *From Madrid to Purgatory: The Art and Craft of Dying in Sixteenth-Century Spain* (1995), which address the religious, intellectual, and social upheaval in Europe as the Enlightenment swept the continent; and *A Very Brief History of Eternity* (2009), a philosophical and historical disquisition on the concept of eternity in Western culture. Eire had always told himself that the revolution he knew firsthand was too close for him to write about objectively.

In 2000, Eire's son turned 11. Elián González, a six-year-old Cuban boy, was rescued from the Florida sea and placed with his relatives in the United States, but then was sent back to Cuba by the U.S. government to be with his biological father. These events prompted Eire to write *Waiting for Snow in Havana: Confessions of a Cuban Boy* (2003), which depicts his life as a child in Cuba in the early days of the Castro revolution, as well as incidents from his childhood and adolescence in the United States, where he spent more than three years in refugee camps and foster homes. Eire wrote this factual account, "my first book without footnotes," as a novel, but his publisher released it as memoir, and *Waiting for Snow in Havana* won the National Book Award in nonfiction. The chapters included here present his father, an eccentric judge who believes that in a previous lifetime he was Louis XVI of France; his mother, who is crippled from polio; his brothers, one of whom will flee Cuba with him; and other people from the world of his childhood. Eire moves backward and forward in time, connecting incidents such as his childish theft of toy soldiers and his later resistance to a bully. When the tropical peace of his Havana neighborhood is shattered, Eire writes, "the world changed while I slept."

---

## FROM WAITING FOR SNOW IN HAVANA

### 1

### Uno

The world changed while I slept, and much to my surprise, no one had consulted me. That's how it would always be from that day forward. Of course, that's the way it had been all along. I just didn't know it until that morning. Surprise upon surprise: some good, some evil, most somewhere in between. And always without my consent.

I was barely eight years old, and I had spent hours dreaming of childish things, as children do. My father, who vividly remembered his prior incarnation as King Louis XVI of France, probably dreamt of costume balls, mobs, and guillotines.[1] My mother, who had no memory of having been Marie Antoi-

---

1. Louis XVI (1754–1793) reigned 1774–92 and was guillotined during the French Revolution.

nette,[2] couldn't have shared in his dreams. Maybe she dreamt of hibiscus blossoms and fine silk. Maybe she dreamt of angels, as she always encouraged me to do. "*Sueña con los angelitos*," she would say: Dream of little angels. The fact that they were little meant they were too cute to be fallen angels.

Devils can never be cute.

The tropical sun knifed through the gaps in the wooden shutters, as always, extending in narrow shafts of light above my bed, revealing entire galaxies of swirling dust specks. I stared at the dust, as always, rapt. I don't remember getting out of bed. But I do remember walking into my parents' bedroom. Their shutters were open and the room was flooded with light. As always, my father was putting on his trousers over his shoes. He always put on his socks and shoes first, and then his trousers. For years I tried to duplicate that nearly magical feat, with little success. The cuffs of my pants would always get stuck on my shoes and no amount of tugging could free them. More than once I risked an eternity in hell and spit out swear words. I had no idea that if your pants are baggy enough, you can slide them over anything, even snowshoes. All I knew then was that I couldn't be like my father.

As he slid his baggy trousers over his brown wingtip shoes, effortlessly, Louis XVI broke the news to me: "Batista[3] is gone. He flew out of Havana early this morning. It looks like the rebels have won."

"You lie," I said.

"No, I swear, it's true," he replied.

Marie Antoinette, my mother, assured me it was true as she applied lipstick, seated at her vanity table. It was a beautiful piece of mahogany furniture with three mirrors: one flat against the wall and two on either side of that, hinged so that their angles could be changed at will. I used to turn the side mirrors so they would face each other and create infinite regressions of one another. Sometimes I would peer in and plunge into infinity.

"You'd better stay indoors today," my mother said. "God knows what could happen. Don't even stick your head out the door." Maybe she, too, had dreamt of guillotines after all? Or maybe it was just sensible, motherly advice. Perhaps she knew that the heads of the elites don't usually fare well on the street when revolutions triumph, not even when the heads belong to children.

That day was the first of January 1959.

The night before, we had all gone to a wedding at a church in the heart of old Havana. On the way home, we had the streets to ourselves. Not another moving car in sight. Not a soul on the Malecón, the broad avenue along the waterfront. Not even a lone prostitute. Louis XVI and Marie Antoinette kept talking about the eerie emptiness of the city. Havana was much too quiet for a New Year's Eve.

I can't remember what my older brother, Tony, was doing that morning or for the rest of the day. Maybe he was wrapping lizards in thin copper wire and hooking them up to our Lionel train transformer. He liked to electrocute them. He liked it a lot. He was also fond of saying: "Shock therapy, ha! That should cure them of their lizard delusion." I don't want to remember what my adopted brother, Ernesto, was doing. Probably something more monstrous than electrocuting lizards.

2. Wife of Louis XVI (1755–1793), guillotined nine months after her husband.　3. Fulgencio Batista y Zaldívar (1901–1973), Cuban soldier; president of Cuba 1940–44, 1952–59.

My older brother and my adopted brother had both been Bourbon princes[4] in a former life. My adopted brother had been the Dauphin, the heir to the French throne. My father had recognized him on the street one day, selling lottery tickets, and brought him to our house immediately. I was the outsider. I alone was not a former Bourbon. My father wouldn't tell me who I had been. "You're not ready to hear it," he would say. "But you were very special."

My father's sister, Lucía, who lived with us, spent that day being as invisible as she always was. She, too, had once been a Bourbon princess. But now, in this life, she was a spinster: a lady of leisure with plenty of time on her hands and no friends at all. She had been protected so thoroughly from the corrupt culture of Cuba and the advances of the young men who reeked of it as to have been left stranded, high and dry, on the lonely island that was our house. Our island within the island. Our safe haven from poor taste and all unseemly acts, such as dancing to drumbeats. She had lived her entire life as a grown woman in the company of her mother and her maiden aunt, who, like her, had remained a virgin without vows. When her mother and aunt died, she moved to a room at the rear of our house and hardly ever emerged. Whether she had any desires, I'll never know. She seemed not to have any. I don't remember her expressing any opinion that day on the ouster of Batista and the triumph of Fidel Castro and his rebels. But a few days later she did say that those men who came down from the mountains needed haircuts and a shave.

Our maid worked for us that day, as always. Her name was Inocencia, and her skin was a purple shade of black. She cooked, cleaned the house, and did the laundry. She was always there. She seemed to have no family of her own. She lived in a room that was attached to the rear of the house but had no door leading directly into it. To enter our house she had to exit her small room and walk a few steps across the patio and through the backdoor, which led to the kitchen. She had a small bathroom of her own too, which I sometimes used when I was playing outdoors.

Once, long before that day when the world changed, I opened the door to that bathroom and found her standing inside, naked. I still remember her shriek, and my shock. I stood there frozen, a child of four, staring at her mountainous African breasts. A few days later, at the market with my mother, I pointed to a shelf full of eggplants and shouted *"Tetas de negra!"* Black women's tits! Marie Antoinette placed her hand over my mouth and led me away quickly as the grocers laughed and made lewd remarks. I couldn't understand what I had done wrong. Those eggplants did look just like Inocencia's breasts, right down to the fact that both had aureolas and nipples. The only difference was that while Inocencia's were bluish black, those of the eggplants were green. Later in life I would search for evidence of God's presence. That resemblance was my first proof for the existence of God. And eggplants would forever remind me of our nakedness and shame.

A few months after that New Year's Day, Inocencia quit working for us. She was replaced by a thin, wiry woman named Caridad, or Charity, who was angry and a thief. My parents would eventually fire her for stealing. She loved Fidel, and she listened to the radio in the kitchen all day long. It was the only Cuban music I ever heard. My father, the former Louis XVI,

---

4. I.e., members of the French family to which Louis XVI and Marie Antoinette (by marriage) belonged.

would not allow anything but classical music to be played in the main part of the house. He remembered meeting some of the composers whose music he played, and he pined for those concerts at Versailles.[5] Cuban music was restricted to the kitchen and the maid's room.

Caridad loved to taunt me when my parents weren't around. "Pretty soon you're going to lose all this." "Pretty soon you'll be sweeping my floor." "Pretty soon I'll be seeing you at your fancy beach club, and you'll be cleaning out the trash cans while I swim." With menacing smirks, she threatened that if I ever told my parents about her taunts, she would put a curse on me.

"I know all sorts of curses. Changó listens to me; I offer him the best cigars, and plenty of firewater. I'll hex you and your whole family. Changó and I will set a whole army of devils upon you."

My father had warned me about the evil powers of Changó and the African gods. He spoke to me of men struck dead in the prime of life, of housewives driven mad with love for their gardeners, of children horribly disfigured. So I kept quiet. But I think she put a curse on me anyway, and on my whole family, for not allowing her to steal and taunt until that day, "pretty soon," when she could take over the house. Her devils swooped down on all of us, with the same speed as the rebels that swept across the whole island on that day.

The lizards remained oblivious to the news that day, as always. Contrary to what my brother Tony liked to say as he administered shock treatments to them, the lizards were not deluded in the least. They knew exactly what they were and always would be. Nothing had changed for them. Nothing would ever change. The world already belonged to them whole, free of vice and virtue. They scurried up and down the walls of the patio, and along its brightly colored floor tiles. They lounged on tree branches, sunned themselves on rocks. They clung to the ceilings inside our house, waiting for bugs to eat. They never fell in love, or sinned, or suffered broken hearts. They knew nothing of betrayal or humiliation. They needed no revolutions. Dreaming of guillotines was unnecessary for them, and impossible. They feared neither death nor torture at the hands of children. They worried not about curses, or proof of God's existence, or nakedness. Their limbs looked an awful lot like our own, in the same way that eggplants resembled breasts. Lizards were ugly, to be sure—or so I thought back then. They made me question the goodness of creation.

*I could never kiss a lizard*, I thought. *Never.*

Perhaps I envied them. Their place on earth was more secure than ours. We would lose our place, lose our world. They are still basking in the sun. Same way. Day in, day out.

## 2

## Dos

I shouldn't have been surprised that New Year's morning. There had been plenty of signs of trouble brewing, of changes to come. Even a sheltered

5. Royal palace in France.

child should have known something was about to snap. Later in life I would think back to that morning and try to link it to earlier events, just to make sense of what had gone wrong with all our lives.

Quite often, my wondering would come back to the day we almost died.

We were only a few blocks from my grandmother's house when the shooting started. It was near the botanical gardens of the Quinta de los Molinos. At first it sounded like a few firecrackers going off in the distance, *pop, pop, pop.* But within one minute, the pops were joined by *bangs* and *rat-tat-tats,* in a mounting crescendo. And the noise kept getting closer and closer. And louder.

My mother began to scream. "A shoot-out, a shoot-out! Oh my God, we're all going to get killed! Stop the car, Antonio, stop the car right here."

Antonio was my father's name in this life. Antonio Juan Francisco Nieto Cortadellas. This time around, my mother was called Maria Azucena Eiré González. Quite a comedown from Louis XVI and Marie Antoinette, but still quite high on the food chain. Marie Antoinette had been stricken by polio just before her first birthday in this lifetime, and her right leg was totally useless. Apparently being imprisoned in the Bastille and losing her head in 1793 had not been enough to settle her Karmic debts.

"If I stop the car now, we'll be killed for sure," said my father. "Stop shouting, you're frightening the kids."

It didn't seem to occur to him that the gunfire might be scary enough.

"Stop, stop, I beg you stop . . . we can get out of the car right here. I know the family that lives in that house right there," said Marie Antoinette, pointing a little ways down the street. In this neighborhood the buildings were all very close together, flush with the sidewalk. No front or side yards. Jumping out of the car and making a mad dash into a house was not too bad an idea.

"What if your friends aren't home?" Louis XVI asked. *Pop, pop, rat-tat-tat, bang!*

"They're not friends; I just know who they are," Marie Antoinette replied. "They're friends of friends of my sister." *Bang, pop, bang, rat-tat-tat, bang!* "And where else would they be on a Sunday evening?" *Pop, ka-pop, bang!* "My God, we're all going to die!" *Pop, bang, ka-blam!*

My brother Tony and I looked at each other in disbelief. This was just like a war movie! Finally, we were lucky enough to be involved in real gunplay. We had heard it in films, and often far in the distance, especially around bedtime, but never this close. It was so much louder! I thought of Audie Murphy in *To Hell and Back,*[6] shooting dead all those evil Nazis and blowing up their tanks. My brother and I must have seen that movie at least a dozen times. Both of us wanted to be Audie Murphy, the most highly decorated American soldier in World War II. Since our father was a judge, we could go to any movie theater in Havana for free, and we went often.

"There are very good shows on television tonight," my brother chimed in. *Rat-tat-tat, bang, pop, pop, ka-blam!* "They're probably watching *Rin Tin Tin.*"

*KA-BLAM! KA-BLAM! KA-BLAM!*

---

6. Murphy (1926?–1971), a real-life war hero, plays himself in this movie version of his autobiography.

"But grown-ups don't watch *Rin Tin Tin*. Grown-ups don't like shows about dogs," I said.

*KA-BLAM! BOOM! BANG! RAT-TAT-TAT!*

"Oh my God, Oh my God, Oh Mary Mother of God in Heaven. Oh Virgin of Charity! Stop the car! Stop the car! STOP!" Mom shouted even louder, over the sound of gunfire.

Maybe it was my overactive imagination, but I could have sworn I also heard a *Ka-ping*. A ricochet. The sound of a bullet bouncing off buildings, just like a war movie. Impressive. Then I heard a dull *thud*. Bullets penetrating buildings. Even more impressive.

Antonio Nieto Cortadellas swung the car over to the curb and stopped abruptly in front of the house my mother had pointed out. My brother and I were thrown forward against the front seat of the car. No one had seatbelts back in those days.

Maria Azucena Eiré González opened her door first.

Then it happened. Before she could swing out her good leg, a man bolted from the shadows. He grabbed my mother by both arms, crouching so low to the ground that his face was lower than hers.

"Save me! Hide me, please! They're after me! They're going to kill me!" The man's voice was shaky.

He started to push Mom back into the car.

"I beg you. For the love of God, hide me. Hide me, please, I beg you! *Por favor, se lo ruego!*"

I popped my head up above the front seat and got a good look at him. He had a round face and dark curly hair, and he was very sweaty. His shirt was open to mid-chest. He must have been in his thirties. I couldn't tell, though. All grown-ups looked the same age until they turned into old people.

The gunfire became ever louder. It made my hair stand on end, for the first time in my life. I heard more dull thuds and *ka-pings*, followed by sirens. Marie Antoinette gave a bloodcurdling shriek, just like the ones in horror films.

In the meantime, Tony had jumped out of the car, without having seen the man. As he rounded the car, the man grabbed him and held him tightly with one arm.

"For the sake of this boy, hide me!" he said through clenched teeth.

Louis XVI shouted: "Get away from us! You're going to get us killed! Can't you see my wife is crippled and that I'm trying to save my kids' lives? Go away! There's nothing we can do for you! Let go of my boy, now! Go! Run!"

The man looked straight at me. I had seen eyes like that before, on paintings and statues of Jesus Christ.

I had also seen them in my dreams. Very often, I used to dream that Jesus would appear at the dining room window, carrying his cross while we were eating dinner. He would just stand there and stare at me, blood trickling down his face. And only I could see him. He didn't have to speak. I knew what he wanted and it frightened me to death. The rest of the family kept eating, oblivious. Then he would simply vanish.

And this man's eyes stared at me exactly the same way.

I ducked back down to avoid the man's gaze.

Then the man took a look at my mother's leg, released my brother, and ran away. As quickly as he had appeared, he disappeared. My brother would say forty-two years later, on the day that I wrote this, that he had never seen anyone run so fast.

We bolted out of the car, not even bothering to close its doors. Tony and I bent close to the ground, just like the soldiers in war movies. All those hours at the movie theater and in front of the television were finally paying off.

"Oh my God, oh my God, oh my God! *Ay, Dios mío!*" Marie Antoinette prayed, limping all the way to the door of the house.

*KA-BLAM, BANG, BANG, RAT-TAT-TAT!*

The noise was deafening. I heard the sound of bullets whizzing past us, too.

*SWOOOOOOSH! KA-PIIING!*

Marie Antoinette and Louis XVI started banging on the door loudly. King Louis used the door knocker, Queen Marie Antoinette pounded with her cane. The banging seemed to last an eternity, but finally a silver-haired woman opened the door a crack. Without saying a word, Marie Antoinette crashed through the door, and the rest of us followed in her wake.

"I guess she really does know these people," Tony said.

"Please, please, you've got to let us stay here until the shooting stops," said Marie Antoinette, as she limped past the living room. Without asking the woman's permission, she herded us to the first bedroom she could find and said: "Get under the bed, quickly."

Tony and I crawled under the bed and huddled together, shaking. I remember the bedspread was brown, and the marble floor was nice and cool. Our mother sat on the bed above us like a hen over her chicks, saying Our Fathers and Hail Marys under her breath. Our father and the lady who lived in the house came into the room too.

The grown-ups just sat, or stood, in silence. My mother's prayers had become inaudible. Outside, the sound of gunfire diminished gradually, moving farther and farther away. And then it stopped, as suddenly as it had started.

My parents thanked the silver-haired lady profusely and talked for a while in that boring way that grown-ups talk. Tony and I emerged from under the bed, and the lady gave us some candy.

And we went home.

That night I didn't fall asleep in the backseat, as I often did. We got home, our parents tucked us into bed, and sleep crept up on us slowly.

That night I didn't dream about Jesus and his cross.

The next day my parents read in the newspaper about the escaped prisoners who had been shot dead near the Quinta de los Molinos. Our desperate man was only one of several who had escaped from the prison at the El Príncipe fortress, a relic from colonial times.

"You know that man who asked us to save him last night? They shot him dead," said my father.

"The police killed him," added my mother.

Louis XVI wouldn't show us the newspaper, but somehow my brother and I managed to get our hands on it later. That's how we got to see the gory photo. He was sprawled on the ground, one arm horribly twisted the wrong way, bloodstains on his shirt, and a pool of blood under his body. A thin stream of blood trickled from his mouth. His eyes were open. But they didn't look the same as when he had looked straight at me. They looked empty.

Cuban newspapers were full of such pictures in the waning days of Batista's regime. Dead rebels. Dead escaped prisoners. Dead innocent bystanders. Blood everywhere. Flies, even.

We were live innocent bystanders. Not a drop of our blood had been shed. What good luck, and at how great a price for that man we turned away in his most desperate hour.

That's what the world was like before it changed. I should have seen it coming.

The year was 1958. Earlier that day, we had held a bon voyage party for my mother's sister, Lily, who was off with a tour group to the United States and Canada. We had gone down to the harbor to see her board the Havana-Miami ferry. It was a lot of fun to watch the cars drive into the huge ship. But it took a long time, and the fun wore off. I had brought only one comic book with me, and it was a bad one. Elastic Man. What a stupid superhero. All he could do was stretch. And he had a very stupid looking red suit without a cape.

As I lay on the cold marble floor under the silver-haired lady's bed, listening to murmured prayers and gunfire, I thought of Elastic Man. How would he have reacted to a shoot-out? By stretching himself completely flat against the ground? Or maybe by stretching himself so thin as to become nearly invisible? He certainly wouldn't have hidden under a bed, not even to avoid being ridiculed for his costume.

I was no superhero, for sure. Nor was anyone else in my family.

The seas were rough that day. So rough that my aunt was seasick all the way to Miami. After she returned to Havana, I was very impressed when she told us about the huge waves and the violent rocking of the ferry, and about how green her cabin mate's face had turned. I imagined my aunt Lily leaning her own green head out of a porthole, puking into the waves. One hundred and twenty miles of vomit. Very impressive. More impressive than her stories about New York City, Niagara Falls, and the Canadian Mounted Police.

Almost as impressive as the sound of bullets whizzing past my head, and the sight of Jesus at my dining room window, cross and all.

## 14

### Catorce

"Bless me Father, for I have sinned . . ."

I was practicing my first confession before my family, who sat in stunned silence. They didn't want to hear it, but they seemed to me the most appropriate audience. After all, they were the people with whom I screwed up most often. I was seated at the dining room table, with my back to the Jesus window, the same table under which my brother Tony had once, years before, smoked a cigarette stolen from our grandfather Amador and gotten so sick that Dr. Portilla was summoned for a house call.

"Come quickly," I remember my mom saying on the phone. "I think one of my boys is dying."

It had all started so suddenly. There we were, watching a Popeye cartoon on television, and my brother started to make groaning noises behind me, from the couch.

"Ooooooh. Ooouuuarrghhh. Ououoooh."

I turned around to look, from my rocking chair, and was shocked by what I saw. Tony's face was actually greeen. As green as a dead, rotting chameleon, I swear. And he was holding his stomach.

Maria Theresa saw the whole thing. If you can find the portrait,[7] just ask her. I'm sure she'd give you a very colorful account.

Our next-door neighbor, Chachi's father, figured out what had happened before Dr. Portilla showed up, black bag in hand. Only someone in the cigar business could have made that instant diagnosis.

My mom had summoned Oscar. Just for company, in an hour of need, because my dad was not at home and there was no man in the house. In Cuba, you see, neighbors always came to your aid. Oscar, "*Quinientos Pesos,*" did his duty and took his turn at hand-holding. Well, not literally. Cubans don't like that. If you ask Cubans to actually hold hands, especially Cuban men, you might get punched in the face, or worse.

How I hate being forced to hold hands with people other than my wife and kids at Mass during the Our Father,[8] Sunday after Sunday. It's not intended as a penitential rite, but it's one of the harshest punishments ever imposed on me by the Church. Stupid American custom. I'm sure if I checked into it, I'd find out it was started by a heretic.

"I think this kid smoked some tobacco," *Quinientos Pesos* said. "Search the house for a cigarette or cigar butt. I bet you'll find one. Look for a place where he could hide to smoke it. This shade of green comes only from tobacco, I'll bet five hundred pesos on it."

We called Chachi's father *Quinientos Pesos* because everything he boasted about seemed to be worth exactly that much—five hundred pesos. His air conditioner had cost *quinientos pesos*, his television, his sofa, his dog, and on and on. Everything, even the most expensive items, such as his Cadillac, had cost exactly five hundred pesos. This was more than some Cubans brought home in a year.

He loved to boast. He built himself a wondrous house right on the seashore, miles west of Havana, way past Sugar Boy's mansion. The only problem was that construction began about the same time that Fidel rode into Havana on a Sherman tank. By the time this house was finished—and how splendid it was, how modern; it looked like a spaceship, or something from a science-fiction film—he and his family got to live in it for only a year or so. Then they left it behind, and all of its furnishings, and fled to Tampa.[9]

Leaving something like that for the sake of principle must be tough. Especially if you're over the age of forty and you've spent all of your life boasting. Even tougher if all you have to look forward to is a crappy apartment and a menial job in another country where almost everyone thinks that all you're

7. Maria Theresa of Austria was the mother of Maria Antoinette; hence a portrait in the home of one who believes he is the reincarnation of Louis XVI.

8. The paternoster, or the Lord's Prayer, the best-known Christian prayer.

9. City in Florida.

good for is mopping floors and cleaning out urinals. Not easy, the transformation into a spic. Not at all like a chameleon changing his color.

How well I remember that day in sixth grade, at Everglades Elementary School in Miami, when some freckle-faced kid named Curtis told me to keep my "stinkin' mitts" off his lunch tray.

"What are mitts?" I asked, in my still-accented English.

"Dumb shit spic, yer all so stinkin' dumb, why don't y'all go back to yer stinkin' country," was his reply. One of those "stinkin's" was really another English word that begins with "f." I had never heard it before.

It was our maid, Inocencia, who found the cigarette butt under the dining room table. The table had a very long wine red velvet tablecloth, which reached all the way to the marble floor. Tony had hidden under there to puff on his stolen cigarette, and the smoke had all been trapped under the table. Keep in mind these were Cuban cigarettes. Unfiltered. They made Camels and Lucky Strikes seem like kids' toys.

Tony stole cigarettes from *Abuelo* Amador and smoked them in secret at the age of eight. I didn't ever do that—though I took a few puffs from Tony's cigarettes now and then—but I was a sinner too, and had amassed all sorts of blotches on my soul. Now, in second grade, it was time to come clean. I had to confess my sins to a priest, I had to lay out my whole sordid seven-year-old past.

"These are my sins, Father . . ." I began my mock confession.

No one dared play the role of the priest, but they all listened to my sins, wide-eyed, as I read them off one by one. They remained as silent as stones, there, at that table, within sight of the Jesus window, under the eighteenth-century French tapestry that depicted a hunting scene. It was the *Bois de something-or-other*, my dad said, with authority. After all, he had been there, in that very same forest, chasing the prey, hadn't he?

"See those hounds? I loved my hounds. They were so sweet, so smart. But the revolutionaries slaughtered them all and ate them. You know what else they did? They broke into the chapel of Saint Denis, the birthplace of Gothic architecture, that jewel built by Abbot Suger in the twelfth century, and they desecrated the tombs of all the French kings. They ripped the heart out of the corpse of my grandfather, Louis XIV, and ate it. They ate his heart. His dead, dead heart."

What a neat little list of sins I had. But I don't think pride was anywhere on that list, not even in disguise. Just the opposite, in fact: I was so, so proud of the list.

A list. Things you check off as you read the items, one by one. Groceries, things to do, wishes, blots on your soul.

Taco sauce, milk, sponges, orange juice, razor blades, cat litter.

Fix the faucet, mow the lawn, rake the leaves, adjust the brakes on the bicycle, clean out the gutters, renew the passport, fire all the secretaries.

New cars with ten-year warranties, a toolshed, a rooftop apartment in Paris overlooking the Île de la Cité,[1] bathrooms that never need cleaning, a way to undo the past, an end to death.

Lies, bad words, bad thoughts, disobedience, theft.

---

1. Island on the Seine River in the city of Paris.

I knew theft was just about the worst sin on the list after bad words, and I might have actually felt sorry for it. I say "might" because I'm not sure I felt any genuine remorse. I loved to steal. Busy little kleptomaniac I had been. Toys, mostly. What was this deal where the store made you pay for the stuff on the shelves? If they had the toys out in the open, where anyone could grab them, why make you hand over this stuff called money? Especially when they had so many other copies of the same thing you were putting in your pocket. In a bin full of army men or cowboys or cars, what difference does one less make?

"Hey, where did you get that?" The question always seemed to surprise me. How did my mom know I didn't have this toy already? But every single time she caught me. And every time I was shocked by her omniscience.

"Uh . . . what do you mean?"

"Where did that toy come from?"

"Uh . . . I've had it for a long time. You just don't remember it."

"Are you sure?"

"Yes, of course."

After the first question-and-answer session, Marie Antoinette would usually walk away. Then she would return a minute or two later.

"I don't think I ever saw that toy before. Are you stealing again?"

"No. I told you, I've had this soldier for a long time."

Then came the stare. That piercing stare that went straight to the core of the soul. The same gaze you see on some Byzantine icons of Christ. That gaze that says "I know what you've done, and you're a big liar."

What could I do when pierced by those all-knowing eyes? Confess, of course.

"Well . . . sí, I took this from the soldier bin at Woolworth's yesterday."

"I thought so. How did you do it? I was watching you carefully."

"I waited until you started talking to that lady with the blue hair. By the way, why do so many old ladies have blue hair? How does it get that way?"

"Don't change the subject. It's hair dye. You know stealing is wrong, don't you? It's a mortal sin."

"Yes, I do. I'm sorry." Sheepish look on my face, with no genuine inner contrition. I knew I'd do it again as soon as I had the chance.

"Next time you do this, you're in for a big surprise."

I'd heard that one before, and the surprise never came. I knew she was bluffing.

But the surprise finally came one day. It was at the Plaza de Marianao, that awful, stinking hellhole with all the butcher shops where they slaughtered animals right in front of your eyes and the air itself seemed soaked in blood. I always found myself breathing through my mouth so I wouldn't have to smell the blood. I also walked around with my fingers in my ears to block out the sounds emitted by animals as they are turned into food.

So different the meat at the Plaza, so unlike the silent, odorless hunks of flesh wrapped in plastic at the Stop & Shop or the Piggly Wiggly.[2] Freshly slaughtered animals, cut up or whole, hanging from hooks, dripping hot blood.

My mom really liked one butcher shop at the Plaza, and we went there too often.

---

2. I.e., at grocery stores in the United States.

There was a toy stand at the Plaza, tucked away in a corner on the upper level that actually received some sunlight and didn't smell too bad. The toys were awful, like the rest of the place, but they were toys. And they cried out to me:

"We're yours for the taking. Take us. We know you don't like us, but please take us home with you. We'll feel so much better in your sweet-smelling house. Do us a favor, please, take us away from here. Save us. It's not just the smell, you know, but also the screams of the pigs and chickens that drive us insane within this dusty bin. Look at the dust, too. No one ever brings kids here to buy us. We linger here, unloved, unwanted, surrounded by death, suffocating in the stench of blood and freshly cut flesh. Take us, please. Put us in your pocket."

Who could resist such a heartrending plea?

I glanced around for watchful eyes, found none, plunged my hand into a bin without looking down, and put some Cossacks in my pocket. Yes, Cossacks. Dad had told me what they were called, but I still had no idea what they were, really.

Anyway, I walked out of there with Cossacks in my pocket. But how many had I freed? I had to know. So the great Cossack liberator made the mistake of attempting a body count in the backseat of the car as we were driving away from the Plaza. I pulled up the booty to the edge of my pocket and peered down. One, two, three. Great! I didn't even care that these were really ugly toy soldiers. I could always make use of them, maybe by setting them on fire or blowing them up with firecrackers.

"What are you doing?" came the question from the front seat. Marie Antoinette was looking straight at me.

"Uh . . . nothing . . . just looking at my pocket, that's all." I've always been a very unimaginative liar.

"What's that red thing sticking out of your pocket?"

It was there all right. The tall skinny Cossack was sticking halfway out of my pocket, and his red jacket was hard to miss. I didn't even try to lie.

"It's a Cossack . . . I took it." I hardly ever said that I "stole" anything. I merely "took" things.

"This is it." She pointed her index finger straight at me without raising her voice. She never raised her voice.

"Antonio, turn the car around, we're going back to the Plaza."

"What for?"

"Carlos stole some toys again, and we're going to make him give them back to the store from which he took them."

"Okay, good idea." The judge agreed, and turned the car around immediately.

"You're in big trouble now," observed my brother.

"No, no, please. Don't make me do this. I promise, I won't ever do it again. I promise. No, no . . . Can't you or *Papa* take them back for me? I promise, I won't take toys again."

"It's time you learned this lesson," said Louis XVI.

Once back at the Plaza de Marianao, I was sent back in to return the stolen Cossacks. I had very clear instructions: I was supposed to confess to the woman minding the store and hand the Cossacks back, one by one. But I was sent in all on my own, and entrusted with this painful, impossible task. Neither of my parents went with me to ensure that the penance would be performed. You can guess what I did. As soon as I was back in the toy store, I simply reversed my tactics: I looked around for witnesses, and, finding none, pulled the Cossacks out of my pocket and dumped them back in their dusty bin, all the while breathing through my mouth.

How that place stunk. Good God, how it reeked of death.

And how I ran.

I got back into our brown Chrysler, panting.

"Did you hand back the toys?"

"Did you do as we asked?"

"Sí," was my simple reply. No elaboration on this falsehood.

"Good. We're so proud of you," said Mom.

"I guess you'll never steal again after this," added Dad.

Not bad, for a bad liar.

A few months later, perhaps even just a few weeks, I found myself at a very small *quincalla*, a store that sold odds and ends, and the toy soldiers called out to me again from their dusty bin. It was a store named Saxony. Once again I couldn't resist the pleas of the poor, neglected toy soldiers. These weren't Cossacks. They were American army men. Nice and green. I had all of them already: bazooka guy, radio-telephone guy, crawling-with-rifle guy, standing-up-shooting guy, kneeling-shooting guy, grenade guy, bayonet guy, binoculars guy, pistol guy, flamethrower guy, mortar guy, minesweeper guy, pointing guy. But it didn't matter that I had others like them. They called out to me.

"Take us home. We're yours. We belong to you. Free us. We will fight for you."

Using my well-honed skills, I pocketed a few green army men. Freed them from imprisonment in a store named after the land of Martin Luther.[3] Freed them from captivity in the land of arch-heretics, without knowing it.

This time I was much more careful. I knew better than to inspect my pockets in the car. But I got caught at home, damn it, as I was playing war on the marble floor.

"Hey, where did you get those soldiers?" Marie Antoinette, as always.

"What do you mean? I've had these for a while."

"But I thought you only had two grenade guys. I see you have four now."

"Uh . . . no. I've had four all along."

"No, I don't think so. I put them away all the time, and I know you only have two. Where did the other two come from?"

"Uh . . . oh, now I remember: Jorge lent them to me."

"Are you sure? I haven't seen Jorge around for a few days. When did he give them to you?"

"He gave them to me last Saturday."

"But we spent the day at Grandma and Grandpa's house last Saturday."

Then came the stare. That all-knowing gaze. Laser beams aimed straight at the conscience.

"Tell me the truth, come on."

What could I do but confess?

This time around the penance imposed on me was the same as at the Plaza de Marianao, but with a wicked twist. This time, when I went back to the store, both of my parents followed me into the store.

---

3. German priest and theologian (1483–1546); leader of the Protestant Reformation.

"My son has something he wants to tell you," King Louis informed the clerk behind the sales counter at Saxony. Louis XVI put his hand on my shoulder. I remember the way his hand seemed to have no weight at all and an awful lot of weight at the same time. Light as a feather. And as heavy as my conscience, which finally, at that very instant, seemed to have sprung to life.

Everything that happened in the store after my dad put his hand on my shoulder is now in my vault of oblivion. No details left. This means, of course, it was a reverse peak experience, a Mariana Trench[4] of the soul. I only know that I did what I was supposed to do because my parents praised me for it and wagged their fingers at me some more.

"I bet this cures him," Marie Antoinette said to King Louis as he started the car.

"How bad was it?" asked my brother, who had wisely refused to go into the store.

Silence from me. I couldn't talk for a long time. Maybe even the rest of the day.

I felt genuine remorse for the first time in my life. Or at least I felt embarrassed. Ashamed. Humiliated. Exposed as a thief. Is that the same as remorse? I still don't know.

But I do know that from that day forward I never stole anything. Not even when I was slowly starving in Miami, at that foster home for juvenile delinquents where Tony and I were fed only once a day, at five in the afternoon.

How wonderful those Twinkies and Moon Pies looked on the store shelves. How they sang out to me.

"Take us! Unwrap us! Touch us! Squeeze us! Taste us! Eat us! We belong inside of you. Hear that rumbling in your gut? Listen to that. That's no rumbling, it's a roar. Listen more closely. Hear that nearly imperceptible sound? Those are your bones. They're gasping, bending, growing crooked. And, by the way, when is the last time you went to a doctor, or had a dessert?"

Tempted as I was by the song of the Twinkies, I resisted their siren call. Stealing was wrong, but not just because it was a sin. Stealing was an affront to the mother and father who had driven me back to Saxony and stood with me as I confessed my sin. Stealing was a betrayal of those memories that mattered most to me.

Stealing seemed so wrong that I couldn't bring myself to go along with some of the thugs who lived with me and wanted me to help them steal stuff. Couldn't do it, even when they threatened me with harm. One of them, Miguel, got it into his head to steal an outboard motor from a boat moored at the Miami River, not far from our foster home. We used to go there often to watch fishermen catch nothing or, every now and then, fight off water moccasins with their rods. The place was crawling with all sorts of snakes.

Miguel wanted me and Tony to help him steal this outboard motor and carry it all seven blocks to our foster home, and he threatened to hurt us if we refused. What he wanted to do with that motor, I'll never know. We had as much chance of gaining access to a boat as we did of having an air

4. Depression in the western Pacific Ocean, east of the Mariana Islands; the deepest location on the surface of the Earth's crust.

conditioner installed in our room, or of winning the Spanish lottery. Tony and I refused to join Miguel, but he ended up finding someone to help him and somehow managed to lift it up onto the flat roof of our orphanage.

Social workers called it a "foster home," but it was really an orphanage. Twelve children living in a rundown, three-bedroom house infested with roaches, mice, and scorpions, under the care of two adults who didn't really care for us. Four or five kids to a room. Two in the glassed-in porch. One in the living room. No air-conditioning, no fans. In Miami, mind you. One tiny bathroom for all of us. One meal a day, and plenty of menial labor. Physical and mental abuse from adults and housemates alike.

Anyway, Miguel got his outboard motor. And one evening, as I was in the backyard throwing out the trash, Miguel snuck up behind me and hit me as hard as he could above the knees with a huge, crudely made club, larger than a baseball bat. I think he was aiming for the knees.

"I broke your legs! I broke your legs! Ha, that'll teach you!"

I thought he had broken my legs for real, it hurt so much. He laughed loudly and swung the club over his head as he did some kind of dance all around me, chanting.

Well, he didn't really break my legs. I managed to get up off the ground about ten minutes later. But I did get the largest bruises I'd ever seen, and I had trouble sitting down for a while.

Miguel ended up getting caught by the police a few days after he whacked me. They came to our house, found the outboard motor on the roof, and took him off to jail. His partner had ratted on him.

Very odd, how my conscience gained the upper hand and prevailed. I still resent that victory, deep down. And that, my friend,[5] is a very big problem. After all, a huge chunk of the message delivered unto Moses by God Himself had to do with keeping your stinkin' mitts off things that belonged to others. Check out Exodus 20:15–17: "Do not steal."

"Do not desire another man's house; do not desire his wife, his slaves, his cattle, his donkeys, or anything else that he owns."

Good God in heaven. Even desire is forbidden. Is this harsh or what? Especially the part about donkeys? You can't crave what belongs to others, ever. If you do, your soul is stained. And if it's stained, you're in big trouble.

That's how the Christian Brothers[6] explained it to us. In order to get to heaven, your soul needs to be pure. Think of it as pure whiteness, that's what they told us. Blazing, blinding white, that's how God wants your soul to be. Just one large stain is enough to land you in hell for eternity. One stolen toy, that's all it takes. One covetous glance at a pair of nice new shoes, or the person wearing them, or whatever belongs to someone else. That's all it takes to be plunged into a sulfurous burning pit, where you will be horribly tortured by hideous demons for eternity.

But there's a remedy, we were told. Your soul can be made pristine, scrubbed white, as pure white as a consecrated host. You can make that

5. Addressed to the reader, not to a specific person.
6. Or the Congregation of Christian Brothers (Latin: *Congregatio Fratrum Christianorum*), a worldwide religious community within the Catholic Church, devoted chiefly to the evangelization and education of youth.

happen by receiving the sacrament of Penance, by going to confession, and exposing each of your stains to a priest.

And confess I did, after rehearsing in front of my family. Since I was a male I had to face the priest directly in the confessional box. Only girls and women got to hide behind a wicker screen. At the time I didn't know that the screen was there to protect the priest from temptation. I thought women were getting another unfair break.

I read my list of sins to the priest, at San Antonio de Miramar, that cool, air-conditioned Art Deco church surrounded by beautiful homes, bathed in light straight from the highest heaven.

Theft was high on my list. Bad words were nowhere on the list, of course. They frightened me so much, they were never a temptation back then. Bad thoughts? You bet. Nearly everything was a bad thought if you dwelt on it long enough. Lots of malice towards others, especially. Wishing lizards harm, and making your wishes come true. No naked women, though, no dirty magazines. Nothing to do with that troublesome *ecce unde*[7] down yonder, not yet, not really. But I confessed that sin anyway, just in case I hadn't understood Brother Alejandro correctly. Maybe I had. After all, you had to touch it every time you peed. Disobedience? Of course. All the time. Lying? Every single day. My whole life was one big, stupid lie. A transparent lie, too, especially to my mother.

"For all of these sins and any others I have overlooked I am heartily sorry."

"*Una confesión muy buena, hijo.*" That was a very good confession, my boy. Go in peace, your sins are forgiven.

Much to my surprise, I did feel relieved as I stepped away from that confessional. I felt as if some weight had been lifted off my shoulders, maybe the weight of a father's hand.

I also felt proud. So proud of myself for making such a good confession and being spotless inside. If they'd been able to assign grades for this exercise, I was sure the Christian Brothers would have given me the highest possible mark, *Sobresaliente*, Outstanding.

I didn't tell any lies that day or the next, and I didn't kill any lizards either. I managed to resist temptation at many turns, and to make it to my First Communion two days later with a fairly white soul and a perfectly tailored, perfectly bleached white suit, white gloves, and white shoes. The white suit looked oddly out of place at the beach later, at the reception that was held at the Havana Yacht Club. Odd, but as white as my soul.

Or so I thought, standing on the pier of the Yacht Club, sweating profusely in the blazing sunshine, feeling the sharp edge of the starched collar against my neck, looking down at my white shoes rather than at the sea, eating a ham salad sandwich, a perfect triangle of white bread, all white on the outside and pink inside, every trace of the brown crust carefully excised.

One stain had been missed, though. Forgiven, of course, under the rubric of "any other sins I have overlooked." It was the stain of pride.

I remember thinking how nice it was to be at the Havana Yacht Club, how well it suited me, my classmates, and our families. I knew at that age

---

7. Behold the place (Latin); from the teachings of the Christian Church father St. Augustine (AD 354–430), bishop of Hippo Regius.

that I was lucky and thought God owed me that luck simply because I richly deserved it. Deserved it more than others.

I would have Fidel to thank for pointing out this pride to me, and "stinkin' mitts" Curtis too, who made me realize for the first time in my life that I was a Cuban.

Thanks, guys. *Muchas gracias.* You gave me what I truly deserved.

And thanks also to the heresiarch who came up with the idea of having everyone in church hold hands during the Our Father. You have no idea how you wound my pride and remind me that I am Cuban. Every Sunday you put me in touch with the abysmal root of all my problems.

I can see that monstrous root now in a way I never could at the age of seven. My first stab at confession was like a leap off a cliff, blindfolded. I rehearsed with my family in the same way Evel Knievel[8] did before any of his motorcycle stunts, with the likelihood of a crash landing in mind, but no real acceptance of the chasm about to be spanned, or the pull of gravity.

"That was an excellent confession," said Marie Antoinette as I finished my rehearsal at the dinner table. Everyone else remained silent.

"Did I leave anything out?"

"No, you didn't. If you confess like that later this week, you'll have covered everything. And you don't have to say you're a thief. You're not anymore."

"Are you sure?" I looked at Marie Antoinette, and then at the others. Everyone but my mother looked away or pretended not to be at the table. Tony hid his face in his armpit.

My mother looked me straight in the eye and said, "Yes, I'm sure."

Total silence. Everyone got up and left the dining room. Tony zipped out of his chair at the speed of light. I remained glued to my seat for a while.

Fast-forward forty-three years. I am confessing to a priest, face to face, cataloguing my soul's dark stains in a sunlit room. The worst ones get the most attention, and this time around they happen to be as dark as they come. Jesus H. Crucified Christ, the gloom inside me is formidable. I recognize these blots for what they are: states of mind and deeds that I am attached to, or even love, but which cause pain to others and diminish me in the process. I am brought face to face with my desire for what's wrong and my dogged avoidance of what's right. Can I really repent for things I don't feel totally sorry about?

I say I'm sorry for not being truly sorry.

The priest looks me in the eye the same way my mother did forty-three years before and says: "Go in peace, your sins are forgiven."

All I can say—all I am supposed to say—is what I say every time: "Thank you, Father."

What I should add, but don't, is: "*Hasta luego, Padre.*" See you again soon, Father.

2003

---

8. American motorcycle daredevil (Robert Craig Knievel, 1938–2007), famous between the late 1960s and early 1980s.

# ROBERTO G. FERNÁNDEZ
## b. 1951

A native of Cuba, Roberto G. Fernández immigrated to the United States with his parents and brother in 1961. He earned his doctorate in linguistics from Florida State University, in Tallahassee, in 1977. He later joined the faculty there, and in 2001 he was named the Dorothy Lois Breen Hoffman Professor of Modern Languages and Linguistics. Fernández has received a Florida Artists Fellowship and a Cintas Fellowship.

Perhaps more than any other Cuban American writer, Fernández writes to preserve a moment in time by focusing on the lives of the first generation of exiles who left their homeland for Miami, Florida, in the early days of the Castro regime, and who are now ending their days in Little Havana. Struggling with the trauma of displacement, his characters resist assimilation into the mainstream of American society as they hold on to the language and the customs of the old country. Fernández's fiction depicts how the past is reinvented, and reality is distorted, by time and nostalgia. It satirizes exiles' typical mythologizing of their homeland, but also shows a profound compassion for the people whose lives are being chronicled.

In the mid-1970s, Fernández published two collections of stories, both written in Spanish, about the Cuban-exile community in Miami: *Cuentos sin rumbo* (Stories without Direction, 1975) and *El jardín de la luna* (The Garden of the Moon, 1976). His first novel, *La vida es un special* (Life on Sale, 1981), expands upon the stories by detailing how, in re-creating their lost island home, the exiles in Miami grotesquely deform Cuban institutions, traditions, and cultural icons. The title reflects the cheapening of life that results from the realization that everything can be purchased, preferably on sale. The novel *La montaña rusa* (Rollercoaster, 1985) again portrays a world in which the mythical Cuba of memory is more real than the stagnant society that exists in exile.

*Raining Backwards* (1988)—Fernández's first novel written in English—develops and builds on these themes. As the exile experience is satirized and parodied, colorful characters invent a mythology to explain their increasingly chaotic lives in their multiple worlds. The narrative employs shifting points of view, letters, song lyrics, telephone calls, radio programs, and advertising slogans to depict the transformation of memories into fantasies. In the chapter included in this anthology, Eloy, a young Cuban American boy in search of his Cuban heritage, is held spellbound by Mirta, who spins tales of a fantastic, golden island peopled by characters from Spanish literature, Greek mythological figures, and religious icons. In *Holy Radishes!* (1995), a chapter of which is also included here, Fernández's manic and heartbreaking exiles try to escape even their memories, seeking an imaginary kingdom in which history does not exist. The primary character, Nellie Pardo, forced by violence, rape, and the murder of her father to leave her home in mythical Xawa, goes to work in a radish packing plant. Like the novel's other exiles, she represses the trauma and dislocation in creating a new version of her life story. Again, the narrative is nonlinear, filled with varied points of view and hyperbolic, carnivalesque monologues. In his most recent novels, *En la Ocho y la Doce* (On 8th Street and 12th Avenue, 2001), and *Entre dos aguas* (Between Two Shores, 2006), the latter his first work to be published in Cuba, Fernández returns to Spanish as he continues his dissection of the Cuban-exile community.

Fernández's English-language novels attempt to reach a broader audience than were reached by the older generations of Cuban-exile writing, which were addressed primarily to other Cuban exiles. At the same time, Fernández's novels contain a multitude of references to idioms, proverbs, poems, music, persons, places, and things intelligible only to Spanish speakers, and mainly to Hispanophone Cuban exiles.

Rather than simply using Spanglish, Fernández translates literally into English his Spanish references, producing comic, often bizarre utterances, such as "I threw the house out the window." His characters' varying levels of expertise in English reflect an exile culture that incorporates many languages but seems at times to contain no intelligible language. The enumeration of elements of Cuban culture affirms their significance, but renaming them in English—*Xawa* substituted for the name of Fernández's hometown, Sagua la Grande; *Faithful Chester* used for Fidel Castro— demonstrates their loss of meaning as signifiers in the new, American world.

---

## FROM RAINING BACKWARDS

### Retrieving Varadero[1]

It had been raining non-stop for months and Eloy was doing his best to swat the palmetto bugs, mosquitoes and gnats which, drunk with rain and crashing against each other, were emerging from the puddles and trying to nest in Mirta's wavy bronze mane.

"Faster! They're driving me crazy. Faster! C'mon, you can do better than that. Fan me faster. Go to the bathroom closet and get the ostrich feather. Maybe it'll help. But be careful with it. It's the only thing my mother left me."

Eloy had been serving Mirta faithfully for the last two months in exchange for tidbits of the past. He was thirsty for information on those golden cities, those fabulous places in that enchanted island his aunt refused to mention because they were so sacred. He wanted to savor tidbits from that past he longed to relive somehow and share it in his old age with his grandchildren.

The evenings with Mirta had begun before the deluge. It all started one afternoon when Eloy, tired of folding clothes for his aunt, the laundry woman, and realizing the futility of trying to retrieve any information from her, pressed his ear against the wall and listened astonished to the discussion that Mirta was having with the radio on the other side of the wall.

"Why do you go on with your lies? Everyone knows that Varadero was the most beautiful beach, not only in the world but in the whole universe! The waters were forever changing colors, the sand had the texture of baby powder, the breezes were always warm but never hot. So how dare you say that Cancún or Sanibel[2] are better and more beautiful. Liar! Communists! And there you go again. Isn't it enough just to say it once. You're getting me mad. I'd love to turn your program off, but you know I'm waiting for Julio's latest hit with German Garcia.[3] But I'm losing my patience! I swear on my mother's grave that I've had it with you. I'm going to silence you forever. Liar! You're forcing me to do it."

---

1. Large resort town in the province of Matanzas, Cuba, east of Havana.
2. Sanibel Island, in the Gulf of Mexico off the coast of southwestern Florida. *Cancún*: coastal city on the Yucatán Peninsula, in eastern Mexico.
3. A Cuban singer (birth date unknown). *Julio*: Julio Iglesias (b. 1943), Spanish singer.

Eloy heard a crashing noise and, overtaken by his curiosity, he sneaked out and knocked on Mirta's door. Mirta refused to open, but managed to stick her head through the kitchen window and shout in anguish: "What do you want?" She was afraid of a rapist or, even worse, the Mastercard collector. Quickly, she muttered: "She's in Disney World in Orlando. Very, very far away from here." In her nervousness, Mirta had failed to recognize her little neighbor, the laundry woman's nephew.

After he explained to her who he was, Mirta opened the door and, somewhat surprised by his visit, offered him a few pieces of candy which were left over from Halloween. After this first meeting, Eloy developed the need to talk to her every evening after school and Mirta had finished her daily factory routine. Gradually, Mirta intoxicated his mind with her maze of remembrances.

"Yes. That's right, the water was always changing colors like a kaleidoscope. Each time that wind changed course the water changed color. When the wind was blowing strongly it turned into an intense violet, and when it was calm, it was as green as Ireland."

"What's Ireland?"

"It's a deodorant soap. But that's not really important. Our ocean was so delicious that even Aristotle, who is a very cultured gentleman, and who can't practice here because he never passed the board, when he tasted a sip of our waters, he left all his knowledge aside and started shacking up with El Cid, who was this enormous black woman that sold coconuts carved in the image of Mary Magdalene,[4] but had the faces made out of bread in El Cid's own image."

"And the sand? Was it like Clearwater's?"[5]

"You must be kidding! In all the beaches in Cuba the sand was made out of grated silver, though in Varadero it was also mixed with diamond dust. And it was definitely finer than Mennen's Baby Powder, the one with the baby inside the rose. I'm going to tell you something no one has ever told you, so you are going to become a very special person because there're only a few people that know this. Are you ready?"

"Yes, ma'am."

"The sun rose in the North and set in the South."

And thus, the days became weeks and the weeks months and Eloy came religiously every morning at dusk to hear Mirta. Very slowly, Mirta came to realize that her words had a narcotic effect upon the youth, and shrewdly opted to trade her remembrances of memories for practical favors that could ease the burden of living. She would send Eloy to Pepe's Grocery to buy a bottle of Seven-Up, or to Cabrera's Pharmacy to buy librium without prescription or benadryl to calm the constant itching that had plagued her since puberty.

One drenching afternoon, Eloy arrived and, as usual, he wiped off the mud that covered his shoes. Mirta greeted him with a list of errands; buy one jar of Bella Aurora cream; go to Clavo, the numbers man,[6] and place

4. Mary Magdalene, identified in the New Testament as a disciple of Jesus, venerated as a saint in branches of Christianity such as the Roman Catholic Church. This paragraph includes playful references to Irish Spring soap, the ancient Greek philosopher Aristotle, and the eleventh-century Spanish soldier and hero El Cid.
5. Beach on the Gulf of Mexico, in central-western Florida.
6. *Numbers*: a kind of gambling in which people bet on combinations of digits, such as regularly published ones.

$5 on 5-9-80; stop by the bank and tell them that there's a mistake in my checkbook, that my name is Miss Mirta Maria Vergara, not Mrs. Mirtha Verga; and fill out my insurance papers that I don't understand. While Eloy read the list, Mirta promised more tales from her seemingly inexhaustible vein. Suddenly, Mirta sneezed and Eloy rushed to wipe her nose.

"Thank you, child. You are the living image of St. Gabriel the Archangel,[7] because you're more beautiful than all the other angels. And now go and wipe the sofa cushion once more, because it still has a lot of dirt, and then go to my room and vacuum it . . ." and the breezes were warm but never hot and there was no need for suntan lotion nor sun screens because the breezes carried the properties of aloe and they even unclogged your nose while moisturizing your skin. Now, let me tell you something very important. I watched everything from the porch. It had the best view of the beach. Besides, my mother never allowed me to go down to the beach because she said I was going to get dirty if I mixed with trash. I remember that at times, when it thundered, El Cid would take off her clothes and, with her two big breasts dancing in the air, stretch her arms, imitating a crucified martyr, and shout: "Mary Madgalene, blessed virgin. Deliver us from thunder and lightning." And then the thunder would cease and my mother would come to cover my eyes so I wouldn't see the naked Cid.

"Eloy, Eloy are you in there? Do you want to play some baseball? C'mon out."

"I can't. I'm busy."

"Could you tell me some more, Miss Mirta? I'll bet my friends don't know about El Cid."

"There were giant penguins and white seals that roamed the beach . . ."

"Excuse me. Miss Mirta. I think it's my aunt calling me. I've got to go now. I have to help her."

"If you stay a little longer I'll tell you about Foquie, the seal with the bright green eyes. Stay, stay . . ."

"Okay, but just a little bit more."

"But could you first squeeze the blackheads on my back, and also those little pimples that are really itching. Could you? I can't see them."

As Eloy groomed her, Mirta felt, without knowing why, a deep pleasure with each exposed blackhead, with each popped pimple.

". . . and the white seals came around the Cape of Horn[8] only because they had heard about the pleasures of Varadero, the most beautiful beach in the world. Once they got there, they would be driven mad by the one hundred waterfalls that bordered the beach and they would slide and play with the swimmers and dive for fish and pearls in exchange for bananas and papayas and could you pour some boric acid on my back and take a damp towel and put it right on my shoulder blade, and while you are at it, rub my swollen thigh with Ben-Gay."

"Really, ma'am, I've got to go. My aunt is calling me and I have to help her fold the laundry and then do my homework because last year I flunked the seventh grade."

---

7. In Judaism, Christianity, and Islam, Gabriel is an angel who serves as God's messenger.

8. Cape Horn island, the most southerly point of South America.

"Why don't you bathe me before you go? I'm so tired with so much over-time at the factory that I can hardly hold the soap. Just a little shower, okay?"

"But Miss Mirtha!"

"It's not Mirtha, it's Mirta. C'mon! Be a good boy. I can even be more than your mother. Stop that nonsense and get the sponge, the avocado soap and the cologne. They're in the closet."

"Okay, Miss Mirta, but tell me more. Tell me more. Do you know about my reading aunt's farm, the one that ended where the rainbow ends?"

Mirta could only think about the pleasures that Eloy's hands would exert on her back as he bathed her, and started to tremble thinking that she would have to turn around and face Eloy in order to reach the towel that hung from the door nail. Just this thought made her salivate so profusely that the dribble threatened to innundate her neck. While Mirta was getting undressed to dive into the old tub, Eloy commenced lathering the sponge without realizing that many years later he would forbid his wife to use a sponge to do the dishes, much less to bathe the kids. That strange sponge-phobia would last throughout his life. Not even Dr. Kings, with her potions, balms and incantations, would be able to cure this malady. Eloy approached the tub and urged her to continue dispensing stories of the by-gone days.

"It was on Varadero Beach that I met my only fiancé. It was a week after the 1943 storm,[9] two days before my fifteenth birthday. He was sunbathing, but he never knew that I was his sweetheart. I treasured our love with all my soul. His hair was the color of mahogany, like yours, but wavier, and when I came over here I sent him love messages in a bottle three times a week. They always read: 'I love you. Yours forever, MV' . . . MV is me, Mirta Vergara . . . and the breezes were warm . . . a little bit more to the right, lather me right down there . . . but the breezes were never hot and you didn't need suntan lotion and the white seals would play happily with the swimmers and they slid through the falls that surrounded Varadero and when it rained, it rained molasses and rice so you just needed to open your mouth and eat and if you wanted more to eat you just simply said: 'Sea crea-tures, I'm hungry,' and the fish and the mollusks would jump from the water to your pan and the sand had the texture of baby powder and the breezes were warm but . . ."

"Miss Mirta, you already told me about the breezes and the sand," shouted Eloy, exasperated, as he retrieved the sponge and used it to wipe the sweat drops that covered his forehead.

"I'm tired, Miss Mirta. I'm tired," Eloy kept saying.

For the first time, Mirta realized that the well of remembrances that she had been exploiting was about to run dry at the precise moment when she need to feel the skeletons of those magnificent corals, which had sacrificed their lives for her happiness, to form that joy-giving sponge.

"Yes, child, continue lathering down there," said Mirta at the same time that she turned around smiling like an old rabbit, and exposing her two udders which had sagged with the weight of virginity and were trying to rest on her reddish bush. Eloy looked at her indifferently for the first time and defiantly said, "Tell me more! If you don't continue, I won't either."

9. A hurricane that swept across Cuba and into the Gulf of Mexico.

Mirta, alarmed by his attitude, tried to lure him again with her all but exhausted memories.

"The white seals then came accompanied by yodelers shouting their yodel-eeps. The women on the beach who greeted the yodelers were dressed in straw skirts and moved their hips incessantly while singing: 'waha, waha, trum, trum, waha, waha, trum trum.' And the men had wide, bronzed shoulders and were always blowing these enormous sea shells. They were sounding them to appease the volcano which stood majestically at a distance and which would let a plume of smoke escape as a sign of gratitude for the shell sounds which pleased him so much. The name of the volcano was 'Pan de Matanzas,' the Killing Bread. It got that name from the many bakers who had thrown themselves from its summit. El Cid's coconut figurines with their heads made out of bread drove the bakers mad with love, for they wanted to possess the immense maiden who denied them her body. Between the lagoon and the sea there was a mountain all covered with snow. Mama, after finishing her cleaning duties at Señora Nelia's would swim towards the mountain to pack some snow and make herself a rum ice cream. She died evoking that mountain and whispering my father's name. He was a very rich merchant from Venice whom I never met and ah, ah, ahhhh."

"What's the matter, ma'am? What's the matter, Miss Mirta? You're sweating! Are you okay? Do you want me to call my aunt?"

"It's nothing. It's just that I get excited when I remember so many beautiful memories. But please, please don't stop lathering me, but now a little bit toward the left . . . please."

"But Miss Mirta. I'm too tired and my aunt . . ."

"I'll tell you more, my love. I'll tell you so much . . . and when a visitor arrived they placed leis around his neck and would whisper in his ear: 'tiare, tiare haere mai, haere mai,' and at that same time their hips would go crazy and they would take him to a heavenly hotel all made of ivory, gold and coral called El Oasis. There they would take their skirts off and, with only hibiscuses on their heads, would dive into the waves carrying with them bananas and plantains for the white seals, yodelers and penguins. Keep lathering, please keep lathering me and I will tell you how the white seals came up to the beach and how they ate from your hand and how Mama followed Señora Nelia when she left for Miami and Mama embraced each room in the house, telling them that she had loved them more than her own family and as a souvenir she plucked an ostrich feather from a hat which the Señora had left forgotten on her bed and how the sand had the texture of baby powder and how the breeze tanned your skin and the waters were technicolor and Aristotle and El Cid were wrestling naked on the sand. Why don't you stay to sleep with me?"

Eloy didn't answer. Mirta got out of the tub, ready to force him to stay if so required. Then a cloud of palmetto bugs landed on her body, covering her nakedness like a robe. This time Eloy didn't even try to swat the gnats that were trying to invade her nostrils. Worn out, he grabbed a folding chair and sat quietly observing and listening to the emerging Mirta, who screaming madly, told him that his mother was a tramp, that his aunts slept together with his uncle in the same bed, that his father had been in jail for being a drug-pushing cuckold and that above all he was ungrateful, for if it weren't for her he would never have known about the past.

Eloy, baffled, used the sponge which he was still holding in his hands to wipe his sweaty face once more. Mirta misinterpreted his gesture and immediately started to salivate again. She knelt and told him that she would constantly talk to him about the past and the beach, and that there were still many things that he didn't know about, like his reading aunt's (as he called his other aunt) silver boat and rainbow ranch, the singing palm trees and the queen of the lizards. She implored him to stay, promising to buy his aunt a dryer and find his father a good job.

He just smiled, caressing with his right hand the peach fuzz growing on his upper lip, and hiding the sponge behind his back with his left hand, he nodded, murmuring, "Tell me more, Mirta. Tell me more, baby."

1988

## *FROM* HOLY RADISHES!

## The Last Supper[1]

The shots that killed the sniper were drowned out by bells calling the faithful to prayer. With the last rounds, the soldiers finished flushing out the remaining rebels that had mounted the April Fools' offensive from the hillocks surrounding Xawa. Juan Benson, Don Andrés' gardener, thought he heard something interspersed with the tolling bells. He dismissed it in his mind as the buzzing of bees building a new hive to accommodate their queen. Benson was helping the club's gardener to reshape the shrubs damaged by flying shrapnel during the rebels' hasty retreat. Inside the Ladies' Tennis Club's kitchen, the servants toiled with six crates of California apples, apricots, and pears that had arrived a few hours before at the port of Isabella.[2] They were a gift from Floyd Conway to the new president on the occasion of her installation.

The inaugural dinner for the president of the Ladies' Tennis Club was Xawa's most exclusive affair. This year the privilege of wearing the presidential sash had fallen to Mrs. Fanny Fern. Her husband, Mr. Joseph Fern, was Xawa's most respected sugar baron. He was also the man who had convinced the government to conduct saturation bombing in the nearby hills. He had ensured his wife's election by donating a swimming pool to the club, which had helped sway the critical votes. Fanny, who hailed from New Orleans, had met Joseph during his school days at Tulane. She had been impressed by his suave manners and old-world charm at the debutante balls during Mardi Gras.

This year's election had been close. Three separate ballots were required to choose the new leader. Rivalry between Cuquín Valley and Pituca Josende had split the vote, paving the way for Fanny. Her mandate, according to the bylaws, was to last forty-two months and five days.

---

1. In Christianity, Jesus' final meal before his crucifixion.  2. Port city in Sagua la Grande, Cuba.

The dignitaries from outside Xawa had begun to arrive for the occasion. From the port city of Isabella came Mr. Fern's business associate, Benigno "the Basque" Juánez, and his elderly mother, Belinda Zubitegüi. Rumor had it the Basque was still bottle-fed at night by the decaying matron. Mayor Sánchez was picked up at the marina in Mr. Fern's yacht. He had come from the capital city dressed in blue knickerbockers. The mayor came alone. His mistress had registered at the Telegraph Hotel the night before, and his wife, Claribel, too drunk on a bottle of extra-aged dry Bacardi she had started at breakfast, remained at home. Exactly two weeks after the party, she would kill herself by jumping from the World Line Pier into the shark-infested waters of the bay.

The poet laureate, Lisander Pons, arrived with his fiancee, Vicky Rey. He was to delight the exclusive audience with the fruits of his muses. The acclaimed national contralto Aïda Lopez, was in attendance, as was Helen Valdés-Curl, wife of the muriatic acid tycoon Pete Frey. Helen drove the 444 kilometers alone in her red Cadillac convertible, her long scarf floating in the wind.

Father Santos, Xawa's gift to the clergy and the newly appointed Bishop of St. James in the Orient, arrived for the occasion accompanied by four identical Oriental acolytes named Horse, Snake, Monkey and Cat. They held the train of his silk- and gold-thread embroidered cassock at all times. Bishop Santos would come down in history as the man who saved the guerrilla leader, Faithful Chester, unwittingly becoming the destroyer of his own class. The neophyte bishop was Nelson Guiristain's godfather.

Joining the outsiders was the cream of Xawa's society: Don Andrés Pardo, his daughter Nellie, and her pet pig Rigoletto; his son-in-law Nelson Guiristain; the President and Vice President of the Xawa branch of The Royal Bank of Canada; Mr. Floyd Conway and Mr. Howe, respectively; Loly Espino escorted by her younger brother, Cioci (her husband, Senator Zubizarreta, was away at a political rally for his reelection campaign); Mrs. Cuquín Valley and Mr. Valley; María Rosa, her daughter Macuqui, her husband Dr. Gastón and her mother Mrs. Peña (the emeritus president and founding member of the club); Pituca Josende and her husband, Chief Justice Josende, who still limped from the shot he received during the landing at Dunkirk and the only Xawan ever to receive a Purple Heart.[3] All the above arrived in their carriages: Mr. and Mrs. Rudolph Guiristain were driven to the event in their Mercedes.

While the doormen were busy letting the final deliveries in, a number of curious eyes had gathered around the passion-vine-covered chain-link fence to get a glimpse of the celebrities. Struggling to climb all the way to top of the ceiba tree, a pudgy nineteen-year old was inching his way to a commanding view of the party. His name was Rulfo. Below the ceiba, the servants, under the direction of Delfina, were busy setting up the banquet table to accommodate the one-hundred guests and dignitaries invited to the event. Juan Benson had finished his gardening task and chopped up an old avocado tree to feed the club's fireplace. Fanny had insisted on having

3. Dunkirk, France, was the site of a famous World War II battle between Allied (specifically British, French, and Belgian) and German forces. In writing that Chief Justice Josende fought during this battle but also received a Purple Heart, a U.S. military decoration, Fernández is playfully mixing Cuban and U.S. references.

the brick fireplace lit. It reminded her of her childhood mansion in the Crescent City. To counterbalance the effects of the heat radiating from the hearth, exacerbated by Xawa's steamy temperatures, four massive blocks of ice would flank the fireplace once it was lit.

The seating arrangements threatened the delicate harmony of the club membership. After negotiations mediated by Father Santos and Floyd Conway, Pituca Josende finally acceded to be seated to Fanny's left. In return she was given a free hand programming the aquatic events in the new pool and would cut the inaugural ribbon. A beaming Cuquín Valley sat to Fanny's right.

"That's not where the forks go," Delfina thundered. "The forks always to the left, the big ones always closer to the plate. No, no, no," she continued, "the napkins must be folded like butterflies in flight. Please don't make the chairs creak so loudly!" She proceeded to scrutinize the recently delivered sacks of oysters. Contemptuously, she announced to the delivery man that his mollusks weren't fresh enough and that his boss's reputation was at stake. Then she turned to her helper and said, "I wonder what you people would have done if you had to prepare banquet tables for one-thousand guests? When Miss Nellie got married, that's what I did. That was really something! This is nothing in comparison. The whole Telegraph Hotel was booked solid with wedding guests. The Prince of Spain came personally to present Nellie with a sapphire choker which any of these women would kill just to hold in their hands for a few seconds."

Then Delfina looked up at Rulfo and yelled, "Get out of that tree. This is not for ruffians to see. Out of there or I'll call the *rurales*."[4] There was not a word from the arboreal slothlike figure, but what Delfina couldn't see was the stream of orange piss which fell directly into the punch bowl below.

·  ·  ·

The string of guests began to arrive for the cocktail hour preceding the supper. Fanny Fern, with her plump Teutonic face and the firm stomach that goes with a barren womb, greeted her guests at the club's romanesque entrance. By the time Floyd Conway walked in, her hands were already tired and her lips puckered from the numerous greetings and exchanges.

"Floyd Conway. Always so punctual," Fanny said sarcastically.

"I know I'm a bit late," said Floyd, attired in a light-blue frock coat and breeches the color of clay.

"It doesn't really matter. I was being bad. It's so good to see you. You're one of the first in. You know these people have no sense of time, but don't pick up that nasty habit." Fanny's smile found an echo in Floyd's.

"I am a trifle late, but I'm rather distressed by the news about the Queen Mother."[5]

"Ah?"

"She was bitten by a pet corgi after she tried to stop a fight among the royal canines at Windsor Castle."

"Was it serious?"

4. Rurals (Spanish); here, police, from the Mexican *Guardia Rural* (Royal Guard), a mounted-police force from 1861 to 1914.

5. The English queen Elizabeth (1900–2002). The following fictional anecdote refers to the British royal family and associated facts.

"Her Majesty had three stitches on her left hand after the incident. The quarrel involved ten dogs, including two belonging to Princess Margaret. I believe the Lord Chamberlain also was nipped while helping the Princess."

"Well, would you care for some port or sherry to ease your sorrow?"

"I'd rather have some Chivas. It's a mosquito repellant."

"Lazarus, bring Mr. Conway a tall glass of Chivas."

"Yes, Ma'am."

"Floyd, I love your kilt! Who made it? Was it Gloria Olivé, the local seam-stress, or Sarah Bosard, the *hautecouturier*?"[6] Fanny seemed genuinely interested in the garment and its maker.

"Oh, no, my dear. They wouldn't know where to start. My sister, Vera, sent it to me."

"You should come visit. I almost forgot to tell you that we have a Rho-desian Ridgeback. It's a beautiful creature."[7]

"I shall come by tomorrow at tea time. But how did you manage to get such a rare specimen? Was it smuggled?"

"Oh, no. A friend of Joseph's brought it as a gift. Excuse me, Floyd. I see someone at the gate." Fanny walked a few paces toward the main doors, and turning her head around, raised her voice to say, "I do hope the Queen Mother's hand heals in a few days."

"I pray to God it does," added a somewhat solemn Floyd Conway.

Fanny stood under the lintel waiting for Helen Valdés, who was detained at the gate. The arriving guests had a grandiose view of the fifty-two horseshoe arches which delineated the perimeter of the great room, the Mozarabic rugs that hung from the marble walls, and above all, the great staircase flooded by the lights of the candelabras and lined with hibiscuses and performing musicians dressed in their terra-cotta colored suits. Helen Valdés was still held back at the entrance, struggling with the uncoopera-tive gate. The latch was somehow stuck and it wouldn't open. It was obvious Helen was becoming desperate. The orchestra sounds wafted out across the garden and she could hear a dulcet flute shining over Aragón's Orchestra's rendition of "The Constitutional Cadet," Helen's favorite song. She was about to miss her favorite dancing tune and cried for help. But no one came to her rescue. Juan Benson, still busy dismembering the tree, was too far from the gate to hear her cries or the beeping of the horn. Fed up with the situation, Helen got out of the car and shook the gates in despair. Finally, the latch gave way and the gates swung open. Helen was in such a rush, she left her car running and scurried as fast as she could, losing one of her high-heel shoes in her flight. As she ran past Fanny and entered through one of the side doors, her long Cordoban-leather skirt rustled slightly; her tanned, freckled shoulders, glossy hair, and diamonds glittered. Not looking directly at any one, Helen advanced to the dance floor, ignoring the gentle-men who stood silently admiring the beauty of her figure, her full shoul-ders, her bosom, her back. "What an exquisite woman," the fellows said, seeing her.

"It's marvelous to see you, Nellie," Fanny said with fake eagerness and language. "What a lovely blue gown! Your pet is adorable and I love his teal jacket." Nellie didn't pay any attention to Fanny and settled the folds in her

6. Designer of high fashion (French).    7. Dog breed developed in southern Africa.

dress. She had never liked Fanny because she was a foreigner and Nellie would have loved to have been one, too.

Fanny's fleshy hands were patting Rigoletto when she realized Don Andrés and Nelson were standing next to Nellie. "Don Andrés, Nelson! I am so sorry. I didn't see you come in." A look of embarrassment came over Fanny's face. "May I take your cane, Don Andrés?"

"It's quite all right, Fanny. You know how attached Nellie is to Rigo. She made us walk behind Rigo in case he spotted a truffle or two."

"Nellie, I hear rumors you're expecting your first? Is it true?" There was a note of sadness in Fanny's voice.

"Yes, it seems that way. Excuse me, I think Rigo has found something interesting in that pot. See how he has straightened his tail, and his snout is directly pointing down?'

"Some port, Nellie? Gentlemen, a bit of sherry?"

Nellie didn't answer. She was already next to the potted tamarind. Don Andrés and Nelson, each carrying a glass of sherry, walked inside where a group of men had congregated under the rotunda.

"If it isn't Don Andrés Pardo and Nelson Guiristain," shouted a perky Welshman. "Your father was looking for you, Nelson. He asked if we had seen you. He said you were supposed to meet him here at seven."

Nelson's face turned pale. "Excuse me, Don Andrés, Mr. Conway. I must find Daddy." He walked out with a clumsy, pained gesture, holding his stomach, his forehead beaded with sweat.

Nelson headed for the club's grounds. He was sure he would find his father at the handball courts, practicing his serve. Inside the club, the conversation continued.

"So, Mr. Conway, what's your opinion of the rebel attack?" asked Don Andrés.

"The usual. Nothing to be alarmed about. I've lived through ten of these insurgencies since I settled in Xawa. I don't worry about them anymore. Besides, these things tend to fizzle out like seltzer water, and if the rebels are ready to face martyrdom, so much the better. I have no respect for martyrs. It's sheer idiocy. Don't lose any sleep over this. You know very well, Andrés, that with money, there's nothing one can't cure. I'm certain last week's bombing has turned the rebels into mashed *pomme de terre*.[8] Oh, I see Peter Frey coming in our direction."

"Is he coming alone? I saw his wife getting out of a red convertible as we drove in."

"They always travel separately to avoid kidnappers. There are some big concerns, like Gravi Laboratories, that are pressuring Pete to sell them his new formula for muriatic acid with Pirey."

"Hi, boys!" Pete Frey greeted the circle, impeccable in the latest Italian-style suit, though his hair seemed to have been hastily finger-combed. It was smooth in the front but sticking out behind like a sea urchin.

"Hello, Pete," the men responded.

"How's business?" Conway hurried to ask.

"Boys, I'm going to make a big request today," he said, gulping his highball. "I drove four-hundred kilometers to be away from all that, to have some fun. I don't want to hear about it. So let's ask the poet to recite for us."

8. Potato (French).

"He usually does it during the after-dinner drinks," Benigno the Basque intervened.

"Well, tell him I want to listen to an early recital. Tell him it's Pete Frey who wants to listen to his muse."

"Lazarus," ordered Don Andrés, "tell Mr. Pons, the man wearing the leaves around his head, that I must tell him something."

"Yes, sir."

A few minutes later, the poet laureate acquiesced to Pete's request, and the circle tightened under the dome.

Lisander cleared his throat with a shot of cognac to feed the muse.

> "I've seen wings come forth
> from firm women's shoulders
> seen butterflies fly out
> of trash heaps."

The poet made a pause, cracked his bony fingers and continued,

> "I come from everywhere
> To everywhere I go:
> I'm art among the arts
> and in the mountains,
> I'm a mountain."

And then, with his eyes focused on the dome, in rapture, his lips parted, he took a deep breath before his final verse.

> "My poems please the strong
> my poems which are sincere and brief
> they're as rugged
> as the steel used
> to forge a sword."

"To forge a sword" was still echoing through the clubhouse when a rather inebriated Pete Frey embraced the poet, impregnating his linen shirt with the stench of winy sweat, and mumbled, "I really love your poems, pal. It's the absolute truth when you say your poems please the strong, and that's why I like them. I'm strong! I'm a sword myself and I'll slice like a piece of Swiss cheese any motherfucker who wants to mess with me." Then Pete looked Lisander straight in the eyes and said, "Buddy, there's something I don't quite understand—that art and mountain stuff."

Lisander, who was obviously pleased, proceeded to explain. "It means that I'm at ease talking to the president of the Royal Bank, for instance, or to my maid."

"No shit, Lisander! I feel just the same." Pete let go of the embrace and, shaking the poet's hand, said, "Next time you're in the capital, give me a call. I'm going to show you the best time of your life. And now I have to take a leak."

The men continued talking about their favorite subjects, women and business, but were careful not to offend Don Andrés with their crude remarks. Don Andrés cleared his throat every so often to signal his displeasure if the boys got carried away. He was regarded as a man of high moral standards, a true gentleman, a man of dignity.

Lisander partook of the conversation for a few minutes and excused himself, promising Pete more poems at the prescribed time. His face still beamed from the adulations as he walked back to his fiance, Vicky, who waved from the bar. Vicky was carrying on an intense conversation with her friend Loly and her child-prodigy brother, Cioci. The group was discussing Cioci's discovery of a presumed extinct amphibian in a cave near the hamlet of Small Corral. Lisander joined the ongoing conversation and took a genuine interest in Cioci's discovery.

"A literary genius," Don Andrés said to Mayor Sánchez, who had joined the group a bit late and had caught the last two lines of the last poem.

"Yes, it's amazing. I've heard him a few times at the Athenaeum. I especially enjoyed one called 'Errant Love.'"

"What's the view in the capital on the uprising we experienced in this region a few weeks ago? I read Faithful Chester's manifesto, *History Will Absorb You*, and I must admit it has distressed me a bit." It seemed to be Don Andrés' opening remark to everyone he spoke with that evening.

"We don't think Faithful Chester, the guerrilla leader, has a chance in Hell. The minute the armed forces coordinate their efforts, he'll be history, running with his tail between his legs. If you excuse me a minute, Don Andrés, I have to telephone my sugar at the Telegraph. Tell the waiter when he comes by I'm low on my libation. I'll be right back."

Outside, Nelson had looked everywhere for his father. He had checked by the handball courts and the croquet lawn and was about to give up his quest after he passed the badminton net when he spotted something shining by the pool.

"Daddy, Daddy," Nelson shouted when he saw his father near the pool. "I've been looking for you everywhere. I thought you'd be at the handball courts. Luckily, something was shining that led me here."

"Don't shout! I am not deaf! Well, it was no star of Bethlehem that brought you here. Probably my gold watch." Rudolph barely glanced at his son, took a final puff from his Havana cigar, and threw it in the pool. "Where were you? I told you at seven. You have this tendency to muddle and spoil." He sounded angry.

"I know, Daddy, but Nellie wasn't feeling well. You know she's pregnant."

"That's no excuse," he said in a gruff voice. "You're a man and she's a woman. It's her job to be pregnant and yours to come on time when I tell you and to carry out in exact detail what I have said. I hate careless people! Did you complete the business consolidations I asked you to do?"

"Yes, sir. Here they are." Nelson took out a long piece of paper filled with official seals and stamps. He waited for his father's praise. There was none. The old man read the paper, told him to file it, and turned around.

"I'll file it tomorrow, Daddy."

"What do you mean, tomorrow? Go to the office right now and file it. And not a word out of you!"

"But, Daddy, the dinner is about to begin and Nellie . . ."

"I said not a word. You're too fat anyway." At that moment Rudolph Guiristain longed to break something.

"Yes, Daddy!"

• • •

The club still hummed like a beehive and a fine mist had started falling outside when there was a sudden stir and all conversation hushed. The crowd rushed sideways and then moved apart to let Fanny walk to the strains of the orchestra, which struck up at once "Pomp and Circumstance."[9] Behind the regal Fanny walked Mrs. Peña, Cuquín Valley and Pituca Josende. The space where Nellie should have walked, but refused, was filled by Helen Valdés-Curl. Fanny walked slowly, waving to the guests as though trying to prolong the first moments of her mandate. At Joseph Fern's request, the musicians changed the tune and played "When The Saints Go Marching In,"[1] a bit of nostalgia from her native land. When Fanny finally reached the banquet table, her face beaming with bliss, the orchestra switched melodies again to the Club's alma mater, lyrics by Mrs. Rudolph Guiristain set to music by Ernest Lecuona and sung with gusto by the invitees and Aïda Lopez, whose deep voice overpowered the rest.

The Little Father, as Father Santos was affectionately called by his friends, stood up and asked the visitors to keep quiet and bow their heads in sign of respect, if not repentance, as he gave the invocation:

*In spiritu humilitatis, et in animo contrito suscipiamur a te, Domine: et sic fiat sacrificium nostrum in conspectu tuo hodie, ut placeat tibi, Domine Deus.*[2]

The hungry guests sat down at the U-shaped table after a resounding "amen," but parted with the blessing, which was to produce a soothing effect on the friendly souls.

No sooner had the guests settled down to eat after the Bishop's benediction, when Mrs. Peña offered a toast in honor of the newly elected President Fanny de Fern. The octogenarian raised her glass and, in a thunderous voice that was out of character, said, "To Fanny, a seed from far away that has rooted deep in the red clay of Xawa."

"To Fanny, To Fanny, Viva Fanny, To Fanny," echoed the walls of the large ballroom.

Only Nellie had remained conspicuously silent and had refused to stand up for the toast. "What's the fuss about her being a seed from far away? I was practically born overseas myself, and I don't make a big deal about it," she whispered to Rigo, who was seated by her feet; Nelson hadn't returned from his errand.

The waiters bustled, and the room was full of noise and movement following Delfina's orders to bring in the evening's courses. The tiny scrolls with the menu in miniature gothic script were bound with sterling silver rings and placed inside the empty crystal water glasses engraved with the club's crest. As each guest retrieved the menu, his glass was immediately filled with sparkling Amaro mineral water. If anyone could read lips, it would have been easy to decipher the menu. Helen Valdés was reciting it to herself:

9. Famous march written by Edward Elgar (1857–1934), English composer; source of the tune for the British patriotic song "Land of Hope and Glory."

1. American gospel hymn, traditionally used in New Orleans as a funeral march.

2. Humbled in mind, and contrite of heart, may we find favor with Thee, O Lord; and may the sacrifice we this day offer up be well pleasing to Thee, Who art our Lord and our God [part of the liturgy of the Latin Mass].

| Appetizers: | Oysters Vieux Carré Fanny |
| | Alligator Tail Fingers |
| Soups: | Creole Turtle Soup |
| | Filé Gumbo |
| Entrees: | Venison Churchill |
| | with Mulled Wine |
| | Quail Fricandeau |
| | with Chianti Classico |
| | Crawfish Fanny |
| | with Riscal White |
| | Bison Tongue in Green Mayonnaise |
| | with Barolo Red |
| | Yeux du Pompano aux Fines Herbes |
| | with Moroccan Bordelaise |
| Vegetables: | Almond Rice |
| | Braised Belgium Endive With Walnuts |
| Desserts: | California Apricots, Pears, Apples |
| | Fidenza Belforti Parmigiano Reggiano |

"The oysters are delicious," remarked Pituca as she finished devouring the last dozen in record time, the empty shells scattered around the plate.

"Yes, they are quite good," answered Floyd, though Pituca's statement was meant for Belinda. "I understand its one of Fanny's family recipes. And Mrs. Josende, if I may say so, you do have a healthy appetite."

Pituca felt embarrassed as all eyes focused on her shell-filled plate. "I'm afraid I've a weakness for oysters," she said, although she had the reputation of not letting a single dish pass her way without sacking it completely.

"It seems more like a passion," interjected Loly Espino as the waiters were bringing the soup.

There was absolute silence for a few minutes. Only the clatter of spoons could be heard as the diners touched and emptied the bowls.

"When is Nelson returning?" Don Andrés asked his daughter as he savored the mulled wine.

"I have no idea, Papá! But I don't think Rigo likes this party. I think he wants to go home."

"Nellie, don't make a scene. We will leave as soon as your husband returns."

Don Andrés went back to enjoying the wine and tilted his head to the right to address Rudolph Guiristain. "How much longer until Nelson returns, Rudolph?"

Guiristain, Sr. laughed out loud. "Ha, ha, ha, it should take him five minutes, but in Nelson's case probably two hours, especially after he married into your family." Mrs. Guiristain pinched him under the table.

Don Andrés pretended not to hear him and added, "I hear rumors the communists have infiltrated the guerrilla movement . . ."

"Such a morbid subject war is. You can talk about it later," Mrs. Guiristain said to be polite, thinking her husband wasn't going to answer Don Andrés.

A tipsy Rudolph with vacant eyes waited a few more seconds to answer him, as if he was ransacking his brains to find the proper words.

"You know what I think of the guerrillas." And without anyone else noticing him but Don Andrés, he grabbed his balls in defiance and shook them
for a while, laughing contemptuously.

Don Andrés, taken by surprise, didn't wait for the garçon and poured
himself another glass of mulled wine, and at a loss for words said, "The
venison is particularly tender, Mr. Guiristain."

"I have an important announcement to make," said Helen. "I have convinced my husband, Pete, to donate a new hardwood dancing floor for the
club."

There was loud applause.

"On behalf of the Ladies' Tennis Club, and in my capacity as President
and as my first official act, we thank you and Peter from the bottom of our
hearts."

"I also have an announcement," Mrs. Peña said as she washed down the
quail with a flood of Chianti. "The Sacred Heart of Jesus Jesuit School will
hold its first sixth-grade swimming meet in our new pool facility."

The next round of applause was about to start when Pituca Josende stood
up and yelled in anger.

"I am the only one with the power to authorize any aquatic activity. I was
promised that if I . . ."

Floyd Conway didn't let her finish her statement, shouting, "Silence,
please. Silence. This is nothing more than a simple misunderstanding, Mrs.
Josende. Do you give your permission to hold the Jesuit swimming meet at
the Ladies' Tennis Club?"

Once more all eyes were on Pituca, and feeling the pressure, she responded,
"I do." Floyd's quick maneuvering caught Pituca by surprise. "But all further
events must be approved by me one month in advance."

"And now, I propose a toast to the new pool." Floyd raised his glass.

"To the new pool," answered the crowd.

. . .

The great cornucopia that had provided the banquet lay empty, and the
guests busied themselves discreetly repositioning their false teeth or chatting with each other with the serenity and good will that only a full belly
can induce.

"Isn't it a lovely clock?" said Vicky to her poet.

"Yes, indeed. But the beauty of that chronometer cannot match my love for
thee." Lisander kissed Vicky's hands, leaving green mayonnaise residue on
her palms. She blushed and, under Cupid's spell, kept her eyes fixed inquir-
ingly on Lisander's black pupils. She was moved by a spirit and burst out,
"How do I love thee, Lis? Let me count the ways. I love you when you brush
your teeth. I love you when you sleep. I love you in the shower. I love you at
the tennis courts. I love you when you gargle. But above all, I love how you
love me!"

"Did you have a nice ride, Mrs. Frey? Ours was a bit bumpy," inquired
Benigno the Basque, looking at Helen.

"Please don't call me Mrs. Frey. Everybody calls me Helen," she said as
she rearranged her bedouin shawl to cover half of her face. "My ride was
awful but uneventful! The roads are filled with potholes, but I had some fun
running over two roosters and a pig."

"How's your daughter, María Rosa?" asked Cuquín, turning sharply around. "Is she better from her illness?"

"Macuqui is a little better, but she could be much better if she were to listen to Dr. Cabrera and take her medicine properly. I told her not to take her clothes off with the windows open. It was the draft that made her sick."

"I understand perfectly. I know how defiant teenagers can be. I have four myself."

"And your mom, Cuquín, still living at Miramar?"[3]

"Oh, no. She lives with us. She lost her mind and doesn't remember anything, not even me. She only remembers the days of the week in French. You know she lived in Blois as a child when my grandfather served as consul in that Gallic city."

"It saddens me to hear it. Loneliness is the only prevention against the outrages of pain."

Cuquín didn't quite understand, but feeling the conversation was getting too personal, she quickly excused herself with the pretext she had to introduce the night's performers.

"Ladies and gentlemen, I have the honor of presenting our nation's leading contralto, Aïda[4] Lopez. She will delight us this evening with her most famous pieces. Immediately following, our poet laureate will enchant us with his latest inspirations."

"Music, maestro." Aïda cleared her throat, and in her husky voice thanked Cuquín Valley, who had introduced her, Aïda was in the middle of one of her favorite renditions, "Martha, Tiny Rose Bud"[5]—at the precise moment when her voice was reaching the crescendo, ". . . Martha from my garden you're the flower . . ."—when a thundering noise was heard and some of the chandeliers came crashing to the floor. Then all the lights went off and the confused screams of the guests rang out.

"The guerrillas! It's another attack. It must be Faithful Chester!"

"My leg. You're sitting on my leg."

"Rigoletto, Rigo, where are you, baby?"

"Let the rebels know that I'm the only one who can arrange the aquatic bookings."

"The government will drive them out of here in no time. Be calm. There's no need to worry . . ."

Aïda kept on singing without the orchestra. She wasn't about to let them spoil her evening. Then she heard a voice ordering her to the floor, and when she ignored it, she was forced down by a blow to her knees. Immediately, the guests heard the sounds of someone being dragged along the ballroom towards one of the side doors. There was silence when Rudolph Guiristain gathered enough courage to stand up and, grouping through the room, reached the wall and flipped on the emergency lights. Then a scream was heard.

"Pete! They have taken Pete! My Peteeeeeeeee! I knew it, I knew it." Helen was sobbing deeply and beating her chest.

"Those awful guerrillas. I thought the soldiers had swept them away." Fanny crawled to her side to comfort her.

---

3. This could be Miramar, Florida, or Miramir, Cuba.
4. A playful reference to the Italian opera *Aida* (1871), by the composer Giuseppe Verdi (1813–

1901) and the librettist Antonio Ghizlanzoni (1824–1893).
5. The English title of a famous Cuban ballad, "Marta, capullito de rosa."

"It wasn't the guerrillas. I begged him to stay home. They wanted the formula." She sighed in pain, "Oh, Peteeeee!" She cried, holding her red shawl in her hands, lifting it from time to time to wipe the mixture of tears and eyeliner as it crept down her cheeks.

"Someone bring this woman a glass of sherry! Let the orchestra play. Maestro, please. Nothing has happened here. The party must go on," ordered Floyd. "Carry on, carry on."

1995

# FRANKLIN GUTIÉRREZ
## b. 1951

Franklin Gutiérrez was born in the Dominican Republic. He earned his bachelor's and master's degrees in education and Latin American literature from the Autonomous University of Santo Domingo, a master's in Spanish and Latin American literatures from the City College of the City University of New York, and a doctorate in Spanish and Latin American literatures from the City University of New York Graduate Center. Since then, he has taught in the City University of New York system and currently is a professor of foreign languages, English as a second language, and humanities at York College, CUNY. He has published several books of poetry, including *Helen* (1986) and *Hábeas Corpus* (1994); edited anthologies, collections of literary essays, and bibliographies, all of these both in Spanish and in English; and has published essays on various Latin American authors. Some of his work is in Spanish and some is in English; most of his books have been published in the Dominican Republic and are available only in Spanish-language bookstores in the United States.

Gutiérrez's widely anthologized poem "Helen" addresses one of the many Dominican women who arrived in the United States in the mid-1960s. Poor, uneducated, and often not knowing any English, these women were forced to fend for themselves in a place vastly different from their homeland and in which they had no experience. As she assimilates, Helen's identity ebbs, and she is left between two worlds, living fully in neither. In crossing the gender line to understand the situations of Helen and women like her, Gutiérrez was ahead of many Dominican poets of his time.

## Helen[1]

How things have changed, Helena,
the anguished cry for a homeland
left behind
the first encounter with
the tall, uniform faded towers of the empire,      5
the wide avenues
buried under immense layers of snow,
the traffic signs,

---

1. Translated by Daisy Cocco de Filippis.

one way, no parking anytime, quarters only.
The daily toils with a heater,                                  10
with feet bumping into sleeping rugs,
and the scar on your left knee,
sad reminder of an escalator's collapse.

No time for letters home, Helena.
now you are enthralled with                                     15
the greatness of the Intrepid Museum,
the aircraft carrier inhabiting
New York's port and the Hudson's waters.[2]
Taken aback only by its greatness
and its illustrious history of wartime deeds                    20
—as the guide books remind us—
its sea voyages
its impressive record of nautical miles.
Take a good look at its walls.
Oh, taken aback only by its greatness.                          25
Its walls smartly decorated
cannot hide the victims of bygone years.

This immense ship once happened to pass by your island
just to see was happening.

How things have changed, Helena,                                30
your mother misses
the final A left out of your name
in your last letter home.
This is how things are now, you tell her,
because your American boyfriend calls you Helen,                35
and you tell your friends
how he beds you
how he stays in your room
how he is free with you
how he never goes out with you                                  40
but, of course, Helena,
what will his friends say of a dark-skinned Mama like you?
And his mother, picture her shame,
unable to understand your English,
much less your Spanish.                                         45
So what? you answer,
you find him nice,
better than those Latin machos,
and so he continues to bed you
while he dates a Northamerican blonde                           50
No, never a Latin man, for
how are you to improve your lot?
Are you forgetting that when Latin are machos
the gringos are . . . Forgive this pause.

2. The Intrepid Sea-Air-Space Museum, founded in 1982, is devoted to military and maritime history. It is housed in the World War II aircraft carrier USS *Intrepid* and is located in the Hudson River, at a pier on the West Side of Manhattan.

Ah, Helen,     55
I find it difficult to call you by that name
—the missing A.
You must understand my fondness for your folks.

Pedro—mi amigo—would have long called you
una puta     60
for confusing stupidity
with improving your lot.

How things have changed, Helena,
the radio cassette, remote control,
la washing machine, la dishwasher,     65
treasures beyond your finest dreams.
*Comida, fiesta, letrina,*[3]
never again to be found in your conversation.
Now you speak of lunch, parties, and toilet,
rock, tours of the U.S. of A     70
and other countries
and, of course, your mink coat,
inseparable companion even in your summer days.

How things have changed, Helena,
far away many are still dreaming     75
and awaiting your next trip
to Tokyo, Paris, or Frankfurt.
Letters from the beloved homeland
tearfully left behind
are torn     80
before they are read
because you think that they will ask you for money
and your income for the next three years
has already been spent.

Oh, Helena,     85
impatiently awaiting
Thanksgiving and
Halloween.

One would never believe, Helena,
what your birth certificate states:     90
Cabimota,
a sector of Jimayaco
between much hunger and little land,
province of La Vega,
half a life away from civilization,     95
República Dominicana.

1986

3. Food, party, outhouse.

*Melody (from When the World Was Good)* (2002), where he explores his passion for music through a protagonist who is a Sephardic Jew interned in a concentration camp by the Nazis during World War II.

Hijuelos's novel for young adults, *Dark Dude* (2008), relates the coming-of-age of Rico Fuentes, the "palest Cubano who ever existed on the planet," his light skin and light hair making him stand out in his Harlem neighborhood. Rico flees to the Midwest, where he searches for and ultimately finds his ethnic identity.

---

## FROM THE MAMBO KINGS PLAY SONGS OF LOVE

## Chapter 1

It was a Saturday afternoon on La Salle Street,[1] years and years ago when I was a little kid, and around three o'clock Mrs. Shannon, the heavy Irish woman in her perpetually soup-stained dress, opened her back window and shouted out into the courtyard, "Hey, Cesar, yoo-hoo, I think you're on television, I swear it's you!" When I heard the opening strains of the *I Love Lucy* show I got excited because I knew she was referring to an item of eternity, that episode in which my dead father and my Uncle Cesar had appeared, playing Ricky Ricardo's singing cousins fresh off the farm in Oriente Province, Cuba, and north in New York for an engagement at Ricky's nightclub, the Tropicana.

This was close enough to the truth about their real lives—they were musicians and songwriters who had left Havana for New York in 1949, the year they formed the Mambo Kings, an orchestra that packed clubs, dance halls, and theaters around the East Coast—and, excitement of excitements, they even made a fabled journey in a flamingo-pink bus out to Sweet's Ballroom in San Francisco, playing on an all-star mambo night, a beautiful night of glory, beyond death, beyond pain, beyond all stillness.

Desi Arnaz had caught their act one night in a supper club on the West Side, and because they had perhaps already known each other from Havana or Oriente Province, where Arnaz, like the brothers, was born, it was natural that he ask them to sing on his show. He liked one of their songs in particular, a romantic bolero written by them, "Beautiful María of My Soul."

Some months later (I don't know how many, I wasn't five years old yet) they began to rehearse for the immortal appearance of my father on this show. For me, my father's gentle rapping on Ricky Ricardo's door has always been a call from the beyond, as in Dracula films, or films of the walking dead, in which spirits ooze out from behind tombstones and through the cracked windows and rotted floors of gloomy antique halls: Lucille Ball,[2] the lovely redheaded actress and comedienne who played Ricky's wife, was housecleaning when she heard the rapping of my father's knuckles against that door.

"I'm commmmmming," in her singsong voice.

---

1. In the Morningside Heights neighborhood of Manhattan.     2. (1911–1989).

Standing in her entrance, two men in white silk suits and butterfly-looking lace bow ties, black instrument cases by their side and black-brimmed white hats in their hands—my father, Nestor Castillo, thin and broad-shouldered, and Uncle Cesar, thickset and immense.

My uncle: "Mrs. Ricardo? My name is Alfonso and this is my brother Manny . . ."

And her face lights up and she says, "Oh, yes, the fellows from Cuba. Ricky told me all about you."

Then, just like that, they're sitting on the couch when Ricky Ricardo walks in and says something like "Manny, Alfonso! Gee, it's really swell that you fellas could make it up here from Havana for the show."

That's when my father smiled. The first time I saw a rerun of this, I could remember other things about him—his lifting me up, his smell of cologne, his patting my head, his handing me a dime, his touching my face, his whistling, his taking me and my little sister, Leticia, for a walk in the park, and so many other moments happening in my thoughts simultaneously that it was like watching something momentous, say the Resurrection, as if Christ had stepped out of his sepulcher, flooding the world with light—what we were taught in the local church with the big red doors—because my father was now newly alive and could take off his hat and sit down on the couch in Ricky's living room, resting his black instrument case on his lap. He could play the trumpet, move his head, blink his eyes, nod, walk across the room, and say "Thank you" when offered a cup of coffee. For me, the room was suddenly bursting with a silvery radiance. And now I knew that we could see it again. Mrs. Shannon had called out into the courtyard alerting my uncle: I was already in his apartment.

With my heart racing, I turned on the big black-and-white television set in his living room and tried to wake him. My uncle had fallen asleep in the kitchen—having worked really late the night before, some job in a Bronx[3] social club, singing and playing the horn with a pickup group of musicians. He was snoring, his shirt was open, a few buttons had popped out on his belly. Between the delicate-looking index and forefingers of his right hand, a Chesterfield cigarette burning down to the filter, that hand still holding a half glass of rye whiskey, which he used to drink like crazy because in recent years he had been suffering from bad dreams, saw apparitions, felt cursed, and, despite all the women he took to bed, found his life of bachelorhood solitary and wearisome. But I didn't know this at the time, I thought he was sleeping because he had worked so hard the night before, singing and playing the trumpet for seven or eight hours. I'm talking about a wedding party in a crowded, smoke-filled room (with bolted-shut fire doors), lasting from nine at night to four, five o'clock in the morning, the band playing one-, two-hour sets. I thought he just needed the rest. How could I have known that he would come home and, in the name of unwinding, throw back a glass of rye, then a second, and then a third, and so on, until he'd plant his elbow on the table and use it to steady his chin, as he couldn't hold his head up otherwise. But that day I ran into the kitchen to wake him up so that he could see the episode, too, shaking him gently and tugging at his elbow, which was a mistake, because it was as if I had pulled loose the support columns of a five-hundred-year-old church: he simply fell over and crashed to the floor.

3. A New York City borough north of Manhattan.

A commercial was running on the television, and so, as I knew I wouldn't have much time, I began to slap his face, pull on his burning red-hot ears, tugging on them until he finally opened one eye. In the act of focusing he apparently did not recognize me, because he asked, "Nestor, what are you doing here?"

"It's me, Uncle, it's Eugenio."

I said this in a really earnest tone of voice, just like that kid who hangs out with Spencer Tracy in the movie of *The Old Man and the Sea*,[4] really believing in my uncle and clinging on to his every word in life, his every touch like nourishment from a realm of great beauty, far beyond me, his heart. I tugged at him again, and he opened his eyes. This time he recognized me.

He said, "You?"

"Yes, Uncle, get up! Please get up! You're on television again. Come on."

One thing I have to say about my Uncle Cesar, there was very little he wouldn't do for me in those days, and so he nodded, tried to push himself off the floor, got to his knees, had trouble balancing, and then fell backwards. His head must have hurt: his face was a wince of pain. Then he seemed to be sleeping again. From the living room came the voice of Ricky's wife, plotting as usual with her neighbor Ethel Mertz about how to get a part on Ricky's show at the Tropicana, and I knew that the brothers had already been to the apartment—that's when Mrs. Shannon had called out into the courtyard—that in about five more minutes my father and uncle would be standing on the stage of the Tropicana, ready to perform that song again. Ricky would take hold of the microphone and say, "Well, folks, and now I have a real treat for you. Ladies and gentlemen, Alfonso and Manny Reyes, let's hear it!" And soon my father and uncle would be standing side by side, living, breathing beings, for all the world to see, harmonizing in a duet of that *canción*.

As I shook my uncle, he opened his eyes and gave me his hand, hard and callused from his other job in those days, as superintendent, and he said, "Eugenio, help me. Help me."

I tugged with all my strength, but it was hopeless. Still he tried: with great effort he made it to one knee, and then, with his hand braced on the floor, he started to push himself up again. As I gave him another tug, he began miraculously to rise. Then he pushed my hand away and said, "I'll be okay, kid."

With one hand on the table and the other on the steam pipe, he pulled himself to his feet. For a moment he towered over me, wobbling as if powerful winds were rushing through the apartment. Happily I led him down the hallway and into the living room, but he fell over again by the door—not fell over, but rushed forward as if the floor had abruptly tilted, as if he had been shot out of a cannon, and, wham, he hit the bookcase in the hall. He kept piles of records there, among them a number of the black and brittle 78s he had recorded with my father and their group, the Mambo Kings. These came crashing down, the bookcase's glass doors jerking open, the records shooting out and spinning like flying saucers in the movies and splintering into pieces. Then the bookcase followed, slamming into the floor beside him: the songs "*Bésame Mucho*," "*Acércate Más*," "*Juventud*," "Twilight in Havana," "Mambo Nine," "Mambo Number Eight," "Mambo for a Hot Night," and their fine version of "Beautiful María of My Soul"—all these were smashed up. This

---

4. In this 1958 Hollywood movie, the American actor Spencer Tracy (1900–1967) plays The Old Man. The Cuban actor Felipe Pazos (b. 1944) plays The Boy.

crash had a sobering effect on my uncle. Suddenly he got to one knee by himself, and then the other, stood, leaned against the wall, and shook his head.

"*Bueno*," he said.

He followed me into the living room, and plopped down on the couch behind me. I sat on a big stuffed chair that we'd hauled up out of the basement. He squinted at the screen, watching himself and his younger brother, whom, despite their troubles, he loved very much. He seemed to be dreaming.

"Well, folks," Ricky Ricardo said, "and now I have a real treat for you . . . ."

The two musicians in white silk suits and big butterfly-looking lace bow ties, marching toward the microphone, my uncle holding a guitar, my father a trumpet.

"Thank you, thank you. And now a little number that we composed . . ." And as Cesar started to strum the guitar and my father lifted his trumpet to his lips, playing the opening of "Beautiful María of My Soul," a lovely, soaring melody line filling the room.

They were singing the song as it had been written—in Spanish. With the Ricky Ricardo Orchestra behind them, they came into a turnaround and began harmonizing a line that translates roughly into English as: "What delicious pain love has brought to me in the form of a woman."

My father . . . He looked so alive!

"Uncle!"

Uncle Cesar had lit a cigarette and fallen asleep. His cigarette had slid out of his fingers and was now burning into the starched cuff of his white shirt. I put the cigarette out, and then my uncle, opening his eyes again, smiled. "Eugenio, do me a favor. Get me a drink."

"But, Uncle, don't you want to watch the show?"

He tried really hard to pay attention, to focus on it.

"Look, it's you and Poppy."

"*Coño*,[5] *sí* . . ."

My father's face with his horsey grin, arching eyebrows, big fleshy ears—a family trait—that slight look of pain, his quivering vocal cords, how beautiful it all seemed to me then . . .

And so I rushed into the kitchen and came back with a glass of rye whiskey, charging as fast as I could without spilling it. Ricky had joined the brothers onstage. He was definitely pleased with their performance and showed it because as the last note sounded he whipped up his hand and shouted "*Olé*," a big lock of his thick black hair falling over his brows. Then they bowed and the audience applauded.

The show continued on its course. A few gags followed: a costumed bull with flowers wrapped around its horns came out dancing an Irish jig, its horn poking into Ricky's bottom and so exasperating him that his eyes bugged out, he slapped his forehead and started speaking a-thousand-words-a-Second Spanish. But at that point it made no difference to me, the miracle had passed, the resurrection of a man, Our Lord's promise which I then believed, with its release from pain, release from the troubles of this world.

1989

_____
5. Damn.

### FROM MR. IVES' CHRISTMAS

## On Madison and Forty-First Street

Buying a chocolate bar in the lobby, Ives stepped out through the revolving doors into the street: the sky was a clean wintry blue—the blue of deeply processed magazine ads, the blue of poster art for seaside vacations in Hawaii and Havana, a blue that, reminiscent of water, seemed dense and inviting, a blue of light diffused through crystal. It was bitterly cold, the temperature way below freezing, thanks to some northeasterly winds that had come down from Canada, he remembered, cold enough so that clouds of steam billowed out of the manholes of the street and oozed out of the very pavement. But a good and clear day, all the same, in fact so clear that Ives had the surprising impression that his slightly myopic vision, never one hundred percent—he disliked wearing glasses—had suddenly improved to a remarkable degree. He had eaten about half of the chocolate bar and was savoring its aftertaste when several of his fellow workers came out of the building, and while he nodded in his usual friendly manner, he could not even begin to entertain the idea of a conversation with them. When Tilly, the receptionist, saw Ives standing by himself, and asked, "Mr. Ives, you feel like taking a walk?" he could barely bring himself to answer. "Maybe tomorrow."

And she walked on.

Then something else unusual happened: walking down the street toward the impossibly crowded avenue, and standing shoulder to shoulder amid a throng of shoppers on the corner, Ives was waiting for the light to change, when he blinked his eyes and, in a moment of pure clarity that he would always remember, began to feel *euphoria*, all the world's goodness, as it were, spinning around him.

At the same time, he began to feel certain physical sensations: the sidewalk under him lifting ever so slightly, and the avenue, dense with holiday traffic, fluttering like an immense carpet, and growing wider and stretching onward as if it would continue to do so forever, an ever-expanding river of life. And the skyscrapers that lined Madison Avenue—beginning with the Young & Rubicam building just across the street, with its streams of employees rushing in and out of its revolving doors—began to waver, the buildings bowing as if to recognize Ives, bending as if the physical world were a grand joke. And in those moments he could feel the very life in the concrete below him, the ground humming—pipes and tangles of cables and wires beneath him, endless ticking, moving, animated objects. Why, it was as if he could hear molecules grinding, light shifting here and there, the vibrancy of things and spirit everywhere.

In one slip of a second, anything seemed possible—had the moon risen and started to sing, had pyramids appeared over the Chrysler building weeping, Ives would have been no more surprised.

Then, not knowing whether to shout from ecstasy or fear, he looked up and saw the sun, glowing red and many times its normal size, looming over the avenue, a pink and then flaring yellow corona bursting from it. And then, in all directions the very sky filled with four rushing, swirling winds, each defined by a different-colored powder like strange Asian spices: one was cardinal red, one the color of saffron, another gray like mothwing, the last a brilliant violet, and these came from four directions, spinning like a great pinwheel over Madison Avenue and Forty-first Street. Leaning back, nearly falling, Ives was on the verge of running for his life when, just like that, a great calm returned, the sun receding, the blue sky utterly tranquil. The traffic light clicked on and the light changed, traffic and commerce resuming as usual.

As a cop in a helmeted, visored, vaguely medieval-looking rain suit directed traffic, waving pedestrians into the street, Ives's fear left him and he began to experience a thorough love for all things. In the glow of such feelings people truly seemed blessed; truck and car horns sounded like heavenly trumpets, the murmur of the crowds and all the other voices fell upon his ears like music; the enormous visage of a dapper-looking fellow smoking a cigarette in an advertisement on the side of a bus seemed like some evidence of the absolute. Then there were the swirls of green wire and Christmas lights, those that tipped over and bubbled, those whose glowing filaments pirouetted like ballerinas, those whose collars resembled cherry necklaces—those lights, entangled or cleverly strung, adorning store windows, twinkling with benevolence, and, it seemed to Ives, nearly breathing, like everything else in the world.

Catching his own reflection in a window, Ives, nondescript in an overcoat, hat, and scarf, judged himself a most pleasant-looking, perhaps saintly, fellow. His face like a sphinx's in one moment, the next like Saint Paul's, as it might have been when he was stricken with a divine light.[1] With a renewed appreciation he considered the mechanisms of his own body, the littlest turn of his artistic hands, the twitch of nose, all splendid. To hear, to smell, to see, to feel, all were miraculous.

It was on Forty-ninth and Fifth that Ives saw an old woman struggling down a stairway to a subway station,[2] and he stopped to help her along. He was whistling and seemed so cheerful that the old woman said, "My, you really do enjoy this holiday, don't you?" and Ives said, "Yes, I do, very much, but you see, ma'am, it's just not this time of the year; you see, ma'am, I've just had the most unusual kind of experience, though it's not anything I can really explain, except to say that about half an hour ago I had a vision of God's presence in the world. And it still makes me feel joy." Then: "Well, good luck to you, ma'am. And Merry Christmas."

The woman, leaning forward on a cane, moved slowly through the turnstile, Ives a little hurt by her expression, which, as he read it, seemed to say that he was a very nice man, but one who was not playing with a full deck of cards.

An afternoon spent keeping things in. A vision was a vision, he supposed, not understanding why it had happened to him. It wasn't his nature to talk

---

1. According to New Testament texts that he wrote, St. Paul (also known as Paul of Tarsus, Paul the Apostle, and the Apostle Paul; ca. 5 BC–ca. 67 AD) was converted to Christianity on the road to Damascus. He became one of the most significant early Christian missionaries.
2. Poetic license is at work here, because no subway station exists at 49th St. and 5th Ave., nor does any subway line run there.

about such things. When he got back to the office, around three-thirty, and someone asked, "How was your lunch?" he smiled, shrugged, and said, "Fine, thanks." Someone, having heard from the doorman about Ives getting stuck in the elevator, had told everyone in the office, so that many a person came by to chat about it, only to find him sitting behind his drawing board, hands folded on his lap, a puzzled and troubled expression upon his face.

He tried to call Annie at home, but she wasn't there. Then, attempting to work and finding that he could not concentrate, he made his way out of the office, even though it was only four o'clock.

Heading uptown on foot, he decided to visit Saint Patrick's Cathedral, beginning to tremble the moment he approached its doors. Visiting the church on that afternoon seemed oddly difficult. Too many supernatural forces seemed to be swarming everywhere around him, and though he found himself doting, as he always had, over the benevolent images of Christ and the Holy Mother—particularly of the crèche—he began to feel a slight weariness and apprehension, partly harking back to his natural disposition, and partly due to a question that he had started to ask himself: "If I had a vision, then why did it not seem Christian?"

Like Saint Paul struck by a heavenly beam of light, or Teresa de Avila with her vision of the celestial mansions of God, or Constantine with his fiery cross in the sky?[3]

1995

3. Constantine I (d. AD 337), Roman emperor 306–37, reputedly saw a fiery cross in the sky before an important battle. *Teresa de Avila*: Spanish nun, writer, and mystic (1515–1582), who was inspired to write her book *El Castillo Interior* or *Las Moradas* (The Interior Castle or The Mansions, 1577) after reputedly receiving a vision from God of a crystal, castle-shaped globe containing seven mansions.

# JIMMY SANTIAGO BACA
## b. 1952

Jimmy Santiago Baca's poetic voice is brutal yet tender. He was born in New Mexico to a Chicano father and an Indian mother. His parents abandoned him, and initially he was raised by his grandparents, but after his grandfather's death he was sent to an orphanage. As an illiterate 21-year-old, he was sentenced to five years in a maximum security prison for selling drugs. He began to turn his life around by learning to read and write and unearthing a voracious passion for poetry. During a conflict with another inmate, Baca was shaken by the voices of the two towering figures in twentieth-century literature: the Chilean poet Pablo Neruda and the Spanish poet and dramatist Federico García Lorca. Frantically, even magically, he wrote a set of autobiographical poems that speak of injustice and alienation. His characters are young males handcuffed by poverty, with "nothing to do, nowhere to go."

Baca sent three of his poems to the American poet Denise Levertov, then the poetry editor of *Mother Jones* magazine. Levertov later described Baca's characters as people who witness brutality and degradation yet retain "an innocent eye—a wild creature's eye—and deep and loving respect for the earth." After being printed in *Mother Jones*, the poems became part of Baca's collection *Immigrants in Our Own Land* (1979, rev. 1990), published the year he was released from prison. He earned his general equivalency diploma (GED) later that same year. In 1984, he earned a bachelor's degree in English from the University of New Mexico, in Albuquerque.

For a decade, Baca steadily produced work about the tortured experiences of Chicanos. The reader senses a poet ready to denounce, and to do so angrily, but careful not to turn his poetry into an organ of propaganda: "I Am with Those / Whose blood has spilled the streets too often, / Surprising bystanders in hushed fear," he writes in one poem. "I am dangerous. I am a fool to you all. / Yes, but I stand as I am, / I am food for the future."

*Martín & Meditations on the South Valley* (1987) is a 45-page exploration of the life of an adolescent Chicano who, abandoned by his parents, travels across the United States and confronts his limitations. Some Chicano critics—displeased with Baca's depictions of alcoholism, violence, and narcotic escapes—accused Baca of pushing down his people by stressing the ugly aspects of life. In the essay "Q-Vo" (the title is a phonetic redraw of *¿Qué hubo?*, or What's up?), Baca responded:

> [In the critics' view] Chicanos have never betrayed each other, we never have fought each other, never sold out; nor have we ever experienced poverty or suffering, wept, made mistakes. I never responded to these absurdities. Such narrowness and stupidity is its own curse.

Baca was writing in the aftermath of the Chicano Movement, as the country moved away from activism. Change had been fought for, but it remained intangible. In exposing the tension between whites and Mexicans in the Southwest, Baca's anger spoke to the unredeemed and nonaffiliated and also to a mainstream audience aware of the social limitations remaining in the wake of the civil rights era. In 1992, he published a collection of pugnacious stories and essays from this period: *Working in the Dark: Reflections of a Poet of the Barrio*. Baca has also written screenplays.

*Black Mesa Poems* (1989) signaled a shift in Baca's concerns, from crime and conflict to barrio life; rustic life, the latter in particular on his New Mexico ranch; community; the redemptive power of love; motherhood; and rivers and *piñón* trees. *Healing Earthquakes: A Love Story in Poems* (2001) consists of five symmetrical sections that range from adulthood to rebirth and back. Baca shapes this semiautobiographical series as a quest for balance in an eminently unbalanced universe. The narrator lusts after women, tangible and chimerical; explores myths and archetypes that come from Mesoamerican civilization; reflects on his imperfections; runs into trouble; and ultimately finds dignity not in religion but in morality.

Most of Baca's memoir, *A Place to Stand: The Making of a Poet* (2001), deals with his very early life: First his father leaves, and then his mother becomes involved with a man who persuades her to leave her children, mask her Mexican ancestry, and begin a WASP family in California. By the time Baca has left the orphanage and begun living on the street, he fears and is suspicious of adults. His race helps make him a societal pariah. Perennially harassed by the police, he is adrift and disoriented. Eventually, he is incarcerated briefly on a false murder charge. Upon his release, he fails to gain his footing and, selling drugs, rambles from San Diego to Arizona. After being arraigned again, he ends up in solitary confinement. Baca enters jail as a lost soul and leaves it empowered; in the early fragments of the book he is a *vato loco*, a crazy dude, but after the second imprisonment, he is an unapologetic, ideologically defined Chicano. In the epilogue, Baca's mother returns to her Mexican identity, but her second husband stops her short with five bullets in her face. In presenting this horrific image of defeat, Baca seems more philosophical than angry.

*A Place to Stand* is about a sense of place in the most encompassing, most flexible sense of the term: as home, as the soil of one's roots, but also as the literary pantheon in which one fits. In the latter sense, the book belongs to the subgenre of prison tales for which the twentieth century was fertile ground, from *The Autobiography of Malcolm X* to the diaries of Václav Havel, the Czech playwright-and-dissident-turned-president. Among the Latinos writing in this genre are Piri Thomas (see p. 812), Miguel Piñero (p. 1372), Reinaldo Arenas (p. 1520), and Luis J. Rodríguez (p. 2047).

Baca's later books include the poetry volumes *Set This Book on Fire* (1999), *C-train (Dream Boy's Story) & Thirteen Mexicans* (2002), *Winter Poems along the Rio Grande* (2004), and *Spring Poems along the Rio Grande* (2007); the story collection *The Importance of a Piece of Paper* (2004); and the novel *A Glass of Water* (2009). A bilingual selection of his poetry was published in 2009. He has received a Pushcart Prize, the American Book Award, the International Hispanic Heritage Award, the International Award, the Cornelius P. Turner Award, and an honorary doctorate from the University of New Mexico. Baca lives in Albuquerque.

The three poems included in this anthology illustrate his stylistic development. "From Violence to Peace," from *Black Mesa Poemsi*, narrates the killing of a bull and the immediate and larger existential implications of the event. "Sixteen," the sixteenth section of *C-Train (Dream Boy's Story) & Thirteen Mexicans*, meditates on labor, migration, and the American Dream. "ChicaIndio," from *Spring Poems along the Rio Grande*, is about the poet's dual identity.

## From Violence to Peace

Twenty-eight shotgun pellets
crater my thighs, belly and groin.
I gently thumb each burnt bead,
fingering scabbed stubs with ointment.

Could have neutered me, made extinct                    5
the volatile, romantic man I am.
"He's dead,"
doctor at emergency room
could've easily told my wife that night.
Instead, "Soak him in a bath twice a day. Apply          10
this ointment to the sores. Here's a month's supply
of pain killers." I remember the deep guttural groan
I gave, when the doctor pressed my groin.
        Assured
I could still make love, morphine drowsed me             15
and in a dull stupor I don't remember
police visiting my bed, or laughing so hard,
they scowled for a serious answer.
I howled a U.F.O. shot me along the Río Grande,
and they cursed and left.                                20

In the summer of '88
I'd traded alfalfa for a bull calf.
Still smelling of milk udders,
I tied it to the truck rack and drove off.
Its hooves teethed                                       25

at pink roots
'til the whole lush field went bare dirt.
A magnificent bull.
Glowing wheel of heart
breathed brimming stream of white flame at dawn.                30
He wrangled his black brawn
like a battleshield to challenge the sun,
reared thick neck down and sideways,
lunged at me with dart and snort,
hoof-stamped and nostrilled dirt,                               35
      'til I growled him back
      whipping air
      with a limber willow branch,
      poured grain in trough
      and spread alfalfa.                               40
I respected his horns
and he the whistling
menace of willow.

One afternoon my cousin Patricio
helped me band the bull's scrotum,                              45
usurp swollen sap
in his testicle sack. It withered
to a pink wattle and seeded
the garden to drive cornstalks
to bear hardy, golden horns.                                    50

Thereafter, he grazed the fenceline,
with the tempered lust and peaceful grace
of a celibate priest.
His bearing now arranged itself
elegant as a wild flower                                        55
sprung over night.

           ———————

Perfecto shot it.
Rasping on a black rope of blood
round its neck, it staggered,
bouldering convulsions.                                         60
Blood exploding
in bright lash of earthquaked air,
it stumble-butted stock trailer fender—
second and third shots glowed
its death.                                                      65
A quivering shadow of life-flame
darkened the air and it sputtered
a last drop of blood.
I drank long swigs
of whiskey and, thinking it was dead,                           70
turned to walk away,
then

it gave a tremendous groan, tremendous groan,
a birth-letting groan . . . a moon groan . . .
blood spurted out, thick, thick, thick                                          75
alleys of dead star blood

and I turned and said aloud to myself,
              "That's the moon's voice!
              That's the moon's voice!"

And the white moon was in the sky,                                            80
and I looked at the moon for a long time.

-------

I sat on the ground
and gulped whiskey, drank the steer's death
still warm in my throat.
A beautiful animal! I allowed to be butchered.                                85
When it trounced and galloped in the field,
its body was a dark, windy cliff edge,
and its eyes were doorways of a dream—
              now it bled a charred scroll
              of ancient chant in gravel, I would never know,       90
              and its blackened logs of blood
              smoldered dying vowels, I would never hear.
My heart's creak-n-tremble rage
milled the steer's death to red grist,
I grieved,                                                                     95
I wept drunkenly
that no one cared,
              that humankind betrayed him,
              that we were all cowards.

-------

Perfecto, Valasquez and the butcher                                           100
tried to stop me
from driving,
              but now was the time to settle
              a bad feud with another friend.
              Redeem the bull's blood with ours.                              105
       I drove to Felipe's house,
       anger knotted in me
       tight as the rope tied
       to the stock trailer
       steer strained against.                                               110
       I pulled, but could not free myself.
       (I had a dream night before—
       I crossed black-iron footbridge,
       partially collapsed by sea storm.
       Left-hand railing swept out to sea,                                   115
       I gripped bolt-studded right-hand railing,

finger-clutched wire netting sides,
carefully descended waist-high water. Waded
through slowly and ascended other side—
but had lost my sunglasses and wallet,                                        120
went back, groped bottom, found them and ascended
    again.)

Had to cross that bridge again.
Full of significance . . . tonight,
deepest part of flooded bridge was danger . . . drowning . . .
represented years of my life collapsed                                       125
and destroyed, water the cleansing element,
my ascent from had me healed, onto firm ground,
but I went back, to re-live
destruction . . .

       "Felipe!" I yelled, porch light                                   130
       flicked on, illuminating the yard.
       "Came to fight," I said, "take off
       your glasses."

Bug-eyes glazed
bewildered, then gray slits of lips                                          135
snarled, "You motherless dog!"
He withdrew in darkness a moment,
reappeared on porch, serrated saw of his voice
cut the chill dark,
       "¡Hijo de su pinche madre!                                      140
       ¡Mátalo! ¡Mátalo!!"[1]

First shot framed darkness round me
with a spillway of bright light,
eruption of sound, and second shot roared
a spray of brilliance and the third                                          145
gave an expanded halo-flash.
My legs woozed, and then
I buckled to the ground.
       (I thought, holy shit, what ever happened
       to the old yard-style fight between estranged friends!)   150

I groaned with the steer,
and crawled my dead legs
to the truck, lunged on elbows into cab,
hand lifting the dead stone beneath my waist
to clutch and brake.                                                         155

Following morning calls came,
"Tell us who did it Gato!"
"Our rifles are loaded!"
       I said,   "Leave it alone. What would you do
         if a drunk man came into your yard,                        160
         threatened to beat you?"

---

1. Son of your wretched mother! / Kill him! Kill him!

I wanted peace,
wanted to diffuse the immovable core
of vengeance in my heart,
I had carried since a child,                                165
dismantle the bloody wheel of violence
I had ridden since a child.

During my week in bed,
pellets pollinated me
with a forgotten peace,                                     170
and between waking thoughts of anger and vengeance,
sleep was a small meadow of light,
a clearing I walked into and rested. Fragrance of peace
filled me as fragrance
of flowers and dirt permeate hands                         175
that work in the garden all day.

*Curandero*[2] came to visit, and said,
"The bull in ancient times was the symbol of females.
Did you know that? Killing the bull,
is killing the intuitive part of yourself,                 180
the feminine part. Did you realize,
when Jesus was raising Lazarus,[3]
he groaned in his spirit and that bull groaned,
and when you killed the bull, it was raising you.
The dying bull gave birth to you and now you are either    185
blessed or cursed. The flood of that bull's blood,
is either going to drown you or liberate you,
but it will not be wasted."

                                                           1989

---

## *From* A Place to Stand

## One

When I was a boy, my father always wore a pained expression and kept his head down, as if he couldn't shake what was bothering him. He snapped irritably at the slightest infraction of his rules and argued continuously with Mother. He drank every day and she sank deeper into sadness and anger. To escape their fighting, and the gossiping of villagers in my Grandma Baca's kitchen, I often bellied into the crawl space under our shack to be alone in my own world. I felt safe in this peaceful refuge. The air was moist and smelled like apples withering in a gunnysack in the cellar at my Uncle Max's

---

2. Quack.
3. Lazarus of Bethany, also known Lazarus of the Four Days; according to the Gospel of John, in the

New Testament, Lazarus died and was miraculously brought back to life by Jesus four days later.

ranch in Willard.[1] A stray dog might be waiting when I entered. Happy to see me, he would roll on the cool earth, panting, his tail wagging, and lick my face. After playing with him, I'd lie on the dirt and close my eyes and float out of my skin into stories my grandfather, Pedro Baca, told me—about those of our people who rode horses across the night prairie on raiding parties, wearing cloth over their heads, as they burned outsiders' barns, cut fences, and poisoned wells, trying to expel the gringo intruders and recover the land stolen from our people. This happened on prairie ranches all over New Mexico, from the late 1800s to the 1940s, when my grandfather was a young man herding sheep on the range.

I don't remember much before the age of five; my memories are of Grandma and Grandpa Baca in the kitchen, whispering sleepily as the coffee pot percolates on the woodstove; at night, their voices become guarded, talking about Father's drinking, concerned by Mother's absence, and worried that there's never enough money. People come and go; behind their conversations, a Motorola radio under the cupboards by the sink drones Mexican *corridos* or mass rosaries. Then tensions rupture in a night of rebukes. Uncle Santiago cuffs his younger brother, Uncle Refugio, for coming home drunk again, and Grandpa scolds Father for *his* drunkenness. I remember wondering if those fights had something to do with what I saw one hot summer afternoon.

I was six years old, in my crawl space under the shack—or La Casita, as we called it—where it was cool and quiet. I was drifting in a reverie when I was jolted back to the present by a door creaking open above me. I scooted to a dark corner and peeked up through a crack in the floorboards. A strange man entered La Casita and sat on the bed. Mother came in behind him, and he embraced her. His shiny wingtip shoes scraped grit into my eyes. They watered painfully, but I forced myself to watch as he raised her skirt and ran his hands along her thighs.

She protested, wrenching to one side and then to the other, pushing him away. But the bedsprings creaked as he pinned her and said, "I love you."

They made love with their clothes on.

She cried, struggling.

His voice trembled.

I wanted to race into the shack and seize him but fear disabled me. I scratched at the ground with my fingers and shook my head to blur what was happening. Dizzy and terrified, all I could do was brace my knees to my chest and hug myself in fear as their bodies bucked back and forth and the iron legs of the bed scratched on the wood floor. She shrieked and he groaned, and then all of a sudden they stopped, gasping for air and sighing.

After he departed, she waited awhile and then left too. I lay in the dark, shaking uncontrollably. The ground trembled. In the distance, a train was braking into the railyard, either to load up sacks of beans or deposit milled lumber or field equipment. An hour or so later, feeling vibrations as it pulled out, I wished it could have taken all our family problems away with it. I didn't know what this affair meant at the time, except I knew it was wrong, and I carried the secret of it like a fresh wound in my heart.

Days passed in anguish. I never told Father and I never let on to my mother that I knew. I feared Father would find out what Mother had done and was glad he hadn't been home for a week.

---

1. Village in New Mexico.

Mother and I were napping one afternoon when I heard his car pull up outside, tires crunching gravel. She ran out to the car. "Where've you been?"

"You m'jailer?" he countered sarcastically. He'd been drinking again.

"Just stay away!" She had tried many times to avoid fights by ignoring his carousing, but when I looked out at her I saw no trace of the vulnerable bride. Her face reddening, she screamed, "You're a drunk!"

He scoffed. "You love to use the past against me, don't you? It's your weapon; you stab and turn and dig it in!" His bloodshot eyes glared with resentment. "I never wanted to marry you!"

"You raped me," she said, and seemed stifled by her words.

"Liar," he growled. "From the very first day you chased after me. Waiting at school, at the dance, at my house! You trapped me, you wanted it! You can't make love or cook! The whole town's laughing behind my back!"

She turned and came into the house, speaking to herself. "You were so drunk you don't even remember." Tears streamed down her cheeks.

•

My mother grew up in Willard, New Mexico, with four sisters and three brothers on a forty-acre ranch with no water. Her father, Leopoldo, a Spanish Comanchero,[2] was a renowned cabinetmaker whom I never met, because he died of alcoholism before I was born. His wife, whom I called Grandma Weaver, raised my mother and her seven siblings. They were poor cowboys and cowgirls. When they weren't competing in regional rodeos, they worked long hours outside in the unbearably cold winters and hot sand-blowing summers, milking cows, feeding pigs and horses, filing ax blades, and chopping wood.

Being the youngest and prettiest, my mother, Cecilia, was shielded from much of the harsh work; she stayed indoors with her mother and cooked, canned fruits and vegetables, darned old clothes, and did housework. Her older sisters planned on marrying railroad workers, diesel mechanics, or cowboys, but Cecilia had set her sights above such a mean life. Although her family was Spanish and poor, she was fair-skinned, green-eyed, and black-haired. Her family expected her to marry a well-off gringo with a big ranch, but her heart was set on Damacio Baca, a Mexican from a neighboring village, Estancia, whose parents were landless peasants. When she first saw him in his new car passing her school bus on her way to school, she knew they were going to get married. At fifteen, he wore store-bought clothes and was already working part-time in the local grocery and feed store as stocker and cashier.

Her opportunity to meet him came when he made the high school basketball team and she joined the cheerleading squad. He was the team star and she the head cheerleader. It was the perfect match. Cecilia didn't mind his stopping at Francisco's pool hall to hustle hicks or play poker with older guys in the back room. After school, he usually gave her a ride home, and they would often park in an isolated field, hidden by windrow trees, to drink Seagram's and make out. They went steady for several months; she got pregnant, and they dropped out of school to get married.

Despite the early marriage, most people in Estancia were happy for them and pitched in to make their wedding a memorable one. Grandma and

---

2. A New Mexican who made a living by trading with the nomadic plains tribes in northeastern New Mexico and West Texas, primarily with the Comanche tribe.

Grandpa Weaver, though indignant and against the marriage, gave them La Casita, which they trucked from Willard to Estancia and set up on blocks in the lot beside his parents' house.

The first few months my parents lived in La Casita next to Grandma Baca's house, but after my sister, Martina, was born, in 1950, Father took a job in Santa Fe, about an hour's drive north. They rented a house in Santa Fe, where they lived during the week, and then on weekends they'd stay in La Casita at Estancia. People liked my father and urged him to work his way into politics and one day run for office. A year later my brother, Mieyo, was born, and when Father was not on the road—he was employed by the DMV to deliver license plates to rural villages—he was with politicos in Santa Fe, drinking at the Toro cantina.

One year after that, in 1952, I was born, and it was about this time that Father's drinking and his absences first became an issue. He was having trouble getting the jobs that the politicians promised him. Also, unlike his village, where everyone respected him, in the urban cities of Santa Fe and Albuquerque, the whites looked down on Mexicans. Mother's frustration began to show. La Casita, with its two tar-papered cardboard rooms, one bed where we all slept, woodstove, and cold water spigot, wasn't the white picket-fenced house in a tree-lined city suburb she'd dreamed of. We had no furniture or dishes; we ate at Grandma's—Martina, Mieyo, and me tugging at Mother's skirt, fighting and crying. Mother tried to care for us, but she didn't know how. She and Damacio were only sixteen when they got married, and with him gone most of the time she had her hands full. Grandma Weaver kept after Mother to divorce him, claiming Father was nothing but a drunk and a womanizer. Her brothers swore they'd shoot him if they ever caught him and blamed her for dishonoring the family by marrying a "damn Mexican."

I remember him being two men. When sober, he looked boyish in pressed trousers, dress jacket, and white shirt, his appearance giving no trace of alcoholism. When he was drunk, he became vulgar and abusive, reducing himself to a pitiful phantom of the man he was when sober. When he was supposed to show up on Friday night, Mother made herself all pretty, and we'd go to the park pond and she'd push me on the swing. She'd chase us across the grass, wrestling us down with hugs, laughing and enchanting us with her girlish enthusiasm. We'd picnic on the grass, her green eyes sparkling with happiness as she told us how we were going to buy a nice house, toys and clothes. But later, waiting for Father, when he didn't arrive, her disappointment would deepen into surly pouting and when I did something wrong, she'd yell, saying she wished I was never born. I thought her sadness was my fault and I'd curl up on the floor in a corner and cry. Later, though, in bed, I'd weave her fingers around mine, kissing and tasting them as she caressed my face, apologized, whispered that everything was going to be fine.

We went back and forth between Santa Fe and Estancia more often once Martina and Mieyo started school in Estancia. I didn't want to go, and they didn't insist, so I played at home. In Santa Fe, although times were hard and we didn't have any money, neighbors sometimes came with canned staples and flour for tortillas. To show her gratitude for their kindness, Mother made me sit as they preached. "What is written in the Bible will come to pass!" they cried, as they stood above me in the middle of the room. "Infidels and sinners! The Lord will dash every idol and take upon himself proud ones and crush them!" I didn't say anything, but I thought they were strange and I was glad their visits were rare.

Not all Christians were the same. Sometimes, when a man named Richard took Mother out, she left me with a kind lady, Señora Valdez. Richard had sneaky ways and I didn't trust him. He was always whispering to my mother. When I asked what he had said, Mother told me I wasn't supposed to ask questions, and I didn't want to cause problems so I was quiet. Anyway, being with Señora Valdez allayed my anxiety about Richard. I often walked with her to the butcher shop for scraps to give stray dogs. At a small stream at the park by the plaza, we'd stand and toss bones to the starving creatures. She'd croon in an archaic voice, "*Bendice El Señor; El Señor perdona tus pecados, y cura tus enfermedades.*"[3] Her voice was warm and reassuring. I believed God listened to her prayers and made the dust storms stop, so I asked her to pray for my parents.

Whether we were in Estancia or Santa Fe, Dad would still come in late at night, smelling of whiskey and perfume. When I was six or seven, I was usually in bed right after sundown, but I stayed awake, waiting for him to come home. I would brace myself for a fight, as anything could happen when he was drunk. Many times I hid under my covers, my body tense, as he threatened my mother, hurling a spindle-back chair at her and roaring.

Mom would scream at him to get out. I often wept with fear, hoping he would not hurt her. Some nights he rushed drunkenly into my room and yanked me out of bed. I always looked desperately at my sister and brother as he carried me out, but they couldn't help me. Mom usually hid, afraid for her own safety. He would toss me into the car and drive away. I never knew where we were going. We usually drove for hours on country roads. I looked at the stars, I listened to the Mexican music on the radio, I glanced at him swigging from his whiskey bottle, and I tried to pretend that none of this was happening. I snuggled deep into the suit coat that covered me. The hum of the engine, the drone of the heater, and the wind blowing past his open window made me drowsy, and eventually I would fall asleep, helpless and sad.

On good days he tried to be conciliatory, promising to stay home more and not drink or womanize. On such days he always had surprises to show that life was going to get better. Once, to make us proud of him, he showed us a creased photograph of the governor of New Mexico shaking his hand on the capitol steps. He was excited, saying the governor was going to hire him soon. Often, after sharing good news with us, he'd say he had to run errands and would be right back. And just when I thought he might be sincere, he would return hours later, drooling drunk and crying with remorse. I pretended to ignore his repulsive drunkenness but was deeply disappointed. He always returned, and after slobbering all over me, saying what a good boy I was, how I was his favorite and someday I would be a great boxer, he would then stagger out for the night and not return until the bars were closing.

I didn't know which was worse, eagerly expecting him, but never knowing when he might barge drunkenly through the door late at night to fight with Mom, or fearing he would never come home again at all.

•

---

3. Bless God; God forgives your sins, and he cures your illnesses.

Because father almost never came around, and when he did he was drunk, Mother had taken a job as a cashier at a Piggly Wiggly grocery store. We almost never saw her. I was too young to have understood, when we were living in Santa Fe, what it meant when this guy Richard kept coming over. I knew, though, the night we went to visit his parents, that something was up. I'd always distrusted this thin pimply-faced man from the "other world" who would drive up to our barrio shack in a shiny car and new suit, bearing chocolates and flowers, dresses, blouses, and other presents for Mom. I pretended to be indifferent to the candy he placed on the table and waited until they'd left before I tore it open and stuffed myself. I was only a child, but I understood in the way children do that Mother enjoyed the new standard of living that Richard was giving her. She'd bleached her hair, wore jewelry he'd given her, and always had money. She'd been changing in other ways too. She quit speaking Spanish and told us not to speak it around Richard.

Riding around in the car Richard had given her, she'd point to white-skinned, blue-eyed children and say I should be like them. When she dressed us, she mentioned that we should look like normal American kids. I had no idea how to do this. She would get mad at me for getting dirty playing in the dusty yard; when Richard was around, we had to stay clean and behave and sit quietly in a chair and say nothing. Richard would get mad when I asked for beans, chile, and tortilla, saying, "It's time you started eating American food." I knew Mom was trying to impress him with her "white ways," but it made her look silly.

It wasn't so with my father; he spoke Spanish and used English only when he had to. He listened to Mexican music, and all his friends were Mexicans. I never saw him with an Anglo. He never said anything bad about them, but he made a point to stay away from them. I remember riding around with him and saying, "No, don't want to go in there, too many gringos." I sensed that if he was around them, he'd be placing himself in harm's way. Ever since I could remember, my Baca grandparents mistrusted whites. When they came to Grandma's with official papers, we hid in the back rooms. Grandma said to be polite but warned me not to talk to them more than necessary. Uncle Santiago said they cheated Uncle Refugio out of his pay. When Grandpa was under the tree by the fence with his friends, I'd hear them talk about whites who used lawyers to pass laws to steal land or intimidated poor folks with their money.

That was why I was nervous the afternoon Richard took us to meet his rich parents. We were going into their world. Mom sat up front all made up, wearing a pretty pink dress and red high heels. Mieyo, Martina, and I huddled in the back. When we were almost there, Richard turned to Mom and explained that, since his parents were old-fashioned, it would be best if she said she was Anglo and that she was just babysitting us for a girlfriend. From where I sat I could see Mother bite her bottom lip as she stared straight ahead. I expected her to say something back to him, but instead she said to us, "You better be on your best behavior." And we were, for the whole boring afternoon; all we did was sit on big soft chairs in the living room as still as we had been in the car, afraid to touch the fancy food on small plates on the table unless it was offered, afraid to speak unless asked to speak, afraid to do anything but sit there and pick our fingernails. When we finally said our good-byes and pulled the car door closed, she turned to Richard and asked, "How'd I do?"

"A-plus," he replied, pleased with her. I remember looking at Mother again and noticing that a bit of lipstick that had smudged her bright teeth when she bit her lip was still there. I felt an odd satisfaction.

The next day, driving out of Santa Fe, Mother forced a smile and told us we were going to Estancia. Her voice was tight. She lit cigarette after cigarette, the lighter in her hand trembling. I could feel a mounting tension in Richard. He would press the gas pedal, making the engine hum higher, and then he would release it, and a few minutes later he would press down on the pedal again. I watched his eyes in the rearview mirror. They were hiding something. I felt Richard was going to do something bad to us, and all I could do was sit and wait for it to happen. I wanted to hit him and take control of the situation somehow, but how does a seven-year-old do that? I fidgeted instead, feeling my pulse throbbing in my fingertips, the seat springs against my butt. I looked up and caught Richard's eyes darting in and out of the mirror, looking at me. I picked my cuticles until they were bleeding. I was thinking of grabbing the steering wheel and begging Mother to stop the car and take us back to Santa Fe; or to leave Richard and just let the four of us live together. I looked out the window at endless miles of cactus and sage. In the window was my sister's reflection, her hand running a hair ribbon through her nervous palm, and Mieyo fingering a roll of caps.

"It's your fault," Martina hissed.

I turned and saw her and Mieyo looking at me. Mieyo's face was white, his neck artery engorged, dark eyes full of fear. "Told you," he said, pinching me. I sucked my breath back to hold my tears in but they came anyway. Maybe they were blaming me because I cried too much. "Crybaby," Mieyo said, and then the engine slowed and Richard backhanded him across the face.

"Stop that or I'll throw you out!" he yelled, and the car swayed forward again, picking up speed. "Do something with them, they're your kids," he told Mom.

"I hate you!" I screamed at Richard. Mieyo grabbed the door handle and flung it open. Richard braked, and we lunged forward as the car skidded in the roadside gravel.

Mom turned and slammed the door shut. "What is the matter with you! Don't ever do that again!" I'd peed in my pants, my blood drumming in my head and my heart beating wildly. I kept my head down to hide my tears.

Richard kept mumbling, "I'll be so happy . . . so happy." Why was he going to be so happy? Maybe we were going to picnic at the park pond. Maybe we were going to eat some good beans and hot buttered tortillas at Grandma's. Maybe he was dropping Mom and us off. Maybe he was going away.

After a while, we drove down Main Street. Trucks brimming with potatoes were parked by the track warehouses. There were men working in a big hole, standing around in that easy manner of small-town workers, talking and laughing. We turned off down a dirt road and pulled into Grandma's yard. She came outside and stood in the yard, her long gray hair braided, her apron splotched with flour. Mother brought us to her and kissed us briskly on the cheeks and said she'd be back. As I watched her leave, hearing the tires whir away on pavement, I felt weightless, sucked into a lifeless, paralyzing emptiness. I couldn't breathe and my legs were shaking. An intensely bright, luminous ball of fire was streaming into my eyes and blinding me.

I tried to pull free of Grandma's hand, and I heard her say, "*Mañana sera mejor con el favor de Dios.*" Tomorrow will be a better day with God's help. But as she led us into the house, I knew tomorrow would never be better. Something in my life had changed forever.

•

We lived with Grandma and Grandpa Baca. Grandpa said it was only temporary and reassured us that our parents would return to pick us up once they settled into our new home. I looked forward to that day, fantasizing about how happy we'd all be. Little did I know that my mother had eloped to San Francisco with Richard, fleeing into a white world as "Sheila," where she could deny her past, hide her identity, and lie about her cultural heritage. I was also ignorant of my father's alcoholic oblivion, in which he pawned every last possession to get a bus ticket to San Francisco to try and find her.

We were resilient, as most children tend to be, and while we awaited their return, my Uncle Santiago took Mieyo and me everywhere with him—to milk his cows, ride his horses, feed the pigs, gather wood in the mountains, and hunt deer. I started to enjoy living with my grandparents again in Estancia. With my friend Mocoso, who came over when his mother Juanoveva visited Grandma, I spent the whole day roaming the village. We crossed fields, played in trees, tracked coyotes, built mud forts in ditch banks, and watched giant frogs crush our dirt village; we spent days in the barn teasing spiders out of webs, trapping mice, climbing up in the loft and making towns out of gunnysacks and tool crates; spying out of wood cracks at people who visited Grandma. When Mocoso wasn't around, I went over to the high school and hung out with Grandpa, who was a janitor. I followed him everywhere through the halls, pushing the dust mop; later we went to irrigate a farmer's bean fields; and I walked home with him in the dusk.

Then, suddenly, Grandpa died. Except for my immediate family, I had loved him the most. When my parents left, it was Grandpa who kept life stable as possible for us. He was always reassuring me that things would turn out fine. Grandpa ordered my father and Uncle Carlos to stop arguing, and they did. Grandpa had often come over to La Casita and brought us candy, food, or other surprises. He was a gentle man, and my mother trusted him.

Before I could come to terms with Grandpa's unexpected death, Mieyo and I were taken to St. Anthony's Boys' Home in Albuquerque. Martina stayed in Estancia to help Grandma. It was June 1959.

At seven years old, I could never accept that my parents had abandoned us. What a shock! Thinking we were going to join them, Mieyo and I were driven instead to an orphanage and dropped off. Nuns escorted us up a flight of stairs into a dark, creaky third-floor dorm with kids in cots lined up on each side of the long room. I was scared and confused, weeping and clinging to Mieyo, begging to be taken back to my grandparents' in Estancia because my parents were coming to get us. No matter how hard the nuns tried to explain, not a day passed that I didn't expect my parents to come.

We were not coddled or given any special treatment at the orphanage, nor did anyone tell us anything about our parents. In the snap of a finger I found myself in a different world, among hundreds of strangers, with each minute planned out for me. The first few months, we slept on the condemned third floor. It rained almost every night, and the roof was leaking everywhere, soaking the bedsheets hanging between the bunks. Thunder roared and lightning revealed me weeping on my bunk at night. Mieyo would come and cradle me, and I clung to him as if we were one person.

At 4:30 A.M. we marched in columns to the chapel for mass on the second floor. After mass we went downstairs to the ground-floor dining room for breakfast. After eating, the older kids scattered out to do their chores and then go to school, and at noon we had lunch. The younger kids went to the playroom most of the morning, then napped or played on the playground. After supper the older kids did evening chores and us young kids got to watch TV for an hour; then we washed up and got ready for bed at 6:30 P.M. Six months after our arrival, new dorms had been completed and we moved into them. Groups were divided into age groups. I was in the 200s, the five-, six-, and seven-year-olds; Mieyo was in the 300s, the group of eight-, nine-, and ten-year-olds. I saw him in the dining room and at mass, but after that he went with older kids to do different chores and sit in different classrooms.

I'd always looked up to Mieyo, since he knew how to read people. At the orphanage he soon had the keys to the soda storeroom and the pantry, stocked with fresh-baked sweet rolls; he had a milk can full of marbles; he had the best clothes; and he worked as a barn boy, which gave him a lot more freedom to come and go as he wished. He knew the answers to things. He had comforted me when Mom and Dad fought.

When I asked the nuns if my parents were coming back, I was told the matter was in God's hands and children shouldn't ask such questions. God knew what he was doing. I should consider myself blessed, because God had something special in store for me. I felt lost and confused around grown-ups. They never told the truth. They were always hiding something that would eventually hurt me. I stayed in the field, away from them, playing with other boys—in the wind or on the teeter-totter with Big Noodle, dizzying myself on the merry-go-round with Peanut Head, shooting marbles or spinning tops with Coo-Coo Clock. Those blissful afternoons made me forget my circumstances. I was the happiest when I was by myself playing in the dirt under an elm tree. I'd notice big rigs and cars on I-40 in the distance, running parallel to the back boundary fence, and wonder if any of them might be carrying my parents. I felt a painful longing for Estancia. In the back of my mind, I always hoped that my parents would come for Mieyo and me.

## Two

My parents never did come, and at thirteen years old I found myself behind bars for the first time, in a detention center for boys. The bars weren't there to keep us in so much as to remind us that we weren't really wanted anywhere else. I must have run away from the orphanage a dozen times, and each time an aunt or an uncle would take me back. The last time, however, instead of calling Saint Anthony's, as they had in the past, they notified the police, who took me to the detention center. When we arrived, my Aunt Charlotte, my mother's sister, was there. The receptionist slid the official papers to her and asked her to sign them, "Here and here," relinquishing custody. I knew she didn't know what the words *relinquishing custody* meant, but I felt her relief at getting rid of me when she hurriedly put pen to paper and signed. Perhaps she was ashamed to do what in her heart she knew wasn't right, because she walked away without even a good-bye.

I sat on the bench until a tall lean man came out and greeted me.

"Hello, I'm Nestor." He was tall and thin, soft-spoken, in a brown sports jacket and brown slacks, with black hair meticulously combed and parted on one side. "Let's get some information on you, son. Remember, you're not here because you did something wrong. It's only because you don't have a home."

"How long do I have to stay?"

"Until we contact your father and arrange for you to live with him."

I celled with six other Chicanos. The fluorescent lighting made the apprehension in their faces obvious, but they concealed their curiosity about who I was, where I came from, and what I was here for with a hard-faced indifference. I wasn't prepared for their stony silence. Estancia kids like Mocoso had a kindheartedness that invited spontaneous participation in play or idle talk. Even the kids at the orphanage generously included you in games and asked you to play; they hadn't lost hope. These boys worried about revealing any information that others might take as a weakness or use against them. Suspicion helped them to survive, as did denying their feelings, especially fear. At night, a heaviness lay over the cells; the kids, perhaps sensing their lives falling apart, were distressed and withdrawn.

Hardly anyone blinked the next morning when a kid in the dining room leaped across one of the long stainless-steel tables with a fork and stabbed another kid in the neck. Even as blood ran through the wounded kid's fingers and down his arm, his eyes announced that it didn't hurt, it was nothing, he had no feelings. Everyone looked, but after the two kids had been removed by guards, the rest went on eating their oatmeal. I was too alarmed to eat, unsettled by the victim's nonchalance. If I stayed here long enough, I too would be trained to feel nothing. After being stripped of everything, all these kids had left was pride—a pride that was distorted, maimed, twisted, and turned against them, a defiant pride that did not allow them to admit that they were human beings and had been hurt.

They reminded me of my brother, Mieyo. After Mother's sudden departure he'd become inaccessible and distant. He had started on a process of change, often beating me up for nothing. I let him because I didn't want him leaving me; he was all I had left. One thing for sure: He wasn't the same brother I'd once had. Instead of his usual candor and curiosity, he became cagey and manipulative. I think he learned to dislike himself. He did things at the orphanage that all kids do—pilfer food from the kitchen cart, cheat in class, fudge at marbles—but he didn't get caught. Determined not to be a victim, he'd lie, deceive, and steal. But having spent six years in the orphanage, he was afraid of the outside world and decided against running away. He stayed at the orphanage, while I landed in the detention center.

He was right, of course; it was worse outside the orphanage. But wherever we were, I believed in my naive way that he was figuring a way to rescue me, because he knew how to do stuff like that—he could lie with such pious sincerity anybody would believe him, and he always knew how to get what he wanted. I pictured him pulling off my escape and embracing me after I was free. I knew he'd be waiting one day at the front office, a nod of the head to welcome me back.

During the day, at the D-Home, we mostly lounged in cells, playing dominoes, checkers, chess, or cards; some kids went into the mat room to box and work out on the speed and body bags, while others went outside to stroll or relax in the sun against the fence or play basketball. I joined those against the fence and we talked about girls or our barrios, falling to the ground in between and pumping off push-ups and sit-ups. I was from the orphanage, which drew their sympathy. The fact that I was alone in the world had some significance to them. It took real guts to be out in the world at thirteen. We'd lie on our backs staring up at the clouds and talk without looking at each other. It was better not to look into each other's eyes.

Low-Blow was one of the guys in my cell, a big muscled Chicano whose fighting abilities were renowned. He took me under his wing. Strutting down the halls or in the rec room, he told me, "Never talk to guards. If anybody looks at you wrong, tries to touch you, mess him up. What's a wrong look?" he asked and answered his own question. "It's when they stare at you like you owe money. Like you did 'em wrong and they're holding a grudge against you. The way starved dogs look at each other over a piece of meat and none of 'em wanna share." During chores one day, Low-Blow decked a guy and was put in isolation. With my partner gone, I had to assume an attitude of fearlessness, walk the walk, even though I desperately wanted Mieyo to come. I waited as the days blurred into boring weeks, planning that when my father and brother and I finally got together, I'd work at a gas station or as a laborer and make money. Without Mother or Martina it wouldn't be the same, but at least I'd have Mieyo and my father. As the warm, sunny days passed, I kept myself busy, hoping for the best. I made my bunk every morning and swept the cell, and when Low-Blow came out, he bunked next to me and we both mopped the halls, washed windows, and exercised. It wasn't that bad, except during the night when I worried about my brother and father, fearing something might have happened to them. I prayed to God to help them, as the halls echoed with the ominous reports of the guard's boots as he checked to see if we were all in our bunks and counted. I felt sorry for the kids in for murder, grand theft auto, or drug possession, because they were headed for Springer, a prison for teenagers. Low-Blow was going there for assault with a deadly weapon, and even though he said he wasn't afraid, I knew he was.

With no word from my brother or my father, the director decided it was time for me to go to school. Since the detention center had no educational facility, I was enrolled at Harrison Junior High. It was still dark and cold when he unlocked the main door one morning and led me out into the cold dawn to the street curb. He told me to wait for a woman to pick me up and offered a brief pep talk about doing my best and the virtues of education. After he left, I was afraid but excited. Snuggled in my jacket, under the streetlamp, I waited for my ride. I could hear the crickets and frogs on the ditch bank across the street. I glanced at every car and truck passing, but the drivers kept moving. I jumped, trying to catch a moth fluttering above me, and when a stray dog came over from the ditch, I gave it my peanut-butter-and-jelly sandwich from my sack lunch. It followed me to the ditch, where I threw mud clods at the water. Here I was, with no restraints, legally free, for the first time in a long while. No cops, nuns, aunts, or uncles looking for me to tell me what I'd done wrong. It felt great being on the ditch as the sun was rising, but just as I was wondering whether I should head for the orphanage to find my brother, a lady drove up under the streetlamp and waved to me. I went toward her running, eager to warm my hands and feet by the car heater. The dog followed, but since I couldn't take it, I gave it my other sandwich, which it gobbled up before we had even turned and pulled away onto the street.

School wasn't anything like I expected. Within a week I faked being sick in order to stay out. The real reason was I was ashamed, not only of my old patched clothes but also because I didn't know anything the teachers were talking about. I couldn't talk to the kids because they were so much smarter than I was. They were the kind of kids my mother pointed to, saying I should be like them. I already half believed that I was a sinner and they were not; at least the nuns had told me so. And because of all the trouble in my family, having no parents, the alcoholism and fights, I also believed there was something basically wrong with me. I didn't think anyone else had the kind of problems I had. So it seemed that everything that happened to me justified their view.

I was trying to redeem myself, but my stint at Harrison only seemed to complicate and confuse my efforts. I was more interested in my cell life and my homeboys and what we talked about—doing time, stealing stuff, recalling things that people had done to us and what we were going to do to pay them back. My homeboys wanted me to get addresses of the girls from school, but I was too shy. They didn't understand how crazy it was. After Mrs. Sanchez let me out, I'd get lost in the riotous commotion of buses and parents dropping off kids. Freedom intimidated me. The ease with which the other kids laughed and roughhoused intimidated me. They'd group behind the gym and I'd be by myself, staring at the dusty track and football field. I dreaded going back into class when the bell rang because I'd have to sit in the back and hope the teacher didn't call my name. I hated every hour, restraining my impulse to flee from the classroom. When I was going through the cafeteria line, unable to make up my mind about what I wanted because there was too much to choose from, kids behind me said things to embarrass me and smirked at my social awkwardness. They wouldn't dare if they were back at the D-Home, because I'd bust them up, but I couldn't do anything to them here.

When Mrs. Sanchez asked why I wasn't bringing my schoolbooks, I told her I'd forgotten. She seemed to understand what I was really feeling, so she led me one morning to the gym and told Coach Tracy who I was and where I lived. He was a good guy—outgoing, square-jawed, buzz-cut, and tough as a marine drill sergeant.

Later that day, when I was behind the gym during lunch, sitting on the dirt eating my sandwich, someone called me. When I turned, it was Coach Tracy. He squatted on his toes and slapped my knee, smiling. "You oughta be out there playing football for us! Just look at those shoulders and arms!" I felt embarrassed. "Come on out this afternoon," he continued. "I'll be waiting for you." He looked at my bologna sandwich and said, "Don't blame you, not eating in the cafeteria. Food'll make you gag. Meet me in the locker room after classes."

I asked him, "What about Mrs. Sanchez? I'll get in trouble if I'm not there."

He patted my shoulder. "I talked to her and the director. I'll take you back after practice." He was the nicest man I ever met, I thought, as he walked away, slightly hunched in the shoulders, wearing gray khakis and black-and-white Converse sneakers, his body hard and rugged.

He assigned me my own locker, piled my arms with pants and jersey, shoulder pads, helmet, cleats, and mouthpiece, and after I dressed I trailed the team out to the field in a slow trot. Coach slapped me on the butt and clapped his hands, rousing me to do my best. I felt thankful but uncomfortable with his considerable kindness, but once on the field, my discomfiture evaporated as I tackled and crushed my teammates into the grass. Coach kept smacking my pads, saying to the others, "You see that! That's how I want you to hit! Get over here, Rudy, on all fours—Jimmy, show them how it's done." I got down, and when Coach blew the whistle I hit Rudy so hard he went backwards and groaned over on his belly. I'd forearmed his face mask and given him a bloody nose. "That's how you linemen should be hitting!"

I felt proud of myself because the rest of the guys were looking at me impressed, and some were saying, "Wow, we're going to win some games now," their admiration mixed with trepidation. They studied me with the curiosity of someone viewing a strange oddity. Who is he? Where did he come from? And while I felt satisfied with myself and equal to them on the field, the difference between us became apparent in the locker room, where they put on nice clothes, watches, rings, new shoes. I lied when they asked where I lived and if I needed a ride home, telling them my mother was picking me up and I lived close by. They talked about going to movies on dates with girlfriends, and they tried to be friendly, inviting me to hang out with them, to go for sodas and burgers after practice, but I didn't have any money. On the insides of their lockers they had family photos, cars they were fixing up with their dads and friends, team pennants, posters of rock heroes. I kept to myself, being quiet as I could so as not to invite questions or attention.

Primarily to please the coach and Mrs. Sanchez, I started playing the part of a student by bringing my books. I'd sit in the last row of each class and look at the pictures, to which I added illustrations of my own: a mustache to the moon, penciled flowers on Nebraska cornfields, a sinister grin and an eye patch on George Washington. I hadn't told anybody that I couldn't read and that looking at the words and math problems made me feel dumb. For a while, though, I was the talk of school. I may have been a dummy in class but I was a hero on the field. I was a good football player, which made girls flirt with me and guys look to me as a leader. I was invited to parties, over to kids' houses, swimming, but since I couldn't go or explain why I couldn't go, I lied that I had things to do, places to go, and generally gave them the impression that my life was full of activities. I must have looked like a fool; my poverty and aloneness in life was apparent. People don't like liars, and after a while they quit inviting me. But what was I going to do, invite them to the D-Home to meet the guards and watch TV with the rest of my homeboys behind bars in a cell? I'm sure they would've enjoyed getting patted down, and escorted to a cell, filled with a bunch of guys who saw them as the enemy. I was ashamed to admit that I was a ward of the state, a piece of property with official papers attached. At any time, I could be swept up by the state, put in handcuffs, and given over to a stranger. I was at the mercy of state officials—state-clothed, housed, and fed, a number on a case file in an office. I was going to wake up here, go to sleep here, eat and live here.

Life at the D-Home was as predictable as it had been at the orphanage. New kids came and went. We woke up at the same time every day and went to bed at the same time every night. Every weekend visitors came and visited their loved ones for an hour. And just as I had done at the Boys' Home, every night, before falling asleep, I'd imagine my mother's voice whispering good night to me. I'd think of my father and brother; I'd see in my mind the carefree kids at school, older than at the Boys' Home but laughing and playing the same, and gradually I'd fall asleep, pretending that tomorrow would be the day when everything was going to turn out well in my life.

Coach Tracy pulled me out of class one day and took me over to the gym. In his office, he sat behind his desk and said he was concerned because I was failing every class. At that time, I'd close up anytime an adult asked me questions; I didn't trust them. And though Coach Tracy was different, I stared out the window, thinking of my brother and resenting the coach's intrusion. He should have just been a coach and not worried about me or my grades. So what if I was failing? I was out of place here. The students were not from my world and I was not part of theirs.

I knew Coach Tracy was trying to be a good friend, so I said I'd try harder. He smiled. "Just give it a shot, that's all I'm asking." But after that he sought me out when I was going from class to class, asking, "How's it going? Keep at them books, Jimmy, it'll pay off." Sometimes, expecting a response, he'd pause, but I never said anything. He'd prod. "Everything okay? Something bothering you?" I played him off, saying I was doing fine, but it was a lie; I wasn't studying at night.

I hated books, I hated reading, I hated everything about school except football. So far we were undefeated. I was a fullback, trampling opponents with relish; on defense I was headhunter, roaming behind the linemen and following the ball carrier, whom I demolished. I was also the extra-point kicker. I kicked the ball so far one time that the refs had to stop the game to go and find it, over the fence in the weeds. We were on our way to becoming city champs.

After one important game, Coach Tracy surprised me by announcing I was staying at his house for the weekend. He was taking me to his home to meet his family.

I didn't know it at the time, but it was a trial run for future adoption. I met his wife and two sons, ages five and eight. They lived in a moderate-sized red-brick house down a street bordered with elm trees in a middle-class neighborhood. He took me in and showed me the bedroom where I'd sleep that night. I felt detached and confused and anxious. Was this a ploy to get me away from my father and brother? Was I being taken away again, this time by myself? Ever since I was seven I'd been boarding in a state rental, and now at fourteen I was being offered my own bedroom. I forced a smile of appreciation but I was self-conscious about being regarded with such attentive courtesy. Over supper, the kids innocently questioned me, while his pretty wife stacked pork chops and string beans and mashed potatoes on my plate. Coach Tracy was telling me that if I could get a handle on the books and keep a good grade average, it'd be no problem getting a college scholarship for football. I didn't want to go to college. I ate stiffly, feeling constrained by their deference, so unfamiliar. These were the kind of people I had a grudge against; if they knew that, they wouldn't be so nice to me. These were the people I'd assumed didn't care about us street kids. They were a part of the white world that had helped to destroy my family, made my father suffer, made my grandpa and grandma work in their fields dawn to dusk. If I lived with them, wouldn't I be betraying everything I had been taught to believe in? I'd be going against my father and brother. I was sitting in the living room with the enemy, and yet in my heart I liked them; they were not harming me in any way. The fact that they were so generous made me feel worse for my bad thoughts. In my world, they represented everything bad, and yet they were not prejudiced, mean, greedy, or money-hungry. I decided that not all white people were the same, but it still didn't make my stay any more comfortable.

I'd begun to feel early on that the state and society at large considered me a stain on their illusion of a perfect America. In the American dream there weren't supposed to be children going hungry or sleeping under bridges. In me, the state—and society by extension—had yet another mouth to feed, another body to clothe. I felt like a nuisance; I suspected that if basic human decency didn't warrant it, society would gladly dismiss me. Yet there were people like Coach Tracy and his family who went against the grain. And while I didn't want to hurt them and was willing to go along for a while, there was no way I could let myself be adopted into a white family. It just couldn't happen. I'd be like my mother then, turning my back on my people—my grandparents, my father, my brother and sister—and living a lie about who I really was. I was not going anywhere. My grandpa had always prided himself in his loyalty to his customs and traditions and people. I'd rather live on the streets and keep my loyalty, my memories and stories, than take on the gringo's way of living, which tried to make me forget where I came from, and sometimes even put down my culture and ridiculed my grandparents as lazy foreigners.

Friday night I'd had bad dreams of my brother dying, and Saturday morning, after breakfast, I decided to walk to the park up the street. I took the younger kid with me. When I stopped to light a cigarette, cradling him in one arm, a floating ash burned his cheek and he screamed. I don't know why his scream affected me so deeply. Perhaps it echoed the sentiments of my mother and the nuns, who insinuated that I was the cause of all the pain and hurt in my family's life. Perhaps, it was the same chilling scream that was buried in me and never came out, the hot cry I stifled throughout my mother's departure, my father's violence, my brother's absence, my terror of being alone in the world. I was not able to put my feelings or thoughts in words, but feeling guilty as hell, I sat on the street curb and kept telling the kid I was sorry, I didn't mean to burn his cheek, it was an accident. He wanted to go home so I carried him back, thinking the whole time I belonged in the D-Home.

Coach Tracy and his wife begged me to tell them what was wrong. My silence aggravated their confusion, and they appealed all the more for an explanation, imploring me to say something. Even if I could've expressed myself, I was confused about what I was supposed to say or not say, and my response to any question was always "I don't know."

That's exactly what I told Coach Tracy and his wife: I didn't know why, I just wanted to go back. On Sunday afternoon, Coach Tracy drove me down. We said very little. His eyes were red, his face drawn from exhaustion. I was tremendously sad when I said good-bye and shut the car door and walked to the entrance of the D-Home. I thought I had spoiled everything for him and I wanted to apologize, but I didn't know how to explain myself. I wasn't strong enough to admit that I felt worthless and was nothing but a trouble-maker. I quit school the next day.

I lived at the detention center for a few months more until one cold December morning when Mieyo came by on a brand-new motorcycle. I was so excited to see him that I begged Nestor, the D-Home director, to let me go with him for the day. I told him that Christmas and my fifteenth birthday, January 5, were around the corner, and that spending a day with Mieyo would be all the Christmas and birthday present I would ever want. Nestor sensed my elation and kindly agreed to let me go for the day, warning me to be back by supper. Mieyo had brought extra gloves, a coat, and a beanie cap. I put them on, and we roared out of the D-Home parking lot. I knew I was not coming back.

It didn't take me long to graduate to the kind of jails where the bars were meant to keep me in. Fortunately, I was never there for very long. I was still a juvenile, and the charges never got more serious than disturbing the peace, vagrancy, or petty theft, none of which they were very good at proving. I'd be held for a while, have a few conversations with child welfare authorities or a probation officer, and then be released into the custody of my father, who was supposed to be taking care of me but whom I never saw.

My father had lost his job with the DMV and now got his drinking money selling shoes. He spent his nights at cantinas and hardly ever came back to the shack in Albuquerque that Mieyo and I were calling home. I couldn't believe he was still searching for my mother. She still haunted him. He even questioned us to see if we knew where she was. When he did show up he'd be drunk, and if Mieyo and I were around we'd keep our distance, because we might get beaten up.

We stayed in a gardener's shack, more or less like the one I'd grown up in, converted into sleeping quarters for the three of us. Mieyo and I would eat at friends' houses, and we roamed around town with a group of like-minded kids with equally unsavory pasts. Mieyo was fifteen and trying to go to school and sometimes worked as a hotel bellboy; I was fourteen and worked occasionally, but school wasn't for me. Mostly we cruised, looking for something to do, any kind of action. We'd steal a bicycle or a tire and resell it, or earn enough—digging ditches for a plumbing contractor, cleaning yards, washing windows, or painting—to put something in our stomachs and then party. When my brother had picked me up at the D-Home, I was surprised that he had already started drinking. I followed suit. Soon there were other things: LSD, pot, harder stuff. We'd get high, cruise around, maybe get in a fight, stoke up again, and then crash wherever we could—abandoned shacks, someone's car, or on a bench or under a tree in the town square. Occasionally, I would wake up in jail.

I don't know when the process of criminalization began for any one of the kids I hung out with or woke up with in a prison cell. For me, it was when my mother first dropped my brother and sister and me off in Estancia; it was reinforced when Mieyo and I were driven through the gates of Saint Anthony's, and it started to take on a more antisocial reality at the detention center. It was at the detention center that I first learned how to intimidate others with my stare, how to lie to the authorities with a smile, how to join a group and think of myself as me against the others. It was at the detention center that I first came in contact with boys who were already well on their way to becoming criminals; whose friendship taught me I was more like them than like the boys outside the cells, living in a society that would never accept me, in a world made of parents, nice clothes, and loving care. You could see the narrowing of life's possibilities in the cold, challenging eyes of the homeboys in the detention center; you could see the numbing of their hearts in their swaggering postures. All of them had been wounded, hurt, abused, ignored; already, aggression was in their talk, in the way they let off steam over their disappointments, in the way they expressed themselves. It was all they allowed themselves to express, for each of them knew they could be hurt again if they tried anything different. So instead they refined what they did know to its own kind of perfection.

I watched and listened and learned in the detention center. I understood that if I was to get by on the streets I would have to do it by fighting. If only through my experience on the football field, I knew I had enough frustrated anger in me to funnel into destructive behavior. But it wasn't until Mieyo told me that he'd been raped during our separation that my world suddenly shifted from passive observer to violent engagement. I was not going to let the world trample my brother and me down like dogs in the street. My faith in the goodness of people began to tremble around the edges until it shattered like glass subjected to a high-pitched sound. My hope that society would one day invite us in was gone. The world was against us. Rather than let the world beat us down, I had to fight back, and I did, on the day Mieyo finally came to get me.

He fetched me on his new motorcycle, and we went over to where he was living. He told me that when I was taken to the detention center, the nuns had located our father and released Mieyo into his care. Father was living in a small shack with barely enough room for two people. He drank all the time. There was never any food, and Mieyo was sometimes beaten. So he left and was living on the streets until one day two older white men picked him up and treated him to a big meal, bought him some clothes, and invited him to their house when he didn't have a place to stay. He thought they were simply being kind, but they raped him and used legal jargon to threaten him. He would go to prison for breaking and entering, they said. They would accuse him of robbing them. Besides, who would believe a young Chicano kid anyway—certainly not over the word of two successful white men with good jobs, a nice house, and social standing.

I had known boys who had been raped before, both in the orphanage and in the detention center. But this was my brother. I found his shame excruciating to bear. I wanted to protect him—I was willing to do anything to protect him—and I began to lash out at every opportunity. We had a kind of gang going; no colors, no rules or rituals, just a bunch of us boys who had already been cast off and who didn't have much else to do but cruise around together and get in trouble. We fought other gangs, white kids mostly, and more and more I would step out and be the point man in any fight situation.

I was good at it, just like my father had said I would be on those nights when he drank and we watched the Gillette fights,[4] or at Grandma's when I was small. Crouching down and protecting my face and ribs, I'd lash out with jabs and kicks on street corners and in alleys; the difference was that now my fighting was fueled by my rage at the world. I wouldn't stop until I was panting with exhaustion as I stared at my opponent bleeding on the pavement. I fought for my brother because I knew that inside him he was hurting in a way that only someone who gets raped can hurt. I wanted to take his hurt away by hurting others, but it never seemed to work. When I finished a fight and we were alone again, he would explode. To vent his anger, he berated and demeaned me, and then he beat me, and I let him. I knew it wasn't right, but in all the confusion of my life I felt this one thing was helping him live. And somewhere along the line I started fighting just for the sake of fighting, because I was good at it and it felt good to beat other people up.

Fighting, drinking, and getting high, driving around, this was my life for three or four years. We'd rent a cheap apartment in a bad section of town, get drunk, burn down the apartment, and take off, a bunch of wild kids in cars prowling affluent white neighborhoods, looking to steal something or break a car window just for something to do. We'd hang out at a burger joint looking to fight other gangs or we'd cruise around to score some drugs, get off, sleep it off until late in the afternoon, and then start all over again.

I'd ride out to Estancia sometimes to visit Grandma, but it didn't feel right. La Casita made me think of my mother and father and the few good memories we had. Her being with me at the park, us lying in bed and talking, but mostly of her at the window, worried and waiting for my father. I never did hear from her after she dropped us off, and I wondered bitterly whether she thought of us and, if so, in what way. With remorse? Gladness? Or, living a carefree life in California, had she completely forgotten we were ever born? Grandma was shrinking with age. She was blind but still caring for Refugio, who came in drunk each night. Martina married at fifteen, a guy from another village, and lived in a trailer in Albuquerque. Jesusita, Julian, and Carlos came on weekends to visit, but Santiago still lived in Estancia, caring for Grandma and working at Grandpa's old job as janitor at the high school. When Grandma asked about my father and brother, I lied and said they were okay. I didn't tell her that occasionally, late at night, I'd see my father stumbling down the sidewalk on his way to the next cantina. I'd be in the backseat of someone's car, and I'd swing my head to the window to catch the expression on his face as we cruised by. It was always the same, but even through my stoned haze I'd feel the same welling of contempt with a weird measure of satisfaction that I had already surpassed him. I was going farther than he'd ever dared.

⋅

4. Televised boxing matches sponsored by Gillette.

My brother and I were alone in the world. I was fifteen and he sixteen, and we were accountable to no one. All I had to do was not get caught doing petty crimes, and I could continue to wander with no direction, going along on a day-to-day basis with any suggestion or impulse a friend might come up with. It wasn't so bad. Each day was a new adventure. But there were hard times, too—waking up on the ground with nothing but a stubbed-out cigarette, a half-finished beer warming in the morning sun, and a full, absolutely empty day before me. I felt as lost and useless as I ever had before or have since.

Mieyo got tired of our poverty because he liked money: having nice clothes and new Converse sneakers, eating out, buying things. He was always looking for one job or another, and still trying to go to school, but he had to quit to put food in his stomach. For a long time he had a job at the Desert Sands Hotel on Central as a bellboy. I'd go by and he'd give me tip change to buy burgers or we'd eat together. He got to see another side of life while working there, meeting people who traveled and stayed in hotels. Their exciting lives made him dream of achieving the same. He talked a lot about being a millionaire and buying a house and car.

With Mieyo always working, occasionally the formlessness of my own existence would become so boring and tiresome I'd try to get it together for a while and take a job. I was a laborer at Walker Plumbing, jackhammering concrete all day or crawling under scorpion- and spider-infested trailers or digging trenches. I'd work pumping gas or walk onto a construction site and do some manual labor. Once I had a job out at the airport, unloading and loading the food service on the planes on the night shift. It was one of the best jobs I ever had. I remember getting off one quiet windless morning in the middle of winter and stopping my bike at the fence next to a runway covered with fresh snow, the red and blue runway lights glimmering like Christmas bulbs in the distance. I stood there for the longest time, my fingers cold as I gripped the metal fence, my breath hovering about me like a small cloud, wondering why my life couldn't have been different.

Throughout those years I always had an appreciation for beautiful, quiet scenes. I just never told anybody. I'd always had a secret longing to have a place in the desert, all alone with the wind and the coyotes, or in the mountains by a stream, the forest beyond my door full of wildlife: birds, deer, elk, mountain lions, wolves. That was the happiest scene I could imagine. When I really needed to feel safe, I'd go out to the mountains and hang out with nature. The ponderosa pines and running streams appealed to me, but I always had to come back to the city, where I never lasted long on jobs. I resented the way I was treated, and when someone would call me a dumb spic or insult me another way, I'd storm off or get in a fight. I didn't understand how my brother could be content carrying suitcases and meals and washing floors for the convenience of people who didn't even look at him. Sometimes I'd try to convince him to quit, and when he wouldn't, when he'd just go back to emptying ashtrays or delivering laundry, I'd run out and hook up with the old crew. I'd get in a fight, steal something, get busted, and end up in jail again.

.

During my last year in Albuquerque, when I was seventeen, I ended up getting picked up and charged with murder. Some guy got himself killed at a gas station, and I was walking along the street with my T-shirt wrapped around my arm, trying to staunch the blood pouring from a gash I'd gotten from punching a windshield in anger. The police took me to the hospital, had a doctor sew my arm up with eighty-two stitches, and then hauled me down to the station, booked me, and showed me into a cell. I didn't say a word from the time I was picked up to being locked up, but I had an alibi. I didn't protest because I knew that sooner or later I would get out. The police always accused me and my friends of crimes we didn't commit. With no money for a lawyer, and no family to challenge the injustice, we were easy targets for the police to hang something on. It gave them the illusion they were fighting crime and winning. Besides, three meals a day and a warm cot with a roof over my head was a vacation. It was often better in jail than on the streets; I didn't have to worry for a while about surviving.

This time, however, I was moody and dark-tempered because I'd just had my heart broken by a woman I believed I loved, and I didn't want to talk to anyone. It made me pissed and sad that I was in the same place my father had been in when I came to visit him. Except I was even worse, because while he was always thrown in the drunk tank, I was in a cell for felons accused of a capital offense.

After being released, I had a brief period where things went okay. I was off the streets and working for a vending machine company. I'd even been able to rent myself a room in a boardinghouse, with a small fridge and its own bathroom. My own car was parked outside. My life was good enough that I'd even started to allow myself the thought that things could get even better, that I was on my way to the kind of existence I imagined others had. I'd forged a birth certificate to make me over eighteen and old enough to be bonded. When I wasn't in Santa Fe I'd be on the road, traveling all over northern New Mexico, servicing vending machines in the small one-cantina towns that clung to the dry hills or perched on the banks of the brown rivers that flowed through the high desert. Those long stretches between stops gave me my first opportunities to truly relax. I was good with people. Every time I went into a bar or a café to refill the cigarettes or the Coke machine, they'd offer me a free meal or soda and ask where I'd been keeping myself. It was like I was just one of the regular guys. I looked forward to dropping by and bullshitting with waitresses and customers. The scenery relaxed me— broad fields with Queen Anne's lace, hefty sunflowers, and wind-blown grasses, poplars, and cottonwoods, shimmering creeks snaking through canyons—it offered me a placid repose from the hectic pace of urban life. I'd let the mountains and prairie beauty empty my mind of all its anxious worry and look forward to seeing my girlfriend, Theresa, waiting for me back in Albuquerque.

I'd met Theresa in the aftermath of a fight when my brother had called me down to Albuquerque. Three guys had been threatening him, and by the time I showed up two more had joined them, all white guys, and one of them had a knife. I had a big old wrench handy and went after them in my fashion and only stopped when police sirens sounded in the distance. Afterward, Theresa was waiting by my car, a brown-skinned, brown-eyed, black-haired Chicana who quietly asked me for a ride. I took her home and we began to see each other. She went to Highland High School and was impressed with my toughness and independence, and I by her beauty, kisses, and high-spirited nature. She was a normal high school girl, with parents and an older brother and sister. She was my first girlfriend.

Nothing could have been sweeter at first. We went to drive-ins, burger joints, parties, bars, campsites, and we necked late into the night in her parents' basement. But I had a difficult time getting along with her friends. They were middle-class Hispanics, whose parents made good money and bought them what they wanted, and they couldn't speak Spanish and had never been in a cell. They'd known each other since childhood, and I felt left out of their collective experience. They'd laugh about what had happened to someone in the past and I would stare at them, wanting to be included, wishing I knew what they were referring to. The only way I seemed to impress them was by my fighting. It was what had attracted Theresa in the first place, and she, and then her friends, began to encourage me to step out with just about anyone they didn't like the look of. I didn't mind it at first; my fighting skills made me somewhat of a hero in their eyes and I liked being feared and respected. But later it made me feel like the reason they ever invited me anywhere with them was to see if I could keep my unbeaten record intact. I was always fighting guys who had bullied them or made them afraid. I'd fight like a pit bull, my violence fueled by the fact that I had nothing to lose. I provided entertainment only; when it came to social gatherings, they ignored me unless there was a fight. Most of the guys I was fighting were big Anglos, and I guess in some way I was taking up where my grandfather left off. He used to fight in barns and sheds against farm-circuit prizefighters to make extra money for his family. I wasn't getting anything out of it except back slaps and free beer.

This went on for some time until I realized I was feeling used, and I began to resent the people Theresa hung out with. They were a bunch of cowards, spineless spoiled brats who had had everything given to them. To gain Theresa's affection, I was willing to oblige them, even though it undermined my self-respect. But when the dust settled and Theresa and I were left alone, we didn't grow any closer. I didn't know how to nurture a friendship, let alone love. We really didn't have much in common except violence and drinking. She wasn't interested in talking about crime, and I wasn't interested in talking about my family or my past. Our conversations were usually superficial and glib, and I was shy around her. My silence annoyed her, but it frustrated me even more because for the first time I could sense the possibility of a real closeness, however elusive.

Our meetings became sour, stiff, and unbearably tentative. I grew jealous of her friends who seemed to speak with her so easily, and I was suspicious of anyone she even looked at. A month after I turned seventeen I had bought a used trailer, hoping to persuade her to move in with me. It was a snowy February afternoon. I was asleep when she walked in. "I hear you been acting stupid again!" she said. I knew she was referring to her friends, whom I had recently threatened to beat up. I was tired of how they reveled in my fighting prowess and afterward sniggered openly at my desperation to make Theresa love me. I'd found out that she was sleeping around. She looked at me with hate in her eyes. She accused me of being a romantic fool, someone who made sex into something special. It was plain and simple fucking, not love. She didn't want an intimate relationship. She just wanted to have fun, to fuck and be done with it, with no attachment or commitment.

I put on my shirt and laced my boots up, hoping she'd want to go out for hot cocoa and a burger, but when I stood in front of her, she slapped me. Again and again, until she yelled, "Slap me back! Why don't you hit me?" She slapped me until her hand was red and puffy. In the silence between us, her eyes simmered with festering resentment. She wanted me to accept her desire to make love to other guys; she wanted to quit hiding it; she even wanted to break off our relationship. And my naïveté rankled and disgusted her. She found my meekness repulsive, my torment indecent, my loyalty vulgar and obscene. In her eyes, everything about me was repugnant. I lived in a stupid imaginary world where I worshiped her as the most beautiful woman ever. To her, it was the pitiful fantasy of a child. She wanted to be free of me. My faithfulness to her was keeping her from enjoying life. She had to hide and lie, hating herself for what she was doing. Our love meant nothing more to her than licking the bottom of every moment's pleasure. She wanted to punish me for my fidelity; she wanted me to be more like her. She gripped my arms and screamed, "Hit me back!"

But I was at the trailer door already. I fled. As I started off in a jog, the chill air and snow felt good. Dogs barked. People stared out their windows. Guys working in driveways on cars looked up. I was running to the foothills of the Sandias. The mountains would make me forget what happened. Sitting up there I could have some peace of mind and try to figure the situation out. I glanced behind me. She was following, screaming, "Get back here! I hate you! I hate you!" I was surprised to find myself among the piñons and juniper trees already. I was scared and confused, but free of her for the moment. I could see her still in pursuit and behind her the trailer park. It was snowing harder. I hid behind a piñon tree and watched her in sorrow. As she neared the foothills, she fell and yelled out, "Help, I can't walk! I broke my ankle! My foot's stuck, help me!"

For a second I thought it was a trap but then decided she needed me; she was in pain. I skidded down, jumped over rocks, and was at her side instantly. My first thought was right. She lashed out, grabbed my foot, and snarled, full of malice, "You bastard!" She bit my calf, and I kicked to release her grasp, then sprang back, terrified. My adrenaline shot up and I dashed up the hill into the dense thickets. I could barely hear her yelling. I didn't understand why she was doing this, why she hated me.

Not until she had walked away and I saw her car leave, toward dusk, did I venture back to the trailer park. In case she might return, I got behind a Dumpster, hugged my knees to my chest to keep warm, and waited until dark to enter my trailer. The light and shadows played games in the snow, and I saw her wandering again in the fields, a woman wearing a white calf-skin hide, dressed in feathers and moccasins, beads and shells, doing a ritual dance. The snow fell seamlessly around her and the air grew darker until she was gone.

I knew Theresa loved me but she was as afraid as I was of intimacy. I leaned against the cinder-block wall, understanding nothing. I reached down sadly and tied my bootlace, wondering if I should go see her and act like this never had happened. I waited until the next day. When I called from the road she seemed uninterested in me. Dreading another abandonment, I clung to her all the tighter, telling myself that I would be able to hold on to her if only I wanted to enough. I was in love—no, not in love, but possessed with her. I prayed to the stars every night that God would make things good between us again.

I drove down to Albuquerque unannounced to visit her. When I arrived I could feel that she was uncomfortable with my being there. She was busy, she said, and recoiled from my touch. I begged her to come out for a Coke or a ride so we could talk things through. She relented and got in but immediately seemed bored and offended by my intensity. Before I had even turned the corner, she wanted me to take her back. Feeling powerless to convey to her how much I loved her, convinced that if she only knew this she would fall back into my arms, I finally got so desperate I told her I was kidnapping her. She didn't believe me at first, but when we left the city limits and kept going on the interstate, she became quieter. I told her we were going to live in another city and love each other and start new lives together. I kept driving. In between long smoldering stretches of silence, I repeated my plans for us. We were in El Paso[5] by nightfall, when she finally agreed to give us another chance. I turned around and drove straight back to Albuquerque. Not a word passed between us the entire time. But just as we neared her neighborhood she told me she wanted me out of her life. I pulled over, and the next thing I knew there was blood everywhere. I had shattered the windshield, put my arm through it. There was a deep ugly gash to the bone in my left forearm. She ran off and I got out of the car, wrapped my T-shirt around my arm, and started walking toward St. Joseph's emergency room.

When the cops picked me up I didn't care what they did; it didn't matter anymore. I figured I had lost Theresa for good. After I was stitched up, the cops returned and told me I was being booked on suspicion of first-degree murder. I didn't respond to their questions. I agreed to everything with an indifferent nod. I was taken to Montessa Park to await trial and stayed there for about four months, until one day my number was called and a guard informed me that I was being released. Outside, Mieyo was waiting for me. He told me he had joined the army. We spent a couple of days together, partying, drinking, and smoking weed with friends. I wasn't saying much when I walked him downtown to the recruiting station, but I hugged him before he went to join the other recruits who were waiting for a bus to take them to basic training camp. He said he'd see me in a year, when he got out.

2001

## Sixteen

Thirteen Mexicans,
each having paid from two fifty to five hundred
to the coyote to smuggle them in the United States to work,
crashed into the back end of a sixteen-wheeler
and died last night—
      the youngest thirteen.
They died wanting to work,
would have done anything for you—

5

5. City in Texas.

washed your dirty clothes, dishes, scrubbed toilets—
        yet this morning no one thinks about them,          10
        no one cares who they were, what songs they had in their hearts,
        what their dreams were, who their parents were,
        just a bunch of wetbacks—
their blood, freezing on the highway pavement,
        reflects your indifference,          15
        marinates your food,
their disfigured, unrecognizable corpses,
        scattered heads and limbs and torsos
are remembered in the white-knuckle clenched fist I raise
to you          20
        who need your crops cut, fields hoed,
        houses cleaned, yards landscaped,
        children cared for—
thirteen of them last night,
        thousands more in growers' fields,          25
        restaurants,
        all-night gas stations
        and construction companies,
offered no medical care, no education, no sanitary living quarters;
dogs, cats, birds, and rats are treated kinder,          30
and no Georgia mule ever worked harder
than my Mexican brothers and sisters,
lacking citizenship papers but with heart, soul, and mind
        full of dreams,
        worked and not paid, greeted when needed          35
but, after their work is finished,
crowded into cattle cars, truck beds, vans, jail cells, livestock pens,
shot, electrocuted, beaten, exiled, robbed, jeered at, blamed,
because they believe in the American Dream
we take for granted.          40
        Don't tell me slavery has ended,
        don't tell me there's no prejudice,
        or that judges rule fairly—
handcuffs, pepper Mace, cells, police, and the INS
were not created for the rich corporate executives.          45
Imagine having worked from dawn until dusk,
        then being cheated out of your pay,
        and when you get back to your freezing tent,
        the boss calls Immigration
        to drag you away so he doesn't have to pay?          50
Imagine your kids working all day in factory sweatshops,
        then being herded into paddy wagons
        and deposited on the border.
What hypocrisy,
        what a sham your prayers are at Sunday services,          55
        assuming you're more entitled to live and breathe and eat
        by exploiting the less fortunate.

        2002

## ChicaIndio

Brown-eyed, black-haired
spirit violated as a boy,
I learned to violate myself as a man,
fucking to cope with loss,
reduce the ache of my fragmented self                              5
to disassociate,
repress my insecurities—
      paralyzed by panic,
      unable to trust,
      labeling love a psychosis,                          10
      fearing commitment,
my heart bellied up
          in an oil spill of arctic deceptions.
I betrayed myself again
    in bed with you                                          15
    at Jackson Hole, Wyoming,
        my rib cage
        a hangman's platform,
        lynched bodies
               swayed from,                              20
               clacking their death spell
               between us,
the words *I love you*
corpse worms wriggling beneath my tongue.

2007

---

# PAT MORA
## b. 1952

Pat Mora's birthplace, El Paso, Texas, and its sister city, Juárez, Mexico, are present throughout her poetry, nonfiction, and children's books. The border region, with its desert environment and thoroughly mixed Texan and Mexican traditions, plays as big a role in her work as do the sympathetic portraits of relatives, friends, and members of the Mexican American and Latino communities that nurtured her as a student and, later, as a teacher in public schools, community colleges, and the University of Texas in El Paso. Mora believes passionate identification with the desert and its mysteries is a source of strength for Mexican Americans.

Mora's poetry is often published in bilingual format. Her work—in volumes such as *Chants* (1984), *Communion* (1991), *Aunt Carmen's Book of Practical Saints* (1997), and *Adobe Odes* (2006)—focuses on the ancestral traditions of *mexicano* culture in Texas. As the five poems selected for this anthology attest, what makes Mora's voice moving is her optimism, her attention to detail, and her love of place, people, and culture. In "A Child, a child," she celebrates birth and motherhood. In "La dulceria," she depicts the customers in a candy store defined by the aromas and tastes of Mexico. In "Coatlicue's Rules: Advice from an Aztec Goddess," "Malinche's

Tips: Pique from Mexico's Mother," and "Consejos de Nuestra Señora de Guadalupe: Counsel from the Brown Virgin," she takes on the voices of mythological and
historical figures to offer advice about gender relations.

In her volume *Nepantla: Essays from the Land in the Middle* (1993), Mora reflects,
in part, on the challenges she faces as a Mexican American author and educator. In
her memoir *House of Houses* (1997), she intertwines reality and fantasy, fact and
myth, in imagining a house in the desert between El Paso and Sante Fe. The
founder of El día de los niños/El día de los libros, Children's Day/Book Day, an effort
to develop literacy among Latinos sponsored by the American Library Association,
Mora has written more than 30 children's books. *Tomás and the Library Lady* (2000)
is based on an event in the life of the writer Tomás Rivera (see p. 1077), a colleague
of Mora's at the University of Texas in El Paso (1979–80), who during his childhood
received from a librarian an encyclopedia that represented the opening of a new
world of information.

In 1988, Mora was admitted to the *El Paso Herald Post*'s Writers Hall of Fame. The
same year, she was inducted into the Texas Institute of Letters. Among the awards
she has received are a Civitella Ranieri Fellowship (2003) to write in Umbria, Italy;
the National Hispanic Cultural Center Literary Award (2006); and an Honorary Doctorate of Letters from State University of New York at Buffalo (2006). She lives in
Santa Fe, New Mexico.

## A Child, a Child[1]

You held your breath
for months it seemed,
feared each phone ring,
her voice saying,
"Can't give you this baby."                                              5

Then the unexpected:
    "Breech."
Together, you sat the hours
    the baby in her
heavy between his mothers,                                               10

oblivious, as children often are,
of the talking, tears
not new to either of you,
hers, resignation,
this parting, final,                                                     15
yours, fear so loud
you strained to hear her words.

Four mother hands
held him those first days,
and you watched her every move,                                          20
knew it was you she held.

---

1. The Christmas carol "Do You Hear What I
Hear?," a celebration of the birth of Jesus Christ,
includes the lines "A Child, a Child / Shivers in
the cold / Let us bring Him silver and gold / Let
us bring Him silver and gold / . . . The Child, the
Child / Sleeping in the night / He will bring us
goodness and light / He will bring us goodness
and light."

The last day there was talk
of love, and she placed him
in your arms. Privately, you
altered fate, woman-to-woman.                                    25

Your mouth formed that new word,
*son*, and his breath began slipping into you,
warm, steady, those breaths,
tiny puffs filling you,
like those Japanese streamers                                    30
flown on Boy's Day Festival,[2]
carp banners, hardy fish
that charge upstream,
good male spirit.

Good spirit, I say, yours,                                       35
those babybreaths filling
you. Your joy streaming forth proclaiming
at long last, let the celebration begin.

                                                                 1995


## La dulcería[1]

Released into the season
of wildflowers, zumban.[2]
Bees burst into petal scent,
gossip rumors of sweet platters,
glazed faraway place brimming                                    5
mountains of sugary crystals.

                    Zumban.

The swarm pursues an orange aroma
of pumpkins, figs, tejocote[3]
simmering in syrups,                                             10
globes rolling in huge cauldrons
dark bubblings and brewings, gold
juices released in heat.

Bodies bumping and bruising,
zumban, hundreds fly through tree                                15
soughings, toward leche quemada,[4]
pause only briefly to sip
fields flowering their yellow,
spinning perfumes to the sun.

---

2. Or Tango-no-Sekku, the Japanese celebration, on May 5, of the healthy growth and development of young boys.
1. The candy store.
2. Buzz.

3. Berries from a species of hawthorn native to Mexico.
4. Mexican candy that includes brown sugar and deeply caramelized milk.

Zumban. Zumban.                    20

They careen down streets and round
corners, veer at last, *zum-zum*,
into la dulcería
round fruit gleaming like jewels, slide
on *ate de guayaba*                    25
sink into brown pools of cajeta.[5]

Zumban y zumban.

Buzzing bodies nuzzle coco
and jamoncillo as la dueña
en su delantal[6] brushes              30
bee bumpings with "Es la temporada,"[7]
season of suckings and burrowings,
nectar irresistible.

1995

## Coatlicue's[1] Rules: Advice from an Aztec Goddess

Rule 1: Beware of offers to make you famous.

I, pious Aztec mother lost in housework,
am pedestaled, "She of the Serpent Skirt,"
necklace dangling hearts and hands, faceless
statue, two snakes eye-to-eye on my shoulders,      5
goddess of earth, also death, which leads to

Rule 2: Retain control of your own publicity.

Past is present. Women are women.
I'm not competitive and motherhood isn't
about numbers, but four hundred sons and a daughter   10
may be a record even without the baby.
There's something wrong in this world
if a woman isn't safe even when she sweeps
her own house, when any speck can enter even through
the eye, I'll bet, and become a stubborn tenant.      15

Rule 3: Protect your uterus.

Conceptions, immaculate and otherwise, happen.
Women swallow sacred stones that fill their bellies
with elbows and knees. In Guatemala, a skull dangling

---

5. Jelly candy or nougat. *Ate de guayaba*: guava
paste.
6. The lady in her apron. *Jamoncillo*: Mexican
candy that includes pecans.

7. It's the time; it's the season.
1. Also known as Tetoinan; Aztec goddess who
gave birth to the moon, stars, and Huitzilopochtli, the god of the sun and war.

from a tree whispers, "Touch me," 20
to a young girl, and a clear drop
drips on her palm, disappears. Dew
drops in, if you know what I mean.
Saliva moved in her, the girl says. Moved in, I say,
settled into that empty space, and grew. Men know. 25
They stay full of themselves, keeps occupancy down.

Rule 4: Avoid housework.

Remember, I was sweeping, humming, actually,
high on Coatepec, our Serpent Mountain, humming loud
so I wouldn't hear all those sighs inside. 30
I was sweeping slivers, gold and jade, picking up
after four hundred sons who think they're gods,
and their spoiled sister. I was sweeping
when feathers fell on me, brushed my face,
first light touch in years, like in a dream. 35

At first, I just blew them off, then I saw
the prettiest ball of tiny plumes, glowing
green and gold. Gently, I gathered it. Oh,
it was soft as baby hair, brought back mother-
shivers when I pressed it to my skin. I nestled it 40
like I used to nestle them, here,
when they finished nursing. Maybe I even stroked
the roundness. I have since heard that feathers
aren't that unusual at annunciations, but I was innocent.

After sweeping, I looked in vain inside 45
my clothes, but the soft ball had vanished, well,
descended. I think I showed within the hour,
or so it seemed. They noticed first, of course.

Rule 5: Avoid housework. It bears repeating.

I was too busy washing, cooking, sweeping again, 50
worrying about my daughter, Painted with Bells,
when I began to bump into their frowns
and mutterings. They kept glancing at my stomach,
started pointing. I got so hurt and mad, I started crying.
Why do they get to us? One wrong word or look 55
from any one of them doubles me over,
and I've had four hundred and one, no anesthetic.
Near them I'm like a snail with no shell on a sizzling day.
They started yelling, "Wicked, wicked," and my daughter,
right there with them, my wannabe warrior boy. 60

The yelling was easier than the whispers, "Kill. Kill.
Kill. Kill." Kill me? Their mother?
One against four hundred and one? All I'd done
was press that feathered softness into me.

Rule 6: Listen to inside voices.                                            65

You mothers know about the baby in a family, right?
Even if he hadn't talked to me from deep inside,
he would have been special. Maybe the best.
But as my name is Coatlicue, he did.
That unborn child, that started as a ball of feathers            70
all soft green and gold, heard my woes, and spoke to me.
A thoughtful boy. And formal too. He said, "Do not be afraid,
I know what I must do." So I stopped shaking.

Rule 7: Verify that the inside voice is yours.

I'll spare you the part about the body hacking                   75
and head rolling. But he was provoked, remember.
All this talk of gods and goddesses distorts.

This planet wasn't big enough for all of us,
but my whole family has done well for itself, I think.
I'm the mother of stars. My daughter's white head               80
rolls round the heavens each night, and my sons
wink down at me. What can I say—a family
of high visibility. The baby? Up there also, the sun,
the real thing. Such a god he is, of war unfortunately,
and the boy never stops, always racing across the sky,          85
every day of the year, a ball of fire since birth.
But I think he has forgotten me. You sense my ambivalence.
I'm blinded by his light.

Rules 8: Insist on personal interviews.

Past is present, remember. Men carved me,                       90
wrote my story, and Eve's, Malinche's, Guadalupe's,
Llorona's,[2] snakes everywhere, even in our mouths.

Rule 9: Be selective about what you swallow.

                                                              1995

## Malinche's Tips: Pique from Mexico's Mother[1]

My face isn't red
from blushing or lust,

---

2. La Llorona (The Weeping Woman); a popular legend in Spanish-speaking cultures in the Americas, generally about a beautiful woman who kills her children to be with a man, is rejected by him, and then wanders, weeping, searching for children and, in some versions of the tale, ready to kidnap wandering children. For a text of the legend, see p. 2452; for a variation on it, see p. 2454. *Malinche's*: La Malinche, also known as Malintzin and Doña Marina (ca. 1496 or 1505–ca. 1529), aboriginal mistress of and translator for the

Spanish conquistador Hernán Cortés (1485–1547), who led the conquest of the Aztecs. *Guadalupe's*: Nuestra Señora de Guadalupe (Our Lady of Guadalupe), also known as *La Virgen de Guadalupe*, the matron saint of Mexico; a sixteenth-century *mestiza* icon of the Virgin Mary, perhaps Mexico's most popular religious and cultural image, it has come to symbolize Catholic Mexicans and Mexico itself.

1. See identification in note 2, above.

flush of wild, swarming
unconstricted blood.

Tip 1: In an unfriendly country,                                          5
wear a mask.
You will see more.

I hear your sticks-and-stones:
whore, traidora, slut.
What happened to mother?                                              10

My reputación
precedes me. I come
from a long line of women
much maligned,
hija de Eva,[2]                                                                    15
rumors of gardens,
crushed flowery scent
heavy as sprawling, tangled
branches, scarlet breeze
velvetmoist with petals,                                               20
piel, fruitflesh, ripe
tempting tongue,
sweet juice of
words, plural hiss
of languagessssss,                                                        25
serpents,
arms tasting
apple-red, mouth
and eyes wide,
ripe legs,                                                                     30
ribbons of blood,
birth, you, blesséd fruit
of my warm redwomb.

Tip 2: Write
your own rumors                                                           35
or hire your own historians.

They say my father,
a Náhuatl prince,
died, and my mother
remarried, of course.                                                     40
We're so redhot
our skin burns
in moonlight
like our eyes, blazing
cats, blacksilk,                                                             45
wickedslink.
My mother sold me,
bundled my body

2. Daughter of Eve.

off to the Maya,
women and competition                                    50
of piel, the flesh.
Prince of a father,
witch of a mother,
bruja.[3]
Sound familiar?                                          55

Tip 3: Re-view
folklore typology
and then reread
hisstory.

Women. Snakes.                                           60
Snakes and tongues. Snake-haired
women. Loose-haired women. Loose-tongued
women. Open-mouthed women. Open
women. Whores. Mothersssss.
Virgin mothers.                                          65
Women of closed
uterus. Women
of closed
mouths. Women
of covered                                               70
hair. Women
of cloaked
bodies. Women
who crush
víboras.[4] Women                                        75
who crush their
own tongues.
Silent women.
Altared women.

Tip 4: Alter                                             80
the altared women.

I became bilingual,
learned to roll
palabras[5] in my mouth
just to taste them,                                      85
chew, swallow,
fruta dulce.[6]

Eva, Sor Juana,[7]
and I remember
words' velvet in our                                     90
mouths. We tasted
their power and red

3. Witch, sorceress.            6. Sweet fruit.
4. Vipers.                      7. Sor Juana Inés de la Cruz (1648 or 1651–1695),
5. Words.                       Mexican nun, scholar, writer, and poet.

sting, long before
"English Only," fearssss
of contagion from                                    95
tangled lenguas,[8]
of verbal intertwinings,
like the uncontrollable
breedings of snakes.

Tip 5: Remember:                                     100
monolinguals know
about linguistics
like atheists know
about theology.

I was given to                                       105
Cortés, flesh gift,
ripe-red
gift, shared
uterus, my hair
flowing, flowing like                                110
snakes sizzling,

like blood rivers, my tongue carrying him
and his men into a world smeared scarlet,
raping and flaming tongues devouring pages.
and children's bones, fire higher than pyramids      115
fueled by my historic lengua, *rat-rattle* of my evil.

Tip 6: Beware
historians citing
only themselves.

But, mis hijas e hijos,[9]                            120
you live. I'm the proud
mother of mexicanos,
brown as I am.
Conceptions happen,
remember? But,                                       125
the blesséd fruit
of my womb spits
my name.

I hear
prostitute, puta, hooker, bitch.                     130
Try saying mamá.

Tip 7: Watch your tongues.

I try to hold you,
to wrap my arms and hair
around my children,                                  135

8. Tongues, languages.                    9. My daughters and sons.

to say, I am
a daughter, abused
woman, abuser,
no saint, human,
sold, slave, sexual                                    140
woman, raped
woman, invisible
translator, mother
but, no virgin,
never immaculate                                        145
enough, never
fleshless enough,
never silent
enough, my eyes—
Mexico's troubled,                                      150
buried mirror.

Tip 8: If you remove your mask,
mirror, mirror won't lie.

Look. Do you see? We.
Inseparable.                                            155

Tip 9: Children are
not bastards;
children are children.

I'm in you, in
your quips, books,                                      160
analysessssssss,
snakey sueños,[1]
carved red
masks of your mother
long-haried for                                         165
prostitution, wantonness,
lizards on my cheeks,
creatures of land,
water, symbols
of sex and divining.                                    170

En agua,[2] I see
your mouths and eyes
opening, my children,
like waterlilies.

Tip 10: Face it:                                        175
Hating your mother
ruins your skin.

1995

1. Sleeps, dreams.          2. In water.

## Consejos de Nuestra Señora de Guadalupe:[1]
## Counsel from the Brown Virgin

You seem surprised that I've appeared.
You gape like Juan Diego[2] as I hovered in a cloud
that December morning above dry Tepeyac.[3] Mortals lack faith
and imagination, fear flying. Hijas,[4] be unpredictable.

> Como la flor de rosa.          5
> Como el arco iris.
> Como las nubes de gloria.
> Como la luna espléndida.[5]

Do not be insistent. I raise neither my voice nor eyes—
yet. Bodies, even celestial, are creatures of habit.          10
Hijas, what we repeat becomes our nature. Beware.
Goddesses fade in and out of fashion.

> Como la flor de rosa.
> Como el arco iris.
> Como las nubes de gloria:          15
> Como la luna espléndida.

Names and images are converted. Now I'm moon-rider
in repose, body concealed in flowing cocoon,
hands, mouth, eyes folded, cloaked in stars.
Hijas, consistent trappings can release us for internal work.          20

> Como la flor de rosa.
> Como el arco irisi.
> Como las nubes de gloria.
> Como la luna espléndida.

You analyze the persistence of my image, how I don't fade.          25
Too much analysis inhibits wisdom, hijas. You fear
flying. A muse amused, I am used everywhere, auto-shops,
buses, bars, slender mother but virgen pura, no Malinche.[6]

> Como la flor de rosa.
> Como el arco iris.          30
> Como las nubes de gloria.
> Como la luna espléndida.

Hijas, beware of altars and rumors of legends.
Holy men altered me, Aztec goddess to Reina[7] de las Américas,

---

1. See identification in note 2, p. 1854.
2. Saint Juan Diego Cuauhtlatoatzin (1474–1548), Mexican religious icon, possibly mythical.
3. Now the site, in Mexico City, of the Basilica of Guadalupe; in December 1531, Juan Diego reputedly met the Virgin of Guadalupe on the hill there. Tepeyac may also have been a site for worship of the pre-Columbian mother-goddess Tonantzin.
4. Daughters.
5. Like the pink flower. / Like the rainbow. / Like the clouds of glory. / Like the splendid moon.
6. See the preceding poem and the identification in note 2, p. 1854.
7. Queen.

pyramid to cathedral. They say I called sweet as birdsong          35
to Juan Diego rushing to the curling hum of holy incense.

> Como la flor de rosa.
> Como el arco iris.
> Como las nubes de gloria.
> Como la luna espléndida.          40

Send men clear signs. They need them, hijas.
In deserts, I favor scarlet roses. Come.
Rise. Practice solitary levitation. Rise,
but ignore halos, hovering men who look like angelitos.

> Como la flor de rosa.          45
> Como el arco iris.
> Como las nubes de gloria.
> Como la luna espléndida.

Hijas, value contemplation. Alone, I write
my own legends. My lines improve. Play the symbols.          50
I loan my cape to women in tennis shoes who fly
back and forth across the Río Grande.

> Como la flor de rosa.
> Como el arco iris.
> Como las nubes de gloria.          55
> Como la luna espléndida.

Listen to this buzz of litanies. Endless praise inhibits musing.
Hijas, silence can be pregnant. My voice rose like a beam
of sunlight, entered Juan. Remember, conceptions,
immaculate and otherwise, happen. He knelt, full of me.          60

> Como la flor de rosa.
> Como el arco iris.
> Como las nubes de gloria.
> Como la luna espléndida.

1995

---

# CHERRÍE MORAGA
## b. 1952

Cherríe Moraga's father is Anglo, her mother Mexican. She was raised in San Gabriel,
California. After earning her bachelor's degree from Immaculate Heart College, in
Los Angeles, California, Moraga taught for two years but found teaching unfulfilling.
In 1977, she moved to San Francisco, where she felt free to declare her lesbianism. As

she pursued her writing career and supported herself with part-time jobs, the spirit of the Bay Area in the late 1970s heavily influenced Moraga's work and her politics. Her best-known publications—the essay collection *Loving in the War Years* (1983), the play *Giving Up the Ghost: Teatro in Two Acts* (1984), and the collection of plays *Heroes and Saints* (1986)—focus on lesbian relationships. Moraga's years-long, in-depth exploration of her identity as a Chicana feminist and lesbian broke ground in Mexican American letters. Her commitment to lesbian letters continues to involve using her own voice and not relying on Anglo norms.

While doing graduate work at San Francisco State University in 1980, Moraga met her fellow Chicana lesbian Gloria Anzaldúa, who proposed gathering writings by women of color, hitherto voiceless. She also contributed the essay "La Güera" (The Light-Skinned Woman) to the collection, and the writing of this piece proved both difficult and liberating, in that she revealed previously private and hidden things about herself as a writer of color and as a lesbian. Moraga moved to New York City to try to sell the book to a mainstream publisher. In 1981, she decided to take the direct route and cofounded Kitchen Table/Women of Color Press, which published the now-seminal collection she and Anzaldúa edited, *This Bridge Called My Back: Writings by Radical Woman of Color* (1981). Moraga served as an editor and administrator at the press. Joined in collaboration with other women writers, she lived in New York for four years.

During this time, Moraga came to think of herself as a Chicana and a Latina, and she determined to work with other Latina writers. In 1983, Kitchen Table/ Women of Color published the first-ever anthology of writing by Latina feminists, *Cuentos: Stories by Latinas*, edited by Moraga, Alma Gómez, and Mariana Romo Carmona. That same year, Moraga collected essays she had written from 1976 onward in *Loving in the War Years*. That collection's subtitle, *lo que nunca pasó por sus labios* (what never passed through her lips), refers to words unspoken, to denial by lesbians afraid to take a stand. Included in the book is a groundbreaking essay Moraga wrote in New York, "A Long Line of Vendidas" (Sellouts).

In this piece, which is steeped in Mexican history and Chicano history, Moraga focused on Malantzín Tenepal, popularly called La Malinche, a sixteenth-century aboriginal woman who served as translator for the Spanish conquistador Hernán Cortés and became his mistress. Moraga views La Malinche, the mother of children by Cortés, as the first *vendida*. She also calls herself, as the daughter of an Anglo and a Mexican, a sellout. Included in this wide brushstroke are all Mexican and Chicana women who subjugate themselves to men. Moraga *chose* her sexuality, she explains, to exclude all men, specifically Chicano men. This highly personal essay liberated lesbians who had married men and had dedicated their lives to their husbands. It also pointed the way for the unification of all Chicana writers. Moraga's forthright statements, honesty, and vivid writing provided for Chicano men a liberating sense as well, and gay Latino men felt encouraged to declare their sexuality.

Moraga's exploration of her Chicana roots inspired her to use more and more Spanish in her works. *Giving Up the Ghost*, included here in its entirety, is primarily in English, but Spanish and Spanglish phrases contribute to each character's development. The action takes place in East Los Angeles, a largely Mexican American neighborhood. The three main characters are tough, working-class Chicanas: Marisa, who is in her late 20s; Corky, who is Marisa's younger self at age 11 and later at age 17; and Amalia, who is Mexican-born and in her late forties. In long monologues, which all the characters can hear and to which they can react, the characters explain themselves, their doubts, and their questioning of what it means to be a woman in a "man's world." Rather than rebelling or accepting, the characters become aware of themselves as worthy people who have found self-respect. The language is faithful to the characters' background, mixing innocence and cynicism, tenderness and brutality. Marisa and Corky use hip slang of the 1960s. Amalia's vocabulary is more conservative.

In 1988, Moraga collaborated with with the writer Ana Castillo and the critic Norma Alarcón in translating *This Bridge Called My Back* into Spanish as *Este puente, mi espalda: Voces de mujeres tercermundistas en los Estados Unidos*. She continued to explore lesbianism and female intimacy in *The Last Generation* (1993) and *Waiting in the Wings: A Portrait of Queer Motherhood* (1997). Her plays *Watsonville, Some Place Not Here, Circle in the Dirt*, and *El pueblo de East Palo Alto* were collected in a single volume in 2002. Among her literary awards, the most important is the American Book Award from the Before Columbus Foundation (1986).

---

# GIVING UP THE GHOST: TEATRO IN TWO ACTS

## The Characters

MARISA  *Chicana in her late 20s*
CORKY  MARISA's *younger self, at 11 and 17 years old*
AMALIA  *Chicana in her late 40s, born in México*
THE PEOPLE  *Those viewing* THE PERFORMANCE

CORKY *is "una chaparrita"[1] who acts tough, but has a wide open sincerity in her face which betrays the toughness. She dresses in the "cholo style" of her period (the '60s): khakis with razor-sharp creases; pressed white undershirt; hair short and slicked back.*

MARISA, *over 10 years later, wears her toughness less self-consciously, a little closer to the bone. The sincerity is more guarded. She appears in levis, tennis shoes, and a dark shirt. Her hair is short.*

AMALIA *is "soft" in just the ways that* MARISA *is "hard." Her clothes give the impression of being draped, as opposed to worn. Shawl-over-blouse-over-skirt—all of Mexican Indian design. Her hair is long and worn down or loosely braided. There is nothing frivolous about this woman.*

The STAGE SET *should be black with as few props as possible. Crates, platforms, or simple wooden chairs, for example, should be used to represent "the street," a "bed," "kitchen," etc. Lighting should be the main feature in providing setting. Throughout the long monologues (unless otherwise stated), the lighting should give the impression that the* ACTORS *are within hearing range of one another; that* THEY *in fact know what the other is saying (thinking), even when there is no obvious response from the "listener."*

The ACTION *(story) takes place (not chronologically) over a period of months.*

The place:  *East Los Angeles*

The year:  *1980*

---

1. A shorty.

# Act One: "La Pachuca"

*Dedicación*

*Don't know where this woman and I*
*will find each other again,*
*but I am grateful to her   to something*
*that feels like a blessing*

*that I am, in fact,*
*not trapped*

*which brings me to the question of prisons*
*politics*
*sex.*

[*Music.*

*Voice from the dark.*]
MARISA:
   I'm only telling you this to stay my hand.
     [*Lights slowly come up on* MARISA *downstage center, facing* THE
     PEOPLE. CORKY *sits back-to-back with* MARISA. SHE *is not yet visible.*]
   But why, cheezus, why me?
   Why'd I hafta get into a situation
   where all my ghosts come to visit?

   I always see that man—thick-skinned, dark, muscular.
   He is a boulder between us.
   I cannot lift him and her, too, carrying him.

   He is a ghost, always haunting her . . .
   lingering.
     [MARISA *slowly exits.*
     *'60s Chicano-style rock 'n' roll can be heard as* CORKY *turns to face*
     THE PEOPLE. SHE *"moves with it" until it slowly fades out.*]
CORKY (1963):
   *the smarter I get the older I get the meaner I get*
   *tough   a tough cookie my mom calls me*
   *sometimes I even pack a blade   no one knows*
   *I never use it or nut'ing but can feel it there*
   *there in my pants pocket   run the pad of my thumb over it*
   *to remind me I carry some'ting   am sharp   secretly*
   *always envy those batos[2] who get all cut up at the weddings*
   *getting their rented tuxes all bloody*
   *that red 'n' clean color against the white*
   *starched collars   I love that shit!*

2. Dudes.

the best part is the chicks
all climbing into the ball of the fight
Chuey déjalo!   leave him go, Güero!
tú sabes[3]   you know how the chicks get
all excited 'n' upset 'n' stuff
they always pulling on the carnales[4] 'n' getting
nowhere 'cept messed up themselves 'n' everybody
looks so like they digging the whole t'ing   tú sabes
their dresses ripped here 'n' there . . . like a movie

it's all like a movie
when I was a little kid I useta love the movies
every saturday you could find me there
my eyeballs glued to the screen
then during the week my friend Tudy and me
we'd make up our own movies
one of our favorites was this cowboy one
where we'd be out in the desert
'n' we'd capture these chicks 'n' hold 'em up
for ransom   we'd string 'em up 'n'
make 'em take their clothes off
jus' pretend a'course but it useta make me feel
real tough
strip   we'd say to the wall
all cool-like

funny now when I think about how little I was
at the time   and a girl
but in my mind   I was big 'n' tough 'n' a dude
in my mind   I had all their freedom
the freedom to really see a girl
kinda   the way   you see
an   animal   you know?

like imagining
they got a difernt set
of blood vessels
or somet'ing   like   so
when you mess with 'em
it don' affect 'em
the way   it do   you
like   like they got a difernt
gland system   or somet'ing   that
that   makes their pain cells
more dense

hell I dunno

3. You know. *Chuey déjalo:* Bro (brother), leave him alone. *Güero:* blondie.
4. Bro's.

*but you see*
*I never could*
*quite*
*pull it off*

*always knew I was a girl*
*deep down inside*
*no matter how*
*I tried to pull the other*
*off*

*I knew*

*always knew*

*I was an animal that kicked back*

*cuz it hurt*
　　[*Black out.*]
　　[MARISA *is sitting on top of her "bed" stage left, rubbing her calves.*]
MARISA:
I'm not tryin' to make no big deal outta this.
In fact, I been avoiding making any deal at all.
But when I go to sleep my legs stiffen up on me
like they got rocks in them.
I mean it. No kinda stretching can release the rock
ball of hardness I got locked between my knees 'n' ankles.

I stretch them.
Dig my bone fingers into the meat of the calf to work it out.
Me duele pero[5] there's no relaxing them.
I'm forced outta bed with the pain.
Marta finds me cruisin' the house like a damn
　　　　　　　　　　　　　　　　sleep-walking zombie.
"You can't sleep, Marisa?" she tries.
"No, I can't," I cry
cuz I'm fighting in my legs what I know.
I'm standing firm on the ground even when I'm layin'
　　　　　　　　　　　　　　　　sideways up in bed
cuz I'm sure to fly away in this anger,
no root to it at all.
Bottomless.
Bottomless.

What *is* betrayal?
Let me tell you about it, it is not clean, nothing neat.
It's about a battle I will never win and never stop fighting.
The dick beats me every time.

---

5. It hurts but.

I know I'm not supposed to be sayin' this
cuz it's like confession,
it's like still cryin' your sins to a priest you long ago
stopped believing was god or god's sit-in.
And you? Pues,[6] you aint no soldier of christ,
but still confessing what long ago you hoped
would be forgiven in you, that prison
that passion
to beat them
at their own game.

AMALIA: [*Entering stage right.*]
I worry about La Pachuca.
That's my nickname for her.
I have trouble calling her by her christian name, Marisa.
It's a beautiful name, really, but she defies it at every turn.
In fact, I change her name at regular intervals
just to stay abreast with her.
La quiero mucho.
She doesn't always know it,
pero hay parte de ella misma que lo sabe perfectamente.[7]

I worry about La Pachuca.
I worry what will happen to the beautiful corn
                                        she is growing
if it continues to rain so hard and much.

CORKY: [*Downstage center, sitting.*]
*one time Tudy and me did it for real*
*strip    I mean*
*we been playing these movie capture games 'n' all*
*'n' getting ourselves all worked-up*
*I mean we could play these games for days!*

*anyway there was this minister 'n' his family down the street*
*they was presbyterians or methodists or somet'ing*
*you know one of those gringo religions*
*and they had a bunch a kids*
*the oldest was named Lisa or somet'ing lightweight like that*
*and the littlest was about three or so named Chrissy*
*I mean you couldn't really complain about Chrissy*
*cuz she wasn't old enough yet to be a pain in the cola[8]*
*but you knew that was coming*

*Lisa'd be hassling me and my sister Patsy all the time*
*tell us how we wernt really christians cuz cath-lics*
*worshipped the virgin mary or somet'ing*

6. So.
7. But there's a part of her that she knows perfectly. *La quiero mucho*: I love her very much.
8. Butt.

*I dint let this worry me too much though cuz*
*we was being tole at school how being cath-lic was*
*the one true numero uno church 'n' all*
*so I just let myself be real cool with her*
*'n' the rest of her little pagan baby brothers 'n' sisters*
*that's all they was to me as far as I was concerned*

*they dint even have no mass    jus' some paddy preaching*
*up on their altar with a dark suit on*
*very weird*
*not a damn candle for miles*
*dint seem to me that there was any god*
                              *happening in that place at all*
*so back to Tudy and me*
*one day Tudy comes up with this idea how we should strip for real*
*well    I wasn't that hot on the idea but still go along with him*
*hopping from backyard to backyard looking for prey*
*then we run into Chrissy*
*so Tudy 'n' me eye each other 'n' figure*
*she's the perfect victim*
*for our sick little fantasies*

*the trouble is    I'm still not completely sold on the idea*
*but Tudy was always too stupid to pull anything off by himself*
*so I end up working out the whole damn thing*
          *the boy lacked imagination if you know what I mean*

*Chrissy is hanging out in her backyard*
*they have this kinda shed there*
*with a buncha junk in it that nobody used for nut'ing*
*so I say to her real simple-minded like    all syrupy-mouthed*
*come heeeeere Chrissy    we got somet'ing to shoooooow you*
*well a'course the kid comes cuz I was a big kid 'n' all*
*so we take her into the shed*

*I have her hand 'n' Tudy tells her*
      [As if suddenly remembering.]
          *no    I told her this*
*I tell her we think she's got somet'ing wrong with her*
*"down there"*
*I think    I think I said she had a coco[9] or somet'ing*
*'n' Tudy 'n' me had to check it out*
*so I pull her little shorts down*
*'n' then her chonas*
*'n' then jus' as we catch a glimple of her little*
          *fuchi fachi . . .*[1]
          *it was so tender-looking*

9. Bogeyman.
1. *Fuchi fachi*: slang for female genitalia. *Chonas*: underwear.

all pink 'n' real sweet
like a bun
'n' then Tudy like a pendejo[2]
goes 'n' sticks his dirty finger on it
like it was burning hot
'n' jus' at that moment . . .

I see this little Chrissy-kid look up at me
    like
    like I was her mom or somet'ing
    like   tú sabes
she has this little kid's frown on her face
    like
    like she knew

somet'ing was wrong with what we was up to
'n' was looking at me to reassure her
that everything was cool
'n' regular 'n' all

what a pendeja I felt like

so I swipe Tudy's stupid hand away 'n' say
"let's get outta here!"
'n' pull up her shorts 'n' whisper to her
"no no you're fine   really
there's nothing wrong with you
but don' tell nobody we looked
it's a secret
we don' want nobody to worry
about you"
      what else was I supposed to say?
[to herself]   tonta
'n' Tudy 'n' me make a beeline into the alley
'n' outta there
      [Long pause, coming toward THE PEOPLE.]
the weird thing was
that after that I was like a maniac all summer
snotty Lisa kept harassing me about the virgin mary
'n' all 'n' jus' in general being a pain in the coolie[3]

things began to break down when me 'n' Patsy stopped
going to their church meetings on wednesday nights
we'd only go cuz they had cookies 'n' treats
after all the bible stuff
'n' sometimes had arts 'n' crafts where you got to paint
little clay statues of blonde Jesus in a robe
'n' the little children coming to him

2. An asshole.
3. Butt.

*anyway the reason we stopped going was cuz*
*one time during these "prayer meetings" they called 'em*
*where everybody'd stand in a circle*
*squeezing hands and each kid'd say a little prayer*
*you know like for the starving people in china*
      *Patsy and me always passed*
      *jus' shaked our heads no when we got squeezed*
      *cuz it was against our religion 'n' all to pray with them*
*well one time this Lisa punk has the nerve to pray*
*that Patsy 'n' me would*
*[Mimicking.]  "come to the light*
*of the one true christian faith"*
*shi-it   can you get to that?*
*'course we never went again*
*I 'member coming home 'n' telling my mom*
*'n' she says "it's better mi'jitas*[4]
*I think if you don' go no more"*

*'n' it was so nice to hear her voice*
*so warm like she loved us a lot*

*'n' that night*
*being cath-lic felt like my mom*

*real warm 'n' dark 'n' kind*

MARISA: [*Long pause.*]
  I hate men.
  Ya, I said it.
  Like my roommate, Marta, she said it too yesterday
  ironing her blouse for work
  the one I had just fixed a hole in,
  "You know Marisa, men are truly not worth
  getting your hands dirty."
  This time she hates them because she jerked
  one of our co-workers off, just this nobody
  guy with muscles on the night-shift,
  literally, with her free hand on her free time
  and now he thinks he's got something over on her
  and it was the easiest thing jerking him around.
  "Men are easy," she says, "always easier than women."
  No challenge to them at all.
  I never wanted to be a man
  I only wanted a woman to want me that bad.
  And they have, you know, plenty of them,
  but there's always that one you can't pin down
  who's undecided.

---

4. My little daughters, my little girls; contraction of *mi hijitas*. *Mi'ja*, below, means my daughter or my
girl.

My mother was a heterosexual
I couldn't save her.
My failures follow thereafter.

AMALIA: [*Seated in her "kitchen" stage right.*]
I am a failure.
I see them.
Their security. Their houses. Their dogs.
Their children are happy. They are not *un*-happy.
Sure they have their struggles, their problemas, but . . .

It's a life.
I always say this.
"It's a life."

MARISA:
Marta bought her mother a house.
After the family talked bad about her
for leaving Chihuahua with a gavacha[5]
she returned cash in hand and bought her mother a casita[6]
kinda on the outskirts of town
ten grand was all it took, that's nothing here
but it did save her mother from the poverty
her dead father left behind.
Her brother didn't do that.
La admiro.[7]
For the first time wished my father dead
so I could do my mother that kind
of rescue routine.

She, the one I could never pin down,
said to me very sweetly-like . . .

AMALIA:
I feel like the little bird that was nesting
in the palm of my hand has flown away.

MARISA:
That's me, the pajarita[8] with legs like steel planks in my bed.
[*Rubbing.*] Is it my anger that keeps me bolted to this planet?

The women I have loved the most
have always loved the man more than me,
even in their hatred of them.
I'm queer I am. Sí soy jota[9]
because I have never ever been crazy about a man.

---

5. Gringa. *Chihuahua:* capital of the state of Chihuahua, northern Mexico.
6. Little house.
7. I admire it.
8. Literally, a female bird; figuratively, a lesbian.
9. I'm a lesbian.

My friend Sally, the hooker,
she still calls herself that even though she aint doin it
no more, she told me the day she decided
to stop tricking was when once, by accident
a john made her come.
That was strickly forbidden, she explained to me,
how her co-workers who were also dykes had this pact.
She'd forgotten to resist.
To keep business, business.
She had let herself go.
It was very *un*-professional
and dangerous.
No, I've never been in love with a man.
I never understood women who were,
although I've certainly been around
to pick up the pieces.
[CORKY *approaches* MARISA. THEY *count off in unison.*]
My sister was in love with my brother.
My mother loved her father.
My first woman, the man who put her away.


CORKY:

*The crazy house. Camarillo, Califas.[1] 1968.*


MARISA:

When I come to get Norma, she has eyes
like saucers    spinning black and glass
I can see through them
my face    my name
she says,
        "I am buddha."


*How'd you get those black eyes*
*is all I wanna know.*


        "¿Quién te pegó?"[2] I ask.
        "I am buddha."
        [*Black out.*]
CORKY: [*Downstage center.*]
*since that prayer meeting night*
*Lisa had been on the warpath*
*her nose getting higher 'n' higher in the air*
*one day Patsy 'n' her are playing dolls*
*up on the second-story porch of Mrs. Rodriguez' house*
*it was nice up there cuz Mrs. R would let you*
*move the tables 'n' chairs 'n' stuff around*

1. *Camarillo*: city in southwestern California.
*Califas*: contraction of "California Sur," referring
to California and especially Southern California;
used predominantly by Latinos there.
2. Who paid you?

so you could really make it like a house if you wanted to
my sister had jus' gotten this nice doll for her birthday
it had this great curly hair
Lisa had only this kinda stupid doll with plastic
painted-on hair 'n' only one leg
she'd always hafta wear long dresses on it
to disguise the missing leg but we all knew it was gone
anyway one day this brat Lisa throws my sister's new doll
into this mud puddle right down from Mrs. R's porch
Patsy comes back into our yard crying like crazy
her doll's all muddy and the hair has turned bone straight
I mean like an arrow!
I wanted to kill that punk Lisa!
so me 'n' Patsy go over to Lisa's house where we find the little creep
all pleased with herself I mean not even feeling bad

suddenly I see her bike which is really her tricycle
but it's huge . . . I mean hu-u-uge!
to this day I never seen a trike that big
don't even think they make 'em that big no more
no more babies big enough
it useta irritate me to no end that she wasn't even trying
to learn to ride a two-wheeler
so all of a sudden that bike and Lisa's wimpiness
comes together in my mind and I got that t'ing and threw
the sucker into the middle of the street
I dint even wreck it none

but it was the principle of the t'ing.

the drag was a'course she goes 'n' tells her mom on me
'n' this lady who by my mind don' even seem like a mom
she dint wear no makeup 'n' was real skinny 'n' tall
'n' wore her hair all long 'n' tied up in some kind of dumb bun
anyway she has the nerve to call my mom 'n' tell her what I done
so a'course my mom calls me on the carpet wants to know the story
'n' I tell her 'bout the doll 'n' Pasty 'n' the principle of the t'ing
'n' Patsy's telling the same story 'n' I can see in my mom's eye
she don' really believe I did nothing so bad
but she tells me how she wants to keep peace in the neighborhood
cuz we was already getting hassles from some of the paddy neighbors
about how my mom hollered too much at us kids . . . her own kids!
I mean if you can't yell at your own kids who can you yell at?
but she don' let on that this is the reason but I could tell
by the way my mom wasn't looking me in the face when she tells me
I hafta go over to the minister's house 'n' apologize
she jus' kinda turns back to the stove 'n' keeps on with
what she was doing telling me "ándale[3] mi'ja dinner's almost ready."

---

3. Let's go.

*so a'course I go . . . I remember . . . I go by myself*
*with no one to watch me to see if I really do it*
*but my mom knows I will cuz she tole me to*
*'n' I ring the doorbell 'n' Mrs. Minister answers*
*'n' as I begin to talk I guess the little wimp hears my voice*
*'n' runs up behind her mother's skirt 'n' peeks out at me*
*from behind it with the ugliest most snottiest shit-eating grin*
*I'd ever seen in a person.*

*all the while I say I'm sorry*
*'n' as the door shuts in front of my face*
*I vow I'll never make a mistake like that again . . .*

*I'll never show anybody how mad I can get.*
        [*Black out.* CORKY *exits.*]
MARISA:
  I have a very long memory.
  I try to warn people how when I get hurt,
  I don't forget it
  never really let it go.
  I use it against them.

  I blame women for everything,
  for my mistakes
  missed opportunities
  for my grief.
  I usually leave just before I wanna lay a woman flat.
  When I feel that rise up in me,
  that vengeance
  that getting-backness,
  I run muddy river.
  I book.
  Hop a train.
  Split.
  Desert.

AMALIA:
  Desert. Desierto.
  Maybe in the desert, it could have turned out
  differently between La Pachuca and me.
  I *had* intended to take her there,
  to México.

  She would never have gone alone,
  sin gente allí.[4]

  For some reason, I could always picture
  her in the desert

4. Without people there.

amid the mesquite y nopal.
Always when I closed my eyes to search for her,
it was in the desert where I found her,

but once with eyes open
I actually did see her there,
en el desierto
there in the body of a little girl.
I was on a bus headed south
traveling through what turned
from U.S. desert to México,
but all was México
     my bones remembered.
   [*Sadly.*]
     It was to be my last trip.
     I felt this, for some reason, unspeakably.

But there was my niña,[5]
her head stuck all the way out of the bus window,
drinking in the hot desert air.
Her hair
flapping in the wind of it
black and dancing.

She is singing and I am putting
La Pachuca's words in her mouth
   [AMALIA *comes up behind* MARISA, *wraps her arms around her neck,*
   *sings.*]
     "Desierto de la Sonora
     Tierra de mi memoria"[6]

Sí
Sí ésas son tu raíces mi chula.
   [*Whispering.*]
Cántales. Cántales.
Same chata face. Yaqui.
   [*Almost like a chant.*]
La luz del atardecer.
Las sierras son azules y lloran en esta luz.
Hay un silencio que habla de cosas ancianas.
Secretos enterrados.
Nada se mueve,
como yo,
pero todo suspira
"Mi chata.
Mi amor."[7]

5. Aunt.
6. "Sonora Desert / Land of my memory."
7. If those are your roots, my dear. / Sing to them.
Sing to them. / Same cutie face. Yaqui. / The light
of dusk. / The sierras are blue and are crying under this light. / There is a silence that speaks of
ancient things. / Nothing moves, / like me, / but
everything sighs / "Mi cutie. / My love."

MARISA: [*Unmoved.*]
I've just never believed
a woman capable of loving a man
was capable of loving a woman
me.

Some part of me remains amazed
that I'm not the only lesbian in the world
and that over the years I can always manage
to find someone
to love me.

But I am never satisfied
because there are always those women left,
unloved.

I don't get it.
I just feel there is a cruel unfairness
in this world, this division
between love
and labor.
> [AMALIA *drops her hands from* MARISA'S *shoulders, coming toward*
> THE PEOPLE. *Long pause.*]

AMALIA:
I've only gone crazy over one man in my life.
He was nothing special.
Pescador. Indio.[8]
Worked the same waters his whole life.
Once we took a drive out of the small town he lived in,
and he was like a baby, terrified.

Era increíble.[9]
I'm driving through the mountains
and he's squirming in his seat,
"Amalia, ¿pa' dónde vamos?[1] Are you sure you know
where we're going?" he kept asking.
I was so amused to see this big macho break
out into a cold sweat
just from going no more than twenty some miles
from his home town.

Pero, ¡Ay Dios! How I loved that man!
I still ask myself what I saw in him, really.
[*Pause.*] He was one of the cleanest people I had ever met.
Took two, three baths a day.
You have to, you know.
That part of la costa is like steam baths some seasons.

---

8. Fisherman. Indian.                    1. Where are we going?
9. It was incredible.

I remember how he'd even put powder in his shorts
and under his huevos[2] to keep dry.
He was *that* clean.
I always loved knowing that when I touched him,
I would find him like a saint.
Pure, somehow.
That no matter where he had been or who he had been with,
he would have washed himself for me.
He always smelled . . . como flor.[3]

Me volví loca[4] over this man, literally.
When I returned home after so many years,
                                        I had never dreamed

of falling in love,
too many damn men under the bridge.

I can see them all floating down the river
like so many sacks of potatoes.
To me, each one . . .
*making love* they call it
was like having sex with children.
They rub your chi-chis[5] a little,
put their finger in you to get you a little wet,
then they stick it in you.
Nada más.
It's all over in a few minutes.
Un río de cuerpos muertos.[6]

MARISA: [*To* AMALIA.]
Sometimes I only see the other river on your face.
I see it running behind your eyes.
Remember the time we woke up together
and your eye was a bowl of blood.
I thought the river had broken open inside you.
AMALIA:
I was crazy about Alejandro. Muy loca.
Now I wonder how it was he put up with me.
But what I loved was not so much him,
I loved his children.
I loved the part of México that was my home with him,

the way he had made México my home again.

Los pájaros eran Alejandro.
El Alejandro was the birds, the insects that
that first summer never bit me.

2. Eggs, i.e., balls.                      5. Tits.
3. Like a flower.                          6. A river of dead bodies.
4. I went crazy.

I, on the other hand, was not clean,
forgot sometimes to wash.
Not when I was around others,
pero con mi misma, I became like the animals
uncombed, el olor del suelo.[7]

MARISA:

I remember the story she told me about the village children,
how they had put a muñeca[8] under the door of her casita
how she had found it there.
It was the first time she had appeared
mad to herself.

So, we take each other in doses.
I learn to swallow my desire,
work my fear slowly through
the strands of her hair.

> [*To* AMALIA.]
> When I saw the seaweed in long thick
> strands swaying back and forth
> a deep blue brown against green ocean
> and foaming lip of white,
>
> I saw *you* there
> underwater
>
> the seaweed era tu pelo
> heavy with movement
> ola y piedra[9]
> and I nearly lost my balance
> on the salt cliff
> that held me

But when the fear gripped me, that sharp stab
of panic you get in the pit of your belly,
I suddenly saw you so different.
The hair pulled from your face,
the head dangling, suspended.

*Bruja*, pensé.
*Vieja.*
*Mala suerte.*[1]
I felt so ashamed to see you like that,
if only in my mind.
Can you forgive me?

---

7. The smell of soil. *Pero con mi misma*: but with myself.
8. Doll.

9. Wave and stone. *Era tu pelo*: it was your hair.
1. Witch, I thought. / Old woman. / Bad luck.

AMALIA:
   Am I your confessor?
   Your priest?

MARISA:
   No, it's only that I felt I had betrayed you
   in my thoughts.

AMALIA:
   Your thoughts are yours.
   They speak of you, not me
   mi corazón.[2]

MARISA:
   But then was the beautiful woman
   in the mirror of the water
   you or me?

   Who do I make love to?
   Who do I see in the ocean of our bed?

         [*Long pause.*]
AMALIA: [*Sitting, to* THE PEOPLE.]
   When I learned of Alejandro's death,
   I died too, weeks later.
   I just started bleeding and the blood wouldn't stop,
   not until his ghost had passed through me
   or was born in me
   I don't know which.

   [*Pause.*] Except since then,
   I feel him living in me
   every time I touch la Marisa
   I don't know he's been there
   until I put my teeth to her flesh.

   That morning I awoke to find the sheets red with blood.
   It had come out in torrents and then
   in thick clots that looked close to a fetus.
   But I had not been pregnant,
   my tubes tied for years now.
   And lying there among the cool dampness of my own blood
   I felt my womanhood leave me.
   Does this make sense?
   And it was Alejandro being born in me.
   I can't say exactly why or how I knew this,
   except again for the smell, the unmistakable
   smell of the sex of the man

---

2. My heart.

as if we had just made love
el olor estaba en el aire
alrededor de la cama[3]
and coming from my lips was *his* voice
"¡Ay mi Marisa! ¡Te deseo! ¡Te deseo!"[4]

MARISA:
   If I had been a man,
   things would of been a lot simpler between us,
   except for one thing . . .
   she never would of wanted me.
   I mean she would of seen me more and all,
   fit me more conveniently into her life
   but she never would of, tú sabes . . .
   *wanted* me.

   It's odd being queer.
   It's not that you don't want a man,
   you just don't want a man in a man.
   You want a man in a woman.
   The woman-part goes without saying.
   That's what you always learn to want first.
   Maybe the first time you see
   your Dad touch your Mom
   in that way . . .

CORKY: [*Entering.*]
   *Eeeho! I remember the first time I got hip to that!*
   *my mom standing at the stove making chile colorado or somet'ing*
   *she asking my dad did he want another tortilla*
   *"¿quieres otro viejo?" she asks*
   *kinda like she's sorta hassled 'n' being poquito fría[5]*
   *tú sabes    but she's really digging my dad to no end*
   *'n' he knows it and nods 'n' jus' as she comes over to him*
   *kinda flipping the tort onto the plate he grabs her*
   *between her step 'n' slides his hand up the inside of her thigh*
   *cheeezus!    I coulda died!*
   *I musta been only 'bout nine or so but I got that tingling*
   *tú sabes    that now I know what it means . . .*
         [CORKY *throws chin out to* MARISA *bato-style.* MARISA, *amused,*
         *returns it.* CORKY *exits.*]
MARISA: [*Watching* AMALIA.]
   Cuando Amalia me dijo . . . [6]

AMALIA: [*To* MARISA.]
   Quítate tus pantalones.

---

3. The smell was in the air / around the bed.
4. I desire you!
5. A little cool. *¿Quieres otro viejo?*: Do you want another old one?
6. When Amalia calls me . . .

MARISA: [*To* THE PEOPLE.]
  I obey and slide off my pants.
  Me siento como un joven lleno de deseo.[7]

  The worn denim and metal buttons
  are cotton and cool ice on my skin.
  I move on top of her, she wants this
  and she is full of slips and lace and stockings
  and yet it is *she* who's taking *me*.

      [*Watching* AMALIA.]
      Hay un hombre en esa mujer
      lo he sentido
      la miro, haciendo café para nosotras
      frente a hornilla
      pienso . . .
      *¿ como puedo ver un hombre en una persona*
      *tan hembra?*[8]

      El pelo
      sus movimientos
      de una quietud imposible describir
      la voz que me acaricia con cada palabra
      tan suave, tan rica.[9]

      Pienso en mi mamá.
      Había un hombre en mi mamá también.[1]

      [*Pause, to* THE PEOPLE.]
  After the last tequila and the first long kiss
  into the side of her grey face, she warned . . .

AMALIA:
  Don't do that. I just can't afford to feel it now.

MARISA:
  . . . and I wanted to plunge my hands into every opening
  her body knew.

  But it's not the desire for my touch which drives her,
  but the need to touch me.
  "Let's go home," I say.

      [*Coming toward* AMALIA.]

---

7. I feel like a young man full of desire.
8. There's a man in that woman / I've felt it / I look at her, making coffee before us / before the oven / I think . . . / how can I see a man in such a feminine / person?

9. The hair / her movements / of tranquility impossible to describe / the voices caressing me with each word / so soft, so rich.
1. I think of my mother. / There was a man with my mom too.

I held the moment.
Strained, that if I looked long and hard enough
at the woman's hand full inside me
if beneath the moon blasting through the window
I could picture and hold pictured in my mind

      [MARISA *takes* AMALIA's *hand.*]
how that hand buried in the wool of my hair
her working it, herself, into me
how everything was changing at that moment
in both of us.

MARISA and AMALIA: [*To each other.*]
How everything was changing
in both of us.

     [*Black out.*

     *End of Act One.*]


## Act Two: "La Salvadora"


*Dedicación 2*

*I have this rock in my hand*
*it is my memory*
*no one can take it away from me*

*the weight is dense, solid*
*in my palm    it cannot fly away*

*and I still remember*
*that*
*woman*
    *not my savior*
    *but an angel*
    *with wings*
    *that did once lift me*
    *to another*
    *self.*

    [*Voices from the dark, like a memory.*]
AMALIA:
You have the rest of your life to forgive me.

MARISA:
Forgive you for what?

AMALIA:
>    My ways.
>    [*Music.*
>    *It is 1969.*
>    CORKY *enters to downstage center, straddling a crate. Something in*
>    *her appearance or style should give the impression that she is now*
>    *six years older. She is slightly more subdued.*
>
>    *The music gradually subsides. After a pause,* CORKY *begins slowly.*]
> Got raped once.
> When I was a kid.
> Taken me a long time to say that was exactly what happened,
> but that was exactly what happened.
> Makes you more aware than ever that you are one hunerd percent
> female, just in case you had any doubts
> one hunerd percent female whether you act it or like it or not.
>
> Y'see I never ever really let myself think about it
> the possibility of rape        even after it happened.
> Not like other girls I dint walk down the street
> like they was men lurking everywhere every corner to devour you.
> Yeah, the street was a war zone but for difernt reasons,
> for muggers, Mexicanos sucking their damn lips at you,
> gringo stupidity, drunks like old garbage sacks
>                                        thrown around the street,
> and the rape of other women and the people I loved.
> They wernt safe and I worried each time they left the house,
> but never never me.
>
> I guess I never wanted to believe I was raped.
> If it could happen to me, I'd rather think it was something else
> like "unprovoked" sex or something        hell I dunno.
> But if someone took me that bad, I wouldn't really want to think
> I was took        you follow me?
>
> But the truth is . . . I was took.
>    [CORKY *begins to walk about downstage as she tells "the story."*]
> I was about twelve years old,
> can even see my little body back then.
> Chaparrita.
> We wore these kind of jumpers, tú sabes, the kind
> they always have for cath-lic school.
> They looked purty shitty on the seventh 'n' eighth grade girls
> cuz here we was getting chi-chis 'n' all 'n' still trying
> to shove 'em into the tops of these jumpers.
> I wasn't too big, tú sabes, pero the big girls looked te-rri-ble!
>
> Anyway in the seventh grade I was trying to mend my ways
> so would hang after school 'n' try to be helpful 'n' all to the nuns.
> I guess cuz my older cousin Norma got straight A's

'n' was taking me into her bed by then
so I figured . . . that was the way to go.

She'd get really pissed when I fucked up in school,
threatened to "take it away" tú sabes if I dint behave.
Can you get that? ¡Qué fría! ¿no?

Anyway Norma was the only one I ever told about the custodian
doing it to me 'n' then she took it away for good.
I'd still like to whip her butt for that
her 'n' her goddamn hubby 'n' kids now      shi-it
puros gavachos      little blonde-haired blue-eyed things.
The oldest is a little joto if you ask me.
Sure, he's barely four years old, but you can already tell
the way he goes around primping all over the place.
Please me to no end.
What goes around, comes around.
"Jason," they call him.
No, not "Hasón," pero "Jay-sun."
Puro gringo.

Anyway so I was walking by Sister Mary Dominic's classroom,
"The Hawk" we called her cuz she had a nose 'n' attitude like one
when this man, a mexicano, motions to me to come on inside.
I'm looking for this girl Rosie who said she'd meet me
cuz she has something "very important" to tell me.
So this guy calls me, "Ven p'aca,"[2] he says.
He's about in his late thirties, I dint recognize him
but the parish was always hiring mexicanos to work
around the grounds 'n' stuff I guess cuz they dint need
to know English 'n' the priests dint need to pay 'em much.
They'd do it "por Dios" tú sabes.
So he asks me if I speak Spanish.
"Señorita ¿hablas español?" muy humilde y todo
'n' I answer, "Sí, poquito," which I always say to strangers
cuz I dunno how much will be expected of me.

"Ven p'aca," he says otra vez 'n' I do outta respect
for my primo Enrique cuz he looks alot like him, real neatly dressed.
He had work clothes on 'n' all I remember but they wernt dirty
or wrinkled or nuthin like they shoulda been
if he'd been working all day
but he has this screwdriver in his hand
so I figure he must be legit.
But something was funny, and his Spanish . . .
I couldn't quite make it out cuz he mumbled alot
which made me feel kinda bad about myself tú sabes
that I was Mexican too but couldn't understand him that good.

2. Come here.

So, I mostly jus' catch on by his body movements
what he wants me to do.

He's tryin' to fix this drawer that's loose in the Hawk's desk.
I knew already about the drawer cuz she was always bitching
'n' moaning about it getting stuck cuz the bottom kept falling out.
So, he tells me he needs someone to hold the bottom
of the drawer up so he can screw the sides in
which makes sense to me, but the problem is . . .
I don' see no screws.
Looked to me like the whole damn thing was glued together.
¡Qué tonta soy![3] ¿no?

But standing to the side, I lean over
and hold the drawer up with my hand, así.
    [CORKY demonstrates.]
Then he says all frustrated-like, "No, así, así."
It turns out he wants me to stand in front of the drawer
with my hands holding each side up 'n' my legs apart,
así. [SHE demonstrates.]
'n' believe it or not, I do
'n' believe it or not, this hijo de la chingada madre[4]
sits behind me on the floor 'n' reaches his arm up
between my legs that I'm straining to keep closed
even though he keeps saying all business-like
"Abrete más, por favor, las piernas. Abrete poco más, señorita."
Still all polite 'n' like a pendeja . . . I do.
Little by little, he gets my legs open.
I feel my face getting hotter 'n' I can kinda feel him
jiggling the drawer pressed up against my front part.
I'm staring straight ahead don' wanna look at what's happening
then worry how someone would see us like this this guy's arm
up between my legs 'n' then it begins to kinda brush
past the inside of my thigh his arm   I can feel the hair
that first   then the heat of his skin 'n' I keep wishing 'n' dreading
that my stupid friend Rosie with her stupid secret might come by.

The skin
the skin is so soft I hafta admit
young kinda . . . like a girl's like . . . Norma's shoulder.
I try to think about Norma 'n' her shoulders
to kinda pass the time hoping to hurry things along
while he keeps saying, "casi término, casi término"
'n' I keep saying back,
"señor me tengo que ir mi mamá me espera"
still all polite como mensa[5]

---

3. How foolish I am!
4. Son of a bitch.
5. Like a dummy. *Casi término*: I'm also finished.

*Señor me tengo que ir mi mamá me espera*: Sir, I
have to leave my mother is waiting for me.

*until finally I feel the screwdriver by my leg like ice*
*then suddenly the tip of it    it feels like to me*
*is against the cotton of my chonas.*

*"Don't move," he tells me. In English. His accent gone.*
*'n' I don.'*
          [SHE *moves right down to the center of* THE PEOPLE.]
*From then on all I see in my mind's eye . . .*
          were my eyes shut?
*is this screwdriver he's got in his sweaty palm*
*yellow    glass    handle*
*shiny    metal*
*the kind my father useta use to fix things around the house*
*remembered how I'd help him*
*how he'd take me on his jobs with him*
*'n' I kept getting him confused in my mind this man 'n' his arm*
*with my father    kept imagining him my father returned*
*come back*
*the arm was so soft        but this other thing . . .*
*hielo    hielo    ice*
*I wanted to cry "papá papá" 'n' then I started crying for real*
*cuz I knew I musta done something real wrong to get myself*
*in this mess.*

*I figure he's gonna shove the damn thing up me*
*he's trying to get my chonas down 'n' I jus' keep saying*
*"por favor señor no please don'"*
*but I can hear my voice through my own ears*
*not from the inside out but the other way around*
*'n' I know I'm not fighting this one I know*
*I don' even sound convinced.*

*"¿Dónde 'stás papá?" I keep running through my mind*
*"¿dónde 'stás?"*
*'n' finally I imagine the man answering*
*"aquí estoy.    soy tu papá."*
*'n' this gives me permission to go 'head*
*to not hafta fight.*

*By the time he gets my chonas down to my knees*
*I suddenly feel like I'm walking on air*
*like I been exposed to the air    like I have no kneecaps*
*my thing kinda not attached to no body*
*flapping in the wind like a bird*
*a wounded bird.*
*I'm relieved when I hear the metal drop to the floor*
*only worry    who will see me doing this?*
*get-this-over-with-get-this-over-with*
*'n' he does gracias a dios bringing his hand up*
*bringing me down to earth*

linoleum floor    cold
the smell of wax polish.

Y ya 'stoy lista[6] for what long ago waited for me
there was no surprise
"open your legs" me dijo otra vez
'n' I do cuz I'm not useta fighting
what feels
like resignation

what feels
like the most natural thing in the world
to give in

'n' I open my legs wide wide open
for the angry animal that springs outta the opening
in his pants 'n' all I wanna do is have it over
so I can go back to being myself 'n' a kid again.

Then he hit me with it
into what was supposed to be a hole
that I remembered had to be cuz Norma had found it
once wet 'n' forbidden 'n' showed me too
how wide 'n' deep like a cueva[7]
hers got when she wanted it to
only with me she said [Pause.]
"Only with you, Corky."
But with this one
there was no hole
he had to make it
'n' I saw myself down there like a face
with no opening
a face with no features
no eyes no nose no mouth
only little lines where they shoulda been
so I dint cry

I never cried as he shoved the thing
into what was supposed to be a mouth
with no teeth
with no hate
with no voice
only a hole. A Hole!
        [Gritando.[8]]
HE MADE ME A HOLE!
        [Black out.]
MARISA: [Upstage, after a pause.]
    I don't regret it.
    I don't regret nuthin.

6. And I'm ready.                        8. Shouting.
7. Cave.

He only convinced me of my own name.
From an early age you learn to live with it,
being a woman . . .
I only got a head start over some.

And then, years later
after I got to be with some other men,
I admired how their things had no opening,
only a tiny tiny pinhole dot to pee from, to come from.
I thought . . . how lucky they were
that they could release all that stuff,
all that pent-up shit from the day
through a hole
that nobody . . . could get into.
        [MARISA *turns away from* THE PEOPLE *and slowly exits. Silence.*]
AMALIA: [*Entering "the street" downstage.*]
En la Zona Rosa, the sky remains pink in light
in night life.
My novio[9] from many years ago is beside me.
I link my arm into his.
        [*Begins to walk as if with a "partner."*]
We have found each other once again
in the country of our birth.
Somos mexicanos still returning.
I am pleased that we have run into each other
no need to explain
what kind of almas perdidas somos.[1]
At least, tonight
no need to explain.
Carlos is cardboard,
not because he has no feeling,
but I attribute no feeling to him. His eyes
may bleed in their want
to know, sorrow to see me
suffer so.
I am shocked it is so visible on my skin
pero no puedo sentirlo.[2]
No puedo.

But we walk together arm in arm
with the generosity of old lovers.
He asks nothing of me and I pray
the cobblestones beneath my feet
la memoria de la piedra abajo[3]
will return the life to me
        [*Pause.*]
but I have already lost this life,
this man.
Ya me abandoné.

9. Boyfriend.
1. Lost souls we are.

2. I can't feel it.
3. The memory of the stone below.

So I stop him in the middle of our walk,
grab his two hands in mine,
and ask him to make love to me
the best way he knows how.
He is a beautiful passionate man, really.
I can see this on the screen of his face,
muy mexicano.
He was my first latino lover and it is true
this makes a difference . . . older now,
both of us, gris y maduro[4]
like this ground that weeps
beneath these buildings,
campo frágil
con memoria tan violenta que
podría destruir todos de estos edificios.[5]
U.S. Embassy. Banco Serfin.[6] Cocktail lounge.
Curio shop.

"Regresaré." La Tierra nos recuerda.
"Regresaré." Nos promote.[7]

When they "discovered" El Templo Mayor[8]
beneath the walls of this city,
they had not realized that it was she
who discovered them.
Nothing remains buried forever.
Not even memory.
Especially, not even memory.

Pero, Carlos . . .
Carlos takes me back to my hotel room.
I credit him with a power only his race remembers.
In spite of himself, todavía lo tiene.
La Raza recuerda.[9]

He is a good lover, we enter our bed confidently.
He takes me into his arms . . . first with his clothes on
which mexicanos are likely to do. We love
the ritual of the unveiling.
He is already stirring beneath
the flannel of his professor's pants.
He is still a boy after all.
Me encanta for his sake.
Men go from boys to viejos . . . todavía es chavo.[1]

---

4. Gray and ripe.
5. Easy field / with an ever so violent memory / it could destroy all these buildings.
6. A bank in Mexico.
7. "I shall return." / The Earth remembers us. / "I shall return." / It promises us.

8. The Great Temple; in Mexico City.
9. It still has him. / La Raza remembers [i.e., the people remember].
1. It is still young. Me encanta: I love it. Viejos: old men.

I wonder for a moment . . . *what moves him?*
¿La memoria?
¿La nostalgia para nuestra juventud?
¿La esperanza para alguna mujer mágica
que lo puede salvar de su propia vergüenza?[2]

We take to bed the gavacha wife
the twenty-five-year-old marriage.
What breed of man we produce!
For a moment, he is like my son and I fear
I should have taken better care with him.
Men go from boys to viejos
[*Sighing.*] so soon.

I don't stop thinking of the wife.
I offer to her through his hungry rose mouth
my pezones,[3] withered as they are.
I offer them
that someone
might keep watch
continue dreaming
that our mouths and tongues and enflaming nerves
can cleanse us of our feelings,
our shame.
Carlos tells me,
'Te quiero, Amalia.
Todavía te quiero.
Siempre te querré."

And I know he is not lying,
only dreaming.
Ay, how I wish I remembered
how to dream this way!
        [*Long pause.*]
        [*Voice from the dark, like a memory.*]
MARISA:
I'll keep driving if you promise not to stop touching me.

AMALIA: [*Onstage.*]
You want me to stop touching you?

MARISA: [*From the dark.*]
No.
If you promise *not* to stop.

AMALIA: [*Long pause.*]
All I was concerned about
                        was getting my health back together.

---

2. The hope for a magic woman / that can save him of her own shame? ¿La nostalgia para nue- stra juventud?: nostalgia for our youth?
3. Nipples.

It was not so much that I had been sick,
only I lacked energy.
Possibly it was the "change" coming on,
but the women in my familia did not
                              go through the "change"
so young . . . I, not even fifty.

I thought, *maybe it was the American influence*
*that causes the blood to be sucked dry from you*
*so early.*
Nothing was wrong with me, really.
My bones ached. That was it.
I needed rest.

*Nothing México couldn't cure*, I thought.
        [*Starts to exit.*]
MARISA: [*Sitting on the "cliff."*]
For the whole summer, I watched the people fly
in bright-colored sails over the califas sea[4]
waiting for her.
        [AMALIA *stops suddenly as if hearing this for the first time, turns,*
        *watches* MARISA.]
MARISA: [*To* THE PEOPLE.]
Red and gold and blue striped wings with black
letters blazing the sky.
Lifting off the sandy cliffs,
                        dangling gringo legs.

Always imagined myself up there in their place,
flying for real
never coming back
down to earth
leaving
my body
behind.

One morning I awoke to find a bird
dead on the beach.
I knew it wasn't a rock because it was light
enough to roll with the tide.
I saw this from a distance.

Later that day, they found a woman
dead there at the very same spot, I swear.
Una viejita.

A crowd gathered 'round her
as a young man in a blue swimsuit
tried to spoon the sand from her throat

---

4. California sea.

with his finger.
Putting his breath to her was too late.

I know it's crazy to say . . .
but I have never seen a dead person.
I mean . . . a live one, just recently dead.
She was so very very grey and wet,
gris y mojada
como la arena.[5]

She was a Mexican
I could tell by her house dress.
How *did* she drown?

      [*Looking to* AMALIA.]
Then I remembered what Amalia had told me
about omens.
I stopped going
waiting.

AMALIA: [*To* MARISA.]
  [*Pause.*] I had a dream once . . .

You and I, Chata, were indias, baking something
maybe bread, maybe clay pots
on a wide expanse of beach.
We were very happy.

And then . . . suddenly . . . the dream changes.
The mood is dark, clouded.
I am in my hut . . . alone.
I remember being crouched down in terror.
In our village, something . . . [*Remembering.*]
some terrible taboo had been broken. That was it.
And everyone, in fear for their lives
had returned to their homes.
Suddenly, there is a furious pounding at my door.
"Let me in! Let me in!" And it is *your* voice, Chatita.
But I am unable to move when I realize it is you
who has gone against the code del pueblo.

Funny . . . I was not afraid of being punished.
I was not afraid the gods would enact their wrath
against our pueblo for the breaking of the taboo.
It was merely . . . that the taboo . . . *could* be broken.

And if this law nearly transcribed in blood
could go . . .
then, what else?

5. Like the sand.

What *was* there to hold to?
What immovable truths were left?
　　　　[*Silence.* AMALIA *and* MARISA *look directly at each other, sustain it.*]
AMALIA: [*To the people.*]
Sometimes I think, with me
that she only wanted to feel herself
so much a woman
that she would no longer be hungry for one.
[*Pause.*] Pero, siempre tiene hambre.
Siempre tiene pena.

　　　　[*Black out.*

　　　　*Long pause. As lights gradually come up again,* MARISA *appears on
　　　　her "bed," rubbing her calves.*]
I woke up this morning the same way I have for months.
Sometimes I'm so mad, I can't even hear the birds
　　　　　　　　　　　　　　　　outside my window.
I wake instead to this fluttering inside my chest
this heat
like the wings of birds are batting up a war dance
stomping out a fire in there.
[*Pause.*] I still wake up imagining touching her . . .
waiting to be touched.
　　　　[*Pause.*]
I must admit, I wanted to save her.
That's probably the whole truth of the story.
And the problem is . . . sometimes I actually believed
I could and *sometimes* she did, too.
She'd look at me that way, you know, with hope
in her eyes and it would light up her whole face
. . . especially when we made love.
Sometimes that look would make me very nervous
but usually I tried to look past it
tried to get to the heart of the matter
of what we were doing and not get all locked up
*thinking* about what we were doing.
Thinking always made me nervous and her scared.

When she wasn't thinking, she'd come to me,
I swear, like heat on wheels!
I'd open the door and find her there, wet
from the outta-nowhere June rains
and without her even opening her mouth
I knew what she had come for.

I never knew when to expect her this way
just like the rains
never ever when *I* wanted it asked for it begged for it
only when *she* decided.

But she would lay herself down and wide open for me
like no woman I'd ever had before.
I think it was in the quality of her skin.
Some people, you know, their skin is like a covering.
They're supposed to be showing you something
when the clothes fall into a heap around your four ankles,
but nothing is lost . . . you know what I mean?
They just don' give up nuthin.
Pero Amalia . . . Eeeholay![6]

She was never fully naked in front of me,
always had to keep some piece of clothing on . . .
a shirt or something always wrapped up around her throat,
her arms all outta it and flying . . .
but she'd never want it all the way off.

What she did reveal, however . . .
each item of clothing removed was a gift,
I swear, a small offering
a *suggestion* of all
that could be lost and found in our making love
together.
It was like she was saying to me,
"I'll lay down my underslip, mi amor . . .
¿y tú? ¿Qué me vas a dar?"[7]
and I'd give her the palm of my hand to warm
the spot she had just exposed.

Everything was a risk.
Everything took time . . . was slow
and painstaking.
I'll never forget after the first time we made love
I felt . . . mucho orgullo y todo de eso[8] . . . like a good lover
and she says to me . . .

AMALIA [*From the dark, like a memory.*]
    You make love to me like worship.

MARISA:
    and I nearly died, it was so powerful
    what she was saying.
    And I wanted to say but didn't . . .
    "Sí. La mujer es mi religión."
    [*To herself.*] If only sex coulda saved us.

    You know sometimes when me and her was
                                in the middle of it,

6. I.e., *Híjole!*: Aww, man!             8. Much pride and all of that.
7. . . . And you? What are you going to give me?

making love . . . I'd look up at her face, kinda grey
from being indoors so much in that cave of a house
                                        she lived in.
But when we were together, I'd see it change, turn
this real deep color of brown and olive
like she was cookin inside . . .
[*Remembering.*] tan linda.[9]
Kind. Very very very kind to me to herself
                            to the pinche[1] planet
and I'd watch it move from outside the house
where that crazy espíritu of hers had been out makin tracks.
I'd watch it come inside through the door
watch it travel all through her own private miseries
and settle itself finally right there in the room with us.
This bed. [*She pounds it.*]
This fucking dreary season.
This cement city.
With us.
With me.
No part of her begging to get outta this.
Have it over. Forget.

And I could feel all the parts of her move into operation.
Waiting. Held. Suspended.
Praying for me to put my mouth to her
and I knew she knew we would find her como fuego
hot hot hot mojada mi mujer
and she could be mi muchachita y mi mujer
en el mismo momento[2]
and just as I pressed my mouth to her, I'd think . . .
*I could save your life.*

It's not often you get to see people that way
in all their puss and glory
and *still* love them.
It makes you feel so good,
like your hands are weapons of war
and as they move up into el corazón de esta mujer
you are making her body remember
it didn't hafta be that hurt, ¿me entiendes?[3]
It was not natural or right
that she got beat down so damn hard
and that all those crimes had *nothing* to do
with the girl she once was two, three, four
decades ago.

It's like making familia from scratch
each time all over again . . . with strangers

---

9. So beautiful.
1. Fucking.
2. Like fire / hot hot hot wet my woman / and she

could be my little girl and my woman / at once.
3. You understand me?

if I must.
If I must, I will.

I am preparing myself for the worst,
so I cling to her in my heart,
my daydream with pencil in my mouth,
when I put my fingers
to my own
forgotten places.

[MARISA *slowly rises and exits. The lights fade out in silence. Music.*

*End of Act Two.*

*Fin.*]

1984

# JUDITH ORTIZ COFER
## b. 1952

Judith Ortiz Cofer was born in Hormigueros, Puerto Rico, and moved with her family to the United States in 1955. Hormigueros, a small, semi-urban town, is the site of the basilica of the black *Virgen de Monserrate*, visited by thousands of devoted pilgrims every year. In her first novel, *The Line of the Sun* (1989), Ortiz Cofer presents the irreverent, passionate, and often hypocritical inhabitants of her Puerto Rican hometown as a counterpoint to the protagonist, who grows up in a tenement in Paterson, New Jersey.

*The Line of the Sun*, shortlisted for the Pulitzer Prize, added an important feminist dimension to the genre of the Latina bildungsroman. Far from the kind of bleak street narratives being written by many male Latinos, this novel is a composite of family members' memories, their interconnections with the island and people left behind, and their new lives in Paterson. In a 1993 interview with the critic Edna Acosta-Belén, Ortiz Cofer made clear that, while many aspects of the novel mirror parts of her life, the story is not strictly autobiographical: "I never lived in a tenement called 'El Building,' but an 'El Building' was central to the Puerto Rican life of Paterson. When I wrote about those lives lived in poverty, those lived in naiveté and fear in Paterson, what I was doing was presenting a picture of the difficulties of Puerto Rican life in that city."

Ortiz Cofer spent most of her childhood in Paterson and thus became the first Puerto Rican writer to relate coming-of-age experiences in a Puerto Rican community outside of New York City. Her father served in the U.S. Navy and was stationed in New York City, but he was frequently away at sea for long periods. Her mother remained nostalgic for Puerto Rico, and so Ortiz Cofer spent some of her childhood commuting with her mother between Hormigueros and Paterson. At different times, she lived at her grandmother's house in Hormigueros and attended the town's schools, but she received most of her early schooling in New Jersey. The back-and-forth movement between her two cultures would later become a vital part of Ortiz Cofer's writing.

At age 16, Ortiz Cofer moved with her family to Augusta, Georgia. There, she earned her bachelor's degree in English from Augusta College. A few years later, she earned her master's in English from Florida Atlantic University, in Boca Raton. She began her writing career as a poet, and one of her early chapbooks, *Peregrina* (1985), won the Riverstone International Poetry Competition. Two years later, she published the poetry collections *Terms of Survival* and *Reaching for the Mainland*.

Ortiz Cofer's *Silent Dancing: A Partial Remembrance of a Puerto Rican Childhood* (1990) received the 1991 PEN Martha Albrand Special Citation for Non-Fiction and was awarded a Pushcart Prize. This book of memoirs draws on oral tradition and includes poems that highlight the major themes of the prose pieces. In her interview with Acosta-Belén, Ortiz Cofer explained why she often includes several genres—poetry, fictional stories, and essays—in a single work:

> They are different ways of seeing. Poetry allows you to delve into the depths of language. Prose is looser. Poetry is a probe to plumb the depths of language, to explore the hidden meaning of words. Poetry is to me the first discipline. It empowers me. In a sense one is like a microscope, and the other like a telescope.

In that same interview, Ortiz Cofer said that she inherited the art of storytelling from her grandmother:

> When my *abuela* sat us down to tell a story, we learned something from it, even though we always laughed. That was her way of teaching. So early on I instinctively knew storytelling was a form of empowerment, that the women in my family were passing on power from one generation to another through fables and stories. They were teaching each other to cope with life in a world where women led restrictive lives.

Ortiz Cofer's most powerful characters are Puerto Rican women trying to break away from restrictive cultural and social conventions or developing survival strategies to deal with the sexism in their culture. She has made it a goal to try "to replace the old pervasive stereotypes and myths about Latinas with a much more interesting set of realities."

"The Story of My Body"—one of five Ortiz Cofer selections in this anthology that are taken from *The Latin Deli* (1993), a collection of poetry, short stories, and personal essays—describes how Ortiz Cofer's skin color, physical appearance, and ethnicity weighed on her and brought rejection and heartbreak during her high school years. However, the author clearly recognizes that these painful experiences were crucial to developing her sense of self-worth. The poem "The Latin Deli: An Ars Poetica," first published in 1992, conjures up a poetic space at the neighborhood deli, where all kinds of cultural exchanges take place and where the smells and tastes of native foods, along with the sounds of music and of the Spanish language satisfy, at least temporarily, the migrants' longing for the distant homeland and their need to connect with others like them. In the poem "The Chameleon," Ortiz Cofer affirms her sense of identity despite all the assimilative pressures on her. "Hostages to Fortune" and "To a Daughter I Cannot Console" express motherly love and the pain that can come from watching a child grow up and experience heartbreak. In "Anniversary," the poet evokes the love, memories, and generational connections with her husband of many years, in addition to the experiences they shared during the tumultuous events of the 1960s, among them the Vietnam War.

Much of Ortiz Cofer's writing—including many of the pieces in *An Island Like You: Stories of the Barrio* (1995), which received the 1995 Pura Belpré Award and was listed among the best books for Young Adults by the American Library Association—focus on the lives of Puerto Rican teenagers, straddling the Puerto Rican culture of their parents and community and an alienating U.S. culture blinded by its own prejudices. Also aimed at a young-adult readership are Ortiz Cofer's nonautobiographical coming-of-age-in-the-United-States novels *The Meaning of Consuelo* (2003) and *Call Me María* (2004) and her edited volume *Riding Low through the Streets of Gold: Latino Literature for Young Adults* (2004), books widely used in secondary schools for studying the rich cultural and racial mix within the United States.

In her multigenre memoir *Woman in Front of the Sun: On Becoming a Writer* (2000)—from which the selections "The Gift of a *Cuento*" and "And May He Be Bilingual" are taken—Ortiz Cofer describes how she blossomed and matured as a writer, reflecting also on the creative process and the role of ethnic literature in the United States. Once again, she links the art of storytelling to her talkative Puerto Rican relatives, who often shared stories—about their homeland, their travels, and their experiences—as a form of entertainment. The mixture of poetry and memoir in the selection "And May He Be Bilingual" underscores the powerlessness and alienation often experienced by non-English-speaking immigrants in the United States.

In collections such as *The Year of Our Revolution: New and Selected Stories and Poems* (1998) and *A Love Story Beginning in Spanish* (2005), Ortiz Cofer continues to employ a combination of poems, personal essays, and short fiction to recall her formative years as an individual and as a writer. Ortiz Cofer is currently the Franklin Professor of English and Creative Writing at the University of Georgia, in Athens. She frequently lectures and does readings at universities throughout the United States and Puerto Rico.

# The Story of My Body

Migration is the story of my body.
—Víctor Hernández Cruz[1]

## Skin

I was born a white girl in Puerto Rico but became a brown girl when I came to live in the United States. My Puerto Rican relatives called me tall; at the American school, some of my rougher classmates called me Skinny Bones, and the Shrimp because I was the smallest member of my classes all through grammar school until high school, when the midget Gladys was given the honorary post of front row center for class pictures and scorekeeper, bench warmer, in P.E. I reached my full stature of five feet in sixth grade.

I started out life as a pretty baby and learned to be a pretty girl from a pretty mother. Then at ten years of age I suffered one of the worst cases of chicken pox I have ever heard of. My entire body, including the inside of my ears and in between my toes, was covered with pustules which in a fit of panic at my appearance I scratched off my face, leaving permanent scars. A cruel school nurse told me I would always have them—tiny cuts that looked as if a mad cat had plunged its claws deep into my skin. I grew my hair long and hid behind it for the first years of my adolescence. This was when I learned to be invisible.

1. See p. 1718.

## Color

In the animal world it indicates danger: the most colorful creatures are often the most poisonous. Color is also a way to attract and seduce a mate. In the human world color triggers many more complex and often deadly reactions. As a Puerto Rican girl born of "white" parents, I spent the first years of my life hearing people refer to me as *blanca*, white. My mother insisted that I protect myself from the intense island sun because I was more prone to sunburn than some of my darker, *trigueño* playmates. People were always commenting within my hearing about how my black hair contrasted so nicely with my "pale" skin. I did not think of the color of my skin consciously except when I heard the adults talking about complexion. It seems to me that the subject is much more common in the conversation of mixed-race peoples than in mainstream United States society, where it is a touchy and sometimes even embarrassing topic to discuss, except in a political context. In Puerto Rico I heard many conversations about skin color. A pregnant woman could say, "I hope my baby doesn't turn out *prieto*" (slang for "dark" or "black") "like my husband's grandmother, although she was a good-looking *negra* in her time." I am a combination of both, being olive-skinned—lighter than my mother yet darker than my fair-skinned father. In America, I am a person of color, obviously a Latina. On the Island I have been called everything from a *paloma blanca*, after the song (by a black suitor), to *la gringa*.

My first experience of color prejudice occurred in a supermarket in Paterson, New Jersey. It was Christmastime, and I was eight or nine years old. There was a display of toys in the store where I went two or three times a day to buy things for my mother, who never made lists but sent for milk, cigarettes, a can of this or that, as she remembered from hour to hour. I enjoyed being trusted with money and walking half a city block to the new, modern grocery store. It was owned by three good-looking Italian brothers. I liked the younger one with the crew-cut blond hair. The two older ones watched me and the other Puerto Rican kids as if they thought we were going to steal something. The oldest one would sometimes even try to hurry me with my purchases, although part of my pleasure in these expeditions came from looking at everything in the well-stocked aisles. I was also teaching myself to read English by sounding out the labels in packages: L&M cigarettes, Borden's homogenized milk, Red Devil potted ham, Nestlé's chocolate mix, Quaker oats, Bustelo coffee, Wonder bread, Colgate toothpaste, Ivory soap, and Goya (makers of products used in Puerto Rican dishes) everything—these are some of the brand names that taught me nouns. Several times this man had come up to me, wearing his blood-stained butcher's apron, and towering over me had asked in a harsh voice whether there was something he could help me find. On the way out I would glance at the younger brother who ran one of the registers and he would often smile and wink at me.

It was the mean brother who first referred to me as "colored." It was a few days before Christmas, and my parents had already told my brother and me that since we were in Los Estados now, we would get our presents on December 25 instead of Los Reyes, Three Kings Day, when gifts are exchanged in Puerto Rico. We were to give them a wish list that they would take to Santa Claus, who apparently lived in the Macy's store downtown—at least that's where we had caught a glimpse of him when we went shopping. Since my parents were timid about entering the fancy store, we did not approach the huge man in the red suit. I was not interested in sitting on a stranger's lap anyway. But I did covet Susie, the talking schoolteacher doll that was displayed in the center aisle of the Italian brothers' supermarket. She talked when you pulled a string on her back. Susie had a limited repertoire of three sentences: I think she could say: "Hello, I'm Susie Schoolteacher," "Two plus two is four," and one other thing I cannot remember. The day the older brother chased me away, I was reaching to touch Susie's blonde curls. I had been told many times, as most children have, not to touch anything in a store that I was not buying. But I had been looking at Susie for weeks. In my mind, she was my doll. After all, I had put her on my Christmas wish list. The moment is frozen in my mind as if there were a photograph of it on file. It was not a turning point, a disaster, or an earth-shaking revelation. It was simply the first time I considered—if naively—the meaning of skin color in human relations.

I reached to touch Susie's hair. It seems to me that I had to get on tiptoe, since the toys were stacked on a table and she sat like a princess on top of the fancy box she came in. Then I heard the booming "Hey, kid, what do you think you're doing!" spoken very loudly from the meat counter. I felt caught, although I knew I was not doing anything criminal. I remember not looking at the man, but standing there, feeling humiliated because I knew everyone in the store must have heard him yell at me. I felt him approach, and when I knew he was behind me, I turned around to face the bloody butcher's apron. His large chest was at my eye level. He blocked my way. I started to run out of the place, but even as I reached the door I heard him shout after me: "Don't come in here unless you gonna buy something. You PR kids put your dirty hands on stuff. You always look dirty. But maybe dirty brown is your natural color." I heard him laugh and someone else too in the back. Outside in the sunlight I looked at my hands. My nails needed a little cleaning as they always did, since I liked to paint with watercolors, but I took a bath every night. I thought the man was dirtier than I was in his stained apron. He was also always sweaty—it showed in big yellow circles under his shirt-sleeves. I sat on the front steps of the apartment building where we lived and looked closely at my hands, which showed the only skin I could see, since it was bitter cold and I was wearing my quilted play coat, dungarees, and a knitted navy cap of my father's. I was not pink like my friend Charlene and her sister Kathy, who had blue eyes and light brown hair. My skin is the color of the coffee my grandmother made, which was half milk, *leche con café* rather than *café con leche*. My mother is the opposite mix. She has a lot of café in her color. I could not understand how my skin looked like dirt to the supermarket man.

I went in and washed my hands thoroughly with soap and hot water, and borrowing my mother's nail file, I cleaned the crusted watercolors from underneath my nails. I was pleased with the results. My skin was the same color as before, but I knew I was clean. Clean enough to run my fingers through Susie's fine gold hair when she came home to me.

### Size

My mother is barely four feet eleven inches in height, which is average for women in her family. When I grew to five feet by age twelve, she was amazed and began to use the word tall to describe me, as in "Since you are tall, this dress will look good on you." As with the color of my skin, I didn't consciously think about my height or size until other people made an issue of it. It is around the preadolescent years that in America the games children play for fun become fierce competitions where everyone is out to "prove" they are better than others. It was in the playground and sports fields that my size-related problems began. No matter how familiar the story is, every child who is the last chosen for a team knows the torment of waiting to be called up. At the Paterson, New Jersey, public schools that I attended, the volleyball or softball game was the metaphor for the battlefield of life to the inner city kids—the black kids versus the Puerto Rican kids, the whites versus the blacks versus the Puerto Rican kids; and I was 4F,[2] skinny, short, bespectacled, and apparently impervious to the blood thirst that drove many of my classmates to play ball as if their lives depended on it. Perhaps they did. I would rather be reading a book than sweating, grunting, and running the risk of pain and injury. I simply did not see the point in competitive sports. My main form of exercise then was walking to the library, many city blocks away from my barrio.

Still, I wanted to be wanted. I wanted to be chosen for the teams. Physical education was compulsory, a class where you were actually given a grade. On my mainly all A report card, the C for compassion I always received from the P.E. teachers shamed me the same as a bad grade in a real class. Invariably, my father would say: "How can you make a low grade for *playing games*?" He did not understand. Even if I had managed to make a hit (it never happened) or get the ball over that ridiculously high net, I already had a reputation as a "shrimp," a hopeless nonathlete. It was an area where the girls who didn't like me for one reason or another—mainly because I did better than they on academic subjects—could lord it over me; the playing field was the place where even the smallest girl could make me feel powerless and inferior. I instinctively understood the politics even then; how the *not* choosing me until the teacher forced one of the team captains to call my name was a coup of sorts—there, you little show-off, tomorrow you can beat us in spelling and geography, but this afternoon you are the loser. Or perhaps those were only my own bitter thoughts as I sat or stood in the sidelines while the big girls were grabbed like fish and I, the little brown tadpole, was ignored until Teacher looked over in my general direction and shouted, "Call Ortiz," or, worse, "Somebody's *got* to take her."

No wonder I read Wonder Woman comics and had Legion of Super Heroes daydreams. Although I wanted to think of myself as "intellectual," my body was demanding that I notice it. I saw the little swelling around my once-flat nipples, the fine hairs growing in secret places; but my knees were still bigger than my thighs, and I always wore long- or half-sleeve blouses to hide my bony upper arms. I wanted flesh on my bones—a thick layer of it. I saw a new product advertised on TV. Wate-On. They showed skinny men and women before and after taking the stuff, and it was a transformation like the ninety-seven-pound-weakling-turned-into-Charles-Atlas[3] ads that I

---

2. "Not qualified for military service due to medical reasons," in the terminology of the U.S. Selective Service (i.e., the ranking for a military draft).
3. Italian-born American bodybuilder (b. Angelo

Siciliano, 1892–1972), whose company, Charles Atlas Ltd., has since 1929 marketed, for the "97-pound weakling," a combination bodybuilding method and exercise program.

saw on the back covers of my comic books. The Wate-On was very expensive. I tried to explain my need for it in Spanish to my mother, but it didn't translate very well, even to my ears—and she said with a tone of finality, eat more of my good food and you'll get fat—anybody can get fat. Right. Except me. I was going to have to join a circus someday as Skinny Bones, the woman without flesh.

Wonder Woman was stacked. She had a cleavage framed by the spread wings of a golden eagle and a muscular body that has become fashionable with women only recently. But since I wanted a body that would serve me in P.E., hers was my ideal. The breasts were an indulgence I allowed myself. Perhaps the daydreams of bigger girls were more glamorous, since our ambitions are filtered through our needs, but I wanted first a powerful body. I daydreamed of leaping up above the gray landscape of the city to where the sky was clear and blue, and in anger and self-pity, I fantasized about scooping my enemies up by their hair from the playing fields and dumping them on a barren asteroid. I would put the P.E. teachers each on their own rock in space too, where they would be the loneliest people in the universe, since I knew they had no "inner resources," no imagination, and in outer space, there would be no air for them to fill their deflated volleyballs with. In my mind all P.E. teachers have blended into one large spiky-haired woman with a whistle on a string around her neck and a volleyball under one arm. My Wonder Woman fantasies of revenge were a source of comfort to me in my early career as a shrimp.

I was saved from more years of P.E. torment by the fact that in my sophomore year of high school I transferred to a school where the midget, Gladys, was the focal point of interest for the people who must rank according to size. Because her height was considered a handicap, there was an unspoken rule about mentioning size around Gladys, but of course, there was no need to say anything. Gladys knew her place: front row center in class photographs. I gladly moved to the left or to the right of her, as far as I could without leaving the picture completely.

## Looks

Many photographs were taken of me as a baby by my mother to send to my father, who was stationed overseas during the first two years of my life. With the army in Panama when I was born, he later traveled often on tours of duty with the navy. I was a healthy, pretty baby. Recently, I read that people are drawn to big-eyed round-faced creatures, like puppies, kittens, and certain other mammals and marsupials, koalas, for example, and, of course, infants. I was all eyes, since my head and body, even as I grew older, remained thin and small-boned. As a young child I got a lot of attention from my relatives and many other people we met in our barrio. My mother's beauty may have had something to do with how much attention we got from strangers in stores and on the street. I can imagine it. In the pictures I have seen of us together, she is a stunning young woman by Latino standards: long, curly black hair, and round curves in a compact frame. From her I learned how to move, smile, and talk like an attractive woman. I remember going into a bodega for our groceries and being given candy by the proprietor as a reward for being *bonita*, pretty.

I can see in the photographs, and I also remember, that I was dressed in the pretty clothes, the stiff, frilly dresses, with layers of crinolines underneath, the glossy patent leather shoes, and, on special occasions, the skull-hugging little hats and the white gloves that were popular in the late fifties and early sixties. My mother was proud of my looks, although I was a bit too thin. She could dress me up like a doll and take me by the hand to visit relatives, or go to the Spanish mass at the Catholic church, and show me off. How was I to know that she and the others who called me "pretty" were representatives of an aesthetic that would not apply when I went out into the mainstream world of school?

In my Paterson, New Jersey, public schools there were still quite a few white children, although the demographics of the city were changing rapidly. The original waves of Italian and Irish immigrants, silk-mill workers, and laborers in the cloth industries had been "assimilated." Their children were now the middle-class parents of my peers. Many of them moved their children to the Catholic schools that proliferated enough to have leagues of basketball teams. The names I recall hearing still ring in my ears: Don Bosco High versus St. Mary's High, St. Joseph's versus St. John's. Later I too would be transferred to the safer environment of a Catholic school. But I started school at Public School Number 11. I came there from Puerto Rico, thinking myself a pretty girl, and found that the hierarchy for popularity was as follows: pretty white girl, pretty Jewish girl, pretty Puerto Rican girl, pretty black girl. Drop the last two categories; teachers were too busy to have more than one favorite per class, and it was simply understood that if there was a big part in the school play, or any competition where the main qualification was "presentability" (such as escorting a school visitor to or from the principal's office), the classroom's public address speaker would be requesting the pretty and/or nice-looking white boy or girl. By the time I was in the sixth grade, I was sometimes called by the principal to represent my class because I dressed neatly (I knew this from a progress report sent to my mother, which I translated for her) and because all the "presentable" white girls had moved to the Catholic schools (I later surmised this part). But I was still not one of the popular girls with the boys. I remember one incident where I stepped out into the playground in my baggy gym shorts and one Puerto Rican boy said to the other: "What do you think?" The other one answered: "Her face is OK, but look at the toothpick legs." The next best thing to a compliment I got was when my favorite male teacher, while handing out the class pictures, commented that with my long neck and delicate features I resembled the movie star Audrey Hepburn.[4] But the Puerto Rican boys had learned to respond to a fuller figure: long necks and a perfect little nose were not what they looked for in a girl. That is when I decided I was a "brain." I did not settle into the role easily. I was nearly devastated by what the chicken pox episode had done to my self-image. But I looked into the mirror less often after I was told that I would always have scars on my face, and I hid behind my long black hair and my books.

After the problems at the public school got to the point where even non-confrontational little me got beaten up several times, my parents enrolled

4. Belgian-born British actress (Audrey Kathleen Ruston, 1929–1993).

me at St. Joseph's High School. I was then a minority of one among the Italian and Irish kids. But I found several good friends there—other girls who took their studies seriously. We did our homework together and talked about the Jackies. The Jackies were two popular girls, one blonde and the other red-haired, who had women's bodies. Their curves showed even in the blue jumper uniforms with straps that we all wore. The blonde Jackie would often let one of the straps fall off her shoulder, and although she, like all of us, wore a white blouse underneath, all the boys stared at her arm. My friends and I talked about this and practiced letting our straps fall off our shoulders. But it wasn't the same without breasts or hips.

My final two and a half years of high school were spent in Augusta, Georgia, where my parents moved our family in search of a more peaceful environment. There we became part of a little community of our army-connected relatives and friends. School was yet another matter. I was enrolled in a huge school of nearly two thousand students that had just that year been forced to integrate. There were two black girls and there was me. I did extremely well academically. As to my social life, it was, for the most part, uneventful—yet it is in my memory blighted by one incident. In my junior year, I became wildly infatuated with a pretty white boy. I'll call him Ted. Oh, he was pretty: yellow hair that fell over his forehead, a smile to die for—and he was a great dancer. I watched him at Teen Town, the youth center at the base where all the military brats gathered on Saturday nights. My father had retired from the navy, and we had all our base privileges— one other reason we had moved to Augusta. Ted looked like an angel to me. I worked on him for a year before he asked me out. This meant maneuvering to be within the periphery of his vision at every possible occasion. I took the long way to my classes in school just to pass by his locker, I went to football games, which I detested, and I danced (I too was a good dancer) in front of him at Teen Town—this took some fancy footwork, since it involved subtly moving my partner toward the right spot on the dance floor. When Ted finally approached me, "A Million to One"[5] was playing on the jukebox, and when he took me into his arms, the odds suddenly turned in my favor. He asked me to go to a school dance the following Saturday. I said yes, breathlessly. I said yes, but there were obstacles to surmount at home. My father did not allow me to date casually. I was allowed to go to major events like a prom or a concert with a boy who had been properly screened. There was such a boy in my life, a neighbor who wanted to be a Baptist missionary and was practicing his anthropological skills on my family. If I was desperate to go somewhere and needed a date, I'd resort to Gary. This is the type of religious nut that Gary was: when the school bus did not show up one day, he put his hands over his face and prayed to Christ to get us a way to get to school. Within ten minutes a mother in a station wagon, on her way to town, stopped to ask why we weren't in school. Gary informed her that the Lord had sent her just in time to find us a way to get there in time for roll call. He assumed that I was impressed. Gary was even good-looking in a bland sort of way, but he kissed me with his lips tightly pressed together. I think Gary probably ended up marrying a native woman from wherever he

5. The song has been recorded by many artists. This version was probably the 1960 hit by Jimmy Charles (b. 1942), an American singer from (coincidentally) Paterson, New Jersey.

may have gone to preach the Gospel according to Paul.[6] She probably believes that all white men pray to God for transportation and kiss with their mouths closed. But it was Ted's mouth, his whole beautiful self, that concerned me in those days. I knew my father would say no to our date, but I planned to run away from home if necessary. I told my mother how important this date was. I cajoled and pleaded with her from Sunday to Wednesday. She listened to my arguments and must have heard the note of desperation in my voice. She said very gently to me: "You better be ready for disappointment." I did not ask what she meant. I did not want her fears for me to taint my happiness. I asked her to tell my father about my date. Thursday at breakfast my father looked at me across the table with his eyebrows together. My mother looked at him with her mouth set in a straight line. I looked down at my bowl of cereal. Nobody said anything. Friday I tried on every dress in my closet. Ted would be picking me up at six on Saturday: dinner and then the sock hop at school. Friday night I was in my room doing my nails or something else in preparation for Saturday (I know I groomed myself nonstop all week) when the telephone rang. I ran to get it. It was Ted. His voice sounded funny when he said my name, so funny that I felt compelled to ask: "Is something wrong?" Ted blurted it all out without a preamble. His father had asked who he was going out with. Ted had told him my name. "Ortiz? That's Spanish, isn't it?" the father had asked. Ted had told him yes, then shown him my picture in the yearbook. Ted's father had shaken his head. No. Ted would not be taking me out. Ted's father had known Puerto Ricans in the army. He had lived in New York City while studying architecture and had seen how the spics lived. Like rats. Ted repeated his father's words to me as if I should understand *his* predicament when I heard why he was breaking our date. I don't remember what I said before hanging up. I do recall the darkness of my room that sleepless night and the heaviness of my blanket in which I wrapped myself like a shroud. And I remember my parents' respect for my pain and their gentleness toward me that weekend. My mother did not say "I warned you," and I was grateful for her understanding silence.

In college, I suddenly became an "exotic" woman to the men who had survived the popularity wars in high school, who were now practicing to be worldly: they had to act liberal in their politics, in their lifestyles, and in the women they went out with. I dated heavily for a while, then married young. I had discovered that I needed stability more than social life. I had brains for sure and some talent in writing. These facts were a constant in my life. My skin color, my size, and my appearance were variables—things that were judged according to my current self-image, the aesthetic values of the times, the places I was in, and the people I met. My studies, later my writing, the respect of people who saw me as an individual person they cared about, these were the criteria for my sense of self-worth that I would concentrate on in my adult life.

1993

---

6. St. Paul (also known as Paul of Tarsus, Paul the Apostle, and the Apostle Paul; ca. 64–65), author of New Testament texts and one of the most significant early Christian missionaries.

## The Latin Deli: An Ars Poetica

Presiding over a formica counter,
plastic Mother and Child magnetized
to the top of an ancient register,
the heady mix of smells from the open bins
of dried codfish, the green plantains                    5
hanging in stalks like votive offerings,
she is the Patroness of Exiles,
a woman of no-age who was never pretty,
who spends her days selling canned memories
while listening to the Puerto Ricans complain           10
that it would be cheaper to fly to San Juan
than to buy a pound of Bustelo coffee[1] here,
and to Cubans perfecting their speech
of a "glorious return" to Havana—where no one
has been allowed to die and nothing to change until then;  15
to Mexicans who pass through, talking lyrically
of *dólares* to be made in El Norte—
                              all wanting the comfort
of spoken Spanish, to gaze upon the family portrait
of her plain wide face, her ample bosom                  20
resting on her plump arms, her look of maternal interest
as they speak to her and each other
of their dreams and their disillusions—
how she smiles understanding,
when they walk down the narrow aisles of her store      25
reading the labels of packages aloud, as if
they were the names of lost lovers: *Suspiros,
Merengues,*[2] the stale candy of everyone's childhood.
                              She spends her days
slicing *jamón y queso* and wrapping it in wax paper     30
tied with string: plain ham and cheese
that would cost less at the A&P, but it would not satisfy
the hunger of the fragile old man lost in the folds
of his winter coat, who brings her lists of items
that he reads to her like poetry, or the others,        35
whose needs she must divine, conjuring up products
from places that now exist only in their hearts—
closed ports she must trade with.

                                          1993


## The Chameleon

I caught a chameleon
in my backyard,
and to amuse myself
moved him from a green leaf

---

1. Café Bustelo, a brand of coffee made for
espresso, originally manufactured by a Latino
company and aimed at the Latino market.

2. A kind of meringue cookie, as are Suspiros
(Spanish for sighs).

to a tree's brown bark,                                    5
then to my yellow porch
where he froze as himself
his eyes on me as if waiting
for me to change.

But I stayed the same.                                     10

I stayed the same,
and kept him behind a screen
until he had shown me his rainbow,
until he had given me
every color he possessed.                                  15

Then I opened the door,
but he wouldn't move.
He just kept his eyes on me
as if waiting for me to change.

                                                        1993

## Hostages to Fortune

In three days, I would have to send her down
into the ground, which treats no differently
excrement, snakeskin, daughter, worm—

if a dream of flight took her too far to return,
as if blown off course by a storm. Trembling,           5
at 3:00 A.M., I am standing by her bed
and her body is too still. Yet,
I hesitate to place my hand on her chest,

to feel it rise and fall with her breath,
as I did in her childhood, waking like this,            10
as I used to often, nearly sleepwalking,
even when her sleep was full and deep
after a day's hard play.

Now she wears a bone-tight skin of nerves.

How would I survive this: touching a cool,              15
alabaster statue in the morning; or the vision
of tan skin melting like wax from her bones,
of her long, slim body—a ruin for study—
female human, sixteen years of age, maybe older.

She was clearly in good health, they will say,          20
strong—no evidence of having given
any hostages to fortune.

                                                        1993

## To a Daughter I Cannot Console

Last night I called my mother long distance
to talk about your sadness. After years
of separation, our tone is forgiving,
our word choices careful; the turmoil
of our kinship now in subscript to the text                    5
of our separate sorrows.
                          I told her of the tears
that keep pouring out of that infinite well
that a broken heart is at sixteen. She spoke
the inevitable "it will pass," asking me                       10
to remember the boy I had cried over for days.
I could not for several minutes
recall that face.

And her consolation was true.
It has to do with time—what we both know now                   15
as enemy to the flesh; also
as the healer of wounds. But for you,
there are no words that will help. Time to you
is a slow clock measuring the rise of beauty,
the deepening of feeling.                                      20
                        It is too late
for the tokens of motherhood; the distraction
of a new toy, a bedtime story, a hug; too soon
to convince you that the storm surging within
will abate—like all acts of God.                               25
                       And the heart,
like a well-constructed little boat, will resume
its course toward hope.

                                    1993

## Anniversary

Lying in bed late, you will sometimes read to me
about a past war that obsesses you;
about young men, like our brothers once,
who each year become more like our sons
because they died the year we met,                             5
or the year we got married
or the year our child was born.
                        You read to me
about how they dragged their feet through a green maze
where they fell, again and again, victims                      10
to an enemy wily enough to be the critter hero
of some nightmare folktale, with his booby traps
in the shape of human children, and his cities
under the earth; and how, even when they survived,
these boys left something behind                               15

in the thick brush or muddy swamp where no one
can get it back—caught like a baseball cap
on a low-hanging tree branch.

        And I think about you and me,
nineteen, angry, and in love, in that same year           20
when America broke out in violence
like a late-blooming adolescent, deep in a turmoil
it could neither understand nor control;
how we marched in the rough parade
decorated with the insignias of our rebellion:          25
peace symbols and scenes of Eden
embroidered on our torn and faded jeans,
necks heavy with beads we did not count on
for patience, singing *Revolution*[1]—
a song we misconstrued for years.                 30
                   Death was a slogan
to shout about with raised fists or hang on banners.

But here we are,
listening more closely than ever to the old songs,
sung for new reasons by new voices. We are survivors    35
of an undeclared war someone might decide to remake
like a popular tune. Sometimes, in the dark, alarmed
by too deep a silence, I will lay my hand on your chest,
for the familiar, steady beat to which I have attuned
my breathing for so many years.              40

                                1993

# The Gift of a *Cuento*[1]

This is the story of a *cuento* that was given to me once upon a time, and
then again. *Una vez y dos son tres.* I was thirteen. It was the year when I
began to feel like a Cinderella whose needs were being totally ignored by
everyone, including the fairy *madrinas* I fantasized would bring me a new,
exciting life with the touch of a magic wand. I had read all of the virtue-
rewarded-by-marriage-to-a-handsome-prince tales at the Paterson Public
Library and was ready for something miraculous to happen to me: beautiful
clothes, an invitation to a great party, love. Unfortunately there was a dearth
of princes in my life, and I was not exactly the most popular girl at a school
socially dominated by Italian and Irish American princesses. Also, that year
I was in the throes of the most severe insecurity crisis of my life: besides
being extremely thin—"skinny-bones" was my nickname in the barrio—I
was the new girl at the Catholic high school where I had been enrolled that
fall, one of two Puerto Rican girls in a small, mostly homogenous social

---

1. The Beatles' song "Revolution" (1968).

1. Story, tale. To preserve the combination of cultures in this essay, most of the Spanish terms herein have not been translated.

world, and I had also recently been prescribed glasses, thick lenses supported by sturdy black frames. After wearing them for only a few weeks, I developed a semipermanent ridge on my nose. I tried to make up for my physical deficiencies by being well read and witty. This worked fine within my talkative *familia* but not at school, among my peers, who did not value eloquence in girls—not more than a well-developed body and prominent social status, anyway.

That Christmas season, the *cuentista* of our family entered my life. My mother's younger brother, who lived in New York, was the black sheep of the family, with a trail of family *cuentos* about his travels, misadventures, and womanizing behind him—which made him immensely attractive to me. His arrival filled our house with new talk, old stories, and music. Tío liked to tell *cuentos*, and he also liked playing his LPs. My mother and he danced to merengues fresh from the Island—which he seemed to be able to acquire before anyone else, and which he carried with him as if they were precious crystal wrapped in layers of newspaper. He was the spirit of Navidad in our house, with just a hint of the Dionysian about him. Tío enjoyed his Puerto Rican rum, too, so his visits were as short as the festivities because his bachelor habits eventually wore down my mother's patience.

Tío must have sensed my loneliness that year, for he took it upon himself to spend a lot of time with me the week before Christmas. We went for walks around the gray city, now decked out in lights and ornaments like an overdressed woman, and for pizza downtown. He asked me about my social life and I confessed that my *príncipe* had not appeared on our block yet, so I had none.

"Why do you need a prince to have fun?" my uncle asked, laughing at my choice of words. Unlike other adults, he seemed to really listen. Later I understood this was how he learned to tell a story. He told me that I had inherited his and my *abuela*'s gift of the *cuento*. And because he was so unlike my other *cariñoso* relatives, who poured the sweet words on us kids without discrimination or restraint (or honesty, I thought), I believed him. I knew how to tell a good story. My mother had warned me that it was Tío's charm, his ability to flatter and to persuade, that usually got him into trouble. I wanted that power for myself, too. The seductiveness and the power of words enticed me.

His appeal had little to do with physical beauty: he was short, wiry, with a Taíno Indian face. But he was generous to a fault, completely giving of himself. Our family dreaded his recklessness, but we also adored him for the many sacrifices he had made for our sake, the good deeds that I heard about, along with the spicy *cuentos* and the gossip about his complex love life.

"I guess I was thinking of Cinderella." I didn't want Tío to think me a child, but I also wanted him to understand me in a way no one else could. I wanted magic in my life. Poised between a sheltered childhood and the yearnings of approaching adolescence, my dreams were hopelessly entangled with fairy-tale fantasies. The prince was the prize I had learned to want from the things I heard and saw around me.

"La Cinderella. That girl has really made trouble for us men," Tío laughed.

We were standing in front of the drugstore where my mother bought her twenty-five-cent Corín Tellado[2] romances—which I also avidly read. My uncle took my hand and guided me inside the store. The rack of Spanish-language *novelas* was a Christmas tree of romance. Passionate couples kissing on every cover.

"See what women read?" My uncle gave the rack a turn, making it go round and round, creating the illusion of a moving picture of embraces and phrases like "*la pasión*," "*corazón y alma*," "*besos*," and the constant refrain of "*el amor, el amor, el amor.*"

"Mami reads these," I confessed, "and sometimes I do, too."

"They are all Cinderella stories. Every one of them." Tío gave the rack another turn. "The plot is always the same: Poor or unfortunate girl meets rich, unattainable man. After many hardships he discovers that the shoe will fit only the girl whose beauty he had not ever really seen because of her rags. If he is an alcoholic, he stops drinking; if he's a miser, he turns generous; if he's short and fat . . ."

"Don't tell me—he gets skinny and tall!"

"Or at least he learns to act as if he were perfect in every other way."

"So what's wrong with that?"

"*La vida no es así.*" My uncle looked uncharacteristically solemn when he told me that the expectations of Cinderella and her female followers were simply not the way life really was for men and women, not even when they were in love.

But I didn't hear him. I knew only that my charming *tío* smelled enticingly of liquor and cigarettes when he leaned down to kiss me, and that he had other vices I could not yet name. But all of that made him alluring to me—the good Catholic girl waiting for life to begin happening for her. He was the mysterious man in one of my mother's *novelas*. I thought he was so much more interesting than my dull, hardworking father and my other male relatives. I didn't know of my *tío*'s lifelong battle with alcoholism, or of the throat cancer that would silence his seductive voice forever before he was much older than I am now.

I remember walking with him past the decorated storefronts of downtown Paterson one evening. My uncle made a game of asking me if I wanted this or that for Christmas: a Thumbelina doll like I had desperately wished for last year? No. I had received a hard plastic doll from one of my grandmothers in Puerto Rico, and my parents had decided that that was enough dolls for me. Only Tío had understood that the Thumbelina baby doll *felt* like a real flesh-and-blood baby. We had gone into the store and held it. He had not bought it for me because that year was one of his *años pobres*, when he was between jobs, holing up or drying out at a relative's apartment somewhere, waiting until he could get together enough money to return to *la Isla*. But this year he had money for gifts, he said. Did I want jewelry? We looked at all the shiny baubles in the jewelry store window. No. An *azabache* to wear around my neck to ward off the evil eye? No. I laughed. I was too sophisticated then for such superstitious nonsense.

"Surprise me, Tío."

2. María del Socorro Tellado López (1927–2009), aka Corín Tellado, Spanish writer of over 4,000 romance novels and photonovels, many of them best sellers in Spanish-language countries.

That week before Nochebuena[3] I stayed close to his magical presence, taking in his masculine appeal, watching women's faces soften when he cast his dark eyes on them, smelling his dangerous other life when he kissed me on the cheek as he said good night and went off like the sleek cat he was to prowl the streets and return in the morning to my mother's kitchen, where his face revealed that he had been *doing* exciting things while the rest of us only dreamed about them.

Mami would frown through her first cup of coffee, then break down in girlish giggles when Tío told us a new joke or *cuento* he had picked up in his wanderings. I gathered these stories in my memory and brought them out during the loneliest times of my life. They nourished and comforted me as they had my mother, who was always hungry for words in Spanish during those first years away from the Island. I had no idea then that my uncle was using his storytelling in a similar way: to trade for attention, time, even affection from others.

"*Mira*, it was like this," he would say, sitting across from my mother at her little Formica table, both of them smoking cigarettes and drinking coffee. "The girl needed attention and I gave her some. I will tell you from the beginning so that you know I am not the scoundrel you think. This is *la verdad, la pura verdad*."

This phrase was a key to their family joke. Whenever any of my *abuela's* children started a story with the announcement that it was the pure, unadulterated truth, as the old lady always did before one of her *cuentos*, we all knew that it was going to be a good one. A whopper. No holds barred.

"And how was I to know that she was married? All I knew was that her big brown eyes, like my *sobrina's* there, were beckoning to me from across the dance floor. *Socorro. Ayuda*, they said to me, save me from this lonely life. . . ."

"She had very eloquent eyes." My mother might comment in mock seriousness.

"What could I do but respond to her silent cries for help?"

"If someone's eyes cry out for help, *pues*, you must do what you have to do, *hombre*." My mother fell easily into the straight-man role that played such a large part in these entertainments. Their jokes and *cuento*-tellings were more like little plays extemporized by people who knew each other well.

"I did what any man with a heart would have done. I danced a few numbers with her. I bought her a drink. I asked her if she would like me to escort her home. You know the streets of this city . . ."

"Are crawling with criminals!" my mother offered.

"Exactly. Well, that's when she thanked me by telling me that her fiancé was getting off from a late shift at any moment. And . . . well, wasn't that him at the door now? Yes, it was the fiancé at the door, and he looked more like King Kong than any other man I have ever seen. *Hija*, he was covered with black fur from head to toe, and he was so huge that he had to squeeze in through the double doors. Good thing that slowed him down enough so I could end my dance with the lovely *señorita* as quickly as possible."

"But how did you get the egg on your forehead, *hermano*? Did you bump it on your way out?"

3. Good Night, i.e., Christmas Eve.

"¡*Ay, bendito!* King Kong gave me this little gift. You see there was no back door. And for a big ape, the fiancé moved fast. The only thing I regret is that he wasted a perfectly good bottle of Bacardi by using it as a weapon on my head."

"Maybe it was not all wasted," my mother was giggling and I was, too, by then. "I think it may have seeped into your brain through your pores."

While I listened to my mother and my uncle talk, I saw how all their daily struggles ceased for the time it took to tell the *cuento*, how pleased they were with their own wit, their ability to laugh at disappointments and hurts and, best of all, to transform any ordinary episode into an adventure.

On Christmas Eve the family gathered in our living room. My mother and I had polished the green linoleum floor until it was a mirror reflecting the multicolored lights of the Christmas tree, which had done its job of perfuming our apartment with the aroma of evergreen. I was wearing a red party dress my mother had let me choose from her closet and a pair of her pumps. I looked at least eighteen, I thought. I put some of Tío's *pachanga* records on our turntable and waited anxiously for him to come through the door with my gift. What I expected it to be was in the airy realm of a dream. But it would, I knew without a doubt, be magical.

It was late when he finally showed up bearing a brown grocery bag full of gifts and a bleached-blond woman on his arm. After kissing his sisters, waving to me from across the room, and wishing everyone *Felices Pascuas*, he and his partner left for another party. My mother and aunts shook their heads at their brother's latest caprice. My feet hurt in the high-heeled shoes, so I sat out the dances and read one of my mother's books. Sometime around midnight I was handed my gifts. Among them there was an unwrapped box of perfume with a card from my uncle. The perfume was Tabu. The card read: "*La Cenisosa* from our Island does not get a prince as a reward. She has another gift given to her. I heard a woman tell this *cuento* once. Maybe you can find it in the library or ask Mamá to tell it to you when you visit her next time."

My mother thought the perfume was too strong for a girl my age and would not let me wear it. I was disappointed by the gift, but I would occasionally spray on the perfume anyway. I discovered that its wilted-flower scent triggered my imagination. I could imagine myself in many different ways when I smelled it. It was the kind of perfume no one else would give me.

I did not find the *cuento* of *La Cenisosa* in the Paterson Public Library, nor in any other book collection for many years. Recently I ran across an anthology of *cuentos folklóricos* from Puerto Rico, and there it was: *La Cenisosa*. In *La Cenisosa* of Puerto Rico, Cinderella is rewarded by a family of three *hadas madrinas*, fairy godmothers, for her generosity of spirit, but her prize is not the hand of a prince. Instead, she is rewarded with diamonds and pearls that fall from her mouth whenever she opens it to speak. And she finds that she can be brave enough to stand up to her wicked stepmother and stepsisters and clever enough to banish them from her home forever. Around the time when I translated this folktale my mother wrote to say that my uncle was dying from cancer of the throat back on the Island, where they had both returned years before. She said that his voice was almost totally gone but not his indomitable spirit. He knew he had little time left to give us the words he wanted us to remember. He had my mother write to me and tell me that he had read my novel and wanted me to know that my stories gave him pleasure. He sent me his *bendición*. I took his blessing to mean that he had accepted my gift of words.

2000

# And May He Be Bilingual

*Latin Women Pray*

Latin women pray
In incense sweet churches
They pray in Spanish
To an Anglo God
With a Jewish heritage.
And this Great White Father
Imperturbable
In his marble pedestal
Looks down upon
His brown daughters
Votive candles shining like lust
In his all seeing eyes
Unmoved
By their persistent prayers.
Yet year after year
Before his image they kneel
Margarita, Josefina, María, and Isabel
All fervently hoping
That if not omnipotent
At least He be bilingual.

In this early poem I express the sense of powerlessness I felt as a non-native speaker of English in the United States. Non-native. Non-participant in the mainstream culture. *Non*, as in no, not, nothing. This little poem is about the non-ness of the non-speakers of the ruling language making a pilgrimage to the only One who can help, hopeful in their faith that someone is listening, yet still suspicious that even He doesn't understand their language. I grew up in the tight little world of the Puerto Rican community in Paterson, New Jersey, and later moved to Augusta, Georgia, where my "native" universe shrank even further to a tiny group of us who were brought to the Deep South through the military channels our fathers had chosen out of economic necessity. I wrote this ironic poem years ago, out of a need to explore the loneliness, the almost hopelessness, I had felt and observed in the other non-native speakers, many my own relatives, who would never master the English language well enough to be able to connect with the native speakers in as significant ways as I did.

Having come to age within the boundaries of language exiles, and making only brief forays out into the vast and often frightening landscape called *the mainstream*, it's easy for the newcomer to become ethnocentric. That's what Little Italy, Little Korea, Little Havana, Chinatown, and barrios are, centers of ethnic concerns. After all, it's a natural human response to believe that there is safety only within the walls around the circle of others who look like us, speak like us, behave like us: it is the animal kingdom's basic rule of survival—if whatever is coming toward you does not look like you or your kin, either fight or fly.

It is this primal fear of the unfamiliar that I have conquered through education, travel, and my art. I am an English teacher by profession and a writer by vocation. I have written several books of prose and poetry based mainly on my experiences in growing up Latina in the United States. Until a few years ago, when multiculturalism became part of the American political agenda, no one seemed to notice my work; suddenly I find myself a Puerto Rican/American (Latina)/Woman writer. Not only am I supposed to share my particular vision of American life, but I am also supposed to be a role model for a new generation of Latino students who expect me to teach them how to get a piece of the proverbial English language pie. I actually enjoy both of these public roles, in moderation. I love teaching literature. Not my own work, but the work of my literary ancestors in English and American literature—my field, that is, the main source of my models as a writer. I also like going into my classrooms at the University of Georgia, where my English classes at this point are still composed mainly of white American students, with a sprinkling of African American and Asian American, and only occasionally a Latino, and sharing my bicultural, bilingual views with them. It is a fresh audience. I am not always speaking to converts.

I teach American literature as an outsider in love with the Word—whatever language it is written in. They, at least some of them, come to understand that my main criterion when I teach is excellence and that I will talk to them about so-called minority writers whom I admire in the same terms as I will the old standards they know they are supposed to honor and study. I show them why they should admire them, not blindly, but with a critical eye. I speak English with my Spanish accent to these native speakers. I tell them about my passion for the genius of humankind, demonstrated through literature: the power of language to affect, to enrich, or to diminish and destroy lives, its potential to empower someone like me, someone like them. The fact that English is my second language does not seem to matter beyond the first few lectures, when the students sometimes look askance at one another, perhaps wondering whether they have walked into the wrong classroom and at any moment this obviously "Spanish" professor will ask them to start conjugating regular and irregular verbs. They can't possibly know this about me: in my classes, everyone is safe from Spanish grammar recitation. Because almost all of my formal education has been in English, I avoid all possible risk of falling into a discussion of the uses of the conditional or of the merits of the subjunctive tense in the Spanish language: Hey, I just *do* Spanish, I don't explain it.

Likewise, when I *do* use my Spanish and allude to my Puerto Rican heritage, it comes from deep inside me where my imagination and memory reside, and I do it through my writing. My poetry, my stories, and my essays concern themselves with the coalescing of languages and cultures into a vision that has meaning first of all for me; then, if I am served well by my craft and the transformation occurs, it will also have meaning for others as art.

My life as a child and teenager was one of constant dislocation. My father was in the U.S. Navy, and we moved back to Puerto Rico during his long tours of duty abroad. On the Island, my brother and I attended a Catholic school run by American nuns. Then it was back to Paterson, New Jersey, to try to catch up, and sometimes we did, academically, but socially it was a different story altogether. We were the perennial new kids on the block. Yet when I write about these gypsy days, I construct a continuity that allows me to see my life as equal to any other, with its share of chaos, with its own system of order. This is what I have learned from writing as a minority person in America that I can teach my students: Literature is the human search for meaning. It is as simple and as profound as that. And we are all, if we are thinking people, involved in the process. It is both a privilege and a burden.

Although as a child I often felt resentful of my rootlessness, deprived of a stable home, lasting friendships, the security of one house, one country, I now realize that these same circumstances taught me some skills that I use today to adapt in a constantly changing world, a place where you can remain in one spot for years and still wake up every day to strangeness wrought by technology and politics. We can stand still and find ourselves in a different nation created overnight by decisions we did not participate in making. I submit that we are all becoming more like the immigrant and can learn from her experiences as a stranger in a strange land. I know I am a survivor in language. I learned early that possessing the secret of words was to be my passport into mainstream life. Notice I did not say "assimilation" into mainstream life. This is a word that has come to mean the acceptance of loss of native culture. Although I know for a fact that to survive everyone "assimilates" what they need out of many different cultures, especially in America, I prefer to use the term "adapt" instead. Just as I acquired the skills to adapt to American life, I have now come to terms with a high-tech world. It is not that different. I learned English to communicate, but now I know computer language. I have been greedy in my grasping and hoarding of words. I own enough stock in English to feel secure in almost any situation where my language skills have to serve me; and I have claimed my rich Puerto Rican culture to give scope and depth to my personal search for meaning.

As I travel around this country I am constantly surprised by the diversity of its peoples and cultures. It is like a huge, colorful puzzle. And the beauty is in its complexity. Yet there are some things that transcend the obvious differences: great literature, great ideas, and great idealists, for example. I find Don Quixote plays[1] almost universal; after all, who among us does not have an Impossible Dream? Shakespeare's wisdom is planetary in its appeal; Gandhi's and King's message[2] is basic to the survival of our civilization, and most people know it; and other voices that are like a human racial memory speak in a language that can almost always be translated into meaning.

And genius doesn't come in only one package: The Bard happened to be a white gentleman from England, but what about our timid Emily Dickinson?[3] Would we call on her in our class, that mousy little girl in the back of the

1. Such as *Man of La Mancha*, a musical origi- nally produced on Broadway in 1965, based on the novel *Don Quixote* (1605, 1616), by the Span- ish writer Miguel de Cervantes (1547–1616). Its main and most popular song is "The Impossible Dream (The Quest)."

2. Mahatma Gandhi (Mohandas Karamchand Gandhi, 1869–1948), Indian nationalist leader, and the Reverend Martin Luther King Jr. (1929– 1968), American clergyman, advocated non- violent resistance to injustice.
3. American poet (1830–1886).

room squinting at the chalkboard and blushing at everything? We almost lost her art to neglect. Thank God poetry is stronger than time and prejudices.

This is where my idealism as a teacher kicks in: I ask myself, who is to say that at this very moment there isn't a Native American teenager gazing dreamily at the desert outside her window as she works on today's assignment, seeing the universe in a grain of sand, preparing herself to share her unique vision with the world. It may all depend on the next words she hears, which may come out of my mouth, or yours. And what about the African American boy in a rural high school in Georgia who showed me he could rhyme for as long as I let him talk. His teachers had not been able to get him to respond to literature. Now they listened in respectful silence while he composed an ode to his girl and his car extemporaneously, in a form so tight and so right (contagious too) that when we discuss the exalted Alexander Pope's[4] oeuvre, we call it heroic couplets. But he was intimidated by the manner in which Pope and his worthy comrades in the canon had been presented to him and his classmates, as gods from Mt. Olympus, inimitable and incomprehensible to mere mortals like himself. He was in turn surprised to see, when it was finally brought to his attention, that Alexander Pope and he shared a good ear.

What I'm trying to say is that the phenomenon we call culture in a society is organic, not manufactured. It grows where we plant it. Culture is our garden, and we may neglect it, trample on it, or we may choose to cultivate it. In America we are dealing with varieties we have imported, grafted, cross-pollinated. I can only hope the experts who say that the land is replenished in this way are right. It is the ongoing American experiment, and it has to take root in the classroom first. If it doesn't succeed, then we will be back to praying and hoping that at least He be bilingual.

2000

4. English poet (1688–1744).

# ALBERTO ÁLVARO RÍOS
## b. 1952

Alberto Álvaro Ríos was born in Nogales, Arizona, to a Mexican father and an English mother. Spanish was his first language, but he learned English in kindergarten and had forgotten his Spanish by the time he entered middle school. Because he had been punished in school if he spoke Spanish, Ríos felt ashamed of being Latino and embarrassed by his culture and his Spanish-speaking relatives. To reimmerse himself in family and ethnic life, he relearned Spanish in high school and in college. As a result, he became proud of his language and heritage. He also began to write poetry.

Ríos earned a bachelor's degree in English from the University of Arizona, in Tucson, in 1974, then remained in school and earned a bachelor's in psychology. He enrolled in law school but dropped out after two semesters to pursue a Master of

Fine Arts degree in creative writing. He received the degree in 1979, the year that the University of California at Berkeley Press published his first collection of poetry, *Elk Heads on the Wall*.

The following year, Ríos won a National Endowment for the Arts Fellowship, which allowed him to write and publish the poetry collection *Sleeping on Fists* (1981), which he followed with *Whispering to Fool the Wind: Poems* (1982). He became widely known and began to do readings across the country. His next publication, *The Iguana Killer: Twelve Stories of the Heart* (1984), brought him high praise and the Western States Book Award for fiction. The stories in *The Iguana Killer* take place in various parts of Arizona and the state of Sonora, Mexico. In the title story, included in this anthology, the young protagonist, Sapito, raised in the tropics of southern Mexico and an expert iguana killer, visits his grandmother in Nogales. He is called Sapito (Spanish for little toad) because of his bulging eyes. When he sees snow for the first time, he becomes frightened, but this event ultimately helps him begin to move past childhood.

In the story collections *Five Indiscretions* (1985), *The Lime Orchard Woman* (1988), *Teodoro Luna's Two Kisses* (1990), *Pig Cookies* (1995), *The Curtain Trees* (1999), *The Smallest Muscle in the Human Body* (2002), and *The Theater of Night* (2006), and in *Capirotada: A Nogales Memoir* (1999), Ríos continues to explore the blended culture that exists on the U.S.-Mexico border. He is the Katharine C. Turner Distinguished Chair in English and Regents' Professor at Arizona State University, in Tempe. Among the awards he has received are a Guggenheim Fellowship, a Latino Hall of Fame Award, a National Book Award nomination, several Pushcart Prizes, the Walt Whitman Award, and the PEN Beyond Margins Award. In 2002, Janet Napolitano, then governor of Arizona, requested that Ríos write and deliver a poem for a visit to the state by Vicente Fox, then the president of Mexico.

The three Ríos poems included in this anthology are reminiscences of physical aspects of the past. "Morning" is about the way that the poet's father's beard defined his father as a person. "The Man Who Became Old" is about a man, his teeth, and how they both connected him to and detached him from other people. And "Mayates," a series of instructions, explores the tactile contact between human and insect.

# Morning

He cradled his head in those hands
who might have kept it,
who might have grown into part of his head
but I would come in, and call him, *daddy*,
and they would let go.                                        5
Every day I saw a man
who wore one suit
and had a beard hid under his skin.
It was black.
I could see it in the light                                  10
see its darkness
as it came out first through his eyes
precisely in their centers
when he looked at me.
Under his suit, under his shirt                              15
and undershirt, it started coming
through his chest too, and on his back.

He thought about his beard
because it was tangled in his head.
It made him unhappy,                                    20
his head was heavy
and sometimes he rested it in those hands
letting his beard come out through
their backs, through the backs
of his palms, the backs of his fingers,                25
through the backs of things lost.

1982

## The Man Who Became Old

For every year, he grew a new tooth
and this, at least among his friends,
created around him a kind of fame,
but the kind that everyone gets used to
so that it was only occasionally enjoyable.          5
And his mouth kept getting bigger
or really, his jawbone, so that he
began taking on the aspect of a wolf
though roughly his teeth were equally sized.
And then it came that he was forty-five              10
and spent his nights still unmarried.
He looked now like the old cartoon wolf
in a zoot suit flipping a coin and whistling,
and his friends all abandoned him.
He could barely remember them.                       15
With each new tooth, a friend left,
the same way that in the early days
a friend came, so that for fifteen years, now
he was alone, and could find no work.
People ran when he walked the streets                20
so he stayed in his apartment
almost entirely, and ordered take-out.
His friends said it was better this way,
then remembered they were no longer
friends, that it didn't matter.                      25
He dreamed about the half-dressed tooth fairy
every night, and finally she took him.

1982

## Mayates[1]

Take thread any color
the length of yourself,

1. Dung beetles.

that he must take advantage, but very carefully. Iguanas can see in almost all directions at once. Unlike human eyes, both iguana eyes do not have to center in on the same thing. One eye can look forward, and one backward, like a clown, so that they can detect almost any movement. Sapito knew this and was always careful to check both eyes before striking. Squinting his own eyes which always puffed out even more when he was excited, he would not draw back his club. That would waste time. It was already kept high in the air all these minutes. When he was ready, he would send the bat straight down as hard and as fast as he could. Just like that. And if he had done all these things right, he would take his prize home by the tail to skin him for eating that night.

Iguanas were prepared like any other meat, fried, roasted, or boiled, and they tasted like tough chicken no matter which way they were done. In Tabasco, and especially in Villahermosa, iguanas were eaten by everybody all the time, even tourists, so hunting them was very popular. Iguana was an everyday supper, eaten without frowning at such a thing, eating lizard. It was not different from the other things eaten here, the turtle eggs, *cahuamas*,[1] crocodile meat, river snails. And when iguanas were killed, nobody was supposed to feel sad. Everybody's father said so. Sapito did, though, sometimes. Iguanas had puffed eyes like his.

But, if Sapito failed to kill one of these iguanas, he would run away as fast as he could—being sad was the last thing he would think of. Iguanas look mean, they have bloodshot eyes, and people say that they spit blood. Sapito and his friends thought that, since no one they knew had ever been hurt by these monsters, they must not be so bad. This was what the boys thought in town, talking on a summer afternoon, drinking coconuts. But when he missed, Sapito figured that the real reason no one had ever been hurt was that no one ever hung around afterward to find out what happens. Whether iguanas were really dangerous or not, nobody could say for certain. Nobody's parents had ever heard of an iguana hurting anyone, either. The boys went home one day and asked. So, no one worried, sort of, and iguanas were even tamed and kept as pets by the old sailors in Villahermosa, along with the snakes. But only by the sailors.

The thought of missing a hit no longer bothered Sapito, who now began carrying his baseball bat everywhere. His friends were impressed more by this than by anything else, even candy in tin boxes, especially when he began killing four and five iguanas a day. No one could be that good. Soon, not only Chachi, but the rest of the boys began following Sapito around constantly just to watch the scourge of the iguanas in action.

By now, the bat was proven. Sapito was the champion iguana-provider, always holding his now-famous killer-bat. All his friends would come to copy it. They would come every day asking for measurements and questioning him as to its design. Chachi and the rest would then go into the jungle and gather fat, straight roots. With borrowed knives and machetes, they tried to whittle out their own iguana-killers, but failed. Sapito's was machine made, and perfect.

This went on for about a week, when Sapito had an idea that was to serve him well for a long time. He began renting out the killer-bat for a *centavo* a

---

1. Giant sea turtles.

day. The boys said yes yes right away, and would go out and hunt at least two or three iguanas to make it worth the price, but really, too, so that they could use the bat as much as possible.

For the next few months, the grown-ups of Villahermosa hated Sapito and his bat because all they ate was iguana. But Sapito was proud. No one would make fun of his bulging eyes now.

Sapito was in Nogales in the United States visiting his grandmother for the first time, before going back to Tabasco, and Villahermosa. His family had come from Chiapas on the other side of the republic on a relative-visiting vacation. It was still winter, but no one in Sapito's family had expected it to be cold. They knew about rain, and winter days, but it was always warm in the jungle, even for these things.

Sapito was sitting in front of the house on Sonoita Avenue, on the side-walk. He was very impressed by many things in this town, especially the streetlights. Imagine lighting up the inside *and* the outside. It would be easy to catch animals at night here. But most of all, he was impressed by his rather large grandmother, whom he already loved very much. He had remembered to thank her for the iguana-killer and the ball. She had laughed and said, "*Por nada, hijo.*" As he sat and thought about this, he wrapped the two blankets he had brought outside with him tighter around his small body. Sapito could not understand or explain to himself that the weather was cold and that he had to feel it, everyone did, even him. This was almost an unknown experience to him since he had never been out of the tropics before. The sensation, the feeling of cold, then, was very strange, especially since he wasn't even wet. It was actually hurting him. His muscles felt as if he had held his bat up in the air for an hour waiting for an iguana. Of course, Sapito could have gone inside to get warm near the wood-burning stove, but he didn't like the smoke or the smell of the north. It was a different smell, not the jungle.

So Sapito sat there. Cold had never been important in his life before, and he wasn't going to let it start now. With blankets he could cover himself up and it would surely pass. Covered up for escape, he waited for warmness, pulling the blankets over his head. Sometimes he would put out his foot to see if it was okay yet, the way the lady iguana would come out first.

Then, right then in one fast second, Sapito seemed to feel, with his foot on the outside, a very quiet and strange moment, as if everything had slowed. He felt his eyes bulge when he scrunched up his face to hear better. Something scary caught hold of him, and he began to shiver harder. It was different from just being cold, which was scary enough. His heartbeat was pounding so much that he could feel it in his eyes.

He carefully moved one of the blankets from his face. Sapito saw the sky falling, just like the story his grandmother had told him the first day they had been there. He thought she was joking, or that she didn't realize he was already eight, and didn't believe in such things anymore.

Faster than hitting an iguana Sapito threw his blankets off, crying as he had not cried since he was five and they had nicknamed him and teased him. He ran to the kitchen and grabbed his mother's leg. Crying and shiver-ing, he begged, "¡*Mamá, por favor, perdóneme!*" He kept speaking fast, ask-ing for forgiveness and promising never to do anything wrong in his life ever again. The sky was falling, but he had always prayed, really he had.

The Río Grijalva comes down from the Sierra Madre mountains, down through the state of Tabasco, through Villahermosa, emptying through Puerto Alvarado several miles north into the Gulf of Mexico. The boys looked over at the Casimira *choza*, then backward at this great river, where the paddle boat was getting ready to make its first trip of the day to Puerto Alvarado. They ran after it, fast enough to leave behind their shadows.

Sapito and his friends had been in Alvarado for about an hour when they learned that a *cahuama*, a giant sea turtle, was near by. They were on the rough beach, walking toward the north where the rocks become huge. Some palm trees nodded just behind the beach, followed by the jungle, as always. Sometimes Sapito thought it followed him, always moving closer.

Climbing the mossy rocks, Chachi was the one who spotted the *cahuama*. This was strange because the turtles rarely came so close to shore. In Villahermosa, and Puerto Alvarado, the money situation was such that anything the boys saw, like iguanas or the *cahuama*, they tried to capture. They always tried hard to get something for nothing, and here was their chance—not to mention the adventure involved. They all ran together with the understood intention of dividing up the catch.

They borrowed a rope from the men who were working farther up the shore near the palm trees. "¡*Buena suerte!*" one of the men called, and laughed. Sapito and Chachi jumped in a *cayuco*, a kayak built more like a canoe, which one of the fishermen had left near shore. They paddled out to the floating turtle, jumped out, and managed to get a rope tied around its neck right off. Usually, then, a person had to hop onto the back of the *cahuama* and let it take him down into the water for a little while. Its burst of strength usually went away before the rider drowned or let go. This was the best fun for the boys, and a fairly rare chance, so Sapito, who was closest, jumped on to ride this one. He put up one arm like a tough cowboy. This *cahuama* went nowhere.

The two boys climbed back into the *cayuco* and tried to pull the turtle, but it still wouldn't budge. It had saved its strength, and its strong flippers were more than a match for the two boys now. Everyone on shore swam over to help them after realizing that yells of how to do it better were doing no good. They all grabbed a part of the rope. With pure strength against strength, the six boys sweated, but finally outpulled the stubborn *cahuama*, dragging it onto the shore. It began flopping around on the sand until they managed to tip it onto its back. The turtle seemed to realize that struggling was a waste of its last fat-man energy, and started moving like a slow motion robot, fighting as before but, now, on its back, the flippers and head moved like a movie going too slow.

The *cahuama* had seemed huge as the boys were pulling it, fighting so strong in the water, but it was only about three feet long when they finally took a breath and looked. Yet, they all agreed, this *cahuama* was very fat. It must have been a grandfather.

Chachi went to call one of the grown-ups to help. Each of the boys was sure that he could kill a *cahuama* and prepare it, but this was everybody's, and they wanted it cut right. The men were impressed as the boys explained. The boys were all nervous. Maybe not nervous—not really, just sometimes they were sad when they caught *cahuamas* because they had seen what happens. Like fish, or iguanas, but bigger, and bigger animals are different.

Sad, but they couldn't tell anyone, especially not the other boys, or the men. Sapito looked at their catch.

These sailors, or men who used to be sailors, all carried short, heavy machetes, specially made for things taken from the sea. Chachi came back with a man who already had his in hand. The blade was straight because there was no way to shape metal, no anvil in Alvarado. The man looked at Sapito. "*Préstame tu palo*," he said, looking at Sapito's iguana-killer. Sapito picked it up from where he had left it and handed it to the man, carefully. The fisherman beat the turtle on the head three times fast until it was either dead or unconscious. Then he handed the bat back to Sapito, who was sort of proud, and sort of not.

The man cut the *cahuama's* head off. Some people eat the head and its juice, but Sapito and his friends had been taught not to. No one said anything as it was tossed to the ground. The flippers continued their robot motion.

He cut the side of the turtle, where the underside skin meets the shell. He then pulled a knife out of his pocket, and continued where the machete had first cut, separating the body of the turtle from the shell. As he was cutting he told the boys about the freshwater sac that *cahuamas* have, and how, if they were ever stranded at sea, they could drink it. They had heard the story a hundred times, but nobody knew anybody who really did it. The boys were impatient. Then he separated the underpart from the inside meat, the prize. It looked a little redder than beef. The fins were then cut off—someone would use their leather sometime later.

The man cut the meat into small pieces. The boys took these pieces and washed them in salt water to make the meat last longer. Before cooking them, they would have to be washed again, this time in fresh water to get all the salt off. In the meantime, the saltwater would keep the meat from spoiling. One time Sapito forgot, or really he was in too much of a hurry, and he took some *cahuama* home but forgot to tell his mother. It changed colors, and Sapito had to go get some more food, with everybody mad at him. The boys knew that each part of the *cahuama* was valuable, but all they were interested in now was what they could carry. This, of course, was the meat.

The man gave each of the boys some large pieces, and then kept most of it for himself. The boys were young, and could not argue with a grownup. They were used to this. The fisherman began to throw the shell away.

"*No, por favor, dámelo*," Sapito called to him. The man laughed and handed the shell to Sapito, who put his pieces of meat inside it and, with the rest of the boys, wandered back to the river to wait for the paddle boat. The shell was almost too big for him. The boys were all laughing and joking, proud of their accomplishment. They asked Sapito what he was going to do with the shell, but he said that he wasn't sure yet. This wasn't true. Of course, he was already making big, very big, plans for it.

They got back early in the afternoon, and everyone went home exhausted. Sapito, before going home, went into the jungle and gathered some green branches. He was not very tired yet—he had a new idea, so Sapito spent the rest of the afternoon polishing the shell with sand and the hairy part of some coconuts, which worked just like sandpaper.

When it was polished, he got four of the best branches and whittled them to perfection with his father's knife. Sapito tied these into a rectangle using some *mecate*, something in between rope and string, which his mother had given him. The shell fit halfway down into the opening of the rectangle. It was perfect. Then, onto this frame, he tied two flat, curved branches across the bottom at opposite ends. It moved back and forth like a drunk man. He had made a good, strong crib. It worked, just right for a new-born baby girl.

Sapito had worked hard and fast with the strength of a guilty conscience. Señora Casimira just might have needed something, after all. It was certainly possible that her husband might have had to work today. All the boys had known these facts before they had left, but had looked only at the paddle boat—and it had waved back at them.

Sapito took the crib, hurrying to beat the jungle dusk. Dusk, at an exact moment, even on Sundays, owned the sky and the air in its own strange way. Just after sunset, for about half an hour, the sky blackened more than would be normal for the darkness of early night, and mosquitoes, like pieces of sand, would come up out of the thickest part of the jungle like tornadoes, coming down on the town to take what they could. People always spent this half hour indoors, Sundays, too, even with all the laughing, which stopped then. This was the signal for the marimba's music to take over.

Sapito reached the *choza* as the first buzzings were starting. He listened at the Casimira's door, hearing the baby cry like all babies. The cradle would help. He put it down in front of the wooden door without making any noise, and knocked. Then, as fast as he could, faster than that even, he ran back over the hill, out of sight. He did not turn around. Señora Casimira would find out who had made it. And he would be famous again, thought Sapito, famous like the other times. He felt for the iguana-killer that had been dragging behind him, tied to his belt, and put it over his right shoulder. His face was not strong enough to keep away the smile that pulled his mouth, his fat eyes all the while puffing out.

1984

# GARY SOTO
## b. 1952

Gary Soto was born and raised in Fresno, California. Part of a working-class Mexican American family, he labored in a factory during his teenage years. Soto did poorly in school, but in high school he became interested in poetry. He started writing at Fresno State College; earned his bachelor's degree from California State University, Fresno, in 1972; and earned his master's from the University of California, Irvine, in 1976, having already received an Academy of American Poets Prize and the Discovery-Nation Award.

Soto's first book of poems, *The Elements of San Joaquin* (1977), presents grim pictures of Mexican American life in California's Central Valley. His second book, *The Tale of Sunlight* (1978), which juxtaposes various narrative devices (including dramatic monologues), was a finalist for the Leonore Marshall Poetry Award. The following year, Soto received a Guggenheim Fellowship and traveled in Mexico. *Living Up the Street: Narrative Recollections* (1985), a collection of autobiographical vignettes about Latino life in the Southwest, received the American Book Award. *Black Hair* (1985) also speaks to skin color. In 1985, Soto joined the faculty at the University of California, Berkeley, where he taught in the English and Chicano Studies Departments.

Soto's subsequent writing—often autobiographical, but striving for universality in addressing issues such as poverty, alienation, and ethnic relations—has been featured in periodicals such as *The New Yorker, Partisan Review, The Paris Review,* and *The Nation.* It has been collected in books such as *Lesser Evils: Ten Quartets* (1988), *Home Course in Religion: New Poems* (1991), *A Natural Man* (1999), *One Kind of Faith* (2003), and *Partly Cloudy: Poems of Love and Longing* (2008). A television adaptation of his novel *The Pool Party* (1993)—about a working-class Mexican's invitation to a wealthy classmate's home—received the Andrew Carnegie Medal. His play for young adults, *Nerdlandia* (1999)—a kind of Chicano *Grease* set in the Los Angeles barrio—was produced by the Los Angeles Opera.

While Soto had stopped teaching in 1994 to write full-time, he returned to teaching in 2003 with a post at the University of California, Riverside. He has received the Literature Award from the Hispanic Heritage Foundation, a National Education Association Fellowship, the Levinson Award from *Poetry* magazine, the Tomás Rivera Children's Literature Award, the Author-Illustrator Civil Rights Award from the National Education Association, and the PEN Center West Book Award. He lives in Berkeley, California, and serves as Young People's Ambassador for the California Rural Legal Assistance (CRLA) and the United Farm Workers of America (UFW).

The six Soto poems included in this anthology are representative of their author's look at life in the United States from a minority observer's viewpoint. "The Level at Which the Sky Begins" is about workers traveling to their jobs in the early morning. "How an Uncle Became Gray" pays homage to the kind of magical realism associated with the Colombian fiction writer, screenwriter, and journalist Gabriel García Márquez. "At the Cantina" depicts the scene at a bar from the bartender's perspective. "Catalina Treviño Is Really from Heaven" explores the incandescence of sexual attraction. In "What Are You Speaking?" a Mexican impersonates an Italian. And in "The Charity of La Señora Lara," an old woman exploits and then sympathizes with a Mexican boy when she finds out his ancestry.

The story "We Ain't Asking Much" presents one of the three down-and-out male protagonists in Soto's collection *Nickel and Dime* (2000). Here, Roberto Silva loses his job, finds his circumstances greatly reduced, and yet remains hopeful.

## The Level at Which the Sky Begins

> Hunched in the green weather of a pine
> Above a theater of steaming roofs
> And all there was to see
>
> I saw the sun take
> Its first step
> Above the water tower at Sun-Maid Raisin     5
> And things separate from the dark
> And lean on their new shadows

Through the streets
Cars fleeced in a light frost                         10
Smoke lifting above the houses

A boy porching
The newspapers that would unfold like a towel
Over coffee   over an egg
Going brown   over the radio saying                   15
*It's 6:05   this is the music of America*

Where the young got up hungry
Roosters cleared
What was caught in their throats
All night                                             20

Where a door slammed
A cane refused
The weight of the hand that carved it

On the horizon
Parting this hour from another                        25
The shelved clouds pulled a cargo of rain
East into the full light that would soon fall
To meet us wherever we turned

                                              1977


## How an Uncle Became Gray

*to García Márquez*

One day his room fluttered
Like a neon
With the butterflies
That had followed him,
A herd of vague motion                                5
He came to think
Was a cloud spread thin
And bearing
A blank message of rain.
They settled                                          10
Along his sleeve
And linked each finger
With the scent
The wind's tongue
Forgot to lick.                                       15
They opened and closed
Their wings, revealing
The bright circles
That focused like pupils
On the pure light                                     20

That stares through
The trees and beyond
The drift of summers
Rivers still trace.
When he shrugged                                    25
Them from his shoulders,
Unhooked their antennas
From his beard,
They gave off
The silver dust                                     30
A coin couldn't match,
The silver that laddered
His sideburns,
Tipped his brows
With something like snow.                            35
So this moment arrived
With its eyes open,
Streaking his pompadour
The color caught
Between two branches                                 40
On a winter day,
The clarity
He would embrace like a tree.

                                                   1978


## At the Cantina

In the cantina
Of six tables
A woman fingers
The ear lobe
Of a bank teller.                                    5
It is late,
And this place is empty
As a crushed hat.
A galaxy of flies
Circles the lamp.                                    10
Manuel wipes the counter,
Flicking ashes
Onto the floor.
The voices of
That couple                                          15
With the faces of oxen
On a hot day
Reach over his shoulder
And vanish
Into the mirror.                                     20
Finally they leave
Without nodding good-bye,
His hand on

Her right breast,
Her thumb hooked                                        25
In his watch pocket.
Manuel locks up,
Uncorks a bottle
And sits at a table.
All night he drinks                                    30
And his hands fold
And unfold,
Against the light,
A kingdom of animal shadows—
The Jackal,                                            35
The Hummingbird,
The sleepy-eyed Llama,
An Iguana munching air—
While the rooster stretches
To the day not there yet.                              40

1976                                                 1978


## Catalina Treviño Is Really from Heaven

Last night
At Mother Tomas's,
We danced the
Chicken-with-its-head-chopped-off,
Her hands on my buttocks,                               5
My crotch puffed
Like a lung
And holding its breath.
This wonderful woman
Stitched my neck                                       10
With kisses
And told secrets—
The silverware she stole,
Her spinster aunt
Living in Taxco,[1] a former lover                     15
With a heart condition.
I in turn, being educated
And a man of
Absolutely no wealth,
Whispered a line                                       20
Of bad poetry
And bit her left ear lobe.
Afterwards we left
Arm in arm
For my room, for our clothes                           25
Piled in a chair, and she
Fingering my bellybutton,

1. Taxco de Alarcón, a small city and municipality in the state of Guerrero, Mexico.

I opening her
Like a large Bible,
The kingdom of hair.                                              30

1978


## What Are You Speaking?

A friend said it was OK to be someone else,
That you didn't always have
To be Mexican. So,
During Lent[1] I wanted to be Italian,
A change that would bring me closer to the Pope.        5
The next day I listened
To my friend Little John, then his mother,
A woman from the old country.
His mother said, "Whatsa madda?"
I heard this when Little John peeled skin                 10
From his finger, when he meant to peel potato.
Little John bowed his head and started crying,
A spark of blood leaping behind his fingers.
Again she asked, this time louder: "Whatsa madda?"
He then really cried,                                      15
And I left my job
Of peeling shrimp and ran out of the house.
I thought she would start hitting him
For crying, and that maybe his mother
Would look at me and think I needed some too.              20
I walked down the street, and repeated,
"What is the matter? What's a matter?"
Whats madder. Madda! Whatsa madda
Madda." I stomped out these words
On a cement as hard as the front of my head.              25
I sucked in the spring air, dizzy with blossoms.
I could feel that I was someone else,
And that maybe I could stay this
Way for a week, then go back to who I was.
When a boy on a tricycle ran over                         30
My shoes, I shot, "Whatsa madda, madda!"
For two blocks I thought
I was speaking Italian,
And that if the Pope, by miracle, showed up
On our street he would recognize me                       35
As one of his own. He would ask,
"Whatsa madda, Gary?" I would suck
In the plugs of my dirty nose,
And answer, "Madda? Little John's
A madda." Since the Pope probably knew a lot,            40

1. In Roman Catholicism and other branches of Christianity, the 40 weekdays from Ash Wednesday to
Easter; generally a period of penitence and abstaining from some foods.

He would know madda was happening
At Little John's house
And some at mine.
The Pope would pat my head
And put me on his bouncing knee                    45
For a long story, Biblical and dangerous,
Baby Jesus between two dry humps
Of a camel, and fleeing two thousand years
From madda.

1976                                                                          1978


## The Charity of La Señora Lara

Once I worked
For a nearly deaf *vieja*,[1]
And she worked to get in my way,
Her grin chattering over my shoulders.
I raked an already raked yard,                      5
Gathered dropped plums into a bag, swept
And hoed the life out of a flowerbed.
I roofed the doghouse with flattened tuna cans
And beat the mites from a rug.
Later, on the lawn, we stood together              10
And stared at a wobbly sprinkler throwing out cool seed
Of water. I worked two hours,
Screamed in her good ear for my pay,
And then walked home,
Musing over the value of unearned money.           15

She was more than *loca*
When I returned, weeks later, and she asked
From the porch, "*¿Quién es?* Who are you?"
Plastic fruit clacked in her straw hat
And the autumn wind rippled her print dress        20
And her furry slippers. She clicked her fingers,
"You're the barber's boy, no?"
I shook my head. I was neither the barber's boy
Nor the preacher's spoiled son.
I was neither Italian nor Jew,                     25
Syrian nor Armenian. I was neither the lost lamb
Nor a stray child walking in the sandals of a gracious god.

I made a raking motion with my hands.
She giggled, remarked, "I am a woman,"
And scratched the one hair on her chin.            30
I gathered invisible oranges,

---

1. Old woman.

Shoveled a flower bed, spanked rugs on a clothesline,
And hammered boards for the rain shook from a cloud.
She shook her head, eyes clear as the zeros
Plugged through a road sign.                                    35

"You know, *señora*," I screamed, "I'm your working boy."
Her smile rattled the banana and cherries on her hat.
"*Mi'jo*,"[2] she wept into my shoulders, "welcome home!"

1997

---

## *FROM* NICKLE AND DIME

## We Ain't Asking Much

For six years Roberto Silva had worked as a security guard at the Walnut
Bank in Oakland,[1] worked in close proximity to large amounts of money
stained with the juices of life, torn and invisibly tainted with cocaine, marijuana, and God knows what other drugs. Roberto surmised that the money
was dirty, or why would these greenbacks fly from hands so nervously? He
added another theory. The lower denominations—fives and tens—gave off
the peculiar odor of old men; still, he figured that the bills were worth more
than the salt mines that gathered under his arms at the end of a workday.
He lamented that the money belonged to other people, some of them feeble-
minded, sourpusses, income-tax cheats, or would-be killers in glossy red
pumps. Some belonged to misers stingy even in offering a smile. That
would have required a blast of energy, a minimum of six calories to lift up
the corners of their mouths. Life's not fair, Roberto thought while he
watched old Mr. Berger lean to his right side as he exited the bank. He was
a regular customer whose colorful ties were wide as bibs. Roberto suspected that the old man's leaning posture was to counter the weight of
money in his jacket's top left pocket; he could imagine no other reason.
    Mr. Berger hurried past Roberto without a nod, a faint smile of recogni-
tion, or even an abrupt "excuse me." The old bugger rushed past within
inches—no, a fraction of an inch, the width of an eyelash—of brushing
against him. He risked a collision that would have proven that his awkward
posture was indeed the result of hoarding twenties in his pocket.
    "*Cabrón!*"[2] Roberto thought, then admonished himself for this silent and
uncharitable outburst. But the man should know better than to run down
the people who guarded his money. Guarded it with their lives, mind you!
    Roberto had spent the morning in front of the bank, pacing from the
cement planter box to the iron bench along with Gus Hernandez, the other
security guard, their steps grinding a path toward blithering boredom. Neither looked at the other for, as in a bad marriage, they had seen too much

2. My son (contraction of *mi* and *hijo*).          2. Bastard.
1. City in west-central California.

of each other in the course of years. Neither found the other worthy of comment.

Roberto fought the urge to plop himself on that bench. The corns on his little toes throbbed. His mind was dulled, lacking even one elementary thought to turn over like a shiny coin. Still, he had to keep pace with Gus.

He caught himself watching a dog the color of an old mop urinate on a parking meter. "This is stupid," he mumbled. It wasn't this beastly spectacle that bothered him, but his silent gambling whether the urine would slip over the curb in a sort of waterfall. The urine puddled impressively, but its mass was not large enough to create a flow over the edge.

During Roberto's tenure as a security guard, his countless yawns had permanently creased his face and stretched his lips until they were slack as a child's jump rope. At thirty-three he appeared older, somewhere in his early forties, his life more than half over, his stomach and precious innards still chugging along but losing speed.

This was how Roberto felt when the bank manager, Mr. Wallace, called him into his office, a cubicle adorned with snapshots of his family. Mr. Wallace's chair squeaked like a metal fart before the bank manager asked if Roberto would be willing to retire.

"Do I look that old?" Roberto asked, worried that perhaps he had indeed withered on the vine of life. He sat erect while asking the question. True, he had noticed that he left more hair on his pillow, that his front teeth, never really white, had yellowed like candles, and that actually—a pathetic admission—he had recently begun to use both hands to push himself out of his La-Z-Boy recliner. And true, unlike a great many tunnel-visioned oldsters, he had saved very little. He was banking that he would get married, sometime soon, and that he and this wife, whoever this delicate love might be, would care deeply for each other. At least for the first three or four years.

"No, *retire* is the wrong word." Mr. Wallace corrected his lax use of language. He explained that with the advent of better security—he pointed vaguely at the video cameras bolted to the four corners of the bank—one of the two security guards had to go. He employed the word *cost-effective*.

"But Gus is older than me," Roberto argued, his back slowly buckling to gravity and hurt though he strained to keep it straight, soldierly. After all, they were talking about his life.

The chair let out another metallic fart when Mr. Wallace opened the desk drawer and brought out a thick envelope. Roberto licked his lips and swallowed. He anticipated a packet of money. Instead Roberto watched with fascination as Mr. Wallace unfolded a form that, from all appearances, was in triplicate, possibly more.

"Yes, Gus is older," Mr. Wallace remarked. "And that's why we want to keep him." He bit the cap off his pen and for a moment let the cap remain in the corner of his mouth like a stogie.

Roberto blinked at his boss. He didn't understand.

Mr. Wallace leaned toward Roberto, a conspirator, and removed the cap from his mouth.

"You see, this job of yours is going nowhere," he whispered, then leaned back to wait for Roberto to size up the meaning. He waited longer than Mr.

Wallace expected, who was prompted to say, "You don't want to be like Gus, do you?"

"What do you mean?" Roberto asked.

"I mean you have a future!" Mr. Wallace brayed as he leaned back, his hands now behind his head like a holdup victim.

I have a future? Roberto wondered. He had dropped out of Fremont High School when a classmate tried to crack a chair over his head, an act of violence precipitated by Roberto's refusal to share his answers during a history test that he failed miserably. After a series of jobs cutting lawns and hauling debris, he lucked into a job at a foundry in Oakland. First he pushed a time-whittled broom from one end of the factory to the other, and soon he was taught to operate a lathe. He would have kept on shaving metal rods into surgical tools thin as chopsticks except one afternoon at the lathe, a curl of metal shaving leaped into his mouth, the carpet of his tongue gargling the still-heated object. He remembered the struggle to cough up the shaving, his head bowed and his hand squeezing the tube of his own throat. But the shaving simply wiggled down his throat, momentarily lodging in his esophagus before settling in his stomach—all while the lathe continued to throw out a confetti of metal shavings. He remembered moaning, "Oh, God!" and a fellow worker slapping him on the back and shouting over the noise of the machines, "Throw it up! Cough it up!" But he had swallowed the shaving. When the incident was reported, Roberto was let go. The foreman didn't want to risk keeping a machinist who couldn't keep his mouth closed while doing his job.

But that was years ago. While nothing happened to him internally—Roberto feared his stomach might blossom open from the razorlike shaving—his life seemed to hang in delicate balance between one paycheck and the next. Now Mr. Wallace was saying that he had a future, an impression he had held about himself all along.

"Listen," Mr. Wallace said, his hands and arms coming down from behind his head. He looked furtively about the cubicle before he confessed in a near hiss, "I'm getting out, too." He divulged this news while gazing at his family of snapshots, teeth bared, though some might call it a smile. He then really smiled. "Roberto, get out while you're young! We'll pay you for a month, plus here's this packet of money as a gift of appreciation." His eyes cut to his desk drawer. With his teeth bared, he said with a chuckle, "You like money, don't you?"

That's how Roberto came to leave his job at the Walnut Bank.

Even before the prompting from Mr. Wallace, Roberto had thought of quitting. He couldn't imagine spending another year, let alone his life, up against the wall, his punishment for not cooperating with that thug in history class. He signed the forms. He shook Mr. Wallace's hand. The grip was nearly pressureless because, at heart, Mr. Wallace didn't care one way or another if Roberto dropped off the face of the earth.

Roberto spent the remainder of the day nearly prancing in front of the bank. He threw himself onto the comfort of the bench. He taunted Gus, a serious and loyal employee, one who raised the set of flags each day and more than once permitted tears to flood his eyes. For this really old fellow, the whip of flags was a solemn sight. Plus he took pride in protecting other people's money.

meager savings and a few odd jobs. These jobs let loose a reservoir of sweat he didn't know was inside him. As a security guard, he had used up his legs and part of his brain from boredom. But crawling on a pitched roof that summer and raising a hammer for eight hours, he discovered the horrors of real work. He hadn't known the body could take such punishment.

By late summer Roberto had to vacate his one-bedroom apartment after the electricity was cut off and the landlord began to bang on the front door as well as the back, shouting for him to get the hell out, that he wasn't playing anymore, that his brother-in-law was a cop who enjoyed breaking heads for sport. Roberto was poorer than the ants that marched darkly across the kitchen sink.

"I messed up," he confessed to his hands, which lay on the dining table like gavels in judgment of his unwise career move. If they had minds of their own, the hands would have clutched Roberto's throat and strangled him.

Roberto wiped his eyes. It was late afternoon, and darkness was coming into the unlit dining room where he sat. He felt more worthless than those straight ahead, no-bullshit ants, which at least knew their purpose. They could bed down in the ground while he, a man with a stone in each shoe, had to hike down a long road.

Roberto cursed his luck and scolded himself for believing Mr. Wallace's cheery talk about a future. In Mr. Wallace's world, destiny really existed. Early in their sabbatical from forty-hour work weeks, he and Manny had talked about applying at Circuit City, an electronics store, both convinced that all that was required—aside from a clean criminal record—was a coat and tie. They hadn't figured on needing a high school diploma.

Having no job was one dilemma; finding a place to house his troubles was another. Roberto stayed at a friend's house for a few weeks during the summer but was asked to leave at the beginning of autumn. He lived with another friend for a week and then moved into a car whose engine just stopped while he was hauling cans to the recycler. Friendless, Roberto resorted to making a home of an abandoned Quonset hut in the middle of a vacant lot not far from a shopping mall. He moved there with his clothes, a few sticks of furniture, an ice chest, and a treasury of records from the 1970s—Santana, War, the Bee Gees, the Supremes, Grand Funk Railroad, Fleetwood Mac—timeless music that would outlast plutonium, it was so good.

He swatted a broom at the wooden floor, rounding up a cloud of dust that he prompted into a far corner, where the floorboards themselves were pinched nearly to dust by termites. With a swooping motion he wiped the hut's one window with an ancient newspaper and then sat down to consider its headlines. One headline said THE CHALLENGER EXPLODES![5] The astronauts were reduced to a human grit endlessly orbiting the earth. He sighed at this tragic news. And while he didn't wish to show those lost souls disrespect, he used the newspaper to close a hole in the wall where the wind whistled.

The third day he woke to the finger tap of rain on the metal roof. For a moment, confused, he thought he was bedded down inside a snare drum, the way the rain clanged. He dragged his hands down his face like a washcloth, his first cleaning for the day. He yawned, stretched until a bone in his

---

5. In 1986, the U.S. space shuttle *Challenger* broke apart about a minute after takeoff; its seven crew members were killed by the explosion.

back clicked, and sucked on a back molar pasted with crackers, a late snack from the night before. Roberto hadn't spoken to anyone in two days, and he opened and closed his mouth, for he had to keep those body parts of his working. He swabbed his mouth with his tongue in readiness for his first words of the day. He sighed and said, "Oh, God."

He stood up, sat back down, and glanced wearily at the cover of Santana's first album, a pen-and-ink drawing of a lion. Any other day, Roberto had surmised that the kingly beast was roaring, but now the lion appeared to be yawning. At him.

He slipped into his shoes, curled from rain and age, and walked in a circle, his one way of stoking a fire inside what a religious brother on the street called his God-given temple. A fire was what he needed—that and a cup of coffee laced with cream and perhaps a glazed doughnut or two would make things all right. He actually pursed his lips, the bud of his mouth deepening with lines.

"Oh, God, I need coffee," he said desperately.

Instead he drank water from a red-plaid-printed thermos and paced back and forth, admonishing himself because he could have done the same thing in front of the Walnut Bank and gotten paid for his time. But here on the edge of nowhere, he just raised a faint stink of dust as he toured the meager confines of his new lodgings. He found a pile of newspapers but was frightened to rifle through them, for the headlines might be even more unsavory than the *Challenger*'s explosion.

The window was rain beaded and foggy. He wiped the glass for a better view. He could stride in the direction of the new mall or chance the old commercial area of Fruitvale. It was a matter of a toss of a coin, nothing more.

Breakfast was a few moist crackers and a single tangerine. He risked stepping outside for his personal business behind a wind-whipped oleander and trotted briskly back into the Quonset, shuddering from the cold. He put on an extra sweater and scanned his home of two days, then left the hut, using a piece of cardboard as an umbrella. He trudged through the vacant lot, mud sucking his shoes, and headed toward East 14th and Fruitvale Avenue, the crossroads for Chinese, Vietnamese, and Latino immigrants. He knew life thrived among its bustle of merchants and shoppers but was clueless what to do once he got there. Still, he trusted that if he just mingled with others, shoulder to shoulder, his grin to theirs, his outlook would improve. If nothing else, he could pick up body heat from these people.

Lately he had begun to count his steps, one to a hundred and over again, an obsession that dried his lips from the repetition of numbers. But this morning when he found himself chattering numbers, his mind an adding machine gone haywire, he scolded himself to be quiet. He forced himself to turn his mind somewhere else. His vision fell on a faraway street where he noticed a car stalled in the intersection. Two men—worker ants—were pushing the vehicle to the side of the road.

"I wish I had a car," he said absently. He looked down at his shoes, two rodents moving through weeds and mud. "And a new pair of shoes."

He found his mind short circuiting, whirling with ideas and silly notions, images that, if held up to the world, would make little sense. He blamed his hunger, his lack of sleep, the high school thug who had nearly whacked him with that chair, and finally his years as a security guard, where his brain sought desperately for sustenance. His mind, he judged harshly, had become a large bowl of shapeless mush. And this mush inside his head demanded stirring. He promised himself that he would start reading books.

The rain stopped, and suddenly the sun broke through the clouds above the former Sears building, long abandoned. The jagged edges of its industrial-sized windows were lit with this new sunshine. The sun broke expansively in the east, bringing joy to Roberto that quickened his steps. He threw down his makeshift umbrella and leaped over a puddle, feeling that he was headed toward something good.

Walking among people further deepened his sense of joy. Some were herding children to school, and others were limping toward La Clinica de la Raza, a hospital. Others blew on plastic foam cups of coffee while they waited for the bus. He crossed the street at East 14th and halted in front of Alfredo's, a mom-and-pop market that took no chances—it sold both Mexican and Asian food, plus a few club-shaped ham hocks for its black clientele. Raindrops leaked from the striped cloth awning over the storefront, one striking Roberto's knuckle, the sign of a blessing. He opened up his palms and gathered additional drops to wash his face.

The produce was set out in bins on the street. The shoppers pinched high-priced tomatoes and pears, held up paddles of nopales, peeked under the skirts of lettuce, and quizzed the mangoes with the press of their thumbs. While he didn't have a coin to speak of, he felt obligated to assess the produce. What harm would result? He sniffed a lemon, an acidic scent that was a meal itself, and inquired of a Salvadoran woman, over whom he towered like a banana tree, "The prices are going up, no?"

The woman was unresponsive to his friendly overture. Instead she continued to bag the lemons quickly, her hands the flittering hands of a factory worker moving without thought.

His stomach grumbled, and something seemed to fall off the inside of his ribs—the last of the taco he ate yesterday? The noisy stomach continued groaning for the food that was within reach; all Roberto had to do was pick up an apple and bring it to his mouth. I'm no thief, he thought, and scolded his stomach for tempting him to crime.

His attention returned to the short woman, now toying with peanuts. He suspected that she was ignoring him because she thought he was a street person without a single coin in his pocket. He tried again to establish a rapport with the woman because he understood from her, as well as others, that he was a mere apparition with no more substance than the glare on a windshield. "I said the prices are going up because of the frost." She raised her face—and said, "No speak English."

To this, Roberto, his spirit once again revived, remarked in Spanish that weren't the lemons a bargain and, hey, the jicama was overpriced but what a crunchy taste! The woman smiled the ruins of her teeth, which were trimmed in gold, cracked, and blue with shadows. Any other day, Roberto would have been shaken by this display, but today he was encouraged. If this woman could smile through the wreckage of her mouth, then there was hope.

He sniffed the produce, one piece at a time, and left when Alfredo, the owner, came out, wiping his hands on a red apron. Roberto didn't want to risk his relationship with this woman or Alfredo or the colorful flood of fruits and vegetables.

He walked three blocks to Sanborn Park, where he sat in the wickery shadows of a sycamore stripped of leaves. He rested his feet, but not for long. From across the lawn, a needle-thin junkie approached, twirling on a finger a sombrero gaffed from the wall of a Mexican restaurant.

"I got this hat here, my man," the junkie in bedroom slippers announced. "And I ain't asking much."

Roberto proceeded toward the library but saw that it was closed, though a light burned behind half-open blinds. He felt small in front of this ivy-shrouded building, small, suddenly weak, and almost delirious. He had a vision of the walls of the library opening and the books pouring out onto the street. He rubbed his eyes. He rubbed them until a light sparked behind their lids and a terror leaped upon him: he envisioned an avalanche of books smothering him with words and pure learning, dictionaries and encyclopedias belting him for his own good. He raised his hands as if in protection and let out a cry. He grimaced and sensed a burning in his stomach. The curl of metal shaving, rusted as a fishhook, about to surface after all these years? His face grayed to the color of river rock, and the latches of his knees buckled.

Two women approaching from the other direction gave him room on the sidewalk. They feared that he was drunk or, worse, another crazy on display. But within minutes, the pain in his stomach receded like the tide. He adjusted his coat, and in its improved fit, he felt a lot better.

The sun was now sucking up puddles and the river coursing along twig-dammed gutters. The wind moved the litter along, and the people at the bus stop were gone. His happiness was all too brief. He meandered down Fruitvale and onto Foothill, a street that, except for the occasional upheaval of cracked sidewalks, was perfectly flat. He was baffled how a street could be called Foothill when there was no hill to speak of. Where were the fruits, too, as in Fruitvale? His mind speculated about a past when village life had the kindly locals eating right off the trees. Aeons ago, these locals wished for nothing more than what they could fit in their mouths.

He was prepared to return to Sanborn Park, where he could marshal these thoughts on a park bench, when his gaze made a roving turn. He spotted some Christmas trees on the side of a closed-up thrift shop. He paused and regarded this mysterious find, his hand massaging his stubbled chin. What are they doing there? he wondered. He walked past the thrift shop, stopped, and returned, his shoe kicking a pebble, for a second peek. They're abandoned, he surmised. Or why else would they be there?

Roberto scanned his surroundings, sizing up the feeble artistry of poor businesses and shabby houses dressing themselves for Christmas. Some storefronts were brightly lit with a lasso of Christmas tree lights, their windows white with the buildup of fake frost. Red bows hung in a black beauty parlor, and painted on the windows of one liquor store, a roly-poly snowman was tipping back a cold beer. On a distant roof, Santa and his sleigh were blown over but still pulsating a string of festive lights.

"It's my lucky day," he said to himself, and shuddered.

He approached the Christmas trees, glancing left and right, conscious of the gravel under his feet, and sidled up to them. He stood next to them, hands wrist deep in his pockets, and did his best to whistle. His whistling didn't last more than three seconds before the melody died, and he had to breathe deeply to get the song cooking again. He then faced the trees. If the trees had had hands, he would have shaken them. Instead he touched their limbs, his fondling hand exciting a scent of pine. He mustered up a scheme to peddle these three trees, each one shorter than the next, this family of trees, all orphans, two brothers and one sister. Yes, they're orphans, he agreed with himself, trees looking for cozy homes.

He hustled the two largest away, rushing wildly down Foothill while the rain-tipped branches slapped and scratched his cheek. He felt like a kidnapper, devious. He cut across Foothill onto 23rd Avenue and finally Ford Avenue, a cul-de-sac with older but tidy homes. The trees were heavy to carry without accidentally snapping a lower branch against the kick of his running knees. This took strength, and he had almost none. His breath flowered before him.

"I'm going to find you dudes a home," he said to the trees. "Then I'm going back and get your sister a place to stay."

He was convinced that he hadn't really stolen the trees but rescued them from oblivion. Time would whittle them to twigs and scattered needles, but before their earthly lives ended, he contended, wouldn't it be beautiful to be dressed up with bulbs and lights, Santas and candy canes, icing and popcorn needled on kite string? He cooed sweet words to the trees and, sufficiently rested, raised them up and continued. He walked halfway down the street, a dog bark prompting more than one curtain to part.

He halted to debate which house to try first. He ran a hand down his sweaty face, salted from his enterprising work. He caught his breath and climbed the steps of a house that appeared naked and in need of the Christmas spirit. He knocked lightly, then with gusto when no one answered.

A voice boomed like a gunshot, "Go away, fool!" and he didn't have to be asked twice and couldn't disagree with the man's appraisal of his scheme. To the hightailing Roberto, the voice belonged to someone at least eight feet tall with the girth of an ancient redwood. His next attempt was a neighboring house with tall black stairs. He knocked and the door opened immediately, albeit not wide. Behind the shadow of the screen door stood an elderly woman, small as a child. She was wearing a sweater and a housecoat and below those articles of clothing an apron with tidy creases.

She examined Roberto, who began his sales pitch brightly. "I got trees." He then remembered the line from the junkie with the sombrero. "And I ain't asking much."

She opened the door wider, a pot roast scent rushing the porch. Roberto's nose flared. His eyes widened and saliva bathed the buds of his tongue. He swallowed. This smell kicked Roberto's stomach into another painful mood swing.

"My husband died," the woman stated calmly. She unlatched the screen door and came out on the porch. "My children can go to hell. I never see them. Why do I need a tree?"

Roberto stepped back to give her room, swinging the trees away from her as he waltzed them against the porch rail. He was unsure what to make of the dead father and the children. He didn't know where to take his sales pitch. So he observed, "Everyone has a tree. Rich families often have two."

"The rich can go to hell. My children are rich, and do I see them?" The woman made this remark without an outburst or a gesture of flung-up-in-the-air hands. Her voice was flat. Her eyes were blue, their clearness suggesting more a child just learning her colors than someone who was at least seventy. And her face was like her apron, neatly creased.

"Ma'am, I need to sell these."

She measured Roberto's despair, her gaze first stopping at his shoes and then settling on his dirty knees. She didn't need to go higher.

"How about twelve dollars?" he asked.

She blinked at Roberto.

"They're special trees," Roberto tried. He remembered Manny drunk on the telephone. "They're Grandma Moses trees. You ever hear of that kind? They grow them in Portugal but also some here. In mountains we never heard of." He licked his lips, worried that he had done a half-assed job of describing the genus of the tree. When he started to add a historical touch by saying that Grandma Moses trees were popular with Democratic presidents, she told him to be quiet and went back into the house. He was set to drag the trees down the steps when she came out of the house.

"Where are you going?" She waved a coin purse at him.

The elderly woman bought a tree and invited Roberto in to help her string it with lights and hang a five-pointed star on top. The limbs sagged under the red bulbs.

"Go outside and look," she asked.

He did what he was told; after all, she was his first customer. He climbed down the black steps, rubbed his hands in the cold, and looked at the house for two minutes. On his return, he chirped, "Beautiful! The bulbs make it stand out. You can't go wrong with a Grandma Moses tree."

He sold the tree for six dollars and went away with a ham-and-cheese sandwich, the meat hanging like tongues from the corners of the bread. He devoured the sandwich while he carried the other tree in his free hand. He next tried Myrtle Street, which was less tidy; in fact, as he walked farther into the neighborhood, he realized it was junky. He was spooked as he passed dogs behind chain-link fences and saw a youth standing on a porch, a cigarette half hidden behind his cupped hand.

"What you got there?" the teenager asked. He wore a knit cap and baggy pants that hung from his hips. Any lower and the cops might haul him for in indecent exposure.

"A tree." He averted his eyes from the teenager.

"Yeah, like duh, motherfucker," the teenager sneered. Smoke flowed from his nose and then was pulled back in, as though in his fierce nastiness he kept everything to himself.

"It's Christmas," Roberto said without missing a stride. The teenager took a bold step down the stairs. He let the smoke drift upward and real flames seemed to from flare his nose, flames from way down in the belly. The teenager continued to taunt Roberto, but Roberto didn't listen. He was going places.

The street was poor, but at the end of block he sold the tree to a woman named Peaches.

"That's a nice tree," she cried as she clapped her large and work-worn hands. Roberto could tell she meant it. He felt blessed to have such an enthusiastic customer.

Her husband was blind. Still, with his suspenders down and his slippers nearly off alligator-long feet, he followed Roberto and Peaches as they scavenged a closet in the hallway for the Christmas ornaments—four crosses of Jesus and some lights, alongside Bibles, broken candles, and hymnals almost as ancient as the Dead Sea Scrolls.[6] The husband trailed them into the kitchen, where Peaches searched for replacements for the burned-out lights. He caught up with them when they returned to the overheated living room. His eyelids fluttered, and his mouth muttered something that might have been a prayer because he uttered the word, "Amen."

The husband hummed as the two fashioned a beautiful Christmas tree. When they finished, he asked Roberto in stutters if the tree was pretty.

"You should see it," Roberto chimed. He guided the old man's hand over the limbs as together they touched the bulbs, one by one, and on tiptoes a star shiny as a new spoon.

"Amen, I can see it!" the husband said, and Roberto caught himself saying amen for selling the tree for four dollars, mostly in change.

When he had left and crossed the street, Roberto broke into a jog. His pant pockets jingled like tambourines, the quarters slapping in time to his stride. They jingled the music of a man making a comeback in life.

Roberto fetched the little sister tree from the closed-up thrift shop and made a pilgrimage to Alfredo's market. He bought fruit, bottled water, and two hog-sized burritos, which he took back to his Quonset hut. It was nearly dark, and the sky was boiling with a new front of rain clouds. The threat of rain made people retreat into their homes, including Roberto.

He stood the tree in the corner and stripped off his two sweaters, then put one back on when his body began to cool from the long walk home.

"Your brothers got nice, cozy homes," Roberto informed the tree. "And you're going to have one too. A warm place for the holiday."

He ate his burritos and drank the water while remembering a previous Christmas when he was a boy in Texas. His aunt Virginia, snake mean, had prodded him and his cousins to visit Santa Claus at a department store. That's where her ex, Uncle Peter, worked as Santa, ho-hoing to the children. They were all brown skinned in that border town, where the sun had stained them the color of walnuts. Uncle Peter was five months behind on his alimony plus child support, though he had been seen driving one of the first air-conditioned cars in town. His aunt forced young Roberto, a sparrow of a child, to climb into Santa's lap on a Saturday morning when he should have been home watching cartoons. Roberto had just sat there, two fingers in mouth, scared not because it was his first visit with Santa, but because of what his aunt had told him to say. He recalled how Santa—Uncle Pete behind that beard—asked if he had been a good boy. He nodded and sucked harder on his fingers. When Santa pulled them out, Roberto shook his head and shoved back them back in like candies with their own natural sugar. When Santa asked what he would like for Christmas, he took his wet fingers out of his mouth and pointed to his aunt hiding near the Christmas tree. In a baby voice, he said, "Auntie says give her the money." He recalled how he was bumped from Santa's lap and Auntie jumped on her ex, pulling off his beard and scratching his face, tough as a leather baseball mitt, which was

6. Nearly a thousand manuscripts found on the northwest shore of the Dead Sea, generally dating to 150 BC–AD 70 and including texts from the Hebrew Bible.

painted pink instead of its normal brown. While the two fought, Roberto reached under a chair for Santa's candies, a fistful, which his aunt let him keep because she was so proud of him. The department store ruckus even made the newspaper—"Santa slapped by former Mrs. Santa." Roberto shuddered at the childhood memory and drank his water.

The dark bullied itself into his abode, and he lit two candles. He admired the tree, fresher than he could ever expect to be. He got up from his cot and sniffed the needles.

"You smell good, little sister," he said. He pulled a needle from a limb and fit it into his mouth. "And you taste good, too!"

A profitable idea, rainlike, tapped him on the forehead. He could cut the tree down, strip its long and short limbs, and twist and bend them into wreaths, perhaps even brightened with ribbons and shiny things. His enterprising future stretched ahead. He took off his sweater, for his ambition produced an unnatural heat.

He took a knife, sawed through a lower limb, and bent it bow shaped. It sprang back like a car antenna. He took the knife up again and practiced on another limb. Some of the needles rained to the floor, but most survived, seemingly dedicated to his design. He cut another limb and then wove the three limbs into a halo-shaped wreath. With the limbs struggling to break apart, to snap back into their natural shape, he tied the entire prototype with wire. The limbs behaved and were newly transformed.

"You're looking nice," he cooed. He recalled how as a boy in Texas he had glued Popsicle sticks to a toilet roll in an effort to make a pencil holder. But the glue couldn't stand up to the summer heat and the Popsicle sticks came off; he ended up just trumpeting nonsense through the toilet roll until his mother told him to knock it off. Many years later, however, he was proving himself an artisan. There was definitely no heat in the Quonset hut to ruin his industry.

He hung the wreath on a nail on the wall and stepped back to admire his creation. It was good enough to adorn a door or a window or possibly the front of a car—he had seen a Volvo just a few days before with a wreath wired to the grille.

He twisted two wreaths and stripped off the small remaining limbs that would not bend. He had a use for them, too. He glowed over his handiwork, though he was saddened at the sight of what remained: a long torso of the Christmas tree nailed to a cross-shaped stand. It looked naked, nearly scandalous.

"Looks like you ain't going to get a home." His voice grieved for the sister tree.

It was scarcely light when Roberto woke to hear a pigeon walking across the metal roof, a grating sound that worked on his nerves. He read an old newspaper until it was time for the stores to open. He ventured forth with his three wreaths hooked on his right arm and a few of the short limbs in the crook of his left arm. On East 14th, he made his way to a variety store that he had spotted a week before. Like Alfredo's, the store sported a striped awning. But unlike Alfredo's, the place was empty of customers, a single bulb announcing to the public that the shop was open. A tiny bell chimed on the doorknob when Roberto pushed open the door, which stuck from the cold weather. He entered after wiping his shoes on a straw mat, for they had picked up enough mud to grow tomatoes. He scanned the hodgepodge of goods in the store. There were galvanized buckets and dread-locked mops, buttons and pins, chrome toasters and heating pads, aprons with forty-eight states—stuff that had more chance of moving from an earthquake tremor than actual customers. Time and commerce had stopped, and Roberto was persuaded that he was in the right place. He could get a good deal.

"You got any ribbon?" Roberto called as he advanced toward the owner, whose eyes were large, luminous, and wet. He was seated behind a glass counter filled with packets of cheap screwdrivers and questionable batteries.

The owner, unfolding his hands, asked, "What for?"

Roberto was baffled by the question, but he remained committed to his simple cause. "I'm selling these wreaths."

The man's attention fell to the wreaths on Roberto's arm before he asked, "What color?"

"Christmas color," Roberto sang, now getting somewhere. "Red. A spool of red."

The owner disappeared behind a curtain door and reported back with a single spool. He held it up like a chalice.

"But that's pink," Roberto argued.

"Red." The owner showed him the end of the spool, which was printed with Red. Made in America.

Roberto was certain that the spool of ribbon had been there since the variety store opened. He took the spool and examined it.

"It's faded," Roberto pointed out at last. This was the best he could argue.

"But it's still red," the owner mumbled, his mouth barely moving.

Roberto pinched his nose. He could see there was no arguing with this man, who hadn't caught up with the sixties, let alone the nineties. "So how much?"

"Two dollars for the spool."

Roberto rocked on his heels.

"But it's faded! You can see that, can't you?"

"It's still red. You stand by the wall over there and you'll think it's red." The owner's hand shooed him away. "Go stand over there and see."

Roberto was tempted to follow the owner's instruction, but he stood his ground, pondering the price of the spool. In fact, both men were pondering the spool when a drop of what appeared to be water fell on the glass counter. Roberto winced at the drop, then raised his gaze toward the ceiling. His stare was so high, his mouth fell open. He leveled his aim on the owner, who appeared older than Roberto had first suspected—age spots overwhelmed his hands and face, and his chest had collapsed. The drop had fallen from one of the old man's eyes, and his sadness swayed Roberto. Two dollars didn't seem like too much for a spool of faded ribbon.

He paid and left with the roll of pinkish ribbon. On the street he unraveled a portion and was happy to discover that the ribbon was redder inside. He chewed off a length of pale ribbon and spit it in the air.

On a bench at Sanborn Park he wove the ribbon among the branches of the first wreath. His work was clumsy, and he had to strip the ribbon from the wreath and start over. However, his perseverance paid off, and soon all three wreaths were dressed up. He next tied ribbon around the short sticks with the intention of selling them as "ornaments."

"You guys are looking good," he piped to the wreaths and Christmas ornaments propped up on the bench. He stepped back to admire his inspired production.

It was then the junkie with the sombrero materialized. This time, instead of slippers, he was plodding along sockless in brown shoes too big for his feet. His appearance was as disheveled as the day before, except he was more fully dressed.

"Hey, hombre, I'm selling this hat your kind of people like," the junkie said, then halted. "Hey, man, how come you got strings on those sticks? What you into?"

"They're ornaments," Roberto said.

"What you mean?"

Roberto gathered up the wreaths and ornaments in his arms, reluctantly explaining that Christmas wreaths were popular, and bounded away with the junkie begging to trade the sombrero for one of the wreaths.

"It'll look good on you, homeboy," the junkie claimed. He demonstrated by putting it on his own head. With the brim down near his eyes, his face was thrown into shadow.

But Roberto broke into a run and outran this lowlife sidekick, jogging to keep up, the sombrero jumping on his head.

Convinced that he had to get out of the barrio to the richer areas to sell the wreaths, he took a bus to Piedmont,[7] where white people and Koreans lived in stately homes as tall and possibly as old as clipper ships. He got off at Grand Avenue and Holly, but not before he sold one of his ornaments for fifty cents to a woman walking with a cane. It'll look nice in your lapel, he told her. He poked the ornament into her buttonhole and crowed how pretty it looked against the backdrop of her red face. He sniffed the foresty scent of pine needles. "Smells good, too. Save you on perfume." He sold it while the bus driver had his eyes lifted to the mirror, watching Roberto's every move. The eyes were bloodshot, but stern. He was the sort of large man who ate his sandwiches in two bites.

Roberto was excited by the two quarters joining the loose change in his pocket. Walking briskly, he could hear his success in the form of jingling money. He slapped his thigh and the money rang out like thunder.

He walked three blocks, smiling, but stopped his giddiness when a Piedmont police cruiser slowed to a crawl. The cruiser braked, its taillights glowing, sinister. Roberto was aware that the cop was sizing him up. Roberto's mouth went dry from fear. He and Manny had once been pushed around by these police, who had caught them peeing in a bush. They had pointed out that the bush was nearly dead, but that didn't stop the single cop with no witnesses from throwing them into the back of the cruiser. First he bounced their heads off the hood. He complained that the hood was now dented and drove what he called their "sorry asses" out of the city limits. Piedmont was rich, and Roberto knew it was not to be played with.

He kept a nonchalant pace, and at last the cruiser drove away, trailing blue smoke.

"Shit," Roberto said under his breath. He heeded the cop's silent warning and kept walking.

---

7. Affluent city surrounded by Oakland.

He reached Magnolia Park, where he gathered small pinecones while sparrows hopped about his feet in search of fodder to keep them going through winter. He pocketed six cones. Shivering from the dewy rain falling from the tree, he hurried to a wooden bench the length of a coffin. There he tied a few of the cones onto the wreaths, happy with his floral touch. He gathered acorns under another tree. He pocketed a few and quarreled with a squirrel, well padded with fat and with a tail as tall as a bush.

"You can't have everything," he yelled at the squirrel. "Greedy *ratón.*"[8]

He couldn't tie the acorns to the ornaments, so he decided to offer them as bonuses with each sale. He departed, leaving the squirrel still chattering.

The climb to the richer homes of Piedmont was steep. His legs burned, his nose ran in the cold, and his breathing became shallow. The sky was gray as flint and looked ready to rain ice as sharp as flint. He was convinced that rich people dwelt in the hills because poor people couldn't climb there without either hurting themselves or using up so much energy that they just turned around in defeat.

He paused in front of a two-story colonial with a fat wreath in each of six leaded windows. He judged the wreaths hooked on his arms. They seemed like stuff raked from a gutter, and his confidence lost some of its air, an inner tube with a pinprick.

"Forget this house." He would have patted his wreaths to console them, except he feared that they might cough up a portion of their needles. They needed to remain full-bodied when he sold them, that or so pathetically naked that people would just throw him coins for trying. He had continued his excursion down the street when, by chance, a Volvo pulled into a driveway. He halted with his heart beating fast. It was now or never to parlay his crafts into bills and coins. He approached the man who was getting out of the Volvo. He was in his midthirties, quick to smile, and dressed in khakis and a windbreaker with leather moccasins. His hair was sandy, just starting to go gray. A second person got out of the Volvo; it was his son, a shock of very blond hair showing under his baseball cap.

"Sir," Roberto called.

The man stopped, a bag of groceries in his arms. He waited for Roberto to add to his one-word revelry.

"I think a wreath on your nice car there would . . ." he started before his mouth stalled. His mind searched for a word, something as elegant as this neighborhood, something educated and appropriate. "Would . . . knock 'em dead." Immediately Roberto could have eaten one of the wreaths. His sales pitch had come out all wrong.

The man swung his groceries from one arm to the other, a sort of exercise, Roberto supposed, to build up his appetite for the goodies the bag held. Surely this man had to burn some calories.

"Let me see," the man requested.

By then the boy was next to Roberto, tiptoeing and eyeing the wreaths.

"How come he's selling sticks?" the boy asked. His eyes floated to his father's for an answer.

The father chuckled as his free arm snaked around his son's shoulders. His smirk burned up a few more calories.

8. Mouse.

"Those are ornaments," Roberto corrected the boy. His face flushed at the accurate description. He knew the boy, neither vicious nor snide, was calling them as he saw them.

The three eyeballed the selections until Roberto, suddenly brave beyond his own imagination, took the best one of the bunch and pressed it against the grill of the Volvo. A gust of engine heat warmed up his frosty mitts. Roberto was elated. If he didn't sell one, at least he might bring the circulation back into his hands.

"How does it look?"

The man smiled but didn't let his teeth show. He rummaged through his pocket, and for a minute Roberto thought he was looking for his wallet. Instead he brought out keys in a leather pouch that matched his leather moccasins. He triggered the car alarm, which sounded with a two-syllable chirp, and opened the door of his car for a package he had forgotten.

"Jason, go on," the father instructed, handing him the keys.

"Aw, come on, Dad," the boy cried. "Buy one."

"It's in style," Roberto said. He realized the depth of his mistake. No one in this neck of the rich woods followed the likes of Roberto. They led, and others followed lamely along, provided that they had the money or credit cards.

"Come on," the boy yammered again. "Mom'll like it!"

The father pulled down the bill of his son's cap.

So one was sold for six dollars, and Roberto wired it to the grill of the Volvo while the man disappeared to put away his groceries. By the time he returned, Roberto was done. His mitts were now heated up.

The boy watched, bent over, hands on his knees.

"You made these, huh?" the boy asked.

"Yeah, how'd you know?"

"They don't look new."

Roberto thought the kid was a wiseass but had to admit that he was describing the wreath to a T. He liked the kid, who didn't back away from whatever made Roberto stink.

The father returned.

"So what do you think?" Roberto asked.

The dad offered a glance, nothing more. He paid with eight quarters and four one-dollar bills warm from his wallet. Roberto assumed that this Piedmont father nested on his butt all day, a rooster on a money egg. He assumed that he wouldn't want a free ornament or a bonus acorn. He had bought the wreath for his son, not for the beauty of Roberto's handiwork.

Roberto thanked the man, turned to go, then shuffled back and repeated his thanks with a "Merry Christmas." He was out of there within seconds, fearing that the father might cancel the whole order because the wreath was slightly off center and the needles were beginning to drop, drying on the prickly stem.

On the next block he wound his way up a curving flagstone walk. From the picture window, a grandfatherly man with a rolled newspaper in his hands snarled at him. Wrong house. He did an about-face and couldn't hurry down the path fast enough.

But at one brick house he was accepted with open arms when an elderly woman greeted him before he even knocked. She clapped at his presence and immediately beamed at the two wreaths on his arms and the bushel of ornaments.

"Ma'am," Roberto started.

"I know why you're here!" she sang. "It's Christmas!"

He was beckoned into the foyer of her large house but didn't dare take a step on the white carpet. The curtains were white and frilly, and the lamps on the maple end tables glowed without even being on.

"Come here," the woman called from the dining room.

"No, ma'am," Roberto said. "My shoes are dirty."

The woman considered them.

"You're a nice boy."

Her smile is too wide for an old lady, Roberto thought, and noticed that the buttons of her sweater were in the wrong holes. He also noticed that no one else was home, the refrigerator in the kitchen eating up most of the silence. Then an aged poodle, sporting a sweater, appeared. Its teeth were crooked and an oil-dark sludge leaked from its eyes. Roberto could tell the poodle, stuck-up little beast, didn't like him. Still, he chirped, "Hey, boy! Hey, girl!"

"That's Francis," the woman said as an introduction. "Come on over here."

He wasn't sure if the woman was talking to him or the dog. Neither moved. Then the dog turned, seemingly disgusted with the visitor. Roberto observed that the pucker of its asshole was dusted with talcum powder. The dog, Roberto knew, had smelled something primordial in the folds of his dirty clothes.

The woman repeated a third time, "Come over here."

Roberto grew scared. A transient such as he was didn't belong in an old woman's house. Nevertheless, he stepped out of his shoes when she insisted that he hang the wreaths in the dining room. A swamp smell hovered around his nose when he wiggled his toes. He hadn't bathed in a week, and with all his walking in rain and mud, the smell would have scared away a den of rats.

"*Chingado*,"[9] he muttered. To the woman, who had returned to clapping with excitement because she was going to see a wreath in her home, he called, "Ma'am, I got to go!"

But she pulled him into the dining room and forced him to prop the wreath on a cabinet with a glass front holding a treasure of wineglasses, pink-tinted champagne flutes, and Royal Copenhagen china. She forced him to rummage through a drawer for a hammer and nails. She forced him to raise that hammer and spike that nail into a wall. He hung his last wreath, which had now begun to rain a sizable portion of its needles. And finally she forced him to stand his ornaments in a vase of water. The vase was cut crystal, heavy.

"These are dead sticks, ma'am," Roberto argued. "They don't belong in water!"

In the vase, the ribbons were bleeding their pinkish dye.

"Robin, they're beautiful."

"No, my name is Roberto," he corrected. Immediately he realized the folly of giving his name away. Maybe she didn't hear, he thought, and hooking a thumb at himself, said, "Yeah, my name is Robin."

"That's my daughter's name. She's coming home soon. You want pea soup?" Again her smile was too wide and her clapping too loud.

9. Fuck.

Roberto knew there was something wrong with the elderly woman. Maybe she was demented or on the bottle. He would have liked a swig from whatever she was drinking, for his despair was deep as a river. He was scared, his bowels grumbling and suddenly loosening a fart that was forceful and not worth hiding. If he had been standing near the front window, the curtains would have moved.

"Excuse me. I didn't hear that," she said.

"My stomach, ma'am." He stepped back when he admitted his moment of disgrace. He could have taken the hammer and struck himself on the head to end his troubles. From the look of things, something was going to happen that would sink him to the bottom of the murky river. And no sooner did he think this than a car pulled up the driveway with the knocking noise of a diesel.

The woman paused, nose twitching, and inquired, "Do you smell something?"

"Ma'am, I got to leave." He wanted to snatch the wreaths from their places, but he controlled himself. It was not a time to hog his creations.

"Why? Have some soup with Robin."

There was no time for questions and answers, no time to pry a few dollars from this woman. Roberto was already at the front door, slipping into his shoes. As he worked them frantically onto his feet, the soles smudged the carpet black. He struggled to open the front door and scampered down the tall steps, just ahead of the woman. He saw from the corner of his eye the other woman closing the trunk of her Mercedes.

Shoes unlaced, he was down the steps and not looking back. As he raced to get away, coins jumped from his pocket. He stopped to pick up a quarter but saw the daughter—Robin was her name?—watching him. Mouth open, her face had a baffled look.

"Shit," he hissed.

He trotted two blocks, spilling coins that paved the already rich streets with more money. With his lungs speared from exhaustion, he slowed to a stop. One of his shoelaces was gone, torn off by the speed of his fleeing. He sat on a curb but stood up when a dog barked behind an ornate gate. Like Francis the poodle, this one also sported a sweater.

Roberto glimpsed over his shoulder a house whose lawn and flower beds were spiked with ADT security signs. Someone with a cellular phone was standing in the window.

"Nah, man, don't call the police," Roberto whined.

He strolled away, sweat bathing his face, and turned on Magnolia Street near the park in time to see a car approaching down the tree-lined street. At first he assumed the car had only one headlight centered in the middle of its grille. The car accelerated smoothly through the scattering leaves, its one eye growing bigger. But on closer scrutiny Roberto jumped, his fear shaking out more coins from his pockets. It was the Volvo with the wreath, and the wreath was on fire from the heat of the engine. The fire was eating at the needles, the ribbon, the pinecone, and Roberto's dream to make something of himself.

The smiling father tooted the horn, and the boy, cap turned backward, waved. Apparently neither of them was aware that the front of the car was on fire.

"Shit," Roberto repeated a second time in less than five minutes. He was never really one to cuss, but there was no other word to elaborate his fear. He repeated it for good measure and hustled away but stopped almost immediately when he heard a prolonged skid. The Volvo, turned profile, was in the middle of the street. A hurricane-shape funnel of smoke was rising from the hood.

In the distance a police car wailed, no doubt summoned by the daughter of the elderly woman with his two wreaths and the smudge of his shoe-prints on a white carpet, evidence of a new scam going around like the flu. And the ruckus brought people out onto their porches, an unusual crisis in quiet Piedmont.

Roberto scurried away, losing an unlaced shoe as he banked around a corner. He stopped to gather the shoe but didn't stop to fit it onto his foot. He clopped along, a runaway mule from a circus. His circuitous route brought him to Magnolia Park, where he hid in the bushes. The sirens of the fire engines, now also getting into the action, howled. He lay in the bushes with his heart beating fast and sweat slowly cooling his poor and punished body.

He could hear the slow, leaf-crunching tires of a police cruiser making its rounds. He closed his eyes and saw only black behind his eyelids, nothing to dream about, until a light frisked the bushes and his eyes saw a bloodred color behind his eyelids. He realized that he was blood and bone and the cops wanted some, if not all, of it.

Twenty minutes passed before the cruiser left in a roar of exhaust. He rolled onto his belly under the bushes and, head lifted, crawled like an alligator from the growth of one bush to the next, determined to slither out of town if need be. He spotted two idling cruisers but kept crawling. He spotted the faraway lights of Oakland and could hear—was it possible? he wondered—a mariachi trumpet. Was it was playing taps for him or calling him home?

"How far do I crawl?" he asked himself. He patted his pockets. Most of the coins had fallen out. It took money to get into Piedmont, and ordinary people, like himself, had to leave it at the city limits. The rich intended to keep it all.

Thus, on his belly, Roberto made his way out of Piedmont.

Roberto stayed in his Quonset hut for two days, squabbling with the mice that had sniffed out his box of crackers. He risked only a brief departure to buy bottled water and a cheap takeout lunch of Chinese food. The sloshing rain erased his footsteps, and he was glad for the anonymity of his trekking. Still, in spite of his distance from Piedmont, he imagined his footprint exposed like an x ray on the white carpet, evidence to jail him for making poor wreaths. He could still see the Volvo on fire, though the rain if nothing else would certainly have extinguished it by now.

He had only been in trouble with the police twice: that time lashing the dead bush with his pee and once in Texas when he and a kid named Ralphie siphoned gas from the pumps. It was a Sunday. The gas station was closed, and while the pumps were locked, the hoses could be taken out of their cradles. So he and Ralphie emptied as much gas they could from those black, elephant-trunk hoses, each splashing a plentiful swallow of gas. There were six pumps, and altogether they nearly filled a gallon can. As they were

leaving, a dusty patrol car stopped the boys. The cop got out and scolded them furiously, mentioning some of Roberto's no-good family members and dwelling at length on Uncle Jorge. Roberto argued that the gas was just left over in the hoses and therefore free. The cop shouted, "Free, my ass!" Stubborn Roberto said he was going to tell his uncle Jorge, and the cop, furious at this threat, exploded more fiercely than the gas can. He collared Roberto and shook him like a tree. Still, a sobbing Roberto swore that he was going to tell his uncle. The cop pushed Roberto, who staggered backward and fell to the ground. He cried but stopped when the cop raised him to his feet, twisted Roberto's arm behind his back, and shoved him on his way. Roberto ran halfway down the block, turned, and shouted, "I'm going to tell Uncle Jorge. You cow shit!" But he couldn't tell his uncle until ten years later. At the time, Uncle Jorge was bedding in a prison in Arizona.

He shuddered at this memory. He next considered the remains of sister tree's poor naked trunk nailed to a wooden stand. Fiercely he yanked off the stand and swung the trunk down on his bed. He recalled reading of such therapy, of a patient beating an object until he was cured of what ailed his heart. He whipped his bed, but it just brought up a cloud of dust, which made him sneeze for a few minutes. He threw the tree trunk—little sister— aside and read a magazine.

Roberto was reading when the walls began to vibrate. A helicopter? Tanks and mud-splashed jeeps all because of one lousy wreath that burned a Volvo? The window darkened for a moment, then flashed back to a dull gray. He stepped outside, prepared to raise his dirt-peppered hands or drop to his weak knees, a position that he had assumed regularly since he returned from Piedmont—prayer was one way of repairing a poor soul. But hovering in the sky near the coliseum was the Goodyear blimp. The Raiders were playing that weekend.

On Monday, when the sky was clear except for a renegade cloud stalled near the old Sears building, Roberto walked over to the library, for he had promised himself to beef up his brain. His pace was languid until he passed Sanborn Park, where the junkie with the sombrero reigned. Roberto picked up speed, though from the corner of his eye he scrutinized the area and saw only pigeons, the hoodlums of all parks, gathered by the monkey bars, their breathing harking up into the air.

The library was warm and well lit, and the atmosphere was enlivened by the electrical juices of computers humming at the four terminals. It was a school day, so there were no kids, only a few mothers who rocked babies in their laps. Roberto noticed that one mother had a baby in her lap and beneath her clothes another in her belly. He acknowledged that Mexicans sure could make babies and happy and pretty ones to boot. This baby was singing, already a little mariachi.

The dictionaries were heavy as bricks and so thick that he was frightened by his puny vocabulary. At the table, he opened one to gaze at unfamiliar words that were like an altogether different language. He closed the dictionary and sat admiring the young woman reshelving books. He admired her because she was in her early twenties and intent on getting her job done. His imagination indulged his curiosity. He saw her as a college student with fairly good grades but not so smart as to scare away average-looking boys. He laughed then—to no one except the little freaky gentleman inside

his own head—and said, "Oops!" He laughed because if he had her job, he would have coordinated the placement of the books by color. The blue books would go over there by the wall, and the red ones would go near the bank of windows. He would put the yellows near the bathroom and the mixed bag of colors would be placed by the computers. Thus, shoulders jerking, he laughed at the stupidity of his organization. His mind was delirious and swimming in his own silly notion of librarianship. He slapped his hand over his mouth to stop his giddiness. To become more serious, he turned to the rack of newspapers. He placed in his lap the *Oakland Tribune*, the Sunday edition. The weight was like a blanket over his legs. He propped the newspaper there, studied the headlines until his eyes adjusted to the small print, and then threw the newspaper into the air. He stood up, crying, "Ahhhhhhh!"

The librarian had been watching Roberto ever since he first entered with his cargo of street smells. She beaded a stare on his skimpy figure when he began to chuckle without control—another loony from the street? She furrowed her face with lines, mouth puckered as though from stashing pins there while sewing. She strode toward him and snapped, "If you're going to be disruptive, you'll have to leave. Understand?"

He nodded. He couldn't leave at that very moment.

"I'll behave," he said weakly.

When she had wheeled around and departed, he picked up the newspaper from the floor. He snapped the newspaper, coughed, and started to read the local news. What brought him to scream was the photograph of James K. Wallace, banker. He was found dead in a river in Yuba County[1] with his pockets filled with twenty-dollar bills and some floating downstream. In Roberto's mind, the money was trying to get back to Oakland. The article said that he had apparently embezzled $39,000, possibly more, and had taken his life after a long-distance call to his wife. The photograph showed him wearing the same suit he had worn when, nine months earlier, he had confided in Roberto that he, too, was getting out. Roberto felt dizzy and his heart skipped. Roberto would never have translated Mr. Wallace speaking of "getting out" to mean the taking of his own life.

Roberto moaned at learning of this suicide, moaned and cursed, "*Chingado*," an outburst that he assumed was under his breath. But apparently the gust of that word was loud enough to echo off the walls. It deepened the librarian's dislike of him. She returned, pointed to the exit, and snapped, "Get out!"

"Can I have the newspaper?" he begged. He wanted to read the article once again and lick a thumb and rifle his way to the obituaries. Perhaps there were added details regarding Mr. Wallace's family or service.

"No, you can't! *Ándale!*"[2] She stomped her foot, and her mouth puckered. Roberto could see how she might suck on needles on her days off.

Out on the street, he leaned his back against the sycamore in front of the library and prayed that the librarian would come stomping out, hurl a dictionary at him, and knock him silly with words he would never know. Knowledge sometimes hurt, as he had learned that morning. He turned and scraped a scab of bark from the tree and would have stood there, facing the

1. Northeast of Oakland.    2. Let's go.

tree, a bad boy who had used a bad word in a public place, except his mind turned a rusty gear. He decided to head off to his old employer, the Walnut Bank, and ask Gus why Mr. Wallace would have stolen such an amount only to drown himself without spending any of it. When Roberto fondled his pockets for change, he discovered a crushed dollar bill plus sixty-three cents.

"This is messed up," he declared to his open palm. A raindrop loosened and fell from the limb of the sycamore into his palm. Startled, he sent the nickels and dimes spilling onto the sidewalk. When he bent to pick them up, his fingers reached for a coin-shaped drop of rainwater. He tried to pick up the rain repeatedly.

He rode a squeaky bus to the Walnut Bank. He got off to stand momentarily in the black exhaust of an accelerating bus. When the smoke cleared, the air became sweet as candy and, as he learned quickly, was more promising than candy. Luck had placed him in front of a pastry shop. His stomach groaned, and if his hunger could have spoken syllables clearly, it would have shouted, "The peach pie! Get the peach pie, dude!" He swallowed a sour deluge of saliva. No, what sort of meal is that? Roberto wondered. He observed customers enter the pastry shop and exit carrying dainty white bags in their pudgy fingers. They don't need to eat, he told himself. He touched his belly and thought he felt the metal shaving, except it was a rib.

He punished himself by lingering in front of the pastry shop, sniffing freely like a dog. He tooted his happiness at the chocolate chip cookies and the carrot cake and appreciated highly the lemon custard in a plastic cup. He praised the sight of a tiered wedding cake with ropes of icing and the bride and groom knee-deep in frosting. Marriage looks so sweet, he mused.

Unable to stand the display of gleaming delicacies, he strode off to the Walnut Bank, where, as he suspected, Gus was standing with his hands behind his back, a captive to time. For Roberto, it was a homecoming. He was happy to see his old friend, so happy that his stride became an actual jog.

"Gus, *compa*,"[3] Roberto boomed.

Gus tilted his head at Roberto, baffled.

"It's me, *carnal*," Roberto boomed even louder. His joy was wild, and he would have given Gus a hug but knew the old man wasn't that kind of fellow, even if he was Mexican and *un abrazo* was loving affection between men, men and sometimes their animals—horse, dog, or squealing pig.

"Roberto?"

Roberto nodded. "I'm here to see you, you ol' goat, but also—"

Suddenly the glass door of the bank swung open. Mr. Berger emerged with his body leaning far to the right, the gravity of his dollars packed somewhere in his front pocket. Mr. Berger passed without a nod or a perfunctory smile. When he was out of view, Roberto continued. "I'm here because I read—"

Gus held a finger to his lips and shook his head. His heavy eyebrows knitted a shadow over his somber eyes.

"I know what you're going to say."

Gus stated that the embezzlement was a simple matter of greed. True, Mr. Wallace had stolen a large amount of money and perhaps could have gotten away with it, except guilt is a dog that follows you to the end. It took

3. Pal.

ays since he had eaten something other than the three cookies
try shop.

pted to head off to the transmission shop to see Manny, his one
only hope to fatten his sides. He scheduled his arrival for the
He arrived at eleven-thirty. With time to kill, he entered a Big
shop to look around and, if the opportunity presented itself,
one of its chairs and warm up. The thrift shop was run by a
roup, so when he was greeted with, "Hello, brother," he wasn't
nd didn't argue about the familiar use of "brother." He nodded
ing black fellow ironing ties at the checkout counter.

ed the air. The faint smell of soup perfumed the air, and this
ked Roberto's stomach into a cage of growling animals. Just
had left the Quonset hut, he'd devoured the last of the soggy
which broke to pieces when he thrust his hand into the box. But
y counted as sustenance because most of the crackers just stuck
h and wouldn't wash down to nourish his weakening body.

he young man at the counter smiled, Roberto felt inclined to
s presence. "Just looking. I need some new clothes." He fingered
"This has just about had it."

ped down an aisle of white shirts, some of them so large that the
iched the floor. A full-length mirror glinted at the end of the aisle.
inslinger, Roberto walked slowly toward the mirror but stepped
this showdown, for the figure that loomed in front of him was
handful of ash. Roberto was disturbed by his sorry appearance.
like shit," he whispered to himself.

was in the right place to alter his ragged appearance. He consid-
coats and pants and rifled through the shoes, his own shoes having
ten by rain, mud, and the crawl out of Piedmont. He intended to
hoelace for his left shoe and would have except he was encircled by
rkers. They appeared without warning, like smoke.

to was astonished that they could read his mind. "I didn't do any-
Roberto remarked a bit too loudly. He was ready to plunge his hands
pockets and turn them inside out. He had nothing to hide.

e all done something," said the young black man. His voice was like
He had cropped hair and wore brown glasses that blended with his
brown skin.

e all sinners here together," said another, a baritone, his chest as
a tuba. A large, older man with his pants pulled up to his chest, he
ed Humpty-Dumpty. But unlike that eggshell of a folk character,
son was black and very real.

rto winced. The cryptic utterance "We're all sinners here together"
nake sense even after it was repeated by the white person in the trio of
s brothers. It didn't make sense until he suddenly felt his hand being
and saw the three of them closing their eyes, heads down, for a spur-
noment prayer. Roberto, not knowing what to do since his other hand
ptured by his brotherly neighbor, decided to close his eyes, too.

w to you feel?" the black brother with the syrupy voice asked when
ayer ended.

erto blinked in the hazy light of the thrift shop. He surveyed the three
g faces.

no more than thirty seconds to sum
thirty seconds for Gus to kick a peb
then, "Roberto, there is another matte

Roberto scratched an ear, ready
explained that the police had puzzled
Roberto's departure—a sly connectio
inquiries about Roberto's character.

"I spoke up for you," Gus said wit
Roberto to know that he had vouched
back-stabbing tellers and the assistant
portrait of him. One of the tellers said
lid on a bottle of wine while on the job.

Roberto's jaw fell open, and his mind
"Do I look like I got money?" Roberto
him back in front of the bank. "Anyhow,

"I told the police that. I told them that
fled his feet, opened his wallet, and bro
thing to eat."

Roberto took the money with a simple
him to offer a hearty thank-you or a broth
fused, his mind once again dizzy. Why wo
the ability to walk out of a bank with mono
get his bimonthly paycheck out of the off
twenties.

"I'm getting out," Roberto said, then sw
words. Those were the words Mr. Wallac
months before, and Roberto was now certai
tried: "I'm leaving. Why is this always happe
last phrase, wondering why every piece of ba
was god-awful living on the street, but being

"You be good," Gus suggested.

Roberto ignored the suggestion. His moo
in the library without getting in trouble." He
a fat helping of fear. "If the cops come lookir
'em I look like shit and I couldn't possibly hav

Roberto hustled back to the pastry shop,
Heavenly Delights. He sized up the pastries,
perhaps they were concocted by angels. He had
back home or eat two dollars' worth of somethin
swabbed his teeth for a morsel of sustenance ar
and entered the pastry stop, which was indee
heaven.

The morning pounded Oakland with rain that
where the Quonset hut sat. Roberto woke to th
if there was sufficient water to drown himself.
facedown in, like Mr. Wallace, a river to sweep
the window and peeked outside at the rain.

The acids of his stomach groped for somethin
of bread, a peanut, a coin of carrot. Starving, he

number of
from the pa

Roberto
friend, his
noon hour.
Hope thrif
lounge in
Christian g
surprised a
at the smil

He sniff
aroma kic
before he
crackers,
they hardl
to his teet

When
explain hi
his collar.

He step
sleeves to
Like a gu
away fror
gray as a

"I look

But he
ered the
been bea
swipe a s
three wo

Rober
thing," I
into his

"We'v
syrup. I
creamy

"We'r
huge as
resembl
this per

Robe
didn't r
religiou
groped
of-the-
was ca

"Ho
the pr

Rob
smilin

number of days since he had eaten something other than the three cookies from the pastry shop.

Roberto opted to head off to the transmission shop to see Manny, his one friend, his only hope to fatten his sides. He scheduled his arrival for the noon hour. He arrived at eleven-thirty. With time to kill, he entered a Big Hope thrift shop to look around and, if the opportunity presented itself, lounge in one of its chairs and warm up. The thrift shop was run by a Christian group, so when he was greeted with, "Hello, brother," he wasn't surprised and didn't argue about the familiar use of "brother." He nodded at the smiling black fellow ironing ties at the checkout counter.

He sniffed the air. The faint smell of soup perfumed the air, and this aroma kicked Roberto's stomach into a cage of growling animals. Just before he had left the Quonset hut, he'd devoured the last of the soggy crackers, which broke to pieces when he thrust his hand into the box. But they hardly counted as sustenance because most of the crackers just stuck to his teeth and wouldn't wash down to nourish his weakening body.

When the young man at the counter smiled, Roberto felt inclined to explain his presence. "Just looking. I need some new clothes." He fingered his collar. "This has just about had it."

He stepped down an aisle of white shirts, some of them so large that the sleeves touched the floor. A full-length mirror glinted at the end of the aisle. Like a gunslinger, Roberto walked slowly toward the mirror but stepped away from this showdown, for the figure that loomed in front of him was gray as a handful of ash. Roberto was disturbed by his sorry appearance.

"I look like shit," he whispered to himself.

But he was in the right place to alter his ragged appearance. He considered the coats and pants and rifled through the shoes, his own shoes having been beaten by rain, mud, and the crawl out of Piedmont. He intended to swipe a shoelace for his left shoe and would have except he was encircled by three workers. They appeared without warning, like smoke.

Roberto was astonished that they could read his mind. "I didn't do anything," Roberto remarked a bit too loudly. He was ready to plunge his hands into his pockets and turn them inside out. He had nothing to hide.

"We've all done something," said the young black man. His voice was like syrup. He had cropped hair and wore brown glasses that blended with his creamy brown skin.

"We're all sinners here together," said another, a baritone, his chest as huge as a tuba. A large, older man with his pants pulled up to his chest, he resembled Humpty-Dumpty. But unlike that eggshell of a folk character, this person was black and very real.

Roberto winced. The cryptic utterance "We're all sinners here together" didn't make sense even after it was repeated by the white person in the trio of religious brothers. It didn't make sense until he suddenly felt his hand being groped and saw the three of them closing their eyes, heads down, for a spur-of-the-moment prayer. Roberto, not knowing what to do since his other hand was captured by his brotherly neighbor, decided to close his eyes, too.

"How to you feel?" the black brother with the syrupy voice asked when the prayer ended.

Roberto blinked in the hazy light of the thrift shop. He surveyed the three smiling faces.

no more than thirty seconds to sum up Mr. Wallace's folly and another thirty seconds for Gus to kick a pebble between them. Silence followed; then, "Roberto, there is another matter."

Roberto scratched an ear, ready to listen. Gus breathed deeply and explained that the police had puzzled over Mr. Wallace's embezzlement and Roberto's departure—a sly connection between the two? There were also inquiries about Roberto's character.

"I spoke up for you," Gus said with his chest pushed out. He wanted Roberto to know that he had vouched for him but that there were others, back-stabbing tellers and the assistant bank manager, who painted a dark portrait of him. One of the tellers said that she had seen him unscrew the lid on a bottle of wine while on the job.

Roberto's jaw fell open, and his mind spun.

"Do I look like I got money?" Roberto pleaded after his dizziness planted him back in front of the bank. "Anyhow, I left a long time ago."

"I told the police that. I told them that you were a good man." Gus shuffled his feet, opened his wallet, and brought out two dollars. "Get something to eat."

Roberto took the money with a simple nod; the amount didn't encourage him to offer a hearty thank-you or a brotherly handshake. Plus he was confused, his mind once again dizzy. Why would the police think that he had the ability to walk out of a bank with money in his pocket? He could barely get his bimonthly paycheck out of the office, let alone stacks of tens and twenties.

"I'm getting out," Roberto said, then swallowed the last vapors of those words. Those were the words Mr. Wallace used that late morning many months before, and Roberto was now certain what he meant by them. So he tried: "I'm leaving. Why is this always happening to me?" He considered the last phrase, wondering why every piece of bad luck was reserved for him. It was god-awful living on the street, but being connected to a robbery?

"You be good," Gus suggested.

Roberto ignored the suggestion. His mood turned dark. "I can't even sit in the library without getting in trouble." He swallowed this pitiful fact and a fat helping of fear. "If the cops come looking, tell 'em I'm a nice guy. Tell 'em I look like shit and I couldn't possibly have money."

Roberto hustled back to the pastry shop, which he noticed was called Heavenly Delights. He sized up the pastries, some of them so dainty that perhaps they were concocted by angels. He had money to either take the bus back home or eat two dollars' worth of something sweet. With his tongue, he swabbed his teeth for a morsel of sustenance and, finding none, he shrugged and entered the pastry stop, which was indeed filled with the delights of heaven.

The morning pounded Oakland with rain that made lakes in the vacant lot where the Quonset hut sat. Roberto woke to this drumming and wondered if there was sufficient water to drown himself. Was there a river to float facedown in, like Mr. Wallace, a river to sweep him to oblivion? He wiped the window and peeked outside at the rain.

The acids of his stomach groped for something to latch onto, like an iota of bread, a peanut, a coin of carrot. Starving, he held up three fingers, the

"I feel good."

They led him into the back room, filled with donations, mostly boxes of clothes but also chairs and sofas, televisions and computers from another era. There were also a few bicycles with flat tires and rust-pitted chrome handlebars.

"Go wash up, brother," said the white brother, who sported a crew cut and was skinny as a pitchfork. "We have a shower if you care to clean up." He hesitated, then confessed, "I was on the street for three years. Did everything against the Lord's wishes. Called him names I wouldn't call the devil." A hand fell on the seat of a bicycle. "And now this is where the Lord has sent me to fix such things."

Roberto blinked at this white brother. His shirtsleeves were rolled halfway up his arms, exposing a swirl of tattoos, some featuring skimpily clad women. The brother rolled down his sleeves and professed, "We can help you through God."

The syrupy-voiced brother sidled up to Roberto and said in a near whisper, "Let's clean up. Let's take a shower."

Roberto couldn't argue with the suggestion. But a conniving thought crept in. He could shower, jump out of the shower, and say with hair wet that he had forgotten something so important that he had to leave. He didn't know what excuse his mind would fumble with, but he would come up with a pretense by the time he toweled off. But Roberto's will melted like the bar of soap in his hands. The hot water was luxurious, the needlelike spray picking at the crust from his toes and the dark shadow of grime circling his neck and wrists. Reluctantly he turned off the shower when a voice called from outside the door. The call was a gentle call to hurry up.

In front of the fogged mirror, he was tempted to rub the soap on his furtartared teeth. But he just scrubbed his teeth with the up-and-down motion of a fingernail. After that, as he was stepping into his old clothes, so sour that he had to close his eyes as he fit a spindly leg into his underwear, a knock sounded on the door. It was like heaven knocking.

"Here are fresh clothes," the white brother said as he pushed open the door. He presented him with khakis fitted with a belt, a T-shirt, heavy wool socks, and Jockey underwear. The clothes were warm, having just been ironed, and folded as carefully as vestments.

"Thanks," Roberto said, touched. He asked the person's name.

"I'm Robert."

"We share the same name," Roberto remarked, letting that piece of dispatch hang in the air mysteriously. He added: "Roberto. That's me."

They shook hands, and Brother Robert closed the door behind him.

Roberto was beginning to like this place called Big Hope thrift shop. He dressed and came out of the bathroom, a new man with sweat beaded on his forehead from the hot shower, and was further outfitted with a reddish sweater and a coat. Shoes were handed him, and Roberto was surprised that these people knew his size.

"We know a lot about people," the syrupy-voiced brother piped. "And by the way, I'm Brother Marvin." Referring to the baritone brother, he said, "That's Brother Julius. And this here is—"

"Robert," Roberto interrupted. "We got the same name except I got an *o* on the end of mine."

Brother Marvin touched his chin. He clicked his fingers. "That makes you 'Roberto.'"

Roberto liked hearing his name from someone who was good. Lately no one had spoken his name, and if they had, the tone would have been a torturing scold.

He was fed chicken noodle soup, which he balanced on his knees as he ate on a wobbly stool by the sink. While the others returned, one by one, to the front of the store, he slurped those noodles with dice-sized chunks of chicken and broke apart saltine crackers. He licked his fingers; an hour ago, the notion of putting his grimy fingers into his mouth would have disgusted him, not to mention possibly laying him low with cholera or TB. But licking the tips of his fingers, he was proud of his own flesh.

Toward evening, six men and two women came into the thrift shop. They were all clean, electric with God—two had hair that was standing on end. From all appearances, they were outfitted from the very ranks of the used clothes that they had washed and ironed. Roberto greeted them with a "Hello, brother. Hello, sister." And they greeted him likewise.

There was a prayer group before dinner, then dinner of more chicken noodle soup ladled into mismatched bowls from the shelves in the store. But there was also a tray of sandwiches and as many potato chips as he could fit in his mouth. Afterward everyone competed to get to the sink and be the one to clean up. It was a playful moment; all shared the enthusiasm of putting out a little elbow grease to show their affection for God and one another.

"Out of my way. Let me in there!" Brother Julius bumped his large hips as he pushed his way between the others at the sink.

Roberto was scraping his bowl while he watched them fight over the honor of doing dishes. He considered the remains in another person's bowl but checked himself, as he was certain that there was a passage in the Bible that scolded street gluttons such as himself about slurping leftover chicken noodle soup.

When the dishes were done, there was a prayer in the kitchen and discussion about their sordid pasts. Some admitted being former drug addicts, while Brother Robert admitted his old racist mind-set—he rolled up his sleeves and showed Nazi insignia. He could have such hateful messages lasered, he explained, but was inclined to keep his tattoos as reminders of his past. "But I wash my hands of those days," Robert said, nearly crying. "What was in me was the devil." He gripped the skin on his wrists, distorting the tattoo of a grinning skull. "And the devil is sometimes white."

There were a lot of "amens" and "praise Jesuses."

Roberto was asked to witness.

"Like all of you, I've sinned," he began meekly as he rose to his feet.

"Speak up, brother," someone called.

Inwardly Roberto wished he could give back his new clothes and the hot food they piled on him. He didn't like talking about himself in such a naked manner.

"I didn't like my job because it was so boring," he began at last. He informed his friends that he had worked as a security guard at the Walnut Bank. He asked his friends if they knew the bank, but they all shook their heads. He licked his lips as he searched his mind for a sin to recant. He told them that one day when he was truly bored, he lowered himself to his haunches and thumbed ants to their oily deaths. He punished the ants for getting in his way, for making him feel small, for their dedication to doing what they were asked—genetically speaking—without complaint. Further, how dare they walk in front of him! How dare they mingle their simple shadows with his! He told them that ants were low creatures and they hurt when they bite. With one of the brothers yawning at his confession, Roberto picked up steam by saying that he once thought of robbing the bank and would have except he didn't have a gun or the nerve. When two others yawned, he used the word *fuck* twice in his storytelling, but no one lifted an eyebrow.

"What else, brother?" someone asked.

"Well, I had hate in my heart when this dude tried to kill me with a chair." He recounted how he had failed to share history answers with a classmate in high school. He didn't tell these brothers and sisters that his answers were flat wrong and that he would have had the same results if he had left the entire test blank. He didn't know them that well.

Roberto was offered a cot in the loft near a window that leaked cold air. He slept uneasily with snoring men who rolled, mumbled, and gnashed their teeth all night. The next morning, he was assigned with Robert to pick up clothes and furniture in the van. The thrift shop was in the business of saving souls plus refurbishing goods, for idle hands were the first to pick up a bottle and drink, among other ghastly amusements.

But before they left, Roberto wanted to say hello to Manny, since the transmission shop was just two storefronts away. He left the thrift store and traveled not more than sixteen strides to the transmission shop. He heard the hiss of a welder, the metallic whine of a ratchet gun, and, behind those sounds, the tinkle of wrenches on metal. When the ratchet gun stopped, Roberto yelled, "Is Manny here?" The shop darkened when a Samoan showed his face and body. Not yet eight-thirty in the morning and his face was streaked with grease. There was even grease around his mouth, and Roberto believed the mighty fellow might have enjoyed lug nuts with his coffee. But he kept this bit of conjecture to himself.

"What do you want?" the Samoan asked.

"Is Manny here?" Roberto's voice was weak as tea, and he sensed his anemic stature next to the Samoan. So he asked again but louder, spreading his legs slightly apart.

The Samoan studied Roberto. Then he pointed vaguely at someone in the pit, arms up in the air as if he were trying to swim out of his miserable station in life, and sneered at Roberto while he proceeded to pick up a transmission with one hand and walk away with only the slightest suggestion that it was heavy. He carried it at his side like a bowling ball.

"Manny, it's me!" Roberto called into the pit that was hell itself, except there were no flames to roast his sorry plight.

"Roberto?" The whites of his eyes were the cleanest thing on Manny's grimy face. Manny hopped out of the pit, his hands bleeding transmission oil. He stepped toward Roberto as he wiped his hands. He asked, "What are you doing here?"

"Ain't you glad to see me?"

"I'm working."

"I came because I was going to ask you for *dinero*." He said this while rubbing his thumb and index finger together, the international sign of "I need money."

"Just like you."

Roberto didn't feel insulted. Already he could feel a religious spirit in his soul.

"But I don't have to." He paused and waited to see if Manny would ask, How come? When he didn't, he volunteered, "And you know why?"

Manny shook his head.

"I'm with the Big Hope thrift shop, and my brothers and sisters are going to save me. It doesn't take much to be saved. Three days, I think."

Manny looked over Roberto's shoulder at the thrift shop. "You're with those losers?"

Roberto would have argued over that piece of slander, except the Samoan returned and glared at Manny. "What the fuck is this? You're here to work, not to talk to bums." The Samoan eyed Roberto to see if he objected. The Samoan wasn't mad, just trying to chum up in his own way. Roberto knew better than to open his mouth and disagree with this description. Truth is, Roberto reflected, I am a bum, but he hoped not for long. Not with the help of my brothers and sisters of the Big Hope thrift shop.

"I'll see you around," Roberto told Manny. He left, taking steps that were longer than the ones that had gotten him there. When he turned for one last glance, he saw the Samoan lecturing Manny with a large tool in his hand. A second, more attentive inspection showed that it was a finger, not a wrench.

Roberto joined Robert in a white van idling roughly in the driveway on the side of the thrift shop.

"It takes a while to warm it up." Robert gunned the engine, booting up a load of black smoke.

They were scheduled to pick up clothes, kitchen utensils, and furniture on their morning run. The van stalled as they rolled down the curb. Robert pressed the gas pedal. "Lord, it's us, it's us, Lord," Robert chanted. He turned the ignition, and the motor sputtered alive and the exhaust pipe popped. Robert smiled at Roberto. "He's listening. And we have to listen, too."

Roberto didn't know what to make of the last pronouncement. How could he or Robert or anyone else listen to God if he never showed himself? Roberto didn't question Robert. He gazed out the window as the business section of Laurel Heights quickly became residential. He liked seeing nice houses, liked seeing roofs and lawns, imagining intact families that would break bread together in the evening. He liked that somehow he was moving in a better crowd. And while the van chugged along, the red traffic lights turned to green; nothing was going to stop their Christian duty. Their first pickup was at a large white house with a yard carpeted with leaves from twin maple trees. The leaves were lifeless, the rain having bullied them into submission.

Roberto was sure that the donation would be large to match the size of the residence. Instead they picked up a single cardboard box of clothes and a wastebasket full of squares of frayed fabric, panty hose, and old *TV Guides*. The next stop had them hauling a small sofa smothered in cat fur. With Roberto shuffling in front and Robert in back, they loaded the sofa into the van. Both sneezed from the cat fur and told the other, "Bless you." They honked their noses using the fabric in the wastebasket.

The woman came out in her robe and pointed at two plastic bags. "Can you take those?"

Roberto marched over to the bags. When he lifted them, they rattled like cornflakes. They were light, not heavy with wool sweaters and men's suits. "What's in here?"

"Leaves. From my gardening."

"Oh, ma'am, we can't take them." Roberto set them back down.

The woman argued that she was giving them a good sofa of antique value, and what was the big deal about taking a few bags of leaves? Roberto turned to Robert for a sign. Robert nodded.

They drove off with a sofa, the bags of leaves, and a sneezing fit from the cat fur. The normal-sized homes of Oakland abruptly gave away to stately homes made of stone and bricks no wolf could blow over. They were two and three stories, and some were castlelike, spitting out rainwater from their gargoyles. A few homes were gated, but others were fringed with white picket fences, a comeback from the 1940s. Roberto noticed this shift to opulent living and gripped his seat when the van banked noisily around Magnolia Park. In the park, a few of the trees were strung with Christmas lights. Two mothers were jogging with their babies in designer strollers. And behind these mothers were Irish setters keeping pace.

"Where are we going next?" Roberto asked nervously. The drive brought back a childhood memory of his annual doctor's checkup at a cinder-block office on the edge of town. He remembered that if his mother turned right at First Street, that meant they were going home. If she turned left, it meant a visit to the doctor's office, where a penguin-shaped nurse in a white dress lay in wait with a tray of syringes. That and other embarrassing pokings with his underwear around his ankles.

The van turned left.

Again Roberto asked his brother.

"We're going to . . ." He peered at the clipboard. "We're going to a street called Frazier."

Roberto couldn't recall whether his last tramping through Piedmont had taken him to Frazier Street. But when he peeked out the window, fogged from Robert's Christian humming, he could swear that they were just passing the house where the father and son and burning Volvo dwelt. But the homes looked the same, well kept and with more imports than all of Europe. He closed his eyes and envisioned the Volvo with its single eyeball—his Christmas wreath!—on fire.

"What's wrong?" Robert asked.

Roberto pinched his nose. The brief deflation of his nostrils made him answer nasally. "I'm getting a cold."

But life had turned more serious than a cold when Robert, after consulting the address on his clipboard, braked suddenly, lodged the van into reverse, and backed up two houses. Gunning the engine, he pulled into a driveway.

"Oh, shit!" Roberto screamed.

Robert eyed Roberto.

"Brother?"

Roberto had heard how thieves characteristically return to the scene of their crimes. He had heard of this sort of blunder, even witnessed it in movies and movies made for TV. While he was no thief, he saw himself fitting the bill when the van came to a halt. The engine shook like a dog before it let out something like a sigh.

There was no mistake. It was the house where Roberto had nailed wreaths onto the wall, placed his "ornaments" in a vase, and left an incriminating shoe print smudge. It was the house where the dog in the sweater and powdered butt lived, far more comfortably than his own sort. It was the house where the old woman was senile, possibly an Alzheimer's case, and the daughter's name was Robin, a springtime name. Yes, he remembered her name and the moment when she pulled unexpectedly into the driveway, not unlike their own arrival. He remembered his shoelace had come undone and was eventually lost in his own terror-infused run for his life.

"You okay?" Robert asked. The engine shuddered one more time, like the dead shaking out their last quiver of tension. In the quiet, Robert touched Roberto's shoulders. "Don't worry, Roberto. Work is a foreign country. You just got to go visit it."

Roberto couldn't make sense of yet another cryptic utterance from his brother. Nor could he make sense of a startling sight—hands cupped around her face, the old woman peered into his window with her lips pressed like a starfish against the glass and her nose, sluglike, moistening the surface. Roberto's shoulders jumped at this sight. The lips peeled away, leaving the imprint of an old woman's kiss. She stepped away from the van and waved.

To Robert, he said shakily, "My cold is worse. Can I stay here? In the van?"

Robert looked at the clipboard.

"It says we got to move a desk and . . . a thing called an 'armory.'" He scratched his cheek, baffled. "How do you say that word, brother?"

Roberto leaned toward the clipboard. He studied the word and expressed his opinion. "Yeah, 'armory.' Just like it's written is how it sounds."

The word was *armoire*, and to Robert it sounded heavy, like armor or army or the army's armor. He had hurt his back two weeks before and didn't wish to repeat the experience.

"Come on," Robert said, opening his door. "Let's go get the armory thing."

Roberto sat with his worry for a moment before he opened his door and stepped out with his face lowered. He was immediately greeted by the old woman.

"You're back!" Her face was red from too much blush, and her hair was wildly teased. "Is that your brother?" she asked of Robert, who was already marching up the two-tiered steps. He hadn't seen the woman on the side of the van.

Roberto grinned hard. He couldn't think of anything to say except, "Pretend I was never here."

The woman smiled false teeth smeared with lipstick. "I like your brother."

"That's good. But can we pretend like I never saw you and you never saw me?" He grinned again.

"I like you and your brother," she answered. "Christmas is a nice time, but we don't have those beautiful wreaths. My daughter got rid of them."

"But we don't know each other."

"Oh, that's nice." She clapped and stabbed her hands wickedly into her hair.

With the old woman in tow, Roberto climbed the steps to Robert, who was at the top of the landing and already knocking on the front door. Robert regarded Roberto and the woman, baffled at the pair.

"Are you the woman of the house?" he asked.

She nodded. "I'm coming."

Robert helped her up the five steps, a StairMaster for the aged, a workout for anyone with a bad hip. When she reached the porch's landing, she marched until her feet were in line and stood at attention. Roberto thought she was going to salute. Instead she pulled her hair and blurted, "It hurts! Christ, it hurts!"

Robert looked at Roberto, who said, "She's, you know . . ."

The woman led the two inside the house, but not before Robert undid his shoes.

"Looks like they got a real white carpet," Robert said.

Roberto kicked off his shoes and followed the woman and Robert into the house. Shivering, he complained of a chill, of the rain and the cold weather ahead. He inspected the carpet. His shoe print was nowhere in sight. And when he walked into the dining area, the wreath on the cabinet was gone as well as the one on the wall. He went up to the wall and ran a hand down the unblemished wall. He searched for the vase that held his ornaments. It was gone, and so was the old woman, though her chatter carried into the dining room, where he and Robert stood. But she returned tugging her daughter Robin. The daughter was tall and as wide as the armoire they were scheduled to haul away. Her wrists jangled bracelets, handcuffs to Roberto's way of thinking. He saw himself in those cuffs and his head slamming against the hood of a police car. He saw himself bleeding.

"Here's that young man and his brother," the old woman cried happily with a clap. "Make me a wreath! Robin threw the others out."

Roberto smiled at the business of the wreath. But his stomach soured with worry when the old woman repeated that she wanted a wreath and would pull her hair until one was hung on the wall. Her hands jumped into her hair and she started to yank at the hair at her temples. The pulling distorted her eyes and twisted up her mouth.

Roberto backed up first one step, then another when the old woman screamed, "Make me a wreath!"

She sobbed as her hands came out of her hair like bats. A few strands floated to the carpet, where the dog sat, panting from just being alive in a crazy house.

The daughter told her mother to behave, to quit acting like a child. Her stare darted to Roberto. She placed her own hands on her hips, banging a music from her bracelets. Her suspicion showed up as a shiny flake of anger in her eyes.

Roberto backed up three more steps. He wheeled around, hurried to the front door for his shoes, and skipped in his socks down the steps, heedless as Robert called, "Brother, where are you going? We got the 'armory' to haul." On the leafy sidewalk, he didn't glance back. His survival was somewhere in front of him.

"Shit!" he said, the curse word that could explain all bleak moments. The rain patted his shoulders and frisked them for their small dents where the skin lay over the bone. When he put on the shoes, he discovered that they were Robert's, not his, far too big on his own feet. He couldn't run without their coming off.

"Shit," he repeated. He clopped down the street, nearly skidding on leaves and the branches the storm had brought down. He leaped over toys and trikes left on the sidewalk and waved at the few neighbors who thought he was out for a brave jog in the rain. He slowed to a stop after he distanced himself from the old woman's house. When he stopped, he found himself panting in front of the house where the Volvo family lived. There was now a new car without plates sitting in the driveway, rain beading up on its shine. Even from where Roberto stood, he could smell its leathery newness.

"Shit," he said for the third time in as many minutes when the father came out, skipping lightly, already beeping the car alarm on his new Volvo in the driveway. The father halted and locked a gaze on Roberto, who, like a rabbit in headlights, couldn't move.

"You should get a better job than making wreaths," he advised. He offered this bit of wisdom calmly, without spite for burning up his family car. Still, he reached into his pocket for his cellular phone, for advice was one thing and police action another.

There was no retort from Roberto. This was the best advice he had had in a long time. He stomped away in the sleds of his big shoes, and when he heard the wail of a police car, he was already jogging across Magnolia Park. He cut into some bushes and lay on his back, his side hurting either from exhaustion or that piece of metal shaving swallowed years ago. He lay appraising the misfortune that awaited him. It wasn't that Mr. Wallace, now buried, was responsible for his present stature, currently the height of a salamander as he hid in bushes. It wasn't the kid who tried to bring a chair down on his head. There was someone bigger pulling the strings. There was someone else, invisible as the wind, mighty as rock, cynical as a clown. There was some god who set him on his back and now had him rolling on his stomach in the rain.

"Oh, shit." He uttered this cry when he could breath again and the pain let go its grip on his side. His eyelashes dripped rain. The tip of his nose held a raindrop. His eyes jerked left and right. An alligator, a reptile from another, nastier time, he ventured out of the swampy ambiance of ferns and thorny bushes. He moved on elbows and knees, mud on his belly and rain on his back. He crawled out of Piedmont and back into Oakland, his familiar homeland.

The Quonset hut was surrounded by a bulldozer, three trucks remarkably clean despite their roll through the watery trenches of the vacant lot, and five burly men, two of them surveyors in orange vests. They told Roberto about a parking lot for the mall. He received this news with his body as muddy as a toad, and one of the surveyors, saddened by this sight, opened up his lunch box and brought out a thermos. He poured what remained of his coffee and offered a sandwich to go along with the drink. Roberto accepted these gifts and ate and drank while watching the men point in the four directions. One even jabbed a finger toward the sky—a takeover of heaven? Was the entire world being paved with malls? The men's consideration boosted his confidence, that and what ended up as his last meal of the day, which he ate standing up. He felt better. If malls expanded, the chances of his getting another job as a security guard increased.

Clouds rolled overhead, but no rain fell. Wind plucked at the matted grass and pushed at the litter. Roberto judged that his tramping toward immigrant Fruitvale and East 14th had been misdirected. He should have jumped over the fence and progressed toward the mall. After all, weren't the lights brighter there? Weren't the people better dressed and every other person white?

The man who had shared his sandwich and coffee told Roberto to leave by tomorrow morning. They were going to bulldoze the Quonset hut and start leveling the ground. When the men left, only the sound of wind through the cracks in the walls disturbed the night.

The next morning, Roberto changed into the clothes he had stashed for such a time. Dressed in an orange sweater and green pants, a warm if mismatched combination, he decided that in order to start over, to rekindle his life, he would sell his collection of vintage records plus the chairs that his mother had lent him (and thus ultimately given him) many years ago. They were old and black where working hands had gripped the back to pull them from the dining table. Wobbly now, the chairs had borne the weight of a lot of men and women.

"I'm out of here," he said to a mouse that had come out of the wall. The mouse chewed nervously at the floor, dust and splinters of wood its breakfast.

He hooked the chairs on his arm and, with his thirty-plus records, he kicked open the door and left the hut just as some of the men from the previous day were arriving. Roberto would have waved good-bye, but his arms were full. With big shoes flopping, he stepped over the rain puddles and set his mind on selling his wares—his last belongings—at Sanborn Park, where there was sidewalk traffic. He walked past the old Sears building and stopped for a moment in front of Goodwill. He stared at a truck whose back end was overflowing with clothes and furniture. He was disheartened at the sight; with such an abundance of goods, why would anyone buy from him? Still, he pressed ahead with his plan. He walked to Sanborn Park, praying the sombrero junkie would not be there. He stopped once to catch his breath and rest his arms where the weight of the chairs pressed into his flesh. He continued toward the park and was relieved when the junkie was nowhere in sight; just a few men lingered near the slide and swings, talking quietly, their occasional laughter sending up white bursts of their breathing.

Roberto displayed his goods, propping the albums on the chair and around its legs. The passersby spoke Spanish, and his selections of rock didn't mean anything except another obstacle to walk around. They walked past, far more taken with his orange sweater than his wares.

"Se venden discos, sillas, discos y sillas!" he yelled through his cupped hands, his words reaching halfway down the street, over the sound of car horns, crying babies in strollers, and the roar of accelerating buses. He stressed in Spanish that the records were classic and that the chairs were antiques. His shout was more like a scold. He attracted only a teenage boy rolling an ice cream cart, who parked next to Roberto. The two scrutinized each other, and when the boy finally said in Spanish, "I'll trade you an ice cream for a record," Roberto jumped at this exchange. He snagged a coconut Popsicle, and the boy took an old Kiss album. The boy chuckled; he said the rocker with his tongue sticking out nearly down to his chin was really funny.

"I'll trade you a *bad* Fleetwood Mac," Roberto suggested when he was not yet half done with his Popsicle.

"Who are they?" the boy asked as he stuck his hand inside the cover of a Supremes album. It looked as though he was trying to stick his hand down Diana Ross's sequined blouse.

Roberto employed the "bad" over and over and flogged the teenager by repeating that he hadn't really lived until he heard "Rhiannon." With that ventilation of reason and a quick lesson on how to pronounce "Rhiannon," he won a strawberry Popsicle just as he was finishing work on the coconut Popsicle. He wiped his fingers on his pants and ate.

The teenager rolled his cart away when he realized that Roberto wasn't going to attract customers. Still, Roberto remained faithful to his merchandising plan, especially when two older women asked him to remove the records from the chairs. They sat in the chairs, their bottoms nearly overflowing the sides. They smiled at each other, their teeth embedded with gold, and got up and traded places. They laughed at the spectacle of themselves sitting in kitchen chairs on the sidewalk.

"How much?" one finally asked after she dismounted the chair. She clutched her purse.

"*Diez dolares*,"[4] Roberto said.

The woman made a face. She said it was too much, and who did he think he was to try to fool someone like her? She knew the costs of used things.

"*Mujer!*"[5] he countered. He explained that they were his mother's chairs and if he sold them, he sold a piece of himself. He was giving his family history, and family was a hard thing to give away. The woman was unmoved. She proceeded to whittle the price to four dollars for both chairs. Soon after the two women left, the junkie with the sombrero appeared in shoes that were oversized, barely on his feet. He appeared to be shrinking; even his coat hung loosely on his body.

"Shit," Roberto said as he bent and started to gather his records.

"My man," the junkie called. He clopped over to Roberto with the sombrero pressed to his chest. "What you doing today?"

"Nothing."

"Couple a days ago you was selling goddamn leaves and shit." The junkie laughed and slapped the sombrero against his twig-thin thigh. "That's a good one. I never known your kind of people selling leaves. That a motherfuckin' scam!" He looked up toward the leafless sycamore that bore against the sky the outlines of three empty nests. He pointed. "I'm going to sell me some sticks myself, motherfucker!"

He cackled as Roberto tucked his records under his arm and started toward the rest room, his bladder full as a water bottle. The junkie followed for a few steps but stopped when someone by the swings called out to him. The person called him Sammy.

The rest room was dark and moist with the beastly breathings of overflowing toilets. Roberto did his best to aim at the urinal, but it was futile.

4. Ten dollars.　　　　　　　　　5. Woman.

He zipped up, left the rest room, and was walking down the cement toward the street when he saw a cop with one knee in Sammy the junkie's back. It was a raid. Other cops were searching the park—the druggies had scattered along with the pigeons and sparrows. Even the litter tried to move in the wind of the activity.

"Damn!" Roberto yelled. Immediately he wished that he hadn't cussed so loudly because a cop wheeled around and started toward him. Roberto considered hopping the fence that led to someone's backyard, but his best course, he judged from the bulky hustle of an immense cop, was just to be calm and seemingly uninvolved. He touched his fly to see if he was zipped and continued his stroll. After all, what had he done?

"You!" a cop called. "Get your ass over here!"

"Why?" Roberto had stopped, and his eyes picked up the commotion of other cops as they were rounding up druggies, winos, and those such as himself, the luckless. One cop had even collared a dog.

"Don't 'why' me, you bum!" The cop snorted his anger and started after Roberto, who hugged his records and cried that he didn't do anything except pee on the rest-room floor and he was sorry about that. The cop's belly jiggled under his shirt and, in spite of his bulk, after a zigzagging cat-and-mouse chase across the lawn, he brought Roberto down with a tackle. One of Roberto's shoes flew off and the albums skipped out of his arms—some of the discs jumped from the album covers and rolled on the sidewalk in their own attempt at a getaway. The cop pressed a knee into Roberto's back and brought both arms behind in a chicken wing. He clamped Roberto's spindly wrists in handcuffs.

"But I didn't do nothing," Roberto cried into the lawn. He wiggled a naked foot, aware that his shoe had kicked off during the race around the park.

The cop left to help subdue a cranked-up druggie, returned, sat Roberto up, and asked what *he* was on.

"I ain't on nothing but my two feet."

The cop laughed as he yanked him to his feet. "You're right about that."

"I need my shoe." Roberto looked frantically about, but it was nowhere in sight. He worried that it had been carried away by the dogs that had come out of the bushes. "I'm going to get a cold. And my records are ruined. I'm just trying to get a job like everybody else."

The cop laughed, picked up two album covers, and led him toward an idling cruiser. When he pressed the top of Roberto's head and shoved him in the back of the cruiser, he tossed the album covers as a follow-up, adding, "Here are your records. I hope they're better than the one downtown."

"I don't got no record!" Roberto fumed. When he turned to the person next to him, he jumped in his seat: he was paired off with Sammy the junkie, who was wearing his sombrero. The sombrero came down over his eyes.

"Shit!" Roberto cried.

"Now why you talk like that?" his new companion whispered. "This here cop is a motherfucker, and I seen him tear up people." Sammy laughed, stomped his shoes, and lowered his gaze on one of the album covers. "Now who is that white man?" He was staring at the muddy photo of Joe Cocker.

Roberto ignored the question. He gazed out his grimy window at the park, where a few people had gathered to watch their exodus. He saw the teenager with the ice cream cart gathering up the albums. He didn't blame him; he would have done the same.

"Now, I ain't into white music," Sammy started in Roberto's left ear. "But you ever listen to George Clinton? That brother be wiser than the president. And when he ain't wise, he's out there and crazy like you and me. You hear what I'm saying?"

"I ain't out there!" He turned a fierce face toward Sammy, and his brow touched the brim of the sombrero.

Sammy sparked. "What you mean? You think you better or something?" He smirked and stepped on the album cover. "You selling leaves and shit, and you think you ain't out there?" He laughed, and the sombrero jumped on his head. "You got only one shoe—what kind of man goes around walking like that in the street, except one who's out there?"

Roberto grumbled and pressed his shoulder against the door, as far as he could get from the scolding.

"And that orange you got on! What kinda people wear orange sweaters except those going off to jail, motherfucker!" His companion laughed. "And you say they ain't something wrong with you!" He stomped the Joe Cocker album cover.

Roberto grew sullen. He had to admit that perhaps he had gone wrong somewhere. He wiggled his toes to keep himself busy.

As the cruiser pulled away, Roberto took one last peek at Sanborn Park. All he wanted was to renew his life, and here he was sitting next to a person he had tried smartly to avoid. The cruiser gunned down the street and banked around a corner, the road chewing at the tires. Luck had it that they drove past the vacant lot where the Quonset hut was now rubble. Two men were stepping among the muddy ruins. A seagull was pecking at a brown bag.

The cruiser picked up speed, and soon they were on the 880 freeway.

"Listen, Officer," Sammy said, leaning toward the Plexiglas window that separated them. "Me and my man here ain't done nothing that you can call wrong. What's wrong with sitting in a park? Birds go there. We ain't hurt nobody but ourselves. Ain't that true?" He nudged Roberto, who nodded.

The cop's eyes filled the rearview mirror, then returned to the slow freeway traffic.

"Listen, my friend here got no shoe, plus nothing to brag about, really. We need to deal, Officer." He rolled his eyes toward his sombrero. "We need to establish what you call a rapport. You heard of the word? *Rapport* is French, and those kinda people know how to work things out."

Roberto was impressed with Sammy's vocabulary and command of history. Perhaps there was something to learn from his companion, something valuable to learn about negotiating with the law. And not to be kept quiet, he added to the fund of their sorry state: "Officer, I got no shoe and I'm cold and like Sammy says it's time to rapport." He purposely shivered and sucked up the moisture in his nose.

"Officer, the rapport between us poor lives and your good life is something to consider." Sammy nodded to his own pronouncement.

"Consider, huh?" the officer asked flatly.

Then Sammy smiled his terrible teeth at Roberto. They were getting somewhere. He turned his attention to the officer, who seemed attentive.

"So I'm willing to sell this Mexican hat for real cheap. Look nice on a wall at home. You got a family, don't you, Officer?" He waited for the cop to raise his eyes and fill the rearview mirror. But instead of his eyes, his teeth appeared with what might have been a smile or a snarl.

"This hat is a antique," Sammy pronounced, and let that statement hang in the air before he added, "And I ain't asking much."

The cruiser pulled off the freeway in the direction of the police station. Neither Roberto nor Sammy would find out if they had reached a deal until they arrived, or if the teeth in the rearview mirror were a smile or a snarl.

"Yes, Officer," Roberto tried. He was pumped up with confidence and regretted not knowing Sammy earlier. "It's a really old sombrero that maybe my grandpa wore when he was on a horse and the police were on horses." He licked his lips, certain that he was reaching the officer's heart, that the art of bargaining was finally sinking in. He elbowed Sammy's ribs. His eyes glistened with hope. He wet his lips again and added, "And like my friend says, we ain't asking much."

2000

# GIANNINA BRASCHI
## b. 1953

Born into the upper class in Puerto Rico, Giannina Braschi is a leading literary critic, poet, and prose-fiction writer. Before she went to college, she had become the youngest female tennis champion in the history of Puerto Rico. She studied comparative literature in Madrid, Rome, and Paris, and the experimental and cosmopolitan nature of her creative writing partly reflects these European intellectual influences. But Braschi is also attuned to Latin American literary traditions and to those of U.S. Latino literature. She moved to New York City in the mid-1970s and earned her doctorate from the State University of New York at Stony Brook (now Stony Brook University) in 1980. She has taught at Rutgers University, in New Brunswick, New Jersey, and the City University of New York, and in 1997 she held the position of Distinguished Chair of Creative Writing at Colgate University.

Most of Brasci's writing was available only in Spanish until 1994, when her collection *El imperio de los sueños* (1988) was translated into English as *Empire of Dreams*. Straddling the boundary between poetry and fiction, this book captures some aspects of the marginalized immigrant experience in the United States. In the introduction to the English translation, the American feminist poet and scholar Alicia Ostriker defines Braschi as

> an artist of the avant-garde, a classical type, an artist of the self-reflective, self-mocking, self-absorbed post-modern eighties. Not personal, but allegorical. Not a protest poet, though deeply aware of politics and power. Not of this or that continent, but a swirling amalgam of Puerto Rican, European, and Manhattanite. And not a feminist, or an advocate of gay and lesbian sexuality, but certainly a voracious woman and a major tease.

All of the above qualities are present in Brasci's novel *Yo-Yo Boing!* (1998), a chapter of which is also included here. In the novel's introduction, the scholars

Doris Sommer and Alexandra Vega-Merino describe this work as "a linguistic roller-coaster," because the narrative oscillates among paragraphs in Spanish, in English, and in Spanglish. The word *yo-yo* in the title refers as much to this bilingual contact and oscillation as to the performing antics, humorous wit, and popular allure of the Puerto Rican comedian Luis Antonio Rivera aka Yoyo Boing. Affirming the deeply rooted Latino presence in U.S. society, the novel requires the reader to be bilingual in English and Spanish and to code switch as easily as the narrator does.

Braschi is a passionate proponent of Spanglish. She has described her text "Pelos en la lengua" (the title is a Spanish idiom that literally means not having hairs on your tongue; the closest English equivalents are "to not mince words" and "to tell it like it is") as a "manifiesto de los huevos poéticos" (manifesto of poetic balls). In this text, also included here, she defines bilingualism as "una estética [an aesthetic] bound to double business," words inspired by the French literary critic René Girard's book *To Double Business Bound* (1978). Like Girard, Braschi is an iconoclast drawn to intertextuality and mimesis. Braschi's writing involves linguistic interplay, brash comedy and sardonic humor, creative experimentation, and the transgression of linguistic and literary boundaries. Spanglish is not only a hybrid means of expression for her, but also an existential, ideological, and social condition.

## *FROM* YO-YO BOING!

—Abrela tú

—¿Por qué yo? Tú tienes las keys. Yo te las entregué a ti.

Además, I left mine adentro.

—¿Por qué las dejaste adentro?

—Porque I knew you had yours.

—¿Por qué dependes de mí?

—Just open it, and make it fast. Y lo peor de todo es cuando te levantas por las mañanas y te vas de la casa y dejas la puerta abierta. Y todo el dinero ahí, desperdigado encima de una gaveta en la cocina, al lado de la entrada. Y ni te das cuenta que me pones en peligro. Yo duermo hasta las diez. Y entonces me levanto y me visto rápidamente y cuando voy a abrir la puerta me doy cuenta que está abierta. Es un descuido de tu parte. Dejar la puerta abierta. Alguien puede entrar y robarme y violarme. Y tú tan Pancho, Sancho,[1] ni te importa.

—Claro que me importa. Eso sí fue un descuido.

—Sí, ¿y lo otro no lo es? Scratch the knob and I'll kill you.

—No, lo otro no lo es. Yo tengo mi forma de hacer las cosas.

—Ah, sí, pero cuando estás conmigo tienes que hacerlo my way. O quieres que llame a los vecinos para que vean lo torpe que tú eres. Imagínate, si hasta las mismas cerraduras se burlan de la forma que tú tienes de entrar. La próxima vez no voy a hacerte caso cuando me toques el timbre. Tú te crees que a mí me gusta cuando me tocas el timbre. No, no me gusta cuando me tocas el timbre. Si tienes keys, ¿por qué no la abres?

---

1. Probably references to Francisco "Pancho" Villa (1878–1923), Mexican revolutionary leader, and Sancho Panza, a major character in the novel *Don Quixote* (1605, 1616), by the Spanish writer Miguel de Cervantes (1547–1616).

—Porque tú estás adentro. ¿Por qué si toco el timbre, no me abres la puerta?

—Porque me da rabia que estando yo adentro, y escuchando el roído de las keys roer la cerradura, y anhelando con toda la pasión que la abras, con toda la pasión, después de hacer ping-pong, un minuto, sin ninguna fuerza, me vengas a tocar el timbre, como si yo estuviera adentro esperándote todo el día, qué sabes tú si hay alguien por dentro. Y si estoy leyendo, why do I have to get up para hacerte el gran favor de abrirte la puerta. Do I look like a doorman. Besides, you have the keys and they fit, they sure do. You just have to learn how to handle them. It's no big deal. You're always making a fuss.

—Shut up.

—You shut up. Step aside.

—Gladly.

—Watch and learn to handle the locks, effortlessly. The rusty one for the bottom hole, a jiggle to the left, and this skinny one for the top slot. You do this just to annoy me. And you do. You certainly do. Nunca. Oíste. No estoy enamorada. Miento. Abúlicamente. No te quiero. Me entiendes. A veces te digo que to quiero, por la noche, la intimidad, digo, antes de acostarme, te veo tan puro roncar, y entonces, un perro manso, cómo lo pude haber tratado tan mal. Maybe it's then that I forget what I'm missing in life. But of course, it's like seeing a corpse, of course, all the good things appear, and I breathe heavy, and murmur deep into your ears: *I love you.* And you continue sleeping but dándome la espalda, acomodándote con mis patas por el medio, la tripa, que sube y que baja, y el dedo pulgar en la boca, te volviste bebé, chupándote el dedo, lulipup, qué manganzón, el zángano éste, tan grande y tan bribón. I shake my head no, no, no, no, but I love you, I guess I do, at least that's what I feel and think when I see you sleeping. Maybe it's a way of convincing myself that I do. Jabalí had something, a pushing something, a driving energy, even with all his short cuts and lies. But you, my buddy-buddy, busy-body, are indulgent with me. Sweet and complacent. Why do I always have to throw a hairy conniption to provoke a reaction. If I had another room, if I could close myself away from you, if I would not have to hear you snoring, lights out, dozing dog. I don't have the energy to sit at my desk and write two simple words. I crawl back in bed, breathing heavy on your cheeks. When I see you dead like that I realize how much we have in common. Where is my aspiration? To feel inspired one must aspire. What do I aspire to be: to be inspired, or at least to have a freehold set of mind, free from mental blocks. A house too small, a bad excuse but one nonetheless. Nothing on the road so keep walking, bad and good times, anxiety raining on me—don't get upset by the downpour, drenching the brain, think clear—but I can't. The problem comes when I realize I have done nothing and I'm still in bed rocking—waiting for Godot[2] or a change of climate. I get so angry at myself that I stand up and write my rage and feel good again and I change, and I change, and I change, but I never really change. Oh, I skim through the book and I say it's growing. So strong. So beautiful. I forgive myself momentarily as I do when I look at my big nose in the mirror. If I stare at it long enough sometimes I can

---

2. A reference to the play *Waiting for Godot* (1953), by Samuel Beckett (1906–1986), Irish playwright who lived in Paris.

fix it, or at least accept it, depending on my mood. I would like to see myself in the mirror always the same, or maybe like a stranger in the street at whom I smile and stare because I see in him something I see in myself. I always stare to make sure I'm not lost. Do you recognize me. You're staring at me and you smile, why? Do you like me? I'd like to ask you a question. Would you smile at me the same way if you knew who I am? Would you still smile so sweet? Y tú sabes lo que para mí significa levantarme azorada a media noche, y primero, hace un calor enervante que me sofoca, y luego que he apagado el heater, me voy al baño y veo ahí mismo, frente a frente a mis ojos, las puertas del closet no sólo abiertas, peor aún, de sus gavetas cuelgan unas sábanas, the incarnation of my nightmare, esos muertos despiertos, y no son los buenos. Intento cerrar la puerta, y se atora, y los ghosts guindando. Y te lo he pedido, por favor, hay que limpiar los closets, hieden los zapatos, y el olor a gato sudado que tienen los sweatshirts. Y voy a la cocina porque tengo la garganta reseca, coño, tú sabes, el calor, abro la nevera, y mi botella de agua, ¿dónde está el tapón de mi botella de agua? Tú no sabes que le entran germs, pierde el fizz, y no me gusta que el agua huela como tu chicken curry sandwich, ésta ya no sirve, ya nadie toma agua de esta botella. I forbid it. I'm throwing it out. Me acerco al maldito dishwasher, y ahí mismo, los trastos desbordándose del fregadero, millones de años sin lavarse, llenos de carrot peels y globs of brie pegados de sus rims. Y esto ya es demasiado para mí. Ya no aguanto más. Esas malditas keys abriendo y cerrando las cerraduras. Y durante los weekends, tu insolencia es inaudita. At least, durante la semana, soy dichosa, when I hear you leave at eight. *Libertad*—me digo a mí misma, con los ojos entrecerrados. Puedo leer en paz. Y si veo a Bloom mirando desde un risco a Gerty,[3] y se toca su prepucio, y me dan ganas, no tengo más que cerrar la cortina que acabo de abrir, y dejarme ir. Qué rico. Una distracción de tu careta. Pero ahora, si yo no me levanto, tú no te levantas, pones el alarm para nada, just to piss me off, and snore some more, hasta las diez. Porque eso sí, yo tengo un alarm por dentro. Cuando me despierto, tú sabes que estás en peligro y me dices:

> —*Breakfast? Orange juice? Croissant?*
> —*No*—I say—*today I want fruit and bacon.*
> —*Okay*—you say—*coming right up.*

Y entonces, te vas, te tardas una hora para hacerme sentir culpable de que te dejé ir sin mí. Escucho las sirenas, horrible, pienso:

> —*Cruzó la calle to bring home the bacon y lo espacharró una guagua. Qué hago ahora yo. Ya solo tengo enough in the checking to cover un mes de la renta, y luego lo tengo que vender todo, salirme de aquí. Qué hago.*

Y lo peor de todo, en la oscuridad, porque a ti no se te ocurre encender las luces, sentada, meciéndome, pensando en tu muerte, y después llegas, no te lo voy a negar, se me alivia el corazón, pero entonces me dan ganas de matarte, cuando veo y escucho, no veo, escucho, la vacilación de las keys en la puerta, y la oscuridad, la maldita oscuridad. Pero el aroma del café me aguanta las ganas que tengo de insultarte. *Bendito*—me digo—*after all, he*

---

3. In one chapter of the novel *Ulysses* (1922), by the Irish writer James Joyce (1882–1941), the main character, Leopold Bloom, a middle-aged man, masturbates at a beach while looking at Gerty MacDowell, a young woman, from a distance.

*risked his life for me. Breakfast*—you say with a smile on your face. You open the white paper bag, and out of the rustling comes . . .

—*What is this?*
—*Chocolate. Oh, it's too late for breakfast, Chipa, it's lunchtime. No bacon. No eggs. Have a chocolate bar. Quick energy. I brought you vitamins. Take a swig. They're good for your bones.*
—*Where is my orange juice?*
—*No orange juice. Vitamin C. It's the same thing.*
—*Not to me.*
—*No seeds. No pulp.*
—*I want my orange juice. Juicy red with its pepas.*
—*Seeds.*
—*And I want fresh squeezed. I don't want chocolate. It gives me grains.*
—*Pimples.*

Why. Tell me, why do you insist on bringing me breakfast in bed when you can never satisfy me. I am sure that there are oranges and bacon and scrambled eggs out there. It's just that you're too eager to disappoint me. As if I couldn't walk to the corner on my own two legs and buy my own breakfast. It's a pleasure for me to wake up in the morning, alone, find $5 and my keys in the kitchen, dress up, brush my teeth, wash and dry my face with a towel, open the door as my stomach growls, ride the elevator, check the bills in the mailbox, relieved that I don't have to pay them, buy *The Post* at the nearest newsstand, head to the Greek, read the gossips with the pleasure of a toasted bran muffin with melted butter and a cup of coffee, relax, come home, and start working. Good old times, not so old after all. But here you are, again, interrupting my creative process. Y cuando me llevas a Toritos, después de estar todo el día sin comer para guardar la línea, lo primero que haces es abrir el menú, y soltarte una carraspera.

—*¿Qué tienes? Mijo. Una tosecita. Toma un poco de agua.*

Sospecho algo de esa tos. Carraspera. Catarro. No. Atoramiento. Se te sube la sangre a la cabeza. Cada vez que Jabalí tosía era porque estaba entrampándome de alguna u otra forma. Ahí mismo. Cuando aparecía la tosecita, aparecía la mentira.

—*Hoy tengo que salir—decía Jabalí—Ahem. Department meetings. Ahem. Tú comprenderás. Ahem. No puedes venir conmigo. Ahem. Son profesores.*

Asuntos amorosos. Metido en ese lío con esa chilla. Y yo sabía que me mentía. Y disfrutaba su mentira. Porque sabía que me mentía. Pero ahora, ahem, qué me trae esta nueva tosecita. Estamos en el booth, y te lo juro, me siento bien a tono con los Mariachis y las velas.

—*¿Qué pido? Chipo.*
—*Pide lo que quieras, Chipa.*
—*No sé si pedir el bifsteak gaucho o el trío dinámico.*
—*Pide lo que quieras, Chipa, ¿Cuál crees tú que debo comer?*
—*Pide lo que quieras, Chipo.*
—*Ahí viene la waitress.*

—*Pues que se espere. We haven't decided yet.*
—*I know what I want, el gaucho.*
—*Ahem, but it comes with garlic bread and fries. Ahem. You are on a diet. Let me see if I have enough to cover it. Sorry. Ahem. You'll have it next time. Or you'll have to select between the steak or the piña colada.*
—*Piña colada, then.*
—*But you understand, we'll have to share the piña colada.*
—*Hurry up, please, it's time.*[4]
—*Just a moment, please. We haven't made up our minds. For the time being, please, ahem, bring the lady a piña colada.*
—*Just one?*
—*Yes, with two straws, and for me, ahem, a frosty glass of tap water with crushed ice, no cubes.*
—*You see, ahem, if you hadn't ordered the piña colada we could have had two dishes. Now, ahem, I'm running short. Plus the tip. I need a better job. Eating out every night. Did I send out my student loan payments last week?*
—*I told you to.*
—*Or was it this week? Wait, I made a deposit last week, which means no problem, it's due next week.*
—*Have you decided what you want?*
—*I'll have a steak.*
—*Ahem, no, we'll have fajitas instead. It's the same beef, but we can share fajitas.*
—*Yes, fajitas, thank you.*
—*How about another drink?*
—*Just water, please, and the bill. How much do I leave for a tip. 15% plus tax. Do you know if I paid the credit cards. Kika, we must stop eating out. You should learn how to cook. It would be so much healthier and we would save so much time and money.*

Para que me invitas a comer y me dejas con hambre, insatisfecha. No puedo escoger el plato que quiero del menú. Esta es la impotencia, la insatisfacción. Tú insatisfacción, tú duda. Mira lo que has hecho con mis cubiertos de plata. Yo te lo dije, no los uses. ¿Por qué no usas la plata que robaste de mi hermano? Esta plata es de mi abuela. Quiero tener recuerdos. Y motivos para ser respetada. Si no tengo plata, ya me respetan menos, y si no tengo hijos, menos y menos. Siempre hay que tener algo que ofrecer, para que te cuiden, o se acuerden de ti cuando estés vieja. Son delicados, hay que cuidarlos.

—I wanted to surprise you but you didn't even notice.
—You promised me you wouldn't use them again except for special occasions.
—A champagne dinner for two to celebrate the publication of the book by Yale. You didn't even notice the silver then, when you were supposed to, you went ahead and called Mona, and just talked and devoured without tasting the meat. Did you even notice that I left the table?

---

4. In part 2 of the poem *The Waste Land* (1922), by the American-born British poet T(homas) S(tearns) Eliot (1888–1965), this line is a bar- tender's call to clear the bar at closing time. It is repeated, but without punctuation, four times.

—I'm sorry. Listen, I'm sorry. Don't make me feel guilty.

—Did you notice how tender the fillet was?

—I'm sorry. But today I wake up, and breakfast is served on the table, you are not there, and I look at the bagel with cheese, and I see my silver fork tarnished. What? My silver used for bagels? You don't respect my wishes. You do whatever you please. Whatever you damn well please.

—You said you weren't hungry, then you wanted more.

—Cheese.

—Why didn't you tell me. I could have cooked you rice and beans.

—Okay.

—Rice and beans?

1998

## Pelos en la lengua

El bilingüismo es una estética bound to double business. O, 'tis most sweet when in one line two crafts directly meet. To be and not to be.[1] Habla con la boca llena and from both sides of its mouth. Está con Dios y con el Diablo. Con el punto y con la coma. Es un purgatorio, un signo grammatical interme-dio, entre heaven and earth, un semicolon entre la independencia y la estadi-dad, un estado libre asociado, un mamarracho multicultural. No tiene cláu-sulas ni subterfugios, no anda con gríngolas ni con muletas, no es artrítico, no se queja—aúlla como un perro al infinito y pide maná del cielo que caiga como lluvia—no se ahoga en un vaso de agua, no deja que le doren la píl-dora—no anda con yeso, saltando como un güimo con muletas de aquí pá allá—no es el canario que se balancea en el columpio dentro de la jaula comiendo los pistachos—se ha ido y se sigue yendo de todas las jaulas como Pedro por su casa y no ha vuelto a mirar hacia atrás. No tiene 10 mandamien-tos porque no tiene pelos en la lengua, pero tiene huevos—yo los he venido poniendo desde toda mi obra que es una sola—y la llamo el manifiesto de los huevos poéticos—se hace mostrando los huevos, metiendo la pata, pisseando aquí y pisseando allá. Nace del fuego popular, del pan, de la tierra, y de la libertad. Es un perro realengo atravesando un puente entre el norte y el sur, entre el siglo XX y el siglo XXI, entre Segismundo y Hamlet, entre Neruda y Whitman, entre Dickinson y Sor Juana, entre Darío y Stein, entre Sarmiento y Melville—entre los dos yo's en choque está el Yo-Yo Boing![2]

2000

1. A play on Shakespeare's *Hamlet*, Act 3, scene 1, line 58: "To be, or not to be." The previous sentence is Act 3, scene 4, lines 185.8–.9 (num-bering per *The Norton Shakespeare*).
2. See p. 1972. Herman Melville (1819–1891), American author. *Segismundo*: like Hamlet, a deeply troubled prince in a classic play—*La vida es sueño* (Life Is a Dream, 1635–36), by the Span-ish dramatist Pedro Calderón de la Barca (1600–1681). *Neruda*: Pablo Neruda (1904–1973), Chil-ean poet and diplomat. *Whitman*: Walt Whitman (1819–1892), American poet. *Dickinson*: Emily Dickinson (1830–1886), American poet. *Sor Juana*: Sor Juana Inés de la Cruz (1648 or 1651–1695), Mexican nun, scholar, and writer. *Darío*: Rubén Darío (1867–1916), Nicaraguan poet. *Stein*: Gertrude Stein (1874–1946), American writer. *Sarmiento*: Domingo Faustino Sarmiento Albarracín (1811–1888), Argentinian activist, in-tellectual, and writer; president of Argentina 1868–74.

# ANA CASTILLO
## b. 1953

Ana Castillo was born in the Chicago inner city. After graduating from Jones Commercial High School, she attended Chicago City College for two years before entering Northeastern Illinois University, where she earned her bachelor's degree in 1975. Castillo went on to earn a master's in Latin American and Caribbean Studies at the University of Chicago and a doctorate in American Studies from the University of Bremen, Germany, in 1991. She was on the faculty at DePaul University, in Chicago, until she moved to New Mexico.

Castillo started writing poetry, in Spanish, in college. Her collection *The Invitation* (1979) included Spanish-language originals along with English translations by Carol Maier. National recognition came with the collection *Women Are Not Roses* (1984). *The Mixquiahuala Letters*, an experimental epistolary novel about obsession and betrayal, was published by a small press in 1986 and republished by Doubleday in 1992.

*The Mixquiahuala Letters*, three sections of which are included in this anthology, asks the reader to take an active role in shaping the plot. Castillo's aesthetic strategy resembles that of the Argentinian writer Julio Cortázar in his classic experimental novel *Rayuela* (Hospcotch, 1963) in that it provides different sequences in which to read the sections. Castillo provides one sequence for the conformist, one for the cynic, and one for the quixotic person. The narrator—the letter writer—is a Mayan woman from Chicago, her correspondent is an Anglo friend, and their dialogue spans a decade. The plot revolves around the conflict between genders: A strong woman faces a man weakened by desire and trapped between two cultures.

In 1988, Castillo collaborated with the playwright Cherríe Moraga and the literary critic Norma Alarcón in translating the anthology *This Bridge Called My Back: Writings by Radical Woman of Color* (1981), edited by Moraga and the theorist Gloria Anzaldúa, into Spanish as *Este puente mi espalda: Voces de mujeres tercermundistas en los Estados Unidos* (This Bridge Called My Back: Voices of Third World Woman in the United States, 1988). Two years later, in the experimental verse novel *Sapogonia (An Anti-Romance in 3/8 Meter)* (1990), Castillo explored the destructive powers of heterosexual relationships as well as the importance of women as keepers and transmitters of culture and the sense of tradition at the heart of *mestizo* civilization. In her seminal book *Massacre of Dreamers: Essays on Xicanisma* (1994), Castillo presented a theoretical framework through which to understand the plight of Latina women, particularly those of Mexican American descent. In her view, the Chicano Movement achieved important political changes but left women's roles untouched. The philosophy of *Xicanisma*—its playful name refers in part to the Mexicas in pre-Columbian Mexico—is meant to be a call to a spiritual but also erotic life, with an acknowledgment of traditional healing and of the "mother-bond principle" that is repressed in the process of becoming an adult. Her views have made Castillo, like Moraga and Anzaldúa, an influential thinker among feminist women of color.

Castillo regularly denounces the troublesome place *lo mexicano* has in the American imagination, the inhumanity her people are often subjected to. Throughout her work—from the novel *So Far from God* (1993) to the story collection *Loveboys* (1996) to the play *Psst . . . I Have Something to Tell You, Mi Amor* (2005)—she has also explored themes such as adolescence as a rite of passage involving drugs, violence, and gang participation; the transit of people across the border; motherhood, especially as a single parent; and the role of Catholicism among Chicanos.

In her novel *The Guardians* (2007), a chapter of which appears in this anthology, the characters are part of a community devastated by death and longing. Regina, a widow, is in charge of the education of her nephew, Gabo, a young man whose religious devotion increasingly pushes him into hallucinatory states. The plot revolves around the search for Rafa, who is Regina's brother and Gabo's father. Each of the ten chapters is divided into sections where characters speak in the first person, offering their sides of the story. Throughout, Castillo combines English, Spanish, and Spanglish, sometimes by conceiving an idea in one language and delivering it in another. She offers no glossary and makes no apologies for infusing *el español* into her work. Neither condescendingly nor self-righteously, she seeks to illustrate the elasticity of language in the United States.

---

## *FROM* THE MIXQUIAHUALA[1] LETTERS

## Letter Seven

Poor Alicia,

A high school diploma in art, no marketable skills and such depth of loneliness that you spent the winter refuged in your bedroom in that wonderful home of your childhood. If you didn't look out at the greyness of the suburban street and only painted, you wouldn't have to face the disoriented future you'd begun to create.

You wouldn't have to think of Rodney, your boyfriend from Harlem. Rodney, always down or high on something, who never kept an appointment on time, remembered to call, or told the truth unless it was to his advantage.

So your passion poured itself into watercolors, pale and removed, like the memories of a few luscious weeks in Acapulco, a brown-skinned man who'd sung lullabys in a native dialect and told folktales of his righteous ancestors. It would've all been relegated to your powerful dreamworld had it not been for one letter.

He probably wondered for a long time afterward, since of course there had been no return address, where that scribbled envelope he had mailed so far away would finally rest.

He might've imagined a woman, as pale as you, but older, with hair the color of straw in the sun (not black like yours since you inherited your coloring from your Andalucian[2] grandmother) and her eyes would be the color of the sky on a troubled day. She would climb the stairs (like the ones he saw in a Pedro Infante[3] film when he first moved to Acapulco) to your room where you'd be at the window, sobbing now and then into a perfumed hanky, nursing a broken heart.

His fantasy wouldn't have been all that absurd or out of bounds with reality because, in fact, it had been your mother who'd brought up the letter; her eyes are the color of the sky when it's about to storm, and you had sobbed with a broken heart, onto your sketch pad if not into a hanky.

The Indian who had played lovers' games with a complacent wife and a hot, young gringa would've found it all as glamorous as the film he'd seen long ago because this scene would include him as the star.

Did you keep the letter after reading it twice, under your pillow, or in the bureau drawer with the mementos of your adolescence? Did you take it out

---

1. A town in central-eastern Mexico.
2. From Andalusia, a region of southern Spain.

3. José Pedro Infante Cruz (1917–1957), Mexican movie actor and singer.

nights when you couldn't sleep or paint, or when Rodney had stood you up in the subway, and wistfully hope for the Indian wife's death so that you might return to your paradise niche overlooking the sea and embraced by the sky?

At the start of the new summer you picked up and took the bus to Chicago, pallid and all tied up in a knot like a pretzel from Central Park.[4]

It was not destined to be a particularly good summer for either of us.

i took my final exams and finished at the university. You stayed with me in my mother's flat, sleeping on the floor of my room. She wasn't pleased a second daughter had split with her husband and we tried to keep out of each other's way. Stones of silent condemnation were thrown from every direction, relatives and friends who believed "bad wives" were bad people.

My husband had moved to California, a move that held more promise than being unemployed without a goal or aim in Chicago. One would've thought i'd sentenced him to hard labor in Siberia.[5]

For all our summer had not been, we managed to have our special days because we were bound in that yet undefined course known as The New Woman's Emergence.

At a pier, i read poems and passages out of books aloud while you painted and commented that the lake seemed immense enough to take us as far as China.

My mother had been close to female companions only during her adolescence. My older sisters never maintained close relationships with women after marriage. When a woman entered the threshold of intimacy with a man, she left the companions of her sex without looking back. Her needs had to be sustained by him. If not, she was to keep her emptiness to herself.

We included in our clandestine chats and activities the sister who'd dared to declare a separation from her husband of a decade. We invited her dancing with us, to view avant-garde films, picket supermarkets, and she went eagerly.

She was enthusiastic about all our suggestions because for the first time in her life she had a choice, expressed an opinion and was able to decide what she wanted to do on a Saturday night.

What we could not offer my sister was acceptance into society, her raison d'être. At the end of the summer, she went back to her husband. i packed a duffel bag with jeans, poems, and a few books, and went to follow mine too.

Always,

T.

## Letter Fifteen

So Alicia, as you may reluctantly recall:

California ended one summer day. The separation from my husband, the meager salary from a part-time job, the eviction out of the apartment, all pointed to an unavoidable exile.

4. Grand public park in Manhattan.
5. Area of northern Asia in Russia; i.e., a remote, isolated place.

There was a definite call to find a place to satisfy my yearning spirit, the Indian in me that had begun to cure the ails of humble folk distrustful of modern medicine; a need for the sapling woman for the fertile earth that nurtured her growth.

Ever the butterfly, not spared of mortality, and California could offer no more than an end if i stayed.

No aimless rambler, or total free spirit that could be blown in the wind's preferred direction, i searched for my home, be it a cave alongside a barren cliff, a ranch of chickens and pigs, a city, with a multitude of familiar faces as confused and hungry as me. i chose Mexico.

Books and curiosity gave me substantial reason to seek the past by visiting the wealth of ancient ruins that recorded awesome yet baffling civilization. i planned out a route: afterward, i would settle in Mexico City.

Our "love affair" was at its height and the idea of the journey that would lead from ruin to ruin offered your creativity new dimensions, so before returning to New York—of course, you joined me in the new adventure.

Not so long ago, as we rinsed out late night tea cups, yawned and scratched, prepared for bed, when i stopped to see you for a few days on my way from one place to another, you mentioned *Mexico Revisited*.[6] Wearily, you muttered, never having been able to pull apart its entanglement in your memory. You sensed, in the end, it all had to have meant something, that, if we were able to analyze, it would be pertinent, not just to benefit our lives, but womanhood.

i nodded, alert, having already begun to open the sealed passages to those months. "i'm writing about it," i confessed. You shuddered, went to bed.

## Letter Twenty-One

¿Sabes?

Nearly a month has gone by since i began to remember the Yucatán[7] saga. The conclusion must be the cause of this heartburn and not the chicharrón[8] in hot sauce i had three weeks ago. To be rid of it, i must create distance:

### Un cuento sin ritmo/Time is Fluid

The two women arrived on the first ferry that morning. They were bombarded by a dozen urchins wanting to carry their bags, direct them to the best place to stay, eat, swim. None got the chance, nor so much as a smile.

The sea was sapphire, a fluid orchid. Sea birds swooped and skimmed along its surface. Men, whose gold-capped teeth caught glimmers of sun as they gave pitches for a great day at the Garrafón,[9] swallowed the women with their black unfriendly eyes. No one heard the women speak. They didn't smile. Behind a wall of opaque glass, they were left alone

---

6. Possibly the 1955 book by the American writer Erna Fergusson (1888–1964).
7. Peninsula connecting southeastern Mexico with northern Central America.
8. Fried pork rind.
9. El Garrafón Natural Reef Park, on Isla Mujeres, in the Mexican Caribbean.

but were watched from a distance, followed. Boys called to them. "Hey, gringas! ¡Oye, chula!"[1] The men who leaned against entrances to the souvenir shops snickered, elbowed each other and whispered, threw obscene kisses in the air.

The women didn't see this. They didn't hear. They were protected by an invisible amulet, a spiritual guardian whose great wings enfolded them as they trudged over the hot sands.

One wears faded blue jeans rolled over the ankles, the other, army fatigues; both have bandanas to hide their hair. Their bags are unstylish and show wear. A woman pulls her small child back into the cafe where she cooks, casts a cynical look their way. She is glad she's not them. Still she wonders, her eagle squint says.

The days were long. There are three, not evident by a calendar or newspaper but by the three identical suns the women witness rise each day before they take the ferry away from the island.

There are voices everywhere, but they are unintelligible sounds, not syllables that form words, messages, but sounds just the same, a grating sound that blends with other sounds blended with that of the sea that eventually becomes a single drone.

It isn't obvious that the women have little money. It is obvious that they're foreigners and typical of the youth of the day, travellers rather than tourists. It isn't surprising that they stop at the first shabby motel they pass.

A young man, perhaps only seventeen, shows them to a room. A girl, with a watermelon belly and an infant perfectly formed but tinier than an elf who clings to her skirt, hides behind a door and watches her husband take the women's bags to the first of many empty rooms along the stretch of sand.

Once the curtains are drawn and the women are left alone, they undress and rinse off in the shower that has only cold water. They put on swimsuits and carefully hide passports and travelers' checks under a loose tile on the floor. They have done this without saying a word. They do not even smile when they're alone.

Out in the blaring sun they choose a road, any will lead to the sea. The one with the legs of a male adolescent, ahead. She jumps rocks, occasionally stops to examine something that has crashed with the waves against the jutting rocks of the sea. The other goes steadily. She's not agile, but robust, full.

1986, 1992

## FROM THE GUARDIANS

### From Regina

It was raining all night hard and heavy, making the land shiver—all the bare ocotillo and all the prickly pear. In the morning we found a tall yucca collapsed in the front yard. Everything is wet and gray so the day has not

---

1. Hey, cutie!

made itself known yet. It is something in between. As usual, I'm anxious. Behind the fog are los Franklins.[1] Behind those mountains is my brother. Waiting. On this side we're waiting, too, my fifteen-year-old nephew, Gabo, and his dog, la Winnie.

Winnie has one eye now. She got it stuck by a staghorn cactus that pulled it right out. Blood everywhere that day. By the time Gabo got home from his after-school bagger's job at el Shur Sav, I was back from the vet's with Winnie, rocking her like a baby. You couldn't blame the dog for being upset, losing her eye and all.

I kept Gabo this time around because I want him to finish high school. I don't care what the authorities say about his legal status. We'll work it out, I say to Gabo, who, when he was barely walking I changed his diapers, which I also tell him. He's still embarrassed to be seen in his boxers. That's okay. I'm embarrassed to be seen in mine, too. Thirty years of being widowed, you better believe I dress for comfort.

"Stop all this mourning," my mamá used to say. "You were only married six months. The guy was a drug addict, por Dios!" She actually would say that and repeat it even though Junior died fighting for his country. That's why we got married. He was being shipped off to Vietnam. If the coroner suggested he had needle tracks, well, I don't know about that.

Mamá always had a way of turning things around for me, to see them in the worst light possible. It's probably not a nice thing to say you are glad your mother's dead. But I am glad she's not around. Can I say that and not worry about a stretch in purgatory? Then I'll say that.

We've been waiting a week, me and Gabo—for his dad to come back. He's been back and forth across that desert, dodging the Border Patrol so many times, you'd think he wouldn't even need a coyote[2] no more. The problem is the coyotes and narcos[3] own the desert now. You look out there, you see thorny cactus, tumbleweed, and sand soil forever and you think, No, there's nothing out there. But you know what? They're out there—los mero-mero cabrones.[4] The drug traffickers and body traffickers. Which are worse? I can't say.

So the problem is Rafa, my brother, can't just come across without paying somebody. Eight days ago we got a call. It was a woman's voice. She said in Spanish that Rafa was all right and that he was coming in a few days so we had better have the balance of the money ready. Who did those people think they were, I asked myself. That woman on the phone acted so damn cocky. I swear, if I knew who she was, I'd report her to the authorities, lock her up for five years. How dare she treat people like that? Take advantage of their poverty and laws that force people to crawl on their bellies for a chance to make it.

Truth is Rafa should have just stayed here last time he came to work the pecans. That's when he finally let me keep his son. Someone in the family's got to finish high school, I said to him. Poor Rafa, all alone like that now, going back and forth, even though I think he has a new wife down in

---

1. Small mountain range that extends from El Paso, Texas, to New Mexico. Regina and Gabo live in the fictitious town of Cabuche, New Mexico.
2. Smuggler of immigrants across the U.S.-Mexico border.
3. Here, drug smugglers. *Narcs* can also refer to narcotics officers.
4. The very true bastards.

Chihuahua.[5] He won't say nothing out of respect for Gabo's dead mother. Just the mention of Ximena and the boy falls apart. It's been almost seven years now but Gabo was just a child. His mind sort of got stuck in that time when his mother didn't make it. He was here with me that winter, too. When Rafa and Ximena were returning they got separated. The coyotes said no, the women had to go in another truck. Three days later the bodies of four women were found out there in that heat by the Border Patrol. All four had been mutilated for their organs. One of them was Ximena. It was in all the news.

I've been fighting to keep my sobrino since then but my brother gets terco[6] about it and keeps insisting on taking him back to the other side. What for? I tell him. Because he's Mexican, Rafa says. As if I'm not, because I choose to live on this side. He's got to know his grandparents— meaning Ximena's folks. He's not gonna become a gringo and forget who he is, my brother says of his only son, as if getting an education would erase the picture the boy keeps in his head of how his mother died.

I stayed and worked here in Cabuche, first in the pecans and cotton. Because of marrying Junior, I got his army benefits. I could stay and not hide in the shadows no more. This meant no more picking, no more peeling chiles, and no more canning. Instead, I got up my courage one year and signed up for night classes at the community college. I did pretty good in my classes. I really liked being in a classroom. I liked the desks, the smell of the chalk and erasers, the bulletin boards with messages about holidays like Valentine's Day and Martin Luther King Day. So later I got more courage and applied for a job as a teacher's aide in the middle school. That's how I bought my casita, here on the mesa, where I can't see los Franklins this morning. But I know they are out there, playing with me. Like giants, they take the sun and play with people's eyes, changing colors. Like shape-shifters, they change the way they look, too. They let the devoted climb up along their spines to crown them with white crosses and flowers and mementos. They give themselves that way, those guardians between the two countries.

I do not know what Rafa is talking about his son becoming a gringo. These lands, this unmerciful desert—it belonged to us first, the Mexicans. Before that it belonged to los Apaches. Los Apaches were mean, too. They knew how to defend themselves. And they're still not too happy about losing everything, despite the casinos up by their land. "Keep right on going," they'll tell tourists when they try to pull over on the highway that cuts across it during dry season.

Ha. I wish I could say that out here whenever some stupid hunter wanders near my property. It's just me and the barbed-wire fence between the hunter and government land where he can do what he pleases, all dressed up like if he was in the National Guard.

One day we héard some shots. It wasn't even dawn yet, that Sunday. Winnie went nuts—the way heelers do at the sign of something amiss. Gabo got up—pulling up his jeans, tripping on the hems of them, barefoot. "What was that, Tía?" he said, all apurado[7] and the dog, meanwhile, barking, barking. This was before the accident, when she could practically see in the dark. I let her go out, and la Winnie ran toward the fence that divides my property

---

5. State in northern Mexico; the city of Chihuahua is the state capital.

6. Stubborn. *Sobrino*: nephew.
7. In a hurry.

and BLM land.[8] "HEY, HEY!" was all my poor nephew called out. He always freezes up. I think he remembers his mother.

Over in El Paso people have asked me if I'm not afraid of the coyotes and rattlers living right next to the wide-open spaces kept by the Bureau of Land Management. The worse snakes and coyotes, I always say, are the ones on two legs. People think that's funny.

"Hey-Hey," Gabo called out again in the dark of the new day out there, with a little less conviction the second time. But la Winnie kept right on barking-barking. I went in the house and got my rifle. When I came out I went up to the fence and pointed the rifle somewhere I couldn't see. What were they shooting anyway? We don't got any deer around here. "YOU ARE WAY TOO CLOSE TO MY LAND!" I yelled like I was Barbara Stanwyck or Doña Bárbara or somebody and I took a shot that rang out like a 30-30.[9] It must've woken up la gente all the way in town. A little while after that I heard Jeeps taking off.

We couldn't go back to sleep after that so I made us some atole[1] and put on the TV. I needed to fold up the laundry I'd left in the dryer anyway. Winnie didn't come in like she would have normally, ready to be fed. She stayed outside roaming the grounds.

"Your father will come back," I said to Gabo that morning at the table about my kid brother who you'd think was way older than me, his mind full of the beliefs of another time, another era, belonging to the Communist Party and all that. He's so proud of it, too.

Gabo's older sister ran off a long time ago with a guy over there in Chihuahua and no one's heard from her since then. So all Gabo has to count on is his father.

And me, of course, his tía Regina.

But he's lost way too much already in his short life to know that for sure. So that's what I'm doing right now, trying to do something good—for my brother and Gabo but for me, too—to see that my sobrinito gets a chance. One day I'm gonna take him to Washington, D.C.

"What the hell for?" Rafa asked me when I mentioned it.

"To see where the Devil makes his deals," I said.

One day I'm gonna take my nephew to New York, too, where I've never been but it's on my list—my very long list—of places to see in this life. I may even take him to Florence, Italy, to see the David.[2] Well, actually I'm the one that wants to see the statue of David but it won't hurt for Gabo to know a little something about great art. What? Why not? All our lives we have to be stuck to the ground like desert centipedes? My nephew doesn't show any signs of interest in the arts. He don't talk about girls. He goes to Mass every Sunday down in Cabuche. If I don't drive him or let him take my truck, he walks. He observes all the holy days of obligation. My biggest fear is he's gonna become a priest. Wait 'til Rafa hears about it. He'll be so disappointed.

---

8. Public land administed by the Bureau of Land Management, an agency within the U.S. Department of Interior.
9. Thirty-caliber cartridge used in a sporting rifle, typically used to hunt deer. *Barbara Stanwyck*: American actress (1907–1990); one of her major roles was as the head of a frontier family on the television series *The Big Valley* (1965–69); Doña Bárbara would be the Mexican American version of Stanwyck in that role.
1. Cornstarch-based hot drink.
2. Famous statue by the Italian artist Michelangelo (1475–1564).

* * *

Gabo found a hawk. It was young, you could tell. It was the most beautiful thing you ever saw, brown and near-white with dashes of black on the wings. Nature is so geometrically precise. If you look real close at birds and fish, too, you see how everything—every feather, fin, wing, gill, is colored just so.

Somewhere I heard that baby hawks have a high mortality rate. This one didn't make it. It must've been trying to take flight when it got hit on the road. Its neck was broken but otherwise it looked like it was sleeping, as they say about people when they're in their coffins. (Except for Mamá. The mortician had painted on such bright orange lipstick and powder too light for her complexion she looked dead for sure.)

"What are you going to do with it?" I asked my nephew. He looked so sad. You'd think he had killed the hawk himself. He'd found it on the road. He was driving my truck back from work. I let him take the truck since he comes home after dark. When he saw it, he pulled over and put it on the passenger seat. "I'm going to bury it, Tía," Gabo replied solemnly, the way he speaks most of the time, "with your permission." My nephew is so polite to the point of being antiquated. True, humble Mexican kids have better manners than American Mexican kids, but Gabo sounds like a page out of Lope de Vega.[3] Lope de Vega, the prince of Spain's Golden Age. I haven't read anything of his; I heard the Spanish teacher at the school talking to the students about him. But Spain's Golden Age of literature is on my list of things to read—my very long list. I've done some reading on my own, García Márquez,[4] for example. *One Hundred Years of Solitude* was assigned in one of the classes I took at the community college and then I looked for other books of his, like the story of Eréndira and her wicked grandmother, that, in some ways, reminded me of my own life with Mamá in the desert. I read the newspaper every day. But now with Gabo here I have become more conscious of the importance of broadening the mind through reading. The next book fair the school has I'm going to buy us everything we see that we think we'll like. We'll treat it like a candy store. I'll have to assure my considerate nephew, who behaves as if he may be overstaying his visit—the way he tiptoes around and hardly eats, although I'm not sure why; it's not because of anything I've said or done, I hope—that I have saved up for such a splurge. Otherwise, he'll hesitate to get anything, even if he sees something he really wants.

The hawk was on Gabo's dresser. He brought home a white veladora.[5] He got it for a dollar with his discount at work. It took exactly seven days to burn through. When the candle was done, Gabo said he would bury the hawk. Every night he prayed over it. "You look like some kind of shaman," I told him when I peeked in to say good night and there he was, standing in the glow of the flame, head bowed, hands suspended just above the dead bird. It looked as if he were trying to resurrect it, although I'm sure that's not what he was trying to do.

When the candle had burned out I found it in the trash. Where was the bird, I asked Gabo. Had he buried it already? Where? When? I thought we were going to hold a funeral for it. I felt a little left out of his ceremonies.

---

3. Or Félix Lope de Vega y Carpio (1562–1635), Spanish playwright and poet.
4. Gabriel García Márquez (b. 1927), Colombian fiction writer, screenwriter, and journalist.
5. Short, thick candle used by Mexicans in religious ceremonies.

"Yes," he said.

Later that day, I saw a hawk perched on the fence post by the gate. The front gate is about an eighth of a mile from the front door. It was brown with near-white feathers, black dashes on the wings. It looked a lot like our dead hawk. Maybe it was its mother or some other relation.

"Where did you say you buried that bird?" I asked Gabo when he came to the kitchen to make a sandwich for his school lunch. He refuses the money I offer so that he can eat in the cafeteria or go out with some of the kids. He saves his work money, spends only on what he needs. He offered his whole check to me at the beginning, but I looked at him as if he were crazy and told him to use it on himself. His sandwiches are very frugal, too—one slice of meat between two slices of ninety-nine-cent whole wheat bread.

"I didn't," Gabo replied.

"You didn't what?" I asked. "You didn't say or you didn't bury it?"

"No," was all he said.

"Maybe that bird was carrying that virus, Gabo," I said. "How much did you handle it anyway?"

"Do not worry yourself so much, Tía," he said.

As far as teenagers go, from what I hear at the school and from the students' parents, Gabo could get a lot worse on my nerves.

This is not why I am so anxious all the time—having a teenager to look out for now. It was not even part of the Change, like the doctor down in Juárez[6] told me last year. The anxiety is just part of me. On any given day, a person can find several reasons to be anxious. If you don't find it in your own life at that moment, all you have to do is pick up a newspaper and read the headlines. Being a fifty-plus-year-old woman alone for so long, widowed thirty years, that could be cause enough. Every paycheck covers the bills to the penny—when I'm lucky.

Every three months or so I come up with another get-rich-quick idea that ends up not making me much money and sometimes ends up costing me some. I've delivered groceries for people out here in the boonies who can't or don't want to drive into town every week. I've taken orders for curtains and sewed quite a few up. Over the years, I've dog-sat, old people–sat, house-sat. I sold Amway, Avon, and Mary Kay products, even though I am allergic to most anything with a chemical scent. I had Tupperware parties. I sold red candy apples and pecan bread in the parking lot of el Shur Sav. For a time, I had a little business out of my troca selling pizzas. I'd buy them wholesale down the road at a place across from the police station. Then I'd drive them to an empty lot on Main Street and put out my sign. People didn't really want to bother ordering a pizza ahead of time. Just drive up and I hand them one into their car or troca or maybe they were on foot. On weekends I'd make a killing. Then a guy started doing it, right next to me, out of his car. He gave away free Cokes, so he ran me out of business. A long time ago I went door to door selling bibles, the King James version. Then my mother found out and told Padre Juan Bosco and he had one of his talks with me, so I felt morally inclined to quit. All these jobs I had in addition to whatever other full-time work I was putting in somewhere. And all of it caused me anxiety.

6. City in the state of Chihuahua.

I keep almost nothing from my nephew now, except what I might look like in a swimsuit, but why he would care to see his fat old aunt half naked I wouldn't know, but nearly everything in my heart or that crosses my mind I share with him. He's been God-sent that way, I think. I had no idea how lonely I was until one day I found myself at my Singer stitching up his jeans, talking my head off, and he, so patiently, sitting nearby listening to it all. Or at least he looked like he was listening.

One thing I won't tell Gabo about is my money worries. He'd run off so as not to be another burden on me. The other topic I cannot bring myself to approach is the fact that we haven't heard from his papá yet. It isn't as if Gabo himself hasn't noticed. I heard him crying into his pillow one night. He probably envisions his father being killed by a coyote and left in the desert like what happened to his mother. It isn't like Rafa not to get word to me somehow, but then again, I wouldn't be terribly surprised if he changed his mind about coming. That coyote woman on the phone was horrid—he may not have wanted to pay them all that they wanted. The fact is, all Gabo and I can do is wait.

In the meantime I discovered where he buried the hawk. It was right near the fallen yucca. La one-eyed Winnie, or Tuerta, as I am calling her now, dug it up. My Mescalero Apache friend, Uriel, told me over the phone that Gabo's finding the hawk was very good luck for him. She said the hawk is good protection medicine. I wonder if finding where it was buried and digging it up was good luck for la Tuerta. Poor little hawk—with so many now trying to benefit from its death. I reburied it this time between two huge chollas, where I don't think the dog will go, seeing that she's cautious now about getting too near anything with thorns.

• • •

I'd rather be pricked by a thousand thorns than have to think about what my little brother may have endured. The fact is, however, that I don't know what exactly he had to endure. Sometimes I like to think he is back in Chihuahua with a pregnant wife and that we just never heard from him because he became too selfish and didn't care about Gabo no more or his past life with Ximena.

Another week went by when a foco[7] went on in my head and I realized that the phone number of that nasty coyote woman that called me might be on the caller-ID box. We don't get many calls. All the numbers of anyone who has ever called since I put in the caller ID right around the time Rafa left my nephew here were still on there. We never erased them. Most of the time we didn't even pay attention to it. Without saying nothing to Gabo, I checked and, sure enough, there was a call from El Paso the very same day la coyota had called me.

"Bueno," she answered when I tried it. I knew it was her. It was a voice full of intriga and bad tidings.

I went on to tell her who I was and that we were still waiting for Rafa. "I don't know what you are talking about," she said and hung up on me, proving all the more that she very well did.

---

7. Spotlight.

My heart started breaking with the sound of the dial tone on the other end and I knew that my brother had been done some awful wrong. Still, without mentioning my concern to my nephew, the next day I took someone into my confidence at the school. I consider most of the teachers much more intelligent than me, with their college education and all. One of them could give me some advice, I thought, but it would have to be someone I could trust, since my brother trying to cross without papers was obviously against the law. Most of the teachers at the school are Mexican or at least of Mexican heritage although half of them call themselves "Hispanic," which means they don't want to be considered Mexican. Or at least that is how Rafa and I feel about the word. It is one of the few political points we agree on.

Mr. Betancourt, the history teacher, calls himself "Chicano." He wears a long ponytail and while he obliges the system with a nice shirt and tie, he always has on jeans. All this about Betancourt told me I could trust him with my fears about Rafa, so I pulled him aside the very next day and told him what I thought.

"We might be able to find an address for that phone number," Betancourt told me. He said there was a phone number that you could call where, if the number you had was listed, you'd get a name and maybe an address. I thought I would try it when I got home, but he took out a cell phone from inside his jean jacket and, to my surprise, within ten minutes had obtained the woman's information for me.

"Will you go to her house?" he asked me.

Betancourt is about thirty-five but most of his hair has gone white. He looks old and young at the same time. I remember when I was in my thirties, I felt like that—old and young at the same time. Now I'm middle-aged and I feel old and really old at the same time. Yes, I told him that I would, that I would have gotten in my truck and gone right then and there but that my nephew would need it for work in an hour. Betancourt nodded. He looked at his watch and then he said, "Let me move some things around. I can meet you somewhere in an hour or I can go pick you up at your house. I'll take you. It's probably not wise for you to go there alone."

Miguel. That's his name. He told me to call him Miguel or Mike but to please not call him Mr. Betancourt no more. I never called him just plain Betancourt to his face but that's how the teachers called him in the lounge. Especially a couple of the young women teachers said it like they meant something more by it. Sometimes a single man is as likely to be the object of a lot of unprofessional interest as a single woman, in particular the attractive ones, of which, at the school, I can count only four. I look around, too. I may not say nothing, being a fifty-plus-year-old widow, but I still look.

Miguel was handsome in his own way but more important, for the purposes of our errand, tall and very strong-looking. When he showed up at my house he was still wearing his tie. He decided to keep it on, he said, because it made him look like he might be someone of authority. "I mean, I'm not gonna say I'm with La Migra[8] or anything but it wouldn't hurt if they think we have some pull."

8. A term, derived from *inmigración* (Spanish) by Spanish-speaking U.S. communities, referring to Immigration and Customs Enforcement, Border Patrol, and similar agencies.

The woman's house was very close to the customs bridge going into Juárez. It was a little house like others on that block, nothing special about it, and if my brother was in there, if they were holding him for ransom, never in a million years would I have guessed it would have been in such an ordinary place and right there in the middle of everything. The woman herself opened the door. She looked us up and down, especially Miguel, who did start to look like some kind of agent all of a sudden, with his Serpico long hair and bigotes.[9]

At first she denied knowing anything, even the fact that she was the one who had called. Then Miguel took me by surprise. He pushed her, and next thing I knew, we were all in the house, in a dark, tiny, crowded living room with a dirty beige couch and two little kids, one in Pampers, in a playpen. "Listen," he said right in her face, "you are going to tell us what happened to this woman's brother or you are going right to jail—today. Do you understand? Do you understand?" He pushed her again so that she went reeling back until she hit a wall. She started crying. She might've been around thirty or so, with a bulging midriff from babies, and her breasts already sagging. The house smelled of stale cigarette smoke. The TV was blaring a Spanish channel. I felt sorry for the babies, who looked startled but hadn't started to cry. It was funny that they didn't cry when the mother was crying. Then she got hold of herself and looked me up and down. "What would I know about your brother?" she said to me with that same sneer I imagined that time she had called me. "Have you tried calling your family back in México? He's probably there."

Before I could even say nothing, Miguel took her by the shoulders and shook her so hard her head went back and forth like it was on a spring. "I'm only going to ask you one more time," he said. And before he asked again, she looked at me and with spittle coming out of the corners of her mouth and with more hate than I have ever felt from a human being, she seemed even glad to tell me, "Your brother must be dead, stupid. Why else do you think you never heard anything again? Do you think they come and tell *me* what goes on out there? I only know about the ones who make it. They come here until their people pay what they owe. Your brother? What do I know of him? They most likely left him to rot out in the desert because he was a tonto or maybe for being a pendejo[1] he got himself killed. What do I know? Now get out of here before I tell my husband you were here and you'll both be sorry you came."

It was like a movie. In movies about drug traficantes they have women like that, in their nightgowns in daytime in gloomy rooms and living an obscure existence. And they have guys like the one who drove up just as we were leaving, wearing a big anchor on a chain around his neck and a diamond earring in one ear. They—everything, even their frightened little kids who wouldn't cry—looked like they were right out of a bad drug video.

El coyote looked at Miguel as we left as if he was memorizing him, taking a mental photograph in case he ever saw him again. But neither said a word to the other.

I turned around and took a last glance at the woman, who stayed inside in the shadows. She knew something about my brother's fate. I felt it in my

9. Whiskers. *Serpico*: Frank Serpico (b. 1936), real-life plainclothes New York Police Department officer played by Al Pacino in the movie

*Serpico* (1973).
1. Coward, jerk, dummy. *Tonto*: fool.

heart. She could have given me some piece of information, however small, a gold nugget to take back to Gabo so that the poor boy would somehow, someday, find closure.

I wanted to go back in and shake her myself. Shake her until her stupid head fell off. Until her neck snapped and we'd carry her lifeless body to Gabo so that he could pray over it for seven days. Then he'd find a place to bury it even though his father had gotten no such consideration. And when la Tuerta Winnie sniffed up the corpse and started digging, fine; she could dig all she wanted. I'd let her dig up that estúpida's body so that all the coyotes that wanted to come on my little bit of land that I protected so well could feed off of her stupid flesh and lick her stupid bones clean. And then we'd all, me and Winnie and Gabo and Miguel, too, if he wanted, and even the coyotes with four feet, could go out to the BLM land and scatter the bones out there to dry in the sun, for sands and wind to wash over. And Rafa, wherever they had left him, would no longer be alone out there.

Then I felt Miguel take my hand. He had to pull me with him. "Come on," he muttered close to my ear. "We'd better get the hell out of here while we can."

2007

# EDUARDO MACHADO
## b. 1953

The playwright Eduardo Machado creates probing, often funny, sometimes disturbing anatomies of Cuban history and culture. Born in Havana into a well-to-do family, Machado moved with his family to the United States at age eight. He grew up in Southern California and has lived in New York City since 1980. The recipient of three National Endowment for the Arts fellowships and a Rockefeller grant, Machado is currently the head of the playwriting program at Columbia University's School of the Arts. Most of his dramatic works—over two dozen plays and several musicals—have been produced. Among the most recent are the plays *The Cook* (2004) and *Kissing Fidel* (2006). He has also written a memoir, *Tastes Like Cuba: An Exile's Hunger for Home* (2007).

Machado's best-known works are *The Floating Island Plays* (1991), a tetralogy that chronicles the lives of several interconnected families in Cuba and the United States. Set in the 1920s, the first play in the cycle, *The Modern Ladies of Guanabacoa* (1984), depicts a conservative and status-conscious family that is thrown into crisis when its patriarch is mysteriously murdered. The next two plays, *Fabiola* (1985) and *In the Eye of the Hurricane* (1989), show the impact of the Cuban Revolution on a wealthy family whose possessions are nationalized and many of whose members have to go into exile. Set in California in 1979, the last play in the cycle, *Broken Eggs* (1984)—the first act of which is excerpted here—is a black comedy about a well-off Cuban American family whose material prosperity cannot conceal the fact that, as a result of squabbles, divorces, and drugs, the family structure has been shattered. A condensed fictional history of twentieth-century Cuba, *The Floating Island Plays* pay homage to the author's cultural heritage even as they expose the myths that underlie it.

## FROM BROKEN EGGS

### CHARACTERS

SONIA MARQUEZ HERNANDEZ, a Cuban woman
LIZETTE, Sonia's daughter, nineteen years old
MIMI, Sonia's daughter
OSCAR, Sonia's son
MANUELA RIPOLL, Sonia's mother
OSVALDO MARQUEZ, Sonia's ex-husband
MIRIAM MARQUEZ, Osvaldo's sister
ALFREDO MARQUEZ, Osvaldo's and Miriam's father

### Time

A hot January day, 1979.

### Place

A country club in Woodland Hills, California, a suburb of Los Angeles.

## From Act One

A waiting room off the main ballroom of a country club in Woodland Hills, California, a suburb of Los Angeles. The room is decorated for a wedding. Up center, sliding glass doors leading to the outside; stage right, a hallway leading to the dressing room; stage left, an archway containing the main entrance to the room and a hallway leading to the ballroom. A telephone booth in one corner. Two round tables, one set with coffee service and the other for the cake.

In the dark, we hear MIMI whistling the wedding march. As the lights come up, LIZETTE is practicing walking down the aisle. MIMI is drinking a Tab and watching LIZETTE. They are both dressed in casual clothes.

MIMI: I never thought that any of us would get married, after all—
LIZETTE: Pretend you come from a happy home.
MIMI: We were the audience to one of the worst in the history of the arrangement.
LIZETTE: Well, I'm going to pretend that Mom and Dad are together for today.
MIMI: That's going to be hard to do if that mustached bitch, whore, cunt, Argentinian Nazi shows up to your wedding.
LIZETTE: Daddy promised me that his new wife had no wish to be here. She's not going to interfere.
    [MIMI starts to gag.]
    Mimi, why are you doing this.
MIMI: The whole family is going to be here.
LIZETTE: They're our family. Don't vomit again, Mimi, my wedding.
MANUELA: [Offstage.] Why didn't the bakery deliver it?

MIMI: Oh, no!

LIZETTE: Oh my God.

[MIMI *and* LIZETTE *run to the offstage dressing room.*]

MANUELA: [*Offstage.*] Who ever heard of getting up at 6 A.M.?

SONIA: [*Offstage.*] Mama, please—

[MANUELA *and* SONIA *enter.* SONIA *is carrying two large cake boxes.*
MANUELA *carries a third cake box.*]

MANUELA: Well, why didn't they?

SONIA: Because the Cuban bakery only delivers in downtown L.A. They
don't come out this far.

[MANUELA *and* SONIA *start to assemble the cake.*]

MANUELA: Then Osvaldo should have picked it up.

SONIA: It was my idea.

MANUELA: He should still pick it up, he's the man.

SONIA: He wanted to get a cake from this place, with frosting on it. But I
wanted a cake to be covered with meringue, like mine.

MANUELA: You let your husband get away with everything.

SONIA: I didn't let him have a mistress.

MANUELA: Silly girl, she ended up being his wife!

SONIA: That won't last forever.

MANUELA: You were better off with a mistress. Now you're the mistress.

SONIA: Please, help me set up the cake. . . . Osvaldo thought we should serve
the cake on paper plates. I said no. There's nothing worse than paper
plates. They only charge a dime a plate for the real ones and twenty dollars for the person who cuts it. I never saw a paper plate till I came to
the USA.

MANUELA: She used witchcraft to take your husband away, and you did
nothing.

SONIA: I will.

MANUELA: Then put powder in his drinks, like the witch lady told you to
do.

SONIA: I won't need magic to get him back, Mama, don't put powders in
his drink. It'll give him indigestion.

MANUELA: Don't worry.

SONIA: Swear to me. On my father's grave.

[*The cake is now assembled.*]

MANUELA: I swear by the Virgin Mary, Saint Teresa my patron saint[1] and
all the saints, that I will not put anything into your husband's food . . . as
long as his slut does not show up. Here. [*She hands* SONIA *a little bottle.*]

SONIA: No.

MANUELA: In case you need it.

SONIA: I won't.

MANUELA: You might want it later. It also gives you diarrhea for at least
three months. For love, you kiss the bottle, and thank the Virgin Mary.
For diarrhea, you do the sign of the cross twice.

SONIA: All right.

---

1. Teresa of Ávila (Teresa Sánchez de Cepeda y
Ahumada, 1515–1582), Spanish nun, mystic,
and writer; venerated as a saint by branches of
Christianity including the Roman Catholic
Church.

MANUELA: If your father was alive, he'd shoot him for you.

SONIA: That's true.

MANUELA: Help me roll the cake out.

SONIA: No. They'll do it. They're getting the room ready now. They don't want us in there. We wait here—the groom's family across the way.

MANUELA: The Jews?

SONIA: The Rifkins. Then we make our entrance.

MANUELA: I see.

SONIA: [*Looks at cake.*] Perfect. Sugary and white . . . pure.

MANUELA: Beautiful.

SONIA: I'm getting nervous.

MANUELA: It's your daughter's wedding. A very big day in a mother's life, believe me.

SONIA: Yes, a wedding is a big day.

MANUELA: The day you got married your father told me, "We are too far away from our little girl." I said to him, "But, Oscar, we live only a mile away." He said, "You know that empty acre on the street where she lives now?" I said, "Yes." He said, "I bought it and we are building another house there, then we can still be near our little girl."

SONIA: He loved me.

MANUELA: Worshipped you.

SONIA: I worshipped him. He'll be proud.

MANUELA: Where's your ex-husband, he's late.

[LIZETTE *enters and makes herself a cup of coffee.* SONIA *helps her.*]

SONIA: So how do you feel, Lizette, my big girl?

LIZETTE: I'm shaking.

MANUELA: That's good. You should be scared.

LIZETTE: Why, Grandma?

MANUELA: You look dark, did you sit out in the sun again?

LIZETTE: Yes, I wanted to get a tan.

MANUELA: Men don't like that, Lizette.

LIZETTE: How do you know?

SONIA: Mama, people like tans in America.

MANUELA: Men like women with white skin.

LIZETTE: That's a lie. They don't.

MANUELA: Don't talk back to me like that.

SONIA: No fights today, please, no fights. Lizette, tell her you're sorry. I'm nervous. I don't want to get a migraine, I want to enjoy today.

LIZETTE: Give me a kiss, Grandma.

[*They kiss.*]

Everything looks so good.

SONIA: It should—eight thousand dollars.

MANUELA: We spent more on your wedding and that was twenty-nine years ago. He should spend money on his daughter.

SONIA: He tries. He's just weak.

MANUELA: Don't defend him.

SONIA: I'm not.

MANUELA: Hate him. Curse him.

SONIA: I love him.

MANUELA: Sonia! Control yourself.

LIZETTE: He's probably scared to see everybody.

MANUELA: Good, the bastard.

[LIZETTE *exits to dressing room.*]

SONIA: Did I do a good job? Are you pleased by how it looks? [*She looks at the corsages and boutonnieres on a table.*] Purples, pinks and white ribbons . . . tulle. Mama, Alfredo, Pedro. . . . No, not Pedro's . . . Oscar's. . . . He just looks like Pedro. Pedro! He got lost. He lost himself and then we lost him.

MANUELA: Sonia!

SONIA: I'll pin yours on, Mama.

MANUELA: Later, it'll wilt if you pin it now.

[MIRIAM *enters. She is wearing a beige suit and a string of pearls.*]

SONIA: Miriam, you're here on time. Thank you, Miriam.

MIRIAM: Sonia, look. [*Points at pearls.*] They don't match. That means expensive. I bought them for the wedding.

MANUELA: Miriam, how pretty you look!

MIRIAM: Do you think the Jews will approve?

MANUELA: They're very nice, the Rifkins. They don't act Jewish. Lizette told me they put up a Christmas tree but what for I said to her?

MIRIAM: To fit in?

MANUELA: Why? Have you seen your brother?

MIRIAM: He picked us up last night from the airport.

MANUELA: Did he say anything to you?

MIRIAM: Yes, how old he's getting. . . . That's all he talks about.

MANUELA: Where's your husband?

MIRIAM: He couldn't come: business.

MANUELA: That's a mistake.

MIRIAM: I'm glad I got away.

MANUELA: But is he glad to be rid of you?

SONIA: Mama, go and see if Lizette needs help, please.

MANUELA: All right. Keep your husband happy, that's the lesson to learn from all this. Keep them happy. Let them have whatever they want. . . . Look at Sonia.

[*She exits to dressing room.*]

SONIA: Thank God for a moment of silence. Osvaldo this, Osvaldo that. Powder. Curse him. Poisons, shit . . .

MIRIAM: Are you all right? That faggot brother of mine is not worth one more tear: coward, mongoloid, retarded creep.

SONIA: Does he look happy to you?

MIRIAM: No.

SONIA: He looks sad?

MIRIAM: He always looked sad. Now he looks old and sad.

SONIA: Fear?

MIRIAM: Doesn't the Argentinian make him feel brave?

SONIA: He'll be mine again. He'll remember what it was like before the revolution. Alfredo and you being here will remind him of that. He'll remember our wedding—how perfect it was; how everything was right . . . the party, the limo, walking through the rose garden late at night, sleeping in the terrace room. I'm so hot I feel like I have a fever.

MIRIAM: "My darling children, do not go near the water, the sharks will eat you up." That's the lesson we were taught.

SONIA: Today I am going to show Osvaldo who's in control. Be nice to him today.

MIRIAM: He left you three months after your father died. He went because he knew you had no defense. He went off with that twenty-nine-year-old wetback. You know, we *had* to come here, but they *want* to come here. And you still want him back?

SONIA: If he apologizes, yes.

MIRIAM: Don't hold your breath. He lets everyone go. Pedro needed him—

SONIA: Don't accuse him of that, he just forgot.

MIRIAM: What? How could he forget. Pedro was our brother.

SONIA: He got so busy here working, that he forgot, he couldn't help him anyway. He was here, Pedro stayed in Cuba, you were in Miami, and I don't think anyone should blame anyone about that. No one was to blame!

MIRIAM: Oh, I'm having an attack . . . [*She shows Sonia her hands.*] See how I'm shaking? It's like having a seizure. Where's water?

[SONIA *gets her a glass of water. She takes two valium.*]

You take one, too.

SONIA: No. Thank you.

[MIMI *enters, goes to the pay phone, dials.*]

MIRIAM: A valium makes you feel like you are floating in a warm beach.

SONIA: Varadero?[2]

MIRIAM: Varadero, the Gulf of Mexico, Santa María del Mar.[3] It's because of these little pieces of magic that I escaped from the path. I did not follow the steps of my brothers and end up an alcoholic.

SONIA: Osvaldo never drank a lot.

MIRIAM: You forget.

SONIA: Well, drinking was not the problem.

MANUELA: [*Entering.*] I made Mimi call the brothel to see why your husband's late.

MIRIAM: Where's Lizette?

MANUELA: Down the hall. It says "Dressing Room."

MIRIAM: I got five hundred dollars, brand-new bills.

[*She exits.*]

SONIA: The world I grew up in is out of style; will we see it again, Mama?

MIMI: [*Comes out of the phone booth.*] She answered. She said, "Yes?" I said, "Where's my father?" She said, "Gone." I said, "Already!" She said, "I'm getting ready for. . . ." I said, "For what? Your funeral?" She hung up on me. She sounded stoned.

MANUELA: Sonia, someday it will be reality again, I promise.

MIMI: What?

SONIA: Cuba. Cuba will be a reality.

MIMI: It was and is a myth. Your life there is mythical.

MANUELA: That's not true. Her life was perfect. In the mornings, after she was married, Oscar would get up at six-thirty and send one of his bus

2. Resort town on the northwestern coast of Cuba.
3. A beach east of Havana.

drivers ten miles to buy bread from her favorite bakery, to buy bread for his little married girl.

SONIA: At around nine, I would wake up and walk out the door through the yard to the edge of the rose garden and call, "Papa, my bread."

MANUELA: The maid would run over, cross the street and hand her two pieces of hot buttered bread . . .

SONIA: I'd stick my hand through the gate and she'd hand me the bread. I'd walk back—into my mother-in-law's kitchen, and my coffee and milk would be waiting for me.

MIMI: Did you read the paper?

SONIA: The papers? I don't think so.

MIMI: Did you think about the world?

SONIA: No. I'd just watch your father sleep and eat my breakfast.

MANUELA: Every morning, "Papa, my bread."

[*She goes to the outside doors and stays there, staring out.*]

MIMI: You will never see it again. Even if you do go back, you will seem out of place; it will never be the same.

SONIA: No? You never saw it.

MIMI: And I will never see it.

SONIA: Never say never!

MIMI: What do you mean, "Never say never"?!

SONIA: Never say never. Never is not real. It is a meaningless word. Always is a word that means something. Everything will happen always. The things that you feared and made your hands shake with horror, and you thought "not to me," will happen always.

MIMI: Stop it!

SONIA: I have thoughts, ideas. Just because I don't speak English well doesn't mean that I don't have feelings. A voice—a voice that thinks, a mind that talks.

MIMI: I didn't say that.

SONIA: So never say never, dear. Be ready for anything. Don't die being afraid. Don't, my darling.

MIMI: So simple.

[MIRIAM *enters.*]

SONIA: Yes, very simple, darling.

MIRIAM: What was simple?

SONIA: Life, when we were young.

MIRIAM: A little embarrassing, a little dishonest, but without real care; that's true. A few weeks ago I read an ad. It said, "Liberate Cuba through the power of Voodoo." There was a picture of Fidel's head with three pins stuck through his temples.

MANUELA: They should stick pins in his penis.

SONIA: Mama!

[*She laughs.*]

MANUELA: Bastard.

MIRIAM: The idea was that if thousands of people bought the product, there would be a great curse that would surely kill him—all that for only $11.99. Twelve dollars would be all that was needed to overthrow the curse of our past.

[LIZETTE *enters wearing a robe.*]

MANUELA: We should try everything, anything.

LIZETTE: Today is my wedding, it is really happening in an hour, here, in Woodland Hills, California, Los Angeles. The United States of America, 1979. No Cuba today please, no Cuba today.

SONIA: Sorry.

MIMI: You want all the attention.

SONIA: Your wedding is going to be perfect. We are going to win this time.

LIZETTE: Win what?

MANUELA: The battle.

MIRIAM: "Honest woman" versus the "whore."

MIMI: But who's the "honest woman" and who's the "whore"?

MANUELA: Whores can be easily identified—they steal husbands.

MIRIAM: They're from Argentina.

SONIA: They say "yes" to everything. The good ones say "no."

LIZETTE: And we're the good ones.

SONIA: Yes. I am happy today. You are the bride, the wedding decorations came out perfect and we are having a party. Oo, oo, oo, oo, oo . . . *uh.*

    [*The women all start doing the conga in a circle. They sing.* OSVALDO *enters.*]

Join the line.

LIZETTE: In back of me, Daddy.

MIRIAM: In front of me, Osvaldo.

    [*They dance.* MIRIAM *gooses* OSVALDO]

OSVALDO: First I kiss my daughter—[*He kisses* LIZETTE.] then my other little girl—[*He kisses* MIMI.] then my sister—

    [*He and* MIRIAM *blow each other a kiss.*]

—then my wife. [*He kisses* SONIA.]

SONIA: Your ex-wife.

OSVALDO: My daughter's mother.

SONIA: That's right.

    [MIRIAM *lights a cigarette and goes outside.*]

MIMI: We were together once, family: my mom, my dad, my big sister, my big brother. We ate breakfast and dinner together and drove down to Florida on our vacations, looked at pictures of Cuba together.

SONIA: And laughed, right?

MIMI: And then Papa gave us up.

OSVALDO: I never gave you up.

MIMI: To satisfy his urge.

MANUELA: Stop right now.

OSVALDO: Don't ever talk like that again.

SONIA: Isn't it true?

OSVALDO: It's more complex than that.

SONIA: More complex—how? No, stop.

LIZETTE: Please stop.

MANUELA: Don't fight.

MIMI: You see, Daddy, I understand you.

OSVALDO: You don't.

MIMI: I try.

OSVALDO: So do I.

MIMI: You don't.

OSVALDO: I'm going outside.

LIZETTE: Come, sit with me.

SONIA: You have to start getting dressed.

LIZETTE: Thank you for making *me* happy.

OSVALDO: I try.

[LIZETTE *and* OSVALDO *exit to dressing room.*]

SONIA: Mimi, no more today. Please, no more.

MIMI: When you're born the third child, the marriage is already half apart, and being born into a family that's half over, half apart, is a disturbing thing to live with.

SONIA: Where did you read that?

MIMI: I didn't read it. It's my opinion. Based on my experience, of my life.

SONIA: We were never half apart.

MIMI: No, but that's what it felt like.

MANUELA: It's unheard of. It's unbelievable—

MIMI: What is she talking about now?

MANUELA: A Catholic does not get a divorce. They have a mistress and a wife but no divorce, a man does not leave everything.

SONIA: [*To* MIMI.] As difficult as it might be for you to understand, we were together, and a family when you were born. I wanted, we wanted, to have you. We had just gotten to the U.S., Lizette was ten months old. Your father had gotten his job as an accountant. We lived behind a hamburger stand between two furniture stores, away from everything we knew, afraid of everything around us. We were alone, no one spoke Spanish. Half of the people thought we were Communist, the other half traitors to a great cause; three thousand miles away from our real lives. But I wanted you and we believed in each other more than ever before. We were all we had.

MIMI: I wish it would have always stayed like that.

SONIA: So do I.

MANUELA: In Cuba, not in California, we want our Cuba back.

MIMI: It's too late for that, Grandma.

MANUELA: No.

MIMI: They like their government.

MANUELA: Who?

MIMI: The people who live there like socialism.

MANUELA: No. Who told you that?

MIMI: He's still in power, isn't he?

MANUELA: Because he oppresses them. He has the guns, Fidel has the bullets. Not the people. He runs the concentration camps. He has Russia behind him. China. We have nothing behind us. My cousins are starving there.

MIMI: At least they know who they are.

MANUELA: You don't? Well, I'll tell you. You're Manuela Sonia Marquez Hernandez. A Cuban girl. Don't forget what I just told you.

MIMI: No, Grandma. I'm Manuela Sonia Marquez, better known as Mimi Mar-kwez. I was born in Canoga Park. I'm a first-generation white Hispanic American.

MANUELA: No you're not. You're a Cuban girl. Memorize what I just told you.

\* \* \*

1984

# KATHLEEN ALCALÁ
## b. 1954

Kathleen Alcalá earned her bachelor's degree in linguistics from Stanford University in 1976 and her master's in English from the University of Washington in 1985. She lives near Seattle, Washington, and is a longstanding member of Los Norteños, a group of Latino writers in western Washington. She is also a board member of Con Tinta, a national group of Latino writers, and of Richard Hugo House, a non-profit community writing center in Seattle. She is a cofounder of and contributing editor to *The Raven Chronicles*, a magazine of multicultural art, literature, and the spoken word, and has been a writer-in-residence at Seattle University and Richard Hugo House and a visiting lecturer at the University of New Mexico. She has received the Pacific Northwest Booksellers Award, the Governor's Writers Award, the Western States Book Award for Fiction, and the Washington State Book Award.

Alcalá has written three novels set in nineteenth-century Mexico: *Spirits of the Ordinary: A Tale of Casas Grandes* (1997), *The Flower in the Skull* (1999), and *Treasures in Heaven* (2000). With Olga Sánchez, she adapted *Spirits of the Ordinary* into a one-act play produced in 2003 by The Miracle Theatre, a Latino theater production company in Portland, Oregon. In addition to fiction, Alcalá has published nonfiction in numerous magazines and a collection of essays, *The Desert Remembers My Name: On Family and Writing* (2007). In 2001, she also wrote the introductions to two anthologies: *Cracking the Earth*, a compendium of feminist writing from the Oregon-based *Calyx Journal*, and *Fantasmas: Supernatural Stories by Mexican American Writers*.

The Alcalá selections in this anthology, "Flora's Complaint" and "Amalia," are from her story collection, *Mrs. Vargas and the Dead Naturalist* (1992). The first is a magical encounter between a woman and a swan; the second, a fantasy about the connections between dreams and reality. In a review of the book, the American science-fiction writer Ursula K. LeGuin described "Alcalá-land" as "this landscape of desert towns and dreaming hearts, of lost sisters and ghost scientists, canary singers, and road readers." From the barest plots, Acalá fashions solid portraits: of multiple generations, social classes, and complex relationships. She describes the stressful family lives of farm laborers and shows women struggling with their roles as mothers, workers, and keepers of family traditions.

---

### FROM MRS. VARGAS AND THE DEAD NATURALIST

### Flora's Complaint

One sunny morning, Flora Morales stepped out her back door to water the potted plants. It was another blazing Southern California day, and if she waited any longer, the plants would wilt in the heat. Flora sensed a shadow overhead. Shading her eyes to look up, Flora saw a dark shape looming closer and closer out of the sky. It looked like an airplane headed for the house.

"No!" she yelled. "Oh, no!" and she ran back inside, where her startled husband was watching television.

"A plane!" she yelled. "It's going to crash!"

They both ran outside to find the largest, blackest bird either of them had ever seen sitting placidly in the little fountain Flora's husband had installed earlier that summer. It was a swan, so big that it covered every inch of water on the surface of the decorative fountain. It was so black that it seemed to absorb light, and made the flowers around it appear pale.

At first Flora was frightened by the bird's size, but it remained still, quietly dipping its red-tipped bill and preening its feathers. She stepped a little closer. It gave off a smell like burnt wood.

Flora's husband brought a piece of bread from the kitchen and tried to feed it, but as he approached, the swan rose majestically and flew away over the treetops.

The next morning the swan was in the yard again, and every morning after that. The neighbors came to peer over the fence at the strange sight, wondering from what exotic estate it might have wandered. But it rose up in an unearthly swirl of wind when others approached. Only Flora could get near enough to feed it, and it followed her like a puppy if no one else was around.

At first, Flora thought that someone might come from a zoo or an amusement park to claim the swan, but no one ever did. Each night it flew away, but was always there in the morning. Its origin remained a mystery, as deep as the black shadows cast by its outstretched wings, or the look in the depths of its smoldering red eye.

Flora took her lawnchair into the backyard in the cool evenings and watched the beautiful bird as it paddled and preened, or regarded her calmly first with one blood-red eye, then the other. It made Flora's mouth set in a straight line of satisfaction.

Her family was afraid of the swan and stayed away from it. The burnt smell was always there, but Flora declared that it came from flying low over chimneys.

One day Flora found a neighbor's child lolling on the grass in the shadow of the black swan. The swan sat contentedly with its feet and wings tucked up. Flora ran forward clapping her hands at them, then pulled the sleepy child to his feet and shook him fiercely.

"Don't go near the swan. It might hurt you."

The black swan took flight over the rooftops.

After that, Flora watched the swan more carefully to make sure that no one got closer to it than she did.

One evening, while her husband was inside watching the season premieres on television, Flora began to talk to the swan in a way that she had never talked to anyone before.

"My life has been so hard," she began. "I have suffered so much, and no one really appreciates me."

She stared at her hands after this confession, but the swan didn't seem to mind. It sat serenely on the grass a few feet away, regarding her through half-closed eyes. Flora ventured to say more.

"I have raised ungrateful children," she continued. "Although I did everything in my power to make them decent, law-abiding citizens, none of them turned out right. My daughters married insolent young men with no respect for their elders, and my sons all married fallen women." Flora paused.

"They wear makeup," she said with distaste, "and let my granddaughters wear pants and play boys' games. The girls should learn how to cook and take care of dolls. I've tried to be friendly to those hussies, but I can tell that they don't care. All they care about is worldly goods, yet they never give me anything that's worth much, after all I've done for them.

"My daughters were never any good. I watched their every move to make sure that they grew up properly. I always punished them when they used slang or acted like boys. And yet they complained when I gave more meat to my sons so that they would grow up stronger. Men want wives who are submissive. I tried to make every one of the girls have a simple, pious spirit. Feminine. That's what men want."

The black swan shifted on the grass. The dim light from the back porch made its long shadow blend with those of the whispering flowers.

"And yet they acted like they couldn't wait to leave the house. Instead of praying in their spare time and embroidering pillowcases for their dowries, they bit their nails and pulled out their eyelashes. They acted as though I was trying to hurt them on purpose when I punished them, instead of realizing it was for their own good."

Flora hitched at her lawnchair and sighed bitterly. "Sometimes they didn't even have the decency to cover up the bruises.

"One of my daughters is even unmarried and," here she paused with embarrassment, "living alone.

"When I couldn't reach her at home one evening, she got upset because I called the police. I only have her welfare in mind."

Flora sighed again. "Decent people are home by ten. I don't know who she thinks she is."

The swan seemed to nod its head in sympathy.

"Even the pastor at my old church didn't understand. He actually had the nerve to take me aside and say that some of the women, he wouldn't give me their names, had complained because I suggested that they hadn't been married nine months before their first babies were born. How dare they say anything to him, when I was just letting them know that other Christians were watching them? He said that it wasn't any of my business. If he had done his job, I wouldn't have to count.

"And then," here Flora lowered her voice to a whisper, "he had the nerve to suggest that I had . . . ." Flora searched for the right phrasing ". . . improperly touched some of the children. Who does he think he is? And who could have told him?"

By now Flora was trembling with indignation. "Imagine that man calling himself a minister of God. That's when I started going to another church."

Flora's voice turned mournful.

"He had the nerve to say, before I left, that I suffered from a sickness of the soul, and need help. Me!" she said, leaning towards the swan, "I who have spent every waking moment trying to enforce God's will!"

The swan ruffled and smoothed its shiny feathers.

"In fact," she added, "if I were a government official, I could make people obey the laws of God." She pondered that thought with pleasure, drumming her fingers on the aluminum arms of her chair.

"Sometimes," she said, "it's hard to see the justice in life. But I know that God has a plan."

The black swan seemed to listen patiently and attentively, resting its bill on its puffy breast as she recited her lamentations. Afterwards, Flora folded her lawnchair against a palm tree and entered the house with a great sense of calm, as though in spite of all she knew, the world was working as it should.

The years passed, and the swan became a fixture in the Morales' backyard. Flora's husband continued to tend the flowers, but retreated to his tool shed whenever the swan came too near, as much to avoid Flora's displeasure as to avoid that fearsome beak. As a result, the formerly manicured garden began to look shaggy.

Flora got old, and prepared to meet her reward. She had lived a long life, and was looking forward to her eternal rest. Her children were called together from their homes all over the country. They arrived one by one at her deathbed, and Flora surveyed them with a form of satisfaction. Only one was missing.

"I have lived a good life," she said to them, "I have never tasted alcohol or touched a cigarette. I have never been in a place where people engage in immoral dancing, or handled a deck of cards. I have never even thought an improper word, or been alone with any man other than my husband."

Mr. Morales looked at his feet and shuffled them on the floor, clearing his throat.

"Because of the pain of raising ungrateful children," Flora continued in a strong voice, "I have suffered long and deep. I count each hardship as a star in my crown. On Judgment Day,[1] which is soon if we can tell by the state of the world, the gold will be separated from the dross, and I will receive my just reward. As will you," she said, glaring at each one of her grown children in turn.

At that, the last daughter arrived. Flora sat up in bed, pointing, and yelled, "That dress is too short!" before she fell back dead.

• • •

When Flora opened her eyes, she was lying on a hard garden bench, her purse clutched tightly over her chest. She blinked at the unfamiliar light, not recognizing the overgrown flowerbeds, or the sharp-smelling hedges at her side.

Flora sat up, trying to recall what had happened. She had been sick, she remembered that, so sick they did not think she would live. Her sons and daughters had been called, arrangements had been made. . . .

It was deadly quiet, except for the droning of insects in the overblown roses and the hedges that stretched out before her. Her feet seemed to rest on firm ground, in her same sensible navy-blue shoes, but the sky above her was a hazy, milky white, the look of late afternoon in late summer. Flora was afraid, and began to cry quietly.

Suddenly, Flora heard a raucous noise to her left and turned to confront a looming black shape.

It was her beloved swan. Flora reached out her hand to stroke it, but the swan bit her hand sharply. With a cry she jumped up, but the swan remained where it sat on the warm sidewalk. Shaken, Flora began to walk away. The

---

1. According to various religions, the day of God's judgment at the end of the world.

swan followed at a distance, keeping one red eye or the other on her every step.

When they came to a listless fountain with a wide, low edge, and green moss growing in its cracks, Flora sat down and turned to the swan.

"Remember your fountain?" she said. "Remember how much you used to like it when we turned the hose on for you?" She splashed her hand invitingly in the tepid water, but the swan remained apart, watching her gravely.

Flora got up and began to walk again, a growing disquiet within her, but she tried to look unconcerned, fanning her hand out a little at her side so that it would dry.

After a time, they came to another fountain with benches, and Flora could make out two women sitting at the far end, talking. They wore luminous robes. As she drew closer, Flora's heart leaped as she saw her dead sister Julia, talking to a woman she faintly recognized.

"Julia?" she said uncertainly, walking up to them.

"Flora!" the woman exclaimed, and stood up and embraced her. Tears of joy streamed down their faces, for it had been many years since Julia had succumbed to cancer and passed on.

"This is la Señorita Barajas, Flora. You remember her?"

"Oh yes, Señorita. How do you do?" she said politely, and la Señorita Barajas, a tiny, white-haired woman, stood up and gave Flora one of her perfectly gloved hands before pecking her lightly on the cheek.

As they calmed down, Flora turned to her sister and finally asked: "Well?"

"Well what?" asked Julia.

"Is this it?"

Julia took in her breath sharply. "What do you mean, is this it?"

Flora began again, not understanding the look in Julia's eyes. "Is this what it's all like?"

Julia was stunned. "What do you mean? What more could you want?"

She was about to say more, but faltered as the black swan stepped up to them. It stood a little too close, and regarded them each in turn with its glittering eye.

As Flora's expression turned to terror, Julia's face softened to pity. She saw Flora's clothing for the first time.

"It is different for each of us," she finally said. "We each find what we have looked for in life."

"But," said Flora, "I didn't look for the swan! It just came to me, while I was still alive! Why is it here? I don't understand!"

By now, the two women were moving away from Flora, the swan standing between her and them. They looked back when she called to them, but did not try to answer her questions.

"We will see you again soon, Flora," her sister called out, "but we must go now."

When she tried to follow, the swan rose up on its toes, unfurled its huge black wings, and hissed in her face. Flora was really afraid of it now, and sat down on a bench and cried for some time, pulling Kleenex from her purse where she always kept a plentiful supply.

She must have fallen asleep, because Flora found herself stretched out on the chipping, wrought-iron bench. When she sat up, she was alone, but felt that she was being watched from a distance. The sky was still a milky white, and the light still that of late afternoon in August or September. Flora knew that she would find other people, other relatives, but that her shame would be almost too much to bear. The black swan would be with her always.

Flora got up, straightened her dress, and began to walk through the endless garden.

## Amalia

She first suspected that something had changed when the yellow roses began to bloom in the weeds at the edge of her porch. Amalia had never noticed the rosebush before, but she was delighted with it. Yellow was her favorite color. She began to water and coddle the roses, humming an old hymn as she worked.

"Here, Jana, you want a pretty flower?" she said to the little neighbor girl. Jana wouldn't look at the rose, only at Amalia's outstretched hand. When the girl turned and ran into her house, frightened, Amalia realized that only she could see the yellow roses.

Amalia had wondered what was going on for years, but the changes had been so small, so subtle, that there hadn't been anything she could point to with certainty.

At the old house, on Valley Avenue in East Los Angeles, nothing had changed for many years. Her brothers and sisters grew up and moved away, her parents died, one after the other, until only she and Rosetta were left. They never married, and the old house, with its musty books and broken-down furniture, was left to them.

At first, she gave piano lessons on the old upright, and Rosetta ran an old hand-cranked printing press in the living-room. This gave them a little income and kept them busy.

But as the paint began to peel on the house, and rain came through the roof and damaged the upstairs rooms, fewer and fewer students made their way past the old, drooping trees in front to study piano with Amalia. Rosetta's back got too bad to run the printing press, and they sold it to their church, the Spanish American Free Evangelical Church of the Resurrection, for sixty dollars. The two aging sisters were left alone with their father's books and the mice which began to make themselves at home in the sagging house.

They lived on crackers, eggs, and Ovaltine, and passed the time reminiscing about their younger days in Mexico and Texas, which remained brighter in their minds than the present. Once in a while, relatives would visit, bringing used clothing or strangers who they claimed were their children, but otherwise the sisters spent days uncluttered by concerns from the outside world. Amalia was happy. As guardian of the family castle, she had a purpose in life. Rosetta's back grew more crooked, but she refused to see a doctor and still smiled radiantly, even if it was at an awkward angle.

Then the neighborhood began to change. Families with more children began renting the houses, and quiet Valley Avenue was loud with the noise of lowriders at night. This did not cause them too much concern until the children began to taunt the two old women.

"¡Bruja, bruja!"[1] they would chant, and eventually the teasing was accompanied by a small rock or two as one or the other of the two women scurried up the long walk to the warped steps of the porch. Amalia wept with fear and frustration, but not until Rosetta was knocked down one day did Amalia dare to tell her brother.

"Carlos, something terrible has happened," she began when he came on one of his monthly visits. He was tacking plastic over one of the broken windows upstairs.

"The children hurt Rosetta."

"What children? What happened?"

"I don't know. A neighbor family. They're always in the street, saying things to us, but yesterday they pushed Rosetta, and she cut her hand."

Carlos went to see his other sister, wedged behind a bookcase downstairs where the sisters now lived, surrounded by the least damaged furniture. She told him the story, and showed him her hands. Finally she even admitted that the children thought they were witches.

Carlos was outraged. He wanted to call the police, but Rosetta and Amalia were afraid that it would just go worse for them. Nothing could be done to the children, and the parents certainly didn't care. It would just be taken out on the two helpless sisters. Reluctantly, Carlos agreed.

Later that evening, Carlos described the situation to his wife, Concha.

"Well, it's no wonder," she said over her shoulder from the sink. "They go around all summer wearing three sweaters and a coat, their stockings falling down, and they never comb their hair. It's no wonder the neighbors think they're witches."

Carlos admitted that she had a point.

The family held a conference, and it was decided to sell the Valley Avenue house and use the proceeds to find the sisters a safer place to live, and help pay their expenses. As it was, each family gave what it could now and then, but it was Carlos who made sure they had groceries and paid the power bill. It was getting too hard to heat the old place, anyway.

Amalia was incensed. How could they do this to the memory of her father, the Reverend Moisés Armadio, founder of over fifty churches throughout Mexico and the Southwest? Who would keep his books? How could they even think of selling the family property? She and Rosetta, of course, would refuse to move. But in the end, the choice wasn't given to them, and Rosetta, it turned out, didn't really care one way or the other. She knew she was not in a position to say. Her back grew a little more crooked, and the two sisters were moved to a duplex on Loma Street.

Some of the old books went with them, in a bookcase with anchors carved in the sides, just to help them feel at home, along with a box full of faded photographs, and the paisley scarf that had covered the piano. The piano itself was given to the church to use in Sunday School.

On Loma, things were a little better, but not much. The roof didn't leak, but the neighborhood was almost as bad. Amalia was so mad at Carlos for selling the old house that she didn't speak to him for four months. Her eyes were rimmed with red, and she sat in a straight-backed chair without moving for hours at a time. Rosetta did not bother her when she was like this,

---

1. Witch, witch!

but went on about her business, moving like a gray crab with her shuffling, sideways walk. Carlos finally got Rosetta to a doctor, but she was told that an operation might or might not correct her ever-bending spine, and would certainly be very painful, if not paralyzing. Rosetta chose to keep her back as it was.

"It doesn't bother me," she said cheerfully. "If this is the way that God wants me to be, then that's the way I'll be. We all have our burdens to bear."

Just as though she carried a great rock on her right shoulder, Rosetta continued to bend more and more sharply down and to the left.

Carlos did the best that he could to keep the two sisters looking decent, but Amalia would wander vacant-eyed down the street, her purse dangling on her arm, her coat buttoned up wrong.

When she finally resumed speaking again, no one paid attention to Amalia. Her sister Rosetta would nod and smile, but often not respond to her questions. Carlos would assure her that the rest of the family was fine and that he would be back in a week, no matter what she said.

"When is my sister Ruth coming to visit?" she would ask. "I have a present for her birthday, which was two weeks ago, and I want to give it to her."

"Ruth is fine," Carlos would say. "Save the present for when she comes at Easter."

Amalia would hold the present, a necklace purchased at the five-and-dime, or found in an old purse, and sit at the window in her straight-backed chair, waiting for Easter.

When the rent was raised at Loma Street, Carlos decided to move the sisters again. He knew it was hard on them, but Amalia had already had her purse snatched once, and the street was too busy for Rosetta to cross alone. It was very hard for her to stand so stooped over and look both ways. She refused to use a cane, because she liked to have both hands free to fend off muggers or overly solicitous people. "Besides," she said, "a cane makes me feel old."

Amalia was angry again, at another move in less than three years, but this brought her to the duplex with the yellow roses. The roses appeared after they had been living on Highland Street for almost a year.

"Look!" she said, running inside with a beautiful bouquet. "Yellow roses just like my mother used to grow in San Antonio!"[2]

Rosetta smiled and went to fetch her a vase, but when the roses had wilted after two days for lack of water, she didn't seem to notice. So Amalia enjoyed her roses by herself, moving her chair out on the narrow porch on warm summer evenings to inhale the delicious fragrance.

One day, maneuvering her chair through the screen door, Amalia was startled to find her nephew Ezekial from Mexico sitting on the steps. He was turning towards the wall, trying to light a cigarette.

"Ezekial!" she said, scandalized. "Does my sister know you smoke?"

"No," he answered, puffing calmly. "But it really doesn't concern anyone anymore."

Amalia was too shocked to say anything, so she sat down on her chair for a minute. It had been so long since she had seen her nephew, years and years, and she tried to think of why he would come.

---

2. City in south-central Texas.

"What brings you to visit?" she finally said. "Did the others come, too? Where is your mother?"

"I've been coming here every day for a long time," he said, sprawled out on the steps, "waiting for you to say something to me."

Amalia was mystified. "I didn't see you!" she said. "Why didn't you say something?"

"It wouldn't have made any difference," he answered languidly. "You would have thought you were hearing voices."

Amalia sat and thought some more. "And how is your family? I haven't seen your mother in years."

"I guess they're okay," said Ezekial. "I really haven't seen much of them since I died. . . . My brother sells Cadillacs."

He blew smoke into the air while Amalia tried to figure out what he was talking about. Finally, she remembered that he had died rather suddenly of typhoid fever almost fifteen years before. All the young girls in Chihuahua[3] had cried at his funeral. Yet here he sat, still handsome and young, his curly brown hair pressed against the side of her duplex.

"Then how can I talk to you?" she managed to ask.

"I'm not sure," he answered. "But I noticed this street one day, and saw you outside, so I thought it would be polite to visit. We can go anywhere we want, you know."

Amalia didn't know. She sat and sat some more, but she couldn't think of anything to say. Finally, it grew too dark to see anything but the glowing tip of Ezekial's cigarette, so she took her chair and went back into the house.

After that, Ezekial came to visit once or twice a week, and Amalia would sit on the porch with him. He refused to go in the house. Eventually, other people came to visit, dear friends and relatives Amalia hadn't seen in thirty, sometimes forty-five years. She sat on the porch and discussed old times with them, the white beaches of Mazatlán, how sweet the water tasted in Los Mochis.[4] The rosebush had grown up and practically screened off the porch from the street, and new flowers of a kind Amalia had never seen before began to appear along the walk. She tried to make sure they got enough water to sustain them through the stifling summer days, but it was hard work.

Amalia tried to get Rosetta to go out on the porch and visit, but she refused, saying she was too busy. If Amalia tried to force her, taking her by the arm, Rosetta would hang on to the doorframe and go even more crooked. Amalia was afraid to hurt her, so she stopped trying to drag her out, apologizing to the visitors for her sister.

They seemed neither surprised nor concerned. "She's just not ready yet," shrugged Estrella, a childhood friend. "When she wants to see us, she will."

That was a wonderful year for Amalia. While before she had been drawn and pale, her face grew rosy and plump with smiles. She combed her hair now, and dressed properly for her little evening porch sessions.

One night, rather late, Ezekial and Estrella showed up and asked Amalia if she wanted to visit dreams. "Come on," said Ezekial. "It only takes a few moments. It's the best way to visit your living relations."

---

3. State in northern Mexico; the city of Chihuahua is the state capital.
4. Like Mazatlán, a coastal city in the state of Sinaloa, Mexico (just south of the state of Chihuahua).

Estrella took her by the hand, and they dropped in on her brother Carlos, tossing in his bed. They stood by impassively as he relived a speeding ticket he had received that day on the freeway, and he woke up confused by their images mixed up with that of the California Highway Patrolman.

They went to two or three other dreams that night—a gardening dream, a church service, preparing food—and they caught up on the nocturnal concerns of their living family. After that, Amalia went along with them now and then, just to see how everyone was getting along.

By the next spring, Amalia was transformed. She carried herself like a young girl, and chattered happily to her brother Carlos when he came to visit. He was relieved that the sisters seemed to like their new home. He gave the next-door neighbors fifteen dollars a month just to keep an eye on them, and this meant that someone often accompanied Amalia to the store, or got groceries for them.

Rosetta seldom left the house now, self-conscious about her back, and now bent so far double that she mostly saw people's shoes, anyway. This took most of the joy out of outdoor walks.

As Amalia grew healthier, she ate less and less. She complained that eggs were too heavy for her, and subsisted almost entirely on crackers and hot cinnamon tea. Her skin was now so translucent, an egg would probably have been visible through her stomach. Her eyes and her curly hair shone.

That May, Amalia looked down the beautiful boulevard of green trees and formal gardens and knew that this wasn't really Highland Street anymore. In fact, it looked like Chapultepec Park,[5] where she had visited as a child. The bushes were shaped like lions and birds, and there was even a statue of her famous ancestor, Manuel Acuña.[6] The droning of bees was the only traffic she could hear.

"Where are we?" she asked. "I mean, really, what is this place?"

"Purgatory," answered her deceased sister Julia, "a way station to heaven."

Amalia was stunned. "But we don't believe in purgatory, do we? That's Catholic!"

"Probably not," sighed Julia. "I've never seen our father here. But it might just be that we haven't been here long enough."

"It seems long enough," said Ezekial. "What's wrong with purgatory, anyway? It's not so bad."

"No, it's not," agreed Amalia, "but our family doesn't know."

"Know what?"

"That we're in purgatory, that purgatory exists."

"You're not, really," said Ezekial to Amalia. "You just visit a lot."

"Oh, I see," said Amalia. A cool breeze blew the scent of jacaranda blossoms across the porch, with just a hint of salt air mixed in.

"Not that we blame you," added Julia. "We love to see you. And we have plenty of time on our hands."

"But we need to tell them!" said Amalia. "They should know!"

"How?" asked Julia. "They wouldn't believe us."

---

5. Large public park on the outskirts of Mexico City.
6. Manuel Acuña Narro (1849–1873), Mexican writer. The monument to him in Chapultepec Park stands in the Rotonda de las Personas Ilustres (Rotunda of the Illustrious Persons).

"No," said Amalia, "no one pays attention to what I say anymore, and I'm still alive. And they're concerned with other things, busy with their own lives. When we visit their dreams, they're full of new cars and work and the faces of children. Where did all those children come from, anyway?"

"That's what happens when you have a big family," said Julia. "Lots of nieces and nephews and second cousins. I'm sorry I never had children. Only Ruth's children were like my own."

"Ruth's children!"

An idea was coming to her. In their nighttime wanderings through the dreams of their relatives, they had come across Ruth's youngest, a young woman who lived in a part of the country where Amalia had never really been. The dreams were cool and wide, full of nights on the desert and luminous skies, rooms full of dusty books, and a fear of the color combination of pink and black.

"Rachel would believe us!" she cried, jumping up. "We can tell my niece Rachel, and she will tell the others!"

"Yes, Rachel," said Julia. "My sweet little Rachel. And she's smart, too. She'll figure out a way to tell them, and make them believe."

"Well, maybe," said Ezekial, doubtful. "Your relatives are all so stubborn," he said, as though they weren't his relatives, too, "that they may just call her a heretic and put her on a prayer list."

"Well, we must try," said Amalia firmly, "and Rachel is our only chance. We will all go to her in a dream," said Amalia. Her mind was made up now. "We will go and tell her that we are all right and we are in purgatory, and that we will see her on the Other Side."

So that's what they did, late that summer, when the last petals were falling off the yellow rosebush, Amalia and Julia and Ezekial. Amalia held Rosetta's hand through the open doorway while they dream-traveled, so she was partially included, too.

Rachel got the message, loud and clear, and waking, was impressed that she could dream so well in Spanish after all these years, for at first she thought that the dream had originated in her own mind. But the longer she thought about it, the stranger it seemed, so she got up and wrote the message down, word for vivid word, and listed everyone she could remember seeing as they stood on the porch, with that swirling garden behind them. It was hard to sleep after that, so she sat awake until the dream faded a little and she could return to her indistinct slumbers.

. . .

And so, not knowing how else to tell it, I have written this story. The Indians in this part of the country, the Northwest, have a term, *sheel-shole*, which means "to thread the bead." It refers to a way of traveling from inland to the ocean by guiding a boat from one interconnected lake to the next. My aunt Amalia is still alive, but it's only a matter of time before she paddles her canoe, yellow roses and all, out into the open sea.

1992

# LORNA DEE CERVANTES
## b. 1954

Lorna Dee Cervantes was born in the Mission District, at the time the largely Latino section of San Francisco, and grew up in an Anglo section of San José, California. Cervantes was raised speaking English—"without language," as she notes in her poem "Refugee Ship," which appeared in her debut collection, *Emplumada* (1981), and is included in this anthology. As a high schooler, she became active in the Chicano Movement and in antinuclear protests. A fledgling actress before turning to poetry as her main source of expression, Cervantes toured California with a theater group and participated in the 1974 international theater festival held in Mexico City. She began her college work in 1972 and, 12 years later, earned her bachelor's degree in creative arts from San José State University. In between, at age 22, Cervantes founded the literary magazine *Mango* and directed it from 1976 to 1982. She completed *Emplumada* thanks, in part, to a 1978 grant from the National Arts Workshop and later by her nine months at the Fine Arts Workshop in Provincetown, Massachusetts.

The book's title includes the word *pluma*, conjuring the plumed serpent Quetzalcóatl, an Aztec symbol of fertility and creativity. The volume is divided in three parts: The first two concern social change; the third is lyrical poetry in which Cervantes struggles with her insecurities regarding language, class, and material things desired but unattained. The poem "Beneath the Shadow of the Frenzy," also included in this anthology, conveys physical and linguistic displacement. In depicting one of the many U.S. roadways that changed the nation's landscape by cutting across working-class neighborhoods, Cervantes provides a metaphor for the nation's obscuring of its ethnic cultures.

In 1982, following the murder of her mother, Cervantes entered into a deep depression. After a long recovery, she continued her education and writing. She pursued graduate studies in the "History of Consciousness" Program at the University of California, Santa Cruz, and then joined the faculty at the University of Colorado at Boulder. In addition to *Emplumada*, she has published the poetry volumes *From the Cables of Genocide: Poems of Love and Hunger* (1991) and *Drive: The First Quartet* (2006). Among the prizes Cervantes has received are the American Book Award (1982) and the Lila Wallace–Reader's Digest Foundation Writer's Award (1995). She teaches at the University of Colorado at Boulder.

# Refugee Ship

Like wet cornstarch, I slide
past my grandmother's eyes. Bible
at her side, she removes her glasses.
The pudding thickens.

Mama raised me without language.                    5
I'm orphaned from my Spanish name.
The words are foreign, stumbling
on my tongue. I see in the mirror
my reflection: bronzed skin, black hair.

I feel I am a captive                                10
aboard the refugee ship.

The ship that will never dock.
*El barco que nunca atraca.*

1981

## Beneath the Shadow of the Freeway

### I

Across the street—the freeway,
blind worm, wrapping the valley up
from Los Altos to Sal Si Puedes.[1]
I watched it from my porch
unwinding. Every day at dusk                                        5
as Grandma watered geraniums
the shadow of the freeway
lengthened.

### II

We were a woman family.
Grandma our innocent Queen;                                        10
Mama the Swift Knight, Fearless Warrior.
Mama wanted to be Princess instead.
I know that. Even now she dreams of taffeta
and foot-high tiaras.

Myself—I could never decide.                                       15
So I turned to books, those staunch, upright men.
I became Scribe, Translator of Foreign Mail
(interpreting letters from the Government,
notices of dissolved marriages

and Welfare stipulations).                                         20
I paid the bills,
did light man-work, fixed faucets,
insured everything
against all leaks.

### III

Before rain I notice seagulls.                                     25
They walk in flocks, cautious across lawns,
splayed toes, indecisive beaks.
Grandma says seagulls mean a storm.

In California in the summer
mockingbirds sing all night.                                       30

---

1. A neighborhood in San José; Los Altos is a nearby city; both are in Santa Clara County, in west-
central California. I.e., from one part of the county to another part.

Grandma says they are singing for their mates
who are nesting.

> "Mockingbirds sing for their wives,
> don't leave their families
> borrachando."[2]                                              35

She likes the ways of birds,
respects how they show themselves
in exchange for toast and a whistle.

She believes in myths and birds,
and trusts only what she has built                              40
with her own hands.

### IV

The fireplace in the back yard,
cocky disheveled masonry,
she built it out of old bricks.
Before that, she lived for twenty five years                    45
with a man who tried to kill her.

Grandma from the hills of Santa Barbara,[3]
I would open my eyes to see her stirring mush
in the morning, hair in loose braids
tucked close around her head                                    50
with a yellow scarf.

Mama said, "It was her own fault,
getting screwed by a man for that long.
She sure as shit wasn't hard."
soft she was                                                    55
soft

### V

in the night I would hear it
glass bottles shattering on the street
words cracking into shrill screams
inside my throat a cold fear                                    60
as it entered the house in hard
unsteady steps stopping at my door
my name   bathrobe   slippers
outside a 3am mist heavy
as a breath full of whiskey                                     65
stop it   come inside   go home
mama if he comes here again
I'll call the police

---

2. Getting drunk.                     3. City on the southwestern coast of California.

inside
a grey kitten    a touchstone                                        70
purring beneath grandma's
hand-sewn quilts    the singing
of mockingbirds

### VI

"You're too soft . . . always were.
You'll get nothing but shit.                                          75
Baby, don't count on nobody . . ."

—a mother's wisdom.
The lines on her face are beginning to show.
The bitter years are all so visible now
as she spends her hours                                              80
washing down the bile.
Soft. I haven't changed,
grown more silent maybe,
more cynical—on the outside.

"O Mama, with what's inside of me                                    85
I could wash that all away . . . I could."

"But Mama, if you're good to them
they'll be good to you back . . ."

Back . . .
The freeway is across the street.                                    90
It's summer now. Every night I sleep with a gentle man
to the hymn of mockingbirds,
and in time, I will plant geraniums.
I will tell myths about birds.
I will tie up my hair into loose braids                              95
and only trust
what I have built
with my own hands.

1981

---

# FRANCISCO GOLDMAN

## b. 1954

Few writers of Central American descent in the United States have had as much
impact on Latino letters as Francisco Goldman has. The son of a Jewish American
father and a Guatemalan mother, Goldman was born in Boston, Massachusetts, and
raised in the Boston suburb of Needham and in Guatemala City. He was educated at

the University of Michigan, in Ann Arbor, after which he began his writing career as a journalist, bringing together literary style and a passionate belief in individual civil rights. From 1982 to 1987, as a contributing editor for *Harper's* magazine, he wrote about Central America. His journalism and short stories have also appeared in periodicals such as *Esquire, The New York Times Magazine,* and *The New Yorker.* He has also translated into English several stories by the contemporary Colombian writer Gabriel García Márquez. Goldman was a Guggenheim Fellow in 1997 and a Fellow at the New York Public Library's Center for Scholars and Writers in 2000–2001. He is Allan K. Smith Professor of English Language and Literature at Trinity College, in Hartford, Connecticut. He lives in Mexico City and Brooklyn, New York.

Goldman's first novel, *The Long Night of White Chickens* (1992), won the Sue Kaufman Prize for First Fiction from the American Academy of Arts and Letters and was also a finalist for the PEN/Faulkner Award. Set in Guatemala in the 1980s during a particularly repressive period in that country's history, *The Long Night of White Chickens* tells the story of Roger Graetz, who is raised in a suburb of Boston by his aristocratic Guatemalan mother. Roger's grandmother sends a beautiful Guatemalan orphan to live with them, and Roger becomes obsessed with the girl. Many years later, when she is murdered while running an orphanage in Guatemala, Roger investigates and slowly learns about the awful politics from which he had been sheltered by his upbringing. (The American filmmaker John Sayles has said that a story Goldman told him about Goldman's Guatemalan uncle was partly an inspiration for Sayles's 1997 film, *Men with Guns.* The uncle, a doctor, became involved in an international health program in Guatemala. He later found that most of his students, whom he had sent off in good faith to serve as barefoot doctors in the poor communities, had been murdered by the very government that claimed to support the program.)

Goldman's second novel, *The Ordinary Seaman* (1997), was also a finalist for the PEN/Faulkner Award and the IMPAC Dublin International Literary Prize, and was named one of the 100 Best American Books of the Century by the *Hungry Mind Review. The Ordinary Seaman,* the third chapter of which is included here, is about a group of Central American seamen who are tricked into signing on with a failing cargo ship, the *Urus,* bound for New York. Once in New York, they are stranded, unable to leave the ship because they do not have the proper entry papers, unpaid because the ship's owner has gone bankrupt, and unable to return to their homeland. They become stateless individuals, slowly wasting away just inches from opportunities in the United States. As the individual and the political become entwined, the story focuses on the interaction between the ordinary seaman Esteban and the denizens of an onshore beauty parlor that he visits secretly late one night. Goldman's third novel, *The Divine Husband* (2004), is set in nineteenth-century Central America. It tells the fact-based story of María de las Nieves Moran, a nun, a translator for the British ambassador, and a woman involved with four men—one of whom, José Martí (see p. 265), may have been the father of her illegitimate child.

Goldman's *The Art of Political Murder: Who Killed the Bishop?* (2007) is a nonfictional account of the "Gerardi affair," which shook Guatemala in the late 1990s. Across chronological lines, the book interweaves conversations, statements, and innuendos about the murder, in 1998, of Bishop Juan Gerardi Conedera, general vicar of the Guatemala City archdiocese and the founding director of the archdiocese's Office of Human Rights. A couple of days before being bludgeoned to death, Bishop Gerardi had released a 1,400-page report by the Recovery of Historical Memory Project, a commission over which he presided. The report was about the culture of violence in Guatemala during the previous three decades, when approximately 200,000 people had been killed in a civil war, which formally ended in 1996. Goldman concludes that justice is a mirage in Latin America.

## FROM THE ORDINARY SEAMAN

### 3

He's crossed under the expressway, climbed into Brooklyn. In this neighborhood, there are many signs in Spanish. *Paco Naco's Tacos.* A place that arranges money transfers and telephone calls to Mexico and the Caribbean and all the Central American countries. There are people out on the streets, lots of men, many mestizo looking, wearing baseball hats, bulky, plastic-looking jackets of different colors, who seem to be in a hurry to get wherever they're going, to work probably. Many descend stairs that lead beneath the sidewalk to the underground trains—he can feel and hear the pavement thundering under his feet. Nobody looks at him in a friendly way. It's nearly dawn, but he finds a little corner restaurant that is open, drab blue walls, steam tables in the window, some of the dishes he recognizes—arroz con pollo,[1] looking like it's been sitting there all night—and others he doesn't. He wishes he had some money so he could go in, order a cup of coffee, get out of the cold. The greasy smell of food, a smell of sauce-saturated chicken, fish, and overripe fruit, makes his stomach rumble; mixing with bus exhaust and the chilly, faintly briny breeze channeling up the long street from the harbor.

He's never stayed out this long. By now, they must be waking up on the ship, wondering where he is. On a side street he finds a puzzling sign, a white sheet of paper covered with photocopied handwriting taped to the glass behind the bars of a lowered shutter: someone has lost a cat named Dolores and is offering a fifty-dollar reward. There is a photocopied picture of Dolores, too smudgy and gray to help you distinguish this cat from most others. But here is the rare thing: the cat's color is listed as "aceituna." But olives can be black or green. If black olive, why list the cat's color as olive and not black? And who's ever heard of an olive green cat?

"Tu, güey!"[2]

He turns and sees this golden-curly-haired muchacha glaring at him, slight and pretty, holding keys to the lock in the door to this place that has lost its cat. She has a soft, almost nougat-hued face, her eyes big, stormy pools framed by blue eyeliner and long, black lashes. Small, puffy nose. Pert, lipsticked mouth, pouting angrily at him. "You're the güey that's been urinating in this doorway, no? Pinche asqueroso!"[3] And now her affronted brown eyes are *pulsing* at him.

"No!" exclaims Esteban. "I've never been here before!"

"Ah no?" accusingly.

"No!"

He can smell her perfume. How old is she? Young. About his own age, no? She's wearing a long, blue wool coat with a collar that looks made of coarse lamb's wool, skinny ankles in whitish tights descending from the coat, into glossy black, sturdy high heels. Now she's looking him up and down.

"Qué triste,[4] güey," she says, with impassioned mockery. "Letting yourself go around looking like that. Güey, you're too young to be homeless. Any

---

1. Literally, rice with chicken.
2. You, bro (brother).
3. Fucking stinker!
4. How sad.

güey can find some type of job. Bueno. What can you do? Otro desgraciado sinvergüenza."[5] She shrugs, looks at him with exaggerated pity, shakes her head. "En fin."[6]

He gapes at her. Her lips look blistered, chapped, through her lipstick— and the way she talks, hombre, it's no wonder!

And she turns back towards the door, and stops, and then she starts up again, mouth working like an agitated choir singer's, keeping her own temperamental rhythm with the keys in her hand, flopped up and down: ". . . Hijos de la chingada, patanes,[7] come and stand in the doorway all night pissing, drinking beer, smoking marijuana, leaving their piggishness all over. Y la policia, qué hacen? Cabrones de mierrrda.[8] Absolutamente nada! No, no, I can't take this anymore. It's too much to ask. Starting your day having to step through *this* porquería. No! Pinche degenarados . . ."[9]

She's stepped backwards, for a moment isn't even facing him anymore as she orates at the doorway, and then she spins around, glaring at him again. He laughs, he can't help it, and she says, "Ah, sí, güey? Go ahead and laugh. Laugh all the way to the homeless shelter, ándale."[1]

"Chocho," he blurts, "Qué agresiva!"[2]

"*Qué!* Vulgarote!"[3]

"Bueno. *OK!*"—flinging his arms out. Amazed at himself, standing on a sidewalk in Brooklyn, arguing with this loca![4] A corner of her lower lip tucked between her teeth while she glares at him like some infuriated abuela[5] again. But what eyes!

Finally, seemingly calmed down a little, she says, "Don't you feel embarrassment, going around like that? Not to mention the cold. You're going to catch something. Bueno, what's it to me? . . . Except you could catch tuberculosis, güey, and give it to somebody else. That happens, you know. It's been on the news."

And he says, "I'm not a vago. I *have* a job. I'm a marinero. I've been stuck on this ship down in the harbor for almost four months now, with no pay, hardly anything to eat, working. The whole crew looks like this. Down there." And he gestures towards the harbor.

"That doesn't happen here," she says flatly. "Four months with no pay? Güey, that's not very intelligent. And I can tell you're not stupid. It's a story. I don't believe a word of it."

"Va, pues,[6] don't believe me, what's it to me?" he says, suddenly angry. "We thought we were going to be paid. Vos,[7] we thought we'd be sailing in a few days. And instead they put us to work repairing this old, broken ship. They keep telling us that when the ship is fixed, we'll sail and we'll get paid. Puta,[8] what were we supposed to do? No one has the money even to go home. We hardly even know where we are." Suddenly he pulls some of the tools from his pocket, holds a wire-splicing pin and the wire cutters out to her. "What do you think these are?"

---

5. Another fucking bastard.
6. So.
7. Sons of bitches, ruffians.
8. And the police, what do they do? Fucking bastards.
9. Fucking degenerates. *Porquería*: stinking thing.
1. Go ahead.

2. How aggressive! *Chocho*: old man.
3. *What!* Barbarian!
4. Crazy woman.
5. Grandmother.
6. Go, then.
7. You.
8. Fuck.

"Qué sé yo?[9] Burglars' tools. You break into parked cars, no? Police catch you with those, you'll see what happens to you, güey"—and she shakes her head. "Just the pretext they'll need to leave you in a bloody pulp."

"These are mariners' tools," he says, thinking, Puta, I guess they are burglars' tools.

She looks at the tools, and then up at him. "You have a funny accent," she finally says. "What's all that with the *vos*?"

"Soy de Nicaragua," he answers. "Esteban Gaitán. Mucho gusto. Y usted?"

"Joaquina," she says warily. "Encantado,"[1] she says with a certain sarcasm and a slight smile. "Bueno. En fin," she says sternly, and lifts the keys towards the door again, grimacing as she steps towards it. "Hasta luego, marinero."

"How can a cat be olive colored?" Esteban points at the sign in the window. "Why doesn't it just say black?"

She steps back from the door again, smiling quizzically, a little slice of a smile that suddenly widens: her smile so lights up her face that suddenly she looks about eight years old.

"I've never thought of that," she says. "Gonzalo thinks Dolores is olive green. Claro,[2] she isn't. More like muddy gray. Maybe he's color blind and hides it. But imagine. You think women are going to come here to get their hair dyed if they know he's color blind? But my jefe,[3] bueno, that's what he's like, full of inventions." She chuckles softly. "Like you, verdad?"[4]

"This is where you work?"

"Pues, claro," she says, as if suddenly annoyed by him again. "I'm the one who has to come and open it up in the morning. Can't you read?" and she points at the sign over the door: *Salón de Belleza Tropicana—Unisex.*

"I can read," he says.

She's looking at him thoughtfully now, not angrily like before. "You're really a marinero?"

"Sí, pues."

"Then you must be good with a mop, no? Isn't that what marineros are always doing, mopping the deck?"

"Sometimes."

"Bueno, te propongo algo.[5] If you mop and sweep the doorway here, I'll make you a cup of coffee. Órale?" Her eyebrows go up.

He smiles. Doesn't understand that word. "Órale?" he repeats.

"Papas!" she says. Potatoes? And she steps forward and opens the door, turning various keys in various locks. As she's going inside, she looks at him standing dumbly on the sidewalk. "Ven!"

He follows Joaquina inside, into the almost noxiously sweet-smelling salon, the gray glow of mirrors in the dark; he stands inside the door while she crosses the room to the light switches. The light comes on, and she disappears behind a red-yellow printed curtain into the back. He hears water pouring against metal, filling a pail. He gapes at himself in the mirror, appalled at his beggar aspect of long, dirty hair and light beard, his hollowed face and frightened eyes: he looks like one of those boys raised by wolves. The water stops; she steps back out through the curtain, she's taken

9. Do I know?
1. Delighted to meet you.
2. Of course.
3. Boss.
4. Right?
5. I propose something to you.

off her coat and is wearing a pleated gray-black wool skirt, a pink cardigan sweater over a white blouse with a lacy collar. She gestures to him. "Ven," she says. "You carry it out, güey."

He follows her through the curtain, into a corridor with three closed doors, a coat rack hung with her coat and blue smocks, supplies arrayed along shelves, an industrial sink. Joaquina is pouring ammonia from a plastic bottle into the metal pail, and when she's done, she carefully twists the cap back on, holding the bottle away from herself. He notices an earring, a small, glassy-purple star, on her lobe. She hands him a mop and a broom, steps out through the curtain; he follows her out, carrying the broom between biceps and rib, the mop in one hand and the sloshing pail in the other.

"I could use a haircut," he says, wanting to make a kind of self-dignifying joke. "And a shave, pues."

"Pinche güey!" she exclaims, darting her eyes at him. "You're out of luck. I'm just the manicurist."

He's walking to the door when he hears her say, "Bueno, I can also wax your legs. Even your bikini line, güey. Ja!"

He turns to look at her, her back to him as she fumbles with the coffee maker on a side table against the wall. She says, "Gonzalo will cut your hair for ten dollars." The hem of her sweater falls like a soft bell over her slender rear. "Clean everything well, güey, and I'll let you have a pastelito[6] too."

The reek of urine is strong in front of the door. He thinks, Bocona, mandona.[7] He really doesn't like the way she speaks to him, mouthy, bossy, patronizing, eh? He picks up two empty quart bottles of beer standing in paper bags between the salon's door and another door with affixed buzzers and scrawled numbers on a battered metal sheet, carries the bottles to the trash cans on the curb, and laying them in, prods open the tear in a plastic bag, sees it full of hair, mainly dark hues of hair. Hairy wax, he remembers, la Marta.[8] Sweeps cigarette butts, a few tiny marijuana butts in pinched pink paper, all the way across the sidewalk—people hurry around and past him on the sidewalk. He stares down at his boots with the broom in his hands. Thinks, This is totally strange, no? His scuffed, grease-stained black boots, made in the Soviet Union, laced with electrical wire, which accompanied him all the way through the war, which la Marta unlaced and tugged off his feet more than once, which that German tracking dog sniffed with its nose of sorrow, boots that stood in a pile of tumbling bullet cartridges as he returned blistering fire through trunk planks during the Zompopera ambush and got soaked with the blood of compas while somehow he wasn't killed; and then went home to Corinto with him and walked through the shitty, steaming, salty mud of its streets and which, oddly yet typically, his Tío Nelson and not his mamá used to like to clean and polish for him; boots which watched his pathetic freak-out with that puta in the burdel,[9] standing empty by her bed, stinking up the already smelly little room and filling it with silent howls of fucked up grief, and then a week later went away to sea with him: and now, vos, here they are, while he sweeps up outside a beauty salon in Brooklyn, these boots like a last living witness to his life, like the only proof he has of the life of Esteban Gaitán . . . He gazes up the ramshackle row house–lined

6. Pastry.
7. Big-mouth, tyrant.
8. La Marta was Esteban's lover, killed in battle during the Nicaraguan revolutionary insurgency.
9. Whorehouse bitch.

street—brick, wood, concrete, and aluminum-sided facades, some with tiny, littered gardens out front behind corroded gates—past trash cans and parked cars, at the avenue flashing busily with traffic and pedestrians now. These people passing, they're probably thinking, Look at that dirty beggar, sweeping up in front of a salon, he must be mentally retarded or a drunk, working for just a few pennies. Puta. Y qué? He finishes sweeping, nudges the small pile between two trash cans. Then he mops vigorously and thoroughly, wringing the mop out with his hands, breathing in the strong scent of ammonia, slapping water all over the place, from the door all the way out to the curb—

"Oye, chamaco,"[1] Joaquina says, standing in the door. "Did I ask you to mop all of Brooklyn?"

Inside, they sit on folding chairs against the wall, a white cardboard box holding a few pastries on the chair between them, sipping their coffee. So how should he talk to her? Like she's his boss?

"Y usted, where are you from?"

"México," she says, yawning, lifting the back of her hand to her mouth. "And you don't have to say *usted*."[2] She gestures at the box. "These are left from yesterday, so they're a little stale."

She's already explained to him about how she made the coffee in that machine over there, told him it's real coffee. Sí pues, like the coffee he had on the airplane. The first of any kind in months, since their officers stopped bringing them jars of instant coffee, which apparently isn't real coffee. He savors the strong, muddy taste, feels the warmth and caffeine hitting inside, feels his intestines cringe. He looks around at the salon, the glossy color photographs of men and women with different hairdos; a framed picture of La Virgen del Cobre against a red backdrop with lighthouse and palms painted in, seashells glued to it; and another framed photograph of a man dressed like Pedro Picapiedra,[3] in a tunic that looks made of leopard skin, holding a spread-eagled, platinum blonde woman in a silvery leotard over his head in muscular arms.

"I don't usually have to come in this early," Joaquina is saying, "but I have a customer coming in for a special appointment."

"Ajá,"[4] he says softly, not looking at her. He reaches for one of the pastelitos, crescent shaped, glazed, and sugar sprinkled, bites into the chewy crust, jam squirts into his mouth. Dismally, he watches himself chewing in the mirrors.

"So you're a náufrago, güey," she says. "De veras?"

A shipwrecked sailor—that's true enough. "Sí, pues," he says, "it's true. But my name isn't güey, it's Esteban. Our capitán always calls us güey."

"He's a chilango?"

He asks what a chilango is, and she tells him it's someone from México, el Distrito Federal. "*May-ksee-koh Ceetee*," she says, trying to imitate a gringo accent.

---

1. Boy.
2. I.e., he doesn't have to use the formal form of *you* (the informal form is *tú*).
3. The Spanish-language name of the cartoon character Fred Flintstone. *La Virgen del Cobre*: literally, the Virgin of Copper; also known as *La Virgen de la Caridad* (the Virgin of Charity); a

statue of the Virgin Mary in the mining town of El Cobre, outside Santiago in southwest Cuba. The site is the most important religious shrine on the island; in 1916, the pope declared the Virgin of Charity the patron saint of Cuba.
4. Okay.

"No, I don't think so. Bueno, he's a pendejo,[5] wherever he's from. Americano. Inglés. Griego. Las Amazonas. I guess he's from all those places." He shrugs. "Is that where you're from in Mexico?"

"Sí. No. Zacatecas.[6] But I lived there for a few years, that's where I went to beautician school, and worked awhile, before I came up here to live with my brothers. We all lived there, for a while."

"It's a big city, no?"

"Sí, güey, it's a big city. Much bigger than this one, they say, though it doesn't seem like it."

"Is it difficult to live here as an immigrant?"

For some reason this makes her laugh, a brief, airy giggle. "Más o menos. Bueno, es bonito[7] . . . *Esteban*." She sips her coffee, eyes beaming as if she's said something funny; holding her cup with her little finger out, chin up, gazing off with a tight-lipped little smirk, as if she's savoring the taste of whatever it is she thinks is so funny and not just the coffee.

They fall into a silence while she holds the cup up to her lips in both hands, taking steady little sips. Her fingernails cut short, neat, glossy. She sits, bent over her coffee, with her legs straight out and a little apart, her feet pointed up in her high heels and gently rocking, the fabric of her tights wrinkled around the straps over the ankles. He lets his eyes coast quickly over her slender, curving calves. He inhales with his mouth closed, slowly drawing in her perfume and faint soapy scent, along with the coffee, all the salon smells. In a nose full of *Urus*, no? Corroded nostrils that by now must be like portable bits of the *Urus*: rust and paint, old diesel oil from the depths of the ship, his unwashed compañeros. No wonder he's a little dizzy, perspiring from the cold, frothy ache in his bowels. And her perfume is beginning to affect his breathing, making his breathing passages feel wooly.

He's finished his coffee, sees that there's more in the pot. Should he ask for more? Doesn't think he wants any more. Can't think of anything to say. Shouldn't he ask to use the toilet? Doesn't dare, what if he stinks the place up. Golden curls partly tucked behind her ears, falling down around her thin neck and lacy collar, a fine silver chain dangling over her small chest, disappearing under the sweater; she has one of those little stars on both lobes. She has a surprisingly low, chesty, womanly voice that goes shrill when she's excited. Kind of a baby face, for all her haughtiness and mouthiness. How old is she? Maybe even younger than he, because all that makeup must make her look older than she is. Hair must be dyed. Decides not to like her, much. Compared with la Marta, he decides, she seems stuck-up and artificial.

"So you like it here," he says.

"Síí. 'stá padre, 'stá chingón."[8]

Uses too much strange slang.

"So what are you going to do?" she asks.

"When?"

"On your *boat*, güey."

"Maybe I'll leave," he says. "Try to get a job here in the city. Of course, I'll need a haircut first. Some clothes." Wonders if he can find some way to sell all those Parcheesis, and the swimming goggles too.[9]

---

5. An asshole.
6. State in north-central Mexico; also the name of the state capital.

7. More or less. Well, it's nice.
8. It's good, it's first-rate.
9. I.e., cargo on the ship.

"Claro," she says.

"But I think I should try to find the United Nations first. See if they can do something to resolve our situation. Do you know how to get there?"

"I think it's somewhere in Manhattan," she says, seemingly unimpressed by this bold, new plan. "I'm sure you can get there by subway. Claro, you can't go there looking like that, though, they'll think you're a terrorist. I'd lend you some clothes, but— My brothers have clothes, but they're shorter than you, and wider, and I don't think they'd like me to be giving away their clothes."

"Bueno," he says. "Thanks for thinking of it."

"Por nada," she says. "Anyway, there are places that sell very inexpensive clothing, secondhand, sometimes you find some nice things . . . Ah! Here's my customer! Esteban, you have to go now."

He looks up and sees a broad-shouldered, tall, yet squarely built man in a bright red, white-trimmed jogging suit outside the door; ebony hair slickly smoothed back over a broad, sharp-featured indio face. Joaquina opens the door for him, and he bends down to embrace her, they give each other kisses on the cheek, she says, "Chucho, corazón, cómo te va, eh?"

"Joaquina, ángel de mi alma," his voice a gruff singsong. "I haven't made you get up too early, I hope. In this pinche cold."

"Sí, 'sta friolín, no?"

Chucho looks down at Esteban, his briefly puzzled glance resolving into an unfriendly stare through narrowing eyes, his chin seeming to pull back into his brawny neck. He is wearing shiny black ankle boots tucked up into his sweatpants; three gem-studded gold rings on one hand, a big, gold-banded gold watch peeking out from under a red sleeve.

"This is Esteban," says Joaquina, glancing over at him and scoldingly widening her eyes. "He's a shipwrecked marinero. Imagine."

"Ah," says Chucho. "Don't tell me."

"Mucho gusto," says Esteban, rising from his seat.

"Sí, pues," says Chucho, and he looks over at Joaquina.

"Really, it's true," says Joaquina, flustered, taking Chucho's arm in two hands and tugging him lightly across the room—she walks, thinks Esteban, as if her shoes are both too heavy and loose fitting for her, yet with a certain elastic rhythm and grace—and starting to explain how she found Esteban outside. ". . . He wanted to know how a cat could be green like an olive. Isn't that cute? When he said that I knew I didn't have to be afraid of him. He cleaned the doorway"—laughing, guiding Chucho to a leather-backed metal chair with leather armrests, next to a footstool, and a small, wheeled cart loaded with bottles of nail polish and other potions, delicate, silvery tools laid out across it, and a cup holding emery board files that remind Esteban of tongue depressors in a doctor's office. And when she has him seated she breathlessly says, "Chucho, un momentito y ya," and Chucho says he's in a hurry, guerita,[1] and she says, "Sí, sí, corazón, I just have to let Esteban out," and she glares at Esteban and walks towards the door and he turns and says good-bye to Chucho and follows her out the door, which she holds open with her shoulder. She gives Esteban her hand.

"Oye, gracias por todo," she says. "And good luck with everything, eh? If there's anything I can do to help? Órale?"

1. Blondie.

"Gracias a vos!"

"Por nada, güey. Órale?"

"Órale."

"Papas!" a quick smile, and then she's already turned back into the salon. He watches her hurry back to Chucho, pulling the little stool in front of him, sitting down on it as she smooths her skirt around her, pulling the little trolley cart to her side while Chucho lifts his hand, extends it towards her; he can see them talking as she takes his hand in both of hers. Chucho glances over at him. He'd better go; he goes. Thinking, Qué cosa, qué cosa. That macho prepotente[2] getting a manicure first thing in the morning!

Feeling elated and then bewildered and then a little less elated as he strides down the sidewalk. Wishes he'd asked to use the toilet. Total mandona, though. Mouthy! She and Chucho, y qué? What's so great about how *Chucho* was dressed? She's one of those chicas plásticas. Not the type that sees into your heart, your values, sees who you really are.

1997

2. Abusive macho. *Qué cosa*: oh well.

---

# ELÍAS MIGUEL MUÑOZ
## b. 1954

Elías Miguel Muñoz left his native province of Camagüey, Cuba, for the United States with his family in 1969. Muñoz received his bachelor's degree from California State University; his master's (1979) from the University of California, Irvine; and a doctorate in Spanish from Irvine (1984). He has taught at several U.S. colleges and universities, and he has published textbooks for students of Spanish, essays, works of criticism, fiction, and poetry.

Muñoz's first novel, *Los viajes de Orlando Cachumbambé* (The Voyages of Orlando on the Seesaw, 1984), uses the metaphor of the *cachumbambé* to convey the protagonist's emotional ups and downs as well as his wavering between Cuban and American culture. Muñoz's second novel, *Crazy Love* (1988), experiments with structure and point of view in telling the story of a child coming of age between cultures. In these works, as well as in his novels *The Greatest Performance* (1991), *Brand New Memory* (1998), and *Vida Mía* (2006), Muñoz explores the different generations of exiles: the older people, who live on memories of a lost world, and the younger people, many born in the U.S., who are torn between nostalgia for a country they never really knew and assimilation into American culture. Issues of gender and sexual orientation play a large part, as the characters often defy the machismo of Hispanic culture.

Muñoz's writing has appeared in many anthologies, including *Iguana Dreams: New Latino Fiction* (1992), *Currents from the Dancing River: Contemporary Latino Fiction, Nonfiction, and Poetry* (1994), and *Muy Macho: Latino Men Confront Their Manhood* (1996). In the essay from *Muy Macho* included here, "From the Land of Machos: Journey to Oz with My Father," Muñoz reveals both the love, hatred, and fear he felt for his father and his attempts to break the traditional macho silence between them. His bilingual poetry, published in the collections *En estas tierras/In*

*This Land* (1989) and *No fue posible el sol* (The Sun Was Not Possible, 1989), reflects the personal and collective wounds of exile.

## From the Land of Machos: Journey to Oz with My Father

I drive; he sleeps. Violin music makes him feel drowsy. He doesn't like the arias and concertos I love; he finds them depressing, impenetrable. So he shuts down. And I must resist the temptation to wake him and force him to listen. It's the opera *Don Giovanni*, Mozart's secret homage to his father.[1] The obvious symbolism of this music betrays my hidden agenda: Can my father and I finally face the past, *our* past, and go on from there? Is it too late?

He is snoring, thanks to Wolfgang Amadeus. I'm enthralled by the endless desert and the ghost towns, all so different from the Cuban landscapes of his youth. Exhausted, I drive the rented truck to a rest area. My load consists of five boxes of books (my graduate school collection), wood shelves, my twin bed, an obsolete stereo with eight-track, and my ancient rolltop desk. And memories, which can also weigh you down.

"Thank you for coming along with me, Papi." This is what I should say to Don Elías, using the word most Cubans use for their fathers: Papi. A word that reeks of obedience and submission. An embarrassing, obligatory form of endearment. I hate it, but I don't know what else to call him.

Truth is, I'm grateful, and I promise myself that I will thank him at the end of our journey. On this hot and cloudless August day, 1984, I'm heading for Kansas, Land of Oz, heart of the Bible Belt. An academic position awaits me at an obscure university. I've deluded myself into thinking I'll begin a new life there. For one thing, I'll be far from California. Far from my family, from this man who sleeps beside me.

Watching him, I feel something like pity or compassion. He seems so defenseless. In an hour or two he'll wake up and ask, impatiently, "Do we have a lot further to go?" And I'll tell him a lie, "No. We're almost there." And he'll be the same old Papi, with no doubts about himself, no revelations from his dreams. No questions.

What or whom does my father dream about? What does he think about when he's at work painting walls? His job since he quit the factory, after the accident: painting houses and apartments. He loves having his own business. A far cry from his sales job in Cuba, but nonetheless a perfect occupation for someone who likes to be alone. My father can spend hours without any human contact. How does he fill all that time? I wonder. He probably thinks about all his responsibilities. The bon mot for Papi, indeed: *responsabilidad*.

There are phrases from my childhood, things he said to my mother, that haunt me: "I make all the decisions here! Don't you ever raise your voice to me again! No woman is going to ride *my* horse!" She was his doll, the little woman of the house. Did she love him? I'll never know. However, now I have words to name what in those days was only an intuition: He was self-

---

1. The music for this 1787 opera is by the Austrian composer Wolfgang Amadeus Mozart (1756–1791); the libretto, in Italian, is by the Venetian librettist and poet Lorenzo Da Ponte (1749–1838). The story concerns the destruction of the title character.

ish, aggressive; never giving, never tender with her. Mami obeyed him silently, moving aside whenever his fists fell on my face. Instead of confronting my torturer, she cried. The fear paralyzed her.

Many years later Gladys, my mother, would go from total paralysis to a passionate quest for her redemption. As she began to push sixty, she'd become a warrior of her freedom. Pent-up rancor, countless reproaches sprang from Mami, flooding our home. It was a poisoned stream: water from a past that refused to run a silent course. She would defy my father, confront him, humiliate him. But all of that would be much later—later than now, I mean. Because in the present of this trip to Kansas, my image of her was still that of a gentle, passive creature.

In this present of our trek to Oz, my father and I are away from our common, known places. We'll be able to talk, I hope. This is our first and last chance. I will relate my memories, the painful ones. And he will have no choice but to listen. Who knows, we might even reach a truce. It's hard to never have found the space and time to be alone with him. It's hard to go through life holding a grudge against your father, unable to tell him how you feel.

### The Memory Came

For now let us invent a game. It'll be an easy one to play: All you have to do is answer my questions. What was the name of that guy who used to sell us plantains? And that other man, the Spanish curmudgeon you used to work for, did he stay in Cuba? What about Lalia and Raimundo, our dear old neighbors, what happened to them? (I keep a thought to myself: They must be dead by now.)

Do you remember what I remember, Papi? Our carriage rides down Calle Independencia,[2] our promenades at Parque Juanita. We spent one month each summer at Varadero.[3] Every year, on January 6, the Reyes Magos packed our house full of presents for my brother and me. Do you remember the corner store in Vista Alegre?[4] We called it El Kiosko Bolita, although it had no sign showing its name. There was a jukebox at the kiosk, a *traganíquel* (literally, "swallow-nickels"). It played languid, heartrending boleros that you knew by heart: "*Nosotros,*" "*Lágrimas Negras,*" "*Cuatro Vidas.*" Have you forgotten those songs, Papi?

Our game ends abruptly when a disturbing memory pushes forward, making me lose control of the wheel momentarily. Papi and I are riding the bus home from the park. My father is trying to protect me from the onslaught of passengers who push and shove and press against us. One of these people is a shoeshine boy we've often seen downtown. Through the eyes of my remembrance he looks like a weary old man, though he couldn't have been more than fifteen. He storms onto the bus and bumps me with his box as he passes by me. It's not a big blow, but it surprises me and I let out a slight moan. My father is furious. He attacks the young man verbally and the shoeshine boy retaliates with a threat: "I'm going to break your neck when we get off!"

2. Thoroughfare in Porto Príncipe, Camagüey, Cuba.
3. Resort town on the northwestern coast of Cuba.

4. Residential area of Santiago de Cuba, capital of the Santiago de Cuba province, southeastern Cuba.

Papi and I get out at the stop near our house. I know we're in danger, but I also know I have to trust my father. He's a macho; he flaunts his big *cojones*[5] all the time. My valiant Papi will defend me.

The next scene happens too fast. I've lost track of the time between the moment we stepped down and the onset of combat. Who attacked whom first? Was it a punch, a shove, a kick? All I remember is the sight of my father and the stranger locked in an embrace! They were moving in unison, in circles, not letting go of each other. What kind of a brawl was this? It made no sense! At one point I looked around and noticed the crowd, the bus that hadn't left, a man who was pulling the fighters apart. And a woman who asked Papi, gently, "What are you doing, Elías? Why are you getting involved in something dirty like this?"

Strange, how vividly one recalls phrases, gestures, voices from such a remote past. I was only five or six, but I can still hear that woman's words as if she were whispering them now in my ear. (Who was she?) I can see Papi's face, puffy and contorted; the way he inspected his arm and discovered a patch of bloody skin. Was he more of a man now, more of a macho? I wondered then. His actions, he must've thought, should speak for themselves. What did those actions tell me? I remember thinking that I'd never want to be a father, not if you had to do what Papi had done. Not if it meant being willing to fight and risk getting killed.

I should've felt pride and admiration for him. *¡Viva el valiente Papi!* I should've wished to emulate him. *¡Que viva!* Yet the only truth I'd gleaned from his display of heroism was that I would always be a coward.

### Pipeline to Heaven

Dawn. We're on the road again. One full day of driving ahead. "Where did you say we're going?" he asks, half asleep and half jokingly. "To Wichita, Kansas," I repeat. "We'll arrive tomorrow morning."

Today my father is a man who feels worn out and restless. My father is an exhausted body that snores and farts and aches. The first time he's traveled since our exodus; maybe that's why he seems a little frightened. Twenty years of predictability and repetition. And then this bizarre trip.

I detect his discomfort. Time is harder to kill than we thought. We should stop at a McDonald's and have lunch, take a leak, and recoup, prepare for the next stretch of silence. Or we could just play the Memory Game. (That is, after all, my secret plan.) Does he remember how he proved God's existence to me? How he showed me that the almighty *Dios* was on his side?

We were vacationing in Varadero. The movie *Aladino* (a Mexican version)[6] was showing at a local theater; I was dying to see it, enticed by the fantasy of having my own personal genie and a flying carpet. Papi told me he'd take me on one condition: I had to say, "*Si Dios quiere*," "God willing." I refused to. He warned me: "If you don't say 'God willing' you won't get to see the movie." I continued to say no, just to annoy him, trusting that *Dios* would be too busy to notice Papi's out-of-character attempt. Why did my father wish to make a God-fearing believer out of me, when he wasn't a believer himself? He never prayed, he never went to Mass. Papi wasn't religious at all!

---

5. Balls.
6. Perhaps *Aladino y la lámpara maravillosa*

(1958), a live-action, Spanish-language version of the Aladdin story.

That afternoon we went to the matinee show and found that the film had been canceled. A trio of roving guitar players was entertaining the people who'd been waiting to see *Aladino*. Suddenly, for that multitude, the movie was not as immediate, not as wondrous as the boleros the street musicians played. They were all singing. All happy, except me.

I asked myself questions that were much too profound for a child of ten: Do I deserve the magic of a miracle? Is this supposed to be a message from God? I was dumbfounded, convinced of my father's mysterious pipeline to Heaven.

"Did you know they were going to cancel the movie?" I ask him now, during our trip, but he can't recall the incident. I insist: "Did you have contacts in the theater, people who informed you? Was it just coincidence?" He doesn't know what I'm talking about.

Needing closure, I conclude that the fateful event served my father perfectly. He gave me overwhelming proof of his *poder*. Yes, he had a special power for imposing his will and creating the world—my reality—at his whim. God and my father became the same entity. An omnipotent being with two faces: that of an old man with a white beard, and that of my progenitor; accomplices who incarnated the same stereotype. Both destined to propagate the seed of fear and obedience. Both fated to be machos.

I took communion shortly after that incident, and I was confirmed. But my faith, my devotion, and my prayers were a farce, an unconvincing simulacrum. I didn't deserve the protection of our Father, creator of the universe. In fact, I dared to repudiate him, secretly reproaching him for his *machista* rules. His Heaven was founded on a hierarchy of men, in which women had no voice. This *Padre nuestro*[7] couldn't be a true god, I told myself. Because if he were real, there would be no place for me in Heaven.

Miguelito would eventually burn in Lucifer's cauldrons, I was sure. Surprisingly, though, this prospect didn't scare me. The Devil, in my young imagination, seemed much more plausible and attractive than his counterpart in the Catholic pantheon. I imagined the *Demonio* as a mischievous and fun-loving angel. Only such a creature could protect and welcome a "deviant" male like me.

For the boy I was detested all typical boys' activities. He didn't play baseball and he refused to whistle at the girls—known in Cuban macho circles as *jevitas*, "little broads"—who passed by his house. The boy I should've been, according to my father, would never have spent his afternoons in his room, drawing, writing poems, or just daydreaming. "Boys are supposed to play ball!" Papi would shout, loud enough for the neighbors to hear him.

He wanted a healthy, handsome *niño*.[8] But then I turned out to be something he didn't expect, an oddity with no hope for a dignified future. The boy he'd engendered was an aberration, someone my adolescent father couldn't define or recognize as his own. He looked at me and hated himself because he'd helped create a monster. Worse yet: a *mariquita*.[9]

Yes, I would go to Hell to pay for my crimes. One of these was a mortal sin: not wanting to act like a man, not assuming the authority of my gender. Papi, on the other hand, would probably wander through Purgatory first.

7. Our Father.
8. Son.

9. Sissy, pansy.

Then he'd be tried by a jury of male angels, and by a judge clad in full patriarchal garb; a very masculine and just and normal judge. Amen.

### The Little Devil

"Do you want to drive?" I ask him, hoping he'll accept. In Cuba he owned a Chevrolet Belair, a classy, stylish vehicle painted green and silver. (The car was confiscated by the state soon after the revolution.) As a salesman for a clothing company, my father spent a great deal of time on the road, putting miles on his '55 Chevy. Riding with him, one felt safe. Which is not the way I feel now as I watch him grab the wheel reluctantly. He endures the task because he thinks I'm tired, because he has no other choice.

But he does have a choice. He could say no and I'd gladly take over. Driving is not the reason he came along. Not my reason, anyway. He's here because we have old debts to settle, some unfinished business.

"Why did you punish me so much when I was a kid, Papi?" I ask him, knowing he'll deny everything. "I didn't," he says through clenched teeth. I insist, "Why did you beat me till the blood ran down my face? Why, *coño!*"[1]

He recoils, defensively, and stares out the window. There's only barren terrain, but looking beyond it is better than looking at me. Better than having to meet my eyes. Slowly, painstakingly, he alleges that I was a *diablito* (a rascal; literally, a "little devil"). He says I was disobedient and had a foul mouth, that I talked back and called him names. I wasn't a good son, he says. He punished me only when it was necessary, when there was no other alternative, and neither more nor less than any typical father.

Bullshit! I cry to myself. There *were* other alternatives! There always are. The hurtful exchange resumes in my head: Tell me the truth, Papi. You didn't feel any pleasure when you punished me? When you gave me every bruise, every mark on my skin, on my soul? No pleasure? Not just the beatings. I'm also referring to those days—entire days—that you forced me to spend naked in bed. One of your favorite punishments: exposing me to the glances of my cousins and the neighbor kids, letting them have fun at my expense as they laughed at my shame and my nudity. Why did you invite them to our house, to come and see me, Papi? Why did you torture me this way? I'll bet I know the answer. By doing this, you castigated me for my "effeminate" manners, right? So that I'd get on a "straight" path (your words: *entrar en camino*). At the same time you proved to the observers—to the world—that I had the proper anatomy, big *cojones* like yours; that I, your *machito*, was a "normal" boy.

It is true that I was an unreachable child, that I was reluctant to participate in my father's life. I wouldn't share his joys and daily triumphs. I wouldn't commiserate with him about his burdens. My attitude and my voice and my conduct didn't fit within the molds Papi had envisioned for me. I rejected him passionately. We were dangerous strangers to each other. Enemies. Yet my "mischiefs"—such small crimes!—did not deserve the pain my father caused me.

You might as well admit it, Papi. You took a bizarre kind of pleasure in bending my will, in stripping me of my dignity, in crushing me. Admit it.

---

1. Damn it.

## Days of Aquarius

I play a tape I recorded especially for him. It's a compilation of old songs from scratchy records, the greatest hits of Orquesta Aragón, Beny Moré, Daniel Santos.[2] The music of his adolescence that revives him and propels him. I hear him hum, then sing. He steps on it, commanding the truck like a pro. And it pleases me to watch him take us through the sleepy villages of New Mexico.

This sky is the most intense blue I've ever seen. (Or was my father's Cuban sky more blue and more intense?) A vast and arid landscape appears; it overpowers us. Desert, rocks, hills of a dusty yellow, caves that used to be someone's refuge.

"We're so far, Miguel," I hear him murmur. "Far from where?" I ask. His response: "From everything."

Far from the world as he knew it. Days of Aquarius, a trip with no return in 1969. We were supposed to have arrived in paradise, but Eden was a sad, desolate planet. The empty sidewalks, the endless freeways. Where did one town end and another begin? We couldn't tell. They all merged into one long, indistinguishable country.

The great northern land would never feel like home. My father was to live longing to return. The younger ones—my brother and I—would be easy converts, slipping with little effort into this new, alien culture. (Or so we thought.) Papi would remain anchored in Cuban soil, oblivious to the language and customs and ideas pulsating around him. He'd learn to speak English unwillingly. He'd fade in and out of our present, ill at ease, like a self-conscious shadow. And I, I would reap the fruit of his effacement.

I saw him cry for the first time after our arrival in Los Angeles. My image of the impassive macho was banished temporarily and that of a weak, vulnerable being emerged. He'd cry about anything: a word, a gesture, a song. His siblings' letters made him weep profusely. He got home every day bedraggled and greasy after assembling thousands of parts at the *factoría*. Papi began to look sickly, wilted.

Few chores made him happier than grocery shopping. Such joy to have enough money to buy steaks, all the rice and beans you want, the fancy sauces, coffee, cheese, and rich desserts. No rationing. No shortages. A blissful abundance of every imaginable product. He'd come home from the market loaded up with American goodies for his family: cottage cheese with pineapple, my mother's weakness; ham, a mythical meat; soda crackers, one box per person; glazed doughnuts, a delicious gringo pastry; Coca-Cola, a sweet, purifying potion; and cornflakes (can't grow up to be a true American without them).

We lived in a spacious, two-bedroom apartment, and my father had managed to buy an almost-new car; it was a cream-colored Impala convertible. There is a photo from those days that shows him in the driver's seat, proudly displaying his machine. Things were finally working out. His sons went to school in Hawthorne, the white people's area, and both he and their mother had jobs. Some day they'd buy a house and he'd have

2. Puerto Rican singer and composer of boleros (1916–1992), who lived in Cuba in the late 1940s. *Orquesta Aragón*: Cuban dance band formed in the 1930s. *Beny Moré*: Cuban singer (1919–1963).

his own business. No more factory work for Gladys. No more greasy parts for Elías.

The photo of him at the hospital vividly depicts his next phase. Papi suffered an accident at work, hurt his back—a pinched disc—and had to stay at home, prostrate, for weeks. Long days stuck in a solitary bed while my mother went off to her *factoría*. He must've done a lot of thinking in those days, a lot of staring at the walls, or at the carpet with its revolting olive color. He must've cursed his decision to come to this city of fenced-in lawns and vacant boulevards.

The accident ordeal left him limping, but a richer man, with a lawyer. He sued the company and got some money (a measly sum) out of it. Well-deserved compensation, he probably thought.

By now he'd realized that we weren't going back to Cuba. His children didn't long for his tropical haven, nor did they share his wrenching nostalgia. This was the phase of resignation; our roots had been permanently severed. But he wouldn't give up his dream of *el regreso* without a fight. Resentful, thriving on his uprootedness, he unleashed his wrath against us. A maniac was set loose in our house with his fist in the air. "*¡Castigo!*" he shouted. He resolved to punish the weaklings like my mother and the unruly dissidents like me. "*¡Castigo!*" Punishment for those who dare forget where we came from!

I was already in my late teens and I had stopped fearing his wrath. He couldn't hurt me anymore; I felt strong enough to fight him. This was a time when the desire for vengeance consumed me. I dreamed of torturing and killing him. I begged my mother to divorce him. At the slightest sign of abuse, I'd start slamming doors and screaming loud enough for the neighbors to hear me: "Why did you have a family, *coño*?! So you could mistreat us?" I'd head him off at the pass with a fit of my own. An eye for an eye and a scream for a scream. *¡Coño!*

I started wearing makeup and dying my hair. I'd come home from school barefoot, carrying flowers, wearing colorful necklaces of beads and seashells. I'd be gone for days, staying with friends, while he waited for me at home, worried and ashamed and raging. His son was a hippie! It felt great to defy him. A disgusting *maricón*![3] It was a pleasure to be different from him.

The young man I turned into wasn't solely the by-product of a macho upbringing; I'm quite aware of that. My actions—and my thoughts and my beliefs and my desires—were not just a result of my rejection of Papi. That would be too simple and deterministic. Yet I surprised myself, during my phases of most intense rebellion, thinking: Fuck you, Elías. *¡Jódete!*[4] I'll show you!

### California Dreaming

He grabs the map and scrutinizes it. "We're doing okay, don't worry," I reassure him. "We're not lost. This is the only way to Kansas." He makes a face like a spoiled, impatient kid. "I'm sick and tired of this truck," he whines. So I suggest we take a long break from driving and have a picnic.

---

3. Faggot.          4. Fuck you!

We stop at a roadside park. The span of grass before us is dry and unappealing, but there are tables with benches and some trees. We could sit in silence, observe the other travelers. Or perhaps we could just talk. Is he game?

Papi listens distractedly while I describe one of my recurring dreams. Its meaning is blatantly evident: I'm always a lost child. I find myself in the midst of an unfamiliar scene, a city, a desert, or often a tunnel through which a train runs swiftly. There are people around me, but I feel alone. My parents aren't with me. They've abandoned me. I run and run, though I don't know where I'm going.

"I never dream," he says, crossly, before I have a chance to interpret my nightmare.

"Everybody has dreams," I declare, "but some people forget them." He adds: "I must be one of those cases. When I wake up, all I can think about are real things."

The intangible world of the subconscious—with its frightening, uncontrollable scenarios—is of no import to him. (Or does he negate his nightmares in order not to face what they show him?) No. Real men don't indulge in dreams and illusions.

Once I asked him to go to the cemetery with me. I thought we could put flowers on his mother's grave. Josefina, my paternal grandmother, was the first of our family to die in the United States. Even if only for that reason we should do something in her honor, I thought, a small ritual like lighting a candle or visiting her grave some Sunday.

"I won't do anything like that," he said. "Why not?" I asked. "Because," he replied, "I did everything I could for my mother when she was alive. When it counted."

For Papi, Josefina had ceased to exist completely. There was nothing tangible about her, nothing that needed tending to. Because his world exists—or is worthy of existence—only when he can touch it, shape it, or destroy it. Meanings could never be found here, in the mind, or in one's heart. There is no room for anything *real* in there.

And yet my telling of the dream has made Papi introspective. How could it not? He turns to me and asks, "Do you regret that we left Cuba?" I believe what he really wants to ask me is: Do you regret that I got you out of Cuba? He needs to know that all the good he's done for me—our exodus, this trip to Wichita—is solid and lasting.

Yes, getting us out of Cuba was a big job. Yes, his good deeds have been considered; the great, unselfish acts are all accounted for. I should tell him that I'm grateful for his efforts and his sacrifices. But I won't, can't bring myself to say a simple *gracias*. Instead, I respond: "No, I don't regret having left."

### Over the Rainbow

So much rolling through flat, unwelcoming places. Truck stops with names like "Eats" and "Restaurant" where the best dish is soggy, bland meatloaf and the rest rooms are raunchy. Barren towns like Barstow, California; Kingman, Arizona; Gallup and Tucumcari, New Mexico; Liberal, Kansas. So much driving on forsaken routes to arrive here, in Mid-America. A brand-new exile; only, this one is mine. Miguel alone will invent it.

I resist the temptation to sing "Over the Rainbow." It is an easy-to-resist temptation because Wichita looks nothing like Dorothy's Emerald City.[5] Vast wheat fields extend from the outskirts of this urban enclave that aspires to be a metropolis. We drive along its main artery, Kellogg Street, a nondescript strip where a handful of typical establishments thrives: hamburger chains, hotels, some office buildings.

I resist the temptation to tell my father, "Papi, I don't think we're in Cuba anymore."[6] An enormous truth: *No estamos en Cuba.* Yet there are parallels between the myth of Oz and the myth of our exodus. We, too, were brought here by a tornado. Many of us left behind an Auntie Em. Some of us came here not knowing how or why.

Fifteen years after our flight from communism, my father and I are standing in an empty house where I will be living. Papi seems impressed. "What luxury!" he exclaims. My new home belongs to a professor on sabbatical and is located in Eastborough, an affluent community. (The police will stop me several times to ask me what I'm doing there and where I'm from.) The whole area is a welcome oasis in the Kansas flatness: towering trees, flowers, birds, ponds. Locus Amenus[7] that has nothing to do with the realities I'll have to face Monday, at the university.

But academia belongs in a future unbeknownst to me today. At the moment of this present, my father and I are unloading the truck. He came along in case I needed a hand, so he could help soften the blow of separation, my so-called uprootedness from family and friends. This is his responsibility; he's fulfilling his role of provider. I observe him taking my books out of boxes. Together we install the old stereo, assemble the shelves, and build all my domestic bridges.

Our voyage has ended. Whatever wounds didn't get healed will remain open, bleeding. Did we manage to suture any of them? I tell myself that the journey has been helpful. I'll have to remember it and narrate it some day. Will there be, in my story, a magical yellow brick road and a loving, wise wizard to save us from our worst fears?[8] I wonder. Beyond the rainbow, will there rise an emerald-green enchanted castle? Will the mischievous, friendly munchkins and the benevolent Witch of the North help us find our way?

My optimistic heart wills the Wizard of Oz to exist. I ask the powerful magician to give my father the courage to admit his mistakes, to talk about the damage he did to his family. (He'll be rewarded for this with unconditional love.) For me, the Wiz will concoct the wisdom of oblivion, the power to forgive and forget.

I must forgive him. Love him? He couldn't connect with me, see the world through my eyes. What models were available to a young, uneducated Cuban male in 1954? What could be expected of him? He inherited a mentality founded on absolute patriarchal rule, a legacy of pernicious taboos and absurd notions. To name just a few: masturbation causes stupidity; a man's "milk" (his semen) floods his brain when he doesn't fuck regularly; a healthy,

---

5. In the movie *The Wizard of Oz* (1939), Dorothy sings "Over the Rainbow" and fantasizes about escaping from the Kansas farm where she lives with her Uncle Henry and Auntie Em. She is subsequently knocked unconscious during a tornado and is transported to the land of Oz, the site of the Emerald City.

6. A variation on Dorothy's statement to her dog: "Toto, I have the feeling we're not in Kansas anymore."

7. A pleasant place, Eden-like (Latin).

8. This sentence, the rest of this paragraph, and the following paragraph refer to elements in *The Wizard of Oz.*

normal penis is a *pinga*[9] with a big head and plenty of foreskin; the man is the boss in his home; women are weak; homosexuality is a vice and a sickness; homosexuals are inferior human beings.

Papi, too, was a victim. He, too, had to endure humiliation, beatings, undeserved suffering. His father was a Spanish patriarch who ran his house with an iron fist. Like father, like son. Or, as we say in Spanish, *de tal palo, tal astilla*—"from such a stick, such a sliver." Until I became the sliver and the stick of machismo was crushed. Torn into pieces.

I will never emulate my father. And yet without him, Miguel wouldn't be who he is. The irony doesn't escape me; I wouldn't be obsessed with the ancestral curse of machismo, with the idea of what it means to be or not to be a man. Perhaps I should thank my father also for this: His attitude and his mentality have served me as important lessons. It's as though he's been saying, "Look at me, son, observe my actions carefully. Never be the type of man I've been."

My father will always incarnate machismo, while I will always try to deconstruct the macho archetype. (Yes, even as I listen to Mozart's rewriting of the Don Juan myth.) I'll seek new ways of defining my identity; I'll let alterity "corrupt" me. And my father will always reject those who aren't like him. He'll awaken each morning and know himself to be a true *cubano*, 100 percent *hombre*. As he opens his eyes, he won't remember his dreams.

### Papi's Shoes

He'll be leaving tomorrow on an early flight. He's not looking forward to taking a plane, he says. Proudly, my father informs me that his painting and his responsibilities await him. Soon he'll be back in his world: Mami's cooking and the *café criollo*[1] that he drinks three times a day; his car, in need of repairs; his grocery shopping at the Cuban market; the Mexican *telenovelas*;[2] the old records, songs he still listens to but never sings.

I will write several books (one of them a disguised version of our past) while living in the Emerald City. I'll spend my time—the future that is now upon me—writing, reading, teaching. While my father still struggles to survive in a foreign country.

I'm not sure what I expected to accomplish during this trip. One fact has become absolutely clear: I had never, until now, tried to walk in my father's shoes. Not those of the oppressor, nor the ones worn by the torturer. Not the glamorous slippers whose heels you can click together to transport you. But the shoes of a man who left the world he knew—with a one-way ticket—for the sake of his children. A man who was willing to start over at thirty-five, having no marketable profession and no English skills, so that I would be free. So that I would one day have the freedom to take this job in Kansas and leave my family behind.

Those shoes don't fit me, yet I must wear them. They are invisible but tangible: the shoes of an immigrant. I'll never be able to justify the way Papi tainted my childhood, but I can cease to see him through the gaze of a hurt and frightened child. I must stop thriving on that pain, on that hatred. Only

9. Prick, cock.
1. Espresso.

2. Soap operas.

in a black-and-white world[3] can Papi be my eternal enemy. In the multilayered space of our relationship, nothing is cut and dried. Nothing simple. Only in a one-dimensional universe can I avenge myself, destroy my tormentor.

I remember how tall he used to be; his hair perfectly parted on the left and his thin mustache à la Clark Gable.[4] I remember his strength, his powerful voice when he called me. A young and handsome father, a powerful and abusive father remains there in the bruised corners of my heart. Like a thorn. An image now juxtaposed to the one of a tired old man at a Midwestern airport.

This other father is giving and defenseless; he has tried, in his own way, to undo the wrongs. He's a parent who won't threaten me or hit me, who doesn't want to mold me. This is a father who remembers, even though he denies everything. Forgetting is not easy for him, either. And he doesn't even have the comfort of words. Words to name the love between a father and a son. Words that by naming it could make this emotion a reality.

Two different fathers have taken over the space of my memories. One is virile and manly and is still determined to shape me in his likeness. The other one is learning to express his regrets. This new, kinder image is fragile. Maybe it has arrived too late?

We give each other an uneasy hug at Midcontinent Airport. "Take care of yourself, *mi hijo!*" he whispers, and starts moving clumsily down the jetway. Will he turn around to see me one last time? I have something to tell him, something I forgot to say. He's almost gone. Can he still hear me? "*¡Gracias!*" I yell seconds before he disappears.

1996

3. In *The Wizard of Oz*, the Kansas scenes are in black-and-white, but the Oz scenes are in color.　4. American movie actor (1901–1960).

---

# MICHAEL NAVA
## b. 1954

The mystery/detective novel has generally been the realm of English and Anglo-American writers, but in the 1980s and 1990s, Latinos such as Manuel Ramos and Carolina García-Aguilera began publishing books in that genre. Others, including Rolando Hinojosa (p. 842), Rudolfo A. Anaya (see p. 1160), and Lucha Corpi (p. 1613), have used the genre for broader literary purposes. Among the first Latino writers to develop a series featuring the same character, a staple of the mystery field, was the Mexican American Michael Nava, whose book *The Little Death* (1986) introduced the gay Mexican American lawyer Henry Ríos. Nava has won five Lambda Awards for the Best Gay Mystery.

Nava was born in Stockton, California, and raised in Sacramento. He earned his bachelor's degree in history from Colorado College, in Colorado Springs, in 1976 and a law degree from Stanford University in 1981. He practiced law in the Stanford area for three years before moving to Los Angeles, where most of the Henry Ríos novels are set. In 1995, Nava moved to San Francisco. Four years later, he joined the staff of the California Supreme Court, and since 2004 he has worked for

Justice Carlos R. Moreno, the third Latino to sit on the California high court. In 2002, he Nava received a Doctorate of Humane Letters from Colorado College.

As an investigating attorney, Henry Ríos enters confrontational situations with the potential for violence. As a gay man and a Mexican American, he has the outsider status that is a hallmark of the hardboiled detective. Nava counterposes this dual outsider status to the kind of personal sensitivity that has often marked the California private detective. In fact, Nava's work is solidly in the California school of mystery writing: For example, his characters often have, or develop, a personal stake in solving the central crimes, some of which hark back to Ríos's childhood or an earlier generation; the past, including Ríos's family, and his sister in particular, lies along the edges of his stories. With each book—including *Goldenboy* (1988), *The Hidden Law* (1992), and *The Death of Friends* (1996)—particularly after his entry into mainstream publishing, Nava has refined the subtleties of his approach. In *Rag and Bone* (2001), which Nava said would be the last work in the series, Ríos suffers a heart attack and faces his own mortality.

In the first chapter of *How Town* (1989), included here, Nava introduces Ríos to a new situation and fills in background information about his personal and professional lives.

---

## *From* How Town

## 1

The road to my sister's house snaked through the hills above Oakland, revealing at each curve a brief view of the bay in the glitter of the summer morning. Along the road, houses stood on small woodsy lots. The houses were rather woodsy themselves, of the post and beam school, more like natural outcroppings than structures. Wild roses dimpled the hillsides, small, blowsy flowers stirring faintly in the trail wind of my car. Otherwise, there was no movement. The sky was cloudless, the weather calm and the road ahead of me clear.

Earlier, coming off the Bay bridge I'd taken a wrong turn and found myself in a neighborhood of small pastel houses. Grafitti-gashed walls and a preternatural calm marked it as gang turf. The papers had been full of gang killings that month. When I drove past, a child walking by herself flinched, ready to take cover. None of that was visible from these heights.

This was like living in a garden, I thought, and other associations came to mind: Eden, paradise, a line from "Sunday Morning" that I murmured aloud: "Is there no change in paradise?"[1] I couldn't remember the rest. Elena would know. And she would appreciate the irony. She and I had grown up in a neighborhood called Paradise Slough in a town called Los Robles about an hour's drive from here.

There had been little about our childhood that could be described as paradisiacal. Our alcoholic father was either brutal or sullenly withdrawn. Our mother retaliated with religious fanaticism. As she knelt before plaster

---

1. Partial quotation of line 76 of "Sunday Morning" (1923), by the American poet Wallace Stevens (1879–1955).

images of saints, in the flicker of votive candles, her furious mutter was more like invective than prayer. Their manias kept my parents quite busy, and Elena and I were more or less left to raise ourselves.

This should have made us allies, but it had the opposite effect. We lived in adjoining bedrooms and occasionally as I lay awake listening to one of my father's drunken rampages, and the wail of my mother's prayers, I was aware of Elena next door, also awake, also listening. It never occurred to me to seek shelter with her, though she was five years older and so, by my lights, almost an adult. What she made of all this, I had no idea, as we never discussed what went on in our house. Elena and I were united only in our unspoken determination to show nothing of what we felt about this embarrassment of a life that our parents had visited upon us. In this we succeeded. To the outside world we were simply quiet children, good at school, not very social, a little high-strung.

Consequently her friends and teachers were completely unprepared for her decision to enter a teaching order of nuns after she graduated from high school. I, on the other hand, understood perfectly. She didn't have a vocation. Our mother had ruined us both for religion. What had happened was that our father forced her to refuse admission to Berkeley on the grounds that she had had enough education for a woman. The Church offered her the one way she could defy him. After he died, Elena left her order, got her master's in American literature and took a job at St. Winifred's College, a girls' school where she had now taught for nearly twenty years. She never again referred to the four years she lived as Sister Magdalan, her bride-of-Christ moniker, and since it had all been faintly embarrassing to me—"my sister, the Sister," I called her, never to her face—I didn't raise the subject.

As long as my mother was alive, we maintained the fiction of being a family and I would see Elena once or twice a year. And then, ten years ago, Mother died, and we returned to Los Robles for the funeral. I was startled by how old Elena appeared; the five years she had on me looked more like twenty. If her appearance was due to grief over our mother's passing, it seemed excessive. My mother died of stomach cancer, and her last days on earth were ghastly.

So I could not understand why Elena seemed insensible with pain. On the way back from the cemetery, trying to do my brotherly duty, I took her hand and muttered consoling platitudes. She pulled her hand away, lit a cigarette and told me not to be a fool. We closed up the house and I went back to finish law school.

A few months later I called her on her birthday. The phone was answered by a woman who identified herself as Elena's roommate. When I asked Elena about her, she was evasive and then peremptory, but it was clear that her mood had lightened considerably since the funeral. In later phone calls, the roommate went unmentioned but every now and then Elena would slip pronouns from "I" to "we," and at some point it occurred to me that this woman was her lover.

I wouldn't have assumed this so quickly had I not been in the process of finally accepting my own homosexuality. By turns terrified and euphoric at the discovery that I wasn't crazy but only queer, I couldn't keep my mouth shut about it. I thought it would be wonderful if Elena was also gay, a final joke on our parents. When I told her about myself there was an appalled silence at her end of the line and then a sputtered, vehement lecture, complete with biblical citations, on the evils of homosexuality. Furious, I accused her of hypocrisy, spelling out exactly what I meant. She hung up on me. I did not talk to her again for a year and a half, until we ran into each other in San Francisco.

After that we had fashioned a kind of truce, careful to call each other just often enough so that nothing too dire could be read into periods between. For many years we'd lived within thirty miles of each other, she in Oakland and I on the peninsula. Our calls would terminate in a vapor of promises to meet for lunch or dinner, but we never did. Since moving to Los Angeles a year earlier, I'd not heard from her at all outside of a Christmas card and a note on my birthday. And then there'd been her urgent call two days earlier, the very day that I was leaving for San Francisco to attend a wedding.

I slowed down, searching for an address by which to orient myself. An old-fashioned mailbox on the side of the road bore the name of her street, and its number indicated I was approaching her house. An even clearer sign was the tumble of sensation in my stomach. Although I was acutely attuned to the emotions of those around me, this was merely a skill I'd developed as a defense against being lied to by my clients: very few people evoked my own feelings. Elena was one of them. Toward her I felt—what?—regret? No, nothing quite as settled as that. The truth was, I didn't know what I felt but it was strong enough to bring me here on a mysterious summons against every inclination.

I had never been to her house. I drove across a little wooden bridge that forded a stream, past a windbreak of pine, and came to a stop in front of a brick and redwood split-level perched on the side of a hill. As I got out of the car, it occurred to me just how much time had passed since that summer afternoon in San Francisco when I'd last seen her. She would be 42 now, and I, whom she'd last seen as a stripling of 28, a freshly minted lawyer, was now 37 and had been in some bad neighborhoods since then, and it showed.

I pushed the doorbell. Melodious chimes sounded from within the house. I found myself face to face with my sister. We looked at each other and for a moment it seemed as if we might embrace, but the moment passed.

"Hello, Henry. Come in."

"Hello, Elena."

I stepped into the cool hall. On a small wooden table was an earthenware pot filled with daisies, and above it a mirror in which I saw the back of her tidy head and my own expressionless face.

She shut the door behind me and said, "You look well, Henry."

"You, too."

She smiled briskly. "I don't change, I just get older."

We started down the hall. I said, "It has been a while. We look more alike than ever."

She nodded. "Yes, I noticed that, too."

As children there'd been a sort of generic resemblance between us; we shared our father's dark coloring, his black hair, teary brown eyes, and we each had the same high rounded cheekbones that had led to our grade school nickname, "*los chinitos*." We no longer looked Chinese. There was a truer, more exact resemblance in the way our faces had thinned out with age, revealing the basic structure.

"I can offer you coffee, or would you like a drink?" Elena asked, leading me into a sparsely furnished room that looked out upon a patio and, beyond that, the bay. "Which?"

"Coffee is fine."

I hadn't told her I no longer drank, because I was unwilling to make the admission of weakness that that would imply to her.

While she made coffee in the kitchen I walked to the window. A regatta of sailboats drifted across the water like a cloud. Looking around the room, I observed the clean, hard Nordic surfaces of Elena's surroundings. Even here, in her own home, she worked hard at revealing nothing about herself beyond conventional good taste, but there were clues about her past. A crucifix. A wave-shaped chunk of glass that, on closer inspection, was a stylized Madonna.

An oil painting of a nude above the fireplace showed a desiccated woman with a flat Indian face, standing with her hands at her breasts, as if to protect herself. There was nothing soft about her nudity; its graphic, painful clarity denied any sensuality—she was a Madonna for whom giving birth had been an act of self-obliteration. I wondered if this represented our mother to Elena.

Behind me, glass chinked against glass and I turned to find Elena setting cups and saucers, sugar bowl, creamer and spoons on the coffee table.

"Joanne's work?" I asked, indicating the painting. One of the few things I knew about Elena's roommate was that she taught art at St. Winifred's.

"Yes, that's right." Her tone warned me off that conversational trail. "You take your coffee black?"

"That's fine." I lowered myself into a chrome and leather contraption and watched her measure out a teaspoon of cream into her own cup, like Prufrock, measuring out his life with coffee spoons.[2]

I was reminded of the poem I thought of driving up. "It's so beautiful up here," I said, "I was thinking of that Stevens poem, 'Sunday Morning.' What's the line after, 'Is there no change in paradise?'"

"You're misquoting, Henry." She got up and walked to the bookshelves at the far end of the room, returning with a volume that she flipped through knowingly. In a clear, low voice she read, "'Is there no change of death in paradise? Does ripe fruit never fall? Or do the boughs hang always heavy in that perfect sky . . .'" Shutting the book, she looked up at me. "He makes it sound so dull."

"Don't you think it would be? Everyone sitting around gazing at God for eternity like reporters at a presidential press conference. Even Dante[3] couldn't work up much enthusiasm for paradise."

"You're as cynical as my students, Henry. But they at least have the excuse of being young."

The coffee smelled of hazelnut. I sipped it. "Nice," I said. "You've become quite elegant, Elena."

"And you've been a lawyer too long. Everything you say sounds like innuendo." She reached into a silver case on the table and extracted a long brown cigarette. Putting it to her lips, she asked, "What is this wedding you're here for?"

I lit her cigarette with a crystal lighter. "Two friends," I replied, "a cop and a criminal defense lawyer. It's a little like a gathering of the Hatfields and the McCoys."

2. Reference to line 51 of "The Love Song of J. Alfred Prufrock" (1915, 1917), by the American-born English poet T(homas) S(tearns) Eliot (1888–1965).

3. Dante Alighieri (1265–1321), Italian poet, author of the epic *Divina Commedia* (Divine Comedy, 1308–21).

"Is he with the San Francisco police?"

"She," I replied, "is an assistant chief. He's the lawyer. I introduced them."

She drew lazily at her cigarette. "Are they marrying in a church?"

I shook my head. "A civil ceremony. They've rented out a bed-and-breakfast place on Alamo Square. Josh and I are staying there."

At the mention of my lover's name, she gazed down at the milky surface of her coffee. "Will you be staying long?"

"Until Monday," I said, adding deliberately, "Josh has to get back to school. He's at UCLA."

Brushing the tip of her cigarette against the edge of an ashtray, she said, "Yes, I think you mentioned that once." As if to forestall further discussion of Josh, she asked, "Do you like Los Angeles?"

"Most of the time. Our house is on a hill, too, like yours. I can see the Hollywood sign from the kitchen window. The other day Josh spotted a pair of deer in the underbrush. It's not at all what I expected."

"Deer," she repeated. "That's interesting."

"Do you ever get down to LA?" I asked.

"No," she replied. "I have no reason to."

I thought about that for a moment and let it pass. Tactless remarks were part of the price we paid for remaining strangers. That, and a finite store of small talk. I'd exhausted mine.

"You said you wanted to see me on a professional matter. Something going on?"

She set her cigarette down. "Not with me," she replied. "Do you remember Sara Bancroft? We grew up together."

A dim image formed in my head of a tall, blonde, unlikable girl. "Vaguely."

"She married Paul Windsor. I think you knew his brother Mark."

I remembered Mark Windsor well, his younger brother Paul less well. The Windsors were local gentry in Los Robles. Mark and I had run track in high school. Miler, we called him, after his event. I had been infatuated with him. Paul had just been someone who got in the way when I was trying to be alone with Mark, little good that that did.

"I remember them."

"Paul's been arrested for murder."

This got a startled "Really?" out of me.

"Apparently he needs a lawyer," she said, without a trace of irony. "I told her I'd talk to you."

"Do they still live in Los Robles?"

"Yes."

"There isn't a town in California that's too small not to have too many lawyers," I said, "including Los Robles. I suggest they start there."

Elena stroked her throat, a nervous gesture that went far back into our childhood. "Sara insisted on you."

"Why?"

She put out her cigarette decisively and said, "I don't know very much about it, Henry. Sara was upset, and she'd been drinking when she called me. The man Paul's supposed to have killed was involved in child pornography. The police are saying it was because he was blackmailing Paul. Sara denied it. She—"

"Wait," I said. "Back up. What's the connection between Paul Windsor and child pornography?"

Her fingers tugged her throat. "A few years ago Paul was arrested for—I don't know what it's called—child molesting?" She forced her hand down. "The girl was fifteen, I think, but it had been going on for some time."

"Are you telling me that Paul Windsor is a pedophile?"

"I don't know what that word means."

I had heard her use that tone before. It implied that her ignorance was grounded in superior morality.

"It's a technical term," I replied, "denoting someone who is sexually attracted to children. The street term is 'baby fucker.'"

Her face darkened. "That was cheap."

I shrugged. "Was he convicted?"

"I don't know," she said, "but he didn't go to jail." Clearly uncomfortable, she fiddled with her coffee cup. Elena had arranged her life as tastefully as she had this room. All this talk of murder and child molesting must have been as unpleasant for her as discovering a bowel movement in the center of her coffee table. I felt a tiny bit of pleasure at her discombobulation. Maybe, as she'd said earlier, I'd been a lawyer too long. In any event, I was used to cleaning up other people's shit.

"When did all this happen?" I asked.

"A week, ten days ago."

"Is he in jail?"

"Yes," she said.

"Then he's already been arraigned," I said. "He must've had a lawyer for that."

Elena looked doubtful. "I really don't know the details, Henry. Sara called three days ago. She said she'd read about you in the papers last year when you had that case in Los Angeles. That busboy."

Jim Pears, I thought, a boy who'd been accused of murdering a classmate who had threatened to expose Jim's homosexuality. The case had never gone to trial because Jim killed himself, but I had still been able to establish his innocence. Then it occurred to me why Sara Windsor might have insisted that I defend her husband.

"Does she think that because I'm gay I have some special insight into pedophiles?"

She cast a cool look at me and said, "Not everyone judges people by their sexual practices. Maybe she just thinks you're an able lawyer."

"What do you think, Elena? She's your friend."

"I hadn't spoken to her in years before she called."

I have a good ear for lies, and I'd just been lied to. Elena was apparently embarrassed by her old friendship with the wife of a child molester. It made me think less of her.

Acidly, I said, "Sexual deviance isn't a virus, Elena. It's not catching."

"What are you talking about, Henry?"

"Loyalty to one's friends."

Her face reddened again. "Why else would I have asked you up here?"

"Touché." I picked up my now cold cup of coffee. The faint flavor of hazelnut had soured as it cooled. "I don't defend child molesters."

"That's not what Paul's accused of," she pointed out.

# Dos Ríos

Manhattan, Central Park South, falling
beneath first snow from a bronze
horse three times life, you are dwarfed
by New York. In truth, you wrote about just
one subject: freedom and its monsters.                    5
You went to your death on your first charge
shot from a bronze horse somewhere
between me, November and a few pigeons.

Martí, the bums are watching. Maybe not.
Some of them will finally join the group               10
of exiles already entranced by your oratory.
A second war, a last war, *Patria*
seemed less dangerous a word.
After all, this was the nineteenth century
and though you may not have sounded like it,            15
you must have looked the stiff professor, right
hand pointing in the air, proper if humble suit,
coat over your left wrist. They want action,
not words. You fight, we'll follow.

Playitas, Oriente Province. 1895.                        20
The landing and soon death.
Everyday your words become the flesh
that a nation devours. For a long time
only the bones have been left,
but they will do in famine's hour,                       25
bones like white roses,
passions like bones like white roses.
Yours is, after all, the only century of *patrias*.
I must choose, mustn't I, what century to live in
unless, like you, the choices have been made            30
and one simply finds them in the snow,
between the rivers.¹

                                                    1993

# Frutas

Growing up in Miami any tropical fruit I ate
could only be a bad copy of the Real Fruit of Cuba.
Exile meant having to consume false food,
and knowing it in advance. With joy
my parents and grandmother would encounter              5
Florida-grown *mameyes* and *caimitos* at the market.
At home they would take them out of the American bag
and describe the taste that I and my older sister

---

1. The Hudson River, which runs along Manhattan's West Side, and the East River, which runs along its East Side.

would, in a few seconds, be privileged to experience
for the first time. We all sat around the table                                    10
to welcome into our lives this football-shaped,
brown fruit with the salmon-colored flesh
encircling an ebony seed. "*Mamey*,"
my grandmother would say with a confirming nod,
as if repatriating a lost and ruined name.                                         15
Then she bent over the plate,
slipped a large slice of *mamey* into her mouth,
then straightened in her chair and, eyes shut,
lost herself in comparison and memory.
I waited for her face to return with a judgment.                                   20
"No, not even the shadow of the ones back home."
She kept eating, more calmly,
and I began tasting the sweet and creamy pulp
trying to raise the volume of its flavor
so that it might become a Cuban *mamey*. "The good                                 25
Cuban *mameyes* didn't have *primaveras*," she said
after the second large gulp, knocking her spoon
against a lump in the fruit and winking.
So at once I erased the lumps in my mental mamey.
I asked her how the word for "spring"                                              30
came to signify "lump" in a *mamey*. She shrugged.
"Next you'll want to know how we lost a country."

1993

## Dulce

For eight years Miami was a place to visit
family and friends of my parents just arrived
from Cuba. We drove from Tampa each time.
Dulce, my black grand aunt,
had married one of my father's uncles,                                             5
a provincial doctor with Vivaldi's hair.[1]
Years later, Tata, the family matriarch
and Dulce's mother-in-law, would die in her arms.

Tata was the daughter of a French baroness.
Because her skin was like a pearl, Tata tried to be one.                           10
Receiving visitors erect in her wicker rocking chair,
she smiled as the maid brought steaming trays of porcelain
*café con leche*,[2] especially in summer, and measured
the character of the guests by how they handled the sweat.
Family memory has her always dressed                                               15
in turn of the century white linen and amethysts,
watching her sprawling progeny with a serenity
she never lost, not even in 1933 when Machado fell[3]

1. Antonio Lucio Vivaldi (1678–1741), Italian composer, had shoulder-length, ringletted hair.
2. (Strong) coffee with (scalded) milk.
3. Gerardo Machado y Morales (1871–1939), general during the Cuban War of Independence, served as president of Cuba from 1925 until his toppling in 1933.

and her favorite son, the senator,
died suddenly in Miami. The mobs                                      20
were looting the senators' houses.[4]
Dulce came out of Tata's mansion
and saved the family by confronting the mob,
"The people of this house are our people!"

After 1960 Havana would get so small                                  25
you could see it all in one living room
in Miami. Dulce was in the center of the room,
the new matriarch surrounded by ever widening
rings of reverential white progeny.
She was round and deep and her voice seemed on the brink     30
of a melody I would hear only once and think I actually did.
She called me to her and kissed me on the head.
"You are beautiful enough to be my own son," she said.
The world got tighter than bones and fire.

                                                                     1993


## Charada China

Every image in every dream has a number.
Each digit from 1 to 100 corresponds
to several images. Thanks to us *chinos*.
the Cubans are now ready to win at lottery.
If last night you dreamt of a shark,                                  5
you must play 45, which is also
the number for President,
Suit, Streetcar, School, and Star,
and often comes up in June drawings.
You heard a phone ring in your dream?                                10
Then play 70 as well, especially
if you also dreamt a coconut,
a shot, a barrel, a rainbow, or a bullet.
A scorpion slid down the terrified leg
of a friend or a cow, play 43 in August.                             15
Monkey, Family, Black Man, Supervisor,
and Dove are 34. And my favorite, 100
for Toilet, God, Broom, Automobile,
Bus Stop, and Collapsed Building.
It usually comes up in January.                                      20

I know what you are thinking:
if these numbers work, why hasn't this *chino*
won the lottery a hundred times?
The wise are robed with poverty.
My dreams have been taken over                                       25
by the chart of the *Charada*.

---

4. After the collapse of the Machacho government, dissident students, labor activists, and noncommissioned military officers led a revolution.

You came to the *barrio chino* for advice
on how to play your dreams. Their free images
evoke a random series of lottery numbers.
Cockroach 48, Rabbit 39, Dark Sun 60, Beggar 91.                    30
But last night I started dreaming
of train tracks and automatically
the other images of 72 came into focus:
an old ox, a saw, a necklace, a scepter
and thunder. Since we all have four dreams                          35
each night, my mind divided 72 by 4 and all
the images of 18 came into focus: a small fish,
a church, a siren, a palm tree, men fishing
and a yellow cat. This last image grew larger
and bared huge teeth, and in came all the images for 92:            40
a lion, a high balloon, a suicide, Cuba, an anarchist.
All my dreams boil down to one number, 54,
the number for a dream you dreamt having.
You must never play this number!

There is no freedom in wisdom, only order,                          45
and so my dreams are endless jugglings
which have long ago stopped meaning
the pathway to happiness, or riches.
That is why I don't sell the *Charada*
and all its listings. You need your dreams                          50
as they are. You need them to terrify you
and to promise you kingdoms and lotteries.
Let them betray you and laugh at you.
Do not buy those charts on the street!
They are plagued with errors                                        55
and it would be a disaster to gamble with them.
I see the birth of a dream swirling in your pupils,
the dream you will have tonight and forget by morning.
No, my ethics prevent me from telling you what it is,
but here are its numbers: 6, 46, 82, 23, 17.                        60

                                                               1993

## Return to Havana

What will that day be like, the return
to streets and shadows that have only names
and which I have learned to miss as if my own?

Will I ponder the smashed doorframe, the burnt
field, the cracked wall, the color-gutted pane                      5
and say, this day is like no other, this return

will stand pure and unmatched, a warrior alone
among meek memories because he could sustain
the conviction that only what you miss is your own?

He will be a tired soldier, this thought learned                    10
from a need like air, constant like the beat of rain
that always treads great days. This return

will not be different, will be full of scorn
for the heat, the bugs, the dust and din
of a strange locale, missed without possession,                     15

ensnared in myths. The desperate champion
of memory, faltering, will be happier among ruins
than among questions. Only the days return
to teach him his duty: lose what you fear to own.

1993

# LUIS J. RODRÍGUEZ
## b. 1954

Luis J. Rodríguez was born in El Paso, Texas. With his family, he moved to Juárez, Mexico, and then back north to Los Angeles. As a teenager, Rodríguez sought friends, acceptance, empowerment, and refuge from his unstable home life by joining an East Los Angeles gang. A high school dropout, he was invited in 1972 by Quinto Sol Publications as a guest writer to attend the award ceremony for that year's winner of *el Premio Quinto Sol* (the Fifth Sun prize), the novel *Estampas del Valle y otras obras*, by Rolando Hinojosa (see p. 842). In the mid-1990s, in a conversation with Hinojosa, Rodríguez said that if Quinto Sol had not sent him the plane tickets, he would have ended up in jail. Coincidentally, at the time of the conversation, his son Ramiro was to be tried for murder. Ramiro is now serving a sentence in a California prison.

In his journalism, poetry, and fiction, Rodríguez often focuses on the problems of youth gangs as a way to warn young people about the inherent dangers of joining gangs. His poetry tends to be confessional, but is not simply about gang life, instead presenting appreciations of human life and the beauties to be found in it. Rodríguez's poetry collection *Poems across the Pavement* (1989) received the Poetry Center Book Award from San Francisco State University.

Rodríguez broke into the mainstream with his memoir *Always Running: La vida loca* (1993), which portrays the time he spent during his youth as a gang member in East Los Angeles. The first Latino book to win the Carl Sandburg Award for Non-Fiction, given by the Chicago Public Library, *Always Running* was awarded the First Prose Book Award in 1994 by *The Chicago Sun-Times* and was chosen as a Notable Book by *The New York Times Book Review*. In the first chapter, which is included in this anthology, the narrator introduces the hurdles his immigrant family faces.

In 1994–95, Rodríguez served as Regent's Lecturer at the University of California at Berkeley. In 1998, additional recognition came in the form of the Hispanic Heritage Award for Literature, presented at the John F. Kennedy Center for the Performing Arts. Since then, Rodríguez has produced two books for juveniles, *America Is Her Name* (1996) and *It Doesn't Have to Be This Way: A Barrio Story* (1999), which depict urban life and its dangers to gang members. He has published work in numerous periodicals and in 1989 founded Tía Chucha Press, in Chicago.

He lives in California, where in 2003 he established the Tía Chucha Centro Cultural, a nonprofit cultural center and bookstore in Sylmar.

In novels such as *The Republic of East L.A.* (2002) and *Music of the Mill* (2005), and in his poetry collection *My Nature Is Hunger: New and Selected Poems, 1989–2004* (2005), Rodríguez explores his political activity during the Chicano Movement, such as his joining the East Los Angeles Walkouts in 1968 and his being arrested along with other marchers in the Chicano Moratorium of 1970.

---

## FROM ALWAYS RUNNING: LA VIDA LOCA

### Chapter One

> "Cry, child, for those without tears have a grief
> which never ends."—Mexican saying

This memory begins with flight. A 1950s bondo[1]-spackled Dodge surged through a driving rain, veering around the potholes and upturned tracks of the abandoned Red Line trains on Alameda.[2] Mama was in the front seat. My father was at the wheel. My brother *Rano* and I sat on one end of the back seat; my sisters *Pata* and *Cuca* on the other. There was a space between the boys and girls to keep us apart.

"Amá, mira a[3] Rano," a voice said for the tenth time from the back of the car. "He's hitting me again."

We fought all the time. My brother, especially, had it in for *La Pata*—thinking of Frankenstein, he called her "Anastein." Her real name was Ana, but most of the time we went by the animal names Dad gave us at birth. I am *Grillo*, which means cricket. Rano stands for "rana," the frog. *La Pata* is the duck and *Cuca* is short for *cucaracha*: cockroach.

The car seats came apart in strands. I looked out at the passing cars which seemed like ghosts with headlights rushing past the streaks of water on the glass. I was nine years old. As the rain fell, my mother cursed in Spanish intermixed with pleas to saints and "*la Santísima Madre de Dios*."[4] She argued with my father. Dad didn't curse or raise his voice. He just stated the way things were.

"I'll never go back to Mexico," he said. "I'd rather starve here. You want to stay with me, it has to be in Los Angeles. Otherwise, go."

This incited my mother to greater fits.

We were on the way to the Union train station in downtown L.A. We had our few belongings stuffed into the trunk and underneath our feet. I gently held on to one of the comic books Mama bought to keep us entertained. I had on my Sunday best clothes with chewed gum stuck in a coat pocket. It could have been Easter, but it was a weeping November. I don't remember for sure why we were leaving. I just knew it was a special day. There was no fear or concern on my part. We were always moving. I looked at the newness

---

1. Auto-repair putty.
2. Street in downtown Los Angeles.
3. Mom, look at.
4. Holy Mother of God, i.e., the Virgin Mary.

of the comic book and felt some exhilaration of its feel in my hand. Mama had never bought us comic books before. It had to be a special day.

For months we had been pushed from one house to another, just Mama and us children. Mom and Dad had split up prior to this. We stayed at the homes of women my mom called *comadres*,[5] with streams of children of their own. Some nights we slept in a car or in the living rooms of people we didn't know. There were no shelters for homeless families. My mother tried to get us settled somewhere but all indications pointed to our going back to the land of her birth, to her red earth, her Mexico.

The family consisted of my father, Alfonso; my mom, María Estela; my older brother, José René; and my younger sisters, Ana Virginia and Gloria Estela. I recall my father with his wavy hair and clean-shaven face, his correct, upright and stubborn demeanor, in contrast to my mother, who was heavy-set with Native features and thick straight hair, often laughing heartily, her eyes narrowed to slits, and sometimes crying from a deep tomb-like place with a sound like swallowing mud.

As we got closer to the Union station, Los Angeles loomed low and large, a city of odd construction, a good place to get lost in. I, however, would learn to hide in imaginative worlds—in books; in TV shows, where I picked up much of my English; in solitary play with mangled army men and crumpled toy trucks. I was so withdrawn it must have looked scary.

· · ·

This is what I know: When I was two years old, our family left Ciudad Juárez, Chihuahua,[6] for Los Angeles. My father was an educated man, unusual for our border town, a hunger city filled to the hills with cardboard hovels of former peasants, Indians and dusk-faced children. In those days, an educated man had to be careful about certain things—questioning authority, for example. Although the principal of a local high school, my father failed to succumb to the local chieftains who were linked to the national party which ruled Mexico, as one famous Latin American writer would later say, with a "perfect dictatorship."

When Dad first became principal, there were no funds due to the massive bureaucratic maze he had to get through to get them. The woman he lived with then was an artist who helped raise money for the school by staging exhibitions. My father used his own money to pay for supplies and at one point had the iron fence around the school torn down and sold for scrap.

One year, Dad received an offer for a six-month study program for foreign teachers in Bloomington, Indiana. He liked it so much, he renewed it three times. By then, my father had married his secretary, my mother, after the artist left him. They had their first child, José René.

By the time my father returned, his enemies had mapped out a means to remove him—being a high school principal is a powerful position in a place like Ciudad Juárez. My father faced a pile of criminal charges, including the alleged stealing of school funds. Police arrived at the small room in the *vecindad*[7] where Mama and Dad lived and escorted him to the city jail.

---

5. Godmothers; also, a woman's female pals.
6. City and seat of the municipality of Juárez, in

the state of Chihuahua, Mexico.
7. Neighborhood.

For months my father fought the charges. While he was locked up, they fed him scraps of food in a rusted steel can. They denied him visitors— Mama had to climb a section of prison wall and pick up 2-year-old José René so he could see his father. Finally, after a lengthy trial, my father was found innocent—but he no longer had his position as principal.

Dad became determined to escape to the United States. My mother, on the other hand, never wanted to leave Mexico; she did it to be with Dad.

Mama was one of two daughters in a family run by a heavy-drinking, wife-beating railroad worker and musician. My mother was the only one in her family to complete high school. Her brothers, Kiko and Rodolfo, were pistol-packing womanizers who often crossed the border to find work and came back with stories of love and brawls on the other side.

Their grandmother was a Tarahumara Indian who once walked down from the mountainous area in the state of Chihuahua where her people lived in seclusion for centuries. The Spanish never conquered them. But their grandmother never returned to her people. She eventually gave birth to my grandmother, Ana Acosta.

Ana's first husband was a railroad worker during the Mexican Revolution;[8] he lost his life when a tunnel exploded during a raid. They brought his remains in a box. Ana was left alone with one son, while pregnant with a daughter. Lucita, the daughter, eventually died of convulsions at the age of four, and Manolo, the son, was later blinded after a bout with a deadly form of chicken pox which struck and killed many children in the area.

Later Ana married my grandfather, Mónico Jiménez, who like her first husband worked the railroads. At one point, Mónico quit the rails to play trumpet and sing for bands in various night clubs. Once he ended up in Los Angeles, but with another woman. In fact, Mónico had many other women. My grandmother often had to cross over to the railroad yards, crowded with prostitutes and where Mónico spent many nights singing, to bring him home.

When my parents married, Mama was 27; Dad almost 40. She had never known any other man. He already had four or five children from three or four other women. She was an emotionally-charged, border woman, full of fire, full of pain, full of giving love. He was a stoic, unfeeling, unmoved intellectual who did as he pleased as much as she did all she could to please him. This dichotomous couple, this sun and moon, this *curandera*[9] and biologist, dreamer and realist, fire woman and water man, molded me; these two sides created a life-long conflict in my breast.

By the time Dad had to leave Ciudad Juárez, my mother had borne three of his children, including myself, all in El Paso, on the American side (Gloria was born later in East L.A.'s General Hospital). This was done to help ease the transition from alien status to legal residency. There are stories of women who wait up to the ninth month and run across the border to have their babies, sometimes squatting and dropping them on the pavement as they hug the closest lamppost.

8. A socialist revolution that lasted from 1910 to 1920.

9. Herb healer.

We ended up in Watts, a community primarily of black people except for *La Colonia*, often called The Quarter—the Mexican section and the oldest part of Watts.

Except for the housing projects, Watts was a ghetto where country and city mixed. The homes were mostly single-family units, made of wood or stucco. Open windows and doors served as air conditioners, a slight relief from the summer desert air. Chicken coops graced many a back yard along with broken auto parts. Roosters crowed the morning to birth and an occasional goat peered from weather-worn picket fences along with the millions of dogs which seemed to populate the neighborhood.

Watts fed into one of the largest industrial concentrations in the country, pulling from an almost endless sea of cheap labor; they came from Texas, Louisiana, Mississippi, Oklahoma, Arkansas . . . from Chihuahua, Sonora, Sinaloa and Nayarit.[1] If you moved there it was because the real estate concerns pushed you in this direction. For decades, L.A. was notorious for restrictive covenants—where some areas were off limits to "undesirables."

Despite the competition for jobs and housing, we found common ground there, among the rolling mills, bucket shops and foundries. All day long we heard the pounding of forges and the air-whistles that signaled the shift changes in the factories which practically lay in our backyards.

We moved to Watts at the behest of my oldest sister, really a half-sister, who was already married with two children of her own. Her family eventually joined us a few months later. Her name was Seni, a name my father invented (although rumor has it, it was an inversion of the name Inés, an old girlfriend of his). The name, however, has stayed in the family. Seni's first daughter was named Ana Seni and in later years, one of Ana Seni's daughters became Seni Bea.

When Seni was a child, my father often left her for long intervals with my grandmother Catita, whom she called Mama Piri. One family legend tells of a 9-year-old Seni answering the door during a pouring rain. A man, with soaked hat and coat, stood at the doorway. Seni yelled out: "Mama Piri, Mama Piri—there's a strange man at the door."

"Don't worry, *m'ija*,"[2] Catita said. "He's only your father."

Seni lived in several rentals in Watts until she found a two-story on 111th Street near a block of factories. The place later got razed to build Locke High School. I stayed there a couple of summers, sleeping in a cobweb-infested attic with exposed 2-by-4 studs. Rats and cockroaches roamed freely in that house: huge rats, huge cockroaches. Seni would place a chair at the bottom of the attic steps and she convinced me it could ward off the creatures. I believed it until one night I noticed the chair was gone. I ran down to tell Seni. But she yelled back in Spanish: "Go back to bed . . . that chair couldn't keep nothing away, and only a fool would believe it could."

I was devastated.

Seni was my father's daughter from one of his earlier relationships; her mother died giving birth to her. My father was handsome and athletic as a young man. He was the pole-vaulting champion at one of the schools he

---

1. Like Chihuahua, these last three places are states in Mexico.

2. My daughter, my girl (contraction of *mi* and *hija*).

attended. But his looks apparently got him into a lot of trouble. His father, Cristóbal, then a general in the Mexican army, once disowned him when Dad fell for a woman and neglected his studies in medical school. Dad quit school to be with the woman, who would later become Seni's mother.

I also had two older half-brothers, Alberto and Mario, who lived in Mexico. Another half-sister, Lisa, died as an infant after she accidently ate some *chicharrones*[3] my father was forced to sell on cobblestone streets in Mexico City after his father cut him off. My mother kept a sepia-colored black-and-white death photo of Lisa in a white lace baptism dress, looking like a doll, looking asleep, so peaceful, as she lay in a tiny wood coffin.

Our first exposure in America stays with me like a foul odor. It seemed a strange world, most of it spiteful to us, spitting and stepping on us, coughing us up, us immigrants, as if we were phlegm stuck in the collective throat of this country. My father was mostly out of work. When he did have a job it was in construction, in factories such as Sinclair Paints or Standard Brands Dog Food, or pushing door-bells selling insurance, Bibles or pots and pans. My mother found work cleaning homes or in the garment industry. She knew the corner markets were ripping her off but she could only speak with her hands and in a choppy English.

Once my mother gathered up the children and we walked to Will Rogers Park.[4] There were people everywhere. Mama looked around for a place we could rest. She spotted an empty spot on a park bench. But as soon as she sat down an American woman, with three kids of her own, came by.

"Hey, get out of there—that's our seat."

My mother understood but didn't know how to answer back in English. So she tried in Spanish.

"Look, spic, you can't sit there!" the American woman yelled. "You don't belong here! Understand? This is not your country!"

Mama quietly got our things and walked away, but I knew frustration and anger bristled within her because she was unable to talk, and when she did, no one would listen.

We never stopped crossing borders. The *Río Grande* (or *Río Bravo*, which is what the Mexicans call it, giving the name a power "Río Grande" just doesn't have) was only the first of countless barriers set in our path.

We kept jumping hurdles, kept breaking from the constraints, kept evading the border guards of every new trek. It was a metaphor to fill our lives—that river, that first crossing, the mother of all crossings. The L.A. River, for example, became a new barrier, keeping the Mexicans in their neighborhoods over on the vast east side of the city for years, except for forays downtown. Schools provided other restrictions: Don't speak Spanish, don't be Mexican—you don't belong. Railroad tracks divided us from communities where white people lived, such as South Gate and Lynwood across from Watts. We were invisible people in a city which thrived on glitter, big screens and big names, but this glamour contained none of our names, none of our faces.

The refrain "this is not your country" echoed for a lifetime.

• • •

3. Crackling; pieces of fried pork fat.
4. Will Rogers State Historic Park, once the estate of the American humorist Will Rogers

(1879–1935), in the Santa Monica mountains of Los Angeles.

Although we moved around the Watts area, the house on 105th Street near McKinley Avenue held my earliest memories, my earliest fears and questions. It was a small matchbox of a place. Next to it stood a tiny garage with holes through the walls and an unpainted barn-like quality. The weather battered it into a leaning shed. The back yard was a jungle. Vegetation appeared to grow down from the sky. There were banana trees, huge "sperm" weeds (named that because they stunk like semen when you cut them), foxtails and yellowed grass. An avocado tree grew in the middle of the yard and its roots covered every bit of ground, tearing up cement walks while its branches scraped the bedroom windows. A sway of clothes on some lines filled the little bit of grassy area just behind the house.

My brother and I played often in our jungle, even pretending to be Tarzan (Rano mastered the Tarzan yell from the movies). The problem, however, was I usually ended up being the monkey who got thrown off the trees. In fact, I remember my brother as the most dangerous person alive. He seemed to be wracked with a scream which never let out. His face was dark with meanness, what my mother called *maldad*. He also took delight in seeing me writhe in pain, cry or cower, vulnerable to his own inflated sense of power. This hunger for cruelty included his ability to take my mom's most wicked whippings—without crying or wincing. He'd just sit there and stare at a wall, forcing Mama to resort to other implements of pain—but Rano would not show any emotion.

Yet in the streets, neighborhood kids often chased Rano from play or jumped him. Many times he came home mangled, his face swollen. Once somebody threw a rock at him which cut a gash across his forehead, leaving a scar Rano has to this day.

Another time a neighbor's kid smashed a metal bucket over Rano's head, slicing the skin over his skull and creating a horrifying scene with blood everywhere. My mother in her broken English could remedy few of the injustices, but she tried. When this one happened, she ran next door to confront that kid's mother.

The woman had been sitting on her porch and saw everything.

"¿Qué pasó aquí?" Mama asked.

"I don't know what you want," the woman said. "All I know is your boy picked up that bucket and hit himself over the head—that's all I know."

In school, they placed Rano in classes with retarded children because he didn't speak much English. They even held him back a year in the second grade.

For all this, Rano took his rage out on me. I recall hiding from him when he came around looking for a playmate. My mother actually forced me out of closets with a belt in her hand and made me play with him.

One day we were playing on the rooftop of our house.

"Grillo, come over here," he said from the roof's edge. "Man, look at this on the ground."

I should have known better, but I leaned over to see. Rano then pushed me and I struck the ground on my back with a loud thump and lost my breath, laying deathly still in suffocating agony, until I slowly gained it back.

Another time he made me the Indian to his cowboy, tossed a rope around my neck and pulled me around the yard. He stopped barely before it choked the life out of me. I had rope burns around my neck for a week.

His abuse even prompted neighborhood kids to get in on it. One older boy used to see how Rano tore into me. One day he peered over the fence separating his yard from ours.

"Hey, little dude . . . yeah you. Come over here a minute," he said. "I got something to show you."

This time I approached with caution. Little good that did me: I stepped into a loop of rope on the ground. He pulled on it and dragged me through the weeds and foxtails, up the splintery fence, and tied it down on his side. I hung upside down, kicking and yelling for what seemed like hours until somebody came and cut me down.

The house on 105th Street stayed cold. We couldn't always pay the gas or light bills. When we couldn't, we used candles. We cleaned up the dishes and the table where we ate without any light, whispering because that's what people do in the dark.

We took baths in cold water, and I remember wanting to run out of the bathroom as my mother murmured a shiver of words to comfort me:

"*Así es, así será,*"[5] she explained as she dunked me into the frigid bath.

One night, my parents decided to take us to a restaurant since we had no heat to cook anything with. We drove around for awhile. On Avalon Boulevard we found one of those all-night, ham-eggs-&-coffee places. As we pulled up, I curled up in the seat.

"No, I don't want to go in," I yelled.

"And why not?" my mother demanded. "*Por el amor de Dios*, aren't you hungry?"

I pointed a finger to a sign on the door. It read: "Come In. Cold Inside."

Christmases came with barely a whimper. Once my parents bought a fake aluminum tree, placed some presents beneath it, and woke us up early to open them up. Most of the wrappings, though, had been haphazardly put together because Rano had sneaked into the living room in the middle of the night and torn them open to take a peek. The presents came from a church group which gave out gifts for the poor. It was our first Christmas. That day, I broke the plastic submarine, toy gun and metal car I received. I don't know why. I suppose in my mind it didn't seem right to have things that were in working order, unspent.

My mother worked on and off, primarily as a *costurera* or cleaning homes or taking care of other people's children. We sometimes went with her to the houses she cleaned. They were nice, American, white-people homes. I remember one had a swimming pool and a fireplace and a thing called rugs. As Mama swept and scrubbed and vacuumed, we played in the corner, my sisters and I, afraid to touch anything. The odor of these houses was different, full of fragrances, sweet and nauseating. On 105th Street the smells were of fried lard, of beans and car fumes, of factory smoke and home-made brew out of backyard stills. There were chicken smells and goat smells in grassless yards filled with engine parts and wire and wood planks, cracked and sprinkled with rusty nails. These were the familiar aromas: the funky

5. Thus it is, thus it shall be.

earth, animal and mechanical smells which were absent from the homes my mother cleaned.

Mama always seemed to be sick. For one thing, she was overweight and suffered from a form of diabetes. She had thyroid problems, bad nerves and high blood pressure. She was still young then in Watts, in her thirties, but she had all these ailments. She didn't even have teeth; they rotted away many years before. This made her look much older until later when she finally obtained false ones. Despite this she worked all the time, chased after my brother with a belt or a board, and held up the family when almost everything else came apart.

· · ·

Heavy blue veins streak across my mother's legs, some of them bunched up into dark lumps at her ankles. Mama periodically bleeds them to relieve the pain. She carefully cuts the engorged veins with a razor and drains them into a porcelain-like metal pail called a *tina*. I'm small and all I remember are dreams of blood, me drowning in a red sea, blood on sheets, on the walls, splashing against the white pail in streams out of my mother's ankle. But they aren't dreams. It is Mama bleeding—into day, into night. Bleeding a birth of memory: my mother, my blood, by the side of the bed, me on the covers, and her slicing into a black vein and filling the pail into some dark, forbidden red nightmare which never stops coming, never stops pouring, this memory of Mama and blood and Watts.

· · ·

One day, my mother asked Rano and me to go to the grocery store. We decided to go across the railroad tracks into South Gate. In those days, South Gate was an Anglo neighborhood, filled with the families of workers from the auto plant and other nearby industry. Like Lynwood or Huntington Park, it was forbidden territory for the people of Watts.

My brother insisted we go. I don't know what possessed him, but then I never did. It was useless to argue; he'd force me anyway. He was nine then, I was six. So without ceremony, we started over the tracks, climbing over discarded market carts and tore-up sofas, across Alameda Street, into South Gate: all-white, all-American.

We entered the first small corner grocery store we found. Everything was cool at first. We bought some bread, milk, soup cans and candy. We each walked out with a bag filled with food. We barely got a few feet, though, when five teenagers on bikes approached. We tried not to pay attention and proceeded to our side of the tracks. But the youths pulled up in front of us. While two of them stood nearby on their bikes, three of them jumped off theirs and walked over to us.

"What do we got here?" one of the boys said. "Spics to order—maybe with some beans?"

He pushed me to the ground; the groceries splattered onto the asphalt. I felt melted gum and chips of broken beer bottle on my lips and cheek. Then somebody picked me up and held me while the others seized my brother, tossed his groceries out, and pounded on him. They punched him in the face, in the stomach, then his face again, cutting his lip, causing him to vomit.

I remember the shrill, maddening laughter of one of the kids on a bike, this laughing like a raven's wail, a harsh wind's shriek, a laugh that I would hear in countless beatings thereafter. I watched the others take turns on my brother, this terror of a brother, and he doubled over, had blood and spew on his shirt, and tears down his face. I wanted to do something, but they held me and I just looked on, as every strike against Rano opened me up inside.

They finally let my brother go and he slid to the ground, like a rotten banana squeezed out of its peeling. They threw us back over the tracks. In the sunset I could see the Watts Towers, shimmers of 70,000 pieces of broken bottles, sea shells, ceramic and metal on spiraling points puncturing the heavens, which reflected back the rays of a falling sun. My brother and I then picked ourselves up, saw the teenagers take off, still laughing, still talking about those stupid greasers who dared to cross over to South Gate.

Up until then my brother had never shown any emotion to me other than disdain. He had never asked me anything, unless it was a demand, an expectation, an obligation to be his throwaway boy-doll. But for this once he looked at me, tears welled in his eyes, blood streamed from several cuts—lips and cheeks swollen.

"Swear—you got to swear—you'll never tell anybody how I cried," he said.

I suppose I did promise. It was his one last thing to hang onto, his rep as someone who could take a belt whipping, who could take a beating in the neighborhood and still go back risking more—it was this pathetic plea from the pavement I remember. I must have promised.

It was a warm September day when my mother pulled me out of bed, handed me a pair of pants and a shirt, a piece of burnt toast and dragged me by the arm toward 109th Street School. We approached a huge, dusty brick building with the school's name carved in ancient English lettering across the entrance. Mama hauled me up a row of steps and through two large doors.

First day of school.

I was six years old, never having gone to kindergarten because Mama needed me then to take care of La Pata and Cuca so she could work. When La Pata became old enough to enter kindergarten, it became time for me to go. Mama filled out some papers. A school monitor directed us to a classroom where Mama dropped me off and left to join some parents who gathered in the main hall.

The first day of school said a lot about my scholastic life to come. I was taken to a teacher who didn't know what to do with me. She complained about not having any room, about kids who didn't even speak the language. And how was she supposed to teach anything under these conditions! Although I didn't speak English, I understood a large part of what she was saying. I knew I wasn't wanted. She put me in an old creaky chair near the door. As soon as I could, I sneaked out to find my mother.

I found Rano's class with the retarded children instead and decided to stay there for a while. Actually it was fun; they treated me like I was everyone's little brother. But the teacher finally told a student to take me to the main hall.

After some more paperwork, I was taken to another class. This time the teacher appeared nicer, but distracted. She got the word about my language problem.

"Okay, why don't you sit here in the back of the class," she said. "Play with some blocks until we figure out how to get you more involved."

It took her most of that year to figure this out. I just stayed in the back of the class, building blocks. It got so every morning I would put my lunch and coat away, and walk to my corner where I stayed the whole day long. It forced me to be more withdrawn. It got so bad, I didn't even tell anybody when I had to go the bathroom. I did it in my pants. Soon I stunk back there in the corner and the rest of the kids screamed out a chorus of "P.U.!" resulting in my being sent to the office or back home.

In those days there was no way to integrate the non-English speaking children. So they just made it a crime to speak anything but English. If a Spanish word sneaked out in the playground, kids were often sent to the office to get swatted or to get detention. Teachers complained that maybe the children were saying bad things about them. An assumption of guilt was enough to get one punished.

A day came when I finally built up the courage to tell the teacher I had to go to the bathroom. I didn't quite say all the words, but she got the message and promptly excused me so I didn't do it while I was trying to explain. I ran to the bathroom and peed and felt good about not having that wetness trickle down my pants leg. But suddenly several bells went on and off. I hesitantly stepped out of the bathroom and saw throngs of children leave their classes. I had no idea what was happening. I went to my classroom and it stood empty. I looked into other classrooms and found nothing. Nobody. I didn't know what to do. I really thought everyone had gone home. I didn't bother to look at the playground where the whole school had been assembled for the fire drill. I just went home. It got to be a regular thing there for a while, me coming home early until I learned the ins and outs of school life.

Not speaking well makes for such embarrassing moments. I hardly asked questions. I just didn't want to be misunderstood. Many Spanish-speaking kids mangled things up; they would say things like "where the beer and cantaloupe roam" instead of "where the deer and antelope roam."

That's the way it was with me. I mixed up all the words. Screwed up all the songs.

Eventually I did make friends. My brother often brought home a one-armed Mexican kid named Jaime. Sometimes we all hung out together. Jaime lost his arm when he was a toddler. Somehow he managed to get the arm stuck in the wringer of one of those old washing machines which pulled the clothes through two rollers. It tore his arm off at the socket. But later he made up for it with soccer feet and even won a couple of fights with his one good arm.

And then there was Earl. I didn't really know him until one day when we lined up following recess, he pulled the *trenzas*[6] of a Mexican girl in our class named Gabriela. We all liked Gabriela. But she was also quiet, like me. So Earl pulled on her braids, the girl wailed, turned around and saw me standing there. Just then the teacher ran out of the classroom. Gabriela pointed in my direction. The one who never says anything. Because of this, I suffered through an hour's detention, fuming in my seat the whole time.

6. Braids.

Later that evening, Earl came to my sister's house, where we were visiting. Seni answered the door and looked askance at him.

"What do you want?"

"I want to know if the boy upstairs can play?"

"I don't know, I don't think so."

"Tell him I got some marbles. If it's okay, I'd like him to play with me."

"I don't know, I don't think so."

I looked down from the attic window and saw the tall, thin boy in striped shirt and blue jeans. Under an arm was a coffee can. Inside the can, marbles rattled whenever Earl moved.

But going through Seni was becoming a chore. Earl looked past her to a large, round woman in a print dress: My mom. She looked at the boy and then yelled up the stairs in Spanish.

"Go and play, Grillo," she said. "You stay in the attic all the time. Go and play. Be like other boys. ¡Ya!"

Earl waited patiently as the Rodríguez household quaked and quavered trying to get me downstairs and into the yard. Finally, I came down. Earl smiled broadly and offered me the can of marbles.

"This is for taking the rap today, man."

I looked hard at him, still a little peeved, then reached out for the can and held the best marble collection I had ever seen. I made a friend.

Desert winds swept past the TV antennas and peeling fences, welcome breezes on sweltering dry summer days when people came out to sit on their porches, or beneath a tree in dirt yards, or to fix cars in the street.

But on those days the perils came out too—you could see it in the faces of street warriors, in the play of children, too innocent to know what lurked about, but often the first to fall during a gang war or family scuffle.

103rd Street was particularly hard. It was the main drag in Watts, where most of the businesses were located, and it was usually crowded with people, including dudes who took whatever small change one might have in their pocket.

On days like that Rano, Jaime, Earl and I ventured out to the "third," as 103rd Street was called, or by the factories and railroad tracks playing dirt war with other kids. Other times we played on the rooftop and told stories.

"Did you ever hear the one about the half-man?" Earl asked.

"The what?" Jaime replied. "What's a half-man?"

"Well, he's a dude who got cut in half at the railroad tracks over there by Dogtown."[7]

"Yeah, go on."

"So now he haunts the streets, half of him one place, the other half in another place—and he eats kids."

"Man, that's sick," Rano said. "But I got one for you. It's about *el pie*."

"What the hell is that?"

"*Pie* means foot in Spanish . . . and that's all it is! One big foot, walking around."

Gusts of winds swirled around the avocado tree branches as the moonlight cast uncanny shadows near where we related our tales.

---

7. Nickname for Venice, a district of Los Angeles.

"And you heard about *La Llorona*, right?" Rano continued.

"Oh, yeah, sure . . ."

"She's an old Mexican lady—"

"You mean Mrs. Alvarez?"

We laughed.

"Nah, this lady once got all her children and cut them up into tiny pieces."

"And . . ."

"And then she went all over the neighborhood, sprinkling bits of their bodies everywhere."

"And then . . ."

"So then God saw what she did and cursed her to walk the world, looking for her children—weeping—for all eternity. That's why she's called *La Llorona*, the weeping woman. And you know what, she picks up other kids to make up for the ones she's killed."[8]

The leaves rustled, giving out an eerie sound. All of us jumped up, including Rano. Before anyone could say good night, we stumbled over one another, trying to get out of there, climbed off the roof, and ran through bedsheets and dresses hanging on a line, dashing like mad as we made our way home.

We changed houses often because of evictions. My dad constantly tried to get better work; he tried so many things. Although he was trained as a teacher, graduated with a degree in biology and had published Spanish textbooks in Mexico, in Los Angeles everyone failed to recognize his credentials. In Los Angeles, he was often no more than a laborer.

One day a miracle happened. My dad obtained a substitute teaching job in the San Fernando Valley, at Taft High School in Woodland Hills, teaching Spanish to well-off white children.

My dad must have thought we had struck oil or something. He bought a house in Reseda.[9] In those days, this made us the only Mexican family around. It was a big house. It had three bedrooms, which meant the boys could have their own room, the girls theirs and my parents could be alone. It had two baths, a large, grassy yard and an upstanding, stucco garage.

I went to a school on Shirley Avenue which actually had books. I remember being chased back home a lot by the Anglo kids. But we were so glad to be in Reseda, so glad to be away from South Central Los Angeles.

Even my brother enjoyed success in this new environment. He became the best fighter in the school, all that he went through in Watts finally amounting to something. The big white kids tried to pick on him, and he fought back, hammered their faces with quick hands, in street style, after which nobody wanted to mess with him. Soon the bullies stopped chasing me home when they found out I was José's brother.

My dad went nuts in Reseda. He bought new furniture, a new TV, and he had the gall to throw away the old black & white box we had in Watts. He bought a new car. He was like a starving man in a candy store, partaking of everything, touching whatever he couldn't eat. He sat on a mountain of debt. But his attitude was "who cares?" We were Americans now. We were

8. This legend is popular in Spanish-speaking cultures in the Americas. For a text of "La Llorona," see p. 2452. For a variation on it, see p. 2454.

9. A San Fernando Valley district of Los Angeles.

on our way to having a little bit of that dream. He was even doing it as a teacher, what he was trained for. Oh what a time it was for my father!

My mother, I could tell, was uncomfortable with the whole set-up. She shied away from the neighbors. The other mothers around here were good-looking, fit and well-built. My pudgy mom looked dark, Indian and foreign, no matter what money could buy. Except she got her false teeth. It seemed Mama was just there to pick up the pieces when my father's house of cards fell. She knew it would.

When it happened, it happened fast, decisively. It turned out Taft High School hired my father to teach Spanish on a temporary basis. Apparently the white kids couldn't understand him because of his accent. He wrote letters to the school board proposing new methods of teaching Spanish to American children so he could keep working. They turned them down, and Taft High school let him go.

We weren't in Reseda very long, less than a school year. Then the furniture store trucks pulled into the driveway to take back the new sofas, the washing machine, the refrigerator—even the TV. A "For Sale" sign jabbed into the front lawn. The new car had been repossessed. We pulled out of Reseda in an old beat-up Dodge. Sad faces on our neighbors were our fare-well. I supposed they realized we weren't so bad for being Mexican. We were going back to an old friend—*pobreza*.[1]

We moved in with Seni, her husband, and their two daughters. They were then occupying an apartment just outside East Los Angeles. Seni's girls were about the same age as me, my brother and sisters, although we were their uncles and aunts. They also had nicknames. Ana Seni was called *Pimpos*, which doesn't mean anything I know of. But Rano called her "Bean-head" and that took. Aidé was called *La Banana* because as a baby she had shades of blonde hair. They later had another daughter named Beca, also *güerita*.[2]

Like most Latinos, we had a mixture of blood. My half-brother Alberto looked Caribbean. His mother came from Veracruz on the Caribbean side of Mexico which has the touch of Africa. The rest of us had different shades of Spanish white to Indian brown.

Uprooted again, we stuffed our things in a garage. The adults occupied the only two bedrooms. The children slept on makeshift bedding in the living room. My grandmother Catita also stayed with us. There were eleven of us crushed into that place. I remember the constant fighting. My dad was dumped on for not finding work. Seni accused her husband of having affairs with other women. Mama often stood outside alone, crying, or in the garage next to all our things piled on top of each other.

Rano and I sought refuge in the street.

One night, we came home late after having stocked up on licorice and bubble gum. We walked past police cars and an ambulance. Colored lights whirled across the tense faces of neighbors who stood on patches of grass and driveway. I pushed through low voices and entered the house: Blood was splattered on a far wall.

---

1. Poverty.

2. A little blond.

Moments before, Seni had been brushing Pimpos' hair when, who knows why, she pulled at the long sections. The girl's screams brought in my sister's husband. An argument ensued. Vicious words. Accusations.

Seni then plucked a fingernail file from the bathroom sink. She flashed it in front of my brother-in-law's face. He grabbed for her hand. The nail file plunged into his arm. Mom and Dad rushed in, ramming my sister against the wall; nail file crashed steely bright onto the linoleum floor.

Soon after the incident, the landlord evicted us all. This was when my mother and father broke up. And so we began that car ride to the train station, on the way back to Mexico, leaving L.A., perhaps never to come back.

. . .

We pull into a parking lot at the Union station. It's like a point of no return. My father is still making his stand. Mama looks exhausted. We continue to sit in our seats, quiet now as Dad maneuvers into an empty space. Then we work our way out of the car, straightening our coats, gathering up boxes and taped-over paper bags: our "luggage." Up to this juncture, it's been like being in a storm—so much instability, of dreams achieved and then shattered, of a silence within the walls of my body, of being turned on, beaten, belittled and pushed aside; forgotten and unimportant. I have no position on the issue before us. To stay in L.A. To go. What does it matter? I've been a red hot ball, bouncing around from here to there. Anyone can bounce me. Mama. Dad. Rano. Schools. Streets. I'm a ball. Whatever.

We are inside the vast cavern of the station. Pews of swirled wood are filled with people. We sit with our bags near us, and string tied from the bags to our wrists so nobody can take them without taking us too. My father turns to us, says a faint goodby, then begins to walk away. No hugs. He doesn't even look at us.

"Poncho."

The name echoes through the waiting area.

"Poncho."

He turns. Stares at my mother. The wet of tears covers her face. Mama then says she can't go. She will stay with him. In L.A. I don't think she's happy about this. But what can a single mother of four children do in Mexico? A woman, sick all the time, with factory work for skills in a land where work is mainly with the soil. What good is it except to starve.

"Está bien," Dad says as he nears my mother. "We will make it, mujer.[3] I know it. But we have to be patient. We have to believe."

Mama turns to us and announces we are not leaving. I'm just a ball. Bouncing outside. Bouncing inside. Whatever.

1993

---

3. Woman.

# HELENA MARÍA VIRAMONTES

## b. 1954

Of Mexican descent, Helena María Viramontes was born in East Los Angeles. While working part-time, she earned her undergraduate degree in English literature from Immaculate Heart College, in Los Angeles, in 1975. Two years later, she won first prize for her short story "Requiem for the Poor" in a story contest sponsored by *Statement Magazine*, at the University of California, Los Angeles. The next year, for her story "The Broken Web," she took first prize in the same contest. In 1979, for "Birthday," she won third prize at the more established short-fiction contest at the University of California, Irvine. She enrolled in that university's creative-writing program in 1981.

He work, influenced by the Chicano Movement, centers on the life of itinerant laborers in California and on urban strife. In her first book, the collection *The Moths and Other Stories* (1985), Viramontes addressed themes such as the problems faced by Chicana women in female rites of passage, the cultural transition faced by recent immigrants, the Roman Catholic Church as oppressor, and the bonding of women who resist male domination in Chicano society. Set in the working-class barrio, where unemployment and urban decay lead to frustration and despair, the stories are presented matter-of-factly, without literary adornment.

Viramontes's impressionistic novella *Under the Feet of Jesus* (1995), the second chapter of which appears in this anthology, is about Estrella, a 13-year-old girl in a family of farmworkers in the fruit fields of California's San Joaquin Valley, and her relationship with the teenage boy Alejo. Among the other *piscadores*, or fruit pickers, depicted here are Estrella's mother, Petra, and her stepfather, Perfecto (her biological father abandoned the family). Viramontes dedicates the novel to "my parents, Mary Louise LaBrada Viramontes and Serafin Bermúdez Viramontes, who met in Buttonwillow picking cotton," and to the memory of the Chicano activist César Chávez (see p. 760). Among Chavez's efforts in the later part of his life were campaigns against the kind of pesticide that is used in this selection.

---

## FROM UNDER THE FEET OF JESUS

### From Chapter Two

The white light of the sun worked hard. Even the birds wavered on the crest of the heat waves. Under the leafy grapevines, the grapes hung heavy. She had readied the large rectangular sheet of newsprint paper over an even bed of tractor levelled soil, then placed the wooden frame to hold the paper down. Now, her basket beneath the bunches, Estrella pulled the vine, slit the crescent moon knife across the stem, and the cluster of grapes was guided to the basket below.

Carrying the full basket to the paper was not like the picture on the red raisin boxes Estrella saw in the markets, not like the woman wearing a fluffy bonnet, holding out the grapes with her smiling, ruby lips, the sun a flat orange behind her. The sun was white and it made Estrella's eyes sting like

an onion, and the baskets of grapes resisted her muscles, pulling their magnetic weight back to the earth. The woman with the red bonnet did not
know this. Her knees did not sink in the hot white soil, and she did not know
how to pour the baskets of grapes inside the frame gently and spread the
bunches evenly on top of the newsprint paper. She did not remove the
frame, straighten her creaking knees, the bend of her back, set down another
sheet of newsprint paper, reset the frame, then return to the pisca[1] again
with the empty basket, row after row, sun after sun. The woman's bonnet
would be as useless as Estrella's own straw hat under a white sun so mighty,
it toasted the green grapes to black raisins.

Alejo snipped his own flesh and dropped his knife. He pressed the
wound between his lips, tasted mud and salt and tin and then heard a lost
child's wailing over the hundreds of rows. The vast field of grapevines was
monotonous—without beginning, without ending—always the same to the
piscadores and then to their children. Another child had wandered off and
he could hear the scolding of a mother who was so relieved to find her
daughter, she was angry.

Alejo thought of his own grandmother working in Edinburg, Texas, ironing, babysitting, cleaning houses, cutting cucumbers with lemon, salt, and
powdered chile to sell at the Swap Meets, or making tamarind and hibiscus
juices to sell after Sunday mass. She would do anything to allow her grandson to get schooling. Right this minute, as he pressed his lips to his wound,
he imagined his grandma walking down Chávez Street, cutting across the
park to get to the bus stop. Alejo readjusted his L.A. Dodger cap and tried
to set the wooden frame with one hand. The other, with its torn skin,
seemed painfully useless.

Estrella was not more than four when she first accompanied the mother
to the fields. She remembered crying just as the small girl was wailing now.
The mother showed pregnant and wore large man's pants with the zipper
down and a shirt to cover her drumtight belly. Even then, the mother
seemed old to Estrella. Yet, she hauled pounds and pounds of cotton by the
pull of her back, plucking with two swift hands, stuffing the cloudy bolls
into her burlap sack, the row of plants between her legs. The sack slowly
grew larger and heavier like the swelling child within her.

Today was Alejo's turn to bring the lunch. He had packed burritos made
of fried potato and French's mustard wrapped in flour tortillas, with fresh
jalapeños crunchy like apples, that he and Gumecindo ate quietly under the
shade of the grapevines. His Dodger cap rested on his knee.

Estrella sat under a vine. The sun shone through, making the leaves
translucent. She could see their bones. And she could see the inside of her
water bottle when she held it up to measure its contents. The water was
tepid with particles floating like pieces of exploded stars in space and she
drank in deep gulps, long and hard.

Alejo struggled with a piece of newsprint paper. His grandmother had
reassured him, this field work was not forever. And every time he awoke to
the pisca, he thought only of his last day here and his first day in high
school. He planned to buy a canvas backpack to carry his books, a pencil

1. Harvesting.

sharpener, and Bobcat bookcovers;[2] and planned to major in geology after graduating. He loved stones and the history of stones because he believed himself to be a solid mass of boulder thrust out of the earth and not some particle lost in infinite and cosmic space. With a simple touch of a hand and a hungry wonder of his connection to it all, he not only became a part of the earth's history, but would exist as the boulders did, for eternity.

Estrella remembered the mother trying to keep her awake, but the days were so hot, and the sun wanted her to sleep so badly, she became cranky and angry. Finally, the mother gave in, laid a four-year-old Estrella right on top of her bag of cotton, hushing her to sleep, and Estrella never realized the added weight she must have been on the mother's shoulders as she dragged the bag slowly between the rows of cotton plants. At least this was how she remembered it: being lulled to sleep by the softness of the cotton, palms pressed together under her cheek, and the mother's pull almost gentle and pleasing, remembered how good it felt to close her eyes, to rest, to be this close to the mother's pull.

A young boy of ten hobbled onto Alejo's row. It was the same boy, he recalled, who mimicked the hawk a few days before. Alejo greeted him with a wave of his cap, but the boy continued walking, punching holes in the soft soil with his steps, barely lifting a hand to return the greeting.

Ricky found Estrella's row. He looked feverish and she put down her basket of grapes and pressed the water bottle to his lips, tilted it to the sky, asked him *where is your hat and where are Arnulfo and Perfecto Flores anyways? No sense walking home when the sun is the meanest. You don't know how to work with the sun yet,* she told him and she set him down under the vines. *Sit until you hear the trucks honking, go that way, okay?* Estrella turned and pointed, but her eyes fell on the flatbeds of grapes she had lined carefully, sheet after sheet of grapes down as far as she could see. Her tracks led to where she stood now. Morning, noon, or night, four or fourteen or forty it was all the same. She stepped forward, her body never knowing how tired it was until she moved once again. Don't cry.

Estrella carried the full basket with the help of a sore hip and kneeled before the clusters of grapes. The muscles of her back coiled like barbed wire and clawed against whatever movement she made. She closed her eyes and pulled in the memory of the cool barn, its hard-packed clay floor where she had gathered straw to sit, her knees to her chin. The swallows ticked their claws against the slope of the roof, the breeze wheezing between the planks like wind blowing over the mouth of a crater. All the day's clamped heat, all the cramping of her worked muscles would ease and hum above her like the music of a windpipe and she opened her eyes and spread the grapes and did not cry.

Alejo's grandmother had reassured him; he came from a long line of intelligent people, not like his cabeza de burro[3] father, God rest his stupid soul; seize the chance and make something of yourself in this great and true country. He imagined her at the market by now, carting a few discarded *Reader's Digests* for him to read, fingering the crookneck squash or maroon yam she would roast in foil on top of the comal[4] and eat with a little marga-

---

2. Book covers with images related to the Bobcat Company.

3. Mule-headed.

4. Clay dish used for baking tortillas.

rine for dinner while sipping her daily cup of hot pinole[5] or the cornsilk tea she said was good for her kidneys. His grandmother's hands turned cold at night and if he were home, he would be rubbing them with camphor balsam as thick as vaseline right this minute, then wrapping them with a towel warmed in the oven. He took her words seriously and wanted to do what was needed to continue the line and tried not to think of tomorrow. Alejo hoped she had received his money order.

The piscadores heard the bells of the railroad crossing somewhere in the distance and they stopped to listen. The trabajadores[6] like Señora Josefina, who might be thinking about what to make for dinner; Ricky, his arms clasped over his stomach, thinking of a Blue Bell ice cream sandwich, artificially flavored; or Gumecindo, who might be planning his Saturday night. Piscadores like Florente of the islands, who might be pinching his nostrils to blow his nose; Perfecto Flores, who might be thinking how hard this work is for such an old man; the children, who might be pulling and tugging the rope tied to the waists of their weary mamas so they wouldn't get lost; Arnulfo, who might be afraid of the snakes that loved to jump out at him by surprise; Alejo, who might be searching beyond the vines; and Estrella, who might be kneeling over the grapes with her eyes closed—all of them stopped to listen to the freight train rattling along the tracks swiftly, its horn sounding like the pressing of an accordion. The lone train broke the sun and silence with its growing thunderous roar, and the train reminded the piscadores of destinations, of arrivals and departures, of home and not of home. For they did stop and listen.

Alejo placed the frame atop the sheet of paper haphazardly. He flattened a few vine leaves to watch the freight cars race past him in the distance. Only after the train disappeared did he see Estrella wiping the sweat from the inside of her straw hat with a bandanna. She retied the bandanna across her nose and securely fastened it with large black bobby pins which weighed it down to protect her lungs on days like today, when the fields were becoming dust-swept. All he could see was her bandanna fluttering with her moist breath. Alejo had been working right next to Estrella all along. How could he not have known?

Under his cap, a breeze raked wisps of hair which fell on his forehead and it felt so good on his face. He wanted her to notice him and figured if he hoped enough, she would. But all she did was continue her work, spreading the grapes evenly, then lifting the frame. His own paper slipped from under the slender frame and tossed and bounced away like old news down the long row of grapevines, and he dashed forth to retrieve it.

For a moment, Estrella did not recognize her own shadow. It was hunched and spindly and grew longer on the grapes. Then she noticed another overshadowing her own, loitering larger and about to engulf her and she immediately straightened her knees and rubbed her eyes. She went over to the vine clutching her knife.

She saw a piscador running down the row, as if the person was being chased by something. The hot soil burned through her shoes as she made her way to the other side of the row. There she saw the bend of a back, and at first could not tell whether it was female or male, old or young, and

5. Cornmeal-based drink.
6. Workers.

Estrella called out. The back unfolded and it was Toothless Kawamoto. He pressed his hand on the small of his back and arched. Estrella sensed the awkwardness as he stood there uncertain as to why she called. Estrella thought quickly, and offered him the one peach she had saved to eat after work, a reward to herself. She held it up and he nodded and she tossed it to him, a long arc in the air, and he caught it with crooked fingers and placed it near his water jug with a smile so wide, his mouth looked like a vacant hole. He thanked Estrella, but it was she who was thankful.

The honking signaled the return of the trucks, and the piscadores gathered their tools and jugs and aches and bags and children and pouches and emerged from the fields, a patch quilt of people charred by the sun: brittle women with bandannas over their noses, their salt-and-pepper hair dusted brown; young teens rinsing their faces and running wet fingers through their hair; children bored, tired, and antsy; and men so old they were thought to be dead when they slept. All emerged from the silence of the fields with sighs and mutters and, every now and then, laughter. A mother fingered a kerchief and poked the horns in her son's ear, while another teased the chin of her baby. The piscadores slapped themselves to chase away the dust of the day while children proudly hooked the necks of their fathers. A teenage girl playfully pounced on the shoulders of her boyfriend and laughed.

The Foreman produced a tablet of tables and columns of numbers, scribbled rows completed, names, erased calculations while the piscadores climbed the flatbed trucks. Gumecindo stood on top offering a hand to pull a piscador up. Alejo shoved his cap in his back pocket, fixed his hair in the side view mirror of the truck. He waited near the rear bumper to lift a child up by the waist to the outstretched arms of a mother.

Alejo sought Estrella. The trucks followed the railroad tracks which passed the orchards and fields, rumbled and rocked and jerked to a stop whenever someone knocked on the rear window. Before the last truck departed, Alejo's glance finally fell upon her. He watched her stooped body step on the ties of the railroad track as if she were cautiously climbing a ladder.

Estrella walked because of the playing field, her basket, jug, and knife bundled under the crook of her arm. She waved to the piscadores, and the children waved to her from between the side panels of the trucks, then continued her walk along the tracks, almost regretful she had not taken the ride.

She reached the baseball diamond before dusk, the skies like whipped clouds with linings of ripe nectarine red. Estrella sat on the rail track, still hot from the day's sun, and hugged her knees to her chin. Two Little League teams played on the green of the lawn, behind the tall wire mesh fence. The players had just run out on the chalked boundaries. Parents and other spectators sat on lawn chairs behind the batter's bench or scattered about on the bleachers, ice chests at arm's reach. Estrella wished she had not surrendered her peach and thought how perfect the evening would be if she had the fruit to eat.

She squinted at the batter in his bleached white uniform going up to bat. Number Four. He seemed blurred in the mesh of fence. Her brother Arnulfo had talked about playing baseball. Ricky wanted to fly.

Another truck rolled past, and she waved and they waved until she was alone on the tracks. The remaining sunlight clung to the clouds like a faint trace of lipstick. The sound of contact, of a ball splitting a bat, dull snap of wood, turned her attention to the game, and the spectators cheered and she saw the ball suspended above left field and the players converged, their arms to the sky, the ball like a peach tossed out to hungry hands. The spectators rose, and Estrella jumped to her feet to see mitts form holes like Mr. Kawamoto's mouth readied for the catch. One short player in a blue uniform took the ball out of the cradle of his glove and held it up as she had done with the peach, and the audience broke out in sporadic applause.

Still on her feet, Estrella turned to the long stretch of railroad ties. They looked like the stitches of the mother's caesarean scar as far as her eyes could see. To the north lay the ties and to the south of her, the same, and in between she stood, not knowing where they ended or began.

Estrella gathered her knife and basket. She startled when the sheets of high-powered lights beamed on the playing field like headlights of cars, blinding her. The round, sharp white lights burned her eyes, and she made a feeble attempt to shield them with an arm. The border patrol, she thought, and she tried to remember which side she was on and which side of the wire mesh she was safe in. The floodlights aimed at the phantoms in the field. Or were the lights directed at her? Could the spectators see her from where she stood? Where was home? A ball hit, a blunt instrument against a skull. A player ran the bases for the point. A score. Destination: home plate. Who would catch the peach, who was hungry enough to run the field in all that light? The perfect target. The lushest peach. The element of surprise. A stunned deer waiting for the bullet. A few of the spectators applauded. Estrella fisted her knife and ran, her shadow fading into the approaching night.

—¿Qué diablos te' ta pasando?[7] asked the mother. She kneeled beside the zinc basin filled with water, where the twins were squeezed in and taking a bath. Towels and calzones[8] and trousers and T-shirts dried on a rope tied from a small tree to the pillar of the porch. A silver washboard lay on top the oak stump. Other shirts and pants clung onto the ground scrub surrounding the bungalow. The mother held a steel can full of water over Perla's head, then poured. ¿Por qué corres?[9]

Estrella had run past the cooking pit, the table with its pots and pans and chipped dishes, jumped on the porch of their bungalow almost stumbling on a missed step. She dropped the empty water bottle and basket, and her pisca knife, and a piece of foil she saved to wrap tomorrow's lunch tumbled off the porch.

—Gonna teach someone a lesson.

—¿Qué dices?[1] What?

She opened the tool chest, her breathing hard, and rummaged through Perfecto's tools until she found the thick pry bar.

—Put that away.

—Someone's trying to get me.

—It's La Migra.[2] Everybody's feeling it, the mother explained. The twins began kicking each other over space and the fighting upset the mother

7. What the hell is happening to you?
8. Underpants.
9. Why are you running?
1. What are you saying?

2. A term, derived from *inmigración* by Spanish-speaking U.S. communities, referring to Immigration and Customs Enforcement, Border Patrol, and similar agencies.

more. Te voy a dar un nalgazo con la correa.[3] She fished for Cookie's hand in the murky bath water to smack it, but smacked Perla's by mistake, which caused a wail of injustice and more shoving.

The mother struggled upward, straightening one knee then the other, and Estrella noticed how purple and thick her veins were getting. Like vines choking the movement of her legs. Even the black straight skirt she wore seemed tighter and her belly spilled over the belt of waist, lax muscles of open births, her loose ponytail untidy after the laundry.

Today had been wash day. She had used the last of the ground yucca roots for soap and had to grind more stiff root, which meant more work. Her knuckles were raw white against her coffee skin. The mother used the remaining rinse water to bathe the twins, although night approached.

—How you feeling today, Mama?

—Ya no hay ajo.[4] And this was all she needed to say. The mother ate five cloves of garlic pickled in vinegar every day to loosen her blood and ease her varicose veins; without the garlic, her veins throbbed.

—Maybe we can get some.

—What do you think? she replied. Her body seemed as faded in the dusk as the duck-print apron she wrung her hands in. She held a towel, hooked Cookie's armpit, and Cookie resisted, slapping the water in protest, splashing the mother's face. Yo ya no voy a correr. No puedo más.[5] With one clean sweep, she lifted Cookie out of the basin and walked to the table, her rubber slippers clicking.

—No sense telling La Migra you've lived here all your life, the mother continued as she dried her face with the towel. Cookie dripped like a soaked kitten on the table and whined about being cold and the mother dried her diligently, buffing her hair, her little birdbone chest, moved to her belly, apricot vagina, finally to her rubbery thighs and legs.

—Do we carry proof around like belly buttons?

—Something's out there, Estrella said.

—Ya cállate[6] before you spook the kids.

—Where's Arnulfo? Ricky was sick today.

—Stop it.

—And Perfecto Flores?

—Con eso basta.[7]

Estrella sat on the porch. She laid the crowbar across her lap, grasping it with two fists until her hands began to sweat. Her eyes hurt badly, and she wanted to close them but knew the mother would need help to make dinner. Perla stuck her toes out of the gray water and wriggled them.

—Don't run scared. You stay there and look them in the eye. Don't let them make you feel you did a crime for picking the vegetables they'll be eating for dinner. If they stop you, if they try to pull you into the green vans, you tell them the birth certificates are under the feet of Jesus, just tell them. The mother paused, still not turning around, and Estrella could see the track of bra etched across her T-shirt back.

The mother raised her voice over Cookie's whining.

3. I'll spank your butt with the belt strap.
4. There's no garlic left.
5. I'm not going to run anymore. I'm exhausted.
6. Shut up
7. That's enough

—Tell them que tienes una madre aquí.[8] You are not an orphan, and she pointed a red finger to the earth, Aquí. The mother turned abruptly and fished Perla out next, and the twin began wailing. Estrella watched from the porch as the mother worked to dry Perla, this time jumpy, more concentrated. Cookie, her buttocks like shiny garbanzo beans, tan white against the brown of her skin, climbed down the table, and splashed back into the water.

Estrella closed her eyes, not wanting to open them again.

—¿Y tu primo?[9] asked one of the piscadores. The group waited by the trees for the truck. One of the women pulled her long hair through the circle of a rubber band and her chestnut hair sheened against the bright sun. Some of the piscadores tied triangle bandannas around their heads anticipating the heat.

*   *   *

1995

___

8. That you have a mother here.        9. And your cousin?

# Writers of Latinidad

As the bilingual children of Cuban exiles, the poets Silvia Curbelo, Cecilia Rodríguez Milanés, Adrián Castro, Richard Blanco, and Sandra M. Castillo live between two worlds: the vanished homeland, alive only in memory and nostalgia, and the United States, also sometimes dreamlike in its foreignness. Working with the musical and linguistic rhythms of both worlds, these writers have assembled their families' broken traditions into mosaics of both identity and self-invention.

Silvia Curbelo (b. 1955) immigrated to the United States from Cuba with her family when she was 12. Among her numerous awards are poetry fellowships from the National Endowment for the Arts, the Cintas Foundation, and the Jessica Nobel-Maxwell Memorial Prize from the *American Poetry Review*. Her poetry collection *The Geography of Leaving* (1990) won the Gerald Cable Chapbook Competition, sponsored by Silverfish Review Press, and in 1992 she won the James Wright Poetry Prize, sponsored by the journal *Mid-America Review*. She has also published *The Secret History of Water* (1997), which was the inaugural volume in the Anhinga Press's Florida Poetry Series, and *Ambush* (2004). Curbelo is managing editor of *Organica Quarterly*. Her subtle images evoke a fictional space, an imaginary homeland that contains the past and the present, memory and hope.

Cecilia Rodríguez Milanés was born in Jersey City, New Jersey, in 1961. She holds a doctorate from the University at Albany, State University of New York, and teaches English at the University of Central Florida, in Orlando. In addition to the many poems, stories, and essays she has published in literary magazines, anthologies, and reviews, she is the author of the story collection *Marielitos, Balseros, and Other Exiles* (2009). Her work examines the dislocations of everyday life, the rupturing of cultural memory, and the ways in which generations view each other through the lens of exile. Her prose poem "Muchacha (After Jamaica)"—inspired by "Girl," a short story by the contemporary American writer Jamaica Kincaid—recalls the lessons, messages, and advice provided by older women to younger Latinas.

Adrián Castro was born in Miami, Florida, in 1967 and lives in Miami Beach. He incorporates into his work as a poet and performance artist not just Spanish, English, and Yoruba, but also the music and mythology of Africa, the Caribbean, and North America. Castro has performed at poetry festivals throughout the United States, and his poems have been published in various literary reviews and anthologies. His collections *Cantos to Blood and Honey* (1997) and *Wise Fish: Tales in 6/8 Time* (2005) explore the experiences and memories of the transplanted. In the selection included here, "In the Tradition of Returning," Castro explores the clash of cultures of Africa, the Caribbean, and North America, drawing especially on Afro-Caribbean tradition, mythology, and language.

Richard Blanco was born in Spain in 1968 to Cuban-exile parents who soon emigrated to the United States. He lives in Miami and combines his writing with a career as a consultant engineer. In 1996, he was a finalist in the National Poetry Series Competition, sponsored by the National Poetry Society. His first collection of poetry, *City of a Hundred Fires* (1998), which won the Agnes Lynch Starrett Prize from the University of Pittsburgh Press, draws on Blanco's upbringing in Miami to create subtle, evocative descriptions of the tensions and attachments of growing up the child of working-class exiles. His second book, *Directions to the Beach of the Dead* (2005), part travel diary and part private journal, takes Blanco into new ground, emotionally as well as geographically, as he explores landscapes such as romantic (and unromantic) love. Blanco has also published poems in literary magazines and anthologies, cofounded the poetry-reading series Butterfly Lightning, and cofounded a YMCA children's literary-arts program.

    Sandra M. Castillo (b. 1968) left Cuba for the United States with her parents in 1970. She has lived in Florida since then and teaches at Miami Dade College. Her work has been published in many literary magazines and featured in several anthologies. In her poetry collections *Red Letters* (1991) and *My Father Sings, To My Embarrassment* (2002), she writes of her childhood in Cuba and the shared pain and memories of those who left and those who were left behind.

---

# SILVIA CURBELO
## b. 1955

### Summer Storm

The waitress props open her book
against the sugar bowl
but doesn't read it.
She hums along with the hard rock station,
a song about a brittle love         5
and a piece of someone's heart.

Like a face behind a drawn shade
it has nothing to do with him.
She pours his coffee,
she will do that much.         10

He stares at his hands,
the coffee cup, the door,
saying nothing. She is beautiful.
When she shakes out her hair
he thinks of water spilling out         15
or the last moonlight shaking itself
out of the trees.

Could that be thunder
in the distance
or just the music rattling         20
in his ears? Anyway
he's stopped listening,
even to the radio.

Even the weather station
means nothing to him now.         25
He knows to sit still

and wait for thunder.
He's got time on his hands.
A good rain is worth a hundred years.

She stares out the plate glass windows.                    30
Pinpoints of light
from the next town are blinking on.
He'll look at her now and then,
but not all of her,
a sleeve, a breast,                                        35
a glimpse of hair,
long like the longest night.

                                                        1995


## If You Need a Reason

—for Adrian

The way things move sometimes,
light or air,
the distance between
two points, or a map unfolding
on a table, or wind,                                        5
never mind sadness.
The difference between sky and room,
between geometry and breath,
the sound we hear
when two opposites finally collide,                        10
smashed bottle, country song,
a bell, any bridge, a connection.
The way some stories end in the middle
of a word,
the words themselves,                                      15
galaxies, statuaries, perspectives,
the stone over stone that is life,
never mind hunger.
The way things move, road,
mirror, blind luck. The way                                20
nothing moves sometimes,
a kiss, a glance,
never mind true north.
The difference between history
and desire, between biology                                25
and prayer, any light
to read by, any voice at the bottom
of the stairs, or the sound
of your own name softly, a tiny bone
breaking near the heart.                                   30

                                                        1998

# CECILIA RODRÍGUEZ MILANÉS
## b. 1961

## Muchacha (After Jamaica)

Wash your panties and stockings when you take them off; always carry a perfumed handkerchief in your bosom; fry frituritas de bacalao[1] in shimmering hot oil; ask for a little extra when you buy cloth from the polacos;[2] wearing those pointed shoes will cripple you!; don't let me catch you talking to those boys hanging out on a corner by the empty lot; but I don't talk to 'em; you mustn't refer to papaya as papaya but as fruta bomba because people might think you're indecent; it's all right to call those little rolls bollitos though;[3] now that's nasty; this is the way you embroider a woman's hankie; this is the way you embroider a man's; this is the way you mend a sock; this is the way you iron a guayabera without messing up the pleats; this is the way you starch your fine linen blouses that you embroider; this is the way to take la grasa[4] out of the soup; this is the way you sort the frijoles;[5] this is the way you wash the rice; but madrina[6] doesn't wash the rice; plant the cilantro under the kitchen window so you know when it's ready; these are the herbs and spices for the lechoncito,[7] remember to use sour oranges; juice for the mojo on noche buena;[8] this is how you grind the herbs and spices; don't throw the fruta bomba seeds near the house they grow silvestre;[9] this silvestre is used to calm the nerves; this leaf is cut in the middle and spread on burns to prevent scars, it can be drunk too for the lungs but watercress is the best for the lungs; this one is to ease your cramps; this is how you wash the porch; always soak bloodstains in icy cold water; they still won't come out; don't keep any stained clothing; wrap red rags around your fruit trees to ward off the evil eye; always wear your azabache[1] for the same reason, I will give one to your firstborn; never play music on viernes santos;[2] don't ever let me catch you cruising; but you and . . . ; don't sit with your legs open, it's indecent and you're a decent girl; wash your chocha[3] with that peach tin can from under the sink, always; don't eat at anybody's house; don't give your picture to anyone; do not put your fingers with merengue in the pig's mouth, can't you see that animal has teeth?; don't dance the merengue too close; don't let any man stand behind you on the bus; show your husband everything but your culo,[4] you can never show a man everything; this is how you make flan; this is how to despojarte with branches of the paraiso;[5] this is how you float the gardenias so they don't turn brown, plant them under the bedroom window when they take root so they perfume your nights; don't eat all the anones,[6] other people like them too; this is how you embrace your

5

10

15

20

25

30

35

1. Codfish fritters.
2. European Jews (Cuban slang).
3. In Cuban slang, *papaya* and *bollo* refer to the female genitals.
4. The grease.
5. Beans.
6. Godmother.
7. Roast pork.
8. Good Night, i.e., Christmas Eve. *Mojo*: gravy.
9. A wild herb.

1. Literally, jet (velvet-black coal); an ornament worn as protection against bad luck, the evil eye, illness, and so on.
2. Good Friday (in Christianity, the day on which Jesus was crucified).
3. Pussy, cunt, crotch.
4. Ass.
5. The branches of the paraíso tree are used for spiritual cleansing.
6. A tropical fruit.

child; this is how you embrace someone else's child; I don't have to tell you how to embrace your husband; this is how you embrace other women; always saluda[7] when you walk in anywhere, you're not just anyone, you know; don't wear black bras, you'll look like the fletera[8] from across the street; always use the formal usted[9] when speaking to people you don't know; don't throw dishes at each other when you fight; don't let your in-laws meddle in your matrimony, that doesn't include me; don't talk Spanish at the factory/school/ office; don't throw that house out the window; don't drive the oxcart in front of the oxen; don't make fun of guajiros,[1] your father will be hurt; don't make fun of gallegos,[2] your grandmother will be hurt; this is how you take a bath without running water; this is how to make a cortadito;[3] this is how you save your pennies; this is how you keep your shoes in good condition; you mustn't let the full moon shine on you when you're sleeping; when you call someone on the telephone always say buenos dias or buenas tardes, you have manners, you know; this is how you make camarones enchilados;[4] this is how you avoid being used, if it happens, it's your own fault and don't let it happen again; this is where you place the glasses full of water for the saints; this is where you put their food; this is how you light a candle for the dead; this is how you pray for the living; this is how you will mourn your tierra; but this is my country; this is how you will live in exile; this is how your spirit will rise when your body falls but only after many years, mi hijita,[5] so don't worry about that now.

1995

7. Say hello.
8. Prostitute.
9. Formal form of *you* (the informal form is *tú*).
1. Peasants.
2. Spaniards who emigrated to Cuba from the province of Galicia at the turn of the twentieth

century.
3. An espresso mixed with sugar and a small amount of steamed milk or condensed milk.
4. Shrimp enchiladas.
5. My little daughter, my little girl.

---

# ADRIÁN CASTRO
## b. 1967

## In the Tradition of Returning

Oye mira meng[1]
listen hear—
do not be astonished
when you see a scorpion
cutting sugar cane . . .                                        5
it is the custom of my country
Don Masayá[2] used to say
his voice full of rum
perched between mangos & chirimoyas
falling asleep on a hammock                                    10

1. Hey, look, man.                          2. A made-up character.

A cosmic legacy begun
by three boats
Here big & beautiful negras
queens of wind & cemetery
provoke hurricanes                                    15
merely flapping their skirts
negras provoke(can) huracanes
flapping their skirts
Steel & iron clash
causing blooshed                                      20
causing steel & iron
to feast on blood

Don Masayá's memory drips the image
of that night
a black cape pis-                                     25
tol-whipped him & flew away
with his custom typewriter
with maracas on the keys—
an assassination attempt
on his rhythm                                         30
Don Masayá's memory drips
Don Masayá's memory drips the image
of many letters he received
already opened
of the echo of his parrot who perched                35
on his shoulder who sang divine danzón
the echo of his parrot's throat
slit.
Don Masayá's memory drips
Don Masayá's memory drips as he tumbles              40
off the hammock
startled by the touch of that colonel's
voice that colonel's
voice
tossing him to foreign soil                           45

•  •  •

A brief interruption
to listen to Miguelito Valdes's instruction
& Chano Pozo's[3] percussion
to aid a cultural eruption

•  •  •

The funeral is commencing                             50
what shall we offer the healer of the sick:
17 lavender candles
a half-burned cigar

---

3. Luciano "Chano" Pozo Gonzales (1915–1948), Cuban percussionist, singer, and composer who played a major role in Latin jazz. *Miguelito Val-* *des*: Cuban popular singer known as "Mr. Ba- balú" (b. Miguel Ángel Lázaro Valdés Hernán- dez, 1912–1978).

& a jar
of aguardiente[4]                                                    55
for tossing him to foreign soil
for tossing him to foreign soil

. . .

Do not be astonished
when revolution arrives on a cigar
wearing shokotó[5]                                                   60
& speaking in a trance—
Don Masayá used to say
his voice full of rum
waking from echoes of abuse
chanting his revenge:                                                65
the black cape
shall call me usted[6]
typewriters shall taca-taca in maraca language
letters delivered by doves
macaws & african grays will perch on shoulders                      70
& sing a son(g)
the colonel's voice
the colonel's voice shall be a ring of smoke
a memory of ashes—
tomorrow shall be the sweetest sugar cane                            75

. . .

It was the roosters with
throat in full throttle
kee-keedee-croaking
in Spanglish . . .
it was the shores of Biscayne Bay[7]                                80
peppered with tar
with cans of Goya beans[8]
with needles . . .
it was the belch
of criollo sauces[9]                                                85
from mirrored cafeterias . . .
it was Calle Ocho[1] singing
people screaming
with their hands . . .
it was Pepe, Carmen, Elena, Miguel                                  90
etcétera, etcétera . . .

it was why we shed our guayabera
& grew a tuxedo

4. Firewater, a high-alcohol liquor distilled from sugarcane.
5. Yoruba (African) male trousers, usually combined with a dashiki (tunic).
6. The formal form of *you* (the informal form is *tú*).
7. Bay in Miami, perhaps named after the Bay of Biscay or a man called El Biscaino (from the Biscay region of the Basque Country, in Spain).
8. Goya Foods, a Hispanic-owned U.S. company, specializes in Latino cuisine.
9. In Cuban cuisine, a mixture of olive oil, garlic, citrus juices, and spices, used for marinating meats and fish.
1. South West 8th Street, thoroughfare in the heart of the Little Havana neighborhood of Miami, lined with landmarks of the Cuban-exile community.

shed our guayabera
& grew a tuxedo                                                    95
We are of those who chose exile
from exiles

Yet now here we are
grand marshalls in a parade of roosters
buoying the polluted Biscayne                                      100
our Biscayne
eating enchilada de shrimp
screaming with our hands
looking for Pepe, Carmen, Elena
even Miguel                                                        105
etcétera, etcétera . . .
The tuxedo didn't fit!!!
The tuxedo didn't fit!!!
Ceiba trees
palm trees                                                        110
Cubano-Dominicano-Americano
& all that comes with it
We can see them/
those we can see our pearls
bouncing down 8th Street.                                          115
We can see pearls
surfing on ceiba trees
palm trees
mama we're coming home
Ceiba trees                                                       120
palm trees
mamita we're coming home
mamita we're coming home

1997

---

# RICHARD BLANCO

## b. 1968

### Palmita Mía

You are this:
the free palm
    of my rest,
the impatient rain
    from your fronds                                               5
a river I collect
    in my open hands
and bring to my dry
    useless lip,

you, my thirst, my water          10
    my tranquil shade.

    You are this:
the drawn island lean
    I stretch with you,
my back breaks          15
    against your coast,
you are the exile
    of my exile
you are the red mountain,
    the temperate valley          20
is my mouth open
    waiting for your harvest

    You are this:
the green crib
    the pulse          25
loose in open hand,
    a hummingbird heart
and the sentinel of still stars,
    attentive faith
among the praying palms,          30
    a creed of breezes:
coconut wine, loaves of sand,
    palmita mía.

                                        1988

## Havanasis

In the beginning, before God created Cuba, the earth was chaos, empty of form and without music. The spirit of God stirred over the dark tropical waters and God said, "Let there be music." And a soft *conga* began a one-two beat in background of the chaos.

Then God called-up *Yemayá*[1] and said, "Let the waters under heaven amass together and let dry land appear." It was done. God called the fertile red earth Cuba and the massed waters the Caribbean. And God saw this was good, tapping his foot to the *conga* beat.

Then God said, "Let the earth sprout *papaya* and *coco* and white *coco* flesh; *malanga* roots and mangos in all shades of gold and amber; let there be *tabaco* and *café* and sugar for the *café*; let there be rum; let there be waving plantains and *guayabas* and everything tropical-like." God saw this was good, then fashioned palm trees—His pièce de résistance.

Then God said, "Let there be a moon and stars to light the nights over the Club Tropicana, and a sun for the 365 days of the year." God saw that this was good, he called the night nightlife, the day he called paradise.

---

1. In Santería, a mermaid creation goddess, associated with the *La Virgin of Regla* (the Virgin of Regla), a Christian icon.

Then God said, "Let there be fish and fowl of every kind." And there was spicy shrimp *enchilado*, chicken *fricasé*, cod fish *bacalao* and fritters. But He wanted something more exciting and said, "Enough. Let there be pork." And there was pork—deep fried, whole roasted, pork rinds and sausage. He fashioned goats, used their skins for bongos and *batús*;[2] he made *claves* and *maracas* and every kind of percussion instrument known to man.

Then out of a red lump of clay, God made a Taino and set him in a city He called *Habana*. Then He said, "It is not good that Taino be alone. Let me make him helpmates." And so God created the *mulata* to dance *guaguancó* and *son* with Taino; the *guajiro* to cultivate his land and his folklore, *Cachita*[3] the sorceress to strike the rhythm of his music, and a poet to work the verses of their paradise.

God gave them dominion over all the creatures and musical instruments and said unto them, "Be fruitful and multiply, eat pork, drink rum, make music and dance." On the seventh day, God rested from the labors of his creation. He smiled upon the celebration and listened to their music.

1998

## Mother Picking Produce

She scratches the oranges then smells the peel,
presses an avocado just enough to judge its ripeness,
polishes the Macintoshes searching for bruises.

She selects with hands that have thickened, fingers
that have swollen with history around the white gold     5
of a wedding ring she now wears as a widow.

Unlike the archived photos of young, slender digits
captive around black and white orange blossoms,
her spotted hands now reaching into the colors.

I see all the folklore of her childhood, the fields,     10
the fruit she once picked from the very tree,
the wiry roots she pulled out of the very ground.

And now, among the collapsed boxes of yucca,
through crumbling pyramids of golden mangos,
she moves with the same instinct and skill.     15

This is how she survives death and her son,
on these humble duties that will never change,
on those habits of living which keep a life a life.

2. African drums.
3. *La Virgin de la Caridad del Cobre* (the Virgin of Charity of Cobre), the patron saint of Cuba; in Santería, identified with the god Ochún. *Mulata*: mixed-race female performer; a Cuban arche-type. *Guaguancó*: an Afro-Cuban rhythm. *Son*: a Cuban style of music, combining the structure and elements of Spanish and African music. *Guajiro*: Cuban peasant.

She holds up red grapes to ask me what I think,
and what I think is this, a new poem about her—                    20
the grapes look like dusty rubies in her hands,

what I say is this: *they look sweet, very sweet.*

1998

---

# SANDRA M. CASTILLO
## b. 1968

### Looking South

The moon followed me,
guided me through the park
from Tía Tere's, past the green bench
where Father and I visit each week,
past the darkness, and the chain-link fences                       5
that haunt me in photographs.

Men gathered on 69th Street,
across from the butcher shop
Father traded the military for.
They drank from unmarked flasks                                     10
and played dominoes in the dust.
Their laughter made my walk home longer.

"Esta Revolución es verde, verde como las palmas,"
Fidel said, and Tío Casimiro repeated it often.
He said he didn't want Father to forget.                           15
He said Father's ink-stained hands
made the revolution bleed.

Momma doesn't agree.
She dreams of American shopping carts
and bringing Abuela[1] Isabel to America.                          20
But Abuela Isabel reads Echeverría
and knows that "to emigrate is to die."[2]

1991

---

1. Grandmother.
2. Loose translation of "exiliarse es morir" (to go
into exile is to die), a phrase by Esteban Echeverría (1805–1851), Argentinian writer, cultural
promoter, and political activist.

# GUILLERMO GÓMEZ-PEÑA
## b. 1955

A nonfiction writer and *performero* (Spanish for performance artist), Guillermo Gómez-Peña was born in Mexico City. In 1978, he immigrated to San Diego, California. He earned his bachelor's degree in linguistics from the National Autonomous University of Mexico, in Mexico City, in 1981, and his master's in post-studio art at the California Institute of the Arts, in San Diego, in 1983. Also in San Diego, Gómez-Peña founded the Border Arts Workshop. Through this and other experimental artistic endeavors, he hoped to embrace the urban Chicano experience, specifically to separate *mestizaje* from its roots as a glorification of the mixture of Indian blood and Spanish heritage. He sought not just to define his subculture, but to redefine the dominant culture.

A self-styled transgressor, Gómez-Peña raises questions—in his performance pieces and in his political commentary on National Public Radio—about culture, language, and identity politics. He also seeks to change the image of Mexican Americans as "naturally" inept when dealing with forms of technology. His film and video art projects, completed alone and with others such as Roberto Sifuentes, James Luna, Violeta Luna, and Coco Fusco, include *Mi Otro Yo* (My Other Self, 1988), in which Gómez-Peña guides the audience through an exploration of Chicano art aided by interviews with the playwright Luis Valdez (see p. 1244), the performance artist Harry Gamboa Jr., the muralist Jucy Baca, and the poet José Montoya, and *Border Brujo* (Border Witch, 1990), in which Gómez-Peña transforms himself into the many "types" of people who inhabit the border.

For his work, he has received numerous honors, including a Bessie Award (1989), a MacArthur Fellowship (1991), the Prix de la Parole (1993), and the American Book Award (1996). He is the author of several mixed-media volumes with text in Spanglish, notably *Warrior for Gringostroika: Essays, Performance Texts, and Poetry* (1993); *The New World Border* (1996), a collection of essays drawn from his collaboration on an experimental form of book art with Felicia Rice, who is the director of Moving Parts Press, and the artist Enrique Chagoya; *Friendly Cannibals* (1996), art by Enrique Chagoya; *Codex Espangliensis: From Columbus to the Border Patrol* (1998), with Enrique Chagoya and Felicia Rice; *El Mexterminator: Antropología de un performancero postmexicano* (2002); *Ethno-Techno: Writings on Performance, Activism, and Pedagogy* (2005), edited by Elaine Peña; and *Homo Fronterizus* (2008), a collaboration with the filmmaker Gustavo Vázquez.

Gómez-Peña rejects the idea of a mainstream view in the United States. "Today, if there is a dominant culture," he stated in a 1998 interview in the magazine *Gestos*, "it is border culture. And those who still haven't crossed a border will do it very soon." The concept of borders as artificial separators is also integral to his vision. The essay "Documented/Undocumented," included in this anthology, illustrates Gómez-Peña's syncopated, postmodern style.

## Documented/Undocumented[1]

I live smack in the fissure between two worlds, in the infected wound: half a block from the end of Western Civilization and four miles from the start of the Mexican–American border, the northernmost point of Latin America.

---

[1]. Translated by Rubén Martínez. Bracketed insertions in the text are Martínez's.

In my fractured reality, but a reality nonetheless, there cohabit two histories, languages, cosmologies, artistic traditions, and political systems which are drastically counterposed. Many "deterritorialized" Latin American artists in Europe and the U.S. have opted for "internationalism" (a cultural identity based upon the "most advanced" of the ideas originating out of New York or Paris). I, on the other hand, opt for "borderness" and assume my role: My generation, the *chilangos* [slang term for a Mexico City native], who came to "el norte" fleeing the imminent ecological and social catastrophe of Mexico City, gradually integrated itself into otherness, in search of that other Mexico grafted onto the entrails of the et cetera . . . became Chicano-ized. We de-Mexicanized ourselves to Mexi-understand ourselves, some without wanting to, others on purpose. And one day, the border became our house, laboratory, and ministry of culture (or counterculture).

Today, eight years after my departure [from Mexico], when they ask me for my nationality or ethnic identity, I can't respond with one word, since my "identity" now possesses multiple repertories: I am Mexican but I am also Chicano and Latin American. At the border they call me *chilango* or *mexiquillo*; in Mexico City it's *pocho* or *norteño*; and in Europe it's *sudaca*.[2] The Anglos call me "Hispanic" or "Latino," and the Germans have, on more than one occasion, confused me with Turks or Italians. My wife, Emilia, is Anglo-Italian, but speaks Spanish with an Argentine accent, and together we walk amid the rubble of the Tower of Babel[3] of our American postmodernity.

The recapitulation of my personal and collective topography has become my cultural obsession since I arrived in the United States. I look for the traces of my generation, whose distance stretches not only from Mexico City to California, but also from the past to the future, from pre-Columbian America to high technology and from Spanish to English, passing through "Spanglish."

As a result of this process I have become a cultural topographer, border-crosser, and hunter of myths. And it doesn't matter where I find myself, in Califas or Mexico City, in Barcelona or West Berlin; I always have the sensation that I belong to the same species: the migrant tribe of fiery pupils.

My work, like that of many border artists, comes from two distinct traditions, and because of this has dual, or on occasion multiple, referential codes. One strain comes from Mexican popular culture, the Latin American literary "boom," and the Mexico City counterculture of the '70s . . . the other comes directly from fluxus (a late-'60s international art movement that explored alternative means of production and distribution), concrete poetry, conceptual art, and performance art. These two traditions converge in my border experience and they fuse together.

In my intellectual formation, Carlos Fuentes, Gabriel García Márquez, Oscar Chávez, Felipe Ehrenberg, José Agustín, and Enrique Cisneros were as important as Burroughs, Foucault, Fassbinder, Lacan, Vito Acconci, and Joseph Beuys.[4]

My "artistic space" is the intersection where the new Mexican urban poetry and the colloquial Anglo poetry meet; the intermediate stage somewhere between Mexican street theater and multimedia performance; the silence that snaps in between the *corrido* and punk; the wall that divides *"neográfica"* (a 1970s Mexico City art movement involved in the production of low-budget book art and graphics) and graffiti; the highway that joins Mexico City and Los Angeles; and the mysterious thread of thought and action that puts pan–Latin Americanism in touch with the Chicano movement, and both of these in touch with other international vanguards.

I am a child of crisis and cultural syncretism, half hippie and half punk. My generation grew up watching movies about cowboys and science fiction, listening to *cumbias* and tunes from the Moody Blues, constructing altars and filming in Super-8, reading the *Corno Emplumado* and *Artforum*, traveling to Tepoztlán[5] and San Francisco, creating and de-creating myths. We went to Cuba in search of political illumination, to Spain to visit the crazy grandmother and to the U.S. in search of the instantaneous musico-sexual Paradise. We found nothing. Our dreams wound up getting caught in the webs of the border.

Our generation belongs to the world's biggest floating population: the weary travelers, the dislocated, those of us who left because we didn't fit anymore, those of us who still haven't arrived because we don't know where to arrive at, or because we can't go back anymore.

Our deepest generational emotion is that of loss, which comes from our having left. Our loss is total and occurs at multiple levels: loss of our country (culture and national rituals) and our class (the "illustrious" middle class and upper middle). Progressive loss of language and literary culture in our native tongue (those of us who live in non-Spanish-speaking countries); loss of ideological meta-horizons (the repression against and division of the left) and of metaphysical certainty.

In exchange, what we won was a vision of a more experimental culture, that is to say, a multi-focal and tolerant one. Going beyond nationalisms, we established cultural alliances with other places, and we won a true political conscience (declassicization and consequent politicization) as well as new options in social, sexual, spiritual, and aesthetic behavior.

Our artistic product presents hybrid realities and colliding visions within coalition. We practice the epistemology of multiplicity and a border semiotics. We share certain thematic interests, like the continual clash with

4. German artist and art theorist (1921–1986) whose work ranged from performance art to graphic art to sculpture. *Carlos Fuentes*: Mexican novelist and essayist (b. 1928). *Gabriel García Márquez*: Colombian novelist, short-story writer, screenwriter, and journalist (b. 1927). *Oscar Chávez*: Mexican singer/songwriter and actor (b. 1935). *Felipe Ehrenberg*: Mexican artist, publisher, essayist, teacher, and activist (b. 1943). *José Agustín*: Mexican novelist (b. 1944). *Enrique Cisneros*: unidentified. *Burroughs*: William S. Burroughs (1914–1997), American writer, primarily of experimental fiction. *Foucault*: Michel Foucault (1926–1984), French philosopher, sociologist, and historian. *Fassbinder*: Rainer Werner

Fassbinder (1945–1982), German filmmaker, dramatist, and actor. *Lacan*: Jacques-Marie-Émile Lacan (1901–1981), French psychoanalyst, psychiatrist, philosopher, and literary theorist. *Vito Acconci*: American architect, landscape architect, and installation artist.
5. Town near Mexico City. *Artforum*: international art magazine. *Moody Blues*: English rock band, formed in 1964. *Super-8*: Super 8 mm film, a motion-picture film format used especially for home movies. *Corno Emplumado*: or *The Plumed Horn* (1962–69), bilingual quarterly published in Mexico City, specializing in writing from Latin America and North America.

cultural otherness, the crisis of identity, or, better said, access to trans- or multiculturalism, and the destruction of borders therefrom; the creation of alternative cartographies, a ferocious critique of the dominant culture of both countries, and, lastly, a proposal for new creative languages.

We witness the borderization of the world, by-product of the "deterritorialization" of vast human sectors. The borders either expand or are shot full of holes. Cultures and languages mutually invade one another. The South rises and melts, while the North descends dangerously with its economic and military pincers. The East moves west and vice-versa. Europe and North America daily receive uncontainable migrations of human beings, a majority of whom are being displaced involuntarily. This phenomenon is the result of multiple factors: regional wars, unemployment, overpopulation, and especially in the enormous disparity in North/South relations.

The demographic facts are staggering: The Middle East and Black Africa are already in Europe, and Latin America's heart now beats in the U.S. New York and Paris increasingly resemble Mexico City and São Paulo. Cities like Tijuana[6] and Los Angeles, once socio-urban aberrations, are becoming models of a new hybrid culture, full of uncertainty and vitality. And border youth—the fearsome "cholo-punks," children of the chasm that is opening between the "first" and the "third" worlds, become the indisputable heirs to a new *mestizaje* (the fusion of the Amerindian and European races).

In this context, concepts like "high culture," "ethnic purity," "cultural identity," "beauty," and "fine arts" are absurdities and anachronisms. Like it or not, we are attending the funeral of modernity and the birth of a new culture.

In 1988, the unigeneric and monocultural vision of the world is insufficient. Syncretism, interdisciplinarianism, and multi-ethnicity are sine qua nons of contemporary art. And the artist or intellectual who doesn't comprehend this will be banished and his or her work will not form part of the great cultural debates of the continent.

Art is conceptual territory where everything is possible, and by the same token there do not exist certainties nor limitations within it. In 1988, all the creative possibilities have been explored, and therefore they are all within our reach.

Thanks to the discoveries and advancements of many artists over the last fifteen years, the concept of *metier* is so wide and the parameters of art so flexible that they include practically every imaginable alternative: art as political negotiation (Felipe Ehrenberg—Mexico), as social reform (Joseph Beuys—Germany), as an instrument of multicultural organization (Judy Baca—Los Angeles), or as alternative communication (*Post Arte*—Mexico, and Kit Galloway & Sherri Rabinowitz[7]—USA). Others conceive art as a strategy of intervention aimed at mass media, or as citizen-diplomacy, social chronicle, a popular semiotics, or personal anthropology.

---

6. City in Baja California, Mexico, on the U.S. border. *São Paulo*: largest city in Brazil.
7. American multimedia artists and cofounders, in 1984, of the Electronic Cafe International, a network of technology-related art venues and ventures. *Post-Arte*: Mexico-based international artists group, founded in 1985.

In 1988, our artistic options in terms of the medium, methodology, system of communication, and channels of distribution for our ideas and images are greater and more diverse than ever. Not understanding and practicing this freedom implies operating outside of history, or, worse yet, blindly accepting the restrictions imposed by cultural bureaucracies.

Our experience as Latino border artists and intellectuals in the U.S. fluctuates between legality and illegality, between partial citizenship and full. For the Anglo community we are simply "an ethnic minority," a subculture, that is to say, some kind of pre-industrial tribe with a good consumerist appetite. For the art world, we are practitioners of distant languages that, in the best of cases, are perceived as exotic.

In general, we are perceived through the folkloric prisms of Hollywood, fad literature and publicity; or through the ideological filters of mass media. For the average Anglo, we are nothing but "images," "symbols," "metaphors." We lack ontological existence and anthropological concreteness. We are perceived indistinctly as magic creatures with shamanistic powers, happy bohemians with pretechnological sensibilities, or as romantic revolutionaries born in a Cuban poster from the '70s. All this without mentioning the more ordinary myths, which link us with drugs, supersexuality, gratuitous violence, and terrorism, myths that serve to justify racism and disguise the fear of cultural otherness.

These mechanisms of mythification generate semantic interference and obstruct true intercultural dialogue. To make border art implies to reveal and subvert said mechanisms.

The term Hispanic, coined by techno-marketing experts and by the designers of political campaigns, homogenizes our cultural diversity (Chicanos, Cubans, and Puerto Ricans become indistinguishable), avoids our indigenous cultural heritage and links us directly with Spain. Worse yet, it possesses connotations of upward mobility and political obedience.

The terms *Third World culture*, *ethnic art*, and *minority art* are openly ethnocentric and necessarily imply an axiological vision of the world at the service of Anglo-European culture. Confronted with them, one can't avoid asking the following questions: Besides possessing more money and arms, is it that the "First World" is qualitatively better in any other way than our "underdeveloped" countries? That the Anglos themselves aren't also an "ethnic group," one of the most violent and antisocial tribes on this planet? That the five hundred million Latin American *mestizos* that inhabit the Americas are a "minority"?

Between Chicanos, Mexicans, and Anglos there is a heritage of relations poisoned by distrust and resentment. For this reason, my cultural work (especially in the camps of performance art and journalism) has concentrated itself upon the destruction of the myths and the stereotypes that each group has invented to rationalize the other two.

With the dismantling of this mythology, I look, if not to create an instantaneous space for intercultural communication, at least to contribute to the creation of the groundwork and theoretical principles for a future dialogue that is capable of transcending the profound historical resentments that exist between the communities on either side of the border.

Within the framework of the false amnesty of the Immigration Reform and Control Act[8] and the growing influence of the North American ultra-right, which seeks to close (militarize) the border because of supposed motives of "national security," the collaboration among Chicano, Mexican, and Anglo artists has become indispensable.

Anglo artists can contribute their technical ability, their comprehension of the new mediums of expression and information (video and audio), and their altruist/internationalist tendencies. In turn, Latinos (whether Mexican, Chicano, Caribbean, Central or South American) can contribute the originality of their cultural models, their spiritual strength, and their political understanding of the world.

Together, we can collaborate in surprising cultural projects but without forgetting that *both should retain control of the product*, from the planning stages up through to distribution. If this doesn't occur, then intercultural collaboration isn't authentic. We shouldn't confuse true collaboration with political paternalism, cultural vampirism, voyeurism, economic opportunism, and demogogic multiculturalism.

We should clear up this matter once and for all:

We (Latinos in the United States) don't want to be a mere ingredient of the melting pot. What we want is to participate actively in a humanistic, pluralistic and politicized dialogue, continuous and not sporadic, and that this occur between equals that enjoy the same power of negotiation.

For this "intermediate space" to open, first there has to be a pact of mutual cultural understanding and acceptance, and it is precisely in this that the border artist can contribute. In this very delicate historical moment, Mexican artists and intellectuals as well as Chicanos and Anglos should try to "recontextualize" ourselves, that is to say, search for a "common cultural territory," and within it put into practice new models of communication and association.

1988

8. Also known as the Simpson-Mazzoli Act; a 1986 Act of Congress that made it illegal to knowingly hire or recruit illegal immigrants, required employers to attest to their employees' immigration status, granted amnesty to certain illegal immigrants, and provided a path toward legalization for certain agricultural seasonal workers and immigrants.

# CARLOS MORTON
## b. 1947

Mexican American writers have not enjoyed the same success in the theater as they have in other literary fields. For example, none of the traveling theater groups that made sporadic appearances up to the 1980s have survived. The three major exceptions—the most successful Mexican American playwrights—are Estela Portillo Trambley (see p. 1151), Luis Valdez (p. 1244), and Carlos Morton, a professor of theater at the University of California, Santa Barbara.

Born in Chicago, Morton received his bachelor's degree in English from the University of Texas at El Paso in 1979. The most frequently produced Chicano playwright of the 1980s, he earned a doctorate in drama from the University of Texas at Austin in 1987. Morton's most famous play, *The Many Deaths of Danny Rosales* (1980), about a Texas police chief who faces charges of killing a young burglary suspect, received the Hispanic Playwrights Festival Award at the New York Shakespeare Festival. His *Johnny Tenorio* (1983) is a modern-day version of the Don Juan story, while *The Miser of Mexico* (1989) is a reimagining of *The Miser* (a classic satire by the seventeenth-century French playwright Molière). His major works since then have included the satirical *Rancho Hollywood* (1991); *The Savior* (1992), about Archbishop Oscar Romero; and *Drug, O the Magnificent* (1996), about the drug-related destruction of a family. The author of *Children of the Sun: Scenes and Monologues for Latino Youth* (2008), Morton also creates theater for children. In teaching the history of the Americas, his plays explore issues such as racism, homophobia, stereotypes, and Mexican immigrants' quest for a solid footing in the United States. The works frequently mix reality and fiction, real-life characters and cartoonlike exaggerations. However, continual linguistic code switching often makes it difficult for non–Spanish speaking audiences to appreciate the humor and biting satire.

Presented here in its entirety, *The Many Deaths of Danny Rosales* is a courtroom drama set in a small central-Texas town. Through the back-and-forth of lawyers and witnesses, Morton explores loyalty, anti-Mexican feeling, the use and abuse of authority, and the tensions between the majority and a minority. He has been accused of simplifying a complex situation. In his essay "Celebrating 500 Years of *Mestizaje*" (published in the journal *MELUS*, Fall 1989–90), Morton notes that the play has "been dismissed by some critics as too 'black and white, too simple,' i.e. 'political'. . . . It was turned down at the Alley in Houston, Stage West in Ft. Worth, and Dallas Theater Center. This is more than just sour grapes; the Texas intelligentsia loves our faces, but denigrates our art."

---

# THE MANY DEATHS OF DANNY ROSALES

## Characters

| | |
|---|---|
| ROWENA SALDIVAR | FRED HALL |
| BAILIFF | DANNY ROSALES |
| JUDGE | KIKI VENTURA |
| HAROLD PEARL | GRACE HALL |
| BERTA ROSALES | DEBBIE HALL |
| STEVE PETERS | DEPUTY BILLY JOE DAVIS |

## Scene

*In and around Arroyo County, Texas, 1975.*

## Act I

ROWENA:  In September 1975, on a moonlit gravel road five miles west of town, Fred Hall, the 52-year-old police chief, put the barrel of a 12-gauge sawed-off shotgun under the left armpit of Danny Rosales and pulled the trigger. [*Behind scrim, in silhouette, we see* HALL *struggle with* ROSALES. ROSALES *falls, a shot is heard.*]

BAILIFF: [*Voice, offstage.*]   All rise! Court is now in session!

JUDGE: [*Voice, from above.*]   Good morning, we are here to arraign Fred Hall, you may be seated.

HAROLD:   Your Honor, my client, Fred Hall, is too ill to appear today for the arraignment proceedings. He is suffering from a chronic brain syndrome and neurosurgery is seriously being considered.

BERTA: [*At* ROWENA's *side.*]   Rowena, what is he talking about? I saw the sheriff and his wife grocery shopping in Dallas just two days ago.

ROWENA:   He is trying to make the sheriff out to be crazy, Berta, that way he can be found not guilty by reason of insanity.

HAROLD:   Your Honor, I move that a sanity hearing be set. I propose to call several witnesses who will testify that my client is not mentally competent to stand trial.

ROWENA:   Your Honor, I object to any further postponement of this trial. It has already been nine months since Danny Rosales' death.

JUDGE:   Miss Saldivar, I hear tell that you are a recent graduate of the Harvard University Law School, are you not?

ROWENA:   Yes, I am, your Honor, but I don't see what . . .

JUDGE:   Please bear with us, Miss Saldivar. We here in Texas move at a more leisurely pace than you do up north. But that doesn't mean we are not sticklers for detail. Remember that it is the object of the court to insure that the accused receives a fair trial. Your objection is overruled. A sanity hearing will be set for May 24. Mr. Pearl, will you approach the bench? [*As they talk silently.*]

BERTA:   Rowena, why are they dragging it out so long?

ROWENA:   It's just another tactic on the part of the defense.

BERTA:   What does that mean?

ROWENA:   He's just trying to buy some more time for his client. But don't worry, we'll find Fred Hall sane enough to stand trial.

HAROLD:   Your Honor, I further move for a change of venue from Arroyo County to Jim Bowie County on the grounds that biased publicity has made it impossible for my client to receive a fair trial here.

BERTA:   What's he saying now, Rowena?

ROWENA:   He is trying to have the trial changed from this county, where there is a high percentage of Mexican American voters, to another county where there are none.

BERTA:   No entiendo, explícamelo.

ROWENA:   This means, if he gets his way, there won't be any Chicanos on the jury. [*To the* JUDGE.] Your Honor, is the defense implying that Fred Hall cannot receive a fair trial in your court?

HAROLD:   I am implying no such thing. My motion is based on evidence gathered from this radical Chicano newspaper which pictures my client as a pig and an ogre. There is a climate of racial hatred in Arroyo County that threatens to explode into riot and disorder in the streets.

ROWENA:   Your Honor, of course the community is indignant. But rather than violence they have staged some peaceful demonstrations. I fail to see how that can be labeled riot and disorder.

HAROLD:   Your Honor, my client has been receiving threatening phone calls.

JUDGE: I will order a change of venue in this case. Unfortunately, there are very strong racial overtones in this matter.

ROWENA: Your Honor, I submit that the question deals not so much with race as it does with justice.

JUDGE: Trial will be held in Jim Bowie County.

HAROLD: Thank you, your Honor.

BERTA: Rowena, ¿qué pasó?

ROWENA: The trial is going to be held in a mostly white, Anglo-Saxon Protestant county.

JUDGE: [*A court in Jim Bowie County.*] Now then, how many prospective jurors were called?

BAILIFF: Seventy-six, your Honor.

JUDGE: Are you satisfied with the jurors selected for this trial?

HAROLD: I certainly am, your Honor.

ROWENA: You see, Berta, the lawyers on both sides have the right to exclude, reject, any juror they want. Out of the seventy-six jurors that were called, only three were Chicanos. So the defense rejected them.

BERTA: Is that why the jury is made up of eleven Anglos and one black? It's not fair!

ROWENA: That's the way the law works. If only we would have had more registered voters who were Chicanos in this county! La Raza doesn't vote, Berta. But don't worry, we have all the evidence we need to convict Hall. We have witnesses that heard Hall threaten to kill Danny; we also have witnesses that saw Hall try to cover up the crime. We can't lose.

BERTA: Juana, I've already lost!

ROWENA: [*To the jury.*] Cortezville, where the killing took place, is a small town in Central Texas whose population is two thousand, half of which are Mexican American. Fred Hall, the police chief, was a retired Air Force Master Sergeant who lived with his wife and daughter in a trailer home. Danny Rosales, the victim, lived with his common-law wife in a little one-room shack. He was twenty-five years old at the time of his death. Ladies and gentlemen of the jury, we intend to prove, beyond the shadow of a doubt, that Fred Hall killed Danny Rosales in cold blood and that he is guilty of first-degree murder. For my first witness, I would like to call Berta Rosales to the stand. [*Enter* BERTA.] State your name, please.

BERTA: Berta López Rosales.

ROWENA: Where do you live?

BERTA: Cortezville.

ROWENA: How long have you lived there?

BERTA: Twenty-four years.

ROWENA: How did you first meet Danny Rosales?

BERTA: In a dance in a place called Chevana. It's on Highway 81.

ROWENA: What was your relationship to the deceased?

BERTA: We were living together as man and wife.

ROWENA: Were you married?

BERTA: No, when I first met him in 1967 I was too young to get married, so we just started living together. It has been seven years now.

ROWENA: When was the last time you saw your husband alive?

BERTA: On September 14, 1975, that Sunday night at our home in Cortezville.

ROWENA: Will you please tell the jury what happened there that night?

BERTA: We were watching television and getting ready to go to bed when the Deputy Sheriff drove his car up to our driveway and knocked on the front door. [*Flashback. Enter* DEPUTY.]

DEPUTY: Is Danny Rosales here?

BERTA: [*From the witness stand.*] "Just a minute," I said, "I'll call him. Danny! Es la policía!"

ROWENA: And what did Danny do? [*Enter* DANNY, *dressing.*]

BERTA: He put his pants on and walked to the door.

DEPUTY: That's a mighty nice stereo and TV you got there, pardner. I'm afraid I'm going to have to take you in.

ROWENA: Do you remember what time of night this was?

BERTA: 10:45 p.m.

ROWENA: What happened then?

BERTA: He handcuffed Danny and took him to the squad car. [*To the* DEPUTY.] How much is the bail going to be?

DEPUTY: I don't know, fifty, one-hundred dollars.

BERTA: Please, Deputy, I don't have a car. Can you give me a ride over to my mother-in-law's so I can borrow the money?

DANNY: Berta, ellos no tienen dinero.[1]

BERTA: Deputy, please, can't you give him another break? Can't it wait until morning?

DANNY: Berta, ¡cállate! ¡Deja de rogar![2] [*The* DEPUTY *leads* DANNY *away to the squad car.*]

ROWENA: What happened then?

BERTA: The Deputy put Danny in the squad car and asked me if he could come into the house.

DEPUTY: I have some search warrants.

BERTA: He never showed them to me. And he went in the house and looked in the cabinets, in my kitchen, and stove, and in the bed . . . under the bed. Meanwhile, I was getting some clothes for Danny.

ROWENA: Can you tell us how Danny was dressed?

BERTA: Gray T-shirt, brown pants, brown shoes, black socks.

ROWENA: Did he have the shoes on when he left the house?

BERTA: No, he asked me to get them as he sat handcuffed in the squad car. That and some cigarettes. I had to light it for him. And I also put his shoes on but I didn't have time to tie them.

ROWENA: Mrs. Rosales, I will hand you what has been identified as "State's Exhibit Number 1." Would you look at that please?

BERTA: This is my husband's shoe that I put on him that night.

ROWENA: And when was the last time you saw that shoe?

BERTA: When I found it the next morning next to a pool of blood on the Old Alamo School Road.

ROWENA: Now then, getting back to this stereo and TV, how long had they been in your house?

BERTA: They had been there barely one day, since early Sunday morning.

ROWENA: And how did Danny bring them to the house?

BERTA: He and Kiki brought them in Kiki's car.

---

1. They don't have money.　　　　　　　　2. Berta, shut up! Stop begging!

ROWENA: Who is Kiki?

BERTA: Kiki, Kiki Ventura. He used to be a friend of Danny's. They came into the house just before dawn. [As DANNY *and* KIKI *enter.*] Danny! Where have you been? It's almost morning. I've been worried to death about you.

DANNY: Wouldn't you know it, Kiki's car broke down. We spent all night fixing it.

BERTA: Your hands are dirty. ¿Quieres algo de comer?³ Go wash up. I'll make some chorizo con huevos. Is that Kiki out there? Every time I see him, he's got a different car.

DANNY: Yeah, that's Kiki all right. The Chicano Robin Hood. Entrale, Kiki, Berta's not going to bite your head off.

KIKI: That's what the black widow spider said to her viejo.⁴

BERTA: And why is Kiki the Chicano Robin Hood?

KIKI: Because I take from the rich Gringos and give to the poor Chicanos like me. Hey man, come on, I'm tired. Where do you wanna put the you-know-what?

DANNY: Shhhh!

BERTA: What are you two whispering about?

KIKI: The new stereo and TV. It's a surprise.

DANNY: It was.

BERTA: New stereo and TV!

DANNY: I rented them from a store in Dallas.

BERTA: Are you sure Señor Hood here didn't rip them off? Where did you get the money?

DANNY: Don't worry, viejita, I didn't use any of the money for la renta or la comida. This is extra feria⁵ I made picking watermelons.

KIKI: Hey, at least he didn't get it picking pockets, hey Berta?

DANNY: Kiki, go get the stuff, will you!

KIKI: Okay. Hey, Berta. ¡No te agüites!⁶ [*Exiting.*]

BERTA: Danny, I could have paid off the doctor's bill with that money. Give me the receipt, I'll ride back to Dallas con la comadre⁷ and take it back.

DANNY: Everybody else has a TV, Berta, why can't we? Ah, I haven't got it. I must have left it at the store.

BERTA: Danny, you've got to start saving your receipts, how else are we going to know how much money we spent!

DANNY: Berta!

BERTA: Danny, we'll never get out of the mess we're in unless we save and sacrifice! Si cada día nos endeudamos más y más⁸—those debts will drag us under.

DANNY: I know you're right, it's just that everything was going so good and then . . . I got laid off. You know, all my life, we never had a TV. I used to watch color TV with this little gabachito⁹ friend. His mother would make me a roast beef sandwich. She used to say, "You probably don't get to eat roast beef at your house, do you?"

---

3. Do you want something to eat?
4. Old man.
5. Money.
6. Don't get depressed!

7. With the godmother.
8. If every day we get deeper and deeper in debt.
9. *Gabachito*: little gringo.

BERTA: All right, mi amor, keep the TV for a month, but what do we need a stereo for?

DANNY: That's the surprise. I know how much you like your música ranchera. I couldn't get something for me without getting something for you también.

BERTA: Danny, you could talk me into anything!

KIKI: [*Entering.*] Hey man, why don't you talk that stereo and TV into walking in here! Come on, that stuff is heavy . . .

ROWENA: Mrs. Rosales, I want you to tell the jury, was Danny telling the truth about having rented the stereo and TV from a firm in Dallas?

BERTA: Yes, he was. My husband didn't steal anything. He died for nothing. He was murdered!

HAROLD: Your Honor, I object. The witness is assuming that a murder has been committed.

JUDGE: Mrs. Rosales, please confine your comments to the questions at hand.

ROWENA: I would like to offer this receipt as evidence to be labeled "State's Exhibit 2."

HAROLD: I ask that the Court verify that receipt for its authenticity.

ROWENA: No further questions. Your witness, Mr. Pearl.

HAROLD: Tell us, your husband, or boyfriend, or the man you were living with, did he have a job?

BERTA: Danny had just gotten laid off from construction work.

HAROLD: What kind of education did he have?

BERTA: He went as far as the sixth grade. He quit school to go to work in the fields. His family was very poor.

HAROLD: According to his school records, Danny Rosales was a truant who was constantly in trouble, was he not?

ROWENA: I object, irrelevant and immaterial.

HAROLD: I will show the relevancy, your Honor.

JUDGE: Overruled. Answer the questions, Mrs. Rosales.

BERTA: My husband was in trouble because nobody understood him. He spoke only Spanish until he was ten. So they put him in a school for backwards children.

HAROLD: Even in his later years, wasn't your husband in constant trouble with the law?

BERTA: Only because the Sheriff was always hassling and picking on him.

HAROLD: Take a look at this photograph. Is this a fair and accurate representation of what he looked like, Danny Rosales?

BERTA: Yes, it is. But I don't know when these pictures were taken.

HAROLD: You don't? You weren't with him? What does it say here?

BERTA: "Arroyo County . . ."

HAROLD: "Arroyo County Sheriff's Department." He was charged with burglary.

ROWENA: Your Honor, again, I object, irrelevant and immaterial.

HAROLD: I will show the relevancy.

JUDGE: Overruled. But please get to the point, Mr. Pearl.

HAROLD: Now then, *Mrs.* Rosales, isn't it a fact that your *husband* was sentenced to three years' probation for burglary?

BERTA: I told you that Danny . . .

HAROLD: I would like a simple yes or no in response to my questions. Was he sentenced to three years' probation for burglary?

BERTA: Yes, he was.

HAROLD: Wasn't he picked up for questioning about other robberies?

BERTA: Yes.

ROWENA: Your Honor, I object, Danny Rosales is not on trial here, Fred Hall is!

HAROLD: I am establishing that Mr. Rosales had a criminal record and therefore my client had every right to question him.

JUDGE: Overruled.

ROWENA: Note my objection to the ruling.

HAROLD: Now then, Mrs. Rosales, isn't it true that your husband sold but did not deliver a calf just one month before his death?

BERTA: Yes! But he didn't steal the calf. And he didn't steal the stereo and TV. And even if he had, that was no reason to kill him!

HAROLD: Mrs. Rosales, let's go back to the night your husband was arrested. You said that the Deputy came and handcuffed your husband and put him in the squad car. What happened then?

BERTA: The Police Chief pulled up in his private car and they took him away.

HAROLD: Did you see anyone beat or push or mistreat your husband?

BERTA: No, I was in the house. It was too far away and it was dark.

HAROLD: No further questions.

BERTA: But they didn't take him to the jailhouse like they said they were . . . they took him in the opposite direction.

HAROLD: I have no further questions. You may be excused. [BERTA *exits.*]

ROWENA: I would now like to call Steve Peters to the stand.

BAILIFF: Raise your right hand. Do you swear to tell the truth, the whole truth, and nothing but the truth, so help you God?

STEVE: I do.

ROWENA: State your name, please.

STEVE: Steve Earl Peters.

ROWENA: What is your relationship to Mr. Hall?

STEVE: His daughter and I are engaged to be married.

ROWENA: Why would your future father-in-law involve you in the shooting of Danny Rosales?

STEVE: I was just keeping him company.

ROWENA: You were what?

STEVE: A lot of people ride around with their police friends in town. There ain't nothing else to do.

ROWENA: What were you doing on the night of September 14, 1975?

STEVE: I was at Mr. Hall's home drinking . . . iced tea . . . and watching television.

ROWENA: And what was the reason for your being there at that time?

STEVE: I was going to ask for his daughter's hand in marriage. But I didn't get a chance to, you see. He kept getting all these calls on his police radio. Boy, he was on duty twenty-four hours per day. For instance, the night before, I was with him on a stakeout hoping to catch this Danny Rosales transporting some stolen goods . . . [*Flashback.*]

FRED: Keep your eyes peeled for a '69 burgundy Mustang, Stevie, I don't want 'er slipping by us.

STEVE: Don'tcha worry, Chief, I got eyes like an eagle.

FRED: Where in the heck could they be? That stool pigeon said they'd be here three hours ago.

STEVE: Yeah, we sure been waiting here a long time. These skeeters are something else. Say, Chief, as long as we're waiting out here, doing nothing, how's about if I ask you a real personal question.

FRED: Wait a minute! What if they took the back road into town?

STEVE: Nah, this is the only direct road from Dallas. Now, I was thinking, I just got promoted to Assistant Manager of the Tasty Freeze. I got my pickup truck all paid off and I just saw this out-of-sight apartment near the Cielito Lindo mall . . .

FRED: Wait, that informer said tonight. But did he mean late night, early evening or even late afternoon? You know how they talk in Spanish— they say evening when they mean afternoon!

STEVE: Gee, Mr. Hall, you must want this guy awful bad to stay out here all night waiting for him.

FRED: I'll tell you, Stevie, this is the last time that two-bit thief is going to pull the wool over my eyes. Every time a house gets broken into, he's seen in the vicinity. But every time I go and pick him up for questioning, he's managed to dispose of the goods. Or else he's got a phony alibi. I'm sick and tired of chasing him.

STEVE: Are you sure this here informer is telling the truth?

FRED: He's been right on three different occasions. And we prosecuted all three times. You see, the man is a thief himself. But I got him under control. I even pay him out of my own back pocket.

STEVE: Well, sounds like you oughta teach that Rosales a lesson, Chief.

FRED: I will. I'll teach him a lesson he'll never forget.

STEVE: Say, Chief, if you don't mind my asking, how come you want me coming along with you on these stakeouts?

FRED: Well, Stevie, if you're going to be my son-in-law . . .

STEVE: Wow, Chief, do you really mean it?

FRED: But forget about that Tasty Freeze, Stevie, that's kid stuff. You need a job with a future, one that'll make a man out of you. [*Handing* STEVE *the shotgun.*]

STEVE: Oh, wow, you don't mean . . .

FRED: Why not law enforcement? I could use a new deputy. The one I have now ain't worth a damn.

STEVE: [*Pointing the shotgun at the audience.*] Will you show me how to use this? [*Fade out.*]

GRACE: [*At the home of* FRED HALL.] Debbie! Did you get those spots scrubbed away?

DEBBIE: Mother, I scoured until my fingers ached.

GRACE: You just have to scrub harder, dear.

DEBBIE: But I'm scraping the finish off the pan, which is why the food sticks to it.

GRACE: Nonsense, you polish it until it shines like a mirror. Then, someday, God willing, when you and Stevie have your own home, your kitchen will be as spic and span as mine. Your dishes will be washed after each meal, the table wiped off, the sink shiny white.

DEBBIE: Oh Mom, that's disgusting!

GRACE: What is, dear?

DEBBIE: That whole domestic scene. I mean, the Lord didn't create me to spend the rest of my life in a kitchen cooking for Mr. Stevie Peters, that's for sure.

GRACE: Debbie, darling, a woman's role is with her man. Why do you think Eve was made from the rib of Adam? Besides, aren't you kinda sweet on Stevie?

DEBBIE: Oh gee, it was strictly a high school romance. He was the quarterback of the football team. He's all right, I guess. But I don't want to spend the rest of my life with the manager of the Tasty Freeze.

GRACE: Don't worry, once he comes into this family, your Daddy'll set him straight.

DEBBIE: Mama, you don't understand. I want to go to school and have a career. I don't want to be a dumb old housewife all my life. Oh, don't get me wrong. I'm not putting you down. You just don't realize your own worth. Cooking and cleaning and raising kids is a full-time job and you don't even get paid for it.

GRACE: Debbie, of course I get paid. Not with a check, but with love. And who do you think bought this trailer home and everything in it? Including your little subcompact, young lady.

DEBBIE: Daddy did, of course. And I'm very grateful. I've seen the way some of these black and Mexican kids live and it just about breaks my heart. I guess what I'm trying to say is, I won't have time to be cooking and cleaning and taking care of kids because I'll be too busy working for me.

GRACE: Debbie, listen to me, I know for a fact that this very night Stevie is going to ask your father for your hand in marriage.

DEBBIE: Do you know what? I think weddings are silly. They're like the opposite of a funeral.

GRACE: Debbie, you're just nervous. But wait until you walk down that aisle, with the organ music and the assembled guests, in the eyes of God.

DEBBIE: God!

GRACE: Don't you use the Lord's name in vain! Honey, your Daddy and Stevie are home.

DEBBIE: [Out of hearing range.] Jesus Christ!

STEVE: Hi, Mrs. Hall!

GRACE: Hello, Stevie dear.

STEVE: Debbie, can I talk to you for a minute?

DEBBIE: [Going to her father.] How's my Lone Ranger?

FRED: Not too good, honey, Tonto and me let the wild injuns get away.

STEVE: Debbie.

DEBBIE: Did you play Tonto tonight, Stevie? Hey, do you know that "Tonto" means dumb in Spanish?

FRED: That's pretty funny, eh kimo sabe?

STEVE: Yeah. Hey Debbie, I gotta tell you something.

DEBBIE: What?

STEVE: Your Daddy said we could get married.

DEBBIE: Wonderful.

GRACE: What's the matter, Fred, are you all right?

FRED: I'm okay. Hand me my painkillers. I've been trying to catch this little weasel for days.

GRACE: Fred, forget it, stay home, this is your weekend off.

FRED: No, no, no. I got a hot tip from an informant. I got this character right between the crossbars. Any news from the police radio?

GRACE: Oh, can't we turn this off, even for one night? You're not going out again, you've been getting home so late. And that big bed gets awful cold with only one body warming it.

FRED: My painkillers. Get me my painkillers.

DEBBIE: I'll get 'em for you, Daddy.

GRACE: Debbie, there's a nice tall pitcher of iced tea in the refrigerator. Fix everybody a cold glass.

STEVE: What's the matter with the Chief?

GRACE: He ain't been the same ever since that shoot-out with the two blacks in the liquor store. Did you know that he was wounded three times?

STEVE: I never heard the whole story.

GRACE: Fred was on patrol when he noticed this suspicious looking car parked out in front of Del's Liquor Store. As he went up to the front door two colored guys ran out.

FRED: One went left and one went right. The one on the left I caught and handcuffed. Just then I noticed a colored lady in the car. I ordered her out and was trying to get help through the dispatcher when the other colored guy came up behind me and stuck a knife to my throat.

GRACE: The first colored fellow that Fred had apprehended started hitting him on the head with a rock and with the handcuffs.

FRED: I kind of went semi-conscious and hit the ground as one of them started shooting at me. I rolled over and over on the floor to avoid being shot.

GRACE: They shot him three times.

FRED: Here, I'll show you.

GRACE: No, Fred, please, don't take off your shirt again!

DEBBIE: Oh, Daddy!

GRACE: [At the witness stand.] And that is why my husband has to take painkillers to this day.

HAROLD: What kind of painkillers does Fred take?

GRACE: Valium and percodan.

HAROLD: Have you noticed anything unusual about your husband since this unfortunate accident occurred?

GRACE: I've noticed that his memory has gotten bad. He has also been depressed, moody and given to fits of bad temper.

HAROLD: How long have you been married to the defendant?

GRACE: For twenty-two years.

HAROLD: Anything else about your husband involving his line of work?

GRACE: He tended to do things that were risky, extra risky. If he thought he was going into some dangerous place to apprehend a criminal or if there might be other people there, he would go in and do it. Or if there was a traffic offender on the highway, he would address them while they sat in their car, a practice which is considered dangerous. He said he felt that he didn't care whether any of these people might shoot him or not. And one day he told me he looked forward to being killed in the line of duty.

HAROLD: Anything else, Mrs. Hall? I know that this is painful, but we've got to get this out so everybody will know what kind of condition your husband was in.

GRACE: Well, he became very cold towards me in our personal relationship. It's not that he didn't love me, I could feel that, it's just that he stopped becoming intimate with me. After Fred almost died in that shootout, he said he wanted to rededicate himself to his career in law. He saw himself as someone saving the community from violence, bringing Christ to couples who got into marital conflicts, and ridding the community of drug addicts and thieves so that his children and grandchildren could grow up in a decent community.

ROWENA: Your Honor, I am going to object to this. Didn't we go over this material during the Sanity Hearing?

JUDGE: Sustained.

HAROLD: Thank you, Mrs. Hall, thank you for telling us what kind of a husband and father Fred Hall is. Your witness, Ms. Saldivar.

ROWENA: I have no questions at this time.

JUDGE: You may step down, Mrs. Hall.

BERTA: Aren't you going to question her? She made him out to be a saint.

ROWENA: This is not the time, Berta. We'll get to her and her daughter later.

BERTA: Why didn't they charge her with murder? She helped him to bury Danny's body!

ROWENA: Siéntate,[1] Berta, please, you're making it worse for our case.

HAROLD: I would now like to call Kiki Ventura to the stand. [*Enter* KIKI.]

BAILIFF: Do you swear to tell the truth, the whole truth, and nothing but the truth, so help you God?

KIKI: Yeah, I guess so.

JUDGE: You mean, "yes," don't you, Mr. Ventura?

KIKI: Yes, sir.

HAROLD: Please state your name, age and occupation.

KIKI: Enrique Ventura. But everybody calls me Kiki. I'm almost thirty years old and, uh, what else did you ask me?

HAROLD: Your occupation.

KIKI: Yeah, well, right now, I'm unemployed.

HAROLD: Mr. Ventura, what was your relationship to the deceased, Danny Rosales?

KIKI: He was my friend.

HAROLD: You were also a business associate of Mr. Rosales, were you not? Didn't you move different items of furniture and things like that from one county to another?

KIKI: Nah, nothing like that.

HAROLD: Mr. Ventura, is it not a proven fact that you have quite an extensive criminal record?

KIKI: Yes, but that was in the past, I don't do that anymore. Ask my parole officer.

1. Sit down

HAROLD: You and Danny were just good drinking buddies, huh?

KIKI: Yeah, we would pop a few cold cans of what they call Colorado kool ade.

HAROLD: Now then, Mr. Ventura, were you ever involved in the sale of narcotics?

KIKI: I refuse to answer that on the grounds that it might incriminal me.

HAROLD: Mr. Ventura, just answer my question, yes or no.

KIKI: Don't I have the right to talk to my lawyers?

JUDGE: Answer the questions, Mr. Ventura.

KIKI: Yes, but I served my time.

HAROLD: Now then, isn't it also a fact that you and Mr. Rosales sold a calf and then did not deliver it?

KIKI: No, no, that's not true! Danny sold that calf, not me. No, you can't pin that on me. It was Danny. [*Flashback.*]

DANNY: Kiki, when am I going to get the feria? The farmer wants his money back.

KIKI: Shit, Danny, I'm kind of broke right now. All I got is half a kilo of grass. Acapulco Gold. Worth about $200. You want it?

DANNY: No, I don't.

KIKI: You could sell it to some Gringo college student for $300 easy.

DANNY: I'm not dealing any dope.

KIKI: Well then, let's smoke it!

DANNY: I'm through getting wasted.

KIKI: Hey man, are you turning into a Boy Scout?

DANNY: No, but I'm going to start using my head to think, instead of using it to beat my brains against the wall.

KIKI: What are you going to do, man, go to college or something?

DANNY: Yeah, what's wrong with that? I'm going to get my G.E.D. and then go to the junior college.

KIKI: Come on, man, you been talking to your old lady again? She's been telling you how you could have been a brain surgeon!

DANNY: No, Kiki, I've been talking to myself. And I've decided that twenty-six years old is too old to be playing in the streets, man. I don't want to give Berta a bunch of kids just to watch them do a rerun of my own life. No ves,[2] I'm sick of being poor and of the alcohol and of the food stamps.

KIKI: Hey, well excuse me! What are you gonna do, go live with the Gringos in their part of town?

DANNY: No, but I'm not going to live like a punk kid, either.

KIKI: Simón vato,[3] you do your own thing. [*Turning to go.*] Later.

DANNY: Hey, Kiki, we're still friends, que no?

KIKI: Sure . . .

DEPUTY: [*Entering.*] Which one of you is Danny Rosales?

KIKI: He is.

DEPUTY: I'm Deputy Davis. I have a warrant for your arrest on the charge that you sold but did not deliver a calf. A farmer named Kramer signed the complaint.

---

2. *Ves:* don't you see.                    3. Yes, bro (brother).

KIKI: Hay te watcho,[4] Danny . . .

DANNY: Wait a minute, Kiki, you got some explaining to do.

DEPUTY: No, I think you better start explaining, Rosales.

DANNY: Well, you see, Deputy, I couldn't deliver the calf because Kiki here took it and killed it.

KIKI: Yeah, I killed it, but it was an accident, an emergency.

DEPUTY: An accident?

KIKI: Well, you see, I was trying to fatten it up for him. It was a little underweight, so my Abuelita[5] says to me, "Kiki, that calf looks a little sickly, maybe you should feed it some of this special grain." So I did. A week passes, three weeks passes. One day I wake up and, boom, the calf is patas para arriba,[6] dead. I was feeding it locoweed by mistake. You don't believe me?

DANNY: Tell him what you did with it, Kiki.

KIKI: I ate it.

DEPUTY: Look, whatever the reason, Rosales, you are still responsible. So, when are you going to give Farmer Kramer his money back?

DANNY: I already gave half of it back last week. And I'm going to give him another fifty tonight. I promise to pay back every penny.

DEPUTY: Why should I believe you?

DANNY: Because I don't want to go to jail. Also, if I'm in jail I can't work. And if I can't work, I'll never pay him back.

DEPUTY: That's a good point. I'll tell you what, if you promise to pay $50 a week until you pay off the entire amount, I won't take you in.

DANNY: Thanks a lot, Deputy.

KIKI: Hey man, I wish all the chotas[7] could be like you!

DEPUTY: I don't want to lock you up, Rosales, but if you miss just one payment . . .

DANNY: Don't worry, I won't. Thanks for the break, Deputy!

KIKI: Orale pues![8] Lemme show you the Chicano handshake. [*Going to the* DEPUTY.]

DEPUTY: [*Ignoring* KIKI.] Don't let me down, Rosales. [*Goes to witness stand.*]

KIKI: Pinche[9] pig!

DANNY: Ya ves, Kiki. My luck is changing already! Pero now you know how much I really need that money.

KIKI: Don't worry, you'll get it, you'll get every bit of it. [*Exits.*]

ROWENA: Deputy Davis, can you tell us what happened that Sunday night when you went to arrest Danny Rosales at his home?

DEPUTY: Chief Hall had left instructions for me to serve that theft warrant charge against Rosales.

ROWENA: And when you arrest someone you routinely call into the dispatcher, do you not?

DEPUTY: Yes, Ma'am.

ROWENA: That must have been how Fred Hall knew you were arresting Danny Rosales at exactly 10:30 P.M.

DEPUTY: Yes, that is the only way he could have known.

---

4. See you later.
5. Little grandmother.
6. Legs upside down.

7. Policemen.
8. Okay!
9. Fucking.

ROWENA: In other words, Chief Hall used the misdemeanor theft warrant as an excuse to take Danny out to the Old Alamo School Road to beat him up and shoot him.

HAROLD: Your Honor, I object to this line of questioning.

JUDGE: Sustained! Miss Saldivar, this court is interested in facts, not assumptions. [*Flashback.*]

DEPUTY: That's a might nice stereo and TV you got there, pardner. Maybe you should have used that money to finish paying off that farmer.

DANNY: But I only missed one payment.

DEPUTY: Danny, you have the right to remain silent. You have the right to an attorney. Anything you say may be used against you.

ROWENA: What happened after you read the suspect his rights and searched the house?

DEPUTY: I was getting ready to take him in when Fred Hall pulled up in his private car.

DEPUTY: Okay, Danny, let's go.

FRED: [*Entering.*] Was the stolen stereo and TV in the house, Davis?

DANNY: Stolen?

DEPUTY: Yes, it was. Who is that with you, Fred?

FRED: None of your damn business. All right, Rosales, where did an unemployed Mexican like you who lives in a broken-down shack like this, which ain't even got a telephone, get a brand new stereo and TV?

DANNY: I rented them in Dallas.

FRED: He rented them in Dallas. Huh. Have you got a receipt?

DANNY: No, I don't, you see, I . . .

FRED: You what! You what! [*Striking* DANNY.] Don't lie to me, boy!

DANNY: I'm telling the truth. I rented them from a store.

FRED: You lying piece of shit! [*Kicking* DANNY *to the floor.*] I've had just about enough of you! Stevie, gimme that shotgun. [*Jabbing* DANNY *with the shotgun.*] Now then, are you going to tell me the truth, are you going to confess? I'll kill you, boy!

DEPUTY: Come on, Danny, tell the truth. You don't want Chief Hall to get all upset, do you?

DANNY: I didn't do anything wrong.

FRED: Let the thieving son of a bitch go! Uncuff him and let him run so I can shoot him!

DANNY: I swear to you! I rented them from a store in Dallas.

FRED: I'm gonna kill you! I'm gonna kill you! [*Beating him.*]

DEPUTY: Hey, Fred, what the hell's got into you?

FRED: You lying to me, boy. You've been lying to me all along! But I got you this time . . . dead to rights.

DEPUTY: Take it easy, Fred.

FRED: Davis, put him in the squad car. Let's go to the Old Alamo School Road, maybe his tongue will loosen up along the way.

DEPUTY: Couldn't we just lock him up overnight and call the rental place in the morning?

FRED: Davis, how long you been a law enforcement officer in Arroyo County?

DEPUTY: Six months.

FRED: And you're the dumb son of a bitch who let him go in the first place. What are you, a social worker! I've been doing this for six years.

DEPUTY: But Fred, you can't be beating a prisoner like that.

FRED: I'm only trying to scare him into confessing. Now, play along with me. Tell him I'm going to shoot him if he doesn't tell the truth. I used to do this all the time in the Civilian Investigation Division.

DEPUTY: Okay, Fred, we'll try it your way.

FRED: I'll follow you in my car. And don't let him go this time. Asshole!

ROWENA: Then, you actually heard Fred Hall threaten to kill Danny Rosales? [*Back at the witness stand.*]

DEPUTY: Yes, I did.

ROWENA: How many times?

DEPUTY: At least five times.

ROWENA: Take note: Deputy Davis heard Fred Hall threaten to kill Danny Rosales at least five times that night. No further questions at this time. I pass the witness.

HAROLD: Deputy Davis, what was your exact title out there in Cortezville? Didn't you call yourself Assistant Chief Deputy?

DEPUTY: I believe the title was Deputy Chief of Police.

HAROLD: You had aspirations of becoming Chief of Police, did you not?

DEPUTY: Well, every police officer has ambitions of bettering himself.

HAROLD: You didn't get along with Chief Hall at all, did you?

DEPUTY: We weren't exactly the best of friends. But I never let this get in the way of our work.

HAROLD: Now, that night at the Rosales' home, when you asked Fred who he was with, why did he respond, "none of your damn business?"

DEPUTY: I guess I wasn't supposed to know.

HAROLD: Yet you just told me that in no way did your personal feelings for each other get in the way of your professional duties, is that right?

DEPUTY: Yes, sir.

HAROLD: Okay. Those threats he made to Danny Rosales, things like, "I'm going to kill you," and things of that nature, he told you that was just a bluff, did he not?

DEPUTY: He tried to convince me it was just a bluff.

HAROLD: But you had no reason to doubt that, did you?

DEPUTY: At that time, I had no reason, no, sir.

HAROLD: That was just a ploy to get information out of a suspected burglar, was it not?

DEPUTY: I don't approve of it.

HAROLD: He told you that this was an accepted tactic, this ploy or bluff, in the Civilian Investigation Division of the United States Air Force, did he not?

DEPUTY: He did, but I really wouldn't know about the legality of that.

HAROLD: You wouldn't know, would you? Were you ever enrolled in a police officer's training academy or anything of that sort prior to being hired in Cortezville?

DEPUTY: No, sir, I was not. But I plan to go, sir.

HAROLD: No further questions. I would now like to call Fred Hall to the stand.

BAILIFF: Raise your right hand. Do you swear to tell the truth, the whole truth, and nothing but the truth, so help you God?

FRED: I do.

HAROLD: Tell us your name please.

FRED:   Fred Harold Hall.

HAROLD:   Mr. Hall, I would like for you to tell the jury a little bit about your background, specifically your involvement with any previous police work.

FRED:   Well, I retired from the United States Air Force in 1969 after thirty years of service. I was a Senior Master Sergeant assigned to the Civilian Investigation Division.

HAROLD:   You also served in combat in World War II, the Korean Conflict, and the Vietnam Conflict . . .

ROWENA:   Immaterial and irrelevant.

JUDGE:   Sustained.

HAROLD:   Let's move on to another point. Back to the night of September 12, Friday. Do you recall receiving information from an informant?

FRED:   Yes, sir, it was information pertaining to Danny Rosales . . .

ROWENA:   Objection, hearsay.

HAROLD:   I'm not going into what the informant said, Your Honor, I just wanted to know if he was reliable.

JUDGE:   Proceed.

HAROLD:   Now then, was the informant reliable in the past?

FRED:   Yes, sir, in three different cases we got three different convictions.

HAROLD:   Now then, the outstanding theft warrant, that business about the calf. Why did you decide to activate that warrant against Rosales?

FRED:   I hoped to use it to stop a vehicle that was supposedly driven by Rosales and which supposedly contained stolen property.

HAROLD:   But you weren't out to "get" Rosales, were you?

FRED:   No, there were just all these trails leading to him.

HAROLD:   And did you ever make any disparaging remarks about Mexicans or Chicanos in general?

FRED:   No, I have a great deal of respect for Mexicans and I have many Mexican friends.

HAROLD:   Now then, that Sunday night, September 14th, why did you take your future son-in-law with you, besides just for the company?

FRED:   Well, I had been taking him along regularly, to show him what police work was like. But that particular night I asked him to come along in case I needed a witness in the event that Deputy Davis had erred. I wanted to show his error in police work because he had erred so badly in the past.

HAROLD:   All right, tell us what happened when you went to arrest Danny Rosales at his home.

FRED:   Well, as Stevie and I pulled into the driveway we saw the Deputy struggling to get Rosales into his squad car. [*Flashback.*]

DANNY:   God damn it, let me go!

DEPUTY:   I should have never given you a break, Rosales.

FRED:   Have you read the suspect his rights, Deputy?

DEPUTY:   Yes, sir.

FRED:   Good. Now, Danny, could you please tell us where you got the new stereo and television?

DEPUTY:   It's a Curtis Mathis.

DANNY:   ¡Qué chingaos te importa, pinche güey![1]

---

1. What the fuck do you care, sucker!

FRED: What did he say, Deputy?

DEPUTY: I don't know, Chief, but it don't sound too good.

FRED: Danny, I hate to do this, but I'm afraid we're going to have to take you down to the station.

DANN: You ain't taking me nowhere!

FRED: Put him in the squad car, Davis. Danny Rosales, are you resisting arrest?

DANNY: ¡Hijos de puta!² Police brutality!

FRED: Davis, why don't we take the long way to the jailhouse. Maybe Danny will calm down by the time we get there.

DEPUTY: Good idea, Chief. [*Blackout.*]

HAROLD: And so, you took him down to the Old Alamo School Road to try and talk to him on a personal level, sort of like how a father might relate to his son.

ROWENA: Your Honor, I object, the defense is leading the witness.

JUDGE: Objection sustained.

HAROLD: Very well, then, in your own words, tell us what happened that night.

FRED: The Deputy had left. Stevie was in the car. Rosales and I were by the side of the road. I was still trying to question him.

HAROLD: Now, as a result of this questioning, did he make any gestures towards you?

FRED: Yes, sir, he started coming closer to me and making threatening gestures and I had to push him back.

HAROLD: You had to protect yourself?

FRED: Yes, sir. He tried to grab a hold of the shotgun. But I wasn't going to let him have it, not if I could help it.

HAROLD: Show us how Rosales grabbed the shotgun.

FRED: Like this. He grabbed the barrel and tried to yank it away from me. Then he kicked me. At one point I was off my feet. I'd been kicked just above the pelvis. I was down on one knee.

HAROLD: Mr. Hall, tell us, did you have fear and apprehension for your life?

FRED: I certainly did. The thought flashed back in my mind how my gun had been taken away from me before and how I had been shot three times.

HAROLD: So here was this taller, younger, stronger man kicking you and trying to take your shotgun away. Go on.

ROWENA: Your Honor, the defense is leading the witness again.

JUDGE: Overruled. Continue!

ROWENA: Note my exception to the ruling.

FRED: Thinking about that earlier fight made me struggle all the further. It was dark, he tried to yank the gun away and it went off . . .

HAROLD: Yes . . .

FRED: Accidentally.

HAROLD: Mr. Hall, I want you to look the jury right in the eye. Did you intentionally pull the trigger of that shotgun, sir?

---

2. Bastards!

FRED:   As God is my witness, I never intended to pull the trigger and hurt that man!

HAROLD:   Ladies and gentlemen, I ask you, does this man sitting here look capable of murdering in cold blood?

BERTA:   He's lying! He's lying! He murdered Danny, he murdered him!

JUDGE:   Mrs. Rosales, sit down or I will be forced to remove you from this court.

BERTA:   He's a killer! You're going to let him get away with it!

JUDGE:   Order, order in this court! Bailiff, remove Mrs. Rosales!

ROWENA:   Your Honor, I see no need to have Mrs. Rosales physically removed from this court!

JUDGE:   Don't you raise your voice to me, Miss Saldivar! This court will recess for ten minutes.

ROWENA:   Your Honor, I have not yet cross-examined the witness!

JUDGE:   Court is recessed for ten minutes!

ROWENA:   Your Honor! I protest!

## Act II

JUDGE:   Miss Saldivar, before continuing the proceedings, I want it made perfectly clear that you are to refrain from any further outbursts in this court, is that understood.

ROWENA:   Your Honor, I apologize for having raised my voice in court.

JUDGE:   You may proceed, Miss Saldivar.

ROWENA:   Now then, Mr. Hall, how long did you work for the City of Cortezville as Chief of Police?

FRED:   Approximately six years.

ROWENA:   What was your salary at the time you were released?

FRED:   $450 per month.

ROWENA:   $450 per month. That's not very much for a family of three, is it?

HAROLD:   This is irrelevant, your Honor.

ROWENA:   I will show the relevancy.

JUDGE:   Proceed.

ROWENA:   You had to supplement your income with your pension from the Air Force, did you not?

FRED:   Yes, I did.

ROWENA:   Now, you never went to a professional police training academy prior to being hired by the City of Cortezville, did you?

FRED:   No, I did not.

ROWENA:   And when you worked for the Civilian Investigation Division of the Air Force, you were a clerk, were you not?

FRED:   Yes, but I . . .

ROWENA:   You only worked for them for two years in a clerical capacity, according to your records. Isn't it a fact that the Air Force stationed you at many different jobs in different places during your thirty-year stint?

FRED:   Yes, it was.

ROWENA:   Isn't it a fact that small Texas towns hire retired servicemen because they are the only ones who can afford to take the relatively low-paying jobs?

HAROLD:   That is not a fact, that is an assumption.

JUDGE: Sustained. The jury will ignore that assumption.

ROWENA: Now then, Mr. Hall, in spite of the fact that you had no formal training in police work, you claim that you performed your duties as police chief according to the letter of the law, correct?

FRED: As to the best of my ability.

ROWENA: Then why did you take Danny Rosales to a deserted country road five miles outside of town to interrogate him? Why didn't you take him to your office inside the police station?

FRED: I took him out there because I had every intention of letting him go. I just did it to scare him.

ROWENA: While you were out there in that woodsy, rural area, did you notice any houses?

FRED: Yes, I did.

ROWENA: There were houses. Is that the reason you didn't want any lights turned on?

FRED: I don't recall that.

ROWENA: You don't recall that?

FRED: No.

ROWENA: You don't recall asking Steve Peters where you could bury the body before it even got cold?

FRED: No, I don't.

ROWENA: You don't recall talking to your wife about taking the body to east Texas?

FRED: No, I don't.

ROWENA: Do you mean to tell the ladies and gentlemen of this jury that you don't recall driving around town with the body in the back seat of your automobile?

FRED: No, I don't.

ROWENA: Your Honor, please instruct the witness to answer the questions!

JUDGE: Mr. Hall, I don't need to remind you that you are under oath. Do you or do you not remember what happend that night?

FRED: Your Honor, I can't recall anything that happened after the gun went off. My mind is a total blank.

HAROLD: Your Honor, if I may interject a word here. Mrs. Hall testified earlier regarding my client's loss of memory due to the trauma of the wounds which he suffered in that shoot-out.

ROWENA: I insist that the witness answer my questions in full!

HAROLD: Your Honor, competent physicians have testified that the defendant, Fred Hall, has Alzheimer's Disease or pre-senile dementia. He is a sick man, your Honor.

JUDGE: Mr. Hall, I want you to answer the questions to the best of your ability. Proceed, Miss Saldivar.

ROWENA: All right, let's talk about this so-called beating on your head, Mr. Hall. Did you have any x-rays taken?

FRED: No, I did not.

ROWENA: You mean to say that the doctors didn't think it was important to take x-rays of your head and yet you claim that this is the cause of your amnesia five years later?

FRED: The bullet wounds to my body were the more serious. The problems with my head turned up later.

ROWENA: Now, you testified, and I quote, "as God is my witness, I did not intend to kill that man." How come your thoughts are so clear on that point, yet on other points, points that are damaging to your case, you can't recall.

FRED: Well, as I indicated, my thoughts, even right now, are real scrambled because of the medication I am obliged to take. But I truly believe that it was an accident.

ROWENA: You believe it was an accident. Are you saying you don't know for sure?

FRED: I am saying that the whole thing has gone all kinds of ways through my mind. I even dream about it. I can't actually say yes or no and be positive one way or another, but this is what I feel in my heart.

ROWENA: You only recall the things that you think will help you, but you don't recall the things you think will hurt, right?

FRED: No, that is not correct.

ROWENA: That's what it sounds like to me, Mr. Hall!

HAROLD: I will object to her arguing with the witness, Your Honor.

JUDGE: Disregard the statement, "it sounds like it."

ROWENA: Very well, Mr. Hall, you may step down. Let me call some witnesses who will help you refresh your memory. I would like to recall Steve Earl Peters to the stand. [*Enter* STEVE.] Steve, do you know what an indictment is?

STEVE: That is when someone is charged with a crime.

ROWENA: Are you charged with a crime now by indictment?

STEVE: Yes, I am.

ROWENA: Do you also understand that you are still under oath and that perjury is a punishable offense?

HAROLD: Your Honor, I object, the Prosecution is intimidating the witness.

JUDGE: Objection sustained. Watch your line of questioning, counsel.

ROWENA: Steve, let's go back to that weekend at the home of Fred Hall, prior to Danny Rosales' arrest. [*Flashback.*]

STEVE: Well, we got back from the stakeout late Saturday night. We all sat down and had a cold drink. Of course, I was so excited I could hardly wait to tell Debbie about the wedding.

DEBBIE: Hi, Daddy!

STEVE: Hey, honey pie, guess what! I talked to your Dad!

DEBBIE: Oh, Stevie, you didn't!

STEVE: He said we could get married!

DEBBIE: Wonderful!

FRED: This calls for a drink.

GRACE: Have you set a date for the wedding?

ROWENA: [*From the side.*] How many drinks did you have, Steve?

STEVE: Oh, about three or four. Debbie, I'm going to make you the happiest woman alive!

ROWENA: Exactly what were you drinking?

STEVE: Margaritas! Margaritas! We drank until dawn. How many kids do you want to have?

DEBBIE: Oh, Stevie, lots and lots!

ROWENA: What did you do when you got up?

STEVE: We had some lunch. Then we started drinking again.

ROWENA: Was Fred drinking margaritas that day?

STEVE: No, not margaritas, iced tea! He was drinking iced tea.

ROWENA: You're under oath, Steve.

STEVE: Yes, he was drinking margaritas.

ROWENA: All night and all day and then that night again?

STEVE: Yes.

ROWENA: What kind of condition was he in?

STEVE: He wasn't drunk or anything, he could really hold his liquor.

ROWENA: Was Fred Hall consuming anything other than margaritas that weekend?

GRACE: Fred, what are you doing? You know the doctor told you not to drink and take painkillers at the same time. [*Fadeout.*]

ROWENA: In other words, ladies and gentlemen of the jury, Fred Hall was taking painkillers and washing them down with margaritas for two days prior to Danny Rosales' arrest. And now, Steve, tell us what happened when you pulled into Rosales' driveway that night.

STEVE: The Chief got out of the car and arrested Danny.

ROWENA: Did he beat him?

STEVE: Yeah, I guess so.

ROWENA: Brutally?

HAROLD: Objection.

JUDGE: Sustained.

ROWENA: Did you participate in that beating?

STEVE: Heck no, I was just holding the shotgun.

ROWENA: Did you point the shotgun at Danny Rosales?

STEVE: No! In fact, the Chief took the gun away from me and pointed it at Danny's head.

ROWENA: Is that when Hall threatened to kill Rosales?

STEVE: Yes. We were out by the Old Alamo School Road waiting for Davis to bring the prisoner. [*Flashback.*] Hey, Chief, how come you hit that Meskin so hard?

FRED: You see, Stevie, when you're dealing with these people you gotta be real firm. This [*Holding shotgun.*] is the only language they understand. You gotta get 'em to respect you. And to do that you gotta put the fear a God in 'em.

STEVE: He looked *real* scared. I'll bet he'll come around to talking any minute.

FRED: I'll tell you something, these damn people breed like rabbits and end up having fifteen kids and living on welfare. I don't know how they do it. Before long they'll outnumber us. What we oughta do is deport them. Don't make no difference if they was born here or not. Now this particular guy here is the worst of the lot. Did I tell you that I seen him eyeing Debbie?

STEVE: Eyeing her? What do you mean, eyeing her?

FRED: He was following her around. One time, after I dropped her off at the bus station, I got back in the car and as the bus was pulling away I saw her waving to me. Rosales was sitting next to her, grinning at me.

STEVE: That damn chile dipper!

FRED: [*To the* DEPUTY *as he brings* DANNY *in.*] Well, it's about time you got here! We've been waiting half the night. Now, for the last time, where did you get that stereo and TV?

DANNY:   Mr. Hall, you are making a big mistake. I rented them from a store in Dallas.

FRED:   You lying son of a bitch! [*Striking* DANNY.] Unhandcuff him. Davis, let him run so I can shoot him!

DEPUTY:   Hey, come on, Fred that's enough!

FRED:   I said unhandcuff him! That's an order!

DEPUTY:   All right, let me have the flashlight here so I can see what I am doing.

FRED:   No, no flashlight. I don't want no lights.

DEPUTY:   [*Down on his knees trying to unhandcuff* DANNY.]   But I can't see to get the handcuffs off him.

FRED:   Steve, close that door! I don't want no car lights, no flashlights, no cigarettes. I killed me a Meskin before and I am fixing to kill me another one.

DEPUTY:   There, I got the handcuffs off of him. Now what are you going to do?

FRED:   Go back to Cortezville, Davis.

DEPUTY:   Fred, stop this shit, it ain't working!

FRED   I'm taking over now!

DEPUTY:   But he's my prisoner!

FRED:   [*Threatening the* DEPUTY *with the shotgun.*]   Fuck you! Now, git! [DEPUTY *exits the murder scene and walks into another space, pacing.*] Now then, Mr. Rosales . . . [*Leading* DANNY *aside.*]

ROWENA:   [*Her voice.*]   What was going through your mind when the police chief threatened you with the shotgun and told you to go back to Cortezville?

DEPUTY:   [*As though he were testifying or thinking out loud.*]   Being relatively new on the job and all, I was thinking that maybe he was trying to put me through some kind of test or play some kind of game to see how sharp I was. He had mentioned several times before that he was going to test me to see if I was good enough to stay in the department.

ROWENA:   So you disobeyed his order? [*Her voice.*]

DEPUTY:   Yes. I had the feeling, an intuition, that something was wrong. I drove about 200 yards or so down the road, cut the radio and lights off, and sat there about two or three minutes. That's when I heard what sounded like a shot. [*Shot is heard.*]

ROWENA:   [*Voice.*]   Now, Steve, you were in the car. Could you see what was happening out there?

STEVE:   Pretty well. The moon was pretty bright that night. They were standing behind the car, two or three feet away from each other, talking back and forth. Mr. Hall pushed him with the butt of the gun and then with the barrel of the gun.

ROWENA:   What did Danny Rosales do?

STEVE:   He pushed the barrel of the gun away. Mr. Hall went towards him and then I heard the shot.

ROWENA:   [*Voice.*]   Did you see what happened?

STEVE:   No, they were in my blind spot. [*To* FRED] What was that? Fred! Fred!

FRED:   He wrestled with the gun, Stevie. It went off . . . and it killed him.

STEVE:   Jesus, what are you going to do now?

FRED: I don't know, it was an accident, but nobody will ever believe me.

STEVE: Let's get the hell outa here!

FRED: Wait. There's a light! Somebody's coming. Move away from here. [*They walk in the direction of the* DEPUTY.]

DEPUTY: What happened? I heard a shot. Fred, where's Rosales? I want to know right now, the bullshit's over.

FRED: Stevie, uh, get back in the car. Come here, Davis, I want to tell you something.

DEPUTY: Just cut the bullshit, Fred. What's going on? Where's Rosales?

FRED: If you just shut up, I'll tell you. Well, Davis, I, uh, killed him!

DEPUTY: You what? How did you do it? What happened, where is he?

FRED: No, I didn't kill him. I was just blowing smoke at you. I just winged him is all.

DEPUTY: Where did you "wing" him?

FRED: Right up here, under the left armpit. But hey, he's all right.

DEPUTY: What the hell are you talking about?

FRED: I was just joking.

DEPUTY: I said cut the bullshit. What did you do to Rosales?

FRED: I'll tell you the truth. He tripped me and I fell. That's when the gun went off accidentally. Then he ran away.

DEPUTY: Which way did he go?

FRED: He ran into the woods. He's all right. I just scared him.

DEPUTY: God damn it! You better tell me the truth, Fred.

FRED: I am. Look for yourself. This is the spot where he took off from. If he's here, he'd be in that ditch.

DEPUTY: Come on down here, help me look. [FRED *makes no effort to look.*]

FRED: Is he there?

DEPUTY: I don't see anything.

FRED: He's probably on his way home right now.

DEPUTY: Are you telling me the truth? Why did you tell me you killed him?

FRED: I was just testing you to see how you would handle a situation like this. Say, now, what would you tell the Sheriff's Office? He was supposed to have been at the county jail twenty minutes ago.

DEPUTY: I don't know, what am I supposed to tell them?

FRED: Well, you could call the dispatcher and tell him that your prisoner escaped somewhere off Highway 90.

DEPUTY: Now, what in the hell am I going to do that for? In the first place, we're not anywhere near Highway 90. In the second place, you had charge of the prisoner.

FRED: You're a jerk, do you know that? You're never gonna make it around this police department or any other police department. When a superior officer gives you an order you obey it!

DEPUTY: Look, first you told me you shot the man, then you told me you didn't. And then you told me something else. I don't know whether to believe you or not. But let me tell you something, I'm not going to lie for you or anybody else.

FRED: Okay. Go on, get out of here.

DEPUTY: I'll see you back at the County Jail, *Chief.* [DEPUTY *exits, goes to the stand.*]

HAROLD:   Now then, Deputy Davis, if you were so certain that Chief Hall killed Danny Rosales, why didn't you arrest him right then and there?

DEPUTY:   I couldn't find the body so I couldn't prove anything.

HAROLD:   Did you actually see Fred Hall shoot Danny Rosales?

DEPUTY:   No, but I heard . . .

HAROLD:   You were two hundred yards away in your squad car. How did you know what was going on out there? Just answer yes or no. Did you see Hall shoot Rosales?

DEPUTY:   No, sir.

HAROLD:   One more question: were you granted immunity from prosecution by the State of Texas?

DEPUTY:   Yes, sir, I was.

HAROLD:   So, in return for this immunity you have agreed to come forward with the most damaging testimony you can think of to bury Fred Hall, isn't that right?

DEPUTY:   No, sir, that's not right. The statement I made was written four months before I was granted immunity.

HAROLD:   The District Attorney didn't come along at that time and tell you, "Now, if you behave and be a good boy and tell us what we want to hear, you won't get prosecuted," right?

DEPUTY:   No, sir, that's not true. I made an oath at the very beginning to uphold the laws of the State of Texas. That's exactly what I told Mrs. Rosales when she came looking for her husband at the police station the night he was killed. [*Flashback*.]

BERTA:   Deputy, where's my husband? They say they haven't seen him at the booking desk and it's way past midnight?

DEPUTY:   I honestly don't know where he is, Mrs. Rosales.

BERTA:   What do you mean? You arrested him two hours ago.

DEPUTY:   Mrs. Rosales, there's nothing I can tell you right now, believe me. If any information comes in you'll be the first to know. Now, if you'll excuse me, there's some problems here at the jail, seems like there's a riot going on or something.

BERTA:   You expect us to be treated like this? You arrest my husband and say you're going to take him to jail and he's nowhere to be found!

DEPUTY:   Please, I'm trying to do everything I can to find out what happened to your husband.

BERTA:   No you're not, what do you care? To you Danny is just another Mexican.

DEPUTY:   That's not true, Mrs. Rosales. Less than a month ago I gave Danny a break, not because he was brown or green or any other color, but because I believed he'd live up to his word.

BERTA:   Where's my husband? Is he hurt? Tell me where to look for him.

DEPUTY:   Why don't you ask his *friend*, Kiki Ventura.

BERTA:   I don't care about him, all I care about is what's happened to Danny.

DEPUTY:   You better care. The only difference between Kiki and Judas is that Judas hung himself.[3] But I promise you one thing, everybody's going to get what's coming to them, everybody.

3. According to the New Testament, Judas Iscariot was one of Jesus' 12 Apostles. His betrayal of Jesus to the Roman authorities led to Jesus' crucifixion. However, biblical Books differ as to how Judas died.

DEBBIE: [*Back at the witness stand,* DEBBIE *has been sworn in and has begun her testimony.*] It was late, but Mama and I were sitting up talking . . . Mama, what are you doing up so late?

GRACE: Waiting for your father and reading the Good Book.

DEBBIE: Oh, how exciting.

GRACE: It is dear, it's the best-seller of all time.

DEBBIE: I thought "Gone with the Wind"[4] was.

GRACE: Do you want to know what passage I was reading?

DEBBIE: Sure.

GRACE: 1 Corinthians 6:19. "Know ye not that your body is the temple of the Holy Spirit?"

DEBBIE: Oh, Mama, not again.

GRACE: The Bible says that thou shalt not defile the body with immorality. Debbie, does Stevie ever touch you?

DEBBIE: Of course he touches me, he touches me all the time.

GRACE: Debbie, you know what I mean. Does he touch you . . . you know, where he shouldn't?

DEBBIE: Of course not, I wouldn't let him touch me there.

GRACE: I know he kisses you good night, because I've seen the two of you on the front porch, but does he ever, I don't know how to say this . . . does he ever stick his tongue in your mouth!

DEBBIE: Oh, Mama! Of course not!

GRACE: I know you're a good girl, Debbie, I just want to make sure you save yourself for your wedding night.

DEBBIE: Mama, you know something, I just made up my mind this very night! There ain't gonna be no wedding!

GRACE: Debbie, you can't be serious. We told all our friends and relatives. [*A car pulls into the driveway.* GRACE *reacts.*] Is that your Daddy and Steve?

DEBBIE: Stevie says he wants to start having lots of kids. Sometimes I think the only reason he wants to get married is so he can sleep with me!

GRACE: Debbie, don't say things like that. [*She is looking out the window.* STEVE *runs into the house past* GRACE.] Hello, Stevie dear.

STEVE: Hello, Mrs. Hall. [*He stands nervously by* DEBBIE's *side as she ignores him.*]

GRACE: [*Opening the screen door and going out to the driveway.*] Fred, what are you doing? Did you know there was another disturbance at the county jail? I heard it on the radio.

FRED: [*Sitting behind the wheel, exhausted.*] I can't go.

GRACE: Fred, what's the matter with you? Is your stomach bothering you again? [*She opens the car door.*] You've been working too hard. You're not going out again, are you?

FRED: Have to.

GRACE: Well, at least let me drive, scoot over. [*Noticing the body in the back.*] What's that! Another drunk?

STEVE: [*To* DEBBIE, *inside the house.*] Debbie, did a guy named Danny Rosales ever speak to you or anything?

DEBBIE: Yeah, sure, so what?

4. Novel (1936) by the American writer Margaret Mitchell (1900–1949).

STEVE: Just answer my question.

DEBBIE: I sat with him once on the Greyhound to Dallas. He was kinda nice, uneducated, but nice.

STEVE: Did he ever touch you or try to make a pass at you or anything like that?

DEBBIE: Why are you asking me these questions? What are you, my father or what?!

STEVE: Debbie, your father just killed a man for no reason!

GRACE: [*Enter* FRED, *followed by* GRACE.] Answer my questions? Where is the Deputy? What did you do, tell me? [FRED *sits, silent.*]

DEBBIE: Daddy, are you all right? You look so pale.

GRACE: Stevie, do you know what happened?

STEVE: Fred said it was an accident. I don't really know, I didn't see it.

GRACE: Fred, for the love of God, will you speak up and say something!

DEBBIE: Do you want me to get you your painkillers? [FRED *nods his head "yes."*]

GRACE: Debbie, pour your Daddy some coffee, he needs to think straight.

FRED: Get me a beer.

GRACE: No more drinking, Fred. Now tell me, why are you so worried? You said it was an accident.

FRED: Too many damn witnesses.

STEVE: I think I better go home. Goodnight, Debbie!

GRACE: Stevie Peters, you stay put. Let me tell you something about this family. We stick together, you hear? If you're going to be a part of us, you've got to stick with us come hell or high water, ya hear?

STEVE: Yes 'um.

FRED: Got to dispose of the body.

DEBBIE: Why don't you do what you always do, Daddy, take it to the funeral home.

FRED: I need a drink!

GRACE: I said, no more drinking! Now, listen to me, you and Stevie clean up the back seat of the car and put the body in the trunk. Hurry up, before it gets light.

FRED: You're right, you're right. Come on, Steve. [*They exit.*]

GRACE: Debbie?

DEBBIE: Yes, Mama.

GRACE: You'd do anything for your Daddy, wouldn't you dear?

DEBBIE: Of course, Mama.

GRACE: Your father is very sick, you know that, dear.

DEBBIE: From the shoot-out and the drugs and the liquor?

GRACE: That's right, dear, we have to protect him. Especially when he makes a mistake like tonight.

DEBBIE: What are we going to do, Mama?

GRACE: I think we're going to have to go for a little ride, dear, this very night.

DEBBIE: Can't it wait until morning, Mama, it's awful late?

GRACE: I'm afraid not, dear, you and I are going to have to help your Daddy get rid of that body.

DEBBIE: You and I, Mama? You and I?

STEVE: [*Re-entering.*]   It's all done, we moved the body into the trunk and the Chief's hosing down the back seat. Can I go now, Mrs. Hall?

DEBBIE:   Stevie, Mama needs somebody to help her . . . get rid of that body.

STEVE:   No, I've done more than my share.

DEBBIE:   Stevie, she wants me to go with her!

STEVE:   Mrs. Hall, can't you just go to the county jail and tell them the truth? Fred's the Chief of Police, they'll protect him.

GRACE:   No, there's a Mexican American riot going on there. This could have something to do with it.

STEVE:   Well, I'm sorry. I just can't deal with this anymore, I just can't. [*Steve exits.*]

DEBBIE:   Stevie! Stevie!

FRED:   All done. What now?

GRACE:   Fred, you tell me!

FRED:   Don't know, can't think.

GRACE:   The only place I could think of is my brother's ranch, in Carthage, by the Louisiana border.

FRED:   Five hundred miles away?!

GRACE:   Exactly, no one will ever find it there.

FRED:   I'll clean up and get started.

GRACE:   No, you stay here in case anybody comes looking for you.

DEBBIE:   Daddy, she wants me to go with her.

FRED:   Grace, I don't think this child . . .

GRACE:   I need her to help me with the driving. You stay here and go to work in the morning as though nothing had happened. And call in sick for me at the bank.

FRED:   I knew I could count on you, Grace. [*They embrace and kiss.*]

GRACE:   I love you, Fred.

FRED:   Take this .38 pistol and holster. [*Handing Grace his pistol and holster.*]

DEBBIE:   I don't want to go!

GRACE:   Hush up, girl! From now on we do what I say! [*They exit.*]

KIKI: [*Late at night.*]   Hey, Berta, what are you doing out so late? Sabes qué,[5] I got some money for Danny! Now he can pay off that farmer, here.

BERTA:   Where did you get this money?

KIKI:   My abuelita died and gave it to me.

BERTA:   Does your abuelita wear a badge and carry a shotgun?

KIKI:   What are you talking about, Berta?

BERTA:   I thought you were Danny's friend.

KIKI:   I am. I am his best friend.

BERTA:   Then how could you lie to the police, how could you take their money?

KIKI:   Hey, now, don't be accusing anybody of being a snitch. People can get hurt for less.

BERTA:   Mentiroso![6] You told the police that Danny stole a new stereo and TV.

5. You know what.                6. Liar!

KIKI: That's a lie!

BERTA: And do you know where they took him? To the Old Alamo School Road. You know what they do to boys down there—they beat the hell out of them—and you helped them.

KIKI: Chingao, Berta. Is that what they did, lo llevaron allí?[7] ¡Hijos de puta!

BERTA: What did you tell them about Danny?

KIKI: Nothing. The Sheriff was angry at me for making him wait four hours by the side of the road. All I said was that Danny had a new stereo and TV. I had to tell him *something*.

BERTA: ¡Madre de Dios!

KIKI: He wanted to get Danny, I don't know why. I just told him the first crazy thing that came to the top of my head. I swear, Berta, I didn't mean to hurt Danny. The Sheriff was going to beat me, he was going to throw me in jail.

BERTA: So you turned Danny in to take your place!

KIKI: I couldn't help it. They were going to send me away for a long time. Tú sabes,[8] I have to survive, I live from day to day, sleeping in the back seat of my car half the time. I ain't got nothing, I never had nothing.

BERTA: Neither did Danny. But at least he was trying to go straight. I hate you! I hope you burn in hell! I wish you were dead!

KIKI: Berta, don't you see, I am dead! [*Exit.*]

DEBBIE: [*Back at the witness stand.*] It was the most horrible thing I had ever experienced in all my life. There we were, Mama and me, on the expressway in the middle of the morning rush hour with a dead body in the trunk! Neither of us had had much sleep. We didn't know what had caused the accident. Daddy was in a state of shock. He couldn't answer my mother's questions. She had always depended upon him for everything. The drive took six hours. I remember stopping along the way and buying some shovels and a digger. It was the month of September and it was still very hot in Texas.

GRACE: The sun is so bright today, like a blinding white disk.

DEBBIE: I ain't never seen so many dead animals on the road in all my life.

GRACE: Look how brown and dried the earth is.

DEBBIE: Just like that boy back there.

GRACE: There's the start of my brother's ranch, three hundred acres.

DEBBIE: Mama, what if somebody sees us?

GRACE: Don't worry, I used to play here when I was a little girl. I know a spot no one will ever find.

DEBBIE: I'm not going anywhere near that body!

GRACE: Debbie, I don't expect you to!

DEBBIE: How are you going to do it all by yourself?

GRACE: Simple. I'll back the car up near the space for the grave, wrap the rope around the body, loop it over a tree branch, and hoist it up out of the car trunk.

DEBBIE: How long do you think it's going to take to dig a grave in this hard clay earth?

GRACE: Don't you worry, I'll do all the digging.

---

7. They took him there. *Chingao*: fuck.　　　8. You know.

DEBBIE:   But Mother, why did you bring two shovels?

GRACE:   [*Starting to dig the grave.*]   After all this is over, we'll go up to our cabin at Lake Austin and relax.

DEBBIE:   Mama, what happens to a man's spirit when he dies?

GRACE:   Well, if he believes that Christ is the Saviour, then he'll be with Him. Honey, don't worry yourself about things like that. I know that you're thinking about that boy, but there's nothing we can do to bring him back to life. We have to think of the living.

DEBBIE:   But Mama, there's too many witnesses! Even Daddy said so. Maybe we should just tell the truth.

GRACE:   What is the truth?

DEBBIE:   That it was an accident, that Daddy didn't mean to do it. Don't you see, we're just making matters worse by trying to cover it up. Why don't we just go to a police station and tell them the truth?

GRACE:   Debbie, I got too many things on my mind to argue with you. Besides, the truth will come out in the end, it always does. Now then, I'm going to dig a small grave and conceal the body. This clay earth will protect it until such a time as we need to retrieve it. Hand me some of those plastic bags.

DEBBIE:   What are you going to use them for?

GRACE:   To cover up his face and chest and other portions of his body.

DEBBIE:   What for?

GRACE:   You don't want dirt falling on his face, do you? [*Blackout.*]

DEPUTY:   [*With* BERTA *at the front door of the Hall home.*]   Fred. Fred! Mrs. Rosales wanted to talk to you and asked me to come along with her.

FRED:   Well, good morning, Mrs. Rosales, what can I do for you?

BERTA:   I want to know what you did to my husband.

FRED:   Well, he's in a lot of trouble. Not only did he escape my custody, but he attempted to assault a law officer.

BERTA:   That's a lie. If he had escaped, he would have gotten word to me.

FRED:   Maybe he's out having a little drink with the boys.

BERTA:   You beat him, didn't you? And then you shot him!

FRED:   Mrs. Rosales, I think you'd better get off my property.

BERTA:   What have you done to my husband?

FRED:   The last time I saw him he was high-tailing it through the woods.

BERTA:   Then how do you explain his shoe and the pool of dried blood I found near the side of the road?

FRED:   Is that true, Davis?

DEPUTY:   That's right, Fred, we spent all morning out there. There's dried blood and lots of it.

FRED:   Well, that don't prove nothing. The gun did go off accidentally, I could have wounded him, but he ran off! Besides, there's no body, where's the body?

DEPUTY:   Fred, I think you'd better come down to the station and answer some questions.

FRED:   Yeah, sure, I got nothing to hide.

DEPUTY:   One more thing, Fred, let's see your sawed-off shotgun. [*Blackout.*]

GRACE:   [*Later on that after noon at Lake Austin.*]   There, you see, we made it, safe and sound.

DEBBIE: It was such a *long* drive.

GRACE: Texas is a country all unto itself, darling.

DEBBIE: Who would have thought it would have taken six hours to dig that grave.

GRACE: You didn't get any blood on your clothes, did you?

DEBBIE: Only on my hands.

GRACE: Now then, we have one more little task to do and then we'll be all done.

DEBBIE: What now?

GRACE: The trunk. First we have to get rid of the shovels and digger. Then we have to scrub it down real good.

DEBBIE: Oh no, not again!

GRACE: We'll scrub it until it's clean as a whistle!

DEBBIE: Mama, I still don't understand why we're going through all of this. You say we have every intention of telling the truth, of going back there and uncovering the body and clearing Daddy's name! Why are we here in Lake Austin hiding from everybody?

GRACE: We're not hiding! [*She opens the trunk and takes out the shovels.*] We're just waiting until your father can get his wits back together again and explain this unfortunate incident.

DEBBIE: Mother, I'm going to be sick.

GRACE: Hand me the cleaning detergent and that towel. [*As she pulls out a plastic bag.*]

DEBBIE: What's in there!

GRACE: Just some garbage left over from the picnic last weekend.

DEPUTY: [*Entering rather suddenly.*] Excuse me, are you Mrs. Grace Hall?

GRACE: Oh, my goodness, you startled me! Why, yes, I am, is something the matter, officer?

DEPUTY: Are you Debbie Hall?

DEBBIE: No, I'm Berta Rosales.

GRACE: Debbie! These children have no respect nowadays.

DEPUTY: Mind if I take a look at the inside of your trunk?

GRACE: Why, what ever are you looking for?

DEPUTY: Two shovels and digger. [*Commenting on the tools.*] God, what is that awful smell?

GRACE: Well, you see, officer, we just got done burying an old dog of ours.

DEBBIE: That's right, and his name was Danny Rosales. Only, you know something, we couldn't get his eyes closed! [*Blackout.*]

JUDGE: [*Back at the trial.*] Ladies and gentlemen of the jury, before we begin the closing arguments, I want to remind you once more that this is a two-stage trial and that your first task is to decide on the guilt or innocence of the defendant. Your second task is to assess the punishment. Now, for the first stage you can find the defendant, Fred Hall, (1) guilty of murder in the first degree, or (2) guilty of aggravated assault, or (3) not guilty as charged. Proceed with the closing arguments.

ROWENA: Ladies and gentlemen, this is more than just another case of murder in a small Texas town. This is a trial with international repercussions. What is being tried here is the American system of justice and whether or not all the people have the inalienable rights promised to them by the Constitution of the United States.

HAROLD:  Ladies and gentlemen of the jury, Ms. Saldivar would have us believe that the American judicial system is on trial here. That is not the case, what is on trial here is whether or not an officer of the law has the right to defend himself under attack.

ROWENA:  On the eve of my involvement in this case, I reaffirmed my professional commitment not to identify too closely with my client, a rule which we were taught in law school. But the violent manner in which Danny Rosales died tore away the veil of my impartiality.

HAROLD:  The prosecutor has admitted being blinded by her emotional involvement in this case. Consequently, she has turned this trial into an arena for her political crusading. But she will find no scapegoat here, no sacrifice to appease the masses.

ROWENA:  Danny Rosales was accused of a crime he did not commit, arrested in his home, beaten without cause in his driveway, dragged into the woods, beaten again, and then shot to death at point-blank range by the highest ranking law enforcement officer of the town in which he lived. If this could happen to Danny Rosales, it could happen to me or even to you.

HAROLD:  If my client is guilty of anything, he is guilty of being over-zealous in his dedication to duty; a man who served his country for thirty years in the United States Air Force, a God-fearing family man who almost gave up his life three years ago in an exchange of gunfire with three suspects in a liquor store. And yet the prosecution paints him as a sadistic racist.

ROWENA:  Ladies and gentlemen, if you decide in your wisdom that this was not first degree murder, which I most certainly think it was, then surely Fred Hall can be found guilty of nothing less than aggravated assault in which he caused the death of Danny Rosales through his negligence. According to the coroner's report, the sawed-off double barreled LeFever shotgun was no more than three and a half feet from the point of impact and wadding from the shell was found imbedded in Danny's chest. Was this negligence? No, this was an execution-style murder.

HAROLD:  Let us examine what happened that night. While there is no denying that Fred Hall was carrying a shotgun when he arrested Danny Rosales, there is also no denying that Rosales attacked Hall. There was a struggle; Rosales grabbed the shotgun with both hands, kicked Hall to the ground, and while attempting to seize the weapon, it discharged, accidentally. It was self-defense, not murder.

ROWENA:  Now we come to the gruesome cover-up attempt. And please keep in mind that by your actions today, tomorrow we will judge those who helped Fred Hall cover up the crime. How could this so-called devoted father and husband allow his wife and daughter to become involved in this macabre affair? And to those of you who say that Fred Hall was temporarily out of his mind, I say, he—with the help of his wife—coldly and calculatingly tried to hide the deed by disposing of the evidence 400 miles from the scene of the crime.

HAROLD:  Ladies and gentlemen, if Fred Hall was going to go out there and kill somebody on purpose, do you think he would take this boy who was going to be his son-in-law to witness a killing? Does that make any sense?

ROWENA: Why was Danny Rosales killed? Was it because he was born poor? Was it because he had been caught stealing in the past? Was it because he was too proud to confess to a crime he did not commit? Or was it because he was a Mexican?

HAROLD: Race had nothing to do with this! We give our police officers the right to bear arms. How can we expect them to perform their duties properly if they are brought to trial each and every time there is a confrontation with a common criminal? It is time that we stopped coddling and indulging the criminals and started caring more about the police officers.

ROWENA: But does a badge and uniform give a man the license to kill?

HAROLD: Examine your hearts and find the only possible verdict in this case. Not guilty!

ROWENA: Guilty of first degree murder!

JUDGE: Now then, ladies and gentlemen of the jury, have you arrived at a verdict? Will you please hand it to the Bailiff. [*They do so.*] What is the ruling?

BAILIFF: The jury finds the defendant, Fred Hall, guilty of aggravated assault.

BERTA: Of aggravated assault! Rowena?

ROWENA: It means that Hall caused Danny's death, but it is a term usually associated with traffic accidents.

BERTA: Traffic accidents?

JUDGE: We have now reached the second point of the trial, which is where you, the jury, deliberate and decide upon the appropriate punishment that should be assessed in this case. Counselors will make their final statements.

ROWENA: Ladies and gentlemen, it is not our place to question the wisdom that you have used in arriving at a verdict of guilty of aggravated assault. But I think that the situation in general cries out for punishment in this case and the punishment you have found the defendant guilty of is two-to-ten years in prison. Now, the defense has filed a motion asking that you consider probation for the defendant. This would be like letting Fred Hall go free for the killing of Danny Rosales. Mr. Pearl made the statement that the law allows a man like Mr. Hall to carry a twelve-gauge sawed-off shotgun. That is true, but along with that privilege comes the responsibility to use it with discretion and extreme caution. There is a saying, originally in Latin, that goes, "Who will guard the guards?" I am talking about guards who could preserve any type of oppression they care to. Who will guard your liberty and mine? I think your verdict should speak to that question. Do not probate the sentence of two-to-ten years. Probation is no punishment and without punishment we have no protection. That is our system of justice.

HAROLD: May it please the court, ladies and gentlemen of the jury, the verdict at which you arrived was probably a very just one. You felt that the gun was not handled properly and that it caused the death of a man. That is now history. When I was selecting you, I told you that the defense was going to be looking for the God-like qualities in you. We are created in God's image and we are the only creatures that have the ability to show mercy and compassion, just as God is merciful and compassionate. No matter what we do here today, we cannot bring life back to Danny Rosales. Please, we have heard one terrible tragedy, don't cap it with another. Please, for your sake, don't let another tragedy occur. Each and every one of us has to look at ourselves in the mirror each morning. Make sure what you do here today you can be proud of tomorrow, when you look in that mirror. Fred Hall is a man of good reputation who has never been convicted of a felony, nor has he ever been given probation. I urge you to probate him. Thank you.

JUDGE: Ladies and gentlemen of the jury, have you arrived at a verdict?

BAILIFF: They have, your Honor.

JUDGE: Hand it to the Bailiff, please. I will read the verdict. "The Jury, having found the defendant, Fred Hall, guilty of the offense of aggravated assault, a third degree felony, assesses the defendant's punishment as confinement in the Texas Department of Corrections for a period of not less than two nor more than ten years."

BERTA: What happens now, Rowena? [*The Hall family is congratulating themselves upon hearing the verdict.*]

HAROLD: [*Walking over to* ROWENA.] Congratulations, counselor.

ROWENA: For what?

HAROLD: For winning the case. My client was found guilty.

ROWENA: You know damn well that with time off for good behavior he could be out in twenty months.

HAROLD: True, but he's still going to serve some time. Look, why don't we go have a drink afterwards and talk about the case?

ROWENA: No thanks, I'm going to be too busy filing for a Department of Justice investigation into this case!

HAROLD: Miss Saldivar, you know you can't try a man twice for the same crime.

ROWENA: But you can try a man for violating another man's civil rights.

HAROLD: Don't waste your time, counselor, don't waste your time. [*Exits.*]

BERTA: Civil rights? What does that mean, Rowena? What about his life, can they bring back his life?

ROWENA: Berta, listen to me, we're not through yet, we're going to fight this all the way. Protests, letters to Congress, appeals, radio and television fund drives . . .

BERTA: I don't care what you do, Rowena, I've had it with the courts and the police and the Gringos! Rowena, crees que todavía estás en[9] law school? This is Texas, not Harvard! There is no justice for Chicanos here! [*Exits.*]

DEPUTY: Miss Saldivar.

ROWENA: Yes, Deputy.

DEPUTY: Did you hear? Grace Hall pleaded no contest to the charge of concealing physical evidence. She was fined $49.50 in court costs.

ROWENA: $49.50! If Danny weighed 154 pounds at the time of his death, that means she got off with about thirty cents a pound!

DEBBIE: Stevie and I are getting married next Saturday.

BERTA: They killed my husband many times.

DEBBIE: All my family and friends will be at the wedding.

---

9. You think you're still in.

BERTA: Once when he was born poor.
DEBBIE: A country and western band will be playing.
BERTA: Once when he didn't get a decent education.
DEBBIE: We'll have fajitas and kegs of Lone Star beer.
BERTA: Once with a shotgun at the Old Alamo School Road.
DEBBIE: We're going to Las Vegas for our honeymoon.
BERTA: Once with a pick and shovel near the Louisiana border.
DEBBIE: We plan to have lots of kids.
BERTA: And once in a court of law.
DEBBIE: I'll be dressed in white.
BERTA: I'll be dressed in black.
ROWENA: In 1977, two years after Danny Rosales' death, we realized a great victory. Fred and Grace Hall were indicted by a federal grand jury. They were eventually found guilty of violating Danny Rosales' civil rights. Fred Hall was sentenced to life in prison, and Grace Hall was sentenced to three years in prison. But was this such a great victory? Did you hear what happened in Mejia, Texas, a couple of years ago? Three black men drowned while in police custody. And just last year in San Antonio they shot Héctor Santoscoy and . . .

1980                                                                          1983

---

# JOSÉ RIVERA
## b. 1955

Born in San Juan, Puerto Rico, the oldest of nine children, José Rivera moved to the United States with his family when he was four. The Riveras settled in Holbrook, Long Island, in what was then a semirural environment. The farms and greenery there reminded him of the rural barrio of Arecibo, Puerto Rico, where the family had lived before migrating. However, the family experienced isolation and prejudice in an ethnically Italian community, where the presence of Puerto Ricans was rare and unwelcome. Rivera's parents had little education, and his father held various blue collar jobs while his mother took care of the family and tried to teach herself English.

As a youngster, Rivera dreamed of becoming a writer. In an interview with the arts writer Lucía Mauro, he described his initiation into storytelling: "I grew up in a household with no books—except copies of the Bible—but where everybody told stories. What I learned about writing, I learned from hearing my parents talk." He started writing at age 12. In high school, he wrote comic strips, a novel about baseball, and several plays. He received a scholarship to attend Denison University, in Ohio. He studied acting at Denison, where four plays he wrote during this period were produced. Rivera then moved to New York City and briefly worked in a bookstore before landing a job with a publishing company. After struggling for years to make it as a playwright, he broke through with the semiautobiographical play *The House of Ramón Iglesia* (1983), which won a New Play Award from the Foundation of Dramatists Guild and CBS Inc. A favorable review in *The New York Times* caught the attention of the renowned television producer and director Norman Lear, who was looking for a Latino writer for one of his series. In 1986, after a three-year stint with Lear's company, Embassy Television, in California, Rivera returned to New York.

A few months before Rivera moved back to New York, an adaptation of *The House of Ramón Iglesia* appeared on national television as part of PBS's *American Playhouse* series. In the introduction he wrote for the volume *On New Ground: An Anthology of Hispanic-American Plays* (1987), Rivera notes that he made superficial changes to give the play more of an ethnic flavor, since at one point—while it was being considered for the series—the material was called "not Hispanic enough." Included in its entirety in this anthology, *The House of Ramón Iglesia* was largely influenced by Rivera's efforts to have the life that his parents were not able to have or to provide for their children. Central to the play are the generational conflicts between a Puerto Rican father and his Americanized, college-educated oldest son, who feels some self-hatred about being Puerto Rican and who refuses to return to the island when, after two decades of living on Long Island, the father plans to move the family back to their homeland. Rivera also notes that he sometimes was criticized by young students for portraying some of the Hispanic characters negatively and for having a character that tries to distance himself from his cultural heritage. These critical reactions, however, helped reshape his thinking:

> Their reaction made me think again about my own anger at the time and how unresolved it was. I once felt that in order to transcend my culture, I had to escape it, to run away from it. In the last several years I've realized that the only transcendence possible is through embracing the culture, learning it, growing up out of it.

Rivera has written and produced numerous plays, most of them reflecting the influence of Latin American magical realism. Among his published earlier plays are *The Promise* (1989); *Marisol* (1994), for which he won his first Obie Award; and *Cloud Tectonics* (1997). In 2004, Rivera received an Oscar nomination for his screenplay for the film *The Motorcycle Diaries*, based on the Latin American revolutionary leader Ernesto "Che" Guevara's memoir about his younger years. The play *References to Salvador Dalí Make Me Hot* (2005), first produced in London, gained Rivera his second Obie Award. *Boleros for the Disenchanted* (2008) was inspired by his mother's life experiences. Rivera has been a writer-in-residence at the Royal Court Theatre, in London, and has received fellowships from the National Endowment for the Arts, the Rockefeller Foundation, Fulbright Arts, and the Whiting Foundation.

---

# The House of Ramón Iglesia

SETTING: *Holbrook, Long Island, New York*
TIME: *February, 1980*

## ACT ONE

*Scene 1. An evening in early February, 1980. Iglesia house.*
*Scene 2. Later that night, 1:00 A.M. Same.*
*Scene 3. The next afternoon. Same.*
*Scene 4. A week later, 4:00 A.M. Marine Recruiting Office.*

ACT TWO

Scene 1.    *A few days later. Iglesia house.*
Scene 2.    *Six hours later. Marine Recruiting Office.*
Scene 3.    *That evening. Iglesia house.*
Scene 4.    *Two weeks later, afternoon. Same.*

# Act One

## Scene 1

*The action begins in the living room of the Iglesia house—a small, lower class structure located in Holbrook, New York, about an hour and a half east of New York City. It is a cold evening in February 1980. The living room has a slightly uneven floor, disheveled furniture, windows with towels stuffed around the cracks, scores of photographs on the wall, and a stack of cardboard boxes in one of the [upstage] corners. The [upstage] wall has a window facing out into the street. There are four exits: the front door, an exit to the kitchen, an exit to the upstairs bedrooms, and an exit to the basement. At rise, DOLORES IGLESIA, a Puerto Rican woman of 45, sits at a little home-made altar, dedicated to her deceased daughter Felicia. There are icons everywhere, as well as a photograph of the infant Felicia. DOLORES prays to the photograph and kisses it.*

DOLORES:    Don't worry, angel, we're going home. [*A knock is heard at the front door.* DOLORES *spins around.*] Ramón?

CAROLINE:   [*Off.*]   Hey, Mrs. Iglesia? It's me, Caroline!

DOLORES:    Oh.

CAROLINE:   [*Off.*]   Could you open up? It's *freezing*—!

DOLORES:    [*Crossing to front door.*]   It's Javier's girlfriend . . . DOLORES *opens door.* CAROLINE, *an attractive, eternal adolescent, wearing lots of makeup and chewing gum, enters. She is 28 and irresistible.*] Come in, hurry. Did you see my husband out there? [CAROLINE *smiles.*]

CAROLINE:   I don't know about this weather. [*Takes off coat and earmuffs.*] Oh geez—it's *murder*, you know? I just hate it.

DOLORES:    Excuse me?

CAROLINE:   [*Looking her in the eye.*]   Murder! I just hate it.

DOLORES:    [*Speaking slowly.*]   Caroline, you know I no speak English . . .

CAROLINE:   [*Speaking slowly.*]   Uh . . . the *weather*. It's freezing! [*Pantomimes being cold.*] Esta mucho frio!

DOLORES:    [*Smiles.*]   You don't have to tell me: it's freezing!

CAROLINE:   What?

DOLORES:    It's murder. I wish it would stop!

CAROLINE:   [*Giving up.*]   Look. I want Javier. Your son. [CAROLINE *looks around the room.*] Is he *here*?

DOLORES:    Javier, he's not here.

CAROLINE:   Do you have any idea where he is?

DOLORES:    Whenever Ramón takes an airplane, I become so frightened.

CAROLINE:   *I don't know what you're saying!!* [CAROLINE *sits on sofa.*]

DOLORES: Would you like some coffee?

CAROLINE: What?

DOLORES: Coffee?

CAROLINE: Did you say coffee?

DOLORES: I can make you a cup of . . .

CAROLINE: [Overjoyed.] Coffee! Would be great! Yes! Please, get me some. Thank God for coffee.

DOLORES: I think, I think you're a very pretty girl. But you're not very smart, are you?

CAROLINE: [Totally confused.] . . . What? [DOLORES kisses CAROLINE on the cheek, crosses to the kitchen, and exits. CAROLINE starts walking around the room, looking into all the boxes. She calls to DOLORES.] I bet you guys are really nervous, huh? I think I'd be freaking out if it was me going away. I turn into a real crybaby when it comes to goodbyes and stuff like that. You should see me at weddings. [Laughs.] I should see me at weddings. [She comes across a photograph of JAVIER.] I don't believe it. The stud himself. [She takes the photograph from the box.] And where the frig are you hanging out, anyway? You better have a great explanation for the way you've been acting, you little baby! Selfish, sneaky, rotten . . . cute little baby. Don't give me those eyes!

[The door opens and CHARLIE and JULIO enter. CHARLIE is tall and thin and 16 years old. JULIO, 19, is built like a tank.]

CHARLIE: [Seeing CAROLINE.] Oh, hi. Look who's here.

CAROLINE: Hi, Charlie.

JULIO: Oh great.

CAROLINE: Hello, Julio.

JULIO: Oh wonderful.

CAROLINE: Don't start.

JULIO: [Winking at CHARLIE.] Somebody call the ASPCA, break out the pooper-scoopers, blow the dog-in-heat alert. [CHARLIE crosses to chair, sits.]

CAROLINE: Listen, fatso . . .

JULIO: . . . are you going to start spraying all over the furniture again?

CAROLINE: Are you finished?

JULIO: Fatso?? You should talk. There's more area on those thighs of yours than on the Nimitz[1] flight deck. Did my father come home?

CAROLINE: I don't know.

JULIO: [Shouting into the kitchen.] IS DAD HOME?

CAROLINE: I can't even find Javier . . .

JULIO: Javier went into Manhattan to get laid. DAD, ARE YOU HERE??

DOLORES: [Entering with coffee.] No! He didn't come back yet!

JULIO: Great! Okay! Unpack the boxes again!

DOLORES: Maybe they gave him trouble . . .

[DOLORES crosses to CHARLIE, kisses him.]

JULIO: [Crosses to DOLORES, kisses her.] Maybe he went to the wrong Caribbean island, Mom.

DOLORES: [Exiting to kitchen.] Perez's people always make trouble . . .

[JULIO sits on sofa with CAROLINE.]

1. USS Nimitz, a supercarrier in the U.S. Navy; one of the largest warships in the world.

CHARLIE: [*To* CAROLINE.]   It's colder in here than it is outside.

CAROLINE: [*To* CHARLIE.]   What's Javier doing in Manhattan?

CHARLIE: [*Crossing to thermostat.*] You're asking me? I'm going to turn up the heat, Julio.

JULIO:   Not too far. You'll turn this place into a gas chamber again.

CHARLIE: [*To* CAROLINE.]   He didn't come home Friday night, that's all I know.

JULIO: [*To* CAROLINE.]   Forget him. He's a floozie. [*To* DOLORES.] I told you we shouldn't disconnect the phone so soon; Dad could be calling. [*To* CAROLINE.] Right, Spot?

DOLORES: [*Off.*]   Don't yell to me, it was Ramón's idea . . .

CAROLINE:   You don't know how impossible it is to follow a conversation in this house. You speak in English, she answers in Spanish . . . and I don't know where to put my ears half the time.

JULIO: [*Hanging up coat.*]   Well, you should take your ears, and the rest of you, and pack them off to a convent, and stop screwing up my brother's life.

CAROLINE:   Thank you.

JULIO: [*Crossing to sofa.*]   Javier is not the baby buggy, home-for-dinner, Fred-and-Ethel[2] type. Go marry a nice, stable cop or something.

CAROLINE:   Why don't you give me a straight answer, Julio?

CHARLIE:   Why don't you give Caroline a straight answer, Julio?

JULIO:   Why don't you go outside and shovel the steps, Charlie?

CHARLIE:   You do it, wimp.

JULIO: [*Crossing to* CHARLIE.]   What did you call me?

CHARLIE:   Nothing, faggot.

JULIO:   How would you like to suck the flowers off the wallpaper?

CHARLIE:   Ya big turkey.

JULIO:   YOU'RE TALKING TO A FUTURE MARINE, PUSSY! [JULIO *lunges for* CHARLIE, *catches him, and puts him in a headlock.*] I'm going to use that enormous mouth of yours to shovel out the sidewalk. WHO'S A WIMP??

CAROLINE:   Tell him he is!

CHARLIE:   You are.

JULIO: [*Tightening.*]   DON'T LISTEN TO HER!! WHO'S A WIMP??

CHARLIE: [*Struggling.*]   Me! Me! Me! Me! *Just let go!* [JULIO *releases* CHARLIE, *who whacks* JULIO *on the arm as hard as he can.*] Fool!

JULIO:   Go help your old lady, clone.

CHARLIE:   I'm not a clone, you colossal wimp. [CHARLIE *bolts for the kitchen and exits.*]

CAROLINE:   You're just a plain old T-H-U-G, thug, Julio!

JULIO: [*Flexing.*]   Do you want to see a trap bounce? I bet you'd love to see a nice inspiring pec flex, wouldn't you, girl? I'm gonna dazzle the Marine Corps, woman!!

CAROLINE:   Get away from me, you horse. I like intellectuals.

JULIO:   I don't know. When I first met you, you could appreciate a good healthy lat spread.

CAROLINE:   Julio, if I asked you a serious question would you turn down the gorilla bit and give me a serious answer, please?

2. Fred and Ethel Mertz are characters, an older married couple, on the sitcom *I Love Lucy* (1951–60).

JULIO: [*Looking through* Marines *Magazine.*]    What is it?

CAROLINE:    I want to know what Javier's been telling you about us. And I want to know what he's been doing the last couple of days.

JULIO:    Are you two kids fighting?

CAROLINE:    Fighting? Shit! That'd be a pleasure! All he does these days is act real polite, real nice, like he's hiding something. He doesn't get mad at me or anything, he just smiles a lot! I hate it! [*Beat.*] Oh shit. I don't need this. I'll see ya. [*She gets up and puts on coat.*]

JULIO:    Hey, wait a minute.

CAROLINE:    I hate being in the dark and you people feeling sorry for me. I learned to make rice and beans for him, and he got mad.

JULIO: [*Intercepting her.*]    Whoa . . . wait a minute . . . relax your face, there . . .

CAROLINE:    I'm so *pissed* at him!

JULIO:    Hey, have dinner with us, hang out, and do not judge the Iglesias by that moody Javier, alright, Private? You'll get that sucker yet! And if he's still screwing up your life, I'll talk to him myself.

> [*The front door bursts open and* RAMÓN IGLESIA *comes in. He is 49 years old, Puerto Rican, with a pronounced limp. He looks 59. He is wearing a coat far too thin for the weather and a bright yellow hat. He is carrying a suitcase.*]

RAMÓN:    Hello, hello, hello! [*To* JULIO.] Is that my soldier?

JULIO: [*Crosses to* RAMÓN, *kisses him.*]    Al-right!

CAROLINE:    Hi!

RAMÓN:    How are you today, Caroline?

JULIO: [*Crossing to kitchen.*]    Dad's home!

DOLORES: [*Off.*]    I'll be right there! [DOLORES *and* CHARLIE *enter.* DOLORES *and* RAMÓN *embrace.*] Oh God, Ramón! Thank God you're here! [*Kisses him.*] Look at you! What a pretty hat!

RAMÓN:    Where's Javier?

DOLORES:    In the city.

RAMÓN:    Why he's not here to see me?

DOLORES:    He's angry, Ramón.

RAMÓN: [*Giving suitcase to* CHARLIE.]    Let him be angry! [*Crosses to chair.*] It's cold outside!

DOLORES: [*Exiting to kitchen.*]    Have you eaten . . . ?

CAROLINE: [*To* JULIO.]    What are they saying?

JULIO:    Mom just said, "Is that a papaya in your pocket, or are you just glad to see me?" and Dad just said—.

CAROLINE:    Kiss off, Julio!

JULIO: [*Crossing to sofa, sits.*]    How did you get to the house?

RAMÓN:    I took the Long Island Rail Road from the city and then I took a cab to the house. Simple.

JULIO:    You're a big spender when it comes to Calla's money, aren't you?

CHARLIE: [*Taking* RAMÓN's *hat.*]    Did you do any swimming down there?

RAMÓN:    No time.

JULIO:    Did you have any time to . . . uh . . . you know . . . get a little nookie-nookie while you were down there?

DOLORES: [*Entering with bowl of soup.*]    Julio!

JULIO:    Tell me in English, Dad.

DOLORES: [*Smacking* JULIO.]    Julio! I'll kill you! [*General laughter.* RAMÓN *absently begins to rub his foot with his hand.*]

RAMÓN:    I had no time for nookie-nookie; I was so worried trying to find Doña Perez, and . . . ah . . . I . . .

JULIO:    Are you alright? What's the matter?

RAMÓN:    Nothing.

CHARLIE:    Is it your foot?

RAMÓN:    Let me tell you, when I landed in San Juan—.

JULIO:    Do you want the bucket?

RAMÓN:    No! My brother and I had to go—.

JULIO:    Charlie, get the bucket for Dad.

RAMÓN:    It's okay, there's nothing wrong.

JULIO:    Right. Take off that shoe, Dad, it smells like death . . . [JULIO *bends down and begins to untie* RAMÓN's *shoe.* CHARLIE *crosses to the kitchen and exits.* JULIO *looks at the shoe, then he looks up at* RAMÓN *suspiciously.*] Did you have a lot of alcohol while you were down there?

RAMÓN:    No. I didn't have anything.

JULIO:    You were drinking, weren't you?

DOLORES:    You weren't, Ramón.

JULIO:    You're a diabetic and you promised to stop drinking. You want to lose that foot?

RAMÓN:    Who cares? I have *stories* to tell—.

DOLORES:    Why did you do that? How can you be so stupid, Ramón?

RAMÓN:    I'm trying to tell you . . .

DOLORES:    I knew you'd do something like that! Do I have to watch you like one of the children?

RAMÓN:    Don't talk to me that way! I'll go to Tony's Bar and tell him my stories and drink until I faint!

DOLORES:    You can take your bed to Tony's Bar too!

JULIO:    ALRIGHT, KIDS, KNOCK IT OFF!

RAMÓN:    These are my feet, Dolores!

DOLORES:    Not for long, Ramón!

JULIO:    Mom, yell at him later! Hurry up with that bucket, Charlie! [*To* RAMÓN.] Did you get the deed, or not?

RAMÓN: [*To* DOLORES.]    Kiss me first.

DOLORES:    Never.

JULIO:    I'm gonna strangle them . . .

CAROLINE:    Did he get it, Julio? [CHARLIE *enters with the bucket, puts it in front of* RAMÓN.]

DOLORES:    Talking to you is like talking to a stone. You'll drink until that foot falls off—.

JULIO: [*To* DOLORES.]    Shhh! [*To* RAMÓN.] For God's sakes, what happened down there? Did you bring it? Are you going back or not?

RAMÓN: [*Putting his feet in bucket.*]    When I landed in San Juan, I took a public car to Bayamon, where I met my brother Herminio. From there, we drove to Adjuntas. No Doña Perez there. "Where I can find Doña Perez?" "Utuado," someone told me. Herminio and I drove to the rain forest of Utuado, the jungle in the hills, there was a storm, a waterfall, I remembered the days I explored—.

JULIO:    What about Perez, Dad?

RAMÓN: Doña Perez had given a party for the baptism of a godchild on the day of a local saint, which is bad enough. But she also slaughtered a pig that day, in the baby's honor: a big, red pig that screamed for hours before it died . . .

DOLORES: She shouldn't have done that, Ramón . . .

RAMÓN: The next day, while making a stew, she heard an animal screaming outside her door. When she went outside to look, there was nothing there. But when she returned to her stew, she discovered that the pot had been moved from the stove to the table, all by itself . . . and inside the pot were bright red balls of pig's hair. The poor woman screamed. People came running. She screamed, "The devil has come to my kitchen to punish me!"

JULIO: This is the town you want to go back to?

RAMÓN: Later she discovered pig's hair in the center of a coconut she had *just opened* with a machete. And every night, outside her door, there was the sound of a pig screaming to death. One night, in a full moon, she decided to follow the noise. She got out of bed, left her house, ran towards that terrible noise . . . until it led her, that poor woman, to the pit where the body of her husband was put to rest. That screaming was the tormented cry of Lumin Perez in the grave. [*Beat.*] Doña Perez, they told me, lost her mind and died.

DOLORES: What? She's dead?

RAMÓN: What? She's dead? That's what I said! They said yes: the devil had come to the town and killed Doña Perez.

JULIO: That's incredible.

CAROLINE: I am completely lost, folks . . .

JULIO: Doña Perez died.

CAROLINE: The lady who owned this house?

DOLORES: What did you do, Ramón?

RAMÓN: I felt so sad for her . . . and for us because the proof that this house really belongs to me . . . is gone forever. So I told Herminio to go back home to Bayamon alone. Then I sat under the avocado tree and cried until I fell asleep.

DOLORES: How many others have died while we've been here, Ramón?

RAMÓN: [*Laughing.*] The next morning I was awakened by an old woman pulling on my sleeve. She was saying, "Ramón Iglesia, is that you?" I looked at her and said, Doña Perez, is that *you?*" And suddenly that withered little face grew thirty years younger and that smile came to her and she said, "Yes, Ramóncito, it's me . . ."

CHARLIE: Wait a minute, Pop . . .

RAMÓN: It was Doña Perez!

JULIO: Dead or alive?

RAMÓN: Alive! She was alive! I told her what the villagers had said and she howled and slapped her knees! They all think she's a witch! They think she can fly and bring the dead come to life! They are always making stories about her!

DOLORES: Why did you scare me like that?

RAMÓN: I don't know . . .

JULIO: She signed the deed for her old man?

RAMÓN: Yes, sir!

JULIO:   Did you bring it? Do you have it?

RAMÓN:   [*Standing, pulling out a folded piece of paper.*]   I sure did! Here it is! It's the deed to the house! Our freedom!

DOLORES: [*Taking deed.*]   Ramón . . .

RAMÓN:   We're going home!

JULIO:   I don't believe it!

RAMÓN:   It's signed, it's perfect. She even signed the names of her daughters!

CHARLIE:   Really? Why?

RAMÓN:   And now I can slap this deed down on Calla's lawyer's desk and say, "Take me home, you goddamn wop, take me home!"

JULIO:   Wow, Dad . . . this is great.

DOLORES: [*Hugs and kisses* RAMÓN.]   You fixed it, Ramón.

RAMÓN: [*Laughing.*]   Well . . . I think I want to tell your mother some few bedtime stories. Do you want to hear some few bedtime stories, mother?

DOLORES: [*All smiles.*]   Yes.

JULIO:   Oh brother, what a line.

RAMÓN: [*Soft.*]   Come on.

JULIO: [*To* DOLORES.]   Guess we won't be seeing much of *you* this week . . .

DOLORES:   Julio, stop. [RAMÓN *crosses to the bedroom with* DOLORES.]

CAROLINE:   Do you think it's okay if I sacked out and waited for Javier?

RAMÓN:   You're very welcome.

JULIO: [*Standing, saluting.*]   Hey—Sarge!

RAMÓN:   Hey soldier!

JULIO:   You did good. Real good, Pop. [JULIO *and* CHARLIE *cross to* RAMÓN *and give him a kiss.*]

RAMÓN:   Tell Javier what I did. [RAMÓN *and* DOLORES *exit upstairs.*]

JULIO: [*Crosses to kitchen.*]   Well, hogs, dinner time. Bring that bucket, Charlie.

CHARLIE:   Tote that barge, Charlie, lift that bale, Charlie. [CHARLIE *lifts the bucket, looks inside, drops it.*] I don't believe it . . .

JULIO:   What's in there? Pig's hair?

CHARLIE:   You got the color right.

JULIO:   What is it?

CHARLIE:   It's blood. Dad's foot's bleeding again, look.

JULIO: [*Looking.*]   Jesus God, that's ugly. [*Beat.*] Don't tell Mom.
   [*Black out. End of Scene One.*]


## Scene 2

*Later that night, 1:00 A.M.* CAROLINE *is asleep on the sofa, wrapped in several thick blankets. A small night light burns in the corner. The door opens and* JAVIER *enters. He is 22, of medium height and build. He enters as quietly as he can and locks the door behind him. He is carrying several newspapers and magazines. He checks a small table for mail, finds a letter, rips it open, and reads it rapidly.*

JAVIER:   Oh shit, this is great! [JAVIER *crosses to sofa and sees* CAROLINE. *Smiles. Takes off shoes and unbuttons shirt.*] *The Sleeping Assassin,* take ten! *Ambush of Love,* starring that hot young couple, Javier and Caroline. [*Crosses to sofa, bends down over her, kisses her.*] Guess who's got a friend in high places . . . [*She slaps him hard across the face.*]

CAROLINE: That's for today. [*She swings at him again.*] Here's for *yesterday!* [JAVIER *grabs her hand as it comes towards him. He bites her on the wrist. She cries out.* JAVIER *kisses her and pushes her back down. She struggles underneath him, but only momentarily.*]

JAVIER: Here's for your love, concern, caring, patience . . .

CAROLINE: Bullshit! And don't—*do not*—look at me like I'm supposed to think you're cute!

JAVIER: You're so cute when you're mad: cute suburban rage! Listen, a friend of mine just got a job at the State Department! Isn't that great?

CAROLINE: Which state department is it? The one in Alaska?

JAVIER: There's only one State Department, dummy.

CAROLINE: Don't tell me! *There's fifty friggin' states!*

JAVIER: Okay—time to take you home. [*Gets off sofa, crosses to chair.*] What? Your old man kick you out of the house again?

CAROLINE: I'm the one asking the questions! I want to know where the frig you've been for three days while I'm having friggin' nightmares and ulcers over you!

JAVIER: Frig's a really beautiful word, Caroline, I wish you'd use it more often.

CAROLINE: Fuck you!

JAVIER: Don't you realize what this letter means? This guy was my *roommate!*

CAROLINE: I don't give a damn, Javier! I want you to talk to *me*, not look at your friggin' mail! I haven't seen you for *days* . . .

JAVIER: [*Putting on shoes.*] Look, I'm not up to it tonight. Let me take you home before your old man comes after me with his best shotgun.

CAROLINE: My father happens to think you're nice. He thinks you're honest and thoughtful and all the things *I* used to think. What's happened to you, Javier?

JAVIER: Carrie. I'm sorry. I was thoughtless.

CAROLINE: No shit. You should see me at home, bored, pissed off, hoping Daddy isn't blitzed out of his mind, watching him treat Mom like shit, and I keep thinking: where's Javier? He used to keep me safe from this.

JAVIER: You're still safe . . .

CAROLINE: I want to be safe.

JAVIER: All you have to do is ask me.

CAROLINE: What do you think I'm doing now?

  [JAVIER *holds her and rocks her gently back and forth.*]

JAVIER: I didn't disappear. I was visible the whole time.

CAROLINE: You're a laugh-riot, Javier. [*Beat.*] Don't I keep you safe?

JAVIER: [*Starts kissing her again.*] Of course you do.

CAROLINE: [*Pushing him back.*] Tell me where you were, liar.

JAVIER: Okay. It's Friday afternoon at the warehouse and I've just gotten those zombies to load five thousand units on the trucks before the second coffee break. I tell the guys to break early—but who should come along but Mr. Krinski, the boss, clacking his steel hands . . .

CAROLINE: Oh! He's the one who had his hands chopped off.

JAVIER: What a memory!

CAROLINE: Ten years ago, at the same warehouse!

JAVIER: Right. And now he's president of the company. Not bad for a man who can't type, right? [*Laughs.*]

CAROLINE: [*Laughs.*] Nice guy . . .

JAVIER: Anyways, here he comes: those mean steel hands glistening in the haze of forklift fumes . . . and I'm doing an imitation of Krinski on a date, unhooking a bra, and the guys are rolling on the floor, and Krinski pulls me over, mad as shit. Demands to see my charts. I show him the charts. He grunts. I point to the export column: *five thousand units.* He drools a little. I tell him the guys and I need a break because we're so far ahead of schedule and he flips out. Out of nowhere, he pulls out his computer printout and tells me how my last shipment had sixteen errors because I *rushed* too much! I flip out! I tell him sixteen errors in an order of ten thousand units is so unimportant, it's a waste of time talking about it, and no one gets it out as fast as I do, and besides, I only have two fucking hands! Why didn't they tell me he'd take that personally?

CAROLINE: What a stupid thing to say, Javier.

JAVIER: Don't I know it. He fired me.

CAROLINE: He *what?*

JAVIER: Fired me!! Me! The only college grad that toad's ever met and the best shipping clerk that company's ever had—*fired* by a man growing moss in his crotch! I tell you, this guy has a real thing against Puerto Ricans.

CAROLINE: It's probably your big mouth, ace. Then what?

JAVIER: Then I came home, changed clothes, and took the first train to Manhattan.

CAROLINE: You went to Manhattan without me?

JAVIER: Well . . . it was three o'clock. You were still at the bank.

CAROLINE: I get off at three-thirty on Fridays, you know that.

JAVIER: I couldn't wait any longer! I had to see people who could help me get work.

CAROLINE: You couldn't wait a lousy half hour?

JAVIER: I'm a year behind schedule, Caroline! I've spent a whole year here helping Dad stay dry, giving him money for the house, helping him find better work, thinking maybe he'll pull it together and do something right.

CAROLINE: He did. He got the deed. Now we're all set.

JAVIER: Dad's home with the deed? Great, that's my whole year down the tubes.

CAROLINE: He's not your son—you don't have to fix him up.

JAVIER: Fine, I'll stop. They can go to Puerto Rico and eat green bananas all day. I'm not sticking around here to watch. As long as I have friends at the State Department, it's crazy for me to be here—rotting in Holbrook! I have nothing here! I mean . . . barely nothing . . .

CAROLINE: So who'd you end up staying with?

JAVIER: A person from school.

CAROLINE: Oh—do I know this person from school?

JAVIER: No, you don't know this person.

CAROLINE: What's this person's—gender?

JAVIER: Her gender is female, Caroline sweetheart.

CAROLINE: Her gender is female! What a surprise! Did you sleep with her, Javier?

JAVIER: Of all the things to ask about—

CAROLINE: If you slept with her, I swear, I'm getting my Dad's fattest shotgun and I'm blasting your friggin' rocks off!

JAVIER: Do you kiss your old lady with that mouth?

CAROLINE: *Did you sleep with her or not??*

JAVIER: If I knew I was coming home to this shit, I would have; I wish I had!

CAROLINE: [*Putting on coat.*]  Oh great.

JAVIER: No, I did not sleep with her or any other female during my three terrible days of absence—okay? And if you can't believe that, you can take your monogamous little ass and trot it out of here. [*Stands up, takes off his shoes.* CAROLINE *takes off her shoes and smiles.*] If I were sleeping with someone else, you better believe I'd tell you. You'd get every inch of every detail. Until then, assume that I am yours . . . assume when I come home and want to take someone to bed . . . that I'll knock on your door, come to your room, and make love with you for as long as you can stand it.

[*They embrace and kiss as the lights go down. End of Scene Two.*]

## Scene 3

*The next afternoon. There are half-filled boxes all over the living room, piles of clothes, and garbage. The walls are nearly bare, and some of the clutter of the room has been relieved.* CHARLIE *is playing a radio and packing things into boxes.* JAVIER *enters, putting a shirt on.*

JAVIER: *Charlie* . . .

CHARLIE: Carlos to you, bro.

JAVIER: *Charlie* . . .

CHARLIE: It's Carlos now.

JAVIER: [*Noticing the boxes.*]  When are you going to learn to *spell*?

CHARLIE: What? I can spell.

JAVIER: Did you mark up all the boxes like this? [*Inspects the other boxes.*]

CHARLIE: That's the spelling I got from Mom.

JAVIER: "That's the spelling I got from Mom."

CHARLIE: Hey, you better watch your step, when Julio leaves, *I'm* the beast of the house!

JAVIER: How the hell do you figure that . . . *Charlie?*

CHARLIE: 'Cause I got these. [*Grabs crotch.*] I don't know what you got!

JAVIER: None of you guys have a method for anything. Look at this mess. I wish you guys would check with me before doing stuff like this.

CHARLIE: What stuff?

JAVIER: Sending half your clothes to Doña Perez. Getting rid of half the furniture.

CHARLIE: If we listened to you, we'd never leave.

JAVIER: You guys just go ahead and do these mindless things.

CHARLIE: "You guys."

JAVIER: [*Sitting down to write letters.*]  I mean, I didn't know Dad quit his job last week. No one told me.

CHARLIE: He was afraid you'd have a hemorrhage.

JAVIER: Wouldn't you? Charlie, Dad's spent Calla's downpayment already. What's he going to do for cash after it's gone?

CHARLIE: After today, Calla can pay Dad the balance on the house.

JAVIER: That's not the point. It's just that you guys never plan properly.

CHARLIE: [*Crossing to* JAVIER.] Why do you call everybody "you guys?" It really sucks, Javier. You're part of this family too, you know!

JAVIER: Don't remind me.

CHARLIE: You try to make everybody in the family feel stupid.

JAVIER: I don't try—it just happens. [CHARLIE *gives him a dirty look.*] I'm sorry, Charlie—Carlos—whoever you are this week. I just wish you guys would consult with me sometimes.

CHARLIE: Consult with you! We have trouble eating meals with you.

[JULIO *enters through the basement door, partially covered in soot, carrying a flashlight and screwdriver.*]

JULIO: [*To* JAVIER.] Hey, look who's working!

JAVIER: Pull this one, buddy.

JULIO: [*Crossing to kitchen.*] I don't know about you and Caroline. Lots of funny forest noises coming from this side of the house last night.

JAVIER: How nice of you to listen! How's it going down there?

JULIO: [*Off.*] We might have heat by July.

CHARLIE: [*Taking book from box; to* JAVIER]. Did you put this in my box?

JULIO: [*Off.*] What'd you put in Charlie's box, Javier?

JAVIER: A book.

JULIO: [*Laughs.*] A book! He put a book in Charlie's box . . . !

CHARLIE: [*Reading.*] *Decline of the West.* Spengler.[3] [*Throws book on floor.*]

JAVIER: [*To* CHARLIE.] You said you'd try to finish it.

CHARLIE: I tried and it's boring.

JULIO: [*Entering.*] You're just a boring guy, Javier. [JULIO *exits through basement door, eating.*]

JAVIER: Where did I go wrong? Where did I fail?

CHARLIE: You went wrong by calling everybody in the family "you guys." [*They continue packing boxes.*] Man, I don't know where you get all your hemorrhoids from. This is the best thing that could happen to Mom and Dad.

JAVIER: To Mom, maybe.

CHARLIE: You don't go shopping with Mom—me and Dad got to talk to everybody in the store for her. She don't read English. Dad drives her everywhere. This place is worse than San Quentin[4] to her.

JAVIER: It's her own fault. She could have learned English: she still can.

CHARLIE: I think it's neat she don't know English.

JAVIER: Doesn't know English.

CHARLIE: It's pure of her. And I think it would be great if you got happy for them, encourage them—.

JAVIER: I don't like encouraging people to quit—.

CHARLIE: I mean, Dad wanted to go back five years ago, but he said, "No, Javier's got to go to college first."

3. Oswald Spengler (1880–1936), German historian and philosopher; in his best-known book, *Der Untergang des Abendlandes* (The Decline of the West, 1918), he presents a cyclical theory of the rise and decline of civilizations.

4. State prison in San Quentin, Marin County, California.

JAVIER: Am I going to be tormented because of my education?

CHARLIE: Because you forgot where it came from!

JAVIER: It came from *me* buddyboy—*me*, busting my ass, seeking out financial aid. If I hadn't taken the time to ask the right—.

CHARLIE: And where'd you get the time? From Dad!

JAVIER: Oh Christ . . .

CHARLIE: *Dad*, who went around ripped-up and filthy-dirty because he worked two jobs so you wouldn't have to work *any*. Dad bent down to clean floors so you'd be able to . . . to . . . walk all over his back, wipe your feet, and go . . . [*They work for a few moments longer.*] Anyway, I think Puerto Rico will be fun. Jungles and farms—you can't get that in Holbrook. And Mom says we can buy a horse down there—something else you can't get in Holbrook.

JAVIER: You can't get malaria in Holbrook either . . .

CHARLIE: . . . and hang out at the beach all day long . . .

JAVIER: . . . or tarantulas and hurricanes . . .

CHARLIE: . . . and all those pretty girls to fall in love with.

JAVIER: Early marriage, lots of brats, and a fat middle age!

CHARLIE: Racist!

JAVIER: [*Laughing.*] Mom hates it when she asks, "Why don't you marry a nice Latin girl?" and I always say back, "Nice Latin girls are fat and mean by the time they're twenty-nine."

CHARLIE: Mom thinks that . . . you really dislike our people.

JAVIER: Is that how it looks?

CHARLIE: Well. Yeah. I mean, you hardly speak Spanish anymore, you don't kiss Dad . . .

JAVIER: Charlie, I love you guys, you know I do. It's just "our people" I don't know about. I don't even know what "our people" even *means*. Is it some mass of Latin Americans on Eighth Avenue? Is it all the Puerto Ricans hanging out on Avenue D?[5] Christ, it's so weird! Whenever I see some poor old Puerto Rican stumbling around drunk, acting like a fool, I think of Dad. If I see a bunch of guys with their numb-chucks[6] and radios, I think of our cousins. I mean, I know exactly how these people think, what they like and dislike, what they need . . . and something in me feels like its got to help them . . . and I will someday . . . but for now, I just want to be as far away as possible.

CHARLIE: That's mixed up, Javier.

JAVIER: Charlie, it's just me. Too many things got in between me and them.

CHARLIE: Like what?

JAVIER: Oh Charlie, like . . . I don't know . . . all the times Dad brought a live pig home and slaughtered it in the backyard the way they used to do it in Puerto Rico. And lucky me gets to hold the bucket to catch the blood I'd eat later that night in blood sausages . . .

CHARLIE: I love blood sausages.

JAVIER: [*Beat.*] There was my Christmas at drunk, crazy Uncle Wilfred's, who beat the living shit out of his son, cousin Javier, that day. I'll never forget Javier crying, twisting around on the floor, bleeding and vomiting

5. Like Eighth Avenue, a thoroughfare in Manhattan.
6. I.e., nunchakus, weapons that consist of two

hardwood sticks joined by rawhide, a cord, or a chain.

all over the Christmas nativity thing, a little plastic doodad the Department of Welfare had given to them. [*Beat.*] Or my first sexual flight to heaven. Another cousin, I won't tell you which, Charlie, the shock would kill you. She stalked into my bed one night, I was ten, she was curious, I faked sleeping, she found her way into my pants, I was scared and quiet; she was very warm. Or my second sexual flight. Another cousin, a male, who crawled into the bathtub I was innocently bathing in—he pushed me face down into the water—I was eleven, Charlie—I almost drowned—terrified—I was ripped up the way you rip up paper—then I was blasted from here to God. [*A knock is heard at the door.*] Who's that?

CALLA: [*Off.*] Calla!

CHARLIE: [*To* JAVIER.] I hear you.

CALLA: [*Off.*] Open up!

JAVIER: [*To* CHARLIE.] Did Calla get the deed yet—?

CALLA: [*Off.*] I want to talk to you! [JAVIER *opens the front door and* NICK CALLA, *a tall, rough Italian in his 40's, enters.*] Javier—I want your father! I have to talk to that brilliant businessman!

JAVIER: He and my mother are—.

CALLA: *Ramón, are you in this house??*

JAVIER: He and my mother are—.

CALLA: Days and days go by. I'm only next door. Why don't you people come to me?

JAVIER: This morning they went—.

CALLA: I swear little children are easier to keep track of than you Puerto Ricans!

JAVIER: *Mr. Calla—*.

CALLA: No telephone! No telephone! [*Crosses to the upstairs exit.*] *Are you upstairs?*

JAVIER: [*Soft, to* CHARLIE.] I think I need Julio.

CALLA: You need an accountant. You need a lawyer. An interpreter. A sense of business. A *plan.* Look, I gave your father a downpayment for this house, one thousand bucks, and he told me he was going to give me the deed *right away.*

JAVIER: Dad's showing it to your lawyer—.

CALLA: So why doesn't he get in touch with *me?* Javier, I've got people waiting for me: repair people, insurance people, my family, creditors. What do I tell them?

JAVIER: I don't know.

CALLA: You don't know! Do you know that I could have kept that money in the bank, *earning me interest??* Do you know that?

JAVIER: We've been having some trouble—!

CALLA: *I've* been having some trouble! I've got a brother-in-law out in Brooklyn who has already broken his lease because he thinks he's moving into this house April first! What the hell am I going to tell him?

JAVIER: I don't know, Nick—.

CALLA: I mean, we're talking *real estate*—people uprooting themselves and promises I gotta keep. Meanwhile, I'm putting out money on trust and I've got my old lady in the hospital with a spastic colon, a weak bladder, a skin rash, and you people got me in this *limbo*! Don't you

realize if I don't buy this dump no one goes back to Puerto Rico? I swear
you people would have been up the devil's asshole if it wasn't for me!

JAVIER: You should be canonized, Nick!

CALLA: I've given you money every time you needed it!

JAVIER: And we're giving you the best real estate deal since the Italians
stole America from the Spanish!

CALLA: *I'll be damned if I give you people one penny more!* [*Pow! A loud
explosion rocks the house. Smoke pours into the living room through the
basement door.*] What the hell—?

JAVIER: Oh shit.

CALLA: What is that smell?

CHARLIE: Julio!

JAVIER: [*Realizing.*] Oh *shit!*

CALLA: What is that . . . ?

JAVIER: That's my brother working on the furnace.

CALLA: The furnace? What's wrong with it? What's wrong with the
furnace?

JAVIER: I'll catch you later, Nick! [JAVIER *exits through basement door.*]

CALLA: I'm losing my shirt on this deal, and NOW I'M GOING TO
LOSE MY MIND!! I swear, I'm going to have a goddamn stroke because
of you people!

CHARLIE: Last time the furnace did this, it was thirty below zero with
the wind chill.

CALLA: Do you hear that noise? That's my brain revving up for a stroke!
[CHARLIE *crosses to basement door, looks in.*] I'm basically a good person.
I'm honest. I'm not a yelling person. You people are making me into a
yelling person. [CALLA *sits, his head in his hands.*]

CHARLIE: I better open up the windows. [CHARLIE *crosses to windows.*]
When the oil fumes come up here, it's the most incredible smell of your
life. [CHARLIE *crosses to* CALLA.] We had to evacuate the house once. Do
you know that if you push against the walls or slam a door, you can feel
the house *give*? [CALLA *walks away from* CHARLIE.]

CALLA: I love it. Tell me more.

CHARLIE: Just wait 'till it's summer and you have to deal with the cess-
pool out back!

CALLA: I'd rather deal with my wife's colon condition, thank you. [*Crosses
to* CHARLIE.] Look, Charlie, tell your father to tell your father's *brain*
that I came by and to get in touch with me real fast—or next time he
sees me, I'm bringing my big Italian buddies.

CHARLIE: Javier says there hasn't been a smart Italian since they stabbed
Caesar.[7] [CALLA *crosses to the front door, stops, turns around, looks at*
CHARLIE, *smiles.*]

CALLA: Everybody in this house has a decent wit, but nobody in this
house has a brain. [CALLA *crosses to* CHARLIE.] You people have to learn
that time is money. I swear, you're so poor only 'cause you're so *slow*.
[CALLA *exits.* CHARLIE *crosses to the basement door and looks in. No more
smoke is coming out of it.*]

---

7. Julius Caesar (100–44 BC), Roman general, statesman, and writer.

CHARLIE: [*Calling into the basement.*] Are you guys alive? [*The door opens.* JULIO *and* JAVIER *enter. They are both covered in soot.*]

JAVIER: Oh God . . .

CHARLIE: What happened down there?

JULIO: Aarggh . . . arrghargarrrrrgh . . .

JAVIER: [*To* JULIO.] Why don't you go clean up?

JULIO: Aarrgharghargh . . .

JAVIER: Wash your face, you'll feel better. [JULIO *exits into the kitchen.*]

CHARLIE: What happened?

JAVIER: Where's Calla?

CHARLIE: He went home to do something to his wife.

JAVIER: [*Sitting.*] I tell you, that basement's a scene right out of Fellini.[8]

JULIO: [*Off.*] SHIT!! SHIT MOTHERFUCKER!! SHIT MOTHER-FUCKER PISS!!

JAVIER: What's wrong . . . ?

JULIO: [*Off.*] I CAN'T BELIEVE THIS PLACE!!

JAVIER: What's wrong?

JULIO: [*Off.*] SHIT ON YOUR MOTHER'S FACE!!

JAVIER: Julio! What is it? [JULIO *enters, wiping his face on a dry towel.*]

JULIO: Everybody better enjoy the way they smell right now—Javier, do you enjoy the way you smell right now—?

JAVIER: What happened?

JULIO: I just used the last, final drops of water in our well. There is now . . . no water . . . not a *drop* . . . coming from the faucet.

JAVIER: You're kidding me.

JULIO: I HATE THIS GODDAMN PLACE! Oh God, thank you, thank you, in one week I will be in boot camp and boot camp will be a luxury paradise compared to this! [JULIO *throws the towel to* JAVIER.] Here. I spit on this. You can use it to bathe with. GODDAMMIT WHY IS IT SO COLD IN HERE??

CHARLIE: I opened all the windows.

JULIO: *Close* them! It's *winter*!! *Christ,* Charlie!

CHARLIE: It was smoking and smelling in here.

JULIO: It's not smoking in here any pissing longer! IS IT?? [CHARLIE *scrambles around, closing windows.*] I'm surrounded by fools, lunkheads, dolts, a natural leader like me.

JAVIER: I bet there's a short circuit; that's why there's no water.

JULIO: WELL CHECK ON IT! Do you expect the beast to do *everything* around here?

JAVIER: Well listen to *her!*

JULIO: I'm not a her!

JAVIER: [*Baby talk.*] Is the big girl overworked?

JULIO: Javier, I swear . . .

JAVIER: Just sit there and rest your ovaries for a while, sweetie.

JULIO: A warning, bro.

JAVIER: Don't call me bro. I'm not a bro.

[*The front door opens and* DOLORES *enters, crying, sits.*]

---

8. Federico Fellini (1920–1993), Italian filmmaker famous for scenes of decadence and decay.

JAVIER:   Aaaaaand—it's mamacita . . .

JULIO:   Oh boy, have we got good news for you, Mom.

DOLORES: [*Holding back her tears.*]   Hello . . .

CHARLIE:   Hi beautiful. [CHARLIE *crosses to her and gives her a kiss.*]

JULIO:   So what's the news?

JAVIER:   Where's Dad—?

DOLORES:   Out—.

CHARLIE:   Mom, why are you crying?

DOLORES:   I'm not crying—.

CHARLIE:   What's the matter?

DOLORES:   Nothing—.

> [RAMÓN *enters and he slams the front door hard behind him.*]

JULIO:   What's going on?

DOLORES:   Ramón—for the sake of God in heaven—.

JULIO:   What's up?

DOLORES:   —don't slam the door that way!

RAMÓN: [*To* DOLORES.]   Don't tell me what to do! If I want to slam the door, I'll slam the door! [*He opens the door again and slams it hard.*]

JULIO:   Dad—.

CHARLIE:   You'll shatter the *glass*—.

RAMÓN: [*To* DOLORES.]   I'll break anything I want to!

DOLORES:   Don't make noise! Just don't make noise!

RAMÓN:   *Noise?*

JULIO:   Hey, kids—.

RAMÓN:   Noise? Noise?

> [*He goes over to one of the taped up boxes, rips it open, and turns it upside down. Pots, pans, and utensils spill out all over the floor.*]

JULIO:   Dad, what the hell are you doing?

CHARLIE:   Dad, you're going to break that stuff!

JULIO:   What the hell happened out there?

RAMÓN:   Look at this stuff. Look at this junk. All of this is the junk that came from my big business, my big diner. Do you know something? I'm stupid . . .

JULIO: [*To* JAVIER.]   Say something to him—.

RAMÓN:   —stupid about money, about friends, everything. [*He finds a plate among the debris and shatters it on the floor,* DOLORES *screams.*]

JULIO:   Alright, Dad, that's *it*—.

JAVIER:   Oh God, this family . . .

CHARLIE: [*To* RAMÓN.]   ARE YOU GOING TO KEEP BREAKING ALL THIS STUFF??

RAMÓN: [*To* CHARLIE.]   DON'T YOU DARE TALK TO ME THAT WAY!!

JULIO:   EVERYBODY STOP SHOUTING!

CHARLIE: [*To* JULIO.]   Are you going to let him have a tantrum all over the house?

JULIO:   I WANT EVERYBODY—QUIET—NOW!

DOLORES: [*Crying openly.*]   None of this is our fault, we never hurt anybody.

JULIO:   We know, we know, we know . . . everyone's okay . . . let's all be *calm* right now. [RAMÓN *walks over to the TV and takes out a bottle of rum. He pours himself a shot of it and drinks.*]

CHARLIE: [*To* RAMÓN.]    What the hell are you doing now, Dad?

RAMÓN: [*To* CHARLIE.]    I want you to go to the liquor store, or go to Tony's, and get me another bottle of this—.

DOLORES:    Ramón, what are you doing?

RAMÓN: [*To* CHARLIE.]    Did you hear what I just told you?

JULIO:    No drinking, Dad. Alcohol's just gonna— [*To* JAVIER.] SAY SOMETHING—YOU'RE HIS SON!

DOLORES: [*To* RAMÓN.]    If you're going to drink in this house tonight, I'm not going to stay here, that's a promise . . .

RAMÓN:    Your promises are full of shit, old lady.

DOLORES:    You're going to squeeze the breath out of me.

RAMÓN:    Don't talk that way to me, or I swear I'll—I'll—.

DOLORES:    You'll what?? What are you going to do to me??

RAMÓN:    I'll show you!! [RAMÓN *goes for* DOLORES: *She screams.* JULIO *intercepts him.*]

JULIO:    You put one hand on her, and I'm going to make you wish you never had sons—!

RAMÓN:    I'm going to punish her— nobody should talk to a man the way that bitch talks to me—!

[DOLORES *falls to the floor.*]

JAVIER:    Oh no . . .

JULIO: [*Rushing to* DOLORES.]    Mom . . .

JAVIER:    Mom, *Mom* . . .

JULIO:    Mom, cut it out . . .

CHARLIE: [*To* RAMÓN.]    See what you did? [RAMÓN, *numb, sits on the stairs, and drinks some more while* JULIO *and* JAVIER *attempt to revive* DOLORES.]

JULIO:    Mom, please . . .

JAVIER:    Can you hear me . . . ?

CHARLIE:    Oh God, Mom, stop this—!

JULIO:    Mom . . .

JAVIER:    *Mom* . . .

JULIO:    Pick her up. [JULIO *and* JAVIER *lift* DOLORES *and put her on the sofa. Her breathing is loud and irregular. She thrashes about.* RAMÓN *is quietly crying.*] Dammit, old lady, stop.

CHARLIE:    Call a doctor!

JAVIER:    She'll be okay, don't worry.

CHARLIE: [*To* JULIO.]    Don't you know any Marine life saving shit?

JULIO:    I'm not a Marine, yet moron!

JAVIER:    Shut up, Charlie! She'll be okay!

CHARLIE:    What if she stops breathing?

JAVIER:    She won't.

RAMÓN:    You should have heard me trying to talk your mother into coming to the beautiful United States with me. All the lies I had to tell her! [JULIO *crosses to* RAMÓN *and tries to quietly take the bottle from him throughout this scene.* RAMÓN *resists him.*]

JULIO: [*To* RAMÓN.]    *Si*, Papi, *si, si* . . .

RAMÓN:    We moved to Holbrook when Grundy Avenue was still a dirt road. We pulled up to the house—it looked like a witch's cap—and your mother started laughing when she saw it, she thought I was making a joke.

JAVIER:    See? She's coming out of it.

JULIO: There better be a great reason for all this hitting around here.

CHARLIE: [*To* RAMÓN.]   *Will you stop drinking?*

RAMÓN: [*To* CHARLIE.]   Charlie, learn what I learned: it's right for a man to drink a drop of rum for every drop of water he has cried. *Two* drops if he can get away with it! [*Drinks shot.*] Good! This shot's for success! [*Drinks.*] For Ramón Iglesia! Cook! Janitor! Manager of a failed, greasy diner!

JULIO: Shut up, Dad.

RAMÓN: For welfare! Welfare lines. Welfare meat. Welfare beans. Christmas welfare.

JAVIER: Son of welfare.

JULIO: For Godsakes, Dad, cool out!

RAMÓN: Find work, they told me. Good janitor work. Slop sinks and oil mops. In the same school of my sons. And your mother at the window, day after day—the clock in her head counting the slow years until our return to Puerto Rico. Each year I *lied*; I said, "This year we go back." But she didn't know how the kids loved me at the school I cleaned. The comic, the funny Ramón!

[DOLORES *has come out of her fit and is opening her eyes.*]

JAVIER: Can you see me, Mom?

DOLORES: Yes.

JAVIER: Do you want to sit up?

DOLORES: I'm okay. [RAMÓN *takes another shot of rum, sits.*]

CHARLIE: [*To* RAMÓN.]   Will you put that junk away?

RAMÓN: Leave me alone—show some respect.

CHARLIE: Who can respect you the way you down that shit, and Mom's all hurt?

JULIO: Mom . . . what *is* it? What the hell happened to you guys?

CHARLIE: [*To* RAMÓN.]   Everybody lets you get away with murder!

JULIO: Charlie, will you calm down??

CHARLIE: [*Stands.*]   Look at him! Look at him! *That's* why we're in one mess after another! That's why his foot's gonna burst right open someday! [CHARLIE *goes to* RAMÓN *and pulls the bottle from his hand.*] Will you leave this shit alone?

RAMÓN: WHO THE HELL DO YOU THINK YOU ARE?? [RAMÓN *stands up and slaps* CHARLIE *across the face.* CHARLIE *pulls back and cocks his fist as if to strike back.* JULIO *grabs* CHARLIE's *wrist and twists it behind his back. He pushes* CHARLIE *offstage.*]

JULIO: WHY DON'T YOU JUST CALM DOWN??

CHARLIE: LET GO OF ME!!

JULIO: ARE YOU GOING TO CALM DOWN?!

[JAVIER *crosses to the exit and pulls* JULIO *back onstage as best he can.*]

JAVIER: Come on, Julio, knock it off.

JULIO: He was going to hit Dad!

JAVIER: Come on.

JULIO: He was going to hit your father!

JAVIER: Is that such a bad idea?

JULIO: Alright, *stop pulling me!* AL-RIGHT! [JULIO *pulls free of* JAVIER. *No one moves for a few moments. The two of them look at each other.*] Charlie. [CHARLIE *enters, wiping his eyes.*]

CHARLIE:  I'm sorry—.

JULIO:  Go give Dad a kiss and tell him you're sorry, go. [CHARLIE *crosses to* RAMÓN *and kisses him on the cheek.*] Put that shit away Dad. [RAMÓN *caps the bottle and puts it away.* JULIO *crosses to* DOLORES.] Are you going to live, sweetie?

DOLORES:  I think so.

JULIO:  Okay, good. I like the way the house sounds right now, nice and *silent*. Okay, I want to know what happened.

DOLORES:  They won't let us go. We can't sell the house.

JULIO:  Why?

DOLORES:  Because the deed to this house was not legally signed and Calla's lawyer won't accept it.

JULIO:  What's wrong with it?

DOLORES:  Doña Perez had to get the signatures of her two daughters because they were co-owners—*are* co-owners—of this house. So she signed for them.

JULIO:  It's a forgery. It's a fucking forgery.

RAMÓN:  That's exactly what the lawyer said . . .

JAVIER:  [*Crossing to* RAMÓN.]  And you knew about this, Dad?

RAMÓN:  Knew? Of course I knew. It was my idea. I thought it would save time.

JAVIER:  [*Taking deed away to look at it.*]  You thought you were going to get away with this? [*No answer.*] How can you be so stupid, Dad?

RAMÓN:  Please don't yell at me—I wasn't thinking.

DOLORES:  Nobody blames you. The boys don't blame you.

JULIO:  [*Crosses to* RAMÓN.]  What's the problem? You send this to Doña Perez today, she'll get the girls to sign the stupid thing.

RAMÓN:  This came in the mail today. [*Shows letter.*] It's a letter from Mercedez Terron and Perdita Santoval. They say they won't put their names to any deed that doesn't give them every penny that comes from the sale of the house. They're getting lawyers to make sure they're not cheated. [*Beat.*] It's somebody else's house, children. Again. [RAMÓN *stands up, puts on a coat and crosses to the front door.*] Charlie, clean up this mess. I'm going to Tony's Bar. If anybody wants to stop me, they can try.

  [RAMÓN *exits.* CHARLIE *begins to pick up the garbage. Lights fade. End of Scene Three.*]

### Scene 4

*A week later, outside in front of the Marine Corps Recruiting Office in Holtsville,[9] New York. It's 4:00 A.M. It's very cold.* JULIO *and* JAVIER *enter, carrying bags.*

JAVIER:  God, Julio.

JULIO:  This is it.

JAVIER:  God, Julio.

JULIO:  Stop being a pussy.

JAVIER:  *God*, Julio.

JULIO:  Go stay in the car if you're so cold.

---

9. Town on Long Island just east of Holbrook.

JAVIER:   You had to pick the coldest damn night of the millennium, didn't you?

JULIO:   Go back in the car if you're so cold.

JAVIER:   I don't want to sit in there by myself—.

JULIO:   I don't want to miss anybody—.

JAVIER:   No one's stupid enough to be out here this early, in this freezing weather . . .

JULIO:   Well, you wanted to come out with me—.

JAVIER:   I thought you would have the good sense to stay in the *car*.

JULIO:   A Marine's got to get used to the cold, wimp!

JAVIER:   Oh, Mother of God, spare me. [JULIO *puts his bags down and looks around. He checks his watch.*]

JULIO:   Nobody.

JAVIER:   Who's supposed to come?

JULIO:   Sergeant Overbaby.

JAVIER:   Who?

JULIO:   Overbaby.

JAVIER:   You're giving your future to a man named *Overbaby*?

JULIO: [*Looking into the office.*]   It's not quite four; I'm early . . .

JAVIER:   He's probably in a snowbank doing pushups in the nude . . .

JULIO:   I think he told me he has to come in from Hempstead.[1]

JAVIER:   "I sing of Olaf, glad and big."[2] Do you know that poem?

JULIO:   Maybe I should give him a call . . .

JAVIER:   "I sing of Olaf, glad and big."

JULIO:   Who's Olaf, your boyfriend?

JAVIER:   He was a Swede, a pacifist, and got the life kicked out of him in a poem because he would not kiss your fucking flag.

JULIO: [*Looking at* JAVIER.]   Sometimes I think you have the basic mentality of a handball.

JAVIER:   I'm going to give your recruiting officer a copy of it . . .

JULIO:   Great. They'll have me shot for having a flake for an older brother. Why don't you stop living in the 60's? Be like me! Adjust to the times! Be a beast!

JAVIER:   I'd rather be in bed, thank you. [JAVIER *walks over to the recruiting office and looks inside the window.*] That's interesting. Hmmmmm-mmm. That's very, *very* interesting. Wow.

JULIO:   What is it?

JAVIER:   Well. Up against the wall. In there. Are all these little boxes . . .

JULIO:   I sense something profoundly stupid coming on.

JAVIER:   . . . *and* above each of the little boxes is a name, rank, and serial number . . . and inside each of the little boxes—let me make sure— [*He looks into the window.*] Yep! Inside each of the little boxes is a pair . . . of human testicles . . . little Marine testicles.

JULIO:   Har. Har. Har. Yuck. Yuck.

JAVIER:   Isn't that part of the Deal? You give Uncle Sam your balls, and what's left of your nervous system, and they zap you and turn you into a grunt!

---

1. Town on Long Island some 35 miles west of Holtsville and Holbrook.

2. Poem (1931) by the American poet E(dward) E(stlin) Cummings (1894–1962).

JULIO: I'm not going to be a grunt—I'm going to be a technician, asshole, a hydraulics *technician*.

JAVIER: Right. Exactly like the ads. "Highschool dropout? Can't read English or do long division? Join the Marines and become a neutron physicist!" Ha!

JULIO: It's not like that, Bolshevik![3]

JAVIER: "Learn bio-warfare and global defoliation!"

JULIO: Hey, at least I didn't waste four years in some obscure little college, learning political science, just so I can come home and hang my brain on the loading dock of a warehouse! *That's* good! That's real progress!

JAVIER: Leave me alone.

JULIO: I, howsoever, am getting my brain together in a big way, with a future, and a job, out in the world where the real power is.

JAVIER: *Nuts!*

JULIO: True!

JAVIER: The real world? You're going right from Mommy's bosom to Uncle Sam's! Fed, clothed, and told what to do. *And* you might get killed in the process. Might get mistaken for a Southeast Asian and blown to bits—.

JULIO: Javier, for Chrissakes, it's 1980, it's *peacetime!*

JAVIER: Accidents can happen in peacetime!

JULIO: Accidents *don't* happen in peacetime! Not to Marines!

JAVIER: And promise me you won't develop a drug habit, or go to Iran.

JULIO: Promise me you'll never run for public office! You're so hopeless! What a mother hen! I can't believe you! Javier, you're such an old nurse . . . .

JAVIER: I am not.

JULIO: You are. You're an old nurse. You're a den mother.

JAVIER: I am *not*.

JULIO: I know the real Javier. Nonviolent, nonalcoholic, boring, abnormal . . .

JAVIER: Listen, have a great military career. I'll see you later.

JULIO: Javier the Saint. The unhappy Javier.

JAVIER: Leave me alone.

JULIO: Awwwww, I know one of the things he's unhappy about. I know why he broods. What does Caroline want from your ass this time? What is the evil woman doing to our hero now?

JAVIER: Nothing. She's . . . been looking for furniture, that's all. [*Beat.*] Do you think Overbaby will let me join the Corps?

JULIO: The Corps don't take the mentally ill . . . the castrated . . . or the pussy-whipped, and you, dear bro, show signs of becoming all three. [JULIO *walks away from* JAVIER.]

JAVIER: [*Lost in thought.*] Don't call me bro. [*Looking at* JULIO.] Do you remember *Patton?*[4] [*Takes* JULIO's *arm, imitates George C. Scott.*] "When you put your hand into a mess of goo that ten seconds ago was your best friend's face, you'll know what to do!"

JULIO: [*Smiling.*] And the line from *Apocalypse Now?*

---

3. Communist; from the term for members of the early-twentieth-century Russian Communist Party.

4. Movie (1970) starring George C. Scott as the American general George Smith Patton (1885–1945).

TOGETHER: [*Imitating Robert Duvall.*][5]  "I love the smell of napalm in the morning. It smells like victory!" [*They laugh.*]

JULIO: [*Beat.*]  So. What are you going to do about Dad?

JAVIER: I don't know. He told me he wants to start a restaurant down in Arecibo[6]—but he hasn't even found a place to live yet. He hasn't even sold the house.

JULIO: Listen, don't fuck with his dreams. When I'm gone you have to keep that house together. That's the only thing I can tell you. It's your *job.*

JAVIER: I don't want that job. I want to solve my problems—not Dad's, not Mom's, not Caroline's: mine. I always used you to protect myself—. [*A car can be heard pulling up.*] Wait; listen—. [JULIO *looks out into the distance.*] Yep. The Marines have landed.

JULIO: Already? Really? [*Getting his stuff together.*] This is it, my friend.

JAVIER: Dammit. I had—so many things I wanted to tell you. Ideas and advice—all sorts of things.

JULIO: Well, unless you can say them in ten words or less you better just say good-bye. I can feel myself turning into government property even as we speak.

JAVIER: I'm going to miss you.

JULIO: I'm going to miss you too. Hey, the truth—doesn't that Overbaby look like a grim guy?

JAVIER: Terrifying. Awesome.

JULIO: You take care of everybody—and make sure they write—and keep Mom from getting too excited—and for Godsakes, why don't you make it big already? I mean, doesn't that Overbaby look like a *really grim guy*? [JULIO *salutes* JAVIER *and exits.* JAVIER *waves to* JULIO. JULIO *re-enters the stage and embraces* JAVIER. *Blackout.*]

### END OF ACT ONE

## Act Two

### *Scene 1*

*Later that week. As the lights come up we see* DOLORES *sitting on the sofa, writing a letter.* JAVIER *enters, partially dressed.*

JAVIER: Did we run out of water again?

DOLORES: I had to wash some clothes for your father.

JAVIER: Mom, I need water. I have to take a bath.

DOLORES: They went out for water. They'll be back soon.

JAVIER: Why hasn't Dad called a repairman? Get some guy to fix the pump and we'll have water like civilized people do.

DOLORES: Wash what you can.

---

5. American actor (b. 1931) who plays Lieutenant Colonel Bill Kilgore in the Vietnam War movie *Apocalypse Now* (1979).

6. Municipality on the northern midwest coast of Puerto Rico.

JAVIER:   Mom, I have an interview today with the campaign manager of a guy running for Congress.

DOLORES:   I wish you'd speak to me in Spanish sometime!

JAVIER:   What for? You're deaf in Spanish too!

DOLORES:   Besides, we're moving. The pump is Calla's problem!

JAVIER:   You'd rather see Dad go from house to house begging for water?

DOLORES:   Javier, in Puerto Rico he'd walk from his house in Miraflores[7] to my house in Arecibo with two barrels of water—one on this shoulder, one on this shoulder! In the sun. Barefoot.

JAVIER:   That's because Dad would do anything for a date, Mom.

DOLORES:   Javier! He was a good boy.

JAVIER:   I'm sure he was a very good boy, Mom. And you were a good girl too, right?

DOLORES:   Yes. I was. [JAVIER laughs.] Javier!

[The door opens. CHARLIE enters carrying a bucket of water.]

CHARLIE:   Man oh man oh man . . .

JAVIER:   Little water boy!

CHARLIE:   [Crossing to kitchen.]   Thanks for the help, Javier. Jesus, it is freezing out there! I think this bucket froze—put your face in it, Javier, find out for me. [CHARLIE exits into kitchen.]

RAMÓN:   [Entering with bucket of water.]   Jesus, it's freezing out there! There's a wind you can't believe.

DOLORES:   I was telling Javier how you used to carry water to my house in Arecibo. So strong!

RAMÓN:   Still strong! Right, Javier?

JAVIER:   Strong like mule and just as stubborn.

CHARLIE:   [Re-entering.]   How would you like to be drowning in this bucket, Javier?

JAVIER:   Two buckets of water for bathing, cooking, cleaning, and drinking. Of all the goddamn days! [JAVIER takes bucket of water and exits upstairs.]

CHARLIE:   Julio's gone a week, and everybody falls apart. Hey, Dad, I'm going next door to watch some TV, okay?

RAMÓN:   You should read those books Javier gave you, instead.

CHARLIE:   Come on, Dad, Wide World of Sports is on.

RAMÓN:   Alright. Don't stay out too long. Your mother needs you here.

CHARLIE:   Just save me water to brush my teeth with. I feel like I got a roll of old pennies in my mouth. [CHARLIE exits outside. DOLORES continues to write. RAMÓN sits.]

RAMÓN:   [Suspiciously.]   What are you writing?

DOLORES:   Nothing, Ramón, it's nothing.

RAMÓN:   Dolores, what is it?

DOLORES:   I'm writing to Doña Perez. I'm writing about . . . how much I'm sad about Julio. How much I miss him, Ramón.

RAMÓN:   He had to do what he had to do. There was nothing for Julio to do in Holbrook.

DOLORES:   He could die where he's going. What if he dies?

RAMÓN:   He's not going to die. Julio is a beast!

---

7. Rural barrio, within the municipality of Arecibo but at a distance from the center of the city.

DOLORES: If they hurt my little boy, I don't know what I'll do . . .

RAMÓN: [*Crossing to* DOLORES.] Come on, old lady, stop.

DOLORES: [*Crossing to sofa, sits.*] He never *relaxed*, Ramón. He worked after school every day—.

RAMÓN: [*Reading her letter.*] He loves responsibility. Loves to give orders!

DOLORES: [*Packing clothes in a box.*] Was he angry with us, Ramón?

RAMÓN: Mamacita, please . . . [RAMÓN *crumples her letter and puts it in his pocket.*] I don't want you talking about this and writing it in your letters! You have no proof, Dolores!

DOLORES: Javier is my proof! When he came home from school he was a stranger. The same will happen to Julio: they'll change him.

RAMÓN: Shhhhhh, Javier will hear.

DOLORES: Javier doesn't kiss you goodnight anymore. Up to the day he left he kissed you at night. That made me feel so good.

RAMÓN: I don't know what's wrong with him, but he's still my Javier! Maybe he'll come to Puerto Rico one day.

DOLORES: No, he won't. And we won't beg him! Do you hear? I'll never beg for my son's affection and neither will you!

[*A knock is heard.*]

RAMÓN: Come in, it's open! [CALLA *enters with two huge buckets of water.* RAMÓN *stands and crosses to* CALLA.] I was going to come see you today! [CALLA *puts buckets down.*]

CALLA: Why didn't you tell me you had no water?

RAMÓN: I didn't want to bother you.

CALLA: How long has it been like this?

RAMÓN: A week.

CALLA: Excuse me, Dolores—*that's really stupid, Ramón!*

RAMÓN: I planned to call a repairman today!

CALLA: Sure you did! Here! From Nick Calla, your local neighborhood Red Cross. Free of charge.

RAMÓN: That's very kind, Mr. Calla.

CALLA: Look, if you want more water, hook up a hose to my spigot out there, alright? Do you have a hose?

RAMÓN: No.

CALLA: No. Well, I'll lend you mine. It's stupid to be without water, Ramón. [CALLA *crosses (downstage) away from* DOLORES, *motions to* RAMÓN *to follow him.* RAMÓN *crosses to* CALLA.] What's new with the deed, anything?

RAMÓN: Doña Perez talks to Santoval and Terron every day.

CALLA: And?

RAMÓN: They don't want to change their minds.

CALLA: I don't know how much longer I can wait. I'll level with you: I'm gonna look at another house today. I don't want to, I want *this* one, but you don't leave me much choice, do you?

RAMÓN: [*Taking crumpled letter from pocket.*] My wife is writing her another letter!

CALLA: *Letters!* Christ, sometimes I think your heart's not really in it.

RAMÓN: How's your wife? Still sick?

CALLA: She's getting there. It's tough for her sometimes—I'm an ox, but she's a bird. I know she'd feel better if this was over with.

RAMÓN: It should be soon.

CALLA: [*Crossing to door.*] Let me know *very* soon. Good to see you again, Dolores.

DOLORES: [*To* RAMÓN.] Tell him I hope she feels better soon.

RAMÓN: She says she hopes your wife feels better soon.

CALLA: Thanks. Be in touch. [*exits.* RAMÓN *takes bucket, crosses to kitchen.*]

DOLORES: I heard what he said, Ramón—.

RAMÓN: You always understand when you want to understand, don't you?

DOLORES: You can't let him buy another house! He has to take this one! This house!

RAMÓN: This house is Ramón Iglesia's house.

DOLORES: Ramón Iglesia's house is in Puerto Rico.

RAMÓN: [*Crossing to* DOLORES.] Do you really think I can start a little business down there? Can you really see us going back there? Back to the little farms and the hills and the people who never left? What I'm going to do down there? [DOLORES *crosses away from* RAMÓN.] I thought about this all week, about my house, about the way it's grown with things, for nineteen years, all the bits and pieces of Ramón Iglesia. Even the accidents—.

DOLORES: Not accidents, Ramón: mistakes.

RAMÓN: Mistakes, then. What. The night I lost the diner and the boys and I filled the station wagon with all the food and things we could save from it. Brought it here. Boxes of pots and plates and bags of rice. The house was full and fat and beautiful.

DOLORES: I swear on the spirit of my little Felicia, if you keep me here another year, it'll be our last year together. Every year you promise me we'll go back and every year you break your promise. No more, Ramón! I let you do what you want to do for nineteen years, now I do what I want. If you don't, Ramón, I'll leave you. I'll go home by myself.

RAMÓN: *We don't have any money!*

DOLORES: There's somebody in this house with enough money to help you.

RAMÓN: I'm not going to go to him. I can't go to him.

DOLORES: [*Pointing offstage.*] He's right there. He knows what we need. When he returned from school what did we hear but some big, big talk about helping the poor? Giving to the poor! Well, Ramón, *we* are the poor. You and me.

RAMÓN: I can't take from him, Dolores, will you listen to what I say!

DOLORES: No! Because it's only fear talking to me. You're so afraid of him, I turn red with shame thinking about it!

RAMÓN: I'm not afraid of Javier—.

DOLORES: You're afraid of him and he's ashamed of you!

RAMÓN: Javier is not ashamed of his father! I wouldn't let him live in the house—!

DOLORES: You let him live in the house! You let him eat your food and spit it back in your face! You let him keep you in this country because you're afraid of him!

RAMÓN: Dolores, don't you use that word with me again!

DOLORES: Coward! Coward!

JAVIER: [*Enters dressed in three-piece suit.*] Hi, folks! I'm on my way, wish me luck! [JAVIER *begins to get his stuff ready.* DOLORES *pokes* RAMÓN.]

DOLORES: Ramón!

RAMÓN: [*Crossing to* JAVIER.] Javier!

JAVIER: [*Crossing to door.*] I've got a train to catch, I'll talk to you later.

RAMÓN: [*Intercepting* JAVIER.] You look very nice, Javier! I've never seen you wearing that!

JAVIER: [*Smiling.*] I bought it at school. Cost me a bundle. It's wool, Dad.

RAMÓN: When is your talk?

JAVIER: Talk?

RAMÓN: Eh—your talking—your *speaking*—.

JAVIER: Interview? It's not for a while. If I catch the one-thirty train, I'll be in at three, have lunch with a friend from school whose gender is female, and the interview is at five. Do I look alright, Mom?

DOLORES: Maybe you'll be governor of Puerto Rico!

JAVIER: This job's not that good. This guy's running for re-election in Brooklyn; I'd be on the field team.

RAMÓN: Kissing babies?

JAVIER: That comes a lot later, Dad.

DOLORES: Is there any money?

JAVIER: Very little. The man's not rich, but he's organized rent strikes and gotten people heat for their apartments.

RAMÓN: We need him in Holbrook! [JAVIER *attempts to exit.* DOLORES *grabs him and sits him down.*]

DOLORES: I'm going to make you lunch better than that rabbit food you college kids eat.

JAVIER: I don't have time for that! [DOLORES *exits quickly.* JAVIER *looks at* RAMÓN.] What's up?

RAMÓN: What's up? Doña Perez wrote and said she can't convince her daughters to sign the deed. I have to go home and talk to them. I need money to go home. I'm broke.

JAVIER: Well, you can take out a loan, Dad. That's what banks are for.

RAMÓN: No bank on Long Island will give me a loan at this point, you know that.

JAVIER: [*Crossing to* RAMÓN.] Dad, how many times did I urge you to get out of that school and get a better-paying job? Do you see, finally, why I kept pushing you?

RAMÓN: Javier—.

JAVIER: You've spent all of Calla's downpayment, haven't you?

RAMÓN: Yes! I had debts!

JAVIER: If you had listened to me about learning English . . . [DOLORES *enters from kitchen.*] You know what I think? I think it's good—this whole Doña Perez thing. It's your chance to change your mind.

DOLORES: [*Gives* JAVIER *tray of food.*] He's not going to change his mind!

JAVIER: Why not? Because you haven't given your permission?

RAMÓN: Nobody tells me what I can or cannot do!

JAVIER: [*Putting tray on floor.*] What do you *really* want, Dad? All you do is what someone else wants. You moved to the States because everyone else was doing it! Now that everyone's going back, you're going back. It's so accidental, so random—.

RAMÓN:  Nobody tells me what to do!

JAVIER:  Bullshit. Jump, fetch, and carry your whole life long. And when Calla knocks, you shit water! When Mom snaps her fingers, you faint. And if you don't faint, she does!

DOLORES:  *Will you speak to us in Spanish or not??*

JAVIER:  Spanish and English have a word in common Mom, and that word is no. No, I will not give you money to go back *there.* [*Beat.*] When I graduated, I had a choice, Mom: take a job offer in D.C., or come back home and help you guys. I came because of all your emotional letters for help. The house! The car! Ramón's foot! So I came and took a job I hated and tried to get Dad to take a civil service test, dry out a little, start a savings account—*but I never got through!* [JAVIER *turns away from* RAMÓN *and* DOLORES.] *Mañana*, Javier, *mañana!*

DOLORES:  You did only what you *had* to do—as a son! An Iglesia!

JAVIER:  I didn't *have* to do anything!

DOLORES:  I thought you came back out of love.

JAVIER:  Liar! You thought I came back out of obligation—.

RAMÓN:  [*Crossing to* JAVIER.]  *Are you calling your mother a liar??*

JAVIER:  I was twenty-one, I wasn't obliged—!

RAMÓN:  *Did you hear me?*

JAVIER:  I HEARD YOU!!

DOLORES:  *Don't yell at your father! Respect your father!*

JAVIER:  I wouldn't have returned if I didn't respect him. But I don't respect him now! Going back to Puerto Rico means you have failed, Dad. I want out. I want my freedom.

DOLORES:  Freedom from being Puerto Rican?

JAVIER:  Freedom from . . . stupidity. From thinking like a peasant.

RAMÓN:  WHAT'S WRONG WITH BEING A PEASANT?? What's wrong to be Puerto Rican? What's wrong with you? We have the same blood . . .

JAVIER:  Excuse me, your selfish son has a train to catch . . . [JAVIER *crosses to front door.* RAMÓN *intercepts him.*]

RAMÓN:  Sorry, Javier, please lend me this money, I'll fix the deed, sell the house, and pay you back.

JAVIER:  No, you won't. You'll go down there and those people will over-whelm you—and you'll fuck everything up, the way you always do.

RAMÓN:  [*Crossing to front door.*]  I'm getting out of here. [*To* DOLORES.] He's ashamed of me.

DOLORES: [*To* JAVIER.]  Apologize to him!

JAVIER: [*To* RAMÓN.]  Put on a pair of boots!

RAMÓN:  I don't have a pair of boots!

JAVIER:  So buy a pair! Wait, I forgot! You're broke! You have debts! You can't make a janitor's salary stretch between lotteries, numbers, horses, alcohol, and, once in a blue moon, *necessities for the family!*

RAMÓN: [*Exploding.*]  *ME CAGO EN DIOS, CARAJO!!*[8] [RAMÓN *crosses to* JAVIER.] I want you to move out, don't wait until the house will be sold. I can't live with you if you don't love me. Don't be here when I'm getting back. [RAMÓN *exits the house.*]

8. I shit on God, dammit!

JAVIER: [*Gathering his stuff.*]  Fine with me . . .

DOLORES:  Where are you going?

JAVIER: [*Crossing to front door.*]  I've got an interview, Mom. I've got to kiss babies!

DOLORES:  Stay here and talk to me!

JAVIER:  I have no time.

DOLORES:  You have time for me—!

JAVIER: [*Starts for door again.*]  I have a train to—!

DOLORES:  DON'T TALK TO ME ABOUT TRAINS! [DOLORES *grabs* JAVIER *from behind but can't hold him. She spins around and staggers* (downstage), *her eyes closed.*] I can't see, Javier! I can't see! [JAVIER *looks at her and shakes his head. She staggers around.*] You've betrayed him, Javier . . .

JAVIER: [*Crossing to* DOLORES.]  I haven't betrayed anybody . . .

DOLORES: [*Eyes closed.*]  . . . that poor old man, what's he going to do . . . ? [JAVIER *takes* DOLORES *by the shoulders and takes her to the sofa. He sits her down.*]

JAVIER: [*Holds out his hand.*]  Let's go, Helen Keller.[9] How many fingers do I have up? Huh?

DOLORES: [*Pushing his hand away.*]  It's a hoof.

JAVIER: [*Rubbing her shoulders.*]  Okay, it's a hoof. How many tails do I have? How many horns?

DOLORES:  Many, many.

JAVIER:  U-huh. Many, many. And you are a major goose. [*Checks watch.*] Are you going to be okay, or what?

DOLORES:  I'll never be okay until I go home again.

JAVIER: [*Crossing to chair.*]  Oh Mom . . .

DOLORES:  You don't remember! You were just a baby! But I remember. Son, I want to see chickens run across my yard, all year round. I want to hear my language spoken by everyone I meet, even little children. I left everything I cared about when I left Puerto Rico.

JAVIER:  Hasn't this ever been home?

DOLORES:  Never. This place has never been good to any of us—.

JAVIER:  It's been good to me, Mom. I'm going to do well here . . . [JAVIER *crosses to* DOLORES *and takes her hand.*]

DOLORES:  I know, love. I don't doubt it for a moment.

JAVIER:  So why can't you accept this place the way I accept it?

DOLORES: [*Crosses to her altar.*]  Because it took away my Felicia . . .

JAVIER:  Mom, you've got to let her go! You've got to bury her! You can't blame this house for that—!

DOLORES:  Yes, I can!

JAVIER:  It would have happened down there. She would have died down there—.

DOLORES:  For six days she lived here! This cold house killed her!

JAVIER:  She was born sickly, Mom; anything could've—.

DOLORES:  She was strong! I could feel how strong she was! I could feel it in her hands. I could see it in her busy, red face. I heard it when she cried. [*Trying not to cry.*] I came to her. I warmed her. I held her against

9. American lecturer (1880–1968), deaf and blind.

me, keeping her from the cold air in this dying house. For six days Ramón worked on the furnace, trying to start it, but it wouldn't start. One day, as I was making coffee, while Ramón was at work, she died. I . . . stood by that window for a whole day, facing Puerto Rico. And poor Ramón. He almost went crazy. [*She starts to cry openly.*]

JAVIER: Oh Mom, don't do that.

DOLORES: Every room is absent with my little girl!

JAVIER: Come on, Mom . . .

DOLORES: My little Felicia would have stayed with me after all the boys have gone . . . [*A knock is heard at the door.*] I better go—.

JAVIER: Don't go—.

DOLORES: [*Crossing to upstairs exit.*] I don't want anyone to see—.

JAVIER: Mom . . . [DOLORES *exits upstairs. Door knock is heard again.*] Come in! It's open! [CAROLINE *enters.*]

CAROLINE: Hi.

JAVIER: You have fucking incredible timing!

CAROLINE: [*Exiting.*] Bye.

JAVIER: You knocked. Get over here.

CAROLINE: [*Enters, closes door.*] If somebody had a phone, somebody else would have better timing.

JAVIER: Alright, okay, I'm sorry, alright, I'm sorry, okay?

CAROLINE: [*Noticing his clothes.*] So who's the date with?

JAVIER: Destiny.

CAROLINE: Does she have big tits?

JAVIER: Enormous. What are you *doing* here?

CAROLINE: A: I came to see you, which I know is pretty selfish. After all, I shouldn't presume I can just pop over any old friggin' time I get the itch—.

JAVIER: Caroline, knock it off.

CAROLINE: B: I came to give your parents a house present. [*Takes out a small glass ball, with a house and snow in it.*] Isn't it cute? I got it at a boutique. It's a house with snow. They can shake it up and make winter.

JAVIER: [*Smiles weakly.*] How clever. How are you?

CAROLINE: Lonely.

JAVIER: Forget I asked . . .

CAROLINE: [*Smiles, crosses to* JAVIER.] Hey, you look kind of nice, bro. Don't dress up for *me*, of course . . .

JAVIER: [*Pulling away.*] These are job hunting clothes, not seduction clothes . . .

CAROLINE: [*Putting arms around him.*] Oh, I don't know . . .

JAVIER: [*Crossing [downstage].*] Look, I've just had a stupid, ugly screaming scene with my Mom and Dad. My mother just laid her usual heavy trip on me. My father kicked me out of the house. There's no heat, very little water, I'm late for my fucking interview—and I'm about to lose my shit!

CAROLINE: [*Crossing to* JAVIER.] So let it down; talk to me. Come on, boy, loosen up! Loosen up that face! You're such a troll!

JAVIER: [*Pulling away.*] Caroline, just don't *touch* me, okay?

CAROLINE: I bet you let your friend from school touch you, huh? Your little college girlfriend! How's she doing, anyway?

JAVIER: She's fine. She's been a real sweetheart about helping me find a place to live. So much of it is word-of-mouth.

CAROLINE: I bet she's good at word-of-mouth.

JAVIER: And . . . I think we've found a place to live—for me, not for her, she already has her own place.

CAROLINE: Is it nice?

JAVIER: Yes, it's nice, and why don't you go home?

CAROLINE: I want to know if your place is nice!

JAVIER: It's everything a man could ask of four tortured walls, four flights of stairs, and waterbugs big as my shoes!

CAROLINE: You're really climbing that ladder! I knew you'd make it big someday! So when are you going to let me break it in?

JAVIER: Do what?

CAROLINE: Break it in. You know, after it's all fixed up, comfy, civilized, you have your Bobby Kennedy[1] poster on the wall . . . and a few tough nights have gone by. I'll come over, bring some beer, and we'll do it: break it in. Do you know what I'm talking about?

JAVIER: I'm afraid you're too subtle for me.

CAROLINE: And I'll break it in for as long as you can stand it . . . [CAROLINE *attempts an embrace.* JAVIER *walks away.*]

JAVIER: That's just about the most generous thing I've heard all day, but there's a problem.

CAROLINE: What?

JAVIER: You can't help me break it in.

CAROLINE: What?

JAVIER: The apartment.

CAROLINE: Why?

JAVIER: Because you're not going to know where it is. [*No response.*] I'm not giving you my new address. I don't want you to visit me, cook for me, sleep with me, or even call me up.

CAROLINE: What are you talking about?

JAVIER: I'm talking about it's over. You and me, us; it's *over*; did you hear that?

CAROLINE: [*Beat.*] Why? What have I ever done to hurt you?

JAVIER: Nothing. Nothing was ever *done*. Do you remember that concert in Stony Brook?[2] The New Year's Eve Rock-n-Roll Blitz?

CAROLINE: Yeah . . .

JAVIER: You had just frosted your hair and you were so excited because you had this great dope. The whole concert came and went and all I could do was stare at you—.

CAROLINE: If you didn't have fun, we could have gone home . . .

JAVIER: You were chewing gum, smoking grass, jumping up and down on your seat and I realized, I didn't love this. Not these people. This music. This wasted time—.

CAROLINE: Wasted time?

---

1. Robert Francis Kennedy (1925–1968), American politician, attorney general 1961–64; associated with liberal activism.
2. Town north of Holbrook; here, probably, the town as the site of the State University of New York at Stony Brook (now Stony Brook University).

JAVIER:  You know what I felt? I felt like your parent and you were my retarded teenage daughter! I felt sick to my stomach, Caroline!

CAROLINE:  Hey, thanks.

JAVIER: [*Crossing to* CAROLINE.]  Carrie, you've been great to me. But I can't live on sex, drugs, and rock-n-roll any more!

CAROLINE:  Sex, drugs, *and* rock-n-roll? You're giving me a dab too much credit, aren't you? Of course I can't do half the things your college girl can do! I can't fuck and do trig at the same time!

JAVIER:  Why don't you go home, Caroline?

CAROLINE:  Yeah, just go home! Forget this whole year! Forget how I fell in love with you, said yes to you, listened to all your ambitions, your high horse bullshit—.

JAVIER:  *I am tired, Caroline! I don't wish to see you any more!* THIS IS THE END OF THE CONVERSATION!

CAROLINE:  This is not the end of the conversation!

JAVIER:  Oh shit . . .

CAROLINE:  Forget all the serious balling we did! Just so you can move out, find a place, disappear out of my life without wiping your bloody jaws—without saying, "Thanks for the meal, bitch!" Without even wondering, what do *you* think, Caroline? *Do* you think, Caroline? Do you *feel? Sex, drugs, and rock-n-roll??* Who the frig do you think you are anyway?? [*Beat.*] Ask me the capital of Spain! Huh? Will you? What about square roots? Ask me about square roots. I can do those. Ask me how to make babies. How love is made. Ask! Ask me who's been mother, sister, and whorehouse to you for the toughest, loneliest year of your life, and you tell me you didn't get enough *nourishment*?? [*Beat.*] I thought you were full of sympathy and mystery and fun and I gave you everything I could without dropping dead and you don't think you got enough. You think you can do better than me, don't you?

JAVIER:  I know I can do better than you. That's the problem. [CAROLINE *puts on her coat and crosses to front door.* JAVIER *tries to stop her.*] Wait a—.

CAROLINE:  *Fuck you, alright?* [CAROLINE *exits.* JAVIER *screams.*]

JAVIER:  SHIT!! [JAVIER *gets his stuff together.*] Hello, Congressman, no, I didn't read your article in the *Times*, I was too busy breaking up with my whorehouse! Goddammit, Caroline. Goddammit, Mom. Goddammit, Julio. Goddammit, Charlie. Where the fuck are you, Dad? [JAVIER *puts on gloves and scarf. He tears up train schedule.*] Here I come, Dad—again.
    [JAVIER *exits. Black out. End of Scene One.*]

## Scene 2

*About six hours later. Outside in front of the Marine Recruiting Office in Holtsville.* RAMÓN *enters, limping, disoriented. He stumbles around for a few moments. He has been drinking. He knocks on the window of the office. He walks away from it and falls in the snow. He sits there for a moment or two, dazed. He gets up and walks toward the recruiting office again. He collapses against the brick wall, barely holding himself up.* JAVIER *comes running on.*]

JAVIER:  Dad . . . ! Dad . . . ! Oh, Jesus, Dad . . . what did you think you were going to do here? [*He tries to pull* RAMÓN *to his feet.*]

RAMÓN: No . . . no . . .

JAVIER: Come on, get away from there . . .

RAMÓN: Tell my son, tell my Julio, to come get me . . .

JAVIER: Julio's long gone, Dad, the smart one took off and left you . . .

RAMÓN: Who are you?

JAVIER: Let's just *go* . . .

RAMÓN: Who are you?

JAVIER: Javier. Your son.

RAMÓN: Javier Iglesia! That's what you are . . .

JAVIER: Yes. Come *on.* You'll *freeze* . . .

RAMÓN: Let go of me . . .

JAVIER: Dad, you're going to freeze here!

RAMÓN: I'd rather freeze to death than go anywhere with you!

JAVIER: Oh . . . Dad . . . don't say that . . .

RAMÓN: I'd rather lie right here, Javier, turn over in the snow, right now, right in front of you, and just die.

JAVIER: Why do you say that?

RAMÓN: You've left me alone . . .

JAVIER: I just want to do for *myself* . . .

RAMÓN: Turned your back . . .

JAVIER: . . . I don't want the world to leave me behind, Dad . . .

RAMÓN: You're going to be left behind, like me . . .

JAVIER: No, I'm not! No, I'm not!

RAMÓN: When you're not as young as you are now. When you're no longer the angel so easy to forgive.

JAVIER: I don't want to be forgiven. I just want to be allowed to forget the old world, *your* old world, Dad. Because that world has killed you and the new world doesn't want you. And I won't let that happen to me too!

RAMÓN: It'll happen. Do you think they really love you? It'll happen to you *worst*, Javier, worst than me.

JAVIER: No, Dad . . .

RAMÓN: You've made them so important! You eat their food, wear their clothes, love their women, talk their language, but you're still their little Puerto Rican, Javier. You're their entertainment, their fun. Something new. Dance for us, Javier! Salsa for us, Javier! Wear the clothes, Javier! Fool yourself, Javier! Keep fooling yourself, Javier! You're a little Puerto Rican, Javier! LET GO OF MY ARM! [JAVIER *lets him go.* RAMÓN *crosses to the Marine Recruiting Office window. He leans against it, disoriented.*]

JAVIER: I can just leave you here! You know that? I'll just leave you here and you can die in the cold! I'll leave you here if I want!

RAMÓN: Leave me alone . . .

JAVIER: Half of me wants to do that! Lie right down there, Dad! Cover yourself up! Go to sleep! Let them find you tomorrow morning! You'll be doing me a favor! I won't have to be pointing to you saying, "That's my father, that janitor there!" See the bent old man with the mop? The old slave dragging his feet? That's my proud old man! [RAMÓN *falls in the snow.*] GET UP, FOR CHRISSAKES! *Don't you have any pride at all?* Are you going to let this snow kill you while I stand here watching you? If you don't get up, I'll walk, I'll leave, I swear! [*Bending down over his father.*] WHY CAN'T YOU HELP YOURSELF? [*Yells.*] WHY?? [*Low.*]

Why can't you help . . . yourself. You should never have bent down so I could wipe my feet on your back. I never asked you to do that for me. Why did you do that for me? Why were you that way for me? Why did you suffer so fucking *quietly*?

> [JAVIER *runs off.* RAMÓN *remains on the ground a few seconds. He struggles to his feet and attempts to exit in the opposite direction. He falls again.* JAVIER *runs on, lifts him, and carries him off. End of Scene Two.*]

### Scene 3

*A few hours later, the Iglesia house. As the lights come up,* DOLORES *and* CHARLIE *enter through the front door.* CHARLIE *crosses to the kitchen while* DOLORES *rushes upstairs.*

CHARLIE:  Dad! [*Crosses to the basement door, opens it.*] Javier! Dad!

DOLORES: [*Coming down stairs.*]   Where are they? If they're not here, where are they?

CHARLIE:  Calla says we should call the cops.

DOLORES:  We have to call Julio.

CHARLIE:  Julio's in South Carolina, Mom.

DOLORES:  We need Julio!

CHARLIE:  You can only get him through the Red Cross, for an emergency.

DOLORES:  *This* is an emergency! It's supposed to get *colder* tonight! [*The front door opens.* JAVIER *enters.*]

JAVIER:  Well, look who's here!

DOLORES:  Where's Ramón?

JAVIER:  Dad's fine, Mom, don't worry.

CHARLIE:  You found him?

JAVIER:  Yeah, I finally caught up with him.

DOLORES:  Why isn't he with you?

JAVIER:  Because he's at the hospital, Mom.

DOLORES:  He's dead!

JAVIER:  No, he's not dead . . .

DOLORES:  He was hit by a car!

JAVIER:  Mom, he's okay. Listen, Dad went on a long walk. He walked to Tony's Bar, then he started wandering all over Holbrook.

CHARLIE:  Calla took us everywhere. Up to Sunrise,[3] to Grundy Avenue.

JAVIER:  Did he take you to the Marine Recruiting Office?

CHARLIE:  He went all the way out *there*?

JAVIER:  That's where I found him, wandering around, drunk. He said he was looking for Julio.

DOLORES:  Javier . . . he misses his boy.

JAVIER:  I know, I know.

DOLORES: [*Almost crying.*]   That poor old man, I have to see him.

JAVIER:  You can't, Mom, visiting hours are over. They're holding him for observation.

DOLORES:  Why?

---

3. Sunrise Highway, a major thoroughfare.

JAVIER: You can't have diabetes, go around drinking beer all the time, and expect your foot to withstand a lot of cold. They're afraid he might be severely frostbitten, so they're going to hold him a while.

DOLORES: I told him! Didn't I tell him day after day!?

JAVIER: He's okay now. It's all cleaned out and bandaged and he's in a big, clean bed, nice and warm, flirting with all the nurses already. Alright, Mom?

DOLORES: It was your fault, you know. You upset him.

JAVIER: I know I did. I talked to him. I said I was sorry.

DOLORES: He wants your blessings in what he does.

JAVIER: I know, Mom. He's okay. Everything's alright. [DOLORES turns away from JAVIER.]

DOLORES: Everything's not alright. [DOLORES crosses to the window and looks out. JAVIER looks at CHARLIE.]

CHARLIE: Calla doesn't want to buy the house no more, Javier.

JAVIER: You're kidding.

CHARLIE: He's been cheating on Dad! He says he's looking at another house . . .

DOLORES: Maybe if you talked to him, Javier.

JAVIER: What do you propose I tell him, Mom?

DOLORES: That he has to take this house!

JAVIER: Mom, I told you before. I don't believe in this move to Puerto Rico. I can't talk to Calla.

CHARLIE: Javier, don't be a shit.

JAVIER: I'm trying to do what's best, Charlie.

CHARLIE: Best? For who?

DOLORES: Charlie, please . . .

JAVIER: For you! For Mom! Everybody!

CHARLIE: You're doing it because you don't want to tell your college friends your parents couldn't hack it in America!

DOLORES: Charlie, don't talk that way to him.

CHARLIE: Why not? *Somebody's* got to! All he does is complain!

DOLORES: He's your big brother!

JAVIER: Charlie, I'm doing it for you!

CHARLIE: Me?

JAVIER: You.

CHARLIE: ME??

JAVIER: YEAH, YOU!! You have to have a good education! Without that you won't get anywhere.

CHARLIE: How do you know, Javier? You're not my father! How do you know I can't learn things down there? Besides, what if, what if I don't want to learn what *you* know?? You never asked me! What if I don't care about *Decline of the West* or the *New York Times* or that other beat shit you never use? Your father went out in the snow and nearly got killed because he knew something you don't: *loyalty,* man! If I learn that by going to *my* home, *then fuck you, alright*??!

JAVIER: You'll go down there and end up in the goddamn Marine Corps!

CHARLIE: If I do, it's my business!

JAVIER: Go down there and vegetate and cop out like Julio did!

CHARLIE: DON'T YOU JUDGE, JULIO!!

JAVIER: He'd be the first to admit it!

CHARLIE: JULIO DOESN'T COP OUT!

DOLORES: *Charlie, stop it—!*

JAVIER: HE *WIMPED* OUT! HE *PUSSIED* OUT!

DOLORES: Javier, for God's sakes—!

CHARLIE: I'LL BUST YOUR FACE, MAN! [CHARLIE *lunges at* JAVIER. DOLORES *screams. They struggle.* DOLORES *pounds them and they separate.*]

JAVIER: Mom!

DOLORES: I don't want to see my boys hurt each other.

CHARLIE: [*Crossing to sofa.*] We're just playing—.

DOLORES: [*To* JAVIER.] Javier, what's wrong with you? The first sky you saw was a Puerto Rican sky. Your first drink of water was Puerto Rican water. But Puerto Rico isn't good any more! It hurts Ramón and separates my children. So I must be wrong!

CHARLIE: You're not wrong, *he* is!

DOLORES: And if I'm wrong, we'll stay here. Is that good, Javier?

JAVIER: Mom, please, just do what you want . . .

DOLORES: I'll stop dreaming about that stupid island! You can bury us here while you're at it! The baby's spirit wants to go home . . . [DOLORES *crosses to the little altar, takes Felicia's picture and gives it to* JAVIER.] *You tell her we can't go home—you tell her!* [JAVIER *takes the picture. A brief pause. He places the picture back in the altar.*]

JAVIER: Just one thing and I'll talk to Calla, alright? Make Charlie work hard, *push* him, push him hard.

CHARLIE: Nothing's free, huh, Javier?

JAVIER: Charlie, when you go to Puerto Rico, you will not stop reading books or newspapers, you will not stop asking questions and seeking action. Do you hear me?

DOLORES: What will you do?

JAVIER: I'll go to Puerto Rico in Dad's place and get Santoval and Terron to sign the deed.

CHARLIE: With *your* Spanish?

JAVIER: I'll pretend I didn't hear that. [*To* DOLORES.] Alright?

DOLORES: Yes. Yes, Javier.

JAVIER: It's a deal, then. Charlie, go get Calla.

CHARLIE: Oh man . . . !

JAVIER: Hurry before I change my mind! [CHARLIE *crosses to the door.*] Charlie. You better come through for me.

CHARLIE: Carlos will come through! [CHARLIE *exits the house.*]

DOLORES: Thank you, Javier.

JAVIER: This doesn't mean I think you're right, Mom. Don't think I believe in what's going on.

DOLORES: Are you really going to Puerto Rico?

JAVIER: *Si.* Christ, I wish my Spanish was better!

DOLORES: You have to go to Miraflores!

JAVIER: What's in Miraflores?

DOLORES: You were born there! And you have to go to Utuado,[4] it's beautiful.

4. Municipality in the mountains south of Arecibo (and thus of Miraflores).

JAVIER: Okay, I will.

DOLORES: And when you meet Santoval and Terron, yell at them for me.

JAVIER: I'll strangle them for you. [*The door opens.* CHARLIE *enters, pulling* CALLA, *wearing a tee-shirt and holding a shirt.*]

CHARLIE: Company!

JAVIER: Oh boy, oh boy . . .

CALLA: Charlie, Christ, what the hell are you doing . . . ?

JAVIER: . . . company . . .

CALLA: You people are really pushing me to the edge of my—.

CHARLIE: Safe and unsound.

JAVIER: [*Putting arm around* CALLA.] Hi, Nick.

CALLA: —of my brain. [*Pulling away from* JAVIER.] For Chrissakes, let go!

DOLORES: Ask him if he wants a cup of coffee.

JAVIER: My mother would like to know if you want a cup of coffee.

CALLA: [*Putting on shirt.*] I want an explanation, thank you, tell her that.

JAVIER: [*To* DOLORES.] He would love a cup of coffee, Mom. [DOLORES *exits into kitchen.*]

CALLA: Hey, wait, I think I just suffered in the translation—.

JAVIER: I'm sorry if this is a little sudden, but I'm afraid I've got some news for you—.

CALLA: Wait. Hold it. Whoa. I'm afraid I have a little news for *you*, Javier. Are you ready for this?

JAVIER: What is it?

CALLA: I've found another house to buy.

JAVIER: That's bullshit.

CALLA: At the edge of town, right by the tracks, you might have seen it.

JAVIER: No, you're lying . . .

CALLA: . . . it's smaller than this, no upstairs, but I won't have to sink a whole lot of extra money into it—the furnace there doesn't explode every ten minutes, I mean—.

JAVIER: I don't believe you.

CALLA: . . . and the people don't have this helter-skelter way of stumbling around with other people's time and money . . .

JAVIER: You're lying, Nick . . .

CALLA: This is the truth! I'm telling you the truth! I went there today, talked to the gentleman, *he* didn't produce a piece of paper with forgeries all over it, *he* didn't run around without having a plan or a method. I admit—it's going to cost me more initially, true, it hurts, but almost any price is worth it to get you people out of my stomach for good!

JAVIER: Oh Nick . . .

CALLA: I'm sorry, you weren't fast enough. But that, as they say, is life! Please excuse me if I'm being flip.

JAVIER: Nick, you have to buy this house.

CALLA: No way!

JAVIER: Nick, I have a plan. I have a plan to get the house to you.

CALLA: Too late.

JAVIER: Have you paid these people yet?

CALLA: No.

JAVIER: Have you signed anything?

CALLA:   No, and I don't care! I just want to be untangled from you people once and for all. The man there speaks my language.

JAVIER:   You're not dealing with my father any more, Mr. Calla, you're dealing with me.

CALLA:   Excuse me, I'm not impressed.

JAVIER:   You're dealing with *me*, Mr. Calla, not with Ramón!

CALLA:   There's a difference? I don't see a difference! Like father, like son: losers breed losers. It's like some assembly line in Heaven got stuck one day and turned out a whole island of you: these little Spanish people who don't know shit about the world. There's this *smell* coming from you people, Javier, the smell of fear, and it's even all over you, don't tell me it ain't. You just don't know how things get done in the world.

JAVIER:   I won't tell you I'm not afraid, because I am! Just like Ramón! I AM! I am more afraid than my father is. I'm afraid for them because I don't know what's going to happen in the future. And I'm afraid of people like you who say, "Losers breed losers." Alright. But you were afraid too, like me, maybe worse. So now it's your turn to be brave for me.

CALLA:   That's just words, Javier. [*Rubs his fingers together to indicate money.*] Words.

JAVIER:   Okay. [*Crosses to desk, gets his checkbook.*] You gave Dad a one-thousand-dollar down payment on this house. It's gone; he spent it. Here, Nick, your down payment back: but in exchange, I want three days in Puerto Rico so I can clear up this mess with the deed. [JAVIER *writes check.*]

CALLA:   Three days? [JAVIER *gives him check. He examines it.*] Okay. But if you fail you may be living in the bottom of the Long Island Sound, and believe me, my family will put you there. [CALLA *exits.* DOLORES *enters with coffee.*]

CHARLIE:   *GOOD-BYE, LONG ISLAND!*
        [*Blackout. End of Scene Three.*]


## Scene 4

*Two weeks later. The Iglesia house.* JULIO *enters, wearing a Marine uniform. He salutes the audience and delivers his letter directly to the audience, in a slight Southern accent. During his speech,* CHARLIE *and* JAVIER *enter the house and begin removing all the furniture and boxes from the house in silence.*

JULIO:   Dear family. Well, folks, it's the beast again writing to you from the world of green, drabby underwear and bad food. In my last letter you got an ache-by-ache tour of Hell's Armpit, also known as Parris Island,[5] but today things are even funnier. Everybody is hot to trot for the possibility of being sent to Iran to kick the Ayatollah's ass around.[6] These bozos are actually looking forward to combat pay! What does the

---

5. Marine Corps Recruit Depot Parris Island, Marine training center in South Carolina.
6. In 1979, Ayatollah Rouhollah Mousavi Khomeini (1902–1989), Iranian religious and political leader, helped lead the Iranian Revolution and then established a theocratic rule over Iran. During the "Iranian hostage crisis" (1979–81)

between Iran and the United States, Khomeini supported the group of Islamist students and militants who took over the American embassy in Iran and held 53 Americans hostage. The one U.S. attempt to rescue the hostages—in 1979, involving helicopters flown from the USS *Nimitz*—failed.

beast think of all this? He's looking forward to tending the Marine Corps Library as far from bullets, shells, and the criminally stupid as possible. Wait until I catch the swindler who told me it was peacetime! [*Beat.*] Well, that's about it from here. I'm thrilled about the sale of the house. But tell Calla that if he doesn't treat that house with respect I'm going to go there and rip his forehead off. And tell Judas[7]—that's you, Javier—that you better write to me very, incredibly soon. Or you'll have one beastly bro standing on your face when next we meet. Kisses and flowers, Julio. The beast. [JULIO *salutes audience and marches off. Lights up full on the house.*]

CHARLIE: [*Looking around the room.*]   This place. It's so different, empty. I hadn't realized how little it was.

JAVIER:   Yeah? Wait'll you take a look at some of the huts out on that little paradise you're going to.

CHARLIE:   I thought you said there were some things that were really nice about Puerto Rico.

JAVIER:   One or two. It's great if you love polyester, food stamps, babies, mosquitos, radios . . .

CHARLIE:   You're being a jerk, you promised not to be a jerk today. You could say *something* nice about Puerto Rico.

JAVIER:   Yes! I don't live there. [*Laughs.*] No, Charlie, I'm kidding. There were things . . . some of the smells . . . the lightning . . . the buzz of the rain forest all night long . . . some beautiful women . . . simple and direct and sweet . . . Just remember, Charlie, that if you need any kind of help, call me up. Alright? And keep a really close eye on those two.
    [CAROLINE *enters and stands by the doorway.*]

CAROLINE:   Hi!

JAVIER:   Caroline . . .

CAROLINE:   Oh, *muchas gracias, señor!*

JAVIER:   I didn't expect to see you.

CAROLINE:   *Muchas gracias, señor!*

JAVIER:   Oh, please . . . [CAROLINE *enters.*]

CAROLINE:   Now, look, I almost had an accident getting here, I skidded half a mile avoiding a boy on a sled, so don't yell at me.

JAVIER:   Who yelled? Did I yell?

CAROLINE:   Your eyebrows are yelling at me. [CHARLIE *takes a box and exits through front door.* CAROLINE *crosses to* JAVIER.] How'd it go in Puerto Rico?

JAVIER: [*Smiles.*]   Well, I ran around like a chicken with its head cut off. I spent a lot of time and a lot of money doing business—and I use the term very loosely—with crazy people. What did you do for two weeks?

CAROLINE:   I gave up drinking. Totally. I never drink any more. And I don't say "frig." And I told Daddy that if he smacks my mother one more time, I'm going to have him arrested. But . . . I still get high because getting high is part of life, so fuck you. [CHARLIE *enters, gets box, exits.*] Are things settled?

JAVIER:   Settled.

---

7. According to the New Testament, Judas Iscariot was one of Jesus' 12 Apostles. His betrayal of Jesus to the Roman authorities led to Jesus' crucifixion.

CAROLINE: Where are you staying tonight?

JAVIER: My options are simple: the Y on 92nd Street, thank you very much, a Central Park[8] bench, or I can sack out here as long as I get out before Calla's brother-in-law arrives tomorrow morning.

CAROLINE: No apartment?

JAVIER: No money.

CAROLINE: Oh. Isn't that interesting. Good thing I brought this along, isn't it? [*She goes to her coat and pulls out a sizeable roll of money.*] Somebody sold a lot of dope this week to get this money together, not to mention her savings, so if you turn it down I'll cream you. [*Smiles.*] This is my loan.

JAVIER: After all the shit—?

CAROLINE: Yes. You need some help—.

JAVIER: Why are you giving me things?

CAROLINE: This money will get you a place to live, where you can live with nothing for a while. No girlfriend, no Mommy and Daddy, no Julio, nothing but your dear, depressing, judgmental, boring self. I'm giving this to you hoping that your next few months are *miserable*. [*Beat.*] You need it, you selfish . . . [*Beat.*] But for now, I guess, all you need is a kiss good-bye and my best, best wishes. [CAROLINE *crosses to* JAVIER, *gives him a light kiss. He tries to embrace her and she pulls away. She crosses to the door, stops.*] You'll forget me, won't you, Javier? [CAROLINE *exits.* RAMÓN *enters down the stairs, with cane and suitcase, wearing his hat from Scene One, Act One.* JAVIER *crosses to* RAMÓN *and takes suitcase.*]

JAVIER: So this is the big day.

RAMÓN: The big day . . .

JAVIER: Goddamn, my nerves are murdering me. How's that foot feeling?

RAMÓN: Better. Doesn't itch now.

JAVIER: Did you clean it out today?

RAMÓN: I cleaned it out today.

JAVIER: Did you clean it out the way they showed you?

RAMÓN: Yes, exactly the way they showed me.

JAVIER: Good. Jesus, I wish my stomach would stop.

RAMÓN: You better take care of that.

JAVIER: You better get Mom. [RAMÓN *crosses to stairs, calls.*]

RAMÓN: Mamacita? Dolores?

DOLORES: [*Off.*] One minute, Ramón, please. [CHARLIE *enters.*]

CHARLIE: Me and Calla got the car all packed and the furniture's in the garage—.

JAVIER: Calla and I. [*Holds out a pack of cigarettes.* CHARLIE *and* JAVIER *take cigarettes.*]

RAMÓN: I want a smoke too. [JAVIER *gives* RAMÓN *cigarette.* JAVIER *flicks on lighter and the three men light up simultaneously.* DOLORES *enters, seemingly a new woman, beautifully dressed and finally content. She smiles at* RAMÓN *and crosses to Felicia's altar to pack the pictures and icons. She lights incense and puts it on a small tray.*]

---

8. Grand public park in Manhattan. Y *on 92nd St.:* the 92nd Street Young Men's and Young Women's Hebrew Association (YM-YWHA), a cultural institution and community center on the Upper East Side of Manhattan.

JAVIER:  Tickets and money, Dad?

RAMÓN:  Everything.

JAVIER:  Well, if there's nothing left . . .

RAMÓN:  Wait, there's one thing . . .

JAVIER:  . . . Calla is waiting . . .

RAMÓN:  . . . one small thing . . .

JAVIER:  . . . I don't know how you fit all that stuff in his car . . .

RAMÓN:  . . . one thing I've been afraid to ask for, but I have to ask . . .

CHARLIE:  Javier, Dad's talking to you.

JAVIER:  I'm sorry . . . what is it, Dad?

RAMÓN:  Could you do me a favor?

JAVIER:  I haven't a single penny left . . .

RAMÓN:  Could you come over to me?

JAVIER:  What for?

RAMÓN:  Come over to me and give me a kiss goodbye.

JAVIER:  Why?

RAMÓN:  Because it would be nice. [JAVIER crosses to RAMÓN and kisses him. A car's horn is heard. CHARLIE crosses to the front door. DOLORES lights incense.]

CHARLIE:  WE'LL BE RIGHT THERE, MR. CALLA! [JAVIER and RAMÓN break their embrace. RAMÓN exits through the front door. CHARLIE and JAVIER embrace.] Oh Christ, my stomach is turning into oatmeal-diarrhea-soup.

JAVIER:  What a lovely image, Charlie. Let's go, you big wimp.

CHARLIE:  Turkey!

JAVIER:  You have the basic mentality of a handball!

CHARLIE:  Yeah—just wait—next time you see me, *I'm going to be a beast!* [CHARLIE exits through front door. DOLORES crosses to center of the living room with incense.]

DOLORES:  [*To* JAVIER.]  Get down. [JAVIER kneels on the floor. DOLORES passes the incense over JAVIER's head, once.] God bless you. Get up. [JAVIER stands. They embrace. DOLORES exits through front door.]

[JAVIER crosses to window to wave goodbye. He finds CHARLIE's tape recorder and turns it on. Salsa plays. JAVIER smiles. He closes his eyes and suddenly starts to sway his hips and dance. JAVIER stops dancing and sits in the empty living room. The lights begin to dim, throwing long shadows around JAVIER. The music continues. He looks around and shivers slightly.]

JAVIER:  Dance for us, Javier. [*Lights continue to dim.*] Salsa for us . . . Javier.

[*Lights to black. Salsa music continues. End of play.*]

THE END

1983

# LUIS ALBERTO URREA
## b. 1955

Luis Alberto Urrea was born in Tijuana, Mexico, to a Mexican father and an American mother, who registered him at the American consulate as an American citizen. His family tree includes Teresita Urrea (1873–1906)—a *curandera* (healer) known as the Saint of Cabora (a town in Sinaloa, Mexico), though she was never canonized by the Roman Catholic Church—and he depicts her life in his novel *The Hummingbird's Daughter* (2005). Urrea's first language was Spanish, but he learned English while growing up, in San Diego, California. Because of his parents' turbulent marriage, Urrea lived with his godparents, who appear as fictional characters in his poetry collection *The Fever of Being* (1994) and his novel *In Search of Snow* (1994). At the University of California, San Diego, Urrea became the first member of his family to graduate from college, earning his bachelor's degree in writing. He later did graduate work at the University of Colorado at Boulder. After doing relief work—in garbage dumps and orphanages—in Baja (northern Mexico), he taught expository writing at Harvard University. He is a professor of fiction, nonfiction, and poetry in the English Department at the University of Illinois, in Chicago.

Urrea's publishing career began when the Mexican American poet Alurista included some of Urrea's poetry in the literary journal *Maize*. During his years in New England, Urrea and the Mexican American poet Tino Villanueva cofounded the literary journal *Imagine*, for which Urrea served as associate editor from 1984 to 1990. In 1991, he collaborated with the director/writer Jorge Huerta on the drama *Un puño de tierra: A Handful of Dust* at the Teatro Máscara Mágica, in San Diego.

Urrea was the first writer to be nominated twice in a row for the Kiriyama Prize, sponsored by the Pacific Rim Voices, winning it for *The Hummingbird's Daughter*. His nonfiction book *The Devil's Highway: A True Story* (2004)—the first chapter of which, "The Rules of the Game," is excerpted in this anthology—was a finalist for the Pulitzer Prize and won the Lannan Literary Award. Urrea has also won the American Book Award, the Christopher Award, the Western States Book Award, and the Colorado Center for the Book Award. His additional publications include the nonfictional volumes *Across the Wire: Life and Hard Times on the Mexican Border* (1993) and *By the Lake of Sleeping Children* (1996), the poetry collection *Vatos* (2000), the short-story collection *Six Kinds of Sky* (2002), and the memoir *Nobody's Son: Notes from an American Life* (2002). His novel *Into the Beautiful North* (2009)—a variation on the classic Western *The Magnificent Seven* (1960) set in a coastal Mexican town—satirizes the idol-worshiping frenzy of a superhero-infested culture. His graphic novel *Mr. Mendoza's Paintbrush* (2010), illustrated by Christopher Cardinale, is based on a short story in *Six Kinds of Sky* that pokes fun at magical realism.

Urrea often details the lives of the downtrodden in the San Diego–Tijuana border area, using humor to avoid stereotypes as he writes about poverty, disease, and violence. "A Lake of Sleeping Children," a personal essay from *By the Lake of Sleeping Children* that is included here, evokes Tijuana through the image of "a loveable dump," a vision of hell in the form of suspended development. The essay ends with references to Proposition 187, a 1994 ballot initiative in California that prohibited illegal immigrants from receiving social services, health care, and public education in that state (passed by the voters but later found unconstitutional by a federal court; for the text, see Appendix 2: Treaties, Acts, and Propositions, p. A15), and to the building of a wall between Mexico and the United States, an idea that became a priority during George W. Bush's presidency. "The Rules of the Game," a piece of investigative journalism that includes personal anecdotes, analyzes "the politics of stupidity" as it follows the path of 26 undocumented Mexican men who, seeking a better life in the United States, battled the elements in the Arizona desert. Only 12 of these men survived.

# A Lake of Sleeping Children

Just when you think you've seen it all, Tijuana comes up with something so unexpected that you may not, at first, be sure what you're seeing. And then, when you do figure it out, likely as not you'll be stunned into silence and have to just stand there, staring. It's happened again: Tijuana threw me a curveball.

Since I am lately seen as some kind of expert on Tijuana's poverty, I often find myself leading mini-safaris to the southland's favorite representation of hell. You know the drill by now: we go to some shacks, maybe stop at an orphanage or two, gobble fish tacos and go to Tacos El Paisano, then gird ourselves for the Tijuana dump. Everybody loves the dump—cameras fly out of purses, and wanderers walk into the trash, furtively glancing at me over their shoulders so they can be sure they're not *really* in danger.

If there aren't a million gulls, some living-dead pit-bull mongrel bitches, or overwhelming stenches rising in eye-watering clouds, the tourists feel cheated and blue. But the sight of an open and festering wound say, on a garbage-picker's hand . . . well! That sends them right over the moon. Pus Polaroids for the apocalypse scrapbook.

It seems to me that the gringos at the King Kong Group, those sultans of NAFTA[1] trash operating the dump and siphoning easy millions off the efforts of these hungry *basureros*,[2] could open an amusement park ride right here. Hieronymus Bosch Land: The Garden of Earthly Delights Ride in 3-D Stinkovision![3]

And there I was, leading a small safari yet again. And when I got to the lake of sleeping children, it took me a while to see what I was looking at. And of course I'm exaggerating: it wasn't nearly a lake; it was a pond, a lagoon. And the smell was as vivid as we'd all hoped. And later, when I tried to sleep, I knew the thing had seeped into me. It gets into you, you know—it gets in through the eyes. You find pieces of it drifting in your head as you sleep, and you're infected. I dreamed, later, of the children. They were waking up. They were sitting up. The filthy water was cascading out of their eye sockets. They opened their mouths to call my name, and black water jetted out, like fountains.

And, my God, *they wanted to play with me.*

Those of us who worked with the poor all those years in Baja saw so many astounding things that we could each make a full album of them. Things at once horrific and sly, with a kind of Salvador Dalí[4] sense of demonic humor. Droll sights, and almost metaphoric in their richness.

Like the day when I came across the refrigerator in the Barrio of Shallow Graves (near the blinking TV antennas you can see from San Diego, ghostly over the middle ground of Tijuana). I opened the door—it wasn't connected

1. North American Free Trade Agreement (1994), between Mexico, the United States, and Canada.
2. Trash collectors.
3. *The Garden of Earthly Delights* (1503–04), the best-known work by the Dutch painter Hieronymus Bosch (ca. 1450–ca. 1516), is a triptych. The left panel depicts the Garden of Eden. The center panel is a rendering of nude figures engaged in fantastical, partly grotesque, and largely erotic activity. The right panel is a vision of hell. Lakes appear in all three panels, but in hell the water is black or bloodred.
4. Spanish Catalan surrealist painter (1904–1989).

to any power source, just sitting on the edge of a dirty alley, more Magritte[5] than Dalí—and sitting on the middle shelf, in the middle of the middle shelf, on a small tin serving tray, was one curled, perfectly formed human turd. Presented tastefully, as if it were some kind of evil finger sandwich.

Like the woman who swore she was suffering from the evil eye. And when the *curandera*[6] came to cast out the demons, a small viper fell out of the straw seat of the kitchen chair she was sitting on and writhed in the dirt beneath her. "I feel better," the woman said.

Like the man who lived in a washing-machine box. He didn't like sleeping on the dirt, so he carpeted the floor with cast-off avocados. He slept in a blackening swamp of guacamole.

Like the time Negra was given a pair of pigs as a gift. Now, Negra is quite a farmer; she has a knack for growing flowers in the trash, for bringing up various creatures and selling them—dogs, cats, crows, geese, pigs. The pigs in question were those cute little potbellied fellows, about the size of small cats when she first got them. When I first saw them in the corner of her house, I mistook them for puppies. I was startled to pick one up and have it shriek, "Greet! Greeeeet!"

It never occurred to the giver, nor to me, that Negra and all her neighbors had never heard of a mini-pig. In fact, the very concept of a mini-pig was so extraordinary as to be indecipherable to them. When I tried to explain what kind of pigs these were, she looked at me as if I were crazy.

Needless to say, the pigs refused to grow into fat giant porkers. Negra fed and fed them—overfed them, in fact. Gave them vitamins. And then, when it was obvious that an evil curse had been put on these shoats ("They stay babies no matter what we do!" Negra said), she called in the handy witch-doctor, who used up most of her family savings casting spell after spell, trying to break the powerful black hoodoo curse that kept these potential bacon factories chained to infancy.

Tony, a United pilot and book dealer, was in town for his mother's wedding. We had met through the book business and were starting a friendship. Because of the nature of the writing life, you travel about once a month, or more, and end up in all kinds of unlikely places. You're seldom home, or at least I have been seldom home, and a United pilot is a good guy to have for a friend, since he's able to show up in many of the cities you're visiting. It is always good to see a friendly face—or, I should say, a face you know. All the faces are usually friendly: everybody but the Tijuana police, Pat Buchanan, and the Nestor Militia[7] likes an author. (One night I was standing around in the lobby of a hotel in San Francisco, chatting with a bunch of really pleasant British bankers. All of them gray-haired, vaguely weathered, wearing jackets and Oxford shirts and saying "Lovely" and "Quite right." It was only when the elevator doors were closing that I realized I'd been chatting with Pink Floyd.)[8]

And Tony had read about the *dompe* and wanted to see it. I think he may have wanted to compare it with his mental pictures of Saigon.[9] I think his

---

5. René Magritte (1898–1967), Belgian surrealist painter.
6. (Female) healer; quack.
7. *Nestor*: a tiny town between Tijuana and San Diego. *Pat Buchanan*: Patrick Joseph "Pat" Buchanan (b. 1938), American conservative syndi-

cated columnist, politician, broadcaster, and author.
8. English rock band, formed 1965.
9. Or Ho Chi Minh City, the largest city in Vietnam.

nose was secretly longing for that weird tropical rot you get stuck in there: mangoes and mud and something dead and some sewage mixed in with flowers.

The dump was quiet.

Once a gaping Grand Canyon, it gradually filled with the endless glacier of trash until it rose, rose, swelling like a filling belly. The canyon filled and formed a flat plain, and the plain began to grow in bulldozed ramps, layers, sections, battlements. New American garbology affected the basic Mexican nature of the place. From a disorderly sprawl of *basura* to a kind of Tower of Babel[1] of refuse.

Still, the poor Mexicans, transformed now by NAFTA into a kind of squadron of human tractors, made their way through the dump, lifting, sifting, bagging, hauling, carting, plucking, cutting, recycling. The original *dompe* rules, a set of ordinances that sprang up organically from the people who have to work the garbage, prevailed. A set of rules, by the way, that are extraordinarily humane and sane.

In the midsection of the *dompe*, the big trucks drop off their loads, and the towering orange tractors, roaring and farting and crushing the mounds with nasty steel wheels sporting *Mad Max* knobs and spikes,[2] pass by with the seeming arrogance of a *T. rex* hunting party.

There, of course, the best stuff is to be found. The strong and the young work this dangerous zone. Anything is possible here. The freshest produce, the undented cans, the unbroken televisions, the bursting bags, the brightest stenches, the runniest of the rotted wads of refuse, the startling explosions of dead dogs, cats, horses, jump out of the tumbling comic books and soda cans and soggy Pampers like some strange carnal jack-in-the-box.

You sometimes have to drop down into the trash. There are gaps in the piles. And if you get down into the gap, into the *basura* fault line, you have a side view of strata. You might find a six-pack of Dole pineapple juice lodged in there like trilobites. It's part mining, part farming, part archaeology. (Some visitors to Negra's house declined water on a hot day, so she graciously broke out some cool cans of orange juice. "Don't tell them," she said, "I got those out of the trash with a shovel.")

When you do drop down in there, you put up a pole with a rag tied at the end. This alerts the tractor-pilots, who would never see you otherwise, to veer away from your hole and spare your life.

Rule #1: Watch for heavy machinery. Those who do not become mulch.

Rule #2: No children in the trash.

Rule #3: Women are equal to men in the trash.

Rule #4: Old-timers and kids are allowed to work the outer edges of the trash, where the tractors push things down the slopes and the slopes themselves act as sifters, rolling the best things out across the face of the new King Kong pyramid.

---

1. In the biblical Book of Genesis, an immense tower in the city of Babel (Hebrew for "Babylon"), dedicated to the glory of man. Angered by the arrogance of the builders and inhabitants, God made them speak many conflicting languages rather than a universal one and scattered the people around the earth.

2. I.e., features resembling the industrial-trash aesthetic of the postapocalyptic science fiction movie *Mad Max* (1979) and its sequels, *Mad Max 2: The Road Warrior* (1981) and *Mad Max Beyond Thunderdome* (1985).

Rule #5: A special safe area is set up by the healthy workers. This area is set apart, avoided by the trucks and the tractors. It has inviolate boundaries, could almost be roped off. And everybody honors it. The occasional truck-load is directed over there, or young men carry a few bags there and toss them in. In this special section, the disabled and the old are allowed to do their share. They can work all day, safely, aside, not competed with or jostled or in harm's way. But working hard, nonetheless.

There is no welfare in the dump, but there is work, care, sweat, and dignity.

The dump could be described as a series of arcs.

There is the small arc of a hill that hides the dump from view. This hill sits between the dump and the view of San Diego. Running along the other side of this hill is a curving road that leads down to barrios at one end and Tijuana at the other.

Behind this hill, the next arc: the narrow village that has sprung up. These homes are where the majority of the modern garbage-pickers dwell. And Tony pointed out that it seemed a pretty well-off community. Certainly better off than Vietnam had been. (*Yeah, no napalm[3]—yet.*) After all, there are chickens and dogs, kites rattling in the power lines; there are power lines!

The next arc: the potter's field. At the top of a rise the crematorium, and in the middle distance the adult graves, and then at the lower end the babies. The graves with cribs for headstones, where parents bring their small daughters and sons and scratch out their final beds in the yellow dirt. *Niña, 3 días*, the crooked wooden crosses say. Or *María de los Angeles, Julio 3–Julio 5*. Or *Hijo. Un día*. Or the cribs, forlorn and somehow fright-ening, still vaguely cheery in their colors as they come apart in the ele-ments, fade, break, slump. Playpens, And a board hammered onto the side that bears the sad, minuscule life history of yet another *niña* or *niño*.

Then the final arc, a sort of bull's-eye: the dump.

We walked along, looking, and then we saw the lake and stopped and it started to lap at the edges of our minds, the dark water, the realization of what it was we were seeing, the strange shore of a land so far from home, so far from Tijuana even, that we could have been glimpsing the lip of the underworld. We could have been wading in the feces-scented waters of the River Styx.

Miraculously peculiar things abound in the dump, too. If you have an eye for the perversely beautiful, you can have a wonderful day looking around. I have seen tornados of garbage rising thirty feet in the air. I have seen piles of money tumbling in the landslide of shattering windows and dancing shoes. Three-legged dogs? All the time. Try a two-legged dog, running at full speed balanced on his two legs and zooming into the distance like a living rollerblade.

One day I thought I was seeing little geysers or volcanoes. But Negra pointed out that a subterranean trash fire had started. But it hadn't remained in the trash: it had crept into the graves. And the dry carcasses of these dear

3. An incendiary weapon, notorious for its use by the U.S. military during the Vietnam War.

people were igniting underground. Sometimes, when it rained, the ground actually broke open and flames leapt up for a moment.

This day, somehow, there had been a flood.

Tony the pilot first saw it. One end of the dump had been closed off by the new trash mountain. A small valley had been sealed at one end, where the runoff would have originally formed a nostalgic little waterfall into the little Edward Abbey[4] desert canyon and run on to the sea. Deer would have frolicked at its base; jackrabbits, coyotes, foxes, hawks, owls, rattlesnakes, tarantulas, three kinds of daisies, locoweed, gourds, raccoons, lizards, tortoises, skunks, wild goats, cottonwoods, berries, grapes, small fish, crawdads, butterflies, pottery shards, arrowheads, lions, morning glories, corn, Queen Anne's lace would have flourished along this glittering little creek. Now, however, the northern arm of the landfill had cut off the vale and the small bed of the waterway. The canyon itself, as we know, was long gone. Kotex, Keds, Kalimán[5] comic books, and ketchup bottles frolicked there now.

The slopes of this vale, small as it was, were crowded with the sad wooden crosses of the dead children's graves. The whole area was full of nameless, abandoned, forgotten, sleeping little corpses. Plastic flowers faded from blue to pink by the sun. A toy or two. Cribs.

From somewhere this flood had come. And the vale filled with water. And the water ate away at the slope, the clay and sand coming loose and the little crosses toppling and falling into the water to float around like model sailboats. And other crosses, those in the bottom of the vale, stood in the water at angles, reflecting on the still surface. It looked like a Pink Floyd album cover, actually.

And all around the edge of this lake (I always think of it as a *lake*, not a pond, a pool) was stinking mud, and stuck to the mud at every angle were more crosses. Broken crosses. Crooked crosses. Scattered crosses. Fallen crosses. Names on some, peering up at me from the lapping water's edge: Juan, Hija, Nena, Linda.

At one side, three vast tractor tires. They marched into the water in a row. The one farthest out we couldn't see into. The middle one was empty, save for some dark water and some blown trash. The one on the shore had become an impromptu outhouse: it was well loaded, the shit falling on crosses. Shit on the painstakingly handpainted letters: *Diciembre 21–Dic. 25*; *Mi Hijo*; *Alfonsina, 10 días y 4 horas*.

And crowding the shore, gulls. Many, many gulls. Gulls fighting, pushing, raising their wings but not flying. Fat and noisy gulls. We stood there watching them, this white snowdrift of gulls. And they'd waddle to the water and heave themselves into it. Filthy water. Black at first, but with a clear blue overlay of sky. Floating with wads of paper and bits of wood and these gulls and the reflections and shadows of the crosses standing out there like mangroves in a swamp.

And the gulls dipped their heads into the water and brought up small tidbits and flung their heads back and gulped.

And the water revealed small brown and green and reddish objects. A kind of layer beneath the surface, like seaweed. Like the clouds of stuff in

4. American writer (1927–1989) known for environmental activism and for exploring landscapes of the American West in novels such as *The*

*Monkey Wrench Gang* (1975) and works of nonfiction such as *Desert Solitaire* (1968).
5. Mexican comic-book hero.

miso soup. Like algae, but not algae. And we looked: looked at the shore, where the ground was swelling with this noxious water and crumbling. And we looked in, deep, where the bed of the lake was mud, and the mud was drifting up, and the rotten soil was broken, and the coffins, the cardboard boxes, the pillowcases, the wooden crates, the winding sheets, were coming up. They were coming up. The children themselves were rising, expanding into the water, and the gulls were eating them.

The gulls had grown too fat to fly on the flesh of these sleeping children.

The sky above was yet another perfect southern California blue. The blue of a stained glass window. Clouds as bright as electric signs over our heads. And that same sky, spreading farther than any of us can know, shading different colors in different places, covered the garbage dump in Mexico City, the garbage dump in Manila, the garbage dumps in El Salvador, Guatemala, Zaire, Rwanda, Honduras, Mexicali, Matamoros, Juárez, Belize, Ho Chi Minh City, Patpong, Calcutta, Sarajevo, Tripoli, New Jersey, and Three Mile Island, Pennsylvania.[6]

*Proposition 187? A new Berlin Wall at the border? California citizen identification cards? Microchips injected into the backs of our hands, read by circling Landsat spy satellites? Two thousand Border Patrol guards augmented by T-1000 Terminator Droids armed with nuclear shotguns and laser-sighting eyeballs?[7]*

*You think they're going to work? You think they can possibly work? Swim in this lake for a minute, then tell me you can keep these people on its shore. Jump in—you own it: it's Lake Nafta.*

1996

6. In 1979, the Three Mile Island Nuclear Generating Station underwent a partial meltdown, the worst nuclear accident in U.S. history. *El Salvador, Guatemala*: countries in Central America. *Zaire, Rwanda*: countries in Africa. *Honduras*: republic in Central America. *Mexicali, Matamoros, Juárez*: cities in Mexico. *Belize*: country in Central America. *Patpong*: district in Bangkok, Thailand. *Calcutta*: city in India. *Sarajevo*: capital of Bosnia and Herzegovina. *Tripoli*: capital of Libya.
7. This paragraph lists some proposed methods— and some fanciful methods based on science fiction scenarios—to limit the illegal immigration of Mexicans into the United States. *Berlin Wall*: the physical, multifaceted boundary that, from 1961 to 1989, completely separated East Berlin from West Berlin, Germany. *Landsat*: program jointly run by the U.S. Geological Survey and the National Aeronautics and Space Administration (NASA), using satellites to obtain images of Earth from space.

## FROM THE DEVIL'S HIGHWAY: A TRUE STORY

### From 1. The Rules of the Game

Five men stumbled out of the mountain pass so sunstruck they didn't know their own names, couldn't remember where they'd come from, had forgotten how long they'd been lost. One of them wandered back up a peak. One of them was barefoot. They were burned nearly black, their lips huge and cracking, what paltry drool still available to them spuming from their mouths in a salty foam as they walked. Their eyes were cloudy with dust, almost too dry to blink up a tear. Their hair was hard and stiffened by old sweat, standing in crowns from their scalps, old sweat because their bodies were no longer sweating. They were drunk from having their brains baked in the pan, they were seeing God and devils, and they were dizzy from drinking their own urine, the poisons clogging their systems.

They were beyond rational thought. Visions of home fluttered through their minds. Soft green bushes, waterfalls, children, music. Butterflies the size of your hand. Leaves and beans of coffee plants burning through the morning mist as if lit from within. Rivers. Not like this place where they'd gotten lost. Nothing soft here. This world of spikes and crags was as alien to them as if they'd suddenly awakened on Mars. They had seen cowboys cut open cacti to find water in the movies, but they didn't know what cactus among the many before them might hold some hope. Men tore their faces open chewing saguaros and prickly pears, leaving gutted plants that looked like animals had torn them apart with their claws. The green here was gray.

They were walking now for water, not salvation. Just a drink. They whispered it to each other as they staggered into parched pools of their own shadows, forever spilling downhill before them: *Just one drink, brothers. Water. Cold water!*

They walked west, though they didn't know it; they had no concept anymore of destination. The only direction they could manage was through the gap they stumbled across as they cut through the Granite Mountains of southern Arizona. Now canyons and arroyos shuffled them west, toward Yuma, though they didn't know where Yuma was and wouldn't have reached it if they did.

They came down out of the screaming sun and broke onto the rough plains of the Cabeza Prieta wilderness, at the south end of the United States Air Force's Barry Goldwater bombing range,[1] where the sun recommenced its burning. Cutting through this region, and lending its name to the terrible landscape, was the Devil's Highway, more death, another desert. They were in a vast trickery of sand.

In many ancient religious texts, fallen angels were bound in chains and buried beneath a desert known only as Desolation. This could be the place.

In the distance, deceptive stands of mesquite trees must have looked like oases. Ten trees a quarter mile apart can look like a cool grove from a distance. In the western desert, twenty miles looks like ten. And ten miles can kill. There was still no water; there wasn't even any shade.

Black ironwood stumps writhed from the ground. Dead for five hundred years, they had already been two thousand years old when they died. It was a forest of eldritch bones.

The men had cactus spines in their faces, their hands. There wasn't enough fluid left in them to bleed. They'd climbed peaks, hoping to find a town, or a river, had seen more landscape, and tumbled down the far side to keep walking. One of them said, "Too many damned rocks." *Pinches piedras*, he said. Damned heat. Damned sun.

Now, as they came out of the hills, they faced the plain and the far wall of the Gila Mountains. Mauve and yellow cliffs. A volcanic cone called Raven's Butte that was dark, as if a rain cloud were hovering over it. It looked as if

1. Named after Goldwater (1909–1998), American politician.

you could find relief on its perpetually shadowy flanks, but that too was an illusion. Abandoned army tanks, preserved forever in the dry heat, stood in their path, a ghostly arrangement that must have seemed like another bad dream. Their full-sun 110-degree nightmare.

* * *

"The Devil's Highway" is a name that has set out to illuminate one notion: *bad medicine.*

The first white man known to die in the desert heat here did it on January 18, 1541.

Most assuredly, others had died before. As long as there have been people, there have been deaths in the western desert. When the Devil's Highway was a faint scratch of desert bighorn hoof marks, and the first hunters ran along it, someone died. But the brown and red men who ran the paths left no record outside of faded songs and rock paintings we still don't understand.

Desert spirits of a dark and mysterious nature have always traveled these trails. From the beginning, the highway has always lacked grace—those who worship desert gods know them to favor retribution over the tender dove of forgiveness. In Desolation, doves are at the bottom of the food chain. Tohono O'Odham poet Ofelia Zepeda[2] has pointed out that rosaries and Hail Marys don't work out here. "You need a new kind of prayers," she says, "to negotiate with this land."

The first time the sky and earth came together, Elder Brother, I'itoi, was born. He still resides in a windy cave overlooking the western desert, and he resents uninvited visitors. Mountains are called do'ags. In the side of one do'ag can be found the twin caves where the spirit of the evil witch, Ho'ok, hides. The coyote-spirit of the place is called Ban, and he works his wicked pranks in the big open spaces.

* * *

The plants are noxious and spiked. Saguaros, nopales, the fiendish chollas. Each long cholla spike has a small barb, and they hook into the skin, and they catch in elbow creases and hook forearm and biceps together. Even the green mesquite trees have long thorns set just at eye level.

Much of the wildlife is nocturnal, and it creeps through the nights, poisonous and alien: the sidewinder, the rattlesnake, the scorpion, the giant centipede, the black widow, the tarantula, the brown recluse, the coral snake, the Gila monster. The kissing bug bites you and its poison makes the entire body erupt in red welts. Fungus drifts on the valley dust, and it sinks into the lungs and throbs to life. The millennium has added a further danger: all wild bees in southern Arizona, naturalists report, are now Africanized. As if the desert felt it hadn't made its point, it added killer bees.

* * *

Today, the ancient Hohokam have vanished, like the Anasazi, long gone in the north. Their etchings and ruins still dot the ground; unexplained radiating lines lead away from the center like ghost roads in the shape of a great

---

2. Professor of linguistics at the University of Arizona and poet laureate of Tucson (b. 1952). *Tohono O'Odham*: a group of Native Americans who live primarily in the Sonoran Desert (in southeastern Arizona and northwest Mexico); their name means "People of the Desert."

star. Not all of these paths are ancient. Some of the lines have been made by the illegals, cutting across the waste to the far lights of Ajo, or Sells, or the Mohawk rest area on I-8. Others are old beyond dating, and no one knows where they lead. Footprints of long-dead cowboys are still there, wagon ruts and mule scuffs. And beneath these, the prints of the phantom Hohokam themselves.

In certain places, boulders form straight lines, arrayed along compass directions on the burning plains. Among these stones are old rock piles in the shapes of arrows. They were left by well-wishers in 1890, aiming at a *tinaja* (water hole) hidden among crags. Cairns that serve as mysterious sign-posts for messages long forgotten mix with ancient graves. Etchings made in the hardpan with feet or sticks form animals centuries old and only visible from the air. Some of these cairns have been put in place by Border Patrol signcutters (trackers), and they are often at the junction of two desert paths, but the cutters just smile when you ask what they mean. One more secret of Desolation.

When the white men came, they brought with them their mania for record keeping. They made their way across the land, subduing indigenous tribes, civilizing the frontier. Missionaries brought the gentle word of the Lamb.[3] Cavalrymen bravely tamed the badlands, built military outposts, settlements, ranches, and towns. Cowboys rode like the wind. Gunslingers fell. The worst bandits you could imagine drank rotgut and shot sheriffs, yet lived on in popular mythology and became the subjects of popular songs and cheap fictions. Railroads followed, and the great cattle drives, and the dusty range wars, and the discovery of gold and silver. In the great north woods, lumberjacks collected the big trees. The Alamo. The Civil War[4] took out countless citizens in its desperate upheaval.

Every Tijuana schoolkid knows it: it's the history of Mexico.

· · ·

If the North American continent was broad ("high, wide, and lonesome"), then Mexico was tall. High, narrow, and lonesome. Europeans conquering North America hustled west, where the open land lay. And the Europeans settling Mexico hustled north. Where the open land was.

Immigration, the drive northward, is a white phenomenon.

White Europeans conceived of and launched El Norte mania, just as white Europeans inhabiting the United States today bemoan it.

They started to complain after the Civil War. The first illegal immigrants to be hunted down in Desolation by the earliest form of the Border Patrol were Chinese. In the 1880s, American railroad barons needed cheap skilled labor to help "tame our continent." Mexico's Chinese hordes could be hired for cheap, yet they could earn more in the United States than in Mexico, even at cut rates. Jobs opened, word went out, the illegals came north.

Sound familiar?

---

3. *Lamb*: i.e., Jesus Christ.
4. The war between the United States (the Union) and the Confederate States of America (1861–65). *The Alamo*: In 1836, during the Texas Revolution, at the now legendary chapel-fort in San Antonio called the Alamo, about 180 Texans were defeated by thousands of Mexicans led by the Mexican general Antonio López de Santa Anna (1794–1876).

Americans panicked at the "yellowing" of America. A force known as the Mounted Chinese Exclusionary Police took to the dusty wasteland. They chased the "coolies" and deported them.

And today?

Sinful frontier towns with bad reputations. Untamed mountain ranges, bears, lions, and wolves. Indians. A dangerous border. Inhabitants speak with a cowpoke twang, listen to country music, dance the two-step, favor cowboy hats, big belt buckles, and pickup trucks. That ain't Texas, it's Sonora.[5]

* * *

January 18, 1541.

Sonoita (also known as Sonoyta) was perhaps not much more than sticks and mud, but it was a stopping point for a Spanish expedition in search of, what else, gold. Even in 1541, Sonoita was the unwilling host of killers and wanderers. The leader of this clanking Spaniard patrol was a firebrand known as Melchior Díaz. He didn't especially want to spend his holidays in the broiling dust of Sonoita, but he was deep into hostile territory. It was commonly believed that the natives of the Devil's Highway devoured human children. The Spaniards weren't planning on settling—spread the cross around, throw up a mission, and hit the road in search of better things.

Melchior Díaz was trying to reach the Sea of Cortez,[6] lying between the Mexican mainland and Baja California. Perhaps he knew that ahead of him lay the most hellish stretch of land in the entire north. The dirt paths he rode his horse down on that day are now the paved and semipaved barrio lanes of modern Sonoita. Some of the hubcap-popping boulders in Sonoita's hillside alleys are the same rocks on which Melchior's horse's shoes struck sparks.

He died trying to kill a dog.

He probably didn't have anything against canines—his troop had dogs that they used to hunt down game and humans. But there were also the feral creatures that dashed in from the outskirts of the settlement to slaughter his sheep. Melchior Díaz kept his sheep in small brush corrals, attended by his Indian slaves. But the wild dogs had a way of sneaking off with lambs when nobody was looking.

And Melchior was cranky. He had spent his holidays far from home, among the savages, and even Tucson was only a small scattering of huts and lean-tos. He couldn't have been farther from Mexico City or Spain. Sonoita was the end of the world. A Christmas in this outpost did not inspire joy. Besides, conquistadores were notoriously short on joie de vivre.

Melchior rode well, and he rode well armed. He certainly carried a sword and a fighting dagger. He probably carried a harquebus and a long metal-tipped lance, the M16 of the day.

Melchior was a strong man and a powerful fighter. In the narratives of the Coronado expedition, we see him plying his trade: ". . . the horsemen began to overtake [the Indians] and the lances cut them down mercilessly . . . until not a man was to be seen."

5. State in northwestern Mexico.
6. Named after Hernán Cortés (1485–1547), Spanish conquistador.

This rout of natives serves as the preface to the story of death that begins with Melchior Díaz.

. . .

We know that he was riding his horse down one of the settlement paths. We can project the smells swirling around him: horse, dirt, his own stink, chickens, smoke, dung. Not all that different from the smells of today.

He was approaching his sheep pen, perhaps where the Así Es Mi Tierra taco shop, or a Pemex station stands today. Melchior squinted ahead and— Damn it to hell!—those lazy slaves of his had allowed a dog to get in the pen! *Perro desgraciado!*

No record states how Melchior entered the pen, but it doesn't seem likely he stopped to open a gate. Not Melchior. He jumped over the fence, and in jumping, somehow he bobbled his lance throw and missed the dog entirely. You can see the dog yipping and sidestepping and making tracks for the horizon, casting wounded looks over his shoulder. And here is where Melchior Díaz died.

The record states that Melchior, somehow, "passed over" the lance. Did he fall from the horse? No one knows, but the lance managed to penetrate his gut and rip him open.

The desert ground must have seemed terribly hard as he hit it. As Melchior died (it took twenty gruesome days) on his stinking cot, he burned and howled. Flies settled in his entrails. Maybe the very dog that killed him drew near to sniff the rich meaty scent. The fallen angels of Desolation came out of the Cabeza Prieta, folded their hands over him, and smiled.

. . .

The land had been haunted before Melchior died, and it remained haunted afterward; 150 years after his death, Catholic apparitions plagued the tribes. Various peoples had alarming encounters with meddlesome white women who flew above their heads. In the lands of the O'Odham, a white woman bearing a cross came drifting down the Devil's Highway itself. The warriors who saw her immediately did the only practical thing they could: they filled her with arrows. They said she refused to die. Kept on flying. Her story was written down in 1699, but the scribe who wrote this history tells us it had happened so long ago that the tribe had already forgotten her.

Fifty years after this Blessed Virgin UFO, a female prophet came out of the desert. She was known as *La Mujer Azul*. The Blue Woman. They filled her full of arrows, too. This time, she died.

Jesuits rolled in. They made the People as unhappy as the mysterious spirit-women, and Pimas raided the town to bludgeon its missionary to death. Angry Yumas by the Colorado River dragged a Jesuit out into the light and beat him to death.

It was the nineteenth century, however, that really got the modern era of death rolling.

The Yumas got stirred up again and massacred the evil scalphunting Glanton gang by the banks of the river in the mid 1840s. Then, in 1848–49, the California gold rush began. Mexicans weren't immune to the siren call of treasure. By now, the Cabeza Prieta/Devil's Highway had been trod by white men and mestizos for 307 years. It was still little more than a rough dirt trail—it is still a rough dirt trail—but it was slyly posing as a handy southern route through Arizona. White Arizonans and Texans hove to and dragged their wagons. Thousands of travelers went into the desert, and piles of human bones revealed where many of them fell. Though the bones are gone, wagon ruts can still be found, and near these ruts, piles of stone still hide the remains of those who fell.

One writer who has focused on this desert, Craig Childs, tells of a pair of old bullet casings found out there. They were jammed together, and when pried apart, an aged curl of paper fell out. On the paper, someone had written, "Was it worth it?"

. . .

The Sand Papagos[7] saw the endless lines of scraggly Mexicans as a rolling supermarket. Their strategy was similar to their approach to the floating virgin: shoot arrows. Wagon train after wagon train was slaughtered. Besieged Mexicans begged their own army to protect them, but the Sand Papagos and their leader, a warrior named Quelele, the Carrion-Hawk, were ready for them, too.

Just to make sure the Mexicans got the point, Quelele let it be known that his favorite snack was dead Mexican. "I don't need the wagons!" he boasted. "Bring on the Mexican army! I am the Carrion-Hawk! I'm hungry for Mexican meat!"

Between Quelele and the harsh landscape, the numbers of dead soared beyond counting. Human skeletons were found lying beside the road, and eerie cattle and horses, reduced to blanched mummies, were reported to be standing out among the ironwood trees. Graves surrounded some waterholes, up to twenty-seven around one pothole alone.

A westerner named Francisco Salazar seems to have been the first to keep an eyewitness record of this phase of the killing fields. By 1850, he wrote, the Devil's Highway was ". . . a vast graveyard of unknown dead . . . the scattered bones of human beings slowly turning to dust . . . the dead were left where they were to be sepulchered by the fearful sand storms that sweep at times over the desolate waste."

In the following years, over four hundred people died of heat, thirst, and misadventure. It became known as the most terrible place in the world.

And it's beautiful. Edward Abbey, the celebrated iconoclast and writer,[8] loved the place. He chose to be buried there, illegally, among the illegal Mexicans he despised.

\* \* \*

The men walked onto the end of a dirt road. They couldn't know it was called the Vidrios Drag. Now they had a choice. Cross the road and stagger along the front range of the mountains, or stay on the road and hope the Border Patrol would find them. The Border Patrol! Their nemesis. They'd

---

7. Among the names of the Hia C-ed O'Odham ("Sand Dune People"), Native American peoples whose traditional homeland was in southeastern Arizona and northwest Mexico. They are unrecognized by the United States and Mexico, but the Tohono O'Odham (named Papagos by conquistadors) hold land in trust for them and consider issues relating to them.
8. See note 4, p. 2167.

walked into hell trying to escape the Border Patrol, and now they were praying to get caught.

In their state, a single idea was too complex, and they looked upon it with uncertainty. They shuffled around. It was ten o'clock in the morning, 104 degrees. Dust devils, dead creosote rattling like diamondbacks, the taunting icy chip of sunlight reflected off a high-flying plane. Weird sounds in the landscape: voices, coughs, laughter, engines. It was the desert haunting they'd been hearing all along. When they heard the engine coming, it sounded like locusts flying overhead, cicadas, wind. And the dust rising could have been smoke from small fires. The flashes of white out there, heading toward them, popping out from behind saguaros and paloverde trees—well, it could have been ghosts, flags, a parade. It could have been anything. They didn't know if they should hide or stand their ground and face whatever was coming their way.

When the windshield flashed in the morning sun, they stood, they walked, ran, tripped, fell. Toward the truck, the white truck. The unlikely geometry of disaster once again worked them into its eternal ciphers.

Border Patrol agent Mike F., at the tail end of another dull drag, was driving his Explorer at a leisurely pace. No fresh sign anywhere on the ground. Boredom. He was about to pull a U and head back to 25E, the dirt road that cut down from Interstate 8 to the Devil's Highway and the Mexican border beyond, looked up, and beheld the men as they walked out of the light. Nothing special. You got lost walkers all the time, people begging for a drink. They often gave themselves up when they realized the western desert had gotten the better of them. Sometimes, you beat them down with your baton, and sometimes everybody just laughed and drank your water.

Only one of the walkers stepped forward. The rest hid under trees. They were watching Mike F. like deer in the shadows.

He took in the scene as he rolled toward them.

He stopped, put the truck in park, and opened his door. He put out a foot and gestured for them with one hand to stay put while he got the radio mike with the other and called in to Wellton Station. Cops tend to assess a situation at first glance—people are always up to something. In the desert, they were often involved in some form of dying. Most of them, if not in trouble, were sneaky. If they weren't illegals, or smugglers, or narco mules, they were trespassing on the military base in some Ed Abbey desert fantasy, or they were cactus thieves, swiping young saguaros for their Scottsdale[9] gardens. Gringos caused more alarm out there than Mexicans. And the OTMs— Other Than Mexicans—were so hapless and weird that you'd just laugh. Like the time they found a large group of Arabs in matching slacks and neckties, like some demented terrorist Jehovah's Witness neighborhood canvass. "Oh? Are we here illegally? Oh! This is, you say, the United States? Right here? No, we did not know that. Praise to God. We were taking a walk, *Allahu Akbar*."[1]

Bad guys had cornered the market on trying to look casual and "innocent." Mexicans, when not giving up, when not running like maniacs, often got wide-eyed, like a two-year-old stealing cookies. I didn't do nothin'! I was just out here looking around! The more innocent they acted, the more ner-

9. Upscale city in south-central Arizona. *Narco mules*: hired carriers of drugs (narcotics).

1. God is great; a common Arabic expression.

vously slouchy and devil-may-care or childlike in their sinlessness, the more hinky the whole scene was, and the cop would start fingering his sidearm.

\* \* \*

Arrests of illegals are often slightly wry, vaguely embarrassing events. The relentless border war is often seen as a highly competitive game that can even be friendly when it's not frightening and deadly. Agents often know their clients, having apprehended them several times already. Daytime arrests have a whole different tone than lone midnight busts, out there in an abandoned landscape where the nearest backup might be a hundred hard miles away. But night or day, the procedure tends to be the same. The cop gets out of the truck and adjusts his gunbelt and puts his hands on his hips and addresses the group in Spanish: "Hola, amigos! Estan arrestados." The Border Patrol so terrifies some of them that they give up immediately. Things happen. Stories burn all along the borderlands of Border Patrol men taking prisoners out into the wasteland and having their way with them. Women handcuffed, then groped and molested. Coyotes[2] shot in the head.

Texas Rangers allegedly handcuff homeboys and toss them into irrigation canals to drown, though the walkers can't tell the Border Patrol apart from the Rangers or any other mechanized hunt squad: they're all cowboys. Truncheons. Beatings. Shootings. Broken legs. Torn panties. Blood. Tear gas. Pepper spray. Kicked ribs. Rape. These are the words handed from border town to border town, a savage gospel of the crossing. And the dark image of the evil Border Patrol agent dogs every signcutter who goes into the desert in his truck. It's the tawdry legacy of the human hunt—ill will on all sides. Paranoia. Dread. Loathing. Mexican-American Border Patrol agents are feared even more by the illegals than the gringos, for the Mexicans can ascribe to them only a kind of rabid self-hatred. Still, when the walkers are dying, they pray to be found by the Boys in Green.

\* \* \*

The five men rushed toward the truck.

"They're dying," they gasped.

"Who's dying?"

"Men. Back there. Amigos."

Seventeen men, they said.

Agent F. gave them water. They gulped. They puked the water back out and didn't care. They drank more.

"Muertos! Muertos!"

Seventeen. Then thirty. One man thought there were seventy bodies fallen behind them.

When Agent F. called it in to Wellton, the station's supervisory officer said, "Oh, shit."

For a long time, the Border Patrol had worried that something bad was coming. Something to match or outstrip the terrible day in 1980 when a group of Salvadorans was abandoned in Organ Pipe Cactus National Monument, and thirteen of them died. If it was the Border Patrol's job to

---

2. Smugglers of illegal immigrants.

apprehend lawbreakers, it was equally their duty to save the lost and the dying.

The guys at Wellton knew the apocalypse had finally come.

. . .

Southern Arizona is divided into two Border Patrol sectors, Tucson and Yuma. Fifteen hundred agents patrol Tucson sector; three hundred work Yuma. Tucson handles the eastern half of the state, starting at the small city of Ajo and covering Tucson, Nogales, Douglas, Patagonia, and so on. Yuma sector patrols the west, all the way to the Colorado River and beyond. They are responsible for Gila Bend, Dateland, Wellton, San Luis, and Yuma. Strangely enough, they also patrol into California's Imperial County. This has caused legal tribulations with the Mexican consulate in Calexico, California: illegals apprehended in eastern California should be tried in San Diego, but they are transported to Phoenix, where their cases are heard. Responsibility for these people can stretch from San Diego to Calexico to Tucson and finally to Phoenix. It only adds to the general chaos that rules the border, a chaos that the Tucson consul calls "the politics of stupidity."

Both Border Patrol sectors had been hammered by growing tidal waves of illegals. Urban crossings had been sealed off, and now smaller rural crossings were systematically clamping down. Operation Gatekeeper, the final solution to the border crossings, introduced by California in the late nineties, had ushered in a new era of secure urban borders and trampled wilderness. San Diego, Calexico, Yuma, El Paso, Nogales, Douglas, they were all becoming harder to get through. This looked great for the politicians of the cities. Voila! No more Mexicans!

Bigger fences, floodlights, a Border Patrol truck every half-mile, sensors, infrared spy videos, night vision cameras, Immigration and Naturalization Service checkpoints on all major freeways in and out of town, more agents.

But now, smaller, rougher places were becoming hot spots. The drug-smuggling village of Naco, for example. The small chicken-scratch settlement of Sasabe. The Tohono O'Odham reservation's small villes.

And astounding numbers of humans were moving through their deserts. Organ Pipe Cactus National Monument, a relatively compact portion of Tucson sector, was withering under two hundred thousand walkers passing through every year. Deaths were on the rise: in the half decade before Mike F. found the five walkers on Vidrios Drag, more than two thousand people had died along the Mexican border. Death by sunlight, hyperthermia, was the main culprit. But illegals drowned, froze, committed suicide, were murdered, were hit by trains and trucks, were bitten by rattlesnakes, had heart attacks.

The unofficial policy was to let them lie where they were found, resting in peace where they fell. Any fan of Joseph Wambaugh[3] books or cop shows on TV can figure out the rest of the story. All cases, for all cops; require paperwork. The Border Patrol is no different. Each corpse generates a case file. Every unidentified corpse represents one case forever left open—you can never close the case if you can never find out who the dead walker was or

---

3. American writer (b. 1937) who specializes in fictional and nonfictional accounts of police work in the United States.

where he or she came from. But uncollected—unreported—bones generate no files. Besides, how do the agents know if the bones are one hundred years old?

The Arizona Border Patrol's beat included this deadly western desert, a region enclosing Organ Pipe and the Cabeza Prieta wilderness, the Papago (Tohono O'Odham) reservation, the northern fingers of the Mexican Pinàcate desert, the Goldwater bombing range, and the dreaded Camino del Diablo—the Devil's Highway. It is a vast trapezoid of land, bound by I-19 to the east, and the Colorado River to the west; I-8 to the north, and Mexican Route 2 and the imaginary border to the south.

. . .

You'd be hard pressed to meet a Border Patrol agent in either southern Arizona sector who had not encountered death. It would be safe to say that every one of them, except for the rankest probie just out of the academy, had handled at least one dead body. And they all knew the locations of unidentified skeletons and skulls. Bones peppered the entire region.

All the agents seem to agree that the worst deaths are the young women and the children. Pregnant women with dying fetuses within them are not uncommon; young mothers have been found dead with infants attached to their breasts, still trying to nurse. A mother staggers into a desert village carrying the limp body of her son; doors are locked in her face. The deaths, however, that fill the agents with deepest rage are the deaths of illegals lured into the wasteland and then abandoned by their Coyotes. When the five dying men told Agent F. they'd been abandoned, he called in the information.

The dispatcher responded with a Banzai Run.

. . .

The town of Wellton is in a wide plain on I-8. It is tucked between Yuma's mountain ranges and the Mohawk Valley, with its strange volcanic upthrusts. The American Canal cuts through the area, and a bombing range is to the south. Running just below I-8 is the railway line that carries freight from Texas to California. Most train crews have learned to carry stores of bottled water to drop out of their locomotives at the feet of staggering illegals.

Wellton Station sits atop a small hill north of the freeway. It is isolated enough that some car radios can't pick up a signal on either AM or FM bands. Cell phones often show "Out of Service Area" messages and go mute.

Many agents, borderwide, commute a fair distance to their stations. Drives of twenty, forty, even seventy miles are common. But the trips to and from work afford them a period of quiet, of wind-down or wind-up time. It is not always easy to leap from bed and go hunt people. Besides, the old-timers have learned to really love the desert, the colors in the cliffs, the swoop of a red-tailed hawk, the saffron dust devils lurching into the hills.

For most agents, it works this way: you get up at dawn and put on your forest green uniform. As you get to work, you pull in behind the station to the fenced lot. You punch in your code on the keypad, and you park beside the other machines safe from your enemies behind the chain-link. Your station is a small Fort Apache.[4] On one side, the agents line up their trucks and sports cars, and on the other side sits the fleet of impeccably maintained Ford Explorers. Border Patrol agents are often military men, and they are spit-and-polish. Their trucks are clean and new; their uniforms are sharp; and their offices are busy but generally squared away. The holding cells in the main building—black steel mesh to the far left of the main door—sparkle. Part of this is, no doubt, due to the relentless public focus on the agency. In Calexico, the Mexican consulate has upped the ante by placing a consulate office inside the actual station: prisoners are greeted by the astounding sight of a service window with Mexican flags and Mexican government signs.

Inside, Wellton Station is a strange mix of rundown police precinct and high-tech command center. Old wood paneling, weathered tables. Computers and expensive radios at each workstation. In the back building, supervisory officer and mainstay of the station Kenny Smith has a couple of radios going, which he listens to, and a couple of phones ringing every few minutes, which he generally ignores. A framed picture of a human skull lying in the desert hangs on the wall. It has a neat hole in the forehead, above one eye socket. "Don't get any cute ideas," one of the boys says. "We didn't shoot that guy."

A computer is on all the time, and GPS satellite hardware bleeps beside it. Above Kenny's desk is a huge topo map showing the region. He sits in a swivel chair and reigns over his domain. He has an arrow with its notched end stuffed into a gas station antenna ball. He holds the ball in his fist and uses the arrow to point out various things of interest on the map.

On the wall is the big call-chart. Names and desert vectors are inked onto a white board in a neat grid. Agents' last names are linked to their patrol areas. In the morning, you check the board, banter with Kenny, say good morning to the station chief, stop by to say hello to Miss Anne, who runs the whole shebang from her neat desk in the big main room out front.

The town of Wellton is farms and dirt, dirt and farms. New agents, fresh from the East or West coasts, amuse the old boys by asking where they can find an espresso or a latte. Kenny Smith tells them, "Well, you can go down to Circle K and get a sixteen-ounce coffee. Then put some flavored creamer in it." That one never fails to get a laugh out of the old boys. An agent, sipping his stout coffee, is mid-story: ". . . And here comes Old José," he says, "all armed-up on some girlie!" Old José seems to be the archetypal tonk[5] who shows up in stories. The listener, a steroidal-looking Aryan monster with a military haircut and a bass voice, notes: "Brutal." He turns to his computer keyboard and plugs away with giant fingers.

Everybody speaks Spanish. Several of the agents are Mexican Americans. Quite a few in each sector who aren't "Hispanic" are married to Mexican women.

Wellton Station is considered a good place to work. The old boys there are plain-spoken and politically incorrect. INS[6] and Border Patrol ranks are overrun with smooth-talking college boys mouthing carefully worded sound

---

4. In the 1948 Western *Fort Apache*, an isolated U.S. cavalry post located within the real-life Indian reservation in Arizona also called Fort Apache.
5. According to an omitted part of the selection,

*tonk* is a Border Patrol epithet for an illegal immigrant. It is "based on the stark sound of a flashlight breaking over a human head."
6. The U.S. Immigration and Naturalization Service.

bites. Not so in Wellton. Agents will tell you that the only way to get a clear picture of the real border world is to find someone who has been in service over four years. A ten-year veteran is even better. Wellton has its share of such veterans, but any agent who has been in service for ten years knows better than to talk to you about his business.

A great compliment in the Border Patrol is: "He's a good guy." Wellton's agents are universally acknowledged by other agents as good guys. Jerome Wofford, they say, will give you the shirt off his back; the station chief will lend you his cherry SUV if you have special business.

Like the other old boys of Wellton Station, you love your country, you love your job, and though you would never admit it, you love your fellow officers. Civilians? They'll just call you jackbooted thugs, say you're doing a bad job, confuse you with INS border guards. You're not a border guard, you're a beat cop. Your station chief urges you not to hang out in small-town restaurants, not to frequent bars. Don't go out in uniform. Don't cross the border. Don't flash your badge. Don't speed, and if you do and get tagged for a ticket, don't use your badge to try to get out of it. Don't talk to strangers. In hamlets like Naco, San Luis, Nogales, civilians often won't make eye contact. Chicanos don't like you. Liberals don't like you. Conservatives mock and insult you. And politicians . . . politicians are the enemy.

There's always someone working in the office, early or late, every day and every night of every year. They're guarding the cells, monitoring the radios, writing reports. Sometimes, you can't sleep. You can always come in to the clubhouse and find someone to talk to. Somebody who votes like you, talks like you. Believes in Christ or the Raiders[7] like you. You can make coffee for the illegals in the cage, flirt with the señoritas—though with all the sexual assault and rape charges that dog the entire border, you probably don't. Human rights groups are constantly lodging complaints, so you watch yourself. The tonks supposedly have phones in their holding pens so they can call lawyers to come slaughter you if you do anything wicked. You pull up one of the rolling office chairs, turn your back to them, and sit at a radio and listen to the ghostly voices of your partners out in the desert night, another American evening passing by.

• • •

But that's later. Now you get your assignment and you head out. You're usually alone. You pick up your vehicle from the yard. The station has its own gas pump, so you use your government card and fill the tank. You have a thermal jug of cool water. Sometimes you have a military map tube with topo maps. You have a GPS unit, and a radio on your belt. You have cuffs, pepper spray, and a baton. You carry a .40 caliber sidearm in a holster at your hip. It has a clip loaded with hollow-point rounds. "You shoot a guy to kill him, not to hurt him." That's the mantra. You carry extra clips.

The Explorers are nice. You go out there four-wheeling in an SUV that has been retrofitted by felons in a Texas prison. (Ain't that rich. The only thing you think would be richer would be if illegals in some Ford plant in Ohio fitted out your rig.) The Explorer has a cage behind the back seat, and a mounted radio down between the front seats, and a shotgun rack behind your seat, but

---

7. Phoenix Raiders, semiprofessional football team in Arizona.

separated from the wets[8] by heavy mesh. An upright pump is usually clipped into the rack. They designed the truck without asking you. For a while there, they put radios in the trucks with the mike on the opposite side from the driver. You had to lean over the whole unit and feel around on the passenger's side. And some genius has designed the shotgun rack to go on the far side of the back seat, over by the door, so by the time you've bent back and struggled with it, the bad guy has busted caps in you. As it is, the mike on the radio is now exactly level with your right knee, so if you're not careful, you'll lean into it and punch the button and either jam the entire channel or transmit your own singing, farting, talking to yourself. The trucks weigh ten thousand pounds, so even in four wheel drive you can hit a sand pit and sink. You come out of that little crisis covered in dust like flour, looking like a ghost, and the assholes back at the station just about fall down laughing.

If they'd just let the beat cops run the asylum, you think, a lot of things would change.

The trucks have two standard features that everyone finds indispensable: a killer AC unit and a strong FM radio. With ground temperatures soaring to 130 on sunny days, and on certain nights dropping only as low as 98, the air conditioner is a lifesaver—literally. You can cool down a burning body right quick with the AC blasting, and with AC and a water jug, you can keep an illegal alive until the BORSTAR (Border Patrol Search, Trauma and Rescue) lifesavers swoop in with their helicopters. They're the Border Patrol's Air Cav.[9] Cute red T-shirts. You save the wets and the boys in red fly in and get all the glory. You crap behind a bush, trying to keep it off your shoes, but BORSTAR goes on ABC nightly news.

As for the FM . . . driving 150 miles at thirty miles an hour, alone, scanning the ground for sign, is boring. Even the night runs, once your probie nerves wear off, are boring. Old boys try to liven them up for you. When you're new, they tell you the Chupacabras[1] is out there on Vidrios Drag, and he sucks blood from lone wanderers. Or Bigfoot's been seen coming out of the Tinajas Altas pass. Or there are ghosts of dead walkers creeping around the Camino del Diablo. Sometimes the bastards will even sneak up on you and shout, right around 3:00 A.M. when you're sleepy, but that's a good way to get shot, so most of them don't bother. The FM keeps morale elevated. Radio calls to base often have a classic rock soundtrack—Van Halen and Led Zeppelin bleed through the call-ins. Sometimes, newbies will be blasting the radio so loud they can't hear calls from dispatch.

"Ten, base, ten. I'm twentied at the Pinacate Lava Flow. I'M GONNA GIVE YOU EVERY INCH OF MY LOVE![2] Over."

One nonstandard lifesaver fits into the space between the base radio and the passenger seat. A roll of toilet paper. It beats a handful of cactus.

• • •

You grab a coffee at Circle K, microwave a burrito, then cross I-8 on the old bridge and head south on 25E. To the west, 29E parallels you. It is the actual terminus of the Devil's Highway. The twin E's take you to the Mexican

---

8. Wetbacks; derogatory slang for illegal immigrants from Mexico.
9. Air Cavalry.
1. Literally, in Spanish, goat sucker; a murder-

ous creature said to exist in various parts of the Americas.
2. The capitalized sentence is a line from Led Zeppelin's "Whole Lotta Love" (1969).

border, crossing miles of a sere and mysterious bombing range. Your ironist's eye loves to pick out crazy things. Right near the Devil's Highway itself is a mutated saguaro that rises ten feet into the sky. Its main body is thick, and the top is a scarred, messed-up ball of tissue. It looks for all the world like an arm raising a fist. And wouldn't you know it, the "ears," or branches, that stick out form an index finger and a little finger. The Devil's Highway throws up a heavy metal devil sign to announce itself. The only thing missing is Ozzy Osbourne.[3]

The aforementioned Army tanks molder in the eastern end of the basin. When no one is around (and no one is ever around) you can shoot at them for fun. On the west end, under Raven's Butte, there's an abandoned squadron of jet fighters. Rounds penetrate their skin easily. (You can't hardly even chip the paint off the tanks, though.) Sometimes, jet jockeys target the Border Patrol trucks and dog them from on high, vectoring in on their white roofs. Many of the Wellton guys enjoy flipping them the bird out the window, or even jumping from the truck in the middle of the faux strafing run and raising the finger at the startled pilots.

\* \* \*

There are other games the Border Patrol guys play. Sometimes they toss a recently shot rattlesnake, dead but still writhing and rattling, into the cage with the captured wets. Ha ha—that's a funny sight, watching them go apeshit in the back of the truck. And they get it, right? Old José has a good sense of humor about it. He pissed his pants and screamed at first, but then he laughed and called the agent "Pinche Migra!"[4] and swear to God, he peeled that snake right there and ate it!

An agent out of Wellton once pulled a classic practical joke on his load of clients out near 25E. One of his boys had been taking potshots in the desert, and he'd plugged a jackrabbit. "Hey," the agent told him, "I've got an idea." He took the big jack and tucked it into some bushes near the road.

Later in the day, he had some Mexicans in the back, and he was tooling along, taking them back to the station holding pens.

Suddenly, he stopped the car and said, "Muchachos, un conejo!" A rabbit!

They crowded the front of the cage and said, "Donde?"

"Allí, allí. Mira. Es grande!"

They squinted and frowned, but nobody saw no stinking rabbit.[5]

"Right there, man!" the agent cried.

A vast plain of saguaro and dry brush and ironwood stumps.

"I'm going to shoot it," he told them. "I'll show you how good the Migra is with our *pistolas*."

He hopped out of the truck and squeezed off a shot with his pistol.

"*Chinga'o!*[6] He's shooting!" They flinched. Ducked. He holstered his weapon and got in the truck.

---

3. John Michael "Ozzy" Osbourne (b. 1948), English singer/songwriter, longtime lead singer of the heavy metal band Black Sabbath (formed 1968); his songs' imagery and his personal iconography often draw on the occult.
4. *Pinche*: fucking. *Migra*: a term, derived from *inmigración* by Spanish-speaking U.S. commu-

nities, referring to Immigration and Customs Enforcement, Border Patrol, and similar agencies.
5. A play on the famous line "We don't need no stinkin' badges!" in the 1948 Western *The Treasure of the Sierra Madre*.
6. Fuck.

"Got him!" he said. "Let's go see."

He drove—they thought it was fifty yards, maybe. But he drove past that. And then he drove a mile. They were muttering and whistling. Then another mile. Then another damn mile. He pulled up to the saguaro cluster where he'd stashed the carcass, parked again, jumped out and dug the rabbit out of the bushes. He held it up so they could see it.

They cried out in shock and awe.

"I told you the Migra were good shots!" he told them.

The guys at the station laughed for years about that one.

• • •

Drags are created by bundles of five car tires attached to a frame, looking somewhat like the Olympic rings. Every few days, a truck chains a drag to its back end and drives the roads, ironing the sand into a smooth surface. The drags tend to cut east/west. Since the illegals head north, they are forced, sooner or later, to cross a drag. The Devil's Highway itself is the Mother of All Drags.

The fiendish ploys of the Coyotes offer you many opportunities to hone your signcutting skills. The whole game for their team is to pass by invisibly, and the team on this side is paid to see the invisible. The Coyotes score when they make it, and the Migra scores when they don't. Like pro wrestling, there is a masked invader who regularly storms the field to disrupt the game. This, of course, is La Muerte.[7]

The illegals try to leap across the drags, but the drags are often wide enough to make jumpers hit the ground at least once. They walk backward, hoping to confuse cutters. You have to be good to confuse a veteran. An Indian reservation cop says, "Them trackers can probably tell you what color the guy's hair was, and that he had eighty-nine cents in his left pocket. Then they can tell you the last time he got laid."

Lately, foamers have been walking the desert. Foamers tape blocks of foam rubber to their feet, thus leaving no prints. Or so they think. Foam blocks make small right-angle dents in the soil at their corners. And sooner or later, the heel of the walker will wear through the foam, and the cutter can see a weird pattern, like a small half-moon hoof in a picture frame. Your classic foamer sign.

Every Coyote team relies on the old Apache trick of the brush-out. Last man through walks backward, brushing the tracks away with a branch of some bush. It's such a standard move that Border Patrol agents call giving civilians and media types evasive answers a brush-out. The Washington, D.C., desk jockeys are considered the ultimate brush-out masters.

There is room, in this desert world, for scholarship as well as sport.

Cutters read the land like a text. They search the manuscript of the ground for irregularities in its narration. They know the plots and the images by heart. They can see where the punctuation goes. They are landscape grammarians, got the Ph.D. in reading dirt.

On lava, a displaced stone will reveal a semicircle of lighter ground underneath. Likewise a pebble kicked out of place on the hardpan, where the desert varnish that accumulates on the ground reveals a crescent of paler

7. Death.

sand. In-ground sensors are buried in places known only to the Border Patrol. These sensors are known as Oscars. A Coyote would give his teeth to get hold of this information.

Sometimes, the sensors are very cleverly placed—their little antennas stick up in the middle of creosote bushes. Cutters know that saguaros, the signature big cactus of the region, always grow among sheltering shrubs. So a stately old saguaro will not only serve as a signpost for the walkers, but a landmark for the cutters, and the landmark has a scribble of handy bushes around it to hide the wire.

When the truck goes by on the drag, the Oscar sends a message to base. Base radios: "Oscar 21? Oscar 21?" The cutter answers, and he's cleared. If base doesn't clear him at his Oscar, he'll call home. "Base, did you catch an Oscar just now?"

Oscar 25 follows Oscar 21; Oscar 35 follows Oscar 25. If a cutter vanishes between Oscar 25 and Oscar 35, they know something might be wrong. They go to look for him. If an Oscar bleeps and no cutter is nearby, they know somebody done snuck into the country.

Often the drag will have what Kenny Smith calls "hither thither." Hither thither is a scrabble of pebbles and twigs and dirt on the clean face of the drag. It's knocked from the tiny berms that the tire drags raise on either side of the road, and they tell you that someone tried to hop over. You look out beyond hither thither for true sign.

Signcutters know most walkers pass between 11:00 at night and 3:00 the next morning. They can tell how old a track is by its sharpness—even in the desert, dirt holds some humidity, and it is this humidity that defines the track's edges. As a track ages, it dries, and as it dries, its edges soften. Bug-sign is created when small creatures begin to scurry about just before dawn. Often, this hour is the only comfortable moment of the day, and in a burst of breakfast exuberance, lizards, rats, and insects set off in a willy-nilly marathon.

If bug-sign crosses over a walker's footprint, the cutter knows the walker has passed nearer to midnight than to dawn. If, however, the footstep flattens the bug-sign, the cutter knows the walker has recently passed, and is in the immediate area, and is probably in trouble. The sun is up, the temperature is rising, and the day will only get more brutal.

When the cutter sees criss-crossing sign on the drag, he radios another unit. That agent drives to the next drag north and cuts. If he finds sign, he calls the first unit to leapfrog north to the next drag. He cuts it. Sooner or later, the sign runs out, and they have the walkers boxed in between them.

It's when the walkers get far off the drags that all the trouble starts.

Mike F.'s walkers were not only off the drag, they were off the map.

• • •

Kenny Smith was working the trailer trash radio, sending more and more units on the Banzai Run. Everybody was heading out there, every truck that could move. They were even thinking of sending out the water-buffaloes, the big water-tank trucks in the fleet. It was a mad scramble as they raced the heat.

From Vidrios Drag, the signcutters started back into the wasteland, cutting, cutting. They started finding corpses. They read the ground and found,

The women tell you that they go home with the smell on their skin, in their hair and clothing. Sometimes, when several packets have arrived in their office, they can't wash it off, even hours later. A year after death, files still reek faintly of spoiled flesh. The incense of their death takes over the room.

So the women light candles.

Once their candles are lit, they bend to the task of trying to find the families back in Mexico so they can deliver their grim news. Many dead walkers come from places with no phones, homes with no addresses. The best the consulate can do is call the village phone booth and hope a passerby will answer. Or they track down the mayor of the nearest town, and he then either does or does not find the widows.

In the back office of the consulate, the chemical scent of jasmine, musk, vanilla, fights the smell of corruption. One of the secretaries utters the Mexican phrase for *yuck*. "Guácala." It sounds like something you eat.

The chief of consular security waves her off.

He says, "When forensic evidence fails us, we are forced to register circumstantial evidence."

Forensic evidence would consist of such things as fingerprints. But the nature of desert death is such that forensic evidence is quickly obliterated. The body mummifies. In one of the million ironies of the desert, those who die of thirst become waterproof. Their fingers turn to stiff leather, and the prints are unreadable. On the day the consulate reopens the files of the Yuma 14, they have four bodies undergoing hydration at the coroner's lab. A new corpse, Juan Doe #78, is cooling in their company. The coroners pump fluids into their reluctant tissue, sometimes for days, to try to plump up the desiccated skin enough to raise a usable print.

\* \* \*

Many of the dead have gold or gold-rimmed or missing teeth, and their photographs offer the final indignity: they have white rubber-clad fingers jammed in their mouths, pulling their lips apart in maniacal grimaces, to reveal these orthodontic details. For these few, it has to be the teeth; there is literally nothing else.

The bodies that are identified are ultimately processed by the Adair Funeral Home in Tucson. They are embalmed, then placed in a cloth-covered wooden casket. This undertaking costs $650. If they are to be flown home, the "air-tray" to hold the casket costs an extra $50. The Mexican consulates pay for the embalming, and other parties—sometimes the governments of the walkers' home states—pay for the flights. For more than 80 percent of the dead, it is the most expensive gift they have ever gotten.

Those who are never identified are registered by the United States. Under their new government-bestowed number, they are interred in the potter's field at the Ft. Lowell cemetery in Tucson. They each get a small marker with metal serial numbers. These Juan Doe burials cost Pima County $760 each.

What of others? What of the phantom walkers from the Wellton 26? Stories float among the survivors that three men walked away. Some call it the Wellton 30. One survivor still maintains there were seventy in the original group.

"They are gone," the Mexican consul in Tucson says. "No, no."

He looks out the window.

"You will never find them."
He rests his hands on the desk and looks at them.
"Perhaps a scrap of clothing."
He sighs.
"In the desert, Levis last longer than meat."
Six coins and four pills, a green handkerchief.
The candles flicker.

\* \* \*

The majority of the group came from tropical Veracruz.[1] No terrorists, ex-cons, or drug mules. Mostly, small-plot farmers, coffee growers, a schoolboy and his dad. Some of them were used to seeing up to sixty inches of rain a year—the Devil's Highway would be lucky to get sixty inches in a decade. They walked into the desert carrying soft drinks. Most of them had never seen a desert. Several of them had never ridden on a train, an elevator, or an escalator. Some had never driven a car. Some of them had never even eaten flour tortillas; to them, that was exotic food.

There are two fairly common jokes told about America among "undocu-mented entrants"—A) Don't drink the water, and B) For good American food, go to Taco Bell.

What we take for granted in the United States as being Mexican, to those from southern Mexico, is almost completely foreign. Rural Mexicans don't have the spare money to drown their food in melted cheese. They don't smother their food in mounds of sour cream. Who would pay for it? They have never seen "nachos." In some regions of the south, they eat soup with bananas; some tribal folks not far from Veracruz eat termite tacos; turkey, when there are turkeys, is not filled with "stuffing"—but with dried pine-apples, papaya, pecans. Meat is killed behind the house, or it is bought, dripping and flyblown, off a wooden plank in the village market. They eat cheeks, ears, feet, tails, lips, fried blood, intestines filled with curdled milk. Southerners grew up eating corn tortillas, and they never varied in their diet. You find them eating food the Aztecs once ate. Flour tortillas, burri-tos, chimichangas—it's foreign food to them, invented on the border.

They were aliens before they ever crossed the line.

2004

1. State in southeastern Mexico.

# ROBERTO VALERO
## 1955–1994

Like Reinaldo Arenas, the Cuban-born poet Roberto Valero moved to the United States as part of the Mariel boatlift, in 1980. The next year, he and Arenas—who knew each other in Cuba—cofounded the journal *Mariel*, which served as an out-let for the writers and artists of what came to be called "The Mariel Generation."

In Cuba, Valero had been expelled from the University of Havana for his vocal opposition to the dictatorship of Fidel Castro. Once in the United States, he settled in Washington, D.C., where he earned his doctorate from Georgetown University in 1988 and taught at George Washington University from then until his death.

Valero's substantial body of poetry, all in Spanish, appeared in collections including *Desde un oscuro ángulo* (From a Dark Corner, 1982), *En fin la noche* (Finally the Night, 1984), *Dharma* (1985), *Venias* (You Were Coming, 1990), and *No estaré en tu camino* (Not in Your Way, 1991). Valero also published the novel *Este viento de cuaresma* (1991) and a critical study, *El desamparado humor de Reinaldo Arenas* (The Desperate Humor of Reinaldo Arenas, 1990), which won the Letras de Oro essay prize, sponsored by the Spanish Ministry of Culture and the University of Miami, in 1989. While Valero's writing does not have the manic originality of Arenas's, his work is in some respects more humane and accessible than that of his mentor and friend.

Ranging in style from the simple to the surreal, and in tone from the sentimental to the sardonic, Valero's poetry unites personal and political preoccupations. Political cataclysms are refracted through private losses: homelessness, disease, separation from loved ones. In "Phone Call" and "Exile," Valero writes of his longing for his wife and daughter to join him in the United States and of the way their bonds were strained and broken by separation. In "Roberto," Valero creates a wry self-portrait. And in "Islands Are Evil and Nobody Knows It," he writes of the pain of those who leave their island and the grim lives of those who remain there.

## Roberto[1]

And God said: "Make him a malcontent, make him a wanderer, let him discover all the hidden paths of the soul, let him love a lot and hurt a lot, open his chest"—and the eager angels opened his chest—"so that he may bleed, and put poetry in his heart and give him two large hands"—and the eager angels smiled—"and let him also have the despair of adolescents and their 5 passions, put a beard on him and strong legs, and have him rise and walk." It was all done, but the last angel asked what to do with all the doubt that was left over, and God, annoyed by the question, said, "add that too." And God saw that it was good, and it was morning and evening the next day.[2]

1983

## Phone Call[1]

Once again your voice
crossing the Caribbean,
crossing Florida
(which you've seen only in pictures),
the Carolinas, 5
Virginia (they say it's the state for lovers),[2]

1. Translated by Gustavo Pérez Firmat.
2. Cf. chapter 1 of the biblical Book of Genesis.
1. Translated by Gustavo Pérez Firmat.

2. Since 1969, "Virginia Is for Lovers" has been the state's travel and tourism slogan.

your voice crossing spring, summer, fall,
reaching the peaceful shores of the Potomac.[3]

Your voice climbing up my building,
waking me. We tremble, we lie                                            10
to each other with silly, hopeful words.
¡So much love in the hands of bureaucrats,
the worst lovers!
Permissions, signatures, paper and pointless ink.

Your voice entering D.C.,                                                15
playing under the cherry trees,
eating grapes
on the red sidewalks of Georgetown,
while you're buying toys
that broke twenty years ago.                                             20

Give our daughter kisses,
strawberries, dolls, flowers.
In four hours I'll be in Manhattan,
where the Cloisters[4] will be waiting for you.
Soon the snow will have covered every inch of autumn.                    25
And still your small voice, sounding in my ear:
"They won't let me leave."

                                                                    1984


## Exile[1]

Darling, your heart arrived today
in an envelope someone searched.
I see that our daughter is growing up
looking at photographs.
Mother, I know you'd rather die                                          5
than not see me,
I've always known that it would kill you
and yet I had to leave,
had to abandon the roads you travelled,
the scent of your cooking,                                               10
your kiss in the mornings.
I had to leave to find myself.
But I haven't.

New York, November 21, 1980                                         1984

---

3. River in the mideastern United States; it flows
through Washington, D.C.
4. A branch of the Metropolitan Museum of Art,
devoted to European art of the Middle Ages.
1. Translated by Gustavo Pérez Firmat.

# Islands Are Evil and Nobody Knows It[1]

> How can one go on living
> with two tongues, two nostalgias,
> two worries, and two melancholies?
>
> Heberto Padilla[2]

Islands are lovely and sad,
their inhabitants are always dreaming
of a day, a date,
the instant when the sea will part
and their lives will divide,                   5
their pasts will be torn in two.
Islanders try to memorize the flowers,
the faces of their neighbors,
the cemetery at the town's entrance.
They know that the foam will separate them.     10

Each island worships its own demons,
it can't get used to other gods.
There are islands that don't know green
or sea shells
or the simple sobs of a child.             15
One day all the tombs will capsize
and the bones of the dead will dance on the waves,
birds will play with the remains of dreams,
with the offal of passions.
At night sea birds will devour corpses     20
and witness the birth of volcanic islands.

We must leave this pile of rocks,
venture into the mainland fearlessly,
run away from the sea:
the sea corrodes,                     25
it never leaves you,
and we must hate it even if our dreams are blue.
I have blue nightmares
where sharks fly
and block all the exits.               30

Once you've seen snow on the mountains,
once you've travelled inside continents
there's no going back.
The shipwrecked, their ships,
their letters in unintelligible languages     35
wash up on islands.
Coasts hide among the cliffs,
the sharp edges of islets wound the seagulls
and scar the seals.
Those who can't escape perish        40

---

1. Translated by Gustavo Pérez Firmat.     2. See p. 1002.

dreaming about Italy or commit suicide
by jumping from Chicago skyscrapers.

One day all the islands will go downstream
bumping into each other,
falling off the edge of the world into the last abyss                45
and the angels will witness a shower of stars.
Islands aren't kind,
islands are evil,
they rise from the sea already tired,
they choke on air,                                                   50
rain distresses them,
they will turn into dust.

Once you have put a sea between two lives
don't try to return,
you'll never find what you lost.                                     55
Mother may look the same,
your friends will praise the sea spray
and no one will have seen the blue heart
of your treacherous island.

1998

---

# RUTH BEHAR
## b. 1956

Ruth Behar was born in Havana, Cuba, the grandaughter of immigrants from Europe and the Middle East. In 1962, after the Castro Revolution, she emigrated with her family to the United States. Behar earned her bachelor's degree in anthropology from Wesleyan University, in Middletown, Connecticut. In 1983, she earned her doctorate in the same subject from Princeton University, in Princeton, New Jersey. The recipient of Guggenheim and MacArthur fellowships, she has been a member of the Anthropology Department of the University of Michigan, in Ann Arbor, since 1986.

Behar's first book, *Santa María del Monte: The Presence of the Past in a Spanish Village* (1986), is an anthropological study of cultural continuity in a Spanish village shifting into modernity. In her second book, *Translated Woman: Crossing the Border with Esperanza's Story* (1993), Behar reconstructs the biography of Esperanza, a Mexican–Native American woman, a story that mirrors the author's identity as a "translated woman." Deliberately blurring the line between social science and personal narrative, Behar creates a voice that represents herself and her subject, even as she recognizes the "editing" that inevitably occurs in translation and ethnography. In her next book, *The Vulnerable Observer: Anthropology That Breaks Your Heart* (1996), Behar continues her "personal ethnography" in essays that mingle observer and observed, Jewishness and *Cubanidad*. Behar explores the idea of *Jubanidad* further in her autobiographical documentary for television, *Adio Kerida: Goodbye My Dear Love* (2002), and in her book *An Island Called Home: Returning to a Jewish Cuba* (2007), with photographs by Humberto Mayol.

Jewish Cuban identity is the focus of the two Behar selections in this anthology: The essay "Juban América," first published in *Poetics Today* (1995), meditates on personal, ethnic, and national identity. The poem "The Hebrew Cemetery of Guabanacoa," originally included in *Little Havana Blues: A Cuban-American Literature Anthology* (1996), movingly recalls Behar's experience looking for the tombstone of a relative during one of her trips to the island.

## *From* Juban América

Shortly before his death in Miami Beach in 1987, my maternal grandfather, Maximo Glinsky, stapled an old photograph to a small piece of cardboard. On the cardboard, by way of explanation, he wrote, "*Recuerdo de Linka de a donde yo nació en 1901, esto era nuestra casa y atras un jardin verde.*" His words were intended for his descendants, now living English-speaking lives in North America: "Souvenir of Linka, where I was born in 1901, this was our house with its garden in back." The picture, indeed, shows a house, or something rather more like a homestead. Three boys in knickers and hats, their faces dim and indistinct, cluster together just off-center; perhaps one of them was my grandfather. The ground is covered with snow.

As a good archivist and granddaughter, I have had this image carefully mounted on acid-free cardboard, put under glass and framed with simple, etched wood. Naturally, I removed the staples, which were beginning to rust. The picture now hangs in a quiet domestic space, above our used, $150 mahogany piano, where I sit almost every night with my kindergarten-age son, Gabriel, begging him to practice his lessons. I had wanted terribly to learn piano as a child during the years after we arrived in the United States from Cuba, but my parents told me they didn't have the space or the money; besides, they thought it wiser for me to learn to play a more portable instrument like the accordion or the guitar, an instrument you could take anywhere. I could not understand then how for my parents, who were in their late twenties when they decided to leave Cuba in 1961, all sense of permanence had been ruptured. Although they were themselves children of immigrants, they had never expected to have to leave Cuba; *nunca me ha ido*, I have never left. A piano in the drawing room—that, for me, is the epitome of a settled, bourgeois existence: the life of people whose citizenship documents are in order and who therefore have no reason to harbor an immigrant's fears, the life of people who don't expect a revolution to occur overnight and challenge their hold on the things of the world. And yet, what if, at a moment's notice, I had to leave? What would I take with me? I think of the picture above the piano, which traveled through two exiles, from Russia to Cuba and from Cuba to America. That picture, which by itself would have said very little, became, with the addition of my grandfather's words, an image of displacement, of deterritorialization.

The image-text harks back to a lost home in Byelorussia, the old country. That this home is undeniably lost is evident not only in my grandfather's use of the past tense, but in the fact that he tells the story of its loss in Spanish, which became the language of his reterritorialization in the New World. The brief, seemingly uncomplicated statement that my grandfather inscribed under the photograph of his birthplace, in which he locates himself as a minority speaker of Spanish, is redolent with politics and history. His Spanish embodies too many contradictions of territoriality and deterritorialization.[1]

As any educated speaker of Spanish knows, my grandfather's text reflects a nonstandard use of the language. Following the Yiddish usage, he disregarded the difference between the first and third person, using the grammatically incorrect "yo nació" instead of the proper "yo nací." It seems eerie to me that he placed himself in the interface between the first person and the third person, as if already imagining himself no longer here in the world of the living, no longer speaking as "I" but being spoken of, by someone else, as "he," already edging toward the third person of biography, of the narrator, of his own granddaughter's text.

Spanish was not my grandfather's "mother tongue." He was a stepson of the language, yet he claimed it as his own. He spoke Spanish to his children and grandchildren; the Yiddish that he spoke with my grandmother and others of their generation failed to get passed on, while English, learned in a second exile, never entered his veins. My relationship with my grandfather, a man of the Jewish European Old World, was lived entirely in Spanish. To be more exact, it was lived in a combination of Spanish and silence. My grandfather did not talk very much. He was suspicious of people who talked too much. He spoke telegraphically. His most memorable utterances were his jokes, tellable only in Spanish, a Spanish that showed a stepson's tenuous kinship to the language. His jokes were really questions, such as "¿Cómo ando?" to which he would answer, "Con los pies"; or "¿Cómo te sientes?" to which the reply was, "En la silla."[2] These jokes—which were also the actual replies that he'd give when asked the Spanish equivalent of "How are you?"—encoded his refusal to say how he was "doing," his refusal to admit that he was "fine, thank you."

It is these refusals, so characteristic of how he spoke and didn't speak, that make me think my grandfather was acutely conscious that his was a colonized voice. The "sound" of a colonized voice, it seems to me, carries traces of the effort to resist speaking, to resist speaking "as usual." The locus of enunciation is challenged before any speaking can even occur. For the colonized speaker, language is never taken for granted; you cannot go into automatic drive. My grandfather's literal enunciations served as a continual brake on our becoming too comfortable in the language of our colonization, and yet, curiously, these enunciations were so thoroughly rooted in Spanish idiomatic phrases as to be untranslatable. Después de todo,[3] Spanish was my grandfather's language, in much the same convoluted way that it is mine now.

\* \* \*

1. His Spanish seems to be dressed in "a Harlequin costume in which very different factions of language and distinct centers of power are played out, blurring what can be said and what can't be said" (Gilles Deleuze and Félix Guattari, *Kafka: Toward a Minor Literature*, Minneapolis: University of Minnesota Press, 1986: 26). For a feminist rereading of Deleuze and Guattari that has informed my interpretation, see Caren Kaplan, "Deterritorializations: The Rewriting of Home and Exile in Western Feminist Discourse," in *The Nature and Context of Minority Discourse*, edited by Abdul R. JanMohamed and David Lloyd, 357–68, New York: Oxford University Press, 1990. [Behar's note]

2. Plays on words; literally, "How am I going?" (meaning "How am I doing?") "With the feet" and "How are you sitting?" (meaning "How do you feel?") "On the chair."

3. After all.

Poor boy,
he got left behind
with the few living Jews
and all the dead ones
for whom the doves pray.                                        40

I reach for my camera
but the shutter won't click.
Through ninety long miles
of burned bridges I've come
and Henry Levin won't smile.                                    45

I have to return another day
to Henry Levin's grave
with a friend's camera.
Mine is useless for the rest
of the trip, transfixed, dead.                                  50

Only later I learn
why Henry Levin
rejected me
a latecomer
to his grave.                                                   55

My aunt and uncle were wrong.
Henry Levin is not abandoned.
Your *criada*,[2] the black woman
who didn't marry to care for him,
tends his grave.                                                60

Tere tells me she can't forget
Henry, he died in her arms.
Your family left you, cousin,
so thank God for a black woman
who still visits your little bones.                             65

1994                                                            1996

2. Maid.

# SUSANA CHÁVEZ-SILVERMAN
## b. 1956

A professor at Pomona College, in Claremont, California, Susana Chávez-Silverman is the daughter of a New York City–born Jewish *hispanista* and a Chicana teacher. She grew up bilingually and triculturally in Los Angeles; Madrid, Spain; and Guadalajara, México. She then spent years peripatetically, in Boston, Massachusetts; Los

Angeles and Berkeley, California; Spain; and South Africa. She earned her bachelor's degree in Spanish from the University of California, Irvine (1977); her master's in Romance languages from Harvard University, in Cambridge (1979); and her doctorate in Spanish from the University of California, Davis (1991). Between 1982 and 1984, she taught at the University of South Africa, in Pretoria.

Along with Tato Laviera (see p. 1399), Alurista (p. 1657), Giannina Braschi (p. 1971), and Guillermo Gómez-Peña (p. 2081), Chávez-Silverman is a prime proponent of Spanglish as a literary vehicle of expression. Her book *Killer Crónicas: Bilingual Memories* (2004) consists of a series of bilingual, code-switching *crónicas*, or firsthand accounts. Filled with overwrought descriptions of daily events, these missives are based on actual e-mail exchanges Chávez-Silverman had while living in Buenos Aires in 2000 and 2001. In 2010, she published a sequel of sorts, *Scenes from la Cuenca de Los Angeles and Other Natural Disasters*.

Typical of Chávez-Silverman's wordplay, which often involves faux or deliberately bad translations, is the "killer" in the title of "*Killer* Crónica," included in this anthology. The word refers to the short story "El matadero" (The Slaughterhouse, written 1839, published 1871), a political allegory by the Argentinian writer, cultural promoter, and political activist Esteban Echeverría (1805–1851), one of Latin America's most important Romantic authors. In Chávez-Silverman's chronicle, the narrator describes a long taxi ride to the outskirts of Buenos Aires in search of the real Argentina. In the Mataderos *barrio* (neighborhood), she happens upon a working-class arts and crafts fair. Several friends criticize the fair as tacky and a tourist trap, but the narrator becomes entranced by a rustic horserace, smoking grills piled high with beef, and impromptu dancing by young and old.

---

## *FROM* KILLER CRÓNICAS: BILINGUAL MEMORIES

### *Killer* Crónica

**26 febrero, 2001**
*Buenos Aires*
*Para María Gabriela Mizraje y*
*para Pablo "Hugo" Zambrano*

"Saquen Uds. *Killer*, por favor" dije, sin immutarme, a mis estudiantes. Ellos tampoco se inmutaron not even a hair, acostumbrados a que yo invente palabras, cree interlingual giros neológicos y *faux* traducciones sin pestañear. And they obeyed. They took out obediently *El matadero* de Esteban Echeverría, reconociendo estar en un curso survey de literatura hispanoamericana, primer semestre, College norteamericano that shall remain nameless, pero sabiendo también, que a pesar de la cononicidad de dicha obra, they weren't in Kansas anymore,[1] and maybe not even in Argentina either, sino somewhere in-between, liminal, interstitial.

---

1. In the movie *The Wizard of Oz* (1939), Dorothy and her dog, Toto, are transported from a Kansas farm to the land of Oz. Dorothy says, "Toto, I have the feeling we're not in Kansas anymore."

Y ahora, dos años después: ¿escribir o dormir? Overwhelmed by the lassitude that only the hottest verano en 10 años—or the hottest February en 30 (according to *La Nación y Clarín*)[2]—in Buenos Aires can impose (is it *really* that hot? O es, en vez, just another instance of typical porteño queja?), me debato listlessly entre el sueño y la escritura. Which could bring relief? Which more pleasure? Which more pain?

0800-555-0016 (Oficina de Turismo); 4374-1251 (Fervor de Buenos Aires); 4687-5602 (Info. Mataderos, de 11–19 horas); 4372-5831 (Centro Cultural); 4373-5839 (Museo de Artes Arg.). All these numbers (and then some) llamamos, tratando in vain to get information sobre la Feria de Mataderos.[3] Como pasa muchas veces en la Argentina, we heard this cheerful but firm message: "el número que Ud. ha marcado no corresponde a . . ." Finally, since our trusty año 2000 version of "Wayne," aka *The Lonely Planet Guide to Argentina* (edited by un tal Wayne Bernhardson, Ph.D. en geografía from Berkeley no less), ponía que la Feria in Killer se daba los fines de semana, from 11–6, nos lanzamos toward Killer last Sunday, a la tarde. Era, creo, nuestro viaje más largo en taxi since arriving in Buenos Aires. No hablo de esos lonely, desperate y desconcertantes viajes desde "cheto-ville," las northern suburbs, cuando nos transportábamos desde La Lucila, from Dayna's apartment, near the Stok family mansion en Victoria, toward the center of Buenos Aires by a combination of tren y subte, looking for an apartment to rent back in August. No. Hablo de within the boundaries de la ciudad de Buenos Aires proper.

Desplazándonos desde El Botánico de Palermo toward Mataderos, bajando por Pueyrredón, toward Independencia and then out west on J. B. Alberdi,[4] pude confirmar una vez más y con suma satisfacción para mí (con estupefacción quizás pa' mi amigo español, Pablo) que lo que dijo Borges en los 40s es exactly (still) true: *nadie ignora que el sur empieza del otro lado de Rivadavia.*[5] That wilder, more forlorn, more mythical geografía. Suena quizás estereotípico, but really it is profound and beautiful (o escuálido y cutre, según). J. B. Alberdi widens and flattens out. Not wide in that cosmopolitan, Parisian manner they fetishize here sino too-flat, too much sky, after the turn-of-the-century sumptuousness of the Recoleta, Palermo, Belgrano, and Colegiales, the funky quaintness of San Telmo and Monserrat.[6] Alberdi opens out into un-charming, jarring cobblestone where wagons once must have jostled; buildings now squat low and mean where once only dust swirled out toward the pampas.

Me recuerda los outskirts de alguna ciudad mucho más . . . qué sé sho, latinoamericana, el D.F.,[7] por ejemplo, Santiago de Chile, even Los Angeles. I feel comforted and disconcerted. I am pierced by recognition. Continuamos y continuamos. Casi diría it's getting boring, except for the occasional outrage-inducing interruption, entre parrillas populares y kioskos, de Blockbuster Video. Finalmente, after miles and miles of someplace that could be, casi, the San Fernando Valley de Califas[8] back when I grew up in it—with

2. Argentinian newspaper.
3. Street fair in Mataderos that highlights traditional *gaucho* culture, especially handicrafts, cuisine, and equestrian skills.
4. Street in Buenos Aires.
5. The italicized sentence is the first line of "El Sur" (The South), a short story by Jorge Luis

Borges (1899–1986), Argentinian writer.
6. Five of Buenos Aires's many neighborhoods, each of which has its own distinctive character.
7. Mexico City, also known as Distrito Federal.
8. An urbanized valley in Southern California ("Califas").

that blowsy, sun-addled energy, all TG & Y stores, no-name brand drive-in chicken places, abandoned warehouses and pumpkin patches—doblamos a la izquierda en Lisandro de la Torre,[9] en la frontera entre los barrios de Mataderos y Liniers, frontera también con la provincia occidental de Buenos Aires. Después de pasar unos menacing, grafitti-covered tenements, un enorme parque abandonado y una pulcra y moderna fábrica, arribamos a una somnolienta plaza, surrounded by these warehouse-looking buildings que me doy cuenta contain residential apartments indicated—and demarcated—by dingy laundry on the second floor. Hay una estatua de algún gaucho hero I am somewhat mortified not to recognize, una estatua de la Virgen de Luján[1] in a glass cage. Tengo la repentina sensación de ese personaje de Borges, I think in "El Sur" or is it "El hombre muerto"?[2] (Ni modo, Never have been that good with names and dates on a longterm basis). Pero anyway, ese personaje. Cuando acaricia el gato, de estar fuera del tiempo. Or at least, I share both his awareness de que los gatos are out of time *and* the very feline out-of-timeness itself.

Al bajar del taxi it is immediately clear we've come on the wrong day. No hay feria. No hay nada. Tampoco importa. It feels slow and too-bright. An oddly menacing haze. Cicadas. On the building surrounding the plaza hay letreros que anuncian la Feria de Mataderos, in circus-elegant, elaborate *filete* scroll. Doesn't say what days or times or where. Olor a parrilla, humo, algunos vecinos sitting at tables on the alcove-shrouded veredas, tomando vino tinto barato (y bueno), eating serving after serving de carne: asado, vacío, bife de chorizo, plus of course chinchulines, mollejas, morcilla and all that other mad-vaca (or at least cholesterol-carrying) offal.

Al rato tomamos, medio wistfully, para Palermo Viejo,[3] to return to the culinary adventures (or safety?) of that medio-*paqueto*, pseudo-multiculti barrio (nicknamed Palermo Soho by local cognoscenti: Borges se moriría, creo, to see *his* Palermo tan yuppified) just blocks from our own (just plain Palermo, a secas). Había esperado algo mucho más . . . místico, qué sé sho, olor a ganado (live, no en una parrisha . . . ), real gauchos, alguna destreza equina, no sé . . .

### Mataderos, The Real Thing
### (24-II-01):

Fortificados por un vecino de Killer (who had informed us en nuestra previa visita abortiva que la Feria se daba los sábados a la noche en verano), y además habiendo preguntado a una bola de taxistas, remiseros y vecinos, we arrived last night, medio aplastaditos con Pablo y Gabriela, habiendo subido en Palermo con un pobre taxista senior citizen NO profesional que se extravió varias veces on the way and whom I myself had to instruct as to the recovecos de las one-way streets en Killer! This time, to our complete amazement, una animada feria artesanal y barrial bien rustic desbordó enteramente la plaza central. En un huge stand, vendían todo tipo de artículo gauchesco: sillas de

9. Wide thoroughfare that divides the predominantly working-class neighborhoods of Mataderos and Liniers.
1. Seventeenth-century icon of the Virgin Mary, housed in the Basilica of Luján, Argentina, and considered miraculous.

2. Another short story by Borges.
3. Palermo is the largest of Buenos Aires's *barrios*. Palermo Soho, reminiscent of New York City's SoHo, is a subdivision of a charming old section of the neighborhood, called Palermo Viejo.

montar, botas, látigos, bombachas, fustas, boleadoras, fajas bordadas a mano, chalecos, sombreros, facones, alpargatas, bridles, bits. A wonderfully acrid smell arose in the slight stir of wind que punzaba los nubarrones color plomo. Olor a humo, a parrilla, a grupa de caballo y a montura.

Si la Feria Rural en Palermo, en agosto, había sido una magníficamente local encarnación of Flaubert's agricultural fair in *Madame Bovary* (my image will always be la insouciant and freckled, placid, slightly bovine yet intensely lovely face of Isabelle Huppert—una de mis actrices predilectas, desde "The Lacemaker"—as Emma, en la película), Mataderos is a wonderfully pueblo, porteño version of the equestrian show in Florence[4] I saw years ago, con mi hermana Laura y con mis padres. Then, wearing heavy woolens against the early spring chill and, unconscious of my incipient myopia, I strained forward to distinguish the thrilling blurs as impeccably elegant Tuscan horsemen cleared the hurdles (mostly). Now, en plena negación de mi (todavía light, conste) miopía, I flat out refuse to wear gafas en público, si no son uno de los miles de pares de designer sunglasses que uso. "Por coquetería" dirían aquí. Odio ese tan gender-loaded term. No, es que simplemente rechazo la excesiva nitidez a la que me obligan las gafas. La oftamóloga argentina se rió cuando le confesé eso; es más me felicitó la turn of phrase. Pablo entiende lo que digo: usando casi la idéntica receta, ambos preferimos la vida no corregida, with blurred edges.

Around the plaza, the restaurants that had been sleepy last Sunday, reluctantly sirviendo asado y parrishada to a few local vecinos, ahora rebosaban de vida: ofrecían everything from panchos (hot dogs), gaseosas e "ingredientes" (stale peanuts and potato chips) to full meals. Nos sentamos con Pablo y Gaby; pedimos tres Gancio con limón, un *Ehprite* pal Juvenil y agua mineral, of course, for Gaby. Even Gaby's a veces exasperantemente decimonónico nacionalismo (y en ehto, claaaro, she's anything but alone), her standing up to sing the himno nacional and her teary eyes when the (desflecada, por cierto) bandera was raised high above the plaza, por ejemplo, couldn't dampen the surge de pura magia que sentí cuando comenzaron a tocar chacareras y los vecinos—*all* of them, fat, skinny, old, young, dark, light—comenzaron a bailar, swirling hankies adorably, provocatively above their heads con infinita pasión y skill.

Gaby insiste en que *right here*, even where we sit, is the real, historical place, where "Killer" took place. Le pregunto, medio tímidamente, pues where's the Bajo? Where's the river? Y ella balbucea "y . . . (pausa porteña) bueno, todo es diferente ahora; el Río ha cambiado de curso." Yeah right . . . *No way* is this where *El matadero* took place, pienso pa' mis adentros. Pero, it doesn't matter. This feeling, these sights—avid vendors, smoke burning the eyes, music, fierce, hand-forged knives, animals, drink, was what I had been waiting almost eight months for. This was, perhaps, what I had *really* come to Argentina for. Ay dios mío, and here I go. Despite all my investigación académica en contra de los estereotipos, here I go, *tropicalizing* a los argentinos. Bueno . . . eso no es posible. OK, dale, gauchificándoles, or whatever. Quiero decir: am I not bringing back from their PoMo, Culti Studies graves the very maniqueísmos I have fought so hard against for

4. City in Tuscany, Italy. The French actress Isabelle Huppert (b. 1953) played Emma Bovary in the 1991 film adaptation of the 1857 novel by the French writer Gustave Flaubert (1821–1880).

years? What is *with* me? The old brain-body split. Pero mirá voh . . . ¿querré que los argentinos sigan siendo gauchos? ¿Jinetes? That this sweat-, aserrín- and meat-filled barrio fiesta be THE REAL THING? ¿Qué me pasa? Qué boludez.

So incredibly anxiety-filled lately, I must acknowledge how much Buenos Aires is a brain-driven city, a city where everybody hyper-intellectualizes, rationalizes. Pero TODOS, eh? From shop keepers to taxi drivers and ni fucking modo los academics. ¡Podridos! The worst of all. Not a step without asking (or explaining) why. Un vómito de palabras. Y eso que yo hablo, eh . . . Ob-vio.

Me di cuenta, de golpe, de que sólo una o dos personas, desde que estoy aquí, parecen tener un verdadero, recíproco y a veces hasta pasional interes en la plática de sus interlocutores, parecen siquiera darse cuenta de que la conversación is a two-way street, joder! La curiosidad, la curiosidad les falta, sustituida por el miedo, quizás. La aprensión. Suspicion. En general, hacen una perfunctory question, ¿de dónde sos? (used principalmente as a way to segue into elaborate stories about *their* ancestors, usually Italian) And then they're OFF! Like a pack of galgos chasing the lure, que la crisis económica, que la poesía no se publica no se vende no se lee que los políticos ladrones, *coimeros*, lavadores de dinero que el calor que ehtoy tan mal, sabéh? que I've gotta get out of here gotta get out . . . It hits me right smack in the face, por primera vez, que quizás mucho de lo que escribió Alejandra Pizarnik[5] (quizás—probablemente—sin querer) *is* quintessentially Argentine after all, like this: "el tesoro de los piratas enterrado en mi primera persona del singular." But . . . (pausa porteñísima) am *I* any different? Have I ever been? ¿Fui argentina en una vida pasada, o qué onda?

Lined up al lado de la vereda, crowded right up against the ramshackle announcer's platform (a mí los caballos siempre me han inspirado una mezcla de admiración y terror, tipo *Equus*), we wait for the contestants in the sortija-race to assemble. Los jinetes, vestidos de riguroso gaucho-ensemble: bombachas, faja, blusa blanca y chaleco negro, sombrero afelpado, boots and spurs. Many with the facón thrust into the faja. Vienen a caballo to sign themselves up with the announcer. Grupas, pezuñas, nervous liquid eyes, all shifting hooves and quivering flesh just inches from us. No entiendo por qué no estoy más aterrada. A chunky beige and white dappled bay, ridden by an equally portly older gaucho, está nervioso, skittish. Stomping, snorting, breaking into a furious run, bowing and bucking, head up, eyes rolling. We are right beside the finish line, una especie de construcción con un little stick hanging down in the middle, de la cual pende una sortija que el jinete tiene que stab with a stick as his horse rushes under the construction. Nos reímos de lo imposible que parece. Son como unos diez jinetes (una es mujer), y cada uno tendrá unas ocho tandas.

Sin demasiado fanfare, far down the cobblestone, sawdust-covered street, escuchamos the sudden, tremendous gathering of force mientras el primer jinete, un gaucho mayor pero con cierto *morbo* canchero, espolea a su rather ordinary-looking mount. In a split second he is under the ring; extiende su palito confidently, and he's got it. Todo es demasiado rápido for our urban

5. Argentine poet (1936–1972) well-known for her often anguished, hermetic, inwardly focused poetic universe.

eyes; creo que ni nos habríamos dado cuenta de su contundente triunfo si no fuera por los wild aplausos del público y los gritos del announcer. Le siguen otros jinetes menos showy y—por cierto—mucho menos diestros. Nobody else gets it for a while. La mujer is slow, slow and hesitant y siento vergüenza ajena as I hear her emotionally urging her steed on (versus el estoico, concentrado silencio que presentan los machos). Parece casi slow motion compared to the others. Qué pena.

Observo un grupo de rather West Virginia-ish children playing together, trepados a la plataforma del announcer. Todos se conocen aquí. El announcer agarra a una, una niñita rubia de Down syndrome, y la coloca ante el micrófono. Papito, papi, she bellows, mi papiiiito. And sure enough, para relevar al *sortijero*, aquí viene daddy, un fornido cowboy bigotudo montado en un commanding cinnamon-colored steed, blowing kisses to his offspring. De repente, about 50 yards away, a huge wheat-colored stallion goes crazy, y acomete contra el público. Instinctively, I shove the Juvenile toward the vereda (él ya está más que aburrido, "Mom, there's horseshit everywhere, this is boooring" . . . se queja, not even realizing he could be in imminent danger), and move myself, casi detrás de la flimsy plataforma. El rogue horse spins and thrashes, hooves clicking sharp, bucking, nearly throwing his rider against the rundown wall of a building.

El único otro jinete notable, además del primero (que logra ensortijar su palito al menos dos veces más) es un delicado adolescente de unos 14 o 15 años quizás, riding an equally petite palomino. An incredible clattering of hoofs announces him, such smallness in such an intense burst of speed. Just feet before the ring, el joven se pone de pie en los estribos, standing completely upright one perfect second extiende el palo y *zas*, he has it. El truco is not *only* to get the ring on the stick, but also not to let it fly off (which it does with disheartening regularity) and of course, not to fall off the horse.

It is late en la sultry noche porteña de barrio. We begin to walk away, right next to the foam-flecked horses (they sweat right down to their hooves; rico el olor). Nos damos cuenta de que la perspectiva desde el comienzo de la carrera es, si cabe, even more thrilling. From here, we can sense the anticipation of riders and their mounts; the horses turn and twitch, reluctant or bored, y los jinetes intentan contenerlos, inspirarlos. They take off like a shot, four legs pumping together, rider crouched down on the haunches and then rising up, some of them, nearly vertical. Algunos caballos fustigados to within an inch of their lives, it seems—*thwack* se escucha el crop—mientras otros run like hell, simplemente porque sí. No látigo required.

The dancers have moved from chacarera and samba to tango now; la plaza está más atestada que nunca. The night is just beginning para los vecinos de Mataderos, but an hour-long taxi ride awaits us (thrill of his life pal conservative, father of "three non-drug taking teens" taxista que nos ha tocado). From the end of the earth—or at least, the end of Capital Federal[6]—up through all the suburban and sleepy residential barrios that begin with "Villa," dropping off Gaby in Villa Urquiza, and finally back to Palermo. Palermo a secas. Our Palermo. Pero that ride, like they say, es otra historia.

2004

6. What *porteños* (Buenos Aires's residents) call the city of Buenos Aires.

# DIONISIO MARTÍNEZ

## b. 1956

Dionisio Martínez Cañas was born in Cuba. After his family was exiled from Cuba, Martínez lived in Spain and southern California, and he now lives in Tampa, Florida. His poetry reflects the many environments and cultures in which he has lived. Navigating the U.S. vernacular, it addresses diverse subjects such as the 1930s American actress Jean Harlow, the 1989 massacre in China's Tiananmen Square, childhood, *Gone with the Wind* (the movie and the novel), and earthquakes. It also exhibits the exile's poignant sense of displacement and grief. For example, in his poem "Burden," Martínez writes of his mother's conviction that "happiness / is the language of another season in another country," and of the bereavement felt when one lives in one language and loves or remembers in another.

Martínez has published four poetry collections: *Dancing at the Chelsea* (1992); *History as a Second Language* (1993); *Bad Alchemy* (1995), one of 25 titles included in the New York Public Library's 1995 "Books to Remember List"; and *Climbing Back* (2001), selected for the 1999 National Poetry Series. He has received numerous awards—including the Whiting Writer's Award, *The Mid-American Review* James Wright Poetry Prize, and the Ohio State University Press/*The Journal* Poetry Award—and fellowships from the National Endowment for the Arts and the Guggenheim Foundation. His work has appeared in periodicals such as *The American Poetry Review, Iowa Review,* and *Kenyon Review* and in anthologies such as *The Best American Poetry* (1992 and 1994), *Walk on the Wild Side: Urban American Poetry since 1975* (1994), *Little Havana Blues: A Cuban-American Literature Anthology* (1996), and *The Norton Anthology of Poetry* (2005).

In 1999, Martínez was invited by Robert Pinsky, then the U.S. poet laureate, to read at the Library of Congress and record his poems for the library's archives. In 2001, Martínez was an artist-in-residence at the Seaside Institute (Seaside, Florida) and participated in *Prairie Schooner* magazine's 75th Anniversary Celebration at the University of Nebraska, in Lincoln. Martínez conducts writing workshops for the YMCA National Writer's Voice, and his essays and reviews appear in the *Atlanta Journal-Constitution,* the *Miami Herald,* and the *St. Petersburg Times.*

In the selections included here—"In a Duplex Near the San Andreas Fault," "Je te veux," "The Cultivation of Orchids," and "History as a Second Language"— Martínez writes of exile, banishment and grief, small moments of intimacy, and the infinite possibilities of language and silence.

## History as a Second Language

I grew up hearing the essence
of conversations in the next room.
My father and his friends conspired
in the next room. The new regime
succeeded in spite of their plot.          5
The next room is usually dark. People
whisper in it. You hear only so much.
Just enough if you know what to listen for.
I thought I heard a murder in the next
room. It was the radio. I thought          10
I heard a murder long after the radio

had been thrown against the wall and smashed
to bits. It was a whore at the end of
a long day. Families like mine
always managed to have a whore or two                    15
as "good" friends. It made us look
less rich, less whatever being rich meant.
In those days things became
the meanings we gave them and not the other
way around, not like today. The next room          20
meant the room next door. If you looked
hard enough, you could see through the wall.

1993                                                                    1996


## In a Duplex Near the San Andreas Fault

When she tells him about the lump in her breast,
he kisses her on the shoulder for the first time—a natural
reflex twenty-some years in the making. Suddenly,

their entire vocabulary revolves around *benign*
and *malignant*—words reserved                                    5
for these occasions—though they will say

very little now, then nothing for a long time. His hands
are just as pale and nearly as fragile as rice paper,
but she's not familiar with rice paper

and what she wants most desperately now                    10
is a point of reference. Calla lilies bloom
like some glorious, abandoned music out on the lawn.

She takes one of his hands and thinks
of the spathe, which has the responsibility
of being leaf and petal, content and shape: without it          15

there would be no calla lily to remember,
nothing to see when she closes
her eyes and places his hand on her breast.

1995


## Je te veux

To want is to desire. One who desires, however, is not necessarily one who
wants. This is the logic of the heart. Romance languages will argue that
wanting may imply love to some degree. Desire, they will tell you, knows its

place and takes no risks. If a man is banished from a country of desire, he acquires an accent that is always foreign. He becomes susceptible to distances. Wherever he goes, vague references to love fall in his path. He will learn to say I *want* in many languages, always with an accent that even he will find alien. Desire will step gracefully out of the picture, leaving no words for the voice in the man's heart. And until the absence of desire is the only thing left to grasp, he will not know that a man with an accent is marked for life.

1995

# The Cultivation of Orchids

This boy with the eyes of an owl
will not grow wings.
Instead, a man who lives on air will grow
inside him. In time, many arms
will sprout from the boy's                                        5
body, which knows how to adapt
from one life to the next. When the man
grows too large for the space he occupies

and the boy starts to ache and complain,
the man will learn to twist one foot, bend            10
his knees just so, relax the neck
until his head comes down and rests
between the shoulders.
With the man correctly positioned, the boy

can lie down, his skin draped tightly                      15
over his rib cage, and we will not notice
this other life inside him.
He will need all his arms to carry
himself, to keep the two lives from coming
in contact with one another.                                      20
In time, the boy will outgrow the man.
His arms, having become unobtrusive

and ordinary, will welcome
the sleeves of heavy coats.
His eyes will look progressively smaller.             25
The man will give himself a voice
and a name. The boy will begin to hold
his breath and eavesdrop
on conversations between the man
and the woman who has come                                30
to draw him out.

1995

# ACHY OBEJAS
## b. 1956

Born in Cuba, Achy Obejas immigrated to the United States with her family at age six. She earned her bachelor's degree from Indiana University and, in 1993, her Master of Fine Arts degree from Warren Wilson College, near Asheville, North Carolina. In 1986, Obejas was a National Endowment for the Arts poetry fellow. For over 10 years, she worked for *The Chicago Tribune*, writing about arts and culture but also reporting on events such as Pope John Paul II's 1998 visit to Cuba, the incarceration at the Guantánamo Bay detention facility of captured Al Qaeda members, the murder of the fashion designer Gianni Versace, and the AIDS epidemic. In 2001, she received a Pulitzer Prize as part of a *Chicago Tribune* staff team. She now regularly writes about Latin music for *The Washington Post* and about books for *In These Times* magazine. Obejas has been the Springer Writer-in-Residence at the University of Chicago and the Distinguished Writer in Residence at the University of Hawaii. She is the Sor Juana Visiting Writer at DePaul University in Chicago.

Her first book, the collection *We Came All the Way from Cuba So You Could Dress Like This?* (1994), blends memoir and essay in depicting a vulnerable urban population of lesbians, gays, Cuban boat people, and addicts. In exploring the meaning of exile and outsider status, Obejas draws on her past as a penniless immigrant child, her lesbian identity, and her sense of displacement. "Wrecks," included in this anthology, is the story of a woman whose series of automobile accidents echoes her breakups with lovers. "I have to be sure I have the right insurance," she tells us, as she also searches for a romantic safety net.

In Obejas's debut novel, *Memory Mambo* (1996), the heroine searches for love and truth, both in her lesbian relationship and in her family's nostalgia for their lost life in Cuba. Her second novel, *Days of Awe* (2001), is a coming-of-age story about a young woman who discovers that she has Jewish ancestors. For each novel, Obejas won the Lambda Literary Award in the lesbian fiction category. Obejas's poetry collection *This Is What Happened in Our Other Life* (2007) explores the collision of sexual and ethnic identities.

Obejas is the editor of *Havana Noir* (2007), a collection of crime stories set in the Cuban capital, and she has rendered the work of the Cuban *negrismo* poet Nicolás Guillén into English. In 2008, she translated Junot Díaz's Pulitzer Prize–winning novel, *The Brief and Wondrous Life of Oscar Wao*, into Spanish. Her novel *Ruins* (2009) is about a weary, aging revolutionary whose world, in Havana in 1994, is collapsing around him.

## Wrecks

I have to be sure I have the right insurance—that is, collision as well as liability. I simply can't afford not to be able to pay for whatever car repairs I might need, and I'm afraid that sooner or later (and probably sooner) I'm going to be sitting in a mechanic's waiting room, right there next to the Coke machine and the faded road maps, flipping through some weathered copy of *Time* or *Popular Mechanics*, waiting to be told what my insurance will and won't cover.

This is very important to me right now because I always have an automobile accident after a break-up, and Sandra, my lover of five years, just left me for some babe who lives in San Francisco, the promised land of fruit and nuts. We were one of those couples everyone envied—good-looking, funny, successful—so I'm still trying to figure out how this happened, and why. Sandra's dark, jealous, and bird-like, as impatient and breathtaking as a nestling, and the new babe is tall and wooden. I know I shouldn't dwell on it—it's not good for me—but I *know* they don't fit.

Since Sandra moved out on me in order to pump up her phone bill and become a free and frequent flyer, I've been trying to take the bus and train everywhere—to work, to the post office, even to the grocery store, which I hate doing because, since I can't carry ten bags of stuff with the same ease with which I can pack them into the VW, I end up having to do some shopping every time I leave the house. Since I'm trying to be environmentally conscious and use paper bags, which don't have handles, this is doubly tough on the five block walk from the store to my apartment.

The last time this happened was about seven years ago. It had been three and a half years of utter hell with Loretta, but I still couldn't believe she'd really left, so in my grief and disbelief I wrapped my car around a tree in a south Chicago suburb. I did it the minute Loretta left for Los Angeles, a city in which no one is actually born but to which millions are drawn like moths to a fire. Loretta was lithe, a singer with an immense and angry voice. I'd always thought we shared a cosmic connection of some sort: after all, we fought and fucked like minks. But she said she had to go because she'd imagined women would be kinder than men, and my sarcasm was wearing on her sense of sisterhood.

To make matters worse, after I'd wrapped my car around the tree, I refused to believe it was inoperable, so I did my damndest to start it, sending the fan blades tearing through the radiator, which had been pushed up a good six inches. The entire mess cost me around two thousand dollars, including the towing fee back to the city. I should have just chucked the car—a beat up mustard-colored Dodge Valiant—but I didn't. I just kept going. So did Loretta, who married the corporate lawyer for Hughes Aircraft. They have two daughters now, one inexplicably named after me. I confess it does give me comfort: it's evidence of sorts that I had an effect on that girl after all.

Before that, when Doris left me for membership in a lesbian separatist living collective somewhere in the hills of Arkansas, I made a point of not seeing the steel post holding up the chain around one of Chicago's lakefront parks. I knew Doris and I had problems living together—she smoked with the same fatal simmer of an arsoned building, leaving powdery ash sculptures everywhere—but it seemed extreme that my nagging should drive her to repentance in a place where no cigarettes, polyester, or dairy products are allowed.

After Doris left, I'd wanted just to drive leisurely and miserably through the park, which was—wisely, I suppose—closed for the winter. I just wanted to get a look at the lake, frozen with the waves mid-roll. I knew they'd remind me of all those little ash tubes, gray and mindless, that Doris had left around the house. But I never made it to the lakefront. I ended up sliding on some ice on the road and sort of hopping onto one of the little posts that held up the keep-out chain, ramming the post through the transmission of my car and causing total vehicular loss. Ultimately, I didn't mind so much. I hadn't yet noticed car accidents as a post-relationship pattern, and I'd never much liked that car anyway, a green and white Gremlin that looked like a pimp shoe.

To be honest, I think the whole accident/relationship thing really started after a brief affair with a former sports writer for the *Chicago Sun-Times* who everybody thinks is bisexual but who is really a lesbian. She'd cover Bulls games by watching them in her peripheral vision on TV while lying on top of me on her bed. After she moved to Washington, D.C., to cover society happenings, I ran my old Chevy van into the line of taxis waiting across the street from the *Sun-Times* building, giving the domino theory a whole new twist.

I don't drive anything as lethal as a van now, but rather my more benign, if not just plain cartoonish, VW bug, one of the original Beetles, red and rusty, but still dependable. Of course, I don't actually drive it much these days, since I'm convinced that getting behind the wheel will be eventually, inevitably, disastrous.

. . .

The fact is, I can't stay away from cars when I'm heartbroken. Even when I tell myself I shouldn't drive, I end up hanging out at fancy used car lots, where they use terms like "vintage" and "pre-owned," just staring at those fine machines and dreaming about getaways.

A few days after Sandra left, I saw a 1956 vanilla-colored Porsche 356, the same kind of car in which Jimmy Dean spun right out of this world,[1] and I swear I would have sold my mother to get it. But my mother's dead, Sandra was gone, and with her, every technological gadget I might ever have hocked for more than a hundred dollars, so I didn't have much with which to bargain with the devil, much less a car salesman. So I just balanced my two paper bags full of groceries and stared at the Porsche. I touched it a few times until, finally, one of the sales guys came out to the showroom and told me to go home. He said I looked like I was going to cry and offered to get me a cab, which he even paid for. That was very nice, but not as nice as driving myself would have been. The thing about cabs is that even if you're rich enough to pay the meter, they still have their limits.

And the idea after a break-up, of course, is to have no limits. I think that's why I like the notion of cars when I'm going through emotional angst. They provide this very cool, very American answer to pain: Even if you follow all the right directions from Chicago to San Francisco, all you need is one wrong turn—one little fuck-up—and you wind up in Mississippi, where there are no lesbians. It's so inevitable that you may as well enjoy the ride—the wind in your hair; the truck stop waitresses who've always been curious but have never been with other women other than in their fantasy letters about threesomes to *Penthouse Forum*; the radio blasting away with great rock 'n' roll songs, then great tear-jerking Country and Western songs, and then, when the tinny static stuff comes on while you're daredeviling through the swamps, you can always pop on a Philip Glass[2] tape and think yourself really courageous.

---

1. The American actor James Dean (1931–1955) died in a car crash.

2. American composer (b. 1937) associated with minimalist music based on repetition.

I'm no fool, though. I know all this romantic posturing about wide-open spaces, the adventurous South, and on-the-road possibilities; all these images and metaphors for freedom are inspired by men, jaded men like Jack Kerouac[3]—that repressed homosexual who never really found love and died a pathetic mess of a human being. It's all a cover-up for just one thing: desperation.

I know from personal experience that, ultimately, no matter how many road maps I study, how many pairs of lacy underwear I pack for travel, how many times I tell myself that there are girls with Creole accents just waiting for me in New Orleans or Miami, all I'm going to do is drive around my ex-lover's house and have an accident. Sandra may pine for San Francisco, but she lives only one block away from me now. That's how crazy this is.

. . .

Of course, I've seen a therapist about this but all I remember is that she recommended I not see *Fatal Attraction*,[4] which offended me terribly because, as a lesbian and a feminist, I would *never* resort to that sort of thing. Instead, I drive around and around and around Sandra's building, like a crazy wind-up toy that's *too* wound up and careens off into the furniture. I always want to throw up, but I don't—my stomach knots up and short-circuits the whole idea. It's like everything else about her and me: one false start after another.

We met through a mutual friend, a woman we were both crushed out on but who didn't want either of us. It took Sandra and me two dates to kiss, which is pretty typical by lesbian standards but a little slow by mine. By the time we made it to bed, it was more formality than desire: we already knew we were completely incompatible and went through it, I think, just so we could say we had.

Six months later we were both still prowling performing arts spaces and foreign movie houses as single lesbians. When we ran into each other again, we both seemed to glow with the right aura, kiss with lips that fit perfectly into each other's mouths, and make love with complementary rhythms. At first, even though it was very nice, I thought that it would be not a casual affair, but a *transient* relationship; I just wasn't sure we'd fall in love. But after another six months, even though I still had doubts about our romantic possibilities, she'd packed her little pointy boots, her Cuisinart, and her cats and re-settled them in my Uptown apartment.

That didn't quite work out, though. She wanted more closet space. She didn't like the posters I had on the walls. She thought my Mexican rugs were cheap. So after six months we moved into another apartment, one that was *ours* from the start, in which no decision could be made without the other's approval. It should have been suffocating, but it wasn't. There was a funny comfort, an uncanny understanding to the way our furniture fit together and our clothes began to match.

Of course, there still were little problems. I liked to stay up until the wee hours; she was up before dawn. I liked rock; she liked *salsa*. I liked sex in public places; she considered it an adventure to do it in our own kitchen.

---

3. American writer (1922–1969).
4. American movie (1987) in which a woman takes revenge on her former lover.

But slowly, almost imperceptibly, we began to behave in ways that said we wanted to be together for a long, long time: My clothes no longer rested on the exercycle, but got hung up at night; her dishes didn't sit for days but got washed as soon as she finished her meals. I opened a savings account; she named me as her spouse on her American Express and got me a card.

If life was too mundane to be heaven, it didn't matter; it was heaven on earth, or heaven enough. We had a long, train-like apartment with so much light we had to cover our eyes when we woke up. And on Sunday mornings, sitting in bed reading the paper while drinking coffee and soaking in Sandra's sleepy musk, I was as happy as I might ever have been.

It's true, I could never tell her about my weird Catholicism, or the way my heart hurt from pleasure sometimes, but I could confess to her my foulest fears, my most awful memories, and I knew they'd be safe. I don't know what she couldn't tell me, but I know no one had ever listened to her with quite the same rapture, or held her as fiercely when she was afraid. I know because she told me so, and to this day I believe her about these things.

All of that changed when Sandra took a business trip to San Francisco. She has told me what happened during that week a million times now, but even though I know too well how one thing led to another, I still don't see *how*—I don't understand why suddenly we didn't make sense, and why *they* did. She explained it by telling me she realized she wasn't in love with me anymore, and that she hadn't been for a long time. She talked about smoking cigarettes for the first time in years, and enjoying it; about walking on the beach; about going to bed at the same time every night with this new babe. She has told me far more than I ever wanted to know about what happened, but try as she might, she's been unable to make me understand how the gears stopped working for us, how the machinery went rusty without our knowing, and how one day the motor simply wouldn't turn over.

When it finally happened—when it became inevitable—I thought that, after five years together, the splitting would be agonizing. I worried about all the everyday things I might have lost sense of; I wondered, really, if I might not walk into walls or the middle of traffic, like a mental patient who thinks she wants freedom but really wants only to be out of the dark and into the light.

I feared the division of our possessions more than anything, not because they were so many but because they were so few and so precious. We were professionals, though, as efficient as the keenest of lawyers: cool, rational, shamelessly unsentimental. We went through the business of furniture without argument, and then we did the same with the dishes and kitchen appliances. After that, the few items of clothing that might have been debatable fell right into place with one or the other's wardrobe, almost as if they—and not we—knew instinctively where they belonged. Her CDs and my CDs gathered in perfect, separate piles.

Even the photo albums were simple to divide. We peeled back the plastic pages and plucked each image, one by one, laughing, and sometimes crying (actually, Sandra didn't cry; she hasn't cried once during this whole thing), remembering our trips to Santa Fe, and to Mexico City, and the good times in Tulsa.[5] I was struck by how few pictures there were of *us*, but how many

5. City in Oklahoma. *Santa Fe*: city in New Mexico. *Mexico City*: capital of Mexico.

of her, standing beside this or that interesting tourist site; and of me, driving with that crazy look in my eyes, or leaning happily against the fender of a rented roadster. I always made us rent sports cars, no matter how inconvenient for luggage or sleeping, because there's nothing like driving at night, very fast, very sure, in a car that does absolutely everything you want it to. I think it's patriotic as hell. And I look corn-fed in those pictures, all of which she kept.

When I visit Sandra now, her cats eye me as if I were some long-lost relative, funny uncle, or divorced parent. It takes them a while to remember me, and I never know if they're reflecting her or acting on their own. I envy them nonetheless, their little brains, and that they get to sleep with her every night. The trouble is, most of the time—not all of the time, not when I'm out dancing with friends or watching TV—I still want her and our life back. I still want to go on long rides with her with the windows open, the radio blasting. I still want her to tell me stories, to fall asleep with her head in my lap while I drive. It's true that I didn't ever really know where we were going, but we *were* going, and it was steady, and it mattered. The trip itself was always as vital, as sunny, and as difficult as wherever we might end up.

Now, whenever I drive by, I look up at Sandra's apartment. I don't stare. I don't lunge out the window. I'm very subtle, the picture of calm. I check my gas gauge. I check my heat vents. I check my mirrors and hope no one has noticed that this is my millionth time around the block, and I'm wearing a groove into the street. Actually, I never have any idea of how many times I've gone around the block. I lose track; I *really* lose track. I get lost, not on the street but inside my own head. Then I get fucking terrified that someone will see me when I'm trying to be casual about checking my mirrors and that they won't believe me, they won't buy my act, and maybe they'll call the cops or the neighborhood crime watch.

I always imagine that I do it right, though: I reach outside the car to adjust my side view mirror, and then, right at that moment, I look up, casually of course, to see if Sandra's light is on, if the cats are poised on the window sill. I hope that maybe, just maybe, she'll pick that same moment to interrupt the flickering of the TV light with a few steps across the window frame, to the kitchen for more scotch or coffee, or to the bedroom to get her robe because it's cold and she misses me, or maybe, just maybe, to come to the damn window to look for me because she knows—I mean, she just absolutely *knows*—that I'm here, adjusting my mirrors outside her window, and needing her.

But, of course, it never works out that way. I don't see anything, or if I do it's all in a split second, an instant, that harrowing and fragile crack between the past and the future. I lose momentary control of the car, threaten the life of some neighborhood kid with the shrill of brakes and screaming car horns, and then drive as fast and far away as I possibly can—to the lake, to the Loop, to Kankakee[6]—anywhere, just as long as I can hide my shame and panic when I get there.

• • •

When Sandra first left, my friend Lourdes kept up my spirits by saying stupid things. "Women," she declared, cozy in the bosom of a seven-year relationship with a woman who is both a cook and a carpenter. "You can't live

---

6. City in Illinois, southwest of Chicago. *The Loop*: the historical center of downtown Chicago.

with 'em, and you can't live without 'em." I thought this was particularly insensitive of her, kind of arrogant actually, but so blatantly dumb that it never failed to get at least one demented, disgusted laugh out of me.

One day, as I contemplated buying materials for a hex to cause California to fall off the earth and thus eliminate all chances of happiness for Sandra and her new babe, Lourdes came up with what then seemed like an epiphany.

"You don't need any of this *santería* stuff," she said. "You're a good egg; you just need a good chick to lay you."

I took her advice. I went on a sex binge, although it was difficult because I don't like to spend the night in a stranger's home, and I felt it was too soon to bring anybody to my home where the bed had been our bed, Sandra's and my cozy little love nest. So instead, I took girls out to Montrose Harbor, to the concrete circle that overlooks the lake and the best, most brilliant view of the city skyline. Even for natives, this can be breathtaking. We looked at the skyscrapers, at the long circuits of car lights on Lake Shore Drive, and at the way the sky divides into layers of blue and gray and pink, depending on the temperature, the pollution, and the cloud formations.

But instead of staring at clouds and trying to make sense of their shapes, we stared at the frozen waves and the little pieces of ice—all looking suspiciously like California floating out into the ocean—and tried to make sense of the terribly awkward situation we had put ourselves in. Inevitably, though, we would make love in my VW, an idea I successfully sold to each girl with the promise of "lesbianizing" high school necking experiences.

The first time was pretty hard. I came up breathless, convinced that I was surely doomed, that whatever drool I was wiping off my chin had just sealed the absolute hopelessness of any potential recovery of my relationship with Sandra. I realized then that every time I closed my eyes, I kept hoping to open them to one of those safe Sunday mornings in bed with Sandra, our bodies tangled together, the cats on either side of us purring. I stared off into the darkness of the lake outside my car window, watched the rats skip between the fogged cars around us, and hyperventilated. I don't think I'd ever felt so alone in my life.

Then I noticed the girl I was with. I wish I could say I felt guilty for not remembering her until that moment, for having blanked her out so completely, but I didn't. Instead, I felt a kind of relief, a strange connection with all the other wretched souls of the earth—whether they were reckless macho men or women—who woke up from their own selfish pain and suddenly realized they were about to inflict it on an innocent bystander whose only desire was love, or comfort, or maybe even something as simple as fun.

When I finally looked at this girl, I didn't know what the hell was going on, but it was pretty clear that she didn't need or want to hear my hellish confessions. She was fine, suffering not one little shrapnel of guilt or regret, popping a tape into the VW's stereo, singing along, offering me more cheap wine. I wanted to say: *Don't you realize what we've just done?* But she just kept singing, perfectly at home there with her elbow in my stomach and my breast crushed by her shoulder.

I knew I'd hit bottom when I realized what I really wanted was to confess to Sandra what I'd done, and to beg forgiveness for this and any other transgression, real or imagined. I wanted to explain to the girl in my car that this could never, ever, happen again because, for heaven's sake, I was an unhappily-processing-my-primary-relationship-lesbian, and this, this thing that had just happened between us—which was, of course, beautiful and powerful and just plain great—was still, well, adultery. As soon as I dropped her off, I had every intention of going home to that long train-like apartment, kicking out any strangers who might have wandered in, and throwing myself at Sandra's mercy.

But I didn't say anything, and I didn't do anything either. I stared out the car window, thinking the city looked extraordinarily innocent, and eventually came to my senses. I moaned a few times, then forgave myself for the temporary insanity that let me forget the block of cozy bungalows that now exists between my mailbox and Sandra's, that we'd need marriage as a precondition for adultery, and that lesbians can only have, at best, a pseudo-marriage. I told the girl I was pseudo-separated, and surely headed for pseudo-divorce. Nonetheless, she never went out with me again, although she did buy me a scale model VW and attached a very charming note thanking me for helping her remember how much fun it used to be to park.

I've been back to Montrose Harbor numerous times since, but when I got her note I rubbed my tender muscles, climbed into my very real VW, and started doing circles around the block.

. . .

I know exactly when the accidents will happen. I also know that, short of being tossed around and bruised by the steering wheel and shoulder belt, I won't be seriously hurt. And I know, as sure as I know that when I find true love again I will forget all of this misery and dive head-first into it, that the next time—the very next time I get behind the wheel—I will experience my post-Sandra accident.

That's why I've been taking public transportation. It's why I've bought insurance—not in a conscientious way, but in a totally ignorant, sure-to-be exploited way. I simply filled out a form I found tucked into the weekly *Chicago Reader* and sent it off with a sixty-dollar down-payment to a company whose phone number spells I-N-S-U-R-E-D. I don't know what came over me; I just know that I needed insurance right there and then.

When I told Lourdes, she suggested that if I *know* the accident is imminent, and that if having the accident is the only way out of this post-Sandra depression, then maybe I need to just get it over with and run over a newspaper boy, ram a mailbox, or hit a station wagon filled with suburbanites. She said that maybe by avoiding the accident I'm delaying the healing process, sidestepping the very idea that Sandra and I are as dead as disco.

Just yesterday I went over to Sandra's—an official visit to drop off a few things she'd forgotten in the move (a bottle of contact lens solution, a box of postcards, and a couple of pairs of cotton panties, all carried over in a paper grocery bag)—and for a few minutes everything seemed fine between us. We hugged when I arrived and, although she seemed smaller in my arms than ever before, her skin was as familiar and painful as ever.

Still, we talked without effort, laughed without embarrassment. It was almost like old times. Then the phone rang. Even before Sandra's answering machine picked it up, we both knew it was San Francisco calling. We stood there, listening to the whir of the tape, the click, and then the voice that has replaced mine at those times when only whispers matter.

I know I was lucky: Sandra picked up the phone and very carefully said she'd call back in a bit, that we were chatting. She could have gloated; she could have smirked; she could have laughed nervously. All of that might have fit. But she didn't. She did everything the sensitive-relationship manuals say to do: She exhibited patience, grace, and even gave me a little squeeze on the arm and a wet little peck on my cheek. She looked as sad and understanding as if she were my best friend, not the woman who'd dumped me. There was no question in my mind she was *trying*.

But it didn't matter. I'd already clenched my teeth, my fists, all of my muscles, and there was nothing that could loosen them up again.

I still haven't been able to get the episode out of my mind. And that's the part I don't understand. I know I've accepted the situation. I know that to go back would require a blinding absolution on both our parts, of which we're both totally incapable. I'm not asking for another chance. I've accepted we're over. I've even accepted, on some deep and awful level, that we are and will be with others. What I want is an answer of another sort: How long will this nag at me? How long will it hurt?

• • •

I've decided to take Lourdes's advice again, so I'm driving my car and looking for trouble. I'm listening to new tapes, tapes I bought on a lark at the 7-Eleven around the corner from my apartment. The place was blazing in fluorescence, humming right along when I went in, moved aside the little American flags that hung from the shelves, and picked out every third tape across the top row. I wound up with some heavy metal, Loretta Lynn, and a collection of the Archies[7] greatest hits, but I will survive all of their flaws and find beauty in them if it kills me.

My new insurance card is in the back pocket of my jeans. I've got a tall, cool take-out Coke between my legs, and I'm pressing down on the accelerator and singing along whenever possible with Metallica. I'm in complete control. I pass a Jeep on Montrose Avenue, right at the intersection with Broadway, and leave behind a mess of pedestrians waving their fists in the air. At Marine Drive I shift and laugh, sending a man in a raincoat chasing after his frightened dog on the perfect lawn around Lake Shore Drive. I'm in the fourth lane and my radio is so damn loud I can't hear my own voice singing along. My hair whips all over my face, a crazy dance of snakes. Before I know it, I'm leaning hard, away from the S-curve, rounding up to the Loop, and I realize I'm running out of prime city concrete.

I'm thinking, yeah, the interstate looks good, and I change lanes and climb the entrance ramp off Lake Shore Drive to I-55, pumping the VW, sure that everything I need will be taken care of in a matter of miles, even before the tape turns itself over. I'm thinking, yeah, San Francisco; I could drive there in a straight line if I wanted to. I'm thinking all this, thinking crazy, murderous thoughts when everything—absolutely everything—comes to a dead halt right there on the entrance ramp, right there in front of me, in one overwhelming wall of excruciating sound and light. I feel my head graze the windshield, like some kind of slow-motion heavenly knocking—immediate and exquisite and over with before I know what's actually happened.

---

7. American bubblegum-pop group, formed 1968. *Loretta Lynn:* American country singer (b. 1935).

But I'm fine, and nothing has happened. Nothing, that is, except that the belt has practically cut my shoulder with the sheer force of how I descended on the brakes, all one hundred and twenty pounds of me, as soon as I saw the red lights going wild in front of my face. I stopped on a dime—*on a dime*. The guy behind me landed on his horn, releasing one long, petulant whine. I sneered at him in the mirror but he threw his hands in the air to apologize, and I realized I had to forgive him, I had no other choice. The guy behind him, I'm sure, kissed his bumper. I don't know after that. I look in the mirror again, but there's no sign of the end to this loose, dangerous train of cars on the ramp, all stopped for god knows what.

I jerk on the emergency brake, unbuckle, rub my shoulder, and leap out of the VW to find, literally, less than an inch between me and the car in front of me, a black BMW from which a gaggle of preschoolers improbably scatters. There are lights everywhere: red and terrible white lights from all the cars, blue lights threatening epileptic seizures from a cop car that's backing up on the shoulder of the interstate. I try to cover my eyes from all the glare and notice a stream of liquid running between my shoes and down the ramp's incline: green anti-freeze, water maybe, with a thread of something vivid and red that looks like blood. My shoes are soaked with it before I can move.

I walk up, maneuvering from small child to small child, all of them curious and straining to get a look at what's under the wheel of the BMW. A woman's voice tells them not to look, causing every one of them to stare even more intently. "Wow," says one, his eyes as wide as saucers. "Disgusting," says another, her face greenish. A man in a dark trench coat is pacing right in front of the car. "Oh my god," he says. "Oh my god," over and over and over again. He has a perfect haircut and his lower lip curls like he's about to cry. I can't see anything except that the liquid flowing down the concrete ramp is almost black now. The lights are so bright, and everything's so confusing.

"Did the dog belong to anybody here?" asks one of the cops, averting his gaze from the scene of the crime.

I look at the colossal, mangled heap under the BMW's wheel and make out a blondish mutt, one eye like blue glass, the other black with blood from the ruptured sclera. His huge body is torn apart, and he looks like the devil. He's wearing no tags, no collar, nothing. His hair is soaked with dirt and all the liquids pouring from the car's engine.

"It's my dog," I lie, reaching out tentatively to the still warm paw, as open as a catcher's mitt.

"Well, what was he doing on the highway?" asks the same cop. "How come he doesn't have a collar? I mean, I'm really sorry and everything but . . . jesus . . . you got any identification, huh?"

I pat my jacket for my wallet, not finding it, finally reach back to my jeans pocket, pull out my insurance card, and hand it to the cop. His partner, as faceless as he is, directs traffic around my bug and the BMW. Since I'm squatting, the headlights blaze right into my face, and for an instant I feel like a criminal caught in some horrible act. One of the preschoolers, a little girl with a stammer, tells me she's real sorry her dad ran over my dog. I just stare at her, and she backs off, bumping right into the cop.

"You know this won't pay for the dog, right?" the cop says, handing me back my insurance card. "I mean, you're still responsible for whatever damage to his car, but I don't think you can get anything on the dog."

"She's irreplaceable," I tell him, and let go of the demon mutt's paw. I stand up and cover my eyes. The cop, who thinks I'm crying, squeezes my shoulder.

Now the cop's partner is in the squad car, making noises on the police radio. The squad's blue lights keep going around and around and around. The man in the trench coat, who can't seem to meet my eyes, keeps apologizing to me. "I'm sorry; I'm really sorry," he says, biting his lip until it finally bleeds. I squeeze his shoulder, and we make out a police report together. I think I'm going to owe him some money, but he says no, that he killed my dog, that he can't take my money for what little damage the dog may have done to his car. We're talking hundreds, maybe thousands of dollars here, but he insists.

Just my luck, I think, I've stumbled upon the last Good Samaritan in the universe, and driving a BMW no less. I can barely keep from laughing.

. . .

When I get back in the VW, I check my emergency brake, my gas gauge, then I look in the mirror. My face is smudged and wet, a strange combination of dirt, sweat and, maybe, tears. I really don't know. I sit in silence for a while, just watching the cars go around me and the BMW. I watch them disappear, not so much into the flow of traffic as into the night, beyond the slope of I-55, into the long line of boarded-up houses and old factories, neglected lawns, and loose dogs around the interstate.

I remember seeing Sandra for the first time, dressed in black, somber, and a little scared, and making her laugh. I have no idea what it was I said. It's all behind me now.

Eventually, a huge blue city truck pulls up, followed by a tow truck. The city workers, all men with rough voices whose breath I can see, scrape the dog from under the BMW and hook the car to the tow truck. They hose down the concrete as the man in the trench coat and his family climb into a taxi. Before the taxi's off the ramp, the water has frozen, and workers are sprinkling salt over it. Finally, it's just me and the cops on the ramp. They turn off their blue lights, flick on their turn signal, and wait for me to mainstream into traffic.

1994

---

# MARTÍN ESPADA
## b. 1957

Martín Espada was born in a public-housing project in Brooklyn, New York. He holds a bachelor's degree in history from the University of Wisconsin–Madison and a law degree from Northeastern University, in Boston. Before receiving his law degree, he worked as a paralegal in the areas of welfare rights and mental health. As a lawyer, he continued representing the poor as an advocate of tenants' rights. These experiences—and the various jobs he held before completing his college education, such as night-desk clerk at a transient hotel, bouncer, gas-station attendant, and bindery worker in a printing plant—partly explain the empathetic connections with the less privileged, and with those victimized by political persecution or socio-economic exploitation, that permeate his poetry.

A professor of English at the University of Massachusetts Amherst, Espada has taught courses in Latino poetry and creative writing. His first published collection of poetry, *The Immigrant Iceboy's Bolero* (1982), includes photographs of barrio life taken by his father, Frank Espada, that provide visual images of the social and cultural milieu that inspired the author's poetic imagery. In his second collection, *Trumpets from the Islands of Their Eviction* (1987), Espada continued to capture the dislocations of Puerto Rican migrant life in New York City. His third book, the bilingual collection *Rebellion Is the Circle of a Lover's Hands/Rebelión es el giro de manos del amante* (1990), pays tribute to all kinds of rebels: workers fighting to make a living, Puerto Rican nationalists fighting to liberate their country, Puerto Rican migrants fighting against racism and poverty. The manuscript earned Espada a PEN/Revson Foundation Fellowship for Poetry, and the published volume earned him the Paterson Poetry Prize.

As a radio journalist, Espada visited Nicaragua during the early years of the Sandinista government and coproduced the series *Nicaragua: Three Years after Somoza.* Many of his poems have been inspired by his various travels to Latin American countries. He translated and edited *The Blood That Keeps Singing* (1991), a selection of poems by the Puerto Rican nationalist poet and former political prisoner Clemente Soto Vélez, who lived in New York for many decades. He also edited the anthologies *Poetry Like Bread: Poets of the Political Imagination from Curbstone Press* (1994) and *El Coro: A Chorus of Latino and Latina Poetry* (1997). Among his more recent poetry volumes are *Imagine the Angels of Bread* (1996), winner of an American Book Award and a finalist for the National Book Critics Circle Award; *A Mayan Astronomer in Hell's Kitchen* (2000); *Alabanza: New and Selected Poems, 1982–2002* (2003), which received a Paterson Award for Sustained Literary Achievement and was designated a Notable Book of the Year by the American Library Association; and *The Republic of Poetry* (2006), which was a finalist for the Pulitzer Prize. Many of Espada's poems have been translated into other languages. He has also published two books of essays: *Zapata's Disciple* (1998) and *The Lover of a Subversive Is Also a Subversive* (2010). Among Espada's other honors are a Massachusetts Artists' Foundation Fellowship, a National Endowment for the Arts Creative Writing Fellowship, a National Hispanic Cultural Center Literary Award, a PEN/Revson Fellowship, and a Guggenheim Fellowship.

Inspired by the nineteenth-century American poet Walt Whitman and the twentieth-century Chilean poet Pablo Neruda, Espada's poems often combine autobiography with ideological struggle and resistance. His training in history is also evident in his poetry, especially in his challenges to official historical documents that neglect to insert the experiences and struggles of the less fortunate working masses into history. His writing and interviews make clear that Espada believes in poetry as a form of revolutionary practice, a consciousness-raising and empowering tool that brings dignity, redemption, and hope to the oppressed.

Two of the poems selected for this anthology, "Revolutionary Spanish Lesson" and "Niggerlips," are among the autobiographical poems in *Rebellion Is a Circle in a Lover's Hands.* In the first, the poet expresses the anger and desire for retribution he feels every time his Spanish name is mispronounced by Anglos. In the second, he recounts the name-calling and intimidation he was subjected to in high school because of his racially mixed heritage. "Imagine the Angels of Bread," also included here, is the signature poem of the collection that bears the same title. It captures the anger, the desire for retribution, but also the compassion created by the painful experiences of those who historically have endured social, racial, and ethnic persecution. "My Name Is Espada," from *A Maya Astronomer,* reflects on the meaning of the poet's last name, "sword" in Spanish. The sword represents the violence and bloodshed inflicted by Europeans on indigenous and black slave populations during the Spanish Colonial period, but it also was the weapon used by these populations in their struggles for emancipation. "Alabanza: In Praise of Local 100" eulogizes the many Latino restaurant workers who died at the World Trade Center in the terrorist attacks of September 11, 2001. After this poem was published in *The Nation*, Espada received a letter of gratitude from the executive board of the union that represented the slain workers. Finally, "The Republic of Poetry" was inspired by Espada's visit to Chile during the Neruda centennial celebrations in 2004.

## Revolutionary Spanish Lesson

Whenever my name
is mispronounced,
I want to buy a toy pistol,
put on dark sunglasses,
push my beret to an angle,                          5
comb my beard to a point,
hijack a busload
of Republican tourists
from Wisconsin,
force them to chant                                 10
anti-American slogans
in Spanish,
and wait
for the bilingual SWAT team
to helicopter overhead,                             15
begging me
to be reasonable

1990

## Niggerlips

Niggerlips was the high school name
for me.
So called by Douglas
the car mechanic, with green tattoos
on each forearm,                                    5
and the choir of round pink faces
that grinned deliciously
from the back row of classrooms,
droned over by teachers
checking attendance too slowly.                     10

Douglas would brag
about cruising his car
near sidewalks of black children
to point an unloaded gun,
to scare niggers                                    15
like crows off a tree,
he'd say.

My great-grandfather Luis
was un negrito too,
a shoemaker in the coffee hills          20
of Puerto Rico, 1900.
The family called him a secret
and kept no photograph.
My father remembers
the childhood white powder          25
that failed to bleach
his stubborn copper skin,
and the family says
he is still a fly in milk.

                                                              1990


# Imagine the Angels of Bread

This is the year that squatters evict landlords,
gazing like admirals from the rail
of the roofdeck
or levitating hands in praise
of steam in the shower;          5
this is the year
that shawled refugees deport judges
who stare at the floor
and their swollen feet
as files are stamped          10
with their destination;
this is the year that police revolvers,
stove-hot, blister the fingers
of raging cops,
and nightsticks splinter          15
in their palms;
this is the year
that darkskinned men
lynched a century ago
return to sip coffee quietly          20
with the apologizing descendants
of their executioners.

This is the year that those
who swim the border's undertow
and shiver in boxcars          25
are greeted with trumpets and drums
at the first railroad crossing
on the other side;
this is the year that the hands
pulling tomatoes from the vine          30
uproot the deed to the earth that sprouts the vine,
the hands canning tomatoes
are named in the will

that owns the bedlam of the cannery;
this is the year that the eyes                                        35
stinging from the poison that purifies toilets
awaken at last to the sight
of a rooster-loud hillside,
pilgrimage of immigrant birth;
this is the year that cockroaches                                    40
become extinct, that no doctor
finds a roach embedded
in the ear of an infant;
this is the year that the food stamps
of adolescent mothers                                                45
are auctioned like gold doubloons,
and no coin is given to buy machetes
for the next bouquet of severed heads
in coffee plantation country.

If the abolition of slave-manacles[1]                                50
began as a vision of hands without manacles,
then this is the year;
if the shutdown of extermination camps[2]
began as imagination of a land
without barbed wire or the crematorium,                              55
then this is the year;
if every rebellion begins with the idea
that conquerors on horseback
are not many-legged gods, that they too drown
if plunged in the river,                                             60
then this is the year.

So may every humiliated mouth,
teeth like desecrated headstones,
fill with the angels of bread.

1993                                                              1996


## My Name Is Espada

*Espada*: the word for sword in Spain
wrought by fire and the hammer's chime,
name for the warrior reeling helmet-hooded
through the pandemonium of horses in mud,
or the face dreaming on a sarcophagus,                               5
hands folded across the hilt of stone.

Espada: sword in el Caribe,
rapier tested sharp across the bellies of Indios, steel tongue
lapping blood like a mastiff gorged on a runaway slave,

---

1. The abolition of slavery in the United States, through the passage of the Thirteenth Amendment to the Constitution (1865).

2. In Nazi Germany, by the Allied Forces during World War II.

god gleaming brighter than the god nailed to the cross,                    10
forged at the anvil with chains by the millions
tangled and red as the entrails of demons.

Espada: baptizing Taíno or Congolese,
name they stuttered in the barking language
of priests and overseers, slave's finger pressed to the blade            15
with the pulsing revelation that a Spaniard's throat
could seep blood like a fingertip, sabers for the uprising
smuggled in the hay, slave of the upraised saber
beheaded even as the servants and field hands
murmured he is not dead, he rides a white horse at night,              20
his sword is a torch, the master cannot sleep,
there is a dagger under the pillow.

Espada: cousin to the machete, peasant cutlass
splitting the cane like a peasant's backbone,
cousin to the kitchen knife skinning a plátano.                          25
Swords at rest, the machetero or cook
studied their blisters as if planets
to glimpse the hands of their father the horseman,
map the hands of their mother the serf.

Espada: sword in Puerto Rico, family name of bricklayers               30
who swore their trowels fell as leaves from iron trees;
teachers who wrote poems in galloping calligraphy;
saintcarvers who whittled a slave's gaze and a conqueror's beard;
shoemaker spitting tuberculosis, madwoman
dangling a lantern to listen for the cough;                             35
gambler in a straw hat inhabited by mathematical angels;
preacher who first heard the savior's voice
bleeding through the plaster of the jailhouse;
dreadlocked sculptor stunned by visions of birds,
sprouting wings from his forehead, earthen wings in the fire.          40

So the face dreaming on a sarcophagus,
the slave of the saber riding a white horse by night
breathe my name, tell me to taste my name: Espada.

2000

# Alabanza: In Praise of Local 100

*for the 43 members of Hotel Employees and Restaurant Employees*
*Local 100, working at the Windows on the World restaurant,[1]*
*who lost their lives in the attack on the World Trade Center*

*Alabanza.* Praise the cook with a shaven head
and a tattoo on his shoulder that said *Oye,*

---

1. Located on the top floors of the North Tower of the World Trade Center.

a blue-eyed Puerto Rican with people from Fajardo,[2]
the harbor of pirates centuries ago.
Praise the lighthouse in Fajardo, candle                                    5
glimmering white to worship the dark saint of the sea.
*Alabanza.* Praise the cook's yellow Pirates cap
worn in the name of Roberto Clemente, his plane
that flamed into the ocean loaded with cans for Nicaragua,
for all the mouths chewing the ash of earthquakes.[3]                       10
*Alabanza.* Praise the kitchen radio, dial clicked
even before the dial on the oven, so that music and Spanish
rose before bread. Praise the bread. *Alabanza.*

Praise Manhattan from a hundred and seven flights up,
like Atlantis[4] glimpsed through the windows of an ancient aquarium.    15
Praise the great windows where immigrants from the kitchen
could squint and almost see their world, hear the chant of nations:
*Ecuador, México, República Dominicana,*
*Haiti, Yemen, Ghana, Bangladesh.*
*Alabanza.* Praise the kitchen in the morning,                              20
where the gas burned blue on every stove
and exhaust fans fired their diminutive propellers,
hands cracked eggs with quick thumbs
or sliced open cartons to build an altar of cans.
*Alabanza.* Praise the busboy's music, the chime-chime                     25
of his dishes and silverware in the tub.
*Alabanza.* Praise the dish-dog, the dishwasher
who worked that morning because another dishwasher
could not stop coughing, or because he needed overtime
to pile the sacks of rice and beans for a family                            30
floating away on some Caribbean island plagued by frogs.
*Alabanza.* Praise the waitress who heard the radio in the kitchen
and sang to herself about a man gone. *Alabanza.*

After the thunder wilder than thunder,
after the shudder deep in the glass of the great windows,                   35
after the radio stopped singing like a tree full of terrified frogs,
after night burst the dam of day and flooded the kitchen,
for a time the stoves glowed in darkness like the lighthouse in Fajardo,
like a cook's soul. Soul I say, even if the dead cannot tell us
about the bristles of God's beard because God has no face,                  40
soul I say, to name the smoke-beings flung in constellations
across the night sky of this city and cities to come.
*Alabanza* I say, even if God has no face.

*Alabanza.* When the war began, from Manhattan and Kabul[5]
two constellations of smoke rose and drifted to each other,                 45
mingling in icy air, and one said with an Afghan tongue:

---

2. City on the eastern coast of Puerto Rico.
3. Roberto Clemente (1934–1972), Puerto Rican
right fielder for the Pittsburgh Pirates—and the
first Latin American player elected to the Baseball Hall of Fame—died while attempting to fly
relief supplies to the victims of an earthquake in
Nicaragua. His plane crashed after taking off
from San Juan, Puerto Rico.
4. Legendary or mythical ancient island that sank
into the sea.
5. Capital of Afghanistan.

*Teach me to dance. We have no music here.*
And the other said with a Spanish tongue:
*I will teach you. Music is all we have.*

2002                                                                 2003

## The Republic of Poetry

*For Chile*

In the republic of poetry,
a train full of poets
rolls south in the rain
as plum trees rock
and horses kick the air,                                             5
and village bands
parade down the aisle
with trumpets, with bowler hats,
followed by the president
of the republic,                                                     10
shaking every hand.

In the republic of poetry,
monks print verses about the night
on boxes of monastery chocolate,
kitchens in restaurants                                              15
use odes for recipes
from eel to artichoke,
and poets eat for free.

In the republic of poetry,
poets read to the baboons                                            20
at the zoo, and all the primates,
poets and baboons alike, scream for joy.

In the republic of poetry,
poets rent a helicopter
to bombard the national palace                                       25
with poems on bookmarks,
and everyone in the courtyard
rushes to grab a poem
fluttering from the sky,
blinded by weeping.                                                  30

In the republic of poetry,
the guard at the airport
will not allow you to leave the country
until you declaim a poem for her
and she says *Ah! Beautiful.*                                        35

2004                                                                 2006

# ROLANDO PÉREZ
## b. 1957

A native of Cuba, Rolando Pérez immigrated with his family to Spain in 1967 and to the United States a year later. He holds a bachelor's degree in philosophy from the College of New Jersey, in Ewing Township; a master's in Spanish and philosophy from the State University of New York at Stony Brook (now Stony Brook University); and a master's in library science from Rutgers, the State University of New Jersey; and a doctorate from the Graduate Center, City University of New York. Pérez works as the romance languages and philosophy bibliographer at Hunter College of the City University of New York and teaches in universities around New York. His critical writings include *Severo Sarduy and the Religion of the Text* (1988), on the Cuban French writer; and *On An(archy) and Schizoanalysis* (1990), an analysis of *Anti-Oedipus* (1972), by the French philosophers Gilles Deleuze and Félix Guattari.

Pérez's literary writing, which began with *The Odyssey* (1990), is boldly experimental, often collapsing the distinctions between poetry and prose, fiction and nonfiction. Unusual among Latino writers for his avoidance of "ethnic" subjects, Pérez derives inspiration from diverse sources such as the visual arts, medieval literature, and information theory. *The Lining of Our Souls* (1995), for example, is a book of prose poems—three of which are included here—inspired by the paintings of the twentieth-century American artist Edward Hopper. In "New York Movie," we hear the frenzied thoughts of the silent usherette as the movie she has seen and heard many times plays yet again. In "Hotel Room," a dejected traveler repeatedly reads the letter that spells the end of her love affair. And in "Summer Evening," the ambiguous silence between a couple is broken by the sounds of crickets. *The Divine Duty of Servants* (1999) is a collage of poems, stories, quotations, photographs, and drawings, based on sadomasochistic drawings by the twentieth-century Polish writer/ artist Bruno Schulz. In "First Experience," included here, the narrator relives the exquisite birth of his obsessive fetish. *The Electric Comedy* (2000) is a modern version of Dante Alighieri's epic *Divina Commedia* (Divine Comedy, 1308–21); here, Pérez portrays modern technology as a form of hell. In the selection included here, "Canto 10," the poet's quest for the meaning of life uses the vocabulary of an advanced search on a computer. In addition to his critical and literary writings, Pérez has also written for the stage and published three books of plays: *Plays and Playthings* (eight one-act plays, 1990), *The House That Ate Their Brains* (1992), and *H Is for Box* (1993), a comedy about the farce of stereotyping.

## New York Movie

Snow-covered 'mountains' appear majestically on the screen. An elderly gentleman, dressed in his best weekend clothes, watches the film . . . inside a great movie palace, with its massive columns, in a violent struggle with nature. Our usherette has seen this movie countless times this month. Holding a flashlight in her hand, she stands by herself against the yellow wall, beneath a lamp and its shadow, lost in a movie all of her own: to thoughts she cannot reconcile.

These are the moments she dreads—when time becomes visible, all too visible to bear in all its cruelty. And she is forced to hear the screaming silence between the shows.

"We should go somewhere tonight," he suggested.

"I'd like to, but I can't, I have work to do," she said . . . almost aloud, repeating a line from an earlier scene.

(The elderly gentleman: Sssshhh.)

Anything to get away from him: from his passion, from his suffocating love, from her turmoil, and from that terrible decision that she will soon have to make. "Anything," she said to herself, "to keep my mind off things. I'll know what to do after the picture show. I'll know the right answer."

Ten minutes to go.

The second feature is almost over. Soon the lights will be turned on and she will have to return to work: ushering the new crowd . . . into their electric purgatory.

A > B > C. Once she has looked at all the angles . . . with rational and logical precision, she will have her answer: undoubtably perfect . . . for all eternity. But like Stella, her cousin, math was never her best subject.

*Damn all these triangles and their respective triangulations! she thinks.*

When the time comes she will call for the death penalty—with a clear conscience, of course. Not to mention, with all the kindness and concern that a loving executioner can call up from the bottom of her soul on execution day. Clean, honest, and bloodless, everyone will go, willingly and happily to their respective corners, embracing their fates like lambs to the slaughter.

But for now she remains standing. (*The flashlight doesn't work.*) Alone. Against the wall . . . standing next to the red curtains and the stairs leading to the balcony above.

1995

## Hotel Room

> She said 'soon'—
> 'soon' a bit too often.
> And when 'soon' finally came,
> it was all a bit too late,
> and everything was over.

After so many delays and detours she finally arrived, dizzy with anticipation. "Inclement weather in Northern Nebraska. . . ." Another cold city along the way.

"There is a message here for you," said the manager at the front desk. With trembling hands she folded it, she put it in her pocket, and followed the bell boy up to her room.

Now, half-undressed, suitcases still unopened, she sits on a perfectly made bed in this modest hotel, in a town she has often imagined, in a town she'll never see again. Her skirt hangs over a chair, her hat upon the dresser, and her shoes on the floor. She was just about to go to sleep when she remembered the letter.

She has traveled from one end of the country to the other for this . . . and now . . . and now . . . she reads the first three sentences word . . . by . . . word. She reads them again. (*Her heart has stopped.*) Again, from left to right. (*The abyss is calling.*) And again, she reads the letter . . . trying to

To be a fetishist is to be obsessed with time. Both the fetishist and the hysteric share this obsession. But while the hysteric runs away from time, the fetishist runs towards it and embraces the time "when . . .", and tries to re-live it with every "repetition" of it.

In my own story, as I'm sure, in the stories of others like myself, it all happened very suddenly: one afternoon while W— and I played together. For though I was already taken in by the beauty of her hair, her lips, her eyes, her girlishly rosy cheeks, never until then, had I given her feet even a passing glance—those delicate little feet of hers. But then, what normal 13-year-old would look at a girl's feet with lust?

Yet I had.

Maybe it was because she had brushed my leg with the sole of her foot. Perhaps. It was a bit like discovering a door I had always passed through, for the first time.

I couldn't believe that this was happening to me, and yet my new experience filled me with all kinds of strange and inexplicable desires.

W—'s feet were white, milky smooth. They were the feet of those angelic nymphs in Pre-Raphaelite paintings of the 19th century. And I wanted nothing more at that moment than to take her feet in my hands and kiss them. Her toes, so pretty, so delicate, the soles of her feet had the appearance of white velvet, such that whenever I come across a reproduction of Ingres' *Grande Odalisque*,[4] I always think of those exquisite feet that so long ago opened up a world for me. For without her realizing it, she changed my life, that quiet, peaceful, summer afternoon in my parents' house; that afternoon when we played together on the floor, and she was barefoot.

It was she and she alone that brought religion to my life. Without her I would, no doubt, have remained—even at that young age—a mere atheist, lacking in spirit, deprived like so many others in our century of a worthy object of worship; ignorant, even of that most spiritual of all books, Mr. Schulz's *Booke of Idolatry*.[5]

1999

## Canto 10

> What is the meaning of life?
> Why is there something rather than nothing?
> Why is the world made of water?
> Why can't you step into the same river twice?[1]

---

4. Also known as *Une Odalisque* or *La Grande Odalisque*; 1814 painting, by the French neo-classical painter Jean-Auguste-Dominique Ingres (1780–1867), of a nude woman (odalisque, or courtesan) reclining.

5. ". . . when the servants of David we come to Ab'i-gail to Carmel, they spake unto her, saying, David sent us unto thee, to take thee to him to wife. And she arose, and bowed herself on her face to the earth, and said, Behold, let thine handmaid be a servant to wash the feet of the servants of my lord." I Samuel, 25:40–41. [Author's note, referring to the biblical Book of Samuel]

*Mr. Schulz's* Booke of Idolatry: Bruno Schulz's *Sklepy Cynamonowe* (Cinnamon Shops, 1934)—an illustrated book of linked stories, commonly known in English as *The Street of Crocodiles*—includes references to a mythical *Book of Idolatry*. [Anthology editors' note]

1. Questions like these date back to the ancient Greek philosophers. For example, Thales of Miletus (625?–?547 BC) stated that water constituted the principle (source, substance) of all things. Heracleitus (ca. 540–ca. 480) stated that one cannot step into the same river twice.

These silly, old questions                                                    5
echo through the leaning tower of knowledge:[2]
vast and empty these days.
You want an answer?
You don't need the tower for that.
An engine named                                                              10
after the hated YAHOOS[3] of yesterday,
will help you navigate
and swallow the bits,
fast and easy like soup.
Search: MEANING AND LIFE                                                     15
Search: SOMETHING AND NOTHING
Search: WORLD AND WATER
Search: RIVER AND TWICE

In nanoseconds
the most recent results                                                      20
come up first!
The newest! The very latest!!!
One need not get lost in
the labyrinthian halls of
the old tower with all those                                                 25
arborescent dusty scribbles
when the *Scientia* of the rhizomes
is so much easier to digest.
The complex logic of A AND B
makes it possible for anyone                                                 30
to see the questions on a screen.
No need to think of it:
the created natures slew Minerva[4]
not so long ago.
Dante, for instance, had to undergo a journey,                               35
but that's because he lacked an engine
named after his guide.[5]
Today with VIRGILIO. IT
he could Search: SIN AND REDEMPTION.
And presto! The time he could have saved!                                    40

What is the meaning of life?

2000

2. Playful combination of the leaning tower of Pisa, Italy, and the Tower of Babel (in the biblical Book of Genesis, an immense tower in the city of Babel, dedicated to the glory of man; angered by the arrogance of the builders and inhabitants, God made them speak many conflicting languages rather than a universal one and scattered the people around the earth).

3. A brutish race in *Gulliver's Travels* (1726, 1735), satire by the Anglo-Irish writer Jonathan Swift (1667–1745).
4. Roman goddess of wisdom.
5. In the *Divine Comedy*, the Roman poet Virgil (70–19 BC) guides Dante through the underworld.

# CAROLINA HOSPITAL
## b. 1957

Carolina Hospital was born in Havana, Cuba. After moving with her family to the United States in 1961, she spent her childhood in the exile community in Miami, Florida. She earned her bachelor's and master's degrees in English from the University of Florida, in Gainesville. She has taught in the Miami public schools and currently teaches English at Miami Dade College.

In 1988, Hospital edited one of the first anthologies of Cuban American poetry, *Cuban American Writers: Los atrevidos*, in which she explored and discussed the works of what she termed "the children of exile," that is, Cubans who came to the United States in early childhood and write in English, Spanish, and Spanglish about Cuba and the United States, nostalgia and assimilation, loss and renewal.

Hospital's poetry and fiction have been published in many literary reviews and anthologies, including *Looking for Home: Women Writing about Exile* (1990), *Paper Dance: 55 Latino Poets* (1995), and *American Diaspora: Poetry of Displacement* (2001). Her poems have been collected in *A Child of Exile: A Poetry Memoir* (2004). Under the pseudonym C. C. Medina and in collaboration with her husband, Carlos Medina, Hospital wrote the well-received novel *Little Love* (2000), centered on the lives of several Latinas in Miami.

In the poem included here, "How the Cubans Stole Miami," Hospital writes with irony of the tensions that erupted in Miami with the large influx of Cuban refugees in the early 1960s. After mentioning earlier settlers of South Florida, she lists the substantial contributions to the city made by Cubans during their decades of exile.

## How the Cubans Stole Miami

The Cubans have stolen Miami.
("Will the last one to leave
bring the American flag?")
And from whom did we steal it?

From the Basque sailor who                                5
gave Biscayne its name?[1]
Or perhaps from the Spanish missionaries who lived
with the mosquitoes by the swampy bay?

In all fairness, we must admit
we stole it from the Tequesta or the Seminoles.[2]       10
natives, driven north by
Andrew Jackson[3] or south into the sea.

No, perhaps we stole it from the Spaniards
sent back to Havana after 300 years
of calling Florida home.                                 15

---

1. Biscayne Bay, in Miami, is perhaps named after the Bay of Biscay or a man called El Biscaino (from the Biscay region of the Basque Country, in Spain). 2. Native American tribes who occupied an area along the Atlantic coast of Florida.

3. American general (1767–1845), U.S. president 1829–37; during the First Seminole War, he led a campaign in Georgia. He also seized parts of Florida from the Spanish and, in 1821, became the territory's military governor.

(And we complain about still being
in exile after only thirty-four.)

If we didn't steal it from the Indians or the Spaniards
it must have been the Conks,
Bahamians who built the railroads with hands of coal          20
while being told to be more Negro like their
neighbors to the north.

I know, we stole it from
Flagler, Tuttle, Merrick and Fisher[4]
who catered to the rich but never to the Jewish.              25
(Only in Miami is a Jew an Anglo.)
If I see one more photo of Domino Park[5]
I'll turn into a Jew.
Was it he, papi, who stole Miami?
He, who engineered from the Bacardi building to               30
One Biscayne Tower[6]
and every school addition from Edison
to Homestead High?[7]

No, it must have been my mother.
(What was it Joan Didion[8] wrote,                            35
"a mango with jewels"?
poor mother, so lean and trim.)
She spent 34 years volunteering
(Sacándole el kilo,[9] my father would sneer.)

The Museum of Science,                                        40
Viscaya,
The Youth Center,
The Archdiocese,
Ballet Concerto,
La Liga Contra el Cancer,                                     45
The Mailman Center.[1]
(A tour of Miami, you ask?)

Enough! says my dad,
locking up his checkbook tight.

---

4. Henry Morrison Flagler (1830–1913), Julia De-
Forest Tuttle (1848–1898), George Edgar Merrick
(1886–1942), and Carl Graham Fisher (1874–
1939), among the early developers of Miami and
Miami Beach.
5. A tourist attraction in Little Havana where elderly exiles congregate.
6. Office skyscraper in downtown Miami; a symbol of prosperity for the Cuban-exile community.
*Bacardi building*: the headquarters of the Bacardi
liquor company, one of the finest examples of
Latin American modernist architecture.
7. Large secondary schools in Miami.
8. American writer (b. 1934) whose books include the travel narrative *Miami* (1987).
9. Getting their money's worth.

1. The Mailman Center for Child Development,
at the University of Miami Miller School of
Medicine. *Museum of Science*: a popular tourist
attraction. *Viscaya*: an Italian Renaissance–style
villa and formal gardens, built in 1916 as a private home. *The Youth Center*: located in the suburb of Coral Gables and providing programs
devoted to sports, arts, and culture. *The Archdiocese*: the Archdiocese of Miami, which serves
the large Catholic community of South Florida.
*Ballet Concerto*: a ballet company and school
founded by Cuban exiles. *La Liga Contra el Can-
cér*: The League against Cancer, a community-
based organization providing free medical care
to cancer patients in need.

"We're retiring out of Miami."                                    50
A new phenomenon.
"Cuban Flight,"
not to be confused with "White Flight."

If the Cubans have stolen Miami
and it's time they paid their dues,                                55
then . . .

If I see one more photograph of Domino Park
who knows what I might do.

1996

---

# CRISTINA GARCÍA
## b. 1958

Cristina García, one of the most widely read and highly esteemed contemporary
Latino novelists, was born in Havana, Cuba. After immigrating to the United States
with her parents in 1960, she grew up in New York City. She earned her bachelor's
degree in political science from Barnard College, in Manhattan, and a master's
degree in international affairs from Johns Hopkins University, in Baltimore. She
writes about the impact of the Cuban Revolution on the lives of Cuban families,
especially of women in a male-centered society, giving a feminist Latina voice to
contemporary fiction's engagement with history.

After working for several years as a reporter and correspondent for *Time* magazine,
García became a full-time writer. Her first novel, *Dreaming in Cuban* (1992)—two
chapters of which are included in this anthology—was a National Book Award finalist. Refracted through the eyes of Pilar, a young Cuban American woman loosely
based on García, the book tells the story of three generations of a Cuban family. The
oldest generation, in Cuba, is represented by Celia, the matriarch of the family and
an ardent supporter of the Revolution, who spends her evenings watching out for
invaders and fantasizing about being ravished by *El Líder*, Fidel Castro. Celia marries a man she does not love, with whom she has two daughters, Lourdes and Felicia,
and a son, Javier. Felicia marries a sailor from whom she contracts syphilis; the disease
makes her mentally unbalanced, and she eventually comes to a tragic end. Raped by
one of Castro's soldiers, Lourdes goes into exile in the United States, where she runs
a bakery, joins the Neighborhood Watch, and participates in anti-Castro activities.
Her daughter, Pilar, who is born in the same year as the Revolution (1959) and grows
up in New York City alienated from her rabidly anti-Communist parents, longs to
reestablish ties with the grandmother who stayed in Cuba.

Like *Dreaming in Cuban*, García's second novel, *The Agüero Sisters* (1997) chronicles the rifts in a family torn apart by the Cuban Revolution. Characterized by the
use of magical realism, the mixing of fact and fantasy, and a sensuous, evocative
prose style, the narrative centers on two sisters, Constancia and Reina, who find
themselves on opposite sides of the Florida Straits. Constancia, the exile, is a prudish woman who has become wealthy peddling a line of cosmetics made from tropical
fruits and vegetables. Reina, who lives in Cuba, is a traveling electrician renowned
for her beauty and uninhibited sexuality. Reunited in Miami, the sisters piece

together a longstanding family puzzle that leads them to discover the circumstances of their mother's violent death at the hands of her husband, Ignacio Agüero, a respected naturalist whose journals serve as the hidden subtext of the sisters' lives (*agüero* is Spanish for omen). The sisters, their father, their children, their lovers, and their husbands take turns narrating the family's story. Reina narrates the chapter included here, "Dulce Fuerte."

As García has matured as a novelist, her plots have focused on the passionate lives of characters defined by major historical events. García's third novel, *Monkey Hunting* (2003), is a multigenerational saga about the Chinese Cuban experience, Chinese being an important minority in the history of immigration into Cuba from the nineteenth century onward. (The author's first husband, the father of her daughter, is of Chinese origin.) Traversing two centuries and four countries—set in Havana; Shanghai, China; Phnom Penh, Cambodia; and other places—the novel addresses topics such as slavery, the Chinese leader Mao Tse-tung's Cultural Revolution, and Fidel Castro's Communist regime. *A Handbook of Luck* (2007), García's fourth novel, follows Cuban, Salvadoran, and Iranian characters as they face the upheavals of migration. One of the protagonists, the nine-year-old Enrique Florit, moves with his father from Cuba to Las Vegas, where he becomes obsessed with gambling. Marta Claros, a Salvadoran girl, sells used clothes and hopes to move to the United States. And Leila Rezvani is a wealthy girl in Tehran. The three story lines eventually connect.

García has edited the anthologies *Cubanísimo!: The Vintage Book of Contemporary Cuban Literature* (2003) and *Bordering Fires: The Vintage Book of Mexican and Chicano Literature* (2006). Her poetry collection is *The Lesser Tragedy of Death* (2010).

---

## FROM DREAMING IN CUBAN

### Ocean Blue

Celia del Pino, equipped with binoculars and wearing her best housedress and drop pearl earrings, sits in her wicker swing guarding the north coast of Cuba. Square by square, she searches the night skies for adversaries then scrutinizes the ocean, which is roiling with nine straight days of unseasonable April rains. No sign of *gusano*[1] traitors. Celia is honored. The neighborhood committee has voted her little brick-and-cement house by the sea as the primary lookout for Santa Teresa del Mar. From her porch, Celia could spot another Bay of Pigs invasion[2] before it happened. She would be feted at the palace, serenaded by a brass orchestra, seduced by El Líder himself on a red velvet divan.

Celia brings the binoculars to rest in her lap and rubs her eyes with stiffened fingers. Her wattled chin trembles. Her eyes smart from the sweetness of the gardenia tree and the salt of the sea. In an hour or two, the fishermen will return, nets empty. The *yanquis*, rumors go, have ringed the island with nuclear poison, hoping to starve the people and incite a counterrevolution.

---

1. Literally, worm; jargon for U.S.-based Cuban traitor.
2. Known in Cuba as *La Batalla de Girón* or *Playa Girón*; unsuccessful attempt, in April 1961, by a CIA-trained force of Cuban exiles with support from U.S. armed forces, to invade southern Cuba and overthrow Castro.

They will drop germ bombs to wither the sugarcane fields, blacken the rivers, blind horses and pigs. Celia studies the coconut palms lining the beach. Could they be blinking signals to an invisible enemy?

A radio announcer barks fresh conjectures about a possible attack and plays a special recorded message from El Líder: "Eleven years ago tonight, *compañeros*, you defended our country against American aggressors. Now each and every one of you must guard our future again. Without your support, *compañeros*, without your sacrifices, there can be no revolution."

Celia reaches into her straw handbag for more red lipstick, then darkens the mole on her left cheek with a black eyebrow pencil. Her sticky graying hair is tied in a chignon at her neck. Celia played the piano once and still exercises her hands, unconsciously stretching them two notes beyond an octave. She wears leather pumps with her bright housedress.

Her grandson appears in the doorway, his pajama top twisted off his shoulders, his eyes vacant with sleep. Celia carries Ivanito past the sofa draped with a faded mantilla, past the water-bleached walnut piano, past the dining-room table pockmarked with ancient history. Only seven chairs remain of the set. Her husband smashed one on the back of Hugo Villaverde, their former son-in-law, and could not repair it for all the splinters. She nestles her grandson beneath a frayed blanket on her bed and kisses his eyes closed.

Celia returns to her post and adjusts the binoculars. The sides of her breasts ache under her arms. There are three fishing boats in the distance—the *Niña*, the *Pinta*, and the *Santa María*. She remembers the singsong way she used to recite their names. Celia moves the binoculars in an arc from left to right, the way she was trained, and then straight across the horizon.

At the far end of the sky, where daylight begins, a dense radiance like a shooting star breaks forth. It weakens as it advances, as its outline takes shape in the ether. Her husband emerges from the light and comes toward her, taller than the palms, walking on water in his white summer suit and Panama hat. He is in no hurry. Celia half expects him to pull pink tea roses from behind his back as he used to when he returned from his trips to distant provinces. Or to offer her a giant eggbeater wrapped in brown paper, she doesn't know why. But he comes empty-handed.

He stops at the ocean's edge, smiles almost shyly, as if he fears disturbing her, and stretches out a colossal hand. His blue eyes are like lasers in the night. The beams bounce off his fingernails, five hard blue shields. They scan the beach, illuminating shells and sleeping gulls, then focus on her. The porch turns blue, ultraviolet. Her hands, too, are blue. Celia squints through the light, which dulls her eyesight and blurs the palms on the shore.

Her husband moves his mouth carefully, but she cannot read his immense lips. His jaw churns and swells with each word, faster, until Celia feels the warm breeze of his breath on her face. Then he disappears.

Celia runs to the beach in her good leather pumps. There is a trace of tobacco in the air. "Jorge, I couldn't hear you. I couldn't hear you." She paces the shore, her arms crossed over her breasts. Her shoes leave delicate exclamation points in the wet sand.

Celia fingers the sheet of onion parchment in her pocket, reads the words again, one by one, like a blind woman. Jorge's letter arrived that morning, as if his prescience extended even to the irregular postal service between the United States and Cuba. Celia is astonished by the words, by the disquieting ardor of her husband's last letters. They seemed written by a younger, more passionate Jorge, a man she never knew well. But his handwriting, an ornate script he learned in another century, revealed his decay. When he wrote this last missive, Jorge must have known he would die before she received it.

A long time ago, it seems to her, Jorge boarded the plane for New York, sick and shrunken in an ancient wheelchair. "Butchers and veterinarians!" he shouted as they pushed him up the plank. "That's what Cuba is now!" *Her* Jorge did not resemble the huge, buoyant man on the ocean, the gentleman with silent words she could not understand.

Celia grieves for her husband, not for his death, not yet, but for his mixed-up allegiances.

For many years before the revolution, Jorge had traveled five weeks out of six, selling electric brooms and portable fans for an American firm. He'd wanted to be a model Cuban, to prove to his gringo boss that they were cut from the same cloth. Jorge wore his suit on the hottest days of the year, even in remote villages where the people thought he was crazy. He put on his boater with its wide black band before a mirror, to keep the angle shy of jaunty.

Celia cannot decide which is worse, separation or death. Separation is familiar, too familiar, but Celia is uncertain she can reconcile it with permanence. Who could have predicted her life? What unknown covenants led her ultimately to this beach and this hour and this solitude?

She considers the vagaries of sports, the happenstance of El Líder, a star pitcher in his youth, narrowly missing a baseball career in America. His wicked curveball attracted the major-league scouts, and the Washington Senators were interested in signing him but changed their minds. Frustrated, El Líder went home, rested his pitching arm, and started a revolution in the mountains.

Because of this, Celia thinks, her husband will be buried in stiff, foreign earth. Because of this, their children and their grandchildren are nomads.

Pilar, her first grandchild, writes to her from Brooklyn in a Spanish that is no longer hers. She speaks the hard-edged lexicon of bygone tourists itchy to throw dice on green felt or asphalt. Pilar's eyes, Celia fears, are no longer used to the compacted light of the tropics, where a morning hour can fill a month of days in the north, which receives only careless sheddings from the sun. She imagines her granddaughter pale, gliding through paleness, malnourished and cold without the food of scarlets and greens.

Celia knows that Pilar wears overalls like a farmhand and paints canvases with knots and whorls of red that resemble nothing at all. She knows that Pilar keeps a diary in the lining of her winter coat, hidden from her mother's scouring eyes. In it, Pilar records everything. This pleases Celia. She closes her eyes and speaks to her granddaughter, imagines her words as slivers of light piercing the murky night.

The rain begins again, softly this time. The finned palms record each drop. Celia is ankle deep in the rising tide. The water is curiously warm, too warm for spring. She reaches down and removes her pumps, crimped and puckered now like her own skin, chalked and misshapen from the saltwater. She wades deeper into the ocean. It pulls on her housedress like weights on her hem. Her hands float on the surface of the sea, still clutching her shoes, as if they could lead her to a new place.

She remembers something a *santera*[3] told her nearly forty years ago, when she had decided to die: "Miss Celia, there's a wet landscape in your palm." And it was true. She had lived all these years by the sea until she knew its every definition of blue.

Celia turns toward the shore. The light is unbearably bright on the porch. The wicker swing hangs from two rusted chains. The stripes on the cushions have dulled to gray as if the color made no difference at all. It seems to Celia that another woman entirely sat for years on those weathered cushions, drawn by the pull of the tides. She remembers the painful transitions to spring, the sea grapes and the rains, her skin a cicatrix.

She and Jorge moved to their house in the spring of 1937. Her husband bought her an upright walnut piano and set it by an arched window with a view of the sea. He stocked it with her music workbooks and sheaves of invigorating Rachmaninoff, Tchaikovsky, and a selection of Chopin. "Keep her away from Debussy,"[4] she overheard the doctors warn him. They feared that the Frenchman's restless style might compel her to rashness, but Celia hid her music to *La Soirée dans Grenade*[5] and played it incessantly while Jorge traveled.

Celia hears the music now, pressing from beneath the waves. The water laps at her throat. She arches her spine until she floats on her back, straining to hear the notes of the Alhambra[6] at midnight. She is waiting in a flowered shawl by the fountain for her lover, her Spanish lover, the lover before Jorge, and her hair is twisted with high combs. They retreat to the mossy riverbank and make love under the watchful poplars. The air is fragrant with jasmine and myrtle and citrus.

A cool wind stirs Celia from her dream. She stretches her legs but she cannot touch the sandy bottom. Her arms are heavy, sodden as porous wood after a storm. She has lost her shoes. A sudden wave engulfs her, and for a moment Celia is tempted to relax and drop. Instead, she swims clumsily, steadily toward shore, sunk low like an overladen boat. Celia concentrates on the palms tossing their headdresses in the sky. Their messages jump from tree to tree with stolen electricity. No one but me, she thinks, is guarding the coast tonight.

Celia peels Jorge's letter from her housedress pocket and holds it in the air to dry. She walks back to the porch and waits for the fishermen, for daylight.

3. Female practitioner of the Afro-Caribbean religious tradition Santería.
4. (Achille-)Claude Debussy (1862–1918), French composer. *Rachmaninoff*: Sergey Vasilyevich Rachmaninoff (1873–1943), Russian composer, pianist, and conductor. *Tchaikovsky*: Pyotr Ilich Tchaikovsky (1840–1893), Russian composer.

*Chopin*: Frédéric François Chopin (1810–1849), Polish pianist and composer.
5. Solo-piano composition (1903) by Debussy.
6. Moorish fort in Granada, Spain; perhaps a reference to "Recuerdos de la Alhambra" (1896), by the Spanish composer and guitarist Francisco Tárrega (1852–1909).

## Felicia del Pino

Felicia del Pino, her head a spiky anarchy of miniature pink rollers, pounds the horn of her 1952 De Soto as she pulls up to the little house by the sea. It is 7:43 A.M. and she has made the seventeen-mile journey from Havana to Santa Teresa del Mar in thirty-four minutes. Felicia screams for her mother, throws herself onto the backseat and shoulders open the car's only working door. Then she flies past the rows of gangly bird of paradise, past the paw-paw tree with ripening fruit, and loses a sandal taking the three front steps in an inelegant leap.

"I know already," Celia says, rocking gently in her wicker swing on the porch. Felicia collapses on her mother's lap, sending the swing lurching crazily, and wails to the heavens.

"He was here last night." Celia grips the wicker armrests as if the entire swing would fly off of its own accord.

"Who?" Felicia demands.

"Your father, he came to say good-bye."

Felicia abruptly stops her lament and stands up. Her pale yellow stretch shorts slide into the crease of her fleshy buttocks.

"You mean he was in the neighborhood and didn't even stop by?" She is pacing now, pushing a fist into her palm.

"Felicia, it was not a social visit."

"But he's been in New York four years! The least he could have done was say good-bye to me and the children!"

"What did your sister say?" Celia asks, ignoring her daughter's outburst.

"The nuns called her at the bakery this morning. They said Papi rose to heaven on tongues of fire. Lourdes was very upset. She's convinced it's a resurrection."

Ivanito stretches his arms around his mother's plump thighs. Felicia, her face softening, looks down at her son. "Your grandfather died today, Ivanito. I know you don't remember him, but he loved you very much."

"What happened to Abuela?" Ivanito asks.

Felicia turns to her mother as if seeing her for the first time. Seaweed clings to her skull like a lethal plant. She is barefoot and her skin, encrusted with sand, is tinged a faint blue. Her legs are cold and hard as marble.

"I went for a swim," Celia says irritably.

"With your clothes on?" Felicia tugs on her mother's damp sleeve.

"Yes, Felicia, with my clothes on." The edge in Celia's voice would end any conversation save with her daughter. "Now, listen to me. I want you to send a telegram to your brother."

Celia hasn't spoken to her son since the Soviet tanks stormed Prague four years ago.[7] She cried when she heard his voice and the sounds of the falling city behind him. What was he doing so far from the warm seas swimming with gentle manatees? Javier writes that he has a Czech wife now and a baby girl. Celia wonders how she will speak to this granddaughter, show her how to catch crickets and avoid the beak of the tortoise.

---

7. I.e., in summer 1968, when the U.S.S.R. put a stop to the "Prague Spring," a brief period of social and political freedom in (then-Communist) Czechoslovakia, of which Prague was the capital (it is now the capital of the Czech Republic).

"What should I say?" Felicia asks her mother.

"Tell him his father died."

. . .

Felicia climbs into the front seat of her car, crosses her arms over the steering wheel, and stares out the windshield. The heat rises from the green hood, reminding her of the ocean the day before it wiped the beach clean of homes, God's bits of wood. It was 1944. Felicia was only six, her brother wasn't even born yet, but she remembers that day with precision. The sea's languid retreat into the horizon and the terrible silence of its absence. The way the she-crabs scurried after their young. The stranded dolphin towed out to sea by the Muñoz brothers, and the majestic shells, thousands of them, with intricate mauve chambers, arranged on a cemetery of wet sand. Felicia set aside pails of them but selected only one, a mother-of-pearl shell, a baroque Spanish fan with which later to taunt her suitors.

Her mother hurriedly wrapped gold-rimmed goblets with newspaper and packed them into a scuffed leather suitcase, all the while listening to the warnings on the radio. "I told you not to bring shells into this house," she reprimanded when Felicia held up her prize. "They bring bad luck."

Felicia's father was away on business in Oriente province when the tidal wave hit. He was always away on business. This time, he had promised to bring his wife a Jamaican maid from the east coast of the island so that she could spend her days resting on the porch, as the doctors ordered, and find solace in the patterns of the sea. Felicia's father didn't return with a maid but he brought back a signed baseball for her sister, Lourdes, that made her jump in place with excitement. Felicia didn't recognize the name.

The sea took more than seventy wooden homes from their stretch of coast. The del Pinos' house survived because it was sturdily built of brick and cement. When they returned, it was like an undersea cave, blanched by the ocean. Dried algae stuck to the walls, and the sand formed a strange topography on the floors. Felicia laughed when she remembered how her mother had warned her not to bring shells home. After the tidal wave, the house was full of them.

"Girl, you're going to fry in there!" Herminia Delgado raps on Felicia's car window. She is carrying a basket with an unplucked chicken, four lemons, and a brittle garlic clove. "I'm making a fricassee later. Why don't you come over? Or are you too busy with your naughty daydreams again?"

Felicia, her face and forearms blotchy with heat, looks up at her best friend.

"My father died last night and I have to be at work in an hour. They're going to transfer me back to the butcher's if I'm late again. They're looking for an excuse since I singed Graciela Moreira's hair. They dumped her on me. Nobody likes to do her hair because it's so fine it tears like toilet paper. I've told her a million times she shouldn't get a permanent but does she listen?"

"Did Lourdes call?"

"The nuns told her it was like a Holy Ascension[8] except Papi was dressed to go dancing. Then he shows up at my mother's house and nearly scares her half to death. I think she dove in the ocean after him."

---

8. In Christianity, the rising of a soul to heaven after death.

Felicia turns away.

"He didn't even say good-bye." The last time Felicia saw her father, he had smashed a chair over her ex-husband Hugo's back. "If you leave with that sonofabitch, don't ever come back!" her father had shouted as they fled.

"Maybe his spirit is still floating free. You must make your peace with him before he's gone for good. I'll call La Madrina.[9] We'll have an emergency session tonight."

"I don't know, Herminia." Felicia believes in the gods' benevolent powers, she just can't stand the blood.

"Listen, girl, there's always new hope for the dead. You must cleanse your soul of this or it will trail you all your days. It may even harm your children. Just a small offering to Santa Bárbara,"[1] Herminia coaxes. "Be there at ten and I'll take care of the rest."

"Well, okay. But please, tell her no goats this time."

That night, Felicia guides her car along a rutted road in the countryside a few miles from Santa Teresa del Mar. Her headlights have not worked since 1967, but she shines an oversized flashlight up the dirt pathway, startling two guinea hens and a dwarf monkey in a bamboo cage. The beam of light moves through the yard to the giant ceiba, thick as six lesser trees. Several identical red handkerchiefs are tied together around the trunk, midway up. The head of a freshly slaughtered rooster juts from one knot. Its beak hangs open, giving the bird a look of surprised indignation.

Herminia motions to her from a side door of the run-down house. She is wearing a cream-yellow blouse with a collar the luster of the absent moon. Her plump black arms stir the darkness. "Hurry up! La Madrina is ready!"

Felicia slides to the backseat of her car and opens the door with a scrape. Ferns and chicken feathers graze her ankles as she tiptoes in backless sandals toward her friend.

"*Por Dios*, we've been waiting for you for over an hour! What took you so long?" Herminia grabs Felicia's arm and pulls her to the door. "Let's go in before you make the gods angry."

She steers Felicia down an airless passageway lit on one side with red votive candles set on wooden tables coated with hardened wax. At the end of the corridor, long strands of shells hang in an arched doorway, the mollusks separated by odd-shaped bits of polished onyx.

"*Bienvenida, hija*," La Madrina beckons in a voice hoarse with a vocation to the unfortunate. "We have been expecting you."

She gestures with upturned palms in an arc around her. Her face is an almond sheen of sweat under her white cotton turban, and her lace blouson, settled off her shoulders, reveals duplicate moles, big and black as beetles, at the base of her throat. Layers of gauze skirts, delicate as membranes, brush her feet, which are bare on the cold cement floor. The low-ceilinged sea-green room wavers with the flames and incense of a hundred candles.

9. The *santera*, or female leader, who guides believers through initiation and in religious issues. 1. In Santería, the African gods are represented by Christian saints. The god Changó, black god of thunder, was identified with Saint Barbara (ca. third century), a martyr venerated by Catholic and Orthodox Christians.

Against the back wall, an ebony statue of Santa Bárbara, the Black Queen, presides. Apples and bananas sit in offering at her feet. Fragrant oblations crowd the shrines of the other saints and gods: toasted corn, pennies, and an aromatic cigar for Saint Lazarus, protector of paralytics; coconut and bitter kola for Obatalá, King of the White Cloth; roasted yams, palm wine, and a small sack of salt for Oggún,[2] patron of metals.

In the front of the room, Elleguá, god of the crossroads, inhabits the clay eggs in nine rustic bowls of varying sizes. The eggs have cowrie-shell eyes and mouths, and soak in an elixir of herbs and holy water. Four mulattas, wearing gingham skirts and aprons, kneel before the shrines, praying. One man, a pure blue-black Yoruban, stands mute in the center of the room, a starched cotton fez on his head.

"Herminia has told us of your dystopia." La Madrina is fond of melodious words, although she doesn't always know what they mean. She places a hand heavily ringed with ivory and bezoar stones on Felicia's shoulder and motions toward the *santero*. "He has traveled many hours from the south, from the mangroves, to be with us, to cleanse you of your infelicities. He will bring you and your father peace, a peace you never knew while he lived on this earth."

"Elleguá wants a goat," the *santero* says, his lips barely moving.

"Oh no, not another goat!" Felicia cries and turns to her friend accusingly. "You promised!"

"You have no choice," Herminia implores. "You can't dictate to the gods, Felicia. Elleguá needs fresh blood to do the job right."

"We will open the future to you, *hija*, you will see," La Madrina assures her. "We have a friendly contact with the complicated surfaces of the globe."

La Madrina gathers the believers around Felicia. They wrap her in garlands of beads and stroke her face and eyelids with branches of rosemary. The *santero* returns with the goat, its mouth and ears tied with string. Felicia takes a mouthful of shredded coconut and spits it on the goat's face, kissing its ears as it whines quietly. She rubs her breasts against its muzzle. "*Kosí ikú, kosí arun, kosí araye*," the women sing.

The *santero* leads the goat over the offerings and quickly pierces its neck with a butcher knife, directing the stream of blood onto the clay eggs. The goat quivers, then is still. The *santero* shakes a box of salt on its head, then pours honey over the offering.

Felicia, reeling from the sweet scent of the blood and the candles and the women, faints on La Madrina's saint-room floor, which is still warm with sacrifice.

---

2. Deity in belief systems such as Haitian voodoo, Yoruba mythology, and Santería. *Saint Lazarus*: reputed first bishop of Marseille (d. second half of first century), who died and was brought back to life by Jesus, according to the New Testament; venerated as a saint by branches of Christianity such as the Roman Catholic Church; in Santería, a healer of physical and spiritual pain. *Obatalá*: in belief systems such as Yoruba mythology and Santería, the maker of human beings; he always wears white.

# The Meaning of Shells

## (1974)

Felicia del Pino cannot remember why she is marching in the Sierra Maestra[1] this hot October afternoon. The camouflage helmet feels like a metal ring around her head, and the rifle, slung over her left shoulder, keeps bumping up against it, making the space behind her eyes reverberate with pain. The cheap Russian boots pinch her feet as she trudges, the last of a single file of would-be guerrillas, up the intolerably fragrant mountainside. "Let's talk in green," her son would have told her, trying to distract her from her misery.

"*Vámonos, vámonos!*" a petite mulatta roars ten yards ahead of Felicia. Lieutenant Xiomara Rojas has an undershot jaw, and her jumble of yellowish teeth is visible when she shouts. "El Líder never slowed down in these mountains! For him it was a matter of life and death, not a Sunday outing! Keep moving!"

Felicia looks down at the trail of moist trampled grasses. Her face is flushed and sweaty, and she can't tell whether the salt in her eyes is from perspiration or involuntary tears. Lieutenant Rojas is from these parts, Felicia thinks, that's why she doesn't sweat. Nobody from Santiago de Cuba ever sweated. It's a known fact.

"Compañera del Pino, you must keep up the rear! It's the most vulnerable position after the leader!" Lieutenant Rojas bellows, not unkindly.

Felicia's calves feel like baseballs below her knees. The earth, muddy and pliable, sucks at her feet. Every tendon is straining, stretched taut like the muscles of cows at the butcher shop that had died in fear. Their meat was never as tender as the flesh of the animals that hadn't anticipated death. Felicia fumbles for her canteen. She twists off the cap, attached by a chain to its neck. Her hands are a stranger's, swollen and coarse, her fingernails dirty.

"Fatherland or death!" Lieutenant Rojas shouts, as Felicia tips the water toward her mouth.

"Fatherland or death!" the guerrillas echo, all except Felicia, who wonders whether all this shouting wouldn't alert the enemy in a real war.

At the makeshift camp, the guerrillas set up their tents and open cans of pinto beans and pressed meat the color of dung. It's their fifth day of this food and it's given some of the soldiers diarrhea, others constipation, and all of them gas. Only Lieutenant Rojas seems unaffected and eats with enthusiasm. Felicia looks around at the others in her mostly middle-aged brigade. Everyone is there for the same reason, whether they admit it or not. They are a unit of malcontents, a troop of social misfits. It is Lieutenant Rojas's mission to reshape them into revolutionaries.

Felicia is there because she nearly killed herself and her son. She doesn't remember this, but everyone has told her it is so. "Why did you do it?" her mother asked her sadly, stretching her hands on the starched white bed. "Why did you do it?" the psychiatrist with the severe pageboy questioned her, as if Felicia were a willful child. "Why, Felicia?" her best friend,

---

1. Mountain range in southeast Cuba.

Herminia, beseeched her, all the while rubbing Felicia's forehead with herbs behind the nurse's back.

But each time Felicia reached for the memory, a white light burned in its place.

The doctors deemed Felicia an "unfit mother," and accused her of irreparably damaging her son that summer on Palmas Street.[2] Nobody knows if Ivanito understands what happened to him. The boy never speaks of it. But the doctors, her mother, even her coworkers at the beauty parlor finally persuaded Felicia to send Ivanito to boarding school. To toughen him up, to catch up with boys his own age, to integrate him. That was the word everyone used. Integrate.

"Don't you love me anymore?" Ivanito called to her from the bus window with eyes that strafed her with grief.

Felicia visits her son the first Sunday of each month at his school in the potato fields outside San Antonio de los Baños.[3] They say little in the hours allotted them. The emotion of their reunions exhausts them so that they often nap together under a tree, or in Ivanito's narrow bunk bed. They speak mainly with their eyes and with their hands, which never stop touching.

Everyone tells Felicia that she must find meaning in her life outside of her son, that she should give the revolution another try, become a New Socialist Woman. After all, as her mother points out, the only thing Felicia ever did for the revolution was pull a few dandelions during the weed-eradication campaign in 1962, and then only reluctantly. Her lack of commitment is a source of great rancor between them.

Felicia tries to shake off her doubts, but all she sees is a country living on slogans and agitation, a people always on the brink of war. She scorns the militant words blaring on billboards everywhere. WE SHALL OVERCOME . . . AS IN VIETNAM . . . CHANGE DEFEAT INTO VICTORY . . . Even the lowly weed pullers had boasted a belligerent name: The Mechanized Offensive Brigade. Young teachers are Fighters for Learning. Students working in the fields are the Juvenile Column of the Centenary. Literacy volunteers are The Fatherland or Death Brigade. It goes on and on, numbing her, undermining her willingness to fight for the future, hers or anybody else's. If only her son could be with her.

Felicia pulls a rusted nail file and a small plastic bottle of hand cream from her knapsack, and gets to work. She pushes back her cuticles with the rounded edge of the file, then expertly picks and scrapes under her nails until they are spotless. With short, brisk strokes she evens the broken nail on her left thumb. Then she squirts the pink lotion onto the backs of her hands, massages it in with a circular motion, and rubs her palms together until her hands are soft and slightly greasy again.

The other members of the troop, except for Lieutenant Rojas, who is listening to a crackling radio in her tent, watch Felicia attentively, as if witnessing an intricate ritual they'll be required to duplicate, like the dismantling and

---

2. Street where Celia, Felicia's mother, lives, in the fictitious town of Santa Teresa del Mar.     3. City in the province of La Habana.

reassembling of their rifles. When Felicia finishes, they turn away, clumping together in twos or threes to talk.

"It was my daughter who turned me in for insisting we say grace at the dinner table," Silvia Lores complains. "That's what they teach her at school, to betray her parents. Now I'm considered an 'antisocial.'"

"It could be worse," a genial man named Paco consoles her. "My neighbor's son was sent off to the marble quarries on the Isle of Pines[4] because he listened to American jazz and wore his hair too long. Now I'm not in favor of long hair, mind you, but hard labor? In that sun?"

"They send the seminarians there, too. They say the church is reactionary," Silvia Lores says.

"The leaders forget what they looked like themselves fifteen years ago," the only young man in the group pronounces. "Today, they'd be thrown in a Social Disgrace Unit with drug addicts and *maricones*.[5] Look at me. They say I'm rebellious, but it was rebels who made the revolution!"

"Calm down, *chico*, calm down. She might hear you," Paco cautions, gesturing toward Lieutenant Rojas's tent.

"Chances are, one of us is a spy anyway," the young man says contemptuously. "It's impossible to hide here."

Felicia listens to the conversation as she rolls a cigarette of strong black tobacco. She took up smoking again in the psychiatric hospital. It gave her something to do with her hands. Now she longs for the satisfying burning it produces deep in her lungs.

The others in her troop tried to draw her out during their first days in the mountains, but Felicia refused to say anything. She doesn't know these people and has no reason to trust them. Perhaps they think *she* is the spy.

Felicia volunteers again for night duty. In the dark, in the moonless jungle, the fissures are not so visible, the hypocrisies and lies less disturbing. Her eyes, she decides, could get accustomed to this darkness. Perhaps she should have lived in the night all along, with the owls and bats and other nocturnal creatures. Herminia told her once of the gods that rule the night, but Felicia cannot remember their names. It was to these gods that the slaves had prayed to preserve a shred of their souls. It had strengthened them for the indignities of their days.

Celia, too, once prayed in the night, rocking in her wicker swing until dawn. Sometimes, when Felicia was a child and couldn't sleep, she'd join her mother on the porch. They'd sit together for hours listening to the rhythm of the sea and the poems her mother recited as if in a dream.

> *Por las ramas del laurel*
> *vi dos palomas oscuras.*
> *La una era el sol,*
> *la otra la luna.*[6]

---

4. *Isla de la Juventud* (Isle of Youth), the second largest Cuban island; called *Isla de Pinos* (Isle of Pines) until 1978.
5. Faggots.

6. On the branches of a laurel tree / I saw two dark doves. / One was the sun, / the other was the moon.

Felicia learned her florid language on those nights. She would borrow freely from the poems she'd heard, stringing words together like laundry on a line, connecting ideas and descriptions she couldn't have planned. The words sounded precisely right when she said them, though often people told her she didn't make any sense at all. Felicia misses those peaceful nights with her mother, when the sea had metered their intertwined thoughts. Now they fight constantly, especially about El Líder. How her mother worships him! She keeps a framed photograph of him by her bed, where her husband's picture used to be. But to Felicia, El Líder is just a common tyrant. No better, no worse than any other in the world.

In fact, Felicia can't help feeling that there is something unnatural in her mother's attraction to him, something sexual. She has heard of women offering themselves to El Líder, drawn by his power, by his unfathomable eyes, and it is said he has fathered many children on the island. But there is a coldness to El Líder, a bitterness she doesn't trust. They say his first wife, his one great love, betrayed him while he was imprisoned on the Isle of Pines, after his ill-fated attack on the Moncada barracks.[7] She accepted money from the government, the government he was trying to overthrow. El Líder never forgave her, and they divorced. There's been another woman in his life since his days in these very mountains, but everyone knows she's only a companion—a mother, a sister, not a true lover. El Líder, it seems, saves his most ardent passions for the revolution.

Still, Felicia muses, what would he be like in bed? Would he remove his cap and boots? Leave his pistol on the table? Would guards wait outside the door, listening for the sharp pleasure that signaled his departure? What would his hands be like? His mouth, the hardness between his thighs? Would he churn inside her slowly as she liked? Trail his tongue along her belly and lick her *there*? Felicia slips her hand down the front of her army fatigue pants. She feels his tongue moving faster, his beard against her thighs. "We need you, Compañera del Pino," she hears him murmur sternly as she comes.

#### (1975)

It is the first Thursday in December. Nearly three hundred people squeeze into Santa Teresa del Mar's only movie theater, sharing seats, cigarettes, and soft drinks. The town has arrived for what promises to be a lively fight: Ester Ugarte, the postmaster's wife, has accused Loli Regalado of seducing her husband, a charge that Loli vehemently denies. On nights like these, nobody minds missing the theater's ordinary fare of grainy Cuban films.

Celia del Pino settles on a folding chair behind a card table facing the audience. It is her third year as a civilian judge. Celia is pleased. What she decides makes a difference in others' lives, and she feels part of a great historical unfolding. What would have been expected of her twenty years ago? To sway endlessly on her wicker swing, old before her time? To baby-sit her grandchildren and wait for death? She remembers the gloomy letters she used to write to Gustavo before the revolution, and thinks of how different the letters would be if she were writing today.

---

7. This event is discussed in the "Upheaval" introduction, p. 585.

Since her husband's death, Celia has devoted herself completely to the revolution. When El Líder needed volunteers to build nurseries in Villa Clara province, Celia joined a microbrigade, setting tiles and operating a construction lift. When he launched a crusade against an outbreak of malaria, Celia inoculated schoolchildren. And every harvest, Celia cut the sugarcane that El Líder promised would bring prosperity. Three nights per month, too, Celia continues to protect her stretch of shore from foreign invaders. She still dresses up for these all-night vigils, putting on red lipstick and darkening the mole on her cheek, and imagines that El Líder is watching her, whispering in her ear with his warm cigar breath. She would gladly do anything he asked.

Celia has judged 193 cases since she was elected to the People's Court, from petty thievery and family disputes to more serious crimes of medical malpractice, arson, and counterrevolutionary activities. But she delights in judging juvenile cases most of all. Reform, not punishment, is her modus operandi, and Celia has succeeded in converting many young delinquents into productive revolutionaries. One girl, Magdalena Nogueras, who at sixteen was caught stealing a pig and a wrench from her neighbor, went on to become a principal actress with the National Theater Company of Cuba. Later, Celia would learn with sadness that the girl had defected while on tour in Oaxaca and was playing a psychotic housewife on a popular Mexican *novela*.[8]

Celia signals the opening of tonight's case with four taps of her hammer, wobbly on its handle. It is her make-do gavel. She senses the audience is evenly split in its support of one woman or the other. Everyone, it seems, has a stake in the outcome.

Since the Family Code passed earlier this year, more and more people are turning to the courts with their problems. Women who claim their husbands are not doing their share of their housework or who want to put a stop to an extramarital affair bring the matter before a judge. Very few men, however, take their complaints to the People's Court for fear of appearing weak or, unthinkably, as cuckolds. Celia dislikes these cases. To her, such matters are private and should not be settled before a public hungry for entertainment. Besides, after all the negotiating, divorce is nearly always the solution. Perhaps if she had to choose again, she herself would have followed her Tía Alicia's example and never married at all.

"I was borrowing a cup of corn flour when her husband threw off his bathrobe and pushed himself on me." Loli Regalado is a curvaceous woman in her early thirties. Her dyed blond hair is pulled back in a high ponytail.

"That's not true!" Ester Ugarte shrieks. "She was seducing my Rogelio! She had on a tight dress that came up to here, with a neckline to there!" Ester indicates her navel both times.

"That wouldn't leave much of a dress, now would it, Compañera Ugarte?" Celia asks, and the audience erupts with laughter.

Loli then recounts how Ester rushed at her with an ironing board and chased her into the stairwell of their building, knocking her against the wall and holding her there like a prisoner.

---

8. Or *telenovela*, Mexican soap opera.

"She called me a *puta*,"[9] Loli complains angrily.

"I never called her a *puta*! Though God knows she deserves it!"

"Everyone knows your husband doesn't love you because you're so jealous," Loli taunts. "He puts the moves on every woman in the neighborhood."

"Liar!"

Celia pounds her hammer on the card table to quiet the spectators, who are hissing and hollering as if it were a boxing match. But Celia knows, as everyone does in Santa Teresa del Mar, that what Loli says is true. Rogelio Ugarte, like his father and his father before him, cannot keep his ungual hands to himself. It's a genetic trait, like his widow's peak and his slow brown eyes and the job he inherited at the post office. Celia remembers the rumors about Rogelio, how he sent off to Chicago for a carton of little rubber tips for his penis that made women crazy with pleasure. That was before the blockade. Celia always wondered how those tips stayed in place.

Several witnesses give their statements, but their information is so contradictory that it proves almost useless. Celia's arm tires from banging her hammer and her voice is hoarse from calling for order. Incredibly, she hears some *desgraciado*[1] selling peanuts in the back of the theater. Before she can throw him out, another voice breaks through the commotion.

"Let's try that sonofabitch postmaster! *He's* the one that should be here!" Nélida Grau yells from the third row, and in an instant the spectators are on their feet, arguing in every direction.

By the time Celia restores a tenuous calm, she has come to a decision.

"Compañera Grau has a point," Celia begins, silencing a heckler, a cousin of Rogelio's, with a harsh look. "It seems to me, *compañeras*, that your problem is not with each other, but with Rogelio."

"What do you expect with someone like her coming around to tempt him? He's only human!" Ester protests.

"Ha!" Loli sneers. "He should be licking his stamps instead of his chops! Maybe then we'd get some mail around here!"

"I'm not going to pass judgment on someone who isn't here," Celia announces over a fresh round of bickering. "You!" She points a finger at Rogelio's cousin, Ambrosio Ugarte, who is surrounded by a circle of angry women. "Bring Rogelio here. You have five minutes."

The auditorium vibrates with discord. Every combination of argument is going full tilt. Husbands against wives. Married women against the single and divorced. The politicized against the apolitical. The fight between Loli Regalado and Ester Ugarte is an excuse for everyone to unleash frustrations at family members, neighbors, the system, their lives. Old wounds are reopened, new ones inflicted.

Celia looks out at the unrest that is Santa Teresa del Mar. She is disheartened. It seems to her that so much of Cuba's success will depend on what doesn't exist, or exists only rarely. A spirit of generosity. Commitments without strings. Are these so against human nature?

Suddenly, all eyes turn to the back door. Rogelio Ugarte has arrived. He stands in the doorway, hesitant to enter. His slow brown eyes search the audience for friends.

---

9. Whore.   1. A wretched, luckless person.

"Please come to the front, *compañero*," Celia orders.

There is none of Rogelio's easy manner, none of his usual bantering or joking. He looks like a forlorn puppet jerking woodenly down the aisle.

"Now we'll get to the bottom of this!" Ester crows, and pandemonium breaks out anew.

As Celia pounds the card table, the head of her hammer finally gives way and flies backward, tearing a hole the size of a fist in the movie screen. It is most effective in securing the audience's attention.

"Compañero Ugarte, you are responsible for causing a great deal of division among your neighbors," Celia resumes loudly. "It has become clear to the court that it is you—not your wife or Compañera Regalado—who must stand before us with an explanation. Now please answer truthfully. Did you or did you not attempt to seduce Compañera Regalado against her will on the afternoon of October twenty-third?"

"Yes."

"Yes what?"

"I did try to seduce her."

The audience cheers, each person for his or her own reasons. It's as if Rogelio's response has justified every polemic.

"Liar!" Ester screams, flushed and trembling. Then in a spectacular leap that no one thought her capable of, Ester knocks her husband to the ground, pulls at his hair, and bites his cheek. By the time her friends pry her away, Ester is crying uncontrollably.

Celia steps onto her metal folding chair and stands over the crowd until no sound can be heard except the steady wheezing of Ester's sobs.

"I have come to a decision," Celia says deliberately. "Rogelio Ugarte, I sentence you to one year of volunteer work at the state nursery in Santa Teresa del Mar."

"What?" Rogelio looks up from the floor, still dazed from his wife's attack.

"The nursery is short-staffed, and our *compañeras* need help changing diapers, warming milk, washing linen, and organizing the children's playtime. You will be the first man to ever work there, *compañero*, and I will be checking up to see that your behavior is one of a model Socialist man in all respects. This case is adjourned."

Celia's decision wins her both bravos and more full-throated squabbling.

"Why don't you send him to Africa?" Nélida Grau shouts, one hand on her hip, the other indicating the direction.

Loli Regalado, while pleased with her exoneration, complains that putting Rogelio with the *compañeras* at the state nursery is akin to dropping the fox off at the henhouse with a knife and fork.

Celia watches, dispirited, as her neighbors file out of the auditorium, already merrily expectant for next month's "love motel" case. In January, Hilario and Vivian Ortega, who live down the street from Celia, will defend themselves against charges that they have been illegally renting by the hour two rooms of their beachfront home. Celia fears that the citizens of Santa Teresa del Mar once again will consider the court as hardly more than occasion for a live soap opera.

Outside the theater, the peanut vendor continues to work the crowd. He offers Celia a packet, and she accepts it without reproaching him. Then she walks unhurriedly back to her brick-and-cement house by the sea, chewing the peanuts one by one.

. . .

Later that night, Celia rocks in her wicker swing and considers the star-inscribed sky, as if its haphazard arrangements might reveal something to her. But tonight it is as formal and unilluminating as a tiara.

Celia enters her kitchen and warms a little milk on the stove, then sweet-ens it with a few lumps of sugar. How is it possible that she can help her neighbors and be of no use at all to her children? Lourdes and Felicia and Javier are middle-aged now and desolate, deaf and blind to the world, to each other, to her. There is no solace among them, only a past infected with disillusion.

Her daughters cannot understand her commitment to El Líder. Lourdes sends her snapshots of pastries from her bakery in Brooklyn. Each glisten-ing éclair is a grenade aimed at Celia's political beliefs, each strawberry shortcake proof—in butter, cream, and eggs—of Lourdes's success in America, and a reminder of the ongoing shortages in Cuba.

Felicia is no less exasperating. "We're *dying* of security!" she moans when Celia tries to point out the revolution's merits. No one is starving or denied medical care, no one sleeps in the streets, everyone works who wants to work. But her daughter prefers the luxury of uncertainty, of time unplanned, of waste.

If only Felicia could take an interest in the revolution, Celia believes, it would give her a higher purpose, a chance to participate in something larger than herself. After all, aren't they part of the greatest social experi-ment in modern history? But her daughter can only wallow in her own discomforts.

Nothing shakes Felicia's settled indifference. Not the two weeks she spent guerrilla training in the mountains. Not the day and a half she lasted cut-ting sugarcane. Felicia returned from the fields complaining of her wrenched back, her shredded hands, of the clumps of dust she'd swallowed. After that, she vowed to drink her coffee bitter. No more sugar.

Felicia's doctors recommended that she join a theater group, saying that many malcontents had finally made their peace with the revolution through acting. But Felicia showed no aptitude for the stage. Her daughter's talents, Celia realized ruefully, lay in her unsurpassed drama for the everyday. In the post office, in the plaza, or in the beauty shop where she worked, Felicia could have earned standing ovations and showers of red carnations.

Celia rummages through her nightstand drawer for her favorite photograph of her son. He is tall and pale as she is, with a mole on his left cheek identi-cal to hers. Javier is wearing his Pioneers[2] uniform, bright and new as the revolution, as his optimistic face. She cannot imagine him any older than he is in this picture.

Her son was almost thirteen when the revolution triumphed. Those first years were difficult, not because of the hardships or the rationing that Celia

2. *Los Pioneros*, or the José Martí Pioneer Orga-nization, a political organization of primary and secondary students, established in 1961 and named for the Cuban writer and nationalist hero José Martí (see p. 265).

knew were necessary to redistribute the country's wealth, but because Celia and Javier had to mute their enthusiasm for El Líder. Her husband would not tolerate praise of the revolution in his home.

Javier never fought his father openly. His war was one of silent defiance, and he left for Czechoslovakia secretly in 1966, without saying good-bye to anyone.

Javier wrote her a long letter after his father died three years ago, and said he'd finally become a professor of biochemistry at the University of Prague, lecturing in Russian, German, and Czech. He didn't mention his wife, not even in passing, but he wrote that he spoke Spanish to his little girl so she'd be able to talk with her grandmother someday. This touched Celia, and she wrote a special note to Irinita encouraging her to keep up her Spanish and promising to teach her how to swim.

Over the years, her son had written her only sporadically, quick notes jotted down, it seemed to Celia, between his lectures. Rarely did he write anything of substance, as if only the most superficial news was suitable for her. What she learned most about Javier came from the family picture her daughter-in-law, Irina, dutifully sent every Christmas. Celia saw her son age in these photographs, watched his mouth acquire his father's obstinate expression. And yet there was something vulnerable in his eyes that heartened Celia, that reminded her of her little boy.

In bed, Celia adjusts her breasts so she can sleep comfortably on her stomach. Every morning she wakes up on her back, her arms and legs spread, the cover sheet on the floor. She cannot account for her inquietude. Her dreams seem to her mere sparks of color and electricity, cut off from the current of her life.

Celia closes her eyes. She doesn't like to admit to herself that, despite all her activities, she sometimes feels lonely. Not the loneliness of previous years, of a reluctant life by the sea, but a loneliness borne of the inability to share her joy. Celia remembers the afternoons on the porch when her infant granddaughter seemed to understand her very thoughts. For many years, Celia spoke to Pilar during the darkest part of the night, but then their connection suddenly died. Celia understands now that a cycle between them had ended, and a new one had not yet begun.

1992

## FROM THE AGÜERO SISTERS

### Dulce Fuerte

#### Havana

Sex is the only thing they can't ration in Havana. It's the next-best currency after dollars, and much more democratic, if you ask me. The biggest problem is competition. Then policemen. Almost everyone I know my age, male or female, turns a trick once in a while. It's the easiest thing in the world, and most of the time you can convince yourself it's just a date that went a little too far. The foreigners like us because there isn't supposed to be any AIDS in Cuba. That's probably El Comandante's[1] most successful propaganda campaign yet. But it's just that. Propaganda.

Take a stroll with me down the Malecón,[2] and you'll see what I'm talking about. It's a fucking safari. And anybody with a pair of brand-name sneakers or sunglasses is the big game. See those jineteros[3] over there? I know them. Very ambitious. They make a living from the hustling. With their dollars and closets of tourist-shop gifts, they're the perfect go-betweens for ordinary Cuban citizens. Don't be so shocked. What the hell else are people supposed to do? Do you really think a family of five can live on one scrawny chicken a month? ¡Por favor!

Despite what my mother suspects. I'm not a professional. I only buy what I need. I only buy what I *need*. Right now, I'm out here earning pocket money until my visa comes through for Spain.

Like I said, it takes an occasional *novio*[4] to get by. Mamá doesn't understand this. She's immune from the day-to-day hassles because she's had that bureaucrat lackey lover of hers since the dawning of *la revolución*. Every night, Pepín brings her a feast from God knows where. Fresh steamed lobsters. Steaks thick as my thumb. Mangoes so perfectly ripe and sweet—not the stringy stuff you get with coupons—they're a kind of ecstasy. He also brings her shampoo that doesn't glue your hair together like the local brand, when you can find it. Let's just say the woman hasn't had to wait in a line since the Year of Ten Million,[5] when the whole country went crazy cutting sugarcane.

Mamá isn't the most fervent revolutionary on the island, but she's basically tolerant of the system. She and Pepín say that young people today are spoiled and don't appreciate all we have, that we should've seen how things were before the revolution to understand deprivation. Everybody I know is sick of these arguments, sick of picking potatoes and building dormitories, only to find no meaningful work in the careers we trained for. Sick of not washing our hands after we shit because there isn't any soap. Sick of the blackouts and dry faucets. Sick of having nothing to do, period. At minimum, it can make a person permanently irritable.

You can never work hard enough here, either. Cuba is like an evil stepmother, abusive and unrewarding of effort. More, more, and more for more nothing. Until last month, when they fired me for fraternizing with a foreigner, I was the volleyball coach at José Martí High School[6] (we came in sixth last year at the national championships), and I earned one hundred eighteen pesos a month. *Créeme*,[7] it's not easy staying in shape on sugar-and-lard

---

1. Fidel Castro's.
2. A seawall, road, and promenade that stretches along the northern coastline of Havana from Havana Harbor to Vedado; a famous landmark.
3. Cuban term derived from *jinetes*, horse jockeys; people who surround tourists with the intention of steering them toward transactions, such as purchases of souvenirs, cigars, or sex.
4. Boyfriend.

5. In 1970, *El año de la zafra de los diez millones* (The Year of Ten Million Tons of Sugar), countless workers, including professionals such as doctors and lawyers, were called upon to harvest sugar to fulfill Castro's pledge to produce a record yield.
6. Named for the Cuban writer and nationalist hero José Martí (see p. 265).
7. Believe me.

sandwiches. At least this way, I make a few dollars. That's how it breaks down here—those with dollars and those without. Dollars mean privileges. A roll of toilet paper. A bottle of rum. Pesos mean *te jodes*. You're fucked. It's that simple.

Come here. Look at this view, this harbor, this gorgeous curve of coast. Men from all over the world tell me that Havana is the most beautiful city they've ever seen. So when will we get it back? When will it be truly ours again? *Coño*, El Caballo[8] has four broken legs, and no one has the courage to put him out of his misery.

My father, José Luís Fuerte, was one of the original revolutionaries. He was at Moncada and in the Sierra Maestra[9] side by side with you-know-who. Part of a museum display in Santiago de Cuba is devoted to his exploits. Mamá took me there when I was a kid. There was a blown-up photograph of him with a rifle across his back. He's smoking a too-big cigar and has a beaded bracelet on his wrist. The odd thing was that he seemed very familiar to me, even though I'd never seen him before. Then I realized it was because I'd inherited his face.

All the while I was growing up and misbehaving, Mamá used to say: What would your father think if he were still alive? It used to shame me for the moment. I have a tattoo on my shoulder, three twisting vines intertwined with the name of my first boyfriend, coincidentally also named José Luís. When I was fourteen and got pregnant by him, my father was the first person I thought of. Mamá never found out, or she would've insisted I have the kid. She was sixteen when I was born and says she couldn't have imagined her life otherwise. Mamá's been after me to have a child. And for what? So she can coo over the kid before shipping him off to some boarding school in *el campo*[1] like she did with me? Forget about it.

These days, I find myself wondering not what my father would think of me but what he would think of his revolution and his former heroes.

People know my father was José Luís Fuerte, and so it makes it difficult sometimes. They expect more from me. I used to be friends with Che Guevara's[2] son in high school. We used to joke about our respective revolutionary burdens. Last I heard, he was a heavy-metal musician, pierced everywhere and trying to leave the country.

I thought of leaving too. At night on an inner tube with other *balseros*, from the beach at Jaimanitas or Santa Fé.[3] A friend of mine from junior high, Lupita Núñez, tried it in 1989, but she got picked up by the Cuban coast guard and sentenced to three years in jail. Others get eaten by sharks or go insane from the thirst. The people who make it to Miami become the real heroes of the revolution. My friends and I listen to the shortwave or spend hours trying to tune in to Radio Martí[4] to get the news. Or if we're really lucky, a TV report from south Florida.

---

8. The Horse, a nickname for Fidel Castro. *Coño*: damn.
9. Mountain range in southeastern Cuba; Castro's revolutionaries began guerilla warfare here. *Moncada*: discussed in the "Upheaval" introduction, p. 585.
1. The country.
2. Ernesto "Che" Guevara (1928–1967), Argentinian-born revolutionary leader in Latin

America.
3. Both beaches are in Havana. *Balseros*: rafters who flee the island using primitive boats made from inner tubes, scraps of wood, and other salvaged materials.
4. Miami-based radio broadcast, established in 1983 and financed by the U.S. government, that transmits 24-hour Spanish-language programming to Cuba.

Leaving. Leaving and dollars. That's all anybody ever talks about any-more. ¡Basta ya![5]

Sometimes, late at night, I wonder how my life would've been different if Mamá had left for the United States with her sister. Tía Constancia lives in New York and has two grown children. I like to imagine how cold it gets there. I'd like to wrap myself in fur and skate endlessly on frozen lakes. Round and round I'd go, my breath a trace of vapor behind me. In Cuba, there aren't any lakes. And only the future is frozen.

When I'm not out here on the Malecón, I ride my bicycle to pass the time. Not by choice, believe me. The damn island ran out of gas, and then the government started importing these bulky black bikes from China and tried to convince everyone that it was good for their health. Well, for once they were right. People started losing weight and having more energy for sex— not that there's ever a shortage of *that* here. Now something like a million bicycles clog Havana, and total chaos reigns in the streets. It's as if cars never existed.

I like to take my bike out of the city and ride for hours in the countryside. On weekends I've gone clear across to the Viñales Valley in Pinar del Río province.[6] There are fields of tobacco everywhere you look. Mamá tells me her father's family came from there, that they were refined people who recited poetry and played music every night. She still has the handmade violin my great-grandfather Reinaldo brought with him from Spain in 1903. Every now and then, Mamá takes the violin out of its little coffin and rubs the horsehair bow with a speck of rosin. I often think of my great-grandfather as I ride, suspended low over the earth, skimming along just fast enough to notice anything important.

My boyfriends come from everywhere. But the Canadian tourists are the easiest tricks, because they want to believe everything you tell them. Like that guy over there. Look how he can't keep his eyes off that trashy number in the hot pants. ¡Que nalgotas![7] Something happens to their brains when they hit Cuba. My theory is that it's the ratio of sunlight to oxygen to ocean here. Ninety percent of their cells are dormant until they arrive and see a good-looking habanera.[8] Then all hell breaks loose. Unfortunately, they're so sexually deprived, they make you work harder than anyone else on the planet.

From what I can tell, the only people making a decent living here are the babalawos.[9] There's one around the corner from my building who's redone his entire house with money from santería initiations. Only a couple of years ago, everyone knew where to find Lisardo Cuenca if he was needed, but it was all very hushed. His house looked like any other on the street, peeling with old paint. The occasional bleating of an illegal goat or the appearance of a horde of paralytics on his doorstep was the only clue to the secret power inside.

Now you should see the place. A thirty-foot statue of San Lázaro[1] stands on his minuscule lawn, and his house is painted white with bright-blue

5. Enough!
6. The western coast of Cuba. Viñales Valley: a national park and a UNESCO World Heritage Site.
7. What an ass!

8. Woman from Havana.
9. Priest in the Afro-Caribbean religious tradition Santería.
1. Saint Lazarus: reputed first bishop of Marseille (d. second half of first century), who died

stripes. Seventeen matching flags surround it, and people come from all over, openly carrying pigeons, sacks of beans, and toasted corn. Cuenca's best clients are referred to him by the government: foreigners who want an authentic initiation. Cuenca charges them a fortune, too. Four thousand dollars in cash is what I've heard. The government, of course, gets its cut. Anything in the name of foreign exchange.

You know things have gotten desperate when the Party needs to buy off the *babalawos*. I don't care if a white dove came to rest on El Comandante's shoulder during his inauguration speech, or that he was clearly the gods' chosen one. I don't think anybody, god or mortal, could have imagined how bad things would get here, to what depths people would stoop for a pork leg or a rusty saw. You always hear how the revolution divided families left and right. But what's going on now is worse than anything that preceded it. I heard of one family committing their grandmother to an asylum to get her apartment in Old Havana, of a brother killing his twin over a used battery for his Chevrolet.

•   •   •

*The Malecón's* been getting rough lately with lowlifes and black marketeers. The hustlers carry knives now, work the strip in pairs. You have to be careful. They don't appreciate girls like me, who come out only occasionally and give them competition. See this scar on my stomach? Some bitch came after me with a metal nail file when her French boyfriend dared look me over. That's when I decided to try my luck at the Habana Libre Hotel. No Cuban woman worth her salt would wear the ugly sandals and calf-length skirts I see on the tourists, so that's what I put on to pass for an *extranjera*.[2] My English is pretty convincing too, for about ninety seconds, just enough to get me a seat at the rooftop bar. That's where I met Abelardo.

At first, I thought he might be an undercover cop, on account of his exaggerated Castilian[3] accent (one of their stupider tricks). But he started off by telling me how he lives with his widowed sister in a tiny high-rise apartment in Madrid. His left hand is partially withered, and he held it up in what little intermittent light reflected off the revolving mirrored ball, as if to say, *Are you sure you still want to talk to me?* He seemed surprised when I did.

Then he told me he had a tumor the size of a plum on his balls, but the doctors assured him it was benign. I almost lost my nerve right then, but he took my hand and told me, sincerely, I thought, that I was the most beautiful woman he'd ever seen, and the kindest, and would I give him the pleasure and honor of becoming his wife.

The old man scared the hell out of me, and it must have shown, because he pulled back, apologized profusely, and—¡Coño! ¡Cojones! ¡Hijo de la gran puta que es tu madre![4]—he began to cry. Not a little disappointed snuffling but loud, heartrending sobs. Everyone turned to stare at me. The room

---

and was brought back to life by Jesus, according to the New Testament; venerated as a saint by branches of Christianity such as the Roman Catholic Church; in Santería, a healer of physical and spiritual pain.

2. Foreigner.
3. The dialect of the region of Castile, Spain.
4. Damn! Balls! Son of the great whore that is your mother!

became utterly still. Out. Out. Get out of there. But I was glued to my seat like an idiot while Abelardo wailed on. Hotel security arrived three abreast and arrested me. *I was arrested at the bar of a Cuban hotel because I couldn't produce a foreign passport.*

The rest is too tedious to tell in detail, but here's the bottom line: I got booked for prostitution, lost my job coaching volleyball, worked two hours in a cement plant with no cement before walking out, and decided to marry Abelardo.

1997

# ALICIA GASPAR DE ALBA
## b. 1958

Born in El Paso, Texas, Alicia Gaspar de Alba attended Loretto Academy and earned a bachelor's degree from the University of Texas in El Paso (1980), a master's in creative writing from the same institution (1983), and a doctorate in American Studies from the University of New Mexico, in Albuquerque (1994). Her doctoral dissertation, *"Mi casa [no] es su casa": The Cultural Politics of the Chicano Art: Resistance and Affirmation, 1965–1985,"* received the Ralph Henry Gabriel Award for Best Dissertation in American Studies in 1994. Gaspar de Alba's poetic voice emerged vibrantly and intimately in the volume *Three Times a Woman: Chicana Poetry* (1989), which also includes contributions by Demetria Martínez and María Herrera-Sobek. *The Mystery of Survival and Other Stories* (1993), Gaspar de Alba's debut as a fiction writer, focuses on the border region. Gaspar de Alba's graduate work led to her historical novel *Sor Juana's Second Dream* (1999), from which the selection in this anthology, "Bishop's Pawn," is taken.

Based on the life and works of Sor Juana Inés de La Cruz, the seventeenth-century nun, poet, playwright, protofeminist, and frequent source of irritation to the Catholic Church in colonial New Spain (later called Mexico), it presents the nun's rebellion, independence, and creative outbursts as the model for Chicana women. In "Bishop's Pawn," set in June 1693 and part of a section called "Fianchetto," the dialogue between Don Manuel Fernández de Santa Cruz y Sahagún, bishop of Puebla; his archenemy, Archbishop Francisco Aguiar y Seijas; and the middleman Padre Antonio Núñez de Miranda, Sor Juana's confessor, reflects the tortured dealings of the Holy Office of the Inquisition in New Spain regarding Sor Juana. Her fame as a distinguished writer and thinker and as a woman put her at odds with the oppressive male establishment.

Gaspar de Alba's other major works of fiction are *Desert Blood: The Juárez Murders* (2005), about a mass killing of Mexican women in the border town, and *Calligraphy of the Witch* (2007), a historical novel set in the seventeenth-century, about a girl who lives in a convent, is captured by pirates and sold into slavery, and ultimately becomes caught up in the Massachusetts Bay Colony witch hunt. Gaspar de Alba is a professor of English and Chicano Studies at the University of California, Los Angeles. Among her honors are the Premio Aztlán (1994), the Latino Literary Hall of Fame Award for Best Historical Fiction (2000), the International Latino Book Award for Best English-Language Mystery (2005), and the Lambda Literary Award for Best Lesbian Mystery (2005).

## FROM SOR JUANA'S SECOND DREAM

### Bishop's Pawn

"Get out of my sight, you brazen harlot!" thundered His Ilustrísima, Archbishop Aguiar y Seijas, his blue eyes blazing in horror. He hurled his cup at the girl walking through the door with a pot of chocolate. Startled, the girl dropped the pot on the bare flagstones of the library, and Don Manuel Fernández de Santa Cruz, Bishop of Puebla, covered his ears against the sound of shattering porcelain.

The Archbishop got to his feet. "This is a disgrace! How many times need I tell you, Padre Antonio, that no woman is ever to attend me? I'll not stay here a minute longer."

Padre Antonio rose, but Don Manuel remained seated, cleaning his nails with a fork tine. "Forgive me, Ilustrísima," Padre Antonio said. "I forgot to ring for the steward instead of the maid. It was an old man's mistake. No harm was done."

"You allowed the room to be defiled by a woman's presence. You know that causes irreparable damage to my liver."

"Forgive me, Ilustrísima," Padre Antonio repeated. "It will never happen again. I shall have that girl flogged for coming in here, but I beg you not to leave yet. We must discuss the chronicle that Sor Juana's Superior has proposed. Mother Andrea has been waiting for an answer since before Lent, and it's already Pentecost.[1] I find it awkward, Ilustrísima, to continue rendering my services at San Jerónimo[2] without broaching the subject with her."

"Nothing could force me to stay in this room," the Archbishop insisted.

"Why don't we move to your private patio, Antonio?" suggested the Bishop. "I know you allow no servants access to that inner sanctum of yours. And perhaps we could lunch on something salty after this—" He gestured disdainfully at the platter of apricot empanadas, of which he had already consumed half. "All this soft, sweet food makes my teeth hurt."

The patio's rose garden had been the only thing motivating Padre Antonio during the long weeks of his illness. He rose for the holy Offices as was his obligation, not even bothering to slip on his shoes or comb the wisps of his hair, disciplined himself three times a day, and even managed to write lectures for the weekly meeting of the Brotherhood of Mary, although it was Sigüenza who delivered them in his place. But he offered no Masses, heard no confessions, gave no sermons, prepared no lessons for his pupils, and ministered to none of his charities, preferring to stay indoors reading the lives of the saints or sweeping the church and the friary. He knew the city needed him after the devastations of the previous summer, but he had lost the strength to care about anything. Only the thought of his roses withering in the drought after all those years of cultivating them, pruning them,

---

1. She has been waiting over three months. In Christianity, Lent is the 40-day period from Ash Wednesday (which can fall on any Wednesday from February 4 to March 22) to Easter (which can fall on any Sunday from March 10 to April 25); Pentecost is the seventh Sunday after Easter.
2. Convent of Santa Paula of the Order of San Jerónimo, in the southern section of Mexico City; Sor Juana Inés de la Cruz lived there.

talking to God through them, experimenting with different strains brought from Valencia and Castile,[3] kept him from submitting to the illness altogether, clippers or watering pail dutifully in hand.

It was his one and only luxury, for which he scourged himself almost as vehemently as for his pride. Here he liked to sit with his rosary every morning, here he liked to take his lunch, here he liked to visit with his closest friends and pupils. He winced at the thought of sharing his private sanctuary with the Archbishop, expecting to be criticized for his indulgence in roses. To his surprise, the Archbishop was a great admirer of well-grown blooms and cultivated a few rose trees of his own.

"What surprises me about Sor Juana's offer to write a new chronicle," Don Manuel called out from the bench on which he installed himself with the plate of bread and sliced sausage that the cook had prepared for their midday repast, "is that she knows it will be used against her. After the *Carta aténagorica*,[4] how could she not?" He held out the plate. "Will you have some, Ilustrísima?"

The Archbishop grimaced at the smell of the sausage and shook his head, settling himself on the bench across from the Bishop, in the shade of a fig tree. Padre Antonio sat between them on the ledge of the fountain, trailing one hand in the water.

"Do you not see, Padre Antonio, how that woman is trying to trick us into regaining her writing privileges with that chronicle?" asked the Archbishop.

"Undoubtedly, that is her ploy, Ilustrísima. But I trust Mother Andrea implicitly, and know that she would make sure Juana did not stray from the margin. Besides, I think she will seal her own fate with this document. I don't see how it could hurt the Church for her to write down her sins."

"Must we read another document?" asked the Bishop. "Haven't we collected enough testimonies from the other sisters that may be submitted for the Tribunal's review? Along with her books and those letters, we have plenty of evidence of Juana's sins, Antonio."

"Am I mistaken," said Padre Antonio, "or did you once have a friendship with Juana, Don Manuel?"

"An intellectual understanding, perhaps, but never a friendship," said the Bishop, sopping his crust in the oil. "She used to be a favorite of mine, that is true, and I remain an admirer of some of her early work, but more and more I am repulsed by her insolence with the written word. And I daresay she hates men. I found even myself being swayed by her logic against my own kind. The woman's rhetoric is dangerous, Padre Antonio. She could persuade the Pope himself."

"And what could she persuade us of if she writes a chronicle of her sins? We already know that she is a sinner."

"As the recipient of one of her chronicles," said the Bishop, "I can assure you that she will most expertly twist logic and history around to her own benefit. She has the power of the verb, and is a master rhetorician. She

3. Regions of Spain.
4. Athenagoric Letter; a document, written in 1690 at the request of the bishop of Puebla, in which Sor Juana refuted the 1650 argument of

the Portuguese Jesuit priest Antonio de Vieyra about Jesus Christ's loving acts of kindness, known in Spanish as *finezas*.

might even sway the Inquisition.[5] Not to mention the fact that she has a publisher in Spain."

"Since when is the Holy Office easily swayed? Master rhetorician or not, she's nothing but a woman and a nun. Only someone with a weak will can be persuaded by what she says."

"Are you suggesting that a Spaniard's will like mine is weaker than a criollo's?"[6]

"I didn't dress myself up in a nun's identity to reprimand her," retorted Padre Antonio.

"You're the one who took her back after *she* renounced *you* over a decade ago. If she had sent the petition to me, I would have returned it immediately without bothering to break the seal."

"Don Manuel, *por favor*, we all know that you were her friend, and you just called yourself her admirer. You couldn't have been a very objective audience."

"I beg to differ. It was I, after all, who drew her out."

"You were playing games with her, assuming the persona of this Sor Filotea, chastising her through a veiled identity only to see your words in print. You had no intention of drawing her out."

"Brothers, please," interrupted the Archbishop, "let us not resort to the unmanly practice of bickering. The question is, Padre Antonio, what are *you* going to do to help us straighten out the infamous Juana Inés de la Cruz?"

"You may trust me completely to guide her back to the straight and narrow, Ilustrísima."

"Don't be a fool! I don't want you to save her. You have to bring her down. Why waste your time on that infidel? Once she is stripped of the sacraments she'll be none of your concern."

"I beg your pardon, Señores," said Padre Antonio, "but are we attempting here to purify or crucify Mary Magdalene?[7] It was my understanding from discussing this matter at some length with my colleagues in the Holy Office that what they want is a recantation, not an excommunication. That is why I have gone to the trouble of getting her on the roster of penitents for the *octava*[8]—"

The Bishop was chuckling behind his napkin. "Crucify Mary Magdalene? You do mix your metaphors, Antonio!"

Padre Antonio clenched his fist in the water of the fountain, quelling the instinct to douse the Bishop's face. How dare he stuff himself with my food and insult me in my own garden, he thought. He felt trickles of sweat slip under his hair shirt, and his skin began to itch, for which he was thankful.

"I am talking about a woman's soul, sir, not a primer on rhetoric!"

The Archbishop threw a fig at him, and it splattered on his cassock. "Padre Antonio, you will do me the kindness of never putting those two

---

5. A notoriously harsh tribunal established in 1478 by the Spanish monarchs to punish the Jews and Muslims who had converted to Catholicism but were insincere; formally abolished in 1834. It had powerful branches in the Americas.
6. Sor Juana was born out of wedlock; her father was from the Basque region of Spain, and her mother was a *criolla*.

7. Identified in the New Testament as a disciple of Jesus, venerated as a saint in branches of Christianity such as the Roman Catholic Church, and for centuries misidentified as an adulteress and repentant prostitute.
8. A religious observance in Catholic liturgy that takes place over eight days.

words together again in my presence. Women have no souls. But this one has a brain, and I will not allow the possibility of her publishing yet another treatise that she will use to our disadvantage. It would be the final drop in the cup of bile she has been serving me since I arrived in New Spain. Every word she writes is fodder for my enemies. Don't be a fool!"

"But, Ilustrísima, why must we complicate matters to such a degree? This is a simple case of a nun's renewal of her vows. A Silver Jubilee."[9]

"What it is, Padre Antonio," said the Archbishop, "is our only opportunity to make her pay for the offenses she has committed against the faith and against mankind. The Bishop has already taken the first step with the publication of that blasphemous *Carta*. Now I want her library expurgated and every single text she owns compared against the Index.[1] As a censor for the Inquisition, Padre Antonio, you must weed out all her banned books. I shall take care of dispossessing her of all she values. Can I trust you to be our ally in this endeavor?"

But my eyes, Padre Antonio wanted to say, I can't see anything with these eyes. "I don't see the need to go to all this trouble when all that's necessary is a rigorous confession and a complete renunciation of her past. I can achieve that, Eminence, I know I can."

"I have had it up to here with your nescience, Antonio. We want her to submit to the Church, once and for all. Can you help us do that?" A white froth had gathered in the corners of the Archbishop's mouth.

"Calm yourself, Eminence," said the Bishop.

"But why excommunication, Ilustrísima? Do you really want her cast out into the world with nothing to guide her? No husband. No vows."

The Archbishop's cane hit him in the knees. "Tell me, Padre Antonio, you who were rebuffed by this daughter of a *criolla* whore, does she not spite the very patriarchs of our faith with every word she scribbles? Those plays! Those love poems directed not at Our Savior but at vicereines and viceroys. That scandalous *respuesta*![2] And now those books! Two volumes of her writings circulating in Spain! One of them comes with a warning, a *warning*, mind you, about the secret influence of the stars that motivated her affections for the Countess of Paredes.[3] And another bears the signature of seven Spaniards who agree with her critique of Vieyra. Do you know how that makes me look to my friends in Spain and Portugal, that the Archbishop of Mexico is being told how to interpret the Bible by one of his own nuns? Are you so blind that you really believe this woman can recant?"

"I believe salvation is always possible, Eminence."

"Don't you understand, Padre Antonio? There is no room for women in God's community."

"But Juana is no heretic, Ilustrísima. I can vouch for that. She is completely misguided, and for that I must take a measure of responsibility for having abandoned her at a critical time. But to make her anathema, Eminence, is a grave mistake."

---

9. A celebration of her 25th year as a nun.
1. Formerly, the Roman Catholic Church's published list of books it prohibited or restricted the reading of.
2. Answer, response.
3. María Luis Manrique de Lara y Gonzaga,

Countess of Paredes and Marquesa of La Laguna, known as "Lysis" in Sor Juana's writing, was Sor Juana's close friend and confidant. Some biographers have suggested a lesbian relationship between them.

"Are you daring to correct me, Padre Antonio?"

"Forgive me, Eminence, that was not my intent. But we all know that Juana is not the equal of any nun. She is more than a woman. The very theologians that you refer to agree to that. Didn't one of them say that she was a man in every respect? Would we excommunicate a priest for doing what she has done, for writing, for publishing, for indulging in a life of the mind? She has committed no heresies."

"You're contradicting yourself, Antonio," interjected Don Manuel through a mouthful of sausage. "Earlier you said she was just a woman and a nun, and now you say she's more than a woman. You may be right. It isn't just the mind that she's been indulging. We've collected plenty of evidence to suggest that Juana and our former Vicereine were engaged in a, shall we say, particularly intimate friendship."

"Please, Manuel. Don't sour my appetite," said the Archbishop, grimacing again. "We can hear about it at the confession."

"I know nothing of a confession," said Padre Antonio, "save the one that she and I have been working on for the last seven weeks."

"We've decided—that is, the Bishop of Puebla and I have decided—that instead of the written chronicle that her Superior requested we permit her to write, there shall be a public confession, in the chambers of the Tribunal, to last as many days as it takes to divulge all of her sins and humiliate her before the world. That should take care of our *tenth muse*."

"But it is not a trial, Señores. Only a confession. And confessions are private."

"Not this one, Padre Antonio. Not if she wants to continue wearing the habit of Saint Jerome."

"Penitence and absolution are all she needs, Ilustrísima."

The Bishop burped behind his hand, then got to his feet and stood before Padre Antonio, thrusting his belly in the Jesuit's face. He reeked of garlic and cured meat, and there were oil stains on his sash.

"As her father confessor, *you* are in charge of administering the penitence, Antonio. We will let the Tribunal decide if she is worthy of absolution. All we need to know is that we can count on your influence with the inquisitors."

Padre Antonio scratched vigorously at his hair shirt and dared not look up lest the Bishop see the anger in his eyes. He had to accept that this was the penitence Juana's own sinfulness had sown. And no doubt it would be his last act of salvation before the merciful darkness closed over his eyes and returned him to his Maker.

"I am nothing but a soldier of Christ," he said, staring at the frayed hem of his cassock. "Who am I to question your command?"

1999

# NILO CRUZ
## b. 1959

The first Latino to win a Pulitzer Prize for drama, Nilo Cruz was born in Matanzas, Cuba. He moved with his family to the United States in 1970 and settled in the Little Havana section of Miami, Florida. After studying theater at what was then Miami-Dade Community College, he moved to New York City, where he studied under the Havana-born playwright María Irene Fornés (see p. 950). Fornés recommended his work to the American playwright Paula Vogel, who was teaching at Brown University, in Rhode Island. Cruz joined Brown's Master of Fine Arts Program, and he earned his degree in 1994. While playwright-in-residence at the New Theatre in Coral Gables, Florida, he wrote *Anna in the Tropics* (2002), a drama about the tobacco industry in Florida. The play won a Pulitzer Prize in 2003 without having been staged. After being staged in Miami, it was awarded the American Theatre Critics/Steinberg Award for Best New Play. In 2004, it opened on Broadway, starring the American actor Jimmy Smits as Juan Julian, a lector in a Tampa cigar factory. (A lector's job was to read to the cigar rollers as they worked.) *Anna in the Tropics*, included in its entirety in this anthology, is set in the late 1920s, when new manufacturing methods threatened to supplant both the Cubans who hand-rolled each cigar and their lectors.

Among the prolific Cruz's other plays are *A Park in Our House* (1996), *A Bicycle Country* (1999), *Two Sisters and a Piano* (1999), *Hortensia and the Museum of Dreams* (2001), and *Beauty of the Father* (2003). He has rendered into English *Doña Rosita* and *The House of Bernarda Alba*, both by the twentieth-century Spanish dramatist Federico García Lorca, and *Life Is a Dream*, by the seventeenth-century Spanish dramatist Pedro Calderón de la Barca. He has also adapted "A Very Old Man with Enormous Wings," a short story by the contemporary Colombian writer and Nobel Prize–winner Gabriel García Márquez, into a children's play. Cruz has taught playwriting at Brown; the University of Iowa, in Iowa City; and Yale University, in New Haven, Connecticut. He lives in New York City.

---

## ANNA IN THE TROPICS

### Characters

SANTIAGO   Owner of a cigar factory, late fifties
CHECHÉ   His half-brother; half-Cuban, half-American, early forties
OFELIA   Santiago's wife, fifties
MARELA   Ofelia and Santiago's daughter, twenty-two
CONCHITA   Her sister, thirty-two
PALOMO   Her husband, forty-one
JUAN JULIAN   The lector, thirty-eight
ELIADES   Local gamester, runs cockfights, forties

### Time and Place

1929. Tampa, Florida. A small town called Ybor City.

## Set

An old warehouse.

## Costumes

These workers are always well dressed.

They use a lot of white and beige linen and their clothes are always well pressed and starched.

## Playwright's Note

After 1931, the lectors were removed from the factories, and what remained of the cigar rollers consisted of low-paid American workers who operated machines.

The end of a tradition.

# Act One

## Scene 1

*Sounds of a crowd at a cockfight.* SANTIAGO *and* CHECHÉ *are betting their money on cockfights. They've been drinking, but are not drunk. They wear typical, long-sleeve, white linen shirts (guayabera), white pants and two-tone shoes.* ELIADES *collects the money and oversees all the operations of this place.*

ELIADES: Cockfights! See the winged beauties fighting in midair! Cockfights! I'll take five, ten, fifteen, twenty dollars on Picarubio. Five, ten, twenty on Espuela de Oro. Picarubio against Espuela de Oro. Espuela de Oro against Picarubio.

SANTIAGO: I'll bet a hundred on Picarubio.

ELIADES: A hundred on Picarubio.

CHECHÉ: Eighty on Espuela de Oro.

ELIADES: Eighty on Espuela de Oro.

SANTIAGO: Ten more on Picarubio.

ELIADES: Ten more on Picarubio. Ten more on Espuela de Oro?

CHECHÉ: No, that's enough.

ELIADES: I'll take five, ten, twenty dollars. Picarubio against Espuela de Oro. Espuela de Oro against Picarubio.

> [*Sound of a ship approaching the harbor.* MARELA, CONCHITA *and their mother,* OFELIA, *are standing by the seaport. They are holding white handkerchiefs and are waiting for a ship to arrive.*]

MARELA: Is that the ship approaching in the distance?

CONCHITA: I think it is.

OFELIA: It's the only ship that's supposed to arrive around this time.

MARELA: Then that must be it. Oh, I'm so excited! Let me look at the picture again, Mamá.

OFELIA: How many times are you going to look at it?

MARELA:   Many times. We have to make sure we know what he looks like.

CONCHITA:   You just like looking at his face.

MARELA:   I think he is elegant and good looking.

[OFELIA *opens a letter and takes out a photograph.*]

OFELIA:   That he is. But what's essential is that he has good vocal chords, deep lungs and a strong voice.

CONCHITA:   What's more important is that he has good diction when he reads.

MARELA:   As long as he reads with feeling and gusto, I'm content. [*Looks at the photo.*] Look at his face and the way he signs his name.

[*Sounds of a crowd at a cockfight.*]

ELIADES:   We have a winner! We have a winner! Espuela de Oro is the winner! Espuela de Oro!

CHECHÉ:   Winner here.

ELIADES: [*Counting money.*]   Ten, twenty, thirty, forty, fifty, sixty.

SANTIAGO:   You're a lucky man.

ELIADES:   Next fight! I'll take five, ten, fifteen, twenty dollars . . . Cuello de Jaca against Uñaroja. Uñaroja against Cuello de Jaca.

SANTIAGO:   Eighty on Cuello de Jaca.

ELIADES:   Eighty on Cuello de Jaca.

CHECHÉ:   Eighty on Uñaroja.

ELIADES:   Eighty on Uñaroja. [*To the audience.*] Uñaroja against Cuello de Jaca! Cuello de Jaca against Uñaroja!

[*Sound of a ship approaching the harbor.*]

OFELIA:   Don't tell your father, but I took some money from the safe to pay for the lector's trip.

CONCHITA:   You did well, Mamá.

OFELIA:   Oh, I don't feel a bit guilty. Doesn't your father spend his money gambling? Then I'll do as I wish with my money. I'll spend my money on the best lector we can get. The gentleman who recommended him says that he is the best lector west of Havana.

MARELA:   Well, I'm glad, because poor old Teodoro used to spit a little too much when he read to us. Sometimes it felt like sprinkles of rain were coming out of his mouth.

OFELIA:   Marela! The poor man was eighty years old.

MARELA:   That he was!

OFELIA:   Have more respect—he died three months ago.

MARELA:   Oh, I respect him, but let the truth be told.

OFELIA:   The poor fellow, for ten years he read to us.

MARELA: [*With satire.*]   Oh, I loved him . . . I loved him, like an uncle, like a grandfather. May he rest in peace! But he should've given up being a lector a long time ago. His heart couldn't take the love stories. He couldn't take the poetry and tragedy in the novels. Sometimes he had to sit down after reading a profound and romantic passage.

CONCHITA:   Oh, that's why I liked him, because I knew that he read to us with his heart.

MARELA:   But it was too much. It took him three months to read the last novel to us.

OFELIA: Ah! But it was *Wuthering Heights*,[1] and none of us wanted it to end, including you.

CONCHITA: Well, I hope this new lector turns out to be as good as Teodoro, because the one who replaced him didn't last . . .

MARELA: Look, the ship is getting closer. Oh, I'm so excited, I just want him to disembark and have him here once and for all.

CONCHITA: [*Looking into the distance.*] He's probably going to bring a lot of new books from Argentina and Spain and France, because so many ships make stops in Cuba.

    [*Sounds of a crowd at a cockfight.*]

ELIADES: We have a winner! We have a winner! Uñaroja! Uñaroja is the winner!

CHECHÉ: Winner here. Uñaroja.

    [ELIADES *pays* CHECHÉ, *then continues announcing the next fight.*]

ELIADES: Twenty, forty, sixty, eighty, one hundred . . . Twenty, forty, sixty . . . Ready for the next fight! We have Colabrava against Falcón de Acero. I'll take five, ten, fifteen, twenty dollars . . . Colabrava against Falcón de Acero . . . [*Continuing his announcement.*]

SANTIAGO: Lend me some money, Cheché.

CHECHÉ: How much?

SANTIAGO: Two hundred.

CHECHÉ: I don't lend any money when I'm gambling, and I don't lend any money when I'm drinking.

SANTIAGO: Are you going to make me walk home to get more money?

CHECHÉ: Ah, just give it up!

SANTIAGO: Are you going to make me walk back to my house?

CHECHÉ: It's not a good night for you! You've lost all your money.

SANTIAGO: Lend me some money, Cheché. I'll pay you back.

CHECHÉ: You're drunk, Santiago.

SANTIAGO: Give me some money and I'll show you my luck. Come on, you've got the lucky money! With your lucky money I'll show you what I can do.

CHECHÉ: And when are you going to pay me back?

SANTIAGO: I guarantee you that I'll pay you back.

CHECHÉ: You got to give me your word.

SANTIAGO: I'll give you my word. Give me a paper. I'll sign a paper. You got paper?

CHECHÉ: No, I don't have any paper.

SANTIAGO: Then lift up your foot.

CHECHÉ: What do you mean lift up my foot?

SANTIAGO: [*Grabbing* CHECHÉ'S *leg.*] Lift up your foot, hombre!

CHECHÉ: What the hell? . . .

SANTIAGO: Let me have the sole of your shoe.

    [SANTIAGO *takes out a knife.*]

CHECHÉ: What are you going to do? [*Lifting up his foot.*]

SANTIAGO: I'm signing my name on the sole of your shoe.

    [SANTIAGO *carves his name on* CHECHÉ'S *shoe.*]

CHECHÉ: What for?

---

1. Novel (1847) by the English writer Emily Brontë (1818–1848).

SANTIAGO: Proof. Testament that I'll pay you back. See here: "S" for Santiago. How much are you going to lend me?

CHECHÉ: Twenty.

SANTIAGO: Twenty? Cheapskate. I'm writing a hundred.

CHECHÉ: A hundred?

SANTIAGO: A hundred. There you go.

CHECHÉ: A hundred?

SANTIAGO: A hundred. That's what I wrote.

CHECHÉ: Are you . . . ?

SANTIAGO: I'll pay you back. I'm your brother, for God's sake!

[Sound of a ship approaching the harbor.]

OFELIA: There is the ship. Wave your handkerchief.

MARELA: Do you see him?

CONCHITA: All the men look the same with their hats.

OFELIA: Oh, why do I get so emotional every time I see a ship?

MARELA: Don't get mad at me, Mamá, but I wrote the lector's name on a piece of paper and placed it in a glass of water with brown sugar and cinnamon.

OFELIA: What for?

MARELA: Carmela, the palm reader, told me that if I sweeten his name, the reader would come our way.

OFELIA: That's like casting a spell on him.

MARELA: It's only sugar and cinnamon. And it worked.

OFELIA: I told you about playing with spells. It's not right, Marela. One should never alter other people's destiny.

MARELA: I didn't alter his destiny. With a little sugar I sweetened his fate.

CONCHITA: That's how witches get started—with brown sugar. Then they begin to play with fire. Look at what happened to Rosario, she put a spell on her lover and the man died. And not only did she lose her man; she's gone to hell herself.

OFELIA: [To MARELA.] Did you hear that?

CONCHITA: They say she couldn't stop crying after her lover's death. That her whole face became an ocean of tears, and the father had to take her back to Cuba, to see if she would get better. But a fever would possess the girl at night. They say she'd run to the sea naked. She'd run there to meet the dead lover.

MARELA: Now you're making me feel awful.

[Sounds of a crowd at a cockfight.]

ELIADES: Kikiriki . . . Ready for the next fight! We have Diamante Negro against Crestafuerte . . . I'll take five, ten, fifteen, twenty dollars . . . Diamante Negro against Crestafuerte. Crestafuerte against Diamante Negro.

SANTIAGO: Lift up your foot again.

CHECHÉ: What for?

SANTIAGO: Lift up your foot and let me see the sole of your shoe.

CHECHÉ: What for?

[SANTIAGO carves something on the sole of CHECHÉ's shoe.]

SANTIAGO: I'm borrowing two hundred more.

CHECHÉ: No. You can't. You're jinxed tonight.

SANTIAGO: I'll pay you back. It's written on your shoe already.

CHECHÉ: Then cross it out.

SANTIAGO: I can't cross it out. I've got my totals there. If I don't pay you, part of the factory is yours.

[*Immediately* CHECHÉ *takes off his shoe.*]

CHECHÉ: Then write it down. Write it down. I want it in writing.

SANTIAGO: I'll write it down. [*Takes the knife and carves out his promise.*] There you go.

[CHECHÉ *looks at the sole of his shoe. He gives* SANTIAGO *more money.*]

CHECHÉ: Here. Let's go.

SANTIAGO: Well, put on your shoe, hombre!

CHECHÉ: No, I'm not putting it on.

SANTIAGO: Why not?

CHECHÉ: Because this here is our contract, and I don't want it erased.

SANTIAGO: And you're going to walk with just one shoe.

CHECHÉ: Yes!

SANTIAGO: You bastard!

[*Sound of a ship approaching.*]

OFELIA: Well, there's no sign of him. Let's see if you spoiled it for us.

MARELA: Ah, don't say that!

I'm so nervous I think I'm going to pee-pee on myself.

CONCHITA: Is he that man waving his hat?

OFELIA: Is it? I can't see very well from here.

CONCHITA: No. He's got to be younger.

MARELA: How is he going to recognize us?

OFELIA: I told him that I was going to wear a white hat.

MARELA: Oh Lord! There are more than fifty women with white hats.

OFELIA: But I told him that my hat would have a gardenia.

CONCHITA: Is it the man with the blue suit?

MARELA: No, too fat.

OFELIA: When you get home take his name out of that sweet water.

MARELA: Oh Lord, I feel awful. He's nowhere to be found. I'm going home. I'm going home. I've ruined it. [*Starts to exit.*]

OFELIA: Marela!

MARELA: No. I've ruined it.

OFELIA: Come back here. A little bit of sugar can't do any harm.

[*The lector,* JUAN JULIAN, *enters. He is wearing a Panama hat and a white linen suit.*]

MARELA: I don't want to spoil it.

OFELIA: Marela, don't be foolish.

JUAN JULIAN: Señora Ofelia?

OFELIA: [*Turning to look.*] Yes . . .

JUAN JULIAN: The gardenia on your hat, am I correct? Señora Ofelia.

[JUAN JULIAN *takes off his hat.*]

OFELIA: [*Dumbstruck.*] Oh!

CONCHITA: Say yes, Mamá!

OFELIA: Ah, yes! I'm Ofelia.

JUAN JULIAN: Juan Julian Rios, at your service!

OFELIA: Ah! Ofelia . . . Ofelia Alcalar. What an honor!

[*We hear* MARELA *pee on herself from nervousness. There is an awkward pause. All of them notice.*]
[*Dissimulating.*] Oh! Do you have everything, Señor Juan Julian? Do you have your luggage?

JUAN JULIAN:   I'll have to tell the steward that I found you.

OFELIA:   Go find him . . . We'll wait here.

[JUAN JULIAN *runs off.*]

[*Turning to* MARELA.] Marela, what happened?

MARELA: [*Dumbstruck.*]   I don't know.

OFELIA:   Oh dear! But you've wet yourself, like a child.

MARELA:   I couldn't hold it in, Mamá.

[*Music plays. Lights change.*]


### Scene 2

*The cigar factory.* JUAN JULIAN *is holding a few books strapped with a belt.* CHECHÉ *enters. He wears one shoe and holds the other in his hand.*

CHECHÉ:   Are you here to see someone?

JUAN JULIAN:   I'm here to see Ofelia.

CHECHÉ:   Ofelia hasn't come yet. Can I help you?

JUAN JULIAN:   She told me she'd be here around this time.

CHECHÉ:   She should be getting here soon. Can I be of any service?

JUAN JULIAN:   No, thank you. I'll wait.

CHECHÉ:   What are you, a lector?

JUAN JULIAN:   Yes, I am. I just arrived from the island. Today is my first day . . .

CHECHÉ:   If you're looking for a job, we're not hiring . . .

JUAN JULIAN:   No, I'm . . . I'm the new lector. Doña Ofelia—

CHECHÉ:   I heard. You just arrived and I'm telling you we're not hiring . . .

JUAN JULIAN:   Well, I imagine you are not hiring because Señora Ofelia . . .

[OFELIA *and her daughters enter.*]

CHECHÉ:   Ofelia, the señor . . . this gentleman is here to see you. I told him we're not hiring . . .

OFELIA: [*With conviction.*]   He's been hired by me, Chester.

CHECHÉ:   Oh, I see. I see. [*Pause.*] Oh, well.

[CHECHÉ *exits.*]

OFELIA:   Welcome, Juan Julian. Some of the cigar rollers who work in front told me they already met you. They're very excited that you're here.

JUAN JULIAN:   Ah yes. I was talking to the gentleman wearing the fedora who sits all the way to the right.

OFELIA:   Peppino Mellini. He's the best buncher we have. He is from Napoli.[2] He has a soft spot for the love stories.
He is the one that sings Neapolitan songs at the end of the day.

JUAN JULIAN:   And I also met Palomo, the gentleman with the Panama hat.

CONCHITA:   My husband. He is a roller like us.

---

2. Or Naples, city in southwestern Italy.

OFELIA: And did you meet Manola?

JUAN JULIAN: Is she the lady with the picture of Valentino[3] on top of her table?

OFELIA: Yes, she does the stuffing. Oh, she's delighted that you are here. Sometimes she's a sea of tears when she listens to the stories.

JUAN JULIAN: And the gentleman with the handkerchief around his neck?

OFELIA: Ah, that's Pascual Torino from Spain. He does the wrapping. A nostalgic at heart, wants to go back to his country and die in Granada.[4]

JUAN JULIAN: And the gentleman that was just here?

MARELA: Chester is a clown.

[CONCHITA and MARELA laugh.]

OFELIA: Marela! We call him Cheché. He is my husband's half-brother. We didn't know he was part of the family, but one day he showed up at the factory with a birth certificate and said he was my father-in-law's son. So we took him in, and ever since, he's been part of the family. But he is really from a town up north. [Laughs.] My father-in-law got around.

JUAN JULIAN: I think that my presence offends him.

MARELA: Oh, that can't be. Don't pay him any mind.

JUAN JULIAN: When I entered the factory this morning he turned his back on me and then he . . .

MARELA: Cheché thinks he owns the factory. [Breaks into laughter.]

OFELIA: My husband has given him a little too much power. But it's my husband who really runs the factory.

CONCHITA: Don't mind him. Cheché has a knack for turning the smallest incident into a loud and tragic event.

JUAN JULIAN: But I didn't do anything to the man.

MARELA: He doesn't like lectors.

OFELIA: He doesn't understand the purpose of having someone like you read stories to the workers.

JUAN JULIAN: But that has always been the tradition.

CONCHITA: He's from another culture.

MARELA: He thinks that lectors are the ones who cause trouble.

JUAN JULIAN: Why? Because we read novels to the workers, because we educate them and inform them?

MARELA: No. It's more complicated than that. His wife ran away from home with a lector.

OFELIA: Marela! He doesn't need to know these things!

MARELA: But it's true. She disappeared one day with the lector that was working here. She was a southern belle from Atlanta and he was from Guanabacoa.[5] Her skin was pale like a lily and he was the color of saffron.

And of course, now Cheché is against all lectors and the love stories they read.

JUAN JULIAN: But he can't put the blame . . .

MARELA: Cheché thinks the love stories got under her skin. That's why she left him.

---

3. Rudolph Valentino (1895–1926), Italian-born American actor and sex symbol; known as "the Latin Lover."

4. A province in the autonomous community of Andalusia, Spain; also the capital of that province.

5. A municipality in Havana. Atlanta: capital of the U.S. state of Georgia.

OFELIA: That's enough, Marela! When all this happened the poor man was desperate, angry and sad. He couldn't accept reality, so he blamed the lectors and the love stories for his misfortune.

CONCHITA: If he's ever disrespectful you should talk to our father.

OFELIA: Don't you worry. I'll take care of him.

MARELA: What are you planning to read to us?

JUAN JULIAN: First, Tolstoy, *Anna Karenina*.[6]

MARELA: *Anna Karenina*. I already like the title. Is it romantic?

JUAN JULIAN: Yes. Quite romantic.

MARELA: Ah, *Anna Karenina* will go right to Cheché's heart. The poor man. He won't be able to take it.

JUAN JULIAN: I could pick another book. I've brought many.

CONCHITA: No, read *Anna Karenina* if that's the book that you chose.

MARELA: He needs to listen to another love story and let the words make nests in his hair, so he can find another woman.

OFELIA: And how do you like Tampa so far, Juan Julian?

JUAN JULIAN: Well, I . . . I . . . It's very . . . It seems like it's a city in the making.

OFELIA: That it is. We are still trying to create a little city that resembles the ones we left back in the island.

JUAN JULIAN: It's curious, there are no mountains or hills here. Lots of sky I have noticed . . . And clouds . . . The largest clouds I've ever seen, as if they had soaked up the whole sea. It's all so flat all around. That's why the sky seems so much bigger here and infinite. Bigger than the sky I know back home. And there's so much light. There doesn't seem to be a place where one could hide.

MARELA: One can always find shade in the park. There's always a hiding place to be found, and if not, one can always hide behind light.

JUAN JULIAN: Really. And how does one hide behind light?

[*The women laugh nervously.*]

MARELA: Depends what you are hiding from.

JUAN JULIAN: Perhaps light itself.

MARELA: Well, there are many kinds of light. The light of fires. The light of stars. The light that reflects off rivers. Light that penetrates through cracks. Then there's the type of light that reflects off the skin. Which one?

JUAN JULIAN: Perhaps the type that reflects off the skin.

MARELA: That's the most difficult one to escape.

[*The women laugh.* CHECHÉ *enters. He is still holding the shoe in his hand.*]

CHECHÉ: Ofelia, why didn't Santiago come to work today?

OFELIA: He went to Camacho's house. Is there a problem, Cheché?

CHECHÉ: No, I'd just like to talk about . . . Will he come by later?

OFELIA: I don't know. What's wrong with your foot?

CHECHÉ: Oh, it's a long story. You see . . . I . . .

OFELIA: Did you fall? Did you hurt yourself?

CHECHÉ: No. I . . . It's nothing.

OFELIA: I know my feet are worse each day. If it isn't a bunion hurting, it's an ingrown nail.

---

6. Novel (1873–77) by the Russian writer Leo Tolstoy (1828–1910).

CHECHÉ:  No, Ofelia. Nothing of the sort.

OFELIA:  Then why are you walking . . . ?

CHECHÉ:  Well, you see . . . My shoes for work . . . I . . . I took them to the shoemaker yesterday and they weren't ready today.

OFELIA:  So, these are new shoes and they hurt your feet.

CHECHÉ:  No, you see . . . I mean . . . Last night Santiago and I . . . We . . . You see, we went to the cockfights.

OFELIA:  Ha! That explains it. You lost all your money and your shoes.

CHECHÉ:  No, I didn't lose my money. Your husband lost all his money and some of mine.

[OFELIA *laughs.*]

OFELIA:  So are you giving me this shoe so I can throw it at him and break his head?

[*The women laugh.*]

CHECHÉ:  No, Ofelia . . . I . . .

OFELIA:  So what's with the shoe? Are you collecting alms? Instead of passing the bucket or the hat are you passing the shoe?

CHECHÉ:  Well, I'm sort of passing it to you.

OFELIA:  I don't have any money, Cheché.

CHECHÉ:  I'm not asking you for money.

[JUAN JULIAN *and the sisters exit.*]

OFELIA:  Then why are you pointing this thing at me?

CHECHÉ:  You see here. Right here, on the sole of my shoe, Santiago wrote how much he owes me.

OFELIA:  And how much does he owe you?

CHECHÉ:  The total is here.

[OFELIA *looks at the shoe.*]

OFELIA:  That's a lot of money.

CHECHÉ:  That's how much he owes me.

OFELIA:  Where did you get so much money?

CHECHÉ:  I was winning.

OFELIA:  And you drank and gave it all away.

CHECHÉ:  No. I . . . Well, he wanted to continue playing. He didn't want to walk home to get more money, so I lent him what I had. And he told me he'd sign my shoe and write the totals. And I trust that he'll pay me back.

OFELIA:  So what do you want me to do?

CHECHÉ:  Well, this here is a bill. A document.

OFELIA:  You're not serious!

CHECHÉ:  No. This here is an agreement. If he doesn't pay me . . . You see here. You see his initials . . . He signed this! He signed it! He told me that if he didn't pay me, another share of the factory would be mine.

OFELIA:  Get this thing out of my sight.

CHECHÉ:  But Ofelia . . .

OFELIA:  Get it out my sight, I said.

CHECHÉ:  But Ofelia . . .

OFELIA:  I don't know what went on between you and your brother, but I don't have anything to do with it. And you better go to a shoemaker and get your shoes mended.

[*Music plays. Lights change.*]

## Scene 3

JUAN JULIAN *strides around the cigar workers reading from Tolstoy's* Anna Karenina. *He reads with passion and fervor. The cigar workers roll, but are completely immersed in the story.*

JUAN JULIAN: [*Reading.*]

Looking at him, Anna Karenina felt a physical humiliation and could not say another word. Her beloved felt what a killer must feel when he looks at the body he has deprived of life. The body he had deprived of life was their love, the beginning of their love. There was something dreadful and revolting in the recollection of what had been paid for by this awful price of shame. The shame Anna sensed from their spiritual nakedness destroyed her and affected him. But in spite of the killer's horror when he faces the body of his victim, the killer must cut the body to pieces and conceal it, and he must make use of what he has gained by his crime. And with the same fury and passion as the killer throws himself upon the body and drags it and cuts it, he covered her face and shoulders with kisses. "Yes, these kisses—these kisses are what have been bought by my shame."[7]
　　[JUAN JULIAN *closes the book.*]
That's all for today from *Anna Karenina.*
　　[*The workers applaud.*]

MARELA: [*Still enraptured by the story.*]　Why does he always end when he gets to the good part?

OFELIA:　To keep us in suspense.

CONCHITA:　To keep us wanting more.

MARELA:　He's really a fine lector.

OFELIA:　That's why he's called the Persian Canary, because it's like hearing a bird sing when he reads.

MARELA:　And can you smell the cologne from his handkerchief every time he dries his forehead? The fragrance wraps itself around the words like smoke.

CHECHÉ: [*To* PALOMO.]　Oh Lord! Exactly what I expected. Now they'll sigh and chat about the love story for hours.

MARELA:　I heard that, Cheché.

CHECHÉ:　Oh, but this is the part I like the most, when you start discussing things. For some reason I never hear the story the same way that you do.

PALOMO:　Neither do I, but maybe that's because we're men.

MARELA:　You're being cynical.

CONCHITA:　Don't pay them any mind.

PALOMO:　No. I'd like to hear what you have to say.

CONCHITA:　Mamá, you did well in sending for him.

OFELIA:　Only a fool can fail to understand the importance of having a lector read to us while we work.

MARELA:　Well, Cheché is not very happy with him.

OFELIA:　That's because Cheché is a fool.

---

7. Part 2, Chapter 11. [Cruz's note]

CHECHÉ: Now I haven't said—

OFELIA: I heard what you told Palomo this morning and we're not going to do away with the lector.

CHECHÉ: All I said—

OFELIA: When I lived in Havana I don't remember ever seeing a tobacco factory without a lector. As a child I remember sitting in the back and listening to the stories. That has always been our pride. Some of us cigar workers might not be able to read or write, but we can recite lines from *Don Quixote* or *Jane Eyre*.[8]

CHECHÉ: All I said was that I'm afraid we're in for another tragic love story.

PALOMO: I like love stories.

MARELA: Me, too.

CHECHÉ: I would've preferred a detective story.

MARELA: They're not very literary, Chester.

CONCHITA: Well. I don't know about you, but ever since he started reading *Anna Karenina* my mind wanders to Russia.

MARELA: Me, too. I have dreams and they are full of white snow, and Anna Karenina is dancing waltzes with Vronsky. Then I see them in a little room, and all the snow melts from the heat of their bodies and their skin. And I just want to borrow a fur coat from my friend Cookie Salazar and go to Russia.

OFELIA: He chose the right book. There is nothing like reading a winter book in the middle of summer. It's like having a fan or an icebox by your side to relieve the heat and the caloric nights.

CHECHÉ: [*To* PALOMO.] Help me with the boxes.

[*The men exit.*]

MARELA: What was that last line? "And, as with fury and passion the killer throws himself upon . . ."

CONCHITA: "Upon the body," he said, "and drags it and cuts it, he covered her face and shoulders with kisses."

MARELA: Does it mean that when you're in love your body is stolen from life?

CONCHITA: No. The body robbed of life was their love. The love of Anna and her beloved.

OFELIA: It must be terrible living that way.

MARELA: Why?

OFELIA: How the three of them live! Anna, the husband and the lover. It must be a nightmare.

MARELA: Of course not!

[CONCHITA *refers to the story, but also to her own life.*]

CONCHITA: Yes. Anna said it herself. It's like a curse, she said. She was talking about it at the end, when she said that his kisses have been bought by her shame. She's got to be miserable.

MARELA: Miserable? Enraptured maybe.

OFELIA: You don't listen to the story, Marela.

MARELA: Of course I listen to the story.

---

8. Novel (1847) by the English writer Charlotte Brontë (1816–1855). *Don Quixote*: novel (1605, 1615) by the Spanish writer Miguel de Cervantes (1547–1616).

CONCHITA: Then you ought to know that it is misery for her. It's pure agony for Anna's husband and for the lover, too. They probably couldn't endure it any longer, if it weren't for some kind of hope.

MARELA: Then why would she take on a lover?

OFELIA: She has no choice. It's something she can't escape. That's why the writer describes love as a thief. The thief is the mysterious fever that poets have been studying for years. Remember Anna Karenina's last words.

CONCHITA: She never remembers anything.

MARELA: I do. I just don't cling to every word the way you do. I don't try to understand everything they say. I let myself be taken. When Juan Julian starts reading, the story enters my body and I become the second skin of the characters.

OFELIA: Don't be silly.

MARELA: We can always dream.

OFELIA: Ah yes. But we have to take a yardstick and measure our dreams.

MARELA: Then I will need a very long yardstick. The kind that could measure the sky.

CONCHITA: How foolish you are, Marela!

MARELA: [To CONCHITO.] No, everything in life dreams. A bicycle dreams of becoming a boy, an umbrella dreams of becoming the rain, a pearl dreams of becoming a woman, and a chair dreams of becoming a gazelle and running back to the forest.

OFELIA: But, my child, people like us . . . We have to remember to keep our feet on the ground and stay living inside our shoes and not have lofty illusions.

[A bell rings. PALOMO enters.]

Ah, workday has come to an end. Good. I rolled more than two hundred cigars today.

MARELA: And I've wedded more than a thousand. That's what I like about putting the bands around the cigars. It's like marrying all these men without actually seeing them.

OFELIA: Men marry their cigars, my dear, and the white smoke becomes the veil of their brides. My mother used to say, "When a man marries, he marries two women, his bride and his cigar." Are you coming, Conchita?

CONCHITA: No. Palomo and I are working till late.

OFELIA: We'll see you for dinner. Adios.

CONCHITA: Adios.

OFELIA: Till later, Palomo.

PALOMO: Adios.

MARELA: Adios.

PALOMO: Is your father in trouble again and that's why . . . ?

CONCHITA: He is.

PALOMO: How much did he lose this time?

CONCHITA: Plenty.

PALOMO: Plenty can be a lot of money.

CONCHITA: Yes, you're right. And I don't know what good he gets from losing all that money.

PALOMO: Oh, that's something we'll never know. [Beginning to roll.]

CONCHITA: And how do you like the novel that Juan Julian is reading to us?

PALOMO: I like it very much.

CONCHITA: Doesn't it make you uncomfortable?

PALOMO: Why would it make me uncomfortable?

CONCHITA: The part about the lover.

PALOMO: It seems like in every novel there's always a love affair.

CONCHITA: And do you ever think about everything that's happening between Anna Karenina and her husband?

PALOMO: I do . . . But I . . .

CONCHITA: So what goes through your mind when you listen to the story?

PALOMO: I think of the money all those people have.

CONCHITA: You would say something like that.

PALOMO: Why? Because I like money?

CONCHITA: I'm talking about literature and you talk about money.

PALOMO: And what do you want me to say?

CONCHITA: I want you to talk about the story, the characters . . .

PALOMO: Wouldn't you like to have all the money they have? So you don't have to spend the whole day rolling cigars and working after hours so we can save money and have our own business.

CONCHITA: I don't mind rolling cigars.

PALOMO: And what's so good about rolling cigars?

CONCHITA: My mind wanders to other places.

PALOMO: What places?

CONCHITA: Places and things money can't buy.

PALOMO: Money can buy everything.

CONCHITA: Not the places I go to in my mind.

PALOMO: And what kind of places are you talking about?

CONCHITA: Places made of dreams.

PALOMO: [Laughs; becoming playful.] You're a strange creature, Conchita. I don't know why I married you.

CONCHITA: You married me because the day you met me, I gave you a cigar I had rolled especially for you and when you smoked it, you told me I had slipped into your mouth like a pearl diver.

PALOMO: I told you that?

CONCHITA: Yes, you did. After blowing a blue ring of smoke out of your mouth. And the words lingered in the air like a zeppelin and I thought to myself, I could fall in love with that mouth.

PALOMO: As far as I can remember, I married you because I couldn't untie your father's hands from around my neck.

CONCHITA: Ah, the truth comes out. That explains everything. You never really cared for me.

PALOMO: Are you trying to start a fight?

CONCHITA: No. I asked you a simple question about a love story and you're being foolish.

PALOMO: Never mind.

CONCHITA: You don't care about anything, do you? Juan Julian could be reading a book by José Martí[9] or Shakespeare and everything goes in one ear and out the other.

9. See p. 265.

PALOMO:  I pay attention to what he reads.
I just don't take everything to heart the way you do.
CONCHITA:  Well, you should. Do you remember that part of the book in which Anna Karenina's husband is suspicious of her having an affair with Vronsky? Remember when he paces the room, like a lost animal.
PALOMO:  I know what you're getting at.
CONCHITA:  I just want to have a civilized conversation. The same way the characters speak to each other in the novel. I've learned many things from this book.
PALOMO:  Such as?
CONCHITA:  Jealousy. For Anna's husband jealousy is base and almost animalistic. And he's right. He would never want Anna to think that he's capable of such vile and shameful emotions.
PALOMO:  But you can't help being jealous. It's part of your nature.
CONCHITA:  Not anymore.
PALOMO:  Well, that's a change.
CONCHITA:  Oh, I could see the husband so clear in the novel. How the thoughts would take shape in his mind, as they have in my own mind. I mean, not the same . . . No, no . . . Not the same, because he's an educated man, surrounded by culture and wealth, and I'm just a cigar roller in a factory. He is well bred and sophisticated. I barely get by in life.
But with this book I'm seeing everything through new eyes. What is happening in the novel has been happening to us.
No. Don't look at me that way. You might not want to admit it, but Anna and her husband remind me of us. Except I'm more like the husband.
PALOMO:  So what does that make me then, Anna Karenina?
CONCHITA:  You are the one who has the secret love, not me.
PALOMO:  Oh, come on. It's late. Let's go home. I can't work like this.
CONCHITA:  That's exactly what Anna said when the husband confronted her about the lover: "It's late. Let's go to sleep."
PALOMO:  I think you're taking this a little too far.
CONCHITA:  Am I? Have you ever heard the voice of someone who's deaf? The voice is crude and ancient, because it has no sense of direction or place, because it doesn't hear itself and it doesn't know if anybody else in the world hears it. Sometimes I want to have a long conversation with you, like this. Like a deaf person. As if I couldn't hear you or myself. But I would just talk and talk, and say everything that comes to my mind, like a shell that shouts with the voice of the sea and it doesn't care if anybody ever hears it. That's how I want to speak to you, and ask you things.
PALOMO:  And what's the use of talking like this? What sort of things do you want to ask me?
CONCHITA:  Things that you wouldn't tell me, afraid that I might not understand.
PALOMO:  Like what?
CONCHITA:  I'd like to know what she's like. And what does she do to make you happy?
PALOMO:  Ah, let's go home.
CONCHITA:  Why?
PALOMO: [Abruptly.]  Because I don't want to talk about these things!
     [A pause.]

CONCHITA: So what's going to happen to us, Palomo?

PALOMO: I don't know. Do you want a divorce? We could travel to Reno[1] and be divorced in six weeks. But your family will be opposed to it, and the same with mine. So divorce is out of the question.

CONCHITA: And if I tell you that I want to cut my hair, change the way I dress and take on a lover.

PALOMO: Say that again?

CONCHITA: What I just said.

PALOMO: You want to have a lover?

CONCHITA: Yes, like you do.

PALOMO: Ave Maria purissima!

CONCHITA: I have the same right as you do.

PALOMO: This book will be the end of us.

CONCHITA: Don't you think we've already come to the end?

PALOMO: No . . . I . . .

CONCHITA: You don't make love to me like you used to.

PALOMO: Well, we . . . You and I . . . We . . .

CONCHITA: It's all right, Palomo. It's all right. [*She touches his arm.*] There's something that Anna Karenina said and I keep repeating it to myself: "If there are as many minds as there are heads, then there are as many kinds of love as there are hearts."[2] I can try to love you in a different way. I can do that. And you should try to do the same.

[*Music plays. Lights change.*]

## Scene 4

*A square of light on the floor suggests the interior of the family's house.* OFELIA *and* SANTIAGO *are not on speaking terms. She sits on one side of the room, he sits on the other.* MARELA *stands by* SANTIAGO. *The dialogue moves fast.* MARELA *runs back and forth as a communicator.*

SANTIAGO: Ask your mother for some money to buy me a pack of cigarettes. She's not talking to me.

MARELA: Papá wants money for a pack of cigarettes.

OFELIA: Ask him when is he going back to work.

MARELA: She wants to know when you're going back to work.

SANTIAGO: Tell her as soon as I get money from Camacho to pay Cheché.

MARELA: He says as soon as he gets money from Camacho to pay Cheché.

OFELIA: Tell him to give up smoking till then, that I'm not giving him any money.

SANTIAGO: What did she say?

MARELA: She says—

SANTIAGO: I heard her. [*In loud voice, to* OFELIA.] Tell her that she's insane!

MARELA: He says you're insane.

OFELIA: And tell him he's a drunk, a thief and a-good-for-nothing gambler.

MARELA: She says—

1. City in Nevada.    2. Part 2, Chapter 7. [Cruz's note]

SANTIAGO: I heard.

MARELA: He heard you, Mamá.

OFELIA: Good!

MARELA: Good, she says.

SANTIAGO: You're a crazy woman! Crazy woman!

OFELIA: Tell him I didn't hear that. I told him I don't want him to talk to me.

SANTIAGO: Ah, she heard me!

OFELIA: Tell him I don't want to hear his barbarisms.

MARELA: Did you hear that, Papá? She doesn't want to hear your barbarisms.

SANTIAGO: Tell her . . .

[MARELA *starts to walk toward her father.*]

OFELIA: [*Infuriated.*] Come here, Marela . . .

[MARELA *walks toward her mother.*]

SANTIAGO: Marela, come here . . .

MARELA: Wait! It's not your turn, Mamá.

OFELIA: Marela . . .

MARELA: Stop! I can't be here and there at the same time!

[*Silence.* OFELIA *and* SANTIAGO *shake their heads as if giving up on the whole thing.*] ⏐

OFELIA AND SANTIAGO: This is insane!

MARELA: Well, you both heard that.

[MARELA *tries to put in a word, but they don't give her a chance.*]

SANTIAGO: Tell her I'm going to a pawnshop to sell my wedding ring. ⏐

OFELIA: Tell him he should've done that a long time ago.

SANTIAGO: She's right, I should've done it a long time ago.

OFELIA: Yes, before his finger got numb.

SANTIAGO: She's right, my finger got numb.

OFELIA: You see, I was right. Numb, like everything else.

SANTIAGO: She's wrong. Not like everything else.

OFELIA: Nothing works on his body. Just his rotten teeth to chew away money.

MARELA: I'm leaving.

OFELIA: Marela!

SANTIAGO: Marela!

MARELA: You can fight without me!

[MARELA *walks out of the room. Silence.*

*Then,* OFELIA *and* SANTIAGO *begin to speak to each other without looking at each other.*]

SANTIAGO: I've been listening to the new lector from up here.

OFELIA: You have?

SANTIAGO: He's good. He has a solid voice, and I like the novel that he's reading.

OFELIA: Yes, a solid voice he has, and I like the novel, too.

SANTIAGO: I 'specially like the character that lives in the countryside.

OFELIA: [*With delight.*] Yes.

SANTIAGO: Yes, him.

OFELIA: The one that has the farm?

SANTIAGO: Yes. The one that has the farm. What is his name?

OFELIA: His name is Levin.

SANTIAGO: That's right, Levin.

OFELIA: The one that lives in the forest surrounded by trees.

SANTIAGO: That Levin reminds me of when I was young and my father left me to run the factory. It seems as if Levin has dedicated his whole life to his farm.

OFELIA: Yes, he's a dedicated man.

SANTIAGO: I used to be like him.

OFELIA: Yes, you used to be like him.

SANTIAGO: I like the part of the book when Anna's brother is going to sell the estate next to Levin's property and Levin counsels him not to sell it.

OFELIA: Yes, that's a good part. And I can't believe that you almost gave another share of the factory to Cheché.

SANTIAGO: You're right, I lost my mind. I shouldn't drink.

OFELIA: That's right, drink you shouldn't. That's an idiotic thing to do, give away another share of the business. Cheché doesn't know what he's doing. He's like a scarecrow. He's been talking about bringing machines and replacing some of the workers. You need to go back to the factory.

SANTIAGO: Yes, you're right. To the factory I need to go back.

[OFELIA *looks at him.*]

OFELIA: Santiago, what's eating you? You haven't gone to work. You don't eat. You don't sleep well.

SANTIAGO: I've acted like a fool, Ofelia. I'm ashamed of myself and I'm angry and bitter. And I can't shake off this damn agony!

OFELIA: Do you want me to call a doctor?

SANTIAGO: No. I don't need a doctor.

OFELIA: But you can't go on like this. Sooner or later you have to go back and face the workers.

SANTIAGO: I will. When I get the money and I can face Cheché.

OFELIA: And are you going to stay here until then?

SANTIAGO: Yes.

OFELIA: That's silly.

SANTIAGO: That's the way I am.

OFELIA: Well, I'm going to bed.

[OFELIA *starts to exit.*]

SANTIAGO: Ofelia.

OFELIA: Yes.

SANTIAGO: Stay up a while longer.

OFELIA: I'm tired. You didn't work like I did today.

SANTIAGO: Talk to me about the novel. I can't always hear very well from up here. This fellow, Levin . . . This character that I admire . . . He's the one who is in love with the young girl in the story, isn't he?

OFELIA: [*A burst of energy.*] Ah yes! He's in love with Kitty. Levin is in love with Kitty, and Kitty is in love with Vronsky. And Vronsky is in love with Anna Karenina. And Anna Karenina is married, but she's in love with Vronsky. Ay, everybody is in love in this book!

SANTIAGO: But for Levin . . . For Levin there's only one woman.

OFELIA: Yes, for him there's only one woman.

SANTIAGO: [*Full of love, he looks at her.*] Ofelia.

OFELIA: Yes.

[SANTIAGO *swallows the gulp of love.*]

SANTIAGO: No. Nothing.

OFELIA: [*Fanning herself.*] Ah, the night breeze is making its way to us again. There's nothing like this Tampa breeze, always a punctual visitor around this time.

SANTIAGO: You know, Ofelia, when I gamble I try to repeat the same motions . . . I try to repeat everything I did the day I won. And when I lose I try to take inventory of what I did wrong. I think to myself, Did I get up from bed with my left foot first? Did I forget to polish my shoes? Did I leave the house in a state of disorder? Was I unkind to someone, and that's why luck didn't come my way? Lately, I've been in a fog and I don't know what to do.

Every time I lose, I feel that something has been taken from me. Something bigger than money. And I see a line of little ants carrying breadcrumbs on their backs. But the crumbs they are taking away are my pride and my self-respect. My dignity. [*Looks at her again.*] Have I lost you too, Ofelia? Have I lost you?

OFELIA: If you had lost me, I wouldn't be here. If you had lost me, I wouldn't be by your side. How can you say that you've lost me! [*She hugs him.*]

[*Music plays. Lights change.*]

, Scene 5

JUAN JULIAN, MARELA *and* CONCHITA *at the factory.*

JUAN JULIAN: I don't really like cities. In the country one has freedom. When I'm in a city I feel asphyxiated. I feel constriction in my lungs. The air feels thick and dense, as if the buildings breathe and steal away the oxygen. As my father used to say, living in a city is like living inside the mouth of a crocodile, buildings all around you like teeth. The teeth of culture, the mouth and tongue of civilization. It's a silly comparison, but it makes sense to me.

Every time I go to a park, I'm reminded of how we always go back to nature. We build streets and buildings. We work five to six days a week, building and cementing our paths and down come tumbling trees and nests, a whole paradise of insects. And all for what? On Sundays we return to a park where we could still find greenery. The verdure of nature.

CONCHITA: You're right. I don't know what I would do without my walks to the park. Why did you choose to read Tolstoy?

JUAN JULIAN: Because Tolstoy understands humanity like no other writer does.

CONCHITA: That's a good enough reason to read him.

JUAN JULIAN: Someone told me that at the end of his life, when he knew he was going to die, he abandoned his house and he was found dead at a train station. The same as . . .

Oh, perhaps I shouldn't tell you this.

CONCHITA: He was probably on his way to visit God.

JUAN JULIAN: That has always been my suspicion.

MARELA: Pardon me, but I must go. [*She exits.*]

[*There is an awkward pause as* JUAN JULIAN *and* CONCHITA *watch* MARELA *leave.*]

CONCHITA: How did you become a lector?

JUAN JULIAN: I discovered books one summer. My father owed a lot of money to a creditor and we had to close ourselves up in our house and hide for a while. For my family, keeping up appearances was important. We had to pretend that we had gone away on a trip. We told neighbors that my mother was ill and she had to recuperate somewhere else. We stayed in that closed-up house for more than two months, while my father worked abroad. I remember it was hot and all the windows were kept closed. The heat was unbearable. The maid was the only one who went out to buy groceries. And while being closed up in our own home my mother read books to the family. And that's when I became a listener and I learned to appreciate stories and the sound of words. [*Smiles.*] Have you ever been to New England?

CONCHITA: No.

JUAN JULIAN: I always wanted to go there. I wonder what New Englanders are like. Here I have met workers from other parts of the world, but I haven't met anybody from up North.

CONCHITA: Cheché is from up North.

JUAN JULIAN: Cheché is from a world of his own.

CONCHITA: I knew a fellow from New London.[3] He was modest and reserved. So shy was this boy, that when he expressed any sort of feeling, he would excuse himself. [*Laughs.*] One day I gave him a braid that I'd cut from my hair and told him to bury it under a tree. I explained to him that back in the island most women cut their hair once a year on the 2nd of February, when plants and trees are pruned, for the feast of Saint Candelaria.[4] I told him how women offer their hair to the earth and the trees, for all the greenery and fruits to come. And I gave him my little braid in a box and told him to choose a tree in the park.

And the boy looked at me with a strange face and said that he would feel embarrassed digging a hole in the middle of the park, in front of everybody. And that's when I took my braid back from him, took a shovel, dug a hole and put him to shame. From then on he never talked to me again. So he's the only person from New England that I've met.

[PALOMO *enters. He watches from a distance.*]

JUAN JULIAN: [*Laughs.*] And do you still cut your hair every 2nd of February?

CONCHITA: Yes. My father always does me the honor of burying it.

JUAN JULIAN: Your father! And why not your husband? It should be an honor for any man . . . If I were your husband I would find an old, wise, banyan tree and I would bury your hair by its roots, and I'm sure it would accept the offering like rainwater.

CONCHITA: Well, I'm cutting my hair short like Clara Bow,[5] and that will be the end of the ritual.

---

3. City in Connecticut.
4. *Nuestra Señora de la Candelaria* (Our Lady of Candelaria); in the Afro-Caribbean religious tradition Santería, identified with Oya, the African

female warrior and spirit of wind, storm, and magic.
5. American movie actress (1905–1965) famous for wearing her hair in a bob.

JUAN JULIAN:   I would offer to find a strong-looking tree. But the ritual won't count if it's not done on February 2nd.

CONCHITA:   I believe everything counts if you have faith.

JUAN JULIAN:   So are you telling me that I should pick a strong-looking tree?

CONCHITA:   Yes, if you wish.

JUAN JULIAN:   And why me?

CONCHITA:   Because you offer to. And you are the reader of the love stories, and anybody who dedicates his life to reading books believes in rescuing things from oblivion.

JUAN JULIAN:   So is there a story in your hair?

CONCHITA:   There will be the day I cut it, and that story will come to an end.

JUAN JULIAN:   And how does one read the story of your hair?

CONCHITA:   The same way one reads a face or a book.

JUAN JULIAN:   Then we shouldn't bury your hair under a tree. We should place it inside a manuscript. The same way Victorian women used to press flowers or a lock of hair between the pages of a book.

CONCHITA:   Then I would leave it to you to choose the book.

JUAN JULIAN:   How about this one?

CONCHITA:   My hair will be in good company with *Anna Karenina*.

JUAN JULIAN:   Then close your eyes and choose a page.

[CONCHITA *closes her eyes. She opens the book and chooses a page.* JUAN JULIAN *reads:*]

At first Anna sincerely thought that she was annoyed because he insisted on pursuing her; but very soon after her return from Moscow, when she went to an evening party where she expected to see him, but which he did not attend, she came to the realization by the sadness that overwhelmed her, that she was deceiving herself.[6]

CONCHITA:   Then here, cut my hair.

[CONCHITA *hands him the scissors. She loosens her hair and turns her back to him. He combs her hair with his fingers. He kisses her shoulder. She then turns around to return his kiss.*]

## Act Two

### Scene 1

*Darkness. Music.*

*As the lights start to come up, we hear the recorded voice of the lector narrating a passage from* Anna Karenina.

JUAN JULIAN:   [*Recorded voice.*]

Anna Karenina had stepped into a new life and she could not convey through words her sense of shame, rapture and horror, and she did not

---

6. Part 2, Chapter 4. [Cruz's note]

want to talk about it and profane this feeling through simple words. And as time passed by, the next day and the next, she still could not find the proper words to express the complexity of her feelings, and could not even find thoughts with which to reflect on all that was in her soul.[7]

[JUAN JULIAN *and* CONCHITA *are at the factory making love. She is lying on top of a table, half naked, her skirt tucked up. He is there between her legs, shirtless and full of sweat. They have transgressed the limits of their bodies, and he now kisses her gently.*]
I'd like to stop seeing you here.

CONCHITA: And where do you want to meet?

JUAN JULIAN: In my room where we could be—

CONCHITA: That would be impossible.

[*They start dressing.*]

JUAN JULIAN: Then we should meet in a hotel.

CONCHITA: Hotels are cold and impersonal like hospitals.

JUAN JULIAN: Like hospitals?

CONCHITA: Yes. Every guest is looking for a remedy, whether it's a temporary relief from the world or a temporary rest from life.

JUAN JULIAN: [*Touching her face playfully.*] Then we should meet in a hospital, because sometimes I detect sad trees in your eyes after we make love.

CONCHITA: Then I must have a terrible malady.

JUAN JULIAN: Yes, and I recommend that you buy a canary and hear it sing five minutes a day . . . [*He starts kissing her neck.*]

CONCHITA: And what if I can't find a canary?

JUAN JULIAN: Then you must come hear me sing when I take a shower.

[*We hear people outside.*]

CONCHITA: Go . . . Go . . . Someone's coming . . . Go . . .

[*We hear* CHECHÉ *in an argument.* JUAN JULIAN *takes his shirt and rushes out.* CONCHITA *fixes her dress and her hair, then runs to sit at her table.*]

CHECHÉ: Wait . . . wait . . . You don't let me finish!!! You don't let me finish!!! That's one of the problems that we have, I own shares in this factory and now that your husband . . .

[*The cigar workers enter and gather around* CHECHÉ. *Next to him is a large machine wrapped in paper.*

*There is a heated controversy over the machine. We hear the workers complaining.*]

OFELIA: I'm the owner of the factory and I have the last word . . .

CHECHÉ: But Ofelia . . .

OFELIA: Someone go upstairs and call Santiago!

CHECHÉ: Ofelia . . . All I'm trying to say is that all these other companies are succeeding . . .

PALOMO: But, Cheché, that has nothing to do with machines . . .

OFELIA: I don't want to listen to this. He's not the owner of this factory. Will someone call my husband!

[CHECHÉ *stands up on a chair and addresses the crowd:*]

---

7. Part 2, Chapter 11. [Cruz's note]

CHECHÉ: Just let me talk!!! Let's back up here! I'm trying to make a point, and you don't let me speak . . .

MARELA: Let the man talk, Mamá!

CHECHÉ: Ofelia . . . Ofelia . . . All these other cigar companies have the leads. I can name them all: Caprichos, Entreactos, Petit Bouquet, Regalia de Salón, Coquetas, Conchas Finas . . . They all have the leads . . .

OFELIA: Bah! They don't roll cigars like we do.

CHECHÉ: It doesn't matter how they roll their cigars. That's what I'm trying to tell you.

OFELIA: It matters to us.

CHECHÉ: Then we're never going to get anywhere.

OFELIA: And who's in a hurry to get anywhere? Are you going somewhere, Conchita?

CONCHITA: No.

OFELIA: Are you going somewhere, Palomo?

PALOMO: I wouldn't mind going to the Canary Islands[8] to see my grandma . . .

    *[Laughter from the crowd.]*

OFELIA: In that case I want to go to Spain . . .

MARELA: And I'd like to go to Russia . . .

    *[Laughter from the crowd.]*

    JUAN JULIAN *enters.]*

CHECHÉ: I'm not joking. I'm talking about the modern world. Modernity. Progress. Advancement.

OFELIA: If working with machines means being modern then we're not interested in the modern world.

    *[Applause from the workers.]*

CONCHITA: Bravo!

CHECHÉ: Do you want to see our sales records? Do you want to see our records?

OFELIA: I don't have to see the sales records. I know how much we sell, and we're not doing that badly.

CHECHÉ: How can we be doing well when we had to let go of two employees?

MARELA: One employee, Cheché. The other one was your wife, and she left of her own accord.

    *[Laughter from the workers.]*

CHECHÉ: My point is that machines . . .

PALOMO: Machines are stealing our jobs.

MARELA: That's right.

    *[The crowd is getting anxious.]*

CHECHÉ: I've been given more shares in this factory. I'm—*[He is interrupted.]* Wait a second. And from now on I'm going to set things straight. *[Another interruption.]* Hold on! Do you want to know the problems we have with our factory? Do you want to know? We are stuck in time. And why are we stuck in time? We are operating in the same manner that we were twenty, thirty, fifty years ago . . . *[Another interruption.]* Hold on . . . Hold on . . . And why are we stuck? We are stuck because we are

8. Archipelago in the Atlantic Ocean, off North Africa, that belongs to Spain.

not part of the new century. Because we are still rolling cigars the same way that Indians rolled them hundreds of years ago. I mean, we might as well wear feathers and walk half naked with bones in our noses. There are machines that do tobacco stuffing at the speed of light: bunching machines, stripping machines . . .

OFELIA: And with all those machines, do they have any workers left?

CHECHÉ: Are you kidding me! The workers operate the machines. The workers run the machines.

PALOMO: Leonardo over at the Aurora factory says . . .

CHECHÉ: Ah, Leonardo is a lector! What does he know about machines?

PALOMO: He doesn't talk about machines like you do. But I can tell you what he says. He's always talking about maintaining our ways. Our methods. The old process we use. What we brought with us from the island. [*Raises his hands.*] We brought these to roll our cigars, so we don't need an apparatus or whatever you want to call it . . .

[*Assertive comments from the crowd.*]

CHECHÉ: Leonardo is a lector. That's why he doesn't value machines. The lectors are being fired from all the factories, because nobody can hear them read over the sound of the machines. And that's another thing I wanted to talk about. I don't know about the rest of you, but I'm not interested in giving any more money from my pocket, from my wages to listen to a lector read me romantic novels.

CONCHITA: It's literature, Cheché.

[PALOMO *looks at his wife, then turns to look at* JUAN JULIAN.]

CHECHÉ: Literature, romance novels . . . It's all the same to me . . .

MARELA: No. It's not the same. We learn things. And the words he reads are like a breeze that breaks the monotony of this factory.

CHECHÉ: Well, some of these companies have done away . . .

JUAN JULIAN: Señor Chester, allow me to say something. My father used to say that the tradition of having readers in the factories goes back to the Taino Indians. He used to say that tobacco leaves whisper the language of the sky. And that's because through the language of cigar smoke the Indians used to communicate to the gods. Obviously I'm not an Indian, but as a lector I am a distant relative of the Cacique, the Chief Indian, who used to translate the sacred words of the deities. The workers are the oidores. The ones who listen quietly, the same way Taino Indians used to listen. And this is the tradition that you're trying to destroy with your machine. Instead of promoting and popularizing machines, why don't you advertise our cigars? Or are you working for the machine industry?

OFELIA: He's right. We need more advertising, so we can sell more cigars.

JUAN JULIAN: Let's face it, Chester, workers, cigars aren't popular anymore. Moving pictures now feature their stars smoking cigarettes: Valentino, Douglas Fairbanks[9] . . . They are all smoking little fags[1] and not cigars. You can go to Hollywood and offer our cigars to producers.

CHECHÉ: You're being cynical . . .

JUAN JULIAN: No, I'm warning you. This fast mode of living with machines and moving cars affects cigar consumption. And do you want to know

---

9. American movie actor (1883–1939).      1. Slang for cigarettes.

why, Señor Chester? Because people prefer a quick smoke, the kind you get from a cigarette. The truth is that machines, cars, are keeping us from taking walks and sitting on park benches, smoking a cigar slowly and calmly. The way they should be smoked. So you see, Chester, you want modernity, and modernity is actually destroying our very own industry. The very act of smoking a cigar.

[*All the workers applaud except for* CHECHÉ *and* PALOMO.]

OFELIA: Bravo!

JUAN JULIAN: I can certainly step out of the room if you want to take a vote.

[JUAN JULIAN *puts his hat on and starts to exit.*]

OFELIA: You don't have to go out of the room. It's obvious that we want you to stay.

JUAN JULIAN: No, let's do it the democratic way. We are in America. I'll step out of the room and you vote. Go ahead, Chester.

[SANTIAGO *enters.*]

SANTIAGO: What's going on here?

OFELIA: Ah, good! I'm glad you're here. We are about to take a vote.

SANTIAGO: What are you voting for?

OFELIA: Machines. Cheché brought a stuffing machine.

SANTIAGO: And do the workers want machines?

WORKERS: [*In unison.*] No.

SANTIAGO: So what are you voting for?

OFELIA: To do it the American way.

SANTIAGO: And what's the American way if everybody said no?

OFELIA: You talk to Cheché. Everything has gone up to his head. He also wants to get rid of the lector.

CHECHÉ: Wait a minute . . .

SANTIAGO: Is that true, Cheché?

CHECHÉ: I asked the workers if they wanted to continue to pay for the lector. That's all I did.

JUAN JULIAN: And I was about to go out, so the workers could vote.

SANTIAGO: You don't have to go anywhere. You stay here. I am glad to meet you. I am Santiago.

JUAN JULIAN: Juan Julian Rios, at your service

SANTIAGO: [*To the workers.*] I've heard that many factories are getting rid of their lectors. But is this what we want, workers? Let's raise our hands if this is what we want.

[CHECHÉ *and* PALOMO *are the only ones who raise their hands.* CONCHITA *is shocked to see* PALOMO's *decision.*]

Two votes. Then that's the answer. We are not getting rid of Juan Julian. And I have good news, workers. We are coming up with a new cigar brand and it will be called Anna Karenina.

OFELIA: Bravo!

SANTIAGO: And Marela, if you will do us the honor, I would like you to pose as Anna Karenina for the label.

MARELA: Me?

SANTIAGO: If you like.

MARELA: Of course!

SANTIAGO: Here are some clothes for you to wear.

[SANTIAGO *gives her a box. She opens the box, which contains an elegant winter coat with fur trimming and a fancy fur hat.*]

MARELA:  I'll go try them on. [*She exits.*]

[SANTIAGO *addresses the workers:*]

SANTIAGO:  Tomorrow we will start making plans for production. We have much work ahead of us, workers. But I promise that we will all benefit from the fruit of our work. I'm glad to be back.

[*Applause from the workers. They exit.* CHECHÉ *pulls* SANTIAGO *aside.* SANTIAGO *hands him an envelope.*]

What are you voting for?

CHECHÉ:  Santiago, what is this new cigar brand that you're talking about? We don't have the money . . .

SANTIAGO:  And what is this apparatus that you've brought to our factory?

CHECHÉ:  Santiago, the sales are down. You haven't been here . . . The price of tobacco coming from Cuba is sky high . . .

SANTIAGO:  Should we spend our money buying machines then?

CHECHÉ:  We can benefit . . .

SANTIAGO:  It's out of the question. Return that apparatus to the factory where you got it from. And get me a calendar.

CHECHÉ:  But Santiago. . . .

SANTIAGO:  Here's your money. I got a loan, Cheché. This time I'm betting my money on the factory. Get me a calendar, I said.

[CHECHÉ *runs to get a calendar. He hands it to* SANTIAGO.]

What's today's date?

CHECHÉ:  The twenty-first.

SANTIAGO:  How can it be the twenty-first when you've already crossed out the twenty-first on the calendar?

CHECHÉ:  That's how I do it.

SANTIAGO:  You've already crossed out today's date!

CHECHÉ:  I know.

SANTIAGO:  You might have a problem, Cheché.

CHECHÉ:  And what kind of problem do you think I might have?

SANTIAGO:  You are crossing out the new day before you start taking part in it.

CHECHÉ:  What's the use anyway when nothing changes in this place?

SANTIAGO:  That's not a good attitude.

CHECHÉ:  Then what do you want me to do?

SANTIAGO:  For one thing, get rid of this crap. Why don't you get the kind of calendar I have? The kind that you tear off the pages.

CHECHÉ:  And do you think the page of a calendar can make a difference in one's life?

SANTIAGO:  Of course. Something as simple as crossing out your days before you live them can have an effect on the mind. It can cause apprehension, anxiety and even despair.

CHECHÉ:  Then I'm going straight to hell, 'cause everything here feels the same. Today feels like yesterday and the day before that.

SANTIAGO:  What in the world is wrong with you, Cheché?

CHECHÉ:  This factory. I can't stand it. Working here is like hitting my head against a wall . . . I try to make changes, modernize this place. But it's like facing a wall of concrete every time I try to do something.

SANTIAGO:  Is that what it is, Chester?

CHECHÉ:  Well, then there's Mildred. Ever since she left me I'm not the same. Something is missing. Have you ever seen the tail of a lizard when it's been cut off? The tail twists and moves from side to side like a worm that's been removed from the soil. The thing moves on its own, like a nerve that still has life and it's looking for the rest of the body that's been slashed away. That's how I feel sometimes. I turn from side to side on my bed at night.

I wake up in the morning looking for her in the kitchen, thinking that she's there making coffee. I look for her in the garden. And then when I come here there's this moron reading the same story every day to remind me of her.

And I hate it! I hate him! It's like there's no end to it, and I just want to . . .

> [MARELA *enters wearing the elegant coat and fur hat. She does a turn, feeling the smooth material of the coat, enjoying the warmth it provides.*]

MARELA:  How do I look, Papá?

SANTIAGO:  You'll make a great Anna. But you have to wear a flower in your hair and make her look like one of our women. I'll get you a flower, my dear.

We'll talk later, Chester. We need to talk.

> [SANTIAGO *exits.* CHECHÉ *turns to* MARELA. *He contemplates her beauty.* MARELA *looks at her clothes and then she does a turn, as if she were dancing a waltz.*]

MARELA:  Well, do you think I can pose for the label?

CHECHÉ:  You look beautiful.

> [JUAN JULIAN *enters.*]

JUAN JULIAN:  Ah, who is this Russian lady?

MARELA:  Do I pass the test?

JUAN JULIAN:  You look wonderful. Your father is right in choosing you. It's going to be a great picture.

I'm looking for my book. I think I left it here.

MARELA:  I didn't see it.

JUAN JULIAN: [*Looking around.*]  No. It's not here. I must've left it outside. [*He exits.*]

> [MARELA *takes off the coat and hat. Then she takes out a box and starts pasting magazine cutouts on her work table.*]

CHECHÉ:  Are you staying until late tonight?

MARELA:  I am.

CHECHÉ:  I'm going over the books. And you?

MARELA:  I'm decorating my table with pictures I like. Photographs of movie stars, and this of a street in Moscow, so I can picture the people in the novel walking through it.

CHECHÉ:  You're really obsessed with this book.

MARELA:  I am.

CHECHÉ:  Just the book or the lector?

MARELA:  That's none of your business.

CHECHÉ:  But it is. I've been watching you while you work.

MARELA:  And what are you doing looking at me when I work?

CHECHÉ:  You have to pay less attention to the reader and more attention to what you're doing.

MARELA: Oh, you're just trying to find any excuse to get rid of the lector. Next thing, you'll tell my father that he's distracting all the workers.

CHECHÉ: As a matter of fact he is. He is distracting you. Some of the cigars you rolled today were faulty, and you're going to get the same dickens that everyone gets.

MARELA: Yes. The new lector is getting to you with *Anna Karenina*.

CHECHÉ: I don't let any book or lector get to me.

MARELA: Sure. You probably remember your wife every time he reads a page.

CHECHÉ: My wife's dead to me.

MARELA: Dead behind your eyes, so everywhere you look you see her.

CHECHÉ: Do you want to see all the cigars you've ruined?

MARELA: Show me. I pride myself in my work. I'm one of the fastest rollers in this whole place.

[CHECHÉ *pulls out a bag of cigars.*]

CHECHÉ: But fast isn't always good, Marela.

MARELA: Nothing's wrong with it.

CHECHÉ: Here. Feel it. Hollow. A soft spot.

MARELA: Thank you, Chester. Is there anything else? Can I start pasting . . . ?

CHECHÉ: As a matter of fact there's something else . . .

MARELA: What, Chester?

CHECHÉ: Sometimes you get so distracted by the Russian story that I've seen you take shortcuts when you're rolling.

MARELA: What kind of shortcuts?

CHECHÉ: Sometimes you bring a cigar to your mouth and you bite the end of it, instead of reaching for the knife.

MARELA: You've seen me do that?

CHECHÉ: Yes, I've seen you do that and a lot more.

MARELA: Really?

CHECHÉ: Yes. When your mind wanders away from your work and you go far to your own little Russia. You forget the paste jar and you lick the last tobacco leaf, as if you were sealing a letter to a lover or playing with the mustache of a Russian man. Is that what it is, little Marela, you're playing with some man in your mind and you forget that you're bringing a cigar to your mouth and licking it, instead of pasting it?

MARELA: [*Laughs.*] Oh, Chester . . .

CHECHÉ: Do you actually forget that you are working in a little factory where it gets real hot in the summer, and we have to wet the tobacco leaves, because they get dry from the heat and they need moisture, like the wet lick of your tongue.

MARELA: Don't look at me that way, Chester.

CHECHÉ: [*Touching her hair.*] And how do you want me to look at you?

MARELA: Don't touch me.

[*She moves away. He follows her.*]

CHECHÉ: Why not?

MARELA: Because I don't like it.

CHECHÉ: But I do. Every time I listen to that story I do see my wife . . .

[*He moves closer to her.*]

MARELA: Get away from me!

[*He tries to kiss her. She struggles to get away from him.*]
CHECHÉ: Marela, please. Come close . . . You don't know . . .
MARELA: Get away from me! Get away from me!
[*She pushes him away. He falls to the floor.*]
Don't you ever touch me again!
[MARELA *exits.* CHECHÉ *remains on the floor. Music plays. Lights change.*]

### Scene 2

*Spotlight on* JUAN JULIAN *sitting on a chair. He begins to recite a passage from* Anna Karenina. *He remains isolated from the action of the scene.*

JUAN JULIAN:

Anna Karenina's husband did not see anything peculiar or improper in his wife's sitting together with Vronsky at a separate table and having a lively conversation with him; but he noticed that the others sitting in the drawing room considered it peculiar and improper, and so it seemed improper to him, too. He decided that he must have a conversation with his wife about it.[2]

[CONCHITA *enters. She goes to her table and begins to roll cigars.* PALOMO *enters. He is like a lost animal.* JUAN JULIAN *continues to read in silence.*]
PALOMO: At what time do you meet your lover?
CONCHITA: At the agreed time.
PALOMO: And what time is that?
CONCHITA: It changes like the moon.
PALOMO: Where do you meet besides this place?
CONCHITA: I can't tell you these things.
PALOMO: Why not?
CONCHITA: Because that's the way it is.
PALOMO: Does he read to you?
CONCHITA: Sometimes when he says that I look sad.
PALOMO: You get sad.
CONCHITA: It's not sadness. Sometimes I feel frightened.
PALOMO: Frightened of what?
CONCHITA: Frightened of something I have never felt or done before.
PALOMO: But isn't this what you wanted?
CONCHITA: Yes. But sometimes I can't help the guilt.
PALOMO: And how does he respond when you tell him this?
CONCHITA: He tells me that we have to make love all over again. That I have to get used to it. To him. To his body.
PALOMO: And what else does he say to you?
CONCHITA: He says things a woman likes to hear.
PALOMO: Like what?
CONCHITA: That I taste sweet and mysterious like the water hidden inside fruits and that our love will be white and pure like tobacco flowers. And it will grow at night, the same way that tobacco plants grow at night.

2. Part 2, Chapter 8. [Cruz's note]

PALOMO: And what else does he tell you?

CONCHITA: Private things.

PALOMO: Like what?

CONCHITA: Obscenities.

PALOMO: And you like that?

CONCHITA: He knows when and how to say them.

PALOMO: And when does he talk to you this way?

CONCHITA: When we're both deep inside each other and we could almost surrender to death. When he pounds so hard inside me as if to kill me. As if to revive me from that drowning place, from that deep place where he takes me.

PALOMO: I see.

CONCHITA: Why so curious, Palomo?

PALOMO: Because I don't know . . . Because . . . You seem different. You've changed.

CONCHITA: It happens when lovers do what they are supposed to do.

PALOMO: Do you ever talk to him about me?

CONCHITA: Yes. He wanted to know why you stopped loving me.

PALOMO: And what did you tell him?

CONCHITA: I told him that it just happened one day, like everything else in life.

PALOMO: And what was his response?

CONCHITA: He wanted to know what I felt, and I told him the truth. I told him that I desire and love you just the same.

PALOMO: And was he fine with that?

CONCHITA: He told me to show him how I love you. To show him on his body.

PALOMO: And what did you do?

CONCHITA: It was terrifying.

PALOMO: What was terrifying?

CONCHITA: I thought it would be impossible. That nobody could occupy that space in me. But he did. He did. And everything seemed so recognizable, as if he had known me all along. His room became a theatre and his bed a stage, and we became like actors in a play. Then I asked him to play my role, to pretend to be me and I dressed him in my clothes. And he was compliant. It was as if I was making love to myself, because he knew what to do, where to go and where to take me.

PALOMO: Show me.

CONCHITA: Show you what?

PALOMO: Show me . . . Show me what he did to you and how he did it.

CONCHITA: You would have to do as actors do.

PALOMO: And what is that?

CONCHITA: Actors surrender. They stop playing themselves and they give in. You would have to let go of yourself and enter the life of another human being, and in this case it would be me.

PALOMO: Teach me then.

CONCHITA: Here, in the factory?

PALOMO: Yes, back there, where you meet him.

[*Soft music plays.* CONCHITA *traces* PALOMO's *neck and shoulders with her hand. He leads her out of the room. Lights change.* JUAN JULIAN *closes the book. The soft music fades.*]

## Scene 3

*A danzón plays. It's the inauguration of the new cigar brand. There's a party. The workers start filing in, dressed in their best clothes.* SANTIAGO *and* OFELIA *enter with two bottles of rum and glasses.*

OFELIA:   Did you get enough rum, Santiago?
SANTIAGO:   Did I get enough rum? Tell her how much rum I got, Juan Julian.
JUAN JULIAN:   He's got enough rum to get an elephant drunk.
OFELIA:   Then give me some before anybody gets here, so I can calm my nerves.
SANTIAGO:   What are you nervous about?
OFELIA:   Oh, I have the heart of a seal and when I get excited it wants to swim out of my chest.
   [SANTIAGO *gives her a drink.*]
SANTIAGO:   Let's have a drink, the three of us. We ought to have a private toast before anybody gets here.
   [SANTIAGO *serves drinks.*]
   We really haven't done that badly this year. Sales were down last month, but we're still staying above water.
OFELIA:   We'll do well, Santiago. People need to blow out smoke and vent themselves.
SANTIAGO: [*Toasting.*]   That's right, salud!
OFELIA:   Salud.
JUAN JULIAN:   Salud.
OFELIA:   Let's bring out the lanterns.
   [*The three of them exit.* CHECHÉ *and* PALOMO, *both elegantly dressed, enter with palm leaves to decorate the factory. They are engaged in conversation.*]
PALOMO:   Sometimes I don't know what to do . . . I can feel it. Or it's just me. My mind. At night I can't sleep. I lie there awake thinking, imagining the two of them together. I can still smell him on her skin, her clothes and her handkerchief. I can see him on her face and her eyes, and I don't know what to do . . .
CHECHÉ:   You should move up North to Trenton[3] and start a new life. Take her away from here. That's what I wanted to do with Mildred. I'd figure we could live up North. The two of us could work in a cigar factory. There are plenty of them in Trenton. And there are no lectors and no good-for-nothing love stories, which put ideas into women's heads and ants inside their pants . . .
   [JUAN JULIAN *enters with a garland of Chinese lanterns.*]
JUAN JULIAN:   Would you give me a hand with the lanterns?
PALOMO:   Ah, we were just talking about the love stories.
JUAN JULIAN:   It's obvious that you don't care much for them. You almost made me lose my job the other day.
PALOMO:   Oh, I'm curious as to how the story ends.
CHECHÉ:   Yeah! Does the husband ever think of killing the lover? [*Laughs.*] I would've killed the bastard a long time ago.

3. Capital of New Jersey.

JUAN JULIAN: The husband would probably choose a duel, instead of killing the lover in cold blood.

CHECHÉ: I would've shot the son of a bitch a long time ago.

JUAN JULIAN: But that's not the way things were done in those days.

CHECHÉ: Then the husband is a coward and a stinker.

PALOMO: Oh, I don't see the husband as a coward. He might be more clever than the three of us. Wouldn't you say so, Juan Julian?

JUAN JULIAN: Well, the husband is acting according to his status. He is a man of power. He has one of the most important positions in the ministry. And we're talking about Saint Petersburg society—everyone knows each other, and he doesn't want Anna's affair to turn into a big scandal.

CHECHÉ: The husband is a pansy, if you ask me.

PALOMO: So what character do you identify with in the novel?

JUAN JULIAN: I like them all. I learn things from all of them.

PALOMO: And what have you learned from Anna's lover?

JUAN JULIAN: Oh, I don't know . . . I . . .

PALOMO: I'm intrigued as to how he became interested in her.

[JUAN JULIAN *knows where* PALOMO *is trying to go with this.*]

JUAN JULIAN: Well, it's very obvious in the novel.

PALOMO: And what's your personal opinion?

JUAN JULIAN: She came to him because she thought that he could help her.

PALOMO: Help her how?

JUAN JULIAN: Help her to love again. Help her to recognize herself as a woman all over again. She had probably known only one man, and that was the husband. With the lover she learns a new way of loving. And it's this new way of loving that makes her go back to the lover over and over again. But that's my interpretation.

[SANTIAGO *and* OFELIA *enter.*]

SANTIAGO: Good! You are all here. We are celebrating the whole day today. Let's have another drink.

OFELIA: Remember you have a speech to make.

SANTIAGO: [*Lifting the bottle.*] This will inspire me.

OFELIA: At the rate we're going we'll be drunk before the party gets started.

SANTIAGO: [*Laughs.*] Enjoy yourself. Today I'm the happiest man on earth.

[CONCHITA *enters. She's dressed in a chiffon paisley dress.*]

CONCHITA: Are you drinking without me?

SANTIAGO: Of course not. Come have a drink with us. Where's your sister? You look beautiful in that dress, my child. I've never seen you wear it.

CONCHITA: Papá, just a month ago I wore it. We were invited to a party. I remember as if it were yesterday. [*She looks at her mother.*] Mamá hates paisleys.

OFELIA: No, I don't, my child.

CONCHITA: You said I looked like an old lady the last time I wore it.

OFELIA: Frankly, I just didn't think much of it when you had it made. But now that you cut your hair and you look so different, it's actually very becoming.

PALOMO: You do look beautiful, my love.

OFELIA: I like paisleys.

CONCHITA: They remind me of gypsies and bohemians.

PALOMO: You actually look very bohemian.

JUAN JULIAN: It's true. Paisleys look dreamy, as if they come from a floating world.

[PALOMO *looks at* JUAN JULIAN. JUAN JULIAN *lifts his glass.*
PALOMO *brings* CONCHITA *close to him and wraps his arm around
her.*]

Señores, one question. As an outsider, as a foreigner in this country, I
have something to ask. Why do Americans prohibit something as divine
as whiskey and rum?

SANTIAGO: Because Americans become socialists when they drink.

[*Laughter from the crowd.*]

PALOMO: I have another answer to your question. Alcohol is prohibited in
this country because alcohol is like literature. Literature brings out the
best and the worst part of ourselves. If you're angry it brings out your
anger. If you are sad, it brings out your sadness. And some of us are . . .
Let's just say, not very happy.

[OFELIA, *who is a little tipsy, taps her glass to make a speech.*]

OFELIA: [*Doing a dance step.*] Ah, but rum brings out your best steps if
you are a good dancer. If you have two left feet, it's better if you don't
dance at all. So let's face it, señores, Americans are good at making
movies, radios and cars, but when it comes to dancing, it's better if . . .
With the exception of the colored folks, of course. They've got what it
takes to dance up a storm. That's why I think alcohol is prohibited,
because most Americans don't know how to dance.

[*Grabbing* SANTIAGO *by the hand.*] Let's go, I feel like dancing.

SANTIAGO: No. We can't dance yet, because I have an announcement to
make. Where's Marela?

OFELIA: She must be putting on her costume.

SANTIAGO: Well, señoras y señores, today we've taken time from work to
drink and dance, and to celebrate the new cigar brand we are launching
into the market. [*He takes out a cigar from his shirt pocket.*] This well-
crafted cigar is wrapped in the finest leaves from Vuelta Abajo in Pinar
del Río, the tip of the island of Cuba. The length of this new cigar is six
and one-eighth inches. The ring gauge is fifty-two. I truly believe this is
our finest toro.[4]

Where's Marela? She should be here.

[MARELA *enters dressed in an elegant black gown. She is like Anna
on the night of the ball.*]

MARELA: I'm here, Papá.

SANTIAGO: Let me look at you, my little blue sky.

OFELIA: But my child, you look beautiful.

SANTIAGO: You came just in time . . . I was just about to say that since
most cigars are named after women and romantic love stories, today we
are baptizing our new cigar with the name Anna Karenina! This cigar
will sell for ten cents and we are hoping this new brand will bring us
fortune and prosperity. So now that we are all gathered here, I would
like to ask my beloved Ofelia to do us the honor of officially lighting the
first Anna Karenina.

---

4. Literally, bull; a term for a standard size and shape of cigar.

[*Applause from the crowd. The cigar is passed to* OFELIA. SANTIAGO *lights it with a match.* OFELIA *takes a puff and blows out a ring of smoke.*]

Well?

OFELIA: It's . . . It's . . . Aaaah! It burns like a blue dream.

[*The crowd applauds.*]

PALOMO: Bravo! Bravo!

[OFELIA *passes the cigar to* SANTIAGO, *and he gives it to* MARELA.]

SANTIAGO: And to the youngest one in the family, our very own Anna.

[MARELA *takes a puff, coughs a little. She laughs. She passes the cigar to another. This person presents it to* SANTIAGO.]

MARELA: Mhm! Lovely!

[SANTIAGO *takes a puff.*]

SANTIAGO: Ah! It's glorious. Perfecto.

[*Applause from the crowd.*]

Chester.

[SANTIAGO *hands the cigar to someone, who passes it to* CHECHÉ. *He takes a puff.*]

CHECHÉ: Burns well. Pleasant aroma. I detect a little bit of cherry. I think it's our finest horse.

[*Applause. The cigar is passed to* PALOMO. PALOMO *passes it to* CONCHITA. *She takes a puff.*]

CONCHITA: Ah! It speaks of forests and orchids.

[*Applause.* CONCHITA *hands the cigar to* MARELA. MARELA *gives it* PALOMO. *He takes a puff.*]

PALOMO: Mhm! Magnifico! Definitely like aged rum. Sweet like mangoes.

[PALOMO *passes it to* SANTIAGO.]

SANTIAGO: You forgot Juan Julian.

PALOMO: Ah, yes we can't forget our lector, who brought us the world of *Anna Karenina.*

[SANTIAGO *passes the cigar back to* PALOMO. PALOMO *takes off his hat and gives* JUAN JULIAN *the cigar. This is an offense since the cigar should never be handed directly to the person that is supposed to smoke. There has to be a mediator to facilitate communication with the gods.*

JUAN JULIAN *smiles. He smells the cigar, looks up and makes a gesture to the gods.*]

JUAN JULIAN: Sweet aroma. [*Taking a puff.*] It sighs like a sunset and it has a little bit of cocoa beans and cedar. I believe we have a cigar, señores!

SANTIAGO: We do have a cigar, señores! We have a champion!

OFELIA: [*A little tipsy.*] Indeed we have a champion!

MARELA: Papá, let's go out into the streets and tell the world about our cigar. Let's give our new cigars to the people.

SANTIAGO: And go bankrupt, my child! No, I propose a gunshot!

OFELIA: A gunshot! Santiago, you're drunk. Stop drinking.

SANTIAGO: No inauguration is complete without the breaking of a bottle or a gunshot.

MARELA: I propose two gunshots then!

SANTIAGO: Can't have two gunshots. It's got to be three.

MARELA: Then I'll shoot the third one.
[*Laughter.*]
SANTIAGO: Let's go. Let's shoot!
OFELIA: Just make sure you aim up high, but don't shoot the moon!
[*They all laugh. The workers bring the party outside. As* CONCHITA *starts to leave,* PALOMO *grabs her by the arm.*]
PALOMO: Where are you going?
CONCHITA: Outside.
PALOMO: You've been looking at him the whole night. You're still in love with this man.
CONCHITA: Maybe just as much as you are.
PALOMO: I don't like men.
[*Sound of a celebratory gunshot. Laughter.*]
CONCHITA: Then why do you always want me to tell you what I do with him?
PALOMO: Because it's part of the old habit we have of listening. We are listeners.
CONCHITA: No, there's something else.
PALOMO: You're right there's something else. And it's terrible sometimes.
CONCHITA: Then nothing makes sense to me anymore.
[*Another gunshot. More laughter.*]
PALOMO: [*Grabbing her arm.*] I want you to go back to him and tell him you want to make love like a knife.
CONCHITA: Why a knife?
PALOMO: Because everything has to be killed.
[*Another gunshot. More laughter.* OFELIA, SANTIAGO, MARELA *and* JUAN JULIAN *reenter.*]
OFELIA: Señores, I have a confession to make. When I was seventeen, and that was yesterday, I was chosen to pose for a cigar brand that was called Aida, like the opera.[5] And, of course, just the thought of my face being on a cigar ring and in so many men's hands and lips, my mother was scandalized. You see, we weren't cigar people, we were in the guava jelly business. So when my mother forbid me to pose for the label, I told her that I wanted a picture of my face on a can of guava marmalade. And it was only fair. So, they dressed me up in a red dress and I had a red carnation behind my ear. They had me looking lovely sitting in a hammock and a parrot by my side . . .
[*Everyone laughs.*]
SANTIAGO: Let's go, my dear. We have smoked, we have fired a gun and you've had too much to drink.
OFELIA: Bah, you just want to take advantage of me because I'm drunk.
MARELA: [*Embarrassed.*] Mamá!
[SANTIAGO *laughs. He takes* OFELIA *by the hand. They start to exit.*]
SANTIAGO: Good night!
MARELA: Good night!
OFELIA: Marela, are you coming with us?
MARELA: I'll be there in a minute.

---

5. Italian opera (1871) by the composer Giuseppe Verdi (1813–1901) and the librettist Antonio Ghislanzoni (1824–1893).

OFELIA: Don't be too long. [*They exit.*]

PALOMO: [*Grabbing Conchita's hand.*]   Let's go home. [*To the others.*] We'll see you tomorrow.

JUAN JULIAN:   Adios!

CONCHITA:   Adios!

[CONCHITA *and* PALOMO *exit, leaving* MARELA *and* JUAN JULIAN *alone.*]

MARELA:   Oh, I don't want this night to end. I could stay up all night. I don't want to sleep. We sleep too much. We spend more than a third of our lives sleeping, sleeping. Darkness descends and everything is a mystery to us. We don't know if trees really walk at night, as I've heard in legends. We don't really know if statues and spirits dance in the squares unbeknown to us. And how would we ever know if we sleep? We sleep and sleep . . .

JUAN JULIAN:   Oh, I want to have what you drank. What did you drink?

MARELA:   Oh, I didn't drink. I just feel gladness.

Papá was so happy. I like to see him that way. And Mamá was so full of joy. [*Laughs.*] She's the one who drinks a little too much.

JUAN JULIAN:   It's good to drink a little once in a while.

[CHECHÉ *reenters. He stays at a distance, watching.*]

MARELA:   Yes, we deserve a little drink. We work hard enough. We deserve all that life offers us, and life is made of little moments. Little moments as small as violet petals. Little moments I could save in a jar and keep forever, like now talking to you.

JUAN JULIAN: [*Playfully.*]   Ah! So you are a collector. And what sort of things do you like to collect besides a night like this one?

MARELA:   The first time you read and the day you walked me to the pharmacy.

JUAN JULIAN:   So I'm in one of your jars.

MARELA:   In many.

JUAN JULIAN: [*Smiles.*]   Many. [*Beat. Looks at her tenderly.*]   You are clear and fresh as water. Did anybody ever tell you this?

MARELA:   No, never.

JUAN JULIAN:   Then people are blind.

MARELA:   Blind? Do you think so? And how can one teach the blind to see?

JUAN JULIAN:   I wouldn't know. I'm not blind.

MARELA:   But we are all blind in the eyes of those who can't see.

JUAN JULIAN:   You're right.

MARELA:   We just have to learn to use our eyes in the dark. We have to learn to see through words and sound, through our hands. [*Touches his hand.*]

JUAN JULIAN:   I'm sure those who are blind will see your beauty once they touch your face. [*Touches her face tenderly.*]

I must go now. Sleep well.

MARELA:   Adios.

JUAN JULIAN:   Adios.

[*Just as* JUAN JULIAN *is about to exit:*]

MARELA:   Juan Julian . . .

JUAN JULIAN:   Yes.

MARELA:   Lend me the book.

JUAN JULIAN: [*Not realizing that he is holding it.*] What book?
MARELA: The book in your hand.
JUAN JULIAN: Oh!
MARELA: I promise not to get ahead of the story.
JUAN JULIAN: Bring it tomorrow morning or I won't have a book to read.
MARELA: May you dream of angels!
JUAN JULIAN: [*Kissing her face.*] You, too.
> [*As* JUAN JULIAN *exits,* MARELA *stays looking at him in the distance.*
> *She brings the book to her chest, then she opens it and reads, as if to*
> *find consolation, the sort one seeks in the lonely hours of the night.*]
MARELA:

Anna Karenina prepared herself for the journey with joy and willfulness. With small, skillful hands she opened a red bag and took out a little cushion, which she placed on her knees before closing the bag.[6]

> [CHECHÉ *emerges from the shadows. He takes a handkerchief from his*
> *pocket and dries his face. He looks at* MARELA. *He comes close to her*
> *and touches her arm. She is startled and runs out.* CHECHÉ *stands*
> *alone for a moment, then exits in a different direction. Lights change.*]

## *Scene 4*

PALOMO *enters the factory carrying a couple of heavy boxes.* CONCHITA *is*
*clearing up the mess from the night before.*

PALOMO: Where's Cheché?
CONCHITA: He hasn't come in yet.
PALOMO: I hope someone gets here with the keys to the safe. The boy
who delivered these boxes is out there, and he wants to get paid.
CONCHITA: I'll go to the house and ask Mamá for the keys.
PALOMO: No. You got to help me take inventory of all these boxes. [*Hands*
*her some papers.*]
CONCHITA: As soon as I finish with this.
I wonder why Papá isn't here.
PALOMO: He's probably still in bed. He did drink . . .
CONCHITA: Yes, you're right. Mamá must be putting cold compresses on
his forehead. It always happens.
> [SANTIAGO *and* OFELIA *enter.* SANTIAGO *is trying to get rid of his*
> *hangover by rubbing his forehead.*]
OFELIA: Morning!
CONCHITA: Morning!
PALOMO: Santiago, I need the key to the safe. I have to pay for this
delivery.
SANTIAGO: Ofelia has them.
OFELIA: I just left them at the office on top of the desk.
> [PALOMO *exits.* OFELIA *sits down and starts rolling cigars.*]
SANTIAGO: Where's Cheché?
CONCHITA: He hasn't arrived yet.

6. Part 1, Chapter 29. [Cruz's note]

SANTIAGO: I don't blame him. I would've stayed in bed myself. But your mother is like a rooster. When she gets up from bed nobody . . .

OFELIA: I didn't wake you up.

SANTIAGO: I didn't say you did. It's those slippers you use to walk around the house. They are louder than a running train. [*Makes noise.*] Shoo . . . Shoo . . . Everywhere . . . One day I'm going to throw them out the window.

OFELIA: You do that and I'll give your Sunday shoes to the chimney cleaner.

SANTIAGO: See, now the pain got worse! This woman, how she likes to bother me! Ay!

CONCHITA: Do you want my bottle of spirits, Papá?

SANTIAGO: Give me anything you have, my child. Your mother doesn't take care of me.

> [CONCHITA *gives him the bottle of spirits. He sniffs.*
> MARELA *enters wearing the long coat. She goes to her table and starts to roll cigars.*]

MARELA: Morning!

CONCHITA: Marela, why are you wearing that coat? Aren't you warm? . . .

MARELA: No. Some coats keep winter inside them. You wear them and you find pockets full of December, January and February. All those months that cover the earth with snow and make everything still. That's how I want to be, layered and still.

OFELIA: My child, are you all right?

MARELA: I'm fine, Mamá. Don't worry about me.

> [JUAN JULIAN *enters.*]

JUAN JULIAN: Good morning!

ALL: Good morning!

MARELA: Here's your book. [*Hands him the book.*]

> [JUAN JULIAN *notices* MARELA's *coat, and that she seems to be in a state of dismay.*]

JUAN JULIAN: Thank you.

> [PALOMO *reenters.*]

PALOMO: Has Cheché come in yet?

CONCHITA: No. He's just late. Sit down. Juan Julian is going to read to us.

JUAN JULIAN: Today I'll begin by reading Part 3, Chapter 13, of *Anna Karenina*:

In his youth Anna Karenina's husband had been intrigued by the idea of dueling because he was physically a coward and was well aware of this fact. In his youth this terror had often forced him to think about dueling and imagining himself in a situation in which it was necessary to endanger his life.

> [CHECHÉ *enters unnoticed. His head is heavy with dark thoughts.*]

This old ingrained feeling now reasserted itself. Let's suppose I challenge him. Let's suppose someone teaches me how to do it, he went on thinking.

> [CHECHÉ *pulls out a gun.*]

They put us in position, I squeeze the trigger, he said to himself, and it turns out I've killed him. He shook his head to drive away such silly thoughts. What would be the sense of killing a man in order to define one's own relations with a woman . . .

[CHECHÉ *shoots* JUAN JULIAN. *Then shoots again. The sound of the gun echoes and echoes as* JUAN JULIAN *falls to the floor.*
*The workers are shocked. Some of them look up to see where the shot came from. The shot still echoes throughout the room as* MARELA *reaches out to touch the dying lector.*
*The lights fade to black.*]

## Scene 5

*Three days have passed. The factory workers are rolling cigars and organizing the tobacco leaves by their proper size and shape.* MARELA *is still wearing her coat.*

OFELIA: What silence! I never knew that silence could have so much weight. Can someone say something? Can someone read? We are listeners! We are oidores! I can't get used to this silence all around us. It's as if a metal blanket has fallen on us.
PALOMO: The same silence we had when our last reader died.
OFELIA: No, this silence is louder. Much louder. Much louder.
SANTIAGO: That's because Juan Julian died before his time, and the shadows of the young are heavier and they linger over the earth like a cloud.
MARELA: I should write his name on a piece of paper and place it in a glass of water with brown sugar, so his spirit knows that he is welcomed in this factory, and he can come here and drink sweet water. And nobody better tell me that it's wrong for me to do this! You hear me, Mamá! [*For the first time tears come to her eyes.*]
SANTIAGO: Your mother hasn't said anything, my child.
MARELA: I know she hasn't. But we must look after the dead, so they can feel part of the world. So they don't forget us and we could count on them when we cross to the other side.
CONCHITA: We should continue reading, Papá!
MARELA: Yes, we should continue reading the story in his honor, so he doesn't feel that he left his job undone. He should know that we're still his faithful listeners.
CONCHITA: If I could, I would read, but I know that if I open that book I'll be weak.
MARELA: We shouldn't cry. Tears are for the weak that mourn the knife and the killer, and the trickle of blood that streams from this factory all the way to the house where he was born.
OFELIA: Could someone read?
[*Pause.*]
PALOMO: I will read.
OFELIA: That's it, read, so we can get rid of this silence and this heat. And we can pause over a few lines and sigh and be glad that we are alive.
SANTIAGO: Read something cheerful.

MARELA: Stories should be finished, Papá. Let him finish the book.
CONCHITA: She's right. Stories should be finished or they suffer the same fate as those who die before their time.
      [PALOMO *opens the book. He looks at* CONCHITA.]
PALOMO: *Anna Karenina.* Part 3, Chapter 14:

> By the time he arrived in Petersburg, Anna Karenina's husband was not only completely determined to carry out his decision, but he had composed in his head a letter he would write to his wife.
> [*He looks up from the book and stares at* CONCHITA.]

> In his letter he was going to write everything he'd been meaning to tell her.
> [*The lights begin to fade.*]

END OF PLAY

2002

---

# DEMETRIA MARTÍNEZ
## b. 1960

Demetria Martínez was born in Albuquerque, New Mexico. She earned her bachelor's degree from the Woodrow Wilson School of Public and International Affairs at Princeton University, in New Jersey. In Albuquerque, she is active with Enlace Comunitario, an immigrants' rights group that serves Spanish-speaking victims of domestic violence. Martínez teaches at the annual June writing workshop at the William Joiner Center for the Study of War and Social Consequences at the University of Massachusetts Boston, and she has taught at Arizona State University and Colorado College. Since 1988, she has written a regular column for the *National Catholic Reporter*.

Martínez's novel, *Mother Tongue* (1994), was a best seller and won the Western States Book Award. It is based in part on her 1988 trial for conspiracy against the U.S. government in connection with transporting Salvadoran refugees into the country, a charge that with others carried a 25-year prison sentence. As a religion reporter covering the Sanctuary movement—a multidenominational group of about 500 congregations that from 1982 to 1992 helped shelter Central American refugees from Immigration and Naturalization Services—she was found not guilty on First Amendment grounds.

Martínez has published the poetry collections *Breathing between the Lines* (1997) and *The Devil's Workshop* (2002). She generally writes about feminism, politics, bilingualism, and the healing power of love. "Fragmentos/Fragments," the first of three Martínez selections in this anthology, is a meditation on the embarrassment among Latinos of not knowing Spanish well enough. The poem is popular with so-called Heritage Speakers, second-generation Latinos who grew up bilingual in Spanish-speaking households but whose oral and written skills in the language of their immigrant parents are not fully developed. "The Devil's Workshop" is not a love poem; it is a poem about writing a poem that is about love. And "Ars Poetica" uses an ephemeral item, a restaurant flier, to elaborate the author's philosophy of poetry writing.

In 1987, Martínez received the University of California at Irvine's Chicano Literature Prize. For *Confessions of a Berlitz-Tape Chicana* (2004), a collection of autobiographical essays, she received the International Latino Book Award for Best Biography (2006). With Rosalee Montoya-Reed, she wrote the children's book *Grandpa's Magic Tortilla* (2010).

## Fragmentos/Fragments

*Escribo esta cartita en español*
*y es como conducir sin manos,*
*es como el sueño de volar,*
*un sentido de poder, el temor*
*de caer. Inglés. Mi máscara,*                                    5
*mi espada. En su lugar, este*
*kimono de palabras, este huipil.[1]*
*Palabras que dejan que entre viento y*
*sol. Toco la seda, toco el algodón.*
*¿Quién es la mujer en el espejo?*                                10
*Quiero conocerla.*

I write this letter in Spanish, and it is
like driving without hands, a dream
of flight, a feeling of power, a fear
of falling. English. My mask, my                                 15
sword. In its place, this kimono of
words, this *huipil*. Words that let in
wind and sun. I touch the silk, the
cotton. Who is the woman in the
mirror? I want to know her.                                      20

*Cada*
*palabra*
*que escribo*
*en español*
*es una luna*                                                    25

hole punched in the dark
with a pen

*mi cara en*
*esta luz*
*mis ojos*                                                       30
*mis labios*
*¿seré yo?*

Each
word
I write                                                         35

1. A Mayan tunic or blouse worn by indigenous people in Mesoamerica, the region encompassing southern Mexico and Central America.

in Spanish
is a moon

hole punched in the dark
with a pen

my face                                                    40
in this light
my eyes
my lips
is it really me?

Sometimes frightened,                                      45
I run back to the familiar
streets of English.

I go about my usual business,
making things go my way
at the bank, store, government office,                      50

moving mountains in English
not by faith but by precision,
words aimed between eyes.

In moments of grace,
poetry or prayer,                                          55
English uses me.

But most of the time, I use it.
I do not always like what I
have become in this tongue.

*Es distinto en español.*                                  60
*Escribo esta carta, paso a paso*
*por fe, en esta media luz,*
*algunas veces parando*
*para pedir direcciones.*

*Cuando no conozca una palabra*                            65
*dejo un blank _____ así.*
*Llevo estos blanks conmigo*
*como velas hasta que alguien*
*me ayude con un fósforo.*
*Y estos blanks.*                                          70
*se transforman*
*en gotas de luz para guiarme*
*hasta que pueda dejar*
*las velas al lado del camino,*
*una ofrenda, una constelación*                            75
*de sueños para los que siguen.*

It is different in Spanish
I write this letter, step by step,

by faith, in this half-light,
at times stopping 80
to ask for directions.

And when I don't know a word
I leave a blank _____ like this.
I carry these blanks with me
like candles until someone 85
stops to help, lights a match.
Emptiness giving way
to light that guides me
so that I can leave the candles
at the side of the road, 90
an offering, a constellation
of dreams for those who follow.

*Hablarte*
*en esta lengua*
*es como desnudarme* 95
*por la primera vez*
*ante tus ojos.*
*Temor, deseo,*
*sin volver . . .*

Speaking to you 100
in this tongue is like
undressing for the first time
before your eyes.
Fear, desire,
No turning back . . . 105

—gracias a Teresa Márquez[2]

1997


# The Devil's Workshop

They were right,
Our mothers and all
Their mothers before them.
Idleness is the devil's workshop.
Instead of writing a poem, I am thinking 5
About writing a poem: about you, of all people,
Who drove my pen like a tanker onto the rocks
Of the Galapagos,[1] who ordered my pen
To lift off when I most needed
To circle the runway. Read my 10
Rap sheet. I could not write

2. Professor Emerita of the University of New
Mexico General Library.

1. Islands in the Pacific Ocean, about 600 miles
off the coast of Ecuador.

A straight line the years we
Were lovers, the years the
Devil made his most
Acclaimed paintings                                    15
Out of my spilt ink.

2002

## Ars Poetica

(a found poem, from a flier at a Tucson *taquería*)

Concrete
Done
With
Quality
And                                                    5
Honor

20 Years' Experience

Slabs
Sidewalks
Driveways                                              10
Garages
Exposed Aggregates

Big or Small

I'll Take It!

2002

---

# ABRAHAM RODRIGUEZ
## b. 1961

Abraham Rodriguez (aka Abraham Rodriguez Jr.) was born to Puerto Rican parents in
the South Bronx, one of New York City's oldest ethnic neighborhoods, during one of
the community's worst periods of physical decay. He dropped out of high school at age
16 to lead a punk rock band for which he played guitar and wrote songs. After touring
with the band for eight years, Rodriguez earned his high school equivalency diploma
and then earned a bachelor's degree in English at City College of New York (CCNY).
During this period, he began writing short stories and, for three consecutive years,
received the first prize in the Goodman Fund Short Story Awards competition, held by
CCNY's English Department. His short narratives appeared in the journal *StoryQuarterly* in the late 1980s and in the anthology *Best Stories from New Writers* (1989).

Rodriguez's first short-story collection, *The Boy without a Flag: Tales of the South Bronx* (1992), powerfully depicts some of the disturbing realities experienced by Puerto Rican and African American youth in the poor inner-city barrios. In the title story, included in this anthology, a precocious young man refuses to salute the American flag, in part to attract the attention of his stern father. In his second book, the novel *Spidertown* (1993), Rodriguez chronicled teenagers in New York involved in gang warfare and crack dealing. Underlying his writing in these works were the author's outrage at and frustration with the inability of many U.S. Puerto Ricans to overcome the destructive effects of poverty, racism, and the colonial status of Puerto Rico. In a 1997 interview with Carmen Dolores Hernández, a cultural columnist in Puerto Rico, Rodriguez explained that "The United States is an integral part of me, just like Puerto Rico is. Puerto Rico was always the smaller part. I kept going back and sort of reclaiming that, reexperiencing it, trying to understand what it means to be Puerto Rican in these times and what kind of context can I be Puerto Rican, in a society like this."

In his second novel, *The Buddha Book* (2001), Rodriguez uses an underground comic book to depict the lives and mishaps of people caught in the turbulent world of the South Bronx, described in this narrative as "the place where young kids faded into brick like old TAGS [i.e., graffiti] under whitewashed walls." His most recent work of fiction is the detective story *South by South Bronx* (2008).  ✔

# The Boy without a Flag

—To Ms. Linda Falcón,
wherever she is

Swirls of dust danced in the beams of sunlight that came through the tall windows, the buzz of voices resounding in the stuffy auditorium. Mr. Rios stood by our Miss Colon, hovering as if waiting to catch her if she fell. His pale mouse features looked solemnly dutiful. He was a versatile man, doubling as English teacher and gym coach. He was there only because of Miss Colon's legs. She was wearing her neon pink nylons. Our favorite.

We tossed suspicious looks at the two of them. Miss Colon would smirk at Edwin and me, saying, "Hey, face front," but Mr. Rios would glare. I think he knew that we knew what he was after. We knew, because on Fridays, during our free period when we'd get to play records and eat stale pretzel sticks, we would see her way in the back by the tall windows, sitting up on a radiator like a schoolgirl. There would be a strange pinkness on her high cheekbones, and there was Mr. Rios, sitting beside her, playing with her hand. Her face, so thin and girlish, would blush. From then on, her eyes, very close together like a cartoon rendition of a beaver's, would avoid us.

Miss Colon was hardly discreet about her affairs. Edwin had first tipped me off about her love life after one of his lunchtime jaunts through the empty hallways. He would chase girls and toss wet bathroom napkins into classrooms where kids in the lower grades sat, trapped. He claimed to have seen Miss Colon slip into a steward's closet with Mr. Rios and to have heard all manner of sounds through the thick wooden door, which was locked (he tried it). He had told half the class before the day was out, the boys sniggering behind grimy hands, the girls shocked because Miss Colon was married, so married that she even brought the poor unfortunate in one morning as a kind of show-and-tell guest. He was an untidy dark-skinned Puerto Rican type in a colorful dashiki. He carried a paper bag that smelled like glue. His eyes seemed sleepy, his Afro an uncombed Brillo pad. He talked about protest marches, the sixties, the importance of an education. Then he embarrassed Miss Colon greatly by disappearing into the coat closet and falling asleep there. The girls, remembering him, softened their attitude toward her indiscretions, defending her violently. "Face it," one of them blurted out when Edwin began a new series of Miss Colon tales, "she married a bum and needs to find true love."

"She's a slut, and I'm gonna draw a comic book about her," Edwin said, hushing when she walked in through the door. That afternoon, he showed me the first sketches of what would later become a very popular comic book entitled "Slut At The Head Of The Class." Edwin could draw really well, but his stories were terrible, so I volunteered to do the writing. In no time at all, we had three issues circulating under desks and hidden in notebooks all over the school. Edwin secretly ran off close to a hundred copies on a copy machine in the main office after school. It always amazed me how copies of our comic kept popping up in the unlikeliest places. I saw them on radiators in the auditorium, on benches in the gym, tacked up on bulletin boards. There were even some in the teachers' lounge, which I spotted one day while running an errand for Miss Colon. Seeing it, however, in the hands of Miss Marti, the pig-faced assistant principal, nearly made me puke up my lunch. Good thing our names weren't on it.

It was a miracle no one snitched on us during the ensuing investigation, since only a blind fool couldn't see our involvement in the thing. No bloody purge followed, but there was enough fear in both of us to kill the desire to continue our publishing venture. Miss Marti, a woman with a battlefield face and constant odor of Chiclets, made a forceful threat about finding the culprits while holding up the second issue, the one with the hand-colored cover. No one moved. The auditorium grew silent. We meditated on the sound of a small plane flying by, its engines rattling the windows. I think we wished we were on it.

It was in the auditorium that the trouble first began. We had all settled into our seats, fidgeting like tiny burrowing animals, when there was a general call for quiet. Miss Marti, up on stage, had a stare that could make any squirming fool sweat. She was a gruff, nasty woman who never smiled without seeming sadistic.

Mr. Rios was at his spot beside Miss Colon, his hands clasped behind his back as if he needed to restrain them. He seemed to whisper to her. Soft, mushy things. Edwin would watch them from his seat beside me, giving me the details, his shiny face looking worried. He always seemed sweaty, his fingers kind of damp.

"I toldju, I saw um holdin hands," he said. "An now lookit him, he's whispering sweet shits inta huh ear."

He quieted down when he noticed Miss Marti's evil eye sweeping over us like a prison-camp searchlight. There was silence. In her best military bark, Miss Marti ordered everyone to stand. Two lone, pathetic kids, dragooned by some unseen force, slowly came down the center aisle, each bearing a huge flag on a thick wooden pole. All I could make out was that great star-spangled unfurling, twitching thing that looked like it would fall as it approached over all those bored young heads. The Puerto Rican flag walked beside it, looking smaller and less confident. It clung to its pole.

"The Pledge," Miss Marti roared, putting her hand over the spot where her heart was rumored to be.

That's when I heard my father talking.

He was sitting on his bed, yelling about Chile, about what the CIA had done there. I was standing opposite him in my dingy Pro Keds. I knew about politics. I was eleven when I read William Shirer's book on Hitler.[1] I was ready.

"All this country does is abuse Hispanic nations," my father said, turning a page of his *Post*,[2] "tie them down, make them dependent. It says democracy with one hand while it protects and feeds fascist dictatorships with the other." His eyes blazed with a strange fire. I sat on the bed, on part of his *Post*, transfixed by his oratorical mastery. He had mentioned political things before, but not like this, not with such fiery conviction. I thought maybe it had to do with my reading Shirer. Maybe he had seen me reading that fat book and figured I was ready for real politics.

Using the knowledge I gained from the book, I defended the Americans. What fascism was he talking about, anyway? I knew we had stopped Hitler. That was a big deal, something to be proud of.

"Come out of fairy-tale land," he said scornfully. "Do you know what imperialism is?"

I didn't really, no.

"Well, why don't you read about that? Why don't you read about Juan Bosch and Allende,[3] men who died fighting imperialism? They stood up against American big business. You should read about that instead of this crap about Hitler."

"But I like reading about Hitler," I said, feeling a little spurned. I didn't even mention that my fascination with Adolf led to my writing a biography of him, a book report one hundred and fifty pages long. It got an A-plus. Miss Colon stapled it to the bulletin board right outside the classroom, where it was promptly stolen.

"So, what makes you want to be a writer?" Miss Colon asked me quietly one day, when Edwin and I, always the helpful ones, volunteered to assist her in getting the classroom spiffed up for a Halloween party.

"I don't know. I guess my father," I replied, fiddling with plastic pumpkins self-consciously while images of my father began parading through my mind.

When I think back to my earliest image of my father, it is one of him sitting behind a huge rented typewriter, his fingers clacking away. He was a frustrated poet, radio announcer, and even stage actor. He had sent for diplomas from fly-by-night companies. He took acting lessons, went into broadcasting, even ended up on the ground floor of what is now Spanish radio, but his fam-

1. *The Rise and Fall of the Third Reich: A History of Nazi Germany* (1960) and *The Rise and Fall of Adolf Hitler* (1961) were among the nonfiction accounts by the American journalist, novelist, and historian William L. Shirer (1904–1993).
2. The tabloid newspaper *New York Post*.
3. Salvador Isabelino Allende Gossens (1908–1973), Chilean physician; democratically elected Marxist socialist president of Chile from 1970 until a successful, U.S.-backed coup d'état in 1973.

*Juan Bosch*: Juan Emilio Bosch Gaviño (1909–2001), Dominican historian, educator, and writer; founder and leader of two political parties opposed to the military dictatorship of Rafael Leonidas Trujillo (1891–1961), who ruled the Dominican Republic for over three decades; president of the Dominican Republic in 1963, Bosch was deposed in a military coup d'état after less than a year in office.

ily talked him out of all of it. "You should find yourself real work, something substantial," they said, so he did. He dropped all those dreams that were never encouraged by anyone else and got a job at a Nedick's on Third Avenue.[4] My pop the counterman.

Despite that, he kept writing. He recited his poetry into a huge reel-to-reel tape deck that he had, then he'd play it back and sit like a critic, brow furrowed, fingers stroking his lips. He would record strange sounds and play them back to me at outrageous speeds, until I believed that there were tiny people living inside the machine. I used to stand by him and watch him type, his black pompadour spilling over his forehead. There was energy pulsating all around him, and I wanted a part of it.

I was five years old when I first sat in his chair at the kitchen table and began pushing down keys, watching the letters magically appear on the page. I was entranced. My fascination with the typewriter began at that point. By the time I was ten, I was writing war stories, tales of pain and pathos culled from the piles of comic books I devoured. I wrote unreadable novels. With illustrations. My father wasn't impressed. I guess he was hard to impress. My terrific grades did not faze him, nor the fact that I was reading books as fat as milk crates. My unreadable novels piled up. I brought them to him at night to see if he would read them, but after a week of waiting I found them thrown in the bedroom closet, unread. I felt hurt and rejected, despite my mother's kind words. "He's just too busy to read them," she said to me one night when I mentioned it to her. He never brought them up, even when I quietly took them out of the closet one day or when he'd see me furiously hammering on one of his rented machines. I would tell him I wanted to be a writer, and he would smile sadly and pat my head, without a word.

"You have to find something serious to do with your life," he told me one night, after I had shown him my first play, eighty pages long. What was it I had read that got me into writing a play? Was it Arthur Miller? Oscar Wilde?[5] I don't remember, but I recall my determination to write a truly marvelous play about combat because there didn't seem to be any around. "This is fun as a hobby," my father said, "but you can't get serious about this." His demeanor spoke volumes, but I couldn't stop writing. Novels, I called them, starting a new one every three days. The world was a blank page waiting for my words to recreate it, while the real world remained cold and lonely. My schoolmates didn't understand any of it, and because of the fat books I carried around, I was held in some fear. After all, what kid in his right mind would read a book if it wasn't assigned? I was sick of kids coming up to me and saying, "Gaw, lookit tha fat book. Ya teacha make ya read tha?" (No, I'm just reading it.) The kids would look at me as if I had just crawled out of a sewer. "Ya crazy, man." My father seemed to share that opinion. Only my teachers understood and encouraged my reading, but my father seemed to want something else from me.

Now, he treated me like an idiot for not knowing what imperialism was. He berated my books and one night handed me a copy of a book about Albizu Campos,[6] the Puerto Rican revolutionary. I read it through in two sittings.

4. Thoroughfare in Manhattan. *Nedick's*: fast-food chain.
5. Irish writer (1854–1900) who worked in vari-
ous genres. *Arthur Miller*: American writer (1915–2005), primarily of plays.
6. Pedro Albizu Campos (see p. 445).

"Some of it seems true," I said.

"Some of it?" my father asked incredulously. "After what they did to him, you can sit there and act like a Yankee flag-waver?"

I watched that Yankee flag making its way up to the stage over indifferent heads, my father's scowling face haunting me, his words resounding in my head.

"Let me tell you something," my father sneered. "In school, all they do is talk about George Washington, right? The first president? The father of democracy? Well, he had slaves. We had our own Washington,[7] and ours had real teeth."

As Old Glory reached the stage, a general clatter ensued.

"We had our own revolution," my father said, "and the United States crushed it with the flick of a pinkie."

Miss Marti barked her royal command. Everyone rose up to salute the flag.

Except me. I didn't get up. I sat in my creaking seat, hands on my knees. A girl behind me tapped me on the back. "Come on, stupid, get up." There was a trace of concern in her voice. I didn't move.

Miss Colon appeared. She leaned over, shaking me gently. "Are you sick? Are you okay?" Her soft hair fell over my neck like a blanket.

"No," I replied.

"What's wrong?" she asked, her face growing stern. I was beginning to feel claustrophobic, what with everyone standing all around me, bodies like walls. My friend Edwin, hand on his heart, watched from the corner of his eye. He almost looked envious, as if he wished he had thought of it. Murmuring voices around me began reciting the Pledge while Mr. Rios appeared, commandingly grabbing me by the shoulder and pulling me out of my seat into the aisle. Miss Colon was beside him, looking a little apprehensive.

"What is wrong with you?" he asked angrily. "You know you're supposed to stand up for the Pledge! Are you religious?"

"No," I said.

"Then what?"

"I'm not saluting that flag," I said.

"What?"

"I said, I'm not saluting that flag."

"Why the . . . ?" He calmed himself; a look of concern flashed over Miss Colon's face. "Why not?"

"Because I'm Puerto Rican. I ain't no American. And I'm not no Yankee flag-waver."

"You're supposed to salute the flag," he said angrily, shoving one of his fat fingers in my face. "You're not supposed to make up your own mind about it. You're supposed to do as you are told."

"I thought I was free," I said, looking at him and at Miss Colon.

"You are," Miss Colon said feebly. "That's why you should salute the flag."

"But shouldn't I do what I feel is right?"

7. I.e., Albizu Campos.

"You should do what you are told!" Mr. Rios yelled into my face. "I'm not playing no games with you, mister. You hear that music? That's the anthem. Now you go stand over there and put your hand over your heart." He made as if to grab my hand, but I pulled away.

"No!" I said sharply. "I'm not saluting that crummy flag! And you can't make me, either. There's nothing you can do about it."

"Oh yeah?" Mr. Rios roared. "We'll see about that!"

"Have you gone crazy?" Miss Colon asked as he led me away by the arm, down the hallway, where I could still hear the strains of the anthem. He walked me briskly into the principal's office and stuck me in a corner.

"You stand there for the rest of the day and see how you feel about it," he said viciously. "Don't you even think of moving from that spot!"

I stood there for close to two hours or so. The principal came and went, not even saying hi or hey or anything, as if finding kids in the corners of his office was a common occurrence. I could hear him talking on the phone, scribbling on pads, talking to his secretary. At one point I heard Mr. Rios outside in the main office.

"Some smart-ass. I stuck him in the corner. Thinks he can pull that shit. The kid's got no respect, man. I should get the chance to teach him some."

"Children today have no respect," I heard Miss Marti's reptile voice say as she approached, heels clacking like gunshots. "It has to be forced upon them."

She was in the room. She didn't say a word to the principal, who was on the phone. She walked right over to me. I could hear my heart beating in my ears as her shadow fell over me. Godzilla over Tokyo.

"Well, have you learned your lesson yet?" she asked, turning me from the wall with a finger on my shoulder. I stared at her without replying. My face burned, red hot. I hated it.

"You think you're pretty important, don't you? Well, let me tell you, you're nothing. You're not worth a damn. You're just a snotty-nosed little kid with a lot of stupid ideas." Her eyes bored holes through me, searing my flesh. I felt as if I were going to cry. I fought the urge. Tears rolled down my face anyway. They made her smile, her chapped lips twisting upwards like the mouth of a lizard.

"See? You're a little baby. You don't know anything, but you'd better learn your place." She pointed a finger in my face. "You do as you're told if you don't want big trouble. Now go back to class."

Her eyes continued to stab at me. I looked past her and saw Edwin waiting by the office door for me. I walked past her, wiping at my face. I could feel her eyes on me still, even as we walked up the stairs to the classroom. It was close to three already, and the skies outside the grated windows were cloudy.

"Man," Edwin said to me as we reached our floor, "I think you're crazy."

The classroom was abuzz with activity when I got there. Kids were chattering, getting their windbreakers from the closet, slamming their chairs up on their desks, filled with the euphoria of soon-home. I walked quietly over to my desk and took out my books. The other kids looked at me as if I were a ghost.

I went through the motions like a robot. When we got downstairs to the door, Miss Colon, dismissing the class, pulled me aside, her face compassionate and warm. She squeezed my hand.

"Are you okay?"

I nodded.

"That was a really crazy stunt there. Where did you get such an idea?"

I stared at her black flats. She was wearing tan panty hose and a black miniskirt. I saw Mr. Rios approaching with his class.

"I have to go," I said, and split, running into the frigid breezes and the silver sunshine.

At home, I lay on the floor of our living room, tapping my open notebook with the tip of my pen while the Beatles blared from my father's stereo. I felt humiliated and alone. Miss Marti's reptile face kept appearing in my notebook, her voice intoning, "Let me tell you, you're nothing." Yeah, right. Just what horrible hole did she crawl out of? Were those people really Puerto Ricans? Why should a Puerto Rican salute an American flag?

I put the question to my father, strolling into his bedroom, a tiny M-1 rifle that belonged to my G.I. Joe strapped to my thumb.

"Why?" he asked, loosening the reading glasses that were perched on his nose, his newspaper sprawled open on the bed before him, his cigarette streaming blue smoke. "Because we are owned, like cattle. And because nobody has any pride in their culture to stand up for it."

I pondered those words, feeling as if I were being encouraged, but I didn't dare tell him. I wanted to believe what I had done was a brave and noble thing, but somehow I feared his reaction. I never could impress him with my grades, or my writing. This flag thing would probably upset him. Maybe he, too, would think I was crazy, disrespectful, a "smart-ass" who didn't know his place. I feared that, feared my father saying to me, in a reptile voice, "Let me tell you, you're nothing."

I suited up my G.I. Joe for combat, slipping on his helmet, strapping on his field pack. I fixed the bayonet to his rifle, sticking it in his clutching hands so he seemed ready to fire. "A man's gotta do what a man's gotta do." Was that John Wayne?[8] I don't know who it was, but I did what I had to do, still not telling my father. The following week, in the auditorium, I did it again. This time, everyone noticed. The whole place fell into a weird hush as Mr. Rios screamed at me.

I ended up in my corner again, this time getting a prolonged, pensive stare from the principal before I was made to stare at the wall for two more hours. My mind zoomed past my surroundings. In one strange vision, I saw my crony Edwin climbing up Miss Colon's curvy legs, giving me every detail of what he saw.

"Why?" Miss Colon asked frantically. "This time you don't leave until you tell me why." She was holding me by the arm, masses of kids flying by, happy blurs that faded into the sunlight outside the door.

"Because I'm Puerto Rican, not American," I blurted out in a weary torrent. "That makes sense, don't it?"

"So am I," she said, "but we're in America!" She smiled. "Don't you think you could make some kind of compromise?" She tilted her head to one side and said, "Aw, c'mon," in a little-girl whisper.

8. American actor and icon (Marion Mitchell Morrison, 1907–1979).

"What about standing up for what you believe in? Doesn't that matter? You used to talk to us about Kent State[9] and protesting. You said those kids died because they believed in freedom, right? Well, I feel like them now. I wanna make a stand."

She sighed with evident aggravation. She caressed my hair. For a moment, I thought she was going to kiss me. She was going to say something, but just as her pretty lips parted, I caught Mr. Rios approaching.

"I don't wanna see him," I said, pulling away.

"No, wait," she said gently.

"He's gonna deck me," I said to her.

"No, he's not," Miss Colon said, as if challenging him, her eyes taking him in as he stood beside her.

"No, I'm not," he said. "Listen here. Miss Colon was talking to me about you, and I agree with her." He looked like a nervous little boy in front of the class, making his report. "You have a lot of guts. Still, there are rules here. I'm willing to make a deal with you. You go home and think about this. Tomorrow I'll come see you." I looked at him skeptically, and he added, "to talk."

"I'm not changing my mind," I said. Miss Colon exhaled painfully.

"If you don't, it's out of my hands." He frowned and looked at her. She shook her head, as if she were upset with him.

I re-read the book about Albizu. I didn't sleep a wink that night. I didn't tell my father a word, even though I almost burst from the effort. At night, alone in my bed, images attacked me. I saw Miss Marti and Mr. Rios debating Albizu Campos. I saw him in a wheelchair with a flag draped over his body like a holy robe. They would not do that to me. They were bound to break me the way Albizu was broken, not by young smiling American troops bearing chocolate bars, but by conniving, double-dealing, self-serving Puerto Rican landowners and their ilk, who dared say they were the future. They spoke of dignity and democracy while teaching Puerto Ricans how to cling to the great coat of that powerful northern neighbor. Puerto Rico, the shining star, the great lap dog of the Caribbean. I saw my father, the Nationalist hero, screaming from his podium, his great oration stirring everyone around him to acts of bravery. There was a shining arrogance in his eyes as he stared out over the sea of faces mouthing his name, a sparkling audacity that invited and incited. There didn't seem to be fear anywhere in him, only the urge to rush to the attack, with his arm band and revolutionary tunic. I stared up at him, transfixed. I stood by the podium, his personal adjutant, while his voice rang through the stadium. "We are not, nor will we ever be, Yankee flag-wavers!" The roar that followed drowned out the whole world.

The following day, I sat in my seat, ignoring Miss Colon as she neatly drew triangles on the board with the help of plastic stencils. She was using colored chalk, her favorite. Edwin, sitting beside me, was beaning girls with spitballs that he fired through his hollowed-out Bic pen. They didn't cry out. They simply enlisted the help of a girl named Gloria who sat a few desks behind him. She very skillfully nailed him with a thick wad of gum. It stayed in his hair until Edwin finally went running to Miss Colon. She used her

9. Or the Kent State shootings; at Kent State University, in Kent, Ohio, on May 4, 1970, the Ohio National Guard shot 13 unarmed college students, killing four and wounding nine. Some of the students were protesting the U.S. invasion of Cambodia; others were bystanders.

huge teacher's scissors. I couldn't stand it. They all seemed trapped in a world of trivial things, while I swam in a mire of oppression. I walked through lunch as if in a trance, a prisoner on death row waiting for the heavy steps of his executioners. I watched Edwin lick at his regulation cafeteria ice cream, sandwiched between two sheets of paper. I was once like him, laughing and joking, lining up for a stickball game in the yard without a care. Now it all seemed lost to me, as if my youth had been burned out of me by a book.

Shortly after lunch, Mr. Rios appeared. He talked to Miss Colon for a while by the door as the room filled with a bubbling murmur. Then, he motioned for me. I walked through the sudden silence as if in slow motion.

"Well," he said to me as I stood in the cool hallway, "have you thought about this?"

"Yeah," I said, once again seeing my father on the podium, his voice thundering.

"And?"

"I'm not saluting that flag."

Miss Colon fell against the door jamb as if exhausted. Exasperation passed over Mr. Rios' rodent features.

"I thought you said you'd think about it," he thundered.

"I did. I decided I was right."

"*You* were right?" Mr. Rios was losing his patience. I stood calmly by the wall.

"I told you," Miss Colon whispered to him.

"Listen," he said, ignoring her, "have you heard of the story of the man who had no country?"

I stared at him.

"Well? Have you?"

"No," I answered sharply; his mouse eyes almost crossed with anger at my insolence. "Some stupid fairy tale ain't gonna change my mind anyway. You're treating me like I'm stupid, and I'm not."

"Stop acting like you're some mature adult! You're not. You're just a puny kid."

"Well, this puny kid still ain't gonna salute that flag."

"You were born here," Miss Colon interjected patiently, trying to calm us both down. "Don't you think you at least owe this country some respect? At least?"

"I had no choice about where I was born. And I was born poor."

"So what?" Mr. Rios screamed. "There are plenty of poor people who respect the flag. Look around you, dammit! You see any rich people here? I'm not rich either!" He tugged on my arm. "This country takes care of Puerto Rico, don't you see that? Don't you know anything about politics?"

"Do you know what imperialism is?"

The two of them stared at each other.

"I don't believe you," Mr. Rios murmured.

"Puerto Rico is a colony," I said, a direct quote of Albizu's. "Why I gotta respect that?"

Miss Colon stared at me with her black saucer eyes, a slight trace of a grin on her features. It encouraged me. In that one moment, I felt strong, suddenly aware of my territory and my knowledge of it. I no longer felt like a boy but like some kind of soldier, my bayonet stained with the blood of my enemy. There was no doubt about it. Mr. Rios was the enemy, and I was beating him. The more he tried to treat me like a child, the more defiant I became, his arguments falling like twisted armor. He shut his eyes and pressed the bridge of his nose.

"You're out of my hands," he said.

Miss Colon gave me a sympathetic look before she vanished into the classroom again. Mr. Rios led me downstairs without another word. His face was completely red. I expected to be put in my corner again, but this time Mr. Rios sat me down in the leather chair facing the principal's desk. He stepped outside, and I could hear the familiar clack-clack that could only belong to Miss Marti's reptile legs. They were talking in whispers. I expected her to come in at any moment, but the principal walked in instead. He came in quietly, holding a folder in his hand. His soft brown eyes and beard made him look compassionate, rounded cheeks making him seem friendly. His desk plate solemnly stated: Mr. Sepulveda, PRINCIPAL. He fell into his seat rather unceremoniously, opened the folder, and crossed his hands over it.

"Well, well, well," he said softly, with a tight-lipped grin. "You've created quite a stir, young man." It sounded to me like movie dialogue.

"First of all, let me say I know about you. I have your record right here, and everything in it is very impressive. Good grades, good attitude, your teachers all have adored you. But I wonder if maybe this hasn't gone to your head? Because everything is going for you here, and you're throwing it all away."

He leaned back in his chair. "We have rules, all of us. There are rules even I must live by. People who don't obey them get disciplined. This will all go on your record, and a pretty good one you've had so far. Why ruin it? This'll follow you for life. You don't want to end up losing a good job opportunity in government or in the armed forces because as a child you indulged your imagination and refused to salute the flag? I know you can't see how child-ish it all is now, but you must see it, and because you're smarter than most, I'll put it to you in terms you can understand.

"To me, this is a simple case of rules and regulations. Someday, when you're older," he paused here, obviously amused by the sound of his own voice, "you can go to rallies and protest marches and express your rebellious tendencies. But right now, you are a minor, under this school's jurisdiction. That means you follow the rules, no matter what you think of them. You can join the Young Lords[1] later."

I stared at him, overwhelmed by his huge desk, his pompous mannerisms and status. I would agree with everything, I felt, and then, the following week, I would refuse once again. I would fight him then, even though he hadn't tried to humiliate me or insult my intelligence. I would continue to fight, until I . . .

"I spoke with your father," he said.

I started. "My father?" Vague images and hopes flared through my mind briefly.

---

1. See p. 1426.

"Yes. I talked to him at length. He agrees with me that you've gotten a little out of hand."

My blood reversed direction in my veins. I felt as if I were going to collapse. I gripped the armrests of my chair. There was no way this could be true, no way at all! My father was supposed to ride in like the cavalry, not abandon me to the enemy! I pressed my wet eyes with my fingers. It must be a lie.

"He blames himself for your behavior," the principal said. "He's already here," Mr. Rios said from the door, motioning my father inside. Seeing him wearing his black weather-beaten trench coat almost asphyxiated me. His eyes, red with concern, pulled at me painfully. He came over to me first while the principal rose slightly, as if greeting a head of state. There was a look of dread on my father's face as he looked at me. He seemed utterly lost.

"Mr. Sepulveda," he said, "I never thought a thing like this could happen. My wife and I try to bring him up right. We encourage him to read and write and everything. But you know, this is a shock."

"It's not that terrible, Mr. Rodriguez. You've done very well with him, he's an intelligent boy. He just needs to learn how important obedience is."

"Yes," my father said, turning to me, "yes, you have to obey the rules. You can't do this. It's wrong." He looked at me grimly, as if working on a math problem. One of his hands caressed my head.

There were more words, in Spanish now, but I didn't hear them. I felt like I was falling down a hole. My father, my creator, renouncing his creation, repentant. Not an ounce of him seemed prepared to stand up for me, to shield me from attack. My tears made all the faces around me melt.

"So you see," the principal said to me as I rose, my father clutching me to him, "if you ever do this again, you will be hurting your father as well as yourself."

I hated myself. I wiped at my face desperately, trying not to make a spectacle of myself. I was just a kid, a tiny kid. Who in the hell did I think I was? I'd have to wait until I was older, like my father, in order to have "convictions."

"I don't want to see you in here again, okay?" the principal said sternly. I nodded dumbly, my father's arm around me as he escorted me through the front office to the door that led to the hallway, where a multitude of children's voices echoed up and down its length like tolling bells.

"Are you crazy?" my father half-whispered to me in Spanish as we stood there. "Do you know how embarrassing this all is? I didn't think you were this stupid. Don't you know anything about dignity, about respect? How could you make a spectacle of yourself? Now you make us all look stupid."

He quieted down as Mr. Rios came over to take me back to class. My father gave me a squeeze and told me he'd see me at home. Then, I walked with a somber Mr. Rios, who oddly wrapped an arm around me all the way back to the classroom.

"Here you go," he said softly as I entered the classroom, and everything fell quiet. I stepped in and walked to my seat without looking at anyone. My cheeks were still damp, my eyes red. I looked like I had been tortured. Edwin stared at me, then he pressed my hand under the table.

"I thought you were dead," he whispered.

Miss Colon threw me worried glances all through the remainder of the class. I wasn't paying attention. I took out my notebook, but my strength ebbed away. I just put my head on the desk and shut my eyes, reliving my father's betrayal. If what I did was so bad, why did I feel more ashamed of him than I did of myself? His words, once so rich and vibrant, now fell to the floor, leaves from a dead tree.

At the end of the class, Miss Colon ordered me to stay after school. She got Mr. Rios to take the class down along with his, and she stayed with me in the darkened room. She shut the door on all the exuberant hallway noise and sat down on Edwin's desk, beside me, her black pumps on his seat.

"Are you okay?" she asked softly, grasping my arm. I told her everything, especially about my father's betrayal. I thought he would be the cavalry, but he was just a coward.

"Tss. Don't be so hard on your father," she said. "He's only trying to do what's best for you."

"And how's this the best for me?" I asked, my voice growing hoarse with hurt.

"I know it's hard for you to understand, but he really was trying to take care of you."

I stared at the blackboard.

"He doesn't understand me," I said, wiping my eyes.

"You'll forget," she whispered.

"No, I won't. I'll remember every time I see that flag. I'll see it and think, 'My father doesn't understand me.'"

Miss Colon sighed deeply. Her fingers were warm on my head, stroking my hair. She gave me a kiss on the cheek. She walked me downstairs, pausing by the doorway. Scores of screaming, laughing kids brushed past us.

"If it's any consolation, I'm on your side," she said, squeezing my arm. I smiled at her, warmth spreading through me. "Go home and listen to the Beatles," she added with a grin.

I stepped out into the sunshine, came down the white stone steps, and stood on the sidewalk. I stared at the towering school building, white and perfect in the sun, indomitable. Across the street, the dingy row of tattered uneven tenements where I lived. I thought of my father. Her words made me feel sorry for him, but I felt sorrier for myself. I couldn't understand back then about a father's love and what a father might give to insure his son safe transit. He had already navigated treacherous waters and now couldn't have me rock the boat. I still had to learn that he had made peace with The Enemy, that The Enemy was already in us. Like the flag I must salute, we were inseparable, yet his compromise made me feel ashamed and defeated. Then I knew I had to find my own peace, away from the bondage of obedience. I had to accept that flag, and my father, someone I would love forever, even if at times to my young, feeble mind he seemed a little imperfect.

1992

# RUBÉN MARTÍNEZ
## b. 1962

Born and raised in Silver Lake, an arts-oriented and ethnically diverse neighborhood in Los Angeles, California, Rubén Martínez is a journalist, author, and musician of Mexican American and Salvadoran descent. In Los Angeles, he has served as news editor of the *LA Weekly*; bureau chief of the Pacific News Service; and the Emmy Award–winning host of the politics and culture series *Life & Times*, on the local PBS affiliate, KCET-TV. He has written for *The New York Times, The Washington Post, Los Angeles Times, San José Mercury News, Salon, The Village Voice, The Nation, Spin, Sojourners,* and *Mother Jones,* among other periodicals. As a political commentator, he has appeared on ABC's *Nightline* and *Politically Incorrect,* PBS's *Frontline,* NPR's *All Things Considered,* and CNN. He has received a Lannan Foundation Fellowship, a Loeb Fellowship from Harvard University's Graduate School of Design, a Freedom of Information Award from the American Civil Liberties Union, and a Greater Press Club of Los Angeles Award of Excellence.

  *The Other Side: Notes from the New L.A., Mexico City and Beyond* (1993) consists of his columns from the *LA Weekly* on topics such as the 1986 earthquake in El Salvador, Mexican immigrants to California, gang life, and the Latino music scene. "A Death in the Family," the first of two Martínez selections in this anthology, is an exploration of the impact of AIDS on the Mexican community of Los Angeles, with a focus on religion and the family. The poem "Manifesto," from the same book, touches the wound where the so-called First and Third Worlds collide.

  *Eastside Stories: Gang Life in East L.A.* (1998), with photographs by Joseph Rodríguez, offers views of street violence. *Crossing Over: A Mexican Family on the Migrant Trail* (2001), the prologue of which is the third Martínez selection in this anthology, is stunning reportage based on on-site ethnographic interviews with Mexican laborers who migrate from their places of origin through the desert and on to different locations in the Southwest. *The New Americans: Seven Families Journey to Another Country* (2004), also with photographs by Rodríguez, is a portrait of the changing multiethnic face of the United States in the twenty-first century. *Flesh Life: Sex in Mexico City* (2006), with an introduction and essay by Martínez and photos by Rodríguez, is a meditation on carnal encounters in the globe's most crowded metropolis.

  Martínez teaches creative writing at the University of Houston, in Texas. As a musician, he has played with artists such as Concrete Blonde, Los Illegals, and Suzzy and Maggie Roche.

---

*From* The Other Side: Notes from the New L.A., Mexico City and Beyond

## A Death in the Family

*Los Angeles, March 1988*

*Sergio is wearing jeans with two jagged holes at the knees, a T-shirt with suspenders, and a red bandana headband: he's both punk and* vato.[1] *His face is*

---

1. Dude (Mexican slang).

*expressive and mercurial: a hard look gives way to a quirky smile, blends into a distant gaze.*

Daniel Lara presses the fast-forward button on the VCR. He eases himself back in his chair and props his head upon his hand, silently watching the accelerated images of Sergio's birthday party ripple across the screen. He says that he is looking for a specific image that will show me Sergio "at his best." He lets the tape roll at normal speed for a few moments.

*Sergio's family and friends are gathered in the backyard of a modest barrio home on a sunny afternoon. The children shout and dash about. Someone puts on some music—a cumbia rhythm. Sergio beams. He gets up to dance.*

"This is what I wanted you to see," says Daniel.

*Only a few people follow Sergio's lead. The rest are still seated, content to watch. As he bends his knees, his skin shows through the holes in his Levis. He smiles, tosses his head back like an outrageously proud macho, and then he swings his hips exaggeratedly, sensually.*

"Isn't that incredible?" says Daniel. "Here he is, being, what's the word? So *fruity*. And yet his family—they're completely okay with it!"

*Closeups on the faces of the family members seated around the impromptu dance floor. There is some laughter, perhaps from mild embarrassment, but not a single face betrays ill feelings. Sergio closes his eyes, stretches his arms wide, opens his palms and twirls about . . .*

The offices of AIDS Project Los Angeles (APLA) don't exactly make you feel you're in a protective environment; they have a corporate feel to them, and you could mistake the ambience for that of an insurance firm. In Daniel Lara's office (he is program manager for community education here) the strains of a Mexican *balada* emerge from a small tape deck. Atop a small end table, there is more of Mexico: potted cactus plants and some pre-Columbian figurines.

Daniel had met Sergio five years ago, and soon afterward they began living together, he tells me, his face slightly pale above the growth of a new beard. They had come from completely different worlds. Sergio grew up in Mexico City's *barrios*, a boy who became aware of being different at an early age. And it was as if Sergio's very body was at the center of the relentless conflict of growing up gay in such an eminently anti-gay environment as Mexico—from his early years, he suffered from numerous physical maladies. At age ten, there was rheumatic fever. Before he was out of his teens, he'd suffered a heart attack. Later there was open heart surgery, two strokes.

"He knew that if he were ever going to be truly happy with himself, he would have to be somewhere where he could be free of the prejudices and negative stereotypes about gay men in Mexico," says Daniel.

In coming to Los Angeles and meeting Daniel, Sergio had been able to establish his independence firmly. But that success had not been achieved overnight. Once here, Sergio followed a path familiar to many, if not most, Latin American immigrants. Although he finished a *preparatoria* education in Mexico (equivalent to junior college in the United States) and attained a degree in accounting, the language barrier and the fact that his credentials weren't transferable meant that Sergio found himself on the bottom rung of the socioeconomic ladder. He worked as a short-order cook at a Burrito King to make ends meet. But his ambitious nature led him to take night courses at Roosevelt Bilingual School, where he polished his English. Classes at East Los Angeles College came next. His goal was a management-level job.

When finally he landed a job as a telephone operator at the Department of Motor Vehicles (DMV), it wasn't exactly management, but it was a start. Sergio fell ill around that time, however. Although he soon recovered from what he would later discover had been the beginning of an ARC (AIDS-Related Complex) condition, he lost his job at the DMV. The official diagnosis of full-blown AIDS came in August 1986.

"He looked at AIDS—and I've never been able to reconcile myself with this—as a gift," says Daniel. "He said that AIDS for him was an affirmation, a sign that God had not abandoned him." Sergio's traditional Catholicism—highly ironic, considering the Church's official anti-gay attitude—was a catalyst for Daniel. He had grown up in the States and flirted with Chicano Movement politics[2] in its heyday, but had ultimately opted for a secular and professional existence well within the American mainstream. Meeting Sergio, Daniel says, was like "hitting a brick wall."

"He was very tied to religion. He had his *velas* [votive candles], and he had his *santos* [Saints], and he had his *medallas* [religious medallions], his *hierbas*, his holy water and his *oraciones*; all of these were things that I'd lost." Daniel smiles as he recites the list in Spanish. "I now have the *velas*, I have Sergio's *santos*, I have his *hierbas*."

When Sergio's mother came up from Mexico City to visit her son soon after his AIDS diagnosis, she faced his homosexuality openly for the first time. She told him that she would not speak to him until after he "changed his lifestyle," Daniel remembers. More than a year would pass without contact between mother and son. Sergio's father never knew about his son's gay lifestyle, nor would he ever learn that he had AIDS.

As his health worsened, Sergio came more and more into contact with a health establishment little prepared to handle the AIDS crisis. At the time of his diagnosis, APLA was practically the only resource available to persons with AIDS, regardless of ethnic or class background. And in Sergio's view, APLA was doing little, if anything at all, for Latinos with AIDS. He began to complain—to anyone who'd listen—about what he saw as a discriminatory situation.

Sergio's illness and activist sentiment spurred Daniel to take action by offering his services to APLA. Although the agency is considered by many activists to be part of the AIDS "establishment," Daniel felt that the best way to influence it was by working within the system, accepting its sometimes sluggish nature. But Sergio, always the rebel, took the opposite approach.

"Whereas we would say, 'You have to deal with the system,' he would say, 'No you don't, you can fight.'" Sergio often went straight to APLA's top administration—over Daniel's head—demanding, among other things, that APLA bilingualize its services. Sergio also lobbied for bereavement counseling in Spanish to help an AIDS victim's family deal with the impact of the disease, something he considered essential for family-oriented Latino culture and its particular brand of homophobia.

2. See the discussion in the "Upheaval" introduction, p. 588.

Sergio literally took his message to the streets. He gave dozens of public *platicas*, informal talks, on AIDS at churches, schools, hospitals, "anywhere they'd take us," says Daniel. He would talk about his life experiences, about the poor treatment he'd received in hospitals, about the need for more education and AIDS services for Latinos. But most important, says Daniel, Sergio's message was "that his goal was to live, and, cliché as it sounds, that AIDS was the disease, and that faith was the cure."

In the fall, Daniel began noticing that Sergio was suffering lapses of memory and other signs of dementia. Still, Sergio mustered enough strength to join the hundreds of thousands of gay men and women who marched on Washington, DC in October, calling for a government response to the AIDS crisis.

It was in November, Daniel says, that he lost the Sergio he'd known and loved. By December, Sergio was bedridden, almost continually delirious. Daniel phoned Sergio's mother in Mexico City and she was soon at her son's bedside, no longer complaining about his "lifestyle" but taking care of his every need as she did when he was a baby.

Sergio's mother and Daniel decided to place him on a morphine drip, without any other treatment, as a way of letting him die without any more unnecessary suffering. On December 12, a traditional Mexican holiday in honor of the Virgen de Guadalupe,[3] Sergio was lucid for a few hours. Daniel took the opportunity to tell him of their decision. "He put both of his hands on my face," Daniel says, now placing his hands on his cheeks. "He said to me, 'How can you help me to live, if you are so negative? You have to believe me when I tell you that I will get over this, that this will pass, and I can't do it unless you're on my side.'"

One day in early January, Sergio told Daniel: "You don't believe me when I tell you that I won't die." In retrospect, Daniel says, "I think he meant it in the spiritual sense. That his spirit would continue to be here. I only focused on the physical."

Sergio died the next day.

At the service, there was anything but morbidity. Daniel had wanted a celebration, and there indeed was one, with mariachi music and a large gathering of friends. Daniel had thought that only such a ceremony would befit what Sergio would surely have believed was his passing into the Afterlife.

Daniel boarded the plane in Los Angeles dressed in black. Sergio's family greeted him at the airport in Mexico City dressed in black. He had known that the "celebration of life" in L.A. was the opposite of what he would encounter in Mexico. The open grief that he found among Sergio's family was anathema to Daniel. He feared that if he gave in to the sorrow, he wouldn't be able to control himself . . . and then what? Have the family about him wonder why he cried like a wife over a dead husband?

Daniel accompanied Sergio's family and friends to the mausoleum to place the ashes in the crypt. En route, he carried the box containing the

---

3. *Nuestra Señora de Guadalupe* (Our Lady of Guadalupe), a sixteenth-century icon of the Virgin Mary; perhaps Mexico's most popular religious and cultural image, it has come to symbolize Catholic Mexicans and Mexico itself.

ashes in his lap. He held it all the way to the mausoleum, causing an invisible but extremely uncomfortable tension between him and Sergio's mother. "May I have my son?" she asked Daniel in front of the crypt. Daniel hesitated. He ran his hand along the box, and slowly handed it to her. She placed the ashes in the crypt, knelt and said her goodbyes. Sergio's father did the same, then his sister. Two workers were about to set in place the stone that would seal the crypt forever when Daniel asked them to wait. He knelt down, and with his hand reached into the space for a moment, as if to retrieve Sergio. But his hand came out empty, and with it he drew the sign of the cross before the crypt.

# Manifesto

*Can anyone tell me what time it is?*
*¿O es que nadie lo sabe?*
*Doesn't anyone know?*
*¡Vamos, across the continent, North y Sur!*
*What time is it in downtown L.A.*      5
*when the LAPD raids the sanctuary at La Placita?*[1]
*And in the city that bans santería*[2] *sacrifices,*
*a thousand Pollo Loco stands notwithstanding?*
*What time is it where little Saigon meets little Havana*
    *meets little Tokyo meets little Armenia and we all meet*      10
    *the sea speaking in tongues?*

*Can you feel the earth shudder?*
*This generation's shaky, bro',*
*dancing a San Andreas*[3] *cumbia!*
*It is 1991 and I live and die*      15
*in Guatemala, San Salvador, Mexico City*
*Tijuana*[4] *and L.A.*
*This is not 1969 and Marx*[5]
*has a bad rap on the international scene,*
*but there's the FMLN in downtown San Salvador,*      20
*(and the death squads*[6] *are in L.A.)*
*and*
*¡Híjole! There goes the Berlin* mauer[7] *down!*
*Can anyone tell me what time it is*

---

1. In the 1980s, La Placita Church, the oldest Catholic Church in Los Angeles, defied the U.S. Immigration and Naturalization Service by declaring itself a sanctuary for refugees from the civil wars in Central America. *LAPD*: Los Angeles Police Department.
2. An Afro-Caribbean religious tradition.
3. The San Andreas Fault is a roughly 800-mile tectonic boundary within California; the site of notable earthquakes, including one in 1989.
4. City in Mexico, bordering San Diego, California.
5. Karl Marx (1818–1883), German political philosopher and socialist.

6. During the Salvadoran Civil War (1980–92), the military-led government employed paramilitary death squads to eliminate its opponents, including many civilians. *FMLN*: Farabundo Martí National Liberation Front, a coalition of five left-wing militias that opposed the Salvadoran government during the Civil War. *San Salvador*: capital of El Salvador.
7. Wall (German); from 1961 until its destruction in 1989, a massive, multilayered wall, built and maintained by the Communist government of East Germany, completely separated East Berlin from (non-Communist) West Berlin. *Híjole*: Jeez (an expression of astonishment).

in the great cities of the States                                                    25
where Third World kids etch the walls
with a message clear
as civil war:
wildstyle, a violent
rainbow, a pistol pointed at your head!                                             30

And what time is it in L.A. when
a guatemalteco[8] wears an Africa Now T-shirt
and a black kid munches carnitas[9] and all
together now dance to Eazy-E. and B.D.P.,[1]
crossing every border ever held sacred?                                             35

But it's live ammunition
on the streets of Southcentral L.A.
and in Westwood[2] and San Salvador
and East L.A.;
as real as video.                                                                   40

This is war, and the battle
will be block to block wherever
the Wes and Theys face off.
Third World in the First:
that's what time it is.                                                             45

History is on fast forward
it's the age of synthesis
which is not to say
that the Rainbow Coalition[3] is
heaven on earth and let's party.                                                    50
This be neither a rehash of
the Summer of Love or
Fidel and Che.[4]
All kinds of battles are yet to come
(race and class rage bullets and blood);                                            55
choose your weapons . . .
just know that everyone is everywhere now
so careful how you shoot.

Los Angeles, 1989                                                                    1993

---

8. Guatemalan.
9. Literally, little meats; braised or roasted pork, in Mexican cuisine.
1. Boogie Down Productions (1989–1992), a hip-hop group. *Eazy-E*.: Eric "Eazy-E." Wright (1964–1995), a rapper.
2. Los Angeles neighborhood that at the time, like South Central and East L.A., had a national reputation for gang violence. To avoid the connotations of its name, South Central is now officially known as South Los Angeles.
3. Or the National Rainbow Coalition, a political

organization that emerged from the 1984 U.S. presidential campaign of the Reverend Jesse Jackson (b. 1941); the Rainbow Coalition was devoted to the promotion of social programs, voting rights, affirmative action, and similar issues.
4. Fidel Castro (b. 1926), Cuban revolutionary and Communist leader, and Ernesto "Che" Guevara (1928–1967), Argentinian-born Latin American revolutionary leader. *The Summer of Love*: summer 1967, seen as a paradisiacal period of free expression and social experimentation.

### FROM CROSSING OVER: A MEXICAN FAMILY ON THE MIGRANT TRAIL

## Prologue: The Passion

I am close to the line.

The mostly invisible line that stretches two thousand miles along sand, yellow dirt dotted with scrub brush, and the muddy waters of the Rio Grande. Invisible, save for certain stretches near San Diego, Nogales, and El Paso,[1] where the idea of the U.S.-Mexico border takes physical form through steel, chain links, barbed wire, concrete, and arc lamps that light the barren terrain at night. At these three crossing points—San Diego being the busiest port of entry in the world—the Border Patrol has cleared the land for miles around, so that the human figures who try to breach the line stand in stark relief and cast shadows. The Border Patrol swallows as many shadows as it can.

It is late summer in California and the hills that line I-15 in southern Riverside County[2] are tinged rusty brown; the brilliant green wild grass of spring is a distant memory. This is one of my least favorite stretches of California highway, an interminable, mostly barren valley corridor.

I-15 is a necessary route for travelers and truckers shuttling between the Inland Empire and San Diego. It is also the preferred route of the "coyotes," the smugglers of human cargo who charge $1,000 a head or more to foil the designs of the Border Patrol and get their migrant clients on the road to their American future.

I am in the badlands of Southern California, en route to an appointment with the dead. I'm headed to Temecula, a growing city on the edge of Riverside County. It is arid country here, the westernmost point of the vast desert that spreads from the California beach all the way to the Gulf Coast of Texas.

For the American migrants who rode the wagon trains westward, California was once the "other side," just as it is today for the migrants heading north. Up from the fine yellow dust of these hills rise imported laurels, palms, sycamores, avocados, willows, oleander, eucalyptus. There are even apple and citrus orchards. But now and again, the old desert, a reminder of Mexican, or even Indian, California, appears in the form of an ancient, lonely stand of nopal cactus.

I take the exit at Rancho California Road. Temecula is picturesque, with its Western wagon-wheel décor. The elite live in the hills above town, in huge, recently built homes of the faux California Mission variety: red tile roofs, beige stucco, wrought iron. There are rose gardens and the occasional artificial pond gracing the spacious yards. One of the local realty agencies is called Sunshine Properties.

I head west along a winding two-lane that climbs into the Santa Rosa Mountains, a range that runs southward and eventually crosses the international line. The Santa Rosas are beautiful and bizarre: gently rolling hills

1. San Diego, California; Nogales, Arizona; and El Paso, Texas, three U.S. cities on the border with Mexico.
2. A rectangular area that stretches across Cali-

fornia, from near the southwestern coast to the eastern border with Arizona; part of the Southern California Inland Empire region.

of green give way suddenly to boulder-strewn peaks and chasms. On the Mexican side, the landscape is precipitous—and infamous. There, a stretch of Mexico Federal Highway 2 known as La Rumorosa (The Whispering One, for the haunted winds that blow through the canyons) has been the site of hundreds of fatal wrecks over the decades.

My destination is the intersection of Calle Capistrano and Avenida Del Oro. The names are, of course, Spanish—appropriated by the whites to romance their idyll with a dash of old California. The street signs are rendered in faux rustic, engraved wood. Most of the whites who live here now were once migrants themselves, belonging to subsequent waves of American wanderers—the Depression-era and postwar generations that pulled up stakes in the Midwest and on the East Coast to spend their lives in balmy paradise. This land was a final destination for them, the consummation of their California dream. You don't leave paradise once you've found it.

But for the Mexican migrants, Temecula is a stopover, not a final destination. Sure, there are Mexican gardeners tending to the rose bushes, cleaning the swimming pools, washing and folding the clothes, cooking the meals; brown women sing lullabies in Spanish to white babies. But the Mexicans are here for just as long as they have to be. They are mostly young and don't think of retiring, not only because they have no money to do so but also because they can't imagine themselves old yet. Most of the Mexicans in Temecula are literally just passing through, crammed into pickup trucks and vans driven by the coyotes. Temecula is just another of the hundred places they will blow through en route to St. Louis, Los Angeles, Houston, New York, Chicago, Decatur. But even these are not final destinations. The migrants will follow trails determined by America's labor economy: they will keep moving, from one coast to another, from picking the fields to working in hotels and restaurants, from cities to heartland towns.

Temecula was long a quiet town. But to the retirees' dismay, it is now a staging area for the battle of the border, in which two armies face off, usually under cover of darkness. It is a battle in which, occasionally, blood is spilled, though usually only on one side.

I turn right at Avenida Del Oro and pick up speed on a steep downhill grade. The road begins a long curve between hills dotted with rural mansions and avocado orchards. At the bottom of the gully, at the intersection with Calle Capistrano, I stop the car. The sun has fallen behind the hills to the west but still illuminates the higher terrain with a lush, classic California gold. Silvery plumes from the irrigation sprinklers arc over the fields.

This is where it happened. Where Benjamín, Jaime, and Salvador Chávez and five others, all of them undocumented Mexican migrants, "illegals," died crammed in a truck that sped along this rural road four and a half years ago.

I clamber down into the drainage ditch below the road. Yellow dirt and sickly weeds. I find a screen from the window of the truck's camper shell and a blue piece of plastic from the shell itself, about a foot long and six inches wide. And another piece of black plastic: a fragment of the truck's running board. I pick up and examine a faded, crumpled tube of Colgate toothpaste, its ingredients listed in Spanish. There is an equally faded and torn McDonald's medium-size Coca-Cola cup.

Above the ditch, an anonymous artisan has built a small altar by taking the trunk of a California oak, slicing it in half, and carving out seven small crosses that he has filled in with light blue paint. (There should be eight crosses; the artisan was apparently unaware of the last victim's death in a nearby hospital several days after the accident.) It is a simple, beautiful monument.

I walk a ways up the hill, the bed of dead avocado leaves crunching underfoot. There is very little traffic and it is quiet, except for the leaves of the avocados rustling in the warm wind and, suddenly and eerily, the voices of men. Men speaking in Spanish. It sounds like they are nearby, but it takes me a while to spot them, high on a hill south of me. They are Mexican farmworkers, chatting casually as they pick avocados. They are a good half mile away, but the wind has brought their voices very close. These men traveled the same road that Benjamín and his brothers did. They are farmworkers now. Benjamín, Salvador, and Jaime Chávez are not. This is where their road ended.

It is five o'clock in the morning on Saturday, April 6, 1996. Two weeks before Easter, two more weeks of Lent before the Passion.[3] The sun will soon break over the Temecula valley. The moon is a little less than half full, dipping low into the southwestern sky. The stars have dimmed with the approach of the sun. Only the planet Jupiter is visible, and it is just about to fall into the leaves of a stand of avocados on the south side of Avenida Del Oro. It is a clear and dry morning, and although it is early spring, the temperature is already seventy degrees; it will reach into the nineties at midday.

Avenida Del Oro is an east-west rural two-lane road of pitch-black asphalt and a bright solid yellow dividing line that runs for several hundred feet across the intersection with Calle Capistrano. Here, Avenida Del Oro falls into a steep gully along a long, sharp curve, the kind that creeps up on you and causes you to instinctively hit the brakes as you come to the bend. Calle Capistrano is a smaller road that runs north toward a few residences and orchards. The point at which the two streets join is precisely the bend in Avenida Del Oro's curve.

Deck lights glow amber from a ranch house high up on a hill to the east. There is no breeze. Occasionally there is the sound of an avocado falling, at first slithering through the branches, then hitting the thick bed of dry dead leaves below with a loud, brittle crash.

At five-fifteen the eastern sky is pale yellow. Shades of dusty pink rise into blue-greens and finally into deep blue at the zenith and in the west. A 1989 GMC truck, blue with silver trim, equipped with a camper shell of darkly tinted windows, speeds westward down Avenida Del Oro. Twenty-seven people are inside, twenty-five of them in the camper and two in the front seat. All are undocumented Mexican migrants.

The reason the coyote is on this isolated rural road is the inauguration of the U.S. Border Patrol interdiction effort known as Operation Gatekeeper. In 1994, a massive new steel wall was built along several miles of the border running east from the beach at Tijuana.[4] After the Border Patrol claimed success with Operation Gatekeeper, it followed with similar measures in

---

3. In Christianity, the suffering of Jesus during the Last Supper; during his crucifixion, on a hill at a site called Golgotha; and during his prayers the night before the crucifixion, at a garden called Gethsemane. Christians commemorate the Passion on Easter Sunday, which is preceded by the 40-day period called Lent.
4. City in Mexico, bordering San Diego.

Nogales, Arizona (Operation Safeguard), El Paso, Texas (Operation Hold the Line), and McAllen, Texas (Operation Rio Grande). Consequently, the Mexican coyotes, not to be outdone by gringo technology, have chosen more circuitous routes through rugged terrain eastward. These new routes are extremely dangerous. Dozens of migrants have died of exposure in the torrid heat and bitter cold of the Colorado Desert since 1994. There are hundreds of such crossings between the beaches of Southern California and the Gulf Coast of Texas, and the cat-and-mouse game between the coyotes and the Border Patrol is never-ending.

A Border Patrol truck spots the GMC several miles south of the intersection of Avenida Del Oro and Calle Capistrano. What the BP agents see is a vehicle clearly overloaded, its fenders practically scraping the tires. From this point on, there are differing versions as to what occurred. The BP maintains that their personnel followed the vehicle at a discreet distance, with its emergency lights off. Lawyers representing the victims say that the BP wrecklessly and needlessly endangered the lives of the migrants by engaging in a high-speed pursuit.

For most of the hour-long ride up from the border, Benjamín, Jaime, and Salvador Chávez and their compatriots in the camper shell see nothing, not even one another's faces, because very little of the approaching dawn's light penetrates the camper's tinted windows.

When the coyote notices the BP truck in his side mirrors (he couldn't have seen much in the rearview mirror, given the dark glass and the twenty-five bodies piled like a cord of wood in the back), he speeds up, the tires screeching on the curves.

Inside the camper, panic rules. Those closest to the small window that looks in on the cab of the truck pound on it and scream at the coyote to stop. Several survivors recall that Benjamín Chávez shouted the loudest, a deep-throated yell. But it is to no avail. The coyote has been drinking. He has been snorting coke. He is hunched over the steering wheel, oblivious to everything but the BP truck behind him and the dark, winding road ahead.

Increasingly desperate, the migrants pop the camper's rear window open. They throw their small travel bags, their water bottles, and even a tire jack in the direction of the BP vehicle, but these fall harmlessly by the side of the road. They make dramatic hand gestures at the agents, imploring them to give up the pursuit, not because they want to avoid apprehension but because they want their driver to slow down. They are in fear for their lives.

The Chávez brothers, crunched against one another in the truck bed, see very little even when the rear window is opened. They are deep inside the camper, hemmed in by twenty-three other bodies. They only feel the lurching of the truck and hear the men's groans as they are slammed about on the curves.

The GMC hurtles down Avenida Del Oro at close to seventy miles an hour. About three hundred feet from Calle Capistrano, the coyote realizes he can't negotiate the curve and slams on the brakes. The realization comes too late.

There is a long skid, and the truck spins 180 degrees.

Then there is silence for a split second, as the truck flies off the road and turns over in the air.

And now a thousand sounds at once: the crumpling, the breaking, the crushing, and the snapping of glass, metal, plastic, and bone. The truck comes down roof-first in the ditch. Most of the bodies inside the camper shell spill out. Not all are completely ejected. Several are crushed underneath the mangled chassis of the truck. A cloud of dust rises from the impact.

The sun crests the horizon in the east now. It is possible that one of the last things some of the migrants saw, for just a fraction of a second, was the yellow glow on the horizon. Or maybe some of them saw the dust from the crash hanging in the air and heard the silence of the desert return as the groans of the dying faded.

Benjamín, Jaime, and Salvador were crushed under the truck. They had departed their home in Cherán, an Indian town in the highlands of Michoacán,[5] a few days earlier and were on their way to Watsonville, California, to their usual stint of seasonal work picking strawberries in the fertile hills east of Santa Cruz.[6] The accident made headlines in the United States for the enormity of the tragedy (eight people killed, nineteen injured, many critically) and because just a few days earlier another incident involving Mexican migrants had attracted attention. A videotape reminiscent of the Rodney King footage[7] had aired on the evening news showing Riverside sheriff's deputies beating unarmed Mexican migrants, none of them visibly resisting, by the side of a Southern California freeway at rush hour.

Over the last decade, the numbers of casualties at the U.S.-Mexico line have begun to look like the tallies from a low-intensity conflict in a corner of the developing world. A University of Houston study counted some three thousand deaths in the last half of the 1990s, a conservative figure. Many bodies, the researchers concluded, will never be found. The bones of these migrants are hidden in the sludge at the bottom of the Rio Grande and scattered across the open desert.

And yet the migrants continue to cross, because ideals of paradise die hard, especially for Mexicans, who for several decades have regarded the Rio Grande as a river of life more than of death, notwithstanding accidents like the one at Temecula. They continue to cross despite the tragedies and despite Operation Gatekeeper because the odds remain in their favor. To truly "hold the line," as American politicians say, the United States would have to spend hundreds of billions of dollars—currently it is spending some four billion a year—to either build the Great Wall of America or amass all along the line, like at the border between North and South Korea or at the old divide between East and West Berlin,[8] thousands of troops and all manner of physical obstacles, weaponry, and technology. Despite continuing anti-immigrant sentiment in the United States, there are no credible proposals to do so at this time. After all the rhetoric, the line is still more an idea than a reality. Most of the border between the United States and Mexico is represented not by Operation Gatekeeper's twelve-foot-tall steel barriers but by barbed-wire fences often little more than a few feet high. In hundreds of places, the wire has been cut. You can stand on the line through most of California, Arizona, New Mexico, and Texas and hop from one side to the

5. State on the southwestern coast of Mexico.
6. City and county in west-central California.
7. In 1991, a bystander videotaped the beating of Rodney King (b. 1965), an African American, by

Los Angeles police officers with their batons. News agencies around the world showed a portion of the footage, which created an uproar.
8. See note 7, p. 2321.

other, screaming at the top of your lungs, and no one will see you, except perhaps a desert tortoise or a real coyote.

In publicity campaigns aimed at deterring prospective migrants, the BP has tried to use the dead as a cautionary symbol—even as an example. But the migrants' awareness of unscrupulous coyotes and the BP's determination to stop the migrant flow is not nearly enough of a deterrent. The reason is very simple. In 1994, Mexico was crippled by a profound—and prolonged— economic crisis that sent a flood of refugees north. The United States, on the other hand, enjoyed throughout the late 1990s a historic boom in practically every corner of its economy, and among the fastest-growing was the "service sector." Its jobs—typically in hotels and restaurants—along with hundreds of thousands of seasonal agricultural jobs, are largely filled by a vast pool of illegal, unskilled migrant labor. It is an arrangement that keeps U.S. employers, migrants, and the Mexican government generally content.

This state of mutual dependence has existed for the better part of a century, but the migrant business has not always been conducted this way. After the Mexican Revolution of 1910, some 700,000 migrants were received in the United States legally. And during the 1940s, a federally sponsored *bracero*, or guest worker, program imported hundreds of thousands of Mexicans—again, legally—to relieve wartime labor shortages.[9] Then in 1965 the U.S. increased quotas from Latin America, and in 1986 the Immigration Reform and Control Act granted amnesty to millions of undocumented migrants, allowing them to legalize and bring family members north.

The one sensible binational policy that recognizes the presence of Mexican workers is the INS's[1] border resident identification program, which grants a limited number of Mexican nationals living in border towns a safe-conduct pass to cross into U.S. territory for a certain distance (depending on the region, up to fifty miles) for business purposes. The program acknowledges that, without cross-border commerce, the towns on the American side would wither away. These days, hundreds of cities and towns in the American interior would probably suffer without the presence of the hard-working illegals. But the idea of U.S.-Mexico integration—as in the radical libertarian proposal to simply open the border and allow market forces to regulate the migratory flow—would cause too much conflict on both sides of the line.

Only a handful of faith communities and human rights organizations have questioned America's contemporary immigration policies, despite the growing number of deaths on the border during the 1990s. Yet the United States pulls, with its job-magnets, its porous border, and its selective enforcement of the immigration code: every migrant and practically every major employer of illegals in the country can tell you that the INS usually puts the heat on only after the crops are picked and on their way to market. For decades the message has been: We have a job for you. Today it is: We have a job for you but you'll have more trouble getting across the line.

From the migrant perspective, the Chávez brothers and the thousands of other migrants who have died over the past decade in car wrecks or by

9. See the discussions in the "Acculturation" introduction, pp. 363 and 365.
1. The Immigration and Naturalization Service's.

drowning or from exposure have become martyrs in a cause: to have the freedom to move, or at least to get the hell out of provincial towns like Cherán, whose timber-based economy is in tatters. Like Indian Joads,[2] they have fled the Mexican dustbowl.

To move, to make some money, to buy some gold chains, or a 1984 Plymouth with 145,000 miles on it but a nice interior, or an Osterizer food processor so that your *madrecita*[3] back home doesn't have to chop-chop the vegetables every night, or some snazzy snakeskin boots for yourself—or hell, to just come back home with a wad of greenbacks in your billfold, enough to peel off a few Jacksons and pin them on the statue of your patron saint and buy a dozen bottles of Bacardi rum, enough to get your entire block drunk for at least one night.

And then, after a winter's rest, to return to California . . . to Arkansas . . . to Wisconsin . . . to North Carolina . . .

This migrant trail is a loop not only in space but in time. The future lies in America, the past in Mexico. The past is tolerable only for so long, especially in the impoverished lands of the south. But the future can also be painful for a migrant in America; the distance from loved ones in the homeland can become unbearable.

It all works out perfectly for the migrant who shuttles between the two. It is best to stay on the road, to keep moving.

Lent in the Year of Our Lord 1996 was, for Mexicans, the darkest hour before the dawn. Certainly they hoped it was the darkest hour. The thought that there could actually be more suffering visited upon their country was too much to bear; Mexicans always prefer to invoke the resurrection.

This was the third consecutive Lent observed in a time of crisis. Since New Year's Day 1994, the stock market had plunged alongside the peso, the jobless rate had soared, and the black market had exploded. The rich tightened their belts, the middle class strained under massive debt. For the Mexican worker or peasant, it was yet another round of survival. The streets of Mexico City were choked as never before with street vendors, prostitutes, pickpockets, and incipient youth gangs aping their counterparts in Compton and East L.A.[4] And then there were the poorest of the poor, the Indians living in the provinces, a good many of whom had become convinced that, in the face of such adversity, revolution was the only recourse. That or crossing the border.

In the border states, narco[5]-wars raged. Mob-style hits were carried out on the streets in broad daylight. Much of Mexican airspace was ruled by a man nicknamed El Señor de los Cielos, the Lord of the Skies, aka Amado Carrillo Fuentes, a cartel godfather who shipped his cargo, by the tons, on chartered jet planes.

Despite forecasts of better times (the Clinton administration even chipped in $50 billion in credit to prop up its free-trade partner), the darkness lingered on. Assassinations, corruption, street crime. In everyday

2. In the novel *The Grapes of Wrath* (1939), by the American writer John Steinbeck (1902–1968), the Joads are a poor family forced, especially by the economic hardship caused by the Great Depression, to leave their farm in Oklahoma. They travel west, through drought-stricken states, in search of agricultural work in California.
3. Dear little mother.
4. Respectively, a city in Los Angeles County and a neighborhood in the city of Los Angeles, known as sites of gang violence.
5. Narcotics.

conversation, Mexicans referred to the phenomenon as, simply, "*la crisis*." They uttered the phrase with almost sentimental familiarity, as if referring to a long-lost relative who unexpectedly shows up on one's doorstep. People said that *la crisis* was responsible for every malady that afflicted them, a deus ex machina that was cause, not effect. "Because of *la crisis*, I lost my job . . ." Because of *la crisis*, you borrowed a thousand dollars and risked your life sneaking across the U.S.-Mexico border.

I spent the better part of Lent adjusting to life in Mexico City, the biggest metropolis on earth, to which I had just moved. I wasted endless hours in bureaucratic queues (phone company, water and power, immigration) that looked more like soup lines. In the evenings, I sat in my apartment writing at a desk next to soot-streaked windows that looked down upon strangely empty streets—strange for the fact that there were some twenty million souls in the immediate vicinity.

And yet Mexico City, capital of a nation in tatters, approached Easter with rapturous anticipation; holy was the great highland city whose belly button the gods tickle to remind it that no matter how poor, crowded, contaminated, or violent, it was still just an inch below heaven. If you stared into the zinc-tinted pall hanging over the valley long enough, celestial forms came into view, writhing in the smog-ether.

But the actual heavens were something else again. There had been several smog alerts since Ash Wednesday.[6] Pigeons fell from the skies, asphyxiated. Head pounding, I wandered the labyrinth, breathing in Volkswagen fumes and smoking Mexican Marlboros, at one with one of the world's last armies of True Smokers. Mexico City dwellers love to show off their tobacco prowess despite, or precisely because of, the fact that they live in the most polluted city on earth. I spat black balls into my handkerchief.

*La crisis* was, above all else, a public event. Yes, there was brooding and violence inside homes, within families—in the tabloids, we were treated to the typical tales of husbands chopping up their wives and sons killing their parents. In this family-values country, you could rest assured that if you were murdered the last face you'd see would be that of a friend or relative.

But the pressure of *la crisis* was too great to bear in private. Every two weeks, *la quincena* came, the bimonthly payday, and we spilled into the streets, into cantinas and dance halls and strip joints. God knows where the money came from. But I'd seen it before, this end-of-the-world excess, in the barrios of San Salvador during the darkest days of the civil war, in Managua at the height of the U.S. embargo against the Sandinista regime, in Havana back when Castro prohibited mention of the word *glasnost* and quarantined the island from contact with the outside world.[7] When apocalypse is at hand there's nothing left to lose, and inhibitions fall. There might not have been enough money to pay the rent, buy clothes, or even eat decently, but, by God, there was enough for a round of drinks. Solidarity.

---

6. The first day of Lent.
7. The events in this sentence took place during the 1980s; see, e.g., note 6, p. 2321. *Managua*: capital of Nicaragua. *Sandinista regime*: The Sandinista National Liberation Front (*Frente* *Sandinista de Liberación Nacional*, or FSLN), a socialist political party, ruled Nicaragua from 1979 until 1990. *Glasnost*: literally, publicity (Russian); a Soviet policy, ca. 1986, of permitting open discussion of social and political issues.

Thus, Mexicans escaped *la crisis* through the spectacle of public ritual. No one ever did anything alone. If you had a doctor's appointment, you called up your best friend; he'd take the day off from work to escort you, and stand by your side even during the embarrassing rubber-gloved examination. Same thing for trips to the bank, to get a haircut, to buy groceries. There was always great chatter as people lined up to do their business.

The ultimate Mexican public ritual, the fiesta, derives its tremendous energy from the tension between spirit and flesh, between Indian and Iberian, between Christianity and pagan pantheism—in a word, from Mexico's "mestizo," or mixed blood and culture. *La crisis* only poured fuel on the fire. In 1995, December 12 (the Virgin of Guadalupe's feast day),[8] 24, and 31 were days of national paroxysm. On Valentine's Day, practically every hotel in the country, from the swank joints to the barrio hovels, hung a No Vacancy sign and ecstatic shrieks echoed along the halls: a national fuck. The provinces partied as hard as the capital; every town has a patron saint and the feast days were excuses for weeklong bacchanals on the order of decadent Rome. In the Indian territories, pagan agricultural rites only thinly disguised as Catholic were celebrated as never before. What all these fiestas had in common was that we celebrated the spirit *through* the flesh. We alternated between the extremes of mortified piety and Dionysian abandon.

And then there was Easter.

Throughout Lent, Mexicans performed the Catholic rote of abstinence and fasting, physically representing the economic collapse with their very bodies. Economic forces, after all, are invisible but for the effect they have on our physical form: where we live, what we eat, what we wear, how we dance. As Lent drew to a close, Mexico prepared to nail itself to the cross.

A gray wind blows in Iztapalapa. The rains of summer are months away and the dust of ancient, infertile earth rises in choking clouds. Lying on a fallow plain south of downtown Mexico City, the district of Iztapalapa, by the looks of things, was a rough-and-tumble barrio long before the Spaniards arrived. It has the color of old poverty: dark brown, almost chocolate-brown skin, the color of little or no crossbreeding. Iztapalapa's Indian population was poor around the time of the Conquest, and it's poor now.

I come up from the bowels of the metro into a plaza adorned with graffiti murals, of the officially sanctioned variety. There are ecosensitive messages, tributes to the dead of the great quake of 1985. And a monument to *la crisis*: ESTAMOS EN LAS MANOS DE DIOS (We Are in the Hands of God), reads a banner flowing above the two hands of the Great One, which cradle a cityscape rendered postapocalyptically with skyscrapers become tombstones and a blood glow tinting the twilight sky.

Iztapalapa is famous for two things: a soaring crime rate inspired by *la crisis* (which led authorities to temporarily deploy regular army troops on its streets) and the best *representación* of the Passion in all of Mexico. The pageantry of the event is on the order of Cecil B. DeMille[9]—practically every barrio resident plays a part. In the United States right now, people are

spectacular epics, such as the biblical story *The Ten Commandments* (1956).

watching *The Ten Commandments* and *The Greatest Story Ever Told* on television, preparing for quiet Passover[1] or Easter family gatherings and religious services. But in Mexico, half the population, from the capital to the Indian countryside, is starring in its own version of the Passion.

It is the 153rd annual *representación* in Iztapalapa (there is a region in the state of Guerrero where the ritual goes back four hundred years), and locals speak of *la tradición* with mystical reverence. The peso may have tumbled, we can't buy ham for Easter, my son was mugged last night, but we're keeping tradition alive! Just because there's a Price Club in every major city doesn't mean that Mexico has lost its essence. If Mexico didn't stop being an Indian nation five hundred years ago—mestizo identity, after all, is at least half pre-Columbian—why should it now? Still, Iztapalapa is a place contaminated by the germ of restlessness. Indians migrate from the countryside looking for the better life in the city; often, after a generation or two of urban poverty, they hit the road again, trying their luck in the States.

The barrio is decked out for the Passion: fully costumed Roman soldiers, Samaritan women, Pharisees walk the streets, snacking and smoking, shooting the breeze. But it's the *nazarenos*, the Nazarenes, who are omnipresent, roving packs of teenage boys who've built their own crosses and had their mothers stitch together simple white robes with purple sashes so they can play Jesus as penance. Five thousand or so *nazarenos* trudge along the streets of Iztapalapa this year, straining under crosses weighing up to ninety kilos. Many of the kids have been training for months.

There are dozens of simultaneous *representaciones*. A mega-spectacle plays out in the plaza on a stage about fifty yards long, floodlit by arc lamps and ringed by a bevy of Televisa remote trucks that transmit the performances live nationwide.

The *representación* of the Last Supper takes place. There are easily 100,000 people gathered in the plaza before the stage, but the concentration on the scene is absolute; the only sound that can be heard, aside from the dialogue, is the hum of the remote trucks. Judas[2] rises from the table. He frets, wrings his hands. He paces back and forth interminably, throwing anguished looks at Jesus, at the disciples, at us. The roles are taken so seriously by the residents of Iztapalapa that the brave souls who play Judas are occasionally shunned by their neighbors, as if by representing Judas they're actually betraying Jesus himself.

The Last Supper table is carted away by stagehands; foam rocks and potted trees are rolled in for the Gethsemane scene. The Iztapalapa resident who has played Jesus for the last six years pleads, with old-school theatricality, to "let this cup pass from me" while the disciples lie sleeping a few feet away.

Then the chaos: Pharisees and scribes rush in, Judas offers his last kiss, a sword is drawn, an ear is lopped off, the disciples scatter, and finally Pilate: "Which of the two do you wish that I release to you?" And the

---

1. A Jewish holiday that commemorates the Jewish people's release from slavery in ancient Egypt. *The Greatest Story Ever Told*: Hollywood movie (1965) about the life of Jesus.
2. According to the New Testament, Judas Iscariot was one of Jesus' 12 Apostles. His betrayal of Jesus (called the Nazarene, because he was from Nazareth) to the Roman authorities led to Jesus' cruci-
fixion. In the following paragraphs, Mexicans re-enact scenes from biblical accounts of the last days of Jesus' life, such as when Pontius Pilate, the Roman prefect (governor) who ordered Jesus' crucifixion, commuted the death sentence of the insurrectionist Barabbas rather than that of Jesus. Pilate reportedly did so at the request of the crowd at the Passover celebration in Jerusalem.

entire plaza, every last man, woman, and child, as per *tradición*, shouts: "BARABBAS!"

Afterward, the crowd begins to disperse, but thousands of people remain in the plaza overnight, laying down blankets and passing around *champurrado* and *atole*, hot beverages that predate the Conquest. These fervent Indian Catholics will stay up with the Savior on the longest night of his life, the night before his death. They will also get the best seats for his crucifixion.

Good Friday[3] begins as a startlingly clear day; somehow, we've been given a respite from the smog. Legions of visitors—an estimated two million—descend on Iztapalapa. The army of vendors fares well among the multitudes as the wait for the Crucifixion grows longer and hotter (the Red Cross tends to hundreds of sunstroke victims), selling crucifixes, sunglasses, cardboard visors, caps, mango, papaya, and bottles of Coke, Sprite, and Fanta chilled atop slabs of ice that drip puddles into the gray dust.

I join the *nazarenos* on their serpentine path through the barrios. Five thousand Christs accompanied by the sound of the wood of five thousand crosses dragging along the asphalt. The kids range in age from preteens with crosses only about four feet long to twenty-somethings with several years of *representación* experience, carrying the better part of a tree over their shoulders. Some of the crosses are painted black, others red. Some are carved with flowery designs, others varnished so well they look like they're encased in glass.

The pilgrimage begins at seven in the morning and winds through the better part of Iztapalapa before arriving at Golgotha in the late afternoon. The *nazarenos* start out in high spirits, perhaps guilty just a tad of the sin of pride. But by noon, the Red Cross is carting kids off on stretchers. It's the feet that suffer the most. A good many Christs go barefoot—on asphalt baking in the hot sun and sprinkled with broken glass. Some wear Ace bandages, which soon grow filthy and unravel. Others wear cheap huaraches; these, too, fall apart after a few kilometers. The kids jump onto pieces of cardboard—thrown down on the sizzling street by store owners along the route—and then, wincing, back onto the asphalt.

At times, the procession grows scraggly as, overpowered by the sun, kids fall out of the ranks, but the organizers rush in, shouting and whistling like Romans. I stand in the shade of a corner general store, drinking Pepsi and smoking Marlboros along with the crowd of onlookers, and suddenly there appears before us the most unlikely of *samaritanas*, dressed in a floor-length red velvet cloak but showing an inordinate amount of cleavage, her face made up like a transvestite's. Maybe she *is* a transvestite, who knows? The sight of this sexy Samaritan, eyeliner running down her cheeks, taking uncertain steps in five-inch stilettos is too much for the gaggle of mothers and grandmothers around me. "In *heels!*" cries one of them with glee. "Now that's really a love of art!"

Amazingly, the vast majority of the procession will make it to Golgotha, to Cerro de la Muerte. A fourteen-year-old carrying a cross he claims weighs seventy kilos says: "My father did it, my older brothers did it, now it is my turn to fulfill the tradition." And an eighteen-year-old wearing a real crown

3. According to Christian tradition, the day of Jesus' crucifixion, two days before his resurrection on Easter.

of thorns, drops of dried blood on his temples: "There's no pain that I couldn't bear with my faith in the Lord." Every kid is followed by a support crew of siblings, parents, and grandparents urging them on, carrying water bottles and cotton and alcohol to swab the aching, blistered feet.

Again and again the theme of *la crisis* comes up in snippets of casual conversation. Seems that there are more *nazarenos* since the peso fell. Seems like there are fewer vendors but more *tradición*, more *devoción*. A barrio grandmother sums it up: "It's the crisis that is making people come closer to God. More sinners, more penitents. The problem is, the really big sinners, *los políticos hijos de la chingada*—politico sons of bitches—never do their penance. We wind up doing it for them."

Finally, close to three in the afternoon, the *nazarenos* and *romanos* and *samaritanas* make their tattered, triumphal approach to Cerro de la Muerte. Kids sprint the final yards up the hill, throw down their crosses, collapse, strip off robes and T-shirts. Soon the hill is littered with five thousand crosses and the panting, half-naked bodies of five thousand brown Christs. Three great crosses crown Golgotha, with five thousand *nazareno* crosses scattered helter-skelter at their feet.

Surrounding the hill, held back from the *representación* area by a chainlink fence, are the two million onlookers. The sea of people in all directions is like a huge, unified organism, a great jellyfish, nudging its way ever closer to the *representación*, straining against the fence and the army of cops, Indian kids armed with ancient service revolvers.

Now trumpets blast. Romans on white stallions charge up the hill.

The proclaimer: "And having committed these and many other crimes . . . we condemn him and sentence him to be taken along the streets of the Holy City of Jerusalem, crowned with thorns and with a chain about his neck, carrying his own cross, and accompanied by two criminals, Dismas and Gestas, unto Golgotha, and that there he be crucified between the two criminals, where he will hang until dead."

He is nailed to the cross, the ninety-kilo cross that he himself built, the one that he has dragged in procession through Iztapalapa every day since Palm Sunday. The sound of the hammer resounds through the great banks of speakers. Stage blood spouts from hands and feet. A camera crane moves in close for the dizzying Scorsese shot.[4]

Christ, Dismas, and Gestas writhe on their crosses, and all of Mexico's children see themselves. On Golgotha hangs every dream ever denied in this land: the three crucified might as well be named Benjamín, Jaime, and Salvador Chávez.

In the final moments of the Passion, the gray wind of Iztapalapa rises in great clouds above the massive crowd. It is the gray of the great dust of the city, not just the arid topsoil of the Cerro but particles of ash from the billion cigarettes of the chain-smoking city, refuse from the garbage dumps on every street corner in the barrios, sooty exhaust from the trucks and taxis and the passenger cars of the rich and poor, especially the poor with their jury-rigged eight-cylinder smoking Chevys—the dust of poverty, the dust of corruption, the dust of hell on earth.

---

4. The American filmmaker Martin Scorsese (b. 1942) is famous for the fast-moving camera work in movies such as *The Last Temptation of Christ* (1988).

As we bring handkerchiefs to our faces and rub our eyes, everything that
was white turns gray: the robes of the *nazarenos*, the blocks of ice at the
vending stalls, the pages of my notebook.
On this Good Friday the holy, fallen country has come to watch itself die.
And live.
*It is accomplished.*[5]

Before Easter and after Easter, for many years before *la crisis* and every year
since, a procession of Mexican *penitentes* has marched out of barrios like
Iztapalapa and out of provincial towns throughout the republic. Migrants
heading north, fleeing Egypt for the Canaan[6] just across the Rio Grande, a
million migrant souls searching for redemption and resurrection, a Mexican
Manifest Destiny[7] to be won on streets paved with gold, on American streets.
For over two years I was on the road, following Mexican migrant families. I did not live what the migrants lived, but I saw a bit of what they saw.
I watched that ribbon of highway curl over and over the horizon. I saw a lot of
hard work and a lot of love and a lot of drunken fights and a lot of long separations between lovers, between mothers and daughters and fathers and sons.
And I saw death. I logged some fifty thousand miles on my Chevy Blazer,
most of it in cross-country travel. I suppose when you're on the road all the
time, the chances of running into tragedy increase.
I saw diamonds of glass glittering on the asphalt and stiff cows with legs
skyward.
I saw a Mexican man sitting in the mangled remains of an old Datsun,
just sitting there, oh so relaxed, in the passenger seat, like he was dozing on
the long ride up the eastern seaboard. But he was never going home.
I saw a young Chicano thrown from his truck on I-10. He and his ride were
separated by four freeway lanes when the macabre ballet ended. He looked
down at his leg, marveling that his kneecap was completely turned around,
while I marveled that he was still alive.
I began my journey alongside the migrants in Cherán, Michoacán, the
Indian town that Benjamín, Jaime, and Salvador hailed from. I followed their
ghost steps across the border. And then, across the United States.

2001

---

5. Reportedly Jesus' last words.
6. According to the Bible, the area to which the
Jewish people moved after their escape from

enslavement.
7. See the discussion of Manifest Destiny in the
"Annexations" introduction, pp. 163–64.

---

# VIRGIL SUÁREZ
## b. 1962

Born in Cuba, Virgil Suárez immigrated with his family to Spain in 1970 and to the
United States two years later. He earned his Master of Fine Arts degree in creative
writing from Louisiana State University, in Baton Rouge, and teaches literature

and creative writing at Florida State University, in Tallahassee. The author of four novels, a memoir, and several collections of poems and stories, he is one of the leading voices of contemporary Cuban American literature. In his writings, Suárez explores the strengths and weaknesses of immigrant families, the solace of shared myths and the pain of remembrance. His fiction evokes vividly the everyday lives and surroundings of newly arrived exiles and those who struggle to come to terms with the passing of the years in an adopted country.

The novels *Latin Jazz* (1989) and *The Cutter* (1991) detail the effects of the Revolution and exile on adolescents. *Welcome to the Oasis* (1992), which collects stories and a novella, is about Latino young men coming of age in the United States. The novels *Havana Thursdays* (1995) and *Going Under* (1996) chronicle the conflicted existences of middle-aged Cuban-Americans who have neither cut their ties with Cuba nor assimilated completely into American society. Suárez's memoir, *Spared Angola: Memories from a Cuban-American Childhood* (1997), blends poetry, fiction, and essays in a forceful remembrance of childhood, violence, separation, and loss. One of the most powerful chapters in the book describes the author's relationship with his father, an angry exile who was defeated in the end not by Castro but by a 576-pound factory pallet that broke his body.

A prolific poet, Suárez has published widely in many literary journals. His poems have been collected in volumes such as *Garabato Poems* (1999), *In the Republic of Longing* (2000), and *Guide to the Blue Tongue* (2002). Suárez has also edited or coedited several important anthologies of Latino literature and poetry, including *Iguana Dreams: New Latino Fiction* (1992) with Delia Poey and *Paper Dance: 55 Latino Poets* (1995) with Víctor Hernández Cruz and Leroy V. Quintana. In 2005, Suárez published *90 Miles: Selected and New Poems* (90 miles is the distance between Cuba and Florida), which showcases his central themes: the nature of displacement and of exile, the embrace of poetry as a communal act, and the use of language as a palliative for longing.

In the seven selections included here, Suárez weaves English and Spanish. He presents people from both of his countries—family, friends, and ancestors. He connects the pasts of his parents and grandparents with the lives he and his family now lead. He mixes natural images—manatees and mockingbirds, dusty leaves and coffee beans, cucuyos and orchids, caracoles and lizards—with the emotions and intimate experiences of an exile's existence.

## Tea Leaves, Caracoles, Coffee Beans

My mother, who in those Havana days believed in divination, found her tea
leaves at El Volcán, the Chinese market/apothecary, brought the leaves in a
precious silk paper bundle, unwrapped them as if unwrapping her own skin,
and then she'd boil water to make my dying grandmother's tea, while my
mother read its leaves, I simply saw leaves floating in steaming water, vapor          5
kissed my skin, my nose became moist as a puppy's. My mother did this
because my grandmother, her mother-in-law, believed in all things. Her appetite for knowledge was vast, the one thing we all agreed she passed down to
me, the skinny kid sent to search for caracoles, these snail shells that littered
the underbrush of the empty lot next door. My mother threw them on top of         10
the table, cleaned them of dirt, kept them in a mason jar and every morning
before breakfast, read them on top of the table, their way of falling, some up,
some down, their ridges, swirls of creamy lines, their broken edges . . . every-

thing sheread looked bad, for my grandmother, for us, for staying in our country, this island of suspended disbelief. My mother read coffee beans too, with their wrinkled, fleshy green and red skin. Orange-skinned beans she kept aside. Orange meant death, and my mother didn't want to accept it. I learned mostly of death from the way a sparrow fell when I hit it in the chest with my slingshot and a lead-pellet I made by melting my toy soldiers. The sparrow's eyes always hid behind droopy eyelids, which is how my grandmother died, by closing her eyes to the world, truth became this fading light, a tunnel, as everybody says, but instead of heaven she went in to the ground, to that one place that still nourishes the tea leaves, caracoles, and the coffee beans which, if I didn't know better, I'd claim shone, those red-glowing beans in starlight were the eyes of the dead looking out through the darkness as those of us who believed in such things, walked through life with a lightness of feet, spirit, a vapor-aura that could be read or sung.

1998                                                                    1999

## Ricochet

I'm working the rubber band made from a long strip I cut from my bicycle tire's inner tube. The black, powdery residue of the rubber leaves fingerprints on the surface where I'm doing the work. Trying not to get a tear in the rubber. This is the second time I try. I'm hiding in the back yard, by the sink and faucet where my mother usually does the wash, out of reach so nobody sees me, nobody bothers me. I'm thinking I'm going to have the meanest, bestest slingshot musket in the neighborhood. I'm going to shoot lizards' heads off with bottle caps. Fermán, my black friend at school, showed me the original drawing of the thing itself. I copied it and now I'm building it back here by the chicken coops, using my father's hammer, scissors, and a few furniture tacks I removed from the bottom of the sofa.

Nobody will miss them, and nobody can see the flap of material hanging loose like a dog's ear.

The rubber holds, dangles around my hands like a pair of black snakes. Fine rubber. The best, which I took from the front wheel of my bicycle. I put the tire back on so my father wouldn't see the thing missing. Only a flat tire, and any bike can have that. I just won't ride it, and if they ask me to I'll say I don't feel like it. My father's been gone for two or three days now. The secret police, as my mother called the two civilian-dressed men, came and arrested my father. I'm here in the house with my grandmother.

I haven't seen my parents in a few days.

The G-Dos, secret police, came for my dissident father. My father, the gusano[1]—this much I know is true.

Every time I glance over at my bicycle with its flat front tire, leaning against the gate that separates the chickens from the rabbits, I think of my father. He stands in line for days to get me this bicycle, and I know he'll be angry if he ever finds out. My grandmother tells me he'll be back

1. Literally, worm; jargon for U.S.-based Cuban traitor.

home any minute now, but we haven't heard from him or my mother. The neighbors keep coming by to talk to my grandmother, find out what happened. The next door neighbors, Miriam and her son Chichi, come by and I almost show Chichi my slingshot musket, but then I think better of it. If I show it around everyone will ask questions. They will glimpse its beauty soon enough.

It's almost done, and I've collected enough bottle caps on the way home from school and back to have a real shoot-out war. Everyone in the neighborhood has slingshots, including Chichi, but nobody has this one. I hold the 2×2 piece of wood in my hand, feel its weight on my fingers. I sanded it down on the sides real smooth because I didn't want to get any more splinters in the tips of my fingers. I plan to paint it red or black, like a real pirate's musket I've seen on TV.

My grandmother, who cooks in the kitchen, keeps poking her head out of the kitchen entrance to ask if I need anything. I've been out here for a long time, long enough to get used to the thick, musky smell of the chickens. A rooster hops up to the fence and eyes me the way chickens do. Turns this side first, then the other. I aim the thing at it and pretend I slice its head off. One clean shot. I want to line up the trigger with the front muzzle. I've cut two feet of rubber for each side. I load one side, then the other. Each side holds three bottle cap back-ups, so that I could reload real fast.

Then Ricardito, my friend from the other side of the fence, shows up on top of the fence between his house and mine. I can't hide the musket fast enough.

"What are you doing?" he asks and licks his lips. He always licks his lips when he's nervous.

"Hey, not much." I want to tell him not now, that I don't want to play. But he looks like he isn't going to jump down and leave me alone, so I glare up at him. He's older by two years, but everything we play I always beat him. My mother once told me the story of how when I was three I peed in my bottle and gave Ricardito it to drink from, told him it was delicious orange juice. I don't remember doing it, but my mother says I did.

"Wanna play ball?" he says, his dirty hands gripping the cement at the top of the cinder block wall. His father always threatens to stick broken pieces of bottles up there so we won't jump the fence so often. Ricardito broke his arm once when we used to walk it up and down, balancing ourselves up there like in tightrope acts.

"Not right now."

"Has your father come back?"

My father, the traitor. My father the counter-revolutionary.

"No, not yet." I feel the rubber bands underneath my thighs as I squat over them so Ricardito won't see them. He's my best friend, but once he sees something of mine he can't stop asking questions.

"My father says they can keep him in prison for good," he says. I don't want to think about my father, so I don't say anything.

"They'll make him cut sugar cane." Once you get him going, he can never stop. There's no way to do it unless you get his mind off on something else. I don't because I don't want him to start asking me questions about what I'm doing.

He sits there and dangles his legs over the side. His scuffed shoes scrape against the cement. I can see the worn sole on one shoe, and the crack in the other. He isn't wearing socks, and his ankles and calves are riddled with mosquito bites, whole constellations of them, some red, others crusted over with purple scabs. The sores never go away because he loves to pick off the scabs and look at them real close. He told me once he saves them all in a jar, and I believe him. I believe anything he says when it concerns his body.

One time when we were alone in the house, he called me into the bathroom, where I had found him with a bloody mouth. He kept spitting up blood and saliva, and when I asked him what had happened he showed me his loose tooth. He'd pulled on a tooth long enough to jiggle it loose, and now his gums were bleeding. This was a permanent tooth too.

Whenever he smiles he's got a gap right there. His parents refuse to take him to the dentist, and his father beat him silly because of it.

"What are you going to do if your father doesn't come back?" Ricardito asked.

"He'll come back."

"Not if they don't want him to. You think they'll kill him?"

"My grandmother says he will."

Ricardito hates my grandmother because she always chases him away with a broom. She calls him the little animal, the little pest. "Animalito," she screams at him. "Salte de aquí! Vete ya!"

He sticks his big, candy-stained tongue out at her.

Once he fell as he ran and scraped his knees, but he didn't cry. I thought of him that night, in bed, waiting for the blood to dry, crust up into giant scabs so he could start digging his dirty nails underneath. He says that if you look at the underside of a scab, you can see the patterns of skin as it heals, like when you cut a tree down and count the rings to see how old the tree is. Except his never heal. He bleeds onto his bed sheets, and his mother never asks why, or where the blood comes from. His mother can't see very well. She wears glasses thicker than the bottoms of bottles.

When I realize Ricardito isn't going to go away, I figure I could ask him to get me something. I need a big nail for a trigger. "Does your father have a nail I can use?" I ask.

"What do you want a nail for?"

"I can't tell you. Does he have one?"

"He might. It depends."

"If you get me one I will tell you."

He stares at me with his eyebrows furrowed, like he always does because half of the things I say he never believes, and also because he's too used to my fooling him and pulling his leg all the time. Maybe there's some truth to the bottle of my urine he drank.

No use. I see it in his eyes. He's in one of those lazy moods. I can tell. He doesn't feel like jumping down. What can I do?

"If I tell you what I'm doing," I tell him, "do you promise not to tell?"

"I might, might not."

"Mierda."

He looks hurt because he never likes it when I call him shit. I feel sorry for him all of a sudden.

"All right."

"OK," he says.

"Can't you tell what it is?"

"A slingshot."

"Better than that."

"Where did you get the rubber bands?"

I don't answer, just shrug.

He jumps down now, his feet landing flat and square by the mound of bottle caps. He lands on it and crushes a few. Startled, the chickens flutter into a ruckus.

"Take it easy," I say. "Look where you're jumping."

He apologizes, but it's no use. I can tell. He wants to know more than ever what it is I'm building.

I show him. "See, it's a musket, a rifle, a machine gun of bottle caps."

I explain how I plan to shoot bottle caps at lizards, at birds, at anything I find.

Already he's all hands. I hate that about him, his groping around with his dirty hands and fingernails. He's about to pull on the rubber bands, stretch them for the first time, and I yank them out of his hands.

If I found the nail, and I put the thing together, I could convince Ricardito to play firing squad. I heard one of my parents' friends mention something about it once. One of my father's friends, Guillermo, who rode the motor-cycle—he rode me around a few times, up and down the street, what a great thrill—and he never came home one afternoon. Guillermo was a gusano, my parents always called him. Gusano means worm, maggot. I found out it means dissident, counter-revolutionary, the kind that could get you killed or disappeared in Cuba. When my father called Guillermo gusano, he always shot back: "It takes one to know one." And both he and my father laughed real hard.

I can play firing squad with Ricardito, yeah.

We look around the chicken coop and rabbit hutches until I find the right nail, then I pull it out slowly. With one knee on the ground and Ricardito breathing over my head, I straighten it out. It has a wide enough head for what I need. The wide head holds the bottle cap under the pressure from the rubber band, and then I can flick it easy like flipping a coin up in the air.

I measure one last time, still making sure that Ricardito doesn't touch any more of the bottle caps—I had them counted—and hammer the nail into place.

"It's done," I say and hold up my brand-new musket. "Look how beautiful."

"Can I hold it?" Ricardito licks his dry, cracked lips.

"Not yet," I say and turn away from him until I can load it properly.

The rubber bands stretch just fine, with plenty of tension. I imagine the bottle caps going fast and hard, easily lobbing off the head of any lizard, frog, snake. Great, I think and feel the excitement in my throat.

The rubber band hugs the first three caps, then I load the second one, another three. It's ready.

I want to shoot it before my grandmother hears us.

"Stand against the wall, just straight like that."

"Why?"

"Just do it," I tell him.

He backs up against the dirty lime walls in the patio of our house in Habana. A little nervous, he fidgets. His shoulders slump, his hands flutter about in and out of his pockets.

"Move back more, right up against the wall."

Then I think of the perfect idea. I blindfold him to make it look real enough. Then Ricardito can't see, and he won't know how the thing works, and he'll be too scared to want to shoot it. I figure I could aim for his gut, or his hands.

I find a rag by the sink, take it and fold it over his eyes.

"I can't see," he says.

"That's the idea." I turn him a few times like he's going to beat up a piñata or pin the tail on the donkey.

Then I back him up against the wall. I decide now that since his eyes are covered he won't have to face the wall. He won't know when I fire. He'll only hear and feel the bottle caps bite into his skin, and if I miss, he'll hear them buzz past his ears.

He stands there blindfolded, his head tilted upward as though he's trying to sneak a peek.

I walk back counting twenty paces. I hold my musket between my legs, pull back on the rubber bands, load, and aim.

"What is this called?"

"Firing squad," I say and close one eye.

I bite down on my tongue as I concentrate, all along thinking of the bottle caps as real bullets. The machine gun in my hand. Ricardito isn't my friend anymore, but my father. I hear my father's voice talking about how he wants to leave the country, take me out of it before the government brainwashes me into thinking my own father is my enemy.

My father, tall and thin, learns to study the bullet marks on the walls. He says they tell tragic stories. A whole calligraphic record of those who've been shot, disappeared, for telling the truth about corrupt governments.

An old-fashioned firing squad like the Spanish used with their shiny muskets. With their conquests. With all that rancor and rage in their hearts.

"What's taking so long?" Ricardo speaks and breaks my concentration.

I take aim. My trigger finger trembles against the nail, then steadies, and I open fire.

1999                                                                    1999


## Floridiana

Lugubrious days pass with the amplitude of manatees,
hibiscus unfold their smiling vortex to confused bees,

somewhere near turkey point a crocodile grows a foot
by the day, tourists mistake the big ones for logs,

anhingas play Jesus on the Spanish moss-riddled branches          5
of oaks and junipers, crucified in the sun. Feral Quaker

parrots build nests high up in the banyan trees. Orchids,
capuchin monkeys loosed from an animal distributor

warehouse, memories of the bearded lady and the lizard
man, retired now in Palatka,[1] holding court in the shade        10

of a parasol by their trailer. Russian midgets, rockets
shot into the eye of the moon, this magic of fireflies

zapping their phosphorescence in the night air, jasmine,
gardenia—somewhere a man barbecues 4-inch-thick steaks

in a thing called the Green Egg. A firefighter, a player          15
of handball. When his son visits once a year from Vegas

he asks when will he return to Tampa,[2] his home. Who isn't
lured by so much sun, heat? The permanence of weather—

or by the mystery of sun showers when the sky opens up
and pelts the earth with a momentary lapse of crying.            20

Right now, somewhere in the Everglades,[3] a fish jumps
out of the water and into the mouth of an alligator.

Nobody was there to witness it, but it happens again and again.

2001                                                            2002

## The Trouble with Some Words in English

Tart means a type of pastry shell filled with jam.
Or, acid, sour, sharp in meaning, which I love

because there were other words in English
that bit the tips of our tongues, or rendered

our mouths numb. One such word was dating.                        5
We were already young men and women

in high school, in the world, doors closing
us out, those of us with the wrong clothes, slick

hair, with this awkwardness of speech, accent.
We thought it meant a way to keep track of time,                 10

not the fucking that took place in the back seats
of Novas, Pintos, Impalas. Girls whom we heard

1. City in northern Florida.                    3. Swamp region of southern Florida.
2. City on the west coast of Florida.

speak the word made their eyes glow with it,
a ripe fruit in their mouths. When we asked them

to go out with us on a date (sweet, fleshy fruit          15
of a certain palm tree,) they told us no, they

couldn't because they thought of us as friends.
Friends, which we interpreted to mean no, not us,

those with the dirty finger nails, greasy lips,
complexion riddled with pimples and tiny scars.          20

Friends, which meant we'd have to postpone
our practice of how we'd get close enough

to another, a native speaker, to whisper in their
ears how much we truly wanted to burn, be them.

2002                                                                                   2002


## Cucuyo Ghazal[1] Razzmatazz

after John Balaban[2]

Those Cuban nights of long ago, smoke
    punctuating my father's talk and from tall grass

the cucuyos, fireflies, flashed their beck-and-call
    to me, as I looked, amazed, at the dark grass.

My father, the dissident, persecuted and sad,              5
    knowing he'd leave his country. No more grass

or these insects of the night that illuminated
    my life with silvery flashes atop the swaying grass.

After forty-three years of exile, my father's dead,
    my mother shrinking in widowhood, the grass          10

is no longer as green, dark or filled with fireflies,
    though once in a while I see a ghost-flash in grass

growing wild around the lip of my man-made pond.

2003                                                                                   2004

---

1. A poetic form that originated in the sixth cen-      and a refrain.
tury in Arabic, consisting of rhyming couplets      2. American poet and translator (b. 1943).

# Orthography

My grandmother always strained
to hear the sinsonte's (mockingbird's)
trill, this gunpowder-chested canticle

in the blushed light of the afternoon
before dusk, a yearning to decipher                                        5
the individual notes, "Al estilo, niño,"[1]

Mockingbird language stitched, stolen
from other birds—a court jester, he
who knew the ways of heart language,

or at least kept the court amused.                                         10
Sinsonte, el cantar de los cantores . . .
The way a bird whistles a thousand

meanings to one need, one desire.
This lost melancholia about a child
quieting to hear his own harsh song.                                       15

2003                                                                    2004


# What We Choose of Exile

"We choose exile as a vantage point;
from exile we look back on the rejected,
rejecting place—"to make our poems
out of it and against it."

—Donald Hall, in his preface to
*Above the River: The Complete
Poems of James Wright*[1]

This rock my father brought over from Las Villas,[2]
    the place of his birth and which he kept in his shoe-
cleaning box kit, a copy of his first full paycheck
    in the United States, $110 in 1974, a month's salary

he brought to my mother as an offering of his love                         5
    to us, no? His blue tongue as he lay dying, entubed
throat, heart, his glands knowing so finally the clasp
    and hold of God's hands upon his body. We choose

nothing, and all. This is the way it is for those lost
    into the eternal haze of dust, cobwebs, broken piano                   10
strings, crow-cawing, a shrieking in the ear. A rusted
    car, a 1965 Dodge Dart. A black comb with a couple

---

1. To the style, boy.
1. American poet (1927–1980). *Donald Hall*:
American poet (b. 1928).

2. A province on the north-central coast of
Cuba.

of broken teeth with which to comb the hair, scratch
that mosquito bite behind his arm. The way our elbows
dry out and become scaley. My mother's arthritic hands,                    15
fingers gone numb from years of sewing zippers at piece-

meal wages. Cufflinks, their dull glint inside her jewelry
box, a gift one Valentine's, bought from the Avon lady.
What chooses us, that's what my father wanted to know.
The moment, fate, life? Cold air in Manhattan, a river          20

in Kentucky. The mesas of New Mexico, where I'd love
to die one night only to have owls, crows, wolves, foxes
tear me apart, appease their hunger of place with my stolen
flesh, this exile's heavy, musky meat—our bodies' history

of place, those places left behind and those about to be        25
traversed. We can carry our lanterns to light the way,
or we can walk on with our eyes closed, our tongues tied,
our arms behind our backs, ready to sacrifice or surrender.

2005                                                      2006


# RAFAEL CAMPO
# b. 1963

Born to Cuban parents in Dover, New Jersey, Rafael Campo earned degrees at
Amherst College and Harvard Medical School. He completed his residency in
internal medicine at the University of California, San Francisco. In 1990, between
his third and fourth years of medical school, he took a year off to study poetry at
Boston University with the Nobel Prize–winning Caribbean poet Derek Walcott.
Writing poetry became a journey of self-discovery, an exploration of his identity as
a gay Cuban American and of his connections with his family, his patients, and his
fellow physicians.

The year resulted in the publication of two volumes of verse: *The Other Man
Was Me: A Voyage to the New World* (1994), winner of the American Poetry
Series Open Competition, and *What the Body Told* (1996), winner of a Lambda
Literary Award. With great flexibility and resourcefulness, Campo uses traditional poetic forms—sestinas, villanelles, haikus—as vehicles for self-revelation.
Many poems in *The Other Man Was Me* focus on his search for belonging and on
his tenuous connection with his family's lost homeland. Other poems focus on
the body, not only as the locus of memory and desire, but also as the healing
place for wounds both physical and spiritual. In *What the Body Told*, Campo
writes about illness and the body, sex and AIDS, death and beauty, and his tense
relation to Cuban culture. A sequence of poems explores the lives and deaths of
his patients, dispassionate physicians who view their patients as a collection of
symptoms, and the growth of his empathy and humanity. In connecting the suffering of others to his work, Campo explained in a 2004 interview with the journalist Robert Birnbaum, "When I listen to narratives of my patients I can see

how they negotiate some of their own identities in this troubled world. And so for me that is something I try to reflect back on my own writing and my work with them."

Campo's third volume of poetry, *Diva* (1999), was selected as a finalist for the National Book Critics Circle Award. It displayed a deeper control of craft while distilling some of Campo's motifs and included a series of provocative translations of the twentieth-century Spanish poet and dramatist Federico García Lorca's *Sonetos del amor oscuro* (Sonnets of Dark Love). It was followed by *Landscape with Human Figure* (2002) and *The Enemy* (2007). He has also written a memoir, *The Poetry of Healing* (1997). Campo has received a Guggenheim Fellowship and an Annual Achievement Award from the National Hispanic Academy of Arts and Sciences, among other honors. He works at Beth Israel Deaconess Medical Center, in Boston, Massachusetts. In his practice, he serves mostly Latinos, gay/lesbian/bisexual/transgendered people, and people with HIV.

The five poems selected here map his commitment to literature and healing. In "Elise," Campo writes about the intimacy of language and silence. In "Miss Key West, 1990," he celebrates his homosexuality and the beauty of difference. In "A Poet's Education," he praises the "medicine" of Derek Walcott's teaching, the transcendent beauty of language, and the hard work of reading and writing poetry. In "I Am Mrs. Lorca," an introduction to his translations of *Sonnets of Dark Love*, he explores the elegance of Lorca, who was homosexual. And in "The Changing Face of AIDS," a poem in 12 parts, he presents AIDS as nemesis and as inspiration.

# Elise[1]

I'll name my daughter after you, Elise,
Since naming is what you do best. The heart
You named with poetry; you named with art
As if it were as obvious as peace
The varied torments of the human soul.                      5
I see you pass beneath, as Hardy[2] might,
A lighted window where a girl sits, slight
And wonderful, to watch the falling snow.
You name her all that's joyous in the night,
You name her sorrows all angelic names.                   10
At the edge of a field, you name the ageless scheme—
It's very quiet—of accumulating white.
You name it bottomless, you name it time
And time again. As Hardy might. Elise,
My daughter, name me too. Give me peace.              15
Name the white slum that is my heart sublime.

1996

---

1. This poem is part 2 of the sequence *Canciones de la vida* (Songs of Life), in *What the Body Told Me*. "Miss Key West, 1990," below, is part
13 of the sequence.
2. Thomas Hardy (1840–1928), English novelist and poet.

# Miss Key West, 1990

The competition's keen: ten women, all
Among the most accomplished in the state.
The crowd is elegant, fifty-bucks-a-plate.
We wait. The women's names are sensual,
Implying appetites and certain tastes,                          5
Meringues and chocolates, and sweet champagne.
I'm just a tourist here—I only came
Because I'm curious. But when a toast
Is raised to the performers by a man
In drag, I feel glamorous, that I                               10
Belong beneath some spotlight too, divine,
The baubles dripping from my ears, so tan
I'm drenched in gold, I'm what you see
When light is passing through a bottle of
Perfume, or when you're powerlessly in love:                   15
I'm Cuba's tears, I'm fashion magazines.

1996


# A Poet's Education

*for Derek Walcott*

In fact, the classroom overlooked a street
That ended in a parking lot. "How quaint,"
I thought, a bit annoyed by my small desk.
I wasn't nervous; really, I was mad.
The river they referred to in the ad                           5
Was far enough away—across Bay State[1]
(The asphalt driveway had a name), then down
A grassy knoll that bordered Storrow Drive,[2]
Beyond which, yes, one *"glimpsed"* the briny Charles—[3]
I had a better chance of seeing Cuba                            10

When gazing through that dingy window pane.
Of course, I wanted it to be romantic.
I wanted it to be unlike the stiff
Cadavers I had picked apart in labs
At Harvard Med; I wanted it to be *alive*,                      15
The pounding pulse of iambs telling me
The body's truths in terms I understood.
I thought of Bishop, Lowell, Sexton, Plath—[4]

1. Bay State Road, near the Boston University campus.
2. Major crosstown expressway in Boston, adjacent to the campus.
3. The Charles River, which runs between Boston and Cambridge, Massachusetts.
4. Sylvia Plath (1932–1963), American poet born in Boston. *Bishop*: Elizabeth Bishop (1911–1979), American poet born in Worcester, Massachusetts. *Lowell*: Robert Lowell (1917–1977), American poet born in Boston. *Sexton*: Anne Sexton (1928–1974), American poet born in Newton, Massachusetts.

Their workshops where the heart was bared without
The scalpel's blade, by instruments more sharp.                    20
I wasn't nervous; serious for sure,

And proud I'd gotten in on scholarship.
I'd practiced how I'd introduce myself:
Respectfully, but not obsequious,
Perhaps a droll remark that showed I'd read            25
His work. The street and parking lot below
Provided little inspiration; still,
I thought I could impress him with a line
Or two of his I'd memorized. OK,
It's true, I was afraid of what he'd think            30
Of me—a careless dilettante, a wanna-be,
A fake, a ruffled-pink-sleeved *mariachi*
Who danced a bit too awkwardly, my feet

As much ungainly as they were too broad.
I worried that my peers had planned applause,          35
Or worse, cold apples polished to a shine
So bright that even a St. Lucian[5] might
Be tempted. Mangos and cigars, the buzz
Of black mosquitos, the ocean's wish
To eat the island in its roaring jaws                  40
Of waves—the fruits of my experience,
I hoped despite my nagging reticence,
Might still appeal. Each pun, each lively rhyme
Internalized by all my prison time—
Three years had passed when not a single word          45

Escaped from me to find the freedom of
The page—seemed ready for *his* medicine,
Seemed eager to express a kind of love,
To reinvent my lost Caribbean.
Then suddenly, as if on cue, he entered:               50
So dignified yet rumpled, stifling a yawn.
The words he spoke I wish I still remembered—
I've lost them in the spotlight that my awe
Directed toward the star that took the stage.
He outlined what his expectations were,                55
And warned us if we didn't read, his rage
Would be exacted on our timid verse
Which, by the way, we would not read in class—
Too many *finished* poems awaited us.

So much for my ingratiating chatter.                   60
Hart Crane it was, then Auden, Dickinson—[6]

---

5. Walcott was born in Castries, on the island of
St. Lucia.
6. Emily Dickinson (1830–1886), American poet
born in Amherst, Massachusetts, where she

lived nearly all of her life. *Hart Crane*: American
poet born in Garrettsville, Ohio (1899–1932).
*Auden*: W. H. Auden (1907–1973), British-born,
naturalized American poet.

We memorized, and scanned because it mattered—
Then Dante,[7] xeroxed for us in Italian,
He challenged us to sound it out until
The language and the rhymes had filled                    65
Our mouths with music we could taste, if not
Completely figure out. I learned to see
A loveliness that never tried to be,
The beauty in what once had seemed mundane—
What Mr. Bleaney[8] took so properly                      70
In hand, those prepositions ending lines
While Gunn's sad captains[9] turned away.
Then Meredith's raw sonnets[1] came one day:
So utterly redemptive, mordantly gay,

And written more as drama than as verse.                  75
Performance! Even in a failing marriage,
The strange bravado to acknowledge
That poetry is singing in a voice
Undampened by its small, constricted space—
He said that resoluteness was the key.                    80
My sonnets, sheaves of them, came back to me
With qualified encouragement, his face
Betraying humor when he said he hoped
I'd write a hundred more someday. I sulked
At first, convinced he thought my writing sucked.         85
The last of winter's dirty snow in heaps
Along that semblance of a street, I left
That day pretending I would not return.
Yet something stopped me. Something I had learned.
His dusty classroom beckoned, high aloft.                 90

                                                        1999


# I Am Mrs. Lorca[1]

*for Kim Vaeth and John Vincent*

Dark love is all I've ever known; the dance
is nearly over, but I think the world
will not allow another end. The lights

burn bright, and I am married to romance,
his eyes betraying secrets that his words               5
conceal. He never speaks to me at night,

---

7. Dante Alighieri (1265–1321), Italian poet, author of the epic *Divina Commedia* (Divine Comedy, 1308–21). *Scanned*: analyzed the verse to show its meter.
8. Title character of a 1955 poem by Philip Lar-

kin (1922–1985), English poet.
9. In "My Sad Captains" (1961), by Thom Gunn (1929–2004), Anglo-American poet.
1. *Modern Love* (1862), a sonnet cycle by George Meredith (1828–1901), English poet and novelist.

our bed as arid as the flat interior
of Spain. I love him just the same, the way
he combs his hair straight back, his hands

so womanly in shape. I'd be his whore,                          10
but I am not as young as this new day,
this century we dance around;

I'd be his son, but I am not as sad
as dying is, as any son of his
inherits only death's queer finery;                            15

right now, instead, I'm only going mad,
the dance and any meaning that it has
dissolving to the perfect thing he sees.

                                                           1999

## The Changing Face of AIDS

### I. *The Ghost of Epidemiology*

Aisha got it from her husband Dex
who'd shoot up with his friends when she was gone.
For Gloria, the unprotected sex
she traded for some crack was how. The guilt
of being negative brought Timothy                               5
to that same place where on his knees he first
sucked Larry's cock—the blowing reeds like stilts
the high clouds teetered on above the Fens—[1]
as if the nameless men who fucked his mouth
might help him speak to Larry once again.                       10
I watch them all, but travel unannounced:
The ghost of epidemiology,

composite picture of their human needs,
believe me when I tell you what I know.
I am a kind of angel. Swollen nodes?                            15
I've touched them with my icy fingertips.
The pitch of doubt? I've heard it in the bleat
of respirators churning through the night
so mindlessly it seems it's all for naught.
(I'm not the gentle, optimistic type.)                          20
I'm here to tell you that you're dying now,
my voice disclosing what is underneath,
my voice, revising what you thought you knew.
My voice will drown you, like an undertow.

---

1. Also known as the Back Bay Fens, a parkland in a formerly marshy area of Boston.

## II. *The New York Times, March 11, 1997*

NEW AIDS DRUGS PROMISE CURE, New York—"Before          25
these drugs, the prospects for AIDS sufferers
were truly bleak," says Dr. Jack Kevor-
kian,[2] a world-renowned authority
on terminal disease. Across the country,
hope has been felt even in hospices,                   30
as end-stage wasting patients, formerly
expected to be dead, linger on. Says
AIDS victim "Timothy," infected through
promiscuous fellatio last year,
"It's like I was alive again." The truth               35
about these magic cocktails still seems murky,

however. Blaming government inaction,
ACT UP[3] ex-members loudly criticized
the new advances, warning that reductions
in fear could lead to mass complacency.                40
In San Francisco, protesters drank bleach,
burned condoms, chanting "AIDS drugs not drugs aid!"
while blocking access to a library.
Still others blamed ACT UP for what they said
amounted to "collaboration." One                       45
anonymous gay man was further quoted: "Size
is everything! More sex is hot sex!" None
of Mr. Clinton's stooges could be reached . . .

                                                     1999

2. Armenian American pathologist (b. 1928) famous and infamous for publicly championing eu-
thanasia, the merciful ending of a terminally ill or
terminally injured patient's life.

3. AIDS Coalition to Unleash Power, a group devoted to ending the AIDS crisis through direct
political action.

# JUNOT DÍAZ
## b. 1968

Born in the Dominican Republic and raised there and in New Jersey, a trajectory reflected in his story collection *Drown* (1996) and novel *The Brief Wondrous Life of Oscar Wao* (2007), Junot Díaz was the first Dominican American man to write and publish a book-length work of fiction in English. Díaz earned his bachelor's degree from Rutgers, the State University of New Jersey, and a Master of Fine Arts degree from Cornell University, in Ithaca, New York. At Cornell, Díaz fashioned the stories that appear in *Drown*. By his mid-20s, he had published stories in the magazines *Story* and *The New Yorker*, where he came to the attention of the editor, Tina Brown. Half the stories in *Drown* take place in the Dominican Republic and half in New Jersey; but unlike most writers of immigrant narratives, Díaz mixes the temporal sequence into a back-and-forth narration that mirrors the ability of the immigrant to travel easily between homeland and new home. In the Dominican Republic, the Díaz-like narrator, "Yunior," is shadowed by a boredom that is mitigated only by an almost limitless curiosity: only experience will satisfy such thirst. In "Ysrael," the story included here, Yunior and his brother hear about a young man who wears a mask to hide a face half-eaten by a pig when he was an infant. They decide to see his face for themselves, with unnerving results. Throughout *Drown*, Díaz examines the consequences of awareness and the uses of the past, themes to which he returns in *The Brief Wondrous Life of Oscar Wao*, the first chapter of which is excerpted here.

The novel's title character, Oscar Wao, is Latino, obese, sensitive, needy, a comic-book geek, an intellectual, and a would-be lover. He lives in New Jersey with his mother and sister, who tell their own stories alongside those of Oscar. No matter how hard he works to overcome life's disappointments, no matter the love his mother, sister, and best friend shower upon him, Oscar seems doomed. The past affects everything. The family seems plagued by Dominican politics—still dominated by the specter of the former dictator Rafael Trujillo—and *fukú*, a vague curse with Afro-Caribbean roots. To help the reader understand the Wao family situation (and Díaz as author), Díaz includes footnotes on relevant cultural and political history. Echoing the name of the nineteenth-century Irish writer, aesthete, and exile Oscar Wilde in its protagonist's name, *Oscar Wao* can be seen as an exploration of the various conventions of the immigrant or ethnic novel, especially themes of outsider status. The novel also establishes a dialogue with previous narratives of immigration, in particular the twentieth-century American writer Henry Roth's *Call It Sleep* (1934), about a six-year-old Austrian Jewish boy and his mystical adventures in New York's Lower East Side. However, Díaz's vision represents a break not only from the traditional acculturation story, but also from the ethnic novel. While employing elements of the Latin American *novela del dictador* (dictator novel), Díaz reflects on the way popular culture defines youth in the United States. The cultures and subcultures Oscar imbibes—African, Caribbean, Latino, U.S., musical, sexual, literary, highbrow and lowbrow—balloon him into unwieldy proportions: hero and antihero, he is virtually paralyzed by desire and multiplicity. (Díaz began to explore the theme of desire and abundance in the short story "How to Date a Black Girl, Brown Girl, White Girl, Halfie," included in *Drown*.) Oscar is postethnic, and his story announces the demise of "the novel of the hyphen," of the immigrant as bicultural production of here-or-there assimilation. *The Brief Wondrous Life of Oscar Wao* unapologetically represents the end of Latinidad as manifesto.

Published in 2007, the novel was received with enormous enthusiasm: it was awarded the John Sargent Sr. First Novel Prize, the National Book Critics Circle Award for Best Novel of 2007, the Anisfield-Wolf Award, the 2008 Dayton Literary Peace Price for Fiction, the 2008 Hurston/Wright Legacy Award, and the 2008 Massachusetts Book Prize for Best Fiction. These acolades were crowned with the 2008 Pulitzer Prize for Fiction, marking the second time a Latino novel was chosen for the prize. (The first one was Oscar Hijuelos's *The Mambo Kings Play Songs of Love*; see p. 1813.) Díaz has also received the Eugene McDermott Award, a fellowship from the John Simon Guggenheim Memorial Foundation, a Lila Acheson Wallace–Reader's Digest Award, the 2002 Pen/Malamud Award, the 2003 U.S.-Japan Creative Artist Fellowship from the National Endowment for the Arts, a fellowship at the Radcliffe Institute for Advanced Study at Harvard University, and the Rome Prize from the American Academy of Arts and Letters. He teaches creative writing at the Massachusetts Institute of Technology, in Cambridge.

# Ysrael

## 1.

We were on our way to the colmado[1] for an errand, a beer for my tío,[2] when Rafa stood still and tilted his head, as if listening to a message I couldn't hear, something beamed in from afar. We were close to the colmado; you could hear the music and the gentle clop of drunken voices. I was nine that summer, but my brother was twelve, and he was the one who wanted to see Ysrael, who looked out towards Barbacoa[3] and said, We should pay that kid a visit.

## 2.

Mami shipped me and Rafa out to the campo every summer. She worked long hours at the chocolate factory and didn't have the time or the energy to look after us during the months school was out. Rafa and I stayed with our tíos, in a small wooden house just outside Ocoa;[4] rosebushes blazed around the yard like compass points and the mango trees spread out deep blankets of shade where we could rest and play dominos, but the campo was nothing like our barrio in Santo Domingo.[5] In the campo there was nothing to do, no one to see. You didn't get television or electricity and Rafa, who was older and expected more, woke up every morning pissy and dissatisfied. He stood out on the patio in his shorts and looked out over the mountains, at the mists that gathered like water, at the brucal trees[6] that blazed like fires on the mountain. This, he said, is shit.

Worse than shit, I said.

Yeah, he said, and when I get home, I'm going to go crazy—chinga[7] all my girls and then chinga everyone else's. I won't stop dancing either. I'm going to be like those guys in the record books who dance four or five days straight.

Tío Miguel had chores for us (mostly we chopped wood for the smokehouse and brought water up from the river) but we finished these as easy as we threw off our shirts, the rest of the day punching us in the face. We caught jaivas in the streams and spent hours walking across the valley to see girls who were never there; we set traps for jurones[8] we never caught and toughened up our roosters with pails of cold water. We worked hard at keeping busy.

I didn't mind these summers, wouldn't forget them the way Rafa would. Back home in the Capital, Rafa had his own friends, a bunch of tigres who liked to knock down our neighbors and who scrawled *chocha* and *toto*[9] on walls and curbs. Back in the Capital he rarely said anything to me except Shut up, pendejo.[1] Unless, of course, he was mad and then he had about five hundred routines he liked to lay on me. Most of them had to do with my complexion, my hair, the size of my lips. It's the Haitian, he'd say to his

---

1. Grocery store.
2. Uncle.
3. On the Samana Peninsula, northeastern Dominican Republic.
4. San José de Ocoa, capital of the province of the same name, south-central Dominican Republic.
5. The capital; southeast of Ocoa.
6. More commonly known as *bucayo gigante* in Spanish, mountain immortelle in English; trees often planted for their shade on coffee plantations. One species has reddish-orange flowers.
7. Fuck.
8. In the Dominican Republic, edible mole-like rodents. *Jaivas*: here, freshwater crabs.
9. Like *chocha*, a variation on *coño* (cunt), though not quite as vulgar; pussy.
1. Jackass.

buddies. Hey Señor Haitian, Mami found you on the border and only took you in because she felt sorry for *you*.

If I was stupid enough to mouth off to him—about the hair that was growing on his back or the time the tip of his pinga[2] had swollen to the size of a lemon—he pounded the hell of out me and then I would run as far as I could. In the Capital Rafa and I fought so much that our neighbors took to smashing broomsticks over us to break it up, but in the campo it wasn't like that. In the campo we were friends.

The summer I was nine, Rafa shot whole afternoons talking about whatever chica he was getting with—not that the campo girls gave up ass like the girls back in the Capital but kissing them, he told me, was pretty much the same. He'd take the campo girls down to the dams to swim and if he was lucky they let him put it in their mouths or in their asses. He'd done La Muda[3] that way for almost a month before her parents heard about it and barred her from leaving the house forever.

He wore the same outfit when he went to see these girls, a shirt and pants that my father had sent him from the States last Christmas. I always followed Rafa, trying to convince him to let me tag along.

Go home, he'd say. I'll be back in a few hours.

I'll walk you.

I don't need you to walk me anywhere. Just wait for me.

If I kept on he'd punch me in the shoulder and walk on until what was left of him was the color of his shirt filling in the spaces between the leaves. Something inside of me would sag like a sail. I would yell his name and he'd hurry on, the ferns and branches and flower pods trembling in his wake.

Later, while we were in bed listening to the rats on the zinc roof he might tell me what he'd done. I'd hear about tetas and chochas and leche[4] and he'd talk without looking over at me. There was a girl he'd gone to see, half-Haitian, but he ended up with her sister. Another who believed she wouldn't get pregnant if she drank a Coca-Cola afterwards. And one who was pregnant and didn't give a damn about anything. His hands were behind his head and his feet were crossed at the ankles. He was handsome and spoke out of the corner of his mouth. I was too young to understand most of what he said, but I listened to him anyway, in case these things might be useful in the future.

### 3.

Ysrael was a different story. Even on this side of Ocoa people had heard of him, how when he was a baby a pig had eaten his face off, skinned it like an orange. He was something to talk about, a name that set the kids to screaming, worse than el Cuco or la Vieja Calusa.[5]

I'd seen Ysrael my first time the year before, right after the dams were finished. I was in town, farting around, when a single-prop plane swept in across the sky. A door opened on the fuselage and a man began to kick out tall bundles that exploded into thousands of leaflets as soon as the wind got

---

2. Prick.
3. The Mute.

4. Literally, milk; here, cum. *Tetas*: tits.
5. The Old Witch. *El Cuco*: the bogeyman.

to them. They came down as slow as butterfly blossoms and were posters of wrestlers, not politicians, and that's when us kids started shouting at each other. Usually the planes only covered Ocoa, but if extras had been printed the nearby towns would also get leaflets, especially if the match or the election was a big one. The paper would cling to the trees for weeks.

I spotted Ysrael in an alley, stooping over a stack of leaflets that had not come undone from its thin cord. He was wearing his mask.

What are you doing? I said.

What do you think I'm doing? he answered.

He picked up the bundle and ran down the alley. Some other boys saw him and wheeled around, howling but, coño,[6] could he run.

That's Ysrael! I was told. He's *ugly* and he's got a cousin around here but we don't like him either. And that face of his would make you *sick!*

I told my brother later when I got home, and he sat up in his bed. Could you see under the mask?

Not really.

That's something we got to check out.

I hear it's bad.

The night before we went to look for him my brother couldn't sleep. He kicked at the mosquito netting and I could hear the mesh tearing just a little. My tío was yukking it up with his buddies in the yard. One of Tío's roosters had won big the day before and he was thinking of taking it to the Capital.

People around here don't bet worth a damn, he was saying. Your average campesino[7] only bets big when he feels lucky and how many of them feel lucky?

You're feeling lucky right now.

You're damn right about that. That's why I have to find myself some big spenders.

I wonder how much of Ysrael's face is gone, Rafa said.

He has his eyes.

That's a lot, he assured me. You'd think eyes would be the first thing a pig would go for. Eyes are soft. And salty.

How do you know that?

I licked one, he said.

Maybe his ears.

And his nose. Anything that sticks out.

Everyone had a different opinion on the damage. Tío said it wasn't bad but the father was very sensitive about anyone taunting his oldest son, which explained the mask. Tía said that if we were to look on his face we would be sad for the rest of our lives. That's why the poor boy's mother spends her day in church. I had never been sad more than a few hours and the thought of that sensation lasting a lifetime scared the hell out of me. My brother kept pinching my face during the night, like I was a mango. The cheeks, he said. And the chin. But the forehead would be a lot harder. The skin's tight.

All right, I said. Ya.

---

6. Damn.         7. Farmworker.

The next morning the roosters were screaming. Rafa dumped the ponchera[8] in the weeds and then collected our shoes from the patio, careful not to step on the pile of cacao beans Tía had set out to dry. Rafa went into the smokehouse and emerged with his knife and two oranges. He peeled them and handed me mine. When we heard Tía coughing in the house, we started on our way. I kept expecting Rafa to send me home and the longer he went without speaking, the more excited I became. Twice I put my hands over my mouth to stop from laughing. We went slow, grabbing saplings and fence posts to keep from tumbling down the rough brambled slope. Smoke was rising from the fields that had been burned the night before, and the trees that had not exploded or collapsed stood in the black ash like spears. At the bottom of the hill we followed the road that would take us to Ocoa. I was carrying the two Coca-Cola empties Tío had hidden in the chicken coop.

We joined two women, our neighbors, who were waiting by the colmado on their way to mass.

I put the bottles on the counter. Chicho folded up yesterday's *El Nacional*. When he put fresh Cokes next to the empties, I said, We want the refund.

Chicho put his elbows on the counter and looked me over. Are you supposed to be doing that?

Yes, I said.

You better be giving this money back to your tío, he said. I stared at the pastelitos and chicharrón[9] he kept under a flyspecked glass. He slapped the coins onto the counter. I'm going to stay out of this, he said. What you do with this money is your own concern. I'm just a businessman.

How much of this do we need? I asked Rafa.

All of it.

Can't we buy something to eat?

Save it for a drink. You'll be real thirsty later.

Maybe we should eat.

Don't be stupid.

How about if I just bought us some gum?

Give me that money, he said.

OK, I said. I was just asking.

Then stop. Rafa was looking up the road, distracted; I knew that expression better than anyone. He was scheming. Every now and then he glanced over at the two women, who were conversing loudly, their arms crossed over their big chests. When the first autobus trundled to a stop and the women got on, Rafa watched their asses bucking under their dresses. The cobrador[1] leaned out from the passenger door and said, Well? And Rafa said, Beat it, baldy.

What are we waiting for? I said. That one had air-conditioning.

I want a younger cobrador, Rafa said, still looking down the road. I went to the counter and tapped my finger on the glass case. Chicho handed me a pastelito and after putting it in my pocket, I slid him a coin. Business is business, Chicho announced but my brother didn't bother to look. He was flagging down the next autobus.

---

8. Bucket or basin, perhaps for use as a chamber pot.
9. Small pieces of fried meat, generally chicken.

*Pastelitos*: little pies or turnovers, like empanadas.
1. Conductor.

Get to the back, Rafa said. He framed himself in the main door, his toes out in the air, his hands curled up on the top lip of the door. He stood next to the cobrador, who was a year or two younger than he was. This boy tried to get Rafa to sit down but Rafa shook his head with that not-a-chance grin of his and before there could be an argument the driver shifted into gear, blasting the radio. *La chica de la novela* was still on the charts. Can you believe that? the man next to me said. They play that vaina[2] a hundred times a day.

I lowered myself stiffly into my seat but the pastelito had already put a grease stain on my pants. Coño, I said and took out the pastelito and finished it in four bites. Rafa wasn't watching. Each time the autobus stopped he was hopping down and helping people bring on their packages. When a row filled he lowered the swing-down center seat for whoever was next. The cobrador, a thin boy with an Afro, was trying to keep up with him and the driver was too busy with his radio to notice what was happening. Two people paid Rafa—all of which Rafa gave to the cobrador, who was himself busy making change.

You have to watch out for stains like that, the man next to me said. He had big teeth and wore a clean fedora. His arms were ropy with muscles.

These things are too greasy, I said.

Let me help. He spit in his fingers and started to rub at the stain but then he was pinching at the tip of my pinga through the fabric of my shorts. He was smiling. I shoved him against his seat. He looked to see if anybody had noticed.

You pato,[3] I said.

The man kept smiling.

You low-down pinga-sucking pato, I said. The man squeezed my bicep, quietly, hard, the way my friends would sneak me in church. I whimpered.

You should watch your mouth, he said.

I got up and went over to the door. Rafa slapped the roof and as the driver slowed the cobrador said, You two haven't paid.

Sure we did, Rafa said, pushing me down into the dusty street. I gave you the money for those two people there and I gave you our fare too. His voice was tired, as if he got into these discussions all the time.

No you didn't.

Fuck you I did. You got the fares. Why don't you count and see?

Don't even try it. The cobrador put his hand on Rafa but Rafa wasn't having it. He yelled up to the driver, Tell your boy to learn how to count.

We crossed the road and went down into a field of guineo;[4] the cobrador was shouting after us and we stayed in the field until we heard the driver say, Forget them.

Rafa took off his shirt and fanned himself and that's when I started to cry. He watched for a moment. You, he said, are a pussy.

I'm sorry.

What the hell's the matter with you? We didn't do anything wrong.

I'll be OK in a second. I sawed my forearm across my nose.

2. Crap.
3. Homo.

4. Bananas, often prepared when they are green.

He took a look around, drawing in the lay of the land. If you can't stop crying, I'll leave you. He headed towards a shack that was rusting in the sun.

I watched him disappear. From the shack you could hear voices, as bright as chrome. Columns of ants had found a pile of meatless chicken bones at my feet and were industriously carting away the crumbling marrow. I could have gone home, which was what I usually did when Rafa acted up, but we were far—eight, nine miles away.

I caught up with him beyond the shack. We walked about a mile; my head felt cold and hollow.

Are you done?

Yes, I said.

Are you always going to be a pussy?

I wouldn't have raised my head if God himself had appeared in the sky and pissed down on us.

Rafa spit. You have to get tougher. Crying all the time. Do you think our papi's crying? Do you think that's what he's been doing the last six years? He turned from me. His feet were crackling through the weeds, breaking stems.

Rafa stopped a schoolboy in a blue and tan uniform, who pointed us down a road. Rafa spoke to a young mother, whose baby was hacking like a miner. A little farther, she said and when he smiled she looked the other way. We went too far and a farmer with a machete showed us the easiest loop back. Rafa stopped when he saw Ysrael standing in the center of a field. He was flying a kite and despite the string he seemed almost unconnected to the distant wedge of black that finned back and forth in the sky. Here we go, Rafa said. I was embarrassed. What the hell were we supposed to do?

Stay close, he said. And get ready to run. He passed me his knife, then trotted down towards the field.

## 4.

The summer before, I pegged Ysrael with a rock and the way it bounced off his back I knew I'd clocked a shoulder blade.

You did it! You fucking did it! the other boys yelled.

He'd been running from us and he arched in pain and one of the other boys nearly caught him but he recovered and took off. He's faster than a mongoose, someone said, but in truth he was even faster than that. We laughed and went back to our baseball games and forgot him until he came to town again and then we dropped what we were doing and chased him. Show us your face, we cried. Let's see it just once.

## 5.

He was about a foot bigger than either of us and looked like he'd been fattened on that supergrain the farmers around Ocoa were giving their stock, a new product which kept my tío up at night, muttering jealously, Proxyl Feed 9, Proxyl Feed 9. Ysrael's sandals were of stiff leather and his clothes were Northamerican. I looked over at Rafa but my brother seemed unperturbed.

Listen up, Rafa said. My hermanito's[5] not feeling too well. Can you show us where a colmado is? I want to get him a drink.

There's a faucet up the road, Ysrael said. His voice was odd and full of spit. His mask was handsewn from thin blue cotton fabric and you couldn't help but see the scar tissue that circled his left eye, a red waxy crescent, and the saliva that trickled down his neck.

We're not from around here. We can't drink the water.

Ysrael spooled in his string. The kite wheeled but he righted it with a yank.

Not bad, I said.

We can't drink the water around here. It would kill us. And he's already sick.

I smiled and tried to act sick, which wasn't too difficult; I was covered with dust. I saw Ysrael looking us over.

The water here is probably better than up in the mountains, he said.

Help us out, Rafa said in a low voice.

Ysrael pointed down a path. Just go that way, you'll find it.

Are you sure?

I've lived here all my life.

I could hear the plastic kite flapping in the wind; the string was coming in fast. Rafa huffed and started on his way. We made a long circle and by then Ysrael had his kite in hand—the kite was no handmade local job. It had been manufactured abroad.

We couldn't find it, Rafa said.

How stupid are you?

Where did you get that? I asked.

Nueva York, he said. From my father.

No shit! Our father's there too! I shouted.

I looked at Rafa, who, for an instant, frowned. Our father only sent us letters and an occasional shirt or pair of jeans at Christmas.

What the hell are you wearing that mask for anyway? Rafa asked.

I'm sick, Ysrael said.

It must be hot.

Not for me.

Don't you take it off?

Not until I get better. I'm going to have an operation soon.

You better watch out for that, Rafa said. Those doctors will kill you faster than the Guardia.[6]

They're American doctors.

Rafa sniggered. You're lying.

I saw them last spring. They want me to go next year.

They're lying to you. They probably just felt sorry.

Do you want me to show you where the colmado is or not?

Sure.

Follow me, he said, wiping the spit on his neck. At the colmado he stood off while Rafa bought me the cola. The owner was playing dominos with the beer deliveryman and didn't bother to look up, though he put a hand in

5. Little brother's.
6. *Guardia Nacional Dominicana* (Dominican National Guard), the central government's military force.

the air for Ysrael. He had that lean look of every colmado owner I'd ever met. On the way back to the road I left the bottle with Rafa to finish and caught up with Ysrael, who was ahead of us. Are you still into wrestling? I asked.

He turned to me and something rippled under the mask. How did you know that?

I heard, I said. Do they have wrestling in the States?

I hope so.

Are you a wrestler?

I'm a great wrestler. I almost went to fight in the Capital.

My brother laughed, swigging on the bottle.

You want to try it, pendejo?

Not right now.

I didn't think so.

I tapped his arm. The planes haven't dropped anything this year.

It's still too early. The first Sunday of August is when it starts.

How do you know?

I'm from around here, he said. The mask twitched. I realized he was smiling and then my brother brought his arm around and smashed the bottle on top of his head. It exploded, the thick bottom spinning away like a crazed eyeglass and I said, Holy fucking shit. Ysrael stumbled once and slammed into a fence post that had been sunk into the side of the road. Glass crumbled off his mask. He spun towards me, then fell down on his stomach. Rafa kicked him in the side. Ysrael seemed not to notice. He had his hands flat in the dirt and was concentrating on pushing himself up. Roll him on his back, my brother said and we did, pushing like crazy. Rafa took off his mask and threw it spinning into the grass.

His left ear was a nub and you could see the thick veined slab of his tongue through a hole in his cheek. He had no lips. His head was tipped back and his eyes had gone white and the cords were out on his neck. He'd been an infant when the pig had come into the house. The damage looked old but I still jumped back and said, Please Rafa, let's go! Rafa crouched and using only two of his fingers, turned Ysrael's head from side to side.

6.

We went back to the colmado where the owner and the deliveryman were now arguing, the dominos chattering under their hands. We kept walking and after one hour, maybe two, we saw an autobus. We boarded and went right to the back. Rafa crossed his arms and watched the fields and roadside shacks scroll past, the dust and smoke and people almost frozen by our speed.

Ysrael will be OK, I said.

Don't bet on it.

They're going to fix him.

A muscle fluttered between his jawbone and his ear. Yunior, he said tiredly. They aren't going to do shit to him.

How do you know?

I know, he said.

I put my feet on the back of the chair in front of me, pushing on an old lady, who looked back at me. She was wearing a baseball cap and one of her eyes was milky. The autobus was heading for Ocoa, not for home. Rafa signaled for a stop. Get ready to run, he whispered. I said, OK.

1996

---

FROM THE BRIEF WONDROUS LIFE OF OSCAR WAO

## From 1. GhettoNerd at the End of the World
## 1974–1987

### The Golden Age

Our hero was not one of those Dominican cats everybody's always going on about—he wasn't no home-run hitter or a fly bachatero,[1] not a playboy with a million hots on his jock.

And except for one period early in his life, dude never had much luck with the females (how *very* un-Dominican of him).

He was seven then.

In those blessed days of his youth, Oscar was something of a Casanova. One of those preschool loverboys who was always trying to kiss the girls, always coming up behind them during a merengue and giving them the pelvic pump, the first nigger to learn the perrito and the one who danced it any chance he got. Because in those days he was (still) a "normal" Dominican boy raised in a "typical" Dominican family, his nascent pimp-liness was encouraged by blood and friends alike. During parties—and there were many many parties in those long-ago seventies days, before Washington Heights was Washington Heights, before the Bergenline[2] became a straight shot of Spanish for almost a hundred blocks—some drunk relative inevitably pushed Oscar onto some little girl and then everyone would howl as boy and girl approximated the hip-motism of the adults.

You should have seen him, his mother sighed in her Last Days. He was our little Porfirio Rubirosa.[3]

---

1. *Bachata* is a musical style that emerged from the Dominican countryside. A *bachatero* is either the musician or sometimes one who dances to the music.
2. Bergenline Avenue, a thoroughfare, major commercial district, and largely Latino (especially Cuban and Dominican) neighborhood in the North Hudson section of Hudson County, New Jersey, across the river from Manhattan. *Washington Heights*: a largely Dominican neighborhood in northern Manhattan.
3. In the forties and fifties, Porfirio Rubirosa—or Rubi, as he was known in the papers—was the third-most-famous Dominican in the world (first came the Failed Cattle Thief, and then the Cobra Woman herself, María Montez). A tall, debo-

nair prettyboy whose "enormous phallus created havoc in Europe and North America," Rubirosa was the quintessential jet-setting car-racing polo-obsessed playboy, the Trujillato's "happy side" (for he was indeed one of Trujillo's best-known minions). A part-time former model and dashing man-about-town, Rubirosa famously married Trujillo's daughter Flor de Oro in 1932, and even though they were divorced five years later, in the Year of the Haitian Genocide, homeboy managed to remain in El Jefe's good graces throughout the regime's long run. Unlike his ex-brother-in-law Ramfis (to whom he was frequently connected), Rubirosa seemed incapable of carrying out many murders; in 1935 he traveled to New York to deliver El Jefe's death sentence

All the other boys his age avoided the girls like they were a bad case of Captain Trips.[4] Not Oscar. The little guy loved himself the females, had "girlfriends" galore. (He was a stout kid, heading straight to fat, but his mother kept him nice in haircuts and clothes, and before the proportions of his head changed he'd had these lovely flashing eyes and these cute-ass cheeks, visible in all his pictures.) The girls—his sister Lola's friends, his mother's friends, even their neighbor, Mari Colón, a thirty-something postal employee who wore red on her lips and walked like she had a bell for an ass—all purportedly fell for him. Ese muchacho está bueno! (Did it hurt that he was earnest and clearly attention-deprived? Not at all!) In the DR during summer visits to his family digs in Baní[5] he was the worst, would stand in front of Nena Inca's house and call out to passing women—Tú eres guapa![6] Tú eres guapa!—until a Seventh-day Adventist complained to his grandmother and she shut down the hit parade lickety-split. Muchacho del diablo! This is not a cabaret!

It truly was a Golden Age for Oscar, one that reached its apotheosis in the fall of his seventh year, when he had two little girlfriends at the same time, his first and only ménage à trois. With Maritza Chacón and Olga Polanco.

Maritza was Lola's friend. Long-haired and prissy and so pretty she could have played young Dejah Thoris.[7] Olga, on the other hand, was no friend of the family. She lived in the house at the end of the block that his mother complained about because it was filled with puertoricans who were always hanging out on their porch drinking beer. (What, they couldn't have done that in Cuamo?[8] Oscar's mom asked crossly.) Olga had like ninety cousins, all who seemed to be named Hector or Luis or Wanda. And since her mother was una maldita borracha[9] (to quote Oscar's mom), Olga smelled on some days of ass, which is why the kids took to calling her Mrs. Peabody.

Mrs. Peabody or not, Oscar liked how quiet she was, how she let him throw her to the ground and wrestle with her, the interest she showed in his Star Trek dolls. Maritza was just plain beautiful, no need for motivation there, always around too, and it was just a stroke of pure genius that convinced him to kick it to them both at once. At first he pretended that it was his number-one hero, Shazam,[1] who wanted to date them. But after they agreed he dropped all pretense. It wasn't Shazam—it was Oscar.

Those were more innocent days, so their relationship amounted to standing close to each other at the bus stop, some undercover hand-holding, and

---

against the exile leader Angel Morales but fled before the botched assassination could take place. Rubi was the original Dominican Player, fucked all sorts of women—Barbara Hutton, Doris Duke (who happened to be the richest woman in the world), the French actress Danielle Darrieux, and Zsa Zsa Gabor—to name but a few. Like his pal Ramfis, Porfirio died in a car crash, in 1965, his twelve-cylinder Ferrari skidding off a road in the Bois de Boulogne. (Hard to overstate the role cars play in our narrative.) [Author/narrator's note]

 The Failed Cattle Thief: Trujillo. María Montez: Dominican-born movie actress (1912–1951). The Haitian Genocide: probably Trujillo's massacre, in 1937, of the Haitians living on the border between the Dominican Republic and Haiti (the two sides of Hispaniola). Angel Morales: in the late 1940s, president-in-exile of

the United Front for Dominican Liberation. Barbara Hutton: American socialite (1912–1979). Doris Duke: American heiress (1912–1993). Danielle Darrieux: b. 1917. Zsa Zsa Gabor: Hungarian American actress and socialite (b. 1917). Bois de Boulogne: grand public park in Paris. [Anthology editors' note]
4. Virus in The Stand (1978, 1990), horror/fantasy novel by the American writer Stephen King (b. 1947).
5. Capital of the Peravia Province, south-central Dominican Republic.
6. You're gorgeous!
7. Fictional character in the series of Martian novels by the American writer Edgar Rice Burroughs (1875–1950).
8. Town in south-central Puerto Rico.
9. A goddamn drunk.
1. Comic-book character.

twice kissing on the cheeks very seriously, first Maritza, then Olga, while they were hidden from the street by some bushes. (Look at that little macho, his mother's friends said. Que hombre.)

The threesome only lasted a single beautiful week. One day after school Maritza cornered Oscar behind the swing set and laid down the law, It's either her or *me*! Oscar held Maritza's hand and talked seriously and at great length about his love for her and reminded her that they had agreed to *share*, but Maritza wasn't having any of it. She had three older sisters, knew everything she needed to know about the possibilities of *sharing*. Don't talk to me no more unless you get rid of her! Maritza, with her chocolate skin and narrow eyes, already expressing the Ogún[2] energy that she would chop at everybody with for the rest of her life. Oscar went home morose to his pre–Korean-sweatshop-era cartoons[3]—to the *Herculoids* and *Space Ghost*. What's wrong with you? his mother asked. She was getting ready to go to her second job, the eczema on her hands looking like a messy meal that had set. When Oscar whimpered, Girls, Moms de León nearly exploded. Tú ta llorando por una muchacha?[4] She hauled Oscar to his feet by his ear.

Mami, stop it, his sister cried, stop it!

She threw him to the floor. Dale un galletazo, she panted, then see if the little puta[5] respects you.

If he'd been a different nigger he might have considered the galletazo. It wasn't just that he didn't have no kind of father to show him the masculine ropes, he simply lacked all aggressive and martial tendencies. (Unlike his sister, who fought boys and packs of morena[6] girls who hated her thin nose and straightish hair.) Oscar had like a zero combat rating; even Olga and her toothpick arms could have stomped him silly. Aggression and intimidation out of the question. So he thought it over. Didn't take him long to decide. After all, Maritza was beautiful and Olga was not; Olga sometimes smelled like pee and Maritza did not. Maritza was allowed over their house and Olga was not. (A puertorican over here? his mother scoffed. Jamás![7]) His logic as close to the yes/no math of insects as a nigger could get. He broke up with Olga the following day on the playground, Maritza at his side, and how Olga had cried! Shaking like a rag in her hand-me-downs and in the shoes that were four sizes too big! Snots pouring out her nose and everything!

In later years, after he and Olga had both turned into overweight freaks, Oscar could not resist feeling the occasional flash of guilt when he saw Olga loping across a street or staring blankly out near the New York bus stop, couldn't stop himself from wondering how much his cold-as-balls breakup had contributed to her present fucked-upness. (Breaking up with her, he would remember, hadn't felt like anything; even when she started crying, he hadn't been moved. He'd said, No be a baby.)

What *had* hurt, however, was when Maritza dumped *him*. Monday after he'd fed Olga to the dogs he arrived at the bus stop with his beloved *Planet of the Apes*[8] lunch box only to discover beautiful Maritza holding hands with

2. In Haitian voodoo and Yoruba mythology, a fiery warrior spirit.
3. I.e., some later cartoons were produced in Korean sweatshops.
4. You're cryin' over a girl?
5. Whore. *Dale un galletazo*: Give her a punch to the face.
6. Brunette.
7. No way! (Never!)
8. Science fiction series—of movies, comics, and so on—that started in 1968.

butt-ugly Nelson Pardo, Nelson Pardo who looked like Chaka from *Land of the Lost!*[9] Nelson Pardo who was so stupid he thought the moon was a stain that God had forgotten to clean. (He'll get to it soon, he assured his whole class.) Nelson Pardo who would become the neighborhood B&E[1] expert before joining the Marines and losing eight toes in the First Gulf War. At first Oscar thought it a mistake; the sun was in his eyes, he'd not slept enough the night before. He stood next to them and admired his lunch box, how realistic and diabolical Dr. Zaius[2] looked. But Maritza wouldn't even *smile* at him! Pretended he wasn't there. We should get married, she said to Nelson, and Nelson grinned moronically, turning up the street to look for the bus. Oscar had been too hurt to speak; he sat down on the curb and felt something overwhelming surge up from his chest, scared the shit out of him, and before he knew it he was crying; when his sister, Lola, walked over and asked him what was the matter he'd shaken his head. Look at the mariconcito,[3] somebody snickered. Somebody else kicked his beloved lunch box and scratched it right across General Urko's face. When he got on the bus, still crying, the driver, a famously reformed PCP addict, had said, Christ, don't be a fucking *baby*.

*How had the breakup affected Olga?* What he really was asking was: *How had the breakup affected Oscar?*

It seemed to Oscar that from the moment Maritza dumped him— Shazam!—his life started going down the tubes. Over the next couple of years he grew fatter and fatter. Early adolescence hit him especially hard, scrambling his face into nothing you could call cute, splotching his skin with zits, making him self-conscious; and his interest—in Genres!—which nobody had said boo about before, suddenly became synonymous with being a loser with a capital L. Couldn't make friends for the life of him, too dorky, too shy, and (if the kids from his neighborhood are to be believed) too *weird* (had a habit of using big words he had memorized only the day before). He no longer went anywhere near the girls because at best they ignored him, at worst they shrieked and called him gordo asqueroso! He forgot the perrito,[4] forgot the pride he felt when the women in the family had called him hombre. Did not kiss another girl for a long *long* time. As though almost everything he had in the girl department had burned up that one fucking week.

Not that his "girlfriends" fared much better. It seemed that whatever bad no-love karma hit Oscar hit them too. By seventh grade Olga had grown huge and scary, a troll gene in her somewhere, started drinking 151[5] straight out the bottle and was finally taken out of school because she had a habit of screaming NATAS![6] in the middle of homeroom. Even her breasts, when they finally emerged, were floppy and terrifying. Once on the bus Olga had called Oscar a *cake eater*, and he'd almost said, Look who's talking, puerca, but he was afraid that she would rear back and trample him; his cool-index, already low, couldn't have survived that kind of a paliza,[7] would have put him on par with the handicapped kids and with Joe Locorotundo, who was famous for masturbating in public.

---

9. Cha-Ka was a character on this science fiction/fantasy TV series (1974–76).
1. Breaking and entering.
2. A character in *Planet of the Apes*, as is General Urko (below).
3. Little faggot.

4. Little dog, or puppy. *Gordo asqueroso*: disgusting fatboy.
5. Very strong rum (151 proof).
6. Possibly "cake-eaters!" (well-off people; from *nata*, cream).
7. Blow (from *palo*).

And the lovely Maritza Chacón? The hypotenuse of our triangle, how had she fared? Well, before you could say *Oh Mighty Isis*, Maritza blew up into the flyest guapa in Paterson, one of the Queens of New Peru.[8] Since they stayed neighbors, Oscar saw her plenty, a ghetto Mary Jane, hair as black and lush as a thunderhead, probably the only Peruvian girl on the planet with pelo curlier than his sister's (he hadn't heard of Afro-Peruvians yet, or of a town called Chincha),[9] body fine enough to make old men forget their infirmities, and from the sixth grade on dating men two, three times her age. (Maritza might not have been good at much—not sports, not school, not work—but she was good at men.) Did that mean she had avoided the curse—that she was happier than Oscar or Olga? That was doubtful. From what Oscar could see, Maritza was a girl who seemed to delight in getting slapped around by her boyfriends. Since it happened to her *all the time*. If a boy hit *me*, Lola said cockily, I would bite his *face*.

See Maritza: French-kissing on the front stoop of her house, getting in or out of some roughneck's ride, being pushed down onto the sidewalk. Oscar would watch the French-kissing, the getting in and out, the pushing, all through his cheerless, sexless adolescence. What else could he do? His bedroom window looked out over the front of her house, and so he always peeped her while he was painting his D&D[1] miniatures or reading the latest Stephen King. The only things that changed in those years were the models of the cars, the size of Maritza's ass, and the kind of music volting out the cars' speakers. First freestyle, then Ill Will–era hiphop, and, right at the very end, for just a little while, Héctor Lavoe[2] and the boys.

He said hi to her almost every day, all upbeat and faux-happy, and she said hi back, indifferently, but that was it. He didn't imagine that she remembered their kissing—but of course he could not forget.

## The Moronic Inferno

High school was Don Bosco Tech, and since Don Bosco Tech was an urban all-boys Catholic school packed to the strakes with a couple hundred insecure hyperactive adolescents, it was, for a fat sci-fi–reading nerd like Oscar, a source of endless anguish. For Oscar, high school was the equivalent of a medieval spectacle, like being put in the stocks and forced to endure the peltings and outrages of a mob of deranged half-wits, an experience from which he supposed he should have emerged a better person, but that's not really what happened—and if there were any lessons to be gleaned from the ordeal of those years he never quite figured out what they were. He walked into school every day like the fat lonely nerdy kid he was, and all he could think about was the day of his manumission, when he would at last be set

8. Paterson, a city in northeastern New Jersey, has one of the largest communities of Peruvian immigrants in the United States. *Oh Mighty Isis*: phrase spoken by the cartoon character Adrianna Tomaz to transform herself into the superhero Isis, a spinoff from the *Shazam* comic-book series. *Guapa*: pretty woman.
9. Central city of Chincha, a province in Peru that has a large Afro-Peruvian population. *Mary Jane*: a reference to Mary Jane Watson, the next-door neighbor and love interest of Peter Parker,

aka Spiderman, in the series of comics and movies. *Pelo*: hair.
1. Dungeons & Dragons, a fantasy role-playing game.
2. Stage name of Héctor Juan Pérez Martínez (1946–1993), Puerto Rican salsa singer. *Freestyle*: also known as Latin freestyle or Latin hip-hop, a form of electronic music most prominent from the early 1980s to the early 1990s. *Ill Will*: record label that existed from 1999 until 2004.

free from its unending horror. Hey, Oscar, are there faggots on Mars?—
Hey, Kazoo, catch *this*. The first time he heard the term *moronic inferno* he
knew exactly where it was located and who were its inhabitants.

Sophomore year Oscar found himself weighing in at a whopping 245 (260
when he was depressed, which was often) and it had become clear to everybody, especially his family, that he'd become the neighborhood parigüayo.[3]
Had none of the Higher Powers of your typical Dominican male, couldn't
have pulled a girl if his life depended on it. Couldn't play sports for shit, or
dominoes, was beyond uncoordinated, threw a ball like a girl. Had no knack
for music or business or dance, no hustle, no rap, no G.[4] And most damning
of all: no looks. He wore his semikink hair in a Puerto Rican afro, rocked
enormous Section 8[5] glasses—his "anti-pussy devices," Al and Miggs, his
only friends, called them—sported an unappealing trace of mustache on his
upper lip and possessed a pair of close-set eyes that made him look somewhat
retarded. The Eyes of Mingus.[6] (A comparison he made himself one day
going through his mother's record collection; she was the only old-school
dominicana he knew who had dated a moreno[7] until Oscar's father put an
end to that particular chapter of the All-African World Party.) You have the
same eyes as your abuelo,[8] his Nena Inca had told him on one of his visits to
the DR, which should have been some comfort—who doesn't like resembling
an ancestor?—except this particular ancestor had ended his days in prison.

Oscar had always been a young nerd—the kind of kid who read Tom
Swift, who loved comic books and watched *Ultraman*[9]—but by high school
his commitment to the Genres had become absolute. Back when the rest
of us were learning to play wallball and pitch quarters and drive our older
brothers' cars and sneak dead soldiers[1] from under our parents' eyes, he was
gorging himself on a steady stream of Lovecraft, Wells, Burroughs, Howard, Alexander, Herbert, Asimov, Bova, and Heinlein, and even the Old
Ones who were already beginning to fade—E. E. "Doc" Smith, Stapledon,
and the guy who wrote all the Doc Savage[2] books—moving hungrily from

---

3. The pejorative *parigüayo*, Watchers agree, is a
corruption of the English neologism "party
watcher." The word came into common usage during the First American Occupation of the DR,
which ran from 1916 to 1924. (You didn't know we
were occupied twice in the twentieth century?
Don't worry, when you have kids they won't know
the U.S. occupied Iraq either.) During the First
Occupation it was reported that members of the
American Occupying Forces would often attend
Dominican parties but instead of joining in the
fun the Outlanders would simply stand at the edge
of dances and *watch*. Which of course must have
seemed like the craziest thing in the world. Who
goes to a party to *watch*? Thereafter, the Marines
were parigüayos—a word that in contemporary usage describes anybody who stands outside and
watches while other people scoop up the girls. The
kid who don't dance, who ain't got game, who lets
people clown him—he's the parigüayo.
   If you looked in the Dictionary of Dominican
Things, the entry for *parigüayo* would include a
wood carving of Oscar. It is a name that would
haunt him for the rest of his life and that would
lead him to another Watcher, the one who lamps
on the Blue Side of the Moon. [Author/narrator's
note]
4. Gangsta.

5. Formerly, a category of discharge from the
U.S. military for being mentally unfit to serve
(such as for being guilty of "sexual perversion").
6. Charles Mingus (1922–1979), American jazz
bassist, composer, and bandleader.
7. Here, a black man.
8. Grandfather.
9. Japanese science fiction/superhero/fantasy series. *Tom Swift*: central character in multiple
series, beginning in 1910, of science fiction/
adventure novels for juveniles.
1. Empty containers, usually bottles or cans,
that have held alcoholic beverages.
2. Adventure hero in stories published in American pulp magazines during the 1930s and 1940s;
the original series was written by Lester Dent
(1904–1959) under the pen name Kenneth
Robeson. The science fiction/adventure/fantasy
writers listed above, some English and some
American, are—in addition to Burroughs (see
note 7, p. 2362)—H(oward) P(hillips) Lovecraft
(1890–1950), H(erbert) G(eorge) Wells (1866–
1946), Robert E(rvin) Howard (1906–1936),
Lloyd Alexander (1924–2007), Frank Herbert
(1920–1986), Isaac Asimov (1920–1992), Benjamin Bova (b. 1932), Robert A. Heinlein (1907–
1988), E(dward) E(lmer) Smith (1890–1965),
and (William) Olaf Stapledon (1886–1950).

book to book, author to author, age to age. (It was his good fortune that the libraries of Paterson were so underfunded that they still kept a lot of the previous generation's nerdery in circulation.) You couldn't have torn him away from any movie or TV show or cartoon where there were monsters or spaceships or mutants or doomsday devices or destinies or magic or evil villains. In these pursuits alone Oscar showed the genius his grandmother insisted was part of the family patrimony. Could write in Elvish, could speak Chakobsa, could differentiate between a Slan, a Dorsai, and a Lensman in acute detail, knew more about the Marvel Universe than Stan Lee,[3] and was a role-playing game fanatic. (If only he'd been good at videogames it would have been a slam dunk but despite owning an Atari and an Intellivision he didn't have the reflexes for it.) Perhaps if like me he'd been able to hide his otakuness[4] maybe shit would have been easier for him, but he couldn't. Dude wore his nerdiness like a Jedi wore his light saber or a Lensman her lens. Couldn't have passed for Normal if he'd wanted to.[5]

Oscar was a social introvert who trembled with fear during gym class and watched nerd British shows like *Doctor Who* and *Blake's 7*, and could tell you the difference between a Veritech fighter and a Zentraedi walker,[6] and

---

3. American comic-book writer and editor (b. Stanley Martin Lieber, 1922); the former president and chairman of Marvel Comics. *Elvish*: fictional language used in the *Lord of the Rings* series (beginning in 1937), by the fantasy author J(ohn) R(onald) R(euel) Tolkien (1892–1973). *Chakobsa*: fictional language used in Frank Herbert's *Dune* series (beginning in 1965). *Slan*: fictional race of superbeings in the science fiction novel of the same title (1946), by A(lfred) E(lton) Van Vogt (1912–2000). *Dorsai*: subculture in the novel of the same title (1960) and the series that followed, by Gordon Rupert Dickson (1923–2001). *Lensman*: i.e., user of the Lens, in E. E. Smith's "Lensman" series (beginning in 1934).
4. From *otaku*, a Japanese term for people with obsessive interests, especially in video games and genres such as anime and manga.
5. Where this outsized love of genre jumped off from no one quite seems to know. It might have been a consequence of being Antillean (who more sci-fi than us?) or of living in the DR for the first couple of years of his life and then abruptly wrenchingly relocating to New Jersey—a single green card shifting not only worlds (from Third to First) but centuries (from almost no TV or electricity to plenty of both). After a transition like that I'm guessing only the most extreme scenarios could have satisfied. Maybe it was that in the DR he had watched too much *Spider-Man*, listened to too many of his abuela's spooky stories about el Cuco and la Ciguapa? Maybe it was his first librarian in the U.S., who hooked him on reading, the electricity he felt when he touched that first Danny Dunn book? Maybe it was just the zeitgeist (were not the early seventies the dawn of the Nerd Age?) or the fact that for most of his childhood he had absolutely no friends? Or was it something deeper, something ancestral?

Who can say?

What is clear is that being a reader/fanboy (for lack of a better term) helped him get through the rough days of his youth, but it also made him stick out in the mean streets of Paterson even more than he already did. Victimized by the other boys—punches and pushes and wedgies and broken glasses and brand-new books from Scholastic, at a cost of fifty cents each, torn in half before his very eyes. You like books? Now you got two! Har-har! No one, alas, more oppressive than the oppressed. Even his own mother found his preoccupations nutty. Go outside and play! she commanded at least once a day. Pórtate como un muchacho normal.

(Only his sister, a reader too, supporting him. Bringing him books from her own school, which had a better library.)

You really want to know what being an X-Man feels like? Just be a smart bookish boy of color in a contemporary U.S. ghetto. Mamma mia! Like having bat wings or a pair of tentacles growing out of your chest.

Pa' 'fuera! his mother roared. And out he would go, like a boy condemned, to spend a few hours being tormented by the other boys—Please, I want to stay, he would beg his mother, but she shoved him out—You ain't a woman to be staying in the house—one hour, two, until finally he could slip back inside unnoticed, hiding himself in the upstairs closet, where he'd read by the slat of light that razored in from the cracked door. Eventually, his mother rooting him out again: What is carajo is the matter with you?

(And already on scraps of paper, in his composition books, on the backs of his hands, he was beginning to scribble, nothing serious for now, just rough facsimiles of his favorite stories, no sign yet that these half-assed pastiches were to be his Destiny.) [Author/narrator's note]

*Run Run Shaw*: Chinese producer of movies in Hong Kong (b. 1907). *Danny Dunn*: protagonist in a series of juvenile science fiction/ adventure books (1950s–70s). *El Cuco*: the bogeyman. *La Ciguapa*: legendary female being with long hair and backward feet. *Portate como un muchacho normal*: Act like a normal boy. *Pa' 'fuera!*: Go outside! *Carajo*: here, hell. [Anthology editors' note]
6. In the *Robotech* science fiction franchise, a fighter aircraft and a weapon, respectively.

he used a lot of huge-sounding nerd words like *indefatigable* and *ubiquitous* when talking to niggers who would barely graduate from high school. One of those nerds who was always hiding out in the library, who adored Tolkien and later the Margaret Weis and Tracy Hickman novels (his favorite character was of course Raistlin),[7] and who, as the eighties marched on, developed a growing obsession with the End of the World. (No apocalyptic movie or book or game existed that he had not seen or read or played— Wyndham and Christopher and Gamma World[8] were his absolute favorites.) You get the picture. His adolescent nerdliness vaporizing any iota of a chance he had for young love. Everybody else going through the terror and joy of their first crushes, their first dates, their first kisses while Oscar sat in the back of the class, behind his DM's screen, and watched his adolescence stream by. Sucks to be left out of adolescence, sort of like getting locked in the closet on Venus when the sun appears for the first time in a hundred years. It would have been one thing if like some of the nerdboys I'd grown up with he hadn't cared about girls, but alas he was still the passionate enamorao[9] who fell in love easily and deeply. He had secret loves all over town, the kind of curly-haired big-bodied girls who wouldn't have said boo to a loser like him but about whom he could not stop dreaming. His affection—that gravitational mass of love, fear, longing, desire, and lust that he directed at any and every girl in the vicinity without regard to looks, age, or availability—broke his heart each and every day. Despite the fact that he considered it this huge sputtering force, it was actually most like a ghost because no girl ever really seemed to notice it. Occasionally they might shudder or cross their arms when he walked near, but that was about it. He cried often for his love of some girl or another. Cried in the bathroom, where nobody could hear him.

Anywhere else his triple-zero batting average with the ladies might have passed without comment, but this is a Dominican kid we're talking about, in a Dominican family: dude was supposed to have Atomic Level G, was supposed to be pulling in the bitches with both hands. Everybody noticed his lack of game and because they were Dominican everybody talked about it. His tío Rudolfo (only recently released from his last and final bid in the Justice[1] and now living in their house on Main Street) was especially generous in his tutelage. Listen, palomo:[2] you have to grab a muchacha, y metéselo. That will take care of *everything*. Start with a fea. Coje that fea y metéselo![3] Tío Rudolfo had four kids with three different women so the nigger was without doubt the family's resident metéselo expert.

His mother's only comment? You need to worry about your grades. And in more introspective moments: Just be glad you didn't get my luck, hijo.

What luck? his tío snorted.

Exactly, she said.

His friends Al and Miggs? Dude, you're kinda way fat, you know.

7. Raistlin Majere, physically weak Wizard of High Sorcery in the *Dragonlance* series (beginning in 1984), by the Americans Weis (b. 1948) and Hickman (b. 1955)
8. A science/fantasy role-playing game (beginning in 1978). *Wyndham*: John Wyndham, one pen name of the English science fiction writer John Wyndham Parkes Lucas Beynon Harris

(1903–1969). *Christopher*: John Christopher, one pen name of the English science fiction writer Samuel Youd (b. 1922).
9. One who is smitten or in love.
1. I.e., the justice system; prison.
2. Term of endearment (from *paloma*, dove or pigeon).
3. Find an ugly girl and get on it!

His abuela, La Inca? Hijo, you're the most buenmoso[4] man I know! Oscar's sister, Lola, was a lot more practical. Now that her crazy years were over—what Dominican girl doesn't have those?—she'd turned into one of those tough Jersey dominicanas, a long-distance runner who drove her own car, had her own checkbook, called men bitches, and would eat a fat cat in front of you without a speck of vergüenza.[5] When she was in fourth grade she'd been attacked by an older acquaintance, and this was common knowledge throughout the family (and by extension a sizable section of Paterson, Union City, and Teaneck), and surviving that urikán of pain, judgment, and bochinche[6] had made her tougher than adamantine. Recently she'd cut her hair short—flipping out her mother yet again— partially I think because when she'd been little her family had let it grow down past her ass, a source of pride, something I'm sure her attacker noticed and admired.

Oscar, Lola warned repeatedly, you're going to die a virgin unless you start *changing*.

Don't you think I know that? Another five years of this and I'll bet you somebody tries to name a church after me.

Cut the hair, lose the glasses, exercise. And get rid of those porn magazines. They're disgusting, they bother Mami, and they'll never get you a date.

Sound counsel that in the end he did not adopt. He tried a couple of times to exercise, leg lifts, sit-ups, walks around the block in the early morning, that sort of thing, but he would notice how everybody else had a girl but him and would despair, plunging right back into eating, *Penthouses*, designing dungeons, and self-pity.

I seem to be allergic to diligence, and Lola said, Ha. What you're allergic to is *trying*.

It wouldn't have been half bad if Paterson and its surrounding precincts had been like Don Bosco or those seventies feminist sci-fi novels he sometimes read—an all-male-exclusion zone. Paterson, however, was girls the way NYC was girls, Paterson was girls the way Santo Domingo was girls. Paterson had mad girls, and if that wasn't guapas enough for you, well, motherfucker, then roll south and there'd be Newark, Elizabeth, Jersey City, the Oranges, Union City, West New York, Weehawken, Perth Amboy[7]—an urban swath known to niggers everywhere as Negrapolis One. So in effect he saw girls—Hispanophone Caribbean girls—everywhere.

He wasn't safe even in his own house, his sister's girlfriends were always hanging out, permanent guests. When they were around he didn't need no *Penthouses*. Her girls were not too smart but they were fine as shit: the sort of hot-as-balls Latinas who only dated weight-lifting morenos or Latino cats with guns in their cribs. They were all on the volleyball team together and tall and fit as colts and when they went for runs it was what the track team might have looked like in terrorist heaven. Bergen County's very own cigüapas: la primera was Gladys, who complained endlessly about her chest being too big, that maybe she'd find normal boyfriends if she'd had a

4. Hunkiest.
5. Shame, embarrassment, inhibition.
6. Gossip. *Urikán*: maelstrom, tempest (hurricane). *Teaneck*: township in northeastern New

Jersey, as is Union City.
7. Cities, townships, and towns closer to New York City than to Paterson.

smaller pair; Marisol, who'd end up at MIT and *hated* Oscar but whom Oscar liked most of all; Leticia, just off the boat, half Haitian half Dominican, that special blend the Dominican government swears *no existe*, who spoke with the deepest accent, a girl so good she refused to sleep with *three consecutive boyfriends*! It wouldn't have been so bad if these chickies hadn't treated Oscar like some deaf-mute harem guard, ordering him around, having him run their errands, making fun of his games and his looks; to make shit even worse, they blithely went on about the particulars of their sex lives with no regard for him, while he sat in the kitchen, clutching the latest issue of *Dragon*. Hey, he would yell, in case you're wondering there's a male unit in here.

Where? Marisol would say blandly. I don't see one.

And when they talked about how all the Latin guys only seemed to want to date whitegirls, he would offer, *I* like Spanish girls, to which Marisol responded with wide condescension. That's great, Oscar. Only problem is no Spanish girl would date you.

Leave him alone, Leticia said. I think you're cute, Oscar.

Yeah, right, Marisol laughed, rolling her eyes. Now he'll probably write a book about you.

These were Oscar's furies, his personal pantheon, the girls he most dreamed about and most beat off to and who eventually found their way into his little stories. In his dreams he was either saving them from aliens or he was returning to the neighborhood, rich and famous—It's him! The Dominican Stephen King!—and then Marisol would appear, carrying one each of his books for him to sign. Please, Oscar, marry me. Oscar, drolly: I'm sorry, Marisol, I don't marry ignorant bitches. (But then of course he would.) Maritza he still watched from afar, convinced that one day, when the nuclear bombs fell (or the plague broke out or the Tripods invaded)[8] and civilization was wiped out he would end up saving her from a pack of irradiated ghouls and together they'd set out across a ravaged America in search of a better tomorrow. In these apocalyptic daydreams he was always some kind of plátano[9] Doc Savage, a supergenius who combined world-class martial artistry with deadly firearms proficiency. Not bad for a nigger who'd never even shot an air rifle, thrown a punch, or scored higher than a thousand on his SATs.

### Oscar Is Brave

Senior year found him bloated, dyspeptic, and, most cruelly, alone in his lack of girlfriend. His two nerdboys, Al and Miggs, had, in the craziest twist of fortune, both succeeded in landing themselves girls that year. Nothing special, skanks really, but girls nonetheless. Al had met his at Menlo Park.[1] She'd come onto *him*, he bragged, and when she informed him, after she sucked his dick of course, that she had a girlfriend *desperate* to meet somebody, Al had dragged Miggs away from his Atari and out to a movie and the

---

8. The latter occurs in John Christopher's *Tripods* trilogy (beginning in 1968).
9. Banana, here meaning Dominican rather than

Anglo.
1. In Edison, a township in central-eastern New Jersey.

rest was, as they say, history. By the end of the week Miggs was getting his too, and only then did Oscar find out about any of it. While they were in his room setting up for another "hair-raising" Champions adventure against the Death-Dealing Destroyers. (Oscar had to retire his famous Aftermath! campaign because nobody else but him was hankering to play in the post-apocalyptic ruins of virus-wracked America.) At first, after hearing about the double-bootie coup, Oscar didn't say nothing much. He just rolled his d10's[2] over and over. Said, You guys sure got lucky. It killed him that they hadn't thought to include him in their girl heists; he hated Al for inviting Miggs instead of him and he hated Miggs for getting a girl, period. Al getting a girl Oscar could comprehend; Al (real name Alok) was one of those tall Indian prettyboys who would never have been pegged by anyone as a role-playing nerd. It was Miggs's girl-getting he could not fathom, that astounded him and left him sick with jealousy. Oscar had always considered Miggs to be an even bigger freak than he was. Acne galore and a retard's laugh and gray fucking teeth from having been given some medicine too young. So is your girlfriend cute? he asked Miggs. He said, Dude, you should see her, she's beautiful. Big fucking tits, Al seconded. That day what little faith Oscar had in the world took an SS-N-17[3] snipe to the head. When finally he couldn't take it no more he asked, pathetically, What, these girls don't have any other friends?

Al and Miggs traded glances over their character sheets. I don't think so, dude.

And right there he learned something about his friends he'd never known (or at least never admitted to himself). Right there he had an epiphany that echoed through his fat self. He realized his fucked-up comic-book-reading, role-playing-game-loving, no-sports-playing friends were embarrassed by *him*.

Knocked the architecture right out of his legs. He closed the game early, the Exterminators found the Destroyers' hide-out right away—That was bogus, Al groused. After he showed them out he locked himself in his room, lay in bed for a couple of stunned hours, then got up, undressed in the bathroom he no longer had to share because his sister was at Rutgers, and examined himself in the mirror. The fat! The miles of stretch marks! The tumescent horribleness of his proportions! He looked straight out of a Daniel Clowes comic book. Or like the fat blackish kid in Beto Hernández's Palomar.[4]

Jesus Christ, he whispered. I'm a Morlock.[5]

The next day at breakfast he asked his mother: Am I ugly?

She sighed. Well, hijo, you certainly don't take after me.

Dominican parents! You got to love them!

Spent a week looking at himself in the mirror, turning every which way, taking stock, not flinching, and decided at last to be like Roberto Durán: No más.[6] That Sunday he went to Chucho's and had the barber shave his Puerto

---

2. Dice, for their role-playing game.
3. A type of intermediate-range, submarine-launched, Soviet ballistic missile.
4. Graphic novel (2003) by the American writer and illustrator Gilberto "Beto" Hernandez (b. 1957). *Daniel Clowes*: American writer and il-

lustrator (b. 1961), notably of alternative comic books.
5. Mutants in the Marvel Comics universe.
6. No more; famously said by Dúran (b. 1951), now-retired professional boxer from Panama, in quitting a 1980 fight.

Rican 'fro off. (Wait a minute, Chucho's partner said. *You're* Dominican?) Oscar lost the mustache next, and then the glasses, bought contacts with the money he was making at the lumberyard and tried to polish up what remained of his Dominicanness, tried to be more like his cursing swaggering cousins, if only because he had started to suspect that in their Latin hypermaleness there might be an answer. But he was really too far gone for quick fixes. The next time Al and Miggs saw him he'd been starving himself for three days straight. Miggs said, Dude, what's the matter with *you*?

Changes, Oscar said pseudo-cryptically.

What, are you some album cover now?

He shook his head solemnly. I'm embarking on a new cycle of my life.

Listen to the guy. He already sounds like he's in college.

That summer his mother sent him and his sister to Santo Domingo, and this time he didn't fight it like he had in the recent past. It's not like he had much in the States keeping him. He arrived in Baní with a stack of notebooks and a plan to fill them all up. Since he could no longer be a gamemaster he decided to try his hand at being a real writer. The trip turned out to be something of a turning point for him. Instead of discouraging his writing, chasing him out of the house like his mother used to, his abuela, Nena Inca, let him be. Allowed him to sit in the back of the house as long as he wanted, didn't insist that he should be "out in the world." (She had always been overprotective of him and his sister. Too much bad luck in this family, she sniffed.) Kept the music off and brought him his meals at exactly the same time every day. His sister ran around with her hot Island friends, always jumping out of the house in a bikini and going off to different parts of the Island for overnight trips, but he stayed put. When any family members came looking for him his abuela chased them off with a single imperial sweep of her hand. Can't you see the muchacho's working? What's he doing? his cousins asked, confused. He's being a genius is what, La Inca replied haughtily. Now váyanse. (Later when he thought about it he realized that these very cousins could probably have gotten him laid if only he'd bothered to hang out with them. But you can't regret the life you didn't lead.) In the afternoons, when he couldn't write another word, he'd sit out in front of the house with his abuela and watch the street scene, listen to the raucous exchanges between the neighbors. One evening, at the end of his trip, his abuela confided: Your mother could have been a doctor just like your grandfather was.

What happened?

La Inca shook her head. She was looking at her favorite picture of his mother on her first day at private school, one of those typical serious DR shots. What always happens. Un maldito hombre.

He wrote two books that summer about a young man fighting mutants at the end of the world (neither of them survive). Took crazy amounts of field notes too, names of things he intended to later adapt for science-fictional and fantastic purposes. (Heard about the family curse for like the thousandth time but strangely enough didn't think it worth incorporating into his fiction—I mean, shit, what Latino family doesn't think it's cursed?)

When it was time for him and his sister to return to Paterson he was almost sad. Almost. His abuela placed her hand on his head in blessing. Cuidate mucho, mi hijo. Know that in this world there's somebody who will always love you.

At JFK,[7] almost not being recognized by his uncle. Great, his tío said, looking askance at his complexion, now you look Haitian.

After his return he hung out with Miggs and Al, saw movies with them, talked Los Brothers Hernández, Frank Miller, and Alan Moore[8] with them but overall they never regained the friendship they had before Santo Domingo. Oscar listened to their messages on the machine and resisted the urge to run over to their places. Didn't see them but once, twice a week. Focused on his writing. Those were some fucking lonely weeks when all he had were his games, his books, and his words. So now I have a hermit for a son, his mother complained bitterly. At night, unable to sleep, he watched a lot of bad TV, became obsessed with two movies in particular: *Zardoz* (which he'd seen with his uncle before they put him away for the second time) and *Virus* (the Japanese end-of-the-world movie with the hot chick from *Romeo and Juliet*).[9] *Virus* especially he could not watch to the end without crying, the Japanese hero arriving at the South Pole base, having walked from Washington, D.C., down the whole spine of the Andes,[1] for the woman of his dreams. I've been working on my fifth novel, he told the boys when they asked about his absences. It's *amazing*.

See? What did I tell you? Mr. Collegeboy.

In the old days when his so-called friends would hurt him or drag his trust through the mud he always crawled voluntarily back into the abuse, out of fear and loneliness, something he'd always hated himself for, but not this time. If there existed in his high school years any one moment he took pride in it was clearly this one. Even told his sister about it during her next visit. She said, Way to go, O! He'd finally showed some backbone, hence some pride, and although it hurt, it also felt motherfucking *good*.

*   *   *

2007

7. John F. Kennedy International Airport, in New York City.
8. English comic-book writer (b. 1953). *Los Brothers Hernández*: collective name for the brothers "Beto" (see note 4, p. 2371), Jaime (b. 1959), and Mario (b. 1953), authors of the *Love and Rockets* comic-book series (for a sample of their work, see p. 2435). *Frank Miller*: American writer, comic-

book artist, and film director (b. 1957).
9. The actress Olivia Hussey (b. in Argentina, 1951) played Juliet in the 1968 movie version of Shakespeare's *Romeo and Juliet* and Marit in *Fukkatsu no hi* (1980), also known as *Virus, Day of Resurrection*, and *The End*.
1. Mountain system in South America.

# ANA MENÉNDEZ
## b. 1970

The daughter of Cuban exiles who fled the island in 1964, Ana Menéndez was born in Los Angeles, California, and raised there and in Tampa, Florida. After earning her bachelor's degree in English from Florida International University, in Miami, she began working as a journalist for the *Miami Herald* and at the *Orange County Register*. Her first book of short stories, *In Cuba I Was a German Shepherd* (2001), was a New York Times Notable Book of the Year and has been translated into 11 languages.

*In Cuba I Was a German Shepherd* has been described as a "Cuban Odyssey"; its stories link to capture the elusive space shared by generations of exiles from Cuba, caught between memories of the past and the painful reality of the present. In a 2001 interview, Menéndez stated that though her stories are not related directly to her family's experiences, her understanding of the exile's world comes from her upbringing. Raised speaking Spanish in Los Angeles and Tampa, hearing constantly about the island left behind, and believing that the family would soon return to Cuba, she says, "Growing up, I always felt more Cuban than American." Menéndez's characters are aging exiles who for more than 40 years have endured separation from their homeland, as well as younger Cuban Americans who have assimilated American ways yet share their elders' feelings of longing and loss. In the title story, which won a Pushcart Prize and is included here, an exiled former professor from Havana, retired after his struggle to open and run a small Miami restaurant, plays dominos in Miami's Maximo Gómez Park, telling pain-filled jokes about Fidel Castro, exile, and himself, while guides on the Little Havana tourist trolleys point out the players as "a slice of the past."

Menéndez's second book, *Loving Che* (2003), centers on a young woman who suspects that she is Che Guevara's illegitimate daughter. Menéndez continues to work as a journalist, writing a weekly column for the *Miami Herald*. In 2007, she received the American Society of Newspaper Editors' Distinguished Writing Award for Commentary.

# In Cuba I Was a German Shepherd

The park where the four men gathered was small. Before the city put it on its tourist maps, it was just a fenced rectangle of space that people missed on the way to their office jobs. The men came each morning to sit under the shifting shade of a banyan tree, and sometimes the way the wind moved through the leaves reminded them of home.

One man carried a box of plastic dominos. His name was Máximo, and because he was a small man his grandiose name had inspired much amusement all his life. He liked to say that over the years he'd learned a thing or two about the physics of laughter and his friends took that to mean good humor could make a big man out of anyone. Now Máximo waited for the others to sit before turning the dominos out on the table. Judging the men to be in good spirits, he cleared his throat and began to tell the joke he had prepared for the day.

"So Bill Clinton dies in office and they freeze his body."

Antonio leaned back in his chair and let out a sigh. "Here we go."

Máximo caught a roll of the eyes and almost grew annoyed. But he smiled. "It gets better."

He scraped the dominos in two wide circles across the table, then continued.

"Okay, so they freeze his body and when we get the technology to unfreeze him, he wakes up in the year 2105."

"Two thousand one hundred and five, eh?"

"Very good," Máximo said. "Anyway, he's curious about what's happened to the world all this time, so he goes up to a Jewish fellow and he says, 'So, how are things in the Middle East?' The guy replies, 'Oh wonderful, wonderful, everything is like heaven. Everybody gets along now.' This makes Clinton smile, right?"

The men stopped shuffling and dragged their pieces across the table and waited for Máximo to finish.

"Next he goes up to an Irishman and he says, 'So how are things over there in Northern Ireland now?' The guy says, 'Northern? It's one Ireland now and we all live in peace.' Clinton is extremely pleased at this point, right? So he does that biting thing with his lip."

Máximo stopped to demonstrate and Raúl and Carlos slapped their hands on the domino table and laughed. Máximo paused. Even Antonio had to smile. Máximo loved this moment when the men were warming to the joke and he still kept the punch line close to himself like a secret.

"So, okay," Máximo continued, "Clinton goes up to a Cuban fellow and says, 'Compadre, how are things in Cuba these days?' The guy looks at Clinton and he says to the president, 'Let me tell you, my friend, I can feel it in my bones. Any day now Castro's gonna fall.'"

Máximo tucked his head into his neck and smiled. Carlos slapped him on the back and laughed.

"That's a good one, sure is," he said. "I like that one."

"Funny," Antonio said, nodding as he set up his pieces.

"Yes, funny," Raúl said. After chuckling for another moment, he added, "But old."

"What do you mean old?" Antonio said, then he turned to Carlos. "What are you looking at?"

Carlos stopped laughing.

"It's not old," Máximo said. "I just made it up."

"I'm telling you, professor, it's an old one," Raúl said. "I heard it when Reagan was president."[1]

Máximo looked at Raúl, but didn't say anything. He pulled the double nine from his row and laid it in the middle of the table, but the thud he intended was lost in the horns and curses of morning traffic on Eighth Street.

·

Raúl and Máximo had lived on the same El Vedado[2] street in Havana for fifteen years before the revolution. Raúl had been a government accountant and Máximo a professor at the University, two blocks from his home on L Street. They weren't close friends, but friendly still in that way of people who come from the same place and think they already know the important things about one another.

---

1. Ronald Wilson Reagan (1911–2004), U.S. president 1981–89.
2. Downtown; a vibrant neighborhood.

Máximo was one of the first to leave L Street, boarding a plane for Miami on the eve of the first of January 1961, exactly two years after Batista[3] had done the same. For reasons he told himself he could no longer remember, he said good-bye to no one. He was thirty-six years old then, already balding, with a wife and two young daughters whose names he tended to confuse. He left behind the row house of long shiny windows, the piano, the mahogany furniture, and the pension he thought he'd return to in two years' time. Three if things were as serious as they said.

In Miami, Máximo tried driving a taxi, but the streets were a web of foreign names and winding curves that could one day lead to glitter and another to the hollow end of a pistol. His Spanish and his University of Havana credentials meant nothing here. And he was too old to cut sugarcane with the younger men who began arriving in the spring of 1961. But the men gave Máximo an idea, and after teary nights of promises, he convinced his wife— she of stately homes and multiple cooks—to make lunch to sell to those sugar men who waited, squatting on their heels in the dark, for the bus to Belle Glade[4] every morning. They worked side by side, Máximo and Rosa. And at the end of every day, their hands stained orange from the lard and the cheap meat, their knuckles red and tender where the hot water and the knife blade had worked their business, Máximo and Rosa would sit down to whatever remained of the day's cooking and they would chew slowly, the day unraveling, their hunger ebbing away with the light.

They worked together for years like that, and when the Cubans began disappearing from the bus line, Máximo and Rosa moved their lunch packets indoors and opened their little restaurant right on Eighth Street. There, a generation of former professors served black beans and rice to the nostalgic. When Raúl showed up in Miami one summer looking for work, Máximo added one more waiter's spot for his old acquaintance from L Street. Each night, after the customers had gone, Máximo and Rosa and Raúl and Havana's old lawyers and bankers and dreamers would sit around the biggest table and eat and talk and sometimes, late in the night after several glasses of wine, someone would start the stories that began with "In Cuba I remember." They were stories of old lovers, beautiful and round-hipped. Of skies that stretched on clear and blue to the Cuban hills. Of green landscapes that clung to the red clay of Güines,[5] roots dug in like fingernails in a good-bye. In Cuba, the stories always began, life was good and pure. But something always happened to them in the end, something withering, malignant. Máximo never understood it. The stories that opened in sun, always narrowed into a dark place. And after those nights, his head throbbing, Máximo would turn and turn in his sleep and awake unable to remember his dreams.

Even now, five years after selling the place, Máximo couldn't walk by it in the early morning when it was still clean and empty. He'd tried it once. He'd stood and stared into the restaurant and had become lost and dizzy in

3. Fulgencio Batista y Zaldívar (1901–1973), Cuban soldier; president of Cuba 1940–55, 1952–99 (i.e., before the revolution).
4. A poverty- and violence-stricken city in south-eastern Florida; much of the sugarcane grown in the U.S. comes from the area.
5. Municipality in the province of Havana.

his own reflection in the glass, the neat row of chairs, the tombstone lunch board behind them.

·

"Okay. A bunch of rafters are on the beach getting ready to sail off to Miami."

"Where are they?"

"Who cares? Wherever. Cuba's got a thousand miles of coastline. Use your imagination."

"Let the professor tell his thing, for God's sake."

"Thank you." Máximo cleared his throat and shuffled the dominos. "So anyway, a bunch of rafters are gathered there on the sand. And they're all crying and hugging their wives and all the rafts are bobbing on the water and suddenly someone in the group yells, 'Hey! Look who goes there!' And it's Fidel in swimming trunks, carrying a raft on his back."

Carlos interrupted to let out a yelping laugh. "I like that, I like it, sure do."

"You like it, eh?" said Antonio. "Why don't you let the Cuban finish it."

Máximo slid the pieces to himself in twos and continued. "So one of the guys on the sand says to Fidel, 'Compatriota, what are you doing here? What's with the raft?' And Fidel sits on his raft and pushes off the shore and says, 'I'm sick of this place too. I'm going to Miami.' So the other guys look at each other and say, 'Coño,[6] compadre, if you're leaving, then there's no reason for us to go. Here, take my raft too, and get the fuck out of here.'"

Raúl let a shaking laugh rise from his belly and saluted Máximo with a domino piece.

"A good one, my friend."

Carlos laughed long and loud. Antonio laughed too, but he was careful not to laugh too hard and he gave his friend a sharp look over the racket he was causing. He and Carlos were Dominican, not Cuban, and they ate their same foods and played their same games, but Antonio knew they still didn't understand all the layers of hurt in the Cubans' jokes.

·

It had been Raúl's idea to go down to Domino Park that first time. Máximo protested. He had seen the rows of tourists pressed up against the fence, gawking at the colorful old guys playing dominos.

"I'm not going to be the sad spectacle in someone's vacation slide show," he'd said.

But Raúl was already dressed up in a pale blue guayabera, saying how it was a beautiful day and smell the air.

"Let them take pictures," Raúl said. "What the hell. Make us immortal."

"Immortal," Máximo said like a sneer. And then to himself, The gods' punishment.

It was that year after Rosa died and Máximo didn't want to tell how he'd begun to see her at the kitchen table as she'd been at twenty-five. Watched one thick strand of her dark hair stuck to her morning face. He saw her at thirty, bending down to wipe the chocolate off the cheeks of their two small

6. Damn.

daughters. And his eyes moved from Rosa to his small daughters. He had something he needed to tell them. He saw them grown up, at the funeral, crying together. He watched Rosa rise and do the sign of the cross. He knew he was caught inside a nightmare, but he couldn't stop. He would emerge slowly, creaking out of the shower and there she'd be, Rosa, like before, her breasts round and pink from the hot water, calling back through the years. Some mornings he would awake and smell peanuts roasting and hear the faint call of the manicero[7] pleading for someone to relieve his burden of white paper cones. Or it would be thundering, the long hard thunder of Miami that was so much like the thunder of home that each rumble shattered the morning of his other life. He would awake, caught fast in the damp sheets, and feel himself falling backwards.

He took the number eight bus to Eighth Street and 15th Avenue. At Domino Park, he sat with Raúl and they played alone that first day, Máximo noticing his own speckled hands, the spots of light through the banyan leaves, a round red beetle that crawled slowly across the table, then hopped the next breeze and floated away.

•

Antonio and Carlos were not Cuban, but they knew when to dump their heavy pieces and when to hold back the eights for the final shocking stroke. Waiting for a table, Raúl and Máximo would linger beside them and watch them lay their traps, a succession of threes that broke their opponents, an incredible run of fives. Even the unthinkable: passing when they had the piece to play.

Other twosomes began to refuse to play with the Dominicans, said that tipo[8] Carlos gave them the creeps with his giggling and monosyllables. Besides, any team that won so often must be cheating, went the charge, especially a team one-half imbecile. But really it was that no one plays to lose. You begin to lose again and again and it reminds you of other things in your life, the despair of it all begins to bleed through and that is not what games are for. Who wants to live their whole life alongside the lucky? But Máximo and Raúl liked these blessed Dominicans, appreciated the well-oiled moves of two old pros. And if the two Dominicans, afraid to be alone again, let them win now and then, who would know, who could ever admit to such a thing?

For many months they didn't know much about each other, these four men. Even the smallest boy knew not to talk when the pieces were in play. But soon came Máximo's jokes during the shuffling, something new and bright coming into his eyes like daydreams as he spoke. Carlos' full loud laughter, like that of children. And the four men learned to linger long enough between sets to color an old memory while the white pieces scraped along the table.

One day as they sat at their table closest to the sidewalk, a pretty girl walked by. She swung her long brown hair around and looked in at the men with her green eyes.

"What the hell is she looking at," said Antonio, who always sat with his back to the wall, looking out at the street. But the others saw how he returned the stare too.

---

7. Peanut vendor.        8. Guy.

Carlos let out a giggle and immediately put a hand to his mouth.

"In Santo Domingo,[9] a man once looked at—" But Carlos didn't get to finish.

"Shut up, you old idiot," said Antonio, putting his hands on the table like he was about to get up and leave.

"Please," Máximo said.

The girl stared another moment, then turned and left. Raúl rose slowly, flattening down his oiled hair with his right hand.

"Ay, mi niña."

"Sit down, hombre," Antonio said. "You're an old fool, just like this one."

"You're the fool," Raúl called back. "A woman like that . . ." He watched the girl cross the street. When she was out of sight, he grabbed the back of the chair behind him and eased his body down, his eyes still on the street. The other three men looked at one another.

"I knew a woman like that once," Raúl said after a long moment.

"That's right, he did," Antonio said, "in his moist boy dreams—what was it? A century ago?"

"No me jodas,"[1] Raúl said. "You are a vulgar man. I had a life all three of you would have paid millions for. Women."

Máximo watched him, then lowered his face, shuffled the dominos.

"I had women," Raúl said.

"We all had women," Carlos said, and he looked like he was about to laugh again, but instead just sat there, smiling like he was remembering one of Máximo's jokes.

"There was one I remember. More beautiful than the rising moon," Raúl said.

"Oh Jesus," Antonio said. "You people."

Máximo looked up, watching Raúl.

"Ay, a woman like that," Raúl said and shook his head. "The women of Cuba were radiant, magnificent, wouldn't you say, professor?"

Máximo looked away.

"I don't know," Antonio said. "I think that Americana there looked better than anything you remember."

And that brought a long laugh from Carlos.

Máximo sat all night at the pine table in his new efficiency, thinking about the green-eyed girl and wondering why he was thinking about her. The table and a narrow bed had come with the apartment, which he'd moved into after selling their house in Shenandoah.[2] The table had come with two chairs, sturdy and polished—not in the least institutional—but he had moved the other chair by the bed.

The landlady, a woman in her forties, had helped Máximo haul up three potted palms. Later, he bought a green pot of marigolds he saw in the supermarket and brought its butter leaves back to life under the window's eastern light. Máximo often sat at the table through the night, sometimes reading Martí,[3] sometimes listening to the rain on the tin hull of the air conditioner.

---

9. Capital of the Dominican Republic.
1. Don't fuck with me.
2. A Miami neighborhood (just south of Little

Havana).
3. José Martí (see p. 265).

When you are older, he'd read somewhere, you don't need as much sleep. And wasn't that funny because his days felt more like sleep than ever. Dinner kept him occupied for hours, remembering the story of each dish. Sometimes, at the table, he greeted old friends and awakened with a start when they reached out to touch him. When dawn rose and slunk into the room sideways through the blinds, Máximo walked as in a dream across the thin patterns of light on the terrazzo. The chair, why did he keep the other chair? Even the marigolds reminded him. An image returned again and again. Was it the green-eyed girl?

And then he remembered that Rosa wore carnations in her hair and hated her name. And that it saddened him because he liked to roll it off his tongue like a slow train to the country.

"Rosa," he said, taking her hand the night they met at La Concha while an old danzón played.

"Clavel," she said, tossing her head back in a crackling laugh. "Call me Clavel."

She pulled her hand away and laughed again. "Don't you notice the flower in a girl's hair?"

He led her around the dance floor, lined with chaperones, and when they turned he whispered that he wanted to follow her laughter to the moon. She laughed again, the notes round and heavy as summer raindrops, and Máximo felt his fingers go cold where they touched hers. The danzón played and they turned and turned and the faces of the chaperones and the moist warm air—and Máximo with his cold fingers worried that she had laughed at him. He was twenty-four and could not imagine a more sorrowful thing in all the world.

Sometimes, years later, he would catch a premonition of Rosa in the face of his eldest daughter. She would turn toward a window or do something with her eyes. And then she would smile and tilt her head back and her laughter connected him again to that night, made him believe for a moment that life was a string you could gather up in your hands all at once.

He sat at the table and tried to remember the last time he saw Marisa. In California now. An important lawyer. A year? Two? Anabel, gone to New York? Two years? They called more often than most children, Máximo knew. They called often and he was lucky that way.

·

"Fidel decides he needs to get in touch with young people."

"Ay, ay, ay."

"So his handlers arrange for him to go to a school in Havana. He gets all dressed up in his olive uniform, you know, puts conditioner on his beard and brushes it one hundred times, all that."

Raúl breathed out, letting each breath come out like a puff of laughter. "Where do you get these things?"

"No interrupting the artist anymore, okay?" Máximo continued. "So after he's beautiful enough, he goes to the school. He sits in on a few classes, walks around the halls. Finally, it's time for Fidel to leave and he realizes he hasn't talked to anyone. He rushes over to the assembly that is seeing him off with shouts of 'Comandante!' and he pulls a little boy out of a row. 'Tell me,' Fidel says, 'what is your name?' 'Pepito,' the little boy answers. 'Pepito—

what a nice name,' Fidel says. 'And tell me, Pepito, what do you think of the revolution?' 'Comandante,' Pepito says, 'the revolution is the reason we are all here.' 'Ah, very good, Pepito. And tell me, what is your favorite subject?' Pepito answers, 'Comandante, my favorite subject is mathematics.' Fidel pats the little boy on the head. 'And tell me, Pepito; what would you like to be when you grow up?' Pepito smiles and says, 'Comandante, I would like to be a tourist.'"

Máximo looked around the table, a shadow of a smile on his thin white lips as he waited for the laughter.

"Ay," Raúl said. "That is so funny it breaks my heart."

.

Máximo grew to like dominos, the way each piece became part of the next. After the last piece was laid down and they were tallying up the score, Máximo liked to look over the table as an artist might. He liked the way the row of black dots snaked around the table with such free-flowing abandon it was almost as if, thrilled to be let out of the box, the pieces choreographed a fresh dance of gratitude every night. He liked the straightforward contrast of black on white. The clean, fresh scrape of the pieces across the table before each new round. The audacity of the double nines. The plain smooth face of the blank, like a newborn unetched by the world to come.

"Professor," Raúl began. "Let's speed up the shuffling a bit, sí?"

"I was thinking," Máximo said.

"Well, that shouldn't take long," Antonio said.

"Who invented dominos, anyway?" Máximo said.

"I'd say it was probably the Chinese," Antonio said.

"No jodas," Raúl said. "Who else could have invented this game of skill and intelligence but a Cuban?"

"Coño," said Antonio without a smile. "Here we go again."

"Ah, bueno," Raúl said with a smile stuck between joking and condescending. "You don't have to believe it if it hurts."

Carlos let out a long laugh.

"You people are unbelievable," said Antonio. But there was something hard and tired behind the way he smiled.

.

It was the first day of December, but summer still hung about in the brightest patches of sunlight. The four men sat under the shade of the banyan tree. It wasn't cold, not even in the shade, but three of the men wore cardigans. If asked, they would say they were expecting a chilly north wind and doesn't anybody listen to the weather forecasts anymore. Only Antonio, his round body enough to keep him warm, clung to the short sleeves of summer.

Kids from the local Catholic high school had volunteered to decorate the park for Christmas and they dashed about with tinsel in their hair, bumping one another and laughing loudly. Lucinda, the woman who issued the dominos and kept back the gambling, asked them to quiet down, pointing at the men. A wind stirred the top branches of the banyan tree and moved on without touching the ground. One leaf fell to the table.

Antonio waited for Máximo to fetch Lucinda's box of plastic pieces. Antonio held his brown paper bag to his chest and looked at the Cubans, his

2382 / Ana Menéndez

customary sourness replaced for a moment by what in a man like him could pass for levity. Máximo sat down and began to dump the plastic pieces on the table as he always did. But this time, Antonio held out his hand.

"One moment," he said and shook his brown paper bag.

"¿Qué pasa, chico?" Máximo said.

Antonio reached into the paper bag as the men watched. He let the paper fall away. In his hand he held an oblong black leather box.

"Coñooo," Raúl said.

Antonio set the box on the table, like a magician drawing out his trick. He looked around to the men and finally opened the box with a flourish to reveal a neat row of big heavy pieces, gone yellow and smooth like old teeth. They bent in closer to look. Antonio tilted the box gently and the pieces fell out in one long line, their black dots facing up now like tight dark pupils in the sunlight.

"Ivory," Antonio said. "And ebony. It's an antique. You're not allowed to make them anymore."

"Beautiful," Carlos said and clasped his hands.

"My daughter found them for me in New Orleans," Antonio continued, ignoring Carlos.

He looked around the table and lingered on Máximo, who had lowered the box of plastic dominos to the ground.

"She said she's been searching for them for two years. Couldn't wait two more weeks to give them to me," he said.

"Coñooo," Raúl said.

A moment passed.

"Well," Antonio said, "what do you think, Máximo?"

Máximo looked at him. Then he bent across the table to touch one of the pieces. He gave a jerk with his head and listened for the traffic. "Very nice," he said.

"Very nice?" Antonio said. "Very nice?" He laughed in his thin way. "My daughter walked all over New Orleans to find this and the Cuban thinks it's 'very nice'?" He paused, watching Máximo. "Did you know my daughter is coming to visit me for Christmas, Máximo? Maybe you can tell her that her gift was very nice, but not as nice as some you remember, eh?"

Máximo looked up, his eyes settling on Carlos, who looked at Antonio and then looked away.

"Calm down, hombre," Carlos said, opening his arms wide, a nervous giggle beginning in his throat. "What's gotten into you?"

Antonio waved his hand and sat down. A diesel truck rattled down Eighth Street, headed for downtown.

"My daughter is a district attorney in Los Angeles," Máximo said after the noise of the truck died. "December is one of the busiest months."

He felt a heat behind his eyes he had not felt in many years.

"Feel one in your hand," Antonio said. "Feel how heavy that is."

•

When the children were small, Máximo and Rosa used to spend Noche-buena with his cousins in Cárdenas.[4] It was a five-hour drive from Havana

4. Municipality east of Havana. *Nochebuena*: literally, good night; Christmas Eve.

in the cars of those days. They would rise early on the twenty-third and arrive by mid-afternoon so Máximo could help the men kill the pig for the feast the following night. Máximo and the other men held the squealing, squirming animal down, its wiry brown coat cutting into their gloveless hands. But God, they were intelligent creatures. No sooner did it spot the knife than the animal bolted out of their arms, screaming like Armageddon. It had become the subtext to the Nochebuena tradition, this chasing of the terrified pig through the yard, dodging orange trees and rotting fruit underneath. The children were never allowed to watch, Rosa made sure. They sat indoors with the women and stirred the black beans. With loud laughter, they shut out the shouts of the men and the hysterical pleadings of the animal as it was dragged back to its slaughter.

.

"Juanito the little dog gets off the boat from Cuba and decides to take a little stroll down Brickell Avenue."[5]

"Let me make sure I understand the joke. Juanito is a dog. Bowwow."

"That's pretty good."

"Yes, Juanito is a dog, goddamn it."

Raúl looked up, startled.

Máximo shuffled the pieces hard and swallowed. He swung his arms across the table in wide, violent arcs. One of the pieces flew off the table.

"Hey, hey, watch it with that, what's wrong with you?"

Máximo stopped. He felt his heart beating. "I'm sorry," he said. He bent over the edge of the table to see where the piece had landed. "Wait a minute." He held the table with one hand and tried to stretch to pick up the piece.

"What are you doing?"

"Just wait a minute." When he couldn't reach, he stood, pulled the piece toward him with his foot, sat back down, and reached for it again, this time grasping it between his fingers and his palm. He put it facedown on the table with the others and shuffled, slowly, his mind barely registering the traffic.

"Where was I—Juanito the little dog, right, bowwow." Máximo took a deep breath. "He's just off the boat from Cuba and is strolling down Brickell Avenue. He's looking up at all the tall and shiny buildings. 'Coño,' he says, dazzled by all the mirrors. 'There's nothing like this in Cuba.'"

"Hey, hey, professor. We had tall buildings."

"Jesus Christ!" Máximo said. He pressed his thumb and forefinger into the corners of his eyes. "This is after Castro, then. Let me just get it out for Christ's sake."

He stopped shuffling. Raúl looked away.

"Ready now? Juanito the little dog is looking up at all the tall buildings and he's so happy to finally be in America because all his cousins have been telling him what a great country it is, right? You know, they were sending back photos of their new cars and girlfriends."

"A joke about dogs who drive cars—I've heard it all."

"Hey, they're Cuban super-dogs."

5. The main thoroughfare in downtown Miami.

"All right, they're sending back photos of their new owners or the biggest bones any dog has ever seen. Anything you like. Use your imaginations." Máximo stopped shuffling. "Where was I?"

"You were at the part where Juanito buys a Rolls-Royce."

The men laughed.

"Okay, Antonio, why don't you three fools continue the joke." Máximo got up from the table. "You've made me forget the rest of it."

"Aw, come on, chico, sit down, don't be so sensitive."

"Come on, professor, you were at the part where Juanito is so glad to be in America."

"Forget it. I can't remember the rest now."

Máximo rubbed his temple, grabbed the back of the chair, and sat down slowly, facing the street. "Just leave me alone, I can't remember it." He pulled at the pieces two by two. "I'm sorry. Look, let's just play."

The men set up their double rows of dominos, like miniature barricades before them.

"These pieces are a work of art," Antonio said and laid down a double eight.

The banyan tree was strung with white lights that were lit all day. Colored lights twined around the metal poles of the fence, which was topped with a long loping piece of gold tinsel garland.

The Christmas tourists began arriving just before lunch as Máximo and Raúl stepped off the number eight. Carlos and Antonio were already at the table, watched by two groups of families. Mom and Dad with kids. They were big; even the kids were big and pink. The mother whispered to the kids and they smiled and waved. Raúl waved back at the mother.

"Nice legs, yes," he whispered to Máximo.

Before Máximo looked away, he saw the mother take out a little black pocket camera. He saw the flash out of the corner of his eye. He sat down and looked around the table; the other men stared at their pieces.

The game started badly. It happened sometimes—the distribution of the pieces went all wrong and out of desperation one of the men made mistakes and soon it was all they could do not to knock all the pieces over and start fresh. Raúl set down a double three and signaled to Máximo it was all he had. Carlos passed. Máximo surveyed his last five pieces. His thoughts scattered to the family outside. He looked to find the tallest boy with his face pressed between the iron slats, staring at him.

"You pass?" Antonio said.

Máximo looked at him, then at the table. He put down a three and a five. He looked again; the boy was gone. The family had moved on.

The tour groups arrived later that afternoon. First the white buses with the happy blue letters WELCOME TO LITTLE HAVANA. Next, the fat women in white shorts, their knees lost in an abstraction of flesh. Máximo tried to concentrate on the game. The worst part was how the other men acted out for them. Dominos are supposed to be a quiet game. And now there they were shouting at each other and gesturing. A few of the men had even brought cigars, and they dangled now, unlit, from their mouths.

"You see, Raúl," Máximo said. "You see how we're a spectacle?" He felt like an animal and wanted to growl and cast about behind the metal fence.

Raúl shrugged. "Doesn't bother me."

"A goddamn spectacle. A collection of old bones," Máximo said.

The other men looked up at Máximo.

"Hey, speak for yourself, cabrón,"[6] Antonio said.

Raúl shrugged again.

Máximo rubbed his knuckles and began to shuffle the pieces. It was hot, and the sun was setting in his eyes, backlighting the car exhaust like a veil before him. He rubbed his temple, feeling the skin move over the bone. He pressed the inside corners of his eyes, then drew his hand back over the pieces.

"Hey, you okay there?" Antonio said.

An open trolley pulled up and parked on the curb. A young man with blond hair, perhaps in his thirties, stood up in the front, holding a microphone. He wore a guayabera. Máximo looked away.

"This here is Domino Park," came the amplified voice in English, then Spanish. "No one under fifty-five allowed, folks. But we can sure watch them play."

Máximo heard shutters click, then convinced himself he couldn't have heard, not from where he was.

"Most of these men are Cuban and they're keeping alive the tradition of their homeland," the amplified voice continued, echoing against the back wall of the park. "You see, in Cuba, it was very common to retire to a game of dominos after a good meal. It was a way to bond and build community. Folks, you here are seeing a slice of the past. A simpler time of good friendships and unhurried days."

Maybe it was the sun. The men later noted that he seemed odd. The tics. Rubbing his bones.

First Máximo muttered to himself. He shuffled automatically. When the feedback on the microphone pierced through Domino Park, he could no longer sit where he was, accept things as they were. It was a moment that had long been missing from his life.

He stood and made a fist at the trolley.

"Mierda!"[7] he shouted. "Mierda! That's the biggest bullshit I've ever heard."

He made a lunge at the fence. Carlos jumped up and restrained him. Raúl led him back to his seat.

The man of the amplified voice cleared his throat. The people on the trolley looked at him and back at Máximo; perhaps they thought this was part of the show.

"Well." The man chuckled. "There you have it, folks."

Lucinda ran over, but the other men waved her off. She began to protest about rules and propriety. The park had a reputation to uphold.

It was Antonio who spoke.

"Leave the man alone," he said.

Máximo looked at him. His head was pounding. Antonio met his gaze briefly, then looked to Lucinda.

---

6. Bastard.     7. Shit!

"Some men don't like to be stared at is all," he said. "It won't happen again."

She shifted her weight, but remained where she was, watching.

"What are you waiting for?" Antonio said, turning now to Máximo, who had lowered his head into the white backs of the dominos. "Let's play."

That night Máximo was too tired to sit at the pine table. He didn't even prepare dinner. He slept, and in his dreams he was a green and yellow fish swimming in warm waters, gliding through the coral, the only fish in the sea and he was happy. But the light changed and the sea darkened suddenly and he was rising through it, afraid of breaking the surface, afraid of the pinhole sun on the other side, afraid of drowning in the blue vault of sky.

•

"Let me finish the story of Juanito the little dog."

No one said anything.

"Is that okay? I'm okay. I just remembered it. Can I finish it?"

The men nodded, but still did not speak.

"He is just off the boat from Cuba. He is walking down Brickell Avenue. And he is trying to steady himself, see, because he still has his sea legs and all the buildings are so tall they are making him dizzy. He doesn't know what to expect. He's maybe a little afraid. And he's thinking about a pretty little dog he knew once and he's wondering where she is now and he wishes he were back home."

He paused to take a breath. Raúl cleared his throat. The men looked at one another, then at Máximo. But his eyes were on the blur of dominos before him. He felt a stillness around him, a shadow move past the fence, but he didn't look up.

"He's not a depressive kind of dog, though. Don't get me wrong. He's very feisty. And when he sees an elegant white poodle striding toward him, he forgets all his worries and exclaims, 'O Madre de Dios, si cocinas como caminas . . .'"[8]

The men let out a small laugh. Máximo continued.

"'Si cocinas como caminas . . . ,' Juanito says, but the white poodle interrupts and says, 'I beg your pardon? This is America—kindly speak English.' So Juanito pauses for a moment to consider and says in his broken English, 'Mamita, you are one hot doggie, yes? I would like to take you to movies and fancy dinners.'"

"One hot doggie, yes?" Carlos repeated, then laughed. "You're killing me." The other men smiled, warming to the story as before.

"So Juanito says, 'I would like to marry you, my love, and have gorgeous puppies with you and live in a castle.' Well, all this time the white poodle has her snout in the air. She looks at Juanito and says, 'Do you have any idea who you're talking to? I am a refined breed of considerable class and you are nothing but a short, insignificant mutt.' Juanito is stunned for a moment, but he rallies for the final shot. He's a proud dog, you see, and he's afraid of his pain. 'Pardon me, your highness,' Juanito the mangy dog says.

---

8. If you can cook like you walk.

'Here in America, I may be a short, insignificant mutt, but in Cuba I was a German shepherd."

Máximo turned so the men would not see his tears. The afternoon traffic crawled eastward. One horn blasted, then another. He remembered holding his daughters days after their birth, thinking how fragile and vulnerable lay his bond to the future. For weeks, he carried them on pillows, like jeweled china. Then the blank spaces in his life lay before him. Now he stood with the gulf at his back, their ribbony youth aflutter in the past. And what had he salvaged from the years? Already, he was forgetting Rosa's face, the precise shade of her eyes.

Carlos cleared his throat and moved his hand as if to touch him, then held back. He cleared his throat again.

"He was a good dog," Carlos said and pressed his lips together.

Antonio began to laugh, then fell silent with the rest. Máximo started shuffling, then stopped. The shadow of the banyan tree worked a kaleidoscope over the dominos. When the wind eased, Máximo tilted his head to listen. He heard something stir behind him, someone leaning heavily on the fence. He could almost feel the breath. His heart quickened.

"Tell them to go away," Máximo said. "Tell them, no pictures."

1. 2001

# WILLIE PERDOMO
## b. 1971

Willie Perdomo is among the younger wave of writers who introduced their work at the Nuyorican Poets Cafe (see p. 1344). Perdomo, who grew up in East Harlem, first appeared at the Cafe at age 22. After finishing his elementary public schooling, he received a scholarship to Friends Seminary, a Quaker school in Lower Manhattan. In this largely white environment, the racially mixed Perdomo got into fights, until a sympathetic school employee who wrote poetry mentored him into channeling his energies into more-creative pursuits. He began to write, and as a high school senior he published some of his work in *New Youth Connections*, a publication of the New York Public Library. Perdomo earned his bachelor's degree from Ithaca College, in Ithaca, New York. He has been an artist-in-residence at Workspace, a studio residency program of the Lower Manhattan Cultural Council; a Woolrich fellow in creative writing at Columbia University; and a teacher at Friends Seminary and the Bronx Academy of Letters.

The prominent African American writer Claude Brown has called Perdomo an incarnation of the renowned Harlem Renaissance poet Langston Hughes, and the title of Perdomo's first poetry collection, *Where a Nickel Costs a Dime* (1996), comes from a line in a Hughes poem. Blending the language of the streets with the creative imagination of a skilled poet, *Where a Nickel Costs a Dime* mixes verse, prose, letters, dialogue, and popular songs, all injected with the irreverent Spanglish colloquial style of hip-hop and rap. The book includes a performance CD, on which, in the Nuyorican style, Perdomo dramatizes his work to the beat of Latino musical rhythms. The poem "Nigger-Reecan Blues," included in this anthology, illustrates Perdomo's conversational rhythms and his bold exposure of racial conflict, poverty, and the cultural practices that help the Puerto Rican people endure. "Brother Lo," like other poems in this collection, provides snippets of life in Harlem and of disaffected characters that roam the streets there. "New Boogaloo" uses the language of gospel and boogaloo (a fusion of rhythm and blues, mambo, salsa, son, and soul) to celebrate Nuyorican culture.

Perdomo's subsequent collections include *Postcards of El Barrio* (2002) and *Smoking Lovely* (2004), which also includes a performance CD and which received a PEN America Beyond Margins Award. With the illustrator Bryan Collier, Perdomo collaborated on the children's book *Visiting Langston* (2002), a celebration of Hughes's work. The book received a Coretta Scott King Award from the American Library Association. Perdomo has also received New York Foundation for the Arts Fellowships in fiction and poetry, and he has been a Pushcart Prize nominee.

## Nigger-Reecan Blues

—Hey, Willie. What are you, man? Boricua? Moreno?[1] Que? Are you
    Black? Puerto Rican?
—I am.
—No, silly. You know what I mean: What are you?
—I am you. You are me. We the same. Can't you feel our veins       5
    drinking the same blood?

      —But who said you was a Porta-Reecan?
      —Tu no ere Puerto Riqueño, brother.
      —Maybe Indian like Ghandi-Indian?[2]
      —I thought you was a Black man.      10
      —Is one of your parents white?
      —You sure you ain't a mix of something like Cuban and
      Chinese?
      —Looks like an Arab brother to me.
      —Naahhh, nah, nah . . . You ain't no Porty-Reecan.      15
      —I keep tellin' y'all: That boy is a Black man with an accent.

If you look real close you will see that your spirits are standing right
next to our songs. Yo soy Boricua! Yo soy Africano! I ain't lyin'. Pero
mi pelo is kinky y curly y mi skin no es negro pero it can pass . . .

      —Hey, yo. I don't care what you say. You Black.      20

I ain't Black! Every time I go downtown la madam blankita de
Madison Avenue[3] sees that I'm standing next to her and she holds her
purse just a bit tighter. Cabdrivers are quick to turn on their
*Off-Duty* signs when they see my hand in the air. And the

1. Slang for dark-skinned man. *Boricua*: The native Taíno peoples on Puerto Rico called the island Boriquén and themselves Boricuas.
2. I.e., like the Indian nationalist leader Mahatma Gandhi (Mohandas Karamchand Gandhi, 1869–1948).
3. I.e., south from uptown neighborhoods such as East Harlem to this largely upscale thoroughfare in Manhattan.

newspapers say that if I'm not in front a gun you can bet I'll be      25
behind one. I wonder why . . .

—Cuz you Black, nigger!

Don't call me no nigger. I am not Black, man. I had a conversation
    with my professor and it went just like this:
"So, Willie, where are you from?"      30
"I'm from Harlem."
"Ohhh . . . Are you Black, Willie?"
"No, but we all the same and—"
"Did you know our basketball team is nationally ranked?"

—Te lo estoy diciendo, brother. Ese hombre es un moreno.      35
Miralo!

Mira, pana mía, yo no soy moreno! I just come out of Jerry's Den and
the coconut spray on my new shape-up is smelling fresh all the way
up 125th Street.[4] I'm lookin' slim and I'm lookin' trim and when my
compai Davi saw me he said: "Coño, Papo, te parece como un      40
moreno, pana.[5] Word up, kid, you look just like a light-skin moreno."

—What I told you? You Black my brother.

Damn! I ain't even Black and here I am suffering from the young
Black man's plight / the old white man's burden / and I ain't even
Black, man / a Black man I am not / Boricua I am / ain't never really      45
was / Black / like me . . . [6]

—Y'all leave that boy alone. He got what they call the
"nigger-reecan blues."

I'm a spic! I'm a nigger!
Spic! Spic! Just like a nigger.      50

Neglected, rejected, oppressed and dispossessed
From banana boats to tenements
Street gangs to regiments
Spic, spic, spic. I ain't nooooo different than a nigger!

1989                                                                      1991

4. In Harlem.
5. Friend.
6. *Black Like Me* (1961) is a nonfiction book by
John Howard Griffin (1920–1980), a white journalist from Texas who spent six weeks passing as
a black man in racially segregated Southern
states.

# Brother Lo

A barefoot Brother Lo
came out his hole in the wall
and jumped onto the top of the
blue mailbox on the corner.

He yanked a palm full of strands                                5
from his thick black beard and blew
them against the breeze that warned
of rain.

He stretched his mighty arms toward the
sky and shouted his daily prophecy to the          10
boys standing near the mailbox, listening to
music, drinking beer.

"Go 'head. Laugh at me. Y'all spend all
day laughing and selling that shit. But
I ain't got no time to joke. I speak the          15
truth. The sky is ready to open and rain
fire. Nothin' but ashes gonna be left where
y'all standing."

One boy drank a long swig and said:

"Let it rain. But you better put on some shoes          20
before the sky opens cuz your feet stink, Brother
Lo. They kickin' like Bruce Lee[1] when he's mad!"

A loose Chihuahua ran away from his owner and
let off a nervous bark. Brother Lo leaped off the
mailbox and dashed through the schoolyard. A          25
congregation of born-again Christians were walking
home, singing hymns for our salvation, pressing their
leather Bibles against their hearts.

Brother Lo laughed like thunder having fun. A Metro-
North train was roaring on the elevated tracks, rushing          30
out of Harlem toward New Haven.[2]

No one heard
the sky open.

1993                                                                                1996

---

1. Chinese American martial artist, actor, and filmmaker (1940–1973).
2. City in Connecticut.

# New Boogaloo

There's a disco ball
spinning starlight
on a new boogaloo
tell Sonia
that the bombs                                          5
are ready to drop
that we got soneros[1]
ready to sing
to those flowers
that did not survive                                    10
Operation Green Thumb
tell Dwight
that the renaissance
he's been looking for
is ready to set up shop                                 15
that dreams
are starting to take
responsibility for themselves
tell Marcito
that painters are eating piraguas[2]                    20
sitting on milkcrates
and kickin' it with poets
they are bored
with keeping it real
so they tape words                                      25
to the floor
and let you decide
tell Rosalia
that the reverend
is on the rooftop                                       30
handing out passports
because the spaceship casita
is about to take off
oye mamita
no te apures                                            35
que como like
a Brook Avenue bombaso[3]
we gonna make you dance
que como un cocotaso limpio[4]
we gonna make your head rock                            40
so tell Pachanga
that si no hablas espanol
bienvenido[5]
that si no hablas engles
bienvenido                                              45

1. Salsa singers.
2. Flavored ice cones.
3. Don't worry / because like / a Brook Avenue
bomba and plena festival. *Brook Avenue*: thoroughfare in the Bronx, a New York City borough
north of Manhattan.
4. Because like a sharp slap to the head.
5. Welcome.

porque you see
this shit is a 10
on a scale from 1 to 9
tell Domingo
that we goona shoot it up                50
mainline
mainland
mainstrean
underground
until we catch your vein                 55
so take this sound
to the grave
and tell the whole
fucking block
that a bambula[6]                         60
building session
is about to begin
and it's gonna be like
two church boys
talking loud                             65
on the train
praising the Lord
in espanglish hip-hop speak
pero que son
yo se que fui the Lord son               70
eso que—mira[7]
you know what it is fam[8]
we keep the Bible real kid
tu me entiende[9]
pero que he wants me to learn            75
because he told me
to bring my notebook son
to all the sermons son
and I was like whoa
when the reverend                        80
was waiting for me
with a passport
and he told me
that this time
we gonna die knowing                     85
how beautiful
we are

2001                                    2003

---

6. A spirited dance, popular in the Caribbean, that originated in Guinea, West Africa; the word is used frequently in salsa music for rhythmic purposes.
7. But son / I know it was the Lord, son / that—look.
8. Family.
9. You see what I mean!

# MANUEL MUÑOZ
## b. 1975

Manuel Muñoz was born into a family of field workers in Dinuba, a small town in California's Central Valley. "Beginning in the fourth grade," he once wrote,

> I helped them in the grape harvest, laying down the paper trays and spreading the grapes around for drying into raisins. . . . Though our family struggled, my siblings—once they were able to work on their own—were never expected to contribute all of their earnings into a pool. We were each as self-supporting as possible and were expected to begin working wherever we could as soon as we could. I worked in a school warehouse at age fourteen and from that money came school clothes and supplies.

In 1994, Muñoz earned his bachelor's degree in American literature from Harvard University, in Cambridge. Four years later, he received his Master of Fine Arts degree in creative writing from Cornell University, in Ithaca, New York. At Cornell, he studied under the Mexican American writer Helena María Viramontes (see p. 2062); among his other stylistic influences are minimalist fiction and the Chicano writers José Antonio Villarreal (p. 711), Richard Vázquez (p. 827), and Tomás Rivera (p. 1077). His debut collection of stories, *Zigzagger* (2003), is about Chicanos in California's Central Valley struggling to overcome the outsider status society imposes on them. Family plays a central role, gay life a less important one. The tension between loyalty and independence defines the characters' paths. For example, in the title story, included here, an adolescent has strong relationships with both family and friends but becomes sexually involved with a town outsider. In Muñoz's second collection, *The Faith Healer of Olive Avenue* (2007), family remains at center stage, but the settings are somewhat more urban. Muñoz teaches creative writing at the University of Arizona, in Tucson.

## Zigzagger

By six in the morning, the boy's convulsions have stopped. The light is graying in the window, allowing the boy's bedroom a shadowy calm—they can see without the lamp; and the father rises to turn it out. The boy's mother moves to stop him and the father realizes that she is still afraid, so he leaves it on. The sun seems slow to rise, and the room cannot brighten as quickly as they would like—it will be cloudy today.

The father is a bold man, but even he could not touch his teenage son several hours ago, when his jerking body was at its worst. The father makes the doorways in their house look narrow and small, his shoulders threatening to brush the jambs, yet even he had trouble controlling the boy and his violent sleep. And it was the father who first noticed how the room had become strangely cold to them, and they put on sweaters in the middle of July—the boy's body glistening, his legs kicking away the blankets as he moaned. The mother had been afraid to touch him at all and, even as the sun began rising, still made no move toward the boy.

In the morning light, the boy seems to have returned to health. He is sleeping peacefully now; he has not pushed away the quilts. His face has come back to a dark brown, the swelling around the eyes gone.

"I'll check his temperature," the father tells the mother, and she does not shake her head at the suggestion. She watches her husband closely as he moves to the bed and reaches for the edge of the quilt. She holds her breath. He pulls the quilt back slowly and reveals their son's brown legs, his bare feet. He puts out his hand to touch the boy's calf but doesn't pull away his fingers once he makes contact with the skin. The father turns to the mother, his fingers moving to the boy's hands and face. "I think he's okay now."

The mother sighs and, for the first time in hours, looks away from the bed. She remembers that today is Sunday and, with the encouragement of the coming morning, she rises from her chair to see for herself.

Saturdays in this town are for dancing. The churchgoers think it is a vile day, and when they drive by the fields on their way to morning services, they sometimes claim to see workers swaying their hips as they pick tomatoes or grapes. They say that nothing gets done on Saturday afternoons because the workers go home too early in order to prepare for a long night of dancing. It is not just evenings, but the stretch of day—a whole cycle of temptation—and the churchgoers feel thwarted in their pleadings to bring back the ones who have strayed. They see them in town at the dry cleaners or waxing their cars. They see them buying food that isn't necessary.

The churchgoers have war veterans among them, some of whom serve as administrators for the town's Veterans Hall. They argue with each other about the moral questions of renting out their hall for Saturday's recklessness. The war veterans tell them that theirs is a public building and that the banquet room, the ballroom, and the wing of tidy classrooms are for all sorts of uses. Sometimes the veterans toss out angry stories about Korea, and the more civil of the lot mention how they converted villagers while fighting.[1] But others claim freedom, including their hall, and to mortify the churchgoers, they tell tales of Korean girls spreading their legs for soldiers and the relief it brought. The churchgoers end the conversation there.

By Saturday afternoon, there is always a bus from Texas or Arizona parked in back of the Veterans Hall, and sometimes workers on their way home will catch a glimpse of the musicians descending from the vehicle with accordions and sequined suits and sombreros in tow. Some days it is simply a chartered bus. But other times, it is a bus with the band's name painted along the side—CONJUNTO ALVAREZ, BENNIE JIMÉNEZ Y FUEGO—and the rumor of a more popular group coming through town will start the weekend much earlier than usual. It means people from towns on the other side of the Valley will make the trek. It means new and eager faces.

The churchgoers smart at the sight of young girls walking downtown toward the hall, their arms crossed in front of their breasts and holding themselves, as if the July evening breeze were capable of giving them a chill. For some of them, these young girls with arm-crossed breasts remind them of their own daughters who no longer live in town. They have moved away with babies to live alone in Los Angeles. All over town, the churchgoers know, young girls sneak from their homes to visit the friends their parents already dislike. There, they know, the girls put on skirts that twirl and makeup that might glisten against the dull lights of the makeshift dance

---

1. I.e., in the Korean War (1950–53).

floor. These girls practice walking on high heels, dance with each other in their bedrooms to get the feel in case a man asks them to do a *cumbia*.[2] The churchgoers remember when they were parents and listening to the closed doors and the girls too silent. Or their teenage boys, just as quiet, then leaving with their pockets full of things hidden craftily in their rooms.

And much of this starts early in the day: the general movement of the town, the activity in the streets and shops—women buying panty hose at the last minute, twisting lipsticks at the pharmacy in search of a plum color. Men carry cases of beer home to drink in their front yards. Pumpkin seeds and beef jerky. Taking showers only minutes before it is time to go.

Saturdays in this town are for dancing, have always been. This town is only slightly bigger than the ones around it, but it is the only one with a Veterans Hall, big enough to hold hundreds. By evening, those other little towns are left with bare streets, their lone gas stations shutting down for the night, a stream of cars heading away to the bigger town. They leave only the churchgoers and the old people already in their beds. They leave parents awake, listening for the slide of a window or too many footsteps. They leave the slow blink atop the height of the water tower, a red glow that dulls and then brightens again as if it were any other day of the week.

For a moment, the mother does not know whether to go to the kitchen herself or to send her husband. She does not want to take her eyes away from her son and yet at the same time is afraid to be alone with him. She says to her husband, "*Una crema*,"[3] but doesn't move toward getting the items she needs to make a lotion for the boy. She needs crushed mint leaves from the kitchen. She needs oil and water, rose petals from the yard.

"Do you want me to go?" her husband asks her. On the bed, the boy is sound asleep, and the sight of him in such a peaceful state almost makes her say yes. But she resists.

"No," she tells her husband. "I'll go."

She is sore from so much sitting, and the tension of having stayed awake makes movement all the worse. The rest of the house seems strangely pleasant: the living room bright because it faces east, the large clock ticking contentedly. She wishes she could tell her husband what to do, but she knows they cannot call a doctor and have him witness this. She has considered a priest, but her husband does not go to church. In the face of this indecision, the calm rooms in the rest of the house frustrate her. She wants to make noise, even from simple activity. From the kitchen, she takes a large bowl and searches her windowsill for a few sprigs of mint. She sets out a bottle of olive oil and a cup of cold water from the faucet.

In the front yard, where the roses line the skinny walkway to their door, the day is brighter than it appeared through the windows. It is overcast, but not a ceiling of low clouds, only large ones with spaces in between, and she can see how the sun will be able to shine through them. They appear to be fast-racing clouds, and, once the sun is high enough, they will plummet the town into gray before giving way to light again. Though slight, the day erases the fear in her.

2. A style of Latin American folk dance that originated within a courtship ritual.

3. A cream.

She notices the skinny walkway and the open gate where their son stumbled home, the place where he vomited into the grass. She had watched from the living room window, his friends behind him at a far distance, dark forms in the street, and she had waited for them to go away as her son entered the house, cursing terribly. From her rosebushes, she notices a gathering of flies buzzing around the mess, some of it on the gray stone of their walkway. There's a streak of red in it, she can see. She quickens her pace with the rose petals when the breeze comes up and the smell of the vomit in the grass lifts, reminding her of how ill her son was only hours ago. Dropping the petals into the bowl, she hurries back into the house, trying to get away from that smell.

She is crying in the kitchen, mixing the mint and the oil and the water, and to make it froth, she adds a bit of milk and egg. The concoction doesn't seem right to her anymore, doesn't match what she recalls as a young girl, her grandmother taking down everyday bottles from the cabinets and blessing their cuts and coughs. The mother does it without any knowledge, only guessing, but it makes her feel better despite feeling lost in her inability to remember. She takes the bowl into the bathroom and dumps half a bottle of hand lotion into the bowl, and the mix turns softer and creamy.

Back in the bedroom, her husband is still at their son's bedside, but the boy has not moved. The stale odor of the room reminds her again of outside and the earlier hours and her son's vile language and her husband's frantic struggle to keep the boy in bed, wild as he was. The boy tore off his own clothes, his thin hands ripping through his shirt and even his pants, shredding them, and he stalked into his bedroom naked and growling and strong. Her husband came to tower over him, beat him for coming home this way. The fear crept into her when the boy fought back and challenged and then, only by exhaustion, collapsed on the bed. He was quiet. And then the odor came. The smell was of liquor at first, but then a heavy urine. Then of something rotting. Her husband had yelled at her to open the windows. Even now, the smell lingers in the air.

"He's still sleeping," her husband whispers. "What do you have there?"

"A cure my grandmother used to give us," she says, half expecting her husband to ignore her and the bowl.

"You want to put it on him?" he offers, and she knows that her husband is asking whether or not she is still afraid.

She does not answer him but moves to the bed, setting the bowl on the floor. With her fingertips, she dips into the concoction and then, resisting an impulse to hold her breath, rubs it on her son's bare legs. They are remarkably smooth, and she looks at her husband as if to have him reassure her that what she had seen last night had not been an illusion. Her son's legs are hairless and cool to the touch. There are no raised veins. They are not reddened with welts. They are not laced with deep scratches made with terrible fingers.

The boy spent the early part of Saturday evening with a group of friends, all of them drinking in the backyard at the house of a girl whose parents were visiting relatives in another town. Even before the sun had set, most of the boy's friends had already had enough to drink, and they tried to convince some of the older boys to go back out and buy beer. But by then, the girls put a stop to all of it, saying the hall wouldn't let them in if they smelled beer on them.

The boy liked being with these friends because he did not have to do much. He laughed at other people when the joke was on them, and it made him feel more comfortable about himself. He smoked cigarettes and watched the orange tips get brighter and brighter as the sun went down. He looked at the girls coming in and out of the back door as they got ready for the dance. He did not drink, because he did not like the acrid taste of beer, yet he liked being here with them, knowing that every sip was what their own parents had done at their age. He did not mind seeing the others drunk—after a certain point, he knew that the drunker boys would sit next to him and talk. He would not respond except to smile, because he didn't know what else to do, what to make of their joking, their arms heavy around his shoulders.

They gathered themselves after the girls were ready and they walked to the hall, twos and threes along the sidewalk, some of them chewing big wads of hard pink gum and then spitting them into the grass. He was not as crass as the other boys, who waited to spit until they saw the dark figures of the churchgoers scowling from their porches. They divided mints between them when the hall came into view: the taillights of cars easing into the parking lot, women sitting in passenger seats waiting for their doors to be opened.

The boy got in line with the rest of them, watching as a pair of older women at the ticket table looked disapprovingly at the girls and motioned with their fingers for each of them to extend their arms. They fastened pink plastic bracelets around their wrists, ignoring the odor of alcohol. When the boy made it to them, he tried to move as close as possible, to show he was not like the rest of them, but one of the women only said, "No beer," strapping the pink bracelet tightly and taking his dollar bills.

Inside, his friends had already fractured. A flurry of kids their age milled around the edge of the dance floor while the older couples swayed gently to the band's ballad of horns and *bandeneón*.[4] All he saw were bodies pressed together, light coming through in the spaces cleared for the dance steps of other couples, hips and fake jewelry catching. He saw the smoke blue in the air around the hanging lights; the cigarettes, which he felt contributed to the heat; the men with unbuttoned shirt collars, their hands around the backs of laughing women.

When the song ended, with a long and mournful note on a single horn, the couples separated to applaud, and some of the women went back to their own tables. He saw that people of every situation were there—older, single women sitting at the circular tables, men his father's age with shiny belt buckles and boots. Of his own age, the boys were pestering some of the older men to buy them beer, hiding the telltale pink bands that showed their age, sneaking sips in the darker shadows of the hall's great room.

As the next song began—a wild, brash *ranchera* complete with accordion at full expansion—the milling began again, people alone, people together. He put his hands in his pockets while men removed their hats and cornered women for a dance. Couples with joined hands pushed their way to the

4. Free-reed instrument popular in Argentina.

floor that had only just settled its dust. Some alone, some together. The
music roared its way through the hall, and the boy reasoned that everyone
felt the way he did at the moment—lost and unnoticed, standing in place as
he was.

The boy's mother spreads the concoction more vigorously, her son's legs
giving way where the flesh is soft, reminding her that he is not fully grown,
not a man yet. She believes her rubbing will wake him, and when he doesn't
respond, she looks at her husband, who does nothing but look back.

She speaks to her son. "Are you awake?" she asks him, her hands grasping his legs quickly to shake him, but he only stirs, his head moving to one
side and then stopping. "Are you in pain?"

Her husband stands up to look closely at their son's face and says to her,
"His eyes are open." He waves his hand slowly in front of the boy, but still
he will not speak. "I don't think he sees me."

"Are you awake?" she says again, rising to see for herself. His eyes are
open, just as her husband said, but they don't seem to stare back at her. She
thinks for a moment that his open eyes will begin to water and she waits for
him to blink, but he only closes his eyes once more.

"It's early still," the father says. "Don't worry."

The boy felt as if he had been the only person to notice the man with the
plain silver buckle, a belt that shimmered against the glow of the yellow
bulbs strung across the hall's high rafters. A plain silver buckle that gleamed
like a cold eye, open and watching. Even from a distance, the boy knew it
was plain, that it had no etchings, no tarnish, no scratches. He watched it
tilt at the waist as the man put his boot up on the leg of a stool, leaning
down to one of the girls who had come with the boy, whispering to her.

He felt as if he were the only one watching how the girl flicked her hair
deliberately with her left wrist, as if to show the pink bracelet in a polite
gesture to move on: she was too young.

The boy pictured himself with the same kind of arrogance, the posture
that cocked the man's hips, the offering he suggested to this girl, and he
wondered if he would ever grow into that kind of superiority, being capable
of seducing and tempting. He watched the silver buckle blink at him, as if it
watched back, as if it knew where the boy was looking.

The man finally left the girl alone, but the boy watched him, circling the
dance floor, sometimes losing him between songs as the hall dimmed the
lighting to invite a slow dance. Or losing him when one of the other boys
distracted him with a stolen beer. But he would quickly find him again, the
belt buckle gleaming and catching—a circle of silver light moving through
the dark tables.

The girl from before came up to the boy and said, "That man kept bug-
ging me," as if she expected the boy to do something about it. He turned to
look at her—she was one of the girls who regularly went to church, didn't
know how to behave at a dance, put up her hair because her girlfriends told
her to. And now, with that strange man, she wanted trouble for its own
sake, he thought. He could hear in her voice that she wanted the attention
in some form—his defense, or that man's proposal—so no one would look
at her as the girl with the straight dark hair, a Sunday girl.

So the boy moved, without looking at the girl, keeping his eye on the silver buckle and followed the man, catching up to him toward the back of the hall, where only the couples who could not wait to get home were kissing, leaning against each other, backing into the wall. The man stood next to a woman, facing her and talking among all the bodies rubbing against each other, his silver buckle the only still thing, and the boy noticed that the man wore nothing but black, down to his boots. The man's teeth gleamed as he smiled, watching the boy approach. He smiled as if he expected him and ignored the woman, who disappeared into the dark bodies.

Before the boy could say anything about the girl, the man extended his hand, offering a beer. "My apologies," he said to the boy, his voice clear and strong, and the boy noticed his face—what a handsome man he was, his skin as dark as anyone's in town—but his voice not anchored by the heaviness of accent. He was not like them, the boy knew instantly.

The mother opens all the doors in the house, though the sky doesn't look as if it will break one way or the other. She draws more curtains, all the rooms filled with the muted daylight. Even the closet doors are open, flush against the walls, and she pushes the clothes apart to allow the light in the tight spaces. She thinks of the kitchen cabinets and the drawers, the small knobs that pull out of tables and nightstands, the blankets hiding the dust motes under the beds. The husband lets her do this and then says nothing as she sits in the living room all by herself with her head in her hands.

Because the front door is wide open, she hears the footsteps on the sidewalk long before they approach the house, and she looks to the porch to see a group of her son's friends coming. They walk so close together; they seem afraid and apologetic at the same time. All of them have their heads bowed, the girls and the boys in fresh Sunday church clothes, and she knows they see the mess her son made on the front lawn.

It is odd for her to be sitting on her living room couch and seeing not the television but her own front yard, and she can do nothing but watch as the boys and girls stop at the porch, almost startled that they do not have to knock.

"What do you want?" she hears her husband say, and she turns to see him in the archway to the kitchen, where he must have heard them coming. "What did you give him last night?"

Her husband's voice is filled with rage, but she can see that her son's friends have come out of concern. And she knows they will tell her that her son had not been drinking, that they will deny that he took any drugs, and she will believe them. But she knots her fingers and her hands, trying to build up a false anger, because she is too ashamed and afraid to let them know what she and her husband saw on her boy's body, the things he said in a voice that was not his, how the house seemed to swell and breathe as if it were living itself, the whole space filling out in the same terrible way that her chest wanted to burst forth.

"We didn't give him anything," one of the boys says. "He wouldn't even take one beer."

"He's sick now!" her husband yells at them. "You understand that? *¿Entienden?*"

"Let them go home," the mother says. "They don't need to know anything."

The boys and girls still stand on the porch, because they see she has been talking to her husband and not them, waiting for him to order them away. But the husband does not say anything, and then one of the boys speaks up and says, "I brought him home because we found him sick. Outside the hall. He was just sick. We don't know how."

No one responds, no one asks questions. Not the husband, not the mother. And just when the mother is about to rise from the couch to point her finger to the street, to show them away from the porch, they all know to look in the hall archway leading to the bedroom. There, clad only in his underwear, his skin pale and the dampness of the day swimming through the house, stands the boy.

He is aware of himself in a way that is unsettling, as if he has escaped his body once and for all and yet, exhausted as he feels, knows that his body is his own again. He is aware that the window to his bedroom is open and the day is overcast; the curtains move in a breeze that is chilly and has made the sheets underneath him cold. He shivers.

He hears the voices in the front of the house, the sound of his father's anger, the way only his father can sound, and his mother's hesitations. He hears the sounds of his friends but can't tell how many.

He feels the cold on his legs and he rises from the bed slowly, putting his feet on the floor, and the act of moving—like water, like the leaves outside his bedroom window today—startles him, the ease of it. Looking at his thin legs, the hollow of his own chest, he does not feel ashamed of himself as he once did.

The boy knows what he has done, what has happened, and yet, deep inside, he believes it could not have been. He thinks back to the man in the black clothes and the silver buckle, the offered beer, and the few words they spoke. The man had asked him if he spoke Spanish and when he had said no, the man had looked almost pleased. He does not remember what else they might have spoken of, only that the hall seemed to tilt and sway, the *ranchera* amplified to ten times as loud as he has ever heard, so that the man's voice came from within him. It came from the darkness when he closed his eyes to the hall's dipping and sinking, and when he opened them, it was still dark and he felt the nip of the outside air, the summer night cool compared to the pushed-together bodies of the dance inside. The cool of the sheets beneath him this morning makes him recall that outside air, how he had felt it not against his face but the bare skin of his chest, then his belly, and the metallic touch of the silver belt buckle pressing close. The music was distant—they were away from the hall, away from the cars in the parking lot, where couples were leaving, the engines starting. He recalls now the rough edges of a tree against his back, the bark and the summer sap, the branches a canopy that hid the stars, because he looked up and saw nothing but the spaces between leaves, small stars peeking through to see him.

He had said nothing to this man, remembers how he allowed the man's hands to grab his waist, his entire arm wrapped around, lifting the boy's feet from the ground, the feeling of rising, almost levitating. He felt as if the man rose with him because he felt the hot press of the man's belly, the rough texture of hair, and now he remembers how he had let his hands run down the man's back, the knots on his spine, the fine-worked furrow, their feet on air. He kept looking up, searching for the stars between the branches.

The man, his back broad, grunted heavily. The sound frightens the boy now as he recalls it in broad daylight. The man's sound made him grow, pushing the boy up higher and higher, to where the boy could see himself in the arms of the man who glowed in the darkness of the canopy of branches, his skin a dull red, the pants and boots gone. And though he felt he was in air, he saw a flash of the man's feet entrenched fast in the ground—long, hard hooves digging into the soil, the height of horses when they charge—it was then that the boy remembers seeing and feeling at the same time—the hooves, then a piercing in the depth of his belly that made his eyes flash a whole battalion of stars, shooting and brilliant, more and more of them, until he had no choice but to scream out.

And now, at midmorning, his father and mother in the front of the house, his skin smelling of mint and roses, he knows enough to go forward and send his friends away. He wonders if he will sound different; he wonders if they will see how he carries himself now; he remembers how feeling the furrow of the man's back reminded him of the hard work of picking grapes in the summer months—his father will punish him with it. The hard work and the rattlers under the vines, their forked tongues brushing the air, and the boy remembers that the man's tongue pushed into his with the same vigor, searching him with the same kind of terrible flick.

He rises from the bed and steps, with an unfamiliar grace, to the wide-open door of his bedroom and down the hall.

The mother sees him, the look in his eye, and she wants to say nothing at all. She believes, as she always has, that talking aloud brings moments to light, and she has refused to speak of her mother's death, of her husband's cheating, of the hatred of her brothers and sisters. She sees her son at the doorway and wants to tell him not to speak.

They all stand and wait for the boy to talk, the doors and windows open as wide as possible and every last secret of their home ready to make an easy break to the outside. The curtains swell with a passing breeze.

"You're awake," the father says, and walks toward the boy, and the mother hopes that he will not speak and reveal his voice. She wonders if her husband knows now, if he can tell how the side-to-side swivel of the dancers at the hall and the zigzag of their steps have invited an ancient trouble, if her husband knows the countless stories of midnight goings-on, of women with broken blood vessels streaming underneath their skin from the touch of every strange man.

She keeps wondering, even when her husband turns to the boy's friends and tells them, "See? He's fine. Now go home," and motions them away from the porch and they leave without asking her son anything at all. She wonders now if her husband has ever awakened at night, dreaming of dances where bags of church-blessed rattlesnakes have been opened in the darkness of the place, the mad slithering between feet and the screams, the rightness of that punishment, the snakes that spoke in human voices, the rushed side-to-side movement of the snakes before they coiled underneath tables to strike at ankles.

When her husband turns his back to walk to the porch, watching the boy's friends walk off warily, she takes her chance and rushes to her underwear-clad son in the archway and grabs him by his arms—his flesh cold—and says, under her breath, "I know, I know," and then bravely, without waiting to hear what his voice might sound like, tries to pry open his mouth and check for herself.

2003

---

# DANIEL ALARCÓN
## b. 1977

A child of Peruvian psychiatrists, Daniel Alarcón was born in Lima, Peru. At age three, he moved with his family to Birmingham, Alabama. He earned his bachelor's degree from Columbia University, in New York City; returned to Peru on a Fulbright scholarship; and then earned his Master of Fine Arts degree from the Writing Program at the University of Iowa, in Iowa City. Alarcón's first book, the story collection *War by Candlelight* (2005), was a finalist for the PEN/Hemingway Foundation Award. Throughout the work, characters deal with poverty, corruption, and death. The title story, included in this anthology, takes place in Lima and New York. In the tradition of Latin American political literature, a revolutionary fighter longs for normalcy, struggling to bring together his family duties and his quest for freedom. Alarcón's debut novel, *Lost City Radio* (2007), returns to the theme of one of his first publications, a nonfiction piece in the periodical *Hopscotch* on the disappearance of a relative in Peru at a time when the underground guerrilla group Shinning Path was active in the countryside. In the novel, the host of a popular radio show in an unnamed South American country helps people deal with disappearance and loss; her husband is among those who vanished. In 2007, the journal *Granta* included Alarcón in its list of the 21 Best Young American Novelists. He has received a Whiting Award, a Guggenheim Fellowship, and a Lannan Literary Fellowship. His work also has been published in *The New Yorker*, *Harper's*, *Virginia Quarterly Review*, and *Salon*. Alarcón lives in Oakland, California, and teaches at Mills College.

## War by Candlelight
### I. Oxapampa,[1] 1989

The day before a stray bomb buried him in the Peruvian jungle, Fernando sat with José Carlos and together they meditated on death.

They were childhood friends. Three decades before, you might have found them together on the steps of the cathedral, sharing a piece of bread, tossing pebbles at the stray dogs that came to lick the crumbs at their feet. Or on hands and knees, playing marbles in the dusty courtyard of José Car-

---

1. Province in central Peru; also the name of a district in that province and of a city that is the capital of the province.

los's house on Tarapacá.[2] Such trivial things come to mind now, Fernando thought. A lifetime's supply of meaningless memories. He could make out the dark blue tint of the sky above. Later it would rain.

They sat at the edge of the campsite. Here, hidden in a tangle of vines and leaves and wrapped in a tarp, were the explosives. Fernando and José Carlos had slipped away from the others, had chosen this place to talk. They shared a rolled cigarette and a stale piece of bread, and agreed both were the worst they'd ever tasted. The bread especially. "Tougher than flesh," José Carlos said. "Worse than prison food."

"Worse than your mother's cooking," Fernando added. He watched for a smile spreading across his friend's face.

But José Carlos looked worn, unshaven, and grim, wearing a frayed white shirt and a straw hat that unraveled at its edges. His eyes drifted, unfocused, and his hands, crisscrossed with nicks and scratches, twitched almost imperceptibly. Fernando watched him closely, looking for answers in José Carlos's face, wondering how they had come to this place and why. Though he had tried to forget, it was no use: the heat was murder, the air unbreathable. A kind of paralysis gripped Fernando those last days. He found himself unable to concentrate on the present. Instead his brain was clogged with memories half-eaten by moths and flies, incomplete records of moments in no semblance of order: Arequipa at night, circa 1960, in the middle of the lonely street looking up, all sky and silence; the women who had cared for him, from birth through childhood and beyond; his wife, Maruja, his daughter, Carmen, fragile, beautiful, and above all, his.

It couldn't help to think too much of those he left behind. Each of the previous four mornings Fernando had woken to the prickling tiptoes of insects meandering among legs or arms. Each day, as the jungle closed in on them, they took to the machetes for a half hour in the late afternoon, hacking and swinging and beating it back. The jungle was their greatest enemy. Unattended food vanished in minutes, with living things bursting from the soil to retrieve it, digest it, destroy it. It was not life that he thought of in the jungle, beneath the forest's thick canopy, in the darkness.

"Does this place have a name?" José Carlos wondered aloud. "Have the mapmakers made it here yet?"

Of course they had not. Oxapampa had a name, but it was a three-day hike from here, and along the way they had passed nothing but forest and rising heat.

It was Fernando who suggested they name it. But what kind of name did this patch of earth deserve? Indigenous? Revolutionary? Should they call it Tarapacá, in honor of their old street?

They settled on Paris, where poets lived, and ate their bread in silence.

In the life he had left behind José Carlos was a professor of philosophy, a life he would survive to reclaim. Fernando could see him trying to laugh but unable. "I'm not scared that they'll catch me," José Carlos said. "I'm not afraid to die."

"To die in Paris!" Fernando said.

José Carlos frowned. "I'm not joking, Negro."

---

2. A street in the city of Arequipa (capital of the region of Arequipa, in southern Peru).

Fernando, his clothes soaked with sweat, felt his body melting into the infinite jungle. José Carlos was right: the time for jokes had passed. These conversations about death made him tired. It was all anyone ever spoke of. What point could there be in it? This moment was all they had worked for in the last fifteen years. The country was at war. The crisis they had foreseen in their youth had finally arrived. It was too late to give up, too late to change course. They were less than three weeks from the New Year and a new decade. Fernando was forty-one years old. His daughter, Carmen, whom he would never see again, was two and a half.

"Me neither," he said. "I'm not afraid to die."

## II. War by Candlelight, 1983

They had a plan if they ever came under fire: "scatter."

Not sophisticated or elegant, but real.

This is a coward's war, Fernando thought, when at the first sign of trouble, I am told to run breathlessly into the heart of the jungle, without stopping or looking back.

"You're no good to us dead, Fernando. We have enough martyrs."

There was too much talk of comradeship and brotherhood for those instructions to sit well. He did his work, hoping it would never come to that. But he was touring the camps in the North, in San Martín,[3] when shots were fired. There was no time to think. An army battalion had stumbled upon them in the steep, forested hills. No tactics or strategies involved, only the logic of a war fought blindly in the darkness of the jungle: a scared soldier fires a shot; a frightened rebel shoots back. Both are too young to do little else but bury their doubts in violence, and suddenly everyone is running and the forest is aflame.

Everything he had been taught came to him with the clarity of intuition: "We must only engage the enemy on our terms."

Neither side sees the other.

"Scatter."

In the jungle the trees have fingers and hands, the vines trip you up. You run because death is chasing, because the only way to escape is alone. Fernando fought through the jungle for two days before finding his way to the narrow path along the ridge where they were to regroup. Two days, alone, following trickles of water and minute hints of shadow, calling him first this way, then that. His instincts were urban, made for estimating bus routes and arrival times, not for looking to the skies for clues. He found his way, but not before wondering aloud if this were the place and the moment God had chosen for him to die. He met up with his comrades, they counted heads, quietly mourned the missing without abandoning hope that they might step out of the jungle, shaken but breathing. What had happened? No one knew anything more than he did. They licked their wounds and gathered their resolve. Back into the trees, to wander, to engage the enemy, to fight the people's war.

But Fernando's tour ended there. In five weeks, he had never carried a gun. He had never laid an explosive. The war, he thought—his war—had

3. A region.

amounted to walking circles through the forest, going hungry, and picking insects off his skin each morning. Trying to stay dry. Praying not to be found.

He boarded a bus in a provincial town and began his journey back to the coast. He wondered if people knew, if he would ever feel completely safe again. Three times the bus was emptied while soldiers searched the baggage hold for weapons. His forged identification papers were inspected by police at isolated mountain checkpoints. Each time Fernando tensed, but they let him through. "Go on," the soldiers said, and Fernando did his best not to act surprised, or worse, grateful. The ride home took two days. Fernando ate in minuscule mountain towns, on wooden benches that sagged beneath the weight of a half dozen bleary-eyed passengers. He did his best to sleep, his head bumping against the fogged-over window. He returned to Lima overjoyed to be alive. It was a relief so overwhelming it made him dizzy.

That first night back he told Maruja he wouldn't leave Lima again. She'd thrown her arms around him when he first came in but had almost immediately pulled away. She avoided him, wouldn't even look at him. "What's wrong?" he asked.

There were lines on her face he'd never noticed before. She bit her lip. Her eyes were red. "I thought you were dead," Maruja said.

Their apartment was cramped and small. He sat at the kitchen table while she prepared the candles and the matches. They listened for the rumble of war's progress, for a bomb to scratch out the quiet, the calm. It happened almost every night now. Electrical towers felled by explosives, a hammer and sickle ignited on the hillsides. It was best to be prepared. A pot of water boiled on the stove. He skimmed six weeks' worth of newspapers. She'd saved him the front pages, thrown away the rest. She summarized for him: "While you were dead," Maruja told him, "things got worse."

She wasn't going to forgive him easily. From the stack of scattered pages, she pulled one. It was dated from a week and a half before, and told of the ambush he'd fled. There were photos of the camp, of the weapons seized, and one of six lifeless bodies laid in a neat row. Though their faces were covered, Fernando knew them. They were his men, his friends. They had names. He recognized them by the shoes they wore.

An hour later, they heard it: *boom*.

Lights flickered and faded.

In the tense dark of their apartment, it occurred to him that he wanted a child. It struck him as exactly right. He felt embarrassed to tell Maruja. He said nothing. His entire body ached. They listened in darkness to the radio announcer calmly describing the evening's events. The room glowed orange.

Sometime in the middle of the night, when she was asleep and the candle had gone out, he reached for her.

It took him weeks to regain his courage. The city appeared strange to him, and his two-day walk through the jungle still had the glow of an apparition. Some mornings he woke and caught himself dreaming of insects and flittering birds. Bombs. Running. He caught himself paying attention to strangers' shoes. Every day he thought of the child he wanted. He rode through the city, debating quietly with himself: a child was a preposterous thing to want at a time like this. Absurd. Dangerous. Around him, men and

women were disappearing, people dying. It was no time to indulge in bourgeois fantasies. But he let himself imagine fatherhood and a hundred other
conventional pleasures: a small house with a courtyard, an olive tree, and
a tomato plant, a childhood like the one he'd had. Sometimes Fernando
imagined himself as an old man, the war long since over and nearly forgotten. His children now grown, his grandchildren asking to be told stories.
What stories would he and Maruja tell them? Stories of survival, perhaps:
How we fled Lima, Fernando mused. How we escaped the war.

He was riding a bus one day when a young woman got on. Visibly pregnant, her belly pushed dramatically against her dress. She was pretty, her
lustrous hair in a single braid, woven as thick as rope. He gave her his seat.
She didn't thank him, or notice him hovering over her. The bus stumbled
on, filled past capacity. Fernando kept his right hand in his pocket, holding
his wallet, and the other he placed on the back of the pregnant woman's
seat. What was he expecting? He wanted her to pull out a book of baby
names, or a spool of yarn to knit tiny socks. She didn't. She chewed gum.
There was nothing at all special about her except that beautiful roundness.
Fernando couldn't help but stare. He tensed. Finally, she opened her bag,
pulled out a newspaper, and turned it to the crossword. Then there was a
pushing and a jostling on the bus, and someone was being robbed at that
exact moment. Everyone knew it: a dozen pairs of eyes darting back and
forth, accusing. The pregnant woman sat still, unconcerned, nibbling on
the tip of her plastic pen. By the time he got off, she'd fallen asleep with the
crossword half-done in her lap.

That night, like every night, he and Maruja sat by candlelight, listening
to the radio. But he had heard enough: the news was uniformly dismal, and
it did no good to hear it all. He turned it off. He told her: "Let's have a
baby."

They sat close together and spoke in circles about the child, he saying yes,
she saying no.

He'd already heard her arguments, of course. They were his own. He
suspected they were true, but as she voiced them, they sounded profoundly
pessimistic. Hadn't they always believed in a future? Had they come to this
place so soon: were they this defeated already? He held his head in his
hands and cried, Maruja stroking his hair, wrapping the black curls around
her fingers. Did she have to hurt him like this? She took his glasses and laid
them on the nightstand. Their bed, resting on cinder blocks, creaked as she
stretched. With the flame clinging to the wick, orange light gliding along
the walls, Fernando told her for the first time of the jungle. "I walked for
days. Alone. I could barely see the sky, and I was sure someone was following me."

Maruja touched him, kissed him. She laid him down and undressed him.
Fernando could scarcely keep his eyes open. It wasn't such a terrible thing
to want, was it? The city was full of children.

"We can't, Nano." She sighed deeply. "I can't."

Maruja had two boys from her first marriage, the oldest now nearing fifteen. Fernando was good with her children. He took them to San Miguel[4] or
to the movies. The noise and chaos of parenting seemed to excite him, to

---

4. District on the west-central coast.

energize him, and Fernando would drive the children, singing and shouting. When they played soccer, Fernando would feed the pass that let his step-children shine. They were the youngest players on the field, but he made them feel welcome, wanted. He picked them first. Maruja's children were in love with Fernando. They let him know. All of this, Fernando thought, was proof. Hasn't she seen me with them? "I'd be a good father," he said.

"For how long?" she asked.

### III. Drive, 1987

The call came before dawn, a phone ringing, startling him from dreams. He hoped it wouldn't wake the baby. Maruja didn't stir. It was a man's voice. He seemed to know who Fernando was. "Can you drive?" the voice asked.

Fernando dressed without turning on the lights. The station wagon started on the second try. He drove along deserted city streets, avoiding the known roadblocks, hoping not to stumble upon others. They changed every night. He had documents ready—real ones—and an excuse, a story to tell, if it came to that: "I'm going to pick up my brother. He's a doctor. My little girl is sick."

It was four-thirty in the morning. He idled his car on the fourth block of Avenida Bolivia[5] and waited. He blew hot air on his hands. His neck hurt, his mouth was dry. It was cold, but in an hour, the darkness would lift, and the curfew as well. He closed his eyes and buried his hands in his armpits. A few moments later, a man stepped out of the shadows, glanced up and down the empty avenue, and got in the car. He muttered a greeting and gave an address on the other side of town. With a nod, they were off.

These people, whoever they were, always seemed like ghosts to Fernando. They shared many things, one might suspect, but nothing they could talk about. There was an unreality to this existence, floating from house to house. The art of clandestine life was to be invisible, to leave no trace. Fernando saw it only from the outside, these predawn drives through the backstreets of Lima, a morose stranger in the seat beside him. He could imagine the rooms where they stayed: the bare white walls, the single bed and thin mattress, the creaky chair. He had promised Maruja he would never do it. He had a daughter now, and the thought of that life made him sick. Fernando gripped the steering wheel tightly.

There were no traffic lights at this hour, or at least none that anyone paid attention to. The city was shuttered and asleep. The car rattled noisily. The man took off his knit cap and rubbed his face. He pulled a pack of cigarettes from an inside pocket and offered one to Fernando. They smoked and said nothing. There was no one out, not a soul. The radio had been stolen a few months before, but Fernando had never missed it as much as he did now: a song, a voice, anything to erase this quiet. He ran through a handful of questions in his mind—How long were you at the old house? Do you know José Carlos? Where will you go next?—but they were all wrong. He couldn't ask anything like that. Nice sweater, Fernando nearly said, where did you get it? He was embarrassed by the thought. Was it allowed? Talking about clothes? Soccer? The weather?

5. Thoroughfare in Lima.

"It's cold," Fernando offered.

"Sure is."

It was a terrible life. Fernando felt afraid, as if his passenger were not an anonymous comrade, but the victim of an unnamable illness. Something contagious. He felt revulsion. What did *comrade* mean anyway? Who was this man? He wanted him out of his car, the errand over. He wanted to be home, next to his wife and child, asleep again, away from the misery this man carried with him.

They hadn't spoken for blocks when the man said, "Oh, I know this street." He asked Fernando to stop at the corner.

"This isn't the place."

"Just for a moment." The man turned to him. "Please."

Fernando let the car slow.

"Here," the man said and rolled his window down. The air was cool and damp.

"What are we looking at?" Fernando asked.

The man pointed at a nondescript building across the street. It had a high, rusty fence, the kind a house thief would sneer at. The curtains were drawn, and there were no lights. "Someone you know?" Fernando asked.

"Sure."

They sat like that for a moment. The man was sailing, he was dreaming. Fernando could see it: that despairing look of a man confronted with his vanished life. "Do you want to get out?" Fernando asked.

"Not especially."

"Then we should go," Fernando said after a moment. The spell was broken.

The man shook his head. "That's right, *compadre*," he said. "We should go." He sighed and pulled out another cigarette. This time he didn't offer. "I knew a girl there. Once."

"How long has it been?"

"Since she died."

They rode on. The man left his window down. Fernando didn't complain about the cold. He pushed the gas and the engine groaned. It would be morning soon.

### IV. Mother, 1984

These were the days when his mother was dying. She had in fact stopped living several years before, when her husband passed away. Fernando just out of the university. The children huddled together in Lima, and, over the course of three nights of drinking and storytelling, forgave the old man everything. Fernando's mother sat on her own, alternately accepting and rejecting her children's affections. She had already done her forgiving, of course, but dying was his last betrayal. She moved to her daughter's house, where they made up a small room for her. It had a window looking out on a quiet street, and a terrace where she sat if it wasn't too cold. But she missed him. She confessed to Fernando that she couldn't remember what her life had been like before his father. Grief exposed all her weaknesses and showed her strengths for what they were: circumstance coupled with faith. She fell into dreams. She lost her faith.

"I'll be dead soon," she told her son, but nearly seven years passed this way and she was still alive. She began to forget. In the afternoons, in deep concentration, she sat down to drink her soup, cradling the bowl in her lap with a napkin spread primly across her thin legs. She smiled and nodded her head in greeting on Sundays when Fernando came to see her, but her smile was civil rather than warm. At times, she felt her family's eyes on her and wished that she could disappear. Other days, her daughter's children played in her room and told her jokes that made her laugh. She had to smile at their friendly disposition, even if she wondered who they might be.

Fernando still came by, but his visits were short. He could squeeze in a drink with his brother-in-law, but never two, and tried to be discreet when he looked at his watch over the rim of the raised glass.

There was hardly any time for socializing. Fernando felt weak. He often woke up dizzy, aching, unable to move, as if sleep, having let his mind go free, were jealously refusing to relinquish his body. He kept his eyes closed tightly, trying to blink away the pains that gripped his body. Unable to sleep, unable to wake, he lay on the bed immobile. Maruja worried about him. He wouldn't let anyone see him this way except her. She wrapped ice in an old shirt and pressed it to his forehead. By midmorning, his fever had cooled, and Fernando could stand, slowly. Once he was up, he wouldn't stop moving until the late evening, when, after telling others there was no time to rest and that the time to act was now, he would lie down to sleep, worried and brooding. The war had been killing him for a long time before he died.

This was not the man his mother would have remembered, if within her clouded memory, something had sparked a moment of lucidity. If she could have recalled Fernando, she would have described a young man who made strangers feel instantly comfortable.

"He was a Boy Scout in Arequipa, and an altar boy at the little church on the Plaza San Antonio de Miraflores. We lived in the little house on Tarapacá and walked to church every Sunday." His comrades called him *Negro*, but in the family he was *Nano*, her youngest child, the one who cost her the most heartache and confusion. He had studied at Independencia, like his older brothers, and years later he still sang his alma mater's hymn proudly, fighting sleep with song as he struggled to stay awake on the eighteen-hour drive back to Arequipa from Lima. He told his mother that melody was unforgettable: *En tus aulas se forjaron grandes hombres . . .* In your halls, great men were molded. He had come to Lima, entertaining little hope of being accepted to the university to study engineering. His older brothers and sister had come before him: Oscar, to the army. Elías, to study accounting. Mateo, to the national police. Enrique, to study medicine. Inés, to study pharmacology. His mother would have remembered the way she saw Fernando off at the bus station, the little bag he carried, his unconcerned smile. It was early morning at the bus station, the first shades of purple sky announcing morning in the east; Padre Alfredo, the priest, a family friend, came to see him off, to wish him luck. His mother would have remembered how sad she was to see her youngest go that morning, how she wondered what she would occupy her day with now, if not waiting for little Nano to come home.

That first year in the city, he sent letters home nearly every week. He had refused to live with his brother or sister, wanting to strike out on his own. Of course they sent him money from Arequipa, which he acknowledged gratefully in his letters. His correspondence was full of a young man's awe at living alone, with enthusiastic descriptions of his boardinghouse in Barrios Altos, of the crowded neighborhood with its teeming street life, panegyrics to Lima and the opportunities it seemed to promise. These were letters that Fernando would have been embarrassed to read later, but his mother had held them nearly sacred at the time. Of course both had forgotten them, and perhaps this was just as well.

She might have remembered his childhood friends, his crew of mischievous, quick-witted boys, nearly all of whom made their way to Lima eventually. If Fernando had ever brought José Carlos around to see her, it might have jogged something in her memory—an image, a flicker. The two boys had been inseparable. She'd found them once, not even eight years old, discussing with great seriousness the creation of a superhero who would be a combination of the two of them, an amalgam of their unique virtues. She had lingered in the doorway, listening, laughing to herself. Having humbly appraised their various qualities, the two boys had left the most contentious topic for last: a name for their conqueror.

All this was forgotten, along with a hundred other details, moments, words: she had never thought much of his politics, had avoided the room whenever the heated talk began between father and son. The boy had opinions on everything. She hadn't wanted to notice when his letters took on a different tenor: his new obsession was Lima and its poverty. One long note was spent describing the trials of a destitute newspaper vendor, a wizened man who claimed to carry his meager life savings in a pouch around his neck. He'd lost his family in a landslide, Fernando wrote, but the man held on. He walked to Lima. No one had come to help them. Fernando found it horrifying, or at least his letters said so.

His mother found it appalling as well. "There are poor right here!" she exclaimed as her husband read the letter aloud. She felt pity for Fernando then: he was such a sensitive boy, to let other people's problems upset him so.

Now she was dying. Inés called one Sunday to tell him this fact. She was older than Fernando by eight years, and liked to make that clear. He had been promising to come visit for weeks, had meant to. "Honestly," he said.

"You don't remember us. You don't come around, Nano. Meanwhile your own mother—"

Fernando cut her off. It was early morning, a Sunday. In better times, he might have come by that afternoon, taken Inés's sons to play soccer in the park, filled up the station wagon with Maruja's boys too and made a day of it. Through his bedroom window, he could see the sun peeking through the fog. Maruja sat at the foot of the bed, her hair wet, pulling on a pair of jeans and a sweater. It was the last time he spoke with his sister for over a year. He would remember it clearly. Inés was excitable, given to waves of sentimentality that could come at any time: a mention of Arequipa, a song, an old picture tugging at her heart from behind a dirty glass frame. But her mother— nothing and no one was more sacred or more special than her mother, who had raised her and guided her. "Fernando, we owe her everything."

"Inés, Inésita. *Cálmate . . .*"

His head hurt each morning in a new way. Sometimes the dizziness overcame the pounding, sometimes his body shook with such force that he wondered if others could see he was falling apart. But to Inés, he was whole, composed. He spoke quietly but did not waver.

"Our mother has everything. She has a home to sleep in. She has food to eat. She has a family to care for her. What about the other mothers? The ones who have nothing? Who will visit them?"

"Their children."

"Their children are busy," he said. "They're cleaning your house."

"Go to hell, Nano. I don't need your lectures."

"I can't come today."

"You're cruel." She hung up the phone softly.

### V. Father, 1966

Fernando placed first in the national exam. He was admitted to the university. It came so suddenly, such good news so unexpectedly, that his parents drove to Lima to congratulate him. They met at Elías's house, the family gathering around to toast Fernando, their youngest. His unruly black hair had been shaved down to the scalp. It made him look even younger than he was, seventeen, but it was tradition. Around Lima, on the buses and in the streets, you could spot the bald young men who had just been accepted. At the party, everyone made fun of his bald head. The photos show Fernando smiling happily, his arms slung over his brothers' shoulders, with Mateo's large hands curling over his younger brother's scalp and onto his forehead. Everyone is laughing in the photograph, including Enrique behind tinted frames, and Elías, the oldest, whose smile was a replica of his father's.

Fernando made a toast, to the coming challenges, to his chosen profession, engineering, and to all the people without homes whom he planned to build houses for. There were chuckles all around, but not from Fernando. He meant every word.

And there was no laughter from his father, Don José, who perhaps knew his son best. Fernando, who argued but always listened. Fernando, who threatened his family with his failure just to remind them he was independent. Fernando, who at age four, undersized and quiet, had refused to eat another bite—not for his mother, not for his sister, and not for his brother. "Who will you eat for, Nano?"

"For Guminga," he said emphatically. "For Gu-min-ga."

Dominga, the maid. Even then he was with the people, Don José thought. Dominga was a child herself when she first came to the house, barely eighteen, taking care of the home, cooking, cleaning, and looking after the infant Fernando. She was the first maid the family had been able to afford. Now Dominga lived in a small room, next to the kitchen. She had sewn a curtain out of scraps of fabric and hung it from a rod above the door. If a candle came down the hallway in the middle of the night, she would sit up in bed, peering out into the kitchen to see if she was needed. She was from Puno,[6] from the cold altiplano, where she went every August on her two-week vacation. She wore her hair in two even braids that stretched to the center of her back. Not beautiful, not even pretty, she had an oval face and inky black eyes. Still, the simplicity of her desires gave her an air of satisfaction

---

6. Region, province, capital city in the southeast.

that others spend their lives chasing. A bed, a roof, a little money to send home; that was all, and when she held Fernando, she was somewhere altogether different, and there was nothing ordinary about her life because she was wanted. Don José had seen her, and it amazed him: the child could do that to her, with his searching look, with his conviction that she stand by him, and be near him, before he drifted into sleep. Even now she had sent a small tin of jam wrapped in newspaper, a present, she said, for the young engineer. She still remembered him. "Little Nano," she had said to Don José. "Give him a kiss for me."

Don José, watching his son toast the houses he would build for Peru's homeless, watching his son tremble with emotion at the warmth of the family surrounding him, recognized that Fernando's heart was like his own: nostalgic but combative, caring but suspicious, able to bundle great ideas into intractable knots of personal anxiety. It is the way men begin to carry the world with them, the way they become responsible for it, not through their minds, but through their hearts. And though they shared much, the differences between Don José and his son were also striking, and also a question of heart. Don José saw that as well and did not, as others did, attribute those differences to something as simple as youth.

Don José, as a young man, had been a Communist. It was easy and logical. His brothers and sisters had all taken the well-worn paths that life in the provinces afforded them. Ricardo and Jaime were farm workers and spent their days bent over in fields they did not own. Luis worked in a leather shop, crafting saddles and belts, bags and soccer balls. By the time Fernando entered high school his uncle Luis was nearly blind. Don José's sisters had never had schooling beyond the fifth grade. They had married young, become the kinds of women who tended to their husbands' houses without complaint or worry. They shopped every morning for that day's meals and went to the plaza to have their letters read to them. Life was work. Life was spent living. Don José read books, studied, became a schoolteacher, and eventually a principal. He loved, he married, and he strayed. Mateo, Fernando's half brother, came to live with the family when he was five. Don José found himself, now the gentleman he had always imagined he could be, disappointed in himself, in his lack of drive and desire. Fernando carried within him those qualities that time had conspired to take from his father.

One must understand what it means to be born at the foot of a volcano. Arequipa is less a city than a living temple to El Misti, that imposing mass of rock rising behind the cathedral. Men invoke its name to describe what is right. What does a volcano do to a man but impress upon him the need to dream on a grand scale?

In 1950, when Fernando was two years old, Independencia went on strike. The students closed the doors of the school, locked themselves inside to protest the raising of school fees. Three tense days followed, with skirmishes along the fences and students pulling stones from the courtyard to throw at police. The government sent in the army, a student was killed. The city took to the streets. Every man in Arequipa knew that if the cathedral's bell was ringing, it was time to rally in the square. The city's narrow lanes filled with angry townspeople, farmers, ranchers, merchants, students. In Arequipa, you had a right to be angry. You had a right to demand better: didn't their volcano prove that they were destined for much more? And people listened: as Arequipa went on strike, other cities and towns across Peru followed suit. The crisis came and power changed hands. The stage shifted. If only for a day, a week, a month, those in power were forced to listen to the people. This was how things got done. This was tradition.

The party rose to a boil. Someone had dusted off a guitar, and Mateo was threatening to sing. He had returned from a trip north, bronzed and happy, telling stories of Ecuadorian girls and nights on the beach. Enrique was dancing with Inés, chiding his sister for her lack of rhythm. Don José felt a warmth in his chest, the comforting sensation that everything was going to be fine; that his work, if such a thing existed, was nearly done. He wasn't old, not yet, but look at what he had accomplished! His children stood before him in diverse stages of drunken cheer, and they all seemed like the kind of people he'd like, if he were to meet them as strangers on a train station platform or in a European café. He had raised them well, or his wife had, or maybe they had done it together—but still: he hadn't ruined them! Don José felt like weeping: his children were the sort of people who would make something out of this country, who could redeem this mess they'd inherited. He wanted to touch their faces, to show them off to the world. Could they be real?

Someone called for a toast. The room had the flickering warmth of a silent movie, except suddenly Don José was talking, the words, he feared, pouring forth without poetry, without grace. He was forced to admit he'd lost count of the drinks. His loved ones laughed with him. Fernando stood with his mother, their hands clasped tightly. She had missed him most this year. It was terrible to see her this way, Don José thought. Watching their son from afar held no pleasure for her: she couldn't appreciate the spectacle the way Don José could. Now, their youngest nearly a man, and look at her: holding his hand like a child, and Nano, generous-hearted, letting her.

He was a beautiful boy.

When he finished, Don José found a place on the sofa, a comfortable position from which to gaze at his family. An hour passed and the liquor ran out. Inés apologized, smirking. "I didn't prepare for you hooligans."

Mateo consoled a red-faced Fernando, shouting in his ear as if he were hard of hearing, "No more liquor? It's all right, Nano, we'll drink vinegar!"

To Don José's surprise, his wife joined him after a while. She brought him coffee and sat close to him, their thighs touching for the first time in many months. He took her hand and raised it to his lips. She blushed. Someone was singing—off-key, out of tune—did it matter? Don José kissed his wife's hand softly.

### VI. Pinochet's[7] Graveyard, 1973

In December of 1973, José Carlos arrived from Santiago de Chile,[8] thin, broken, with hands that shook uncontrollably. He stumbled over his words and brooded in long silences, looking away into the distance, the ash from his cigarette floating into his lap.

---

7. Augusto Pinochet Ugarte (1915–2006), Chilean general; president of Chile 1974–90.

8. The capital.

"They killed me, Negro, they killed me," he said, his voice trembling. Fernando met him at the airport; José Carlos staggered off the last airlift of Peruvian citizens from Chile. The rest stayed to die.

"Where did they keep you?"

"In Pinochet's graveyard, in the stadium. We had nothing to defend ourselves with."

The story came out slowly, over many nights. José Carlos was smaller and weaker than Fernando remembered. His movements came haltingly: a finger rubbing his temples, a foot tapping an uneven rhythm. Five years at the university in Santiago. José Carlos had been expelled without papers, without a degree, with nothing.

"What did they do to you, José Carlos?"

"They killed me. They kept us in the stadium. There were thousands of us. I was locked in a dressing room under the stands with two hundred others, mostly students. Communists. They kept the lights on, fluorescent lights, burning our eyes. We slept in groups, took turns standing. Twelve hours at a time, standing with people I'd never met before and others I knew well. It was impossible to sleep. We heard shots sometimes from outside. People were dragged out screaming and never came back. They pulled me out too. I was angry. You're going to die, you piece of shit. *Comunista.* They spat on me. Peruvian dog, you're going to die in Chile today! I told them to go to hell. They were young, the soldiers, just children, but cold. They wouldn't look me in the eye. I remember one of the officers: he was silent, standing behind. He had big hands. Finally, he yelled out, Tie him up, and they did. They put my hands behind my back and then blindfolded me. I spat at them. Say your last words, Communist. Fuck off, I said. I'm ready."

José Carlos spilled the ashtray with a clumsy brush of his arm; he was shaking violently. Fernando moved quickly to sweep the ash into his hands.

"They shot me, Negro! They killed me!" José Carlos brought his hand down hard against the table, slapping it loudly. "They shot me with blanks! They played at killing me!"

"They dragged me back to the dressing room. I smelled from my own piss and shit. My friends there held me. Someone threw water on me. You're alive, they said, but I didn't believe them. No bullet touched you, they said, but I knew I had felt it. I spent three days dead, Fernando. Three days . . ."

José Carlos's voice was thin and smoky. "That's what they're going to do to you."

"What do we do, *Perucho?*"[9] Fernando took his hand and squeezed. "You're home. We're alive."

José Carlos shook his head, and coughing loudly, put out his cigarette. "It's simple, Negro. The side with guns always wins."

## VII. *To Lima, 1965*

Then there was the bus that took Fernando to Lima. It was the kind of contraption held together by ingenuity, built from salvaged parts with the practiced art of making do. Learn what the engine can handle and disregard its feelings, its wishes, and its whims.

9. Nickname for "Pedro."

Repairs were cruel surgeries of convenience, and the bus grew hardened, indifferent, and ran from spite and disgust, crossing Andean passes,[1] wheezing and cursing the broad-bowed freighter that brought it from Germany, the United States, or Sweden. Soon the seats were cracked and choking with dust, the windows rattled with each bump, each pothole, each patch of rough stones. The passengers rode, somehow coaxing sleep from the nauseating pounding of metal and glass, and the murderous odors of diesel.

This is how Fernando came to Lima at age seventeen: wearing a brown sweater over a modest button-up, with blue slacks and black shoes worn thin at the heels. Riding that bus, seated in the back row with six others, a mishmash collection of souls on one or another of life's various errands: to buy, to sell, to visit, to marry, to find, and more than a few, to forget.

Young people climbed onto the bus in the dead of night, leaving behind bankrupt and miserable villages of adobe houses and cold fields of cotton and maize. They carried a change of clothes, a picture, a little food, a plastic comb, a letter of introduction, a bag of coca leaves, or a crucifix. They dropped their bundles in the aisle and stood for twelve hours, until the sun was up and roaring, the bus warm and drowsy with heat, and still they stood, beads of sweat forming on their lips and on their temples. Fernando watched them. They were his contemporaries. His countrymen. He watched them pull a few soles[2] from their pockets, haggle with the driver, shake their heads, and point their fingers. Their skin toughened by the sun and the wind. Some spoke only Quechua and some seemed not to speak at all.

Sometime in the afternoon the driver lost control. In a frightening half-second, the tires slid on the gravel, the road slipping beneath them. With a punishing blow, the bus slammed into the side railing, swerved back toward the mountain, toward safety, and came to rest, half-leaning, half-balancing against the brittle and crumbling earth that overlooked the road. To their right, just beyond the guardrail, a jagged drop-off and the valley below. People picked themselves up slowly. Bags and blankets were pushed aside. Fernando found himself stretched across three strangers. Legs and arms sorted themselves out. Mothers attended to crying children. Someone handed him his glasses with a smile and asked if he was all right. Everyone seemed to be reasonably well, though shaken—except the driver, who had taken it worst of all, perhaps because he had seen that shocking flash of blue across his window as the bus peered over the edge. He knew better than anyone how close they had come. The force of the accident had thrown him from his seat, but he had climbed back up to his perch, pulled the door release, and then sat still, pallid, gripping the wheel, rocking his head back and forth, eyes glazed, reliving the accident. A few people stopped to check on him, to pat him on the shoulder, to urge him outside, but he ignored them.

The men, with Fernando eagerly helping, set about the business of righting the bus. It was leaning precariously against the dirt rock wall of the road, its right tires about two or three feet off the ground. The cargo tied to the racks on the roof of the bus had come loose. Now it draped over the edge of the right-side windows. The tarp that covered the cargo had held, the

1. In the Andes, mountain range in South
America.   2. Peruvian currency.

suitcases, sacks, and crates together still, but dangling dangerously from the top of the bus.

Fernando walked to the edge where the bus had nearly taken flight and looked out over the valley. It was a tremendous sight, a magnificent Andean landscape, a silver-gray sheath of rock, a fierce blue sky, and along the hills, footpaths where man and beast walked. Perhaps the Inca's own messengers had marched along those paths in the days before the Spanish, before Atahualpa tossed Pizarro's Bible to the ground, before the killing began.[3] There was a spectacular loneliness in the mountains, in the grand theater of wind and sky, mountain and water, and so much quiet, Fernando felt ashamed to speak. Perhaps he imagined this, or imposed it on himself, or perhaps he adopted the quiet rectitude of his fellow passengers, who nodded and gestured more than they spoke. Fernando longed to know their language.

Then the driver, still shaken, stepped into the sun-struck day, pointing frantically at the luggage compartment beneath the coach. And suddenly they heard it—the banging, clawing against metal, a sound previously lost in the wind. The men sprang into action, and in an instant, the door was open, and beneath luggage and crates, a man emerged. He had been asleep beneath the bus, having driven all night, waiting to replace the driver at the next town. They pulled him out, his legs kicking, arms flailing, a man being born again, having experienced death blindly.

"Brother," the driver said, rushing toward him. "My brother!"

Fernando could hear the man breathing, pulling in enormous lungs full of oxygen, replenishing himself. The man was crying and fearful. "Oh God, Oh God, Oh God," he murmured. A thin stream of blood curled from his bottom lip. The brothers embraced and Fernando fell in love with his people.

## VIII. Carmen, 1986

His mother died. Lima accepted his sadness and gave him a month of sunless days. At the funeral, Fernando held Inés's hand. The war had worsened. It seemed that the city might fall at any moment. In Lima, people tried to live their lives as if nothing were happening, but no one slept by the windows anymore. Bombs could go off at any moment. Fathers rushed home to beat the curfew. Young people used it as an excuse to stay out all night. Parties had devolved into fatalistic bacchanals.

Sixteen journalists were killed in a faraway mountain village. The peasants had mistaken them for collaborators. News crawled into Lima ten days later. In San Martín, a group of rebels took over a jungle town and waved rifles in the air. Guerrilla leaders, drunk with victory, pulled bandanas from their faces and announced to television cameras that victory was near. A shocked nation stared at its tormentors. The papers called them terrorists. In Lima, Fernando cringed. A backlash would come soon.

On July 13, 1986, Carmen was born on the third floor of the public hospital in central Lima.

---

3. I.e., before the Spanish forces led by the conquistador Francisco Pizarro (ca. 1475–1541) began killing the Incas, who were led by Atahualpa (ca. 1502–1533), the last Inca king of Peru.

With Carmen, Fernando and Maruja were finally alive. It was as if they had been sleeping all along. He had never seen anyone more beautiful than Maruja that morning she gave birth to his child, and when Carmen slept for the first time on his chest, he felt complete. Even as he held her, he realized he was placing a wager on his life: that the war might not spare him long enough to see her grow. Still at the hospital, he confided with Maruja that he was afraid. She said that she had always been.

Carmen was an accident. Maruja had never been convinced, not until that moment that she held the child and discovered that she could love that much again. She told Fernando that she hadn't expected to find that within her once more. Fernando's health reappeared, and he carried Carmen with him everywhere. He relished changing her diapers. He rode the bus with his daughter asleep on his lap. In meetings, while comrades waved fingers and spoke forcefully, Fernando rocked the child and whispered nursery rhymes in her ear, so she wouldn't be afraid of the loud voices.

Maruja brought home a map one day, and they tacked it to their bedroom wall. That evening, once the baby was asleep, they stood hand in hand to marvel at the size of the world. It was comforting to see how little their war was, and to think there were places out there where their struggles were not news.

But in public, they showed no signs of retreat. Maruja stayed with her union. Fernando traveled to the interior and back, lightning trips to visit universities in Piura and union meetings in Huancavelica,[4] returning to Lima on the overnight bus to see his daughter in her crib. His promise—to never leave Lima—was not mentioned.

He took Carmen with him one day when he was called to the home of a murdered syndicalist in San Juan de Lurigancho[5] to offer the Party's condolences. It was daylight and safe, he thought, but he hated this work. The man had lived in that part of the city built of dust. The bus let Fernando off in front of a newspaper stand. It was a warm day, inexplicably sunny. Children in tattered clothing watched Fernando as he passed, while his baby girl slept against his chest, oblivious. He'd been here, to this very home, ages ago, in the dead of night. Fernando had met the murdered man, but no picture came to mind: no toothy smile, no salt-and-pepper hair, no bushy eyebrows or face creased with wrinkles. It worried him. Now he would meet the man's widow, and the prospect of her sadness seemed daunting. He walked on to the house, certain his feet would remember the way. His daughter yawned. Her tiny mouth opening, she blinked, and then fell asleep again. It took only a moment. Her hair had fallen out a few weeks after birth: thin, reddish brown, and straight like her mother's. Fernando held her in his shadow so that the sun wouldn't wake her.

He was walking along a dusty street a few blocks from the bus stop when a boy came toward him with a steady stare. He appeared suddenly from the shadowed doorway of a storefront, as if he'd been waiting. "Hey, mister," he asked, "are you the man from the city?"

He said city as if it were far away. Fernando shook his head and walked on.

---

4. Capital of the Huancavelica region, in the southwest. Piura: capital of the Piura region and province, in the northwest.
5. District in Lima.

But the boy insisted. His voice was deep for his size, or maybe he was small for his age. "She's waiting for you. Señora Aronés."

"The widow?"

"My mother," the boy said flatly. He cupped a hand over his eyes. "She said you were coming."

Fernando followed the boy. "How is she?" he asked.

"The house is just over there."

"Is there anything I can do?"

The boy frowned. "Were you his friend?"

"We worked together."

"I'm not stupid, mister." He rubbed his eyes. "You got him killed."

Fernando stood, dumbstruck. The boy didn't back down. His jaw was set fiercely. He hates me, Fernando thought, and the idea shocked him. "You've misunderstood, son."

But the boy didn't answer. Someone from the house had recognized Fernando, was calling his name, "Negro . . ."

"My mother's in there," the boy said grimly and walked away.

The home was surrounded by mourners. Fernando made his way inside, shaking hands on the way with men who recognized him. No one here seemed to blame him. Still, he felt numb. There were more people crowded inside, forming a circle around the widow. Fernando sat on the dirt floor. The widow thanked him for coming without even glancing up at him. When she finally looked up, she nodded. "You've been here before."

"Your husband was a good friend."

Someone brought him a glass of soda and he drank politely. He was there to watch her cry. He was there to show that she hadn't been forgotten.

"Can I hold her?" she asked after a moment. She meant Camucha. The widow's face was flush and red. He looked around her bare home; all her worldly possessions could fit into a trunk. And now she had lost it all. It was there on her face for anyone to see. Her son would never recover. Fernando passed her his sleeping child. Something like a smile graced the widow's lips, flashed for a moment, and was gone.

## VIII. La Uni, 1977

At La Uni, they were safe. Inside they could speak their minds, wear their affiliations on their sleeves. Students denounced their professors, stormed out of class and into the streets. Some disappeared into the mountains to learn the art of war. Every wall spoke politics: an angry poster announced a meeting; a slogan appeared, scrawled in red across the bricks. With angry partisans looking on, a frightened groundskeeper painted over it all. He did it every week.

Some hid their entire adult lives in and out of halls of La Uni. Fernando knew them. One man, Victor, never stayed in a house very long, two weeks but not more, and came to the university with fake papers to meet his comrades. He had left medical school in his second year and spent some time in Cusco[6] with the peasants during the land takeovers. He plowed the earth with the Indians and carried water for their crops in leaky wooden pails.

6. City in the southeast.

Back in Lima, he threw rocks at the Presidential Palace and broke windows at the Congress building. When the situation allowed, he set fires, and then people began to whisper his name. In 1977, he was already wanted. His friends remarked that the posters made him look even slighter than he was.

Victor fell ill in the early spring. A man came looking for Fernando at La Uni and told him the news. The messenger was paunchy and dark, careful with his words. Each syllable escaped through his teeth, so Fernando was forced to lean close simply to hear him. It was the way people in the movement spoke. "Victor needs a doctor. He says he knows what it is, only he can't operate on himself."

Fernando's brother Enrique was a doctor. He had trained in North America. He would know someone, or he could even see the patient himself. Fernando called him and they met at Inés's house in San Miguel. It was a Saturday afternoon in October. Inés poured drinks while her brothers spoke. Her two boys ran through the living room, screaming and laughing. They attacked their uncles with hugs and jumped into Enrique's lap. "What are you learning in school now, Ciro?"

"Nothing," the boy said, laughing.

"And you, Guillermo?"

"Can't remember."

He was only in first grade, but Fernando was afraid it was true. Public schools in Lima were not like Independencia; they were crowded, chaotic, dirty. Enrique was urging Inés to save for a private school. The boys ran outside to play.

When it was quieter, Fernando told Enrique about Victor. "He's a friend," he said. "He can't go to the hospital."

"Don't ask me to get involved, Nano."

"Involved?" Fernando laughed. "Come on, *hermano*.[7] It's just a small favor."

"I wish I could help."

"It would all be very quiet."

Enrique shook his head. "I'm sorry."

Inés's boys were kicking a deflated plastic ball in front of the house. Ciro waved and smiled through the window, then kicked the ball straight at them. Both Fernando and Enrique flinched, but the ball ricocheted harmlessly off the iron bars in front of the glass. The boys smirked, then Ciro raised his arms and shouted *gol* with such exuberance that Fernando couldn't help but smile.

But Enrique didn't. He turned away from the window.

"Well?" Fernando asked.

"You know what, *hermanito*?" Enrique said in a sharp whisper. "I have a wife. I have two daughters. I have a son on the way."

They had discussed this before, across their father's kitchen table in Arequipa: What will you do when the time comes to act? What is demanded of people like us in a country like this?

"When you're my age you'll understand, Nano."

A radio hummed in the background. They could hear Inés singing along to the old tune from the kitchen. Enrique got up without saying another

7. Brother (*hermanito*, below, meaning little brother).

word. Fernando watched his older brother through the window. Enrique picked up one of the boys and put him on his shoulders. The boy shrieked with delight.

Sometimes Fernando thought they scarcely seemed like brothers at all.

Victor died in a windowless basement apartment in Barrios Altos of complications resulting from acute appendicitis.

### X. Mateo, 1989

Fernando stopped by Mateo's apartment one evening. It was November. Soon the city would be beautiful again. The brothers embraced warmly; though they lived nearby, they had not seen each other in months. Fernando sat down, and Mateo brought him a drink. "This apartment is killing me, Nano," he said.

The curtains were drawn. All the furniture was covered in dust. "You changed the arrangement here, no?" Fernando asked.

"We moved everything toward the center. Away from the window," Mateo said, nodding absentmindedly. "Bombs."

Outside, along the avenue, just one hundred feet from Mateo's window, there was a red brick wall that read NO STOPPING UNDER PENALTY OF DEATH. Behind it, there was an army installation. Every two hundred feet or so, a turret stood above the brick wall, each with an armed soldier inside. Mateo had been pleading with the landlord to let his family move to another apartment, one that wasn't so compromised by its location.

The sofa was set in the middle of the room; two strips of electrical tape made an × across each window. "To keep the glass from blowing inward."

Fernando nodded. He had done the same in his apartment. Mateo's neighbors had moved away. "We try not to look out the window," Mateo said, finishing his drink.

"Someone has been watching me, Mateo."

"Of course."

Mateo knew exactly what his brother was involved in. They had never discussed it, but each assumed that they knew the same people, only from different sides. They were right. Mateo was an officer. Policía Nacional del Perú. "What happened?" he asked.

"My car was stolen, the other day, near the university—"

"Which doesn't in itself mean anything."

"No, of course not." Fernando chuckled. "It's a piece of shit, but still, it's surprising it hasn't happened sooner. But what happened after was strange. I reported it to the police. At the station, they made me wait. Then an officer came out, less than two hours after it had gone, and told me they had found my car."

Stolen cars don't appear in Lima, not like that, not until the piranhas have taken them apart. Mateo knew that. Everyone knew that.

Fernando continued. "They took me right to it, right where I had left it. Exactly as it was before I had reported it missing." He paused, and leaned over the table toward Mateo. "Except my briefcase was missing."

"You're certain?"

"Gone."

"Did you go back for it?"

Fernando nodded.

"You shouldn't have." Mateo shook his head. "What did they tell you?"

"'So, it seems you're some kind of *politico*, no?'"

"And you said?"

Fernando paused, taking a deep, tired breath. He hadn't slept. "I said where's my fucking briefcase."

"Nano!" Mateo stood up with a start. "How could you put yourself in that kind of position? How could you have so little regard for your own life?"

"I don't know. I messed up." He looked down. He wiggled his toes inside his shoes.

"Nano," his brother said. "Look at me. What was in the briefcase? What did you have in there?"

"Documents. Papers. Names. I don't know exactly. Maybe nothing."

"Nothing?"

Fernando was suddenly afraid. "I haven't told Maruja."

"Is she implicated?" Mateo asked.

"No."

"Are you?"

Fernando closed his eyes but didn't answer. Mateo was still standing over him when he opened them again. The brothers stared at each other for a moment, in silence.

Mateo slumped down in his chair again.

"The circle is tightening, Nano. . . . Be careful."

### XI. Oxapampa, 1989

A few weeks before Christmas, the Party called on Fernando to make a trip. He didn't tell Maruja where he was going, although she must have suspected. He didn't inform the university that he was taking leave, nor did he expect to be gone for long. Fernando took a bus to Huancayo,[8] and in the noisy bus station he met his contact, a comrade from the Party. Together, they rode away from Huancayo, north into the valley, and then into the jungle. They spent one night in Oxapampa, registered under false names at a local hotel, and woke with flea bites and neck cramps. They hiked for the next two days and then met another man, who led them even farther. And then, in a clearing, three days from anywhere, Fernando met the combatants. José Carlos had been waiting for him.

The fighters were young and frightened and dwarfed by their weapons. They had scarcely begun to live. They had never read Marx or heard of Castro.[9] Some had never been to Lima. There was little bravado among them, little of that swagger that one would associate with carrying a gun. The forest was dark and damp. In camp, they made space for the visitor from Lima in one of the olive green tents. Fernando thought they looked ill, gaunt, tired. He briefly felt shame.

There was a clearing, where the rebels learned the basics of engagement. In the mornings, they dispersed in squadrons, drifting into the jungle; they ran exercises, learned how to use their guns. They hid from one another and

---

8. Capital of the Huancayo province, in the central highlands.
9. Fidel Castro (b. 1926), Cuban revolutionary leader. *Marx*: Karl Marx (1818–1883), German political philosopher and socialist.

shot the branches off trees from a hundred yards away. They tossed rocks at targets, pretending they were grenades. Fernando watched as they threw, counting—one, two, three, four—and whispered the coming explosion:

*Boom.*

Those who saw him then described Fernando as electric, brilliant, defining the sacrifices that still awaited them, and the injustices that had steeled their resolve. No question animated him more, sparked more passion within him, than why. Why there were no choices; why the time was now; why victory was assured.

It came from his heart, but he spoke with his hands, his arms, his entire body. Why the people had been denied schooling; why their fathers worked land they would never own; why their mothers cleaned houses; why their uncles did not stop working until blindness overwhelmed them. Why the defeated chased happiness in drink; why wealth bred depravity. Why the history was cruel and maniacal; why blood must be shed.

Standing in front of a map of the Americas tacked to the mossy trunk of a jungle tree, Fernando ran his finger up and down the peaks of the Andes, the spine of his continent, and told the tattered and inexperienced group of fighters what he would die believing that very day:

"All of this will be ours once more," he said.

And he smiled as they repeated it with him. He delighted in the sound of their rising voices.

He looked up and caught a glimpse of the swollen sky through the forest's canopy.

"All of this will be ours once more!" he said again.

And the words filled him with an inexplicable joy, even hope.

He was still alive.

1998                                                                                      2003

---

# MARÍA TERESA "MARIPOSA" FERNÁNDEZ
## b. 1977

The literary and artistic movement that developed around the Nuyorican Poets Cafe in the late 1970s (see p. 1344) has been carried on by new generations of writers, artists, and performers. One of the most prominent newer figures is María Teresa (aka Mariposa) Fernández. Born and raised in the New York City borough of the Bronx, Fernández is of Puerto Rican and African ancestry. An organic grassroots poet, performer, visual artist, activist, educator, and community resource specialist at the Center for Family Community and Social Justice, in New York, Fernández earned both her bachelor's degree in women's studies and her master's in special education from New York University. She has been a resident artist at New York's Caribbean Cultural Center/African Diaspora Institute, Poets House, Poets & Writers, the Bronx Writers' Center, and the Teachers & Writers Collaborative. While frequently offering poetry workshops for public school students, she has run the open mike poetry series *Son La Heights*, in New York's Dominican community of Washington Heights, and *Bronx Bohemia*, in the Bronx. Fernández has performed at more than a hundred universities in the United States and Puerto Rico and was highlighted in the acclaimed HBO documentary *Americanos: Latino Life in the U.S.* (2002). Fernández has received a literary fellowship from the Bronx Council for the Arts and an award from the Puerto Rican organization Comité-Noviembre.

As influences, Fernández cites the Nuyorican movement and the work of prominent African American feminist writers/activists, such as Sonia Sanchez and Ntosake Shange. Her poems and articles have appeared in periodicals and newspapers such as *Centro Journal, Newsday, Brownstone Magazine, AHA Hispanic Art News*, and Puerto Rico's *El Nuevo Día* and in the anthology *Resistance in Paradise: Rethinking 100 Years of U.S. Involvement in the Caribbean and the Pacific* (1998). Fernández has published the chapbook *Born Bronxeña: Poems* (2001). As part of the New World Theater's 2001 program, she performed the one-woman play *Diaspo-Rican Dementia*, which recounts her institutionalization and misdiagnosis with bipolar disorder.

The poem "Ode to the Diasporican," the first of three Fernández selections in this anthology, is a classic among the coming-of-age identity poems that are such an important part of the Latino literary tradition. "Boricua Butterfly" and "Poem for my Grifa-Rican Sistah Or Broken Ends Broken Promises" address Fernández's mixed racial heritage. The personal nature of "Boricua Butterfly" is underscored in the poem's title, which alludes to the author's pen name: *mariposa* means butterfly in Spanish. All three poems affirm a new, distinctive, collective sense of Puerto Ricanness, arising from fragmentation and marginality experienced by Puerto Ricans born and raised in the United States. For Fernández, this sense of identity within the diaspora also entails a validation of her African roots. In a personal statement she provided for the Web site of La Peña Cultural Center's Next Generation project for artistic development, Fernández explains that she writes "to look myself in the face, but of course I'm just one person of many of a collective experience. My experience is part of a larger collective experience. So the issues that strike me are going to strike chords in other people."

# Boricua Butterfly[1]

I am the
Meta-morpho-sized
The reborn
The living phoenix
Rising up out of the ashes                                                    5
With my conquered people
Not the lost Puerto Rican soul in search of identity
Not the tragic Nuyorican in search of the land of the palm tree
Not fragmented but whole
Not colonized                                                                10
But free.

1998                                                                      1999

---

1. The native Taíno peoples on Puerto Rico called the island Boriquén and themselves Boricuas.

# Ode to the Diasporican

## (pa' mi gente)[1]

Mira a mi cara Puertorriqueña
Mi pelo vivo
Mis manos morenas
Mira a mi corazón que se llena de orgullo
Y dime que no soy Boricua.[2]                                                    5

Some people say that I'm not the real thing
Boricua, that is
cause I wasn't born on the enchanted island
cause I was born on the mainland
north of Spanish Harlem                                                         10
cause I was born in the Bronx
some people think that I'm not bonafide
cause my playground was a concrete jungle
cause my Río Grande de Loiza[3] was the Bronx River
cause my Fajardo was City Island[4]                                             15
my Luquillo Orchard Beach[5]
and summer nights were filled with city noises
instead of coquis[6]
and Puerto Rico
was just some paradise                                                          20
that we only saw in pictures.

What does it mean to live in between
What does it take to realize
that being Boricua
is a state of mind                                                              25
a state of heart
a state of soul . . .

Mira a mi cara Puertorriqueña
Mi pelo vivo
Mis manos morenas                                                               30
Mira a mi corazón que se llena de orgullo
Y dime que no soy Boricua.

No nací en Puerto Rico.
Puerto Rico nació en mi.[7]

1993                                                                          2001

---

1. For my people.
2. Look at my Puerto Rican face / My nappy hair / My brown-skinned hands / Look into my heart filled with pride / And tell me that I am not Boricua.
3. River in northeastern Puerto Rico, immortalized in the poetry of Julia de Burgos (see p. 595).
4. Small island that is part of Bronx County. *Fajardo*: small city in eastern Puerto Rico. Both

City Island and Fajardo are associated with waterfront property.
5. Public beach in the Bronx. *Luquillo*: Luquillo Beach, public beach in the town of Luquillo, northeastern Puerto Rico.
6. Species of small frogs that make a rhythmic sound at night.
7. I was not born in Puerto Rico. / Puerto Rico was born in me.

# Poem for My Grifa-Rican Sistah
## Or Broken Ends Broken Promises

(for my twin sister, Melissa, who endured it with me)

Braids twist and tie
constrain baby naps never to be free
braids twist and tie
contain / hold in the shame
of not havin' long black silky strands          5
to run my fingers through.
Moños[1] y bobby pins
twist and wrap
Please forgive me for the sin
Of not inheriting Papi's "good hair"          10
moños y bobby pins
twist and wrap
restrain kinky naps
dying to be free
but not the pain          15
of not having a long black silky mane
to run my fingers through.

Clips and ribbons
to hold back and tie
oppressing baby naps          20
never to be free.

Clips and ribbons
to hold back and tie
imprisoning baby naps
never to have the dignity to be.          25

Chemical relaxers
broken ends / broken promises
activator and cream
mixed in with bitterness
mix well . . .          30

Keep away from children
Avoid contact with eyes
This product contains lye and lies
Harmful if swallowed

The ritual *of combing / parting / sectioning*          35
the greasing of the scalp / the neck
the forehead / the ears
the process / and then the burning / the burning

---

1. Hair buns.

"It hurts to be beautiful, 'ta te quieta"[2]
My mother tells me.                                                                    40
"¡Pero mami me pica!"[3]

and then the running / the running to water
to salvation / to neutralizer / to broken ends
and broken promises.

Graduating from Carefree Curl                                                          45
to Kitty curl / to Revlon / to super duper Fabulaxer
different boxes offering us broken ends and broken promises.

"We've come a long way since Dixie Peach,"
my mother tells me as I sit at the kitchen table.

Chemical relaxers to melt away the shame                                               50
until new growth reminds us
that it is time once again
for the ritual and the fear of
scalp burns and hair loss
and the welcoming                                                                      55
of broken ends
and broken
promises.

When the truth is that
Black hair
African textured hair                                                                  60
Care free crazy curly hair
is beautiful.

¡Que viva el pelo libre![4]

¡Que viva!                                                                             65

1995                                                                    2001

---

2. Sit still.
3. But Mommy, it stings!

4. Literally, long live free hair! Figuratively, long
live *grifa* (kinky) hair!

# Popular Dimensions

Rubén Darío, the Nicaraguan poet and founder of *Modernismo* (discussed in the "Annexations" introduction, p. 168), refers to the writer as a prophet, a savant, a "torre de Dios" (divine tower) in touch with the Muses. This ideal—of an individualistic, solitary observer capable of appreciating hidden aspects of reality—derives from the nineteenth-century artistic movement Romanticism. It places the writer in sharp contrast to the collective symphony of spoken voices, what ethnographers call the vernacular, within society.

But the roots of Latino culture reach back far past Romanticism—for example, to pre-Columbian tribal raconteurs. Working with and within the vernacular, these speakers presented community members with the all-encompassing cosmologies of the time. Such communal presentations of knowledge and belief differed in many ways from the Romantic sense of artistic creation. The primary difference was that these speakers depended on the presence of people—a popular audience—to receive and complete their stories. Since their goal was not self-expression as much as enlightenment and entertainment, the speakers would have served no purpose without audiences. In this way, these artists and their works represent the beginning of a vernacular thread that runs through the Latino literary tradition. This section of the anthology is devoted to that thread. It presents audience-focused texts: saying and jokes (meant to be repeated), visual imagery (meant to be displayed), theatrical spectacles (meant to be enacted), folktales and legends (meant to be told), and songs (meant to be performed). Because vernacular expression is infinitely varied and always evolving, this section is a sampling, a window into these vital forms.

Many Latino works intended for popular audiences are examples of folklore. The word *folklore*, of German etymology and coined in 1846, refers to the traditional beliefs, legends, and customs current among the common people. Folklore can be a ballad, a proverb, a cautionary tale, an oral history, or any other verbal demonstration of a common culture. As the ethnographer Richard Bauman puts it in his handbook *Folklore, Cultural Performance, and Popular Entertainments* (1992), folklore emerges from "a bounded, homogeneous, unsophisticated, tradition-oriented group sharing a common language and a collective body of vernacular knowledge, custom, oral tradition, and the like." The author of a piece of folklore is not at center stage, nor does the value of the craft depend on the genius of individual expression. Instead, folklore is a collective endeavor, shaped by many people over a long period, often over several generations. Representing the collective psyche, the work exists not as a "final draft," but as a work-in-progress, in constant flux and mutation.

Scholars divide folklore by Latinos in the United States into categories, such as folk dances, folk costumes, and folk beliefs. The present section represents the category of folk speech through *dichos* (sayings; the synonym *refranes* is more formal) and *chistes* (jokes). The former are ingenious sentences through which wisdom is passed along. The latter are one of Spanish-language culture's idiosyncratic forms of humor. Each *chiste* is a succinct tale, no longer than a few lines, concluding with a strong, emblematic punch line. Each is seldom repeated twice to the same audience, and its success depends on an artful, syncopated delivery.

For centuries, graphic art has been an essential fixture of Latino life—a form of entertainment, a venue for satire, and a means of expressing political dissent. At the end of the nineteenth century and the dawn of the twentieth, the Mexican engraver and illustrator José Guadalupe Posada created provocative lithographs in which he used the folk icon of the skull, the *calavera*, to poke fun at government figures and respond to natural and social disasters. In the twentieth century, his work inspired Diego Rivera, one of the so-called *Tres Grandes*, along with David Alfaro Siqueiros and José Clemente Orozco. The street art of these three legendary Mexican muralists mirrored collective discontent. Their influence on Chicano and Puerto Rican pictorial artists is enormous. A connection also exists between their frescos and the graffiti that appeared in New York, Los Angeles, and other U.S. cities during the hip-hop era. Within the Latino literary tradition, creators of political cartoons, comic strips, or graphic novels with a manifest Hispanic sensibility are known as *cartoonistas*, and this section includes several fine examples of *cartoonistas'* work.

*Teatro popular* (popular theater) has its roots in the folk dramas staged in the Southwest during the Spanish Colonial period. For example, *Moros y cristianos* depicted a battle between Christians and Moors in medieval Spain, and *Los comanches* was about the fight in 1774 between the Comanche tribe and the Spanish settlers of New Mexico. Written texts exist of these anonymous plays, but the performances depended on improvisation, making each enactment different from the previous one. Bringing that tradition up to date is the modern theater group Culture Clash. Culture Clash's creative method is based on extensive, in-the-field interviews the members conduct with ordinary people in the city where the group will be performing. Using this material as background, the group improvises until a collective piece emerges. That piece enters the company's repertoire, but changes in live performance and is continually updated with current news items. Featured here is a segment of Culture Clash's first full-length play, *The Mission* (1988).

*Cuentos* (folktales) and *leyendas* (legends) are usually told by community elders (grandparents, teachers), raconteurs with unique access to the collective memory. The target audience is generally children, and the unequivocal objective is to socialize the young audience. Legends normally carry moral messages. Through the presentations of folktales and legends, the people's history is preserved or recovered.

Latino *canciones* (songs) include corridos (Mexican ballads) and narco-corridos (drug-smuggling ballads) and come from varieties of popular music such as boleros, salsa, merengue, Tejano, Chicano rock, Latin pop, hip-hop, and reggaetón. They reflect a tradition dating to the *trovadores*, itinerant singers of the sacred and popular music of medieval Spain and the *canciones navideñas* that circulated in the Americas during the Spanish colonial period. Every one of the songs selected here tells a narrative—the growth of nostalgia for the abandoned homeland, the misadventures of an out-of-luck thief, a love affair gone sour—invariably about the common folk. Each one, through its narrative, seeks to deliver a message of universality.

Many of the songs and other pieces in "Popular Dimensions" come from anthologies of folklore and of children's tales, compendiums of popular sayings, collectors' albums, recordings, hymnals, and museum collections. Serving as a guide for many of these selections are the works of major folklore scholars: J. Frank Dobie (1888–1964), a liberal journalist and newspaper columnist who taught at Cambridge University, in England, and the University of Texas at Austin, devoted his life to understanding rural Texas traditions. Aurelio M. Espinosa (1880–1958) recognized speech patterns linking the New Mexican population to medieval Spain; with the help of his son, José M. Espinosa (1909–1999), he focused on ballads, religious literature, proverbs, storytelling, and traditional religious and secular popular dramas. Among Aurelio M. Espinosa's students at the University of California, Berkeley, was Juan Bautista Rael (1900–1993), a linguist and ethnographer who taught at Stanford University, in California. Rael studied the people, folktales, and languages of northern New Mexico and southern Colorado, with a particular emphasis on the morphological varieties of New Mexican Spanish. Arthur L. Campa (1905–1978), a professor of modern languages at the University of Denver, in Colorado, and director of its Center for Latin American Studies, approached New Mexican folklore as having its origins in Mexico and not in Spain, as Aurelio M. Espinosa did. The Chicano ethnomusicologist Américo Paredes (see p. 603) pointed at the U.S.-Mexico border as a "contact zone," a region where disparate cultures clash and result in a hybrid that has its own syntactical patterns.

For the many of the selections originally in Spanish, the best available translations have been used, some of them newly created for this anthology. All songs written in English (for example, "Livin' La Vida Loca") appear in English. All songs written in Spanish appear as double-column texts, with the Spanish on the left and an English translation on the right.

The items here and on the Web site wwnorton.com/web/latinolit are not meant to be definitive or exhaustive. Space limitations made it impossible to include myths, *décimas* (10-strophe poems), and a more substantial representation of traditional and contemporary songs, such as "Allá en el Rancho Grande" (Over at Rancho Grande) and "Cuatro milpas" (Four Cornfields), as well as *canciones rancheras*, such as "El Rey" (The King), "No vale nada la vida" (Life Is Worthless), and "Los laureles" (The Laurels). To explore all of the categories further, see the "Popular Dimensions" entry in the selected bibliographies.

# *Dichos*

These manifestations of popular wisdom have their roots in medieval and Renaissance Spain, from where they were transported to the Americas by the conquistadors, explorers, and missionaries. Through a process of transculturation, their meanings have become intertwined with the wisdom of both aboriginal populations and black slaves. The results are a distinctive mixed heritage that speaks to cultural fluidity. The scope of this *mestizaje* knows no boundaries. An individual nation may claim that particular sayings belong to its popular culture, but these sayings are geographically widespread. Incessant migration functions as a communication vessel.

Some examples:

*El que nació pa' tamal, del cielo le caen hojas.*
Every dog has his day.

*Nunca es tarde si la dicha es buena.*
Better late than never.

*De tal palo, tal astilla.*
A chip off the old block.

*El que no habla, Dios no lo oye.*
Fortune favors the bold.

*El diablo sabe más por viejo que por diablo.*
Experience is the best teacher.

*Perro que ladra no muerde.*
A barking dog never bites.

*Eso es harina de otro costal.*
That's a horse of a different color.

*Dime con quién andas y te dire quién eres.*
You can judge a man by the company he keeps.

*Saliste de Guatemala y te metiste en Guatepeor.*
Out of the frying pan, into the fire.

*Camarón que se duerme se lo lleva la corriente.*
Time and tide wait for no man.

*De noche todos los gatos son pardos.*
At night all cats are gray.

# Chistes

*Chistes malos* (bad jokes) differ from *chistes buenos* (good jokes) in terms of delivery style but also the sexual explicitness of the content: One type of *chiste malo* is the *albur*, an explicit oral communication between a male and a female who often do not share a common history and in which the former makes an unwanted sexual pass at the latter. Two other types, *choteo* and *relajo*, are strategies through which authority is challenged and the seriousness of a situation is put in question. (*Indagación del choteo* [Inquiry on Choteo, 1940], by the distinguished Cuban writer and academic Jorge Mañach [1898–1961], is a classic psychocultural analysis of the place of the *choteo* in Cuban culture.) In addition, as in English, black humor is used to treat a serious event irreverently.

*Chistes* among Latinos in the United States often spring from the clash of Hispanic and Anglo cultures. They are often bilingual and include word games, onomatopoeias, and other verbal pyrotechnics. Their elements vary from one national group to another, but these *chistes* tend to be fatalistic and to include an array of innuendo. Repeating characters are *el menso* (the ignoramus); *el que no sabe inglés* (the monolingual); *borrachitos* (drunkards); *el padrecito* and *la monjita* (religious figures); *el ladrón* (the thief); *el cabrón* (the cuckold); *el loquito* (the lunatic); *el nene* (the baby); *el chinito, el judío,* and *el negrito* (ethnic types); *el gringo* (the foreigner); and *el perico, la vaca,* and *el puerco* (various animals).

Some examples:

*Pepito vuelve de la escuela y su mamá le pregunta:*
  *—¿Cómo te va con tus calificaciones?*
  *—Como en el polo norte, mamá.*
  *—¿Cómo? No entiendo. . . .*
  *—Es que todo está bajo cero.*

Pepito returns from school, and his mother asks:
  "How are your grades?"
  "Like the North Pole, Mom."
  "How so? I don't understand. . . ."
  "Everything is below zero."

*—Anda, chica, que no ves que es el tiempo perfecto, ¡déjame que te toque el wiwichu!*
*—No, ¡no te lo permitiré!*
*—Anda chica, es ahora o nunca, deja que te toque el wiwichu. . . .*
*—Bueno, sólo porque me gustas.*
*Entonces el hombre agarra su guitarra y canta: "Wiwichu a merry crismas, wiwichu a merry crismas, wiwichu a merry crismas, and a japy niu yir!"*

"Please, chica, it's the perfect time. Let me touch the wiwichu!"

"No, I won't allow it!"

"Please, chica, now or never. Let me touch the wiwichu. . . ."

"All right, but only because I like you."

Then the man reaches for his guitar and sings: "Wiwichu a merry Crismas, wiwichu a merry Crismas, wiwichu a merry crismas, and a japy niu yir!"

---

*Un mexicano que no sabe inglés visita una cuidad norteamericana. Entra al barrio de mala muerte. Sale una aventurada y le pregunta: "Hey, honey, wanna do it?"*

*El mexicano le contesta: "¿Mande?"*

*Disgustada, la mujer responde: "No, not Monday. Right now!"*

A Mexican who doesn't speak English visits a North American city. He enters a rough neighborhood. An easy woman shows up and asks: "Hey, honey, wanna do it?"

The Mexican responds: "¿Mande?" (Beg your pardon?)

Annoyed, the woman says: "No, not Monday. Right now!"

# Cartoonistas

The father figure among Latino comic-strip artists is Gus Arriola, the Mexican American creator of *Gordo*, which appeared in newspapers around the United States from 1941 through 1985. For a while, Gordo was the only Mexican American cartoon character in mainstream media, and in terms of popularity he might be second among Mexican American cartoon characters only to the mouse Speedy González. The *Gordo* strip is said to have introduced English-language readers to words and expressions such as *amigo, compadre, hasta la vista,* and *hasta mañana.* Arriola was criticized for perpetuating stereotypes, however, and modified his protagonist accordingly. Following directly in Arriola's footsteps were Hector Canú and Carlos Castellanos, who launched *Baldo* in 2000. Their protagonist, Baldomero "Baldo" Bermudez, a teenager interested in girls and cars, has appeared in two books: *The Lower You Ride, The Cooler You Are* (2001) and *Night of the Bilingual Telemarketers* (2002).

Lalo López Alcaraz is among the most distinguished Latino political cartoonists. He began publishing cartoons in a student newspaper, *The Daily Aztec,* at San Diego State University, and since 1985 his cartoons have been syndicated by Hispanic Link News Service. His cartoon *La Cucaracha* is published daily in periodicals nationwide. Juxtaposing ideology with popular culture, Alcaraz uses sharp humor to denounce abuse of Hispanics, addressing issues such as immigration and xenophobia. Among his book publications are *Latino USA: A Cartoon History* (2000), written by Ilan Stavans, and the graphic novel *Leave It to Beaner* (2004).

Arguably the most celebrated *cartoonistas* are the Hernandez Brothers: Mario, Jaime, and Gilberto. They came to love comics while growing up in a large family in Oxnard, California, and first became successful with *Love and Rockets,* a series about the California punk scene. Each brother has since developed an independent series about a group of friends or a fictional town and has published it in the form of a graphic novel, a genre that has evolved rapidly among Latinos since the late 1990s.

Not represented in this anthology but a vital part of Latino popular culture are the superheroes that defend the defenseless in the Spanish-speaking world. Latino superheroes have been created by artists of Mexican, Cuban, Colombian, Argentinian, and Puerto Rican heritage. They include Rocketo, created by Frank Espinoza; El Gato Negro, by Richard Domínguez; and Sonámbuo, by Rafael Navarro.

# GUS ARRIOLA
## 1917–2008

1945

# THE HERNANDEZ BROTHERS
## Mario (b. 1953), Gilberto (b. 1957), and Jaime (b. 1959)

1989

LALO LÓPEZ ALCARAZ
b. 1964

1996

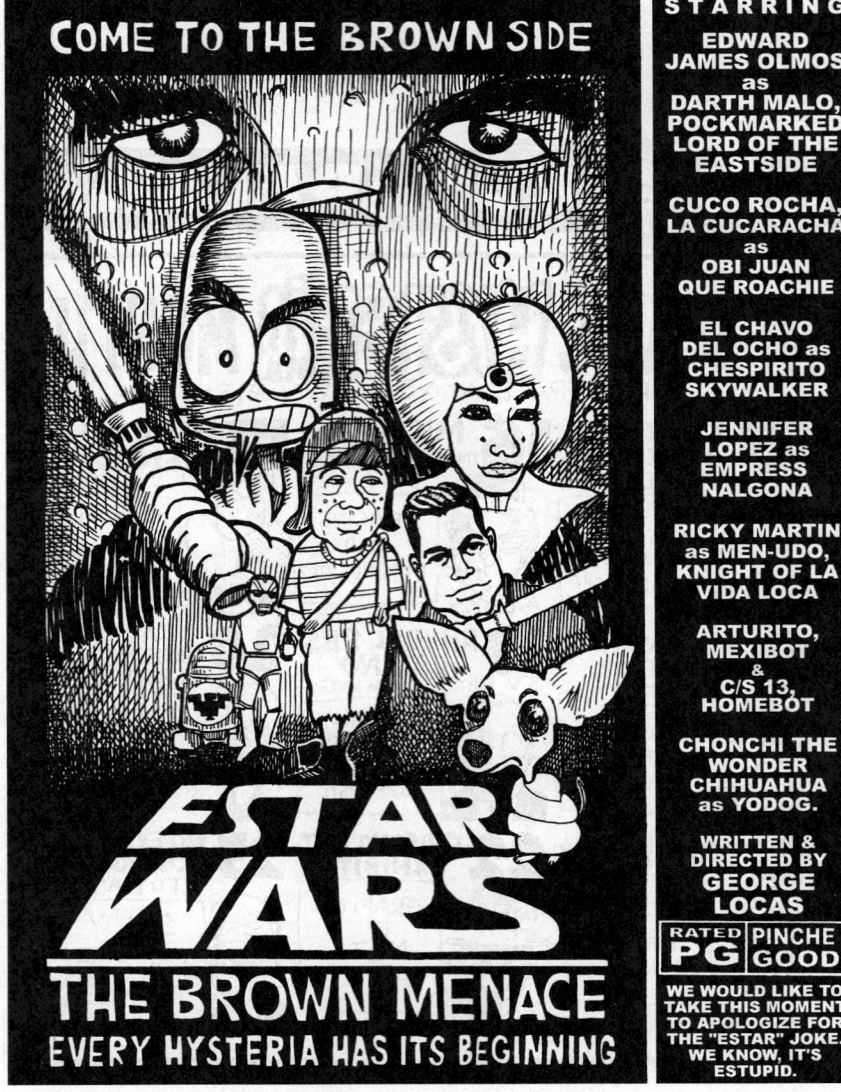

1998

# Teatro Popular

A performance group whose satirical humor is an anarchic response to the spread of Latino stereotypes in mainstream media, Culture Clash descends directly from the colonial folk plays, vaudeville, the *teatro de carpa* (tent theater) of iconic Mexican comedians such as Mario Moreno aka "Cantinflas" and Germán Valdés aka "Tin-Tan," and the Teatro Campesino (Farmworkers' Theater) of Luis Valdez (see p. 1244). Founded on the Mexican holiday Cinco de Mayo (May 5) in 1984, the company originally included Richard Montoya, Ric Salinas, Herbert Siguenza (who in 2001 created a one-man show called *Cantinflas!*), José Antonio Burciaga (p. 1227), Marga Gómez, and Mónica Palacio. Montoya, Salinas, and Siguenza, as a trio, have gone on to make Culture Clash internationally famous. Their play *Radio Mambo* (1995) deals with Latinos in Miami; *Nuyorican Stories* (1999) is about the Latino ethnic rainbow in New York City; *Anthems* (2002) looks at the intersection of ethnicity and politics post–September 11 in Washington, D.C.; and *Chavez Ravine* (2003) is about a community in Los Angeles that was displaced to make way for public housing and later Dodger Stadium. Starting in 1993, Culture Clash made 30 episodes—two seasons—of a television series for Fox Syndication; *Culture Clash in Americca*, a concert film directed by Emilio Estevez, aired in 2005; other works include interactive videos and art pieces. Individual plays have appeared in print or have been compiled in volumes such as *Life, Death, and Revolutionary Comedy* (1998) and *Culture Clash in Americca* (2004). Their play *The Mission* (1988) toured nationally. It is, as Salinas notes in his introduction to the published text,

> a synthesis of many traditions. It is a play about us: Richard, Ric and Herbert, a culmination of three separate lives coming together in a desperate plea to tell the world about our dilemma. It is a semi-autobiographical romp about three frustrated Latino actors from San Francisco's Mission District trying to break into show biz. It opens in 1776 at Mission Dolores, where the sadomasochistic Spanish Father Junipero Serra tries to save his little neophytes with true "Western" culture. The action leaps, via a peyote vision quest, to the present, where we meet three out-of-work actors.

The first scene, included here, gives a taste of the trio's combination of propaganda, agitation, and Monty Pythonesque irreverence.

# CULTURE CLASH

## The Mission[1]

NOTE

*The beginning of the play is set in eighteenth-century San Francisco, California. The upstage center area is used as the Mission courtyard. The downstage center area is flanked by a very contemporary apartment which must not be exposed for the opening "Serra Overture" scene.*

### Act One

#### SCENE ONE

#### Serra Overture, 1776

*Darkness.*

  *Four Mission bells toll and a Native American funeral chant is heard. Moments later two* INDIOS[2] *enter carrying candles. They cross center stage and salute the Four Directions, then turn upstage toward the altar/pedestal.*

  *The* INDIOS *bend down and each light a candle on the floor; then, they each light a candle on the second step of the pedestal. They are precise in observing their ritual. Following the lighting of the candles, the* INDIOS *kneel, each holding a candle at eye-level. They blow the candles out.*

  *The funeral chant music segues into European religious music. As this music builds, the lights slowly expose* FATHER SERRA[3] *on his pedestal—first his feet, then his legs, then his face, and then his hands outstretched to the heavens.*

  FATHER SERRA *descends a step at a time assisted by the* INDIOS, *who remain on their knees until* FATHER SERRA *passes before them. The* INDIOS *rise, turn toward the audience, follow* FATHER SERRA *a step downstage,*

VOICEOVER:    October 9th, 1776. The sixth mission under the direction of Father Junipero Serra was completed in California. San Francisco de Assisi was the crown jewel of all the missions in the Brave New World.

  One man, one vision, one million Indios wiped out by murder, disease and torture. And, at least five known cases of the dreaded jock itch.

  *[One of the* INDIOS *scratches his crotch area.* FATHER SERRA *grabs the* INDIOS *by their ears.]*

Father Serra loved his little savages. No Indian was buried before his time. And, by the grace of God, he set out to make these naked creatures "Men of Reason." The beloved Mission Dolores was built next to the "Stream of Sorrows," known today as the "San Francisco Bathhouse of Sorrows." Thousands of tourists lose their collective chonies[4] there each year in the barrio streets of their mind, de chamberline, hear my rhyme, tecate with lime, commit a crime, do the time, OK, that's enough. Ladies and gentlemen, the anatomy of a Culture Clash—The Mission!

---

1. A predominantly Latino district in San Francisco (good taquerías). The artistic mission of three starving Latino comedians. An OK movie starring Robert DeNiro. [From the "Glossary of Terms" included with the published text]

2. Indio: Spanish for "Native American." [Glossary entry]
3. See p. 129.
4. Underwear (Jockey, usually). [Glossary entry]

[*Music swells, underscoring* FATHER SERRA'*s following monologue.*]
FATHER SERRA: Oh, my little brown ones. What mischief have we been in
today? My little savages, digo[5] my little sheep. When I found these little
creatures they were living in the cracks of the earth. Now, they say no
to crack! Verdad![6]
    [*With that,* FATHER SERRA *yanks the* INDIOS' *heads back by their
    hair.*]
I took away their pagan dances and gave them true culture! La opera, el
ballet, los Gipsy Kings![7] I took away their primitive tongue and taught
them Español, and you better speak Spanish now, my little ones, before
English becomes the official language! I took away their religion; now
they fear God! And, with a little help from the whip, the gun and the
cross . . . [*He pulls a large blade from a cross.*] they respect me, despite
my lisp.
    One day the world will recognize me. In fact, I was almost canonized
by the Pope himself. Yes, I'm feeling a little smug about the whole affair,
and why not? The guilt I have instilled in these Indios is the very same
guilt passed on to future generations of Indios, Mestizos, and struggling
Latino actors. I founded twenty-one California missions. My favorite is
Mission Dolores in San Francisco of a sissy, digo Assisi. I envision a city
here with great bridges, of pyramids, of Forty-Niners and of Giants.
One day they will name hospitals and schools after me. One day they
will construct a stupid statue of me on Highway 280! Yet, there are
people who question whether I have performed any miracles. My
friends, let me show you un milagro.[8]
    [FATHER SERRA *slaps his hand in a command.* INDIO #1 *instinctively
    rolls forward like a trained dog.*[9]]
Parate! Bestia!
    [INDIO #1 *stands.*]
Sing, my little neophyte. Sing, my little California raisin!
INDIO #1: Fa la la la la la . . . [*Turns to* FATHER SERRA *for approval.*]
FATHER SERRA: You were flat like a tortilla. Donde esta mi whip? Sing
again . . . sing . . . sing!
    [FATHER SERRA *begins to flog the* INDIO *with a leather whip.*]
Sing, sing, sing! [*He is in a flogging sadomasochistic frenzy.*] Stop! Stop!
Vale,[1] vale, you have reached your flogging quota for the day. Go!
    [INDIO #1 *turns back upstage to join* INDIO #2. *As he turns, he ex-
    poses to the audience a perfect Tic-Tac-Toe game on his back from
    the bloody flogging.*]
FATHER SERRA: Oh, I don't know what to do with these Indios. I give
them books, college, and I still get ring around the collar. Oh well, I
guess I'll go to the Friars Club and have a smoke. Why do I speak like
Count Chocula?[2] [*Walks upstage to the* INDIOS. *To* INDIO #2:] And, I better not catch you spray-painting graffiti on the mission walls! [*Turns to*

---

5. Speak.
6. Truth!
7. Pop-oriented flamenco group, formed in France
in 1979.
8. A miracle.
9. Stand up! Beast!
1. Okay.

2. The cartoon vampire who is the symbol and
"spokesman" for the breakfast cereal of the same
name; like many versions of Count Dracula, he
has an exaggerated "Transylvanian" accent. *Friars Club*: a private club in New York City, known
for its celebrity "roasts' (public tributes that also
involve comedic insults).

INDIO #1.] And as for you, do not worry about your back. A little lime juice will help.

[*With that,* FATHER SERRA *whips* INDIO #1 *on the back again.* INDIO #1 *contorts in pain.* FATHER SERRA *crosses himself.*]

And God bless you, son. And remember, [*Chanting.*] Dominus Pizza delivers!

[FATHER SERRA *exits.* INDIO #2 *helps* INDIO #1 *from the ground; they struggle.* INDIO #1 *is singing, half-dazed from the whipping.* INDIO #2 *slaps some sense into him.*

INDIO #1 *speaks to* INDIO #2 *in exaggerated sign language.* INDIO #2 *responds with faster sign language.*]

INDIO #1: Wait, wait, my brother; you always go too fast.

[INDIO #2 *slows down.*

*Then, the* INDIOS *stop signing and start speaking in mock English accents.*]

Yes, what you say is true, my hardened-nippled brother. Father Serra is . . . an asshole!

INDIO #2: Why do you refuse to speak in our own language? You are assimilating, and why must you pretend to be a singer? You have told me on numerous occasions that you want to be a stand-up comedian.

INDIO #1: What you say is true, but the friars do not allow me to tell jokes in our native tongue. Why just last night at the Monks' Lounge, I told a joke in our language and I received fifty lashes! Would you like to see the joke? [*He gestures the joke in native sign language.*] Do you like it?

INDIO #2: Yes, but I saw that on Indio Star Search[3] last night.

INDIO #1: I remember a time not long ago when we didn't have to hold in our tummies so hard. A time when our people were proud and unafraid.

INDIO #2: We used to pray to the Grandfather Spirit and we respected Mother Earth.

INDIO #1: And then the Spaniards moved in, high atop their horses, and they tried to fix up everybody's hut and put our children in Montessori schools.[4] And, there went the barrio![5]

INDIO #2: And now our days are filled with hard labor, endless hours of work, pesticides. And we have no medical or dental benefits. Oh, why couldn't César Chávez[6] have been born now?

INDIO #1: Hark! My foolish Jerry Garcia-looking[7] brother, these Spaniards do not understand nonviolent protest. They will kill us for sure! What we need to do is mount an attack, a revolution! We must educate the others. [*Secretive.*] I know a printer in Berkeley who can print us 10,000 flyers for a bushel of corn and a pair of Birkenstocks! What is it, my Three-Dog-Night-looking brother?[8] Why does it appear that you are smelling freshly laid buffalo manure?

---

3. Reference to *Star Search* (1983–95, 2002–04), a television show in the form of a talent search.
4. The name officially refers to alternative educational institutions—primarily preschools and elementary schools—influenced by the child development theories of the Italian educator Maria Montessori (1870–1952); but unrelated schools also use the Montessori name, which is not trademarked.

5. Neighborhood. [Glossary entry]
6. See p. 760.
7. I.e., looking like the singer, songwriter, and guitarist Jerome John Garcia (1941–1995), who cofounded the San Francisco rock band the Grateful Dead in 1965 and is considered a prototypical hippie.
8. Three Dog Night was a Los Angeles pop/rock band formed in 1968.

INDIO #2: Oh, my large-buttocked friend, the flogging has gone to your head like bad peyote.

[INDIO #2 *slaps* INDIO #1 *on his flogged back.*]

INDIO #1: Ouch!

INDIO #2: Sorry. What I am trying to say is that our brothers from the south tried an insurrection and it failed. This is our destiny. History is not on our side. [*Singing.*] Que será, será. Whatever will be, will be.

INDIO #1: The future's not ours to see . . .

INDIO #2: Que Serra, Serra . . .

INDIO #1: There you go again with that Doris Day[9] existential buffalo crap again. I have no time for your Kafka[1] novel. You are falling for the Spanish Manifesto. I will mount a revolution, myself. Because, my Creedence Clearwater Revival[2] Brother, at the end of this tunnel of death, I see a light!

INDIO #2: Light, my brother?

INDIO #1: Bud Lite! [*Pulls out beer can from a sack.*] No! There.

INDIO #2: The exit sign?

INDIO #1: No, higher.

INDIO #2: Hi-yer?

INDIO #1: Hi-yah.

INDIO #2: Hi-yah?

[*They perform a mock Native American chant and dance.*]

INDIO #1: AND #2: Hi-yah, hi-yah, hi-yah, hi-yah.

INDIO #1: Stop that! See, high above the ridge. A thousand points of light, a burning bush and a dead quail.[3] Surely it is a sign. I must warn the others, I must go. [*He exits.*]

INDIO #2: My brother, my brother . . . my heart bleeds for him. Too many floggings, too much MTV. I must transcend this reality. I must call upon the Grandfather Spirit and make contact with future generations and warn them of the evil and slaughter to come.

1988

---

9. Iconic American singer and actress (b. Doris Von Kappelhoff, 1924), whose signature song was "Que Sera Sera (Whatever Will Be, Will Be)."
1. Franz Kafka (1883–1924), Czech-born author whose works, written in German, explore extreme, often ambiguous existential situations.
2. Rock band formed in El Cerrito, California, in 1967.

3. Joking references: to the "thousand points of light" mentioned in speeches by George H. W. Bush (b. 1924) as U.S. president (1989–93); to the burning bush that, according to the biblical Book of Exodus, charged the religious leader, prophet, and lawgiver Moses to lead the Israelites out of Egypt; and to Bush's vice-president, James Danforth "Dan" Quayle (b. 1947).

# *Cuentos* and *Leyendas*

Just as *dichos* and *chistes* deliver worldviews, *cuentos* (folktales) convey emotional, social, and intellectual intricacies. Animals play important roles in *cuentos* that feel like fables in the Aesopian sense. In the United States, Latino oral tradition is rooted in the Southwest, where folktales play a major role in a child's education. *Cuentos* are also important to immigrants from the Caribbean Basin.

*Cuento* also means literary short story, and numerous Latino writers (for example, Ernesto Galarza, Nicholasa Mohr, Julia Alvarez, Gary Soto, and Pat Mora) have written *cuentos* as children's literature. Daniel Venegas uses the style of the *cuento*—innocent, naïve, detached—in his novel *The Adventures of Don Chipote: or, A Sucker's Tale* (see p. 398), and Rudolfo A. Anaya does in his novel *Bless Me, Ultima* (p. 1169).

*Leyendas* (legends) involve characters, such as Juan Chililí and La Llorona, who offer common wisdom. Religion and magic often play important roles, tacitly or overtly.

## Juan Chililí[1]

There was once a man who had three sons, and the youngest was the smartest. In time the three brothers grew up, but they couldn't go out and work because a giant lived nearby. The giant killed all the people who left their houses, but no one could kill the giant.

But finally the two older brothers decided to go out and work anyway. They left home and came to a place near the giant's house and decided to spend the night hiding there. The youngest brother had also left home secretly and followed them, and he got to where the others were hiding and said, "You're cowards. I can go to the giant's house right now." His brothers were scared and said they were staying there because they didn't want to go looking for danger.

The youngest set out alone for the giant's house, and when he got there he found the giant standing in the doorway. When he saw the boy, the giant said, "What are you doing around here, where not even little birds live?"

And the boy, who was named Juan, told him, "I came here to see if you'll give us lodging for the night."

"Yes, I can do that," the giant replied.

"All right," Juan said. "Now I'll go and get my brothers." And he went and told them the giant had given them lodging for the night.

---

1. This and the next four folktales were collected from the oral tradition by J. Manuel Espinosa in *Spanish Folk-Tales from New Mexico* (Memoirs of the American Folklore Society, vol. XXX, 1937), edited and translated by Joe Hayes.

They all went there and the giant told them he had beds all ready for them. The giant was going to kill them that night, but when they lay down, Juan told his brothers, "Now let's go and get the giant's three daughters and leave them sleeping here with our kerchiefs on." And that's what they did.

A little while later the giant went in with his sword and thinking they were the brothers cut his daughters' heads off. In the morning he saw it was his daughters and said to his wife, "The one who had done all this is Juan. But let's not waste them." And they cooked the daughters and ate them.

Then after the three brothers had traveled a long way, Juan got mad at his brothers and left them and went to work at a king's house. And in the palace there was a baker who was very spiteful, and he went to the king and said, "Do you know what Juan says?"

"What?" the king replied.

"He says he can steal the giant's horse."

So Juan was sent for and the king said to him, "Juan, did you say you could steal the giant's horse?"

"I didn't say that, Señor Rey, but if I had said it, I'd do it."

"All right," the king said, "if you don't go and steal it, you'll pay with your life."

Juan Chililí didn't know what else to do. He waited until it was nighttime and then went and stole the horse and the giant didn't even know it. He delivered the giant's horse to the king.

And then the spiteful baker went and told another lie to the king. "Listen, Señor Rey," he said, "Juan has said he can bring you the head of the giant's wife."

Juan was sent for again and the king asked him, "Juan, did you say you can bring me the head of the giant's wife?"

"I didn't say that, but if I had said it, I'd do it," Juan said.

"Well, now you have to bring me the giant's wife's head, and if you don't, you'll pay with your life."

Juan went off to make his plan. He waited until the giant went out hunting, and then he went and found the giantess splitting firewood. He walked up and said, "Good afternoon, ma'am. I'll split that wood for you."

She gave him the ax and he started splitting wood. And when the giantess bent down to pick up the chips, Juan gave her a chop in the neck and killed her. Right away he cut off her head and left with it for the king's house. When he got there and handed it over to the king, everyone was amazed.

Juan Chililí stayed there at the king's house until the king began to think about how much harm the giant was doing. The king sent a party of soldiers to kill him, but the giant killed all the soldiers. And then the baker went to the king with another lie. "Señor Rey," he said, "Juan says he can bring you back the giant alive."

So Juan was called for again, and the king said to him, "Listen, Juan, have you said you can bring me the giant alive?"

"I didn't say that," Juan answered, "but if I had said it, I'd do it."

And the king told him, "Very well then, you have to bring me the giant alive, and if you don't, you'll pay with your life."

Juan told the king, "For that job you'll have to give me a new suit of clothes, a cowboy hat, new boots, a new wagon, heavy chains, and a team of fat oxen." The king gave him all of it, and Juan went to the giant's house.

"Good afternoon," he said.

And the giant replied, "What are you doing here where not even little birds live?"

Juan told him, "You should know, Mr. Giant, that the king has sent me to get one of these cottonwood trees to hollow into a trough to lock Juan Chililí in."

And since the giant didn't know who he was, he said, "All right. I'll help you make the trough myself because Juan Chililí has been doing a lot of bad things to me."

And as they were making the trough, they began to chat. When the trough was almost finished Juan Chililí told the giant, "Did you know that Juan Chililí says he can kill you and that he is the same size as you? We can find out if Juan Chililí will fit in this trough if you'll get in yourself and try it out."

The giant climbed into the trough and said to Juan, "It's a little tight."

"Good," Juan said. "Now let me fasten the top with some nails to see how I'll close it when Juan Chililí is inside."

Juan Chililí drove in a lot of nails, and then shouted, "See if you can open the top."

The giant tried hard, but he couldn't open the top. And then Juan Chililí drove in more nails until he clinched it down tight. Then he tied the chains he had brought around the trough and hitched it to the wagon. He shouted at the oxen and they started at a fast pace.

When he was near the palace, the baker came out and said to him, "Juan, Juan, give me half of the king's reward, because I've done so much for you."

"All right," Juan Chililí told him.

Juan got to the palace and the king came out to meet him. "Here's the giant," Juan told him. "You just have to pry the top of the trough with a strong tool to see that the giant is alive."

They did what Juan Chililí told them to do and found the giant alive. And the king called for Juan Chililí and said, "Now choose whatever you want."

"I don't want money," Juan said. "All I want is to be given three hundred lashes with a whip, but not until I ask for them. For now, I just want the king's baker to be given half the reward I've earned."

The king ordered that Juan's request should be granted. The baker was whipped, and he died before he had received half the lashes, but Juan still hasn't gotten his lashes. And the king has the giant in his power.

## Paloma Blanca[1]

There was once an old man and an old woman who had a son, and the son left home to make his living. He came to a palace that no one dared enter and he went inside and he heard a cat crying. And he began to pet the cat.

The cat talked to him and told him not to be afraid, that she was an enchanted princess and that the time had come for her to be freed from the enchantment and that she had to go to a lake and bathe. The cat told him she had to bathe in the form of a dove and for that reason she was named

1. White Dove.

Paloma Blanca. She fed him and told him he should stay there in the palace, and that the next day when she went to bathe herself he should follow her on a horse he would find in the stable below. The cat gave the boy a rosary and a ring, and she told him to go by the pathway and not by the road. And then the cat disappeared.

The boy slept until morning. He got up and went to saddle one of the best horses he found. He found fine clothes in his room and he dressed himself like a prince. Then he mounted the horse and set out to find Paloma Blanca.

And since he was dressed so fine and riding such a pretty horse, he said to himself, "Dressed like a prince and riding this animal, how can I travel on the path?" And just then he came to a road and he traveled down the road and not the path. And on that road lived the witch who was holding Paloma Blanca under the spell.

The old witch came out and said to him, "Where are you going?"

"I'm going to the lake to find Paloma Blanca."

"Take me with you, grandson. Take me too."

And he said he would take her. So the old woman made a lunch and she rode along with him on the horse's haunches.

When they came to the lake, Paloma Blanca was already bathing. And the old woman got out the lunch and began to eat and said, "Oh, how tasty are the sweet things of the beautiful Paloma Blanca!"

And he said, "Give me some."

The witch gave him sweet cakes and he ate them and fell asleep. And he didn't even remember Paloma Blanca.

When he woke up the old witch had gone. And Paloma Blanca said to him, crying, "If you keep up like this you'll never free me from the spell. I only have three days to bathe. Don't do this again. I want to marry you, but you have to do what I tell you. Come again tomorrow, but by the path and not by the road. Don't listen to that witch. She is the one who enchanted me." And then she told him to go back to the palace.

The next day the boy got up again and saddled the horse and left for the lake. When he got to where the road branched off he said, "Dressed like a prince and on this animal, how can I not travel on the road?" And again he left the path and traveled down the road. Again he came to the witch's house. She had a lunch ready when he got there and said to him, "Come on, grandson, take me to see Paloma Blanca bathing."

And he said all right and took her along on the horse's haunches again. When they got there, Paloma Blanca was already bathing, and the witch got out the lunch and started to eat and said, "Oh, how tasty are the sweet things of the beautiful Paloma Blanca!"

"Give some to me too," the boy said. And the witch gave him some and he fell asleep, and he didn't remember Paloma Blanca or anything.

When he woke up the witch had gone. Paloma Blanca cried and said to him, "You'll never free me from the spell this way. Tomorrow is the last time I'll come to bathe. If you don't free me this time, all will be lost. Don't go by the road, and if you do, don't eat the witch's little cakes." And the boy promised her he would do as she said.

So the next day was the last chance, and the boy got up and dressed like a prince again and saddled his horse and set out. And seeing himself so well dressed and on such a beautiful horse he said, "Dressed like a prince and on this horse, how can I not travel on the road?"

He went by the road again. And the old witch was waiting for him with a lunch and said, "Come on, grandson, take me along again." He took her again on the horse's haunches and soon they arrived. Paloma Blanca was bathing, and the old woman took out the lunch and started to eat. She said, "Oh, how tasty are the sweet things of the beautiful Paloma Blanca!"

"Give me some," the boy told her. And he ate and fell asleep again. And the old witch left. When the boy woke up, Paloma Blanca told him she was going far away and he would never see her again, and she left him there crying. The old witch came and took the princess to a faraway city where there were many rich and handsome princes.

And when the princess got to the city all the princes wanted to marry her because she was so pretty. One of them asked for her hand and the old witch wanted to marry her to him. She told everyone Princess Paloma Blanca was her daughter.

But the boy kept searching and searching for her everywhere, and finally he came to the city where Princess Paloma Blanca and the old witch lived, and the people told him that Paloma Blanca was about to marry a handsome prince. They told him only three days remained before the wedding.

He showed up looking ragged, with his rosary and his ring. Along the way he had bought a violin, and he was also a good singer. He said he wanted to play for the wedding if they would let him, and they agreed. Three years had gone by since he had last seen Paloma Blanca and she didn't even remember him.

The day of the wedding arrived and the stranger came to play. He joined the other musicians and started playing, and when the bride heard the music she was pleased by it and began to remember that she had heard that music when she was living under the spell. Later he sang, and Paloma Blanca remembered even better that she had heard those songs when she was enchanted. And then the boy took out his rosary and his ring and Paloma Blanca saw them and remembered everything. Paloma Blanca ran to hug the boy and cried, "This is my husband! This is my husband!"

"Hooray! Hooray!" said the king. "Paloma Blanca will marry the musician!"

Paloma Blanca married the boy and was freed from the enchantment, and they are living there still. And they killed the old witch.

## Chirlos Birlos[1]

There were once two compadres, one rich and the other poor, and each one had a bay mule. Every time they met up, they wanted each other's mule. The rich man's wife was always very sick. The husband brought in doctors from all over, but no one could cure her. But whenever the husband went off to tend his sheep and didn't see her, she wasn't sick at all and gave parties and everything.

1. A play on words typical of children games ("orejas / parejas, narices / lombrices"); also, a folk reference to a magical medicine that brings back happiness.

One day a friend of the rich man told him, "If you want your wife to get well, go to the sea and bring her chirlos birlos." And so the next day the rich man set out for the sea on his mule to look for chirlos birlos.

He met up with his poor compadre along the way. "Where are you going, compadre?" the other one asked him.

"Well, you see," he said, "my wife is very sick and I'm going to the sea to get chirlos birlos."

"Don't go. I'll give you a medicine so that she won't get sick again," the poor compadre said. "Get into this suitcase and let me carry you back home. And when I shout, 'Suitcase, harken to my whistle!' come out of the suitcase."

"All right," the rich man said, and he got into the suitcase and his poor compadre carried him away.

When he got to the house, the rich man's wife said, "How are you, compadre? Come in. Come in. Have you seen my husband around here?"

"Yes, comadre, he was on his way to the sea to hunt for chirlos birlos."

And the wife saucily began to set the table so that the compadre could eat. And when the table was set, she called her compadre to eat, and she sang:

> My husband has gone to the sea
> to bring chirlos birlos to me.
> Whether or not he ever comes home,
> I won't let the friar leave me alone.

Then the poor compadre said, "Suitcase, harken to my whistle!"
And the rich man came out of the suitcase and cried:

> Even if you get my bay mule from me,
> grab the friar; don't let him get away.

## The Burro and the Coyote

This one is about a poor man who was working in the fields, and at noontime he sent his burro to bring him some food. When the burro was bringing the food back, he met up with a coyote, and the coyote said, "Brother burro, let me climb up on you. My feet are full of stickers and I can't walk."

The burro felt sorry for him and let him climb up, and coyote rode along on the burro's back and ate all the food. Then he said that was as far as he was going and he got down and went away.

The burro went on and came to where his master was working, and when the master saw that the burro hadn't brought any food, he said, "Where's the food?"

And since there was no food, the master gave the burro a good whipping and told him he'd better get something for him to eat. The poor burro went away sadly and didn't know what to do. But then the burro said, "I'm going to punish the coyote for eating all the food when he was riding on me."

The burro went to the cave where the coyote lived with his wife and children. When he got there, he moved up close and opened his asshole wide and put it against the entrance to the cave. The little coyotes saw the burro's asshole and said to their father, "Papa, there's some meat!" and they started howling and saying, "I want the kidneys! I want the heart!"

The coyote went and stuck his head up the burro's ass and the burro closed it tight and caught the coyote, and then dragged him off to his master. The master took the coyote out and skinned him. He released the coyote naked, with just a little skin on his head, like a cap, and on his feet, like shoes.

The poor coyote ran away howling in pain, and the coyote's wife didn't recognize him when she saw him coming. She shouted, "Hey, you with the red cape and the yellow hat and shoes, have you seen my husband around here pulling a steer by the tail?"

## The Pranks of Pedro de Urdemalas

There were once two brothers. One was named Pedro and the other was named Juan. Their mother was very old and very sick. They had some goats, and Juan would tend them one day and Pedro would tend them the other. On the days that Pedro tended the goats, he would blow air up their asses and fill them with wind so they would look fat, with nice round bellies. But on the days Juan tended the goats, they always gave more milk.

One day when it was Juan's turn to tend the goats, Pedro stayed home to look after their mother. He started cooking a pot of cornmeal mush, and when it was ready, he went and gave it to his mother. But since the old woman couldn't eat, he kept stuffing mush into her mouth until she choked. Then he washed her and dressed her and set her up next to the door.

When he saw Juan coming, he told him that their mother was dressed and spinning wool next to the door. Juan went running to see and hit her with the door and knocked her down. Juan thought he had killed her.

"You killed my mom," Pedro said. "Now what are we going to do?"

Poor Juan started to cry.

"Don't cry. I know what we'll do," Pedro told him. And he went and saddled up a horse, and Juan helped him lift their dead mother onto its back. Then they turned the horse loose in the wheat field of a rich man who lived nearby.

When the rich man saw the horse and rider going into his wheat field and tearing everything up, he came out hollering and shouting for them to get out of there. But the horse kept going clear to the middle of the field, ruining everything. The rich man grabbed a sling and hurled a rock that hit the old woman and knocked her from the horse.

Then Pedro ran over to the rich man and told him angrily, "That's my mother! You killed her!"

When the rich man saw what he had done, he begged Pedro to forgive him, saying that he hadn't done it on purpose, that he'd only meant to scare her. But Pedro still acted angry and insisted the rich man had done it on purpose.

The rich man promised he would sponsor a wake for her and pay for the burial, and he even said he'd give the brothers three hundred pesos. So they held a wake for their mother and buried her in the churchyard at the rich man's expense.

But since Pedro de Urdemalas was so bad, God finally sent death to get him. When death got there, she found him sitting on a hilltop. He saw her coming and put a lot of pine tar on the seat next to him. Death arrived and sat on the pine tar and got stuck. She tried to take Pedro but she stayed glued to the spot and couldn't move.

Then God sent another death for Pedro de Urdemalas. But when he saw her coming, Pedro did the same thing as before. He put a lot of pine tar where death would sit and she got there and sat down and was stuck just like the other one.

Then God sent another death for Pedro and told her to watch out for him and not to get stuck in any pine tar. Pedro put a lot of pine tar where he thought she would sit, but this Death didn't sit there and didn't get stuck. She took Pedro to heaven.

When he heard Pedro was there, God told Saint Peter[1] to take him to purgatory. He was taken to purgatory and there Pedro de Urdemalas started whipping all the souls until they couldn't put up with Pedro in purgatory any longer.

God said Pedro de Urdemalas should be taken to limbo. And when he was taken to limbo, Pedro heard the unbaptized babies crying, "Water! Water!" And he started grabbing them and throwing them into the river that was nearby. As soon as they came out of the river, they flew away to heaven because now they were baptized.

And when God saw all the mischief he was doing, he ordered Pedro taken to hell. Along the way Pedro de Urdemalas made a lot of crosses and carried them in his hands, and when he got to hell, the devils took off running from the holy crosses. Pedro de Urdemalas went and put crosses in all the windows and doors and the devils couldn't go in or out.

Finally the main devil got out through the chimney and went to complain to the Lord. The Lord sent for Pedro de Urdemalas again, and when Pedro got to heaven Saint Peter came out to meet him. And Pedro de Urdemalas said, "Saint Peter, open the door for me. Let me look inside."

Saint Peter opened the door a little way so that Pedro de Urdemalas could take a look, and Pedro jumped inside. When he got inside, the Lord saw him and said, "Pedro, you will be a stone."

"But one with eyes," Pedro de Urdemalas said.

And God turned him into a stone with eyes. And Pedro de Urdemalas is still there by the doorway to heaven seeing everyone who comes inside.

# Eyes That Come Out at Night[1]

There was a boy who was told to spend the night with an elderly neighbor woman, for his parents were out of town. The boy gathered his belongings and took them to the old woman's home. He helped her with the chores, and when the time came to go to bed, he would sleep in the living room. The old woman picked up her black cat and put it outside. She went to the

---

1. Simon Peter (ca. AD 1–64), leader of the early Christian Church; according to the New Testament, "keeper of the keys of the kingdom of heaven" (Matthew 16.19).

1. Retold by Teresa Pijoan de Van Etten in her book *Spanish-American Folktales* (1990).

alcove where she slept, just off the living room, and she pulled a curtain across the doorway.

The boy was curious. He tiptoed to the curtain. He ever so cautiously peeked at the old woman. He saw her unscrew her legs and place them under her cot. He saw the old woman scratch her brown eyes so that they fell into her hand. She put them in a round saucer on a table by her bed.

The boy went back to his bed in the living room. He tried to sleep, but the black cat kept clawing at the door and crying at the window. The boy felt sorry for the black cat, and he opened the door. The cat ran into the house, slipped under the curtain, and jumped up on the table by the old woman's cot. The cat leaned over the saucer and ate the brown eyeballs.

The boy was scared and left early in the morning to go home. A day or two later, he met the old woman on the road. Her eyes glowed a deep green. He asked her politely how she was, and she said she had a terrible headache and missed his company. He said he would help her home.

When they got to her house, she invited him in for some cake. He ate the cake, thanked the old woman, and left. Outside, he bumped into the black cat. Its eyes were sunken shut. Its eyes were gone!

The boy ran home, and never went back to the old woman's house again.

## La Llorona[1]

This is a story that the old ones have been telling to children for hundreds of years. It is a sad tale, but it lives strong in the memories of the people, and there are many who swear that it is true.

Long years ago in a humble little village there lived a fine-looking girl named María. Some say she was the most beautiful girl in the world! And because she was so beautiful, María thought she was better than everyone else.

As María grew older, her beauty increased. And her pride in her beauty grew too. When she was a young woman, she would not even look at the young men from her village. They weren't good enough for her!

"When I marry," María would say, "I'll marry the most handsome man in the world."

And then one day, into María's village rode a man who seemed to be just the one she had been talking about. He was a dashing young ranchero—the son of a wealthy rancher from the southern plains.

He could ride like a Comanche! In fact, if he owned a horse, and it grew tame, he would give it away and go rope a wild horse from the plains. He thought it wasn't manly to ride a horse unless it was half wild.

He was handsome! And he could play the guitar and sing beautifully. María made up her mind—this was the man for her! She knew just the tricks to win his attention.

If the ranchero spoke when they met on the pathway, she would turn her head away. When he came to her house in the evening to play his guitar and serenade her, she wouldn't even come to the window. She refused all his costly gifts.

1. Told by Joe Hayes in *La llorona/The Weeping Woman: A Hispanic Legend* (1987).

The young man fell for her tricks. "That haughty girl María," he said to himself. "I can win her heart. That's the girl I'll marry."

And so everything turned out just as María planned. Before long, she and the ranchero became engaged, and soon they were married.

At first, things were fine. They had two children and they seemed to be a happy family together.

But after a few years, the ranchero went back to the wild life of the prairies. He would be leave town and be gone for months at a time. And when he returned home, it was only to visit his children. He seemed to care nothing for the beautiful María. He even talked of setting María aside and marrying a woman of his own wealthy class.

As proud as María was, of course she became very angry with the ranchero. She also began to feel anger toward her children, because he paid attention to them, but just ignored her.

One evening, as María was strolling with her two children on the shady pathway near the river, the ranchero came by in a carriage. An elegant woman sat on the seat beside him. He stopped and spoke to his children, but didn't even look at María. He whipped the horses on up the street.

When she saw that, a terrible rage filled María, and it all turned against her children. And, although it is sad to tell, the story says that in her anger María seized her two children and threw them into the river!

But as they disappeared down the river, she realized what she had done! She ran down the bank of the river, reaching out her arms to them. But they were long gone.

On and on ran María, driven by the fear that filled her heart, until finally she sank to the ground and lay still.

The next morning, a traveler brought word to the villagers that a beautiful woman lay dead on the bank of the river. That is where they found María, and they laid her to rest where she had fallen.

But from the first night she was in the grave, the villagers heard the sound of crying down by the river. At first they thought it was only the wind they were hearing. But when they listened more carefully, they heard words. "Aaaaaiiii . . . my children," a voice sobbed pitifully. "Where are my children?"

And they saw a woman walking up and down the bank of the river, dressed in a long white robe, the way they had dressed María for burial.

On many a dark night, they saw her walk the river bank. But more often, they would hear her cry for her children. And so they no longer spoke of her as María. They called her La Llorona (la yoh-RROHn-a)—the weeping woman. And by that name she is known to this day.

And they still warn the young ones, "When it grows dark, get inside the house. La Llorona may be about, looking for her children. Be careful! She might mistake you for one of her own children."

They tell of many children down through the years who have been chased by the crying ghost—and of some who have even been caught!

Is the story really true? Who knows? Some claim that it is. Others say that it isn't. But the old ones still tell it to the children, just as they heard it themselves when they were young. And in the same way, the children who hear it today will someday tell it to their own children and grandchildren.

# La Llorona[1]

This rendition of the mythic tale of La Llorona takes place in Ciudad Juarez.

She was, as everyone knows, a betrayed woman. After her husband left her without a single centavo, La Llorona and her three children tried to cross the border to the United States. She sold all her belongings in the town not far from Chetumal, the capital of Quintana Roo, where poverty reigns. A distant relative in Arizona (a nephew of her stepfather), to whom she had sent a desperate word, replied several months later saying he wasn't wealthy enough to provide her with the tickets but if she moved to el otro lado, the other side, he knew of a ninera always helpful to Mexican immigrants where she could place the kids during the day while she herself worked as a cleaning maid. He offered her the name and phone number of a coyote[2] who could help her in the task of deceiving the U.S. border police.

The prospect of cleaning other people's dirt didn't appeal to La Llorona, but she was very hungry and so were the kids. She decided to be at the mercy of strangers by traveling to Ciudad Juarez in whichever way she could.

Along the way people were helpful but to a certain degree. They offered an occasional tortilla con frijoles and gave them a ride on the back of a truck. The journey was extremely difficult. By the time they arrived, the second child, only three years old, had contracted diphtheria. La Llorona buried him in an unnamed pit somewhere in northeastern Nuevo Leon.

She decided not to give up, though. She contacted the coyote from a public phone, but he wanted to charge her $750. It was an astronomical amount; she didn't even have a small fraction of it. She begged him by telling the whole truth: that she had not even a roof where to stay overnight and that her children were dying of malnutrition. But the coyote hung up the phone. Many people came to him with the same litany.

On the street La Llorona's children were crying out loud. She began to ask for una lumoznita, a small charity. After a while a passer-by gave her a few pesos. He whispered to her ear that she could get a few more by selling herself once or twice that night. She sobbed in desperation.

Then she saw a feria, a town fair. An idea crossed her mind. She would use the remaining money on amusement rides for her children, and while they were on them, she would run away. The thought overwhelmed her with remorse, but she had no other alternative.

And thus, when the kids were at la rueda de la fortuna, the Ferris wheel, La Llorona escaped without looking back. She had seen some Mexican peasants being taken in the morning in the direction of the border and she followed that same road. When she reached a fence, she jumped it and moved toward a nearby river. Soon after she heard dogs barking and saw a helicopter.

---

1. This fictionalized version is by Alcina Lubitch Domecq and translated by Ilan Stavans.
2. Trafficker of illegal immigrants.

A day later La Llorona was returned to Ciudad Juarez. In punishment for abandoning her children, the Almighty condemned her to wandering eternally in search of them.

Her shrieks are still heard at dawn in the city.

1991                                                                                    1999


## The Flea[1]

Once there was and was not a rich landowner. He loved to laugh; he loved a good joke as well as any fellow. Best of all, he loved to make riddles that no one could answer. One day the rich landowner came back from a long ride across his land. He was hot and tired but in a good mood. As his worker helped him remove his heavy riding jacket, a flea jumped from the jacket to the rich landowner's nose. The rich landowner put up his hands for all to be quiet, and with one swift gesture he caught the flea in his hand.

He smiled gleefully, for now he had a great idea. He told his worker to run quickly for the *mayordomo*, the landowner's steward, and to tell him it was urgent he see him right away. The worker ran, returning with the *mayordomo*, who was anxious to know what was so important that he had to be taken away from his work.

The landowner took the *mayordomo* into his study and talked with him privately. The rich landowner asked the *mayordomo* to put out his hand. The rich landowner put the tiny flea in the *mayordomo*'s hand. "Don't crush it. I want you to feed this flea until it is the size of a cow. Don't tell anyone what it is. You yourself will lose your life if anyone finds out what I have asked of you. Now go, and come back to me when that flea is the size of a cow." The *mayordomo* nodded that he understood and left the rich landowner chuckling to himself.

You can be sure that the *mayordomo* did not tell anyone at all about the flea. First of all, he didn't want anyone to know of such a crazy idea, and second, he did not want to lose his life. He was a married man with seven children, and his job paid well. *Sí, como no.*[2]

Well, the rich landowner's wife gave birth to their first child, a beautiful girl. Shortly after her birth, the landowner's wife became very ill and died, leaving the landowner with the responsibility of raising the daughter himself. She grew quickly and well, and she loved to laugh as much as her father. Soon she was ten, and then her fourteenth birthday arrived and along with it many young men who wanted to court her. Her father became very strict and sent the young men away from the house.

One day the *mayordomo* came to the rich landowner. The rich landowner asked, "What brings you here, my good man?" The *mayordomo* reminded the landowner of the flea.

The landowner laughed and laughed. "Oh, yes, now and then I would think of that flea. Is it as big as a cow?"

---

1. Retold by Teresa Pijoan de Van Etten in her book *Spanish-American Folktales* (1990).     2. Sure, why not.

The *mayordomo* shook his head. "Well," he said, "the flea is as big as a small calf. However, sir, the flea is now very old, and I fear that soon it might die."

The landowner told the *mayordomo* to wait until dark and bring the flea to the barn. There should be no one else, or else.

That night the rich landowner and the *mayordomo* sat in front of the flea. The flea could hardly breathe, it was so fat and so old. The landowner patted the flea and said, "Good-bye, flea. Your life will not be forgotten or wasted. You will still be put to good use."

The flea died, and the rich landowner and the *mayordomo* skinned it. The *mayordomo* saddled up the landowner's best horse, and the landowner rode out into the night. He rode to a small town far to the north, to the home of an Indian drum maker. The old Indian welcomed the landowner, for wealth always followed the landowner. The landowner talked late into the night with the drum maker. Then the landowner rode home.

Three weeks passed, and the landowner saddled his horse late in the night and rode back to the old Indian drum maker. The landowner picked up a perfectly round tambourine, which he kept until his daughter's sixteenth birthday. On that day he gave it to her, telling her it would be the riddle that must be answered if she were to be married.

The daughter invited all her friends to a party, and she danced with her new tambourine. When she finished, her father clapped his hands.

"Whoever can tell me what this tambourine is made of may marry my daughter." The landowner's eyes sparkled with glee.

Many of the young men ran to him and, kneeling, told him that it was made from a goat skin, or a calf skin, or a sheepskin. The landowner laughed and laughed. They were all wrong. The daughter thought this was a good test, for she loved her father and hated the thought of having to leave him if she married.

The riddle lasted a long time—well into the daughter's seventeenth year. The landowner was by now tired of this riddle and of the thoughtlessness of the young men who tried to answer. He decided that anyone who did not answer the question correctly should be horsewhipped. That way they could have some privacy and not be so bothered by suitors. It worked. Very few men came to try the riddle.

Now, up in the hills above Chimayó[3] there happened to be a sheepherder and his family. The youngest of the boys heard of this riddle. He thought that if he answered the question he would have money and a beautiful wife. He had always had to wear his brothers' clothes, eat last, and be the first one blamed if the sheep were lost.

He decided that since he was fourteen, he would like to try his best for the rich landowner's daughter. He said good-bye to his family and put half a tortilla in his pocket. His mother wept at the thought of her little boy getting a whipping.

There is something you should know about this young sheepherder. He had spent most of his life walking up and down mountains, so he had a difficult time walking on the flat path to the rich landowner's home. As the boy walked along, he kept tripping and falling flat. At one point he fell right

3. Place in New Mexico.

down on an ant hill. He lifted his head, and there before him was a large red ant with its stinger straight out, ready to sting him.

The sheepherder said, "Oh, please don't hurt me. I fell by accident. I mean you no harm."

The ant said, "All right, but for the inconvenience of landing on my ant pile, I would like to ask you to carry me to town, for I would like to see what goes on there."

The sheepherder thought for a moment and said, "Well, I am going to the rich landowner's home first, but then I could take you to the town. Here, get in my pocket."

So they started off, and the ant wondered at the sheepherder, for he had not taken a bath in many, many months and the smell was quite strong.

Soon the sheepherder forgot that the land was flat and tripped over his own feet. This time when he fell, he almost hit a tree. On the tree was a fine fat beetle sunning himself. The beetle was frightened at this body coming at him and turned, ready to hide. The sheepherder lifted himself on one elbow and apologized for scaring the beetle.

The beetle asked where he was going, and the sheepherder told him. The beetle asked, "Can I go with you? I would like to see the inside of the rich landowner's home." And so the beetle joined the ant in the sheepherder's pocket. The beetle expressed alarm at the smell of the sheepherder, but then sheepherders are known for not taking baths.

The sheepherder had gone quite a ways when there was a bridge. The boy was so interested in the sides of the bridge that he forgot once again about his feet, and he fell. This time he fell inches away from a field mouse. The field mouse was a brave mouse and ran up to the sheepherder to lecture him about being more careful.

The sheepherder apologized and offered the mouse some of his tortilla in apology. Once the mouse heard of the journey, he wanted to come too. And so the ant, the beetle, and the field mouse shared the half tortilla with the sheepherder. Then they climbed into his pocket.

Before the afternoon sun could give long shadows to the tall trees, they came to the landowner's house. The sheepherder called out to the gate-keeper. The gatekeeper let him in, though he was shaking his head, for this boy was so young it would be a shame if he got a whipping.

The housekeeper opened the door for the shepherd boy. She had tears in her eyes. I am not sure if they were from sympathy or because the boy smelled so strongly.

The rich landowner left his bookkeeper and met the young boy. "Are you sure that you want to do this? You will be whipped if you guess wrong, you know that, don't you?"

The boy nodded.

The daughter came into the room dancing with the tambourine. She danced round and round, careful not to get too close, for the boy smelled disgusting. When she finished, the rich landowner asked the boy if he knew what the skin of the tambourine was—and would he *please* hurry, for the air in the room was thickening.

The boy asked if he could hold the tambourine. As he moved forward to take it from the daughter, he tripped over his feet and fell. The ant was thrown out of his pocket onto his sleeve. The boy got up and took the tambourine. The daughter was so disgusted by this boy that she was ready to cry. The ant crawled down the boy's sleeve onto the tambourine and walked across it. Then the ant crawled back up the sleeve to the collar of the jacket and called to the sheepherder.

"This tambourine is made from a flea's skin. I know flea skin, for one winter I shared my food with one."

The sheepherder studied the tambourine. It looked to him more like sheepskin.

Then the beetle, who wanted to know what was going on, crawled out onto the tambourine. He was climbing the boy's sleeve when the boy started toward the daughter to return the tambourine. As he did so, you can guess, he fell again. With that, the beetle landed up in his hair. The beetle edged down and hid behind the boy's ear.

The rich landowner called to the boy. "What is this tambourine made of, my son?"

The beetle tickled the sheepherder's ear and said, "It is a flea skin. Tell him it is a flea skin. Fleas are my cousins and this is a flea skin."

The sheepherder nodded his head saying, "All right, all right. It is a flea skin. I got it—it is a *flea skin!*" The sheepherder said it twice so that the beetle would stop tickling his ear.

The rich landowner stood up aghast. The daughter threw herself at her father's feet. "Please, please, father, don't make me marry this boy. He is awful. He stinks!"

The sheepherder put out his hand. "Wait a minute. It is up to *me* if I want to marry you or not. Is that not right?"

The father said, "Yes, that is right. Daughter, I am a man of my word. It is up to this boy."

The sheepherder was going to walk over to them, but decided against it. The beetle whispered in the boy's ear. "Don't take this woman. She is spoiled by too many rich things. Besides, she is too old for you. Ask for gold instead."

The boy thought this over and repeated what the beetle advised him. The father and daughter were most relieved. The rich landowner asked the sheepherder how much money he would like to have. The sheepherder pulled his pouch from his pocket. He had always dreamed of having his little pouch filled with money. "I would like money up to the top of my pouch as I stand here holding it."

The landowner called his bookkeeper and told him to bring gold.

The mouse had now awakened because there was no more falling or swaying, and he stuck his head out of the pocket to see what was happening. He heard the last of the sheepherder's request and thought this boy needed his help. The mouse climbed down the sleeve of the sheepherder's jacket and into the pouch. The mouse ate a hole in the bottom of the pouch. As the bookkeeper returned to fill it, the money fell on the boy's feet. The boy did not move, though, for the mouse was now on his shoulder telling him to hold his hands still and not say a word.

The rich landowner was as good as his word. He let the money fall through the hole in the pouch and soon the mountain of money was up as high as the top of the pouch which the patient sheepherder held.

The landowner asked if there was one more request that the sheepherder wanted to ask. The sheepherder listened to the mouse and repeated what he heard. "Yes, I need a nice wagon and two good horses to help me pull this money back to Chimayo."

The landowner was only too happy to have the sheepherder leave.

The sheepherder waved and went on his way. The ant decided that he had had enough excitement and wanted to go home. The beetle was dropped off at the landowner's barn to visit some friends, and the mouse, well, he wanted to go back to Chimayo with the sheepherder.

The young sheepherder married when he was sixteen. He married a girl he had known since he was little, and they lived in a nice modest house and had many children.

## The Boy and the Devil

Once upon a time there was a boy who ran away from home. He wanted to be rich so he left home to find his fortune. On the road he came upon a well-dressed man walking toward him. After exchanging greetings with the stranger he told him he was looking for work. The stranger replied, "I've been looking for a *mozo*, a helper. Do you know how to read?"

"Yes," replied the boy.

"That's too bad," said the stranger. "I want a boy who can't read."

Then the boy said, "Perhaps you will give work to my brother. He's slow and can't read, and he's walking way back behind me. Maybe you will meet him." And with that the boy said goodbye.

The boy then continued in the direction he was going. When he was out of sight of the stranger the boy doubled back on the road. He then put his hat and poncho on backwards and, running as fast as he could, he raced to the road. In no time he encountered the stranger once again.

The señor, or Satan as we know him, greeted the young boy once again. Indeed the devil had been tricked for he really thought this was the brother of the first boy.

"I am looking for work," said the boy.

"Can you read?" asked the devil.

"Oh no, Señor!" replied the boy.

The señor replied, "Boy, you are in luck! I have been looking for a *mozo* to keep my office and library clean. You can work for me."

And so the young boy began his work with the devil.

After a short time the boy began to peek into his master's books and drawings. Then he realized who his master was. Over time the boy began to master the devil's arts.

One day the devil caught the boy reading his book and secrets, and he was furious. In his fury the devil changed himself into the form we know so well and began chasing the boy. And just when it looked like the boy was going to get caught he changed himself into a jackrabbit.

The jackrabbit was too quick for Satan, so Satan changed himself into a fox!

And when it looked like the fox was just about ready to catch the rabbit, the boy turned himself into a dove and flew away from under the devil's very nose!

But the devil was not to be tricked by a mere boy! He suddenly changed himself into a hawk.

Now the race became fast and desperate as the hawk gained on the dove. The hawk, being faster and more skillful in the air was just upon the dove when the dove changed itself into a pebble and began to fall to the earth.

And in a flash the hawk became a grain of rice. And it too fell from the sky right behind the pebble.

When the pebble hit the ground it changed into a rooster and saw the grain of rice land right in front of it, and it ate it!

And that's why, ever since, Satan is on his guard when he's around boys.

# Canciones

Sometimes the provenance of a canción selected for this anthology is clear: a Puerto Rican bolero, a Dominican merengue, a Cuban salsa. But many of these rhythms embrace Latinidad in a way that goes beyond standard categorization. One national group easily influences another. Each piece was selected not because of its music per se or how representative it might be of its own musical genre, but on the relevance of the canción in the literary consciousness of Latinos. For example, a famous bolero by Rafael Hernández Marín, "Lamento Borincano" (Puerto Rican Lament), captures the Depression-era poverty conditions on the island that led thousands of countryside Puerto Ricans to migrate to the United States. A song performed by Celia Cruz, "Burundanga," represents her signature style through its syncopated rhythms and the connections it makes between emotional and spiritual worlds.

## CHILDREN'S SONG

*Canciones infantiles* (children's songs) by Latinos come from various geographical and historical sources. They are decisively moral tales used to educate youngsters. The following selection, "Arroz con leche" (Rice Pudding), which originated in Latin America, emphasizes traditional gender roles and points to the value of urban girls as appropriate spousal partners. The simple, rhyming poetic form makes the song easy to memorize.

### Arroz con leche

Arroz con leche,
me quiero casar
con una señorita de la capital
que sepa cocer
que sepa bordar                     5
que sepa abrir la puerta
para ir a jugar.

Con ésta sí,
con ésta no,

### Rice Pudding[1]

Rice pudding,
I'd like to get married
to a city girl
if she can cook
if she can sew                      5
if she can open the door
to go out to play.

This one yes,
this one no,

1. Translated by Ilan Stavans.

2461

| | | | |
|---|---|---|---|
| con esta señorita | 10 | this is the one | 10 |
| me caso yo. | | with whom I shall go. | |

Cásate conmigo que yo
  te daré
zapatos y medias color
  café.

Marry me, miss, and one day
  you'll own
shoes and stockings the color of
  brown.

---

# FOLK SONG

*Canciones populares* (folk songs) are often about unity and harmony among heterogeneous social groups as well as about an individual facing adversity. The selection below, "De colores" (In Such Colors), is a traditional religious Spanish ballad brought to the Americas during the sixteenth century. In the 1960s, the United Farm Workers union adopted the song as a hymn in its struggle for justice and equality, and since then the song has been recorded by artists such as Los Lobos, Joan Baez, and Tish Hinojosa. The verses consist of quintets, each of which has two repeated lines at the end. The chorus establishes the message: "Variety gives place to unity."

## De colores

De colores, de colores
  se visten los campos
  en la primavera.
De colores, de colores
  son los pajaritos
  que vienen de fuera.
De colores, de colores
  es el arco iris
  que vemos lucir.
Y por eso los grandes amores
  de muchos colores
  me gustan a mí.
Y por eso los grandes amores
  de muchos colores
  me gustan a mí.

Canta el gallo, canta el gallo
  con el kikirikí.
La gallina, la gallina
  con el cara cara cara cara.
Los pollitos, los pollitos
  con el pío pío pío pío.

## In Such Colors[1]

In such colors, in such colors
  the countryside dresses itself
  in spring's graces.
In such colors, in such colors
  the birds come to us from
  such faraway places.
In such colors, in such colors
  the rainbow shines brightly in
  our eyes.
It's enchanting, great love and
  its colors, great love and its
  colors, this love I would see.
It's enchanting, great love and
  its colors, great love and its
  colors, this love I would see.

The cock is crowing, the cock
  crows his cock-doodle-doo.
The hen is clucking, the hen
  clucks her cluck, cluck, cluck.
The chicks are peeping, the
  chicks peep their peep, peep.

5

5

1. Translated by Ilan Stavans and Harold Augenbraum.

Y por eso los grandes amores
  de muchos colores
  me gusta a mí.
Y por eso los grandes amores          10
  de muchos colores
  me gusta a mí.

De colores, de colores
  brillantes y finos
  se viste la aurora.
De colores, de colores
  son los mil reflejos
  que el sol atesora.
De colores, de colores
  se viste el diamante
  que vemos lucir.
Y por eso los grandes amores
  de muchos colores
  me gusta a mí.
Y por eso los grandes amores          15
  de muchos colores
  me gusta a mí.

Jubilosos, jubilosos vivamos
  en gracia
  puesto que se puede.
Saciaremos, saciaremos
  la sed ardorosa del Rey
  que no muere.
Jubilosos, jubilosos
  llevemos a Cristo
  un alma y mil más.
Difundiendo la luz que
  ilumina la gracia divina
  del gran ideal.
Difundiendo la luz                    20
  que ilumina la gracia divina
  del gran ideal.

It's enchanting, great love and
  its colors, great love and its
  colors, this love I would see.
It's enchanting, great love and       10
  its colors, great love and its
  colors, this love I would see.

In such colors, in such colors
  the sky dresses up in its finest
  at sunrise.
In such colors, in such colors
  the sun sends back all the
  treasures we longed for.
In such colors, in such colors a
  diamond dresses itself up in
  our eyes.
It's enchanting, great love and
  its colors, great love and its
  colors, this love I would see.
It's enchanting, great love and       15
  its colors, great love and its
  colors, this love I would see.

Jubilation, jubilation we aim for
  no matter the lives that
  confront us.
We will ease it, we will ease the
  great thirsting of the King
  who's immortal.
Jubilation, jubilation will give
  Christ one soul and many
  thousands more.
As we spread all the light that
  illumines God's grace and His
  great ideals evermore.
As we spread all the light that       20
  illumines God's grace and His
  great ideals evermore.

# CORRIDO

A corrido (from the Spanish *correr*, to run) is a Mexican ballad that tells a story, generally in a gut-wrenching way. The tradition stretches back to the *trovadores*, whose lyrics concerned romantic love. Transferred to the New World during the Spanish colonial period, the tradition spread widely in the nineteenth century and reached its apex during the Mexican Revolution (1910), when political figures such as Pancho Villa and Emiliano Zapata, and prototypes such as the female soldier La Soldadera, became the stuff of the anonymous *corridistas'* imaginations. While these older corridos detail the feats of Mexican American rebels and guerrilla fighters, also including Tiburcio Vázquez and Juan N. Cortina, contemporary corridos treat events and circumstances such as the death of the *tejana* pop star Selena, the career of the revolutionary figure Subcomandante Marcos, the Los Angeles race riots catalyzed by police brutality against Rodney King in 1992, the terrorist attacks of September 11, 2001, and Hurricane Katrina's impact on New Orleans. Corridos also explore the lives of immigrants, love, death, money, alcohol, crime, and cultural forgetfulness. The tradition remains alive wherever Mexicans and Mexican Americans live, and any topic, serious or comical, can find its way into the lyrics.

While corridos are flexible in structure, the most common stanza form consists of four to six lines. The lyrics often start by stating the date, identifying the place where the action transpired, and naming the protagonists. They announce an important historical or personal event, narrate the incidents that led to it, and conclude with a moral message stressing the universal value of the tale. Among the most famous corridos, and the first of two in this anthology, is the one dedicated to Gregorio Cortez, the legendary border Mexican American hero. In his book *With His Pistol in His Hand: A Border Ballad and Its Hero* (1958), Américo Paredes dissected the various versions of it, and the version used here rated first in his hierarchy. Paredes's research inspired the dramatic film *The Ballad of Gregorio Cortez* (1984). Another important corrido, also included here, celebrates Joaquín Murrieta (also spelled Murieta), a legendary Californian Robin Hood active in the late Gold Rush period, whose first appearance in literature was in 1853. Murrieta is the subject of several works, notably a play by the Nobel Prize–winner Pablo Neruda, a fictional account by Isabel Allende (p. 1478), and an essay by Richard Rodriguez (p. 1574).

## Corrido de Gregorio Cortez[1]

| | |
|---|---|
| En el condado del Carmen | In the county of El Carmen |
| miren lo que ha sucedido, | Look what has happened; |
| murió el Cherife Mayor, | The Major Sheriff died, |
| quedando Román herido. | Leaving Román badly wounded. |
| | |
| Otro día por la mañana,    5 | The next day, in the morning,    5 |
| cuando la gente llegó, | When people arrived, |
| unos a los otros dicen: | They said to one another, |
| —No saben quién lo mató. | "It is not known who killed him." |
| | |
| Se anduvieron | They went around asking |
|   informando |   questions, |
| como tres horas después,    10 | About three hours afterward;    10 |
| supieron que el malhechor | They found that the wrongdoer |
| era Gregorio Cortez. | Had been Gregorio Cortez. |
| | |
| Ya insortaron a Cortez | Now they have outlawed Cortez, |
| por toditito el estado, | Throughout the whole state; |
| que vivo o muerto lo    15 | Let him be taken, dead or    15 |
|   aprehendan |   alive; |
| porque a varios ha matado. | He has killed several men. |

1. Translated by Américo Paredes.

Decía Gregorio Cortez
con su pistola en la mano:
—No siento haberlo matado,
al que siento es a mi hermano.　20

Decía Gregorio Cortez
con su alma muy encendida:
—No siento haberlo matado,
la defensa es permitida.

Venían los americanos　25
que por el viento
　volaban
porque se iban a ganar
tres mil pesos que les
　daban.

Tiró con rumbo a Gonzales,
varios cherifes lo vieron,　30
no lo quisieron seguir
porque le tuvieron miedo.

Venían los perros jaunes,
venían sobre la huella,
pero alcanzar a Cortez　35
era seguir a una estrella.

Decía Gregorio Cortez:
—¿Pa' qué se valen de
　planes?
Si no pueden agarrarme
ni con esos perros jaunes.　40

Decían los americanos:
—Si lo alcanzamos ¿qué
　haremos?
Si le entramos por derecho
muy poquitos volveremos.

Se fué de Brownsville　45
　al rancho,
lo alcanzaron a
　rodear,
poquitos más de
　trescientos,
y allí les brincó el
　corral.

Allá por El Encinal,
según lo que aquí se dice,　50
se agarraron a balazos

Then said Gregorio Cortez,
With his pistol in his hand,
"I don't regret that I killed him;
I regret my brother's death."　20

Then said Gregorio Cortez,
And his soul was all aflame,
"I don't regret that I killed him;
A man must defend himself."

The Americans were coming;　25
They seemed to fly through the
　air;
Because they were going to get
Three thousand dollars they
　were offered.

He struck out for Gonzales;
Several sheriffs saw him;　30
They decided not to follow
Because they were afraid of him.

The bloodhounds were coming,
They were coming on the trail,
But overtaking Cortez　35
Was like following a star.

Then said Gregorio Cortez,
"What is the use of your
　scheming?
You cannot catch me,
Even with those bloodhounds."　40

Then the Americans said,
"If we catch up with him, what
　shall we do?
If we fight him man to man,
Very few of us will return."

From Brownsville he went to　45
　the ranch,
They succeeded in surrounding
　him;
Quite a few more than three
　hundred,
But there he jumped their
　corral.

Over by El Encinal,
According to what we hear,　50
They got into a gunfight,

| | |
|---|---|
| y les mató otro cherife. | And he killed them another sheriff. |

Decía Gregorio Cortez
con su pistola en la mano:
—No corran, rinches     55
  cobardes,
con un solo mexicano.

Then said Gregorio Cortez,
With his pistol in his hand,
"Don't run, you cowardly     55
  rangers,
From just one Mexican."

Tiró con rumbo a Laredo
sin ninguna timidez:
—Síganme, rinches cobardes,
yo soy Gregorio Cortez.     60

He struck out for Laredo
Without showing any fear,
"Follow me, cowardly rangers,
I am Gregorio Cortez."     60

Gregorio le dice a Juan
en el rancho del Ciprés:
—Platícame qué hay de nuevo,
yo soy Gregorio Cortez.

Gregorio says to Juan,
At the Cypress Ranch,
"Tell me the news;
I am Gregorio Cortez."

Gregorio le dice a Juan:     65
—Muy pronto lo vas a ver,
anda y díle a los cherifes
que me vengan a aprehender.

Gregorio says to Juan,     65
"You will see it happen soon;
Go call the sheriffs
So they can come and arrest me."

Cuando llegan los cherifes
Gregorio se presentó:     70
—Por la buena sí me
  llevan,
porque de otro modo no.

When the sheriffs arrive,
Gregorio gave himself up,     70
"You take me because I'm
  willing,
But not any other way."

Ya agarraron a Cortez,
ya terminó la cuestión,
la pobre de su familia     75
la lleva en el corazón.

Now they have taken Cortez,
Now matters are at an end;
His poor family     75
Are suffering in their hearts.

Ya con ésta me despido
a la sombra de un ciprés,
aquí se acaba cantando
la tragedia de Cortez.     80

Now with this I say farewell,
In the shade of a cypress,
This is the end of the singing
Of the ballad about Cortez.     80

## Corrido de Joaquín Murrieta[1]

Yo no soy americano
pero comprendo el inglés.
Yo lo aprendí con mi hermano
al derecho y al revés.
A cualquier americano     5
lo hago temblar a mis pies.

I'm not American
but I understand English.
I learned it with my brother
backwards and forwards.
I can make any American     5
cower at my feet.

1. Translated by Ilan Stavans.

| | |
|---|---|
| Cuando apenas era un niño | When I was still a child |
| huérfano a mí me dejaron. | my parents left me an orphan. |
| Nadie me hizo ni un cariño, | I got no affection, |
| a mi hermano lo mataron,    10 | my brother was murdered,    10 |
| y a mi esposa, Carmelita, | and my wife, Carmelita, |
| cobardes la asesinaron. | was murdered by some cowards. |
| | |
| Yo me vine de Hermosillo | I came from Hermosillo[1] |
| en busca de oro y riqueza. | seeking gold and riches. |
| Al indio pobre y sencillo    15 | I fiercely defended    15 |
| lo defendí con fiereza. | the poor and simple Indian. |
| Y a buen precio los sherifes | And sheriffs put |
| pagaban por mi cabeza. | a price on my head. |
| | |
| A los ricos avarientos, | I took money away |
| yo les quité su dinero.    20 | from the greedy rich.    20 |
| Con los humildes y pobres | I took off my hat |
| yo me quité mi sombrero. | to the humble and poor. |
| Ay, qué leyes tan injustas | Oh, these unjust laws |
| fue llamarme bandolero. | that label me a bandit! |
| | |
| A Murrieta no le gusta    25 | Murrieta doesn't like    25 |
| lo que hace no es desmentir. | the lies told about him. |
| Vengo a vengar a mi esposa, | I came to avenge my wife, |
| yo lo vuelvo a repetir, | I'll say it again, |
| Carmelita tan hermosa, | Carmelita so beautiful, |
| cómo la hicieron sufrir.    30 | how they made her suffer.    30 |
| | |
| Por cantinas me metí, | I spent time in cantinas, |
| castigando americanos. | punishing Americans. |
| "Tú serás el capitán | "You would be the captain |
| que mataste a mi hermano. | who killed my brother. |
| Lo agarraste indefenso,    35 | You came upon him unarmed,    35 |
| orgulloso americano." | such a proud American." |
| | |
| Mi carrera comenzó | My career began |
| por una escena terrible. | with a fearful scene. |
| Cuando llegué a setecientos | When I reached seven hundred, |
| ya mi nombre era temible.    40 | my name was infamous.    40 |
| Cuando llegué a mil doscientos | By twelve hundred |
| ya mi nombre era terrible. | my name was terrifying. |
| | |
| Yo soy aquel que domina | I'm the man who subdues |
| hasta leones africanos. | even African lions. |
| Por eso salgo al camino    45 | Which is why I'm on the road    45 |
| a matar americanos. | killing Americans. |
| Ya no es otro mi destino. | It is my destiny: |
| ¡Pon cuidado, parroquianos! | watch out, whoever is nearby. |
| | |
| Las pistolas y las dagas | Pistols and daggers |
| son juguetes para mí.    50 | to me are just toys.    50 |

1. Capital of the state of Sonora, northern Mexico.

| | |
|---|---|
| Balazos y puñaladas, | Gunshots and knifings |
| carcajadas para mí. | just make me laugh. |
| Ahora con medios cortados | Such short work |
| ya se asustan por aquí. | strikes fear around here. |
| | |
| No soy chileno ni extraño    55 | I'm not Chilean or a stranger    55 |
| en este suelo que piso. | on this earth that I walk. |
| De México es California, | California belongs to Mexico |
| porque Dios así lo quiso. | because that's God's will. |
| Y en mi sarape cosida | And in my serape is sewed |
| traigo mi fe de bautismo.    60 | my baptismal certificate.    60 |
| | |
| Qué bonito es California | California is so beautiful |
| con sus calles alineadas, | with its streets all aligned |
| donde paseaba Murrieta | where Murrieta has wandered |
| con su tropa bien formada, | with his formidable gang, |
| con su pistola repleta,    65 | his loaded gun,    65 |
| y su montura plateada. | and his silver saddle. |
| | |
| Me he paseado en California | I've wandered through California |
| por el año de cincuenta, | around the year 1850, |
| con mi montura plateada, | my silver saddle, |
| y mi pistola repleta.    70 | and my loaded gun.    70 |
| Yo soy ese mexicano | I'm that Mexican |
| de nombre Joaquín Murrieta. | they call Joaquín Murrieta. |

# NARCOCORRIDO

A subgenre of the corrido, with the structure and rhyme scheme of traditional corridos, the narcocorrido is a narrative song primarily about drug trafficking. Chronicling the business of drugs, exploits of drug smugglers, and battles between drug smugglers and Federal Agents, it addresses social and political issues such as poverty, injustice, and discrimination. Its most celebrated practitioners are Rosalino "Chalino" Sánchez, Angel González, Francisco Quintero, and Paulino Vargas. In the U.S.-Mexico border area, their music plays on the radio, at birthday parties, and in places such as cantinas, malls, and mechanic shops. González's "Contrabando y traición" (Contraband and Betrayal), included here, is about a pair of Bonnie and Clyde–like narcotraficantes. After they have completed their assignment, the man betrays his female partner, who ends up pocketing the payment.

| Contrabando y traición | Contraband and Betrayal[1] |
|---|---|
| *Written by Angel González* | |
| Salieron de San Isidro, | They left San Isidro, |
| procedentes de Tijuana | coming from Tijuana, |

---

1. Translated by Peermusic III, Ltd. / Peer International Corporation.

| | |
|---|---|
| traían las llantas del carro | bringing their car tires |
| repletas de hierba mala, | full of bad grass, |
| eran Emilio Varela y $\quad$ 5 | they were Emilio Varela and $\quad$ 5 |
| Camelia la tejana. | Camelia the Texan. |
| | |
| Pasaron por San Clemente, | Passing through San Clemente, |
| los paró la inmigración, | customs stopped them, |
| les pidió sus documentos, | he requested documents, |
| les dijo, "¿De dónde son?" $\quad$ 10 | he said, "Where are you from?" $\quad$ 10 |
| Ella era de San Antonio, | She was from San Antonio, |
| una hembra de corazón. | a full-hearted woman. |
| | |
| Una hembra así quiere un hom- | If a woman loves a man, |
| bre, por él puede dar la vida, | she will sacrifice her life, |
| pero hay que tener cuidado si $\quad$ 15 | you better watch out, $\quad$ 15 |
| esa hembra se siente herida, | if that woman is hurt, |
| la traición y el contrabando | betrayal and contraband |
| son cosas incompartidas. | are unshareable things. |
| | |
| A Los Angeles llegaron, | They arrived in Los Angeles, |
| a Hollywood se pasaron, $\quad$ 20 | to Hollywood they went, $\quad$ 20 |
| en un callejón oscuro, | through a dark alley, |
| las cuatro llantas cambiaron, | changing their four tires, |
| allí entregaron la hierba | they delivered the grass |
| y allí también les pagaron. | and so they were paid. |
| | |
| Emilio dice a Camelia, $\quad$ 25 | Emilio tells Camelia, $\quad$ 25 |
| hoy te das por despedida | "Today you should go, |
| con la parte que te toca, | with your share, |
| tú puedes rehacer tu vida. | you can make a new life. |
| Yo me voy pa' San Francisco, | I am goin' to San Francisco |
| con la dueña de mi vida. $\quad$ 30 | With the love of my life." $\quad$ 30 |
| | |
| Sonaron siete balazos, | Seven shots rang out, |
| Camelia a Emilio mataba, | Camelia was killing Emilio, |
| la policía sólo halló | the police found only |
| una pistola tirada, | a discarded gun, |
| del dinero y de Camelia, $\quad$ 35 | of the money and Camelia, $\quad$ 35 |
| nunca más se supo nada. | nobody knew a thing |

---

# BOLERO

The bolero, a traditional kind of Spanish romantic song, has its roots in an eighteenth-century dance. The music, inspired by love poetry, is often saccharine and melodramatic. The instrumental accompaniment consists of guitar and castanets. During the nineteenth and early twentieth centuries, the style became influential across Europe, where it was adapted to classical music and ballets by composers such as

Frédéric Chopin and Maurice Ravel. In the Americas, bolero was shaped into different modalities and became associated with patriotism and nostalgia. The music achieved widespread popularity in the 1950s throughout Cuba, Mexico, and Puerto Rico. Rafael Hernández Marín (1892–1965) fought for the United States in World War I and lived in New York and Mexico. "Lamento Borincano" (Puerto Rican Lament) is about a *jibarito*, a rural worker in Puerto Rico, portrayed in this famous song as an optimist eager to sell his products in the city market.

# Lamento Borincano[1]

### Written by Rafael Hernández Marín

| | | |
|---|---|---|
| Sale loco de contento, | | Happy as can be, |
| con su cargamento, | | with his cargo, |
| para la ciudad, ay, para la | | heading to the |
| ciudad. | | city. |
| Lleva en el pensamiento, | | His thoughts are of a world |
| todo un mundo lleno 5 | | filled with happiness, 5 |
| de felicidad, ay, de felicidad. | | oh, filled with happiness. |
| | | |
| Piensa remediar la situación | | Hoping to bring relief |
| del hogar que es toda su ilusión, | | to his home that is his life, |
| y alegre el jibarito va. | | the Jibarito goes. |
| | | |
| Pensando así, diciendo así, 10 | | And, oh so thinking, 10 |
| cantando así | | so singing, |
| por el camino: | | on his journey: |
| Si yo vendo la carga, mi Dios | | If I sell these goods, my Beloved |
| querido, | | God, |
| un traje a mi viejita yo he de | | I shall buy my wife a new |
| comprar. | | dress. |
| | | |
| Y alegre también su yegua va, 15 | | His mare is equally joyous 15 |
| al presentir que su cantar | | as she realizes his song |
| es todo un himno de alegría. | | is a true hymn to happiness. |
| Y en eso le sorprende la luz del | | And then the light of day amazes |
| día, | | them, |
| y llegan al mercado de la | | and they arrive at the city |
| ciudad. | | market. |
| | | |
| Pasa la mañana entera 20 | | He spends all morning 20 |
| sin que nadie quiera | | Without anyone wanting |
| su carga comprar, ay, | | to buy his goods, oh, |
| su carga comprar. | | buy his goods. |
| Todo, todo está desierto | | Everything, everything is deserted |
| y el pueblo está lleno 25 | | and the town is full 25 |
| de necesidad, de necesidad. | | of need, of need. |

1. Translated by Peermusic III, Ltd. / Peer International Corporation.

Se oye este lamento por doquier
de mi desdichada Borinquen.

Y triste el jibarito va
pensando así, diciendo así,
llorando así
por el camino:
¿Qué será de Borinquen,
mi Dios querido?
¿Qué será de mis hijos y de mi
hogar?

Borinquen, la tierra del Edén,
la que al cantar
el gran Gautier
llamó la Perla de los Mares.
Ahora que tú te mueres con tus
pesares,
déjame que te cante yo también.

Borinquen de mi amor . . .

This lament is heard everywhere
in my unhappy Borinquen.

The Jibarito goes back
thinking, saying,
crying thus,
on his journey:
What shall happen to Borinquen,
my Beloved God?
What shall happen to my children and my home?

Borinquen, Land of Eden,
the one called
"Pearl of the Seas"
by the great Gautier.[2]
Now that you are dying with
your sorrows,
let me sing to you as well.

Borinquen of my love . . .

# SALSA

The music theorist Cristóbal Díaz-Ayala argues that salsa is not only a musical genre but also an approach to making music. "As a sauce," Díaz-Ayala writes, "it reminds one of the different ingredients in it, but the taste is unmistakable—different. As with any sauce, it is capable of infinite changes, as long as one adds or omits some of its components. Thus, jazz, blues, pop, plena, bomba, guaguancó, and many other forms of Latin American music have been added in different combinations." The origins of salsa in the United States go back to New York in the 1920s, but the term *salsa* was not popularized until 1971, when the Fania record label produced a concert album and a series of movies devoted to the form. The publisher and artist Izzy Sanabria promoted the term, to the chagrin of old-timers such as the Puerto Rican musician Tito Puente, who commented: "Salsa is what comes out of a bottle. I play Cuban music." Today, the five principal schools of salsa are defined by their geographical locations: New York, Puerto Rico, Venezuela, Colombia, and Cuba.

Celia Cruz (Úrsula Hilaria Celia Caridad Cruz Alfonso, 1925–2003) was the Cuban diva originally known as "La guarachera de Oriente" (The guaracha singer from the Oriente province of Cuba). She symbolized—ethnically, culturally, musically—the refulgent spirit of the Cuban-exile community. As the lead singer of the group Sonora Matancera, Cruz performed music that represented her background. But as her career flourished, she collaborated with a plethora of artists and groups—among them Tito Puente, Johnny Pacheco, Arsenio Rodríguez, Willie Colón, Larry Harlow,

2. José Gautier Benítez (1851–1880), Puerto Rican Romantic poet who used this phrase in his poem "Puerto Rico."

and Henny Alvarez—her audience became international, and she intentionally symbolized a pan-American identity. During the last few decades of her life, which she spent in the United States, she also became known as "the Queen of Salsa." Cruz's song "Burundanga," written by Oscar Muñoz Bouffartique and included here, is about a potion used in shamanic rituals to induce a trancelike state. The drug is also used by professional criminals to put a victim to sleep while a criminal act is performed. *Burundanga*, an Africanism widely used in Cuba, Puerto Rico, and other parts of the Caribbean, can refer to a worthless thing or piece of junk (probably so, in this song), but it can also describe a messy situation. In Puerto Rico, it is also used to refer to a dish that mixes different things, especially a mixture of root vegetables, such as yuca, chayote, ñame, and malanga.

# Burundanga[1]

*Written by Oscar Muñoz Bouffartique*
*and performed by Celiz Cruz*

| | | | |
|---|---|---|---|
| Songo le dio a Borondongo, | | Songo hit Borondongo, | |
| Borondongo le dio a Bernabé. | | Borondongo hit Bernabé. | |
| Bernabé le pegó a Fuchilanga, | | Bernabé hit Fuchilanga, | |
| le echó a Burundanga. | | she threw Burundunga at him. | |
| Les hinchan los pies. | 5 | His feet are swollen. | 5 |
| | | | |
| Abambele: practica el amor, | | Abambele: practice love, | |
| defiende a tus hermanos | | defend your siblings | |
| porque entre hermanos se vive | | because among siblings we live | |
|    mejor. | |    better. | |
| | | | |
| Abambele: practica el amor, | | Abambele: practice love, | |
| defiende a tus hermanos | 10 | defend your siblings | 10 |
| porque entre hermanos se vive | | because among siblings we live | |
|    mejor. | |    better. | |
| | | | |
| Y nos sigue con: | | And they follow us: | |
| | | | |
| Songo le dio a Borondongo, | | Songo hit Borondongo, | |
| Borondongo le dio a Bernabé. | | Borondongo hit Bernabé. | |
| Bernabé le pegó a Fuchilanga, | 15 | Bernabé hit Fuchilanga, | 15 |
| le echó a Burundanga. | | she threw Burundunga at him. | |
| Les hinchan los pies. | | His feet are swollen. | |
| | | | |
| Monina | | Monina | |
| | | | |
| Songo le dio a Borondongo, | | Songo hit Borondongo, | |
| Borondongo le dio a Bernabé. | 20 | Borondongo hit Bernabé. | 20 |
| Bernabé le pegó a Fuchilanga, | | Bernabé hit Fuchilanga, | |
| le echó a Burundanga. | | she threw Burundunga at him. | |
| Les hinchan los pies. | | His feet are swollen. | |

---

1. Translated by Peermusic III, Ltd. / Peer International Corporation.

| | |
|---|---|
| ¿Por qué fue que Songo le dio a Borondongo? | Why did Songo hit Borondongo? |
| Porque Borondongo le dio a Bernabé.   25 | Because Borondongo hit Bernabé.   25 |
| ¿Por qué Borondongo le dio a Bernabé? | Why did Borondongo hit Bernabé? |
| Porque Bernabé le pegó a Fuchilanga. | Because Bernabé hit Fuchilanga. |
| ¿Por qué Bernabé le pegó a Fuchilanga? | Why did Bernabé hit Fuchilanga? |
| Porque Fuchilanga le echó a Burundanga. | Because Fuchilanga threw Burundunga at him. |
| Porque Fuchilanga le echó a   30 Burundanga. | Because Fuchilanga threw   30 Burundunga at him. |

---

# MERENGUE

Merengue is a lively rhythm, created with a melodeon, a type of diatonic button accordion; a *tambora*, a two-sided drum held on the lap; and a *guiro*, a percussion instrument made from a gourd. It is one of the most popular types of music in the Dominican Republic and is also very popular in Puerto Rico. Famous *merengueros* include Los Hermanos Rosario, Wilfrido Vargas, Fernando Villalona, Johnny Ventura, Cuco Valoy, Elvis Crespo, Olga Tañón, and Juan Luis Guerra. The genre has become a template for stories about Dominican immigrants in the United States. The song "Carnaval del Barrio," written by Lin-Manuel Miranda and part of his Broadway musical hit *In the Heights* (2007), is a symphony of Latino voices in a New York neighborhood.

## Carnaval del Barrio

### *Written by Lin-Manuel Miranda*

DANIELA:
  Hey . . . Hey . . .
  What's this *tontería*[1] that I'm
  Seeing on the street?
  I never thought I'd see the
  Day . . .     5
  Since when are Latin people
  Scared of heat?
  When I was a little girl

---

1. Silliness.

Growing up in the hills of
Vega Alta[2]
My favorite time of year was
Christmas time!                                                    10
Ask me why!

CARLA:
Why?

DANIELA:
There wasn't an ounce of snow                                      15
But oh, the coquito[3] would
Flow

DANIELA:
As we sang the *aguinaldo*,[4]
The *carnaval* would begin to
Grow!                                                              20
Business is closed, and we're
About to go . . .
Let's have a *carnaval del
Barrio!*

PIRAGUA GUY:
*Wepa!*[5]                                                          25

DANIELA:
*Carnaval del barrio!*
*Carnaval del barrio!*
*Carnaval* . . .

PIRAGUA GUY:
*Carnaval!*

DANIELA:
*Del barrio* . . .                                                 30

PIRAGUA GUY:
*Barrio!*

DANIELA:
*Carnaval* . . .

SONNY / PIRAGUA GUY:
*Carnaval!*

DANIELA:
*Del barrio* . . .

SONNY / PIRAGUA GUY:
*Barrio!*                                                          35

DANIELA:
We don't need *electricidad*!
Get off your butt, *avanza*!
*Saca la maraca*,[6] bring your
Tambourine
Come and join the *parranda!*[7]                                   40

PIRAGUA GUY:
*Wepa!*

---

2. Town on the northern coast of Puerto Rico.
3. Puerto Rican drink of the Christmas season,
similar to egg nog but made with rum and coconut.
4. Year-end bonus.
5. Puerto Rican expression meaning yee-hahh.

6. Move forward! / Take out the maraca!
7. Puerto Rican tradition where friends and relatives gather at someone's house during the Christmas season to play musical instruments and sing
holiday music.

DANIELA / COMMUNITY:
    *Carnaval . . .*
        *carnaval!*
    *Del barrio . . .*
        *barrio!*                   45
    *Carnaval . . .*
        *carnaval!*
    *Del barrio . . .*
        *barrio!*
    *Carnaval . . .*                   50
        *carnaval!*
    *Del barrio . . .*
        *barrio!*
    *Carnaval . . .*
        *carnaval!*                55
    *Del barrio . . .*
        *del barrio!*

CARLA:
    Ooh, me me me, Dani I have a
    Question.
    I don't know what you're            60
    *Cantando.*[8]

DANIELA:
    Just make it up as you go
    We are *improvisando:*[9]
    *Lai le lo lai lo le lo lai*
    You can sing anything,            65
    Carla, whatever pops into
    Your head
    Just so long as you sing

CARLA:
    My mom is Dominican-Cuban,
    My dad is from Chile and P.R.,         70
    Which means:
    I'm Chile-Domini-Curican . . . but
    I always say I'm from Queens![1]

PIRAGUA GUY:
    *Wepaaa!*

DANIELA / COMMUNITY:
    *Carnaval . . .*                   75
        *carnaval . . .*
    *Del barrio . . .*
        *barrio . . .*
    *Carnaval . . .*
        *carnaval . . .*            80
    *Del barrio . . .*
        *del barrio . . .*

VANESSA:
    Yo! Why is everyone so happy?
    We're sweating and we have

8. Singing.
9. Improvising.

1. A New York City borough east of Manhattan.

No power!                                                    85
I've gotta get out of here
Soon,
This block's getting worse by
The hour!
You can't even go to a club                                  90
With a friend
Without having somebody
Shove you!
DANIELA:
*Ay, por favor,*
Vanessa, don't pretend that                                  95
Usnavi's your friend, we all
Know
That he love you!
COMMUNITY:
Ohhhh!!
CARLA:
Wow, now that you mention                                   100
That sexual tension it's
Easy to
See!
VANESSA:
Yo, this is bogus . . .
DANIELA:
Haven't you noticed you get                                 105
All your coffee for free?
DANIELA / COMMUNITY:
*Carnaval . . .*
                    *carnaval . . .*
*Del barrio . . .*
                    *barrio . . .*                           110
*Carnaval . . .*
                    *carnaval . . .*
*Del barrio!*
                    *del barrio!*
NEIGHBOR:
Here comes Usnavi!                                           115
USNAVI:
Yo, yo, yo y-y-yo-yo
Now, now, everyone gather
'Round, sit
Down, listen, I got an
Announcement                                                 120
Wow, it involves large
Amounts, it's
Somewhere in the range of
Ninety six thousand!
*Atención*, I'm closin' shop!                                125
Sonny, grab everybody a
Soda-pop!
Yo, grab a bottle, kiss it up

To God,
Cuz Abuela[2] Claudia just won                    130
The lotto!
Abuela Claudia won the lotto
We're bookin' a flight for
D.R. tomorrow!

COMMUNITY:
Oh my Gah!                                        135

COMMUNITY:
*Alza la bandera*
*La bandera dominicana*
*Alza la bandera*
*La bandera puertoriqueña*
*Alza la bandera*                                 140
*La bandera mejicana*
*Alza la bandera*
*La bandera cubana*[3]

PIRAGUA GUY:[4]
*Pa'rriba esa bandera!*
*Alzala donde quiera!*                            145
*Recuerdo de mi tierra!*[5]

COMMUNITY:
Hey!
Hey!

PIRAGUA GUY / USNAVI:
*Me acuerdo de mi tierra . . .*
*Esa bonita bandera!*                             150
*Contiene mi alma entera!*
*Y cuando yo me muera,*
*Entiérrame en mi tierra!*[6]

COMMUNITY:
Hey!
Hey!                                              155

DANIELA:
Everything changes today

COMMUNITY:
Hey!

DANIELA / CARLA:
Usnavi's on his way

COMMUNITY:
Hey!

DANIELA / CARLA:
Off to a better place                             160

COMMUNITY:
Hey!

DANIELA / CARLA:
Look at Vanessa's face!

---

2. Grandma.
3. Raise the flag / The Dominican flag / Raise the
flag / The Puerto Rican flag / Raise the flag / The
Mexican flag / Raise the flag / The Cuban flag.
4. Seller of flavored ice cones.

5. Up with that flag / Raise it everywhere! / A
memento from my homeland.
6. I remember my homeland . . . / This beautiful
flag / It contains my whole soul! / And when I die /
Bury me in my homeland!

BENNY:
Everything changes today . . .
USNAVI:
Hey!
BENNY:
Goodbye, Mr. Rosario . . .                                                    165
USNAVI:
Okay!
BENNY:
I'm taking over the barrio!
USNAVI / DANIELA / CARLA:
We're getting out of the
Barrio!
DANIELA:
Hey, Mr. Benny, have you seen                                                170
Any horses today?
COMMUNITY:
Hey!
BENNY:
What do you mean?
DANIELA:
I heard you and Nina went for
a roll in the . . .                                                          175
COMMUNITY:
Hay! Hey! Ohhhhhh!

| WOMEN | MEN |
|---|---|
| Benny and Nina | |
| | Benny and Nina |
| Sitting in a tree | |
| | Sitting in a tree |  180
| K-i-s-s-i-n-g! | |
| | K-i-s-s-i-n-g! |
| *Qué bochinche!*[7] | |
| | *Qué bochinche!* |
| Nina and Benny! | |  185
| | Nina and Benny! |
| K-i-s-s-i-n-g! | |
| | K-i-s-s-i-n-g! |

SONNY:
Hold up, wait a minute!
GUYS:
Wait a minute!                                                               190
SONNY:
Usnavi's leavin' us for the
Dominican Republic?
And Benny went and stole
The girl
That I'm in love with?                                                       195
She was my babysitter first!
GUYS:
Whoo!

7. What a ruckus!

SONNY:
   Listen up, is this
   What ya'll want?
   We close this bodega,                              200
   The neighborhood is gone!
   They selling the dispatch,
   They closing the salon
   And they'll never turn the
   Lights back on 'cuz—                               205
SONNY / VANESSA:
   We are powerless, we are
   Powerless!
SONNY:
   But y'all keep dancin' and
   Singin' and celebratin'
   But it's gettin' late and this                     210
   Place is disintegratin' and—
SONNY / VANESSA:
   We are powerless, we are
   Powerless!
USNAVI:
   Alright, we're powerless, so
   Light up a candle!                                 215
   There's nothing going on here
   That we can't handle!
SONNY:
   You don't understand, I'm not
   Trying to be funny!
USNAVI:
   We're gonna give a third of                        220
   The money to you, Sonny!
SONNY:
   What?
USNAVI:
   Yeah, yeah . . .
SONNY:
   For real?
USNAVI:
   Yes!                                               225
   Maybe you're right, Sonny.
   Call in the coroners!
   Maybe we're powerless, a
   Corner full of foreigners
   Maybe this neighborhood's                          230
   Changing forever
   Maybe tonight is our last
   Night together, however!
   How do you wanna face it?
   Do you wanna waste it, when                        235
   The end is so close you can
   Taste it?
   Y'all could cry with your
   Head in the sand

I'm a fly this flag that I got
In my hand! 240

PIRAGUA GUY:
*Pa'rriba esa bandera!*

COMMUNITY:
Hey!

PIRAGUA GUY / DANIELA:
*Alzala donde quiera!*

COMMUNITY:
Hey! 245

USNAVI:
Can we raise our voice tonight?
Can we make a little noise
Tonight?

COMMUNITY:
Hey!

PIRAGUA GUY / DANIELA / CARLA:
*Esa bonita bandera!* 250
*Contiene mi alma entera!*

COMMUNITY:
Hey!
Hey!

USNAVI:
In fact, can we sing so loud
And raucous 255
They can hear us across the
Bridge in East Secaucus?[8]

COMMUNITY:
*Pa'rriba esa bandera!*
*Alzala donde quiera!*
                *Carnaval del barrio . . .* 260

USNAVI:
From Puerto Rico to Santo
Domingo,
Wherever we go, we rep our
People and the beat go . . .

COMMUNITY:
*Esa bonita bandera!* 265
*Contiene mi alma entera!*
                *Carnaval del barrio . . .*

USNAVI:
Vanessa, forget about what
Coulda been.
Dance with me, one last 270
Night, in the hood again.

DANIELA/CARLA:
*Wepa!*

COMMUNITY:
*Carnaval del barrio!*
*Carnaval del barrio!*
*Carnaval del barrio!* 275

---

8. A town in New Jersey, across the Hudson River from Manhattan.

DANIELA:
*P'arriba esa bandera!*
COMMUNITY / DANIELA:
*Carnaval del barrio!*
*Oye!*
DANIELA:
*Y cuando yo me muera*
*Entierrame en mi tierra!* 280
COMMUNITY / DANIELA:
*Del barrio!*
*Del barrio!*
COMMUNITY:
*Alza la bandera*
*La bandera dominicana*
COMMUNITY / DANIELA:
*Alza la bandera* 285
*Alza la bandera!*
COMMUNITY:
*La bandera puertoriqueña*
*Alza la bandera*
COMMUNITY / DANIELA:
*La bandera mejicana*
*Adiós, adiós, adiós . . .* 290
COMMUNITY:
*Alza la bandera*
*La bandera*
*La bandera*
*La bandera*
*La bandera* 295
*Alza la bandera!*

(*All cheer*)

---

# CHICANO ROCK

Spanish-language rock, predominantly from the Southwest and West (Houston, Dallas, Los Angeles, San Francisco), infuses songs with ethnically defined themes that spring from the Chicano experience. The genre, sometimes called Chicano rock, includes roughly two currents: one inspired by rhythm and blues, country, and rock and roll, represented by Richie Valens; and another that moves in the direction of heavy rock, blues, and punk, exemplified by Carlos Santana. But since the 1990s, Chicano rock has evolved in various directions, incorporating boleros, funk, and Tejano music. Its most famous singers and groups are Trini López, Mark Guerrero, Sir Douglas Quintet, War, Los Lobos, El Chicano, Los Ilegales, Ozomatli, and Quetzal. The group Los Lobos (The Wolves) was founded in the 1970s. Their lyrics generally address the history and identity of Mexican Americans in Los Angeles. "Good Morning Aztlán" (2002), included here, looks for ways to make the foundational myth of Aztlán tangible today.

# Good Morning Aztlán

*Written by David Hidalgo and Louie Pérez and performed by Los Lobos*

There's a tattoo heart
With an arrow through the middle
Of a name that looks like Joe
And a young girl's looking
At her makeup in the mirror                    5
Puts a little gold ring on her toe

I gotta say one, two, three
More things before I go on

There's a sharp dressed man
Playing something on a fiddle                   10
In the backyard right next door
And everybody's mother
Is cooking something in the kitchen
Got dishes stacked ceiling to floor

I gotta say one, two, three                     15
More things before I go on

You can't run and try to hide away
Here it comes, here comes another day

A red rooster crows
A little Mexican tune                           20
On the chain link fence by the gate
Somebody's daddy's out there
Honkin' on the horn
Hurry up, we're gonna make him late

I gotta say one, two, three                     25
More things before I go on

You can't run and try to hide away
Here it comes, here comes another day
If you're long down that highway
No matter where you are                         30
You're never really far
Good morning Aztlán

There's a big fat heart
With an arrow through the middle
Of this place that I call home                  35
And when I get lost
And don't even got a nickel
There's a piece of dirt I call my own

I gotta say one, two, three
More things before I go on                      40

You can't run and try to hide away
Here it comes, here comes another day
You can't run to try to hide away
Here it comes, here comes another day
Where you are, never really far away                    45
Good morning Aztlán

---

# LATIN POP

Since World War II, pop music has developed new branches in response to the growing diversification of American society. Latin pop, which combines ingredients from musical forms such as salsa (see above), samba, cumbia, banda, flamenco, tango, vallenato, reggae, and norteño, is among the most commercially successful of these new branches. Top performers include Gloria Estefan, Enrique Iglesias, Juan Gabriel, Thalia, Luis Miguel, Marc Anthony, and Shakira, who typically treat romantic themes. The Puerto Rican–born Ricky Martin (Enrique José Martín Morales, b. 1971) was originally part of the Latin boy band Menudo. His single "Livin' la Vida Loca" (2004), written by Desmond Child and Robi Rosa and included here, became an international hit and an unofficial national anthem among young Latinos experiencing angst over life in the United States.

## Livin' la Vida Loca

### Written by Desmond Child and Robi Rosa and performed by Ricky Martin

She's into superstition
Black cats and voodoo dolls
I feel a premonition
That girl's gonna make me fall
She's into new sensation                                5
New kicks in the candlelight
She's got a new addiction
For every day and night

She'll make you take your
Clothes off and go dancing in the rain                  10
She'll make you live her crazy life
But she'll take away your pain
Like a bullet to your brain

Upside inside out
She's livin' la vida loca                                15
She'll push and pull you down
She's livin' la vida loca
Her lips are devil red

And her skin's the color of mocha
She will wear you out                                    20
Livin' la vida loca (c'mon)
Livin' la vida loca (c'mon)
She's livin' la vida loca

Wake up in New York City
In a funky cheap hotel                                   25
She took my heart
And she took my money
She must've slipped me a sleepin' pill

She never drinks the water
Makes you order French Champagne                         30
Once you've had a taste of her
You'll never be the same
Yeah, she'll make you go insane

Upside inside out
She's livin' la vida loca                                35
She'll push and pull you down
She's livin' la vida loca
Her lips are devil red
And her skin's the color of mocha

She will wear you out                                    40
Livin' la vida loca
Livin' la vida loca
She's livin' la vida loca

She'll make you take your
Clothes off and go dancing in the rain                   45
She'll make you live her crazy life
But she'll take away your pain
Like a bullet to your brain

Upside inside out
She's livin' la vida loca                                50
She'll push and pull you down
She's livin' la vida loca
Her lips are devil red
And her skin's the color of mocha
She will wear you out                                    55
Livin' la vida loca

Upside inside out
She's livin' la vida loca
She'll push and pull you down
Livin' la vida loca                                      60
Her lips are devil red
And her skin's the color of mocha
She will wear you out

Livin' la vida loca
Livin' la vida loca                                          65
Livin' la vida loca
Livin' la vida loca

---

# HIP-HOP

Hip-hop is part of an artistic and cultural movement that includes graffiti art and breakdancing. This movement emerged among African Americans and Latinos in New York City in the 1970s, although hip-hop achieved the peak of its popularity in later decades. In hip-hop, one or more rappers deliver spontaneous-seeming autobiographical tales to assonant, syncopated musical rhythms created over backbeats and scratching by a DJ on turntables. The lyrics address drugs, urban violence, and alienation, and they regularly are at the heart of international controversies about the function and impact of music and the role of the artist, especially one from an ethnic minority. Cypress Hill, a hip-hop group from South Gate, California, was the first Latino group to have multiplatinum albums. Its song "Latin Lingo" (1991), included here, is among the most prominent symbols of the dissemination of Spanglish. Delivered in a "broken lingo" that involves neologisms, fluid syntax, and evasive meaning, the lyrics explore the unstable nature of code switching by Latino youth. They suggest that a unique aesthetic, "funky bilingual," has emerged.

## Latin Lingo

*Written by Senen Reyes, Louis Freeze, and Lawrence Muggerud
and performed by Cypress Hill*

Maagghhh, let's start the fuckin' show, ah?

[*Sen Dog*]
Freak to the funk that no one else is bringing
Sen Dog with the funky bilenge
Yeah that's the nombre, heard the homey
Peace to Mellow and Frost en el deporte                      5
Sen Dog is not kid of veterano
I'm down, another fried hispano
One of the many of the Latin de este año
And I got plenty for the Jennies tryin to hound dog
But wait, they're clownin' on me cause of my language         10
I have to tell 'em straight up, it's called Spanglish
Now who's on the pinga tha gringo
Tryin' to get paid, from the funky bilingual

[*Chorus: B-Real and Sen Dog*]
Latin lingo, baby (funky bilingual), funky bilingual
Yeah, funky bilingual!                                        15

Latin lingo, baby (funky bilingual), funky bilingual
It's the latin lingo!

[Sen Dog]
Cuando entro, when I come in, suckers fronted
Me mira another bilingual from villa
Vengo con un ejemplo, check the tiempo                        20
Ahhh . . . esta chingón el instrumento
Ya oiste, como somos
Yo no jodo, I gots the soul dose
And you can hear it, en las congas
Tribal ceremony as the Hill gets stronger                     25
Don't be such a leper, what u got for la cabeza?
Hey homes, pass the cerveza
Before I have to go and push up on your resa
Hhhmm, she's fine, son que fresca
Here, homes, have a hit of this yesca                         30
Di yo enseño the leño lo prendo
Now you know that I am in the centro
Where you live, si tu puedes
Nowadays you ain't shit without your puentes
Something like it's gangbang, vatos quieren BANG BANG!         35
Could of hung out with them, now you callin me a insane
Salte de mi cara, sal de mi camino
Make way for the funky bilingual

[Chorus: B-Real and Sen Dog]
Latin lingo, baby (funky bilingual), funky bilingual
Funky bilinguals, hoe!                                        40
Latin lingo, baby (funky bilingual), funky bilingual
It's the Latin lingo, baby!
Latin lingo, baby (funky bilingual), funky bilingual
Funky bilingual . . .
Some of that old Latin funk, know what I'm sayin?             45

[Sen Dog]
(What's up, homey? Don't you know me?) Simón!
(Ain't you the brother of the más pingón?) Straight up
And I'm down with La Raza
Kid Frost got my back, BOO-YAA! in la casa
Cause everyday things get a little crazier                    50
As I step to the microphone area
First I claim my city, puro Los Angeles
Yeah (you know, homes), that's where the calles is
Vato wouldn't know me, along with the heinas
Catchin' all them slippin', for they such a one-timer         55
So when you see me at the party or the baile
Before I got here I was gaffled in the calle
Troop like a vacho who said I was borracho
Had an attitude, tried to play me macho
Just relax, calmado mijo                                      60
Sen Dog with the funky bilingual

[*Chorus: B-Real and Sen Dog*]
Latin lingo, baby, funky bilingual
Funky bilingual
Latin lingo, baby, funky bilingual
Funky bilingual                                                                   65
Latin lingo, baby, funky bilingual
Funky bilingual . . . funky, baby!

Yeah, I'd like to send peace, to my homeboy B-Real
Mellow Man Ace, Kid Frost, Ralph M the Mexican
And we're out                                                                     70

---

# REGGAETÓN

Reggaetón (also spelled reguetón) originated in Panama, but acquired prominence and its name in Puerto Rico. It mixes Latin and other musical styles that include reggae, bomba, plena, merengue, bachata, rap, hip-hop, electronica, and dancehall. Its lyrics switch from Spanish to English to Spanglish and are sometimes violent, racist, sexually explicit, or demeaning to women and various ethnic groups. But they also capture the anger, skepticism, and rebelliousness of those who have been kept at the fringes of society. Ivy Queen (Martha Ivelisse Pesante, b. 1972) is a Puerto Rican composer and singer known as "La diva," "La gata" (Catwoman), "La caballota" (The Big Mare), and "La reina del reggaetón" (The Queen of Reggaetón). Her debut single "Somos raperos pero no delincuentes" (We're Rappers but Not Delinquents), a hit in the 1990s, is about stereotypes.

| Somos raperos<br>pero no delincuentes | We're rappers<br>but not delinquents[1] |
|---|---|
| *Written and performed by Ivy Queen* | |

(Ivy Queen)
somos raperos pero no
    delincuentes
así que me voy a tirar
    la rima con Vico

(Vico C)
yeah yeahh                                    5
óyeme yo quiero que . . .
    compatir tarima de verdad pa'
    mí es un honor también
y dice

(Ivy Queen)
we're rappers but not
    delinquents
so I'll bust
    a rhyme with Vico

(Vico C)
yeah yeahh                                    5
listen to share . . .
    the stage right here
    is my honor too
and so it goes

---

1. Translated by Ilan Stavans.

| | | | |
|---|---|---|---|
| aquí te tengo | 10 | here i got | 10 |
| un estilo que | | a style | |
| se llama hip-hop | | called hip-hop | |

| | | | |
|---|---|---|---|
| soy un don't stop mi lyrica dice | | i'm a don't stop my lyrics say | |
| patz patz patz | | patz patz patz | |
| aniquilando la maldad | 15 | destroy the evil | 15 |
| de la concorra | | of competition | |
| deberás de hablar demasiado | | need to talk lots | |
| o es astuta como la zorra | | a sharp lady fox | |
| y para que no me tumben | | so i don't drop | |
| y me pulsen tengo que ignorar | 20 | and i don't pop i will ignore | 20 |
| todas las cosas que por envidia | | what their envy | |
| dicen los que | | says and their | |
| maldicen | | curse | |
| pues no han logrado lo | | 'cause they've done worse | |
| que quieren y se dedican | 25 | so they spend their time | 25 |
| a decir palabras que me hieren | | on hurtful words | |
| pero no pueden cumplir a lo que | | and though they want me gone | |
| siempre vienen | | that won't go on | |
| ese deseo de eliminarme | | 'cause i have talent | |
| porque tengo talento | 30 | that they | 30 |
| que no tienen | | don't have | |

| | | | |
|---|---|---|---|
| aprovechando cada conversación | | working conversations | |
| que le de razón | | that seem right | |
| para no exceder a mi condición | | so i stay within myself | |
| usando la química extra peligrosa | 35 | using extra-dangerous chemistry | 35 |
| de los que supieron hoy en día | | from those who knew | |
| todavía lo gozan | | and who use it still | |
| pero aprendí cuando me levanté | | i found out when i came up | |
| para obtener lo que quiero | | to get what i want | |
| que con una mano se pueden | 40 | use an outstretched hand | 40 |
| encontrar a los amigos sinceros | | to find true friends | |
| yeahh y todos aquellos | | yeahh and everybody | |
| que no saben de mí | | who doesn't know me | |
| el que te canta | | the one whose singing | |
| es the V to the I to the C | 45 | is name V then I to the C | 45 |
| y añadiéndole una O | | and add O | |
| soy de tierra | | i'm from the earth | |
| y eso siempre es un orgullo | | and that's my pride | |
| pa' mí chequean | | they check me out | |
| ahora que se guillen por la fama | 50 | 'cause they're into fame | 50 |
| que los sube que no lloren | | 'cause those who rise don't cry | |
| cuando los bajemos | | when we bring them down | |
| de esa nube | | from that cloud | |
| pues el que echa la | | if you toss humility aside | |
| humildad para un lado | 55 | you'll get eaten up made up | 55 |
| termina engabanado, | | surrounded yeahh | |
| maquillado, rodeado yeahh y | | that's what they say | |
| dice asi y dice así Ivy | | this way Ivy | |
| yeahhh gracias!! | | yeahhh thanks!! | |

(Ivy Queen)
un aplauso a Vico                              60
   que esta noche comparte
   conmigo
al maestro Vico C vamos a darle
   un aplauso porque el hombre
   se lo merece                                65

(Ivy Queen)
a hand for Vico                                60
   who is sharing the stage with
   me
the master Vico C let's give him
   a hand cause the man
   deserves it                                 65

# Appendix 1:
# Chronology—Literature and
# History

1492   Christopher Columbus embarks on the first of his four voyages across the Atlantic Ocean. He sails from the Canary Islands to the Bahamas and then onward to Hispaniola (the island that now consists of Haiti and the Dominican Republic). He also arrives at the island he names Juana (Cuba). This same year, Spain expels its Jewish population and defeats the Moors in their last stronghold in Granada. The Spanish lexicographer Antonio de Nebrija publishes the first grammar of the Spanish language.

1493   During his second voyage, Christopher Columbus arrives at the island he names Isla de San Juan Bautista (Puerto Rico).

1508   Juan Ponce de León begins the colonization of Puerto Rico. The next year, he is appointed governor of the island.

1513   Juan Ponce de León lands on Florida's east coast.

1521   Hernán Cortés conquers Tenochtitlán (present-day Mexico City).

1524   The Spanish Crown establishes the Consejo de Indias (Council on the Indies) to help administer the new colonies.

1527   Álvar Núñez Cabeza de Vaca joins the expedition to Florida of *Adelantado* Pánfilo de Narváez. After surviving a shipwreck, Cabeza de Vaca, the Moroccan slave Estevanico, Andrés Dorantes, and Alonso del Castillo Maldonado wander from Florida to Arizona, returning to Mexico City in 1536.

1542   Álvar Núñez Cabeza de Vaca publishes *La relación* (known in English as *Chronicle of the Narváez Expedition*) in Spain.

1552   Fray Bartolomé de Las Casas finishes writing *Brevísima relación de la destrucción de las Indias* (most recently translated as *The Devastation of the Indies*). He is the most vocal opponent of the Spaniards' treatment of the indigenous population in the Americas, behavior known as "the black legend."

1565   The Spanish found St. Augustine, Florida.

1598   Juan de Oñate begins the colonization of New Mexico.

1605   "El Inca" Garcilaso de la Vega publishes *La Florida del Inca* (The Florida of the Inca) in Lisbon.

**1607**   The British found a settlement at Jamestown, Virginia.

**1607–08**   The Spanish found a settlement (La Villa Real de la Santa Fé de San Francisco de Asís) at what becomes Santa Fe.

**1610**   Gaspar Pérez de Villagrá publishes *La historia de la Nueva México* (The History of New Mexico), an epic poem about the conquest of the Acoma Indians in what is now New Mexico.

**1620**   On the *Mayflower*, British Pilgrims travel from Plymouth, England, to the New World.

**1666**   The Spanish found San Antonio (officially known as San Antonio de los Llanos).

**1680**   The Pueblo Revolt unfolds. Spanish forces retreat to El Paso del Norte (today Ciudad Juárez, Mexico).

**1696**   The second Pueblo Revolt takes place.

**1700**   The Jesuit missionary Fray Eusebio Francisco Kino establishes a mission at San Xavier del Bac, near present-day Tucson, Arizona.

**1763**   The Treaty of Paris (1763) is signed, ending the Seven Years' War/ French and Indian War. It transfers ownership of Florida from Spain to England.

**1766**   Spain founds the presidio of San Francisco, its northernmost settlement.

**1767**   The Spanish Crown expels the Jesuits from its empire, including the New World.

**1769**   Captain Gaspar de Portolá and Fray Junípero Serra explore and settle Alta California.

**1774**   Led by Captain Juan Bautista de Anza, an expedition travels from Tubac (south of Tucson, Arizona), along the Gila River to the Colorado River, onward to Alta California, and then back to Tubac.

**1776**   The 13 British colonies sign a declaration of independence, a year after the beginning of hostilities that will become the American Revolutionary War.

**1783**   The Treaty of Versailles ends the Revolutionary War, establishing the United States. The treaty also returns Florida to Spanish control.

**1803**   The Louisiana Purchase virtually doubles the size of the United States.

**1810**   The Mexican War of Independence is among the first attempts in Latin America to break from Spanish control. It concludes with the formation of a short-lived republic. (Throughout the nineteenth century, other nations in Latin America form republics.)

**1819**   The Adams-Onís Treaty, settling a border dispute between the United States and Spain, grants the former most of Florida.

**1822**   Joseph Marion Hernández, a delegate from the Florida territory, becomes the first Latino in the U.S. Congress.

**1823**   The Monroe Doctrine is proclaimed. It states that European nations must not interfere in the activities of the Americas and that the United States will reciprocate by not interfering in the affairs of Europe. This same year, Father Félix Varela is forced to leave Cuba by Spanish colonial authorities. Erasmo Seguín, a Texas delegate to the U.S. Congress, helps pass a colonization act designed to bring more Anglo settlers to Texas.

**1824**   In New York City, Félix Varela starts the separatist newspaper *El Habanero* and José María Heredia writes his poem "Oda al Niágara" (Ode to Niagara). Between this year and 1830 (when, through the April 6

Law, Mexico voids incomplete land contracts and allows immigration to specific sites), thousands of Anglo families enter East Texas. They acquire hundreds of thousands of free acres and buy land cheaply.

**1829** Slavery is abolished in Mexico.

**1833** Mexico secularizes its missions, including those north of the Rio Grande.

**1834** After 350 years, the Holy Office of the Inquisition, active in Spain and the Americas, is officially abolished.

**1835** Félix Varela begins publishing *Cartas a Elpidio sobre la impiedad, la superstición y el fanatismo en sus relaciones con la sociedad* (translated as *Letters to Elpidio*).

**1836** In San Antonio, the Battle of the Alamo is fought between the Mexican government and Texas rebel forces. Texas becomes independent after the Battle of San Jacinto.

**1845** The American editor and columnist John L. O'Sullivan first uses the phrase *manifest destiny*, in an editorial advocating the U.S. annexation of Texas.

**1846–48** The Mexican-American War is fought between the United States and Mexico. For a brief while, U.S. troops occupy Mexico City.

**1848** The Treaty of Guadalupe Hidalgo is signed between the United States and Mexico. It stipulates that for 15 million dollars Mexico gives to the U.S. the territories known today as California, Arizona, Nevada, New Mexico, Colorado, Utah, and Wyoming. The United States now stretches from the Atlantic to the Pacific.

**1851** Antonio María Osio y Higuera finishes writing *La historia de Alta California* (The History of Alta California), the earliest written record of the territory.

**1853** The Gadsden Purchase Treaty, signed by the United States and Mexico, grants the former a parcel of land known as the Mesilla region. This same year, Joaquín Murrieta, a folk hero considered the Mexican American Robin Hood, is killed, allegedly by the California State Rangers, after a $5,000 reward is posted for his head. At locations in California, Murrieta's head is displayed, floating in brandy, and people pay to see it. (The head is lost during the San Francisco Earthquake of 1906.)

**1855** The new American state of California passes "greaser laws," which discriminate against Mexican Americans, American Indians, and African Americans. *El Trovo del Viejo Vilmas y Gracia*, written anonymously, is performed.

**1862** The U.S. government passes the Homestead Act. This legislation allows squatters to settle vacant land—often owned by Mexican Americans fighting legal battles for their ranches—upon the condition of improving it.

**1865** In New York City, Antillean separatists found the Sociedad Republicana de Cuba y Puerto Rico (Republican Society of Cuba and Puerto Rico).

**1867** Puerto Rican patriot Ramón Emeterio Betances issues his proclamation "Los diez mandamientos de los hombres libres" (The Ten Commandments of Free Men), also known as "You Shall Be Free."

**1868** In Puerto Rico on September 23, the *Grito de Lares* independence revolt begins and is crushed by the Spanish army in a few days. In Cuba on October 10, the *Grito de Yara* insurrection begins the Ten Years' War of independence against Spain. During the war, many Puerto Ricans and Cubans seek exile in the United States and other countries.

1869    Eugenio María de Hostos arrives in New York City from Spain and writes for the separatist newspaper *La Revolución*.

1871    Esteban Bellán becomes the first Latino to play on a professional baseball team in the United States, the Troy Haymakers.

1872    María Amparo Ruiz de Burton anonymously publishes *Who Would Have Thought It?*, the first novel by a Latino or Latina written in English.

1876    In Puerto Rico, Lola Rodríguez de Tió publishes her poetry collection *Mis cantares* (My Songs).

1880    Cuban patriot José Martí moves to New York City. He leaves New York shortly thereafter to reside in Caracas, Venezuela, but returns to New York and lives there from 1881 until 1895.

1885    María Amparo Ruiz de Burton publishes her novel *The Squatter and the Don*, which focuses on the land disputes in California that resulted from the Treaty of Guadalupe Hidalgo.

1888    Eugenio María de Hostos publishes his collection of ethical essays *Moral social* (Social Morals).

1889    Sotero Figueroa arrives in New York City from Puerto Rico, joins the Antillean separatist movement, and opens a printing press.

1891    José Martí publishes *Versos sencillos* (Simple Verses). This same year, Arturo Alfonso (Arthur A.) Schomburg and Francisco Gonzalo "Pachín" Marín arrive in New York City from Puerto Rico and join the Antillean separatist movement. Marín starts the revolutionary newspaper *El Postillón*.

1892    In New York, José Martí founds the Partido Revolucionario Cubano (Cuban Revolutionary Party) and its official newspaper, *Patria*. This same year, Lola Rodríguez de Tió joins the separatist émigrés in New York. Eusebio Chacón publishes his stories "El hijo de la tempestad" (The Son of the Storm) and "Tras la tormenta la calma" (The Calm after the Storm). Francisco Gonzalo "Pachín" Marín publishes his poetry collection *Romances*. José Policarpo Rodríguez begins dictating to G. B. Winton his memoir *The Old Guide: Surveyor, Scout, Hunter, Indian Fighter, Ranchman, Preacher: His Life in His Own Words*, which he continues dictating "at odd times" during the following years and finishes in 1897.

1895    The second Cuban War for independence unfolds. José Martí dies in combat on Cuban soil. His oeuvre becomes a symbol of resistance and affirmation among Cubans and throughout the Hispanic world.

1897    Miguel Antonio Otero Jr. becomes governor of the Territory of New Mexico, a position he holds until 1906. He chronicles his life as a frontiersman in *My Life on the Frontier 1864–1882* (1935), *My Life on the Frontier 1882–1897* (1939), and *My Nine Years as Governor of the Territory of New Mexico 1897–1905* (1940).

1898    The Spanish-American War is fought between Spain and the United States, after the latter intervenes in the ongoing war between Spain and Cuba. The Spanish-American War ends with the signing of the Treaty of Paris (1898). Spain, a longstanding colonial empire in the Caribbean Basin, loses its last New World colonies—the territories Cuba and Puerto Rico—and also the Philippine Islands to the United States. The United States becomes the dominant power in the region. This same year, Francisco Gonzalo "Pachín" Marín's poetry volume *En la arena* (On the Sand) is published posthumously. In New York, Eugenio María de Hostos founds the Liga de Patriotas Puertorriqueños (League of Puerto Rican Patriots), with the goal of requesting that the U.S. government allow Puerto Ricans to decide their political future.

**1900**  José Enrique Rodó, Uruguayan man of letters, publishes his ground-breaking essay "Ariel," in which he calls for Latin American youths to resist the temptation of becoming like their counterparts in the United States. This same year, the U.S. government passes the Foraker Act, which establishes a civilian government in Puerto Rico after two years of U.S. military rule.

**1901**  The U.S. government passes the Platt Amendment, which gives the United States control over Cuban foreign affairs and establishes a military base in Guantánamo, Cuba. This same year, Mexican American ranch hand Gregorio Cortez is captured in Texas and thus becomes the subject of legends and corridos. In New York, Luis Muñoz Rivera founds the newspaper *The Puerto Rico Herald*.

**1910**  The Mexican Revolution begins as a refutation of the 32-year dictatorship of Porfirio Díaz. The insurgent leaders, supporting future president Francisco Indalecio Madero, are Francisco "Pancho" Villa and Emiliano Zapata. The number of casualties over the next decade is estimated at around 1.5 million. Mexicans escape by migrating to the United States in waves.

**1913**  In New York City, the Spanish-language newspaper *La Prensa* is founded. (In 1963, it merges with *El Diario*, founded in 1947.)

**1914**  The United States invades Veracruz, Mexico. This same year, the United States completes the Panama Canal. Forty-eight miles long, it connects the Atlantic and Pacific Oceans.

**1916**  Bernardo Vega migrates to New York from Puerto Rico. This same year, the Mexican writer Julio C. Arce, aka Jorge Ulica, starts publishing *Crónicas diabólicas* (Diabolical Tales). He concludes the effort the year of his death, 1926. Vicente J. Bernal's poetry collection *Las primicias* (First Fruits) is published posthumously. U.S. Marines invade the Dominican Republic, purportedly to calm insurrections and bring order; they remain until 1924.

**1917**  The U.S. Congress approves the Jones Act, which grants U.S. citizenship to Puerto Ricans without altering the island's colonial status. Citizenship facilitates Puerto Rican migration to the mainland. This same year, the Immigration Act of 1917, the first U.S. legislation affecting the U.S.-Mexico border, institutes a literacy requirement for immigrants from Mexico.

**1918**  Jesús Colón arrives in New York City from Puerto Rico.

**1919**  U.S. Marines invade Honduras, purportedly to maintain order in an atmosphere of revolution. Beginning this same year, the Volstead Act, officially known as the National Prohibition Act, inadvertently bolsters U.S. tourism to Latin America and the Caribbean Basin.

**1924**  The U.S.-Mexican Border Patrol is established to police the border.

**1925**  José Vasconcelos, a Mexican philosopher and diplomat, publishes his book *The Cosmic Race*, which argues that the *mestizo* race will emerge and eventually lead the globe. This same year, William Carlos Williams publishes his nonfiction book *In the American Grain*.

**1926** Puerto Ricans and other Latinos are attacked by non-Latinos in what is known as the Harlem Riots. Also this year, the Spanish-language newspaper *La Opinión* is founded in Los Angeles.

**1927** In New York City, the Liga Puertorriqueña e Hispana (Puerto Rican and Hispanic League) is founded to unite Latinos, defend their rights, and promote their welfare. This same year, Bernardo Vega purchases the Spanish-language newspaper *Gráfico* and becomes its editor.

**1928** Daniel Venegas publishes *Las aventuras de Don Chipote: o, Cuando los pericos mamen* (Adventures of Don Chipote: or, When Parrots Suckle).

**1929** The League of United Latin American Citizens (LULAC) is founded, in Corpus Christi, Texas. In New York this same year, Federico García Lorca, an Andalusian poet, begins studying English at Columbia University, where he writes his influential collection *Poeta en Nueva York* (Poet in New York).

**1930** With U.S. support, General Rafael Leonidas Trujillo takes control of the Dominican Republic.

**1931** Manuel Gamio, a Mexican anthropologist interested in the indigenous people of Mesoamerica as well as in the flow of labor workers to the United States, having moved north of the Rio Grande to denounce corruption in his native country and working at the Social Science Research Council in Washington, D.C., publishes *The Mexican Immigrant: His Life Story*. The book, which includes autobiographical documents, exerts a strong scholarly influence in the fields of sociology and ethnography.

**1933** The administration of U.S. president Franklin D. Roosevelt reverses the policy of having English as the official language of Puerto Rico. President Roosevelt also establishes the Good Neighbor Policy, which renounces military intervention in Latin America and establishes the idea of Pan-Americanism.

**1934** The Platt Amendment is annulled.

**1936** Felipe Alfau publishes the novel *Locos: A Comedy of Gestures*. This same year, George Santayana—like Alfau, an immigrant from Spain—lands on the cover of *Time* magazine after his novel, *The Last Puritan: A Memoir in the Form of a Novel*, becomes a best seller. Adelina "Nina" Otero-Warren publishes her book *Old Spain in Our Southwest*.

**1937** The U.S. colonial government in Puerto Rico intensifies its campaign against Puerto Rican nationalists. At a rally, many nationalists are killed or wounded in what is known as the Masacre de Ponce (Ponce Massacre). Nationalist leader Pedro Albizu Campos had been sent to prison less than a year before.

**1938** Mexican president Lázaro Cárdenas expropriates U.S. and British oil companies, nationalizing the petroleum industry.

**1942** The United States and Mexico sign the Bracero Agreement, under which the United States admits thousands of Mexican workers to fill the wartime labor shortage in agriculture and public works. This same year, the Sleepy Lagoon Incident takes place. A jury convicts 22 Mexicans of murder, but their conviction is overturned in 1944.

**1943** In Los Angeles, the Zoot Suit Riots unfold.

**1947** The Puerto Rican government initiates *Operación Manos a la Obra* (Operation Put Your Hands to Work), known in the United States as

"Operation Bootstrap," as a development project to encourage U.S.-led industrialization on the island and to help the United States meet the demand for labor after World War II. This project stimulates contract labor and one of the largest mass migrations of displaced workers to the United States.

**1948** Luis Muñoz Marín becomes Puerto Rico's first elected governor.

**1950** Mexican poet and essayist Octavio Paz publishes *El laberinto de la soledad* (The Labyrinth of Solitude), which includes the controversial chapter "The *Pachuco* and Other Extremes." This same year, a nationalist revolt occurs in Puerto Rico. Pedro Albizu Campos is again arrested and imprisoned.

**1951** The first episode of the U.S. television show *I Love Lucy*, starring Lucille Ball and Desi Arnaz, airs on CBS. The show runs for 181 episodes and wins four Emmy Awards. This same year, Guillermo Cotto-Turner publishes *Trópico en Manhattan* (Tropic in Manhattan).

**1952** The Estado Libre Asociado de Puerto Rico, the Commonwealth of Puerto Rico, is officially inaugurated.

**1953** René Marqués's play *La carreta* (The Oxcart) is first staged, in New York City. It is performed in Puerto Rico a year later.

**1954** In the landmark case *Hernández v. Texas*, the U.S. Supreme Court rules that Hispanic Americans are not being treated as "whites." In recognizing Latinos as a class of people suffering profound discrimination, the court paves the way for Latinos to use legal means to attack all types of discrimination. Between this year and 1958, the U.S. Immigration and Nationalization Service deports Mexicans though its Operation Wetback. This same year, Lolita Lebrón and other Puerto Rican nationalists are involved in a shooting at the U.S. House of Representatives in their struggle to free the island from U.S. control; five politicians are wounded. Fabiola Cabeza de Baca Gilbert publishes her novel *We Fed Them Cactus*. José Luis González publishes his short-story collection *En Nueva York y otras desgracias* (In New York and Other Misfortunes). In San Juan, Puerto Rico, Angel Ramos founds the television broadcasting company Telemundo.

**1955** In San Antonio, Texas, KCOR-TV (later KWEX-TV), part of the Spanish International Network, begins broadcasting to the Hispanic community. Cleofas M. Jaramillo publishes her autobiographical tale *Romance of a Little Village Girl*.

**1956** Pedro Juan Soto publishes his short-story collection *Spiks*.

**1956–59** In Cuba, Fidel Castro, Ernesto "Che" Guevara, and other guerrilla fighters lead a successful uprising against dictator Fulgencio Batista, who flees the island on New Year's Eve 1958. Within a few years, Castro implements a Communist government modeled after the Soviet Union's.

**1958** Chicano ethnomusicologist Américo Paredes publishes *With His Pistol in His Hand*, a study of the legends and corridos about ranch hand Gregorio Cortez. The book helps establish the study of folklore by and among Latinos in the United States.

**1959** In Manhattan, the first Puerto Rican Day Parade is held. José Antonio Villarreal publishes his novel *Pocho*.

**1961** U.S. president John F. Kennedy orders the Bay of Pigs invasion, in which U.S.-trained Cuban exiles attempt to topple the Cuban government.

The operation fails. This same year, Jesús Colón publishes his book *A Puerto Rican in New York and Other Sketches*. Rita Moreno becomes the first Latina to win an Oscar, for her performance in the movie musical *West Side Story*.

**1962** The Cuban-Missile Crisis unfolds between Cuba and the United States. This same year, singer Joan Baez, whose father was Mexican, is the first Latino or Latina performer to appear on the cover of *Time* magazine.

**1963** John Rechy publishes *City of Night*, the first gay novel by a Latino. This same year, José Yglesias publishes his first novel, *A Wake in Ybor City*. María Irene Fornés's *There! You Died* (later retitled *Tango Palace*) becomes the first of her plays to be produced.

**1964** Congress passes the Civil Rights Act. The first comprehensive civil rights law since the post–Civil War Reconstruction period, it fosters affirmative action programs nationwide. Sabine R. Ulibarrí publishes *Tierra Amarilla: Cuentos de Nuevo Mexico* (Stories of New Mexico).

**1965** César Chávez, Dolores Huerta, and other activists found the National Farm Workers Association (NFWA). This action helps launch the Chicano Movement, characterized by strikes for better wages for migrant workers, for a larger political representation in city and state leadership, and for a more comprehensive curriculum in elementary, middle and high schools. This same year, U.S. Marines and elements of the Army's Airborne Division invade the Dominican Republic, intervening in a military rebellion.

**1966** A U.S. branch of the Real Academia de la Lengua Española (Royal Academy of the Spanish Language) is established. The branch is incorporated in 1980.

**1967** Piri Thomas publishes his autobiographical novel *Down These Mean Streets*. This same year, Andrew García's *Tough Trip through Paradise*, a nineteenth-century memoir from the Texas frontier, is published posthumously. A small press publishes Rodolfo "Corky" Gonzales's poetry collection, *I Am Joaquín*, which is reprinted by a major publisher in 1972.

**1968** The U.S. Congress passes the Bilingual Education Act, which provides school districts with federal funds to establish educational programs for students with limited English-language proficiency. This same year, the Congress approves a proclamation to celebrate an annual Hispanic Heritage Week, which two decades later is expanded to Hispanic Heritage Month (September 15–October 15). Víctor Hernández Cruz publishes his poetry collection *Snaps*.

**1969** The Chicano Youth Liberation Conference, in Denver, issues *El plan espiritual de Aztlán* (The Spiritual Plan of Aztlán), a manifesto for Chicano activism and independence. This same year, the Chicano Coordinating Council on Higher Education releases the *Plan of Santa Barbara*, pushing for curriculum on Chicanos to be taught in California. The first programs of Chicano Studies are established, including ones at the University of California, Santa Barbara; San Diego State University; California State University, Northridge; and California State University, Fullerton. Chapters of the Puerto Rican Young Lords Organization are formed in Chicago and New York City. The term *Hispanic* is adopted by the U.S. government, when President Richard M. Nixon signs into law the celebration of a Hispanic Heritage Week. The term is then consistently used in government documents as an umbrella category for Spanish-speakers, regardless of their ethnic and national backgrounds. From this year through 1973, several Puerto Rican Studies academic programs are established at the City and State of New York university systems and other U.S. higher education institutions as a result of student and community activism.

1970   A coalition led by the Chicano Moratorium organizes a march in East Los Angeles, drawing some 30,000 demonstrators. The coalition protests the Vietnam War, and it demands justice and equality for Chicanos in general and for students in particular. Journalist Rubén Salazar is killed by a tear gas canister fired by police. This year, guitarist Carlos Santana and his band release their second album, *Abraxas*, which proves highly popular and highly influential.

1971   Pablo Neruda, a Chilean poet and diplomat, receives the Nobel Prize for Literature. This same year, Abelardo Baltazar Heredia Urista, aka "Alurista," publishes his first poetry collection, *Floricanto en Aztlán* (*Flor y canto*, Flower and Song, in Aztlán). Tomás Rivera publishes his novel *. . . y no se lo tragó la tierra* (translated as *This Migrant Earth*). Ricardo Sánchez publishes his poetry collection *Canto y grito mi liberación* (I Sing and Shout My Liberation). Ramona Acosta Bañuelos is appointed U.S. treasurer, the first Latina to hold this position.

1972   Rudolfo A. Anaya publishes his novel *Bless Me, Ultima*. This same year, Alurista publishes his second poetry collection, *Nationchild Plumaroja, 1969–1972*. ABC television journalist Geraldo Rivera wins a Peabody Award for exposing the conditions of neglect and abuse at a New York State school for the mentally disabled; in 1987, he becomes the first Latino to host his own talk show. The journal *Revista Chicano-Riqueña* is first published; it ceases publication in 1999.

1973   Miguel Algarín, Miguel Piñero, Pedro Pietri, and others found the Nuyorican Poets Cafe. This same year, Roberto Clemente becomes the first Latino baseball player to be inducted into the Baseball Hall of Fame by the Baseball Writers of America. (Lefty Gomez had been elected by the Veterans Committee and inducted the previous year.) Pedro Pietri publishes his poetry collection *Puerto Rican Obituary*. José Angel Figueroa publishes his poetry collection *East 110th Street*. Nicholasa Mohr publishes her novel *Nilda*. Rolando Hinojosa publishes his novel *Estampas del valle y otras obras* (published in English as *The Valley*, 1983). Abelardo "Lalo" Delgado circulates *The Chicano Movement: Some Not Too Objective Observations*. The first *floricanto* festival, a gathering of Chicano writers on a U.S. university campus, co-organized by Alurista, takes place at the University of Southern California. Invitees include Hinojosa, Tomás Rivera, and Oscar "Zeta" Acosta. (In subsequent years, *floricantos* take place in Milwaukee, Wisconsin, and Corpus Christi, Texas.) Bilingual Review Press, devoted to publishing established and emerging Latino writers, is founded; it eventually is housed at Arizona State University.

1974   The U.S. Congress passes the Equal Education Opportunity Act, giving Latinos the right to bilingual education. This same year, Oscar "Zeta" Acosta disappears in Mazatlán, Mexico, an event that achieves mythic status among Chicanos. Miguel Algarín publishes his poetry collection *Mongo Affair*. Miguel Piñero's play *Short Eyes* is first staged; it is published the next year and made into a feature film two years later. The Centro de Estudios Puertorriqueños (Center for Puerto Rican Studies) is established at the City University of New York as an outcome of the Puerto Rican Studies movement. Puerto Rican comedian Freddie Prinze stars in the hit NBC sitcom *Chico and the Man*.

**1975** *Nuyorican Poetry: An Anthology of Puerto Rican Words and Feelings*, edited by Miguel Algarín and Miguel Piñero, is published. This same year, Nicholasa Mohr publishes her short-story collection *El Bronx Remembered*. Estela Portillo Trambley publishes *Rain of Scorpions and Other Writings*.

**1976** *The Miami Herald* begins to publish a Spanish-language supplement, *El Herald*, which is relaunched as *El Nuevo Herald* in 1987. This same year, Luis Rafael Sánchez publishes his novel *La guaracha del macho Camacho* (translated as *Macho Camacho's Beat* four years later).

**1977** Gary Soto publishes his poetry collection *The Elements of San Joaquín*. This same year, *Memorias de Bernardo Vega* (Memoirs of Bernardo Vega), written in the 1940s, is published posthumously in Puerto Rico; it is translated into English seven years later. María Irene Fornés first stages her play *Fefu and Her Friends*.

**1978** Luis Valdez, creator of El Teatro Campesino, directs his play *Zoot Suit*, about the Sleepy Lagoon Incident and the Zoot Suit Riots, at the Mark Taper Forum, in Los Angeles.

**1979** Tato Laviera publishes his first poetry collection, *La Carreta Made a U-Turn*. Arte Público Press, eventually the largest U.S. publisher of Latino literature, is founded; from 1980, it is housed at the University of Houston.

**1980** Under the presidency of Jimmy Carter, the Mariel Boatlift brings to Florida thousands of Cuban refugees who had occupied the Peruvian Embassy in Havana, clamoring for escape. This same year, Dade County, Florida, approves the "anti-bilingual ordinance." Sandra María Esteves publishes her poetry collection *Yerba Buena* (The Good Herb).

**1981** Cuban businessman Jorge Más Canosa creates the Cuban American National Foundation to promote the transition from communism to democracy in Cuba. This same year, Lorna Dee Cervantes publishes her first poetry collection, *Emplumada*. *This Bridge Called My Back: Writings by Radical Women of Color*, edited by Gloria Anzaldúa and Cherríe Moraga, is published.

**1982** Richard Rodriguez publishes his memoir *Hunger of Memory: The Education of Richard Rodriguez*. This same year, Evangelina Vigil-Piñón publishes her poetry collection *Thirty an' Seen a Lot*.

**1983** Brian De Palma directs the movie *Scarface*, with Al Pacino as Tony Montana, a Cuban exile turned cocaine lord. This same year, Edward Rivera publishes *Family Installments: Memories of Growing Up Hispanic*. José Rivera's play *The House of Ramón Iglesia* is first produced.

**1984** Robert M. Young directs the movie *The Ballad of Gregorio Cortez*, based on the legends and corridos about this border ranch hand. Sandra Cisneros publishes the coming-of-age novel *The House on Mango Street*.

**1985** Helena María Viramontes publishes her collection *The Moths and Other Stories*. This same year, Luis Rafael Sánchez publishes "La guagua aérea" (translated as "The Airbus").

**1986** The U.S. Congress passes the Immigration Reform and Control Act, which both makes it illegal to knowingly hire or recruit undocumented immigrants and grants a path toward the acquisition of documents by certain immigrants who have been in the country without papers. This same year, Felipe Maximiliano Chacón's *Memoirs*, written in the first half of the twentieth century, is published posthumously. Hallmark Greeting Cards acquires the Spanish International Network and renames it Univisión. Ana Castillo publishes the experimental novel *The Mixquiahuala Letters*.

**1987** Gloria Anzaldúa publishes her nonfiction book *Borderlands/La Frontera: The New Mestiza*. This same year, Martín Espada publishes his poetry collection *Trumpets for the Islands of Their Eviction*. Luz María Umpierre-Herrera publishes *The Margarita Poems*. Judith Ortiz Cofer publishes her poetry collection *Terms of Survival*. Telemundo, the Spanish-language television station in San Juan, Puerto Rico, is consolidated with radio and television stations in cities such as Los Angeles, Miami, and New York; this network becomes a premier producer of Spanish-language telenovelas in the United States.

**1988** U.S. president Ronald Reagan appoints the first Latino secretary of education, Lauro F. Cavazos. This same year, Roberto G. Fernández publishes his novel *Raining Backwards*.

**1989** Judith Ortiz Cofer publishes her novel *The Line of the Sun*. This same year, Cuban-born singer Gloria Estefan releases the best-selling album *Cuts Both Ways*, which includes the Billboard Hot 100 number-one hit "I Don't Wanna Lose You."

**1990** Oscar Hijuelos becomes the first Latino to be awarded the Pulitzer Prize, for his novel *The Mambo Kings Play Songs of Love*. Judith Ortiz Cofer publishes her memoir *Silent Dancing: A Partial Remembrance of a Puerto Rican Childhood*. Sandra María Esteves publishes her poetry collection *Bluestown Mockingbird Mambo*. This same year, President George H. W. Bush appoints the first woman and first Latino or Latina surgeon general of the United States: Antonia C. Novello, from Puerto Rico. Aristeo Brito wins the Western States Award for his novel *The Devil in Texas*.

**1991** Julia Alvarez publishes her autobiographical novel *How the García Girls Lost Their Accents*. Victor Villaseñor publishes his novel *Rain of Gold*. This same year, President George H. W. Bush signs the Cuban Democracy Act—also known as the Torricelli Bill, and heavily backed by Cuban Americans—which bans trade with Cuba by U.S. subsidiary companies in third countries and prohibits ships docking in U.S. ports if they have visited Cuba. The United Nations General Assembly condemns the United States for maintaining its 30-year embargo of Cuba.

**1992** Reinaldo Arenas's memoir, *Before Night Falls*, is published posthumously. This same year, Cristina García publishes her debut novel, *Dreaming in Cuban*. The quincentennial of Columbus's first voyage across the Atlantic Ocean is celebrated amid protests. The Colombian American performer John Leguizamo debuts on Broadway, with his one-man show *Mambo Mouth*. Rosalino "Chalino" Sánchez, a corridista whose songs are about undocumented immigrants in the United States, is killed in Culiacán, Mexico.

**1993** Shortly after receiving the U.S. Medal of Freedom from U.S. president Bill Clinton, César Chávez dies in his sleep, in San Luis, Arizona. This same year, Clinton appoints Federico Peña as secretary of transportation, Henry Cisneros as secretary of housing and urban development, Norma Cantú as assistant secretary for civil rights; all are the first Latinos to hold these positions. Luis Rodríguez publishes his memoir *Always Running: La Vida Loca*. Esmeralda Santiago publishes her memoir *When I Was Puerto Rican*. Abraham Rodriguez publishes his novel *Spidertown*. Tino Villanueva publishes his poetry collection *Scenes from the Movie* Giant.

**1994** California passes Proposition 187, an initiative banning immigrants from receiving public education and benefits such as welfare and subsidized health care; three years later, a federal court overturns this law. This same year, Gustavo Pérez Firmat publishes his study *Life on the Hyphen: The Cuban American Way*. Demetria Martínez publishes her novel *Mother Tongue*. In San Cristóbal de las Casas, Chiapas, Mexico, Mayan guerrillas led by Subcomandante Marcos and calling themselves the Zapatista National Liberation Army stage a revolution, demanding better treatment of Mexico's indigenous population. Denise Chavez publishes her novel *Face of an Angel*. Julia Alvarez publishes her novel *In the Time of the Butterflies*.

**1995** Ilan Stavans publishes his study *The Hispanic Condition*. This same year, Selena Quintanilla, a Tejana singer, is assassinated in Corpus Christi, Texas. Gustavo Pérez Firmat publishes his memoir *Next Year in Cuba*. Rosario Ferré publishes *The House on the Lagoon*, her first novel written in English.

**1996** Junot Díaz publishes his first short-story collection, *Drown*. This same year, Chicana playwright Josefina López publishes her monologue *Real Women Have Curves*, which in 2002 becomes a movie directed by Patricia Cardoso. Willie Perdomo publishes his poetry collection *Where a Nickel Costs a Dime*. Iris Morales releases her documentary *¡Palante, Siempre, Palante!: The Young Lords*.

**1997** Chicano scholar Luis Leal receives the National Humanities Medal from President Bill Clinton. This same year, Virgil Suárez publishes his memoir *Spared Angola: Memories from a Cuban-American Childhood*.

**1998** Giannina Braschi publishes the code-switching novel *Yo-Yo Boing!* This same year, the activist theater troupe Culture Clash publishes the book *Life, Death, and Revolutionary Comedy*. Anthony Muñoz becomes the first Latino inducted into the Football Hall of Fame. Bill Richardson becomes the first Latino to be appointed secretary of energy, by President Clinton.

**2000** Elián González, a Cuban child lost at sea, is reunited with his father in Cuba on orders from U.S. attorney general Janet Reno. This same year, Guillermo Gómez-Peña, with Enrique Chagoya and Felicia Rice, publishes the graphic treatise *Codex Espangliensis: From Columbus to the Border Patrol*. The Latin Grammy Awards are launched and are telecast by CBS. The U.S. Census Bureau begins publicly using the term *Latino* as well as *Hispanic* in documenting the nation's population.

**2001** Ilan Stavans publishes his memoir *On Borrowed Words*. María Teresa "Mariposa" Fernández publishes her first chapbook, *Born Bronxeña: Poems*.

**2002**  Richard Rodriguez publishes *Brown: The Last Discovery of America*, the third installment of his trilogy. Juan Felipe Herrera publishes *Notebooks of a Chile Verde Smuggler*.

**2003**  The U.S. Census Bureau declares that Latinos, in surpassing African Americans and Asians, have become the largest minority in the United States. This same year, salsa singer Celia Cruz dies, in New Jersey. A 6,000-word dictionary, *Spanglish: The Making of a New American Language*, edited by Ilan Stavans and including a translation into Spanglish of the first chapter of Miguel de Cervantes's novel *Don Quixote*, is published. Nilo Cruz becomes the first Latino to win a Pulitzer Prize for drama, with his play *Anna in the Tropics*. Carlos M. N. Eire publishes his memoir *Waiting for Snow in Havana: Confessions of a Cuban Boy*, which becomes the first nonfiction book by a Latino to win the National Book Award.

**2004**  Susana Chávez-Silverman publishes her volume of electronic chronicles *Killer Crónicas: Bilingual Memories*. This same year, José Rivera is nominated for a screenwriting Academy Award for the film *The Motorcycle Diaries*, a biography of Che Guevara as a young man.

**2006**  In the United States, millions of people nationwide march on Labor Day to protest the stern policies toward immigrants of the administration of U.S. president George W. Bush. This same year, a national debate ensues after "The Star-Spangled Banner" is translated into Spanglish. The U.S. Senate votes to make English the country's official language. The television show *Ugly Betty*, an adaptation of the Colombian telenovela *Betty la fea*, premieres, starring America Ferrera.

**2007**  Junot Díaz publishes his first novel, *The Brief Wondrous Life of Oscar Wao*; the next year, the book wins the Pulitzer Prize for fiction. Bill Richardson, governor of New Mexico, becomes the first Latino to run for president of the United States.

**2008**  *An Organizer's Tale*, a collection of César Chávez's speeches, is published. This same year, the compendium *The Last Supper of Chicano Heroes: Selected Works of José Antonio Burciaga* is published posthumously.

**2009**  Sonia Sotomayor, judge on the U.S. District Court for the Southern District of New York and of Puerto Rican descent, becomes the first-ever Latino or Latina justice on the U.S. Supreme Court.

**2010**  Archbishop José Horacio Gómez, a U.S. citizen born in Mexico, becomes the first Latino leader of the Archdiocese of Los Angeles, the largest Roman Catholic Archdiocese in the country. He is also the highest-ranking Latino Catholic bishop in the U.S. This same year, Arizona adopts a highly controversial law requiring police officers to check the immigration status of any person they suspect of being an undocumented alien. The U.S. House of Representatives passes a measure that calls for the citizens of Puerto Rico to vote on whether the island should remain a commonwealth and then to vote on whether it should become the nation's 51st state, retain its current status, become fully independent, or acquire a sovereignty that would entail some association with the United States.

# Appendix 2:
# Treaties, Acts,
# and Propositions

This section consists of five historical documents that have had a defining impact on Latino history. The first three resulted from armed conflicts and treat territorial and governmental issues, while the final two concern immigration.

As discussed in the "Annexations" introduction, the Treaty of Guadalupe Hidalgo was the peace arrangement that concluded the Mexican-American War (1846–48) between the interim military regime in Mexico and the United States. It established the transfer of 525,000 square miles of Mexican land to the United States for $15 million. This portion of land became parts of the modern-day U.S. states of Colorado, Arizona, New Mexico, and Wyoming, as well as the whole of California, Nevada, and Utah. (Other parts of Arizona and New Mexico were ceded in 1853 as part of the Gadsden Purchase.) The treaty also eliminated $3.25 million of Mexico's debt to the United States. Before it was signed, however, the U.S. Senate deleted Article X, which guaranteed the protection of Mexican land grants. The amended treaty was signed on February 2, 1848, in the Mexico City neighborhood of Guadalupe Hidalgo, by representatives of the U.S. president, James K. Polk, and by representatives of the interim Mexican president, Pedro Bernardino María de Anaya.

Similarly—as discussed in the "Annexations" introduction—the Treaty of Paris, signed on December 10, 1898, concluded the Spanish-American War between Spain and the United States. It established that Cuba would become independent from Spain; however, under the Platt Amendment of 1901, Cuba essentially came under the rule of the United States, as did the Caribbean inlet Guantánamo Bay. Spain also ceded Puerto Rico to the United States, which kept the island as an unincorporated colonial territory. Two years later, as discussed in the "Acculturation" introduction, a civilian government was established in Puerto Rico under the Foraker Act (like the Platt Amendment, not included here). In return for $20 million, Spain ceded the Philippines to the United States.

As noted in the "Acculturation" introduction, the Jones-Shafroth Act, also known as the Jones Act—signed on March 2, 1917, by U.S. president

Woodrow Wilson—gave Puerto Ricans U.S. citizenship with the restriction that Puerto Ricans on the island could not (and still cannot) vote for president or have voting representation in the U.S. Congress. It also established on the island a system of government that parallels the one on the mainland, consisting of executive, legislative and judicial branches. According to the Jones Act, the island's governor and other Cabinet officials were to be appointed by the president of the United States with the approval of the U.S. Senate, and Puerto Ricans would elect the members of the island's House of Representatives and Senate. In 1948, Puerto Ricans were also granted the right to elect their own governor. Four years later, the current Estado Libre Asociado de Puerto Rico, the Commonwealth of Puerto Rico, was inaugurated. Under this status, the island has a Constitution, but continues as an unsovereign territory under U.S. jurisdiction. The territorial provisions of the Jones Act remain in effect.

The Bracero Program, again discussed in the "Annexations" introduction, was designed to help the United States cope with a labor shortage during World War II. Signed on August 4, 1942, and revised on April 26, 1943, the Bracero Agreement brought Mexican agricultural workers north of the Rio Grande, initially to harvest sugar beets in Stockton, California. The program soon expanded to cover low-wage field labor, and another agreement (not included here) was signed to cover the U.S. railroad industry.

The final document in this section pertains to immigration in California, the state with the largest percentage of Latinos. Proposition 187 was a 1994 ballot initiative stipulating that, given the limited state budget and the draining of resources from noncitizens, illegal immigrants should be denied social services, health care, and public education. Introduced by Republican assemblyman Dick Mountjoy as part of the "Save Our State" initiative, and supported by then California governor Pete Wilson, Proposition 187 passed with 58.8 percent of the vote but was overturned by a federal court in 1997. Labeled "the last gasp" of white America in California by critics, this crucial piece of legislative history influenced the rhetoric of the "immigration wars" that materialized at the dawn of the twenty-first century.

# The Treaty of Guadalupe Hidalgo

*Treaty of Peace, Friendship, Limits, and Settlement with the Republic of Mexico*

In the name of Almighty God:

The United States of America and the United Mexican States, animated by a sincere desire to put an end to the calamities of the war which unhappily exists between the two republics, and to establish upon a solid basis relations of peace and friendship, which shall confer reciprocal benefits upon the citizens of both, and assure the concord, harmony, and mutual confidence wherein the two people should live, as good neighbors, have for that purpose appointed their respective plenipotentiaries—that is to say, the President of the United States has appointed Nicholas P. Trist, a citizen of the United States, and the President of the Mexican republic has appointed

Don Luis Gonzaga Cuevas, Don Bernardo Couto, and Don Miguel Atristain, citizens of the said republic, who, after a reciprocal communication of their respective full powers, have, under the protection of Almighty God, the author of peace, arranged, agreed upon, and signed the following

*Treaty of Peace, Friendship, Limits, and Settlement between the United States of America and the Mexican Republic.*

### ARTICLE I

There shall be firm and universal peace between the United States of America and the Mexican republic, and between their respective countries, territories, cities, towns, and people, without exception of places or persons.

### ARTICLE II

Immediately upon the signature of this treaty, a convention shall be entered into between a commissioner or commissioners appointed by the General-in-chief of the forces of the United States, and such as may be appointed by the Mexican government, to the end that a provisional suspension of hostilities shall take place, and that, in the places occupied by the said forces, constitutional order may be reëstablished, as regards the political, administrative, and judicial branches, so far as this shall be permitted by the circumstances of military occupation.

### ARTICLE III

Immediately upon the ratification of the present treaty by the government of the United States, orders shall be transmitted to the commanders of their land and naval forces, requiring the latter (provided this treaty shall then have been ratified by the government of the Mexican republic, and the ratifications exchanged) immediately to desist from blockading any Mexican ports; and requiring the former (under the same condition) to commence, at the earliest moment practicable, withdrawing all troops of the United States then in the interior of the Mexican republic, to points that shall be selected by common agreement, at a distance from the seaports not exceeding thirty leagues; and such evacuation of the interior of the republic shall be completed with the least possible delay; the Mexican government hereby binding itself to afford every facility in its power for rendering the same convenient to the troops, on their march and in their new positions, and for promoting a good understanding between them and the inhabitants. In like manner orders shall be despatched to the persons in charge of the custom-houses at all ports occupied by the forces of the United States, requiring them (under the same condition) immediately to deliver possession of the same to the persons authorized by the Mexican government to receive it, together with all bonds and evidences of debt for duties on importations and on exportations, not yet fallen due. Moreover, a faithful and exact account shall be made out, showing the entire amount of all duties on imports and on exports, collected at such custom-houses, or elsewhere in Mexico, by authority of the United States, from and after the day of the ratification of this treaty by the government of the Mexican republic; and also an account of the cost of collection; and such entire amount, deducting only the cost of collection, shall be delivered to the Mexican government, at the city of Mexico, within three months after the exchange of ratifications.

The evacuation of the capital of the Mexican republic by the troops of the United States, in virtue of the above stipulation, shall be completed in one month after the orders there stipulated for shall have been received by the commander of said troops, or sooner if possible.

### ARTICLE IV

Immediately after the exchange of ratifications of the present treaty, all castles, forts, territories, places, and possessions, which have been taken or occupied by the forces of the United States during the present war, within the limits of the Mexican republic, as about to be established by the following article, shall be definitively restored to the said republic, together with all the artillery, arms, apparatus of war, munitions, and other public property, which were in the said castles and forts when captured, and which shall remain there at the time when this treaty shall be duly ratified by the government of the Mexican republic. To this end, immediately upon the signature of this treaty, orders shall be despatched to the American officers commanding such castles and forts, securing against the removal or destruction of any such artillery, arms, apparatus of war, munitions, or other public property. The city of Mexico, within the inner line of intrenchments surrounding the said city, is comprehended in the above stipulations, as regards the restoration of artillery, apparatus of war, & c.

The final evacuation of the territory of the Mexican republic, by the forces of the United States, shall be completed in three months from the said exchange of ratifications, or sooner if possible: the Mexican government hereby engaging, as in the foregoing article, to use all means in its power for facilitating such evacuation, and rendering it convenient to the troops, and for promoting a good understanding between them and the inhabitants.

If, however, the ratification of this treaty by both parties should not take place in time to allow the embarcation of the troops of the United States to be completed before the commencement of the sickly season, at the Mexican ports on the Gulf of Mexico, in such case a friendly arrangement shall be entered into between the General-in-chief of the said troops and the Mexican government, whereby healthy and otherwise suitable places, at a distance from the ports not exceeding thirty leagues, shall be designated for the residence of such troops as may not yet have embarked, until the return of the healthy season. And the space of time here referred to as comprehending the sickly season, shall be understood to extend from the first day of May to the first day of November.

All prisoners of war taken on either side, on land or on sea, shall be restored as soon as practicable after the exchange of ratifications of this treaty. It is also agreed that if any Mexicans should now be held as captives by any savage tribe within the limits of the United States, as about to be established by the following article, the government of the said United States will exact the release of such captives, and cause them to be restored to their country.

ARTICLE V

The boundary line between the two republics shall commence in the Gulf of Mexico, three leagues from land, opposite the mouth of the Rio Grande, otherwise called Rio Bravo del Norte, or opposite the mouth of its deepest branch, if it should have more than one branch emptying directly into the sea; from thence up the middle of that river, following the deepest channel, where it has more than one, to the point where it strikes the southern boundary of New Mexico; thence, westwardly, along the whole southern boundary of New Mexico (which runs north of the town called *Paso*) to its western termination; thence, northward, along the western line of New Mexico, until it intersects the first branch of the River Gila; (or if it should not intersect any branch of that river, then to the point on the said line nearest to such branch, and thence in a direct line to the same;) thence down the middle of the said branch and of the said river, until it empties into the Rio Colorado; thence across the Rio Colorado, following the division line between Upper and Lower California, to the Pacific Ocean.

The southern and western limits of New Mexico, mentioned in this article, are those laid down in the map entitled *"Map of the United Mexican States, as organized and defined by various acts of the Congress of said republic, and constructed according to the best authorities. Revised edition. Published at New York, in 1847, by J. Disturnell."* Of which map a copy is added to this treaty, bearing the signatures and seals of the undersigned plenipotentiaries. And, in order to preclude all difficulty in tracing upon the ground the limit separating Upper from Lower California, it is agreed that the said limit shall consist of a straight line drawn from the middle of the Rio Gila, where it unites with the Colorado, to a point on the coast of the Pacific Ocean distant one marine league due south of the southernmost point of the port of San Diego, according to the plan of said port made in the year 1782 by Don Juan Pantoja, second sailing-master of the Spanish fleet, and published at Madrid in the year 1802, in the Atlas to the voyage of the schooners *Sutil* and *Mexicana*, of which plan a copy is hereunto added, signed and sealed by the respective plenipotentiaries.

In order to designate the boundary line with due precision, upon authoritative maps, and to establish upon the ground landmarks which shall show the limits of both republics, as described in the present article, the two governments shall each appoint a commissioner and a surveyor, who, before the expiration of one year from the date of the exchange of ratifications of this treaty, shall meet at the port of San Diego, and proceed to run and mark the said boundary in its whole course to the mouth of the Rio Bravo del Norte. They shall keep journals and make out plans of their operations; and the result agreed upon by them shall be deemed a part of this treaty, and shall have the same force as if it were inserted therein. The two governments will amicably agree regarding what may be necessary to these persons, and also as to their respective escorts, should such be necessary.

The boundary line established by this article shall be religiously respected by each of the two republics, and no change shall ever be made therein, except by the express and free consent of both nations, lawfully given by the general government of each, in conformity with its own constitution.

### ARTICLE VI

The vessels and citizens of the United States shall, in all time, have a free and uninterrupted passage by the Gulf of California, and by the River Colorado below its confluence with the Gila, to and from their possessions situated north of the boundary line defined in the preceding article; it being understood that this passage is to be by navigating the Gulf of California and the River Colorado, and not by land, without the express consent of the Mexican government.

If, by the examinations which may be made, it should be ascertained to be practicable and advantageous to construct a road, canal, or railway, which should in whole or in part run upon the River Gila, or upon its right or its left bank, within the space of one marine league from either margin of the river, the governments of both republics will form an agreement regarding its construction, in order that it may serve equally for the use and advantage of both countries.

### ARTICLE VII

The River Gila, and the part of the Rio Bravo del Norte lying below the southern boundary of New Mexico, being, agreeably to the fifth article, divided in the middle between the two republics, the navigation of the Gila and of the Bravo below said boundary shall be free and common to the vessels and citizens of both countries; and neither shall, without the consent of the other, construct any work that may impede or interrupt, in whole or in part, the exercise of this right; not even for the purpose of favoring new methods of navigation. Nor shall any tax or contribution, under any denomination or title, be levied upon vessels, or persons navigating the same, or upon merchandise or effects transported thereon, except in the case of landing upon one of their shores. If, for the purpose of making the said rivers navigable, or for maintaining them in such state, it should be necessary or advantageous to establish any tax or contribution, this shall not be done without the consent of both governments.

The stipulations contained in the present article shall not impair the territorial rights of either republic within its established limits.

### ARTICLE VIII

Mexicans now established in territories previously belonging to Mexico, and which remain for the future within the limits of the United States, as defined by the present treaty, shall be free to continue where they now reside, or to remove at any time to the Mexican republic, retaining the property which they possess in the said territories, or disposing thereof, and removing the proceeds wherever they please, without their being subjected, on this account, to any contribution, tax, or charge whatever.

Those who shall prefer to remain in the said territories, may either retain the title and rights of Mexican citizens, or acquire those of citizens of the United States. But they shall be under the obligation to make their election within one year from the date of the exchange of ratifications of this treaty; and those who shall remain in the said territories after the expiration of that year, without having declared their intention to retain the character of Mexicans, shall be considered to have elected to become citizens of the United States.

In the said territories, property of every kind, now belonging to Mexicans not established there, shall be inviolably respected. The present owners, the heirs of these, and all Mexicans who may hereafter acquire said property by contract, shall enjoy with respect to it guaranties equally ample as if the same belonged to citizens of the United States.

### ARTICLE IX

Mexicans who, in the territories aforesaid, shall not preserve the character of citizens of the Mexican republic, conformably with what is stipulated in the preceding article, shall be incorporated into the Union of the United States, and be admitted at the proper time (to be judged of by the Congress of the United States) to the enjoyment of all the rights of citizens of the United States, according to the principles of the constitution; and in the mean time shall be maintained and protected in the free enjoyment of their liberty and property, and secured in the free exercise of their religion without restriction.

### ARTICLE X

[Deleted by the U.S. Senate.]

### ARTICLE XI

Considering that a great part of the territories which, by the present treaty, are to be comprehended for the future within the limits of the United States, is now occupied by savage tribes, who will hereafter be under the exclusive control of the government of the United States, and whose incursions within the territory of Mexico would be prejudicial in the extreme, it is solemnly agreed that all such incursions shall be forcibly restrained by the government of the United States whensoever this may be necessary; and that when they cannot be prevented, they shall be punished by the said government, and satisfaction for the same shall be exacted—all in the same way, and with equal diligence and energy, as if the same incursions were meditated or committed within its own territory, against its own citizens.

It shall not be lawful, under any pretext whatever, for any inhabitant of the United States to purchase or acquire any Mexican or any foreigner residing in Mexico, who may have been captured by Indians inhabiting the territory of either of the two republics, nor to purchase or acquire horses, mules, cattle, or property of any kind, stolen within Mexican territory by such Indians.

And in the event of any person or persons, captured within Mexican territory by Indians, being carried into the territory of the United States, the government of the latter engages and binds itself, in the most solemn manner, so soon as it shall know of such captives being within its territory, and shall be able so to do, through the faithful exercise of its influence and power, to rescue them and return them to their country, or deliver them to the agent or representative of the Mexican government. The Mexican authorities will, as far as practicable, give to the government of the United States notice of such captures; and its agent shall pay the expenses incurred in the maintenance and transmission of the rescued captives; who, in the mean time, shall be treated with the utmost hospitality by the American authorities at the place where they may be. But if the government of the United States, before receiving such notice from Mexico, should obtain intelligence, through any other channel, of the existence of Mexican captives within its territory, it will proceed forthwith to effect their release and delivery to the Mexican agent, as above stipulated.

For the purpose of giving to these stipulations the fullest possible efficacy, thereby affording the security and redress demanded by their true spirit and intent, the government of the United States will now and hereafter pass, without unnecessary delay, and always vigilantly enforce, such laws as the nature of the subject may require. And finally, the sacredness of this obligation shall never be lost sight of by the said government when providing for the removal of the Indians from any portion of the said territories, or for its being settled by citizens of the United States; but on the contrary, special care shall then be taken not to place its Indian occupants under the necessity of seeking new homes, by committing those invasions which the United States have solemnly obliged themselves to restrain.

### ARTICLE XII

In consideration of the extension acquired by the boundaries of the United States, as defined in the fifth article of the present treaty, the government of the United States engages to pay to that of the Mexican republic the sum of fifteen millions of dollars.

Immediately after this treaty shall have been duly ratified by the government of the Mexican republic, the sum of three millions of dollars shall be paid to the said government by that of the United States, at the city of Mexico, in the gold or silver coin of Mexico. The remaining twelve millions of dollars shall be paid at the same place, and in the same coin, in annual instalments of three millions of dollars each, together with interest on the same at the rate of six per centum per annum. This interest shall begin to run upon the whole sum of twelve millions from the day of the ratification of the present treaty by the Mexican government, and the first of the instalments shall be paid at the expiration of one year from the same day. Together with each annual instalment, as it falls due, the whole interest accruing on such instalment from the beginning shall also be paid.

### ARTICLE XIII

The United States engage, moreover, to assume and pay to the claimants all the amounts now due them, and those hereafter to become due, by reason of the claims already liquidated and decided against the Mexican republic, under the conventions between the two republics severally concluded on the eleventh day of April, eighteen hundred and thirty-nine, and on the thirtieth day of January, eighteen hundred and forty-three; so that the

Mexican republic shall be absolutely exempt, for the future, from all expense whatever on account of the said claims.

### ARTICLE XIV

The United States do furthermore discharge the Mexican republic from all claims of citizens of the United States, not heretofore decided against the Mexican government, which may have arisen previously to the date of the signature of this treaty; which discharge shall be final and perpetual, whether the said claims be rejected or be allowed by the board of commissioners provided for in the following article, and whatever shall be the total amount of those allowed.

### ARTICLE XV

The United States, exonerating Mexico from all demands on account of the claims of their citizens mentioned in the preceding article, and considering them entirely and forever cancelled, whatever their amount may be, undertake to make satisfaction for the same, to an amount not exceeding three and one quarter millions of dollars. To ascertain the validity and amount of those claims, a board of commissioners shall be established by the government of the United States, whose awards shall be final and conclusive: provided, that in deciding upon the validity of each claim, the board shall be guided and governed by the principles and rules of decision prescribed by the first and fifth articles of the unratified convention, concluded at the city of Mexico on the twentieth day of November, one thousand eight hundred and forty–three;[1] and in no case shall an award be made in favor of any claim not embraced by these principles and rules.

If, in the opinion of the said board of commissioners, or of the claimants, any books, records, or documents in the possession or power of the government of the Mexican republic, shall be deemed necessary to the just decision of any claim, the commissioners, or the claimants through them, shall, within such period as Congress may designate, make an application in writing for the same, addressed to the Mexican Minister for Foreign Affairs, to be transmitted by the Secretary of State of the United States; and the Mexican government engages, at the earliest possible moment after the receipt of such demand, to cause any of the books, records, or documents, so specified, which shall be in their possession or power, (or authenticated copies or extracts of the same,) to be transmitted to the said Secretary of State, who shall immediately deliver them over to the said board of commissioners: *Provided*, That no such application shall be made by, or at the instance of, any claimant, until the facts which it is expected to prove by such books, records, or documents, shall have been stated under oath or affirmation.

### ARTICLE XVI

Each of the contracting parties reserves to itself the entire right to fortify whatever point within its territory it may judge proper so to fortify, for its security.

1. For these articles, see p. A28.

ARTICLE XVII

The treaty of amity, commerce, and navigation, concluded at the city of Mexico on the fifth day of April, A. D. 1831, between the United States of America and the United Mexican States, except the additional article, and except so far as the stipulations of the said treaty may be incompatible with any stipulation contained in the present treaty, is hereby revived for the period of eight years from the day of the exchange of ratifications of this treaty, with the same force and virtue as if incorporated therein; it being understood that each of the contracting parties reserves to itself the right, at any time after the said period of eight years shall have expired, to terminate the same by giving one year's notice of such intention to the other party.

ARTICLE XVIII

All supplies whatever for troops of the United States in Mexico, arriving at ports in the occupation of such troops previous to the final evacuation thereof, although subsequently to the restoration of the custom-houses at such ports, shall be entirely exempt from duties and charges of any kind; the government of the United States hereby engaging and pledging its faith to establish, and vigilantly to enforce, all possible guards for securing the revenue of Mexico, by preventing the importation, under cover of this stipulation, of any articles other than such, both in kind and in quantity, as shall really be wanted for the use and consumption of the forces of the United States during the time they may remain in Mexico. To this end, it shall be the duty of all officers and agents of the United States to denounce to the Mexican authorities at the respective ports any attempts at a fraudulent abuse of this stipulation which they may know of or may have reason to suspect, and to give to such authorities all the aid in their power with regard thereto; and every such attempt, when duly proved and established by sentence of a competent tribunal, shall be punished by the confiscation of the property so attempted to be fraudulently introduced.

ARTICLE XIX

With respect to all merchandise, effects, and property whatsoever, imported into ports of Mexico whilst in the occupation of the forces of the United States, whether by citizens of either republic, or by citizens or subjects of any neutral nation, the following rules shall be observed:—

1. All such merchandise, effects, and property, if imported previously to the restoration of the custom-houses to the Mexican authorities, as stipulated for in the third article of this treaty, shall be exempt from confiscation, although the importation of the same be prohibited by the Mexican tariff.

2. The same perfect exemption shall be enjoyed by all such merchandise, effects, and property, imported subsequently to the restoration of the custom-houses, and previously to the sixty days fixed in the following article for the coming into force of the Mexican tariff at such ports respectively; the said merchandise, effects, and property being, however, at the

time of their importation, subject to the payment of duties, as provided for in the said following article.

3. All merchandise, effects, and property described in the two rules foregoing shall, during their continuance at the place of importation, and upon their leaving such place for the interior, be exempt from all duty, tax, or impost of every kind, under whatsoever title or denomination. Nor shall they be there subjected to any charge whatsoever upon the sale thereof.

4. All merchandise, effects, and property, described in the first and second rules, which shall have been removed to any place in the interior whilst such place was in the occupation of the forces of the United States, shall, during their continuance therein, be exempt from all tax upon the sale or consumption thereof, and from every kind of impost or contribution, under whatsoever title or denomination.

5. But if any merchandise, effects, or property, described in the first and second rules, shall be removed to any place not occupied at the time by the forces of the United States, they shall, upon their introduction into such place, or upon their sale or consumption there, be subject to the same duties which, under the Mexican laws, they would be required to pay in such cases if they had been imported in time of peace, through the maritime customhouses, and had there paid the duties conformably with the Mexican tariff.

6. The owners of all merchandise, effects, or property described in the first and second rules, and existing in any port of Mexico, shall have the right to reship the same, exempt from all tax, impost, or contribution whatever.

With respect to the metals, or other property, exported from any Mexican port whilst in the occupation of the forces of the United States, and previously to the restoration of the custom-house at such port, no person shall be required by the Mexican authorities, whether general or state, to pay any tax, duty, or contribution upon any such exportation, or in any manner to account for the same to the said authorities.

### ARTICLE XX

Through consideration for the interests of commerce generally, it is agreed, that if less than sixty days should elapse between the date of the signature of this treaty and the restoration of the custom-houses, conformably with the stipulation in the third article, in such case all merchandise, effects, and property whatsoever, arriving at the Mexican ports after the restoration of the said custom-houses, and previously to the expiration of sixty days after the day of the signature of this treaty, shall be admitted to entry; and no other duties shall be levied thereon than the duties established by the tariff found in force at such custom-houses at the time of the restoration of the same. And to all such merchandise, effects, and property the rules established by the preceding article shall apply.

### ARTICLE XXI

If unhappily any disagreement should hereafter arise between the governments of the two republics, whether with respect to the interpretation of any stipulation in this treaty, or with respect to any other particular concerning the political or commercial relations of the two nations, the said governments, in the name of those nations, do promise to each other that they will endeavor, in the most sincere and earnest manner, to settle the differences so arising, and to preserve the state of peace and friendship in which the two countries are now placing themselves; using, for this end, mutual representations and pacific negotiations. And if, by these means, they should not be enabled to come to an agreement, a resort shall not, on this account, be had to reprisals, aggression, or hostility of any kind, by the one republic against the other, until the government of that which deems itself aggrieved shall have maturely considered, in the spirit of peace and good neighborship, whether it would not be better that such difference should be settled by the arbitration of commissioners appointed on each side, or by that of a friendly nation. And should such course be proposed by either party, it shall be acceded to by the other, unless deemed by it altogether incompatible with the nature of the difference, or the circumstances of the case.

### ARTICLE XXII

If (which is not to be expected, and which God forbid!) war should unhappily break out between the two republics, they do now, with a view to such calamity, solemnly pledge themselves to each other and to the world, to observe the following rules; absolutely where the nature of the subject permits, and as closely as possible in all cases where such absolute observance shall be impossible:—

1. The merchants of either republic then residing in the other shall be allowed to remain twelve months, (for those dwelling in the interior,) and six months (for those dwelling at the seaports,) to collect their debts and settle their affairs; during which periods, they shall enjoy the same protection, and be on the same footing, in all respects, as the citizens or subjects of the most friendly nations; and, at the expiration thereof, or at any time before, they shall have full liberty to depart, carrying off all their effects without molestation or hinderance, conforming therein to the same laws which the citizens or subjects of the most friendly nations are required to conform to. Upon the entrance of the armies of either nation into the territories of the other, women and children, ecclesiastics, scholars of every faculty, cultivators of the earth, merchants, artisans, manufacturers, and fishermen, unarmed and inhabiting unfortified towns, villages, or places, and in general all persons whose occupations are for the common subsistence and benefit of mankind, shall be allowed to continue their respective employments unmolested in their persons. Nor shall their houses or goods be burnt or otherwise destroyed, nor their cattle taken, nor their fields wasted, by the armed force into whose power, by the events of war, they may happen to fall; but if the necessity arise to take any thing from them for the use of such armed force, the same shall be paid for at an equitable price. All churches, hospitals, schools, colleges, libraries, and other establishments for charitable and beneficent purposes, shall be respected, and all persons connected with the same protected in the discharge of their duties, and the pursuit of their vocations.

2. In order that the fate of prisoners of war may be alleviated, all such practices as those of sending them into distant inclement or unwholesome

districts, or crowding them into close and noxious places, shall be studiously avoided. They shall not be confined in dungeons, prison-ships, or prisons; nor be put in irons, or bound, or otherwise restrained in the use of their limbs. The officers shall enjoy liberty on their paroles, within convenient districts, and have comfortable quarters; and the common soldier shall be disposed in cantonments, open and extensive enough for air and exercise, and lodged in barracks as roomy and good as are provided by the party in whose power they are for its own troops. But if any officer shall break his parole by leaving the district so assigned him, or any other prisoner shall escape from the limits of his cantonment, after they shall have been designated to him, such individual, officer, or other prisoner, shall forfeit so much of the benefit of this article as provides for his liberty on parole or in cantonment. And if any officer so breaking his parole, or any common soldier so escaping from the limits assigned him, shall afterwards be found in arms, previously to his being regularly exchanged, the person so offending shall be dealt with according to the established laws of war. The officers shall be daily furnished by the party in whose power they are, with as many rations, and of the same articles, as are allowed, either in kind or by commutation, to officers of equal rank in its own army; and all others shall be daily furnished with such ration as is allowed to a common soldier in its own service: the value of all which supplies shall, at the close of the war, or at periods to be agreed upon between the respective commanders, be paid by the other party, on a mutual adjustment of accounts for the subsistence of prisoners; and such accounts shall not be mingled with or set off against any others, nor the balance due on them be withheld, as a compensation or reprisal for any cause whatever, real or pretended. Each party shall be allowed to keep a commissary of prisoners, appointed by itself, with every cantonment of prisoners, in possession of the other; which commissary shall see the prisoners as often as he pleases; shall be allowed to receive, exempt from all duties or taxes, and to distribute, whatever comforts may be sent to them by their friends; and shall be free to transmit his reports in open letters to the party by whom he is employed.

And it is declared that neither the pretence that war dissolves all treaties, nor any other whatever, shall be considered as annulling or suspending the solemn covenant contained in this article. On the contrary, the state of war is precisely that for which it is provided; and during which, its stipulations are to be as sacredly observed as the most acknowledged obligations under the law of nature or nations.

### ARTICLE XXIII

This treaty shall be ratified by the President of the United States of America, by and with the advice and consent of the Senate thereof; by the President of the Mexican republic, with the previous approbation of its General Congress; and the ratifications shall be exchanged in the city of Washington, or at the seat of government of Mexico, in four months from the date of the signature hereof, or sooner if practicable.

In faith whereof, we, the respective plenipotentiaries, have signed this treaty of peace, friendship, limits, and settlement; and have hereunto affixed our seals respectively. Done in quintuplicate, at the city of Guadalupe Hidalgo, on the second day of February, in the year of our Lord one thousand eight hundred and fortyeight.

N. P. Trist, [L.S.]
Luis G. Cuevas, [L.S.]
Bernardo Couto, [L.S.]
Migl. Atristain, [L.S.]

*First and Fifth Articles of the unratified Convention between the United States and the Mexican Republic of the 20th November, 1843*

### ARTICLE I

All claims of citizens of the Mexican republic against the government of the United States, which shall be presented in the manner and time hereinafter expressed, and all claims of citizens of the United States against the government of the Mexican republic, which, for whatever cause, were not submitted to, nor considered, nor finally decided by, the commission, nor by the arbiter appointed by the convention of 1839, and which shall be presented in the manner and time hereinafter specified, shall be referred to four commissioners, who shall form a board, and shall be appointed in the following manner, that is to say: Two commissioners shall be appointed by the President of the Mexican republic, and the other two by the President of the United States, with the approbation and consent of the Senate. The said commissioners, thus appointed, shall, in presence of each other, take an oath to examine and decide impartially the claims submitted to them, and which may lawfully be considered, according to the proofs which shall be presented, the principles of right and justice, the law of nations, and the treaties between the two republics.

### ARTICLE V

All claims of citizens of the United States against the government of the Mexican republic, which were considered by the commissioners, and referred to the umpire appointed under the convention of the eleventh April, 1839, and which were not decided by him, shall be referred to, and decided by, the umpire to be appointed, as provided by this convention, on the points submitted to the umpire under the late convention, and his decision shall be final and conclusive. It is also agreed, that if the respective commissioners shall deem it expedient, they may submit to the said arbiter new arguments upon the said claims.

1848

# The Treaty of Paris

### INTRODUCTION

The United States of America and Her Majesty the Queen Regent of Spain, in the name of her august son Don Alfonso XIII, desiring to end the state of war now existing between the two countries, have for that purpose appointed as plenipotentiaries:

The President of the United States,

William R. Day, Cushman K. Davis, William P. Frye, George Gray, and Whitelaw Reid, citizens of the United States;

And Her Majesty the Queen Regent of Spain,

Don Eugenio Montero Ríos, president of the senate, Don Buenaventura de Abarzuza, senator of the Kingdom and ex minister of the Crown; Don Jose de Garnica, deputy to the Cortes and associate justice of the supreme court; Don Wenceslao Ramirez de Villa-Urrutia, envoy extraordinary and minister plenipotentiary at Brussels, and Don Rafael Cerero, general division;

Who having assembled in Paris, and having exchanged their full powers, which were found to be in due and proper form, have, after discussion of the matters before them, agreed upon the following articles:

### ARTICLE I

Spain relinquishes all claim of sovereignty over the title to Cuba. And as the island is, upon its evacuation by Spain, to be occupied by the United States, the United States will, so long as such occupation shalt last, assume and discharge the obligations that may under international law result from the fact of its occupation, for the protection of life and property.

### ARTICLE II

Spain cedes to the United States the island of Puerto Rico and other islands now under Spanish sovereignty in the West Indies, and the island of Guam in the Marianas or Ladrones.

### ARTICLE III

Spain cedes to the United States the archipelago known as the Philippine Islands, and comprehending the islands lying within the following lines:

A line running from west to east along or near the twentieth parallel of north latitude, and through the middle of the navigable channel of Bachi, from the one hundred and eighteenth (118th) to the one hundred and twenty-seventh (127th) degree meridian of longitude east of Greenwich, thence along the one hundred and twenty-seventh (127th) degree meridian of longitude east of Greenwich to the parallel of four degrees and forty-five minutes (40° 45') north latitude, thence along the parallel of four degrees and forty-five minutes (4° 45') north latitude to its intersection with the meridian of longitude one hundred and nineteen degrees and thirty-five minutes (119° 35') east of Greenwich, thence along the meridian of longitude one hundred and nineteen degrees and thirty-five minutes (119° 35') east of Greenwich to the parallel of latitude seven degrees and forty-five minutes (7° 45') north, thence along the parallel of latitude of seven degrees and forty-five minutes (7° 45') to its intersection with the one hundred and six-teenth (116th) degree meridian of longitude east of Greenwich, thence by a direct line to the intersection of the tenth (10th) degree parallel of north latitude with the one hundred and eighteenth (118th) degree meridian of longitude east of Greenwich, and thence along the one hundred and eighteenth

(118th) degree meridian of longitude east of Greenwich to the point of beginning.

The United States will pay to Spain the sum of twenty million dollars ($20,000,000) within three months after the exchange of the ratifications of the present treaty.

## ARTICLE IV

The United States will, for the term of ten years from the date of the exchange of the ratifications of the present treaty, admit Spanish ships and merchandise to the ports of the Philippine Islands on the same terms as ships and merchandise of the United States.

## ARTICLE V

The United States will, upon the signature of the present treaty, send back to Spain, at its own cost, the Spanish soldiers taken as prisoners of war on the capture of Manila by the American forces. The arms of the soldiers in question shall be restored to them.

Spain will, upon the exchange of the ratifications of the present treaty, proceed to evacuate the Philippines, as well as the island of Guam, on terms similar to those agreed upon by the Commissioners appointed to arrange for the evacuation of Puerto Rico and other islands in the West Indies, under the Protocol of August 12, 1898, which is to continue in force till its provisions are completely executed.

The time within which the evacuation of the Philippine Islands and Guam shall be completed shall be fixed by the two Governments. Stands of colors, uncaptured war vessels, small arms, guns of all calibers, with their carriages and accessories, powder, ammunition, livestock, and materials and supplies of all kinds, belonging to the land and naval forces of Spain in the Philippines and Guam, remain the property of Spain. Pieces of heavy ordnance, exclusive of field artillery, in the fortifications and coast defenses, shall remain in their emplacements for the term of six months, to be reckoned from the exchange of ratifications of the treaty; and the United States may, in the meantime, purchase such material from Spain, if a satisfactory agreement between the two Governments on the subject shall be reached.

## ARTICLE VI

Spain will, upon the signature of the present treaty, release all prisoners of war, and all persons detained or imprisoned for political offenses, in connection with the insurrections in Cuba and the Philippines and the war with the United States.

Reciprocally, the United States will release all persons made prisoners of war by the American forces, and will undertake to obtain the release of all Spanish prisoners in the hands of the insurgents in Cuba and the Philippines.

The Government of the United States will at its own cost return to the United States, Cuba, Puerto Rico and the Philippines, according to the situation of their respective homes, prisoners released or caused to be released by them, respectively, under this article.

### ARTICLE VII

The United States and Spain mutually relinquish all claims for indemnity, national and individual, of every kind, of either Government, or of its citizens or subjects, against the other Government, that may have arisen since the beginning of the late insurrection in Cuba and prior to the exchange of ratifications of the present treaty, including all claims for indemnity for the cost of the war.

The United States will adjudicate and settle the claims of its citizens against Spain relinquished in this article.

### ARTICLE VIII

In conformity with the provisions of Articles I, II, and III of this treaty, Spain relinquishes in Cuba, and cedes in Puerto Rico and other islands in the West Indies, in the island of Guam, and in the Philippines Archipelago all the buildings, wharves, barracks, forts, structures, public highways and other immovable property which, in conformity with law, belong to the public domain, and as such belong to the Crown of Spain.

And it is hereby declared that the relinquishment or cession, as the case may be, to which the preceding paragraph refers, cannot in any respect impair the property or rights which by law belong to the peaceful possession of property of all kinds, of provinces, municipalities, public or private establishments, ecclesiastical or civic bodies, or any other associations having legal capacity to acquire and possess property in the aforesaid territories renounced or ceded, or of private individuals, of whatsoever nationality such individuals may be.

The aforesaid relinquishment or cessions, as the case may be, includes all documents exclusively referring to the sovereignty relinquished or ceded that may exist in the archives of the Peninsula. Where any document in such archives only in part relates to said sovereignty, a copy of such part will be furnished whenever it shall be requested. Like rules shall be reciprocally observed in favor of Spain in respect to documents in the archives of the islands above referred to.

In the aforesaid relinquishment or cession, as the case may be, are also included such rights as the Crown of Spain and its authorities possess in respect of the official archives and records, executive as well as judicial, in the islands above referred to, which relate to said islands or the rights and property of their inhabitants. Such archives and records shall be carefully preserved, and private persons shall without distinction have the right to require, in accordance with law, authenticated copies of the contracts, wills and other instruments forming part of notarial protocols or files, or which may be contained in the executive or judicial archives, be the latter in Spain or in the islands aforesaid.

### ARTICLE IX

Spanish subjects, natives of the Peninsula, residing in the territory over which Spain by the present treaty relinquishes or cedes her sovereignty, may remain in such territory or may remove therefrom, retaining in either event all their rights of property, including the right to sell or dispose of such property or of its proceeds; and they shall also have the right to carry on their industry, commerce and professions, being subject in respect thereof to such laws as are applicable to other foreigners. In case they remain in the territory they may preserve their allegiance to the Crown of Spain by making before a court of record, within a year from the date of the exchange of ratifications of this treaty, a declaration of their decision to preserve such allegiance; in default of which declaration they shall be held to have renounced it and to have adopted the nationality of the territory in which they may reside.

The civil rights and political status of the native inhabitants of the territories hereby ceded to the United States shall be determined by the Congress.

### ARTICLE X

The inhabitants of the territories over which Spain relinquishes or cedes her sovereignty shall be secured in the free exercise of their religion.

### ARTICLE XI

The Spaniards residing in the territories over which Spain by this treaty cedes or relinquishes her sovereignty shall be subject in matters civil as well as criminal to the jurisdiction of the courts of the country wherein they reside, pursuant to the ordinary laws governing the same; and they shall have the right to appear before such courts and to pursue the same course as citizens of the country to which the courts belong.

### ARTICLE XII

Judicial proceedings pending at the time of the exchange of ratifications of this treaty in the territories over which Spain relinquishes or cedes her sovereignty shall be determined according to the following rules:

1. Judgments rendered either in civil suits between private individuals, or in criminal matters, before the date mentioned, and with respect to which there is no recourse or right of review under the Spanish law, shall be deemed to be final, and shall be executed in due form by competent authority in the territory within which such judgments should be carried out.

2. Civil suits between private individuals which may on the date mentioned be undetermined shall be prosecuted to judgment before the court in which they may then be pending or in the court that may be substituted therefor.

3. Criminal actions pending on the date mentioned before the Supreme Court of Spain against citizens of the territory which by this treaty ceases to be Spanish shall continue under its jurisdiction until final judgment; but, such judgment having been rendered, the execution thereof shall be committed to the competent authority of the place in which the case arose.

### ARTICLE XIII

The rights of property secured by copyrights and patents acquired by Spaniards in the Island of Cuba and in Puerto Rico, the Philippines and other ceded territories, at the time of the exchange of the ratification of this treaty, shall continue to be respected. Spanish scientific, literary and artistic works, not subversive of public order in the territories in question, shall continue to be admitted free of duty into such territories, for the period of ten years, to be reckoned from the date of the exchange of the ratifications of this treaty.

### ARTICLE XIV

Spain shall have the power to establish consular officers in the ports and places of the territories, the sovereignty over which has been either relinquished or ceded by the present treaty.

### ARTICLE XV

The Government of each country will, for the term of ten years, accord to the merchant vessels of the other country the same treatment in respect of all port charges, including entrance and clearance dues, light dues, and tonnage duties, as it accords to its own merchant vessels, not engaged in the coastwise trade.

This article may at any time be terminated on six months' notice given by either Government to the other.

### ARTICLE XVI

It is understood that any obligations assumed in this treaty by the United States with respect to Cuba are limited to the time of its occupancy thereof; but it will upon the termination of such occupancy, advise any Government established in the island to assume the same obligations.

### ARTICLE XVII

The present treaty shall be ratified by the President of the United States, by and with the advice and consent of the Senate thereof, and by Her Majesty the Queen Regent of Spain; and the ratifications shall be exchanged at Washington within six months from the date hereof, or earlier if possible.

In faith whereof, we, the respective Plenipotentiaries, have signed this treaty and hereunto affixed our seals.

Done in duplicate at Paris, the tenth day of December, in the year of Our Lord one thousand eight hundred and ninety eight.

(Seal) WILLIAM R. DAY
(Seal) CUSHMAN K. DAVIS
(Seal) WILLIAM P. FRYE
(Seal) GEO. GRAY
(Seal) WHITELAW REID
(Seal) EUGENIO MONTERO RIOS
(Seal) J. DE GARNICA
(Seal) B. DE ABARZUZA
(Seal) W.R. DE VILLA-URRUTIA
(Seal) RAFAEL CERERO

1898

# The Jones Act

## An Act to Provide a Civil Government for Porto Rico, and for Other Purposes

*Be it enacted by the Senate and House of Representatives of the United States of America in Congress assembled,* That the provisions of this Act shall apply to the island of Porto Rico and to the adjacent islands belonging to the United States, and waters of those islands; and the name Porto Rico as used in this Act shall be held to include not only the island of that name but all the adjacent islands as aforesaid.

### BILL OF RIGHTS

SEC. 2. That no law shall be enacted in Porto Rico which shall deprive any person of life, liberty, or property without due process of law, or deny to any person therein the equal protection of the laws.

That in all criminal prosecutions the accused shall enjoy the right to have the assistance of counsel for his defense, to be informed of the nature and cause of the accusation, to have a copy thereof, to have a speedy and public trial, to be confronted with the witnesses against him, and to have compulsory process for obtaining witnesses in his favor.

That no person shall be held to answer for a criminal offense without due process of law; and no person for the same offense shall be twice put in jeopardy of punishment, nor shall be compelled in any criminal case to be a witness against himself.

That all persons shall before conviction be bailable by sufficient sureties, except for capital offenses when the proof is evident or the presumption great.

That no law impairing the obligation of contracts shall be enacted.

That no person shall be imprisoned for debt.

That the privilege of the writ of habeas corpus shall not be suspended, unless when in case of rebellion, insurrection, or invasion the public safety may require it, in either of which events the same may be suspended by the President, or by the governor, whenever during such period the necessity for such suspension shall exist.

That no ex post facto law or bill of attainder shall be enacted.

Private property shall not be taken or damaged for public use except upon payment of just compensation ascertained in the manner provided by law.

Nothing contained in this Act shall be construed to limit the power of the legislature to enact laws for the protection of the lives, health, or safety of employees.

That no law granting a title of nobility shall be enacted, and no person holding any office of profit or trust under the government of Porto Rico shall, without the consent of the Congress of the United States, accept any present, emolument, office, or title of any kind whatever from any king, queen, prince, or foreign State, or any officer thereof.

That excessive bail shall not be required, nor excessive fines imposed, nor cruel and unusual punishments inflicted.

That the right to be secure against unreasonable searches and seizures shall not be violated.

That no warrant for arrest or search shall issue but upon probable cause, supported by oath or affirmation, and particularly describing the place to be searched and the persons or things to be seized.

That slavery shall not exist in Porto Rico.

That involuntary servitude, except as a punishment for crime, whereof the party shall have been duly convicted, shall not exist in Porto Rico.

That no law shall be passed abridging the freedom of speech or of the press, or the right of the people peaceably to assemble and petition the Government for redress of grievances.

That no law shall be made respecting an establishment of religion or prohibiting the free exercise thereof, and that the free exercise and enjoyment of religious profession and worship without discrimination or preference shall forever be allowed, and that no political or religious test other than an oath to support the Constitution of the United States and the laws of Porto Rico shall be required as a qualification to any office or public trust under the government of Porto Rico.

That no public money or property shall ever be appropriated, applied, donated, used, directly or indirectly, for the use, benefit, or support of any sect, church, denomination, sectarian institution or association, or system of religion, or for the use, benefit, or support of any priest, preacher, minister, or other religious teacher or dignitary as such, or for charitable, industrial, educational, or benevolent purposes to any person, corporation, or community not under the absolute control of Porto Rico. Contracting of polygamous or plural marriages hereafter is prohibited.

That one year after the approval of this Act and thereafter it shall be unlawful to import, manufacture, sell, or give away, or to expose for sale or gift any intoxicating drink or drug: *Provided,* That the legislature may authorize and regulate importation, manufacture, and sale of said liquors and drugs for medicinal, sacramental, industrial, and scientific uses only. The penalty for violations of this provision with reference to intoxicants shall be a fine of not less than $25 for the first offense, and for second and subsequent offenses a fine of not less than $50 and imprisonment for not less than one month or more than one year: *And provided further,* That at any general election within five years after the approval of this Act this provision may, upon petition of not less than ten per centum of the qualified electors of Porto Rico, be submitted to a vote of the qualified electors of Porto Rico, and if a majority of all the qualified electors of Porto Rico voting upon such question shall vote to repeal this provision it shall thereafter not be in force and effect; otherwise it shall be in full force and effect.

That no money shall be paid out of the treasury except in pursuance of an appropriation by law, and on warrant drawn by the proper officer in pursuance thereof.

That the rule of taxation in Porto Rico shall be uniform.

That all money derived from any tax levied or assessed for a special purpose shall be treated as a special fund in the Treasury and paid out for such purpose only except upon the approval of the President of the United States.

That eight hours shall constitute a day's work in all cases of employment of laborers and mechanics by and on behalf of the government of the island on public works, except in cases of emergency.

That the employment of children under the age of fourteen years in any occupation injurious to health or morals or hazardous to life of limb is hereby prohibited.

Sec. 3. That no export duties shall be levied or collected on exports from Porto Rico, but taxes and assessments on property, internal revenue, and license fees, and royalties for franchises, privileges, and concessions may be imposed for the purposes of the insular and municipal governments, respectively, as may be provided and defined by the Legislature of Porto Rico; and when necessary to anticipate taxes and revenues, bonds and other obligations may be issued by Porto Rico or any municipal government therein as may be provided by law, and to protect the public credit: *Provided, however,* That no public indebtedness of Porto Rico or of any subdivision or municipality thereof shall be authorized or allowed in excess of seven per centum of the aggregate tax valuation of its property, and all bonds issued by the government of Porto Rico, or by its authority, shall be exempt from taxation by the Government of the United States, or by the government of Porto Rico or of any political or municipal subdivision thereof, or by any State, or by any county, municipality, or other municipal subdivision of any State or Territory of the United States, or by the District of Columbia. In computing the indebtedness of the people of Porto Rico, bonds issued by the people of Porto Rico secured by an equivalent amount of bonds of municipal corporations or school boards of Porto Rico shall not be counted.

Sec. 4. That the capital of Porto Rico shall be at the city of San Juan, and the seat of government shall be maintained there.

Sec. 5. That all citizens of Porto Rico, as defined by section seven of the Act of April twelfth, nineteen hundred, "temporarily to provide revenues and a civil government for Porto Rico, and for other purposes," and all natives of Porto Rico who were temporarily absent from that island on April eleventh, eighteen hundred and ninety-nine, and have since returned and are permanently residing in that island, and are not citizens of any foreign country, are hereby declared, and shall be deemed and held to be, citizens of the United States: *Provided.* That any person hereinbefore described may retain his present political status by making a declaration, under oath, of his decision to do so within six months of the taking effect of this Act before the district court in the district in which he resides, the declaration to be in form as follows:

"I,      , being duly sworn, hereby declare my intention not to become a citizen of the United States as provided in the Act of Congress conferring United States citizenship upon citizens of Porto Rico and certain natives permanently residing in said island."

In the case of any such person who may be absent from the island during said six months the term of this proviso may be availed of by transmitting a declaration, under oath, in the form herein provided within six months of the taking effect of this Act to the executive secretary of Porto Rico: *And provided further,* That any person who is born in Porto Rico of an alien parent and is permanently residing in that island may, if of full age, within six months of the taking effect of this Act, or if a minor, upon reaching his majority or within one year thereafter, make a sworn declaration of allegiance to the United States before the United States District Court for Porto Rico, setting forth therein all the facts connected with his or her birth and residence in Porto Rico and accompanying due proof thereof, and from and after the making of such declaration shall be considered to be a citizen of the United States.

SEC. 6. That all expenses that may be incurred on account of the government of Porto Rico for salaries of officials and the conduct of their offices and departments, and all expenses and obligations contracted for the internal improvement or development of the island, not, however, including defenses, barracks, harbors, lighthouses, buoys, and other works undertaken by the United States, shall, except as otherwise specifically provided by the Congress, be paid by the treasurer of Porto Rico out of the revenue in his custody.

SEC. 7. That all property which may have been acquired in Porto Rico by the United States under the cession of Spain in the treaty of peace entered into on the tenth day of December, eighteen hundred and ninety-eight, in any public bridges, road houses, water powers, highways, unnavigable streams and the beds thereof, subterranean waters, mines or minerals under the surface of private lands, all property which at the time of the cession belonged, under the laws of Spain then in force, to the various harbor works boards of Porto Rico, all the harbor shores, docks, slips, reclaimed lands, and all public lands and buildings not heretofore reserved by the United States for public purposes, is hereby placed under the control of the government of Porto Rico, to be administered for the benefit of the people of Porto Rico; and the Legislature of Porto Rico shall have authority, subject to the limitations imposed upon all its acts, to legislate with respect to all such matters as it may deem advisable: *Provided,* That the President may from time to time, in his discretion, convey to the people of Porto Rico such lands, buildings, or interests in lands or other property now owned by the United States and within the territorial limits of Porto Rico as in his opinion are no longer needed for purposes of the United States. And he may from time to time accept by legislative grant from Porto Rico any lands, buildings, or other interests or property which may be needed for public purposes by the United States.

SEC. 8. That the harbor areas and navigable streams and bodies of water and submerged lands underlying the same in and around the island of Porto Rico and the adjacent islands and waters, now owned by the United States and not reserved by the United States for public purposes, be, and the same are hereby, placed under the control of the government of Porto Rico, to be administered in the same manner and subject to the same limitation as the property enumerated in the preceding section: *Provided,* That all laws of the United States for the protection and improvement of the navigable waters of the United States and the preservation of the interests of navigation and commerce, except so far as the same may be locally inapplicable, shall apply to said island and waters and to its adjacent islands and waters: *Provided further,* That nothing in this Act contained shall be construed so as to affect or impair in any manner the terms or conditions of any authorizations, permits, or other powers heretofore lawfully granted or exercised in or in respect of said waters and submerged lands in and surrounding said island and its adjacent islands by the Secretary of War or other authorized officer or agent of the United States: *And provided further,* That the Act of Congress approved June eleventh, nineteen hundred and six, entitled "An Act to empower the Secretary of War, under certain restrictions, to authorize the construction, extension, and maintenance of wharves, piers, and other structures on lands underlying harbor areas in navigable streams and bodies of water in or surrounding Porto Rico and the islands adjacent thereto," and all other laws and parts of laws in conflict with this section be, and the same are hereby, repealed.

SEC. 9. That the statutory laws of the United States not locally inapplicable, except as hereinbefore or hereinafter otherwise provided, shall have the same force and effect in Porto Rico as in the United States, except the internal-revenue laws: *Provided, however,* That hereafter all taxes collected under the internal-revenue laws of the United States on articles produced in Porto Rico and transported to the United States, or consumed in the island shall be covered into the treasury of Porto Rico.

SEC. 10. That all judicial process shall run in the name of "United States of America, ss, the President of the United States," and all penal or criminal prosecutions in the local courts shall be conducted in the name and by the authority of "The People of Porto Rico"; and all officials shall be citizens of the United States, and, before entering upon the duties of their respective offices, shall take an oath to support the Constitution of the United States and the laws of Porto Rico.

SEC. 11. That all reports required by law to be made by the governor or heads of departments to any official of the United States shall hereafter be made to an executive department of the Government of the United States to be designated by the President, and the President is hereby authorized to place all matters pertaining to the government of Porto Rico in the jurisdiction of such department.

## EXECUTIVE DEPARTMENT

SEC. 12. That the supreme executive power shall be vested in an executive officer, whose official title shall be "The Governor of Porto Rico." He shall be appointed by the President, by and with the advice and consent of the Senate, and hold his office at the pleasure of the President and until his successor is chosen and qualified. The governor shall reside in Porto Rico during his official incumbency and maintain his office at the seat of government. He shall have general supervision and control of all the departments and bureaus of the government in Porto Rico, so far as is not inconsistent with the provisions of this Act, and shall be commander in chief of the militia. He may grant pardons and reprieves and remit fines and forfeitures for offenses against the laws of Porto Rico, and respites for all offenses against the laws of the United States until the decision of the President can be ascertained, and may veto any legislation enacted as hereinafter provided. He shall commission all officers that he may be authorized to appoint. He shall be responsible for the faithful execution of the laws of Porto Rico and of the United States applicable in Porto Rico, and whenever it becomes necessary he may call upon the commanders of the military and naval forces of the United States in the island, or summon the posse comitatus, or call out the militia to prevent or suppress lawless violence, invasion, insurrection, or rebellion, and he may, in case of rebellion or invasion, or imminent danger thereof, when the public safety requires it, suspend the privilege of the writ of habeas corpus, or place the island, or any part thereof, under martial law until communication can be had with the President and the President's decision therein made known. He shall annually, and at such other times as he may be required, make official report of the transactions of the government of Porto Rico to the executive department of the Government of the United States to be designated by the President as herein provided, and his said annual report shall be transmitted to Congress, and he shall perform such additional duties and functions as may in pursuance of law be delegated to him by the President.

SEC. 13. That the following executive departments are hereby created: A department of justice, the head of which shall be designated as the attorney general; a department of finance, the head of which shall be designated as the treasurer; a department of interior, the head of which shall be designated as the commissioner of the interior; a department of education, the head of which shall be designated as the commissioner of education; a department of agriculture and labor, the head of which shall be designated as the commissioner of agriculture and labor; and a department of health, the head of which shall be designated as the commissioner of health. The attorney general and commissioner of education shall be appointed by the President, by and with the advice and consent of the Senate of the United States, to hold office for four years and until their successors are appointed and qualified, unless sooner removed by the President. The heads of the four remaining departments shall be appointed by the governor, by and with the advice and consent of the Senate of Porto Rico. The heads of departments appointed by the governor shall hold office for the term of four years and until their successors are appointed and qualified, unless sooner removed by the governor.

Heads of departments shall reside in Porto Rico during their official incumbency, and those appointed by the governor shall have resided in Porto Rico for at least one year prior to their appointment.

The heads of departments shall collectively form a council to the governor, known as the executive council. They shall perform under the general supervision of the governor the duties hereinafter prescribed, or which may hereafter be prescribed by law and such other duties, not inconsistent with law, as the governor, with the approval of the President, may assign to them; and they shall make annual and such other reports to the governor as he may require, which shall be transmitted to the executive department of the Government of the United States to be designated by the President as herein provided: *Provided*, That the duties herein imposed upon the heads of departments shall not carry with them any additional compensation.

SEC. 14. That the attorney general shall have charge of the administration of justice in Porto Rico; he shall be the legal adviser of the governor and the heads of departments and shall be responsible for the proper representation of the people of Porto Rico or its duly constituted officers in all actions and proceedings, civil or criminal, in the Supreme court of Porto Rico in which the people of Porto Rico shall be interested or a party, and he may, if directed by the governor or if in his judgment the public interest requires it, represent the people of Porto Rico or its duly constituted officers in any other court or before any other officer or board in any action or proceeding, civil or criminal, in which the people of Porto Rico may be a party or be interested. He shall also perform such other duties not inconsistent herewith as may be prescribed by law.

SEC. 15. That the treasurer shall give bond, approved as to form by the attorney general of Porto Rico, in such sum as the legislature may require, not less, however, than the sum of $125,000, with surety or sureties approved by the governor, and he shall collect and be the custodian of public funds, and shall disburse the same in accordance with law, on warrants signed by the auditor and countersigned by the governor, and perform such other duties as may be provided by law. He may designate banking institutions in Porto Rico and the United States as depositaries of the government of Porto Rico, subject to such conditions as may be prescribed by the governor, after they have filed with him satisfactory evidence of their sound financial condition and have deposited bonds of the United States or of the government of Porto Rico or other security satisfactory to the governor in such amounts as may be indicated by him; and no banking institution shall be designated a depositary of the government of Porto Rico until the foregoing conditions have been complied with. Interest on deposits shall be required and paid into the treasury.

SEC. 16. That the commissioner of the interior shall superintend all works of a public nature, have charge of all public buildings, grounds, and lands, except those belonging to the United States, and shall execute such requirements as may be imposed by law with respect thereto, and perform such other duties as may be prescribed by law.

SEC. 17. That the commissioner of education shall superintend public instruction throughout Porto Rico; all proposed disbursements on account thereof must be approved by him, and all courses of study shall be prepared by him, subject to disapproval by the governor if he desires to act. He shall prepare rules governing the selection of teachers, and appointments of teachers by local school boards shall be subject to his approval, and he shall perform such other duties, not inconsistent with this Act, as may be prescribed by law.

SEC. 18. That the commissioner of agriculture and labor shall have general charge of such bureaus and branches of government as have been or shall be legally constituted for the study, advancement, and benefit of agricultural and other industries, the chief purpose of this department being to foster, promote, and develop the agricultural interests and the welfare of the wage earners of Porto Rico, to improve their working conditions, and to advance their opportunities for profitable employment, and shall perform such other duties as may be prescribed by law.

SEC. 19. That the commissioner of health shall have general charge of all matters relating to public health, sanitation, and charities, except such as relate to the conduct of maritime quarantine, and shall perform such other duties as may be prescribed by law.

SEC. 20. That there shall be appointed by the President an auditor, at an annual salary of $5,000, for a term of four years and until his successor is appointed and qualified, who shall examine, audit, and settle all accounts pertaining to the revenues and receipts, from whatever source, of the government of Porto Rico and of the municipal governments of Porto Rico, including public trust funds and funds derived from bond issues; and audit, in accordance with law and administrative regulations, all expenditures of funds or property pertaining to or held in trust by the government of Porto Rico or the municipalities or dependencies thereof. He shall perform a like duty with respect to all government branches.

He shall keep the general accounts of the government and preserve the vouchers pertaining thereto.

It shall be the duty of the auditor to bring to the attention of the proper administrative officer expenditures of funds or property which, in his opinion, are irregular, unnecessary, excessive, or extravagant.

In case of vacancy or of the absence from duty, from any cause, of the auditor, the Governor of Porto Rico may designate an assistant, who shall have charge of the office.

The jurisdiction of the auditor over accounts, whether of funds or property, and all vouchers and records pertaining thereto, shall be exclusive. With the approval of the governor, he shall from time to time make and promulgate general or special rules and regulations not inconsistent with law covering the methods of accounting for public funds and property, and funds and property held in trust by the government or any of its branches: *Provided,* That any officer accountable for public funds or property may require such additional reports or returns from his subordinates or others as he may deem necessary for his own information and protection.

The decisions of the auditor shall be final, except that appeal therefrom may be taken by the party aggrieved or the head of the department concerned within one year, in the manner hereinafter prescribed. The auditor shall, except as hereinafter provided, have like authority as that conferred by the law upon the several auditors of the United States and the Comptroller of the United States Treasury, and is authorized to communicate directly with any person having claims before him for settlement, or with any department, officer, or person having official relations with his office.

As soon after the close of each fiscal year as the accounts of said year may be examined and adjusted, the auditors shall submit to the governor an annual report of the fiscal concerns of the government, showing the receipts and disbursements of the various departments and bureaus of the government and of the various municipalities, and make such other reports as may be required of him by the governor or the head of the executive department of the Government of the United States, to be designated by the President as herein provided.

In the execution of his duties the auditor is authorized to summon witnesses, administer oaths, and to take evidence, and, in the pursuance of these provisions, may issue subpœnas and enforce the attendance of witnesses.

The office of the auditor shall be under the general supervision of the governor and shall consist of the auditor and such necessary assistants as may be prescribed by law.

SEC. 21. That any person aggrieved by the action or decision of the auditor in the settlement of his account or claim may, within one year, take an appeal in writing to the governor, which appeal shall specifically set forth the particular action of the auditor to which exception is taken, with the reason and authorities relied on for reversing such decision. The decision of the governor in such case shall be final, subject to such right of action as may be otherwise provided by law.

Sec. 22. That there shall be appointed by the governor, by and with the advice and consent of the Senate of Porto Rico, an executive secretary at an annual salary of $4,000, who shall record and preserve the minutes and proceedings of the public service commission hereinafter provided for and the laws enacted by the legislature and all acts and proceedings of the governor, and promulgate all proclamations and orders of the governor and all laws enacted by the legislature, and until otherwise provided by the legislature of Porto Rico perform all the duties of secretary of Porto Rico as now provided by law, except as otherwise specified in this Act, and perform such other duties as may be assigned to him by the Governor of Porto Rico. In the event of a vacancy in the office, or the absence, illness, or temporary disqualification of such officer, the governor shall designate some officer or employee of the government to discharge the functions of said office during such vacancy, absence, illness, or temporary disqualification.

Sec. 23. That the Governor of Porto Rico, within sixty days after the end of each session of the legislature, shall transmit to the executive department of the Government of the United States, to be designated as herein provided for, which shall in turn transmit the same to the Congress of the United States, copies of all laws enacted during the session.

Sec. 24. That the President may from time to time designate the head of an executive department of Porto Rico to act as governor in the case of a vacancy, the temporary removal, resignation, or disability of the governor, or his temporary absence, and the head of the department thus designated shall exercise all the powers and perform all the duties of the governor during such vacancy, disability, or absence.

### LEGISLATIVE DEPARTMENT

Sec. 25. That all local legislative powers in Porto Rico, except as herein otherwise provided, shall be vested in a legislature which shall consist of two houses, one the senate and the other the house of representatives, and the two houses shall be designated "the Legislature of Porto Rico."

Sec. 26. That the Senate of Porto Rico shall consist of nineteen members elected for terms of four years by the qualified electors of Porto Rico. Each of the seven senatorial districts defined as hereinafter provided shall have the right to elect two senators, and in addition thereto there shall be elected five senators at large. No person shall be a member of the Senate of Porto Rico who is not over thirty years of age, and who is not able to read and write either the Spanish or English language, and who has not been a resident of Porto Rico for at least two consecutive years, and, except in the case of senators at large, an actual resident of the senatorial district from which chosen for a period of at least one year prior to his election. Except as herein otherwise provided, the Senate of Porto Rico shall exercise all of the purely legislative powers and functions heretofore exercised by the Executive Council, including confirmation of appointments; but appointments made while the senate is not in session shall be effective either until disapproved or until the next adjournment of the senate for the session. In electing the five senators at large each elector shall be permitted to vote for but one candidate, and the five candidates receiving the largest number of votes shall be declared elected.

SEC. 27. That the House of Representatives of Porto Rico shall consist of thirty-nine members elected quadrennially by the qualified electors of Porto Rico, as hereinafter provided. Each of the representative districts hereinafter provided for shall have the right to elect one representative, and in addition thereto there shall be elected four representatives at large. No person shall be a member of the house of representatives who is not over twenty-five years of age, and who is not able to read and write either the Spanish or English language, except in the case of representative at large, who has not been a bona fide resident of the district from which elected for at least one year prior to his election. In electing the four representatives at large, each elector shall be permitted to vote for but one candidate and the four candidates receiving the largest number of votes shall be elected.

SEC. 28. That for the purpose of elections hereafter to the legislature the island of Porto Rico shall be divided into thirty-five representative districts, composed of contiguous and compact territory and established, so far as practicable, upon the basis of equal population. The division into and the demarcation of such districts shall be made by the Executive Council of Porto Rico. Division of districts shall be made as nearly as practicable to conform to the topographical nature of the land, with regard to roads and other means of communication and to natural barriers. Said Executive Council shall also divide the island of Porto Rico into seven senatorial districts, each composed of five contiguous and compact representative districts. They shall make their report within thirty days after the approval of this Act, which report, when approved by the governor, shall be final.

SEC. 29. That the next election in Porto Rico shall be held in the year nineteen hundred and seventeen upon the sixteenth day of July. At such election there shall be chosen senators, representatives, a Resident Commissioner to the United States, and two public-service commissioners, as herein provided. Thereafter the elections shall be held on the first Tuesday after the first Monday in November, beginning with the year nineteen hundred and twenty, and every four years thereafter, and the terms of office of all municipal officials who have heretofore been elected and whose terms would otherwise expire at the beginning of the year nineteen hundred and nineteen are hereby extended until the officials who may be elected to fill such offices in nineteen hundred and twenty shall have been duly qualified: *Provided, however,* That nothing herein contained shall be construed to limit the right of the Legislature of Porto Rico at any time to revise the boundaries of senatorial and representative districts and of any municipality, or to abolish any municipality and the officers provided therefor.

SEC. 30. That the term of office of senators and representatives chosen by the first general election shall be until January first, nineteen hundred and twenty-one, and the terms of office of senators and representatives chosen at subsequent elections shall be four years from the second of January following their election. In case of vacancy among the members of the senate or in the house of representatives, special elections may be held in the districts wherein such vacancy occurred, under such regulations as may be prescribed by law, but senators or representatives elected in such cases shall hold office only for the unexpired portion of the term wherein the vacancy occurred, and no senator or representative shall, during the time for which he shall have been elected, be appointed to any civil office under the government of Porto Rico, nor be appointed to any office created by Act of the legislature during the time for which he shall have been elected until two years after his term of office shall have expired.

Sec. 31. That members of the Senate and House of Representatives of Porto Rico shall receive compensation at the rate of $7 per day for the first ninety days of each regular session and $1 per day for each additional day of such session while in session, and mileage for each session at the rate of 10 cents per kilometer for each kilometer actually and necessarily traveled in going from their legislative districts to the capital and therefrom to their place of residence in their districts by the usual routes of travel.

Sec. 32. That the senate and house of representatives, respectively, shall be the sole judges of the elections, returns, and qualifications of their members, and they shall have and exercise all the powers with respect to the conduct of their proceedings that usually pertain to parliamentary legislative bodies. Both houses shall convene at the capital on the second Monday in February following the next election, and organize by the election of a speaker or a presiding officer, a clerk, and a sergeant at arms for each house, and such other officers and assistants as may be required.

Sec. 33. That the first regular session of the Legislature of Porto Rico, provided for by this Act, shall convene on the twenty-eighth day after the first election provided for herein, and regular sessions of the legislature shall be held biennially thereafter, convening on the second Monday in February of the year nineteen hundred and nineteen, and on the second Monday in February of each second year thereafter. The governor may call special sessions of the legislature or of the senate at any time when in his opinion the public interest may require it, but no special session shall continue longer than ten days, not including Sundays and holidays, and no legislation shall be considered at such session other than that specified in the call, and he shall call the senate in special session at least once each year on the second Monday in February of those years in which a regular session of the legislature is not provided for.

Sec. 34. That the enacting clause of the laws shall be as to acts, "Be it enacted by the Legislature of Porto Rico," and as to joint resolutions, "Be it resolved by the Legislature of Porto Rico." Except as hereinafter provided, bills and joint resolutions may originate in either house. The governor shall submit at the opening of each regular session of the legislature a budget of receipts and expenditures, which shall be the basis of the ensuing biennial appropriation bill. No bill shall become a law until it be passed in each house by a majority yea-and-nay vote of all of the members belonging to such house and entered upon the journal and be approved by the governor within ten days thereafter. If when a bill that has been passed is presented to the governor for his signature he approves the same, he shall sign it; or if not, he shall return it, with his objections, to the house in which it originated, which house shall enter his objections at large on its journal and proceed to reconsider it. If, after such reconsideration, two-thirds of all the members of that house shall agree to pass the same it shall be sent, together with the objections, to the other house, by which it shall likewise be reconsidered, and if approved by two-thirds of all the members of that house it shall be sent to the governor, who, in case he shall then not approve, shall transmit the same to the President of the United States. The vote of each house shall be by yeas and nays, and the names of the members voting for and against shall be entered on the journal. If the President of the United States approve the same he shall sign it and it shall become a law. If he shall not approve same he shall return it to the governor so stating, and it shall not become a law: *Provided,* That the President of the United States shall approve or disapprove an Act submitted to him under the provisions of this section within ninety days from and after its submission for his approval; and if not approved within such time it shall become a law the same as if it had been specifically approved. If any bill presented to the governor contains several items of appropriation of money, he may object to one or more of such items, or any part or parts, portion or portions thereof, while approving of the other portion of the bill. In such case he shall append to the bill, at the time of signing it, a statement of the items, parts or portions thereof to which he objects, and the appropriation so objected to shall not take effect. If any bill shall not be returned by the governor within ten days (Sundays excepted) after it shall have been presented to him, it shall be a law in like manner as if he had signed it, unless the legislature by adjournment prevents its return, in which case it shall be a law if signed by the governor within thirty days after receipt by him; otherwise it shall not be a law. All laws enacted by the Legislature of Porto Rico shall be reported to the Congress of the United States, as provided in section twenty-three of this Act, which hereby reserves the power and authority to annual the same. If at the termination of any fiscal year the appropriations necessary for the support of the government for the ensuing fiscal year shall not have been made, the several sums appropriated in the last appropriation bills for the objects and purposes therein specified, so far as the same may be applicable, shall be deemed to be reappropriated item by item; and until the legislature shall act in such behalf the treasurer may, with the advice of the governor, make the payments necessary for the purposes aforesaid.

Each house shall keep a journal of its proceedings, and may, in its discretion, from time to time publish the same, and the yeas and nays on any question shall, on the demand of one-fifth of the members present, be entered on the journal.

The sessions of each house and of the committees of the whole shall be open.

Neither house shall, without the consent of the other, adjourn for more than three days, nor to any other place than that in which the two houses shall be sitting.

No law shall be passed except by bill, and no bill shall be so altered or amended on its passage through either house as to change its original purpose.

No act of the legislature except the general appropriation bills for the expenses of the government shall take effect until ninety days after its passage, unless in case of emergency (which shall be expressed in the preamble or body of the act) the legislature shall by a vote of two-thirds of all the members elected to each house otherwise direct. No bill, except the general appropriation bill for the expenses of the government only, introduced in either house of the legislature after the first forty days of the session, shall become a law.

No bill shall be considered or become a law unless referred to a committee, returned therefrom, and printed for the use of the members: *Provided,*

That either house may by a majority vote discharge a committee from the consideration of a measure and bring it before the body for consideration.

No bill, except general appropriation bills, shall be passed containing more than one subject, which shall be clearly expressed in its title; but if any subject shall be embraced in any act which shall not be expressed in the title, such act shall be void only as to so much thereof as shall not be so expressed.

No law shall be revived, or amended, or the provisions thereof extended or conferred by reference to its title only, but so much thereof as is revived, amended, extended, or conferred shall be reenacted and published at length.

The presiding officer of each house shall, in the presence of the house over which he presides, sign all bills and joint resolutions passed by the legislature, after their titles shall have been publicly read, immediately before signing; and the fact of signing shall be entered on the journal.

The legislature shall prescribe by law the number, duties, and compensation of the officers and employees of each house; and no payment shall be made for services to the legislature from the treasury, or be in any way authorized to any person, except to an acting officer or employee elected or appointed in pursuance of law.

No bill shall be passed giving any extra compensation to any public officer, servant or employee, agent or contractor, after services shall have been rendered or contract made.

Except as otherwise provided in this Act, no law shall extend the term of any public officer, or increase or diminish his salary or emoluments after his election or appointment, nor permit any officer or employee to draw compensation for more than one office or position.

All bills for raising revenue shall originate in the house of representatives, but the senate may propose or concur with amendments, as in case of other bills.

The general appropriation bill shall embrace nothing but appropriations for the ordinary expenses of the executive, legislative, and judicial departments, interest on the public debt, and for public schools. All other appropriations shall be made by separate bills, each embracing but one subject.

Every order, resolution, or vote to which the concurrence of both houses may be necessary, except on the question of adjournment, or relating solely to the transaction of business of the two houses, shall be presented to the governor, and before it shall take effect be approved by him, or, being disapproved, shall be repassed by two-thirds of both houses, according to the rules and limitations prescribed in case of a bill.

Any person who shall, directly or indirectly, offer, give, or promise any money or thing of value, testimonial, privilege, or personal advantage to any executive or judicial officer or member of the legislature to influence him in the performance of any of his public or official duties, shall be deemed guilty of bribery, and be punished by a fine not exceeding $5,000, or imprisonment not exceeding five years, or both.

The offense of corrupt solicitation of members of the legislature, or of public officers of Porto Rico, or of any municipal division thereof, and any occupation or practice of solicitation of such members or officers to influence their official action, shall be defined by law, and shall be punished by fine and imprisonment.

In case the available revenues of Porto Rico for any fiscal year, including available surplus in the insular treasury, are insufficient to meet all the appropriations made by the legislature for such year, such appropriations shall be paid in the following order, unless otherwise directed by the governor:

First class. The ordinary expenses of the legislative, executive, and judicial departments of the State government, and interest on any public debt, shall first be paid in full.

Second class. Appropriations for all institutions, such as the penitentiary, insane asylum, industrial school, and the like, where the inmates are confined involuntarily, shall next be paid in full.

Third class. Appropriations for education and educational and charitable institutions shall next be paid in full.

Fourth class. Appropriations for any other officer or officers, bureaus or boards, shall next be paid in full.

Fifth class. Appropriations for all other purposes shall next be paid.

That in case there are not sufficient revenues for any fiscal year, including available surplus in the insular treasury, to meet in full the appropriations of said year for all of the said classes of appropriations, then said revenues shall be applied to the classes in the order above named, and if, after the payment of the prior classes in full, there are not sufficient revenues for any fiscal year to pay in full the appropriations for that year for the next class, then, in that event, whatever there may be to apply on account of appropriations for said class shall be distributed among said appropriations pro rata according as the amount of each appropriation of that class shall bear to the total amount of all of said appropriations for that class for such fiscal year.

No appropriation shall be made, nor any expenditure authorized by the legislature, whereby the expenditure of the Government of Porto Rico during any fiscal year shall exceed the total revenue then provided for by law and applicable for such appropriation or expenditure, including any available surplus in the treasury, unless the legislature making such appropriation shall provide for levying a sufficient tax to pay such appropriation or expenditure within such fiscal year.

SEC. 35. That at the first election held pursuant to this Act the qualified electors shall be those having the qualifications of voters under the present law. Thereafter voters shall be citizens of the United States twenty-one years of age or over and have such additional qualifications as may be prescribed by the legislature of Porto Rico: *Provided,* That no property qualification shall ever be imposed upon or required of any voter.

SEC. 36. That the qualified electors of Porto Rico shall at the next general election choose a Resident Commissioner to the United States, whose term of office shall begin on the date of the issuance of his certificate of election and shall continue until the fourth of March, nineteen hundred and twenty-one. At each subsequent election, beginning with the year nineteen hundred and twenty, the qualified electors of Porto Rico shall choose a Resident Commissioner to the United States, whose term of office shall be four years from the fourth of March following such general election, and who shall be entitled to receive official recognition as such Commissioner by all of the departments of the Government of the United States, upon presentation, through the Department of State, of a certificate of election of the Governor of Porto Rico. The Resident Commissioner shall receive a salary, payable monthly by the United States, of $7,500 per annum. Such Commissioner shall be allowed the same sum for stationery and for the pay of necessary clerk hire as is now allowed to Members of the House of Representatives of the United States; and he shall be allowed the sum of $500 as mileage for each session of the House of Representatives and the franking privilege granted Members of Congress. No person shall be eligible to election as Resident Commissioner who is not a bona fide citizen of the United States and who is not more than twenty-five years of age, and who does not read and write the English language. In case of a vacancy in the office of Resident Commissioner by death, resignation, or otherwise, the governor, by and with the advice and consent of the senate, shall appoint a Resident Commissioner to fill the vacancy, who shall serve until the next general election and until his successor is elected and qualified.

SEC. 37. That the legislative authority herein provided shall extend to all matters of a legislative character not locally inapplicable, including power to create, consolidate, and reorganize the municipalities so far as may be necessary, and to provide and repeal laws and ordinances therefor; also the power to alter, amend, modify, or repeal any or all laws and ordinances of every character now in force in Porto Rico or municipality or district thereof in so far as such alteration, amendment, modification, or repeal may be consistent with the provisions of this Act.

No executive department not provided for in this Act shall be created by the legislature, but the legislature may consolidate departments, or abolish any department, with the consent of the President of the United States.

SEC. 38. That all grants of franchises, rights, and privileges of a public or quasi public nature shall be made by a public-service commission, consisting of the heads of executive departments, the auditor, and two commissioners to be elected by the qualified voters at the first general election to be held under this Act, and at each subsequent general election thereafter. The terms of said elective commissioners elected at the first general election shall commence on the twenty-eighth day following the said general election, and the terms of the said elective commissioners elected at each subsequent general election shall commence on the second day of January following their election; they shall serve for four years and until their successors are elected and qualified. Their compensation shall be $8 for each day's attendance on the sessions of the commission, but in no case shall they receive more than $400 each during any one year. The said commission is also empowered and directed to discharge all the executive functions relating to public-service corporations heretofore conferred by law upon the executive council. Franchises, rights, and privileges granted by the said commission shall not be effective until approved by the governor, and shall be reported to Congress, which hereby reserves the power to annual or modify the same.

The interstate-commerce Act and the several amendments made or to be made thereto, the safety-appliance Acts and the several amendments made or to be made thereto, and the Act of Congress entitled "An Act to amend an Act entitled 'An Act to regulate commerce,' approved February fourth, eighteen hundred and eighty-seven, and all Acts amendatory thereof, by providing for a valuation of the several classes of property of carriers subject thereto and securing information concerning their stocks, bonds, and other securities," approved March first, nineteen hundred and thirteen, shall not apply to Porto Rico.

The Legislative Assembly of Porto Rico is hereby authorized to enact laws relating to the regulation of the rates, tariffs, and service of public carriers by rail in Porto Rico, and the Public-Service Commission hereby created shall have power to enforce such laws under appropriate regulation.

Sec. 39. That all grants of franchises and privileges under the section last preceding shall provide that the same shall be subject to amendment, alteration, or repeal, and shall forbid the issue of stocks or bonds except in exchange for actual cash or property at a fair valuation to be determined by the public-service commission equal in amount to the par value of the stocks or bonds issued, and shall forbid the declaring of stock or bond dividends, and in the case of public-service corporations shall provide for the effective regulation of charges thereof and for the purchase or taking of their property by the authorities at a fair and reasonable valuation.

That nothing in this Act contained shall be so construed as to abrogate or in any manner impair or affect the provision contained in section three of the joint resolution approved May first, nineteen hundred, with respect to the buying, selling, or holding of real estate. That the Governor of Porto Rico shall cause to have made and submitted to Congress at the session beginning the first Monday in December, nineteen hundred and seventeen, a report of all the real estate used for the purposes of agriculture and held either directly or indirectly by corporations, partnerships, or individuals in holdings in excess of five hundred acres.

## JUDICAL DEPARTMENT

Sec. 40. That the judicial power shall be vested in the courts and tribunals of Porto Rico now established and in operation under and by virtue of existing laws. The jurisdiction of said courts and the form of procedure in them, and the various officers and attachés thereof, shall also continue to be as now provided until otherwise provided by law: *Provided, however,* That the chief justice and associate justices of the supreme court shall be appointed by the President, by and with the advice and consent of the Senate of the United States, and the Legislature of Porto Rico shall have authority, from time to time as it may see fit, not inconsistent with this Act, to organize, modify, or rearrange the courts and their jurisdiction and procedure, except the District Court of the United States for Porto Rico.

Sec. 41. That Porto Rico shall constitute a judicial district to be called "the district of Porto Rico." The President, by and with the advice and consent of the Senate, shall appoint one district judge, who shall serve for a term of four years and until his successor is appointed and qualified and whose salary shall be $5,000 per annum. There shall be appointed in like manner a district attorney, whose salary shall be $4,000 per annum, and a marshal for said district, whose salary shall be $3,500 per annum, each for a term of four years unless sooner removed by the President. The district court for said district shall be called "the District Court of the United States for Porto Rico," and shall have power to appoint all necessary officials and assistants, including the clerk, interpreter, and such commissioners as may be necessary, who shall be entitled to the same fees and have like powers and duties as are exercised and performed by United States commissioners. Such district court shall have jurisdiction of all cases cognizable in the district courts of the United States, and shall proceed in the same manner. In addition said district court shall have jurisdiction for the naturalization of aliens and Porto Ricans, and for this purpose residence in Porto Rico shall be counted in the same manner as residence elsewhere in the United States. Said district court shall have jurisdiction of all controversies where all of the parties on either side of the controversy are citizens or subjects of a foreign State or States, or citizens of a State, Territory, or District of the United States not domiciled in Porto Rico, wherein the matter in dispute exceeds, exclusive of interest or cost, the sum or value of $3,000, and of all controversies in which there is a separable controversy involving such jurisdictional amount and in which all of the parties on either side of such separable controversy are citizens or subjects of the character aforesaid: *Provided,* That nothing in this Act shall be deemed to impair the jurisdiction of the District Court of the United States for Porto Rico to hear and determine all controversies pending in said court at the date of the approval of this Act. Upon the taking effect of this Act the salaries of the judge and officials of the District Court of the United States for Porto Rico, together with the court expenses, shall be paid from the United States revenues in the same manner as in other United States district courts. In case of vacancy or of the death, absence, or other legal disability on the part of the judge of the said District Court of the United States for Porto Rico, the President of the United States is authorized to designate one of the judges of the Supreme Court of Porto Rico to discharge the duties of judge of said court until such absence or disability shall be removed, and thereupon such judge so designated for said service shall be fully authorized and empowered to perform the duties of said office during such absence or disability of such regular judge, and to sign all necessary papers and records as the acting judge of said court, without extra compensation.

Sec. 42. That the laws of the United States relating to appeals, writs of error and certiorari, removal of causes, and other matters or proceedings as between the courts of the United States and the courts of the several States shall govern in such matters and proceedings as between the district court of the United States and the courts of Porto Rico. Regular terms of said United States district court shall be held at San Juan, commencing on the first Monday in May and November of each year, and also at Ponce on the second Monday in February of each year, and special terms may be held at Mayaguez at such stated times as said judge may deem expedient. All pleadings and proceedings in said court shall be conducted in the English language. The said district court shall be attached to and included in the first circuit of the United States, with the right of appeal and review by said circuit court of appeals in all cases where the same would lie from any district court to a circuit court of appeals of the United States, and with the right of appeal and review directly by the Supreme Court of the United States in all cases where a direct appeal would be from such district courts.

Sec. 43. That writs of error and appeals from the final judgments and decrees of the Supreme Court of Porto Rico may be taken and prosecuted to the Circuit Court of Appeals for the First Circuit and to the Supreme Court of the United States, as now provided by law.

Sec. 44. That the qualifications of jurors as fixed by the local laws of Porto Rico shall not apply to jurors selected to serve in the District Court of the United States for Porto Rico; but the qualifications required of jurors in said court shall be that each shall be of the age of not less than twenty-one years and not over sixty-five years, a resident of Porto Rico for not less than one year, and have a sufficient knowledge of the English language to enable him to serve as a juror; they shall also be citizens of the United States. Juries for the said court shall be selected, drawn and subject to exemption in accordance with the laws of Congress regulating the same in the United States courts in so far as locally applicable.

Sec. 45. That all such fees, fines, costs, and forfeitures as would be deposited to the credit of the United States if collected and paid into a district court of the United States shall become revenues of the United States when collected and paid into the District Court of the United States for Porto Rico: *Provided*, That $500 a year from such fees, fines, costs, and forfeitures shall be retained by the clerk and expended for law library purposes under the direction of the judge.

Sec. 46. That the Attorney General of the United States shall from time to time determine the salaries of all officials and assistants appointed by the United States district court, including the clerk, his deputies, interpreter, stenographer, and other officials and employees, the same to be paid by the United States as other salaries and expenses of like character in United States courts.

Sec. 47. That jurors and witnesses in the District Court of the United States for Porto Rico shall be entitled to and receive 15 cents for each mile necessarily traveled over any stage line or by private conveyance and 10 cents for each mile over any railway in going to and returning from said courts. But no constructive or double mileage fees shall be allowed by reason of any person being summoned both as witness and juror or as witness in two or more cases pending in the same court and triable at the same term thereof. Such jurors shall be paid $3 per day and such witnesses $1.50 per day while in attendance upon the court.

Sec. 48. That the supreme and district courts of Porto Rico and the respective judges thereof may grant writs of habeas corpus in all cases in which the same are grantable by the judges of the district courts of the United States, and the district courts may grant writs of mandamus in all proper cases.

Sec. 49. That hereafter all judges, marshals, and secretaries of courts now established or that may hereafter be established in Porto Rico, and whose appointment by the President is not provided for by law, shall be appointed by the governor, by and with the advice and consent of the Senate of Porto Rico.

## MISCELLANEOUS PROVISIONS

Sec. 50. That, except as in this Act otherwise provided, the salaries of all the officials of Porto Rico not appointed by the President, including deputies, assistants, and other help, shall be such and be so paid out of the revenues of Porto Rico as shall from time to time be determined by the Legislature of Porto Rico and approved by the governor; and if the legislature shall fail to make an appropriation for such salaries, the salaries theretofore fixed shall be paid without the necessity of further appropriations therefor. The salaries of all officers and all expenses of the offices of the various officials of Porto Rico appointed as herein provided by the President shall also be paid out of the revenues of Porto Rico on warrant of the auditor, countersigned by the governor. The annual salaries of the following-named officials appointed by the President and so to be paid shall be: The governor, $10,000; in addition thereto he shall be entitled to the occupancy of the buildings heretofore used by the chief executive of Porto Rico, with the furniture and effects therein, free of rental; heads of executive departments, $5,000; chief justice of the supreme court, $6,500; associate justices of the supreme court, $5,500 each.

Where any officer whose salary is fixed by this act is required to give a bond, the premium thereof shall be paid from the insular treasury.

SEC. 51. That the provisions of the foregoing section shall not apply to municipal officials; their salaries and the compensation of their deputies, assistants, and other help, as well as all other expenses incurred by the municipalities, shall be paid out of the municipal revenues, in such manner as the legislature shall provide.

SEC. 52. That wherever in this Act offices of the insular government of Porto Rico are provided for under the same names as in the heretofore existing Acts of Congress affecting Porto Rico, the present incumbents of those offices shall continue in office in accordance with the terms and at the salaries prescribed by this Act, excepting the heads of those departments who are to be appointed by the governor and who shall continue in office only until their successors are appointed and have qualified. The offices of secretary of Porto Rico and director of labor, charities, and correction are hereby abolished. Authority is given to the respective appointing authorities to appoint and commission persons to fill the new offices created by this Act.

SEC. 53. That any bureau or office belonging to any of the regular departments of the government, or hereafter created, or not assigned, may be transferred or assigned to any department by the governor with the approval of the Senate of Porto Rico.

SEC. 54. That deeds and other instruments affecting land situate in the District of Columbia, or any other territory or possession of the United States, may be acknowledged in Porto Rico before any notary public appointed therein by proper authority, or any officer therein who has ex officio the powers of a notary public: *Provided,* That the certificate by such notary shall be accompanied by the certificate of the executive secretary of Porto Rico to the effect that the notary taking such acknowledgment is in fact such notarial officer.

SEC. 55. That nothing in this Act shall be deemed to impair or interrupt the jurisdiction of existing courts over matters pending therein upon the approval of this Act, which jurisdiction is in all respects hereby continued, the purpose of this Act being to preserve the integrity of all of said courts and their jurisdiction until otherwise provided by law, except as in this Act otherwise specifically provided.

SEC. 56. That this Act shall take effect upon approval, but until its provisions shall severally become operative, as hereinbefore provided, the corresponding legislative and executive functions of the government in Porto Rico shall continue to be exercised and in full force and operation as now provided by law; and the Executive Council shall, until the assembly and organization of the Legislature of Porto Rico as herein provided, consist of the attorney general, the treasurer, the commissioner of the interior, the commissioner of education, the commissioner of health, and the commissioner of agriculture and labor, and the five additional members as now provided by law. And any functions assigned to the Senate of Porto Rico by the provisions of this Act shall, until this said senate has assembled and organized as herein provided, be exercised by the Executive Council as thus constituted: *Provided, however,* That all appointments made by the governor, by and with the advice and consent of the Executive Council as thus constituted, in the Executive Council as authorized by section thirteen of this Act or in the office of Executive Secretary of Porto Rico, shall be regarded as temporary and shall expire not later than twenty days from and after the assembly and organization of the legislature hereinbefore provided, unless said appointments shall be ratified and made permanent by the said Senate of Porto Rico.

SEC. 57. That the laws and ordinances of Porto Rico now in force shall continue in force and effect, except as altered, amended, or modified herein, until altered, amended, or repealed by the legislative authority herein provided for Porto Rico or by Act of Congress of the United States; and such legislative authority shall have power, when not inconsistent with this Act, by due enactment to amend, alter, modify, or repeal any law or ordinance, civil or criminal, continued in force by this Act as it may from time to time see fit.

SEC. 58. That all laws or parts of laws applicable to Porto Rico not in conflict with any of the provisions of this Act, including the laws relating to tariffs, customs, and duties on importations into Porto Rico prescribed by the Act of Congress entitled "An Act temporarily to provide revenues and a civil government for Porto Rico, and for other purposes," approved April twelfth, nineteen hundred, are hereby continued in effect, and all laws and parts of laws inconsistent with the provisions of this Act are hereby repealed.

March 2, 1917

# The Bracero Agreement[1]

*For the temporary migration of Mexican agricultural workers to the United States. As revised April 26, 1943, by an exchange of notes between the American embassy at Mexico City and the Mexican Ministry for Foreign Affairs.*

## GENERAL PROVISIONS

1) It is understood that Mexicans contracting to work in the United States shall not be engaged in any military service.

1. This agreement was formalized on July 23, 1942, revised on August 4, and subsequently further modified. In the version here, released on April 26, 1943, revised passages in the body are in italics. The original agreement was signed by representatives from Mexico: Ernesto Hidalgo, representative of the Foreign Affairs Ministry, and Abraham J. Navas, Esq., representative of the Ministry of Labor; and from the United States: Joseph F. McGurk, Counsel of the American Embassy in Mexico, John Walker, Deputy Administrator of the Farm Security Administration, United States Department of Agriculture (USDA), and David Mecker, Deputy Director of War Farming Operations (also USDA).

2) Mexicans entering the United States as result of this understanding shall not suffer discriminatory acts of any kind in accordance with the Executive Order No. 8802 issued at the White House June 25, 1941.

3) Mexicans entering the United States under this understanding shall enjoy the guarantees of transportation, living expenses and repatriation established in Article 29 of the Mexican Federal Labor Law as follows:

Article 29.—All contracts entered into by Mexican workers for lending their services outside their country shall be made in writing, legalized by the municipal authorities of the locality where entered into and visaed by the Consul of the country where their services are being used. Furthermore, such contract shall contain, as a requisite of validity of same, the following stipulations, without which the contract is invalid.

I. Transportation and subsistence expenses for the worker, and his family, if such is the case, and all other expenses which originate from point of origin to border points and compliance of immigration requirements, or for any other similar concept, shall be paid exclusively by the employer or the contractual parties.

II. The worker shall be paid in full the salary agreed upon, from which no deduction shall be made in any amount for any of the concepts mentioned in the above sub-paragraph.

III. The employer or contractor shall issue a bond or constitute a deposit in cash in the Bank of Workers, or in the absence of same, in the Bank of Mexico, to the entire satisfaction of the respective labor authorities, for a sum equal to repatriation costs of the worker and his family, and those originated by transportation to point of origin.

IV. Once the employer established proof of having covered such expenses or the refusal of the worker to return to his country, and that he does not owe the worker any sum covering salary or indemnization to which he might have a right, the labor authorities shall authorize the return of the deposit or the cancellation of the bond issued.

*It is specifically understood that the provisions of Section III of Article 29 above-mentioned shall not apply to the Government of the United States notwithstanding the inclusion of this section in the agreement, in view of the obligations assumed by the United States government under Transportation (a) and (c) of this agreement.*

4) Mexicans entering the United States under this understanding shall not be employed to displace other workers, or for the purpose of reducing rates of pay previously established.

In order to implement the application of the general Principles mentioned above the following specific clauses are established:

(When the word "employer" is used hereinafter it shall be understood to mean the Farm Security Administration of the Department of Agriculture of the United States of America; the word "sub-employer" shall mean the owner or operator of the farm or farms in the United States on which the Mexican will be employed; the word "worker" hereinafter used shall refer to the Mexican Farm laborer entering the United States under this understanding.)

### CONTRACTS

a) Contracts will be made between the employer and the worker under the supervision of the Mexican Government. (Contracts must be written in Spanish.)

b) The employer shall enter into a contract with the sub-employer, with a view to proper observance of the principles embodied in this understanding.

### ADMISSION

a. The Mexican health authorities will, at the place whence the worker comes, see that he meets the necessary physical conditions.

### TRANSPORTATION

a. All transportation and living expenses from the place of origin to destination, and return, as well as expenses incurred in the fulfillment of any requirements of a migratory nature shall be met by the Employer.

b. Personal belongings of the workers up to a maximum of 35 kilos per person shall be transported at the expense of the Employer.

c. In accord with the intent of Article 29 of Mexican Federal Labor Law, quoted under General Provisions (3) above, it is expected that the employer will collect all or part of the cost accuring under (a) and (b) of Transportation from the sub-employer.

### WAGES AND EMPLOYMENT

a. (1) Wages to be paid the worker shall be the same as those paid for similar work to other agricultural laborers under the same conditions within the same area, in the respective regions of destination. Piece rates shall be so set as to enable the worker of average ability to earn the prevailing wage. In any case wages for piece work or hourly work will not be less than 30 cents per hour.

b. (2) On the basis of prior authorization from the Mexican Government salaries lower than those established in the previous clause may be paid those emigrants admitted into the United States as members of the family of the worker under contract and who, when they are in the field, are able also to become agricultural laborers but who, by their condition of age or sex, cannot carry out the average amount of ordinary work.

c. The worker shall be exclusively employed as an agricultural laborer for which he has been engaged; any change from such type of employment or any change of locality shall be made with the express approval of the worker and with the authority of the Mexican Government.

d. There shall be considered illegal any collection by reason of commission or for any other concept demanded of the worker.

e. Work of minors under 14 years shall be strictly prohibited, and they shall have the same schooling opportunities as those enjoyed by children of other agricultural laborers.

f. Workers domiciled in the migratory labor camps or at any other place of employment under this understanding shall be free to obtain articles for their personal consumption, or that of their families, wherever it is most convenient for them.

g. *The Mexican workers will be furnished without cost to them with hygienic lodgings, adequate to the physical conditions of the region of a type used by a common laborer of the region and the medical and sanitary services enjoyed also without cost to them will be identical with those furnished to the other agricultural workers in the regions where they may lend their services.*

h. Workers admitted under this understanding shall enjoy as regards occupational diseases and accidents the same guarantees enjoyed by other agricultural workers under United States legislation.

i. Groups of workers admitted under this understanding shall elect their own representatives to deal with the Employer, but it is understood that all such representatives shall be working members of the group.

*The Mexican Consuls, assisted by the Mexican Labor Inspectors, recognized as such by the Employer will take all possible measures of protection in the interest of the Mexican workers in all questions affecting them, within their corresponding jurisdiction, and will have free access to the places of work of the Mexican workers. The Employer will observe that the sub-employer grants all facilities to the Mexican Government for the compliance of all the clauses in this contract.*

j. For such time as they are unemployed under a period equal to 75% of the period (exclusive of Sundays) for which the workers have been contracted they shall receive a subsistence allowance at the rate of $3.00 per day.

Should the cost of living rise this will be a matter for reconsideration.

The master contracts for workers submitted to the Mexican government shall contain definite provisions for computation of subsistence and payments under the understanding.

k. The term of the contract shall be made in accordance with the authorities of the respective countries.

l. At the expiration of the contract under this understanding, and if the same is not renewed, the authorities of the United States shall consider illegal, from an immigration point of view, the continued stay of the worker in the territory of the United States, exception made of cases of physical impossibility.

### SAVINGS FUND

a. The respective agencies of the Government of the United States shall be responsible for the safekeeping of the sums contributed by the Mexican workers toward the formation of their Rural Savings Fund, until such sums are transferred to *the Wells Fargo Bank and Union Trust Company of San Francisco for the account of the Bank of Mexico, S.A., which will transfer such amounts to the Mexican Agricultural Credit Bank. This last shall assume responsibility for the deposit, for the safekeeping and for the application, or in the absence of these, for the return of such amounts.*

b. The Mexican Government through the Banco de Crédito Agrícola will take care of the security of the savings of the workers to be used for payment of the agricultural implements, which may be made available to the Banco de Crédito Agrícola in accordance with exportation permits for shipment to Mexico with the understanding that the Farm Security Administration will recommend priority treatment for such implements.

### NUMBERS

As it is impossible to determine at this time the number of workers who may be needed in the United States for agricultural labor employment, the employer shall advise the Mexican Government from time to time as to the number needed. The Government of Mexico shall determine in each case the number of workers who may leave the country without detriment to its national economy.

### GENERAL CONSIDERATIONS

It is understood that, with reference to the departure from Mexico of Mexican workers, who are not farm laborers, there shall govern in understandings reached by agencies to the respective Governments the same fundamental principles which have been applied here to the departure of farm labor.

It is understood that the employers will cooperate with such other agencies of the Government of the United States in carrying this understanding into effect whose authority under the laws of the United States are such as to contribute to the effectuation of the understandings.

Either Government shall have the right to renounce this understanding, given appropriate notification to the other Government 90 days in advance.

This understanding may be formalized by an exchange of notes between the Ministry of Foreign Affairs of the Republic of Mexico and the Embassy of the United States of America in Mexico.

August 4, 1942

# California Proposition 187

This initiative measure is submitted to the people in accordance with the provisions of Article II, Section 8 of the Constitution.

This initiative measure adds sections to various codes; therefore, new provisions proposed to be added are printed in *italic type* to indicate that they are new.

## *Proposed Law*

### SECTION 1. FINDINGS AND DECLARATION

The People of California find and declare as follows:

That they have suffered and are suffering economic hardship caused by the presence of illegal aliens in this state.

That they have suffered and are suffering personal injury and damage caused by the criminal conduct of illegal aliens in this state.

That they have a right to the protection of their government from any person or persons entering this country unlawfully.

Therefore, the People of California declare their intention to provide for cooperation between their agencies of state and local government with the federal government, and to establish a system of required notification by and between such agencies to prevent illegal aliens in the United States from receiving benefits or public services in the State of California.

### SECTION 2. MANUFACTURE, DISTRIBUTION OR SALE OF FALSE CITIZENSHIP OR RESIDENT ALIEN DOCUMENTS: CRIME AND PUNISHMENT

Section 113 is added to the Penal Code, to read:

*113. Any person who manufactures, distributes or sells false documents to conceal the true citizenship or resident alien status of another person is guilty of a felony, and shall be punished by imprisonment in the state prison for five years or by a fine of seventy-five thousand dollars ($75,000).*

### SECTION 3. USE OF FALSE CITIZENSHIP OR RESIDENT ALIEN DOCUMENTS: CRIME AND PUNISHMENT

Section 114 is added to the Penal Code, to read:

*114. Any person who uses false documents to conceal his or her true citizenship or resident alien status is guilty of a felony, and shall be punished by imprisonment in the state prison for five years or by a fine of twenty-five thousand dollars ($25,000).*

### SECTION 4. LAW ENFORCEMENT COOPERATION WITH INS

Section 834b is added to the Penal Code, to read:

834b. (a) Every law enforcement agency in California shall fully cooperate with the United States Immigration and Naturalization Service regarding any person who is arrested if he or she is suspected of being present in the United States in violation of federal immigration laws.

(b) With respect to any such person who is arrested, and suspected of being present in the United States in violation of federal immigration laws, every law enforcement agency shall do the following:

(1) Attempt to verify the legal status of such person as a citizen of the United States, an alien lawfully admitted as a permanent resident, an alien lawfully admitted for a temporary period of time or as an alien who is present in the United States in violation of immigration laws. The verification process may include, but shall not be limited to, questioning the person regarding his or her date and place of birth, and entry into the United States, and demanding documentation to indicate his or her legal status.

(2) Notify the person of his or her apparent status as an alien who is present in the United States in violation of federal immigration laws and inform him or her that, apart from any criminal justice proceedings, he or she must either obtain legal status or leave the United States.

(3) Notify the Attorney General of California and the United States Immigration and Naturalization Service of the apparent illegal status and provide any additional information that may be requested by any other public entity.

(c) Any legislative, administrative, or other action by a city, county, or other legally authorized local governmental entity with jurisdictional boundaries, or by a law enforcement agency, to prevent or limit the cooperation required by subdivision (a) is expressly prohibited.

### SECTION 5. EXCLUSION OF ILLEGAL ALIENS FROM PUBLIC SOCIAL SERVICES

Section 10001.5 is added to the Welfare and Institutions Code, to read:

10001.5. (a) In order to carry out the intention of the People of California that only citizens of the United States and aliens lawfully admitted to the United States may receive the benefits of public social services and to ensure that all persons employed in the providing of those services shall diligently protect public funds from misuse, the provisions of this section are adopted.

(b) A person shall not receive any public social services to which he or she may be otherwise entitled until the legal status of that person has been verified as one of the following:

*(1) A citizen of the United States.*

*(2) An alien lawfully admitted as a permanent resident.*

*(3) An alien lawfully admitted for a temporary period of time.*

*(c) If any public entity in this state to whom a person has applied for public social services determines or reasonably suspects, based upon the information provided to it, that the person is an alien in the United States in violation of federal law, the following procedures shall be followed by the public entity:*

*(1) The entity shall not provide the person with benefits or services.*

*(2) The entity shall, in writing, notify the person of his or her apparent illegal immigration status, and that the person must either obtain legal status or leave the United States.*

*(3) The entity shall also notify the State Director of Social Services, the Attorney General of California, and the United States Immigration and Naturalization Service of the apparent illegal status, and shall provide any additional information that may be requested by any other public entity.*

### SECTION 6. EXCLUSION OF ILLEGAL ALIENS FROM PUBLICLY FUNDED HEALTH CARE

Chapter 1.3 (commencing with Section 130) is added to Part 1 of Division 1 of the Health and Safety Code, to read:

*Chapter 1.3. Publicly-Funded Health Care Services*

*130. (a) In order to carry out the intention of the People of California that, excepting emergency medical care as required by federal law, only citizens of the United States and aliens lawfully admitted to the United States may receive the benefits of publicly-funded health care, and to ensure that all persons employed in the providing of those services shall diligently protect public funds from misuse, the provisions of this section are adopted.*

*(b) A person shall not receive any health care services from a publicly-funded health care facility, to which he or she is otherwise entitled until the legal status of that person has been verified as one of the following:*

*(1) A citizen of the United States.*

*(2) An alien lawfully admitted as a permanent resident.*

*(3) An alien lawfully admitted for a temporary period of time.*

*(c) If any publicly-funded health care facility in this state from whom a person seeks health care services, other than emergency medical care as required by*

*federal law, determines or reasonably suspects, based upon the information provided to it, that the person is an alien in the United States in violation of federal law, the following procedures shall be followed by the facility:*

*(1) The facility shall not provide the person with services.*

*(2) The facility shall, in writing, notify the person of his or her apparent illegal immigration status, and that the person must either obtain legal status or leave the United States.*

*(3) The facility shall also notify the State Director of Health Services, the Attorney General of California, and the United States Immigration and Naturalization Service of the apparent illegal status, and shall provide any additional information that may be requested by any other public entity.*

*(d) For purposes of this section "publicly-funded health care facility" shall be defined as specified in Sections 1200 and 1250 of this code as of January 1, 1993.*

### SECTION 7. EXCLUSION OF ILLEGAL ALIENS FROM PUBLIC ELEMENTARY AND SECONDARY SCHOOLS

Section 48215 is added to the Education Code, to read:

*48215. (a) No public elementary or secondary school shall admit, or permit the attendance of, any child who is not a citizen of the United States, an alien lawfully admitted as a permanent resident, or a person who is otherwise authorized under federal law to be present in the United States.*

*(b) Commencing January 1, 1995, each school district shall verify the legal status of each child enrolling in the school district for the first time in order to ensure the enrollment or attendance only of citizens, aliens lawfully admitted as permanent residents, or persons who are otherwise authorized to be present in the United States.*

*(c) By January 1, 1996, each school district shall have verified the legal status of each child already enrolled and in attendance in the school district in order to ensure the enrollment or attendance only of citizens, aliens lawfully admitted as permanent residents, or persons who are otherwise authorized under federal law to be present in the United States.*

*(d) By January 1, 1996, each school district shall also have verified the legal status of each parent or guardian of each child referred to in subdivisions (b) and (c), to determine whether such parent or guardian is one of the following:*

*(1) A citizen of the United States.*

*(2) An alien lawfully admitted as a permanent resident.*

*(3) An alien admitted lawfully for a temporary period of time.*

(e) *Each school district shall provide information to the State Superintendent of Public Instruction, the Attorney General of California, and the United States Immigration and Naturalization Service regarding any enrollee or pupil, or parent or guardian, attending a public elementary or secondary school in the school district determined or reasonably suspected to be in violation of federal immigration laws within forty-five days after becoming aware of an apparent violation. The notice shall also be provided to the parent or legal guardian of the enrollee or pupil, and shall state that an existing pupil may not continue to attend the school after ninety calendar days from the date of the notice, unless legal status is established.*

(f) *For each child who cannot establish legal status in the United States, each school district shall continue to provide education for a period of ninety days from the date of the notice. Such ninety day period shall be utilized to accomplish on orderly transition to a school in the child's country of origin. Each school district shall fully cooperate in this transition effort to ensure that the educational needs of the child are best served for that period of time.*

## SECTION 8. EXCLUSION OF ILLEGAL ALIENS FROM PUBLIC POSTSECONDARY EDUCATIONAL INSTITUTIONS

Section 66010.8 is added to the Education Code, to read:

66010.8. (a) *No public institution of postsecondary education shall admit, enroll, or permit the attendance of any person who is not a citizen of the United States, an alien lawfully admitted as a permanent resident in the United States, or a person who is otherwise authorized under federal law to be present in the United States.*

(b) *Commencing with the first term or semester that begins after January 1, 1995, and at the commencement of each term or semester thereafter, each public postsecondary educational institution shall verify the status of each person enrolled or in attendance at that institution in order to ensure the enrollment or attendance only of United States citizens, aliens lawfully admitted as permanent residents in the United States, and persons who are otherwise authorized under federal law to be present in the United States.*

(c) *No later than 45 days after the admissions officer of a public postsecondary educational institution becomes aware of the application, enrollment, or attendance of a person determined to be, or who is under reasonable suspicion of being, in the United States in violation of federal immigration laws, that officer shall provide that information to the State Superintendent of Public Instruction, the Attorney General of California, and the United States Immigration and Naturalization Service. The information shall also be provided to the applicant, enrollee, or person admitted.*

## SECTION 9. ATTORNEY GENERAL COOPERATION WITH THE INS

Section 53069.65 is added to the Government Code, to read:

53069.65. *Whenever the state or a city, or a county, or any other legally authorized local governmental entity with jurisdictional boundaries reports the presence of a person who is suspected of being present in the United States in violation of federal immigration laws to the Attorney General of California, that report shall be transmitted to the United States Immigration and Naturalization Service. The Attorney General shall be responsible for maintaining on-going and accurate records of such reports, and shall provide any additional information that may be requested by any other government entity.*

### SECTION 10. AMENDMENT AND SEVERABILITY

The statutory provisions contained in this measure may not be amended by the Legislature except to further its purposes by status passed in each house by rollcall vote entered in the journal, two-thirds of the membership concurring, or by a statute that becomes effective only when approved by the voters.

In the event that any portion of this act or the application thereof to any person or circumstance is held invalid, that invalidity shall not affect any other provision or application of the act, which can be given effect without the invalid provision or application, and to that end the provisions of this act are severable.

1994

# Appendix 3:
# Influential Essays by Latin American Writers

Latin Americans have long been fascinated with the United States, a neighboring nation with epic ambitions and uniquely heterogeneous DNA. There is no dominating Latin American opinion on *El Coloso del Norte*, but Latin Americans' fascination tends to differ from its equivalent among Europeans. While Europeans often envy the openness, creativity, and tradition-breaking that characterize U.S. culture, Latin Americans often view that same culture with a wistfulness cut with horror. Rubén Darío, the Nicaraguan poet and founder of *Modernismo* (discussed in the "Annexations" introduction), put it best in his poem to the U.S. president Theodore Roosevelt, published in 1904. In an English-language version by Greg Simon and Steven F. White:

> The U.S. is a country that is powerful and strong.
> When the giant yawns and stretches, the earth feels a tremor
> ripping through the enormous vertebrae of the Andes
>     [mountain range in South America].
> If you shout, the sound you make is a lion's roar.
> . . . You're so rich, you
> join the cult to Hercules [ancient Greek hero famous
>     for his strength] with the cult to Mammon [material wealth,
>     possessions, especially as a debasing influence].
> And lighting the broad straight path that leads to easy conquests
> Lady Liberty raises her torch in New York City.

Other intellectuals south of the Rio Grande—among them, Ezequiel Martínez Estrada, Samuel Ramos, Germán Arciniegas, Carlos Fuentes, and Mario Vargas Llosa—have analyzed the United States by focusing on aspects such as the natural environment, the educational system, and the political challenges ahead. Domingo Faustino Sarmiento, the Argentinian writer of works such as *Facundo: Civilización y barbarie* (Civilization and Barbarism, 1845) and president of Argentina from 1868 to 1874, was amazed by the geographical expansion and entrepreneurial spirit he witnessed on a visit to the United States in 1847 and while he was his country's ambassador to the United States in 1864. (President Andrew Johnson received him at the White House.) The Chilean poet and diplomat Pablo Neruda, in "I Wish the Woodcutter Would Wake Up," part of his collection *Canto General* (1934–45), admired the average American, whom he saw as dressed simply, hardworking, and invariably enthusiastic, with a humbleness regularly preyed upon by politicians. Jorge Luis Borges, the Argentinian librarian and author of story collections such as *Ficciones* (Fictions, 1944), empathized with the New England transcendentalists Ralph Waldo Emerson, Nathaniel Hawthorne, and Henry David Thoreau.

In Latin American writers' intellectual disquisitions, Latinos in the United States are a controversial topic commanding attention, particularly after World War II. (During the war, larger numbers of Mexican Americans and Puerto Ricans were in the U.S. armed forces than ever before. Beginning in this period, as discussed in the "Acculturation" introduction, the Bracero Program and the Great Migration brought about major demographic changes in the United States.) Questions regarding policy and identity acquired urgency: Are Latinos an extremity of Latin America, a Hispanic nation within an Anglo nation? How do they experience acculturation? Are they victims of or agents of colonialism? To what extent are they willing and able to remain loyal, especially after successive generations, to their immigrant cultures? How do they differ from other immigrants? Some Latin American writers, concerned with history and politics, concentrate on national groups, such as the Cuban exiles who fled to Miami after Fidel Castro's revolution in 1958–59 or the Central American refugees who escaped civil wars and arrived in Texas in the 1980s. Other writers spotlight cultural realms such as cuisine, fashion, music, and sports (baseball, in particular). Perhaps inspired by the work of poet and activist José Martí (see p. 265), in particular the essay "Nuestra América" (Our America, 1891), many writers now stress a hemispheric brotherhood. (Note, though, that Martí omits Anglos from his proposed union, suggesting that the languages Spanish, Portuguese, French, and Creole have a synchronicity on this side of the Atlantic Ocean not shared by English and its speakers.) Over time, simplistic profiles of Latinos north of the border have given way to the belief that a fresh type of *mestizaje*, a cultural crossbreeding, is forming a dynamic new civilization.

This appendix consists of four canonical texts that reflect such issues or address them directly:

José Enrique Rodó (1872–1917), a Uruguayan thinker and man of letters, was one of the torchbearers of *Modernismo*. This movement was defined by the Spanish-American War, which brought to a close Spain's colonial domination of the Caribbean Basin and began the U.S. geopolitical domination in the region. Rodó's most famous work, the groundbreaking essay "Ariel" (1900), excerpted here, takes the form of an open letter—a figurative speech—to Latin American youth: "I want each of you to be aware. . . ." Calling for a rejection of U.S. culture for its infatuation with earthly possessions, Rodó draws on Shakespeare's play *The Tempest*, in which the characters Ariel and Caliban represent the idealistic and materialistic aspects of human nature. Rodó embraces Ariel as a benign symbol of endurance. In his view, the United States "is effecting a kind of moral conquest among us. Admiration for its greatness and power is making impressive inroads in the minds of our leaders and, perhaps even more, in the impressionable minds of the masses, who are awed by its incontrovertible victories." He cautions against this effect, warning that "in the ambience of American democracy, the spirit of vulgarity encounters no barriers to slow its rising waters, and it spreads and swells as if flooding across an endless plain." Still, "although I do not love" those in the United States, Rodó admits, "I admire them."

José Vasconcelos (1882–1959) was a Mexican philosopher and politician, secretary of education, and presidential candidate in the 1929 elections. He was instrumental in the development of Mexico into a modern nation. Of Portuguese and Native American ancestry, Vasconcelos spent part of his childhood in the border town of Piedras Negras, where he came into contact with U.S. culture. In his adulthood, after a feud with the Mexican president Venustiano Carranza, he lived as an exile in the United States for several periods. Vasconcelos's exposure to Anglo ways left a deep imprint on him. In his multivolume memoirs, which he composed over two decades— *Creole Ulysses* (1935) is the only volume available in English translation—he analyzes the racism directed at Latinos and Native Americans. Such behavior inspired his controversial essay "Mestizaje," which, as discussed in the "Annexations" introduction, is the first of the three sections of his book *The Cosmic Race* (1925). In "Mestizaje," which is excerpted here, Vasconcelos states that *mestizos*, the Brown Race created by the union of Iberians with the indigenous populations of Central and South America, will dominate the world and thereby usher in an age of harmony.

Vasconcelos's theories spring from the work of two nineteenth-century thinkers: the English naturalist Charles Darwin, whose ideas about inherited traits he opposed, and the German philosopher Friedrich Nietzsche, whose ideas about the *Übermensch* (superman or overman) he embraced. He argues that mixed marriages, racial miscegenation, result not in the detriment but in the improvement of society—in a "fitter" race. Vasconcelos admires "the vigorous drive" of the United States, placing Argentina, another modern country made of immigrants, in close second. But he creates a racial hierarchy that is unsustainable, even dangerous, arguing that mestizos, Indians, and blacks are superior to whites in numerous ways. Since the scientific method used by the sociologists of his time does not serve his purpose, Vasconcelos calls for it to be revamped—that is, for the birth of a new science capable of justifying his theory. "Mestizaje," despite its spurious claims, became an ideological touchstone for the Chicano Movement, in the late 1960s and throughout the 1970s, and for pan-Latino thinkers through the 1990s. It is now seen as a discredited but historically important document.

Octavio Paz (1914–1998) was a Mexican poet, essayist, translator, editor, and diplomat. One of the commanding intellectuals of the twentieth century, he received the Nobel Prize for Literature in 1990. In numerous books and his monthly magazine *Vuelta*, he explored the connections between Mexico and the rest of the world. His studies on Romantic poetry and his translations into Spanish of French, American, Japanese, and Hindu poems opened up new vistas in Latin American literary circles. His contacts with William Carlos Williams, Elizabeth Bishop, Irving Howe, and other writers in the United States established a bridge across the U.S.-Mexican border through symposia, academic exchanges, and collaborations in periodicals.

As discussed in the "Acculturation" introduction, Paz's psychosociological book *El Laberinto de la soledad* (published in 1950, translated in 1961 as *The Labyrinth of Solitude*) analyzes the Mexican character. Inspired by the kind of socially oriented psychoanalysis practiced by Alfred Adler, one of Sigmund Freud's disciples, Paz sees his compatriots as suffering from an inferiority complex, a defiance of death, and a sense of cosmic confusion.

First published as a series of essays in periodicals, the book opens with a polemic, "The *Pachuco* and Other Extremes," written while Paz lived in Los Angeles and included here. Earlier in the decade, the Sleepy Lagoon Incident and the Zoot Suit Riots had radicalized young Mexican Americans, and Paz reacted negatively to the "anguished tension" of Pachuco culture. He describes Chicanos as having "this stubborn desire to be different" and "the lone Mexican" as "an orphan lacking both protectors and positive values." From this starting point, Paz proceeds to an elaborate comparison of the Mexican and the North American. He then extrapolates his ideas about these peoples to humans generally. His essay has been used as proof that Latin American intellectuals are unable to accurately understand the plight of Latinos in the United States. Chicano identity, say Paz's critics, is not a deformation of its Mexican counterpart but a dramatic reformulation, a new *mestizo*.

Roberto Fernández Retamar (b. 1930), a Cuban writer, was for years the editor-in-chief of the publishing house Casa de las Américas, in Havana, Cuba. He is best-known for his essay "Caliban: Notes Toward a Discussion of Culture in our America." A response of sorts to Rodó's argument against U.S. materialism, "Caliban" suggests that everything the United States touches turns into evil. The first three of the essay's eight parts are included here.

Fernández Retamar's viewpoint developed during Cuba's turbulent political situation in the late 1960s and early 1970s, as the Communist dictator Fidel Castro continued restructuring society on the foundation he built via the Cuban Revolution. The only place in the Western Hemisphere where a Communist regime has survived, the island had resisted the 1961 invasion of the Bay of Pigs (specifically at the beach Playa Girón) by Cuban exiles trained by American troops, ordered by U.S. president John F. Kennedy. Immediately after this incident, Cuba became subject to a stern, ongoing economic embargo by the United States. By the time Fernández Retamar published his essay in the magazine *Casa de las Américas,* in 1971, the feeling in Cuba of defiance toward the United States had evolved into a national sport. Fernández Retamar ponders how issues such as *mestizaje* and colonialism define Latin American identity. In his opinion, European and American abusers treat Latin America as a backwater. The time has come to resist the invasion, to turn subalterns into masters.

Fernández Retamar rejects Ariel and instead embraces Caliban— "Shakespeare's anagram for 'cannibal,'" a word in turn derived from *Caribe*—as a symbol of Latin America. He argues:

> This is something that we, the *mestizo* inhabitants of these same isles where Caliban lived, see with particular clarity: Prospero [the master/ wizard in *The Tempest*] invaded the islands, killed our ancestors, enslaved Caliban, and taught him his language to make himself understood. What else can Caliban do but use that same language—today he

has no other—to curse him, to wish that the "red plague" would fall on him? I know no other metaphor more expressive of our cultural situation, of our reality.

While these four foundational texts are more about the United States generally than about Latinos, they have been at the heart of heated discussions about Latinos. In Latin America, the question is whether U.S. culture has deracinated Latinos north of the border or whether Latinos represent communicating vessels that establish hemispheric continuity from south to north and back. In the United States, Latino activists, educators, journalists, and intellectuals have shaped a collective consciousness partly by supporting or opposing the ideas in these pieces. For instance, Rodó's invitation to the youth of Latin America to embrace Ariel, not Caliban, and Fernández Retamar's furthering of that argument from the ranks of the Cuban Revolution were subtly echoed in the anti-imperialist rhetoric of Latino intellectuals in the 1970s. Likewise, the vision expressed in Vasconcelos's "Mestizaje" served leaders of the Chicano Movement such as Rodolfo "Corky" Gonzales (see p. 787) and Reies López Tijerina—as well as lawyers, poets, and memorialists such as Oscar "Zeta" Acosta (p. 1039), Ricardo Sánchez (p. 1323), and Alurista (p. 1657)—as support for the idea that La Raza was more than a political stand: It was utopia with the mythical Aztlán at its heart. Feminist theorists such as Gloria Anzaldúa (p. 1490), with her vision of "the new mestiza," and Ana Castillo (p. 1978) were also inspired by Vasconcelos, as was the essayist Richard Rodriguez (p. 1574), whose understanding of the concept of "brownness" is directly related to *The Cosmic Race*. Indeed, the notion of cultural and racial hybridity has been essential in the construction of ethnic and panethnic Latino identities in the United States, and it has been celebrated in the social and political thought of U.S. Latino writers of diverse origins. Some of these writers refer to *mestizaje* not only in terms of indigenous influences among Chicanos, but also in terms of African influences. Along the same lines, the shaping of a Chicano sense of self, in the 1960s, grew in opposition to Paz's misconceptions in "The *Pachuco* and Other Extremes."

These four texts represent a sample of a larger canon, one predominantly shaped by male intellectuals. Among the Latin American women of this period who were thinking along these same lines was the Nobel Prize–winner Gabriela Mistral. In her poems, articles, and speeches, Mistral celebrated *mestizaje*, empathized with the conditions of impoverished Latin Americans, and worked for equal education for all (topics central to U.S. Latino writers). She lived and taught in the United States for brief periods, was an ambassador to the League of Nations (a precursor to the United Nations), promoted international collaboration, and had a high profile internationally. She also worked with Vasconcelos in Mexico. However, Mistral's essays do not have canonical status in Latin America.

# JOSÉ ENRIQUE RODÓ
## 1872–1917

### *From* Ariel[1]

* * *

The inextricably linked concepts of utilitarianism as a concept of human destiny and egalitarian mediocrity as a norm for social relationships compose the formula for what Europe has tended to call the spirit of *Americanism*. It is impossible to ponder either inspiration for social conduct, or to compare them with their opposites, without their inevitable association with that formidable and productive democracy to our North. Its display of prosperity and power is dazzling testimony to the efficacy of its institutions and to the guidance of its concepts. If it has been said that "utilitarianism" is the word for the spirit of the English, then the United States can be considered the embodiment of the word. And the Gospel of that word is spread everywhere through the good graces of its material miracles. Spanish America is not, in this regard, entirely a land of heathens. That powerful federation is effecting a kind of moral conquest among us. Admiration for its greatness and power is making impressive inroads in the minds of our leaders and, perhaps even more, in the impressionable minds of the masses, who are awed by its incontrovertible victories. And from admiring to imitating is an easy step. A psychologist will say that admiration and conviction are passive modes of imitation. "The main seat of the imitative part of our nature is our belief," said Bagehot.[2] Common sense and experience should in themselves be enough to establish this simple relationship. We imitate what we believe to be superior or prestigious. And this is why the vision of an America de-Latinized of its own will, without threat of conquest, and reconstituted in the image and likeness of the North, now looms in the nighmares of many who are genuinely concerned about our future. This vision is the impetus behind an abundance of similar carefully thought-out designs and explains the continuous flow of proposals for innovation and reform. We have our *USAmania*. It must be limited by the boundaries our reason and sentiment jointly dictate.

When I speak of boundaries, I do not suggest absolute negation. I am well aware that we find our inspirations, our enlightenment, our teachings, in the example of the strong; nor am I unaware that intelligent attention to external events is singularly fruitful in the case of a people still in the process of forming its national entity. I am similarly aware that by persevering in the educational process we hope to modulate the elements of society that must be adapted to new exigencies of civilization and new opportunities in life, thus balancing the forces of heritage and custom with that of innovation. I do not, however, see what is to be gained from denaturalizing the character—the *personality*—of a nation, from imposing an identification with a foreign model, while sacrificing irreplaceable uniqueness. Nor do I see anything to

---

1. Translated by Margaret Sayers Peden. Bracketed insertions in the text are the translator's.

2. Walter Bagehot (1826–1877), British businessman, economist, essayist, and journalist.

be gained from the ingenuous belief that identity can somehow be achieved through artificial and improvised imitation. Michelet[3] believed that the mindless transferral of what is natural and spontaneous in one society to another where it has neither natural nor historical roots was like attempting to introduce a dead organism into a living one by simple implantation. In a social structure, as in literature and art, forced imitation will merely distort the configuration of the model. The misapprehension of those who believe they have reproduced the character of a human collectivity in its essence, the living strength of its spirit, as well as the secret of its triumphs and prosperity, and have exactly reproduced the mechanism of its institutions and the external form of its customs, is reminiscent of the delusion of naïve students who believe they have achieved the genius of their master when they have merely copied his style and characteristics.

In such a futile effort there is, furthermore, an inexpressible ignobility. Eager mimicry of the prominent and the powerful, the successful and the fortunate, must be seen as a kind of political *snobbery*; and a servile abdication—like that of some snobs condemned by Thackeray in *The Book of Snobs*[4] to be satirized for all eternity—lamentably consumes the energies of those who are not blessed by nature or fortune but who impotently ape the caprices and foibles of those at the peak of society. Protecting our *internal* independence—independence of personality and independence of judgment—is a basic form of self-respect. Treatises on ethics often comment on one of Cicero's[5] moral precepts, according to which one of our responsibilities as human beings is zealously to protect the uniqueness of our personal character—whatever in it that is different and formative—while always respecting Nature's primary impulse: that the order and harmony of the world are based on the broad distribution of her gifts. The truth of this precept would seem even greater when applied to the character of human societies. Perhaps you will hear it said that there is no distinctive mark or characteristic of the present ordering of our peoples that is worth struggling to maintain. What may perhaps be lacking in our collective character is a sharply defined "personality." But in lieu of an absolutely distinct and autonomous particularity, we Latin Americans have a heritage of race, a great ethnic tradition, to maintain, a sacred place in the pages of history that depends upon us for its continuation. Cosmopolitanism, which we must respect as a compelling requisite in our formation, includes fidelity both to the past and to the formative role that the genius of our race must play in recasting the American of tomorrow.

More than once it has been observed that the great epochs of history, the most luminous and fertile periods in the evolution of humankind, are almost always the result of contemporaneous but conflicting forces that through the stimulus of concerted opposition preserve our interest in life, a fascination that would pale in the placidity of absolute conformity. So it was that the most genial and civilizing of cultures turned upon an axis supported by the poles of Athens and Sparta.[6] America must continue to

---

3. Jules Michelet (1798–1874), French historian.
4. A comic analysis of snobs, by "One of Themselves," the English writer William Makepeace Thackeray (1811–1863).

5. Marcus Tullius Cicero (106–43 BC), Roman statesman, orator, and writer.
6. Ancient Greek cities representing, respectively, democracy and militarism.

maintain the dualism of its original composition, which re-creates in history the classic myth of the two eagles released simultaneously from the two poles in order that each should reach the limits of its domain at the same moment. Genial and competitive diversity does not exclude but, rather, tolerates, and even in many aspects favors, solidarity. And if we could look into the future and see the formula for an eventual harmony, it would not be based upon the *unilateral imitation*—as Gabriel Tarde[7] would say—of one people by another, but upon a mutual exchange of influences, and the fortuitous fusion of the attributes that gave each its special glory.

In addition, a dispassionate examination of the civilization that some consider to be the only perfect model will reveal no less powerful reasons to temper the enthusiasms of those who demand idolatrous devotion, reasons other than those based on the thesis that to reject everything original is both unworthy and unjustifiable. And now I come to the direct relation between the theme of my talk and the spirit of imitation.

Any criticism of the Americans to our north should always be accompanied, as in the case of any worthy opponent, with the chivalrous salute that precedes civilized combat. And I make that bow sincerely. But to ignore a North American's defects would seem to me as senseless as to deny his good qualities. Born—calling upon the paradox that Baudelaire[8] employed in a different context—with the *innate experience* of freedom, they have remained faithful to the laws of their origins and with the precision and sureness of a mathematical progression have developed the basic principles of their formation. Subsequently, their history is characterized by a uniformity that, although it may lack diversity in skills and values, does possess the intellectual beauty of logic. The traces of their presence will never be erased from the annals of human rights. From tentative essays and utopian visions, they were the first to evoke our modern ideal of liberty, forging imperishable bronze and living reality from concepts. With their example they have demonstrated the possibility of imposing the unyielding authority of a republic upon an enormous national organism. With their federation they have demonstrated—recalling de Tocqueville's[9] felicitous expression—how the brilliance and power of large states can be reconciled with the happiness and peace of the small. Some of the boldest strokes in the panorama of this century, deeds that will be recorded through all time, are theirs. Theirs, too, the glory of having fully established—by amplifying the strongest note of moral beauty in our civilization—the grandeur and power of work, that sacred power that antiquity degraded to the abjectness of slave labor, and that today we identify with the highest expression of human dignity, founded on the awareness of its intrinsic worth. Strong, tenacious, believing that inactivity is ignominious, they have placed in the hands of the mechanic in his shop and the farmer in his field the mythic club of Hercules and have given human nature a new and unexpected beauty by girding onto it the blacksmith's leather apron. Each of them marches forward to conquer life in the same way the first Puritans set out to tame the wilderness. Persevering devotees of that cult of individual energy that makes each man the author of his own destiny,

---

7. Jean-Gabriel de Tarde (1843–1904), French social psychologist and criminologist.
8. Charles Baudelaire (1821–1867), French poet.

9. Alexis de Tocqueville (1805–1859), French historian and political thinker.

they have modeled their society on an imaginary assemblage of Crusoes[1] who, after gaining their crude strength by looking out for their self-interests, set to weaving the stout cloth of their society. Without sacrificing the sovereign concept of individualism, they have at the same time created from the spirit of association the most admirable instrument of their grandeur and empire. Similarly, from the sum of individual strengths subordinated to a plan of research, philanthropy, and industry, they have achieved marvelous results that are all the more remarkable, considering that they were obtained while maintaining the absolute integrity of personal autonomy. There is in these North Americans a lively and insatiable curiosity and an avid thirst for enlightenment. Professing their reverence for public education with an obsessiveness that resembles monomania—glorious and productive as it may be— they have made the school the hub of their prosperity, and a child's soul the most valued of all precious commodities. Although their culture is far from being refined or spiritual, it is admirably efficient as long as it is directed to the practical goal of realizing an immediate end. They have not added a single general law, a single principle, to the storehouse of scientific knowledge. They have, however, worked magic through the marvels of their application of general knowledge. They have grown tall as giants in the domains of utility; and in the steam engine and electric generator they have given the world billions of invisible slaves to serve the human Aladdin, increasing a hundredfold the power of the magic lamp. The extent of their greatness and strength will amaze generations to come. With their prodigious skill for improvisation, they have invented a way to speed up time; and by the power of will in one day they have conjured up from the bosom of absolute solitude a culture equal to the work of centuries. The liberty of Puritanism, still shedding its light from the past, joined to that light the heat of a piety that lives today. Along with factories and schools, their strong hands have also raised the churches from which rise the prayers of many millions of free consciences. They have been able to save from the shipwreck of all idealisms the highest idealism, keeping alive the tradition of a religion that although it may not fly on wings of a delicate and profound spiritualism does, at least, amid the harshness of the utilitarian tumult, keep a firm grip on the reins of morality. Surrounded by the refinements of civilized life, they have also been able to maintain a certain robust primitivism. They have a pagan cult of health, of skill, of strength; they temper and refine the precious instrument of will in muscle; and obliged, by their insatiable appetite for dominance, to cultivate all human activities with obsessive energy, they build an athlete's torso in which to shelter the heart of free man. And from the concord of their civilization, from the harmonious mobility of their culture, sounds a dominant note of optimism and confidence and faith that expands their hearts; they advance toward the future under the power of a stubborn and arrogant expectation. This is the note of Longfellow's "Excelsior" and "A Psalm of Life,"[2] which their poets, in the philosophy of strength and action, have advocated as an infallible balm against all bitterness.

1. I.e., embodiments of Robinson Crusoe, title character of a 1719 novel, by the English writer Daniel Defoe (ca. 1659–1731), about the adventures of a castaway who spends three decades on a remote tropical island near Venezuela.

2. Poems by the American educator and poet Henry Wadsworth Longfellow (1807–1882), originally included in his collection *Ballads and Other Poems* (1842).

Thus their titanic greatness impresses even those who have been fore-warned by the enormous excesses of their character or the recent violence of their history. As for me, you have already seen that, although I do not love them, I admire them. I admire them, first of all, for their formidable strength of *volition* and, as Philarète Chasles[3] said of their English fore-bears, I bow before the "school of will and work" they have instituted.

*In the beginning was Action.* A future historian of that powerful republic could begin the still-to-be-concluded Genesis of their national existence with these famous words from *Faust*.[4] Their genius, like the universe of the Dyna-mists, could be defined as *force in motion.* Above all else, they have the capacity, the enthusiasm, and the blessed vocation for action. Will is the chisel that has sculptured these peoples in hard stone. Their outstanding characteristics are the two manifestations of the power of will: originality and boldness. Their history, in its entirety, has been marked by paroxysms of vigorous activity. Their typical figure, like Nietzsche's *superman*, is named *I Will It.* If something saves him, collectively, from vulgarity, it is that extraordinary show of energy that leads to achievement and that allows him to invest even the struggles of self-interest and materialism with a certain aura of epic grandeur. Thus Paul Bourget[5] could say that the speculators of Chicago and Minneapolis are like heroic warriors whose skills of attack and defense are comparable to those of Napoleon's veteran *grognards*.[6] And this supreme energy that seems to permit North American genius—audacious and hypnotic as it is—to cast spells and the power of suggestion over the Fates is to be found even in those peculiarities of their civilization that we consider exceptional or divergent. For example, no one will deny that Edgar Allan Poe[7] is one such anomalous and rebellious individual. He is of the elect who resist assimilation into the national soul, a person who successfully, if in infinite solitude, struggled among his fellows for self-expression. And yet—as Baudelaire has so tellingly pointed out—the basic characteristic of Poe's heroes is still the superhuman persistence, the indom-itable stamina, of their will. When Poe conceived Ligeia,[8] the most mysteri-ous and adorable of his creatures, he symbolized in the inextinguishable light of her eyes the hymn of the triumph of Will over Death.

With my sincere recognition of all that is luminous and great in its genius, I have won the right to complete a fair appraisal of this powerful nation; one vital question, however, remains to be answered. Is that society achieving, or at least partially achieving, the concept of rational conduct that satisfies the legitimate demands of intellectual and moral dignity? Will this be the soci-ety destined to create the closest approximation of the "perfect state"? Does the feverish restlessness that seems to magnify the activity and intensity of their lives have a truly worthwhile objective, and does that stimulus jus-tify their impatience?

Herbert Spencer,[9] voicing his sincere and noble tribute to American democracy at a banquet in New York City, identified this same unrestrain-

3. Victor-Euphémien-Philarète Chasles (1798–1873), French critic and man of letters.
4. Two-part tragic play (1808, 1832) by the Ger-man writer Johann Wolfgang von Goethe (1749–1832).
5. French novelist and critic (1852–1935).
6. Literally, grumblers (French); members of the French Army's Imperial Guard under Napoléon Bonaparte (1769–1821), emperor of France 1804–15.
7. American writer (1809–1849).
8. Title character of an 1838 short story by Poe.
9. English philosopher and political theorist (1820–1903).

able restiveness as the fundamental characteristic of the lives of North Americans, an agitation manifest in their infinite passion for work and their drive toward material expansion in all its forms. And then he observed that such an atmosphere of activity exclusively subordinated to the immediate proposals of utility denoted a concept of life that might well be acceptable as a provisional quality of a civilization, or as the preliminary stage of a culture. Such a concept, however, demands subsequent revision, for unless that tendency is curbed, the result will be to convert utilitarian work into an end, into the supreme goal of life, when rationally it can be only one among numbers of elements that facilitate the harmonious development of our being. Then Spencer added that it was time to preach to North Americans the "gospel of relaxation." And as we identify the ultimate meaning of those words with the classic concept of *otium*,[1] as it was dignified by the moralists of antiquity, we would include among the chapters of gospel those tireless workers should heed, everything concerned with the ideal, the use of time for other than selfish purposes, and any meditation not directed toward the immediate ends of utility.

North American life, in fact, perfectly describes the vicious circle identified by Pascal:[2] the fervent pursuit of well-being that has no object beyond itself. North American prosperity is as great as its inability to satisfy even an average concept of human destiny. In spite of its titanic accomplishments and the great force of will that those accomplishments represent, and in spite of its incomparable triumphs in all spheres of material success, it is nevertheless true that as an entity this civilization creates a singular impression of insufficiency and emptiness. And when following the prerogative granted by centuries of evolution dominated by the dignity of classicism and Christianity we ask, what is its directing principle, what its ideal *substratum*, what the ultimate goal of the present Positivist interests surging through that formidable mass, we find nothing in the way of a formula for a definitive ideal but the same eternal preoccupation with material triumphs. Having drifted from the traditions that set their course, the peoples of this nation have not been able to replace the inspiring idealism of the past with a high and selfless concept of the future. They live for the immediate reality, for the present, and thereby subordinate all their activity to the egoism of personal and collective well-being. Of the sum of their riches and power could be said what Bourget said of the intelligence of the Marquis de Norbert, a figure in one of his books: that it is like a well-laid fire to which no one has set a match. What is lacking is the kindling spark that causes the flame of a vivifying and exciting ideal to blaze from the abundant but unlighted wood. Not even national egoism, lacking a higher motivation, not even exclusiveness and pride of nationhood, which is what in antiquity transfigured and exalted the prosaic severity of Roman life, can engender glimmers of idealism and beauty in a people in whom cosmopolitan confusion and the *atomism* of a poorly understood democracy impede the formation of a true national consciousness.

It could be said that when the Positivism of the mother country was transmitted to her emancipated children in America, it suffered a distilling

---

1. Leisure or ease (Latin).
2. Blaise Pascal (1623–1662), French philosopher.

process that filtered out the emollient idealism, reducing it to the harshness that previous excessive passion and satire had attributed to English Positivism. But beneath the hard utilitarian shell, beneath the mercantile cynicism, beneath the Puritanical severity, the English spirit masks—you must never doubt it—a poetic genius and a profound veneration for sensitivity. All this, in Taine's[3] opinion, reveals that the primitive, the Germanic, essence of that people, later diluted by the pressures of conquest and commercial activities, was one of an extraordinary exaltation of sentiment. The American spirit did not inherit the ancestral poetic instinct that bursts like a crystalline stream from the heart of Britannic rock when smitten by an artistic Moses. In the institution of their aristocracy—as anachronistic and unjust as it may be in the realm of politics—the English people possess a high and impregnable bulwark against the attacks of mercantilism and the encroachment of the prosaic. This bulwark is so high and so impregnable that Taine himself states that, since the age of the Greek city-states, history has not seen an example of a way of life more propitious to heightening a sense of human nobility. In the ambience of American democracy, the spirit of vulgarity encounters no barriers to slow its rising waters and it spreads and swells as if flooding across an endless plain.

Sensibility, intelligence, customs—everything in that enormous land is characterized by a radical ineptitude for selectivity which, along with the mechanistic nature of its materialism and its politics, nurtures a profound disorder in anything having to do with idealism. It is all too easy to follow the manifestations of that ineptitude, beginning with the most external and apparent, then arriving at those that are more essential and internal. Prodigal with his riches—because in his appetites, as Bourget has astutely commented, there is no trace of Molière's miserly Harpagon[4]—the North American has with his wealth achieved all the satisfaction and vanity that come with sumptuous magnificence—but good taste has eluded him. In such an atmosphere, true art can exist only in the form of individual rebellion. Emerson and Poe, in that situation, are like plants cruelly uprooted from their natural soil by the spasms of a geologic catastrophe. Bourget, in *Outre mer*,[5] speaks of the solemnity with which the word *art* trembles on the lips of the North Americans who have courted fortune. In such sycophancy, the hearty and righteous heroes of *self-help* hope to crown, by assimilating refinement, the labor of their tenaciously won eminence. But never have they conceived of the divine activity they so emphatically profess as anything other than a new way to satisfy their pervading restiveness, and as a trophy for their vanity. They ignore in art all that is selfless and selective. They ignore it, in spite of the munificence with which private fortunes are employed to stimulate an appreciation of beauty; in spite of the splendid museums and exhibitions their cities boast; in spite of the mountains of marble and bronze they have sculptured into statues for their public squares. And if a word may some day characterize their taste in art, it will be a word that negates art itself: the grossness of affectation, the ignorance of all that is subtle and exquisite, the

---

3. Hippolyte-Adolphe Taine (1828–1893), French philosopher and critic.
4. Protagonist of the satirical comedy *The Miser* (1668), by the French actor and dramatist Molière

(Jean-Baptiste Poquelin, 1622–1673).
5. *Outre-Mer: Notes sur l'Amérique* (1895), Bourget's journal of his 1893 visit to the United States.

cult of false grandeur, the *sensationalism* that excludes the serenity that is irreconcilable with the pace of a feverish life.

The idealism of beauty does not fire the soul of a descendant of austere Puritans. Nor does the idealism of truth. He scorns as vain and unproductive any exercise of thought that does not yield an immediate result. He does not bring to science a selfless thirst for truth, nor has he ever shown any sign of revering science for itself. For him research is merely preparation for a utilitarian application. His grandiose plans to disseminate the benefits of popular education were inspired in the noble goal of communicating rudimentary knowledge to the masses; but although those plans promote the growth of education, we have seen no sign that they contain any imperative to enhance selective education, or any inclination to aid in allowing excellence to rise above general mediocrity. Thus the persistent North American war against ignorance has resulted in a universal *semi*-culture, accompanied by the diminution of high culture. To the same degree that basic ignorance has diminished in that gigantic democracy, wisdom and genius have correspondingly disappeared. This, then, is the reason that the trajectory of their intellectual activity is one of decreasing brilliance and originality. While in the period of independence and the formation of their nation many illustrious names emerged to expound both the thought and the will of that people, only a half century later de Tocqueville could write of them, *the gods have departed.* It is true, however, that even as de Tocqueville was writing his masterpiece, the rays of a glorious pleiad of universal magnitude in the intellectual history of this century were still beaming forth from Boston, the *Puritan citadel,* the city of learned traditions. But who has come along to perpetuate the bequest of a William Ellery Channing,[6] an Emerson, a Poe? The bourgeois leveling process, ever-swifter in its devastation, is tending to erase what little character remains of their precarious intellectualism. For some time now North American literature has not been borne to heights where it can be perceived by the rest of the world. And today the most genuine representation of American taste in belle lettres is to be found in the gray pages of a journalism that bears little resemblance to that of the days of the *Federalist.*[7]

In the area of morality, the mechanistic thrust of utilitarianism has been somewhat regulated by the balance wheel of a strong religious tradition. We should not, nevertheless, conclude that this tradition has led to true principles of selflessness. North American religion, a derivation from and exaggeration of English religion, actually serves to aid and enforce penal law that will relinquish its hold only on the day it becomes possible to grant to moral authority the religious authority envisioned by John Stuart Mill. Benjamin Franklin[8] represents the highest point in North American morality: a philosophy of conduct whose ideals are grounded in the normality of honesty and the utility of prudence. His is a philosophy that would never give rise to either sanctity or heroism, one that although it may—like the cane that habitually supports its originator—lend conscience support along the

---

6. American transcendentalist poet (1818–1901).
7. Two-volume compilation (1788) of the Federalist Papers, 85 articles advocating the ratification of the U.S. Constitution, 77 of which were first published serially in two New York newspapers.
8. American statesman and philosopher (1706–1790). *John Stuart Mill*: English philosopher and economist (1806–1873).

everyday paths of life is a frail staff indeed when it comes to scaling the peaks. And these are the heights; consider the reality to be found in the valleys. Even were the moral criterion to sink no lower than Franklin's honest and moderate utilitarianism, the inevitable consequence—already revealed in de Tocqueville's sagacious observation—of a society educated in such limitations of duty would not inevitably be that state of proud and magnificent decadence that reveals the proportions of the satanic beauty of evil during the dissolution of empires; it would, instead, result in a kind of pallid and mediocre materialism and, ultimately, the lassitude of a lusterless enervation resulting from the quiet winding-down of all the mainsprings of moral life. In a society whose precepts tend to place the demonstration of self-sacrifice and virtue outside the realm of obligation, the bounds of that obligation will constantly be pushed back. And the school of material prosperity—always an ordeal for republican austerity—that captures minds today has carried the simplistic concept of rational conduct even farther. In their frankness other codes have surpassed even Franklin as an expression of the national wisdom. And it is not more than five years ago that in all of North America's cities public opinion consecrated, with the most unequivocal demonstration of popular and critical acclaim, the new moral law: from the Boston of the Puritans, Orison Swett Marden wrote a learned book entitled *Pushing to the Front*,[9] solemnly announcing that *success* should be considered the supreme goal of life. His "revelation" echoed even in the bosom of Christian fellowship, and once was cited as being comparable to Thomas à Kempis' *The Imitation of Christ*.[1]

Public life, of course, does not escape the consequences of the spread of the germ of disorganization harbored in the entrails of that society. Any casual observer of its political customs can relate how the obsession of utilitarian interests tends progressively to enervate and impoverish the sense of righteousness in the hearts of its citizens. Civic valor, that venerable Hamiltonian[2] virtue, is a forgotten sword that lies rusting among the cobwebs of tradition. Venality, which begins in the polling places, spreads through the workings of the institution. A government of mediocrity discourages the emulation that exalts character and intelligence and relates those qualities to the efficacy of power. Democracy, which consistently has resisted the regulator of a noble and instructive notion of human excellence, has always tended toward an abominable slavishness to numbers that undervalues the greatest moral benefits of liberty and nullifies respect for the dignity of others. Today, furthermore, a formidable force is rising up to emphasize the absolutism of numbers. The political influence of a plutocracy represented by the all-powerful allies of the trust, the monopolizers of production and masters of the economy, is undoubtedly one of the most significant features in the present physiognomy of that great nation. The formation of this plutocracy has caused some to recall, with good reason, the rise of the arrogant and wealthy class that in the waning days of the Roman republic was one of the visible

---

9. *Pushing to the Front; or, Success under Difficulties* (1894) was the first of several books on success, willpower, and positive thinking, by Marden (1850–1924), American writer, doctor, and businessman.

1. Widely read book about Christian devotion (ca. 1418), originally in Latin and probably by Thomas (ca. 1380–1471), a Catholic monk.
2. Reference to the American statesman Alexander Hamilton (1755–1804).

signs of the decline of liberty and the tyranny of the Caesars.[3] And the exclusive concern for material gain—the numen of that civilization—imposes its logic on political life, as well as on all other areas of activity, granting the greatest prominence to Alphonse Daudet's[4] bold and astute *Struggle-for-lifer*, become, by dint of brutal efficiency, the supreme personification of national energy: a postulant for Emerson's *representative man*, or for Taine's *personnage régnant* [leading personage].

There is a second impulse corresponding to the one that in the life of the spirit is speeding toward utilitarian egoism and the disintegration of idealism, and that is the physical impulse the multitudes and the initiatives of an astounding population explosion are pushing Westward toward the boundless territory that throughout the period of the Independence was still a mystery hidden by the forests of the Mississippi. In fact, it is in this extemporaneous West—beginning to be so formidable to the interests of the original Atlantic states, and threatening in the near future to demand its hegemony—that we find the most faithful representation of contemporary North American life. It is in the West that the definitive results, the logical and natural fruits, of the spirit that has led this powerful democracy away from its origins stand out so clearly, allowing the observer to picture the face of the immediate future of this great nation. As a representative type, the Yankee and Virginian have been replaced by the tamer of the only-yesterday-deserted Plains, those settlers of whom Michel Chevalier said, prophetically, a half-century ago, "the last shall be first."[5] In that man of the West, a utilitarianism void of any idealism, a kind of universal *in*definition and the leveling process of an ill-conceived democracy will reach their ultimate triumph. Everything noble in that civilization, everything that binds it to magnanimous memories and supports its historic dignity—the heritage of the *Mayflower*, the memory of patrician Virginians and New England gentry, the spirit of the citizens and the legislators of the emancipation—will live on in the original States, there where in Boston and Philadelphia "the palladium of Washingtonian tradition" is still upheld. It is Chicago that now rears its head to rule. And its confidence in its superiority over the original Atlantic states is based on the conviction that they are too reactionary, too European, too traditional. History confers no titles when the election process entails auctioning off the purple.

To the degree that the generic utilitarianism of that civilization assumes more defined, more open, and more limiting characteristics, the intoxication of material prosperity increases the impatience of its children to propagate that doctrine and enshrine it with the historical importance of a Rome. Today, North Americans openly aspire to preeminence in universal culture, to leadership in ideas; they consider themselves the forgers of a type of civilization that will endure forever. The semi-ironic speech that Réné Lefebvre Laboulaye[6] places in the mouth of a student in his Americanized Paris to signify the superiority that experience has conceded to whatever favors

3. Powerful ancient Roman family, including the statesman/dictator Julius (100–44 BC) and his grandnephew, the emperor Augustus (63 BC–AD 14).
4. French novelist (1840–1897).
5. Translated quotation from this French engi-neer, statesman, and economist (1806–1879), in "Letter X.: The Yankee and the Virginian" (*Society, Manners and Politics in the United States: Being a Series of Letters on North America*, 1839).
6. Édouard-René-Lefèvre de Laboulaye (1811–1883), French jurist, historian, politician, and poet.

the pride of nationalism would today be accepted by any patriotic North American as absolute truth. At the base of the Americans' open rivalry with Europe there is an ingenuous disdain, and the profound conviction that Americans will in a very brief time obscure the intellectual superiority and glory of Europe, once again fulfilling in the evolution of human civilization the harsh law of the ancient mysteries in which the initiate always killed his initiator. It would be futile to attempt to convince a North American that, although the contribution his nation has made to the evolution of liberty and utility has undoubtedly been substantial, and should rightly qualify as a universal contribution, indeed, as a contribution to *humanity*, it is not so great as to cause the axis of the world to shift in the direction of a new Capitol. It would be similarly futile to attempt to convince him that the enduring achievements of the European Aryans, who dwelt along the civilizing shores of the Mediterranean that more than three thousand years ago jubilantly displayed the garland of its Hellenic cities—achievements that survived until today, and whose traditions and teachings we still adhere to—form a sum that cannot be equaled by the formula *Washington plus Edison*.[7] Given the opportunity, they would gladly revise *Genesis*, hoping to gain a place "in the beginning."[8] But, in addition to the relative modesty of their role in the enlightenment of humanity, their very character denies them the possibility of hegemony. Nature has not gifted them either with a genius for persuasion or with the vocation of the apostle. They lack the supreme gift of *amiability*, given the highest meaning of the word, that is, the extraordinary power of sympathy that enables nations endowed by Providence with the gift and responsibility for educating to instill in their culture something of the beauty of classic Greece, beauty of which all cultures hope to find some trace. That civilization may abound—undoubtedly it does abound—in proposals and productive examples. It may inspire admiration, amazement, and respect. But it is difficult to believe that when a stranger glimpses their enormous symbol from the high seas—Bartholdi's Statue of Liberty,[9] triumphantly lifting her torch high above the port of New York City—it awakens in his soul the deep and religious feeling that must have been evoked in the diaphanous nights of Attica by the sight of Athena high upon the Acropolis,[1] her bronze sword, glimpsed from afar, gleaming in the pure and serene atmosphere.

I want each of you to be aware that when in the name of the rights of the spirit I resist the mode of North American utilitarianism, which they want to impose on us as the summa and model of civilization, I do not imply that everything they have achieved in the sphere of what we might call *the interests of the soul* has been entirely negative. Without the arm that levels and constructs, the arm that serves the noble work of the mind would not be free to function. Without a certain material well-being, the realm of the spirit and the intellect could not exist. The aristocratic idealism of Renan[2] accepts this fact when it exalts—in relation to the moral concerns

---

7. I.e., George Washington (1732–1799), U.S. president 1789–97, plus Thomas Alva Edison (1847–1931), American inventor.
8. First words of the biblical Book of Genesis, the Judeo-Christian Creation story.
9. The statue was designed by the French sculptor Frédéric-Auguste Bartholdi (1834–1904).
1. Ancient Greek monument in Athens (chief city of the state of Attica), site of a temple to the goddess Athena.
2. Joseph-Ernest Renan (1823–1892), French philologist and historian.

of the species and its future spiritual selection—the importance of the utilitarian work of this century. "To rise above necessity," the master adds, "is to be redeemed." In the remote past, the effects of the prosaic and self-interested actions of the merchant who first put one people in contact with others were of incalculable value in disseminating ideas, since such contacts were an effective way to enlarge the scope of intelligence, to polish and refine customs, even, perhaps, to advance morality. The same positive force reappears later, propitiating the highest idealism of civilization. According to Paul de Saint-Victor,[3] the gold accumulated by the mercantilism of the Italian republics financed the Renaissance. Ships returning from the lands of the Thousand and One Nights laden with spices and ivory to fill the storehouses of the Florentine merchants made it possible for Lorenzo de Medici to renew the Platonic feast.[4] History clearly demonstrates a reciprocal relationship between the progress of utilitarianism and idealism. And in the same way that utility often serves as a strong shield for the ideal, frequently (as long as it is not specifically intended) the ideal evokes the useful. Bagehot, for example, observed that mankind might never have enjoyed the positive benefits of navigation had there not in primitive ages been idle dreamers—surely misunderstood by their contemporaries—who were intrigued by contemplating the movement of the planets. This law of harmony teaches us to respect the arm that tills the inhospitable soil of the prosaic and the ordinary. Ultimately, the work of North American Positivism will serve the cause of Ariel. What that Cyclopean nation, with its sense of the useful and its admirable aptitude for mechanical invention, has achieved directly in the way of material well-being, other peoples, or they themselves in the future, will effectively incorporate into the process of selection. This is how the most precious and fundamental of the acquisitions of the spirit—the alphabet, which lends immortal wings to the word—was born in the very heart of Canaanite trading posts, the discovery of a mercantile civilization that used it for exclusively financial purposes, never dreaming that the genius of superior races would transfigure it, converting it into a means of communicating mankind's purest and most luminous essence. The relationship between material good and moral and intellectual good is, then, according to an analogy offered by Fouillée,[5] nothing more than a new aspect of the old equivalence of forces; and, in the same way that motion is transformed into heat, elements of spiritual excellence may also be obtained from material benefits.

As yet, however, North American life has not offered us a new example of that incontestable relationship, nor even afforded a glimpse of a glorious future. Our confidence and our opinion must incline us to believe, however, that in an inferred future their civilization is destined for excellence. Considering that under the scourge of intense activity the very brief time separating them from their dawn has witnessed a sufficient expenditure of

3. Paul Bins, comte de Saint-Victor (1827–1881), French writer.
4. I.e., Lorenzo de' Medici (1449–1492), ruler of the Florentine Republic during the Italian Renaissance, continued the higher traditions of ancient Greece as represented by the philosopher Plato (ca. 428–348 or 347 BC). *Thousand and One Nights*: collection of Middle Eastern and South Asian stories and folk tales compiled in Arabic (ninth–fifteenth centuries); often known in English as the *Arabian Nights*.
5. Alfred Jules Émile Fouillée (1838–1912), French philosopher.

life forces to effect a great evolution, their past and present can only be the prologue to a promising future. Everything indicates that their evolution is still very far from definitive. The assimilative energy that has allowed them to preserve a certain uniformity and a certain generic character in spite of waves of ethnic groups very different from those that have until now set the tone for their national identity will be vitiated in increasingly difficult battles. And in the utilitarianism that so effectively inhibits idealism, they will not find an inspiration powerful enough to maintain cohesion. An illustrious thinker who compared the slave of ancient societies to a particle undigested by the social system might use a similar comparison to characterize the situation of the strong Germanic strain now identifiable in the Mid- and Far West. There, preserved intact—in temperament, social organization, and customs—are all the traits of a German nature that in many of its most profound and most vigorous specificities must be considered to be antithetical to the American character. In addition, a civilization destined to endure and expand in the world, a civilization that has not, in the manner of an Oriental empire, become mummified, or lost its aptitude for variety, cannot indefinitely channel its energies and ideas in one, and only one, direction. Let us hope that the spirit of that titanic society, which has until today been characterized solely by *Will* and *Utility*, may one day be known for its intelligence, sentiment, and idealism. Let us hope that from that enormous crucible will ultimately emerge the exemplary human being, generous, balanced, and select, who Spencer, in a work I have previously cited, predicted would be the product of the costly work of the melting pot. But let us not expect to find such a person either in the present reality of that nation or in its immediate evolution. And let us refuse to see an exemplary civilization where there exists only a clumsy, though huge, working model that must still pass through many corrective revisions before it acquires the serenity and confidence with which a nation that has achieved its perfection crowns its work—the powerful ascent that Leconte de Lisle describes in "Le sommeil du condor" [The Dream of the Condor][6] as an ascent that ends in Olympian tranquility.

1900

---

6. Poem by the French poet Charles Marie René Leconte de Lisle (1818–1894).

# JOSÉ VASCONCELOS
## 1882–1959

*FROM* THE COSMIC RACE

*From* Mestizaje[1]

*I*

In the opinion of respectable geologists, the American continent includes some of the most ancient regions of the world. The Andes are, undoubtedly, as old as any other mountain range on earth. And while the land itself is ancient, the traces of life and human culture also go back in time beyond any calculations. The architectural ruins of legendary Mayans, Quechuas, and Toltecs are testimony of civilized life previous to the oldest foundations of towns in the Orient and Europe.[2] As research advances, more support is found for the hypothesis of Atlantis as the cradle of a civilization that flourished millions of years ago in the vanished continent and in parts of what is today America.[3] The thought of Atlantis evokes the memory of her mysterious predecessors. The Hiperborean continent, vanished without trace, other than the vestiges of life and culture sometimes discovered under the snows of Greenland; the Lemurians or the black race from the south; the Atlantean civilization of the red men; immediately afterwards, the emergence of the yellow races, and finally the civilization of the white men.[4] This profound legendary hypothesis explains the evolution of the races better

1. Translated by Didier T. Jaén. Except as indicated, all footnotes are Jaén's. Two of his notes have been omitted.
2. According to scientific data, urban civilization in the Old World can be traced back to the third and second millenium B.C., approximately 2740 B.C. in Egypt, 2000 B.C. in Mesopotamia, and 2000 B.C. in India; in America, however, the Maya civilization can be traced only as far back as 292 A.D. and the Inca to 1200 A.D. Vasconcelos' statement makes sense only if we take into account theories such as those put forth by the Theosophists (see note 4), which trace Maya, Quechua, and Toltec cultures to Atlantean origins, millions of years B.C. Needless to say, no scientific basis for such theories exists, or is claimed.
3. It is difficult to determine to what "research" Vasconcelos was referring, although at the beginning of the XX century the existence of Atlantis was still a much debated issue. * * *
4. Vasconcelos' allusion to the "mysterious" continents, predecessors of Atlantis, originates in the ideas of the Theosophists, the occultist movement founded by Helena P. Blavatsky (1831–1891), author of, among other books, a six volume work, *The Secret Doctrine: The Synthesis of Science, Religion, and Philosophy* (Adyar: Theosoph. Pub. House, 1888–1936). The title

alone suggests Vasconcelos' attempt at a philosophical synthesis of the different branches of intellectual and spiritual knowledge.

* * *

* * * In this introductory paragraph to *La raza cósmica*, Vasconcelos evidently makes use of Theosophist cosmogony. According to Blavatsky, Humanity has evolved in seven stages or cycles, each characterized by a different race. The first race, a sort of astral body, inhabited the "Imperishable Sacred Land". The second race inhabited the Hyperborean continent in the Arctic. The third race was the Lemurian, hermaphrodites, inhabitants of the lost Lemuria, the sunken continent that joined South Africa and India. The fourth race was the Atlantean, very similar to the present human races. The fifth race is the present day Human, while the sixth and seventh races are still to come. * * *

* * *

However, Vasconcelos' summary mentions only four races and is closer to one found in Edouard Schuré, whose work, *The Great Initiates* (Paris, 1889) attained popularity in Latin America, especially in Argentina and Mexico. * * *

* * *

than the elucubrations of geologists like Ameghino,[5] who places the origin of man in Patagonia, a land which, it is well known, is of recent geological formation. On the other hand, the hypothesis of prehistoric ethnic empires finds extraordinary support in Wegener's theory of the translation of continents.[6] According to this thesis, all the lands were previously united into a single continent, which has since been breaking apart. Thus, it is easy to assume that in a particular region of a continuous land mass, a race would develop which, after progress and decline, would be substituted by another, instead of having recourse to the hypothesis of migrations from one continent to another by means of disappearing land bridges. It is also interesting to note another coincidence of the ancient tradition with the most recent facts from geology: According to Wegener, the communication between Australia, India, and Madagascar was interrupted before the communication between South America and Africa. This amounts to a corroboration of the theory that the site of the Lemurian civilization disappeared before the flourishing of Atlantis, and also, that the last continent to disappear was Atlantis, since scientific explorations have come to demonstrate that the Atlantic Ocean is the sea of most recent formation.

Although the origins of this theory remain more or less confused within a tradition as obscure as it is rich in meaning, the legend still remains of a civilization born in our forests, or spread to them after a powerful growth. Traces of it are still visible in Chichén Itzá and Palenque,[7] and in all the sites where the Atlantean mystery prevails: The mystery of the red men who, after dominating the world, had the precepts of their wisdom engraved on the Emerald Table,[8] perhaps a marvelous Colombian emerald, which at the time of the telluric upheavals was taken to Egypt, where Hermes[9] and his adepts learned and transmitted its secrets.

If we are, then, geologically ancient, as well as in respect to the tradition, how can we still continue to accept the fiction, invented by our European fathers, of the novelty of a continent that existed before the appearance of the land from where the discoverers and conquerors came?

The question has paramount importance to those who insist in looking for a plan in History. The confirmation of the great antiquity of our continent may seem idle to those who see nothing in the chain of events but a fateful repetition of meaningless patterns. With boredom we should regard the work of contemporary civilization, if the Toltec palaces would tell us nothing

5. Florentino Ameghino (1854–1911). Argentinian paleontologist. One of his contentions was that all mammals of the world, including man, had their origin in Argentina and the South American continent.
6. Alfred L. Wegener (1880–1930). German geophysicist, author of the theory of the translation of continents, expounded in his work, *The Origin of Continents and Oceans* (1915; translated into Spanish in 1924). * * *

Vanconcelos' contention, that this theory supports the idea of the existence of Atlantis, seems questionable, since, to the scientific theory, the separation of the continents was completed during the Pleistocene, long before the appearance of human civilizations. On the other hand, Theosophists and Anthroposophists date the origin of pre-human races in millions of years, and the

age of Atlantis from 75000 to the date of the last catastrophe in 9564 B.C. * * *
7. * * * Maya ruins in Yucatan and southern Mexico whose art and decorations are strikingly reminiscent of Indian and Egyptian art and architecture. The origin and decline of the Maya civilization still remains a mystery.
8. * * * Famous alchemical text of the Middle Ages, first translated from Arabic to Latin at about 1144 by Hugh of Santalla. * * *

* * *

9. Hermes Trismegistus (Hermes Thrice-Great). Mythical-historical character identified with Greek god Hermes (Mercury), and with Egyptian god Thoth. * * *

* * *

else but that civilizations pass away leaving no other fruit than a few carved stones piled upon each other or forming arched vaults or roofs of two planes intersecting at an angle. Why begin again, if within four or five thousand years other new immigrants will distract their leisure by pondering upon the remains of our trivial contemporary architecture? Scientific history becomes confused and leaves unanswered all these ruminations. Empirical history, suffering from myopia, loses itself in details, but it cannot determine a single antecedent for historical times. It flees from general conclusions, from transcendental hypotheses, to fall into the puerility of the description of utensils and cranial indices and so many other, merely external, minutiae that lack importance when seen apart from a vast and comprehensive theory.

Only a leap of the spirit, nourished with facts, can give us a vision that will lift us above the micro-ideology of the specialist. Then we can dive deeply into the mass of events in order to discover a direction, a rhythm, and a purpose. Precisely there, where the analyst discovers nothing, the synthesizer and the creator are enlightened. Let us, then, attempt explanations, not with the fantasy of the novelist, but with an intuition supported by the facts of history and science.

The race that we have agreed to call Atlantean prospered and declined in America. After its extraordinary flourishment, after having completed its cycle and fulfilled its particular mission, it entered the silence and went into decline until being reduced to the lesser Aztec and Inca empires, totally unworthy of the ancient and superior culture. With the decline of the Atlanteans, the intense civilization was transported to other sites and changed races: It dazzled in Egypt; it expanded in India and Greece, grafted onto new races. The Aryans mixed with the Dravidians[1] to produce the Hindustani, and at the same time, by means of other mixtures, created Hellenic culture.

Greece laid the foundations of Western or European civilization; the white civilization that, upon expanding, reached the forgotten shores of the American continent in order to consummate the task of re-civilization and re-population. Thus we have the four stages and the four racial trunks: the Black, the Indian, the Mongol, and the White. The latter, after organizing itself in Europe, has become the invader of the world, and has considered itself destined to rule, as did each of the previous races during their time of power. It is clear that domination by the whites will also be temporary, but their mission is to serve as a bridge. The white race has brought the world to a state in which all human types and cultures will be able to fuse with each other. The civilization developed and organized in our times by the whites has set the moral and material basis for the union of all men into a fifth universal race, the fruit of all the previous ones and amelioration of everything past.

White culture is migratory, yet it was not Europe as a whole that was in charge of initiating the reintegration of the red world into the modality of preuniversal culture, which had been represented for many centuries by the white man. The transcendental mission fell upon the two most daring

---

1. ° ° ° Peoples of south and middle India where a Dravidian language is spoken. The term is purely linguistic since Dravidian-speaking peoples are of many different genetic types. ° ° ° However, in general, Dravidians were dark skinned races that populated India previous to the Aryan invasion in the second millenium B.C. ° ° °

branches of the European family, the strongest and most different human types: the Spanish and the English.

. . .

From the start, from the time of the discovery and the conquest, * * * the Castilians and the British (or the Latins and the Anglo-Saxons, if we include the Portuguese, on one side, and the Dutch, on the other) * * * accomplished the task of beginning a new period of history by conquering and populating the new hemisphere. Although they may have thought of themselves simply as colonizers, as carriers of culture, in reality, they were establishing the basis for a period of general and definitive transformation. The so-called Latins, well endowed with genius and courage, seized the best regions, the ones they thought were the richest, while the English had to be satisfied with what was left to them by a more capable people. Neither Spain nor Portugal allowed the Anglo-Saxons to come near their domains, and I do not mean for reasons of war, but not even to take part in commerce. Latin predominance was unquestionable at the beginning. No one would have suspected at the time of the Papal arbitration which divided the New World between Spain and Portugal[2] that, a few centuries later, the New World would no longer be Spanish nor Portuguese but English. No one would have imagined that the humble colonists of the Hudson and the Delaware,[3] so peaceful and diligent, would go on taking over, step by step, the best and largest expansions of land, until they formed a republic which today constitutes one of the largest empires in History.

Our age became, and continues to be, a conflict of Latinism against Anglo-Saxonism; a conflict of institutions, aims and ideals. It marks the climax of a secular fight that begins with the disaster of the Invincible Armada and gets worse with the defeat of Trafalgar.[4] Since then, the location of the conflict began to change and was transferred to the new continent, where it still had fateful episodes. The defeats of Santiago de Cuba, Cavite, and Manila[5] were distant but logical echoes of the catastrophes of the Invincible and Trafalgar. Now the conflict is set entirely in the New World. In History, centuries tend to be like days; thus it is not strange at all that we still cannot completely discard the impression of defeat. We are going through times of despair, we continue to lose not only geographic sovereignty, but moral power. Far from feeling united in the face of disaster, our determina-

2. In 1493, Pope Alexander I (Rodrigo Borgia, 1431–1503, from Spain) issued a papal bull that gave Africa and India to Portugal and the lands further west to Spain. (The next year, the Treaty of Tordesillas moved the dividing line further west.) [Anthology editors' note]
3. Rivers, respectively, in New York State and running south from New York State to Delaware Bay. [Anthology editors' note]
4. In 1588, the *Invincible Armada*, sent by the Spanish king, Phillip II, to attack England under the reign of Elizabeth I, was battered by a tempest off the English coast and defeated by the smaller and more maneuverable English fleet. This defeat marked the decline of Spanish, and the rise of English, sea power.
    In 1805, the English fleet under [Viscount Horatio Nelson (1758–1805), British admiral] de-

feated the French-Spanish fleets near the cape of Trafalgar, on the Spanish Atlantic coast. England's victory insured her power at sea and the security of her island against the European conquests by [Napoléon Bonaparte (1769–1821), emperor of France 1804–15].
    Two years earlier, Napoleon had sold Louisiana to the United States, although he had sworn to the Spanish king never to cede this colony to any other power but Spain.
5. Santiago de Cuba, Cavite, and Manila mark locations of Spanish defeats during the Spanish American War in 1898, both on the Cuban (Santiago) and the Asian (Cavite and Manila) fronts. As a result, Spain lost Cuba, Puerto Rico, and the Philippines, marking the end of the Spanish empire and the farthest extension of American imperial policy.

tion is dispersed in search of small and vain goals. Defeat has brought us the confusion of values and concepts; the victor's diplomacy deceives us after defeating us; commerce conquers us with its small advantages. Despoiled of our previous greatness, we boast of an exclusively national patriotism and we do not even see the dangers that threaten our race as a whole. We deny ourselves to each other. Defeat has debased us to the point that, without even being aware of it, we serve the ends of the enemy policy of defeating us one by one; of offering particular advantages to some of our brothers while the vital interests of the others are sacrificed. Not only were we defeated in combat; ideologically, the Anglos continue to conquer us. The greatest battle was lost on the day that each one of the Iberian republics went forth alone, to live her own life apart from her sisters, concerting treaties and receiving false benefits, without tending to the common interests of the race. The founders of our new nationalism were, without knowing it, the best allies of the Anglo-Saxons, our rivals in the possession of the continent. The unfurling of our twenty banners at the Pan American Union[6] in Washington, should be seen as a joke played by skillful enemies. Yet, each of us takes pride in our humble rags, expression of a vain illusion, and we do not even blush at the fact of our discord in the face of the powerful North American union. We ignore the contrast presented by Anglo-Saxon unity in opposition to the anarchy and solitude of the Ibero American emblems. We keep ourselves jealously independent from each other, yet one way or another we submit to, or ally ourselves with, the Anglo-Saxon union. Not even the national unity of the five Central American states has been possible, because a stranger has not granted us his approval and because we lack the true patriotism to sacrifice the present for the future. A lack of creative thinking and an excess of critical zeal, which we have certainly borrowed from other cultures, takes us to fruitless discussions in which our common aspirations are denied as often as they are ascertained. Yet, we do not realize that, in times of action, and despite all the doubts of English thinkers, the English seek the alliance of their American or Australian brothers, and the Yankee feels as English as the Englishman from England. We shall not be great as long as the Spaniard from America does not feel as much a Spaniard as the sons of Spain. This does not preclude that we may differ whenever necessary, as long as we do not drift away from the higher common mission. This is the way we have to act, if we are to allow the Iberian culture to finish producing all its fruits; if we are going to keep Anglo-Saxon culture from remaining triumphant in America without opposition. It is futile to imagine other solutions. Civilization is neither improvised nor curtailed, nor can it grow out of the paper of a political constitution. It always derives from a long, secular preparation and purification of elements that are transmitted and combined from the beginning of History. For that reason, it is stupid to initiate our patriotism with Father Hidalgo's cry of independence,[7] or the conspiration of

6. In 1889, the *International Union of American Republics* was founded in Washington at the initiative of the United States. In 1910, the name was changed to *Pan American Union*, and in 1948, to its present name, *Organization of American States*.

7. Father Miguel Hidalgo y Costilla (1753–1811). Mexican revolutionary hero. On the morning of September 15, 1810, he rallied a group of parishioners in front of his church in Dolores under the banner of the Virgin of Guadalupe, and to the cry of, "Long live Independence! Long live

*Must know the roots for origins in order to proudly yell independence*

*high interest of race ≠ Marti*

Quito,[8] or the feats of Bolívar,[9] because if we do not root it in Cuauhtémoc[1] and Atahualpa,[2] it will have no support. At the same time, it is necessary to trace our patriotism back to our Hispanic fountainhead and educate it on the lessons we should derive from the defeats, which are also ours, of Trafalgar and the Invincible Armada. If our patriotism is not identified with the different stages of the old conflict between Latins and Anglo-Saxons, it shall never overcome a regionalism lacking in universal breadth. We shall fatefully see it degenerate into the narrowness and myopia of parochialism, or into the impotent inertia of a mollusk attached to its rock.

So that we shall not be forced to deny our own fatherland, it is necessary that we live according to the highest interests of the race, even though this may not be yet in the highest interest of humanity. It is true that the heart is not satisfied with less than a full-fledged internationalism, but given the present world conditions, internationalism would only serve to consummate the triumph of the strongest nations; it would only serve the aims of the English. Even the Russians, with their two hundred million population, have had to postpone their theoretical internationalism, in order to devote themselves to the support of oppressed nationalities such as India and Egypt. At the same time, they have strengthened their own nationalism in order to defend themselves against a disintegration which could only favor the great imperialist states. It would, then, be puerile for weak countries like ours, to start denying what is rightfully theirs in the name of aims that could not crystalize in reality. The present state of civilization still imposes patriotism on us as a necessity for the defense of material and moral interests; but it is indispensable for this patriotism to seek vast and transcendental aims. Its mission was cut short, in a sense, with independence. Now it is necessary to bring it back to the flow of its universal historical destiny.

The first stage of the profound conflict was decided in Europe and we lost. Afterwards, when all the advantages were on our side in the New World, since Spain had conquered America, the Napoleonic stupidity gave Louisiana away to the Englishmen from this side of the ocean, to the Yankees; this decided the fate of the New World in favor of the Anglo-Saxons. The "genius of war" could see no farther than the miserable boundary disputes between puny European states, and did not realize that the cause of Latinism, which he claimed to represent, was defeated on the same day that the Empire was proclaimed, by the sole fact that the common destiny was placed in the hands of an incompetent. On the other hand, European prejudice hid the fact that, in America, the conflict that Napoleon could not comprehend in its full transcendence had already acquired universal dimensions. Napoleon, in his foolishness, was not able to surmise that the destiny of the European races was going to be decided in the New World. When, in the most thoughtless manner, he destroyed French power in

---

Our Lady of Guadalupe! Death to the Gachupines!" (Grito de Dolores), initiated the fight for Mexican independence.

8. * * * Patriotic conspiration that proclaimed the independence of Ecuador from Spain on August 10, 1809.

9. Simón Bolívar (1783–1830). Father of South American independence. Liberator of Venezuela, Colombia, Ecuador, Perú, and Bolivia, he tried to unite all of Latin America into a federation like the United States.

1. Cuauhtémoc (1494?–1525). Nephew of Moctezuma and last Aztec emperor of Mexico, who resisted the siege of Tenochtitlán (Mexico City) by Hernán Cortés [(1485–1547). Conqueror of Mexico], but finally was captured and tortured by the Spaniards. * * * Later he was executed by hanging, upon the order of Cortés.

2. * * * Last *Inca* of Perú, was born at the beginning of the XVI century and died in 1533. * * *

America, he also weakened the Spaniards. He betrayed us and placed us at the mercy of the common enemy. Without Napoleon, the United States would not exist as a world empire, and Louisiana, still French, would have to be part of the Latin American Confederation. The defeat of Trafalgar, then, would have been irrelevant. None of these facts were even considered because the destiny of the race was in the hands of a fool, because caesarism is the scourge of the Latin race.

Napoleon's betrayal of the global destiny of France mortally wounded the Spanish empire in America at the moment of its greatest weakness. The English-speaking people took possession of Louisiana without combat, reserving their ammunitions for the now easy conquest of Texas and California. Without the base of the Mississippi, the English, who call themselves Yankees out of a simple richness of expression, would not have been able to take possession of the Pacific; they would not be the masters of the continent today; they would have remained in a sort of Netherlands transplanted to America, and the New World would be Spanish and French. Bonaparte made it Anglo-Saxon.

It is clear, of course, that not merely the external causes, the treaties, wars, and policies, determine the destinies of nations. Figures like Napoleon are nothing but marks of vanity and corruption. The decadence of manners, the loss of public liberties, and the general ignorance have the effect of paralyzing the energy of a whole race at any given time.

The Spaniards went to the New World with the overflow of vigor left after the success of the Reconquest.[3] Free men like Cortez, Pizarro,[4] Alvarado,[5] and Belalcázar[6] were not caesars nor lackeys, but great captains that joined destructive impetus to creative genius. Immediately after victory, they traced the plans of the new cities and wrote the statutes of their foundation. Later, at the hour of bitter disputes with the metropolis, they knew how to return insult for insult, as did one of the Pizarros in a famous trial. They all felt equal before the king, like the Cid, like the great writers of the Golden Age[7] felt, as all free men feel during epochs of greatness.

But as the conquest was being completed, the new organization began to fall into the hands of courtiers and favorites of the king: Incompetent men, not only for conquest, but even for the defense of what others had conquered with their talent and courage; degenerate courtiers, capable of oppressing and humiliating the natives, but submissive before the royal power. They and their masters did nothing else but spoil the work of Spanish genius in America. The portentous work started by iron-willed conquerors and consummated by wise and selfless missionaries was gradually annulled. A series of foreign monarchs, so justly painted by Velázquez[8] and

---

3. Following the Islamic conquest of the Iberian Peninsula (AD 711–18), an 800-year period during which several Christian kingdoms retook the Peninsula. [Anthology editors' note]
4. Francisco Pizarro (1475–1541). Conqueror of Peru.
5. Pedro de Alvarado (1485?–1541). Companion of Cortés in the conquest of Mexico, and later conqueror of Guatemala, where he founded Santiago de los Caballeros de Guatemala (Guatemala City).
6. Sebastián de Belalcázar (1495–1551). Conqueror of present day Ecuador, and founder of

Quito and Guayaquil. * * *
7. The Spanish Golden Age, a period in which the arts and literature flourished in Spain; roughly from the end of the Reconquest to the late seventeenth century. The Cid: Rodrigo Díaz de Vivar aka El Cid (ca. 1043–1099), Spanish soldier and hero. [Anthology editors' note]
8. Diego Rodríguez de Silva y Velázquez (1599–1660). Royal painter to Phillip IV, a Hapsburg. Beginning in 1516, with the Emperor Charles V, this German royal family ruled Spain up to 1714. * * *

Goya[9] in the company of dwarfs, buffoons, and courtiers, completed the disaster of colonial administration. The mania for imitating the Roman empire, which has caused so much harm in Spain, as well as in Italy and France, with its militarism and absolutism, brought about our decadence. At the same time our rivals, strengthened by virtue, grew and expanded in freedom.

Along with their growth in material strength, their practical ingenuity and intuition of success increased. The old colonists of New England and Virginia severed themselves from England only to grow better and become stronger. Political separation has never been an obstacle between England and her former colonies to maintain their unity and agreement in regards to the business of their common ethnic mission. Emancipation, instead of debilitating the great race, made it branch off, multiply, and spread, all-powerful, over the whole world, out of the impressive nucleus of one of the largest empires of all times. Since then, what is not conquered by the English of the Isles, is taken over and kept by the English of the new continent.

On the other hand, we Spaniards by blood or by culture, began by denying our traditions at the moment of our emancipation. We broke off with the past, and some even denied their blood saying it would have been better if the conquest of our regions had been accomplished by the English. Such words of treason may be excused only as actions brought about by tyranny and as the blindness engendered by defeat, but to lose the historical sense of a race in this way borders on the absurd. It is the same as denying our strong and wise parents when it is we, and not them, who are guilty of our decadence.

At any rate, the anti-Hispanic preaching and the corresponding anglicizing, skillfully spread by the English themselves, perverted our judgment from the beginning. It made us forget that we also have our share in the affront of Trafalgar. The meddling of English officers in the high ranks of our armies of independence would have ended by dishonoring us, were it not for the old pride of blood that came back to life in the face of insult and punished the pirates of Albion[1] each time they approached with the intention of perpetrating a raid. Our ancestral rebelliousness knew how to reply with cannonades, in Buenos Aires as well as in Veracruz, Havana, Campeche and Panama,[2] every time the English corsair attacked. Disguised as pirates in order to avoid the responsibilities of defeat, the English were confident of attaining, if victorious, a place of honor among the British nobility.

Despite this firm unity against an invading enemy, our war of independence was limited by provincialism and by the absence of transcendental plans. The race that had dreamed of a world empire, that presumed to be descendents of the Roman glory, fell into the puerile satisfaction of creating little nations and sovereign principalities, encouraged by mentalities that

9. Francisco José de Goya y Lucientes (1746–1828). Court painter to Charles III and to his son Charles IV, descendants of the French house of Bourbon, the ruling family in Spain from 1714 to the XX century. * * *
1. * * * Ancient Greek and Roman name for Britain. * * *
2. Buenos Aires was attacked in 1587, by the English pirate Thomas Cavendish, later knighted by Queen Elizabeth; Veracruz was looted in 1683; Havana was attacked without success by Sir Francis Drake, and suffered many other attacks by English, French and Dutch pirates; Campeche, in Yucatan, was plundered by English pirates in 1680; Panama was sacked and destroyed by Henry Morgan in 1671. These were but a few of the attacks suffered by Spanish colonies during the XVI and XVII centuries.

saw a wall and not a summit in each mountain range. Our liberators, with the illustrious exceptions of Bolívar and Sucre,[3] the black Petion,[4] and no more than half a dozen others, were dreaming of Balkan glories. The rest, obsessed with the local outlook and entangled in a confused pseudo-revolutionary phraseology, simply busied themselves in belittling a conflict that could have been the beginning of the awakening of a whole continent. To divide, to tear to pieces the dream of a great Latin confederation, seemed to have been the goal of some of the ignorant practical men who fought for independence. Although they deserve their place of honor in this movement, they did not know how to follow, or did not even want to listen to the wise warnings of Bolívar.

It is clear that in every social development, the profound, inevitable causes that determine a given moment have to be taken into account. Our geography, for example, was and continues to be an obstacle to unity, but if we are to overcome this obstacle, first it will be necessary that we put order in our spirit by purifying our ideas and delineating precise orientations. As long as we are not able to correct our concepts, it will not be possible to influence the physical environment to make it serve our purposes.

In Mexico, for instance, except for Mina,[5] almost no one thought of the interests of the continent; worse yet, for a whole century the vernacular patriotism taught that we had triumphed over Spain thanks to the indomitable valor of our soldiers. At the same time, the Cortes of Cádiz and the uprisings against Napoleon,[6] which electrified the whole race, went almost without mention, as did the victories and sufferings of the sister nations of the continent. This error, common to all of our countries, is the result of times when history is written in order to please the despots. Boastful patriotism is not satisfied with presenting its heroes as unities of a continental movement, but as autonomous, not realizing that in acting this way, it belittles rather than exalts them.

Such aberrations may also be explained because the indigenous element had not, and has not yet been fused in its totality with the Spanish blood. But this discord is more apparent than real: Should one talk to the most exalted Indianist of the convenience of adapting ourselves to Latinism, he will raise no questions; but tell him that our culture is Spanish and he will immediately bring up counter arguments. The stain from the spilled blood still remains. It is an accursed stain that centuries have not erased, but which the common danger must annul. There is no other recourse. Even the pure Indians are Hispanized, they are Latinized, just as the environment itself is Latinized. Say what one may, the red men, the illustrious Atlanteans from

---

3. Antonio José de Sucre (1795–1830). South American general, born in Venezuela, who fought with Bolívar for the Independence of Perú, Ecuador and Bolivia, and supported Bolívar's idea of a Latin American Union. This failed, though, and the continent became divided into smaller nations, like the Balkan Peninsula.
4. Alejandro Sabes Petion (1770–1818). Father of Haitian Independence. ° ° °
5. Francisco Xavier Mina (1789–1817). Spanish liberal and revolutionary who fought against Napoleon in Spain, and later in Mexico for the cause of Mexican independence from Spain.
6. Cortes of Cádiz. A parliamentary body con-

vened by Spanish liberals in 1812, after the abdication of Ferdinand VII, the legitimate sovereign, in favor of Napoleon's brother, Joseph Bonaparte. The Cortes met in Cádiz to form a legitimate and Independent government for Spain, and to organize the fight against Napoleon. It proclaimed a liberal constitution, creating a parliamentary monarchy for Spain. Elsewhere in Spain, the people took arms against Napoleon and, with English help ° ° ° eventually succeeded in driving back the French. ° ° ° This Napoleonic defeat in Spain, together with the retreat from the Russian front, marked the decline of Napoleonic power in Europe.

whom Indians derive, went to sleep millions of years ago, never to awaken. There is no going back in History, for it is all transformation and novelty. No race returns. Each one states its mission, accomplishes it, and passes away. This truth rules in Biblical times as well as in our times; all the ancient historians have formulated it. The days of the pure whites, the victors of today, are as numbered as were the days of their predecessors. Having fulfilled their destiny of mechanizing the world, they themselves have set, without knowing it, the basis for a new period: The period of the fusion and mixing of all peoples. The Indian has no other door to the future but the door of modern culture, nor any other road but the road already cleared by Latin civilization. The white man, as well, will have to depose his pride and look for progress and ulterior redemption in the souls of his brothers from other castes. He will have to diffuse and perfect himself in each of the superior varieties of the species, in each of the modalities that multiply revelation and make genius more powerful.

· · ·

In the process of our ethnic mission, the war of emancipation from Spain signals a dangerous crisis. I do not mean that this war should not have been waged or should not have succeeded. In certain epochs, the transcendental end must be postponed: The race can wait while the fatherland presses upon us, and the fatherland is the immediate and indispensable present. It was impossible to continue depending on a sceptre which from mishap to mishap, and from misfortune to embarrassment had been going down until it fell into the dishonored hands of a Ferdinand VII.[7] The organization of a free Castilian Federation could have been worked out at the *Cortes* of Cádiz. The monarchy could not have been answered except by the defeat of its envoys. On this point, Mina's vision was complete: First, to establish freedom in the New World, and later, to overthrow the monarchy in Spain. Since the imbecility of the times kept this genial design from fulfillment, at least, let us try to keep it present in our minds. Let us recognize that it was a disgrace not to have proceeded with the cohesion demonstrated by those to the north, that prodigious race which we are accustomed to lavish with insults only because they have won each hand at the secular fight. They triumph because they join to their practical talents the clear vision of a great destiny. They keep present the intuition of a definite historical mission, while we get lost in the labyrinth of verbal chimeras. It seems as if God Himself guided the steps of the Anglo-Saxon cause, while we kill each other on account of dogma or declare ourselves atheists. How those mighty empire builders must laugh at our groundless arrogance and Latin vanity! They do not clutter their mind with the Ciceronian[8] weight of phraseology, nor have they in their blood the contradictory instincts of a mixture of dissimilar races, *but they committed the sin of destroying those races, while we*

---

7. Ferdinand VII (1784–1883). King of Spain during the Napoleonic invasion. Both he and his father, Charles IV, were forced by Napoleon to abdicate in favor of Napoleon's brother, Joseph Bonaparte. The Spaniards rejected the Napoleonic rule and fought the invaders in the so-called "War of Independence" to return Ferdinand VII to the throne. In the interim, most of Latin America declared independence from Spain. Ferdinand VII repaid his subjects by rejecting the liberal constitution proclaimed by the Cortes of Cádiz and by persecuting the liberals. 8. In the mode of Marcus Tullius Cicero (106–43 BC), Roman statesman, orator, and writer. [Anthology editors' note]

*assimilated them, and this gives us new rights and hopes for a mission without precedent in History.*

For this reason, adverse obstacles do not move us to surrender, for we vaguely feel that they will help us to discover our way. Precisely in our differences, we find the way. If we simply imitate, we lose. If we discover and create, we shall overcome. The advantage of our tradition is that it has greater facility of sympathy towards strangers. This implies that our civilization, with all defects, may be the chosen one to assimilate and to transform mankind into a new type; that within our civilization, the warp, the multiple and rich plasma of future humanity is thus being prepared. This mandate from History is first noticed in that abundance of love that allowed the Spaniard to create a new race with the Indian and the Black, profusely spreading white ancestry through the soldier who begat a native family, and Occidental culture through the doctrine and example of the missionaries who placed the Indians in condition to enter into the new stage, the stage of world One. Spanish colonization created mixed races, this signals its character, fixes its responsibility, and defines its future. The English kept on mixing only with the whites and annihilated the natives. Even today, they continue to annihilate them in a sordid and economic fight, more efficient yet than armed conquest. This proves their limitation and is indication of their decadence. The situation is equivalent, in a larger scale, to the incestuous marriages of the pharaohs which undermined the virtues of the race; and it contradicts the ulterior goals of History to attain the fusion of peoples and cultures. To build an English world and to exterminate the red man, so that Northern Europe could be renovated all over an America made up with pure whites, is no more than a repetition of the triumphant process of a conquering race. This was already attempted by the red man and by all strong and homogeneous races, but it does not solve the human problem. America was not kept in reserve for five thousand years for such a petty goal. The purpose of the new and ancient continent is much more important. Its predestination obeys the design of constituting the cradle of a fifth race into which all nations will fuse with each other to replace the four races that have been forging History apart from each other. The dispersion will come to an end on American soil; unity will be consummated there by the triumph of fecund love and the improvement of all the human races. In this fashion, the synthetic race that shall gather all the treasures of History in order to give expression to universal desire shall be created.

The so-called Latin peoples, because they have been more faithful to their divine mission in America, are the ones called upon to consummate this mission. Such fidelity to the occult design is the guarantee of our triumph.

Even during the chaotic period of independence, which deserves so much censure, one can notice, however, glimpses of that eagerness for universality which already announced the desire to fuse humanity into a universal and synthetic type. Needless to say, Bolívar, partly because he realized the danger into which we were falling by dividing ourselves into isolated nationalities, and partly because of his gift for prophecy, formulated the plan for an Ibero-American Federation which some fools still question today.

It is true that, in general, the other leaders of Latin American independence did not have a clear conception of the future. Carried away by a provincialism that today we call patriotism, or by a limitation that today is dubbed national sovereignty, every one of them was only concerned with the immediate fate of their own people. Yet, it is also surprising to observe that almost all of them felt animated by a humane and universal sentiment which coincides with the destiny that today we assign to the Latin American continent. Hidalgo, Morelos,[9] Bolívar, Petion the Haitian, the Argentinians in Tucumán,[1] Sucre, all were concerned with the liberation of the slaves, with the declaration of the equality of all men by natural right, and with the civil and social equality of Whites, Blacks and Indians. In a moment of historical crisis, they formulated the transcendental mission assigned to that region of the globe: The mission of fusing all peoples ethnically and spiritually.

Thus, what no one even thought of doing on the Anglo-Saxon area of the continent was done on the Latin side. In the north, the contrary thesis continued to prevail: The confessed or tacit intention of cleaning the earth of Indians, Mongolians or Blacks, for the greater glory and fortune of the Whites. In fact, since that time, the systems which, continuing to the present, have placed the two civilizations on opposing sociological fields were very well defined. The one wants exclusive dominion by the Whites, while the other is shaping a new race, a synthetic race that aspires to engulf and to express everything human in forms of constant improvement. If it were necessary to adduce proof, it would be sufficient to observe the increasing and spontaneous mixing which operates among all peoples in all of the Latin continent; in contrast with the inflexible line that separates the Blacks from the Whites in the United States, and the laws, each time more rigorous, for the exclusion of the Japanese and Chinese from California.[2]

The so-called Latins insist on not taking the ethnic factor too much into account for their sexual relations, perhaps because from the beginning they are not, properly speaking, Latins but a conglomeration of different types and races. Whatever opinions one may express in this respect, and whatever repugnance caused by prejudice one may harbor, the truth is that the mixture of races has taken place and continues to be consummated. It is in this fusion of ethnic stocks that we should look for the fundamental characteristic of Ibero-American idiosyncrasy. It may happen sometimes and, in fact, it has already happened, that economic competition may force us to close our doors, as is done by the Anglo-Saxons, to an unrestrained influx of Asians. But, in doing so, we obey reasons of economic order. We recognize that it is not fair that people like the Chinese, who, under the saintly guidance of Confucian morality multiply like mice, should come to degrade the human condition precisely at the moment when we begin to understand that intelligence serves to refrain and regulate the lower zoological instincts, which are contrary to a truly religious conception of life. If we reject the Chinese, it is because man, as he progresses, multiplies less, and feels the

---

9. José María Morelos y Pavón (1765–1815). Mexican Catholic priest who continued the fight for Mexican Independence from Spain initiated by Father Hidalgo, who was executed in 1811.
1. In 1816, Argentinian representatives met in Tucumán to officially declare independence from Spain and draft a new constitution (which, among other things, abolished slavery).
2. During the latter part of the XIX century, the United States gradually reversed their previously liberal attitude towards immigration, partly due to economic and political reasons, but also to current theories of Anglo-Saxon racial

superiority.
The U.S. Congress began the legal change by excluding further Chinese immigration in 1882. Exclusion of Japanese laborers was effected in 1908. Finally in 1921, and 1924, the United States adopted a frankly "racial" policy and established immigration quotas for different ethnic groups. Asian immigrants were excluded altogether. This system, with minor amendments after 1940 to allow Asian nationalities small quotas, survived until 1965 in spite of the discrediting of its racial theory in the 1930's and 1940's * * *.

horror of numbers, for the same reason that he has begun to value quality. In the United States, Asians are rejected because of the same fear of physical overflow, characteristic of superior stocks; but also because Americans simply do not like Asians, even despise them, and would be incapable of intermarriage with them. The ladies of San Francisco have refused to dance with officials of the Japanese Navy, who are men as clean, intelligent, and, in their way, as handsome as those of any other navy in the world. Yet, these ladies will never understand that a Japanese may be handsome. Nor is it easy to convince the Anglo-Saxon that if the yellow and the black races have their characteristic smell, the Whites, for a foreigner, also have theirs, even though we may not be aware of it. In Latin America, the repulsion of one blood that confronts another strange blood also exists, but infinitely more attenuated. There, a thousand bridges are available for the sincere and cordial fusion of all races. The ethnic barricading of those to the north in contrast to the much more open sympathy of those to the south is the most important factor, and at the same time, the most favorable to us, if one reflects even superficially upon the future, because it will be seen immediately that we belong to tomorrow, while the Anglo-Saxons are gradually becoming more a part of yesterday. The Yankees will end up building the last great empire of a single race, the final empire of White supremacy. Meanwhile, we will continue to suffer the vast chaos of an ethnic stock in formation, contaminated by the fermentation of all types, but secure of the avatar into a better race. In Spanish America, Nature will no longer repeat one of her partial attempts. This time, the race that will come out of the forgotten Atlantis will no longer be a race of a single color or of particular features. The future race will not be a fifth, or a sixth race, destined to prevail over its ancestors. What is going to emerge out there is the definitive race, the synthetical race, the integral race, made up of the genius and the blood of all peoples and, for that reason, more capable of true brotherhood and of a truly universal vision.

In order to come near this sublime purpose, it is necessary to keep on creating, so to speak, the cellular tissue which will serve as the flesh and support of this new biological formation. In order to create that Protean, malleable, profound, ethereal, and essential tissue, it will be necessary for the Ibero-American race to permeate itself with its mission and embrace it as a mysticism.

Perhaps there is nothing useless in historical developments. Our own physical isolation and the mistake of creating nations, together with the original mixture of bloods, has served to keep us from the Anglo-Saxon limitation of constituting castes of pure races. History shows that these prolonged and rigorous selections produce types of physical refinement, interesting but lacking in vigor. They have a strange beauty, like that of the Brahmanic caste, but are decadent in the end. Never have they been seen to surpass other men, neither in talent, in goodness, or in strength. The road we have initiated is much more daring. It breaks away from ancient prejudices, and it would be almost unexplainable if it were not grounded on a sort of clamor that reaches from a remote distance, a distance which is not that of the past, but that mysterious distance from where the presage of the future comes.

If Latin America were just another Spain, to the same extent that the United States is another England, then the old conflict of the two stocks would do nothing else but to repeat its episodes on a vaster territory, and one of the two rivals would end up prevailing and imposing itself. But this is not the natural law of conflicts, neither in mechanics nor in life. Opposition and fight, particularly when transposed to the field of the spirit, serve to better define the contenders, to take each one to the summit of its destiny and, in the end, to join them into a common and victorious superiority.

The Anglo-Saxon mission has been accomplished sooner than ours because it was more immediate and was already known to History. In order to accomplish it, all that was necessary was to follow the example of other victorious people. Being mere continuators of Europe in the region of the continent they occupied, the values of the Whites reached the zenith. This is why the history of North America is like the uninterrupted and vigorous allegro of a triumphal march.

How different the sounds of the Ibero-American development! They resemble the profound scherzo of a deep and infinite symphony: Voices that bring accents from Atlantis; depths contained in the pupil of the red man, who knew so much, so many thousand years ago, and now seems to have forgotten everything. His soul resembles the old Mayan cenote[3] of green waters, laying deep and still, in the middle of the forest, for so many centuries since, that not even its legend remains any more. This infinite quietude is stirred with the drop put in our blood by the Black, eager for sensual joy, intoxicated with dances and unbridled lust. There also appears the Mongol, with the mystery of his slanted eyes that see everything according to a strange angle, and discover I know not what folds and newer dimensions. The clear mind of the White, that resembles his skin and his dreams, also intervenes. Judaic striae hidden within the Castilian blood since the days of the cruel expulsion[4] now reveal themselves, along with Arabian melancholy, as a remainder of the sickly Muslim sensuality. Who has not a little of all this, or does not wish to have all? There is the Hindu, who also will come, who has already arrived by way of the spirit, and although he is the last one to arrive, he seems the closest relative . . . So many races that have come and others that will come. In this manner, a sensitive and ample heart will be taking shape within us; a heart that embraces and contains everything and is moved with sympathy, but, full of vigor, imposes new laws upon the world. And we foresee something like another head that will dispose of all angles in order to fulfill the miracle of surpassing the sphere.

## II

After examining the close and the remote possibilities of the mixed race that inhabits the Ibero-American continent, as well as the destiny that drives it to become the first synthetic race of the earth, it is necessary to inquire if the physical milieu within which this human stock is being developed corresponds to the ends determined by its bionomy. The territorial expanse already at its disposal is enormous. There is no land problem, then. The fact

3. * * * Natural wells, typical of Yucatan, formed by subterranean rivers. These caverns and wells where the rivers came to the surface were used by the Maya Indians as sacred places for sacrifice or for bathing and watering. Their appearance is often striking since some of them occur as a sudden circular depression reaching great depths on an otherwise generally flat land.
4. The Alhambra Decree (also known as the Edict of Expulsion), issued in March 1492 by the Catholic monarchs of Spain, ordered the expulsion of Jews from the Spanish Empire by July of that year. [Anthology editors' note]

that its coasts do not have many first rate harbors is of almost no importance, given the ever increasing engineering advances. On the other hand, all the essential elements are, without doubt, abundant in quantities that surpass those of any other region on earth: Natural resources, arable land, water, and favorable climate. In regards to the latter factor, some will raise, of course, an objection: The climate, it will be said, is adverse to the new race, because the greatest part of the available land is located in the hottest region of the earth. However, this is precisely the advantage and the secret of the future. The great civilizations began in the Tropics and the final civilization will return to the Tropics. The new race will begin to fulfill its destiny as new means are invented to combat the heat insofar as it is adverse to man, yet leaving intact its benefic power for the production of life. The triumph of the Whites began with the conquest of snow and cold. The basis of white civilization is fuel. First, it served as a protection against the long winters. Then, it was discovered that its power could be used not only for warmth, but also for work; and the motor was born. And so it is that, from the hearth and the stove proceed all the machinery that is transforming the world. A similar invention would have been impossible in warm Egypt and, in fact, did not occur there, despite the fact that the Egyptians infinitely surpassed the intellectual capacity of the English race. To corroborate the last statement, it is sufficient to compare the sublime metaphysics of the *Book of the Dead*[5] of the Egyptian priests, with the vulgarity of Spencerian Darwinism. The chasm that separates Spencer[6] from Hermes Trismegistus cannot be crossed by the blond dolichocephalics even in another thousand years of training and selection.

On the other hand, the English ship, that marvelous machine that proceeds from the Vikings of the north, was not even dreamed of by the Egyptians. The rude fight against the environment forced the Whites to devote their aptitudes to the conquest of temporal nature, and it is precisely this what constitutes their contribution to the civilization of the future. The Whites taught the control of matter. The science of the Whites will some day revert the method employed to attain control over fire and, instead, will make use of condensed snows, electrochemical currents, or subtle magic gases to destroy flies and pests and dissipate the sultry weather and the fevers. Then the whole world will spread over the Tropics and, in the solemn immensity of its landscapes, souls will conquer plenitude.

*　　*　　*

Perhaps the traits of the white race will predominate among the characteristics of the fifth race, but such a supremacy must be result of the free choice of personal taste, and not the fruit of violence or economic pressure. The superior traits of culture and nature will have to triumph, but that triumph will be stable only if it is based on the voluntary acceptance by conscience and on the free choice of fantasy. Up to this date, life has received its character from man's lower faculties; the fifth branch will be the fruit of the superior faculties. The fifth race does not exclude but accumulates life.

5. * * * A collection of ancient Egyptian magical formulas preserved in papyrus scrolls buried with the dead, to guide them safely to the gates of the underworld. * * *
6. Herbert Spencer (1820–1903), English philosopher, political theorist, and sociological theorist. After reading Darwin's *On the Origin of Species* (1859), he coined the phrase "survival of the fittest" and, by applying that concept to society, created Social Darwinism. [Anthology editors' note]

For this reason, the exclusion of the Yankee, like the exclusion of any other human type, would be equivalent to an anticipated mutilation, more deadly even than a later cut. If we do not want to exclude even the races that might be considered inferior, it would be much less sensible to keep from our enterprise a race full of vigor and solid social virtues.

Now that we have expressed the theory of the formation of the future Ibero-American race, and the manner in which it will be able to take advantage of the environment in which it lives, only the third factor of the transformation which is taking place in our continent remains to be considered: The spiritual factor, which has to direct and consummate this extraordinary enterprise. Some may think, perhaps, that the fusion of the different contemporary races into a new race that will fulfill and surpass all the others is going to be a repugnant process of anarchic hybridization. By comparison, the English practice of marrying only within the same stock may be seen as an ideal of refinement and purity. The primitive Aryans from Hindustan attempted precisely that English system, in order to keep themselves from mixing with the colored races. However, since those dark races possessed a wisdom necessary to complement that of the blond invaders, the true Hindu culture was not produced until after the centuries had completed the mixture, in spite of all written prohibitions. Furthermore, the fateful mixture was useful not only for cultural reasons, but because the physical specimen itself needs to be renovated in its kin. North Americans have held very firmly to their resolution to maintain a pure stock, the reason being that they are faced with the Blacks, who are like the opposite pole, like the antithesis of the elements to be mixed. In the Ibero-American world, the problem does not present itself in such crude terms. We have very few Blacks, and a large part of them is already becoming a mulatto population. The Indian is a good bridge for racial mixing. Besides, the warm climate is propitious for the interaction and gathering of all peoples. On the other hand, and this is essential, interbreeding will no longer obey reasons of simple proximity as occurred in the beginning when the white colonist took an indian or black woman because there were no others at hand. In the future, as social conditions keep improving, the mixture of bloods will become gradually more spontaneous, to the point that interbreeding will no longer be the result of simple necessity but of personal taste or, at least, of curiosity. Spiritual motivation, in this manner, will increasingly superimpose itself upon the contingencies of the merely physical. By spiritual motivation, we should understand, rather than reflective thinking, the faculty of personal taste that directs the mysterious selection of one particular person out of the multitude.[7]

1925

7. In the third and final part of "Mestizaje," Vasconcelos studies what in his view are the three social stages through which humankind finds liberation: the material or warlike, the intellectual or political, and the spiritual or aesthetic. "If we acknowledge that Humanity is gradually approaching the third period of its destiny," Vasconcelos writes, "we shall see that the work of racial fusion is going to take place in the Ibero-American continent according to a law derived from the fruition of the highest faculties." He adds: "A mixture of races accomplished according to the laws of social well-being, sympathy, and beauty, will lead to the creation of a type infinitely superior to all that have previously existed. . . . The Hispanic race, in general, still has ahead of it [the] mission of discovering new regions of the spirit." He concludes by describing a mural he once commissioned, which visualized the birth of "the final race, the cosmic race." [Anthology editors' note]

# OCTAVIO PAZ
## 1914–1998

### FROM THE LABYRINTH OF SOLITUDE

### *From* Chapter One. The *Pachuco* and Other Extremes[1]

All of us, at some moment, have had a vision of our existence as something unique, untransferable and very precious. This revelation almost always takes place during adolescence. Self-discovery is above all the realization that we are alone: it is the opening of an impalpable, transparent wall—that of our consciousness—between the world and ourselves. It is true that we sense our aloneness almost as soon as we are born, but children and adults can transcend their solitude and forget themselves in games or work. The adolescent, however, vacillates between infancy and youth, halting for a moment before the infinite richness of the world. He is astonished at the fact of his being, and this astonishment leads to reflection: as he leans over the river of his consciousness, he asks himself if the face that appears there, disfigured by the water, is his own. The singularity of his being, which is pure sensation in children, becomes a problem and a question.

Much the same thing happens to nations and peoples at a certain critical moment in their development. They ask themselves: What are we, and how can we fulfill our obligations to ourselves as we are? The answers we give to these questions are often belied by history, perhaps because what is called the "genius of a people" is only a set of reactions to a given stimulus. The answers differ in different situations, and the national character, which was thought to be immutable, changes with them. Despite the often illusory nature of essays on the psychology of a nation, it seems to me there is something revealing in the insistence with which a people will question itself during certain periods of its growth. To become aware of our history is to become aware of our singularity. It is a moment of reflective repose before we devote ourselves to action again. "When we dream that we are dreaming," Novalis[2] wrote, "the moment of awaking is at hand." It does not matter, then, if the answers we give to our questions must be corrected by time. The adolescent is also ignorant of the future changes that will affect the countenance he sees in the water. The mask of an old man is as indecipherable at first glance as a sacred stone covered with occult symbols: it is the history of various amorphous features that only take shape, slowly and vaguely, after the profoundest contemplation. Eventually these features are seen as a face, and later as a mask, a meaning, a history.

At one time I thought that my preoccupation with the significance of my country's individuality—a preoccupation I share with many others—was pointless and even dangerous. Instead of asking ourselves questions, it

---

1. Translated by Lysander Kemp. Except as indicated, all footnotes are Paz's. Two of his notes have been omitted.

2. German writer and philosopher (Georg Philipp Friedrich Freiherr von Hardenberg, 1772–1801). [Anthology editors' note]

would be better, I felt, to create, to work with the realities of our situation. We could not alter those realities by contemplation, only by plunging ourselves into them. We could distinguish ourselves from other peoples by our creations rather than by the dubious originality of our character, which was the result, perhaps, of constantly changing circumstances. I believed that a work of art or a concrete action would do more to define the Mexican—not only to express him but also, in the process, to recreate him—than the most penetrating description. Therefore I considered my questions, like those of others, to be a cowardly excuse for not facing reality; I also felt that all our speculations about the supposed character of the Mexican were nothing but subterfuges of our impotence as creators. I agreed with Samuel Ramos[3] that an inferiority complex influenced our preference for analysis, and that the meagerness of our creative output was due not so much to the growth of our critical faculties at the expense of our creativity as it was to our instinctive doubts about our abilities.

But the adolescent cannot forget himself—when he succeeds in doing so, he is no longer an adolescent—and we cannot escape the necessity of questioning and contemplating ourselves. I am not trying to say that the Mexican is by nature critical, merely that he goes through a reflective stage. It is natural that the Mexican should withdraw into himself after the explosive phase of the Revolution, to spend a few moments in self-contemplation. The questions we all ask ourselves today will probably be incomprehensible fifty years from now. Different circumstances are likely to produce different reactions.

My thoughts are not concerned with the total population of our country, but rather with a specific group made up of those who are conscious of themselves, for one reason or another, as Mexicans. Despite general opinion to the contrary, this group is quite small. Our territory is inhabited by a number of races speaking different languages and living on different historical levels. A few groups still live as they did in prehistoric times. Others, like the Otomíes, who were displaced by successive invasions, exist on the outer margins of history. But it is not necessary to appeal to these extremes: a variety of epochs live side by side in the same areas or a very few miles apart, ignoring or devouring one another. "Catholics of Peter the Hermit and Jacobins of the Third Era," with their different heroes, customs, calendars and moral principles, live under the same sky. Past epochs never vanish completely, and blood still drips from all their wounds, even the most ancient. Sometimes the most remote or hostile beliefs and feelings are found together in one city or one soul, or are superimposed like those pre-Cortesian pyramids that almost always conceal others.[4]

3. Mexican philosopher (1897–1959), author of the sociopsychological study *El perfil del hombre y la cultura en México* (Profile of Man and Culture in Mexico, 1934). [Anthology editors' note]
4. In our recent history there are many examples of this superimposition, as well as of the existence of different historical levels: the neofeudalism of the Porfirio Díaz regime, using positivism (a bourgeois philosophy) to justify itself historically; Antonio Caso and José Vasconcelos, the intellectual initiators of the Revolution, using the ideas of Boutroux and Bergson to combat positivism; socialist education in a country at least incipiently capitalist; revolutionary murals on government walls; etc. These apparent contradictions all demand a new examination of our history and also of our culture, which is a mingling of many currents and epochs. [Paz's note]

*Pre-Cortesian*: preceding the arrival in the New World of the Spanish conquistador Hernán Cortés (1485–1547). *Porfirio Díaz*: Mexican general (1830–1915), president of Mexico 1877–80 and 1884–1911. *Antonio Caso*: Antonio Caso

The minority of Mexicans who are aware of their own selves do not make up a closed or unchanging class. They are the only active group, in comparison with the Indian-Spanish inertia of the rest, and every day they are shaping the country more and more into their own image. And they are also increasing. They are conquering Mexico. We can all reach the point of knowing ourselves to be Mexicans. It is enough, for example, simply to cross the border: almost at once we begin to ask ourselves, at least vaguely, the same questions that Samuel Ramos asked in his *Profile of Man and Culture in Mexico*. I should confess that many of the reflections in this essay occurred to me outside of Mexico, during a two-year stay in the United States. I remember that whenever I attempted to examine North American life, anxious to discover its meaning, I encountered my own questioning image. That image, seen against the glittering background of the United States, was the first and perhaps the profoundest answer which that country gave to my questions. Therefore, in attempting to explain to myself some of the traits of the present-day Mexican, I will begin with a group for whom the fact that they are Mexicans is a truly vital problem, a problem of life or death.

When I arrived in the United States I lived for a while in Los Angeles, a city inhabited by over a million persons of Mexican origin. At first sight, the visitor is surprised not only by the purity of the sky and the ugliness of the dispersed and ostentatious buildings, but also by the city's vaguely Mexican atmosphere, which cannot be captured in words or concepts. This Mexicanism—delight in decorations, carelessness and pomp, negligence, passion and reserve—floats in the air. I say "floats" because it never mixes or unites with the other world, the North American world based on precision and efficiency. It floats, without offering any opposition; it hovers, blown here and there by the wind, sometimes breaking up like a cloud, sometimes standing erect like a rising skyrocket. It creeps, it wrinkles, it expands and contracts; it sleeps or dreams; it is ragged but beautiful. It floats, never quite existing, never quite vanishing.

Something of the same sort characterizes the Mexicans you see in the streets. They have lived in the city for many years, wearing the same clothes and speaking the same language as the other inhabitants, and they feel ashamed of their origin; yet no one would mistake them for authentic North Americans. I refuse to believe that physical features are as important as is commonly thought. What distinguishes them, I think, is their furtive, restless air: they act like persons who are wearing disguises, who are afraid of a stranger's look because it could strip them and leave them stark naked. When you talk with them, you observe that their sensibilities are like a pendulum, but a pendulum that has lost its reason and swings violently and erratically back and forth. This spiritual condition, or lack of a spirit, has given birth to a type known as the *pachuco*. The *pachucos* are youths, for

Andrade (1883–1946), Mexican philosopher and university rector; cofounded with José Vasconcelos (see p. A67) the Ateneo de la Juventud, a humanist group against philosophical positivism. *Boutroux*: Étienne Émile Marie Boutroux (1845–1921), French philosopher of science and reli-gion, opposed to materialism in science. *Bergson*: Henri-Louis Bergson (1859–1941), French philosopher who studied, among other things, the relation between science and metaphysics. [Anthology editors' note]

the most part of Mexican origin, who form gangs in Southern cities; they can be identified by their language and behavior as well as by the clothing they affect. They are instinctive rebels, and North American racism has vented its wrath on them more than once. But the *pachucos* do not attempt to vindicate their race or the nationality of their forebears. Their attitude reveals an obstinate, almost fanatical will-to-be, but this will affirms nothing specific except their determination—it is an ambiguous one, as we will see—not to be like those around them. The *pachuco* does not want to become a Mexican again; at the same time he does not want to blend into the life of North America. His whole being is sheer negative impulse, a tangle of contradictions, an enigma. Even his very name is enigmatic: *pachuco*, a word of uncertain derivation, saying nothing and saying everything. It is a strange word with no definite meaning; or, to be more exact, it is charged like all popular creations with a diversity of meanings. Whether we like it or not, these persons are Mexicans, are one of the extremes at which the Mexican can arrive.

Since the *pachuco* cannot adapt himself to a civilization which, for its part, rejects him, he finds no answer to the hostility surrounding him except this angry affirmation of his personality.[5] Other groups react differently. The Negroes, for example, oppressed by racial intolerance, try to "pass" as whites and thus enter society. They want to be like other people. The Mexicans have suffered a less violent rejection, but instead of attempting a problematical adjustment to society, the *pachuco* actually flaunts his differences. The purpose of his grotesque dandyism and anarchic behavior is not so much to point out the injustice and incapacity of a society that has failed to assimilate him as it is to demonstrate his personal will to remain different.

It is not important to examine the causes of this conflict, and even less so to ask whether or not it has a solution. There are minorities in many parts of the world who do not enjoy the same opportunities as the rest of the population. The important thing is this stubborn desire to be different, this anguished tension with which the lone Mexican—an orphan lacking both protectors and positive values—displays his differences. The *pachuco* has lost his whole inheritance: language, religion, customs, beliefs. He is left with only a body and a soul with which to confront the elements, defenseless against the stares of everyone. His disguise is a protection, but it also differentiates and isolates him: it both hides him and points him out.

His deliberately aesthetic clothing, whose significance is too obvious to require discussion, should not be mistaken for the outfit of a special group or sect. *Pachuquismo* is an open society, and this in a country full of cults and tribal costumes, all intended to satisfy the middle-class North American's desire to share in something more vital and solid than the abstract morality of the "American Way of Life." The clothing of the *pachuco* is not a uniform or a ritual attire. It is simply a fashion, and like all fashions it is based on novelty—the mother of death, as Leopardi[6] said—and imitation.

---

5. Many of the juvenile gangs that have formed in the United States in recent years are reminiscent of the post-war *pachucos*. It could not have been otherwise: North American society is closed to the outside world, and at the same time it is inwardly petrified. Life cannot penetrate it, and being rejected, squanders itself aimlessly on the outside. It is a marginal life, formless but hoping to discover its proper form.

6. Giacomo Taldegardo Francesco di Sales Saverio Pietro Leopardi (1798–1837), Italian poet, essayist, philosopher, and philologist. [Anthology editors' note]

Its novelty consists in its exaggeration. The *pachuco* carries fashion to its ultimate consequences and turns it into something aesthetic. One of the principles that rules in North American fashions is that clothing must be comfortable, and the *pachuco*, by changing ordinary apparel into art, makes it "impractical." Hence it negates the very principles of the model that inspired it. Hence its aggressiveness.

This rebelliousness is only an empty gesture, because it is an exaggeration of the models against which he is trying to rebel, rather than a return to the dress of his forebears or the creation of a new style of his own. Eccentrics usually emphasize their decision to break away from society—either to form new and more tightly closed groups or to assert their individuality—through their way of dressing. In the case of the *pachuco* there is an obvious ambiguity: his clothing spotlights and isolates him, but at the same time it pays homage to the society he is attempting to deny.

This duality is also expressed in another, perhaps profounder way: the *pachuco* is an impassive and sinister clown whose purpose is to cause terror instead of laughter. His sadistic attitude is allied with a desire for self-abasement which in my opinion constitutes the very foundation of his character: he knows that it is dangerous to stand out and that his behavior irritates society, but nevertheless he seeks and attracts persecution and scandal. It is the only way he can establish a more vital relationship with the society he is antagonizing. As a victim, he can occupy a place in the world that previously had ignored him; as a delinquent, he can become one of its wicked heroes.

I believe that the North American's irritation results from his seeing the *pachuco* as a mythological figure and therefore, in effect, a danger. His dangerousness lies in his singularity. Everyone agrees in finding something hybrid about him, something disturbing and fascinating. He is surrounded by an aura of ambivalent notions: his singularity seems to be nourished by powers that are alternately evil and beneficent. Some people credit him with unusual erotic prowess; others consider him perverted but still aggressive. He is a symbol of love and joy or of horror and loathing, an embodiment of liberty, of disorder, of the forbidden. He is someone who ought to be destroyed. He is also someone with whom any contact must be made in secret, in the darkness.

The *pachuco* is impassive and contemptuous, allowing all these contradictory impressions to accumulate around him until finally, with a certain painful satisfaction, he sees them explode into a tavern fight or a raid by the police or a riot. And then, in suffering persecution, he becomes his true self, his supremely naked self, as a pariah, a man who belongs nowhere. The circle that began with provocation has completed itself and he is ready now for redemption, for his entrance into the society that rejected him. He has been its sin and its scandal, but now that he is a victim it recognizes him at last for what he really is: its product, its son. At last he has found new parents.

The *pachuco* tries to enter North American society in secret and daring ways, but he impedes his own efforts. Having been cut off from his traditional culture, he asserts himself for a moment as a solitary and challenging figure. He denies both the society from which he originated and that of North America. When he thrusts himself outward, it is not to unite with what surrounds him but rather to defy it. This is a suicidal gesture, because the *pachuco* does not affirm or defend anything except his exasperated will-not-to-be. He is not divulging his most intimate feelings: he is revealing an ulcer, exhibiting a wound. A wound that is also a grotesque, capricious, barbaric adornment. A wound that laughs at itself and decks itself out for the hunt. The *pachuco* is the prey of society, but instead of hiding he adorns himself to attract the hunter's attention. Persecution redeems him and breaks his solitude: his salvation depends on his becoming part of the very society he appears to deny. Solitude and sin, communion and health become synonymous terms.[7]

If this is what happens to persons who have long since left their home-land, who can hardly speak the language of their forebears, and whose secret roots, those that connect a man with his culture, have almost with-ered away, what is there to say about the rest of us when we visit the United States? Our reaction is not so unhealthy, but after our first dazzled impres-sions of that country's grandeur, we all instinctively assume a critical atti-tude. I remember that when I commented to a Mexican friend on the loveli-ness of Berkeley, she said: "Yes, it's very lovely, but I don't belong here. Even the birds speak English. How can I enjoy a flower if I don't know its right name, its English name, the name that has fused with its colors and petals, the name that's the same thing as the flower? If I say *bugambilia* to you, you think of the bougainvillaea vines you've seen in your own village, with their purple, liturgical flowers, climbing around an ash tree or hanging from a wall in the afternoon sunlight. They're a part of your being, your culture. They're what you remember long after you've seemed to forget them. It's very lovely here, but it isn't mine, because whatever saying it for me . . . or to me, either."

Yes, we withdraw into ourselves, we deepen and aggravate our awareness of everything that separates or isolates or differentiates us. And we increase our solitude by refusing to seek out our compatriots, perhaps because we fear we will see ourselves in them, perhaps because of a painful, defensive unwillingness to share our intimate feelings. The Mexican succumbs very easily to sentimental effusions, and therefore he shuns them. We live closed up within ourselves, like those taciturn adolescents—I will add in passing that I hardly met any of the sort among North American youths—who are custodians of a secret that they guard behind scowling expressions, but that only waits for the opportune moment in which to reveal itself.

I am not going to expand my description of these feelings or discuss the states of depression or frenzy (or often both) that accompany them. They are all apt to lead to unexpected explosions, which destroy a precarious equilib-rium based on the imposition of forms that oppress or mutilate us. Our sense of inferiority—real or imagined—might be explained at least partly by the reserve with which the Mexican faces other people and the unpredict-able violence with which his repressed emotions break through his mask of impassivity. But his solitude is vaster and profounder than his sense of infe-riority. It is impossible to equate these two attitudes: when you sense that you are alone, it does not mean that you feel inferior, but rather that you feel

---

7. No doubt many aspects of the *pachuco* are lacking in this description. But I am convinced that his hybrid language and behavior reflect a physic oscillation between two irreducible worlds—the North American and the Mexican—which he vainly hopes to reconcile and conquer. He does not want to become either a Mexican or a Yankee. * * *

you are different. Also, a sense of inferiority may sometimes be an illusion, but solitude is a hard fact. We are truly different. And we are truly alone.

This is not the moment to analyze our profound sense of solitude, which alternately affirms and denies itself in melancholy and rejoicing, silence and sheer noise, gratuitous crimes and religious fervor. Man is alone everywhere. But the solitude of the Mexican, under the great stone night of the high plateau that is still inhabited by insatiable gods, is very different from that of the North American, who wanders in an abstract world of machines, fellow citizens and moral precepts. In the Valley of Mexico man feels himself suspended between heaven and earth, and he oscillates between contrary powers and forces, and petrified eyes, and devouring mouths. Reality—that is, the world that surrounds us—exists by itself here, has a life of its own, and was not invented by man as it was in the United States. The Mexican feels himself to have been torn from the womb of this reality, which is both creative and destructive, both Mother and Tomb. He has forgotten the word that ties him to all those forces through which life manifests itself. Therefore he shouts or keeps silent, stabs or prays, or falls asleep for a hundred years.

The history of Mexico is the history of a man seeking his parentage, his origins. He has been influenced at one time or another by France, Spain, the United States and the militant indigenists of his own country, and he crosses history like a jade comet, now and then giving off flashes of lightning. What is he pursuing in his eccentric course? He wants to go back beyond the catastrophe he suffered: he wants to be a sun again, to return to the center of that life from which he was separated one day. (Was that day the Conquest? Independence?) Our solitude has the same roots as religious feelings. It is a form of orphanhood, an obscure awareness that we have been torn from the All, and an ardent search: a flight and a return, an effort to re-establish the bonds that unite us with the universe.

Nothing could be further from this feeling than the solitude of the North American. In the United States man does not feel that he has been torn from the center of creation and suspended between hostile forces. He has built his own world and it is built in his own image: it is his mirror. But now he cannot recognize himself in his inhuman objects, nor in his fellows. His creations, like those of an inept sorcerer, no longer obey him. He is alone among his works, lost—to use the phrase by José Gorostiza[8]—in a "wilderness of mirrors."

Some people claim that the only differences between the North American and ourselves are economic. That is, they are rich and we are poor, and while their legacy is Democracy, Capitalism and the Industrial Revolution, ours is the Counter-reformation, Monopoly and Feudalism. But however influential the systems of production may be in the shaping of a culture, I refuse to believe that as soon as we have heavy industry and are free of all economic imperialism, the differences will vanish. (In fact, I look for the opposite to happen, and I consider this possibility one of the greatest virtues of the Revolution of 1910.) But why search history for an answer that only we ourselves can give? If it is we who feel ourselves to be different, what makes us so, and in what do the differences consist?

---

8. Mexican poet, educator, and diplomat (1901–1973). [Anthology editors' note]

I am going to suggest an answer that will perhaps not be wholly satisfactory. I am only trying to clarify the meaning of certain experiences for my own self, and I admit that what I say may be worth no more than a personal answer to a personal question.

When I arrived in the United States I was surprised above all by the self-assurance and confidence of the people, by their apparent happiness and apparent adjustment to the world around them. This satisfaction does not stifle criticism, however, and the criticism is valuable and forthright, of a sort not often heard in the countries to the south, where long periods of dictatorship have made us more cautious about expressing our points of view. But it is a criticism that respects the existing systems and never touches the roots. I thought of Ortega y Gasset's[9] distinction between uses and abuses, in his definition of the "revolutionary spirit." The revolutionary is always a radical, that is, he is trying to correct the uses themselves rather than the mere abuses of them. Almost all the criticisms I heard from the lips of North Americans were of the reformist variety: they left the social or cultural structures intact and were only intended to limit or improve this or that procedure. It seemed to me then, and it still does, that the United States is a society that wants to realize its ideals, has no wish to exchange them for others, and is confident of surviving, no matter how dark the future may appear. I am not interested in discussing whether this attitude is justified by reason and reality; I simply want to point out that it exists. It is true that this faith in the natural goodness of life, or in its infinite wealth of possibilities, cannot be found in recent North American literature, which prefers to depict a much more somber world; but I found it in the actions, the words and even the faces of almost everyone I met.

On the other hand, I heard a good deal of talk about American realism and also about American ingenuousness, qualities that would seem to be mutually exclusive. To us a realist is always a pessimist. And an ingenuous person would not remain so for very long if he truly contemplated life realistically. Would it not be more accurate to say that the North American wants to use reality rather than to know it? In some matters—death, for example—he not only has no desire to understand it, he obviously avoids the very idea. I met some elderly ladies who still had illusions and were making plans for the future as if it were inexhaustible. Thus they refuted Nietzsche's statement condemning women to an early onset of skepticism because "men have ideals but women only have illusions." American realism, then, is of a very special kind, and American ingenuousness does not exclude dissimulation and even hypocrisy. When hypocrisy is a character trait it also affects one's thinking, because it consists in the negation of all the aspects of reality that one finds disagreeable, irrational or repugnant.

In contrast, one of the most notable traits of the Mexican's character is his willingness to contemplate horror: he is even familiar and complacent in his dealings with it. The bloody Christs in our village churches, the macabre humor in some of our newspaper headlines, our wakes, the custom of eating skull-shaped cakes and candies on the Day of the Dead,[1] are habits inherited

9. José Ortega y Gassett (1883–1955), Spanish writer and philosopher. [Anthology editors' note]
1. El Día de los Muertos, also known as All Souls' Day, a holiday celebrated in Mexico and by Latinos in the United States and Canada; family members and friends gather to remember and pray for those who have died. [Anthology editors' note]

from the Indians and the Spaniards and are now an inseparable part of our being. Our cult of death is also a cult of life, in the same way that love is a hunger for life and a longing for death. Our fondness for self-destruction derives not only from our masochistic tendencies but also from a certain variety of religious emotion.

And our differences do not end there. The North Americans are credulous and we are believers; they love fairy tales and detective stories and we love myths and legends. The Mexican tells lies because he delights in fantasy, or because he is desperate, or because he wants to rise above the sordid facts of his life; the North American does not tell lies, but he substitutes social truth for the real truth, which is always disagreeable. We get drunk in order to confess; they get drunk in order to forget. They are optimists and we are nihilists—except that our nihilism is not intellectual but instinctive, and therefore irrefutable. We are suspicious and they are trusting. We are sorrowful and sarcastic and they are happy and full of jokes. North Americans want to understand and we want to contemplate. They are activists and we are quietists; we enjoy our wounds and they enjoy their inventions. They believe in hygiene, health, work and contentment, but perhaps they have never experienced true joy, which is an intoxication, a whirlwind. In the hubbub of a fiesta night our voices explode into brilliant lights, and life and death mingle together, while their vitality becomes a fixed smile that denies old age and death but that changes life to motionless stone.

What is the origin of such contradictory attitudes? It seems to me that North Americans consider the world to be something that can be perfected, and that we consider it to be something that can be redeemed. Like their Puritan ancestors, we believe that sin and death constitute the ultimate basis of human nature, but with the difference that the Puritan identifies purity with health. Therefore he believes in the purifying effects of asceticism, and the consequences are his cult of work for work's sake, his serious approach to life, and his conviction that the body does not exist or at least cannot lose—or find—itself in another body. Every contact is a contamination. Foreign races, ideas, customs, and bodies carry within themselves the germs of perdition and impurity. Social hygiene complements that of the soul and the body. Mexicans, however, both ancient and modern, believe in communion and fiestas: there is no health without contact. Tlazolteotl, the Aztec goddess of filth and fecundity, of earthly and human moods, was also the goddess of steam baths, sexual love and confession. And we have not changed very much, for Catholicism is also communion.

These two attitudes are irreconcilable, I believe, and, in their present form, insufficient. I would not be telling the truth if I were to say that I had ever seen guilt feelings transformed into anything other than hatred, solitary despair or blind idolatry. The religious feelings of my people are very deep—like their misery and helplessness—but their fervor has done nothing but return again and again to a well that has been empty for centuries. I would also not be telling the truth if I were to say that I can believe in the fertility of a society based on the imposition of certain modern principles. Contemporary history invalidates the belief in man as a creature whose essential being can be modified by social or pedagogical procedures. Man is not simply the result of history and the forces that activate it, as is now claimed; nor is history simply the result of the human will, a belief on which the North

American way of life is implicitly predicated. Man, it seems to me, is not *in* history: he *is* history.

The North American system only wants to consider the positive aspects of reality. Men and women are subjected from childhood to an inexorable process of adaptation; certain principles, contained in brief formulas, are endlessly repeated by the press, the radio, the churches and the schools, and by those kindly, sinister beings, the North American mothers and wives. A person imprisoned by these schemes is like a plant in a flowerpot too small for it: he cannot grow or mature. This sort of conspiracy cannot help but provoke violent individual rebellions. Spontaneity avenges itself in a thousand subtle or terrible ways. The mask that replaces the dramatic mobility of the human face is benevolent and courteous but empty of emotion, and its set smile is almost lugubrious: it shows the extent to which intimacy can be devastated by the arid victory of principles over instincts. The sadism underlying almost all types of relationships in contemporary North American life is perhaps nothing more than a way of escaping the petrifaction imposed by that doctrine of aseptic moral purity. The same is true of the new religions and sects, and the liberating drunkenness that opens the doors of "life." It is astonishing what a destructive and almost physiological meaning this word has acquired: to live means to commit excesses, break the rules, go to the limit (of what?), experiment with sensations. The act of love is an "experience" (and therefore unilateral and frustrating). But it is not to my purpose to describe these reactions. It is enough to say that all of them, like their Mexican opposites, seem to me to reveal our mutual inability to reconcile ourselves to the flux of life.

\* \* \*

1950

---

# ROBERTO FERNÁNDEZ RETAMAR
## b. 1930

### *From* Caliban: Notes Toward a Discussion of Culture in Our America[1]

#### A Question

A European journalist, and moreover a leftist, asked me a few days ago, "Does a Latin-American culture exist?" We were discussing, naturally enough, the recent polemic regarding Cuba that ended by confronting, on the one hand, certain bourgeois European intellectuals (or aspirants to that

1. Translated by Roberto Márquez and David Arthur McMurray. Except as indicated, all footnotes are Fernández Retamar's, with slight emendations by the translators. Three of his notes have been omitted. Except as indicated, all bracketed insertions in the text are Fernández Retamar's.

state) with a visible colonialist nostalgia; and on the other, that body of Latin-American writers and artists who reject open or veiled forms of cultural and political colonialism. The question seemed to me to reveal one of the roots of the polemic and, hence, could also be expressed another way: "Do you exist?" For to question our culture is to question our very existence, our human reality itself, and thus to be willing to take a stand in favor of our irremediable colonial condition, since it suggest that we would be but a distorted echo of what occurs elsewhere. This elsewhere is of course the metropolis, the colonizing centers, whose "right wings" have exploited us and whose supposed "left wings" have pretended and continue to pretend to guide us with pious solicitude—in both cases with the assistance of local intermediaries of varying persuasions.

While this fate is to some extent suffered by all countries emerging from colonialism—those countries of ours that enterprising metropolitan intellectuals have ineptly and successively termed *barbarians, peoples of color, underdeveloped countries, Third World*—I think the phenomenon achieves a singular crudeness with respect to what Martí called "our *mestizo* America." Although the thesis that every man and even every culture is *mestizo* could easily be defended and although this seems especially valid in the case of colonies, it is nevertheless apparent that in both their ethnic and their cultural aspects capitalist countries long ago achieved a relative homogeneity. Almost before our eyes certain readjustments have been made. The white population of the United States (diverse, but of common European origin) exterminated the aboriginal population and thrust the black population aside, thereby affording itself homogeneity in spite of diversity and offering a coherent model that its Nazi disciples attempted to apply even to other European conglomerates—an unforgivable sin that led some members of the bourgeoisie to stigmatize in Hitler what they applauded as a healthy Sunday diversion in westerns and Tarzan films. Those movies proposed to the world—and even to those of us who are kin to the communities under attack and who rejoiced in the evocation of our own extermination—the monstrous racial criteria that have accompanied the United States from its beginnings to the genocide in Indochina.[2] Less apparent (and in some cases perhaps less cruel) is the process by which other capitalist countries have also achieved relative racial and cultural homogeneity at the expense of *internal* diversity.

Nor can any necessary relationship be established between *mestizaje* ["racial intermingling, racial mixture"—ed. note] and the colonial world. The latter is highly complex[3] despite basic structural affinities of its parts. It has included countries with well-defined millennial cultures, some of which have suffered (or are presently suffering) direct occupation (India, Vietnam), and others of which have suffered indirect occupation (China). It also comprehends countries with rich cultures but less political homogeneity, which have been subjected to extremely diverse forms of colonialism (the Arab world). There are other peoples, finally, whose fundamental structures were savagely dislocated by the dire activity of the European despite which

2. Peninsular region in Southeast Asia that includes Vietnam. Fernández Retamar is referring to the Vietnam War (aka the Second Indochina War, 1959–75), but genocide was not part of that conflict. [Anthology editors' note]
3. See Yves Lacoste, *Les pays sous-développés* [The Underdeveloped Countries] (Paris, 1959), 82–84.

they continue to preserve a certain ethnic and cultural homogeneity (black Africa). (Indeed, the latter has occurred despite the colonialists' criminal and unsuccessful attempts to prohibit it.) In these countries *mestizaje* naturally exists to a greater or lesser degree, but it is always accidental and always on the fringe of the central line of development.

But within the colonial world there exists a case unique to *the entire planet*: a vast zone for which *mestizaje* is not an accident but rather the essence, the central line: ourselves, "our mestizo America." Martí, with his excellent knowledge of the language, employed this specific adjective as the distinctive sign of our culture—a culture of descendants, both ethnically and culturally speaking, of aborigines, Africans, and Europeans. In his "Letter from Jamaica" (1815), the Liberator, Simón Bolívar,[4] had proclaimed, "We are a small human species: we possess a world encircled by vast seas, new in almost all its arts and sciences." In his message to the Congress of Angostura (1819),[5] he added:

> Let us bear in mind that our people is neither European nor North American, but a composite of Africa and America rather than an emanation of Europe; for even Spain fails as a European people because of her African blood, her institutions, and her character. It is impossible to assign us with any exactitude to a specific human family. The greater part of the native peoples has been annihilated; the European has mingled with the American and with the African, and the African has mingled with the Indian and with the European. Born from the womb of a common mother, our fathers, different in origin and blood, are foreigners; all differ visibly in the epidermis, and this dissimilarity leaves marks of the greatest transcendence.

Even in this century, in a book as confused as the author himself but full of intuitions (*La raza cósmica*, 1925), the Mexican José Vasconcelos pointed out that in Latin America a new race was being forged, "made with the treasure of all previous ones, the final race, the cosmic race."[6]

This singular fact lies at the root of countless misunderstandings. Chinese, Vietnamese, Korean, Arab, or African cultures may leave the Euro-North American enthusiastic, indifferent, or even depressed. But it would never occur to him to confuse a Chinese with a Norwegian, or a Bantu with an Italian; nor would it occur to him to ask whether they exist. Yet, on the other hand, some Latin Americans are taken at times for apprentices, for rough drafts or dull copies of Europeans, including among these latter whites who constitute what Martí called "European America." In the same way, our entire culture is taken as an apprenticeship, a rough draft or a copy of European bourgeois culture ("an emanation of Europe," as Bolívar said). This last error is more frequent than the the the first, since confusion of a Cuban with an Englishman, or a Guatemalan with a German, tends to be impeded by a certain ethnic tenacity. Here the *rioplatenses*[7] appear to be less ethnically, although not culturally, differentiated. The confusion lies in the

4. South American liberator (1783–1830). [Anthology editors' note]
5. Meeting of 26 delegates in Angostura (now Ciudad Bolívar), Venezuela, summoned by Bolívar during the wars of Independence of Colombia and Venezuela; it ended in 1821. [Anthology editors' note]
6. José Vasconcelos, *La raza cósmica* [The Cosmic Race] (1925).
7. People living in and around the Río de la Plata basin (or River Plate region), between Argentina and Uruguay. [Anthology editors' note]

root itself, because as descendants of numerous Indian, African, and European communities, we have only a few languages with which to understand one another: those of the colonizers. While other colonials or ex-colonials in metropolitan centers speak among themselves in their own language, we Latin Americans continue to use the languages of our colonizers. These are the linguas francas capable of going beyond the frontiers that neither the aboriginal nor Creole languages succeed in crossing. Right now as we are discussing, as I am discussing with those colonizers, how else can I do it except in one of their languages, which is now also *our* language, and with so many of their conceptual tools, which are now also *our* conceptual tools? This is precisely the extraordinary outcry that we read in a work by perhaps the most extraordinary writer of fiction who ever existed. In *The Tempest*, William Shakespeare's last play, the deformed Caliban—enslaved, robbed of his island, and trained to speak by Prospero—rebukes Prospero thus: "You taught me language, and my profit on't/ Is, I know how to curse. The red plague rid you/ For learning me your language!" (1.2.362–64).

## Toward the History of Caliban

Caliban is Shakespeare's anagram for "cannibal," an expression that he had already used to mean "anthropophagus," in the third part of *Henry VI* and in *Othello* and that comes in turn from the word *carib*. Before the arrival of the Europeans, whom they resisted heroically, the Carib Indians were the most valiant and warlike inhabitants of the very lands that we occupy today. Their name lives on in the name Caribbean Sea (referred to genially by some as the American Mediterranean, just as if we were to call the Mediterranean the Caribbean of Europe). But the name *carib* in itself—as well as in its deformation, *cannibal*—has been perpetuated in the eyes of Europeans above all as a defamation. It is the term in this sense that Shakespeare takes up and elaborates into a complex symbol. Because of its exceptional importance to us, it will be useful to trace its history in some detail.

In the *Diario de Navegación* [Navigation logbooks] of Columbus[8] there appear the first European accounts of the men who were to occasion the symbol in question. On Sunday, 4 November 1492, less than a month after Columbus arrived on the continent that was to be called America, the following entry was inscribed: "He learned also that far from the place there were men with one eye and others with dogs' muzzles, who ate human beings."[9] On 23 November, this entry: "[the island of Haiti], which they said was very large and that on it lived people who had only one eye and others called cannibals, of whom they seemed to be very afraid." On 11 December it is noted ". . . that *caniba* refers in fact to the people of El Gran Can," which explains the deformation undergone by the name *carib*—also used by Columbus. In the very letter of 15 February 1493, "dated on the caravelle

---

8. Christopher Columbus (1451–1506), Spanish admiral and explorer from Genoa. [Anthology editors' note]
9. Cited along with subsequent references to the *Diario* [Logbook], by Julio C. Salas, in *Etnografía americana: Los indios caribes—Estudio sobre el origen del mito de la antropofagia* [Latin-American Ethnography: The Carib Indians—A

Study of the Origin of the Myth of Anthropophagy] (Madrid, 1920). The book exposes "the irrationality of [the] charge that some American tribes devoured human flesh, maintained in the past by those interested in enslaving [the] Indians and repeated by the chroniclers and historians, many of whom were supporters of slavery" (211).

off the island of Canaria" in which Columbus announces to the world his "discovery," he writes: "I have found, then, neither monsters nor news of any, save for one island [Quarives], the second upon entering the Indies, which is populated with people held by everyone on the islands to be very ferocious, and who eat human flesh."[1]

This *carib/cannibal* image contrasts with another one of the American man presented in the writings of Columbus: that of the *Arauaco* of the Greater Antilles—our *Taino* Indian primarily—whom he describes as peaceful, meek, and even timorous and cowardly. Both visions of the American aborigine will circulate vertiginously throughout Europe, each coming to know its own particular development: The Taino will be transformed into the paradisical inhabitant of a utopic world; by 1516 Thomas More will publish his *Utopia*,[2] the similarities of which to the island of Cuba have been indicated, almost to the point of rapture, by Ezequiel Martínez Estrada.[3] The Carib, on the other hand, will become a *cannibal*—an anthropophagus, a bestial man situated on the margins of civilization, who must be opposed to the very death. But there is less of a contradiction than might appear at first glance between the two visions; they constitute, simply, options in the ideological arsenal of a vigorous emerging bourgeoisie. Francisco de Quevedo[4] translated "utopia" as "there is no such place." With respect to these two visions, one might add, "There is no such man." The notion of an Edenic creature comprehends, in more contemporary terms, a working hypothesis for the bourgeois left, and, as such, offers an ideal model of the perfect society free from the constrictions of that feudal world against which the bourgeoisie is in fact struggling. Generally speaking, the utopic vision throws upon these lands projects for political reforms unrealized in the countries of origin. In this sense its line of development is far from extinguished. Indeed, it meets with certain perpetuators—apart from its radical perpetuators, who are the consequential revolutionaries—in the numerous advisers who unflaggingly propose to countries emerging from colonialism magic formulas from the metropolis to solve the grave problems colonialism has left us and which, of course, they have not yet resolved in their own countries. It goes without saying that these proponents of "There is no such place" are irritated by the insolent fact that the place *does* exist and, quite naturally, has all the virtues and defects not of a project but of genuine reality.

As for the vision of the *cannibal*, it corresponds—also in more contemporary terms—to the right wing of that same bourgeoisie. It belongs to the ideological arsenal of politicians of action, those who perform the dirty work in whose fruits the charming dreamers of utopias will equally share. That the Caribs were as Columbus (and, after him, an unending throng of followers) depicted them is about as probable as the existence of one-eyed men, men with dog muzzles or tails, or even the Amazons mentioned by the

1. *La carta de Colón anunciando el descubrimiento del nuevo mundo, 15 de febrero–14 de marzo 1493* [Columbus's Letter Announcing the Discovery of the New World, 15 February–14 March 1493] (Madrid, 1956), 20.
2. Work of fiction, in which More (1478–1535) depicts an island society. [Anthology editors' note]
3. Ezequiel Martínez Estrada, "El Nuevo Mundo, la Isla de Utopía y la Isla de Cuba" [The New World, the Island of Utopia, and the Island of Cuba], *Casa de las Américas* 33 (November–December 1965); this issue is entitled *Homenaje a Ezequiel Martínez Estrada*.
4. Francisco Gómez de Quevedo y Santibáñez Villegas (1580–1645), Spanish nobleman, politician, and writer. [Anthology editors' note]

explorer in pages where Greco-Roman mythology, the medieval bestiary, and the novel of chivalry all play their part. It is a question of the typically degraded vision offered by the colonizer of the man he is colonizing. That we ourselves may have at one time believed in this version only proves to what extent we are infected with the ideology of the enemy. It is typical that we have applied the term *cannibal* not to the extinct aborigine of our isles but, above all, to the African black who appeared in those shameful Tarzan films. For it is the colonizer who brings us together, who reveals the profound similarities existing above and beyond our secondary differences. The colonizer's version explains to us that owing to the Caribs' irremediable bestiality, there was no alternative to their extermination. What it does not explain is why even before the Caribs, the peaceful and kindly Arauacos were also exterminated. Simply speaking, the two groups suffered jointly one of the greatest ethnocides recorded in history. (Needless to say, this line of action is still more alive than the earlier one.) In relation to this fact, it will always be necessary to point out the case of those men who, being on the fringe both of utopianism (which has nothing to do with the actual America) and of the shameless ideology of plunder, stood in their midst opposed to the conduct of the colonialists and passionately, lucidly, and valiantly defended the flesh-and-blood aborigine. In the forefront of such men stands the magnificent figure of Father Bartolomé de las Casas,[5] whom Bolívar called "the apostle of America" and whom Martí extolled unreservedly. Unfortunately, such men were exceptions.

One of the most widely disseminated European utopian works is Montaigne's[6] essay "De los caníbales" [On Cannibals; in French, "Des cannibales"], which appeared in 1580. There we find a presentation of those creatures who "retain alive and vigorous their genuine, their most useful and natural, virtues and properties."[7]

Giovanni Floro's English translation of the *Essays* was published in 1603. Not only was Floro a personal friend of Shakespeare, but the copy of the translation that Shakespeare owned and annotated is still extant. This piece of information would be of no further importance but for the fact that it proves beyond a shadow of doubt that the *Essays* was one of the direct sources of Shakespeare's last great work, *The Tempest* (1612). Even one of the characters of the play, Gonzalo, who incarnates the Renaissance humanist, at one point closely glosses entire lines from Floro's Montaigne, originating precisely in the essay on cannibals. This fact makes the form in which Shakespeare presents his character *Caliban/cannibal* even stranger. Because if in Montaigne—in this case, as unquestionable literary source for Shakespeare—"there is nothing barbarous and savage in that nation . . . , except that each man calls barbarism whatever is not his own practice,"[8] in Shakespeare, on the other hand, *Caliban/cannibal* is a savage and deformed slave who cannot be degraded enough. What has happened is simply that in depicting Caliban, Shakespeare, an implacable realist, here takes *the other option* of the emerging bourgeois world. Regarding the utopian vision, it does indeed exist in the work but is unrelated to Caliban; as was said

5. See p. 13. [Anthology editors' note]
6. Michel de Montaigne (1533–1592), French essayist. [Anthology editors' note]

7. *The Complete Essays of Montaigne*, trans. Donald Frame (Stanford, Calif., 1965), 152.
8. Ibid.

before, it is expressed by the harmonious humanist Gonzalo. Shakespeare thus confirms that both ways of considering the American, far from being in opposition, were perfectly reconcilable. As for the concrete man, present him in the guise of an animal, rob him of his land, enslave him so as to live from his toil, and at the right moment exterminate him; this latter, of course, only if there were someone who could be depended on to perform the arduous tasks in his stead. In one revealing passage, Prospero warns his daughter that they could not do without Caliban: "We cannot miss him: he does make our fire,/ Fetch in our wood, and serves in offices/ that profit us" (1.2.311–13). The utopian vision can and must do without men of flesh and blood. After all, *there is no such place.*

There is no doubt at this point that *The Tempest* alludes to America, that its island is the mythification of one of our islands. Astrana Marín,[9] who mentions the "clearly Indian (American) ambience of the island," recalls some of the actual voyages along this continent that inspired Shakespeare and even furnished him, with slight variations, with the names of not a few of his characters: Miranda, Fernando, Sebastian, Alonso, Gonzalo, Setebos.[1] More important than this is the knowledge that Caliban is our Carib.

We are not interested in following all the possible readings that have been made of this notable work since its appearance,[2] and shall merely point out some interpretations. The first of these comes from Ernest Renan, who published his drama *Caliban: Suite de "La Tempête"* in 1878.[3] In this work, Caliban is the incarnation of the people presented in their worst light, except that this time his conspiracy against Prospero is successful and he achieves power—which ineptitude and corruption will surely prevent him from retaining. Prospero lurks in the darkness awaiting his revenge, and Ariel disappears. This reading owes less to Shakespeare than to the Paris Commune, which had taken place only seven years before.[4] Naturally, Renan was among the writers of the French bourgeoisie who savagely took part against the prodigious "assault of heaven."[5] Beginning with this event, his antidemocratic feeling stiffened even further. "In his *Philosophical Dialogues*," Lidsky tells us, "he believes that the solution would lie in the creation of an *élite* of intelligent beings who alone would govern and posses the secrets of science."[6] Characteristically, Renan's aristocratic and prefascist elitism and his hatred of the common people of his country are united with an even greater hatred for the inhabitants of the colonies. It is instructive to hear him express himself along these lines.

9. Luis Astrana Marín (1889–1959), Spanish biographer, journalist, essay writer, and translator. [Anthology editors' note]
1. In William Shakespeare, *Obras completas*, trans. Luis Astrana Marín (Madrid, 1961), 107–8.
2. For example, Jan Kott notes that "there have been learned shakespearian scholars who tried to interpret *The Tempest* as a direct autobiography, or as an allegorical political drama" (*Shakespeare, Our Contemporary*, trans. Boleslaw Taborski, 2d ed. (London, 1967), 240.
3. Ernest Renan, *Caliban: Suite de "La Tempête." Drame Philosophique* [Caliban: "The Tempest" Suite. A philosophical Drama] (Paris, 1878). [Fernández Retamar's note]

Joseph-Ernest Renan (1823–1892), French philologist, historian, and political theorist. [Anthology editors' note]
4. This government—the city council and, as such, a representative of the working class—ruled Paris for two months in 1871. [Anthology editors' note]
5. See V. Arthur Adamov. *La Commune de Paris (8 mars–28 mars 1871): Anthologie* [The Paris Commune (8 March–28 March 1871): An Anthology] (Paris, 1959); and, especially, Paul Lidsky, *Les écrivains contre la Commune* [Writers Against the Commune] (Paris, 1970).
6. Lidsky, Paul, *Les écrivains contre la Commune*, 82.

We aspire [he says] not only to equality but to domination. The country of a foreign race must again be a country of serfs, of agricultural laborers or industrial workers. It is not a question of eliminating the inequalities among men but of broadening them and making them law.[7]

And on another occasion:

The regeneration of the inferior or bastard races by the superior races is within the providential human order. With us, the common man is nearly always a *declassé* nobleman, his heavy hand is better suited to handling the sword than the menial tool. Rather than work he chooses to fight, that is, he returns to his first state. *Regere imperio populos—* that is our vocation. Pour forth this all-consuming activity onto countries which, like China, are crying aloud for foreign conquest. . . . Nature has made a race of workers, the Chinese race, with its marvelous manual dexterity and almost no sense of honor; govern them with justice, levying from them, in return for the blessing of such a government, an ample allowance for the conquering race, and they will be satisfied; a race of tillers of the soil, the black . . . a race of masters and soldiers, the European race. . . . *Let each do that which he is made for, and all will be well.*[8]

It is unnecessary to gloss these lines, which, as Césaire rightly says, came from the pen not of Hitler[9] but of the French humanist Ernest Renan.

The initial destiny of the Caliban myth on our own American soil is a surprising one. Twenty years after Renan had published his *Caliban*—in other words, in 1898—the United States intervened in the Cuban war of independence against Spain and subjected Cuba to its tutelage, converting her in 1902 into her first *neocolony* (and holding her until 1959), while Puerto Rico and the Philippines became colonies of a traditional nature. The fact—which had been anticipated by Martí years before—moved the Latin-American *intelligentsia*. Elsewhere I have recalled that "ninety-eight" is not only a Spanish date that gives its name to a complex group of writers and thinkers of that country, but it is also, and perhaps most importantly, a Latin-American data that should serve to designate a no less complex group of writers and thinkers on this side of the Atlantic, generally known by the vague name of *modernistas*.[1] It is "ninety-eight"—the visible presence of North American imperialism in Latin America—already foretold by Martí, which informs the later work of someone like Darío or Rodó.[2]

---

7. Cited by Aimé Césire in *Discours sur le colonialisme* [An Address on Colonialism], 3d ed. (Paris 1955), 13. This is a remarkable work, and I have made extensive use of its main ideas in this essay. (A part of it has been translated into Spanish in *Casa de las Américas* 36–37 [May–August 1966], an issue dedicated to *Africa en América* [Africa in Latin America]). [The bracketed insertion is Fernández Retamar's. —Anthology editors' note]
8. Ibid., 14–15.
9. Adolf Hitler (1889–1945), Austrian-born founder of Nazism, leader of Germany 1933–45. *Césaire*: Aimé Césaire (1913–2008), Afro-

Martinican poet, playwright, and politician who wrote in French. [Anthology editors' note]
1. See Roberto Fernández Retamar, "Modernismo, noventiocho, subdesarrollo" [Modernism, the Generation of 1898, Underdevelopment], paper read at the Third Congress of the International Association of Hispanists, Mexico City, August 1968; collected in *Ensayo de otro mundo* [Essay on a Different World], 2d ed. (Santiago, 1969).
2. Both writers are discussed in the introduction to Appendix 3; the historical events in this paragraph are discussed in the "Acculturation" introduction. [Anthology editors' note]

In a speech given by Paul Groussac[3] in Buenos Aires on 2 May 1898, we have an early example of how Latin-American writers of the time would react to this situation:

> Since the Civil War and the brutal invasion of the West [he says], the *Yankee* spirit had rid itself completely of its formless and "Caliban-esque" body, and the Old World has contemplated with disquiet and terror the newest civilization that intends to supplant our own, declared to be in decay.[4]

The Franco-Argentine writer Groussac feels that "our" civilization (obviously understanding by that term the civilization of the "Old World," of which we Latin Americans would, curiously enough, be a part) is menaced by the Calibanesque Yankee. It seems highly improbable that the Algerian or Vietnamese writer of the time, trampled underfoot by French colonialism, would have been ready to subscribe to the first part of such a criterion. It is also frankly strange to see the Caliban symbol—in which Renan could with exactitude see, if only to abuse, the people—being applied to the United States. But nevertheless, despite this blurred focus—characteristic, on the other hand, of Latin America's unique situation—Groussac's reaction implies a clear rejection of the Yankee danger by Latin-American writers. This is not, however, the first time that such a rejection was expressed on our continent. Apart from cases of Hispanic writers such as Bolívar and Martí, among others, Brazilian literature presents the example of Joaquín de Sousa Andrade, or Sousândrade,[5] in whose strange poem, *O Guesa Errante*, stanza 10 is dedicated to "O inferno Wall Street," "a *Walpurgisnacht* of corrupt stockbrokers, petty politicians, and businessmen."[6] There is besides José Verissimo, who in an 1890 treatise on national education impugned the United States with his "I admire them, but I don't esteem them."

We do not know whether the Uruguayan José Enrique Rodó—whose famous phrase on the United States, "I admire them, but I don't love them," coincides literally with Verissimo's observation—knew the work of that Brazilian thinker but it is certain that he was familiar with Groussac's speech, essential portions of which were reproduced in *La Razón* of Montevideo[7] on 6 May 1898. Developing and embellishing the idea outlined in it, Rodó published in 1900, at the age of twenty-nine, one of the most famous works of Latin-American literature: *Ariel*. North American civilization is implicitly presented there as Caliban (scarcely mentioned in the work), while Ariel would come to incarnate—or should incarnate—the best of what Rodó did not hesitate to call more than once "our civilization" (223, 226). In his words, just as in those of Groussac, this civilization was identified not only with "our Latin America" (239) but with ancient Romania, if not with the Old World as a whole. The identification of Caliban with the United States, proposed by Groussac and popularized by Rodó, was cer-

---

3. Paul-François Groussac (1848–1929), French-born Argentinian writer, literary critic, historian, and librarian. [Anthology editors' note]
4. Quoted in José Enrique Rodó, *Obras completas* [Complete Works], ed. Emir Rodríguez Monegal (Madrid, 1957), 193; this volume will hereafter be cited by page number in the text. [The bracketed insertion is Fernández Retamar's. —Anthology

editors' note]
5. Brazilian writer (1833–1902). [Anthology editors' note]
6. See Jean Franco, *The Modern Culture of Latin America: Society and the Artist* (London, 1967), 49.
7. City in Uruguay. [Anthology editors' note]

tainly a mistake. Attacking this error from one angle, José Vasconcelos commented that "if the Yankees were only Caliban, they would not represent any great danger."[8] But this is doubtless of little importance next to the relevant fact that the danger in question had clearly been pointed out. As Benedetti[9] rightly observed, "Perhaps Rodó erred in naming the danger, but he did not err in his recognition of where it lay."[1]

Sometime afterward, the French writer Jean Guéhenno[2]—who, although surely aware of the work by the colonial Rodó, knew of course Renan's work from memory—restated the latter's Caliban thesis in his own *Caliban parle* [Caliban speaks], published in Paris in 1929. This time, however, the Renan identification of Caliban *with* the people is accompanied by a positive evaluation of Caliban. One must be grateful to Guéhenno's book—and it is about the only thing for which gratitude is due—for having offered for the first time an appealing version of the character. But the theme would have required the hand or the rage of a Paul Nizan to be effectively realized.[3]

Much sharper are the observations of the Argentine Aníbal Ponce,[4] in his 1935 work *Humanismo burgués y humanismo proletario*. The book—which a student of Che's[5] thinking conjectures must have exercised influence on the latter[6]—devotes the third chapter to "Ariel; or, The Agony of an Obstinate Illusion." In commenting on *The Tempest*, Ponce says that "those four beings embody an entire era: Prospero is the enlightened despot who loves the Renaissance; Miranda, his progeny; Caliban, the suffering masses [Ponce will then quote Renan, but not Guéhenno]; and Ariel, the genius of the air without any ties to life."[7] Ponce points up the equivocal nature of Caliban's presentation, one that reveals "an enormous injustice on the part of a master." In Ariel he sees the intellectual, tied to Prospero in "less burdensome and crude a way than Caliban, but also in his service." His analysis of the conception of the intellectual ("mixture of slave and mercenary") coined by Renaissance humanism, a concept that "taught as nothing else could an indifference to action and an acceptance of the established order" and that even today is for the intellectual in the bourgeois world "the educational ideal of the governing classes," constitutes one of the most penetrating essays written on the theme in our America.

But this examination, although made by a Latin American, still took only the European world into account. For a new reading of *The Tempest*—for a new consideration of the problem—it was necessary to await the emergence of the colonial countries, which begins around the time of the Second World War. That abrupt presence led the busy technicians of the United Nations to invent, between 1944 and 1945, the term *economically underdeveloped*

8. José Vasconcelos, *Indología* [Indology], 2d ed. (Barcelona, n.d.), XXIII.
9. Mario Benedetti (1920–2009), Uruguayan novelist, playwright, novelist, and poet. [Anthology editors' note]
1. Mario Benedetti, *Genio y figura de José Enrique Rodó* [A Portrait of José Enriqué Rodó] (Buenos Aires, 1966), 95.
2. Marcel-Jules-Marie Guéhenno, known as Jean Guéhenno (1890–1978), essayist and literary critic. [Anthology editors' note]
3. French writer and philosopher (1905–1940). [Anthology editors' note]

4. Essayist, psychologist, professor, and politician (1898–1938) [Anthology editors' note]
5. Ernesto "Che" Guevara (1928–1967), Argentinian-born Latin American revolutionary leader. [Anthology editors' note]
6. See Michael Lowy, *La pensée de Che Guevara* [Che Guevara's Thought] (Paris, 1970), 19.
7. Aníbal Ponce, *Humanismo burgués y humanismo proletario* [Bourgeois Humanism and Proletarian Humanism] (Havana, 1962), 83. [The bracketed insertion is Fernández Retamar's. —Anthology editors' note]

*area* in order to dress in attractive (and profoundly confusing) verbal garb what had until then been called *colonial area*, or *backward areas*.[8]

Concurrently with this emergence there appeared in Paris in 1950 O. Mannoni's[9] book *Psychologie de la colonisation*. Significantly, the English edition of this book (New York, 1956) was to be called *Prospero and Caliban: The Psychology of Colonization*. To approach his subject, Mannoni has created, no less, what he calls the "Prospero complex," defined as "the sum of those unconscious neurotic tendencies that delineate at the same time the 'picture' of the paternalist colonial and the portrait of 'the racist whose daughter has been the object of an [imaginary] attempted rape at the hands of an inferior being.'"[1] In this book, probably for the first time, Caliban is identified with the colonial. But the odd theory that the latter suffers from a "Prospero complex" that leads him neurotically to require, even to anticipate, and naturally to accept the presence of Prospero/colonizer is roundly rejected by Frantz Fanon[2] in the fourth chapter ("The So-Called Dependence Complex of Colonized Peoples") of his 1952 book *Black Skin, White Masks*.

Although he is (apparently) the first writer in our world to assume our identification with Caliban, the Barbadian writer George Lamming[3] is unable to break the circle traced by Mannoni:

> Prospero [says Lamming] has given Caliban language; and with it an unstated history of consequences, an unknown history of future intentions. This gift of language meant not English, in particular, but speech and concept as a way, a method, a necessary avenue towards areas of the self which could not be reached in any other way. It is this way, entirely Prospero's enterprise, which makes Caliban aware of possibilities. Therefore, all of Caliban's future—for future is the very name of possibilities—must derive from Prospero's experiment, which is also his risk. Provided there is no extraordinary departure which explodes all of Prospero's premises, then Caliban and his future now belong to Prospero . . . Prospero lives in the absolute certainty that Language, which is his gift to Caliban, is the very prison in which Caliban's achievements will be realized and restricted.[4]

In the decade of the 1960s, the new reading of *The Tempest* ultimately established its hegemony. In *The Living World of Shakespeare* (1964), the Englishman John Wain[5] will tell us that Caliban

> has the pathos of the exploited peoples everywhere, poignantly expressed at the beginning of a three-hundred-year wave of European colonization; even the lowest savage wishes to be left alone rather than be "educated" and made to work for someone else, and there is an undeniable justice in his complaint: "For I am all the subjects that you

8. J. L. Zimmerman, *Países pobres, países ricos: La brecha que se ensancha* [Poor Countries, Rich Countries: The Breech That Is Widening], trans. G. González Aramburo (Mexico City, 1966), 7.
9. Dominique-Octave Mannoni (1899–1989), French psychoanalyst and author. [Anthology editors' note]
1. O. Mannoni, *Psychologie de la colonisation* [The Psychology of Colonialism] (Paris, 1950), 71; quoted by Frantz Fanon, in *Peau noire, masques blancs* [Black Skin, White Masks], 2d

ed. (Paris [c. 1965]), 106.
2. Martinican psychiatrist, philosopher, revolutionary, and writer (1925–1961). [Anthology editors' note]
3. Novelist, poet, and scholar (b. 1927). [Anthology editors' note]
4. George Lamming, *The Pleasures of Exile* (London, 1960), 109.
5. Poet, novelist, critic, and journalist (1925–1994). [Anthology editors' note]

have,/ Which once was mine own king." Prospero retorts with the inevitable answer of the colonist: Caliban has gained in knowledge and
skill (though we recall that he already knew how to build dams to catch
fish, and also to dig pig-nuts from the soil, as if this were the English
countryside). Before being employed by Prospero, Caliban had no language: ". . . thou didst not, savage,/ Know thy own meaning, but
wouldst gabble like/ A thing most brutish." However, this kindness has
been rewarded with ingratitude. Caliban, allowed to live in Prospero's
cell, has made an attempt to ravish Miranda. When sternly reminded of
this, he impertinently says, with a kind of slavering guffaw, "Oh ho! Oh
ho!—would it have been done!/ Thou didst prevent me; I had peopled
else/ This isle with Calibans." Our own age [Wain concludes], which is
much given to using the horrible word "miscegenation," ought to have no
difficulty in understanding this passage.[6]

At the end of that same decade, in 1969, and in a highly significant manner, Caliban would be taken up with pride as our symbol by three Antillian
writers—each of whom expresses himself in one of the three great colonial
languages of the Caribbean. In that year, independently of one another, the
Martinican writer Aimé Césaire published his dramatic work in French
*Une tempête: Adaptation de "La Tempête" de Shakespeare pour un théâtre
nègre*; the Barbadian Edward Brathwaite,[7] his book of poems *Islands*, in
English, among which there is one dedicated to "Caliban" and the author of
these lines, an essay in Spanish, "Cuba hasta Fidel," which discusses our
identification with Caliban.[8] In Césaire's work the characters are the same
as those of Shakespeare. Ariel, however, is a mulatto slave, and Caliban is
a black slave; in addition, Eshzú, "a black god-devil" appears. Prospero's
remark when Ariel returns, full of scruples, after having unleashed—following
Prospero's orders but against his own conscience—the tempest with which
the work begins is curious indeed: "Come now!" Prospero says to him, "Your
crisis! It's always the same with intellectuals!" Brathwaite's poem called
"Caliban" is dedicated, significantly, to Cuba: "In Havana that morning . . ."
writes Brathwaite, "It was December second, nineteen fifty-six./ It was the
first of August eighteen thirty-eight./ It was the twelfth October fourteen
ninety-two./ How many bangs how many revolutions?"

## Our Symbol

Our symbol then is not Ariel, as Rodó thought, but rather Caliban. This is
something that we, the *mestizo* inhabitants of these same isles where Caliban lived, see with particular clarity: Prospero invaded the islands, killed
our ancestors, enslaved Caliban, and taught him his language to make himself understood. What else can Caliban do but use that same language—
today he has no other—to curse him, to wish that the "red plague" would fall
on him? I know no other metaphor more expressive of our cultural situation,

6. John Wain, *the Living World of Shakespeare*
(New York, 1964), 226–27. * * * [The bracketed
insertion is Fernández Retamar's. —Anthology
editors' note]
7. Edward Kamau Brathwaite (b. 1930), poet and
scholar. [Anthology editors' note]
8. See Aimé Césaire, *Une tempête: Adaptation*

*de "La Tempête" de Shakespeare pour un théâtre
nègre* [A Tempest: An Adaptation of Shakespeare's
"The Tempest" for a Black Theater] (Paris, 1969);
Edward Brathwaite, *Islands* (London, 1969); Ro-
berto Fernández Retamar, "Cuba hasta Fidel"
[Cuba until Fidel], *Bohemia*, 19 September 1969.

of our reality. From Túpac Amaru, *Tiradentes*, Toussaint-Louverture, Simón Bolívar, Father Hidalgo, José Artigas, Bernardo O'Higgins, Benito Juárez, Antonio Maceo, and José Martí, to Emiliano Zapata, Augusto César Sandino, Julio Antonio Mella, Pedro Albizu Campos, Lázaro Cárdenas, Fidel Castro, and Ernesto Che Guevara, from the Inca Garcilaso de la Vega, the *Aleijadinho*, the popular music of the Antilles, José Hernández, Eugenio María de Hostos, Manuel González Prada, Rubén Darío (yes, when all is said and done), Baldomero Lillo, and Horacio Quiroga, to Mexican muralism, Heitor Villa-Lobos, César Vallejo, José Carlos Mariátegui, Ezequiel Martínez Estrada, Carlos Gardel, Pablo Neruda, Alejo Carpentier, Nicolás Guillén, Aimé Césaire, José María Arguedas, Violeta Parra, and Frantz Fanon[9]— what is our history, what is our culture, if not the history and culture of Caliban?

As regards Rodó, if it is indeed true that he erred in his symbols, as has already been said, it is no less true that he was able to point with clarity to the greatest enemy of our culture in his time—and in ours—and that is enormously important. Rodó's limitations (and this is not the moment to elucidate them) are responsible for what he saw unclearly or failed to see at all.[1] But what is worthy of note in his case is what he did indeed see and what continued to retain a certain amount of validity and even virulence.

> Despite his failings, omissions, and ingenuousness [Benedetti has also said], Rodó's vision of the Yankee phenomenon, rigorously situated in its historical context, was in its time the first launching pad for other less ingenuous, better informed and more foresighted formulations to come. . . . the almost prophetic substance of Rodó's Arielism still retains today a certain amount of validity.[2]

These observations are supported by indisputable realities. We Cubans become well aware that Rodó's vision fostered later, less ingenuous, and more radical formulations when we simply consider the work of our own Julio Antonio Mella,[3] on whose development the influence of Rodó was decisive. In "Intelectuales y tartufos" [Intellectuals and Tartuffes] (1924), a vehement work written at the age of twenty-one, Mella violently attacks the false intellectual values of the time—opposing them with such names as Unamuno, José Vasconcelos, Ingenieros, and Varona.[4] He writes, "The intellectual is the worker of the mind. The worker! That is, the only man who in Rodó's judgment is worthy of life, . . . he who takes up his pen against iniquity just as others take up the plow to fecundate the earth, or the sword to liberate peoples, or a dagger to execute tyrants."[5]

9. In this list, Fernández Retamar highlights people, works, and genres important in Latin American political and cultural history from the Spanish colonial period to his time. Some of the people are discussed in this essay, some of them are discussed or included in this anthology, and many of them are annotated at various points in the anthology. [Anthology editors' note]

1. "It is improper," Benedetti has said, "to confront Rodó with present-day structures, statements, and ideologies. His time was different from ours[;] . . . his true place, his true temporal homeland was the nineteenth century" (*Genio y figura de José Enrique Rodó*, 128). [The bracketed insertion is Fernández Retamar's. —Anthology editors' note]

2. Ibid., 109. * * *

3. Cuban Marxist revolutionary, cofounder of the Cuban Communist Party (1903–1929). [Anthology editors' note]

4. Enrique José Varona (1849–1933), Cuban philosopher and professor, vice-president of Cuba 1913–17. *Unamuno*: Miguel de Unamuno y Jugo (1864–1936), Spanish philosopher and writer. *Ingenieros*: José Ingenieros (1877–1925), Argentinian physician, philosopher, and writer. [Anthology editors' note]

5. *Hombres de la revolucion: Julio Antonio Mella* [Men of the Revolution: Julio Antonio Mella] (Havana, 1971), 12.

Mella would again quote Rodó with devotion during that year[6] and in the following year he was to help found the Ariel Polytechnic Institute in Havana.[7] It is opportune to recall that in this same year, 1925, Mella was also among the founders of Cuba's first Communist party. Without a doubt, Rodó's *Ariel* served as a "launching pad" for the meteoric revolutionary career of this first organic Marxist-Leninist in Cuba (who was also one of the first on the continent.)

As further examples of the relative validity that Rodó's anti-Yankee argument retains even in our own day, we can point to enemy attempts to disarm such an argument. A strange case is that of Emir Rodríguez Monegal,[8] for whom *Ariel*, in addition to "material for philosophic or sociological mediation, *also* contains pages of a polemic nature on political problems *of the moment*. And it was precisely this *secondary* but undeniable condition that determined its immediate popularity and dissemination." Rodó's essential position against North American penetration would thus appear to be an afterthought, a *secondary* fact in the work. It is known, however, that Rodó conceived it immediately after American intervention in Cuba in 1898, *as a response to the deed*. Rodríguez Monegal says:

> The work thus projected was *Ariel*. In the final version *only two direct allusions* are found to the historical fact that was its primary motive force; . . . both allusions enable us to appreciate how Rodó has *transcended* the initial historical circumstance to arrive fully at the essential problem: the proclaimed decadence of the Latin race.[9]

The fact that a servant of imperialism such as Rodríguez Monegal, afflicted with the same "Nordo-mania" that Rodó denounced in 1900, tries so coarsely to emasculate Rodó's work, only proves that it does indeed retain a certain virulence in its formulation—something that we would approach today from other perspectives and with other means. An analysis of *Ariel*—and this is absolutely not the occasion to make one—would lead us also to stress how, despite his background and his antiJacobinism,[1] Rodó combats in it the antidemocratic spirit of Renan and Nietzsche (in whom he finds "an abominable, reactionary spirit" [224]) and exalts democracy, moral values, and emulation. But undoubtedly the rest of the work has lost the immediacy that its gallant confrontation of the United States and the defense of our values still retains.

Put into perspective, it is almost certain that these lines would not bear the name they have were it not for Rodó's book, and I prefer to consider them also as a homage to the great Uruguayan, whose centenary is being celebrated this year. That the homage contradicts him on not a few points is not strange. Medardo Vitier[2] has already observed that "if there should be a return to Rodó, I do not believe that it would be to adopt the solution he offered concerning the interests of the life of the spirit, but rather to reconsider the problem."[3]

6. Ibid., 15.

7. See Erasmo Dumpierre, *Mella* (Havana, c. 1965), 145; see also José Antonio Portunondo, "Mella y los intelectuales" [Mella and the Intellectuals] [1963], which is reproduced in *Casa de las Américas*, no. 68 (1971).

8. Uruguayan scholar, literary critic, and editor of Latin American literature (1921–1985). [Anthology editors' note]

9. Emir Rodríguez Monegal, ed., *Rodó* (Madrid, 1957), 192–93; my emphasis.

1. Opposition to revolutionary opinions (from the Jacobin Club, a political club during the French Revolution). [Anthology editors' note]

2. Medardo Vitier y Guanche (1886–1960), Cuban scholar and writer. [Anthology editors' note]

3. Medardo Vitier, *Del ensayo americano* [On the Latin-American Essay] (Mexico City, 1945), 117.

In proposing Caliban as our symbol, I am aware that it is not entirely ours, that it is also an alien elaboration, although in this case based on our concrete realities. But how can this alien quality be entirely avoided? The most venerated word in Cuba—*mambí*—was disparagingly imposed on us by our enemies at the time of the war for independence, and we still have not totally deciphered its meaning. It seems to have an African root, and in the mouth of the Spanish colonists implied the idea that all *independentistas* were so many black slaves—emancipated by that very war for independence— who of course constituted the bulk of the liberation army. The *independentistas*, white and black, adopted with honor something that colonialism meant as an insult. This is the dialectic of Caliban. To offend us they call us *mambí*, they call us *black*; but we reclaim as a mark of glory the honor of considering ourselves descendants of the *mambí*, descendants of the rebel, runaway, *independentista* black—*never* descendants of the slave holder. Nevertheless, Propero, as we well know, taught his language to Caliban and, consequently, gave him a name. But is this his true name? Let us listen to this speech made in 1971:

> To be completely precise, we still do not even have a name; we still have no name; we are practically unbaptized—whether as Latin Americans, Ibero-Americans, Indo-Americans. For the imperialists, we are nothing more than despised and despicable peoples. At least that was what we were. Since Girón they have begun to change their thinking. Racial contempt—to be a Creole, to be a mestizo, to be black, to be simply, a Latin American, is for them contemptible.[4]

This, naturally, is Fidel Castro on the tenth anniversary of the victory at Playa Girón.

To assume our condition as Caliban implies rethinking our history from the *other* side, from the viewpoint of the *other* protagonist. The *other* protagonist of *The Tempest* (or, as we might have said ourselves, *The Hurricane*) is not of course Ariel but, rather, Prospero.[5] There is no real Ariel-Caliban polarity: both are slaves in the hands of Prospero, the foreign magician. But Caliban is the rude and unconquerable master of the island, while Ariel, a creature of the air, although also a child of the isle, is the intellectual—as both Ponce and Césaire have seen.

\* \* \*

1971

4. Fidel Castro, speech, 19 April 1971.
5. See Kott, *Shakespeare, Our Contemporary*, 269.

# Selected Bibliographies

This list is meant to serve as a wide-ranging, comprehensive resource for understanding the Latino literary tradition in its social and historical contexts. The opening section, "Panoramic Views," offers bibliographical references about the tradition, such as thematic studies and collections of interviews. Subsequent sections are organized by period and, within each period, alphabetically by author, except for "Popular Dimensions," where the material is arranged thematically. Each section opens with a thematic list of references defining that period: the Spanish-American War, the Bracero Program, the Chicano Movement, the Cuban Revolution, and so on. Since the target reader of *The Norton Anthology of Latino Literature* is in the United States, the bibliographical focus is on English-language books. References to anthologies, interviews, and academic articles are limited to the most significant. This is the first major publication for a number of authors featured in the anthology, especially some from the nineteenth century; thus the scarcity of information about them.

## PANORAMIC VIEWS

As discussed in the introduction, "The Search for Wholeness," the Latino literary tradition in the United States was firmly established in the 1980s, when, for economic, political, social, and cultural reasons, the various national groups constituting the minority (Mexicans, Cubans, Puerto Ricans, Dominicans, and others) began to perceive themselves as a unit.

Engaging, all-encompassing historical discussions about Latinos, exploring social, psychological, economic, political, cultural, and linguistic issues, include *Latinos: A Biography of the People* (1992), by Earl Shorris; *Ethnic Labels, Latino Lives* (1995), by Suzanne Oboler; *The Hispanic Condition: Reflections on Culture and Identity in America* (1995, rev. 2001), by Ilan Stavans; *Strangers in the Land: How Latino Immigration Is Transforming America* (1998), by Roberto Suro; *Harvest of Empire: A History of Latinos in America* (2000), by Juan González; *Latino USA: A Cartoon History* (2000), by Ilan Stavans, illustrated by Lalo López Alcaraz; *Latinos, Inc.: The Marketing and Making of a People* (2001), by Arlene Dávila; *Livin' in Span-*

*glish: The Search for a New Latino Identity* (2002), by Ed Morales; *Translation Nation: Defining a New American Identity in the Spanish-Speaking United States* (2005), by Héctor Tobar; and *The Companion to Latina/o Studies* (2007), edited by Juan Flores and Renato Rosaldo. Valuable resources include the four-volume *Encyclopedia Latina* (2005), edited by Ilan Stavans; *Latinas in the United States: A Historical Encyclopedia* (2006), edited by Vicki L. Ruiz and Virginia Sánchez Korrol; *Voices of the U.S. Latino Experience* (2008), edited by Rodolfo F. Acuña and Guadalupe Compeán; *Icons of Latino America: Latino Contributions to American Culture* (2008), by Roger Bruns; *Latinos and the Nation's Future* (2009), edited by Henry G. Cisneros with John Rosales; and the Web site *lae.greenwood.com.*

Significant anthologies of Latino literature in the United States include *Iguana Dreams: New Latino Fiction* (1992), edited by Virgil Suárez and Delia Poey; *Growing Up Latino: Memoirs and Stories* (1993), edited by Harold Augenbraum and Ilan Stavans; *Short Fiction by*

*Hispanic Writers of the United States* (1993), edited by Nicolás Kanellos; *Barrios and Borderlands: Cultures of Latinos and Latinas in the United States* (1994), edited by Denis Lynn Daly Heyck; *Currents from the Dancing River: Contemporary Latino Fiction, Nonfiction, and Poetry* (1994), edited by Ray González; *Paper Dance: 55 Latino Poets* (1995), edited by Víctor Hernández Cruz, Leroy V. Quintana, and Virgil Suárez; *El Coro: A Chorus of Latino and Latina Poetry* (1997), edited by Martín Espada; *Hispanic American Literature: An Anthology* (1997), edited by Rodolfo J. Cortina; *Máscaras* (1997), edited by Lucha Corpi; *New World: Young Latino Writers* (1997), edited by Ilan Stavans; *The Latino Reader* (1997), edited by Harold Augenbraum and Margarite Fernández-Olmos; *Latino Heretics* (1999), edited by Tony Díaz; *Wáchale!: Poetry and Prose about Growing Up Latino in America* (2001), edited by Ilan Stavans; *Herencia: An Anthology of Hispanic Literature of the United States* (2002), edited by Nicolás Kanellos; *The Prentice Hall Anthology of Latino Literature* (2002), edited by Eduardo R. del Río; *Under the Fifth Sun: Latino Literature from California* (2002), edited by Rick Heide; *U.S. Latino Literature Today* (2005), edited by Gabriela Baeza Ventura; *Latino Boom: An Anthology of U.S. Latino Literature* (2006), edited by John S. Christie and José B. González; *Lengua Fresca: Latinos Writing on the Edge* (2006), edited by Harold Augenbraum and Ilan Stavans; *Telling Tongues: A Latin@ Anthology on Language Experience* (2007), edited by Louis G. Mendoza and Toni Nelson Herrera; *Latinos in Lotusland: An Anthology of Contemporary Southern California Literature* (2008), edited by Daniel A. Olivas; and *The Chicano/Latino Literary Prize* (2008), edited by Stephanie Fetta.

Influential general studies on Latino literature, dealing with topics such as national identity, ethnicity, religion, gender, eroticism, and linguistic choices, are *Breaking Boundaries: Latina Writing and Critical Readings* (1989), edited by Asunción Horno-Delgado et al.; *Dance between Two Cultures: Latino Caribbean Literature Written in the United States* (1997), by William Luis; *Show and Tell: Identity as Performance in U.S. Latina/o Fiction* (1997), by Karen Christian; *Latino Fiction and the Modernist Imagination: Literature of the Borderlands* (1998), by John S. Christie; *Latino American Literature in the Classroom* (2002), by Delia Poey; *Latino Literature in America* (2003), by Bridget Kevane; *Tongue Ties: Logo-Eroticism in Anglo-Hispanic Literature* (2003), by Gustavo Pérez Firmat; *Killing Spanish: Literary Essays on Ambivalent U.S. Latino/a Identity* (2004), by Lyn Di Iorio Sandín; *Redreaming America: Toward a Bilingual American Culture* (2005), by Debra A. Castillo; *Strangers in Our Own Land: Religion in Contemporary*

*U.S. Latina/o Literature* (2005), by Héctor Avalos; *El ambiente nuestro: Chicano/Latino Homoerotic Writing* (2006), by David William Foster; *On Latinidad: U.S. Latino Literature and the Construction of Ethnicity* (2007), by Marta Caminero-Santángelo; *Technofuturos: Critical Interventions in Latina/o Studies* (2007), edited by Nancy Raquel Mirabal and Agustín Laó-Montes; *The Latino/a Canon and the Emergence of Post-Sixties Literature* (2007), by Raphael Dalleo and Elena Machado Sáenz; *Latino Spin: Public Image and the Whitewashing of Race* (2008), by Arlene Dávila; *Latinos in America: Philosophy and Social Identity* (2008), by Jorge J. E. Gracia; *The Latino Threat: Constructing Immigrants, Citizens, and the Nation* (2008), by Leo R. Chavez; *Homecoming Queers: Desire and Difference in Chicana/Latina Cultural Production* (2009), by Marivel T. Danielson; *How the United States Racializes Latinos: White Hegemony and Its Consequences* (2009), edited by José A. Cobas, Jorge Duany, and Joe R. Feagin; *Imagined Transnationalism: U.S. Latina/o Literature, Culture, and Identity* (2009), edited by Kevin Concannon, Francisco A. Lomelí, and Marc Priewe; and *Latina/o Sexualities: Probing Powers, Passions, Practices, and Policies* (2010), by Marysol Asencio. Useful resources are *U.S. Latino Literature: A Critical Guide for Students and Teachers* (2000), edited by Harold Augenbraum and Margarite Fernández-Olmos; *Hispanic Literature of the United States: A Comprehensive Reference* (2003), by Nicolás Kanellos; and the two-volume *Latino and Latina Writers* (2004), edited by Alan West-Durán.

The handful of bibliographies showcasing the Latino literary tradition include *American Ethnic Literatures: Native American, African American, Chicano/Latino, and Asian American Writers and Their Backgrounds: An Annotated Bibliography* (1992), edited by David R. Peck; *Latinos in English: A Selected Bibliography of Latino Fiction Writers of the United States* (1992), edited by Harold Augenbraum, with research compiled by Hilda Mundo-López, introduction by Ilan Stavans; *U.S. Latino Literature: An Essay and Annotated Bibliography* (1992), edited by Marc Zimmerman; *The Hispanic Literary Companion* (1997), edited by Nicolás Kanellos; *Bibliographic Guide to Chicana and Latina Narrative* (2003), edited by Kathy S. Leonard; and *Latina and Latino Voices in Literature: Lives and Works* (2003), edited by Frances Ann Day.

Important academic studies on Mexican American literature include *Occupied America: The Chicano's Struggle toward Liberation* (1972; rev. 1981, 1988), by Rodolfo F. Acuña; *Images of the Mexican American in Fiction and Film* (1980), by Arthur G. Pettit, edited with an afterword by Dennis E. Showalter; *Introduction to the Chicano Novel* (1982), by Marvin A.

Lewis; *Chicano Poetry: A Critical Introduction* (1986), by Cordelia Candelaria; *Contemporary Chicano Fiction: A Critical Survey* (1986), edited by Vernon E. Lattin; *Understanding Chicano Literature* (1988), by Carl R. Shirley and Paula W. Shirley; *The Children of the Sun: Mexican-Americans in the Literature of the United States* (1989), by Marcienne Rocard, translated by Edward G. Brown Jr.; *Chicano Narrative: The Dialectics of Difference* (1990), by Ramón Saldívar; *RetroSpace: Collected Essays on Chicano Literature, Theory, and History* (1990), by Juan Bruce-Novoa; *Criticism in the Borderlands: Studies in Chicano Literature, Culture, and Ideology* (1991), edited by Héctor Calderón and José David Saldívar, with a foreword by Rolando Hinojosa; *Mexican Ballads, Chicano Poems: History and Influence in Mexican-American Social Poetry* (1992), by José E. Limón; *Chicana Critical Issues* (1993), edited by Norma Alarcón et al.; *Movements in Chicano Poetry: Against Myths, Against Margins* (1995), by Rafael Pérez-Torres; *Rethinking the Borderlands: Between Chicano Culture and Legal Discourse* (1995), by Carl Gutiérrez-Jones; *Women Singing in the Snow: A Cultural Analysis of Chicana Literature* (1995), by Tey Diana Rebolledo; *Contemporary Mexican-American Women Novelists: Toward a Feminist Identity* (1996), by María C. González; *Daughters of Self-Creation: The Contemporary Chicana Novel* (1996), by Annie O. Eysturoy; *Home Girls: Chicana Literary Voices* (1996), by Alvina E. Quintana; *Tender Accents of Sound: Spanish in the Chicano Novel in English* (1996), by Ernst Rudin; *Chicano Poetics: Heterotexts and Hybridities* (1997), by Alfred Arteaga; *Migrant Song: Politics and Process in Contemporary Chicano Literature* (1997), by Teresa McKenna; *American Encounters: Greater Mexico, the United States, and the Erotics of Culture* (1998), by José E. Limón; *Tolerating Ambiguity: Ethnicity and Community in Chicano/a Writing* (1998), by Wilson Neate; *Mexicanos: A History of Mexicans in the United States* (1999, rev. 2009), by Manuel G. Gonzales; *Barrio-Logos: Space and Place in Urban Chicano Literature and Culture* (2000), by Raul Homero Villa; *Chicano Drama: Performance, Society, and Myth* (2000), by Jorge Huerta; *Understanding Contemporary Chicana Literature* (2000), by Deborah L. Madsen; *Extinct Lands, Temporal Geographies: Chicana Literature and the Urgency of Space* (2002), by Mary Pat Brady; *Nuevomexicano Cultural Legacy: Forms, Agencies, and Discourse* (2002), edited by Francisco A. Sorell, Víctor A. Sorell, and Genaro M. Padilla; *Life in Search of Readers: Reading (in) Chicano/a Literature* (2003), by Manuel M. Martín-Rodríguez; *When We Arrive: A New Literary History of Mexican America* (2003), by José F. Aranda Jr.; *Border Confluences: Borderland Narratives from the Mexican War to the Present* (2004), by Rosemary A. King; *Narratives*

*of Greater Mexico: Essays on Chicano Literary History, Genre, and Borders* (2004), by Héctor Calderón; *Brown on Brown: Chicano/a Representations of Gender, Sexuality, and Ethnicity* (2005), by Frederick Luis Aldama; *Chicano and Chicana Literature: Otra voz del pueblo* (2006), by Charles M. Tatum; and *Mexican American Literature: The Politics of Identity* (2006), by Elizabeth Jacobs.

Among the valuable anthologies on Mexican American literature are *Aztlán: An Anthology of Mexican-American Literature* (1972), edited by Luis Valdez and Stan Steiner; *Voices of Aztlán: Chicano Literature of Today* (1974), edited by Dorothy E. Harth and Lewis M. Baldwin; *Chicanos: Antología histórica y literaria* (1980), edited by Tino Villanueva; *Voces: An Anthology of Nuevo Mexicano Writers* (1987), edited by Rudolfo A. Anaya; *Aztlán: Essays on the Chicano Homeland* (1989), edited by Rudolfo A. Anaya and Francisco A. Lomelí; *North of the Rio Grande: The Mexican-American Experience in Short Fiction* (1992), edited by Edward Simmen; *Infinite Divisions: An Anthology of Chicana Literature* (1993), edited by Tey Diana Rebolledo and Eliana S. Rivero; *Pieces of the Heart: New Chicano Fiction* (1993), edited by Gary Soto; *Literatura Chicana, 1965–1995: An Anthology in Spanish, English, and Caló* (1997), edited by Manuel de Jesús Hernández-Gutiérrez and David William Foster; *Pláticas: Conversations with Hispano Writers of New Mexico* (2000), by Nasario García; *The Chicano Studies Reader: An Anthology of Aztlán, 1970–2000* (2002), edited by Chon A. Noriega et al.; and *Hecho en Tejas: An Anthology of Texas-Mexican Literature* (2006), edited by Dagoberto Gilb.

Important bibliographies of Chicano literature include *Chicano Perpsectives in Literature: A Critical and Annotated Bibliography* (1976), edited by Francisco A. Lomelí and Donaldo Urioste; *Chicano Literature: An Introduction and Annotated Bibliography* (1977), edited by Carlota Cárdenas de Dwyer; *A Bibliography of Criticism of Contemporary Chicano Literature* (1980–82), edited by Ernestina N. Eger; *Mexican American Literature: A Preliminary Bibliography of Literary Criticism* (1981), edited by Mike Anzaldúa; *A Decade of Chicano Literature (1970–1979): Critical Essays and Bibliography* (1982), edited by Roberto G. Trujillo and Raquel Quiroz de González; *Literatura Chicana: A Comprehensive Bibliography: 1980–1984* (1984), edited by Roberto G. Trujillo, A. A. Rodríguez, and Richard Kiy; and "An Essay on Collection Development and Bibliography of Chicano Literature Published 1980–1984," in *Chicano Literature: A Reference Guide* (1985), edited by Julio Martínez and Francisco A. Lomelí. See also the extensive bibliographical essay in *Chicana Creativity and Criticism: New Frontiers in American Literature*

(2nd ed., 1996), edited by María Herrera-Sobek and Helena María Viramontes.

Regarding Puerto Rican literature on the mainland, important academic studies include *The Nuyorican Experience: Literature of the Puerto Rican Minority* (1982), by Eugene V. Mohr; *Divided Borders: Essays on Puerto Rican Identity* (1993), by Juan Flores; *La memoria rota* (1993) and *El arte de bregar: Ensayos* (2000), by Arcadio Díaz Quiñones; *Puerto Rican Voices in English* (1997), by Carmen Dolores Hernández; *Partes de un todo* (1999), by Efraín Barradas; *From Bomba to Hip-Hop: Puerto Rican Culture and Latino Identity* (2000), by Juan Flores; *Boricua Literature: A Literary History of the Puerto Rican Diaspora* (2001), by Lisa Sánchez González; *Kissing the Mango Tree: Puerto Rican Women Rewriting American Literature* (2002), by Carmen S. Rivera; *Humor and the Eccentric Text in Puerto Rican Literature* (2005), by Israel Reyes; *Para romper con el insularismo: Letras puertorriqueñas en comparación* (2006), edited by Efraín Barradas and Rita De Maeseneer; *Writing Off the Hyphen: New Perspectives on the Literature of the Puerto Rican Diaspora* (2008), edited by José L. Torres-Padilla and Carmen Haydeé Rivera; and *The Diaspora Strikes Back: Caribeño Tales of Learning and Turning* (2009), by Juan Flores.

Influential anthologies about Puerto Rican literature on the mainland (some with material from the island) include *Borinquen: An Anthology of Puerto Rican Literature* (1974), edited by María Teresa Babín and Stan Steiner; *Nuyorican Poetry: An Anthology of Puerto Rican Words and Feelings* (1975), edited by Miguel Algarín and Miguel Piñero, photographs by Gil Méndez; *Herejes y mitificadores: Muestra de poesía puertorriqueña en Estados Unidos* (1980), edited by Efraín Barradas and Rafael Rodríguez; *Inventing a Word: An Anthology of Twentieth-Century Puerto Rican Poetry* (1980), edited by Julio Marzán; *Papiros de Babel* (1991), edited by Pedro López Adorno; *Puerto Rican Writers at Home in the USA: An Anthology* (1991), edited by Faythe Turner; *Aloud: Voices from the Nuyorican Poets Cafe* (1994), edited by Miguel Algarín and Bob Holman; *Nuestro New York: An Anthology of Puerto Rican Plays* (1994), edited by John V. Antush; *Boricuas: Influential Puerto Rican Writings—An Anthology* (1995), edited by Roberto Santiago; *Action: The Nuyorican Poets Cafe Theater Festival* (1997), edited by Miguel Algarín and Lois Griffith; and *Growing Up Puerto Rican: An Anthology* (1997), edited and with an introduction by Joy L. De Jesús, foreword by Ed Vega. A valuable bibliographical resource is *Puerto Rican Literature: A Bibliography of Secondary Sources* (1982), by David William Foster.

Regarding Cuban American literature, important academic studies include *The Cuban Condition: Translation and Identity in Modern Cuban Literature* (1989) and *Life on the Hyphen: The Cuban-American Way* (1994), both by Gustavo Pérez Firmat; *Cuban-American Literature of Exile: From Person to Person* (1998), by Isabel Alvarez-Borland; *La literatura cubano americana y su imagen* (2004), by José Manuel García; *Discursos desde la diáspora* (2005), by Eliana Rivero; *Generational Traumas in Contemporary Cuban-American Literature* (2006), by Rafael Miguel Montes; and *Cultural Erotics in Cuban America* (2007), by Ricardo L. Ortiz.

Anthologies dedicated to Cuban Americans are *Cuban American Writers: Los atrevidos* (1988), edited and with an introduction by Carolina Hospital; *Cuban American Theater* (1991), edited by Rodolfo J. Cortina; *Bridges to Cuba/Puentes a Cuba* (1995), edited by Ruth Behar; *Little Havana Blues: A Cuban-American Literature Anthology* (1996), edited by Delia Poey and Virgil Suárez; *ReMembering Cuba: Legacy of a Diaspora* (2001), edited by Andrea O'Reilly Herrera; *Burnt Sugar/Caña quemada: Contemporary Cuban Poetry in English and Spanish* (2006), edited by Oscar Hijuelos and Lori Carlson; and *The Portable Island: Cubans at Home in the World* (2008), edited by Ruth Behar and Lucía M. Suárez. A useful bibliography of Cuban American literature is *Cuban-American Fiction in English: An Annotated Bibliography of Primary and Secondary Sources* (2005), by M. Delores Carlito.

Regarding Dominican American literature, important academic studies include *A Visa for a Dream: Dominicans in the United States* (1995), by Patricia R. Pessar; *The Dominican Americans* (1998), by Silvio Torres-Saillant and Ramona Hernández; *El retorno de las yolas: Ensayos sobre diáspora, democracia y dominicanidad* (1999), *Introduction to Dominican Blackness* (1999), and *Diasporic Disquisitions: Dominicanists, Transnationalism, and the Community* (2000), all by Silvio Torres-Saillant; *Language, Race, and Negotiation of Identity: A Study of Dominican Americans* (2002), by Benjamin H. Bailey; and *A Tale of Two Cities: Santo Domingo and New York after 1950* (2008), by Jesse Hoffnung-Garskof. Useful anthologies on Dominican American literature include *Historias de Washington Heights y otros rincones del mundo: Cuentos* (1994) and *Literatura dominicana en los Estados Unidos: Presencia temprana, 1900–1950* (2001), both edited by Daisy Cocco de Filippis and Franklin Gutiérrez.

## COLONIZATION: 1534–1809

Bibliographical references in this section address exclusively the conquest and exploration of the territories that eventually became parts of the United States. All other material by authors such as Fray Bartolomé de Las Casas and "El Inca" Garcilaso de la Vega is not included.

The leading study of the age of exploration remains *Spanish Exploration in the Southwest 1542–1706* (1908), by Herbert Eugene Bolton. See also *The Colonization of North America, 1492–1783* (1920), by Herbert Eugene Bolton and Thomas Maitland Marshall. Equally valuable are *Historia de los caminos del nuevo mundo: Expansión de la cultura hispánica en América* (1945), by Ricardo Carrasco, with a prologue by Enrique de Gandía; *Anglo-Spanish Rivalry in North America* (1971), by J. Leitch Wright Jr.; *The Invasion Within: The Contest of Cultures in Colonial North America* (1985) and *Beyond 1492: Encounters in Colonial North America* (1992), both by James Axtell; *When Jesus Came, the Corn Mother Went Away* (1991), by Ramón Gutiérrez; *The Spanish Frontier in North America* (1992), by David Weber; *Reconstructing a Chicano/a Literary Heritage: Hispanic Colonial Literature of the Southwest* (1993), by María Herrera-Sobek; *The Backcountry and the City: Colonization and Conflict in Early America* (2005), by Ed White; and *Empires of the Atlantic World: Britain and Spain in America, 1492–1830* (2006), by J. H. Elliott.

### Juan Bautista de Anza

The most valuable editions of and studies on de Anza's journey are Pedro Font's *The Anza Expedition of 1775–1776* (1913), edited by Frederick J. Teggart; *Anza's California Expeditions* (1930), by Herbert Eugene Bolton; *Outpost of Empire: The Story of the Founding of San Francisco* (1931), by Herbert Eugene Bolton; *Forgotten Frontiers: A Study of the Spanish Indian Policy of Don Juan Bautista de Anza, Governor of New Mexico, 1777–1787* (1932), translated and edited by Alfred Barnaby Thomas; and *Anza Conquers the Desert: The Anza Expeditions from Mexico to California and the Founding of San Francisco, 1774 to 1776* (1971), by Richard F. Pourade.

### Álvar Núñez Cabeza de Vaca

There is a plethora of editions in English of Álvar Núñez Cabeza de Vaca's account of his journey across the North American hinterland. The first one appeared in *Spanish Explorers in the Southern United States, 1528–1543* (1907), divided into three parts: *Álvar Núñez Cabeza de Vaca*, edited by Frederick W. Hodge; *The Narrative of the Expedition of Hernando de Soto, by the Gentleman of Elvas*, edited by Theodore H. Lewis; and *The Narrative of the Expedition of Coronado, by Pedro de Castañeda*, edited by Frederick W. Hodge. The most established early translation is featured in *The Journey of Álvar Núñez Cabeza de Vaca*

*and His Companions from Florida to the Pacific, 1528–1536* (1922), translated by Fanny Bandelier, introduction by Adolph F. Bandelier. Then there are *Álvar Núñez Cabeza de Vaca: The Journey and Route of the First European to Cross the Continent of North America, 1534–1536* (1940), translated by Cleve Hallenbeck; *Cabeza de Vaca's Adventures in the Unknown Interior of America* (1961), translated and annotated by Cyclone Covey, epilogue by William T. Pilkington; *Castaways: The Narrative of Álvar Núñez Cabeza de Vaca* (1993), translated by Frances M. López-Morillas, edited by Enrique Pupo-Walker; *The Account: Álvar Núñez Cabeza de Vaca's Relación* (1993), translated by Martín A. Favata and José B. Hernández; *Álvar Núñez Cabeza de Vaca: His Account, His Life, and the Expedition of Pánfilo de Narváez* (1999), edited and translated by Rolena Adorno and Patrick Charles Pautz; and *Chronicle of the Narváez Expedition* (2002), revised by Harold Augenbraum from Fanny Bandelier's translation, introduction by Ilan Stavans.

A study of Cabeza de Vaca's adventures is *A Land So Strange: The Epic Journey of Cabeza de Vaca, the Extraordinary Tale of a Shipwrecked Spaniard Who Walked across America in the Sixteenth Century* (2007), by Andrés Reséndez. A film based on Cabeza de Vaca's writings, released to coincide with the quincentennial of Columbus's arrival to the Americas in 1492, is *Cabeza de Vaca* (1993), directed by Nicolás Echevarría. The documentary *Conquistadors* (2001), directed by Michael Wood, includes a section on Cabeza de Vaca.

### Pedro Castañeda de Nájera

See *Spanish Explorers in the Southern United States, 1528–1543* (1907), divided into three parts: *Álvar Nuñez Cabeza de Vaca*, edited by Frederick W. Hodge; *The Narrative of the Expedition of Hernando de Soto, by the Gentleman of Elvas*, edited by Theodore H. Lewis; and *The Narrative of the Expedition of Coronado*, by Pedro Castañeda de Nájera, edited by Frederick W. Hodge.

### Fray Juan Crespi

A bilingual edition of Crespi's journals is included in *A Description of Distant Roads: Original Journals of the First Expedition into California, 1769–1770* (2001), edited and translated by Alan K. Brown. Some excerpts also appear in *A World Transformed: Firsthand Accounts of California before the Gold Rush* (1999), edited with an introduction by Joshua Paddison. An anthology and study of Crespi's work is *Fray Juan Crespi: Missionary Explorer on the Pacific Coast, 1769–1774* (1927), by Herbert Eugene Bolton.

## Juan de Castellanos

The first edition of Juan de Castellanos's epic poem, *Elegías de varones ilustres de Indias* (1589), was published in Spain. A subsequent annotated edition, by Isaac Pardo, was published and reprinted by Venezuela's Academia Nacional de la Historia (1962, 1987). An English translation by Muna Lee of the sixth elegy appears in *La gesta de Puerto Rico: Elegías de varones ilustres de Indias, elegía VI* (1974), by María Teresa Babín. There is no English translation of the full poem. Castellanos's writings are collected in *Obras de Juan de Castellanos* (1930). Major studies of his work include *Juan de Castellanos: Estudio de las Elegías de varones ilustres de Indias* (1961), by Isaac J. Pardo; *Estudio sobre Juan de Castellanos* (1972), by Giovanni Meo Zilio; *Juan de Castellanos: Tradición española y realidad americana* (1972), by Manuel Alvar; and *Las auroras de sangre: Juan de Castellanos y el descubrimiento poético de América* (1999), by William Ospina.

## Fray Bartolomé de Las Casas

The earliest English translation of Fray Bartolomé de Las Casas's work is *An Account of the First Voyages and Discoveries Made by the Spaniards in America* (1699). See also *History of the Indies* (1971), translated and edited by Andrée Collard; *A Short Account of the Destruction of the Indies* (1992), edited by Nigel Griffin, introduction by Anthony Pagden; *The Devastation of the Indies: A Brief Account* (1992), translated by Herma Briffault, introduction by Bill M. Donovan; and *An Account, Much Abbreviated, of the Destruction of the Indies, with Related Texts* (2003), translated by Andrew Hurley, edited with an introduction by Franklin W. Knight. A useful anthology of his work is *Fray Bartolomé de Las Casas: A Selection of his Writings* (1971), translated and edited by George Sanderlin. Also useful is *Western Expansion and Indigenous Peoples: The Heritage of Las Casas* (1977), edited by Elías Sevilla-Casas.

## Fray Marcos de Niza

De Niza's report appears in *The Journey of Alvar Núñez Cabeza de Vaca and His Companions from Florida to the Pacific, 1528–1536, Together with the Report of Father Marcos of Nizza* [sic] *and a Letter from the Viceroy Mendoza* (1922), translated by Fanny Bandelier, introduction by Adolph F. Bandelier.

## Hernando de Soto

See *Spanish Explorers in the Southern United States, 1528–1543* (1907), divided into three parts: *Alvar Núñez Cabeza de Vaca*, edited by Frederick W. Hodge; *The Narrative of the Expedition of Hernando de Soto, by the Gentleman of Elvas*, edited by Theodore H. Lewis; and *The Narrative of the Expedition of Coronado, by Pedro de Castañeda*, edited by Frederick W. Hodge.

## "El Inca" Garcilaso de la Vega

In Spanish, there are multiple editions of "El Inca" Garcilaso de la Vega's work, including those of Ayacucho (1985), Cátedra (1996), and Castalia (2000). In English, the *Comentarios* have appeared as *The Incas: The Royal Commentaries of the Inca, Garcilaso de la Vega* (1961), translated by Alain Gheerbrant, and *Royal Commentaries of the Incas, and General History of Peru* (1969), translated by H. V. Livermore. *The Florida of the Inca* (1951) was translated and edited by John Grier Varner and Jeannette Johnson Varner. For studies of "El Inca" Garcilaso de la Vega, see *Language, Authority and Indigenous History in the Comentarios Reales de los Incas* (1968), by Margarita Zamora; *La Florida del Inca and the Struggle for Social Equality in America* (2005), by Jonathan Steigman; and *Beyond Books and Borders: Garcilaso de la Vega and La Florida del Inca* (2006), by Raquel Chang-Rodríguez.

## Fray Eusebio Francisco Kino

The bibliography on Fray Eusebio Francisco Kino's political, geographical, scientific, and cartographic efforts is extensive. His own work is available in *Kino's Historical Memoir of Pimería Alta: A Contemporary Account of the Beginnings of California, Sonora, and Arizona* (1919), edited by Herbert Eugene Bolton; *Father Kino at La Paz, April 1683: A Translation of the "Relación Puntual" of 1683* (1952), edited by Charles N. Rudkin; *Kino's Biography of Francisco Javier Saeta, S.J.* (1961), edited by Ernest J. Burrus; and *Plan for the Development of Pimería Alta, Arizona, and Upper California: A Report to the Mexican Viceroy* (1961), edited by Ernest J. Burrus. His diaries are featured in *First from the Gulf to the Pacific: The Diary of the Kino-Atondo Peninsular Expedition, December 14, 1684–January 13, 1685* (1969), edited by W. Michael Mathes. His correspondence is found in *Kino Reports to Headquarters: Correspondence from New Spain with Rome* (1954), *Correspondencia del P. Kino con los generales de la Compañía de Jesús, 1682–1707* (1961), and *Kino Writes to the Duchess: Letters of Eusebio Francisco Kino, S.J., to the Duchess of Aveiro* (1965), all edited by Ernest J. Burrus, and *Eusebio Francesco Chini: Epistolario, 1670–1710* (1998), edited by Domenico Calarco. Kino is the subject of several biographies: *Pioneer Padre: The Life and Times of Eusebio Francisco Kino* (1935), by Rufus Kay Wyllys; *Rim of Christendom: A Biography of Eusebio Francisco Kino,*

*Pacific Coast Pioneer* (1936), by Herbert Eugene Bolton; *A Kino Guide: A Life of Eusebio Francisco Kino, Arizona's First Pioneer and A Guide to His Missions and Monuments* (1968), by Charles W. Polzer; *Pioneer Padre: A Biography of Eusebio Francisco Kino S.J., Missionary, Discoverer, Scientist, 1645–1711* (1968), by Boniface Bolognani; and *Missionary-Discoverer: Padre Eusebio Kino* (1978), by Thaddeus P. Jost. Studies of his legacy include *Il Padre Eusebio Chini: Esploratore missionario della California e dell'Arizona* (1930), by Eugenia Ricci; *Story of the Spanish Missions of the Middle Southwest, with a Complete Survey of the Missions Founded by Padre Eusebio Francisco Kino in the Seventeenth Century and Later Enlarged and Beautified by the Franciscan Fathers during the Last Part of the Eighteenth Century* (1934), by Frank Cummins Lockwood; *With Padre Kino on the Trail* (1934), by Frank Cummins Lockwood; *El padre Kino, misionero y gobernante* (1945), by F. Ibarra de Anda; *The Padre on Horseback* (1963), by Herbert Eugene Bolton; *Kino and the Cartography of Northwestern New Spain* (1965), by Ernest J. Burrus; *Father Kino in Arizona* (1966), by Fay Jackson Smith; *Kino and Manje, Explorers of Sonora and Arizona: Their Vision of the Future* (1971), by Ernest J. Burrus; *El padre Kino: Misionero itinerante y ecuestre* (1973), by Alfonso Trueba; *Kino alla conquista dell'America* (1980), by Annamaria Kelly; *Der reitende Padre: Auf den Spuren des Welschtiroler Jesuitenmissionars Eusebio Kino in Amerika* (1995), by Hubert Gundolf; *L'apostolo dei Pima: Il metodo di evangelizzazione di Eusebio Francesco Chini missionario gesuita pioniere delle coste del Pacifico (1645–1711)* (1995), by Domenico Calarco; and *Kino, a Legacy: His Life, His Works, His Missions, His Monuments* (1998), by Charles W. Polzer.

### Juan de Oñate

The most valuable studies on Juan de Oñate's expedition, some of which include translations of primary documents, are *Don Juan de Oñate and the Founding of New Mexico: A New Investigation into the Early History of New Mexico* (1927), by George Peter Hammond; *The Fight for the Pueblo: The Story of Oñate's Expedition and the Founding of Santa Fe, 1598–1609* (1934), by Cornelia James Cannon; *The Habit of Empire* (1939), by Paul Horgan; *Don Juan de Oñate, Colonizer of New Mexico: 1595–1628* (1953), by

George Peter Hammond and Agapito Rey; *Juan de Oñate's Colony in the Wilderness: An Early History of the American Southwest* (1990), by Robert McGeagh; *The Last Conquistador: Juan de Oñate and the Settling of the Far Southwest* (1991), by Marc Simmons; *Into the Wilderness Dream: Exploration Narratives of the American West, 1500–1805* (1994), edited by Donald A. Barclay, James H. Maguire, and Peter Wild; *The Hispanic Presence in North America from 1492 to Today* (1999), by Carlos M. Fernández-Shaw; *Oñate: Conquistador de Nuevo México* (2003), by Concepción López Valles; and *Following the Royal Road: A Guide to the Historic Camino Real de Tierra Adentro* (2006), by Hal E. Jackson. Juan de Oñate is featured in *Historia de la Nueva México* (1610), by Gaspar Pérez de Villagrá. His treks are fictionalized in *Two Lives for Oñate* (1997), by Miguel Encinias.

### Fray Junípero Serra

An anthology of Serra's work, *Writings of Junípero Serra* (1955), was translated and edited by Father Antonine Tibesar. *A Letter of Junípero Serra to the Reverend Father Preacher Fray Fermín Francisco de Lasuén* (1970) was translated and edited by Francis J. Weber.

### Gaspar Pérez de Villagrá

There are two English editions of Pérez de Villagrá's work: *History of New Mexico* (1933), translated by Gilberto Espinosa, with introduction and notes by F. W. Hodge; and *Historia de la Nueva México* (1992), translated and edited by Miguel Encinias, Alfred Rodríguez, and Joseph P. Sánchez, published in bilingual format. A valuable essay on Villagrá by Luis Leal appears in *A Luis Leal Reader* (2007), edited by Ilan Stavans.

### Sebastián Vizcaíno

The only volume available in English is *A Natural and Civil History of California* (1758), translated by Miguel Venegas, which contains, as Appendix 2, the "Narrative of the Voyage of Captain Sebastián Vizcaíno in the Year 1602 for Surveying the Outward or Western Coast of California on the South-Sea." A study of Vizcaíno's odyssey is *Vizcaíno and Spanish Expansion in the Pacific Ocean: 1580–1630* (1968), by W. Michael Mathes.

## ANNEXATIONS: 1811–1898

The Latino literature of the nineteenth century has received scant attention. Consequently, the works of only a handful of the authors in the "Annexations" section of this anthology have been published in book form. *Recovering*

*the U.S. Hispanic Literary Heritage*, a scholarly series done at the University of Houston, has opened new vistas into the Latino literary tradition. Several of the volumes—I (1993) was edited by Ramón Gutiérrez and Genaro Padilla, II

(1996) by Erlinda Gonzales-Berry and Charles Tatum, III (2000) by María Herrera-Sobek and Virginia Sánchez Korrol, IV (2002) by José Aranda Jr. and Silvio Torres-Saillant, V (2006) by Kenya Dworkin-Méndez and Agnes Lugo-Ortiz, and VI (2007) by Antonia I. Castañeda and A. Gabriel Meléndez—include material from the nineteenth century.

Important resources about journalists and artists in New Mexican newspapers are *My History, Not Yours: The Formation of Mexican American Autobiography* (1993), by Genaro M. Padilla; *Speaking for Themselves: Neomexicano Cultural Identity and the Spanish-Language Press, 1880–1920* (1996), by Doris Meyer; *So All Is Not Lost: The Poetics of Print in Nuevomexicano Communities, 1834–1958* (1997), by A. Gabriel Meléndez; and *Hispanic Periodicals in the United States* (2000), by Nicolás Kanellos and Helvetia Martell. Beyond these volumes, no material is available for the writers in the "Frontier Memoirs" cluster (Juan Nepomuceno Seguín, José Policarpo Rodríguez, and Andrew García) and those in the "Southwestern Newspaper Poetry" cluster (Juan B. Hijar y Jaro, J. M. Vigil, José Rómulo Ribera, Luis A. Torres, and Luis Tafoya aka X.X.X.).

Valuable resources on the Mexican-American War and the selling of Mexican territory to the United States in the Treaty of Guadalupe Hidalgo are *Occupied America: The Chicano's Struggle toward Liberation* (1972; rev. 1981, 1988), by Rodolfo F. Acuña; *The Mexican War, 1846–1848* (1974), by K. Jack Bauer; *The Great Land Grab: The Mexican-American War, 1846–1848* (1975), by Orlando Martínez; *To the Halls of the Montezumas: The Mexican War in the American Imagination* (1985), by Robert W. Johannsen; *Army of Manifest Destiny: The American Soldier in the Mexican War, 1846–1848* (1992), by James M. McCaffrey; *Olive Branch and Sword: The United States and Mexico, 1845–1848* (1997), by Dean B. Mahin; *The Mexican War, 1846–1848* (2003), by Douglas V. Meed; *Echoes of the Mexican-American War* (2004), by Krystyna M. Libura, Luis Gerardo Morales Moreno, and Jesús Velasco Márquez, translated by Mark Fried; *Wars within War: Mexican Guerrillas, Domestic Elites, and the United States of America, 1846–1848* (2005), by Irving W. Levinson; *The Mexican War* (2006), by David S. Heidler and Jeanne T. Heidler; and *Invading Mexico: America's Continental Dream and the Mexican War, 1846–1848* (2007), by Joseph Wheelan.

The Spanish-American War continues to generate substantial scholarly reflection. Important sources referring to the rise of U.S. power in the world and Latinos in the United States include *The Spanish-Cuban-American War and the Birth of American Imperialism* (1972), by Philip S. Foner; *The Mirror of War: American Society and the Spanish-American War* (1974), by Gerald F. Linderman; *The Splendid Little War* (1974), by Frank Burt Freidl; *1898: La guerra hispanoamericana en caricaturas/The Spanish American War in Cartoons* (1992), edited by Manuel Méndez Saavedra; *Crucible of Empire: The Spanish-American War and Its Aftermath* (1993), edited by James C. Bradford; *The Spanish War: An American Epic, 1898* (1994), by G. J. A. O'Toole; *The Spanish-American War: Conflict in the Caribbean and the Pacific, 1895–1902* (1995), by Joseph Smith; *Teddy Roosevelt at San Juan: The Making of a President* (1997), by Peggy Samuels and Harold Samuels; *1898: The Birth of the American Century* (1998), by David Traxel; *Empire by Default: The Spanish-American War and the Dawn of the American Century* (1998), by Ivan Musicant; *The War of 1898* (1998), by Louis Pérez Jr.; *The Reckless Decade: America in the 1890s* (2002), by H. W. Brands; *The Spanish-American War* (2003), by Kenneth E. Hendrickson Jr.; *Uncle Sam's War of 1898 and the Origins of Globalization* (2003), by Thomas Schoonover, foreword by Walter LaFeber; *Power and Progress: American National Identity, the War of 1898, and the Rise of American Imperialism* (2006), by Paul T. McCartney; and *Global Intrigues: The Era of the Spanish-American War and the Rise of the United States to World Power* (2007), by Juan R. Torruella. A useful compendium of the literature of the Spanish-American War is *The Literature of the Spanish-American War: An Anti-Imperialist Anthology* (1974), edited by Roger James Bresnahan.

Cuban-exile poetry in the United States in the nineteenth century is featured in the anthology *El laúd del desterrado*. A modern critical edition was published in 1995 under the editorship of Matías Montes-Huidobro. The original and the modern edition are in Spanish.

## Julio G. Arce

See the entry for Jorge Ulica, below.

## Isidoro Armijo

A profile of Isidoro Armijo as a newspaper editor appears in *Speaking for Themselves: Neomexicano Cultural Identity and the Spanish-Language Press, 1880–1920* (1996), by Doris Meyer.

## Ramón Emeterio Betances

Few of Betances's writings in Spanish or French have been translated into English. The most complete collection of his writings is the multivolume *Ramón Emeterio Betances: Obras Completas* (2007, 2008, 2009), edited by Félix Ojeda Reyes and Paul Estrade, with Spanish translations of the works Betances published in France. Ojeda Reyes published two studies, *La manigua en Paris: Correspondencia diplomática de Betances* (1984) and *Peregrinos de la libertad* (1992), that document the activities of Betances and other Puerto Rican separatists. He also authored a Betances biography, *El desterrado de Paris* (2001). *Las Antillas para los antillanos* (1975), edited with an introduction and notes by Carlos M. Rama, includes some Spanish translations of Betances's writings in French.

## Eusebio Chacón

Portions of Eusebio Chacón's *Hijo de la tempestad* have appeared in an English translation by Doris Sommer in *The Multilingual Anthology of American Literature* (2000), edited by Marc Shell and Werner Sollors. Another version, by Amy Diane Prince, is featured in *The Latino Reader: From 1542 to the Present* (1997), edited by Harold Augenbraum and Margarite Fernández-Olmos. A valuable resource is *Eusebio Chacón: Eslabón temprano de la novela chicana* (2004), by Francisco A. Lomelí. *Legacy of Honor: The Life of Rafael Chacón, a Nineteenth-Century New Mexican* (1986), the autobiography of Eusebio and Felipe Maximiliano Chacón's relative, was edited by Jacqueline Dorgan Meketa.

## Felipe Maximiliano Chacón

None of Felipe Maximiliano Chacón's work is available in English. A Spanish edition, *Obras de Felipe Maximiliano Chacón, El Cantor Neomexicano: Poesía y prosa* (1924), has a prologue by Benjamin M. Read. *Legacy of Honor: The Life of Rafael Chacón, a Nineteenth-Century New Mexican* (1986), the autobiography of Eusebio and Felipe Maximiliano Chacón's relative, was edited by Jacqueline Dorgan Meketa. A useful resource on Felipe Maximiliano Chacón is "Two Texts for a New Canon: Vicente Bernal's *Las primicias* and Felipe Maximiliano Chacón's *Poesía y prosa*," by Erlinda Gonzáles-Berry, in *Recovering the U.S. Hispanic Literary Project*, vol. I (1993).

## Gaspar Betancourt Cisneros

Little of Betancourt Cisneros's work is available in English. A substantial segment of his writing is included in *Escenas cotidianas* (1950) and *Cartas del lugareño* (1951). *Gaspar Betancourt Cisneros: El lugareño* (1938), by Federico Córdova, is a study of his life and work.

## José Escobar

Escobar's work remains buried in nineteenth-century New Mexican newspapers. Efforts at recovery were done by Doris Meyer in *Speaking for Themselves: Neomexicano Cultural Identity and the Spanish-Language Press, 1880–1920* (1996) and by A. Gabriel Meléndez in *So All Is Not Lost: The Poetics of Print in Nuevomexicano Communities, 1834–1958* (1997).

## Fabio Fiallo

Fallo's *Cuentos frágiles* (1908) and *Poesías* (1931) are unavailable in English. New editions of his work are *La canción de una vida* (1992) and *Cuentos frágiles y Las manzanas de Mefisto* (1992), both edited by José Enrique García.

## Sotero Figueroa

Figueroa's writings are unavailable in English. In Spanish, his six-part essay, *La verdad de la historia* (1892), was first published in the New York separatist newspaper *Patria* and later edited by Carlos Ripoll in 1977. It also appeared in *Puerto Rico en "Patria"* (1996), by Edgardo Meléndez. Figueroa's writings and political activities are extensively discussed in *Peregrinos de la libertad* (1992), by Félix Ojeda Reyes. Extensive biographical information appears in *Sotero Figueroa, editor de Patria: Apuntes para una biografía* (1985), by Josefina Toledo.

## José María Heredia

Heredia's work is available in Spanish, French, and English. The most complete edition in Spanish is *Obra poética* (1993, rev. 2003), edited by Angel Augier. An English edition of his poems is *Torrente prodigioso: A Cuban Poet at Niagara Falls* (1998), translated by Keith Ellis, with an essay by Eliseo Diego. An early study of Heredia's poetics is *The Odes of Bello, Olmedo and Heredia* (1920), with an introduction by Elijah Clarence Hills.

## Eugenio María de Hostos

Hostos's works have not been collected in English. His essay "At the Tomb of Segundo Ruiz Belvis," translated by Harry Morales, appears in *The Oxford Book of Latin American Essays* (1987), edited by Ilan Stavans. The Spanish-language *Obras completas* (1939) was reprinted in 1988. Julio César López edited a selection, *Obra literaria selecta* (1988). Manuel Maldonado-Denis edited two influential volumes: the novel *La peregrinación de Bayoán* (1863, repr. 1970) and the essay collection *Moral social/Sociología* (1888, repr. 1982 with the original and other sociological essays). *Ideario de Eugenio María de Hostos* (2003), by Elida Jiménez Victorio, is a study of Hostos's ideas. His contributions to the separatist movement are discussed in *Peregrinos de la libertad* (1992), by Félix Ojeda Reyes.

## Francisco Gonzalo "Pachín" Marín

A valuable compendium of "Pachín" Marín's oeuvre in Spanish is *Pachín Marín: Poeta en libertad* (2001), edited by Ramón Luis Acevedo. Most of his work is unavailable in English. The essay "New York from Within: One Aspect of Its Bohemian Life" (1892) was first published in New York's separatist newspaper *La Gaceta del Pueblo* and translated by Lizabeth Paravisini-Gebert for *The Latino Reader* (1997), edited by Harold Augenbraum and Margarite Fernández-Olmos. His contributions to the separatist movement are discussed in *Peregrinos de la libertad* (1992), by Félix Ojeda Reyes.

## José Martí

Martí's multivolume *Obras Completas* (1963) was published in Havana. In Spanish, his writing on the United States is also featured in *Estados Unidos* (1944), edited by Dardo Cúneo; *En los Estados Unidos* (1968), edited by Andrés Sorel; *Lecturas norteamericanas de José Martí: Emerson y el socialismo contemporáneo (1880–1887)* (1995), edited by José Ballón Aguirre; and *En los Estados Unidos: Periodismo de 1881 a 1892* (2003), edited by Roberto Fernández Retamar and Pedro Pablo Rodríguez.

In English, there are *The America of José Martí: Selected Writings* (1953), translated by Federico de Onís; *Martí on the U.S.A.* (1966), edited by Luis A. Baralt, foreword by J. Cary David; *Our America: Writings on Latin America and the Struggle for Cuban Independence* (1977), translated by Elinor Randall, Juan de Onís, and Roslyn Held Foner, edited by Philip S. Foner; *On Education: Articles on Educational Theory and Pedagogy, and Writings for Children from The Age of Gold* (1979), translated by Elinor Randall, edited by Philip S. Foner; the bilingual edition of *Thoughts on Liberty, Government, Art, and Morality/Pensamientos sobre la libertad, la política, el arte, y la moral* (1980), edited by Carlos Ripoll; *José Martí: Major Poems* (1982), also a bilingual edition, with English translations by Elinor Randall, edited by Philip S. Foner; *Versos sencillos/Simple verses* (1997), translated by Manuel A. Tellechea; *A José Martí Reader: Writings on the Americas* (1999), edited by Deborah Shnookal and Mirta Muniz; *Versos sencillos* (2000, rev. 2005), translated by Anne Fountain, foreword by Pete Seeger; *José Martí: Selected Writings* (2002), edited and translated by Esther Allen; *The Complete Poems of José Martí/Obra poética completa* (2003), translated by Jack Agüeros; and *Ismaelillo* (2007), translated by Tyler Fisher, foreword by Virgil Suárez.

A selection in English of Martí's pieces on the United States appears in *Inside the Monster: Writings on the United States and American Imperialism* (1975), translated by Elinor Randall, with additional translations by Luis A. Baralt, Juan de Onís, and Roslyn Held Foner, edited by Philip S. Foner; and *Political Parties and Elections in the United States* (1988), translated by Elinor Randall, edited by Philip S. Foner.

Important academic studies on Martí in English are *José Martí: Cuban Patriot* (1962), by Richard Burler Gray, and *The Cuban Republic and José Martí: Reception and Use of a National Symbol* (2006), edited by Mauricio A. Font and Alfonso W. Quiroz. A Spanish-language reference resource is *La gran enciclopedia martiana* (1978), edited by Ramón Cernuda.

## Luis Muñoz Rivera

Muñoz Rivera's complete poetry and writings in Spanish appear in his *Obras completas* (1960–68), edited by Lidio Cruz Monclova. No English translations of his work have been published in book form.

## Antonio María Osio y Higuera

Osio's historical account has appeared in English as *History of Alta California: A Memoir of Mexican California* (1996), translated by Rose Marie Beebe and Robert M. Senkewicz. Beebe's introduction to the volume is a valuable resource about Osio's career and writings.

## Miguel Antonio Otero

Otero is the author of *My Life on the Frontier, 1864–1882* (1935); its sequel, *My Life on the Frontier, 1882–1897* (1939); and its conclusion, *My Nine Years as Governor of the Territory of New Mexico, 1897–1906* (1940). The trilogy was reissued in a single volume in 1974. A 1998 reissue of *The Real Billy the Kid* (1936) was edited by John-Michael Rivera. A valuable essay on Otero appears in *A Luis Leal Reader* (2007), edited by Ilan Stavans.

## Jesse Pérez

Because Pérez's manuscript has never been published, very little has been written about it. In his book *My History, Not Yours: The Formation of Mexican American Autobiography* (1993), Genaro M. Padilla sets this and other works into the overall context of Mexican American memoir.

## Eulalia Pérez

Pérez's autobiography is featured in *The Memoirs of Mexican California: Carlos N. Hijar, Eulalia Pérez, and Agustín Escobar*, as recorded in 1877 by Thomas Savage or under his supervision (1988), translated by Vivian C. Fisher and others.

## Lola Rodríguez de Tió

Rodríguez de Tió's works in Spanish appeared as *Obras Completas* (1968). Some uncollected writings appeared in the New York separatist newspaper *Patria*. Most of her writings are unavailable in English. An essay on her life and works, by Edna Acosta-Belén, appears in *Latina Legacies: Identity, Biography, and Community* (2005), edited by Vicki L. Ruiz and Virginia Sánchez Korrol. Her contributions to the separatist cause are discussed in *Peregrinos de la libertad* (1992), by Félix Ojeda Reyes.

## María Amparo Ruiz de Burton

Ruiz de Burton's writings are undergoing a revival. Her novels *Who Would Have Thought It?* (1872) and *The Squatter and the Don* (1885) have been reprinted in editions (1995 and 1992, respectively) edited by Rosaura Sánchez and Beatrice Pita. Another version of *The Squatter and the Don* (2004) has an introduction by Ana Castillo. *Conflicts of Interest: The Letters of María Amparo Ruiz de Burton* (2001) was edited by Rosaura Sánchez and Beatrice Pita. A critical study on her work, *María Amparo Ruiz de Burton: Critical and Pedagogical Perspectives* (2004), was edited by Amelia María de la Luz Montes and Anne Elizabeth Goldman.

## Manuel M. Salazar

Salazar's work remains buried in nineteenth-century New Mexican newspapers. Efforts at recovery were done by Doris Meyer in *Speaking for Themselves: Neomexicano Cultural Identity and the Spanish-Language Press, 1880–1920* (1996) and by A. Gabriel Meléndez in *So All Is Not Lost: The Poetics of Print in Nuevomexicano Communities, 1834–1958* (1997).

## Jorge Ulica

Ulica's *Obras completas* (1982), in Spanish, was edited by Juan Rodríguez.

## Félix Varela

Varela's *Letters to Elpidio*, edited by Felipe J. Estévez, was published in 1989. A critical edition of his anonymously published novel *Jicoténcatl*, edited by Luis Leal and Rodolfo J. Cortina, was published in 1995 in Spanish. *Xicoténcatl: An Anonymous Historical Novel about the Events Leading Up to the Conquest of the Aztec Empire* (1999) is an English translation by Guillermo I. Castillo-Feliú. A valuable essay on Varela appears in *A Luis Leal Reader* (2007), edited by Ilan Stavans.

## ACCULTURATION: 1899–1945

The Bracero Program and immigration continue to define Latino lives in the United States. Valuable resources on these subjects are *Occupied America: The Chicano's Struggle toward Liberation* (1972; rev. 1981, 1988), by Rodolfo F. Acuña; *The Bracero Experience: Elitelore versus Folklore* (1979), by María Herrera-Sobek, introduction by James W. Wilkie; *Crossing Over: A Mexican Family on the Migrant Trail* (2001) and *The New Americans: Seven Families Journey to Another Country* (2004), both by Rubén Martínez, the latter with photographs by Joseph Rodríguez; and *There's No José Here: Following the Hidden Lives of Mexican Immigrants* (2007), by Gabriel Thompson. For information on Puerto Rican contract labor and migration to the United States, see *Labor Migration under Capitalism: The Puerto Rican Experience* (1979), by the Centro de Estudios Puertorriqueños; *The Puerto Rican Diaspora* (2005), edited by Carmen Teresa Whalen and Víctor Vázquez-Hernández; and *Puerto Ricans in the United States: A Contemporary Portrait* (2006), by Edna Acosta-Belén and Carlos E. Santiago.

## Pedro Albizu Campos

Albizu Campos's writings in Spanish are featured in the four-volume *Obras Escogidas* (1923–36), edited by J. Benjamín Torres. Valuable Spanish-language sources for his life and work are *Pedro Albizu Campos y el nacionalismo puertorriqueño* (1990), by Luis Angel Ferrao, and *La palabra como delito: Los discursos que condenaron a Pedro Albizu Campos* (1993), by Ivonne Acosta. Most of Albizu Campos's writings are unavailable in English.

## Felipe Alfau

Alfau's book of children's stories is *Old Tales from Spain* (1929). His novels are *Locos: A Comedy of Gestures* (1936, repr. 1988) and *Chromos* (1990). His poetry is collected in *Sentimental Songs/La poesía cursi* (1992), edited by Ilan Stavans. An interview with him appears in *Conversations with Ilan Stavans* (2005). A special issue of the *Review of Contemporary Fiction*, Georges Perec/Felipe Alfau: 13.1 (Spring 1993), includes essays by Carmen Martín Gaite, Charles Simmons, Chandler Brossard, Gregory Rabassa, and Paul West. A personal reminiscence with useful research material is "Felipe Alfau," by Ilan Stavans, in *Art and Anger: Essays on Politics and the Imagination* (2001). Alfau's archives, with approximately a dozen interviews, are in the Ilan Stavans Collection at Frost Library, Amherst College.

## Vicente J. Bernal

Bernal's *Las primicias* (1916), partly in English and partly in Spanish, was published in the *Telegraph-Herald* in Dubuque, Iowa, edited by Robert McLean and Bernal's brother, Luis Bernal. A useful resource on Bernal is "Two Texts for a New Canon: Vicente Bernal's *Las Primicias* and Felipe Maximiliano Chacón's *Poesía y prosa*," by Erlinda Gonzales-Berry, in *Recovering the U.S. Hispanic Literary Project* (1993), vol. I.

## Fabiola Cabeza de Baca Gilbert

Cabeza de Baca Gilbert's memoir appeared posthumously as *We Fed Them Cactus* (1954), with drawings by Dorothy L. Peters. It was reprinted in 1994 with an introduction by Tey Diana Rebolledo.

## Fray Angélico Chávez

Chávez is the author of *Clothed with the Sun* (1939); *Seraphic Days: Franciscan Thoughts and Affections on the Principal Feats of Our Lord and Our Lady and All the Saints of the Three Orders of the Seraph of Assisi* (1940); *New Mexico Triptych: Being Three Panels and Three Accounts: 1. The Angel's New Wings; 2. The Penitente Thief; and 3. Hunchback Madonna* (1940); *Eleven Lady-Lyrics and Other Poems* (1945); *Our Lady of the Conquest* (1948); *The Single Rose: The Rose Única and Commentary of Fray Manuel de Santa Clara* (1948); *Origins of New Mexico Families in the Spanish Colonial Period: In Two Parts: The Seventeenth (1598–1693) and the Eighteenth (1693–1821) Centuries* (1954); *La Conquistadora: The Autobiography of an Ancient Statue* (1954); *Archives of the Archdiocese of Santa Fe, 1678–1900* (1957); *From an Altar Screen, El Retablo: Tales from New Mexico* (1957); *The Virgin of Port Lligat* (1959); *The Lady from Toledo* (1960); *Coronado's Friars* (1968); *Selected Poems with an Apologia* (1969); *The Song of Francis* (1973); *My Penitente Land: Reflections on Spanish New Mexico* (1974); *But Time and Chance: The Story of Padre Martínez de Taos, 1793–1867* (1981); *Très Macho—He Said: Padre Gallegos of Albuquerque, New Mexico's First Congressman* (1985); *The Short Stories of Fray Angélico Chávez* (1987), edited by Genaro M. Padilla; *Chávez: A Distinctive American Clan of New Mexico* (1989); *Cantares: Canticles and Poems of Youth, 1925–1932* (2000), edited by Nasario García, foreword by E. A. Morales; *Wake for a Fat Vicar: Father Juan Felipe Ortiz, Archbishop Lamy, and the New Mexican Catholic Church in the Middle of the Nineteenth Century* (2004), coauthored with Thomas E. Chávez. Chávez also translated *Missions of New Mexico, 1776, A Description by Fray Francisco Atanasio Domínguez. With Other Contemporary Documents* (1956), translated and annotated with Eleanor B. Adams; *The Oroz Codex: Or, Relation of the Description of the Holy Gospel Province in New Spain and the Lives of the Founders and Other Note-worthy Men of Said Province. Composed by Fray Pedro Oroz: 1584–1586* (1972); and *The Domínguez-Escalante Journal: Their Expedition through Colorado, Utah, Arizona, and New Mexico in 1776* (1976), translated by Fray Angélico Chávez and edited by Ted J. Warner. A valuable study of Chávez's oeuvre is *Fray Angélico Chávez: Poet, Priest, and Artist* (2000), edited by Ellen McCracken.

## Jesús Colón

Colón's sketches and vignettes are included in *A Puerto Rican in New York and Other Sketches* (1961, repr. 1982) and *The Way It Was and Other Writings by Jesús Colón* (1993), the latter edited with an introductory essay by Edna Acosta-Belén and Virginia Sánchez Korrol. In Spanish, Colón's journalistic writings are included in the volume *Lo que el pueblo me dice . . . : Crónicas de la colonia puertorriqueña en Nueva York* (2001), edited by Edwin Karli Padilla Aponte. Colón's work is also featured in the anthology *Growing Up Latino: Memoirs and Stories* (1993), edited by Harold Augenbraum and Ilan Stavans, and *The Latino Reader: From 1542 to the Present* (1997), edited by Harold Augenbraum and Margarite Fernández-Olmos.

## José Dávila Semprit

Dávila Semprit published the poetry collections *Brazos bronce* (1933) and *Poemario de la madre* (1958). The poems he published in Spanish-language newspapers in New York City are unavailable in English.

## Eugenio Florit

Florit's publications include the poetry collections *Poema mío* (1947), *Conversación a mi padre* (1948), *Asonante final y otros poemas* (1950), *Hábito de esperanza* (1965), *Versos pequeños* (1977), *A pesar de todo* (1987), *Hasta luego* (1992), and *Lo que queda* (1995), as well as critical essays, textbooks, and anthologies such as *Antología penúltima* (1970). Florit's multivolume *Obras completas* (1982–2000) was published by the Society of Spanish and Spanish-American Studies, at the University of Nebraska. In English, Florit edited *Invitation to Spanish Poetry* (1964, rev. 1991). No book-length English translation of his poetry has been published. Scholarly studies include *Tierra, mar y cielo en la poesía de Eugenio Florit* (1976), by María Castellanos Collins; *Eugenio Florit y su poesía* (1977), by Mario Parajón; and *The Quest for Harmony: The Dialectics of Communication in the Poetry of Eugenio Florit* (1979), by Mirella Servodidio.

### Ernesto Galarza

Galarza is most famous for his memoir, *Barrio Boy* (1971). His books for children are *La historia verdadera de una botella de leche* (1972) and *Poems, pe-que, pe-que, pe-que-ñitos/Very Very Short Nature Poems* (1972). His other publications are *The Roman Catholic Church as a Factor in the Political and Social History of Mexico* (1928); *Labor Trends and Social Welfare in Latin America* (1939–42); *Strangers in Our Fields* (1958); *Merchants of Labor: The Mexican Bracero Story. An Account of the Managed Migration of Mexican Farm Workers to California, 1492–1960* (1964), preface by Ernest Gruening; *Mexican Americans in the Southwest* (1969), with Herman Gallegos and Julián Zamora, photographs by George Ballis; and *Spiders in the House, Workers in the Field* (1970). Interviews with Galarza appear in *Action Research: In Defense of the Barrio* (1974), edited by Mario Barrera and Geralda Vialpando.

### Jovita González de Mireles

González's works, which became available posthumously, are *Caballero: A Historical Novel* (1996), with Eve Raleigh, edited by José E. Limón and María Eugenia Cotera, foreword by Thomas H. Kreneck; *Dew on the Thorn* (1997), edited by José E. Limón; *The Woman Who Lost Her Soul and Other Stories* (2000), edited by Sergio Reyna; and *Life along the Border: A Landmark Tejana* (2000), edited by María Eugenia Cotera.

### Cleofas M. Jaramillo

Jaramillo's memoir is *Romance of a Little Village Girl* (1955; repr. 2000). She also authored *Shadows of the Past* (1941, repr. 1972), in which she juxtaposes folklore, customs, and personal experiences. Her recipes are featured in *The Genuine New Mexico Tasty Recipes: Potajes sabrosos* (1939, repr. 1981). Some of Jaramillo's culinary recommendations appear in *A Thousand Years over a Hot Stove: A History of American Women Told through Food, Recipes, and Remembrances* (2003), edited by Laura Schenone. She is the topic of contextual analysis in the anthology *Infinite Divisions: An Anthology of Chicana Literature* (1993), edited by Eliana S. Rivero and Tey Diana Rebolledo.

### Luis Leal

Leal published critical studies such as *México: Civilizaciones y culturas* (1955), *Mariano*

Azuela* (1967), *Juan Rulfo* (1983), and *Aztlán y México: Perfiles literarios e históricos* (1985). He edited the anthology *Cuentistas hispanoamericanos del siglo XX* (1972). *A Luis Leal Reader* (2007), edited by Ilan Stavans, is a comprehensive survey of Leal's essays on Mexican and Mexican American culture. *Luis Leal: Una vida y dos culturas* (1998), by Víctor Fuentes, and *Luis Leal: An Auto/biography* (2000), by Mario T. García, are book-long interviews with Leal. *Luis Leal: A 100 Year Journey/Luis Leal: Un camino de 100 años* (2007), is an English-language film about Leal's life and works, directed by Janette García.

### María Cristina Mena

Mena published stories in *Century Magazine*, *Cosmopolitan*, *Household*, and *Monthly Criterion*. Her children's books are *The Water-Carrier's Secrets* (1942), *The Two Eagles* (1943), *The Bullfighter's Son* (1944), *The Three Kings* (1946), and *Boy Heroes of Chapultepec: A Story of the Mexican War* (1953). Mena's adult fiction is collected in *The Collected Stories of María Cristina Mena* (1997), edited by Amy Doherty. A valuable essay on Mena appears in *A Luis Leal Reader* (2007), edited by Ilan Stavans.

### Luis Muñoz Marín

Muñoz Marín published several articles in English in U.S. newspapers and magazines, but no book by him has appeared in English. His literary writing is compiled in *La obra literaria de Luis Muñoz Marín: Poesía y prosa, 1915–1968* (1999), edited by Marcelino J. Canino Salgado. His autobiography, *Memorias: Autobiografía pública, 1898–1940* (1982), has a prologue by Jaime Benítez. His speeches are collected in *Discursos* (1999). His account of the making of the Partido Popular Democrático is *Historia del Partido Popular Democrático* (1984). Muñoz Marín's late diaries appear in *Diario, 1972–1974* (1999). His correpondence appears in *Luis Muñoz Marín: Servidor público y humanista: Cartas en su centenario, 1898–1998* (1998), edited by Carmelo Rosario Natal. A handful of Muñoz Marín's letters are featured in *Historia de mi vida política en la fundación del Partido Popular Democrático* (1986), by Ernesto Juan Fonfrías. Jonathan Cohen edited the work of Muñoz Marín's first wife as *A Pan-American Life: Selected Poetry and Prose by Muna Lee* (2004).

### Josefina Niggli

Niggli's works until the mid-1940s are collected (along with *Mexican Silhouettes*) in *The Plays of Josefina Niggli* (2007), edited by William Orchard and Yolanda Padilla. Her one-act plays

Tooth or Shave, Soldadera, The Red Velvet Goat, Azteca, and Sunday Costs Five Pesos, most of which had previously been published in book form, were collected in Niggli's Mexican Folk Plays (1938), edited by Frederick H. Koch. Niggli's fiction appears in two volumes: Mexican Village (1945, repr. 1994 with an introduction by María Herrera-Sobek), with drawings by Marion Fitzsimmons, translated into Spanish in 1949 by Justin Ruiz-de-Conde; and Step Down, Elder Brother (1947). These five plays and two novels are included in Mexican Village and Other Works (2008), introduction by Ilan Stavans. Niggli is also the author of the folktale A Miracle for Mexico (1964), with paintings by Alejandro Rangel Hidalgo, and the writing manual Pointers on Playwriting (1945). Her papers, which include correspondence, newspaper clippings, journals, manuscripts, and classroom notes, are located at Western Carolina University's Hunter Library. See also Josefina Niggli, Mexican American Writer: A Critical Biography (2007), by Elizabeth Coonrod Martínez.

### Adelina "Nina" Otero-Warren

Old Spain in Our Southwest (1936) is Otero-Warren's only publication. A valuable resource is Nina Otero-Warren of Santa Fe (1994), by Charlotte Whaley.

### Arthur A. Schomburg

Schomburg's writings are featured in Arthur A. Schomburg: A Puerto Rican's Quest for His Black Heritage (1989), edited by Flor Piñeiro de Rivera, foreword by Ricardo E. Alegría. Arthur Alfonso Schomburg: Black Bibliophile and Collector (1989) is a biography by Elinor Des Verney Sinnette.

### Bernardo Vega

The Spanish version of Vega's memoirs (1977) was edited by César Andreu Iglesias. The English version, Memoirs of Bernardo Vega: A Contribution to the History of the Puerto Rican Community in New York (1984), was translated by Juan Flores. Vega's extensive writings for several Spanish-language newspapers in New York remain uncollected.

### Daniel Venegas

The Spanish edition of Venegas's only known novel is Las aventuras de don Chipote: o, Cuando los pericos mamen (1984). The English version, The Adventures of Don Chipote: or, When Parrots Breast-Feed (2000), was translated by Ethriam Cash Brammer and has an introduction by Nicolás Kanellos.

### Leonor Villegas de Magnón

Villegas de Magnón's memoir was published as The Rebel (1994), edited by Clara Lomas.

### William Carlos Williams

Williams's writing connected to his Puerto Ricanness is included in the two-volume The Collected Poems of William Carlos Williams (1986–88), edited by A. Walton Litz and Christopher MacGowan, and The Collected Stories of William Carlos Williams (1996), introduction by Sherwin B. Nuland. Williams wrote the novels White Mule (1937), In the Money (1940), and The Build-Up (1952). His nonfiction, memoirs, and autobiographies include In the American Grain (1925); Autobiography (1951, repr. 1967 as The Autobiography of William Carlos Williams); Selected Essays (1954); I Wanted to Write a Poem: The Autobiography of the Works of a Poet (1958), edited by Edith Heal; and Yes, Mrs. Williams: A Personal Record of My Mother (1959).

Interviews appear in William Carlos Williams: "Speaking Straight Ahead" (1976), edited by Linda Welshimer Wagner. Of relevance to Williams's Latino identity are his Selected Letters (1957), edited by John C. Thirlwall. A useful resource is The William Carlos Williams Reader (1966), edited by M. L. Rosenthal.

The Spanish American Roots of William Carlos Williams (1994), by Julio Marzán, foreword by David Ignatow, places Williams's Puerto Rican and Latino selves in context. Also valuable is William Carlos Williams and the Language of Poetry (2002), edited by Burton Hatlen and Demetres Tryphonopoulos.

## UPHEAVAL: 1946–1979

Important studies on the Chicano Movement are Occupied America: The Chicano's Struggle toward Liberation (1972; rev. 1981, 1988), A Community under Siege: A Chronicle of Chicanos East of the Los Angeles River, 1945–1975 (1984), Anything but Mexican: Chicanos in Contemporary Los Angeles (1996), and Sometimes There Is No Other Side: Chicanos and the Myth of Equality (1998), all by Rodolfo F. Acuña; United We Win: The Rise and Fall of La Raza Unida Party (1989) and Chicanismo: The Forging of a Militant Ethos among Mexican Americans (1997), both by Ignacio M. García; Youth, Identity, Power: The Chicano Movement (1989, rev. 2007), by Carlos Muñoz Jr.; Chicano Politics: Reality and Promise, 1940–1990 (1990), by Juan Gómez-Quiñones; Mexican Americans: The Ambivalent Minority (1993), by Peter

Skerry; *Memories of Chicano History: The Life and Narrative of Bert Corona* (1994), edited by Mario T. García; and *La Raza Unida Party: A Chicano Challenge to the U.S. Two-Party Dictatorship* (2000), by Armando Navarro. An important resource by and about the martyred *Los Angeles Times* reporter Rubén Salazar is *Border Correspondent: Selected Writings, 1955–1970* (1995), edited by Mario T. García.

The essay collection *The Puerto Rican Movement: Voices from the Diaspora* (1998), edited by Andrés Torres and José E. Velázquez, covers the civil rights and other political activism of Puerto Ricans on the mainland during the 1960s and 1970s. Other important sources on Puerto Rican history and social and cultural movements in the United States are *From Colonia to Community: The History of Puerto Ricans in New York City, 1917–1948* (1983, 1994), by Virginia Sánchez Korrol; *Puerto Ricans Born in the USA* (1989), by Clara E. Rodríguez; *The Puerto Rican Diaspora* (2005), edited by Carmen Teresa Whalen and Víctor Vázquez-Hernández; and *Puerto Ricans in the United States: A Contemporary Portrait* (2006), by Edna Acosta-Belén and Carlos E. Santiago.

Important studies and resources on the Cuban Revolution are *Cubans in Exile: Disaffection and the Revolution* (1968), by Richard R. Fagen, Richard A. Brody, and Thomas J. O'Leary; *Response to Revolution: The United States and the Cuban Revolution, 1959–1961* (1985), by Richard E. Welch Jr.; *Miami* (1987), by Joan Didion; *The Exile: Cuba in the Heart of Miami* (1993), by David Rieff; *The Limits of Hegemony: The United States and the Cuban Revolution* (1996), by Thomas G. Paterson; *Castro and the Cuban Revolution* (1999), by Thomas M. Leonard; *The Cuban Revolution: Origins, Course, and Legacy* (1999), by Marifeli Pérez-Stable; and *The Cuban Revolution: Past, Present, and Future Perspectives* (2004), by Geraldine Lievesley. *Fidel Castro: My Life* (2008), an oral autobiography written with Ignacio Ramonet, was translated by Andrew Hurley.

### Oscar "Zeta" Acosta

Acosta published the autobiographical novels *The Autobiography of a Brown Buffalo* (1972) and *The Revolt of the Cockroach People* (1973). As a character, he is featured in two Hollywood films based on Hunter S. Thompson's nonfiction account *Fear and Loathing in Las Vegas: A Savage Journey to the Heart of the American Dream* (1971): *Where the Buffalo Roam* (1980), starring Peter Boyle and directed by Art Linson, and *Fear and Loathing in Las Vegas* (1998), starring Benicio del Toro and directed by Terry Gilliam. Alberto Baltazar Heredia Urista, also known as "Alurista," wrote his doctoral dissertation on Acosta in 1983, at the University of

California, San Diego. *Bandido: The Death and Resurrection of Oscar "Zeta" Acosta* (1995, rev. 2004) is an impressionistic biographical meditation on Acosta, by Ilan Stavans. Stavans also edited *Oscar "Zeta" Acosta: The Uncollected Works* (1996). Acosta's work is featured in the anthology *Growing Up Latino: Memoirs and Stories* (1993), edited by Harold Augenbraum and Ilan Stavans. Also relevant is *Chicano Controversy: Oscar Acosta and Richard Rodríguez* (2002), by Paul Guajardo.

### Jack Agüeros

Agüeros's fiction includes *Correspondence between the Stonehaulers* (1991) and *Dominoes and Other Stories from the Puerto Rican* (1993). His poetry volumes are *Sonnets from the Puerto Rican* (1996) and *Lord, Is This a Psalm?* (2002). His essay on growing up in the United States is part of the collection of autobiographical pieces *The Immigrant Experience: The Anguish of Becoming American* (1971), edited by Thomas C. Wheeler. He collected and translated Julia de Burgos's poetry in *Song of the Simple Truth: Obra poética completa/The Complete Poems of Julia de Burgos* (1997), and José Martí's in *Come, Come, My Boiling Blood: The Complete Poems of José Martí* (2007). An interview with Agüeros appears in *Puerto Rican Voices in English* (1997), by Carmen Dolores Hernández.

### Miguel Algarín

Algarín's poetry collections include *Mongo Affair* (1974); *On Call* (1980), with photographs by Geoffrey Biddle; *Body Bee Calling from the 21st Century* (1982); *The Time Is Now/Ya es tiempo* (1984); *Love Is Hard Work: Memorias de Loisaida/Poems* (1997); and the selection *Survival Supervivencia* (2009), edited by T. Marc Newell. With Tato Laviera, he coauthored the play *Olú Clemente, the Philosopher of Baseball* (1973). Algarín also published three anthologies: *Nuyorican Poetry: An Anthology of Puerto Rican Words and Feelings* (1975), edited with Miguel Piñero, photographs by Gil Méndez; *Aloud: Voices from the Nuyorican Poets Cafe* (1994), edited with Bob Holman; and *Action: The Nuyorican Poets Cafe Theater Festival* (1997), edited with Lois Griffith. An interview with Algarín appears in *Puerto Rican Voices in English* (1997), by Carmen Dolores Hernández.

### Rudolfo A. Anaya

Anaya's fiction includes *Bless Me, Ultima* (1972), *Heart of Aztlán* (1976), *The Silence of El Llano* (1982), *The Legend of La Llorona* (1984), *The Legend of Juan Chicaspatas* (1985), *Lord of the Dawn: The Legend of Quetzalcóatl* (1987),

*Tortuga* (1988), *Alburquerque* (1992), *Jalamanta: A Message from the Desert* (1996), *Serafina's Stories* (2004), *Curse of the Chupa Cabra* (2006), and *The Man Who Could Fly and Other Stories* (2006). Anaya is the author of the Sonny Baca mysteries, which include *Zia Summer* (1995), *Rio Grande Fall* (1996), *Shaman Winter* (1999), and *Jemez Spring* (2005). His nonfiction book is *A Chicano in China* (1986). His books for children are *The Farolitos of Christmas: A New Mexico Christmas Story* (1987); *Maya's Children: The Story of La Llorona* (1996), illustrated by María Baca; *Farolitos for Abuelo* (1998), illustrated by Edward González; *My Land Sings: Stories from the Río Grande* (1999), illustrated by Amy Córdova; *Elegy on the Death of César Chávez* (2000), illustrated by Gaspar Enríquez; *Roadrunner's Dance* (2000), illustrated by David Díaz; *The Santero's Miracle: A Bilingual Story* (2004), illustrated by Amy Córdova, Spanish translation by Enrique Lamadrid; and *The First Tortilla: A Bilingual Story* (2007), illustrated by Amy Córdova, Spanish translation by Enrique R. Lamadrid. A valuable compendium is *A Rudolfo Anaya Reader* (1995). Anaya's essays are collected in *Rudolfo Anaya: The Essays* (2009).

Anaya edited the anthologies *Cuentos Chicanos* (1980), with Antonio Márquez; *Voices: An Anthology of New Mexican Writers* (1987); *Aztlán: Essays on the Chicano Homeland* (1989), with Francisco A. Lomelí; *Tierra: Contemporary Short Fiction of New Mexico* (1989); *Flow of the River* (2nd ed., 1992); *Descansos: An Interrupted Journey* (1995), with Denise Chávez and Juan Estevan Arellano; and *Chicano/a Studies: Writing into the Future* (1999), edited with Robert Con Davis-Undiano. He adapted New Mexican folktales by Juan B. Rael in *Cuentos: Tales from the Hispanic Southwest* (1980), edited by José Griego y Maestas, illustrated by Jaime Valdez.

Useful scholarly resources are *The Magic of Words: Rudolfo A. Anaya and His Writings* (1982), edited by Paul Vassallo; *Rudolfo A. Anaya: Focus on Criticism* (1990), edited by César A. González-T.; and *Rudolfo A. Anaya: A Critical Companion* (1999), by Margarite Fernández-Olmos. Also important is the volume of interviews *Conversations with Rudolfo Anaya* (1998), edited by Bruce Dick and Silvio Sirias. A valuable essay on Anaya appears in *A Luis Leal Reader* (2007), edited by Ilan Stavans.

### José Antonio Burciaga

Burciaga's nonfiction includes the volumes *Restless Serpents* (1976), with Beatríz Zamora; *Weedee Peepo: A Collection of Essays* (1988); *Drink Cultura: Chicanismo* (1993); and *Spilling the Beans* (1995). Burciaga's poetry includes the book *Undocumented Love: A Personal Anthology of Poetry* (1992). A short story, "Emilio's Revenge: 1960," appeared in the *Massachusetts Review* (1996). The unfinished manuscript of the anthology *In Few Words: A Compendium of Latino Folk Wit and Wisdom* (1997) was completed, in bilingual format, by Carol and Thomas Christensen. *The Last Supper of Chicano Heroes: Selected Works of José Antonio Burciaga* (2008), edited by Mimi R. Gladstein and Daniel Chacón, is a selection of Burciaga's writings, including an excerpt of his unfinished novel, *The Temple Gang*.

### Nash Candelaria

Candelaria has published seven volumes of fiction: *Memories of the Alhambra* (1977), *Not by the Sword* (1982), *Inheritance of Strangers* (1985), *The Day the Cisco Kid Shot John Wayne* (1988), *Leonor Park* (1991), *Uncivil Rights and Other Stories* (1998), and *A Daughter's a Daughter* (2008). Candelaria's work is featured in the anthology *Growing Up Latino: Memoirs and Stories* (1993), edited by Harold Augenbraum and Ilan Stavans.

### Jaime Carrero

Carrero is the author of the novels *Raquelo tiene un mensaje* (1970), *Los nombres* (1972), and *El hombre que no sudaba* (1982). The 1973 volume *Flag Inside* includes the plays *Captain F4C*, *Pipo Subway no sabe reir*, and *El caballo de Ward*. The volume *Teatro* (1992) consists of his play *A cuchillo de palo* and Roberto Ramos-Perea's *Melodía salvaje*. Carrero is also the author of *Jet neorriqueño/Neo-Rican Jetliner* (1964), a collection of poems in Spanish, in English, and in Spanglish.

### Lourdes Casal

Casal published the poetry collection *Palabras juntan revolución* (1981). She edited a study on the Heberto Padilla affair, *El caso Padilla: Literatura y revolución en Cuba* (1971), and co-wrote a monograph, *The Position of Blacks in Brazilian and Cuban Society* (1979), with Anani Dzidzienyo. Casal also published *The Cuban Minority in the U.S.* (1980).

### César Chávez

Chávez's ordeals as leader of the farmworkers are recounted in several oral histories and biographical accounts, including *César Chávez: Autobiography of La Causa* (1975, repr. 2007), by Jacques E. Levy; *César Chávez: A Brief Biography with Documents* (2002), edited with an introduction by Richard W. Etulain; and *César Chávez: A Biography* (2005), by Roger Bruns. Journalistic reminiscences include *Sal Si*

*Puedes (Escape If You Can): César Chávez and the New American Revolution* (1969), originally written for *The New Yorker* by Peter Matthiessen, with a foreword by Ilan Stavans and a postscript by the author; and *Delano: The Story of the California Grape Strike* (1971, repr. 2008), originally written for the *Saturday Evening Post* by John Gregory Dunne, photographs by Ted Streshinsky, foreword by Ilan Stavans. Also valuable are *The Words of César Chávez* (2002), edited by Richard J. Jensen and John C. Hammerback, and *The Gospel of César Chávez: My Faith in Action* (2007), edited by Mario T. García.

Studies on Chávez's labor and rhetorical strategies are *César Chávez: The Rhetoric of Nonviolence* (1975), by Winthrop Yinger; *Chávez and the Farm Workers* (1975), by Ronald B. Taylor; *César Chávez: A Triumph of Spirit* (1995), by Richard Griswold del Castillo and Richard A. García; *The Fight in the Fields: César Chávez and the Farmworkers Movement* (1997), by Susan Ferriss and Ricardo Sandoval; and *The Moral Vision of César Chávez* (2003), by Frederick John Dalton. *César Chávez: An Organizer's Tale* (2008), edited by Ilan Stavans, is a selection of Chávez's speeches. *Cesar Chavez: A Photographic Essay* (2010), by Ilan Stavans, is a pictorial exploration. The César E. Chávez Foundation (*www.chavezfoundation.org*) promotes his legacy.

### Guillermo Cotto-Thorner

Cotto-Thorner's two novels are *Trópico en Manhattan* (1967), with a prologue by Mariano Picón-Salas, and *Gambeta* (1971). A chapter of *Trópico en Manhattan* was translated into English as well as edited with an introduction by Juan Flores in *Divided Arrival: Narratives of the Puerto Rican Migration, 1920–1950* (1987, rev. 1998). Uncollected are the articles Cotto-Thorner published in several Spanish-language periodicals in New York City.

### Julia de Burgos

An important anthology of de Burgos's poetry in Spanish is *Antología poética* (1968), edited by Emilio M. Colón. Other volumes include her *Julia de Burgos: Poesía* (1964), with engravings by José A. Torres Martinó; the collection *Julia de Burgos: Yo misma fui mi ruta* (1986), edited by María M. Solá; *Amor y soledad* (1994), edited by Manuel de la Puebla; and *Obra poética* (2005), edited by Consuelo Burgos and Juan Bautista Pagán. In English, some of de Burgos's poems appear in the selection *Roses in the Mirror* (1992), translated by Carmen D. Lucca. *Song of the Simple Truth: Obra completa poética/ The Complete Poems of Julia de Burgos* (1997) is a bilingual volume of her collected poetry,

translated by Jack Agüeros. Useful Spanish-language studies of de Burgos's work are *Dos poetisas de América: Clara Lair, Julia de Burgos* (1968), by Isabel Cuchi Coll, and *Julia en blanco y negro* (2000), by Juan Antonio Rodríguez Pagán. *The Life and Poetry of Julia de Burgos* (1979) is a film documentary of de Burgos's life and legacy, directed by José García Torres, in Spanish with English subtitles.

### Angela de Hoyos

De Hoyos's poetry volumes include *Arise, Chicano: and Other Poems* (1975); *Chicano Poems for the Barrio* (1976); *Selected Poems/ Selecciones* (1979), a bilingual publication translated by Mireya Robles; and *Woman, Woman* (1985). She coedited, with Bryce Milligan and Mary Guerrero Milligan, *Daughters of the Fifth Sun: A Collection of Latina Fiction and Poetry* (1995) and *Floricanto, Sí: A Collection of Latina Poetry* (1998). De Hoyos also translated *Time, the Artisan* (1975), by Mireya Robles.

### Abelardo "Lalo" Delgado

Delgado's books include *Chicano: 25 Pieces of a Chicano Mind* (1969); *Los cuatro* (1971), with Ricardo Sánchez, Raymundo "Tigre" Pérez, and Magdaleno Avila (aka Juan Valdez); *The Chicano Movement: Some Not Too Objective Observations* (1973); *It's Cold: 52 Cold-Thoughts Poems of Abelardo* (1974); *A Thermos Bottle Full of Self Pity: 25 Bottles by Abelardo* (1975); *Under the Skirt of Lady Justice: 43 Skirts* (1978); *El niño del migrante* (1979); *Mortal Sin Kit* (n.d); *Reflexiones* (n.d.); *Totoncaxihuitle, a Laxative: 25 Laxatives of Abelardo* (1981); and *Letters to Louise* (1982).

### Sandra María Esteves

Esteves has published the poetry collections *Yerba Buena: Dibujos y poemas* (1980), *Tropical Rains: A Bilingual Downpour* (1984), *Bluestown Mockingbird Mambo* (1990), *Undelivered Love Poems* (1997), *Finding Your Way: Poems for Young Folks* (1999), *Poems in Concert* (2006), and *Portal, A Journey in Poetry* (2007). An interview with her is included in *Puerto Rican Voices in English* (1997), by Carmen Dolores Hernández.

### Rosario Ferré

In Spanish, Ferré's fiction includes *Papeles de Pandora* (1976); *La caja de cristal* (1978); *La muñeca menor* (1980); *La mona que le pisaron la cola* (1981); *Fábulas de la garza desangrada* (1982); *Maldito amor* (1986); *El coloquio de las perras* (1990); *Las dos Venecias* (1992); *La batalla de las vírgenes* (1993); *La casa de la laguna*

(1997); and *Vecindarios excéntricos* (1998). Edgardo Rodríguez Juliá edited *Antología personal: Rosario Ferré* (2009). Ferré's essays include *El acomodador: Una lectura fantástica de Felisberto Hernández* (1986); *Sitio a Eros: Quince ensayos literarios* (1986); *El árbol y sus sombras* (1989); *Cortázar: El romántico en su observatorio* (1990); *A la sombra de tu nombre* (2001); and *Las puertas del placer* (2005). Her poetry includes *Sonatinas* (1989), *Fábulas de la garza desangrada* (1980), and *Fisuras* (2006), the latter with a prologue by Julio Ortega.

In English, Ferré's books are *Sweet Diamond Dust* (1988), her translation of *Maldito amor*; *Youngest Doll* (1991), a translation of *Papeles de Pandora*, with a foreword by Jean Franco; the novels *The House on the Lagoon* (1995), *Eccentric Neighborhoods* (1998), and *Flight of the Swan* (2001); and the bilingual volume *Language Duel/Duelo de lenguaje* (2002). Ferré's books for children include *Medio Pollito* (1977), *Los cuentos de Juan Bobo* (1981), and *La cucarachita Martina* (1990).

### José Angel Figueroa

Figueroa has published the poetry collections *East 110th Street* (1973); *Noo Jork* (1978), translated into Spanish in 1981; and *Hypocrisy Held Hostage* (2007).

### María Irene Fornés

Fornés's plays appear in her volumes *Promenade and Other Plays* (1971), *Plays* (1986, with a preface by Susan Sontag), *Lovers and Keepers* (1987), *Fefu and Her Friends* (1990), and *Letters from Cuba* (2000). She has translated the work of the Cuban writer Virgilio Piñera into English as *Cold Air* (1985).

### Rodolfo "Corky" Gonzales

Gonzales's poetry collection, *I Am Joaquín*, was first published in 1967 and was reprinted in 1972. *Yo soy Joaquín/I Am Joaquín* (1969) is a documentary directed by Luis Valdéz. An anthology of Gonzales's work, *Message to Aztlán: Selected Writings of Rodolfo "Corky" Gonzales* (2001), was edited by Antonio Esquibel and has a foreword by Rodolfo F. Acuña.

### José Luis González

In Spanish, González's volumes of fiction include *En la sombra* (1943); *Cinco cuentos de sangre* (1945); *El hombre en la calle* (1948); *Paisa* (1950); *En este lado* (1954); *En Nueva York y otras degracias* (1954, repr. 1981); *Mambrú se fue a la guerra y otros relatos* (1972); *Cuento de cuentos y once más* (1973); *Balada de otro tiempo* (1978), illustrated by Antonio

Martorell; *La llegada: Crónica con "ficción"* (1980); *La galería y otros cuentos* (1982); *La tercera llamada y otros relatos* (1983); *Las caricias del tigre* (1984); *La luna no era de queso: Memorias de infancia* (1988); and *Historia de vecinos y otras historias* (1993), with a prologue by Gustavo Luis Carrera. González's essay collections on the formation of Puerto Rican national culture are *El país de cuatro pisos y otros ensayos* (1980) and *Literatura y sociedad en Puerto Rico* (1976). A selection of González's writing is included in *Antología personal* (1990; 2009, edited by Edgardo Rodríguez Juliá). A valuable resource is *Conversación con José Luis González* (1976), by Arcadio Díaz Quiñones. In English, González's writing is available in *Ballad of Another Time* (1987), translated by Asa Zatz, and *Puerto Rico: The Four-Storeyed Country and Other Essays* (1990), a translation by Gerald Guinness of *El país de cuatro pisos y otros ensayos*.

### Pablo Guzmán

Guzmán has published numerous articles in *The Village Voice*. His account of his experience with the Young Lords appears in *Palante: Young Lords Party* (1971), photographs by Michael Abramson, and *The Puerto Rican Movement: Voices from the Diaspora* (1998), edited by Andrés Torres and José E. Velázquez.

### Rolando Hinojosa

Hinojosa's books of fiction are *Estampas del valle y otras obras* (1973; English version: *The Valley*, 1983), *Klail City y sus alrededores* (1976; English version: *Klail City*, 1987), *Korean Love Songs* (1978), *Mi querido Rafa* (1981, English version: *Dear Rafe*, 1985), *Rites and Witnesses* (1982), the bilingual *Claros varones de Belken/Fair Gentlemen of Belken County* (1986), *Becky and Her Friends* (1990; Spanish version: *Los amigos de Becky*, 1991), *Partners in Crime* (1985), *The Useless Servants* (1993), *Ask a Policeman* (1998), and *We Happy Few* (2006). Hinojosa rendered Tomás Rivera's novel, . . . *Y no se lo tragó la tierra*, into English as *This Migrant Earth* (1987).

Useful resources are *The Rolando Hinojosa Reader: Essays Historical and Critical* (1985), edited by José David Saldívar; the Spanish-language *Rolando Hinojosa y su "Cronicón" chicano: Una novela del lector* (1993), by Manuel M. Martín Rodríguez; *Rolando Hinojosa and the American Dream* (1997), by Joyce Glover Lee; and *Rolando Hinojosa: A Reader's Guide* (2001), by Klaus Zilles. His work in detective fiction is analyzed in *Brown Gumshoes: Detective Fiction and the Search for Chicana/o Identity* (2005), by Ralph E. Rodríguez.

A valuable essay on Hinojosa appears in *A Luis Leal Reader* (2007), edited by Ilan Stavans.

Interviews appear in *Conversations with Ilan Stavans* (2005) and *Conversations with Contemporary Chicana and Chicano Writers* (2007), the latter by Hector A. Torres. His fiction is featured in *Growing Up Latino: Memoirs and Stories* (1993), edited by Harold Augenbraum and Ilan Stavans, and *Wáchale!: Poetry and Prose about Growing Up Latino in America* (2001), edited by Ilan Stavans.

## Arturo Islas

Islas's books include *The Rain God: A Desert Tale* (1984); *Migrant Souls* (1990); and *La Mollie and the King of Tears* (1996), edited by Paul Skenazy. *Arturo Islas: The Uncollected Works* (2003), edited by Frederick Luis Aldama, is a selection of Islas's unpublished writing. Aldama also published *Critical Mappings of Arturo Islas's Fiction* (2005) and *Dancing with Ghosts: A Critical Biography of Arturo Islas* (2006). An interview with Islas is featured in *Conversations with Contemporary Chicana and Chicano Writers* (2007), by Hector A. Torres.

## José Kozer

Kozer has published over 20 volumes of poetry in Spanish, among them *Padres y otras profesiones* (1972), *Este judío de números y letras* (1975), *Y así tomaron posesión en las ciudades* (1978), *Jarrón de las abreviaturas* (1980), *La rueca de los semblantes* (1980), *Bajo este cien* (1983), *La garza sin sombras* (1985), *El carillón de los muertos* (1987), *Carece de causa* (1988), *De donde oscilan los seres en sus proporciones* (1990), *Dípticos* (1998), *Mezcla para dos tiempos* (1999), *Un caso llamado FK* (2002), *No buscan reflejarse* (2002), and *Y del esparto la invariabilidad* (2005). His English-language poetry includes *The Ark upon the Number* (1982) and *Stet: Selected Poems* (2006). His poetry is also included in the anthology *Burnt Sugar/Caña quemada: Contemporary Cuban Poetry in English and Spanish* (2006), edited by Oscar Hijuelos and Lori Carlson. His work has been analyzed in *La poesía de José Kozer* (1994), by Aida Heredia; *Life on the Hyphen: The Cuban American Way* (1994), by Gustavo Pérez Firmat; and *La voracidad grafómana—José Kozer: Crítica, entrevistas y documentos* (2002), edited by Jacobo Sefamí.

## Tato Laviera

Laviera has published the poetry collections *La Carreta Made a U-Turn* (1979), *Enclave* (1981), *AmeRícan* (1985), *Mainstream Ethics (Etica corriente)* (1988), and *Mixturado and Other Poems* (2008), which include poems in Spanish, in English, and in Spanglish. With Miguel Algarín, he coauthored the play *Olú Clemente, the Philosopher of Baseball* (1973).

Valuable studies on Laviera's aesthetics appear in *Divided Borders: Essays on Puerto Rican Identity* (1993), by Juan Flores, and *Janus Identities and Forked Tongues: Two Caribbean Writers in the United States* (2004), by Rosanna Rivero Marín. An interview with Laviera is included in *Puerto Rican Voices in English* (1997), by Carmen Dolores Hernández.

## René Marqués

Marqués's plays include *El hombre y sus sueños* (1948, repr. 1971); *Los soles truncos* (1959), translated into English by Willis Knapp Jones as *The House of the Setting Suns* (1964); *Un niño azul para esa sombra* (1956); *El sol y los McDonald* (1957, repr. 1971); *La muerte no entrará en palacio* (1959, repr. 1970); *Las casa sin reloj* (1962); *El apartamiento* (1965); *Mariana o el alba* (1965); *Sacrificio en el Monte Moriah* (1969); and *David y Jonatán; Tito y Berenice* (1970). Marqués's most celebrated play concerning Puerto Rican migration is *La carreta* (1952, repr. 1961), translated into English by Charles Pilditch as *The Oxcart* (1969). His English-language play, *Palm Sunday* (1949), remains unpublished. Marqués's novels include *La víspera del hombre* (1959, repr. 1970) and *La mirada* (1976), the latter translated into English by Charles Pilditch as *The Look* (1983). His stories are collected in *Otro día nuestro* (1955), *En una ciudad llamada San Juan* (1960), and *Inmersos en el silencio* (1976); these volumes remain untranslated. Marqués edited the anthology *Cuentos puertorriqueños de hoy* (1959, rev. 1971). His essays are gathered in *Ensayos (1953–1966)* (1966) and *El puertorriqueno dócil y otros ensayos: 1953–1971* (1977), the latter translated by Barbara Bockus Aponte as *The Docile Puerto Rican: Essays* (1976).

## Jesús "Papoleto" Meléndez

Meléndez has published the poetry collections *Casting Long Shadows* (1970), *Street Poetry and Other Poems* (1972), and *Concertos on Market Street: Poems* (1993). He also wrote the play *The Junkies Stole the Clock* (1974).

## Nicholasa Mohr

Mohr's books include *Nilda* (1973); *El Bronx Remembered: A Novella and Stories* (1975, repr. 1993); *In Nueva York* (1977, repr. 1988); *Felita* (1979, repr. 1999); *Rituals of Survival: A Woman's Portfolio* (1985); *Going Home* (1986, repr. 1999); *In My Own Words: Growing Up inside the Sanctuary of My Imagination* (1994); *The Song of El Coquí and Other Tales of Puerto Rico* (1995), with Antonio Martorell; *Old Letivia and the Mountain of Sorrows* (1996), illustrated by Rudy G. Gutiérrez; and *A*

*Matter of Pride and Other Stories* (1997). Her work is featured in *Growing Up Latino: Memoirs and Stories* (1993), edited by Harold Augenbraum and Ilan Stavans. An interview with Mohr appears in *Puerto Rican Voices in English* (1997), by Carmen Dolores Hernández.

### Iris Morales

Morales produced the documentary *¡Palante, Siempre Palante!: The Young Lords* (1996) based on the history of the group and their political activism. Accounts of her experiences as a Puerto Rican growing up in New York and as a member of the Young Lords appear in *Palante: Young Lords Party* (1971), photographs by Michael Abramson, and *The Puerto Rican Movement: Voices from the Diaspora* (1998), edited by Andrés Torres and José E. Velázquez. The oral history *Reminiscences of Iris Morales* (1984) is available at the New York State Archives.

### Rosario Morales and Aurora Levins Morales

Aurora Levins Morales is the author of *Medicine Stories: History, Culture, and the Politics of Integrity* (1998) and *Remedios: Stories of Earth and Iron from the History of Puertorriqueñas* (1998). With her mother, Rosario Morales, she coauthored the poetry collection *Getting Home Alive* (1986). Their poetry also appears in *This Bridge Called My Back: Writings by Radical Women of Color* (1981), edited by Cherríe Moraga and Gloria Anzaldúa.

### Heberto Padilla

Padilla's Spanish-language poetry collections are *El justo tiempo humano* (1962), *La hora* (1964), *Fuera del juego* (1968), *Provocaciones* (1973), and *El hombre junto al mar* (1981). English-language volumes are *Sent Off the Field: A Selection from the Poetry of Heberto Padilla* (1972), translated by J. M. Cohen; *Legacies: Selected Poems* (1982), translated by Alastair Reid and Andrew Hurley; and *A Fountain, a House of Stone* (1991), translated by Alastair Reid and Alexander Coleman. Padilla's novel, *En mi jardín pastan los héroes* (1981), was translated into English by Andrew Hurley as *Heroes Are Grazing in My Garden* (1984). His autobiography, *La mala memoria* (1989), was translated into English by Alexander Coleman as *Self-Portrait with the Other* (1990).

### Américo Paredes

Paredes's most celebrated scholarly work is the classic *With His Pistol in His Hand: A Border Ballad and Its Hero* (1958). In 1982, Robert M. Young directed a made-for-television movie based on it. Paredes's collection of articles, *Folklore and Culture on the Texas-Mexican Border* (1993), was edited by Richard Bauman. Paredes edited *Folktales of Mexico* (1970), with a foreword by Richard M. Dorson; *The Urban Experience and Folk Tradition* (1971), with Ellen J. Stekert; *Toward New Perspectives in Folklore* (1972), with Richard Bauman; *A Texas-Mexican Cancionero: Folksongs of the Lower Border* (1976); and *Uncle Remus con Chile* (1993). Paredes's fiction includes *George Washington Gómez: A Mexicotexan Novel* (1990); *The Hammon and the Beans and Other Stories* (1994), introduction by Ramón Saldívar; and *The Shadow* (1998). *Between Two Worlds* (1991) is a poetry collection. Paredes's work appears in the anthology *Growing Up Latino: Memoirs and Stories* (1993), edited by Harold Augenbraum and Ilan Stavans. A valuable essay on Paredes is in *A Luis Leal Reader* (2007), edited by Ilan Stavans. A comprehensive study of Paredes's life and work is *The Borderlands of Culture: Américo Paredes and the Transnational Imaginary* (2006), by Ramón Saldívar. "Américo Paredes: A Tribute," a bibliographical essay on Paredes's work, appears in *Mexican Studies/Estudios Mexicanos* (2000), by María Herrera-Sobek.

### Pedro Pietri

Pietri published the poetry collections *Puerto Rican Obituary* (1973), translated into Spanish by Alfredo Matilla Rivas in 1977, and *Traffic Violations* (1983); the play *The Masses Are Asses* (1984); and the essay *Perdido en el Museo de Historia Natural/Lost in the Museum of Natural History* (1981). Other plays appear in *Illusions of a Revolving Door* (1992), edited by Alfredo Matilla Rivas. An interview with Pietri is included in *Puerto Rican Voices in English* (1997), by Carmen Dolores Hernández.

### Miguel Piñero

Piñero's short plays are collected in *Outrageous One-Act Plays* (1986). *Plays* (1984) includes *The Sun Always Shines for the Cool, Midnight Moon at the Greasy Spoon,* and *Eulogy for a Small Time Thief.* Piñero's poetry is collected in *La Bodega Sold Dreams* (1980), with photographs by Dominique [sic]. He acted in several movies, including *Deal of the Century* (1983), *Alphabet City* (1984), and *Fort Apache the Bronx* (1981). He also acted in and wrote for television series, including *Kojak* and *Miami Vice.* With Miguel Algarín, Piñero coedited the anthology *Nuyorican Poetry: An Anthology of Puerto Rican Words and Feelings* (1975), photographs by Gil Méndez. A 1977 movie based on the play *Short Eyes* (1974) was directed by Robert M. Young. *Piñero* (2001), a film based on Piñero's life, was directed by León Ichazo.

**Mary Helen Ponce**

Ponce has published the story collections *Recuerdo: Short Stories of the Barrio* (1983) and *Taking Control* (1987); a novel, *The Wedding* (1989); and her autobiography, *Hoyt Street: Memories of a Chicana Childhood* (1993).

**Estela Portillo Trambley**

Portillo Trambley's fiction is included in *Trini* (1986, repr. 2005) and *Rain of Scorpions and Other Stories* (1975, repr. 1993). Her plays are collected in *The Day of the Swallows* (1970) and *Sor Juana and Other Plays* (1983).

**John Rechy**

Rechy's novels are *City of Night* (1963), *Numbers* (1967), *This Day's Death* (1970), *The Vampires* (1978), *Rushes* (1981), *The Fourth Angel* (1983), *Marilyn's Daughter* (1988), *Gómez* (1991), *The Miraculous Day of Amalia Gómez* (1991, repr. 2001), *Our Lady of Babylon* (1996), *The Coming of the Night* (1999), *Bodies and Souls* (2001), and *The Life and Adventures of Lyle Clemens* (2003). Rechy's nonfiction includes *The Sexual Outlaw: A Documentary* (1985) and *Beneath the Skin: The Collected Essays of John Rechy* (2004). His plays are *Tigers Wild (The Fourth Angel)*, *Rushes*, and *Momma as She Became—But Not as She Was. About My Life and the Kept Woman* (2008) is a memoir. Charles Casillo wrote a useful biography, *Outlaw: The Lives and Careers of John Rechy* (2002).

**Tomás Rivera**

The three English translations of Rivera's novel, *. . . y no se lo tragó la tierra*, are *. . . And the Earth Did Not Part* (1971), by Rivera, although the translation credit is in question; *This Migrant Earth* (1985), by Rolando Hinojosa; and the most established, *And the Earth Did Not Devour Him* (1987), by Evangelina Vigil-Piñón. In 1994, Severo Pérez directed a made-for-television movie based on the book. Rivera's short stories appear in *The Harvest* (1989). His poems appear in *Always and Other Poems* (1973) and *The Searchers* (1990), the latter edited by Julián Olivares. Olivares also edited *Tomás Rivera: The Complete Works* (1991). Valuable essays on Rivera appear in *The Identification and Analysis of Chicano Literature* (1979), edited by Francisco Jiménez, and *A Luis Leal Reader* (2007), edited by Ilan Stavans. An important resource is *International Studies in Honor of Tomás Rivera* (1986), edited by Julián Olivares.

**Luis Rafael Sánchez**

Among Sánchez's best-known writings are the novel *La guaracha del macho Camacho* (1976, repr. 2000), translated into English by Gregory Rabassa as *Macho Camacho's Beat* (1980); the play *Los ángeles se han fatigado* (1976); the collection of plays *Sol 13, interior* (1976); the play *La pasión según Antígona Pérez* (1978); the play *Quíntuples* (1985), translated into English by Diana Vélez in 1989; the collection of narratives *La guagua aérea* (1994); the essay collections *No llores por nosotros, Puerto Rico* (1998) and *Devórame otra vez: Artículos de primera necesidad* (2004); the novel *La importancia de llamarse Daniel Santos* (2000); and the novel *Indiscreciones de un perro gringo* (2007). Sánchez's story "La guagua aérea" was translated into English by Diana Vélez and Elpidio Laguna. In 1995, Luis Molina directed a movie based on it.

**Ricardo Sánchez**

Sánchez's poetry is included in *Canto y grito mi liberación (y lloro mis desmadrazgos: Pensamientos, gritos, angustias, orgullos, penumbras poéticas, ensayos, historietas, hechizos almales del son de mi existencia* (1971); *Hechizospells: Poetry/Stories/Vignettes/Articles/Notes on the Human Condition of Chicanos* (1976); *Amsterdam: Cantos y poemas pistos* (1982); *Eagle-Visioned/Feathered Adobes: Manito Sojourns and Pachuco Ramblings* (1990); and *Amerikan Journeys/Jornadas americanas* (1994). Compilations of his work are *Selected Poems* (1985), *The Loves of Ricardo* (1997), and *The Ricardo Sánchez Reader* (2000), edited by Arnoldo Carlos Vento. Sánchez is the subject of *West of the American Dream: An Encounter with Texas* (2001), by Paul Christensen. An analysis of his poetry appears in *Chicano Timespace: The Poetry and Politics of Ricardo Sánchez*, by Miguel R. López (2001). Sánchez's papers are archived at the University of Texas at Austin and Stanford University.

**Pedro Juan Soto**

In Spanish, Soto's books include the novels *Usmail* (1959, repr. 1970), *Ardiente suelo, fría estación* (1961, repr. 1978), *El francotirador* (1969), *Temporada de duendes* (1970), and *Un oscuro pueblo sonriente* (1982). His collections of stories are *Spiks* (1956, repr. 1970) and *Un decir: Cuentos* (1976). Soto also edited the bilingual volume *Puerto Rico: La nueva vida/The New Life* (1966), with Nina Kaiden and Andrew Vladimir. An anthology of Soto's writing, *Palabras al vuelo* (1990), was edited by Emilio Jorge Rodríguez. Available in English are the novel *Hot Land, Cold Season* (1973), translated by Helen R. Lane; *Usmail* (2007), translated by Charlie Connelly and Myrna Pagán; and *Spiks: Stories* (1973), translated by Victoria Ortiz.

## Mario Suárez

All of Suárez's stories are collected in *Chicano Sketches: Short Stories* (2004), edited by Francisco A. Lomelí, Cecilia Cota-Robles Suárez, and Juan José Casillas-Núñez.

## Carmen Tafolla

Tafolla's publications include the poetry collections *Get Your Tortillas Together* (1976), *Curandera* (1983), *Sonnets to Human Beings and Other Selected Works* (1995), and *Sonnets and Salsa* (2004); the story collection *The Holy Tortilla and a Poet of Beans* (2008); and the mixed-genre collection *To Split a Human: Mitos, machos, y la mujer chicana* (1985). Her bilingual books for children are *Patchwork Colcha* (1987), *The Dog Who Wanted to Be a Tiger* (1996), *Baby Coyote and the Old Woman* (2000), *My House Is Your House* (2000), *Somebody Stole My Smile!* (2005), *What Can You Do with a Rebozo* (2008), *That's Not Fair!: Emma Tenayuca's Struggle for Justice* (2008), *What Can You Do with a Paleta?* (2009), and *Fiesta Babies* (2010). With Laura Tafolla, Tafolla coedited the autobiography of her great-grandfather Santiago Tafolla, *A Life Crossing Borders: Memoir of a Mexican-American Confederate* (2009).

## Piri Thomas

Thomas has published the autobiographical memoirs *Down These Mean Streets* (1967), *Savior, Savior, Hold My Hand* (1972), and *Seven Long Times* (1974) and the short-fiction collection *Stories from El Barrio* (1978). On the compact discs *Sounds of the Street, Barrio Blues,* and *Creations without Hesitations,* he reads some of his poems with musical accompaniment. Interviews with Thomas appear in *Puerto Rican Voices in English* (1997), by Carmen Dolores Hernández, and *Conversations with Ilan Stavans* (2005). *Every Child Is Born a Poet: The Life and Work of Piri Thomas* (1993) is a made-for-television documentary. In 1998, Thomas's wife, Suzanne Dod Thomas, translated *Down These Mean Streets* into Spanish.

## Sabine R. Ulibarrí

Ulibarrí's volumes of fiction include *Tierra Amarilla: Stories of New Mexico/Tierra Amarilla: Cuentos de Nuevo México* (1964, repr. 1993); *My Grandma Smoked Cigars and Other Stories of Tierra Amarilla/Mi abuela fumaba puros y otros cuentos de Tierra Amarilla* (1977);

*First Encounters/First Encounters* (1982); *Governor Glu Glu and Other Stories/El gobernador Glu Glu y otros cuentos* (1988); *El Cóndor, and Other Stories* (1989); *Corre el río* (1992); *Sueños/Dreams* (1994); and *Mayhem Was Our Business* (1997). His two volumes of poetry, *Al cielo se sube a pie* (1961) and *Amor y Ecuador* (1966), have not been translated into English. He also wrote *Kissing Cousins: 1,000 Words Common to English and Spanish* (1991). Dick Gerdes edited *The Best of Sabine R. Ulibarrí: Selected Stories* (1993). A valuable resource is *Sabine R. Ulibarrí: Critical Essays* (1995), edited by María I. Duke dos Santos and Patricia de la Fuente.

## Luis Valdez

Valdez's plays are collected in three volumes: *Early Works* (*Actos, Bernabé,* and *Pensamiento serpentino,* 1990); *Zoot Suit and Other Plays* (*Zoot Suit, Bandido!,* and *I Don't Have to Show You No Stinking Badges!,* 1992); and *Mummified and Other Plays* (*Mummified Deer, Mundo Mata,* and *The Shrunken Head of Pancho Villa,* 2005). Several of his films, including *Zoot Suit* and *La Bamba,* are available on DVD. With Stan Steiner, he edited *Aztlán: An Anthology of Mexican American Literature* (1972).

## Richard Vázquez

Vázquez published the novels *Chicano* (1970, repr. 2005 with an introduction by Rubén Martínez), *The Giant Killer* (1978), and *Another Land* (1982).

## Evangelina Vigil-Piñón

Vigil-Piñón has published the poetry collections *Nade y nade* (1978), *Thirty an' Seen a Lot* (1982), and *The Computer Is Down* (1987). She edited *Woman of Her Word: Hispanic Women Write* (1983) and translated Tomás Rivera's novel, *. . . y no se lo tragó la tierra,* into English as *. . . And the Earth Did Not Devour Him* (1987).

## José Antonio Villarreal

Villarreal is the author of three novels: *Pocho* (1959), translated into Spanish by Roberto Cantú in 1994; *The Fifth Horseman* (1974); and *Clemente Chacón* (1984). He published three stories: "Some Turn to God" in *Pegasus* (1947), "A Pot of Pink Beans Boiling" in *San Francisco Review* (1959), and "The Conscripts" in *Puerto del Sol* (1973). Two sketches by Villarreal, "The Last Minstrel in California" and "The Laughter of My Father," appear in *Iguana Dreams: New Latino Fiction* (1992), edited by Virgil Suárez and Delia Poey. Villarreal's work is featured in the anthology *Growing Up*

*Latino: Memoirs and Stories* (1993), edited by Harold Augenbraum and Ilan Stavans.

### Victor Villaseñor

Villaseñor's volumes of fiction are *Macho!* (1973, 1991) and *Walking Stars: Stories of Magic and Power* (1998). His volume of nonfiction is *Jury: The People vs. Juan Corona* (1977). His memoirs are *Rain of Gold* (1991), *Wild Steps of Heaven* (1996), *Thirteen Senses: A Memoir* (2001), and *Burro Genius* (2004). Among his children's books are *The Frog and His Friends Save Humanity* and *Little Crow to the Rescue* (both 2005).

### José Yglesias

Yglesias's novels are *A Wake in Ybor City* (1963), *The Truth about Them* (1971), *Home Again* (1987), and *Tristan and the Hispanics* (1989). His short-story collection is *The Guns in the Closet* (1996). His works of nonfiction are *The Goodbye Land* (1967), *In the Fist of the Revolution: Life in a Cuban Country Town* (1968), *Down There* (1970), and *The Franco Years* (1977). Uncollected are many articles, stories, and reviews. *José Yglesias: Latino Literature's Founding Father* (2002) is a documentary film directed by Kenya Dworkin y Méndez and Jane Duncan.

## INTO THE MAINSTREAM: 1980–PRESENT

About the role of language in the Latino literary tradition, Spanglish in particular, see the scholarly studies *Estudios sobre el español de Nuevo Méjico* (1930), by Aurelio M. Espinosa, edited by Amado Alonso and Angel Rosenblat; *Spanish and Portuguese Languages in the United States* (1980), edited by Carlos E. Cortés; *A Dictionary of New Mexico and Southern Colorado Spanish* (2003), by Rubén Cobos; *Bilingual Games: Some Literary Investigations* (2003), edited by Doris Sommer; *Spanglish: The Making of a New American Language* (2003), by Ilan Stavans; *Tongue Ties: Logo-Eroticism in Anglo-Hispanic Literature* (2003), by Gustavo Pérez Firmat; *Bilingual Aesthetics: A New Sentimental Education* (2004), by Doris Sommer; *How I Learned English* (2007), edited by Tom Miller; and *Enciclopedia del español en los Estados Unidos* (2009), edited by Humberto López Morales.

### Daniel Alarcón

Alarcón has published the story collection *War by Candlelight* (2005) and the novel *Lost City Radio* (2007).

### Kathleen Alcalá

Alcalá has published the story collection *Mrs. Vargas and the Dead Naturalist* (1992); the novels *Spirits of the Ordinary: A Tale of Casas Grandes* (1997), *The Flower in the Skull* (1999), and *Treasures in Heaven* (2000); and the essay collection *The Desert Remembers My Name: On Family and Writing* (2007).

### Isabel Allende

Allende's volumes of fiction are *The House of the Spirits* (1985), *Eva Luna* (1987), *Of Love and Shadows* (1987), *The Stories of Eva Luna* (1991), *The Infinite Plan* (1993), *Daughter of Fortune* (1999), *Portrait in Sepia* (2001), *Zorro* (2005), and *Inés of My Soul* (2006). Allende has also published a memoir about her daughter, *Paula* (1994); a culinary book, *Aphrodite: A Memoir of the Senses* (1998); and a travel book, *The Invented Country: A Nostalgic Journey through Chile* (2003). Her fantasy novels for young adults are *City of the Beasts* (2002), *The Kingdom of the Golden Dragon* (2003), and *Forest of the Pygmies* (2005). In 1993, Bille August wrote and directed a Hollywood adaptation of *The House of the Spirits*.

Valuable resources, some in Spanish and some in English, are *Los libros tienen sus propios espíritus: Estudios sobre Isabel Allende* (1986), edited by Marcelo Coddou; *Para leer a Isabel Allende: Introducción a* La casa de los espíritus (1988), by Marcelo Coddou; *Narrative Magic in the Fiction of Isabel Allende* (1989), by Patricia Hart; *Critical Approaches to Isabel Allende's Novels* (1991), edited by Sonia Riquelme Rojas and Edna Aguirre Rehbein; *Isabel Allende: Vida y espíritu* (1998), by Celia Correas Zapata; *Allende, Buitrago, Luiselli: Aproximaciones teóricas al concepto del "Bildungsroman" femenino* (2000), by Leasa Y. Lutes; *Isabel Allende: Hija de la fortuna: Rediagramación fronteriza del saber histórico* (2001), by Marcelo Coddou; *Isabel Allende* (2002), by Linda Gould Levine; *Isabel Allende: La casa de los espíritus* (2002), edited by Lloyd Davies; *Isabel Allende Today: An Anthology of Essays* (2002), edited by Rosemary G. Feal and Yvette E. Millar; *Isabel Allende: A Critical Companion* (2003), edited by Karen Castellucci Cox; and *Isabel Allende: Eva Luna & Cuentos de Eva Luna* (2003), edited by Stephen M. Hart.

John Rodden's *Conversations with Isabel Allende* (1999, rev. 2004) includes samples of Allende's feelings about her work. An interview with Allende about her beginnings as a writer appears in *Conversations with Ilan Stavans* (2005).

## René Alomá

Aloma has published his play A Little Something to Ease the Pain (1981), also included in the anthology Cuban American Theater (1991), edited by Rodolfo J. Cortina.

## Alberto Baltazar Heredia Urista aka Alurista

Alurista's books of poetry are Floricanto en Aztlán (1971), art by Judith Hernández; Nationchild plumaroja, 1969–1972 (1972); Cantares arrullos (1975); Timespace Huracán: Poems, 1972–1975 (1976); Spik in Glyph? (1981); Return: Poems Collected and New (1982); Z Eros (1995); Et tú . . . Raza? (1996); and Chorizo Tonguefire (1999), a compilation of his previous collections. Alurista is also the author of the novel as our barrio turns: who the yoke b on? (2000). He edited or coedited Herberto Espinoza's short-story collection Viendo morir a Teresa y otros relatos (1983), translated from Spanish by D. J. Espinoza, and the anthologies Festival de flor y canto: An Anthology of Chicano Literature (1976) and Southwest Tales: A Contemporary Collection (1986), the latter with Xelina Rojas-Urista. Alurista also edited the literary journal Maize. El plan espiritual de Aztlán (The Spiritual Plan of Aztlán), cowritten by Alurista, appears in bilingual form in the first issue of the journal Aztlán. The Alurista papers (1968–78) are archived in the Benson Library, at the University of Texas at Austin.

## Julia Alvarez

Alvarez's novels are How the García Girls Lost Their Accents (1991); In the Time of the Butterflies (1995), which was adapted into a made-for-television movie (2001) directed by Mariano Barroso; ¡Yo! (1997); In the Name of Salomé (2000), translated into Spanish in 2002 by Dolores Prida; and Saving the World (2006). Her poetry collections include Homecoming (1994), The Other Side/El otro lado (1995), Seven Trees (1998), and The Woman I Kept to Myself (2004). She has also published the essay collection Something to Declare (1998) and the ethnographic volume Quinceañera (2007). Her books for children are The Secret Footprint (2000); A Cafecito Story (2001), afterword by Bill Eichner, woodcuts by Belkis Ramírez; Before We Were Free (2002); Finding Miracles (2004); The Gift of Gracias: The Legend of Altagracia (2005); and The Best Gift of All: The Legend of La Vieja Belén (2008). Alvarez's books for young readers are How Tía Lola Came to Stay (2001), Return to Sender (2009), and How Tía Lola Learned to Teach (2010). An interview with Alvarez appears in Conversations with Ilan Stavans (2005). Useful resources are Julia Alvarez: A Critical Companion (2001), by Silvio Sirias, and Julia Alvarez: Writing a New Place on the Map (2005), by Kelli Lyon Johnson.

## Gloria Anzaldúa

Anzaldúa wrote Borderlands/La Frontera: The New Mestiza (1987; rev. 1999, 2007). She edited volumes such as This Bridge Called My Back: Writings by Radical Women of Color (1981), with Cherríe Moraga; Making Face, Making Soul/Haciendo Caras: Creative and Critical Perspectives by Feminists of Color (1990); This Bridge We Call Home: Radical Visions for Transformation (2002), with AnaLouise Keating; and The Gloria Anzaldúa Reader (2009), with AnaLouise Keating. A volume of conversations with Anzaldúa, Interviews/Entrevistas (2000), was edited by AnaLouise Keating. An interview with Anzaldúa is featured in Conversations with Contemporary Chicana and Chicano Writers (2007), by Hector A. Torres. She also wrote three books for children: Prietita Has a Friend (1991), Friends from the Other Side/Amigos del Otro Lado (1993), and Prietita y La Llorona (1996). Her published and unpublished manuscripts, among other archival resources, form part of the Benson Latin American Collection, at the University of Texas at Austin.

## Reinaldo Arenas

In Spanish, Arenas's novels and novellas are Celestino antes del alba (1967, repr. 1982 as Cantando en el pozo), El mundo alucinante: Una novela de aventuras (1969), La vieja Rosa (1980), El palacio de las blanquísimas mofetas (1980), Otra vez el mar (1982), Arturo, la estrella más brillante (1984), La loma del ángel (1987), El portero (1989), El asalto (1991), El color del verano (1991), and Viaje a la Habana: Novela en tres viajes (1991). Con los ojos cerrados (1972), Termina el desfile (1981), and Adiós Mamá: De la Habana a Nueva York (1996) are short-story collections. Arenas's poetry volumes include El central (1981), Leprosorio (1990), Voluntad de vivir manifestándose (1989), and Infierno (2001), the latter with a prologue by Juan Abreu. His memoir is Antes que anochezca (1992). Persecución: Cinco piezas de teatro experimental (1986) is a collection of plays, and Necesidad de libertad: Testimonios de un intelectual disidente (1986) is a collection of political writings.

In English, Arenas's books are Hallucinations: Being an Account of the Life and Adventures of Fray Servando Teresa de Mier (1971), translated by Gordon Botherston (retranslated in 1987 by Andrew Hurley as The Ill-Fated Peregrinations of Fray Servando); Farewell to the Sea (1986), translated by Andrew Hurley; Graveyard of Angels (1986), translated by Alfred

MacAdam; *The Assault* (1994), translated by Andrew Hurley; *El Central: A Cuban Sugar Mill* (1984), translated by Anthony Kerrigan; *Singing from the Well* (1987), translated by Andrew Hurley; *Old Rosa: A Novel in Two Stories* (1989), translated by Ann Tashi Slater and Andrew Hurley; *The Palace of White Skunks* (1990), translated by Andrew Hurley; *The Doorman* (1991), translated by Dolores M. Koch; *The Color of Summer: or, The New Garden of Earthly Delights* (2000), translated by Andrew Hurley; and *Mona and Other Tales* (2001), translated by Dolores M. Koch. Arenas's memoir was translated as *Before Night Falls* (1993) by Dolores M. Koch. Julian Schnabel directed the film adaptation in 2000. Arenas's poetry is included in the anthology *Burnt Sugar/Caña quemada: Contemporary Cuban Poetry in English and Spanish* (2006), edited by Oscar Hijuelos and Lori Carlson.

Valuable scholarly resources in Spanish are *Reinaldo Arenas: Narrativa de transgresión* (1986), by Perla Rozencvaig; *La textualidad de Reinaldo Arenas* (1987), by Eduardo Béjar; *El desamparado humor de Reinaldo Arenas* (1991), by Roberto Valero; *La escritura de la memoria* (1992), by Otmar Ette; *Reinaldo Arenas: Recuerdo y presencia* (2004), by Reinaldo Sánchez; *Reinaldo Arenas: The Pentagonía* (1994), by Francisco Soto; *La alucinación y los recursos literarios en las novelas de Reinaldo Arenas* (1995), by Félix Lugo Nazario; and *Desviación y verdad: La re-escritura en Arenas y la Avellaneda* (1999), by Carolina Alzate Cadavid. English-language resources are *Reinaldo Arenas* (1998), a brief general study of Arenas's life and work by Francisco Soto; *Cuba's Political and Sexual Outlaw: Reinaldo Arenas* (2003), by Rafael Ocasio; and *A Gay Cuban Activist in Exile: Reinaldo Arenas* (2007), also by Rafael Ocasio.

## Octavio Armand

Armand's poetry collections are *Horizonte no es siempre lejanía* (1970); *Cosas pasan* (1975); *Cómo escribir con erizo* (1982); *With Dusk* (1984), translated by Carol Maier; *Origami* (1987); *El pez volador* (1997); and *Son de ausencia* (1999). His essay collections are *Superficies* (1980); *Hacer la tradición* (1984); *Refractions* (1994), translated by Carol Maier; and *El aliento del dragón* (2005). He edited the volume *Toward an Image of Latin American Poetry* (1982).

## Jimmy Santiago Baca

Baca's poetry collections are *Immigrants in Our Own Land* (1979, rev. 1990); *What's Happening* (1982); *Poems from My Yard* (1986); *Martín & Meditations on the South Valley*

(1987); *Black Mesa Poems* (1989); *Set This Book on Fire* (1999); *Healing Earthquakes: A Love Story in Poems* (2001); *C-train (Dream Boy's Story) & Thirteen Mexicans* (2002); *Winter Poems along the Rio Grande* (2004); *Spring Poems along the Rio Grande* (2007); and *Selected Poems* (2009), introduction by Ilan Stavans. He has also published the nonfiction volume *Working in the Dark: Reflections of a Poet of the Barrio* (1992), the memoir *A Place to Stand: The Making of a Poet* (2001), the story collection *The Importance of a Piece of Paper* (2004), and the novel *A Glass of Water* (2009).

## Ruth Behar

Behar has published a number of anthropological studies, starting with *Santa María del Monte: The Presence of the Past in a Spanish Village* (1986). Her book *Translated Woman: Crossing the Border with Esperanza's Story* (1993) offers an insightful use of oral history. She is also the author of *The Vulnerable Observer: Anthropology That Breaks Your Heart* (1996) and *An Island Called Home: Returning to a Jewish Cuba* (2007), the latter with photographs by Humberto Mayol. In Spanish, Behar published the bilingual poetry collections *Poemas que vuelven a Cuba/Poems Returned to Cuba* (1995) and *Todo lo que guardé/Everything I Kept* (2001). She edited *Bridges to Cuba/Puentes a Cuba* (1995); *Women Writing Culture* (1995), with Deborah A. Gordon; and *The Portable Island: Cubans at Home in the World* (2008), with Lucía M. Suárez. She also created the autobiographical made-for-television documentary *Adio Kerida: Goodbye My Dear Love* (2002). Her work is featured in anthologies such as *Little Havana Blues: A Cuban-American Literature Anthology* (1996), edited by Delia Poey and Virgil Suárez; *King David's Harp: Autobiographical Essays by Jewish American Writers* (1999), edited by Steven Sadow; and *Wáchale!: Poetry and Prose about Growing Up Latino in America* (2001), edited by Ilan Stavans. Useful resources on Behar's work are "Ruth Behar," in *Uncertain Travelers: Conversations with Jewish Women Immigrants to America* (1999), edited by Marjorie Agosín; an essay in *Current Biography* (May 2005); and "Writing, Teaching, and Filming Material Lives: A Conversation between Ruth Behar and Circe Sturm," in *Transformations: A Journal of Inclusive Scholarship and Pedagogy* (Fall 2007/Winter 2008).

## Richard Blanco

Blanco's poetry collections are *City of Hundred Fires* (1998) and *Directions to the Beach of the Dead* (2005).

### Giannina Braschi

Braschi has published the fiction-and-poetry volume *Empire of Dreams* (1994), translated by Tess D'Dwyer, with an introduction by Alicia Ostriker; and the novel *Yo-Yo Boing!* (1998). Her Spanglish manifesto, "Pelos en la lengua," was published in the anthology *Lengua Fresca* (2006), edited by Harold Augenbraum and Ilan Stavans.

### Rafael Campo

Campo's poetry collections are *The Other Man Was Me: A Voyage to the New World* (1994), *What the Body Told* (1996), *Diva* (1999), *Landscape with Human Figure* (2002), and *The Enemy* (2007). His memoir, *The Desire to Heal: A Doctor's Education in Empathy, Identity, and Poetry* (1998), was published in paperback as *The Poetry of Healing* (1999).

### Ana Castillo

Castillo's poetry collections are *The Invitation* (1979), with English translations by Carol Maier, illustrated by Marina Gutiérrez; *Women Are Not Roses* (1984); *My Father Was a Toltec and Selected Poems, 1973–1988* (1988); and *I Ask the Impossible* (2001). Her fiction volumes are the epistolary novel *The Mixquiahuala Letters* (1986, repr. 1992), the novel *So Far from God* (1993), the story collection *Loverboys* (1996), the novel *Peel My Love Like an Onion* (1999), and the novel *The Guardians* (2007). Her verse novels are *Sapogonia: An Anti-Romance in 3/8 Meter* (1990) and *Watercolor Women, Opaque Men: A Novel in Verse* (2005). *Psst . . . I Have Something to Tell You, Mi Amor* (2005) consists of two versions of her play, with a preface by Sister Dianna Ortiz. Her criticism includes *Keats, Poe, and the Shaping of Cortázar's Mythopoesis* (1981) and *Massacre of the Dreamers: Essays on Xicanisma* (1994). Castillo edited *The Sexuality of Latinas* (1993), with Norma Alarcón and Cherríe Moraga, and *Goddess of the Americas/La diosa de las Américas: Writings on the Virgin of Guadalupe* (1996). Her manuscripts and other materials are archived in the Chicano Studies Library at the University of California, Santa Barbara.

### Sandra M. Castillo

Castillo's poetry collections are *Red Letters* (1991) and *My Father Sings, To My Embarrassment* (2002).

### Adrián Castro

Castro's poetry collections are *Cantos to Blood and Honey* (1997) and *Wise Fish: Tales in 6/8 Time* (2005). His work appears in the anthology *Burnt Sugar/Caña quemada: Contemporary Cuban Poetry in English and Spanish* (2006), edited by Oscar Hijuelos and Lori Carlson.

### Lorna Dee Cervantes

Cervantes's poetry collections are *Emplumada* (1981), *From the Cables of Genocide: Poems of Love and Hunger* (1991), and *Drive: The First Quartet* (2006).

### Denise Chávez

Chávez has published the story collection *The Last of the Menu Girls* (1986), the children's book *The Woman Who Knew the Language of Animals* (1992), the novels *Face of an Angel* (1994) and *Loving Pedro Infante* (2001), and the memoir-cum-recipe book *A Taco Testimony: Meditations on Family, Food and Culture* (2006). Her numerous plays include *Novitiates* (1973), *The Flying Tortilla Man* (1975), *The Mask of November* (1975), *Elevators* (1977), *The Adobe Rabbit* (1980), *Nacimiento* (1980), *Santa Fe Charm* (1980), *An Evening of Theater* (1981), *El Santero de Córdova* (1981), *How Junior Got Throwed in the Joint* (1981), *Sí, Hay Posada* (1981), *The Green Madonna* (1982), *Francis!* (1983), *Hecho en México* (1983), *La Morenita* (1983), *Plaza* (1984), *Plague-Time* (1985), *Novena Narrative* (1987), *The Step* (1987), *Language of Vision* (1988), and *Women in the State of Grace* (1989). Valuable resources on Chávez's work include "Displaced Abjection and States of Grace: Denise Chávez's *The Last of the Menu Girls*," by Douglas Anderson, in *American Women Short Story Writers: A Collection of Critical Essays* (1995), edited by Julie Brown; and "Narrative and Traumatic Memory in Denise Chávez's *Face of an Angel*," by Maya Socolovsky, in *MELUS: The Journal of the Society for the Study of the Multi-Ethnic Literature of the United States* (Winter 2003).

### Susana Chávez-Silverman

Chávez-Silverman has published *Killer Crónicas: Bilingual Memories* (2004), with a foreword by Paul Allatson, and *Scenes from la Cuenca de Los Angeles and Other Natural Disasters* (2010). Her creative work also appears in the anthology *Lengua Fresca* (2006). She has edited the academic books *Tropicalizations: Transcultural Representations of Latinidad* (1997), with Frances R. Aparicio, and *Reading and Writing the Ambiente: Queer Sexualities in Latino, Latin American, and Spanish Culture* (2000), with Librada Hernández.

### Lucha Corpi

Corpi's poetry collections are *Palabras de mediodía/Noon Words* (1980) and *Variaciones sobre una tempestad/Variations on a Storm* (1990). Her novels are *Delia's Song* (1989), *Eulogy for a Brown Angel* (1992), *Cactus Blood* (1995), *Black Widow's Wardrobe* (1999), *Crimson Moon* (2004), and *Death at Solstice* (2009). Corpi edited *Máscaras* (1997), an anthology of Latina writing. She was featured in *Firefight: Three Latin American Poets, Elsie Alvarado de Ricord, Lucha Corpi, and Concha Michel* (1976), translated by Catherine Rodríguez-Nieto.

Corpi is featured in *Chicana Ways: Conversations with Ten Chicana Writers* (2002), by Karin Rosa Ikas, and *Spilling the Beans in Chicanolandia: Conversations with Writers and Artists* (2006), by Frederick Luis Aldama. Corpi's work in detective fiction is analyzed in *Multicultural Detective Fiction: Murder from the "Other" Side* (1999), edited by Adrienne Johnson Gosselin; *Brown Gumshoes: Detective Fiction and the Search for Chicana/o Identity* (2005), by Ralph E. Rodríguez; and *Race and Religion in the Postcolonial British Detective Story: Ten Essays* (2005), edited by Julie H. Kim.

### Nilo Cruz

Cruz's published plays are *A Bicycle Country* (1999), *Two Sisters and a Piano* (1999), *Hortensia and the Museum of Dreams* (2001), *Anna and the Tropics* (2002), and *Beauty of the Father* (2003). His translations of *Life Is a Dream*, by Pedro Calderón de la Barca, and *Doña Rosita the Spinster*, by Federico García Lorca, were published in 2008 and 2009, respectively.

### Silvia Curbelo

Curbelo's poetry collections are *The Geography of Leaving* (1990), *The Secret History of Water* (1997), and *Ambush* (2004).

### Junot Díaz

Díaz has published two books: *Drown* (1996), a collection of interrelated stories, translated into Spanish as *Negocios* (1997), and the novel *The Brief Wondrous Life of Oscar Wao* (2007). An interview with him appears in *Conversations with Ilan Stavans* (2005).

### Ariel Dorfman

In addition to those listed in the headnote, Dorfman's novels, some in Spanish and some in English, include *The Last Song of Manuel Sendero* (1987), *Máscara* (1988), *Widows* (1989), and *Blake's Therapy* (2001). His nonfiction includes *How to Read Donald Duck: Imperialist Ideology in the Disney Comic* (1975), with Armand Mattelart, translated by David Kunzle; *The Empire's Old Clothes: What the Lone Ranger, Babar, and Other Innocent*

*Heroes Do to Our Minds* (1983); *Exorcising Terror: The Incredible Unending Trial of General Augusto Pinochet* (2002); and *Other Septembers, Many Americas* (2004).

Dorfman's plays include *Death and the Maiden* (1991), made into a film by Roman Polanski in 1994; *Widows* (1991, with Tony Kushner), adapted from Dorfman's 1989 novel; *Reader* (1995); and *Purgatorio, The Other Side*, and *Picasso's Closet* (all 2006). His poems—some in Spanish, some in English, and some in both languages—have been collected into *In Case of Fire in a Foreign Land: New and Collected Poems from Two Languages* (2002). Some of his poems have been set to music for chorus and organ as *Cantos sagrados* (1992), by James MacMillan. Dorfman collaborated with the composer and lyricist Eric Woolfson on the musical *Dancing Shadows* (2007). His memoir *Heading South, Looking North* (1998) was adapted into a feature documentary film directed by Peter Raymont, *A Promise to the Dead: The Exile Journey of Ariel Dorfman* (2007).

Useful resources are *La obra de Ariel Dorfman: Ficción y crítica* (1992), by Salvador A. Oropesa, and *The Dialectics of Exile: Nation, Time, Language, and Space in Hispanic Literatures* (2004), by Sophia A. McClennen. An interview with Dorfman appears in *Conversations with Ilan Stavans* (2005).

### Carlos M. N. Eire

Eire has published several scholarly books on religion and faith in Europe, including *War against the Idols: the Reformation of Worship from Erasmus to Calvin* (1986) and *From Madrid to Purgatory: The Art and Craft of Dying in Sixteenth-Century Spain* (1995). In *A Very Brief History of Eternity* (2009), Eire traces the idea of eternity in Western culture. He has published the memoir *Waiting for Snow in Havana: Confessions of a Cuban Boy* (2003).

### Martín Espada

Espada's poetry collections are *The Immigrant Iceboy's Bolero* (1982), with photographs by Frank Espada; *Trumpets from the Islands of Their Eviction* (1987); *Rebellion Is the Circle of a Lover's Hands/Rebelión es el giro de manos del amante* (1990), Spanish translation by Camilo Pérez-Bustillo and the author; *City of Coughing and Dead Radiators* (1993); *Imagine the Angels of Bread* (1996); *A Mayan Astronomer in Hell's Kitchen* (2000); *Alabanza: New and Selected Poems, 1982–2002* (2003); and *The Republic of Poetry* (2006). His essay collections are *Zapata's Disciple* (1998) and *The Lover of a Subversive Is Also a Subversive* (2010). With Camilo Pérez-Bustillo, he translated and edited *The*

*Blood That Keeps Singing: Selected Poems of Clemente Soto Vélez* (1991). He also edited the anthologies *Poetry Like Bread: Poets of the Political Imagination* from Curbstone Press (1994) and *El Coro: A Chorus of Latino and Latina Poetry* (1997). Interviews with Espada appear in *Puerto Rican Voices in English* (1997), by Carmen Dolores Hernández, and *Conversations with Ilan Stavans* (2005).

### María Teresa "Mariposa" Fernández

Fernández has published the chapbook *Born Bronxeña: Poems* (2001). She is featured in the HBO documentary *Americanos: Latino Life in the U.S.* (2002).

### Roberto G. Fernández

Fernández's story collections include *Cuentos sin rumbo* (1975), *En la Ocho y la Doce* (2001), and *Entre dos aguas* (2006). His novels are *La vida es un special 1.5* (1981), *La montaña rusa* (1985), *Raining Backwards* (1988), and *Holy Radishes!* (1995). A valuable resource on Fernández is *Janus Identities and Forked Tongues: Two Caribbean Writers in the United States* (2004), by Rosanna Rivero Marín.

### Cristina García

García's novels are *Dreaming in Cuban* (1992), *The Agüero Sisters* (1997), *Monkey Hunting* (2003), and *A Handbook of Luck* (2007). Her poetry collection is *The Lesser Tragedy of Death* (2010). She edited the anthologies *Cubanísimo!: The Vintage Book of Contemporary Cuban Literature* (2003) and *Bordering Fires: The Vintage Book of Mexican and Chicano Literature* (2006).

### Alicia Gaspar de Alba

Gaspar de Alba's poetry is featured in *Three Times a Woman: Chicana Poetry* (1989), along with poems by Demetria Martínez and María Herrera Sobek. Her poetry collection is *La Llorona on the Longfellow Bridge: Poetry y otras movidas, 1985–2001* (2003). Her fiction volumes include *The Mystery of Survival and Other Stories* (1993); *Sor Juana's Second Dream* (1999); *Desert Blood: The Juárez Murders* (2005), based on her pamphlet *The Maquiladora Murders: or, Who Is Killing the Women of Juárez, Mexico?* (2003); and *Calligraphy of the Witch* (2007). Her academic works are *Chicano Art Inside/Outside the Master's House* (1998) and *Velvet Barrios: Popular Culture and Chicana/o Sexualities* (2003).

### Dagoberto Gilb

Gilb's story collections are *Winners on the Pass Line* (1985), *The Magic of Blood* (1993), and *Woodcuts of Women* (2001). His novels are *The Last Known Residence of Mickey Acuña* (1994) and *The Flowers* (2008). He has also published the essay collection *Gritos* (2003) and edited *Hecho en Tejas: An Anthology of Texas-Mexican Literature* (2006). His work appears in the anthologies *Muy Macho!: Latino Men Confront Their Manhood* (1996), edited by Ray González, and *Lengua Fresca* (2006), edited by Harold Augenbraum and Ilan Stavans. Gilb's papers are housed in the Southwestern Writers Collection at Texas State University.

### Francisco Goldman

Goldman's novels are *The Long Night of White Chickens* (1992), *The Ordinary Seaman* (1997), and *The Divine Husband* (2004). His nonfiction book, about the assassination of the Guatemalan bishop Juan Gerardi Conedera, is *The Art of Political Murder: Who Killed the Bishop?* (2007). An interview with Goldman appears in *Conversations with Ilan Stavans* (2005).

### Guillermo Gómez-Peña

Gómez-Peña is the author of *Mi Otro Yo* (1988); *Border Brujo* (1990); *Warrior for Gringostroika: Essays, Performance Texts, and Poetry* (1993); *Friendly Cannibals* (1996), art by Enrique Chagoya; *Temple of Confessions: Mexican Beasts and Living Santos* (1996); *The New World Border* (1996); *Codex Espangliensis: From Columbus to the Border Patrol* (1998), with Enrique Chagoya and Felicia Rice; *Dangerous Border Crossers: The Artist Talks Back* (2000); *El Mexterminator: Antropología de un performancero postmexicano* (2002); *Ethno-Techno: Writings on Performance, Activism, and Pedagogy* (2005), edited by Elaine Peña; and *Homo Fronterizus* (2008), with Gustavo Vázquez.

### Franklin Gutiérrez

Gutiérrez's poetry collections are *Cantos a mi pueblo sufrido* (1973), *Hojas de octubre* (1982), *Inriri* (1984), *Helen* (1986), and *Hábeas Corpus* (1994). His story collection is *Seis historias casi falsas* (1993). His essay collections are *Los areitos en la cultura taína* (1985), *Reflexiones sobre la literatura latinoamericana* (1986), *Aproximaciones a la narrativa de Juan Bosch* (1987), *Enriquillo: Radiografía de un héroe galvaniano* (1999), and *Palabras de ida y vuelta: Ensayos literarios* (2002). He edited the anthologies *Historias de Washington Heights y otros rincones del mundo* (1994), with Daisy Cocco de Filippis; *Antología histórica de la poesía dominicana del siglo XX: 1912–1995* (1995); *Literatura dominicana en los Estados Unidos: Presencia temprana, 1900–1950* (2001), with Daisy Cocco de Filippis; *Treinta y tres historiadores dominicanos: Bibliografías* (2002); and *Diccionario de la literatura dominicana* (2004).

## Víctor Hernández Cruz

Hernández Cruz's poetry collections include *Snaps* (1969), *Mainland* (1973), *Tropicalization* (1976), *By-Lingual Wholes* (1982), *Red Beans* (1991), *Panoramas* (1997), *Rhythm, Content and Flavor* (1998), *Maraca: New and Selected Poems, 1966–2000* (2001), and *The Mountain in the Sea* (2006). He has edited two anthologies: *Stuff: A Collection of Poems, Visions & Imaginative Happenings from Young Writers in Schools—Opened & Closed* (1970), with Herbert Kohl, illustrations by Sean Chappell and Phillip Crowder; and *Paper Dance: 55 Latino Poets* (1995), with Leroy V. Quintana and Virgil Suárez. An interview with Hernández Cruz, produced by the Lannan Foundation in 1998, is available on videocassette. Other interviews appear in *Puerto Rican Voices in English* (1997), by Carmen Dolores Hernández, and *A Poet's Truth: Conversations with Latino/Latina Poets* (2003), by Bruce A. Dick.

## Juan Felipe Herrera

Herrera's books for adults are *Rebozos of Love* (1974); *Exiles of Desire* (1985); *Facegames* (1987); *Akrílica* (1989); *Night Train to Tuxtla: New Stories and Poems* (1994); *The Roots of a Thousand Embraces: Dialogues* (1994); *Love after the Riots* (1996); *Mayan Drifter: Chicano Poet in the Lowlands of America* (1997); *Border-Crosser with a Lamborghini Dream* (1999); *Loteria Cards & Fortune Poems* (1999); *Thunderweavers* (2000); *Giraffe on Fire* (2001); *Notebooks of a Chile Verde Smuggler* (2002); *187 Reasons Mexicanos Can't Cross the Border: Undocuments 1970–2007* (2007); and *Half the World in Light: New and Selected Poems* (2008), introduction by Francisco Lomelí.

For young adults, Herrera has published *Crash Boom Love: A Novel in Verse* (1999), *Cinnamon Girl: Letters Found inside a Cereal Box* (2005), *Downtown Boy* (2005), and *Put a Poem Wherever You Go!* (2008). For children, he has published the bilingual volumes *Calling the Doves/Canto a Las Palomas* (1995), *The Upside Down Boy/El Niño de Cabeza* (2000), *Grandma & Me at the Flea/Los meros meros remateros* (2002), *Cilantro Girl/La superniña del cilantro* (2003), *Featherless/Desplumado* (2004), and *Coralito's Bay/La bahía de Coralito* (2004). A useful resource is Santiago Vaquera-Vásquez's essay "Juan Felipe Herrera," in *Latino and Latina Writers* (2004), edited by Alan West-Durán. Herrera's papers are archived at Stanford University.

## Oscar Hijuelos

Hijuelos is the author of the novels *Our House in the Last World* (1983), *The Mambo Kings Play Songs of Love* (1989), *The Fourteen Sisters of Emilio Montez O'Brien* (1993), *Mister Ives' Christmas* (1995), *Empress of the Splendid Season* (1999), and *A Simple Habana Melody (From When the World Was Good)* (2002). *Dark Dude* (2008) is his novel for young adults. With Lori Carlson, he edited the anthology *Burnt Sugar/Caña quemada: Contemporary Cuban Poetry in English and Spanish* (2006). His work is analyzed in *Life on the Hyphen: The Cuban American Way* (1994), by Gustavo Pérez Firmat. His fiction is included in *Growing Up Latino: Memoirs and Stories* (1993), edited by Harold Augenbraum and Ilan Stavans. An interview with Hijuelos appears in *Conversations with Ilan Stavans* (2005).

## Carolina Hospital

Hospital's poetry collection is *The Child of Exile: A Poetry Memoir* (2004). Under the pseudonym C. C. Medina and with her husband, Carlos Medina, she published the novel *Little Love* (2000). She edited the anthology *Cuban-American Writers: Los Atrevidos* (1988). Her poetry and fiction have appeared in many literary reviews and anthologies.

## Eduardo Machado

Machado's plays include *Once Removed* (1988), *The Burning Beach* (1988), *The Cook* (2004), and *Kissing Fidel* (2006). *The Floating Island Plays* (1991) includes *Broken Eggs* (1984), *The Modern Ladies of Guanabacoa* (1984), *Fabiola* (1985), and *In the Eye of the Hurricane* (1989). His memoir is *Tastes Like Cuba: An Exile's Hunger for Home* (2007).

## Jaime Manrique

Manrique's volumes of fiction include *El cadáver de papá y versiones poéticas* (1978), *Colombian Gold: A Novel of Power and Corruption* (1983), *Latin Moon in Manhatan* (1992), *Twilight at the Equator* (1997), and *Our Lives Are the Rivers* (2006). His poetry collections are *Los adoradores de la luna* (1976); *Scarecrow* (1990); the bilingual *My Night with Federico García Lorca/Mi noche con Federico García Lorca* (1997), translated by Edith Grossman and Eugene Richie; *Mi cuerpo y otros poemas* (1999); and *Tarzán / My Body / Christopher Columbus* (2001), translated by Margaret Sayers Peden. With Jesse Doris, he edited the anthology *Bésame Mucho: New Gay Latino Fiction* (1999). With Joan Larkin, he translated and edited *Sor Juana's Love Poems/Poemas de amor de Sor Juana* (1997). Manrique has also published the semiautobiographical study

*Eminent Maricones: Arenas, Lorca, Puig, and Me* (1999).

## Demetria Martínez

Martínez's poetry collections are *Breathing between the Lines* (1997) and *The Devil's Workshop* (2002). Her poetry is featured in *Three Times a Woman: Chicana Poetry* (1989), which also includes poems by Alicia Gaspar de Alba and María Herrera-Sobek, and *Wáchale!: Poetry and Prose about Growing Up Latino in America* (2001), edited by Ilan Stavans. She has also published the novel *Mother Tongue* (1994), the essay collection *Confessions of a Berlitz-Tape Chicana* (2004), and the children's book *Grandpa's Magic Tortilla* (2010). Interviews with Martínez are featured in *A Poet's Truth: Conversations with Latino/Latina Poets* (2003), by Dick Bruce, and *Conversations with Contemporary Chicana and Chicano Writers* (2007), by Hector A. Torres. Useful resources on Martínez's work are *New Latina Narrative: The Feminine Space of Postmodern Ethnicity* (1995), by Ellen McCracken; *Chicana (W)riters on Word and Film* (1995), by María Herrera-Sobek and Helena María Viramontes; and *Women Singing in the Snow: A Cultural Analysis of Chicana Literature* (1995), by Tey Diana Rebolledo.

## Dionisio D. Martínez

Martínez's poetry collections are *Dancing at the Chelsea* (1992), *History as a Second Language* (1993), *Bad Alchemy* (1995), and *Climbing Back* (2001). His poetry appears in numerous anthologies, such as *The Best American Poetry* (1992), edited by Charles Simic and David Lehman; *The Best American Poetry* (1994), edited by A. R. Ammons and David Lehman; *Walk on the Wild Side: Urban American Poetry since 1975* (1994), edited by Nicholas Christopher; *Little Havana Blues: A Cuban-American Literature Anthology* (1996), edited by Delia Poey and Virgil Suárez; *Wáchale!: Poetry and Prose about Growing Up Latino in America* (2001), edited by Ilan Stavans; *The Norton Anthology of Poetry* (5th ed., 2005), edited by Margaret Ferguson, Mary Jo Salter, and Jon Stallworthy; and *Burnt Sugar/Caña quemada: Contemporary Cuban Poetry in English and Spanish* (2006), edited by Oscar Hijuelos and Lori Carlson.

## Rubén Martínez

Martínez's collection of journalistic dispatches published in the *LA Weekly*, *The Other Side: Fault Lines, Guerrilla Saints, and the True Heart of Rock 'n' Roll* (1992), was retitled in paperback *The Other Side: Notes from the New L.A., Mexico City, and Beyond* (1993). His study of Mexican migrant workers is *Crossing Over: A Mexican Family on the Migrant Trail* (2001).

Martínez has also published *East Side Stories: Gang Life in East L.A.* (1998), with photographs by Joseph Rodríguez, interview with Luis J. Rodríguez; *The New Americans: Seven Families Journey to Another Country* (2004), photographs by Joseph Rodríguez; and *Flesh Life: Sex in Mexico City* (2006), photographs by Joseph Rodríguez. In 2005, Martínez wrote the introduction to a new edition of Richard Vázquez's novel *Chicano* (1970). An interview with Martínez appears in *Conversations with Ilan Stavans* (2005).

## Pablo Medina

Medina's poetry collections are *Pork Rind and Cuban Songs* (1975), *Arching into the Afterlife* (1991), *The Floating Island* (1999), and the bilingual *Points of Balance/Puntos de apoyo* (2005). His poetry is featured in the anthology *Burnt Sugar/Caña quemada: Contemporary Cuban Poetry in English and Spanish* (2006), edited by Oscar Hijuelos and Lori Carlson. Medina has also published the memoir *Exiled Memories: A Cuban Childhood* (1990) and the novels *The Marks of Birth* (1994), *The Return of Felix Nogara* (2000), and *The Cigar Roller* (2005). With Mark Statman, he translated Federico García Lorca's *Poet in New York* (2008), foreword by Edward Hirsch. Useful analyses of Medina's writing appear in *Cuban American Literature of Exile* (1998), by Isabel Alvarez Borland, and *Encounters in Exile* (2006), by Belén Rodríguez Meruelo.

## Ana Menéndez

Menéndez has published the story collection *In Cuba I Was a German Shepherd* (2001) and the novel *Loving Che* (2003).

## Pat Mora

Mora's poetry collections are *Chants* (1984), *Borders* (1986), *Communion* (1991), *Agua Santa/Holy Water* (1995), *Aunt Carmen's Book of Practical Saints* (1997), and *Adobe Odes* (2006). Her books for children, some of them bilingual volumes, are *A Birthday Basket for Tía* (1992); *Agua, Agua, Agua* (1994); *Pablo's Tree* (1994); *The Desert Is My Mother/El desierto es mi madre* (1994), art by Daniel Lechón; *The Gift of the Poinsetta/El regalo de la Flor de Nochebuena* (1995); *The Race of Toad and Deer* (1995); *Confetti: Poems for Children* (1996); *Uno, Dos, Tres: One, Two, Three* (1996); *Delicious Hullabaloo/Pachanga deliciosa* (1998); *The Big Sky* (1998); *The Rainbow Tulip* (1999); *La noche que se cayó la luna/The Night the Moon Fell* (2000); *My Own True Name: New and Selected Poems for Young Adults, 1984–1999* (2000); *Tomás and the Library Lady* (2000); and *Doña Flor: A Tall Tale about a Giant Woman with a Great Big Heart* (2005), illustrated by Raul Colón. Mora's nonfiction appears in *Nepantla: Essays from the Land in the Middle* (1993). Her memoir is *House of Houses* (1998). An interview with her appears in *Conversations with Contemporary Chicana and Chicano Writers* (2007), by Hector A. Torres.

## Cherríe Moraga

Moraga's volumes of plays are *Giving Up the Ghost: Teatro in Two Acts* (1986), *Heroes and Saints and Other Plays* (1994), and *Watsonville/ Circle in the Dirt: Watsonville: Some Place Not Here and Circle in the Dirt: El Pueblo de East Palo Alto* (2002). Her nonfiction is collected in *Loving in the War Years: Lo que nunca pasó por sus labios* (1983), *The Last Generation: Prose and Poetry* (1993), *Waiting in the Wings: A Portrait of Queer Motherhood* (1997), and *The Hungry Woman* (2001). Moraga edited the anthologies *This Bridge Called My Back: Writings by Radical Women of Color* (1981), with Gloria Anzaldúa; *Cuentos: Stories by Latinas* (1983), with Alma Gómez and María Romero-Carmona; and *The Sexuality of Latinas* (1993), with Norma Alarcón and Ana Castillo.

An important piece by Moraga, "Anatomy Lesson," appears in *Gender Violence: Interdisciplinary Perspectives* (2007), edited by Laura L. O'Toole, Jessica R. Schiffman, and Margie L. Kiter Edwards. A conversation with her is featured in *Spilling the Beans in Chicanolandia: Conversations with Writers and Artists* (2006), by Frederick Luis Aldama. Useful sources on Moraga are *Unveiling the body in Hispanic Women's Literature: From 19th Century Spain to 21st Century United States* (2006), edited by Renée Sum Scott and Arleen Chiclana y González, and *Remembering Maternal Bodies: Melancholy in Latina and Latin American Women's Writing* (2006), by Benigno Trigo.

## Carlos Morton

Morton's books of plays include *The Many Deaths of Danny Rosales and Other Plays* (1983), *Johnny Tenorio and Other Plays* (1992), *and Dreaming on a Sunday in the Alameda and Other Plays* (2004). Collected in *The Fickle Finger of Lady Death and Other Plays* (1996) are Morton's translations into English of works by four Latin American playwrights: *The Tree*, by Elena Garro; *Profane Games*, by Carlos Olmos; *Fickle Finger of Lady Death*, by Eduardo Rodríguez Solís; and *Murder with Malice*, by Víctor Hugo Rascón Banda. He has also published *Children of the Sun: Scenes and Monologues for Latino Youth* (2008).

## Elías Miguel Muñoz

Muñoz has published the novels *Los viajes de Orlando Cachumbambé* (1984), *Crazy Love* (1988), *The Greatest Performance* (1991), *Brand New Memory* (1998), and *Vida mía* (2006); the bilingual poetry collections *En estas tierras/In This Land* (1989) and *No fue posible el sol* (1989); and the critical studies *Desde esta orilla: Poesía cubana del exilio* (1988) and *El discurso utópico de la sexualidad en Manuel Puig* (1988). Muñoz's writing has appeared in many anthologies, including *Iguana Dreams: New Latino Fiction* (1992), edited by Virgil Suárez and Delia Poey; *Currents from the Dancing River: Contemporary Latino Fiction, Nonfiction, and Poetry* (1994), edited by Ray González; and *Muy Macho!: Latino Men Confront Their Manhood* (1996), edited by Ray González.

## Manuel Muñoz

Muñoz has published the story collections *Zigzagger* (2003) and *The Faith Healer of Olive Avenue* (2007).

## Michael Nava

Nava has published the novels *The Little Death* (1986), *Goldenboy* (1988), *How Town* (1989), *The Hidden Law* (1992), *The Death of Friends* (1996), *The Burning Plain* (1997), and *Rag and Bone* (2001). With Robert Dawidoff, he edited *Created Equal: Why Gay Rights Matter to America* (1994).

## Achy Obejas

Obejas's first book, *We Came All the Way from Cuba So You Could Dress Like This?* (1994), blends memoir and essay. Her novels are *Memory Mambo* (1996); *Days of Awe* (2001), published with an interview with her by Ilan Stavans; and *Ruins* (2009). Her poetry collection is *This Is What Happened in Our Other Life* (2007). Her poetry also appears in the anthology *Burnt Sugar/Caña quemada: Contemporary Cuban Poetry in English and Spanish* (2006), edited by Oscar Hijuelos and Lori Carlson. Obejas edited the volume *Havana Noir* (2007). She translated Junot Díaz's novel *The Brief and Wondrous Life of Oscar Wao* (2008) into Spanish as *La breve y maravillosa vida de Óscar Wao* (2008).

## Judith Ortiz Cofer

Ortiz Cofer's first book publication was the poetry volume *Triple Crown: Chicano, Puerto Rican, and Cuban-American Poetry* (1987), with work by Roberto Durán and Gustavo Pérez Firmat. Her subsequent books include the poetry collection *Terms of Survival* (1987), the novel *The Line of the Sun* (1989), the memoir *Silent Dancing: A Partial Remembrance of a Puerto Rican Childhood* (1991), *The Latin Deli: Poems and Prose* (1993), *Reaching for the Mainland and Selected New Poems* (1995), *The Year of*

*Our Revolution: New and Selected Stories and Poems* (1998), *Woman in Front of the Sun: On Becoming a Writer* (2000), *A Love Story Beginning in Spanish* (2005), and the novel *Call Me María* (2006). For young adults, Ortiz Cofer has published *An Island Like You: Stories of the Barrio* (1995) and the novel *The Meaning of Consuelo* (2004) and edited the anthology *Riding Low on the Streets of Gold: Latino Literature for Young Adults* (2003). An interview with her is included in *Puerto Rican Voices in English* (1997), by Carmen Dolores Hernández.

The University of Puerto Rico Press published *La línea del sol* (1997), a translation of *The Line of the Sun*. Fondo de Cultura Económica, in México, published *Una isla como tú* (1997), a translation of *An Island Like You*. Arte Público Press published *Bailando en silencio: Escenas de una niñez puertorriqueña* (1997), a translation of *Silent Dancing* and *El año de nuestra revolución* (2006), a translation of *The Year of Our Revolution*. The University of Georgia Press published *El Deli Latino* (2006), a translation of *The Latin Deli*. All the Spanish translations were done by Elena Olazagasti-Segovia.

### Ricardo Pau-Llosa

Pau-Llosa's poetry collections are *Veinticinco poemas* (1973), *Sorting Metaphors* (1983), *Bread of the Imagined* (1991), *Cuba* (1993), *Vereda tropical* (1999), *The Mastery Impulse* (2003), and *Parable Hunter* (2008). His poetry is included in the anthology *Burnt Sugar/Caña quemada: Contemporary Cuban Poetry in English and Spanish* (2006), edited by Oscar Hijuelos and Lori Carlson. Pau-Llosa edited the volume *Outside Cuba: Contemporary Cuban Visual Artists* (1989), with Ileana Fuentes-Pérez and Graciella Cruz-Taura.

### Willie Perdomo

Perdomo's poetry collections are *Postcards of El Barrio* (1992), a bilingual edition translated into Spanish by Mayra Santos Febres and Rafael Franco; *Where a Nickel Costs a Dime* (1996); and *Smoking Lovely* (2004). He has also published the children's book *Visiting Langston* (2002), illustrated by Bryan Collier. His poetry is included in *Wáchale!: Poetry and Prose about Growing Up Latino in America* (2001), edited by Ilan Stavans.

### Rolando Pérez

Pérez's academic works include *Severo Sarduy and the Religion of the Text* (1988) and *On An(archy) & Schizoanalysis* (1990). His other publications, which blend genres such as nonfiction and poetry, include *The Odyssey* (1990), *The Lining of Our Souls: Excursions into Se-*

*lected Paintings of Edward Hopper* (1995), and *The Electric Comedy* (2000). He has also published the play collections *Plays and Playthings* (1990), *The House That Ate Their Brains* (1992), and *H Is for Box* (1993).

### Dolores Prida

Prida's plays are collected in the volume *Beautiful Señoritas and Other Plays* (1991), edited by Judith Weiss. She has translated into Spanish several novels, most notably Julia Alvarez's *In Search of Salomé* (2002). Her poetry is included in the anthology *Burnt Sugar/Caña quemada: Contemporary Cuban Poetry in English and Spanish* (2006), edited by Oscar Hijuelos and Lori Carlson.

### Alberto Alvaro Ríos

Ríos's poetry collections are *Sleeping on Fists* (1981) and *Whispering to Fool the Wind* (1982). His story collections are *The Iguana Killer: Twelve Stories of the Heart* (1984, repr. 1998), etchings by Antonio Pazos; *Five Indiscretions* (1985); *The Lime Orchard Woman* (1988); *Teodoro Luna's Two Kisses* (1990); *Pig Cookies and Other Stories* (1995); *The Curtain Trees* (1999), *The Smallest Muscle in the Human Body* (2002), and *The Theater of Night* (2006). His autobiography is *Capirotada: A Nogales Memoir* (1999).

### Edward Rivera

Rivera has published *Family Installments: Memories of Growing Up Hispanic* (1983). His autobiographical essay "Stable Manners: or, How the Publication of *Family Installments* was Stalled for Three Years and $3,000" appeared in the *Massachusetts Review* in 1996.

### José Rivera

Rivera's books of plays are *The House of Ramón Iglesia* (1983), *The Promise* (1989), *Giants Have Us in Their Books: Six Naive Plays* (1997), *Marisol and Other Plays* (1997), and *References to Salvador Dalí Make Me Hot and Other Plays* (2005). He also wrote the Academy Award–nominated screenplay for the film *The Motorcycle Diaries* (2004), directed by Walter Salles and based on the early life of Ernesto "Che" Guevara.

### Abraham Rodriguez

Rodriguez has published four books of fiction: *The Boy without a Flag: Tales of the South Bronx* (1992), *Spidertown* (1993), *The Buddha Book* (2001), and *South by South Bronx* (2008). An interview with him appears in *Puerto Ri-*

can Voices in English (1997), by Carmen Dolores Hernández.

## Luis J. Rodríguez

Rodríguez has published the memoir Always Running: La vida loca (1993), translated into Spanish as La vida loca: El testimonio de un pandillero en Los Angeles (1996); the nonfiction book Hearts and Hands: Creating Community in Violent Times (2001); and the novels The Republic of East L.A. (2002) and Music of the Mill (2005). His poetry is collected in Poems across the Pavement (1989), The Concrete River (1991), Trochemoche (1998), and My Nature Is Hunger: New and Selected Poems, 1989–2004 (2005). He has published two books for children: América Is Her Name (1997), illustrations by Carlos Vázquez, and It Doesn't Have to Be This Way: A Barrio Story (1999). He edited the anthology Power Lines: A Decade of Poetry from Chicago's Guild Complex (1999), with Julie Parson-Nesbitt and Michael Warr. An interview with him, produced by the Lannan Foundation in 1993, is available on videocassette. A later interview with him appears in East Side Stories: Gang Life in East L.A. (1998), with photographs by Joseph Rodríguez and an essay by Rubén Martínez. Also valuable is Rodríguez's interview in Conversations with Ilan Stavans (2005).

## Richard Rodriguez

Rodriguez's trilogy consists of the books Hunger of Memory: The Education of Richard Rodriguez (1982), Days of Obligation: An Argument with My Mexican Father (1992), and Brown: The Last Discovery of America (2002). Rodriguez contributes essays to the PBS show The NewsHour with Jim Lehrer. He contributed an essay to the art catalogue Martín Ramírez: The Last Works (2008), by Brooke Davis Anderson. An interview with him appears in Conversations with Ilan Stavans (2005).

## Cecilia Rodríguez Milanés

Rodríguez Milanés has published the story collection Marielitos, Balseros, and Other Exiles (2009). She has published poems, stories, and essays in many literary magazines, anthologies, and reviews, including Iguana Dreams: New Latino Fiction (1992), edited by Virgil Suárez and Delia Poey, preface by Oscar Hijuelos; and New World: Young Latino Writers (1997), edited by Ilan Stavans.

## Esmeralda Santiago

Santiago's autobiographical volumes include When I Was Puerto Rican (1993), translated by the author as Cuando era puertorriqueña (1994); Almost a Woman (1998); and The Turkish Lover (2004). These last two works were translated into Spanish by Nina Torres-Vidal as Casi una mujer (1999) and El amante turco (2005). In 1996, Santiago published a novel in English, America's Dream, and also her own Spanish version, El sueño de América. With Joie Davidow, she edited the anthologies Las Christmas: Favorite Latino Authors Share Their Holiday Memories (1998) and Las Mamis: Favorite Latino Authors Remember Their Mothers (2000). Interviews with Santiago appear in Puerto Rican Voices in English (1997), by Carmen Dolores Hernández, and Conversations with Ilan Stavans (2005). In 2001, Santiago adapted Almost a Woman for the PBS series Masterpiece Theater.

## Gary Soto

Soto's poetry collections include The Elements of San Joaquin (1977), The Tale of Sunlight (1978), Small Faces (1986), Lesser Evils: Ten Quartets (1988), A Fire in My Hands: A Book of Poems (1990), Who Will Know Us? (1990), Home Course in Religion: New Poems (1991), Taking Sides (1991), Pacific Crossing (1992), Local News (1993), Jesse (1994), New and Selected Poems (1995), A Natural Man (1999), Buried Onions (1999), Poetry Lover (2001), One Kind of Faith (2003), and Partly Cloudy: Poems of Love and Longing (2009). His volumes of fiction include A Summer Life (1990), Baseball in April and Other Stories (1990), Junior College (1997), Nickel and Dime (2000), and Amnesia in a Republican Country (2003). His memoirs are Black Hair (1985), Living Up the Street: Narrative Recollections (1985), The Effects of Knut Hamsun on a Fresno Boy: Recollections and Short Essays (2000), and Petty Crimes (2006). His books for children are The Cat's Meow (1987), illustrated by Carolyn Soto; Neighborhood Odes (1992), illustrated by David Díaz; The Skirt (1992), illustrated by Eric Velasquez; The Old Man and His Door (1996), illustrated by Joe Cepeda; Snapshots from the Wedding (1997), illustrated by Stephanie García; Chato and the Party Animals (2000), illustrated by Susan Guevara; and If the Shoes Fit (2002), illustrated by Terry Widener. Soto wrote the libretto of an opera for young adults, Nerdlandia (1999).

He edited the anthologies California Childhood: Recollections and Stories of the Golden State (1988) and Pieces of the Heart: New Chicano fiction (1993). An interview with him, produced by the Lannan Foundation in 1995, is available on videocassette. His work has appeared in numerous anthologies, including Wáchale!: Poetry and Prose about Growing Up

Latino in America (2001), edited by Ilan Stavans.

## Virgil Suárez

Suárez's poetry collections are You Come Singing (1998), Garabato Poems (1999), In the Republic of Longing (1999), Banyan (2001), Palm Crows (2001), Guide to the Blue Tongue (2002), and 90 Miles: Selected and New Poems (2005). His poetry is featured in the anthologies Wáchale!: Poetry and Prose about Growing Up Latino (2001), edited by Ilan Stavans, and Burnt Sugar/Caña quemada: Contemporary Cuban Poetry in English and Spanish (2006), edited by Oscar Hijuelos and Lori Carlson. His volumes of fiction are Latin Jazz (1989, repr. 2002), The Cutter (1991), Welcome to the Oasis and Other Stories (1992), Havana Thursdays (1995), and Going Under (1996). His memoirs are Spared Angola: Memories from a Cuban-American Childhood (1997) and Infinite Refuge (2002). He edited the anthologies Iguana Dreams: New Latino Fiction (1993), with Delia Poey, preface by Oscar Hijuelos; Paper Dance: 55 Latino Poets (1995), with Víctor Hernández Cruz and Leroy V. Quintana; Little Havana Blues: A Cuban-American Literature Anthology (1996), with Delia Poey; American Diaspora: Poetry of Displacement (2001), with Ryan G. Van Cleave; Like Thunder: Poets Respond to Violence in America (2002), with Ryan G. Van Cleave; and Red, White, and Blues: Poets on the Promise of America (2004), with Ryan G. Van Cleave.

## Luz María Umpierre-Herrera

Umpierre-Herrera's poetry collections are Una puertorriqueña en Penna (1979), En el país de las maravillas (1982), the bilingual Y otras desgracias/And Other Misfortunes (1985), The Margarita Poems (1987), and For Christine (1995). Her books of criticism are Ideología y novela en Puerto Rico: Un estudio de la narrativa de Zeno, Laguerre y Soto (1982) and Nuevas aproximaciones críticas a la literatura puertorriqueña contemporánea (1983).

## Luis Alberto Urrea

Urrea's poetry collections include Frozen Moments (1977), Ghost Sickness (1977), The Fever of Being (1994), and Vatos (2000). Urrea's fiction volumes are In Search of Snow (1994), Six Kinds of Sky (2002), The Hummingbird's Daughter (2005), Into the Beautiful North (2009), and the graphic novel Mr. Mendoza's Paintbrush (2010), illustrated by Christopher Cardinale. His nonfiction volumes include Across the Wire: Life and Hard Times on the Mexican Border (1993), By the Lake of Sleeping Children: The Secret Life of the Mexican Border (1996), No-

body's Son: Notes from an American Life (1998), Wandering Time: Western Notebooks (1999), and The Devil's Highway: A True Story (2004). He also wrote the play Un puño de tierra: A Handful of Dust (1991). Urrea's work is included in the anthology Lengua Fresca (2006). An interview with Urrea appears in Conversations with Ilan Stavans (2005).

## Roberto Valero

Valero's poetry collections include Desde un oscuro ángulo (1982), En fin la noche (1984), Dharma (1985), Venias (1990), and No estaré en tu camino (1991). He has also published the novel Este viento de cuaresma (1991) and the critical study El desamparado humor de Reinaldo Arenas (1990).

## Sherezada "Chiqui" Vicioso

Vicioso has published almost two dozen books. Her poetry collections are Viaje desde el agua (1981), Un extraño ulular traía el viento (1985), and Internamiento (1992). Her essay collections include Volver a vivir: ensayos sobre Nicaragua (1985), Algo que decir: Ensayos sobre literatura femenina, 1981–1991 (1991), and Julia de Burgos la nuestra (1992).

## Alma Luz Villanueva

Villanueva's poetry collections are Bloodroot (1977), Planet with Mother, May I? (1978), La Chingada (1985), Life Span (1985), Desire (1998), Vida (2002), and Soft Chaos (2008). Her volumes of fiction are Ultraviolet Sky (1988), Naked Ladies (1994), Weeping Woman: La Llorona and Other Stories (1994), and Luna's California Poppies (2002).

## Tino Villanueva

Villanueva's poetry collections are Hay otra voz: Poems, 1968–1971 (1972); Shaking Off the Dark (1984, rev. 1998); Crónica de mis años peores (1987); Scene from the Movie Giant (1993; Spanish ed., 2005); Chronicle of My Worst Years/Crónica de mis años peores (1994, rev. 2001), a bilingual volume with Spanish translation by James Hoggard; and Primera causa/First Cause (1999), a bilingual volume with Spanish translation by Lisa Horowitz. A compendium of Villanueva's poetry is Il canto del cronista: Antología poética (2002). His criticism includes Tres poetas de posguerra: Celaya, González y Caballero Bonald (1988). Villanueva edited the Spanish-language anthology Chicanos: Antología histórica y literaria (1980) and the magazine Imagine: International Chicano Poetry Journal, published from 1984 to 1990. He translated into Spanish Luis J. Rodríguez's América Is Her Name (1997). Villanueva's papers are in the

Southwestern Writers Collection at Texas State University–San Marcos.

**Helena María Viramontes**

Viramontes's fiction includes *The Moths and Other Stories* (1985) and the novels *Under the* *Feet of Jesus* (1995) and *The Dog Came with Them* (2007). Her academic work appears in *Chicana Creativity and Criticism: Charting New Frontiers in American Literature* (1988) and *Chicana Creativity and Criticism: New Frontiers in American Literature* (1996), both edited with María Herrera-Sobek.

## POPULAR DIMENSIONS

The study of folklore and oral tradition in Latino culture dates from the early decades of the twentieth century, with explorations focusing on the Southwest. For a comprehensive overview of the Mexican American tradition, see *Chicano Folklore: A Handbook* (2006), by María Herrera-Sobek.

Aurelio M. Espinosa is an early distinguished folklorist devoted to the New Mexican tradition. His work includes *Spanish Folklore in New Mexico* (1926); *España en Nuevo Méjico: Lecturas elementales sobre la historia de Nuevo Méjico y su tradición española* (1937, rev. 1969); *Romancero de Nuevo Méjico* (1953); and, listed above, Espinosa's magnum opus, *The Folklore of Spain in the American Southwest: Traditional Spanish Folk Literature in Northern New Mexico and Southern Colorado* (1985), edited by his son J. Manuel Espinosa. Aurelio M. Espinosa also edited *Folklore puertorriqueño: Adivinanzas* (1965), by J. Alden Mason. A second distinguished folklorist from New Mexico is Arthur León Campa, author of *Spanish Folk Poetry in New Mexico* (1946); *Hispanic Culture in the Southwest* (1979); and *Treasure of the Sangre de Cristo: Tales and Traditions of the Spanish Southwest* (1994), foreword by J. Manuel Espinosa and paintings by Joe Beeler.

In the 1950s, a new concentration on the Chicano tradition was pioneered by Américo Paredes, the "father" of Mexican American folklore studies. In his critical writings, he concentrated almost exclusively on the U.S.-Mexican border. Important works by Paredes on the topic are *Folktales of Mexico* (1970), translated and edited by Américo Paredes, foreword by Richard M. Dorson; *The Urban Experience and Folk Tradition* (1971), edited with Ellen J. Stekert; *Toward New Perspectives in Folklore* (1972), edited with Richard Bauman; and *Folklore and Culture on the Texas-Mexican Border* (1993), edited with and with an introduction by Richard Bauman. (For more entries by Paredes, see his entry above and the section below on corridos and narcocorridos.)

Also valuable are the groundbreaking works on folklore by Aurora Lucero-White, especially *The Folkore of New Mexico, Volume 1: Romances, Corridos, Cuentos Proverbios, Dichos, Adivinanzas* (1941); *Los Hispanos: Five Essays on the Folkways of the Hispanos as Seen through the Eyes of One of Them* (1947), illustrated by James Morris; *Literary Folklore of the Hispanic Southwest* (1953); and *Juan Bobo* (1966), adapted from the Spanish folktale "Bertoldo" by Aurora Lucero-White, illustrated by Jaime Morris.

Other important scholarly volumes on the Southwest include *Coronado's Children: Tales of Lost Mines and Buried Treasure of the Southwest* (1930), edited by J. Frank Dobie; *A Treasury of Mexican Folkways* (1947), by Frances Toor; *Mexican Folk Narratives from the Los Angeles Area* (1973), by Elaine K. Miller; *Hispano Folklife of New Mexico: The Lorin W. Brown Federal Writers' Project Manuscripts* (1978), by Lorin W. Brown, with Charles L. Briggs and Marta Weigle; *Recuerdos de los viejitos/Tales of the Río Puerco* (1987), edited by Nasario García; *The Lore of New Mexico* (1988), by Marta Weigle and Peter White; *Mexican American Folklore: Legends, Songs, Festivals, Proverbs, Crafts, Tales of Saints, of Revolutionaries, and More* (1988), edited by John O. West; *Cuentos from My Childhood: Legends and Folktales of Northern New Mexico* (1991), by Paulette Atencio, translated by Rubén Cobos; *Abuelitos: Stories of the Río Puerco Valley* (1992), edited by Nasario García; *Comadres: Hispanic Women of the Río Puerco Valley* (1997), edited by Nasario García; *Tales of Witchcraft and the Supernatural in the Pecos Valley* (1999), edited by Nasario García; *Women's Tales from the New Mexico WPA: La diabla a pie* (2000), edited by Tey Diana Rebolledo and María Teresa Márquez; *Chicano Folklore: A Guide to the Folktales, Traditions, Rituals and Religious Practices of Mexican-Americans* (2001), by Rafaela G. Castro; *Chicana Traditions: Continuity and Change* (2002), by Norma Cantú; *Old Las Vegas: Hispanic Memories from the New Mexico Meadowlands* (2005), translated and edited by Nasario García; and *Cantemos al alba: Origins of Songs, Sounds, and Liturgical Drama of Hispanic New Mexico* (2007), by Tomás Lozano, edited and translated by Rima Montoya.

Important bibliographical resources on the Mexican American oral tradition are "Bibliography of Spanish Ballads in Spanish America," in *Homenaje a Menéndez Pidal* (3 vols., 1925); "Bibliography of Spanish American Folklore," in *Journal of American Folklore* (1928), by Arthur Lesser; *Bibliography of Latin American Folklore* (1940), by Ralph Steele Boggs; *An Annotated Bibliography of Spanish Folklore in New Mexico and Southern Colorado* (1950), by

Marjorie F. Tully and Juan B. Rael; *A Bibliography of the Romance and Related Forms in Spanish America* (1963), by Merle E. Simmons; *Index of Mexican Folktales: Including Narrative Texts from Mexico, Central America and the Hispanic United States* (1973), by Stanley L. Robe; *An Annotated Bibliography of Chicano Folklore from the Southwestern United States* (1977), by Michael Heisley; and *Chicano Folklore: A Handbook* (2006), by María Herrera-Sobek, which includes an extensive bibliography.

The foremost ethnographers of Cuban folklore are Fernando Ortiz and Lydia Cabrera. In various ways, their work intersects with the Cuban American oral tradition. In Spanish, their collected works span dozens of volumes. Ortíz's only book translated into English is *Cuban Counterpoint: Tobacco and Sugar* (1947, repr. 1997), translated by Harriet de Onís, with an introduction by Bronislaw Malinowski. Cabrera's only work available in English is *Afro-Cuban Tales/Cuentos negros de Cuba* (2004), translated by Alberto Hernández-Chiroldes and Lauren Yoder, with an introduction by Isabel Castellanos. A valuable resource is *Pioneros de la etnografía afrocubana: Fernando Ortiz, Rómulo Lachatañeré, Lydia Cabrera* (2003), by Jorge Castellanos.

Among the earliest efforts to collect Puerto Rican folklore is *Myths and Legends of Our New Possessions and Protectorate* (1900), by Charles M. Skinner. Further efforts to examine the oral tradition on the island and mainland include *Raíces de la tierra: Colección de cuentos populares y tradiciones* (1941), by María Cadilla de Martínez; *Folklore puertorriqueño: Adivinanzas* (1960), by J. Alden Mason, edited by Aurelio M. Espinosa; *El cantar folklórico de Puerto Rico* (1974), by Marcelino J. Canino; *Esencia del folklore portorriqueño* (1979), by Juan Angel Tió Nazario; *De arañas, conejos y tortugas: Presencia de Africa en la cuentística de tradición oral en Puerto Rico* (1995), by Julia Cristina Ortiz Lugo. From her post at the New York Public Library, the Puerto Rican librarian Pura Belpré dedicated most of her life to collecting Puerto Rican children's folktales and publishing them in bilingual editions, which include *Pérez and Martina* (1932), *Juan Bobo and the Queen* (1962), and *Tiger and the Rabbit and Other Tales* (1965).

An important resource on the Puerto Rican oral tradition is *Bibliografía del folklore de Puerto Rico* (1991), by Alberto Arroyo Gómez.

### Canciones

Important English- and Spanish-language resources on Latino music are *The Latin Tinge: The Impact of Latin American Music on the United States* (1979), by John Storm Roberts; *La plena: Origen, sentido y desarrollo en el folklore puertorriqueño* (1984), by Félix Echevarría Alvarado; *Los Mariachis! An Introduction to Mexican Mariachi Music* (1990), by Patricia Harpole; *My Music Is My Flag: Puerto Rican Musicians and Their New York Communities, 1917–1940* (1997), by Ruth Glasser; *Cuando salí de la Habana, 1898–1997: Cien años de música cubana por el mundo* (3rd ed., 1999), by Cristóbal Díaz Ayala; *Musica! Salsa, Rumba, Merengue, and More: The Rhythm of Latin America* (1999), by Sue Steward, foreword by Willie Colón; *From Bomba to Hip-Hop: Puerto Rican Culture and Latino Identity* (2000), by Juan Flores; *Island Sounds in the Global City: Caribbean Popular Music and Identity in New York* (2001), by Ray Allen and Lois Wilken; *From Tejano to Tango: Latin American Popular Music* (2002), edited by Walter Aaron Clark; *Musical Migrations* (2002), by Frances Aparicio and Cándida F. Jaquez; *Música cubana: Del areyto al rap cubano* (4th ed., 2003), by Cristóbal Díaz Ayala; *The Latin Beat: The Rhythms and Roots of Latin Music from Bossa Nova to Salsa and Beyond* (2003), by Ed Morales; *Cocinando!: Fifty Years of Latin Album Cover Art* (2005), by Pablo Ellicott Yglesias, foreword by Izzy Sanabria; *Arsenio Rodríguez and the Transnational Flows of Latin Popular Music* (2006), by David F. García; *Los contrapuntos de la música cubana* (2006), by Cristóbal Díaz Ayala; and *Oye como va!: Hybridity and Identity in Latino Popular Music* (2010), by Deborah Pacini Hernández. Paquito D'Rivera has written a memoir, *My Sax Life* (2005), foreword by Ilan Stavans. A valuable resource is the two-DVD television documentary *Latin Music USA* (2009), produced by Adriana Bosch.

In Spanish, Vicente T. Mendoza wrote fundamental studies on canciones, including *La décima en México* (1947), *La canción mexicana: Ensayo de clasificación y antología* (1961), and *Estudio y clasificación de la música tradicional hispánica de Nuevo México* (1986). See also the bibliography in *Chicano Folklore: A Handbook* (2006), by María Herrera-Sobek.

Valuable sources on corridos and narcocorridos are *El corrido mexicano* (1954, 1974, 1976) and *El corrido de la Revolución Mexicana* (1956), both by Vicente T. Mendoza; *The Mexican Corrido as a Source for Interpretive Study of Modern Mexico, 1870–1950* (1957), by Merle Edwin Simmons; *With His Pistol in His Hand: A Border Ballad and Its Hero* (1958) and *A Texas-Mexican Cancionero: Folksongs of the Lower Border* (1976), both by Américo Paredes; *The Kennedy Corridos: A Study of the Ballads of a Mexican American Hero* (1978), by Dan William Dickey; *The Mexican Corrido: A Feminist Analysis* (1990) and *Northward Bound: The Mexican Immigrant Experience in Ballad and Song* (1993), both by María

Herrera-Sobek; *Narcocorrido: A Journey into the Music of Drugs, Guns, and Guerrillas* (2001), by Elijah Wald; *Jefe de Jefes: Corridos y narcocultura en México* (2002), by José Manuel Valenzuela; *El narcocorrido:¿Tradición o mercado?* (2004), by Rubén Tinajero Medina and María del Rosario Hernández Iznaga; and *Corridos in Migrant Memory* (2006), by Martha I. Chew Sánchez.

Encyclopedic studies on the bolero are *Cien años de boleros: Su historia, sus compositores, sus mejores intérpretes y 600 boleros inolvidables* (1993), by Jaime Rico Salazar, and *La poética del bolero en Cuba y Puerto Rico* (2000), by Alinaluz Santiago Torres.

Valuable resources on salsa in the United States, the Caribbean Basin, and Colombia are *El libro de la salsa: Crónica de la música del Caribe urbano* (1980), by César Miguel Rondón; *Salsa!: The Rhythm of Latin Music* (1989), by Charley Gerard with Marty Sheller; *La salsa en Cali* (1992), by Alejandro Ulloa; *Salsa!: Havana Heat, Bronx Beat* (1995), by Hernando Calvo Ospina, translated by Nick Caistor; *Listening to Salsa: Gender, Latin Popular Music, and Puerto Rican Cultures* (1998), by Frances Aparicio; *¡Salsa, sabor y control!: Sociología de la música "tropical"* (1998), by Angel G. Quintero Rivera; *Situating Salsa: Global Markets and Local Meanings in Latin Popular Music* (2002), edited by Lise Waxer; *The City of Musical Memory: Salsa, Record Grooves, and Popular Culture in Cali, Colombia* (2002), by Lise A. Waxer; *Encuentros sincopados: El Caribe contemporáneo a través de sus prácticas musicales* (2003), by Lara Ivette López de Jesús; *La máquina de la salsa: Tránsitos del sabor* (2004), by Juan Carlos Quintero Herencia; *Salsa Talks: A Musical Heritage Uncovered* (2005), by Mary Kent; and *From Afro-Cuban Rhythms to Latin Jazz* (2006), by Raúl A. Fernández. Celia Cruz's autobiography, *Celia: My Life* (2004), was written with Ana Cristina Reymundo and translated from the Spanish by José Lucas Badué; it has a foreword by Maya Angelou.

Thought-provoking disquisitions on Latino rap, hip-hop, and reggaetón are *From Bomba to Hip-Hop: Puerto Rican Culture and Latino Identity* (2000), by Juan Flores; *The 'Hood Comes First: Race, Space, and Place in Rap and Hip-Hop* (2002), by Murray Forman; *New York Ricans from the Hip Hop Zone* (2003), by Raquel Z. Rivera; *That's the Joint!: The Hip-Hop Studies Reader* (2004), edited by Murray Forman and Mark Anthony Neal; *Can't Stop, Won't Stop: A History of the Hip-Hop Generation* (2005), by Jeff Chang, introduction by DJ Kool Herc; *Total Chaos: The Art and Aesthetics of Hip-Hop* (2006), edited by Jeff Chang; *Icons of Hip Hop: An Encyclopedia of the Movement, Music, and Culture* (2007), edited by Mickey Hess; *Hip-Hop Revolution: The Culture and Politics of Rap* (2007), by Jeffrey O. G. Ogbar; *Other People's Property: A Shadow History of Hip-Hop in White America* (2007), by Jason Tanz; and *Reggaetón* (2009), by Raquel Z. Rivera, Wayne Marshall, and Deborah Pacini Hernández.

### Cartoonistas

Gus Arriola's work is featured and analyzed in *Accidental Ambassador Gordo: The Comic Strip Art of Gus Arriola* (2000), by Robert C. Harvey. The work of the Hernández Brothers (Jaime, Gilberto, and Mario) is featured in numerous graphic volumes, including *Love and Rockets*, vol. 1 (1982–96) and *Love and Rockets*, vol. 2 (2000–2007). Lalo López Alcaraz is the illustrator of *Latino U.S.A.: A Cartoon History* (2000, written by Ilan Stavans), *La Cucaracha* (2004), *Leave It to Beaner* (2004), and *Migra Mouse: Political Cartoons on Immigration* (2004). With Alex Rivera, Alcaraz made a series of short animated films, *Animaquiladora* (1997).

Cartoonistas' work is studied in *Your Brain on Latino Comics* (2009), by Frederick Luis Aldama, and *Redrawing the Nation: National Identity in Latin/o American Comics* (2009), edited by Héctor Fernández L'Hoeste and Juan Poblete. The Latin American perspective appears in *How to Read Donald Duck* (1971), by Ariel Dorfman and Armand Mattelart, and *From Mafalda to Los Supermachos: Latin American Graphic Humor as Popular Culture* (1989), by David William Foster. Ilan Stavans discusses cartoon art in *The Riddle of Cantinflas: Essays on Hispanic Popular Culture* (1998).

### Chistes

Important compilations and studies of Latino humor are *Uncle Remus con chile* (1993), edited by Américo Paredes, and *Selected Proceedings of the First International Conference on Hispanic Humor* (1998), edited by Paul W. Seaver Jr. See also *Raza Humor: Chicano Joke Tradition in Texas* (n.d.), by José Reyna.

### Cuentos and Leyendas

For important collections of Latino folktales, see the opening paragraphs under "Popular Dimensions," above.

### Dichos

Extensive work on the proverb and tall tale was done by Shirley Arora in *Proverbial Comparisons and Related Expression in Spanish* (1977). The best anthology of Latino proverbs from the Southwest is Aurelio M. Espinosa's

*The Folklore of Spain in the American Southwest: Traditional Spanish Folk Literature in Northern New Mexico and Southern Colorado* (1985), edited by his son J. Manuel Espinosa. Also available are the bilingual edition of *Southwestern Spanish Proverbs/Refranes españoles del sudoeste* (1974, rev. 1985), edited by Rubén Cobos; *Children's Riddling* (1979), by John McDowell; *A Dictionary of Mexican American Proverbs* (1987), by Mark Glazer; *Refranes usados en Puerto Rico* (1994), edited by María Elisa Díaz Rivera; *In Few Words: A Compendium of Latino Folk Wit and Wisdom/En pocas palabras* (1997), by José Antonio Burciaga, edited by Carol and Thomas Christensen; *A Spanish/English Dictionary of Proverbs, Sayings, Maxims, and Adages/Diccionario de refranes, proverbios, dichos, adagios* (1998), by Delfín Carbonell Basset; *Los que dicen ¡ay bendito!: Dichos modismos y expresiones del habla coloquial puertorriqueña* (1999), by Rosario Núñez de Ortega and Isabel Delgado de Laborde; and *Speaking Boricua!* (2005), by Jared Romey.

## Teatro Popular

Important sources on *teatro popular* are "*Los Comanches*: A New Mexican Folk Drama," edited by Arthur L. Campa, included in *University of New Mexico Bulletin* (Language Series, April 1942); *Los Tejanos*: A New Mexican Spanish Popular Dramatic Composition of the Middle of the Nineteenth Century," edited by Aurelio M. Espinosa and J. Manuel Espinosa, in *Hispania* 27 (1944); the anonymous "Moros y cristianos," in *Literary Folklore of the Hispanic Southwest* (1953), edited by Aurora Lucero-White; and "A History of the Matachines Dance," by Adrián Treviño and Barbara Gilles, in *New Mexico Historical Review* 69 (April 1994).

Culture Clash's plays are collected in *Culture Clash: Life, Death, and Revolutionary comedy* (1997) and *Culture Clash in America: Four Plays* (2003). The group has made the films *Culture Clash's Bowl of Beings* (1992) and, with Lourdes Portillo, *Columbus on Trial* (1992).

## APPENDIX 2: TREATIES, ACTS, AND PROPOSITIONS

See "Panoramic Views," above.

## APPENDIX 3: INFLUENTIAL ESSAYS BY LATIN AMERICAN WRITERS

Important comparative volumes on Latin American and U.S. literatures are *Writing the Apocalypse: Historical Vision in Contemporary U.S. and Latin American Fiction* (1989), by Lois Parkinson Zamora; *Do the Americas Have a Common Literature?* (1990), edited by Gustavo Pérez Firmat; and *Mutual Impressions: Writers from the Americas Reading One Another* (1999), edited by Ilan Stavans.

José Enrique Rodó's writings in Spanish appear in his four-volume *Obras Completas* (1945–58). Rodó's "Ariel" is available in English in the 1922 translation by F. J. Stimson; the 1967 translation by Gordon Brotherston; and the 1988 translation by Margaret Sayers Peden, with a foreword by James W. Symington and a prologue by Carlos Fuentes.

José Vasconcelos's writings in Spanish appear in his four-volume *Obras Completas* (1957–61). In English, he published *Mexico* (1928), written with Guy Stevens. One volume of his autobiography appears as *A Mexican Ulysses* (1963), translated and abridged by W. Rex Crawford. The only available English edition of *The Cosmic Race* was done in bilingual format in 1997 by Didier T. Jaén, afterword by Joseba Gabilondo.

Octavio Paz's writings in Spanish appear in his 14-volume *Obras Completas* (1994–2004). His writings have been generously rendered into English. His chapter "The Pachuco and Other Extremes" comes from *The Labyrinth of Solitude: Life and Thought in Mexico* (1961), translated by Lysander Kemp. An expanded edition of this volume, *The Labyrinth of Solitude and the Other Mexico* (1985), translated by Lysander Kemp, Yara Milos, and Rachel Phillips Belash, also includes "Return to the Labyrinth of Solitude," "Mexico and the United States," and "The Philanthropic Ogre."

Roberto Fernández Retamar's writings in Spanish appear in almost 50 volumes. His only writings rendered into English appear in *Caliban and Other Essays* (1989), translated by Edward Baker, foreword by Fredric Jameson.

# PERMISSIONS ACKNOWLEDGMENTS

A161

Houston, 1985). "lady liberty" from *Mainstream Ethics* by Tato Laviera is reprinted with permission from the publisher (Houston: Arte Público Press–University of Houston, 1988).

**Leal, Luis**: "In Search of Aztlán," translated by Gladys Leal. First published in *Aztlán: Essays on the Chicano Homeland*, ed. Rudolfo A. Anaya and Francisco Lomelí (Albuquerque, New Mexico: Academia/El Norte Publications). Copyright © 1989 by Gladys Leal. Used by permission of the estate of Gladys Leal.

**Levins Morales, Aurora**: Selections from *Getting Home Alive* by Aurora Levins Morales and Rosario Morales, Firebrand Books, Milford, Connecticut. Copyright © 1986.

**Machado, Eduardo**: Excerpt from Act 1 of *The Floating Island Plays* by Eduardo Machado. Copyright © 1991 by Eduardo Machado. Published by Theatre Communications Group. Used by permission of Theatre Communications Group.

**Manrique, Jaime**: "Little Columbia, Jackson Heights" from *Latin Moon in Manhattan*. Copyright © Jamie Manrique. Reprinted with the permission of the author.

**Marín, Francisco Gonzalo "Pachín"**: "New York from Within." Reprinted with the permission of the translator, Lisa Paravisini-Gebert.

**Marqués, René**: Act 3 from *The Oxcart* by René Marqués. © Reprinted by permission of Pearson Education, Inc., Upper Saddle River, NJ. "The Function of the Puerto Rican Writer Today" from *The Docile Puerto Rican: Essays* by René Marqués, translated with an introduction by Barbara Bockus Aponte. Copyright © 1976 by Temple University Press. Used by permission of Barbara B. Lunden.

**Martí, José**: "Our America" from *José Martí: Selected Writings* by José Martí, introduction by Roberto González Echevarria, edited by Esther Allen, translated by Esther Allen. Copyright © 2002 by Esther Allen. Used by permission of Viking Penguin, a division of Penguin Group (USA) Inc. *Marti on the USA* by Luis A. Baralt. Copyright © 1966 by Southern Illinois University Press. Reprinted by permission.

**Martínez, Demetria**: "Fragmentos/Fragments" from *Breathing between the Lines* by Demetria Martínez. Copyright © 1997 Demetria Martínez. Reprinted by permission of the University of Arizona Press. "The Devil's Workshop" and "Ars Poetica" from *The Devil's Workshop* by Demetria Martínez. Copyright © 2002 Demetria Martínez. Reprinted by permission of the University of Arizona Press.

**Martínez, Dionisio**: "History as a Second Language." Originally published in *History as a Second Language* (Ohio State University Press, 1993). Reprinted with the permission of the author. "In a Duplex Near the San Andreas Fault," "Je te veux," and "The Cultivation of Orchids" from *Bad Alchemy* by Dionisio D. Martínez. Copyright © 1995 by Dionisio D. Martínez. Used by permission of W. W. Norton & Company, Inc.

**Martínez, Rubén**: "A Death in the Family" and "Manifesto" from *The Other Side*. Reprinted with the permission of Verso Publishers. "Prologue: The Passion" from *Crossing Over: A Mexican Family on the Migrant Trail*. Copyright © 2001 by Rubén Martínez. Published in paperback by Picador USA, and originally in hardcover by Metropolitan Books/Henry Holt & Co. Reprinted by permission of Susan Bergholz Literary Services, New York, NY, and Lamy, NM. All rights reserved.

**Medina, Pablo**: "Arrival: 1960" from *Exiled Memories: A Cuban Childhood* by Pablo Medina (University of Texas Press © 1990, Persea Books 2002). "Calle de la Amargura" and "Nothing Nietzsche" originally appeared in *The Floating Island*. Buffalo, NY, White Pine Press, 1999. Reprinted with the permission of the author. From *The Return of Felix Nogara* by Pablo Medina. Copyright © 2000 by Pablo Medina. Reprinted by Permission of Persea Books, Inc., New York. "A Dictionary of Guatemalan Bird Calls" from *Points of Balance* (New York, NY: Four Way Books, 2005).

**Meléndez, Jesús "Papoleto"**: "of a butterfly in el barrio or a stranger in paradise" first appeared in *Street People and Other Poems*, Barlenmir House Publishers. Copyright © 1972 by Jesús "Papoleto" Meléndez.

**Menéndez, Ana**: "In Cuba I Was a German Shepherd" from *In Cuba I Was a German Shepherd* by Ana Menéndez. Copyright © 2001 by Ana Menéndez. Used by permission of Grove/Atlantic, Inc.

**Miranda, Lin-Manuel**: "Carnaval del Barrio." Music and Lyrics by Lin-Manuel Miranda. Copyright © 2008 Miranda. Administered by Williamson Music, An Imagem Company (ASCAP). International copyright secured. All rights reserved. Used by permission.

**Mohr, Nicholasa**: "May, 1945" from *Nilda: A Novel*, "Aunt Rosana's Rocker (Zoraida)," and "A Journey toward a Common Ground: The Struggle and Identity of Hispanics in the USA." Nicholasa Mohr was born in Manhattan's El Barrio, of Puerto Rican parentage. She is the author of numerous essays and books for adults, young adults, and children. Among them are *Nilda*, *Rituals of Survival: A Woman's Portfolio*, *A Matter of Pride*, *El Bronx Remembered*, *Felita*, and *Going Home*. Her many awards include an Honorary Doctorate from the State University of New York, Hispanic Heritage Award for Literature, National Book Award finalist, and the Raúl Juliá Award for creative commitment. "The Wrong Lunch Line: Early Spring 1946." Copyright © 1975 by Nicholasa Mohr. Used by permission of HarperCollins Publishers.

**Mora, Pat**: All selections copyright © 1994 by Pat Mora. Currently published in *Agua Santa/Holy Water*, published by the University of Arizona Press. Reprinted by permission of Curtis Brown, Ltd.

**Moraga, Cherríe**: "Giving Up the Ghost" from *Heroes and Saints and Other Plays*. Copyright © 1995 by Cherríe L. Moraga. Reprinted with the permission of West End Press, Albuquerque, New Mexico. All rights reserved.

**Morales, Iris**: "PALANTE, SIEMPRE PALANTE!: The Young Lords" article contributed by Iris Morales. Reprinted with the permission of the author.

**Morales, Rosario**: Selections from *Getting Home Alive* by Aurora Levins Morales and Rosario Morales, Firebrand Books, Milford, Connecticut. Copyright © 1986. Reprinted by permission of the publisher.

**Morton, Carlos**: *The Many Deaths of Danny Rosales* from *The Many Deaths of Danny Rosales and Other Plays* by Carlos Morton is reprinted with permission from the publisher (Houston: Arte Público Press–University of Houston, 1983).

**Muñoz, Elías Miguel**: "From the Land of Machos: Journey to Oz with My Father" from *Muy Macho*, ed. Ray Gonzalez (New York: Doubleday, 1996). Reprinted with the permission of Writer's House, Inc.

**Muñoz, Manuel**: "Zigzagger." From *Zigzagger*. Evanston: Northwestern University Press, 2003. Pp. 1–17.

**Muñoz Marín, Luis**: "The Sad Case of Porto Rico" and "Speech." Reprinted by permission of the Enoch Pratt Free Library, Baltimore, in accordance with the terms of the bequest of H. L. Mencken.

**Nava, Michael**: Chapter 1 from *How Town*. Copyright © 1990 by Michael Nava. Used by permission of Jed Mattes Inc.

**Rodriguez, Abraham**: "The Boy without a Flag" from *The Boy without a Flag: Tales of the South Bronx* (Minneapolis: Milkweed Editions, 1999). Copyright © 1992, 1999 by Abraham Rodriguez Jr. Reprinted with the permission of Milkweed Editions.

**Rodríguez, Luis J.**: Chapter 1 from *Always Running: La vida loca* by Luis J. Rodriguez (Curbstone Press, 1993). Reprinted with the permission of Curbstone Press.

**Rodriguez, Richard**: Part 1, "Aria," from *Hunger of Memory: The Education of Richard Rodriguez* by Richard Rodriguez. Reprinted by permission of David R. Godine, Publisher, Inc. Copyright © 1982 by Richard Rodriguez. Chapter 2, "Late Victorians," from *Days of Obligation* by Richard Rodriguez. Copyright © 1992 by Richard Rodriguez. Used by permission of Viking Penguin, a division of Penguin Group (USA) Inc. "Preface" from *Brown: The Last Discovery of America* by Richard Rodriguez. Copyright © 2002 by Richard Rodriguez. Used by permission of Viking Penguin, a division of Penguin Group (USA) Inc.

**Rodríguez de Tió, Lola**: "The Song of Borinquen" and "Cuba and Puerto Rico" from *Borinquen: An Anthology of Puerto Rican Literature*. We have made diligent efforts to contact the copyright holder to obtain permission to reprint this selection. If you have information that would help us, please write to College Permissions Department, W. W. Norton & Company, Inc., 500 Fifth Avenue, New York, NY 10110.

**Rodríguez Milanés, Cecilia**: "Muchacha (After Jamaica)" from *Paper Dance*. Copyright © 1995. Reprinted with the permission of the author.

**Sánchez, Luis Rafael**: "The Airbus" from *Caribbean Review* 13, no. 3 (1984) and "The New Yorkian Quartet," both translated by Diana L. Vélez. Reprinted with the permission of the author and Diana L. Vélez.

**Sánchez, Ricardo**: "Indict Amerika," "Stream," "Teresa, last night," "Fridays Belong to Friends, Sometimes," and "And Would That I Could" by Dr. Ricardo Sánchez. Reprinted by permission of Maria Teresa Sánchez.

**Santiago, Esmeralda**: "The American Invasion of Macún" from *When I Was Puerto Rican* by Esmeralda Santiago. Copyright © 1993 by Esmeralda Santiago. Reprinted by permission of Perseus Books PLC, a member of Perseus Books, LLC. "Island of Lost Causes." Reprinted by permission of Esmeralda Santiago.

**Serra, Fray Junípero**: "Writings of Junipero Serra" from *Writings of Junípero Serra*. Copyright © 1966. Reprinted with the permission of the Academy of American Franciscan History.

**Soto, Gary**: "The Level at Which the Sky Begins." Copyright © 1977 by Gary Soto. Used by permission of the author. "How an Uncle Became Gray." Copyright © 1977 by Gary Soto. Used by permission of the author. "At the Cantina," "Catalina Treviño Is Really from Heaven," "What Are You Speaking?" and "The Charity of La Señora Lara" from *Junior College*. Copyright © 1997 by Gary Soto. Used by permission of Chronicle Books LLC, San Francisco. Visit ChronicleBooks.com. "We Ain't Asking Much" from *Nickel and Dime*. Copyright © 2000 University of New Mexico Press.

**Soto, Pedro Juan**: "The Innocents," "The Champ," "Scribbles," and "Bayaminiña" from *Spiks: Stories* by Pedro Juan Soto. Copyright © 1974. Reprinted by permission of Monthly Review Press.

**Suárez, Mario**: "El Hoyo" and "Señor Garza" from *Chicano Sketches: Short Stories* by Mario Suárez, edited by Francisco A. Lomeli, Cecilia Cota-Robles Suárez, and Juan José Casillas-Núñez. Copyright © The Arizona Board of Regents. Reprinted by permission of the University of Arizona Press.

**Suárez, Virgil**: All selections reprinted with the permission of the author.

**Tafolla, Carmen**: "Compliments," "Marked," and "Letter to Ti" by Carmen Tafolla. "Myths, Machos and the Movies: Will the Real Chicana Please Stand Up?" from *To Split a Human: Mitos, Machos y La Mujer Chicana* by Carmen Tafolla (Mexican-American Cultural Center, 1985). Copyright © 1985 by Carmen Tafolla. Reprinted by permission of the author.

**Thomas, Piri**: "Alien Turf" from *Down These Mean Streets* by Piri Thomas. Copyright © 1967 by Piri Thomas. Copyright renewed 1995 by Piri Thomas. Used by permission of Alfred A. Knopf, a division of Random House, Inc. "The Konk" from *Stories from El Barrio*. Reprinted by permission of Piri Thomas, author.

**Ulibarrí, Sabine R.**: "My Grandma Smoked Cigars" and "El Apache." Reprinted with the permission of Connie L. Ulibarrí on behalf of Sabine R. Ulibarrí.

**Umpierre-Herrera, Luz María**: "Immanence" and "No Hatchet Job" from *The Margarita Poems*. Copyright © 1987 by Luz María Umpierre-Herrera. Reprinted with the permission of the author.

**Urista, Alberto Baltazar Heredia, aka Alurista**: "a bone" and "labyrinth of scarred hearts" from *Nationchild Plumaroja, 1969–1972*. Copyright © 1972 by Centro Cultural de la Raza. Reprinted with the permission of the author. "sometime war" from *Timespace Huracán: Poems, 1972–1975*. Copyright © 1976 by Pajarito Publications. Reprinted with the permission of the author. "juan" from *as our barrio turns . . . who the yoke b on?* Copyright © Alurista. From *Nationchild Plumaroja 1969–1972*. Reprinted with the permission of the author.

**Urrea, Luis Alberto**: "A Lake of Sleeping Children" from *By the Lake of Sleeping Children: The Secret Life of the Mexican Border* by Luis Urrea. Copyright © 1996 by Luis Urrea. Used by permission of Doubleday, a division of Random House, Inc. Excerpt from Chapter 1 of *The Devil's Highway* by Luis Urrea. Copyright © 2004 by Luis Urrea. Used by permission of Little, Brown and Company.

**Valdez, Luis**: *Zoot Suit* from *Zoot Suit and Other Plays* by Luis Valdez is reprinted with permission from the publisher (Houston: Arte Público Press–University of Houston, 1992).

**Valero, Roberto**: Selections from *En Fin la Noche*. Reprinted with the permission of Maria Valero. "Las islas son malvades y nadie lo sospecha" (Islands Are Evil and Nobody Knows It) from *Encuentro*. Reprinted with the permission of Asociación Encuentro de La Cubana.

**Varela, Félix**: Excerpts from *Letters to Elpidio*, edited by Félipe Estevez. Copyright © 1989. Used by permission of Paulist Press, *www.paulistpress.com*.

**Vasconcelos, José**: *The Cosmic Race/La raza cosmica*. Pp. 7–27, 83–94. Translation and annotation by Didier T. Jaén. Copyright © 1979 California State University, Los Angeles. Afterword by Joseba Gabilondo. Copyright © 1997 the Johns Hopkins University Press. Reprinted with the permission of the Johns Hopkins University Press.

**Vázquez, Richard**: Chapter 1 from *Chicano*. Copyright © 1970. Reprinted with the permission of Richard Vázquez's daughter Sylvia Vázquez.

# Index

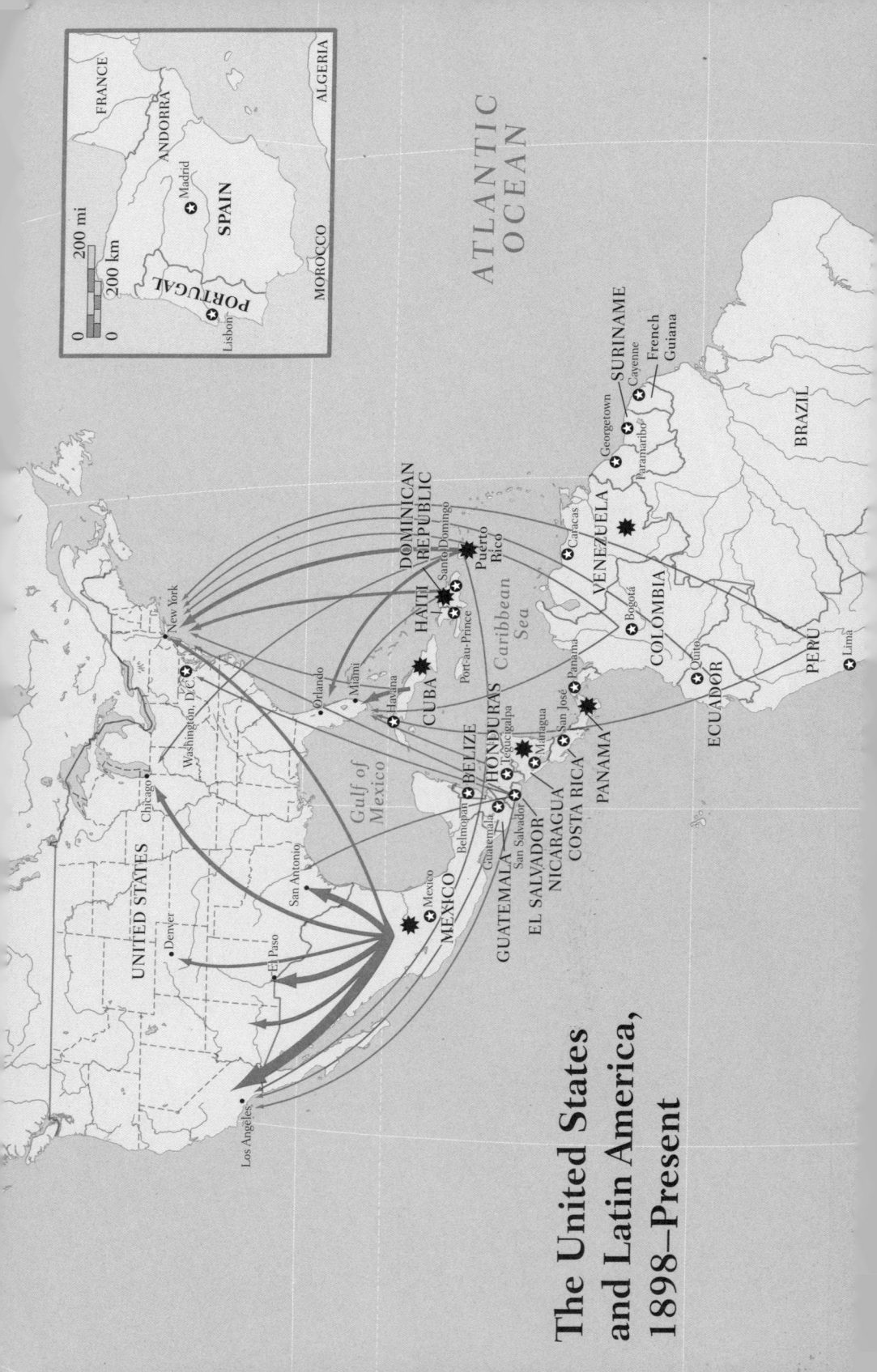

# The United States and Latin America, 1898–Present

FRANCE

ANDORRA

SPAIN

• Madrid

PORTUGAL

Lisbon •

MOROCCO

ALGERIA

200 mi

200 km

0

ATLANTIC OCEAN

SURINAME

Georgetown

Cayenne

Paramaribo

French Guiana

BRAZIL

VENEZUELA

• Caracas

COLOMBIA

• Bogotá

• Quito

ECUADOR

PERU

• Lima

DOMINICAN REPUBLIC

Santo Domingo

Puerto Rico

HAITI

Port-au-Prince

Caribbean Sea

CUBA

Havana

New York

Washington, D.C.

Orlando

Miami

Chicago

San Antonio

Denver

El Paso

Los Angeles

UNITED STATES

Gulf of Mexico

Mexico

MEXICO

BELIZE

Belmopan

Guatemala

GUATEMALA

San Salvador

EL SALVADOR

Tegucigalpa

HONDURAS

Managua

NICARAGUA

San José

COSTA RICA

Panamá

PANAMA